THE NORTON ANTHOLOGY OF

ENGLISH
LITERATURE

NINTH EDITION

VOLUME 1

THE NORTON ANTHOLOGY OF
ENGLISH
LITERATURE

NINTH EDITION

Stephen Greenblatt, *General Editor*

COGAN UNIVERSITY PROFESSOR OF THE HUMANITIES

HARVARD UNIVERSITY

VOLUME 1

W · W · NORTON & COMPANY

NEW YORK · LONDON

W. W. Norton & Company has been independent since its founding in 1923, when William Warder Norton and Mary D. Herter Norton first published lectures delivered at the People's Institute, the adult education division of New York City's Cooper Union. The firm soon expanded its program beyond the Institute, publishing books by celebrated academics from America and abroad. By midcentury, the two major pillars of Norton's publishing program—trade books and college texts—were firmly established. In the 1950s, the Norton family transferred control of the company to its employees, and today—with a staff of four hundred and a comparable number of trade, college, and professional titles published each year—W. W. Norton & Company stands as the largest and oldest publishing house owned wholly by its employees.

Editor: Julia Reidhead
Associate Editor: Carly Fraser Doria
Managing Editor, College: Marian Johnson
Manuscript Editors: Susan Joseph, Jennifer Harris, Katharine Ings,
Pam Lawson, and Jack Borrebach
Electronic Media Editor: Eileen Connell
Marketing Manager, Literature: Kimberly Bowers
Production Manager: Benjamin Reynolds
Photo Editor: Michael Fodera
Editorial Assistants: Hannah Blaisdell, Jennifer Barnhardt
Permissions Manager: Megan Jackson
Permissions Clearing: Nancy J. Rodwan
Text Design: Jo Anne Metsch
Art Director: Rubina Yeh
Composition: The Westchester Book Group
Manufacturing: R. R. Donnelley & Sons—Crawfordsville, IN

The text of this book is composed in Fairfield Medium with the display set in Aperto.

Library of Congress Cataloging-in-Publication Data

The Norton anthology of English literature. v. 1 / Stephen Greenblatt, general editor;
M. H. Abrams, founding editor emeritus. — 9th ed.
    p. cm.
Includes bibliographical references and indexes.
Complete in 2 volumes.
ISBN 978-0-393-91247-0 (v. 1 : pbk.) — ISBN 978-0-393-91248-7 (v. 2 : pbk.)
1. English literature. 2. Great Britain—Literary collections. I. Greenblatt,
Stephen, 1943– II. Abrams, M. H. (Meyer Howard), 1912–
    PR1109.N6 2012
    820.8—dc23   2011046008

W. W. Norton & Company, Inc., 500 Fifth Avenue, New York, NY 10110-0017
wwnorton.com

W. W. Norton & Company Ltd., Castle House, 75/76 Wells Street, London W1T 3QT

3 4 5 6 7 8 9 0

Contents*

* To explore the table of contents of the Supplemental Ebook, visit wwnorton.com/nael.

The Sixteenth Century (1485–1603)

WILLIAM SHAKESPEARE (1564–1616) 1166

The Early Seventeenth Century (1603–1660)

The Restoration and
the Eighteenth Century (1660–1785)

Preface to the Ninth Edition

A great anthology of English literature is a compact library for life. Its goal is to bring together works of enduring value and to make them accessible, comprehensible, and pleasurable to a wide range of readers. Its success depends on earning the reader's trust, trust in the wisdom of the choices, the accuracy of the texts, and the usefulness and good sense of the apparatus. It is not a place for the display of pedantry, the pushing of cherished theories, or the promotion of a narrow ideological agenda. If it succeeds, if it manages to give its readers access to many of the most remarkable works written in English during centuries of restless creative effort, then it furthers a worthwhile democratic cause, that of openness. What might have been a closed pleasure ground, jealously guarded as the preserve of a privileged elite, becomes open to all. Over fifty years and nine editions, *The Norton Anthology of English Literature* has served this important goal.

The works anthologized here generally form the core of courses that are designed to introduce students to English literature. The selections reach back to the earliest moments of literary creativity in English, when the language itself was still molten, and extend to some of the most recent experiments, when, once again, English seems remarkably fluid and open. That openness—a recurrent characteristic of a language that has never been officially regulated and that has constantly renewed itself—helps to account for the sense of freshness that characterizes the works brought together here.

One of the joys of literature in English is its spectacular abundance. Even within the geographical confines of England, Scotland, Wales, and Ireland, where the majority of texts in this collection originated, one can find more than enough distinguished and exciting works to fill the pages of this anthology many times over. But English literature is not confined to the British Isles; it is a global phenomenon. This border-crossing is not a consequence of modernity alone. It is fitting that among the first works here is *Beowulf*, a powerful epic written in the Germanic language known as Old English about a singularly restless Scandinavian hero. *Beowulf*'s remarkable translator in *The Norton Anthology of English Literature*, Seamus Heaney, is one of the great contemporary masters of English literature—he was awarded the Nobel Prize for Literature in 1995—but it would be potentially misleading to call him an "English poet" for he was born in Northern Ireland and is not in fact English. It would be still more misleading to call him a "British poet," as if the British Empire were the most salient fact about the language he speaks and writes in or the culture by which he was shaped. What matters is that the language in which Heaney writes is English, and this fact links him powerfully with the authors assembled in these volumes, a linguistic community that stubbornly refuses to fit comfortably within any firm geographical or ethnic or national boundaries. So too, to glance at other authors and writings in the anthology, in the twelfth century, the noblewoman Marie de France wrote her short stories in an Anglo-Norman dialect at home on both sides of the channel; in the sixteenth century William Tyndale, in exile in the Low Countries and inspired by German religious reformers, translated the New Testament from Greek and thereby changed the course of the English language; in the seventeenth century Aphra Behn touched readers with a story that moves from Africa, where its hero is born, to South America, where Behn herself may have witnessed some of the tragic events she describes; and early in the twentieth century Joseph Conrad, born in Ukraine of Polish parents, wrote in eloquent English a celebrated novella whose ironic vision of European empire gave way by the century's end to the voices of those over whom the empire, now in ruins, had once hoped to rule: the Caribbean-born Claude McKay, Louise Bennett, Derek Walcott, Kamau Brathwaite, V. S. Naipaul, and Grace Nichols; the African-born Chinua Achebe, Wole Soyinka, J. M. Coetzee, and Ngugi Wa Thiong'o; and the Indian-born A. K. Ramanujan and Salman Rushdie.

A vital literary culture is always on the move. This principle was the watchword of M. H. Abrams, the distinguished literary critic who first conceived *The Norton Anthology of English Literature,* brought together the original team of editors, and, with characteristic insight, diplomacy, and humor, oversaw seven editions and has graciously offered counsel on subsequent editions. Abrams wisely understood that new scholarly discoveries and the shifting interests of readers constantly alter the landscape of literary history. To stay vital, the anthology, therefore, would need to undergo a process of periodic revision, guided by advice from teachers, as well as students, who view the anthology with a loyal but critical eye. As with past editions, we have benefited from detailed information on the works actually assigned and suggestions for improvements from 155 reviewers. Their participation has been crucial as the editors grapple with the task of strengthening the selection of more traditional texts while adding texts that reflect the expansion of the field of English studies.

The great challenge (and therefore the interest) of the task is inevitably linked to space constraints. The virtually limitless resources of the Web make some of the difficult choices less vexing: in addition to the print anthology, we have created for our readers a supplemental ebook, with more than one thousand texts from the Middle Ages to the turn of the twentieth century. The expansion of the anthology's range by means of this ebook is breathtaking: at no additional cost, readers have access to remarkable works, edited, glossed, and annotated to the exacting scholarly standards and with the sensitivity to classroom use for which the Norton Anthology is renowned. Hence teachers who wish to extend the selections from major authors included in the print anthology will find hundreds of further readings—Milton's *Comus* and *Samson Agonistes,* for example, or Conrad's *Youth*—in the supplemental ebook. At the same time, the ebook contains marvelous works that might otherwise be lost from view: among them, to cite several of my personal favorites, Gascoigne's "Woodmanship," Wycherley's *The Country Wife*, Mary Robinson's "The Camp," and Edward Lear's "The Jumblies."

In addition, there are many fascinating topical clusters—"The First Crusade: Sanctifying War," "Genius," "Romantic Literature and Wartime," "Victorian Issues: Education," "Imagining Ireland," to name only a few—all designed to draw readers into larger cultural contexts and to expose them to a wide spectrum of voices.

With each edition, *The Norton Anthology of English Literature* has offered a broadened canon without sacrificing major writers and a selection of complete longer texts in which readers can immerse themselves. Perhaps the most emblematic of these great texts are the epics *Beowulf* and *Paradise Lost*. Among the many other complete longer works in the Ninth Edition are *Sir Gawain and the Green Knight* (new in Simon Armitage's spectacular translation), Sir Thomas More's *Utopia*, Sir Philip Sidney's *Defense of Poesy*, William Shakespeare's *Twelfth Night* and *King Lear*, Samuel Johnson's *Rasselas*, Aphra Behn's *Oroonoko*, Robert Louis Stevenson's *The Strange Case of Dr. Jekyll and Mr. Hyde*, Rudyard Kipling's *The Man Who Would Be King*, Joseph Conrad's *Heart of Darkness*, Virginia Woolf's *Mrs. Dalloway*, James Joyce's *Portrait of the Artist as a Young Man*, Samuel Beckett's *Waiting for Godot*, Harold Pinter's *The Dumb Waiter*, and Tom Stoppard's *Arcadia*. To augment the number of complete longer works instructors can assign, and—a special concern—better to represent the achievements of novelists, the publisher is making available the full list of Norton Critical Editions, more than 220 titles, including such frequently assigned novels as Jane Austen's *Pride and Prejudice*, Mary Shelley's *Frankenstein*, Charles Dickens's *Hard Times*, and Chinua Achebe's *Things Fall Apart*. A Norton Critical Edition may be packaged with either volume or any individual paperback-split volume for free.

We have in this edition continued to expand the selection of writing by women in several historical periods. The sustained work of scholars in recent years has recovered dozens of significant authors who had been marginalized or neglected by a male-dominated literary tradition and has deepened our understanding of those women writers who had managed, against considerable odds, to claim a place in that tradition. The First Edition of the Norton Anthology included 6 women writers; this Ninth Edition includes 74, of whom 8 are newly added and 9 are reselected or expanded. Poets and dramatists whose names were scarcely mentioned even in the specialized literary histories of earlier generations—Aemilia Lanyer, Lady Mary Wroth, Elizabeth Cary, Margaret Cavendish, Mary Leapor, Anna Letitia Barbauld, Charlotte Smith, Letitia Elizabeth Landon, Mary Elizabeth Coleridge, Mina Loy, and many others—now appear in the company of their male contemporaries. There are in addition four complete long prose works by women—Aphra Behn's *Oroonoko*, Eliza Haywood's *Fantomina*, Jane Austen's *Love and Friendship*, and Virginia Woolf's *Mrs. Dalloway*—along with new selections from such celebrated fiction writers as Maria Edgeworth, Jean Rhys, Katherine Mansfield, Doris Lessing, Margaret Atwood, Kiran Desai, and Zadie Smith.

Building on an innovation introduced as early as the First Edition, the editors have expanded the array of clusters that gather together short texts illuminating the cultural, historical, intellectual, and literary concerns of each of the periods. We have designed these clusters with three aims: to make them lively and accessible, to ensure that they are possible to teach effectively in a class meeting or two, and to heighten their relevance to the surrounding works of literature. Hence, for example, in the Sixteenth Century section, a new cluster on "Renaissance Love and Desire" enables readers to situate the celebrated achievements of Sidney and Shakespeare in the larger context of a culture obsessed with the fashioning of passionate lyrics. Similarly, in the Eighteenth Century section, a grouping of texts called "Low People and High People" provides perspective on the system of rank and class and brings together such celebrated elite writers as Fielding and Sterne with the working-class Stephen Duck and Mary Collier. And in the Romantic Period, a new cluster on "The Slave Trade and the Literature of Abolition" joins Olaudah Equiano's searing autobiographical account of enslavement with powerful texts by William Cowper, Hannah More, Samuel Taylor Coleridge, and others that together mobilized popular support for abolition. These are only a few of the clusters in print and in the supplemental ebook. Across the volumes the clusters provide an exciting way to broaden the field of the literary and to set masterpieces in a wider cultural, social, and historical framework

Now, as in the past, cultures define themselves by the songs they sing and the stories they tell. But the central importance of visual media in contemporary culture has heightened our awareness of the ways in which songs and stories have always been closely linked to the images that societies have fashioned and viewed. The Ninth Edition of *The Norton Anthology of English Literature* features sixty pages of color plates (in seven color inserts) and more than 120 black-and-white illustrations throughout the volumes. In selecting visual material—from the Sutton Hoo treasure of the seventh century to Yinka Shonibare's *Nelson's Ship in a Bottle* in the twenty-first century— the editors sought to provide images that conjure up, whether directly or indirectly, the individual writers in each section; that relate specifically to individual works in the anthology; and that shape and illuminate the culture of a particular literary period. We have tried to choose visually striking images that will interest students and provoke discussion, and our captions draw attention to important details and cross-reference related texts in the anthology.

Period-by-Period Revisions

The Middle Ages, edited by James Simpson and Alfred David, has taken on a striking new look, with a major revision and expansion of its selections. The heart of the Anglo-Saxon portion is the great epic *Beowulf,* in an acclaimed translation, specially commissioned for *The Norton Anthology of English Literature,* by Seamus Heaney. The array of Anglo-Saxon texts includes Alfred David's new verse translations of the poignant, visionary *Dream of the Rood,* the elegiac *Wanderer,* and *The Wife's Lament.* A new Irish Literature selection features a tale from *The Tain* and a group of vivid ninth-century lyrics. The Anglo-Norman section—a key bridge between the Anglo-Saxon period and the time of Chaucer—includes an illuminating cluster on the Romance, with three stories by Marie de France (two of them new and all three from a newly chosen translation) and *Sir Orfeo,* a comic version of the Orpheus and Eurydice story. The Middle English section centers, as always, on Chaucer, with a generous selection of texts carefully glossed and annotated so as to heighten their accessibility. New to the Ninth

Edition is a brilliant, specially revised verse translation of *Sir Gawain and the Green Knight* by Simon Armitage, one of the foremost poets and translators of our time. In addition, we include for the first time Thomas Hoccleve's *Compleinte*, a startlingly personal account of Hoccleve's attempt to reintegrate himself with his readership after a period of mental instability. Among the highlights of the revised and expanded medieval section of the ebook— too extensive to enumerate here—is a new, fully annotated edition of the great fifteenth-century morality play, *Mankind*.

The Sixteenth Century, edited by Stephen Greenblatt and George Logan, features seven complete longer texts: More's *Utopia* (with two letters from More to Peter Giles), Book 1 of Spenser's *Faerie Queene*, Marlowe's *Hero and Leander* and *Doctor Faustus*, Shakespeare's *Twelfth Night* and *King Lear*, and—in response to many requests—the whole of Sidney's *Defense of Poesy*. A new cluster, "Renaissance Love and Desire," enables readers to sample the emotional range of Tudor love lyrics and to savor the astonishingly high level of skill reached under the influence of Petrarch and of native English traditions. The ebook further enriches this topic by providing the originals (in Italian and modern English translation) of key Petrarchan poems by Wyatt and Surrey. Also new to the ebook are Skelton's brooding, paranoidal vision of life in the orbit of Henry VIII, "The Bowge of Court," and a greatly expanded cluster of texts of exploration and discovery in "The Wider World."

The Early Seventeenth Century. At the heart of this section, edited by Katharine Eisaman Maus and Barbara Lewalski, is John Milton's *Paradise Lost*, presented in its entirety. Other complete longer works include John Donne's soul-searching *Satire 3* and, new to this edition, his hauntingly eloquent *The Anatomy of the World: The First Anniversary*; Aemilia Lanyer's country-house poem "The Description of Cookham"; Ben Jonson's *Volpone* and the Cary-Morison ode; John Webster's tragedy *The Duchess of Malfi*; and Milton's "Lycidas." Significant additions have been made to the works of Mary Wroth and Robert Burton; the Puritan William Gouge added to the topic "Gender Relations: Conflict and Counsel"; and William Harvey (on the circulation of the blood) added to the topic "Inquiry and Experience." Headnotes, introductions, and bibliographies have all been revised. And among the highlights of the ebook are a substantial selection from Donne's startling defense of suicide, the *Biathanatos*; Ben Jonson's *Masque of Blackness*; and the complete text of the first tragedy in English from the pen of a woman, Elizabeth Cary's *The Tragedy of Mariam*.

The Restoration and the Eighteenth Century. The impressive array of complete longer texts in this section, edited by James Noggle and Lawrence Lipking, includes Dryden's satires *Absalom and Achitophel* and *MacFlecknoe*; Aphra Behn's novel *Oroonoko*; Congreve's comedy *The Way of the World*; Pope's *Essay on Criticism*, *The Rape of the Lock*, and *Epistle to Dr. Arbuthnot*; Gay's *Beggar's Opera*; Eliza Haywood's sly novella of sexual role-playing, *Fantomina*; Hogarth's graphic satire "Marriage A-la-Mode"; Johnson's *Vanity of Human Wishes* and *Rasselas*; Gray's "Elegy Written in a Country Churchyard"; and Goldsmith's "The Deserted Village." There are new texts by Henry Fielding, Samuel Johnson, Matthew Prior, and Lawrence Sterne. Thomas Chatterton, the doomed poet and forger, is represented for the first time, as are Mary Barber and Mary Jones, who join the ranks of such distinguished women writers as Aphra Behn, Mary Astell, Anne Finch, Eliza Haywood, Lady Mary Wortley Montagu (with a new selection of Turkish Embassy letters), Anne Ingram, Mary Leapor, and Frances Burney. An exciting new topical cluster, "Low People and High People"—the phrase comes from Fielding's *Joseph Andrews*—enables readers to sample the new kinds of writings, many by middle- and lower-class authors, that were produced in this period to appeal to the emerging phenomenon of "the common reader." Among the many features of the corresponding ebook section are extensive readings in eighteenth-century aesthetics (with texts on grace, on the general and the particular, and on genius); topical clusters on daily life in London, slavery and the slave trade, the plurality of worlds, and travel, trade, and the expansion of empire; and the complete text of William Wycherley's scandalous Restoration comedy *The Country Wife*.

The Romantic Period, edited by Deidre Shauna Lynch and Jack Stillinger, has been extensively revised; every text, headnote, and annotation has been reconsidered. The result is a dramatic reimagining of the entire period, from the lively and illuminating opening selection of popular ballads to the new inclusion at the close of Letitia Landon's "Fairy of the Fountains," a poem of female revenge and female monstrosity that enigmatically rewrites Keats's *Lamia* and Coleridge's *Christabel*. There are new works in this edition for almost every author, from Wordsworth's "Goody Blake and Harry Gill," where the stylistic revolution of the *Lyrical Ballads* is at its most apparent, to Felicia Hemans's ambitious and exciting dramatic monologue "Properzia Rossi." The addition of Byron's *Vision of Judgment* and Shelley's *The Mask of Anarchy* provides eloquent evidence that the genius of Romantic poets was often at its height when they threw themselves into the tumult of the era, writing for political causes or scoring points against their polemical enemies. Other additions—including selections from Coleridge's *Table Talk*, Shelley's *Keepsake* essay "On Love," and Hazlitt's "Coriolanus"— make it clear that an era scholars used to represent solely in terms of the glory of its poetry was also distinctive for exciting experiments in prose.

The revision of this period in the anthology is not only a matter of brilliant additions. The facing-page comparison in the new section on "Versions of *The Prelude*" allows readers to see Wordsworth as a reviser and to gauge the significance of the changes he wrought. By replacing the 1850 *Prelude* with the 1805 *Prelude*, the Norton Anthology provides a text that shows Wordsworth immediately engaged with his Romantic contemporaries. This sense of engagement—as if windows in an ornate room had been thrown open to the world outside—extends to the new topical cluster on "The Slave Trade and the Literature of Abolition," which joins "The Revolution Controversy and the 'Spirit of the Age,'" with the addition of Gillray's searing political prints, and "The Gothic and the Development of a Mass Readership." A new ebook topic, "Reviewer vs. Poet in the Romantic Period," conveys the rough-and-tumble of literary battles, while another new ebook topic, "Romantic Literature and Wartime," documents Romantic writers' pointed efforts to make literature do justice to the wider world.

The Victorian Age, edited by Catherine Robson and Carol Christ, opens with a revised introduction that features expanded discussions of fiction and the cultural role of poetry. A new cluster on the Pre-Raphaelites extends the impressive coverage of poetry and the visual arts. Among the many complete longer works included here are major poems by Elizabeth Barrett Browning, Alfred, Lord Tennyson, Robert Browning, Dante Gabriel Rossetti, Christina Rossetti, William Morris, Algernon Charles Swinburne, Gerard Manley Hopkins, and Ernest Dowson. Plays include Oscar Wilde's *The Importance of Being Earnest* and Bernard Shaw's controversial drama on prostitution, *Mrs Warren's Profession.* New among the prose selections is Arthur Conan Doyle's *The Speckled Band*, the thriller that the author himself chose as his favorite. The piece joins a distinguished array of complete prose works, including Elizabeth Gaskell's *The Old Nurse's Story*, Robert Louis Stevenson's *The Strange Case of Dr. Jekyll and Mr. Hyde,* and Rudyard Kipling's *The Man Who Would Be King.* From the inception of the Norton Anthology, the Victorian section has been innovative in bringing together a wide array of texts—works of poetry and fiction, proclamations, official reports, autobiographical memoirs, scientific papers, and the like—that enable readers to grapple with the period's most resonant and often fiercely contentious issues. Among the areas of focus are evolution, industrialism, gender and sexuality, and empire. The eminently teachable clusters are supplemented in the extensive ebook section by a new topic on Victorian education that brings together powerful reflections by Newman, Mill, and others with key passages from such works as *Hard Times, Alice's Adventures in Wonderland,* and *Jude the Obscure.*

The Twentieth Century and After. The editors, Jahan Ramazani and Jon Stallworthy, have undertaken a root-and-branch reconsideration, leading to a dramatic revision of the entire section. Its spine, as it were, consists of three modernist masterpieces: Virginia Woolf's *Mrs. Dalloway,* James Joyce's *Portrait of the Artist as a Young Man*, and Samuel Beckett's *Waiting for Godot.* These complete works are surrounded by a dazzling choice of other fiction and drama, including, among others, Joseph Conrad's *Heart of Darkness;* powerful stories by D. H. Lawrence, Katherine Mansfield, Jean Rhys, Doris Lessing, and Nadine Gordimer; and Harold Pinter's *The Dumb Waiter* and Tom Stoppard's *Arcadia.* A generous representation of poetry centers on a substantial selection of key works by Thomas Hardy, William Butler Yeats, and T. S. Eliot, and extends out to a wide array of other poets, from A. E. Housman, Wilfred Owen, and W. H. Auden to Philip Larkin, Derek Walcott, and Seamus Heaney. New to the cluster on "Modernist Manifestos" is Mina Loy's much-requested "Songs to Joannes," and there are new poems by Grace Nichols, Carol Ann Duffy, Paul Muldoon, Margaret Atwood, and Les Murray. Other new fiction includes works by Jean Rhys, Chinua Achebe, Margaret Atwood, Ian McEwan, Hanif Kureishi, Kiran Desai, and Zadie Smith. There are also new images, including those in the topical cluster on World War II, and new nonfiction selections, including texts by Salman Rushdie, Hanif Kureishi, and, in a daring experimental vein, M. Nourbese Philip. The much-praised cluster "Nation, Race, and Language" has been expanded. The voices in this cluster—Claude McKay, Louise Bennett, Kamau Brathwaite, Wole Soyinka, Ngugi Wa Thiong'o, M. Nourbese Philip, Salman Rushdie,

Grace Nichols, and Hanif Kureishi—bear eloquent witness to the global diffusion of English, the urgency of unresolved issues of nation and identity, and the rich complexity of literary history.

Editorial Procedures and Format

The Ninth Edition adheres to the principles that have always characterized *The Norton Anthology of English Literature*. Period introductions, headnotes, and annotations are designed to enhance students' reading and, without imposing an interpretation, to give students the information they need to understand each text. The aim of these editorial materials is to make the anthology self-sufficient, so that it can be read anywhere—in a coffeeshop, on a bus, under a tree.

The *Norton Anthology of English Literature* prides itself on both the scholarly accuracy and the readability of its texts. To ease students' encounter with some works, we have normalized spelling and capitalization in texts up to and including the Romantic period—for the most part they now follow the conventions of modern English. We leave unaltered, however, texts in which such modernizing would change semantic or metrical qualities. From the Victorian period onward, we have used the original spelling and punctuation. We continue other editorial procedures that have proved useful in the past. After each work, we cite the date of first publication on the right; in some instances, this date is followed by the date of a revised edition for which the author was responsible. Dates of composition, when they differ from those of publication and when they are known, are provided on the left. We have used square brackets to indicate titles supplied by the editors for the convenience of readers. Whenever a portion of a text has been omitted, we have indicated that omission with three asterisks. If the omitted portion is important for following the plot or argument, we have provided a brief summary within the text or in a footnote. Finally, we have reconsidered annotations throughout and increased the number of marginal glosses for archaic, dialect, or unfamiliar words.

Thanks to the thorough work of James Simpson, with help from Lara Bovilsky of the University of Oregon, the Ninth Edition provides a more useful "Literary Terminology" appendix, recast as a quick-reference alphabetical glossary with examples from works in the anthology. We have also overhauled and updated the General Bibliography that appears in the print volumes, as well as the period and author bibliographies, which now appear in the supplemental ebook, where they can be more easily searched and updated.

Additional Resources from the Publisher

For students using *The Norton Anthology of English Literature*, the publisher provides a wealth of resources on the free StudySpace website (wwnorton. com/nael). Students who activate the free password included in each new copy of the anthology gain access both to the supplemental ebook and to StudySpace, where they will find approximately fifty multiple-choice reading-comprehension quizzes on widely taught individual works with extensive feedback; summaries of the period introductions; period review quizzes with feedback; a new "Literary Places" feature that uses images, maps, and

Google Tours tools to offer students a practical way to (virtually) visit the Lake District, Dover Beach, Canterbury, and other literary places; art galleries—one per period—including author portraits, interactive timelines, and over three hours of spoken-word and musical recordings. The rich gathering of content on StudySpace is designed to help students understand individual works and appreciate the places, sounds, and sights of literature.

The publisher also provides extensive instructor-support materials. Designed to enhance large or small lecture environments, the Instructor Resource Disc, expanded for the Ninth Edition, features more than 300 images with explanatory captions; PowerPoint slides for each period introduction and for most topic clusters; and audio recordings (MP3). Much praised by both new and experienced instructors, *Teaching with* The Norton Anthology of English Literature: *A Guide for Instructors* by Sondra Archimedes (University of California–Santa Cruz), Laura Runge (University of South Florida), Philip Schwyzer (University of Exeter), Leslie Ritchie (Queen's University), and Scott-Morgan Straker (Queen's University) provides extensive help, from planning a course and developing a syllabus and course objectives to preparing exams. Guide entries provide a "hook" to start class discussion; a Quick Read section to refresh instructors on essential information about a text or author; Teaching Suggestions that call out interesting textual or contextual features; Teaching Clusters of suggested groups or pairs of texts; and Discussion Questions. To help instructors integrate the anthology's rich supplemental ebook, the Guide features new entries for online texts and clusters. The Guide also offers revised material on using technology in the classroom, with suggestions for teaching the anthology's multimedia with the texts and for incorporating the media into traditional or distance-learning courses. For the first time, the Guide will also be made available in a searchable online format. Finally, Norton Coursepacks bring high-quality Norton digital media into a new or existing online course. The coursepacks include all content from the StudySpace website, short-answer questions with suggested answers, and a bank of discussion questions adapted from the Guide. Norton's Coursepacks are available in a variety of formats, including Blackboard/WebCT, Desire2Learn, Angel, and Moodle at no cost to instructors or students.

The editors are deeply grateful to the hundreds of teachers worldwide who have helped us to improve *The Norton Anthology of English Literature*. A list of the instructors who replied to a detailed questionnaire follows, under Acknowledgments. The editors would like to express appreciation for their assistance to Elizabeth Anker (University of Virginia), Paul B. Armstrong (Brown University), Derek Attridge (University of York, UK), Homi Bhabha (Harvard University), Glenn Black (Oriel College, Oxford), Gordon Braden (University of Virginia), Mary Ellen Brown (Indiana University), Sandie Byrne (Oxford University), Sarita Cargas (University of New Mexico), Joseph W. Childers (University of California, Riverside), Jason Coats (University of Virginia), Kathleen Coleman (Harvard University), Daniel Cook (University of California, Davis), Guy Cuthbertson (University of St. Andrews), Pamela Dalziel (University of British Columbia, Vancouver), Linda David, Roy Davids (Oxford University), Jed Esty (University of Pennsylvania), Christopher Fanning (Queen's University), Laura Farwell Blake (Harvard University Library, who provided invaluable and expert help with the General Bibliography), Jamie H. Ferguson (University of Houston), Anne Fernald (Fordham University), William Flesch (Brandeis University), Robert Folkenflik (University of California, Irvine), Ryan Fong (University of California, Davis), Robert D. Fulk (Indiana University), Hans Walter Gabler (University of Munich), Kevis Goodman (University of California, Berkeley), Susannah Gottlieb (Northwestern University), Omaar Hena (University of Virginia), Heather Jackson (University of Toronto), Anuj Kapoor (University of Virginia), Tom Keirstead (University of Toronto), Theresa Kelley (University of Wisconsin, Madison), Tim Kendall (University of Exeter), Shayna Kessel (University of Southern California), Scott Klein (Wake Forest University), Cara Lewis (University of Virginia), Joanna Lipking (Northwestern University), Ian Little (Liverpool University), Tricia Lootens (University of Georgia), Lynne Magnusson (University of Toronto), Laura Mandell (Texas A & M University), Steven Matthews (Oxford Brookes University), Peter McDonald (Oxford University), Tara McDonald (University of Toronto), Edward Mendelson (Columbia University), Erin Minear (Harvard University), Andrew Motion, Elaine Musgrave (University of California, Davis), J. Morgan Myers (University of Virginia), Kate Nash (University of Virginia), Bernard O'Donoghue (Oxford University), Paul O'Prey (Roehampton University), Daniel O'Quinn (University of Guelph), Ruth Perry (M.I.T.), Emily Peterson (Harvard University), Kate Pilson (Harvard University), Adela Pinch (University of Michigan), Jane Potter (Oxford Brookes University), Leah Price (Harvard University), Mark Rankin (James Madison University), Angelique Richardson (Exeter University), Ronald Schuchard (Emory University), Philip Schwyzer (Exeter University), John W. Sider (Westmont College), Claire Marie Stancek (University of California, Berkeley), Paul Stevens (University of Toronto), Ramie Targoff (Brandeis University), Elisa Tersigni (University of Toronto), and Daniel White (University of Toronto). We also thank the many people at Norton who contributed to the Ninth Edition: Julia Reidhead, who served not only as the inhouse supervisor but also as an unfailingly wise and effective collaborator in every aspect of planning and accomplishing this Ninth Edition; Marian Johnson, managing editor for college books; Carly Fraser, associate editor and Course Guide editor; Eileen Connell, electronic media editor; Susan Joseph, Jennifer Harris, Pam Lawson, Jack Borrebach, and Katharine Ings, manuscript editors; Ben Reynolds, senior production manager; Nancy Rodwan, permissions; Jo Anne Metsch, designer; Mike Fodera, photo editor; and Hannah Blaisdell and Jennifer Barnhardt, editorial assistants. All these friends provided the editors with indispensable help in meeting the challenge of representing the unparalleled range and variety of English literature.

STEPHEN GREENBLATT

Acknowledgments

The editors would like to express appreciation and thanks to the hundreds of teachers who provided reviews:

Robert Anderson (Oakland University); Stephen Arata (University of Virginia); Patricia Ard (Ramapo College of NJ, AIS); Oliver Arnold (Princeton University); Donna Berliner (University of Texas at Dallas); Jennifer Black (Boise State University); Scott Black (University of Utah); Martin (Rob) Blain (Houston Community College, Southeast); Robert Bleil (Penn State University); Melissa Bloom (St. John Fisher College); Dr. Erik Bond (University of Michigan–Dearborn); Rebecca Borden (University of Maryland); Ken Bugajski (University of Saint Francis); Miriam Burstein (College at Brockport, State University of New York); Michael Carson (University of Evansville); Gregory Castle (Arizona State University); William Ching-chi Chen (National Kaohsiung Normal University); Kai Chong Cheung (Shih Hsin University); Deborah Christie (University of Miami); Elizabeth Claussen (Miami University Hamilton); Thomas F. Connolly (Suffolk University); Tony Cousins (Macquarie University); Eugene Crook (Florida State University); Pamela Dalziel (University of British Columbia); Kristine Dassinger (Genesee Community College); Alan Dilnot (Monash University); James C. Dixon (Elizabethtown Community and Technical College); Graham N. Drake (SUNY Geneseo); Darlene Farabee (Temple University); Thomas J. Farrell (Stetson University); Robert Felgar (Jacksonville State University); Maryanne Felter (Cayuga Community College); Andrew Franta (University of Utah); Lee Garver (Butler University); Michael Given (Stephen F. Austin State University); Esther Godfrey (University of South Carolina Upstate); Jason Goldsmith (Butler University); S. E. Gontarski (Florida State University); Evan Gottlieb (Oregon State University); Robin Grey (University of Illinois–Chicago); Emily Griesinger (Azusa Pacific University); Marlene San Miguel Groner (SUNY Farmingdale); Alexander Gourlay (Rhode Island School of Design); Lisa Hager (University of Florida); George Hahn (Towson University); Roxanne Harde (University of Alberta, Augustana Campus); Rebecca Cole Heinowitz (Bard College); Jack Heller (Huntington University); Carrie Hintz (Queens/CUNY); Erin Hollis (California State University, Fullerton); Tom Howerton (Johnston Community College); Elizabeth Huston (Eastfield College); Farhad Idris (Frostburg State University); Jamison Brenner Kantor (University of Maryland); George Klawitter (St. Edward's University); Scott Kleinman (California State University, Northridge); Marta Kvande (Valdosta State University);

Barbara Laman (Dickinson State University); Mitchell R. Lewis (Elmira College); Christopher Madson (University at Buffalo); Joseph Marohl (Wake Technical Community College); Nicholas Mason (Brigham Young University); Rebecca A. McLaughlin (University of Vermont); Darin A. Merrill (Brigham Young University–Idaho); Frank Molloy (Charles Sturt University); Deborah Murray (Kansas State University); Jeff Myers (Goucher College); Hilary Nanda (Suffolk University); Anne-Marie Obilade (Alcorn State University); George O'Brien (Georgetown University); John O'Brien (University of Virginia); J. L. Ollenquist (Ferris State University); Patrick O'Malley (Georgetown University); David Paddy (Whittier College); John Peters (University of North Texas); Trey Philpotts (Arkansas Tech University); Albert Pionke (University of Alabama); James W. Pipkin (University of Houston); Derrick Pitard (Slippery Rock University); S. D. Powell (University of Guelph); Richard Preiss (University of Utah); Kevin Rahimzadeh (Eastern Kentucky University); Mark Rankin (James Madison University); Hugh Reid (Carleton University); Robert L. Reid (Emory & Henry College); Mary P. Richards (University of Delaware); Jill Rubinson (University of Maine at Augusta); David Ruiter (University of Texas at El Paso); Treadwell Ruml (California State University, San Bernardino); Lisa Schnell (University of Vermont); Peter C. Schwartz (Elmira College); Lisa M. Schwerdt (California University of Pennsylvania); Michael Scrivener (Wayne State University); Linda Shires (Syracuse University); Gerald F. Snelson (Frostburg State University); Cindy Soldan (Lakehead University); Brooke A. Stafford (Creighton University); Tom Stillinger (University of Utah); Jessica Straley (University of Utah); Joyce Sutphen (Gustavus Adolphus College); Alison Taufer (California State University, Los Angeles); Ryan Trimm (University of Rhode Island); Thomas Trzyna (Seattle Pacific University/University Design Consultants); Deborah Uman (St. John Fisher College); Janine Utell (Widener University); Timothy Viator (Rowan University); Bente Videbaek (SUNY Stony Brook); John N. Wall (North Carolina State University); Tracy Ware (Queen's University); Michael Weiser (Thomas Nelson Community College); Barry Weller (University of Utah); Lisa Wellinghoff (West Virginia University); Jacqueline Wilkotz (Towson University); Lea Williams (Norwich University); Tara Williams (Oregon State University); Brett D. Wilson (College of William & Mary); Mark Womack (University of Houston); Shannon R. Wooden (University of Southern Indiana)

Congratulations to Brittany McDaniel, Carmen Daniels, Emily Wood, Jordan Massey, Karyn Lord, Joann Le, and Roman Kuschev of Troy University Dothan, winners of the 2010 Norton Anthology Student Video Contest.

THE NORTON ANTHOLOGY OF

ENGLISH LITERATURE

NINTH EDITION

VOLUME 1

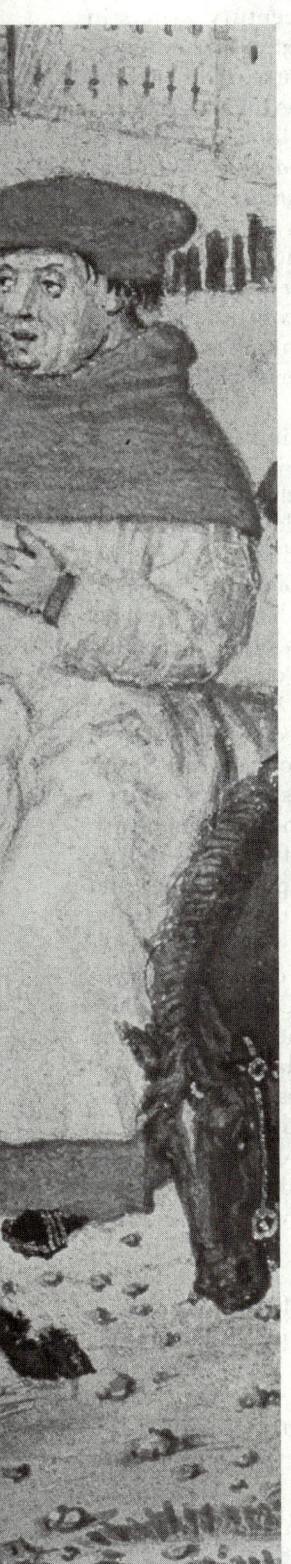

The Middle Ages to ca. 1485

43–ca. 420:	Roman invasion and occupation of Britain
ca. 450:	Anglo-Saxon Conquest
597:	St. Augustine arrives in Kent; beginning of Anglo-Saxon conversion to Christianity
871–899:	Reign of King Alfred
1066:	Norman Conquest
1154–1189:	Reign of Henry II
ca. 1200:	Beginnings of Middle English literature
1360–1400:	Geoffrey Chaucer; *Piers Plowman*; *Sir Gawain and the Green Knight*
1485:	William Caxton's printing of Sir Thomas Malory's *Morte Darthur*, one of the first books printed in England

The Middle Ages designates the time span roughly from the collapse of the Roman Empire to the Renaissance and Reformation. The adjective "medieval," coined from Latin *medium* (middle) and *aevum* (age), refers to whatever was made, written, or thought during the Middle Ages. The Renaissance was so named by nineteenth-century historians and critics because they associated it with an outburst of creativity attributed to a "rebirth" or revival of Latin and, especially, of Greek learning and literature. The word "Reformation" designates the powerful religious movement that began in the early sixteenth century and repudiated the supreme authority of the Roman Catholic Church. The Renaissance was seen as spreading from Italy in the fourteenth and fifteenth centuries to the rest of Europe, whereas the Reformation began in Germany and quickly affected all of Europe to a greater or lesser degree. The very idea of a Renaissance or rebirth, however, implies something dormant or lacking in the preceding era. More recently, there have been two nonexclusive tendencies in our understanding of the medieval period and what follows. Some scholars emphasize the continuities between

Pilgrims leaving Canterbury, ca. 1420. For more information about this image, see the color insert in this volume.

the Middle Ages and the later time now often called the Early Modern Period. Others emphasize the ways in which sixteenth-century writers in some sense "created" the Middle Ages, in order to highlight what they saw as the brilliance of their own time. Medieval authors, of course, did not think of themselves as living in the "middle"; they sometimes expressed the idea that the world was growing old and that theirs was a declining age, close to the end of time. Yet art, literature, and science flourished during the Middle Ages, rooted in the Christian culture that preserved, transmitted, and transformed classical tradition.

The works covered in this section of the anthology encompass a period of more than eight hundred years, from Cædmon's *Hymn* at the end of the seventh century to *Everyman* at the beginning of the sixteenth. The date 1485, the year of the accession of Henry VII and the beginning of the Tudor dynasty, is an arbitrary but convenient one to mark the "end" of the Middle Ages in England.

Although the Roman Catholic Church provided continuity, the period was one of enormous historical, social, and linguistic change. To emphasize these changes and the events underlying them, we have divided the period into three primary sections: Anglo-Saxon Literature, Anglo-Norman Literature, and Middle English Literature in the Fourteenth and Fifteenth Centuries. The Anglo-Saxon invaders, who began their conquest of the southeastern part of Britain around 450, spoke an early form of the language we now call Old English. Old English displays its kinship with other Germanic languages (German or Dutch, for example) much more clearly than does contemporary British and American English, of which Old English is the ancestor. As late as the tenth century, part of an Old Saxon poem written on the Continent was transcribed and transliterated into the West Saxon dialect of Old English without presenting problems to its English readers. In form and content Old English literature also has much in common with other Germanic literatures with which it shared a body of heroic as well as Christian stories. The major characters in *Beowulf* are pagan Danes and Geats, and the only connection to England is an obscure allusion to the ancestor of one of the kings of the Angles.

The changes already in progress in the language and culture of Anglo-Saxon England were greatly accelerated by the Norman Conquest of 1066. The ascendancy of a French-speaking ruling class had the effect of adding a vast number of French loan words to the English vocabulary. The conquest resulted in new forms of political organization and administration, architecture, and literary expression. In the twelfth century, through the interest of the Anglo-Normans in British history before the Anglo-Saxon Conquest, not only England but all of Western Europe became fascinated with a legendary hero named Arthur who makes his earliest appearances in Celtic literature. King Arthur and his knights became a staple subject of medieval French, English, and German literature. Selections from Latin, French, and Old Irish, as well as from Early Middle English have been included here to give a sense of the cross-currents of languages and literatures in Anglo-Norman England and to provide background for later English literature in all periods.

Literature in English was performed orally and written throughout the Middle Ages, but the awareness of and pride in a uniquely *English* literature

did not actually exist before the late fourteenth century. In 13
began a war to enforce his claims to the throne of France; the
intermittently for more than one hundred years until finally the
driven from all their French territories, except for the port of Cal.
One result of the war and these losses was a keener sense on
England's nobility of their English heritage and identity. Toward t
the fourteenth century English finally began to displace French a
guage for conducting business in Parliament and much official co
dence. Although the high nobility continued to speak French by pre
they were certainly bilingual, whereas some of the earlier Norman kir
known no English at all. It was becoming possible to obtain patron
literary achievement in English. The decision of Chaucer (d. 1400) to
late French and Italian poetry in his own vernacular is an indication o
change taking place in the status of English, and Chaucer's works v.
greatly to enhance the prestige of English as a vehicle for literature of high
ambition. He was acclaimed by fifteenth-century poets as the embellisher
of the English tongue; later writers called him the English Homer and the
father of English poetry. His friend John Gower (ca. 1330–1408) wrote long
poems in French and Latin before producing his last major work, the *Confessio Amantis* (The Lover's Confession), which in spite of its Latin title is composed in English.

The third and longest of the three primary sections, Middle English Literature in the Fourteenth and Fifteenth Centuries, is thus not only a chronological and linguistic division but implies a new sense of English as a
literary medium that could compete with French and Latin in elegance and
seriousness.

Book production throughout the medieval period was an expensive
process. Until the invention of moveable type in the mid-fifteenth century
(introduced into England by Caxton in 1476), medieval books were reproduced by hand in manuscript (literally "written by hand"). While paper
became increasingly common for less expensive manuscripts in the fifteenth century, manuscripts were until then written on carefully prepared
animal (usually calf or sheep) skin, known as parchment or vellum. More
expensive books could be illuminated both by colored and calligraphic let-
tering, and by visual images.

The institutions of book production developed across the period. In the
Anglo-Saxon period monasteries were the main centers of book production
and storage. Until their dissolution in the 1530s, monastic and other religious houses continued to produce books, but from the early fourteenth
century, particularly in London, commercial book-making enterprises came
into being. These were loose organizations of various artisans such as parch-
mentmakers, scribes, flourishers, illuminators, and binders, who usually
lived in the same neighborhoods in towns. A bookseller or dealer (usually
a member of one of these trades) would coordinate the production of books
to order for wealthy patrons, sometimes distributing the work of copying
to different scribes, who would be responsible for different gatherings, or
quires, of the same book. Such shops could call upon the services of professional scribes working in the bureaucracies of the royal court.

The market for books also changed across the period: while monasteries,
other religious houses, and royal courts continued to fund the production

6 ... om the Anglo-Norman period books were also produced for (and ... s by) noble and gentry households. From the fourteenth century of br ...et was widened yet further, with wealthy urban patrons also order- ...sks. Some of these books were dedicated to single works, some largely ...gle genres; most were much more miscellaneous, containing texts of ...y kinds and (particularly in the Anglo-Norman period) written in differ- ... languages (especially Latin, French, and English). Only a small propor- ...on of medieval books survive; large numbers were destroyed at the time of the dissolution of the monasteries in the 1530s.

Texts in Old English, Early Middle English, the more difficult texts in later Middle English (*Sir Gawain and the Green Knight, Piers Plowman*), and those in other languages are given in translation. Chaucer and other Middle English works may be read in the original, even by the beginner, with the help of marginal glosses and notes. These texts have been spelled in a way that is intended to aid the reader. Analyses of the sounds and grammar of Middle English and of Old and Middle English prosody are presented on pages 19–25.

ANGLO-SAXON LITERATURE

From the first to the fifth century, England was a province of the Roman Empire and was named Britannia after its Celtic-speaking inhabitants, the Britons. The Britons adapted themselves to Roman civilization, of which the ruins survived to impress the poet of *The Wanderer*, who refers to them as "the ancient works of giants." The withdrawal of the Roman legions during the fifth century, in a vain attempt to protect Rome itself from the threat of Germanic conquest, left the island vulnerable to seafaring Germanic invad- ers. These belonged primarily to three related tribes, the Angles, the Saxons, and the Jutes. The name *English* derives from the Angles, and the names of the counties Essex, Sussex, and Wessex refer to the territories occupied by the East, South, and West Saxons.

The Anglo-Saxon occupation was no sudden conquest but extended over decades of fighting against the native Britons. The latter were, finally, largely confined to the mountainous region of Wales, where the modern form of their language is spoken alongside English to this day. The Britons had become Christians in the fourth century after the conversion of Emperor Constan- tine along with most of the rest of the Roman Empire, but for about 150 years after the beginning of the invasion, Christianity was maintained only in the remoter regions where the as yet pagan Anglo-Saxons failed to penetrate. In the year 597, however, a Benedictine monk (afterward St. Augustine of Can- terbury) was sent by Pope Gregory as a missionary to King Ethelbert of Kent, the most southerly of the kingdoms into which England was then divided, and about the same time missionaries from Ireland began to preach Christi- anity in the north. Within 75 years the island was once more predominantly Christian. Before Christianity there had been no books. The impact of Chris- tianity on literacy is evident from the fact that the first extended written specimen of the Old English (Anglo-Saxon) language is a code of laws pro- mulgated by Ethelbert, the first English Christian king.

In the centuries that followed the conversion, England produced many distinguished churchmen. One of the earliest of these was Bede, whose Latin *Ecclesiastical History of the English People*, which tells the story of the conversion and of the English church, was completed in 731; this remains one of our most important sources of knowledge about the period. In the next generation Alcuin (735–804), a man of wide culture, became the friend and adviser of the Frankish emperor Charlemagne, whom he assisted in making the Frankish court a great center of learning; thus by the year 800 English culture had developed so richly that it overflowed its insular boundaries.

Lindisfarne Gospels. Opening of Gospel of St. Matthew, ca. 698. The veil of mysteries is drawn aside, and the author of the gospel text copies his book as if by divine dictation.

In the ninth century the Christian Anglo-Saxons were themselves subjected to new Germanic invasions by the Danes who in their longboats repeatedly ravaged the coast, sacking Bede's monastery among others. Such a raid late in the tenth century inspired *The Battle of Maldon*, the last of the Old English heroic poems. The Danes also occupied the northern part of the island, threatening to overrun the rest. They were stopped by Alfred, king of the West Saxons from 871 to 899, who for a time united all the kingdoms of southern England. This most active king was also an enthusiastic patron of literature. He himself translated various works from Latin, the most important of which was Boethius's *Consolation of Philosophy*, a sixth-century Roman work also translated in the fourteenth century by Chaucer. Alfred probably also instigated a translation of Bede's *History* and the beginning of the *Anglo-Saxon Chronicle*: this year-by-year record in Old English of important events in England was maintained at one monastery until the middle of the twelfth century. Practically all of Old English poetry is preserved in copies made in the West Saxon dialect after the reign of Alfred.

Old English Poetry

The Anglo-Saxon invaders brought with them a tradition of oral poetry (see "Bede and Cædmon's *Hymn*," p. 29). Because nothing was written down before the conversion to Christianity, we have only circumstantial evidence of what that poetry must have been like. Aside from a few short inscriptions on small artifacts, the earliest records in the English language are in manuscripts produced at monasteries and other religious establishments, beginning in the seventh century. Literacy was mainly restricted to servants of the church, and so it is natural that the bulk of Old English literature deals with religious subjects and is mostly drawn from Latin sources. Under the expensive conditions of manuscript production, few texts were written down that did not pertain directly to the work of the church. Most of Old English poetry is contained in just four manuscripts.

Germanic heroic poetry continued to be performed orally in alliterative verse and was at times used to describe current events. *The Battle of Brunanburh*, which celebrates an English victory over the Danes in traditional alliterative verse, is preserved in the *Anglo-Saxon Chronicle*. *The Battle of Maldon* (in the supplemental ebook) commemorates a Viking victory in which the Christian English invoke the ancient code of honor that obliges a warrior to avenge his slain lord or to die beside him.

These poems show that the aristocratic heroic and kinship values of Germanic society continued to inspire both clergy and laity in the Christian era. As represented in the relatively small body of Anglo-Saxon heroic poetry that survives, this world shares many characteristics with the heroic world described by Homer. Nations are reckoned as groups of people related by kinship rather than by geographical areas, and kinship is the basis of the heroic code. The tribe is ruled by a chieftain who is called *king*, a word that has "kin" for its root. The *lord* (a word derived from Old English *hlaf*, "loaf," plus *weard*, "protector") surrounds himself with a band of retainers (many of them his blood kindred) who are members of his household. He leads his men in battle and rewards them with the spoils; royal generosity was one of the most important aspects of heroic behavior. In return, the retainers are obligated to fight for their lord to the death, and if he is slain, to avenge him or die in the attempt. Blood vengeance is regarded as a sacred duty, and in poetry, everlasting shame awaits those who fail to observe it.

Even though the heroic world of poetry could be invoked to rally resistance to the Viking invasions, it was already remote from the Christian world of Anglo-Saxon England. Nevertheless, Christian writers like the *Beowulf* poet were fascinated by the distant culture of their pagan ancestors and by the inherent conflict between the heroic code and a religion that teaches that we should "forgive those who trespass against us" and that "all they that take the sword shall perish with the sword." The *Beowulf* poet looks back on that ancient world with admiration for the courage of which it was capable and at the same time with elegiac sympathy for its inevitable doom.

For Anglo-Saxon poetry, it is difficult and probably futile to draw a line between "heroic" and "Christian," for the best poetry crosses that boundary. Much of the Christian poetry is also cast in the heroic mode: although the Anglo-Saxons adapted themselves readily to the ideals of Christianity, they did not do so without adapting Christianity to their own heroic ideal. Thus Moses and St. Andrew, Christ and God the Father are represented in the style of heroic verse. In *The Dream of the Rood*, the Cross speaks of Christ as "this young man, . . . strong and courageous." In Cædmon's *Hymn* the creation of heaven and earth is seen as a mighty deed, an "establishment of wonders." Anglo-Saxon heroines, too, are portrayed in the heroic manner. St. Helena, who leads an expedition to the Holy Land to discover the true Cross, is described as a "battle-queen." The biblical narrative related in the Anglo-Saxon poem *Judith* is recast in the terms of Germanic heroic poetry. Christian and heroic ideals are poignantly blended in *The Wanderer*, which laments the separation from one's lord and kinsmen and the transience of all earthly treasures. Love between man and woman, as described by the female speaker of *The Wife's Lament*, is disrupted by separation, exile, and the malice of kinfolk.

The world of Old English poetry is often elegiac. Men are said to be cheerful in the mead hall, but even there they think of war, of possible triumph but more possible failure. Romantic love—one of the principal topics of later literature—appears hardly at all. Even so, at some of the bleakest moments, the poets powerfully recall the return of spring. The blade of the magic sword with which Beowulf has killed Grendel's mother in her sinister underwater lair begins to melt, "as ice melts / when the Father eases the fetters off the frost / and unravels the water ropes, He who wields power."

The poetic diction, formulaic phrases, and repetitions of parallel syntactic structures, which are determined by the versification, are difficult to reproduce in modern translation. A few features may be anticipated here and studied in the text of Cædmon's *Hymn*, printed below (pp. 29–32) with interlinear translation.

Poetic language is created out of a special vocabulary that contains a multiplicity of terms for *lord, warrior, spear, shield*, and so on. Synecdoche and metonymy are common figures of speech, as when "keel" is used for *ship* or "iron" for *sword*. A particularly striking effect is achieved by the kenning, a compound of two words in place of another as when *sea* becomes "whale-road" or *body* is called "life-house." The figurative use of language finds playful expression in poetic riddles, of which about one hundred survive. Common (and sometimes uncommon) creatures, objects, or phenomena are described in an enigmatic passage of alliterative verse, and the reader must guess their identity. Sometimes they are personified and ask, "What is my name?"

Because special vocabulary and compounds are among the chief poetic effects, the verse is constructed in such a way as to show off such terms by creating a series of them in apposition. In the second sentence of Cædmon's *Hymn*, for example, God is referred to five times appositively as "he," "holy Creator," "mankind's Guardian," "eternal Lord," and "Master Almighty." This use of parallel and appositive expressions, known as *variation*, gives the verse a highly structured and musical quality.

The overall effect of the language is to formalize and elevate speech. Instead of being straightforward, it moves at a slow and stately pace with steady indirection. A favorite mode of this indirection is irony. A grim irony pervades heroic poetry even at the level of diction where *fighting* is called "battle-play." A favorite device, known by the rhetorical term *litotes*, is ironic understatement. After the monster Grendel has slaughtered the Danes in the great hall Heorot, it stands deserted. The poet observes, "It was easy then to meet with a man / shifting himself to a safer distance."

More than a figure of thought, irony is also a mode of perception in Old English poetry. In a famous passage, the Wanderer articulates the theme of *Ubi sunt?* (where are they now?): "Where did the steed go? Where the young warrior? Where the treasure-giver? . . ." *Beowulf* is full of ironic balances and contrasts—between the aged Danish king and the youthful Beowulf, and between Beowulf, the high-spirited young warrior at the beginning, and Beowulf, the gray-haired king at the end, facing the dragon and death.

The formal and dignified speech of Old English poetry was always distant from the everyday language of the Anglo-Saxons, and this poetic idiom remained remarkably uniform throughout the roughly three hundred years that separate Cædmon's *Hymn* from *The Battle of Maldon*. This clinging to old forms—grammatical and orthographic as well as literary—by the Anglo-Saxon church and aristocracy conceals from us the enormous changes that were taking place in the English language and the diversity of its dialects. The dramatic changes between Old and Middle English did not happen overnight or over the course of a single century. The Normans displaced the English ruling class with their own barons and clerics, whose native language was a dialect of Old French that we call Anglo-Norman. Without a ruling literate class to preserve English traditions, the custom of transcribing vernacular texts in an earlier form of the West-Saxon dialect was abandoned, and both language and literature were allowed to develop unchecked in new directions.

For examples of Irish medieval literature, see the excerpt from the Old Irish epic *Táin Bó Cuailnge* (The Cattle Raid of Cooley) and some delightful monastic lyrics.

ANGLO-NORMAN LITERATURE

The Normans, who took possession of England after the decisive Battle of Hastings (1066), were, like the Anglo-Saxons, descendants of Germanic adventurers, who at the beginning of the tenth century had seized a wide part of northern France. Their name is actually a contraction of "Norsemen." A highly adaptable people, they had adopted the French language of the land they had settled in and its Christian religion. Both in Normandy and in Britain they were great builders of castles, with which they enforced their political dominance, and magnificent churches. Norman bishops, who held land and castles like the barons, wielded both political and spiritual authority. The earlier Norman kings of England, however, were often absentee rulers, as much concerned with defending their Continental possessions as with ruling over their English holdings. The English Crown's French territories were enormously increased in 1154 when Henry II, the first of England's Plantagenet kings, ascended the throne. Through his marriage with Eleanor of Aquitaine, the divorced wife of Louis VII of France, Henry had acquired vast provinces in the southwest of France.

The presence of a French-speaking ruling class in England created exceptional opportunities for linguistic and cultural exchange. Four languages coexisted in the realm of Anglo-Norman England: Latin, as it had been for Bede, remained the international language of learning, used for theology, science, and history. It was not by any means a written language only but also a lingua franca by which different nationalities communicated in the church and the newly founded universities. The Norman aristocracy for the most part spoke French, but intermarriage with the native English nobility and the business of daily life between masters and servants encouraged bilingualism. Different branches of the Celtic language group were spoken in Scotland, Ireland, Wales, Cornwall, and Brittany.

Inevitably, there was also literary intercourse among the different languages. The Latin Bible and Latin saints' lives provided subjects for a great deal of Old English as well as Old French poetry and prose. The first medi-

King Harold Fatally Struck in the Eye. Bayeux Tapestry, textile, ca. 1070–80. The decisive historical moment is captured as Harold falls victim to irrepressible horizontal attack. Note the dead being stripped of their armor, in the margins.

eval drama in the vernacular, *The Play of Adam*, with elaborate stage directions in Latin and realistic dialogue in the Anglo-Norman dialect of French, was probably produced in England during the twelfth century.

The Anglo-Norman aristocracy was especially attracted to Celtic legends and tales that had been circulating orally for centuries. The twelfth-century poets Thomas of England, Marie de France, and Chrétien de Troyes each claim to have obtained their narratives from Breton storytellers, who were probably bilingual performers of native tales for French audiences. *Sir Orfeo* may represent the kind of lay that served as a model for Marie. "Breton" may indicate that they came from Brittany, or it may have been a generic term for a Celtic bard. Marie speaks respectfully of the storytellers, while Thomas expresses caution about their tendency to vary narratives; Chrétien accuses them of marring their material, which, he boasts, he has retold with an elegant fusion of form and meaning. Marie wrote a series of short romances, which she refers to as "lays" originally told by Bretons. Her versions are the most original and sophisticated examples of the genre that came to be known as the Breton lay, represented here by Marie's *Milun*, *Lanval*, and *Chevrefoil*. It is very likely that Henry II is the "noble king" to whom she dedicated her lays and that they were written for his court. Thomas composed a moving, almost operatic version of the adulterous passion of Tristran and Ysolt, very different from the powerful version of the same story by Beroul, also composed in the last half of the twelfth century. Chrétien is the principal creator of the romance of chivalry in which knightly adventures are a means of exploring psychological and ethical dilemmas that the knights must solve, in addition to displaying martial prowess in saving ladies from monsters, giants, and wicked knights. Chrétien, like Marie, is thought to have spent time in England at the court of Henry II.

Thomas, Marie, and Chrétien de Troyes were innovators of the genre that has become known as "romance." The word *roman* was initially applied in French to a work written in the French vernacular. Thus the thirteenth-century *Roman de Troie* is a long poem about the Trojan War in French. While this work deals mainly with the siege of Troy, it also includes stories about the love of Troilus for Cressida and of Achilles for the Trojan princess Polyxena. Eventually, "romance" acquired the generic associations it has for us as a story about love and adventure.

Romance was the principal narrative genre for late medieval readers. Insofar as it was centrally concerned with love, it developed ways of representing psychological interiority with great subtlety. That subtlety itself provoked a sub-genre of questions about love. Thus in the late twelfth century, Andreas Capellanus (Andrew the Chaplain) wrote a Latin treatise, the title of which may be translated *The Art of Loving Correctly* [*honeste*]. In one part, Eleanor of Aquitaine, her daughter, the countess Marie de Champagne, and other noble women are cited as a supreme court rendering decisions on difficult questions of love—for example, whether there is greater passion between lovers or between married couples. Whether such "courts of love" were purely imaginary or whether they represent some actual court entertainment, they imply that the literary taste and judgment of women had a significant role in fostering the rise of romance in France and Anglo-Norman England.

In Marie's *Lanval* and in Chrétien's romances, the court of King Arthur had already acquired for French audiences a reputation as the most famous center of chivalry. That eminence is owing in large measure to a remarkable book in Latin, *The History of the Kings of Britain*, completed by Geoffrey of Monmouth, ca. 1136–38. Geoffrey claimed to have based his "history" on a book in the British tongue (i.e., Welsh), but no one has ever found such a book. He drew on a few earlier Latin chronicles, but the bulk of his history was probably fabricated from Celtic oral tradition, his familiarity with Roman history and literature, and his own fertile imagination. The climax of the book is the reign of King Arthur, who defeats the Roman armies but is forced to turn back to Britain to counter the treachery of his nephew Mordred. In 1155 Geoffrey's Latin was rendered into French rhyme by an Anglo-Norman poet called Wace, and fifty or so years later Wace's poem was turned by Layamon, an English priest, into a much longer poem that combines English alliterative verse with sporadic rhyme.

Layamon's work is one of many instances where English receives new material directly through French sources, which may be drawn from Celtic or Latin sources. There are two Middle English versions of Marie's *Lanval*, and the English romance called *Yvain and Gawain* is a cruder version of Chrétien's *Le Chevalier au Lion* (The Knight of the Lion). A marvelous English lay, *Sir Orfeo*, is a version of the Orpheus story in which Orpheus succeeds in rescuing his wife from the other world, for which a French original, if there was one, has never been found. Romance, stripped of its courtly, psychological, and ethical subtleties, had an immense popular appeal for English readers and listeners. Many of these romances are simplified adaptations of more aristocratic French poems and recount in a rollicking and rambling style the adventures of heroes like Guy of Warwick, a poor steward who must prove his knightly worth to win the love of Fair Phyllis. The ethos of many romances, aristocratic and popular alike, involves a knight proving his worthiness through nobility of character and brave deeds rather than through high birth. In this respect romances reflect the aspirations of a lower order of the nobility to rise in the world, as historically some of these nobles did. William the Marshall, for example, the fourth son of a baron of middle rank, used his talents in war and in tournaments to become tutor to the oldest son of Henry II and Eleanor of Aquitaine. He married a great heiress and became one of the most powerful nobles in England and the subject of a verse biography in French, which often reads like a romance.

Of course, not all writing in Early Middle English depends on French sources or intermediaries. The *Anglo-Saxon Chronicle* continued to be written at the monastery of Peterborough. It is an invaluable witness for the changes taking place in the English language and allows us to see Norman rule from an English point of view. *The Owl and the Nightingale* (?late twelfth century) is a witty and entertaining poem in which these two female birds engage in a fierce debate about the benefits their singing brings to humankind. The owl grimly reminds her rival of the sinfulness of the human condition, which her mournful song is intended to amend; the nightingale sings about the pleasures of life and love when lord and lady are in bed together. The poet, who was certainly a cleric, is well aware of the fashionable new romance literature; he specifically has the nightingale allude to Marie de France's lay *Laüstic*, the Breton word, she says, for "rossignol" in French and "nightingale" in English. The poet does not side with either bird; rather he has amusingly created the sort of dialectic between the discourses of religion and romance that is carried on throughout medieval literature.

There is also a body of Early Middle English religious prose aimed at women. Three saints' lives celebrate the heroic combats of virgin martyrs who suffer dismemberment and death; a tract entitled *Holy Maidenhead* paints the woes of marriage not from the point of view of the husband, as in standard medieval antifeminist writings, but from that of the wife. Related to these texts, named the Katherine Group after one of the virgin martyrs, is a religious work also written for women but in a very different spirit. The *Ancrene Wisse* (Anchoresses' Guide) is one of the finest works of English religious prose in any period. It is a manual of instruction written at the request of three sisters who have chosen to live as religious recluses. The author, who may have been their personal confessor, addresses them with affection, and, at times, with kindness and humor. He is also profoundly serious in his analyses of sin, penance, and love. In the selection included here from his chapter on penance, he imagines the enclosed life in richly metaphorical ways, mixing pleasure strangely with pain.

MIDDLE ENGLISH LITERATURE IN THE FOURTEENTH AND FIFTEENTH CENTURIES

The styles of *The Owl and the Nightingale* and *Ancrene Wisse* show that around the year 1200 both poetry and prose were being written for sophisticated and well-educated readers whose primary language was English. Throughout the thirteenth and early fourteenth centuries, there are many kinds of evidence that, although French continued to be the principal language of Parliament, law, business, and high culture, English was gaining

The City. Ambrogio Lorenzetti, *Effects of Good Government in the City,* 1338–39. The extraordinary energies of urban culture are set in a dynamic relation of peace and competition: the external walls of the city protect against outside invasion, even as the skyscrapers compete for space and power within the city.

ground. Several authors of religious and didactic works in English state that they are writing for the benefit of those who do not understand Latin or French. Anthologies were made of miscellaneous works adapted from French for English readers and original pieces in English. Most of the nobility were by now bilingual, and the author of an English romance written early in the fourteenth century declares that he has seen many nobles who cannot speak French. Children of the nobility and the merchant class were now learning French as a second language. By the 1360s the linguistic, political, and cultural climate had been prepared for the flowering of Middle English literature in the writings of Chaucer, Gower, Langland, and the *Gawain* poet.

The Fourteenth Century

War and disease were prevalent throughout the Middle Ages but never more devastatingly than during the fourteenth century. In the wars against France, the gains of two spectacular English victories, at Crécy in 1346 and Poitiers in 1356, were gradually frittered away in futile campaigns that ravaged the French countryside without obtaining any clear advantage for the English. In 1348 the first and most virulent epidemic of the bubonic plague—the Black Death—swept Europe, wiping out a quarter to a third of the population. The toll was higher in crowded urban centers. Giovanni Boccaccio's description of the plague in Florence, with which he introduces the *Decameron,* vividly portrays its ravages: "So many corpses would arrive in front of a church every day and at every hour that the amount of holy ground for burials was certainly insufficient for the ancient custom of giving each body its individual place; when all the graves were full, huge trenches were dug in all of the cemeteries of the churches and into them the new arrivals were dumped by the hundreds; and they were packed in there with dirt, one on top of another, like a ship's cargo, until the trench was filled." The resulting scarcity of labor and a sudden expansion of the possibilities for social mobility fostered popular discontent. In 1381 attempts to enforce wage controls and to collect oppressive new taxes provoked a rural uprising in Essex and Kent that dealt a profound shock to the English ruling class. The participants were for the most part tenant farmers, day laborers, apprentices, and rural workers not attached to the big manors. A few of the lower clergy sided with the rebels against their wealthy church superiors; the priest John Ball was among the leaders. The movement was quickly suppressed, but not before sympathizers in London had admitted the rebels through two city gates, which had been barred against them. The insurgents burned down the palace of the hated duke of Lancaster, and they summarily beheaded the archbishop of Canterbury and the treasurer of England, who had taken refuge in the Tower of London. The church had become the target of popular resentment because it was among the greatest of the oppressive landowners and because of the wealth, worldliness, and venality of many of the higher clergy.

These calamities and upheavals nevertheless did not stem the growth of international trade and the influence of the merchant class. In the portrait of Geoffrey Chaucer's merchant, we see the budding of capitalism based on credit and interest. Cities like London ran their own affairs under politically powerful mayors and aldermen. Edward III, chronically in need of money to finance his wars, was obliged to negotiate for revenues with the Commons in the English Parliament, an institution that became a major political force during this period. A large part of the king's revenues depended on taxing the profitable export of English wool to the Continent. The Crown thus became involved in the country's economic affairs, and this involvement led to a need for capable administrators. These were no longer drawn mainly from the church, as in the past, but from a newly educated laity that occupied a rank somewhere between that of the lesser nobility and the upper bourgeoisie. The career of Chaucer, who served Edward III and his successor Richard II in a number of civil posts, is typical of this class—with the exception that Chaucer was also a great poet.

In the fourteenth century, a few poets and intellectuals achieved the status and respect formerly accorded only to the ancients. Marie de France and Chrétien de Troyes had dedicated their works to noble patrons and, in their role as narrators, address themselves as entertainers and sometimes as instructors to court audiences. Dante (1265–1321) made himself the protagonist of *The Divine Comedy*, the sacred poem, as he called it, in which he revealed the secrets of the afterlife. After his death, manuscripts of the work were provided with lengthy commentaries as though it were Scripture, and public readings and lectures were devoted to it. Francis Petrarch (1304–1374) won an international reputation as a man of letters. He wrote primarily in Latin and contrived to have himself crowned "poet laureate" in emulation of the Roman poets whose works he imitated, but his most famous work is the sonnet sequence he wrote in Italian. Giovanni Boccaccio (1313–1375) was among Petrarch's most ardent admirers and carried on a literary correspondence with him.

Chaucer read these authors along with the ancient Roman poets and drew on them in his own works. Chaucer's *Clerk's Tale* is based on a Latin version Petrarch made from the last tale in Boccaccio's *Decameron*; in his prologue, the Clerk refers to Petrarch as "lauriat poete" whose sweet rhetoric illuminated all Italy with his poetry. Yet in his own time, the English poet Chaucer never attained the kind of laurels that he and others accorded to Petrarch. In his earlier works, Chaucer portrayed himself comically as a diligent reader of old books, as an aspiring apprentice writer, and as an eager spectator on the fringe of a fashionable world of courtiers and poets. In *The House of Fame*, he relates a dream of being snatched up by a huge golden eagle (the eagle and many other things in this work were inspired by Dante), who transports him to the palace of the goddess Fame. There he gets to see phantoms, like the shades in Dante's poem, of all the famous authors of antiquity. At the end of his romance *Troilus and Criseyde*, Chaucer asks his "litel book" to kiss the footsteps where the great ancient poets had passed before. Like Dante and Petrarch, Chaucer had an ideal of great poetry and, in his *Troilus* at least, strove to emulate it. But in *The House of Fame* and in his final work, *The Canterbury Tales*, he also views that ideal ironically and distances himself from it. The many surviving documents that record Geoffrey Chaucer's career as a civil servant do not contain a single word to show that he was also a poet. Only in the following centuries would he be canonized as the father of English poetry.

Chaucer is unlikely to have known his contemporary William Langland, who says in an autobiographical passage (see pp. 392–95), added to the third and last version of his great poem *Piers Plowman*, that he lived in London on Cornhill (a poor area of the city) among "lollers." "Loller" was a slang term for the unemployed and transients; it was later applied to followers of the religious and social reformer John Wycliffe, some of whom were burned at the stake for heresy in the next century. Langland assailed corruption in church and state, but he was certainly no radical. It is thought that he may have written the third version of *Piers Plowman*, which tones down his attacks on the church, after the rebels of 1381 invoked Piers as one of their own. Although Langland does not condone rebellion and his religion is not revolutionary, he nevertheless presents the most clear-sighted vision of social and religious issues in the England of his day. *Piers Plowman* is also a painfully honest search for the right way that leads to salvation. Though learned himself, Langland and the dreamer who represents him in the poem arrive at the insight that learning can be one of the chief obstacles on that way.

Langland came from the west of England, and his poem belongs to the "Alliterative Revival," a final flowering in the late fourteenth century of the verse form that goes all the way back to Anglo-Saxon England. Anglo-Saxon traditions held out longest in the west and north, away from London, where Chaucer and his audience were more open to literary fashions from the Continent.

John Gower is a third major late fourteenth-century English poet. While his first and second large works are written in French and Latin verse respectively, his *Confessio Amantis* (1390) is written in English four-stress couplets. Gower's first two works are severe satires; the *Confessio*, by contrast, broaches political and ethical issues from an oblique angle. Its primary narrative concerns the treatment of a suffering lover. His therapy consists of listening to, and understanding, many other narratives, many of which are drawn from classical sources. Like Chaucer, Gower anglicizes and absorbs classical Latin literature.

Admiration for the poetry of both Chaucer and Gower and the controversial nature of Langland's writing assured the survival of their work in many manuscripts. The work of a fourth major fourteenth-century English poet, who remains anonymous, is known only through a single manuscript, which contains four poems all thought to be by a single author: *Cleanness* and *Patience*, two biblical narratives in alliterative verse; *Pearl*, a moving dream vision in which a grief-stricken father is visited and consoled by his dead child, who has been transformed into a queen in the kingdom of heaven; and *Sir Gawain and the Green Knight*, the finest of all English romances. The plot of *Gawain* involves a folklore motif of a challenge by a supernatural visitor, first found in an Old Irish tale. The poet has made this motif a challenge to King Arthur's court and has framed the tale with allusions at the beginning and end to the legends that link Arthur's reign with the Trojan War and the founding of Rome and of Britain. The poet has a sophisticated awareness of romance as a literary genre and plays a game with both the hero's and the reader's expectations of what is supposed to happen in a romance. One could say that the broader subject of *Sir Gawain and the Green Knight* is "romance" itself, and in this respect the poem resembles Chaucer's *Canterbury Tales* in its author's interest in literary form.

Julian of Norwich is a fifth major writer of this period. The first known woman writer in the English vernacular, the anchoress Julian participates in a Continental tradition of vision- ary writings, often by women. She spent a good deal of her life medi- tating and writing about a series of visions, which she called "show- ings," that she had received in 1373, when she was thirty years old. While very carefully negotiating the dangers of writing as a woman, and of writing sophisticated theology in the vernacular, Julian manages to produce visionary writing that is at once penetrating and serene.

The Fifteenth Century

In 1399 Henry Bolingbroke, the duke of Lancaster, deposed his cousin Richard II, who was mur- dered in prison. As Henry IV, he successfully defended his crown against several insurrections and passed it on to Henry V, who briefly united the country once more and achieved one last apparently deci- sive victory over the French at the Battle of Agincourt (1415). The pre- mature death of Henry V in 1422, however, left England exposed to the civil wars known as the Wars of the Roses, the red rose being the emblem of the house of Lancaster;

The Seasons. Limbourg Brothers, "Febru- ary," from *Les Très Riches Heures du Duc de Berry* (ca. 1411–16). The calm inevitability of cosmic, seasonal change is set above the uncertain yet inventive struggle of peasants, for heat and food, in the main frame.

the white, of York. These wars did not end until 1485, when Henry Tudor defeated Richard III at Bosworth Field and acceded to the throne as Henry VII.

The most prolific poet of the fifteenth century was the monk John Lydgate (1371?–1449), who produced dream visions; a life of the Virgin; translations of French religious allegories; a *Troy Book*; *The Siege of Thebes*, which he framed as a "new" Canterbury tale; and a thirty-six-thousand-line poem called *The Fall of Princes*, a free translation of a French work, itself based on a Latin work by Boccaccio. The last illustrates the late medieval idea of tragedy, namely that emperors, kings, and other famous men enjoy power and fortune only to be cast down in misery. Lydgate shapes these tales as a "mirror" for princes, i.e., as object lessons to the powerful men of his own day, several of whom were his patrons. A self-styled imitator of Chaucer, Lydgate had a reputation almost equal to Chaucer's in the fifteenth century. The other significant poet of the first half of the fifteenth century is Thomas Hoccleve (1367?–1426). Like Lydgate, Hoccleve also wrote for powerful Lancastrian patrons, but his poetry is strikingly private, painfully concerned as it often is with his penury and mental instability. The searing poem *My Compleinte* is an example of his work.

Religious works of all kinds continued to be produced in the fifteenth century, but under greater surveillance. The Lancastrian authorities responded to the reformist religious movement known as "Lollardy" in draconian ways. They introduced a statute for the burning of heretics (the first such statute) in 1401, and a series of measures designed to survey and censor theology in English in 1409. Despite this, many writers continued to produce religious works in the vernacular. Perhaps the most remarkable of these writers is Margery Kempe (who records her visit to Julian of Norwich in about 1413). Kempe made pilgrimages to the Holy Land, Rome, Santiago, and to shrines in Northern Europe. These she records, in the context of her often fraught and painful personal life, in her *Book of Margery Kempe*. Both Julian of Norwich and Margery Kempe, in highly individual ways, allow us to see the medieval church and its doctrines from female points of view.

Social, economic, and literary life continued as they had throughout all of the previously mentioned wars. The prosperity of the towns was shown by performances of the mystery plays—a sequence or "cycle" of plays based on the Bible and produced by the city guilds, the organizations representing the various trades and crafts. The cycles of several towns are lost, but those of York and Chester have been preserved, along with two other complete cycles, one possibly from Wakefield in Yorkshire, and the other titled the "N-Town" Cycle. Under the guise of dramatizing biblical history, playwrights such as the Wakefield Master manage to comment satirically on the social ills of the times. The century also saw the development of the morality play, in which personified vices and virtues struggle for the soul of "Mankind" or "Everyman." Performed by professional players, the morality plays were precursors of the professional theater in the reign of Elizabeth I.

The best of Chaucer's imitators was Robert Henryson, who, in the last quarter of the fifteenth century, wrote *The Testament of Cresseid*, a continuation of Chaucer's great poem *Troilus and Criseyde*. He also wrote the *Moral Fabilis of Esope,* among which *The Cock and the Fox,* included here, is a remake of Chaucer's *Nun's Priest's Tale.*

The works of Sir Thomas Malory (d. 1471) gave the definitive form in English to the legend of King Arthur and his knights. Malory spent years in prison Englishing a series of Arthurian romances that he translated and abridged chiefly from several enormously long thirteenth-century French prose romances. Malory was a passionate devotee of chivalry, which he personified in his hero Sir Lancelot. In the jealousies and rivalries that finally break up the round table and destroy Arthur's kingdom, Malory saw a distant image of the civil wars of his own time. A manuscript of Malory's works fell into the hands of William Caxton (1422?–1492), who had introduced the new art of printing by movable type to England in 1476. Caxton divided Malory's tales into the chapters and books of a single long work, as though it were a chronicle history, and gave it the title *Morte Darthur*, which has stuck to it ever since. Caxton also printed *The Canterbury Tales*, some of Chaucer's earlier works, and Gower's *Confessio Amantis*. Caxton himself translated many of the works he printed for English readers: a history of Troy, a book on chivalry, Aesop's fables, *The History of Reynard the Fox*, and *The Game and Playe of Chesse*. The new technology extended literacy and made books more easily accessible to new classes of readers. Printing made the production of literature a business and made possible the bitter political and doctrinal disputes that, in the sixteenth century, were waged in print as well as on the field of battle.

MEDIEVAL ENGLISH

The medieval works in this anthology were composed in different states of our language. Old English, the language that took shape among the Germanic settlers of England, preserved its integrity until the Norman Conquest radically altered English civilization. Middle English, the first records of which date from the early twelfth century, was continually changing. Shortly after the introduction of printing at the end of the fifteenth century, it attained the form designated as Early Modern English. Old English is a very heavily inflected language. (That is, the words change form to indicate changes in function, such as person, number, tense, case, mood, and so on. Most languages have some inflection—for example, the personal pronouns in Modern English have different forms when used as objects—but a "heavily inflected" language is one in which almost all classes of words undergo elaborate patterns of change.) The vocabulary of Old English is almost entirely Germanic. In Middle English, the inflectional system was weakened, and a large number of words were introduced into it from French, so that many of the older Anglo-Saxon words disappeared. Because of the difficulty of Old English, all selections from it in this book have been given in translation. So that the reader may see an example of the language, Cædmon's *Hymn* has been printed in the original, together with an interlinear translation. The present discussion, then, is concerned primarily with the relatively late form of Middle English used by Chaucer and the East Midland dialect in which he wrote.

The chief difficulty with Middle English for the modern reader is caused not by its inflections so much as by its spelling, which may be described as a rough-and-ready phonetic system, and by the fact that it is not a single standardized language, but consists of a number of regional dialects, each with its own peculiarities of sound and its own systems for representing sounds in writing. The East Midland dialect—the dialect of London and of Chaucer, which is the ancestor of our own standard speech—differs greatly from the dialect spoken in the west of England (the original dialect of *Piers Plowman*), from that of the northwest (*Sir Gawain and the Green Knight*), and from that of the north (*The Second Shepherds' Play*). In this book, the long texts composed in the more difficult dialects have been translated or modernized, and those that—like Chaucer, Gower, *Everyman,* and the lyrics—appear in the original, have been re-spelled in a way that is designed to aid the reader. The remarks that follow apply chiefly to Chaucer's East Midland English, although certain non-Midland dialectal variations are noted if they occur in some of the other selections.

I. *The Sounds of Middle English: General Rules*

The following general analysis of the sounds of Middle English will enable the reader who does not have time for detailed study to read Middle English aloud and preserve some of its most essential characteristics, without, however, worrying too much about details. The next section, "Detailed Analysis," is designed for the reader who wishes to go more deeply into the pronunciation of Middle English. The best way to absorb the sound of Middle English pronunciation is to listen to it; the StudySpace offers recordings of selections as an aid to this end.

Middle English differs from Modern English in three principal respects: (1) the pronunciation of the long vowels *a, e, i* (or *y*), *o,* and *u* (spelled *ou, ow*); (2) the fact that Middle English final *e* is often sounded; and (3) the fact that all Middle English consonants are sounded.

1. LONG VOWELS

Middle English vowels are long when they are doubled (*aa, ee, oo*) or when they are terminal (*he, to, holy*); *a, e,* and *o* are long when followed by a single consonant plus a vowel (*name, mete, note*). Middle English vowels are short when they are followed by two consonants.

Long *a* is sounded like the *a* in Modern English "father": *maken, madd.*

Long *e* may be sounded like the *a* in Modern English "name" (ignoring the distinction between the close and open vowel): *be, sweete.*

Long *i* (or *y*) is sounded like the *i* in Modern English "machine": *lif, whit; myn, holy.*

Long *o* may be sounded like the *o* in Modern English "note" (again ignoring the distinction between the close and open vowel): *do, soone.*

Long *u* (spelled *ou, ow*) is sounded like the *oo* in Modern English "goose": *hous, flowr.*

Note that in general Middle English long vowels are pronounced like long vowels in modern European languages other than English. Short vowels and diphthongs, however, may be pronounced as in Modern English.

2. FINAL E

In Middle English syllabic verse, final *e* is sounded, like the *a* in "sofa," to provide a needed unstressed syllable: *Another Nonnë with hire haddë she.* But (cf. *hire* in the example) final *e* is suppressed when not needed for the meter. It is commonly silent before words beginning with a vowel or *h*.

3. CONSONANTS

Middle English consonants are pronounced separately in all combinations—*gnat: g-nat; knave: k-nave; write: w-rite; folk: fol-k.* In a simplified system of pronunciation the combination *gh* as in *night* or *thought* may be treated as if it were silent.

II. The Sounds of Middle English: Detailed Analysis

1. SIMPLE VOWELS

Sound	Pronunciation	Example
long *a* (spelled *a, aa*)	*a* in "father"	*maken, maad*
short *a*	*o* in "hot"	*cappe*
long *e* close (spelled *e, ee*)	*a* in "name"	*be, sweete*
long *e* open (spelled *e, ee*)	*e* in "there"	*mete, heeth*
short *e*	*e* in "set"	*setten*
final *e*	*a* in "sofa"	*large*
long *i* (spelled *i, y*)	*i* in "machine"	*lif, myn*
short *i*	*i* in "wit"	*wit*
long *o* close (spelled *o, oo*)	*o* in "note"	*do, soone*
long *o* open (spelled *o, oo*)	*oa* in "broad"	*go, goon*
short *o*	*o* in "oft"	*pot*
long *u* when spelled *ou, ow*	*oo* in "goose"	*hous, flowr*
long *u* when spelled *u*	*u* in "pure"	*vertu*
short *u* (spelled *u, o*)	*u* in "full"	*ful, love*

Doubled vowels and terminal vowels are always long, whereas single vowels before two consonants other than *th, ch* are always short. The vowels *a, e,* and *o* are long before a single consonant followed by a vowel: *nāmë, sēkë* (sick), *hōly*. In general, words that have descended into Modern English reflect their original Middle English quantity: *līven* (to live), but *līf* (life).

The close and open sounds of long *e* and long *o* may often be identified by the Modern English spellings of the words in which they appear. Original long close *e* is generally represented in Modern English by *ee*: "sweet," "knee," "teeth," "see" have close *e* in Middle English, but so does "be"; original long open *e* is generally represented in Modern English by *ea*: "meat," "heath," "sea," "great," "breath" have open *e* in Middle English. Similarly, original long close *o* is now generally represented by *oo*: "soon," "food," "good," but also "do," "to"; original long open *o* is represented either by *oa* or by *o*: "coat," "boat," "moan," but also "go," "bone," "foe," "home." Notice that original close *o* is now almost always pronounced like the *oo* in "goose," but that original open *o* is almost never so pronounced; thus it is often possible to identify the Middle English vowels through Modern English sounds.

The nonphonetic Middle English spelling of *o* for short *u* has been preserved in a number of Modern English words ("love," "son," "come"), but in others *u* has been restored: "sun" (*sonne*), "run" (*ronne*).

For the treatment of final *e*, see "General Rules," "Final *e*."

2. DIPHTHONGS

Sound	Pronunciation	Example
ai, ay, ei, ay	between *ai* in "aisle" and *ay* in "day"	*saide, day, veine, preye*
au, aw	*ou* in "out"	*chaunge, bawdy*
eu, ew	*ew* in "few"	*newe*
oi, oy	*oy* in "joy"	*joye, point*
ou, ow	*ou* in "thought"	*thought, lowe*

Note that in words with *ou, ow* that in Modern English are sounded with the *ou* of "about," the combination indicates not the diphthong but the simple vowel long *u* (see "Simple Vowels").

3. CONSONANTS

In general, all consonants except *h* were always sounded in Middle English, including consonants that have become silent in Modern English, such as the *g* in *gnaw*, the *k* in *knight*, the *I* in *folk*, and the *w* in *write*. In noninitial *gn*, however, the *g* was silent as in Modern English "sign." Initial *h* was silent in short common English words and in words borrowed from French and may have been almost silent in all words. The combination *gh* as in *night* or *thought* was sounded like the *ch* of German *ich* or *nach*. Note that Middle English *gg* represents both the hard sound of "dagger" and the soft sound of "bridge."

III. Parts of Speech and Grammar

1. NOUNS

The plural and possessive of nouns end in *es*, formed by adding *s* or *es* to the singular: *knight, knightes; roote, rootes*; a final consonant is frequently doubled before *es: bed, beddes*. A common irregular plural is *yën*, from *yë*, eye.

2. PRONOUNS

The chief comparisons with Modern English are as follows:

Modern English	East Midlands Middle English
I	*I, ich* (*ik* is a northern form)
you (singular)	*thou* (subjective); *thee* (objective)
her	*hir(e), her(e)*
its	*his*
you (plural)	*ye* (subjective); *you* (objective)
they	*they*
their	*hir* (*their* is a Northern form)
them	*hem* (*them* is a Northern form)

In formal speech, the second-person plural is often used for the singular. The possessive adjectives *my, thy* take *n* before a word beginning with a vowel or *h: thyn yë, myn host*.

3. ADJECTIVES

Adjectives ending in a consonant add final *e* when they stand before the noun they modify and after another modifying word such as *the, this, that*, or nouns or pronouns in the possessive: *a good hors*, but *the (this, my, the kinges) goode hors.* They also generally add *e* when standing before and modifying a plural noun, a noun in the vocative, or any proper noun: *goode men, oh goode man, faire Venus.*

Adjectives are compared by adding *er(e)* for the comparative, *est(e)* for the superlative. Sometimes the stem vowel is shortened or altered in the process: *sweete, swettere, swettest; long, lenger, lengest.*

4. ADVERBS

Adverbs are formed from adjectives by adding *e, ly,* or *liche*; the adjective *fair* thus yields *faire, fairly, fairliche.*

5. VERBS

Middle English verbs, like Modern English verbs, are either "weak" or "strong." Weak verbs form their preterites and past participles with a *t* or *d* suffix and preserve the same stem vowel throughout their systems, although it is sometimes shortened in the preterite and past participle: *love, loved; bend, bent; hear, heard; meet, met.* Strong verbs do not use the *t* or *d* suffix, but vary their stem vowel in the preterite and past participle: *take, took, taken; begin, began, begun; find, found, found.*

The inflectional endings are the same for Middle English strong verbs and weak verbs except in the preterite singular and the imperative singular. In the following paradigms, the weak verbs *loven* (to love) and *heeren* (to hear), and the strong verbs *taken* (to take) and *ginnen* (to begin) serve as models.

	Present Indicative	Preterite Indicative
I	*love, heere*	*loved(e), herde*
	take, ginne	*took, gan*
thou	*lovest, heerest*	*lovedest, herdest*
	takest, ginnest	*tooke, gonne*
he, she, it	*loveth, heereth*	*loved(e), herde*
	taketh, ginneth	*took, gan*
we, ye, they	*love(n) (th), heere(n) (th)*	*loved(e) (en), herde(n)*
	take(n) (th), ginne(n) (th)	*tooke(n), gonne(n)*

The present plural ending *eth* is southern, whereas the *e(n)* ending is Midland and characteristic of Chaucer. In the north, *s* may appear as the ending of all persons of the present. In the weak preterite, when the ending *e* gave a verb three or more syllables, it was frequently dropped. Note that in certain strong verbs like *ginnen* there are two distinct stem vowels in the preterite; even in Chaucer's time, however, one of these had begun to replace the other, and Chaucer occasionally writes *gan* for all persons of the preterite.

	Present Subjunctive	Preterite Subjunctive
Singular	*love, heere*	*lovede, herde*
	take, ginne	*tooke, gonne*
Plural	*love(n), heere(n)*	*lovede(n), herde(n)*
	take(n), ginne(n)	*tooke(n), gonne(n)*

In verbs like *ginnen*, which have two stem vowels in the indicative preterite, it is the vowel of the plural and of the second person singular that is used for the preterite subjunctive.

The imperative singular of most weak verbs is *e: (thou) love*, but of some weak verbs and all strong verbs, the imperative singular is without termination: *(thou) heer, taak, gin*. The imperative plural of all verbs is either *e* or *eth*: *(ye) love(th), heere(th), take(th), ginne(th)*.

The infinitive of verbs is *e* or *en: love(n), heere(n), take(n), ginne(n)*.

The past participle of weak verbs is the same as the preterite without inflectional ending: *loved, herd*. In strong verbs the ending is either *e* or *en: take(n), gonne(n)*. The prefix *y* often appears on past participles: *yloved, yherd, ytake(n)*.

OLD AND MIDDLE ENGLISH PROSODY

All the poetry of Old English is in the same verse form. The verse unit is the single line, because rhyme was not used to link one line to another, except very occasionally in late Old English. The organizing device of the line is alliteration, the beginning of several words with the same sound ("Foemen fled"). The Old English alliterative line contains, on the average, four principal stresses and is divided into two half-lines of two stresses each by a strong medial caesura, or pause. These two half-lines are linked to each other by the alliteration; at least one of the two stressed words in the first half-line, and often both of them, begin with the same sound as the first stressed word of the second half-line (the second stressed word is generally nonalliterative). The fourth line of *Beowulf* is an example (*sc* has the value of modern *sh*; þ is a runic symbol with the value of modern *th*):

> Oft Scyld Scefing   sceaþena þreatum.

For further examples, see Cædmon's *Hymn*. It will be noticed that any vowel alliterates with any other vowel. In addition to the alliteration, the length of the unstressed syllables and their number and pattern is governed by a highly complex set of rules. When sung or intoned—as it was—to the rhythmic strumming of a harp, Old English poetry must have been wonderfully impressive in the dignified, highly formalized way that aptly fits both its subject matter and tone.

The majority of Middle English verse is either in alternately stressed rhyming verse, adapted from French after the conquest, or in alliterative verse that is descended from Old English. The latter preserves the caesura of Old English and in its purest form the same alliterative system, the two stressed words of the first half-line (or at least one of them) alliterating with the first stressed word in the second half-line. But most of the alliterative poets allowed themselves a number of deviations from the norm. All four stressed words may alliterate, as in the first line of *Piers Plowman*:

> In a summer season   when soft was the sun.

Or the line may contain five, six, or even more stressed words, of which all or only the basic minimum may alliterate:

> A fair field full of   folk found I there between.

There is no rule determining the number of unstressed syllables, and at times some poets seem to ignore alliteration entirely. As in Old English, any vowel may alliterate with any other vowel; furthermore, since initial *h* was silent or lightly pronounced in Middle English, words beginning with *h* are treated as though they began with the following vowel.

There are two general types of stressed verse with rhyme. In the more common, unstressed and stressed syllables alternate regularly as x X x X x X or, with two unstressed syllables intervening as x x X x x X x x X or a combination of the two as x x X x X x x X (of the reverse patterns, only X x X x X x is common in English). There is also a line that can only be defined as containing a predetermined number of stressed syllables but an irregular number and pattern of unstressed syllables. Much Middle English verse has to be read without expectation of regularity; some of this was evidently composed in the irregular meter, but some was probably originally composed according to a strict metrical system that has been obliterated by scribes careless of fine points. One receives the impression that many of the lyrics—as well as the *Second Shepherds' Play*—were at least composed with regular syllabic alternation. In the play *Everyman*, only the number of stresses is generally predetermined but not the number or placement of unstressed syllables.

In pre-Chaucerian verse the number of stresses, whether regularly or irregularly alternated, was most often four, although sometimes the number was three and rose in some poems to seven. Rhyme in Middle English (as in Modern English) may be either between adjacent or alternate lines, or may occur in more complex patterns. Most of the *Canterbury Tales* are in rhymed couplets, the line containing five stresses with regular alternation—technically known as iambic pentameter, the standard English poetic line, perhaps introduced into English by Chaucer. In reading Chaucer and much pre-Chaucerian verse, one must remember that the final *e,* which is silent in Modern English, could be pronounced at any time to provide a needed unstressed syllable. Evidence seems to indicate that it was also pronounced at the end of the line, even though it thus produced a line with eleven syllables. Although he was a very regular metricist, Chaucer used various conventional devices that are apt to make the reader stumble until he or she understands them. Final *e* is often not pronounced before a word beginning with a vowel or *h,* and may be suppressed whenever metrically convenient. The same medial and terminal syllables that are slurred in Modern English are apt to be suppressed in Chaucer's English: *Canterb'ry* for *Canterbury; ev'r* (perhaps *e'er*) for *evere.* The plural in *es* may either be syllabic or reduced to *s* as in Modern English. Despite these seeming irregularities, Chaucer's verse is not difficult to read if one constantly bears in mind the basic pattern of the iambic pentameter line.

THE MIDDLE AGES

TEXTS	CONTEXTS
	43–ca. 420 Romans conquer Britons; Brittania a province of the Roman Empire
	307–37 Reign of Constantine the Great leads to adoption of Christianity as official religion of the Roman Empire
ca. 405 St. Jerome completes *Vulgate,* Latin translation of the Bible that becomes standard for the Roman Catholic Church	
	432 St. Patrick begins mission to convert Ireland
	ca. 450 Anglo-Saxon conquest of Britons begins
523 Boethius, *Consolation of Philosophy* (Latin)	
	597 St. Augustine of Canterbury's mission to Kent begins conversion of Anglo-Saxons to Christianity
ca. 658–80 Cædmon's *Hymn,* earliest poem recorded in English	
731 Bede completes *Ecclesiastical History of the English People*	
? ca. 750 *Beowulf* composed	
	ca. 787 First Viking raids on England
871–99 Texts written or commissioned by Alfred	**871–99** Reign of King Alfred
ca. 1000 Unique manuscript of *Beowulf* and *Judith*	
	1066 Norman Conquest by William I establishes French-speaking ruling class in England
	1095–1221 Crusades
ca. 1135–38 Geoffrey of Monmouth's Latin *History of the Kings of Britain* gives pseudohistorical status to Arthurian and other legends	
	1152 Future Henry II marries Eleanor of Aquitaine, bringing vast French territories to the English crown
1154 End of *Peterborough Chronicle,* last branch of the *Anglo-Saxon Chronicle*	
? ca. 1165–80 Marie de France, *Lais* in Anglo-Norman French from Breton sources	
ca. 1170–91 Chrétien de Troyes, chivalric romances about knights of the Round Table	**1170** Archbishop Thomas Becket murdered in Canterbury Cathedral

TEXTS	CONTEXTS
? ca. 1200 Layamon's *Brut*	1182 Birth of St. Francis of Assisi
? ca. 1215–25 *Ancrene Wisse*	1215 Fourth Lateran Council requires annual confession. English barons force King John to seal Magna Carta (the Great Charter) guaranteeing baronial rights
ca. 1304–21 Dante Alighieri writing *Divine Comedy*	
ca. 1340–1374 Giovanni Boccaccio active as writer in Naples and Florence	ca. 1337–1453 Hundred Years' War
	1348 Black Death ravages Europe
ca. 1340–1374 Francis Petrarch active as writer	1362 English first used in law courts and Parliament
1368 Chaucer, *Book of the Duchess*	
	1372 Chaucer's first journey to Italy
1373–93 Julian of Norwich, *Book of Showings*	
ca. 1375–1400 *Sir Gawain and the Green Knight*	
	1376 Earliest record of performance of cycle drama at York
1377–79 William Langland, *Piers Plowman* (B-Text)	
ca. 1380 Followers of John Wycliffe begin first complete translation of the Bible into English	
	1381 People's uprising briefly takes control of London before being suppressed
ca. 1385–87 Chaucer, *Troilus and Criseyde*	
ca. 1387–99 Chaucer working on *The Canterbury Tales*	
ca. 1390–92 John Gower, *Confessio Amantis*	
	1399 Richard II deposed by his cousin, who succeeds him as Henry IV
	1400 Richard II murdered
	1401 Execution of William Sawtre, first Lollard burned at the stake under new law against heresy
ca. 1410–49 John Lydgate active	
ca. 1420 Thomas Hoccleve, *My Compleinte*	1415 Henry V defeats French at Agincourt
ca. 1425 *York Play of the Crucifixion*	
	1431 English burn Joan of Arc at Rouen
ca. 1432–38 Margery Kempe, *The Book of Margery Kempe*	

TEXTS	CONTEXTS
ca. 1450–75 Wakefield mystery cycle, *Second Shepherds' Play*	
	1455–85 Wars of the Roses
ca. 1470 Sir Thomas Malory in prison working on *Morte Darthur*	
ca. 1475 Robert Henryson active	
	1476 William Caxton sets up first printing press in England
1485 Caxton publishes *Morte Darthur*, one of the first books in English to be printed	**1485** The earl of Richmond defeats the Yorkist king, Richard III, at Bosworth Field and succeeds him as Henry VII, founder of the Tudor dynasty
ca. 1510 *Everyman*	**1575** Last performance of mystery plays at Chester

Anglo-Saxon Literature

BEDE (ca. 673–735) and CÆDMON'S *HYMN*

The Venerable Bede (the title by which he is known to posterity) became a novice at the age of seven and spent the rest of his life at the neighboring monasteries of Wearmouth and Jarrow. Although he may never have traveled beyond the boundaries of his native district of Northumbria, he achieved an international reputation as one of the greatest scholars of his age. Writing in Latin, the learned language of the era, Bede produced many theological works as well as books on science and rhetoric, but his most popular and enduring work is the *Ecclesiastical History of the English People* (completed 731). The *History* tells about the Anglo-Saxon conquest and the vicissitudes of the petty kingdoms that comprised Anglo-Saxon England; Bede's main theme, however, is the spread of Christianity and the growth of the English church. The latter were the great events leading up to Bede's own time, and he regarded them as the unfolding of God's providence. The *History* is, therefore, also a moral work and a hagiography—that is, it contains many stories of saints and miracles meant to testify to the grace and glory of God.

The story we reprint preserves what is probably the earliest extant Old English poem (composed sometime between 658 and 680) and the only biographical information, outside of what is said in the poems themselves, about any Old English poet. Bede tells how Cædmon, an illiterate cowherd employed by the monastery of Whitby, miraculously received the gift of song, entered the monastery, and became the founder of a school of Christian poetry. Cædmon was clearly an oral-formulaic poet, one who created his work by combining and varying formulas—units of verse developed in a tradition transmitted by one generation of singers to another. In this respect he resembles the singers of the Homeric poems and oral-formulaic poets recorded in the twentieth century, especially in the Balkan countries. Although Bede tells us that Cædmon had never learned the art of song, we may suspect that he concealed his skill from his fellow workmen and from the monks because he was ashamed of knowing "vain and idle" songs, the kind Bede says Cædmon never composed. Cædmon's inspiration and the true miracle, then, was to apply the meter and language of such songs, presumably including pagan heroic verse, to Christian themes.

Although most Old English poetry was written by lettered poets, they continued to use the oral-formulaic style. The *Hymn* is, therefore, a good short example of the way Old English verse, with its traditional poetic diction and interwoven formulaic expressions, is constructed. Eight of the poem's eighteen half-lines contain epithets describing various aspects of God: He is *Weard* (Guardian), *Meotod* (Measurer), *Wuldor-Fæder* (Glory-Father), *Drihten* (Lord), *Scyppend* (Creator), and *Frea* (Master). God is *heofonrices Weard* or *mancynnes Weard* (heaven's or mankind's Guardian), depending on the alliteration required. This formulaic style provides a richness of texture and meaning difficult to convey in translation. As Bede said about his own Latin paraphrase of the *Hymn*, no literal translation of poetry from one language to another is possible without sacrifice of some poetic quality.

Several manuscripts of Bede's *History* contain the Old English text in addition to Bede's Latin version. The poem is given here in a West Saxon form with a literal interlinear translation. In Old English spelling, æ (as in Cædmon's name and line 3) is a vowel symbol that represents the vowel of Modern English *cat*; þ (line 2) and ð (line 7) both represented the sound *th*. The spelling *sc* (line 1) = *sh*; ġ (line 1) = *y* in *yard*; ċ (line 1) = *ch* in *chin*; c (line 2) = *k*. The large space in the middle of the line indicates the caesura. The alliterating sounds that connect the half-lines are printed in bold italics.

From An Ecclesiastical History of the English People

[THE STORY OF CÆDMON]

Heavenly grace had especially singled out a certain one of the brothers in the monastery ruled by this abbes[1] for he used to compose devout and religious songs. Whatever he learned of holy Scripture with the aid of interpreters, he quickly turned into the sweetest and most moving poetry in his own language, that is to say English. It often happened that his songs kindled a contempt for this world and a longing for the life of Heaven in the hearts of many men. Indeed, after him others among the English people tried to compose religious poetry, but no one could equal him because he was not taught the art of song by men or by human agency but received this gift through heavenly grace. Therefore, he was never able to compose any vain and idle songs but only such as dealt with religion and were proper for his religious tongue to utter. As a matter of fact, he had lived in the secular estate until he was well advanced in age without learning any songs. Therefore, at feasts, when it was decided to have a good time by taking turns singing, whenever he would see the harp getting close to his place,[2] he got up in the middle of the meal and went home.

Once when he left the feast like this, he went to the cattle shed, which he had been assigned the duty of guarding that night. And after he had stretched himself out and gone to sleep, he dreamed that someone was standing at his side and greeted him, calling out his name. "Cædmon," he said, "sing me something."

And he replied, "I don't know how to sing; that is why I left the feast to come here—because I cannot sing."

"All the same," said the one who was speaking to him, "you have to sing for me."

"What must I sing?" he said.

And he said, "Sing about the Creation."

At this, Cædmon immediately began to sing verses in praise of God the Creator, which he had never heard before and of which the sense is this:

Nu sculon **h**eriġean	**h**eofonriċes Weard
Now we must praise	heaven-kingdom's Guardian,

---

1. Abbess Hilda (614–680), a grandniece of the first Christian king of Northumbria, founded Whitby, a double house for monks and nuns, in 657 and ruled over it for twenty-two years.

2. Oral poetry was performed to the accompaniment of a harp; here the harp is being passed from one participant of the feast to another, each being expected to perform in turn.

Meotodes meahte	and his modgeþanc
the Measurer's might	and his mind-plans,
weorc Wuldor-Fæder	swa he wundra ġehwæs
the work of the Glory-Father,	when he of wonders of every one,
eċe Drihten	or onstealde
eternal Lord,	the beginning established.[3]
He ærest sceop	ielda[4] bearnum
He first created	for men's sons
heofon to hrofe	haliġ Scyppend
heaven as a roof,	holy Creator;
ða middanġeard	moncynnes Weard
then middle-earth	mankind's Guardian,
eċe Drihten	æfter teode
eternal Lord,	afterwards made—
firum foldan	Frea ælmihtiġ
for men earth,	Master almighty.

This is the general sense but not the exact order of the words that he sang in his sleep;[5] for it is impossible to make a literal translation, no matter how well-written, of poetry into another language without losing some of the beauty and dignity. When he woke up, he remembered everything that he had sung in his sleep, and to this he soon added, in the same poetic measure, more verses praising God.

The next morning he went to the reeve,[6] who was his foreman, and told him about the gift he had received. He was taken to the abbess and ordered to tell his dream and to recite his song to an audience of the most learned men so that they might judge what the nature of that vision was and where it came from. It was evident to all of them that he had been granted the heavenly grace of God. Then they expounded some bit of sacred story or teaching to him, and instructed him to turn it into poetry if he could. He agreed and went away. And when he came back the next morning, he gave back what had been commissioned to him in the finest verse.

Therefore, the abbess, who cherished the grace of God in this man, instructed him to give up secular life and to take monastic vows. And when she and all those subject to her had received him into the community of brothers, she gave orders that he be taught the whole sequence of sacred history. He remembered everything that he was able to learn by listening, and turning it over in his mind like a clean beast that chews the cud,[7] he converted it into

---

3. I.e., established the beginning of every one of the wonders.
4. The later manuscript copies read eorpan, "earth," for ælda (West Saxon ielda), "men's."
5. Bede is referring to his Latin translation, for which we have substituted the Old English text with interlinear translation.

6. Superintendent of the farms belonging to the monastery.
7. In Mosaic law "clean" animals, those that may be eaten, are those that both chew the cud and have a cloven hoof (cf. Leviticus 11.3 and Deuteronomy 14.6).

sweetest song, which sounded so delightful that he made his teachers, in their turn, his listeners. He sang about the creation of the world and the origin of the human race and all the history of Genesis; about the exodus of Israel out of Egypt and entrance into the promised land; and about many other stories of sacred Scripture, about the Lord's incarnation, and his passion,[8] resurrection, and ascension into Heaven; about the advent of the Holy Spirit and the teachings of the apostles. He also made many songs about the terror of the coming judgment and the horror of the punishments of hell and the sweetness of heavenly kingdom; and a great many others besides about divine grace and justice in all of which he sought to draw men away from the love of sin and to inspire them with delight in the practice of good works.[9] * * *

8. The suffering of Christ between the night of the Last Supper and his death.
9. The great majority of extant Old English poems are on religious subjects like those listed here, but most are thought to be later than Cædmon.

THE DREAM OF THE ROOD

Ruthwell Cross, Ruthwell, Scotland, ca. 8th century. Not only is the cross sculpted with Christian images; it also has lines from *The Dream of the Rood* inscribed in runic letters. They may have been added at a later date.

The Dream of the Rood (i.e., of the Cross) is considered the finest of a large number of religious poems in Anglo-Saxon. Neither the author nor its date of composition is known. It appears in a late tenth-century manuscript located in Vercelli in northern Italy, a manuscript made up of Old English religious poems and sermons. The poem may antedate its manuscript, because some passages from the Rood's speech were carved, with some variations, in runes on a stone cross at some time after its construction early in the eighth century; this is the famous Ruthwell Cross, preserved near Dumfries in southern Scotland. The precise relation of the poem to this cross is, however, uncertain.

The experience of the Rood, often called "tree" in the poem—its humiliation at the hands of those who cut it down and made it into an instrument of punishment for criminals and its humility when the young hero Christ mounts it—has a suggestive relevance to the condition of the Dreamer. His isolation and melancholy is typical of exile figures in Anglo-Saxon poetry. For the Rood, however, glory has replaced torment, and at the end, the Dreamer's description of Christ's entry into heaven with the souls he has liberated from Hades reflects the Dreamer's response to the hope that has been brought to him. Christ and the Rood both act in keeping with, and yet diametrically opposed to, a code of heroic action: Christ is both heroic in mounting and passive in suffering on the Rood, while the Rood is loyal to its lord, yet must participate in his death.

The Dream of the Rood[1]

Attend to what I intend to tell you
a marvelous dream that moved me at night
when human voices are veiled in sleep.
In my dream I espied the most splendid tree.
5 looming aloft with light all around,
the most brilliant beam. That bright tree was
covered with gold; gemstones gleamed
fairly fashioned down to its foot, yet another five were standing[2]
high up on the crossbeam —the Lord's angel beheld them—[3]
10 cast by eternal decree. Clearly this was no criminal's gallows,[4]
but holy spirits were beholding it there,
men on this earth, all that mighty creation.
That tree was triumphant and I tarnished by sin,
begrimed with evil. I beheld Glory's trunk
15 garnished with grandeur, gleaming in bliss,
all plated with gold; precious gemstones
had gloriously graced the Lord God's tree.
Yet I could see signs of ancient strife:
beneath that gold it had begun
20 bleeding on the right side.[5] I was all bereft with sorrows;
that splendid sight made me afraid. I beheld the sign rapidly
changing clothing and colors. Now it was covered with moisture,
drenched with streaming blood, now decked in treasure.
Yet I, lying there for a long time,
25 sorrowfully beheld the tree of our Savior
until I could hear it call out to me,
the best of all wood began speaking words:
"That was years ago —I yet remember—
that I was cut down at the edge of the forest
30 torn up from my trunk. There powerful enemies took me,
put me up to make a circus-play to lift up and parade their criminals.
Soldiers bore me on their shoulders till they set me up on a mountain;
more than enough foes made me stand fast. I saw the lord of mankind
coming with great haste so that he might climb up on me.

1. The translation by Alfred David is based on *Eight Old English Poems*, 3rd ed., edited by John C. Pope, revised by R. D. Fulk (2000).
2. This longer line and the two following, as well as lines 20–23, 30–34, 39–43, 46–49, 59–70, 75–76, and 133, contain additional stresses and are designated as "hypermetric." Less than 500 such lines survive in the corpus of Anglo-Saxon poetry.
3. The translation follows R. D. Fulk's emenda-tion: "beheold on þam engel dryhtnes."
4. Constantine the Great, emperor from 306 to 337, erected a jeweled cross at the site of the crucifixion, transforming the Roman "felon's gallows" from a symbol of shame into a universal icon of Christian art.
5. According to biblical tradition, following John 19.34, Christ was wounded by the centurion's lance on the right side.

35   Then I did not dare   act against the Lord's word
      bow down or fall to pieces   when I felt the surface
      of the earth trembling.[6]   Although I might
      have destroyed the foes,   I stood in place.
Then this young man stripped himself   —that was God Almighty—
40 strong and courageous;   he climbed up on the high gallows,
brave in the sight of many,   as he set out to redeem mankind.
I trembled when the man embraced me;   I dared not bow down to earth,
stoop to the surface of the ground,   but I had to stand fast.
    I was reared a rood;   I raised up a mighty king,
45   the heavens' lord;   I dared not bow in homage.
They drove dark nails into me;   the dints of those wounds can still be seen,
open marks of malice;   but I did not dare maul any of them in return.
They mocked both of us.   I was moistened all over with blood,
shed from the man's side   after he had sent up his spirit.
50   On that mountain   I have endured many
      cruel happenings.   I saw the God of hosts
      direly stretched out.   Shades of darkness
      had clouded over   the corpse of the Lord,
      the shining radiance;   shadows went forth
55   dark under clouds.   All creation wept,
      mourning the king's fall: Christ was on the cross.
      "Yet from afar   fervent men came
      to that sovereign.   I saw all that.
I was badly burdened with grief   yet bowed down to their hands,
60 submissive with most resolve.   There they took up almighty God,
lifted him from that cruel torment.   Then the warriors left me there
standing, blood all over me,   pierced everywhere with arrows.
They laid him there, limb-wearied;   they stood at the head of his lifeless
      body.
65 There they beheld the lord of heaven,   and he rested there for a while,
spent after that great struggle.   Then they set about to construct a sepulcher
warriors in the slayer's[7] sight.   Out of bright stone they carved it;
they laid the lord of victories into it.   They began singing a lay of sorrow,
warriors sad as night was falling,   when they wished to journey back
70 wearily far from that famous lord;   he rested there with few followers.[8]
    We,[9]grieving there   for a good while,
      stood still in place;   the soldiers' voices
      faded away.   Finally men brought axes
      to fell us to earth.   That was a frightful destiny!
75 They buried us in a deep pit.   But thanes° of the Lord,   *retainers*
friends learned about me[1]* * *
    * * *adorned me   with gold and silver.
    "Now, man so dear to me,   you may understand
    that I have gone through   grievous sufferings,
80   terrible sorrows.   Now the time has come

---

6. According to Matthew 27.51, the earth quaked at the crucifixion.
7. I.e., the Cross. See John 19.41–42.
8. An example of Anglo-Saxon litotes, ironically expressing something by its contrary. In fact, Christ's tomb is now deserted.

9. I.e, Christ's Cross and those on which the two thieves had been crucified.
1. The reference in this gap in the manuscript must be to the discovery of the Cross by St. Helena.

so that far and wide   men worship me
everywhere on earth,   and all creation,
pray to this sign.   On me the son of God
suffered a time;   therefore I now tower
85 in glory under heaven,   and I may heal
any one of those   in awe of me.
Long ago I became   the most cruel punishment,
most hated by men,   until I made open
the right way of life   to language-bearers.
90 So the lord of glory,   guardian of Heaven,
exalted me then   over all forest-trees,
as Almighty God   before all humankind
exalted over   all the race of women
His own mother,   Mary herself.
95   "Now I command you,   my man so dear,
to tell others   the events you have seen;
find words to tell   it was the tree of glory
Almighty God   suffered upon
for mankind's   so many sins
100 and for that ancient   offense of Adam.
There he tasted death;   yet the Redeemer arose
with his great might   to help mankind.
Then he rose to Heaven.   He will come again
to this middle-earth   to seek out mankind
105 on Judgment Day,   the Redeemer himself,
God Almighty   and his angels with him,
so that He will judge,   He who has power of the Judgment,
all humanity   as to the merits each
has brought about   in this brief life.
110 Nor may anyone   be unafraid
of the last question   the Lord will ask.
Before the multitude   he will demand
where a soul might be   who in the Savior's name
would suffer the death   He suffered on that tree.
115 But they shall fear   and few shall think
what to contrive   to say to Christ.
But no one there   need be afraid
who bears the best   sign on his breast.
And on this earth   each soul that longs
120 to exist with its savior   forevermore
must seek His kingdom   through that cross."
      Then compelled by joy,   I prayed to that tree
with ardent zeal,   where I was alone
with few followers.   Then my heart felt
125 an urge to set forth;   I have suffered
much longing since.   Now I live in hope,
venturing after   that victory-tree,
alone more often   than all other men,
to worship it well.   The will to do so
130 is much in my heart;   my protection
depends on the rood.   I possess but few
friends on this earth.   But forth from here

they have set out from worldly joys   to seek the King of Glory.
They dwell in Heaven now   with the High-father
135 living in glory,   and I look forward
constantly toward   that time the Lord's rood
which I beheld before   here on this earth
shall fetch me away   from this fleeting life
and bring me then   where bliss is eternal
140 to joy in Paradise   where the Lord's people
are joined at that feast   where joy lasts forever
and seat me there   where evermore
I shall dwell in glory,   together with the saints
share in their delights.   May the Lord be my friend,
145 who on earth long ago   on the gallows-tree
suffered agony   for the sins of men:
he redeemed us   and gave us life,
a home in Heaven.   Hope was made new
and blossomed with bliss   to those burning in fire.[2]
150 The Son was victorious   in venturing forth,
mighty and triumphant   when he returned with many,
a company of souls   to the Kingdom of God,
the Almighty Ruler,   to the joy of angels,
and all those holy ones   come to Heaven before.[3]
155 to live in glory,   when their Lord returned,
the Eternal King   to His own country.

2. This line and those following refer to the so-called Harrowing of Hell. After his death on the Cross, Christ descended into hell, from which he released the souls of certain patriarchs and prophets, conducting them into heaven (see *Piers Plowman*, Passus 18). The analogy is to the triumphal procession of a Roman emperor returning from war.
3. The line probably refers to a belief that God had sanctified a chosen few before the crucifixion.

BEOWULF

B eowulf, the oldest of the great long poems written in English, may have been composed more than twelve hundred years ago, in the first half of the eighth century, although some scholars would place it as late as the tenth century. As is the case with most Old English poems, the title has been assigned by modern editors, for the manuscripts do not normally give any indication of title or authorship. Linguistic evidence shows that the poem was originally composed in the dialect of what was then Mercia, the Midlands of England today. But in the unique late-tenth-century manuscript preserving the poem, it has been converted into the West-Saxon dialect of the southwest in which most of Old English literature survives. In 1731, before any modern transcript of the text had been made, the manuscript was seriously damaged in a fire that destroyed the building in London that housed the extraordinary collection of medieval English manuscripts made by Sir Robert Bruce Cotton (1571–1631). As a result of the fire and subsequent deterioration, a number of lines and words have been lost from the poem.

It is possible that *Beowulf* may be the lone survivor of a genre of Old English long epics, but it must have been a remarkable and difficult work even in its own day. The poet was reviving the heroic language, style, and pagan world of ancient Germanic oral poetry, a world that was already remote for his contemporaries and that is stranger to the modern reader, in many respects, than the epic world of Homer and Virgil. With the help of *Beowulf* itself, a few shorter heroic poems in Old English, and later poetry and prose in Old Saxon, Old Icelandic, and Middle High German, we can only conjecture what Germanic oral epic must have been like when performed by the Germanic *scop*, or bard. The *Beowulf* poet himself imagines such oral performances by having King Hrothgar's court poet recite a heroic lay at a feast celebrating Beowulf's defeat of Grendel. Many of the words and formulaic expressions in *Beowulf* can be found in other Old English poems, but there are also an extraordinary number of what linguists call *hapax legomena*—that is, words recorded only once in a language. The poet may have found them elsewhere, but the high incidence of such words suggests that he was an original wordsmith in his own right.

Although the poem itself is English in language and origin, it deals not with native Englishmen but with their Germanic forebears, especially with two south Scandinavian tribes, the Danes and the Geats, who lived on the Danish island of Zealand and in southern Sweden. Thus the historical period the poem concerns—insofar as it may be said to refer to history at all—is some centuries before it was written—that is, a time after the initial invasion of England by Germanic tribes in the middle of the fifth century but before the Anglo-Saxon migration was completed. The one datable fact of history mentioned in the poem is a raid on the Franks in which Hygelac, the king of the Geats and Beowulf's lord, was killed, and this raid occurred in the year 520. Yet the poet's elliptical references to quasihistorical and legendary material show that his audience was still familiar with many old stories, the outlines of which we can only infer, sometimes with the help of later analogous tales in other Germanic languages. This knowledge was probably kept alive by other heroic poetry, of which little has been preserved in English, although much may once have existed.

It is now widely believed that *Beowulf* is the work of a single poet who was a Christian and that his poem reflects well-established Christian tradition. The conversion of the Germanic settlers in England had been largely completed during the seventh century. The Danish king Hrothgar's poet sings a song about the Creation (lines 87–98) reminiscent of Cædmon's *Hymn*. The monster Grendel is said to be a descendant of Cain. There are allusions to God's judgment and to fate (*wyrd*) but none to pagan deities. References to the New Testament are notably absent, but Hrothgar and Beowulf often speak of God as though their religion is monotheistic. With sadness the poet relates that, made desperate by Grendel's attacks, the Danes pray for help at heathen shrines—apparently backsliding as the children of Israel had sometimes lapsed into idolatry.

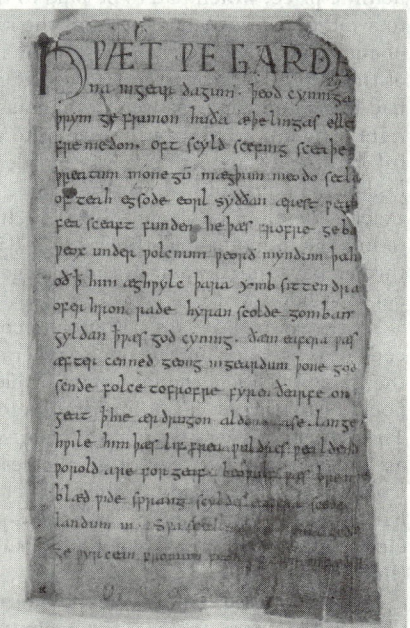

Beowulf. The opening page. Note the charred edges, caused by a fire in 1731.

Anglo-Saxon helmet, 6th to 7th centuries. Excavated at Sutton Hoo, Suffolk.

Although Hrothgar and Beowulf are portrayed as morally upright and enlightened pagans, they fully espouse and frequently affirm the values of Germanic heroic poetry. In the poetry depicting this warrior society, the most important of human relationships was that which existed between the warrior—the thane—and his lord, a relationship based less on subordination of one man's will to another's than on mutual trust and respect. When a warrior vowed loyalty to his lord, he became not so much his servant as his voluntary companion, one who would take pride in defending him and fighting in his wars. In return, the lord was expected to take care of his thanes and to reward them richly for their valor; a good king, one like Hrothgar or Beowulf, is referred to by such poetic epithets as "ring-giver" and as the "helmet" and "shield" of his people.

The relationship between kinsmen was also of deep significance to this society. If one of his kinsmen had been slain, a man had a moral obligation either to kill the slayer or to exact the payment of *wergild* (man-price) in compensation. Each rank of society was evaluated at a definite price, which had to be paid to the dead man's kin by the killer if he wished to avoid their vengeance—even if the killing had been an accident. In the absence of any legal code other than custom or any body of law enforcement, it was the duty of the family (often with the lord's support) to execute justice. The payment itself had less significance as wealth than as proof that the kinsmen had done what was right. The failure to take revenge or to exact compensation was considered shameful. Hrothgar's anguish over the murders committed by Grendel is not only for the loss of his men but also for the shame of his inability either to kill Grendel or to exact a "death-price" from the killer. "It is always better / to avenge dear ones than to indulge in mourning" (lines 1384–85), Beowulf says to Hrothgar, who has been thrown back into despair by the revenge-slaying of his old friend Aeschere by Grendel's mother.

Yet the young Beowulf's attempt to comfort the bereaved old king by invoking the code of vengeance may be one of several instances of the poet's ironic treatment of the tragic futility of the never-ending blood feuds. The most graphic example in the poem of that irony is the Finnsburg episode, the lay sung by Hrothgar's hall-poet. The Danish princess Hildeburh, married to the Frisian king Finn—probably to put an end to a feud between those peoples—loses both her brother and her son when a bloody fight breaks out in the hall between a visiting party of Danes and her husband's men. The bodies are cremated together on a huge funeral pyre: "The glutton element flamed and consumed / the dead of both sides. Their great days were gone" (lines 1124–25).

Such feuds, the staple subject of Germanic epic and saga, have only a peripheral place in the poem. Instead, the poem turns on Beowulf's three great fights against preternatural evil, which inhabits the dangerous and demonic space surrounding human society. He undertakes the fight against Grendel to save the Danes from the monster and to exact vengeance for the men Grendel has slain. Another motive is to demonstrate his strength and courage and thereby to enhance his personal glory. Hrothgar's magnificent gifts become the material emblems of that glory. Revenge and glory also motivate Beowulf's slaying of Grendel's mother. He undertakes his last battle against the dragon, however, only because there is no other way to save his own people.

A somber and dignified elegiac mood pervades *Beowulf*. The poem opens and closes with the description of a funeral and is filled with laments for the dead. Our first view of Beowulf is of an ambitious young hero. At the end, he has become an old king, facing the dragon and death. His people mourn him and praise him, as does the poet, for his nobility, generosity, courage, and, what is less common in Germanic heroes, kindness to his people. The poet's elegiac tone may be informed by something more than the duty to "praise a prince whom he holds dear / and cherish his memory when that moment comes / when he has to be convoyed from his bodily home" (lines 3175–77). The entire poem could be viewed as the poet's lament for heroes like Beowulf who went into the darkness without the light of the poet's own Christian faith.

The present verse translation is by the Irish poet Seamus Heaney, who received the Nobel Prize for literature in 1995. Selections from Heaney's own poems appear in Volume 2 of the anthology.

TRIBES AND GENEALOGIES

1. The Danes (Bright-, Half-, Ring-, Spear-, North-, East-, South-, West-Danes; Shield-ings, Honor-, Victor-, War-Shieldings; Ing's friends)

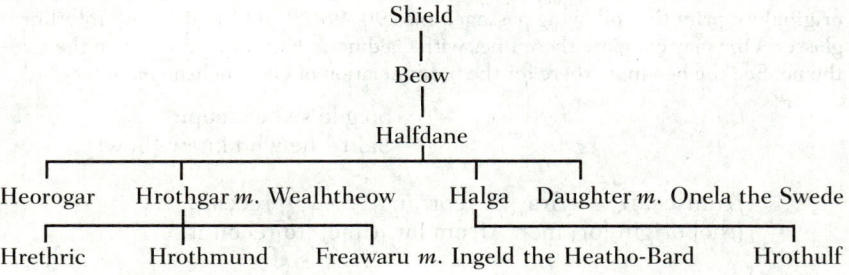

2. The Geats (Sea-, War-, Weather-Geats)

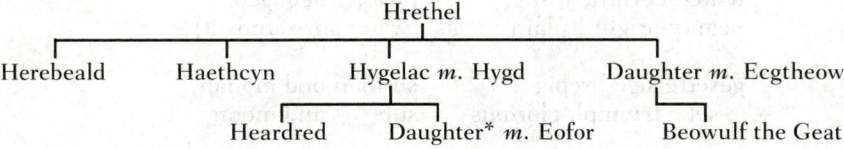

---

*The daughter of Hygelac who was given to Eofor may have been born to him by a former wife, older than Hygd.

3. *The Swedes*

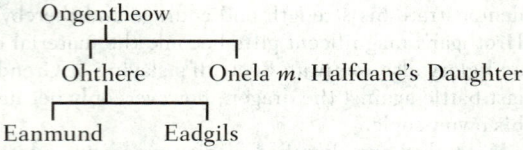

4. *Miscellaneous*

A. The Half-Danes (also called Shieldings) involved in the fight at Finnsburg may represent a different tribe from the Danes described above. Their king Hoc had a son, Hnaef, who succeeded him, and a daughter Hildeburh, who married Finn, king of the Jutes.

B. The Jutes or Frisians are represented as enemies of the Danes in the fight at Finnsburg and as allies of the Franks or Hugas at the time Hygelac the Geat made the attack in which he lost his life and from which Beowulf swam home. Also allied with the Franks at this time were the Hetware.

C. The Heatho-Bards (i.e., "Battle-Bards") are represented as inveterate enemies of the Danes. Their king Froda had been killed in an attack on the Danes, and Hrothgar's attempt to make peace with them by marrying his daughter Freawaru to Froda's son Ingeld failed when the latter attacked Heorot. The attack was repulsed, although Heorot was burned.

The Poet's Song in Heorot

To give the reader a sample of the language, style, and texture of *Beowulf* in the original we print the following passage, lines 90–98, in Old English with interlinear glosses. One may compare these lines with Cædmon's *Hymn* (pp. 28–32) on the same theme. See the headnote there for the pronunciation of Old English characters.

> Sægde se þe cuþe
> Said he who knew [how]

> *f*rumsceaft *f*ira *f*eorran reccan,
> [the] origin [of] men from far [time] [to]recount,

> cwæð þæt se Ælmightiga *eo*rðan worhte,
> said that the Almighty [the] earth wrought

> *w*lite-beorhtne *w*ang, swa *w*æter bebugeð,
> beauty-bright plain as water surrounds[it]

> gesette sige-hreþig sunnan ond monan,
> set triumph-glorious sun and moon

> *l*eoman to *l*eohte *l*andbuendum,
> beacons as light [for] land-dwellers

> ond ge*f*rætwade *f*oldan sceatas
> and adorned [of]earth[the]grounds

> *l*eomum ond *l*eafum, *l*if eac gesceop
> [with]limbs and leaves, life also[he]created

cynna   gehwylcum*   þara ðe   cwice hwyrfaþ.
[of]kinds [for]each   [of]those who living move about

A NOTE ON NAMES

Old English, like Modern German, contained many compound words, most of which have been lost in Modern English. Most of the names in *Beowulf* are compounds. Hrothgar is a combination of words meaning "glory" and "spear"; the name of his older brother, Heorogar, comes from "army" and "spear"; Hrothgar's sons Hrethric and Hrothmund contain the first elements of their father's name combined, respectively, with *ric* (kingdom, empire; Modern German *Reich*) and *mund* (hand, protection). As in the case of the Danish dynasty, family names often alliterate. Masculine names of the warrior class have military associations. The importance of family and the demands of alliteration frequently lead to the designation of characters by formulas identifying them in terms of relationships. Thus Beowulf is referred to as "son of Ecgtheow" or "kinsman of Hygelac" (his uncle and lord).

The Old English spellings of names are mostly preserved in the translation. A few rules of pronunciation are worth keeping in mind. Initial *H* before *r* was sounded, and so Hrothgar's name alliterates with that of his brother Heorogar. The combination *cg* has the value of *dg* in words like "edge." The first element in the name of Beowulf's father "Ecgtheow" is the same word as "edge," and, by the figure of speech called synecdoche (a part of something stands for the whole), *ecg* stands for *sword* and Ecgtheow means "sword-servant."

For more information about *Beowulf*, see "The Linguistic and Literary Contexts of *Beowulf*," in the supplemental ebook.

Beowulf

[PROLOGUE: THE RISE OF THE DANISH NATION]

So. The Spear-Danes[1] in days gone by
and the kings who ruled them had courage and greatness.
We have heard of those princes' heroic campaigns.
    There was Shield Sheafson,[2] scourge of many tribes,
5   a wrecker of mead-benches, rampaging among foes.
This terror of the hall-troops had come far.
A foundling to start with, he would flourish later on
as his powers waxed and his worth was proved.
In the end each clan on the outlying coasts
10   beyond the whale-road had to yield to him
and begin to pay tribute. That was one good king.

---

*Modern syntax would be "for each of kinds." In Old English, the endings *-a* and *-um* indicate that *gewylcum* is an indirect object and *cynna*, a possessive plural.

1. There are different compound names for tribes, often determined by alliteration in Old English poetry. Line 1 reads, *"Hwæt, we Gar-dena in gear-dagum,"* where alliteration falls on *Gar* (spear) and *gear* (year). Old English hard and soft g (spelled *y* in Modern English) alliterate. The compound

geardagum derives from "year," used in the special sense of "long ago," and "days" and survives in the archaic expression "days of yore."
2. Shield is the name of the founder of the Danish royal line. Sheafson translates *Scefing*, i.e., *sheaf* + the patronymic suffix-*ing*. Because Sheaf was a "foundling" (line 7: *feasceaft funden*, i.e., found destitute) who arrived by sea (lines 45–46), it is likely that as a child Shield brought with him only a sheaf, a symbol of fruitfulness.

Afterward a boy-child was born to Shield,
a cub in the yard, a comfort sent
by God to that nation. He knew what they had tholed,[3]
15   the long times and troubles they'd come through
without a leader; so the Lord of Life,
the glorious Almighty, made this man renowned.
Shield had fathered a famous son:
Beow's name was known through the north.
20   And a young prince must be prudent like that,
giving freely while his father lives
so that afterward in age when fighting starts
steadfast companions will stand by him
and hold the line. Behavior that's admired
25   is the path to power among people everywhere.
    Shield was still thriving when his time came
and he crossed over into the Lord's keeping.
His warrior band did what he bade them
when he laid down the law among the Danes:
30   they shouldered him out to the sea's flood,
the chief they revered who had long ruled them.
A ring-whorled prow rode in the harbor,
ice-clad, outbound, a craft for a prince.
They stretched their beloved lord in his boat,
35   laid out by the mast, amidships,
the great ring-giver. Far-fetched treasures
were piled upon him, and precious gear.
I never heard before of a ship so well furbished
with battle-tackle, bladed weapons
40   and coats of mail. The massed treasure
was loaded on top of him: it would travel far
on out into the ocean's sway.
They decked his body no less bountifully
with offerings than those first ones did
45   who cast him away when he was a child
and launched him alone out over the waves.[4]
And they set a gold standard up
high above his head and let him drift
to wind and tide, bewailing him
50   and mourning their loss. No man can tell,
no wise man in hall or weathered veteran
knows for certain who salvaged that load.
    Then it fell to Beow to keep the forts.
He was well regarded and ruled the Danes
55   for a long time after his father took leave
of his life on earth. And then his heir,
the great Halfdane,[5] held sway
for as long as he lived, their elder and warlord.
He was four times a father, this fighter prince:

---

3. Suffered, endured.
4. See n. 2, above. Since Shield was found destitute, "no less bountifully" is litotes or understatement; the ironic reminder that he came with

nothing (line 43) emphasizes the reversal of his
fortunes.
5. Probably named so because, according to one
source, his mother was a Swedish princess.

60 one by one they entered the world,
Heorogar, Hrothgar, the good Halga,
and a daughter, I have heard, who was Onela's queen,
a balm in bed to the battle-scarred Swede.

The fortunes of war favored Hrothgar.
65 Friends and kinsmen flocked to his ranks,
young followers, a force that grew
to be a mighty army. So his mind turned
to hall-building: he handed down orders
for men to work on a great mead-hall
70 meant to be a wonder of the world forever;
it would be his throne-room and there he would dispense
his God-given goods to young and old—
but not the common land or people's lives.[6]
Far and wide through the world, I have heard,
75 orders for work to adorn that wallstead
were sent to many peoples. And soon it stood there
finished and ready, in full view,
the hall of halls. Heorot was the name[7]
he had settled on it, whose utterance was law.
80 Nor did he renege, but doled out rings
and torques at the table. The hall towered,
its gables wide and high and awaiting
a barbarous burning.[8] That doom abided,
but in time it would come: the killer instinct
85 unleashed among in-laws, the blood-lust rampant.[9]

[HEOROT IS ATTACKED]

Then a powerful demon,[1] a prowler through the dark,
nursed a hard grievance. It harrowed him
to hear the din of the loud banquet
every day in the hall, the harp being struck
90 and the clear song of a skilled poet
telling with mastery of man's beginnings,
how the Almighty had made the earth
a gleaming plain girdled with waters;
in His splendor He set the sun and the moon
95 to be earth's lamplight, lanterns for men,
and filled the broad lap of the world
with branches and leaves; and quickened life
in every other thing that moved.

So times were pleasant for the people there
100 until finally one, a fiend out of hell,
began to work his evil in the world.
Grendel was the name of this grim demon

---

6. The king could not dispose of land used by all, such as a common pasture, or of slaves.
7. I.e., "Hart," from antlers fastened to the gables or because the crossed gable-ends resembled a stag's antlers; the hart was also an icon of royalty.
8. An allusion to the future destruction of Heorot by fire, probably in a raid by the Heatho-Bards.

9. As told later (lines 2020–69), Hrothgar plans to marry a daughter to Ingeld, chief of the Heatho-Bards, in hopes of resolving a long-standing feud. See previous note.
1. The poet withholds the name for several lines. He does the same with the name of the hero as well as others.

haunting the marches, marauding round the heath
and the desolate fens; he had dwelt for a time
105   in misery among the banished monsters,
Cain's clan, whom the Creator had outlawed
and condemned as outcasts.[2] For the killing of Abel
the Eternal Lord had exacted a price:
Cain got no good from committing that murder
110   because the Almighty made him anathema
and out of the curse of his exile there sprang
ogres and elves and evil phantoms
and the giants too who strove with God
time and again until He gave them their reward.
115   So, after nightfall, Grendel set out
for the lofty house, to see how the Ring-Danes
were settling into it after their drink,
and there he came upon them, a company of the best
asleep from their feasting, insensible to pain
120   and human sorrow. Suddenly then
the God-cursed brute was creating havoc:
greedy and grim, he grabbed thirty men
from their resting places and rushed to his lair,
flushed up and inflamed from the raid,
125   blundering back with the butchered corpses.
      Then as dawn brightened and the day broke,
Grendel's powers of destruction were plain:
their wassail was over, they wept to heaven
and mourned under morning. Their mighty prince,
130   the storied leader, sat stricken and helpless,
humiliated by the loss of his guard,
bewildered and stunned, staring aghast
at the demon's trail, in deep distress.
He was numb with grief, but got no respite
135   for one night later merciless Grendel
struck again with more gruesome murders.
Malignant by nature, he never showed remorse.
It was easy then to meet with a man
shifting himself to a safer distance
140   to bed in the bothies[3] for who could be blind
to the evidence of his eyes, the obviousness
of the hall-watcher's hate? Whoever escaped
kept a weather-eye open and moved away.
      So Grendel ruled in defiance of right,
145   one against all, until the greatest house
in the world stood empty, a deserted wallstead.
For twelve winters, seasons of woe,
the lord of the Shieldings[4] suffered under
his load of sorrow; and so, before long,
150   the news was known over the whole world.

---

2. See Genesis 4.9–12.
3. Huts, outlying buildings. Evidently Grendel
wants only to dominate the hall.

4. The descendants of Shield, another name for
the Danes.

Sad lays were sung about the beset king,
the vicious raids and ravages of Grendel,
his long and unrelenting feud,
nothing but war; how he would never
155 parley or make peace with any Dane
nor stop his death-dealing nor pay the death-price.[5]
No counselor could ever expect
fair reparation from those rabid hands.
All were endangered; young and old
160 were hunted down by that dark death-shadow
who lurked and swooped in the long nights
on the misty moors; nobody knows
where these reavers from hell roam on their errands.
    So Grendel waged his lonely war,
165 inflicting constant cruelties on the people,
atrocious hurt. He took over Heorot,
haunted the glittering hall after dark,
but the throne itself, the treasure-seat,
he was kept from approaching; he was the Lord's outcast.
170   These were hard times, heartbreaking
for the prince of the Shieldings; powerful counselors,
the highest in the land, would lend advice,
plotting how best the bold defenders
might resist and beat off sudden attacks.
175 Sometimes at pagan shrines they vowed
offerings to idols, swore oaths
that the killer of souls[6] might come to their aid
and save the people. That was their way,
their heathenish hope; deep in their hearts
180 they remembered hell. The Almighty Judge
of good deeds and bad, the Lord God,
Head of the Heavens and High King of the World,
was unknown to them. Oh, cursed is he
who in time of trouble has to thrust his soul
185 in the fire's embrace, forfeiting help;
he has nowhere to turn. But blessed is he
who after death can approach the Lord
and find friendship in the Father's embrace.

[THE HERO COMES TO HEOROT]

    So that troubled time continued, woe
190 that never stopped, steady affliction
for Halfdane's son, too hard an ordeal.
There was panic after dark, people endured
raids in the night, riven by the terror.
    When he heard about Grendel, Hygelac's thane
195 was on home ground, over in Geatland.
There was no one else like him alive.

---

5. I.e., *wergild* (man-price); monetary compensation for the life of the slain man is the only way, according to Germanic law, to settle a feud peacefully.

6. I.e., the devil. Heathen gods were thought to be devils.

In his day, he was the mightiest man on earth,
highborn and powerful. He ordered a boat
that would ply the waves. He announced his plan:
200   to sail the swan's road and seek out that king,
the famous prince who needed defenders.
Nobody tried to keep him from going,
no elder denied him, dear as he was to them.
Instead, they inspected omens and spurred
205   his ambition to go, whilst he moved about
like the leader he was, enlisting men,
the best he could find; with fourteen others
the warrior boarded the boat as captain,
a canny pilot along coast and currents.
210   Time went by, the boat was on water,
in close under the cliffs.
Men climbed eagerly up the gangplank,
sand churned in surf, warriors loaded
a cargo of weapons, shining war-gear
215   in the vessel's hold, then heaved out,
away with a will in their wood-wreathed ship.
Over the waves, with the wind behind her
and foam at her neck, she flew like a bird
until her curved prow had covered the distance,
220   and on the following day, at the due hour,
those seafarers sighted land,
sunlit cliffs, sheer crags
and looming headlands, the landfall they sought.
It was the end of their voyage and the Geats vaulted
225   over the side, out on to the sand,
and moored their ship. There was a clash of mail
and a thresh of gear. They thanked God
for that easy crossing on a calm sea.
     When the watchman on the wall, the Shieldings' lookout
230   whose job it was to guard the sea-cliffs,
saw shields glittering on the gangplank
and battle-equipment being unloaded
he had to find out who and what
the arrivals were. So he rode to the shore,
235   this horseman of Hrothgar's, and challenged them
in formal terms, flourishing his spear:
"What kind of men are you who arrive
rigged out for combat in your coats of mail,
sailing here over the sea-lanes
240   in your steep-hulled boat? I have been stationed
as lookout on this coast for a long time.
My job is to watch the waves for raiders,
any danger to the Danish shore.
Never before has a force under arms
245   disembarked so openly—not bothering to ask
if the sentries allowed them safe passage
or the clan had consented. Nor have I seen
a mightier man-at-arms on this earth

than the one standing here: unless I am mistaken,
250 he is truly noble. This is no mere
hanger-on in a hero's armor.
So now, before you fare inland
as interlopers, I have to be informed
about who you are and where you hail from.
255 Outsiders from across the water,
I say it again: the sooner you tell
where you come from and why, the better."
    The leader of the troop unlocked his word-hoard;
the distinguished one delivered this answer:
260 "We belong by birth to the Geat people
and owe allegiance to Lord Hygelac.
In his day, my father was a famous man,
a noble warrior-lord named Ecgtheow.
He outlasted many a long winter
265 and went on his way. All over the world
men wise in counsel continue to remember him.
We come in good faith to find your lord
and nation's shield, the son of Halfdane.
Give us the right advice and direction.
270 We have arrived here on a great errand
to the lord of the Danes, and I believe therefore
there should be nothing hidden or withheld between us.
So tell us if what we have heard is true
about this threat, whatever it is,
275 this danger abroad in the dark nights,
this corpse-maker mongering death
in the Shieldings' country. I come to proffer
my wholehearted help and counsel.
I can show the wise Hrothgar a way
280 to defeat his enemy and find respite—
if any respite is to reach him, ever.
I can calm the turmoil and terror in his mind.
Otherwise, he must endure woes
and live with grief for as long as his hall
285 stands at the horizon on its high ground."
    Undaunted, sitting astride his horse,
the coast-guard answered: "Anyone with gumption
and a sharp mind will take the measure
of two things: what's said and what's done.
290 I believe what you have told me, that you are a troop
loyal to our king. So come ahead
with your arms and your gear, and I will guide you.
What's more, I'll order my own comrades
on their word of honor to watch your boat
295 down there on the strand—keep her safe
in her fresh tar, until the time comes
for her curved prow to preen on the waves
and bear this hero back to Geatland.
May one so valiant and venturesome
300 come unharmed through the clash of battle."

So they went on their way. The ship rode the water,
broad-beamed, bound by its hawser
and anchored fast. Boar-shapes[7] flashed
above their cheek-guards, the brightly forged
305 work of goldsmiths, watching over
those stern-faced men. They marched in step,
hurrying on till the timbered hall
rose before them, radiant with gold.
Nobody on earth knew of another
310 building like it. Majesty lodged there,
its light shone over many lands.
So their gallant escort guided them
to that dazzling stronghold and indicated
the shortest way to it; then the noble warrior
315 wheeled on his horse and spoke these words:
"It is time for me to go. May the Almighty
Father keep you and in His kindness
watch over your exploits. I'm away to the sea,
back on alert against enemy raiders."
320   It was a paved track, a path that kept them
in marching order. Their mail-shirts glinted,
hard and hand-linked; the high-gloss iron
of their armor rang. So they duly arrived
in their grim war-graith[8] and gear at the hall,
325 and, weary from the sea, stacked wide shields
of the toughest hardwood against the wall,
then collapsed on the benches; battle-dress
and weapons clashed. They collected their spears
in a seafarers' stook, a stand of grayish
330 tapering ash. And the troops themselves
were as good as their weapons.
                    Then a proud warrior
questioned the men concerning their origins:
"Where do you come from, carrying these
decorated shields and shirts of mail,
335 these cheek-hinged helmets and javelins?
I am Hrothgar's herald and officer.
I have never seen so impressive or large
an assembly of strangers. Stoutness of heart,
bravery not banishment, must have brought you to Hrothgar."
340   The man whose name was known for courage,
the Geat leader, resolute in his helmet,
answered in return: "We are retainers
from Hygelac's band. Beowulf is my name.
If your lord and master, the most renowned
345 son of Halfdane, will hear me out
and graciously allow me to greet him in person,
I am ready and willing to report my errand."
    Wulfgar replied, a Wendel chief

---

7. Carved images of boars were placed on helmets, probably as charms to protect the warriors.
8. "Graith": archaic for apparel.

renowned as a warrior, well known for his wisdom
350   and the temper of his mind: "I will take this message,
      in accordance with your wish, to our noble king,
      our dear lord, friend of the Danes,
      the giver of rings. I will go and ask him
      about your coming here, then hurry back
355   with whatever reply it pleases him to give."
          With that he turned to where Hrothgar sat,
      an old man among retainers;
      the valiant follower stood foursquare
      in front of his king: he knew the courtesies.
360   Wulfgar addressed his dear lord:
      "People from Geatland have put ashore.
      They have sailed far over the wide sea.
      They call the chief in charge of their band
      by the name of Beowulf. They beg, my lord,
365   an audience with you, exchange of words
      and formal greeting. Most gracious Hrothgar,
      do not refuse them, but grant them a reply.
      From their arms and appointment, they appear well born
      and worthy of respect, especially the one
370   who has led them this far: he is formidable indeed."
          Hrothgar, protector of Shieldings, replied:
      "I used to know him when he was a young boy.
      His father before him was called Ecgtheow.
      Hrethel the Geat[9] gave Ecgtheow
375   his daughter in marriage. This man is their son,
      here to follow up an old friendship.
      A crew of seamen who sailed for me once
      with a gift-cargo across to Geatland
      returned with marvelous tales about him:
380   a thane, they declared, with the strength of thirty
      in the grip of each hand. Now Holy God
      has, in His goodness, guided him here
      to the West-Danes, to defend us from Grendel.
      This is my hope; and for his heroism
385   I will recompense him with a rich treasure.
      Go immediately, bid him and the Geats
      he has in attendance to assemble and enter.
      Say, moreover, when you speak to them,
      they are welcome to Denmark."
                              At the door of the hall,
390   Wulfgar duly delivered the message:
      "My lord, the conquering king of the Danes,
      bids me announce that he knows your ancestry;
      also that he welcomes you here to Heorot
      and salutes your arrival from across the sea.
395   You are free now to move forward
      to meet Hrothgar in helmets and armor,
      but shields must stay here and spears be stacked

---

9. Hygelac's father and Beowulf's grandfather.

until the outcome of the audience is clear."
    The hero arose, surrounded closely
400   by his powerful thanes. A party remained
under orders to keep watch on the arms;
the rest proceeded, led by their prince
under Heorot's roof. And standing on the hearth
in webbed links that the smith had woven,
405   the fine-forged mesh of his gleaming mail-shirt,
resolute in his helmet, Beowulf spoke:
"Greetings to Hrothgar. I am Hygelac's kinsman,
one of his hall-troop. When I was younger,
I had great triumphs. Then news of Grendel,
410   hard to ignore, reached me at home:
sailors brought stories of the plight you suffer
in this legendary hall, how it lies deserted,
empty and useless once the evening light
hides itself under heaven's dome.
415   So every elder and experienced councilman
among my people supported my resolve
to come here to you, King Hrothgar,
because all knew of my awesome strength.
They had seen me boltered[1] in the blood of enemies
420   when I battled and bound five beasts,
raided a troll-nest and in the night-sea
slaughtered sea-brutes. I have suffered extremes
and avenged the Geats (their enemies brought it
upon themselves; I devastated them).
425   Now I mean to be a match for Grendel,
settle the outcome in single combat.
And so, my request, O king of Bright-Danes,
dear prince of the Shieldings, friend of the people
and their ring of defense, my one request
430   is that you won't refuse me, who have come this far,
the privilege of purifying Heorot,
with my own men to help me, and nobody else.
I have heard moreover that the monster scorns
in his reckless way to use weapons;
435   therefore, to heighten Hygelac's fame
and gladden his heart, I hereby renounce
sword and the shelter of the broad shield,
the heavy war-board: hand-to-hand
is how it will be, a life-and-death
440   fight with the fiend. Whichever one death fells
must deem it a just judgment by God.
If Grendel wins, it will be a gruesome day;
he will glut himself on the Geats in the war-hall,
swoop without fear on that flower of manhood
445   as on others before. Then my face won't be there
to be covered in death: he will carry me away
as he goes to ground, gorged and bloodied;

1. Clotted, sticky.

he will run gloating with my raw corpse
and feed on it alone, in a cruel frenzy
450 fouling his moor-nest. No need then
to lament for long or lay out my body:[2]
if the battle takes me, send back
this breast-webbing that Weland[3] fashioned
and Hrethel gave me, to Lord Hygelac.
455 Fate goes ever as fate must."
    Hrothgar, the helmet of Shieldings, spoke:
"Beowulf, my friend, you have traveled here
to favor us with help and to fight for us.
There was a feud one time, begun by your father.
460 With his own hands he had killed Heatholaf
who was a Wulfing; so war was looming
and his people, in fear of it, forced him to leave.
He came away then over rolling waves
to the South-Danes here, the sons of honor.
465 I was then in the first flush of kingship,
establishing my sway over the rich strongholds
of this heroic land. Heorogar,
my older brother and the better man,
also a son of Halfdane's, had died.
470 Finally I healed the feud by paying:
I shipped a treasure-trove to the Wulfings,
and Ecgtheow acknowledged me with oaths of allegiance.
    "It bothers me to have to burden anyone
with all the grief that Grendel has caused
475 and the havoc he has wreaked upon us in Heorot,
our humiliations. My household guard
are on the wane, fate sweeps them away
into Grendel's clutches—but God can easily
halt these raids and harrowing attacks!
480   "Time and again, when the goblets passed
and seasoned fighters got flushed with beer
they would pledge themselves to protect Heorot
and wait for Grendel with their whetted swords.
But when dawn broke and day crept in
485 over each empty, blood-spattered bench,
the floor of the mead-hall where they had feasted
would be slick with slaughter. And so they died,
faithful retainers, and my following dwindled.
Now take your place at the table, relish
490 the triumph of heroes to your heart's content."

[FEAST AT HEOROT]

    Then a bench was cleared in that banquet hall
so the Geats could have room to be together
and the party sat, proud in their bearing,

---

2. I.e., for burial. Hrothgar will not need to give
Beowulf an expensive funeral.

3. Famed blacksmith in Germanic legend.

strong and stalwart. An attendant stood by
495 with a decorated pitcher, pouring bright
helpings of mead. And the minstrel sang,
filling Heorot with his head-clearing voice,
gladdening that great rally of Geats and Danes.
From where he crouched at the king's feet,
500 Unferth, a son of Ecglaf's, spoke
contrary words. Beowulf's coming,
his sea-braving, made him sick with envy:
he could not brook or abide the fact
that anyone else alive under heaven
505 might enjoy greater regard than he did:
"Are you the Beowulf who took on Breca
in a swimming match on the open sea,
risking the water just to prove that you could win?
It was sheer vanity made you venture out
510 on the main deep. And no matter who tried,
friend or foe, to deflect the pair of you,
neither would back down: the sea-test obsessed you.
You waded in, embracing water,
taking its measure, mastering currents,
515 riding on the swell. The ocean swayed,
winter went wild in the waves, but you vied
for seven nights; and then he outswam you,
came ashore the stronger contender.
He was cast up safe and sound one morning
520 among the Heatho-Reams, then made his way
to where he belonged in Branding country,
home again, sure of his ground
in strongroom and bawn.[4] So Breca made good
his boast upon you and was proved right.
525 No matter, therefore, how you may have fared
in every bout and battle until now,
this time you'll be worsted; no one has ever
outlasted an entire night against Grendel."
Beowulf, Ecgtheow's son, replied:
530 "Well, friend Unferth, you have had your say
about Breca and me. But it was mostly beer
that was doing the talking. The truth is this:
when the going was heavy in those high waves,
I was the strongest swimmer of all.
535 We'd been children together and we grew up
daring ourselves to outdo each other,
boasting and urging each other to risk
our lives on the sea. And so it turned out.
Each of us swam holding a sword,
540 a naked, hard-proofed blade for protection
against the whale-beasts. But Breca could never
move out farther or faster from me

---

4. Fortified outwork of a court or castle. The word was used by English planters in Ulster to describe
fortified dwellings they erected on lands confiscated from the Irish [Translator's note].

than I could manage to move from him.
Shoulder to shoulder, we struggled on
545   for five nights, until the long flow
and pitch of the waves, the perishing cold,
night falling and winds from the north
drove us apart. The deep boiled up
and its wallowing sent the sea-brutes wild.
550   My armor helped me to hold out;
my hard-ringed chain-mail, hand-forged and linked,
a fine, close-fitting filigree of gold,
kept me safe when some ocean creature
pulled me to the bottom. Pinioned fast
555   and swathed in its grip, I was granted one
final chance: my sword plunged
and the ordeal was over. Through my own hands,
the fury of battle had finished off the sea-beast.
      "Time and again, foul things attacked me,
560   lurking and stalking, but I lashed out,
gave as good as I got with my sword.
My flesh was not for feasting on,
there would be no monsters gnawing and gloating
over their banquet at the bottom of the sea.
565   Instead, in the morning, mangled and sleeping
the sleep of the sword, they slopped and floated
like the ocean's leavings. From now on
sailors would be safe, the deep-sea raids
were over for good. Light came from the east,
570   bright guarantee of God, and the waves
went quiet; I could see headlands
and buffeted cliffs. Often, for undaunted courage,
fate spares the man it has not already marked.
However it occurred, my sword had killed
575   nine sea-monsters. Such night dangers
and hard ordeals I have never heard of
nor of a man more desolate in surging waves.
But worn out as I was, I survived,
came through with my life. The ocean lifted
580   and laid me ashore, I landed safe
on the coast of Finland.
                              Now I cannot recall
any fight you entered, Unferth,
that bears comparison. I don't boast when I say
that neither you nor Breca were ever much
585   celebrated for swordsmanship
or for facing danger on the field of battle.
You killed your own kith and kin,
so for all your cleverness and quick tongue,
you will suffer damnation in the depths of hell.
590   The fact is, Unferth, if you were truly
as keen or courageous as you claim to be
Grendel would never have got away with
such unchecked atrocity, attacks on your king,

havoc in Heorot and horrors everywhere.
595 But he knows he need never be in dread
of your blade making a mizzle of his blood
or of vengeance arriving ever from this quarter—
from the Victory-Shieldings, the shoulderers of the spear.
He knows he can trample down you Danes
600 to his heart's content, humiliate and murder
without fear of reprisal. But he will find me different.
I will show him how Geats shape to kill
in the heat of battle. Then whoever wants to
may go bravely to mead, when the morning light,
605 scarfed in sun-dazzle, shines forth from the south
and brings another daybreak to the world."
　　　Then the gray-haired treasure-giver was glad;
far-famed in battle, the prince of Bright-Danes
and keeper of his people counted on Beowulf,
610 on the warrior's steadfastness and his word.
So the laughter started, the din got louder
and the crowd was happy. Wealhtheow came in,
Hrothgar's queen, observing the courtesies.
Adorned in her gold, she graciously saluted
615 the men in the hall, then handed the cup
first to Hrothgar, their homeland's guardian,
urging him to drink deep and enjoy it
because he was dear to them. And he drank it down
like the warlord he was, with festive cheer.
620 So the Helming woman went on her rounds,
queenly and dignified, decked out in rings,
offering the goblet to all ranks,
treating the household and the assembled troop,
until it was Beowulf's turn to take it from her hand.
625 With measured words she welcomed the Geat
and thanked God for granting her wish
that a deliverer she could believe in would arrive
to ease their afflictions. He accepted the cup,
a daunting man, dangerous in action
630 and eager for it always. He addressed Wealhtheow;
Beowulf, son of Ecgtheow, said:
"I had a fixed purpose when I put to sea.
As I sat in the boat with my band of men,
I meant to perform to the uttermost
635 what your people wanted or perish in the attempt,
in the fiend's clutches. And I shall fulfill that purpose,
prove myself with a proud deed
or meet my death here in the mead-hall."
This formal boast by Beowulf the Geat
640 pleased the lady well and she went to sit
by Hrothgar, regal and arrayed with gold.
　　　Then it was like old times in the echoing hall,
proud talk and the people happy,
loud and excited; until soon enough
645 Halfdane's heir had to be away

to his night's rest. He realized
that the demon was going to descend on the hall,
that he had plotted all day, from dawn light
until darkness gathered again over the world
650 and stealthy night-shapes came stealing forth
under the cloud-murk. The company stood
as the two leaders took leave of each other:
Hrothgar wished Beowulf health and good luck,
named him hall-warden and announced as follows:
655 "Never, since my hand could hold a shield
have I entrusted or given control
of the Danes' hall to anyone but you.
Ward and guard it, for it is the greatest of houses.
Be on your mettle now, keep in mind your fame,
660 beware of the enemy. There's nothing you wish for
that won't be yours if you win through alive."

[THE FIGHT WITH GRENDEL]

Hrothgar departed then with his house-guard.
The lord of the Shieldings, their shelter in war,
left the mead-hall to lie with Wealhtheow,
665 his queen and bedmate. The King of Glory
(as people learned) had posted a lookout
who was a match for Grendel, a guard against monsters,
special protection to the Danish prince.
And the Geat placed complete trust
670 in his strength of limb and the Lord's favor.
He began to remove his iron breast-mail,
took off the helmet and handed his attendant
the patterned sword, a smith's masterpiece,
ordering him to keep the equipment guarded.
675 And before he bedded down, Beowulf,
that prince of goodness, proudly asserted:
"When it comes to fighting, I count myself
as dangerous any day as Grendel.
So it won't be a cutting edge I'll wield
680 to mow him down, easily as I might.
He has no idea of the arts of war,
of shield or sword-play, although he does possess
a wild strength. No weapons, therefore,
for either this night: unarmed he shall face me
685 if face me he dares. And may the Divine Lord
in His wisdom grant the glory of victory
to whichever side He sees fit."
Then down the brave man lay with his bolster
under his head and his whole company
690 of sea-rovers at rest beside him.
None of them expected he would ever see
his homeland again or get back
to his native place and the people who reared him.
They knew too well the way it was before,

695 how often the Danes had fallen prey
to death in the mead-hall. But the Lord was weaving
a victory on His war-loom for the Weather-Geats.
Through the strength of one they all prevailed;
they would crush their enemy and come through
700 in triumph and gladness. The truth is clear:
Almighty God rules over mankind
and always has.
                Then out of the night
came the shadow-stalker, stealthy and swift.
The hall-guards were slack, asleep at their posts,
705 all except one; it was widely understood
that as long as God disallowed it,
the fiend could not bear them to his shadow-bourne.
One man, however, was in fighting mood,
awake and on edge, spoiling for action.
710   In off the moors, down through the mist-bands
God-cursed Grendel came greedily loping.
The bane of the race of men roamed forth,
hunting for a prey in the high hall.
Under the cloud-murk he moved toward it
715 until it shone above him, a sheer keep
of fortified gold. Nor was that the first time
he had scouted the grounds of Hrothgar's dwelling—
although never in his life, before or since,
did he find harder fortune or hall-defenders.
720 Spurned and joyless, he journeyed on ahead
and arrived at the bawn.[5] The iron-braced door
turned on its hinge when his hands touched it.
Then his rage boiled over, he ripped open
the mouth of the building, maddening for blood,
725 pacing the length of the patterned floor
with his loathsome tread, while a baleful light,
flame more than light, flared from his eyes.
He saw many men in the mansion, sleeping,
a ranked company of kinsmen and warriors
730 quartered together. And his glee was demonic,
picturing the mayhem: before morning
he would rip life from limb and devour them,
feed on their flesh; but his fate that night
was due to change, his days of ravening
735 had come to an end.
                Mighty and canny,
Hygelac's kinsman was keenly watching
for the first move the monster would make.
Nor did the creature keep him waiting
but struck suddenly and started in;
740 he grabbed and mauled a man on his bench,
bit into his bone-lappings, bolted down his blood
and gorged on him in lumps, leaving the body

5. See p. 52, n. 4.

utterly lifeless, eaten up
hand and foot. Venturing closer,
745 his talon was raised to attack Beowulf
where he lay on the bed, he was bearing in
with open claw when the alert hero's
comeback and armlock forestalled him utterly.
The captain of evil discovered himself
750 in a handgrip harder than anything
he had ever encountered in any man
on the face of the earth. Every bone in his body
quailed and recoiled, but he could not escape.
He was desperate to flee to his den and hide
755 with the devil's litter, for in all his days
he had never been clamped or cornered like this.
Then Hygelac's trusty retainer recalled
his bedtime speech, sprang to his feet
and got a firm hold. Fingers were bursting,
760 the monster back-tracking, the man overpowering.
The dread of the land was desperate to escape,
to take a roundabout road and flee
to his lair in the fens. The latching power
in his fingers weakened; it was the worst trip
765 the terror-monger had taken to Heorot.
And now the timbers trembled and sang,
a hall-session[6] that harrowed every Dane
inside the stockade: stumbling in fury,
the two contenders crashed through the building.
770 The hall clattered and hammered, but somehow
survived the onslaught and kept standing:
it was handsomely structured, a sturdy frame
braced with the best of blacksmith's work
inside and out. The story goes
775 that as the pair struggled, mead-benches were smashed
and sprung off the floor, gold fittings and all.
Before then, no Shielding elder would believe
there was any power or person upon earth
capable of wrecking their horn-rigged hall
780 unless the burning embrace of a fire
engulf it in flame. Then an extraordinary
wail arose, and bewildering fear
came over the Danes. Everyone felt it
who heard that cry as it echoed off the wall,
785 a God-cursed scream and strain of catastrophe,
the howl of the loser, the lament of the hell-serf
keening his wound. He was overwhelmed,
manacled tight by the man who of all men
was foremost and strongest in the days of this life.
790   But the earl-troop's leader was not inclined
to allow his caller to depart alive:

6. In Hiberno-English the word "session" (*seissiún* in Irish) can mean a gathering where musicians and singers perform for their own enjoyment [Translator's note].

he did not consider that life of much account
to anyone anywhere. Time and again,
Beowulf's warriors worked to defend
795 their lord's life, laying about them
as best they could, with their ancestral blades.
Stalwart in action, they kept striking out
on every side, seeking to cut
straight to the soul. When they joined the struggle
800 there was something they could not have known at the time,
that no blade on earth, no blacksmith's art
could ever damage their demon opponent.
He had conjured the harm from the cutting edge
of every weapon.[7] But his going away
805 out of this world and the days of his life
would be agony to him, and his alien spirit
would travel far into fiends' keeping.
      Then he who had harrowed the hearts of men
with pain and affliction in former times
810 and had given offense also to God
found that his bodily powers failed him.
Hygelac's kinsman kept him helplessly
locked in a handgrip. As long as either lived,
he was hateful to the other. The monster's whole
815 body was in pain; a tremendous wound
appeared on his shoulder. Sinews split
and the bone-lappings burst. Beowulf was granted
the glory of winning; Grendel was driven
under the fen-banks, fatally hurt,
820 to his desolate lair. His days were numbered,
the end of his life was coming over him,
he knew it for certain; and one bloody clash
had fulfilled the dearest wishes of the Danes.
The man who had lately landed among them,
825 proud and sure, had purged the hall,
kept it from harm; he was happy with his nightwork
and the courage he had shown. The Geat captain
had boldly fulfilled his boast to the Danes:
he had healed and relieved a huge distress,
830 unremitting humiliations,
the hard fate they'd been forced to undergo,
no small affliction. Clear proof of this
could be seen in the hand the hero displayed
high up near the roof: the whole of Grendel's
835 shoulder and arm, his awesome grasp.

[CELEBRATION AT HEOROT]

      Then morning came and many a warrior
gathered, as I've heard, around the gift-hall,
clan-chiefs flocking from far and near
down wide-ranging roads, wondering greatly

---

7. Grendel is protected by a charm against metals.

840   at the monster's footprints. His fatal departure
     was regretted by no one who witnessed his trail,
     the ignominious marks of his flight
     where he'd skulked away, exhausted in spirit
     and beaten in battle, bloodying the path,
845   hauling his doom to the demons' mere.[8]
     The bloodshot water wallowed and surged,
     there were loathsome upthrows and overturnings
     of waves and gore and wound-slurry.
     With his death upon him, he had dived deep
850   into his marsh-den, drowned out his life
     and his heathen soul: hell claimed him there.
        Then away they rode, the old retainers
     with many a young man following after,
     a troop on horseback, in high spirits
855   on their bay steeds. Beowulf's doings
     were praised over and over again.
     Nowhere, they said, north or south
     between the two seas or under the tall sky
     on the broad earth was there anyone better
860   to raise a shield or to rule a kingdom.
     Yet there was no laying of blame on their lord,
     the noble Hrothgar; he was a good king.
        At times the war-band broke into a gallop,
     letting their chestnut horses race
865   wherever they found the going good
     on those well-known tracks. Meanwhile, a thane
     of the king's household, a carrier of tales,
     a traditional singer deeply schooled
     in the lore of the past, linked a new theme
870   to a strict meter.[9] The man started
     to recite with skill, rehearsing Beowulf's
     triumphs and feats in well-fashioned lines,
     entwining his words.
                   He told what he'd heard
     repeated in songs about Sigemund's exploits,[1]
875   all of those many feats and marvels,
     the struggles and wanderings of Waels's son,[2]
     things unknown to anyone
     except to Fitela, feuds and foul doings
     confided by uncle to nephew when he felt
880   the urge to speak of them: always they had been
     partners in the fight, friends in need.
     They killed giants, their conquering swords
     had brought them down.
                 After his death
     Sigemund's glory   grew and grew

---

8. A lake or pool, although we learn later that it
has an outlet to the sea. Grendel's habitat.
9. I.e., an extemporaneous heroic poem in alliterative verse about Beowulf's deeds.
1. Tales about Sigemund, his nephew Sinfjotli
(Fitela), and his son Sigurth are found in a 13th-

century Old Icelandic collection of legends
known as the *Volsung Saga*. Analogous stories
must have been known to the poet and his audience, though details differ.
2. Waels is the father of Sigemund.

885 *because of his courage   when he killed the dragon,*
the guardian of the hoard.   Under gray stone
he had dared to enter   all by himself
to face the worst   without Fitela.
But it came to pass   that his sword plunged
890 *right through   those radiant scales*
and drove into the wall.   The dragon died of it.
His daring had given him   total possession
of the treasure-hoard,   his to dispose of
however he liked.   He loaded a boat:
895 *Waels's son   weighted her hold*
with dazzling spoils.   The hot dragon melted.
*   Sigemund's name   was known everywhere.*
He was utterly valiant   and venturesome,
a fence round his fighters   and flourished therefore
900 *after King Heremod's[3]   prowess declined*
and his campaigns slowed down.   The king was betrayed,
ambushed in Jutland,   overpowered
and done away with.   The waves of his grief
had beaten him down,   made him a burden,
905 *a source of anxiety   to his own nobles:*
that expedition   was often condemned
in those earlier times   by experienced men,
men who relied   on his lordship for redress,
who presumed that the part   of a prince was to thrive
910 *on his father's throne   and defend the nation,*
the Shielding land   where they lived and belonged,
its holdings and strongholds.   Such was Beowulf
in the affection of his friends   and of everyone alive.
But evil entered   into Heremod.
915   They kept racing each other, urging their mounts
down sandy lanes. The light of day
broke and kept brightening. Bands of retainers
galloped in excitement to the gabled hall
to see the marvel; and the king himself,
920 guardian of the ring-hoard, goodness in person,
walked in majesty from the women's quarters
with a numerous train, attended by his queen
and her crowd of maidens, across to the mead-hall.
    When Hrothgar arrived at the hall, he spoke,
925 standing on the steps, under the steep eaves,
gazing toward the roofwork and Grendel's talon:
"First and foremost, let the Almighty Father
be thanked for this sight. I suffered a long
harrowing by Grendel. But the Heavenly Shepherd
930 can work His wonders always and everywhere.
Not long since, it seemed I would never
be granted the slightest solace or relief
from any of my burdens: the best of houses

---

3. Heremod was a bad king, held up by the bard as the opposite of Beowulf, as Sigemund is held up as a heroic prototype of Beowulf.

glittered and reeked and ran with blood.
935   This one worry outweighed all others—
a constant distress to counselors entrusted
with defending the people's forts from assault
by monsters and demons. But now a man,
with the Lord's assistance, has accomplished something
940 none of us could manage before now
for all our efforts. Whoever she was
who brought forth this flower of manhood,
if she is still alive, that woman can say
that in her labor the Lord of Ages
945 bestowed a grace on her. So now, Beowulf,
I adopt you in my heart as a dear son.
Nourish and maintain this new connection,
you noblest of men; there'll be nothing you'll want for,
no worldly goods that won't be yours.
950 I have often honored smaller achievements,
recognized warriors not nearly as worthy,
lavished rewards on the less deserving.
But you have made yourself immortal
by your glorious action. May the God of Ages
955 continue to keep and requite you well."
    Beowulf, son of Ecgtheow, spoke:
"We have gone through with a glorious endeavor
and been much favored in this fight we dared
against the unknown. Nevertheless,
960 if you could have seen the monster himself
where he lay beaten, I would have been better pleased.
My plan was to pounce, pin him down
in a tight grip and grapple him to death—
have him panting for life, powerless and clasped
965 in my bare hands, his body in thrall.
But I couldn't stop him from slipping my hold.
The Lord allowed it, my lock on him
wasn't strong enough; he struggled fiercely
and broke and ran. Yet he bought his freedom
970 at a high price, for he left his hand
and arm and shoulder to show he had been here,
a cold comfort for having come among us.
And now he won't be long for this world.
He has done his worst but the wound will end him.
975 He is hasped and hooped and hirpling with pain,
limping and looped in it. Like a man outlawed
for wickedness, he must await
the mighty judgment of God in majesty."
    There was less tampering and big talk then
980 from Unferth the boaster, less of his blather
as the hall-thanes eyed the awful proof
of the hero's prowess, the splayed hand
up under the eaves. Every nail,
claw-scale and spur, every spike
985 and welt on the hand of that heathen brute

was like barbed steel. Everybody said
there was no honed iron hard enough
to pierce him through, no time-proofed blade
that could cut his brutal, blood-caked claw.
990   Then the order was given for all hands
to help to refurbish Heorot immediately:
men and women thronging the wine-hall,
getting it ready. Gold thread shone
in the wall-hangings, woven scenes
995   that attracted and held the eye's attention.
But iron-braced as the inside of it had been,
that bright room lay in ruins now.
The very doors had been dragged from their hinges.
Only the roof remained unscathed
1000   by the time the guilt-fouled fiend turned tail
in despair of his life. But death is not easily
escaped from by anyone:
all of us with souls, earth-dwellers
and children of men, must make our way
1005   to a destination already ordained
where the body, after the banqueting,
sleeps on its deathbed.
                   Then the due time arrived
for Halfdane's son to proceed to the hall.
The king himself would sit down to feast.
1010   No group ever gathered in greater numbers
or better order around their ring-giver.
The benches filled with famous men
who fell to with relish; round upon round
of mead was passed; those powerful kinsmen,
1015   Hrothgar and Hrothulf, were in high spirits
in the raftered hall. Inside Heorot
there was nothing but friendship. The Shielding nation
was not yet familiar with feud and betrayal.[4]
    Then Halfdane's son presented Beowulf
1020   with a gold standard as a victory gift,
an embroidered banner; also breast-mail
and a helmet; and a sword carried high,
that was both precious object and token of honor.
So Beowulf drank his drink, at ease;
1025   it was hardly a shame to be showered with such gifts
in front of the hall-troops. There haven't been many
moments, I am sure, when men exchanged
four such treasures at so friendly a sitting.
An embossed ridge, a band lapped with wire
1030   arched over the helmet: head-protection
to keep the keen-ground cutting edge
from damaging it when danger threatened
and the man was battling behind his shield.

---

4. Probably an ironic allusion to the future usurpation of the throne from Hrothgar's sons by Hrothulf,
although no such treachery is recorded of Hrothulf, who is the hero of other Germanic stories.

Next the king ordered eight horses
1035 with gold bridles to be brought through the yard
into the hall. The harness of one
included a saddle of sumptuous design,
the battle-seat where the son of Halfdane
rode when he wished to join the sword-play:
1040 wherever the killing and carnage were the worst,
he would be to the fore, fighting hard.
Then the Danish prince, descendant of Ing,
handed over both the arms and the horses,
urging Beowulf to use them well.
1045 And so their leader, the lord and guard
of coffer and strongroom, with customary grace
bestowed upon Beowulf both sets of gifts.
A fair witness can see how well each one behaved.
       The chieftain went on to reward the others:
1050 each man on the bench who had sailed with Beowulf
and risked the voyage received a bounty,
some treasured possession. And compensation,
a price in gold, was settled for the Geat
Grendel had cruelly killed earlier—
1055 as he would have killed more, had not mindful God
and one man's daring prevented that doom.
Past and present, God's will prevails.
Hence, understanding is always best
and a prudent mind. Whoever remains
1060 for long here in this earthly life
will enjoy and endure more than enough.
       They sang then and played to please the hero,
words and music for their warrior prince,
harp tunes and tales of adventure:
1065 there were high times on the hall benches,
and the king's poet performed his part
with the saga of Finn and his sons, unfolding
the tale of the fierce attack in Friesland
where Hnaef, king of the Danes, met death.[5]
1070 *Hildeburh*
              had little cause
to credit the Jutes:
              son and brother,
she lost them both
              on the battlefield.
She, bereft
              and blameless, they

---

5. The bard's lay is known as the Finnsburg Episode. Its allusive style makes the tale obscure in
many details, although some can be filled in from
a fragmentary Old English lay, which modern editors have entitled *The Fight at Finnsburg*. Hildeburh, the daughter of the former Danish king
Hoc, was married to Finn, king of Friesland, presumably to help end a feud between their peoples.
As the episode opens, the feud has already broken
out again when a visiting party of Danes, led by
Hildeburh's brother Hnaef, who has succeeded
their father, is attacked by a tribe called the Jutes.
The Jutes are subject to Finn but may be a clan
distinct from the Frisians, and Finn does not
seem to have instigated the attack. In the ensuing
battle, both Hnaef and the son of Hildeburh and
Finn are killed, and both sides suffer heavy losses.

foredoomed, cut down
               and spear-gored. She,
1075   the woman in shock,
               waylaid by grief,
Hoc's daughter—
               how could she not
lament her fate
               when morning came
and the light broke
               on her murdered dears?
And so farewell
               delight on earth,
1080   war carried away
               Finn's troop of thanes
all but a few.
               How then could Finn
hold the line
               or fight on
to the end with Hengest,
               how save
the rump of his force
               from that enemy chief?
1085   So a truce was offered
               as follows:[6] first
separate quarters
               to be cleared for the Danes,
hall and throne
               to be shared with the Frisians.
Then, second:
               every day
at the dole-out of gifts
               Finn, son of Focwald,
1090   should honor the Danes,
               bestow with an even
hand to Hengest
               and Hengest's men
the wrought-gold rings,
               bounty to match
the measure he gave
               his own Frisians—
to keep morale
               in the beer-hall high.
1095   Both sides then
               sealed their agreement.
With oaths to Hengest
               Finn swore
openly, solemnly,
               that the battle survivors
would be guaranteed
               honor and status.

6. The truce was offered by Finn to Hengest, who succeeded Hnaef as leader of the Danes.

No infringement
        by word or deed,
1100   no provocation
        would be permitted.
Their own ring-giver
        after all
was dead and gone,
        they were leaderless,
in forced allegiance
        to his murderer.
So if any Frisian
        stirred up bad blood
1105   with insinuations
        or taunts about this,
the blade of the sword
        would arbitrate it.
A funeral pyre
        was then prepared,
effulgent gold
        brought out from the hoard.
The pride and prince
        of the Shieldings lay
1110   awaiting the flame.
        Everywhere
there were blood-plastered
        coats of mail.
The pyre was heaped
        with boar-shaped helmets
forged in gold,
        with the gashed corpses
of wellborn Danes—
        many had fallen.
1115   Then Hildeburh
        ordered her own
son's body
        be burnt with Hnaef's,
the flesh on his bones
        to sputter and blaze
beside his uncle's.
        The woman wailed
and sang keens,
        the warrior went up.[7]
1120   Carcass flame
        swirled and fumed,
they stood round the burial
        mound and howled
as heads melted,
        crusted gashes
spattered and ran
        bloody matter.

7. The meaning may be that the warrior was placed up on the pyre, or went up in smoke. "Keens": lamentations or dirges for the dead.

The glutton element
                flamed and consumed
1125   the dead of both sides.
                          Their great days were gone.
Warriors scattered
                to homes and forts
all over Friesland,
                fewer now, feeling
loss of friends.
                Hengest stayed,
lived out that whole
                resentful, blood-sullen
1130   winter with Finn,
                          homesick and helpless.
No ring-whorled prow
                could up then
and away on the sea.
                Wind and water
raged with storms,
                wave and shingle
were shackled in ice
                until another year
1135   appeared in the yard
                          as it does to this day,
the seasons constant,
                the wonder of light
coming over us.
                Then winter was gone,
earth's lap grew lovely,
                longing woke
in the cooped-up exile
                for a voyage home—
1140   but more for vengeance,
                          some way of bringing
things to a head:
                his sword arm hankered
to greet the Jutes.
                So he did not balk
once Hunlafing
                placed on his lap
Dazzle-the-Duel,
                the best sword of all,[8]
1145   whose edges Jutes
                knew only too well.
Thus blood was spilled,
                the gallant Finn
slain in his home
                after Guthlaf and Oslaf[9]

---

8. Hunlafing may be the son of a Danish warrior called Hunlaf. The placing of the sword in Hengest's lap is a symbolic call for revenge.
9. It is not clear whether the Danes have traveled home and then returned to Friesland with reinforcements, or whether the Danish survivors attack once the weather allows them to take ship.

back from their voyage
                    made old accusation:
the brutal ambush,
                    the fate they had suffered,
1150   *all blamed on Finn.*
                    The wildness in them
had to brim over.
                    The hall ran red
with blood of enemies.
                    Finn was cut down,
the queen brought away
                    and everything
the Shieldings could find
                    inside Finn's walls—
1155   *the Frisian king's*
                    gold collars and gemstones—
swept off to the ship.
                    Over sea-lanes then
back to Daneland
                    the warrior troop
bore that lady home.

                    The poem was over,
the poet had performed, a pleasant murmur
1160   started on the benches, stewards did the rounds
with wine in splendid jugs, and Wealhtheow came to sit
in her gold crown between two good men,
uncle and nephew, each one of whom
still trusted the other;[1] and the forthright Unferth,
1165   admired by all for his mind and courage
although under a cloud for killing his brothers,
reclined near the king.
                    The queen spoke:
"Enjoy this drink, my most generous lord;
raise up your goblet, entertain the Geats
1170   duly and gently, discourse with them,
be open-handed, happy and fond.
Relish their company, but recollect as well
all of the boons that have been bestowed on you.
The bright court of Heorot has been cleansed
1175   and now the word is that you want to adopt
this warrior as a son. So, while you may,
bask in your fortune, and then bequeath
kingdom and nation to your kith and kin,
before your decease. I am certain of Hrothulf.
1180   He is noble and will use the young ones well.
He will not let you down. Should you die before him,
he will treat our children truly and fairly.
He will honor, I am sure, our two sons,
repay them in kind, when he recollects

1. See n. 4, p. 62.

1185 all the good things we gave him once,
the favor and respect he found in his childhood."
She turned then to the bench where her boys sat,
Hrethric and Hrothmund, with other nobles' sons,
all the youth together; and that good man,
1190 Beowulf the Geat, sat between the brothers.
The cup was carried to him, kind words
spoken in welcome and a wealth of wrought gold
graciously bestowed: two arm bangles,
a mail-shirt and rings, and the most resplendent
1195 torque of gold I ever heard tell of
anywhere on earth or under heaven.
There was no hoard like it since Hama snatched
the Brosings' neck-chain and bore it away
with its gems and settings to his shining fort,
1200 away from Eormenric's wiles and hatred,[2]
and thereby ensured his eternal reward.
Hygelac the Geat, grandson of Swerting,
wore this neck-ring on his last raid;[3]
at bay under his banner, he defended the booty,
1205 treasure he had won. Fate swept him away
because of his proud need to provoke
a feud with the Frisians. He fell beneath his shield,
in the same gem-crusted, kingly gear
he had worn when he crossed the frothing wave-vat.
1210 So the dead king fell into Frankish hands.
They took his breast-mail, also his neck-torque,
and punier warriors plundered the slain
when the carnage ended; Geat corpses
covered the field.
Applause filled the hall.
1215 Then Wealhtheow pronounced in the presence of the company:
"Take delight in this torque, dear Beowulf,
wear it for luck and wear also this mail
from our people's armory: may you prosper in them!
Be acclaimed for strength, for kindly guidance
1220 to these two boys, and your bounty will be sure.
You have won renown: you are known to all men
far and near, now and forever.
Your sway is wide as the wind's home,
as the sea around cliffs. And so, my prince,
1225 I wish you a lifetime's luck and blessings
to enjoy this treasure. Treat my sons
with tender care, be strong and kind.
Here each comrade is true to the other,
loyal to lord, loving in spirit.

---

2. The necklace presented to Beowulf is compared to one worn by the goddess Freya in Germanic mythology. In another story it was stolen by Hama from the Gothic king Eormenric, who is treated as a tyrant in Germanic legend, but how Eormenric came to possess it is not known.
3. Later we learn that Beowulf gave the necklace to Hygd, the queen of his lord Hygelac. Hygelac is here said to have been wearing it on his last expedition. This is the first of several allusions to Hygelac's death on a raid up the Rhine, the one incident in the poem that can be connected to a historical event documented elsewhere.

1230 The thanes have one purpose, the people are ready:
having drunk and pledged, the ranks do as I bid."
She moved then to her place. Men were drinking wine
at that rare feast; how could they know fate,
the grim shape of things to come,
1235 the threat looming over many thanes
as night approached and King Hrothgar prepared
to retire to his quarters? Retainers in great numbers
were posted on guard as so often in the past.
Benches were pushed back, bedding gear and bolsters
1240 spread across the floor, and one man
lay down to his rest, already marked for death.
At their heads they placed their polished timber
battle-shields; and on the bench above them,
each man's kit was kept to hand:
1245 a towering war-helmet, webbed mail-shirt
and great-shafted spear. It was their habit
always and everywhere to be ready for action,
at home or in the camp, in whatever case
and at whatever time the need arose
1250 to rally round their lord. They were a right people.

[ANOTHER ATTACK]

They went to sleep. And one paid dearly
for his night's ease, as had happened to them often,
ever since Grendel occupied the gold-hall,
committing evil until the end came,
1255 death after his crimes. Then it became clear,
obvious to everyone once the fight was over,
that an avenger lurked and was still alive,
grimly biding time. Grendel's mother,
monstrous hell-bride, brooded on her wrongs.
1260 She had been forced down into fearful waters,
the cold depths, after Cain had killed
his father's son, felled his own
brother with a sword. Branded an outlaw,
marked by having murdered, he moved into the wilds,
1265 shunned company and joy. And from Cain there sprang
misbegotten spirits, among them Grendel,
the banished and accursed, due to come to grips
with that watcher in Heorot waiting to do battle.
The monster wrenched and wrestled with him,
1270 but Beowulf was mindful of his mighty strength,
the wondrous gifts God had showered on him:
he relied for help on the Lord of All,
on His care and favor. So he overcame the foe,
brought down the hell-brute. Broken and bowed,
1275 outcast from all sweetness, the enemy of mankind
made for his death-den. But now his mother
had sallied forth on a savage journey,
grief-racked and ravenous, desperate for revenge.

She came to Heorot. There, inside the hall,
1280 Danes lay asleep, earls who would soon endure
a great reversal, once Grendel's mother
attacked and entered. Her onslaught was less
only by as much as an amazon warrior's
strength is less than an armed man's
1285 when the hefted sword, its hammered edge
and gleaming blade slathered in blood,
razes the sturdy boar-ridge off a helmet.
Then in the hall, hard-honed swords
were grabbed from the bench, many a broad shield
1290 lifted and braced; there was little thought of helmets
or woven mail when they woke in terror.
The hell-dam was in panic, desperate to get out,
in mortal terror the moment she was found.
She had pounced and taken one of the retainers
1295 in a tight hold, then headed for the fen.
To Hrothgar, this man was the most beloved
of the friends he trusted between the two seas.
She had done away with a great warrior,
ambushed him at rest.
                              Beowulf was elsewhere.
1300 Earlier, after the award of the treasure,
the Geat had been given another lodging.
There was uproar in Heorot. She had snatched their trophy,
Grendel's bloodied hand. It was a fresh blow
to the afflicted bawn. The bargain was hard,
1305 both parties having to pay
with the lives of friends. And the old lord,
the gray-haired warrior, was heartsore and weary
when he heard the news: his highest-placed adviser,
his dearest companion, was dead and gone.
1310 Beowulf was quickly brought to the chamber:
the winner of fights, the arch-warrior,
came first-footing in with his fellow troops
to where the king in his wisdom waited,
still wondering whether Almighty God
1315 would ever turn the tide of his misfortunes.
So Beowulf entered with his band in attendance
and the wooden floorboards banged and rang
as he advanced, hurrying to address
the prince of the Ingwins, asking if he'd rested
1320 since the urgent summons had come as a surprise.
Then Hrothgar, the Shieldings' helmet, spoke:
"Rest? What is rest? Sorrow has returned.
Alas for the Danes! Aeschere is dead.
He was Yrmenlaf's elder brother
1325 and a soul-mate to me, a true mentor,
my right-hand man when the ranks clashed
and our boar-crests had to take a battering
in the line of action. Aeschere was everything
the world admires in a wise man and a friend.

1330 Then this roaming killer came in a fury
and slaughtered him in Heorot. Where she is hiding,
glutting on the corpse and glorying in her escape,
I cannot tell; she has taken up the feud
because of last night, when you killed Grendel,
1335 wrestled and racked him in ruinous combat
since for too long he had terrorized us
with his depredations. He died in battle,
paid with his life; and now this powerful
other one arrives, this force for evil
1340 driven to avenge her kinsman's death.
Or so it seems to thanes in their grief,
in the anguish every thane endures
at the loss of a ring-giver, now that the hand
that bestowed so richly has been stilled in death.
1345 "I have heard it said by my people in hall,
counselors who live in the upland country,
that they have seen two such creatures
prowling the moors, huge marauders
from some other world. One of these things,
1350 as far as anyone ever can discern,
looks like a woman; the other, warped
in the shape of a man, moves beyond the pale
bigger than any man, an unnatural birth
called Grendel by the country people
1355 in former days. They are fatherless creatures,
and their whole ancestry is hidden in a past
of demons and ghosts. They dwell apart
among wolves on the hills, on windswept crags
and treacherous keshes, where cold streams
1360 pour down the mountain and disappear
under mist and moorland.
                                        A few miles from here
a frost-stiffened wood waits and keeps watch
above a mere; the overhanging bank
is a maze of tree-roots mirrored in its surface.
1365 At night there, something uncanny happens:
the water burns. And the mere bottom
has never been sounded by the sons of men.
On its bank, the heather-stepper halts:
the hart in flight from pursuing hounds
1370 will turn to face them with firm-set horns
and die in the wood rather than dive
beneath its surface. That is no good place.
When wind blows up and stormy weather
makes clouds scud and the skies weep,
1375 out of its depths a dirty surge
is pitched toward the heavens. Now help depends
again on you and on you alone.
The gap of danger where the demon waits
is still unknown to you. Seek it if you dare.
1380 I will compensate you for settling the feud

as I did the last time with lavish wealth,
coffers of coiled gold, if you come back."

[BEOWULF FIGHTS GRENDEL'S MOTHER]

Beowulf, son of Ecgtheow, spoke:
"Wise sir, do not grieve. It is always better
1385   to avenge dear ones than to indulge in mourning.
For every one of us, living in this world
means waiting for our end. Let whoever can
win glory before death. When a warrior is gone,
that will be his best and only bulwark.
1390   So arise, my lord, and let us immediately
set forth on the trail of this troll-dam.
I guarantee you: she will not get away,
not to dens under ground nor upland groves
nor the ocean floor. She'll have nowhere to flee to.
1395   Endure your troubles today. Bear up
and be the man I expect you to be."
    With that the old lord sprang to his feet
and praised God for Beowulf's pledge.
Then a bit and halter were brought for his horse
1400   with the plaited mane. The wise king mounted
the royal saddle and rode out in style
with a force of shield-bearers. The forest paths
were marked all over with the monster's tracks,
her trail on the ground wherever she had gone
1405   across the dark moors, dragging away
the body of that thane, Hrothgar's best
counselor and overseer of the country.
So the noble prince proceeded undismayed
up fells and screes, along narrow footpaths
1410   and ways where they were forced into single file,
ledges on cliffs above lairs of water-monsters.
He went in front with a few men,
good judges of the lie of the land,
and suddenly discovered the dismal wood,
1415   mountain trees growing out at an angle
above gray stones: the bloodshot water
surged underneath. It was a sore blow
to all of the Danes, friends of the Shieldings,
a hurt to each and every one
1420   of that noble company when they came upon
Aeschere's head at the foot of the cliff.
    Everybody gazed as the hot gore
kept wallowing up and an urgent war-horn
repeated its notes: the whole party
1425   sat down to watch. The water was infested
with all kinds of reptiles. There were writhing sea-dragons
and monsters slouching on slopes by the cliff,
serpents and wild things such as those that often
surface at dawn to roam the sail-road

1430 and doom the voyage. Down they plunged,
lashing in anger at the loud call
of the battle-bugle. An arrow from the bow
of the Geat chief got one of them
as he surged to the surface: the seasoned shaft
1435 stuck deep in his flank and his freedom in the water
got less and less. It was his last swim.
He was swiftly overwhelmed in the shallows,
prodded by barbed boar-spears,
cornered, beaten, pulled up on the bank,
1440 a strange lake-birth, a loathsome catch
men gazed at in awe.
                 Beowulf got ready,
donned his war-gear, indifferent to death;
his mighty, hand-forged, fine-webbed mail
would soon meet with the menace underwater.
1445 It would keep the bone-cage of his body safe:
no enemy's clasp could crush him in it,
no vicious armlock choke his life out.
To guard his head he had a glittering helmet
that was due to be muddied on the mere bottom
1450 and blurred in the upswirl. It was of beaten gold,
princely headgear hooped and hasped
by a weapon-smith who had worked wonders
in days gone by and adorned it with boar-shapes;
since then it had resisted every sword.
1455 And another item lent by Unferth
at that moment of need was of no small importance:
the brehon[4] handed him a hilted weapon,
a rare and ancient sword named Hrunting.
The iron blade with its ill-boding patterns
1460 had been tempered in blood. It had never failed
the hand of anyone who hefted it in battle,
anyone who had fought and faced the worst
in the gap of danger. This was not the first time
it had been called to perform heroic feats.
1465   When he lent that blade to the better swordsman,
Unferth, the strong-built son of Ecglaf,
could hardly have remembered the ranting speech
he had made in his cups. He was not man enough
to face the turmoil of a fight under water
1470 and the risk to his life. So there he lost
fame and repute. It was different for the other
rigged out in his gear, ready to do battle.
    Beowulf, son of Ecgtheow, spoke:
"Wisest of kings, now that I have come
1475 to the point of action, I ask you to recall
what we said earlier: that you, son of Halfdane
and gold-friend to retainers, that you, if I should fall

4. One of an ancient class of lawyers in Ireland [Translator's note]. The Old English word for Unferth's office, *thyle*, has been interpreted as "orator" and "spokesman."

and suffer death while serving your cause,
would act like a father to me afterward.

1480 If this combat kills me, take care
of my young company, my comrades in arms.
And be sure also, my beloved Hrothgar,
to send Hygelac the treasures I received.
Let the lord of the Geats gaze on that gold,

1485 let Hrethel's son take note of it and see
that I found a ring-giver of rare magnificence
and enjoyed the good of his generosity.
And Unferth is to have what I inherited:
to that far-famed man I bequeath my own

1490 sharp-honed, wave-sheened wonder-blade.
With Hrunting I shall gain glory or die."
    After these words, the prince of the Weather-Geats
was impatient to be away and plunged suddenly:
without more ado, he dived into the heaving

1495 depths of the lake. It was the best part of a day
before he could see the solid bottom.
    Quickly the one who haunted those waters,
who had scavenged and gone her gluttonous rounds
for a hundred seasons, sensed a human

1500 observing her outlandish lair from above.
So she lunged and clutched and managed to catch him
in her brutal grip; but his body, for all that,
remained unscathed: the mesh of the chain-mail
saved him on the outside. Her savage talons

1505 failed to rip the web of his war-shirt.
Then once she touched bottom, that wolfish swimmer
carried the ring-mailed prince to her court
so that for all his courage he could never use
the weapons he carried; and a bewildering horde

1510 came at him from the depths, droves of sea-beasts
who attacked with tusks and tore at his chain-mail
in a ghastly onslaught. The gallant man
could see he had entered some hellish turn-hole
and yet the water there did not work against him

1515 because the hall-roofing held off
the force of the current; then he saw firelight,
a gleam and flare-up, a glimmer of brightness.
    The hero observed that swamp-thing from hell,
the tarn-hag in all her terrible strength,

1520 then heaved his war-sword and swung his arm:
the decorated blade came down ringing
and singing on her head. But he soon found
his battle-torch extinguished; the shining blade
refused to bite. It spared her and failed

1525 the man in his need. It had gone through many
hand-to-hand fight, had hewed the armor
and helmets of the doomed, but here at last
the fabulous powers of that heirloom failed.
    Hygelac's kinsman kept thinking about

1530   his name and fame: he never lost heart.
Then, in a fury, he flung his sword away.
The keen, inlaid, worm-loop-patterned steel
was hurled to the ground: he would have to rely
on the might of his arm. So must a man do
1535   who intends to gain enduring glory
in a combat. Life doesn't cost him a thought.
Then the prince of War-Geats, warming to this fight
with Grendel's mother, gripped her shoulder
and laid about him in a battle frenzy:
1540   he pitched his killer opponent to the floor
but she rose quickly and retaliated,
grappled him tightly in her grim embrace.
The sure-footed fighter felt daunted,
the strongest of warriors stumbled and fell.
1545   So she pounced upon him and pulled out
a broad, whetted knife: now she would avenge
her only child. But the mesh of chain-mail
on Beowulf's shoulder shielded his life,
turned the edge and tip of the blade.
1550   The son of Ecgtheow would have surely perished
and the Geats lost their warrior under the wide earth
had the strong links and locks of his war-gear
not helped to save him: holy God
decided the victory. It was easy for the Lord,
1555   the Ruler of Heaven, to redress the balance
once Beowulf got back up on his feet.
    Then he saw a blade that boded well,
a sword in her armory, an ancient heirloom
from the days of the giants, an ideal weapon,
1560   one that any warrior would envy,
but so huge and heavy of itself
only Beowulf could wield it in a battle.
So the Shieldings' hero hard-pressed and enraged,
took a firm hold of the hilt and swung
1565   the blade in an arc, a resolute blow
that bit deep into her neck-bone
and severed it entirely, toppling the doomed
house of her flesh; she fell to the floor.
The sword dripped blood, the swordsman was elated.
1570   A light appeared and the place brightened
the way the sky does when heaven's candle
is shining clearly. He inspected the vault:
with sword held high, its hilt raised
to guard and threaten, Hygelac's thane
1575   scouted by the wall in Grendel's wake.
Now the weapon was to prove its worth.
The warrior determined to take revenge
for every gross act Grendel had committed—
and not only for that one occasion
1580   when he'd come to slaughter the sleeping troops,
fifteen of Hrothgar's house-guards

surprised on their benches and ruthlessly devoured,
and as many again carried away,
a brutal plunder. Beowulf in his fury
1585 now settled that score: he saw the monster
in his resting place, war-weary and wrecked,
a lifeless corpse, a casualty
of the battle in Heorot. The body gaped
at the stroke dealt to it after death:
1590 Beowulf cut the corpse's head off.
  Immediately the counselors keeping a lookout
with Hrothgar, watching the lake water,
saw a heave-up and surge of waves
and blood in the backwash. They bowed gray heads,
1595 spoke in their sage, experienced way
about the good warrior, how they never again
expected to see that prince returning
in triumph to their king. It was clear to many
that the wolf of the deep had destroyed him forever.
1600   The ninth hour of the day arrived.
The brave Shieldings abandoned the cliff-top
and the king went home; but sick at heart,
staring at the mere, the strangers held on.
They wished, without hope, to behold their lord,
Beowulf himself.
1605   Meanwhile, the sword
began to wilt into gory icicles
to slather and thaw. It was a wonderful thing,
the way it all melted as ice melts
when the Father eases the fetters off the frost
1610 and unravels the water-ropes, He who wields power
over time and tide: He is the true Lord.
  The Geat captain saw treasure in abundance
but carried no spoils from those quarters
except for the head and the inlaid hilt
1615 embossed with jewels; its blade had melted
and the scrollwork on it burned, so scalding was the blood
of the poisonous fiend who had perished there.
Then away he swam, the one who had survived
the fall of his enemies, flailing to the surface.
1620 The wide water, the waves and pools,
were no longer infested once the wandering fiend
let go of her life and this unreliable world.
  The seafarers' leader made for land,
resolutely swimming, delighted with his prize,
1625 the mighty load he was lugging to the surface.
His thanes advanced in a troop to meet him,
thanking God and taking great delight
in seeing their prince back safe and sound.
Quickly the hero's helmet and mail-shirt
1630 were loosed and unlaced. The lake settled,
clouds darkened above the bloodshot depths.
  With high hearts they headed away

along footpaths and trails through the fields,
roads that they knew, each of them wrestling
1635 with the head they were carrying from the lakeside cliff,
men kingly in their courage and capable
of difficult work. It was a task for four
to hoist Grendel's head on a spear
and bear it under strain to the bright hall.
1640 But soon enough they neared the place,
fourteen Geats in fine fettle,
striding across the outlying ground
in a delighted throng around their leader.
    In he came then, the thanes' commander,
1645 the arch-warrior, to address Hrothgar:
his courage was proven, his glory was secure.
Grendel's head was hauled by the hair,
dragged across the floor where the people were drinking,
a horror for both queen and company to behold.
1650 They stared in awe. It was an astonishing sight.

[ANOTHER CELEBRATION AT HEOROT]

    Beowulf, son of Ecgtheow, spoke:
"So, son of Halfdane, prince of the Shieldings,
we are glad to bring this booty from the lake.
It is a token of triumph and we tender it to you.
1655 I barely survived the battle under water.
It was hard-fought, a desperate affair
that could have gone badly; if God had not helped me,
the outcome would have been quick and fatal.
Although Hrunting is hard-edged,
1660 I could never bring it to bear in battle.
But the Lord of Men allowed me to behold—
for He often helps the unbefriended—
an ancient sword shining on the wall,
a weapon made for giants, there for the wielding.
1665 Then my moment came in the combat and I struck
the dwellers in that den. Next thing the damascened
sword blade melted; it bloated and it burned
in their rushing blood. I have wrested the hilt
from the enemies' hand, avenged the evil
1670 done to the Danes; it is what was due.
And this I pledge, O prince of the Shieldings:
you can sleep secure with your company of troops
in Heorot Hall. Never need you fear
for a single thane of your sept or nation,
1675 young warriors or old, that laying waste of life
that you and your people endured of yore."
    Then the gold hilt was handed over
to the old lord, a relic from long ago
for the venerable ruler. That rare smithwork
1680 was passed on to the prince of the Danes
when those devils perished; once death removed

that murdering, guilt-steeped, God-cursed fiend,
eliminating his unholy life
and his mother's as well, it was willed to that king
1685   who of all the lavish gift-lords of the north
was the best regarded between the two seas.
    Hrothgar spoke; he examined the hilt,
that relic of old times. It was engraved all over
and showed how war first came into the world
1690   and the flood destroyed the tribe of giants.
They suffered a terrible severance from the Lord;
the Almighty made the waters rise,
drowned them in the deluge for retribution.
In pure gold inlay on the sword-guards
1695   there were rune-markings correctly incised,
stating and recording for whom the sword
had been first made and ornamented
with its scrollworked hilt. Then everyone hushed
as the son of Halfdane spoke this wisdom:
1700   "A protector of his people, pledged to uphold
truth and justice and to respect tradition,
is entitled to affirm that this man
was born to distinction. Beowulf, my friend,
your fame has gone far and wide,
1705   you are known everywhere. In all things you are even-tempered,
prudent and resolute. So I stand firm by the promise of friendship
we exchanged before. Forever you will be
your people's mainstay and your own warriors'
helping hand.
               Heremod was different,
1710   the way he behaved to Ecgwela's sons.
His rise in the world brought little joy
to the Danish people, only death and destruction.
He vented his rage on men he caroused with,
killed his own comrades, a pariah king
1715   who cut himself off from his own kind,
even though Almighty God had made him
eminent and powerful and marked him from the start
for a happy life. But a change happened,
he grew bloodthirsty, gave no more rings
1720   to honor the Danes. He suffered in the end
for having plagued his people for so long:
his life lost happiness.
             So learn from this
and understand true values. I who tell you
have wintered into wisdom.
             It is a great wonder
1725   how Almighty God in His magnificence
favors our race with rank and scope
and the gift of wisdom; His sway is wide.
Sometimes He allows the mind of a man
of distinguished birth to follow its bent,
1730   grants him fulfillment and felicity on earth

and forts to command in his own country.
He permits him to lord it in many lands
until the man in his unthinkingness
forgets that it will ever end for him.
1735 He indulges his desires; illness and old age
mean nothing to him; his mind is untroubled
by envy or malice or the thought of enemies
with their hate-honed swords. The whole world
conforms to his will, he is kept from the worst
1740 until an element of overweening
enters him and takes hold
while the soul's guard, its sentry, drowses,
grown too distracted. A killer stalks him,
an archer who draws a deadly bow.
1745 And then the man is hit in the heart,
the arrow flies beneath his defenses,
the devious promptings of the demon start.
His old possessions seem paltry to him now.
He covets and resents; dishonors custom
1750 and bestows no gold; and because of good things
that the Heavenly Powers gave him in the past
he ignores the shape of things to come.
Then finally the end arrives
when the body he was lent collapses and falls
1755 prey to its death; ancestral possessions
and the goods he hoarded are inherited by another
who lets them go with a liberal hand.
    "O flower of warriors, beware of that trap.
Choose, dear Beowulf, the better part,
1760 eternal rewards. Do not give way to pride.
For a brief while your strength is in bloom
but it fades quickly; and soon there will follow
illness or the sword to lay you low,
or a sudden fire or surge of water
1765 or jabbing blade or javelin from the air
or repellent age. Your piercing eye
will dim and darken; and death will arrive,
dear warrior, to sweep you away.
    "Just so I ruled the Ring-Danes' country
1770 for fifty years, defended them in wartime
with spear and sword against constant assaults
by many tribes: I came to believe
my enemies had faded from the face of the earth.
Still, what happened was a hard reversal
1775 from bliss to grief. Grendel struck
after lying in wait. He laid waste to the land
and from that moment my mind was in dread
of his depredations. So I praise God
in His heavenly glory that I lived to behold
1780 this head dripping blood and that after such harrowing
I can look upon it in triumph at last.
Take your place, then, with pride and pleasure,

and move to the feast. Tomorrow morning
our treasure will be shared and showered upon you."
1785   The Geat was elated and gladly obeyed
the old man's bidding; he sat on the bench.
And soon all was restored, the same as before.
Happiness came back, the hall was thronged,
and a banquet set forth; black night fell
1790   and covered them in darkness.
                        Then the company rose
for the old campaigner: the gray-haired prince
was ready for bed. And a need for rest
came over the brave shield-bearing Geat.
He was a weary seafarer, far from home,
1795   so immediately a house-guard guided him out,
one whose office entailed looking after
whatever a thane on the road in those days
might need or require. It was noble courtesy.

[BEOWULF RETURNS HOME]

    That great heart rested. The hall towered,
1800   gold-shingled and gabled, and the guest slept in it
until the black raven with raucous glee
announced heaven's joy, and a hurry of brightness
overran the shadows. Warriors rose quickly,
impatient to be off: their own country
1805   was beckoning the nobles; and the bold voyager
longed to be aboard his distant boat.
Then that stalwart fighter ordered Hrunting
to be brought to Unferth, and bade Unferth
take the sword and thanked him for lending it.
1810   He said he had found it a friend in battle
and a powerful help; he put no blame
on the blade's cutting edge. He was a considerate man.
    And there the warriors stood in their war-gear,
eager to go, while their honored lord
1815   approached the platform where the other sat.
The undaunted hero addressed Hrothgar.
Beowulf, son of Ecgtheow, spoke:
"Now we who crossed the wide sea
have to inform you that we feel a desire
1820   to return to Hygelac. Here we have been welcomed
and thoroughly entertained. You have treated us well.
If there is any favor on earth I can perform
beyond deeds of arms I have done already,
anything that would merit your affections more,
1825   I shall act, my lord, with alacrity.
If ever I hear from across the ocean
that people on your borders are threatening battle
as attackers have done from time to time,
I shall land with a thousand thanes at my back
1830   to help your cause. Hygelac may be young

to rule a nation, but this much I know
about the king of the Geats: he will come to my aid
and want to support me by word and action
in your hour of need, when honor dictates
1835 that I raise a hedge of spears around you.
Then if Hrethric should think about traveling
as a king's son to the court of the Geats,
he will find many friends. Foreign places
yield more to one who is himself worth meeting."
1840   Hrothgar spoke and answered him:
"The Lord in his wisdom sent you those words
and they came from the heart. I have never heard
so young a man make truer observations.
You are strong in body and mature in mind,
1845 impressive in speech. If it should come to pass
that Hrethel's descendant dies beneath a spear,
if deadly battle or the sword blade or disease
fells the prince who guards your people
and you are still alive, then I firmly believe
1850 the seafaring Geats won't find a man
worthier of acclaim as their king and defender
than you, if only you would undertake
the lordship of your homeland. My liking for you
deepens with time, dear Beowulf.
1855 What you have done is to draw two peoples,
the Geat nation and us neighboring Danes,
into shared peace and a pact of friendship
in spite of hatreds we have harbored in the past.
For as long as I rule this far-flung land
1860 treasures will change hands and each side will treat
the other with gifts; across the gannet's bath,
over the broad sea, whorled prows will bring
presents and tokens. I know your people
are beyond reproach in every respect,
1865 steadfast in the old way with friend or foe."
    Then the earls' defender furnished the hero
with twelve treasures and told him to set out,
sail with those gifts safely home
to the people he loved, but to return promptly.
1870 And so the good and gray-haired Dane,
that highborn king, kissed Beowulf
and embraced his neck, then broke down
in sudden tears. Two forebodings
disturbed him in his wisdom, but one was stronger:
1875 nevermore would they meet each other
face to face. And such was his affection
that he could not help being overcome:
his fondness for the man was so deep-founded,
it warmed his heart and wound the heartstrings
1880 tight in his breast.
                    The embrace ended
and Beowulf, glorious in his gold regalia,

stepped the green earth. Straining at anchor
and ready for boarding, his boat awaited him.
So they went on their journey, and Hrothgar's generosity
1885   was praised repeatedly. He was a peerless king
until old age sapped his strength and did him
mortal harm, as it has done so many.

    Down to the waves then, dressed in the web
of their chain-mail and war-shirts the young men marched
1890   in high spirits. The coast-guard spied them,
thanes setting forth, the same as before.
His salute this time from the top of the cliff
was far from unmannerly; he galloped to meet them
and as they took ship in their shining gear,
1895   he said how welcome they would be in Geatland.
Then the broad hull was beached on the sand
to be cargoed with treasure, horses and war-gear.
The curved prow motioned; the mast stood high
above Hrothgar's riches in the loaded hold.

1900   The guard who had watched the boat was given
a sword with gold fittings, and in future days
that present would make him a respected man
at his place on the mead-bench.

                      Then the keel plunged
and shook in the sea; and they sailed from Denmark.

1905   Right away the mast was rigged with its sea-shawl;
sail-ropes were tightened, timbers drummed
and stiff winds kept the wave-crosser
skimming ahead; as she heaved forward,
her foamy neck was fleet and buoyant,
1910   a lapped prow loping over currents,
until finally the Geats caught sight of coastline
and familiar cliffs. The keel reared up,
wind lifted it home, it hit on the land.

    The harbor guard came hurrying out
1915   to the rolling water: he had watched the offing
long and hard, on the lookout for those friends.
With the anchor cables, he moored their craft
right where it had beached, in case a backwash
might catch the hull and carry it away.
1920   Then he ordered the prince's treasure-trove
to be carried ashore. It was a short step
from there to where Hrethel's son and heir,
Hygelac the gold-giver, makes his home
on a secure cliff, in the company of retainers.

1925   The building was magnificent, the king majestic,
ensconced in his hall; and although Hygd, his queen,
was young, a few short years at court,
her mind was thoughtful and her manners sure.
Haereth's daughter behaved generously
1930   and stinted nothing when she distributed
bounty to the Geats.

                Great Queen Modthryth

perpetrated terrible wrongs.[5]
If any retainer ever made bold
to look her in the face, if an eye not her lord's[6]
1935   stared at her directly during daylight,
the outcome was sealed: he was kept bound,
in hand-tightened shackles, racked, tortured
until doom was pronounced—death by the sword,
slash of blade, blood-gush, and death-qualms
1940   in an evil display. Even a queen
outstanding in beauty must not overstep like that.
A queen should weave peace, not punish the innocent
with loss of life for imagined insults.
But Hemming's kinsman[7] put a halt to her ways
1945   and drinkers round the table had another tale:
she was less of a bane to people's lives,
less cruel-minded, after she was married
to the brave Offa, a bride arrayed
in her gold finery, given away
1950   by a caring father, ferried to her young prince
over dim seas. In days to come
she would grace the throne and grow famous
for her good deeds and conduct of life,
her high devotion to the hero king
1955   who was the best king, it has been said,
between the two seas or anywhere else
on the face of the earth. Offa was honored
far and wide for his generous ways,
his fighting spirit and his farseeing
1960   defense of his homeland; from him there sprang Eomer,
Garmund's grandson, kinsman of Hemming,[8]
his warriors' mainstay and master of the field.

   Heroic Beowulf and his band of men
crossed the wide strand, striding along
1965   the sandy foreshore; the sun shone,
the world's candle warmed them from the south
as they hastened to where, as they had heard,
the young king, Ongentheow's killer
and his people's protector,[9] was dispensing rings
1970   inside his bawn. Beowulf's return
was reported to Hygelac as soon as possible,

---

5. The story of Queen Modthryth's vices is abruptly introduced as a foil to Queen Hygd's virtues. A transitional passage may have been lost, but the poet's device is similar to that of using the earlier reference to the wickedness of King Heremod to contrast with the good qualities of Sigemund and Beowulf.

6. This could refer to her husband or her father before her marriage. The story resembles folktales about a proud princess whose unsuccessful suitors are all put to death, although the unfortunate victims in this case seem to be guilty only of looking at her.

7. I.e., Offa I, a legendary king of the Angles. We know nothing about Hemming other than that

Offa was related to him. Offa II (757–96) was king of Mercia, and although the story is about the second Offa's ancestor on the Continent, this is the only English connection in the poem and has been taken as evidence to date its origins to 8th-century Mercia.

8. I.e., Eomer, Offa's son. See previous note. Garmund was presumably the name of Offa's father.

9. I.e., Hygelac. Ongentheow was king of the Swedish people called the Shylfings. This is the first of the references to wars between the Geats and the Swedes. One of Hygelac's war party named Eofer was the actual slayer of Ongentheow.

news that the captain was now in the enclosure,
his battle-brother back from the fray
alive and well, walking to the hall.
1975 Room was quickly made, on the king's orders,
and the troops filed across the cleared floor.
        After Hygelac had offered greetings
to his loyal thane in a lofty speech,
he and his kinsman, that hale survivor,
1980 sat face to face. Haereth's daughter
moved about with the mead-jug in her hand,
taking care of the company, filling the cups
that warriors held out. Then Hygelac began
to put courteous questions to his old comrade
1985 in the high hall. He hankered to know
every tale the Sea-Geats had to tell:
"How did you fare on your foreign voyage,
dear Beowulf, when you abruptly decided
to sail away across the salt water
1990 and fight at Heorot? Did you help Hrothgar
much in the end? Could you ease the prince
of his well-known troubles? Your undertaking
cast my spirits down, I dreaded the outcome
of your expedition and pleaded with you
1995 long and hard to leave the killer be,
let the South-Danes settle their own
blood-feud with Grendel. So God be thanked
I am granted this sight of you, safe and sound."
        Beowulf, son of Ecgtheow, spoke:
2000 "What happened, Lord Hygelac, is hardly a secret
any more among men in this world—
myself and Grendel coming to grips
on the very spot where he visited destruction
on the Victory-Shieldings and violated
2005 life and limb, losses I avenged
so no earthly offspring of Grendel's
need ever boast of that bout before dawn,
no matter how long the last of his evil
family survives.
                When I first landed
2010 I hastened to the ring-hall and saluted Hrothgar.
Once he discovered why I had come,
the son of Halfdane sent me immediately
to sit with his own sons on the bench.
It was a happy gathering. In my whole life
2015 I have never seen mead enjoyed more
in any hall on earth. Sometimes the queen
herself appeared, peace-pledge between nations,
to hearten the young ones and hand out
a torque to a warrior, then take her place.
2020 Sometimes Hrothgar's daughter distributed
ale to older ranks, in order on the benches:
I heard the company call her Freawaru

as she made her rounds, presenting men
with the gem-studded bowl, young bride-to-be
2025 to the gracious Ingeld,[1] in her gold-trimmed attire.
The friend of the Shieldings favors her betrothal:
the guardian of the kingdom sees good in it
and hopes this woman will heal old wounds
and grievous feuds.
But generally the spear
2030 is prompt to retaliate when a prince is killed,
no matter how admirable the bride may be.
"Think how the Heatho-Bards are bound to feel,
their lord, Ingeld, and his loyal thanes,
when he walks in with that woman to the feast:
2035 Danes are at the table, being entertained,
honored guests in glittering regalia,
burnished ring-mail that was their hosts' birthright,
looted when the Heatho-Bards could no longer wield
their weapons in the shield-clash, when they went down
2040 with their beloved comrades and forfeited their lives.
Then an old spearman will speak while they are drinking,
having glimpsed some heirloom that brings alive
memories of the massacre; his mood will darken
and heart-stricken, in the stress of his emotion,
2045 he will begin to test a young man's temper
and stir up trouble, starting like this:
'Now, my friend, don't you recognize
your father's sword, his favorite weapon,
the one he wore when he went out in his war-mask
2050 to face the Danes on that final day?
After Withergeld[2] died and his men were doomed,
the Shieldings quickly claimed the field;
and now here's a son of one or other
of those same killers coming through our hall
2055 overbearing us, mouthing boasts,
and rigged in armor that by right is yours.'
And so he keeps on, recalling and accusing,
working things up with bitter words
until one of the lady's retainers lies
2060 spattered in blood, split open
on his father's account.[3] The killer knows
the lie of the land and escapes with his life.
Then on both sides the oath-bound lords
will break the peace, a passionate hate
2065 will build up in Ingeld, and love for his bride
will falter in him as the feud rankles.
I therefore suspect the good faith of the Heatho-Bards,
the truth of their friendship and the trustworthiness

---

1. King of the Heatho-Bards; his father, Froda, was killed by the Danes.
2. One of the Heatho-Bard leaders.
3. I.e., the young Danish attendant is killed because his father killed the father of the young Heatho-Bard who has been egged on by the old veteran of that campaign.

of their alliance with the Danes.

But now, my lord,

2070 I shall carry on with my account of Grendel,
the whole story of everything that happened
in the hand-to-hand fight.

After heaven's gem

had gone mildly to earth, that maddened spirit,
the terror of those twilights, came to attack us
2075 where we stood guard, still safe inside the hall.
There deadly violence came down on Hondscio
and he fell as fate ordained, the first to perish,
rigged out for the combat. A comrade from our ranks
had come to grief in Grendel's maw:
2080 he ate up the entire body.
There was blood on his teeth, he was bloated and dangerous,
all roused up, yet still unready
to leave the hall empty-handed;
renowned for his might, he matched himself against me,
2085 wildly reaching. He had this roomy pouch,
a strange accoutrement, intricately strung
and hung at the ready, a rare patchwork
of devilishly fitted dragon-skins.
I had done him no wrong, yet the raging demon
2090 wanted to cram me and many another
into this bag—but it was not to be
once I got to my feet in a blind fury.
It would take too long to tell how I repaid
the terror of the land for every life he took
2095 and so won credit for you, my king,
and for all your people. And although he got away
to enjoy life's sweetness for a while longer,
his right hand stayed behind him in Heorot,
evidence of his miserable overthrow
2100 as he dived into murk on the mere bottom.
    "I got lavish rewards from the lord of the Danes
for my part in the battle, beaten gold
and much else, once morning came
and we took our places at the banquet table.
2105 There was singing and excitement: an old reciter,
a carrier of stories, recalled the early days.
At times some hero made the timbered harp
tremble with sweetness, or related true
and tragic happenings; at times the king
2110 gave the proper turn to some fantastic tale;
or a battle-scarred veteran, bowed with age,
would begin to remember the martial deeds
of his youth and prime and be overcome
as the past welled up in his wintry heart.
2115   "We were happy there the whole day long
and enjoyed our time until another night
descended upon us. Then suddenly
the vehement mother avenged her son

and wreaked destruction. Death had robbed her,
2120 Geats had slain Grendel, so his ghastly dam
struck back and with bare-faced defiance
laid a man low. Thus life departed
from the sage Aeschere, an elder wise in counsel.
But afterward, on the morning following,
2125 the Danes could not burn the dead body
nor lay the remains of the man they loved
on his funeral pyre. She had fled with the corpse
and taken refuge beneath torrents on the mountain.
It was a hard blow for Hrothgar to bear,
2130 harder than any he had undergone before.
And so the heartsore king beseeched me
in your royal name to take my chances
underwater, to win glory
and prove my worth. He promised me rewards.
2135 Hence, as is well known, I went to my encounter
with the terror-monger at the bottom of the tarn.
For a while it was hand-to-hand between us,
then blood went curling along the currents
and I beheaded Grendel's mother in the hall
2140 with a mighty sword. I barely managed
to escape with my life; my time had not yet come.
But Halfdane's heir, the shelter of those earls,
again endowed me with gifts in abundance.
    "Thus the king acted with due custom.
2145 I was paid and recompensed completely,
given full measure and the freedom to choose
from Hothgar's treasures by Hrothgar himself.
These, King Hygelac, I am happy to present
to you as gifts. It is still upon your grace
2150 that all favor depends. I have few kinsmen
who are close, my king, except for your kind self."
Then he ordered the boar-framed standard to be brought,
the battle-topping helmet, the mail-shirt gray as hoar-frost,
and the precious war-sword; and proceeded with his speech:
2155   "When Hrothgar presented this war-gear to me
he instructed me, my lord, to give you some account
of why it signifies his special favor.
He said it had belonged to his older brother,
King Heorogar, who had long kept it,
2160 but that Heorogar had never bequeathed it
to his son Heoroward, that worthy scion,
loyal as he was. Enjoy it well."
    I heard four horses were handed over next.
Beowulf bestowed four bay steeds
2165 to go with the armor, swift gallopers,
all alike. So ought a kinsman act,
instead of plotting and planning in secret
to bring people to grief, or conspiring to arrange
the death of comrades. The warrior king
2170 was uncle to Beowulf and honored by his nephew:

each was concerned for the other's good.
    I heard he presented Hygd with a gorget,
the priceless torque that the prince's daughter,
Wealhtheow, had given him; and three horses,
2175   supple creatures brilliantly saddled.
The bright necklace would be luminous on Hygd's breast.
    Thus Beowulf bore himself with valor;
he was formidable in battle yet behaved with honor
and took no advantage; never cut down
2180   a comrade who was drunk, kept his temper
and, warrior that he was, watched and controlled
his God-sent strength and his outstanding
natural powers. He had been poorly regarded
for a long time, was taken by the Geats
2185   for less than he was worth:[4] and their lord too
had never much esteemed him in the mead-hall.
They firmly believed that he lacked force,
that the prince was a weakling; but presently
every affront to his deserving was reversed.
2190   The battle-famed king, bulwark of his earls,
ordered a gold-chased heirloom of Hrethel's[5]
to be brought in; it was the best example
of a gem-studded sword in the Geat treasury.
This he laid on Beowulf's lap
2195   and then rewarded him with land as well,
seven thousand hides; and a hall and a throne.
Both owned land by birth in that country,
ancestral grounds; but the greater right
and sway were inherited by the higher born.

[THE DRAGON WAKES]

2200   A lot was to happen in later days
in the fury of battle. Hygelac fell
and the shelter of Heardred's shield proved useless
against the fierce aggression of the Shylfings:[6]
ruthless swordsmen, seasoned campaigners,
2205   they came against him and his conquering nation,
and with cruel force cut him down

---

4. There is no other mention of Beowulf's unpromising youth. This motif of the "Cinderella hero"
and others, such as Grendel's magic pouch, are
examples of folklore material, probably circulating orally, that made its way into the poem.
5. Hygelac's father and Beowulf's grandfather.
6. There are several references, some of them
lengthy, to the wars between the Geats and the
Swedes. Because these are highly allusive and not in
chronological order, they are difficult to follow and
keep straight. This outline, along with the Genealo-
gies (p. 32), may serve as a guide. *Phase 1:* After the
death of the Geat patriarch, King Hrethel (lines
2462–70), Ohthere and Onela, the sons of the
Swedish king Ongentheow, invade Geat territory
and inflict heavy casualties in a battle at Hreosnahill (lines 2472–78). *Phase 2:* The Geats invade
Sweden under Haethcyn, King Hrethel's son who

has succeeded him. At the battle of Ravenswood,
the Geats capture Ongentheow's queen, but Ongentheow counterattacks, rescues the queen, and kills
Haethcyn. Hygelac, Haethcyn's younger brother,
arrives with reinforcements; Ongentheow is killed
in savage combat with two of Hygelac's men; and the
Swedes are routed (lines 2479–89 and 2922–90).
Phase 3: Eanmund and Eadgils, the sons of Ohthere
(presumably dead), are driven into exile by their
uncle Onela, who is now king of the Swedes. They
are given refuge by Hygelac's son Heardred, who has
succeeded his father. Onela invades Geatland and
kills Heardred; his retainer Weohstan kills Eanmund; and after the Swedes withdraw, Beowulf
becomes king (lines 2204–8, which follow, and
2379–90). *Phase 4:* Eadgils, supported by Beowulf,
invades Sweden and kills Onela (lines 2391–96).

so that afterwards
          the wide kingdom
reverted to Beowulf. He ruled it well
for fifty winters, grew old and wise

2210 as warden of the land
            until one began
to dominate the dark, a dragon on the prowl
from the steep vaults of a stone-roofed barrow
where he guarded a hoard; there was a hidden passage,
unknown to men, but someone[7] managed

2215 to enter by it and interfere
with the heathen trove. He had handled and removed
a gem-studded goblet; it gained him nothing,
though with a thief's wiles he had outwitted
the sleeping dragon. That drove him into rage,

2220 as the people of that country would soon discover.
    The intruder who broached the dragon's treasure
and moved him to wrath had never meant to.
It was desperation on the part of a slave
fleeing the heavy hand of some master,

2225 guilt-ridden and on the run,
going to ground. But he soon began
to shake with terror;[8] . . . . . . in shock
the wretch . . . .
. . . . panicked and ran

2230 away with the precious . . . . . .
metalwork. There were many other
heirlooms heaped inside the earth-house,
because long ago, with deliberate care,
some forgotten person had deposited the whole

2235 rich inheritance of a highborn race
in this ancient cache. Death had come
and taken them all in times gone by
and the only one left to tell their tale,
the last of their line, could look forward to nothing

2240 but the same fate for himself: he foresaw that his joy
in the treasure would be brief.
              A newly constructed
barrow stood waiting, on a wide headland
close to the waves, its entryway secured.
Into it the keeper of the hoard had carried

2245 all the goods and golden ware
worth preserving. His words were few:
"Now, earth, hold what earls once held
and heroes can no more; it was mined from you first
by honorable men. My own people

2250 have been ruined in war; one by one
they went down to death, looked their last

---

7. The following section was damaged by fire. In lines 2215–31 entire words and phrases are missing or indicated by only a few letters. Editorial attempts to reconstruct the text are conjectural and often disagree.

8. Lines 2227–30 are so damaged that they defy guesswork to reconstruct them.

on sweet life in the hall. I am left with nobody
to bear a sword or to burnish plated goblets,
put a sheen on the cup. The companies have departed.
2255 The hard helmet, hasped with gold,
will be stripped of its hoops; and the helmet-shiner
who should polish the metal of the war-mask sleeps;
the coat of mail that came through all fights,
through shield-collapse and cut of sword,
2260 decays with the warrior. Nor may webbed mail
range far and wide on the warlord's back
beside his mustered troops. No trembling harp,
no tuned timber, no tumbling hawk
swerving through the hall, no swift horse
2265 pawing the courtyard. Pillage and slaughter
have emptied the earth of entire peoples."
And so he mourned as he moved about the world,
deserted and alone, lamenting his unhappiness
day and night, until death's flood
2270 brimmed up in his heart.
                  Then an old harrower of the dark
happened to find the hoard open,
the burning one who hunts out barrows,
the slick-skinned dragon, threatening the night sky
with streamers of fire. People on the farms
2275 are in dread of him. He is driven to hunt out
hoards under ground, to guard heathen gold
through age-long vigils, though to little avail.
For three centuries, this scourge of the people
had stood guard on that stoutly protected
2280 underground treasury, until the intruder
unleashed its fury; he hurried to his lord
with the gold-plated cup and made his plea
to be reinstated. Then the vault was rifled,
the ring-hoard robbed, and the wretched man
2285 had his request granted. His master gazed
on that find from the past for the first time.
    When the dragon awoke, trouble flared again.
He rippled down the rock, writhing with anger
when he saw the footprints of the prowler who had stolen
2290 too close to his dreaming head.
So may a man not marked by fate
easily escape exile and woe
by the grace of God.
                  The hoard-guardian
scorched the ground as he scoured and hunted
2295 for the trespasser who had troubled his sleep.
Hot and savage, he kept circling and circling
the outside of the mound. No man appeared
in that desert waste, but he worked himself up
by imagining battle; then back in he'd go
2300 in search of the cup, only to discover
signs that someone had stumbled upon

the golden treasures. So the guardian of the mound,
the hoard-watcher, waited for the gloaming
with fierce impatience; his pent-up fury
2305 at the loss of the vessel made him long to hit back
and lash out in flames. Then, to his delight,
the day waned and he could wait no longer
behind the wall, but hurtled forth
in a fiery blaze. The first to suffer
2310 were the people on the land, but before long
it was their treasure-giver who would come to grief.

    The dragon began to belch out flames
and burn bright homesteads; there was a hot glow
that scared everyone, for the vile sky-winger
2315 would leave nothing alive in his wake.
Everywhere the havoc he wrought was in evidence.
Far and near, the Geat nation
bore the brunt of his brutal assaults
and virulent hate. Then back to the hoard
2320 he would dart before daybreak, to hide in his den.
He had swinged the land, swathed it in flame,
in fire and burning, and now he felt secure
in the vaults of his barrow; but his trust was unavailing.

    Then Beowulf was given bad news,
2325 the hard truth: his own home,
the best of buildings, had been burned to a cinder,
the throne-room of the Geats. It threw the hero
into deep anguish and darkened his mood:
the wise man thought he must have thwarted
2330 ancient ordinance of the eternal Lord,
broken His commandment. His mind was in turmoil,
unaccustomed anxiety and gloom
confused his brain; the fire-dragon
had razed the coastal region and reduced
2335 forts and earthworks to dust and ashes,
so the war-king planned and plotted his revenge.
The warriors' protector, prince of the hall-troop,
ordered a marvelous all-iron shield
from his smithy works. He well knew
2340 that linden boards would let him down
and timber burn. After many trials,
he was destined to face the end of his days,
in this mortal world, as was the dragon,
for all his long leasehold on the treasure.
2345   Yet the prince of the rings was too proud
to line up with a large army
against the sky-plague. He had scant regard
for the dragon as a threat, no dread at all
of its courage or strength, for he had kept going
2350 often in the past, through perils and ordeals
of every sort, after he had purged
Hrothgar's hall, triumphed in Heorot
and beaten Grendel. He outgrappled the monster

and his evil kin.
                    One of his crudest
2355   hand-to-hand encounters had happened
when Hygelac, king of the Geats, was killed
in Friesland: the people's friend and lord,
Hrethel's son, slaked a swordblade's
thirst for blood. But Beowulf's prodigious
2360   gifts as a swimmer guaranteed his safety:
he arrived at the shore, shouldering thirty
battle-dresses, the booty he had won.
There was little for the Hetware[9] to be happy about
as they shielded their faces and fighting on the ground
2365   began in earnest. With Beowulf against them,
few could hope to return home.
    Across the wide sea, desolate and alone,
the son of Ecgtheow swam back to his people.
There Hygd offered him throne and authority
2370   as lord of the ring-hoard: with Hygelac dead,
she had no belief in her son's ability
to defend their homeland against foreign invaders.
Yet there was no way the weakened nation
could get Beowulf to give in and agree
2375   to be elevated over Heardred as his lord
or to undertake the office of kingship.
But he did provide support for the prince,
honored and minded him until he matured
as the ruler of Geatland.
                      Then over sea-roads
2380   exiles arrived, sons of Ohthere.[1]
They had rebelled against the best of all
the sea-kings in Sweden, the one who held sway
in the Shylfing nation, their renowned prince,
lord of the mead-hall. That marked the end
2385   for Hygelac's son: his hospitality
was mortally rewarded with wounds from a sword.
Heardred lay slaughtered and Onela returned
to the land of Sweden, leaving Beowulf
to ascend the throne, to sit in majesty
2390   and rule over the Geats. He was a good king.
    In days to come, he contrived to avenge
the fall of his prince; he befriended Eadgils
when Eadgils was friendless, aiding his cause
with weapons and warriors over the wide sea,
2395   sending him men. The feud was settled
on a comfortless campaign when he killed Onela.
    And so the son of Ecgtheow had survived
every extreme, excelling himself
in daring and in danger, until the day arrived
2400   when he had to come face to face with the dragon.
The lord of the Geats took eleven comrades

---

9. A tribe of the Franks allied with the Frisians.   1. See p. 88, n. 6, Phases 3 and 4.

and went in a rage to reconnoiter.
By then he had discovered the cause of the affliction
being visited on the people. The precious cup
2405 had come to him from the hand of the finder,
the one who had started all this strife
and was now added as a thirteenth to their number.
They press-ganged and compelled this poor creature
to be their guide. Against his will
2410 he led them to the earth-vault he alone knew,
an underground barrow near the sea-billows
and heaving waves, heaped inside
with exquisite metalwork. The one who stood guard
was dangerous and watchful, warden of the trove
2415 buried under earth: no easy bargain
would be made in that place by any man.
    The veteran king sat down on the cliff-top.
He wished good luck to the Geats who had shared
his hearth and his gold. He was sad at heart,
2420 unsettled yet ready, sensing his death.
His fate hovered near, unknowable but certain:
it would soon claim his coffered soul,
part life from limb. Before long
the prince's spirit would spin free from his body.
2425   Beowulf, son of Ecgtheow, spoke:
"Many a skirmish I survived when I was young
and many times of war: I remember them well.
At seven, I was fostered out by my father,
left in the charge of my people's lord.
2430 King Hrethel kept me and took care of me,
was openhanded, behaved like a kinsman.
While I was his ward, he treated me no worse
as a wean[2] about the place than one of his own boys,
Herebeald and Haethcyn, or my own Hygelac.
2435 For the eldest, Herebeald, an unexpected
deathbed was laid out, through a brother's doing,
when Haethcyn bent his horn-tipped bow
and loosed the arrow that destroyed his life.
He shot wide and buried a shaft
2440 in the flesh and blood of his own brother.
That offense was beyond redress; a wrongfooting
of the heart's affections; for who could avenge
the prince's life or pay his death-price?
It was like the misery endured by an old man
2445 who has lived to see his son's body
swing on the gallows. He begins to keen
and weep for his boy, watching the raven
gloat where he hangs: he can be of no help.
The wisdom of age is worthless to him.
2450 Morning after morning, he wakes to remember
that his child is gone; he has no interest

2. A young child [Northern Ireland; Translator's note].

in living on until another heir
is born in the hall, now that his first-born
has entered death's dominion forever.
2455 He gazes sorrowfully at his son's dwelling,
the banquet hall bereft of all delight,
the windswept hearthstone; the horsemen are sleeping,
the warriors under ground; what was is no more.
No tunes from the harp, no cheer raised in the yard.
2460 Alone with his longing, he lies down on his bed
and sings a lament; everything seems too large,
the steadings and the fields.
                              Such was the feeling
of loss endured by the lord of the Geats
after Herebeald's death. He was helplessly placed
2465 to set to rights the wrong committed,
could not punish the killer in accordance with the law
of the blood-feud, although he felt no love for him.
Heartsore, wearied, he turned away
from life's joys, chose God's light
2470 and departed, leaving buildings and lands
to his sons, as a man of substance will.
    "Then over the wide sea Swedes and Geats
battled and feuded and fought without quarter.
Hostilities broke out when Hrethel died.[3]
2475 Ongentheow's sons were unrelenting,
refusing to make peace, campaigning violently
from coast to coast, constantly setting up
terrible ambushes around Hreosnahill.
My own kith and kin avenged
2480 these evil events, as everybody knows,
but the price was high: one of them paid
with his life. Haethcyn, lord of the Geats,
met his fate there and fell in the battle.
Then, as I have heard, Hygelac's sword
2485 was raised in the morning against Ongentheow,
his brother's killer. When Eofor cleft
the old Swede's helmet, halved it open,
he fell, death-pale: his feud-calloused hand
could not stave off the fatal stroke.
2490   "The treasures that Hygelac lavished on me
I paid for when I fought, as fortune allowed me,
with my glittering sword. He gave me land
and the security land brings, so he had no call
to go looking for some lesser champion,
2495 some mercenary from among the Gifthas
or the Spear-Danes or the men of Sweden.
I marched ahead of him, always there
at the front of the line; and I shall fight like that
for as long as I live, as long as this sword
2500 shall last, which has stood me in good stead

3. See p. 88, n. 6, Phases 1 and 2.

late and soon, ever since I killed
Dayraven the Frank in front of the two armies.
He brought back no looted breastplate
to the Frisian king but fell in battle,
2505   their standard-bearer, highborn and brave.
No sword blade sent him to his death:
my bare hands stilled his heartbeats
and wrecked the bone-house. Now blade and hand,
sword and sword-stroke, will assay the hoard."

[BEOWULF ATTACKS THE DRAGON]

2510   Beowulf spoke, made a formal boast
for the last time: "I risked my life
often when I was young. Now I am old,
but as king of the people I shall pursue this fight
for the glory of winning, if the evil one will only
2515   abandon his earth-fort and face me in the open."
Then he addressed each dear companion
one final time, those fighters in their helmets,
resolute and highborn: "I would rather not
use a weapon if I knew another way
2520   to grapple with the dragon and make good my boast
as I did against Grendel in days gone by.
But I shall be meeting molten venom
in the fire he breathes, so I go forth
in mail-shirt and shield. I won't shift a foot
2525   when I meet the cave-guard: what occurs on the wall
between the two of us will turn out as fate,
overseer of men, decides. I am resolved.
I scorn further words against this sky-borne foe.
"Men-at-arms, remain here on the barrow,
2530   safe in your armor, to see which one of us
is better in the end at bearing wounds
in a deadly fray. This fight is not yours,
nor is it up to any man except me
to measure his strength against the monster
2535   or to prove his worth. I shall win the gold
by my courage, or else mortal combat,
doom of battle, will bear your lord away."
Then he drew himself up beside his shield.
The fabled warrior in his war-shirt and helmet
2540   trusted in his own strength entirely
and went under the crag. No coward path.
Hard by the rock-face that hale veteran,
a good man who had gone repeatedly
into combat and danger and come through,
2545   saw a stone arch and a gushing stream
that burst from the barrow, blazing and wafting
a deadly heat. It would be hard to survive
unscathed near the hoard, to hold firm
against the dragon in those flaming depths.

2550　Then he gave a shout. The lord of the Geats
　　　unburdened his breast and broke out
　　　in a storm of anger. Under gray stone
　　　his voice challenged and resounded clearly.
　　　Hate was ignited. The hoard-guard recognized
2555　a human voice, the time was over
　　　for peace and parleying. Pouring forth
　　　in a hot battle-fume, the breath of the monster
　　　burst from the rock. There was a rumble under ground.
　　　Down there in the barrow, Beowulf the warrior
2560　lifted his shield: the outlandish thing
　　　writhed and convulsed and viciously
　　　turned on the king, whose keen-edged sword,
　　　an heirloom inherited by ancient right,
　　　was already in his hand. Roused to a fury,
2565　each antagonist struck terror in the other.
　　　Unyielding, the lord of his people loomed
　　　by his tall shield, sure of his ground,
　　　while the serpent looped and unleashed itself.
　　　Swaddled in flames, it came gliding and flexing
2570　and racing toward its fate. Yet his shield defended
　　　the renowned leader's life and limb
　　　for a shorter time than he meant it to:
　　　that final day was the first time
　　　when Beowulf fought and fate denied him
2575　glory in battle. So the king of the Geats
　　　raised his hand and struck hard
　　　at the enameled scales, but scarcely cut through:
　　　the blade flashed and slashed yet the blow
　　　was far less powerful than the hard-pressed king
2580　had need of at that moment. The mound-keeper
　　　went into a spasm and spouted deadly flames:
　　　when he felt the stroke, battle-fire
　　　billowed and spewed. Beowulf was foiled
　　　of a glorious victory. The glittering sword,
2585　infallible before that day,
　　　failed when he unsheathed it, as it never should have.
　　　For the son of Ecgtheow, it was no easy thing
　　　to have to give ground like that and go
　　　unwillingly to inhabit another home
2590　in a place beyond; so every man must yield
　　　the leasehold of his days.
　　　　　　　　　　　　　Before long
　　　the fierce contenders clashed again.
　　　The hoard-guard took heart, inhaled and swelled up
　　　and got a new wind; he who had once ruled
2595　was furled in fire and had to face the worst.
　　　No help or backing was to be had then
　　　from his highborn comrades; that hand-picked troop
　　　broke ranks and ran for their lives
　　　to the safety of the wood. But within one heart
2600　sorrow welled up: in a man of worth

the claims of kinship cannot be denied.
His name was Wiglaf, a son of Weohstan's,
a well-regarded Shylfing warrior
related to Aelfhere.[4] When he saw his lord
2605   tormented by the heat of his scalding helmet,
he remembered the bountiful gifts bestowed on him,
how well he lived among the Waegmundings,
the freehold he inherited from his father[5] before him.
He could not hold back: one hand brandished
2610   the yellow-timbered shield, the other drew his sword—
an ancient blade that was said to have belonged
to Eanmund, the son of Ohthere, the one
Weohstan had slain when he was an exile without friends.
He carried the arms to the victim's kinfolk,
2615   the burnished helmet, the webbed chain-mail
and that relic of the giants. But Onela returned
the weapons to him, rewarded Weohstan
with Eanmund's war-gear. He ignored the blood-feud,
the fact that Eanmund was his brother's son.[6]
2620   Weohstan kept that war-gear for a lifetime,
the sword and the mail-shirt, until it was the son's turn
to follow his father and perform his part.
Then, in old age, at the end of his days
among the Weather-Geats, he bequeathed to Wiglaf
2625   innumerable weapons.
                  And now the youth
was to enter the line of battle with his lord,
his first time to be tested as a fighter.
His spirit did not break and the ancestral blade
would keep its edge, as the dragon discovered
2630   as soon as they came together in the combat.
    Sad at heart, addressing his companions,
Wiglaf spoke wise and fluent words:
"I remember that time when mead was flowing,
how we pledged loyalty to our lord in the hall,
2635   promised our ring-giver we would be worth our price,
make good the gift of the war-gear,
those swords and helmets, as and when
his need required it. He picked us out
from the army deliberately, honored us and judged us
2640   fit for this action, made me these lavish gifts—
and all because he considered us the best
of his arms-bearing thanes. And now, although
he wanted this challenge to be one he'd face
by himself alone—the shepherd of our land,

4. Although Wiglaf is here said to be a Shylfing (i.e., a Swede), in line 2607 we are told his family are Waegmundings, a clan of the Geats, which is also Beowulf's family. It was possible for a family to owe allegiance to more than one nation and to shift sides as a result of feuds. Nothing is known of Aelfhere.
5. I.e., Weohstan, who, as explained below, was the slayer of Onela's nephew Eanmund. Possibly,

Weohstan joined the Geats under Beowulf after Eanmund's brother, with Beowulf's help, avenged Eanmund's death on Onela and became king of the Shylfings. See p. 88, n. 6, Phase 2.
6. An ironic comment: since Onela wanted to kill Eanmund, he rewarded Weohstan for killing his nephew instead of exacting compensation or revenge.

2645 a man unequaled in the quest for glory
and a name for daring—now the day has come
when this lord we serve needs sound men
to give him their support. Let us go to him,
help our leader through the hot flame
2650 and dread of the fire. As God is my witness,
I would rather my body were robed in the same
burning blaze as my gold-giver's body
than go back home bearing arms.
That is unthinkable, unless we have first
2655 slain the foe and defended the life
of the prince of the Weather-Geats. I well know
the things he has done for us deserve better.
Should he alone be left exposed
to fall in battle? We must bond together,
2660 shield and helmet, mail-shirt and sword."
Then he waded the dangerous reek and went
under arms to his lord, saying only:
"Go on, dear Beowulf, do everything
you said you would when you were still young
2665 and vowed you would never let your name and fame
be dimmed while you lived. Your deeds are famous,
so stay resolute, my lord, defend your life now
with the whole of your strength. I shall stand by you."
        After those words, a wildness rose
2670 in the dragon again and drove it to attack,
heaving up fire, hunting for enemies,
the humans it loathed. Flames lapped the shield,
charred it to the boss, and the body armor
on the young warrior was useless to him.
2675 But Wiglaf did well under the wide rim
Beowulf shared with him once his own had shattered
in sparks and ashes.
                        Inspired again
by the thought of glory, the war-king threw
his whole strength behind a sword stroke
2680 and connected with the skull. And Naegling snapped.
Beowulf's ancient iron-gray sword
let him down in the fight. It was never his fortune
to be helped in combat by the cutting edge
of weapons made of iron. When he wielded a sword,
2685 no matter how blooded and hard-edged the blade,
his hand was too strong, the stroke he dealt
(I have heard) would ruin it. He could reap no advantage.
        Then the bane of that people, the fire-breathing dragon,
was mad to attack for a third time.
2690 When a chance came, he caught the hero
in a rush of flame and clamped sharp fangs
into his neck. Beowulf's body
ran wet with his life-blood: it came welling out.
        Next thing, they say, the noble son of Weohstan
2695 saw the king in danger at his side

and displayed his inborn bravery and strength.
He left the head alone,[7] but his fighting hand
was burned when he came to his kinsman's aid.
He lunged at the enemy lower down
2700 so that his decorated sword sank into its belly
and the flames grew weaker.

                       Once again the king
gathered his strength and drew a stabbing knife
he carried on his belt, sharpened for battle.
He stuck it deep in the dragon's flank.
2705 Beowulf dealt it a deadly wound.
They had killed the enemy, courage quelled his life;
that pair of kinsmen, partners in nobility,
had destroyed the foe. So every man should act,
be at hand when needed; but now, for the king,
2710 this would be the last of his many labors
and triumphs in the world.

                     Then the wound
dealt by the ground-burner earlier began
to scald and swell; Beowulf discovered
deadly poison suppurating inside him,
2715 surges of nausea, and so, in his wisdom,
the prince realized his state and struggled
toward a seat on the rampart. He steadied his gaze
on those gigantic stones, saw how the earthwork
was braced with arches built over columns.
2720 And now that thane unequaled for goodness
with his own hands washed his lord's wounds,
swabbed the weary prince with water,
bathed him clean, unbuckled his helmet.

    Beowulf spoke: in spite of his wounds,
2725 mortal wounds, he still spoke
for he well knew his days in the world
had been lived out to the end—his allotted time
was drawing to a close, death was very near.

    "Now is the time when I would have wanted
2730 to bestow this armor on my own son,
had it been my fortune to have fathered an heir
and live on in his flesh. For fifty years
I ruled this nation. No king
of any neighboring clan would dare
2735 face me with troops, none had the power
to intimidate me. I took what came,
cared for and stood by things in my keeping,
never fomented quarrels, never
swore to a lie. All this consoles me,
2740 doomed as I am and sickening for death;
because of my right ways, the Ruler of mankind
need never blame me when the breath leaves my body
for murder of kinsmen. Go now quickly,

7. I.e., he avoided the dragon's flame-breathing head.

dearest Wiglaf, under the gray stone
2745 where the dragon is laid out, lost to his treasure;
hurry to feast your eyes on the hoard.
Away you go: I want to examine
that ancient gold, gaze my fill
on those garnered jewels; my going will be easier
2750 for having seen the treasure, a less troubled letting-go
of the life and lordship I have long maintained."
    And so, I have heard, the son of Weohstan
quickly obeyed the command of his languishing
war-weary lord; he went in his chain-mail
2755 under the rock-piled roof of the barrow,
exulting in his triumph, and saw beyond the seat
a treasure-trove of astonishing richness,
wall-hangings that were a wonder to behold,
glittering gold spread across the ground,
2760 the old dawn-scorching serpent's den
packed with goblets and vessels from the past,
tarnished and corroding. Rusty helmets
all eaten away. Armbands everywhere,
artfully wrought. How easily treasure
2765 buried in the ground, gold hidden
however skillfully, can escape from any man!
    And he saw too a standard, entirely of gold,
hanging high over the hoard,
a masterpiece of filigree; it glowed with light
2770 so he could make out the ground at his feet
and inspect the valuables. Of the dragon there was no
remaining sign: the sword had dispatched him.
Then, the story goes, a certain man
plundered the hoard in that immemorial howe,
2775 filled his arms with flagons and plates,
anything he wanted; and took the standard also,
most brilliant of banners.
                              Already the blade
of the old king's sharp killing-sword
had done its worst: the one who had for long
2780 minded the hoard, hovering over gold,
unleashing fire, surging forth
midnight after midnight, had been mown down.
    Wiglaf went quickly, keen to get back,
excited by the treasure. Anxiety weighed
2785 on his brave heart—he was hoping he would find
the leader of the Geats alive where he had left him
helpless, earlier, on the open ground.
    So he came to the place, carrying the treasure
and found his lord bleeding profusely,
2790 his life at an end; again he began
to swab his body. The beginnings of an utterance
broke out from the king's breast-cage.
The old lord gazed sadly at the gold.
    "To the everlasting Lord of all,

2795 to the King of Glory, I give thanks
that I behold this treasure here in front of me,
that I have been allowed to leave my people
so well endowed on the day I die.
Now that I have bartered my last breath
2800 to own this fortune, it is up to you
to look after their needs. I can hold out no longer.
Order my troop to construct a barrow
on a headland on the coast, after my pyre has cooled.
It will loom on the horizon at Hronesness[8]
2805 and be a reminder among my people—
so that in coming times crews under sail
will call it Beowulf's Barrow, as they steer
ships across the wide and shrouded waters."
        Then the king in his great-heartedness unclasped
2810 the collar of gold from his neck and gave it
to the young thane, telling him to use
it and the war-shirt and gilded helmet well.
"You are the last of us, the only one left
of the Waegmundings. Fate swept us away,
2815 sent my whole brave highborn clan
to their final doom. Now I must follow them."
        That was the warrior's last word.
He had no more to confide. The furious heat
of the pyre would assail him. His soul fled from his breast
2820 to its destined place among the steadfast ones.

[BEOWULF'S FUNERAL]

        It was hard then on the young hero,
having to watch the one he held so dear
there on the ground, going through
his death agony. The dragon from underearth,
2825 his nightmarish destroyer, lay destroyed as well,
utterly without life. No longer would his snakefolds
ply themselves to safeguard hidden gold.
Hard-edged blades, hammered out
and keenly filed, had finished him
2830 so that the sky-roamer lay there rigid,
brought low beside the treasure-lodge.
        Never again would he glitter and glide
and show himself off in midnight air,
exulting in his riches: he fell to earth
2835 through the battle-strength in Beowulf's arm.
There were few, indeed, as far as I have heard,
big and brave as they may have been,
few who would have held out if they had had to face
the outpourings of that poison-breather
2840 or gone foraging on the ring-hall floor
and found the deep barrow-dweller

---

8. A headland by the sea. The name means "Whalesness."

on guard and awake.
              The treasure had been won,
bought and paid for by Beowulf's death.
Both had reached the end of the road
2845   through the life they had been lent.
                        Before long
the battle-dodgers abandoned the wood,
the ones who had let down their lord earlier,
the tail-turners, ten of them together.
When he needed them most, they had made off.
2850   Now they were ashamed and came behind shields,
in their battle-outfits, to where the old man lay.
They watched Wiglaf, sitting worn out,
a comrade shoulder to shoulder with his lord,
trying in vain to bring him round with water.
2855   Much as he wanted to, there was no way
he could preserve his lord's life on earth
or alter in the least the Almighty's will.
What God judged right would rule what happened
to every man, as it does to this day.
2860   Then a stern rebuke was bound to come
from the young warrior to the ones who had been cowards.
Wiglaf, son of Weohstan, spoke
disdainfully and in disappointment:
"Anyone ready to admit the truth
2865   will surely realize that the lord of men
who showered you with gifts and gave you the armor
you are standing in—when he would distribute
helmets and mail-shirts to men on the mead-benches,
a prince treating his thanes in hall
2870   to the best he could find, far or near—
was throwing weapons uselessly away.
It would be a sad waste when the war broke out.
Beowulf had little cause to brag
about his armed guard; yet God who ordains
2875   who wins or loses allowed him to strike
with his own blade when bravery was needed.
There was little I could do to protect his life
in the heat of the fray, but I found new strength
welling up when I went to help him.
2880   Then my sword connected and the deadly assaults
of our foe grew weaker, the fire coursed
less strongly from his head. But when the worst happened
too few rallied around the prince.
    "So it is good-bye now to all you know and love
2885   on your home ground, the open-handedness,
the giving of war-swords. Every one of you
with freeholds of land, our whole nation,
will be dispossessed, once princes from beyond
get tidings of how you turned and fled
2890   and disgraced yourselves. A warrior will sooner
die than live a life of shame."

Then he ordered the outcome of the fight to be reported
to those camped on the ridge, that crowd of retainers
who had sat all morning, sad at heart,
2895   shield-bearers wondering about
the man they loved: would this day be his last
or would he return? He told the truth
and did not balk, the rider who bore
news to the cliff-top. He addressed them all:
2900   "Now the people's pride and love,
the lord of the Geats, is laid on his deathbed,
brought down by the dragon's attack.
Beside him lies the bane of his life,
dead from knife-wounds. There was no way
2905   Beowulf could manage to get the better
of the monster with his sword. Wiglaf sits
at Beowulf's side, the son of Weohstan,
the living warrior watching by the dead,
keeping weary vigil, holding a wake
2910   for the loved and the loathed.
                    Now war is looming
over our nation, soon it will be known
to Franks and Frisians, far and wide,
that the king is gone. Hostility has been great
among the Franks since Hygelac sailed forth
2915   at the head of a war-fleet into Friesland:
there the Hetware harried and attacked
and overwhelmed him with great odds.
The leader in his war-gear was laid low,
fell among followers: that lord did not favor
2920   his company with spoils. The Merovingian king
has been an enemy to us ever since.
    "Nor do I expect peace or pact-keeping
of any sort from the Swedes. Remember:
at Ravenswood,[9] Ongentheow
2925   slaughtered Haethcyn, Hrethel's son,
when the Geat people in their arrogance
first attacked the fierce Shylfings.
The return blow was quickly struck
by Ohthere's father.[1] Old and terrible,
2930   he felled the sea-king and saved his own
aged wife, the mother of Onela
and of Ohthere, bereft of her gold rings.
Then he kept hard on the heels of the foe
and drove them, leaderless, lucky to get away
2935   in a desperate rout into Ravenswood.
His army surrounded the weary remnant
where they nursed their wounds; all through the night
he howled threats at those huddled survivors,
promised to axe their bodies open

---

9. The messenger describes in greater detail the
Battle of Ravensword. See the outline of the
Swedish wars on p. 88 n. 6.
1. I.e., Ongentheow.

2940 when dawn broke, dangle them from gallows
to feed the birds. But at first light
when their spirits were lowest, relief arrived.
They heard the sound of Hygelac's horn,
his trumpet calling as he came to find them,
2945 the hero in pursuit, at hand with troops.
  "The bloody swathe that Swedes and Geats
cut through each other was everywhere.
No one could miss their murderous feuding.
Then the old man made his move,
2950 pulled back, barred his people in:
Ongentheow withdrew to higher ground.
Hygelac's pride and prowess as a fighter
were known to the earl; he had no confidence
that he could hold out against that horde of seamen,
2955 defend his wife and the ones he loved
from the shock of the attack. He retreated for shelter
behind the earthwall. Then Hygelac swooped
on the Swedes at bay, his banners swarmed
into their refuge, his Geat forces
2960 drove forward to destroy the camp.
There in his gray hairs, Ongentheow
was cornered, ringed around with swords.
And it came to pass that the king's fate
was in Eofor's hands,[2] and in his alone.
2965 Wulf, son of Wonred, went for him in anger,
split him open so that blood came spurting
from under his hair. The old hero
still did not flinch, but parried fast,
hit back with a harder stroke:
2970 the king turned and took him on.
Then Wonred's son, the brave Wulf,
could land no blow against the aged lord.
Ongentheow divided his helmet
so that he buckled and bowed his bloodied head
2975 and dropped to the ground. But his doom held off.
Though he was cut deep, he recovered again.
  "With his brother down, the undaunted Eofor,
Hygelac's thane, hefted his sword
and smashed murderously at the massive helmet
2980 past the lifted shield. And the king collapsed,
the shepherd of people was sheared of life.
Many then hurried to help Wulf,
bandaged and lifted him, now that they were left
masters of the blood-soaked battle-ground.
2985 One warrior stripped the other,
looted Ongentheow's iron mail-coat,
his hard sword-hilt, his helmet too,
and carried the graith[3] to King Hygelac,

2. I.e., he was at Eofor's mercy. Eofor's slaying of Ongentheow was described in lines 2486–89, where no mention is made of his brother Wulf's part in the battle. They are the sons of Wonred. *Eofor* means boar; *Wulf* is the Old English spelling of wolf.
3. Possessions, apparel.

he accepted the prize, promised fairly
2990   that reward would come, and kept his word.
For their bravery in action, when they arrived home,
Eofor and Wulf were overloaded
by Hrethel's son, Hygelac the Geat,
with gifts of land and linked rings
2995   that were worth a fortune. They had won glory,
so there was no gainsaying his generosity.
And he gave Eofor his only daughter
to bide at home with him, an honor and a bond.
    "So this bad blood between us and the Swedes,
3000   this vicious feud, I am convinced,
is bound to revive; they will cross our borders
and attack in force when they find out
that Beowulf is dead. In days gone by
when our warriors fell and we were undefended,
3005   he kept our coffers and our kingdom safe.
He worked for the people, but as well as that
he behaved like a hero.
              We must hurry now
to take a last look at the king
and launch him, lord and lavisher of rings,
3010   on the funeral road. His royal pyre
will melt no small amount of gold:
heaped there in a hoard, it was bought at heavy cost,
and that pile of rings he paid for at the end
with his own life will go up with the flame,
3015   be furled in fire: treasure no follower
will wear in his memory, nor lovely woman
link and attach as a torque around her neck—
but often, repeatedly, in the path of exile
they shall walk bereft, bowed under woe,
3020   now that their leader's laugh is silenced,
high spirits quenched. Many a spear
dawn-cold to the touch will be taken down
and waved on high; the swept harp
won't waken warriors, but the raven winging
3025   darkly over the doomed will have news,
tidings for the eagle of how he hoked and ate,
how the wolf and he made short work of the dead."[4]
    Such was the drift of the dire report
that gallant man delivered. He got little wrong
3030   in what he told and predicted.
                 The whole troop
rose in tears, then took their way
to the uncanny scene under Earnaness.[5]
There, on the sand, where his soul had left him,
they found him at rest, their ring-giver

---

4. The raven, eagle, and wolf—the scavengers who will feed on the slain—are "the beasts of battle," a common motif in Germanic war poetry. "Hoked": rooted about [Northern Ireland, Translator's note].
5. The site of Beowulf's fight with the dragon. The name means "Eaglesness."

3035 from days gone by. The great man
had breathed his last. Beowulf the king
had indeed met with a marvelous death.
    But what they saw first was far stranger:
the serpent on the ground, gruesome and vile,
3040 lying facing him. The fire-dragon
was scaresomely burned, scorched all colors.
From head to tail, his entire length
was fifty feet. He had shimmered forth
on the night air once, then winged back
3045 down to his den; but death owned him now,
he would never enter his earth-gallery again.
Beside him stood pitchers and piled-up dishes,
silent flagons, precious swords
eaten through with rust, ranged as they had been
3050 while they waited their thousand winters under ground.
That huge cache, gold inherited
from an ancient race, was under a spell—
which meant no one was ever permitted
to enter the ring-hall unless God Himself,
3055 mankind's Keeper, True King of Triumphs,
allowed some person pleasing to Him—
and in His eyes worthy—to open the hoard.
    What came about brought to nothing
the hopes of the one who had wrongly hidden
3060 riches under the rock-face. First the dragon slew
that man among men, who in turn made fierce amends
and settled the feud. Famous for his deeds
a warrior may be, but it remains a mystery
where his life will end, when he may no longer
3065 dwell in the mead-hall among his own.
So it was with Beowulf, when he faced the cruelty
and cunning of the mound-guard. He himself was ignorant
of how his departure from the world would happen.
The highborn chiefs who had buried the treasure
3070 declared it until doomsday so accursed
that whoever robbed it would be guilty of wrong
and grimly punished for their transgression,
hasped in hell-bonds in heathen shrines.
Yet Beowulf's gaze at the gold treasure
3075 when he first saw it had not been selfish.
    Wiglaf, son of Weohstan, spoke:
"Often when one man follows his own will
many are hurt. This happened to us.
Nothing we advised could ever convince
3080 the prince we loved, our land's guardian,
not to vex the custodian of the gold,
let him lie where he was long accustomed,
lurk there under earth until the end of the world.
He held to his high destiny. The hoard is laid bare,
3085 but at a grave cost; it was too cruel a fate
that forced the king to that encounter.

I have been inside and seen everything
amassed in the vault. I managed to enter
although no great welcome awaited me
3090   under the earthwall. I quickly gathered up
a huge pile of the priceless treasures
handpicked from the hoard and carried them here
where the king could see them. He was still himself,
alive, aware, and in spite of his weakness
3095   he had many requests. He wanted me to greet you
and order the building of a barrow that would crown
the site of his pyre, serve as his memorial,
in a commanding position, since of all men
to have lived and thrived and lorded it on earth
3100   his worth and due as a warrior were the greatest.
Now let us again go quickly
and feast our eyes on that amazing fortune
heaped under the wall. I will show the way
and take you close to those coffers packed with rings
3105   and bars of gold. Let a bier be made
and got ready quickly when we come out
and then let us bring the body of our lord,
the man we loved, to where he will lodge
for a long time in the care of the Almighty."
3110   Then Weohstan's son, stalwart to the end,
had orders given to owners of dwellings,
many people of importance in the land,
to fetch wood from far and wide
for the good man's pyre:
                    "Now shall flame consume
3115   our leader in battle, the blaze darken
round him who stood his ground in the steel-hail,
when the arrow-storm shot from bowstrings
pelted the shield-wall. The shaft hit home.
Feather-fledged, it finned the barb in flight."
3120   Next the wise son of Weohstan
called from among the king's thanes
a group of seven: he selected the best
and entered with them, the eighth of their number,
under the God-cursed roof; one raised
3125   a lighted torch and led the way.
No lots were cast for who should loot the hoard
for it was obvious to them that every bit of it
lay unprotected within the vault,
there for the taking. It was no trouble
3130   to hurry to work and haul out
the priceless store. They pitched the dragon
over the cliff-top, let tide's flow
and backwash take the treasure-minder.
Then coiled gold was loaded on a cart
3135   in great abundance, and the gray-haired leader,
the prince on his bier, borne to Hronesness.
      The Geat people built a pyre for Beowulf,

stacked and decked it until it stood foursquare,
hung with helmets, heavy war-shields
3140 and shining armor, just as he had ordered.
Then his warriors laid him in the middle of it,
mourning a lord far-famed and beloved.
On a height they kindled the hugest of all
funeral fires; fumes of woodsmoke
3145 billowed darkly up, the blaze roared
and drowned out their weeping, wind died down
and flames wrought havoc in the hot bone-house,
burning it to the core. They were disconsolate
and wailed aloud for their lord's decease.
3150 A Geat woman too sang out in grief;
with hair bound up, she unburdened herself
of her worst fears, a wild litany
of nightmare and lament: her nation invaded,
enemies on the rampage, bodies in piles,
3155 slavery and abasement. Heaven swallowed the smoke.
    Then the Geat people began to construct
a mound on a headland, high and imposing,
a marker that sailors could see from far away,
and in ten days they had done the work.
3160 It was their hero's memorial; what remained from the fire
they housed inside it, behind a wall
as worthy of him as their workmanship could make it.
And they buried torques in the barrow, and jewels
and a trove of such things as trespassing men
3165 had once dared to drag from the hoard.
They let the ground keep that ancestral treasure,
gold under gravel, gone to earth,
as useless to men now as it ever was.
Then twelve warriors rode around the tomb,
3170 chieftains' sons, champions in battle,
all of them distraught, chanting in dirges,
mourning his loss as a man and a king.
They extolled his heroic nature and exploits
and gave thanks for his greatness; which was the proper thing,
3175 for a man should praise a prince whom he holds dear
and cherish his memory when that moment comes
when he has to be convoyed from his bodily home.
So the Geat people, his hearth-companions,
sorrowed for the lord who had been laid low.
3180 They said that of all the kings upon earth
he was the man most gracious and fair-minded,
kindest to his people and keenest to win fame.

JUDITH

iblical narrative inspired Anglo-Saxon poetry from its earliest recorded beginnings: the poet Cædmon (p. 32) is said, for example, to have composed poetry on biblical subjects from Genesis to the Last Judgment. Although those texts do not survive, up to one third of surviving Anglo-Saxon poetic texts are translations of biblical material. Prose writers also produced ambitious biblical translations: at the end of the tenth century Ælfric, Abbot of Eynsham (died ca. 1010), made partial translations of many texts that he worked into sermon material; an Anglo-Saxon version of the Pentateuch (the first five books of the Old Testament) was compiled at about the same time. The prose translations are more or less faithful to the biblical text. The poetic translations, on the other hand, are much freer: they take liberties with the narrative and style of the biblical sources, reshaping narratives and placing the stories within a recognizably Germanic cultural setting.

One of the biblical books from which Ælfric drew material was the Book of Judith. This book was regarded as apocryphal (i.e., not authentically a part of the Old Testament) by Protestant churches from the sixteenth century, but for all pre- and post-Reformation Catholic readers it was an authentic part of the Hebrew Bible. The narrative recounts the campaign of the Babylonian king Nebuchadnezzar to punish many subject peoples who had refused to join him in his successful war against Media (another ancient empire). Nebuchadnezzar's general Holofernes plunders and razes many cities that resist his army, and others capitulate to him. He lays siege to the strategic Israelite town of Bethulia, which blocks his route to Jerusalem (Bethulia no longer exists, and its location in biblical times is uncertain). The leaders of the suffering and thirsty population of Bethulia are almost ready to surrender, but the pious, wealthy, and beautiful widow Judith rebukes them for their faintness of heart and promises to liberate them if they will hold out a few days longer. After praying to God in sackcloth and ashes, Judith dresses and adorns herself sumptuously. With only one servant she enters the enemy camp, where all, and especially Holofernes himself, are amazed at her beauty. She pretends to be fleeing a doomed people and persuades Holofernes that she will lead him to victory over all the Israelite cities. The Old English text begins four days after Judith's arrival, with Holofernes's invitation to his principal warriors to a banquet, after which he plans to go to bed with the beautiful Israelite. Judith, however, has other plans.

The poet of *Judith* translated from the Latin text of the Bible (the so-called "Vulgate" Bible, produced in the late fourth century). We do not know the date for this rendering of the Book of Judith into Anglo-Saxon poetry, but it was probably composed sometime in the tenth century (the one surviving text appears in the same late tenth-century manuscript that contains *Beowulf*). Neither do we know the motives for this translation. Ælfric, writing in the late tenth century, made his translation of Judith to encourage the Anglo-Saxons in defense of their territory against the invading Vikings. The text is, he says, "set down in our manner in English, as an example to you people that you should defend your land with weapons against the invading army."[*]

The opening of the poem is lost (scholars estimate that some one hundred lines are missing), but from the remainder we can see that the poet has freely reshaped the biblical source and set the narrative within terms intelligible to an Anglo-Saxon audience. The poet has stripped the geographical, historical, and political complexity of

---

The Old English Heptateuch, ed. S. J. Crawford, Early English Text Society 160 (London, 1922), p. 48.

the story down to its bare essentials: the confrontation between Judith and Holofernes. Judith is the leader of an embattled people up against an exultant and terrifying enemy. Her only resources are her unfailing courage, her wits, and her faith in God. Within this concentrated narrative, the poet colors certain episodes by employing the traditional language and formulas of Anglo-Saxon poetry. Holofernes, for example, becomes riotous at the feast; "the beasts of battle" anticipate and enjoy *their* feast (cf. *Beowulf*, lines 3023–27); Judith is rewarded with Holofernes's battle gear, not with his household treasures as in the biblical narrative. Perhaps the most penetrating touch added by the Anglo-Saxon poet is the account of the net surrounding Holofernes's bed, from which he can see out but cannot be seen inside. This technology of tyrannical power undermines Holofernes's army in the end, since his men, waiting nervously around his bed because they are afraid to wake up their leader, lose precious time under attack from the Israelites.

Like the Abbess Hilda (see p. 30), Judith is one of the women of power in Anglo-Saxon history and literature. Another is St. Helen, the mother of the emperor Constantine the Great: in the poem *Elene* she leads a Roman army to the Holy Land to discover the cross on which Christ was crucified.

Judith[1]

      . . . She doubted
  gifts in this wide earth; there she readily found
  protection from the glorious Lord, when she had most need
  of favour from the highest Judge, so that he, the Lord of creation,
5 defended her against the greatest terror. The glorious Father in the
      skies
  granted her request, since she always possessed true faith
  in the Almighty. I have heard then that Holofernes
  eagerly issued invitations to a feast and provided all types of
  magnificent wonders for the banquets; to it the lord of men
      summoned
10 the most experienced retainers. The warriors obeyed
  with great haste; they came to the powerful lord and
  proceeded to the leader of people. That was the fourth day
  after Judith, prudent in mind,
  this woman of elfin beauty first visited him.
15   They went into the feast to sit down,
  proud men at the wine-drinking, bold mail-coated warriors,
  all his companions in misfortune. There, along the benches,
  deep bowls were carried frequently; full cups and pitchers
  were also carried to the sitters in the hall. They received those,
      doomed to die,
20 brave warriors, though the powerful man did not expect it,
  that terrible lord of heroes. Then Holofernes,
  the gold-giving friend of his men, became joyous from the drinking.
  He laughed and grew vociferous, roared and clamoured,
  so that the children of men could hear from far away,
25 how the fierce one stormed and yelled;
  arrogant and excited by mead, he frequently admonished

1. The translation is by Elaine Treharne, *Old and Middle English: An Anthology* (2000).

the guests that they enjoy themselves well.
So, for the entire day, the wicked one,
the stern dispenser of treasures,
30 drenched his retainers with wine until they lay unconscious,
the whole of his troop were as drunk as if they had been struck
     down in death,
drained of every ability. So, the men's lord commanded
the guests to be served, until the dark night approached
the children of men. Then corrupted by evil,
35 he commanded that the blessed maiden should be hastily fetched
to his bed, adorned with bracelets,
decorated with rings. The retainers quickly did
as their lord, the ruler of warriors,
commanded them. They stepped into the tumult
40 of the guest-hall where they found the wise Judith,
and then quickly
the warriors began to lead the
illustrious maiden to the lofty tent,
where the powerful man Holofernes, hateful to the Saviour,
45 rested himself during the night.
There was a beautiful
all-golden fly-net[2] that the commander
had hung around the bed, so that the wicked one,
the lord of warriors, could look through
50 on each of those sons of men who came in there,
but not one of the race of mankind could look
on him, unless, brave man, he commanded one
of his very iniquitous men to come
nearer to him for secret consultation. They quickly brought to bed
55 the prudent woman. Then the resolute heroes
went to inform their lord that the holy maiden
had been brought into his tent. Then the notorious one, that lord of
     cities,
became happy in his mind: he intended to violate
the bright woman with defilement and with sin. The Judge of glory,
60 the majestic Guardian, the Lord, Ruler of hosts, would not consent to
     that,
but he prevented him from that thing. Then the diabolical one,
the wanton and wicked man, departed
with a troop of his men to find his bed, where he would lose his life
forthwith within that one night. He had attained his violent end
65 on earth, just as he had previously deserved,
this severe lord of men, since he had dwelled under the roof
of clouds in this world. The mighty man then fell into the middle
of his bed, so drunk with wine that he possessed no sense
in his mind. The warriors stepped
70 out from that place with great haste,
men sated with wine, who led the traitor,
that hateful tyrant, to bed

2. Book of Judith 10.21: "A mosquito-net of purple interwoven with gold, emerald, and precious
stones." Here the "fly-net" is a kind of screen
enabling Holofernes to see outside his bed without being seen.

for the last time. Then the Saviour's
glorious handmaiden was very mindful
75 of how she could deprive the terrible one
of life most easily, before the impure and
foul one awoke. Then the Creator's maiden,
with her braided locks, took a sharp sword,
a hard weapon in the storms of battle, and drew it from the sheath
80 with her right hand. She began to call the Guardian of heaven
by name, the Saviour of all
the inhabitants of earth, and said these words:
"God of creation, Spirit of comfort,
Son of the Almighty, I want to beseech you
85 for your mercy on me in my time of need,
glorious Trinity.[3] My heart is intensely
inflamed within me now, and my mind is troubled,
greatly afflicted with sorrows. Give me, Lord of heaven,
victory and true belief so I might cut down this bestower of torment
90 with this sword. Grant me my salvation,
mighty Lord of men: I have never had more need
of your mercy than now. Avenge now, mighty Lord,
eminent Bestower of glory, that which is so grievous in my mind,
so fervent in my heart." Then the highest Judge
95 inspired her immediately with great zeal, as he does to each
of the dwellers on earth who seek help from him
with reason and with true faith. Then she felt relief in her mind,
hope was renewed for the holy woman. She seized the heathen man
securely by his hair, pulled him shamefully towards her
100 with her hands, and skilfully placed
the wicked and loathsome man
so that she could most easily manage the miserable one
well. Then, the woman with braided locks struck
the enemy, that hostile one,
105 with the shining sword, so that she cut through half
of his neck, such that he lay unconscious,
drunk and wounded. He was not dead yet,
not entirely lifeless. The courageous woman
struck the heathen hound energetically
110 another time so that his head rolled
forwards on the floor. The foul body lay
behind, dead; the spirit departed elsewhere
under the deep earth and was oppressed there
and fettered in torment forever after,
115 wound round with serpents, bound with punishments,
cruelly imprisoned in hell-fire
after his departure. Enveloped in darkness,
he had no need at all to hope that he should get out from
that serpent-hall, but there he must remain
120 always and forever, henceforth without end,
in that dark home deprived of the joy of hope.

---

3. Anglo-Saxon "Drynesse," "threeness." In lines 83–84, the heroine prays to the three persons of the
Trinity. In the Apocrypha, she invokes the "Lord, God of Israel."

    Judith had won illustrious glory
    in the battle as God, the Lord of heaven,
    granted it so when he gave her her victory.
125 Then the prudent woman immediately placed
    the warrior's head still bloody
    into the sack in which her attendant,
    a woman of pale complexion, an excellent handmaiden,
    had brought food for them both; and then Judith
130 put it, all gory, into the hands of her
    thoughtful servant to carry home.
    Then both the courageous women
    went from there straightaway,
    until the triumphant women, elated,
135 got away out from that army
    so that they could clearly see
    the beautiful city walls of Bethulia
    glitter. Then, ring-adorned,
    they hurried forwards along the path
140 until, glad at heart, they had reached
    the rampart gate. Warriors were sitting,
    men watching, and keeping guard
    in that stronghold, just as Judith the wise maiden
    had asked, when she had previously
145 departed from the sorrowful people,
    the courageous woman. The beloved woman had returned again
    to the people, and the prudent woman
    soon asked one of the men
    from the spacious city to come towards her,
150 and hastily to let them in
    through the gate of the city-wall; and she spoke these words
    to the victorious people: "I am able to tell you
    a memorable thing so that you need no longer
    mourn in your minds. The Ruler, the Glory of kings,
155 is well disposed towards you. It had become revealed
    throughout this wide world that glorious and triumphant success
    is approaching and that honour has been granted by fate to you
    because of the afflictions that you have long suffered."
    Then the city-dwellers were joyful
160 when they heard how the holy one spoke
    over the high city-wall. The army was joyous
    and people hurried to the fortress gate,
    men and women, in multitudes and crowds,
    groups and troops pressed forward and ran
165 towards the Lord's maiden in their thousands,
    old and young. The mind of each one of the people
    in that rejoicing city was gladdened
    when they perceived that Judith had returned
    to her native land; and then hastily
170 and reverently, they let her in.
    Then the prudent woman, adorned with gold, asked
    her attentive handmaiden
    to uncover the warrior's head

and to display it, bloodied, as proof
175 to the citizens of how she had been helped in battle.
Then the noble woman spoke to all the people:
"Victorious heroes, here you can gaze clearly
on the leader of the people, on this head
of the most hateful of heathen warriors,
180 of the unliving Holofernes,
who, among men, inflicted on us the worst torments,
grievous afflictions, and wished to add to these
even more; but God would not grant him
a longer life so that he could plague us
185 with wrongs. I deprived him of life
through God's help. Now I intend to ask
each of the men of these citizens,
each of the warriors, that you immediately
hasten to battle, as soon as the God of creation,
190 that glorious King, sends his radiant beam of light
from the east. Go forward carrying shields,
shields in front of your breasts and corslets,
gleaming helmets, into the troop of enemies;
fell the commanders, those leaders doomed to die
195 with shining swords. Your enemies
are condemned to death, and you will possess glory,
honour in conflict, just as mighty God has
given you that sign by my hand."
    Then a host of brave and keen men prepared quickly
200 for the battle. Noble warriors and retainers
stepped out; they carried triumphant banners;
heroes in helmets went forward to battle straightaway
from that holy city
at dawn of that same day. Shields clashed,
205 resounded loudly. The lean wolf rejoiced
in the forest, as did the dark raven,
a bloodthirsty bird: they both knew
that the warriors intended to provide them
with a feast from those doomed to die; but behind them flew
210 the eagle eager for food, dewy-winged
with dark plumage; the horn-beaked bird
sang a battle-song.[4] The warriors advanced,
men to battle, protected by shields,
hollow wooden shields, those who previously
215 had suffered the insolence of foreigners,
the insult of heathens. In the spear-play,
that was all grievously requited to
the Assyrians, when the Israelites
under their battle-banners had gone
220 to that camp. Then they boldly
let showers of arrows fly forwards,
battle arrows from horned bows,
firm arrows. Angry warriors

---

4. See *Beowulf*, lines 3024–27, n. 4 (p. 105).

roared loudly, sent spears
225 into the midst of the cruel ones. The native heroes
were angry against the hateful race,
resolute, they marched, determined,
they violently aroused their ancient enemies
who were drunk with mead. With their hands,
230 the retainers drew brightly adorned swords from their sheaths,
excellent sword-edges, zealously killed
the Assyrian warriors,
those evil schemers. They did not spare one
man's life from that army, neither the
235 lowly nor the powerful whom they could overcome.
    So, in the morning, the retainers
pursued the foreign people the entire time,
until the chief leaders of that army,
of those who were the enemies, perceived
240 that the Hebrew men had shown violent sword-brandishing
to them. They went to reveal
all that in words to the most
senior retainers, and they aroused the warriors
and announced fearfully to those drunk with mead
245 the dreadful news, the morning's terror,
the terrible battle. Then, I have heard, immediately
the warriors, doomed to perish, cast off sleep,
and the subdued men thronged in crowds
to the tent of the wicked man,
250 Holofernes. They intended to announce
the battle to their lord at once,
before the terrible force of the Israelites
came down on them. They all supposed
that the leader of the warriors and the bright maiden
255 were together in that beautiful tent:
Judith the noble one, and the licentious one,
terrible and fierce. There was not a single one of the men
who dared to wake the warrior
or inquire how the warrior
260 had got on with the holy maiden,
the Lord's woman. The armed force of the Israelites
approached; they fought vigorously
with hard swords, violently requited
their ancient grudges, that old conflict,
265 with shining swords. The Assyrian's
glory was destroyed in that day's work,
their pride humbled. Warriors stood
about their lord's tent very uneasy
and sombre in spirit. Then together they all
270 began to cough, to cry out loudly,
to gnash their teeth, suffering grief,
to no avail. Then their glory, success and brave deeds
were at an end. The men considered how to awaken
their lord; it did them no good.
275   It got later and later when one of the warriors

became bold in that he daringly risked going
into the tent, as need compelled him to.
He found on the bed his pale lord,
lying deprived of spirit,
280   devoid of life. Immediately, he fell
frozen to the floor, and began to tear at his hair
and clothing, wild in mind,
and he spoke these words to the warriors
who were outside, dejected:
285   "Here our own destruction is made clear,
the future signified, that the time of troubles
is pressing near when we shall now lose,
shall perish at the battle together. Here lies our protector
cut down and beheaded by the sword." Sorrowful, they
290   threw their weapons down then, and departed from him
        weary-spirited
to hasten in flight. The mighty people
fought them from behind, until the greatest part
of the army lay destroyed in battle
on that field of victory, cut down by swords
295   as a pleasure for the wolves and also as a joy
to bloodthirsty birds. Those who still lived fled
from the wooden weapons of their enemies. Behind them
came the army of the Hebrews, honoured with victory,
glorified with that judgement. The Lord God, the almighty Lord,
300   helped them generously with his aid.
Then quickly the valiant heroes
made a war-path through the hateful enemies
with their shining swords; cut down shields,
and penetrated the shield-wall. The Hebrew missile-throwers
305   were enraged in the battle,
the retainers at that time greatly desired
a battle of spears. There in the sand fell
the greatest part of the total number
of leaders of the Assyrians,
310   that hateful nation. Few returned
alive to their native land. The brave warriors
turned back to retreat among the carnage,
the reeking corpses. There was an opportunity for
the native inhabitants to seize from the most hateful
315   ancient enemies, the unliving ones,
bloody plunder, beautiful ornaments,
shield and broad sword, shining helmets,
precious treasures. The guardians of the country
had gloriously conquered their foes,
320   the ancient enemy, on that battlefield,
executed them with swords. Those who had been
the most hateful of living men while alive
rested in their tracks. Then the entire nation,
the greatest of tribes, the proud braided-haired ones,
325   for the space of one month carried and led
to the bright city of Bethulia

helmets and hip-swords, grey corslets,
men's armour decorated with gold,
more illustrious treasures than any man
330 among the wise could say.
All of that was earned by the warriors' glory,
bold under the banners and in battle
through the prudent counsel of Judith,
the daring maiden. The brave warriors
335 brought as her reward from that expedition
the sword of Holofernes and his gory helmet,
and likewise his ample mail-coat
adorned with red gold, and everything that the arrogant
lord of warriors owned by way of treasures or personal heirlooms,
340 rings and bright riches; they gave that to the bright
and ready-witted woman. For all of this Judith said
thanks to the Lord of hosts, who had given her honour
and glory in the kingdom of this earth, and also as her reward in
      heaven,
the reward of victory in heaven's glory, because she possessed true
      faith
345 in the Almighty. Indeed, at the end she did not doubt
in the reward which she had long yearned for. For that be glory
to the beloved Lord for ever and ever, who created wind and air,
the heavens and spacious earth, likewise the raging seas
and joys of heaven through his own individual grace.

THE WANDERER

The lament of *The Wanderer* is an excellent example of the elegiac mood so common in Anglo-Saxon poetry. Such poems look back to a time when oral poets performed heroic songs in the meter preserved, practiced, and recorded in original works by their Christian descendants. In celebration of Beowulf's victory over Grendel, Hrothgar's court poet performs a heroic lay about the Germanic hero Sigemund (lines 883–914). The elegiac tone common to *Beowulf* and these later poems, however, expresses the poets' profound feelings toward their ancestors who lived before St. Augustine brought the "good news" to Kent and initiated the conversion. Nowhere are those feelings expressed more poignantly than in *The Wanderer*.

As is true of most Anglo-Saxon elegiac laments, both the language and the structure of *The Wanderer* are difficult. At the beginning, the speaker (whom the poet identifies as an "earth-treader") voices hope of finding comfort after his many tribulations. After the poet's interruption, the Wanderer continues to speak—to himself—of his long search for a new home, describing how he must keep his thoughts locked within him while he makes that search. But these thoughts form the most vivid and moving part of his soliloquy—how, floating on the sea, dazed with sorrow and fatigue, he imagines that he sees his old companions, and how, as he wakens to reality, they vanish on the water like seabirds. The second part of the poem, beginning

"Therefore I don't know why," expands the theme from one man to all human beings in a world wasted by war and time. He derives such cold comfort as he can from asking the old question, Where are they now, who were once so glad in the mead-hall?

The Wanderer is preserved only in the Exeter Book, a manuscript of about 975 (although the poem may be much earlier), which contains the largest surviving collection of Anglo-Saxon poetry.

The Wanderer[1]

"Often the lone-dweller[2]   longs for relief,
the Almighty's mercy,   though melancholy,
his hands turning   time and again
the ocean's currents,   the ice-cold seas,
following paths of exile.   Fate is firmly set."
   So spoke the Wanderer,[3]   weary of hardships,
cruel combats,   the death of kinsmen.
   "Often alone,   always at daybreak
I must lament my cares;   not one remains alive
to whom I could utter   the thoughts in my heart,
tell him my sorrows.   In truth, I know that
for any eorl[4]   an excellent virtue
is to lock tight   the treasure chest
within one's heart,   howsoever he may think.
A downcast heart   won't defy destiny,
nor the sad spirit   give sustenance.
And therefore those   who thirst for fame
often bind fast   their breast chamber.
   "So I must hold in   the thoughts of my heart—
though often wretched,   bereft of my homeland,
far from kinfolk—   bind them with fetters,
since in days long past   with darkness of earth
I covered my gold-friend,[5]   and I fared from there
over the waves' bed,   winter-weary,
longing for a hall   and a lord of rings,
where near or far   I might find one
in the mead-hall   remembering me and my kin,
or else show favor   to a friendless man,
requite me with comfort.   One acquainted with pain
understands how cruel   a traveling companion
sorrow is for someone   with few friends at his side.
Exile attends him,   not twisted gold rings,
Heart-freezing frost,   not fruits of the earth.
He recalls tablemates   and treasure distributed,

5
10
15
20
25
30

---

1. The translation by Alfred David is based on *Eight Old English Poems*, 3rd ed., edited by John C. Pope, revised by R. D. Fulk. The translation is also indebted to comments by Professor Fulk.
2. Old English *an-haga*=one+hedge, enclosure—i.e., one who dwells alone in some sort of confinement.
3. Old English *eard-stapa*=earth+treader. The modern title—there is no title in the manuscript—derives from this compound noun.
4. *Eorl*=warrior. Only later did the Old English word come to designate a member of the British nobility.
5. Old English *gold-wine*=gold-friend, one of the many formulas applied to the lord, here in his role as dispenser of treasure to his retainers.

35 how from the first his friend and lord
 helped him to the feast. That happy time is no more.
  "This, indeed, anyone forced to forgo for long
 the beloved counsel of his lord knows well.
 Often when sorrow and sleep together
40 bind the poor lone-dweller in their embrace,
 he dreams he clasps and that he kisses
 his liege-lord again, lays head and hands
 on the lord's knees as he did long ago,
 enjoyed the gift-giving in days gone by.
45 Then the warrior, friendless, awakens again,
 sees before him the fallow waves,
 seabirds on the water spreading their wings,
 snow and hail falling and sleet as well.
 Then the heart's wounds grow heavier,
50 sadness for dear ones. Sorrow returns.
 Then through his mind pass memories of kinsmen—
 joyfully he greets them, eagerly gazes—
 his fellow warriors, the floating spirits,
 fade on their way. They fail to bring
55 much familiar talk —trouble is renewed—
 for any man who must often send
 his weary spirit over the waves' bed.
  "Therefore I don't know why my woeful heart
 should not wax dark in this wide world
60 when I look back on the life of eorls,
 how quickly they quit the mead-hall's floor,
 brave young men. So this middle-earth
 from day to day dwindles and fails;
 therefore no one is wise without his share of winters
65 in the world's kingdom. A wise man must be patient,
 not too hot of heart nor hasty of speech,
 not reluctant to fight nor too reckless,
 not too timid nor too glad, not too greedy,
 and never eager to commit until he can be sure.
70 A man should hold back his boast until
 that time has come when he truly knows
 to direct his heart on the right path.
  "A wise man must know the misery of that time
 when the world's wealth shall all stand waste,
75 just as in our own day all over middle-earth
 walls are standing wind-swept and wasted,
 downed by frost, and dwellings covered with snow.
 The mead-hall crumbles, its master lies dead,
 bereft of pleasures, all the warrior-band[6] perished,
80 boldly by the wall. Battle took some,
 bore them away; a bird carried one
 above the high waves; the gray wolf took another,
 divided him with death; dreary-spirited

---

6. Old English *duguth*=generally something that affords benefit or advantage, but here it specifically
applies to a band of warriors.

an eorl buried another   in an earthen pit.
85   "Mankind's Creator   laid waste this middle-earth
till the clamor of city-dwellers   ceased to be heard
and ancient works of giants   stood empty.
He who wisely   contemplates this wall-stead,
and considers deeply   the darkness of this life,
90   mature in years,   remembers many
bloody battlegrounds   and so begins:
    'Where did the steed go? Where the young warrior?   Where the
        treasure-giver?
Where the seats of fellowship?   Where the hall's festivity?
Alas bright beaker!   Alas burnished warrior!
95   Alas pride of princes!   How the time has passed,
gone under night-helm   as if it never was!
A towering wall,   traced with serpent shapes,[7]
endures instead   of the dear warrior-band.
Strength of ash-spears   destroyed warriors,
100   slaughter-greedy weapons,   overwhelming fate,
and storms beat against   these stone-faced cliffs,
snow descending   seals up the ground,
drumming of winter   when darkness falls,
night shadows darken,   from the north send down
105   fierce hail-showers   in hatred of men.
All is wretchedness   in the realm of earth;
fate's work lays low   the world under heaven.
Here wealth is fleeting,   here friend is fleeting,
here family is fleeting,   here humankind is fleeting.
110   All this resting-place Earth   shall become empty.'"
    So said the wise man   as he sat in meditation.
A good man holds his words back,   tells his woes not too soon,
baring his inner heart   before knowing the best way,
an eorl who acts with courage.   All shall be well for him who seeks
        grace,
115   help from our Father in heaven   where a fortress stands for us all.

7. The reference is to a kind of serpentine ornamentation; examples from Roman times survive in Britain.

THE WIFE'S LAMENT

I n modern English translation, the speaker of this poem sounds much like the speaker in *The Wanderer*, lamenting his exile, isolation, and the loss of his lord. But in Old English the grammatical gender of the pronouns reveals that this speaker is a woman; the man she refers to as "my lord" must, therefore, be her husband. The story behind the lament remains obscure. All that can be made out for certain is that the speaker was married to a nobleman of another country; that her husband has left her (possibly forced into exile as a result of a feud); that his kinsmen are hostile to her; and that she is now living alone in a wilderness. Although the circumstances are shadowy, it is reasonable to conjecture that the wife may have been a "peace-weaver" (a woman married off to make peace between warring tribes), like Hildeburh and Freawaru, whose politically inspired marriages only result in further bloodshed (see *Beowulf*, pp. 63 and 82). The obscurity of the Old English text has led to diametrically opposed interpretations of the husband's feeling toward his wife. One interpretation holds that, for unexplained reasons, possibly because of his kinsmen's hostility to her, he has turned against her. The other, which is adopted in this translation, is that, in her mind at least, they share the suffering of his exile and their separation. Thus in the line here rendered "I must suffer the feud of my much-beloved," *fæhðu* (feud) is read by some as the technical term for a blood feud—the way it is used in *Beowulf* when Hrothgar says he settled a great feud started by Beowulf's father with *feo* (fee), i.e., monetary compensation (p. 51). Others take the word in a more general sense as referring to the man's enmity toward his wife. In either case, the woman's themes and language resemble those of male "wræccas" (outcasts or exiles; the Old English root survives in modern *wretch* and *wretched*) in the Old English poems called "elegies" because of their elegiac content and mood.

The Wife's Lament[1]

Full of sorrow,   I shall make this song
about me, my own fate.   Surely I can tell
what sufferings I endured   since I came of age,
both the new and old,   never more than now.
5   I must endure without end   the misery of exile.
    First my lord[2] departed   from his people
over tossing waves;   I worried when day came
in what land   my liege-lord could be.
Then I set out,   a friendless exile,
10   to seek a place   for my sore need.
My husband's kin   had hatched a plot,
conspiring secretly   to separate us,
so that we[3] widest apart   in the world's realms
lived in most misery,   and I languished.
15   My lord commanded me   to keep house here;
in this dwelling-place;   I had few dear ones,
devoted friends.   Therefore I feel downcast.
Then I learned my lord   was like myself—
down on his luck,   dreary-spirited,
20   secretly minding   murder in his heart.
A happy pair   we had promised each other,
that death alone   would ever divide us,
and nothing else.   All that is changed;
our nearness once   is now as though
25   it never had been.   Now, far or near, I must

---

1. The translation by Alfred David is based on *Eight Old English Poems*, 3rd ed., edited by John C. Pope, revised by R. D. Fulk (2000). I am indebted to Professor Fulk for his advice on my translation.

2. A woman would refer to her husband as her "lord."
3. Old English *wit*, an example of the dual form, used for two persons.

bear the malice   of the man I loved.
   I was told to live   in a grove of trees,
under an oak   in an earthen cave.
That earth-hall is old;   yearning overcomes me.
30   These dales are dark   and the dunes high,
bitter bulwarks   overgrown with briers,
a joyless place.   Here my lord's departure
afflicts me cruelly.   Friends here on earth,
lovers lying together,   lounge in bed,
35   while at daybreak   I abandon
this earthen-pit   under the oak
to sit alone   the summer-long day.
There I may bewail   my many woes,
suffering of exile,   for I can never
40   obtain comfort   for all my cares
nor all the longing   this life brought me.
   If ever anyone   should feel anguish,
harsh pain at heart,   she[4] should put on
a happy appearance   while enduring
45   endless sorrows—   should she possess
all the world's bliss,   or be banished far away
from her homeland.   I believe my lord sits
by a stony   storm-beaten cliff,
that water-tossed   my weary friend
50   sits in a desolate home.   He must suffer
much in his mind,   remembering too often
a happier place.   Woe unto him
who languishing   waits for a loved one.

---

4. Old English *geong-man*. The identity of the speaker has been debated, but most recent opinion holds it to be the wife herself, speaking impersonally. The translation takes the liberty of using "she" in reference to the speaker.

IRISH LITERATURE

The changes European literature underwent during the twelfth and thirteenth centuries were greatly indebted to Celtic influences. The legends about King Arthur and his knights, although they were assimilated to the feudal culture of the Anglo-Normans and transmitted by texts written in Latin, French, and English (see p. 12), were originally products of Celtic myth and legend. The folkloric otherworld elements and the major role played by women in those stories profoundly shaped and colored the literature we now think of as "romance." The French Tristran romances, the romances of Marie de France and Chrétien de Troyes, and even the legends of the Holy Grail could not have been imagined without their Celtic components.

   The Celts overran central Europe, Spain, and the British Isles during the first millennium B.C.E. On the Continent and in Great Britain, south of the wall built by the emperor Hadrian (see the map inside the front cover), they were absorbed into the Roman Empire. However, the Celtic vernacular continued to be spoken as the native language, and Ireland never became a Roman province. The Anglo-Saxon invasions in the fifth and early sixth centuries, and the Danish invasions after the eighth, displaced Celts in England, but Celtic language and culture continued to flourish in Wales (Welsh), in Cornwall (Cornish), across the English Channel in Brittany (Breton), and, of course, in Ireland (Gaelic). While still part of the Roman Empire, Britain and, in consequence, Ireland had been converted to Christianity. As portrayed in the Arthurian legend, the Christian Britons fought against barbaric Germanic invaders. Irish and Welsh missionaries, along with Roman ones, brought about the conversion of the Anglo-Saxons.

The earliest Celtic literature, like that of the Anglo-Saxons, was transmitted orally and little was copied down before the twelfth century. Nevertheless, the surviving monuments indicate its richness and its significance for the development of French and English medieval literature.

What follows are two examples of Irish literature, an excerpt from the Old Irish epic *Táin Bó Cuailnge* (The Cattle Raid of Cooley) and some delightful monastic lyrics written between the sixth and the ninth centuries.

CÚCHULAINN'S BOYHOOD DEEDS

Cúchulainn (koo-chúll-in), nephew of Ulster's king Conchobor, is the hero of the Old Irish epic *Táin Bó Cuailnge* (The Cattle Raid of Cooley), which tells of a great war between the kingdoms of Connacht and Ulster. The cause of the war that gives this epic work its title is the desire of Queen Medb of Connacht to obtain possession of the brown bull of Ulster to match one owned by her husband, King Ailill. The tales go back to ancient oral literature; the best surviving manuscript, pieced together in the twelfth century from different sources, although seriously defective, nevertheless tells powerful tales. This excerpt is part of the answer Medb and Ailill, leading the invading army, are given to the query "What sort of man . . . is this Hound of Ulster?"

Cúchulainn's Boyhood Deeds[1]

'There was another deed he did,' Fiacha Mac Fir Febe said. 'Cathbad the druid was staying with his son, Conchobor mac Nesa. He had one hundred studious men learning druid lore from him—this was always the number that Cathbad taught.

'One day a pupil asked him what that day would be lucky for. Cathbad said if a warrior took up arms for the first time that day his name would endure in Ireland as a word signifying mighty acts, and stories about him would last forever.

1. The translation is by Thomas Kinsella, *The Táin* (1969). For "The Exile of the Sons of Uísliu," see the supplemental ebook.

'Cúchulainn overheard this. He went to Conchobor and claimed his weapons. Conchobor said:

"By whose instruction?"

"My friend Cathbad's," Cúchulainn said.

"We have heard of him," Conchobor said, and gave him shield and spear. Cúchulainn brandished them in the middle of the house, and not one piece survived of the fifteen sets that Conchobor kept in store for new warriors or in case of breakage. He was given Conchobor's own weapons at last, and these survived. He made a flourish and saluted their owner the king and said:

"Long life to their seed and breed, who have for their king the man who owns these weapons."

'It was then that Cathbad came in and said:

"Do I see a young boy newly armed?"

"Yes," Conchobor said.

"Then woe to his mother's son," he said:

"What is this? Wasn't it by your own direction he came?" Conchobor said.

"Certainly not," Cathbad said.

"Little demon, why did you lie to me?" Conchobor said to Cúchulainn.

"It was no lie, king of warriors," Cúchulainn said. "I happened to hear him instructing his pupils this morning south of Emain, and I came to you then."

"Well," Cathbad said, "the day has this merit: he who arms for the first time today will achieve fame and greatness. But his life is short."

"That is a fair bargain," Cúchulainn said. "If I achieve fame I am content, though I had only one day on earth."

'Another day came and another druid asked what that day would be lucky for.

"Whoever mounts his first chariot today," Cathbad said, "his name will live forever in Ireland."

Cúchulainn overheard this also, and went to Conchobor and said:

"Friend Conchobor, my chariot!"

'A chariot was given to him. He clapped his hand to the chariot between the shafts, and the frame broke at his touch. In the same way he broke twelve chariots. At last they gave him Conchobor's chariot and that survived him.

'He mounted the chariot beside Conchobor's charioteer. This charioteer, Ibor by name, turned the chariot round where it stood.

"You can get out of the chariot now," the charioteer said.

"You think your horses are precious," Cúchulainn said, "but so am I, my friend. Drive round Emain now, and you won't lose by it."

'The charioteer set off.

'Cúchulainn urged him to take the road to the boy-troop, to greet them and get their blessing in return. After this he asked him to go further along the road. Cúchulainn said to the charioteer as they drove onward:

"Use your goad on the horses now."

"Which direction?" the charioteer said.

"As far as the road will take us!" Cúchulainn said.

'They came to Sliab Fuait. They met Conall Cernach there—for to Conall Cernach had fallen the care of the province boundary that day. Each of Ulster's heroic warriors had his day on Sliab Fuait, to take care of every man who came that way with poetry, and to fight any others. In this way everyone was challenged and no one slipped past to Emain unnoticed.

"May you prosper," Conall said. "I wish you victory and triumph."

"Conall, go back to the fort," Cúchulainn said, "and let me keep watch here a little."

"You would do for looking after men of poetry," Conall said. "But you are a little young still for dealing with men of war."

"It might never happen at all," Cúchulainn said. "Let us wander off, meanwhile," he said, "to view the shore of Loch Echtra. Warriors are often camped there."

"It is a pleasant thought," Conall said.

'They set off. Suddenly Cúchulainn let fly a stone from his sling and smashed the shaft of Conall Cernach's chariot.

"Why did you cast that stone, boy?" Conall said.

"To test my hand and the straightness of my aim," Cúchulainn said. "Now, since it is your Ulster custom not to continue a dangerous journey, go back to Emain, friend Conall, and leave me here on guard."

"If I must," Conall said.

'Conall Cernach wouldn't go beyond that point.

'Cúchulainn went on to Loch Echtra but found no one there. The charioteer said to Cúchulainn that they ought to go back to Emain, that they might get there for the drinking.

"No," Cúchulainn said. "What is that peak there?"

"Sliab Mondairn," the charioteer said.

"Take me there," Cúchulainn said.

'They travelled on until they got there. On arriving at the mountain, Cúchulainn asked:

"That white heap of stones on the mountain-top, what is it called?"

"The look-out place, Finncarn, the white cairn," the charioteer said.

"That plain there before us?" Cúchulainn said.

"Mag mBreg, Breg Plain," the charioteer said.

'In this way he gave the name of every fort of any size between Temair and Cenannos. And he recited to him also all fields and fords, all habitations and places of note, and every fastness and fortress. He pointed out at last the fort of the three sons of Nechta Scéne, who were called Foill (for deceitfulness) and Fannall (the Swallow) and Tuachell (the Cunning). They came from the mouth of the river Scéne. Fer Ulli, Lugaid's son, was their father and Nechta Scéne their mother. Ulstermen had killed their father and this is why they were at enmity with them.

"Is it these who say," Cúchulainn said, "that they have killed as many Ulstermen as are now living?"

"They are the ones," the charioteer said.

"Take me to meet them," Cúchulainn said.

"That is looking for danger," the charioteer said.

"We're not going there to avoid it," Cúchulainn said.

'They travelled on, and turned their horses loose where bog and river met, to the south and upstream of their enemies' stronghold. He took the spancel-hoop of challenge from the pillar-stone at the ford and threw it as far as he could out into the river and let the current take it—thus challenging the ban of the sons of Nechta Scéne.

'They took note of this and started out to find him.

'Cúchulainn, after sending the spancel-hoop downstream, lay down by the pillar-stone to rest, and said to his charioteer:

"If only one man comes, or two, don't wake me, but wake me if they all come."

'The charioteer waited meanwhile in terror. He yoked the chariot and pulled off the skins and coverings that were over Cúchulainn, trying not to wake him, since Cúchulainn had told him not to wake him for only one.

'Then the sons of Nechta Scéne came up.

"Who is that there?" said one.

"A little boy out in his chariot today for the first time," the charioteer said.

"Then his luck has deserted him," the warrior said. "This is a bad beginning in arms for him. Get out of our land. Graze your horses here no more."

"I have the reins in my hand," the charioteer said.

Then Ibor said to the warrior:

"Why should you earn enmity? Look, the boy is asleep."

"A boy with a difference!" cried Cúchulainn. "A boy who came here to look for fight!"

"It will be a pleasure," the warrior said.

"You may have that pleasure now, in the ford there," Cúchulainn said.

"You would be wise," the charioteer said, "to be careful of the man who is coming against you. Foill is his name," he said. "If you don't get him with your first thrust, you may thrust away all day."

"I swear the oath of my people that he won't play that trick on an Ulsterman again when my friend Conchobor's broad spear leaves my hand to find him. He'll feel it like the hand of an outlaw!"

'He flung the spear at him, and it pierced him and broke his back. He removed the trophies, and the head with them.

"Watch this other one," the charioteer said. "Fannall is his name, and he treads the water no heavier than swan or swallow."

"I swear he won't use that trick on an Ulsterman again," Cúchulainn said. "You have seen how I foot the pool in Emain."

'They met in the ford, and he killed the man and took away the trophies and the head.

"Watch this next one advancing against you," the charioteer said. "Tuachell is his name, and he wasn't named in vain. He has never fallen to any weapon."

"I have the *del chliss* for him, a wily weapon to churn him up and red-riddle him," Cúchulainn said.

'He threw the spear at him and tore him asunder where he stood. He went up and cut off his head. He gave the head and trophies to his charioteer.

'Then a scream rose up behind them from the mother, Nechta Scéne. Cúchulainn lifted the trophies off the ground and brought the three heads with him into the chariot, saying:

"I won't let go of these trophies until we reach Emain Macha."

'They set out for Emain Macha with all his spoils. Cúchulainn said to his charioteer:

"You promised us great driving. We'll need it now after our fight, with this chase after us."

'They travelled onward to Sliab Fuait. So fleet their haste across Breg Plain, as he hurried the charioteer, that the chariot-horses overtook the wind and the birds in flight, and Cúchulainn could catch the shot from his sling before it hit the earth.

'When they got to Sliab Fuait they found a herd of deer before them.

"What are those nimble beasts there?" Cúchulainn said.

"Wild deer," the charioteer said.

Cúchulainn said:

"Which would the men of Ulster like brought in, a dead one or a live one?"

"A live one would startle them more," the charioteer said. "It isn't every-one who could do it. Every man there has brought home a dead one. You can't catch them alive."

"I can," Cúchulainn said. "Use your goad on the horses, over the marsh."

'The charioteer did so until the horses bogged down. Cúchulainn got out and caught the deer nearest to him, the handsomest of all. He lashed the horses free of the bog and calmed the deer quickly. Then he tethered it between the rear shafts of the chariot.

'The next thing they saw before them was a flock of swans.

"Would the men of Ulster prefer to have these brought in alive or dead?" Cúchulainn said.

"The quickest and the most expert take them alive," the charioteer said.

'Cúchulainn immediately flung a little stone at the birds and brought down eight of them. Then he flung a bigger stone that brought down twelve more. He did this with his feat of the stunning-shot.

"Gather in our birds now," Cúchulainn said to his charioteer. "If I go out to them this wild stag will turn on you."

"But it's no easier if I go," the charioteer said. "The horses are so mad-dened that I can't get past them. I can't get over the two iron rims of the chariot wheels, they are so sharp. And I can't get past the stag; his antlers fill all the space between the chariot's shafts."

"Step out onto the antlers," Cúchulainn said. "I swear the oath of Ulster's people, I'll turn my head on him with such a stare, I'll fix him with such an eye, that he won't dare to stir or budge his head at you."

'He did this. Cúchulainn tied the reins and the charioteer gathered up the birds. Then Cúchulainn fastened the birds to the cords and thongs of the chariot. It was in this manner that they came back to Emain Macha: a wild stag behind the chariot, a swan-flock fluttering above, and the three heads of Nechta Scéne's sons inside the chariot.

'They came to Emain.

"A man in a chariot advancing upon us," cried the watcher in Emain Macha. "He'll spill the blood of the whole court unless you see to him and send naked women to meet him."

'Cúchulainn turned the left chariot-board toward Emain in insult, and he said:

"I swear by the oath of Ulster's people that if a man isn't found to fight me, I'll spill the blood of everyone in this court."

"Naked women to him!" Conchobor said.

'The women of Emain went forth, with Mugain the wife of Conchobor mac Nesa at their head, and they stripped their breasts at him.

"These are the warriors you must struggle with today," Mugain said.

'He hid his countenance. Immediately the warriors of Emain seized him and plunged him in a vat of cold water. The vat burst asunder about him. Then he was thrust in another vat and it boiled with bubbles the size of fists. He was placed at last in a third vat and warmed it till its heat and cold were equal. Then he got out and Mugain the queen gave him a blue cloak to go round him with a silver brooch in it, and a hooded tunic. And he sat on Conchobor's knee, and that was his seat ever after.

'What wonder,' Fiacha mac Fir Febe said, 'that the one who did this in his seventh year should triumph against odds and beat his match today, when he is fully seventeen years old?'

EARLY IRISH LYRICS

Monastic Irish scribes were also composers of beautiful lyrics, inspired by both the study and what could be seen from the study.

The Scholar and His Cat

I and white Pangur practice each of us his special art: his mind is set on hunting, my mind on my special craft.

I love (it is better than all fame) to be quiet beside my book, diligently pursuing knowledge. White Pangur does not envy me: he loves his childish craft.

When the two of us (this tale never wearies us) are alone together in our house, we have something to which we may apply our skill, an endless sport.

It is usual, at times, for a mouse to stick in his net, as a result of warlike battlings. For my part, into my net falls some difficult rule of hard meaning.

He directs his bright perfect eye against an enclosing wall. Though my clear eye is very weak I direct it against keenness of knowledge.

He is joyful with swift movement when a mouse sticks in his sharp paw. I too am joyful when I understand a dearly loved difficult problem.

Though we be thus at any time, neither of us hinders the other: each of us likes his craft, severally rejoicing in them.

He it is who is master for himself of the work which he does every day. I can perform my own work directed at understanding clearly what is difficult.

The Scribe in the Woods

A hedge of trees overlooks me; a blackbird's lay sings to me (an announcement which I shall not conceal); above my lined book the birds' chanting sings to me.

A clear-voiced cuckoo sings to me (goodly utterance) in a grey cloak from bush fortresses. The Lord is indeed good to me: well do I write beneath a forest of woodland.

The Lord of Creation

Let us adore the Lord, maker of wondrous works, great bright Heaven with its angels, the white-waved sea on earth.

My Hand Is Weary with Writing

My hand is weary with writing; my sharp great point is not thick; my slender-beaked pen juts forth a beetle-hued draft of bright blue ink.

A steady stream of wisdom springs from my well-colored neat fair hand; on the page it pours its draft of ink of the green-skinned holly.

I send my little dripping pen unceasingly over an assemblage of books of great beauty, to enrich the possessions of men of art—whence my hand is weary with writing.

Anglo-Norman Literature

The Myth of Arthur's Return

During the twelfth century, three authors, who wrote in Latin, Anglo-Norman French, and Middle English, respectively, created a mostly legendary history of Britain for their Norman overlords (see p. 11). This "history" was set in the remote past, beginning with a foundation myth—a heroic account of national origins—modeled on Virgil's *Aeneid* and ending with the Anglo-Saxon conquest of the native islanders, the Britons, in the fifth and sixth centuries. The chief architect of the history is Geoffrey of Monmouth, who was writing his *History of the Kings of Britain* in Latin prose ca. 1136–38. His work was freely translated into French verse by Wace in 1155, and Wace in turn was translated into English alliterative poetry by Layamon in his *Brut* (ca. 1190).

Geoffrey of Monmouth and Wace wrote their histories of Britain primarily for an audience of noblemen and prelates who were descendants of the Norman conquerors of the Anglo-Saxons. Geoffrey wrote several dedications of his *History*, first to supporters of Matilda, the heiress presumptive of Henry I, and, when the Crown went instead to Stephen of Blois, to the new king's allies and to Stephen himself. Layamon tells us that Wace wrote his French version for Eleanor of Aquitaine, queen of Stephen's successor, Henry II. The prestige and power of ancient Rome still dominated the historical and political imagination of the feudal aristocracy, and the legendary history of the ancient kings of the Britons, especially of King Arthur, who had defeated Rome itself, served to flatter the self-image and ambitions of the Anglo-Norman barons. Perhaps the destruction of Arthur's Kingdom also provided a timely object lesson of the disastrous consequences of civil wars such as those over the English succession in which these lords were engaged.

Folklore and literature provide examples of a recurrent myth about a leader or hero who has not really died but is asleep somewhere or in some state of suspended life and will return to save his people. Evidently, the Bretons and Welsh developed this myth about Arthur in oral tradition long before it turns up in medieval chronicles. Geoffrey of Monmouth, Wace, and Layamon, and subsequent writers about Arthur, including Malory (see p. 480), allude to it with varying degrees of skepticism.

The selections from Geoffrey of Monmouth and Wace are translated by Alfred David. The Layamon selection is translated by Rosamund Allen. For more information about Arthur, see the "King Arthur" topic in the supplemental ebook.

Geoffrey of Monmouth: *From* The History of the Kings of Britain

But also the famous King Arthur himself was mortally wounded. When he was carried off to the island of Avalon to have his wounds treated, he bestowed the crown on his cousin Constantine, the son of Duke Cador in the year 542 after the Incarnation of our lord. May his soul rest in peace.

WACE: *From* Roman de Brut

Arthur, if the story is not false, was mortally wounded; he had himself carried to Avalon to be healed of his wounds. He is still there and the Britons expect him as they say and hope. He'll come from there if he is still alive. Master Wace, who made this book, won't say more about Arthur's end than the prophet Merlin rightly said once upon a time that one would not know whether or not he were dead. The prophet spoke truly: ever since men have asked and shall always ask, I believe, whether he is dead or alive. Truly he had himself taken to Avalon 542 years after the Incarnation. It was a pity that he had no offspring. He left his realm to Constantine, the son of Cador of Cornwall, and asked him to reign until his return.

LAYAMON: *From* Brut

Arthur was mortally wounded, grievously badly;
To him there came a young lad who was from his clan,
He was Cador the Earl of Cornwall's son;
The boy was called Constantine; the king loved him very much.
14270 Arthur gazed up at him, as he lay there on the ground,
And uttered these words with a sorrowing heart:
"Welcome, Constantine; you were Cador's son;
Here I bequeath to you all of my kingdom,
And guard well my Britons all the days of your life
14275 And retain for them all the laws which have been extant in my days
And all the good laws which there were in Uther's days.
And I shall voyage to Avalon, to the fairest of all maidens,
To the Queen Argante, a very radiant elf,
And she will make quite sound every one of my wounds,
14280 Will make me completely whole with her health-giving potions.
And then I shall come back to my own kingdom
And dwell among the Britons with surpassing delight."
    After these words there came gliding from the sea
What seemed a short boat, moving, propelled along by the tide
14285 And in it were two women in remarkable attire,
Who took Arthur up at once and immediately carried him
And gently laid him down and began to move off.
And so it had happened, as Merlin said before:
That the grief would be incalculable at the passing of Arthur.
14290 The Britons even now believe that he is alive
And living in Avalon with the fairest of the elf-folk,
And the Britons are still always looking for when Arthur comes
        returning.
Yet once there was a prophet and his name was Merlin:
He spoke his predictions, and his sayings were the truth,
14295 Of how an Arthur once again would come to aid the English.

THOMAS OF ENGLAND

The tragic love story of Tristran and Ysolt, the wife of Tristran's maternal uncle King Mark, derives mainly from Breton, Welsh, and Irish sources although it also incorporates motifs of eastern tales that were probably transmitted to Europe from India via Arabic Spain. The romance of Tristran and Ysolt entered the mainstream of Western European literature through the Old French version in octosyllabic couplets by a twelfth-century author who identifies himself only as "Thomas" and of whom practically nothing else is known for certain. Only 3,143 lines (roughly a sixth) of the poem survive in nine separate fragments. But we can reconstruct the story from the *Tristrams saga* (1226), a relatively faithful translation into Old Norse, and the Middle High German adaptation *Tristan und Isolde* (also early thirteenth century) by Gottfried von Strassburg, who names the author of his major source "Thomas of Britain."

Thomas's *Tristran* is written in a dialect of western France containing Anglo-Norman forms; he is likely to have composed the romance for the court of Henry II. Borrowings from Wace's *Brut* (see p. 131) prove that he wrote after 1155, probably some time before 1170. As Thomas himself tells his audience, "My lords, this tale is told in many ways." Comparisons with other early versions in French and German suggest that he was following a lost text from which he eliminated episodes he considered improbable or coarse and to which he added new courtly and psychological dimensions. Thomas's work proved enormously influential not only by way of Gottfried's important poem (the source of Richard Wagner's opera *Tristan und Isolde*), but it may well have provided the inspiration and model for the love affair of Lancelot and Guinevere. That relationship first appears (already in progress) in Chrétien de Troye's romance *The Knight of the Cart* (see "King Arthur," in the supplemental ebook).

The romance of Tristran was drawn into the orbit of Arthurian romance where Sir Tristran is the only knight who can match Sir Lancelot. After fighting a five-hour duel to a draw, they become fast friends. Tristran is thus a champion in war and tournaments, but in Thomas and in other Tristran romances he has other attributes as well: he is a master of the hunt, chess, and several languages; he is a gifted harp player; and he and Ysolt make an expert team in the art of deceiving a jealous husband.

Tristran starts life as an orphan. His own story is preceded by the romance of his parents: Rivalen and Blancheflor, the sister of King Mark. Rivalen is killed in battle before Tristran's birth; Blancheflor dies in childbirth. Tristran is fostered by his father's steward until he is kidnapped by merchants who lure the handsome youth aboard their ship to play chess and then set sail. A storm they blame on the kidnapping causes them to strand the youth on a deserted coast of his uncle's kingdom. Tristran's gifts and charm lead Mark to adopt him as a trusted servant, who is identified as his nephew when Tristran's foster-father arrives at the court in search of him. Mark contracts to marry the king of Ireland's daughter Ysolt and sends Tristran to escort the bride to England. On the return voyage, Tristran and Ysolt become lovers after they unwittingly drink a love potion her mother had prepared for Ysolt and Mark. On Ysolt's wedding night, her maid Brengvein takes her place in the marriage bed. Tristran and Ysolt scheme repeatedly to meet secretly and devise ways to allay Mark's suspicions and frustrate his attempts to surprise them. Finally, however, Tristran is exiled from Britain for good and pursues wars on the Continent. Eventually, fearing that Ysolt no longer loves him and hoping that he will get over his love for her, he marries a second Ysolt, "Ysolt of the White Hands," the sister of Tristran's young friend and admirer Caerdin. Tristran, however, cannot bring himself to consummate the marriage, and the second Ysolt remains an unwilling virgin. When Tristran is wounded by a poisoned spear, Caerdin sets sail for England to fetch the first Ysolt who alone has it in her power to save Tristran's life.

Tristan and Isolde, French ivory, ca. 1350. The image depicts a night scene in which the reflection of the face of King Mark, hiding in the tree above, is spotted by the lovers in the pool below (note Ysolt's pointing finger).

Medieval people believed that given names sometimes foreshadowed one's destiny, and the French authors of Tristran's story interpreted *trist*, the Celtic root of the name, as French *triste* (sad). The sense of a tragic illicit love whose passion finds an ultimate fulfillment in death haunts the story of Tristran and Ysolt in Thomas and in the different versions that derive from it.

The geography of the Tristran romances varies from version to version. Tristran's homeland Lyonesse may originally have been Lothian in Scotland. In Marie de France's *Chevrefoil* (see pp. 167–69), it is in Wales. In Thomas it is Brittany, and the sea voyages across the English Channel and Irish Sea are episodes in which the sea itself plays a pivotal and symbolic role. The names Tristran and Ysolt vary according to the language of different versions. They are adopted here from the translation by A. T. Hatto (1960).

From Le Roman de Tristran

[THE DEATHS OF TRISTRAN AND YSOLT]

When Ysolt hears this message there is anguish in her heart, and pain, and sorrow, and grief—never yet has she known greater. Now she ponders deeply, and sighs and longs for Tristran, her lover. But she does not know how to come to him. She goes to speak with Brengvein. She tells her the whole story of the poisoned wound, the pain he is in and the misery, and how he lies there languishing, how and through whom he has sent for her—else his wound will never be healed. She has described all his torment and then asks advice what to do. And as they talk there begins a sighing, complaining, and weeping, and pain, sorrow, sadness, and grief, for the pity which they have on his account. Nevertheless they have discussed the matter and finally decide to set out on their journey and go away with Caerdin to treat Tristran's illness and succour him in his need.

They make ready towards evening and take what they will require. As soon as the others are all asleep, they leave very stealthily under cover of night by a lucky postern in the wall overlooking the Thames. The water has come up to it with the rising tide. The boat is all ready and the Queen has gone aboard it. They row, they sail with the ebb—quickly they fly before the wind. They make a mighty effort and keep on rowing till they are alongside the big ship. They hoist the yard and then they sail. They run before the waves as long as they have wind behind them. They coast along the foreign land past the port of Wissant, and then Boulogne, and Treport. The wind is strong and favourable and the ship that bears them is fleet. They sail past Normandy. They sail happily and joyfully, since they have the wind they want.

Tristran lies on his bed languishing of his wound. He can find no succour in anything. Medicine cannot avail him; nothing that he does affords him any aid. He longs for the coming of Ysolt, desiring nothing else. Without her he can have no ease—it is because of her that he lives so long. There, in his bed, he pines and he waits for her. He has high hopes that she will come and heal his malady, and believes that he will not live without her. Each day he sends to the shore to see if the ship is returning, with no other wish in his heart. And many is the time that he commands his bed to be made beside the sea and has himself carried out to it, to await and see the ship—what way she is making, and with what sail? He has no desire for anything, except for the coming of Ysolt: his whole mind, will, and desire are set on it. Whatever the world holds he rates of no account unless the Queen is coming to him. Then he has himself carried back again from the fear which he anticipates, for he dreads that she may not come, may not keep her faith with him, and he would much rather hear it from another than see the ship come without her. He longs to look out for the ship, but does not wish to know it, should she fail to come. There is anguish in his heart, and he is full of desire to see her. He often laments to his wife but does not tell her what he longs for, apart from Caerdin, who does not come. Seeing him delay so long Tristran greatly fears that Caerdin has failed in his mission.

Now listen to a pitiful disaster and a most sad mishap which must touch the hearts of all lovers! You never heard tell of greater sorrow arising from such love and such desire. Just there where Tristran is waiting and the lady is eager to arrive and has drawn close enough to see the land—gay they are on board and they sail lightheartedly—a wind springs up from the south and strikes them full in the middle of the yard, checking the whole ship in its course. The crew run to luff and turn the sail, they turn about whether they wish to or not. The wind gains in force and raises the swell, the deep begins to stir; the weather grows foul and the air thick, the waves rise, the sea grows black, it rains and sleets as the storm increases. Bowlines and shrouds snap. They lower the yard and drift along with the wind and waves. They had put out their boat on the sea, since they were close to their own country, but by ill luck they forgot it and a wave has smashed it to pieces. This at least they have now lost, and the tempest has grown so in violence that the best of sailors could never have kept his feet. All on board weep and lament and give vent to great grief, so afraid are they.

"Alas, poor me," cried Ysolt. "God does not wish me to live until I see my lover Tristran.—He wants me to be drowned in the sea! Tristran, if only I had spoken with you, I would not mind if I had then died. Dear love, when you hear that I am dead I know you will never again be consoled. You will be so afflicted by my death, following your long-drawn sufferings, that you will never be well again. My coming does not rest with me. God willing, I would come and take charge of your wound. For I have no other sorrow than that you are without aid; this is my sorrow and my grief. And I am very sad at heart, my friend, that you will have no support against death, when I die. My own death matters nothing to me—if God wills it, so be it. But when at last you learn of it, my love, I know that you will die of it. Such is our love, I can feel no grief unless you are in it. You cannot die without me, nor can I perish without you. If I am to be shipwrecked at sea, then you, too, must drown. But you cannot drown on dry land, so you have come to sea to seek me! I see your death before my eyes and know that I am soon to die. Dear friend, I fail in my desire, since I hoped to die in your arms and to be buried in one coffin with you. But now we have failed to achieve it. Yet it may still happen so: for if I am to drown here, and you, as I think, must also drown, a fish could swallow us, and so, my love, by good fortune we should share one sepulture, since it might be caught by someone who would recognize our bodies and do them the high honour befitting our love. But what I am saying cannot be.—Yet if God wills it, it must be!—But what would you be seeking on the sea? I do not know what you could be doing here. Nevertheless I am here, and here shall I die. I shall drown here, Tristran, without you. Yet it is a sweet comfort to me, my darling, that you will not know of my death. From henceforward it will never be known and I do not know who should tell it. You will live long after me and await my coming. If it please God you may be healed—that is what I most desire. I long for your recovery more than that I should come ashore. So truly do I love you, dear friend, that I must fear after my death, if you recover, lest you forget me during your lifetime or console yourself with another woman, Tristran, when I am dead. My love, I am indeed much afraid of Ysolt of the White Hands, at least. I do not know whether I ought to fear her; but, if you were to die before me, I would not long survive you. I do not know at all what to do, but you I do desire above all things. God grant we come together so that I may heal you, love, or that we two may die of one anguish!"

As long as the storm endures Ysolt gives vent to her sorrow and grief. The storm and foul weather last on the sea for five days and more; then the wind drops and it is fair. They have hoisted the white sail and are making good speed, when Caerdin espies the coast of Brittany. At this they are gay and light-hearted, they raise the sail right up so that it can be seen what sail it is, the white or the black. Caerdin wished to show its colour from afar, since it was the last day of the term that lord Tristran had assigned when they had set out for England.

While they are happily sailing, there is a spell of warm weather and the wind drops so that they can make no headway. The sea is very smooth and still, the ship moves neither one way nor the other save so far as the swell draws it. They are also without their boat. And now they are in great distress. They see the land close ahead of them, but have no wind with which to reach it. And so up and down they go drifting, now back, now forward. They cannot make any progress and are very badly impeded. Ysolt is much afflicted by it. She sees the land she has longed for and yet she cannot reach it: she all but dies of her longing. Those in the ship long for land, but the wind is too light for them. Time and again, Ysolt laments her fate. Those on the shore long for the ship, but they have not seen it yet. Thus Tristran is wretched and sorrowful, he often laments and sighs for Ysolt, whom he so much desires. The tears flow from his eyes, he writhes about, he all but dies of longing.

While Tristran endures such affliction, his wife Ysolt comes and stands before him. Meditating great guile she says: "Caerdin is coming, my love! I have seen his ship on the sea. I saw it making hardly any headway but nevertheless I could see it well enough to know that it is his. God grant it brings news that will comfort you at heart!"

Tristran starts up at this news. "Do you know for sure that it is his ship, my darling?" he asks. "Tell me now, what sort of sail is it?"

"I know it for a fact!" answered Ysolt. "Let me tell you, the sail is all black! They have hoisted it and raised it up high because they have no wind!"

At this Tristran feels such pain that he has never had greater nor ever will, and he turns his face to the wall and says: "God save Ysolt and me! Since you will not come to me I must die for your love. I can hold on to life no longer. I die for you, Ysolt, dear love! You have no pity for my sufferings, but you will have sorrow of my death. It is a great solace to me that you will have pity for my death."

Three times did he say "Dearest Ysolt." At the fourth he rendered up his spirit.

Thereupon throughout the house the knights and companions weep. Their cries are loud, their lament is great. Knights and serjeants rise to their feet and bear him from his bed, then lay him upon a cloth of samite and cover him with a striped pall.

And now the wind has risen on the sea. It strikes the middle of the sailyard and brings the ship to land. Ysolt has quickly disembarked, she hears the great laments in the street and the bells from the minsters and chapels. She asks people what news? and why they toll the bells so? and the reason for their weeping? Then an old man answers: "My lady, as God help me, we have greater sorrow than people ever had before. Gallant, noble Tristran, who was a source of strength to the whole realm, is dead! He was generous to the needy, a great succour to the wretched. He has died just now in his bed of a wound that his body received. Never did so great a misfortune befall this realm!"

As soon as Ysolt heard this news she was struck dumb with grief. So afflicted is she that she goes up the street to the palace in advance of the others, without her cloak. The Bretons have never seen a woman of her beauty; in the city they wonder whence she comes and who she may be. Ysolt goes to where she sees his body lying, and, turning towards the east, she prays for him piteously. "Tristran, my love, now that I see you dead, it is against reason for me to live longer. You died for my love, and I, love, die of grief, for I could not come in time to heal you and your wound. My love, my love, nothing shall ever console me for your death, neither joy nor pleasure nor any delight. May this storm be accursed that so delayed me on the sea, my sweetheart, so that I could not come! Had I arrived in time, I would have given you back your life and spoken gently to you of the love there was between us. I should have bewailed our fate, our joy, our rapture, and the great sorrow and pain that have been in our loving. I should have reminded you of this and kissed you and embraced you. If I had failed to cure you, then we could have died together. But since I could not come in time and did not hear what had happened and have come and found you dead, I shall console myself by drinking of the same cup. You have forfeited your life on my account, and I shall do as a true lover: I will die for you in return!"

She takes him in her arms and then, lying at full length, she kisses his face and lips and clasps him tightly to her. Then straining body to body, mouth to mouth, she at once renders up her spirit and of sorrow for her lover dies thus at his side.

Tristran died of his longing, Ysolt because she could not come in time. Tristran died for his love; fair Ysolt because of tender pity.

Here Thomas ends his book. Now he takes leave of all lovers, the sad and the amorous, the jealous and the desirous, the gay and the distraught, and all who will hear these lines. If I have not pleased all with my tale, I have told it to the best of my power and have narrated the whole truth, as I promised at the beginning. Here I have recounted the story in rhyme, and have done this to hold up an example, and to make this story more beautiful, so that it may please lovers, and that, here and there, they may find some things to take to heart. May they derive great comfort from it, in the face of fickleness and injury, in the face of hardship and grief, in the face of all the wiles of Love.

ANCRENE WISSE
(GUIDE FOR ANCHORESSES)

In the twelfth and thirteenth centuries, there was a movement toward a more solitary religious life and a more personal encounter with God. In the early days of Christianity, monasticism had originated with the desert fathers, men who withdrew to the wilderness in order to lead a life of prayer and meditation. The fifth and sixth centuries saw the growth and spread of religious orders, men and women living in religious communities, especially the Benedictine order of monks, founded in Italy by St. Benedict. New orders founded in the eleventh and twelfth centuries—the Cistercians, for example—emphasized a more actively engaged and individual spirituality. The Dominican and Franciscan orders of friars were not confined to their houses but were preaching and teaching orders who staffed the newly founded universities.

Along with the new orders, a number of both men and women chose to become anchorites or hermits, living alone or in small groups. In his *Rule*, St. Benedict had described such solitaries with a military metaphor: "They have built up their strength and go from the battle line in the ranks of their brothers to the single combat of the desert. Self-reliant now, without the support of another, they are ready with God's help to grapple single-handed with the vices of body and mind." Benedict's battle imagery anticipates the affinities between this solitary kind of spirituality and the literary form of romance, both of which were developing in the twelfth and thirteenth centuries. The individual soul confined in its enclosure fights temptation, as Sir Gawain rides out alone in the wilderness to seek the Green Chapel and encounters temptation along the way. The wilderness in romance often contains hermits, who may be genuinely holy men, or they may be enchanters like Archimago, disguised as a holy hermit, in the *Faerie Queene*. The influence of romance on religion and of religion on romance is also strikingly seen in portrayals of Christ as a knight who jousts for the love and salvation of human souls, which is a motif common to *Ancrene Wisse*, William Herebert's poem "What is he, this lordling, that cometh from the fight" (p. 409), and *Piers Plowman* (see p. 397).

Anchoress (the feminine form of *anchorite*, from the Greek *anachoretes*, "one who retires") refers to a religious recluse who, unlike a hermit, lives in an enclosure, attached to a church, from which she never emerges. Anchoresses and anchorites might live singly, like Julian of Norwich (see p. 412) or in small groups. *Ancrene Wisse* (ca. 1215) was originally written for three young sisters, who, the author says in an aside in one manuscript, come from a noble family with ample means to support them. The author of *Ancrene Wisse* addresses the sisters in a colloquial, urbane, and personal prose style that distinguishes the guide both as a book of religious instruction and as a literary achievement of Early Middle English. Note in particular the richly metaphorical transformations of pleasure and pain.

The excerpt comes from Part 6, to which the author gave the title "Penitence."[1]

From Ancrene Wisse (Guide for Anchoresses)

[THE SWEETNESS AND PAINS OF ENCLOSURE]

Now perhaps someone complains that she cannot feel any sweetness from God or sweetness within herself. Let her not wonder in the least if she is not Mary, for she must buy sweetness with exterior bitterness; but not with bitterness of any kind at all, for some lead away from God, for example every worldly grief that does not make for health in the soul. Thus it is written in the Gospel, of the three Marys, *that coming, they might anoint Jesus,*[2] *not going.* These Marys, it says, these bitternesses, were coming to anoint Our Lord. The bitter things which we suffer for His love come to anoint Our Lord, who reaches out toward us like one who has been anointed, and makes himself soft and sweet to touch. And was not He Himself a recluse in Mary's womb? These two things belong properly to an anchoress: narrowness of room, and bitterness; for the womb, where Our Lord was a recluse, is a narrow dwelling, and this word "Mary", as I have often said, means "bitterness". If you then suffer bitter things in a narrow place you are His fellow-recluses, since He was a recluse in Mary's womb. Are you confined within four great walls? He was confined in a narrow cradle, confined when He was nailed to the cross, and fast enclosed in a sepulchre of stone. Mary's womb and this sepulchre were His anchor-houses. In neither was He a Man mingling with the world, but as it were apart from the world, to show anchoresses that with the world they should have nothing in common. "Yes," you

---

1. The translation is from *The Ancrene Riwle*, translated by M. B. Salu (Exeter: University of Exeter Press, 1990; first published 1955).
2. Mark 16.1.

will answer me, "but He went out of both." Yes, then go you out of both your anchor-houses too, as He did, without breaking them, and leave them both whole. That is what will happen when the spirit goes out at the end, without any breaking, without making any scar on its two houses. One is the body, the other is its outer house which is like the outer wall about the castle.

All that I have said about mortification of the flesh is not intended for you, my dear sisters, who sometimes suffer more than I would have you, but for some who are quite likely to read this and who treat themselves too gently. Nonetheless, young trees are encircled about with thorns for fear animals will feed on them while they are tender. You are young trees planted in God's orchard. The hardships which I have spoken of are the thorns, and it is necessary for you to be encircled with them, so that the beast of hell, when he sneaks towards you, intending to bite you, may be hurt by their sharpness and turn back frightened by all those hardships. Be glad and be well content if there is not much talk about you, and if you are of little account, for a thorn is sharp and unnoticeable. Be encircled, then, by these two things. You ought not, however, to allow any evil reports about yourselves. Giving scandal is a mortal sin, that is, saying or doing something in such a way that a bad interpretation may easily be put upon it, resulting in sins of evil thought or evil speech on the part of those who misinterpret, and on the part of others, and sins also of deed. You should be content that there be no talk of you at all, any more than there is of the dead, and if you incur disdain from Slurry, the cook's boy, who washes and dries the dishes in the kitchen, you should be happy in your hearts. Then you will be mountains lifted up towards heaven, for see what is said by the lady in the sweet Book of Love, *My beloved cometh, leaping upon the mountains, skipping over the hills.*[3] "My love comes leaping," she says, "upon the mountains, that is, he treads them underfoot, making them vile, allows them to be trodden on, to be outrageously chastised, and shows on them his own footmarks, so that by them people might follow him, and discover how he was trodden upon, as his traces show." These are the high mountains, like Montjoy and the mountains of Armenia. The hills, which are lower, and which the lady herself says He skips over, He had no confidence in, because of their weakness; they might not be able to bear such a tread and He skips over them, leaves them alone and avoids them until they grow higher, out of hills into mountains. Only His shadow passes over them and covers them as He skips over them; that is, He lays over them some likeness of His earthly life, His shadow as it were; but the mountains receive the impression of His own feet and in their lives they show what His life was like, how and where He went, in what lowliness and in what sorrow He led His earthly life. The good Paul spoke of such mountains and said with humility: *We are cast down: but we perish not. Bearing about in our body the mortification of Jesus, that the life also of Jesus may be made manifest in our bodies.*[4] "We suffer," he said, "all tribulation and all shame, but that is our happiness, to bear upon our body the mortification of Jesus Christ, so that in us there may be made plain the kind of life that was His on earth." God knows, they who do this prove to us their love of Our Lord. "Lovest thou me?" Then show it, for love does show itself in exterior actions. St Gregory says,

3. Song of Solomon 2.8.   4. 2 Corinthians 4.9–10.

The proof of love is the manifestation of its effect.[5] However hard a thing may be, true love lightens it and makes it easy and sweet. *Love makes all things easy.* What do men and women suffer for false love and for unclean love? And how much more they would still be willing to suffer! And what is more strange than that true, real love, sweet beyond all other, cannot drive us forward as the love of sin does? And yet, I know one man who wears at the same time a heavy coat of mail and a hair-shirt fastened painfully about his waist, thighs, and arms with broad, thick bands of iron; to bear the sweat which this causes is agony; he fasts, watches, and performs great labours, and yet, Christ knows, laments that this gives him no pain at all, and he often asks me to teach him some means of mortifying his body. All that is bitter he finds sweet in the love of Our Lord. God knows, he still weeps to me and says that God has forgotten him because He has not sent him any great illness. These, God knows, are the effects of love, for as he often says to me, no evil thing that God might do to him, even though He should cast him into hell with those who are lost, could ever, he believes, make him love Him any the less. Anyone who imagines that it could, is more confounded than a thief taken with his theft. I know a woman too, who suffers not much less than this. We can only thank God for the strength which He gives them and humbly acknowledge our own weakness. Let us love what is good in them and thus it comes to belong to us, for, as St Gregory says, love is of such great power that it makes others' good our own, without any effort on our part, as has been said before.[6] We have arrived now, I think, at the seventh part, which is entirely concerned with love, which makes the heart pure.

---

5. Gregory the Great, *Homilies* 30.1 (*Patrologia Latina* 76.1220).

6. See Gregory, *Moralia in Job* 6.10 (*Patrologia Latina* 76.461).

ROMANCE

Romances satisfy our deepest imaginative desires. If we most fear loss of identity in separation from what we hold dearest and from what makes us what we are, romances allay that fear. As they imagine narratives of separation, errancy, and loss, they therapeutically deliver endings of reintegration, recovery, and return. That which was lost is found.

The word *romans* was originally a simple linguistic designation, meaning "French," since French was derived from Latin, the language of Rome. In the twelfth century, however, the word narrowed in meaning, coming to designate narrative (forms of *roman* still mean "novel" in French, Italian, and German). The word then became particularly associated with a genre of narrative. It came to designate stories of separation and return, disintegration and reintegration.

Certainly classical Greek literature has examples of "romance" narrative, stories that involve separation, testing, and travel, all the prelude to, and premise of, a final homecoming and recognition. Homer's *Odyssey* is fundamentally a romance; five later Greek narratives of this kind also survive (first to fourth centuries CE). The broader modal commitment of romance to "comedy" (a story with a happy ending) also has classical roots. Romances are "comic" stories not because they make us laugh but, rather, like Shakespeare's comedies, they make us feel good through happy endings.

The dynamic French-speaking court cultures of twelfth-century France and England gave the genre its most powerful, undying impetus. Chrétien de Troyes (fl. 1160–90) is its greatest exponent in his Arthurian romances, but the rich set of Tristran materials, and the lais of Marie de France, are also of exceptional importance. The genre, once deeply planted in the twelfth century in French, flourishes anew in all European vernacular languages and in each historical period of European and American culture. It remains energetically immune to the literary plant killers of moralistic objection, high literary disdain for escapist entertainment, and satire.

The Dance of Mirth. *The Romance of the Rose,* ca. 1500. The scene illustrates a moment in the thirteenth-century French poem. Note the splendor and circularity of this aristocratic performance of amorous ritual.

The fundamental characteristic of romances is structural, not stylistic. They can be short or long, oral or literary, but to be romances they must have, or adapt, a particular story structure. Romances classically have a tripartite structure: integration (or implied integration); disintegration; and reintegration. They begin in, or at least imply, a protected, civilized state of some integrated social unit (e.g., family). That state is disrupted, expelling a member of the unit (the hero or heroine of the story, who is usually young) into a wild place. Undergoing the tests of that wild place is the premise of return to the integrated, civilized state of familial and/or social unity. Successfully undergoing tests in the wild often results in marriage, in which case return to home and family is also return to an enlarged home and family.

This story pattern is characteristic of many fairy stories, medieval romances, Shakespearean comedies, novels, and popular movies. It not only represents desire but activates desire in its readers: the pleasure we take in such stories derives from our desire for the reintegration of lives in a coherent and constructive narrative. The desired pattern can also, of course, be adapted in many variations. In particular, it can be activated in order to be frustrated: some protagonists, particularly adulterous ones like Tristan and Ysolt, never reach home, forever needing to defer that unreachable happy ending of recognition.

Romances, then, are symbolic stories, replaying and allaying the fears of the young as they face the apparently insuperable challenges of the adult world. Their deepest wisdom is this: civilization is not a unitary concept. To enter and remain in the world of civilized order, we must, say romances, have commerce with all that threatens it. To regain Rome at the center, we must first be tested in the marginal wilds of romance. To be recognized and found, we must first be lost.

The romances offered here exemplify different possibilities derived from this story structure. *Sir Orfeo* is the only classic example, true in almost every respect to the model sketched above. *Sir Gawain and the Green Knight* and Chaucer's *Wife of Bath's Tale*, following this cluster, play fascinating games with classic romance structure. *Milun* and *Lanval* suggest different possibilities for romance within the tight and suffocating context of the medieval court. *Chevrefoil* expresses the way the aspiration to achieve a happy ending is all the more painfully intense because impossible. The earlier sample from Thomas's *Tristran* underlines the inevitable end of such an impossible passion.

MARIE DE FRANCE

Much of twelfth-century French literature was composed in England in the Anglo-Norman dialect (see p. 10). Prominent among the earliest poets writing in the French vernacular, who shaped the genres, themes, and styles of later medieval European poetry, is the author who, in an epilogue to her *Fables*, calls herself Marie de France. That signature tells us only that her given name was Marie and that she was born in France, but circumstantial evidence from her writings shows that she spent much of her life in England. A reference to her in a French poem written in England around 1180 speaks of "dame Marie" who wrote "lais" much loved and praised, read, and heard by counts, barons, and knights and indicates that her poems also appealed to ladies who listened to them gladly and joyfully.

Three works can be safely attributed to Marie, probably written in the following order: the *Lais* [English "lay" refers to a short narrative poem in verse], the *Fables*, and *St. Patrick's Purgatory*. Marie's twelve lays are short romances (they range from 118 to 1,184 lines), each of which deals with a single event or crisis in the affairs of noble lovers. In her prologue, Marie tells us that she had heard these *performed*, and in several of the lays she refers to the Breton language and Breton storytellers—that is, professional minstrels from the French province of Brittany or the Celtic parts of Great Britain. Marie's lays provide the basis of the genre that came to be known as the "Breton lay." In the prologue Marie dedicates the work to a "noble king," who is most likely to have been Henry II of England, who reigned from 1154 to 1189.

The portrait of the author that emerges from the combination of these works is of a highly educated noblewoman, proficient in Latin and English as well as her native French, with ideas of her own and a strong commitment to writing. Scholars have proposed several Maries of the period who fit this description to identify the author. A likely candidate is Marie, abbess of Shaftesbury, an illegitimate daughter of Geoffrey of Anjou and thus half-sister of Henry II. Correct or not, such an identification points to the milieu in which Marie moved and to the kind of audience she was addressing.

Many of Marie's lays contain elements of magic and mystery. Medieval readers would recognize that *Lanval* is about a mortal lover and a fairy bride, although the word "fairy" is not used in the tale. In the Middle Ages fairies were not thought of as the small creatures they became in Elizabethan and later literature. Fairies are supernatural, sometimes dangerous, beings who possess magical powers and inhabit another world. Their realm in some respects resembles the human (fairies have kings and queens), and fairies generally keep to themselves and disappear when humans notice them. But the tales are often about crossovers between the human and fairy worlds. *Sir Orfeo* and Chaucer's *Wife of Bath's Tale* are such stories.

Marie's narrative *Milun* has a tight family unit at its core, but that unit is divided in time and space by an oppressive marital system. Testing consists of long deferral;

ability to recognize signs; and intergenerational violence, between father and son, that turns out to be constructive.

Chevrefoil, the shortest of Marie's lays, tells of a brief encounter between Tristran and Ysolt. The lay exemplifies the pain of their separation as well as the stratagems by which the lovers are forced to communicate and meet. The title refers to an image from the natural world that serves as a symbol of the inextricable and fatal character of the love that binds them to one another.

Marie wrote in eight-syllable couplets, which was the standard form of French narrative verse, employed also by Wace and Chrétien de Troyes. Here is what the beginning of Marie's prologue to the *Lais* says about her view of a writer's duty and, implicitly, of her own talent:

Ki Deu ad duné escïence	He to whom God has given knowledge
E de parler bon' eloquence	And the gift of speaking eloquently,
Ne s'en deit taisir ne celer,	Must not keep silent nor conceal the gift.
Ainz se deit volunters mustrer.	But he must willingly display it.

All translations of Marie's *Lais* are by Robert Hanning and Joan Ferrante.

Milun

    Whoever wants to tell a variety of stories
ought to have a variety of beginnings,
and speak so intelligently
that people will enjoy listening.
5 Now I'll begin *Milun*
and show, in a brief discourse,
why and how the *lai*
called by that name was written.[1]
    Milun was born in South Wales.
10 From the day he was dubbed knight
he couldn't find a single opponent
who could knock him off his horse.
He certainly was a good knight:
generous and strong, courteous and proud.
15 He won fame in Ireland,
in Norway and Gothland;
in Logres and in Albany
many envied him.
He was well beloved
20 and honored by many princes.
    There was a baron in his country—
I don't know his name—
who had a daughter,
a beautiful and most refined girl.
25 She had heard of Milun,
and began to love him.
She sent a messenger to him,

---

1. The French term, *trovez*, translated here as "written," could also be rendered "composed," if Marie is referring to a musical setting.

to say that, if it pleased him, she would love him.
Milun was happy with the news,
30 and thanked the girl;
he willingly granted her his love,
and said he would never leave her;
his response to her was very courtly,
and he gave rich gifts to the messenger,
35 promising him his friendship.
"My friend," he said, "please undertake
to help me speak to my beloved
and to keep our communications secret.
Carry my gold ring to her
40 and tell her on my behalf:
whenever she wants, she can send you for me
and I'll go with you."
The messenger took his leave and soon went away;
he returned to his lady.
45 He gave her the ring and told her
that he had done what she had asked.
The girl was delighted
at the love she was being offered.
Outside her room, in a grove
50 where she went to amuse herself,
she and Milun, very often,
had a rendezvous.
Milun came there so often and loved her so much
that the girl became pregnant.
55 When she realized this,
she sent for Milun and made her lament.
She told him what had happened;
she had lost her honor and her good name
when she got herself into this situation.
60 She would be grievously punished:
tortured by the sword
or sold into slavery in another land.
Such were the ancient customs
observed in those days.
65 Milun answered that he would do
whatever she counseled.
"When the child is born," she said,
"you must bring him to my sister,
who is married and living in Northumbria;
70 she is a rich woman, worthy and prudent.
And send word to her, in writing
and also orally
that this child belongs to her sister,
who has endured great grief because of him.
75 She should make sure that he's well nourished,
whatever it may be, son or daughter.
I shall hang your ring around his neck
and send a letter with it,

in which will be written his father's name
80 and the unfortunate story of his mother.[2]
When he is full grown,
and has arrived at the age
when he can listen to reason,
she should give him the ring and the letter
85 and command him to keep them
so that he can find his father."
    They abided by this plan,
and the time eventually came
for the girl to have her baby.
90 An old woman who watched over her,
to whom she had disclosed her entire situation,
covered things up so well
that she was never discovered,
by her words or appearance.
95 The girl had a beautiful son.
They hung the ring around his neck,
and also a silken wallet
with the letter in it, so that no one could see it.
Then they laid the child in a little cradle,
100 wrapped in a white linen cloth;
beneath his head
they placed a fine pillow
and over him a coverlet,
hemmed all around with marten fur.
105 The old nurse gave him to Milun,
who was waiting for her in the grove.
He turned the child over to some trustworthy retainers
who would take him to his destination.
As they traveled from town to town,
110 they stopped to rest seven times a day;
they had the child nursed,
changed, and bathed.
They took their job so seriously
that they had brought a wet nurse with them.
115 They stayed on the right road
until they reached the sister and gave the child to her.
She took him from them, and was very pleased with him.
She also took the letter with its seal.
When she knew who he was,
120 she cherished him even more.
Then the men who had brought the child
returned to their own land.
    Milun left his homeland
to seek honor through martial exploits.[3]
125 His mistress remained at home
and her father gave her in marriage

---

2. Marie uses the key term *aventure*.
3. The text uses the term *sudees*, meaning paid military service.

to a rich lord of the region,
a powerful man of great repute.
When she found out about this turn of events,[4]
130 she was grief-stricken,
and she cried for Milun.
She was especially worried about being blamed
for having had a child already;
her husband would discover that soon enough.
135 "Alas," she said, "what can I do?
Must I be married? How can I?
I'm no longer a virgin,
I'll have to be a servant all my life.
I didn't know it would be like this;
140 rather, I thought I could have my love,
that we could keep it a secret between us,
that I'd never hear it bruited about.
Now I'd rather die than live,
but I'm not even free to do that,
145 since I have guardians all around me,
old and young; my chamberlains,
who hate a noble love,
and take their delight in sadness.
Now I have to suffer like this—
150 if only I could die!"
The time came for her to be married,
and her father led her to the altar.
    Milun came back to his land;
he was sad and upset—
155 he gave himself up to grief.
He took some comfort from the fact
that the one he loved so much
was still in her country, nearby.
Milun undertook to plan
160 how he could send word to her—
without being discovered—
that he had come home.
He wrote a letter and sealed it.
He had a swan of which he was very fond;
165 he tied the letter to its neck,
hid it among the feathers.
He summoned one of his squires
and made him his messenger.
"Go immediately and change your clothes," he said.
170 "I want you to go to my mistress' castle,
and take my swan with you.
Make arrangements
for the swan to be given to her
by a servant or a maid."

4. French: *aventure*.

175   The squire did his duty.
He went off quickly, taking the swan with him;
by the most direct route he knew
he came to the castle.
He went through the village
180   directly to the main gate,
called out to the porter:
"Friend," he said, "listen!
This is how I make a living:
I go around catching birds.
185   In a meadow outside Caerleon
I captured a swan in my net.
To earn her goodwill and support,
I want to make a present of it to the lady of the castle,
so that I won't be bothered
190   while I'm working in this area."
The porter replied,
"Friend, no one can speak to her;
but nonetheless, I'll go find out:
if I can find a place
195   that I can bring you to,
I'll arrange for you to speak with her."
    The porter went to the main hall
and found only two knights there,
seated at a big table
200   amusing themselves at chess.
Quickly he returned to the messenger,
and brought him in in such a way
that he wasn't seen
or disturbed by anyone.
205   He came to the lady's chamber, and called;
a girl opened the door for them.
They came into the lady's presence,
presented her with the swan.
She called one of her valets
210   and said to him, "Make it your business
to take good care of my swan;
be sure he has enough food."
"My lady," said the messenger who brought the swan,
"No one but you should have him;
215   this is indeed a royal present—
see how fine and handsome a bird he is!"
He placed the bird in her hands.
She accepted it quite willingly,
petted its neck and head,
220   and felt the letter among the feathers.
Her blood ran cold; she shivered,
realizing the letter was from her lover.
She had some money given to the messenger,
and told him to go.
225   When the chamber was empty

she called one of her maids.
She detached the letter,
broke the seal.
She read at the top of the sheet, "Milun,"
230   and when she saw her lover's name
she kissed it a hundred times, crying,
before she could read further.
At the beginning of the letter she read
what he had written
235   of the great sadness
from which he was suffering night and day.
Now it was entirely in her power
to kill or cure him.
If she could think of a scheme
240   whereby he could speak with her,
she should let him know in a letter
and send the swan back to him.
First she should have the swan well guarded,
then keep him fasting
245   three days without any food.
Then the letter should be hung on his neck,
and he should be released; he would fly
to where he had formerly lived.
When she had looked at the whole letter,
250   and heard the contents,
she had the swan well taken care of
with abundant food and drink;
she kept him in her chamber for a month.
Now listen to what happened!
255   She used her ingenuity so well
that she obtained some ink and parchment;
she wrote the letter she wanted to,
and sealed it with a ring.
Then she made the swan go hungry,
260   hung the letter on his neck, released him.
The bird was famished—
he really wanted food;
so he quickly returned
to where he had come from—
265   the same town, the same household—
there he landed at Milun's feet.
When Milun saw him, he was very joyful;
he quickly grabbed him by the wings,
he called his steward,
270   had him give the swan some food,
and meanwhile took the letter from his neck.
He read it from one end to the other,
noting all the words that he found in it,
and rejoicing at her message:
275   "She couldn't have any pleasure without him,
and now he should send back his feelings to her,

by the swan, the same way she had done."
He'll do that right away!
      For twenty years they lived like this,
280 Milun and his mistress.
The swan was their messenger,
they had no other means of communication,
and they always made him fast
before they let him go on his errand;
285 whoever the bird came to,
you can be sure, fed it well.
      They met together several times.
(No one can be so constrained
or so closely guarded
290 that he can't find a way out.)
      Meanwhile, the lady who had raised their son
had him dubbed a knight;
he had been with her long enough
to come of age.
295 He had become a fine young man.
She gave him the letter and the ring,
told him who his mother was,
and his father's story as well:
how his father was a good knight,
300 so bold, hardy, and proud
that there was none who exceeded him
in worth or valor anywhere.
When the lady had told him all this
and he'd listened carefully to her,
305 he rejoiced in his father's virtues;
he was delighted with what he had learned.
He said to himself,
"A man oughtn't to think he's worth much,
being born in such a manner
310 and having such a famous father,
if he doesn't seek out even greater renown
away from home, in foreign lands."
He had everything he needed;
he didn't stay beyond that night,
315 but took his leave next morning.
His foster mother admonished him,
urging him to do good deeds;
she also gave him plenty of money.
      He went to Southampton to get under way;
320 as quickly as he could he set out to sea.
He arrived at Barfleur
and went right to Brittany.
There he spent lavishly and tourneyed,
and became acquainted with rich men.
325 In every joust he entered,
he was judged the best combatant.
He loved poor knights;

what he gained from rich ones
he gave to them and thus retained them in his service;
330 he was generous in all his spending.
He would never willingly stay long in one place;
in all those foreign lands
he won renown for his heroic virtues.
He also excelled in refined and honorable behavior.
335 Because of his excellence and fame
the news spread to his own country
that a young knight of that land,
who had gone abroad to seek honor,
had so excelled in prowess,
340 goodness, and generosity
that those who didn't know his name
called him, everywhere, "the knight without equal."
Milun heard this stranger praised
and his virtues recounted.
345 He was saddened, and complained to himself
about this knight who was worth so much
that, so long as he traveled,
fought in tournaments, and bore arms,
no one else born in that land
350 would be praised or honored.
Milun came to a decision:
he would quickly cross the sea
and joust with this knight,
in order to do some harm to him and his reputation.
355 Anger spurred him on
to try to unhorse the knight—
that would put him to shame!
Then he would go look for his son
who had left the country;
360 Milun did not know what had become of him.
    He let his mistress know his scheme,
and asked her leave to go;
he revealed his intentions
by sending her a sealed letter,
365 by the swan, I believe;
now she had to let him know how she felt.
When she heard his wish,
she thanked him, expressing her gratitude
that he wanted to leave the country
370 to find their son,
and to find out about his fortunes;
she wouldn't interfere with his plans.
Milun got her message,
then dressed himself richly
375 and went over to Normandy,
whence he traveled to Brittany.
He made many acquaintances,
sought out many tournaments;
his lodgings were usually luxurious,

380 and he gave suitably generous gifts.
    Through an entire winter, I believe,
Milun stayed in that land.
He obtained the services of many good knights,
until Easter came,
385 when tournaments began again,
as well as wars and other battles.[5]
A tournament was held at Mont Saint Michel;
Normans and Bretons,
Flemings and Frenchmen all came,
390 though there were few English knights.
Milun came early,
good knight that he was.
He inquired after the knight without equal;
there were plenty of knights who could tell him
395 where he had come from.
By his arms and shield
he was pointed out to Milun,
who observed him carefully.
    The tournament began.
400 Whoever wanted to joust quickly found the opportunity;
he need only search the ranks a bit
to find a companion
in the quest for victory or defeat.
This much I'll tell you about Milun:
405 it went very well with him in combat
and he was highly praised that day.
But the young man of whom I've told you—
he was acclaimed beyond all others;
none could equal him
410 in tourneying and jousting.
Milun watched him perform,
riding and attacking so well;
although he was Milun's rival,
he pleased Milun greatly.
415 Milun rushed into the ranks against him,
and the two jousted together.
Milun struck him so hard
that his lance splintered,
but he didn't unhorse him.
420 The other knight struck Milun so hard
that he knocked him right off his steed.
Beneath Milun's visor,
he saw his beard and white hair;
he was sorry to have made him fall.
425 He took Milun's horse by the reins,
and presented it to him,
saying, "My lord, remount;
I'm saddened

5. During much of the Middle Ages, the times of year when the church permitted warfare and tournaments were strictly limited by the concept of the "truce of God." Lent, the period of penance before Easter, was one such time of truce. (The church's ban was not always observed.)

that I should have so humiliated
430   a man of your age."
Milun leaped up, highly pleased,
for he had recognized the ring on the other's finger
when he gave Milun his horse.
He spoke to the young man.
435   "My friend," he said, "listen to me!
For the love of almighty God
tell me your father's name!
What is yours? Who is your mother?
I want to know the truth about this.
440   I've seen a lot, wandered a lot,
searched in many lands
in tournaments and wars;
I never once fell from my war-horse
because of a blow from another knight.
445   You knocked me down in a joust—
I could love you a great deal."
The other answered, "I'll tell you
about my father, as much as I know of him.
I think he was born in Wales
450   and is named Milun.
He loved the daughter of a rich man
and secretly conceived me with her.
I was sent to Northumbria,
and there I was raised and educated
455   by my aunt.
She kept me with her,
then gave me a horse and my arms,
and sent me to this land,
where I have long resided.
460   It is my desire and intent
to go back across the sea quickly
and return to my own land;
I wish to find out who my father is,
and how he is behaving toward my mother.
465   I'll show him my gold ring
and tell him my story;
he will certainly not reject me,
rather, as a loving father he'll make much of me."
When Milun heard him say all this
470   he didn't wait to hear any more;
he quickly leapt forward
and took the other by the skirt of his hauberk.
"God!" he cried, "I'm a new man!
By my faith, friend, you are my son!
475   It was to look for you
that I left my homeland this year."
When the young knight heard him, he got down from his horse
and kissed his father warmly.
They both looked so happy
480   and said such things to each other

that all the others watching them
began to cry from joy and pity.
　　When the tournament broke up,
Milun went away, very anxious
485　to speak at leisure with his son,
to find out what his pleasure was.
They spent the night in a hostel
where there was much celebrating
being done by a large number of knights.
490　Milun told his son
how he loved the boy's mother,
and how her father had given her
to a baron of that region,
and how he had continued loving her,
495　and she him, with all her heart,
and how he used the swan as a messenger,
having the bird carry his letters,
since he couldn't trust anyone else.
The son responded, "Indeed, my good father,
500　I'll bring you and my mother together;
I shall kill her husband
and see you married."
　　They spoke no more about it;
the next day they made ready to leave.
505　They said good-bye to their friends,
and returned to their own land.
Their crossing was speedy,
thanks to a good strong wind.
As they went on their way
510　they met a boy
coming from Milun's mistress;
he was on his way to Brittany,
for she had dispatched him to go there.
Now his trip was shortened.
515　She was sending Milun a sealed letter
with a message telling him
that he should come to her without delay:
her husband was dead—now was the time to make haste!
Milun heard the news,
520　and it seemed wonderful to him.
Then he told his son.
Nothing held them back now;
they pushed on until they came
to the lady's castle.
525　She was delighted with her son,
who was so worthy and well behaved.
Without consulting any relatives,
with no advice from anyone else,
their son brought them together,
530　gave his mother to his father.
In great happiness and well-being
they lived happily ever after.

The ancients made a *lai*
about their love and good fortune;
535 and I who have put it down in writing
have thoroughly enjoyed retelling it.

1154–89

Lanval

I shall tell you the adventure of another *lai*,
just as it happened:
it was composed about a very noble vassal;
in Breton, they call him Lanval.

5 Arthur, the brave and the courtly king,
was staying at Cardoel,
because the Scots and the Picts
were destroying the land.
They invaded Logres[1]
10 and laid it waste.
At Pentecost, in summer,[2]
the king stayed there.
He gave out many rich gifts:
to counts and barons,
15 members of the Round Table—
such a company had no equal[3] in all the world—
he distributed wives and lands,
to all but one who had served him.
That was Lanval; Arthur forgot him,
20 and none of his men favored him either.
For his valor, for his generosity,
his beauty and his bravery,
most men envied him;
some feigned the appearance of love
25 who, if something unpleasant happened to him,
would not have been at all disturbed.
He was the son of a king of high degree
but he was far from his heritage.
He was of the king's household
30 but he had spent all his wealth,
for the king gave him nothing
nor did Lanval ask.
Now Lanval was in difficulty,
depressed and very worried.
35 My lords, don't be surprised:
a strange man, without friends,
is very sad in another land,

1. England.
2. In medieval poetry the feast of Pentecost is frequently the starting point of an Arthurian adventure.
3. Equal in number as well as in worth.

when he doesn't know where to look for help.
The knight of whom I speak,
40 who had served the king so long,
one day mounted his horse
and went off to amuse himself.
He left the city
and came, all alone, to a field;
45 he dismounted by a running stream
but his horse trembled badly.
He removed the saddle and went off,
leaving the horse to roll around in the meadow.
He folded his cloak beneath his head
50 and lay down.
He worried about his difficulty,
he could see nothing that pleased him.
As he lay there
he looked down along the bank
55 and saw two girls approaching;
he had never seen any lovelier.
They were richly dressed,
tightly laced,
in tunics of dark purple;
60 their faces were very lovely.
The older one carried basins,
golden, well made, and fine;
I shall tell you the truth about it, without fail.[4]
The other carried a towel.
65 They went straight
to where the knight was lying.
Lanval, who was very well bred,
got up to meet them.
They greeted him first
70 and gave him their message:
"Sir Lanval, my lady,
who is worthy and wise and beautiful,
sent us for you.
Come with us now.
75 We shall guide you there safely.
See, her pavilion is nearby!"
The knight went with them;
giving no thought to his horse
who was feeding before him in the meadow.
80 They led him up to the tent,
which was quite beautiful and well placed.
Queen Semiramis,
however much more wealth,
power, or knowledge she had,
85 or the emperor Octavian
could not have paid for one of the flaps.

---

4. Cf. lines 178–79, where these articles are used. Washing one's hands before meals indicates aristocratic luxury and refinement. Marie makes a mock pretense that her listeners could hardly imagine these splendors of the other world.

There was a golden eagle on top of it,
whose value I could not tell,
nor could I judge the value of the cords or the poles
90 that held up the sides of the tent;
there is no king on earth who could buy it,
no matter what wealth he offered.
The girl was inside the tent:
the lily and the young rose
95 when they appear in the summer
are surpassed by her beauty.
She lay on a beautiful bed—
the bedclothes were worth a castle—
dressed only in her shift.
100 Her body was well shaped and elegant;
for the heat, she had thrown over herself,
a precious cloak of white ermine,
covered with purple alexandrine,
but her whole side was uncovered,
105 her face, her neck and her bosom;
she was whiter than the hawthorn flower.
The knight went forward
and the girl addressed him.
He sat before the bed.
110 "Lanval," she said, "sweet love,
because of you I have come from my land;
I came to seek you from far away.
If you are brave and courtly,
no emperor or count or king
115 will ever have known such joy or good;
for I love you more than anything."
He looked at her and saw that she was beautiful;
Love stung him with a spark
that burned and set fire to his heart.
120 He answered her in a suitable way.
"Lovely one," he said, "if it pleased you,
if such joy might be mine
that you would love me,
there is nothing you might command,
125 within my power, that I would not do,
whether foolish or wise.
I shall obey your command;
for you, I shall abandon everyone.
I want never to leave you.
130 That is what I most desire."
When the girl heard the words
of the man who could love her so,
she granted him her love and her body.
Now Lanval was on the right road!
135 Afterward, she gave him a gift:
he would never again want anything,
he would receive as he desired;
however generously he might give and spend,

she would provide what he needed.
140 Now Lanval is well cared for.
The more lavishly he spends,
the more gold and silver he will have.
"Love," she said, "I admonish you now,
I command and beg you,
145 do not let any man know about this.
I shall tell you why:
you would lose me for good
if this love were known;
you would never see me again
150 or possess my body."
He answered that he would do
exactly as she commanded.
He lay beside her on the bed;
now Lanval is well cared for.
155 He remained with her
that afternoon, until evening
and would have stayed longer, if he could,
and if his love had consented.
"Love," she said, "get up.
160 You cannot stay any longer.
Go away now; I shall remain
but I will tell you one thing:
when you want to talk to me
there is no place you can think of
165 where a man might have his mistress
without reproach or shame,
that I shall not be there with you
to satisfy all your desires.
No man but you will see me
170 or hear my words."
When he heard her, he was very happy,
he kissed her, and then got up.
The girls who had brought him to the tent
dressed him in rich clothes;
175 when he was dressed anew,
there wasn't a more handsome youth in all the world;
he was no fool, no boor.
They gave him water for his hands
and a towel to dry them,
180 and they brought him food.
He took supper with his love;
it was not to be refused.
He was served with great courtesy,
he received it with great joy.
185 There was an entremet[5]
that vastly pleased the knight
for he kissed his lady often

---

5. French *entremès*: a side dish served between main courses; an interlude between acts. Marie may well intend a double-entendre involving both meanings.

and held her close.
When they finished dinner,
190   his horse was brought to him.
The horse had been well saddled;
Lanval was very richly served.
The knight took his leave, mounted,
and rode toward the city,
195   often looking behind him.
Lanval was very disturbed;
he wondered about his adventure
and was doubtful in his heart;
he was amazed, not knowing what to believe;
200   he didn't expect ever to see her again.
He came to his lodging
and found his men well dressed.
That night, his accommodations were rich
but no one knew where it came from.
205   There was no knight in the city
who really needed a place to stay
whom he didn't invite to join him
to be well and richly served.
Lanval gave rich gifts,
210   Lanval released prisoners,
Lanval dressed jongleurs,[6]
Lanval offered great honors.
There was no stranger or friend
to whom Lanval didn't give.
215   Lanval's joy and pleasure were intense;
in the daytime or at night,
he could see his love often;
she was completely at his command.

In that same year, it seems to me,
220   after the feast of St. John,
about thirty knights
were amusing themselves
in an orchard beneath the tower
where the queen was staying.
225   Gawain was with them
and his cousin, the handsome Yvain;
Gawain, the noble, the brave,
who was so loved by all, said:
"By God, my lords, we wronged
230   our companion Lanval,
who is so generous and courtly,
and whose father is a rich king,
when we didn't bring him with us."
They immediately turned back,
235   went to his lodging
and prevailed on Lanval to come along with them.
At a sculpted window

6. Performers.

the queen was looking out;
she had three ladies with her.
240 She saw the king's retinue,
recognized Lanval and looked at him.
Then she told one of her ladies
to send for her maidens,
the loveliest and the most refined;
245 together they went to amuse themselves
in the orchard where the others were.
She brought thirty or more with her;
they descended the steps.
The knights came to meet them,
250 because they were delighted to see them.
The knights took them by the hand;
their conversation was in no way vulgar.
Lanval went off to one side,
far from the others; he was impatient
255 to hold his love,
to kiss and embrace and touch her;
he thought little of others' joys
if he could not have his pleasure.
When the queen saw him alone,
260 she went straight to the knight.
She sat beside him and spoke,
revealing her whole heart:
"Lanval, I have shown you much honor,
I have cherished you, and loved you.
265 You may have all my love;
just tell me your desire.
I promise you my affection.
You should be very happy with me."
"My lady," he said, "let me be!
270 I have no desire to love you.
I've served the king a long time;
I don't want to betray my faith to him.
Never, for you or for your love,
will I do anything to harm my lord."
275 The queen got angry;
in her wrath, she insulted him:
"Lanval," she said, "I am sure
you don't care for such pleasure;
people have often told me
280 that you have no interest in women.
You have fine-looking boys
with whom you enjoy yourself.
Base coward, lousy cripple,
my lord made a bad mistake
285 when he let you stay with him.
For all I know, he'll lose God because of it."
When Lanval heard her, he was quite disturbed;
he was not slow to answer.
He said something out of spite

290   that he would later regret.
"Lady," he said, "of that activity
I know nothing,
but I love and I am loved
by one who should have the prize
295   over all the women I know.
And I shall tell you one thing;
you might as well know all:
any one of those who serve her,
the poorest girl of all,
300   is better than you, my lady queen,
in body, face, and beauty,
in breeding and in goodness."
The queen left him
and went, weeping, to her chamber.
305   She was upset and angry
because he had insulted her.
She went to bed sick;
never, she said, would she get up
unless the king gave her satisfaction
310   for the offense against her.
The king returned from the woods,
he'd had a very good day.
He entered the queen's chambers.
When she saw him, she began to complain.
315   She fell at his feet, asked his mercy,
saying that Lanval had dishonored her;
he had asked for her love,
and because she refused him
he insulted and offended her:
320   he boasted of a love
who was so refined and noble and proud
that her chambermaid,
the poorest one who served her,
was better than the queen.
325   The king got very angry;
he swore an oath:
if Lanval could not defend himself in court
he would have him burned or hanged.
The king left her chamber
330   and called for three of his barons;
he sent them for Lanval
who was feeling great sorrow and distress.
He had come back to his dwelling,
knowing very well
335   that he'd lost his love,
he had betrayed their affair.
He was all alone in a room,
disturbed and troubled;
he called on his love, again and again,
340   but it did him no good.
He complained and sighed,

from time to time he fainted;
then he cried a hundred times for her to have mercy
and speak to her love.
345 He cursed his heart and his mouth;
it's a wonder he didn't kill himself.
No matter how much he cried and shouted,
ranted and raged,
she would not have mercy on him,
350 not even let him see her.
How will he ever contain himself?
The men the king sent
arrived and told him
to appear in court without delay:
355 the king had summoned him
because the queen had accused him.
Lanval went with his great sorrow;
they could have killed him, for all he cared.
He came before the king;
360 he was very sad, thoughtful, silent;
his face revealed great suffering.
In anger the king told him:
"Vassal, you have done me a great wrong!
This was a base undertaking,
365 to shame and disgrace me
and to insult the queen.
You have made a foolish boast:
your love is much too noble
if her maid is more beautiful,
370 more worthy, than the queen."
Lanval denied that he'd dishonored
or shamed his lord,
word for word, as the king spoke:
he had not made advances to the queen;
375 but of what he had said,
he acknowledged the truth,
about the love he had boasted of,
that now made him sad because he'd lost her.
About that he said he would do
380 whatever the court decided.
The king was very angry with him;
he sent for all his men
to determine exactly what he ought to do
so that no one could find fault with his decision.[7]
385 They did as he commanded,
whether they liked it or not.
They assembled,
judged, and decided,
than Lanval should have his day;
390 but he must find pledges for his lord

7. The trial of Lanval shows precise knowledge of 12th-century legal procedure concerning the respective rights of the king and his barons.

to guarantee that he would await the judgment,
return, and be present at it.
Then the court would be increased,
for now there were none but the king's household.[8]
395 The barons came back to the king
and announced their decision.
The king demanded pledges.
Lanval was alone and forlorn,
he had no relative, no friend.
400 Gawain went and pledged himself for him,
and all his companions followed.
The king addressed them: "I release him to you
on forfeit of whatever you hold from me,
lands and fiefs, each one for himself."
405 When Lanval was pledged, there was nothing else to do.
He returned to his lodging.
The knights accompanied him,
they reproached and admonished him
that he give up his great sorrow;
410 they cursed his foolish love.
Each day they went to see him,
because they wanted to know
whether he was drinking and eating;
they were afraid that he'd kill himself.
415 On the day that they had named,
the barons assembled.
The king and the queen were there
and the pledges brought Lanval back.
They were all very sad for him:
420 I think there were a hundred
who would have done all they could
to set him free without a trial
where he would be wrongly accused.
The king demanded a verdict
425 according to the charge and rebuttal.
Now it all fell to the barons.
They went to the judgment,
worried and distressed
for the noble man from another land
430 who'd gotten into such trouble in their midst.
Many wanted to condemn him
in order to satisfy their lord.
The Duke of Cornwall said:
"No one can blame us;
435 whether it makes you weep or sing
justice must be carried out.
The king spoke against his vassal
whom I have heard named Lanval;
he accused him of felony,

8. The case is important enough to require judgment by all of Arthur's vassals, not just the immediate household. Hence the delay of the trial.

440   charged him with a misdeed—
      a love that he had boasted of,
      which made the queen angry.
      No one but the king accused him:
      by the faith I owe you,
445   if one were to speak the truth,
      there should have been no need for defense,
      except that a man owes his lord honor
      in every circumstance.[9]
      He will be bound by his oath,
450   and the king will forgive us our pledges
      if he can produce proof;
      if his love would come forward,
      if what he said,
      what upset the queen, is true,
455   then he will be acquitted,
      because he did not say it out of malice.
      But if he cannot get his proof,
      we must make it clear to him
      that he will forfeit his service to the king;
460   he must take his leave."
      They sent to the knight,
      told and announced to him
      that he should have his love come
      to defend and stand surety for him.
465   He told them that he could not do it:
      he would never receive help from her.
      They went back to the judges,
      not expecting any help from Lanval.
      The king pressed them hard
470   because of the queen who was waiting.
      When they were ready to give their verdict
      they saw two girls approaching,
      riding handsome palfreys.
      They were very attractive,
475   dressed in purple taffeta,
      over their bare skin.
      The men looked at them with pleasure.
      Gawain, taking three knights with him,
      went to Lanval and told him;
480   he pointed out the two girls.
      Gawain was extremely happy, and begged him
      to tell if his love were one of them.
      Lanval said he didn't know who they were,
      where they came from or where they were going.
485   The girls proceeded
      still on horseback;
      they dismounted before the high table

9. Lanval's denial of the queen's accusation of improper advances (lines 371–74) is accepted, but he is nevertheless guilty of dishonoring his lord unless he can prove the claims about his mistress to which he has admitted.

at which Arthur, the king, sat.
They were of great beauty,
490 and spoke in a courtly manner:
"King, clear your chambers,
have them hung with silk
where my lady may dismount;
she wishes to take shelter with you."
495 He promised it willingly
and called two knights
to guide them up to the chambers.
On that subject no more was said.
The king asked his barons
500 for their judgment and decision;
he said they had angered him very much
with their long delay.
"Sire," they said, "we have decided.
Because of the ladies we have just seen
505 we have made no judgment.
Let us reconvene the trial."
Then they assembled, everyone was worried;
there was much noise and strife.
While they were in that confusion,
510 two girls in noble array,
dressed in Phrygian silks
and riding Spanish mules,
were seen coming down the street.
This gave the vassals great joy;
515 to each other they said that now
Lanval, the brave and bold, was saved.
Gawain went up to him,
bringing his companions along.
"Sire," he said, "take heart.
520 For the love of God, speak to us.
Here come two maidens,
well adorned and very beautiful;
one must certainly be your love."
Lanval answered quickly
525 that he did not recognize them,
he didn't know them or love them.
Meanwhile they'd arrived,
and dismounted before the king.
Most of those who saw them praised them
530 for their bodies, their faces, their coloring;
each was more impressive
than the queen had ever been.
The older one was courtly and wise,
she spoke her message fittingly:
535 "King, have chambers prepared for us
to lodge my lady according to her need;
she is coming here to speak with you."
He ordered them to be taken
to the others who had preceded them.

540 There was no problem with the mules.
When he had seen to the girls,
he summoned all his barons
to render their judgment;
it had already dragged out too much.
545 The queen was getting angry
because she had fasted so long.
They were about to give their judgment
when through the city came riding
a girl on horseback:
550 there was none more beautiful in the world.
She rode a white palfrey,
who carried her handsomely and smoothly:
he was well apportioned in the neck and head,
no finer beast in the world.
555 The palfrey's trappings were rich;
under heaven there was no count or king
who could have afforded them all
without selling or mortgaging lands.
She was dressed in this fashion:
560 in a white linen shift
that revealed both her sides
since the lacing was along the side.
Her body was elegant, her hips slim,
her neck whiter than snow on a branch,
565 her eyes bright, her face white,
a beautiful mouth, a well-set nose,
dark eyebrows and an elegant forehead,
her hair curly and rather blond;
golden wire does not shine
570 like her hair in the light.
Her cloak, which she had wrapped around her,
was dark purple.
On her wrist she held a sparrow hawk,
a greyhound followed her.
575 In the town, no one, small or big,
old man or child,
failed to come look.
As they watched her pass,
there was no joking about her beauty.
580 She proceeded at a slow pace.
The judges who saw her
marveled at the sight;
no one who looked at her
was not warmed with joy.
585 Those who loved the knight
came to him and told him
of the girl who was approaching,
if God pleased, to rescue him.
"Sir companion, here comes one
590 neither tawny nor dark;
this is, of all who exist,

the most beautiful woman in the world."
Lanval heard them and lifted his head;
he recognized her and sighed.
595 The blood rose to his face;
he was quick to speak.
"By my faith," he said, "that is my love.
Now I don't care if I am killed,
if only she forgives me.
600 For I am restored, now that I see her."
The lady entered the palace;
no one so beautiful had ever been there.
She dismounted before the king
so that she was well seen by all.
605 And she let her cloak fall
so they could see her better.
The king, who was well bred,
rose and went to meet her;
all the others honored her
610 and offered to serve her.
When they had looked at her well,
when they had greatly praised her beauty,
she spoke in this way,
she didn't want to wait:
615 "I have loved one of your vassals:
you see him before you—Lanval.
He has been accused in your court—
I don't want him to suffer
for what he said; you should know
620 that the queen was in the wrong.
He never made advances to her.
And for the boast that he made,
if he can be acquitted through me,
let him be set free by your barons."
625 Whatever the barons judged by law
the king promised would prevail.
To the last man they agreed
that Lanval had successfully answered the charge.
He was set free by their decision
630 and the girl departed.
The king could not detain her,
though there were enough people to serve her.
Outside the hall stood
a great stone of dark marble
635 where heavy men mounted
when they left the king's court;
Lanval climbed on it.
When the girl came through the gate
Lanval leapt, in one bound,
640 onto the palfrey, behind her.
With her he went to Avalun,
so the Bretons tell us,
to a very beautiful island;

there the youth was carried off.
645 No man heard of him again,
and I have no more to tell.

1154–89

Chevrefoil (The Honeysuckle)

I should like very much
to tell you the truth
about the lai men call *Chevrefoil*—
why it was composed and where it came from.
5 Many have told and recited it to me
and I have found it in writing,
about Tristan and the queen
and their love that was so true,
that brought them much suffering
10 and caused them to die the same day.
King Mark was annoyed,
angry at his nephew Tristan;
he exiled Tristan from his land
because of the queen whom he loved.
15 Tristan returned to his own country,
South Wales, where he was born,
he stayed a whole year;
he couldn't come back.
Afterward he began to expose himself
20 to death and destruction.
Don't be surprised at this:
for one who loves very faithfully
is sad and troubled
when he cannot satisfy his desires.
25 Tristan was sad and worried,
so he set out from his land.
He traveled straight to Cornwall,
where the queen lived,
and entered the forest all alone—
30 he didn't want anyone to see him;
he came out only in the evening
when it was time to find shelter.
He took lodging that night,
with peasants, poor people.
35 He asked them for news
of the king—what he was doing.
They told him they had heard
that the barons had been summoned by ban.
They were to come to Tintagel
40 where the king wanted to hold his court;
at Pentecost they would all be there,
there'd be much joy and pleasure,

and the queen would be there too.
Tristan heard and was very happy;
45   she would not be able to go there
without his seeing her pass.
The day the king set out,
Tristan also came to the woods
by the road he knew
50   their assembly must take.
He cut a hazel tree in half,
then he squared it.
When he had prepared the wood,
he wrote his name on it with his knife.
55   If the queen noticed it—
and she should be on the watch for it,
for it had happened before
and she had noticed it then—
she'd know when she saw it,
60   that the piece of wood had come from her love.
This was the message of the writing[1]
that he had sent to her:
he had been there a long time,
had waited and remained
65   to find out and to discover
how he could see her,
for he could not live without her.
With the two of them it was just
as it is with the honeysuckle
70   that attaches itself to the hazel tree:
when it has wound and attached
and worked itself around the trunk,
the two can survive together;
but if someone tries to separate them,
75   the hazel dies quickly
and the honeysuckle with it.
"Sweet love, so it is with us:
You cannot live without me, nor I without you."
The queen rode along;
80   she looked at the hillside
and saw the piece of wood; she knew what it was,
she recognized all the letters.
The knights who were accompanying her,
who were riding with her,
85   she ordered to stop:
she wanted to dismount and rest.
They obeyed her command.
She went far away from her people
and called her girl

---

1. There are several possible explanations of this line: that Tristan had sent a message to her before she arrived in the forest, which seems least likely since it is not otherwise mentioned; that his name on the wood told her everything because of the understanding that existed between them; that the message was written on the wood in runic inscriptions which only the specially trained could read.

90　Brenguein, who was loyal to her.
　　She went a short distance from the road;
　　and in the woods she found him
　　whom she loved more than any living thing.
　　They took great joy in each other.
95　He spoke to her as much as he desired,
　　she told him whatever she liked.
　　Then she assured him
　　that he would be reconciled with the king—
　　for it weighed on him
100　that he had sent Tristan away;
　　he'd done it because of the accusation.
　　Then she departed, she left her love,
　　but when it came to the separation,
　　they began to weep.
105　Tristan went to Wales,
　　to wait until his uncle sent for him.
　　For the joy that he'd felt
　　from his love when he saw her,
　　by means of the stick he inscribed
110　as the queen had instructed,
　　and in order to remember the words,
　　Tristan, who played the harp well,
　　composed a new lai about it.
　　I shall name it briefly:
115　in English they call it *Goat's Leaf*
　　the French call it *Chevrefoil*.
　　I have given you the truth
　　about the lai that I have told here.

1154–89

SIR ORFEO
ca. 1300

S ir Orfeo is a reworking of the classical, tragic myth of Orpheus and his wife, Eurydice. When Eurydice died of a snake bite, Orpheus followed her to the underworld. Having so pleased Pluto and Proserpina with his music, Orpheus was granted Eurydice's release, on condition he not look back to his wife as she followed him from Hades. Orpheus did look back, and so lost his wife. The medieval narrative evokes this tragedy to replace it with the comedy of reunification, not only of husband and wife but also of king and subjects. Orfeo's abdication, his entry into the forest and the underworld, his charming of the faery kingdom with his music: all permit the rescue of his paralyzed, lacerated wife, Eurydice, and their joyful return home.

　　The poem was probably translated from a French romance of the kind called a Breton lay. The English translation was likely made before 1300, but it has survived in only three manuscripts of later date. Some scholars believe that the best of these, the Auchinleck manuscript, might once have been read by Chaucer, whose *Frank-lin's Tale* is also a Breton lay.

The text presented here is flexibly based on the Auchinleck manuscript. The metrical form is the four-stress couplet, the standard English form used to translate French octosyllabic couplets.

Sir Orfeo

We reden ofte and finden ywrite—
As thise clerkes doon° us wite°—   *cause / to learn*
The layes that been of harping[1]
Been yfounde° of freely° thing.   *composed / pleasant*
5 Some been of werre° and some of wo,   *war*
And some of joye and mirthe also,
And some of trecherye and of gile;
And some of happes° that fellen° while,° *events / occurred / once*
And some of bourdes° and ribaudye,°   *jokes / ribaldry*
10 And manye been of faïrye.[2]
Of alle thing that men may see,
Most of love forsoothe they be.
In Britain° thise layes been wrought,   *Brittany*
First yfounde° and forth ybrought.   *composed*
15 Of aventures that felle° by dayes[3]   *occurred*
The Britons° therof maden layes: *Bretons*
Whan they mighte owher° yheere°   *anywhere / hear*
Of any merveiles that ther were,
They tooken hem hir harpes with game,°   *pleasure*
20 Maden layes and yaf° hem name.   *gave*
 Of aventures that han bifalle
I can some telle, but nought alle.
Herkneth, lordinges° that been trewe,   *gentlemen*
I wol you telle of Sir Orfewe.
25 Orfeo was a riche° king,   *noble*
In Engelond an heigh lording,
A stalworth° man and hardy bo,°   *valiant / both*
Large° and curteis° he was also, *generous / courteous*
His fader was come of King Pluto,
30 And his moder of King Juno,
That somtime were as goddes yholde°   *considered*
For aventures that they dide and tolde.
 This king sojourned in Traciens°   *Thrace*
That is a citee of noble defens°   *fortification*
35 (For Winchester was cleped° tho°   *called / then*
Traciens withouten no°).   *denial*
Orfeo most of any thing
Loved the glee° of harping: *music*

---

1. I.e., composed to be sung to the harp.
2. Fairyland and, more commonly, the other- world and its supernatural inhabitants.
  3. Once.

Siker° was every good harpour   *certain*

40   Of him to have muche honour.

Himself he lerned for to harpe,

And laide° theron his wittes sharpe;°   *applied / keenly*

He lerned so ther nothing was

A bettre harpour in no plas.°   *place*

45   In al the world was no man bore°   *born*

That ones° Orfeo sat bifore,   *once*

And° he mighte of his harping heere,   *if*

But he sholde thinke that he were

In oon of the joyes of Paradis,

50   Swich melodye in his harping is.

    Orfeo hadde a queene of pris°   *excellence*

That was ycleped° Dame Heurodis,   *named*

The fairest lady for the° nones°   *that / matter*

That mighte goon° on body and bones,   *walk*

55   Ful of love and of goodnesse—

But no man may telle hir fairnesse.

    Bifel so, the comsing° of May,   *beginning*

When merye and hot is the day,

And away been winter showres,

60   And every feeld is ful of flowres,

And blosme breme° on every bough   *glorious*

Overal° wexeth° merye ynough,   *everywhere / grows*

This eeche° queene Dame Heurodis   *same*

Took with hire two maides of pris°   *excellence*

65   And wente in the undertide°   *forenoon*

To playe in an orchard-side,

To see the flowres sprede° and-springe   *open*

And to heere the fowles singe.

    They setten hem down alle three

70   Faire° under an impe-tree;°   *fairly / grafted fruit tree*

And wel soone this faire queene

Fel on sleepe upon the greene.

The maidens durste hire not awake,

But lete hire lie and reste take.

75   So she slepte til afternoon

That undertide was al ydoor.°   *passed*

But as soone as she gan wake

She cried and loothly bere° gan make: *outcry*

She frotte° hir hondes and hir feet   *tore at*

80   And cracched° hir visage—it bledde weet;°   *scratched / wet*

Hir riche robe she al torit,°   *tears apart*

And was ravised° out of her wit.   *ravished*

The two maidenes hire biside

Ne durste with hire no leng° abide,   *longer*

85   But runne to the palais right

And tolde bothe squier and knight

That hir queene awede° wolde,   *go mad*

And bad hem go and hire atholde.°   *restrain*

Knightes runne and ladies also,

90   Damiseles sixty and mo,°   *more*

In th' orchard to the queene they come,
And hire up in armes nome,°   took
And broughte hire to bed at laste,
And heelde hire there fine° faste.   very
95   But evere she heeld° in oo° cry,   continued / one
And wolde uppe° and awy.°   get up / go away
   Whan the king herde that tiding
Nevere him nas worse for no thing:
Orfeo cam with knightes tene°   ten
100 To chambre right bifore the queene,
And looked and saide with greet° pitee,   great
"O leve° lif, what aileth thee?—   dear
That evere yit hast been so stille,
And now thou gredest° wonder shille.°   cry out / shrilly
105 Thy body that was so whit ycore°   excellent
With thine nailes is all totore.°   torn
Allas, thy rode° that was so reed°   complexion / red
Is as wan as thou were deed.°   dead
And also thy fingres smale
110 Been al bloody and al pale.
Allas, thy lovesome yën two
Looketh so° man dooth on his fo.   as
A, dame, ich° biseeche mercy—   I
Lete been al this reweful° cry,   pitiful
115 And tel me what° thee is and how,   what the matter with
And what thing may thee helpe now."
   Tho° lay she stille at the laste,   then
And gan to weepe swithe° faste,°   very / hard
And saide thus the king unto:
120 "Allas, my lord Sir Orfeo,
Sitthen° we first togider were   since
Ones wrothe° nevere we nere,   angry
But evere ich have yloved thee
As my lif, and so thou me.
125 But now we mote° deele° atwo—   must / separate
Do thy best, for I moot° go."   must
   "Allas," quath he, "forlorn ich am!
Whider wilt thou go and to wham?°   whom
Whider thou goost ich wil with thee,
130 And whider I go thou shalt with me."
"Nay, nay, sire, that nought nis.[4]
Ich wil thee telle al how it is:
As ich lay this undertide°   forenoon
And slepte under oure orchard-side,
135 Ther come to me two faire knightes,
Wel y-armed al to rightes,
And bad me comen on hying°   in haste
And speke with hir lord the king;
And ich answerede at° wordes bolde   in
140 That I ne durste nought ne I nolde.°   would not

---

4. I.e., that's no use.

They prikked again as they mighte drive.[5]
Tho° cam hir king also blive°   *then / straightway*
With an hundred knightes and mo,
And damiseles an hundred also,
145 Alle on snow-white steedes;
As white as milk were hir weedes:°   *clothes*
I ne seigh° nevere yit bifore   *saw*
So faire creatures ycore.°   *splendid*
The king hadde a crown on his heed:°   *head*
150 It nas of silver n'of gold reed,°   *red*
But it was of a precious stoon;
As brighte as the sonne it shoon.
And as soone as he to me cam,
Wolde ich, nolde ich, he me nam°   *took*
155 And made me with him to ride
Upon a palfrey him biside,
And broughte me to his palais
Wel attired° in eech a ways,°   *equipped / way*
And shewed me castels and towrs,
160 Riveres, foreestes, frith° with flowres,   *meadow*
And his riche steedes eechcon,
And sitthen° broughte me again hoom   *afterwards*
Into oure owene orche-yard,°   *orchard*
And saide to me thus afterward,
165 'Looke tomorwe that thou be
Right here under this impe-tree,
And thanne thou shalt with us go,
And live with us everemo.°   *evermore*
And if thou makest us ylet,°   *resistance*
170 Where° thou be, thou worst° yfet.°   *wherever / shall be / fetched*
And al totore° thy limes al   *torn apart*
That no thing thee helpe shal.
And though thou beest so totorn,
Yit thou worst° with us yborn.'"°   *shall be / carried off*
175   When king Orfeo herde this cas,°   *circumstance*
"O, weel"° quath he, "allas, allas!   *woe*
Lever me were to lete° my lif   *leave*
Than thus to lese° the queene my wif."   *lose*
He asked conseil at° eech a man,   *from*
180 But no man him helpe can.
    Amorwe° the undertide is come,   *next day*
And Orfeo hath his armes ynome,°   *taken*
And wel ten hundred knightes with him,
Eech y-armed, stout and grim.
185 And with the queene wenten he°   *they*
Right unto that impe-tree.
They made sheltrom° in eech a side,   *military formation*
And saide they wolde ther abide
And die there everichoon,
190 Er the queene sholde from hem goon.

5. I.e., they rode as fast as they could.

And yit amiddes hem full right
The queene was away ytwight,°   *snatched*
With° faïrye forth ynome:°   *by / taken*
Men wiste nevere wher she was bicome.[6]

195   Tho° was ther crying, weep and wo;   *then*
The king into his chambre is go
And ofte swooned upon the stoon,°   *floor*
And made swich dool and swich moon[7]
That nye° his lif was yspent°—   *nearly / finished*
200   Ther was noon amendement.°   *remedy*
    He clepte° togider his barouns,   *called*
Eerles, lordes of renouns,°   *great names*
And whan they alle yeomen were,
"Lordinges," he saide, "bifor you here
205   Ich ordaine myn heigh steward
To wite° my kingdom afterward;   *keep*
In my stede been he shal
To keepe my londes overal.°   *everywhere*
For now I have my queene ylore,°   *lost*
210   The faireste lady that evere was bore,°   *born*
Nevere eft° I nil° no womman see;   *again / will not*
In wildernesse now wil ich tee°   *go*
And live ther for everemore,
With wilde beestes in holtes° hore.°   *woods / gray*
215   And whan ye wite° that I be spent,°   *learn / dead*
Make you than a parlement
And chese° you° a newe king: *choose / for yourselves*
Now dooth youre best with al my thing."
    Tho° was ther weeping in the halle,   *then*
220   And greet° cry among hem alle;   *great*
Unnethe° mighte olde or yong   *scarcely*
For weeping speke a word with tonge.
They kneeled alle adown in fere°   *together*
And prayede him if his wille were,
225   That he ne sholde from hem go.
"Do way," quath he, "it shal be so."
    Al his kingdom he forsook;
But° a sclavin° on him he took: *only / pilgrim's cloak*
He hadde no kirtel° ne noon hood,   *short coat*
230   Shert ne yit noon other good.
But his harp he took algate,°   *at any rate*
And dide him barefoot out at yate:°   *gate*
No man moste° with him go.   *must*
    O way,° what° ther was weep and wo,   *alas / how*
235   Whan he that hadde been king with crown
Wente so poorelich out of town.
Thrugh the wode° and over heeth   *wood*
Into the wildernesse he geeth.°   *goes*
Nothing he fint° that him is aise,°   *finds / easy*

6. No one knew what had become of her.
7. And made such lamentation and such complaint.

240 But evere he liveth in greet malaise.
   He that hadde wered° the fowe and gris,[8]   *worn*
   And on bed the purper° bis,°   *purple / linen*
   Now on harde heeth he lith,°   *lies*
   With leves and grasse he him writh.°   *covers*
245 He that hadde had castels and towres,
   Rivere foreest, frith° with flowres,   *meadow*
   Now though it ginne snowe and freese,
   This king moot° make his bed in meese.°   *must / moss*
   He that hadde had knightes of pris,°   *renown*
250 Bifore him kneeling and ladis,
   Now seeth he nothing that him liketh,°   *pleases*
   But wilde wormes° by him striketh.°   *snakes / glide*
   He that hadde yhad plentee
   Of mete and drinke, of eech daintee,
255 Now may he alday° digge and wrote°   *constantly / scrounge*
   Er he finde his fille of roote.
   In somer he liveth by wilde fruit
   And berien° but goode lite,[9]°   *berries*
   In winter may he nothing finde
260 But roote, grasses, and the rinde.°   *bark*
   Al his body away was dwined°   *wasted*
   For misaise, and al tochined.°   *scarred*
   Lord, who may telle of the sore
   This king suffered ten yeer and more?
265 His heer of his beerd, blak and rowe,°   *rugged*
   To his girdel-stede° was growe.   *waist*
   His harp wheron was al his glee
   He hidde in an holwe tree,
   And whan the weder was cleer and bright,
270 He took his harp to him wel right,
   And harped at his owene wille:°   *pleasure*
   In al the woode the soun gan shille,°   *resound*
   That wilde beestes that ther beeth
   For joy abouten him they teeth;°   *draw*
275 And alle the fowles that ther were
   Come and sete on eech a brere°   *briar*
   To here his harping afine,°   *to the end*
   So muche melodye was therine.
   When he his harping lete° wolde,   *leave off*
280 No beest by him abide nolde.
      Ofte he mighte see him bisides
   In the hote undertides°   *mornings*
   The king of fairy with his route°   *company*
   Come to hunte him al aboute
285 With dinne, cry, and with blowing,
   And houndes also with him berking.
   But no beeste they ne nome°   *took*
   Ne nevere he niste wher they bicome.[1]

8. White and gray fur; i.e., royal ermine.   1. Nor did he ever learn what happened to them.
9. Little good.

And otherwhile he mighte see,
290 As a greet oost° by him tee,°.   host / passed
Wel atourned° ten hundred knightes,   equipped
Eech y-armed to his rightes,°   fittingly
Of countenance stout and fiers,°   fierce
With manye displayed° baners,   unfurled
295 And eech his swerd ydrawe holde,
But nevere he niste° wher they wolde,   knew not
And somwhile he seigh° other thing: saw
Knightes and ladies come dauncing,
In quainte° atir, degisely,°   elegant / wonderfully
300 Quainte pas° and softely.   step
Tabours° and trumpes yede° him by,   drums / went
And al manere mïnstracy.°   minstrelsy
    And on a day he seigh° biside   saw
Sixty ladies on horse ride,
305 Gentil and jolif° as brid° on ris°—   pretty / bird / bough
Nought oo man amonges hem nis.
And eech a faucon on hond beer,°   bore
And riden on hawking by river.
Of game they founde wel good haunt,°   plenty
310 Maulardes,° hairoun,° and cormeraunt.   mallards / herons
The fowles of° the water ariseth;   from
The faucons hem wel deviseth:°   descry
Eech faucon his preye slough.°   slew
That seigh° Orfeo and lough:°   saw / laughed
315 "Parfay!"° quath he, "ther is fair game!   by faith
Thider ich wil,° by Goddes name.   will go
Ich was ywon° swich° werk to see."   accustomed / such
He aroos and thider gan tee.°   draw
To a lady he was ycome,
320 Biheeld, and hath wel undernome,°   understood
And seeth by al thing that it is
His owene queene Dame Heurodis,
Yerne° biheeld hire and she him eke,°   eagerly / also
But neither to other a word ne speke.
325 For misaise that she on him seigh°   saw
That hadde been so riche and heigh,
The teres felle out of hir ye.
The othere ladies this ysye°   saw
And maked hire away to ride:
330 She moste° with him no lenger° abide.   must / longer
    "Allas," quath he, "now me is wo.
Why nil° deeth now me nought slo?°   will not / slay
Allas, wrecche,° that I ne mighte   wretched one
Die now after this sighte.
335 Allas, too longe last° my lif   lasts
Whan I ne dar nought to my wif—
Ne she to me—oo word ne speke.
Allas, why nil myn herte breke?
Parfay,"° quath he, "tide what bitide,   by faith
340 Whider so thise ladies ride

The selye° waye ich wil strecche:°　　　　　　　　　*same / go*
Of lif ne deeth me nothing recche."°　　　　　　　　*care*
　　His sclavin° he dide on also spak°　　　　　*cloak / at once*
And heeng° his harp upon his bak,　　　　　　　　*hung*
345　And hadde wel good wil to goon:
He ne spared neither stub ne stoon.[2]
In at a roche° the ladies rideth　　　　　　　　*rock, cave*
And he after and nought abideth.
　　Whan he was in the roche ago
350　Wel three mile other° mo,　　　　　　　　　　*or*
He cam into a fair countrey,
As bright so° sonne on somers day,　　　　　　　　*as*
Smoothe and plain° and alle greener:　　　　　　*flat*
Hil ne dale nas ther noon seene.
355　Amidde the lond a castel he seigh,°　　　　　　*saw*
Riche and real° and wonder heigh.　　　　　　　*royal*
Al the utemoste° wal　　　　　　　　　　　　*outmost*
Was cleer° and shined as crystal.　　　　　　　　*bright*
An hundred towres ther were aboute,
360　Degiseliche,° and batailed[3] stoute.　　　　*wonderful*
The butres° cam out of the diche　　　　　　　*buttress*
Of reed gold y-arched riche.[4]
The vousour° was anourned° al　　　*vaulting / adorned*
Of eech manere divers aumal.°　　　　　　　　*enamel*
365　Within ther were wide wones,°　　　　　　　*halls*
And alle were fulle of precious stones.
The worste pilar on to biholde
Al it was of burnist golde.
Al that land was evere light,
370　For when it sholde be therk° and night　　　　*dark*
The riche stones lighte gonne[5]
As brighte as dooth at noon the sonne.
No man may telle ne thinke in thought
The riche werk that ther was wrought.
375　By alle thing him thinkth it is
The proude court of Paradis.
　　In this castel the ladies alighte:
He wolde in after, if he mighte.
Orfeo knokketh at the yate:°　　　　　　　　　*gate*
380　The porter was redy therate
And asked what he wolde have ydo.°　　　　　　*done*
"Parfay,° ich am a minstrel, lo,　　　　　　　*by faith*
To solace° thy lord with my glee　　　　　　　*delight*
If[6] his sweete wille be."
385　The porter undide the gate anoon
And lete him into the castel goon.
　　Than he gan looke aboute al
And seigh,° lying within the wal,　　　　　　　*saw*

2. I.e., neither stump nor stone prevented him.
3. I.e., furnished with battlements.
4. I.e., made of red gold that arched splendidly:
gold was commonly described as red in Middle
English.
5. Did light it.
6. If it.

Of folk that ther were thider ybrought,
390 And thoughte° dede,° and nere nought:[7]   *seemed / dead*
Some stoode withouten hade,°   *head*
And some none armes hade,
And some thurgh the body hadde wounde,
And some laye woode° ybounde;   *mad*
395 And some armed on horse sete,
And some astrangled as they ete,
And some were in watre adreint,°   *drowned*
And some with fire al forshreint,°   *shriveled*
Wives ther laye on child-bedde,
400 Some dede and some awedde.°   *driven mad*
And wonder fele° ther laye bisides   *many*
Right as they slepte hir undertides°   *forenoons*
Each was thus in this world ynome,°   *taken*
With° faïrye thider ycome.   *by force of*
405 Ther he seigh his owene wif,
Dame Heurodis, his leve° lif,   *dear*
Sleepe under an impe-tree:
By hir clothes he knew it was she.
    Whan he hadde seen thise mervailes alle
410 He wente into the kinges halle.
Than seigh he ther a seemly sighte:
A tabernacle[8] wel ydight°—   *arrayed*
Hir maister king therinne sete,
And hir queene fair and sweete.
415 Hir crownes, hir clothes shoon so brighte
That unnethe° he biholde hem mighte.   *with difficulty*
    Whan he hadde seen al this thing,
He kneeled adoun bifor the king:
"O lord," he saide, "if thy wil were,
420 My minstracye thou sholdest yheere."°   *hear*
The king answerede, "What man art thou
That art hider yeomen now?
Ich, ne noon that is with me,
Ne sente never after thee.
425 Sith° that ich here regne° gan   *since / reign*
I ne foond° nevere so hardy man   *found*
That hider to us durste wende
But° that ich him wolde ofsende."°   *unless / send for*
"Lord," quath he, "ye trowe° wel   *may believe*
430 I nam but a poore minstrel,
And, sire, it is the maner of us
To seeche many a lordes hous.
And theigh° we not welcome be,   *though*
Yit we mote° profere forth oure glee."°   *must / music*
435   Bifor the king he sat adown
And took his harp so merye of soun,
And tempreth° it as he wel can.   *tunes*
And blisful notes he ther gan

---

7. Were not.   8. I.e., an alcove.

That alle that in the palais were
440   Come to him for to heere,
And lieth adown to his feete,
Hem thinkth his melodye so sweete.
The king herkneth and sit° ful stille: *sits*
To heere his glee he hath good wille.
445   Good bourde° he hadde of his glee: *entertainment*
The riche queene also hadde she.
    Whan he hadde stint° of his harping,   *ceased*
Then saide to him the riche king,
"Minstrel, me liketh wel thy glee.
450   Now aske of me what it may be—
Largeliche° ich wil thee paye   *generously*
Now speke and thou might it assaye."
"Sire," he saide, "ich praye thee
That thou woldest yive me
455   The eeche° lady, bright on blee,°   *very / of hue*
That sleepeth under the impe-tree."
"Nay," quath the king, "that nought nere:[9]
A sory couple of you it were;
For thou art lene,° rowe,° and blak,   *lean / rough*
460   And she is lovesom, withoute lak.°   *blemish*
A loothly tiling it were forthy°   *therefore*
To seen hire in thy compaigny."
    "O sire," he saide, "gentil king,
Yit were it a wel fouler thing
465   To heere a lesing° of thy mouthe.   *lie*
So, sire, as ye saide nouthe°   *now*
What ich wolde aske, have I wolde,
A kinges word moot° needes be holde."   *must*
"Thou sayest sooth," the king saide than,
470   "And sith° I am a trewe man,   *since*
I wol wel that it be so:
Taak hire by the hond and go.
Of hire ich wol that thou be blithe."
    He kneeled adown and thanked him swithe;° *quickly*
475   His wif he took by the hond
And dide him swithe out of that lond,
And wente° him out of that thede:°   *turned / country*
Right as he cam the way he yede.°   *went*
    So longe he hath the way ynome°   *taken*
480   To Winchester he is ycome,
That somtime was his owene citee,
But no man knew that it was he.
No forther than the townes ende
For knoweleche[1] he durste wende.
485   But in a beggeres bild° ful narwe°   *house / small*
Ther he hath take his herbarwe°   *lodging*
(To him and to his owene wife),
As a minstrel of poore lif,

---

9. I.e., that wouldn't do.   1. I.e., for fear of being recognized.

And asked tidinges of that lond,
490 And who the kingdom heeld in hond.
The poore begger in his cote°   *hovel*
Tolde him everich° a grote°—   *every / bit*
How hir queene was stole awy,°   *away*
Ten yeer goon, with° faïry.   *by*
495 And now hir king in exile yede°   *went*
But no man wiste° in which thede;°   *knew / country*
And how the steward the lond gan holde,
And othere many thinges him tolde.
   Amorwe ayain the noon-tide[2]
500 He maked his wif ther abide,
And beggeres clothes he borwed anoon,°   *straightaway*
And heeng° his harp his rigge° upon,   *hung / back*
And wente him into that citee,
That men mighte him biholde and see.
505 Bothe eerles and barouns bolde,
Burgeis° and ladies him gan biholde: *burgesses*
"Lord," they saide, "swich° a man!   *such*
How longe the heer° him hangeth upon!   *hair*
Lo, how his beerd hangeth to his knee!
510 He is yclungen° also° a tree!"   *withered / as*
   And as he yede° in the streete,   *walked*
With his steward he gan meete.
And loude he sette him on a cry,
"Sir steward," he saide, "grant mercy!
515 Ich am an harpour of hethenesse:°   *heathen country*
Help me now in this distresse."
The steward saide, "Com with me, com:
Of that I have thou shalt have som.
Eech harpour is welcome me to
520 For my lordes love, Sir Orfeo."
   Anoon they wente into the halle,
The steward and the lordes alle.
The steward wessh° and wente to mete,   *washed*
And manye lordes by him sete.
525 Ther were trumpours° and tabourers,°   *trumpeters / drummers*
Harpours fele,° and crouders:°   *many / fiddlers*
Muche melodye they maked alle.
And Orfeo sat stille in halle.
And herkneth; whan they been al stille,
530 He took his harp and tempered° shille°—   *played / loudly*
The blisfullest notes he harped there
That evere man yherde with ere.
Eech man liked wel his glee.
   The steward looked and gan ysee,
535 And the harp knew also blive.°   *right away*
"Minstrel," he saide, "so mote° thou thrive,   *may*
Where haddest thou this harp and how?
I praye that thou me telle now."

2. In the morning toward noontime.

"Lord," quath he, "in uncouthe° thede,°   *strange / country*
540 Thurgh a foreest as I yede,°   *walked*
I foond° lying in a dale   *found*
A man with° lions totorn° smale,   *by / torn to bits*
And wolves him frette° with teeth so sharp.   *bit*
By him I foond this eeche° harp   *very*
545 Wel ten yeer it is ago."
"O," quath the steward, "now me is wo!
That was my lord Sir Orfeo.
Allas, wrecche, what shal I do
That have swich° a lord ylore?°   *such / lost*
550 A, way,° that evere ich was ybore°   *woe / born*
That him was so harde grace y-yarked,°   *ordained*
And so vile deeth ymarked."°   *appointed*
Adown he fel aswoone to grounde.
His barouns him tooke up that stounde°   *time*
555 And telleth him how that it geeth:°   *goes*
It is no boote° of mannes deeth.   *remedy*
    King Orfeo knew wel by than°   *that*
His steward was a trewe man
And loved him as him oughte to do,
560 And stondeth up and saith thus, "Lo,
Steward, herkne now this thing:
If ich were Orfeo the king
And hadde ysuffered ful yore°   *long*
In wildernesse muche sore,
565 And hadde ywonne my queene awy°   *away*
Out of the lond of faïry,
And hadde ybrought the lady hende°   *gracious*
Right here to the townes ende,
And with a begger hir in° ynome,°   *lodging / taken*
570 And were myselve hider ycome
Poorelich to thee thus stille,°   *secretly*
For to assaye° thy goode wille,   *test*
And° ich founde thee thus trewe,   *if*
Thou ne sholdest it nevere rewe:°   *regret*
575 Sikerliche,° for love or ay,°   *surely / dread*
Thou sholdest be king after my day.
If thou of my deeth haddest been blithe,
Thou sholdest have voided° also swithe." *been dismissed*
    Tho° alle tho° that therinne sete   *then / those*
580 That is was Orfeo underyete,°   *understood*
And the steward wel him knew:
Over and over the boord° he threw   *table*
And fel adown to his feete.
So dide eech lord that ther sete,
585 And alle they saide at oo° crying,   *one*
"Ye beeth oure lord, sire, and oure king."
Glade they were of his live:
To chambre they ladde him as blive,°   *at once*
And bathed him and shaved his beard,
590 And tired° him as a king apert.°   *dressed / openly*

And sith° with greet processioun   *after*
They broughte the queene into the town,
With alle manere minstracye.
Lord, ther was greet melodye:
595 For joye they wepte with hir yë
That hem so sound° yeomen sye.°   *healthy / saw*
  Now Orfeo newe corouned° is,   *crowned*
And his queene Dame Heurodis,
And lived longe afterward,
600 And sitthen° king was the steward.   *afterward*
  Harpours in Britain after than°   *that*
Herde how this merveile bigan
And made a lay of good liking,°   *well-pleasing*
And nempned° it after the king.   *named*
605 That lay is "Orfeo" yhote:°   *called*
Good is the lay, sweete is the note.
  Thus cam Sir Orfeo out of his care:
God grante us alle wel to fare.

SIR GAWAIN AND THE GREEN KNIGHT
ca. 1375–1400

Between the *Ancrene Wisse* and the later fourteenth century, writers deployed English for many genres, especially for saints' lives and romances. The finest Arthurian romance in English survives in only one manuscript, which also contains three religious poems—*Pearl, Patience*, and *Purity*—generally believed to be by the same poet. Nothing is known about the author except what can be inferred from the works. The dialect of the poems locates them in a remote corner of the northwest midlands between Cheshire and Staffordshire, and details of Sir Gawain's journey north show that the author was familiar with the geography of that region. But if author and audience were provincials, *Sir Gawain* and the other poems in the manuscript reveal them to have been highly sophisticated and well acquainted both with the international culture of the high Middle Ages and with ancient insular traditions.

Sir Gawain belongs to the so-called Alliterative Revival. After the Norman Conquest, alliterative verse doubtless continued to be recited by oral poets. At the beginning, the *Gawain* poet pretends that this romance is an oral poem and asks the audience to "listen" to a story, which he has "heard." Alliterative verse also continued to appear in Early Middle English texts. Layamon's *Brut* (see pp. 131–32) is the outstanding example. During the late fourteenth century there was a renewed flowering of alliterative poetry, especially in the north and west of Britain, which includes *Piers Plowman* and a splendid poem known as *The Alliterative Morte Darthur*.

The *Gawain* poet's audience evidently valued the kind of alliterative verse that Chaucer's Parson caricatures as "Rum-Ram-Ruf by lettre" (see p. 341 line 43). They would also have understood archaic poetic diction surviving from Old English poetry such as *athel* (noble) and words of Scandinavian origin such as *skete* (quickly) and *skifted* (alternated). They were well acquainted with French Arthurian romances and the latest fashions in clothing, armor, and castle building. In making Sir Gawain, Arthur's sister's son, the preeminent knight of the Round Table, the poet was faithful to an older tradition. The thirteenth-century French romances, which in the next century became the main sources of Sir Thomas Malory, had made Sir Lancelot the best of Arthur's knights and Lancelot's adultery with Queen Guinevere the central event on which the fate of Arthur's kingdom turns. In *Sir Gawain* Lancelot is only one name in a list of Arthur's knights. Arthur is still a youth, and the court is in its springtime. Sir Gawain epitomizes this first blooming of Arthurian chivalry, and the reputation of the court rests upon his shoulders.

Ostensibly, Gawain's head is what is at stake. The main plot belongs to a type folklorists classify as the "Beheading Game," in which a supernatural challenger offers to let his head be cut off in exchange for a return blow. The earliest written occurrence

Baronial Feasting. Limbourg Brothers, "January," from *Les Très Riches Heures du Duc de Berry,* ca. 1411–16. This wall hanging depicts the Trojan War as if it were invading the protected space of the duke's feast.

of this motif is in the Middle Irish tale of *Bricriu's Feast.* The *Gawain* poet could have encountered it in several French romances as well as in oral tradition. But the outcome of the game here does not turn only on the champion's courage as it does in *Bricriu's Feast.* The *Gawain* poet has devised another series of tests for the hero that link the beheading with his truth, the emblem of which is the pentangle—a five-pointed star—displayed on Gawain's coat of arms and shield. The word *truth* in Middle English as in Chaucer's ballade of that name (see p. 344), and in *Passus 1 of Piers Plowman* (see p. 376), means not only what it still means now—a fact, belief, or idea held to be "true"—but what is conveyed by the old-fashioned variant from the same root: *troth*—that is, faith pledged by one's word and owed to a lord, a spouse, or anyone who puts someone else under an obligation. In this respect, Sir Gawain is being measured against a moral and Christian ideal of chivalry. Whether or not he succeeds in that contest is a question carefully left unresolved—perhaps as a challenge for the reader.

The poet has framed Gawain's adventure with references in the first and last stanzas to what are called the "Brutus books," the foundation stories that trace the origins of Rome and Britain back to the destruction of Troy. See, for example, the selection from Geoffrey of Monmouth's *History of the Kings of Britain* (pp. 131). A cyclical sense of history as well as of the cycles of the seasons of the year, the generations of humankind, and of individual lives runs through *Sir Gawain and the Green Knight.*

The poem is written in stanzas that contain a group of alliterative lines (the number of lines in a stanza varies). The line is longer and does not contain a fixed number or pattern of stresses like the classical alliterative measure of Old English poetry. Each stanza closes with five short lines rhyming *a b a b a.* The first of these rhyming lines contains just one stress and is called the "bob"; the four three-stress lines that follow are called the "wheel." For details on alliterative verse, see "Old and Middle English Prosody" (pp. 24–25) The opening stanza is printed below in Middle English with an interlinear translation. The stressed alliterating sounds have been italicized.

> **S**ithen the **s**ege and the **a**ssaut was **s**esed at Troye,
> After the siege and the assault was ceased at Troy,
>
> The **b**orgh **b**rittened and **b**rent to **b**rondes and askes,
> The city destroyed and burned to brands and ashes,

The *t*ulk that the *t*rammes of *t*resoun ther wroght
The man who the plots of treason there wrought

Was *t*ried for his *t*richerie, the *t*rewest on erthe.
Was tried for his treachery, the truest on earth.

Hit was Ennias the *a*thel and his *h*ighe kynde,
It was Aeneas the noble and his high race,

That sithen de*p*reced *p*rovinces, and *p*atrounes bicome
Who after subjugated provinces, and lords became

*W*elneghe of al the *w*ele in the *w*est iles.
Wellnigh of all the wealth in the west isles.

Fro *r*iche *R*omulus to *R*ome *r*icchis hym swythe,
Then noble Romulus to Rome proceeds quickly,

With gret *b*obbaunce that *b*urghe he *b*iges upon fyrst
With great pride that city he builds at first

And *n*evenes hit his aune *n*ome, as hit *n*ow hat;
And names it his own name, as it now is called;

*T*icius to *T*uskan and *t*eldes bigynnes,
Ticius (goes) to Tuscany and houses begins,

*L*angaberde in *L*umbardie *l*yftes up homes,
Longbeard in Lombardy raises up homes,

And *f*er over the French *f*lod, Felix Brutus
And far over the English Channel, Felix Brutus

On mony *b*onkkes ful *b*rode Bretayn he settes
On many banks very broad Brittain he sets

>   *W*yth *w*ynne,
>   With joy,

*W*here *w*erre and *w*rake and *w*onder
Where war and revenge and wondrous happenings

Bi sythes has wont therinne,
On occasions have dwelled therein

And oft *b*othe *b*lysse and *b*lunder
And often both joy and strife

Ful *s*kete has *s*kyfted synne.
Very swiftly have alternated since.

Sir Gawain and the Green Knight[1]

FITT i

Once the siege and assault of Troy had ceased,
with the city a smoke-heap of cinders and ash,
the traitor who contrived such betrayal there
was tried for his treachery, the truest on earth;[2]
5   Aeneas, it was, with his noble warriors
who went conquering abroad, laying claim to the crowns
of the wealthiest kingdoms in the western world.
Mighty Romulus[3] quickly careered towards Rome
and conceived a city in magnificent style
10 which from then until now has been known by his name.
Ticius constructed townships in Tuscany
and Langobard[4] did likewise building homes in Lombardy.
And further afield, over the Sea of France,
Felix Brutus[5] founds Britain on broad banks
15   most grand.
              And wonder, dread and war
              have lingered in that land
              where loss and love in turn
              have held the upper hand.

20 After Britain was built by this founding father
a bold race bred there, battle-happy men
causing trouble and torment in turbulent times,
and through history more strangeness has happened here
than anywhere else I know of on Earth.
25 But most regal of rulers in the royal line
was Arthur, who I heard is honored above all,
and the inspiring story I intend to spin
has moved the hearts and minds of many—
an awesome episode in the legends of Arthur.
30 So listen a little while to my tale if you will
and I'll tell it as it's told in the town where it trips from
              the tongue;
              and as it has been inked
              in stories bold and strong,
35   through letters which, once linked,
              have lasted loud and long.

It was Christmas at Camelot—King Arthur's court,
where the great and the good of the land had gathered,
the right noble lords of the ranks of the Round Table
40 all roundly carousing and reveling in pleasure.

---

1. This translation is by Simon Armitage.
2. The treacherous knight is Aeneas, who was a traitor to his city, Troy, according to medieval tradition, but Aeneas was actually tried by the Greeks for his refusal to hand his sister Polyxena over to them.
3. Like Aeneas, the legendary founder of Rome

is here given Trojan ancestry.
4. The reputed founder of Lombardy. Ticius is not otherwise known.
5. Great-grandson of Aeneas and legendary founder of Britain, not elsewhere given the name *Felix* (Latin, "happy").

Time after time, in tournaments of joust,
they had lunged at each other with leveled lances
then returned to the castle to carry on their caroling,
for the feasting lasted a full fortnight and one day,
45 with more food and drink than a fellow could dream of.
The hubbub of their humor was heavenly to hear:
pleasant dialogue by day and dancing after dusk,
so house and hall were lit with happiness
and lords and ladies were luminous with joy.
50 With all the wonder in the world they gathered there as one:
the most chivalrous and courteous knights known to Christendom;
the most wonderful women to have walked in this world;
the handsomest king to be crowned at court.
Fine folk with their futures before them, there in
55   that hall.
          Their highly honored king
          was happiest of all:
          no nobler knights had come
          within a castle's wall.

60 With New Year so young it still yawned and stretched
helpings were doubled on the dais that day.
And as king and company were coming to the hall
the choir in the chapel fell suddenly quiet,
then a chorus erupted from the courtiers and clerks:
65 "Noel," they cheered, then "Noel, Noel,"
"New Year Gifts!" the knights cried next
as they pressed forwards to offer their presents,
teasing with frivolous favors and forfeits,
till those ladies who lost couldn't help but laugh,
70 and the undefeated were far from forlorn.[6]
Their merrymaking rolled on in this manner until mealtime,
when, worthily washed, they went to the table,
and were seated in order of honor, as was apt,
with Guinevere in their gathering, gloriously framed
75 at her place on the platform, pricelessly curtained
by silk to each side, and canopied across
with tasteful tapestries of Toulouse and Tharsia,
studded with stones and stunning gems
beyond pocket or purse, beyond what pennies
80   could buy.
          But not one stone outshone
          the quartz of the queen's eyes;
          with hand on heart, no one
          could argue otherwise.

85 But Arthur would not eat until all were served.
He brimmed with ebullience, being almost boyish
in his love of life, and what he liked the least
was to sit still watching the seasons slip by.

6. The forfeit that made the ladies who lost laugh was in all likelihood a kiss.

His blood was busy and he buzzed with thoughts,
90 and the matter which played on his mind at that moment
was his pledge to take no portion from his plate
on such a special day until a story was told:
some far-fetched yarn or outrageous fable,
the tallest of tales, yet one ringing with truth,
95 like the action-packed epics of men-at-arms.
Or till some chancer had challenged his chosen knight,
dared him, with a lance, to lay life on the line,
to stare death face-to-face and accept defeat
should fortune or fate smile more favorably on his foe.
100 Within Camelot's castle this was the custom,
and at feasts and festivals when the fellowship
would meet.
With features proud and fine
he stood there tall and straight,
105 a king at Christmastime
amid great merriment.

And still he stands there just being himself,
chatting away charmingly, exchanging views.
Good Sir Gawain is seated by Guinevere,
110 and at Arthur's other side sits Agravain the Hard Hand,
both nephews of the king and notable knights.
At the head of the board sat Bishop Baldwin,
with Ywain, son of Urien, to eat beside him.
First those sitting on the dais[7] were splendidly served,
115 then those stalwarts seated on the benches to the sides.
The first course comes in to the fanfare and clamor
of blasting trumpets hung with trembling banners,
then pounding double-drums and dinning pipes,
weird sounds and wails of such warbled wildness
120 that to hear and feel them made the heart float free.
Flavorsome delicacies of flesh were fetched in
and the freshest of foods, so many in fact
there was scarcely space to present the stews
or to set the soups in the silver bowls on
125 the cloth.
Each guest received his share
of bread or meat or broth;
a dozen plates per pair—
plus beer or wine, or both.

130 Now, on the subject of supper I'll say no more
as it's obvious to everyone that no one went without.
Because another sound, a new sound, suddenly drew near,
which might signal the king to sample his supper,
for barely had the horns finished blowing their breath
135 and with starters just spooned to the seated guests,

---

7. A raised platform. Although the Round Table is referred to (line 39), the king and queen, along with
the most prominent members of the court, are seated above the rest.

a fearful form appeared, framed in the door:
a mountain of a man, immeasurably high,
a hulk of a human from head to hips,
so long and thick in his loins and his limbs
140   I should genuinely judge him to be a half giant,
or a most massive man, the mightiest of mortals.
But handsome, too, like any horseman worth his horse,
for despite the bulk and brawn of his body
his stomach and waist were slender and sleek.
145   In fact in all features he was finely formed
            it seemed.
        Amazement seized their minds,
        no soul had ever seen
        a knight of such a kind—
150   entirely emerald green.

And his gear and garments were green as well:
a tight fitting tunic, tailored to his torso,
and a cloak to cover him, the cloth fully lined
with smoothly shorn fur clearly showing, and faced
155   with all-white ermine, as was the hood,
worn shawled on his shoulders, shucked from his head.
On his lower limbs his leggings were also green,
wrapped closely round his calves, and his sparkling spurs
were green-gold, strapped with stripy silk,
160   and were set on his stockings, for this stranger was shoeless.
In all vestments he revealed himself veritably verdant!
From his belt hooks and buckle to the baubles and gems
arrayed so richly around his costume
and adorning the saddle, stitched onto silk.
165   All the details of his dress are difficult to describe,
embroidered as it was with butterflies and birds,
green beads emblazoned on a background of gold.
All the horse's tack—harness strap, hind strap,
the eye of the bit, each alloy and enamel
170   and the stirrups he stood in were similarly tinted,
and the same with the cantle and the skirts of the saddle,
all glimmering and glinting with the greenest jewels.
And the horse: every hair was green, from hoof
           to mane.
175   A steed of pure green stock.
        Each snort and shudder strained
        the hand-stitched bridle, but
        his rider had him reined.

The fellow in green was in fine fettle.
180   The hair of his head was as green as his horse,
fine flowing locks which fanned across his back,
plus a bushy green beard growing down to his breast,
which hung with the splendid hair from his head
and was lopped in a line at elbow length
185   so half his arms were gowned in green growth,

crimped at the collar, like a king's cape.
The mane of his mount was groomed to match,
combed and knotted into curlicues
then tinseled with gold, tied and twisted
190 green over gold, green over gold.
The fetlocks were finished in the same fashion
with bright green ribbon braided with beads,
as was the tail—to its tippety-tip!
And a long, tied thong lacing it tight
195 where bright and burnished gold bells chimed clearly.
No waking man had witnessed such a warrior
or weird warhorse—otherworldly, yet flesh
        and bone.
        His look was lightning bright
200   said those who glimpsed its glow.
        It seemed no man there might
        survive his violent blow.

Yet he wore no helmet and no hauberk either,
no armored apparel or plate was apparent,
205 and he swung no sword nor sported any shield,
but held in one hand a sprig of holly—
of all the evergreens the greenest ever—
and in the other hand held the mother of all axes,
a cruel piece of kit I kid you not:
210 the head was an ell in length at least
and forged in green steel with a gilt finish;
its broad-edged blade brightly burnished,
it could shear a man's scalp and shave him to boot.
The handle which fitted that fiend's great fist
215 was inlaid with iron, end to end,
with green pigment picking out impressive designs.
From stock to neck, where it stopped with a knot,
a lace was looped the length of the haft,
trimmed with tassels and tails of string
220 fastened firmly in place by forest-green buttons.
And he kicks on, canters through that crowded hall
towards the top table, not the least bit timid,
cocksure of himself, sitting high in the saddle.
"And who," he bellows, without breaking breath,
225 "is governor of this gaggle? I'll be glad to know.
It's with him and no one else that I'll hold
        a pact."
        He held them with his eyes,
        and looked from right to left,
230   not knowing, of those knights,
        which person to respect.

The guests looked on. They gaped and they gawked
and were mute with amazement: what did it mean
that human and horse could develop this hue,
235 should grow to be grass-green or greener still,

like green enamel emboldened by bright gold?
Some stood and stared then stepped a little closer,
drawn near to the knight to know his next move;
they'd seen some sights, but this was something special,
240   a miracle or magic, or so they imagined.
Yet several of the lords were like statues in their seats,
left speechless and rigid, not risking a response.
The hall fell hushed, as if all who were present
had slipped into sleep or some trancelike state.
245   No doubt
          not all were stunned and stilled
          by dread, but duty bound
          to hold their tongues until
          their sovereign could respond.

250   Then the king acknowledged this curious occurrence,
cordially addressed him, keeping his cool.
"A warm welcome, sir, this winter's night.
My name is Arthur, I am head of this house.
Won't you slide from that saddle and stay awhile,
255   and the business which brings you we shall learn of later."
"No," said the knight, "by Him in highest heaven,
I'm not here to idle in your hall this evening.
But because your acclaim is so loudly chorused,
and your castle and brotherhood are called the best,
260   the strongest men to ever mount the saddle,
the worthiest knights ever known to the world,
both in competition and true combat,
and since courtesy, so it's said, is championed here,
I'm intrigued, and attracted to your door at this time.
265   Be assured by this holly stem here in my hand
that I mean no menace. So expect no malice,
for if I'd slogged here tonight to slay and slaughter
my helmet and hauberk wouldn't be at home
and my sword and spear would be here at my side,
270   and more weapons of war, as I'm sure you're aware;
I'm clothed for peace, not kitted out for conflict.
But if you're half as honorable as I've heard folk say
you'll gracefully grant me this game which I ask for
                by right."
275   Then Arthur answered, "Knight
          most courteous, you claim
          a fair, unarmored fight.
          We'll see you have the same."

"I'm spoiling for no scrap, I swear. Besides,
280   the bodies on these benches are just bum-fluffed bairns.
If I'd ridden to your castle rigged out for a ruck
these lightweight men wouldn't last a minute.
But it's Yuletide—a time of youthfulness, yes?
So at Christmas in this court I lay down a challenge:
285   if a person here present, within these premises,

is big or bold or red-blooded enough
to strike me one stroke and be struck in return,
I shall give him as a gift this gigantic cleaver
and the axe shall be his to handle how he likes.
290   I'll kneel, bare my neck and take the first knock.
So who has the gall? The gumption? The guts?
Who'll spring from his seat and snatch this weapon?
I offer the axe—who'll have it as his own?
I'll afford one free hit from which I won't flinch,
295   and promise that twelve months will pass in peace,
         then claim
        the duty I deserve
        in one year and one day.
        Does no one have the nerve
300   to wager in this way?"

Flustered at first, now totally foxed
were the household and the lords, both the highborn and
      the low.
Still stirruped, the knight swiveled round in his saddle
looking left and right, his red eyes rolling
305   beneath the bristles of his bushy green brows,
his beard swishing from side to side.
When the court kept its counsel he cleared his throat
and stiffened his spine. Then he spoke his mind:
"So here is the House of Arthur," he scoffed,
310   "whose virtues reverberate across vast realms.
Where's the fortitude and fearlessness you're so famous for?
And the breathtaking bravery and the big-mouth bragging?
The towering reputation of the Round Table,
skittled and scuppered by a stranger—what a scandal!
315   You flap and you flinch and I've not raised a finger!"
Then he laughed so loud that their leader saw red.
Blood flowed to his fine-featured face and he raged
      inside.
      His men were also hurt—
320   those words had pricked their pride.
      But born so brave at heart
      the king stepped up one stride.

"Your request," he countered, "is quite insane,
and folly finds the man who flirts with the fool.
325   No warrior worth his salt would be worried by your words,
so in heaven's good name hand over the axe
and I'll happily fulfill the favor you ask."
He strides to him swiftly and seizes his arm;
the man dismounts in one mighty leap.
330   Then Arthur grips the axe, grabs it by its haft
and takes it above him, intending to attack.
Yet the stranger before him stands up straight,
highest in the house by at least a head.
Quite simply he stands there stroking his beard,

335 fiddling with his coat, his face without fear,
 about to be bludgeoned, but no more bothered
 than a guest at the table being given a goblet
    of wine.
    By Guinevere, Gawain
340   now to his king inclines
    and says, "I stake my claim.
    This melee must be mine."

 "Should you call me, courteous lord," said Gawain to
   his king,
 "to rise from my seat and stand at your side,
345 politely take leave of my place at the table
 and quit without causing offence to my queen,
 then I shall come to your counsel before this great court.
 For I find it unfitting, as my fellow knights would,
 when a deed of such daring is dangled before us
350 that you take on this trial—tempted as you are—
 when brave, bold men are seated on these benches,
 men never matched in the mettle of their minds,
 never beaten or bettered in the field of battle.
 I am weakest of your warriors and feeblest of wit;
355 loss of my life would be least lamented.
 Were I not your nephew my life would mean nothing;
 to be born of your blood is my body's only claim.
 Such a foolish affair is unfitting for a king,
 so; being first to come forward, it should fall to me.
360 And if my proposal is improper, let no other person
    stand blame."
    The knighthood then unites
    and each knight says the same:
    their king can stand aside
365   and give Gawain the game.

 So the sovereign instructed his knight to stand.
 Getting to his feet he moved graciously forward
 and knelt before Arthur, taking hold of the axe.
 Letting go of it, Arthur then held up his hand
370 to give young Gawain the blessing of God
 and hope he finds firmness in heart and fist.
 "Take care, young cousin, to catch him cleanly,
 use full-blooded force then you needn't fear
 the blow which he threatens to trade in return."
375 Gawain, with the weapon, walked towards the warrior,
 and they stood face-to-face, not one man afraid.
 Then the green knight spoke, growled at Gawain:
 "Before we compete, repeat what we've promised.
 And start by saying your name to me, sir,
380 and tell me the truth so I can take it on trust."
 "In good faith," said the knight, "Gawain is my name.
 I heave this axe, and whatever happens after,
 in twelvemonth's time I'll be struck in return

with any weapon you wish, and by you and you
385   alone."
            The green man speaks again:
            "I swear on all I know,
            I'm glad it's you, Gawain,
            who'll drive the axe-head home."

390 "Gawain," said the green knight, "by God, I'm glad
the favor I've called for will fall from your fist.
You've perfectly repeated the promise we made
and the terms of the contest are crystal clear.
Except for one thing: you must solemnly swear
395 that you'll seek me yourself; that you'll search me out
to the ends of the earth to earn the same blow
as you'll dole out today in this decorous hall."
"But where will you be? Where's your abode?
You're a man of mystery, as God is my maker.
400 Which court do you come from and what are you called?
There is knowledge I need, including your name,
then I shall use all my wit to work out the way,
and keep to our contract, so cross my heart."
"But enough at New Year. It needs nothing more,"
405 said the warrior in green to worthy Gawain.
"I could tell you the truth once you've taken the blow;
if you smite me smartly I could spell out the facts
of my house and home and my name, if it helps,
then you'll pay me a visit and vouch for our pact.
410 Or if I keep quiet you might cope all the better,
loafing and lounging here, looking no further. But
            we stall!
            Now grasp that gruesome axe
            and show your striking style."
415   He answered, "Since you ask,"
            and touched the tempered steel.

In the standing position he prepared to be struck,
bent forward, revealing a flash of green flesh
as he heaped his hair to the crown of his head,
420 the nape of his neck now naked and ready.
Gawain grips the axe and heaves it heavenwards,
plants his left foot firmly on the floor in front,
then swings it swiftly towards the bare skin.
The cleanness of the strike cleaved the spinal cord
425 and parted the fat and the flesh so far
that the bright steel blade took a bite from the floor.
The handsome head tumbles onto the earth
and the king's men kick it as it clatters past.
Blood gutters brightly against his green gown,
430 yet the man doesn't shudder or stagger or sink
but trudges towards them on those tree-trunk legs
and rummages around, reaches at their feet
and cops hold of his head and hoists it high,

and strides to his steed, snatches the bridle,
435 steps into the stirrup and swings into the saddle
still gripping his head by a handful of hair.
Then he settles himself in his seat with the ease
of a man unmarked, never mind being minus
         his head!
440   He wheeled his bulk about,
     that body which still bled.
     They cowered in the court
     before his speech was said.

For that scalp and skull now swung from his fist;
445 to the noblest at the table he turned the face
and it opened its eyelids, stared straight ahead
and spoke this speech, which you'll hear for yourselves:
"Sir Gawain, be wise enough to keep your word
and faithfully follow me until you find me,
450 as you vowed in this hall within hearing of these horsemen.
You're charged with getting to the Green Chapel,
to reap what you've sown. You'll rightfully receive
that what is due to be dealt to you as New Year dawns.
Men know my name as the Green Chapel knight,
455 and even a fool couldn't fail to find me.
So come, or be called a coward forever."
With a tug of the reins he twisted around
and, head still in hand, galloped out of the hall,
so the hooves brought fire from the flame in the flint.
460 Which kingdom he came from they hadn't a clue,
no more than they knew where he made for next.
         And then?
     Well, with the green man gone
     they laughed and grinned again.
465   And yet such goings-on
     were magic to those men.

And although King Arthur was awestruck at heart
no sign of it showed. Instead he spoke
to his exquisite queen with courteous words:
470 "Dear lady, don't be daunted by this deed today,
it's in keeping that such strangeness should occur at Christmas
between sessions of banter and seasonal song,
amid the lively pastimes of ladies and lords.
And at least I'm allowed to eat at last,
475 having witnessed such wonder, wouldn't you say?"
Then he glanced at Gawain and spoke gracefully:
"Now hang up your axe[8]—one hack is enough."
So it dangled from the drape behind the dais
so that men who saw it would be mesmerized and amazed,
480 and give voice, on its evidence, to that stunning event.
Then the two of them turned and walked to the table,

8. A colloquial expression equivalent to "bury the hatchet," but here with an ironic literal sense.

the monarch and his knight, and men served the meal—
double dishes apiece, rare delicacies,
all manner of food—and the music of minstrels.
485 And they danced and sang till the sun went down
              that day.
          But mind your mood, Gawain,
          lest dread make you delay,
          or lose this lethal game
490   you've promised you will play.

FITT ii

This happening was a gift—just as Arthur had asked for
and had yearned to hear of while the year was young.
And if guests had no subject as they strolled to their seats,
now this serious concern sustained their chatter.
495 And Gawain had been glad to begin the game,
but don't be so shocked should the plot turn pear-shaped:
for men might be merry when addled with mead
but each year, short lived, is unlike the last
and rarely resolves in the style it arrived.
500 So the festival finishes and a new year follows
in eternal sequence, season by season.
After lavish Christmas come the lean days of Lent
when the flesh is tested with fish and simple food.
Then the world's weather wages war on winter:
505 cold shrinks earthwards and the clouds climb;
sun-warmed, shimmering rain comes showering
onto meadows and fields where flowers unfurl;
woods and grounds wear a wardrobe of green;
birds burble with life and build busily
510 as summer spreads, settling on slopes as
              it should.
          Now every hedgerow brims
          with blossom and with bud,
          and lively songbirds sing
515   from lovely, leafy woods.

So summer comes in season with its subtle airs,
when the west wind sighs among shoots and seeds,
and those plants which flower and flourish are a pleasure
as their leaves let drip their drink of dew
520 and they sparkle and glitter when glanced by sunlight.
Then autumn arrives to harden the harvest
and with it comes a warning to ripen before winter.
The drying airs arrive, driving up dust
from the face of the earth to the heights of heaven,
525 and wild sky wrestles the sun with its winds,
and the leaves of the lime lie littered on the ground,
and grass that was green turns withered and gray.
Then all which had risen over-ripens and rots
and yesterday on yesterday the year dies away,

530 and winter returns, as is the way of the world
through time.
At Michaelmas[9] the moon
stands like that season's sign,
a warning to Gawain
535 to rouse himself and ride.

Yet by All Saints' Day[1] he was still at Arthur's side,
and they feasted in the name of their noble knight
with the revels and riches of the Round Table.
The lords of that hall and their loving ladies
540 were sad and concerned for the sake of their knight,
but nevertheless they made light of his load.
Those joyless at his plight made jokes and rejoiced.
Then sorrowfully, after supper, he spoke with his uncle,
and openly talked of the trip he must take:
545 "Now, lord of my life, I must ask for your leave.
You were witness to my wager. I have no wish
to retell you the terms—they're nothing but a trifle.
I must set out tomorrow to receive that stroke
from the knight in green, and let God be my guide."
550 Then the cream of Camelot crowded around:
Ywain and Eric and others of that ilk,
Sir Dodinal the Dreaded, the Duke of Clarence,
Lancelot, Lionel, Lucan the Good,
and Sir Bors and Sir Bedevere—both big names,
555 and powerful men such as Mador de la Port.
This courtly committee approaches the king
to offer up heartfelt advice to our hero.
And sounds of sadness and sorrow were heard
that one as worthy and well liked as Gawain
560 should suffer that strike but offer no stroke in
reply.
Yet keeping calm the knight
just quipped, "Why should I shy
away. If fate is kind.
565 or cruel, man still must try."

He remained all that day and in the morning he dressed,
asked early for his arms and all were produced.
First a rug of rare cloth was unrolled on the floor,
heaped with gear which glimmered and gleamed,
570 and the stout knight steps onto it and handles the steel.
He tries on his tunic of extravagant silk,
then the neatly cut cloak, closed at the neck,
its lining finished with a layer of white fur.
Then they settled his feet into steel shoes
575 and clad his calves, clamped them with greaves,
then hinged and highly polished plates
were knotted with gold thread to the knight's knees.

9. September 29.   1. November 1.

Then leg guards were fitted, lagging the flesh,
attached with thongs to his thick-set thighs.
580 Then comes the suit of shimmering steel rings
encasing his body and his costly clothes:
well burnished braces to both of his arms,
good elbow guards and glinting metal gloves,
all the trimmings and trappings of a knight tricked out
585   to ride:
        a metal suit that shone;
        gold spurs which gleam with pride;
        a keen sword swinging from
        the silk belt to his side.

590 Fastened in his armor he seemed fabulous, famous,
every link looking golden to the very last loop.
Yet for all that metal he still made it to mass,
honored the Almighty before the high altar.
After which he comes to the king and his consorts
595 and asks to take leave of the ladies and lords;
they escort and kiss him and commended him to Christ.
Now Gringolet is rigged out and ready to ride
with a saddle which flickered with fine gold fringes
and was set with new studs for the special occasion.
600 The bridle was bound with stripes of bright gold,
the apparel of the panels was matched in appearance
to the color of the saddlebows and cropper and cover,
and nails of red gold were arrayed all around,
shining splendidly like splintered sunlight.
605 Then he holds up his helmet and hastily kisses it;
it was strongly stapled and its lining was stuffed,
and sat high on his head, fastened behind
with a colorful cloth to cover his neck
embroidered and bejeweled with brilliant gems
610 on the broad silk border, and with birds on the seams
such as painted parrots perched among periwinkles
and turtle doves and true lover's knots, tightly entwined
as if women had worked at it seven winters
             at least.
615   The diamond diadem
        was greater still. It gleamed
        with flawless, flashing gems
        both clear and smoked, it seemed.

Then they showed him the shining scarlet shield
620 with its pentangle painted in pure gold.[2]
He seized it by its strap and slung it round his neck;
he looked well in what he wore, and was worthy of it.
And why the pentangle was appropriate to that prince
I intend to say, though it will stall our story.

2. A five-pointed star, formed by five lines drawn without lifting the pencil from the paper; as Solomon's sign (line 625), a mystical significance was attributed to it.

625 It is a symbol that Solomon once set in place
and is taken to this day as a token of fidelity,
for the form of the figure is a five-pointed star
and each line overlaps and links with the last
so is ever eternal, and when spoken of in England
630 is known by the name of the endless knot.
So it suits this soldier in his spotless armor,
fully faithful in five ways five times over.
For Gawain was as good as the purest gold—
devoid of vices but virtuous, loyal
635   and kind,
            so bore that badge on both
            his shawl and shield alike.
            A prince who talked the truth:
            known as the noblest knight.

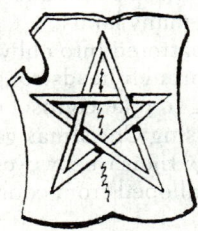

640 First he was deemed flawless in his five senses;
and secondly his five fingers were never at fault;
and thirdly his faith was founded in the five wounds
Christ received on the cross, as the creed recalls.
And fourthly, if that soldier struggled in skirmish
645 one thought pulled him through above all other things:
the fortitude he found in the five joys
which Mary had conceived in her son, our Savior.[3]
For precisely that reason the princely rider
had the shape of her image inside his shield,
650 so by catching her eye his courage would not crack.
The fifth set of five which I heard the knight followed
included friendship and fraternity with fellow men,
purity and politeness that impressed at all times,
and pity, which surpassed all pointedness. Five things
655 which meant more to Gawain than to most other men.
So these five sets of five were fixed in this knight,
each linked to the last through the endless line,
a five-pointed form which never failed,
never stronger to one side or slack at the other,
660 but unbroken in its being from beginning to end
however its trail is tracked and traced.
So the star on the spangling shield he sported
shone royally, in gold, on a ruby red background,

3. The Annunciation, Nativity, Resurrection, Ascension, and Assumption. These overlap but are not similar to the Five Joyful Mysteries of the Rosary, which were not formally established until the 16th century.

the pure pentangle as people have called it
665   for years.
         Then, lance in hand, held high,
         and got up in his gear
         he bids them all good-bye
         one final time, he fears.

670 Spiked with the spurs the steed sped away
with such force that the fire-stones sparked underfoot.
All sighed at the sight, and with sinking hearts
they whispered their worries to one another,
concerned for their comrade. "A pity, by Christ,
675 if a lord so noble should lose his life.
To find his equal on earth would be far from easy.
Cleverer to have acted with caution and care,
deemed him a duke—a title he was due—
a leader of men, lord of many lands;
680 better that than being battered into oblivion,
beheaded by an ogre, through headstrong pride.
Whoever knew any king to take counsel of a knight
in the grip of an engrossing Christmas game?"
Warm tears welled up in their weepy eyes
685 as gallant Sir Gawain galloped from court
           that day.
         He sped from home and hearth
         and went his winding way
         on steep and snaking paths,
690   just as the story says.

Now through England's realm he rides and rides,
Sir Gawain, God's servant, on his grim quest,
passing long dark nights unloved and alone,
foraging to feed, finding little to call food,
695 with no friend but his horse through forests and hills
and only our Lord in heaven to hear him.
He wanders near to the north of Wales
with the Isles of Anglesey off to the left.
He keeps to the coast, fording each course,
700 crossing at Holy Head and coming ashore
in the wilds of the Wirral, whose wayward people
both God and good men have quite given up on.[4]
And he constantly enquires of those he encounters
if they know, or not, in this neck of the woods,
705 of a great green man or a Green Chapel.
No, they say, never. Never in their lives.
They know of neither a chap nor a chapel
           so strange.
         He trails through bleak terrain.
710   His mood and manner change

---

4. Gawain travels from Camelot north to the northern coast of Wales, opposite the islands of Anglesey, where he turns east across the Dee to the forest of Wirral in Cheshire.

at every twist and turn
towards that chosen church.

In a strange region he scales steep slopes;
far from his friends he cuts a lonely figure.
715 Where he bridges a brook or wades through a waterway
it's no surprise to find that he faces a foe
so foul or fierce he is bound to use force.
So momentous are his travels among the mountains
to tell just a tenth would be a tall order.
720 Here he scraps with serpents and snarling wolves,
here he tangles with wodwos causing trouble in the crags,
or with bulls and bears and the odd wild boar.
Hard on his heels through the highlands come giants.
Only diligence and faith in the face of death
725 will keep him from becoming a corpse or carrion.
And the wars were one thing, but winter was worse:
clouds shed their cargo of crystallized rain
which froze as it fell to the frost-glazed earth.
Nearly slain by sleet he slept in his armor,
730 bivouacked in the blackness amongst bare rocks
where meltwater streamed from the snow-capped summits
and high overhead hung chandeliers of ice.
So in peril and pain Sir Gawain made progress,
crisscrossing the countryside until Christmas
735 　　　　Eve. Then
　　　at that time of tiding,
　　　he prayed to highest heaven.
　　　Let Mother Mary guide him
　　　towards some house or haven.

740 Next morning he moves on, skirts the mountainside,
descends a deep forest, densely overgrown,
with vaulting hills to each half of the valley
and ancient oaks in huddles of hundreds.
Hazel and hawthorn are interwoven,
745 decked and draped in damp, shaggy moss,
and bedraggled birds on bare, black branches
pipe pitifully into the piercing cold.
Under cover of the canopy he girded Gringolet
through mud and marshland, a man all alone,
750 concerned and afraid in case he should fail
in the worship of our Deity, who, on that date
was born the Virgin's son to save our souls.
He prayed with heavy heart. "Father, hear me,
and Lady Mary, our mother most mild,
755 let me happen on some house where mass might be heard,
and matins in the morning; meekly I ask,
and here I utter my pater, ave
　　　　and creed."
　　　He rides the path and prays,
760 　　　dismayed by his misdeeds,

and signs Christ's cross and says,
"Be near me in my need."

No sooner had he signed himself three times
than he became aware, in those woods, of high walls
765   in a moat, on a mound, bordered by the boughs
of thick-trunked timber which trimmed the water.
The most commanding castle a knight ever kept,
positioned in a site of sweeping parkland
with a palisade of pikes pitched in the earth
770   in the midst of tall trees for two miles or more.
He stopped and stared at one side of that stronghold
as it sparkled and shone within shimmering oaks,
and with helmet in hand he offered up thanks
to Jesus and Saint Julian,[5] both gentle and good,
775   who had courteously heard him and heeded his cry.
"A lodging at last. So allow it, my Lord."
Then he girded Gringolet with his gilded spurs,
and purely by chance chose the principal approach
to the building, which brought him to the end of the bridge
780   with haste.
          The drawbridge stood withdrawn,
          the front gates were shut fast.
          Such well-constructed walls
          would blunt the storm wind's blast.

785   In the saddle of his steed he halts on the slope
of the delving moat with its double ditch.
Out of water of wondrous depth, the walls
then loomed overhead to a huge height,
course after course of crafted stone,
790   then battlements embellished in the boldest style
and turrets arranged around the ramparts
with lockable loopholes set into the lookouts.
The knight had not seen a more stunning structure.
Further in, his eye was drawn to a hall
795   attended, architecturally, by many tall towers
with a series of spires spiking the air
all crowned by carvings exquisitely cut.
Uncountable chimneys the color of chalk
sprutted from the roof and sparkled in the sun.
800   So perfect was that vision of painted pinnacles
clustered within the castle's enclosure
it appeared that the place was cut from paper.[6]
Then a notion occurred to that noble knight:
to seek a visit, get invited inside,
805   to be hosted and housed, and all the holy days
          remain.
          Responding to his call
          a pleasant porter came,

5. Patron saint of hospitality.
6. Paper castles were a common table decoration at feasts.

a watchman on the wall,
810   who welcomed Sir Gawain.

"Good morning," said Gawain, "will you go with a message
to the lord of this house to let me have lodging?"
"By Saint Peter," said the porter, "it'll be my pleasure,
and I'll warrant you'll be welcome for as long as you wish."
815   Then he went on his way, but came back at once
with a group who had gathered to greet the stranger;
the drawbridge came down and they crossed the ditch
and knelt in the frost in front of the knight
to welcome this man in a way deemed worthy.
820   Then they yielded to their guest, yanked open the gate,
and bidding them to rise he rode across the bridge.
He was assisted from the saddle by several men
and the strongest amongst them stabled his steed.
Then knights, and the squires of knights, drew near,
825   to escort him, with courtesy, into the castle.
As he took off his helmet, many hasty hands
stretched to receive it and to serve this noble knight,
and his sword and his shield were taken aside.
Then he made himself known to nobles and knights
830   and proud fellows pressed forwards to confer their respects.
Still heavy with armor he was led to the hall
where a fire burned bright with the fiercest flames.
Then the master of the manor emerged from his chamber,
to greet him in the hall with all due honor,
835   saying, "Behave in my house as your heart pleases.
To whatever you want you are welcome, do what
          you will."
        "My thanks," Gawain exclaimed,
        "May Christ reward you well."
840   Then firmly, like good friends,
        arm into arm they fell.

Gawain gazed at the lord who greeted him so gracefully,
the great one who governed that grand estate,
powerful and large, in the prime of his life,
845   with a bushy beard as red as a beaver's,
steady in his stance, solid of build,
with a fiery face and fine conversation:
and it suited him well, so it seemed to Gawain,
to keep such a castle and captain his knights.
850   Escorted to his quarters the lord quickly orders
that a servant be assigned to assist Gawain,
and many were willing to wait on his word.
They brought him to a bedroom, beautifully furnished
with fine silken fabrics finished in gold
855   and curious coverlets lavishly quilted
in bright ermine and embroidered to each border.
Curtains ran on cords through red-gold rings,
tapestries from Toulouse and Turkistan

were fixed against walls and fitted underfoot.
860 With humorous banter Gawain was helped out
of his chain-mail coat and costly clothes,
then they rushed to bring him an array of robes
of the choicest cloth. He chose, and changed,
and as soon as he stood in that stunning gown
865 with its flowing skirts which suited his shape
it almost appeared to the persons present
that spring, with its spectrum of colors, had sprung;
so alive and lean were that young man's limbs
a nobler creature Christ had never created, they declared.
870   This knight,
           whose country was unclear,
           now seemed to them by sight
           a prince without a peer
           in fields where fierce men fight.

875 In front of a flaming fireside a chair
was pulled into place for Gawain, and padded
with covers and quilts all cleverly stitched,
then a cape was cast across the knight
of rich brown cloth with embroidered borders,
880 finished inside with the finest furs,
ermine, to be exact, and a hood which echoed it.
Resplendently dressed he settled in his seat;
as his limbs thawed, so his thoughts lightened.
Soon a table was set on sturdy trestles
885 covered entirely with a clean white cloth
and cruets of salt and silver spoons.
In a while he washed and went to his meal.
Staff came quickly and served him in style
with several soups all seasoned to taste,
890 double helpings as was fitting, and a feast of fish,
some baked in bread, some browned over flames,
some boiled or steamed, some stewed in spices
and subtle sauces which the knight savored.
Four or five times he called it a feast,
895 and the courteous company happily cheered him
           along:
           "On penance plates you dine—[7]
           there's better board to come."
           The warming, heady wine
900   then freed his mind for fun.

Now through tactful talk and tentative enquiry
polite questions are put to this prince;
he responds respectfully, and speaks of his journey
from the Court of Arthur, King of Camelot,
905 the royal ruler of the Round Table,

---

7. "Penance" because, although sumptuous, the meal consists of fish dishes appropriate to a fasting day.

and he says they now sit with Gawain himself,
who has come here at Christmastime quite by chance.
Once the lord has gathered that his guest is Gawain
he likes it so well that he laughs out loud.

910 All the men of that manor were of the same mind,
being happy to appear promptly in his presence,
this person famed for prowess and purity,
whose noble skills were sung to the skies,
whose life was the stuff of legend and lore.

915 Then knight spoke softly to knight, saying
"Watch now, we'll witness his graceful ways,
hear the faultless phrasing of flawless speech;
if we listen we will learn the merits of language
since we have in our hall a man of high honor.

920 Ours is a graceful and giving God
to grant that we welcome Gawain as our guest
as we sing of His birth who was born to save us.
        We few
            shall learn a lesson here
925   in tact and manners true,
            and hopefully we'll hear
            love's tender language, too."

Once dinner was done Gawain drew to his feet
and darkness neared as day became dusk.

930 Chaplains went off to the castle's chapels
to sound the bells hard, to signal the hour
of evensong, summoning each and every soul.
The lord goes alone, then his lady arrives,
concealing herself in a private pew.

935 Gawain attends, too; tugged by his sleeve
he is steered to a seat, led by the lord
who greets Gawain by name as his guest.
No man in the world is more welcome, are his words.
For that he is thanked. And they hug there and then,

940 and sit as a pair through the service in prayer.
Then she who desired to see this stranger
came from her closet with her sisterly crew.
She was fairest amongst them—her face, her flesh,
her complexion, her quality, her bearing, her body,

945 more glorious than Guinevere, or so Gawain thought,
and in the chancel of the church they exchanged courtesies.
She was hand in hand with a lady to her left,
someone altered by age, an ancient dame,
well respected, it seemed, by the servants at her side.

950 Those ladies were not the least bit alike:
one woman was young, one withered by years.
The body of the beauty seemed to bloom with blood,
the cheeks of the crone were wattled and slack.
One was clothed in a kerchief clustered with pearls

955 which shone like snow—snow on the slopes
of her upper breast and bright bare throat.

The other was noosed and knotted at the neck,
her chin enveloped in chalk-white veils,
her forehead fully enfolded in silk
960 with detailed designs at the edges and hems;
nothing bare, except for the black of her brows
and the eyes and nose and naked lips
which were chapped and bleared and a sorrowful sight.
A grand old mother, a matriarch she might
965   be hailed.
   Her trunk was square and squat,
   her buttocks bulged and swelled.
   Most men would sooner squint
   at her whose hand she held.

970 Then Gawain glanced at the gracious-looking woman,
and by leave of the lord he approached those ladies
saluting the elder with a long, low bow,
holding the other for a moment in his arms,
kissing her respectfully and speaking with courtesy.
975 They request his acquaintance, and quickly he offers
to serve them unswervingly should they say the word.
They take him between them and talk as they walk
to a hearth full of heat, and hurriedly ask
for specially spiced cakes, which are speedily fetched,
980 and wine filled each goblet again and again.
Frequently the lord would leap to his feet
insisting that mirth and merriment be made:
hauling off his hood he hoisted it on a spear—
a prize, he promised, to the person providing
985 most comfort and cheer at Christmastime.
"And my fellows and friends shall help in my fight
to see that it hangs from no head but my own."
So the laughter of that lord lights up the room,
and Gawain and the gathering are gladdened by games
990   till late.
   So late, his lordship said,
   that lamps should burn with light.
   Then, blissful, bound for bed,
   Sir Gawain waved good night.

995 So the morning dawns when man remembers
the day our Redeemer was born to die,
and every house on earth is joyful for Lord Jesus.
Their day was no different, being a diary of delights:
banquets and buffets were beautifully cooked
1000 and dutifully served to diners at the dais.
The ancient elder sat highest at the table
with the lord, I believe, in the chair to her left;
the sweeter one and Gawain took seats in the center
and were first at the feast to dine; then food
1005 was carried around as custom decrees
and served to each man as his status deserved.

There was feasting, there was fun, and such feelings of joy
as could not be conveyed by quick description,
yet to tell it in detail would take too much time.
1010 But I'm aware that Gawain and the beautiful woman
found such comfort and closeness in each other's company
through warm exchanges of whispered words
and refined conversation free from foulness
that their pleasure surpassed all princely sports
1015   by far.
          Beneath the din of drums
          men followed their affairs,
          and trumpets thrilled and thrummed
          as those two tended theirs.

1020 They drank and danced all day and the next
and danced and drank the day after that,
then Saint John's Day[8] passed with a gentler joy
as the Christmas feasting came to a close.
Guests were to go in the grayness of dawn,
1025 so they laughed and dined as the dusk darkened,
swaying and swirling to music and song.
Then at last, in the lateness, they upped and left
toward distant parts along different paths.
Gawain offered his good-byes, but was ushered by his host
1030 to his host's own chamber and the heat of its chimney,
waylaid by the lord so the lord might thank him
profoundly and profusely for the favor he had shown
in honoring his house at that hallowed season
and lighting every corner of the castle with his character.
1035 "For as long as I live my life shall be better
that Gawain was my guest at God's own feast."
"By God," said Gawain, "but the gratitude goes to you.
May the High King of Heaven repay your honor.
Your requests are now this knight's commands.
1040 I am bound by your bidding, no boon is too high
        to say."
          At length his lordship tried
          to get his guest to stay.
          But proud Gawain replied
1045   he must now make his way.

Then the lord of the castle inquired courteously
of what desperate deed in the depth of winter
should coax him from Camelot, so quickly and alone,
before Christmas was over in his king's court.
1050 "What you ask," said the knight, "you shall now know.
A most pressing matter prized me from that place:
I myself am summoned to seek out a site
and I have not the faintest idea where to find it.
But find it I must by the first of the year, and not fail

8. December 27.

1055 for all the acres in England, so the Lord help me.
Consequently this inquiry I come to ask of you:
that you tell me, in truth, if you have heard the tale
of a green chapel and the ground where it stands,
or the guardian of those grounds who is colored green.
1060 For I am bound by a bond agreed by us both
to link up with him there, should I live that long.
As dawn on New Year's Day draws near,
if God sees fit, I shall face that freak
more happily than I would the most wondrous wealth!
1065 With your blessing, therefore, I must follow my feet.
In three short days my destiny is due,
and I would rather drop dead than default from duty."
Then laughing the lord of the house said, "Stay longer.
I'll direct you to your rendezvous when the time is right,
1070 you'll get to the green chapel, so give up your grieving.
You can bask in your bed, bide your time,
save your fond farewells till the first of the year
and still meet him by midmorning to do as you might.
　　　　So stay.
1075 　　A guide will get you there
　　　at dawn on New Year's Day.
　　　The place you need is near,
　　　two miles at most away."

Then Gawain was giddy with gladness, and declared,
1080 "For this more than anything I thank you thoroughly,
and shall work to do well at whatever you wish,
until that time, attending every task."
The lord squeezed Gawain's arm and seated him at his side,
and called for the ladies to keep them company.
1085 There was pleasure aplenty in their private talk,
the lord delighting in such lively language,
like man who might well be losing his mind.
Then speaking to Gawain, he suddenly shouted:
"You have sworn to serve me, whatever I instruct.
1090 Will you hold to that oath right here and now?"
"You may trust my tongue," said Gawain, in truth,
"for within these walls I am servant to your will."
The lord said warmly, "You were weary and worn,
hollow with hunger, harrowed by tiredness,
1095 yet joined in my reveling right royally every night.
You relax as you like, lie in your bed
until mass tomorrow, then go to your meal
where my wife will be waiting; she will sit at your side
to accompany and comfort you in my absence from court.
1100 　　　So lounge:
　　　at dawn I'll rise and ride
　　　to hunt with horse and hound."
　　　The gracious knight agreed
　　　and, bending low, he bowed.

1105 "Furthermore," said the master, "let's make a pact.
Here's a wager: what I win in the woods will be yours,
and what you gain while I'm gone you will give to me.
Young sir, let's swap, and strike a bond,
1110 let a bargain be a bargain, for better or worse."
"By God," said Gawain, "I agree to the terms,
and I find it pleasing that you favor such fun."
"Let drink be served and we'll seal the deal,"
the lord cried loudly, and everyone laughed.
1115 So they reveled and caroused uproariously,
those lords and ladies, for as long as they liked;
then with immaculate exchanges of manners and remarks
they slowed and they stood and they spoke softly.
And with parting kisses the party dispersed,
1120 footmen going forward with flaring torches,
and everybody was brought to their bed at long last,
to dream.
Before they part the pair
repeat their pact again.
1125 That lord was well aware
of how to host a game.

FITT iii

Well before sunrise the servants were stirring;
the guests who were going had called for their grooms,
and they scurried to the stables to strap on the saddles,
trussing and tying all the trammel and tack.
1130 The high-ranking nobles got ready to ride,
jumped stylishly to their saddles and seized the reins,
then cantered away on their chosen courses.
The lord of that land was by no means last
to be rigged out for riding with the rest of his men.
1135 After mass he wolfed down a meal, then made
for the hills in a hurry with his hunting horn.
So as morning was lifting its lamp to the land
his lordship and his huntsmen were high on horseback,
and the canny kennel men had coupled the hounds
1140 and opened the cages and called them out.
On the bugles they blew three long, bare notes
to a din of baying and barking, and any dogs
which wandered at will where whipped back into line
by a hundred hunters, or so I heard tell,
1145 at least.
The handlers hold their hounds,
the huntsmen's hounds run free.
Each bugle blast rebounds
between the trunks of trees.

1150 As the cry went up the wild creatures quaked.
The deer in the dale, quivering with dread

The Temptation of Sir Gawain by Bertilak's Wife. Gawain may think he is protected, but bedrooms are dangerous places.

hurtled to high ground, but were headed off
by the ring of beaters who bellowed boisterously.
The stags of the herd with their high-branched heads
1155 and the broad-horned bucks were allowed to pass by,
for the lord of the land had laid down a law
that man should not maim the male in close season.
But the hinds were halted with hollers and whoops
and the din drove the does to sprint for the dells.
1160 Then the eye can see that the air is all arrows:
all across the forest they flashed and flickered,
biting through hides with their broad heads.
What! They bleat as they bleed and they die on the banks,
and always the hounds are hard on their heels,
1165 and the hunters on horseback come hammering behind
with stone-splitting cries, as if cliffs had collapsed.
And those animals which escaped the aim of the archers
were steered from the slopes down to rivers and streams
and set upon and seized at the stations below.
1170 So perfect and practiced were the men at their posts
and so great were the greyhounds which grappled with the deer
that prey was pounced on and dispatched with speed
and force.
The lord's heart leaps with life.
1175 Now on, now off his horse
all day he hacks and drives.
And dusk comes in due course.

So through a lime-leaf border the lord led the hunt,
while good Gawain lay slumbering in his sheets,
1180 dozing as the daylight dappled the walls,
under a splendid cover, enclosed by curtains.

And while snoozing he heard a slyly made sound,
the sigh of a door swinging slowly aside.
From below the bedding he brings up his head
1185 and lifts the corner of the curtain a little
wondering warily what it might be.
It was she, the lady, looking her loveliest,
most quietly and craftily closing the door,
nearing the bed. The knight felt nervous;
1190 lying back he assumed the shape of sleep
as she stole towards him with silent steps,
then cast up the curtain and crept inside,
then sat down softly at the side of his bed.
And awaited his wakening for a good long while.
1195 Gawain lay still, in his state of false sleep,
turning over in his mind what this matter might mean,
and where the lady's unlikely visit might lead.
Yet he said to himself, "Instead of this stealth
I should openly ask what her actions imply."
1200 So he stirred and stretched, turned on his side,
lifted his eyelids and, looking alarmed,
crossed himself hurriedly with his hand, as if saving
          his life.
          Her chin is pale, her cheeks
1205   are ruddy red with health;
          her smile is sweet, she speaks
          with lips that love to laugh:

"Good morning, Sir Gawain," said the graceful lady,
"You sleep so soundly one might sidle in here.
1210 You're tricked and trapped! But let's make a truce,
or I'll bind you in your bed, and you'd better believe me."
The lady laughed, making light of his quandary.
"Good morning, madam," Gawain said merrily.
I'll contentedly attend whatever task you set,
1215 and in serving your desires I shall seek your mercy,
which seems my best plan, in the circumstances!"
And he loaded his light-hearted words with laughter.
"But my gracious lady, if you grant me leave,
will you pardon this prisoner and prompt him to rise,
1220 then I'll quit these covers and pull on my clothes,
and our words will flow more freely back and forth."
"Not so, beautiful sir," the sweet lady said.
"Bide in your bed—my own plan is better.
I'll tuck in your covers corner to corner,
1225 then playfully parley with the man I have pinned.
Because I know your name—the knight Sir Gawain,
famed through all realms whichever road he rides,
whose princely honor is highly praised
amongst lords and ladies and everyone alive.
1230 And right here you lie. And we are left all alone,
with my husband and his huntsmen away in the hills
and the servants snoring and my maids asleep

and the door to this bedroom barred with a bolt.
I have in my house an honored guest
1235 so I'll make the most of my time and stay talking
        a while.
      You're free to have my all,
      do with me what you will.
      I'll come just as you call
1240   and swear to serve you well."

"In-good faith," said Gawain, "such gracious flattery,
though in truth I'm not now such a noble knight.
I don't dare to receive the respect you describe
and in no way warrant such worthy words.
1245 But by God, I'd be glad, if you give me the right,
to serve your desires, and with action or speech
bring you perfect pleasure. It would be pure joy."
Said the gracious lady, "Sir Gawain, in good faith,
how improper on my part if I were to imply
1250 any slur or slight on your status as a knight.
But what lady in this land wouldn't latch the door,
wouldn't rather hold you as I do here—
in the company of your clever conversation,
forgetting all grief and engaging in joy—
1255 than hang on to half the gold that she owns?
I praise the Lord who upholds the high heavens,
for I have what I hoped for above all else by
      His grace."
      That lovely looking maid,
1260   she charmed him and she chased.
      But every move she made
      he countered, case by case.

"Madam," said our man, "may Mary reward you,
in good faith, I have found your fairness noble.
1265 Some fellows are praised for the feats they perform;
I hardly deserve to receive such respect.
It is you who is genuinely joyful and generous."
"By Mary," she declared, "it's quite the contrary.
Were I the wealthiest woman in the world
1270 with priceless pearls in the palm of my hand
to bargain with and buy the best of all men,
then for all the signs you have shown me, sir,
of kindness, courtesy and exquisite looks—
a picture of perfection now proved to be true—
1275 no person on this planet would be picked before you."
"In fairness," said Gawain, "you found far better.
But I'm proud of the price you would pay from your purse,
and will swear to serve you as my sovereign lady.
Let Gawain be your servant and Christ your Savior."
1280 Then they muse on many things through morning and midday,
and the lady stares with a loving look,
but Gawain acts graciously and remains on guard,

and although no woman could be warmer or more winning,
he is cool in his conduct, on account of the scene he
1285   foresees:
            the strike he must receive,
            as cruel fate decrees.
            The lady begs her leave—
            at once Gawain agrees.

1290   She glanced at him, laughed and gave her good-bye,
        then stood, and stunned him with astounding words:
        "May the Lord repay you for your prize performance.
        But I know that Gawain could never be your name."
        "But why not?" the knight asked nervously,
1295   afraid that some fault in his manners had failed him.
        The beautiful woman blessed him, then rebuked him:
        "A good man like Gawain, so greatly regarded,
        the embodiment of courtliness to the bones of his being,
        could never have lingered so long with a lady
1300   without craving a kiss, as politeness requires,
        or coaxing a kiss with his closing words."
        "Very well," said Gawain, "Let it be as you wish.
        I shall kiss at your command, as becomes a knight,
        and further, should it please you, so press me no more."
1305   The lady comes close, cradles him in her arms,
        leans nearer and nearer, then kisses the knight.
        Then they courteously commend one another to Christ,
        and without one more word the woman is away.
        Rapidly he rises and makes himself ready,
1310   calls for his chamberlain, chooses his clothes,
        makes himself ready then marches off to mass.
        Then he went to a meal which was made and waiting,
        and was merry and amused till the moon had silvered
                    the view.
1315   No man felt more at home
                tucked in between those two,
                the cute one and the crone.
                Their gladness grew and grew.

        And the lord of the land still led the hunt,
1320   driving hinds to their death through holts and heaths,
        and by the setting of the sun had slaughtered so many
        of the does and other deer that it beggared belief.
        Then finally the folk came flocking to one spot
        and quickly they collected and counted the kill.
1325   Then the leading lords and their loyal men
        chose the finest deer—those fullest with fat—
        and ordered them cut open by those skilled in the art.
        They assessed and sized every slain creature
        and even on the feeblest found two fingers worth of fat.
1330   Through the sliced-open throat they seized the stomach
        and the butchered innards were bound in a bundle.
        Next they lopped off the legs and peeled back the pelt

and hooked out the bowels through the broken belly,
but carefully, being cautious not to cleave the knot.
1335 Then they clasped the throat, and clinically they cut
the gullet from the windpipe, then garbaged the guts.
Then the shoulder blades were severed with sharp knives
and slotted through a slit so the hide stayed whole.
Then the beasts were prized apart at the breast,
1340 and they went to work on the gralloching again,
riving open the front as far as the hind fork,
fetching out the offal, then with further purpose
filleting the ribs in the recognized fashion.
And the spine was subject to a similar process,
1345 being pared to the haunch so it held as one piece
then hoisting it high and hacking it off.
And its name is the numbles, as far as I know, and
                    just that.
                Its hind legs pulled apart
1350   they slit the fleshy flaps,
                then cleave and quickly start
                to break it down its back.

Then the heads and necks of hinds were hewn off,
and the choice meat of the flanks chopped away from the chine,
1355 and a fee for the crows was cast into the copse.
Then each side was skewered, stabbed through the ribs
and heaved up high, hung by its hocks,
and every person was paid with appropriate portions.
Using pelts for plates, the dogs pogged out
1360 on liver and lights and stomach linings
and a blended sop of blood and bread.
The kill horn was blown and the bloodhounds bayed.
Then hauling their meat they headed for home,
sounding howling wails on their hunting horns,
1365 and as daylight died they had covered the distance
and had come to the castle where the knight was ensconced,
                    adjourned
                in peace, with fires aflame.
                The huntsman has returned,
1370   and when he greets Gawain
                warm feelings are confirmed.

Then the whole of the household was ordered to the hall,
and the women as well with their maids in waiting.
And once assembled he instructs the servants
1375 that the venison be revealed in full view,
and in excellent humor he asked that Gawain
should see for himself the size of the kill,
and showed him the side slabs sliced from the ribs.
"Are you pleased with this pile? Have I won your praise?
1380 Does my skill at this sport deserve your esteem?"
"Yes indeed," said the other. "It's the hugest haul
I have seen, out of season, for several years."

"And I give it all to you, Gawain," said the master,
"for according to our contract it is yours to claim."
1385 "Just so," said Gawain, "and I'll say the same,
for whatever I've won within these walls
such gains will be graciously given to you."
So he held out his arms and hugged the lord
and kissed him in the comeliest way he could.
1390 "You're welcome to my winnings—to my one profit,
though I'd gladly have given you any greater prize."
"I'm grateful," said the lord, "and Gawain, this gift
would carry more worth if you cared to confess
by what wit you won it. And when. And where."
1395 "That wasn't our pact," he replied. "So don't pry.
You'll be given nothing greater, the agreement we have
       holds good!"
     They laugh aloud and trade
     wise words which match their mood.
1400   When supper's meal is made
     they dine on dainty food.

Later, they lounged by the lord's fire,
and were served unstintingly with subtle wines
and agreed to the game again next morning
1405 and to play by the rules already in place:
any takings to be traded between the two men
at night when they met, no matter what the merchandise.
They concurred on this contract in front of the court,
and drank on the deal, and went on drinking
1410 till late, when they took their leave at last,
and every person present departed to bed.
By the third cackle of the crowing cock
the lord and his liegemen are leaping from their beds,
so that mass and the morning meal are taken,
1415 and riders are rigged out ready to run as
       day dawns.
     They leave the levels, loud
     with howling hunting horns.
     The huntsmen loose the hounds
1420   through thickets and through thorns.

Soon they picked up a scent at the side of a swamp,
and the hounds which first found it were urged ahead
by wild words and shrill shouting.
The pack responded with vigor and pace,
1425 alert to the trail, forty lurchers at least.
Then such a raucous din rose up all around them
it ricocheted and rang through the rocky slopes.
The hounds were mushed with hollers and the horn,
then suddenly they swerved and swarmed together
1430 in a wood, between a pool and a precipice.
On a mound, near a cliff, on the margins of a marsh
where toppled stones lay scattered and strewn,

they coursed towards their quarry with huntsmen at heel.
Then a crew of them ringed the hillock and the cliff,
1435 until they were certain that inside their circle
was the beast whose being three bloodhounds had sensed.
Then they riled the creature with their rowdy ruckus,
and suddenly he breaks the barrier of beaters,
—the biggest of wild boars has bolted from his cover—
1440 ancient in years and estranged from the herd,
savage and strong, a most massive swine,
truly grim when he grunted. And the group were aggrieved,
for three were thrown down by the first of his thrusts;
then he fled away fast without further damage.
1445 The other huntsmen bawled "hi" and "hay, hay,"
blasted on their bugles, blew to regroup,
so the dogs and the men made a merry din,
tracking him nosily, testing him time and time
again.
1450   The boar would stand at bay
    and aim to maul and maim
    the thronging dogs, and they
    would yelp and yowl in pain.

Then the archers advanced with their bows and took aim,
1455 shooting arrows at him which were often on target,
but their points could not pierce his impenetrable shoulders
and bounced away from his bristly brow.
The smooth, slender shafts splintered into pieces,
and the heads glanced away from wherever they hit.
1460 Battered and baited by such bombardment,
in frenzied fury he flies at the men,
hurts them horribly as he hurtles past
so that many grew timid and retreated a tad.
But the master of the manor gave chase on his mount,
1465 the boldest of beast hunters, his bugle blaring,
trumpeting the tally-ho and tearing through thickets
till the setting sun slipped from the western sky.
So the day was spent in pursuits of this style,
while our lovable young lord had not left his bed,
1470 and, cosseted in costly quilted covers, there he
remained.
    The lady, at first light,
    did not neglect Gawain,
    but went to wake the knight
1475   and meant to change his mind.

She approaches the curtains, parts them and peeps in,
at which Sir Gawain makes her welcome at once,
and with prompt speech she replies to the prince,
settling by his side and laughing sweetly,
1480 looking at him lovingly before launching her words.
"Sir, if you truly are Gawain it seems wondrous to me

that a man so dedicated to doing his duty
cannot heed the first rule of honorable behavior,
which has entered through one ear and exited the other;
1485 you have already lost what yesterday you learned
in the truest lesson my tongue could teach."
"What lesson?" asked the knight. "I know of none,
though if discourtesy has occurred then blame me, of course."
"I encouraged you to kiss," the lady said kindly,
1490 "and to claim one quickly when one is required,
an act which ennobles any knight worth the name."
"Dear lady," said the other, "don't think such a thing,
I dare not kiss in case I am turned down.
If refused, I'd be at fault for offering in the first place."
1495 "In truth," she told him, "you cannot be turned down.
If someone were so snooty as to snub your advance,
a man like you has the means of his muscles."
"Yes, by God," said Gawain, "what you say holds good.
But such heavy-handedness is frowned on in my homeland,
1500 and so is any gift not given with grace.
What kiss you command I will courteously supply,
have what you want or hold off, whichever
    the case."
    So bending from above
1505   the fair one kissed his face.
    The two then talk of love:
    its grief; also its grace.

"I would like to learn," said the noble lady,
"and please find no offence, but how can it follow
1510 that a lord so lively and young in years,
a champion in chivalry across the country—
and in chivalry, the chiefmost aspect to choose,
as all knights acknowledge, is loyalty in love,
for when tales of truthful knights are told
1515 in both title and text the topic they describe
is how lords have laid down their lives for love,
endured for many days love's dreadful ordeal,
then vented their feelings with avenging valor
by bringing great bliss to a lady's bedroom—
1520 and you the most notable knight who is known,
whose fame goes before him . . . yes, how can it follow
that twice I have taken this seat at your side
yet you have not spoken the smallest syllable
which belongs to love or anything like it.
1525 A knight so courteous and considerate in his service
really ought to be eager to offer this pupil
some lessons in love, and to lead by example.
Why, are you, whom all men honor, actually ignorant,
or do you deem me too dull to hear of dalliances?
1530   I come
    to learn of love and more,

a lady all alone.
Perform for me before
my husband heads for home."

1535 "In faith," said Gawain, "may God grant you fortune.
It gives me great gladness and seems a good game
that a woman so worthy should want to come here
and take pains to play with your poor knight,
unfit for her favors—I am flattered indeed.
1540 But to take on the task of explaining true love
or touch on the topics those love tales tell of,
with yourself, who I sense has more insight and skill
in the art than I have, or even a hundred
of the likes of me, on earth where I live,
1545 would be somewhat presumptuous, I have to say.
But to the best of my ability I'll do your bidding,
bound as I am to honor you forever
and to serve you, so let our Savior preserve me!"
So the lady tempted and teased him, trying
1550 to entice him to wherever her intentions might lie.
But fairly and without fault he defended himself,
no sin on either side transpiring, only happiness
that day.
At length, when they had laughed,
1555 the woman kissed Gawain.
Politely then she left
and went her own sweet way.

Roused and risen he was ready for mass,
and then men sumptuously served the morning meal.
1560 Then he loitered with the ladies the length of the day
while the lord of the land ranged left and right
in pursuit of that pig which stampeded through the uplands,
breaking his best hounds with its back-snapping bite
when it stood embattled . . . then bowmen would strike,
1565 goading it to gallop into open ground
where the air was alive with the huntsman's arrows.
That boar made the best men flinch and bolt,
till at last his legs were like lead beneath him,
and he hobbled away to hunker in a hole
1570 by a stony rise at the side of a stream.
With the bank at his back he scrapes and burrows,
frothing and foaming foully at the mouth,
whetting his white tusks. The hunters waited,
irked by the effort of aiming from afar
1575 but daunted by the danger of daring to venture
too near.
So many men before
had fallen prey. They feared
that fierce and frenzied boar
1580 whose tusks could slash and tear.

Till his lordship hacks up, urging on his horse,
spots the swine at standstill encircled by men,
then handsomely dismounts and unhands his horse,
brandishes a bright sword and goes bounding onwards,
1585 wades through the water to where the beast waits.
Aware that the man was wafting a weapon
the hog's hairs stood on end, and its howling grunt
made the fellows there fear for their master's fate.
Then the boar burst forward, bounded at the lord,
1590 so that beast and hunter both went bundling
into white water, and the swine came off worst,
because the moment they clashed the man found his mark,
knifing the boar's neck, nailing his prey,
hammering it to the hilt, bursting the hog's heart.
1595 Screaming, it was swept downstream, almost slipping
beneath.
At least a hundred hounds
latch on with tearing teeth.
Then, dragged to drier ground,
1600 the dogs complete its death.

The kill was blown on many blaring bugle
and the unhurt hunters hollered and whooped.
The chief amongst them, in charge of the chase,
commanded the bloodhounds to bay at the boar,
1605 then one who was wise in woodland ways
began carefully to cut and carve up the carcass.
First he hacks off its head and hoists it aloft,
then roughly rives it right along the spine;
he gouges out the guts and grills them over coals,
1610 and blended with bread they are tidbits for the bloodhounds.
Next he fetches out the fillets of glimmering flesh
and retrieves the intestines in time-honored style,
then the two sides are stitched together intact
and proudly displayed on a strong pole.
1615 So with the swine swinging they swagger home,
the head of the boar being borne before the lord
who had fought so fiercely in the ford till the beast
was slain.
The day then dragged, it seemed,
1620 before he found Gawain,
who comes when called, most keen
to countenance the claim.

Now the lord is loud with words and laughter
and speaks excitedly when he sees Sir Gawain;
1625 he calls for the ladies and the company of the court
and he shows off the meat slabs and shares the story
of the boar's hulking hugeness, and the full horror
of the fight to the finish as it fled through the forest.
And Gawain is quick to compliment the conquest,

1630 praising it as proof of the lord's prowess,
for such prime pieces of perfect pork
and such sides of swine were a sight to be seen.
Then admiringly he handles the boar's huge head,
feigning fear to flatter the master's feelings.
1635 "Now Gawain," said the lord, "I give you this game,
as our wager warranted, as well you remember."
"Certainly," said Sir Gawain. "It shall be so.
And graciously I shall give you my gains in exchange."
He catches him by the neck and courteously kisses him,
1640 then a second time kisses him in a similar style.
"Now we're even," said Gawain, "at this eventide;
the clauses of our contract have been kept and you have what
        I owe."
    "By Saint Giles," the just lord says,
1645   "You're now the best I know.
    By wagering this way
    your gains will grow and grow."

Then the trestle tables were swiftly assembled
and cast with fine cloths. A clear, living light
1650 from the waxen torches awakened the walls.
Places were set and supper was served,
and a din arose as they reveled in a ring
around the fire on the floor, and the feasting party
made much pleasant music at the meal and after,
1655 singing seasonal songs and carol dancing
with as much amusement as a mouth could mention.
The young woman and Gawain sat together all the while.
And so loving was that lady towards the young lord,
with stolen glances and secret smiles
1660 that the man himself was maddened and amazed,
but his breeding forbade him rebuking a lady,
and though tongues might wag he returned her attention
        all night.
    Before his friends retire
1665   his lordship leads the knight,
    heads for his hearth and fire
    to linger by its light.

They supped and swapped stories, and spoke again
of the night to come next, which was New Year's Eve.
1670 Gawain pleaded politely to depart by morning,
so in two days' time he might honor his treaty.
But the lord was unswerving, insisting that he stayed:
"As an honest soul I swear on my heart,
you shall find the Green Chapel to finish your affairs
1675 long before dawn on New Year's Day.
So lie in your room and laze at your leisure
while I ride my estate, and, as our terms dictate,
we'll trade our trophies when the hunt returns.
I have tested you twice and found you truthful.

1680 But think tomorrow *third time throw best*.
Now, a lord can feel low whenever he likes,
so let's chase cheerfulness while we have the chance."
So those gentlemen agreed that Gawain would stay,
and they took more drink, then by torchlight retired to
1685   their beds.
         Our man then sleeps, a most
         reposed and peaceful rest.
         As hunters must, his host
         is up at dawn and dressed.

1690 After mass the master grabs a meal with his men
and asks for his mount on that marvelous morning.
All those grooms engaged to go with their lord
were high on their horses before the hall gates.
The fields were dazzling, fixed with frost,
1695 and the crown of sunrise rose scarlet and crimson,
scalding and scattering cloud from the sky.
At the fringe of the forest the dogs were set free
and the rumpus of the horns went ringing through the rocks.
They fall on the scent of a fox, and follow,
1700 turning and twisting as they sniff out the trail.
A young harrier yowls and a huntsman yells,
then the pack come panting to pick up the scent,
running as a rabble along the right track.
The fox scurries ahead, they scamper behind,
1705 and pursue him at speed when he comes within sight,
haranguing him with horrific ranting howls.
Now and then he doubles back through thorny thickets,
or halts and harkens in the hem of a hedge,
until finally, by a hollow, he hurdles a fence,
1710 and carefully he creeps by the edge of a copse,
convinced that his cunning has conned those canines!
But unawares he wanders where they lie in wait,
where greyhounds are gathered together, a group
         of three.
1715   He springs back with a start,
         then twists and turns and flees.
         With heavy, heaving heart
         he tracks towards the trees.

It was one of life's delights to listen to those hounds
1720 as they massed to meet him, marauding together.
They bayed bloodily at the sight of his being,
as if clustering cliffs had crashed to the ground.
Here he was ambushed by bushwhacking huntsmen
waiting with a welcome of wounding words;
1725 there he was threatened and branded a thief,
and the team on his tail gave him no time to tarry.
Often, in the open, the pack tried to pounce,
then that crafty Reynard would creep into cover.
So his lordship and his lords were merrily led

1730   in this manner through the mountains until midafternoon,
      while our handsome hero snoozed contentedly at home,
      kept from the cold of the morning by curtains.
      But love would not let her ladyship sleep
      and the fervor she felt in her heart would not fade.
1735   She rose from her rest and rushed to his room
      in a flowing robe that reached to the floor
      and was finished inside with fine-trimmed furs.
      Her head went unhooded, but heavenly gems
      were entwined in her tresses in clusters of twenty.
1740   She wore nothing on her face; her neck was naked,
      and her shoulders were bare to both back and breast.
      She comes into his quarters and closes the door,
      throws the window wide open and wakes Gawain,
      right away rouses him with ringing words for
1745   his ear.
          "Oh, sir, how can you sleep
          when morning comes so clear?"
          And though his dreams are deep
          he cannot help but hear.

1750   Yes he dozes in a daze, dreams and mutters
      like a mournful man with his mind on dark matters—
      how destiny might deal him a death blow on the day
      when he grapples with the guardian of the Green Chapel;
      of how the strike of the axe must be suffered without struggle.
1755   But sensing her presence there he surfaces from sleep,
      comes quickly from the depths of his dreams to address her.
      Laughing warmly she walks towards him
      and finds his face with the friendliest kiss.
      In a worthy style he welcomes the woman
1760   and seeing her so lovely and alluringly dressed,
      every feature so faultless, her complexion so fine,
      a passionate heat takes hold in his heart.
      They traded smiles and speech tripped from their tongues,
      and a bond of friendship was forged there, all blissful
1765   and bright.
          They talk with tenderness
          and pride, and yet their plight
          is perilous unless
          sweet Mary minds her knight.

1770   For that noble princess pushed him and pressed him,
      nudged him ever nearer to a limit where he needed
      to allow her love or impolitely reject it.
      He was careful to be courteous and avoid uncouthness,
      and more so for the sake of his soul should he sin
1775   and be counted a betrayer by the keeper of the castle.
      "I shall not succumb," he swore to himself.
      With affectionate laughter he fenced and deflected
      all the loving phrases which leapt from her lips.
      "You shall bear the blame," said the beautiful one,

1780 "if you feel no love for the lady you lie with,
and wound her, more than anyone on earth, to the heart.
Unless, of course, there is a lady in your life
to whom you are tied and so tightly attached
that the bond will not break, as I must now believe.
1785 So in honesty and trust now tell me the truth;
for all the love alive, do not lessen the truth
          with guile."
       "You judge wrong, by Saint John,"
       he said to her, and smiled.
1790   "There is no other one
       nor will be for this while!"

"Those words," said the woman, "are the worst of all.
But I asked, and you answered, and now I ache.
Kiss me as I wish and I shall walk away
1795 in mourning like a lady who loved too much."
Stooping and sighing she kisses him sweetly,
then withdraws from his side, saying as she stands,
"But before we part will you find me some small favor?
Give me some gift—a glove at least,
1800 that might leaven my loss when we meet in my memory."
"Well it were," said Gawain. "I wish I had here
my most precious possession as a present for your love,
for over and over you deserve and are owed
the highest prize I could hope to offer.
1805 But I would not wish on you a worthless token,
and it strikes me as unseemly that you should receive
nothing greater than a glove as a keepsake from Gawain.
I am here on an errand in an unknown land
without men bearing bags of beautiful things,
1810 which my regard for you, lady, makes me regret;
but man must live by his means, and neither mope
         nor moan."
       The pretty one replies:
       "Nay, knight, since you decline
1815   to pass to me a prize.
       you must have one of mine."

She offers him a ring of rich, red gold,
and the stunning stone set upon it stood proud,
beaming and burning with the brightness of the sun;
1820 what wealth it was worth you can well imagine.
But he would not accept it, and said straight away,
"By God, no tokens will I take at this time;
I have nothing to give, so nothing will I gain."
She insists he receive it but still he resists,
1825 and swears, on his name as a knight, not to swerve.
Snubbed by his decision, she said to him then,
"You refuse my ring because you find it too fine,
and don't care to be deeply indebted to me;
so I give you my girdle, a lesser thing to gain."

1830　From around her body she unbuckled the belt
　　　which fastened the frock beneath her fair mantle,
　　　a green silk girdle trimmed with gold,
　　　exquisitely edged and hemmed by hand.
　　　And she sweetly beseeched Sir Gawain to receive it,
1835　in spite of its slightness, and hoped he would accept.
　　　But still he maintained he intended to take
　　　neither gold nor girdle, until by God's grace
　　　the challenge he had chosen was finally achieved.
　　　"With apologies I pray you be not displeased,
1840　but end all your offers, for always against them
　　　　　　　I am.
　　　　　　For all your grace I owe
　　　　　　a thousand thank-you's, ma'am.
　　　　　　I shall through sun and snow
1845　　　　remain your loyal man."

　　　"And now he spurns my silk," the lady responded,
　　　"so simple in itself, or so it appears,
　　　so little and unlikely, worth nothing, or less.
　　　But the knight who knew of the power knitted in it
1850　would pay a high price to possess it, perhaps.
　　　For the body which is bound within this green belt,
　　　as long as it is buckled robustly about him,
　　　will be safe against anyone who seeks to strike him,
　　　and all the slyness on earth wouldn't see him slain."
1855　The man mulled it over, and it entered his mind
　　　it might just be the jewel for the jeopardy he faced
　　　and save him from the strike in his challenge at the chapel.
　　　With luck, it might let him escape with his life.
　　　So relenting at last he let her speak,
1860　and promptly she pressed him to take the present,
　　　and he granted her wish, and she gave with good grace,
　　　though went on to beg him not to whisper a word
　　　of this gift to her husband, and Gawain agreed;
　　　those words of theirs within those walls
1865　　　　　　should stay.
　　　　　　His thanks are heartfelt, then.
　　　　　　No sooner can he say
　　　　　　how much it matters, when
　　　　　　the third kiss comes his way.

1870　Then the lady departed, leaving him alone,
　　　for no more merriment could be had from that man.
　　　And once she has quit he clothes himself quickly,
　　　rises and dresses in the richest of robes,
　　　stowing the love-lace safely aside,
1875　hiding it away from all hands and eyes.
　　　Then he went at once to the chapel of worship,
　　　privately approached the priest and implored him
　　　to allow his confession, and to lead him in life

so his soul might be saved when he goes to his grave.
1880 Then fully and frankly he spoke of his sins,
no matter how small, always seeking mercy,
beseeching the counselor that he receive absolution.
The priest declares him so clean and so pure
that the Day of Doom could dawn in the morning.
1885 Then in merrier mood he mingled with the ladies,
caroling and carousing and carrying on
as never before, until nightfall. Folk feel
     and hear
     and see his boundless bliss
1890   and say, "Such charm and cheer;
     he's at his happiest
     since his arrival here."

And long let him loiter there, looked after by love.
Now the lord of the land was still leading his men,
1895 finishing off the fox he had followed for so long.
He vaults a fence to flush out the victim,
hearing that the hounds are harrying hard.
Then Reynard scoots from a section of scrub
and the rabble of the pack rush right at his heels.
1900 Aware of its presence the wary lord waits,
then bares his bright sword and swishes at the beast,
which shirks from its sharpness, and would have shot away
but a hound flew forward before it could flee
and under the hooves of the horses they have him,
1905 worrying the wily one with wrathful baying.
The lord hurtles from his horse and heaves the fox up,
wrestles it from the reach of those ravenous mouths,
holds it high over head and hurrahs manfully
while the bloodthirsty bloodhounds bay and howl.
1910 And the other huntsmen hurried with their horns
to catch sight of the slaughter and celebrate the kill.
And when the courtly company had come together
the buglers blew with one mighty blast,
and the others hallooed with open throats.
1915 It was the merriest music ever heard by men,
that rapturous roar which for Reynard's soul
     was raised.
     The dogs, due their reward,
     are patted, stroked and praised.
1920   Then red fur rips—Reynard
     out of his pelt is prised.

Then with night drawing near they headed homewards,
blaring their bugles with the fullness of their breath.
And at last the lord lands at his lovely home,
1925 to find, by the heat of the fireside, his friend
the good Sir Gawain, in glad spirits
on account of the company he had kept with the ladies.

His blue robe flowed as far as the floor,
his soft-furred surcoat suited him well,
1930 and the hood which echoed it hung from his shoulders.
Both hood and coat were edged in ermine.
He meets the master in the middle of the room,
greets him graciously, with Gawain saying:
"I shall first fulfill our formal agreement
1935 which we fixed in words when the drink flowed freely."
He clasps him tight and kisses him three times
with as much emotion as a man could muster.
"By the Almighty," said the master, "you must have had luck
to profit such a prize—if the price was right."
1940 "Oh fiddlesticks to the fee," said the other fellow.
"As long as I have given the goods which I gained."
"By Mary," said the master, "mine's a miserable match.
I've hunted for hours with nothing to my name
but this foul-stinking fox—fling its fur to the devil—
1945 so poor in comparison with such priceless things,
these presents you impart, three kisses perfect
                and true."
          "Enough!" the knight entreats,
          "I thank you through and through."
1950   The standing lord then speaks
          of how the fox fur flew!

And with meals and mirth and minstrelsy
they made as much amusement as any mortal could,
and among those merry men and laughing ladies
1955 Gawain and his host got giddy together;
only lunatics and drunkards could have looked more delirious.
Every person present performed party pieces
till the hour arrived when revelers must rest,
and the company in that court heard the call of their beds.
1960 And lastly, in the hall, humbly to his host,
our knight says good night and renews his gratitude.
"Your uncountable courtesies have kept me here
this Christmas—be honored by the High King's kindness.
If it suits, I submit myself as your servant.
1965 But tomorrow morning I must make a move;
if you will, as you promised, please appoint some person
to guide me, God willing, towards the Green Chapel,
where my destiny will dawn on New Year's Day."
"On my honor," he replied. "With hand on heart,
1970 every promise I made shall be put into practice."
He assigns him a servant to steer his course,
to lead him through the land without losing time,
to ride the fastest route between forest
                and fell.
1975   Gawain will warmly thank
          his host in terms that tell;
          towards the womenfolk
          the knight then waves farewell.

It's with a heavy heart that guests in the hall
1980 are kissed and thanked for their care and kindness,
and they respond with speeches of the same sort,
commending him to our Savior with sorrowful sighs.
Then politely he leaves the lord and his household,
and to each person he passes he imparts his thanks
1985 for taking such trouble in their service and assistance
and such attention to detail in attendance of duty.
And every guest is grieved at the prospect of his going,
as if honorable Gawain were one of their own.
By tapering torchlight he was taken to his room
1990 and brought to his bed to be at his rest.
But if our knight sleeps soundly I couldn't say,
for the matter in the morning might be muddying
        his thoughts.
    So let him lie and think,
1995   in sight of what he sought.
    In time I'll tell if tricks
    work out the way they ought.

FITT iv

Now night passes and New Year draws near,
drawing off darkness as our Deity decrees.
2000 But wild-looking weather was about in the world:
clouds decanted their cold rain earthwards;
the nithering north needled man's very nature;
creatures were scattered by the stinging sleet.
Then a whip-cracking wind comes whistling between hills
2005 driving snow into deepening drifts in the dales.
Alert and listening, Gawain lies in his bed;
his lids are lowered but he sleeps very little
as each crow of the cock brings his destiny closer.
Before day had dawned he was up and dressed
2010 for the room was livened by the light of a lamp.
To suit him in his metal and to saddle his mount
he called for a servant, who came quickly,
bounded from his bedsheets bringing his garments.
He swathes Sir Gawain in glorious style,
2015 first fastening clothes to fend off the frost,
then his armor, looked after all the while by the household:
the buffed and burnished stomach and breastplates,
and the rings of chain mail, raked free of rust,
all gleaming good as new, for which he is grateful
2020   indeed.
    With every polished piece
    no man shone more, it seemed
    from here to ancient Greece.
    He sent then for his steed.

2025 He clothes himself in the costliest costume:
his coat with the brightly emblazoned badge

mounted on velvet; magical minerals
inside and set about it; embroidered seams;
a lining finished with fabulous furs.
2030 And he did not leave off the lady's lace girdle;
for his own good, Gawain won't forget that gift.
Then with his sword sheathed at his shapely hips
he bound himself twice about with the belt,
touchingly wrapped it around his waist.
2035 That green silk girdle truly suited Sir Gawain
and went well with the rich red weaves that he wore.
But our man bore the belt not merely for its beauty,
or the appeal of its pennants, polished though they were,
or the gleam of its edges which glimmered with gold,
2040 but to save his skin when presenting himself,
without shield or sword, to the axe. To its swing
        and thwack!
      Now he is geared and gowned
      he steps outside and thinks
2045   those nobles of renown
      are due his thorough thanks.

Then his great horse Gringolet was got up ready.
The steed had been stabled in comfort and safety
and snorted and stamped in readiness for the ride.
2050 Gawain comes closer to examine his coat,
saying soberly to himself, swearing on his word:
"There are folk in this castle who keep courtesy to the forefront;
their master maintains them—happiness to them all.
And let his lordship's lady be loved all her life.
2055 That they chose, out of charity, to cherish a guest,
showing kindness and care, then may heaven's King
who reigns overall reward them handsomely.
For as long as I live in the lands of this world
I shall practice every means in my power to repay him."
2060 Then he steps in the stirrup and vaults to the saddle
and his servant lifts his shield which he slings on his shoulder,
then he girds on Gringolet with his golden spurs
who clatters from the courtyard, not stalling to snort
        or prance.
2065   His man was mounted, too,
      who lugged the spear and lance.
      "Christ keep this castle true,"
      he chanted. "Grant good chance."

The drawbridge was dropped, and the double-fronted gates
2070 were unbarred and each half was heaved wide open.
As he clears the planking he crosses himself quickly,
and praises the porter, who kneels before the prince
and prays that God be good to Gawain.
Then he went on his way with the one whose task
2075 was to point out the road to that perilous place
where the knight would receive the sorry stroke.

They scrambled up bankings where branches were bare,
clambered up cliff faces where the cold clings.
The clouds which had climbed now cooled and dropped
2080 so the moors and the mountains were muzzy with mist
and every hill wore a hat of mizzle on its head.
The streams on the slopes seemed to fume and foam,
whitening the wayside with spume and spray.
They wandered onwards through the wildest woods
2085 till the sun, at that season, came skyward, showing
its hand.
On hilly heights they ride,
snow littering the land.
The servant at his side
2090 then has them slow and stand.

"I have accompanied you across this countryside, my lord,
and now you are near the site you have named
and have steered and searched for with such singleness of mind.
But there's something I should like to share with you, sir,
2095 because upon my life, you're a lord that I love,
so if you value your health you'll hear my advice:
the place you proceed to is held to be perilous.
In that wilderness lives a wildman, the worst in the world,
he is brooding and brutal and loves bludgeoning people.
2100 He's more powerful than any person alive on this earth
and four times the figure of any fighting knight
in Arthur's house, or Hector or any other hero.
This grizzliness goes on at the green chapel,
and to pass through that place unscathed is impossible,
2105 for he deals out death blows by dint of his hands,
a man without measure who shows no mercy.
Be it chaplain or churl who rides by the chapel,
monk or priest, whatever man or person,
he loves murdering more than he loves his own life.
2110 So I say, just as sure as you sit in your saddle,
if you come there you'll be killed, of that there's no question.
Trust me, he could trample you twenty times over
or more.
He's lurked about too long
2115 engaged in grief and gore.
His hits are swift and strong—
he'll fell you to the floor."

"Therefore, good Sir Gawain, let the man go,
and for God's sake travel an alternate track,
2120 ride another road, and be rescued by Christ.
I'll head off home, and with hand on heart
I shall swear by God and all his good saints,
and on all earthly holiness, and other such oaths,
that your secret is safe, and not a soul will know
2125 that you fled in fear from the fellow I described."
"Many thanks," said Gawain, in a terse tone of voice,

"and for having my interests at heart, be lucky.
I'm certain such a secret would be silent in your keep.
But as faithful as you are, if I failed to find him
2130 and were to flee in fear in the fashion you urge,
I'd be christened a coward, and could not be excused.
So I'll trek to the chapel and take my chances,
say my piece to that person, speak with him plainly,
whether fairness or foulness follows, however fate
2135   behaves.
      He may be stout and stern
      and standing armed with stave,
      but those who strive to serve
      our Lord, our Lord will save."

2140 "By Mary," said the servant, "you seem to be saying
you're hell-bent on heaping harm on yourself
and losing your life, so I'll delay you no longer.
Set your helmet on your head and your lance in your hand
and ride a route through that rocky ravine
2145 till you're brought to the bottom of that foreboding valley,
then look towards a glade a little to the left
and you'll see in the clearing the site itself,
and the hulking person who inhabits the place.
Now God bless and good-bye, brave Sir Gawain;
2150 for all the wealth in the world I wouldn't walk with you
or go further in this forest by a single footstep."
With a wrench on the reins he reeled around
and heel-kicked the horse as hard as he could,
and was gone from Gawain, galloping hard
2155   for home.
      "By Christ, I will not cry,"
      announced the knight, "or groan,
      but find my fortune by
      the grace of God alone."

2160 Then he presses ahead, picks up a path,
enters a steep-sided grove on his steed
then goes by and by to the bottom of a gorge
where he wonders and watches—it looks a wild place:
no sign of a settlement anywhere to be seen
2165 but heady heights to both halves of the valley
and set with saber-toothed stones of such sharpness
no cloud in the sky could escape unscratched.
He stalls and halts, holds the horse still,
glances side to side to glimpse the green chapel
2170 but sees no such thing, which he thinks is strange,
except at mid-distance what might be a mound,
a sort of bald knoll on the bank of a brook
where fell water surged with frenzied force,
bursting with bubbles as if it had boiled.
2175 He heels the horse, heads for that mound,
grounds himself gracefully and tethers Gringolet,

looping the reins to the limb of a lime.
Then he strides forwards and circles the feature,
baffled as to what that bizarre hill could be:
2180   it had a hole at one end and at either side,
and its walls, matted with weeds and moss, ← decay
enclosed a cavity, like a kind of old cave
or crevice in the crag—it was all too unclear to
       declare.
2185   "Green Church?" chunters the knight.
       "More like the devil's lair
       where, at the nub of night,
       he makes his morning prayer."

"For certain," he says, "this is a soulless spot,
2190   a ghostly cathedral overgrown with grass,
the kind of kirk where that camouflaged man
might deal in devotions on the devil's behalf.
My five senses inform me that Satan himself
has tricked me in this tryst, intending to destroy me.
2195   This is a haunted house—may it go to hell.
I never came across a church so cursed."
With head helmeted and lance in hand
he scrambled towards skylight in that strange abyss.
Then he heard on the hillside, from behind a hard rock
2200   and beyond the brook, a blood-chilling noise.
What! It cannoned though the cliffs as if they might crack,
like the scream of a scythe being ground on a stone.
What! It whined and wailed, like a waterwheel.
What! It rasped and rang, raw on the ear.
2205   "My God," cried Gawain, "that grinding is a greeting.
My arrival is honored with the honing of an axe
       up there.
       Then let the Lord decide.
       'Oh well,' won't help me here.
2210   I might well lose my life
       but freak sounds hold no fear."

Then Gawain called as loudly as his lungs would allow,
"Who has power in this place to honor his pact?
Because good Gawain now walks on this ground.
2215   If anyone wants anything then hurry and appear
to do what he needs—it's now or it's never."
"Abide," came a voice from above the bank.
"You'll cop for what's coming to you quickly enough."
Yet he went at his work, whetting the blade,
2220   not showing until it was sharpened and stropped.
Then out of the crags he comes, through the cave mouth,
whirling into view with a wondrous weapon,
a Danish-style axe for dealing the dint,
with a brute of a blade curving back to the haft
2225   filed on a stone, a four footer at least
by the look of the length of its shining lace.

And again he was green, as a year ago,
with green flesh, hair and beard, and a fully green face,
and firmly on green feet he came stomping forwards,
2230 the handle of that axe like a staff in his hand.
At the edge of the water, he will not wade
but vaults the stream with the shaft, and strides
with an ominous face onto earth covered over
        with snow.
2235   Our brave knight bowed, his head
        hung low—but not too low!
        "Sweet Sir," the green man said,
        "Your visit keeps your vow."

The green knight spoke again, "God guard you, Gawain.
2240 Welcome to my world after all your wandering.
You have timed your arrival like a true traveler
to begin this business which binds us together.
Twelvemonths ago at this time you took what was yours,
and with New Year come you are called to account.
2245 We're very much alone, beyond view in this valley,
no person to part us—we can do as we please.
Pull your helmet from your head and take what you're owed.
Show no more struggle than I showed myself
when you severed my head with a single smite."
2250 "No," said good Gawain, "by my life-giving God,
I won't gripe or begrudge the grimness to come,
so keep to one stroke and I'll stand stock-still,
won't whisper a word of unwillingness, or one
        complaint."
2255   He bowed to take the blade
        and bared his neck and nape,
        but, loath to look afraid,
        he feigned a fearless state.

Suddenly the green knight summons up his strength,
2260 hoists the axe high over Gawain's head,
lifts it aloft with every fiber of his life
and begins to bring home a bone-splitting blow.
Had he seen it through as thoroughly as threatened
the knight, being brave, would have died from the blow.
2265 But glimpsing the axe at the edge of his eye
bringing death earthwards as it arced through the air,
and sensing its sharpness, Gawain shrank at the shoulders.
The swinging axman swerved from his stroke,
and reproached the young prince with some proud words:
2270 "Call yourself good Sir Gawain?" he goaded,
"who faced down every foe in the field of battle
but now flinches with fear at the foretaste of harm.
Never have I known such cowardice in a knight.
Did I budge or even blink when you aimed the axe,
2275 or carp or quibble in King Arthur's castle,
or flap when my head went flying to my feet?

But entirely untouched, you are terror struck.
I'll be found the better fellow, since you were so feeble
    and frail."
2280   Gawain confessed, "I flinched
    at first, but will not fail.
    Though once my head's unhitched
    it's off once and for all!"

"So be brisk with the blow, bring on the blade.
2285 Deal me my destiny and do it out of hand,
and I'll stand the stroke without shiver or shudder
and be wasted by your weapon. You have my word."
"Take this then," said the other, throwing up the axe,
with a menacing glare like the gaze of a maniac.
2290 Then he launches his swing but leaves him unscathed,
withholds his arm before harm could be done.
And Gawain was motionless, never moved a muscle,
but stood stone-still, or as still as a tree stump
anchored in the earth by a hundred roots.
2295 Then the warrior in green mocked Gawain again:
"Now you've plucked up your courage I'll dispatch you properly.
May the honorable knighthood heaped on you by Arthur—
if it proves to be powerful—protect your neck."
That insulting slur drew a spirited response:
2300 "Thrash away then, thug, your threats are hollow.
Such huffing and fussing—you'll frighten your own heart."
"By God," said the green man, "since you speak so grandly
there'll be no more shilly-shallying, I shall shatter you
    right now."
2305   He stands to strike, a sneer
    from bottom lip to brow.
    Who'd fault Gawain if fear
    took hold. All hope is down.

Hoisted and aimed, the axe hurtled downwards,
2310 the blade baring down on the knight's bare neck,
a ferocious blow, but far from being fatal
it skewed to one side, just skimming the skin
and finely snicking the fat of the flesh
so that bright red blood shot from body to earth
2315 Seeing it shining on the snowy ground
Gawain leapt forward a spear's length at least,
grabbed hold of his helmet and rammed it on his head,
brought his shield to his side with a shimmy of his shoulder,
then brandished his sword before blurting out brave words,
2320 because never since birth, as his mother's babe,
was he half as happy as here and now.
"Enough swiping, sir, you've swung your swing.
I've borne one blow without backing out,
go for me again and you'll get some by return,
2325 with interest! Hit out, and be hit in an instant,
    and hard.

One axe attack—that's all.
Now keep the covenant
agreed in Arthur's hall
2330 and hold the axe in hand."

The warrior steps away and leans on his weapon,
props the handle in the earth and slouches on the head
and studies how Gawain is standing his ground,
bold in his bearing, brave in his actions,
2335 armed and ready. In his heart he admires him.
Then remarking merrily, but in a mighty voice,
with reaching words he rounded on the knight:
"Be a mite less feisty, fearless young fellow,
you've suffered no insulting or heinous incident
2340 beyond the game we agreed on in the court of your king.
One strike was promised—consider yourself well paid!
From any lingering loyalties you are hereby released.
Had I mustered all my muscles into one mighty blow
I would have hit more harshly and done you great harm.
2345 But my first strike fooled you—a feint, no less—
not fracturing your flesh, which was only fair
in keeping with the contract we declared that first night,
for with truthful behavior you honored my trust
and gave up your gains as a good man should.
2350 Then I missed you once more, and this for the morning
when you kissed my pretty wife then kindly kissed me.
So twice you were truthful, therefore twice I left
                        no scar.
            The person who repays
2355   will live to feel no fear.
            The third time, though, you strayed,
            and felt my blade therefore."

"Because the belt you are bound with belongs to me;
it was woven by my wife so I know it very well.
2360 And I know of your courtesies, and conduct, and kisses,
and the wooing of my wife—for it was all my work!
I sent her to test you—and in truth it turns out
you're by the far the most faultless fellow on earth.
As a pearl is more prized than a pea which is white,
2365 in good faith, so is Gawain, amongst gallant knights.
But a little thing more—it was loyalty that you lacked:
not because you're wicked, or a womanizer, or worse,
but you loved your own life; so I blame you less."
Gawain stood speechless for what seemed a great while,
2370 so shocked and ashamed that he shuddered inside.
The fire of his blood brought flames to his face
and he shrank out of shame at what the other had said.
Then he tried to talk, and finding his tongue, said:
"A curse upon cowardice and covetousness.
2375 They breed villainy and vice, and destroy all virtue."
Then he grabbed the girdle and ungathered its knot

and flung it in fury at the man before him.
"My downfall and undoing; let the devil take it.
Dread of the death blow and cowardly doubts
2380 meant I gave in to greed, and in doing so forgot
the freedom and fidelity every knight knows to follow.
And now I am found to be flawed and false,
through treachery and untruth I have totally failed," said
        Gawain.
2385   "Such terrible mistakes,
       and I shall bear the blame.
       But tell me what it takes
       to clear my clouded name."

The green lord laughed, and leniently replied:
2390 "The harm which you caused me is wholly healed.
By confessing your failings you are free from fault
and have openly paid penance at the point of my axe.
I declare you purged, as polished and as pure
as the day you were born, without blemish or blame.
2395 And this gold-hemmed girdle I present as a gift,
which is green like my gown. It's yours, Sir Gawain,
a reminder of our meeting when you mix and mingle
with princes and kings. And this keepsake will be proof
to all chivalrous knights of your challenge in this chapel.
2400 But follow me home. New Year's far from finished—
we'll resume our reveling with supper and song.
       What's more
       my wife is waiting there
       who flummoxed you before.
2405   This time you'll have in her
       a friend and not a foe."

"Thank you," said the other, taking helmet from head,
holding it in hand as he offered his thanks.
"But I've loitered long enough. The Lord bless your life
2410 and bestow on you such honor as you surely deserve.
And mind you commend me to your fair wife,
both to her and the other, those honorable ladies
who kidded me so cleverly with their cunning tricks.
But no wonder if a fool finds his way into folly
2415 and be wiped of his wits by womanly guile—
it's the way of the world. Adam fell because of a woman,
and Solomon because of several, and as for Samson,
Delilah was his downfall, and afterwards David
was bamboozled by Bathsheba and bore the grief.
2420 All wrecked and ruined by their wrongs; if only
we could love our ladies without believing their lies.
And those were foremost of all whom fortune favored,
excellent beyond all others existing under heaven,"
       he cried.
2425   "Yet all were charmed and changed
       by wily womankind.

> I suffered just the same,
> but clear me of my crime."

"But the girdle," he went on, "God bless you for this gift.
2430 And I shall wear it with good will, but not for its gold,
nor its silks and streamers, and not for the sake
of its wonderful workmanship or even its worth,
but as a sign of my sin—I'll see it as such
when I swagger in the saddle—a sad reminder
2435 that the frailty of his flesh is man's biggest fault,
how the touch of filth taints his tender frame.
So when praise for my prowess in arms swells my pride,
one look at this love-lace will lessen my ardor.
But I will ask one thing, if it won't offend:
2440 since I stayed so long in your lordship's land
and was hosted in your house—let Him reward you
who upholds the heavens and sits upon high—
will you make known your name? And I'll ask nothing else."
"Then I'll treat you to the truth," the other told him,
2445 "Here in my homelands they call me Bertilak de Hautdesert.
And in my manor lives the mighty Morgan le Fay,
so adept and adroit in the dark arts,
who learned magic from Merlin—the master of mystery—
for in earlier times she was intimately entwined
2450 with that knowledgeable man, as all you knights know
> back home.
> Yes, 'Morgan the Goddess'—
> I will announce her name.
> There is no nobleness
2455 > she cannot take and tame."

"She guided me in this guise to your great hall
to put pride on trial, and to test with this trick
what distinction and trust the Round Table deserves.
She imagined this mischief would muddle your minds
2460 and that grieving Guinevere would go to her grave
at the sight of a specter making ghostly speeches
with his head in his hands before the high table.
So that ancient woman who inhabits my home
is also your aunt—Arthur's half sister,
2465 the daughter of the duchess of Tintagel; the duchess
who through Uther, was mother to Arthur, your king.
So I ask you again, come and greet your aunt
and make merry in my house; you're much loved there,
and, by my faith, I am as fond of you my friend
2470 as any man under God, for your great truth."
But Gawain would not. No way would he go.
So they clasped and kissed and made kind commendations
to the Prince of Paradise, and then parted in the cold,
> that pair.
2475 > Our man, back on his mount
> now hurtles home from there.

> The green knight leaves his ground
> to wander who-knows-where.

So he winds through the wilds of the world once more,
2480 Gawain on Gringolet, by the grace of God,
under a roof sometimes and sometimes roughing it,
and in valleys and vales had adventures and victories
but time is too tight to tell how they went.
The nick to his neck was healed by now;
2485 thereabouts he had bound the belt like a baldric—
slantwise, as a sash, from shoulder to side,
laced in a knot looped below his left arm,
as a sign that his honor was stained by sin.
So safe and sound he sets foot in court,
2490 and great joy came to the king in his castle
when tidings of Gawain's return had been told.
The king kissed his knight and so did the queen,
and Gawain was embraced by his band of brothers,
who made eager enquiries, and he answered them all
2495 with the tale of his trial and tribulations,
and the challenge at the chapel, and the great green chap,
and the love of the lady, which led to the belt.
And he showed them the scar at the side of his neck,
confirming his breach of faith, like a badge
2500   of blame.
> He grimaced with disgrace,
> he writhed in rage and pain.
> Blood flowed towards his face
> and showed his smarting shame.

2505 "Regard," said Gawain, as he held up the girdle,
"the symbol of sin, for which my neck bears the scar;
a sign of my fault and offence and failure,
of the cowardice and covetousness I came to commit.
I was tainted by untruth. This, its token,
2510 I will drape across my chest till the day I die.
For man's crimes can be covered but never made clean;
once sin is entwined it is attached for all time."
The king gave comfort, then the whole of the court
allow, as they laugh in lovely accord,
2515 that the lords and ladies who belong to the Table,
every knight in the brotherhood, should bear such a belt,
a bright green belt worn obliquely to the body,
crosswise, like a sash, for the sake of this man.
So that slanting green stripe was adopted as their sign,
2520 and each knight who held it was honored ever after,
as all the best books on romance remind us:
an adventure which happened in Arthur's era,
as the chronicles of this country have stated clearly.
Since fearless Brutus first set foot
2525 on these shores, once the siege land assault at Troy
           had ceased,

our coffers have been crammed
with stories such as these.
Now let our Lord, thorn-crowned,
2530   bring us to perfect peace. AMEN.

HONY SOYT QUI MAL PENCE[9]

9. "Shame be to the man who has evil in his mind." This is the motto of the Order of the Garter, founded ca. 1350; apparently a copyist of the poem associated this order with the one founded to honor Gawain.

GEOFFREY CHAUCER
ca. 1343–1400

Medieval social theory held that society was made up of three "estates": the nobility, composed of a small hereditary aristocracy, whose mission on earth was to rule over and defend the body politic; the church, whose duty was to look after the spiritual welfare of that body; and everyone else, the large mass of commoners who were supposed to do the work that provided for its physical needs. By the late fourteenth century, however, these basic categories were layered into complex, interrelated, and unstable social strata among which birth, wealth, profession, and personal ability all played a part in determining one's status in a world that was rapidly changing economically, politically, and socially. Chaucer's life and his works, especially *The Canterbury Tales*, were profoundly influenced by these forces. A growing and prosperous middle class was beginning to play increasingly important roles in church and state, blurring the traditional class boundaries, and it was into this middle class that Chaucer was born.

Chaucer was the son of a prosperous wine merchant and probably spent his boyhood in the mercantile atmosphere of London's Vintry, where ships docked with wines from France and Spain. Here he would have mixed daily with people of all sorts, heard several languages spoken, become fluent in French, and received schooling in Latin. Instead of apprenticing Chaucer to the family business, however, his father was apparently able to place him, in his early teens, as a page in one of the great aristocratic households of England, that of the countess of Ulster who was married to Prince Lionel, the second son of Edward III. There Chaucer would have acquired the manners and skills required for a career in the service of the ruling class, not only in the role of personal attendant in royal households but in a series of administrative posts. (For Chaucer's portrait, see the color insert in this volume.)

We can trace Chaucer's official and personal life in a considerable number of surviving historical documents, beginning with a reference, in Elizabeth of Ulster's household accounts, to an outfit he received as a page (1357). He was captured by the French and ransomed in one of Edward III's campaigns during the Hundred Years War (1359). He was a member of King Edward's personal household (1367) and took part in several diplomatic missions to Spain (1366), France (1368), and Italy (1372). As controller of customs on wool, sheepskins, and leather for the port of London (1374–85), Chaucer audited and kept books on the export taxes, which were one of the Crown's main sources of revenue. During this period he was living in a rent-free apartment over one of the gates in the city wall, probably as a perquisite of the customs job. He served as a justice of the peace and knight of the shire (the title given to members of Parliament) for the county of Kent (1385–86) where he moved after giving up the controllership. As clerk of the king's works (1389–91), Chaucer was responsible for the maintenance of numerous royal residences, parks, and other holdings; his duties included supervision of the construction of the nave of Westminster Abbey and of stands and lists for a celebrated tournament staged by Richard II. While the records show Chaucer receiving many grants and annuities in addition to his salary for these services, they also show that at times he was being pressed by creditors and obliged to borrow money.

These activities brought Chaucer into association with the ruling nobility of the kingdom, with Prince Lionel and his younger brother John of Gaunt, duke of Lancaster, England's most powerful baron during much of Chaucer's lifetime; with their father, King Edward; and with Edward's grandson, who succeeded

Middle-class Prosperity. Jan van Eyck, *The Arnolfini Portrait*, 1434. Note the way the religious elements of the scene are secondary to the fine, rich qualities of fabric represented here.

to the throne as Richard II. Near the end of his life Chaucer addressed a comic *Complaint to His Purse* to Henry IV—John of Gaunt's son, who had usurped the crown from his cousin Richard—as a reminder that the treasury owed Chaucer his annuity. Chaucer's wife, Philippa, served in the households of Edward's queen and of John of Gaunt's second wife, Constance, daughter of the king of Castile. A Thomas Chaucer, who was probably Chaucer's son, was an eminent man in the next generation, and Thomas's daughter Alice was married successively to the earl of Salisbury and the duke of Suffolk. The gap between the commoners and the aristocracy would thus have been bridged by Chaucer's family in the course of three generations.

None of these documents contains any hint that this hardworking civil servant wrote poetry, although poetry would certainly have been among the diversions cultivated at English courts in Chaucer's youth. That poetry, however, would have been in French, which still remained the fashionable language and literature of the English aristocracy, whose culture in many ways had more in common with that of the French nobles with whom they warred than with that of their English subjects. Chaucer's earliest models, works by Guillaume de Machaut (1300?–1377) and Jean Froissart (1333?–1400?), the leading French poets of the day, were lyrics and narratives about courtly love, often cast in the form of a dream in which the poet acted as a protagonist or participant in some aristocratic love affair. The poetry of Machaut and Froissart derives from the thirteenth-century *Romance of the Rose,* a long dream allegory in which the dreamer suffers many agonies and trials for the love of a symbolic rosebud. Chaucer's apprentice work may well have been a partial translation of the twenty-one-thousand-line *Romance.* His first important original poem is *The Book of the Duchess,* an elegy in the form of a dream vision commemorating John of Gaunt's first wife, the young duchess of Lancaster, who died in 1368.

The diplomatic mission that sent Chaucer to Italy in 1372 was in all likelihood a milestone in his literary development. Although he may have acquired some knowledge of the language and literature from Italian merchants and bankers posted in London, this visit and a subsequent one to Florence (1378) brought him into direct contact with the Italian Renaissance. Probably he acquired manuscripts of works by Dante, Petrarch, and Boccaccio—the last two still alive at the time of Chaucer's visit, although he probably did not meet them. These writers provided him with models of new verse forms, new subject matter, and new modes of representation. *The House of Fame,* still a dream vision, takes the poet on a journey in the talons of a gigantic eagle to the celestial palace of the goddess Fame, a trip that at many points affectionately parodies Dante's journey in the *Divine Comedy.* In his dream vision *The Parliament of Fowls,* all the birds meet on St. Valentine's Day to choose their mates; their "parliament" humorously depicts the ways in which different classes in human society think and talk about love. Boccaccio provided sources for two of Chaucer's finest poems—although Chaucer never mentions his name. *The Knight's Tale,* the first of *The Canterbury Tales,* is based on Boccaccio's romance *Il Teseida* (The Story of Theseus). His longest completed poem, *Troilus and Criseyde* (ca. 1385), which tells the story of how Trojan Prince Troilus loved and finally lost Criseyde to the Greek warrior Diomede, is an adaptation of Boccaccio's *Il Filostrato* (The Love-Stricken). Chaucer reworked the latter into one of the greatest love poems in any language. Even if he had never written *The Canterbury Tales, Troilus* would have secured Chaucer a place among the major English poets.

A final dream vision provides the frame for Chaucer's first experiment with a series of tales, the unfinished *Legend of Good Women.* In the dream, Chaucer is accused of heresy and antifeminism by Cupid, the god of love himself, and ordered to do penance by writing a series of "legends," i.e., saints' lives, of Cupid's martyrs, women who were betrayed by false men and died for love. Perhaps a noble patron, possibly Queen Anne, asked the poet to write something to make up for telling about Criseyde's betrayal of Troilus.

Throughout his life Chaucer also wrote moral and religious works, chiefly translations. Besides French, which was a second language for him, and Italian, Chaucer also read Latin. He made a prose translation of the Latin *Consolation of Philosophy,* written by the sixth-century Roman statesman Boethius while in prison awaiting execution for crimes for which he had been unjustly condemned. The *Consolation* became a favorite book for the Middle Ages, providing inspiration and comfort through its lesson that worldly fortune is deceitful and ephemeral and through the platonic doctrine that the body itself is only a prison house for the soul that aspires to eternal things. The influence of Boethius is deeply ingrained in *The Knight's Tale* and *Troilus.* The ballade *Truth* compresses the Boethian and Christian teaching into three stanzas of homely moral advice.

Thus long before Chaucer conceived of *The Canterbury Tales,* his writings were many faceted: they embrace prose and poetry; human and divine love; French, Italian, and Latin sources; secular and religious influences; comedy and philosophy. Moreover, different elements are likely to mix in the same work, often making it difficult to extract from Chaucer simple, direct, and certain meanings.

This Chaucerian complexity owes much to the wide range of Chaucer's learning and his exposure to new literary currents on the Continent but perhaps also to the special social position he occupied as a member of a new class of civil servants. Born into the urban middle class, Chaucer, through his association with the court and service of the Crown, had attained the rank of "esquire," roughly equivalent to what would later be termed a "gentleman." His career brought him into contact with overlapping bourgeois and aristocratic social worlds, without his being securely anchored in either. Although he was born a commoner and continued to associate with commoners in his official life, he did not live as a commoner; and although his training and service at court, his wife's connections, and probably his poetry brought him into contact with the nobility, he must always have been conscious of the fact that he did not really belong to that society of which birth alone could make one a true member. Situated at the intersection of these social worlds, Chaucer had the gift of being able to view with both sympathy and humor the behaviors, beliefs, and pretensions of the diverse people who comprised the levels of society. Chaucer's art of being at once involved in and detached from a given situation is peculiarly his own, but that art would have been appreciated by a small group of friends close to Chaucer's social position—men like Sir Philip de la Vache, to whom Chaucer addressed the humorous envoy to *Truth*. Chaucer belongs to an age when poetry was read aloud. A beautiful frontispiece to a manuscript of *Troilus* pictures the poet's public performance before a magnificently dressed royal audience, and he may well have been invited at times to read his poems at court. But besides addressing a listening audience, to whose alleg- edly superior taste and sensibility the poet often ironically defers (for example, *The General Prologue*, lines 745–48), Chaucer has in mind discriminating readers whom he might expect to share his sense of humor and his complex attitudes toward the company of "sondry folk" who make the pilgrimage to Canterbury.

The text given here is from E. T. Donaldson's *Chaucer's Poetry: An Anthology for the Modern Reader* (1958, 1975) with some modifications. For *The Canterbury Tales* the Hengwrt Manuscript has provided the textual basis. The spelling has been altered to improve consistency and has been modernized in so far as is possible without distorting the phonological values of the Middle English. A discussion of Middle English pronunciation, grammar, and prosody is included in the introduc- tion to "The Middle Ages" (pp. 19–25).

The Canterbury Tales

Chaucer's original plan for *The Canterbury Tales*— if we assume it to be the same as that which the fictional Host proposes at the end of *The General Prologue*—projected about one hundred twenty stories, two for each pilgrim to tell on the way to Canterbury and two more on the way back. Chaucer actually completed only twenty-two and the beginnings of two others. He did write an ending, for the Host says to the Parson, who tells the last tale, that everyone except him has told "his tale." Indeed, the pilgrims never even get to Canterbury. The work was probably first conceived in 1386, when Chaucer was living in Green- wich, some miles east of London. From his house he might have been able to see the pilgrim road that led toward the shrine of the famous English saint, Thomas Becket, the archbishop of Canterbury who was murdered in his cathedral in 1170. Medieval pilgrims were notorious tale tellers, and the sight and sound of the bands riding toward Canterbury may well have suggested to Chaucer the idea of using a fictitious pilgrimage as a framing device for a number of stories. Collections of sto- ries linked by such a device were common in the later Middle Ages. Chaucer's con- temporary John Gower had used one in his *Confessio Amantis* (see p. 346). The most famous medieval framing tale besides Chaucer's is Boccaccio's *Decameron*, in which ten different narrators each tell a tale a day for ten days. Chaucer could have known the *Decameron*, which contains tales with plots analogous to plots found also in *The Canterbury Tales*, but these stories were widespread, and there is no proof that Chaucer got them from Boccaccio.

Chaucer's artistic exploitation of the device is, in any case, altogether his own. Whereas in Gower a single speaker relates all the stories, and in Boccaccio the ten speakers—three young gentlemen and seven young ladies—all belong to the same sophisticated social elite, Chaucer's pilgrim narrators represent a wide spectrum of ranks and occupations. This device, however, should not be mistaken for "realism." It is highly unlikely that a group like Chaucer's pilgrims would ever have joined together and communicated on such seemingly equal terms. That is part of the fiction, as is the tacit assumption that a group so large could have ridden along listening to one another tell tales in verse. The variety of tellers is matched by the diversity of their tales: tales are assigned to appropriate narrators and juxtaposed to bring out contrasts in genre, style, tone, and values. Thus the Knight's courtly romance about the rivalry of two noble lovers for a lady is followed by the Miller's fabliau of the seduction of an old carpenter's young wife by a student. In several of *The Canterbury Tales* there is a fascinating accord between the narrators and their stories, so that the story takes on rich overtones from what we have learned of its teller in *The General Prologue* and elsewhere, and the character itself grows and is revealed by the story. Chaucer conducts two fictions simultaneously—that of the individual tale and that of the pilgrim to whom he has assigned it. He develops the second fiction not only through *The General Prologue* but also through the "links," the interchanges among pilgrims connecting the stories. These interchanges some-times lead to quarrels. Thus *The Miller's Tale* offends the Reeve, who takes the fig-ure of the Miller's foolish, cuckolded carpenter as directed personally at himself, and he retaliates with a story satirizing an arrogant miller very much like the pilgrim Miller. The antagonism of the two tellers provides comedy in the links and enhances the comedy of their tales. The links also offer interesting literary commentary on the tales by members of the pilgrim audience, especially the Host, whom the pilgrims have declared "governour" and "juge" of the storytelling. Further dramatic interest is created by the fact that several tales respond to topics taken up by previous tellers. The Wife of Bath's thesis that women should have sovereignty over men in marriage gets a reply from the Clerk, which in turn elicits responses from the Merchant and the Franklin. The tales have their own logic and interest quite apart from the fram-ing fiction; no other medieval framing fiction, however, has such varied and lively interaction between the frame and the individual stories.

The composition of none of the tales can be accurately dated; most of them were written during the last fourteen years of Chaucer's life, although a few were prob-ably written earlier and inserted into *The Canterbury Tales*. The popularity of the poem in late medieval England is attested by the number of surviving manuscripts: more than eighty, none from Chaucer's lifetime. It was also twice printed by Wil-liam Caxton, who introduced printing to England in 1476, and often reprinted by Caxton's early successors. The manuscripts reflect the unfinished state of the poem—the fact that when he died Chaucer had not made up his mind about a num-ber of details and hence left many inconsistencies. The poem appears in the manu-scripts as nine or ten "fragments" or blocks of tales; the order of the poems within each fragment is generally the same, but the order of the fragments themselves varies widely. The fragment containing *The General Prologue;* the Knight's, Mill-er's, and Reeve's tales; and the Cook's unfinished tale, always comes first, and the fragment consisting of *The Parson's Tale* and *The Retraction* always comes last. But the others, such as that containing the Wife of Bath, the Friar, and the Summoner or that consisting of the Physician and Pardoner or the longest fragment, consisting of six tales concluding with the Nun's Priest's, are by no means stable in relation to one another. The order followed here, that of the Ellesmere manuscript, has been adopted as the most nearly satisfactory.

THE GENERAL PROLOGUE

Chaucer did not need to make a pilgrimage himself to meet the types of people that his fictitious pilgrimage includes, because most of them had long inhabited literature as well as life: the ideal Knight, who had taken part in all the major expeditions and battles of the crusades during the last half-century; his fashionably dressed son, the Squire, a typical young lover; the lady Prioress, the hunting Monk, and the flattering Friar, who practice the little vanities and larger vices for which such ecclesiastics were conventionally attacked; the prosperous Franklin; the fraudulent Doctor; the lusty and domineering Wife of Bath; the austere Parson; and so on down through the lower orders to that spellbinding preacher and mercenary, the Pardoner, peddling his paper indulgences and phony relics. One meets all these types throughout medieval literature, but particularly in a genre called estates satire, which sets out to expose and pillory typical examples of corruption at all levels of society. (For more information on estates satire, see the "Medieval Estates and Orders" topic in the supplemental ebook.) A remarkable number of details in *The General Prologue* could have been taken straight out of books as well as drawn from life. Although it has been argued that some of the pilgrims are portraits of actual people, the impression that they are drawn from life is more likely to be a function of Chaucer's art, which is able to endow types with a reality we generally associate only with people we know. The salient features of each pilgrim leap out randomly at the reader, as they might to an observer concerned only with what meets the eye. This imitation of the way our minds actually perceive reality may make us fail to notice the care with which Chaucer has selected his details to give an integrated sketch of the person being described. Most of these details give something more than mere verisimilitude to the description. The pilgrims' facial features, the clothes they wear, the foods they like to eat, the things they say, the work they do are all clues not only to their social rank but to their moral and spiritual condition and, through the accumulation of detail, to the condition of late-medieval society, of which, collectively, they are representative. What uniquely distinguishes Chaucer's prologue from more conventional estates satire, such as the *Prologue* to *Piers Plowman*, is the suppression in all but a few flagrant instances of overt moral judgment. The narrator, in fact, seems to be expressing chiefly admiration and praise at the superlative skills and accomplishments of this particular group, even such dubious ones as the Friar's begging techniques or the Manciple's success in cheating the learned lawyers who employ him. The reader is left free to draw out the ironic implications of details presented with such seeming artlessness, even while falling in with the easygoing mood of "felaweship" that pervades Chaucer's prologue to the pilgrimage.

FROM THE CANTERBURY TALES

The General Prologue

Whan that April with his° showres soote°	*its / fresh*
The droughte of March hath perced to the roote,	
And bathed every veine[1] in swich° licour,°	*such / liquid*
Of which vertu[2] engendred is the flowr;	
5 Whan Zephyrus eek° with his sweete breeth	*also*
Inspired[3] hath in every holt° and heeth°	*grove / field*
The tendre croppes,° and the yonge sonne[4]	*shoots*
Hath in the Ram his halve cours yronne,	
And smale fowles° maken melodye	*birds*
10 That sleepen al the night with open yë°—	*eye*
So priketh hem° Nature in hir corages[5]—	*them*
Thanne longen folk to goon° on pilgrimages,	*go*
And palmeres for to seeken straunge strondes	
To ferne halwes,[6] couthe° in sondry° londes;	*known / various*

1. I.e., in plants.
2. By the power of which.
3. Breathed into. "Zephyrus": the west wind.
4. The sun is young because it has run only halfway through its course in Aries, the Ram—the first sign of the zodiac in the solar year.

5. Their hearts.
6. Far-off shrines. "Palmeres": palmers, wide-ranging pilgrims—especially those who sought out the "straunge strondes" (foreign shores) of the Holy Land.

15 And specially from every shires ende
  Of Engelond to Canterbury they wende,
  The holy blisful martyr[7] for to seeke
  That hem hath holpen° whan that they were seke.°   *helped / sick*
   Bifel° that in that seson on a day,   *It happened*
20 In Southwerk[8] at the Tabard as I lay,
  Redy to wenden on my pilgrimage
  To Canterbury with ful° devout corage,   *very*
  At night was come into that hostelrye
  Wel nine and twenty in a compaignye
25 Of sondry folk, by aventure° yfalle   *chance*
  In felaweshipe, and pilgrimes were they alle
  That toward Canterbury wolden° ride.   *would*
  The chambres and the stables weren wide,
  And wel we weren esed° at the beste.[9]   *accommodated*
30 And shortly,° whan the sonne was to reste,[1]   *in brief*
  So hadde I spoken with hem everichoon°   *every one*
  That I was of hir felaweshipe anoon,°   *at once*
  And made forward[2] erly for to rise,
  To take oure way ther as[3] I you devise.°   *describe*
35 But nathelees,° whil I have time and space,[4] *nevertheless*
  Er° that I ferther in this tale pace,°   *before / proceed*
  Me thinketh it accordant to resoun[5]
  To telle you al the condicioun
  Of eech of hem, so as it seemed me,
40 And whiche they were, and of what degree,°   *social rank*
  And eek° in what array that they were inne: *also*
  And at a knight thanne° wol I first biginne.   *then*
   A Knight ther was, and that a worthy man,
  That fro the time that he first bigan
45 To riden out, he loved chivalrye,
  Trouthe and honour, freedom and curteisye.[6]
  Ful worthy was he in his lordes werre,°   *war*
  And therto hadde he riden, no man ferre,°   *farther*
  As wel in Cristendom as hethenesse,[7]
50 And[8] evere honoured for his worthinesse.
   At Alisandre[9] he was whan it was wonne;

---

7. St. Thomas à Becket, murdered in Canterbury Cathedral in 1170.
8. Southwark, site of the Tabard Inn, was then a suburb of London, south of the Thames River.
9. In the best possible way.
1. Had set.
2. I.e., (we) made an agreement.
3. Where.
4. I.e., opportunity.
5. It seems to me according to reason.
6. Courtesy. "Trouthe": integrity. "Freedom": generosity of spirit.
7. Heathen lands. "Cristendom" here designates specifically only crusades waged by the nations of Roman Catholic Western Europe in lands under other dispensations, primarily Arabic, Turkish, and Moorish Islam but also, as indicated in the list of the Knight's campaigns given below, the Christian Eastern Orthodox Church. Conspicu-

ous by absence is any reference to major battles in the Hundred Years War, fought between French and English Catholics. For excerpts from Christian, Jewish, and Arabic texts on the First Crusade, see the supplemental ebook.
8. I.e., and he was.
9. The capture of Alexandria in Egypt (1365) was considered a famous victory, although the Crusaders abandoned the city after a week of looting. Below: "Pruce" (Prussia), "Lettow" (Lithuania), and "Ruce" (Russia) refer to campaigns by the Teutonic Order of Knights on the shores of the Baltic Sea in northern Europe against the Eastern Orthodox Church, "Gernada" (Granada), "Algezir" (Algeciras), and "Belmarye" (Belmarin), to northern Spain and Morocco; "Lyeis" (Ayash, seaport near Antioch, modern Syria), "Satalye," "Palatye" (Antalya and Balat, modern Turkey), "Tramyssene" (Tlemcen, modern Algeria).

Ful ofte time he hadde the boord bigonne[1]
Aboven alle nacions in Pruce;
In Lettou had he reised,° and in Ruce,   *campaigned*
55 No Cristen man so ofte of his degree;
In Gernade° at the sege eek hadde he be   *Granada*
Of Algezir, and riden in Belmarye;
At Lyeis was he, and at Satalye,
Whan they were wonne; and in the Grete See°   *Mediterranean*
60 At many a noble arivee° hadde he be.   *military landing*
    At mortal batailes[2] hadde he been fifteene,
And foughten for oure faith at Tramissene
In listes[3] thries,° and ay° slain his fo.   *thrice / always*
    This ilke° worthy Knight hadde been also   *same*
65 Sometime with the lord of Palatye[4]
Again° another hethen in Turkye;   *against*
And everemore he hadde a soverein pris.°   *reputation*
And though that he were worthy, he was wis,[5]
And of his port° as meeke as is a maide.   *demeanor*
70 He nevere yit no vilainye° ne saide   *rudeness*
In al his lif unto no manere wight:[6]
He was a verray,° parfit,° gentil° knight.   *true / perfect / noble*
But for to tellen you of his array,
His hors° were goode, but he was nat gay.[7]   *horses*
75 Of fustian° he wered° a gipoun[8]   *thick cloth / wore*
Al bismotered with his haubergeoun,[9]
For he was late° come from his viage,°   *lately / expedition*
And wente for to doon his pilgrimage.
    With him ther was his sone, a yong Squier,[1]
80 A lovere and a lusty bacheler,
With lokkes crulle° as° they were laid in presse.   *curly / as if*
Of twenty yeer of age he was, I gesse.
Of his stature he was of evene° lengthe,   *moderate*
And wonderly delivere,° and of greet° strengthe.   *agile / great*
85 And he hadde been som time in chivachye[2]
In Flandres, in Artois, and Picardye,
And born him wel as of so litel space,[3]
In hope to stonden in his lady° grace.   *lady's*
    Embrouded° was he as it were a mede,[4]   *embroidered*
90 Al ful of fresshe flowres, white and rede;°   *red*
Singing he was, or floiting,° al the day: *whistling*
He was as fressh as is the month of May.
Short was his gowne, with sleeves longe and wide.
Wel coude he sitte on hors, and faire ride;

---

1. Sat in the seat of honor at military feasts.
2. Tournaments fought to the death.
3. Lists, tournament grounds.
4. A Moslem: alliances of convenience were often made during the Crusades between Christians and Moslems.
5. I.e., he was wise as well as bold.
6. Any sort of person. In Middle English, negatives are multiplied for emphasis, as in these two lines: "nevere," "no," "ne," "no."
7. I.e., gaily dressed.

8. Tunic worn underneath the coat of mail.
9. All rust-stained from his hauberk (coat of mail).
1. The vague term "Squier" (Squire) here seems to be the equivalent of "bacheler" (line 80), a young knight still in the service of an older one.
2. On cavalry expeditions. The places in the next line are sites of skirmishes in the constant warfare between the English and the French.
3. I.e., considering the little time he had been in service.
4. Mead, meadow.

95   He coude songes make, and wel endite,°   *compose verse*
     Juste[5] and eek° daunce, and wel portraye° and write.   *also / sketch*
     So hote° he loved that by nightertale[6]   *hotly*
     He slepte namore than dooth a nightingale.
     Curteis he was, lowely,° and servisable,   *humble*
100 And carf biforn his fader at the table.[7]
       A Yeman hadde he[8] and servants namo°   *no more*
     At that time, for him liste[9] ride so;
     And he[1] was clad in cote and hood of greene.
     A sheef of pecok arwes,° bright and keene,   *arrows*
105 Under his belt he bar° ful thriftily;°   *bore / properly*
     Wel coude he dresse° his takel° yemanly:[2]   *tend to / gear*
     His arwes drouped nought with fetheres lowe.
     And in his hand he bar a mighty bowe.
     A not-heed° hadde he with a brown visage.   *close-cut head*
110 Of wodecraft wel coude° he al the usage.   *knew*
     Upon his arm he bar a gay bracer,[3]
     And by his side a swerd° and a bokeler,[4]   *sword*
     And on that other side a gay daggere,
     Harneised° wel and sharp as point of spere;   *mounted*
115 A Cristophre[5] on his brest of silver sheene;°   *bright*
     An horn he bar, the baudrik[6] was of greene.
     A forster° was he soothly,° as I gesse.   *forester / truly*
       Ther was also a Nonne, a Prioresse,
     That of hir smiling was ful simple and coy.[7]
120 Hir gretteste ooth was but by sainte Loy!°   *Eloi*
     And she was cleped° Madame Eglantine.   *named*
     Ful wel she soong° the service divine,   *sang*
     Entuned° in hir nose ful semely;[8]   *chanted*
     And Frenssh she spak ful faire and fetisly,°   *elegantly*
125 After the scole° of Stratford at the Bowe[9]—   *school*
     For Frenssh of Paris was to hire unknowe.
     At mete° wel ytaught was she withalle:°   *meals / besides*
     She leet° no morsel from hir lippes falle,   *let*
     Ne wette hir fingres in hir sauce deepe;
130 Wel coude she carye a morsel, and wel keepe°   *take care*
     That no drope ne fille° upon hir brest.   *should fall*
     In curteisye was set ful muchel hir lest.[1]
     Hir over-lippe° wiped she so clene   *upper lip*
     That in hir coppe° ther was no ferthing° seene   *cup / bit*
135 Of grece,° whan she dronken hadde hir draughte;   *grease*
     Ful semely after hir mete she raughte.°   *reached*
     And sikerly° she was of greet disport,[2]   *certainly*

5. Joust, fight in a tournament.
6. At night.
7. It was a squire's duty to carve his lord's meat.
8. I.e., the Knight. The "Yeman" (Yeoman) is an independent commoner who acts as the Knight's military servant.
9. It pleased him to.
1. I.e., the Yeoman.
2. In a workmanlike way.
3. Wrist guard for archers.
4. Buckler (a small shield).

5. St. Christopher medal.
6. Baldric (a supporting strap).
7. Sincere and shy. The Prioress is the mother superior of her nunnery.
8. In a seemly, proper manner.
9. The French learned in a convent school in Stratford-at-the-Bow, a suburb of London, was evidently not up to the Parisian standard.
1. I.e., her chief delight lay in good manners.
2. Of great good cheer.

	And ful plesant, and amiable of port,°	*mien*
	And pained hire to countrefete cheere[3]	
140	Of court, and to been statlich° of manere,	*dignified*
	And to been holden digne[4] of reverence.	
	But, for to speken of hir conscience,	
	She was so charitable and so pitous°	*merciful*
	She wolde weepe if that she saw a mous	
145	Caught in a trappe, if it were deed° or bledde.	*dead*
	Of[5] smale houndes hadde she that she fedde	
	With rosted flessh, or milk and wastelbreed;°	*fine white bread*
	But sore wepte she if oon of hem were deed,	
	Or if men smoot it with a yerde smerte;[6]	
150	And al was conscience and tendre herte.	
	Ful semely hir wimpel° pinched° was,	*headdress / pleated*
	Hir nose tretis,° hir yën° greye as glas,	*well-formed / eyes*
	Hir mouth ful smal, and therto° softe and reed,°	*moreover / red*
	But sikerly° she hadde a fair forheed:	*certainly*
155	It was almost a spanne brood,[7] I trowe,°	*believe*
	For hardily,° she was nat undergrowe.	*assuredly*
	Ful fetis° was hir cloke, as I was war;°	*becoming / aware*
	Of smal° coral aboute hir arm she bar	*dainty*
	A paire of bedes, gauded all with greene,[8]	
160	And theron heeng° a brooch of gold ful sneene,°	*hung / bright*
	On which ther was first writen a crowned A,[9]	
	And after, *Amor vincit omnia*.[1]	
	Another Nonne with hire hadde she	
	That was hir chapelaine,° and preestes three.[2]	*secretary*
165	A Monk ther was, a fair for the maistrye,[3]	
	An outridere[4] that loved venerye,°	*hunting*
	A manly man, to been an abbot able.°	*worthy*
	Ful many a daintee° hors hadde he in stable,	*fine*
	And whan he rood,° men mighte his bridel heere	*rode*
170	Ginglen° in a whistling wind as clere	*jingle*
	And eek° as loude as dooth the chapel belle	*also*
	Ther as this lord was kepere of the celle.[5]	
	The rule of Saint Maure or of Saint Beneit,	
	By cause that it was old and somdeel strait[6]—	
175	This ilke° Monk leet olde thinges pace,°	*same / pass away*
	And heeld° after the newe world the space.°	*held / course*
	He yaf° nought of that text a pulled hen[7]	*gave*
	That saith that hunteres been° nought holy men,	*are*
	Ne that a monk, whan he is recchelees,[8]	
180	Is likned til° a fissh that is waterlees—	*to*
	This is to sayn, a monk out of his cloistre;	

---

3. And took pains to imitate the behavior.
4. And to be considered worthy.
5. I.e., some.
6. If someone struck it with a rod sharply.
7. A handsbreadth wide.
8. Provided with green beads to mark certain prayers. "A paire": string (i.e., a rosary).
9. An *A* with an ornamental crown on it.
1. "Love conquers all."
2. The three get reduced to just one nun's priest.

3. I.e., a superlatively fine one.
4. A monk charged with supervising property distant from the monastery. Monasteries obtained income from large landholdings.
5. Prior of an outlying cell (branch) of the monastery.
6. Somewhat strict. St. Maurus and St. Benedict were authors of monastic rules.
7. He didn't give a plucked hen for that text.
8. Reckless, careless of rule.

But thilke° text heeld he nat worth an oystre.   *that same*
And I saide his opinion was good:
What° sholde he studye and make himselven wood°   *why / crazy*
185 Upon a book in cloistre alway to poure,°   *pore*
Or swinke° with his handes and laboure,   *work*
As Austin bit?[9] How shal the world be served?
Lat Austin have his swink to him reserved!
Therefore he was a prikasour° aright.   *hard rider*
190 Grehoundes he hadde as swift as fowl in flight.
Of priking° and of hunting for the hare   *riding*
Was al his lust,° for no cost wolde he spare.   *pleasure*
I sawgh his sleeves purfiled° at the hand   *fur lined*
With gris,° and that the fineste of a land;   *gray fur*
195 And for to festne his hood under his chin
He hadde of gold wrought a ful curious[1] pin:
A love-knotte in the grettere° ende ther was.   *greater*
His heed was balled,° that shoon as any glas,   *bald*
And eek his face, as he hadde been anoint:
200 He was a lord ful fat and in good point;[2]
His yën steepe,° and rolling in his heed,   *protruding*
That stemed as a furnais of a leed,[3]
His bootes souple,° his hors in greet estat°   *supple / condition*
Now certainly he was a fair prelat.[4]
205 He was nat pale as a forpined° gost: *wasted away*
A fat swan loved he best of any rost.
His palfrey° was as brown as is a berye.   *saddle horse*
      A Frere ther was, a wantoune° and a merye,   *jovial*
A limitour,[5] a ful solempne° man.   *ceremonious*
210 In alle the ordres foure is noon that can°   *knows*
So muche of daliaunce° and fair langage: *sociability*
He hadde maad ful many a mariage
Of yonge wommen at his owene cost;
Unto his ordre he was a noble post.[6]
215 Ful wel biloved and familier was he
With frankelains over al[7] in his contree,
And with worthy wommen of the town—
For he hadde power of confessioun,
As saide himself, more than a curat,°   *parish priest*
220 For of° his ordre he was licenciat.[8]   *by*
Ful swetely herde he confessioun,
And plesant was his absolucioun.
He was an esy man to yive penaunce
Ther as he wiste to have[9] a good pitaunce;°   *donation*
225 For unto a poore ordre for to yive

---

9. I.e., as St. Augustine bids. St. Augustine had
written that monks should perform manual labor.
1. Of careful workmanship.
2. In good shape, plump.
3. That glowed like a furnace with a pot in it.
4. Prelate (an important churchman).
5. The "Frere" (Friar) is a member of one of the
four religious orders whose members live by begging; as a "limitour" he has been granted by his
order exclusive begging rights within a certain
limited area.
6. I.e., pillar, a staunch supporter.
7. I.e., with franklins everywhere. Franklins
were well-to-do country men.
8. I.e., licensed to hear confessions.
9. Where he knew he would have.

Is signe that a man is wel yshrive,[1]
For if he yaf, he dorste make avaunt°   *boast*
He wiste° that a man was repentaunt;   *knew*
For many a man so hard is of his herte
230   He may nat weepe though him sore smerte:[2]
Therfore, in stede of weeping and prayeres,
Men mote° yive silver to the poore freres.[3]   *may*
      His tipet° was ay farsed° ful of knives   *hood / stuffed*
And pinnes, for to yiven faire wives;
235   And certainly he hadde a merye note;
Wel coude he singe and playen on a rote;°   *fiddle*
Of yeddinges he bar outrely the pris.[4]
His nekke whit was as the flowr-de-lis;°   *lily*
Therto he strong was as a champioun.
240   He knew the tavernes wel in every town,
And every hostiler° and tappestere,°   *innkeeper / barmaid*
Bet° than a lazar or a beggestere.[5]   *better*
For unto swich a worthy man as he
Accorded nat, as by his facultee,[6]
245   To have with sike° lazars aquaintaunce: *sick*
It is nat honeste,° it may nought avaunce,°   *dignified / profit*
For to delen with no swich poraile,[7]
But al with riche, and selleres of vitaile;°   *foodstuffs*
And over al ther as[8] profit sholde arise,
250   Curteis he was, and lowely of servise.
Ther was no man nowher so vertuous:°   *effective*
He was the beste beggere in his hous.°   *friary*
And yaf a certain ferme for the graunt;[9]
Noon of his bretheren cam ther in his haunt.[1]
255   For though a widwe° hadde nought a sho,°   *widow / shoe*
So plesant was his *In principio*[2]
Yit wolde he have a ferthing° er he wente;   *small coin*
His purchas was wel bettre than his rente.[3]
And rage he coude as it were right a whelpe;[4]
260   In love-dayes[5] ther coude he muchel° helpe,   *much*
For ther he was nat lik a cloisterer,
With a thredbare cope, as is a poore scoler,
But he was lik a maister[6] or a pope.
Of double worstede was his semicope,°   *short robe*
265   And rounded as a belle out of the presse.°   *bell mold*
Somwhat he lipsed° for his wantounesse°   *lisped / affectation*

1. Shriven, absolved.
2. Although he is sorely grieved.
3. Before granting absolution, the confessor must be sure the sinner is contrite; moreover, the absolution is contingent on the sinner's performance of an act of satisfaction. In the case of Chaucer's Friar, a liberal contribution served both as proof of contrition and as satisfaction.
4. He absolutely took the prize for ballads.
5. "Beggestere": female beggar. "Lazar:" leper.
6. It was not suitable because of his position.
7. I.e., poor trash. The oldest order of friars had been founded by St. Francis to administer to the spiritual needs of precisely those classes the Friar avoids.
8. Everywhere.
9. And he paid a certain rent for the privilege of begging.
1. Assigned territory.
2. A friar's usual salutation: "In the beginning [was the Word]" (John 1.1).
3. I.e., the money he got through such activity was more than his proper income.
4. And he could flirt wantonly, as if he were a puppy.
5. Days appointed for the settlement of lawsuits out of court.
6. A man of recognized learning.

To make his Englissh sweete upon his tonge;
And in his harping, whan he hadde songe,°   *sung*
His yën twinkled in his heed aright
270 As doon the sterres° in the frosty night.   *stars*
This worthy limitour was cleped Huberd.
  A Marchant was ther with a forked beerd,
In motelee,[7] and hye on hors he sat,
Upon his heed a Flandrissh° bevere hat,   *Flemish*
275 His bootes clasped faire and fetisly.°   *elegantly*
His resons° he spak ful solempnely,   *opinions*
Souning° alway th' encrees of his winning.°   *implying / profit*
He wolde the see were kept for any thing[8]
Bitwixen Middelburgh and Orewelle.
280 Wel coude he in eschaunge sheeldes[9] selle.
This worthy man ful wel his wit bisette:°   *employed*
Ther wiste° no wight° that he was in dette,   *knew / person*
So statly° was he of his governaunce,[1]   *dignified*
With his bargaines,° and with his chevissaunce.°   *bargainings / borrowing*
285 Forsoothe° he was a worthy man withalle;   *in truth*
But, sooth to sayn, I noot° how men him calle.   *don't know*
  A Clerk[2] ther was of Oxenforde also
That unto logik hadde longe ygo.[3]
As lene was his hors as is a rake,
290 And he was nought right fat, I undertake,
But looked holwe,° and therto sobrely.   *hollow*
Ful thredbare was his overeste courtepy,
For he hadde geten him yit no benefice,[4]
Ne was so worldly for to have office.°   *secular employment*
295 For him was levere[5] have at his beddes heed
Twenty bookes, clad in blak or reed,
Of Aristotle and his philosophye,
Than robes riche, or fithele,° or gay sautrye.[6]   *fiddle*
But al be that he was a philosophre[7]
300 Yit hadde he but litel gold in cofre;°   *coffer*
But al that he mighte of his freendes hente,°   *take*
On bookes and on lerning he it spente,
And bisily gan for the soules praye
Of hem that yaf him wherwith to scoleye.°   *study*
305 Of studye took he most cure° and most heede.   *care*
Nought oo° word spak he more than was neede,   *one*
And that was said in forme[8] and reverence,
And short and quik,° and ful of heigh sentence:[9]   *lively*

7. Motley, a cloth of mixed color.
8. I.e., he wished the sea to be guarded at all costs. The sea route between Middelburgh (in the Netherlands) and Orwell (in Suffolk) was vital to the Merchant's export and import of wool—the basis of England's chief trade at the time.
9. Shields were units of transfer in international credit, which he exchanged at a profit.
1. The management of his affairs.
2. The Clerk is a student at Oxford; to become a student, he would have had to signify his intention of becoming a cleric, but he was not bound to proceed to a position of responsibility in the church.
3. Who had long since matriculated in philosophy.
4. Ecclesiastical living, such as the income a parish priest receives. "Courtepy": outer cloak.
5. He would rather.
6. Psaltery (a kind of harp).
7. The word may also mean alchemist, someone who tries to turn base metals into gold. The Clerk's "philosophy" does not pay either way.
8. With decorum.
9. Elevated thought.

Souning° in moral vertu was his speeche,   *resounding*
310 And gladly wolde he lerne, and gladly teche.
    A Sergeant of the Lawe, war and wis,[1]
That often hadde been at the Parvis[2]
Ther was also, ful riche of excellence.
Discreet he was, and of greet reverence—
315 He seemed swich, his wordes weren so wise.
Justice he was ful often in assise°   *circuit courts*
By patente[3] and by plein° commissioun.   *full*
For his science° and for his heigh renown   *knowledge*
Of fees and robes hadde he many oon.
320 So greet a purchasour° was nowher noon;   *speculator in land*
Al was fee simple[4] to him in effect—
His purchasing mighte nat been infect.[5]
Nowher so bisy a man as he ther nas;°   *was not*
And yit he seemed bisier than he was.
325 In termes hadde he caas and doomes[6] alle
That from the time of King William[7] were falle.
Therto he coude endite and make a thing,[8]
Ther coude no wight pinchen° at his writing;   *cavil*
And every statut coude° he plein° by rote.[9]   *knew / entire*
330 He rood but hoomly° in a medlee cote,[1]   *unpretentiously*
Girt with a ceint° of silk, with barres[2] smale.   *belt*
Of his array telle I no lenger tale.
    A Frankelain[3] was in his compaignye:
Whit was his beerd as is the dayesye;°   *daisy*
335 Of his complexion he was sanguin.[4]
Wel loved he by the morwe a sop in win.[5]
To liven in delit° was evere his wone,°   *sensual delight / wont*
For he was Epicurus[6] owene sone,
That heeld opinion that plein° delit   *full*
340 Was verray° felicitee parfit.°   *true / perfect*
An housholdere and that a greet was he:
Saint Julian[7] he was in his contree.
His breed, his ale, was always after oon;[8]
A bettre envined° man was nevere noon.   *wine-stocked*
345 Withouten bake mete was nevere his hous,
Of fissh and flessh, and that so plentevous°   *plenteous*
It snewed° in his hous of mete° and drinke,   *snowed / food*
Of alle daintees that men coude thinke.

---

1. Wary and wise. The Sergeant is not only a practicing lawyer but one of the high justices of the nation.
2. The Paradise, the porch of St. Paul's Cathedral, a meeting place for lawyers and their clients.
3. Royal warrant.
4. Owned outright without legal impediments.
5. Invalidated on a legal technicality.
6. Law cases and decisions. "By termes": i.e., by heart.
7. I.e., the Conqueror (reigned 1066–87).
8. Compose and draw up a deed.
9. By heart.
1. A coat of mixed color.
2. Transverse stripes.

3. The "Frankelain" (Franklin) is a prosperous country man, whose lower-class ancestry is no impediment to the importance he has attained in his county.
4. A reference to the fact that the Franklin's temperament, "humor," is dominated by blood as well as to his red face (see p. 253, n. 8).
5. I.e., in the morning he was very fond of a piece of bread soaked in wine.
6. The Greek philosopher whose teaching is popularly believed to make pleasure the chief goal of life.
7. The patron saint of hospitality.
8. Always of the same high quality.

After° the sondry sesons of the yeer   *according to*
350 So chaunged he his mete° and his soper.°   *dinner / supper*
Ful many a fat partrich hadde he in mewe,°   *cage*
And many a breem,° and many a luce° in stewe[9]   *carp / pike*
Wo was his cook but if his sauce were
Poinant° and sharp, and redy all his gere.   *spicy*
355 His table dormant in his halle alway
Stood redy covered all the longe day.[1]
At sessions ther was he lord and sire.
Ful ofte time he was Knight of the Shire.[2]
An anlaas° and a gipser° al of silk   *dagger / purse*
360 Heeng at his girdel,[3] whit as morne° milk.   *morning*
A shirreve° hadde he been, and countour.[4]   *sheriff*
Was nowhere swich a worthy vavasour.[5]
    An Haberdasshere and a Carpenter,
A Webbe,° a Dyere, and a Tapicer°—   *weaver / tapestry maker*
365 And they were clothed alle in oo liveree[6]
Of a solempne and greet fraternitee.
Ful fresshe and newe hir gere apiked° was;   *trimmed*
Hir knives were chaped° nought with bras,   *mounted*
But al with silver; wrought ful clene and weel
370 Hir girdles and hir pouches everydeel.°   *altogether*
Wel seemed eech of hem a fair burgeis°   *burgher*
To sitten in a yeldehalle° on a dais.   *guildhall*
Everich, for the wisdom that he can,[7]
Was shaply° for to been an alderman.   *suitable*
375 For catel° hadde they ynough and rente,°   *property / income*
And eek hir wives wolde it wel assente—
And elles certain were they to blame:
It is ful fair to been ycleped° "Madame,"   *called*
And goon to vigilies all bifore,[8]
380 And have a mantel royalliche ybore.[9]
    A Cook they hadde with hem for the nones,[1]
To boile the chiknes with the marybones,°   *marrowbones*
And powdre-marchant tart and galingale.[2]
Wel coude he knowe° a draughte of London ale.   *recognize*
385 He coude roste, and seethe,° and broile, and frye,   *boil*
Maken mortreux,° and wel bake a pie.   *stews*
But greet harm was it, as it thoughte° me,   *seemed to*
That on his shine a mormal° hadde he,   *ulcer*
For blankmanger,[3] that made he with the beste.
390   A Shipman was ther, woning° fer by weste—°   *dwelling / in the west*
For ought I woot,° he was of Dertemouthe.[4]   *know*

---

9. Fishpond.
1. Tables were usually dismounted when not in use, but the Franklin kept his mounted and set ("covered"), hence "dormant."
2. County representative in Parliament. "Sessions": i.e., sessions of the justices of the peace.
3. Hung at his belt.
4. Auditor of county finances.
5. Feudal landholder of lowest rank; a provincial gentleman.
6. In one livery, i.e., the uniform of their "frater-

nitee" or guild, a partly religious, partly social organization.
7. Was capable of.
8. I.e., at the head of the procession. "Vigiles": feasts held on the eve of saints' days.
9. Royally carried.
1. For the occasion.
2. "Powdre-marchant" and "galingale" are flavoring materials.
3. A white stew or mousse.
4. Dartmouth, a port in the southwest of England.

He rood upon a rouncy° as he couthe,[5]   *large nag*
In a gowne of falding° to the knee.   *heavy wool*
A daggere hanging on a laas° hadde he   *strap*
395 Aboute his nekke, under his arm adown.
The hote somer hadde maad his hewe° al brown;   *color*
And certainly he was a good felawe.
Ful many a draughte of win hadde he drawe[6]
Fro Burdeuxward, whil that the chapman sleep:[7]
400 Of nice° conscience took he no keep;°   *fastidious / heed*
If that he faught and hadde the hyer° hand,   *upper*
By water he sente hem hoom to every land.[8]
But of his craft, to rekene wel his tides,
His stremes° and his daungers° him bisides,[9]   *currents / hazards*
405 His herberwe° and his moone, his lodemenage,[1]   *anchorage*
There was noon swich from Hulle to Cartage.[2]
Hardy he was and wis to undertake;[3]
With many a tempest hadde his beerd been shake;
He knew alle the havenes° as they were   *harbors*
410 Fro Gotlond to the Cape of Finistere,[4]
And every crike° in Britaine° and in Spaine.   *inlet / Brittany*
His barge ycleped was the Maudelaine.°   *Magdalene*
    With us ther was a Doctour of Physik:°   *medicine*
In al this world ne was ther noon him lik
415 To speken of physik and of surgerye.
For° he was grounded in astronomye,°   *because / astrology*
He kepte° his pacient a ful greet deel[5]   *tended to*
In houres by his magik naturel.[6]
Wel coude he fortunen the ascendent
420 Of his images[7] for his pacient.
He knew the cause of every maladye,
Were it of hoot or cold or moiste or drye,
And where engendred and of what humour:[8]
He was a verray parfit praktisour.[9]
425 The cause yknowe,° and of his° harm the roote,   *known / its*
Anoon he yaf the sike man his boote.°   *remedy*
    Ful redy hadde he his apothecaries
To senden him drogges° and his letuaries,°   *drugs / medicines*
For eech of hem made other for to winne:
430 Hir frendshipe was nought newe to biginne.

---

5. As best he could.
6. Drawn, i.e., stolen.
7. Merchant slept. "Fro Burdeuxward": from Bordeaux; i.e., while carrying wine from Bordeaux (the wine center of France).
8. He drowned his prisoners.
9. Around him.
1. Pilotage, art of navigation.
2. From Hull (in northern England) to Cartagena (in Spain).
3. Shrewd in his undertakings.
4. From Gotland (an island in the Baltic) to Finisterre (the westernmost point in Spain).
5. Closely.
6. Natural—as opposed to black—magic. "In houres": i.e., the astrologically important hours (when conjunctions of the planets might help his

recovery).
7. Assign the propitious time, according to the position of stars, for using talismanic images. Such images, representing either the patient himself or points in the zodiac, were thought to be influential on the course of the disease.
8. Diseases were thought to be caused by a disturbance of one or another of the four bodily "humors," each of which, like the four elements, was a compound of two of the elementary qualities mentioned in line 422: the melancholy humor, seated in the black bile, was cold and dry (like earth); the sanguine, seated in the blood, hot and moist (like air); the choleric, seated in the yellow bile, hot and dry (like fire); the phlegmatic, seated in the phlegm, cold and moist (like water).
9. True perfect practitioner.

Wel knew he the olde Esculapius.[1]
And Deiscorides and eek Rufus,
Olde Ipocras, Hali, and Galien,
Serapion, Razis, and Avicen,
435 Averrois, Damascien, and Constantin,
Bernard, and Gatesden, and Gilbertin.
Of his diete mesurable° was he,   *moderate*
For it was of no superfluitee,
But of greet norissing° and digestible.   *nourishment*
440 His studye was but litel on the Bible.
In sanguin° and in pers° he clad was al,   *blood red / blue*
Lined with taffata and with sendal;°   *silk*
And yit he was but esy of dispence;°   *expenditure*
He kepte that he wan in pestilence.[2]
445 For° gold in physik is a cordial,[3]   *because*
Therfore he loved gold in special.
   A good Wif was ther of biside Bathe,
But she was somdeel deef,° and that was scathe.°   *a bit deaf / a pity*
Of cloth-making she hadde swich an haunt,°   *skill*
450 She passed° hem of Ypres and of Gaunt.[4]   *surpassed*
In al the parissh wif ne was ther noon
That to the offring[5] bifore hire sholde goon,
And if ther dide, certain so wroth° was she   *angry*
That she was out of alle charitee.
455 Hir coverchiefs° ful fine were of ground°—   *headcovers / texture*
I dorste° swere they weyeden° ten pound   *dare / weighed*
That on a Sonday weren° upon hir heed.   *were*
Hir hosen° weren of fin scarlet reed,°   *leggings / red*
Ful straite yteyd,[6] and shoes ful moiste° and newe.   *supple*
460 Bold was hir face and fair and reed of hewe.
She was a worthy womman al hir live:
Housbondes at chirche dore[7] she hadde five,
Withouten° other compaignye in youthe—   *not counting*
But therof needeth nought to speke as nouthe.°   *now*
465 And thries hadde she been at Jerusalem;
She hadde passed many a straunge° streem;   *foreign*
At Rome she hadde been, and at Boloigne,
In Galice at Saint Jame, and at Coloigne:[8]
She coude° muchel of wandring by the waye: *knew*
470 Gat-toothed[9] was she, soothly for to saye.

---

1. The Doctor is familiar with the treatises that the Middle Ages attributed to the "great names" of medical history, whom Chaucer names: the purely legendary Greek demigod Aesculapius; the Greeks Dioscorides, Rufus, Hippocrates, Galen, and Serapion; the Persians Hali and Rhazes; the Arabians Avicenna and Averroës; the early Christians John (?) of Damascus and Constantine Afer; the Scotsman Bernard Gordon; the Englishmen John of Gatesden and Gilbert, the former an early contemporary of Chaucer.
2. He saved the money he made during the plague time.
3. A stimulant. Gold was thought to have some medicinal properties.
4. Ypres and Ghent ("Gaunt") were Flemish clothmaking centers.
5. The offering in church, when the congregation brought its gifts forward.
6. Tightly laced.
7. In medieval times, weddings were performed at the church door.
8. Rome, Boulogne (in France), St. James (of Compostella) in Galicia (Spain), and Cologne (in Germany) were all sites of shrines much visited by pilgrims.
9. Gap-toothed, thought to be a sign of amorousness.

Upon an amblere[1] esily she sat,
Ywimpled° wel, and on hir heed an hat   *veiled*
As brood as is a bokeler or a targe,[2]
A foot-mantel° aboute hir hipes large,   *riding skirt*
475 And on hir feet a paire of spores° sharpe.   *spurs*
In felaweshipe wel coude she laughe and carpe:°   *talk*
Of remedies of love she knew parchaunce,°   *as it happened*
For she coude of that art the olde daunce.[3]
        A good man was ther of religioun,
480 And was a poore Person° of a town,   *parson*
But riche he was of holy thought and werk.
He was also a lerned man, a clerk,
That Cristes gospel trewely° wolde preche;   *faithfully*
His parisshens° devoutly wolde he teche.   *parishioners*
485 Benigne he was, and wonder° diligent,   *wonderfully*
And in adversitee ful pacient,
And swich he was preved° ofte sithes.°   *proved / times*
Ful loth were him to cursen for his tithes,[4]
But rather wolde he yiven, out of doute,[5]
490 Unto his poore parisshens aboute
Of his offring[6] and eek of his substaunce:°   *property*
He coude in litel thing have suffisaunce.°   *sufficiency*
Wid was his parissh, and houses fer asonder,
But he ne lafte° nought for rain ne thonder,   *neglected*
495 In siknesse nor in meschief,° to visite   *misfortune*
The ferreste° in his parissh, muche and lite,[7]   *farthest*
Upon his feet, and in his hand a staf.
This noble ensample° to his sheep he yaf   *example*
That first he wroughte,[8] and afterward he taughte.
500 Out of the Gospel he tho° wordes caughte,°   *those / took*
And this figure° he added eek therto: *metaphor*
That if gold ruste, what shal iren do?
For if a preest be foul, on whom we truste,
No wonder is a lewed° man to ruste.   *uneducated*
505 And shame it is, if a preest take keep,°   *heed*
A shiten° shepherde and a clene sheep.   *befouled*
Wel oughte a preest ensample for to yive
By his clennesse how that his sheep sholde live.
He sette nought his benefice[9] to hire
510 And leet° his sheep encombred in the mire   *left*
And ran to London, unto Sainte Poules,[1]
To seeken him a chaunterye[2] for soules,
Or with a bretherhede to been withholde,[3]

1. Horse with an easy gait.
2. "Bokeler" and "targe": small shields.
3. I.e., she knew all the tricks of that trade.
4. He would be most reluctant to invoke excommunication in order to collect his tithes.
5. Without doubt.
6. The offering made by the congregation of his church was at the Parson's disposal.
7. Great and small.
8. I.e., he practiced what he preached.

9. I.e., his parish. A priest might rent his parish to another and take a more profitable position.
1. St. Paul's Cathedral.
2. Chantry, i.e., a foundation that employed priests for the sole duty of saying masses for the souls of wealthy deceased persons. St. Paul's had many of them.
3. Or to be employed by a brotherhood; i.e., to take a lucrative and fairly easy position as chaplain with a parish guild (see this page, n. 6).

But dwelte at hoom and kepte wel his folde,
515 So that the wolf ne made it nought miscarye:[4]
He was a shepherde and nought a mercenarye.
And though he holy were and vertuous,
He was to sinful men nought despitous,°   *scornful*
Ne of his speeche daungerous° ne digne,°   *disdainful / haughty*
520 But in his teching discreet and benigne,
To drawen folk to hevene by fairnesse
By good ensample—this was his bisinesse.
But it° were any persone obstinat,   *if there*
What so he were, of heigh or lowe estat,
525 Him wolde he snibben° sharply for the nones:[5]   *scold*
A bettre preest I trowe° ther nowher noon is.   *believe*
He waited after[6] no pompe and reverence,
Ne maked him a spiced conscience,[7]
But Cristes lore° and his Apostles twelve   *teaching*
530 He taughte, but first he folwed it himselve.
   With him ther was a Plowman, was his brother,
That hadde ylad° of dong° ful many a fother[8]   *carried / dung*
A trewe swinkere° and a good was he,   *worker*
Living in pees° and parfit charitee.   *peace*
535 God loved he best with al his hoole° herte   *whole*
At alle times, though him gamed or smerte,[9]
And thanne his neighebor right as himselve.[1]
He wolde thresshe, and therto dike° and delve,°   *work hard / dig*
For Cristes sake, for every poore wight,
540 Withouten hire, if it laye in his might.
His tithes payed he ful faire and wel,
Bothe of his propre swink[2] and his catel.°   *property*
In a tabard° he rood upon a mere.°   *workman's smock / mare*
   Ther was also a Reeve° and a Millere,   *estate manager*
545 A Somnour, and a Pardoner[3] also,
A Manciple,° and myself—ther were namo.   *steward*
   The Millere was a stout carl° for the nones.   *fellow*
Ful big he was of brawn° and eek of bones—   *muscle*
That preved[4] wel, for overal ther he cam
550 At wrastling he wolde have alway the ram.[5]
He was short-shuldred, brood,° a thikke knarre.[6]   *broad*
Ther was no dore that he nolde heve of harre,[7]
Or breke it at a renning° with his heed.°   *running / head*
His beerd as any sowe or fox was reed,°   *red*
555 And therto brood, as though it were a spade;
Upon the cop right[8] of his nose he hade
A werte,° and theron stood a tuft of heres,   *wart*

---

4. See John 10.11–13.
5. On the spot, promptly.
6. I.e., expected.
7. Nor did he assume an overfastidious conscience, a holier-than-thou attitude.
8. Load.
9. Whether he was pleased or grieved.
1. Matthew 22.36–40.
2. His own work.
3. "Somnour" (Summoner): server of summonses

to the ecclesiastical court. "Pardoner": dispenser of papal pardons (see p. 257, n. 1, and p. 259, 2nd n. 7).
4. Proved, i.e., was evident.
5. A ram was frequently offered as the prize in wrestling, a village sport.
6. Sturdy fellow.
7. He would not heave off (its) hinge.
8. Right on the tip.

Rede as the bristles of a sowes eres;°   *ears*
His nosethirles° blake were and wide.   *nostrils*
560 A swerd and a bokeler° bar° he by his side.   *shield / bore*
His mouth as greet was as a greet furnais.°   *furnace*
He was a janglere° and a Goliardais,[9]   *chatterer*
And that was most of sinne and harlotries.°   *obscenities*
Wel coude he stelen corn and tollen thries[1]—
565 And yit he hadde a thombe[2] of gold, pardee.°   *by heaven*
A whit cote and a blew hood wered° he.   *wore*
A baggepipe wel coude he blowe and soune,°   *sound*
And therwithal° he broughte us out of towne.   *therwith*
    A gentil Manciple[3] was ther of a temple,
570 Of which achatours° mighte take exemple   *buyers of food*
For to been wise in bying of vitaile;°   *victuals*
For wheither that he paide or took by taile,[4]
Algate he waited so in his achat[5]
That he was ay biforn and in good stat.[6]
575   Now is nat that of God a ful fair grace
That swich a lewed° mannes wit shal pace°   *uneducated / surpass*
The wisdom of an heep of lerned men?
Of maistres° hadde he mo than thries ten   *masters*
That weren of lawe expert and curious,°   *cunning*
580 Of whiche ther were a dozeine in that hous
Worthy to been stiwardes of rente° and lond   *income*
Of any lord that is in Engelond,
To make him live by his propre good[7]
In honour dettelees but if he were wood,[8]
585 Or live as scarsly° as him list° desire,   *economically / it pleases*
And able for to helpen al a shire
In any caas° that mighte falle° or happe,   *event / befall*
And yit this Manciple sette hir aller cappe![9]
    The Reeve was a sclendre° colerik[1] man;   *slender*
590 His beerd was shave as neigh° as evere he can;   *close*
His heer was by his eres ful round yshorn;
His top was dokked[2] lik a preest biforn;°   *in front*
Ful longe were his legges and ful lene,
Ylik a staf, ther was no calf yseene.°   *visible*
595 Wel coude he keepe° a gerner° and a binne—   *guard / granary*
Ther was noon auditour coude on him winne.[3]
Wel wiste° he by the droughte and by the rain   *knew*
The yeelding of his seed and of his grain.
His lordes sheep, his neet,° his dayerye,°   *cattle / dairy herd*
600 His swin, his hors, his stoor,° and his pultrye   *stock*

---

9. Goliard, teller of ribald stories.
1. Take toll thrice—i.e., deduct from the grain far more than the lawful percentage.
2. Thumb. Ironic allusion to a proverb: "An honest miller has a golden thumb."
3. The Manciple is the business agent of a community of lawyers in London (a "temple").
4. By tally, i.e., on credit.
5. Always he was on the watch in his purchasing.
6. Financial condition. "Ay biforn": i.e., ahead of the game.

7. His own money.
8. Out of debt unless he were crazy.
9. This Manciple made fools of them all.
1. Choleric describes a person whose dominant humor is yellow bile (choler)—i.e., a hot-tempered person. The Reeve is the superintendent of a large farming estate.
2. Cut short; the clergy wore the head partially shaved.
3. I.e., find him in default.

Was hoolly° in this Reeves governinge,   *wholly*
And by his covenant yaf[4] the rekeninge,
Sin° that his lord was twenty-yeer of age.   *since*
There coude no man bringe him in arrerage.[5]

605 Ther nas baillif, hierde, nor other hine,
That he ne knew his sleighte and his covine[6]
They were adrad° of him as of the deeth.°   *afraid / plague*
His woning° was ful faire upon an heeth;°   *dwelling / meadow*
With greene trees shadwed was his place.

610 He coude bettre than his lord purchace.°   *acquire goods*
Ful riche he was astored° prively.°   *stocked / secretly*
His lord wel coude he plesen subtilly,
To yive and lene° him of his owene good,°   *lend / property*
And have a thank, and yit a cote and hood.

615 In youthe he hadde lerned a good mister:°   *occupation*
He was a wel good wrighte, a carpenter.
This Reeve sat upon a ful good stot°   *stallion*
That was a pomely° grey and highte° Scot.   *dapple / was named*
A long surcote° of pers° upon he hade,[7]   *overcoat / blue*
620 And by his side he bar° a rusty blade.   *bore*
Of Northfolk was this Reeve of which I telle,
Biside a town men clepen Baldeswelle.°   *Bawdswell*
Tukked[8] he was as is a frere aboute,
And evere he rood the hindreste of oure route.[9]

625   A Somnour[1] was ther with us in that place
That hadde a fir-reed° cherubinnes[2] face,   *fire-red*
For saucefleem° he was, with yën narwe,   *pimply*
And hoot° he was, and lecherous as a sparwe,°   *hot / sparrow*
With scaled° browes blake and piled[3] beerd: *scabby*
630 Of his visage children were aferd.°   *afraid*
Ther nas quiksilver, litarge, ne brimstoon,
Boras, ceruce, ne oile of tartre noon,[4]
Ne oinement that wolde dense and bite,
That him mighte helpen of his whelkes° white,   *pimples*
635 Nor of the knobbes° sitting on his cheekes.   *lumps*
Wel loved he garlek, oinons, and eek leekes,
And for to drinke strong win reed as blood.
Thanne wolde he speke and crye as he were wood;°   *mad*
And whan that he wel dronken hadde the win,
640 Thanne wolde he speke no word but Latin:
A fewe termes hadde he, two or three,
That he hadde lerned out of som decree;
No wonder is—he herde it al the day,
And eek ye knowe wel how that a jay°   *parrot*

---

4. And according to his contract he gave.
5. Convict him of being in arrears financially.
6. There was no bailiff (i.e., foreman), shepherd, or other farm laborer whose craftiness and plots he didn't know.
7. He had on.
8. With clothing tucked up like a friar.
9. Hindmost of our group.
1. The "Somnour" (Summoner) is an employee of the ecclesiastical court, whose duty is to bring to court persons whom the archdeacon—the justice of the court—suspects of offenses against canon law. By this time, however, summoners had generally transformed themselves into corrupt detectives who spied out offenders and blackmailed them by threats of summonses.
2. Cherubs, often depicted in art with red faces.
3. Uneven, partly hairless.
4. These are all ointments for diseases affecting the skin, probably diseases of venereal origin.

645 Can clepen "Watte"[5] as wel as can the Pope—
But whoso coude in other thing him grope,°   *examine*
Thanne hadde he spent all his philosophye;[6]
Ay *Questio quid juris*[7] wolde he crye.
     He was a gentil harlot° and a kinde;   *rascal*
650 A bettre felawe sholde men nought finde:
He wolde suffre,° for a quart of win,   *permit*
A good felawe to have his concubin
A twelfmonth, and excusen him at the fulle;[8]
Ful prively° a finch eek coude he pulle.[9]   *secretly*
655 And if he foond° owher° a good felawe   *found / anywhere*
He wolde techen him to have noon awe
In swich caas of the Ercedekenes curs,[1]
But if[2] a mannes soule were in his purs,
For in nis purs he sholde ypunisshed be.
660 "Purs is the Ercedekenes helle," saide he.
     But wel I woot he lied right in deede:
Of cursing° oughte eech gilty man him drede,   *excommunication*
For curs wol slee° right as assoiling° savith—   *slay / absolution*
And also war him of a *significavit*.[3]
665   In daunger[4] hadde he at his owene gise°   *disposal*
The yonge girles of the diocise,
And knew hir conseil,° and was al hir reed.[5]   *secrets*
A gerland hadde he set upon his heed
As greet as it were for an ale-stake,[6]
670 A bokeler hadde he maad him of a cake.
     With him ther rood a gentil Pardoner[7]
Of Rouncival, his freend and his compeer,°   *comrade*
That straight was comen fro the Court of Rome.[8]
Ful loude he soong,° "Com hider, love, to me."   *sang*
675 This Somnour bar to him a stif burdoun:[9]
Was nevere trompe° of half so greet a soun.   *trumpet*
     This Pardoner hadde heer as yelow as wex,
But smoothe it heeng° as dooth a strike° of flex;°   *hung / hank / flax*
By ounces[1] heenge his lokkes that he hadde,
680 And therwith he his shuldres overspradde,°   *overspread*
But thinne it lay, by colpons,° oon by oon;   *strands*
But hood for jolitee° wered° he noon,   *nonchalance / wore*
For it was trussed up in his walet:°   *pack*

5. Call out: "Walter"—like modern parrots' "Polly."
6. I.e., learning.
7. "What point of law does this investigation involve?" A phrase frequently used in ecclesiastical courts.
8. Fully. Ecclesiastical courts had jurisdiction over many offenses that today would come under civil law, including sexual offenses.
9. "To pull a finch" (pluck a bird) is to have sexual relations with a woman.
1. Archdeacon's sentence of excommunication.
2. Unless.
3. And also one should be careful of a *significavit* (the writ that transferred the guilty offender from the ecclesiastical to the civil arm for pun-

ishment).
4. Under his domination.
5. Was their chief source of advice.
6. A tavern was signalized by a pole ("ale-stake"), rather like a modern flagpole, projecting from its front wall; on this hung a garland, or "bush."
7. A Pardoner dispensed papal pardon for sins to those who contributed to the charitable institution that he was licensed to represent; this Pardoner purported to be collecting for the hospital of Roncesvalles ("Rouncival") in Spain, which had a London branch.
8. The papal court.
9. I.e., provided him with a strong bass accompaniment.
1. I.e., thin strands.

	Him thoughte he rood al of the newe jet.°	*fashion*
685	Dischevelee° save his cappe he rood al bare.	*with hair down*
	Swiche glaring yën hadde he as an hare.	
	A vernicle² hadde he sowed upon his cappe,	
	His walet biforn him in his lappe,	
	Bretful° of pardon, come from Rome al hoot.°	*brimful / hot*
690	A vois he hadde as smal° as hath a goot;°	*high-pitched / goat*
	No beerd hadde he, ne nevere sholde have;	
	As smoothe it was as it were late yshave:	
	I trowe° he were a gelding³ or a mare.	*believe*
	But of his craft, fro Berwik into Ware,⁴	
695	Ne was ther swich another pardoner;	
	For in his male° he hadde a pilwe-beer°	*bag / pillowcase*
	Which that he saide was Oure Lady veil;	
	He saide he hadde a gobet° of the sail	*piece*
	That Sainte Peter hadde whan that he wente	
700	Upon the see, til Jesu Crist him hente.°	*seized*
	He hadde a crois° of laton,° ful of stones,	*cross / brassy metal*
	And in a glas he hadde pigges bones,	
	But with thise relikes⁵ whan that he foond°	*found*
	A poore person° dwelling upon lond,⁶	*parson*
705	Upon° a day he gat° him more moneye	*in / got*
	Than that the person gat in monthes twaye;	
	And thus with feined° flaterye and japes°	*false / tricks*
	He made the person and the peple his apes.°	*dupes*
	But trewely to tellen at the laste,	
710	He was in chirche a noble ecclesiaste;	
	Wel coude he rede a lesson and a storye,°	*liturgical narrative*
	But alderbest° he soong an offertorye,⁷	*best of all*
	For wel he wiste° whan that song was songe,	*knew*
	He moste° preche and wel affile° his tonge	*must / sharpen*
715	To winne silver, as he ful wel coude—	
	Therefore he soong the merierly° and loude.	*more merrily*
	Now have I told you soothly in a clause⁸	
	Th'estaat, th'array, the nombre, and eek the cause	
	Why that assembled was this compaignye	
720	In Southwerk at this gentil hostelrye	
	That highte the Tabard, faste° by the Belle;⁹	*close*
	But now is time to you for to telle	
	How that we baren us¹ that ilke° night	*same*
	Whan we were in that hostelrye alight;	
725	And after wol I telle of oure viage,°	*trip*
	And al the remenant of oure pilgrimage.	
	But first I praye you of youre curteisye	
	That ye n'arette it nought my vilainye²	

2. Portrait of Christ's face as it was said to have been impressed on St. Veronica's handkerchief, i.e., a souvenir reproduction of a famous relic in Rome.
3. A neutered stallion, i.e., a eunuch.
4. I.e., from one end of England to the other.
5. Relics, i.e., the pigs' bones that the Pardoner represented as saints' bones.

6. Upcountry.
7. Part of the mass sung before the offering of alms.
8. I.e., in a short space.
9. Another tavern in Southwark.
1. Bore ourselves.
2. That you do not attribute it to my boorishness.

Though that I plainly speke in this matere
730 To telle you hir wordes and hir cheere,°   *behavior*
Ne though I speke hir wordes proprely;°   *accurately*
For this ye knowen also wel as I:
Who so shal telle a tale after a man
He moot° reherce,° as neigh as evere he can,   *must / repeat*
735 Everich a word, if it be in his charge,°   *responsibility*
Al speke he[3] nevere so rudeliche and large,°   *broadly*
Or elles he moot telle his tale untrewe,
Or feine° thing, or finde° wordes newe;   *make up / devise*
He may nought spare[4] although he were his brother:
740 He moot as wel saye oo word as another.
Crist spak himself ful brode° in Holy Writ,   *broadly*
And wel ye woot no vilainye° is it;   *rudeness*
Eek Plato saith, who so can him rede,
The wordes mote be cosin to the deede.
745   Also I praye you to foryive it me
Al° have I nat set folk in hir degree   *although*
Here in this tale as that they sholde stonde:
My wit is short, ye may wel understonde.
     Greet cheere made oure Host[5] us everichoon,
750 And to the soper sette he us anoon.°   *at once*
He served us with vitaile° at the beste.   *food*
Strong was the win, and wel to drinke us leste.°   *it pleased*
A semely man oure Hoste was withalle
For to been a marchal[6] in an halle;
755 A large man he was, with yën steepe,°   *prominent*
A fairer burgeis° was ther noon in Chepe[7]—   *burgher*
Bold of his speeche, and wis, and wel ytaught,
And of manhood him lakkede right naught.
Eek therto he was right a merye man,
760 And after soper playen he bigan,
And spak of mirthe amonges othere thinges—
Whan that we hadde maad oure rekeninges[8]—
And saide thus, "Now, lordinges, trewely,
Ye been to me right welcome, hertely.°   *heartily*
765 For by my trouthe, if that I shal nat lie,
I sawgh nat this yeer so merye a compaignye
At ones in this herberwe° as is now.   *inn*
Fain° wolde I doon you mirthe, wiste I[9] how.   *gladly*
And of a mirthe I am right now bithought,
770 To doon you ese, and it shal coste nought.
     "Ye goon to Canterbury—God you speede;
The blisful martyr quite you youre meede.[1]
And wel I woot as ye goon by the waye
Ye shapen you[2] to talen° and to playe,   *converse*
775 For trewely, confort ne mirthe is noon

---

3. Although he speak.
4. I.e., spare anyone.
5. The landlord of the Tabard Inn.
6. Marshal, one who was in charge of feasts.
7. Cheapside, business center of London.

8. Had paid our bills.
9. If I knew.
1. Pay you your reward.
2. Intend.

To ride by the waye domb as stoon;°   *stone*
And therefore wol I maken you disport
As I saide erst,° and doon you som confort;   *before*
And if you liketh alle, by oon assent,
780   For to stonden at[3] my juggement,
And for to werken as I shall you saye,
Tomorwe whan ye riden by the waye—
Now by my fader° soule that is deed,   *father's*
But° ye be merye I wol yive you myn heed!°   *unless / head*
785   Holde up youre handes withouten more speeche."
     Oure counseil was nat longe for to seeche;°   *seek*
Us thought it was not worth to make it wis,[4]
And graunted him withouten more avis,°   *deliberation*
And bade him saye his voirdit° as him leste.[5]   *verdict*
790   "Lordinges," quod he, "now herkneth for the beste;
But taketh it nought, I praye you, in desdain.
This is the point, to speken short and plain,
That eech of you, to shorte° with oure waye   *shorten*
In this viage, shal tellen tales twaye°—   *two*
795   To Canterburyward, I mene it so,
And hoomward he shal tellen othere two,
Of aventures that whilom° have bifalle;   *once upon a time*
And which of you that bereth him best of alle—
That is to sayn, that telleth in this cas
800   Tales of best sentence° and most solas°—   *meaning / delight*
Shal have a soper at oure aller cost,[6]
Here in this place, sitting by this post,
Whan that we come again fro Canterbury.
And for to make you the more mury°   *merry*
805   I wol myself goodly° with you ride—   *kindly*
Right at myn owene cost—and be youre gide.
And who so wol my juggement withsaye°   *contradict*
Shal paye al that we spende by the waye.
And if ye vouche sauf that it be so,
810   Telle me anoon, withouten wordes mo,°   *more*
And I wol erly shape me[7] therefore."
     This thing was graunted and oure othes swore
With ful glad herte, and prayden[8] him also
That he wolde vouche sauf for to do so,
815   And that he wolde been oure governour,
And of oure tales juge and reportour,°   *accountant*
And sette a soper at a certain pris,°   *price*
And we wol ruled been at his devis,°   *disposal*
In heigh and lowe; and thus by oon assent
820   We been accorded to his juggement.
And therupon the win was fet° anoon;   *fetched*
We dronken and to reste wente eechoon°   *each one*
Withouten any lenger° taryinge.   *longer*

---

3. Abide by.
4. We didn't think it worthwhile to make an issue of it.
5. It pleased.
6. At the cost of us all.
7. Prepare myself.
8. I.e., we prayed.

Amorwe° whan that day bigan to springe   *in the morning*
825 Up roos oure Host and was oure aller cok,[9]
And gadred us togidres in a flok,
And forth we riden, a litel more than pas,°   *walking pace*
Unto the watering of Saint Thomas;[1]
And ther oure Host bigan his hors arreste,°   *halt*
830 And saide, "Lordes, herkneth if you leste:°   *it please*
    Ye woot youre forward° and it you recorde:[2]   *agreement*
If evensong and morwesong° accorde,°   *morning song / agree*
Lat see now who shal telle the firste tale.
As evere mote° I drinken win or ale,   *may*
835 Who so be rebel to my juggement
Shal paye for al that by the way is spent.
Now draweth cut er that we ferrer twinne:[3]
He which that hath the shorteste shal biginne.
    "Sire Knight," quod he, "my maister and my lord,
840 Now draweth cut, for that is myn accord.°   *will*
Cometh neer," quod he, "my lady Prioresse,
And ye, sire Clerk, lat be youre shamefastnesse°—   *modesty*
Ne studieth nought. Lay hand to, every man!"
    Anoon to drawen every wight bigan,
845 And shortly for to tellen as it was
Were it by aventure, or sort, or cas,[4]
The soothe° is this, the cut fil° to the Knight;   *truth / fell*
Of which ful blithe and glad was every wight,
And telle he moste° his tale, as was resoun,   *must*
850 By forward and by composicioun,[5]
As ye han herd. What needeth wordes mo?
And whan this goode man sawgh that it was so,
As he that wis was and obedient
To keepe his forward by his free assent,
855 He saide, "Sin° I shal biginne the game,   *since*
What, welcome be the cut, in Goddes name!
Now lat us ride, and herkneth what I saye."
And with that word we riden forth oure waye,
And he bigan with right a merye cheere°   *countenance*
860 His tale anoon, and saide as ye may heere.

[*The Knight's Tale* is a romance of 2,350 lines, which Chaucer had written before beginning *The Canterbury Tales*—one of several works assumed to be earlier that he inserted into the collection. It is probably the same story, with only minor revisions, that Chaucer referred to in *The Legend of Good Women* as "al the love of Palamon and Arcite." These are the names of the two heroes of *The Knight's Tale*, kinsmen and best friends who are taken prisoner at the siege and destruction of ancient Thebes by Theseus, the ruler of Athens. Gazing out from their prison cell in a tower, they fall in love at first sight and almost at the same moment with Theseus's sister-in-law, Emily, who is taking an early-morning walk in a garden below their window. After a bitter

9. Was rooster for us all.
1. A watering place near Southwark.
2. You recall it.
3. Go farther. "Draweth cut": i.e., draw straws.
4. Whether it was luck, fate, or chance.
5. By agreement and compact.

rivalry, they are at last reconciled through a tournament in which Emily is the prize. Arcite wins the tournament but, as he lies dying after being thrown by his horse, he makes a noble speech encouraging Palamon and Emily to marry. The tale is an ambitious combination of classical setting and mythology, romance plot, and themes of fortune and destiny.]

The Miller's Prologue and Tale

The Miller's Tale belongs to a genre known as the "fabliau": a short story in verse that deals satirically, often grossly and fantastically as well as hilariously, with intrigues and deceptions about sex or money (and often both these elements in the same story). These are the tales Chaucer is anticipating in *The General Prologue* when he warns his presumably genteel audience that they must expect some rude speaking (see lines 727–44). An even more pointed apology follows at the end of *The Miller's Prologue*. Fabliau tales exist everywhere in oral literature; as a literary form they flourished in France, especially in the thirteenth century. By having Robin the Miller tell a fabliau to "quit" (to requite or pay back) the Knight's aristocratic romance, Chaucer sets up a dialectic between classes, genres, and styles that he exploits throughout *The Canterbury Tales*.

The Prologue

	Whan that the Knight hadde thus his tale ytold,	
	In al the route° nas° ther yong ne old	*group / was not*
	That he ne saide it was a noble storye,	
	And worthy for to drawen° to memorye,	*recall*
5	And namely° the gentils everichoon.	*especially*
	Oure Hoste lough° and swoor, "So mote I goon,[1]	*laughed*
	This gooth aright: unbokeled is the male.°	*pouch*
	Lat see now who shal telle another tale.	
	For trewely the game is wel bigonne.	
10	Now telleth ye, sire Monk, if that ye conne,°	*can*
	Somwhat to quite° with the Knightes tale."	*repay*
	The Millere, that for dronken[2] was al pale,	
	So that unnethe° upon his hors he sat,	*with difficulty*
	He nolde° avalen° neither hood ne hat,	*would not / take off*
15	Ne abiden no man for his curteisye,	
	But in Pilates vois[3] he gan to crye,	
	And swoor, "By armes[4] and by blood and bones,	
	I can° a noble tale for the nones,	*know*
	With which I wol now quite the Knightes tale."	
20	Oure Hoste sawgh that he was dronke of ale,	
	And saide, "Abide, Robin, leve° brother,	*dear*
	Som bettre man shal telle us first another.	
	Abide, and lat us werken thriftily."°	*with propriety*
	"By Goddes soule," quod he, "that wol nat I,	
25	For I wol speke or elles go my way."	

1. So might I walk—an oath.
2. I.e., drunkenness.
3. The harsh voice usually associated with the character of Pontius Pilate in the mystery plays.
4. I.e., by God's arms, a blasphemous oath.

Oure Host answerde, "Tel on, a devele way![5]
Thou art a fool; thy wit is overcome."
"Now herkneth," quod the Millere, "alle and some.[6]
But first I make a protestacioun°   *public affirmation*
30 That I am dronke: I knowe it by my soun.°   *tone of voice*
And therfore if that I misspeke° or saye,   *speak or say wrongly*
Wite it[7] the ale of Southwerk, I you praye;
For I wol telle a legende° and a lif   *saint's life*
Bothe of a carpenter and of his wif,
35 How that a clerk hath set the wrightes cappe."[8]
    The Reeve answerde and saide, "Stint thy clappe![9]
Lat be thy lewed° dronken harlotrye.°   *ignorant / obscenity*
It is a sinne and eek° a greet folye   *also*
To apairen° any man or him defame,   *injure*
40 And eek to bringen wives in swich fame.°   *reputation*
Thou maist ynough of othere thinges sayn."
    This dronken Millere spak ful soone again,
And saide, "Leve° brother Osewold,   *dear*
Who hath no wif, he is no cokewold.°   *cuckold*
45 But I saye nat therfore that thou art oon.
Ther ben ful goode wives many oon,°   *a one*
And evere a thousand goode ayains oon badde.
That knowestou wel thyself but if thou madde.°   *rave*
Why artou angry with my tale now?
50 I have a wif, pardee,° as wel as thou,   *by God*
Yit nolde° I, for the oxen in my plough,   *would not*
Take upon me more than ynough°   *enough*
As deemen of myself that I were oon:[1]
I wol bileve wel that I am noon.
55 An housbonde shal nought been inquisitif
Of Goddes privetee,° nor of his wif.   *secrets*
So[2] he may finde Goddes foison° there,   *plenty*
Of the remenant° needeth nought enquere."° *rest / inquire*
    What sholde I more sayn but this Millere
60 He nolde his wordes for no man forbere,
But tolde his cherles tale in his manere.
M'athinketh° that I shal reherce° it here,   *I regret / repeat*
And therefore every gentil wight I praye,
Deemeth nought, for Goddes love, that I saye
65 Of yvel entente, but for° I moot reherse   *because*
Hir tales alle, be they bet° or werse,   *better*
Or elles falsen° som of my matere.   *falsify*
And therfore, whoso list it nought yheere°   *hear*
Turne over the leef,° and chese° another tale, *page / choose*
70 For he shal finde ynowe,° grete and smale,   *enough*
Of storial[3] thing that toucheth gentilesse,°   *gentility*
And eek moralitee and holinesse:
Blameth nought me if that ye chese amis.

5. I.e., in the devil's name.
6. Each and every one.
7. Blame it on.
8. I.e., how a clerk made a fool of a carpenter.
9. Stop your chatter.
1. To think that I were one (a cuckold).
2. Provided that.
3. Historical, i.e., true.

The Millere is a cherl, ye knowe wel this,
75 So was the Reeve eek, and othere mo,
And harlotrye° they tolden bothe two.   *ribaldry*
Aviseth you,[4] and putte me out of blame:
And eek men shal nought maken ernest of game.

The Tale

Whilom° ther was dwelling at Oxenforde   *once upon a time*
80 A riche gnof° that gestes heeld to boorde,[5]   *churl*
And of his craft he was a carpenter.
With him ther was dwelling a poore scoler,
Hadde lerned art[6] but al his fantasye°   *desire*
Was turned for to lere° astrologye,   *learn*
85 And coude a certain of conclusiouns,
To deemen by interrogaciouns,[7]
If that men axed° him in certain houres   *asked*
Whan that men sholde have droughte or elles showres,
Or if men axed him what shal bifalle
90 Of every thing—I may nat rekene hem alle.
This clerk was cleped° hende[8] Nicholas.   *called*
Of derne love he coude, and of solas,[9]
And therto he was sly and ful privee,°   *secretive*
And lik a maide meeke for to see.
95 A chambre hadde he in that hostelrye
Allone, withouten any compaignye,
Ful fetisly ydight[1] with herbes swoote,°   *sweet*
And he himself as sweete as is the roote
Of licoris or any setewale.[2]
100 His *Almageste*[3] and bookes grete and smale,
His astrelabye, longing for[4] his art,
His augrim stones,[5] layen faire apart
On shelves couched° at his beddes heed;   *set*
His presse° ycovered with a faiding reed;[6]   *storage chest*
105 And al above ther lay a gay sautrye,°   *psaltery (harp)*
On which he made a-nightes melodye
So swetely that al the chambre roong,°   *rang*
And *Angelus ad Virginem*[7] he soong,
And after that he soong the *Kinges Note*.[8]
110 Ful often blessed was his merye throte.
And thus this sweete clerk his time spente
After his freendes finding and his rente.[9]

---

4. Take heed.
5. I.e., took in boarders.
6. Who had completed the first stage of university education (the trivium).
7. I.e., and he knew a number of propositions on which to base astrological analyses (which would reveal the matters in the next three lines).
8. Courteous, handy, attractive.
9. I.e., he knew about secret love and pleasurable practices.
1. Elegantly furnished.
2. Setwall, a spice.

3. The 2nd-century treatise by Ptolemy, still the standard astronomy textbook.
4. Belonging to. "Astrelabye": astrolabe, an astronomical instrument.
5. Counters used in arithmetic.
6. Red coarse woolen cloth.
7. "The Angel to the Virgin," an Annunciation hymn.
8. Probably a popular song of the time.
9. In accordance with his friends' provision and his own income.

This carpenter hadde wedded newe° a wif   *lately*
Which that he loved more than his lif.
115 Of eighteteene yeer she was of age;
Jalous he was, and heeld hire narwe in cage,
For she was wilde and yong, and he was old,
And deemed himself been lik a cokewold[1]
He knew nat Caton,[2] for his wit was rude,
120 That bad men sholde wedde his similitude:[3]
Men sholde wedden after hir estat,[4]
For youthe and elde° is often at debat.   *age*
But sith that he was fallen in the snare,
He moste endure, as other folk, his care.
125   Fair was this yonge wif, and therwithal
As any wesele° hir body gent and smal.[5]   *weasel*
A ceint she wered, barred[6] al of silk;
A barmcloth° as whit as morne° milk   *apron / morning*
Upon hir lendes,° ful of many a gore;°   *loins / flounce*
130 Whit was hir smok,° and broiden° al bifore   *undergarment / embroidered*
And eek bihinde, on hir coler° aboute,   *collar*
Of° col-blak silk, withinne and eek withoute;   *with*
The tapes° of hir white voluper°   *ribbons / cap*
Were of the same suite of[7] hir coler;
135 Hir filet° brood° of silk ana set ful hye;   *headband / broad*
And sikerly° she hadde a likerous° yë;   *certainly / wanton*
Ful smale ypulled[8] were hir browes two,
And tho were bent,° and blake as any slo.°   *arching / sloeberry*
She was ful more blisful on to see
140 Than is the newe perejonette° tree,   *pear*
And softer than the wolle° is of a wether;°   *wool / ram*
And by hir girdel° heeng° a purs of lether,   *belt / hung*
Tasseled with silk and perled with latoun.[9]
In al this world, to seeken up and down,
145 Ther nis no man so wis that coude thenche°   *imagine*
So gay a popelote° or swich° a wenche.   *doll / such*
Ful brighter was the shining of hir hewe
Than in the Towr[1] the noble° yforged newe.   *gold coin*
But of hir song, it was as loud and yerne°   *lively*
150 As any swalwe° sitting on a berne.°   *swallow / barn*
Therto she coude skippe and make game°   *play*
As any kide or calf folwing his dame.°   *mother*
Hir mouth was sweete as bragot or the meeth,[2]
Or hoord of apples laid in hay or heeth.°   *heather*
155 Winsing° she was as is a joly° colt,   *skittish / high-spirited*
Long as a mast, and upright° as a bolt.°   *straight / arrow*
A brooch she bar upon hir lowe coler
As brood as is the boos° of a bokeler;°   *boss / shield*

---

1. I.e., suspected of himself that he was like a cuckold.
2. Dionysius Cato, the supposed author of a book of maxims used in elementary education.
3. Commanded that one should wed his equal.
4. Men should marry according to their condition.
5. Slender and delicate.
6. A belt she wore, with transverse stripes.
7. The same kind as, i.e., black.
8. Delicately plucked.
9. I.e., with brassy spangles on it.
1. The Tower of London, the Mint.
2. "Bragot" and "meeth" are honey drinks.

Hir shoes were laced on hir legges hye.
160 She was a primerole,° a piggesnye,³   *primrose*
For any lord to leggen° in his bedde,   *lay*
Or yit for any good yeman to wedde.
    Now sire, and eft° sire, so bifel the cas   *again*
That on a day this hende Nicholas
165 Fil° with this yonge wif to rage° and playe,   *happened / flirt*
Whil that hir housbonde was at Oseneye⁴
(As clerkes been ful subtil and ful quainte),°   *clever*
And prively he caughte hire by the queinte,⁵
And saide, "Ywis,° but° if ich° have my wille,   *truly / unless / I*
170 For derne° love of thee, lemman, I spille,"°   *secret / die*
And heeld hire harde by the haunche-bones,°   *thighs*
And saide, "Lemman,° love me al atones,⁶   *sweetheart*
Or I wol dien, also° God me save."   *so*
And she sproong° as a colt dooth in a trave,⁷   *sprang*
175 And with hir heed she wried° faste away;   *twisted*
She saide, "I wol nat kisse thee, by my fay.°   *faith*
Why, lat be," quod she, "lat be, Nicholas!
Or I wol crye 'Out, harrow,° and allas!'   *help*
Do way youre handes, for your curteisye!"
180   This Nicholas gan mercy for to crye,
And spak so faire, and profred him so faste,⁸
That she hir love him graunted atte laste,
And swoor hir ooth by Saint Thomas of Kent⁹
That she wolde been at his comandement,
185 Whan that she may hir leiser¹ wel espye.
"Myn housbonde is so ful of jalousye
That but ye waite° wel and been privee   *be on guard*
I woot right wel I nam but deed,"² quod she.
"Ye moste been ful derne° as in this cas."   *secret*
190   "Nay, therof care thee nought," quod Nicholas.
"A clerk hadde litherly biset his while,³
But if he coude a carpenter bigile."
And thus they been accorded and ysworn
To waite° a time, as I have told biforn.   *watch for*
195 Whan Nicholas hadde doon this everydeel,°   *every bit*
And thakked° hire upon the lendes° weel,   *patted / loins*
He kiste hire sweete, and taketh his sautrye,
And playeth faste, and maketh melodye.
    Thanne fil° it thus, that to the parissh chirche,   *befell*
200 Cristes owene werkes for to wirche,°   *perform*
This goode wif wente on an haliday:°   *holy day*
Hir forheed shoon as bright as any day,
So was it wasshen whan she leet° hir werk.   *left*
Now was ther of that chirche a parissh clerk,⁴

---

3. A pig's eye, a name for a common flower.
4. A town near Oxford.
5. Elegant (thing); a euphemism for the female genitals.
6. Right now.
7. Frame for holding a horse to be shod.
8. I.e., made such vigorous advances.

9. Thomas à Becket.
1. I.e., opportunity.
2. I am no more than dead, I am done for.
3. Poorly employed his time.
4. Assistant to the parish priest, not a cleric or student.

205	The which that was ycleped° Absolon:	*called*
	Crul° was his heer, and as the gold it shoon,	*curly*
	And strouted° as a fanne⁵ large and brode;	*spread out*
	Ful straight and evene lay his joly shode.⁶	
	His rode° was reed, his yën greye as goos.°	*complexion / goose*
210	With Poules window corven⁷ on his shoos,	
	In hoses° rede he wente fetisly.°	*stockings / elegantly*
	Yclad he was ful smale° and proprely,	*finely*
	Al in a kirtel° of a light waget°—	*tunic / blue*
	Ful faire and thikke been the pointes⁸ set—	
215	And therupon he hadde a gay surplis,°	*surplice*
	As whit as is the blosme upon the ris.°	*bough*
	A merye child° he was, so God me save.	*young man*
	Wel coude he laten blood, and clippe,⁹ and shave,	
	And maken a chartre of land, or acquitaunce;¹	
220	In twenty manere° coude he trippe and daunce	*ways*
	After the scole of Oxenforde tho,°	*then*
	And with his legges casten° to and fro,	*prance*
	And playen songes on a smal rubible;°	*fiddle*
	Therto he soong somtime a loud quinible,²	
225	And as wel coude he playe on a giterne:°	*guitar*
	In al the town nas brewhous ne taverne	
	That he ne visited with his solas,°	*entertainment*
	Ther any gailard tappestere³ was.	
	But sooth to sayn, he was somdeel squaimous°	*a bit squeamish*
230	Of° farting, and of speeche daungerous.⁴	*about*
	This Absolon, that joly° was and gay,	*pretty, amorous*
	Gooth with a cencer° on the haliday,	*incense burner*
	Cencing the wives of the parissh faste,	
	And many a lovely look on hem he caste,	
235	And namely° on this carpenteres wif:	*especially*
	To looke on hire him thoughte a merye lif.	
	She was so propre° and sweete and likerous,⁵	*neat*
	I dar wel sayn, if she hadde been a mous,	
	And he a cat, he wolde hire hente° anoon.	*pounce on*
240	This parissh clerk, this joly Absolon,	
	Hath in his herte swich a love-longinge°	*lovesickness*
	That of no wif ne took he noon offringe—	
	For curteisye he saide he wolde noon.	
	The moone, whan it was night, ful brighte shoon,°	*shone*
245	And Absolon his giterne° hath ytake—	*guitar*
	For paramours° he thoughte for to wake—	*love*
	And forth he gooth, jolif° and amorous,	*pretty*
	Til he cam to the carpenteres hous,	
	A litel after cokkes hadde ycrowe,	

5. Wide-mouthed basket for separating grain from chaff.
6. Parting of the hair.
7. Carved with intricate designs, like the tracery in the windows of St. Paul's.
8. Laces for fastening the tunic and holding up the hose.

9. Let blood and give haircuts. Bleeding was a medical treatment performed by barbers.
1. Legal release. "Chartre": deed.
2. Part requiring a very high voice.
3. Gay barmaid.
4. Prudish about (vulgar) talk.
5. Wanton, appetizing.

250 And dressed him up by a shot-windowe[6]
    That was upon the carpenteres wal.
    He singeth in his vois gentil and smal,°   *dainty*
    "Now dere lady, if thy wille be,
    I praye you that ye wol rewe° on me,"   *have pity*
255 Ful wel accordant to his giterninge.[7]
    This carpenter awook and herde him singe,
    And spak unto his wif, and saide anoon,
    "What, Alison, heerestou nought Absolon
    That chaunteth thus under oure bowres° wal?"   *bedroom's*
260 And she answerde hir housbonde therwithal,
    "Yis, God woot, John, I heere it everydeel."°   *every bit*
      This passeth forth. What wol ye bet than weel?[8]
    Fro day to day this joly Absolon
    So woweth° hire that him is wo-bigoon: *woos*
265 He waketh° al the night and al the day;   *stays awake*
    He kembed° his lokkes brode[9] and made him gay; *combed*
    He woweth hire by menes and brocage,[1]
    And swoor he wolde been hir owene page° *personal servant*
    He singeth, brokking° as a nightingale;   *trilling*
270 He sente hire piment,° meeth,° and spiced ale, *spiced wine / mead*
    And wafres° piping hoot out of the gleede;° *pastries / coals*
    And for she was of towne,[2] he profred meede°— *money*
    For som folk wol be wonnen for richesse,
    And som for strokes,° and som for gentilesse. *blows (force)*
275 Somtime to shewe his lightnesse and maistrye,[3]
    He playeth Herodes[4] upon a scaffold° hye. *platform, stage*
    But what availeth him as in this cas?
    She loveth so this hende Nicholas
    That Absolon may blowe the bukkes horn;[5]
280 He ne hadde for his labour but a scorn.
    And thus she maketh Absolon hir ape,[6]
    And al his ernest turneth til° a jape.°   *to / joke*
    Ful sooth is this proverbe, it is no lie;
    Men saith right thus: "Alway the nye slye
285 Maketh the ferre leve to be loth."[7]
    For though that Absolon be wood° or wroth,   *furious*
    By cause that he fer was from hir sighte,
    This nye° Nicholas stood in his lighte.   *nearby*
      Now beer° thee wel, thou hende Nicholas, *bear*
290 For Absolon may waile and singe allas.
      And so bifel it on a Saterday
    This carpenter was goon til Oseney,
    And hende Nicholas and Alisoun
    Accorded been to this conclusioun,
295 That Nicholas shal shapen° hem a wile°   *arrange / trick*

---

6. Took his position by a hinged window.
7. In harmony with his guitar playing.
8. Better than well.
9. I.e., wide-spreading.
1. By go-betweens and agents.
2. Because she was a town woman.
3. Facility and virtuosity.

4. Herod, a role traditionally played as a bully in the mystery plays.
5. Blow the buck's horn, i.e., go whistle, waste his time.
6. I.e., thus she makes a monkey out of Absolon.
7. Always the sly man at hand makes the distant dear one hated.

This sely[8] jalous housbonde to bigile,
And if so be this game wente aright,
She sholden sleepen in his arm al night—
For this was his desir and hire° also.   *hers*
300 And right anoon, withouten wordes mo,
This Nicholas no lenger wolde tarye,
But dooth ful softe unto his chambre carye
Bothe mete and drinke for a day or twaye,
And to hir housbonde bad hire for to saye,
305 If that he axed after Nicholas,
She sholde saye she niste° wher he was—   *didn't know*
Of al that day she sawgh him nought with yë:
She trowed° that he was in maladye,   *believed*
For for no cry hir maide coude him calle,
310 He nolde answere for no thing that mighte falle.°   *happen*
     This passeth forth al thilke° Saterday   *this*
That Nicholas stille in his chambre lay,
And eet,° and sleep,° or dide what him leste,[9]   *ate / slept*
Til Sonday that the sonne gooth to reste.
315   This sely carpenter hath greet mervaile
Of Nicholas, or what thing mighte him aile,
And saide, "I am adrad,° by Saint Thomas,   *afraid*
It stondeth nat aright with Nicholas.
God shilde° that he deide sodeinly!   *forbid*
320 This world is now ful tikel,° sikerly: *precarious*
I sawgh today a corps yborn to chirche
That now a° Monday last I sawgh him wirche.°   *on / work*
Go up," quod he unto his knave° anoon,   *manservant*
"Clepe° at his dore or knokke with a stoon.°   *call / stone*
325 Looke how it is and tel me boldely."
     This knave gooth him up ful sturdily,
And at the chambre dore whil that he stood
He cride and knokked as that he were wood,°   *mad*
"What? How? What do ye, maister Nicholay?
330 How may ye sleepen al the longe day?"
But al for nought: he herde nat a word.
An hole he foond ful lowe upon a boord,
Ther as the cat was wont in for to creepe,
And at that hole he looked in ful deepe,
335 And atte laste he hadde of him a sighte.
     This Nicholas sat evere caping° uprighte   *gaping*
As he hadde kiked° on the newe moone.   *gazed*
Adown he gooth and tolde his maister soone
In what array° he saw this ilke° man.   *condition / same*
340   This carpenter to blessen him[1] bigan,
And saide, "Help us, Sainte Frideswide![2]
A man woot litel what him shal bitide.
This man is falle, with his astromye,°   *astronomy*
In som woodnesse° or in som agonye.   *madness*

---

8. Poor innocent.
9. He wanted.

1. Cross himself.
2. Patron saint of Oxford.

345 I thoughte ay° wel how that it sholde be: *always*
Men sholde nought knowe of Goddes privetee.°   *secrets*
Ye, blessed be alway a lewed° man   *ignorant*
That nought but only his bileve° can.°   *creed / knows*
So ferde° another clerk with astromye: *fared*
350 He walked in the feeldes for to prye°   *gaze*
Upon the sterres,° what ther sholde bifalle,   *stars*
Til he was in a marle-pit³ yfalle—
He saw nat that. But yit, by Saint Thomas,
Me reweth sore⁴ for hende Nicholas.
355 He shal be rated of⁵ his studying,
If that I may, by Jesus, hevene king!
Get me a staf that I may underspore,°   *pry up*
Whil that thou, Robin, hevest° up the dore.   *heave*
He shal⁶ out of his studying, as I gesse."
360 And to the chambre dore he gan him dresse.⁷
His knave was a strong carl° for the nones,°   *fellow / purpose*
And by the haspe he haaf° it up atones: *heaved*
Into° the floor the dore fil° anoon.   *on / fell*
This Nicholas sat ay as stille as stoon,
365 And evere caped up into the air.
This carpenter wende° he were in despair,   *thought*
And hente° him by the shuldres mightily,   *seized*
And shook him harde, and cride spitously,°   *vehemently*
"What, Nicholay, what, how! What! Looke adown!
370 Awaak and thenk on Cristes passioun!⁸
I crouche⁹ thee from elves and fro wightes."°   *wicked creatures*
Therwith the nightspel saide he anoonrightes¹
On foure halves° of the hous aboute,   *sides*
And on the thresshfold° on the dore withoute: *threshold*
375 "Jesu Crist and Sainte Benedight,°   *Benedict*
Blesse this hous from every wikked wight!
For nightes nerye the White Pater Noster.²
Where wentestou,° thou Sainte Petres soster?°   *did you go / sister*
And at the laste this hende Nicholas
380 Gan for to sike° sore, and saide, "Allas,   *sigh*
Shal al the world be lost eftsoones° now?"   *again*
    This carpenter answerde, "What saistou?
What, thenk on God as we doon, men that swinke."°   *work*
    This Nicholas answerde, "Fecche me drinke,
385 And after wol I speke in privetee
Of certain thing that toucheth me and thee.
I wol telle it noon other man, certain."
    This carpenter gooth down and comth again,

---

3. Pit from which a fertilizing clay is dug.
4. I sorely pity.
5. Scolded for.
6. I.e., shall come.
7. Took his stand.
8. I.e., the Crucifixion.
9. Make the sign of the cross on.
1. The night-charm he said right away (to ward off evil spirits).

2. Pater Noster is Latin for "Our Father," the beginning of the Lord's Prayer. The line is obscure, but a conjectural reading would be, "May the White 'Our Father' (or 'Our White Father') [either a prayer or the personification of a protecting power] defend [*nerye*] (us) against nights." The "nightspel" is a jumble of Christian references and pagan superstition.

And broughte of mighty° ale a large quart,   *strong*
390 And when that eech of hem hadde dronke his part,
This Nicholas his dore faste shette,°   *shut*
And down the carpenter by him he sette,
And saide, "John, myn hoste lief° and dere,   *beloved*
Thou shalt upon thy trouthe° swere me here   *word of honor*
395 That to no wight thou shalt this conseil° wraye;°   *secret / disclose*
For it is Cristes conseil that I saye,
And if thou telle it man,[3] thou art forlore,°   *lost*
For this vengeance thou shalt have therfore,
That if thou wraye me, thou shalt be wood."[4]
400   "Nay, Crist forbede it, for his holy blood,"
Quod tho this sely° man. "I nam no labbe,°   *innocent / tell-tale*
And though I saye, I nam nat lief to gabbe.[5]
Say what thou wilt, I shal it nevere telle
To child ne wif, by him that harwed helle."[6]
405   "Now John," quod Nicholas, "I wol nought lie.
I have yfounde in myn astrologye,
As I have looked in the moone bright,
That now a Monday next, at quarter night,[7]
Shal falle a rain, and that so wilde and wood,°   *furious*
410 That half so greet was nevere Noees° flood.   *Noah's*
This world," he saide, "in lasse° than an hour   *less*
Shal al be dreint,° so hidous is the showr.   *drowned*
Thus shal mankinde drenche° and lese° hir lif."   *drown / lose*
    This carpenter answerde, "Allas, my wif!
415 And shal she drenche? Allas, myn Alisoun!"
For sorwe of this he fil almost[8] adown,
And saide, "Is there no remedye in this cas?"
    "Why yis, for[9] Gode," quod hende Nicholas,
"If thou wolt werken after lore and reed[1]—
420 Thou maist nought werken after thyn owene heed;°   *head*
For thus saith Salomon that was ful trewe,
'Werk al by conseil and thou shalt nought rewe.'°   *be sorry*
And if thou werken wolt by good conseil,
I undertake, withouten mast or sail,
425 Yit shal I save hire and thee and me.
Hastou nat herd how saved was Noee
Whan that oure Lord hadde warned him biforn
That al the world with water sholde be lorn?"°   *lost*
    "Yis," quod this carpenter, "ful yore° ago."   *long*
430   "Hastou nat herd," quod Nicholas, "also
The sorwe of Noee with his felaweshipe?
Er° that he mighte gete his wif to shipe,   *before*
Him hadde levere,[2] I dar wel undertake,
At thilke time than alle his wetheres[3] blake

---

3. To anyone.
4. Go mad.
5. And though I say it myself, I don't like to gossip.
6. By Him that despoiled hell—i.e., Christ.
7. I.e., shortly before dawn.
8. Almost fell.

9. I.e., by.
1. Act according to learning and advice.
2. He had rather.
3. Rams. I.e., he'd have given all the black rams he had.

435 That she hadde had a ship hirself allone.⁴
And therfore woostou° what is best to doone?   *do you know*
This axeth° haste, and of an hastif° thing   *requires / urgent*
Men may nought preche or maken tarying.
Anoon go gete us faste into this in°   *lodging*
440 A kneeding trough or elles a kimelin°   *brewing tub*
For eech of us, but looke that they be large,°   *wide*
In whiche we mowen swimme as in a barge,⁵
And han therinne vitaile suffisaunt⁶
But for a day—fy° on the remenaunt!   *fie*
445 The water shal aslake° and goon away   *diminish*
Aboute prime⁷ upon the nexte day.
But Robin may nat wite° of this, thy knave,   *know*
Ne eek thy maide Gille I may nat save.
Axe nought why, for though thou axe me,
450 I wol nought tellen Goddes privetee.°   *secrets*
Suffiseth thee, but if thy wittes madde,°   *go mad*
To han° as greet a grace as Noee hadde.   *have*
Thy wif shal I wel saven, out of doute.
Go now thy way, and speed thee heraboute.
455 But whan thou hast for hire° and thee and me   *her*
Ygeten us thise kneeding-tubbes three,
Thanne shaltou hangen hem in the roof ful hye,
That no man of oure purveyance° espye.   *preparations*
And whan thou thus hast doon as I have said,
460 And hast oure vitaile faire in hem ylaid,
And eek an ax to smite the corde atwo,
Whan that the water comth that we may go,
And broke an hole an heigh⁸ upon the gable
Unto the gardinward,⁹ over the stable,
465 That we may freely passen forth oure way,
Whan that the grete showr is goon away,
Thanne shaltou swimme as merye, I undertake,
As dooth the white doke° after hir drake.   *duck*
Thanne wol I clepe,° 'How, Alison? How, John?   *call*
470 Be merye, for the flood wol passe anoon.'
And thou wolt sayn, 'Hail, maister Nicholay!
Good morwe, I see thee wel, for it is day!'
And thanne shal we be lordes al oure lif
Of al the world, as Noee and his wif.
475 But of oo thing I warne thee ful right:
Be wel avised° on that ilke night   *warned*
That we been entred into shippes boord
That noon of us ne speke nought a word,
Ne clepe, ne crye, but been in his prayere,
480 For it is Goddes owene heeste dere¹
Thy wif and thou mote hange fer atwinne,²

---

4. The reluctance of Noah's wife to board the ark
is a traditional comic theme in the mystery plays.
5. In which we can float as in a vessel.
6. Sufficient food.
7. 9 A.M.

8. On high.
9. Toward the garden.
1. Precious commandment.
2. Far apart.

For that bitwixe you shal be no sinne—
Namore in looking than ther shal in deede.
This ordinance is said: go, God thee speede.
485 Tomorwe at night whan men been alle asleepe,
Into oure kneeding-tubbes wol we creepe,
And sitten there, abiding Goddes grace.
Go now thy way, I have no lenger space°   *time*
To make of this no lenger sermoning.
490 Men sayn thus: 'Send the wise and say no thing.'
Thou art so wis it needeth thee nat teche:
Go save oure lif, and that I thee biseeche."
    This sely carpenter gooth forth his way:
Ful ofte he saide allas and wailaway,
495 And to his wif he tolde his privetee,
And she was war,° and knew it bet° than he,   *aware / better*
What al this quainte cast was for to saye.[3]
But nathelees she ferde° as she wolde deye,   *acted*
And saide, "Allas, go forth thy way anoon.
500 Help us to scape,° or we been dede eechoon.   *escape*
I am thy trewe verray wedded wif:
Go, dere spouse, and help to save oure lif."
    Lo, which a greet thing is affeccioun!°   *emotion*
Men may dien of imaginacioun,
505 So deepe° may impression be take.   *deeply*
This sely carpenter biginneth quake;
Him thinketh verrailiche° that he may see   *truly*
Noees flood come walwing° as the see   *rolling*
To drenchen° Alison, his hony dere.   *drown*
510 He weepeth, waileth, maketh sory cheere;
He siketh° with ful many a sory swough,°   *sighs / groan*
And gooth and geteth him a kneeding-trough,
And after a tubbe and a kimelin,
And prively he sente hem to his in,°   *dwelling*
515 And heeng° hem in the roof in privetee;   *hung*
His° owene hand he made laddres three,   *with his*
To climben by the ronges° and the stalkes°   *rungs / uprights*
Unto the tubbes hanging in the balkes,°   *rafters*
And hem vitailed,° bothe trough and tubbe,   *victualed*
520 With breed and cheese and good ale in a jubbe,°   *jug*
Suffising right ynough as for a day.
But er° that he hadde maad al this array,   *before*
He sente his knave, and eek his wenche also,
Upon his neede[4] to London for to go.
525 And on the Monday whan it drow to[5] nighte,
He shette° his dore withouten candel-lighte,   *shut*
And dressed° alle thing as it sholde be,   *arranged*
And shortly up they clomben° alle three.   *climbed*
They seten° stille wel a furlong way[6]   *sat*

---

3. What all this clever plan meant.
4. On an errand for him.
5. Drew toward.

6. The time it takes to go a furlong (i.e., a few minutes).

530   "Now, Pater Noster, clum,"[7] saide Nicholay,
And "Clum" quod John, and "Clum" saide Alisoun.
This carpenter saide his devocioun,
And stille he sit° and biddeth° his prayere,   *sits / prays*
Awaiting on the rain, if he it heere.°   *might hear*
535   The dede sleep, for wery bisinesse,
Fil° on this carpenter right as I gesse   *fell*
Aboute corfew time,[8] or litel more.
For travailing of his gost[9] he groneth sore,
And eft° he routeth,° for his heed mislay.[1]   *then / snores*
540   Down of the laddre stalketh Nicholay,
And Alison ful softe adown she spedde:
Withouten wordes mo they goon to bedde
Ther as the carpenter is wont to lie.
Ther was the revel and the melodye,
545 And thus lith° Alison and Nicholas   *lies*
In bisinesse of mirthe and of solas,°   *pleasure*
Til that the belle of Laudes[2] gan to ringe,
And freres° in the chauncel° gonne singe.   *friars / chancel*
     This parissh clerk, this amorous Absolon,
550 That is for love alway so wo-bigoon,
Upon the Monday was at Oseneye,
With compaignye him to disporte and playe,
And axed upon caas a cloisterer[3]
Ful prively after John the carpenter;
555 And he drow him apart out of the chirche,
And saide, "I noot:[4] I sawgh him here nought wirche°   *work*
Sith Saterday. I trowe that he be went
For timber ther oure abbot hath him sent.
For he is wont for timber for to go,
560 And dwellen atte grange[5] a day or two.
Or elles he is at his hous, certain.
Where that he be I can nought soothly sayn."
     This Absolon ful jolif was and light,[6]
And thoughte, "Now is time to wake al night,
565 For sikerly,° I sawgh him nought stiringe   *certainly*
Aboute his dore sin day bigan to springe.
So mote° I thrive, I shal at cokkes crowe   *may*
Ful prively knokken at his windowe
That stant° ful lowe upon his bowres° wal.   *stands / bedroom's*
570 To Alison now wol I tellen al
My love-longing,° for yet I shal nat misse   *lovesickness*
That at the leeste way[7] I shal hire kisse.
Som manere confort shal I have, parfay.°   *in faith*
My mouth hath icched al this longe day:
575 That is a signe of kissing at the leeste.

---

7. Hush (?). "Pater Noster": Our Father.
8. Probably about 8 P.M.
9. Affliction of his spirit.
1. Lay in the wrong position.
2. The first church service of the day, before daybreak.

3. Here a member of the religious order of Osney Abbey. "Upon caas": by chance.
4. Don't know.
5. The outlying farm belonging to the abbey.
6. Was very amorous and cheerful.
7. I.e., at least.

Al night me mette[8] eek I was at a feeste.
Therfore I wol go sleepe an hour or twaye,
And al the night thanne wol I wake and playe."
  Whan that the firste cok hath crowe, anoon
580 Up rist° this joly lovere Absolon,   *rises*
And him arrayeth gay at point devis.[9]
But first he cheweth grain[1] and licoris,
To smellen sweete, er he hadde kembd° his heer.   *combed*
Under his tonge a trewe-love[2] he beer,°   *bore*
585 For therby wende° he to be gracious.°   *supposed / pleasing*
He rometh° to the carpenteres hous,   *strolls*
And stille he stant° under the shot-windowe—   *stands*
Unto his brest it raughte,° it was so lowe—   *reached*
And ofte he cougheth with a semisoun.°   *small sound*
590 "What do ye, hony-comb, sweete Alisoun,
My faire brid,[3] my sweete cinamome?°   *cinnamon*
Awaketh, lemman° myn, and speketh to me.   *sweetheart*
Wel litel thinken ye upon my wo
That for your love I swete° ther I go.   *sweat*
595 No wonder is though that I swelte° and swete: *melt*
I moorne as doth a lamb after the tete.°   *teat*
Ywis, lemman, I have swich love-longinge,
That lik a turtle° trewe is my moorninge: *dove*
I may nat ete namore than a maide."
600   "Go fro the windowe, Jakke fool," she saide.
"As help me God, it wol nat be com-pa-me.°   *come-kiss-me*
I love another, and elles I were to blame,
Wel bet° than thee, by Jesu, Absolon.   *better*
Go forth thy way or I wol caste a stoon,
605 And lat me sleepe, a twenty devele way."[4]
  "Allas," quod Absolon, "and wailaway,
That trewe love was evere so yvele biset.[5]
Thanne kis me, sin that it may be no bet,
For Jesus love and for the love of me."
610   "Woltou thanne go thy way therwith?" quod she.
  "Ye, certes, lemman," quod this Absolon.
  "Thanne maak thee redy," quod she. "I come anoon."
And unto Nicholas she saide stille,°   *quietly*
"Now hust,° and thou shalt laughen al thy fille."   *hush*
615   This Absolon down sette him on his knees,
And said, "I am a lord at alle degrees,[6]
For after this I hope ther cometh more.
Lemman, thy grace, and sweete brid, thyn ore!"°   *mercy*
  The windowe she undooth, and that in haste.
620 "Have do," quod she, "come of and speed thee faste,
Lest that oure neighebores thee espye."
  This Absolon gan wipe his mouth ful drye:
Derk was the night as pich or as the cole,

8. I dreamed.
9. To perfection.
1. Grain of paradise; a spice.
2. Sprig of a cloverlike plant.

3. Bird or bride.
4. In the name of twenty devils.
5. Ill-used.
6. In every way.

And at the windowe out she putte hir hole,
625 And Absolon, him fil no bet ne wers,[7]
But with his mouth he kiste hir naked ers,
Ful savoury,° er he were war of this.   *with relish*
Abak he sterte,° and thoughte it was amis,   *started*
For wel he wiste a womman hath no beerd.°   *beard*
630 He felte a thing al rough and longe yherd,°   *haired*
And saide, "Fy, allas, what have I do?"
   "Teehee," quod she, and clapte the windowe to.
And Absolon gooth forth a sory pas.[8]
   "A beerd, a beerd!"[9] quod hende Nicholas,
635 "By Goddes corpus,° this gooth faire and weel."   *body*
This sely Absolon herde everydeel,°   *every bit*
And on his lippe he gan for anger bite,
And to himself he saide, "I shal thee quite."°   *repay*
Who rubbeth now, who froteth° now his lippes   *wipes*
640 With dust, with sond,° with straw, with cloth, with chippes, *sand*
But Absolon, that saith ful ofte allas?
"My soule bitake° I unto Satanas,°   *commit / Satan*
But me were levere[1] than all this town," quod he,
"Of this despit° awroken° for to be.   *insult / avenged*
645 Allas," quod he, "allas I ne hadde ybleint!"°   *turned aside*
His hote love was cold and al yqueint,°   *quenched*
For fro that time that he hadde kist hir ers
Of paramours he sette nought a kers,[2]
For he was heled° of his maladye.   *cured*
650 Ful ofte paramours he gan defye,°   *renounce*
And weep° as dooth a child that is ybete.   *wept*
A softe paas[3] he wente over the streete
Until° a smith men clepen daun Gervais,[4]   *to*
That in his forge smithed plough harneis:°   *equipment*
655 He sharpeth shaar and cultour[5] bisily.
This Absolon knokketh al esily,°   *quietly*
And saide, "Undo, Gervais, and that anoon."°   *at once*
   "What, who artou?" "It am I, Absolon."
   "What, Absolon? What, Cristes sweete tree!°   *cross*
660 Why rise ye so rathe?° Ey, benedicite,°   *early / bless me*
What aileth you? Som gay girl, God it woot,
Hath brought you thus upon the viritoot.[6]
By Sainte Note, ye woot wel what I mene."
   This Absolon ne roughte nat a bene[7]
665 Of al his play. No word again he yaf:
He hadde more tow on his distaf[8]
Than Gervais knew, and saide, "Freend so dere,
This hote cultour in the chimenee° here,   *fireplace*
As lene[9] it me: I have therwith to doone.

---

7. It befell him neither better nor worse.
8. I.e., walking sadly.
9. A trick (slang), but with a play on line 629.
1. I had rather.
2. He didn't care a piece of cress for woman's love.
3. I.e., quiet walk.
4. Master Gervais.

5. He sharpens plowshare and coulter (the turf cutter on a plow).
6. I.e., on the prowl.
7. Didn't care a bean.
8. I.e., more on his mind.
9. I.e., please lend.

670 I wol bringe it thee again ful soone."
    Gervais answerde, "Certes, were it gold,
Or in a poke nobles alle untold,[1]
Thou sholdest have, as I am trewe smith.
Ey, Cristes fo,[2] what wol ye do therwith?"
675   "Therof," quod Absolon, "be as be may.
I shal wel telle it thee another day."
And caughte the cultour by the colde stele.°   *handle*
Ful softe out at the dore he gan to stele,
And wente unto the carpenteres wal:
680 He cougheth first and knokketh therwithal
Upon the windowe, right as he dide er.°   *before*
    This Alison answerde, "Who is ther
That knokketh so? I warante[3] it a thief."
    "Why, nay," quod he, "God woot, my sweete lief,°   *dear*
685 I am thyn Absolon, my dereling.°   *darling*
Of gold," quod he, "I have thee brought a ring—
My moder yaf it me, so God me save;
Ful fin it is and therto wel ygrave:°   *engraved*
This wol I yiven thee if thou me kisse."
690   This Nicholas was risen for to pisse,
And thoughte he wolde amenden[4] al the jape:°   *joke*
He sholde kisse his ers er that he scape.
And up the windowe dide he hastily,
And out his ers he putteth prively,
695 Over the buttok to the haunche-boon.
    And therwith spak this clerk, this Absolon,
"Speek, sweete brid, I noot nought wher thou art."
This Nicholas anoon leet flee[5] a fart
As greet as it hadde been a thonder-dent°   *thunderbolt*
700 That with the strook he was almost yblent,°   *blinded*
And he was redy with his iren hoot,°   *hot*
And Nicholas amidde the ers he smoot:°   *smote*
Of° gooth the skin an hande-brede° aboute;   *off / handsbreadth*
The hote cultour brende so his toute°   *buttocks*
705 That for the smert° he wende for to[6] die;   *pain*
As he were wood° for wo he gan to crye,   *crazy*
"Help! Water! Water! Help, for Goddes herte!"
    This carpenter out of his slomber sterte,
And herde oon cryen "Water!" as he were wood,
710 And thoughte, "Allas, now cometh Noweles[7] flood!"
He sette him up[8] withoute wordes mo,
And with his ax he smoot the corde atwo,
And down gooth al: he foond neither to selle
Ne breed ne ale til he cam to the celle,[9]
715 Upon the floor, and ther aswoune° he lay.   *in a faint*

---

1. Or gold coins all uncounted in a bag.
2. Foe, i.e., Satan.
3. I.e., wager.
4. Improve on.
5. Let fly.
6. Thought he would.

7. The carpenter is confusing Noah and Noel (Christmas).
8. Got up.
9. He found time to sell neither bread nor ale until he arrived at the foundation, i.e., he did not take time out.

Up sterte hire[1] Alison and Nicholay,
And criden "Out" and "Harrow" in the streete.
The neighebores, bothe smale and grete,
In ronnen for to gauren° on this man   gape
720 That aswoune lay bothe pale and wan,
For with the fal he brosten° hadde his arm;   broken
But stonde he moste° unto his owene harm,   must
For whan he spak he was anoon bore down[2]
With° hende Nicholas and Alisoun: by
725 They tolden every man that he was wood—
He was agast so of Noweles flood,
Thurgh fantasye, that of his vanitee°   folly
He hadde ybought him kneeding-tubbes three,
And hadde hem hanged in the roof above,
730 And that he prayed hem, for Goddes love,
To sitten in the roof, *par compaignye*.[3]
     The folk gan laughen at his fantasye.
Into the roof they kiken° and they cape,°   peer / gape
And turned al his harm unto a jape,°   joke
735 For what so that this carpenter answerde,
It was for nought: no man his reson° herde;   argument
With othes grete he was so sworn adown,
That he was holden° wood in al the town,   considered
For every clerk anoonright heeld with other:
740 They saide, "The man was wood, my leve brother,"
And every wight gan laughen at this strif.°   fuss
Thus swived[4] was the carpenteres wif
For al his keeping° and his jalousye,   guarding
And Absolon hath kist hir nether° yë,   lower
745 And Nicholas is scalded in the toute:
This tale is doon, and God save al the route!°   company

The Man of Law's Epilogue

The Reeve has taken *The Miller's Tale* personally and retaliates with a fabliau about a miller whose wife and daughter are seduced by two clerks. Next the Cook begins yet another fabliau, which breaks off after fifty-five lines, thereby closing Fragment I of *The Canterbury Tales*. Chaucer may never have settled on a final order for the tales he completed, but all modern editors, following many manuscripts, agree in putting *The Man of Law's Tale* next. The Man of Law tells a long moralistic tale about the many trials of a heroine called Constance for the virtue she personifies. This tale is finished, but Fragment II shows that *The Canterbury Tales* reaches us as a work in progress, which Chaucer kept revising, creating many problems for its scribes and editors. In the link that introduces him, the Man of Law says he will tell a tale in prose, but the story of Constance turns out to be in a seven-line stanza called rhyme royal. That inconsistency has led to speculation that at one time the Man of Law was assigned a long prose allegory, which Chaucer later reassigned to his own pilgrim persona. In thirty-five manuscripts *The Man of Law's Tale* is followed by an *Epilogue* omitted in

---

1. Started.
2. Refuted.
3. For company's sake.
4. The vulgar verb for having sexual intercourse.

twenty-two of the manuscripts that contain more or less complete versions of *The Canterbury Tales*. The often-missing link begins with the Host praising the *Man of Law's Tale* and calling upon the Parson to tell another uplifting tale. The Parson, however, rebukes the Host for swearing. The Host angrily accuses the Parson of being a "Lollard," a derogatory term for followers of the reformist polemicist John Wycliffe. This is Chaucer's only overt reference to an important religious and political controversy that anticipates the sixteenth-century English Reformation.

A third speaker, about whose identity the manuscripts disagree (six read "Summoner"; twenty-eight, "Squire"; one, "Shipman"), interrupts with the promise to tell a merry tale. Several modern editions, including the standard one used by scholars, print *The Man of Law's Epilogue* at the end of Fragment II, and begin Fragment III with *The Wife of Bath's Prologue*. Because the third speaker in the former *sounds* like the Wife, an argument has been made that she is the pilgrim who refers to "My joly body" (line 23), who at one time told a fabliau tale in which the narrator speaks of married women in the first person plural ("we," "us," "our"). Chaucer, so the argument goes, later gave that story to the Shipman. If in fact the Wife of Bath did once tell what is now *The Shipman's Tale*, that would be an indication of the exciting new possibilities he discovered in the literary form he had invented.

	Oure Host upon his stiropes stood anoon	
	And saide, "Goode men, herkneth everichoon,	
	This was a thrifty° tale for the nones,°	*proper / occasion*
	Sire parissh Preest," quod he, "for Goddes bones,	
5	Tel us a tale as was thy forward° yore.°	*agreement / earlier*
	I see wel that ye lerned men in lore°	*teaching*
	Can° muche good, by Goddes dignitee."	*know*
	The Person him answerde, "Benedicite,°	*bless me*
	What aileth the man so sinfully to swere?"	
10	Oure Host answerede, "O Jankin, be ye there?[1]	
	I smelle a lollere[2] in the wind," quod he.	
	"Now, goode men," quod oure Hoste, "herkneth me:	
	Abideth, for Goddes digne° passioun,	*worthy*
	For we shal have a predicacioun.°	*sermon*
15	This lollere here wol prechen us somwhat."	
	"Nay, by my fader soule that shal he nat,"	
	Saide the [Wif of Bathe],[3] "here shal he nat preche:	
	He shal no gospel glosen[4] here ne teche.	
	We leven° alle in the grete God," quod [she].	*believe*
20	"He wolde sowen som difficultee	
	Or sprengen cokkel in oure clene corn.[5]	
	And therfore, Host, I warne thee biforn,	
	My joly body shal a tale telle	
	And I shal clinken you so merye a belle	
25	That I shal waken al this compaignye.	
	But it shal nat been of philosophye,	
	Ne physlias[6] ne termes quainte of lawe:	
	There is but litel Latin in my mawe."°	*stomach*

1. Is that where you're coming from? "Jankin": Johnny; derogatory name for a priest.
2. Contemptuous term for a religious reformer considered radical; a heretic.
3. On the speaker here, see discussion in headnote.
4. Gloss, with the sense of distorting the meaning of scripture.
5. Sow tares (impure doctrine) in our pure wheat.
6. No such word exists. The speaker is coining a professional-sounding term in philosophy, law, or medicine.

The Wife of Bath's Prologue and Tale

The Wife of Bath. Illumination from the Ellesmere Manuscript of *The Canterbury Tales*, ca. 1400–1405. Note the whip and the spurs.

In creating the Wife of Bath, Chaucer drew upon a centuries-old tradition of misogynist writing that was particularly nurtured by the medieval church. In their conviction that the rational, intellectual, spiritual, and, therefore, higher side of human nature predominated in men, whereas the irrational, material, earthly, and, therefore, lower side of human nature predominated in women, St. Paul and the early Church fathers exalted celibacy and virginity above marriage, although they were also obliged to concede the necessity and sanctity of matrimony. In the fourth century, a monk called Jovinian wrote a tract in which he apparently presented marriage as a positive good rather than as a necessary evil. That tract is known only through St. Jerome's extreme attack upon it. Jerome's diatribe and other antifeminist and antimatrimonial literature provided Chaucer with a rich body of bookish male "auctoritee" (authority) against which the Wife of Bath asserts her female "experience" and defends her rights and justifies her life as a five-time married woman. In her polemical wars with medieval clerks and her matrimonial wars with her five husbands, the last of whom was once a clerk of Oxenford, the Wife of Bath seems ironically to confirm the accusations of the clerks, but at the same time she succeeds in satirizing the shallowness of the stereotypes of women and marriage in antifeminist writings and in demonstrating how much the largeness and complexity of her own character rise above that stereotype.

The Prologue

	Experience, though noon auctoritee	
	Were in this world, is right ynough for me	
	To speke of wo that is in mariage:	
	For lordinges,° sith I twelf yeer was of age—	gentlemen
5	Thanked be God that is eterne on live—	
	Housbondes at chirche dore[1] I have had five	
	(If I so ofte mighte han wedded be),	
	And alle were worthy men in hir degree.	
	But me was told, certain, nat longe agoon is,	
10	That sith that Crist ne wente nevere but ones°	once
	To wedding in the Cane[2] of Galilee,	
	That by the same ensample° taughte he me	example
	That I ne sholde wedded be but ones.	
	Herke eek,° lo, which° a sharp word for the nones,[3]	also / what
15	Biside a welle, Jesus, God and man,	
	Spak in repreve° of the Samaritan:	reproof

---

1. The actual wedding ceremony was celebrated at the church door, not in the chancel.
2. Cana (see John 2.1).
3. To the purpose.

"Thou hast yhad five housbondes," quod he,

"And that ilke° man that now hath thee   *same*

Is nat thyn housbonde." Thus saide he certain.

20   What that he mente therby I can nat sayn,

But that I axe° why the fifthe man   *ask*

Was noon housbonde to the Samaritan?[4]

How manye mighte she han in mariage?

Yit herde I nevere tellen in myn age

25   Upon this nombre diffinicioun.°   *definition*

Men may divine° and glosen° up and down,   *guess / interpret*

But wel I woot,° expres,° withouten lie,   *know / expressly*

God bad us for to wexe[5] and multiplye:

That gentil text can I wel understonde.

30   Eek wel I woot° he saide that myn housbonde   *know*

Sholde lete° fader and moder and take to me,[6]   *leave*

But of no nombre mencion made he—

Of bigamye or of octogamye:[7]

Why sholde men thanne speke of it vilainye?

35   Lo, here the wise king daun° Salomon: *master*

I trowe° he hadde wives many oon,[8]   *believe*

As wolde God it leveful° were to me   *permissible*

To be refresshed half so ofte as he.

Which yifte[9] of God hadde he for alle his wives!

40   No man hath swich° that in this world alive is.   *such*

God woot this noble king, as to my wit,°   *knowledge*

The firste night hadde many a merye fit°   *bout*

With eech of hem, so wel was him on live.[1]

Blessed be God that I have wedded five,

45   Of whiche I have piked out the beste,[2]

Bothe of hir nether purs[3] and of hir cheste.°   *money box*

Diverse scoles maken parfit° clerkes,   *perfect*

And diverse practikes[4] in sondry werkes

Maken the werkman parfit sikerly:°   *certainly*

50   Of five housbondes scoleying° am I.   *schooling*

Welcome the sixte whan that evere he shal![5]

For sith I wol nat kepe me chast° in al,   *celibate*

Whan my housbonde is fro the world agoon,

Som Cristen man shal wedde me anoon.°   *right away*

55   For thanne th'Apostle[6] saith that I am free

To wedde, a Goddes half, where it liketh me.[7]

He saide that to be wedded is no sinne:

Bet is to be wedded than to brinne.[8]

---

4. Christ was actually referring to a sixth man who was not married to the Samaritan woman (cf. John 4.6ff.).
5. I.e., increase (see Genesis 1.28).
6. See Matthew 19.5.
7. I.e., of two or even eight marriages. The Wife of Bath is referring to successive, rather than simultaneous, marriages.
8. Solomon had seven hundred wives and three hundred concubines (1 Kings 11.3).
9. What a gift.
1. I.e., so pleasant a life he had.

2. Whom I have cleaned out of everything worth while.
3. Lower purse, i.e., testicles.
4. Practical experiences.
5. I.e., shall come along.
6. St. Paul.
7. I please. "A Goddes half": on God's behalf.
8. "It is better to marry than to burn" (1 Corinthians 7.9). Many of the Wife's citations of St. Paul are from this chapter, often secondhand from St. Jerome's tract *Against Jovinian*.

What rekketh me[9] though folk saye vilainye
60 Of shrewed° Lamech[1] and his bigamye?   *cursed*
I woot wel Abraham was an holy man,
And Jacob eek, as fer as evere I can,°   *know*
And eech of hem hadde wives mo than two,
And many another holy man also.
65   Where can ye saye in any manere age
That hye God defended° mariage   *prohibited*
By expres word? I praye you, telleth me.
Or where comanded he virginitee?
I woot as wel as ye, it is no drede,°   *doubt*
70 Th'Apostle, whan he speketh of maidenhede,°   *virginity*
He saide that precept therof hadde he noon:
Men may conseile a womman to be oon,°   *single*
But conseiling nis° no comandement.   *is not*
He putte it in oure owene juggement.
75 For hadde God comanded maidenhede,
Thanne hadde he dampned° wedding with the deede;[2]   *condemned*
And certes, if there were no seed ysowe,
Virginitee, thanne wherof sholde it growe?
Paul dorste nat comanden at the leeste
80 A thing of which his maister yaf° no heeste.°   *gave / command*
The dart[3] is set up for virginitee:
Cacche whoso may, who renneth° best lat see.   *runs*
But this word is nought take of[4] every wight,°   *person*
But ther as[5] God list° yive it of his might.   *it pleases*
85 I woot wel that th'Apostle was a maide,°   *virgin*
But nathelees, though that he wroot and saide
He wolde that every wight were swich° as he,   *such*
Al nis but conseil to virginitee;
And for to been a wif he yaf me leve
90 Of indulgence; so nis it no repreve°   *disgrace*
To wedde me[6] if that my make° die,   *mate*
Withouten excepcion of bigamy[7]—
Al° were it good no womman for to touche[8]   *although*
(He mente as in his bed or in his couche,
95 For peril is bothe fir° and tow° t'assemble—   *fire / flax*
Ye knowe what this ensample may resemble).[9]
This al and som,[1] he heeld virginitee
More parfit than wedding in freletee.°   *frailty*
(Freletee clepe I but if[2] that he and she
100 Wolde leden al hir lif in chastitee.)
I graunte it wel, I have noon envye
Though maidenhede preferre° bigamye:°   *excel / remarriage*
It liketh hem to be clene in body and gost.°   *spirit*

9. What do I care.
1. The first man whom the Bible mentions as having two wives (Genesis 4.19–24); he is cursed, however, not for his marriages but for murder.
2. I.e., at the same time.
3. I.e., prize in a race.
4. Understood for, i.e., applicable to.
5. Where.

6. For me to marry.
7. I.e., without there being any legal objection on the score of remarriage.
8. "It is good for a man not to touch a woman" (1 Corinthians 7.1).
9. I.e., what this metaphor may apply to.
1. This is all there is to it.
2. Frailty I call it unless.

Of myn estaat ne wol I make no boost;
105   For wel ye knowe, a lord in his houshold
Ne hath nat every vessel al of gold:
Some been of tree,° and doon hir lord servise.   *wood*
God clepeth° folk to him in sondry wise,   *calls*
And everich hath of God a propre yifte,[3]
110   Som this, som that, as him liketh shifte.°   *ordain*
Virginitee is greet perfeccioun,
And continence eek with devocioun,
But Crist, that of perfeccion is welle,°   *source*
Bad nat every wight he sholde go selle
115   Al that he hadde and yive it to the poore,
And in swich wise folwe him and his fore:°[4]   *footsteps*
He spak to hem that wolde live parfitly°—   *perfectly*
And lordinges, by youre leve, that am nat I.
I wol bistowe the flour of al myn age
120   In th'actes and in fruit of mariage.
    Telle me also, to what conclusioun°   *end*
Were membres maad of generacioun
And of so parfit wis a wrighte ywrought?[5]
    Trusteth right wel, they were nat maad for nought.
125   Glose° whoso wol, and saye bothe up and down   *interpret*
That they were maked for purgacioun
Of urine, and oure bothe thinges smale
Was eek° to knowe a femele from a male,   *also*
And for noon other cause—saye ye no?
130   Th'experience woot it is nought so.
So that the clerkes be nat with me wrothe,
I saye this, that they been maad for bothe—
That is to sayn, for office° and for ese°   *use / pleasure*
Of engendrure,° ther we nat God displese.   *procreation*
135   Why sholde men elles in hir bookes sette
That man shal yeelde[6] to his wif hir dette?°   *(marital) debt*
Now wherwith sholde he make his payement
If he ne used his sely° instrument?   *innocent*
Thanne were they maad upon a creature
140   To purge urine, and eek for engendrure.
    But I saye nought that every wight is holde,°   *bound*
That hath swich harneis° as I to you tolde,   *equipment*
To goon and usen hem in engendrure:
Thanne sholde men take of chastitee no cure.°   *heed*
145   Crist was a maide° and shapen as a man,   *virgin*
And many a saint sith that the world bigan,
Yit lived they evere in parfit chastitee.
I nil° envye no virginitee: *will not*
Lat hem be breed° of pured° whete seed,   *bread / refined*
150   And lat us wives hote° barly breed—   *be called*
And yit with barly breed, Mark telle can,

3. See 1 Corinthians 7.4–5.
4. Matthew 19.21
5. And wrought by so perfectly wise a maker.
6. I.e., pay. See 1 Corinthians 7.4–5.

Oure Lord Jesu refresshed many a man.[7]
In swich estaat as God hath cleped us
I wol persevere: I nam nat precious.°   *fastidious*
155 In wifhood wol I use myn instrument
As freely° as my Makere hath it sent.   *generously*
If I be daungerous[8], God yive me sorwe:
Myn housbonde shal it han both eve and morwe,°   *morning*
Whan that him list[9] come forth and paye his dette.
160 An housbonde wol I have, I wol nat lette,[1]
Which shal be bothe my dettour° and my thral,°   *debtor / slave*
And have his tribulacion withal°   *as well*
Upon his flessh whil that I am his wif.
I have the power during al my lif
165 Upon his propre° body, and nat he: *own*
Right thus th'Apostle tolde it unto me,
And bad oure housbondes for to love us weel.
Al this sentence° me liketh everydeel.°   *sense / entirely*

[AN INTERLUDE]

Up sterte° the Pardoner and that anoon:°   *started / at once*
170 "Now dame," quod he, "by God and by Saint John,
Ye been a noble prechour in this cas.
I was aboute to wedde a wif: allas,
What° sholde I bye° it on my flessh so dere?   *why / purchase*
Yit hadde I levere° wedde no wif toyere."°   *rather / this year*
175 "Abid," quod she, "my tale is nat bigonne.
Nay, thou shalt drinken of another tonne,°   *tun, barrel*
Er° that I go, shal savoure wors than ale.   *before*
And whan that I have told thee forth my tale
Of tribulacion in mariage,
180 Of which I am expert in al myn age—
This is to saye, myself hath been the whippe—
Thanne maistou chese° wheither thou wolt sippe   *choose*
Of thilke° tonne that I shal abroche;°   *this same / open*
Be war of it, er thou too neigh approche,
185 For I shal telle ensamples mo than ten.
'Whoso that nil° be war by othere men,   *will not*
By him shal othere men corrected be.'
Thise same wordes writeth Ptolomee:
Rede in his *Almageste* and take it there."[2]
190 "Dame, I wolde praye you if youre wil it were,"
Saide this Pardoner, "as ye bigan,
Telle forth youre tale; spareth for no man,
And teche us yonge men of youre practike."°   *mode of operation*
"Gladly," quod she, "sith it may you like;°   *please*

---

7. In the descriptions of the miracle of the loaves and fishes, it is actually John, not Mark, who mentions barley bread (6.9).
8. In romance *dangerous* is a term for disdainfulness with which a woman rejects a lover. The Wife means she will not withhold sexual favors, in emulation of God's generosity (line 156).
9. When he wishes to.
1. I will not leave off, desist.
2. "He who will not be warned by the example of others shall become an example to others." The *Almagest*, an astronomical work by the Greek astronomer and mathematician Ptolemy (2nd century C.E.), contains no such aphorism.

195 But that I praye to al this compaignye,
    If that I speke after my fantasye,[3]
    As taketh nat agrief° of that I saye,   *amiss*
    For myn entente nis but for to playe."

[THE WIFE CONTINUES]

    Now sire, thanne wol I telle you forth my tale.
200 As evere mote I drinke win or ale,
    I shal saye sooth: tho° housbondes that I hadde,   *those*
    As three of hem were goode, and two were badde.
    The three men were goode, and riche, and olde;
    Unnethe° mighte they the statut holde   *scarcely*
205 In which they were bounden unto me—
    Ye woot wel what I mene of this, pardee.
    As help me God, I laughe whan I thinke
    How pitously anight I made hem swinke;°   *work*
    And by my fay,° I tolde of it no stoor:[4]   *faith*
210 They hadde me yiven hir land and hir tresor;
    Me needed nat do lenger diligence
    To winne hir love or doon hem reverence.
    They loved me so wel, by God above,
    That I ne tolde no daintee of[5] hir love.
215 A wis womman wol bisye hire evere in oon[6]
    To gete hire love, ye, ther as she hath noon.
    But sith I hadde hem hoolly in myn hand,
    And sith that they hadde yiven me al hir land,
    What° sholde I take keep° hem for to plese,   *why / care*
220 But it were for my profit and myn ese?
    I sette hem so awerke,° by my fay,   *awork*
    That many a night they songen° wailaway.   *sang*
    The bacon was nat fet° for hem, I trowe,   *brought back*
    That some men han in Essexe at Dunmowe.[7]
225 I governed hem so wel after° my lawe   *according to*
    That eech of hem ful blisful was and fawe°   *glad*
    To bringe me gaye thinges fro the faire;
    They were ful glade whan I *spalt* hem faire,
    For God it woot, I chidde° hem spitously.°   *chided / cruelly*
230 Now herkneth how I bar me° proprely: *bore myself, behaved*
    Ye wise wives, that conne understonde,
    Thus sholde ye speke and here him wrong on honde[8]—
    For half so boldely can ther no man
    Swere and lie as a woman can.
235 I saye nat this by wives that been wise,
    But if it be whan they hem misavise.[9]
    A wis wif, if that she can hir good,[1]

---

3. If I speak according to my fancy.
4. I set no store by it.
5. Set no value on.
6. Busy herself constantly.
7. At Dunmow, a side of bacon was awarded to the couple who after a year of marriage could claim no quarrels, no regrets, and the desire, if freed, to remarry one another.
8. Accuse him falsely.
9. Unless it happens that they make a mistake.
1. If she knows what's good for her.

Shal bere him on hande the cow is wood,[2]
And take witnesse of hir owene maide
240 Of hir assent.[3] But herkneth how I saide:
   "Sire olde cainard,° is this thyn array?[4]   *sluggard*
Why is my neighebores wif so gay?
She is honoured overal° ther she gooth: *wherever*
I sitte at hoom; I have no thrifty° cloth.   *decent*
245 What doostou at my neighebores hous?
Is she so fair? Artou so amorous?
What roune° ye with oure maide, benedicite.[5]   *whisper*
Sire olde lechour, lat thy japes° be.   *tricks, intrigues*
And if I have a gossib° or a freend   *confidant*
250 Withouten gilt, ye chiden as a feend,
If that I walke or playe unto his hous.
Thou comest hoom as dronken as a mous,
And prechest on thy bench, with yvel preef.[6]
Thou saist to me, it is a greet mischief°   *misfortune*
255 To wedde a poore womman for costage.[7]
And if that she be riche, of heigh parage,°   *descent*
Thanne saistou that it is a tormentrye
To suffre hir pride and hir malencolye.°   *bad humor*
And if that she be fair, thou verray knave,
260 Thou saist that every holour° wol hire have: *lecher*
She may no while in chastitee abide[8]
That is assailed upon eech a side.
   "Thou saist som folk desiren us for richesse,
Som[9] for oure shap, and som for oure fairnesse,
265 And som for she can outher° singe or daunce,   *either*
And som for gentilesse and daliaunce,°   *flirtatiousness*
Som for hir handes and hir armes smale°—   *slender*
Thus gooth al to the devel by thy tale![1]
Thou saist men may nat keepe[2] a castel wal,
270 It may so longe assailed been overal.°   *everywhere*
And if that she be foul,° thou saist that she   *ugly*
Coveiteth° every man that she may see;   *desires*
For as a spaniel she wol on him lepe,
Til that she finde som man hire to chepe.°   *bargain for*
275 Ne noon so grey goos gooth ther in the lake,
As, saistou, wol be withoute make;°   *mate*
And saist it is an hard thing for to weelde°   *possess*
A thing that no man wol, his thankes, heelde[3]
Thus saistou, lorel,° whan thou goost to bedde,   *wretch*
280 And that no wis man needeth for to wedde,
Ne no man that entendeth° unto hevene—   *aims*
With wilde thonder-dint° and firy levene°   *thunderbolt / lightning*

---

2. Shall persuade him the chough has gone crazy.
The chough, a talking bird, was popularly supposed to tell husbands of their wives' infidelity.
3. And call as a witness her maid, who is on her
side.
4. I.e., is this how you behave?
5. The Lord bless you.
6. I.e., (may you have) bad luck.

7. Because of the expense.
8. Remain faithful to her husband.
9. "Som," in this and the following lines, means
"one."
1. I.e., according to your story.
2. I.e., keep safe.
3. No man would willingly hold.

Mote thy welked nekke be tobroke!⁴
Thou saist that dropping° houses and eek smoke   *leaking*
285 And chiding wives maken men to flee
Out of hir owene hous: a, benedicite,
What aileth swich an old man for to chide?
Thou saist we wives wil oure vices hide
Til we be fast,⁵ and thanne we wol hem shewe—
290 Wel may that be a proverbe of a shrewe!°   *rascal*
Thou saist that oxen, asses, hors,° and houndes, *horses*
They been assayed° at diverse stoundes;° *tried out / times*
Bacins, lavours,° er that men hem bye,° *washbowls / buy*
Spoones, stooles, and al swich housbondrye,° *household goods*
295 And so be° pottes, clothes, and array°— *are / clothing*
But folk of wives maken noon assay
Til they be wedded—olde dotard shrewe!
And thanne, saistou, we wil oure vices shewe.
Thou saist also that it displeseth me
300 But if° that thou wolt praise my beautee,   *unless*
And but thou poure° alway upon my face,   *gaze*
And clepe me 'Faire Dame' in every place,
And but thou make a feeste on thilke day
That I was born, and make me fressh and gay,
305 And but thou do to my norice° honour,   *nurse*
And to my chamberere within my bowr,⁶
And to my fadres folk, and his allies⁷—
Thus saistou, olde barel-ful of lies.
And yit of our apprentice Janekin,
310 For his crispe° heer, shining as gold so fin,   *curly*
And for° he squiereth me bothe up and down,   *because*
Yit hastou caught a fals suspecioun;
I wil° him nat though thou were deed° tomorwe. *want / dead*
 "But tel me this, why hidestou with sorwe⁸
315 The keyes of thy cheste° away fro me?   *money box*
It is my good° as wel as thyn, pardee.   *property*
What, weenestou° make an idiot of oure dame?⁹ *do you think to*
Now by that lord that called is Saint Jame,
Thou shalt nought bothe, though thou were wood,° *furious*
320 Be maister of my body and of my good:
That oon thou shalt forgo, maugree thine yën.¹
 "What helpeth it of me enquere° and spyen?   *inquire*
I trowe thou woldest loke° me in thy cheste.   *lock*
Thou sholdest saye, 'Wif, go wher thee leste.° *it may please*
325 Taak youre disport² I nil leve° no tales: *believe*
I knowe you for a trewe wif, dame Alis.'
We love no man that taketh keep or charge³
Wher that we goon: we wol been at oure large.⁴

---

4. May thy withered neck be broken!
5. I.e., married.
6. And to my chambermaid within my bedroom.
7. Relatives by marriage.
8. I.e., with sorrow to you.
9. I.e., me, the mistress of the house.

1. Despite your eyes, i.e., despite anything you can do about it.
2. Enjoy yourself.
3. Notice or interest.
4. I.e., liberty.

Of alle men yblessed mote he be
330 The wise astrologen° daun Ptolomee,   *astronomer*
That saith this proverbe in his *Almageste*:
'Of alle men his wisdom is the hyeste
That rekketh° nat who hath the world in honde.[5]   *cares*
By this proverbe thou shalt understonde,
335 Have thou[6] ynough, what thar° thee rekke or care   *need*
How merily that othere folkes fare?
For certes, olde dotard, by youre leve,
Ye shal han queinte[7] right ynough at eve:
He is too greet a nigard that wil werne°   *refuse*
340 A man to lighte a candle at his lanterne;
He shal han nevere the lasse° lighte, pardee.   *less*
Have thou ynough, thee thar nat plaine thee.[8]
     "Thou saist also that if we make us gay
With clothing and with precious array,
345 That it is peril of oure chastitee,
And yit, with sorwe, thou moste enforce thee,[9]
And saye thise wordes in th' Apostles[1] name:
'In habit° maad with chastitee and shame   *clothing*
Ye wommen shal apparaile you,' quod he,
350 'And nat in tressed heer[2] and gay perree,°   *jewelry*
As perles, ne with gold ne clothes riche.'[3]
After thy text, ne after thy rubriche,[4]
I wol nat werke as muchel as a gnat.
Thou saidest this, that I was lik a cat:
355 For whoso wolde senge° a cattes skin,   *singe*
Thanne wolde the cat wel dwellen in his in;°   *lodging*
And if the cattes skin be slik° and gay,   *sleek*
She wol nat dwelle in house half a day,
But forth she wol, er any day be dawed,[5]
360 To shewe her skin and goon a-caterwawed.°   *caterwauling*
This is to saye, if I be gay, sire shrewe,
I wol renne° out, my borel° for to shewe.   *run / clothing*
Sir olde fool, what helpeth[6] thee t'espyen?
Though thou praye Argus with his hundred yën[7]
365 To be my wardecors,° as he can best,   *bodyguard*
In faith, he shal nat keepe° me but me lest:[8]   *guard*
Yit coude I make his beerd,[9] so mote I thee.°   *prosper*
     "Thou saidest eek that ther been thinges three,
The whiche thinges troublen al this erthe,
370 And that no wight may endure the ferthe.°   *fourth*
O leve° sire shrewe, Jesu shorte° thy lif!   *dear / shorten*
Yit prechestou and saist an hateful wif

5. Who rules the world.
6. If you have.
7. Elegant, pleasing thing; a euphemism for sexual enjoyment.
8. I.e., you need not complain.
9. Strengthen your position.
1. I.e., St. Paul's.
2. I.e., elaborate hairdo.
3. See 1 Timothy 2.9.

4. Rubric, i.e., direction.
5. Has dawned.
6. What does it help.
7. Argus was a monster whom Juno set to watch over one of Jupiter's mistresses. Mercury put all one hundred of his eyes to sleep and slew him.
8. Unless I please.
9. I.e., deceive him.

Yrekened° is for oon of thise meschaunces.[1]   *is counted*
Been ther nat none othere resemblaunces
375 That ye may likne youre parables to,[2]
But if° a sely° wif be oon of tho?   *unless / innocent*
    "Thou liknest eek wommanes love to helle,
To bareine° land ther water may nat dwelle;   *barren*
Thou liknest it also to wilde fir—
380 The more it brenneth,° the more it hath desir   *burns*
To consumen every thing that brent° wol be;   *burned*
Thou saist right° as wormes shende° a tree,   *just / destroy*
Right so a wif destroyeth hir housbonde—
This knowen they that been to wives bonde."°   *bound*
385   Lordinges, right thus, as ye han understonde,
Bar I stifly mine olde housbondes on honde[3]
That thus they saiden in hir dronkenesse—
And al was fals, but that I took witnesse
On Janekin and on my nece also.
390 O Lord, the paine I dide hem and the wo,
Ful giltelees, by Goddes sweete pine!°   *suffering*
For as an hors I coude bite and whine;°   *whinny*
I coude plaine° and° I was in the gilt,   *complain / if*
Or elles often time I hadde been spilt.°   *ruined*
395 Whoso that first to mille comth first grint.°   *grinds*
I plained first: so was oure werre stint.[4]
They were ful glade to excusen hem ful blive°   *quickly*
Of thing of which they nevere agilte hir live.[5]
Of wenches wolde I beren hem on honde,[6]
400 Whan that for sik[7] they mighte unnethe° stonde,   *scarcely*
Yit tikled I his herte for that he
Wende° I hadde had of him so greet cheertee.°   *thought / affection*
I swoor that al my walking out by nighte
Was for to espye wenches that he dighte.[8]
405 Under that colour[9] hadde I many a mirthe.
For al swich wit is yiven us in oure birthe:
Deceite, weeping, spinning God hath yive
To wommen kindely° whil they may live.   *naturally*
And thus of oo thing I avaunte me:[1]
410 At ende I hadde the bet° in eech degree,   *better*
By sleighte or force, or by som manere thing,
As by continuel murmur° or grucching;°   *complaint / grumbling*
Namely° abedde hadden they meschaunce: *especially*
Ther wolde I chide and do hem no plesaunce;[2]
415 I wolde no lenger in the bed abide
If that I felte his arm over my side,
Til he hadde maad his raunson° unto me;   *ransom*
Thanne wolde I suffre him do his nicetee.°   *foolishness (sex)*

---

1. For the other three misfortunes see Proverbs 30.21–23.
2. Are there no other (appropriate) similitudes to which you might draw analogies?
3. I rigorously accused my old husbands.
4. Our war brought to an end.
5. Of which they were never guilty in their lives.

6. Falsely accuse them.
7. I.e., sickness.
8. Had intercourse with.
9. I.e., pretense.
1. Boast.
2. Give them no pleasure.

And therfore every man this tale I telle:
420 Winne whoso may, for al is for to selle;
     With empty hand men may no hawkes lure.
     For winning° wolde I al his lust endure,   *profit*
     And make me a feined° appetit—   *pretended*
     And yit in bacon³ hadde I nevere delit.
425 That made me that evere I wolde hem chide;
     For though the Pope hadde seten° hem biside,   *sat*
     I wolde nought spare hem at hir owene boord.°   *table*
     For by my trouthe, I quitte° hem word for word.   *repaid*
     As help me verray God omnipotent,
430 Though I right now sholde make my testament,
     I ne owe hem nat a word that it nis quit.
     I broughte it so aboute by my wit
     That they moste yive it up as for the beste,
     Or elles hadde we nevere been in reste;
435 For though he looked as a wood° leoun,   *furious*
     Yit sholde he faile of his conclusioun.°   *object*
        Thanne wolde I saye, "Goodelief, taak keep,⁴
     How mekely looketh Wilekin,⁵ oure sheep!
     Com neer my spouse, lat me ba° thy cheeke—   *kiss*
440 Ye sholden be al pacient and meeke,
     And han a sweete-spiced° conscience,   *mild*
     Sith ye so preche of Jobes pacience;
     Suffreth alway, sin ye so wel can preche;
     And but ye do, certain, we shal you teche
445 That it is fair to han a wif in pees.
     Oon of us two moste bowen, doutelees,
     And sith a man is more resonable
     Than womman is, ye mosten been suffrable.°   *patient*
     What aileth you to grucche° thus and grone?   *grumble*
450 Is it for ye wolde have my queinte° allone?   *sexual organ*
     Why, taak it al—lo, have it everydeel.°   *all of it*
     Peter,⁶ I shrewe° you but ye° love it weel.   *curse / if you don't*
     For if I wolde selle my bele chose,⁷
     I coude walke as fressh as is a rose;
455 But I wol keepe it for youre owene tooth.°   *taste*
     Ye be to blame. By God, I saye you sooth!"°   *the truth*
     Swiche manere° wordes hadde we on honde.   *kind of*
     Now wol I speke of my ferthe° housbonde.   *fourth*
        My ferthe housbonde was a revelour°   *reveler*
460 This is to sayn, he hadde a paramour°   *mistress*
     And I was yong and ful of ragerye,°   *passion*
     Stibourne° and strong and joly as a pie:°   *untamable / magpie*
     How coude I daunce to an harpe smale,°   *gracefully*
     And singe, ywis,° as any nightingale,   *indeed*
465 Whan I hadde dronke a draughte of sweete win.
     Metellius, the foule cherl, the swin,

---

3. I.e., old meat.
4. Good friend, take notice.
5. I.e., Willie.

6. By St. Peter.
7. French for "beautiful thing"; a euphemism for sexual organs.

That with a staf birafte° his wif hir lif   *deprived*
For° she drank win, though I hadde been his wif,   *because*
Ne sholde nat han daunted° me fro drinke;   *frightened*
470   And after win on Venus moste° I thinke,   *must*
For also siker° as cold engendreth hail,   *sure*
A likerous° mouth moste han a likerous° tail: *greedy / lecherous*
In womman vinolent° is no defence—   *who drinks*
This knowen lechours by experience.

475   But Lord Crist, whan that it remembreth me[8] ✗
Upon my youthe and on my jolitee,
It tikleth me aboute myn herte roote—
Unto this day it dooth myn herte boote°   *good*
That I have had my world as in my time.
480   But age, allas, that al wol envenime,°   *poison*
Hath me biraft[9] my beautee and my pith°—   *vigor*
Lat go, farewel, the devel go therwith!
The flour is goon, ther is namore to telle:
The bren° as I best can now moste I selle;   *bran*
485   But yit to be right merye wol I fonde.°   *strive*
Now wol I tellen of my ferthe housbonde.

[handwritten: ✗ her youth is gone]

    I saye I hadde in herte greet despit
That he of any other hadde delit,
But he was quit,° by God and by Saint Joce: *paid back*
490   I made him of the same wode a croce[1]—
Nat of my body in no foul manere—
But, certainly, I made folk swich cheere[2]
That in his owene grece I made him frye,
For angre and for verray jalousye.
495   By God, in erthe I was his purgatorye,
For which I hope his soule be in glorye.
For God it woot, he sat ful ofte and soong°   *sang*
Whan that his sho ful bitterly him wroong.°   *pinched*
Ther was no wight save God and he that wiste°   *knew*
500   In many wise how sore I him twiste.
He deide whan I cam fro Jerusalem,
And lith ygrave under the roode-beem,[3]
Al° is his tombe nought so curious[4]   *although*
As was the sepulcre of him Darius,
505   Which that Apelles wroughte subtilly:[5]
It nis but wast to burye him preciously.°   *expensively*
Lat him fare wel, God yive his soule reste;
He is now in his grave and in his cheste.°   *coffin*
    Now of my fifthe housbonde wol I telle—
510   God lete his soule nevere come in helle—
And yit he was to me the moste shrewe:[6]
That feele I on my ribbes al by rewe,[7]

---

8. When I look back.
9. Has taken away from me.
1. I made him a cross of the same wood. The proverb has much the same sense as the one quoted in line 493.
2. Pretended to be in love with others.
3. And lies buried under the rood beam (the cru-cifix beam running between nave and chancel).
4. Carefully wrought.
5. Accordingly to medieval legend, the artist Apelles decorated the tomb of Darius, king of the Persians.
6. Worst rascal.
7. In a row.

And evere shal unto myn ending day.
But in oure bed he was so fressh and gay,
515 And therwithal so wel coulde he me glose°   *flatter, coax*
Whan that he wolde han my bele chose,
That though he hadde me bet° on every boon,°   *beaten / bone*
He coude winne again my love anoon.°   *immediately*
I trowe I loved him best for that he
520 Was of his love daungerous[8] to me.
We wommen han, if that I shal nat lie,
In this matere a quainte fantasye:[9]
Waite what[1] thing we may nat lightly° have,   *easily*
Therafter wol we crye al day and crave;
525 Forbede us thing, and that desiren we;
Preesse on us faste, and thanne wol we flee.
With daunger oute we al oure chaffare:[2]
Greet prees° at market maketh dere° ware,   *crowd / expensive*
And too greet chepe is holden at litel pris.[3]
530 This knoweth every womman that is wis.
   My fifthe housbonde—God his soule blesse!—
Which that I took for love and no richesse,
He somtime was a clerk at Oxenforde,
And hadde laft° scole and wente at hoom to boorde   *left*
535 With my gossib,° dwelling in oure town   *confidante*
God have hir soule!—hir name was Alisoun;
She knew myn herte and eek my privetee°   *secrets*
Bet° than oure parissh preest, as mote I thee.°   *better / prosper*
To hire biwrayed° I my conseil° al,   *disclosed / secrets*
540 For hadde myn housbonde pissed on a wal,
Or doon a thing that sholde han cost his lif,
To hire,° and to another worthy wif,   *her*
And to my nece which I loved weel,
I wolde han told his conseil everydeel;°   *entirely*
545 And so I dide ful often, God it woot,
That made his face often reed° and hoot°   *red / hot*
For verray shame, and blamed himself for he
Hadde told to me so greet a privetee.
   And so bifel that ones° in a Lente—   *once*
550 So often times I to my gossib wente,
For evere yit I loved to be gay,
And for to walke in March, Averil, and May,
From hous to hous, to heere sondry tales—
That Janekin clerk and my gossib dame Alis
555 And I myself into the feeldes wente.
Myn housbonde was at London al that Lente:
I hadde the better leiser for to playe,
And for to see, and eek for to be seye°   *seen*
Of lusty folk—what wiste I wher my grace°   *luck*
560 Was shapen° for to be, or in what place?   *destined*

8. I.e., he played hard to get.
9. Strange fancy.
1. Whatever.

2. (Meeting) with reserve, we spread out our merchandise.
3. Too good a bargain is held at little value.

Therfore I made my visitaciouns
To vigilies[4] and to processiouns,
To preching eek, and to thise pilgrimages,
To playes of miracles and to manages,
565 And wered upon[5] my gaye scarlet gites°—   *gowns*
Thise wormes ne thise motthes ne thise mites,
Upon my peril[6] frete° hem neveradeel: *ate*
And woostou why? For they were used weel.
  Now wol I tellen forth what happed me.
570 I saye that in the feeldes walked we,
Til trewely we hadde swich daliaunce,°   *flirtation*
This clerk and I, that of my purveyaunce°   *foresight*
I spak to him and saide him how that he,
If I were widwe, sholde wedde me.
575 For certainly, I saye for no bobaunce,°   *boast*
Yit was I nevere withouten purveyaunce
Of mariage n'of othere thinges eek:
I holde a mouses herte nought worth a leek
That hath but oon hole for to sterte° to,   *run*
580 And if that faile thanne is al ydo.[7]
I bar him on hand[8] he hadde enchaunted me
(My dame° taughte me that subtiltee);   *mother*
And eek I saide I mette° of him al night: *dreamed*
He wolde han slain me as I lay upright,°   *on my back*
585 And al my bed was ful of verray blood—
"But yit I hope that ye shul do me good;
For blood bitokeneth° gold, as me was taught."   *signifies*
And al was fals, I dremed of it right naught,
But as I folwed ay my dames° lore°   *mother's / teaching*
590 As wel of that as othere thinges more.
But now sire—lat me see, what shal I sayn?
Aha, by God, I have my tale again.
  Whan that my ferthe housbonde was on beere,°   *funeral bier*
I weep,° algate,° and made sory cheere,   *wept / anyhow*
595 As wives moten,° for it is usage,°   *must / custom*
And with my coverchief covered my visage;
But for I was purveyed° of a make.°   *provided / mate*
I wepte but smale, and that I undertake.°   *guarantee*
  To chirche was myn housbonde born amorwe;[9]
600 With neighebores that for him maden sorwe,
And Janekin oure clerk was oon of tho.
As help me God, whan that I saw him go
After the beere, me thoughte he hadde a paire
Of legges and of feet so clene[1] and faire,
605 That al myn herte I yaf unto his hold.°   *possession*
He was, I trowe,° twenty winter old,   *believe*
And I was fourty, if I shal saye sooth—
But yit I hadde alway a coltes tooth:[2]

4. Evening service before a religious holiday.
5. Wore.
6. On peril (to my soul), an oath.
7. I.e., the game is up.
8. I pretended to him.
9. In the morning.
1. I.e., neat.
2. I.e., youthful appetites.

Gat-toothed[3] was I, and that bicam me weel;
610 I hadde the prente[4] of Sainte Venus seel.°   *seal*
As help me God, I was a lusty oon,
And fair and riche and yong and wel-bigoon,°   *well-situated*
And trewely, as mine housbondes tolde me,
I hadde the beste quoniam[5] mighte be.
615 For certes I am al Venerien
In feeling, and myn herte is Marcien:[6]
Venus me yaf my lust, my likerousnesse,°   *amorousness*
And Mars yaf me my sturdy hardinesse.
Myn ascendent was Taur[7] and Mars therinne—
620 Allas, allas, that evere love was sinne!
I folwed ay° my inclinacioun   *ever*
By vertu of my constellacioun;[8]
That made me I coude nought withdrawe
My chambre of Venus from a good felawe.
625 Yit have I Martes° merk upon my face,   *Mars's*
And also in another privee place.
For God so wis° be my savacioun,°   *surely / salvation*
I loved nevere by no discrecioun,°   *moderation*
But evere folwede myn appetit,
630 Al were he short or long or blak or whit;
I took no keep,° so that he liked° me,   *heed / pleased*
How poore he was, ne eek of what degree.
What sholde I saye but at the monthes ende
This joly clerk Janekin that was so hende°   *courteous, nice*
635 Hath wedded me with greet solempnitee,°   *splendor*
And to him yaf I al the land and fee°   *property*
That evere was me yiven therbifore—
But afterward repented me ful sore:
He nolde suffre no thing of my list.°   *wish*
640 By God, he smoot° me ones on the list°   *struck / ear*
For that I rente° out of his book a leef,   *tore*
That of the strook° myn ere weex° al deef.   *blow / grew*
Stibourne° I was as is a leonesse,   *stubborn*
And of my tonge a verray jangleresse,°   *chatterbox*
645 And walke I wolde, as I hadde doon biforn,
From hous to hous, although he hadde it[9] sworn;
For which he often times wolde preche,
And me of olde Romain geestes° teche,   *stories*
How he Simplicius Gallus lafte° his wif,   *left*
650 And hire forsook for terme of al his lif,
Nought but for open-heveded he hire sey[1]
Looking out at his dore upon a day.
Another Romain tolde he me by name
That, for his wif was at a someres° game   *summer's*

---

3. Gap-toothed women were considered to be amorous.
4. Print, i.e., a birthmark.
5. Latin for "because"; another euphemism for a sexual organ.
6. Influenced by Mars. "Venerien": astrologi-

cally influenced by Venus.
7. My birth sign was the constellation Taurus, a sign in which Venus is dominant.
8. I.e., horoscope.
9. I.e., the contrary.
1. Just because he saw her bareheaded.

655   Withouten his witing,° he forsook hire eke;   *knowledge*
     And thanne wolde he upon his Bible seeke
     That ilke proverbe of Ecclesiaste[2]
     Where he comandeth and forbedeth faste°   *strictly*
     Man shal nat suffre his wif go roule° aboute;   *roam*
660   Thanne wolde he saye right thus withouten doute:
     "Whoso that buildeth his hous al of salwes,°   *willow sticks*
     And priketh° his blinde hors over the falwes,[3]   *rides*
     And suffreth° his wif to go seeken halwes,°   *allows / shrines*
     Is worthy to be hanged on the galwes."°   *gallows*
665   But al for nought—I sette nought an hawe[4]
     Of his proverbes n'of his olde sawe;
     N' I wolde nat of him corrected be:
     I hate him that my vices telleth me,
     And so doon mo, God woot, of us than I.
670   This made him with me wood al outrely:°   *entirely*
     I nolde nought forbere° him in no cas.   *submit to*
       Now wol I saye you sooth, by Saint Thomas,
     Why that I rente° out of his book a leef,   *tore*
     For which he smoot me so that I was deef.
675   He hadde a book that gladly night and day
     For his disport° he wolde rede alway.   *entertainment*
     He cleped it *Valerie*[5] *and Theofraste,*
     At which book he lough° alway ful faste;   *laughed*
     And eek ther was somtime a clerk at Rome,
680   A cardinal, that highte Saint Jerome,
     That made a book[6] again° Jovinian;   *against*
     In which book eek ther was Tertulan,
     Crysippus, Trotula, and Helouis,[7]
     That was abbesse nat fer fro Paris;
685   And eek the Parables of Salomon,
     Ovides *Art,*[8] and bookes many oon—
     And alle thise were bounden in oo volume.
     And every night and day was his custume,
     Whan he hadde leiser and vacacioun°   *free time*
690   From other worldly occupacioun,
     To reden in this book of wikked wives.
     He knew of hem mo legendes and lives
     Than been of goode wives in the Bible.
     For trusteth wel, it is an impossible°   *impossibility*
695   That any clerk wol speke good of wives,
     But if it be of holy saintes lives,
     N'of noon other womman nevere the mo—

---

2. Ecclesiasticus (25.25).
3. Plowed land.
4. I did not rate at the value of a hawthorn berry.
5. *"Valerie":* i.e., the *Letter of Valerius Concerning Not Marrying,* by Walter Map; *"Theofraste":* Theophrastus's *Book Concerning Marriage.* Medieval manuscripts often contained a number of different works, sometimes, as here, dealing with the same subject.

6. St. Jerome's misogynist *Against Jovinian.*
7. "Tertulan": i.e., Tertullian, author of treatises on sexual modesty. "Crysippus": mentioned by Jerome as an antifeminist. "Trotula": a female doctor whose presence here is unexplained. "Helouis": i.e., Eloise, whose love affair with the great scholar Abelard was a medieval scandal.
8. Ovid's *Art of Love.* "Parables of Salomon": the biblical Book of Proverbs.

Who painted the leon, tel me who?[9]
By God, if wommen hadden writen stories,
700 As clerkes han within hir oratories,°   *chapels*
They wolde han writen of men more wikkednesse
Than al the merk[1] of Adam may redresse.
The children of Mercurye and Venus[2]
Been in hir werking° ful contrarious:°   *operation / opposed*
705 Mercurye loveth wisdom and science,
And Venus loveth riot° and dispence;°   *revelry / spending*
And for hir diverse disposicioun
Each falleth in otheres exaltacioun,[3]
And thus, God woot, Mercurye is desolat
710 In Pisces wher Venus is exaltat,[4]
And Venus falleth ther Mercurye is raised:
Therfore no womman of no clerk is praised.
The clerk, whan he is old and may nought do
Of Venus werkes worth his olde sho,°   *shoe*
715 Thanne sit° he down and writ° in his dotage   *sits / writes*
That wommen can nat keepe hir mariage.
    But now to purpose why I tolde thee
That I was beten for a book, pardee:
Upon a night Janekin, that was our sire,[5]
720 Redde on his book as he sat by the fire
Of Eva first, that for hir wikkednesse
Was al mankinde brought to wrecchednesse,
For which that Jesu Crist himself was slain
That boughte° us with his herte blood again—   *redeemed*
725 Lo, heer expres of wommen may ye finde
That womman was the los° of al mankinde.[6]   *ruin*
    Tho° redde he me how Sampson loste his heres: *then*
Sleeping his lemman° kitte° it with hir sheres,   *lover / cut*
Thurgh which treson-loste he both his yën.
730   Tho redde he me, if that I shal nat lien,
Of Ercules and of his Dianire,[7]
That caused him to sette himself afire.
No thing forgat he the sorwe and wo
That Socrates hadde with his wives two—
735 How Xantippa caste pisse upon his heed:
This sely° man sat stille as he were deed;   *poor, hapless*
He wiped his heed, namore dorste° he sayn   *dared*
But "Er that thonder stinte,° comth a rain."   *stops*
    Of Pasipha[8] that was the queene of Crete—
740 For shrewednesse° him thoughte the tale sweete—   *malice*
Fy, speek namore, it is a grisly thing

---

9. In one of Aesop's fables, the lion, shown a picture of a man killing a lion, asked who painted the picture. Had a lion been the artist, of course, the roles would have been reversed.
1. Mark, sex.
2. I.e., clerks and women, astrologically ruled by Mercury and Venus, respectively.
3. Because of their contrary positions (as planets), each one descends (in the belt of the zodiac) as the other rises, hence one loses its power as

the other becomes dominant.
4. I.e., Mercury is deprived of power in Pisces (the sign of the Fish), where Venus is most powerful.
5. My husband.
6. The stories of wicked women Chaucer drew mainly from St. Jerome and Walter Map.
7. Deianira unwittingly gave Hercules a poisoned shirt, which hurt him so much that he committed suicide by fire.
8. Pasiphaë, who had intercourse with a bull.

Of hir horrible lust and hir liking.°   *pleasure*
Of Clytermistra[9] for hir lecherye
That falsly made hir housbonde for to die,
745 He redde it with ful good devocioun.
    He tolde me eek for what occasioun
Amphiorax[1] at Thebes loste his lif:
Myn housbonde hadde a legende of his wif
Eriphylem, that for an ouche° of gold   *trinket*
750 Hath prively unto the Greekes told
Wher that hir housbonde hidde him in a place,
For which he hadde at Thebes sory grace.
    Of Livia tolde he me and of Lucie:[2]
They bothe made hir housbondes for to die,
755 That oon for love, that other was for hate;
Livia hir housbonde on an even late
Empoisoned hath for that she was his fo;
Lucia likerous° loved hir housbonde so   *lecherous*
That for° he sholde alway upon hire thinke,   *in order that*
760 She yaf him swich a manere love-drinke
That he was deed er it were by the morwe.[3]
And thus algates° housbondes han sorwe.   *in every way*
    Thanne tolde he me how oon Latumius
Complained unto his felawe Arrius
765 That in his garden growed swich a tree,
On which he saide how that his wives three
Hanged hemself for herte despitous.[4]
    "O leve° brother," quod this Arrius,   *dear*
"Yif me a plante of thilke blessed tree,
770 And in my gardin planted shal it be."
    Of latter date of wives hath he red
That some han slain hir housbondes in hir bed
And lete hir lechour dighte[5] hire al the night,
Whan that the cors° lay in the floor upright;°   *corpse / on his back*
775 And some han driven nailes in hir brain
Whil that they sleepe, and thus they han hem slain;
Some han hem yiven poison in hir drinke.
He spak more harm than herte may bithinke,°   *imagine*
And therwithal he knew of mo proverbes
780 Than in this world ther growen gras or herbes:
"Bet° is," quod he, "thyn habitacioun   *better*
Be with a leon or a foul dragoun
Than with a womman using° for to chide."   *accustomed*
"Bet is," quod he, "hye in the roof abide
785 Than with an angry wif down in the hous:
They been so wikked° and contrarious,   *perverse*
They haten that hir housbondes loveth ay."

---

9. Clytemnestra, who, with her lover, Aegisthus, slew her husband, Agamemnon.
1. Amphiaraus, betrayed by his wife, Eriphyle, and forced to go to the war against Thebes.
2. Livia murdered her husband in behalf of her lover, Sejanus. "Lucie": i.e., Lucilla, who was said to have poisoned her husband, the poet Lucretius, with a potion designed to keep him faithful.
3. He was dead before it was near morning.
4. For malice of heart.
5. Have intercourse with.

He saide, "A womman cast° hir shame away   *casts*
When she cast of° hir smok,"[6] and ferthermo,   *off*
790 "A fair womman, but she be chast also,
Is like a gold ring in a sowes nose."
Who wolde weene,° or who wolde suppose   *think*
The wo that in myn herte was and pine?°   *suffering*
 And whan I sawgh he wolde nevere fine°   *end*
795 To reden on this cursed book al night,
Al sodeinly three leves have I plight°   *snatched*
Out of his book right as he redde, and eke
I with my fist so took[7] him on the cheeke
That in oure fir he fil° bakward adown.   *fell*
800 And up he sterte as dooth a wood° leoun,   *raging*
And with his fist he smoot me on the heed°   *head*
That in the floor I lay as I were deed.°   *dead*
And whan he sawgh how stille that I lay,
He was agast, and wolde have fled his way,
805 Til atte laste out of my swough° I braide:°   *swoon / started*
"O hastou slain me, false thief?" I saide,
"And for my land thus hastou mordred° me?   *murdered*
Er I be deed yit wol I kisse thee."
And neer he cam and kneeled faire adown,
810 And saide, "Dere suster Alisoun,
As help me God, I shal thee nevere smite.
That I have doon, it is thyself to wite.°   *blame*
Foryif it me, and that I thee biseeke."°   *beseech*
And yit eftsoones° I hitte him on the cheeke,   *another time*
815 And saide, "Thief, thus muchel am I wreke.°   *avenged*
Now wol I die: I may no lenger speke."
 But at the laste with muchel care and wo
We fille[8] accorded by us selven two.
He yaf me al the bridel° in myn hand,   *bridle*
820 To han the governance of hous and land,
And of his tonge and his hand also;
And made[9] him brenne° his book anoonright tho.   *burn*
And whan that I hadde geten unto me
By maistrye° al the sovereinetee,°   *skill / dominion*
825 And that he saide, "Myn owene trewe wif,
Do as thee lust° the terme of al thy lif;   *it pleases*
Keep thyn honour, and keep eek myn estat,"
After that day we hadde nevere debat.
God help me so, I was to him as kinde
830 As any wif from Denmark unto Inde,°   *India*
And also trewe, and so was he to me.
I praye to God that sit° in majestee,   *sits*
So blesse his soule for his mercy dere.
Now wol I saye my tale if ye wol heere.

---

6. Undergarment.   8. I.e., became.
7. I.e., hit.   9. I.e., I made.

[ANOTHER INTERRUPTION]

835   The Frere lough° whan he hadde herd all this: *laughed*
"Now dame," quod he, "so have I joye or blis,
This is a long preamble of a tale."
And whan the Somnour herde the Frere gale,°   *exclaim*
"Lo," quod the Somnour, "Goddes armes two,
840 A frere wol entremette him[1] everemo!
Lo, goode men, a flye and eek a frere
Wol falle in every dissh and eek matere.
What spekestou of preambulacioun?
What, amble or trotte or pisse or go sitte down!
845 Thou lettest° oure disport in this manere."   *hinder*
    "Ye, woltou so, sire Somnour?" quod the Frere.
"Now by my faith, I shal er that I go
Telle of a somnour swich a tale or two
That al the folk shal laughen in this place."
850   'Now elles, Frere, I wol bishrewe° thy face,"   *curse*
Quod this Somnour, "and I bishrewe me,
But if I telle tales two or three
Of freres, er I come to Sidingborne,[2]
That I shal make thyn herte for to moorne°—   *mourn*
855 For wel I woot thy pacience is goon."
    Oure Hoste cride, "Pees, and that anoon!"
And saide, "Lat the womman telle hir tale:
Ye fare as folk that dronken been of ale.
Do, dame, tel forth youre tale, and that is best."
860   "Al redy, sire," quod she, "right as you lest°—   *it pleases*
If I have licence of this worthy Frere."
"Yis, dame," quod he, "tel forth and I wol heere."

The Tale

As was suggested in the headnote to *The Man of Law's Epilogue,* Chaucer may have originally written the fabliau that became *The Shipman's Tale* for the Wife of Bath. If so, then he replaced it with a tale that is not simply appropriate to her character but that develops it even beyond the complexity already revealed in her *Prologue.* The story survives in two other versions in which the hero is Sir Gawain, whose courtesy contrasts sharply with the behavior of the knight in the Wife's tale. (For excerpts from *The Marriage of Sir Gawain and Dame Ragnell,* see the "King Arthur" topic in the supplemental ebook.) As Chaucer has the Wife tell it, the tale expresses her views about the relations of the sexes, her wit and humor, and her fantasies. Like Marie de France's lay *Lanval* (see p. 154), the Wife's tale is about a fairy bride who seeks out and tests a mortal lover.

    In th'olde dayes of the King Arthour,
    Of which that Britouns speken greet honour,
865   Al was this land fulfild of faïrye:[3]
    The elf-queene° with hir joly compaignye   *queen of the fairies*
    Daunced ful ofte in many a greene mede°—   *meadow*

---

1. Intrude himself.
2. Sittingbourne (a town forty miles from London).
3. I.e., filled full of supernatural creatures.

This was the olde opinion as I rede;
I speke of many hundred yeres ago.
870 But now can no man see none elves mo,
For now the grete charitee and prayeres
Of limitours,[4] and othere holy freres,
That serchen every land and every streem,
As thikke as motes° in the sonne-beem,   *dust particles*
875 Blessing halles, chambres, kichenes, bowres,
Citees, burghes,° castels, hye towres,   *townships*
Thropes, bernes, shipnes,[5] dayeries—
This maketh that ther been no fairies.
For ther as wont to walken was an elf
880 Ther walketh now the limitour himself,
In undermeles° and in morweninges,°   *afternoons / mornings*
And saith his Matins and his holy thinges,
As he gooth in his limitacioun.[6]
Wommen may go saufly° up and down: *safely*
885 In every bussh or under every tree
Ther is noon other incubus[7] but he,
And he ne wol doon hem but[8] dishonour.
     And so bifel it that this King Arthour
Hadde in his hous a lusty bacheler,°   *young knight*
890 That on a day cam riding fro river,[9]
And happed° that, allone as he was born,   *it happened*
He sawgh a maide walking him biforn;
Of which maide anoon, maugree hir heed,[1]
By verray force he rafte° hir maidenheed;   *deprived her of*
895 For which oppression° was swich clamour,   *rape*
And swich pursuite° unto the King Arthour,   *petitioning*
That dampned was this knight for to be deed[2]
By cours of lawe, and sholde han lost his heed—
Paraventure° swich was the statut tho—   *perchance*
900 But that the queene and othere ladies mo
So longe prayeden the king of grace,
Til he his lif him graunted in the place,
And yaf him to the queene, al at hir wille,
To chese° wheither she wolde him save or spille.[3]   *choose*
905 The queene thanked the king with al hir might,
And after this thus spak she to the knight,
Whan that she saw hir time upon a day:
"Thou standest yit," quod she, "in swich array°   *condition*
That of thy lif yit hastou no suretee.°   *guarantee*
910 I graunte thee lif if thou canst tellen me
What thing it is that wommen most desiren:
Be war and keep thy nekke boon° from iren.   *bone*
And if thou canst nat tellen me anoon,°   *right away*

---

4. Friars licensed to beg in a certain territory.
5. Thorps (villages), barns, stables.
6. I.e., the friar's assigned area. His "holy thinges" are prayers.
7. An evil spirit that seduces mortal women.
8. "Ne . . . but": only.

9. Hawking, usually carried out on the banks of a stream.
1. Despite her head, i.e., despite anything she could do.
2. This knight was condemned to death.
3. Put to death.

Yit wol I yive thee leve for to goon
915 A twelfmonth and a day to seeche° and lere°   *search / learn*
An answere suffisant° in this matere,   *satisfactory*
And suretee wol I han er that thou pace,°   *pass*
Thy body for to yeelden in this place."
  Wo was this knight, and sorwefully he siketh.°   *sighs*
920 But what, he may nat doon al as him liketh,
And atte laste he chees° him for to wende,   *chose*
And come again right at the yeres ende,
With swich answere as God wolde him purveye,°   *provide*
And taketh his leve and wendeth forth his waye.
925 He seeketh every hous and every place
Wher as he hopeth for to finde grace,
To lerne what thing wommen love most.
But he ne coude arriven in no coost⁴
Wher as he mighte finde in this matere
930 Two creatures according in fere.⁵
  Some saiden wommen loven best richesse;
Some saide honour, some saide jolinesse;°   *pleasure*
Some riche array, some saiden lust abedde,
And ofte time to be widwe and wedde.
935 Some saide that oure herte is most esed
Whan that we been yflatered and yplesed—
He gooth ful neigh the soothe, I wol nat lie:
A man shal winne us best with flaterye,
And with attendance° and with bisinesse°   *attention / solicitude*
940 Been we ylimed,° bothe more and lesse.   *ensnared*
  And some sayen that we loven best
For to be free, and do right as us lest,°   *it pleases*
And that no man repreve° us of oure vice,   *reprove*
But saye that we be wise and no thing nice.°   *foolish*
945 For trewely, ther is noon of us alle,
If any wight wol clawe° us on the galle,°   *rub / sore spot*
That we nil kike° for° he saith us sooth: *kick / because*
Assaye° and he shal finde it that so dooth.   *try*
For be we nevere so vicious withinne,
950 We wol be holden° wise and clene of sinne.   *considered*
  And some sayn that greet delit han we
For to be holden stable and eek secree,⁶
And in oo° purpos stedefastly to dwelle,   *one*
And nat biwraye° thing that men us telle—   *disclose*
955 But that tale is nat worth a rake-stele.°   *rake handle*
Pardee,° we wommen conne no thing hele:°   *by God / conceal*
Witnesse on Mida.° Wol ye heere the tale?   *Midas*
  Ovide, amonges othere thinges smale,
Saide Mida hadde under his longe heres,
960 Growing upon his heed, two asses eres,
The whiche vice° he hidde as he best mighte   *defect*
Ful subtilly from every mannes sighte,

4. I.e., country.
5. Agreeing together.
6. Reliable and also closemouthed.

That save his wif ther wiste° of it namo.   *knew*
He loved hire most and trusted hire also.
965 He prayed hire that to no creature
      She sholde tellen of his disfigure.°   *deformity*
          She swoor him nay, for al this world to winne,
      She nolde do that vilainye or sinne
      To make hir housbonde han so foul a name:
970 She nolde nat telle it for hir owene shame.
      But nathelees, hir thoughte that she dyde°   *would die*
      That she so longe sholde a conseil° hide;   *secret*
      Hire thoughte it swal° so sore about hir herte   *swelled*
      That nedely som word hire moste asterte,[7]
975 And sith she dorste nat telle it to no man,
      Down to a mareis° faste° by she ran—   *marsh / close*
      Til she cam there hir herte was afire—
      And as a bitore bombleth[8] in the mire,
      She laide hir mouth unto the water down:
980 "Biwray° me nat, thou water, with thy soun,"°   *betray / sound*
      Quod she. "To thee I telle it and namo:°   *to no one else*
      Myn housbonde hath longe asses eres two.
      Now is myn herte al hool,[9] now is it oute.
      I mighte no lenger keep it, out of doute."
985 Here may ye see, though we a time abide,
      Yit oute it moot:° we can no conseil hide.   *must*
      The remenant of the tale if ye wol heere,
      Redeth Ovide, and ther ye may it lere.[1]
          This knight of which my tale is specially,
990 Whan that he sawgh he mighte nat come thereby—
      This is to saye what wommen loven most—
      Within his brest ful sorweful was his gost,°   *spirit*
      But hoom he gooth, he mighte nat sojourne:°   *delay*
      The day was come that hoomward moste° he turne.   *must*
995 And in his way it happed him to ride
      In al this care under° a forest side,   *by*
      Wher as he sawgh upon a daunce go
      Of ladies foure and twenty and yit mo;
      Toward the whiche daunce he drow ful yerne,[2]
1000 In hope that som wisdom sholde he lerne.
      But certainly, er he cam fully there,
      Vanisshed was this daunce, he niste° where.   *knew not*
      No creature sawgh he that bar° lif,   *bore*
      Save on the greene he sawgh sitting a wif°—   *woman*
1005 A fouler wight ther may no man devise.°   *imagine*
      Again[3] the knight this olde wif gan rise,
      And saide, "Sire knight, heer forth lith° no way.°   *lies / road*
      Telle me what ye seeken, by youre fay.°   *faith*
      Paraventure it may the better be:
1010 Thise olde folk conne° muchel thing," quod she.   *know*

---

7. Of necessity some word must escape her.
8. Makes a booming noise. "Bittore": bittern, a heron.
9. I.e., sound.

1. Learn. The reeds disclosed the secret by whispering *"aures aselli"* (ass's ears).
2. Drew very quickly.
3. I.e., to meet.

"My leve moder,"° quod this knight, "certain,   *mother*
I nam but deed but if that I can sayn
What thing it is that wommen most desire.
Coude ye me wisse,° I wolde wel quite youre hire."[4]   *teach*
1015   "Plight° me thy trouthe here in myn hand," quod she,   *pledge*
"The nexte thing that I requere° thee,   *require of*
Thou shalt it do, if it lie in thy might,
And I wol telle it you er it be night."
    "Have heer my trouthe," quod the knight. "I graunte."
1020   "Thanne," quod she, "I dar me wel avaunte°   *boast*
Thy lif is sauf,° for I wol stande therby.   *safe*
Upon my lif the queene wol saye as I.
Lat see which is the pruddeste° of hem alle   *proudest*
That wereth on[5] a coverchief or a calle°   *headdress*
1025   That dar saye nay of that I shal thee teche.
Lat us go forth withouten lenger speeche."
Tho rouned° she a pistel° in his ere,   *whispered / message*
And bad him to be glad and have no fere.
    Whan they be comen to the court, this knight
1030   Saide he hadde holde his day as he hadde hight,°   *promised*
And redy was his answere, as he saide.
Ful many a noble wif, and many a maide,
And many a widwe—for that they been wise—
The queene hirself sitting as justise,
1035   Assembled been this answere for to heere,
And afterward this knight was bode° appere.   *bidden to*
To every wight comanded was silence,
And that the knight sholde telle in audience°   *open hearing*
What thing that worldly wommen loven best.
1040   This knight ne stood nat stille as dooth a best,°   *beast*
But to his question anoon answerde
With manly vois that al the court it herde.
    "My lige° lady, generally," quod he,   *liege*
"Wommen desire to have sovereinetee°   *dominion*
1045   As wel over hir housbonde as hir love,
And for to been in maistrye him above.
This is youre moste desir though ye me kille.
Dooth as you list:° I am here at youre wille."   *please*
    In al the court ne was ther wif ne maide
1050   Ne widwe that contraried° that he saide,   *contradicted*
But saiden he was worthy han° his lif.   *to have*
    And with that word up sterte° that olde wif,   *started*
Which that the knight sawgh sitting on the greene;
"Mercy," quod she, "my soverein lady queene,
1055   Er that youre court departe, do me right.
I taughte this answere unto the knight,
For which he plighte me his trouthe there
The firste thing I wolde him requere°   *require*
He wolde it do, if it laye in his might.
1060   Bifore the court thanne praye I thee, sire knight,"

Quod she, "that thou me take unto thy wif,
For wel thou woost that I have kept° thy lif.   saved
If I saye fals, say nay, upon thy fay."
  This knight answerde, "Allas and wailaway,
1065 I woot right wel that swich was my biheeste.°   promise
For Goddes love, as chees° a newe requeste: choose
Taak al my good and lat my body go."
  "Nay thanne," quod she, "I shrewe° us bothe two.   curse
For though that I be foul and old and poore,
1070 I nolde for al the metal ne for ore
That under erthe is grave° or lith° above,   buried / lies
But if thy wif I were and eek thy love."
  "My love," quod he. "Nay, my dampnacioun!°   damnation
Allas, that any of my nacioun[6]
1075 Sholde evere so foule disparaged° be."   degraded
But al for nought, th'ende is this, that he
Constrained was: he needes moste hire wedde,
And taketh his olde wif and gooth to bedde.
  Now wolden some men saye, paraventure,
1080 That for my necligence I do no cure[7]
To tellen you the joye and al th'array
That at the feeste was that ilke day.
To which thing shortly answere I shal:
I saye ther nas no joye ne feeste at al;
1085 Ther nas but hevinesse and muche sorwe.
For prively he wedded hire on morwe,[8]
And al day after hidde him as an owle,
So wo was him, his wif looked so foule.
  Greet was the wo the knight hadde in his thought:
1090 Whan he was with his wif abedde brought,
He walweth° and he turneth to and fro.   tosses
His olde wif lay smiling everemo,
And saide, "O dere housbonde, benedicite,°   bless me
Fareth° every knight thus with his wif as ye?   behaves
1095 Is this the lawe of King Arthures hous?
Is every knight of his thus daungerous?°   standoffish
I am youre owene love and youre wif;
I am she which that saved hath youre lif;
And certes yit ne dide I you nevere unright.
1100 Why fare ye thus with me this firste night?
Ye faren like a man hadde lost his wit.
What is my gilt? For Goddes love, telle it,
And it shal been amended if I may."
  "Amended!" quod this knight. "Allas, nay, nay,
1105 It wol nat been amended neveremo.
Thou art so lothly° and so old also,   hideous
And therto comen of so lowe a kinde,°   lineage
That litel wonder is though I walwe and winde.°   turn
So wolde God myn herte wolde breste!"°   break

---

6. I.e., family.
7. I do not take the trouble.

8. In the morning.

1110   "Is this," quod she, "the cause of youre unreste?"
     "Ye, certainly," quod he. "No wonder is."
     "Now sire," quod she, "I coude amende al this,
     If that me liste, er it were dayes three,
     So° wel ye mighte bere you[9] unto me.   *provided that*
1115   "But for ye speken of swich gentilesse°   *nobility*
     As is descended out of old richesse—
     That therfore sholden ye be gentilmen—
     Swich arrogance is nat worth an hen.
     Looke who that is most vertuous alway,
1120   Privee and apert,[1] and most entendeth° ay°   *tries / always*
     To do the gentil deedes that he can,
     Taak him for the gretteste° gentilman.   *greatest*
     Crist wol° we claime of him oure gentilesse,   *desires that*
     Nat of oure eldres for hir 'old richesse.'
1125   For though they yive us al hir heritage,
     For which we claime to been of heigh parage,°   *descent*
     Yit may they nat biquethe for no thing
     To noon of us hir vertuous living,
     That made hem gentilmen ycalled be,
1130   And bad[2] us folwen hem in swich degree.
     "Wel can the wise poete of Florence,
     That highte Dant,[3] speken in this sentence;°   *topic*
     Lo, in swich manere rym is Dantes tale:
     'Ful selde° up riseth by his braunches[4] smale   *seldom*
1135   Prowesse° of man, for God of his prowesse   *excellence*
     Wol that of him we claime oure gentilesse.'
     For of oure eldres may we no thing claime
     But temporel thing that man may hurte and maime.
     Eek every wight woot this as wel as I,
1140   If gentilesse were planted natureelly
     Unto a certain linage down the line,
     Privee and apert, thanne wolde they nevere fine°   *cease*
     To doon of gentilesse the faire office°—   *function*
     They mighte do no vilainye or vice.
1145   "Taak fir and beer° it in the derkeste hous   *bear*
     Bitwixe this and the Mount of Caucasus,
     And lat men shette° the dores and go thenne,°   *shut / thence*
     Yit wol the fir as faire lye° and brenne°   *blaze / burn*
     As twenty thousand men mighte it biholde:
1150   His° office natureel ay wol it holde,   *its*
     Up° peril of my lif, til that it die.   *upon*
     Heer may ye see wel how that genterye°   *gentility*
     Is nat annexed° to possessioun,[5]   *related*
     Sith folk ne doon hir operacioun
1155   Alway, as dooth the fir, lo, in his kinde.°   *nature*
     For God it woot, men may wel often finde
     A lordes sone do shame and vilainye;

---

9. Behave.
1. Privately and publicly.
2. I.e., they bade.

3. Dante (see his *Convivio*).
4. I.e., by the branches of a man's family tree.
5. I.e., inheritable property.

And he that wol han pris of his gentrye,[6]
For he was boren° of a gentil° hous,   *born / noble*
1160 And hadde his eldres noble and vertuous,
And nil himselven do no gentil deedes,
Ne folwen his gentil auncestre that deed° is,   *dead*
He nis nat gentil, be he due or erl—
For vilaines sinful deedes maken a cherl.
1165 Thy gentilesse[7] nis but renomee°   *renown*
Of thine auncestres for hir heigh bountee,°   *magnanimity*
Which is a straunge° thing for thy persone.   *external*
For gentilesse[8] cometh fro God allone.
Thanne comth oure verray gentilesse of grace:
1170 It was no thing biquethe us with oure place.
Thenketh how noble, as saith Valerius,[9]
Was thilke Tullius Hostilius
That out of poverte° roos to heigh noblesse.   *poverty*
Redeth Senek° and redeth eek Boece:°   *Seneca / Boethius*
1175 Ther shul ye seen expres that no drede° is   *doubt*
That he is gentil that dooth gentil deedes.
And therfore, leve housbonde, I thus conclude:
Al° were it that mine auncestres weren rude,[1]   *although*
Yit may the hye God—and so hope I—
1180 Graunte me grace to liven vertuously.
Thanne am I gentil whan that I biginne
To liven vertuously and waive° sinne.   *avoid*
"And ther as ye of poverte me repreve,°   *reprove*
The hye God, on whom that we bileve,
1185 In wilful° poverte chees° to live his lif;   *voluntary / chose*
And certes every man, maiden, or wif
May understonde that Jesus, hevene king,
Ne wolde nat chese° a vicious living.   *choose*
Glad poverte is an honeste° thing, certain;   *honorable*
1190 This wol Senek and othere clerkes sayn.
Whoso that halt him paid of[2] his poverte,
I holde him riche al hadde him nat a sherte.°   *shirt*
He that coveiteth[3] is a poore wight,
For he wolde han that is nat in his might;
1195 But he that nought hath, ne coveiteth° have,   *desires to*
Is riche, although we holde him but a knave.°   *peasant*
Verray° poverte it singeth proprely.°   *true / appropriately*
Juvenal saith of poverte, 'Merily
The poore man, whan he gooth by the waye,
1200 Biforn the theves he may singe and playe.'
Poverte is hateful good, and as I gesse,
A ful greet bringere out of bisinesse;[4]
A greet amendere eek of sapience°   *wisdom*
To him that taketh it in pacience;
1205 Poverte is thing, although it seeme elenge,°   *wretched*

6. Have credit for his noble birth.   1. I.e., low born.
7. I.e., the gentility you claim.   2. Considers himself satisfied with.
8. I.e., true gentility.   3. I.e., suffers desires.
9. A Roman historian.   4. I.e., remover of cares.

Possession that no wight wol chalenge;[5]
Poverte ful often, whan a man is lowe,
Maketh[6] his God and eek himself to knowe;
Poverte a spectacle° is, as thinketh me,   *pair of spectacles*
1210 Thurgh which he may his verray° freendes see.   *true*
And therfore, sire, sin that I nought you greve,
Of my poverte namore ye me repreve.°   *reproach*
    "Now sire, of elde° ye repreve me: *old age*
And certes sire, though noon auctoritee
1215 Were in no book, ye gentils of honour
Sayn that men sholde an old wight doon favour,
And clepe him fader for youre gentilesse—
And auctours[7] shal I finde, as I gesse.
    "Now ther ye saye that I am foul° and old: *ugly*
1220 Thanne drede you nought to been a cokewold,°   *cuckold*
For filthe° and elde, also mote I thee,[8]   *ugliness*
Been grete wardeins° upon chastitee.   *guardians*
But nathelees, sin I knowe your delit,
I shal fulfille youre worldly appetit.
1225   "Chees° now," quod she, "oon of thise thinges twaye: *choose*
To han me foul and old til that I deye
And be to you a trewe humble wif,
And nevere you displese in al my lif,
Or elles ye wol han me yong and fair,
1230 And take youre aventure° of the repair[9]   *chance*
That shal be to youre hous by cause of me—
Or in some other place, wel may be.
Now chees youreselven wheither° that you liketh."   *whichever*
    This knight aviseth him[1] and sore siketh;°   *sighs*
1235 But atte laste he saide in this manere:
"My lady and my love, and wif so dere,
I putte me in youre wise governaunce:
Cheseth° youreself which may be most plesaunce°   *choose / pleasure*
And most honour to you and me also.
1240 I do no fors the wheither[2] of the two,
For as you liketh it suffiseth° me."   *satisfies*
    "Thanne have I gete° of you maistrye," quod she,   *got*
"Sin I may chese and governe as me lest?"°   *it pleases*
    "Ye, certes, wif," quod he. "I holde it best."
1245   "Kisse me," quod she. "We be no lenger wrothe.
For by my trouthe, I wol be to you bothe—
This is to sayn, ye, bothe fair and good.
I praye to God that I mote sterven wood.[3]
But° I to you be al so good and trewe   *unless*
1250 As evere was wif sin that the world was newe.
And but I be tomorn° as fair to seene   *tomorrow morning*
As any lady, emperisse, or queene,

---

5. Claim as his property.   9. I.e., visits.
6. I.e., makes him.   1. Considers.
7. I.e., authorities.   2. I do not care whichever.
8. So may I prosper.   3. Die mad.

That is bitwixe the eest and eek the west,
Do with my lif and deeth right as you lest:
1255 Caste up the curtin,[4] looke how that it is."
    And whan the knight sawgh verraily al this,
That she so fair was and so yong therto,
For joye he hente° hire in his armes two;   *took*
His herte bathed in a bath of blisse;
1260 A thousand time arewe° he gan hire kisse,   *in a row*
And she obeyed him in every thing
That mighte do him plesance or liking.°   *pleasure*
And thus they live unto hir lives ende
In parfit° joye. And Jesu Crist us sende   *perfect*
1265 Housbondes meeke, yonge, and fresshe abedde—
And grace t'overbide° hem that we wedde.   *outlive*
And eek I praye Jesu shorte° hir lives   *shorten*
That nought wol be governed by hir wives,
And olde and angry nigardes° of dispence°—   *misers / spending*
1270 God sende hem soone a verray° pestilence!   *veritable*

4. The curtain around the bed.

The Pardoner's Prologue and Tale

As with *The Wife of Bath's Prologue* and *Tale*, *The Pardoner's Prologue* and *Tale* develop in profound and surprising ways the portrait sketched in *The General Prologue*. In his *Prologue* the Pardoner boasts to his fellow pilgrims about his own depravity and the ingenuity with which he abuses his office and extracts money from poor and ignorant people.

The Power of Money. Quinten Metsys, *The Money Lender and His Wife*, 1514. Note the gaze of the wife: she has turned away from her book of devotions toward the more fascinating sight of money being weighed.

The medieval pardoner's job was to collect money for the charitable enterprises, such as hospitals, supported by the church. In return for donations he was licensed by the pope to award token remission of sins that the donor should have repented and confessed. By canon law pardoners were permitted to work only in a prescribed area; within that area they might visit churches during Sunday service, briefly explain their mission, receive contributions, and in the pope's name issue indulgence, which was not considered to be a sale but a gift from the infinite treasury of Christ's mercy made in return for a gift of money. In practice, pardoners ignored the restrictions on their office, made their way into churches at will, preached emotional sermons, and claimed extraordinary power for their pardons.

The Pardoner's Tale is a bombastic sermon against gluttony, gambling, and swearing, which he preaches to the pilgrims to show off his professional skills. The sermon is framed by a narrative that is supposed to function as an *exemplum* (that is, an illustration) of the scriptural text, the one on which the Pardoner, as he tells the pilgrims, always preaches: *"Radix malorum est cupiditas"* (Avarice is the root of evil).

The Introduction

	Oure Hoste gan to swere as he were wood°	*insane*
	"Harrow,"° quod he, "by nailes and by blood,[1]	*help*
	This was a fals cherl and a fals justise.[2]	
	As shameful deeth as herte may devise	
5	Come to thise juges and hir advocats.	
	Algate° this sely° maide is slain, allas!	*at any rate / innocent*
	Allas, too dere boughte she beautee!	
	Wherfore I saye alday° that men may see	*always*
	The yiftes of Fortune and of Nature	
10	Been cause of deeth to many a creature.	
	As bothe yiftes that I speke of now,	
	Men han ful ofte more for harm than prow.°	*benefit*
	"But trewely, myn owene maister dere,	
	This is a pitous tale for to heere.	
15	But nathelees, passe over, is no fors:[3]	
	I praye to God to save thy gentil cors,°	*body*
	And eek thine urinals and thy jurdones,[4]	
	Thyn ipocras and eek thy galiones,[5]	
	And every boiste° ful of thy letuarye°—	*box / medicine*
20	God blesse hem, and oure lady Sainte Marye.	
	So mote I theen,[6] thou art a propre man,	
	And lik a prelat, by Saint Ronian![7]	
	Saide I nat wel? I can nat speke in terme.[8]	
	But wel I woot, thou doost° myn herte to erme°	*make / grieve*
25	That I almost have caught a cardinacle.[9]	
	By corpus bones,[1] but if° I have triacle,°	*unless / medicine*
	Or elles a draughte of moiste° and corny° ale,	*fresh / malty*
	Or but I here anoon° a merye tale,	*at once*
	Myn herte is lost for pitee of this maide.	
30	"Thou bel ami,[2] thou Pardoner," he saide,	
	"Tel us som mirthe or japes° right anoon."	*jokes*
	"It shal be doon," quod he, "by Saint Ronion.	

1. I.e., God's nails and blood.
2. The Host has been affected by the Physician's sad tale of the Roman maiden Virginia, whose great beauty caused a judge to attempt to obtain her person by means of a trumped-up lawsuit in which he connived with a "churl" who claimed her as his slave; in order to preserve her chastity, her father killed her.
3. I.e., never mind.
4. Jordans (chamberpots): the Host is somewhat confused in his endeavor to use technical medical terms. "Urinals": vessels for examining urine.

5. A medicine, probably invented on the spot by the Host, named after Galen. "Ipocras": a medicinal drink named after Hippocrates.
6. So might I prosper.
7. St. Ronan or St. Ninian, with a possible play on "runnion" (sexual organ).
8. Speak in technical idiom.
9. Apparently a cardiac condition, confused in the Host's mind with a cardinal.
1. An illiterate oath, mixing "God's bones" with *corpus dei* ("God's body").
2. Fair friend.

But first," quod he, "here at this ale-stake[3]
I wol bothe drinke and eten of a cake."°   *flat loaf of bread*
35   And right anoon thise gentils gan to crye,
"Nay, lat him telle us of no ribaudye.°   *ribaldry*
Tel us som moral thing that we may lere,°   *learn*
Som wit,[4] and thanne wol we gladly heere."
  "I graunte, ywis,"° quod he, "but I moot thinke   *certainly*
40 Upon som honeste° thing whil that I drinke."   *decent*

The Prologue

  Lordinges—quod he—in chirches whan I preche,
I paine me[5] to han° an hautein° speeche,   *have / loud*
And ringe it out as round as gooth a belle,
For I can al by rote[6] that I telle.
45 My theme is alway oon,[7] and evere was:
Radix malorum est cupiditas.[8]
First I pronounce whennes° that I come,   *whence*
And thanne my bulles shewe I alle and some:[9]
Oure lige lordes seel on my patente,[1]
50 That shewe I first, my body to warente,°   *keep safe*
That no man be so bold, ne preest ne clerk,
Me to destourbe of Cristes holy werk.
And after that thanne telle I forth my tales[2]—
Bulles of popes and of cardinales,
55 Of patriarkes and bisshopes I shewe,
And in Latin I speke a wordes fewe,
To saffron with[3] my predicacioun,°   *preaching*
And for to stire hem to devocioun.
  Thanne shewe I forth my longe crystal stones,°   *jars*
60 Ycrammed ful of cloutes° and of bones   *rags*
Relikes been they, as weenen° they eechoon.   *suppose*
Thanne have I in laton° a shulder-boon   *brass*
Which that was of an holy Jewes sheep.
"Goode men," I saye, "take of my wordes keep:°   *notice*
65 If that this boon be wasshe° in any welle,   *dipped*
If cow, or calf, or sheep, or oxe swelle,
That any worm hath ete or worm ystonge,[4]
Take water of that welle and wassh his tonge,
And it is hool[5] anoon. And ferthermoor,
70 Of pokkes° and of scabbe and every soor°   *pox, pustules / sore*
Shal every sheep be hool that of this welle
Drinketh a draughte. Take keep eek° that I telle: *also*
If that the goode man that the beestes oweth°   *owns*
Wol every wike,° er° that the cok him croweth,   *week / before*

---

3. Sign of a tavern.
4. I.e., something with significance.
5. Take pains.
6. I know all by heart.
7. I.e., the same. "Theme": biblical text on which the sermon is based.
8. Avarice is the root of evil (1 Timothy 6.10).
9. Each and every one. "Bulles": papal bulls,
official documents.
1. I.e., the pope's or bishop's seal on my papal license.
2. I go on with my yarn.
3. To add spice to.
4. That has eaten any worm or been bitten by any snake.
5. I.e., sound.

75	Fasting drinken of this welle a draughte—
	As thilke° holy Jew oure eldres taughte—
	His beestes and his stoor° shal multiplye.
	"And sire, also it heleth jalousye:
	For though a man be falle in jalous rage,
80	Lat maken with this water his potage,°
	And nevere shal he more his wif mistriste,°
	Though he the soothe of hir defaute wiste,[6]
	Al hadde she[7] taken preestes two or three.
	"Here is a mitein° eek that ye may see:
85	He that his hand wol putte in this mitein
	He shal have multiplying of his grain,
	Whan he hath sowen, be it whete or otes—
	So that he offre pens or elles grotes.[8]
	"Goode men and wommen, oo thing warne I you:
90	If any wight be in this chirche now
	That hath doon sinne horrible, that he
	Dar nat for shame of it yshriven° be,
	Or any womman, be she yong or old,
	That hath ymaked hir housbonde cokewold,°
95	Swich° folk shal have no power ne no grace
	To offren to[9] my relikes in this place;
	And whoso findeth him out of swich blame,
	He wol come up and offre in Goddes name,
	And I assoile° him by the auctoritee
100	Which that by bulle ygraunted was to me."
	By this gaude° have I wonne, yeer by yeer,
	An hundred mark[1] sith° I was pardoner.
	I stonde lik a clerk in my pulpet,
	And whan the lewed° peple is down yset,
105	I preche so as ye han herd bifore,
	And telle an hundred false japes° more.
	Thanne paine I me[2] to strecche forth the nekke,
	And eest and west upon the peple I bekke°
	As dooth a douve,° sitting on a berne;°
110	Mine handes and my tonge goon so yerne°
	That it is joye to see my bisinesse.
	Of avarice and of swich cursednesse°
	Is al my preching, for to make hem free°
	To yiven hir pens, and namely° unto me,
115	For myn entente is nat but for to winne,[3]
	And no thing for correccion of sinne:
	I rekke° nevere whan that they been beried°
	Though that hir soules goon a-blakeberied.[4]
	For certes, many a predicacioun°
120	Comth ofte time of yvel entencioun:
	Som for plesance of folk and flaterye,

Glosses (right margin):
- *that same* (line 76)
- *stock* (line 77)
- *soup* (line 80)
- *mistrust* (line 81)
- *mitten* (line 84)
- *confessed* (line 92)
- *cuckold* (line 94)
- *such* (line 95)
- *absolve* (line 99)
- *trick* (line 101)
- *since* (line 102)
- *ignorant* (line 104)
- *tricks* (line 106)
- *nod* (line 108)
- *dove / barn* (line 109)
- *fast* (line 110)
- *sin* (line 112)
- *generous* (line 113)
- *especially* (line 114)
- *care / buried* (line 117)
- *sermon* (line 119)

6. Knew the truth of her infidelity.
7. Even if she had.
8. Pennies, groats, coins.
9. To make gifts in reverence of.

1. Marks (pecuniary units).
2. I take pains.
3. My intent is only to make money.
4. Go blackberrying, i.e., go to hell.

To been avaunced° by ypocrisye,   *promoted*
And som for vaine glorye, and som for hate;
For whan I dar noon otherways debate,°   *fight*
125 Thanne wol I stinge him[5] with my tonge smerte°   *sharply*
In preching, so that he shal nat asterte°   *escape*
To been defamed falsly, if that he
Hath trespassed to my bretheren[6] or to me.
For though I telle nought his propre name,
130 Men shal wel knowe that it is the same
By signes and by othere circumstaunces.
Thus quite° I folk that doon us displesaunces;[7]   *pay back*
Thus spete° I out my venim under hewe°   *spit / false colors*
Of holinesse, to seeme holy and trewe.
135 But shortly myn entente I wol devise:°   *explain*
I preche of no thing but for coveitise;°   *covetousness*
Therfore my theme is yit and evere was
Radix malorum est cupiditas.
      Thus can I preche again that same vice
140 Which that I use, and that is avarice.
But though myself be gilty in that sinne,
Yit can I make other folk to twinne°   *separate*
From avarice, and sore to repente—
But that is nat my principal entente:
145 I preche no thing but for coveitise.
Of this matere it oughte ynough suffise.
      Thanne telle I hem ensamples[8] many oon
Of olde stories longe time agoon,
For lewed° peple loven tales olde—   *ignorant*
150 Swiche° thinges can they wel reporte and holde.[9]   *such*
What, trowe° ye that whiles I may preche,   *believe*
And winne gold and silver for° I teche,   *because*
That I wol live in poverte wilfully?°   *voluntarily*
Nay, nay, I thoughte° it nevere, trewely,   *intended*
155 For I wol preche and begge in sondry landes;
I wol nat do no labour with mine handes,
Ne make baskettes and live therby,
By cause I wol nat beggen idelly.[1]
I wol none of the Apostles countrefete:°   *imitate*
160 I wol have moneye, wolle,° cheese, and whete,   *wool*
Al were it[2] yiven of the pooreste page,
Or of the pooreste widwe in a village—
Al sholde hir children sterve[3] for famine.
Nay, I wol drinke licour of the vine
165 And have a joly wenche in every town.
But herkneth, lordinges, in conclusioun,
Youre liking° is that I shal telle a tale: *pleasure*
Now have I dronke a draughte of corny ale,
By God, I hope I shal you telle a thing

5. An adversary critical of pardoners.
6. Injured my fellow pardoners.
7. Make trouble for us.
8. Exempla (stories illustrating moral principles).

9. Repeat and remember.
1. I.e., without profit.
2. Even though it were.
3. Even though her children should die.

170   That shal by reson been at youre liking;
      For though myself be a ful vicious man,
      A moral tale yit I you telle can,
      Which I am wont to preche for to winne.
      Now holde youre pees, my tale I wol biginne.

The Tale

175 In Flandres whilom° was a compaignye		*once*
Of yonge folk that haunteden° folye—		*practiced*
As riot, hasard, stewes,[4] and tavernes,		
Wher as with harpes, lutes, and giternes°		*guitars*
They daunce and playen at dees° bothe day and night,		*dice*
180 And ete also and drinke over hir might,[5]		
Thurgh which they doon the devel sacrifise		
Within that develes temple in cursed wise		
By superfluitee° abhominable.		*overindulgence*
Hir othes been so grete and so dampnable		
185 That it is grisly for to heere hem swere:		
Oure blessed Lordes body they totere[6]—		
Hem thoughte that Jewes rente° him nought ynough.		*tore*
And eech of hem at otheres sinne lough.°		*laughed*
And right anoon thanne comen tombesteres,°		*dancing girls*
190 Fetis° and smale,° and yonge frutesteres,[7]		*shapely / slender*
Singeres with harpes, bawdes,° wafereres[8]—		*pimps*
Whiche been the verray develes officeres,		
To kindle and blowe the fir of lecherye		
That is annexed unto glotonye:[9]		
195 The Holy Writ take I to my witnesse		
That luxure° is in win and dronkenesse.		*lechery*
Lo, how that dronken Lot[1] unkindely°		*unnaturally*
Lay by his doughtres two unwitingly:		
So dronke he was he niste° what he wroughte.°		*didn't know / did*
200 Herodes, who so wel the stories soughte,[2]		
Whan he of win was repleet° at his feeste,		*filled*
Right at his owene table he yaf his heeste°		*command*
To sleen° the Baptist John, ful giltelees.		*slay*
Senek[3] saith a good word doutelees:		
205 He saith he can no difference finde		
Bitwixe a man that is out of his minde		
And a man which that is dronkelewe,°		*drunken*
But that woodnesse, yfallen in a shrewe,[4]		
Persevereth lenger than dooth dronkenesse.		
210 O glotonye, ful of cursednesse!°		*wickedness*
O cause first of oure confusioun!°		*downfall*
O original of oure dampnacioun,°		*damnation*

---

4. Wild parties, gambling, brothels.
5. Beyond their capacity.
6. Tear apart (a reference to oaths sworn by parts of His body, such as "God's bones!" or "God's teeth!").
7. Fruit-selling girls.
8. Girl cake vendors.
9. I.e., closely related to gluttony.
1. See Genesis 19.30–36.
2. For the story of Herod and St. John the Baptist, see Mark 6.17–29. "Who so . . . soughte": i.e., whoever looked it up in the Gospel would find.
3. Seneca, the Roman Stoic philosopher.
4. But that madness, occurring in a wicked man.

Til Crist hadde bought° us with his blood again!   *redeemed*
Lo, how dere, shortly for to sayn,
215 Abought° was thilke° cursed vilainye;   *paid for / that same*
Corrupt was al this world for glotonye:
Adam oure fader and his wif also
Fro Paradis to labour and to wo
Were driven for that vice, it is no drede.°   *doubt*
220 For whil that Adam fasted, as I rede,
He was in Paradis; and whan that he
Eet° of the fruit defended° on a tree,   *ate / forbidden*
Anoon he was out cast to wo and paine.
O glotonye, on thee wel oughte us plaine!°   *complain*
225   O, wiste a man[5] how manye maladies
Folwen of excesse and of glotonies,
He wolde been the more mesurable°   *moderate*
Of his diete, sitting at his table.
Allas, the shorte throte, the tendre mouth,
230 Maketh that eest and west and north and south,
In erthe, in air, in water, men to swinke,°   *work*
To gete a gloton daintee mete° and drinke.   *food*
Of this matere, O Paul, wel canstou trete:
"Mete unto wombe,° and wombe eek unto mete,   *belly*
235 Shal God destroyen bothe," as Paulus saith.[6]
Allas, a foul thing is it, by my faith,
To saye this word, and fouler is the deede
Whan man so drinketh of the white and rede[7]
That of his throte he maketh his privee°   *toilet*
240 Thurgh thilke cursed superfluitee.°   *overindulgence*
    The Apostle[8] weeping saith ful pitously,
"Ther walken manye of which you told have I—
I saye it now weeping with pitous vois—
They been enemies of Cristes crois,°   *cross*
245 Of whiche the ende is deeth—wombe is hir god!"[9]
O wombe,° O bely, O stinking cod,°   *belly / bag*
Fulfilled° of dong° and of corrupcioun!   *filled full / dung*
At either ende of thee foul is the soun.°   *sound*
How greet labour and cost is thee to finde!°   *provide for*
250 Thise cookes, how they stampe° and straine and grinde,   *pound*
And turnen substance into accident[1]
To fulfillen al thy likerous° talent!°   *greedy / appetite*
Out of the harde bones knokke they
The mary,° for they caste nought away   *marrow*
255 That may go thurgh the golet[2] softe and soote.°   *sweetly*
Of spicerye° of leef and bark and roote   *spices*
Shal been his sauce ymaked by delit,
To make him yit a newer appetit.
But certes, he that haunteth swiche delices°   *pleasures*

5. If a man knew.
6. See 1 Corinthians 6.13.
7. I.e., white and red wines.
8. I.e., St. Paul.
9. See Philippians 3.18.

1. A philosophic joke, depending on the distinction between inner reality (substance) and outward appearance (accident).
2. Through the gullet.

260	Is deed° whil that he liveth in tho° vices.	*dead / those*
	A lecherous thing is win, and dronkenesse	
	Is ful of striving° and of wrecchednesse.	*quarreling*
	O dronke man, disfigured is thy face!	
	Sour is thy breeth, foul artou to embrace!	
265	And thurgh thy dronke nose seemeth the soun	
	As though thou saidest ay,° "Sampsoun, Sampsoun."	*always*
	And yit, God woot,° Sampson drank nevere win.[3]	*knows*
	Thou fallest as it were a stiked swin;°	*stuck pig*
	Thy tonge is lost, and al thyn honeste cure,[4]	
270	For dronkenesse is verray sepulture°	*burial*
	Of mannes wit° and his discrecioun.	*intelligence*
	In whom that drinke hath dominacioun	
	He can no conseil° keepe, it is no drede.°	*secrets / doubt*
	Now keepe you fro the white and fro the rede—	
275	And namely° fro the white win of Lepe[5]	*particularly*
	That is to selle in Fisshstreete or in Chepe:[6]	
	The win of Spaine creepeth subtilly	
	In othere wines growing faste° by,	*close*
	Of which ther riseth swich fumositee°	*heady fumes*
280	That whan a man hath dronken draughtes three	
	And weeneth° that he be at hoom in Chepe,	*supposes*
	He is in Spaine, right at the town of Lepe,	
	Nat at The Rochele ne at Burdeux town;[7]	
	And thanne wol he sayn, "Sampsoun, Sampsoun."	
285	But herkneth, lordinges, oo° word I you praye,	*one*
	That alle the soverein actes,[8] dar I saye,	
	Of victories in the Olde Testament,	
	Thurgh verray God that is omnipotent,	
	Were doon in abstinence and in prayere:	
290	Looketh° the Bible and ther ye may it lere.°	*behold / learn*
	Looke Attila, the grete conquerour,[9]	
	Deide° in his sleep with shame and dishonour,	*died*
	Bleeding at his nose in dronkenesse:	
	A capitain sholde live in sobrenesse.	
295	And overal this, aviseth you[1] right wel	
	What was comanded unto Lamuel[2]—	
	Nat Samuel, but Lamuel, saye I—	
	Redeth the Bible and finde it expresly,	
	Of win-yiving° to hem that har[3] justise:	*wine-serving*
300	Namore of this, for it may wel suffise.	
	And now that I have spoken of glotonye,	
	Now wol I you defende° hasardrye:°	*prohibit / gambling*
	Hasard is verray moder° of lesinges,°	*mother / lies*

3. Before Samson's birth an angel told his mother that he would be a Nazarite throughout his life; persons who took this vow took no strong drink.

4. Care for self-respect.

5. A town in Spain.

6. Fishstreet and Cheapside in the London market district.

7. The Pardoner is joking about the illegal custom of adulterating fine wines of Bordeaux and La Rochelle with strong Spanish wine.

8. Distinguished deeds.

9. Attila was the leader of the Huns who almost captured Rome in the 5th century.

1. Consider.

2. Lemuel's mother told him that kings should not drink (Proverbs 31.4–5).

3. I.e., administer.

And of deceite and cursed forsweringes,°   *perjuries*
305 Blaspheme of Crist, manslaughtre, and wast° also   *waste*
Of catel° and of time; and ferthermo,   *property*
It is repreve° and contrarye of honour   *disgrace*
For to been holden a commune hasardour,°   *gambler*
And evere the hyer he is of estat
310 The more is he holden desolat.[4]
If that a prince useth hasardrye,
In alle governance and policye
He is, as by commune opinioun,
Yholde the lasse° in reputacioun.   *less*
315   Stilbon, that was a wis embassadour,
Was sent to Corinthe in ful greet honour
Fro Lacedomye° to make hir alliaunce,   *Sparta*
And whan he cam him happede° parchaunce   *it happened*
That alle the gretteste° that were of that lond   *greatest*
320 Playing at the hasard he hem foond,°   *found*
For which as soone as it mighte be
He stal him[5] hoom again to his contree,
And saide, "Ther wol I nat lese° my name,   *lose*
N'I wol nat take on me so greet defame°   *dishonor*
325 You to allye unto none hasardours:
Sendeth othere wise embassadours,
For by my trouthe, me were levere[6] die
Than I you sholde to hasardours allye.
For ye that been so glorious in honours
330 Shal nat allye you with hasardours
As by my wil, ne as by my tretee."°   *treaty*
This wise philosophre, thus saide he.
   Looke eek that to the king Demetrius
The King of Parthes,° as the book[7] saith us,   *Parthians*
335 Sente him a paire of dees° of gold in scorn,   *dice*
For he hadde used hasard therbiforn,
For which he heeld his glorye or his renown
At no value or reputacioun.
Lordes may finden other manere play
340 Honeste° ynough to drive the day away.   *honorable*
   Now wol I speke of othes false and grete
A word or two, as olde bookes trete:
   Greet swering is a thing abhominable,
And fals swering is yit more reprevable.°   *reprehensible*
345 The hye God forbad swering at al—
Witnesse on Mathew.[8] But in special
Of swering saith the holy Jeremie,[9]
"Thou shalt swere sooth thine othes and nat lie,
And swere in doom° and eek in rightwisnesse,° *equity / righteousness*
350 But idel swering is a cursednesse."°   *wickedness*

---

4. I.e., dissolute.
5. He stole away.
6. I had rather.
7. The book that relates this and the previous incident is the *Policraticus* of the 12th-century

Latin writer John of Salisbury.
8. "But I say unto you, Swear not at all" (Matthew 5.34).
9. Jeremiah 4.2.

Biholde and see that in the firste Table[1]
Of hye Goddes heestes° honorable   *commandments*
How that the seconde heeste of him is this:
"Take nat my name in idel or amis."
355 Lo, rather° he forbedeth swich swering   *sooner*
Than homicide, or many a cursed thing.
I saye that as by ordre thus it stondeth—
This knoweth that[2] his heestes understondeth
How that the seconde heeste of God is that.
360 And fertherover,° I wol thee telle al plat°   *moreover / plain*
That vengeance shal nat parten° from his hous   *depart*
That of his othes is too outrageous.
"By Goddes precious herte!" and "By his nailes!"°   *fingernails*
And "By the blood of Crist that is in Hailes,[3]
365 Sevene is my chaunce,° and thyn is cink and traye!"[4]   *winning number*
"By Goddes armes, if thou falsly playe
This daggere shal thurghout thyn herte go!"
This fruit cometh of the bicche bones[5] two—
Forswering, ire, falsnesse, homicide.
370 Now for the love of Crist that for us dyde,°   *died*
Lete° youre othes bothe grete and smale.   *leave*
But sires, now wol I telle forth my tale.
    Thise riotoures° three of whiche I telle,   *revelers*
Longe erst er prime[6] ronge of any belle,
375 Were set hem in a taverne to drinke,
And as they sat they herde a belle clinke
Biforn a cors° was caried to his grave.   *corpse*
That oon of hem gan callen to his knave:°   *servant*
Go bet,"[7] quod he, "and axe° redily°   *ask / promptly*
380 What cors is this that passeth heer forby,
And looke° that thou reporte his name weel."°   *be sure / well*
    "Sire," quod this boy, "it needeth neveradeel.[8]
It was me told er ye cam heer two houres.
He was, pardee,° an old felawe of youres,   *by God*
385 And sodeinly he was yslain tonight,°   *last night*
Fordronke° as he sat on his bench upright;   *very drunk*
Ther cam a privee° thief men clepeth° Deeth,   *stealthy / call*
That in this contree al the peple sleeth,°   *slays*
And with his spere he smoot his herte atwo,
390 And wente his way withouten wordes mo.
He hath a thousand slain this° pestilence.   *during this*
And maister, er ye come in his presence,
Me thinketh that it were necessarye
For to be war of swich an adversarye;
395 Beeth redy for to meete him everemore:
Thus taughte me my dame.° I saye namore."   *mother*
    "By Sainte Marye," saide this taverner,

---

1. I.e., the first four of the Ten Commandments,
which specify duties humankind owes to God.
2. I.e., he that.
3. An abbey in Gloucestershire supposed to possess some of Christ's blood.
4. Five and three.
5. I.e., damned dice.
6. Long before 9 A.M.
7. Better, i.e., quick.
8. It isn't a bit necessary.

"The child saith sooth, for he hath slain this yeer,
Henne° over a mile, within a greet village,   *hence*
400   Bothe man and womman, child and hine⁹ and page.
I trowe° his habitacion be there.   *believe*
To been avised° greet wisdom it were   *wary*
Er that he dide a man a dishonour."
        "Ye, Goddes armes," quod this riotour,
405   "Is it swich peril with him for to meete?
I shal him seeke by way and eek by streete,¹
I make avow to Goddes digne° bones.   *worthy*
Herkneth, felawes, we three been alle ones:°   *of one mind*
Lat eech of us holde up his hand to other
410   And eech of us bicome otheres brother,
And we wol sleen this false traitour Deeth.
He shal be slain, he that so manye sleeth,
By Goddes dignitee, er it be night."
        Togidres han thise three hir trouthes plight²
415   To live and dien eech of hem with other,
As though he were his owene ybore° brother.   *born*
And up they sterte,° al dronken in this rage,   *started*
And forth they goon towardes that village
Of which the taverner hadde spoke biforn,
420   And many a grisly ooth thanne han they sworn,
And Cristes blessed body they torente:°   *tore apart*
Deeth shal be deed° if that they may him hente.°   *dead / catch*
        Whan they han goon nat fully half a mile,
Right as they wolde han treden° over a stile,   *stepped*
425   An old man and a poore with hem mette;
This olde man ful mekely hem grette,°   *greeted*
And saide thus, "Now lordes, God you see."³
        The pruddeste° of thise riotoures three   *proudest*
Answerde again, "What, carl° with sory grace,   *fellow*
430   Why artou al forwrapped° save thy face?   *muffled up*
Why livestou so longe in so greet age?"
        This olde man gan looke in his visage,
And saide thus, "For° I ne can nat finde   *because*
A man, though that I walked into Inde,°   *India*
435   Neither in citee ne in no village,
That wolde chaunge his youthe for myn age;
And therefore moot° I han myn age stille,   *must*
As longe time as it is Goddes wille.
        "Ne Deeth, allas, ne wol nat have my lif.
440   Thus walke I lik a resteelees caitif,°   *wretch*
And on the ground which is my modres° gate   *mother's*
I knokke with my staf bothe erly and late,
And saye, 'Leve° moder, leet me in: *dear*
Lo, how I vanisshe, flessh and blood and skin.
445   Allas, whan shal my bones been at reste?
Moder, with you wolde I chaunge° my cheste⁴   *exchange*

9. Farm laborer.   3. May God protect you.
1. By highway and byway.   4. Chest for one's belongings, used here as the
2. Pledged their words of honor.   symbol for life—or perhaps a coffin.

That in my chambre longe time hath be,
Ye, for an haire-clour[5] to wrappe me.'
But yit to me she wol nat do that grace,
450   For which ful pale and welked° is my face.   *withered*
But sires, to you it is no curteisye
To speken to an old man vilainye,°   *rudeness*
But° he trespasse° in word or elles in deede.   *unless / offend*
In Holy Writ ye may yourself wel rede,
455   'Agains[6] an old man, hoor° upon his heed,   *hoar*
Ye shall arise.'[7] Wherfore I yive you reed,°   *advice*
Ne dooth unto an old man noon harm now,
Namore than that ye wolde men dide to you
In age, if that ye so longe abide.[8]
460   And God be with you wher ye go° or ride: *walk*
I moot go thider as I have to go."
    "Nay, olde cherl, by God thou shalt nat so,"
Saide this other hasardour anoon.
"Thou partest nat so lightly,° by Saint John!   *easily*
465   Thou speke° right now of thilke traitour Deeth,   *spoke*
That in this contree alle oure freendes sleeth:
Have here my trouthe, as thou art his espye,°   *spy*
Tel wher he is, or thou shalt it abye,°   *pay for*
By God and by the holy sacrament!
470   For soothly thou art oon of his assent[9]
To sleen us yonge folk, thou false thief."
    "Now sires," quod he, "if that ye be so lief°   *anxious*
To finde Deeth, turne up this crooked way,
For in that grove I lafte° him, by my fay,°   *left / faith*
475   Under a tree, and ther he wol abide:
Nat for youre boost° he wol him no thing hide.   *boast*
See ye that ook?° Right ther ye shal him finde.   *oak*
God save you, that boughte again[1] mankinde,
And you amende." Thus saide this olde man.
480   And everich of thise riotoures ran
Til he cam to that tree, and ther they founde
Of florins° fine of gold ycoined rounde   *coins*
Wel neigh an eighte busshels as hem thoughte—
Ne lenger thanne after Deeth they soughte,
485   But eech of hem so glad was of the sighte,
For that the florins been so faire and brighte,
That down they sette hem by this precious hoord.
The worste of hem he spak the firste word:
    "Bretheren," quod he, "take keep° what that I saye: *heed*
490   My wit is greet though that I bourde° and playe.   *joke*
This tresor hath Fortune unto us yiven
In mirthe and jolitee oure lif to liven,
And lightly° as it cometh so wol we spende.   *easily*
Ey, Goddes precious dignitee, who wende[2]

---

5. Haircloth, for a winding sheet.
6. In the presence of.
7. Cf. Leviticus 19.32.
8. I.e., if you live so long.

9. I.e., one of his party.
1. Redeemed.
2. Who would have supposed.

495 Today that we sholde han so fair a grace?
But mighte this gold be caried fro this place
Hoom to myn hous—or elles unto youres—
For wel ye woot that al this gold is oures—
Thanne were we in heigh felicitee.
500 But trewely, by daye it mighte nat be:
Men wolde sayn that we were theves stronge,°   *flagrant*
And for oure owene tresor doon us honge.[3]
This tresor moste ycaried be by nighte,
As wisely and as slyly as it mighte.
505 Therefore I rede° that cut° amonges us alle   *advise / straws*
Be drawe, and lat see wher the cut wol falle;
And he that hath the cut with herte blithe
Shal renne° to the town, and that ful swithe,°   *run / quickly*
And bringe us breed and win ful prively;
510 And two of us shal keepen° subtilly   *guard*
This tresor wel, and if he wol nat tarye,
Whan it is night we wol this tresor carye
By oon assent wher as us thinketh best."
That oon of hem the cut broughte in his fest°   *fist*
515 And bad hem drawe and looke wher it wol falle;
And it fil° on the yongeste of hem alle,   *fell*
And forth toward the town he wente anoon.
And also° soone as that he was agoon,°   *as / gone away*
That oon of hem spak thus unto that other:
520 "Thou knowest wel thou art my sworen brother;
Thy profit wol I telle thee anoon:
Thou woost wel that oure felawe is agoon,
And here is gold, and that ful greet plentee,
That shall departed° been among us three.   *divided*
525 But nathelees, if I can shape° it so   *arrange*
That it departed were among us two,
Hadde I nat doon a freendes turn to thee?"
    That other answerde, "I noot[4] how that may be:
He woot that the gold is with us twaye.
530 What shal we doon? What shal we to him saye?"
    "Shal it be conseil?"[5] saide the firste shrewe.°   *villain*
"And I shal telle in a wordes fewe
What we shul doon, and bringe it wel aboute."
    "I graunte," quod that other, "out of doute,
535 That by my trouthe I wol thee nat biwraye."°   *expose*
    "Now," quod the firste, "thou woost wel we be twaye,
And two of us shal strenger° be than oon: *stronger*
Looke whan that he is set that right anoon
Aris as though thou woldest with him playe,
540 And I shal rive° him thurgh the sides twaye,   *pierce*
Whil that thou strugelest with him as in game,
And with thy daggere looke thou do the same;
And thanne shal al this gold departed be,

3. Have us hanged.   5. A secret.
4. Don't know.

My dere freend, bitwixe thee and me.
545 Thanne we may bothe oure lustes° al fulfille,   *desires*
And playe at dees° right at oure owene wille."   *dice*
And thus accorded been thise shrewes twaye
To sleen the thridde, as ye han herd me saye.
    This yongeste, which that wente to the town,
550 Ful ofte in herte he rolleth up and down
The beautee of thise florins newe and brighte.
"O Lord," quod he, "if so were that I mighte
Have al this tresor to myself allone,
Ther is no man that liveth under the trone°   *throne*
555 Of God that sholde live so merye as I."
And at the laste the feend oure enemy
Putte in his thought that he sholde poison beye,°   *buy*
With which he mighte sleen his felawes twaye—
Forwhy° the feend° foond him in swich livinge   *because / devil*
560 That he hadde leve° him to sorwe bringe:[6]   *permission*
For this was outrely° his fulle entente,   *plainly*
To sleen hem bothe, and nevere to repente.
    And forth he gooth—no lenger wolde he tarye—
Into the town unto a pothecarye,°   *apothecary*
565 And prayed him that he him wolde selle
Som poison that he mighte, his rattes quelle,°   *kill*
And eek ther was a polcat[7] in his hawe°   *yard*
That, as he saide, his capons hadde yslawe,°   *slain*
And fain he wolde wreke him[8] if he mighte
570 On vermin that destroyed him[9] by nighte.
    The pothecarye answerde, "And thou shalt have
A thing that, also° God my soule save,   *as*
In al this world there is no creature
That ete or dronke hath of this confiture°   *mixture*
575 Nat but the mountance° of a corn° of whete—   *amount / grain*
That he ne shal his lif anoon forlete.°   *lose*
Ye, sterve° he shal, and that in lasse° while   *die / less*
Than thou wolt goon a paas[1] nat but a mile,
The poison is so strong and violent."
580 This cursed man hath in his hand yhent°   *taken*
This poison in a box and sith° he ran   *then*
Into the nexte streete unto a man
And borwed of him large botels three,
And in the two his poison poured he—
585 The thridde he kepte clene for his drinke,
For al the night he shoop him[2] for to swinke°   *work*
In carying of the gold out of that place.
And whan this riotour with sory grace
Hadde filled with win his grete botels three,
590 To his felawes again repaireth he.
    What needeth it to sermone of it more?

---

6. Christian doctrine teaches that the devil may
not tempt people except with God's permission.
7. A weasellike animal.
8. He would gladly avenge himself.

9. I.e., were ruining his farming.
1. Take a walk.
2. He was preparing.

For right as they had cast° his deeth bifore,   *plotted*
Right so they han him slain, and that anoon.
And whan that this was doon, thus spak that oon:
595 "Now lat us sitte and drinke and make us merye,
And afterward we wol his body berye."°   *bury*
And with that word it happed him par cas[3]
To take the botel ther the poison was,
And drank, and yaf his felawe drinke also,
600 For which anoon they storven° bothe two.   *died*
    But certes I suppose that Avicen
Wroot nevere in no canon ne in no *fen*[4]
Mo wonder signes[5] of empoisoning
Than hadde thise wrecches two er hir ending:
605 Thus ended been thise homicides two,
And eek the false empoisonere also.
    O cursed sinne of alle cursednesse!
O traitours homicide, O wikkednesse!
O glotonye, luxure,° and hasardrye!   *lechery*
610 Thou blasphemour of Crist with vilainye
And othes grete of usage° and of pride!   *habit*
Allas, mankinde, how may it bitide
That to thy Creatour which that thee wroughte,
And with his precious herte blood thee boughte,°   *redeemed*
615 Thou art so fals and so unkinde,° allas?   *unnatural*
    Now goode men, God foryive you youre trespas,
And ware° you fro the sinne of avarice: *guard*
Myn holy pardon may you alle warice°—   *save*
So that ye offre nobles or sterlinges,[6]
620 Or elles silver brooches, spoones, ringes.
Boweth your heed under this holy bulle!
Cometh up, ye wives, offreth of youre wolle!°   *wool*
Youre name I entre here in my rolle: anoon
Into the blisse of hevene shul ye goon.
625 I you assoile° by myn heigh power—   *absolve*
Ye that wol offre—as clene and eek as cleer
As ye were born.—And lo, sires, thus I preche.
And Jesu Crist that is oure soules leeche°   *physician*
So graunte you his pardon to receive,
630 For that is best—I wol you nat deceive.

The Epilogue

    "But sires, oo word forgat I in my tale:
I have relikes and pardon in my male°   *bag*
As faire as any man in Engelond,
Whiche were me yiven by the Popes hond.
635 If any of you wol of devocioun
Offren and han myn absolucioun,

3. By chance.
4. The *Canon of Medicine,* by Avicenna, an 11th-century Arabic philosopher, was divided
into sections called "fens."
5. More wonderful symptoms.
6. "Nobles" and "sterlinges" were valuable coins.

Come forth anoon, and kneeleth here adown,
And mekely receiveth my pardoun,
Or elles taketh pardon as ye wende,°   *ride along*
640   Al newe and fressh at every miles ende—
So that ye offre alway newe and newe[7]
Nobles or pens whiche that be goode and trewe.
It is an honour to everich° that is heer   *everyone*
That ye have a suffisant° pardoner   *competent*
645   T'assoile you in contrees as ye ride,
For aventures° whiche that may bitide: *accidents*
Paraventure ther may falle oon or two
Down of his hors and breke his nekke atwo;
Looke which a suretee° is it to you alle   *safeguard*
650   That I am in youre felaweshipe yfalle
That may assoile you, bothe more and lasse,[8]
Whan that the soule shal fro the body passe.
I rede° that oure Hoste shal biginne,   *advise*
For he is most envoluped° in sinne.   *involved*
655   Com forth, sire Host, and offre first anoon,
And thou shalt kisse the relikes everichoon,°   *each one*
Ye, for a grote: unbokele° anoon thy purs."   *unbuckle*
    "Nay, nay," quod he, "thanne have I Cristes curs!
Lat be," quod he, "it shal nat be, so theech!°   *may I prosper*
660   Thou woldest make me kisse thyn olde breech°   *breeches*
And swere it were a relik of a saint,
Though it were with thy fundament° depeint.°   *anus / stained*
But, by the crois which that Sainte Elaine foond,[9]
I wolde I hadde thy coilons° in myn hond,   *testicles*
665   In stede of relikes or of saintuarye.°   *relic-box*
Lat cutte hem of: I wol thee helpe hem carye.
They shal be shrined in an hogges tord."°   *turd*
    This Pardoner answerde nat a word:
So wroth he was no word ne wolde he saye.
670   "Now," quod oure Host, "I wol no lenger playe
With thee, ne with noon other angry man."
    But right anoon the worthy Knight bigan,
Whan that he sawgh that al the peple lough,°   *laughed*
"Namore of this, for it is right ynough.
675   Sire Pardoner, be glad and merye of cheere,
And ye, sire Host that been to me so dere,
I praye you that ye kisse the Pardoner,
And Pardoner, I praye thee, draw thee neer,
And as we diden lat us laughe and playe."
680   Anoon they kiste and riden forth hir waye.

---

7. Over and over.
8. Both high and low (i.e., everybody).
9. I.e., by the cross that St. Helena found. Helena, mother of Constantine the Great, was
reputed to have found the cross on which Christ
was crucified.

The Nun's Priest's Tale

In the framing story, *The Nun's Priest's Tale* is linked to a dramatic exchange that follows *The Monk's Tale*. The latter consists of brief tragedies, the common theme of which is the fall of famous men and one woman, most of whom are rulers, through the reversals of Fortune. Like *The Knight's Tale*, this was probably an earlier work of Chaucer's, one that he never finished. As the Monk's tragedies promise to go on and on monotonously, the Knight interrupts and politely tells the Monk that his tragedies are too painful. The Host chimes in to say that the tragedies are "nat worth a botterflye" and asks the Monk to try another subject, but the Monk is offended and refuses. The Host then turns to the Nun's Priest, that is, the priest who is accompanying the Prioress. The three priests said in *The General Prologue* to have been traveling with her have apparently been reduced to one.

The Nun's Priest's Tale is an example of the literary genre known as the "animal fable," familiar from the fables of Aesop in which animals, behaving like human beings, point to a moral. In the Middle Ages fables often functioned as elementary texts to teach boys Latin. Marie de France's fables in French are the earliest known vernacular translations. This particular fable derives from an episode in the French *Roman de Renard*, a "beast epic," which satirically represents a feudal animal society ruled over by Noble the Lion. Reynard the Fox is a wily trickster hero who is constantly preying upon and outwitting the other animals, although sometimes Reynard himself is outwitted by one of his victims. See also Henryson's brilliant *Cock and the Fox* (p. 501, this volume).

In *The Nun's Priest's Tale*, morals proliferate: both the priest-narrator and his hero, Chauntecleer the rooster, spout examples, learned allusions, proverbs, and sententious generalizations, often in highly inflated rhetoric. The simple beast fable is thus inflated into a delightful satire of learning and moralizing and of the pretentious rhetoric by which medieval writers sometimes sought to elevate their works. Among them, we may include Chaucer himself, who in this tale seems to be making affectionate fun of some of his own works, like the tragedies which became *The Monk's Tale*.

A poore widwe somdeel stape° in age		*advanced*
Was whilom° dwelling in a narwe[1] cotage,		*once upon a time*
Biside a grove, stonding in a dale:		
This widwe of which I telle you my tale,		
5 Sin thilke° day that she was last a wif,		*that same*
In pacience ladde° a ful simple lif.		*led*
For litel was hir catel° and hir rente,°		*property / income*
By housbondrye° of swich as God hire sente		*economy*
She foond° hirself and eek hir doughtren two.		*provided for*
10 Three large sowes hadde she and namo,		
Three kin,° and eek a sheep that highte° Malle.		*cows / was called*
Ful sooty[2] was hir bowr° and eek hir halle.		*bedroom*
In which she eet ful many a sclendre° meel;		*scanty*
Of poinant° sauce hire needed neveradeel:°		*pungent / not a bit*
15 No daintee morsel passed thurgh hir throte—		
Hir diete was accordant to hir cote.°		*cottage*
Repleccioun° ne made hire nevere sik:		*overeating*
Attempre° diete was al hir physik,°		*moderate / medicine*
And exercise and hertes suffisaunce.°		*contentment*

---

1. I.e., small.
2. I.e., her cottage lacked a chimney.

20 The goute lette hire nothing for to daunce,[3]
N'apoplexye shente° nat hir heed.°   *hurt / head*
No win ne drank she, neither whit ne reed:°   *red*
Hir boord° was served most with whit and blak,[4]   *table*
Milk and brown breed, in which she foond no lak;°   *found no fault*
25 Seind° bacon, and somtime an ey° or twaye,   *Broiled / egg*
For she was as it were a manere daye.[5]
A yeerd° she hadde, enclosed al withoute   *yard*
With stikkes, and a drye dich aboute,
In which she hadde a cok heet° Chauntecleer: *named*
30 In al the land of crowing nas° his peer.   *was not*
His vois was merier than the merye orgon
On massedayes that in the chirche goon;[6]
Wel sikerer[7] was his crowing in his logge°   *dwelling*
Than is a clok or an abbeye orlogge;°   *timepiece*
35 By nature he knew eech ascensioun
Of th'equinoxial[8] in thilke town:
For whan degrees fifteene were ascended,
Thanne crew° he that it mighte nat been amended.°   *crowed / improved*
His comb was redder than the fin coral,
40 And batailed° as it were a castel wal;   *battlemented*
His bile° was blak, and as the jeet° it shoon;   *bill / jet*
Like asure[9] were his legges and his toon;°   *toes*
His nailes whitter° than the lilye flowr,   *whiter*
And lik the burned° gold was his colour.   *burnished*
45 This gentil° cok hadde in his governaunce   *noble*
Sevene hennes for to doon al his plesaunce,°   *pleasure*
Whiche were his sustres and his paramours,[1]
And wonder like to him as of colours;
Of whiche the faireste hewed° on hir throte   *colored*
50 Was cleped° faire damoisele Pertelote: *called*
Curteis she was, discreet, and debonaire,°   *meek*
And compaignable,° and bar° hirself so faire,   *companionable / bore*
Sin thilke day that she was seven night old,
That trewely she hath the herte in hold
55 Of Chauntecleer, loken° in every lith.°   *locked / limb*
He loved hire so that wel was him therwith.[2]
But swich a joye was it to heere hem singe,
Whan that the brighte sonne gan to springe,
In sweete accord *My Lief is Faren in Londe*[3]—
60 For thilke time, as I have understonde,
Beestes and briddes couden speke and singe.
     And so bifel that in a daweninge,
As Chauntecleer among his wives alle
Sat on his perche that was in the halle,

3. The gout didn't hinder her at all from dancing.
4. I.e., milk and bread.
5. I.e., a kind of dairywoman.
6. I.e., is played.
7. More reliable.
8. I.e., he knew by instinct each step in the progression of the celestial equator. The celestial equator was thought to make a 360° rotation around the earth every twenty-four hours; therefore, a progression of 15° would be equal to the passage of an hour (line 37).
9. Blue (lapis lazuli).
1. His sisters and his mistresses.
2. That he was well contented.
3. "My Love Has Gone Away," a popular song of the time. See p. 479.

65   And next him sat this faire Pertelote,
    This Chauntecleer gan gronen in his throte,
    As man that in his dreem is drecched° sore.   *troubled*
       And whan that Pertelote thus herde him rore,°   *roar*
    She was agast, and saide, "Herte dere,

70   What aileth you to grone in this manere?
    Ye been a verray slepere,[4] fy, for shame!"
       And he answerde and saide thus, "Madame,
    I praye you that ye take it nat agrief.°   *amiss*
    By God, me mette I was in swich meschief[5]

75   Right now, that yit myn herte is sore afright.
    Now God," quod he, "my swevene recche aright,[6]
    And keepe my body out of foul prisoun!
    Me mette° how that I romed up and down   *dreamed*
    Within oure yeerd, wher as I sawgh a beest,

80   Was lik an hound and wolde han maad arrest[7]
    Upon my body, and han had me deed.[8]
    His colour was bitwixe yelow and reed,
    And tipped was his tail and bothe his eres
    With blak, unlik the remenant° of his heres;°   *rest / hairs*

85   His snoute smal, with glowing yën twaye.
    Yit of his look for fere almost I deye:°   *die*
    This caused me my groning, doutelees."
       "Avoi,"° quod she, "fy on you, hertelees!°   *fie / coward*
    Allas," quod she, "for by that God above,

90   Now han ye lost myn herte and al my love!
    I can nat love a coward, by my faith.
    For certes, what so any womman saith,
    We alle desiren, if it mighte be,
    To han housbondes hardy, wise, and free,°   *generous*

95   And secree,° and no nigard,° ne no fool,   *discreet / miser*
    Ne him that is agast of every tool,°   *weapon*
    Ne noon avauntour.° By that God above,   *boaster*
    How dorste° ye sayn for shame unto youre love   *dare*
    That any thing mighte make you aferd?

100   Have ye no mannes herte and han a beerd?°   *beard*
    Allas, and conne° ye been agast of swevenes?°   *can / dreams*
    No thing, God woot, but vanitee[9] in swevene is!
    Swevenes engendren of replexiouns,[1]
    And ofte of fume° and of complexiouns,°   *gas / bodily humors*

105   Whan humours been too habundant in a wight.[2]
    Certes, this dreem which ye han met° tonight   *dreamed*
    Comth of the grete superfluitee
    Of youre rede colera,[3] pardee,
    Which causeth folk to dreden° in hir dremes   *fear*

110   Of arwes,° and of fir with rede lemes,°   *arrows / flames*

---

4. Sound sleeper.
5. I dreamed that I was in such misfortune.
6. Interpret my dream correctly (i.e., in an auspicious manner).
7. Would have laid hold.
8. I.e., killed me.
9. I.e., empty illusion.

1. Dreams have their origin in overeating.
2. I.e., when humors (bodily fluids) are too abundant in a person. Pertelote's diagnosis is based on the familiar concept that an excess of one of the bodily humors in a person affected his or her temperament (see p. 253, n. 8).
3. Red bile.

Of rede beestes, that they wol hem bite,
Of contek,° and of whelpes grete and lite[4]—   *strife*
Right° as the humour of malencplye[5]   *just*
Causeth ful many a man in sleep to crye
115 For fere of blake beres° or boles° blake,   *bears / bulls*
Or elles blake develes wol hem take.
Of othere humours coude I tell also
That werken many a man in sleep ful wo,
But I wol passe as lightly° as I can.   *quickly*
120 Lo, Caton,[6] which that was so wis a man,
Saide he nat thus? 'Ne do no fors of[7] dremes.'
Now, sire," quod she, "whan we flee fro the bemes,[8]
For Goddes love, as take som laxatif.
Up° peril of my soule and of my lif,   *upon*
125 I conseile you the beste, I wol nat lie,
That bothe of colere and of malencolye
Ye purge you; and for° ye shal nat tarye,   *in order that*
Though in this town is noon apothecarye,
I shal myself to herbes techen you,
130 That shal been for youre hele° and for youre prow,°   *health / benefit*
And in oure yeerd tho° herbes shal I finde,   *those*
The whiche han of hir propretee by kinde°   *nature*
To purge you binethe and eek above.
Foryet° nat this, for Goddes owene love.   *forget*
135 Ye been ful colerik° of complexioun;   *bilious*
Ware° the sonne in his ascencioun   *beware that*
Ne finde you nat repleet° of humours hote;°   *filled / hot*
And if it do, I dar wel laye° a grote   *bet*
That ye shul have a fevere terciane,[9]
140 Or an agu° that may be youre bane.°   *ague / death*
A day or two ye shul han digestives
Of wormes, er° ye take youre laxatives   *before*
Of lauriol, centaure, and fumetere,[1]
Or elles of ellebor° that groweth there,   *hellebore*
145 Of catapuce, or of gaitres beries,[2]
Of herb-ive° growing in oure yeerd ther merye is[3]—   *herb ivy*
Pekke hem right up as they growe and ete hem in.
Be merye, housbonde, for youre fader° kin!   *father's*
Dredeth no dreem: I can saye you namore."
150   "Madame," quod he, "graunt mercy of youre lore,[4]
But nathelees, as touching daun° Catoun,   *master*
That hath of wisdom swich a greet renown,
Though that he bad no dremes for to drede,
By God, men may in olde bookes rede
155 Of many a man more of auctoritee°   *authority*
Than evere Caton was, so mote I thee,°   *prosper*

---

4. And of big and little dogs.
5. I.e., black bile.
6. Dionysius Cato, supposed author of a book of maxims used in elementary education.
7. Pay no attention to.
8. Fly down from the rafters.
9. Tertian (recurring every other day).

1. Of laureole, centaury, and fumitory. These, and the herbs mentioned in the next lines, were all common medieval medicines used as cathartics.
2. Of caper berry or of gaiter berry.
3. Where it is pleasant.
4. Many thanks for your instruction.

That al the revers sayn of his sentence,°   *opinion*
And han wel founden by experience
That dremes been significaciouns
160 As wel of joye as tribulaciouns
That folk enduren in this lif present.
Ther needeth make of this noon argument:
The verray preve[5] sheweth it in deede.
    "Oon of the gretteste auctour[6] that men rede
165 Saith thus, that whilom two felawes wente
On pilgrimage in a ful good entente,
And happed so they comen in a town,
Wher as ther was swich congregacioun
Of peple, and eek so strait of herbergage,[7]
170 That they ne founde as muche as oo cotage
In which they bothe mighte ylogged° be;   *lodged*
Wherfore they mosten° of necessitee   *must*
As for that night departe° compaignye.   *part*
And eech of hem gooth to his hostelrye,
175 And took his logging as it wolde falle.°   *befall*
That oon of hem was logged in a stalle,
Fer° in a yeerd, with oxen of the plough;   *far away*
That other man was logged wel ynough,
As was his aventure° or his fortune,   *lot*
180 That us governeth alle as in commune.
And so bifel that longe er it were day,
This man mette° in his bed, ther as he lay,   *dreamed*
How that his felawe gan upon him calle,
And saide, 'Allas, for in an oxes stalle
185 This night I shal be mordred° ther I lie!   *murdered*
Now help me, dere brother, or I die!
In alle haste com to me,' he saide.
    "This man out of his sleep for fere abraide,°   *started up*
But whan that he was wakened of his sleep,
190 He turned him and took of this no keep:°   *heed*
Him thoughte his dreem nas but a vanitee.°   *illusion*
Thus twies in his sleeping dremed he,
And atte thridde time yit his felawe.
Cam, as him thoughte, and saide, 'I am now slawe:°   *slain*
195 Bihold my bloody woundes deepe and wide.
Axis up erly in the morwe tide,[8]
And atte west gate of the town,' quod he,
'A carte ful of dong° ther shaltou see,   *dung*
In which my body is hid ful prively:
200 Do thilke carte arresten boldely.[9]
My gold caused my mordre, sooth to sayn'
—And tolde him every point how he was slain,
With a ful pitous face, pale of hewe.
And truste wel, his dreem he foond° ful trewe,   *found*
205 For on the morwe° as soone as it was day,   *morning*

5. Actual experience.
6. I.e., one of the greatest authors (perhaps Cicero or Valerius Maximus).
7. And also such a shortage of lodging.
8. In the morning.
9. Boldly have this same cart seized.

To his felawes in° he took the way,   *lodging*
And whan that he cam to this oxes stalle,
After his felawe he bigan to calle.
 "The hostiler° answerde him anoon,   *innkeeper*
210 And saide, 'Sire, youre felawe is agoon:° *gone away*
As soone as day he wente out of the town.'
 "This man gan fallen in suspecioun,
Remembring on his dremes that he mette;° *dreamed*
And forth he gooth, no lenger wolde he lette,° *tarry*
215 Unto the west gate of the town, and foond
A dong carte, wente as it were to donge° lond, *put manure on*
That was arrayed in that same wise
As ye han herd the dede° man devise;   *dead*
And with an hardy herte he gan to crye,
220 'Vengeance and justice of this felonye!
My felawe mordred is this same night,
And in this carte he lith° gaping upright!° *lies / on his back*
I crye out on the ministres,' quod he,
'That sholde keepe and rulen this citee.
225 Harrow,° allas, here lith my felawe slain!' *help*
What sholde I more unto this tale sayn?
The peple up sterte° and caste the carte to grounde, *started*
And in the middel of the dong they founde
The dede man that mordred was al newe.[1]
230 "O blisful God that art so just and trewe,
Lo, how that thou biwrayest° mordre alway! *disclose*
Mordre wol out, that see we day by day:
Mordre is so wlatsom° and abhominable   *loathsome*
To God that is so just and resonable,
235 That he ne wol nat suffre it heled° be,   *concealed*
Though it abide a yeer or two or three.
Mordre wol out: this my conclusioun.
And right anoon ministres of that town
Han hent° the cartere and so sore him pined,[2] *seized*
240 And eek the hostiler so sore engined,°   *racked*
That they biknewe° hir wikkednesse anoon, *confessed*
And were anhanged° by the nekke boon.   *hanged*
Here may men seen that dremes been to drede.[3]
 "And certes, in the same book I rede—
245 Right in the nexte chapitre after this—
I gabbe° nat, so have I joye or blis—   *lie*
Two men that wolde han passed over see
For certain cause into a fer contree,
If that the wind ne hadde been contrarye
250 That made hem in a citee for to tarye,
That stood ful merye upon an haven° side— *harbor's*
But on a day again° the even-tide   *toward*
The wind gan chaunge, and blewe right as hem leste:[4]
Jolif° and glad they wenten unto reste,   *merry*

1. Recently.   3. Worthy of being feared.
2. Tortured.   4. Just as they wished.

255   And casten° hem ful erly for to saile.   *determined*
        "But to that oo man fil° a greet mervaile;   *befell*
    That oon of hem, in sleeping as he lay,
    Him mette[5] a wonder dreem again the day:
    Him thoughte a man stood by his beddes side,
260   And him comanded that he sholde abide,
    And saide him thus, 'If thou tomorwe wende,
    Thou shalt be dreint:° my tale is at an ende.'   *drowned*
        "He wook and tolde his felawe what he mette,
    And prayed him his viage° to lette;°   *voyage / delay*
265   As for that day he prayed him to bide.
        "His felawe that lay by his beddes side
    Gan for to laughe, and scorned him ful faste.°   *hard*
    'No dreem,' quod he, 'may so myn herte agaste°   *terrify*
    That I wol lette for to do my thinges.°   *business*
270   I sette nat a straw by thy dreminges,[6]
    For swevenes been but vanitees and japes:[7]
    Men dreme alday° of owles or of apes,[8]   *constantly*
    And of many a maze° therwithal—   *delusion*
    Men dreme of thing that nevere was ne shal.[9]
275   But sith I see that thou wolt here abide,
    And thus forsleuthen° wilfully thy tide,°   *waste / time*
    God woot, it reweth me,[1] and have good day.'
    And thus he took his leve and wente his way.
    But er that he hadde half his cours ysailed—
280   Noot I nat why ne what meschaunce it ailed—
    But casuelly the shippes botme rente,[2]
    And ship and man under the water wente,
    In sighte of othere shippes it biside,
    That with hem sailed at the same tide.
285   And therfore, faire Pertelote so dere,
    By swiche ensamples olde maistou lere°   *learn*
    That no man sholde been too recchelees°   *careless*
    Of dremes, for I saye thee doutelees
    That many a dreem ful sore is for to drede.
290   "Lo, in the lif of Saint Kenelm[3] I rede—
    That was Kenulphus sone, the noble king
    Of Mercenrike°—how Kenelm mette a thing   *Mercia*
    A lite° er he was mordred on a day.   *little*
    His mordre in his avision° he sey.°   *dream / saw*
295   His norice° him expounded everydeel°   *nurse / every bit*
    His swevene, and bad him for to keepe him[4] weel
    For traison, but he nas but seven yeer old,
    And therfore litel tale hath he told
    Of any dreem,[5] so holy was his herte.
300   By God, I hadde levere than my sherte[6]

---

5. He dreamed.
6. I don't care a straw for your dreamings.
7. Dreams are but illusions and frauds.
8. I.e., of absurdities.
9. I.e., shall be.
1. I'm sorry.
2. I don't know why nor what was the trouble

with it—but accidentally the ship's bottom split.
3. Kenelm succeeded his father as king of Mercia at the age of seven, but was slain by his aunt (in 821).
4. Guard himself.
5. Therefore he has set little store by any dream.
6. I.e., I'd give my shirt.

That ye hadde rad° his legende as have I. — *read*
    "Dame Pertelote, I saye you trewely,
Macrobeus,[7] that writ the *Avisioun*
In Affrike of the worthy Scipioun,
305 Affermeth° dremes, and saith that they been — *confirms*
Warning of thinges that men after seen.
    "And ferthermore, I praye you looketh wel
In the Olde Testament of Daniel,
If he heeld° dremes any vanitee.[8] — *considered*
310   "Rede eek of Joseph[9] and ther shul ye see
Wher° dremes be somtime—I saye nat alle— — *whether*
Warning of thinges that shul after falle.
    "Looke of Egypte the king daun Pharao,
His bakere and his botelere° also, — *butler*
315 Wher they ne felte noon effect in dremes.[1]
Whoso wol seeke actes of sondry remes° — *realms*
May rede of dremes many a wonder thing.
    "Lo Cresus, which that was of Lyde° king, — *Lydia*
Mette° he nat that he sat upon a tree, — *dreamed*
320 Which signified he sholde anhanged° be? — *hanged*
    "Lo here Andromacha, Ectores° wif, — *Hector's*
That day that Ector sholde lese° his lif, — *lose*
She dremed on the same night biforn
How that the lif of Ector sholde be lorn,° — *lost*
325 If thilke° day he wente into bataile; — *that same*
She warned him, but it mighte nat availe:° — *do any good*
He wente for to fighte nathelees,
But he was slain anoon° of Achilles. — *right away*
But thilke tale is al too long to telle,
330 And eek it is neigh day, I may nat dwelle.
Shortly I saye, as for conclusioun,
That I shal han of this avisioun[2]
Adversitee, and I saye ferthermoor
That I ne telle of[3] laxatives no stoor,
335 For they been venimes,° I woot it weel: — *poisons*
I hem defye, I love hem neveradeel.° — *not a bit*
    "Now lat us speke of mirthe and stinte° al this. — *stop*
Madame Pertelote, so have I blis,
Of oo thing God hath sente me large grace:
340 For whan I see the beautee of youre face—
Ye been so scarlet reed° aboute youre yën— — *red*
It maketh al my drede for to dien.
For also siker° as *In principio*,[4] — *certain*
Mulier est hominis confusio,[5]
345 Madame, the sentence° of this Latin is, — *meaning*
'Womman is mannes joye and al his blis.'

7. Macrobius wrote a famous commentary on Cicero's account in *De Republica* of the dream of Scipio Africanus Minor; the commentary came to be regarded as a standard authority on dream lore.
8. See Daniel 7.
9. See Genesis 37.
1. See Genesis 39–41.

2. Divinely inspired dream (as opposed to the more ordinary "swevene" or "dreem").
3. Set by.
4. Beginning of the Gospel of St. John that gives the essential premises of Christianity: "In the beginning was the Word."
5. Woman is man's ruination.

For whan I feele anight youre softe side—
Al be it that I may nat on you ride,
For that oure perche is maad so narwe, allas—
350 I am so ful of joye and of solas°   *delight*
That I defye bothe swevene and dreem."
And with that word he fleigh° down fro the beem,   *flew*
For it was day, and eek his hennes alle,
And with a "chuk" he gan hem for to calle,
355 For he hadde founde a corn° lay in the yeerd.   *grain*
Real° he was, he was namore aferd:°   *regal / afraid*
He fethered⁶ Pertelote twenty time,
And trad hire as ofte er it was prime.⁷
He looketh as it were a grim leoun,
360 And on his toes he rometh up and down:
Him deined⁸ nat to sette his foot to grounde.
He chukketh whan he hath a corn yfounde,
And to him rennen° thanne his wives alle.   *run*
Thus royal, as a prince is in his halle,
365 Leve I this Chauntecleer in his pasture,
And after wol I telle his aventure.
    Whan that the month in which the world bigan,
That highte° March, whan God first maked man,   *is called*
Was compleet, and passed were also,
370 Sin March biran,° thritty days and two,⁹   *passed by*
Bifel that Chauntecleer in al his pride,
His sevene wives walking him biside,
Caste up his yën to the brighte sonne,
That in the signe of Taurus hadde yronne
375 Twenty degrees and oon and somwhat more,
And knew by kinde,° and by noon other lore,   *nature*
That it was prime, and crew with blisful stevene.°   *voice*
"The sonne," he saide, "is clomben¹ up on hevene
Fourty degrees and oon and more, ywis.°   *indeed*
380 Madame Pertelote, my worldes blis,
Herkneth thise blisful briddes° how they singe,   *birds*
And see the fresshe flowers how they springe:
Ful is myn herte of revel and solas."
But sodeinly him fil° a sorweful cas,°   *befell / chance*
385 For evere the latter ende of joye is wo—
God woot that worldly joye is soone ago,
And if a rethor° coude faire endite,°   *rhetorician / compose*
He in a cronicle saufly° mighte it write,   *safely*
As for a soverein notabilitee.²
390 Now every wis man lat him herkne me:
This storye is also° trewe, I undertake,   *as*
As is the book of *Launcelot de Lake*,³
That wommen holde in ful greet reverence.
Now wol I turne again to my sentence.°   *main point*

---

6. I.e., embraced.
7. 9 A.M. "Trad": trod, copulated with.
8. He deigned.
9. The rhetorical time telling yields May 3.

1. Has climbed.
2. Indisputable fact.
3. Romances of the courteous knight Lancelot of the Lake were very popular.

395   A colfox⁴ ful of sly iniquitee,
     That in the grove hadde woned° yeres three,   *dwelled*
     By heigh imaginacion forncast,⁵
     The same night thurghout the hegges° brast°   *hedges / burst*
     Into the yeerd ther Chauntecleer the faire
400   Was wont, and eek his wives, to repaire;
     And in a bed of wortes° stille he lay   *cabbages*
     Til it was passed undren° of the day,   *midmorning*
     Waiting his time on Chauntecleer to falle,
     As gladly doon thise homicides alle,
405   That in await liggen to mordre⁶ men.
     O false mordrour, lurking in thy den!
     O newe Scariot! Newe Geniloun!⁷
     False dissimilour!° O Greek Sinoun,⁸   *dissembler*
     That broughtest Troye al outrely° to sorwe!   *utterly*
410   O Chauntecleer, accursed be that morwe°   *morning*
     That thou into the yeerd flaugh° fro the bemes!   *flew*
     Thou were ful wel ywarned by thy dremes
     That thilke day was perilous to thee;
     But what that God forwoot° moot° needes be,   *foreknows / must*
415   After° the opinion of certain clerkes: *according to*
     Witnesse on him that any parfit° clerk is   *perfect*
     That in scole is greet altercacioun
     In this matere, and greet disputisoun,°   *disputation*
     And hath been of an hundred thousand men.
420   But I ne can nat bulte it to the bren,⁹
     As can the holy doctour Augustin,
     Or Boece, or the bisshop Bradwardin¹—
     Wheither that Goddes worthy forwiting°   *foreknowledge*
     Straineth me nedely² for to doon a thing
425   ("Nedely" clepe I simple necessitee),
     Or elles if free chois be graunted me
     To do that same thing or do it naught,
     Though God forwoot° it er that I was wrought;   *foreknew*
     Or if his wiring° straineth neveradeel,   *knowledge*
430   But by necessitee condicionel³—
     I wol nat han to do of swich matere:
     My tale is of a cok, as ye may heere,
     That took his conseil of his wif with sorwe,
     To walken in the yeerd upon that morwe
435   That he hadde met° the dreem that I you tolde.   *dreamed*
     Wommenes conseils been ful ofte colde,⁴
     Wommanes conseil broughte us first to wo,

---

4. Fox with black markings.
5. Having planned with great cunning.
6. That lie in ambush to murder.
7. I.e., Ganelon, who betrayed Roland to the Saracens (in the medieval French epic *The Song of Roland*). "Scariot": Judas Iscariot.
8. Sinon, who persuaded the Trojans to take the Greeks' wooden horse into their city—with, of course, the result that the city was destroyed.
9. Sift it to the bran, i.e., get to the bottom of it.

1. St. Augustine, Boethius (6th-century Roman philosopher, whose *Consolation of Philosophy* was translated by Chaucer), and Thomas Bradwardine (archbishop of Canterbury, d. 1349) were all concerned with the interrelationship between people's free will and God's foreknowledge.
2. Constrains me necessarily.
3. Boethius's "conditional necessity" permitted a large measure of free will.
4. I.e., baneful.

And made Adam fro Paradis to go,
Ther as he was ful merye and wel at ese.
440 But for I noot° to whom it mighte displese   *don't know*
If I conseil of wommen wolde blame,
Passe over, for I saide it in my game°—   *sport*
Rede auctours where they trete of swich matere,
And what they sayn of wommen ye may heere—
445 Thise been the cokkes wordes and nat mine:
I can noon harm of no womman divine.°   *guess*
    Faire in the sond° to bathe hire merily   *sand*
Lith° Pertelote, and alle hir sustres by,   *lies*
Again° the sonne, and Chauntecleer so free°   *in / noble*
450 Soong° merier than the mermaide in the see—   *sang*
For Physiologus[5] saith sikerly
How that they singen wel and merily.
    And so bifel that as he caste his yë
Among the wortes on a boterflye,°   *butterfly*
455 He was war of this fox that lay ful lowe.
No thing ne liste him[6] thanne for to crowe,
But cride anoon "Cok cok!" and up he sterte,°   *started*
As man that[7] was affrayed in his herte—
For naturelly a beest desireth flee
460 Fro his contrarye[8] if he may it see,
Though he nevere erst° hadde seen it with his yë.   *before*
This Chauntecleer, whan he gan him espye,
He wolde han fled, but that the fox anoon
Saide, "Gentil sire, allas, wher wol ye goon?
465 Be ye afraid of me that am youre freend?
Now certes, I were worse than a feend
If I to you wolde° harm or vilainye.   *meant*
I am nat come youre conseil° for t'espye,   *secrets*
But trewely the cause of my cominge
470 Was only for to herkne how ye singe:
For trewely, ye han as merye a stevene°   *voice*
As any angel hath that is in hevene.
Therwith ye han in musik more feelinge
Than hadde Boece,[9] or any that can singe.
475 My lord your fader—God his soule blesse!—
And eek youre moder, of hir gentilesse,°   *gentility*
Han in myn hous ybeen, to my grete ese.
And certes sire, ful fain° wolde I you plese.   *gladly*
    "But for men speke of singing, I wol saye,
480 So mote I brouke[1] wel mine yën twaye,
Save ye, I herde nevere man to singe
As dide youre fader in the morweninge.
Certes, it was of herte° al that he soong.°   *heartfelt / sang*
And for to make his vois the more strong,

---

5. Supposed author of a bestiary, a book of moralized zoology describing both natural and supernatural animals (including mermaids).
6. He wished.
7. Like one who.
8. I.e., his natural enemy.
9. Boethius also wrote a treatise on music.
1. So might I enjoy the use of.

485 He wolde so paine him² that with bothe his yën
He moste winke,³ so loude wolde he cryen;
And stonden on his tiptoon therwithal,
And strecche forth his nekke long and smal;
And eek he was of swich discrecioun
490 That ther nas no man in no regioun
That him in song or wisdom mighte passe.
I have wel rad° in *Daun Burnel the Asse*⁴   *read*
Among his vers how that ther was a cok,
For a preestes sone yaf him a knok⁵
495 Upon his leg whil he was yong and nice,°   *foolish*
He made him for to lese° his benefice.⁶   *lose*
But certain, ther nis no comparisoun
Bitwixe the wisdom and discrecioun
Of youre fader and of his subtiltee.⁷
500 Now singeth, sire, for sainte° charitee!   *holy*
Lat see, conne° ye youre fader countrefete?"°   *can / imitate*
    This Chauntecleer his winges gan to bete,
As man that coude his traison nat espye,
So was he ravisshed with his flaterye.
505   Allas, ye lordes, many a fals flatour°   *flatterer*
Is in youre court, and many a losengeour°   *deceiver*
That plesen you wel more, by my faith,
Than he that soothfastnesse° unto you saith!   *truth*
Redeth Ecclesiaste⁸ of flaterye.
510 Beeth war, ye lordes, of hir trecherye.
    This Chauntecleer stood hye upon his toos,
Strecching his nekke, and heeld his yën cloos,
And gan to crowe loude for the nones;°   *occasion*
And daun Russel the fox sterte° up atones,   *jumped*
515 And by the gargat° hente° Chauntecleer,   *throat / seized*
And on his bak toward the wode him beer,°   *bore*
For yit ne was ther no man that him sued.°   *followed*
    O destinee that maist nat been eschued!°   *eschewed*
Allas that Chauntecleer fleigh° fro the bemes!   *flew*
520 Allas his wif ne roughte nat of⁹ dremes!
And on a Friday fil° al this meschaunce!   *befell*
    O Venus that art goddesse of plesaunce,
Sin that thy servant was this Chauntecleer,
And in thy service dide al his power—
525 More for delit than world¹ to multiplye—
Why woldestou suffre him on thy day² to die?
    O Gaufred,³ dere maister soverein,
That, whan thy worthy king Richard was slain

---

2. Take pains.
3. He had to shut his eyes.
4. Master Brunellus, a discontented donkey, was the hero of a 12th-century satirical poem by Nigel Wireker.
5. Because a priest's son gave him a knock.
6. The offended cock neglected to crow so that his master, now grown to manhood, overslept, missing his ordination and losing his benefice.

7. His (the cock in the story) cleverness.
8. The Book of Ecclesiasticus, in the Apocrypha.
9. Didn't care for.
1. I.e., population.
2. Friday is Venus's day.
3. Geoffrey of Vinsauf, a famous medieval rhetorician, who wrote a lament on the death of Richard I in which he scolded Friday, the day on which the king died.

With shot,[4] complainedest his deeth so sore,
530 Why ne hadde I now thy sentence and thy lore,[5]
The Friday for to chide as diden ye?
For on a Friday soothly slain was he.
Thanne wolde I shewe you how that I coude plaine°   *lament*
For Chauntecleres drede and for his paine.
535   Certes, swich cry ne lamentacioun
Was nevere of ladies maad when Ilioun°   *Ilium, Troy*
Was wonne, and Pyrrus[6] with his straite° swerd,   *drawn*
Whan he hadde hent° King Priam by the beerd   *seized*
And slain him, as saith us *Eneidos*,[7]
540 As maden alle the hennes in the cloos,°   *yard*
Whan they hadde seen of Chauntecleer the sighte.
But sovereinly° Dame Pertelote shrighte°   *supremely / shrieked*
Ful louder than dide Hasdrubales[8] wif
Whan that hir housbonde hadde lost his lif,
545 And that the Romains hadden brend° Cartage: *burned*
She was so ful of torment and of rage°   *madness*
That wilfully unto the fir she sterte,°   *jumped*
And brende hirselven with a stedefast herte.
    O woful hennes, right so criden ye
550 As, whan that Nero brende the citee
Of Rome, criden senatoures wives
For that hir housbondes losten alle hir lives:[9]
Withouten gilt this Nero hath hem slain.
Now wol I turne to my tale again.
555   The sely° widwe and eek hir doughtres two   *innocent*
Herden thise hennes crye and maken wo,
And out at dores sterten° they anoon,   *leapt*
And sien° the fox toward the grove goon,   *saw*
And bar upon his bak the cok away,
560 And criden, "Out, harrow,° and wailaway,   *help*
Ha, ha, the fox," and after him they ran,
And eek with staves many another man;
Ran Colle oure dogge, and Talbot and Gerland,[1]
And Malkin with a distaf in hir hand,
565 Ran cow and calf, and eek the verray hogges,
Sore aferd° for berking of the dogges   *frightened*
And shouting of the men and wommen eke.
They ronne° so hem thoughte hir herte breke;[2]   *ran*
They yelleden as feendes doon in helle;
570 The dokes° criden as men wolde hem quelle;°   *ducks / kill*
The gees for fere flowen° over the trees;   *flew*
Out of the hive cam the swarm of bees;
So hidous was the noise, a, benedicite,°   *bless me*

---

4. I.e., a missile.
5. Thy wisdom and thy learning.
6. Pyrrhus was the Greek who slew Priam, king of Troy.
7. As the *Aeneid* tells us.
8. Hasdrubal was king of Carthage when it was
destroyed by the Romans.
9. According to the legend, Nero not only set fire to Rome (in 64 C.E.) but also put many senators to death.
1. Two other dogs.
2. Would break.

Certes, he Jakke Straw[3] and his meinee°   *company*
575 Ne made nevere shoutes half so shrille
Whan that they wolden any Fleming kille,
As thilke day was maad upon the fox:
Of bras they broughten bemes° and of box,° *trumpets / boxwood*
Of horn, of boon,° in whiche they blewe and pouped,° *bone / tooted*
580 And therwithal they skriked° and they houped°— *shrieked / whooped*
It seemed as that hevene sholde falle.
  Now goode men, I praye you herkneth alle:
Lo, how Fortune turneth° sodeinly *reverses, overturns*
The hope and pride eek of hir enemy.
585 This cok that lay upon the foxes bak,
In al his drede unto the fox he spak,
And saide, "Sire, if that I were as ye,
Yit sholde I sayn, as wis° God helpe me,   *surely*
'Turneth ayain, ye proude cherles alle!
590 A verray pestilence upon you falle!
Now am I come unto this wodes side,
Maugree your heed,[4] the cok shal here abide.
I wol him ete, in faith, and that anoon.'"
  The fox answerde, "In faith, it shal be doon."
595 And as he spak that word, al sodeinly
The cok brak from his mouth deliverly,° *nimbly*
And hye upon a tree he fleigh° anoon.   *flew*
  And whan the fox sawgh that he was agoon,
"Allas," quod he, "O Chauntecleer, allas!
600 I have to you," quod he, "ydoon trespas,
In as muche as I maked you aferd
Whan I you hente° and broughte out of the yeerd. *seized*
But sire, I dide it in no wikke° entente: *wicked*
Come down, and I shal telle you what I mente.
605 I shal saye sooth to you, God help me so."
  "Nay thanne," quod he, "I shrewe° us bothe two: *curse*
But first I shrewe myself, bothe blood and bones,
If thou bigile me ofter than ones;
Thou shalt namore thurgh thy flaterye
610 Do° me to singe and winken with myn yë. *cause*
For he that winketh° whan he sholde see, *closes both eyes*
Al wilfully, God lat him nevere thee."° *prosper*
  "Nay," quod the fox, "but God yive him meschaunce
That is so undiscreet of governaunce° *self-control*
615 That jangleth° whan he sholde holde his pees." *chatters*
  Lo, swich it is for to be reccheless° *careless*
And necligent and truste on flaterye.
But ye that holden this tale a folye
As of a fox, or of a cok and hen,
620 Taketh the moralitee, goode men.
For Saint Paul saith that al that writen is

3. One of the leaders of the Uprising of 1381, which was partially directed against the Flemings living in London. 4. Despite your head—i.e., despite anything you can do.

To oure doctrine° it is ywrit, ywis:[5]   *teaching*
Taketh the fruit, and lat the chaf be stille.[6]
Now goode God, if that it be thy wille,
625 As saith my lord, so make us alle goode men,
And bringe us to his hye blisse. Amen.

Close of Canterbury Tales

At the end of *The Canterbury Tales*, Chaucer invokes a common allegorical theme, that life on earth is a pilgrimage. As Chaucer puts it in his moral ballade *Truth* (p. 344), "*Here* in noon home . . . / Forth, pilgrim, forth!" In the final fragment, he makes explicit a metaphor that has been implicit all along in the journey to Canterbury. The pilgrims never arrive at the shrine of St. Thomas, but in *The Parson's Tale*, and in its short introduction and in the "Retraction" that follows it, Chaucer seems to be making an end for two pilgrimages that had become one, that of his fiction and that of his life.

In the introduction to the tale we find the twenty-nine pilgrims moving through a nameless little village as the sun sinks to within twenty-nine degrees of the horizon. The atmosphere contains something of both the chill and the urgency of a late autumn afternoon, and we are surprised to find that the pilgrimage is almost over, that there is need for haste to make that "good end" that every medieval Christian hoped for. This delicately suggestive passage, rich with allegorical overtones, introduces an extremely long penitential treatise, translated by Chaucer from Latin or French sources. Although often assumed to be an earlier work, it may well have been written by Chaucer to provide the ending for *The Canterbury Tales*.

In the "Retraction" that follows *The Parson's Tale*, Chaucer acknowledges, lists, revokes, and asks forgiveness for his "giltes" (that is, his sins), which consist of having written most of the works on which his reputation as a great poet depends. He thanks Christ and Mary for his religious and moral works. One need not take this as evidence of a spiritual crisis or conversion at the end of his life. The "Retraction" seems to have been written to appear at the end of *The Canterbury Tales*, without censoring any of the tales deemed to be sinful. At the same time, one need not question Chaucer's sincerity. A readiness to deny his own reality before the reality of his God is implicit in many of Chaucer's works, and the placement of the "Retraction" within or just outside the border of the fictional pilgrimage suggests that although Chaucer finally rejected his fictions, he recognized that he and they were inseparable.

From The Parson's Tale

The Introduction

By that[1] the Manciple hadde his tale al ended,
The sonne fro the south line[2] was descended
So lowe, that he has nat to my sighte
Degrees nine and twenty as in highte.
5 Four of the clokke it was, so as I gesse,
For elevene foot, or litel more or lesse,
My shadwe was at thilke time as there,

---

5. See Romans 15.4.
6. The "fruit" refers to the kernel of moral or doctrinal meaning; the "chaf," or husk, is the narrative containing that meaning. The metaphor was commonly applied to scriptural interpretation.
1. By the time that.
2. I.e., the line that runs some 28° to the south of the celestial equator and parallel to it.

Of swich feet as° my lengthe parted° were   *as if / divided*
In sixe feet equal of proporcioun.[3]

10   Therwith the moones exaltacioun[4]—
I mene Libra—always gan ascende,
As we were entring at a thropes° ende.   *village's*
For which oure Host, as he was wont to gie°   *lead*
As in this caas oure joly compaignye,

15   Saide in this wise, "Lordinges everichoon,
Now lakketh us no tales mo than oon:
Fulfild is my sentence° and my decree;   *purpose*
I trowe° that we han herd of ech degree;   *believe*
Almost fulfild is al myn ordinaunce.

20   I praye to God, so yive him right good chaunce
That telleth this tale to us lustily.
Sire preest," quod he, "artou a vicary,°   *vicar*
Or arte a Person? Say sooth, by thy fay.°   *faith*
Be what thou be, ne breek° thou nat oure play,   *break*

25   For every man save thou hath told his tale.
Unbokele and shew us what is in thy male!°   *bag*
For trewely, me thinketh by thy cheere°   *expression*
Thou sholdest knitte up wel a greet matere.
Tel us a fable anoon, for cokkes bones!"[5]

30   This Person answerde al atones,°   *immediately*
"Thou getest fable noon ytold for me,
For Paul, that writeth unto Timothee,
Repreveth° hem that waiven soothfastnesse,[6]   *reproves*
And tellen fables and swich wrecchednesse.

35   Why sholde I sowen draf° out of my fest,°   *chaff / fist*
Whan I may sowen whete if that me lest?[7]
For which I saye that if you list to heere
Moralitee and vertuous matere,
And thanne that ye wol yive me audience,

40   I wol ful fain,° at Cristes reverence,   *gladly*
Do you plesance leveful° as I can.   *lawful*
But trusteth wel, I am a southren man:
I can nat geeste Rum-Ram-Ruf by lettre[8]—
Ne, God woot, rym holde° I but litel bettre.   *consider*

45   And therfore, if you list—I wol nat glose[9]—
I wol you telle a merye tale in prose
To knitte up al this feeste and make an ende.
And Jesu for his grace wit me sende
To shewe you the way in this viage°   *journey*

50   Of thilke parfit glorious pilgrimage
That highte° Jerusalem celestial.   *is called*
And if ye vouche sauf, anoon I shal
Biginne upon my tale, for which I praye
Telle youre avis:° I can no bettre saye.   *opinion*

---

3. This detailed analysis merely says that the shadows are lengthening.
4. I.e., the astrological sign in which the moon's influence was dominant.
5. Cock's bones, a euphemism for God's bones.
6. Depart from truth (see 1 Timothy 1.4).

7. It pleases me.
8. I.e., I cannot tell stories in the alliterative measure (without rhyme): this form of poetry was not common in southeastern England.
9. I.e., speak in order to please.

55 But nathelees, this meditacioun
I putte it ay under correccioun
Of clerkes, for I am nat textuel:[1]
I take but the sentence,° trusteth wel.   *meaning*
Therefore I make protestacioun°   *public acknowledgment*
60 That I wol stonde to correccioun."
     Upon this word we han assented soone,
For, as it seemed, it was for to doone[2]
To enden in som vertuous sentence,°   *doctrine*
And for to yive him space° and audience;   *time*
65 And bede[3] oure Host he sholde to him saye
That alle we to telle his tale him praye.
     Oure Hoste hadde the wordes for us alle:
"Sire preest," quod he, "now faire you bifalle:
Telleth," quod he, "youre meditacioun.
70 But hasteth you; the sonne wol adown.
Beeth fructuous,° and that in litel space,°   *fruitful / time*
And to do wel God sende you his grace.
Saye what you list, and we wol gladly heere."
And with that word he saide in this manere.

Chaucer's Retraction

Here taketh the makere of this book his leve[4]

Now praye I to hem alle that herkne this litel tretis[5] or rede, that if ther be
any thing in it that liketh[6] hem, that therof they thanken oure Lord Jesu
Crist, of whom proceedeth al wit[7] and al goodnesse. And if ther be any thing
that displese hem, I praye hem also that they arrette it to the defaute of myn
unconning,[8] and nat to my wil, that wolde ful fain[9] have said bettre if I hadde
had conning. For oure book saith, "Al that is writen is writen for oure doctrine,"[1] and that is myn entente. Wherfore I biseeke[2] you mekely, for the
mercy of God, that ye praye for me that Crist have mercy on me and foryive
me my giltes, and namely of my translacions and enditinges[3] of worldly vani-
tees, the whiche I revoke in my retraccions: as is the *Book of Troilus*; the Book
also of *Fame*; the *Book of the Five and Twenty Ladies*;[4] the *Book of the Duch-
esse*; the *Book of Saint Valentines Day of the Parlement of Briddes*; the *Tales of
Canterbury*, thilke that sounen into[5] sinne; the *Book of the Leon*;[6] and many
another book, if they were in my remembrance, and many a song and many
a leccherous lay:[7] that Crist for his grete mercy foryive me the sinne. But of
the translacion of Boece[8] *De Consolatione*, and other bookes of legendes of

---

1. Literal, faithful to the letter.
2. Necessary to be done.
3. I.e., we bade.
4. "Chaucer's Retraction" is the title given to
this passage by modern editors. The heading,
"*Here . . . leve*," which does appear in all manuscripts, may be by Chaucer himself or by a
scribe.
5. Hear this little treatise, i.e., *The Parson's Tale*.
6. Pleases.
7. Understanding.

8. Ascribe it to the defect of my lack of skill.
9. Gladly.
1. Romans 15.4.
2. Beseech.
3. Compositions. "Namely": especially.
4. I.e., the *Legend of Good Women*.
5. Those that tend toward.
6. The *Book of the Lion* has not been preserved.
7. Lyric poem.
8. Boethius.

saintes, and omelies,[9] and moralitee, and devocion, that thanke I oure Lord Jesu Crist and his blisful Moder and alle the saintes of hevene, biseeking hem that they from hennes[1] forth unto my lives ende sende me grace to biwaile my giltes and to studye to the salvacion of my soule, and graunte me grace of ver-ray[2] penitence, confession, and satisfaccion to doon in this present lif, thurgh the benigne grace of him that is king of kinges and preest over alle preestes, that boughte[3] us with the precious blood of his herte, so that I may been oon of hem at the day of doom[4] that shulle be saved. *Qui cum patre et Spiritu Sancto vivit et regnas Deus per omnia saecula.*[5] Amen.

1386–1400

LYRICS AND OCCASIONAL VERSE

In addition to his narrative verse, Chaucer wrote lyric poetry on the models of famous French and Italian poets who made lyric into a medieval art form aimed at learned and aristocratic audiences, an audience that included fellow poets. Chaucer also embedded lyric in narrative poetry. As an example of courtly lyric, we print a "song" that Troilus, the hero of Chaucer's romance *Troilus and Criseyde*, makes up about his violent and puzzling emotions after falling in love. The "song" is actually Chaucer's translation into rhyme royal of one of Petrarch's sonnets, more than a century before Sir Thomas Wyatt introduced the sonnet form itself to England. In the fifteenth century, Troilus's song was sometimes excerpted and included in anthologies of lyric poetry.

Chaucer also wrote homiletic ballades, one of which is entitled *Truth* by modern editors and called "ballade de bon conseil" (ballade of good advice) in some manuscripts. A ballade is a verse form of three or more stanzas, each with an identical rhyme scheme and the same last line, the refrain. Often a ballade ends with a shorter final stanza called an *envoy* in which the poem is addressed or sent to a friend or patron, or, conventionally, to a "prince" or "princes" in general. The good advice of *Truth* is to abandon worldly pursuits of wealth and power and to concentrate on the pilgrimage that leads to our true home in heaven. There are many copies of *Truth* with only this heartfelt advice. The one printed below contains a unique humorous *envoy*, addressed to a "Vache" (French for "cow"), who is probably a Sir Philip de la Vache.

A single stanza *To His Scribe Adam* comically conveys Chaucer's exasperation at the sloppy work of a professional copyist. The *Complaint to His Purse* is a parody of a lover's complaint to his lady: Ladies, like coins, should be golden, and, like purses, they should not be "light" (i.e., fickle). *Purse* survives both without and with an *envoy*. The addressee in the latter case is the recently crowned Henry IV, who is being wittily implored to restore payment of Chaucer's annuity, which had been interrupted by the new king's deposition of Richard II.

9. Homilies.
1. Hence.
2. True.
3. Redeemed.

4. Judgment.
5. Who with the Father and the Holy Spirit livest and reignest God forever.

Troilus's Song[1]

If no love is, O God, what feele I so?
And if love is, what thing and which is he?
If love be good, from whennes cometh my wo?
If it be wikke,° a wonder thinketh° me,   *miserable / it seems to*
5 Whan every torment and adversitee
That cometh of him may to me savory° thinke,°   *pleasant / seem*
For ay° thurste I, the more that ich° drinke.   *always / I*

And if that at myn owene lust° I brenne,°   *desire / burn*
From whennes cometh my wailing and my plainte?°   *complaint*
10 If harm agree° me, wherto plaine° I thenne? *agrees with / complain*
I noot,° ne why unwery° that I fainte.   *know not / not weary*
O quikke° deeth, O sweete harm so quainte,°   *living / strange*
How may° of thee in me swich quantitee,   *can there be*
But if° that I consente that it be?   *unless*

15 And if that I consente, I wrongfully
Complaine: ywis,° thus possed° to and fro   *indeed / tossed*
All stereless° within a boot° am I   *rudderless / boat*
Amidde the see, bitwixen windes two,
That in contrarye stonden everemo.
20 Allas, what is this wonder maladye?
For hoot° of cold, for cold of hoot I die.   *hot*

Truth[1]

Flee fro the prees° and dwelle with soothfastnesse;   *crowd*
Suffise unto° thy thing, though it be smal;   *be content with*
For hoord hath[2] hate, and climbing tikelnesse;°   *insecurity*
Prees hath envye, and wele° blent° overal.   *prosperity / blinds*
5 Savoure° no more than thee bihoove shal;   *relish*
Rule wel thyself that other folk canst rede:°   *advise*
And Trouthe shal delivere,[3] it is no drede.°   *doubt*
Tempest thee nought al crooked to redresse[4]
In trust of hire[5] that turneth as a bal;
10 Muche wele stant in litel bisinesse;[6]
Be war therfore to spurne ayains an al[7]

---

1. *Troilus and Criseyde*, Book 1, lines 400–420. A translation of Petrarch's Sonnet 132, "S'amor non è."

1. Taking as his theme Christ's words to his disciples (in John 8.32), "And ye shall know the truth, and the truth shall make you free," Chaucer plays on the triple meaning that the Middle English word *trouthe* seems to have had for him: the religious truth of Christianity, the moral virtue of integrity, and the philosophical idea of reality. By maintaining one's faith and one's integrity, one rises superior to the vicissitudes of this world and comes eventually to know reality—which is not, however, of this world.
2. Hoarding causes.
3. I.e., truth shall make you free.
4. Do not disturb yourself to straighten all that's crooked.
5. Fortune, who turns like a ball in that she is always presenting a different aspect to people.
6. Peace of mind stands in little anxiety.
7. Awl, i.e., "don't kick against the pricks," wound yourself by kicking a sharp instrument.

Strive nat as dooth the crokke° with the wal.   *pot*
Daunte° thyself that dauntest otheres deede: *master*
And Trouthe shal delivere, it is no drede.

15 That° thee is sent, receive in buxomnesse;°   *what / obedience*
The wrastling for the world axeth° a fal;   *asks for*
Here is noon hoom, here nis° but wildernesse: *is not*
Forth, pilgrim, forth! Forth, beest, out of thy stal!
Know thy countree, looke up, thank God of al.
20 Hold the heigh way and lat thy gost° thee lede: *spirit*
And Trouthe shal delivere, it is no drede.

Envoy

Therfore, thou Vache,[8] leve thyn olde wrecchednesse
Unto the world; leve° now to be thral.   *i.e., cease*
Crye him mercy° that of his heigh goodnesse   *beg him for mercy*
25 Made thee of nought, and in especial
Draw unto him, and pray in general,
For thee and eek for othere, hevenelich meede:[9]
And Trouthe shal delivere, it is no drede.

To His Scribe Adam[1]

Adam scrivain,° if evere it thee bifalle   *scribe*
Boece or *Troilus*[2] for to writen newe,
Under thy longe lokkes thou moste[3] have the scalle,°   *scurf*
But after my making thou write more trewe,[4]
5 So ofte a day I moot° thy werk renewe,   *must*
It to correcte, and eek to rubbe and scrape:
And al is thurgh thy necligence and rape.°   *haste*

Complaint to His Purse

To you, my purs, and to noon other wight,°   *person*
Complaine I, for ye be my lady dere.
I am so sory, now that ye be light,
For certes, but if° ye make me hevy cheere,   *unless*
5 Me were as lief[1] be laid upon my beere;°   *bier*
For which unto youre mercy thus I crye:
Beeth hevy again, or elles moot° I die.   *must*

8. Probably Sir Philip de la Vache, with a pun on the French for "cow."
9. Reward, with a pun on *meadow*.
1. Chaucer had fair copies of longer works made by a professional scribe. This humorous complaint about Adam's sloppy work is written in the verse form of Chaucer's great poem *Troilus and Criseyde*.
2. *Troilus and Criseyde*. "Boece": i.e., Chaucer's translation of Boethius's *De Consolatione*.
3. I.e., may you.
4. Unless you write more accurately what I've composed.
1. I'd just as soon.

Now voucheth sauf° this day er° it be night   *grant / before*
That I of you the blisful soun may heere,
10   Or see youre colour, lik the sonne bright,
That of yelownesse hadde nevere peere.°   *equal*
Ye be my life, ye be myn hertes steere,°   *rudder, guide*
Queene of confort and of good compaignye:
Beeth hevy again, or elles moot I die.

15   Ye purs, that been to me my lives light
And saviour, as in this world down here,
Out of this towne[2] helpe me thurgh your might,
Sith that ye wol nat be my tresorere;°   *treasurer*
For I am shave as neigh as any frere.[3]
20   But yit I praye unto youre curteisye:
Beeth hevy again, or elles moot I die.

Envoy to Henry IV[4]

O conquerour of Brutus Albioun,[4]
Which that by line° and free eleccioun   *lineage*
Been verray° king, this song to you I sende: *true*
25   And ye, that mowen° alle oure harmes amende,   *may*
Have minde upon my supplicacioun.

2. Probably Westminster, where Chaucer had rented a house.
3. Shaved as close as any (tonsured) friar, an expression for being broke.

4. Britain (Albion) was supposed to have been founded by Brutus, the grandson of Aeneas, the founder of Rome.

JOHN GOWER
ca. 1330–1408

Of Gower's life relatively little is known: he was certainly a landowner in Kent, and from about 1377 he seems to have been resident in Southwark, just over the River Thames from the City of London. He had close relations with Chaucer, who sent *Troilus and Criseyde* (ca. 1385) to "moral Gower" for "correction" (5.1856). Indeed, as the co-initiator of a new tradition of English poetry, his reputation throughout the fifteenth century was very nearly on a par with that of Chaucer. He was himself more concerned than Chaucer for his own literary posterity, since he took care that texts of his work would be transmitted in finished, stable form. No contemporary poet matches him for linguistic virtuosity, since Gower wrote in three languages. His main poetic works are as follows: the *Mirour de l'omme* (Mirror of Man) (finished 1376–78), written in Anglo-Norman (the dialect of French spoken in England); the Latin *Vox Clamantis* (Voice of the Crier), written substantially before 1386; and the English *Confessio Amantis* (The Lover's Confession), first published in 1390. The *Mirour* (the last major work written in Anglo-Norman in England) was addressed primarily to an upper-class audience capable of reading both French and English, while the Latin *Vox* was clearly directed to a highly educated audience. The first version of the *Confessio* was dedicated to Richard II. By the time of the third recension (1392–93), Richard had been replaced by Henry Bolingbroke, the future Henry IV, as the poem's dedicatee. Despite these dedications to specific and powerful readers, Gower in fact addressed the *Confessio* to all educated readers, both men and women.

Vox Clamantis refers to the saint whose name Gower bore, John the Baptist, whom all four gospels refer to as "the voice of one crying out in the wilderness" (Matthew 3.3, Mark 1.3, Luke 3.4, John 1.23) who will prepare the way for the Lord, fulfilling the prophecy of Isaiah 40.3. Gower thus identifies himself with the prophetic voice of John the Baptist as well as the apocalyptic voice of John the Evangelist in the Book of Revelation. In keeping with this posture, the *Mirour* and the *Vox* are examples of estates satire, a genre of satire in which the writer addresses and berates each main occupational grouping of society in turn. (For more information on estates satire, see the "Medieval Estates and Orders" topic in the supplemental ebook, in which there are translations of excerpts from the *Mirour* and *Vox*.) In the *Vox*, for example, Gower vigorously attacks the peasantry for their part in the English Uprising of 1381.

While Gower wrote as moralist and satirist in the *Mirour* and the *Vox*, he changed tack in the *Confessio Amantis*. To be sure, the poem is structured as a moral discourse: the Confessor figure Genius hears the confession of the penitent Amans, as if enacting the procedures of the Church's sacrament of penance (one part of which was a formal, confidential confession to a priest). In seven of the poem's eight books, Genius hears Amans's confession concerning a different Deadly Sin (respectively Pride, Envy, Anger, Sloth, Greed, Gluttony, and Lechery). The very names of penitent and confessor themselves suggest, however, that this is no ordinary confession. For Amans (literally "one who loves") is heard by a "genial" aspect of the psyche, Genius, who is the priest of Venus. Far from condemning Amans for his hopeless subjection to erotic desire, Genius as often as not encourages Amans in his passion, or so it would seem initially. The eighty or so stories Genius tells by way of "correcting" Amans are drawn not from penitential treatises; they are rather, on the whole, drawn from secular, classical sources, and often from the poetry of Ovid, the classical poet of erotic love.

As the *Confessio* progresses, however, Genius increasingly registers the social and political disasters that result from solipsistic pursuit of sexual desire. While never abandoning his "genial" perspective altogether, and while never wishing wholly to repress sexual passion, Genius finally brings Amans around, to the point where Amans reintegrates with the psyche of which he is ideally a part. He finally regains his full identity as "John Gower." This recovery of identity involves a very moving self-recognition scene in the poem's finale, in which an aged Gower recognizes his position as a lover, a citizen, and a Christian. The poem is not only about one individual, however: Gower's sexual governance is linked to political governance of the kingdom. Just as Gower must rule yet recognize the proper demands of his body, so too must the king rule and recognize his kingdom.

Many of Genius's narratives relate stories whose violence entirely overshadows the often pathetic, and always hopeless pursuit of Amans for his lady. The narrative of Tereus and Philomela ("Philomene" in Gower's narrative), drawn from Ovid, *Metamorphoses* (6.426–676), is one such frightening text. It tells a story of unremitting domestic violence, relating the "greediness" of rape to the larger concept of greed, the sin treated by Genius in Book 5 of the *Confessio*. A husband (Tereus) rapes and cuts out the tongue of his sister-in-law (Philomela); his wife (Procne) and her sister take their vengeance by murdering and cooking the rapist's child (Itys). Philomela's concern is as much for *publication* of the rape as for vengeance: with her excised tongue, she relies on weaving as a means of writing to communicate the terror of her experience, just as, transformed into a chattering bird at the end of the story, she continues to remind humans of Tereus's disgrace. When Chaucer had recounted the same story in *The Legend of Good Women* (ca. 1386), he omitted the most hair-raising episodes of the Ovidian source. Gower, by contrast, follows the lineaments of Ovid's narrative fairly closely, and does not turn aside from the transformation of suffering women into terrible avengers, as Procne (here "Progne") murders and butchers her own child. Nor does he fail to register the horror of rape, as Philomela feels the inescapable weight of Tereus upon her (lines 96–101).

From The Lover's Confession[1]

The Tale of Philomene and Tereus

GENIUS:

Now list,° my Sone, and thou shalt heere,		*listen*
So as it hath befalle er° this		*before*
In loves cause how that it is		
A man to take be° ravine°		*seize by / rape*
5 The preie° that is femeline.		*prey*
Ther was a real° noble king,		*royal*
And riche of alle worldes thing,		
Which of his propre° inheritance		*own*
Athenes hadde in governance,		
10 And who so° thenke thereupon,		*whoever*
His name was king Pandion.		
Two doughtres° hadde he be his wif,		*daughters*
The whiche he lovede as his lif;		
The firste doughter Progne highte,°		*was called*
15 And the secounde, as she wel mighte,		
Was cleped° faire Philomene,		*called*
To whom fell after° muchel tene.°		*afterward / grief*
The fader of his purveance°		*forethought*
His doughter Progne wolde avance°		*advance*
20 And yaf° hire unto marriage		*gave*
A worthy king of hye lignage,°		*high lineage*
A noble knight eke° of his hond,[2]		*also*
So was he kid° in every lond,		*known*
Of Trace[3] he highte Tereus;		
25 The clerk Ovide[4] telleth thus.		
This Tereus his wif hoom ladde,		
A lusty° lif with hire he hadde;		*agreeable*
Til it befell upon a tide,°		*certain time*
This Progne, as she lay him beside,		
30 Bethoughte hire° how it mighte be		*considered*
That she hir suster mighte see,		
And to hir lord hir will she saide,		
With goodly wordes and him prayde		

1. The text is drawn from *The English Works of John Gower*, edited by G. C. Macaulay, Early English Text Society, extra series 81–82 (London: Oxford University Press, 1900–1901).
2. With respect to himself (in addition to his high lineage).
3. Thrace.
4. Gower's source is the Roman poet Ovid's *Metamorphoses* 4.424–674.

That she to hire mighte go:
35 And if it liked him noght° so,   *if it did not displease him*
That than he wolde himselve wende,°   *go*
Or elles be° some other sende,   *by*
Which mighte hir deere suster greete
And shape° how that they mighten meete.   *arrange*
40 Hir lord anon° to that he herde   *immediately*
Yaf his acord, and thus answerde:
"I wol," he saide, "for thy sake
The way after thy suster take
Myself, and bring hire, if I may."
45 And she with that, ther as he lay,
Began him in hir armes clippe,°   *embrace*
And kist him with hir softe lippe,
And saide, "Sire, grant mercy."°   *thank you*
And he soone° after was redy,   *right away*
50 And took his leve forto go;
In sory° time dide he so.   *sorrowful*
   This Tereus gooth forth to shipe
With him and with his felaweshipe;
By see the righte course he nam,°   *took*
55 Into the contree til he cam,
Wher Philomene was dwellinge,
And of hir suster the tidinge°   *news*
He tolde, and tho° they weren glade,   *then*
And muchel joy of him they made.
60 The fader and the moder bothe
To leve hir doughter weren lothe,
But if they weren in presence[5]
And natheles at reverence°   *with due respect*
Of him, that wolde himself travaile,°   *take the trouble*
65 They wolden noght he sholde faile
Of that he prayed, and yive hire leve:
And she, that wolde noght beleve,°   *remain*
In alle haste made hire yare°   *ready*
Toward hir suster forto fare°   *travel*
70 With Tereus and forth she wente.
And he withal his hool entente,°   *mind*
Whan she was from hir frendes go,
Assoteth° of hir love so,   *is besotted*
His yë° myghte he noght withholde,   *eye*
75 That he ne moste on hire beholde;[6]
And with the sighte he gan desire,
And set his owene herte on fire;
And fir, whan it to tow° aproeheth,   *flax*
To him° anon the strengthe acrocheth,°   *it / draws*
80 Til with his° hete it be devoured,   *its*
The tow ne may noght be socoured.°   *preserved*
And so that tyrant raviner,
Whan that she was in his power,

5. Unless they should be present.   6. Could not keep from looking at her.

And he therto saugh time and place,
85   As he that lost hath alle grace,
Foryat he was a wedded man,
And in a rage on hire he ran,
Right as a wolf which takth[7] his preye.
And she began to crye and praye,
90   "O fader, o mi moder deere,
Now help!" But they ne mighte it heere,
And she was of to litel might
Defense again° so rude° a knight   against / rough
To make, whan he was so wood°   mad
95   That he no reson understood,
But held hire under in such wise,
That she ne myghte noght arise,
But lay oppressed and disesed,°   distressed
As if a goshawk hadde sesed°   seized
100 A brid° which dorste noght for fere° bird / fear
Remue°: and thus this tyrant there   escape
Beraft° hire such thing as men sayn   deprived
May neveremore be yolde° again,   restored
And that was the virginitee:
105 Of such ravine it was pitee.
   But whan she to hirselven cam,
And of hir meschief heede nam,°.   took heed of her misfortune
And knew how that she was no maide,
With wofull herte thus she saide:
110 "O thou of alle men the worste,
Wher was ther evere man that dorste
Do such a dede as thou hast do?
That day shal falle, I hope so,
That I shal telle out al my fille,[8]
115 And with my speeche I shal fulfille
The wide world in brede° and lengthe.   breadth
That° thou hast do to me be strengthe,   that which
If I among the peple dwelle,
Unto the peple I shal it telle;
120 And if I be withinne wall
Of stones closed, than I shal
Unto the stones clepe° and crye,   call
And tellen hem thy felonye;
And if I to the woodes wende,
125 Ther shal I tellen tale and ende,°   the whole story
And crye it to the briddes oute,
That they shul heer it al aboute.
For I so loude it shal reherse,°   repeat
That my vois shal the hevene perce,°   pierce
130 That it shal soune° in goddes ere.   resound
Ha, false man, where is thy fere?°   fear (of the gods)
O more cruel than any beste,

---

7. Gower frequently contracts the third-person present singular of verbs (takth = taketh).

8. I.e., have my fill of telling, tell all.

How hast thou holden thy biheste°   *promise*
Which thou unto my suster madest?
135 O thou, which alle love ungladest,
And art ensample of alle untrewe,
Now wolde God my suster knewe,
Of thin untrouthe, how that it stood!"
    And he than as a lion wood°   *mad*
140 With his unhappy handes stronge
Hire caughte be the tresses longe,
With which he bond ther bothe hir armes—
That was a fieble° deed of armes—   *feeble, cowardly*
And to the grounde anon hire caste,
145 And out he clippeth also faste
Hir tonge with a paire of sheres,°   *shears*
So what with blood and what with teres
Out of hir yë and of hir mouth,
He made hir faire face uncouth:°   *unfamiliar, distorted*
150 She lay swounende° unto the deeth,   *fainting*
Ther was unnethes° any breeth;   *scarcely*
But yit whan he hir tonge refte,
A litel part therof belefte,°   *was left*
But she with al no word may soune,°   *utter*
155 But chitre° as a brid jargoune.°   *twitter / chatters*
And natheles that woode hound
Hir body hent° up fro the ground,   *seized*
And sente hire ther as be his wille
She sholde abide in prison stille
160 For everemo: but now take heede
What after fell of this misdeede.
    Whan al this meschief was befalle,
This Tereus, that foule him falle,
Unto his contree hoom he tye;°   *traveled*
165 And whan he com his paleis nye,
His wif al redy ther him kepte.°   *awaited*
Whan he hire sih,° anon he wepte,   *saw*
And that he dide for deceite,
For she began to axe° him streite,°   *ask / directly*
170 "Wher is my suster?" And he saide
That she was deed; and Progne abraide,°   *started violently*
As she that was a woful wif,°   *woman*
And stood between hir deeth and lif,
Of that she herde such tidinge:
175 But for she sih° hir lord wepinge,   *saw*
She wende° noght but alle trouthe,   *thought*
And hadde wel the more routhe.°   *pity*
The perles weren tho forsake
To hire,[9] and blake clothes take;
180 As she that was gentil and kinde,
In worshipe° of hir sustres minde°   *respect / memory*
She made a riche enterement,°   *funeral*

9. I.e., she gave up jewelry.

For she fond non amendement°   *betterment*
To sighen or to sobbe more:
185 So was ther guile under gore.[1]
        Now leve we this king and queene,
And torne again to Philomene,
As I began to tellen erst.°   *before*
Whan she cam into prison ferst,
190 It thoghte° a kinges doughter straunge   *seemed to*
To maken so sodein a chaunge
Fro welthe unto so greet a wo;
And she began to thenke tho,
Thogh she be mouthe nothing prayde,
195 Withinne hir herte thus she saide:
"O thou, almighty Jupiter,
That hye sits and lookest fer,
Thou suffrest many a wrong doinge,
And yit it is noght thy willinge.
200 To thee ther may nothing been hid,
Thou woost how it is me betid:
I wolde I hadde noght be bore,°   *born*
For thanne I hadde noght forlore°   *lost*
My speeche and my virginitee.
205 But, goode lord, al is in thee,
Whan thou therof wolt do° vengeance   *wish to do*
And shape my deliverance."
And evere among this lady wepte,
And thoghte that she nevere kepte°   *cared*
210 To been a worldes womman more,
And that she wisheth everemore.
But ofte unto hir suster deere
Hir herte spekth in this manere,
And saide, "Ha, Suster, if ye knewe
215 Of myn estat, ye wolde rewe,
I trowe,° and my deliverance   *believe*
Ye wolde shape, and do vengeance
On him that is so fals a man:
And natheles, so as I can,
220 I wol you sende some tokeninge,°   *token*
Whereof ye shul have knowlechinge
Of thing I woot, that shal you lothe,°   *make sick*
The which you toucheth and me bothe."
And tho withinne a while als tit°   *as quickly*
225 She waf° a cloth of silk al whit   *wove*
With lettres and ymagerye,
In which was al the felonye
Which Tereus to hire hath do;
And lappede° it togidre tho   *wrapped*
230 And sette hir signet° therupon   *seal*
And sende it unto Progne anon.

---

1. I.e., deceit under cover. "Gore" is a kind of cloak; the expression is probably proverbial for "deception."

The messager which forth it bar,
What it amounteth° is noght war; *means*
And natheles to Progne he goth
235 And prively takth hire the cloth,
And wente again right as he cam,
The court of him non heede nam.
    Whan Progne of Philomene herde,
She wolde knowe how that it ferde,
240 And openeth that the man hath broght,
And woot therby what hath be wroght
And what meschief ther is befalle.
In swoune° tho she gan doun falle, *faint*
And eft° aroos and gan to stonde, *again*
245 And eft she takth the cloth on honde,
Beheld the lettres and thymages;
But atte laste, "Of such outrages,"
She sayth, "weeping is noght the boote,"° *remedy*
And swerth, if that she live moote,
250 It shal be venged otherwise.
And with that she gan hire avise° *consider*
How ferst she mighte unto hire winne° *get*
Hir suster, that noman withinne,
But only they that were swore,° *sworn (to silence)*
255 It sholde knowe, and shoop° therefore *arranged*
That Tereus nothing it wiste;° *knew*
And yit right as hirselven liste,° *desired*
Hir suster was delivered soone
Out of prison, and be the moone
260 To Progne she was broght be nighte.
    Whan ech of other hadde a sighte,
In chambre, ther they were al one,
They maden many a pitous mone;° *moaning*
But Progne most of sorwe made,
265 Which sih° hir suster pale and fade° *saw / wan*
And speecheles and deshonoured,
Of that she hadde be defloured;
And eke upon hir lord she thoughte,
Of that he so untrewely wroghte
270 And hadde his espousaile broke.
She makth a vow it shal be wroke,° *avenged*
And with that word she kneleth doun
Weeping in greet devocioun:
Unto Cupide and to Venus
275 She prayde, and saide thanne thus:
"O ye, to whom nothing asterte° *escapes*
Of love may, for every herte
Ye knowe, as ye that been above
The god and goddesse of love;
280 Ye witen wel that evere yit
With al my will and al my wit,
Sith ferst ye shoopen me to wedde,
That I lay with my lord abedde,

I have be trewe in my degree,
285 And evere thoghte forto be,
And nevere love in other place,
But al only the king of Trace,
Which is my lord and I his wif.
But now allas this wofull strif!
290 That I him thus againward° finde   *on the contrary*
The most untrewe and most unkinde°   *unnatural*
That evere in lady armes lay.
And wel I woot that he ne may
Amende his wrong, it is so greet;
295 For he to litel of me leet,°   *prized*
Whan he myn owne suster took,
And me that am his wif forsook."
    Lo, thus to Venus and Cupide
She prayed, and furthermore she cryde
300 Unto Appollo the higheste,
And saide, "O mighty god of reste,
Thou do vengeance of this debat.
My suster and al hir estat
Thou woost, and how she hath forlore°   *lost*
305 Hir maidenhood, and I therfore
In al the world shal bere a blame
Of that my suster hath a shame,
That Tereus to hire I sente:
And wel thou woost that myn entente
310 Was al for worship and for goode.
O lord, that yifst° the lives foode   *gives*
To every wight, I pray thee here
Thes wofull sustres that been here,
And let us noght to thee been lothe;°   *hateful*
315 We been thyn owne wommen bothe."
    Thus plaineth Progne and axeth wreche,°   *vengeance*
And thogh hir suster lacke speeche,
To him that alle thinges woot
Hir sorwe is noght the lasse hoot:°   *hot*
320 But he that thanne had herd hem two,
Him oughte have sorwed everemo
For sorwe which was hem betweene.
With signes plaineth Philomene,
And Progne sayth, "It shal be wreke,°   *avenged*
325 That al the world therof shal speke."
And Progne tho° siknesse feineth,   *then*
Wherof unto hir lord she plaineth,
And prayth she most hir chambres keepe,
And as hire liketh wake and sleepe.
330 And he hire granteth to be so;
And thus togidre been they two,
That wolde him but a litel good.
Now herk herafter how it stood
Of wofull auntres° that befelle: *chances*
335 Thes sustres, that been bothe felle°—   *fiercely cunning*

And that was noght on hem along,°   *natural*
But onliche on° the greete wrong   *on account of*
Which Tereus hem hadde do—
They shoopen forto venge hem tho.

340   This Tereus be Progne his wif
A sone hath, which as his lif
He loveth, and Ithis he highte:
His moder wiste wel she mighte
Do Tereus no more grief
345 Than slee this child, which was so lief.°   *dear*
Thus she, that was, as who sayth, mad
Of wo, which hath hir overlad,°   *overborne*
Withoute insighte of moderheede
Foryat pitee and loste dreede,
350 And in hir chambre prively
This child withouten noise or cry
She slou° and hewe° him al to pieces.   *slew / cut*
And after with diverse spices
The flessh, whan that it was tohewe,°   *all cut up*
355 She takth, and makth therof a sewe,°   *stew*
With which the fader at his mete°   *meal*
Was served, til he hadde him ete;
That he ne wiste how it stood,
But thus his owene flessh and blood
360 Himself devoureth again kinde,°   *contrary to nature*
As he that was tofore unkinde.
And thanne, er that he were arise,
For that he sholde been agrise,°   *horrified*
To shewen him the child was deed,
365 This Philomene took the heed
Between two dishes, and al wrothe°   *angry*
Tho comen forth the sustres bothe,
And setten it upon the bord.
And Progne tho began the word,
370 And saide, "O werste of alle wicke,
Of conscience whom no pricke
May stere,° lo, what thou hast do!   *disturb*
Lo, here been now we sustres two;
O raviner, lo here thy preie,°   *prey*
375 With whom so falsliche on the waye
Thou hast thy tyrannye wroght.
Lo, now it is somdel aboght,°   *somewhat repaid*
And bet° it shal, for of thi deede   *better*
The world shal evere singe and rede
380 In remembrance of thy defame:
For thou to love hast do such shame,
That it shal nevere be foryete."
With that he sterte up fro the mete,
And shoof° the bord unto the floor,   *pushed*
385 And caughte a swerd anon and swoor
That they sholde of his handes dye
And they unto the goddess crye

Begunne with so loude a stevene,°   *voice*
That they were herd unto the hevene;
390 And in a twinklinge of an yë
The goddes, that the meschief syë,
Hir formes chaungen alle three.
Echoon of hem in his degree
Was torned into briddes kinde;
395 Diverseliche as men may finde,
After thestat that they were inne,
Hir formes were set atwinne.[2]
And as it telleth in the tale,
The ferst into a nightingale
400 Was shape, and that was Philomene,
Which in the winter is noght sene,
For thanne been the leves falle
And naked been the bushes alle.
For after that she was a brid,
405 Hir will was evere to been hid,
And forto dwelle in privee place,
Than noman sholde seen hir face
For shame which may noght be lassed,°   *diminished*
Of thing that was tofore passed,
410 Whan that she loste hir maidenhede:
For evere upon hir wommanhede,
Thogh that the goddes wolde hire chaunge,
She thenkth, and is the more straunge,
And halt hire cloos[3] the winters day.
415 But whan the winter gooth away,
And that Nature the goddesse
Wole of hir owene free° largesse   *generous*
With herbes and with flowres bothe
The feldes and the medwes° clothe   *meadows*
420 And eke the woodes and the greves°   *groves*
Been heled° al with greene leves,   *covered*
So that a brid hire hide may,
Between Averil° and March and May,   *April*
She that the winter held hire cloos,
425 For pure shame and noght aroos,
Whan that she seeth the bowes thikke,
And that ther is no bare stikke,
But al is hid with leves greene,
To woode comth this Philomene
430 And makth hir ferste yeres flight;
Wher as she singeth day and night,
And in hir song al openly
She makth hir plainte and sayth, "O why,
O why ne were I yit a maide?'°   *virgin*
435 For so these olde wise saide,
Which understooden what she mente,

---

2. I.e., their forms as birds differed from one
another as they had in their human estate or
condition.
3. Keeps herself concealed.

Hir notes been of such entente.°   *meaning*
And eke they saide how in hir song
She makth greet joye and mirthe among,
440 And sayth, "Ha, now I am a brid,
Ha, now my face may been hid:
Though I have lost my maidenhede,
Shal noman see my cheekes rede."
Thus medleth° she with joye wo   *mixes*
445 And with hir sorwe mirthe also,
So that of loves maladye
She makth diverse melodye,
And sayth love is a wofull blisse,
A wisdom which can noman wisse,°   *instruct*
450 A lusty° fevere, a wounde softe: *healthy*
This note she reherseth ofte
To hem, whiche understonde hir tale.
Now have I of this nightingale,
Which erst was cleped Philomene,
455 Told al that evere I wolde mene,
Bothe of hir forme and of hir note,
Wherof men may the storye note.°   *remember*
   And of hir suster Progne I finde,
How she was torned° out of kinde   *transformed*
460 Into a swalwe° swift of winge,   *swallow*
Which eke in winter lith swouninge,°   *lies fainting*
Ther as she may nothing be sene:
But whan the world is woxe° greene   *grown*
And comen is the somertide,
465 Than fleth she forth and ginth° to chide,   *begins*
And chitreth out in hir langage
What falshood is in marriage,
And telleth in a maner speeche
Of Tereus spousebreeche.°   *adultery*
470 She wol noght in the woodes dwelle,
For she wolde openliche telle;
And eke for that she was a spouse,
Among the folk she comth to house,
To do these wives understonde
475 The falshood of hir housbonde,
That they of hem be war also,
For ther been many untrewe of tho.°   *those*
Thus been the sustres briddes bothe,
And been toward the men so lothe,
480 That they ne wole of pure shame
Unto no mannes hand be tame;
For evere it dwelleth in hir minde
Of that they founde a man unkinde,
And that was false Tereus.
485 If such oon be amonges us
I noot,° but his condicioun   *do not know*
Men sayn in every regioun
Withinne toune and eke withoute

Now regneth communliche aboute.
490 And natheles in remembrance
I wol declare what vengeance
The goddess hadden him ordained,
Of that the sustres hadden plained:
For anon after he was chaunged
495 And from his owene kinde straunged,°   *estranged*
A lappewinge made he was,
And thus he hoppeth on the gras,
And on his heed ther stant upright
A creste in tokne he was a knight;
500 And yit unto this day men sayth,
A lappewinge hath lore° his faith   *lost*
And is the brid falseste of alle.
    Bewar my sone, er thee so falle;
For if thou be of such covine,°   *treachery*
505 To get of love be ravine
Thy lust,° it may thee falle thus,   *desire*
As it befell of Tereüs.

AMANS:
My fader, goddes forebode!°   *forbid*
Me were levere be fortrode°   *trodden*
515 With wilde hors and be todrawe,°   *drawn*
Er I again love and his lawe
Dide any thing or loude or stille,
Which were noght my lady wille.
Men sayn that every love hath drede;
520 So folweth it that I hire drede,
For I hire love, and who so dredeth,
To plese his love and serve him needeth.
Thus may ye knowen be this skile°   *argument*
That no ravine doon I wille
525 Again hir will be such a waye;
But while I live, I wol obeye
Abidinge on hir courtesye,
If any mercy wolde hir plye.°   *persuade*
Forthy, my fader, as of this
530 I woot noght I have doon amis:
But furthermore I you beseeche,
Some other point that ye me teche
And axeth forth, if ther be ought,°   *anything*
That I may be the bettre taught.

1390

THOMAS HOCCLEVE
ca. 1367–1426

"Debaat is nowe noon bitwixe me and my wit," declares the first-person narrator, one "Thomas," of Thomas Hoccleve's poem *My Compleinte* (1419–20): "I'm wholly recovered from mental instability" (line 247). The text as a whole, however, tells a much more painful story: Hoccleve's problem is less mental instability and more the fact that his friends think him unstable. Thomas acknowledges that he had a nervous breakdown of sorts five years ago, but now, feeling fully recovered, he remains tortured by his friends' lack of trust. He's so distressed by their distrust, in fact, that it is driving him insane.

The real Thomas Hoccleve corresponds closely to the "Thomas" as represented in Hoccleve's poetry. Hoccleve was a civil servant, working as a skilled clerk in the office of the Privy Seal. In addition to his bureaucratic tasks, he produced poetic texts of a high order, notably the *Regement of Princes* (1410–13) and the so-called *Series* (ca. 1419–21), a compilation of which *My Compleinte* is the first part. He also wrote occasional poems, both subtle petitionary texts (asking for payment) and poetry voicing official policy. He seems to have experienced a period of mental instability in 1414. The detailed evidence for this inference derives only from the *Series*, although it might be relevant that Hoccleve was not paid in Michaelmas 1414.

Hoccleve represents himself in sometimes amusingly, more often painfully, vulnerable ways. He is English poetry's first alienated urban bureaucrat, intellectual, and poet, alienated from his work (for which he is underpaid and paid late, if paid at all) and alienated from his patrons, readers, and friends.

Being thought less than fully sane is a tricky challenge for both a human being and an author. Staying away from company so to avoid suspicion merely provokes suspicion: Thomas's friends will, he reasonably surmises, think him "fallen in again" (line 182). Out in public he overhears the voices of those commenting on his bizarre physical mannerisms; but back home, he retreats to his mirror and searches for signs of instability that he might rectify. In public or alone with his mirror image, Thomas is bounced back and forth by the "people's imagination" (line 380), what others think or say about him, his public image. Maybe reading books of consolation is the answer, books that anchor identity in God, not in society. So ends *My Compleinte*, but, interestingly, Thomas never gets to the end of that book, and besides, his apparent acceptance of its advice is belied by the complex time sequence of *My Compleinte*: he claims

Patronage. Thomas Hoccleve, *Regement of Princes*, 1412. Hoccleve presents his poem to Prince Henry. The author is on his knees to his patron, even if the book he presents is less subservient than the image might suggest.

to have been pacified by the spiritual book *before* the time of bursting out with the complaint. Only Hoccleve's own text might do the trick here, by reintegrating him with his readers, unless of course they examine his work diagnostically, looking for signs in his poetry of uncured madness.

My Compleinte is a searing expression of, and attempted self-therapy for, melancholia. This is the "thoughtful malady" (line 21), or what we might call depression. Hoccleve represents the author in the act of dying, his voice invaded by the distrustful voices of his readers and so-called friends. The painful predicament of the outsider in the claustrophobic society of late medieval court society points forward to early modern court satire (see, for example, Skelton's *Bouge of Court* in the supplemental ebook). It might also point us to that other striking misfit in late medieval English writing, Hoccleve's contemporary Margery Kempe, whose distinctiveness is either saintly or sad.

My Compleinte[1]

	Aftir that hervest° inned° had hise sheves,	*autumn / brought in*
	And that the broun sesoun of Mihelmesse[2]	
	Was come, and gan° the trees robbe° of her° leves,	*proceeded / (to) rob / their*
	That grene had ben and in lusty° freisshenesse,	*pleasing*
5	And hem into colour of yelownesse	
	Had died° and doun throwen undirfoote,	*dyed*
	That chaunge sanke into myn herte° roote.	*heart's*
	For freisshly broughte it to my remembraunce	
	That stablenesse in this worlde is ther noon.	
10	Ther is nothing but chaunge and variaunce.°	*alteration*
	Howe welthi° a man be or wel begoon,	*prosperous*
	Endure it shal not. He shal it forgoon.°	*lose*
	Deeth undirfoote shal him thriste adoun.°	*thrust down*
	That is every wightes° conclusioun,	*person's*
15	Wiche for to weyve° is in no mannes myght,	*avoid*
	Howe° riche he be, stronge, lusty,° freissh and gay.	*however / vigorous*
	And in the ende of Novembre, uppon a night,	
	Sighynge° sore, as I in my bed lay,	*sighing*
	For this and othir thoughtis° wiche many a day,	*thoughts*
20	Byforne,° I tooke, sleep cam noon in myn ye,°	*before / eye*
	So vexid me the thoughtful maladie.°	*i.e., melancholia*
	I sy° wel, sithin° I with siknesse last	*saw / since*
	Was scourgid, cloudy hath bene the favour	
	That shoon° on me ful bright° in times past.	*shone / very brightly*
25	The sunne abated,° and the dirke° shour	*diminished / dark*
	Hilded° doun right on me, and in langour°	*poured / depression*
	Me made swymme, so that my spirite	
	To lyve no lust° had, ne no delyte.	*pleasure*

1. The text is drawn from Thomas Hoccleve, *"My Compleinte" and Other Poems*, edited by Roger Ellis, Exeter Medieval Texts and Studies (Exeter: University of Exeter Press, 2001). Obsolete letter forms have been modernized. Ellis's glosses have been preserved, with some modification.
2. Michaelmas falls on September 29. Note the melancholy inversion of the opening of Chaucer's *Canterbury Tales*.

The greef aboute myn herte so sore swal° — *swelled*
30 And bolned° evere to and to° so sore — *swelled / more and more*
That nedis° oute° I muste therwithal.° — *necessarily / (burst) out / with it*
I thoughte I nolde° kepe it cloos° no more, — *would not / secret*
Ne lete it in me for to eelde° and hore,° — *age / grow gray*
And for to preve° I cam° of a womman, — *prove / was born*
35 I braste oute° on the morwe° and thus bigan. — *burst / next day*

Here endith my prolog and folwith my compleinte.

Almyghty God, as liketh° his goodnesse, — *pleases*
Vesitethe° folke alday,° as men may se, — *visits / continually*
With los of good and bodily sikenesse,
And amonge othir,° he forgat° not me. — *others / forgot*
40 Witnesse uppon the wilde infirmite
Wiche that I hadde, as many a man wel knewe,
And wiche me oute of mysilfe caste and threwe.

It was so knowen° to the peple and kouthe — *familiar*
That counseil° was it noon, ne not be might. — *secret*
45 Howe it with me stood was in every mannes mouthe,
And that ful sore° my frendis affright.° — *sorely / frightened*
They for myn helthe pilgrimages hight,° — *promised*
And soughte hem, somme on hors and somme
    on foote,
God yelde it hem,° to gete me my boote.° — *reward them for it / health*

50 But although the substaunce of my memorie
Wente to pleie as for a certein space,° — *for a time*
Yit° the lorde of vertue, the kyng of glorie, — *yet*
Of his highe myght and his benigne grace,
Made it for to retourne into the place
55 Whens it cam,° whiche at Alle Halwemesse[3] — *went out*
Was five yeere,° neither more ne lesse. — *five years ago*

And evere sithin,° thankid be God oure Lord — *since*
Of° his good and gracious reconsiliacioun, — *for*
My wit and I have bene of suche acord° — *as well agreed*
60 As we were or° the alteracioun — *before*
Of it was, but by my savacioun,° — *salvation*
Sith° that time have I be sore sette on fire — *since*
And lyved in greet turment and martire.° — *suffering*

For though that my wit were hoom come ayein,° — *had returned again*
65 Men wolde it not so undirstonde or take.° — *accept*
With me to dele hadden they disdein.° — *scorn*
A riotous° persone I was and forsake.° — *dissolute / abandoned*
Min oolde frendshipe was al overshake.° — *shaken off*
No wight° with me list make daliaunce.° — *person / pleased to converse*
70 The worlde me made a straunge — *shower*
    countinaunce,° — *the face of a stranger*

3. All Hallowmas, or All Saints Day, falls on November 1.

Wich that myn herte sore gan to tourment,
For ofte whanne I in Westmynstir Halle,
And eke° in Londoun, amonge the prees° went,   *also / crowd*
I sy° the chere abaten° and apalle°   *saw / faces grow dejected / pale*
75 Of hem° that weren wonte° me for to calle   *those / accustomed*
To companie.° Her heed° they caste awry,°   *to join them / their heads / aside*
Whanne I hem mette, as° they not me sy.°   *as if / saw*

As seide is in the sauter° might I sey,   *Psalter*
'They that me sy,° fledden awey fro me.'   *saw*
80 Foryeten° I was al oute of mynde awey,   *forgotten*
As he that deed° was from° hertis cherte.°   *dead / (far) from / love*
To a lost vessel lickned° mighte I be,   *likened*
For manie a wight° aboute me dwelling°   *person / in my vicinity*
Herde I me blame and putte in dispreisyng.°   *and censure*

85 Thus spake manie oone and seide by° me: *about*
'Although from him his sicknesse savage°   *wild*
Withdrawen and passed as for a time be,
Resorte° it wole,° namely° in suche age   *return / will / specially*
As he is of,' and thanne my visage°   *face*
90 Bigan to glowe° for the woo° and fere.°   *burn / grief / fear*
Tho° wordis, hem vnwar,° cam to myn   *those / without their knowledge*
    eere.°   *ear*

'Whanne passinge° hete is,' quod thei, 'trustith° this,   *extreme / believe*
Assaile him wole ayein that maladie.'
And yit, parde,° thei token hem amis.°   *by heaven / were wrong*
95 Noon effecte at al took her° prophecie.   *their*
Manie someris bene° past sithen° remedie   *are / since*
Of that God of his grace° me purveide.°   *in his grace / provided with*
Thankid be God, it shoop° not as thei seide.   *happened*

What° falle shal,° what men so   *whatever / shall happen*
    deme° or gesse,   *judge*
100 To him that woot° every hertis secree,°   *knows / secret*
Reserved is. It is a lewidnesse°   *an ignorance*
Men wiser hem pretende than thei be,   *to pretend themselves*
And no wight° knowith, be it he or she,   *person*
Whom, howe, ne whanne God wole him vesite.°   *visit*
105 It happith often whanne men wene° it lite.°   *expect / not at all*

Somtime I wende° as lite° as any man   *thought / little*
For to han falle° into that wildenesse,   *to have fallen*
But God, whanne him liste,° may, wole and can   *it pleases*
Helthe withdrawe and sende a wight° sicknesse.   *person*
110 Though man be wel this day, no sikernesse°   *certainty*
To hym bihighte° is that it shal endure.   *promised*
God hurte nowe can, and nowe hele° and cure.   *heal*

He suffrith° longe but at the laste he smit.°   *endures / smites*
Whanne that a man is in prosperite,

115   To drede a falle comynge it is a wit.°   *mark of wisdom*
      Whoso° that taketh hede ofte may se   *whoever*
      This worldis chaunge and mutabilite
      In sondry wise,° howe nedith not expresse.°   *different ways / to declare*
      To my mater streite° wole I me dresse.°   *immediately / address myself*

120   Men seiden I loked° as a wilde steer,°   *looked like / ox*
      And so my looke aboute I gan to throwe.°   *cast*
      Min heed° to hie,° anothir seide, I beer.°   *head / high / carried*
      'Full bukkissh° is his brayn, wel may I trowe.'°   *very like a buck / believe*
      And seide the thridde, 'And apt is°   *(he) is fit/*
          in the rowe°   *row (i.e., company)*
125   To site° of hem that a resounles reed°   *sit / senseless piece of advice*
      Can yeve:° no sadnesse° is in his heed.'   *give / soundness*

      Chaunged had I my pas,° somme seiden eke,°   *step / moreover*
      For here and there forthe stirte° I as a roo,°   *started / roe*
      Noon abood,° noon areest,° but al brainseke.°   *resting / stopping / brainsick*
130   Another spake and of° me seide also,   *concerning*
      My feet weren ay wavynge° to and fro,   *moving*
      Whanne that I stonde° shulde and with men   *stand (still)*
          talke,
      And that myn yen° soughten° every halke.°   *eyes / sought / corner (of room)*

      I leide an eere ay to° as I by wente,   *gave an ear to this constantly*
135   And herde al, and thus in myn herte I caste:°   *reflected*
      'Of longe abidinge here I may me repente.
      Lest that of hastinesse° I at the laste   *in hastiness*
      Answere amys,° beste is hens hie faste,°   *wrongly / to depart quickly*
      For if I in this prees° amys me gye,°   *crowd / misbehave myself*
140   To harme wole it me turne and to folie.'°   *and (make me) a laughingstock*

      And this I demed° wel and knewe wel eke,°   *judged / also*
      Whatso° that evere I shulde answere or seie,   *whatever*
      They wolden not han holde° it worth a leke.°   *held / leek*
      Forwhy,° as° I had lost my tunges keie,°   *therefore / as if / tongue's key*
145   Kepte I me cloos,° and trussid me my weie,°   *private / took myself off*
      Droupinge° and hevy and al woo bistaad.°   *drooping / woebegone*
      Smal cause hadde I, methoughte, to be glad.

      My spirites labouriden evere ful bisily
      To peinte countenaunce,° chere and look,°   *appearance / face*
150   For° that men spake of me so wondringly,   *because*
      And for the verry shame and fear I qwook.°   *shook*
      Though° myn herte hadde be dippid° in the   *even if / been plunged*
          brook,
      It weet° and moist was ynow° of my swoot,°   *wet / enough / with my sweat*
      Wiche was nowe frosty colde, nowe firy hoot.°   *hot as fire*

155   And in my chaumbre at home whanne that I was
      Mysilfe aloone I in this wise° wrought.°   *way / did*
      I streite° unto my mirrour and my glas,   *(went) straight*

To loke howe that me of my chere thought,°   *my expression seemed to me*
If any othir° were it than it ought,   *at all other*
160 For fain° wolde I, if it not had bene right,   *gladly*
Amendid° it to° my kunnynge° and myght.   *to have improved / according to/ knowledge*

Many a saute° made I to this mirrour,   *leap*

Thinking, 'If that I looke in this manere
Amonge folke as I nowe do, noon° errour   *no*
165 Of suspecte° look may in my face appere.   *suspicious*
This countinaunce,° I am sure, and this chere,°   *appearance / expression*
If I it forthe° use, is nothing° reprevable°   *abroad / not / objectionable*
To hem that han conceitis° resonable.'   *understandings*

And therwithal° I thoughte thus anoon:°   *thereupon / at once*
170 'Men in her° owne cas° bene blinde alday,°   *their / situation / continually*
As I have herde seie manie a day agoon,°   *before this*
And in that same plite° I stonde may.   *danger*
Howe shal I do? Whiche is the beste way
My troublid spirit for to bringe in rest?
175 If I wiste° howe, fain° wolde I do the best.'°   *knew / gladly / my best*

Sithen° I recovered was, have I ful ofte   *since*
Cause had of anger and inpacience,
Where I borne have it esily° and softe,°   *calmly / gently*
Suffringe° wronge be done to me, and offence,   *enduring*
180 And not answerid ayen,° but kepte silence,   *back*
Leste that men of me deme° wolde, and sein,   *judge*
'Se howe this man is fallen in° ayein.'°   *in (to his sickness) / again*

As that I oones° fro Westminstir⁴ cam,   *once*
Vexid ful grevously with thoughtful hete,°   *burning thought*
185 Thus thoughte I, 'A greet fool I am,
This pavyment adaies° thus to bete,°   *daily / beat (upon)*
And in and oute° laboure faste and swete,°   *everywhere / sweat*
Wondringe and hevinesse to purchace,°   *gain*
Sithen° I stonde out of al favour and grace.'   *since*

190 And thanne thoughte I on that othir side,
'If that I not be sen° amonge the prees,°   *seen / throng*
Men deme° wole that I myn heed hide,   *judge*
And am werse than I am, it is no lees.'°   *lie*
O Lorde, so my spirit was restelees.
195 I soughte reste and I not it fonde,°   *found*
But ay° was trouble redy at myn honde.   *always*

I may not lette° a man to ymagine°   *prevent / from imagining*
Fer° above the mone,° if that him liste.°   *far / moon / please*

---

4. Westminster, a city separate from London proper; Hoccleve's workplace as a royal bureaucrat.

Therby the sothe° he may not determine, *truth*
200 But by the preef° ben thingis knowen and wiste.° *proof / grasped*
Many a doom° is wrappid in° the myste. *judgment / hidden as in*
Man by hise dedis° and not by hise lookes *deeds*
Shal knowen be. As it is writen in bookes,

Bi taaste of fruit men may wel wite° and knowe *know*
205 What that it is. Othir preef° is ther noon. *proof*
Every man woote° wel that, as that I trowe.° *knows / believe*
Right so, thei that deemen° my wit is goon, *judge*
As yit this day ther deemeth many oon° *many a one*
I am not wel, may, as I by hem goo,
210 Taaste and assay° if it be so or noo. *test*

Uppon a look is° harde men hem to grounde° *(it) is / for men to determine*
What a man is. Therby the sothe° is hid. *truth*
Whethir hise wittis° sick bene° or sounde, *wits / are*
By countynaunce is it not wist° ne kid.° *known / made public*
215 Though a man harde have oones been bitid,° *has once experienced hardship*
God shilde° it shulde on him continue alway. *forbid*
By communinge° is the beste assay.° *conversation / test*

I mene, to commune° of thingis mene,° *converse / ordinary*
For I am but right lewide,° douteles, *uneducated*
220 And ignoraunt. My kunnynge° is ful lene.° *knowledge / very slight*
Yit° homely resoun° knowe I neverethelees. *yet / ordinary reasoning*
Not hope° I founden be° so resounlees° *think / (to) be found / foolish*
As men deemen.° Marie,° Crist forbede!° *judge / St Mary / forbid*
I can° no more. Preve° may the dede.° *know / prove (this) / deed*

225 If a man oones° falle in drunkenesse, *once*
Shal he continue therynne everemo?
Nay, though a man do in drinking excesse° *drink to excess*
So ferforthe° that not speke he ne can, ne goo, *far*
And hise witts welny bene refte° him fro, *are almost all taken*
230 And buried in the cuppe; he aftirward
Cometh to hymsilfe ayeine,° ellis were it° hard. *again / otherwise it would be*

Right so, though that my witte were a pilgrim,
And wente fer° from home, he cam° again. *far / returned*
God me devoided° of the grevous venim° *emptied / poison*
235 That had enfectid and wildid° my brain. *maddened*
See howe the curteise leche° moost soverain *doctor*
Unto the seke yeveth° medicine *sick (man) gives*
In nede, and hym releveth of his grevous pine.° *torment*

Nowe lat° this passe. God woot,° many a man *let / knows*
240 Semeth ful wiis° by countenaunce° and chere° *wise / appearance / expression*
Wiche, and he tastid° were what he can,° *tested / knows*
Men mighten licken° him to a fooles peere,° *compare / mate*
And som man loketh in foltisshe manere° *like a fool*

As to the outward doom° and jugement,   *external judgement*
245 That, at the prefe,° discreet° is and prudent.   *when tested / rational*

But algatis,° howe so° be my countinaunce,   *all the same / however*
Debaat° is nowe noon bitwixe° me and my wit,   *disagreement / between*
Although that ther were a disseveraunce,°   *separation*
As for a time, bitwixe me and it.
250 The gretter harme is myn, that nevere yit°   *yet*
Was I wel lettrid,° prudent and discreet.°   *educated / deliberative*
Ther nevere stood yit wiis° man on my feet.   *wise*

The sothe° is this, suche conceit° as I had   *truth / thoughts*
And undirstonding, al° were it but° smal,   *although / only*
255 Bifore that my wittis weren unsad,°   *unstable*
Thanked be oure Lorde Ihesu Crist of al,°   *for all*
Suche have I nowe, but blowe° is ny overal°   *blown / nearly everywhere*
The reverse, wherthorugh° moche is my   *through which*
    mornynge,
Whiche causeth me thus syghe° in compleinynge.   *sigh*

260 Sithen° my good fortune hath chaungid hir chere,°   *since / look*
Hie° tyme is me° to crepe into my grave.   *high / for me*
To lyve joielees,° what do I here?   *joyless*
I in myn herte can no gladnesse have.
I may but smal° seie but if° men deme° I rave.   *only a little / unless / judge*
265 Sithen° othir thing than woo° may I noon gripe,°   *since / woe / grasp*
Unto° my sepulcre am I nowe ripe.°   *for / ready*

My wele,° adieu, farwel, my good fortune.   *wealth*
Oute of youre tables me planed° han ye.   *removed.*
Sithen welny° eny wight° for to commune°   *since almost / person / talk*
270 With me loth° is, farwel prosperite.   *unwilling*
I am no lenger° of youre livere.°   *longer / livery*
Ye have me putte oute of youre retenaunce.°   *retinue*
Adieu, my good aventure and good chaunce.°   *fortune / luck*

And aswithe° aftir, thus bithoughte I me:°   *immediately / reflected*
275 'If that I in this wise me dispeire,
It is purchas° of more adversite.   *purchase*
What nedith it° my feble wit appeire,°   *need is there / to weaken*
Sith° God hath made myn helthe home repeire,°   *since / retum*
Blessid be he? And what° men deme° and speke,   *whatever / judge*
280 Suffre° it thenke° I and me not   *(to) endure / think /*
    on me wreke.'°   *(to) avenge*

But somdel° had I rejoisinge amonge,°   *somewhat / between whiles*
And a gladnesse also in my spirite,
That though the peple took hem° mis° and   *judged / amiss*
    wronge,°   *wrongly*
Me deemyng° of my sicknesse not quite,°   *judging / freed*
285 Yit for they compleined° the hevy plite°   *regretted / plight*

That they had seen me in with tendirnesse
Of hertis cherte,° my greef° was the lesse.   *love / grief*

In hem putte I no defaute° but oon.°   *found no fault / one*
That I was hool,° thei not ne deme° kowde,   *whole / judge*
290 And day by day thei sye° me bi hem goon°   *saw / go*
In hete and coolde, and neither stille or lowde°   *silent or speaking*
Knewe thei me do suspectly.° A dirke° clowde   *(to) act suspiciously / dark*
Hir sight° obscurid withynne and withoute,   *their sight*
And for al that were° ay in suche a doute.°   *(they) were / uncertainty*

295 Axide° han they ful oftesithe,° and freined°   *asked / often / inquired*
Of my felawis° of the Prive Seel,[5]   *fellows*
And preied hem to telle hem with herte unfeined,°   *sincere*
Howe it stood with me, wethir yvel or wel.
And they the sothe tolde hem every del,°   *completely*
300 But thei helden her° wordis not° but lees.°   *reckoned their / nothing / lies*
Thei mighten as wel have holden her pees.°   *kept their peace*

This troubly° liif° hath al to longe endurid.   *troublesome / life*
Not have I wist° how in my skyn to tourne.   *known*
But nowe mysilfe to mysilfe° have ensurid°   *I myself / guaranteed*
305 For no suche wondringe° aftir this to mourne.°   *puzzlement / to be fretful*
As longe as my liif shal in me sojourne°   *remain*
Of such imagining I not ne recche.°   *care*
Lat hem deeme° as hem list° and   *judge / please*
    speke and drecche.°   *speculate*

This othir day a lamentacioun
310 Of a wooful man in a book[6] I sy,°   *saw*
To whom wordis of consolacioun
Resoun yaf° spekynge effectuelly,°   *gave / to good effect*
And wel esid° myn herte was therby,°   *eased / by it*
For whanne I had a while in the book reed,°   *read*
315 With the speche of Resoun was I wel feed.°   *nourished*

The hevy° man wooful and angwisshous°   *depressed / anguished*
Compleined in this wise, and thus seide he:
'My liif is unto me ful encomborus,°   *burdensome*
For whidre or unto what place I flee,
320 My wickidnessis evere folowen me,
As men may se the shadwe° a body sue,°   *shadow / follow*
And in no manere I may hem eschewe.°   *avoid*

'Vexacioun of spirit and turment
Lacke I right noon. I have of hem plente.

---

5. Hoccleve was a clerk in the Office of the Privy Seal, one of three great bureaucratic offices, responsible for the production and issuing of many kinds of official documents. Hoccleve himself pro-duced a set, or "Formulary," of almost 900 model Privy Seal documents.
6. The book can be identified as the *Synonyma* of Isidore of Seville (d. 636).

325 Wondirly° bittir is my taast and sent.°   *amazingly / smell*
    Woo° be the time of my nativite.   *accursed*
    Unhappi man, that evere shulde I be.
    O deeth, thi strook° a salve° is of swetnesse   *stroke / ointment*
    To hem that lyven in suche wrecchidnesse.

330 'Gretter plesaunce were it me° to die,   *pleasure would it be for me*
    By manie foolde° than for to live so.   *many times over*
    Sorwes so manie in me multiplie
    That my liif is to me a verre° foo.°   *very / foe*
    Comforted may I not be of my woo.
335 Of my distresse see noon ende I can.
    No force° howe soone I stinte° to be a man.'   *matter / cease*

    Thanne spake Resoun, 'What meneth al this fare?°   *behavior*
    Though welthe be not frendly to thee, yit°   *yet*
    Oute of thin herte voide° woo and care.'   *cast*
340 'By what skile,° howe, and by what reed°   *strategem / counsel*
      and wit,'°   *skill*
    Seide this wooful man, 'mighte I doon° it?'   *do*
    'Wrastle,'° quod Resoun, 'ayein° hevynesse°   *struggle / against / sadnesses*
    Of the worlde, troublis, suffringe and duresse.°   *hardships*

    'Biholde howe many a man suffrith dissese,
345 As greet as thou and alaway° grettere,   *continually*
    And though it hem° pinche sharply and sese,°   *them / seize*
    Yit paciently thei it suffre° and bere.°   *endure / bear*
    Thinke hereon and the lesse it shal thee dere.°   *injure*
    Suche suffraunce is of mannes gilte clensinge,°   *purification*
350 And hem enableth° to° joie everelastinge.   *enables them (to attain)*

    'Woo, hevinesse and tribulacioun
    Comen° aren to men alle and profitable.   *common*
    Though grevous be mannes temptacioun,
    It sleeth° man not. To hem that° ben suffrable°   *kills / those who / patient*
355 And to whom Goddis strook° is acceptable   *stroke*
    Purveied° joie is, for God woundith tho°   *ordained / those*
    That he ordeined hath to blis to goo.

    'Golde purgid° is, thou seest, in the furneis,   *purified*
    For the finer and clenner° it shal be.   *purer*
360 Of thi dissese the weighte and the peis°   *burden*
    Bere lightly,° for God, to prove thee,   *easily*
    Scourgid the hath with sharpe adversite.
    Not grucche° and seie, "Whi susteine I this?"   *complain*
    For if thou do, thou the takest amis.°   *act wrongly*

365 'But thus thou shuldist thinke in thin herte,
    And seie, "To thee, lorde God, I have agilte°   *done wrong*
    So sore° I moot° for myn offensis smerte,°   *grievously / must / suffer*
    As I am worthi. O Lorde I am spilte,°   *destroyed*
    But° thou to me thi mercy graunte wilte.   *unless*

370   I am ful sure thou maist it not denie.
      Lorde, I me repente, and I the mercy crie.'"°   *beg mercy of you*

      Lenger° I thoughte reed have° in this book,   *longer / to have read*
      But so it shope° that I ne might naught.°   *happened / not*
      He that it oughte° ayen° it to him took,   *owned / back*
375   Me of his hast° vnwar.° Yit have I caught°   *haste / unaware / taken*
      Sum of the doctrine by Resoun taught
      To the man, as above have I said.
      Wel therof° I holde me ful wel apaid,°   *with it / satisifed*

      For evere sithen° sett have I the lesse   *since*
380   By the peples imaginacioun,
      Talkinge this and that of my siknesse
      Which cam of° Goddis visitacioun.   *from*
      Mighte I have be founde in probacioun°   *when tested*
      Not grucching° but han take it in souffraunce,° *complaining / patience*
385   Holsum and wiis° had be° my   *wise / would have been*
          governaunce.°   *self-control*

      Farwel my sorowe, I caste it to the cok.°   *? away (to the cock)*
      With pacience I hensforthe thinke unpike°   *(to) undo*
      Of suche thoughtful dissese° and woo the lok,° *(i.e.) melancholia / lock*
      And lete hem° out that han me made to sike.° *them (my thoughts) / sigh*
390   Hereafter oure Lorde God may, if him like,°   *please*
      Make al myn oolde affeccioun° resorte,°   *feeling / return*
      And in hope of that wole I me comforte.

      Thorugh° Goddis just doom° and his jugement   *through / sentence*
      And for my best,° nowe I take and deeme,° *my greatest (profit) / reckon*
395   Yaf° that good lorde me my punischement.   *gave*
      In welthe I tooke of him noon hede or yeme,°   *attention*
      Him for to plese° and him honoure and queme,° *please / gratify*
      And he me yaf° a boon° on for to gnawe,   *gave / bone*
      Me to correcte and of him to have awe.

400   He yaf° wit and he tooke it away   *gave*
      Whanne that he sy° that I it mis dispente,°   *saw / used it amiss*
      And yaf ayein° whanne it was to his pay°   *again / profit*
      He grauntide me my giltis to repente,
      And hensforwarde to sette myn entente°   *intention*
405   Unto his deitee° to do plesaunce,   *to please his godhead*
      And to amende my sinful governaunce.°   *way of life*

      Laude and honour and thanke unto thee be,
      Lorde God, that salve art to al hevinesse.°   *sadness*
      Thanke of° my welthe and myn adversitee.   *thanks for*
410   Thanke of myn elde° and of my seeknesse.°   *age / sickness*
      And thanke be to thin infinit goodnesse
      And thi yiftis° and benefices° alle,   *gifts / benefits*
      And unto thi mercy and grace I calle.

WILLIAM LANGLAND
ca. 1330–1387

William Langland is agreed by most scholars to be the sole author of a long religious allegory in alliterative verse known as *The Vision of Piers Plowman* or more simply *Piers Plowman*, which survives in at least three distinct versions that scholars refer to as the A-, B-, and C-texts. The first, about twenty-four hundred lines long, breaks off at a rather inconclusive point in the action; the second (from which all but one of the selections here have been drawn) is a revision of the first plus an extension of more than four thousand lines; and the third is a revision of the second. About Langland we know hardly anything except what can be inferred from the poem itself. He came from the west of England and was probably a native of the Malvern Hills area in which the opening of the poem is set. We can never identify the persona of the narrator of a medieval text positively or precisely with its author, especially when we are dealing with allegory. Nevertheless, a passage that was added to the C-text, the last of the selections printed here, gives the strong impression of being at one and the same time an allegory in which the narrator represents willful Mankind and a poignantly ironic self-portrait of the stubborn-willed poet who occasionally plays on his own name: "I have lived in *land* . . . my name is *Long Will*" (15.152). In this new episode the narrator tries to defend his shiftless way of life against Conscience and Reason, presumably his own conscience and reason. Conscience dismisses his specious argument that a clerical education has left him no "tools" to support himself with except for his prayer book and the Psalms with which he prays for the souls of those from whom he begs alms. The entire work conforms well with the notion that its author was a man who was educated to enter the church but who, through marriage and lack of preferment, was reduced to poverty and may well have wandered in his youth like those "hermits" he scornfully describes in the prologue.

Piers Plowman has the form of a dream vision, a common medieval type in which the author presents the story under the guise of having dreamed it. The dream vision generally involves allegory, not only because one expects from a dream the unrealistic, the fanciful, but also because people have always suspected that dreams relate the truth in disguised form—that they are natural allegories. Through a series of such visions it traces the Dreamer-narrator's tough-minded, persistent, and passionate search for answers to his many questions, especially the question he puts early in the poem to Lady Holy Church: "How I may save my soul." Langland's theme is nothing less than the history of Christianity as it unfolds both in the world of the Old and New Testaments and in the life and heart of an individual fourteenth-century Christian—two seemingly distinct realms between which the poet's allegory moves with dizzying rapidity.

Within the larger sequence of the poem, from its beginning until the end of *Passus* 7, the following selections form a thematically coherent narrative. In the Prologue (the first selection), Langland's narrator falls asleep and witnesses a compact vision of the whole of late fourteenth-century English society. Poised between two stark and static possibilities of heaven and hell, an intensely active, mobile earthly life is concentrated into a "field full of folk." Some ideal practitioners of earthly occupations are surrounded and undermined by a much larger set of very energetic social types who exploit their occupations for entirely selfish ends. Langland practices an estates satire, which surveys and excoriates each worldly occupation (cf. Chaucer's very different example of estates satire in the *General Prologue* to the

Between Heaven and Hell. Hieronymus Bosch, *Haywain Triptych*, ca. 1490–95. The calm scene atop the haystack is perilously perched between heaven and hell, and above the furious activity of the world.

Canterbury Tales; for other examples, see the "Medieval Estates and Orders" topic in the supplemental ebook.) He reserves his especial anger for those who abuse ecclesiastical authority, and for the wealthy, pitiless laity (i.e., non-ecclesiastical figures).

Passus, Latin for "step," is the word used for the poem's basic divisions. *Passus 1* (the second selection) promises to give some intellectual and moral purchase on the teeming energies of the Prologue. Holy Church instructs the poem's narrator and dreamer Will in the proper relation of material wealth and spiritual health. In particular, she accentuates the value of the "best treasure," *truthe*, one of Langland's key words: *truthe* is the justice that flows from God; it manifests itself in the exercise of earthly justice and fidelity, and in the correlative poetic value of truthtelling. Will recognizes the force of Holy Church's sermon, but still needs to know it by an interior form of knowledge, grounded in the depths of the self.

It would seem that the rest of the poem is devoted to the discovery of that internalized truth. The first of the poem's large-scale narratives (*Passus 2–4*) represents the attempt of earthly justice to control the disruptive energies of the profit economy. That economy is here represented by the personification "Lady Mede," meaning "reward beyond deserving." After this sequence concerning earthly justice, the poem then turns to the deeper, more personal mechanisms of spiritual justice. In *Passus 5*, accordingly, the seven Deadly Sins confess in turn, before the poem's ideal earthly representative of justice, Piers Plowman, offers to lead a spiritual pilgrimage to the shrine of St. *Truthe* (*Passus 5.507–642*, the third selection).

The ideal of *truthe* takes a local habitation, then, in the model of society that Piers establishes for the conduct of his "pilgrimage." The truest form of pilgrimage is no pilgrimage at all; instead, all classes of society should stay at home and work harmoniously for the production of material food by agricultural workers, with knights helping plowmen and protecting the Church, while priests pray for both workers and knights. This ideal scene is pictured in *Passus 6* (the fourth selection).

Langland's poem might seem, thus far, to be a deeply conservative one, whereby justice is manifest only in a manorial society, within which each person knows his or

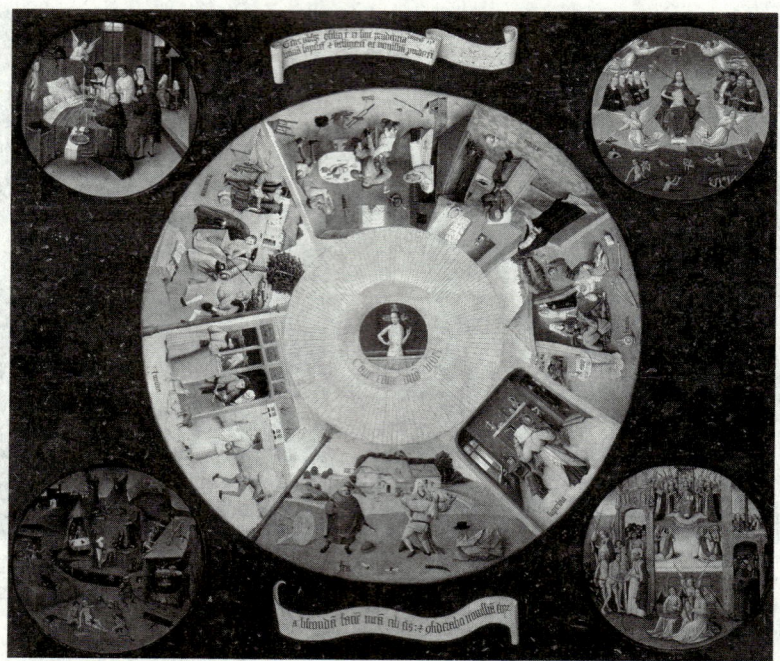

Sin. Hieronymus Bosch, *The Seven Deadly Sins*, ca. 1500. The violence of sin springs from no abstract source but is embedded in the precise social practices and material fabric of this world.

her place, and works harmoniously and obediently with the others. There is, however, a problem with this model: it collapses. In *Passus* 6 the ideal society put into action by Piers fails entirely; workers simply refuse to work, abuse the authority of knights, and respond only to the terrible pressure of Hunger, a punishing, Gargantuan figure who graphically evokes the ravages of famine in the fourteenth century.

In *Passus* 7 (the fifth selection) the limitations of the *truthe* model become dramatically visible. A pardon sent from God as *Truthe* promises no pardon at all, but only retribution for those who fail to meet the standards of God's justice, and reward for those who do not so fail. As the plowing has demonstrated, however, all fail. Such a "pardon" promises nothing but universal damnation. In an exceptionally powerful, dramatic and enigmatic moment, Piers actually tears this pardon in two, as he disputes with a priest about its force. Earlier in the poem it had seemed that all Will had to do was to absorb Holy Church's understanding of *Truthe*; once Piers tears the pardon, however, we realize that the search for *Truthe* modifies the goal. We realize, that is, that *Truthe* cannot be the whole truth. The shortcomings of *Truthe* propel Will to a more urgent search for God's love and forgiveness, beyond justice, in the deepest resources of his own self. This search climaxes in the vision of Christ's Atonement (*Passus* 18; see the selection in this volume, pp. 397–408).

In the last selection from the C-text, Langland presents a moving, if less passionate and conflicted scene than the tearing of *Truthe's* Pardon. In a passage often regarded as autobiographical, Will argues with Conscience and Reason (principles of law, but also, doubtless, Will's own conscience and reason). They reproach him for his way of life in a poor district of London, where Will barely supports his family with alms he gets by praying for the souls of wealthy burghers.

A large number of manuscripts and two sixteenth-century editions show that *Piers Plowman* was avidly read and studied by a great many people from the end of the fourteenth century to the reign of Elizabeth I. Some of these readers have left a record of their engagement with the poem in marginal comments. Almost from the first, it was a controversial text. Within four years of the writing of the second version—which scholars have good evidence to date 1377, the year of Edward III's death and Richard II's accession to the throne—it had become so well known that the leaders of the Uprising of 1381 used phrases borrowed from it as part of the rhetoric of the rebellion (for an example of such rhetoric, see the letter by John Ball, "The Uprising of 1381," in the "Medieval Estates and Orders" topic in the supplemental ebook). Langland's sympathy with the sufferings of the poor and his indignant satire of corruption in Church and State undoubtedly made his poem popular with the rebels. Although he may not have sympathized with the violence of the rebels and their leaders, he recognized that for the Church to be preserved, it needed profound reform. The passionate sympathy for the commoner, idealized in *Piers Plowman*, also appealed to reformers who felt that true religion was best represented not by the ecclesiastical hierarchy but by the humblest orders of society. Many persons reading his poem in the sixteenth century (it was first printed in 1550) saw in *Piers Plowman* a prophecy and forerunner of the English Reformation. Immersed as it is in thorny political and theological controversies of its own day, *Piers Plowman* is arguably the most difficult and, at times, even the most frustrating of Middle English texts, but its poetic, intellectual, and moral complexity and integrity also make it one of the most rewarding.

From The Vision of Piers Plowman[1]

From *The Prologue*

[THE FIELD OF FOLK]

In a summer season when the sun was mild
I clad myself in clothes as I'd become a sheep;
In the habit of a hermit unholy of works,[2]
Walked wide in this world, watching for wonders.
5   And on a May morning, on Malvern Hills,
There befell me as by magic a marvelous thing:
I was weary of wandering and went to rest
At the bottom of a broad bank by a brook's side,
And as I lay lazily looking in the water
10 I slipped into a slumber, it sounded so pleasant.
There came to me reclining there a most curious dream
That I was in a wilderness, nowhere that I knew;
But as I looked into the east, up high toward the sun,
I saw a tower on a hill-top, trimly built,
15 A deep dale beneath, a dungeon tower in it,
With ditches deep and dark and dreadful to look at.
A fair field full of folk I found between them,
Of human beings of all sorts, the high and the low,
Working and wandering as the world requires.
20   Some applied themselves to plowing, played very rarely,

---

1. The translation is by E. T. Donaldson (1990) and is based on *Piers Plowman: The B Version*, edited by George Kane and E. T. Donaldson (1975).

2. For Langland's opinion of hermits, see lines 28–30 and 53–57. The sheep's clothing may suggest the habit's physical resemblance to sheep's wool as well as a false appearance of innocence.

Sowing seeds and setting plants worked very hard;
Won what wasters gluttonously consume.
And some pursued pride, put on proud clothing,
Came all got up in garments garish to see.
25 To prayers and penance many put themselves,
All for love of our Lord lived hard lives,
Hoping thereafter to have Heaven's bliss—
Such as hermits and anchorites that hold to their cells,
Don't care to go cavorting about the countryside,
30 With some lush livelihood delighting their bodies.
And some made themselves merchants—they managed better,
As it seems to our sight that such men prosper.
And some make mirth as minstrels can
And get gold for their music, guiltless, I think.
35 But jokers and word jugglers, Judas' children,[3]
Invent fantasies to tell about and make fools of themselves,
And have whatever wits they need to work if they wanted.
What Paul preaches of them I don't dare repeat here:
Qui loquitur turpiloquium[4] is Lucifer's henchman.
40 Beadsmen[5] and beggars bustled about
Till both their bellies and their bags were crammed to the brim;
Staged flytings[6] for their food, fought over beer.
In gluttony, God knows, they go to bed
And rise up with ribaldry, those Robert's boys.°   *i.e., robbers*
45 Sleep and sloth pursue them always.
        Pilgrims and palmers[7] made pacts with each other
To seek Saint James[8] and saints at Rome.
They went on their way with many wise stories,
And had leave to lie all their lives after.
50 I saw some that said they'd sought after saints:
In every tale they told their tongues were tuned to lie
More than to tell the truth—such talk was theirs.
A heap of hermits with hooked staffs
Went off to Walsingham,[9] with their wenches behind them.
55 Great long lubbers that don't like to work
Dressed up in cleric's dress to look different from other men
And behaved as they were hermits, to have an easy life.
I found friars there—all four of the orders[1]—
Preaching to the people for their own paunches' welfare,
60 Making glosses° of the Gospel that would look good for   *interpretations*
        themselves;
Coveting copes,[2] they construed it as they pleased.
Many of these Masters[3] may clothe themselves richly,

3. Minstrels who deceive with jokes and fantastic stories are regarded as descendants of Christ's betrayer, Judas.
4. Who speaks filthy language. Cf. Ephesians 5.3–4 & 11–12.
5. Prayer sayers, i.e., people who offered to say prayers, sometimes counted on the beads of the rosary, for the souls of those who gave them alms.
6. Contests in which the participants took turns insulting each other, preferably in verse.
7. Virtually professional pilgrims who took

advantage of the hospitality offered them to go on traveling year after year (see p. 243, n. 6).
8. I.e., his shrine at Compostela in Spain.
9. English town, site of a famous shrine to the Virgin Mary.
1. In Langland's day there were four orders of friars in England: Franciscans, Dominicans, Carmelites, and Augustinians.
2. Monks', friars', and hermits' capes.
3. I.e., masters of divinity.

For their money and their merchandise[4] march hand in hand.
Since Charity[5] has proved a peddler and principally shrives lords,
65 Many marvels have been manifest within a few years.
Unless Holy Church and friars' orders hold together better,
The worst misfortune in the world will be welling up soon.
   A pardoner[6] preached there as if he had priest's rights,
Brought out a bull[7] with bishop's seals,
70 And said he himself could absolve them all
Of failure to fast, of vows they'd broken.
Unlearned men believed him and liked his words,
Came crowding up on knees to kiss his bulls.
He banged them with his brevet and bleared their eyes,[8]
75 And raked in with his parchment-roll rings and brooches.
Thus you give your gold for gluttons' well-being,
And squander it on scoundrels schooled in lechery.
If the bishop were blessed and worth both his ears,
His seal should not be sent out to deceive the people.
80 —It's nothing to the bishop that the blackguard preaches,
And the parish priest and the pardoner split the money
That the poor people of the parish would have but for them.
   Parsons and parish priests complained to the bishop
That their parishes were poor since the pestilence-time,[9]
85 Asked for license and leave to live in London,
And sing Masses there for simony,[1] for silver is sweet.

                         * * *

   Yet scores of men stood there in silken coifs
Who seemed to be law-sergeants[2] that served at the bar,
Pleaded cases for pennies and impounded[3] the law,
And not for love of our Lord once unloosed their lips:
215 You might better measure mist on Malvern Hills
Than get a "mum" from their mouths till money's on the table.
Barons and burgesses[4] and bondmen also
I saw in this assemblage, as you shall hear later;
Bakers and brewers and butchers aplenty.
220 Weavers of wool and weavers of linen,
Tailors, tinkers, tax-collectors in markets,
Masons, miners, many other craftsmen.
Of all living laborers there leapt forth some,

4. The "merchandise" sold by the friars for money is shrift, i.e., confession and remission of sins, which by canon law cannot be sold.
5. The ideal of the friars, as stated by St. Francis, was simply love, i.e., charity.
6. An official empowered to pass on from the pope temporal indulgence for the sins of people who contributed to charitable enterprises—a function frequently abused.
7. Papal license to act as a pardoner, endorsed with the local bishop's seals.
8. I.e., pulled the wool over their eyes. "Brevet": pardoner's license.
9. Since 1349 England had suffered a number of epidemics of the plague, the Black Death, which had caused famine and depopulated the countryside.

1. Buying and selling the functions, spiritual powers, or offices of the church. Wealthy persons, especially in London, set up foundations to pay priests to sing masses for their souls and those of their relatives (see the portrait of Chaucer's Parson, pp. 255–56, lines 479–530).
2. Important lawyers (see The General Prologue to The Canterbury Tales, p. 251, lines 311ff.). "Coifs": a silk scarf was a lawyer's badge of office.
3. Detained in legal custody. Pennies were fairly valuable coins in medieval England.
4. Town dwellers who had full rights as the citizens of a municipality. In contrast, barons were members of the upper nobility, and bondmen were peasants who held their land from a lord in return for customary services or rent.

Such as diggers of ditches that do their jobs badly,
225 And dawdle away the long day with *"Dieu save dame Emme."*[5]
Cooks and their kitchen-boys crying, "Hot pies, hot!
Good geese and pork! Let's go and dine!"
Tavern-keepers told them a tale of the same sort:
"White wine of Alsace and wine of Gascony,
230 Of the Rhine and of La Rochelle, to wash the roast down with."
All this I saw sleeping, and seven times more.

Passus 1

[THE TREASURE OF TRUTH]

What this mountain means, and the murky dale,
And the field full of folk I shall clearly tell you.
A lady lovely of look, in linen clothes,
Came down from the castle and called me gently,
5 And said, "Son, are you asleep? Do you see these people,
How busy they're being about the maze?
The greatest part of the people that pass over this earth,
If they have well-being in this world, they want nothing more:
For any heaven other than here they have no thought."
10 I was afraid of her face, fair though she was,
And said, "Mercy, madam, what may this mean?"
"The tower on the hill-top," she said, "Truth[6] is within it,
And would have you behave as his words teach.
For he is father of faith, formed you all
15 Both with skin and with skull, and assigned you five senses
To worship him with while you are here.
And therefore he ordered the earth to help each one of you
With woolens, with linens, with livelihood at need,
In a moderate manner to make you at ease;
20 And of his kindness declared three things common to all:
None are necessary but these, and now I will name them
And rank them in their right order—you repeat them after.
The first is vesture to defend you from the cold;
The second is food at fit times to fend off hunger,
25 And drink when you're dry—but don't drink beyond reason
Or you will be the worse for it when you've work to do.
For Lot in his lifetime because he liked drink
Did with his daughters what the Devil found pleasing,
Took delight in drink as the Devil wished,
30 And lechery laid hold on him and he lay with them both,
Blamed it all on the wine's working, that wicked deed.
> *Let us make him drunk with wine, and let us lie with him,*
> *that we may preserve seed of our father.*[7]
By wine and by women there Lot was overcome
And there begot in gluttony graceless brats.

---

5. "God save Dame Emma," presumably a popular song.
6. Langland plays on three meanings of the term "Truth": (1) fidelity, integrity—as in modern "troth"; (2) reality, actuality, conformity with what is; (3) God, the ultimate truth; see Headnote.
7. Genesis 19.32.

Therefore dread delicious drink and you'll do the better:
35 Moderation is medicine no matter how you yearn.
It's not all good for your ghost[8] that your gut wants
Nor of benefit to your body that's a blessing to your soul.
Don't believe your body for it does the bidding of a liar:
That is this wretched world that wants to betray you;
40 For the Fiend and your flesh both conform to it,
And that besmirches your soul: set this in your heart,
And so that you should yourself be wary I'm giving this advice."
    "Ah, madam, mercy," said I, "your words much please me.
But the money minted on earth that men are so greedy for,
45 Tell me to whom that treasure belongs?"
"Go to the Gospel," she said, "that God himself spoke
When the people approached him with a penny in the temple
And asked whether they should worship[9] with it Caesar the king.
And he asked them to whom the inscription referred
50 'And the image also that is on the coin?'
'Caesaris,'[1] they said, 'we can all see it clearly.'
'Reddite Caesari,' said God, 'what Caesari belongs,[2]
And quae sunt Dei Deo, or else you do wrong.'
For rightfully Reason[3] should rule you all,
55 And Kind Wit be keeper to take care of your wealth
And be guardian of your gold to give it out when you need it,
For economy[4] and he are of one accord."
    Then I questioned her courteously, in the Creator's name,
"The dungeon in the dale that's dreadful to see,
60 What may it mean, madam, I beseech you?"
"That is the Castle of Care: whoever comes into it
Will be sorry he was ever born with body and soul.
The captain of the castle is called Wrong,
Father of falsehood, he founded it himself.
65 Adam and Eve he egged to evil,
Counseled Cain to kill his brother;
He made a joke out of Judas with Jewish silver,[5]
And afterwards on an elder tree hanged him high.
He's a molester of love, lies to every one;
70 Those who trust in his treasure are betrayed soonest."
    Then I wondered in my wits what woman it might be
Who could show from Holy Scripture such wise words,
And I conjured her in the high name, ere she went away,
To say who she really was that taught me so well.
75 "I am Holy Church," she said, "you ought to know me:
I befriended you first and taught the faith to you.

8. Spirit.
9. "Worship" in Middle English often means religious celebration, but the worship of God is only one instance of showing the appropriate honor and respect to someone or something; the word can therefore be used about objects other than God.
1. Caesar's.
2. "Render unto Caesar"; "to Caesar." In the next line the Latin clause means "What are God's unto God." See Matthew 22.15–21.
3. Langland distinguishes the role of reason, as

the distinctive human capacity to reach truth by discursive reasoning, from the functions of a number of other related mental processes and sources of truth, e.g., Kind Wit (next line): natural intelligence, common sense.
4. I.e., prudent management.
5. For the fall of Adam and Eve, see Genesis 3; for Cain's murder of Abel, see Genesis 4. In the next lines, for Judas's betrayal of Jesus, see Matthew 26.14–16; for his death (line 68), see Matthew 27.3–6.

You gave me gages[6] to be guided by my teaching
And to love me loyally while your life lasts."
Then kneeling on my knees I renewed my plea for grace,
80   Prayed piteously to her to pray for my sins,
And advise me how I might find natural faith[7] in Christ,
That I might obey the command of him who made me man.
"Teach me of no treasure, but tell me this one thing,
How I may save my soul, sacred as you are?"
85   "When all treasures are tried, Truth is the best.
I call on *Deus caritas*[8] to declare the truth.
It's as glorious a love-gift as dear God himself.
For whoever is true of his tongue, tells nothing untrue,
Does his work with truth, wishes no man ill,
90   He is a god by the Gospel, on ground and aloft.
And also like our Lord by Saint Luke's words.[9]
Clerks who've been taught this text should tell it all about,
For Christians and non-Christians lay claim to it both.
To keep truth kings and knights are required by reason,
95   And to ride out in realms about and beat down wrong-doers,
Take *transgressores*[1] and tie them up tight
Until Truth has determined their trespass in full.
For David in his days when he dubbed knights[2]
Made them swear on their swords to serve Truth forever.
100   That is plainly the profession that's appropriate for knights,
And not to fast one Friday in five score winters,
But to hold with him and with her who ask for truth,
And never leave them for love nor through a liking for presents,
And whoever passes that point is an apostate to his order.
105   For Christ, King of Kings, created ten orders,[3]
Cherubim and seraphim, seven such and another.
Gave them might in his majesty—the merrier they thought it—
And over his household he made them archangels,
Taught them through the Trinity how Truth may be known,
110   And to be obedient to his bidding—he bade nothing else.
Lucifer with his legions learned this in Heaven,
And he was the loveliest of light after our Lord
Till he broke obedience—his bliss was lost to him
And he fell from that fellowship in a fiend's likeness
115   Into a deep dark hell, to dwell there forever,
And more thousands went out with him than any one could count,
Leaping out with Lucifer in loathly shapes,
Because they believed Lucifer who lied in this way:
I shall set my foot in the north and I shall be like the most high.[4]

6. I.e., pledges (at baptism).
7. The Middle English phrase is "kynde knowynge."
8. "God [is] love": 1 John 4.8.
9. Not Luke, but see 1 John 4.16 and cf. Psalms 81.6. The phrase "a god by the Gospel" is Langland's; what he means by it will be a recurrent theme.
1. Transgressors: the Latin word appears at Isaiah 53.12.
2. Behind the idea that King David created knighthood probably lies his selection of officers for his army (1 Chronicles 12.18) translated into chivalric terms; like other heroes, he was typically portrayed in the Middle Ages as a chivalric figure, just as God's creation of the angels, below, is pictured in terms of a medieval aristocratic household.
3. I.e., ten orders of heavenly beings; seraphim, cherubim, thrones, dominions, virtues, powers, principalities, archangels, angels, and the nameless order that fell with Lucifer.
4. Cf. Isaiah 14.13–14, which has "throne" (*sedem*) where Langland has "foot" (*pedem*).

120 And all that hoped it might be so, no Heaven could hold them,
But they fell out in fiend's likeness fully nine days together,
Till God of his goodness granted that Heaven settle,
Become stationary and stable, and stand in quiet.
When these wicked ones went out they fell in wondrous wise,
125 Some in air, some on earth, some deep in hell,
But Lucifer lies lowest of them all.
For pride that puffed him up his pain has no end.
And all that work with wrong will surely make their way
After their death-day to dwell with that wretch.
130 But those who wish to work well, as holy words direct,
And who end, as I said earlier, in Truth that is the best
May be certain that their souls will ascend to Heaven
Where Truth is in Trinity, bestowing thrones on all who come.
Therefore I say as I said before, by the sense of these texts
135 When all treasures are tried, Truth is the best.
Let unlearned men be taught this, for learned men know it,
That Truth is the trustiest treasure on earth."
   "Yet I've no natural knowledge,"[5] said I, "you must teach me more
      clearly
Through what force faith is formed in my body and where."
140 "You doting dolt," said she, "dull are your wits:
Too little Latin you learned, lad, in your youth.
   Alas, I repine for a barren youth was mine.[6]
It's a natural knowledge that's nurtured in your heart
To love your Lord more dearly than you love yourself,
To do no deadly sin though you should die for it.
145 This I trust is truth: whoever can teach you better,
Look to it that you let him speak, and learn it after.
For thus his word witnesses: do your work accordingly.
For Truth tells us that love is the trustiest medicine in Heaven.
No sin may be seen on him by whom that spice is used.
150 And all the deeds he pleased to do were done with love.
And he[7] taught it to Moses as a matchless thing, and most like Heaven,
And also the plant of peace, most precious of virtues.
For Heaven might not hold it,[8] so heavy it seemed,
Till it had with earth alloyed itself.
155 And when it had of this earth taken flesh and blood,
Never was leaf upon linden lighter thereafter,
And portable and piercing as the point of a needle:
No armor might obstruct it, nor any high walls.
Therefore Love is leader of the Lord's people in Heaven,
160 And an intermediary as the mayor is between community and king.
Just so Love is a leader by whom the law's enforced
Upon man for his misdeeds—he measures the fine.
And to know this naturally, it's nourished by a power
That has its head in the heart, and its high source.

---

5. Instinctive or experiential knowledge; Langland's phrase, a recurrent and important one, is
"kynde knowynge."
6. Proverbial.

7. I.e., Truth.
8. I.e., love, which, as the passage goes on,
becomes embodied in Christ.

165 For a natural knowledge in the heart is nourished by a power
That's let fall by the Father who formed us all,
Looked on us with love and let his son die
Meekly for our misdeeds, to amend us all.
Yet he[9] did not ask harm on those who hurt him so badly,
170 But with his mouth meekly made a prayer for mercy—
For pity for those people who so painfully killed him.
Here you may see examples in himself alone,
How he was mighty and meek, and bade mercy be granted
To those who hanged him high and pierced his heart.

* * *

Love is Life's doctor, and next[1] our Lord himself,
205 And also the strait[2] street that goes straight to Heaven.
Therefore I say as I said before, by the sense of these texts,
When all treasures are tried, Truth is the best.
Now that I've told you what Truth is—there's no treasure better—
I may delay no longer now: our Lord look after you."

From *Passus* 5

[PIERS PLOWMAN SHOWS THE WAY TO SAINT TRUTH]

Then Hope took hold of a horn of *Deus tu conversus vivificabis nos*[3]
And blew it with *Beati quorum remissae sunt iniquitates,*[4]
So that all the saints sang for sinners at once,
*"Men and animals thou shalt save inasmuch as thou hast multiplied thy
  mercy, O God."*[5]
510 A thousand men then thronged together,
Cried upward to Christ and to his clean mother
To have grace to go to Truth—God grant they might!
But there was no one so wise as to know the way thither,
But they blundered forth like beasts over banks and hills
515 Till they met a man, many hours later,
Appareled like a pagan[6] in pilgrims' manner.
He bore a stout staff with a broad strap around it,
In the way of woodbine wound all about.
A bowl and a bag he bore by his side.
520 A hundred holy water phials were set on his hat,
Souvenirs of Sinai and shells of Galicia,
And many a Cross on his cloak and keys of Rome,
And the vernicle in front so folk should know
By seeing his signs what shrines he'd been to.[7]

---

9. I.e., Christ, not the Father as in the sentence before. In such slippery transitions from one subject to another, Langland takes advantage of the greater flexibility of Middle English syntax; and usually, as here, the transition reflects an important connection of ideas, in this case the relationship between God's action and Christ's.
1. Next to.
2. I.e., narrow; see Matthew 7.13–14.
3. O God, you will turn and give us life (from the Mass).

4. Blessed [are they] whose transgressions are forgiven (Psalms 32.1).
5. Psalms 36.6–7.
6. I.e., outlandishly. (Langland's word *paynym* was especially associated with Saracens, i.e., Arabs.)
7. A pilgrim to Canterbury collected a phial of holy water from St. Thomas's shrine; collecting another every time one passed through Canterbury was a mark of a professional pilgrim. "Sinai": souvenirs from the Convent of St. Katharine on Sinai. "Shells": the emblem of St. James at Compostela,

525 These folk asked him fairly from whence he came.
"From Sinai," he said, "and from the Holy Sepulchre.
Bethlehem, Babylon, I've been to both;
In Armenia, in Alexandria,[8] in many other places.
You can tell by the tokens attached to my hat
530 That I've walked far and wide in wet and in dry
And sought out good saints for my soul's health."
"Did you ever see a saint," said they, "that men call Truth?
Could you point out a path to where that person lives?"
"No, so God save me," said the fellow then.
535 "I've never known a palmer with knapsack or staff
To ask after him ere now in this place."
    "Peter!"[9] said a plowman, and put forth his head.
"We're as closely acquainted as a clerk and his books.
Conscience and Kind Wit[1] coached me to his place
540 And persuaded me to swear to him I'd serve him forever,
Both to sow and set plants so long as I can work.
I have been his follower all these forty winters,
Both sowed his seed and overseen his cattle,
Indoors and outdoors taken heed for his profit,
545 Made ditches and dikes, done what he bids.
Sometimes I sow and sometimes I thresh,
In tailor's craft and tinker's, whatever Truth can devise.
I weave wool and wind it and do what Truth says.
For though I say it myself, I serve him to his satisfaction.
550 I get good pay from him, and now and again more.
He's the promptest payer that poor men know.
He withholds no worker's wages so he's without them by evening.
He's as lowly as a lamb and lovely of speech.
And if you'd like to learn where that lord dwells,
555 I'll direct you on the road right to his palace."
"Yes, friend Piers,"[2] said these pilgrims, and proffered him pay.
"No, by the peril of my soul!" said Piers, and swore on oath:
"I wouldn't take a farthing's fee for Saint Thomas's shrine.[3]
Truth would love me the less a long time after.
560   But you that are anxious to be off, here's how you go:
You must go through Meekness, both men and women,
Till you come into Consciences[4] that Christ knows the truth
That you love our Lord God of all loves the most,
And next to him your neighbors—in no way harm them,
565 Otherwise than you'd have them behave to you.

And so follow along a brook's bank, Be-Modest-Of-Speech,
Until you find a ford, Do-Your-Fathers-Honor;
   Honor thy father and thy mother, etc.[5]
Wade in that water and wash yourselves well there
And you'll leap the lighter all your lifetime.
570   So you shall see Swear-Not-Unless-It-Is-For-Need-
And-Namely-Never-Take-In-Vain-The-Name-Of-God-Amighty.
Then you'll come to a croft,[6] but don't come into it:
The croft is called Covet-Not-Men's-Cattle-Nor-Their-Wives
And-None-Of-Your-Neighbor's-Serving-Men-So-As-To-Harm-Them.
575   See that you break no boughs there unless they belong to you.
Two wooden statues stand there, but don't stop for them:
They're called Steal-Not and Slay-Not: stay away from both;
Leave them on your left hand and don't look back.
And hold well your holiday until the high evening.[7]
580   Then you shall blench at a barrow,[8] Bear-No-False-Witness:
It's fenced in with florins and other fees aplenty.
See that you pluck no plant there for peril of your soul.
Then you shall see Speak-The-Truth-So-It-Must-Be-Done-
And-Not-In-Any-Other-Way-Not-For-Any-Man's-Asking.
585   Then you shall come to a castle shining clear as the sun.
The moat is made of mercy, all about the manor;
And all the walls are of wit° to hold will out.   *reason*
The crenelations° are of Christendom to save Christiankind,   *battlements*
Buttressed with Believe-So-Or-You-Won't-Be-Saved;
590   And all the houses are roofed, halls and chambers,
Not with lead but with Love-And-Lowness-As-Brothers-Of-One-
     Womb.
The bridge is of Pray-Properly-You-Will-Prosper-The-More.
Every pillar is of penance, of prayers to saints;
The hooks are of almsdeeds that the gates are hanging on.
595   The gate-keeper's name is Grace, a good man indeed;
His man is called Amend-Yourself, for he knows many men.
Say this sentence to him: 'Truth sees what's true;
I performed the penance the priest gave me to do
And I'm sorry for my sins and shall be so always
600   When I think thereon, though I were a pope.'
Pray Amend-Yourself mildly to ask his master once
To open wide the wicket-gate that the woman shut
When Adam and Eve ate unroasted apples.
   Through Eve it was closed to all and through the Virgin
     Mary it was opened again.[9]
605   For he keeps the latchkey though the king sleep.
And if Grace grants you to go in in this way
You shall see in yourself Truth sitting in your heart

5. Exodus 20.12. Beginning in lines 563–64 with the two "great" commandments (Matthew 22.37–39), Piers's directions include most of the commandments of Exodus 20.
6. A small enclosed field, or a small agricultural holding worked by a tenant.
7. A holiday (i.e., a holy day) lasted until sunset ("high evening"); it was not supposed to be used for work, and drinking and games were forbidden, at least until after attendance at church services.
8. A low hillock or a burial mound.
9. From a service commemorating the Virgin Mary.

In a chain of charity as though you were a child again,[1]
To suffer your sire's will and say nothing against it."

* * *

630   "By Christ," cried a pickpocket, "I have no kin there."
"Nor I," said an ape-trainer, "for anything I know."
"God knows," said a cake-seller, "if I were sure of this,
I wouldn't go a foot further for any friar's preaching."
"Yes!" said Piers Plowman, and prodded him for his good.
635   "Mercy is a maiden there that has dominion over them all,
And she is sib to all sinners, and her son as well,
And through the help of these two—think nothing else—
You might get grace there if you go in time."
"By Saint Paul!" said a pardoner, "possibly I'm not known there;
640   I'll go fetch my box with my brevets and a bull with bishop's letters."
"By Christ!" said a common woman,[2] "I'll keep you company.
You shall say I am your sister." I don't know what became of them.

Passus 6

[THE PLOWING OF PIERS'S HALF-ACRE]

  "This would be a bewildering way unless we had a guide
Who could trace our way foot by foot": thus these folk complained.
Said Perkin[3] the Plowman, "By Saint Peter of Rome!
I have a half-acre to plow by the highway;
5   If I had plowed this half-acre and afterwards sowed it,
I would walk along with you and show you the way to go."
"That would be a long delay," said a lady in a veil.
"What ought we women to work at meanwhile?"
"Some shall sew sacks to stop the wheat from spilling.
10   And you lovely ladies, with your long fingers,
See that you have silk and sendal to sew when you've time
Chasubles[4] for chaplains for the Church's honor.
Wives and widows, spin wool and flax;
Make cloth, I counsel you, and teach the craft to your daughters.
15   The needy and the naked, take note how they fare:
Keep them from cold with clothing, for so Truth wishes.
For I shall supply their sustenance unless the soil fails
As long as I live, for the Lord's love in Heaven.
And all sorts of folk that feed on farm products,
20   Busily abet him who brings forth your food."
  "By Christ!" exclaimed a knight then, "your counsel is the best.
But truly, how to drive a team has never been taught me.
But show me," said the knight, "and I shall study plowing."

1. Cf. Mark 10.15: "whosoever shall not receive the kingdom of God as a little child, he shall not enter therein." This childlike quality is here envisaged as total submissiveness (line 608). "In a chain of charity": either Truth is bound by (that is, constrained by) *caritas* (love) or Truth is enthroned, adorned with *caritas* like a chain of office.
2. Prostitute. "Brevets": pardoner's credentials.
3. A nickname for Piers, or Peter.
4. Garments worn by priests to celebrate Mass. "Sendal": a thin, rich form of silk.

"By Saint Paul," said Perkin, "since you proffer help so humbly,
25   I shall sweat and strain and sow for us both,
And also labor for your love all my lifetime,
In exchange for your championing Holy Church and me
Against wasters and wicked men who would destroy me.
And go hunt hardily hares and foxes,
30   Boars and bucks that break down my hedges,
And have falcons at hand to hunt down the birds
That come to my croft° and crop my wheat."   *small enclosed field*
Thoughtfully the knight then spoke these words:
"By my power, Piers, I pledge you my word
35   To uphold this obligation though I have to fight.
As long as I live I shall look after you."
"Yes, and yet another point," said Piers, "I pray you further:
See that you trouble no tenant unless Truth approves,
And though you may amerce[5] him, let Mercy set the fine,
40   And Meekness be your master no matter what Meed° does.   *bribery*
And though poor men proffer you presents and gifts,
Don't accept them for it's uncertain that you deserve to have them.
For at some set time you'll have to restore them
In a most perilous place called purgatory.
45   And treat no bondman badly—you'll be the better for it;
Though here he is your underling, it could happen in Heaven
That he'll be awarded a worthier place, one with more bliss:
    Friend, go up higher.[6]
For in the charnelhouse[7] at church churls are hard to distinguish,
Or a knight from a knave: know this in your heart.
50   And see that you're true of your tongue, and as for tales—hate them
Unless they have wisdom and wit for your workmen's instruction.
Avoid foul-mouthed fellows and don't be friendly to their stories,
And especially at your repasts shun people like them,
For they tell the Fiend's fables—be very sure of that."
55   "I assent, by Saint James," said the knight then,
"To work by your word while my life lasts."
"And I shall apparel myself," said Perkin, "in pilgrims' fashion
And walk along the way with you till we find Truth."
He donned his working-dress, some darned, some whole,
60   His gaiters and his gloves to guard his limbs from cold,
And hung his seed-holder behind his back instead of a knapsack:
"Bring a bushel of bread-wheat for me to put in it,
For I shall sow it myself and set out afterwards
On a pilgrimage as palmers do to procure pardon.
65   And whoever helps me plow or work in any way
Shall have leave, by our Lord, to glean my land in harvest-time,
And make merry with what he gets, no matter who grumbles.
And all kinds of craftsmen that can live in truth,
I shall provide food for those that faithfully live,
70   Except for Jack the juggler and Jonette from the brothel,
And Daniel the dice-player and Denot the pimp,

---

5. Punish with a fine the amount of which is at the discretion of the judge.
6. Luke 14.10.

7. A house for dead bodies connected to a church graveyard.

And Friar Faker and folk of his order,
And Robin the ribald for his rotten speech.
Truth told me once and bade me tell it abroad:
75 *Deleantur de libro viventium:*[8] I should have no dealings with them,
For Holy Church is under orders to ask no tithes[9] of them.
    For let them not be written with the righteous.[1]
Their good luck has left them, the Lord amend them now."
    Dame-Work-When-It's-Time-To was Piers's wife's name;
His daughter was called Do-Just-So-Or-Your-Dame-Will-Beat-You;
80 His son was named Suffer-Your-Sovereigns-To-Have-Their-Will-
Condemn-Them-Not-For-If-You-Do-You'll-Pay-A-Dear-Price-
Let-God-Have-His-Way-With-All-Things-For-So-His-Word-Teaches.
"For now I am old and hoary and have something of my own,
To penance and to pilgrimage I'll depart with these others;
85 Therefore I will, before I go away, have my will written:
'*In Dei nomine, amen,*[2] I make this myself.
He shall have my soul that has deserved it best,
And defend it from the Fiend—for so I believe—
Till I come to his accounting, as my Creed teaches me—
90 To have release and remission I trust in his rent book.
The kirk° shall have my corpse and keep my bones,   *church*
For of my corn and cattle it craved the tithe:
I paid it promptly for peril of my soul;
It is obligated, I hope, to have me in mind
95 And commemorate me in its prayers among all Christians.
My wife shall have what I won with truth, and nothing else,
And parcel it out among my friends and my dear children.
For though I die today, my debts are paid;
I took back what I borrowed before I went to bed.'
100 As for the residue and the remnant, by the Rood of Lucca,[3]
I will worship Truth with it all my lifetime,
And be his pilgrim at the plow for poor men's sake.
My plowstaff shall be my pikestaff and push at the roots
And help my coulter to cut and cleanse the farrows."
105   Now Perkin and the pilgrims have put themselves to plowing.
Many there helped him to plow his half-acre.
Ditchers and diggers dug up the ridges;
Perkin was pleased by this and praised them warmly.
There were other workmen who worked very hard:
110 Each man in his manner made himself a laborer,
And some to please Perkin pulled up the weeds.
At high prime[4] Piers let the plow stand
To oversee them himself; whoever worked best

8. Let them be blotted out of the book of the living (Psalms 69.28).
9. Because the money they make is not legitimate income or increase derived from the earth; therefore, they do not owe the tithes, or 10 percent taxes, due the church.
1. Psalms 69.28.
2. "In the name of God, amen," customary beginning of a will.
3. An ornate crucifix at Lucca in Italy was a popular object of pilgrimage. "Residue and remnant":

land had to be left to one's natural heirs, although up to one-third of personal property (the "residue and remnant") could be left to the church for Masses for the testator or other purposes; the other two-thirds had to go to the family, one to the widow and the other to the children. Piers's arrangements seem to leave the wife considerably more latitude.
4. 9 A.M., or after a substantial part of the day's work has been done, because laborers start so early.

Should be hired afterward, when harvest-time came.
115 Then some sat down and sang over ale
And helped plow the half-acre with "Ho! trolly-lolly!"[5]
"Now by the peril of my soul!" said Piers in pure wrath,
"Unless you get up again and begin working now,
No grain that grows here will gladden you at need,
120 And though once off the dole you die let the Devil care!"
Then fakers were afraid and feigned to be blind;
Some set their legs askew as such loafers can
And made their moan to Piers, how they might not work:
"We have no limbs to labor with, Lord, we thank you;
125 But we pray for you, Piers, and for your plow as well,
That God of his grace make your grain multiply,
And reward you for whatever alms you will give us here,
For we can't strain and sweat, such sickness afflicts us."
    "If what you say is so," said Piers, "I'll soon find out.
130 I know you're ne'er-do-wells, and Truth knows what's right,
And I'm his sworn servant and so should warn him
Which ones they are in this world that do his workmen harm.
You waste what men win with toil and trouble.
But Truth shall teach you how his team should be driven,
135 Or you'll eat barley bread and use the brook for drink;
Unless you're blind or broken-legged, or bolted° with iron—   *braced*
Those shall eat as well as I do, so God help me,
Till God of his goodness gives them strength to arise.
But you could work as Truth wants you to and earn wages and bread
140 By keeping cows in the field, the corn from the cattle,
Making ditches or dikes or dinging on sheaves,
Or helping make mortar, or spreading muck afield.
You live in lies and lechery and in sloth too,
And it's only for suffrance that vengeance has not fallen on you.
145 But anchorites and hermits that eat only at noon
And nothing more before the morrow, they shall have my alms,
And buy copes[6] at my cost—those that have cloisters and churches.
But Robert Runabout shall have no rag from me,
Nor 'Apostles' unless they can preach and have the bishop's
        permission.
150 They shall have bread and boiled greens and a bit extra besides,
For it's an unreasonable religious life that has no regular meals."
    Then Waster waxed angry and wanted to fight;
To Piers the Plowman he proffered his glove.
A Breton, a braggart, he bullied Piers too,
155 And told him to go piss with his plow, peevish wretch.
"Whether you're willing or unwilling, we will have our will
With your flour and your flesh, fetch it when we please,
And make merry with it, no matter what you do."
Then Piers the Plowman complained to the knight
160 To keep him safe, as their covenant was, from cursed rogues,
"And from these wolfish wasters that lay waste the world,

5. Presumably the refrain of a popular song (note similarly musical loafers in the *Prologue*, lines 224–25).
6. Capes that signify religious callings.

For they waste and win nothing, and there will never be
Plenty among the people while my plow stands idle."
Because he was born a courteous man the knight spoke kindly to
    Waster
165 And warned him he would have to behave himself better:
"Or you'll pay the penalty at law, I promise, by my order!"
"It's not my way to work," said Waster, "I won't begin now!"
And made light of the law and lighter of the knight,
And said Piers wasn't worth a pea or his plow either,
170 And menaced him and his men if they met again.
    "Now by the peril of my soul!" said Piers, "I'll punish you all."
And he whooped after Hunger who heard him at once.
"Avenge me on these vagabonds," said he, "that vex the whole world."
Then Hunger in haste took hold of Waster by the belly
175 And gripped him so about the guts that his eyes gushed water.
He buffeted the Breton about the cheeks
That he looked like a lantern all his life after.
He beat them both so that he almost broke their guts.
Had not Piers with a pease loaf[7] prayed him to leave off
180 They'd have been dead and buried deep, have no doubt about it.
"Let them live," he said, "and let them feed with hogs,
Or else on beans and bran baked together."
Fakers for fear fled into barns
And flogged sheaves with flails from morning till evening,
185 So that Hunger wouldn't be eager to cast his eye on them.
For a potful of peas that Piers had cooked
A heap of hermits laid hands on spades
And cut off their copes and made short coats of them
And went like workmen to weed and to mow,
190 And dug dirt and dung to drive off Hunger.
Blind and bedridden got better by the thousand;
Those who sat to beg silver were soon healed,
For what had been baked for Bayard[8] was boon to many hungry,
And many a beggar for beans obediently labored,
195 And every poor man was well pleased to have peas for his wages,
And what Piers prayed them to do they did as sprightly as
    sparrowhawks.
And Piers was proud of this and put them to work,
And gave them meals and money as they might deserve.
    Then Piers had pity and prayed Hunger to take his way
200 Off to his own home and hold there forever.
"I'm well avenged on vagabonds by virtue of you.
But I pray you, before you part," said Piers to Hunger,
"With beggars and street-beadsmen[9] what's best to be done?
For well I know that once you're away, they will work badly;
205 Misfortune makes them so meek now,
And it's for lack of food that these folk obey me.
And they're my blood brothers, for God bought° us all.   *redeemed*

---

7. The cheapest and coarsest grade of bread, the food of those who cannot get better.
8. Generic name for a horse; a bread made of beans and bran, the coarsest category of bread, was used to feed horses and hounds, but was eaten by people when need was great.
9. Paid prayer sayers.

Truth taught me once to love them every one
And help them with everything after their needs.
210 Now I'd like to learn, if you know, what line I should take
And how I might overmaster them and make them work."
"Hear now," said Hunger, "and hold it for wisdom:
Big bold beggars that can earn their bread,
With hounds' bread and horses' bread hold up their hearts,
215 And keep their bellies from swelling by stuffing them with beans—
And if they begin to grumble, tell them to get to work,
And they'll have sweeter suppers once they've deserved them.
And if you find any fellow-man that fortune has harmed
Through fire or through false men, befriend him if you can.
220 Comfort such at your own cost, for the love of Christ in Heaven;
Love them and relieve them—so the law of Kind° directs.   *Nature*
    Bear ye one another's burdens[1]
And all manner of men that you may find
That are needy or naked and have nothing to spend,
With meals or with money make them the better.
225 Love them and don't malign them; let God take vengeance.
Though they behave ill, leave it all up to God
    Vengeance is mine and I will repay.[2]
And if you want to gratify God, do as the Gospel teaches,
And get yourself loved by lowly men: so you'll unloose his grace."
    Make to yourselves friends of the mammon of unrighteousness.[3]
    "I would not grieve God," said Piers, "for all the goods on earth!
230 Might I do as you say without sin?" said Piers then.
"Yes, I give you my oath," said Hunger, "or else the Bible lies:
Go to Genesis the giant, engenderer of us all:[4]
In sudore[5] and slaving you shall bring forth your food
And labor for your livelihood, and so our Lord commanded.
235 And Sapience says the same—I saw it in the Bible.
Piger propter frigus[6] would plow no field;
He shall be a beggar and none abate his hunger.
Matthew with man's face[7] mouths these words:
'Entrusted with a talent, *servus nequam*[8] didn't try to use it,
240 And earned his master's ill-will for evermore after,
And he took away his talent who was too lazy to work,
And gave it to him in haste that had ten already;
And after he said so that his servants heard it,
He that has shall have, and help when he needs it,
245 And he that nothing has shall nothing have and no man help him,
And what he trusts he's entitled to I shall take away.'
Kind Wit wants each one to work,

---

1. Galatians 6.2.
2. Romans 12.19.
3. Luke 16.9.
4. This puzzling epithet has been explained on the grounds that Genesis is the longest book (except for Psalms) in the Bible and that it recounts the creation of humankind.
5. In the sweat [of thy face shalt thou eat bread] (Genesis 3.19).
6. The sluggard [will not plow] by reason of the cold (Proverbs 20.4). "Sapience": the biblical

"Wisdom Books" attributed to Solomon.
7. Each of the four Evangelists had his traditional pictorial image, derived partly from the faces of the four creatures in Ezekiel's vision (Ezekiel 1.5–12) and partly from those of the four beasts of the Apocalypse (Revelation 4.7): Matthew was represented as a winged man; Mark, a lion; Luke, a winged ox; and John, an eagle.
8. The wicked servant (Luke 19.22; see 17–27). "Talent": a unit of money.

Either in teaching or tallying or toiling with his hands,
Contemplative life or active life; Christ wants it too.
250 The Psalter says in the Psalm of *Beati omnes*,[9]
The fellow that feeds himself with his faithful labor,
He is blessed by the Book in body and in soul."
  The labors of thy hands, etc.[1]
  "Yet I pray you," said Piers, "*pour charité,*° if you know   for charity
Any modicum of medicine, teach me it, dear sir.
255 For some of my servants and myself as well
For a whole week do no work, we've such aches in our stomachs."
"I'm certain," said Hunger, "what sickness ails you.
You've munched down too much: that's what makes you groan,
But I assure you," said Hunger, "if you'd preserve your health,
260 You must not drink any day before you've dined on something.
Never eat, I urge you, ere Hunger comes upon you
And sends you some of his sauce to add savor to the food;
And keep some till suppertime, and don't sit too long;
Arise up ere Appetite has eaten his fill.
265 Let not Sir Surfeit sit at your table;
Love him not for he's a lecher whose delight is his tongue,
And for all sorts of seasoned stuff his stomach yearns.
And if you adopt this diet, I dare bet my arms
That Physic for his food will sell his furred hood
270 And his Calabrian[2] cloak with its clasps of gold,
And be content, by my troth, to retire from medicine
And learn to labor on the land lest livelihood fail him.
There are fewer physicians than frauds—reform them, Lord!—
Their drinks make men die before destiny ordains."
275 "By Saint Parnel,"[3] said Piers, "these are profitable words.
This is a lovely lesson; the Lord reward you for it!
Take your way when you will—may things be well with you always!"
  "My oath to God!" said Hunger, "I will not go away
Till I've dined this day and drunk as well."
280 "I've no penny," said Piers, "to purchase pullets,
And I can't get goose or pork; but I've got two green cheeses,
A few curds and cream and a cake of oatmeal,
A loaf of beans and bran baked for my children.
And yet I say, by my soul, I have no salt bacon
285 Nor any hen's egg, by Christ, to make ham and eggs,
But scallions aren't scarce, nor parsley, and I've scores of cabbages,
And also a cow and a calf, and a cart-mare
To draw dung to the field while the dry weather lasts.
By this livelihood I must live till Lammass[4] time
290 When I hope to have harvest in my garden.
  Then I can manage a meal that will make you happy."
  All the poor people fetched peasepods;[5]

9. Blessed [are] all [who] (Psalms 128.1).
1. Psalms 128.2. Thou shalt eat the labor of thine hands: happy shalt thou be, and it shall be well with thee.
2. Of gray fur (a special imported squirrel fur).
3. Who St. Pernelle was is obscure; other manuscripts and editions read "By Saint Paul."

4. The harvest festival, August 1 (the name derived from Old English *hlaf*, "loaf"), when a loaf made from the first wheat of the season was offered at Mass.
5. Peas in the pod. These, like most foods in the next lines, are early crops.

Beans and baked apples they brought in their skirts,
Chives and chervils and ripe cherries aplenty,
295 And offered Piers this present to please Hunger with.
Hunger ate this in haste and asked for more.
Then poor folk for fear fed Hunger fast,
Proffering leeks and peas, thinking to appease him.
And now harvest drew near and new grain came to market.[6]
300 Then poor people were pleased and plied Hunger with the best;
With good ale as Glutton taught they got him to sleep.
Then Waster wouldn't work but wandered about,
And no beggar would eat bread that had beans in it,
But the best bread or the next best, or baked from pure wheat,
305 Nor drink any half-penny ale[7] in any circumstances,
But of the best and the brownest that barmaids sell.
Laborers that have no land to live on but their hands
Deign not to dine today on last night's cabbage.
No penny-ale can please them, nor any piece of bacon,
310 But it must be fresh flesh or else fried fish,
And that *chaud* or *plus chaud*[8] so it won't chill their bellies.
Unless he's hired at high wages he will otherwise complain;
That he was born to be a workman he'll blame the time.
Against Cato's counsel he commences to murmur:
315 *Remember to bear your burden of poverty patiently.*[9]
He grows angry at God and grumbles against Reason,
And then curses the king and all the council after
Because they legislate laws that punish laboring men.[1]
But while Hunger was their master there would none of them
       complain
320 Or strive against the statute,[2] so sternly he looked.
But I warn you workmen, earn wages while you may,
For Hunger is hurrying hitherward fast.
With waters he'll awaken Waster's chastisement;
Before five years are fulfilled such famine shall arise.
325 Through flood and foul weather fruits shall fail,
And so Saturn[3] says and has sent to warn you:
When you see the moon amiss and two monks' heads,
And a maid have the mastery, and multiply by eight,[4]
Then shall Death withdraw and Dearth be justice,
330 And Daw the diker[5] die for hunger,
Unless God of his goodness grants us a truce.

---

6. Presumably as the new harvest approaches, merchants who have been holding grain for the highest prices release it for sale, because prices are about to tumble.
7. Weak ale diluted with water; in line 309, laborers are too fussy and will no longer accept even penny ale.
8. "Hot" or "very hot."
9. From Cato's *Distichs*, a collection of pithy phrases used to teach Latin to beginning students.
1. Like so many governments, late-14th-century England responded to inflation and the bargaining power of the relatively scarce laborers with wage and price freezes, which had their usual lack of effect. One way landowners, desperate to obtain enough laborers, tried to get around the wage laws was by offering food as well as cash.
2. I.e., anti-inflationary legislation.
3. Planet thought to influence the weather, generally perceived as hostile.
4. This cryptic prophecy has never been satisfactorily explained; the basic point is that it is Apocalyptic.
5. A laborer who digs dikes and ditches.

Passus 7

[PIERS TEARS TRUTH'S PARDON]

Truth heard tell of this and sent word to Piers
To take his team and till the earth,
And procured him a pardon *a poena et a culpa*,[6]
For him and for his heirs for evermore after;
5 And bade him hold at home and plow his land,
And any one who helped him plow or sow,
Or any kind of craft that could help Piers,
Pardon with Piers Plowman Truth has granted.

✳ ✳ ✳

"Piers," said a priest then, "your pardon must I read,
For I'll explain each paragraph to you and put it in English."
And Piers unfolds the pardon at the priest's prayer,
110 And I behind them both beheld all the bull.[7]
In two lines it lay, and not a letter more,
And was worded this way in witness of truth:
They that have done good shall go into life everlasting;
And they that have done evil into everlasting fire.[8]
115 "Peter!" said the priest then, "I can find no pardon here—
Only 'Do well, and have well,' and God will have your soul,
And 'Do evil, and have evil,' and hope nothing else
But that after your death-day the Devil will have your soul."
And Piers for pure wrath pulled it in two
120 And said, *"Though I walk in the midst of the shadow of death*
I will fear no evil; for thou art with me.[9]
I shall cease my sowing and not work so hard,
Nor be henceforth so busy about my livelihood.
My plow shall be of penance and of prayers hereafter,
125 And I'll weep when I should work, though wheat bread fails me.
The prophet[1] ate his portion in penance and sorrow
As the Psalter says, and so did many others.
Who loves God loyally, his livelihood comes easy.
    My tears have been my bread day and night.[2]
And unless Luke lies, he finds another lesson for us
130 In birds that are not busy about their belly-joy:
'Ne soliciti sitis,'[3] he says in the Gospel,
And shows us examples by which to school ourselves.

---

6. This pardon has remained one of the most controversial elements of the poem. "From punishment and from guilt" is a formula indicating an absolute pardon. Strictly speaking, remissions obtained by pilgrimages (and pardons dispensed by pardoners in return for donations) could remit only the *punishment* for sin; note that even Truth's pardon does both only for some people. Christ alone, through the Atonement, had the power to absolve repentant sinners from the *guilt* and delegated it to St. Peter and to the Church through the apostolic succession to be dispensed in the sacrament of confession and in penance. (This pardon also covers, according to another legal formula in the next line, Piers's heirs, which ordinary pardons could not.) The belief, however, that indulgences (especially those obtained from the pope himself) absolved guilt as well as punishment was widespread.
7. A document issued by the pope and sealed with his *bulla*, or seal.
8. From the Athanasian Creed, based on Matthew 25.31–46.
9. Psalms 23.4.
1. David, whose Psalm is quoted below:
2. Psalms 42.3.
3. "Take no thought [for your life]": Matthew 6.25; also Luke 12.22.

The fowls in the firmament, who feeds them in winter?
When the frost freezes they forage for food,
135 They have no granary to go to, but God feeds them all."
"What!" said the priest to Perkin, "Peter, it would seem
You are lettered a little. Who lessoned you in books?"
"Abstinence the abbess taught me my a b c,
And Conscience came after and counseled me better."
140 "If you were a priest, Piers," said he, "you might preach when you
     pleased
As a doctor of divinity, with *Dixit insipiens*,[4] as your text."
"Unlearned lout!" said Piers, "you know little of the Bible;
Solomon's sayings are seldom your reading."
    *Cast out the scorners and contentions with them, lest they
     increase.*[5]
    The priest and Perkin opposed each other,
145 And through their words I awoke and looked everywhere about,
And saw the sun sit due south at that time.
Meatless and moneyless on Malvern Hills,
Musing on my dream, I walked a mile-way.

From *The C-Text*

[THE DREAMER MEETS CONSCIENCE AND REASON][6]

    Thus I awoke, as God's my witness, when I lived in Cornhill,[7]
Kit and I in a cottage, clothed like a loller,[8]
And little beloved, believe you me,
Among lollers of London and illiterate hermits.
5 For I wrote rhymes of those men as Reason taught me.
For as I came by Conscience I met with Reason,
In a hot harvest time when I had my health,
And limbs to labor with, and loved good living,
And to do no deed but to drink and sleep.
10 My body sound, my mind sane, a certain one accosted me;
Roaming in remembrance, thus Reason upbraided me:
    "Can you serve," he said, "or sing in a church?
Or cock hay with my hay-makers, or heap it on the cart,
Mow it or stack what's mown or make binding for sheaves?
15 Or have a horn and be a hedge-guard and lie outdoors at night,
And keep my corn in my field from cattle and thieves?
Or cut cloth or shoe-leather, or keep sheep and cattle,
Mend hedges, or harrow, or herd pigs or geese,

---

4. "The fool hath said [in his heart, There is no God]": Psalms 14.1.
5. Proverbs 22.10.
6. In the C-text, the last of the three versions of *Piers Plowman*, Langland prefixed to the "Confession of the Seven Deadly Sins" (*Passus* 5 of the B-text) an apology by the Dreamer, "Long Will," who is at once long (or tall) and long on willing (or, arguably, willful). Although there is no conclusive historical evidence for doing so, readers of *Piers Plowman* have generally regarded this passage as a source of information about the real author, about whom we otherwise know so

little.
7. An area of London associated with vagabonds, seedy clerics, and people at loose ends.
8. Idler, vagabond. The term was eventually applied to the proto-Protestant followers of John Wycliffe. "Kit": refers to "Kit my wife and Calote [i.e., Colette] my daughter" (B-text, 18.426). The Dreamer seems to be someone with clerical training who has received consecration into minor clerical orders (such as that of deacon) but who is not a priest. Lesser clerics could marry, although marriage blocked their further advancement in the church.

Or any other kind of craft that the commons needs,
20 So that you might be of benefit to your bread-providers?"
    "Certainly!" I said, "and so God help me,
I am too weak to work with sickle or with scythe,
And too long,[9] believe me, for any low stooping,
Or laboring as a laborer to last any while."
25 "Then have you lands to live by," said Reason, "or relations with
        money
To provide you with food? For you seem an idle man,
A spendthrift who thrives on spending, and throws time away.
Or else you get what food men give you going door to door,
Or beg like a fraud on Fridays[1] and feastdays in churches.
30 And that's a loller's life that earns little praise
Where Rightfulness rewards men as they really deserve.
    He shall reward every man according to his works.[2]
Or are you perhaps lame in your legs or other limbs of your body,
Or maimed through some misadventure, so that you might be
        excused?"
    "When I was young, many years ago,
35 My father and my friends provided me with schooling,
Till I understood surely what Holy Scripture meant,
And what is best for the body as the Book tells,
And most certain for the soul, if so I may continue.
And, in faith, I never found, since my friends died,
40 Life that I liked save in these long clothes.[3]
And if I must live by labor and earn my livelihood,
The labor I should live by is the one I learned best.
    [Abide] in the same calling wherein you were called.[4]
And so I live in London and upland[5] as well.
The tools that I toil with to sustain myself
45 Are Paternoster and my primer, *Placebo* and *Dirige*,[6]
And sometimes my Psalter and my seven Psalms.
These I say for the souls of such as help me.
And those who provide my food vouchsafe, I think,
To welcome me when I come, once a month or so,
50 Now with him, now with her, and in this way I beg
Without bag or bottle but my belly alone.
    And also, moreover, it seems to me, sir Reason,
No clerk should be constrained to do lower-class work.
For by the law of Leviticus[7] that our Lord ordained
55 Clerks with tonsured crowns should, by common understanding,
Neither strain nor sweat nor swear at inquests,
Nor fight in a vanguard and defeat an enemy:
    Do not render evil for evil.[8]

---

9. I.e., tall, perhaps a pun on "willfulness." The Dreamer is called "Long Will" in B-text, 15.152.
1. Fast days, because Christ was crucified on a Friday.
2. Matthew 16.27; cf. Psalm 62.12.
3. The long dress of a cleric, not limited to actual priests.
4. 1 Corinthians 7.20, with variations.
5. North of London, in rural country.
6. "I will please [the Lord]" and "Make straight

[my way]" (Psalm 116.9 and 5.8, respectively). *Placebo* and *Dirige* are the first words of hymns based on two of the seven "penitential" Psalms that were part of the regular order of personal prayer. "Paternoster": the Lord's Prayer ("Our father"). The "primer" was the basic collection of private prayers for laypeople.
7. Leviticus 21 sets restrictions on members of the priesthood.
8. 1 Thessalonians 5.15, with variations.

For they are heirs of Heaven, all that have the tonsure,
And in choir and in churches they are Christ's ministers.
   The Lord is the portion of my inheritance. And elsewhere,
      Mercy does not constrain.[9]
60 It is becoming for clerks to perform Christ's service,
And untonsured boys be burdened with bodily labor.
For none should acquire clerk's tonsure unless he claims descent
From franklins[1] and free men and folk properly wedded.
Bondmen and bastards and beggars' children—
65 These belong to labor; and lords' kin should serve
God and good men as their degree requires,
Some to sing Masses or sit and write,
Read and receive what Reason ought to spend.
But since bondmen's boys have been made bishops,
70 And bastards' boys have been archdeacons,
And shoemakers and their sons have through silver become knights,
And lords' sons their laborers whose lands are mortgaged to them—
And thus for the right of this realm they ride against our enemies
To the comfort of the commons and to the king's honor—
75 And monks and nuns on whom mendicants must depend
Have had their kin named knights and bought knight's-fees,[2]
And popes and patrons have shunned poor gentle blood
And taken the sons of Simon Magus[3] to keep the sanctuary,
Life-holiness and love have gone a long way hence,
80 And will be so till this is all worn out or otherwise changed.
Therefore proffer me no reproach, Reason, I pray you,
For in my conscience I conceive what Christ wants me to do.
Prayers of a perfect man and appropriate penance
Are the labor that our Lord loves most of all.
85 *"Non de solo,"* I said, "forsooth *vivit homo,*
Nec in pane et in pabulo;[4] the Paternoster witnesses
Fiat voluntas Dei[5]—that provides us with everything."
   Said Conscience, "By Christ, I can't see that this lies;°   is pertinent
But it seems no serious perfectness to be a city-beggar,
90 Unless you're licensed to collect for prior or monastery."
   "That is so," I said, "and so I admit
That at times I've lost time and at times misspent it;
And yet I hope, like him who has often bargained
And always lost and lost, and at the last it happened
95 He bought such a bargain he was the better ever,
That all his loss looked paltry in the long run,
Such a winning was his through what grace decreed.

9. I.e., "mercy is not restricted," source unknown. The quotation above is from Psalm 16.5.
1. Freemen. By this date, the term did not just mean nonserfs but designated landowners who were becoming members of the gentry class yet were not knights. The distinction Langland seems to make in this line between franklins and freemen may reflect the rising status of certain families of "freedmen," the original meaning of the word *franklins.*
2. The estate a knight held from his overlord in return for military service was called his "fee."
3. Priests who obtained office through bribery or "simony," a term derived from Simon Magus, a magician who offered the apostles money for their power to perform miracles through the Holy Spirit (see Acts 8).
4. "Not solely [by bread] doth man live, neither by bread nor by food"; the verse continues, "but by every word that proceedeth out of the mouth of God": Matthew 4.4, with variations; cf. Deuteronomy 8.3.
5. "God's will be done." The Lord's Prayer reads, "Thy will be done" (Matthew 6.10).

The kingdom of Heaven is like unto treasure hidden in a field.
The woman who found the piece of silver, etc.[6]
So I hope to have of him that is almighty
A gobbet of his grace, and begin a time
100   That all times of my time shall turn into profit."
"And I counsel you," said Reason, "quickly to begin
The life that is laudable and reliable for the soul."
"Yes, and continue," said Conscience, and I came to the church.[7]

6. Matthew 13.44, Luke 15.9–10. Both passages come from parables that compare finding the kingdom of heaven to risking everything you have to get the one thing that matters most.
7. The four lines that follow this passage connect it to the beginning of the second dream (B-text, 5): "And to the church I set off, to honor God; before the Cross, on my knees, I beat my breast, sighing for my sins, saying my Paternoster, weeping and wailing until I fell asleep."

CHRIST'S HUMANITY

The literary and visual representation of the godhead is necessarily, in any religion, a powerful index of religious culture. In some religions, indeed, visual representation of God is such a sensitive issue that it is forbidden altogether. Christian culture has experienced moments of severe hostility to visual representation (for example, in the Reformation period of the sixteenth century), but has, in general, permitted images of God (and especially of God-become-man, Christ). In the later Middle Ages in Europe the bodily representation of Christ became a central preoccupation for writers, readers, and visual artists.

In the late eleventh century St. Anselm of Canterbury (1033–1099) developed a new conception of the Atonement ("at-one-ment"), the act whereby humans are reconciled with God after the separation caused by Original Sin. An earlier theory had posited that the Atonement was the solution to a dispute between God and the Devil concerning property rights over Mankind. In his tract *Why Did Christ Become Man?* Anselm argued instead that the real center of the Atonement was Mankind's moral responsibility to pay God back. Humanity needed to repay God for the sin committed, but was unable to do so. Faced with this impasse, God could either simply abolish the debt, or else *become human,* in order to repay Himself, as it were. God chose this latter route, allowing Christ to suffer and die as a human in order to clear the debt.

Earlier representations of the Crucifixion had tended to place the accent on Christ as impassive King, standing erect on the Cross, come to claim His property of mankind. In *The Dream of the Rood* (see pp. 33–36), for example, Christ's suffering is for the most part absorbed by the Cross itself, while Christ is represented as a conquering, royal hero. Later medieval representations of Christ, by contrast, accentuate the suffering, sagging, lacerated body of a very human God. In this newly conceived theology, Christ's suffering humanity takes center stage. The artistic significance of this massively influential development was itself massive. Certainly the older tradition survived in vital form: compare, for example, the triumphalist lyric "What is He, this Lordling, that Cometh from the Fight?" with the quiet suffering of "Ye that Pasen by the Weye." Langland's Christ, too, comes to claim his property as a conquering hero. It was, nonetheless, the tradition of Christ suffering in His humanity that dominated literary and visual art from the thirteenth century until the Reformation initiated in 1517.

These theological developments had forceful artistic and stylistic consequences. Because the theology was best expressed through visual or verbal images, it fed readily into both painting and a highly pictorial literature. In both painting and literature, a humble style, focusing on the particularities of bodily pain and grief, became the bearer of high theological significance. The painting of Giotto (1266?–1337), for example, broke with a prior tradition of painting that represented an elegant Christ against a splendid gold background; Giotto's inelegant and crucified Christ suffers under the pull of his own weight. Spiritual experience was, in the first instance, something *seen* more than something *thought*. It was also a spirituality rooted in the dramatic present: as one saw Christ, one saw Him in the here and now. Thus works in this almost cinematic mode foreshorten historical and geographical distance: such texts encourage readers, that is, to imagine that they are physically and emotionally present at the crucial scenes of Christ's life. In some examples of the tradition, viewers are encouraged to imagine those around Christ (especially Romans and Jews) as wholly responsible for the infliction of pain; in others, viewers are made to realize that they are themselves responsible for the continued suffering of Christ.

As deployed by the Church, this movement discouraged abstract thought. It did nevertheless have the effect of widening access to spiritual experience, and, in ways unforeseen by official sponsors of such piety, could be the springboard for very sophisticated theology. As the Church attempted to deepen the spiritual literacy of its members from the late twelfth century, emphasis on Christ's humanity in art and literature opened powerful spiritual experience to a much wider audience of readers and viewers. To engage in this spirituality, a public did not need to be versed in detailed matters of doctrine. Instead, a reader or viewer had to develop the capacity for sympathetic response to physical suffering. Such spirituality gained official impetus through the foundation of the Franciscan order of friars (1223), who promoted earthly poverty in imitation of, and emotional response to, Christ's sufferings. The centrality of Christ's living presence in the liturgy was, furthermore, reaffirmed and extended with the establishment, throughout Christendom, of the Feast of Corpus Christi (the Feast of the Body of Christ), first proclaimed by the pope in 1264 and again in 1311. This feast celebrated the Eucharistic host, or wafer, as Christ's body. It grew steadily in popularity and came to involve outdoor processions depicting the biblical foreshadowings of the Eucharist, as a prelude to display of the Eucharist itself. In some medieval English cities this was the day also chosen for the performance of cycle plays, sometimes known as the plays of Corpus Christi.

Female readers in particular, who had been excluded from the Latin-based, textual traditions of theology, discovered fertile ground in this tradition of so-called "affective," or emotional, piety. Through such emotive imagining, one gained an apparently unmediated, and potentially authoritative, relation with Christ. Women working in this tradition did not necessarily remain, however, within its visual, imaginative terms: Julian of Norwich is, for example, capable of developing very subtle and abstract thought, holding the incarnate image in view all the while.

This powerfully emotional piety also provoked wider social applications of the Christian narrative. Whereas "The Parable of the Christ Knight" in the *Ancrene Wisse* (supplemental ebook) presents a suffering Christ as an aristocratic lover for a very select spiritual elite of women, the Christ of Margery Kempe is very much the "homely" husband of a bourgeois woman (see in particular Book I, Chapter 36). On a much larger scale, the mystery plays mark the moment in which urban institutions represent Christ for themselves. In this drama, both Old and New Testament narrative is inflected by the trials of domestic and urban experience (on the origins, civic sponsorship, and production of these plays, see the introduction to "Mystery Plays," p. 447).

WILLIAM LANGLAND

For full information about William Langland, see the headnote on pages 370–73. The following passage (*Passus 18* of *Piers Plowman*) both completes the selections from Langland and serves as the first text of "Christ's Humanity."

Passus 18 describes the central event of Christianity, the Crucifixion, followed by an account of Christ's descent into hell, traditionally called the "Harrowing of Hell." The Dreamer has come a long way in his personal search for truth, and this vision is the most immediate and fulfilling answer to the questions he addressed to Holy Church, although not a final answer, for in Langland's poem the search has no end in this life. Piers, who had assumed aspects of Adam, Moses, and the Good Samaritan (while never ceasing to be the ideal plowman), is now partially identified with Christ. The terms of this identification are rooted in material necessity of food: Christ has come to fetch the "fruit" of Piers Plowman (lines 31 and 34). The "food" that Christ seeks has now become the souls of the patriarchs and prophets, and of all mankind, which must be redeemed from the devil's power. And just as the earthly Piers becomes Christ-like, so too does Christ, in His bodily manifestation, become intensely human. He jousts in the arms (i.e., no arms at all, but the unprotected flesh) of Piers Plowman (line 24); He comes to earth precisely in order to *know* what being human is like (lines 229–32); and He does so precisely because of his co-natural, sympathetic kinship with suffering humanity (lines 408–10).

For all that, Langland does not focus here for long on the grievous suffering of Christ. On the contrary, he addresses the terms of the Atonement through intellectual debate, first through the Four Daughters of God (personifications taken from Psalm 85.10), and then through Christ's direct encounter with Lucifer. Against powerful legal and written evidence to the contrary, first Mercy and Peace and then Christ Himself reveal a divine curiosity and sympathy with imprisoned humanity. This mercy is anterior to, and more powerful than, the law of strict *Truthe* or justice, by which mankind appears to have been irredeemably damned. So far from being a wounded, suffering Christ, Langland's Christ is at once spiritually triumphant and a delighted trickster, by whose divine guile the devil has been fooled.

The Vision of Piers Plowman

Passus 18

[THE CRUCIFIXION AND HARROWING OF HELL]

Wool-chafed[1] and wet-shoed I went forth after
Like a careless creature unconscious of woe,
And trudged forth like a tramp, all the time of my life,
Till I grew weary of the world and wished to sleep again,
5   And lay down till Lent, and slept a long time,

---

1. Scratchy wool was worn next to the body as an act of penance.

Rested there, snoring roundly, till *Ramis-Palmarum*.[2]
    I dreamed chiefly of children and cheers of "*Gloria, laus!*"
And how old folk to an organ sang "*Hosanna!*"
And of Christ's passion and pain for the people he had reached for.
10 One resembling the Samaritan[3] and somewhat Piers the Plowman
Barefoot on an ass's back bootless came riding
Without spurs or spear: sprightly was his look,
As is the nature of a knight that draws near to be dubbed,
To get himself gilt spurs and engraved jousting shoes.
15 Then was Faith watching from a window and cried, "*A, fill David!*"
As does a herald of arms when armed men come to joust.
Old Jews of Jerusalem joyfully sang,
    "*Blessed is he who cometh in the name of the Lord.*"
And I asked Faith to reveal what all this affair meant,
And who was to joust in Jerusalem. "Jesus," he said,
20 "And fetch what the Fiend claims, the fruit of Piers the Plowman."
"Is Piers in this place?" said I; and he pierced me with his look:
"This Jesus for his gentleness will joust in Piers's arms,
In his helmet and in his hauberk, *humana natura*,[4]
So that Christ be not disclosed here as *consummatus Deus*.[5]
25 In the plate armor of Piers the Plowman this jouster will ride,
For no dint will do him injury as *in deitate Patris*.[6]
"Who shall joust with Jesus," said I, "Jews or Scribes?"[7]
"No," said Faith, "but the Fiend and False-Doom°-To-Die.   *sentence*
Death says he will undo and drag down low
30 All that live or look upon land or water.
Life says that he lies, and lays his life in pledge
That for all that Death can do, within three days he'll walk
And fetch from the Fiend the fruit of Piers the Plowman,
And place it where he pleases, and put Lucifer in bonds,
35 And beat and bring down burning death forever.
    O death, I will be thy death."[8]
    Then Pilate came with many people, *sedens pro tribunali*,[9]
To see how doughtily Death should do, and judge the rights of both.
The Jews and the justice were joined against Jesus,
And all the court cried upon him, "*Crucifige!*"[1] loud.
40 Then a plaintiff appeared before Pilate and said,
"This Jesus made jokes about Jerusalem's temple,
To have it down in one day and in three days after
Put it up again all new[2]—here he stands who said it—

2. Palm Sunday (literally, "branches of palms"): the background of this part of the poem is the biblical account of Christ's entry into Jerusalem on this day, when the crowds greeted him crying, "Hosanna (line 8) to the son of David (line 15): Blessed is he that cometh in the name of the Lord (line 17a); Hosanna in the highest" (see Matthew 21.9). "*Gloria, laus*" (line 7) are the first words of an anthem, "Glory, praise, and honor," that was sung by children in medieval religious processions on Palm Sunday.
3. In the previous vision, the Dreamer has encountered Abraham, or Faith (mentioned in lines 15, 18, 28, and 92); Moses, or Hope; and the Good Samaritan, or Charity, who was riding toward a "jousting in Jerusalem" and who now appears as an aspect of Christ.
4. Human nature, which Christ assumed in order to redeem humanity. "Hauberk": coat of mail.
5. The perfect (three-personed) God.
6. In the godhead of the Father: as God, Christ could not suffer but as man, he could.
7. People who made a very strict, literal interpretation of the Old Law and hence rejected teaching of the New.
8. Cf. Hosea 13.14.
9. Sitting as a judge (cf. Matthew 27.19).
1. Crucify him! (John 19.15).
2. See John 2.19–21 and Mark 14.58–59.

And yet build it every bit as big in all dimensions,
45 As long and as broad both, above and below."
"*Crucifige!*" said a sergeant, "he knows sorcerer's tricks."
"*Tolle! tolle!*"[3] said another, and took sharp thorns
And began to make a garland out of green thorn,
And set it sorely on his head and spoke in hatred,
50 "*Ave, Rabbi,*" said that wretch, and shot reeds[4] at him;
They nailed him with three nails naked on a Cross,
And with a pole put a potion up to his lips
And bade him drink to delay his death and lengthen his days,
And said, "If you're subtle, let's see you help yourself.
55 If you are Christ and a king's son, come down from the Cross!
Then we'll believe that Life loves you and will not let you die."
    "*Consummatum est,*"[5] said Christ and started to swoon,
Piteously and pale like a prisoner dying.
The Lord of Life and of Light then laid his eyelids together.
60 The day withdrew for dread and darkness covered the sun;
The wall wavered and split and the whole world quaked.
Dead men for that din came out of deep graves
And spoke of why that storm lasted so long:
"For a bitter battle," the dead body said;
65 "Life and Death in this darkness, one destroys the other.
No one will surely know which shall have the victory
Before Sunday about sunrise"; and sank with that to earth.
Some said that he was God's son that died so fairly:
    Truly this was the Son of God.[6]
And some said he was a sorcerer: "We should see first
70 Whether he's dead or not dead before we dare take him down."
Two thieves were there that suffered death that time
Upon crosses beside Christ; such was the common law.
A constable came forth and cracked both their legs
And the arms afterward of each of those thieves.
75 But no bastard was so bold as to touch God's body there;
Because he was a knight and a king's son, Nature decreed that time
That no knave should have the hardiness to lay hand on him.
    But a knight with a sharp spear was sent forth there
Named Longeus[7] as the legend tells, who had long since lost his sight;
80 Before Pilate and the other people in that place he waited on his
        horse.
For all that he might demur, he was made that time
To joust with Jesus, that blind Jew Longeus.
For all who watched there were unwilling, whether mounted or afoot,
To touch him or tamper with him or take him down from the Cross,
85 Except this blind bachelor that bore him through the heart.
The blood sprang down the spear and unsparred[8] his eyes.
The knight knelt down on his knees and begged Jesus for mercy.

3. Away with him, away with him! (John 19.15).
4. Arrows, probably small ones intended to hurt rather than to kill. "*Ave, Rabbi*": "Hail, master" (Matthew 26.49): these are actually Judas's words when he kissed Christ in order to identify him to the arresting officers.
5. It is finished (John 19.30).

6. Matthew 27.54.
7. Longeus (usually Longinus) appears in the apocryphal Gospel of Nicodemus, which provided Langland with the material for much of his account of Christ's despoiling of hell.
8. Opened; in the original there is a play on words with "spear." "Bachelor": knight.

"It was against my will, Lord, to wound you so sorely."
He sighed and said, "Sorely I repent it.
90 For what I here have done, I ask only your grace.
Have mercy on me, rightful Jesu!" and thus lamenting wept.
    Then Faith began fiercely to scorn the false Jews,[9]
Called them cowards, accursed forever.
"For this foul villainy, may vengeance fall on you!
95 To make the blind beat the dead, it was a bully's thought.
Cursed cowards, no kind of knighthood was it
To beat a dead body with any bright weapon.
Yet he's won the victory in the fight for all his vast wound,
For your champion jouster, the chief knight of you all,
100 Weeping admits himself worsted and at the will of Jesus.
For when this darkness is done, Death will be vanquished,
And you louts have lost, for Life shall have the victory;
And your unfettered freedom has fallen into servitude;
And you churls and your children shall achieve no prosperity,
105 Nor have lordship over land or have land to till,
But be all barren and live by usury,
Which is a life that every law of our Lord curses.
Now your good days are done as Daniel prophesied;
When Christ came their kingdom's crown should be lost:
    When the Holy of Holies comes your anointing shall cease."[1]
110   What for fear of this adventure and of the false Jews
I withdrew in that darkness to *Descendit-ad-Inferna,*[2]
And there I saw surely *Secundum Scripturas*[3]
Where out of the west a wench,[4] as I thought,
Came walking on the way—she looked toward hell.
115 Mercy was that maid's name, a meek thing withal,
A most gracious girl, and goodly of speech.
Her sister as it seemed came softly walking
Out of the east, opposite, and she looked westward,
A comely creature and cleanly: Truth was her name.
120 Because of the virtue that followed her, she was afraid of nothing.
When these maidens met, Mercy and Truth,
Each of them asked the other about this great wonder,
And of the din and of the darkness, and how the day lowered,
And what a gleam and a glint glowed before hell.
125   "I marvel at this matter, by my faith," said Truth,
"And am coming to discover what this queer affair means."
    "Do not marvel," said Mercy, "it means only mirth.
A maiden named Mary, and mother without touching
By any kind of creature, conceived through speech
130 And grace of the Holy Ghost; grew great with child;

---

9. The references in this passage (lines 92–110) and in lines 258–60 appear to reflect a blind anti-Semitism all too prevalent in late-medieval art and literature, brought out especially in portrayals of the Passion. Elsewhere Langland exhibits a more enlightened attitude—for instance, in a passage in which he holds up Jewish charity as an example to Christians. In the present passage he may intend a distinction between those who betrayed and condemned Jesus and the "old Jews of Jerusalem" who welcomed him in the Palm Sunday procession (lines 7–17).

1. Daniel 9.24.
2. He descended into hell (from the Apostles' Creed).
3. According to the Scriptures.
4. The word is Langland's and had much the same connotations in his time as it has in ours.

With no blemish to her woman's body brought him into this world.
And that my tale is true, I take God to witness,
Since this baby was born it has been thirty winters,[5]
Who died and suffered death this day about midday.
135 And that is the cause of this eclipse that is closing off the sun,
In meaning that man shall be removed from darkness
While this gleam and this glow go to blind Lucifer.
For patriarchs and prophets have preached of this often
That man shall save man through a maiden's help,
140 And what a tree took away a tree shall restore,[6]
And what Death brought down a death shall raise up."
    "What you're telling," said Truth, "is just a tale of nonsense.
For Adam and Eve and Abraham and the rest,
Patriarchs and prophets imprisoned in pain,
145 Never believe that yonder light will lift them up,
Or have them out of hell—hold your tongue, Mercy!
Your talk is mere trifling. I, Truth, know the truth,
For whatever is once in hell, it comes out never.
Job the perfect patriarch disproves what you say:
    Since in hell there is no redemption."[7]
150   Then Mercy most mildly uttered these words:
"From observation," she said, "I suppose they shall be saved,
Because venom destroys venom, and in that I find evidence
That Adam and Eve shall have relief.
For of all venoms the foulest is the scorpion's:
155 No medicine may amend the place where it stings
Till it's dead and placed upon it—the poison is destroyed,
The first effect of the venom, through the virtue it possesses.
So shall this death destroy—I dare bet my life—
All that Death did first through the Devil's tempting.
160 And just as the beguiler with guile beguiled man first,
So shall grace that began everything make a good end
And beguile the beguiler—and that's a good trick:
    A trick by which to trick trickery."[8]
    "Now let's be silent," said Truth. "It seems to me I see
Out of the nip[9] of the north, not far from here,
165 Righteousness come running—let's wait right here,
For she knows far more than we—she was here before us both."
    "That is so," said Mercy, "and I see here to the south
Where Peace clothed in patience[1] comes sportively this way.
Love has desired her long: I believe surely
170 That Love has sent her some letter, what this light means
That hangs over hell thus: she will tell us what it means."
When Peace clothed in patience approached near them both,
Righteousness did her reverence for her rich clothing

5. See Luke 3.23.
6. The first tree bore the fruit that Adam and
Eve ate, thereby damning humankind; the second tree is the cross on which Christ was crucified, thereby redeeming humankind.
7. Cf. Job 7.9.
8. From a medieval Latin hymn.
9. The word is Langland's and the sense obscure;

it probably meant "coldness" to him, although an
Old English word similar to *nip* meant "gloom."
1. What Langland envisioned clothes of patience
to look like, aside from their "richness" (line 173),
it is impossible to say; to him any abstraction
could become a concrete allegory without visual
identification.

And prayed Peace to tell her to what place she was going,
175   And whom she was going to greet in her gay garments.
     "My wish is to take my way," said she, "and welcome them all
Whom many a day I might not see for murk of sin.
Adam and Eve and the many others in hell,
Moses and many more will merrily sing,
180   And I shall dance to their song: sister, do the same.
Because Jesus jousted well, joy begins to dawn.
Weeping may endure for a night, but joy cometh in the
     morning.[2]
Love who is my lover sent letters to tell me
That my sister Mercy and I shall save mankind,
And that God has forgiven and granted me, Peace, and Mercy
185   To make bail for mankind for evermore after.
Look, here's the patent," said Peace: "*In pace in idipsum:*
And that this deed shall endure, *dormiam et requiescam.*"[3]
     "What? You're raving," said Righteousness. "You must be really
     drunk.
Do you believe that yonder light might unlock hell
190   And save man's soul? Sister, don't suppose it.
At the beginning God gave the judgment himself
That Adam and Eve and all that followed them
Should die downright and dwell in torment after
If they touched a tree and ate the tree's fruit.
195   Adam afterwards against his forbidding
Fed on that fruit and forsook as it were
The love of our Lord and his lore too,
And followed what the Fiend taught and his flesh's will
Against Reason. I, Righteousness, record this with Truth,
200   That their pain should be perpetual and no prayer should help them,
Therefore let them chew as they chose, and let us not chide, sisters,
For it's misery without amendment, the morsel they ate."
     "And I shall prove," said Peace, "that their pain must end,
And in time trouble must turn into well-being;
205   For had they known no woe, they'd not have known well-being;
For no one knows what well-being is who was never in woe,
Nor what is hot hunger who has never lacked food.
If there were no night, no man, I believe,
Could be really well aware of what day means.
210   Never should a really rich man who lives in rest and ease
Know what woe is if it weren't for natural death.
So God, who began everything, of his good will
Became man by a maid for mankind's salvation
And allowed himself to be sold to see the sorrow of dying.
215   And that cures all care and is the first cause of rest,
For until we meet *modicum,*° I may well avow it,   *small quantity*
No man knows, I suppose, what 'enough' means.
Therefore God of his goodness gave the first man Adam

2. Psalm 30.5.
3. The "patent" or "deed" is a document conferring authority: this one consists of phrases from

Psalm 4.8: "In peace in the selfsame"; "I will sleep
and find rest."

A place of supreme ease and of perfect joy,
220 And then he suffered him to sin so that he might know sorrow,
And thus know what well-being is—to be aware of it naturally.
And afterward God offered himself, and took Adam's nature,
To see what he had suffered in three separate places,
Both in Heaven and on earth, and now he heads for hell,
225 To learn what all woe is like who has learned of all joy.
So it shall fare with these folk: their folly and their sin
Shall show them what sickness is—and succor from all pain.
No one knows what war is where peace prevails,
Nor what is true well-being till 'Woe, alas!' teaches him."
230   Then was there a wight with two broad eyes:
Book was that beaupere's[4] name, a bold man of speech.
"By God's body," said this Book, "I will bear witness
That when this baby was born there blazed a star
So that all the wise men in the world agreed with one opinion
235 That such a baby was born in Bethlehem city
Who should save man's soul and destroy sin.
And all the elements," said the Book, "hereof bore witness.
The sky first revealed that he was God who formed all things:
The hosts in Heaven took *stella comata*[5]
240 And tended her like a torch to reverence his birth.
The light followed the Lord into the low earth.
The water witnessed that he was God for he walked on it;
Peter the Apostle perceived his walking
And as he went on the water knew him well and said,
    'Bid me come unto thee on the water.'[6]
245 And lo, how the sun locked her light in herself
When she saw him suffer that made sun and sea.
The earth for heavy heart because he would suffer
Quaked like a quick° thing and the rock cracked all to pieces.   *living*
Lo, hell might not hold, but opened when God suffered,
250 And let out Simeon's sons[7] to see him hang on Cross.
And now shall Lucifer believe it, loath though he is,
For Jesus like a giant with an engine[8] comes yonder
To break and beat down all that may be against him,
And to have out of hell every one he pleases.
255 And I, Book, will be burnt unless Jesus rises to life
In all the mights of a man and brings his mother joy,
And comforts all his kin, and takes their cares away,
And all the joy of the Jews disjoins and disperses;
And unless they reverence his Rood and his resurrection
260 And believe on a new law be lost body and soul."
    "Let's be silent," said Truth, "I hear and see both
A spirit speaks to hell and bids the portals be opened."

---

4. Fine fellow. The book's two broad eyes suggest the Old and New Testaments. "Wight": creature, person.
5. Hairy star, i.e., comet.
6. Matthew 14.28.
7. Simeon, who was present at the presentation of the infant Jesus in the temple, had been told by the Holy Ghost that "he should not see death" before he had seen "the Lord's Christ" (Luke 2.26). The Apocryphal Gospel of Nicodemus echoes the incident in reporting that Simeon's sons were raised from death at the time of Jesus's crucifixion.
8. A device, probably thought of as a gigantic slingshot, although, of course, Christ needs nothing to break down his enemies but his own authority.

>   *Lift up your gates.*[9]
>   A voice loud in that light cried to Lucifer,
>   "Princes of this place, unpin and unlock,
> 265   For he comes here with crown who is King of Glory."
>   Then Satan[1] sighed and said to hell,
>   "Without our leave such a light fetched Lazarus away:[2]
>   Care and calamity have come upon us all.
>   If this King comes in he will carry off mankind
> 270   And lead it to where Lazarus is, and with small labor bind me.
>   Patriarchs and prophets have long prated of this,[3]
>   That such a lord and a light should lead them all hence."
>   "Listen," said Lucifer, "for this lord is one I know;
>   Both this lord and this light, it's long ago I knew him.
> 275   No death may do this lord harm, nor any devil's trickery,
>   And his way is where he wishes—but let him beware of the perils.
>   If he bereaves me of my right he robs me by force.
>   For by right and by reason the race that is here
>   Body and soul belongs to me, both good and evil.
> 280   For he himself said it who is Sire of Heaven,
>   If Adam ate the apple, all should die
>   And dwell with us devils: the Lord laid down that threat.
>   And since he who is Truth himself said these words,
>   And since I've possessed them seven thousand winters,
> 285   I don't believe law will allow him the least of them."
>   "That is so," said Satan, "but I'm sore afraid
>   Because you took them by trickery and trespassed in his garden,
>   And in the semblance of a serpent sat upon the apple tree
>   And egged them to eat, Eve by herself,
> 290   And told her a tale with treasonous words;
>   And so you had them out, and hither at the last."
>   "It's an ill-gotten gain where guile is at the root,
>   For God will not be beguiled," said Goblin, "nor tricked.
>   We have no true title to them, for it was by treason they were
>   damned."
> 295   "Certainly I fear," said the Fiend,[4] "lest Truth fetch them out.
>   These thirty winters, as I think, he's gone here and there and
>   preached.
>   I've assailed him with sin, and sometimes asked
>   Whether he was God or God's son: he gave me short answer.
>   And thus he's traveled about like a true man these two and thirty
>   winters.
> 300   And when I saw it was so, while she slept I went

---

9. The first words of Psalm 24.9, which reads in the Latin version, "Lift up your gates, O princes, and be ye lift up, ye everlasting doors, and the King of Glory shall come in."

1. Langland, following a tradition also reflected in Milton's *Paradise Lost*, pictures hell as populated by a number of devils: Satan; Lucifer (line 273 ff.), who began the war in heaven and tempted Eve; Goblin (line 293); Belial (line 321); and Ashtoreth (line 404). Lucifer the rebel angel naturally became identified with Satan, a word that in the Old Testament had originally meant an evil adversary; many of the other devils are displaced gods of pagan religions.

2. For Christ's raising of Lazarus from the dead, cf. John 11.

3. E.g., Psalm 68.18, as interpreted in Ephesians 4.8–10.

4. Here and in line 309, "the Fiend" is presumably Lucifer's most articulate critic, Satan, whom Christ names as his tempter in Matthew 4.10.

To warn Pilate's wife what sort of man was Jesus,[5]
For some hated him and have put him to death.
I would have lengthened his life, for I believed if he died
That his soul would suffer no sin in his sight.
305 For the body, while it walked on its bones, was busy always
To save men from sin if they themselves wished.
And now I see where a soul comes descending hitherward
With glory and with great light; God it is, I'm sure.
My advice is we all flee," said the Fiend, "fast away from here.
310 For we had better not be at all than abide in his sight.
For your lies, Lucifer, we've lost all our prey.
Through you we fell first from Heaven so high:
Because we believed your lies we all leapt out.
And now for your latest lie we have lost Adam,
315 And all our lordship, I believe, on land and in hell."
  Now shall the prince of this world be cast out.[6]
 Again the light bade them unlock, and Lucifer answered,
  "Who is that?[7]
What lord are you?" said Lucifer. The light at once replied,
  "The King of Glory.
The Lord of might and of main and all manner of powers:
  The Lord of Powers.
Dukes of this dim place, at once undo these gates
320 That Christ may come in, the Heaven-King's son."
And with that breath hell broke along with Belial's bars;
For° any warrior or watchman the gates wide opened.   *in spite of*
Patriarchs and prophets, *populus in tenebris,*[8]
Sang Saint John's song, *Ecce agnus Dei.*[9]
325 Lucifer could not look, the light so blinded him.
And those that the Lord loved his light caught away,
And he said to Satan, "Lo, here's my soul in payment
For all sinful souls, to save those that are worthy.
Mine they are and of me—I may the better claim them.
330 Although Reason records, and right of myself,
That if they ate the apple all should die,
I did not hold out to them hell here forever.
For the deed that they did, your deceit caused it;
You got them with guile against all reason.
335 For in my palace Paradise, in the person of an adder,
You stole by stealth something I loved.
Thus like a lizard with a lady's face[1]
Falsely you filched from me; the Old Law confirms
That guilers be beguiled, and that is good logic:

---

5. In Matthew 27.19, Pilate's wife warns Pilate to "have nothing to do with that just man [Jesus]," for she has been troubled by a dream about him. Langland has the Fiend admit to having caused the dream so that Pilate's wife should persuade her husband not to harm Jesus and thus keep him safe on earth and not come to visit hell and despoil it.
6. John 12.31. "Prince of this world" is a title for the devil.
7. This and the next two phrases translated from

the Latin are from Psalm 24.8, following immediately on the words quoted in line 262a.
8. "People in darkness," the phrase is from Matthew 4.16, citing Isaiah 9.2, "The people that walked in darkness have seen a great light."
9. Behold the Lamb of God (John 1.36).
1. In medieval art the devil tempting Eve was sometimes represented as a snake (see the "serpent" of line 288) and sometimes as a lizard with a female human face and standing upright.

A tooth for a tooth and an eye for an eye.[2]

340 *Ergo*[3] soul shall requite soul and sin revert to sin,
And all that man has done amiss, I, man, will amend.
Member for member was amends in the Old Law,
And life for life also, and by that law I claim
Adam and all his issue at my will hereafter.

345 And what Death destroyed in them, my death shall restore
And both quicken° and requite what was quenched   revitalize
    through sin.
And that grace destroy guile is what good faith requires.
So don't believe it, Lucifer, against the law I fetch them,
But by right and by reason here ransom my liegemen.
     I have not come to destroy the law but to fulfill it.[4]

350 You fetched mine in my place unmindful of all reason
Falsely and feloniously; good faith taught me
To recover them by reason and rely on nothing else.
So what you got with guile through grace is won back.
You, Lucifer, in likeness of a loathsome adder

355 Got by guile those whom God loved;
And I, in likeness of a mortal man, who am master of Heaven,
Have graciously requited your guile: let guile go against guile!
And as Adam and all died through a tree
Adam and all through a tree return to life,[5]

360 And guile is beguiled and grief has come to his guile:
     And he is fallen into the ditch which he made.[6]
And now your guile begins to turn against you,
And my grace to grow ever greater and wider.
The bitterness that you have brewed, imbibe it yourself
Who are doctor[7] of death, the drink you made.

365   For I who am Lord of Life, love is my drink
And for that drink today I died upon earth.
I struggled so I'm thirsty still for man's soul's sake.
No drink may moisten me or slake my thirst
Till vintage time befall in the Vale of Jehoshaphat,[8]

370 When I shall drink really ripe wine, *Resurrectio mortuorum.*[9]
And then I shall come as a king crowned with angels
And have out of hell all men's souls.
Fiends and fiendkins shall stand before me
And be at my bidding, where best it pleases me.

375 But to be merciful to man then, my nature requires it.
For we are brothers of one blood, but not in baptism all.
And all that are both in blood and in baptism my whole brothers
Shall not be damned to the death that endures without end.
     Against thee only have I sinned, etc.[1]

---

2. See Matthew 5.38 citing Exodus 21.24.
3. Therefore. The Latin conjunction was used in formal debate to introduce the conclusion derived from a number of propositions.
4. See Matthew 5.17.
5. See 1 Corinthians 15.21–22.
6. Psalm 7.15.
7. The ironical use of the word carries the sense both of "physician" and of "one learned in a discipline."

8. On the evidence of Joel 3.2, 12, the site of the Last Judgment was thought to be the Vale of Jehoshaphat.
9. The resurrection of the dead (from the Nicene Creed).
1. Psalm 51.4. The psalm is understood to assign the sole power of judging the sinner to God, because it is only against God that the sinner has acted.

It is not the custom on earth to hang a felon
380 Oftener than once, even though he were a traitor.
And if the king of the kingdom comes at that time
When a felon should suffer death or other such punishment,
Law would he give him life if he looks upon him.[2]
And I who am King of Kings shall come in such a time
385 Where doom to death damns all wicked,
And if law wills I look on them, it lies in my grace
Whether they die or do not die because they did evil.
And if it be any bit paid for, the boldness of their sins,
I may grant mercy through my righteousness and all my true words;
390 And though Holy Writ wills that I wreak vengeance on those
    that wrought evil,
       No evil unpunished, etc.[3]
They shall be cleansed and made clear and cured of their sins,
In my prison purgatory till *Parce*° says 'Stop!'   *Spare!*
And my mercy shall be shown to many of my half-brothers,
For blood-kin may see blood-kin both hungry and cold,
395 But blood-kin may not see blood-kin bleed without his pity:
    I heard unspeakable words which it is not lawful for a man
      to utter.[4]
But my righteousness and right shall rule all hell
And mercy rule all mankind before me in Heaven.
For I'd be an unkind king unless I gave my kin help,
And particularly at such a time when help was truly needed.
    Enter not into judgment with thy servant.[5]
400 Thus by law," said our Lord, "I will lead from here
Those I looked on with love who believed in my coming;
And for your lie, Lucifer, that you lied to Eve,
You shall buy it back in bitterness"—and bound him with chains.
Ashtoreth and all the gang hid themselves in corners;
405 They dared not look at our Lord, the least of them all,
But let him lead away what he liked and leave what he wished.
    Many hundreds of angels harped and sang,
      Flesh sins, flesh redeems, flesh reigns as God of God.[6]
    Then Peace piped a note of poetry:
      As a rule the sun is brighter after the biggest clouds; After
      hostilities love is brighter.
    "After sharp showers," said Peace, "the sun shines brightest;
410 No weather is warmer than after watery clouds;
Nor any love lovelier, or more loving friends,
Than after war and woe when Love and peace are masters.
There was never war in this world nor wickedness so sharp

---

2. I.e., "Law dictates that the king pardon the felon if the king sees him."
3. [He is a just judge who leaves] no evil unpunished [and no good unrewarded]. Not from the Bible but from Pope Innocent III's tract *Of Contempt for the World* (1195).
4. In 2 Corinthians 12.4, St. Paul tells how in a vision he was snatched up to heaven where he heard things that may not be repeated among men. Langland is apparently invoking a similar mystic experience when he puts into Christ's mouth a promise to spare many of his half-brothers, the unbaptized. The orthodox theology of the time taught that all the unbaptized were irredeemably damned, a proposition Langland refused to accept: in his vision he has heard words to the contrary that might not be repeated among men, because they would be held heretical.
5. Psalm 143.2.
6. From a medieval Latin hymn. The source of the two Latin verses immediately below is Alain of Lille, a late 12th-century poet and philosopher.

That Love, if he liked, might not make a laughing matter.
415 And peace through patience puts an end to all perils."
"Truce!" said Truth, "you tell the truth, by Jesus!
Let's kiss in covenant, and each of us clasp other."
"And let no people," said Peace, "perceive that we argued;
For nothing is impossible to him that is almighty."
420 "You speak the truth," said Righteousness, and reverently kissed her,
Peace, and Peace her, *per saecula saeculorum:*[7]
>   *Mercy and Truth have met together; Righteousness and Peace*
>   *have kissed each other.*[8]
Truth sounded a trumpet then and sang *Te Deum Laudamus,*[9]
And then Love strummed a lute with a loud note:
>   *Behold how good and how pleasant, etc.*[1]
Till the day dawned these damsels caroled.
425 When bells rang for the Resurrection, and right then I awoke
And called Kit my wife and Calote my daughter:
>   "Arise and go reverence God's resurrection,
>   And creep to the Cross on knees, and kiss it as a jewel,
>   For God's blessed body it bore for our good,
430 And it frightens the Fiend, for such is its power
That no grisly ghost may glide in its shadow."

---

7. For ever and ever (the liturgical formula).
8. Psalm 85.10.
9. We praise thee, O Lord.

1. Psalm 133.1. The verse continues, "it is for brothers to dwell together in unity."

MIDDLE ENGLISH INCARNATION AND CRUCIFIXION LYRICS

Many religious lyrics were written down and preserved. These were mostly written by anonymous clerics, but in rare instances we know at least the name of an author. Seventeen poems by the Franciscan William Herebert are collected in a single manuscript. In his dramatic lyric printed here, the main speaker is the Christ-knight, returning from the Crucifixion, which is treated as a battle the way it is in *The Dream of the Rood* and in *Passus 18* of *Piers Plowman*. Christ in his blood-stained garments is compared in a famous image from Isaiah 63.2 to one who treads grapes in a winepress, a passage that is also the source of Julia Ward Howe's "grapes of wrath" in "The Battle Hymn of the Republic."

The religious lyrics are for the most part devotional poems that depend on the Latin Bible and liturgy of the church. The passage from Isaiah adapted by Herebert was part of a lesson in a mass performed during Holy Week. But the diction of that poem, though there are a few French loan words, is predominantly of English origin. Many of the poems, like Herebert's, contain an element of drama: "Ye that Pasen by the Weye" is spoken by Christ from the Cross to all wayfarers; similar verses are spoken by the crucified Christ to the crowd (as well as to the audience) in the mystery plays of the Crucifixion.

Among the most beautiful and tender lyrics are those about the Virgin Mary, who is the greatest of all queens and ladies. They celebrate Mary's joys, sorrows, and the mystery of her virgin motherhood. "Sunset on Calvary," a tableau of Mary at the foot of the Cross, contains an implicit play upon English "sun," which is setting, and the "son," who is dying but, like the sun, will rise again. Like love songs the Marian lyrics often celebrate the mysteries of the natural world and thus defy any simple division of medieval lyric into "secular" or "religious" poetry. "I Sing of a Maiden" visualizes the conception of Jesus in terms of the falling dew, and he steals silently to her bower like a lover. "Adam Lay Bound" cheerfully treats the original sin as though it were a child's theft of an apple, which had the happy result of making Mary the Queen of Heaven. "The Corpus Christi Carol" has the form of a lullaby but penetrates by stages to the heart of a mystery similar to the Holy Grail, the chalice that contained Christ's blood, which continues to flow, as it does in this carol, for humanity's salvation.

What is he, this lordling, that cometh from the fight[1]

"What is he, this lordling,[2] that cometh from the fight
With blood-rede wede so grislich ydight,[3]
So faire ycointised,° so semelich in sight,[4]   *appareled*
So stiflich he gangeth,[5] so doughty° a knight?"   *valiant*

5   "Ich° it am, ich it am, that ne speke but right,[6]   *I*
Champioun to helen° mankinde in fight."   *save*

"Why then is thy shroud rede, with blood al ymeind,
As troddares in wringe with must al bespreind?"[7]

"The wring ich have ytrodded al myself one°   *alone*
10   And of° al mankinde was none other wone.°   *for / hope*
Ich hem[8] have ytrodded in wrathe and in grame,°   *anger*
And al my wede is bespreind with here blood ysame,[9]
And al my robe yfouled° to here grete shame.   *soiled*
The day of th'ilke wreche[1] liveth in my thought;

15   The yeer of medes yelding ne foryet ich nought.[2]
Ich looked al aboute some helping mon;[3]
Ich soughte al the route,[4] but help nas ther non.
It was mine owne strengthe that this bote° wrought,   *remedy*
Mine owne doughtinesse that help ther me brought."[5]
20   Ich have ytrodded the folk in wrathe and in grame,
Adreint al with shennesse, ydrawe down with shame."[6]

---

1. The poem, by William Herebert (d. 1333), paraphrases Isaiah 63.1–7, in which the "lordling" (lord's son) is a messianic figure returning from battle against the Edomites.
2. Who is this lord's son?
3. With blood-red garment, so terribly arrayed.
4. So fair to behold.
5. So boldly he goes.
6. Who speaks only what is right.
7. Why then is thy garment red, all stained with blood, like treaders in the winepress all spattered with must (the juice of the grapes).

8. Them, i.e., humankind symbolized by the grapes in the press. Cf. line 20.
9. And my garment is all spattered with their blood together.
1. That same vengeance (perhaps Judgment Day).
2. I do not forget the year of paying wages.
3. I looked all around for some man to help (me).
4. I searched the whole crowd.
5. My own valor brought help to me there.
6. All drowned with ignominy, pulled down with shame.

"On Godes milsfulnesse° ich wil bethenche me,[7] *mercy*
And herien° him in alle thing that he yeldeth° me." *praise / gives*

Ye That Pasen by the Weye

Ye that pasen by the weye,
Abidet a little stounde.° *while*
Beholdet, all my felawes,
Yif° any me lik is founde.[8] *if*
5 To the tre with nailes thre
Wol° fast I hange bounde; *very*
With a spere all thoru my side
To mine herte is made a wounde.

Sunset on Calvary

Now gooth sunne under wode:[9]
Me reweth,[1] Marye, thy faire rode.° *face*
Now gooth sunne under tree:
Me reweth, Marye, thy sone and thee.

I Sing of a Maiden

I sing of a maiden
 That is makelees:[2]
King of alle kinges
 To° her sone she chees.° *as / chose*

5 He cam also° stille *as*
 Ther° his moder° was *where / mother*
As dewe in Aprille
 That falleth on the gras.

He cam also stille
10 To his modres bowr
As dewe in Aprille
 That falleth on the flowr.

He cam also stille
 Ther his moder lay
15 As dewe in Aprille
 That falleth on the spray.

7. I will bethink myself.
8. Lines 1–4 paraphrase Lamentations 1.1–2.
9. Both the woods and the wooden Cross.

1. I pity.
2. Spotless, matchless, and mateless—a triple pun.

    Moder and maiden
      Was nevere noon but she:
      Wel may swich° a lady   *such*
20   Godes moder be.

Adam Lay Bound

Adam lay ybounden, bounden in a bond,
Four thousand winter thoughte he not too long;
And al was for an apple, an apple that he took,
As clerkes finden writen, writen in hire book.
5 Ne hadde[3] the apple taken been, the apple taken been,
Ne hadde nevere Oure Lady ybeen hevene Queen.
Blessed be the time that apple taken was:
Therfore we mown° singen *Deo Gratias.*[4]   *may*

The Corpus Christi Carol

    Lully, lullay, lully, lullay,
    The faucon° hath borne my make° away.   *falcon / mate*

    He bare him up, he bare him down,
    He bare him into an orchard brown.

5   In that orchard ther was an hall
    That was hanged with purple and pall.°   *black velvet*

    And in that hall ther was a bed:
    It was hanged with gold so red.

    And in that bed ther lith° a knight,   *lies*
10   His woundes bleeding by day and night.

    By that beddes side ther kneeleth a may,°   *maid*
    And she weepeth both night and day.

    And by that beddes side ther standeth a stoon°   *stone*
    Corpus Christi[5] writen thereon.

3. Had not.   5. Body of Christ.
4. Thanks be to God.

JULIAN OF NORWICH
1342–ca. 1416

The "Showings," or "Revelations" as they are also called, were sixteen mystical visions received by the woman known as Julian of Norwich. The name may be one that she adopted when she became an anchoress in a cell attached to the church of St. Julian that still stands in that city in East Anglia, then one of the most important English cities. An anchorite (m.) or anchoress (f.) is a religious recluse confined to an enclosure, which he or she has vowed never to leave. At the time of such an enclosing the burial service was performed, signifying that the enclosed person was dead to the world and that the enclosure corresponded to a grave. The point of this confinement was, of course, to pursue more actively the contemplative or spiritual life.

Julian may well have belonged to a religious order at the time that her visions led her to choose the life of an anchoress. We know little about her except what she tells us in her writings. She is, however, very precise about the date of her visions. They occurred, she tells us, at the age of thirty and a half on May 13, 1373. Four extant wills bequeath sums for Julian's maintenance in her anchorage. The most important document witnessing her life is *The Book of Margery Kempe*. Kempe asked Julian whether there might be any deception in Kempe's own visions, "for the anchoress," she says, "was expert in such things." Kempe's description of Julian's conversation accords well with the doctrines and personality that emerge from Julian's own book.

Reading and Vision. *The Hours of Mary of Burgundy*, ca. 1475. This extraordinary and utterly impossible view makes perfect sense as a vision of what the woman envisions from her reading.

A Book of Showings survives in a short and a long version. The longer text, from which the following excerpts are taken, was the product of fifteen and more years of meditation on the meaning of the visions in which much had been obscure to Julian. Apparently the mystical experiences were never repeated, but through constant study and contemplation the showings acquired a greater clarity, richness, and profundity as they continued to be turned over in a mind both gifted with spiritual insight and learned in theology. Her editors document her extensive use of the Bible and her familiarity with medieval religious writings in both English and Latin.

Julian's sixteen revelations are each treated in uneven numbers of Chapters; these groupings of chapters form an extended meditation on a given vision. Each vision is treated with an unpredictable combination of visual description of what Julian saw, the words she was offered, and the meanings she "saw." Her visions are, in her words, "ghostly" (that is, spiritual), "bodily," and subtle combinations of the two. They embrace powerful visual phenomena such as blood drops running from the crown of thorns and revelations that take place in pure mind. All are, nevertheless, "seen"; the spiritualized meanings do not render bodily sights redundant.

Of the selections here, Chapters 3 and 86 are from the opening and closing sequences of the work; Chapters 4, 5, and 7 are from the First Vision; Chapter 27 from the Thirteenth Vision; and Chapters 58, 59, 60, and 61 from the great Fourteenth Vision.

Julian's First Vision is rooted in, but moves beyond, the tradition of affective piety described in the headnote to this section. The vision is provoked by Julian's own bodily approximation to the bodily pains of Christ, as she thinks she is dying. The crucifix offered for her comfort provokes a kinetic, fresh response, as it seems to move into life, bleeding and persuading Julian that the vision is God's unmediated gift to her. Julian moves well beyond this initial sight, however; she sees a sequence of created things: the Virgin Mary as the best creature that God made, and, lower down the scale, the entire world in her palm, "the quantity of an hazelnut." Such a vision might lead away from created things altogether, into a realm of pure essence; significantly, it does not, precisely because Julian never leaves the sight of the wounded, bodily Christ, whose very physical suffering is somehow simultaneous with these almost immaterial visions. Julian strains the tradition of affective piety to its limits, but ends by transforming rather than rejecting it.

The serene optimism Julian's visions express for the material, created world and for fallen creatures extends into the most daring and surprising realms of speculation. "Sin is behovely": these are (Julian's) Christ's own words. They are expressed in the Thirteenth Vision for the first time (Chapter 27), but only in the extended, daring meditation of the Fourteenth Vision (not included in the Shorter Version) are they given their deepest sense. At the heart of Julian's profoundly optimistic theology is a transformative understanding of Christ's Humanity. She develops, without ever mentioning it explicitly, the idea of the felix culpa, the notion that, given its happy consequence in Christ's redemption of mankind, Adam's sin, or culpa, was somehow, "happy" (felix). Christ is so much a part of us, by Julian's account, that He is "the ground of our kind [natural/kind] making" (Chapter 59). He is our Mother, who strains and suffers as He gives birth to our salvation. Julian's concept of Jesus as mother has antecedents in both Old and New Testaments, in medieval theology, and in the writings of medieval mystics (both men and women), but nowhere else in Middle English writing is the concept so subtly and resonantly explored.

Julian was clearly aware of the dangers of expressing such high mysteries as a woman writer. She participates, it is true, in a late medieval tradition of visionary writing, often by women, such as the *Dialogue* of Catherine of Siena (translated into Middle English as the *Orchard of Syon*) and the *Revelations* of St. Bridget of Sweden (also translated into Middle English). Julian, however, does not refer to these figures; instead, she negotiates the difficulties and dangers of writing as a woman with enormous tact and shrewdness, both disclaiming and creating exceptional authority. Part of her strategy is to write with calm lucidity; part is to claim that the vision is not particular to her alone. Precisely by virtue of a common humanity, the visions are common property: "We are all one, and I am sure I saw it for the profit of many other."

From A Book of Showings to the Anchoress
Julian of Norwich[1]

Chapter 3

[JULIAN'S BODILY SICKNESS AND THE WOUNDS OF CHRIST]

And when I was thirty year old and a half, God sent me a bodily sickness in the which I lay three days and three nights; and on the fourth night I took all my rites of holy church, and went[2] not to have liven till day. And after this I lay two days and two nights; and on the third night I weened[3] often-times to have passed,[4] and so weened they that were with me. And yet in this I felt a great loathsomeness[5] to die, but for nothing that was on earth that me liketh to live for, ne[6] for no pain that I was afraid of, for I trusted in God of his mercy. But it was for I would have lived to have loved God better and longer time, that I might by the grace of that living have the more knowing and loving of God in the bliss of heaven. For me thought[7] all that time that I had lived here so little and so short in regard of[8] that endless bliss, I thought: Good Lord, may my living no longer be to thy worship?[9] And I understood by my reason and by the feeling of my pains that I should die; and I assented fully with all the will of my heart to be at God's will.

Thus I endured till day, and by then was my body dead from the middes downward, as to my feeling.[1] Then was I holpen[2] to be set upright, underset[3] with help, for to have the more freedom of my heart to be at God's will, and thinking on God while my life lasted. My curate was sent for to be at my ending, and before he came I had set up my eyen[4] and might not speak. He set the cross before my face and said: "I have brought the image of thy savior; look thereupon and comfort thee therewith." Me thought I was well, for my eyen was set upright into heaven, where I trusted to come by the mercy of God; but nevertheless I assented to set my eyen in the face of the crucifix, if I might, and so I did, for me thought I might longer dure to look even forth than right up.[5] After this my sight began to fail. It waxed as dark about me in the chamber as if it had been night, save in the image of the cross, wherein held a common light; and I wist[6] not how. All that was beside the cross was ugly and fearful to me as[7] it had been much occupied with fiends.

After this the over[8] part of my body began to die so farforth that unneth[9] I had any feeling. My most pain was shortness of breath and failing of life. Then went[1] I verily to have passed. And in this suddenly all my pain was taken from me, and I was as whole, and namely in the over part of my body, as ever I was before. I marvelled of this sudden change, for me thought that it was a privy working of God, and not of kind;[2] and yet by feeling of this

---

1. The text is based on that given by Edmund Colledge, O.S.A., and James Walsh, S. J., for the Pontifical Institute of Mediaeval Studies, Toronto (1978), but it has been freely edited and modern spelling has been used where possible.
2. Thought.
3. Supposed.
4. Died.
5. Reluctance.
6. Nor.
7. I thought, [it] thought me.
8. In comparison with.

9. Glory.
1. As it felt to me.
2. Helped.
3. Supported.
4. Eyes.
5. Endure to look straight ahead than straight up.
6. Knew.
7. As if.
8. Upper.
9. To the extent that scarcely.
1. Thought.
2. Nature.

ease I trusted never more to have lived, ne the feeling of this ease was no full ease to me, for me thought I had liever[3] have been delivered of this world, for my heart was willfully set thereto.

Then came suddenly to my mind that I should desire the second wound of our Lord's gift and of his grace, that my body might be fulfilled with mind and feeling of his blessed passion, as I had before prayed,[4] for I would that his pains were my pains, with compassion and afterward longing to God. Thus thought me that I might with his grace have the wounds that I had before desired; but in this I desired never no bodily sight ne no manner showing of God, but compassion as me thought that a kind soul might have with our Lord Jesu, that for love would become a deadly[5] man. With him I desired to suffer, living in my deadly body, as God would give me grace.

Chapter 4

[CHRIST'S PASSION AND INCARNATION]

And in this suddenly I saw the red blood running down from under the garland, hot and freshly, plenteously and lively, right as it was in the time that the garland of thorns was pressed on his blessed head. Right so, both God and man, the same that suffered for me, I conceived truly and mightily that it was himself that shewed it me without any mean.[6]

And in the same showing suddenly the Trinity fulfilled my heart most of joy, and so I understood it shall be in heaven without end to all that shall come there. For the Trinity is God, God is the Trinity. The Trinity is our maker, the Trinity is our keeper, the Trinity is our everlasting lover, the Trinity is endless joy and our bliss, by our Lord Jesu Christ, and in our Lord Jesu Christ. And this was showed in the first sight and in all, for where Jesu appeareth, the blessed Trinity is understand, as to my sight.[7] And I said, *"Benedicite dominus."*[8] This I said for reverence in my meaning,[9] with a mighty voice, and full greatly was I astoned[1] for wonder and marvel that I had, that he that is so reverend and so dreadful[2] will be so homely[3] with a sinful creature living in this wretched flesh.

Thus I took it for that time that our Lord Jesu of his courteous love would show me comfort before the time of my temptation; for me thought it might well be that I should by the sufferance of God and with his keeping be tempted of[4] fiends before I should die. With this sight of his blessed passion, with the godhead that I saw in my understanding, I knew well that it was strength enough to me, yea, and to all creatures living that should be saved, against all the fiends of hell, and against all ghostly[5] enemies.

In this he brought our Lady Saint Mary to my understanding; I saw her ghostly in bodily likeness, a simple maiden and a meek, young of age, a little waxen above a child,[6] in the stature as she was when she conceived. Also God

3. Rather.
4. Julian had prayed for three gifts: direct experience of Christ's passion, mortal sickness, and the wounds of true contrition, loving compassion, and a willed desire for God.
5. Mortal.
6. Intermediary.
7. Is understood, as I see it.
8. Blessed be the Lord.

9. Intention.
1. Astonished.
2. Awe-inspiring.
3. Familiar, intimate (the quality of being "at home").
4. By.
5. Spiritual.
6. Grown a little older than a child.

showed me in part the wisdom and the truth of her soul, wherein I understood the reverend beholding, that she beheld her God, that is her maker, marvelling with great reverence that he would be born of her that was a simple creature of his making. And this wisdom and truth, knowing the greatness of her maker and the littlehead[7] of herself that is made, made her to say full meekly to Gabriel: "Lo me here, God's handmaiden."[8] In this sight I did understand verily that she is more than all that God made beneath her in worthiness and in fullhead;[9] for above her is nothing that is made but the blessed manhood of Christ, as to my sight.

Chapter 5

[ALL CREATION AS A HAZELNUT]

In this same time that I saw this sight of the head bleeding, our good Lord showed a ghostly sight of his homely loving. I saw that he is to us all thing that is good and comfortable to our help. He is our clothing that for love wrappeth us and windeth us, halseth us[1] and all becloses us, hangeth about us for tender love that[2] he may never leave us. And so in this sight I saw that he is all thing that is good, as to my understanding.

And in this he showed a little thing, the quantity of an hazelnut, lying in the palm of my hand, as me seemed, and it was as round as a ball. I looked thereon with the eye of my understanding, and thought: What may this be? And it was answered generally thus: It is all that is made. I marvelled how it might last, for me thought it might suddenly have fallen to nought for[3] littleness. And I was answered in my understanding: It lasteth and ever shall, for God loveth it; and so hath all thing being by the love of God.

In this little thing I saw three properties. The first is that God made it, the second that God loveth it, the third that God keepeth[4] it. But what beheld I therein? Verily, the maker, the keeper, the lover. For till I am substantially united to him[5] I may never have full rest ne very[6] bliss; that is to say that I be so fastened to him that there be right nought that is made between my God and me.

This little thing that is made, me thought it might have fallen to nought for littleness. Of this needeth us to have knowledge, that us liketh nought all thing that is made, for to love and have God that is unmade.[7] For this is the cause why we be not all in ease of heart and of soul, for we seek here rest in this thing that is so little, where no rest is in, and we know not our God, that is almighty, all wise and all good, for he is very rest. God will be known, and him liketh that we rest us in him; for all that is beneath him suffiseth not to us. And this is the cause why that no soul is in rest till it is noughted of all things that is made.[8] When she is wilfully[9] noughted for love, to have him that is all, then is she able to receive ghostly rest.

---

7. Littleness.
8. See Luke 1.38.
9. Perfection.
1. Envelops us and embraces us.
2. So that.
3. Because of.
4. Looks after.
5. Joined to him in "substance," which Julian

regards as the eternal essence of being.
6. True.
7. I.e., we need to know that we should not be attracted to earthly things, which are made, to love and possess God, who is not made, who exists eternally.
8. Emptied of (its attachment to) all created things.
9. Of its free will.

And also our good Lord showed that it is full great pleasance to him that a sely[1] soul come to him naked, plainly and homely. For this is the kind[2] yearning of the soul by the touching of the Holy Ghost, as by the understanding that I have in this showing: God of thy goodness gave me thyself, for thou art enough to me, and I may ask nothing that is less that may be full worship to thee. And if I ask any thing that is less, ever me wanteth;[3] but only in thee I have all.

And these words of the goodness of God be full lovesome to the soul and full near touching the will of our Lord, for his goodness fulfilleth all his creatures and all his blessed works and overpasseth[4] without end. For he is the endlesshead and he made us only to himself and restored us by his precious passion,[5] and ever keepeth us in his blessed love; and all this is of his goodness.

* * *

Chapter 7

[CHRIST AS HOMELY AND COURTEOUS]

And in all that time that he showed this that I have now said in ghostly sight, I saw the bodily sight lasting of the plenteous bleeding of the head. The great drops of blood fell down fro under the garland like pellets, seeming as it had come out of the veins. And in the coming out they were brown red, for the blood was full thick; and in the spreading abroad they were bright red. And when it came at the brows, there they vanished; and not withstanding the bleeding continued till many things were seen and understanded. Nevertheless the fairhead and livelihead continued in the same beauty and liveliness.

The plenteoushead is like to the drops of water that fall of the evesing[6] of an house after a great shower of rain, that fall so thick that no man may number them with no bodily wit.[7] And for the roundness they were like to the scale of herring in the spreading of the forehead.

These three things came to my mind in the time: pellets for the roundhead[8] in the coming out of the blood, the scale of the herring for the roundhead in the spreading, the drops of the evesing of a house for the plenteoushead unnumerable. This showing was quick[9] and lively and hideous and dreadful and sweet and lovely; and of all the sight that I saw this was most comfort to me, that our good Lord, that is so reverend and dreadful, is so homely and so courteous, and this most fulfilled me with liking and sickerness[1] in soule.

And to the understanding of this he showed this open example. It is the most worship[2] that a solemn king or a great lord may do to a poor servant if he will be homely with him; and namely if he show it himself of a full true meaning[3] and with a glad cheer both in private and openly. Then thinketh this poor creature thus: "Lo, what might this noble lord do more worship and joy to me than to show to me that am so little this marvelous homeliness? Verily, it is more joy and liking to me than if he gave me great gifts and

---

1. Innocent.
2. Natural.
3. I am forever lacking.
4. Surpasses.
5. Suffering.
6. Eaves.
7. Intelligence.
8. Roundness.
9. Vivid.
1. Security.
2. Honor.
3. Intent.

were himself strange in manner." This bodily example was showed so high that this man's heart might be ravished and almost forget himself for joy of this great homeliness.

Thus it fareth by our Lord Jesu and by us, for verily it is the most joy that may be, as to my sight, that he that is highest and mightiest, noblest and worthiest, is lowest and meekest, homeliest and courteousest. And truly and verily this marvelous joy shall be show us all when we shall see him. And this will our good Lord that we believe and trust, joy and like, comfort us and make solace as we may with his grace and with his help, into[4] the time that we see it verily. For the most fullhead of joy that we shall have, as to my sight, is this marvelous courtesy and homeliness of our fader, that is our maker, in our Lord Jesu Christ, that is our brother and oure saviour. But this marvelous homeliness may no man know in this life, but if he have it by special showing of our Lord, or of great plenty of grace inwardly given of the Holy Ghost. But faith and belief with charity deserve the meed,[5] and so it is had by grace. For in faith with hope and charity our life is grounded. The showing is made to whom that God will, plainly teacheth the same opened and declared, with many privy points belonging to our faith and belief which be worshipful to be known. And when the showing which is given for a time is passed and hid, then faith keepeth it by grace of the Holy Ghost into our life's end. And thus by the showing it is none other than the faith, ne less ne more, as it may be seen by our Lord's meaning in the same matter, by then[6] it come to the last end.

Chapter 27

[SIN IS FITTING]

And after this our Lord brought to my mind the longing that I had to him before; and I saw nothing letted[7] me but sin, and so I beheld generally in us all, and me thought that if sin had not been, we should all have been clean[8] and like to our Lord as he made us. And thus in my folly before this time often I wondered why, by the great foreseeing wisdom of God, the beginning of sin was not letted.[9] For then thought me that all should have been well.

This stering[1] was much to be forsaken; and nevertheless mourning and sorrow I made therefore without reason and discretion. But Jesu that in this vision informed me of all that me needed answered by this word and said: "Sin is behovely[2] but all shall be well, and all manner of thing shall be well."[3] In this naked word "Sin," our Lord brought to my mind generally all that is not good, and the shameful despite[4] and the uttermost tribulation that he bore for us in this life, and his dying and all his pains, and passion[5] of all his creatures ghostly and bodily. For we be all in part troubled, and we shall be troubled, following our master Jesu, till we be fully purged of our deadly[6] flesh which be not very good.

---

4. Until.
5. Reward. "Charity": love. See 1 Corinthians 13.13.
6. By the time that.
7. Hindered.
8. Pure.
9. Prevented.
1. Fretting.

2. Fitting.
3. T. S. Eliot quotes this statement, versions of which appear several times in the *Showings*, in the last movement of his *Four Quartets*.
4. Spite.
5. Suffering.
6. Mortal.

And with the beholding of this, with all the pains that ever were or ever shall be, I understood the passion of Christ for the most pain and overpassing.[7] And with all, this was showed in a touch, readily passed over into comfort. For our good Lord would not that the soul were afeared of this ugly sight. But I saw not sin, for I believe it had no manner of substance, ne no part of being,[8] ne it might not be known but by the pain that is caused thereof. And this pain is something, as to my sight, for a time, for it purgeth and maketh us to know ourself and ask mercy; for the passion of our Lord is comfort to us against all this, and so is his blessed will. And for the tender love that our good Lord hath to all that shall be saved, he comforteth readily and sweetly, meaning thus: It is true that sin is cause of all this pain, but all shall be well, and all manner of thing shall be well.

These words were showed full tenderly, showing no manner of blame to me ne to none that shall be safe.[9] Then were it great unkindness of me to blame or wonder on God of my sin, sithen[1] he blameth not me for sin. And in these same words I saw an high marvelous privity[2] hid in God, which privity he shall openly make and shall be known to us in heaven. In which knowing we shall verily see the cause why he suffered sin to come, in which sight we shall endlessly have joy.

Chapters 58, 59, 60, 61

[JESUS AS MOTHER]

From *Chapter 58*

God the blessedful Trinity, which is everlasting being, right as he is endless fro without beginning,[3] right so it was in his purpose endless to make mankind,[4] which fair kind[5] first was dight to[6] for his own son, the second person; and when he would,[7] by full accord of all the Trinity he made us all at once.[8] And in our making he knit us and oned[9] us to himself, by which oneing we be kept as clean[1] and as noble as we were made. By the virtue of that ilke[2] precious oneing we love our maker and like[3] him, praise and thank him, and endlessly enjoy[4] in him. And this is the working which is wrought continually in each soul that shall be saved, which is the godly will before said.

And thus in our making God almighty is our kindly[5] father, and god all wisdom is our kindly mother, with the love and the goodness of the Holy Ghost, which is all one God, one Lord. And in the knitting and in the oneing he is our very true spouse and we his loved wife[6] and his fair maiden, with which wife he was never displeased. For he sayeth: "I love thee and thou lovest me, and our love shall never part in two."

---

7. Exceeding (pain).
8. On "substance" and "being," see chapter 5, p. 416, n. 5.
9. Saved.
1. Since.
2. Secret.
3. I.e., eternal.
4. I.e., his purpose to make humankind is also eternal.
5. Nature.
6. Prepared for.
7. Wanted to.

8. All of us at one and the same time.
9. United. Julian sustains the idea of oneness in the verb *oned* and the noun *oneing*.
1. Pure.
2. Same.
3. Please.
4. Rejoice.
5. Both "kind" and "natural."
6. The relationship between God and humanity is also conceived as a mystical marriage in which Christ is the bridegroom and the human soul his spouse.

I beheld the working of all the blessed Trinity, in which beholding I saw and understood these three properties: The property of the fatherhood, and the property of the motherhood, and the property of the lordship in one God. In our father almighty we have our keeping[7] and our bliss as anemptis[8] our kindly substance which is to us by our making fro without beginning.[9] And in the second person in wit[1] and wisdom we have our keeping as anemptis our sensuality[2] our restoring and our saving, for he is our mother, brother and savior And in our good lord the Holy Ghost we have our rewarding and our yielding[3] for our living and our travail,[4] and endlessly overpassing[5] all that we desire in his marvelous courtesy of his high plenteous grace. For all our life is in three: in the first we have our being, and in the second we have our increasing, and in the third we have our fulfilling. The first is kind,[6] the second is mercy, the third is grace.

For the first[7] I saw and understood that the high might of the Trinity is our father, and the deep wisdom of the Trinity is our mother, and the great love of the Trinity is our lord; and all these have we in kind and in our substantial making. And furthermore I saw that the second person, which is our mother, substantially the same dearworthy person,[8] is now become our mother sensual,[9] for we be double of God's making, that is to say substantial and sensual. Our substance is the higher part, which we have in our father God almighty; and the second person of the Trinity is our mother in kind in our substantial making, in whom we be grounded and rooted, and he is our mother of mercy in our sensual taking.[1]

* * *

From *Chapter* 59

* * *

And thus is Jesu our very[2] mother in kind of our first making, and he is our very mother in grace by taking of our kind made. All the fair working and all the sweet kindly offices of dearworthy motherhood is impropered to[3] the second person, for in him we have this goodly will, whole and safe without end, both in kind and in grace, of his own proper goodness.

I understood three manner of beholdings of motherhood in God. The first is ground of our kind making, the second is taking of our kind, and there beginneth the motherhood of grace, the third is motherhood in working.[4] And therein is a forthspreading[5] by the same grace of length and breadth, of high and of deepness without end. And all is one love.

Chapter 60

But now me behooveth to say a little more of this forthspreading, as I understood, in the meaning of our Lord: how that we be brought again by the

---

7. Protection.
8. With regard to.
9. I.e., our natural created being which is eternal. On *substance* see chapter 5, p. 416, n. 5.
1. Intelligence.
2. With regard to the nature of our sensual being (as opposed to substance).
3. Payment.
4. Life and labor.
5. Surpassing.

6. Nature.
7. For the first time.
8. The same beloved person with regard to our eternal being.
9. Mother of our physical being.
1. Taking on of sensuality.
2. True.
3. Appropriated to.
4. At work.
5. (Infinite) spreading out, expansion.

motherhood of mercy and grace into our kindly stead, where that we were in,[6] made by the motherhood of kind love, which kind love never leaveth us.

Our kind mother, our gracious mother (for he would[7] all wholly become our mother in all thing) he took the ground of his work full low[8] and full mildly in the maiden's womb. And that showed he first, where he brought that meek maiden before the eye of my understanding, in the simple stature as she was when she conceived;[9] that is to say our high god, the sovereign wisdom of all, in this low place he arrayed him and dight him[1] all ready in our poor flesh, himself to do the service, he and the office of motherhood in all thing. The mother's service is nearest, readiest, and surest: nearest for it is most of kind, readiest for it is most of love, and sikerest[2] for it is most of truth. This office ne might nor could never none doon to the full but he alone. We wit[3] that all our mothers bear us to pain and to dying. Ah, what is that? But our very Mother Jesu, he alone beareth us to joy and to endless living, blessed moot[4] he be. Thus he sustaineth us within him in love and travail, into the full time that he would suffer the sharpest thorns and grievous pains that ever were or ever shall be, and died at the last. And when he had done, and so borne us to bliss, yet might not all this make aseeth[5] to his marvelous love. And that showed he in these high overpassing words of love: "If I might suffer more I would suffer more."[6] He might no more die, but he would not stint[7] working.

Wherefore him behooveth to find[8] us, for the dearworthy love of motherhood hath made him debtor to us.[9] The mother may give her child sucken her milk, but our precious mother Jesu, he may feed us with himself, and doth full courteously and full tenderly with the blessed sacrament, that is precious food of very life; and with all the sweet sacraments he sustaineth us full mercifully and graciously, and so meant he in these blessed words, where he said: "I it am that holy church preacheth thee and teacheth thee." That is to say: All the health and the life of sacraments, all the virtue and the grace of my word, all the goodness that is ordained in holy church to thee, I it am.

The mother may lay her child tenderly to her breast, but our tender mother Jesu, he may homely lead us into his blessed breast by his sweet open side,[1] and show us therein in party of[2] the godhead and the joys of heaven with ghostly sureness of endless bliss. And that showed he in the tenth revelation, giving the same understanding in this sweet word where he sayeth: "Lo, how I love thee." * * *

This fair lovely word "Mother," it is so sweet and so kind in itself that it may not verily be said of none ne to none but of him and to him[3] that is very mother of life and of all. To the property of motherhood longeth[4] kind love, wisdom, and knowing, and it is God. For though it be so that our bodily forthbringing be but little, low, and simple in regard[5] of our ghostly forthbringing, yet it is he that doth it in the creatures by whom that it is done. The

---

6. The natural condition, i.e., the state of grace, that we were in originally.
7. Because he wanted to.
8. I.e., he laid the groundwork for his mission in a very humble place.
9. The appearance of the Virgin in Julian's first vision. See chapter 4, p. 415.
1. Arrayed and dressed himself.
2. Surest.
3. Know.
4. May.
5. Bring satisfaction.

6. These and other quotations refer to Julian's earlier revelations.
7. Stop.
8. Nourish, feed.
9. As any mother is obligated to look after her child.
1. The wound inflicted by a soldier in John 19.34.
2. A part of.
3. Other manuscripts read "her," with reference to the Virgin.
4. Belongs.
5. In comparison with.

kind loving mother that woot and knoweth the need of her child, she keepeth it full tenderly as the kind and condition of motherhood will. And ever as it waxeth[6] in age and in stature, she changeth her works but not her love. And when it is waxed of more age, she suffereth it that it be chastised in breaking down of vices to make the child receive virtues and grace. This working with all that be fair and good, our Lord doth it in hem by whom it is done. Thus he is our mother in kind by the working of grace in the lower party for love of the higher. And he will[7] that we know it, for he will have all our love fastened to him; and in this I saw that all debt that we owe by God's bidding to fatherhood and motherhood is fulfilled in true loving of God, which blessed love Christ worketh in us. And this was showed in all, and namely in the words where he sayeth: "I it am that thou lovest."

Chapter 61

And in our ghostly forthbringing he useth more tenderness in keeping without any comparison, by as much as our soul is of more price in his sight. He kindleth our understanding, he prepareth our ways, he easeth our conscience, he comforteth our soul, he lighteth our heart and giveth us in party knowing and loving in his blessedful godhead, with gracious mind in his sweet manhood and his blessed passion, with courteous marveling in his high overpassing goodness, and maketh us to love all that he loveth for his love, and to be well apaid[8] with him and with all his works. And when we fall, hastily he raiseth us by his lovely becleping[9] and his gracious touching. And when we be strengthened by his sweet working, then we wilfully[1] choose him by his grace to be his servants and his lovers, lastingly without end.

And yet after this he suffereth some of us to fall more hard and more grievously than ever we did before, as us thinketh. And then ween[2] we (that be not all wise) that all were nought that we have begun. But it is not so, for it needeth us to fall, and it needeth us to see it; for if we fell not, we should not know how feeble and how wretched we be of ourself, nor also we should not so fulsomely[3] know the marvelous love of our maker.

For we shall verily see in heaven without end that we have grievously sinned in this life; and notwithstanding this we shall verily see that we were never hurt in his love, nor we were never the less of price in his sight. And by the assay of this falling we shall have an high and a marvelous knowing of love in God without an end. For hard and marvelous is that love which may not nor will not be broken for[4] trespass.

And this was one understanding of profit; and other[5] is the lowness and meekness that we shall get by the sight of our falling, for thereby we shall highly be raised in heaven, to which rising we might never have come without that meekness. And therefore it needed us to see it; and if we see it not, though we fell it should not profit us. And commonly first we fall and sithen[6] we see it; and both is of the mercy of God.

6. Grows.
7. Wants.
8. Pleased.
9. Calling (to us).
1. Gladly.

2. Suppose.
3. Fully.
4. Because of.
5. Another.
6. Then.

The mother may suffer the child to fall sometime and be diseased[7] in diverse manner of peril come to her child for love. And though our earthly mother may suffer her child to perish, our heavenly mother Jesu may never suffer us that be his children to perish, for he is all mighty, all wisdom, and all love, and so is none but he, blessed mote he be.

But oft times when our falling and our wretchedness is showed to us, we be so sore adread and so greatly ashamed of ourself that unnethes[8] we wit where that we may hold us. But then will not our courteous mother that we flee away, for him were nothing loather;[9] for then he will that we use[1] the condition of a child. For when it is diseased and afeared, it runneth hastily to the mother; and if it may do no more, it crieth on the mother for help with all the might. So will he that we do as the meek child, saying thus: "My kind mother, my gracious mother, my dearworthy mother, have mercy on me. I have made myself foul and unlike to thee, and I may not nor can amend it but with thine help and grace."

And if we feel us not then eased, as soon be we sure that he useth[2] the condition of a wise mother. For if he see that it be for profit to us to mourn and to weep, he suffereth with ruth[3] and pity, into the best time,[4] for love. And he will then that we use the property of a child that ever more kindly trusteth to the love of the mother in weal and in woe. And he will that we take us mightily to the faith of holy church and find there our dearworthy mother in solace and true understanding with all the blessed common.[5] For one singular person may oftentimes be broken, as it seemeth to the self, but the whole body of holy church was never broken, nor never shall be without end. And therefore a sure thing it is, a good and a gracious, to willen meekly and mightily been fastened and oned to our mother holy church, that is Christ Jesu. For the flood of his mercy that is his dearworthy blood and precious water is plenteous to make us fair and clean. The blessed wounds of our savior be open and enjoy[6] to heal us. The sweet gracious hands of our mother be ready and diligent about us; for he in all this working useth the very office of a kind nurse that hath not else to do but to entend[7] the salvation of her child.

It is his office to save us, it is his worship to do it, and it is his will we know it; for he will we love him sweetly and trust in him meekly and mightily. And this showed he in these gracious words: "I keep thee full surely."

Chapter 86

[CHRIST'S MEANING]

This book is begun by God's gift and his grace, but it is not yet performed,[8] as to my sight. For charity, pray we all together with God's working, thanking, trusting, enjoying, for thus will our good Lord be prayed, but the understanding that I took in all his own meaning, and in the sweet words where he sayeth full merrily: "I am ground of thy beseeching." For truly I saw and understood in our Lord's meaning that he showed it for he will have it known

---

7. Unhappy.
8. Scarcely.
9. Nothing would be more hateful to him.
1. He wants us to experience.
2. Right away we are sure he is practicing.
3. Compassion.

4. Until the right time.
5. Community.
6. Rejoice.
7. Be busy about.
8. Completed.

more than it is. In which knowing he will give us grace to love him and cleave to him, for he beheld his heavenly treasure with so great love on earth that he will give us more light, and solace in heavenly joy, in drawing of our hearts fro sorrow and darkness which we are in.

And fro the time that it was showed, I desired oftentimes to wit[9] in what was our Lord's meaning. And fifteen year after and more, I was answered in ghostly understanding, saying thus: "What, wouldst thou wit thy Lord's meaning in this thing? Wit it well, love was his meaning. Who showeth it thee? Love. What showed he thee? Love. Wherefore showeth he it thee? For love. Hold thee therein, thou shalt wit more in the same. But thou shalt never wit therein other withouten end."

Thus was I learned,[1] that love is our Lord's meaning. And I saw full surely in this and in all, that ere God made us he loved us, which love was never slaked[2] ne never shall. And in this love he hath done all his works, and in this love he hath made all things profitable to us, and in this love our life is everlasting. In our making we had beginning, but the love wherein he made us was in him fro without beginning. In which love we have our beginning, and all this shall we see in God withouten end.

Deo gracias. Explicit liber revelacionum Julyane anacorite Norwyche, cuius anime propicietur deus.[3]

ca. 1390

9. Know.
1. Taught.
2. Abated.

3. Thanks be to God. Here ends the book of revelations of Julian, anchorite of Norwich, on whose soul may god have mercy.

MARGERY KEMPE
ca. 1373–1438

*T*he Book of Margery Kempe is the spiritual autobiography of a medieval laywoman, telling of her struggles to carry out instructions for a holy life that she claimed to have received in personal visions from Christ and the Virgin Mary. The assertion of such a mission by a married woman, the mother of fourteen children, was in itself sufficient grounds for controversy; in addition, Kempe's outspoken defense of her visions as well as her highly emotional style of religious expression embroiled her with fellow citizens and pilgrims and with the Church, although she also won both lay and clerical supporters. Ordered by the archbishop of York to swear not to teach in his diocese, she courageously stood up for her freedom to speak her conscience.

Margery Kempe was the daughter of John Burnham, five-time mayor of King's Lynn, a thriving commercial town in Norfolk. At about the age of twenty she married John Kempe, a well-to-do fellow townsman. After the traumatic delivery of her first child—the rate of maternal mortality in childbirth was high—she sought to confess to a priest whose harsh, censorious response precipitated a mental breakdown, from which she eventually recovered through the first of her visions. Her subsequent conversion and strict religious observances generated a good deal of domestic strife, but she continued to share her husband's bed until, around the age of forty, she negotiated a vow of celibacy with him, which was confirmed before the bishop and left her free to undertake a pilgrimage to the Holy Land. There she experienced visions of Christ's passion and of the sufferings of the Virgin. These visions recurred during the rest of her life, and her noisy weeping at such times made her the object of much scorn and hostility. Her orthodoxy was several times examined, but her unquestioning acceptance of the Church's doctrines and authority, and perhaps also her status as a former mayor's daughter, shielded her against charges of heresy.

Kempe was unable to read or write, but acquired her command of Scripture and theology from sermons and other oral sources. Late in her life, she dictated her story in two parts to two different scribes; the latter of these was a priest who revised the whole text. Nevertheless, it seems likely that the work retains much of the characteristic form and expression of its author.

Kempe's text offers a perspective on the tradition of "affective piety" unlike any other: here that visionary tradition comes to life in the context of vividly realized, often painful psychological and bodily experience. Kempe's own marriage, and her often troubled worldly relations, inform and are informed by her "homely" and sometimes erotic spiritual relations. Her imitation of Christ moves her to travel vast distances to be present at the scenes of Christ's suffering, just as she sees Christ present in male babies or good-looking young men. She sees the living divine presence in the Eucharistic host. "Sir," she says to a skeptic, "His death is as fresh to me as He had died this same day." This form of intensely sympathetic vision has, however, its negative obverse. As in Chaucer's *Prioress's Tale*, where tender feeling for the Blessed Virgin is complemented by hatred for the "cursed Jewes," Christian pathos produces an anti-Semitic reflex (Book 1.79).

From The Book of Margery Kempe[1]

[THE BIRTH OF HER FIRST CHILD AND HER FIRST VISION]

[**Book 1.1**] When this creature[2] was twenty years of age or somewhat more, she was married to a worshipful[3] burgess and was with child within a short time, as nature would. And, after she had conceived, she was labored with great attacks of illness until the child was born, and then, what for the labor she had in childing and for the sickness going before, she despaired of her life, thinking she might not live. And then she sent for her ghostly father,[4] for she had a thing in conscience which she had never shown before that time in all her life. For she was ever hindered by her enemy, the devil, evermore saying to her that, while she was in good health, she needed no confession but could do penance by herself alone, and all should be forgiven, for God is merciful enough. And therefore this creature oftentimes did great penance in fasting on bread and water and other deeds of alms with devout prayers, except she would not show this sin in confession. And, when she was at any time sick or troubled, the devil said in her mind that she should be damned, for she was not shriven[5] of that sin. Wherefore, after her child was born, she, not trusting her life, sent for her ghostly father, as was said before, in full will to be shrive of all her lifetime as nearly as she could. And,

1. The text is based on the unique manuscript, first discovered in 1934, edited by Lynn Staley. Spelling and inflexional forms have in many cases been modernized. Some archaic words have also been silently translated.
2. Throughout the book Kempe refers to herself in the third person as "this creature," a standard way of saying "this person, a being created by God."
3. Worthy.
4. Spiritual father; i.e., a priest.
5. Confessed.

when she came to the point to say that thing which she had so long concealed, her confessor was a little too hasty and began sharply to reprove her before she had fully said her intent, and so she would no more say for aught he might do.

And anon, for the dread she had of damnation on the one side and his sharp reproving on that other side, this creature went out of her mind and was wonderfully vexed and labored with spirits for half a year, eight weeks and some odd days. And in this time she saw, as she thought, devils open their mouths, all inflamed with burning flames of fire as if they should have swallowed her in, sometimes menacing her, sometimes threatening her, sometimes pulling her and hailing her both night and day during the foresaid time. And also the devils cried upon her with great threats and bade her that she should forsake her Christianity, her faith, and deny her God, his mother, and all the saints in heaven, her good works and all good virtues, her father, her mother, and all her friends. And so she did. She slandered her husband, her friends and her own self; she spoke many a reproving word and many a harsh word; she knew no virtue nor goodness; she desired all wickedness; just as the spirits tempted her to say and do, so she said and did. She would have killed herself many a time because of her stirrings and have been damned with them in hell. And as a witness thereof she bit her own hand so violently that it was seen all her life afterward. And also she tore the skin on her body against her heart grievously with her nails, for she had no other instruments, and worse she would have done, save she was bound and kept with strength both day and night so that she might not have her will.

And, when she had long been labored in these and many other temptations, so that men thought she should never have escaped nor lived, then on a time, as she lay alone and her keepers were away from her, our merciful Lord Christ Jesus, ever to be trusted, worshiped be his name, never forsaking his servant in time of need, appeared to his creature, who had forsaken him, in likeness of a man, most seemly, most beautiful, and most amiable that ever might be seen with man's eye, clad in a mantle of purple silk, siting upon her bedside, looking upon her with so blessed a countenance that she was strengthened in all her spirits, said to her these words: "Daughter, why have you forsaken me, and I forsook never you?"

And anon, as soon as he had said these words, she saw verily how the air opened as bright as any lightning, and he rose up into the air, not right hastily and quickly, but fairly and easily so that she might well behold him in the air until it was closed again. And anon the creature was stabled in her wits and in her reason as well as ever she was before, and prayed her husband, as soon as he came to her, that she might have the keys of the buttery[6] in order to take her meat and drink as she had done before.

*　*　*

[MARGERY AND HER HUSBAND REACH A SETTLEMENT]

*　*　*

[Book 1.11] It befell upon a Friday on Midsummer Eve in right hot weather, as this creature was coming from York bearing a bottle with beer in her hand and

6. Pantry.

her husband a loaf in his bosom, he asked his wife this question, "Margery, if there came a man with a sword and would smite off my head unless I should common naturally with you as I have done before, tell me the truth from your conscience—for you say you will not lie—whether would you suffer my head to be smote off or else suffer me to meddle with you again, as I did at one time?"

"Alas, sir," she said, "why move you this matter, and have we been chaste these eight weeks?"

"For I will know the truth of your heart."

And then she said with great sorrow, "Forsooth I had rather see you be slain than we should turn again to our uncleanness."

And he said in reply, "You are no good wife."

And then she asked her husband what was the cause that he had not meddled with her eight weeks before, since she lay with him every night in his bed. And he said he was so made afraid when he would have touched her that he dared do no more.

"Now, good sir, amend yourself and ask God mercy, for I told you nearly three years since that you should be slain suddenly, and now is this the third year, and yet I hope I shall have my desire. Good sir, I pray you grant me what I shall ask, and I shall pray for you that you shall be saved through the mercy of our Lord Jesus Christ, and you shall have more reward in heaven than if you wore a hair cloth or a jacket of mail. I pray you, suffer me to make a vow of chastity in whatever bishop's hand that God will."

"No," he said, "that will I not grant you, for now may I use you without deadly sin and then might I not so."

Then she said again, "If it be the will of the Holy Ghost to fulfill what I have said, I pray God you may consent thereto; and, if it be not the will of the Holy Ghost, I pray God you never consent thereto."

Then went they forth toward Bridlington in right hot weather, the aforesaid creature having great sorrow and great dread for her chastity. And, as they came by a cross, her husband set himself down under the cross, calling his wife unto him and saying these words unto her, "Margery, grant me my desire, and I shall grant you your desire. My first desire is that we shall lie still together in one bed as we have done before; the second, that you shall pay my debts before you go to Jerusalem; and the third, that you shall eat and drink with me on Fridays as you were wont to do."[7]

"No, sir," she said, "to break the Friday I will never grant you while I live."

"Well," he said, "then shall I meddle you again."

She prayed him that he would give her leave to make her prayers, and he granted it well. Then she kneeled down beside a cross in the field and prayed in this manner with great abundance of tears, "Lord God, you know all things; you know what sorrow I have had to be chaste in my body to you all these three years, and now might I have my wish, and I dare not for love of you. For, if I would break that manner of fasting which you commanded me, to keep the Friday without food or drink, I should now have my desire. But, blessed Lord, you know I will not go against your will, and great now is my sorrow unless I find comfort in you. Now, blessed Jesus, make your will known to me, unworthy, so that I may follow thereafter and fulfill it with all my might."

---

7. Christ had told her that keeping a strict Friday fast would allow her to have her wish to end further sexual relations with her husband.

And then our Lord Jesus Christ with great sweetness spoke to this creature, commanding her to go again to her husband and pray him to grant her what she desired. "And he shall have what he desires. For, my worthy daughter, this was the cause that I bade you to fast, for you should the sooner obtain and get your desire, and now it is granted you. I wish no longer for you to fast, therefore I bid you in the name of Jesus eat and drink as your husband does."

Then this creature thanked our Lord Jesus Christ for his grace and his goodness, then rose up and went to her husband, saying unto him, "Sir, if it pleases you, you shall grant me my desire, and you shall have your desire. Grant me that you shall not come in my bed, and I grant you to requite your debts before I go to Jerusalem. And make my body free to God so that you never challenge me by asking the debt of matrimony after this day while you live, and I shall eat and drink on the Friday at your bidding."

Then said her husband again to her, "As free may your body be to God as it has been to me."

This creature thanked God greatly, rejoicing that she had her desire, praying her husband that they should say three Our Father's in the worship of the Trinity for the great grace that he had granted them. And so they did, kneeling under a cross, and afterward they ate and drank together in great gladness of spirit. This was on a Friday on Midsummer Eve.

※　※　※

[MARGERY SEES THE HOST[8] FLUTTER AT MASS]

※　※　※

[**Book 1.20**] One day as this creature was hearing her Mass, a young man and a good priest holding up the sacrament[9] in his hands over his head, the sacrament shook and flickered to and fro is a dove flickers with her wings. And, when he held up the chalice with the precious sacrament, the chalice moved to and fro as though it should have fallen out of his hands. When the consecration was done, this creature had great marvel about the stirring and moving of the blessed sacrament, desiring to see more consecrations, looking if it would do so again. Then said our Lord Jesus Christ to the creature, "You shall no more see it in this manner, therefore thank God that you have seen. My daughter, Bridget[1] saw me never in this manner."

Then said this creature in her thought, "Lord, what does this betoken?"

"It betokens vengeance."

"A, good Lord, what vengeance?"

Then said our Lord in reply to her, "There shall be an earthquake; tell it to whom you wish in the name of Jesus. For I tell you forsooth, right as I spoke to Saint Bridget, right so I speak to you, daughter, and I tell you truly it is true, every word that is written in Bridget's book, and by you it shall be known for very truth. And you shall fare well, daughter, in spite of all your enemies. The more envy they have for you because of my grace, the better shall I love you. I were not a rightful God unless I proved you, for I know

---

8. I.e., the Eucharistic wafer consumed in the sacrament of Communion.
9. A metonymy for the Eucharistic wafer, strictly one of the seven sacraments.

1. Saint Bridget of Sweden (ca. 1303–1373), to whose *Revelations* Margery refers in Book 1.17 and 1.58.

you better than you know yourself, whatever men say of you. You say I have great patience for the sin of the people, and you say the truth, but, if you saw the sin of the people as I do, you would have much more marvel in my patience and much more sorrow in the sin of the people than you have."

Then the creature said, "Alas, worthy Lord, what shall I do for the people?"

Our Lord answered, "It is enough for you to do as you do."

Then she prayed, "Merciful Lord Christ Jesus, in you is all mercy and grace and goodness. Have mercy, pity, and compassion for them. Show your mercy and your goodness upon them. Help them; send them very contrition, and let them never die in their sin."

Our merciful Lord said, "I may no more, daughter, for my rightfulness, do for them than I do. I send them preaching and teaching, pestilence and battles, hunger and famine, loss of their goods with great sickness, and many other tribulations, and they will not believe my words, nor will they know my visitation. And therefore I shall say to them that I made my servants to pray for you, and you despised their works and their living."

*   *   *

[PILGRIMAGE TO JERUSALEM]

*   *   *

[**Book 1.28**] And so they[2] went forth into the Holy Land till they might see Jerusalem. And, when this creature saw Jerusalem, riding on an ass, she thanked God with all her heart, praying him for his mercy that, as he had brought her to see this earthly city Jerusalem, he would grant her grace to see the blissful city Jerusalem above, the city of heaven. Our Lord Jesus Christ, answering to her thought, granted her to have her desire. Then, for joy that she had and the sweetness that she felt in the dalliance of our Lord, she was in point to have fallen off her ass, for she might not bear the sweetness and grace that God wrought in her soul. Then two German pilgrims went to her and kept her from falling, of which one was a priest. And he put spices in her mouth to comfort her, thinking she had been sick. And so they helped her forth to Jerusalem.

And, when she came there, she said, "Sirs, I pray you be not displeased though I weep sorely in this holy place where our Lord Jesus Christ was quick[3] and dead."

Then went they to the Temple[4] in Jerusalem, and they were let in on the one day at evensong time and abided therein till the next day at evensong time.

Then the friars lifted up a cross and led the pilgrims about from one place to another where our Lord had suffered his pains and his passions, every man and woman bearing a wax candle in their hand. And the friars always, as they went about, told them what our Lord suffered in every place. And the foresaid creature wept and sobbed so plenteously as though she had seen our Lord with her bodily eye suffering his Passion at that time. Before her in her soul she saw him verily by contemplation, and that caused her to have compassion. And when they came up onto the Mount of Calvary, she fell down so that she might not stand or kneel but wallowed and twisted with her body,

---

2. The company of pilgrims.
3. Living.

4. The Church of the Holy Sepulcher.

spreading her arms abroad, and cried with a loud voice as though her heart should have burst asunder, for in the city of her soul she saw verily and freshly how our Lord was crucified. Before her face she heard and saw in her ghostly sight the mourning of our Lady, of Saint John and Mary Magdalene,[5] and of many others who loved our Lord. And she had so great compassion and so great pain to see our Lord's pain that she might not keep herself from crying and roaring though she should have died from it.

And this was the first cry that ever she cried in any contemplation. And this manner of crying endured many years after this time for aught that any man might do, and therefore suffered she much despite and much reproof. The crying was so loud and so wonderful that it made the people astonished unless they had heard it before or else they knew the cause of the crying. And she had them so often that they made her right[6] weak in her bodily mights, and, namely, if she heard of our Lord's Passion. And sometimes, when she saw the crucifix, or if she saw a man or a beast, whether[7] it were, had a wound or if a man beat a child before her or smote a horse or another beast with a whip, if she might see it or hear it, she thought she saw our Lord being beaten or wounded just as she saw in the man or in the beast, as well in the field as in the town, and by herself alone, as well as among the people.

First when she had her cryings at Jerusalem, she had them often times, and in Rome also. And, when she came home into England, first at her coming home it came but seldom, as it were once in a month, afterward once in the week, afterward daily, and once she had fourteen on one day, and another day she had seven, and so as God would visit her, sometime in the church, sometime in the street, sometime in the chamber, sometime in the field when God would send them, for she knew never time nor hour when they should come. And they came never without passing great sweetness of devotion and high contemplation.

And, as soon as she perceived that she should cry, she would keep it in as much as she might, so that the people should not have heard it, for it annoyed them. For some said it was a wicked spirit vexed her; some said it was a sickness; some said she had drunk too much wine; some banned her; some wished she had been in the harbor; some would she had been in the sea in a bottomless boat; and so each man as he thought. Other ghostly men loved her and favored her the more. Some great clerks said our Lady cried never so, nor no saint in heaven, but they knew full little what she felt, nor would they not believe that she might have abstained from crying if she wished.

* * *

[MARGERY'S MARRIAGE TO AND INTIMACY WITH CHRIST]

* * *

[Book 1.35] As this creature was in the Apostle's Church at Rome on St. John Lateran's Day,[8] the Father of Heaven said to her, "Daughter, I am well pleased with you, inasmuch as you believe in all the sacraments of Holy Church and in all faith that pertains to it, and specially because you believe in the man-

---

5. Mary, St. John, and Mary Magdalene are traditionally portrayed at the foot of the cross in medieval art. See John 19.25.

6. Especially.
7. Whichever.
8. Saint John Lateran's Day, November 9.

hood of my son and because of the great compassion that you have for his bitter Passion."

Also the Father said to this creature, "Daughter, I will have you wedded to my Godhead, for I shall show you my secrets and my counsels,[9] for you shall dwell with me without end."

Then the creature kept silence in her soul and answered not thereto, for she was full sore afraid of the Godhead, and she had no knowledge of the dalliance of the Godhead, for all her love and all her affection was set on the manhood of Christ and thereof had she good knowledge, and she would for no thing have parted therefrom. She was so much affected by the manhood of Christ that when she saw women in Rome bearing children in their arms, if she might learn that there were any men children, she should then cry, roar, and weep as though she had seen Christ in his childhood. And, if she might have had her will, oftentimes she would have taken the children out from the mother's arms and have kissed them in the place of Christ. And, if she saw a handsome man, she had great pain to look on him in case she might have seen him who was both God and man. And therefore she cried many times and often when she met a seemly man and wept and sobbed full sorely in the manhood of Christ as she went in the streets at Rome, so that those who saw her wondered full much on her, for they knew not the cause.

And therefore it was no wonder if she were silent and answered not the Father of Heaven when he told her that she should be wedded to his Godhead. Then said the second person, Christ Jesus, whose manhood she loved so much, to her, "What say you, Margery, daughter, to my Father of these words that he speaks to you? Are you well pleased that it is so?"

And then she would not answer the second person but wept wonder sore, desiring to have still himself and in no way to be parted from him.

Then the second person in the Trinity answered to his Father for her and said, "Father, have her excused, for she is yet but young and not fully instructed as to how she should answer."

And then the Father took her by the hand in her soul before the Son and the Holy Ghost and the Mother of Jesus and all the twelve apostles and Saint Katherine and Saint Margaret and many other saints and holy virgins, with a great multitude of angels, saying to her soul, "I take you, Margery, for my wedded wife, for fairer, for fouler, for richer, for poorer, as long as you be buxom[1] and obedient to do what I bid you do. For, daughter, there was never a child so buxom to the mother as I shall be to you, both in well and in woe, to help you and comfort you. And thereto I make you surety."

And then the Mother of God and all the saints that were there present in her soul prayed that they might have much joy together. And then the creature with high devotion, with great plenty of tears, thanked God for this ghostly[2] comfort, considering herself in her own feeling right unworthy of any such grace as she felt, for she felt many great comforts, both ghostly comforts and bodily comforts. Sometimes she felt sweet smells with her nose; it was sweeter, she thought, than ever was any sweet earthly thing that she smelled before, nor might she ever tell how sweet it was, for she thought she might have lived thereby if they would have lasted.

---

9. Private deliberations.
1. Submissive.

2. Spiritual.

Sometimes she heard with her bodily ears such sounds and melodies that she might not well hear what a man said to her in that time unless he spoke the louder. These sounds and melodies had she heard nearly every day for the term of twenty-five years when this book was written, and especially when she was in devout prayer, also many times while she was at Rome and in England both.

She saw with her bodily eye many white things flying all about her on every side, as thick in a manner as motes[3] in the sun; they were right delicate and comfortable, and the brighter that the sun shone, the better she might see them. She saw them many different times and in many different places, both in church and in her chamber, at her meal and in her prayers, in field and in town, both going and sitting. And many times she was afraid what they might be, for she saw them as well in nights in darkness as in daylight. Then, when she was afraid of them, our Lord said unto her, "By this token, daughter, believe it is God that speaks in you, for whereso God is, heaven is, and where God is there are many angels, and God is in you and you are in him. And therefore be not afraid, daughter, for this betokens that you have many angels about you to keep you both day and night so that no devil shall have power over you nor no evil man harm you."

Then from that time forward she used to say when she saw them come, "*Benedictus qui venit in nomine domini.*"[4]

Also our Lord gave her another token, which endured about sixteen years, and it increased ever more and more, and that was a flame of fire wonderfully hot and delectable and right comfortable, not wasting but ever increasing of flame, for, though the weather was never so cold, she felt the heat burning in her breast and at her heart, as verily as a man should feel the material fire if he put his hand or his finger therein.

When she felt first the fire of love burning in her breast, she was afraid thereof, and then our Lord answered to her mind and said, "Daughter, be not afraid, for this heat is the heat of the Holy Ghost, which shall burn away all your sins, for the fire of love quenches all sins. And you shall understand by this token that the Holy Ghost is in you, and you know well wherever the Holy Ghost is, there is the Father, and where the Father is, there is the Son, and so you have fully in your soul all the Holy Trinity. Therefore you have great cause to love me right well, and yet you shall have greater cause than ever you had to love me, for you shall hear what you never heard, and you shall see what you never saw, and you shall feel what you never felt.

For, daughter, you are sure of the love of God as God is God. Your soul is more sure of the love of God than of your own body, for your soul shall part from your body, but God shall never part from your soul, for they are joined together without end. Therefore, daughter, you have as great cause to be merry as any lady in this world, and, if you knew, daughter, how much you please me when you suffer me willfully to speak in you, you should never do otherwise, for this is a holy life, and the time is right well spent. For, daughter, this life pleases me more than wearing of the jacket of mail or of the hair shirt or fasting on bread and water, for, if you said every day a thou-

---

3. Specks of dust.
4. "Blessed is he who comes in the name of the

Lord" (Matthew 21.9). A blessing used in the Mass as part of the consecration.

sand Pater Nosters[5] you should not please me as well as you do when you are in silence and suffer me to speak in your soul.

[**Book 1.36**] "Fasting, daughter, is good for young beginners and discreet penance, especially that which their ghostly father gives them or enjoins them to do. And to bid many beads,[6] it is good to those who can do no better, and yet it is not perfect. But it is a good way toward perfection. For I tell you, daughter, those who are great fasters and great doers of penance, they desire that it should be considered the best life; also those who give themselves to say many devotions, they would have that the best life, and those who give many alms, they would that that was held the best life. And I have oftentimes, daughter, told you that thinking, weeping, and high contemplation is the best life on earth. And you shall have more merit in heaven for one year of thinking in your mind than for a hundred years of praying with your mouth, and yet you will not believe me, for you will bid many beads whether I will or not.

"And yet, daughter, I will not be displeased with you whatever you think, say, or speak, for I am always pleased with you. And, if I were on earth as bodily as I was before I died on the cross, I should not be ashamed of you as many other men are, for I should take you by the hand among the people and make you great welcome so that they should well know that I loved you right well. For it is suitable for the wife to be homely with her husband. Be he never so great a lord and she so poor a woman when he wedded her, yet they must lie together and rest together in joy and peace. Right so must it be between you and me, for I take no heed what you have been but what you wish to be. And oftentimes have I told you that I have clean forgiven you all your sins. Therefore must I needs be homely with you and lie in your bed with you. Daughter, you desire greatly to see me, and you may boldly, when you are in your bed, take me to you as your wedded husband, as your most worthy darling, and as your sweet son, for I will be loved as a son should be loved by the mother and will that you love me, daughter, as a good wife ought to love her husband. And therefore you may boldly take me in the arms of your soul and kiss my mouth, my head, and my feet as sweetly as you will.

"And, as often as you think on me or would do any good deed to me, you shall have the same reward in heaven as if you did it to my own precious body which is in heaven, for I ask no more of you but your heart to love what loves you, for my love is ever ready for you."

Then she gave thanks and praise to our Lord Jesus Christ for the high grace and mercy that he showed unto her, an unworthy wretch.

This creature had divers tokens in her bodily hearing. One was a manner of sound as if it had been a pair of bellows blowing in her ear. She, being confounded thereof, was warned in her soul no fear to have, for it was the sound of the Holy Ghost. And then our Lord turned that sound into the voice of a dove, and afterward he turned it into the voice of a little bird which is called a red breast that sang full merrily oftentimes in her right ear. And then should she evermore have great grace after she heard such a token. And she had been used to such tokens about twenty-five years at the writing of this book.

---

5. "Our Father," i.e., the Lord's Prayer.
6. Prayers (the original sense of the word "bedes," applied by association to beads in a rosary).

Then our Lord Jesus Christ said to his creature, "By these tokens may you well know that I love you, for you are to me a very mother, and to all the world, because of that great charity that is in you, and yet I myself am the cause of that charity, and you shall have great reward therefore in Heaven.

[MARGERY'S REACTION TO A PIETÀ[7]]

* * *

[**Book 1.60**] The good priest, of whom it is written before, who was her reader,[8] fell into great sickness, and she was stirred in her soul to take care of him in God's service. And, when she lacked such as was needful for him, she went about to good men and good women and got such thing as was necessary unto him. He was so sick that men trusted nothing for his life, and his sickness was long continuing. Then on a time, as she was in the church hearing her mass and prayed for the same priest, our Lord said to her that he should live and fare right well. Then was she stirred to go to Norwich to Saint Stephen's Church where is buried the good vicar,[9] who died but little before that time, for whom God showed high mercy to his people, and thank him for the recovery of his priest.

She took leave of her confessor, going forth to Norwich. When she came in the churchyard of Saint Stephen's, she cried, she roared, she wept, she fell down to the ground, so fervently the fire of love burnt in her heart. Afterward she rose up again and went forth weeping into the church to the high altar, and there she fell down with violent sobbing, weepings, and loud cries beside the grave of the good vicar, all ravished with spiritual comfort in the goodness of our Lord who wrought so great grace for his servant who had been her confessor and many times heard her confession of all her living,[1] and administered to her the precious sacrament of the altar at divers times. And in so much was her devotion the more increased in that she saw our Lord work such special grace for such a creature as she had been conversant with in his lifetime. She had such holy thoughts and such holy visions that she might not control her weeping nor her crying. And therefore the people had great marvel of her, supposing that she had wept for some fleshly or earthly affection, and said unto her, "What ails you, woman? Why do you fare thus with yourself? We knew him as well as you."

Then were there priests in the same place who knew her manner of working, and they full charitably led her to a tavern and made her drink and made her full high and goodly comfort. Also there was a lady who desired to have the said creature to a meal. And therefore, as good manners required, she went to the church where the lady heard her service, where this creature saw a fair image of our Lady called a *pity*. And through the beholding of that *pity*, her mind was all wholly occupied in the Passion of our Lord Jesus Christ and in the compassion of our Lady, Saint Mary, by which she was compelled to cry full loudly and weep full sorely, as though she should have died.

---

7. An image, painted or sculpted, of the dead Christ laid across the Virgin's lap.
8. Book 1.58 relates how a priest newly arrived in Lynn read to Margery across seven or eight years, from the Bible and from visionary texts.
9. Richard of Caister (d. 1429), who had a reputation for sanctity.
1. Of (sins committed in) her entire life.

Then came to her the lady's priest, saying, "Damsel, Jesus is dead long since."

When her crying was ceased, she said to the priest, "Sir, his death is as fresh to me as if he had died this same day, and so I think it ought to be to you and to all Christian people. We ought ever to have mind of his kindness and ever think of the doleful death that he died for us."

Then the good lady, hearing her communication, said, "Sir, it is a good example to me, and to other men also, the grace that God works in her soul."

And so the good lady was her advocate and answered for her. Afterward she had her home with her to meat and showed her full glad and goodly comfort as long as she would abide there. And soon after, she came home again to Lynn, and the foresaid priest, for whom she went most specially to Norwich, who had read to her for about seven years, recovered and went about where he wished, thanked be almighty God for his goodness.

* * *

[MARGERY NURSES HER HUSBAND IN HIS OLD AGE]

* * *

[Book 1.76] It happened on a time that the husband of the said creature, a man of great age passing three score years,[2] as he would have come down from his chamber barefoot and bare-leg, he slithered or else failed of his footing and fell down to the ground from the steps, with his head under him grievously broken and bruised, insomuch that he had in his head five rolls of soft material in the wounds for many days while his head was healing. And, as God would, it was known to some of his neighbors how he had fallen down the steps, perhaps through the din and the rushing of his falling. And so they came to him and found him lying with his head under him, half on life, all streaked with blood, never likely to have spoken with priest nor with clerk unless by high grace and miracle.[3] Then the said creature, his wife, was sent for, and so she came to him. Then was he taken up and his head was sewn, and he was sick a long time after, so that men thought that he should have been dead. And then the people said, if he died, his wife was worthy to be hanged for his death, forasmuch as she might have kept him and did not.

They dwelled not together; they lay not together, for, as is written before, they both with one assent and with free will of the other had made a vow to live chaste. And therefore to avoid all perils they dwelled and so journed in divers places where no suspicion should be had of their incontinence, for first they dwelled together after they had made their vow, and then the people slandered them and said they used their lust and their liking as they did before their vow-making. And, when they went out on pilgrimage or to see and speak with other ghostly creatures, many evil folk whose tongues were their own, lacking the dread and love of our Lord Jesus Christ, thought and said that they went rather to woods, groves, or valleys to use the lust of their bodies so that the people should not espy it nor know it. They, having knowledge how prone the people were to think evil of them, desiring to avoid all occasion, inasmuch as they might goodly, by their good

2. Sixty years.
3. I.e., unlikely to have confessed to a priest and received rites except by grace.

will and their mutual consent, they parted asunder as touching their board and their chambers, and went to board in divers places. And this was the cause that she was not with him and also that she should not be hindered from her contemplation.

And therefore, when he had fallen and grievously was hurt, as is said before, the people said, if he died, it was worthy that she answer for his death. Then she prayed to our Lord that her husband might live a year and she delivered from slander if it were his pleasure. Our Lord said to her mind, "Daughter, you shall have your boon, for he shall live, and I have wrought a great miracle for you that he was not dead. And I bid you take him home and keep him for my love."

She said, "No, good Lord, for I shall then not tend to you as I do now."

"Yes, daughter," said our Lord, "you shall have as much reward for keeping him and helping him in his need at home as if you were in church to make your prayers. And you have said many times that you would fain keep me. I pray you now keep him for the love of me, for he has sometime fulfilled your will and my will both, and he has made your body free to me so that you should serve me and live chaste and clean, and therefore I will that you be free to help him at his need in my name."

"A, Lord," said she, "for your mercy grant me grace to obey your will and fulfill your will and let never my ghostly enemies have any power to hinder me from fulfilling your will."

Then she took home her husband with her and kept him years after, as long as he lived, and had full much labor with him, for in his last days he turned childish again and lacked reason so that he could not do his own easement by going to a stool, or else he would not, but, as a child, voided his natural digestion in his linen clothes where he sat by the fire or at the table, wherever it might be, he would spare no place. And therefore was her labor much the more in washing and wringing and her expense in making fires and hindered her full much from her contemplation, so that many times she should have been irked at her labor save she bethought herself of how she in her young age had full many delectable thoughts, fleshly lusts, and inordinate loves for his body. And therefore she was glad to be punished with the same person and took it much the more easily and served him and helped him, as she thought, as she would have done Christ himself.

* * *

[MARGERY'S VISION OF THE PASSION SEQUENCE[4]]

* * *

[Book 1.79] Then she beheld in the sight of her soul our blissful Lord Christ Jesus coming toward his Passion, and, before he went, he kneeled down and took his mother's blessing. Then she saw his mother falling down in swooning before her son, saying unto him, "Alas, my dear Son, how shall I suffer this sorrow and have no joy in all this world but you alone. A, dear Son, if you will die anyway, let me die before you and let me never suffer this day of sorrow, for I may never bear this sorrow that I shall have for your

---

4. Margery experiences this vision while participating in a Palm Sunday Mass.

death. I would, Son, that I might suffer death for you so that you should not die, if man's soul might so be saved. Now, dear son, if you have no pity on yourself, have pity on your mother, for you know full well there can no man in all this world comfort me but you alone."

Then our Lord took up his mother in his arms and kissed her full sweetly and said to her, "A, blessed mother, be of a good cheer and of a good comfort, for I have told you full often that I must needs suffer death, otherwise no man should be saved nor ever come into bliss. And mother, it is my father's will that it be so, and therefore I pray you let it be your will also, for my death shall bring me great honor and you and all mankind great joy and profit, for whomever trusts in my passion and works thereafter. And therefore, blessed mother, you must abide here after me, for in you shall rest all the faith of Holy Church, and by your faith Holy Church shall increase in her faith. And therefore I pray you, worthy mother, cease from your sorrowing, for I shall not leave you comfortless. I shall leave here with you John, my cousin, to comfort you instead of me; I shall send my holy angels to comfort you on earth; and I shall comfort you in your soul my own self, for, mother, you know well I have promised you the bliss of heaven and that you are sure thereof. A, worthy mother, what would you better than where I am king you be queen, and all angels and saints shall be obedient to your will?

"And what grace you ask me I shall not deny your desire. I shall give you power over the devils so that they shall be afraid of you and you not of them. And also, my blessed mother, I have said to you beforetime that I shall come for you my own self when you shall pass out of this world with all my angels and all my saints that are in heaven and bring you before my father with all manner of music, melody, and joy. And there shall I set you in great peace and rest without end. And there shall you be crowned as Queen of Heaven, as lady of all the world, and as Empress of Hell. And therefore, my worthy mother, I pray you bless me and let me go do my father's will, for therefore I came into this world and took flesh and blood from you."

When the said creature beheld this glorious sight in her soul and saw how he blessed his mother and his mother him, and then his blessed mother might not speak one word more to him but fell down to the ground, and so they parted asunder, his mother lying still as if she had been dead, then the said creature thought she took our Lord Jesus Christ by the clothes and fell down at his feet, praying him to bless her, and therewith she cried full loudly and wept right sorely, saying in her mind, "A, Lord, what shall become of me? I had far rather that you would slay me than let me abide in the world without you, for without you I may not abide here, Lord."

Then answered our Lord to her, "Be still, daughter, and rest with my mother here, and comfort you in her, for she who is my own mother must suffer this sorrow. But I shall come again, daughter, to my mother and comfort her and you both and turn all your sorrow into joy."

And then she thought our Lord went forth his way, and she went to our Lady and said, "A, blessed Lady, rise up and let us follow your blessed son as long as we may see him so that I may look enough upon him before he dies. A, dear Lady, how may your heart last and see your blissful son see all this woe? Lady, I may not endure it, and yet am I not his mother."

Then our Lady answered and said, "Daughter, you hear well it will not otherwise be, and therefore I must needs suffer it for my son's love."

And then she thought that they followed forth after our Lord and saw how he made his prayers to his father in the Mount of Olives[5] and heard the goodly answer that came from his father and the goodly answer that he gave his father in reply. Then she saw how our Lord went to his disciples and bade them wake; his enemies were near. And then came a great multitude of people with much light and many armed men with staves, swords, and pole-axes to seek our Lord Jesus Christ. Our merciful Lord as a meek lamb saying unto them, "Whom seek you?"

They answered with a sharp spirit, "Jesus of Nazareth."

Our Lord said in reply, "*Ego sum*."[6]

And then she saw the Jews fall down on the ground; they might not stand for dread, but anon they rose again and sought as they had done before. And our Lord asked, "Whom seek you?"

And they said again, "Jesus of Nazareth."

Our Lord answered, "I it am."

And then anon she saw Judas come and kiss our Lord, and the Jews laid hands upon him full violently.

Then had our Lady and she much sorrow and great pain to see the lamb of innocence so contemptibly he held and drawn by his own people that he was specially sent unto. And immediately the said creature beheld with her spiritual eye the Jews putting a cloth before our Lord's eye, beating him and buffeting him in the head and striking him before his sweet mouth, crying full cruelly unto him, "Tell us now who smote you."

They spared not to spit in his face in the most shameful way that they could. And then our Lady and she her unworthy handmaiden for the time wept and sighed full sorely, for the Jews acted so foully and so venomously with her blissful Lord. And they would not spare to pull his blissful ears and pull the hair of his beard. And anon after she saw them draw off his clothes and make him all naked and then draw him forth before them as if he had been the greatest malefactor in all the world. And he went forth full meekly before them, all mother-naked as he was born, to a pillar of stone and spoke no word against them but let them do and say what they would. And there they bound him to the pillar as straight as they could and beat him on his fair white body with switches, with whips, and with scourges. And then she thought our Lady wept wonderfully sorely. And therefore the said creature must needs weep and cry when she saw such ghostly sights in her soul as freshly and as verily as if it had been done in deed in her bodily sight, and she thought that our Lady and she were always together to see our Lord's pains, such ghostly sights had she every Palm Sunday and every Good Friday, and in many other ways for many years together. And therefore cried she and wept full sorely and suffered full much despite and reproof in many a country.

And then our Lord said to her soul, "Daughter, these sorrows and many more suffered I for your love, and divers pains, more than any man can tell on earth. Therefore, daughter, you have great cause to love me right well, for I have bought your love full dearly."

* * *

5. For Christ's betrayal on the Mount of Olives, see Luke 22.39–54 and John 18.3–12.   6. "I am He": John 18.4–8.

THE YORK PLAY OF THE CRUCIFIXION
ca. 1425

The climax of the mystery cycles (on the cycles see the introduction to "Mystery Plays") is reached with a sequence of plays about the passion, or suffering, of Christ. Everything in each cycle leads up to the Crucifixion, the turning point in human history, when the original sin of Adam and Eve is paid for by Christ's suffering and death. No cycle has a more dramatic series of passion plays than that performed at York, the longest of the four extant English cycles. Records of the York mystery plays begin to appear in the last quarter of the fourteenth century when York was, next to London, England's most populous and prosperous city. Richard II came to see the cycle in 1397. Sometime after 1415 the plays of the passion sequence were extensively revised by a gifted playwright referred to by scholars as the York Realist. The *Crucifixion*, although not written in that author's distinctive alliterative style, has sometimes been attributed to him, and is, in any case, a powerful example of late medieval dramatic art. It is also an especially powerful example of the representation of Christ in his suffering humanity that was characteristic of late medieval spirituality.

The York plays leading up to the *Crucifixion* are especially cruel: a silent Jesus is vilified, scourged, crowned with thorns, and battered and mocked in a sadistic game of blind man's bluff. Much of the York *Crucifixion* revolves around the mechanical difficulties the soldiers encounter in nailing Jesus to the Cross. The play focuses on the soldiers; they are villains, to be sure, but ordinary men engaged in what they see as ordinary work. They are not monsters.

The gory details, part of the play's "realism," create a shudder, but the play has larger designs on its audience. While the soldiers are hard at work, the audience see only them, complaining of bad workmanship by those who bored the nail holes too far apart, necessitating the stretching of Christ's arms. Only when Christ is raised does the audience recognize the full extent to which both soldiers and audience have been immune from the pain inflicted by the soldiers' work. When the Cross is finally raised, the actor-Christ speaks to "All men that walk by way or street" (cf. the lyric "Ye that Pasen by the Weye," derived from Lamentations 1.12). He thereby addresses the spectators in the streets of York as though *they* were representing the crowd around the Cross on Calvary, directly involving and implicating them in the drama and its theme of salvation. The soldiers may concentrate on their "work" of nailing Christ to the Cross, but the audience is prompted to reflect on the relation between daily labor and the "works" of mercy incumbent upon each Christian. The meaning of Christ's words is, however, lost on the soldiers, who truly "know not what they do" and proceed to quarrel about possession of Christ's cloak.

The York Play of the Crucifixion

Cast of Characters

Jesus   Four Soldiers

[*Calvary*]

1ST SOLDIER	Sir knights, take heed hither in hie,°	*haste*
	This deed on dergh we may not draw[1]	
	Ye woot° yourself as well as I	*know*
	How lords and leaders of our law	
5	Has given doom that this dote° shall die.	*fool*
2ND SOLDIER	Sir, all their counsel well we know.	
	Sen° we are comen to Calvary,	*since*
	Let ilk° man help now as him awe.°	*each / ought*
3RD SOLDIER	We are all ready, lo,	
10	This forward° to fulfill.	*agreement*
4TH SOLDIER	Let hear how we shall do,	
	And go we tite theretill.[2]	
1ST SOLDIER	It may not help here for to hone,°	*delay*
	If we shall any worship° win.	*honor*
15 2ND SOLDIER	He must be dead needlings° by noon.	*of necessity*
3RD SOLDIER	Then is good time that we begin.	
4TH SOLDIER	Let ding° him down, then is he done:	*strike*
	He shall not dere° us with his din.	*annoy*
1ST SOLDIER	He shall be set and learned soon[3]	
20	With care° to him and all his kin.	*sorrow*
2ND SOLDIER	The foulest dead° of all	*death*
	Shall he die for his deeds.	
3RD SOLDIER	That means cross° him we shall.	*crucify*
4TH SOLDIER	Behold, so right he reads.°	*speaks*
25 1ST SOLDIER	Then to this work us must take heed,	
	So that our working be not wrang.°	*wrong*
2ND SOLDIER	None other note to neven is need,[4]	
	But let us haste him for to hang.	
3RD SOLDIER	And I have gone for gear good speed,[5]	
30	Both hammers and nails large and lang.°	*long*
4TH SOLDIER	Then may we boldly do this deed.	
	Come on, let kill this traitor strong.°	*flagrant*
1ST SOLDIER	Fair might ye fall in fere[6]	
	That has wrought on this wise.	
35 2ND SOLDIER	Us needs not for to lear°	*learn*
	Such faitours° to chastise.	*fakers*

---

1. We may not delay the time of this deed.
2. And let's get to it quickly.
3. He'll be put in his place and taught quickly.
4. There is no need to mention any other business.
5. Quickly.
6. May you all have good luck together.

3RD SOLDIER	Sen ilk a thing is right arrayed,	
	The wiselier° now work may we.	*more skillfully*
4TH SOLDIER	The cross on ground is goodly graid,°	*prepared*
40		And bored[7] even as it ought to be.	
1ST SOLDIER	Look that the lad on length be laid,	
	And made be fest° unto this tree.[8]	*fastened*
2ND SOLDIER	For all his fare he shall be flayed:°	*beaten*
	That on assay[9] soon shall ye see.	
45	3RD SOLDIER	Come forth, thou cursed knave,	
	Thy comfort soon shall keel.°	*grow cold*
4TH SOLDIER	Thine hire here shall thou have.	
1ST SOLDIER	Walk on, now work we weel.°	*well*
JESUS	Almighty God, my Father free,°	*noble*
50		Let these matters be made in mind:	
	Thou bade that I should buxom° be,	*obedient*
	For Adam° plight for to be pined.°	*Adam's / tortured*
	Here to dead° I oblige me[1]	*death*
	Fro° that sin for to save mankind,	*from*
55		And sovereignly beseek I thee,[2]	
	That they for me may favor find.	
	And from the Fiend them fend,°	*defend*
	So that their souls be safe,	
	In wealth° withouten end.	*welfare*
60		I keep° nought else to crave.	*care*
1ST SOLDIER	We,[3] hark, sir knights, for Mahound's blood.	
	Of Adam-kind° is all his thought!	*mankind*
2ND SOLDIER	The warlock waxes worse than wood.[4]	
	This doleful dead° ne dreadeth he nought.	*death*
65	3RD SOLDIER	Thou should have mind, with main and mood,[5]	
	Of wicked works that thou hast wrought.	
4TH SOLDIER	I hope° that he had been as good°	*think / well off*
	Have ceased of saws that he up sought.[6]	
1ST SOLDIER	Those saws° shall rue° him sore	*sayings / repent*
70		For all his sauntering[7] soon.	
2ND SOLDIER	I'll speed them that him spare[8]	
	Till he to dead° be done.	*death*
3RD SOLDIER	Have done belive,° boy, and make thee boun°	*at once / ready*
	And bend thy back unto this tree.	
	[JESUS *lies down.*]	

---

7. I.e., bored with holes for the nails, which were probably wooden.
8. I.e., the Cross. "Fare": behavior.
9. I.e., in actual experience.
1. Render myself liable.
2. And above all I beseech thee.
3. "We": an exclamation of surprise or displeasure. "Mahound's": Muhammad's; the sacred figures of other religions were considered devils by Christians in the Middle Ages; the soldier is swearing by the Devil.
4. This devil grows worse than crazy.
5. You should think, with all your strength and wits.
6. I.e., to have ceased of the sayings that he thought up.
7. Behaving like a saint.
8. Bad luck to them that spare him.

75	4TH SOLDIER	Behold, himself has laid him down,
		In length and breadth as he should be.
	1ST SOLDIER	This traitor here tainted° of treasoun,	convicted
		Go fast and fetch him then, ye three.
		And sen he claimeth kingdom with crown,
80		Even as a king here hang shall he.
	2ND SOLDIER	Now certes I shall not fine°	stop
		Ere his right hand be fest.°	fastened
	3RD SOLDIER	The left hand then is mine:
		Let see who bears him⁹ best.
85	4TH SOLDIER	His limbs on length then shall I lead,°	stretch
		And even unto the bore° them bring.	hole
	1ST SOLDIER	Unto his head I shall take heed,
		And with my hand help him to hing.°	hang
	2ND SOLDIER	Now sen we four shall do this deed,
90		And meddle° with this unthrifty° thing,	deal / unrewarding
		Let no man spare for special speed,¹
		Till that we have made ending.
	3RD SOLDIER	This forward° may not fail,	agreement
		Now are we right arrayed.°	set up
95	4TH SOLDIER	This boy here in our bail°	control
		Shall bide° full bitter braid.°	abide / treatment
	1ST SOLDIER	Sir knights, say, how work we now?
	2ND SOLDIER	Yes, certes, I hope° I hold this hand.	think
		And to the bore I have it brought,
100		Full buxomly° withouten band.°	effortlessly / cord
	1ST SOLDIER	Strike on then hard, for him thee bought.²
	2ND SOLDIER	Yes, here is a stub° will safely stand:	nail
		Through bones and sinews it shall be sought.°	driven
		This work is well, I will warrand.°	warrant
105	1ST SOLDIER	Say, sir, how do we thore?°	there
		This bargain may not blin.³
	3RD SOLDIER	It fails° a foot and more,	falls short
		The sinews are so gone in.°	shrunken
	4TH SOLDIER	I hope that mark° amiss be bored.	hole
110	2ND SOLDIER	Then must he bide° in bitter bale.°	wait / woe
	3RD SOLDIER	In faith, it was over-scantly scored.⁴
		That makes it foully° for to fail.	badly
	1ST SOLDIER	Why carp° ye so? Fast° on a cord	complain / fasten
		And tug him to, by top and tail.⁵
115	3RD SOLDIER	Yea, thou commands lightly° as a lord:	readily
		Come help to haul, with ill hail.⁶

---

9. Handles himself.
1. Let nobody slacken because of his own welfare.
2. Drive the nail in hard, for him who redeemed thee: a splendidly anachronistic oath.
3. This arrangement may not fail: the arrange-

ment is of the four soldiers at the four ends of the cross.
4. It was overcarelessly bored.
5. And stretch him to it, head and toe.
6. With bad luck to you.

	IST SOLDIER	Now certes° that shall I do	*certainly*
		Full snelly° as a snail.	*quickly*
	3RD SOLDIER	And I shall tach° him to	*attach*
120		Full nimbly with a nail.	

This work will hold, that dare I heet,°   *promise*
For now are fest° fast both his hend.°   *fastened / hands*

	4TH SOLDIER	Go we all four then to his feet:	
		So shall our space° be speedly° spend.	*time / well*
125	2ND SOLDIER	Let see, what bourd his bale might beet.[7]	
		Thereto my back now will I bend.	
	4TH SOLDIER	Ow! this work is all unmeet:°	*wrongly done*
		This boring must be all amend.	
	IST SOLDIER	Ah, peace, man, for Mahound,°	*Mohammed*
130		Let no man woot° that wonder,	*know*
		A rope shall rug° him down,	*jerk*
		If all his sinews go asunder.	

	2ND SOLDIER	That cord full kindly can I knit,°	*knot*
		The comfort of this carl° to keel.°	*knave / cool*
135	IST SOLDIER	Fest on then fast that all be fit.	
		It is no force° how fell° he feel.	*matter / badly*
	2ND SOLDIER	Lug on, ye both, a little yit,°	*yet*
	3RD SOLDIER	I shall not cease, as I have seel.[8]	
	4TH SOLDIER	And I shall fond° him for to hit.	*try*
140	2ND SOLDIER	Ow, hail!°	*pull*
	4TH SOLDIER	Ho, now I hold° it weel.°	*think / well*
	IST SOLDIER	Have done, drive in that nail	
		So that no fault be found.	
	4TH SOLDIER	This working would not fail	
		If four bulls here were bound.	

145	IST SOLDIER	These cords have evil° increased his pains	*badly*
		Ere° he were till° the borings brought.	*before / to*
	2ND SOLDIER	Yea, asunder are both sinews and veins	
		On ilk a side, so have we sought.°	*afflicted*
	3RD SOLDIER	Now all his gauds° nothing him gains:	*tricks*
150		His sauntering shall with bale be bought.[9]	
	4TH SOLDIER	I will go say to our sovereigns	
		Of all these works how we have wrought.	
	IST SOLDIER	Nay, sirs, another thing	
		Falls first to you and me:[1]	
155		They bade we should him hing°	*hang*
		On height that men might see.	

	2ND SOLDIER	We woot well so their words were,	
		But sir, that deed will do us dere.°	*harm*

7. Let's see, what trick could increase his suffering.   with pain.
8. As I may have good luck.   1. You and I must do first.
9. His acting like a saint (?) shall be paid for

	1ST SOLDIER	It may nought mend° for to moot° more:	*improve / argue*
160		This harlot° must be hanged here.	*rascal*
	2ND SOLDIER	The mortise² is made fit° therefore.	*ready*
	3RD SOLDIER	Fast on your fingers then, in fere.³	
	4TH SOLDIER	I ween° it will never come there.	*think*
		We four raise it not right to°-year.	*this*
165	1ST SOLDIER	Say, man, why carps thou so?	
		Thy lifting was but light.°	*easy*
	2ND SOLDIER	He means there must be mo°	*more*
		To heave him up on height.	

	3RD SOLDIER	Now certes I hope it shall not need	
170		To call to us more company.	
		Methink we four should do this deed,	
		And bear him to yon hill on high.	
	1ST SOLDIER	It must be done withouten dread:°	*doubt*
		No more, but look ye be ready,	
175		And this part shall I lift and lead.°	*carry*
		On length he shall no longer lie.	
		Therefore now make you boun:°	*ready*
		Let bear him to yon hill.	
	4TH SOLDIER	Then will I bear here down,	
180		And tent his toes untill.⁴	

	2ND SOLDIER	We two shall see till either side,	
		For else this work will wry° all wrang.°	*turn out / wrong*
	3RD SOLDIER	We are ready.	
	4TH SOLDIER	Good sirs, abide,	
		And let me first his feet up fang.°	*take*
185	2ND SOLDIER	Why tent ye so to tales this tide?⁵	
	1ST SOLDIER	Lift up!	
		[*All lift the cross together.*]	
	4TH SOLDIER	Let see!	
	2ND SOLDIER	Ow! Lift along!	
	3RD SOLDIER	From all this harm he should him hide°	*protect*
		And° he were God.	*if*
	4TH SOLDIER	The Devil him hang!	
	1ST SOLDIER	For great harm° I have hent:°	*injury / received*
190		My shoulder is in sunder.	
	2ND SOLDIER	And certes I am near shent,°	*ruined*
		So long have I born under.⁶	

	3RD SOLDIER	This cross and I in two must twin°—	*separate*
		Else breaks my back in sunder soon.	
195	4TH SOLDIER	Lay down again and leave° your din.	*cease*
		This deed for us will never be done.	

2. A hole in the ground shaped to receive the cross.
3. Fasten your fingers on it, all together.
4. Then I'll carry the part down here and attend to his toes.

5. Why are you so intent on talking at a time like this?
6. So long have I borne it up.

		[*They lay it down.*]	
	1ST SOLDIER	Assay,° sirs, let see if any gin°	*try / trick*
		May help him up, withouten hone.°	*delay*
		For here should wight° men worship win,	*strong*
200		And not with gauds° all day to gone.	*pranks*
	2ND SOLDIER	More wighter° men than we	*stronger*
		Full few I hope° ye find.	*think*
	3RD SOLDIER	This bargain° will not be,°	*arrangement / work*
		For certes me wants wind.	
205	4TH SOLDIER	So will° of work never we wore.°	*at a loss / were*
		I hope this carl some cautels cast.[7]	
	2ND SOLDIER	My burden sat° me wonder sore:	*vexed*
		Unto the hill I might not last.	
	1ST SOLDIER	Lift up and soon he shall be thore.°	*there*
210		Therefore fest° on your fingers fast.	*fasten*
	3RD SOLDIER	Ow, lift!	
	1ST SOLDIER	We, lo!	
	4TH SOLDIER	A little more!	
	2ND SOLDIER	Hold then!	
	1ST SOLDIER	How now?	
	2ND SOLDIER	The worst is past.	
	3RD SOLDIER	He weighs a wicked weight.	
	2ND SOLDIER	So may we all four say,	
215		Ere he was heaved on height	
		And raised on this array.°	*way*
	4TH SOLDIER	He made us stand as any stones,	
		So boistous° was he for to bear.	*bulky*
	1ST SOLDIER	Now raise him nimbly for the nones,[8]	
220		And set him by this mortise here;	
		And let him fall in all at once,	
		For certes that pain shall have no peer.°	*equal*
	3RD SOLDIER	Heave up!	
	4TH SOLDIER	Let down, so all his bones	
		Are asunder now on sides sere.[9]	
		[*The cross is raised.*]	
225	1ST SOLDIER	That falling was more fell°	*cruel*
		Than all the harms he had.	
		Now may a man well tell°	*count*
		The least lith° of this lad.	*joint*
	3RD SOLDIER	Methinketh this cross will not abide	
230		Nor stand still in this mortise yit.°	*yet*
	4TH SOLDIER	At the first was it made overwide:	
		That makes it wave, thou may well wit.°	*learn*

7. I think this knave cast some spells.
8. For the purpose.
9. Are pulled apart on every side.

1ST SOLDIER	It shall be set on ilk a side,	
	So that it shall no further flit.°	*move*
235	Good wedges shall we take this tide,°	*time*
	And fast° the foot, then is all fit.	*fasten*
2ND SOLDIER	Here are wedges arrayed°	*prepared*
	For that, both great and small.	
3RD SOLDIER	Where are our hammers laid	
240	That we should work withal?	

4TH SOLDIER   We have them here even at our hand.

2ND SOLDIER   Give me this wedge, I shall it in drive.

4TH SOLDIER   Here is another yit ordand.°   *ready*

3RD SOLDIER   Do take° it me hither belive.°   *give / quickly*

240   1ST SOLDIER   Lay on then fast.

3RD SOLDIER   Yes. I warrand.°   *guarantee*

I thring them sam, so mote I thrive.[1]

Now will this cross ful stably stand:

All if he rave they will not rive.[2]

1ST SOLDIER   Say, sir, how likes thou now

250   The work that we have wrought?

4TH SOLDIER   We pray you, say us how

Ye feel, or faint ye aught?[3]

JESUS   All men that walk by way or street,

Take tent—ye shall no travail tine[4]—

255   Behold mine head, mine hands, my feet,

And fully feel now ere ye fine°   *cease*

If any mourning may be meet

Or mischief° measured unto mine.   *injury*

My Father, that all bales may bete,[5]

260   Forgive these men that do me pine.°   *torment*

What they work woot° they nought: *know*

Therefore my Father I crave

Let never their sins be sought,°   *searched*

But see their souls to save.

265   1ST SOLDIER   We, hark! he jangles like a jay.

2ND SOLDIER   Methink he patters like a pie.°   *magpie*

3RD SOLDIER   He has been doand° all this day,   *doing so*

And made great mening° of mercy.   *talk*

4TH SOLDIER   Is this the same that gun° us say   *did*

270   That he was God's son almighty?[6]

1ST SOLDIER   Therefore he feels full fell affray,[7]

And doomed this day was for to die.

2ND SOLDIER   Vath! *qui destruis templum!*[8]

1. I press them together, so may I thrive.
2. Even if he struggles, they will not budge.
3. Or do you feel somewhat faint?
4. Take heed, you shall not lose your labor.
5. My father, who may remedy all evils.
6. That he was the son of almighty God.
7. For that he suffers a full cruel assault.
8. In Faith thou who destroys the temple (cf. Mark 14.58, John 2.19).

	3RD SOLDIER	His saws° were so, certain.	*sayings*
275	4TH SOLDIER	And, sirs, he said to some	
		He might raise it again.	
	1ST SOLDIER	To muster° that he had no might,	*exhibit*
		For all the cautels° that he could cast;	*charms*
		All if he were in word so wight,[9]	
280		For all his force now is he fast.	
		All Pilate deemed is done and dight:°	*accomplished*
		Therefore I read° that we go rest.	*advise*
	2ND SOLDIER	This race must be rehearsed right[1]	
		Through the world both east and west.	
285	2ND SOLDIER	Yea, let him hang here still	
		And make mows on the moon.[2]	
	4TH SOLDIER	Then may we wend° at will.	*go away*
	1ST SOLDIER	Nay, good sirs, not so soon.	
		For certes us needs another note:[3]	
290		This kirtle would I of you crave.	
	2ND SOLDIER	Nay, nay, sir, we will look° by lot	*see*
		Which of us four falls° it to have.	*chances*
	3RD SOLDIER	I read° we draw cut° for this coat.	*advise / lots*
		Lo, see now soon, all sides to save.[4]	
295	4TH SOLDIER	The short cut° shall win, that well ye woot,	*straw*
		Whether it fall to knight or knave.	
	1ST SOLDIER	Fellows, ye thar not flite,[5]	
		For this mantle is mine.	
	2ND SOLDIER	Go we then hence tite,°	*quickly*
300		This travail here we tine.[6]	

9. Even though he was so clever in words.
1. This course of action must be repeated correctly.
2. And make faces at the moon.
3. For surely we have another piece of business

to settle.
4. See now straightway, to protect all parties.
5. Fellows, you don't need to quarrel.
6. We're wasting our time here.

MYSTERY PLAYS

The increasing prosperity and importance of the towns was shown by performances of the mystery plays—a sequence or "cycle" of plays based on the Bible and produced by the city guilds, the organizations representing the various trades and crafts. The cycles of several towns are lost. Those of York and Chester have been preserved, the latter in a post-Reformation form. The Towneley plays, sometimes connected with Wakefield (Yorkshire), and those that constitute the so-called N-town plays from East Anglia treat comparable material, as do fragmentary survivals from elsewhere.

Medieval mystery plays had an immensely confident reach in both space and time. In York, for example, the theatrical space and time of this urban, amateur drama was that of the entire city, lasting from sunrise throughout the entire long summer holiday. The time represented ran from the Fall of the Angels and the Creation of the World right through to the end of time, in the Last Judgment. Between these extremities of the beginning and end of time, each cycle presents key episodes of Old Testament narrative, such as the Fall and the Flood, before presenting a concentrated sequence of freely interpreted New Testament plays focused on the life and Passion of Christ.

The church had its own drama in Latin, dating back to the tenth century, which developed through the dramatization and elaboration of the liturgy—the regular service—for certain holidays, the Easter morning service in particular. The vernacular drama was once thought to have evolved from the liturgical, passing by stages from the church into the streets of the town. However, even though the vernacular plays at times echo their Latin counterparts and although their authors may have been clerics, the mysteries represent an old and largely independent tradition of vernacular religious drama. As early as the twelfth century a *Play of Adam* in Anglo-Norman French was performed in England, a dramatization of the Fall with highly sophisticated dialogue, characterization, and stagecraft.

During the late fourteenth and the fifteenth centuries, the great English mystery cycles were formed in provincial, yet increasingly powerful and independent cities. They were the production of the city itself, with particular responsibility for staging and performance devolving onto the city guilds. A guild was also known as a "mystery," from Latin *ministerium,* whence the phrase "mystery plays." A guild combined the functions of modern trade union, club, religious society, and political action group. The performance and staging required significant investments of time and money from amateur performers, the status of whose mystery might be at stake in the quality of their performance. Often the subject of the play corresponded to the function of the guild (thus the Pinners, or nail-makers, performed the York Crucifixion, for example).

Most of our knowledge of the plays, apart from the texts themselves, comes through municipal and guild records, which tell us a great deal about the evolution, staging, and all aspects of the production of the cycles. In some of the cities each guild had a wagon that served as a stage. The wagon proceeded from one strategic point in the city to another, and the play would be performed a number of times on the same day. In other towns, plays were probably acted out in sequence on a platform erected at a single location such as the main city square.

The cycles were performed every year at the time of one of two great early summer festivals—Whitsuntide, the week following the seventh Sunday after Easter, or Corpus Christi, a week later (falling somewhere between May 21 and June 24). They served as both religious instruction and entertainment for wide audiences, including unlearned folk like the carpenter in *The Miller's Tale* (lines 405–74), who recalls from them the trouble Noah had getting his wife aboard the ark, but also educated laypeople and clerics, who besides enjoying the sometimes boisterous comedy would find the plays acting out traditional interpretations of Scripture such as the ark as a type, or prefiguration, of the church.

Thus the cycles were public spectacles watched by every layer of society, and they paved the way for the professional theater in the age of Elizabeth I. The rainbow in *Noah's Flood* (lines 356–71; for the text of *Noah's Flood* see the supplemental ebook) and the Angel's *Gloria* in the *Shepherds' Play,* with their messages of mercy and hope, unite actors and audience in a common faith. Yet the first shepherd's opening speech, complaining of taxation and the insolent exploitation of farmers by "gentlery-men," shows how the plays also served as vehicles of social criticism and reveal many of the rifts and tensions in the late-medieval social fabric.

The particular intersection of religious and civic institutions that made the cycles possible was put under strain from the beginning of the Reformation in England from the 1530s. Given the strength of civic institutions, the cycles survived into the reign of Elizabeth, but partly because they were identified with the Catholic Church, were suppressed by local ecclesiastical pressures in each city in the late 1560s and 1570s. The last performance of the York Cycle in 1569 is very nearly coincident with the opening of the first professional theater in Whitechapel (London) in 1567.

On the morality play—the other major form of theater that flourished in England in the fifteenth century and continued on into the sixteenth—see the headnote to *Everyman* (p. 507).

The Wakefield Second Shepherds' Play   In putting on the stage biblical shepherds and soldiers, medieval playwrights inevitably and often quite deliberately gave them the appearance and characters of contemporary men and women. No play better illustrates this aspect of the drama than the *Second Shepherds' Play*, included in the Towneley collection of mystery plays and imaginatively based on scriptural material typical of the cycles. As the play opens, the shepherds complain about the cold, the taxes, and the high-handed treatment they get from the gentry— evils closer to shepherds on the Yorkshire moors than to those keeping their flocks near Bethlehem. The sophisticated dramatic intelligence at work in this and several other of the Wakefield plays belonged undoubtedly to one individual, who probably revised older, more traditional plays some time during the last quarter of the fifteenth century. His identity is not known, but because of his achievement scholars refer to him as the Wakefield Master. He was probably a highly educated cleric stationed in the vicinity of Wakefield. The Wakefield Master had a genius for combining comedy, including broad farce, with religion in ways that make them enhance one another. In the *Second Shepherds' Play*, by linking the comic subplot of Mak and Gill with the solemn story of Christ's nativity, the Wakefield Master has produced a dramatic parable of what the Nativity means in Christian history and in Christian hearts. No one will fail to observe the parallelism between the stolen sheep, ludicrously disguised as Mak's latest heir, lying in the cradle, and the real Lamb of God, born in the stable among beasts. A complex of relationships based on this relationship suggests itself. But perhaps the most important point is that the charity twice shown by the shepherds—in the first instance to the supposed son of Mak and in the second instance to Mak and Gill when they decide to let them off with only the mildest of punishments—is rewarded when they are invited to visit the Christ Child, the embodiment of charity. The bleak beginning of the play, with its series of individual complaints, is ultimately balanced by the optimistic ending, which sees the shepherds once again singing together in harmony.

The *Second Shepherds' Play* is exceptional among the mystery plays in its development of plot and character. There is no parallel to its elaboration of the comic subplot and no character quite like Mak, who has doubtless been imported into religious drama from popular farce. Mak is perhaps the best humorous character outside of Chaucer's works in this period. A braggart of the worst kind, he has something of Falstaff's charm; and he resembles Falstaff also in his grotesque attempts to maintain the last shreds of his dignity when he is caught in a lie. Most readers will be glad that the shepherds do not carry out their threat to have the death penalty invoked for his crime.

Following the 1994 edition of the Early English Text Society, the stanza, traditionally printed as nine lines (with an opening quatrain of four long lines, the first halves of which rhyme with one another) is rendered here as "thirteeners," rhyming *a b a b a b a b c d d d c*.

The Second Shepherds' Play[1]

CAST OF CHARACTERS

COLL	GILL
GIB	ANGEL
DAW	MARY
MAK	

[A field.]

[Enter COLL*]*

COLL   Lord, what° these weathers are cold,   *how*
    And I am ill happed;°   *badly covered*
    I am nearhand dold,°   *numb*
    So long have I napped;
5   My legs they fold,°   *give way*
    My fingers are chapped.
    It is not as I wold,°   *would (wish)*
    For I am all lapped°   *wrapped*
      In sorrow:
10   In storms and tempest,
    Now in the east, now in the west,
    Woe is him that has never rest
      Midday nor morrow!

    But we sely° husbands[2]   *hapless*
15   That walks on the moor,
    In faith we are nearhands°   *nearly*
    Out of the door.°   *homeless*
    No wonder, as it stands
    If we be poor,
20   For the tilth of our lands
    Lies fallow as the floor,[3]
      As ye ken.°   *know*
    We are so hammed,
    Fortaxed, and rammed,
25   We are made hand-tamed
      With these gentlery-men.[4]

    Thus they reave° us our rest—   *rob*
    Our Lady them wary!°   *curse*
    These men that are lord-fest,[5]

---

1. The text is based on the (1994) edition by A. C. Cawley and Martin Stevens, but has been freely edited. Spelling has been normalized except where rhyme makes changes impossible. Because the original text has no indications of scenes and only four stage directions, written in Latin, appropriate scenes of action and additional stage directions have been added; the four original stage directions are identified in the notes.
2. Farmers. The shepherds are also tenant farmers.
3. The arable part of our land lies fallow (as flat) as the floor. Landowners were converting farmland to pasture for sheep.
4. We are so hamstrung, overtaxed, and beaten down [that] we are made to obey these gentry folk. Coll is here complaining about the peasants' hard lot, at the mercy of retainers of the wealthy landowners.
5. Attached to lords.

30   They cause the plow tarry.[6]
    That, men say, is for the best—
    We find it contrary.
    Thus are husbands oppressed
    In point to miscarry.
35   On live.[7]
    Thus hold they us under,
    Thus they bring us in blunder,°   *trouble*
    It were a great wonder
       And° ever should we thrive.   *if*

40   For may he get a paint-sleeve[8]
    Or brooch nowadays,
    Woe is him that him grieve
    Or once again-says.°   *gainsays*
    Dare no man him reprieve,°   *reprove*
45   What mastery he maes.[9]
    And yet may no man lieve°   *believe*
    One word that he says,
       No letter.
    He can make purveyance[1]
50   With boast and bragance,°   *bragging*
    And all is through maintenance[2]
       Of men that are greater.

    There shall come a swain°   *fellow*
    As proud as a po:°   *peacock*
55   He must borrow my wain,°   *wagon*
    My plow also;
    Then I am full fain°   *glad*
    To grant ere he go.
    Thus live we in pain,
60   Anger, and woe,
       By night and by day.
    He must have if he lang° it,   *wants*
    If I should forgang it.[3]
    I were better be hanged
65   Than once say him nay.

    It does me good, as I walk
    Thus by mine one,°   *self*
    Of this world for to talk
    In manner of moan.
70   To my sheep I will stalk,

---

6. Hold up the plow, i.e., interfere with the farm work.
7. In life. "In point to miscarry": to the point of ruin.
8. An embroidered sleeve, part of the livery worn by the landlord's officers as a badge of authority.
9. No matter what force he uses.
1. Requisition (of private property).
2. Practice of retaining servants under a nobleman's protection with the power to lord it over his tenants.
3. Even if I have to do without it.

And hearken anon,
There abide on a balk,[4]
Or sit on a stone,
   Full soon;
75 For I trow,° pardie,°   *think / by God*
True men if they be,
We get more company
   Ere it be noon.[5]

    [*Enter* GIB, *who at first does not see* COLL.]

GIB Bensté and Dominus,[6]
80 What may this bemean?°   *mean*
Why fares this world thus?
Oft have we not seen.
Lord, these weathers are spiteous°   *cruel*
And the winds full keen,
85 And the frosts so hideous
They water mine een,°   *eyes*
   No lie.
Now in dry, now in wet,
Now in snow, now in sleet,
90 When my shoon° freeze to my feet   *shoes*
   It is not all easy.

But as far as I ken,°   *see*
Or yet as I go,°   *walk*
We sely° wedmen°   *hapless / married men*
95 Dree° mickle° woe;   *suffer / much*
We have sorrow then and then°—   *constantly*
It falls oft so.
Sely Copple, our hen,[7]
Both to and fro
100   She cackles;
But begin she to croak,
To groan or to cluck,
Woe is him is our cock,
   For he is in the shackles.

105 These men that are wed
Have not all their will:
When they are full hard stead°   *beset*
They sigh full still;°   *constantly*
God wot° they are led   *knows*
110 Full hard and full ill;
In bower nor in bed

---

4. A raised strip of grassland dividing parts of a field.
5. I.e., if the other shepherds keep their promise to meet Coll.
6. Bless us and Lord.
7. Silly Copple, our hen, i.e., Gib's wife, who henpecks him.

They say nought theretill.°   *against that*
  This tide°   *time*
My part have I fun;°   *found, learned*
115 I know my lesson:
Woe is him that is bun,°   *bound (in wedlock)*
  For he must abide.

But now late in our lives—
A marvel to me,
120 That I think my heart rives°   *splits*
Such wonders to see;
What that destiny drives
It should so be[8]—
Some men will have two wives,
125 And some men three
  In store.[9]
Some are woe° that has any,   *miserable*
But so far can° I,   *know*
Woe is him that has many,
130   For he feels sore.

But young men a-wooing,
For God that you bought,°   *redeemed*
Be well ware of wedding
And think in your thought:
135 "Had I wist"° is a thing   *known*
That serves of nought.
Mickle° still° mourning   *much / continual*
Has wedding home brought,
  And griefs,
140 With many a sharp shower,°   *fight*
For thou may catch in an hour
That° shall sow° thee full sour°   *that which / vex / bitterly*
  As long as thou lives.

For as ever read I 'pistle,[1]
145 I have one to my fere[2]
As sharp as a thistle,
As rough as a brere;°   *briar*
She is browed like a bristle,
With a sour-loten cheer;[3]
150 Had she once wet her whistle
She could sing full clear
  Her Pater Noster.[4]
She is great as a whale;
She has a gallon of gall:

---

8. What destiny causes must occur.
9. I.e., by remarrying after being widowed.
1. Epistle, i.e., part of the church service.
2. As my mate.

3. She has brows like pig's bristles and a sour-looking face.
4. "Our Father," or the Lord's Prayer.

155 By him that died for us all,
   I would I had run to° I lost her.   *till*

COLL   God look over the raw!⁵
[*to* GIB] Full deafly ye stand!
GIB   Yea, the devil in thy maw°   *guts*
160   So tariand!⁶
   Saw thou awhere° of Daw?   *anywhere*
COLL   Yea, on a lea-land°   *pasture land*
   Heard I him blaw.°   *blow (his horn)*
   He comes here at hand,
165   Not far.
   Stand still.
GIB   Why?

COLL   For he comes, hope° I.   *think*
GIB   He will make us both a lie
   But if° we be ware.   *unless*

[*Enter* DAW,⁷ *who does not see the others.*]

170 DAW   Christ's cross me speed
   And Saint Nicholas!⁸
   Thereof had I need:
   It is worse than it was.
   Whoso could take heed
175   And let the world pass,
   It is ever in dread°   *doubt*
   And brickie° as glass,   *brittle*
     And slithes.°   *slips away*
   This world foor° never so,   *behaved*
180   With marvels mo° and mo,   *more*
   Now in weal, now in woe,
   And all thing writhes.°   *changes*

   Was never sin° Noah's flood   *since*
   Such floods seen,
185   Winds and rains so rude
   And storms so keen:
   Some stammered, some stood
   In doubt,⁹ as I ween.°   *suppose*
   Now God turn all to good!
190   I say as I mean.
     For ponder:°   *consider (this)*
   These floods so they drown
   Both in fields and in town,

---

5. I.e., God watch over the audience! Coll has been trying to get Gib's attention as the latter harangues the audience.
6. For being so late.
7. Daw (Davy) is a boy working for the older shepherds.
8. May Christ's cross and St. Nicholas help me.
9. Probably refers to people's consternation at the time of Noah's Flood.

And bears all down,
195   And that is a wonder.

We that walk on the nights
Our cattle to keep,°   *keep watch over*
We see sudden° sights   *startling*
When other men sleep.
200 Yet methink my heart lights:°   *feels lighter*
I see shrews peep.[1]

[*He sees the others, but does not hail them*]

Ye are two tall wights.°   *creatures*
I will give my sheep
    A turn.
205 But full ill have I meant:[2]
As I walk on this bent°   *field*
I may lightly° repent,   *quickly*
    My toes if I spurn.°   *stub*

Ah, sir, God you save,
210 And master mine!
A drink fain° would I have,   *gladly*
And somewhat to dine.

COLL   Christ's curse, my knave,
        Thou art a lither° hine!°   *lazy / servant*
215 GIB   What, the boy list rave!
        Abide unto sine.[3]
            We have made it.°   *had dinner*
        Ill thrift on thy pate![4]
        Though the shrew° came late   *rascal*
220   Yet is he in state
            To dine—if he had it.

DAW   Such servants as I,
        That° sweats and swinks,°   *who / toil*
        Eats our bread full dry,
225   And that me forthinks.°   *angers*
        We are oft wet and weary
        When master-men winks,°   *sleep*
        Yet comes full lately°   *tardily*
        Both dinners and drinks.
230   But nately°   *profitably*
        Both our dame and our sire,[5]
        When we have run in the mire,

---

1. I see rascals peeping. Daw is relieved to recognize the other shepherds aren't monstrous apparitions.
2. But that's a very poor idea (to give the sheep a turn).
3. The boy must be crazy! Wait till later.
4. Bad luck on thy head!
5. I.e., mistress and master.

They can nip at our hire,[6]
And pay us full lately.

235 But here my troth, master,
For the fare° that ye make°   *food / provide*
I shall do thereafter:
Work as I take.[7]
I shall do a little, sir,
240 And among° ever lake,°   *betweentimes / play*
For yet lay my supper
Never on my stomach[8]
    In fields.
Whereto should I threap?°   *haggle*
245 With my staff can I leap,°   *run away*
And men say, "Light cheap
    Litherly foryields."[9]

COLL   Thou were an ill lad
To ride a-wooing
250 With a man that had
But little of spending.[1]
GIB   Peace, boy, I bade—
No more jangling,
Or I shall make thee full rad,°   *quickly (stop)*
255 By the heaven's King!
        With thy gauds°—   *tricks*
Where are our sheep, boy?—we scorn.[2]
DAW   Sir, this same day at morn
I left them in the corn°   *wheat*
260   When they rang Lauds.[3]

They have pasture good,
They cannot go wrong.
COLL   That is right. By the rood,°   *cross*
These nights are long!
265 Yet I would, ere we yode,°   *went*
One° gave us a song.   *someone*
GIB   So I thought as I stood,
To mirth° us among.°   *cheer / meanwhile*
DAW   I grant.
270 COLL   Let me sing the tenory.°   *tenor*
GIB   And I the treble so hee.°   *high*
DAW   Then the mean° falls to me.   *middle part*
Let see how you chant.   [*They sing.*]

---

6. They can deduct from our wages.
7. I.e., work (as little) as I am paid.
8. I.e., a full stomach has never weighed me down.
9. A cheap bargain repays badly (a proverb).
1. You would be a bad servant to take wooing for

a man with little money to spend.
2. We scorn (your tricks).
3. The first church service of the day (morn) but
performed while it is still dark.

[Enter MAK *with a cloak over his clothes.]*[4]

	MAK	Now, Lord, for thy names seven,	
275		That made both moon and starns°	stars
		Well mo than I can neven,°	name
		Thy will, Lord, of me tharns.[5]	
		I am all uneven°—	at odds
		That moves oft my harns.[6]	
280		Now would God I were in heaven,	
		For there weep no barns°	children
		So still.°	continually
	COLL	Who is that pipes so poor?	
	MAK	*[aside]* Would God ye wist° how I foor!°	knew / fared
285		*[aloud]* Lo, a man that walks on the moor	
		And has not all his will.	

	GIB	Mak, where has thou gane?°	gone
		Tell us tiding.	
	DAW.	Is he come? Then ilkane	
290		Take heed to his thing.[7]	

[Snatches the cloak from him.]

	MAK	What! Ich[8] be a yeoman,	
		I tell you, of the king,	
		The self and the same,	
		Sond° from a great lording	messenger
295		And sich.°	suchlike
		Fie on you! Goth° hence	go
		Out of my presence:	
		I must have reverence.	
		Why, who be ich?	

300	COLL	Why make ye it so quaint?[9]	
		Mak, ye do wrang.°	wrong
	GIB	But, Mak, list ye saint?	
		I trow that ye lang.[1]	
	DAW	I trow the shrew can paint[2]—	
305		The devil might him hang!	
	MAK	Ich shall make complaint	
		And make you all to thwang°	be flogged
		At a word,	
		And tell even° how ye doth.	exactly
310	COLL	But Mak, is that sooth?	

---

4. Stage direction in the original manuscript.
5. Thy will, Lord, falls short in regard to me.
6. That often disturbs my brains.
7. Each one look to his possessions (lest Mak steal them). The stage direction below is in the manuscript.
8. I (a southern dialect form in contrast with the northern dialect spoken by the Yorkshire shep-

herds). Mak pretends to be an important person from the south.
9. Why are you putting on such airs?
1. Do you want to play the saint? I guess you long (to do so).
2. I think the rascal knows how to put on false colors.

Now take out that Southern tooth,[3]
And set in a turd![4]

GIB   Mak, the devil in your ee!°   *eye*
A stroke would I lean° you!   *give*
315   DAW   Mak, know ye not me?
By God, I could teen° you.   *vex*
MAK   God look° you all three: *guard*
Methought I had seen you.
Ye are a fair company.
320   COLL   Can ye now mean you?[5]
GIB   Shrew, peep![6]
Thus late as thou goes,
What will men suppose?
And thou has an ill nose[7]
325   Of stealing sheep.

MAK   And I am true as steel,
All men wate.°   *know*
But a sickness I feel
That holds me full hate:°   *hot, feverish*
330   My belly fares not weel,
It is out of estate.
DAW   Seldom lies the de'el°   *devil*
Dead by the gate.[8]
MAK   Therefore[9]
335   Full sore am I and ill
If I stand stone-still,
I eat not a needill[1]
       This month and more.

COLL   How fares thy wife? By my hood,
340   How fares sho?°   *she*
MAK   Lies waltering,° by the rood,   *sprawling*
By the fire, lo!
And a house full of brood.°   *children*
She drinks well, too:
345   Ill speed other good
That she will do![2]
       But sho
Eats as fast as she can;
And ilk° year that comes to man   *every*
350   She brings forth a lakan°—   *baby*
       And some years two.

3. I.e., now stop pretending to speak like a southerner.
4. I.e., shut up!
5. Can you now remember (who you are)?
6. Rascal, watch out.
7. Noise, i.e., reputation.

8. Road, i.e., the devil is always on the move.
9. Mak ignores Daw and continues his speech from line 331.
1. As sure as I'm standing here as still as a stone, I haven't eaten a needle (i.e., a tiny bit).
2. I.e., that (drinking) is the only good she does.

But were I now more gracious°   *prosperous*
And richer by far,
I were eaten out of house
355 And of harbar.°   *home*
Yet is she a foul douce,°   *sweetheart*
If ye come nar:³
There is none that trows°   *imagines*
Nor knows a war°   *worse*
360   Than ken° I.   *know*
Now will ye see what I proffer:
To give all in my coffer
Tomorn at next° to offer   *tomorrow*
    Her head-masspenny.⁴

365 GIB I wot° so forwaked⁵   *know*
    Is none in this shire.
    I would sleep if° I taked   *even if*
    Less to my hire.⁶
DAW I am cold and naked
370   And would have a fire.
COLL I am weary forraked°   *from walking*
    And run in the mire.
       Wake thou!⁷   [*Lies down.*]
GIB Nay, I will lie down by,
375   For I must sleep, truly.   [*Lies down beside him.*]
DAW As good a man's son was I
       As any of you.

        [*Lies down and motions to* MAK *to lie between them.*]

But Mak, come hither, between
    Shall thou lie down.
380 MAK Then might I let you bedeen
    Of that ye would rown,⁸
       No dread.°   *doubt*
From my top to my toe,   [*Lies down and prays.*]
    Manus tuas commendo
385 *Pontio Pilato*⁹
       Christ's cross me speed!°   *help*

        [*He gets up as the others sleep and speaks.*]¹

Now were time for a man
That lacks what he wold°   *would, wants*
To stalk privily than°   *then*

---

3. I.e., near the truth.
4. The penny paid to sing a mass for her soul; i.e., I wish she were dead.
5. Exhausted from lack of sleep.
6. I should take a cut in wages.
7. Keep watch.

8. Then I might be in the way if you wanted to whisper together.
9. "Thy hands I commend to Pontius Pilate." A parody of Luke 23.46, "Into thy hands I commend my spirit."
1. One of the original stage directions.

390　　Unto a fold,°　　　　　　　　　　　　　　　　　　　　　 *sheepfold*
　　　And nimbly to work than,
　　　And be not too bold,
　　　For he might abuy° the bargan°　　　　　　　　　　　 *pay for / bargain*
　　　If it were told
395　　　　At the ending.
　　　Now were time for to reel:°　　　　　　　　　　　　　　 *move fast*
　　　But he needs good counseel°　　　　　　　　　　　　　　 *counsel*
　　　That fain would fare weel°　　　　　　　　　　　　　　　 *well*
　　　　And has but little spending.°　　　　　　　　　　　　 *money*

　　　　[*He draws a magic circle around the shepherds and recites
　　　　a spell.*]

400　　But about you a circill,°　　　　　　　　　　　　　　　 *circle*
　　　As round as a moon,
　　　To° I have done that° I will,　　　　　　　　　　 *until / what*
　　　Till that it be noon,
　　　That ye lie stone-still
405　　To° that I have done;　　　　　　　　　　　　　　　　　 *until*
　　　And I shall say theretill°　　　　　　　　　　　　　　　 *thereto*
　　　Of good words a foon:°　　　　　　　　　　　　　　　　　 *few*
　　　　"On hight,
　　　Over your heads my hand I lift.
410　　Out go your eyes! Fordo your sight!"[2]
　　　But yet I must make better shift
　　　　And it be right.[3]

　　　Lord, what° they sleep hard—　　　　　　　　　　　　　 *how*
　　　That may ye all hear.
415　　Was I never a shephard,
　　　But now will I lear.°　　　　　　　　　　　　　　　　　　 *learn*
　　　If the flock be scar'd,
　　　Yet shall I nip near.[4]
　　　How! Draws hitherward![5]　　　　　　　　　[*He catches one.*]
420　　Now mends our cheer
　　　　From sorrow.
　　　A fat sheep, I dare say!
　　　A good fleece, dare I lay!°　　　　　　　　　　　　　　　 *bet*
　　　Eft-quit° when I may,　　　　　　　　　　　　　　　　　　 *repay*
425　　But this will I borrow.

　　　　[*Moves with the sheep to his cottage and calls from outside.*]

　　　How, Gill, art thou in?
　　　Get us some light.
　　　GILL [*inside*]　　Who makes such a din

2. May your sight be rendered powerless.　　　　　　sheep) close.
3. If it is to turn out all right.　　　　　　　　　　　5. Stop! come this way.
4. Even if the flock is alarmed, yet shall I grip (a

This time of the night?
430 I am set for to spin;
I hope not I might
Rise a penny to win[6]—
I shrew° them on height!   *curse*
   So fares
435 A housewife that has been
To be raised thus between:
Here may no note be seen
   For such small chares.[7]

MAK Good wife, open the hek!°   *door*
440 Sees thou not what I bring?
GILL I may thole thee draw the sneck.[8]
Ah, come in, my sweeting.°   *sweetheart*
MAK Yea, thou thar not reck
Of my long standing.[9]

   [*She opens the door.*]

445 GILL By the naked neck
Art thou like for to hing.°   *hang*
MAK Do way!°   *let it be*
I am worthy° my meat,   *worthy of*
For in a strait° I can get   *pinch*
450 More than they that swink° and sweat   *work*
All the long day.

Thus it fell to my lot,
Gill, I had such grace.°   *luck*
GILL It were a foul blot
455 To be hanged for the case.°   *deed*
MAK I have 'scaped,° Jelot,°   *escaped / Gill*
Of as hard a glase.°   *blow*
GILL But "So long goes the pot
To the water," men says,
460   "At last
Comes it home broken."
MAK Well know I the token,°   *saying*
But let it never be spoken!
   But come and help fast.

465 I would he were flain,°   *skinned*
I list° well eat: *wish*
This twelvemonth was I not so fain
Of one sheep-meat.

GILL   Come they ere he be slain,
470   And hear the sheep bleat—
MAK   Then might I be ta'en°—   *taken*
    That were a cold sweat!
      Go spar°   *fasten*
    The gate-door.°   *street door*
GILL   Yes, Mak,
475   For and° they come at thy back—   *if*
MAK   Then might I buy, for all the pack,
    The devil of the war.[1]

GILL   A good bourd° have I spied,   *trick*
    Sin° thou can° none.   *since / know*
480   Here shall we him hide
    To° they be gone,   *until*
    In my cradle. Abide!
    Let me alone,
    And I shall lie beside
485   In childbed and groan.
MAK   Thou red,°   *get ready*
    And I shall say thou was light°   *delivered*
    Of a knave-child° this night.   *boy child*
GILL   Now well is me day bright
490   That ever I was bred.[2]

    This is a good guise°   *method*
    And a far-cast:°   *clever trick*
    Yet a woman's advice
    Helps at the last.
495   I wot° never who spies: *know*
    Again° go thou fast.   *back*
MAK   But° I come ere they rise,   *unless*
    Else blows a cold blast.
     I will go sleep.   *[Returns to the shepherds.]*
500   Yet sleeps all this meny,°   *company*
    And I shall go stalk privily,
    As it had never been I
     That carried their sheep.   *[Lies down among them.]*

        [The shepherds are waking.]

COLL   *Resurrex a mortruus!*[3]
505   Have hold my hand!
    Judas carnas dominus![4]
    I may not well stand.
    My foot sleeps, by Jesus,
    And I waiter° fastand.°   *stagger / (from) fasting*

1. Then I might have to pay the devil the worse
on account of the whole pack of them.
2. Now lucky for me the bright day I was born.

3. A garbled form of "resurrexit a mortuis" (he
arose from the dead) from the Creed.
4. Judas, (in?)carnate lord.

510   I thought we had laid us
       Full near England.
       GIB   Ah; yea?
       Lord, what° I have slept weel!°   *how / well*
       As fresh as an eel,
515   As light I me feel
          As leaf on a tree.

       DAW   Bensté° be herein!   *(God's) blessing*
       So my body quakes,
       My heart is out of skin,
520   What-so° it makes.°   *whatever / causes*
       Who makes all this din?
       So my brows blakes,[5]
       To the door will I win.[6]
       Hark, fellows, wakes!
525   We were four:
       See ye aywhere of Mak now?
       COLL   We were up ere thou.
       GIB   Man, I give God avow
          Yet-yede he naw're.[7]

530   DAW   Methought he was lapped°   *covered*
       In a wolfskin.
       COLL   So are many happed°   *clad*
       Now, namely° within.   *especially*
       DAW   When we had long napped,
535   Methought with a gin°   *snare*
       A fat sheep he trapped,
       But he made no din.
       GIB   Be still!
       Thy dream makes thee wood.°   *crazy*
540   It is but phantom, by the rood.°   *cross*
       COLL   Now God turn all to good,
       If it be his will.

       [*They wake up* MAK *who pretends to have been asleep.*]

       GIB   Rise, Mak, for shame!
       Thou lies right lang.°   *long*
545   MAK   Now Christ's holy name
       Be us amang!°   *among*
       What is this? For Saint Jame,
       I may not well gang.°   *walk*
       I trow° I be the same.   *think*
550   Ah, my neck has lain wrang.°   *wrong*
          [*One of them twists his neck.*]
          Enough!

5. My brow turns pale (with fear).   thinks he's inside.
6. I'll head for the door. Still half-asleep, Daw   7. He's gone nowhere yet.

Mickle° thank! Sin° yestereven   *much / since*
Now, by Saint Stephen,
I was flayed with a sweven—
555   My heart out of slough.[8]

I thought Gill began to croak
And travail° full sad,°   *labor / hard*
Well-near at the first cock,[9]
Of a young lad,
560 For to mend° our flock—   *increase*
Then be I never glad:
I have tow on my rock[1]
More than ever I had.
    Ah, my head!
565 A house full of young tharms!°   *bellies*
The devil knock out their harns!°   *brains*
Woe is him has many barns,°   *children*
    And thereto little bread.

I must go home, by your leave,
570 To Gill, as I thought.°   *intended*
I pray you look° my sleeve,   *examine*
That I steal nought.
I am loath you to grieve
Or from you take aught.
575 DAW   Go forth! Ill might thou chieve!°   *prosper*
Now would I we sought
    This morn,
That we had all our store.[2]
COLL   But I will go before.
Let us meet.
580 GIB   Whore?°   *where*
DAW   At the crooked thorn.

[MAK'S *house.* MAK *at the door.*]

MAK   Undo this door!
GILL   Who is here?
MAK   How long shall I stand?
GILL   Who makes such a bere?°   *clamor*
585 Now walk in the weniand![3]
MAK   Ah, Gill, what cheer?
It is I, Mak, your husband.
GILL   Then may we see here
The devil in a band,[4]
590   Sir Guile!

---

8. I was terrified by a dream—my heart [jumped] out of [my] skin.
9. First cockcrow, i.e., midnight.
1. Flax on my distaff (i.e., trouble, mouths to feed).
2. Now I want us to make sure . . . we have all our stock.
3. Waning of the moon (an unlucky time), i.e., "Go with bad luck!"
4. In a noose (?) Gill perhaps continues to remind Mak that sheep stealing is a hanging offense.

Lo, he comes with a lote°   *sound*
As° he were holden in° the throat: *as if / by*
I may not sit at my note°   *work*
 A hand-long° while.   *short*

595 MAK Will ye hear what fare° she makes *fuss*
 To get her a glose?°   *excuse*
 And does nought but lakes°   *plays*
 And claws° her toes?   *scratches*

 GILL Why, who wanders? Who wakes?
600 Who comes? Who goes?
 Who brews? Who bakes?
 What makes me thus hose?[5]
  And than°   *then*
 It is ruth° to behold,   *pity*
605 Now in hot, now in cold,
 Full woeful is the household
  That wants° a woman.   *lacks*

 But what end has thou made
 With the herds,° Mak?   *shepherds*
610 MAK The last word that they said
 When I turned my back,
 They would look that they had
 Their sheep all the pack.
 I hope they will not be well paid[6]
615 When they their sheep lack.
  Pardie!°   *by God*
 But how-so the game goes,
 To me they will suppose,[7]
  And make a foul nose,°   *noise*
620 And cry out upon me.
 But thou must do as thou hight.° *promised*
 GILL I accord me theretill.[8]
 I shall swaddle him right
 In my cradill.

   [*She wraps up the sheep and puts it in the cradle.*]

625 If it were a greater sleight,
 Yet could I help till.[9]
 I will lie down straight.°   *immediately*
 Come hap° me.   *cover*
 MAK   I will.
  [*Covers her.*]
 GILL Behind

---

5. Hoarse (from shouting at her husband and children).
6. I expect they won't be well pleased.
7. They will suspect me.

8. I agree to that.
9. Even if it were a greater trick, I could still help with it.

630   Come Coll and his marrow,[1]
        They will nip° us full narrow.°   *pinch / closely*
   MAK   But I may cry "Out, harrow,"[2]
        The sheep if they find.

   GILL   Hearken ay when they call—
635   They will come anon.
        Come and make ready all,
        And sing by thine one.°   *self*
        Sing "lullay"° thou shall,   *lullaby*
        For I must groan
640   And cry out by the wall
        On Mary and John
          For sore.°   *pain*
        Sing "lullay" on fast
        When thou hears at the last,[3]
645   And but I play a false cast,[4]
          Trust me no more.

        [*The shepherds meet again.*]

   DAW   Ah, Coll, good morn.
        Why sleeps thou not?
   COLL   Alas, that ever I was born!
650   We have a foul blot:
        A fat wether° have we lorn.°   *ram / lost*
   DAW   Marry, God's forbot!°   *God forbid*
   GIB   Who should do us that scorn?
        That were a foul spot!°   *disgrace*
655   COLL   Some shrew.°   *rascal*
        I have sought with my dogs
        All Horbury[5] shrogs,°   *thickets*
        And of fifteen hogs
          Found I but one ewe.[6]

660   DAW   Now trow° me, if ye will,   *believe*
        By Saint Thomas of Kent,
        Either Mak or Gill
        Was at that assent.[7]
   COLL   Peace, man, be still!
665   I saw when he went.
        Thou slanders him ill—
        Thou ought to repent
          Good speed.°   *speedily*
   GIB   Now as ever might I thee,°   *thrive*
670   If I should even here dee,°   *die*

---

1. Coll and his mate are coming on your tracks.
2. A cry of distress.
3. When at last you hear (them coming).
4. Unless I play a false trick.

5. A village near Wakefield.
6. And with fifteen lambs I found only a ewe (i.e., the wether [ram] was missing).
7. Was a party to it.

I would say it were he
   That did that same deed.

DAW Go we thither, I read,°   *advise*
   And run on our feet.
675 Shall I never eat bread
   The sooth to I weet.[8]
COLL Nor drink in my head,
   With him till I meet.[9]
GIB I will rest in no stead°   *place*
680 Till that I him greet,
    My brother.
   One I will hight:[1]
   Till I see him in sight
   Shall I never sleep one night
685   There I do another.[2]

[*The shepherds approach* MAK's *house.* MAK *and* GILL *within, she in
bed, groaning, he singing a lullaby.*]

DAW Will ye hear how they hack?[3]
   Our sire list° croon.   *wants to*
COLL Heard I never none crack°   *sing loudly*
   So clear out of tune.
   Call on him.
690 GIB   Mak!
   Undo your door soon!°   *at once*
MAK Who is that spake,
   As° it were noon,   *as if*
    On loft?°   *loudly*
695 Who is that, I say?
DAW Good fellows, were it day.[4]
MAK As far as ye may,
   [*opening*] Good,° speaks soft   *good men*

   Over a sick woman's head
700 That is at malease.[5]
   I had liefer° be dead   *rather*
   Ere she had any disease.°   *distress*
GILL Go to another stead!°   *place*
   I may not well wheeze:°   *breathe*
705 Each foot that ye tread
   Goes through my nese.°   *nose*
    So, hee![6]
COLL Tell us, Mak, if you may,

---

8. Until I know the truth.
9. Nor take a drink till I meet with him.
1. One thing will I promise.
2. I'll never sleep in the same place two nights in
a row.
3. Trill; a musical term used sarcastically, as

also "crack" below.
4. Good friends, if it were daylight (i.e., not
friends, since it's still night).
5. Who feels badly.
6. So loudly, i.e., your tramping goes right
through my head.

How fare ye, I say?
710 MAK But are ye in this town today?[7]
    Now how fare ye?

Ye have run in the mire
And are wet yit.
I shall make you a fire
715 If you will sit.
A nurse would I hire.
Think ye on yit?[8]
Well quit is my hire—
My dream this is it—
720   A season.[9]
I have barns,° if ye knew,   *children*
Wel mo° than enew:°   *more / enough*
But we must drink as we brew,
    And that is but reason.

725 I would ye dined ere ye yode.°   *went*
Methink that ye sweat.
GIB Nay, neither mends our mood,
Drink nor meat.[1]
MAK Why sir, ails you aught but good?[2]
730 DAW Yea, our sheep that we get°   *tend*
Are stolen as they yode:°   *wandered*
Our loss is great.
MAK Sirs, drinks!
Had I been thore,°   *there*
735 Some should have bought° it full sore. *paid for*
COLL Marry, some men trows° that ye wore,° *think / were*
    And that us forthinks.°   *displeases*

GIB Mak, some men trows,
That it should be ye.
740 DAW Either ye or your spouse,
So say we.
MAK Now if you have suspouse°   *suspicion*
To Gill or to me,
Come and ripe° the house   *ransack*
745 And then may ye see
    Who had her[3]—
If I any sheep fot,°   *fetched, stole*
Either cow or stot[4]—
And Gill my wife rose not
750   Here sin she laid her.°   *lay down*

---

7. I.e., what brings you to this neighborhood today?
8. Do you still remember (my dream)?
9. Ironic: my season's wages are well paid—my dream (that Gill was giving birth) has come true.

1. Neither food nor drink will improve our mood.
2. Does anything other than good trouble you? I.e., what's wrong?
3. I.e., the sheep.
4. Either female or male.

As I am true and leal,°   *honest*
To God here I pray
That this be the first meal
That I shall eat this day.

755   COLL   Mak, as I have sele,[5]
     Advise thee, I say:
     He learned timely to steal
     That could not say nay.[6]   [*They begin to search.*]

     GILL   I swelt!°   *die*

760   Out, thieves, from my wones!°   *dwelling*
     Ye come to rob us for the nones.[7]
     MAK   Hear ye not how she groans?
       Your hearts should melt.

     GILL   Out, thieves, from my barn!°   *child*
765   Nigh him not thore![8]
     MAK   Wist ye how she had farn,[9]
     Your hearts would be sore.
     You do wrong, I you warn,
     That thus comes before°   *in the presence*
770   To a woman that has farn°—   *been in labor*
     But I say no more.
     GILL   Ah, my middill!°   *middle*
     I pray to God so mild,
     If ever I you beguiled,
775   That I eat this child
       That lies in this cradill.
     MAK   Peace, woman, for God's pain,
     And cry not so!
     Thou spills° thy brain   *harm*
780   And makes me full woe.
     GIB   I trow our sheep be slain.
     What find ye two?
     DAW   All work we in vain;
     As well may we go.
785   But hatters![1]
     I can find no flesh,
     Hard nor nesh,°   *soft*
     Salt nor fresh,
       But two tome° platters.   *empty*

790   Quick cattle but this,[2]
     Tame nor wild,
     None, as I have bliss,
     As loud as he smiled.[3]   [*Approaches the cradle.*]

---

5. As I hope to have salvation.
6. He learned early to steal who could not say no (proverbial).
7. You come for the purpose of robbing us.
8. Don't come close to him there.

9. If you knew how she had fared (in labor).
1. An expression of consternation.
2. Livestock other than this (the baby).
3. Smelled as strongly as he (the missing ram).

GILL No, so God me bliss,°   *bless*
795 And give me joy of my child!
 COLL We have marked° amiss—   *aimed*
  I hold° us beguiled.   *consider*
 GIB Sir, don!°   *totally*
  [*to* MAK] Sir—Our Lady him save!—
800   Is your child a knave?[4]
 MAK Any lord might him have,
  This child, to° his son.   *as*

  When he wakens he kips,°   *snatches, grabs*
  That joy is to see.
805 DAW In good time to his hips,
  And in sely.[5]
  But who were his gossips,°   *godparents*
  So soon ready?
 MAK So fair fall their lips[6]—
810 COLL Hark, now, a lee,°   *lie*
 MAK So God them thank,
  Perkin, and Gibbon Waller, I say,
  And gentle John Horne, in good fay°— *faith*
  He made all the garray°   *quarrel*
815 With the great shank.[7]

 GIB Mak, friends will we be,
  For we are all one.°   *in accord*
 MAK We? Now I hold for me,
  For mends get I none.[8]
820 Farewell all three,
  All glad[9] were ye gone.
 DAW Fair words may there be,
  But love is there none
   This year.   [*They go out the door.*]
825 COLL Gave ye the child anything?
 GIB I trow not one farthing.
 DAW Fast again will I fling.°   *dash*
  Abide ye me there.   [*He runs back.*]

  Mak, take it no grief
830 If I come to thy barn.°   *child*
 MAK Nay, thou does me great reprief,° *shame*
  And foul has thou farn.°   *behaved*
 DAW The child it will not grief,
  That little day-starn.°   *day star*
835 Mak, with your leaf,°   *permission*

---

4. Boy (although Mak takes the alternate meaning of "rascal").
5. Good luck and happiness to him.
6. May good luck befall them.
7. An allusion to a dispute among the shepherds in the author's *First Shepherds' Play.*
8. I'll look out for myself, for I'll get no compensation.
9. I.e., I would be glad.

Let me give your barn
    But sixpence.
MAK Nay, do way! He sleeps.
DAW Methinks he peeps.°   *opens his eyes*
840 MAK When he wakens he weeps.
    I pray you go hence.

[*The other shepherds reenter.*]

DAW Give me leave him to kiss,
    And lift up the clout.°   *cover*
    [*lifts the cover*]
    What the devil is this?
845   He has a long snout!
COLL He is marked amiss.
    We wot ill about.[1]
GIB Ill-spun weft, ywis,
    Ay comes foul out.[2]
850   Aye, so!
    He is like to our sheep.
DAW How, Gib, may I peep?
COLL I trow kind will creep
    Where it may not go.[3]

855 GIB This was a quaint gaud
    And a far-cast.[4]
    It was high fraud.
DAW Yea, sirs, was't.°   *it was*
    Let bren° this bawd°   *burn / evildoer*
860   And bind her fast.
    A false scaud°   *scold*
    Hang at the last:[5]
    So shall thou.
    Will you see how they swaddle
865   His four feet in the middle?
    Saw I never in the cradle
    A horned lad ere now.

MAK Peace bid I! What,
    Let be your fare!°   *fuss*
870   I am he that him gat.°   *begot*
    And yond woman him bare.
COLL What devil shall he hat?[6]
    Lo, God, Mak's heir!
GIB Let be all that!

---

1. He is deformed. We know something fishy is going on around here.
2. An ill-spun web, indeed, always comes out badly (proverbial), i.e., ill work always comes to a bad end.
3. Nature will creep where it can't walk (proverbial), i.e., nature will reveal itself by hook or crook.
4. This was a cunning trick and a clever ruse.
5. Will hang in the end.
6. What the devil shall he be named?

875   Now God give him care°—   *sorrow*
         I sawgh!°   *saw*
   GILL   A pretty child is he
       As sits on a woman's knee,
       A dillydown,° pardie,°   *darling / by God*
880   To gar° a man laugh.   *make*

   DAW   I know him by the earmark—
       That is a good token.
   MAK   I tell you, sirs, hark,
       His nose was broken.
885   Sithen° told me a clerk   *later*
       That he was forspoken.°   *bewitched*
   COLL   This is a false wark.°   *work*
       I would fain be wroken.°   *avenged*
       Get wapen.°   *weapon*
890   GILL   He was taken with an elf[7]
       I saw it myself—
       When the clock struck twelf
       Was he forshapen.°   *transformed*

   GIB   Ye two are well feft
895   Sam in a stead.[8]
   DAW   Sin° they maintain their theft,   *since*
       Let do° them to dead.°   *put / death*
   MAK   If I trespass eft,°   *again*
       Gird° off my head.   *chop*
900   With you will I be left.[9]
   COLL   Sirs, do my read:°   *advice*
       For this trespass
       We will neither ban° ne flite,°   *curse / quarrel*
       Fight nor chite,°   *chide*
905   But have done as tite,°   *quickly*
       And cast him in canvas.

        [*They toss* MAK *in a blanket.*]

           [*The fields*]

   COLL   Lord, what° I am sore,   *how*
       In point for to brist!°   *burst*
       In faith, I may no more—
910   Therefore will I rist.°   *rest*
   GIB   As a sheep of seven score[1]
       He weighed in my fist:
       For to sleep aywhore°   *anywhere*
       Methink that I list.°   *want*

---

7. He was stolen by a fairy, i.e., the baby is a changeling.
8. You two are well endowed in the same place, i.e., you are two of a kind.
9. I put myself at your mercy.
1. I.e., 140 pounds.

915 DAW Now I pray you
    Lie down on this green.
  COLL On the thieves yet I mean.°   *think*
  DAW Whereto should ye teen?°   *be angry*
    Do as I say you.   *[They lie down.]*

      [An ANGEL *sings* Gloria in Excelsis *and then speaks.]*[2]

920 ANGEL Rise, herdmen hend,°   *gracious*
    For now is he born
    That shall take fro the fiend°   *devil*
    That Adam had lorn;[3]
    That warlock° to shend,°   *devil / destroy*
925 This night is he born.
    God is made your friend
    Now at this morn,
      He behestys.°   *promises*
    At Bedlem° go see: *Bethlehem*
930 There lies that free,°   *noble one*
    In a crib full poorly,
      Betwixt two bestys.°   *beasts*

      [The ANGEL *withdraws.]*

  COLL This was a quaint° steven°   *marvelous / voice*
    That ever yet I hard.°   *heard*
935 It is a marvel to neven°   *tell of*
    Thus to be scar'd.°   *scared*
  GIB Of God's Son of heaven
    He spake upward.°   *on high*
    All the wood on a leven
940 Methought that he gard
      Appear.[4]
  DAW He spake of a barn°   *child*
    In Bedlem, I you warn.°   *tell*
  COLL That betokens yond starn.[5]
945   Let us seek him there.

  GIB Say, what was his song?
    Heard ye not how he cracked it?[6]
    Three breves° to a long?   *in triple rhythm*
  DAW Yea, marry, he hacked it.
950 Was no crochet[7] wrong,
    Nor nothing that lacked it.[8]

---

2. This is an original stage direction; "Glory [to God] in the highest" (see Luke 2.14).
3. That [which] Adam had brought to ruin.
4. I thought he made the whole woods appear in a flash of light.
5. That's what yonder star means.
6. Trilled it; a technical musical term, close in meaning to *hacked* and *knacked*: to break (notes), to sing in a lively or ornate manner (cf. lines 685 and 687).
7. A very short note, requiring quick and skillful execution.
8. That it lacked.

COLL   For to sing us among,
      Right as he knacked it,
      I can.°   *know how*

955   GIB   Let see how ye croon!
      Can ye bark at the moon?
    DAW   Hold your tongues! Have done!
    COLL   Hark after, than!   [*Sings.*]

    GIB   To Bedlem he bade
960   That we should gang:°   *go*
      I am full fard°   *afraid*
      That we tarry too lang.°   *long*
    DAW   Be merry and not sad;
      Of mirth is our sang:
965   Everlasting glad°   *joy*
      To meed° may we fang.°   *reward / get*
    COLL   Without nose°   *noise*
      Hie we thither forthy°   *therefore*
      To that child and that lady;
970   If° we be wet and weary,   *though*
        We have it not to lose.[9]

    GIB   We find by the prophecy—
      Let be your din!—
      Of David and Isay,
975   And mo than I min,[1]
      That prophesied by clergy°   *learning*
      That in a virgin
      Should he light° and lie,   *alight*
      To sloken° our sin   *quench*
980   And slake° it,   *relieve*
      Our kind,° from woe,   *humankind*
      For Isay said so:
      Ecce virgo
        Concipiet[2] a child that is naked.

985   DAW   Full glad may we be
      And° we abide that day   *if*
      That lovely to see,
      That all mights may.[3]
      Lord, well were me
990   For once and for ay
      Might I kneel on my knee,
      Some word for to say
        To that child.
      But the angel said

---

9. We must not neglect it.
1. Of David and Isaiah and more than I remember.
2. Behold, a virgin shall conceive (Isaiah 7.14).

3. I.e., when we see that lovely one who is all-powerful.

995 In a crib was he laid,
He was poorly arrayed,
　　Both meaner° and mild.　　　　　　　　　　　　　　*very humbly*

COLL　Patriarchs that has been,
And prophets beforn,°　　　　　　　　　　　*before (our time)*
1000 That desired to have seen
This child that is born,
They are gone full clean—
That have they lorn.[4]
We shall see him, I ween,°　　　　　　　　　　　*think*
1005 Ere it be morn,
　　To token.[5]
When I see him and feel,
Then wot° I full weel°　　　　　　　　　　　*know / well*
It is true as steel
1010 That° prophets have spoken:　　　　　　　　　*what*

To so poor as we are
That he would appear,
First find and declare[6]
By his messenger.
1015 GIB　Go we now, let us fare,
The place is us near.
DAW　I am ready and yare;°　　　　　　　　　　*eager*
Go we in fere°　　　　　　　　　　　　　　*together*
　　To that bright.°　　　　　　　　　　　　*glorious one*
1020 Lord, if thy wills be—
We are lewd° all three—　　　　　　　　　　*ignorant*
Thou grant us some kins glee[7]
　　To comfort thy wight.°　　　　　　　　　*child*

[*They go to Bethlehem and enter the stable.*]

COLL　Hail, comely and clean!°　　　　　　　　*pure*
1025 Hail, young child!
Hail Maker, as I mean,°　　　　　　　　　　*believe*
Of° a maiden so mild!　　　　　　　　　　　*born of*
Thou has waried,° I ween,°　　　　　　　　*cursed / think*
The warlock° so wild.　　　　　　　　　　　*devil*
1030 The false guiler of teen,[8]
Now goes he beguiled.
　　Lo, he merries!°　　　　　　　　　　　*is merry*
Lo, he laughs, my sweeting!
A well fair meeting!
1035 I have holden my heting:°　　　　　　　　*promise*
　　Have a bob° of cherries.　　　　　　　　*bunch*

4. That (sight) have they lost. See Matthew 13.17.　　birth).
5. As a sign.　　　　　　　　　　　　　　　　　　7. Some kind of cheer.
6. Find (us) first (of all), and make known (his　　8. The false grievous deceiver, i.e., the devil.

GIB Hail, sovereign Saviour,
For thou has us sought!
Hail freely food° and flour,°   *noble child / flower*
1040   That all thing has wrought!°   *created*
Hail, full of favour,
That made all of nought!
Hail! I kneel and I cower.°   *crouch*
A bird have I brought
1045   To my barn.°   *child*
Hail, little tiny mop!°   *baby*
Of our creed thou art crop.°   *head*
I would drink on thy cup,
      Little day-starn.°   *day star*

1050 DAW Hail, darling dear,
Full of Godhead!
I pray thee be near
When that I have need.
Hail, sweet is thy cheer°—   *face*
1055   My heart would bleed
To see thee sit here
In so poor weed,°   *clothing*
      With no pennies.
Hail, put forth thy dall!°   *hand*
1060   I bring thee but a ball:
Have and play thee withal,
      And go to the tennis.
MARY The Father of heaven,
God omnipotent,
1065   That set all on seven,[9]
His Son has he sent.
My name could he neven,
And light ere he went.[1]
I conceived him full even
1070   Through might as he meant.[2]
And now is he born.
He° keep you from woe!   *(may) he*
I shall pray him so.
Tell forth as ye go,
1075   And min on° this morn.   *remember*

COLL Farewell, lady,
So fair to behold,
With thy child on thy knee.
GIB But he lies full cold.
1080   Lord, well is me.
Now we go, thou behold.

---

9. Who created everything in seven (days).
1. My name did he name, and alighted (in me) before he went (see Luke 1.28).

2. I conceived him, indeed, through his power, just as he intended.

DAW   Forsooth, already
    It seems to be told
    Full oft.
1085 COLL   What grace we have fun!°   received
GIB   Come forth, now are we won!°   redeemed
DAW   To sing are we bun:°   bound
    Let take on loft.[3]
    [*They sing.*]

3. Let's raise our voices.

MIDDLE ENGLISH LYRICS

I t was only late in the fourteenth century that English began to develop the kinds of aristocratic, formal, learned, and literary types of lyric that had long been cultivated on the Continent by the Troubador poets in the south of France, the Minnesänger in Germany (German *Minne* corresponds to French *fine amour*—that is, refined or aristocratic love), or the Italian poets whose works Dante characterized as the *dolce stil nuovo* (the sweet new style). Chaucer, under the influence of French poets, wrote lovers' complaints, homiletic poetry, and verse letters in the form of ballades, roundels, and other highly stylized lyric types (see pp. 343–346). In the fifteenth century, John Lydgate, Thomas Hoccleve, and others following Chaucer wrote lyrics of this sort, which were praised for embellishing the English language, and these along with Chaucer's were collected in manuscript anthologies that were produced commercially for well-to-do buyers.

Chaucer, his courtly predecessors, and their followers were of course familiar with and influenced by an ancient tradition of popular song from which only a small fraction survives. With one exception, the Middle English lyrics included in this section are the work of anonymous poets and are difficult to date with any precision. Some of these survive in a single manuscript, especially in anthologies of religious poetry and prose. The topics and language in these poems are highly conventional, yet the lyrics often seem remarkably fresh and spontaneous. Many are marked by strong accentual rhythms with a good deal of alliteration. Their pleasure does not come from originality or lived experience but from variations of expected themes and images. Some were undoubtedly set to music, and in a few cases the music has survived. Perhaps the earliest of those printed here, "The Cuckoo Song," is a canon or round in which the voices follow one another and join together echoing the joyous cry, "Cuckou." The rooster and hen in *The Nun's Priest's Tale* sing "My Lief Is Faren in Londe" in "sweet accord." "I Am of Ireland" was undoubtedly accompanied by dancing as well as music.

A frequent topic that lyric shares with narrative is the itemization of the beloved's beauties. The Alisoun of the lyric and Alisoun of *The Miller's Tale* are both dark-eyed, a quality that suggests a sexuality supressed in the conventional gray- or blue-eyed heroines of courtly romance. The lover in the lyric protests, as Nicholas does in *The Miller's Tale*, that he will die if he cannot obtain her love.

The joyous return of spring (the *reverdie*, spring song, or, literally, "regreening") is the subject of many lyrics. In love lyrics the mating of birds and animals in wild nature often contrasts with the melancholy of unrequited or forsaken lovers. These lovers are usually male. We know that some women wrote troubador and court poetry, but we do not know whether women composed popular lyrics; women certainly sang popular songs, just as they are portrayed doing in narrative poetry.

Foweles in the Frith

Foweles° in the frith,°	*birds / forest*
The fisses° in the flod,°	*fishes / sea*
And I mon° waxe wod:°	*must / go mad*
Mulch sorw° I walke with	*much sorrow*
For beste[1] of bon and blod°	*bone and blood*

The Cuckoo Song

Sumer is ycomen in,	
Loude sing cuckou!	
Groweth seed and bloweth meed[1]	
And springth the wode° now.	*wood*
5 Sing cuckou!	
Ewe bleteth after lamb,	
Loweth after calve cow,	
Bulloc sterteth,° bucke verteth,°	*leaps / farts*
Merye sing cuckou!	
10 Cuckou, cuckou,	
Wel singest thou cuckou:	
Ne swik° thou never now!	*cease*

Alison

Bitweene° Merch and Averil,	*in the seasons of*
When spray biginneth to springe,	
The litel fowl hath hire wil°	*pleasure*
On hire leod[1] to singe.	
5 Ich° libbe° in love-longinge	*I / live*
For semlokest° of alle thinge.	*seemliest, fairest*
Heo° may me blisse bringe:	*she*
Ich am in hire baundoun.°	*power*
An hendy hap ich habbe yhent,[2]	
10 Ichoot° from hevene it is me sent:	*I know*

---

1. Most obviously "best," but note possible pun on Middle English "beste," meaning "beast." So one might translate as "creature."

1. The meadow blossoms.
1. In her language.
2. A gracious chance I have received.

From alle[3] wommen my love is lent,°   *removed*
And light° on Alisoun.   *alights*

On hew° hire heer° is fair ynough,   *hue / hair*
Hire browe browne, hire yë° blake;   *eye*
15 With lossum cheere heo on me lough;[4]
With middel smal and wel ymake.
But° heo me wolle to hire take   *unless*
For to been hire owen make,°   *mate*
Longe to liven ichulle° forsake,   *I will*
20 And feye° fallen adown.   *dead*
  An hendy hap, etc.

Nightes when I wende° and wake,   *turn*
Forthy° mine wonges° waxeth wan: *therefore / cheeks*
Levedy,° al for thine sake   *lady*
25 Longinge is ylent me on.[5]
In world nis noon so witer° man   *clever*
That al hire bountee° telle can;   *excellence*
Hire swire° is whittere° than the swan, *neck / whiter*
  And fairest may° in town.   *maid*
30 An hendy, etc.

Ich am for wowing° al forwake,° *wooing / worn out from waking*
Wery so° water in wore.[6]   *as*
Lest any reve me[7] my make
Ich habbe y-yerned yore.[8]
35 Bettere is tholien° while° sore *endure / for a time*
Than mournen evermore.
Geinest under gore,[9]
  Herkne to my roun:°   *song*
  An hendy, etc.

My Lief Is Faren in Londe

My lief is faren in londe[1]—
Allas, why is she so?
And I am so sore bonde°   *bound*
I may nat come her to.
5 She hath myn herte in holde
Wherever she ride or go°—   *walk*
With trewe love a thousand folde.

3. I.e., all other.
4. With lovely face she on me smiled.
5. Longing has come upon me.
6. Perhaps "millpond."
7. Deprive me.
8. I have been worrying long since.
9. Fairest beneath clothing.
1. My beloved has gone away.

Western Wind

Westron wind, when will thou blow?
The small rain down can rain.
Christ, that my love were in my arms,
And I in my bed again.

I Am of Ireland

Ich am of Irlonde,
And of the holy londe
   Of Irlonde.
Goode sire, praye ich thee,
5 For of° sainte charitee,   *sake of*
Com and dance with me
   In Irlonde.

SIR THOMAS MALORY
ca. 1405–1471

Morte Darthur (Death of Arthur) is the title that William Caxton, the first English printer, gave to Malory's volume, which Caxton described more accurately in his Preface as "the noble histories of * * * King Arthur and of certain of his knights." The volume begins with the mythical story of Arthur's birth. King Uther Pendragon falls in love with the wife of one of his barons. Merlin's magic transforms Uther into the likeness of her husband, and Arthur is born of this union. The volume ends with the destruction of the Round Table and the deaths of Arthur, Queen Guinevere, and Sir Lancelot, who is Arthur's best knight and the queen's lover. The bulk of the work is taken up with the separate adventures of the knights of the Round Table.

On the evolution of the Arthurian legend, see the headnote to "The Myth of Arthur's Return," p. 130. During the thirteenth century the stories about Arthur and his knights had been turned into a series of enormously long prose romances in French, and it was these, as Caxton informed his readers, "Sir Thomas Malory did take out of certain books of French and reduced into English." For Caxton's Preface and excerpts from a modern translation of the French *Prose Vulgate Cycle* (Malory's "French books"), see the "King Arthur" topic in the supplemental ebook.

Little was known about the author until the early twentieth century when scholars began to unearth the criminal record of a Sir Thomas Malory of Newbold Revell in Warwickshire. In 1451 he was arrested for the first time to prevent his doing injury—presumably further injury—to a priory in Lincolnshire, and shortly thereafter he was accused of a number of criminal acts. These included escaping from prison after his first arrest, twice breaking into and plundering the Abbey of Coombe, extorting money from various persons, and committing rape. Malory pleaded innocent of all charges. The Wars of the Roses—in which Malory, like the formidable earl of Warwick (the "kingmaker"), whom he seems to have followed, switched sides from Lancaster to York and back again—may account for some of his troubles with the law. After a failed Lancastrian revolt, the Yorkist king, Edward IV, specifically excluded Malory from four amnesties he granted to the Lancastrians.

The identification of this Sir Thomas Malory (there is another candidate with the same name) as the author of the *Morte* was strengthened by the discovery in 1934 of a manuscript that differed from Caxton's text, the only version previously known. The manuscript contained eight separate romances. Caxton, in order to give the impression of a continuous narrative, had welded these together into twenty-one books, subdivided into short chapters with summary chapter headings. Caxton suppressed all but the last of the personal remarks the author had appended to individual tales in the manuscript. At the very end of the book Malory asks "all gentlemen and gentlewomen that readeth this book * * * pray for me while I am alive that God send me good deliverance." The discovery of the manuscript revealed that at the close of the first tale he had written: "this was drawyn by a knight presoner Sir Thomas Malleoré, that God sende him good recover." There is strong circumstantial evidence, therefore, that the book from which the Arthurian legends were passed on to future generations to be adapted in literature, art, and film was written in prison by a man whose violent career might seem at odds with the chivalric ideals he professes.

Such a contradiction—if it really is one—should not be surprising. Nostalgia for an ideal past that never truly existed is typical of much historical romance. Like the slave-owning plantation society of Margaret Mitchell's *Gone with the Wind*, whose southern gentlemen cultivate chivalrous manners and respect for gentlewomen, Malory's Arthurian world is a fiction. In our terms, it cannot even be labeled "historical," although the distinction between romance and history is not one that Malory would have made. Only rarely does he voice skepticism about the historicity of his tale; one such example is his questioning of the myth of Arthur's return. Much of the tragic power of his romance lies in his sense of the irretrievability of past glory in comparison with the sordidness of his own age.

The success of Malory's retelling owes much to his development of a terse and direct prose style, especially the naturalistic dialogue that keeps his narrative close to earth. And both he and many of his characters are masters of understatement who express themselves, in moments of great emotional tension, with a bare minimum of words.

In spite of its professed dedication to service of women, Malory's chivalry is primarily devoted to the fellowship and competitions of aristocratic men. Fighting consists mainly of single combats in tournaments, chance encounters, and battles, which Malory never tires of describing in professional detail. Commoners rarely come into view; when they do, the effect can be chilling—as when pillagers by moonlight plunder the corpses of the knights left on the field of Arthur's last battle. Above all, Malory cherishes an aristocratic male code of honor for which his favorite word is "worship." Men win or lose "worship" through their actions in war and love.

The most "worshipful" of Arthur's knights is Sir Lancelot, the "head of all Christian knights," as he is called in a moving eulogy by his brother, Sir Ector. But Lancelot is compromised by his fatal liaison with Arthur's queen and torn between the incompatible loyalties that bind him as an honorable knight, on the one hand, to his lord Arthur and, on the other, to his lady Guinevere. Malory loves his character Lancelot even to the point of indulging in the fleeting speculation, after Lancelot has been admitted to the queen's chamber, that their activities might have been innocent, "for love that time was not as love is nowadays." But when the jealousy and malice of two wicked knights force the affair into the open, nothing can avert a mighty civil war; the breaking up of the fellowship of the Round Table; and the death of Arthur himself, which Malory relates with somber magnificence as the passing of a great era.

From Morte Darthur[1]

[THE CONSPIRACY AGAINST LANCELOT AND GUINEVERE]

In May, when every lusty[2] heart flourisheth and burgeoneth, for as the season is lusty to behold and comfortable,[3] so man and woman rejoiceth and gladdeth of summer coming with his fresh flowers; for winter with his rough winds and blasts causeth lusty men and women to cower and to sit fast by the fire—so this season it befell in the month of May a great anger and unhap that stinted not[4] till the flower of chivalry of all the world was destroyed and slain. And all was long upon two unhappy[5] knights which were named Sir Agravain and Sir Mordred that were brethren unto Sir Gawain.[6] For this Sir Agravain and Sir Mordred had ever a privy[7] hate unto the Queen, Dame Guinevere, and to Sir Lancelot, and daily and nightly they ever watched upon Sir Lancelot.

So it misfortuned Sir Gawain and all his brethren were in King Arthur's chamber, and then Sir Agravain said thus openly, and not in no counsel,[8] that many knights might hear: "I marvel that we all be not ashamed both to see and to know how Sir Lancelot lieth daily and nightly by the Queen. And all we know well that it is so, and it is shamefully suffered of us all[9] that we should suffer so noble a king as King Arthur is to be shamed."

Then spoke Sir Gawain and said, "Brother, Sir Agravain, I pray you and charge you, move no such matters no more afore[1] me, for wit you well, I will not be of your counsel."[2]

"So God me help," said Sir Gaheris and Sir Gareth,[3] "we will not be known of your deeds."[4]

"Then will I!" said Sir Mordred.

"I lieve[5] you well," said Sir Gawain, "for ever unto all unhappiness, sir, ye will grant.[6] And I would that ye left all this and make you not so busy, for I know," said Sir Gawain, "what will fall of it."[7]

"Fall whatsoever fall may," said Sir Agravain, "I will disclose it to the King."

"Not by my counsel," said Sir Gawain, "for and[8] there arise war and wrack betwixt[9] Sir Lancelot and us, wit you well, brother, there will many

---

1. The selections here are from the section that Caxton called book 20, chaps. 1–4, 8–10, and book 21, chaps. 3–7, 10–12, with omissions. In the Winchester manuscript this section is titled "The Most Piteous Tale of the Morte Arthur Saunz Guerdon" (i.e., the death of Arthur without reward or compensation). The text is based on Winchester, with some readings introduced from the Caxton edition; spelling has been modernized and modern punctuation added.
2. Merry.
3. Pleasant.
4. Misfortune that ceased not.
5. On account of two ill-fated.
6. Gawain and Agravain are sons of King Lot of Orkney and his wife, Arthur's half-sister Mor-

gause. Mordred is the illegitimate son of Arthur and Morgause.
7. Secret.
8. Secret manner.
9. Put up with by all of us.
1. Before. "Move": propose.
2. On your side. "Wit you well": know well, i.e., give you to understand.
3. Sons of King Lot and Gawain's brothers.
4. A party to your doings.
5. Believe.
6. You will consent to all mischief.
7. Come of it.
8. If.
9. Strife between.

kings and great lords hold with Sir Lancelot. Also, brother, Sir Agravain," said Sir Gawain, "ye must remember how often times Sir Lancelot hath rescued the King and the Queen. And the best of us all had been full cold at the heart-root[1] had not Sir Lancelot been better than we, and that has he proved himself full oft. And as for my part," said Sir Gawain, "I will never be against Sir Lancelot for[2] one day's deed, when he rescued me from King Carados of the Dolorous[3] Tower and slew him and saved my life. Also, brother, Sir Agravain and Sir Mordred, in like wise Sir Lancelot rescued you both and three score and two[4] from Sir Tarquin. And therefore, brother, methinks such noble deeds and kindness should be remembered."

"Do as ye list,"[5] said Sir Agravain, "for I will layne[6] it no longer."

So with these words came in Sir Arthur.

"Now, brother," said Sir Gawain, "stint your noise."[7]

"That will I not," said Sir Agravain and Sir Mordred.

"Well, will ye so?" said Sir Gawain. "Then God speed you, for I will not hear of your tales, neither be of your counsel."

"No more will I," said Sir Gaheris.

"Neither I," said Sir Gareth, "for I shall never say evil by[8] that man that made me knight." And therewithal they three departed making great dole.[9]

"Alas!" said Sir Gawain and Sir Gareth, "now is this realm wholly destroyed and mischieved,[1] and the noble fellowship of the Round Table shall be disparbeled."[2]

So they departed, and then King Arthur asked them what noise[3] they made. "My lord," said Sir Agravain, "I shall tell you, for I may keep[4] it no longer. Here is I and my brother Sir Mordred broke[5] unto my brother Sir Gawain, Sir Gaheris, and to Sir Gareth—for this is all, to make it short—how that we know all that Sir Lancelot holdeth your queen, and hath done long; and we be your sister[6] sons, we may suffer it no longer. And all we woot[7] that ye should be above Sir Lancelot, and ye are the king that made him knight, and therefore we will prove it that he is a traitor to your person."

"If it be so," said the King, "wit[8] you well, he is none other. But I would be loath to begin such a thing but[9] I might have proofs of it, for Sir Lancelot is an hardy knight, and all ye know that he is the best knight among us all. And but if he be taken with the deed,[1] he will fight with him that bringeth up the noise, and I know no knight that is able to match him. Therefore, and[2] it be sooth as ye say, I would that he were taken with the deed."

For, as the French book saith, the King was full loath that such a noise should be upon Sir Lancelot and his queen. For the King had a deeming[3] of it, but he would not hear of it, for Sir Lancelot had done so much for him and for the Queen so many times that, wit you well, the King loved him passingly[4] well.

---

1. Would have been dead.
2. On account of.
3. Dismal.
4. I.e., sixty two.
5. You please.
6. Conceal.
7. Stop making scandal.
8. About.
9. Lamentation.
1. Put to shame.
2. Dispersed.

3. Rumor.
4. Conceal.
5. Revealed.
6. Sister's.
7. Know.
8. Know.
9. Unless
1. Unless he is caught in the act.
2. If.
3. Suspicion.
4. Exceedingly.

"My lord," said Sir Agravain, "ye shall ride tomorn[5] on hunting, and doubt ye not, Sir Lancelot will not go with you. And so when it draweth toward night, ye may send the Queen word that ye will lie out all that night, and so may ye send for your cooks. And then, upon pain of death, that night we shall take him with the Queen, and we shall bring him unto you, quick[6] or dead."

"I will well,"[7] said the King. "Then I counsel you to take with you sure fellowship."

"Sir," said Sir Agravain, "my brother, Sir Mordred, and I will take with us twelve knights of the Round Table."

"Beware," said King Arthur, "for I warn you, ye shall find him wight."[8]

"Let us deal!"[9] said Sir Agravain and Sir Mordred.

So on the morn King Arthur rode on hunting and sent word to the Queen that he would be out all that night. Then Sir Agravain and Sir Mordred got to them[1] twelve knights and hid themself in a chamber in the castle of Carlisle. And these were their names: Sir Colgrevance, Sir Mador de la Porte, Sir Guingalen, Sir Meliot de Logres, Sir Petipace of Winchelsea, Sir Galeron of Galway, Sir Melion de la Mountain, Sir Ascamore, Sir Gromore Somyr Jour, Sir Curselayne, Sir Florence, and Sir Lovell. So these twelve knights were with Sir Mordred and Sir Agravain, and all they were of Scotland, or else of Sir Gawain's kin, or well-willers[2] to his brother.

So when the night came, Sir Lancelot told Sir Bors[3] how he would go that night and speak with the Queen.

"Sir," said Sir Bors, "ye shall not go this night by my counsel."

"Why?" said Sir Lancelot.

"Sir," said Sir Bors, "I dread me[4] ever of Sir Agravain that waiteth upon[5] you daily to do you shame and us all. And never gave my heart against no going that ever ye went[6] to the queen so much as now, for I mistrust[7] that the King is out this night from the Queen because peradventure he hath lain[8] some watch for you and the Queen. Therefore, I dread me sore of some treason."

"Have ye no dread," said Sir Lancelot, "for I shall go and come again and make no tarrying."

"Sir," said Sir Bors, "that me repents,[9] for I dread me sore that your going this night shall wrath[1] us all."

"Fair nephew," said Sir Lancelot, "I marvel me much why ye say thus, sithen[2] the Queen hath sent for me. And wit you well, I will not be so much a coward, but she shall understand I will[3] see her good grace."

"God speed you well," said Sir Bors, "and send you sound and safe again!"

So Sir Lancelot departed and took his sword under his arm, and so he walked in his mantel,[4] that noble knight, and put himself in great jeopardy. And so he passed on till he came to the Queen's chamber, and so lightly he was had[5] into the chamber. And then, as the French book saith, the Queen and Sir Lancelot were together. And whether they were abed or at other

---

5. Tomorrow.
6. Alive.
7. Readily agree.
8. Strong.
9. Leave it to us.
1. Gathered to themselves.
2. Partisans.
3. Nephew and confidant of Sir Lancelot.
4. I am afraid.
5. Lies in wait.

6. Never misgave my heart against any visit you made.
7. Suspect.
8. Perhaps he has set.
9. I regret.
1. Cause injury to.
2. Since.
3. Wish to.
4. Cloak. Lancelot goes without armor.
5. Quickly he was received.

manner of disports, me list[6] not thereof make no mention, for love that time[7] was not as love is nowadays.

But thus as they were together there came Sir Agravain and Sir Mordred with twelve knights with them of the Round Table, and they said with great crying and scaring[8] voice: "Thou traitor, Sir Lancelot, now are thou taken!" And thus they cried with a loud voice that all the court might hear it. And these fourteen knights all were armed at all points, as[9] they should fight in a battle.

"Alas!" said Queen Guinevere, "now are we mischieved[1] both!"

"Madam," said Sir Lancelot, "is there here any armor within your chamber that I might cover my body withal? And if there be any, give it me, and I shall soon stint[2] their malice, by the grace of God!"

"Now, truly," said the Queen, "I have none armor neither helm, shield, sword, neither spear, wherefore I dread me sore our long love is come to a mischievous end. For I hear by their noise there be many noble knights, and well I woot they be surely[3] armed, and against them ye may make no resistance. Wherefore ye are likely to be slain, and then shall I be burned! For and[4] ye might escape them," said the Queen, "I would not doubt but that ye would rescue me in what danger that ever I stood in."

"Alas!" said Sir Lancelot, "in all my life thus was I never bestead[5] that I should be thus shamefully slain for lack of mine armor."

But ever in one[6] Sir Agravain and Sir Mordred cried: "Traitor knight, come out of the Queen's chamber! For wit thou well thou art beset so that thou shalt not escape."

"Ah, Jesu mercy!" said Sir Lancelot, "this shameful cry and noise I may not suffer, for better were death at once than thus to endure this pain." Then he took the Queen in his arms and kissed her and said, "Most noblest Christian queen, I beseech you, as ye have been ever my special good lady, and I at all times your poor knight and true unto[7] my power, and as I never failed you in right nor in wrong sithen the first day King Arthur made me knight, that ye will pray for my soul if that I be slain. For well I am assured that Sir Bors, my nephew, and all the remnant of my kin, with Sir Lavain and Sir Urry,[8] that they will not fail you to rescue you from the fire. And therefore, mine own lady, recomfort yourself,[9] whatsoever come of me, that ye go with Sir Bors, my nephew, and Sir Urry and they all will do you all the pleasure that they may, and ye shall live like a queen upon my lands."

"Nay, Sir Lancelot, nay!" said the Queen. "Wit thou well that I will not live long after thy days. But and[1] ye be slain I will take my death as meekly as ever did martyr take his death for Jesu Christ's sake."

"Well, Madam," said Sir Lancelot, "sith it is so that the day is come that our love must depart,[2] wit you well I shall sell my life as dear as I may. And a thousandfold," said Sir Lancelot, "I am more heavier[3] for you than for myself!

---

6. I care. "Disports": pastimes.
7. At that time.
8. Terrifying.
9. Completely, as if.
1. Come to grief.
2. Stop.
3. Securely.
4. If.
5. Beset.

6. In unison.
7. To the utmost of.
8. The brother of Elaine, the Fair Maid of Astolat, and a knight miraculously healed of his wound by Sir Lancelot. "Remnant": rest.
9. Take heart again.
1. If.
2. Come to an end.
3. More grieved.

And now I had liefer[4] than to be lord of all Christendom that I had sure armor upon me, that men might speak of my deeds ere ever I were slain."

"Truly," said the Queen, "and[5] it might please God, I would that they would take me and slay me and suffer[6] you to escape."

"That shall never be," said Sir Lancelot. "God defend me from such a shame! But, Jesu Christ, be Thou my shield and mine armor!" And therewith Sir Lancelot wrapped his mantel about his arm well and surely; and by then they had gotten a great form[7] out of the hall, and therewith they all rushed at the door. "Now, fair lords," said Sir Lancelot, "leave[8] your noise and your rushing, and I shall set open this door, and then may ye do with me what it liketh you."[9]

"Come off,[1] then," said they all, "and do it, for it availeth thee not to strive against us all. And therefore let us into this chamber, and we shall save thy life until thou come to King Arthur."

Then Sir Lancelot unbarred the door, and with his left hand he held it open a little, that but one man might come in at once. And so there came striding a good knight, a much[2] man and a large, and his name was called Sir Colgrevance of Gore. And he with a sword struck at Sir Lancelot mightily. And he put aside[3] the stroke and gave him such a buffet[4] upon the helmet that he fell groveling dead within the chamber door. Then Sir Lancelot with great might drew the knight within[5] the chamber door. And then Sir Lancelot, with help of the Queen and her ladies, he was lightly[6] armed in Colgrevance's armor. And ever stood Sir Agravain and Sir Mordred, crying, "Traitor knight! Come forth out of the Queen's chamber!"

"Sirs, leave[7] your noise," said Sir Lancelot, "for wit you well, Sir Agravain, ye shall not prison me this night. And therefore, and[8] ye do by my counsel, go ye all from this chamber door and make you no such crying and such manner of slander as ye do. For I promise you by my knighthood, and ye will depart and make no more noise, I shall as tomorn appear afore you all and before the King, and then let it be seen which of you all, other else ye all,[9] that will deprove[1] me of treason. And there shall I answer you, as a knight should, that hither I came to the Queen for no manner of mal engine,[2] and that will I prove and make it good upon you with my hands."

"Fie upon thee, traitor," said Sir Agravain and Sir Mordred, "for we will have thee malgré thine head[3] and slay thee, and we list.[4] For we let thee wit we have the choice of[5] King Arthur to save thee other slay thee."

"Ah, sirs," said Sir Lancelot, "is there none other grace with you? Then keep[6] yourself!" And then Sir Lancelot set all open the chamber door and mightily and knightly he strode in among them. And anon[7] at the first stroke he slew Sir Agravain, and after twelve of his fellows. Within a little while he had laid them down cold to the earth, for there was none of the twelve

4. Rather.
5. If.
6. Allow.
7. Bench.
8. Stop.
9. Pleases you.
1. Go ahead.
2. Big.
3. Fended off.
4. Blow.
5. Inside.

6. Quickly.
7. Stop.
8. If.
9. Or else all of you.
1. Accuse.
2. Evil design.
3. In spite of you.
4. If we please.
5. From.
6. Defend.
7. Right away.

knights might stand Sir Lancelot one buffet.[8] And also he wounded Sir Mordred, and therewithal he fled with all his might.

And then Sir Lancelot returned again unto the Queen and said, "Madam, now wit you well, all our true love is brought to an end, for now will King Arthur ever be my foe. And therefore, Madam, and it like you[9] that I may have you with me, I shall save you from all manner adventurous[1] dangers."

"Sir, that is not best," said the Queen, "me seemeth, for[2] now ye have done so much harm, it will be best that ye hold you still with this. And if ye see that as tomorn they will put me unto death, then may ye rescue me as ye think best."

"I will well,"[3] said Sir Lancelot, "for have ye no doubt, while I am a man living I shall rescue you." And then he kissed her, and either of them gave other a ring, and so there he left the Queen and went until[4] his lodging.

[WAR BREAKS OUT BETWEEN ARTHUR AND LANCELOT][5]

Then said King Arthur unto Sir Gawain, "Dear nephew, I pray you make ready in your best armor with your brethren, Sir Gaheris and Sir Gareth, to bring my Queen to the fire, there to have her judgment and receive the death."

"Nay, my most noble king," said Sir Gawain, "that will I never do, for wit you well I will never be in that place where so noble a queen as is my lady Dame Guinevere shall take such a shameful end. For wit you well," said Sir Gawain, "my heart will not serve me for to see her die, and it shall never be said that ever I was of your counsel for her death."

"Then," said the King unto Sir Gawain, "suffer[6] your brethren Sir Gaheris and Sir Gareth to be there."

"My lord," said Sir Gawain, "wit you well they will be loath to be there present because of many adventures[7] that is like to fall, but they are young and full unable to say you nay."

Then spake Sir Gaheris and the good knight Sir Gareth unto King Arthur: "Sir, ye may well command us to be there, but wit you well it shall be sore against our will. But and[8] we be there by your strait commandment, ye shall plainly[9] hold us there excused—we will be there in peaceable wise and bear none harness of war[1] upon us."

"In the name of God," said the King, "then make you ready, for she shall have soon[2] her judgment."

"Alas," said Sir Gawain, "that ever I should endure[3] to see this woeful day." So Sir Gawain turned him and wept heartily, and so he went into his chamber.

---

8. Withstand Sir Lancelot one blow.
9. If it please you.
1. Perilous.
2. Because.
3. Agree.
4. To.
5. Lancelot and Sir Bors mobilize their friends for the rescue of Guinevere. In the morning Mordred reports the events of the night to Arthur who, against Gawain's strong opposition, condemns the queen to be burned, for "the law was such in those days that whatsoever they were, of what estate or degree, if they were found guilty of treason there should be none other remedy but death."
6. Allow.
7. Chance occurrences.
8. If.
9. Openly. "Straight": strict.
1. Armor.
2. Right away.
3. Live.

And then the Queen was led forth without[4] Carlisle, and anon she was dispoiled into[5] her smock. And then her ghostly father[6] was brought to her to be shriven of her misdeeds.[7] Then was there weeping and wailing and wringing of hands of many lords and ladies, but there were but few in comparison that would bear any armor for to strengthen[8] the death of the Queen.

Then was there one that Sir Lancelot had sent unto that place, which went to espy what time the Queen should go unto her death. And anon as[9] he saw the Queen dispoiled into her smock and shriven, then he gave Sir Lancelot warning. Then was there but spurring and plucking up[1] of horses, and right so they came unto the fire. And who[2] that stood against them, there were they slain—there might none withstand Sir Lancelot. So all that bore arms and withstood them, there were they slain, full many a noble knight. * * * And so in this rushing and hurling, as Sir Lancelot thrang[3] here and there, it misfortuned him[4] to slay Sir Gaheris and Sir Gareth, the noble knight, for they were unarmed and unwares.[5] As the French book saith, Sir Lancelot smote Sir Gaheris and Sir Gareth upon the brain-pans, wherethrough[6] that they were slain in the field, howbeit[7] Sir Lancelot saw them not. And so were they found dead among the thickest of the press.[8]

Then when Sir Lancelot had thus done, and slain and put to flight all that would withstand him, then he rode straight unto Queen Guinevere and made a kirtle[9] and a gown to be cast upon her, and then he made her to be set behind him and prayed her to be of good cheer. Now wit you well the Queen was glad that she was escaped from death, and then she thanked God and Sir Lancelot.

And so he rode his way with the Queen, as the French book saith, unto Joyous Garde,[1] and there he kept her as a noble knight should. And many great lords and many good knights were sent him, and many full noble knights drew unto him. When they heard that King Arthur and Sir Lancelot were at debate,[2] many knights were glad, and many were sorry of their debate.

Now turn we again unto King Arthur, that when it was told him how and in what manner the Queen was taken away from the fire, and when he heard of the death of his noble knights, and in especial Sir Gaheris and Sir Gareth, then he swooned for very pure[3] sorrow. And when he awoke of his swoon, then he said: "Alas, that ever I bore crown upon my head! For now have I lost the fairest fellowship of noble knights that ever held Christian king[4] together. Alas, my good knights be slain and gone away from me. Now within these two days I have lost nigh forty knights and also the noble fellowship of Sir Lancelot and his blood,[5] for now I may nevermore hold them together with my worship.[6] Alas, that ever this war began!

---

4. Outside.
5. Undressed down to.
6. Spiritual father, i.e., her priest.
7. For her to be confessed of her sins.
8. Secure.
9. As soon as.
1. Urging forward.
2. Whoever.
3. Pressed. "Hurling": turmoil.
4. He had the misfortune.
5. Unaware.

6. Through which.
7. Although.
8. Crowd.
9. Petticoat.
1. Lancelot's castle in England.
2. Strife.
3. Sheer.
4. That Christian king ever held.
5. Kin.
6. Keep both them and my dignity.

"Now, fair fellows," said the King, "I charge you that no man tell Sir Gawain of the death of his two brethren, for I am sure," said the King, "when he heareth tell that Sir Gareth is dead, he will go nigh out of his mind. Mercy Jesu," said the King, "why slew he Sir Gaheris and Sir Gareth? For I dare say, as for Sir Gareth, he loved Sir Lancelot above all men earthly."[7]

"That is truth," said some knights, "but they were slain in the hurling,[8] as Sir Lancelot thrang in the thickest of the press. And as they were unarmed, he smote them and wist[9] not whom that he smote, and so unhappily[1] they were slain."

"Well," said Arthur, "the death of them will cause the greatest mortal war that ever was, for I am sure that when Sir Gawain knoweth hereof that Sir Gareth is slain, I shall never have rest of him[2] till I have destroyed Sir Lancelot's kin and himself both, other else he to destroy me. And therefore," said the King, "wit you well, my heart was never so heavy as it is now. And much more I am sorrier for my good knights' loss[3] than for the loss of my fair queen; for queens I might have enough, but such a fellowship of good knights shall never be together in no company. And now I dare say," said King Arthur, "there was never Christian king that ever held such a fellowship together. And alas, that ever Sir Lancelot and I should be at debate. Ah, Agravain, Agravain!" said the King, "Jesu forgive it thy soul, for thine evil will that thou and thy brother Sir Mordred haddest unto Sir Lancelot hath caused all this sorrow." And ever among these complaints the King wept and swooned.

Then came there one to Sir Gawain and told him how the Queen was led away with[4] Sir Lancelot, and nigh a four-and-twenty knights slain. "Ah, Jesu, save me my two brethren!" said Sir Gawain. "For full well wist I," said Sir Gawain, "that Sir Lancelot would rescue her, other else he would die in that field. And to say the truth he were not of worship but if he had[5] rescued the Queen, insomuch as she should have been burned for his sake. And as in that," said Sir Gawain, "he hath done but knightly, and as I would have done myself and I had stood in like case. But where are my brethren?" said Sir Gawain. "I marvel that I hear not of them."

Then said that man, "Truly, Sir Gaheris and Sir Gareth be slain."

"Jesu defend!"[6] said Sir Gawain. "For all this world I would not that they were slain, and in especial my good brother Sir Gareth."

"Sir," said the man, "he is slain, and that is great pity."

"Who slew him?" said Sir Gawain.

"Sir Lancelot," said the man, "slew them both."

"That may I not believe," said Sir Gawain, "that ever he slew my good brother Sir Gareth, for I dare say my brother loved him better than me and all his brethren and the King both. Also I dare say, an[7] Sir Lancelot had desired my brother Sir Gareth with him, he would have been with him against the King and us all. And therefore I may never believe that Sir Lancelot slew my brethren."

"Verily, sir," said the man, "it is noised[8] that he slew him."

"Alas," said Sir Gawain, "now is my joy gone." And then he fell down and swooned, and long he lay there as he had been dead. And when he arose out of his swoon, he cried out sorrowfully and said, "Alas!" And forthwith he ran unto the King, crying and weeping, and said, "Ah, mine uncle King Arthur! My good brother Sir Gareth is slain, and so is my brother Sir Gaheris, which were two noble knights."

Then the King wept and he both, and so they fell on swooning. And when they were revived, then spake Sir Gawain and said, "Sir, I will go and see my brother Sir Gareth."

"Sir, ye may not see him," said the King, "for I caused him to be interred and Sir Gaheris both, for I well understood that ye would make overmuch sorrow, and the sight of Sir Gareth should have caused your double sorrow."

"Alas, my lord," said Sir Gawain, "how slew he my brother Sir Gareth? Mine own good lord, I pray you tell me."

"Truly," said the King, "I shall tell you as it hath been told me—Sir Lancelot slew him and Sir Gaheris both."

"Alas," said Sir Gawain, "they bore none arms against him, neither of them both."

"I woot not how it was," said the King, "but as it is said, Sir Lancelot slew them in the thickest of the press and knew them not. And therefore let us shape a remedy for to revenge their deaths."

"My king, my lord, and mine uncle," said Sir Gawain, "wit you well, now I shall make you a promise which I shall hold by my knighthood, that from this day forward I shall never fail[9] Sir Lancelot until that one of us have slain the other. And therefore I require you, my lord and king, dress[1] you unto the wars, for wit you well, I will be revenged upon Sir Lancelot; and therefore, as ye will have my service and my love, now haste you thereto and assay[2] your friends. For I promise unto God," said Sir Gawain, "for the death of my brother Sir Gareth I shall seek Sir Lancelot throughout seven kings' realms, but I shall slay him, other else he shall slay me."

"Sir, ye shall not need to seek him so far," said the King, "for as I hear say, Sir Lancelot will abide me and us all within the castle of Joyous Garde. And much people draweth unto him, as I hear say."

"That may I right well believe," said Sir Gawain, "but my lord," he said, "assay your friends and I will assay mine."

"It shall be done," said the King, "and as I suppose I shall be big[3] enough to drive him out of the biggest tower of his castle."

So then the King sent letters and writs throughout all England, both the length and the breadth, for to summon all his knights. And so unto King Arthur drew many knights, dukes, and earls, that he had a great host, and when they were assembled the King informed them how Sir Lancelot had bereft him his Queen. Then the King and all his host made them ready to lay siege about Sir Lancelot where he lay within Joyous Garde.

---

8. Reported.
9. Give up the pursuit of.
1. Prepare.

2. Appeal to.
3. Strong.

[THE DEATH OF ARTHUR][4]

So upon Trinity Sunday at night King Arthur dreamed a wonderful dream, and in his dream him seemed that he saw upon a chafflet[5] a chair, and the chair was fast to a wheel, and thereupon sat King Arthur in the richest cloth of gold that might be made. And the King thought there was under him, far from him, an hideous deep black water, and therein was all manner of serpents, and worms, and wild beasts, foul and horrible. And suddenly the King thought that the wheel turned upside down, and he fell among the serpents, and every beast took him by a limb. And then the King cried as he lay in his bed, "Help, help!"

And then knights, squires, and yeomen awaked the King, and then he was so amazed[6] that he wist[7] not where he was. And then so he awaked[8] until it was nigh day, and then he fell on slumbering again, not sleeping nor thoroughly waking. So the King seemed[9] verily that there came Sir Gawain unto him with a number of fair ladies with him. So when King Arthur saw him, he said, "Welcome, my sister's son. I weened ye had been dead. And now I see thee on-live, much am I beholden unto Almighty Jesu. Ah, fair nephew and my sister's son, what been these ladies that hither be come with you?"

"Sir," said Sir Gawain, "all these be ladies for whom I have foughten for when I was man living. And all these are tho[1] that I did battle for in righteous quarrels, and God hath given them that grace, at their great prayer, because I did battle for them for their right, that they should bring me hither unto you. Thus much hath given me leave God, for to warn you of your death. For and ye fight as tomorn[2] with Sir Mordred, as ye both have assigned,[3] doubt ye not ye must be slain, and the most party of your people on both parties. And for the great grace and goodness that Almighty Jesu hath unto you, and for pity of you and many mo other good men there[4] shall be slain, God hath sent me to you of his special grace to give you warning that in no wise ye do battle as tomorn, but that ye take a treatise for a month-day.[5] And proffer you largely,[6] so that tomorn ye put in a delay. For within a month shall come Sir Lancelot with all his noble knights and rescue you worshipfully and slay Sir Mordred and all that ever will hold with him."

Then Sir Gawain and all the ladies vanished. And anon the King called upon his knights, squires, and yeomen, and charged them wightly[7] to fetch his noble lords and wise bishops unto him. And when they were come the King told them of his avision,[8] that Sir Gawain had told him and warned him that, and he fought on the morn, he should be slain. Then the King

4. The pope arranges a truce, Guinevere is returned to Arthur, and Lancelot and his kin leave England to become rulers of France. At Gawain's instigation Arthur invades France to resume the war against Lancelot. Word comes to the king that Mordred has seized the kingdom, and Arthur leads his forces back to England. Mordred attacks them upon their landing, and Gawain is mortally wounded and dies, although not before he has repented for having insisted that Arthur fight Lancelot and has written Lancelot to come to the aid of his former lord.
5. Scaffold. "Him seemed": it seemed to him.

6. Confused.
7. Knew.
8. Lay awake.
9. It seemed to the king.
1. Those.
2. If you fight tomorrow.
3. Decided.
4. I.e., who there. "Mo": more.
5. For a month from today. "Treatise": treaty, truce.
6. Make generous offers.
7. Quickly.
8. Dream.

commanded Sir Lucan the Butler[9] and his brother Sir Bedivere the Bold, with two bishops with them, and charged them in any wise to take a treatise for a month-day[1] with Sir Mordred. "And spare not: proffer him lands and goods as much as ye think reasonable."

So then they departed and came to Sir Mordred where he had a grim host of an hundred thousand, and there they entreated[2] Sir Mordred long time. And at the last Sir Mordred was agreed for to have Cornwall and Kent by King Arthur's days,[3] and after that, all England, after the days of King Arthur.

Then were they condescended[4] that King Arthur and Sir Mordred should meet betwixt both their hosts, and everich[5] of them should bring fourteen persons. And so they came with this word unto Arthur. Then said he, "I am glad that this is done," and so he went into the field.

And when King Arthur should depart, he warned all his host that, and[6] they, see any sword drawn, "Look ye come on fiercely and slay that traitor Sir Mordred, for I in no wise trust him." In like wise Sir Mordred warned his host that "And ye see any manner of sword drawn, look that ye come on fiercely, and so slay all that ever before you standeth, for in no wise I will not trust for this treatise." And in the same wise said Sir Mordred unto his host, "For I know well my father will be avenged upon me."

And so they met as their pointment[7] was and were agreed and accorded thoroughly. And wine was fetched and they drank together. Right so came an adder out of a little heath-bush, and it stung a knight in the foot. And so when the knight felt him so stung, he looked down and saw the adder. And anon he drew his sword to slay the adder, and thought[8] none other harm. And when the host on both parties saw that sword drawn, then they blew beams,[9] trumpets, and horns, and shouted grimly. And so both hosts dressed them[1] together. And King Arthur took his horse and said, "Alas, this unhappy day!" and so rode to his party, and Sir Mordred in like wise.

And never since was there never seen a more dolefuller battle in no Christian land, for there was but rushing and riding, foining[2] and striking; and many a grim word was there spoken of either to other, and many a deadly stroke. But ever King Arthur rode throughout the battle[3] of Sir Mordred many times and did full nobly, as a noble king should do, and at all times he fainted[4] never. And Sir Mordred did his devoir[5] that day and put himself in great peril.

And thus they fought all the long day, and never stinted[6] till the noble knights were laid to the cold earth. And ever they fought still till it was near night, and by then was there an hundred thousand laid dead upon the down.[7] Then was King Arthur wood-wroth[8] out of measure when he saw his people so slain from him. And so he looked about him and could see no mo[9] of all

9. "Butler" here is probably only a title of high rank, although it was originally used to designate the officer who had charge of wine for the king's table.
1. By any means necessary to make a treaty for the period of a month.
2. Dealt with.
3. During King Arthur's lifetime.
4. Agreed.
5. Each.
6. If.
7. Arrangement.

8. Meant.
9. A kind of trumpet.
1. Prepared to come.
2. Lunging.
3. Battalion.
4. Lost heart.
5. Knightly duty.
6. Stopped.
7. Upland.
8. Mad with rage.
9. Others.

his host, and good knights left no mo on-live, but two knights: the t'one[1] was Sir Lucan the Butler and [the other] his brother Sir Bedivere. And yet they were full sore wounded.

"Jesu, mercy," said the King, "where are all my noble knights become?[2] Alas that ever I should see this doleful day! For now," said King Arthur, "I am come to mine end. But would to God," said he, "that I wist[3] now where were that traitor Sir Mordred that has caused all this mischief."

Then King Arthur looked about and was ware where stood Sir Mordred leaning upon his sword among a great heap of dead men.

"Now give me my spear," said King Arthur unto Sir Lucan, "for yonder I have espied the traitor that all this woe hath wrought."

"Sir, let him be," said Sir Lucan, "for he is unhappy.[4] And if ye pass this unhappy day ye shall be right well revenged upon him. And, good lord, remember ye of your night's dream, and what the spirit of Sir Gawain told you tonight, and yet God of his great goodness hath preserved you hitherto. And for God's sake, my lord, leave off by this,[5] for, blessed be God, ye have won the field: for yet we been here three on-live, and with Sir Mordred is not one on-live. And therefore if ye leave off now, this wicked day of destiny is past."

"Now, tide[6] me death, tide me life," said the King, "now I see him yonder alone, he shall never escape mine hands. For at a better avail[7] shall I never have him."

"God speed you well!" said Sir Bedivere.

Then the King got his spear in both his hands and ran toward Sir Mordred, crying and saying, "Traitor, now is thy deathday come!"

And when Sir Mordred saw King Arthur he ran until him with his sword drawn in his hand, and there King Arthur smote Sir Mordred under the shield, with a foin[8] of his spear, throughout the body more than a fathom.[9] And when Sir Mordred felt that he had his death's wound, he thrust himself with the might that he had up to the burr[1] of King Arthur's spear, and right so he smote his father King Arthur with his sword holden in both his hands, upon the side of the head, that the sword pierced the helmet and the tay[2] of the brain. And therewith Sir Mordred dashed down stark dead to the earth.

And noble King Arthur fell in a swough[3] to the earth, and there he swooned oftentimes, and Sir Lucan and Sir Bedivere ofttimes heaved him up. And so, weakly betwixt them, they led him to a little chapel not far from the seaside, and when the King was there, him thought him reasonably eased. Then heard they people cry in the field. "Now go thou, Sir Lucan," said the King, "and do me to wit[4] what betokens that noise in the field."

So Sir Lucan departed, for he was grievously wounded in many places. And so as he yede[5] he saw and harkened by the moonlight how that pillers[6] and robbers were come into the field to pill and to rob many a full noble knight of brooches and bees[7] and of many a good ring and many a rich jewel. And who

---

1. That one, i.e., the first.
2. What has become of all my noble knights?
3. Knew.
4. I.e., unlucky for you.
5. I.e., with this much accomplished.
6. Betide.
7. Advantage.
8. Thrust.

9. I.e., six feet.
1. Hand guard.
2. Outer membrane.
3. Swoon.
4. Let me know.
5. Walked.
6. Plunderers.
7. Bracelets.

that were not dead all out there they slew them for their harness[8] and their riches. When Sir Lucan understood this work, he came to the King as soon as he might and told him all what he had heard and seen. "Therefore by my read,"[9] said Sir Lucan, "it is best that we bring you to some town."

"I would it were so," said the King, "but I may not stand, my head works[1] so. Ah, Sir Lancelot," said King Arthur, "this day have I sore missed thee. And alas that ever I was against thee, for now have I my death, whereof Sir Gawain me warned in my dream."

Then Sir Lucan took up the King the t'one party[2] and Sir Bedivere the other party; and in the lifting up the King swooned and in the lifting Sir Lucan fell in a swoon that part of his guts fell out of his body, and therewith the noble knight's heart burst. And when the King awoke he beheld Sir Lucan how he lay foaming at the mouth and part of his guts lay at his feet.

"Alas," said the King, "this is to me a full heavy[3] sight to see this noble duke so die for my sake, for he would have holpen[4] me that had more need of help than I. Alas that he would not complain him for[5] his heart was so set to help me. Now Jesu have mercy upon his soul."

Then Sir Bedivere wept for the death of his brother.

"Now leave this mourning and weeping, gentle knight," said the King, "for all this will not avail me. For wit thou well, and[6] I might live myself, the death of Sir Lucan would grieve me evermore. But my time passeth on fast," said the King. "Therefore," said King Arthur unto Sir Bedivere, "take thou here Excalibur[7] my good sword and go with it to yonder water's side; and when thou comest there I charge thee throw my sword in that water and come again and tell me what thou sawest there."

"My lord," said Sir Bedivere, "your commandment shall be done, and [I shall] lightly[8] bring you word again."

So Sir Bedivere departed. And by the way he beheld that noble sword, that the pommel and the haft[9] was all precious stones. And then he said to himself, "If I throw this rich sword in the water, thereof shall never come good, but harm and loss." And then Sir Bedivere hid Excalibur under a tree. And so, as soon as he might, he came again unto the King and said he had been at the water and had thrown the sword into the water.

"What saw thou there?" said the King.

"Sir," he said, "I saw nothing but waves and winds."

"That is untruly said of thee," said the King. "And therefore go thou lightly again and do my commandment; as thou art to me lief[1] and dear, spare not, but throw it in."

Then Sir Bedivere returned again and took the sword in his hand. And yet him thought[2] sin and shame to throw away that noble sword. And so eft[3] he hid the sword and returned again and told the King that he had been at the water and done his commandment.

8. Armor. "All out": entirely.
9. Advice.
1. Aches.
2. On one side.
3. Sorrowful.
4. Helped.
5. Because.
6. If.
7. The sword that Arthur had received as a young man from the Lady of the Lake; it is presumably she who catches it when Bedivere finally throws it into the water.
8. Quickly.
9. Handle. "Pommel": rounded knob on the hilt.
1. Beloved.
2. It seemed to him.
3. Again.

"What sawest thou there?" said the King.

"Sir," he said, "I saw nothing but waters wap and waves wan."[4]

"Ah, traitor unto me and untrue," said King Arthur, "now hast thou betrayed me twice. Who would have weened that thou that has been to me so lief and dear, and thou art named a noble knight, and would betray me for the riches of this sword. But now go again lightly, for thy long tarrying putteth me in great jeopardy of my life, for I have taken cold. And but if thou do now as I bid thee, if ever I may see thee I shall slay thee mine[5] own hands, for thou wouldest for my rich sword see me dead."

Then Sir Bedivere departed and went to the sword and lightly took it up, and so he went to the water's side; and there he bound the girdle[6] about the hilts, and threw the sword as far into the water as he might. And there came an arm and an hand above the water and took it and clutched it, and shook it thrice and brandished; and then vanished away the hand with the sword into the water. So Sir Bedivere came again to the King and told him what he saw.

"Alas," said the King, "help me hence, for I dread me I have tarried overlong."

Then Sir Bedivere took the King upon his back and so went with him to that water's side. And when they were at the water's side, even fast[7] by the bank hoved[8] a little barge with many fair ladies in it; and among them all was a queen; and all they had black hoods, and all they wept and shrieked when they saw King Arthur.

"Now put me into that barge," said the King; and so he did softly. And there received him three ladies with great mourning, and so they set them[9] down. And in one of their laps King Arthur laid his head, and then the queen said, "Ah, my dear brother, why have ye tarried so long from me? Alas, this wound on your head hath caught overmuch cold." And anon they rowed fromward the land, and Sir Bedivere beheld all tho ladies go froward him.

Then Sir Bedivere cried and said, "Ah, my lord Arthur, what shall become of me, now ye go from me and leave me here alone among mine enemies?"

"Comfort thyself," said the King, "and do as well as thou mayest, for in me is no trust for to trust in. For I must into the vale of Avilion[1] to heal me of my grievous wound. And if thou hear nevermore of me, pray for my soul."

But ever the queen and ladies wept and shrieked that it was pity to hear. And as soon as Sir Bedivere had lost the sight of the barge he wept and wailed and so took the forest, and went[2] all that night. And in the morning he was ware betwixt two holts hoar[3] of a chapel and an hermitage.[4]

* * *

4. The phrase seems to mean "waters wash the shore and waves grow dark."
5. I.e., with mine.
6. Sword belt.
7. Close.
8. Waited.
9. I.e., they sat.
1. A legendary island, sometimes identified with the earthly paradise.
2. Walked. "Took": took to.

3. Ancient thickets of small trees.
4. In the passage here omitted, Sir Bedivere meets the former bishop of Canterbury, now a hermit, who describes how on the previous night a company of ladies had brought to the chapel a dead body, asking that it be buried. Sir Bedivere exclaims that the dead man must have been King Arthur and vows to spend the rest of his life there in the chapel as a hermit.

Thus of Arthur I find no more written in books that been authorized,[5] neither more of the very certainty of his death heard I never read,[6] but thus was he led away in a ship wherein were three queens: that one was King Arthur's sister, Queen Morgan la Fée,[7] the t'other[8] was the Queen of North Wales, and the third was the Queen of the Waste Lands. * * *

Now more of the death of King Arthur could I never find but that these ladies brought him to his burials,[9] and such one was buried there that the hermit bore witness that sometime was Bishop of Canterbury.[1] But yet the hermit knew not in certain that he was verily the body of King Arthur, for this tale Sir Bedivere, a Knight of the Table Round, made it to be written. Yet some men say in many parts of England that King Arthur is not dead, but had[2] by the will of our Lord Jesu into another place. And men say that he shall come again and he shall win the Holy Cross. Yet I will not say that it shall be so, but rather I will say, Here in this world he changed his life. And many men say that there is written upon his tomb this verse: *Hic iacet Arthurus, rex quondam, rexque futurus.*[3]

[THE DEATHS OF LANCELOT AND GUINEVERE][4]

And thus upon a night there came a vision to Sir Lancelot and charged him, in remission[5] of his sins, to haste him unto Amesbury: "And by then[6] thou come there, thou shalt find Queen Guinevere dead. And therefore take thy fellows with thee, and purvey them of an horse-bier,[7] and fetch thou the corse[8] of her, and bury her by her husband, the noble King Arthur. So this avision[9] came to Lancelot thrice in one night. Then Sir Lancelot rose up ere day and told the hermit.

"It were well done," said the hermit, "that ye made you ready and that ye disobey not the avision."

Then Sir Lancelot took his eight fellows with him, and on foot they yede[1] from Glastonbury to Amesbury, the which is little more than thirty mile, and thither they came within two days, for they were weak and feeble to go. And when Sir Lancelot was come to Amesbury within the nunnery, Queen Guinevere died but half an hour afore. And the ladies told Sir Lancelot that Queen Guinevere told them all ere she passed that Sir Lancelot had been priest near a twelve-month:[2] "and hither he cometh as fast as he may to fetch my corse, and beside my lord King Arthur he shall bury me." Wherefore the Queen said in hearing of them all, "I beseech Almighty God that I may never have power to see Sir Lancelot with my worldly eyes."

"And thus," said all the ladies, "was ever her prayer these two days till she was dead."

---

5. That have authority.
6. Tell.
7. The fairy.
8. The second.
9. Grave.
1. Of whom the hermit, who was formerly bishop of Canterbury, bore witness.
2. Conveyed.
3. "Here lies Arthur, who was once king and king will be again."
4. Guinevere enters a convent at Amesbury, where Lancelot, returned with his companions to

England, visits her, but she commands him never to see her again. Emulating her example, Lancelot joins the bishop of Canterbury and Bedivere in their hermitage, where he takes holy orders and is joined in turn by seven of his fellow knights.
5. For the remission.
6. By the time.
7. Provide them with a horse-drawn hearse.
8. Body.
9. Dream.
1. Went.
2. Nearly twelve months.

Then Sir Lancelot saw her visage, but he wept not greatly, but sighed. And so he did all the observance of the service himself, both the *dirige*[3] and on the morn he sang mass. And there was ordained[4] an horse-bier, and so with an hundred torches ever burning about the corse of the Queen, and ever Sir Lancelot with his eight fellows went about[5] the horse-bier, singing and reading many an holy orison,[6] and frankincense upon the corse incensed.[7]

Thus Sir Lancelot and his eight fellows went on foot from Amesbury unto Glastonbury, and when they were come to the chapel and the hermitage, there she had a *dirige* with great devotion.[8] And on the morn the hermit that sometime[9] was Bishop of Canterbury sang the mass of requiem with great devotion, and Sir Lancelot was the first that offered, and then als[1] his eight fellows. And then she was wrapped in cered cloth of Rennes, from the top[2] to the toe, in thirtyfold, and after she was put in a web[3] of lead, and then in a coffin of marble.

And when she was put in the earth Sir Lancelot swooned and lay long still, while[4] the hermit came and awaked him, and said, "Ye be to blame, for ye displease God with such manner of sorrow-making."

"Truly," said Sir Lancelot, "I trust I do not displease God, for He knoweth mine intent—for my sorrow was not, nor is not, for any rejoicing of sin, but my sorrow may never have end. For when I remember of her beaulté and of her noblesse[5] that was both with her king and with her,[6] so when I saw his corse and her corse so lie together, truly mine heart would not serve to sustain my careful[7] body. Also when I remember me how by my defaute and mine orgule[8] and my pride that they were both laid full low, that were peerless that ever was living of Christian people, wit you well," said Sir Lancelot, "this remembered, of their kindness and mine unkindness, sank so to mine heart that I might not sustain myself." So the French book maketh mention.

Then Sir Lancelot never after ate but little meat,[9] nor drank, till he was dead, for then he sickened more and more and dried and dwined[1] away. For the Bishop nor none of his fellows might not make him to eat, and little he drank, that he was waxen by a kibbet[2] shorter than he was, that the people could not know him. For evermore, day and night, he prayed, but sometime he slumbered a broken sleep. Ever he was lying groveling on the tomb of King Arthur and Queen Guinevere, and there was no comfort that the Bishop nor Sir Bors, nor none of his fellows could make him—it availed not.

So within six weeks after, Sir Lancelot fell sick and lay in his bed. And then he sent for the Bishop that there was hermit, and all his true fellows. Then Sir Lancelot said with dreary steven,[3] "Sir Bishop, I pray you give to me all my rights that longeth[4] to a Christian man."

---

3. The first word of the anthem beginning the funeral service (> modern "dirge").
4. Prepared.
5. Around.
6. Reciting many a prayer.
7. Burned frankincense over the body.
8. Earnest reverence.
9. Once.
1. Also. "Offered": made his donation.
2. Head. "Cloth of Rennes": A shroud made of fine linen smeared with wax, produced at Rennes.

3. Afterward she was put in a sheet.
4. Until.
5. Her beauty and nobility.
6. That she and her king both had.
7. Sorrowful.
8. My fault and my haughtiness.
9. Food.
1. Wasted.
2. Grown by a cubit.
3. Sad voice.
4. Pertains. "Rights": last sacrament.

"It shall not need you,"[5] said the hermit and all his fellows. "It is but heaviness of your blood. Ye shall be well mended by the grace of God tomorn."

"My fair lords," said Sir Lancelot, "wit you well my careful body will into the earth; I have warning more than now I will say. Therefore give me my rights."

So when he was houseled and annealed[6] and had all that a Christian man ought to have, he prayed the Bishop that his fellows might bear his body to Joyous Garde. (Some men say it was Alnwick, and some men say it was Bamborough.) "Howbeit," said Sir Lancelot, "me repenteth[7] sore, but I made mine avow sometime that in Joyous Garde I would be buried. And because of breaking[8] of mine avow, I pray you all, lead me thither." Then there was weeping and wringing of hands among his fellows.

So at a season of the night they all went to their beds, for they all lay in one chamber. And so after midnight, against[9] day, the Bishop that was hermit, as he lay in his bed asleep, he fell upon a great laughter. And therewith all the fellowship awoke and came to the Bishop and asked him what he ailed.[1]

"Ah, Jesu mercy," said the Bishop, "why did ye awake me? I was never in all my life so merry and so well at ease."

"Wherefore?" said Sir Bors.

"Truly," said the Bishop, "here was Sir Lancelot with me, with mo[2] angels than ever I saw men in one day. And I saw the angels heave[3] up Sir Lancelot unto heaven, and the gates of heaven opened against him."

"It is but dretching of swevens,"[4] said Sir Bors, "for I doubt not Sir Lancelot aileth nothing but good."[5]

"It may well be," said the Bishop. "Go ye to his bed and then shall ye prove the sooth."

So when Sir Bors and his fellows came to his bed, they found him stark dead. And he lay as he had smiled, and the sweetest savor[6] about him that ever they felt. Then was there weeping and wringing of hands, and the greatest dole they made that ever made men. And on the morn the Bishop did his mass of Requiem, and after the Bishop and all the nine knights put Sir Lancelot in the same horse-bier that Queen Guinevere was laid in tofore that she was buried. And so the Bishop and they all together went with the body of Sir Lancelot daily, till they came to Joyous Garde. And ever they had an hundred torches burning about him.

And so within fifteen days they came to Joyous Garde. And there they laid his corse in the body of the choir,[7] and sang and read many psalters[8] and prayers over him and about him. And ever his visage was laid open and naked, that all folks might behold him; for such was the custom in tho[9] days that all men of worship should so lie with open visage till that they were buried.

And right thus as they were at their service, there came Sir Ector de Maris that had seven year sought all England, Scotland, and Wales, seeking his

---

5. You shall not need it.
6. Given communion and extreme unction.
7. I am sorry.
8. In order not to break.
9. Toward.
1. Ailed him.
2. More.
3. Lift.

4. Illusion of dreams.
5. Has nothing wrong with him.
6. Odor. A sweet scent is a conventional sign in saints' lives of a sanctified death.
7. The center of the chancel, the place of honor.
8. Psalms.
9. Those.

brother, Sir Lancelot. And when Sir Ector heard such noise and light in the choir of Joyous Garde, he alight and put his horse from him and came into the choir. And there he saw men sing and weep, and all they knew Sir Ector, but he knew not them. Then went Sir Bors unto Sir Ector and told him how there lay his brother, Sir Lancelot, dead. And then Sir Ector threw his shield, sword, and helm from him, and when he beheld Sir Lancelot's visage, he fell down in a swoon. And when he waked, it were hard any tongue to tell the doleful complaints that he made for his brother.

"Ah, Lancelot!" he said, "thou were head of all Christian knights. And now I dare say," said Sir Ector, "thou Sir Lancelot, there thou liest, that thou were never matched of earthly knight's hand. And thou were the courteoust[1] knight that ever bore shield. And thou were the truest friend to thy lover that ever bestrode horse, and thou were the truest lover, of a sinful man,[2] that ever loved woman, and thou were the kindest man that ever struck with sword. And thou were the goodliest person that ever came among press of knights, and thou was the meekest man and the gentlest that ever ate in hall among ladies, and thou were the sternest knight to thy mortal foe that ever put spear in the rest."[3]

Then there was weeping and dolor out of measure.

Thus they kept Sir Lancelot's corse aloft fifteen days, and then they buried it with great devotion. And then at leisure they went all with the Bishop of Canterbury to his hermitage, and there they were together more than a month.

Then Sir Constantine that was Sir Cador's son of Cornwall was chosen king of England, and he was a full noble knight, and worshipfully he ruled this realm. And then this King Constantine sent for the Bishop of Canterbury, for he heard say where he was. And so he was restored unto his bishopric and left that hermitage, and Sir Bedivere was there ever still hermit to his life's end.

Then Sir Bors de Ganis, Sir Ector de Maris, Sir Gahalantine, Sir Galihud, Sir Galihodin, Sir Blamour, Sir Bleoberis, Sir Villiars le Valiant, Sir Clarrus of Clermount, all these knights drew them to their countries.[4] Howbeit[5] King Constantine would have had them with him, but they would not abide in this realm. And there they all lived in their countries as holy men.

And some English books make mention that they went never out of England after the death of Sir Lancelot—but that was but favor of makers.[6] For the French book maketh mention—and is authorized—that Sir Bors, Sir Ector, Sir Blamour, and Sir Bleoberis went into the Holy Land, thereas Jesu Christ was quick[7] and dead, and anon as they had stablished their lands;[8] for the book saith so Sir Lancelot commanded them for to do ere ever he passed out of this world. There these four knights did many battles upon the miscreaunts,[9] or Turks, and there they died upon a Good Friday for God's sake.

1. Most courteous.
2. Of any man born in original sin.
3. Support for the butt of the lance.
4. Withdrew themselves to their home districts.
5. However.
6. The authors' bias.
7. Living. "Thereas": where.
8. As soon as they had put their lands in order.
9. Infidels.

Here is the end of the whole book of King Arthur and of his noble knights of the Round Table, that when they were whole together there was ever an hundred and forty. And here is the end of *The Death of Arthur*.[1]

I pray you all gentlemen and gentlewomen that readeth this book of Arthur and his knights from the beginning to the ending, pray for me while I am alive that God send me good deliverance. And when I am dead, I pray you all pray for my soul.

For this book was ended the ninth year of the reign of King Edward the Fourth, by Sir Thomas Malory, knight, as Jesu help him for His great might, as he is the servant of Jesu both day and night.

1469–70   1485

1. By the "whole book" Malory refers to the entire work; the *Death of Arthur*, which Caxton made the title of the entire work, refers to the last part of Malory's book.

ROBERT HENRYSON
ca. 1425–ca. 1500

Robert Henryson is perhaps the greatest of a set of exceptionally accomplished late-fifteenth- and early-sixteenth-century Scots poets. He was an acute reader and critic of Chaucer; his intense poem *The Testament of Cresseid*, which is a sequel to *Troilus and Criseyde*, imagines the fate of Criseyde/Cresseid as she becomes a prostitute in the Greek camp, stricken with both venereal disease and, finally, remorse. This text was routinely printed, in sixteenth-century editions of Chaucer's works, at the end of *Troilus* as its sixth book. *The Cock and the Fox,* one of fourteen fables that constitute another subtle, penetrating work by Henryson, his *Moral Fables*, is a wonderfully original retelling of Chaucer's *Nun's Priest's Tale.* Henryson clearly enjoyed and shared Chaucer's humor, and the animals in his fables speak a grittily colloquial idiom; he also learned and adapted from Chaucer the art of sudden changes of stylistic register. Although Henryson's moral vision is darker and more hard-edged than Chaucer's, he too puts pressure on the simplistic moralizing characteristic of the fable tradition.

Very little is known for certain about Henryson's life. Because he is spoken of as "master," he probably held a master's degree, and evidence points to his having been headmaster of a grammar school founded by monks of the town Dunfermline. As a schoolmaster, Henryson would have regularly used collections of fables to teach boys their Latin. Such a Latin collection by Walter the Englishman served as Henryson's main source for *The Fables*.

One of the chief attractions of Henryson's poetry is the language, which is no more difficult than Chaucer's. The text here is based on the Oxford edition by Denton Fox (1981), but spellings have occasionally been altered for easier comprehension. The notes call attention to some of the main differences between Chaucer's East Midland and Henryson's Scots dialect. The seven-line stanza of *The Fables* and *The Testament of Cresseid*, known as rhyme royal, is the one Chaucer used in his *Troilus and Criseyde*

The Wily Fox. Jost Amman, *Reynard, Disguised as a Monk, Brings the Cock a Sealed Document*, 16th century. A fox disguised as a religious figure makes us think first of the cunning of the fox; only second do we think of the possible cunning of religious figures.

and most of the religious stories in *The Canterbury Tales*. It has been said to derive its name from the fact that a royal poet, King James I of Scotland, wrote *The Kingis Quair* (The King's Book) in that stanza.

The Cock and the Fox

Thogh brutal[1] beestes be irrational,
That is to say, wantand[2] discretioun,
Yit ilk ane° in their[3] kindes natural   *each one*
Has many divers inclinatioun:°   *natural disposition*
5   The bair° busteous,° the wolf, the wylde lyoun,   *bear / rough, rude*
The fox fenyeit,° craftie and cautelous,°   *deceitful / cunning*
The dog to bark on night and keep the hous.

Sa[4] different they are in properteis°   *qualities*
Unknawin° unto man and infinite,   *unknown*
10   In kind havand sa fel° diversiteis,   *having so many*
My cunning° it excedis[5] for to dyte.°   *skill / write*

1. Brute, adj., in the sense of relating to animals, as in "brute beasts."
2. Wanting (i.e., lacking). In the Scottish dialect the normal ending of the present participle is *-and* instead of *-ing.*
3. Note that Scottish dialect uses *their* and *them* where Chaucer's East Midland has the older forms *hire* and *hem.*
4. So. Note that in Scottish dialect long *a* is pronounced for long *o.*
5. Note that the third person singular of verbs ends in *-s* or *-is* instead of *-th* as in Chaucer.

Forthy° as now, I purpose for to wryte   *therefore*
Ane case I fand whilk fell this other yeer[6]
Betwix° ane fox and gentil° Chauntecleer.   *between / noble*

15   Ane widow dwelt intill ane drop they dayis[7]
Whilk wan hir food off[8] spinning on hir rok,°   *distaff*
And na mair° had, forsooth, as the fabill sayis,   *no more*
Except of hennes scho° had ane lyttel flok,   *she*
And them to keep scho had ane jolie cok,
20   Right corageous, that to this widow ay°   *always*
Divided night[9] and crew before the day.

Ane lyttel fra° this foresaid widow's hous,   *from*
Ane thornie schaw° there was of greet defence,   *thicket*
Wherein ane foxe, craftie and cautelous,°   *cunning*
25   Made his repair and daylie residence,
Whilk° to this widow did greet violence   *which*
In pyking off pultrie° baith° day and night,   *poultry / both*
And na way be revengit on him scho might.

This wylie tod,° when that the lark couth sing,[1]   *fox*
30   Full sair° and hungrie unto the toun him   *sorely, painfully*
    drest,°   *proceeded*
Where Chauntecleer, in to the gray dawing,°   *dawn*
Werie for° night, was flowen fra his nest.   *weary of*
Lowrence[2] this saw and in his mind he kest°   *cast, considered*
The jeperdies, the wayes, and the wyle,[3]
35   By what menis° he might this cok begyle.   *means*

Dissimuland in to countenance and cheer,[4]
On knees fell and simuland thus he said,
"Gude morne, my maister, gentil Chantecleer!"
With that the cok start bakwart in ane braid.°   *with a start*
40   "Schir,"° by my saul,° ye need not be effraid,   *sir / soul*
Nor yit for me to start nor flee abak;
I come bot here service to you to mak.

"Wald I not serve to you, it wer bot blame,[5]
As I have done to your progenitouris.
45   Your father oft fulfillit has my wame,°   *belly*
And sent me meit° fra midding° to the muris,°   *food / refuse pile / moors*
And at his end I did my besie curis°   *busy cares*
To held his heed and gif him drinkis warme,
Syne° at the last, the sweit° swelt° in my arme!"   *then / sweet (man) / died*

---

6. A case I found which happened a year or two ago. "Ane": a. The same word as *one*, which functions as the indefinite article.
7. In a village [in] those days.
8. Who made her living (literally: won her food) by.
9. I.e., kept the hours at night by crowing. Cf. *The Miller's Tale*, line 567, and *The Nun's Priest's Tale*, lines 33–38.

1. When the lark could sing, i.e., at dawn.
2. Generic name for a fox, perhaps invented here by Henryson.
3. The stratagems, the devices, and the trickery.
4. Dissimulating in facial expression and manner.
5. It would be just a shame if I were not to serve you. "Serve" has both the feudal sense of service and a second sense.

50   "Knew ye my father?" quad the cok, and leuch.°   *laughed*
     "Yea, my fair son, forsooth I held his heed
     When that he deit° under ane birkin beuch,°   *died / birch bough*
     Syne said the Dirigie[6] when that he was deed.
     Betwix us twa how suld there be ane feid?[7]
55   Wham suld ye traist° bot me, your servitour   *whom should you trust*
     That to your father did so greet honour?

     When I beheld your fedderis° fair and gent,   *feathers*
     Your beak, your breast, your hekill,° and your kame°—   *hackle / comb*
     Schir, by my saul, and the blissit sacrament,[8]
60   My heart warmis, me think I am at hame.
     You for to serve, I wald creep on my wame°   *belly*
     In froist and snaw, in wedder wan and weit°   *dark and wet*
     And lay my lyart° lokkes under your feit."   *gray*

     This fenyeit° fox, fals and dissimulate,   *deceptive*
65   Made to this cok ane cavillatioun:°   *a critical remark*
     "Ye are, me think, changed and degenerate
     Fra your father and his conditioun,
     Of craftie crawing he might beer the croun,[9]
     For he wald on his tais° stand and craw.   *toes*
70   This is no le;° I stude beside and saw."   *lie*

     With that the cok, upon his tais° hie,   *toes*
     Kest up his beak and sang with all his might.
     Quod schir Lowrence, "Well said, sa mot I the.[1]
     Ye are your fatheris son and heir upright,°   *rightful*
75   Bot of his cunning yit ye want ane slight."°   *trick*
     "What?" quad the cok. "He wald, and have na dout,
     Baith wink,° and craw, and turne him thryis about."[2]   *close both eyes*

     The cok, inflate with wind and fals vanegloir,°   *vainglory*
     That mony puttes unto confusioun,
80   Traisting to win ane greet worship° therefoir,   *honor*
     Unwarlie winkand[3] walkit up and doun,
     And syne° to chant and craw he made him boun°—   *then / ready*
     And suddandlie, by° he had crawin ane note   *by the time that*
     The fox was war, and hent° him be the throte.   *seized*

85   Syne to the wood but tarie° with him hyit,°   *without delay / hurried*
     Of countermaund havand but lytil dout.[4]
     With that Pertok, Sprutok, and Coppok cryit,
     The widow heard, and with ane cry come out.
     Seand the case scho sighit and gaif[5] ane schout,

6. *Dirigie* (>modern "dirge"): the first word of the anthem beginning the funeral service, which designates the prayer itself or the whole Office for the Dead: *"Dirige Dominus Deus meus"*— Lead me O Lord my God (Psalm 5.9).
7. Between the two of us how should there be a feud? "Suld": should. The future of "shall" is "sall."
8. The Eucharist.

9. He might bear the crown of skillful crowing.
1. So may I prosper.
2. Crow, and turn himself around thrice.
3. Unwarily shutting his eyes.
4. Having but little fear of prevention.
5. Gave. Note the hard *g* where the Chaucerian form would be *yaf.* "Seand": seeing.

90   "How, murther, reylok!"[6] with ane hiddeous beir,°   *noise*
     "Allas, now lost is gentil Chauntecleer!"

     As scho were wod° with mony yell and cry,   *mad*
     Ryvand hir hair, upon hir breist can beit,[7]
     Syne pale of hew,° half in ane extasy,°   *hue / frenzy*
95   Fell doun for care in swoning° and in sweit.°   *fainting / sweating*
     With that the selie° hennes left their meit,°   *poor / food*
     And whyle this wyfe was lyand thus in swoon,
     Fell of that case in disputacioun.

     "Allas," quod Pertok, makand sair murning,[8]
100 With teeris greet attour hir cheekis fell,[9]
     "Yon was our drowrie° and our day's darling,   *beloved*
     Our nightingal, and als° our orlege° bell,   *also / clock*
     Our walkrife watch,° us for to warne and tell   *wakeful sentinel*
     When that Aurora with hir curcheis° gray   *headcovers, scarves*
105 Put up hir heid° betwix the night and day.   *head*

     "Wha sall° our lemman° be? Who sail us leid?°   *who shall / lover / lead*
     When we are sad wha sall unto us sing?
     With his sweet bill he wald breke us the breid;°   *bread*
     In all this warld was there ane kynder thing?
110 In paramouris° he wald do us plesing,   *making love*
     At his power, as nature list him geif.[1]
     Now efter him, allas, how sall we leif?"°   *live*

     Quod Sprutok than, "Ceis,° sister of your sorrow,   *cease*
     Ye be too mad, for him sic murning mais.[2]
115 We sall fare well, I find Sanct John to borrow;[3]
     The proverb sayis, 'Als gude lufe cummis as gais.'[4]
     I will put on my haly-dayis clais°   *holiday clothes*
     And mak me fresch agane this jolie May,
     Syne chant this sang, 'Was never widow sa gay!'

120 "He was angry and held us ay in aw,°   *always in fear*
     And wounded with the speir° of jelowsy.   *spear*
     Of chalmerglew,[5] Pertok, full well ye knaw,
     Wasted he was, of nature cauld and dry.[6]
     Sen° he is gone, therefore, sister, say I,   *since*
125 Be blythe in baill,[7] for that is best remeid.°   *remedy*
     Let quik° to quik, and deid° ga to the deid."   *living / dead*

     Than Pertok spak, that feinyeit faith° before,   *pretended fidelity*
     In lust but° lufe that set all hir delyte,   *without*

---

6. Ho [Stop], murder, robbery.
7. Tearing her hair, did beat upon her breast.
8. Making sore mourning.
9. While great tears fell down over her cheeks.
1. To the extent of the potency nature was pleased to give him.
2. You are too silly—you make such mourning for him.

3. I take St. John to be my guarantor; an expression used at parting.
4. As good love comes as goes.
5. Chamber-joy, i.e., performance in the bedroom.
6. A preponderance of black bile, the humor that is cold and dry like earth, enfeebled his potency.
7. Be merry in misery.

"Sister, ye wait° of sic° as him ane score   *know / such*
130 Wald not suffice to slake our appetyte.
I hecht° you by my hand, sen ye are quyte,°   *promise / free*
Within ane oulk,° for schame and I durst speik,   *week*
To get ane berne suld better claw oure breik."[8]

Than Coppok like ane curate° spak full crous:°   *priest / smugly*
135 "Yon was ane verray vengeance from the hevin.
He was sa lous° and sa lecherous,   *loose, dissolute*
Ceis coud he noght with kittokis ma than sevin,[9]
But righteous God, haldand the balance evin,[1]
Smytis right sair,° thoght he be patient,   *sore*
140 Adulteraris° that list them not° repent.   *adulterers / do not care to*

"Prydeful he was, and joyit of his sin,
And comptit° not for Goddis favor nor feid.°   *cared / enmity*
Bot traisted ay to rax and sa to rin,[2]
Whil at the last his sinnis can° him leid°   *did / lead*
145 To schameful end and to yon suddand deid.°   *sudden death*
Therefore it is the verray hand of God
That causit him be werryit° with the tod."°   *seized by the throat / fox*

When this was said, this widow fra hir swoun
Start up on fute, and on hir kennettis° cryde,   *small hunting dogs*
150 "How,° Birkye, Berrie, Bell, Bawsie, Broun,   *what*
Rype Schaw, Rin Weil, Curtes, Nuttieclyde!
Togidder all but grunching furth ye glyde![3]
Reskew my nobil cok ere he be slane,°   *slain*
Or ellis to me see ye come never agane!°   *again*

155 With that, but baid, they braidet over the bent,[4]
As fire off flint they over the feildis flaw,°   *flew*
Full wichtlie° they through wood and wateris went,   *swiftly*
And ceissit not, schir Lowrence while they saw.[5]
But when he saw the raches° come on raw,°   *dogs / in a line*
160 Unto the cok in mind° he said, "God sen°   *thought / grant*
That I and thou were fairlie in my den."

Then spak the cok, with sum gude spirit inspyrit,
"Do my counsall[6] and I sail warrand° thee.   *guarantee*
Hungrie thou art, and for greet travel° tyrit,°   *labor / tired*
165 Right faint of force° and may not ferther flee: *strength*
Swyth° turn agane and say that I and ye   *quickly*
Freindes are made and fellowis for ane yeir.°   *year*
Than will they stint,° I stand for it, and not steir."[7]   *stop*

8. If I dare speak, shame not withstanding, to get a man who should better claw our tail.
9. He could not stop [even] with more than seven wenches. "Kittock" is a Scots diminutive for Katherine (as *-ok* is a diminutive in the names of the hens), used here as a generic term for "girl."
1. Holding the scales (of judgment) level.
2. And trusted always to have rule and so to reign.
3. Glide forth all together without grumbling.
4. Without delay they rushed over the ground.
5. And did not stop as long as they saw sir Lowrence.
6. Take my advice.
7. I guarantee it and [will] not move.

This tod, thogh he were fals and frivolous,°   *untrustworthy*
170 And had fraudis, his querrel° to defend,   *cause*
Desavit° was by menis° right marvelous,   *deceived / means*
For falset° failis ay° at the latter end.   *falsehood / always*
He start about, and cryit as he was kend°—   *instructed*
With that the cok he braid° unto a bewch.°   *moved quickly / bough*
175 Now juge ye all whereat schir Lowrence lewch.[8]

Begylit° thus, the tod under the tree   *deceived*
On knees fell, and said, "Gude Chauntecleer,
Come doun agane, and I but meit or fee[9]
Sall be your man and servant for ane yeir."
180 "Na, murther, theif, and revar, stand on reir.[1]
My bludy hekill° and my nek sa bla°   *bloody hackle / blue*
Has partit love for ever betwene us twa.

"I was unwise that winkit° at thy will,   *shut my eyes*
Wherethrough almaist I loissit° had my heid."°   *lost / head*
185 "I was mair fule,"[2] quod he, "coud noght be still,
Bot spake to put my pray into pleid."[3]
"Fare on, fals theef, God keep me fra thy feid."°   *enmity, feud*
With that the cok over the feildis tuke his flight,
And in at the widow's lewer[4] couth he light.

Moralitas°   *moral*

190 Now worthie folk, suppose° this be ane fabill,   *although*
And overheillit with typis figural,[5]
Yit may ye find ane sentence° right agreabill°   *meaning / suitable*
Under their fenyeit termis textual.[6]
To our purpose this cok well may we call
195 Nyce° proud men, woid° and vaneglorious   *foolish / mad*
Of kin and blude, whilk is presumptuous.[7]

Fy, puffed up pride, thou is full poysonabill!°   *poisonous*
Wha favoris thee, on force man have ane fall,[8]
Thy strength is noght, thy stule° standis unstabill.   *stool*
200 Tak witnes of the feyndes infernall,
Whilk° houndit doun was fra that hevinlie° hall[9]   *who / heavenly*
To hellis hole and to that hiddeous hous,
Because in pride they were presumptous.

---

8. Laughed, i.e., he had no reason whatsoever to laugh.
9. Without board or wages.
1. No, murderer, thief, and robber, back off (literally, "stand in the rear").
2. The greater fool (said by the fox).
3. To make my prey a subject of a plea (i.e., a legal argument).
4. Louver, i.e., a hole in a roof for letting out smoke.
5. And covered over with figural symbols, i.e., a hidden allegory.
6. Beneath the feigned words of the text, i.e., referring to the interpretation of scripture allegorically, not by the "letter" but by the "spirit."
7. Of family and bloodline, which (pride) is arrogant.
8. Whoever favors thee necessarily must have a fall.
9. The fallen angels who were cast from heaven into hell because they rebelled against God.

205 This fenyeit foxe may well be figurate°   *serve as a figure for*
To flatteraris with plesand wordis white,
With fals mening and mynd maist toxicate,°   *most poisonous*
To loif and le that settis their hail delyte.[1]
All worthie folk at sic suld haif despite[2]—
For where is there mair perrelous pestilence?—
210 Nor give to learis° haistelie credence.   *liars*

The wickit mind and adullatioun,°   *excessive praise*
Of sucker sweet haifand similitude,[3]
Bitter as gall and full of fell poysoun
To taste it is, wha cleirlie understude,[4]
215 Forthy° as now schortlie to conclude,   *therefore*
Thir° twa sinnis, flatterie and vanegloir.   *these*
Are venomous: gude folk, flee them thairfoir!

1. Who set their whole delight in lauding and lying.
2. Should have contempt for such people.
3. Having resemblance to sweet sugar.
4. Whoever clearly understands it.

EVERYMAN
after 1485

Everyman belongs to the midpoint of the morality play's history. The surviving examples of this genre include only a handful from the fifteenth century (the earliest, *The Pride of Life*, ca. 1400) but more than two dozen from the sixteenth century, dating as late as 1579 (*Marriage between Wit and Wisdom*). Morality plays apparently originated side by side with the mystery plays but were composed individually rather than in cycles and were dominated by allegorical characters. Some morality plays addressed such diverse subjects as social and political satire (e.g., *All For Money*, Skelton's *Magnificence*), philosophy of education (e.g., *The Marriage of Wit and Science*), Protestant polemic (e.g., *The Conflict of Conscience*), prudential morality (e.g., *The Contention between Liberality and Prodigality*), and natural science (e.g., *The Nature of the Four Elements*). From first to last, however, the dominant theme was the struggle of good and evil for the human soul (*psychomachia*), usually depicted in the life span of a representative figure with a name like "Mankind." *Everyman*, untypically, is devoted entirely to the day of judgment that every individual human being must face eventually. The play represents allegorically the forces—both outside the protagonist and within—that can help save Everyman and those that cannot or that obstruct his salvation.

Everyman lacks the broad (even slapstick) humor of many morality plays that portray as clowns the vices that try to lure the Everyman figure away from salvation. The play does contain a certain grim humor in showing the haste with which the hero's fair-weather friends abandon him when they discover what his problem is. The play inculcates its austere lesson by the simplicity and directness of its language and of its approach. A sense of urgency builds—one by one Everyman's supposed resources fail him as time is running out. Ultimately Knowledge teaches him the lesson that every Christian must learn in order to be saved.

The play was written near the end of the fifteenth century. It is probably a translation of a Flemish play, although it is possible that the Flemish play is the translation and the English *Everyman* the original.

Everyman[1]

CAST OF CHARACTERS

MESSENGER	KNOWLEDGE
GOD	CONFESSION
DEATH	BEAUTY
EVERYMAN	STRENGTH
FELLOWSHIP	DISCRETION
KINDRED	FIVE-WITS
COUSIN	ANGEL
GOODS	DOCTOR
GOOD DEEDS	

HERE BEGINNETH A TREATISE HOW THE HIGH FATHER OF HEAVEN SENDETH DEATH TO SUMMON EVERY CREATURE TO COME AND GIVE ACCOUNT OF THEIR LIVES IN THIS WORLD, AND IS IN MANNER OF A MORAL PLAY

[*Enter* MESSENGER.]

MESSENGER   I pray you all give your audience,°   *hearing*
And hear this matter with reverence,°   *respect*
By figure° a moral play.   *in form*
The Summoning of Everyman called it is,
5 That of our lives and ending shows
How transitory we be all day.°   *always*
The matter is wonder precious,
But the intent of it is more gracious
And sweet to bear away.
10 The story saith: Man, in the beginning
Look well, and take good heed to the ending,
Be you never so gay.
You think sin in the beginning full sweet,
Which in the end causeth the soul to weep,
15 When the body lieth in clay.
Here shall you see how fellowship and jollity,
Both strength, pleasure, and beauty,
Will fade from thee as flower in May.

---

1. The text is based on the earliest printing of the play (no manuscript is known) by John Skot about 1530, as reproduced by W. W. Greg (1904). The spelling has been modernized except where modernization would spoil the rhyme, and modern punctuation has been added. The stage directions have been amplified.

For ye shall hear how our Heaven-King
20 Calleth Everyman to a general reckoning.
Give audience and hear what he doth say.

[*Exit* MESSENGER.—*Enter* GOD.]

GOD   I perceive, here in my majesty,
How that all creatures be to me unkind,°   thoughtless
Living without dread in worldly prosperity.
25 Of ghostly° sight the people be so blind,   spiritual
Drowned in sin, they know me not for their God.
In worldly riches is all their mind:
They fear not of my righteousness the sharp rod;
My law that I showed when I for them died
30 They forget clean, and shedding of my blood red.
I hanged between two,[2] it cannot be denied:
To get them life I suffered to be dead.°   allowed myself to die
I healed their feet, with thorns hurt was my head.
I could do no more than I did, truly—
35 And now I see the people do clean forsake me.
They use the seven deadly sins damnable,
As pride, coveitise,° wrath, and lechery[3]   avarice
Now in the world be made commendable.
And thus they leave of angels the heavenly company.
40 Every man liveth so after his own pleasure,
And yet of their life they be nothing sure.
I see the more that I them forbear,
The worse they be from year to year:
All that liveth appaireth° fast.   degenerates
45 Therefore I will, in all the haste,
Have a reckoning of every man's person.
For, and° I leave the people thus alone   if
In their life and wicked tempests,
Verily they will become much worse than beasts;
50 For now one would by envy another up eat.
Charity do they all clean forgeet.
I hoped well that every man
In my glory should make his mansion,
And thereto I had them all elect.°   chosen
55 But now I see, like traitors deject,°   abased
They thank me not for the pleasure that I to° them meant,   for
Nor yet for their being that I them have lent.
I proffered the people great multitude of mercy,
And few there be that asketh it heartily.°   sincerely
60 They be so cumbered° with worldly riches   encumbered
That needs on them I must do justice—

---

2. I.e., the two thieves between whom Christ
was crucified.

3. The other three deadly sins are envy, gluttony, and sloth.

On every man living without fear.
Where art thou, Death, thou mighty messenger?

[*Enter* DEATH.]

DEATH   Almighty God, I am here at your will,
65   Your commandment to fulfill.
GOD   Go thou to Everyman,
And show him, in my name,
A pilgrimage he must on him take,
Which he in no wise may escape;
70   And that he bring with him a sure reckoning
Without delay or any tarrying.
DEATH   Lord, I will in the world go run over all,°   *everywhere*
And cruelly out-search both great and small.

[*Exit* GOD.]

Everyman will I beset that liveth beastly
75   Out of God's laws, and dreadeth not folly.
He that loveth riches I will strike with my dart,
His sight to blind, and from heaven to depart°   *separate*
Except that Almsdeeds be his good friend—
In hell for to dwell, world without end.
80   Lo, yonder I see Everyman walking:
Full little he thinketh on my coming;
His mind is on fleshly lusts and his treasure,
And great pain it shall cause him to endure
Before the Lord, Heaven-King.

[*Enter* EVERYMAN.]

85   Everyman, stand still! Whither art thou going
Thus gaily? Hast thou thy Maker forgeet?°   *forgotten*
EVERYMAN   Why askest thou?
Why wouldest thou weet?°   *know*
DEATH   Yea, sir, I will show you:
90   In great haste I am sent to thee
From God out of his majesty.
EVERYMAN   What! sent to me?
DEATH   Yea, certainly.
Though thou have forgot him here,
95   He thinketh on thee in the heavenly sphere,
As, ere we depart, thou shalt know.
EVERYMAN   What desireth God of me?[4]
DEATH   That shall I show thee:
A reckoning he will needs have

---

4. "What doth the Lord require of thee, but to do justly, and to love mercy, and to walk humbly with thy God?" (Micah 6.8).

100 Without any longer respite.

EVERYMAN   To give a reckoning longer leisure I crave.°   *request*

This blind° matter troubleth my wit.   *unexpected*

DEATH   On thee thou must take a long journay:

Therefore thy book of count° with thee thou bring,   *accounts*

105 For turn again thou cannot by no way.

And look thou be sure of thy reckoning,

For before God thou shalt answer and shew

Thy many bad deeds and good but a few—

How thou hast spent thy life and in what wise,

110 Before the Chief Lord of Paradise.

Have ado that we were in that way,[5]

For weet thou well thou shalt make none attornay.[6]

EVERYMAN   Full unready I am such reckoning to give.

I know thee not. What messenger art thou?

115 DEATH   I am Death that no man dreadeth,[7]

For every man I 'rest,° and no man spareth;   *arrest*

For it is God's commandment

That all to me should be obedient.

EVERYMAN   O Death, thou comest when I had thee least in mind.

120 In thy power it lieth me to save:

Yet of my good° will I give thee, if thou will be kind,   *goods*

Yea, a thousand pound shalt thou have—

And defer this matter till another day.

DEATH   Everyman, it may not be, by no way.

125 I set nought by[8] gold, silver, nor riches,

Nor by pope, emperor, king, duke, nor princes,

For, and° I would receive gifts great,   *if*

All the world I might get.

But my custom is clean contrary:

130 I give thee no respite. Come hence and not tarry!

EVERYMAN   Alas, shall I have no longer respite?

I may say Death giveth no warning.

To think on thee it maketh my heart sick,

For all unready is my book of reckoning.

135 But twelve year and I might have a biding,[9]

My counting-book I would make so clear

That my reckoning I should not need to fear.

Wherefore, Death, I pray thee, for God's mercy,

Spare me till I be provided of remedy.

140 DEATH   Thee availeth not to cry, weep, and pray;

But haste thee lightly° that thou were gone that journay   *quickly*

And prove° thy friends, if thou can.   *test*

For weet° thou well the tide° abideth no man,   *know / time*

And in the world each living creature

145 For Adam's sin must die of nature.[1]

---

5. I.e., let's get started at once.
6. I.e., none to appear in your stead.
7. That fears nobody.

8. I care nothing for.
9. If I might have a delay for just twelve years.
1. Naturally. See Romans 5.12.

EVERYMAN   Death, if I should this pilgrimage take
And my reckoning surely make,
Show me, for saint° charity,   *holy*
Should I not come again shortly?
150 DEATH   No, Everyman. And° thou be once there,   *if*
Thou mayst never more come here,
Trust me verily.
EVERYMAN   O gracious God in the high seat celestial,
Have mercy on me in this most need!
155 Shall I have company from this vale terrestrial
Of mine acquaintance that way me to lead?
DEATH   Yea, if any be so hardy
That would go with thee and bear thee company.
Hie° thee that thou were gone to God's magnificence, *hasten*
160 Thy reckoning to give before his presence.
What, weenest° thou thy life is given thee,   *suppose*
And thy worldly goods also?
EVERYMAN   I had weened so, verily.
DEATH   Nay, nay, it was but lent thee.
165 For as soon as thou art go,
Another a while shall have it and then go therefro,[2]
Even as thou hast done.
Everyman, thou art mad! Thou hast thy wits° five, *senses*
And here on earth will not amend thy live![3]
170 For suddenly I do come.
EVERYMAN   O wretched caitiff! Whither shall I flee
That I might 'scape this endless sorrow?
Now, gentle Death, spare me till tomorrow,
That I may amend me
175 With good advisement.°   *preparation*
DEATH   Nay, thereto I will not consent,
Nor no man will I respite,
But to the heart suddenly I shall smite,
Without any advisement.°   *warning*
180 And now out of thy sight I will me hie:
See thou make thee ready shortly,
For thou mayst say this is the day
That no man living may 'scape away.

[*Exit* DEATH.]

EVERYMAN   Alas, I may well weep with sighs deep:
185 Now have I no manner of company
To help me in my journey and me to keep.° *guard*
And also my writing° is full unready— *ledger*
How shall I do now for to excuse me?
I would to God I had never be geet!° *been begotten*
190 To my soul a full great profit it had be.

---

2. See Luke 12.19–20.   3. In thy life.

For now I fear pains huge and great.
The time passeth: Lord, help, that all wrought!
For though I mourn, it availeth nought.
The day passeth and is almost ago:°   *gone by*
195 I wot° not well what for to do.   *know*
To whom were I best my complaint to make?
What and° I to Fellowship thereof spake,   *if*
And showed him of this sudden chance?
For in him is all mine affiance,°   *trust*
200 We have in the world so many a day
Be good friends in sport and play.
I see him yonder, certainly.
I trust that he will bear me company.
Therefore to him will I speak to ease my sorrow.

[*Enter* FELLOWSHIP.]

205 Well met, good Fellowship, and good morrow!
FELLOWSHIP   Everyman, good morrow, by this day!
Sir, why lookest thou so piteously?
If anything be amiss, I pray thee me say,
That I may help to remedy.
210 EVERYMAN   Yea, good Fellowship, yea:
I am in great jeopardy.
FELLOWSHIP   My true friend, show to me your mind.
I will not forsake thee to my life's end
In the way of good company.
215 EVERYMAN   That was well spoken, and lovingly!
FELLOWSHIP   Sir, I must needs know your heaviness.°   *sorrow*
I have pity to see you in any distress.
If any have you wronged, ye shall revenged be,
Though I on the ground be slain for thee,
220 Though that I know before that I should die.
EVERYMAN   Verily, Fellowship, gramercy.°   *many thanks*
FELLOWSHIP   Tush! by thy thanks I set not a stree.°   *straw*
Show me your grief and say no more.
EVERYMAN   If I my heart should to you break,°   *disclose*
225 And then you to turn your mind fro me,
And would not me comfort when ye hear me speak,
Then should I ten times sorrier be.
FELLOWSHIP   Sir, I say as I will do, indeed.
EVERYMAN   Then be you a good friend at need.
230 I have found you true herebefore.
FELLOWSHIP   And so ye shall evermore.
For, in faith, and° thou go to hell,   *if*
I will not forsake thee by the way.
EVERYMAN   Ye speak like a good friend. I believe you well.
235 I shall deserve° it, and° I may.   *repay / if*
FELLOWSHIP   I speak of no deserving, by this day!
For he that will say and nothing do

Is not worthy with good company to go.
Therefore show me the grief of your mind,
240 As to your friend most loving and kind.
EVERYMAN   I shall show you how it is:
Commanded I am to go a journay,
A long way, hard and dangerous,
And give a strait° count,° without delay,   strict / accounting
245 Before the high judge Adonai.°   God
Wherefore I pray you bear me company,
As ye have promised, in this journay.
FELLOWSHIP   This is matter indeed! Promise is duty—
But, and° I should take such a voyage on me,   if
250 I know it well, it should be to my pain.
Also it maketh me afeard, certain.
But let us take counsel here, as well as we can—
For your words would fear° a strong man.   frighten
EVERYMAN   Why, ye said if I had need,
255 Ye would me never forsake, quick ne dead,
Though it were to hell, truly.
FELLOWSHIP   So I said, certainly,
But such pleasures° be set aside, the sooth to say.   jokes
And also, if we took such a journay,
260 When should we again come?
EVERYMAN   Nay, never again, till the day of doom.
FELLOWSHIP   In faith, then will not I come there!
Who hath you these tidings brought?
EVERYMAN   Indeed, Death was with me here.
265 FELLOWSHIP   Now by God that all hath bought,°   redeemed
If Death were the messenger,
For no man that is living today
I will not go that loath° journay—   loathsome
Not for the father that begat me!
270 EVERYMAN   Ye promised otherwise, pardie.°   by God
FELLOWSHIP   I wot well I said so, truly.
And yet, if thou wilt eat and drink and make good cheer,
Or haunt to women the lusty company,[4]
I would not forsake you while the day is clear,
275 Trust me verily!
EVERYMAN   Yea, thereto ye would be ready—
To go to mirth, solace,° and play: pleasure
Your mind to folly will sooner apply°   attend
Than to bear me company in my long journay.
280 FELLOWSHIP   Now in good faith, I will not that way.
But, and° thou will murder or any man kill,   if
In that I will help thee with a good will.
EVERYMAN   O that is simple° advice, indeed!   foolish
Gentle fellow, help me in my necessity:
285 We have loved long, and now I need—

4. Or frequent the lusty company of women.

And now, gentle Fellowship, remember me!

FELLOWSHIP Whether ye have loved me or no,
 By Saint John, I will not with thee go!

EVERYMAN Yet I pray thee take the labor and do so much for me,
290 To bring me forward,° for saint charity,   *escort me*
 And comfort me till I come without the town.

FELLOWSHIP Nay, and° thou would give me a new gown, *if*
 I will not a foot with thee go.
 But, and° thou had tarried, I would not have left thee so. *if*
295 And as now, God speed thee in thy journay!
 For from thee I will depart as fast as I may.

EVERYMAN Whither away, Fellowship? Will thou forsake me?

FELLOWSHIP Yea, by my fay!° To God I betake° thee. *faith / commend*

EVERYMAN Farewell, good Fellowship! For thee my heart is sore.
300 Adieu forever—I shall see thee no more.

FELLOWSHIP In faith, Everyman, farewell now at the ending:
 For you I will remember that parting is mourning.

   [*Exit* FELLOWSHIP.]

EVERYMAN Alack, shall we thus depart° indeed—   *part*
 Ah, Lady, help!⁵—without any more comfort?
305 Lo, Fellowship forsaketh me in my most need!
 For help in this world whither shall I resort?
 Fellowship herebefore° with me would merry make, *before this*
 And now little sorrow for me doth he take.
 It is said, "In prosperity men friends may find
310 Which in adversity be full unkind."
 Now whither for succor° shall I flee,   *aid*
 Sith° that Fellowship hath forsaken me?   *since*
 To my kinsmen I will, truly,
 Praying them to help me in my necessity.
315 I believe that they will do so,
 For kind will creep where it may not go.⁶
 I will go 'say°—for yonder I see them— *assay*
 Where° be ye now my friends and kinsmen. *whether*

   [*Enter* KINDRED *and* COUSIN.]

KINDRED Here be we now at your commandment:
320 Cousin, I pray you show us your intent
 In any wise, and not spare.

COUSIN Yea, Everyman, and to us declare
 If ye be disposed to go anywhither.
 For, weet° you well, we will live and die together. *know*
325 KINDRED In wealth and woe we will with you hold,
 For over his kin a man may be bold.⁷

---

5. An appeal to the Virgin Mary.
6. For kinship will creep where it cannot walk (i.e., kinsmen will suffer hardship for one another).

7. I.e., for a man may make demands of his kinsmen.

EVERYMAN   Gramercy,° my friends and kinsmen kind.   *much thanks*
    Now shall I show you the grief of my mind.
    I was commanded by a messenger
330   That is a high king's chief officer:
    He bade me go a pilgrimage, to my pain—
    And I know well I shall never come again.
    Also I must give a reckoning strait,°   *strict*
    For I have a great enemy that hath me in wait,[8]
335   Which intendeth me to hinder.
KINDRED   What account is that which ye must render?
    That would I know.
EVERYMAN   Of all my works I must show
    How I have lived and my days spent;
340   Also of ill deeds that I have used
    In my time sith° life was me lent,   *since*
    And of all virtues that I have refused.
    Therefore I pray you go thither with me
    To help me make mine account, for saint° charity.   *holy*
345 COUSIN   What, to go thither? Is that the matter?
    Nay, Everyman, I had liefer fast[9] bread and water
    All this five year and more!
EVERYMAN   Alas, that ever I was bore!°   *born*
    For now shall I never be merry
350   If that you forsake me.
KINDRED   Ah, sir, what? Ye be a merry man:
    Take good heart to you and make no moan.
    But one thing I warn you, by Saint Anne,
    As for me, ye shall go alone.
355 EVERYMAN   My Cousin, will you not with me go?
COUSIN   No, by Our Lady! I have the cramp in my toe:
    Trust not to me. For, so God me speed,°   *prosper*
    I will deceive you in your most need.
KINDRED   It availeth you not us to 'tice.°   *entice*
360   Ye shall have my maid with all my heart:
    She loveth to go to feasts, there to be nice,°   *wanton*
    And to dance, and abroad to start.[1]
    I will give her leave to help you in that journey,
    If that you and she may agree.
365 EVERYMAN   Now show me the very effect° of your mind: *true bent*
    Will you go with me or abide behind?
KINDRED   Abide behind? Yea, that will I and° I may!   *if*
    Therefore farewell till another day.

       [*Exit* KINDRED.]

EVERYMAN   How should I be merry or glad?
370   For fair promises men to me make,
    But when I have most need they me forsake.

---

8. I.e., Satan lies in ambush for me.   1. To go gadding about.
9. I.e., rather fast on.

I am deceived. That maketh me sad.

COUSIN   Cousin Everyman, farewell now,
For verily I will not go with you;
375   Also of mine own an unready reckoning
I have to account—therefore I make tarrying.
Now God keep thee, for now I go.

[Exit COUSIN.]

EVERYMAN   Ah, Jesus, is all come hereto?°   to this
Lo, fair words maketh fools fain:°   glad
380   They promise and nothing will do, certain.
My kinsmen promised me faithfully
For to abide with me steadfastly,
And now fast away do they flee.
Even so Fellowship promised me.
385   What friend were best me of to provide?
I lose my time here longer to abide.
Yet in my mind a thing there is:
All my life I have loved riches;
If that my Good° now help me might,   Goods
390   He would make my heart full light.
I will speak to him in this distress.
Where art thou, my Goods and riches?

GOODS   [within] Who calleth me? Everyman? What, hast thou haste?
I lie here in corners, trussed and piled so high,
395   And in chests I am locked so fast—
Also sacked in bags—thou mayst see with thine eye
I cannot stir, in packs low where I lie.
What would ye have? Lightly° me say.   quickly

EVERYMAN   Come hither, Good, in all the haste thou may,
400   For of counsel I must desire thee.

[Enter GOODS.]

GOODS   Sir, and° ye in the world have sorrow or adversity,[2]   if
That can I help you to remedy shortly.

EVERYMAN   It is another disease° that grieveth me: distress
In this world it is not, I tell thee so.
405   I am sent for another way to go,
To give a strait count general
Before the highest Jupiter° of all.   God
And all my life I have had joy and pleasure in thee:
Therefore I pray thee go with me,
410   For, peradventure, thou mayst before God Almighty
My reckoning help to clean and purify.
For it is said ever among°   now and then
That money maketh all right that is wrong.

GOODS   Nay, Everyman, I sing another song:

2. See John 16.33.

415 I follow no man in such voyages.
     For, and° I went with thee,   *if*
     Thou shouldest fare much the worse for me;
     For because on me thou did set thy mind,
     Thy reckoning I have made blotted and blind,°   *illegible*
420 That thine account thou cannot make truly—
     And that hast thou for the love of me.
     EVERYMAN   That would grieve me full sore
     When I should come to that fearful answer.
     Up, let us go thither together.
425 GOODS   Nay, not so, I am too brittle, I may not endure.
     I will follow no man one foot, be ye sure.
     EVERYMAN   Alas, I have thee loved and had great pleasure
     All my life-days on good and treasure.
     GOODS   That is to thy damnation, without leasing,°   *lie*
430 For my love is contrary to the love everlasting.
     But if thou had me loved moderately during,°   *in the meanwhile*
     As to the poor to give part of me,
     Then shouldest thou not in this dolor be,
     Nor in this great sorrow and care.
435 EVERYMAN   Lo, now was I deceived ere I was ware,
     And all I may wite° misspending of time.   *blame on*
     GOODS   What, weenest° thou that I am thine?   *suppose*
     EVERYMAN   I had weened so.
     GOODS   Nay, Everyman, I say no.
440 As for a while I was lent thee;
     A season thou hast had me in prosperity.
     My condition° is man's soul to kill;   *disposition*
     If I save one, a thousand I do spill.°   *ruin*
     Weenest thou that I will follow thee?
445 Nay, from this world, not verily.
     EVERYMAN   I had weened otherwise.
     GOODS   Therefore to thy soul Good is a thief;
     For when thou art dead, this is my guise°—   *custom*
     Another to deceive in the same wise
450 As I have done thee, and all to his soul's repreef.°   *shame*
     EVERYMAN   O false Good, cursed thou be,
     Thou traitor to God, that hast deceived me
     And caught me in thy snare!
     GOODS   Marry, thou brought thyself in care,°   *sorrow*
455 Whereof I am glad:
     I must needs laugh, I cannot be sad.
     EVERYMAN   Ah, Good, thou hast had long my heartly° love;   *sincere*
     I gave thee that which should be the Lord's above.
     But wilt thou not go with me, indeed?
460 I pray thee truth to say.
     GOODS   No, so God me speed!
     Therefore farewell and have good day.

     [*Exit* GOODS.]

EVERYMAN   Oh, to whom shall I make my moan
For to go with me in that heavy° journay?   *sorrowful*
465   First Fellowship said he would with me gone:°   *go*
His words were very pleasant and gay,
But afterward he left me alone.
Then spake I to my kinsmen, all in despair,
And also they gave me words fair—
470   They lacked no fair speaking,
But all forsake me in the ending.
Then went I to my Goods that I loved best,
In hope to have comfort; but there had I least,
For my Goods sharply did me tell
475   That he bringeth many into hell.
Then of myself I was ashamed,
And so I am worthy to be blamed:
Thus may I well myself hate.
Of whom shall I now counsel take?
480   I think that I shall never speed°   *prosper*
Till that I go to my Good Deed.
But alas, she is so weak
That she can neither go° nor speak.   *walk*
Yet will I venture° on her now.   *gamble*
485   My Good Deeds, where be you?
GOOD DEEDS [*speaking from the ground*]   Here I lie, cold in
     the ground:
Thy sins hath me sore bound
That I cannot stear.°   *stir*
EVERYMAN   O Good Deeds, I stand in fear:
490   I must you pray of counsel,
For help now should come right well.
GOOD DEEDS   Everyman, I have understanding
That ye be summoned, account to make,
Before Messiah of Jer'salem King.
495   And you do by me,[3] that journey with you will I take.
EVERYMAN   Therefore I come to you my moan to make:
I pray you that ye will go with me.
GOOD DEEDS   I would full fain,° but I cannot stand, verily.   *gladly*
EVERYMAN   Why, is there anything on you fall?°   *fallen*
500 GOOD DEEDS   Yea, sir, I may thank you of all:
If ye had perfectly cheered me,
Your book of count full ready had be.

[GOOD DEEDS *shows him the account book.*]

Look, the books of your works and deeds eke,°   *also*
As how they lie under the feet,
505   To your soul's heaviness.°   *distress*
EVERYMAN   Our Lord Jesus help me!

3. I.e., if you do what I say.

For one letter here I cannot see.

GOOD DEEDS   There is a blind° reckoning in time of distress!   *illegible*

EVERYMAN   Good Deeds, I pray you help me in this need,

510   Or else I am forever damned indeed.

Therefore help me to make reckoning

Before the Redeemer of all thing

That King is and was and ever shall.

GOOD DEEDS   Everyman, I am sorry of° your fall   *for*

515   And fain would help you and° I were able.   *if*

EVERYMAN   Good Deeds, your counsel I pray you give me.

GOOD DEEDS   That shall I do verily,

Though that on my feet I may not go;

I have a sister that shall with you also,

520   Called Knowledge, which shall with you abide

To help you to make that dreadful reckoning.

[*Enter* KNOWLEDGE.]

KNOWLEDGE   Everyman, I will go with thee and be thy guide,

In thy most need to go by thy side.

EVERYMAN   In good condition I am now in everything,

525   And am whole content with this good thing,

Thanked be God my Creator.

GOOD DEEDS   And when she hath brought you there

Where thou shalt heal thee of thy smart,°   *pain*

Then go you with your reckoning and your Good Deeds

together

530   For to make you joyful at heart

Before the blessed Trinity.

EVERYMAN   My Good Deeds, gramercy!°   *thanks*

I am well content, certainly,

With your words sweet.

535   KNOWLEDGE   Now go we together lovingly

To Confession, that cleansing river.

EVERYMAN   For joy I weep—I would we were there!

But I pray you give me cognition,°   *knowledge*

Where dwelleth that holy man Confession?

540   KNOWLEDGE   In the House of Salvation:

We shall us comfort, by God's grace.

[KNOWLEDGE *leads* EVERYMAN *to* CONFESSION.]

Lo, this is Confession: kneel down and ask mercy,

For he is in good conceit° with God Almighty.   *esteem*

EVERYMAN [*kneeling*]   O glorious fountain that all

uncleanness doth clarify,°   *purify*

545   Wash from me the spots of vice unclean,

That on me no sin may be seen.[4]

4. See Zechariah 13.1.

I come with Knowledge for my redemption,
Redempt° with heart and full contrition,   *redeemed*
For I am commanded a pilgrimage to take
550   And great accounts before God to make.
Now I pray you, Shrift,° mother of Salvation,   *confession*
Help my Good Deeds for my piteous exclamation.
CONFESSION   I know your sorrow well, Everyman:
Because with Knowledge ye come to me,
555   I will you comfort as well as I can,
And a precious jewel I will give thee,
Called Penance, voider° of adversity.   *expeller*
Therewith shall your body chastised be—
With abstinence and perseverance in God's service.
560   Here shall you receive that scourge of me,
Which is penance strong° that ye must endure,   *harsh*
To remember thy Saviour was scourged for thee
With sharp scourges,[5] and suffered it patiently.
So must thou ere thou 'scape that painful pilgrimage.
565   Knowledge, keep° him in this voyage,   *guard*
And by that time Good Deeds will be with thee.
But in any wise be secure° of mercy—   *certain*
For your time draweth fast—and ye will saved be.
Ask God mercy and he will grant, truly.
570   When with the scourge of penance man doth him° bind,   *himself*
The oil of forgiveness then shall he find.
EVERYMAN   Thanked be God for his gracious work,
For now I will my penance begin.
This hath rejoiced and lighted my heart,
575   Though the knots be painful and hard within.[6]
KNOWLEDGE   Everyman, look your penance that ye fulfill,
What pain that ever it to you be;
And Knowledge shall give you counsel at will
How your account ye shall make clearly.
580   Everyman O eternal God, O heavenly figure,
O way of righteousness, O goodly vision,
Which descended down in a virgin pure
Because he would every man redeem,
Which Adam forfeited by his disobedience;
585   O blessed Godhead, elect and high Divine,°   *divinity*
Forgive my grievous offense!
Here I cry thee mercy in this presence:
O ghostly° Treasure, O Ransomer and Redeemer,   *spiritual*
Of all the world Hope and Conduiter,°   *guide*
590   Mirror of joy, Foundator° of mercy,   *Founder*
Which enlumineth° heaven and earth thereby,   *lights up*
Hear my clamorous complaint, though it late be;
Receive my prayers, of thy benignity.

---

5. See John 19.1.
6. I.e., to my senses. "Knots": i.e., the knots on the scourge (whip) of penance.

Though I be a sinner most abominable,
595　Yet let my name be written in Moses' table.[7]
O Mary, pray to the Maker of all thing
Me for to help at my ending,
And save me from the power of my enemy,
For Death assaileth me strongly.
600　And Lady, that I may by mean of thy prayer
Of your Son's glory to be partner—
By the means of his passion° I it crave.　　　　　　　　*suffering*
I beseech you help my soul to save.
Knowledge, give me the scourge of penance:
605　My flesh therewith shall give acquittance.°　　　*satisfaction for sins*
I will now begin, if God give me grace.
KNOWLEDGE　Everyman, God give you time and space!°　　*opportunity*
Thus I bequeath you in the hands of our Saviour:
Now may you make your reckoning sure.
610　EVERYMAN　In the name of the Holy Trinity
My body sore punished shall be:
Take this, body, for the sin of the flesh!
Also° thou delightest to go gay and fresh,　　　　　　　*as*
And in the way of damnation thou did me bring,
615　Therefore suffer now strokes of punishing!
Now of penance I will wade the water clear,
To save me from purgatory, that sharp fire.
GOOD DEEDS　I thank God, now can I walk and go,
And am delivered of my sickness and woe.
620　Therefore with Everyman I will go, and not spare:
His good works I will help him to declare.
KNOWLEDGE　Now, Everyman, be merry and glad:
Your Good Deeds cometh now, ye may° not be sad.　　　*can*
Now is your Good Deeds whole and sound,
625　Going° upright upon the ground.　　　　　　　　　　*walking*
EVERYMAN　My heart is light, and shall be evermore.
Now will I smite faster than I did before.
GOOD DEEDS　Everyman, pilgrim, my special friend,
Blessed be thou without end!
630　For thee is preparate° the eternal glory.　　　　　　*prepared*
Ye have me made whole and sound
Therefore I will bide by thee in every stound.°[8]　　　*trial*
EVERYMAN　Welcome, my Good Deeds! Now I hear thy voice,
I weep for very sweetness of love.
635　KNOWLEDGE　Be no more sad, but ever rejoice:
God seeth thy living in his throne above.
Put on this garment to thy behove,°　　　　　　　　　*advantage*
Which is wet with your tears—
Or else before God you may it miss

7. "Moses' table" is here the tablet on which are recorded those who have been baptized and have done penance.
8. "Blessed are the dead which die in the Lord

from henceforth: yea, saith the spirit, that they may rest from their labors; and their works do follow them" (Revelation 14.13).

640 When ye to your journey's end come shall.

EVERYMAN   Gentle Knowledge, what do ye it call?

KNOWLEDGE   It is a garment of sorrow;

From pain it will you borrow:°   *redeem*

Contrition it is

645 That getteth forgiveness;

It pleaseth God passing° well.   *surpassingly*

GOOD DEEDS   Everyman, will you wear it for your heal?°   *welfare*

EVERYMAN   Now blessed be Jesu, Mary's son,

For now have I on true contrition.

650 And let us go now without tarrying.

Good Deeds, have we clear our reckoning?

GOOD DEEDS   Yea, indeed, I have it here.

EVERYMAN   Then I trust we need not fear.

Now friends, let us not part in twain.

655 KNOWLEDGE   Nay, Everyman, that will we not, certain.

GOOD DEEDS   Yet must thou lead with thee

Three persons of great might.

EVERYMAN   Who should they be?

GOOD DEEDS   Discretion and Strength they hight,°   *are called*

660 And thy Beauty may not abide behind.

KNOWLEDGE   Also ye must call to mind

Your Five-Wits° as for your counselors.   *senses*

GOOD DEEDS   You must have them ready at all hours.

EVERYMAN   How shall I get them hither?

665 KNOWLEDGE   You must call them all togither,

And they will be here incontinent.°   *at once*

EVERYMAN   My friends, come hither and be present,

Discretion, Strength, my Five-Wits, and Beauty!

[*They enter.*]

BEAUTY   Here at your will we be all ready.

670 What will ye that we should do?

GOOD DEEDS   That ye would with Everyman go

And help him in his pilgrimage.

Advise you:° will ye with him or not in that voyage?   *take thought*

STRENGTH   We will bring him all thither,

675 To his help and comfort, ye may believe me.

DISCRETION   So will we go with him all togither.

EVERYMAN   Almighty God, loved° might thou be!   *praised*

I give thee laud that I have hither brought

Strength, Discretion, Beauty, and Five-Wits—lack I nought—

680 And my Good Deeds, with Knowledge clear,

All be in my company at my will here:

I desire no more to my business.

STRENGTH   And I, Strength, will by you stand in distress,

Though thou would in battle fight on the ground.

685 FIVE-WITS   And though it were through the world round,

We will not depart for sweet ne sour.

BEAUTY   No more will I, until death's hour,
  Whatsoever thereof befall.
DISCRETION   Everyman, advise you first of all:
690   Go with a good advisement° and deliberation.   *preparation*
  We all give you virtuous° monition°   *confident / prediction*
  That all shall be well.
EVERYMAN   My friends, hearken what I will tell;
  I pray God reward you in his heaven-sphere;
695   Now hearken all that be here,
  For I will make my testament,
  Here before you all present:
  In alms half my good° I will give with my hands twain,   *goods*
  In the way of charity with good intent;
700   And the other half, still° shall remain,   *which still*
  I 'queath° to be returned there it ought to be.   *bequeath*
  This I do in despite of the fiend of hell,
  To go quit out of his perel,[9]
  Ever after and this day.
705   KNOWLEDGE   Everyman, hearken what I say:
  Go to Priesthood, I you advise,
  And receive of him, in any wise,°   *at all costs*
  The holy sacrament and ointment° togither;   *extreme unction*
  Then shortly see ye turn again hither:
710   We will all abide you here.
FIVE-WITS   Yea, Everyman, hie° you that ye ready were.   *haste*
  There is no emperor, king, duke, ne baron,
  That of God hath commission
  As hath the least priest in the world being:
715   For of the blessed sacraments pure and bening°   *benign*
  He beareth the keys, and thereof hath the cure°   *care*
  For man's redemption—it is ever sure—
  Which God for our souls' medicine
  Gave us out of his heart with great pine,°   *torment*
720   Here in this transitory life for thee and me.
  The blessed sacraments seven there be:
  Baptism, confirmation, with priesthood° good,   *ordination*
  And the sacrament of God's precious flesh and blood,
  Marriage, the holy extreme unction, and penance:
725   These seven be good to have in remembrance,
  Gracious sacraments of high divinity.
EVERYMAN   Fain° would I receive that holy body,   *gladly*
  And meekly to my ghostly° father I will go.   *spiritual*
FIVE-WITS   Everyman, that is the best that ye can do:
730   God will you to salvation bring.
  For priesthood exceedeth all other thing:
  To us Holy Scripture they do teach,
  And converteth man from sin, heaven to reach;
  God hath to them more power given

9. In order to go free of danger from him.

735 Than to any angel that is in heaven.
    With five words[1] he may consecrate
    God's body in flesh and blood to make,
    And handleth his Maker between his hands.
    The priest bindeth and unbindeth all bands,[2]
740 Both in earth and in heaven.
    Thou ministers° all the sacraments seven;   *administer*
    Though we kiss thy feet, thou were worthy;
    Thou art surgeon that cureth sin deadly;
    No remedy we find under God
745 But all only priesthood.[3]
    Everyman, God gave priests that dignity
    And setteth them in his stead among us to be.
    Thus be they above angels in degree.

       [*Exit* EVERYMAN.]

KNOWLEDGE   If priests be good, it is so, surely.
750 But when Jesu hanged on the cross with great smart,°   *pain*
    There he gave out of his blessed heart
    The same sacrament in great torment,
    He sold them not to us, that Lord omnipotent:
    Therefore Saint Peter the Apostle doth say
755 That Jesu's curse hath all they
    Which God their Saviour do buy or sell,[4]
    Or they for any money do take or tell.[5]
    Sinful priests giveth the sinners example bad:
    Their children sitteth by other men's fires, I have heard;
760 And some haunteth° women's company   *frequents*
    With unclean life, as lusts of lechery.
    These be with sin made blind.
FIVE-WITS   I trust to God no such may we find.
    Therefore let us priesthood honor,
765 And follow their doctrine for our souls' succor.
    We be their sheep and they shepherds be
    By whom we all be kept in surety.
    Peace, for yonder I see Everyman come,
    Which hath made true satisfaction.
770 GOOD DEEDS   Methink it is he indeed.

       [*Re-enter* EVERYMAN.]

EVERYMAN   Now Jesu be your alder speed![6]

---

1. The five words ("For this is my body") spoken by the priest when he offers the wafer at communion.
2. A reference to the power of the keys, inherited by the priesthood from St. Peter, who received it from Christ (Matthew 16.19) with the promise that whatever St. Peter bound or loosed on earth would be bound or loosed in heaven.
3. Except from priesthood alone.
4. To give or receive money for the sacraments is simony, named after Simon, who wished to buy the gift of the Holy Ghost and was cursed by St. Peter. See Acts 8.20.
5. Or who, for any sacrament, take or count money.
6. The prosperer of you all.

I have received the sacrament for my redemption,
And then mine extreme unction.
Blessed be all they that counseled me to take it!
775   And now, friends, let us go without longer respite.
I thank God that ye have tarried so long.
Now set each of you on this rood° your hond   cross
And shortly follow me:
I go before there° I would be. God be our guide!   where
775   STRENGTH   Everyman, we will not from you go
Till ye have done this voyage long.
DISCRETION   I, Discretion, will bide by you also.
KNOWLEDGE   And though this pilgrimage be never so strong,°   harsh
I will never part you fro.
785   STRENGTH   Everyman, I will be as sure by thee
As ever I did by Judas Maccabee.[7]
EVERYMAN   Alas, I am so faint I may not stand—
My limbs under me doth fold!
Friends, let us not turn again to this land,
790   Not for all the world's gold.
For into this cave must I creep
And turn to earth, and there to sleep.
BEAUTY   What, into this grave, alas?
EVERYMAN   Yea, there shall ye consume,° more and lass.[8]   decay
795   BEAUTY   And what, should I smother here?
EVERYMAN   Yea, by my faith, and nevermore appear.
In this world live no more we shall,
But in heaven before the highest Lord of all.
BEAUTY   I cross out all this! Adieu, by Saint John—
800   I take my tape in my lap and am gone.[9]
EVERYMAN   What, Beauty, whither will ye?
BEAUTY   Peace, I am deaf—I look not behind me,
Not and thou wouldest give me all the gold in thy chest.

[*Exit* BEAUTY.]

EVERYMAN   Alas, whereto may I trust?
805   Beauty goeth fast away fro me—
She promised with me to live and die!
STRENGTH   Everyman, I will thee also forsake and deny.
Thy game liketh° me not at all.   pleases
EVERYMAN   Why then, ye will forsake me all?
810   Sweet Strength, tarry a little space.
STRENGTH   Nay, sir, by the rood of grace,
I will hie me from thee fast,
Though thou weep till thy heart tobrast.°   break
EVERYMAN   Ye would ever bide by me, ye said.

---

7. Judas Maccabaeus was an enormously powerful warrior in the defense of Israel against the
Syrians in late Old Testament times.

8. More and less (i.e., all of you).
9. I tuck my skirts in my belt and am off.

815 STRENGTH Yea, I have you far enough conveyed!°   *escorted*
       Ye be old enough, I understand,
       Your pilgrimage to take on hand:
       I repent me that I hither came.
     EVERYMAN Strength, you to displease I am to blame,[1]
820   Yet promise is debt, this ye well wot.°   *know*
     STRENGTH In faith, I care not:
       Thou art but a fool to complain;
       You spend your speech and waste your brain.
       Go, thrust thee into the ground.

       [*Exit* STRENGTH.]

825 EVERYMAN I had weened° surer I should you have found.   *supposed*
       He that trusteth in his Strength
       She him deceiveth at the length.
       Both Strength and Beauty forsaketh me—
       Yet they promised me fair and lovingly.
830 DISCRETION Everyman, I will after Strength be gone:
       As for me, I will leave you alone.
     EVERYMAN Why Discretion, will ye forsake me?
     DISCRETION Yea, in faith, I will go from thee.
       For when Strength goeth before,
835   I follow after evermore.
     EVERYMAN Yet I pray thee, for the love of the Trinity,
       Look in my grave once piteously.
     DISCRETION Nay, so nigh will I not come.
       Farewell everyone!

       [*Exit* DISCRETION.]

840 EVERYMAN O all thing faileth save God alone—
       Beauty, Strength, and Discretion.
       For when Death bloweth his blast
       They all run fro me full fast.
     FIVE-WITS Everyman, my leave now of thee I take.
845   I will follow the other, for here I thee forsake.
     EVERYMAN Alas, then may I wail and weep,
       For I took you for my best friend.
     FIVE-WITS I will no longer thee keep.°   *watch over*
       Now farewell, and there an end!

       [*Exit* FIVE-WITS.]

850 EVERYMAN O Jesu, help, all hath forsaken me!
     GOOD DEEDS Nay, Everyman, I will bide with thee:
       I will not forsake thee indeed;
       Thou shalt find me a good friend at need.

---

1. I'm to blame for displeasing you.

EVERYMAN   Gramercy, Good Deeds! Now may I true friends see.
855   They have forsaken me every one—
I loved them better than my Good Deeds alone.
Knowledge, will ye forsake me also?
KNOWLEDGE   Yea, Everyman, when ye to Death shall go,
But not yet, for no manner of danger.
860   EVERYMAN   Gramercy, Knowledge, with all my heart!
KNOWLEDGE   Nay, yet will I not from hence depart
Till I see where ye shall be come.[2]
EVERYMAN   Methink, alas, that I must be gone
To make my reckoning and my debts pay,
865   For I see my time is nigh spent away.
Take example, all ye that this do hear or see,
How they that I best loved do forsake me,
Except my Good Deeds that bideth truly.
GOOD DEEDS   All earthly things is but vanity.
870   Beauty, Strength, and Discretion do man forsake,
Foolish friends and kinsmen that fair spake—
All fleeth save Good Deeds, and that am I.
EVERYMAN   Have mercy on me, God most mighty,
And stand by me, thou mother and maid, holy Mary!
875   GOOD DEEDS   Fear not: I will speak for thee.
EVERYMAN   Here I cry God mercy!
GOOD DEEDS   Short our end, and 'minish our pain.[3]
Let us go, and never come again.
EVERYMAN   Into thy hands, Lord, my soul I commend:
880   Receive it, Lord, that it be not lost.
As thou me boughtest,° so me defend,   redeemed
And save me from the fiend's boast,
That I may appear with that blessed host
That shall be saved at the day of doom.
885   *In manus tuas*, of mights most,
Forever *commendo spiritum meum*.[4]

[EVERYMAN *and* GOOD DEEDS *descend into the grave.*]

KNOWLEDGE   Now hath he suffered that we all shall endure,
The Good Deeds shall make all sure.
Now hath he made ending,
890   Methinketh that I hear angels sing
And make great joy and melody
Where Everyman's soul received shall be.
ANGEL [*within*]   Come, excellent elect° spouse to Jesu![5]   chosen
Here above thou shalt go
895   Because of thy singular virtue.
Now the soul is taken the body fro,

2. Till I see where you will come to.
3. I.e., make our dying quick and diminish our pain.
4. Into thy hands, O greatest of powers, I commend my spirit forever. Cf. Christ's dying words (Luke 23.46).
5. The soul is often referred to as the bride of Jesus.

Thy reckoning is crystal clear:
Now shalt thou into the heavenly sphere—
Unto the which all ye shall come
900   That liveth well before the day of doom.

[*Enter* DOCTOR.[6]]

DOCTOR   This memorial° men may have in mind: *reminder*
Ye hearers, take it of worth,° old and young,   *prize it*
And forsake Pride, for he deceiveth you in the end.
And remember Beauty, Five-Wits, Strength, and Discretion,
905   They all at the last do Everyman forsake,
Save his Good Deeds there doth he take—
But beware, for and° they be small,   *if*
Before God he hath no help at all—
None excuse may be there for Everyman.
910   Alas, how shall he do than?°   *then*
For after death amends may no man make,
For then mercy and pity doth him forsake.
If his reckoning be not clear when he doth come,
God will say, *"Ite, maledicti, in ignem eternum!"*[7]
915   And he that hath his account whole and sound,
High in heaven he shall be crowned,
Unto which place God bring us all thither,
That we may live body and soul togither.
Thereto help, the Trinity!
920   Amen, say ye, for saint° charity.   *holy*

6. The Doctor is the learned theologian who explains the meaning of the play.

7. Depart, ye cursed, into everlasting fire (Matthew 25.41).

The Sixteenth Century
1485–1603

The ancient Roman poet Virgil characterized Britain as a wild, remote place set apart from all the world, and it must still have seemed so in the early sixteenth century to the inhabitants of cities like Venice, Madrid, and Paris. To be sure, some venturesome Continental travelers crossed the Channel and visited London, Oxford, or Cambridge, bringing home reports of bustling markets, impressive universities, and ambitious nobles vying for position at an increasingly powerful royal court. But these visitors were but a trickle compared with the flood of wealthy young Englishmen (and, to a lesser extent, Englishwomen) who embarked at the first opportunity for the Continent. English travelers were virtually obliged to learn some French, Italian, or Spanish, for

The Life and Death of Sir Henry Unton (detail), anonymous, ca. 1597. For more information about this painting, see the color insert in this volume.

they would encounter very few people who knew their language. On returning home, they would frequently wear foreign fashions—much to the disgust of moralists—and would pepper their speech with foreign phrases.

At the beginning of the sixteenth century, the English language had almost no prestige abroad, and there were those at home who doubted that it could serve as a suitable medium for serious, elevated, or elegant discourse. It is no accident that one of the first works in this selection of English Renaissance literature, Thomas More's *Utopia*, was not written in English: More, who began his great book in 1515 when he was on a diplomatic mission in the Netherlands, was writing for an international intellectual community, and as such his language of choice was Latin. His work quickly became famous throughout Europe, but it was not translated into English until the 1550s. Evidently, neither More himself nor the London printers and booksellers thought it imperative to publish a vernacular *Utopia*. Yet by the century's end there were signs of a great increase in what we might call linguistic self-confidence, signs that at least some contemporary observers were aware that something extraordinary was happening to their language. Though in 1600 England still remained somewhat peripheral to the Continent, English had been fashioned into an immensely powerful expressive medium, one whose cadences in the works of Marlowe, Shakespeare, and the translators of the Bible continue after more than four centuries to thrill readers.

How did it come about that by the century's end so many remarkable poems, plays, and prose works were written in English? The answer lies in part in the spectacular creativity of a succession of brilliant writers, the best of whom are represented in these pages. Still, a vital literary culture is the product of a complex process, involving thousands of more modest, half-hidden creative acts sparked by a wide range of motives, some of which we will briefly explore.

THE COURT AND THE CITY

The development of the English language in the sixteenth century is linked at least indirectly to the consolidation and strengthening of the English state. Preoccupied by violent clashes between the thuggish feudal retainers of rival barons, the English, through most of the fifteenth century, had rather limited time and inclination to cultivate rhetorical skills. The social and economic health of the nation had been severely damaged by the so-called Wars of the Roses, a vicious, decades-long struggle for royal power between the noble houses of York and Lancaster. The struggle was resolved by the establishment of the Tudor dynasty that ruled England from 1485 to 1603. The family name derives from Owen Tudor, an ambitious Welshman who himself had no claim to the throne but who married Catherine of Valois, widow of the Lancastrian king Henry V. Their grandson, the earl of Richmond, who also inherited Lancastrian blood on his mother's side, became the first Tudor monarch: he won the crown by leading the army that defeated and killed the reigning Yorkist king, Richard III, at the battle of Bosworth Field. The victorious Richmond, crowned King Henry VII in 1485, promptly consolidated his rather shaky claim to the throne by marrying Elizabeth of the house of York, hence effectively uniting the two rival factions.

England's barons, impoverished and divided by the dynastic wars, could not effectively oppose the new power of the Crown, and the leaders of the Church also generally supported royal power. The wily Henry VII was therefore able to counter the multiple and competing power structures characteristic of feudal society and to impose a much stronger central authority and order on the nation. Initiated by the first Tudor sovereign, this consolidation progressed throughout the sixteenth century; by the reign of the last Tudor—Henry's granddaughter, Elizabeth I—though the ruler still needed the consent of Parliament on crucial matters (including the all-important one of levying taxes), the royal court had concentrated in itself much of the nation's power.

The court was a center of culture as well as power: court entertainments such as theater and masque (a sumptuous, elaborately costumed performance of dance, song, and poetry); court fashions in dress and speech; court tastes in painting, music, and poetry—all shaped the taste and the imagination of the country as a whole. Culture and power were not, in any case, easily separable in Tudor England. In a society with no freedom of speech as we understand it and with relatively limited means of mass communication, important public issues were often aired indirectly, through what we might now regard as entertainment, and lyrics that to us seem slight and nonchalant could serve as carefully designed manifestations of rhetorical agility by aspiring courtiers.

Whereas in the Middle Ages noblemen had guarded their power by keeping their distance from London and the king, ruling over semi-independent fiefdoms, in the Tudor era the route to power lay in proximity to the royal body. (One of the coveted positions in the court of Henry VIII was Groom of the Stool, "close stool" being the Tudor term for toilet.) The monarch's chief ministers and favorites were the primary channels through which patronage was dispensed to courtiers who competed for offices in the court, the government bureaucracies, the royal household, the army, the church, and the universities, or who sought titles, grants of land, leases, or similar favors. But if proximity held out the promise of wealth and power, it also harbored danger. Festive evenings with the likes of the ruthless Henry VIII were not occasions for relaxation. The court fostered paranoia, and an attendant obsession with secrecy, spying, duplicity, and betrayal.

Tudor courtiers were torn between the need to protect themselves and the equally pressing need to display themselves. For lessons in the art of intrigue, many no doubt turned to Machiavelli's notorious *Il Principe* (The Prince), with its cool guidance on how power may be gained and kept. For advice on the cultivation and display of the self, they could resort to the still more influential *Il Cortegiano* (The Courtier) by Count Baldassare Castiglione. It was particularly important, Castiglione wrote, to conceal the effort that lay behind elegant accomplishments, so that they would seem natural. In this anxious atmosphere, courtiers became highly practiced at crafting and deciphering graceful words with double or triple meanings. Poets had much to learn from courtiers, the Elizabethan critic George Puttenham observed; indeed many of the best poets in the period, Sir Thomas Wyatt, Sir Philip Sidney, Sir Walter Ralegh, and others, *were* courtiers.

If court culture fostered performances for a small coterie audience, other forces in Tudor England pulled toward a more public sphere. Markets expanded significantly, international trade flourished, and cities throughout the realm experienced a rapid surge in size and importance. London's population in particular soared, from 60,000 in 1520, to 120,000 in 1550, to 375,000 a century later, making it the largest and fastest-growing city not only in England but in all of Europe. Every year in the first half of the seventeenth century about 10,000 people migrated to London from other parts of England—wages in London tended to be around 50 percent higher than in the rest of the country—and it is estimated that one in eight English people lived in London at some point in their lives. Elderly Londoners in the 1590s could barely recognize the city of their childhood; London's boom was one factor among many contributing to the sense of a culture moving at increasing velocity away from its historical roots.

About a decade before Henry VII won his throne, the art of printing from movable metal type, a German invention, had been introduced into England by William Caxton (ca. 1422–1491), who had learned and practiced it in the Low Countries. Though reliable statistics are impossible to come by, literacy seems to have increased during the fifteenth century and still more during the sixteenth, when Protestantism encouraged a direct encounter with the Bible. Printing made books cheaper and more plentiful, providing more opportunity to read and more incentive to learn. The greater availability of books may also have reinforced the trend toward silent reading, a practice that gradually transformed what had been a communal experience into a more intimate encounter with a text.

Yet it would be a mistake to imagine these changes as sudden and dramatic. Manuscripts retained considerable prestige among the elite; throughout the sixteenth century and well into the seventeenth, court poets in particular were wary of the "stigma of print" that might mark their verse as less exclusive. Although Caxton, who was an author and translator as well as a printer, introduced printed books, he attempted to cater to courtly tastes by translating works whose tone was more medieval than modern. Fascination with the old chivalric code of behavior is reflected as well in the jousts and tournaments that continued at court for a century, long after gunpowder had rendered them obsolete. As often in an age of alarming novelty, many people looked back to an idealized past. Indeed the great innovations of the Tudor era—intellectual, governmental, and religious—were all presented, at the time, as attempts to restore lost links with ancient traditions.

RENAISSANCE HUMANISM

During the fifteenth century a few English clerics and government officials had journeyed to Italy and had seen something of the extraordinary cultural and intellectual movement flourishing in the city-states there. That movement, generally known as the Renaissance, involved a rebirth of letters and arts stimulated by the recovery of texts and artifacts from classical antiquity, the development of techniques such as linear perspective, and the creation of powerful new aesthetic practices based on classical models. It also unleashed new ideas and new social, political, and economic forces that gradually displaced the spiritual and communal values of the Middle Ages. To Renaissance intellectuals and artists, the achievements of the pagan philosophers of ancient Greece and Rome came to seem more compelling than the subtle distinctions drawn by medieval Christian theologians. In the brilliant, intensely competitive, and vital world of Leonardo da Vinci and Michelangelo, the submission of the human spirit to penitential discipline gave way to unleashed curiosity, individual self-assertion, and a powerful conviction that man was the measure of all things. Yet the superb human figure placed at the center of the Renaissance worldview was also seen as remarkably malleable. "We have made thee neither of heaven nor of earth, neither mortal nor immortal," God tells Adam, in the Florentine Pico della Mirandola's *Oration on the Dignity of Man* (1486), "so that with freedom of choice and with honor, as though the maker and molder of thyself, thou mayest fashion thyself in whatever shape thou shalt prefer." "As though the maker and molder of thyself": this vision of self-fashioning may be glimpsed in the poetry of Petrarch, the sculpture of Donatello, and the statecraft of Lorenzo de' Medici. But in England it was not until Henry VII's reign brought some measure of political stability that the Renaissance could take root, and it was not until the accession of Henry VIII that it began to flower.

This flowering, when it occurred, came not, as in Italy, in painting, sculpture, and architecture. It came rather in the intellectual program and literary vision known as humanism. More's *Utopia* (1516), with its dream of human existence entirely transformed by a radical change in institutional arrangements, is an extreme instance of a general humanist interest in education: in England and elsewhere, humanism was bound up with struggles over the purposes of education and curriculum reform. The great Dutch humanist Erasmus, who spent some time in England and developed a close friendship with More, was a leader in the assault on what he and others regarded as a hopelessly narrow and outmoded intellectual culture based on scholastic hairsplitting and a dogmatic adherence to the philosophy of Aristotle. English humanists, including John Colet (who, as dean of St. Paul's Cathedral, recast its grammar school on humanist principles), Roger Ascham (tutor to Princess Elizabeth), and Sir Thomas Elyot, wrote treatises on education to promote the kind of learning they regarded as the most suitable preparation for public service. That education—predominantly male and conducted by tutors in wealthy families or in grammar schools—was still ordered according to the subjects of the medieval *trivium* (grammar, logic, and rhetoric) and *quadrivium* (arithmetic, geometry, astronomy, and music), but its focus shifted from training for the Church to the general acquisition of "literature," in the sense both of literacy and of cultural knowledge. For some of the more intellectually ambitious humanists, that knowledge extended to ancient Greek, whose enthusiastic adherents began to challenge the entrenched preeminence of Latin.

Still, at the core of the curriculum remained the study of Latin, the mastery of which was in effect a prolonged male puberty rite involving pain as well as pleasure. Though some educators counseled mildness, punishment was an established part of the pedagogy of the age, and even gifted students could rarely escape recurrent flogging. The purpose was to train the sons of the nobility and gentry to speak and write good Latin, the language of diplomacy, of the professions, and of all higher learning. Their sisters were always educated at home or in other noble houses. They chiefly learned modern languages, religion, music, and needlework, but they very seldom received the thorough training in the ancient languages and classical literature so central to the dominant culture. Through this training, Elizabethan schoolmasters sought to impart facility and rhetorical elegance, but the books their students laboriously pored over were not considered mere exhibitions of literary style: from the *Sententiae Pueriles* (Maxims for Children) for beginners on up through the dramatists Terence, Plautus, and Seneca, the poets Virgil and Horace, and the orator Cicero, the classics were also studied for the moral, political, and philosophical truths they contained. Though originating in pagan times, those truths could, in the opinion of many humanists, be reconciled to the moral vision of Christianity. The result, perplexing for some modern readers, is that pagan gods and goddesses flourish on the pages of even such a devoutly Christian poem as Edmund Spenser's *Faerie Queene*.

Humanists committed to classical learning were faced with the question of whether to write their own works in Latin or in English. To many learned men, influenced both by the humanist exaltation of the classical languages and by the characteristic Renaissance desire for eternal fame, the national languages seemed relatively unstable and ephemeral. Intellectuals had long shared a pan-European world of scientific inquiry, so that works by such English scientists as William Gilbert, William Harvey, and Francis Bacon easily joined those by Nicolaus Copernicus, Johannes Kepler, and Andreas Vesalius in the common linguistic medium of Latin. But throughout Europe

Tudor schoolroom. In this lithograph from the sixteenth century, the pupils sit on "forms," or benches, with few if any desks. As an early school statute explains, "When they have to write, let them use their knees for a table." All the lessons, for the different age groups, are taught in the same room: the younger boys (left) are learning their letters, while the students at the upper right are studying music. The schoolmaster, seated, holds a birch, while the usher, or assistant master, is beating a student. The windows of the schoolroom are set high in the walls, to cut down on distractions. Next to the far pillar is an hourglass used in marking time for various lessons. The school's valuable books are kept in a locked chest, behind the schoolmaster.

nationalism and the expansion of the reading public were steadily strengthening the power and allure of the vernaculars. The famous schoolmaster Richard Mulcaster (ca. 1530–1611), Spenser's teacher, captured this emergent sense of national identity in singing the praises of his native tongue:

> Is it not indeed a marvelous bondage, to become servants to one tongue for learning's sake the most of our time, with loss of most time, whereas we may have the very same treasure in our own tongue, with the gain of more time? our own bearing the joyful title of our liberty and freedom, the Latin tongue remembering us of our thralldom and bondage? I love Rome, but London better; I favor Italy, but England more; I honor the Latin, but I worship the English.

These two impulses—humanist reverence for the classics and English pride in the vernacular language—gave rise to many distinguished translations throughout the century: Homer's *Iliad* and *Odyssey* by George Chapman, Plutarch's *Lives of the Noble Grecians and Romans* by Sir Thomas North, and Ovid's *Metamorphoses* by Arthur Golding. Translators also sought to make available in English the most notable literary works in the modern languages: Castiglione's *Il Cortegiano* by Sir Thomas Hoby, Ariosto's *Orlando furioso* (Orlando mad) by Sir John Harington, and Montaigne's *Essais* by John Florio. The London book trade of the sixteenth century was a thoroughly international affair.

THE REFORMATION

There had long been serious ideological and institutional tensions in the religious life of England, but officially, at least, England in the early sixteenth century had a single religion, Catholicism, whose acknowledged head was the pope in Rome. For its faithful adherents the Roman Catholic Church was the central institution in their lives, a universal and infallible guide to human existence from cradle to grave and on into the life to come. They were instructed by its teachings, corrected by its discipline, sustained by its sacraments, and comforted by its promises. At Mass, its most sacred ritual, the congregation could witness a miracle, as the priest held aloft the Host and uttered the words that transformed the bread and wine into the body and blood of God incarnate. A vast system of confession, pardons, penance, absolution, indulgences, sacred relics, and ceremonies gave the unmarried male clerical hierarchy great power, at once spiritual and material, over their largely illiterate flock. The Bible, the liturgy, and most of the theological discussions were in Latin, which few laypeople could understand; however, religious doctrine and spirituality were mediated to them by the priests, by beautiful church art and music, and by the liturgical ceremonies of daily life—festivals, holy days, baptisms, marriages, exorcisms, and funerals.

Several of the key doctrines and practices of the Catholic Church had been challenged in fourteenth-century England by the teachings of John Wycliffe and his followers, known as Lollards. But the heretical challenge had been ruthlessly suppressed, and the embers of dissent lay largely dormant until they were ignited once again in Germany by Martin Luther, an Augustinian monk and professor of theology at the University of Wittenberg. What began in November 1517 as an academic disputation grew with

The Pope as Antichrist. In this satirical woodcut, the pope, riding the seven-headed Beast of the Apocalypse, holds in his hand a banner on which he urges his followers to be traitors and kill their princes. His message, carried by three froglike devils, flies into the gaping mouths of a knight, a bishop, and a monk. The devils are a reference to Revelation 16.13: "And I saw three unclean spirits like frogs come out of the mouth of the dragon, and out of the mouth of the beast, and out of the mouth of the false prophet." From *Fierie Tryall of God's Saints* (1611; author unknown).

amazing speed into a bitter, far-reaching, and bloody revolt that forever ruptured the unity of Western Christendom.

When Luther rose up against the ancient church, he did so in the name of private conscience enlightened by a personal reading of the Scriptures. A person of formidable intellectual energy, eloquence, and rhetorical violence, Luther charged that the pope and his hierarchy were the servants of Satan and that the Church had degenerated into a corrupt, worldly conspiracy designed to bilk the credulous and subvert secular authority. Salvation depended upon destroying this conspiracy and enabling all of the people to regain direct access to the word of God by means of vernacular translations of the Bible. The common watchwords of the Reformation, as the movement Luther sparked came to be known, were *sola scriptura* and *sola fide*: only the Scriptures (not the Church or tradition or the clerical hierarchy) have authority in matters of religion and should determine what an individual must believe and practice; only the faith of the individual (not good works or the scrupulous observance of religious rituals) can effect a Christian's salvation.

These tenets, heretical in the eyes of the Catholic Church, spread and gathered force, especially in northern Europe, where major leaders like the Swiss pastor Ulrich Zwingli in Zurich and the French theologian John Calvin in Geneva, elaborating various and sometimes conflicting doctrinal principles, organized the populace to overturn the existing church and established new institutional structures. In England, however, the Reformation began less with popular discontent and theological disputation than with dynastic politics and royal greed. Henry VIII, who had received from Pope Leo X the title Defender of the Faith for writing a diatribe against Luther, craved a legitimate son to succeed to the throne, and his queen, Catherine of Aragon, failed to give him one. (Catherine had borne six children, but only a daughter, Mary, survived infancy.) After lengthy negotiations, the pope, under pressure from Catherine's powerful Spanish family, refused to grant the king the divorce he sought in order to marry Anne Boleyn.

A series of momentous events followed, as England lurched away from the Church of Rome. In 1531 Henry forced the entire clergy of England to beg pardon for having usurped royal authority in the administration of canon law (the law that governed such matters as divorce). Two years later Henry's marriage to Catherine was officially declared null and void and Anne Boleyn was crowned queen. The king was promptly excommunicated by the pope, Clement VII. In the following year, a parliamentary Act of Succession required an oath from all adult male subjects confirming the new dynastic settlement. Thomas More and John Fisher, the bishop of Rochester, were among the small number who refused. The Act of Supremacy, passed later in the year, formally declared the king to be "Supreme Head of the Church in England" and again required an oath to this effect. In 1535 and 1536 further acts made it treasonous to refuse the oath of royal supremacy or, as More had tried to do, to remain silent. The first victims were three Carthusian monks who rejected the oath—"How could the king, a layman," said one of them, "be Head of the Church of England?"—and in May 1535 were duly hanged, drawn, and quartered. A few weeks later Fisher and More were convicted and beheaded. Between 1536 and 1539, under the direction of Henry's powerful secretary of state, Thomas Cromwell, England's monasteries were suppressed. Their vast wealth was seized by the Crown and transferred, by either gift or sale, to the king's followers.

Royal defiance of the authority of Rome was a key element in the Reformation but did not by itself constitute the establishment of Protestantism in England. On the contrary, in the same year that Fisher and More were martyred for their adherence to Roman Catholicism, twenty-five Protestants, members of a sect known as Anabaptists, were burned for heresy on a single day. Through most of his reign, Henry remained an equal-opportunity persecutor, pitiless to Catholics loyal to Rome and hostile to many of those who espoused Reformation ideas, though these ideas, aided greatly by the printing press, gradually established themselves on English soil.

Upon Henry's death, in 1547, his son, Edward (by his third wife, Jane Seymour), came to the throne. Both the ten-year-old Edward and his successive Protectors, the dukes of Somerset and Northumberland, were staunch Protestants, and reformers hastened to transform the English Church accordingly. During Edward's brief reign, Thomas Cranmer, the archbishop of Canterbury, formulated the forty-two articles of religion which became the core of Anglican orthodoxy and wrote the first *Book of Common Prayer*, which was officially adopted in 1549 as the basis of English worship services.

The sickly Edward died in 1553, only six years after his accession to the throne, and was succeeded by his half-sister Mary (Henry VIII's daughter by his first wife, Catherine), who immediately took steps to return her kingdom to Roman Catholicism. Though she was unable to get Parliament to agree to return church lands seized under Henry VIII, she restored the Catholic Mass, once again affirmed the authority of the pope, and put down a rebellion that sought to depose her. Seconded by her ardently Catholic husband, Philip II, king of Spain, she initiated a series of religious persecutions that earned her (from her enemies) the name Bloody Mary. Hundreds of Protestants took refuge abroad in cities like Calvin's Geneva; almost three hundred less-fortunate Protestants were condemned as heretics and burned at the stake. Yet for thousands of English men and women, Mary's reign came as a liberation; the rapid restoration of old Catholic ornaments to parish churches all over England indicates that they had not in fact been confiscated or destroyed as ordered, but simply hidden away, in hopes of better times.

Mary died childless in 1558, and her younger half-sister, Elizabeth, became queen. Elizabeth's succession had been by no means assured. For if Protestants regarded as invalid Henry VIII's marriage to Catherine and hence deemed Mary illegitimate, so Catholics regarded as invalid his marriage to Anne Boleyn and hence deemed *her* daughter illegitimate. Henry himself seemed to support both views, since only three years after divorcing Catherine he beheaded Anne on charges of treason and adultery and urged Parliament to invalidate the marriage. Moreover, though during her sister's reign Elizabeth outwardly complied with the official Catholic religious observances, Mary and her advisers rightly suspected her of Protestant leanings, and the young princess's life was in grave danger. Poised and circumspect, Elizabeth warily evaded the traps that were set for her. When she ascended the throne, her actions were scrutinized for some indication of the country's future course. During her coronation procession, when a girl in an allegorical pageant presented her with a Bible in English translation—banned under Mary's reign—Elizabeth kissed the book, held it up reverently, and laid it to her breast. By this simple yet profound (and carefully choreographed) gesture, Elizabeth signaled England's return to the Reformation.

Many English men and women, of all classes, remained loyal to the old Catholic faith, but English authorities under Elizabeth moved steadily, if cautiously, toward ensuring at least an outward conformity to the official Protestant settlement. Recusants, those who refused to attend regular Sunday services in their parish churches, were heavily fined. Anyone who wished to receive a university degree, to be ordained as a priest in the Church of England, or to be named as an officer of the state had to swear an oath to the royal supremacy. Commissioners were sent throughout the land to confirm that religious services were following the officially approved liturgy and to investigate any reported backsliding into Catholic practice or, alternatively, any attempts to introduce reforms more radical than the queen and her bishops had chosen to embrace. For the Protestant exiles who streamed back were eager not only to undo the damage Mary had done but also to carry the Reformation much further than it had gone. A minority, who would come to be known as Puritans, sought to dismantle the church hierarchy, to purge the calendar of folk customs deemed pagan and the church service of ritual practices deemed superstitious, to dress the clergy in simple garb, and, at the extreme edge, to smash "idolatrous" statues, crucifixes, and altarpieces. Throughout her long reign, however, Elizabeth remained cautiously conservative and determined to hold religious zealotry in check.

In the space of a single lifetime, England had gone officially from Roman Catholicism, to Catholicism under the supreme headship of the English king, to a guarded Protestantism, to a more radical Protestantism, to a renewed and aggressive Roman Catholicism, and finally to Protestantism again. Each of these shifts was accompanied by danger, persecution, and death. It was enough to make people wary. Or skeptical. Or extremely agile.

A FEMALE MONARCH IN A MALE WORLD

In the last year of Mary's reign, the Scottish Calvinist minister John Knox thundered against what he called "the monstrous regiment of women." After the Protestant Elizabeth came to the throne the following year, Knox and his religious brethren were less inclined to denounce all female rulers, but in England, as elsewhere in Europe, there remained a widespread conviction that women were unsuited to wield power over men. Many men seem to have regarded the capacity for rational thought as exclusively male; women, they assumed, were led only by their passions. While gentlemen mastered the arts of rhetoric and warfare, gentlewomen were expected to display the virtues of silence and good housekeeping. Among upper-class males, the will to dominate others was acceptable and indeed admired; the same will in women was condemned as a grotesque and dangerous aberration.

Apologists for the queen countered these prejudices by appealing to historical precedent and legal theory. History offered inspiring examples of just female rulers, notably Deborah, the biblical prophetess who had judged Israel. In the legal sphere, Crown lawyers advanced the theory of "the king's two bodies." As England's crowned head, Elizabeth's person was mystically divided between her mortal "body natural" and the immortal "body politic." While the queen's natural body was inevitably subject to the failings of human flesh, the body politic was timeless and perfect. In political terms, therefore, Elizabeth's sex was a matter of no consequence, a thing indifferent.

Elizabeth, who had received a fine humanist education and an extended, dangerous lesson in the art of survival, made it immediately clear that she intended to rule in more than name only. She assembled a group of trustworthy advisers, foremost among them William Cecil (later created Lord Burghley), but she insisted on making many of the crucial decisions herself. Like many Renaissance monarchs, Elizabeth was drawn to the idea of royal absolutism, the theory that ultimate power was quite properly concentrated in her person and indeed that God had appointed her to be His deputy in the kingdom. Opposition to her rule, in this view, was not only a political act but also a kind of impiety, a blasphemous grudging against the will of God. Supporters of absolutism contended that God commands obedience even to manifestly wicked rulers whom He has sent to punish the sinfulness of humankind. Such arguments were routinely made in speeches and political tracts and from the pulpits of churches, where they were incorporated into the *Book of Homilies* that clergymen were required to read out to their congregations.

In reality, Elizabeth's power was not absolute. The government had a network of spies, informers, and *agents provocateurs*, but it lacked a standing army, a national police force, an efficient system of communication, and an extensive bureaucracy. Above all, the queen had limited financial resources and needed to turn periodically to an independent and often recalcitrant Parliament, which by long tradition had the sole right to levy taxes and to grant subsidies. Members of the House of Commons were elected from their boroughs, not appointed by the monarch, and though the queen had considerable influence over their decisions, she could by no means dictate policy. Under these constraints, Elizabeth ruled through a combination of adroit political maneuvering and imperious command, all the while enhancing her authority in the eyes of both court and country by means of an extraordinary cult of love.

"We all loved her," Elizabeth's godson Sir John Harington wrote, with just a touch of irony, a few years after the queen's death, "for she said she loved us." Ambassadors, courtiers, and parliamentarians all submitted to Elizabeth's cult of love, in which the queen's gender was transformed from a potential liability into a significant asset. Those who approached her generally did so on their knees and were expected to address her with the most extravagant compliments; she in turn spoke, when it suited her to do so, in a comparable language of love. The court moved in an atmosphere of romance, with music, dancing, plays, and the elaborate, fancy-dress entertainments called masques. The queen adorned herself in dazzling clothes and rich jewels. When she went on one of her summer "progresses," ceremonial journeys through her land, she looked like an exotic, sacred image in a religious cult of love, and her noble hosts virtually bankrupted themselves to lavish upon her the costliest pleasures. England's leading artists, such as the poet Edmund Spenser and the painter Nicholas Hilliard, enlisted themselves in the celebration of Elizabeth's mystery, likening her to the goddesses of mythology and the heroines of the Bible: Diana, Astraea, Cynthia, Deborah. The cultural sources of the cult of Elizabeth were both secular (her courtiers could pine for her as the cruelly chaste mistress celebrated in Petrarchan love poetry) and sacred (the veneration that under Catholicism had been due to the Virgin Mary could now be directed toward England's semi-divine queen).

There was a sober, even grim aspect to these poetical fantasies: Elizabeth was brilliant at playing off one dangerous faction against another, now turning her gracious smiles on one favorite, now honoring his hated rival, now suddenly looking elsewhere and raising an obscure upstart to royal favor. And when she was disobeyed or when she felt that her prerogatives had been challenged, she was capable of an anger that, as Harington put it, "left no doubtings whose daughter she was." Thus when Sir Walter Ralegh, one of the queen's glittering favorites, married without her knowledge and consent, he found himself promptly imprisoned in the Tower of London. Or when the Protestant polemicist John Stubbes ventured to publish a pamphlet stridently denouncing the queen's proposed marriage to the French Catholic duke of Anjou, Stubbes and his publisher were arrested and had their right hands chopped off. (After receiving the blow, the now prudent Stubbes lifted his hat with his remaining hand and cried, "God save the Queen!")

THE KINGDOM IN DANGER

Beset by Catholic and Protestant extremists, Elizabeth contrived to forge a moderate compromise that enabled her realm to avert the massacres and civil wars that poisoned France and other countries on the Continent. But menace was never far off, and there were continual fears of conspiracy, rebellion, and assassination. Suspicion swirled around Elizabeth's second cousin Mary,

Queen of Scots, who had been driven from her own kingdom in 1568 and had taken refuge in England. The presence, under a kind of house arrest, of a Catholic queen with a plausible claim to the English throne was the source of widespread anxiety and helped generate recurrent rumors of plots. Some of these were real enough, others imaginary, still others fabricated by the secret agents of the government's intelligence service under the direction of Sir Francis Walsingham. Fears of Catholic conspiracies intensified greatly after Spanish imperial armies invaded the Netherlands in order to stamp out Protestant rebels (1567), after the St. Bartholomew's Day Massacre of Protestants (Huguenots) in France (1572), and after the assassination of Europe's other major Protestant leader, William of Orange (1584).

The queen's life seemed to be in even greater danger after Pope Gregory XIII's proclamation in 1580 that the assassination of the great heretic Elizabeth (who had been excommunicated a decade before) would not constitute a mortal sin. The immediate effect of the proclamation was to make life more difficult for English Catholics, most of whom were loyal to the queen but who fell under grave suspicion. Suspicion was heightened by the clandestine presence of English Jesuits, trained at seminaries abroad and smuggled back into England to serve the Roman Catholic cause. When, after several botched conspiracies had been disclosed, Elizabeth's spymaster Walsingham unearthed another assassination plot, in the correspondence between the Queen of Scots and the Catholic Anthony Babington, the wretched Mary's fate was sealed. After a public display of vacillation and perhaps with genuine regret, Elizabeth signed the death warrant, and her cousin was beheaded.

The long-anticipated military confrontation with Catholic Spain was now unavoidable. Elizabeth learned that Philip II, her former brother-in-law and one-time suitor, was preparing to send an enormous fleet against her island realm. The Armada was to sail first to the Netherlands, where a Spanish army would be waiting to embark and invade England. Barring its way was England's small fleet of well-armed and highly maneuverable fighting vessels, backed up by ships from the merchant navy. The Invincible Armada reached English waters in July 1588, only to be routed in one of the most famous and decisive naval battles in European history. Then, in what many viewed as an act of God on behalf of Protestant England, the Spanish fleet was dispersed and all but destroyed by violent storms.

As England braced itself to withstand the land invasion that never materialized, Elizabeth appeared in person to review a detachment of soldiers assembled at Tilbury, on the Thames estuary. Dressed in a white gown and a silver breastplate, she declared that though some among her councilors had urged her not to appear before a large crowd of armed men, she would never fail to trust the loyalty of her faithful and loving subjects. Nor did she fear the Spanish armies. "I know I have the body but of a weak and feeble woman," Elizabeth declared, "but I have the heart and stomach [i.e., valor] of a king, and of a king of England too." In this celebrated, carefully publicized speech, Elizabeth displayed many of her most memorable qualities: her self-consciously theatrical command of grand public occasions, her subtle blending of magniloquent rhetoric and the language of love, her strategic appropriation of traditionally masculine qualities, and her great personal courage. "We princes," she once remarked, "are set on stages in the sight and view of all the world."

Armada Portrait. This portrait of Queen Elizabeth, painted ca. 1588–89, is attributed to George Gower. Through the windows to the left and right can be glimpsed the arrival and then the defeat of the Spanish Armada, wrecked in violent storms. The queen, glowing with the pearls that symbolized her chastity, rests her hand on a globe, her fingers in effect claiming the Americas for her empire.

THE ENGLISH AND OTHERNESS

In 1485, most English people would have devoted little thought to their national identity. If asked to describe their sense of belonging, they would probably have spoken of the international community of Christendom and of their local region, such as Kent or Cornwall. The extraordinary events of the Tudor era, from the encounter with the New World to the break with Rome, made many people newly aware and proud of their Englishness. At the same time, they began to perceive those who lay outside the national community in new (and often negative) ways. Like most national communities, the English defined themselves largely in terms of what or who they were not. In the wake of the Reformation, the most prominent "others" were those who had until recently been more or less the same, that is, the Catholics of western Christendom. But other groups were also instrumental in the project of English self-definition.

Elizabethan London had a large population of resident aliens, mainly artisans and merchants and their families, from Portugal, Italy, Spain, Germany, and, above all, France and the Netherlands. Many of these people were Protestant refugees, and they were accorded some legal and economic protection by the government. But they were not always welcome to the local populace. Throughout the sixteenth century, London was the site of repeated demonstrations and, on occasion, bloody riots against the communities of foreign artisans, who were accused of taking jobs away from Englishmen. There was widespread hostility as well toward the Welsh, the Scots, and above all the Irish, whom the English had for centuries been struggling unsuccessfully to subdue. The kings of England claimed to be rulers of Ireland, but in reality they effectively controlled only a small area known as the Pale, extending north from Dublin. The great majority of the Irish population remained stubbornly Catholic and, despite endlessly reiterated English repression, burning of villages, destruction of crops, seizure of land, and massacres, incorrigibly independent.

Medieval England's Jewish population, the recurrent object of persecution, extortion, and massacre, had been officially expelled by King Edward I in 1290—the earliest such mass expulsion in Europe—but Elizabethan England harbored a tiny number of Jews or Jewish converts to Christianity. They were the objects of suspicion and hostility. Elizabethans appear to have been fascinated by Jews and Judaism but quite uncertain whether the terms referred to a people, a foreign nation, a set of strange practices, a living faith, a defunct religion, a villainous conspiracy, or a messianic inheritance. Protestant Reformers brooded deeply on the Hebraic origins of Christianity; government officials ordered the arrest of those "suspected to be Jews"; villagers paid pennies to itinerant fortune-tellers who claimed to be descended from Abraham or masters of kabbalistic mysteries; and London playgoers enjoyed the spectacle of the downfall of the wicked Barabas in Christopher Marlowe's *The Jew of Malta* and the forced conversion of Shylock in Shakespeare's *The Merchant of Venice*. Jews were not officially permitted to resettle in England until the middle of the seventeenth century, and even then their legal status was ambiguous.

Sixteenth-century England also had a small African population, whose skin color was the subject of pseudoscientific speculation and theological debate. Some Elizabethans believed that Africans' blackness resulted from the climate of the regions where they lived, where, as one traveler put it, they were "so scorched and vexed with the heat of the sun, that in many places they curse it when it riseth." Others held that blackness was a

Etching of a black woman, 1645, by Wenceslaus Hollar. The Bohemian-born Hollar lived and worked for most of his career in Antwerp and in London. He drew portraits of many men and women, including this sympathetic depiction of a black woman, probably a servant.

curse inherited from their forefather Cush, the son of Ham (who had, according to Genesis, wickedly exposed the nakedness of his drunken father, Noah). George Best, a proponent of this theory of inherited skin color, reported that "I myself have seen an Ethiopian as black as coal brought into England, who taking a fair English woman to wife, begat a son in all respects as black as the father was, although England were his native country, and an English woman his mother: whereby it seemeth this blackness proceedeth rather of some natural infection of that man."

As the word "infection" suggests, Elizabethans frequently regarded blackness as a physical defect, though the black people who lived in England and Scotland throughout the sixteenth century were also treated as exotic curiosities. At his marriage to Anne of Denmark, James VI of Scotland (the son of Mary, Queen of Scots; as James I of England, he succeeded Elizabeth, in 1603) entertained his bride and her family by commanding four naked black youths to dance before him in the snow. (The youths died of exposure shortly afterward.) In 1594, in the festivities celebrating the baptism of James's son, a "Black-Moor" entered pulling an elaborately decorated chariot that was, in the original plan, supposed to be pulled by a lion. In England there was a black trumpeter in the courts of Henry VII and Henry VIII, while Elizabeth had at least two black servants, one an entertainer, the other a page. Africans became increasingly fashionable as servants in aristocratic and gentle households in the last decades of the sixteenth century.

Some of these Africans were almost certainly slaves, though the legal status of slavery in England was ambiguous. In Cartwright's Case (1569), the court ruled "that England was too Pure an Air for Slaves to breathe in," but there is evidence that black slaves were owned in Elizabethan and Jacobean England. Moreover, by the mid-sixteenth century the English had become involved in the profitable trade that carried African slaves to the New World. In 1562 John Hawkins embarked on his first slaving voyage, transporting some three hundred Africans from the Guinea coast to Hispaniola, where they were sold for ten thousand pounds. Elizabeth is reported to have said that this venture was "detestable, and would call down the Vengeance of Heaven upon the Undertakers." Nevertheless, she invested profitably in Hawkins's subsequent voyages and loaned him ships.

Elizabeth also invested in other enterprises that combined aggressive nationalism and the pursuit of profit. In 1493 the pope had divided the New World between the Spanish and the Portuguese by drawing a line from pole to pole (hence Brazil speaks Portuguese today and the rest of Latin America speaks Spanish): the English were not in the picture. But by the end of Edward VI's reign the Company of Merchant Adventurers was founded, and Englishmen began to explore Asia and North America. Some of these adventurers turned to piracy, preying on Spanish ships that were returning laden with wealth extracted from Spain's New World possessions. (The pope had ruled that the Indians were human beings—and hence could be converted to Christianity—but the ruling did nothing to prevent their enslavement and brutal exploitation.) English acts of piracy soon became a private undeclared war, with the queen and her courtiers covertly investing in the raids but accepting no responsibility for them. The greatest of many astounding exploits was the voyage of Francis Drake (1577–80): he sailed through the Strait of Magellan, pillaged Spanish towns on the Pacific, reached as far north as San Francisco, crossed to the Philippines, and returned around the Cape of Good Hope; he came back with a million pounds in treasure, and his investors earned a dividend of 5,000 percent. Queen Elizabeth knighted him on the deck of his ship, *The Golden Hind.*

WRITERS, PRINTERS, AND PATRONS

The association between literature and print, so natural to us, was less immediate in the sixteenth century. Poetry in particular frequently circulated in manuscript, copied by reader after reader into personal anthologies—commonplace books—or reproduced by professional scribes for a fee. The texts that have come down to us in printed form often bear an uncertain relation to authorial manuscripts, and were frequently published only posthumously. The career of professional writer in sixteenth-century England was almost impossible: there was no such thing as author's copyright, no royalties paid to an author according to the sales of his book, and virtually no notion that anyone could make a decent living through the creation of works of literature. Writers sold their manuscripts to the printer or bookseller outright, for what now seem like ridiculously low prices. The churchyard of St. Paul's Cathedral in London was lined with booksellers' shops: dissolved chantries were taken over by bookshops in the 1540s, church officials leased out their residences near the church's north door to members of the Stationers' Company (the guild whose members had the exclusive right to own printing presses), and eventually bookstores two stories high and more filled the bays between the cathedral's buttresses. St. Paul's was the main center of business in the capital, with the church itself serving as a meeting place, and its columns as bulletin boards; publishers would post there, and elsewhere in the city, the title pages of new books as advertisements. Those title pages listed the wholesaler for the work, but customers could have bought popular books at most of the shops in St. Paul's Yard. The publishing business was not entirely contained in that busy space. Some stationers were only printers, merely working as contractors for publishers, and their printshops were located all over the city, often in the owner's residence.

Freedom of the press did not exist. Before Elizabeth's reign, state control of printed books was poorly organized, although licensing efforts had been underway since 1538. In 1557, however, the Stationers' Company received its charter, and became responsible for the licensing of books. Two years later, the government commanded the stationers to license only books that had been approved by either six privy councilors or the archbishop of Canterbury and the bishop of London. Despite these seemingly strict regulations, "scandalous, malicious, schismatical, and heretical" works were never effectively suppressed. Though there were occasional show trials and horrendous punishments—the printer William Carter was hanged for treason in 1584 because he had published a Catholic pamphlet; the Protestant separatists John Penry, Henry Barrow, and John Greenwood were executed in 1593 under a statute that made it a capital offense to "devise and write, print or set forth, any manner of book . . . letter, or writing containing false, seditious, and slanderous matter to the defamation of the Queen's Majesty"—active censorship was not as frequent or thorough as we might expect.

The censors largely focused their attention on works of history, which often had political implications for the present, and on religious treatises. In this, they shared the public's taste. Plays and secular poetry occasionally sold well (Shakespeare's *Henry IV, Part 1* was printed 7 times in 25 years), but they could not compete with publishing blockbusters such as *The Plain Man's Pathway* (16 editions in 25 years), let alone *The Psalms in English Meter*, published 124 times between 1583 and 1608. Publishers were largely interested in profit margins, and the predominance of devotional texts among the surviving books from the period attests to their greater marketability. The format in which works of literature were usually published is also telling. We normally find plays and poetry in quartos (or octavos), small volumes which had four (or eight) pages printed on each side of a sheet which was then folded twice (or three times) and stitched together with other such folded sheets to form the book. The more imposing folio format (in which the paper was folded only once, at two pages per side of a sheet) tended to be reserved not just for longer works but for those regarded as meriting especially respectful treatment. In 1577, Raphael Holinshed's massive history *The Chronicles of England, Scotlande, and Irelande* appeared in a woodcut-illustrated folio; ten years later, a second edition was published, again in the large format. In contrast, Edmund Spenser's huge poem *The Faerie Queene* was printed as a quarto both in 1590 and in 1596. A decade after his death, though, as the poet's reputation grew, his epic appeared again (1609), this time as a folio.

Elizabethan writers of exalted social standing, like the earl of Surrey or Sir Philip Sidney, thought of themselves as courtiers, statesmen, and landowners; poetry was for them an indispensable social grace and a deeply pleasurable, exalted form of play. Writers of lower rank, such as Samuel Daniel and Michael Drayton, sought careers as civil servants, secretaries, tutors, and clerics; they might take up more or less permanent residence in a noble household, or, more casually, offer their literary work to actual or prospective patrons, in the hope of protection, career advancement, or financial reward. Ambitious authors eager to rise from threadbare obscurity often looked to the court for livelihood, notice, and encouragement, but their great expectations generally proved chimerical. "A thousand hopes, but all nothing," wailed John Lyly, alluding to his long wait for the office of Master of the Revels, "a hundred promises but yet nothing."

Financial rewards for writing prose or poetry came mostly in the form of gifts from wealthy patrons, who sought to enhance their status and gratify their vanity through the achievements and lavish praises of their clients. Some Elizabethan patrons, though, were well-educated humanists motivated by aesthetic interests, and with them, patronage extended beyond financial support to the creation of lively literary and intellectual circles. Poems by Daniel, Ben Jonson, Aemilia Lanyer, and others bear witness to the sustaining intelligence and sophistication, as well as the generosity, of their benefactors. But the experience of Robert Greene is perhaps equally revealing: the fact that he had sixteen different patrons for seventeen books suggests that he did not find much favor or support from any one of them. Indeed, a practice grew up of printing off several dedications to be inserted into particular copies of a book, so that an impecunious author could deceive each of several patrons into thinking that he or she was the uniquely fortunate person to be honored by the volume.

In addition to the court and great families as dispensers of patronage, the city of London and the two universities also had a substantial impact on the period's literature. London was the center of the book trade, the nursery of a fledgling middle-class reading public, and, most important, the home of the public theaters. Before Elizabeth's time, the universities were mainly devoted to educating the clergy, and that remained an important part of their function. But in the second half of the century, the sons of the gentry and the aristocracy were going in increasing numbers to the universities and the Inns of Court (law schools), not in order to take religious orders or to practice law but to prepare for public service or the management of their estates. Other, less affluent students, such as Marlowe and Spenser, attended Oxford or Cambridge on scholarship. A group of graduates, including Thomas Nashe, Robert Greene, and George Peele, enlivened the literary scene in London in the 1590s, but the precarious lives of these so-called "university wits" testify to the difficulties they encountered in their quixotic attempt to survive by their writing skill. The diary of Philip Henslowe, a leading theatrical manager, has entry after entry showing university graduates in prison or in debt or at best eking out a miserable existence patching plays.

Women had no access to grammar schools, the universities, or the Inns of Court. While Protestantism, with its emphasis on reading Scripture, certainly helped to improve female literacy in the sixteenth century, girls were rarely encouraged to pursue their studies. Indeed, while girls were increasingly taught to read, they were not necessarily taught to write, for the latter skill in women was considered to be at the very least useless, at the worst dangerous. When the prominent humanist Sir Thomas Smith thought of how he should describe his country's social order, he declared that "we do reject women, as those whom nature hath made to keep home and to nourish their family and children, and not to meddle with matters abroad, nor to bear office in a city or commonwealth." Then, with a kind of nervous glance over his shoulder, he made an exception of those few in whom "the blood is respected, not the age nor the sex": for example, the queen. Every piece of writing by a woman from this period is a triumph over nearly impossible odds.

TUDOR STYLE: ORNAMENT, PLAINNESS, AND WONDER

Renaissance literature is the product of a rhetorical culture, a culture steeped in the arts of persuasion and trained to process complex verbal signals. (The contemporary equivalent would be the ease with which we deal with complex visual signals, effortlessly processing such devices as fade-out, montage, crosscutting, and morphing.) In 1512, Erasmus published a work called *De copia* that taught its readers how to cultivate "copiousness," verbal richness, in discourse. The work obligingly provides, as a sample, a list of 144 different ways of saying "Thank you for your letter."

In Renaissance England, certain syntactic forms or patterns of words known as "figures" (also called "schemes") were shaped and repeated in order to confer beauty or heighten expressive power. Figures were usually known by their Greek and Latin names, though in an Elizabethan rhetorical manual, *The Arte of English Poesie*, George Puttenham made a valiant if short-lived attempt to give them English equivalents, such as "Hyperbole, or the Overreacher" and "Ironia, or the Dry Mock." Those who received a grammar-school education throughout Europe at almost any point between the Roman Empire and the eighteenth century probably knew by heart the names of up to one hundred such figures, just as they knew by heart their multiplication tables. According to one scholar's count, William Shakespeare knew and made use of about two hundred.

As certain grotesquely inflated Renaissance texts attest, lessons from *De copia* and similar rhetorical guides could encourage prolixity and verbal self-display. Elizabethans had a taste for elaborate ornament in language as in clothing, jewelry, and furniture, and, if we are to appreciate their accomplishments, it helps to set aside the modern preference, particularly in prose, for unadorned simplicity and directness. When, in one of the age's most fashionable works of prose fiction, John Lyly wishes to explain that the vices of his young hero, Euphues, are tarnishing his virtues, he offers a small flood of synonymous images: "The freshest colors soonest fade, the teenest [i.e., keenest] razor soonest turneth his edge, the finest cloth is soonest eaten with moths." Lyly's multiplication of balanced rhetorical figures sparked a small literary craze known as "Euphuism," which was soon ridiculed by Shakespeare and others for its formulaic excesses. Yet the multiplication of figures was a source of deep-rooted pleasure in rhetorical culture, and most of the greatest Renaissance writers used it to extraordinary effect. Consider, for example, the succession of images in Shakespeare's sonnet 73:

> That time of year thou mayst in me behold
> When yellow leaves, or none, or few, do hang
> Upon those boughs which shake against the cold,
> Bare ruined choirs, where late the sweet birds sang.
> In me thou seest the twilight of such day
> As after sunset fadeth in the west;
> Which by and by black night doth take away,
> Death's second self that seals up all in rest.
> In me thou seest the glowing of such fire
> That on the ashes of his youth doth lie,
> As the deathbed whereon it must expire,
> Consumed with that which it was nourished by.
>   This thou perceiv'st, which makes thy love more strong,
>   To love that well, which thou must leave ere long.

What seems merely repetitious in Lyly here becomes a subtle, poignant amplification of the perception of decay, through the succession of images from winter (or late fall) to twilight to the last glow of a dying fire. Each of these images is in turn sensitively explored, so that, for example, the season is figured by bare boughs that shiver, as if they were human, and then these anthropomorphized tree branches in turn are figured as the ruined choirs of a church where services were once sung. No sooner is the image of singers in a church choir evoked than these singers are instantaneously transmuted back into the songbirds who, in an earlier season, had sat upon the boughs, while these sweet birds in turn conjure up the poet's own vanished youth. And this nostalgic gaze extends, at least glancingly, to the chancels of the Catholic abbeys reduced to ruins by Protestant iconoclasm and the dissolution of the monasteries. All of this within the first four lines: here and elsewhere Shakespeare, along with other poets of his time, contrives to freight the small compass and tight formal constraints of the sonnet—fourteen lines of rhymed iambic pentameter—with remarkable emotional intensity, psychological nuance, and imagistic complexity. The effect is what Christopher Marlowe called "infinite riches in a little room."

Elizabethans were certainly capable of admiring plainness of speech—in *King Lear* Shakespeare contrasts the severe directness of the virtuous Cordelia to the "glib and oily art" of her wicked sisters—and such poets as George Gascoigne, Thomas Nashe, and, in the early seventeenth century, Ben Jonson wrote restrained, aphoristic, moralizing lyrics in a plain style whose power depends precisely on the avoidance of richly figurative verbal pyrotechnics. This power is readily apparent in the wintry spareness of Nashe's "A Litany in Time of Plague," with its grim refrain:

> Wit with his wantonness
> Tasteth death's bitterness;
> Hell's executioner
> Hath no ears for to hear
> What vain art can reply.
> I am sick, I must die.
>   Lord, have mercy on us!

Here the linguistic playfulness beloved by Elizabethan culture is scorned as an ineffectual "vain art" to which the executioner, death, is utterly indifferent.

But here and in other plain-style poetry, the somber, lapidary effect depends on a tacit recognition of the allure of the suppleness, grace, and sweet harmony that the dominant literary artists of the period so assiduously cultivated. Poetry, writes Puttenham, is "more delicate to the ear than prose is, because it is more current and slipper upon the tongue [i.e., flowing and easily pronounced], and withal tunable and melodious, as a kind of Music, and therefore may be termed a musical speech or utterance." The sixteenth century was an age of superb vocal music. The renowned composers William Byrd, Thomas Morley, John Dowland, and others scarcely less distinguished, wrote a rich profusion of madrigals (part songs for two to eight voices, unaccompanied) and airs (songs for solo voice, generally accompanied by the lute). These works, along with hymns, popular ballads, rounds, catches, and other forms of song, enjoyed immense popularity, not only in the royal court, where musical skill was regarded as an important accomplishment, and in aristocratic households, where professional musicians were employed as entertainers, but also in less exalted social circles. In his *Plain and Easy Introduction to Practical Music* (1597), Morley tells a story of social humiliation at a failure to perform that suggests that a well-educated Elizabethan was expected to be able to sight-sing. Even if this is an exaggeration in the interest of book sales, there is evidence of impressively widespread musical literacy, a literacy reflected in a splendid array of music for the lute, viol, recorder, harp, and virginal, as well as vocal music.

Many sixteenth-century poems were written to be set to music, but even those that were not often aspire in their metrical and syllabic virtuosity to the complex pleasures of madrigals or to the sweet fluency of airs. In poetry and music, as in gardens, architecture, and dance, Elizabethans had a taste for elaborate, intricate, but perfectly regular designs. They admired form, valued the artist's manifest control of the medium, and took pleasure in the highly patterned surfaces of things. Modern responses to art often evidence a suspicion of surfaces, impatience with order, the desire to rip away the mask in order to discover a hidden core of experiential truth: these responses are far less evident in Renaissance aesthetics than is a delight in pattern. Indeed many writers of the time expressed the faith that the universe itself had in its basic construction the beauty, concord, and harmonious order of a poem or a piece of music. "The world is made by Symmetry and proportion," wrote Thomas Campion, who was both a poet and a composer, "and is in that respect compared to Music, and Music to Poetry." The design of an exquisite work of art is deeply linked in this view to the design of the cosmos.

Such an emphasis on conspicuous pattern might seem to encourage an art as stiff as the starched ruffs that ladies and gentlemen wore around their necks, but the period's fascination with order was conjoined with a profound interest in persuasively conveying the movements of the mind and heart. Syntax in the sixteenth century was looser, more flexible than our own and punctuation less systematic. If the effect is sometimes confusing, it also enabled writers to follow the twists and turns of thought or perception. Consider, for example, Roger Ascham's account, in his book on archery, of a day in which he saw the wind blowing the new-fallen snow:

> That morning the sun shone bright and clear, the wind was whistling aloft, and sharp according to the time of the year. The snow in the highway lay loose and trodden with horse feet: so as the wind blew, it took the loose snow with it, and made it so slide upon the snow in the field which was hard and crusted by reason of the frost overnight, that thereby I might see very well, the whole nature of the wind as it blew that day. And I had a great delight and pleasure to mark it, which maketh me now far better to remember it. Sometime the wind would be not past two yards broad, and so it would carry the snow as far as I could see. Another time the snow would blow over half the field at once. Sometime the snow would tumble softly, by and by it would fly wonderful fast. And this I perceived also, that the wind goeth by streams and not whole together. . . . And that which was the most marvel of all, at one time two drifts of snow flew, the one of the West into the East, the other out of the North into the East: And I saw two winds by reason of the snow the one cross over the other, as it had been two highways. . . . The more uncertain and deceivable the wind is, the more heed must a wise Archer give to know the guiles of it.

What is delightful here is not only the author's moment of sharpened perception but his confidence that this moment—a glimpse of baffling complexity and uncertainty—can be captured in the restless succession of sentences and then neatly summed up in the pithy conclusion. (This effect parallels that of the couplet that sums up the complexities of a Shakespearean sonnet.) A similar confidence emanates from Sir Walter Ralegh's deeply melancholy, deeply ironic apostrophe to Death at the close of *The History of the World*, written when he was a prisoner in the Tower of London:

> O eloquent, just, and mighty Death! Whom none could advise, thou hast persuaded; what none hath dared, thou hast done; and whom all the world hath flattered, thou only hast cast out of the world and despised;

thou hast drawn together all the far-stretched greatness, all the pride, cruelty, and ambition of man, and covered it all over with these two narrow words: *Hic jacet!* [Here lies]

Death is triumphant here, but so is Ralegh's eloquent, just, and mighty language.

The sense of *wonder* that animates both of these exuberant prose passages—as if the world were being seen clearly and distinctly for the first time—characterizes much of the period's poetry as well. The mood need not always be solemn. One can sense laughter, for example, rippling just below the surface of Marlowe's admiring description of the beautiful maiden Hero's boots:

> Buskins of shells all silvered usèd she,
> And branched with blushing coral to the knee,
> Where sparrows perched, of hollow pearl and gold,
> Such as the world would wonder to behold;
> Those with sweet water oft her handmaid fills;
> Which, as she went, would chirrup through the bills.

Seashells were beloved by Renaissance collectors because their intricate designs, functionally inexplicable, seemed the works of an ingenious, infinitely playful craftsman. Typically, the shells did not simply stand by themselves in cabinets but were gilded or silvered and then turned into other objects: cups, miniature ships, or, in Marlowe's fantasy, boots further decorated with coral and mechanical sparrows made of conspicuously precious materials and designed, as he puts it deliciously, to "chirrup." The poet knows perfectly well that the boots would be implausible footwear in the real world, but he invites us into an imaginary world of passion, a world in which the heroine's costume includes a skirt "whereon was many a stain, / Made with the blood of wretched lovers slain" and a veil of "artificial flowers and leaves, / Whose workmanship both man and beast deceives." The veil reflects an admiration for an art of successful imitation—after all, bees are said to look in vain for honey amidst the artificial flowers—but it is cunning illusion rather than realism that excites Marlowe's wonder. Renaissance poetry is interested not in representational accuracy but in the magical power of exquisite workmanship to draw its readers into fabricated worlds.

In his *Defense of Poesy*, the most important work of literary criticism in sixteenth-century England, Sidney claims that this magical power is also a moral power. All other arts, he argues, are subjected to fallen, imperfect nature, but the poet alone is free to range "within the zodiac of his own wit" and create a second nature, superior to the one we are condemned to inhabit: "Her world is brazen, the poets only deliver a golden." The poet's golden world in this account is not an escapist fantasy; it is a model to be emulated in actual life, an ideal to be brought into reality as completely as possible. It is difficult to say, of course, how seriously this project of realization was taken—though the circumstances of Sidney's own death suggest that he may have been attempting to enact on the battlefield an ideal image of Protestant chivalry. A didactic role for poetry is, in any case, urged not by Sidney alone but by most Elizabethan poets. Human sinfulness has corrupted life, robbing it of the sweet wholesomeness that it had once possessed in Eden, but poetry can mark the way back to a more virtuous and fulfilled existence. And not only mark the way: poetry, Sidney and others argue, has a unique persuasive force that shatters inertia and impels readers toward the good they glimpse in its ravishing lines.

This force, attributed to the energy and vividness of figurative language, made poetry a fitting instrument not only for such high-minded enterprises as moral exhortation, prayer, and praise, and for such uplifting narratives as the legends of religious and national heroes, but also for such verbal actions as cursing, lamenting, flattering, and seducing. The almost inexhaustible range of motives was given some order by literary conventions that functioned as shared cultural codes, enabling poets to elicit particular responses from readers and to relate their words to other times, other languages, and other cultures. Among the most prominent of the clusters of conventions in the period were those that defined the major literary modes (or "kinds," as Sidney terms them): pastoral, heroic, lyric, satiric, elegiac, tragic, and comic. They helped to shape subject matter, attitude, tone, and values, and in some cases—sonnet, verse epistle, epigram, funeral elegy, and masque, to name a few—they also governed formal structure, meter, style, length, and occasion. We can glimpse some of the ways in which these literary codes worked by looking briefly at two that are, for modern readers, among the least familiar: pastoral and heroic.

The conventions of the pastoral mode present a world inhabited by shepherds and shepherdesses who are concerned not just to tend their flocks but to fall in love and to engage in friendly singing contests. The mode celebrated leisure, humility, and contentment, exalting the simple country life over the city and its business, the military camp and its violence, the court and its burdens of rule. Pastoral motifs could be deployed in different genres. Pastoral songs commonly expressed the joys of the shepherd's life or his disappointment in love. Pastoral dialogues between shepherds might conceal serious, satiric comment on abuses in the great world under the guise of homely, local concerns. There were pastoral funeral elegies, pastoral dramas, pastoral romances (prose fiction), and even pastoral episodes within epics. The most famous pastoral poem of the period is Marlowe's "The Passionate Shepherd to His Love," an erotic invitation whose promise of gold buckles, coral clasps, and amber studs serves to remind us that, however much it sings of naïve innocence, the mode is ineradicably sophisticated and urban.

With its rustic characters, simple concerns, and modest scope, the pastoral mode was regarded as situated at the opposite extreme from heroic, with its values of honor, martial courage, loyalty, leadership, and endurance, and its glorification of a nation or people. The chief genre here was the epic, typically a long, ambitious poem in the high style, based on a heroic story from the nation's distant past and imitating Homer and Virgil in structure and motifs. Renaissance poets throughout Europe undertook to honor their nations and their vernacular languages by writing this most prestigious kind of poetry. In sixteenth-century England the major success in heroic poetry is Spenser's *Faerie Queene*. Yet the success of *The Faerie Queene* owes much to the fact that the poem is a generic hybrid, in which the conventions of classical epic mingle with those of romance, medieval allegory, pastoral, satire, mythological narrative, comedy, philosophical meditation, and many others in a strange, wonderful blend. The spectacular mixing of genres in Spenser's poem is only an extreme instance of a general Elizabethan indifference to the generic purity admired by writers, principally on the Continent, who adhered to Aristotle's *Poetics*. Where such neoclassicists attempted to observe rigid stylistic boundaries, English poets tended to approach the different genres in the spirit of Sidney's inclusivism: "if severed they be good, the conjunction cannot be hurtful."

THE ELIZABETHAN THEATER

If Sidney welcomed the experimental intertwining of genres in both poetry and prose—and his own *Arcadia*, a prose romance incorporating both pastoral and heroic elements, confirms that he did—there was one place where he found it absurd: the theater. He condemned the conjunction of high and low characters in "mongrel" tragicomedies that mingled "kings and clowns." Moreover, in the spirit of neoclassical advocacy of the "dramatic unities," Sidney disliked the ease with which the action on the bare stage ("where you shall have Asia of the one side, and Afric of the other") violated the laws of time and space. "Now you shall have three ladies walk to gather flowers," he writes in *The Defense of Poesy*, "and then we must believe the stage to be a garden. By and by we hear news of shipwreck in the same place: and then we are to blame if we accept it not for a rock." The irony is that this mocking account, written probably in 1579, anticipates by a few years the stupendous achievements of Marlowe and Shakespeare, whose plays joyously break every rule that Sidney thought it essential to observe.

A permanent, freestanding public theater in England dates only from Shakespeare's own lifetime. A London playhouse, the Red Lion, is first mentioned in 1567, and James Burbage's playhouse, The Theater, was built in 1576. But it is quite misleading to identify English drama exclusively with the new, specially constructed playhouses, for in fact there was a rich and vital theatrical tradition in England stretching back for centuries. Townspeople in late medieval England mounted elaborate cycles of plays (sometimes called "mystery plays") depicting the great biblical stories, from the creation of the world to Christ's Passion and its miraculous aftermath. Many of these plays have been lost, but those that survive, as the selection in this anthology demonstrates, include magnificent and complex works of art. At once civic and religious festivals, the cycles continued to be performed into the reign of Elizabeth, but their close links to popular Catholic piety led Protestant authorities in the later sixteenth century to suppress them.

Early English theater was not restricted to these annual festivals. Performers acted in town halls and the halls of guilds and aristocratic mansions, on scaffolds erected in town squares and marketplaces, on pageant wagons in the streets, and in innyards. By the fifteenth century, and probably earlier, there were organized companies of players traveling under noble patronage. Such companies earned a precarious living providing amusement, while enhancing the prestige of the patron whose livery they wore and whose protection they enjoyed. (Otherwise, by statutes enjoining productive labor, actors without another, ordinary trade could have been classified as vagabonds and whipped or branded.) This practice explains why the professional acting companies of Shakespeare's time, including Shakespeare's own, attached themselves to a nobleman and were technically his servants (the Lord Chamberlain's Men, the Lord Admiral's Men, etc.), even though virtually all their time was devoted to entertaining the public, from whom most of their income derived.

The "Long View" of London, 1647, by Wenceslaus Hollar. In this detail from Hollar's engraving of London, one can glimpse, on the south bank of the Thames, the Globe Theater and an arena for bearbaiting. The labels were accidentally transposed in the original: the Globe is the round structure on the left.

Before the construction of the public theaters, the playing companies often performed short plays called "interludes" that were, in effect, staged dialogues on religious, moral, and political themes. Henry Medwall's *Fulgens and Lucrece* (ca. 1490–1501), for example, pits a wealthy but dissolute nobleman against a virtuous public servant of humble origins, while John Heywood's *The Play of the Weather* (ca. 1525–33) stages a debate among social rivals, including a gentleman, a merchant, a forest ranger, and two millers. The structure of such plays reflects the training in argumentation that students received in Tudor schools and, in particular, the sustained practice in examining both sides of a difficult question. Some of Shakespeare's amazing ability to look at critical issues from multiple perspectives may be traced back to this practice and the dramatic interludes it helped to inspire.

Another major form of theater that flourished in England in the fifteenth century and continued on into the sixteenth was the morality play, a dramatization of the spiritual struggle of the Christian soul. As *Everyman* (included in "The Middle Ages") demonstrates, these dramas derived their power from the poignancy and terror of an individual's encounter with death. Often this somber power was supplemented by the extraordinary comic vitality of the evil character, or Vice.

If such plays sound more than a bit like sermons, it is because they were. The Church was a profoundly different institution from the theater, but its professionals shared some of the same rhetorical skills. It would be grossly misleading to regard churchgoing and playgoing as comparable entertainments, but clerical attacks on the theater sometimes make it sound as if ministers thought themselves to be in direct competition with professional players. The players, for their part, were generally too discreet to present themselves in a similar light, yet they almost certainly understood their craft as relating to sermons, with an uneasy blend of emulation and rivalry. When, in 1610, the theater manager Philip Rosseter was reported to have declared that plays were as good as sermons, he was summoned before the bishop of London to recant; but Rosseter had said no more than what many players must have privately thought.

By the later sixteenth century, many churchmen, particularly those with Puritan leanings, were steadfastly opposed to the theater, but some early Protestant Reformers, such as John Bale, tried their hand at writing plays. Thomas Norton, who with a fellow lawyer, Thomas Sackville, wrote the first English tragedy in blank verse, *Gorboduc, or Ferrex and Porrex* (1561), was also a translator of the great Reformer John Calvin. There is no evidence that Norton felt a tension between his religious convictions and his theatrical interests, nor was his play a private exercise. The five-act tragedy, a grim vision of Britain descending into civil war, was performed at the Inner Temple (one of London's law schools) and subsequently acted before the queen.

Gorboduc was closely modeled on the works of the Roman playwright Seneca, and Senecan influence—including violent plots, resounding rhetorical speeches, and ghosts thirsting for blood—remained pervasive in the Elizabethan theater, giving rise to the subgenre of revenge tragedy, in which a wronged protagonist plots and executes revenge, destroying himself (or herself) in the process. An early, highly influential example is Thomas Kyd's *Spanish Tragedy* (1592), and, despite its unprecedented psychological complexity, Shakespeare's *Hamlet* clearly participates in this kind. A related but distinct kind is the villain tragedy, in which the protagonist is blatantly evil: in his *Poetics,* Aristotle had advised against attempting to use a wicked person as the hero of a tragedy, but Shakespeare's *Richard III* and *Macbeth* amply justify the general English indifference to classical rules. Some Elizabethan tragedies, such as the fine *Arden of Feversham* (whose author is unknown), are concerned not with the fall of great men but with domestic violence; others, such as Christopher Marlowe's *Tamburlaine*, are concerned with "overreachers," larger-than-life heroes who challenge the limits of human possibility. Certain tragedies in the period, such as *Richard III*, intersect with another Elizabethan genre, the history play, in which dramatists staged the great events, most often conspiracies, rebellions, and wars, of the nation. Not all of the events commemorated in history plays were tragic, but they tend to circle back again and again to the act that epitomized what for this period was the ultimate challenge to authority: the killing of a king. When the English cut off the head of their king in 1649, they were performing a deed which they had been rehearsing, literally, for most of a century.

English schoolboys would read and occasionally perform comedies by the great Roman playwrights Plautus and Terence. Shortly before mid-century a schoolmaster, Nicholas Udall, used these as a model for a comedy in English, *Ralph Roister Doister*. At about the same time, another comedy, *Gammar Gurton's Needle*, which put vivid, native English material into classical form, was amusing the students at Cambridge. From the classical models English playwrights derived some elements of structure and content: plots based on intrigue, division into acts and scenes, and type characters such as the rascally servant and the *miles gloriosus* (cowardly braggart soldier). The latter type appears in *Ralph Roister Doister* and is a remote ancestor of Shakespeare's Sir John Falstaff in the two parts of *Henry IV* and *The Merry Wives of Windsor*.

Early plays such as *Gorboduc* and *Ralph Roister Doister* are rarely performed or read today, and with good reason. In terms of both dramatic structure and style, they are comparatively crude. Take, for example, this clumsy expression of passionate love by the title character in *Cambyses, King of Persia*, a popular play written around 1560 by a Cambridge graduate, Thomas Preston:

> For Cupid he, that eyeless boy, my heart hath so enflamed
> With beauty, you me to content the like cannot be named;
> For since I entered in this place and on you fixed mine eyes,
> Most burning fits about my heart in ample wise did rise.
> The heat of them such force doth yield, my corpse they scorch, alas!
> And burns the same with wasting heat as Titan doth the grass.
> And sith this heat is kindled so and fresh in heart of me,
> There is no way but of the same the quencher you must be.

Around 1590, an extraordinary change overcame the English drama, transforming it almost overnight into a vehicle for unparalleled poetic and dramatic expression. Many factors contributed to this transformation, but probably the chief was the eruption onto the scene of Christopher Marlowe. Compare Preston's couplets, written in a meter called "fourteeners," with the lines in Marlowe's *Doctor Faustus* (ca. 1592–93) with which Faustus greets the conjured figure of Helen of Troy:

> Was this the face that launched a thousand ships,
> And burnt the topless towers of Ilium?
> Sweet Helen, make me immortal with a kiss:
> Her lips sucks forth my soul, see where it flies!
> Come Helen, come, give me my soul again.
> Here will I dwell, for heaven be in these lips,
> And all is dross that is not Helena! (Scene 12, lines 81–87)

Marlowe has created and mastered a theatrical language—a superb unrhymed iambic pentameter, or blank verse—far more expressive than anything that anyone accustomed to the likes of Preston could have imagined.

Play-acting, whether of tragedies, comedies, or any of the other Elizabethan genres, took its place alongside other forms of public expression and entertainment as well. Perhaps the most important, from the perspective of the theater, were music and dance, since these were directly and repeatedly incorporated into plays. Moreover, virtually all plays in the period, including Shakespeare's, apparently ended with a dance. Brushing off the theatrical gore and changing their expressions from woe to pleasure, the actors in plays like *Doctor Faustus* and *King Lear* would presumably have received the audience's applause and then bid for a second round by performing a stately pavane or a lively jig.

Plays, music, and dancing were by no means the only shows in town. There were jousts, tournaments, royal entries, religious processions, pageants in honor of newly installed civic officials or ambassadors arriving from abroad; wedding masques, court masques, and costumed entertainments known as Disguisings or Mummings; juggling acts, fortune-tellers, exhibitions of swordsmanship, mountebanks, folk healers, storytellers, magic shows; bearbaiting, bullbaiting, cockfighting, and other blood sports; folk festivals such as Maying, the Feast of Fools, Carnival, and Whitsun Ales. For several years, Elizabethan Londoners were delighted by a trained animal—Banks's Horse—that could, it was thought, do arithmetic and answer questions. And there was always the grim but compelling spectacle of public shaming, mutilation, and execution.

Most English towns had stocks and whipping posts. Drunks, fraudulent merchants, adulterers, and quarrelers could be placed in carts or mounted backward on asses and paraded through the streets for crowds to jeer and throw refuse at. Women accused of being scolds could be publicly muzzled by an iron device called a brank or tied to a "cucking stool" and dunked in the river. Convicted criminals could have their ears cut off, their noses slit, their foreheads branded. Public beheadings and hangings were common. In the worst cases, felons were sentenced to be "hanged by the neck, and being alive cut down, and your privy members to be cut off, and your bowels to be taken out of your belly and there burned, you being alive." In the dismemberment with which Marlowe's *Doctor Faustus* ends, the audience

Scold's bridle, or brank. First recorded in Scotland, the scold's bridle was a device to humiliate and torture women who were regarded as "riotous" or "troublesome" in speech. The metal gag was designed to inflict maximum pain if the victim attempted to speak. In England, unruly women were also humiliated by being dragged through the streets in chairs known as "cucking stools," to be dunked.

was witnessing the theatrical equivalent of the execution of criminals and traitors that they could have also watched in the flesh, as it were, nearby.

Doctor Faustus was performed by the Lord Admiral's Men at the Rose Theater, one of four major public playhouses that by the mid-1590s were feverishly competing for crowds of spectators. These playhouses (including Shakespeare's famous Globe Theater, which opened in 1599) each accommodated some two thousand spectators and generally followed the same design: they were oval in shape, with an unroofed yard in the center where stood the groundlings (apprentices, servants, and others of the lower classes) and three rising tiers around the yard for men and women able to pay a higher price for places to sit and a roof over their heads. A large platform stage jutted out into the yard, surrounded on three sides by spectators (see the conjectural drawing of an Elizabethan playhouse in the appendices to this volume). These financially risky ventures relied on admission charges—it was an innovation of this period to have money advanced in the expectation of pleasure rather than offered to servants afterward as a reward—and counted on habitual playgoing fueled by a steady supply of new plays. The public playhouses were all located outside the limits of the city of London and, accordingly, beyond the jurisdiction of the city authorities, who were generally hostile to dramatic spectacles. Eventually, indoor theaters, artificially lighted and patronized by a more select audience, were also built inside the city, secured under conditions that would allow them some protection from those who wished to shut them down.

Why should what we now regard as one of the undisputed glories of the age have aroused so much hostility? One answer, curiously enough, is traffic: plays drew large audiences, and nearby residents objected to the crowds, the noise, and the crush of carriages. Other, more serious concerns were public health and crime. It was thought that many diseases, including the dreaded bubonic plague, were spread by noxious odors, and the packed playhouses were obvious breeding grounds for infection. (Patrons often tried to protect themselves by sniffing nosegays or stuffing cloves in their nostrils.) The large crowds drew pickpockets, cutpurses, and other scoundrels. On one memorable afternoon a pickpocket was caught in the act and tied for the duration of the play to one of the posts that held up the canopy above the stage. The theater was, moreover, a well-known haunt of prostitutes, and, it was alleged, a place where innocent maids were seduced and respectable matrons corrupted. It was darkly rumored that "chambers and secret places" adjoined the theater galleries, and, in any case, taverns, disreputable inns, and brothels were close at hand.

There were other charges as well. Plays were performed in the afternoon and therefore drew people, especially the young, away from their work. They were schools of idleness, luring apprentices from their trades, law students from their studies, housewives from their kitchens, and potentially pious souls from the sober meditations to which they might otherwise devote themselves. Moralists warned that the theaters were nests of sedition, and religious polemicists, especially Puritans, obsessively focusing on the use of boy actors to play the female parts, charged that theatrical transvestism excited illicit sexual desires, both heterosexual and homosexual.

But the playing companies had powerful allies, including Queen Elizabeth herself, and continuing popular support. One theater historian has estimated that between the late 1560s and 1642, when the playhouses were shut down by the English Civil War, well over fifty million visits were paid to the London theater, an astonishing figure for a city that had, by our standards, a very modest population. Plays were performed without the scene breaks and intermissions to which we are accustomed; there was no scenery and few props, but costumes were usually costly and elaborate. The players formed what would now be called repertory companies—that is, they filled the roles of each play from members of their own group, not employing outsiders. They performed a number of different plays on consecutive days, and the principal actors were shareholders in the profits of the company. Boys were apprenticed to actors just as they were apprenticed to master craftsmen in the guilds; they took the women's parts in plays until their voices changed. The plays might be bought for the company from freelance writers, or, as in Shakespeare's company, the group might include an actor-playwright who could supply it with some (though by no means all) of its plays. The script remained the property of the company, but a popular play was eagerly sought by the printers, and the companies, which generally tried to keep their plays from appearing in print, sometimes had trouble guarding their rights. The editors of the earliest collected edition of Shakespeare, the First Folio (1623), complained about the prior publication of "divers stolen and surreptitious copies" of his plays, "maimed and deformed by the frauds and stealths of injurious imposters."

SURPRISED BY TIME

All of the ways we cut up time into units are inevitably distortions. The dividing line between centuries was not, as far as we can tell, a highly significant one for people in the Renaissance, and many of the most important literary careers cross into the seventeenth century without a self-conscious moment of reflection. But virtually everyone must have been aware, by the end of the 1590s, that the long reign of England's Queen Elizabeth was nearing its end, and this impending closure occasioned considerable anxiety. Childless, the last of her line, Elizabeth had steadfastly refused to name a successor. She continued to make brilliant speeches, to receive the extravagant compliments of her flatterers, and to exercise her authority—in 1601, she had her favorite, the headstrong earl of Essex, executed for attempting to raise an insurrection. But, as her seventieth birthday approached, she was clearly, as Ralegh put it, "a lady surprised by time." She suffered from bouts of ill health and melancholy; her godson Sir John Harington was dismayed to see her pacing through the rooms of her palace, striking at the tapestries with a sword. Her more astute advisers—among them Lord Burghley's son, Sir Robert Cecil, who had succeeded his father as her principal councillor—secretly entered into correspondence with the likeliest claimant to the throne, James VI of Scotland. Though the English queen had executed his Catholic mother, Mary, Queen of Scots, the Protestant James had continued to exchange polite letters with Elizabeth. It was at least plausible, as officially claimed, that in her dying breath, on March 24, 1603, Elizabeth designated James as her successor. A jittery nation that had feared a possible civil war at her death lit bonfires to welcome its new king. But in just a very few years, the English began to express nostalgia for the rule of "Good Queen Bess" and to look back on her reign as a magnificent high point in the history and culture of their nation.

THE SIXTEENTH CENTURY

TEXTS	CONTEXTS
	1485 Accession of Henry VII inaugurates Tudor dynasty
	ca. 1504 Leonardo da Vinci paints the *Mona Lisa*
ca. 1505–07 Amerigo Vespucci, *New World* and *Four Voyages*	**1508–12** Michaelangelo paints Sistine Chapel ceiling
	1509 Death of Henry VII; accession of Henry VIII
1511 Desiderius Erasmus, *Praise of Folly*	**1513** James IV of Scotland killed at Battle of Flodden; succeeded by James V
1516 Thomas More, *Utopia*. Ludovico Ariosto, *Orlando furioso*	**1517** Martin Luther's Ninety-Five Theses; beginning of the Reformation in Germany
ca. 1517 John Skelton, "The Tunning of Elinour Rumming"	**1519** Cortés invades Mexico. Magellen begins his voyage around the world
	1521 Pope Leo X names Henry VIII "Defender of the Faith"
1520s–30s Thomas Wyatt's poems circulating in manuscript	
1525 William Tyndale's English translation of the New Testament	
1528 Baldassare Castiglione, *The Courtier*	**1529–32** More is Lord Chancellor
	1532–34 Henry VIII divorces Catherine of Aragon to marry Anne Boleyn; Elizabeth I born; Henry declares himself head of the Church of England
1532 Niccolò Machiavelli, *The Prince* (written 1513)	**1535** More beheaded
	1537 Establishment of Calvin's theocracy at Geneva
1537 John Calvin, *The Institution of Christian Religion*	**1542** Roman Inquisition. James V of Scotland dies; succeeded by infant daughter, Mary
1543 Copernicus, *On the Revolution of the Spheres*	**1547** Death of Henry VIII; accession of Protestant Edward VI
1547 *Book of Homilies*	
1549 *Book of Common Prayer*	**1553** Death of Edward VI; failed attempt to put Protestant Lady Jane Grey on throne; accession of Catholic Queen Mary, daughter of Catherine of Aragon
	1555–56 Archbishop Cranmer and former bishops Latimer and Ridley burned at the stake
1557 Tottel's *Songs and Sonnets* (printing poems by Wyatt, Surrey, and others)	
	1558 Mary dies; succeeded by Protestant Elizabeth I

TEXTS	CONTEXTS
1563 John Foxe, *Acts and Monuments*	
1565 Thomas Norton and Thomas Sackville, *Gorboduc*, first English blank-verse tragedy (acted in 1561)	
1567 Arthur Golding, translation of Ovid's *Metamorphoses*	**1567–68** Mary, Queen of Scots, forced to abdicate; succeeded by her son James VI; Mary imprisoned in England
	1570 Elizabeth I excommunicated by Pope Pius V
	1572 St. Bartholomew's Day Massacre of French Protestants
	1576 James Burbage's playhouse, The Theater, built in London
	1577–80 Drake's circumnavigation of the globe
1578 John Lyly, *Euphues*	
1579 Edmund Spenser, *The Shepheardes Calender*	
1580 Montaigne, *Essais*	
	1583 Irish rebellion crushed
	1584–87 Sir Walter Ralegh's earliest attempts to colonize Virginia
	1586–87 Mary, Queen of Scots, tried for treason and executed
ca. 1587–90 Marlowe's *Tamburlaine* acted. Shakespeare begins career as actor and playwright	
1588 Thomas Hariot, *A Brief and True Report of . . . Virginia*	**1588** Failed invasion of the Spanish Armada
1589 Richard Hakluyt, *The Principal Navigations . . . of the English Nation*	
1590 Sir Philip Sidney, *Arcadia* (posthumously published); Spenser, *The Faerie Queene*, Books 1–3	
1591 Sidney, *Astrophil and Stella* published	
ca. 1592 John Donne's earliest poems circulating in manuscript	
1595 Sidney, *The Defense of Poesy* published	**1595** Ralegh's voyage to Guiana
1596 Spenser, *The Faerie Queene*, Books 4–6 (with Books 1–3)	
1598 Ben Jonson, *Every Man in His Humor*	
	1599 Globe Theater opens
	1603 Elizabeth I dies; succeeded by James VI of Scotland (as James I), inaugurating the Stuart dynasty

JOHN SKELTON
ca. 1460–1529

John Skelton was not a tame poet. There was something wild about him that continues to provoke, baffle, and fascinate readers. It is difficult to fit the varied pieces of his life together: gifted rhetorician, translator, Latin tutor to the young prince who became Henry VIII, disgruntled courtier, political pamphleteer, visionary, biting satirist, and ordained priest. He was also the major poet of the first quarter of the century, with the title of poet laureate from both Oxford and Cambridge. His poetic achievement, remarkable though it is, is equally difficult to place; as C. S. Lewis observes, Skelton had "no real predecessors and no important disciples." His poetry draws, to be sure, on a long tradition of medieval anticlerical satire and carnivalesque parody, but Skelton brings to his mature works a fresh, often extremely eccentric voice.

His early works were more routinely conventional—ornate compliments, dutiful elegies, pious hymns to the Trinity and the like—but in a satire written at the end of the fifteenth century, *The Bowge of Court* (available in the supplemental ebook), Skelton gave unusually powerful expression to the anxiety of living in the dangerous, viciously competitive precincts of royal power. (The poem's main character is called "Dread.") A few years later, whether self-exiled or sent away by his enemies, Skelton was living far from the court: about 1503 he became the rector of the parish church at Diss, in Norfolk, where he remained for some eight years. By 1512 he had returned to court, appointed king's orator. He moved to a house in the sanctuary of Westminster Abbey in 1518 and shortly thereafter, in a series of satires including *Speak, Parrot; Colin Clout;* and *Why Come Ye Not to Court* (1521–22), began vituperative attacks on Cardinal Wolsey, the great prelate-statesman. Wolsey had Skelton briefly imprisoned but released him and promptly hired his services for himself.

Skelton's poems gain some of their most startling effects by mixing high and low styles and by playing bawdy and scatological verbal games with the Catholic liturgy. The games are not necessarily sacrilegious—for the Catholic Church, prior to the challenge of the Reformation, was capable of tolerating a wide range of expression— but they seem risk-taking and obstreperous, an impression heightened by the way they are written. In the satires, Skelton rejects the ornate rhetorical devices and aureate language that characterized his period's most ambitious poetry; he writes in short, rhymed lines, having from two to five beats, and the lines can keep on rhyming helter-skelter until the resources of the language give out. To many of his poems, with their aggressive and restless energies, this strange verse form is singularly appropriate. "The Tunning of Elinour Rumming" is, for example, a wonderfully clattering, apparently disordered portrait of an alewife, and the "skeltonics," as this way of writing has come to be called, contribute to the effect of disorder. The voice of the narrator of the satires has a breathless urgency that was much admired by twentieth-century poets, while to contemporary ears it is strikingly reminiscent of rap.

The English Reformation, which was set in motion shortly after Skelton's death, would drastically alter the context in which his work was received. English Protestants later in the century had trouble knowing what to make of him. On the one hand, his satires of the cardinal made him ripe for inclusion (with Langland and others) in the honor roll of supposedly proto-Protestant poets. Yet as a foul-mouthed and frivolous priest, Skelton could stand for the alleged corruption of the Catholic clergy. He also became associated with various tales and jests that seemed nostalgically to recall the innocence and "merriment" of pre-Reformation England. (In one of these, Skelton proudly ascends the pulpit to show off his naked illegitimate baby to his astonished parishioners.) For English society, as for English poetry, Skelton quickly came to represent the path not taken.[*]

Mannerly Margery Milk and Ale[1]

	Aye, beshrew° you, by my fay,°	curse / faith
	These wanton clerks[2] be nice° alway,	foolish
	Avaunt, avaunt, my popagay![3]	
	"What, will ye do nothing but play?"	
5	Tilly vally straw, let be I say!	
	Gup,[4] Christian Clout, gup, Jack of the Vale!	
	With Mannerly Margery milk and ale.	
	"By God, ye be a pretty pode,°	toad
	And I love you an whole cartload."	
10	Straw, James Foder, ye play the fode,°	deceiver, flatterer
	I am no hackney° for your rod:°	horse / riding
	Go watch a bull, your back is broad!	
	Gup, Christian Clout, gup, Jack of the Vale!	
	With Mannerly Margery milk and ale.	
15	Ywis° ye deal uncourteously;	truly
	What, would ye frumple° me? now fie!	rumple, tumble
	"What, and ye shall not be my pigsny?"[5]	
	By Christ, ye shall not, no hardily:	
	I will not be japed° bodily!	tricked, deceived
20	Gup, Christian Clout, gup, Jack of the Vale!	
	With Mannerly Margery milk and ale.	
	"Walk forth your way, ye cost me naught;	
	Now have I found that° I have sought:	that which
	The best cheap flesh that ever I bought."	
25	Yet, for his love that hath all wrought,	
	Wed me, or else I die for thought.°	i.e., of distress
	Gup, Christian Clout, your breath is stale!	
	With Mannerly Margery milk and ale!	
	Gup, Christian Clout, gup, Jack of the Vale!	
30	With Mannerly Margery milk and ale.	

ca. 1495   1523

---

[*] For additional poems by Skelton, including *The Bowge of Court* and an excerpt from *Colin Clout* with the author's own account of "skeltonics," see the supplemental ebook.

1. The poem is a song for three voices. The seducer's lines are in quotation marks; Margery sings the rest, except the chorus, which is sung by a bass.

2. Educated men: students, scholars, clergymen.
3. Popinjay, parrot—i.e., vain fellow.
4. "Go on!" (usually applied to horses). "Tilly vally straw": an exclamation of impatience: Nonsense!
5. Pig's eye. Here used as a (rough) term of endearment.

With lullay, lullay, like a child

With lullay, lullay, like a child,
Thou sleepest too long, thou art beguiled.°   *deceived*
"My darling dear, my daisy flower,
Let me," quod° he, "lie in your lap."   *quoth*
5   "Lie still," quod she, "my paramour,°   *lover*
Lie still, hardily,° and take a nap."   *confidently*
His head was heavy, such was his hap,°   *fortune, lot*
All drowsy dreaming, drowned in sleep,
That of his love he took no keep.°   *care*
10   With hey lullay, lullay, like a child,
Thou sleepest too long, thou art beguiled.

With ba, ba, ba! and bas, bas, bas![1]
She cherished him, both cheek and chin,
That he wist° never where he was;   *knew*
15   He had forgotten all deadly sin.
He wanted wit[2] her love to win,
He trusted her payment and lost all his prey;
She left him sleeping and stale° away,   *stole*
With hey lullay, lullay, like a child,
20   Thou sleepest too long, thou art beguiled.

The rivers rowth,° the waters wan,   *rough*
She sparèd not to wet her feet;
She waded over, she found a man
That halsèd° her heartily and kissed her sweet—   *embraced*
25   Thus after her cold she caught a heat.
"My lief,"° she said, "routeth° in his bed;   *lover / snores*
Ywis° he hath an heavy head."   *truly*
With hey lullay, lullay, like a child,
Thou sleepest too long, thou art beguiled.

30   What dreamest thou, drunkard, drowsy pate?°   *head*
Thy lust and liking[3] is from thee gone.
Thou blinkard blowboll,[4] thou wakest too late:
Behold thou liest, luggard,° alone!   *sluggard*
Well may thou sigh, well may thou groan,
35   To deal with her so cowardly.
Ywis, pole-hatchet, she bleared thine eye.[5]

1495–1500   1527

1. Kiss, kiss, kiss. "Ba": the "by" of *lullaby*.
2. Lacked sufficient intelligence.
3. Your pleasure and enjoyment.
4. Blink-eyed drunkard.
5. Deceived you. "Pole-hatchet": a soldier who carried a poleax.

From The Tunning of Elinour Rumming[1]

Secundus Passus[2]

Some have no money
That thither comey,
For their ale to pay;
That is a shrewd array!°   *sorry state of affairs*
5 Elinour sweared, "Nay,
Ye shall not bear away
My ale for nought,
By Him that me bought."
With, "Hey, dog, hey,
10 Have these hogs away!"
With, "Get me a staff,
The swine eat my draff!°   *refuse, dregs*
Strike the hogs with a club,
They have drunk up my swilling-tub!"°   *tub for stirring*
15 For, be there never so much prese,°   *crowd*
These swine go to the high dese;[3]
The sow with her pigs;
The boar his tail wrigs,°   *wriggles*
His rump also he frigs°   *rubs*
20 Against the high bench!
With, "Fo, there is a stench!
Gather up, thou wench;
Seest thou not what is fall?°   *has fallen*
Take up dirt° and all,   *dung*
25 And bear out of the hall:
God give it ill preving°   *ill success*
Cleanly as evil cheving!"°   *bad luck*
    But let us turn plain
There° we left° again.   *where / left off*
30 For as ill a patch° as that   *poor piece of ground*
The hens run in the mash-fat;°   *mixing vat*
For they go to roost
Straight over the ale-joust,°   *ale pot*
And dung, when it comes,
35 In the ale tuns.°   *barrels*
Then Elinour taketh
The mash-bowl, and shaketh
The hens' dung away,
And skommeth° it in a tray   *skims*
40 Whereas the yeast is,
With her mangy fistis,°   *fists*
And sometime she blens
The dung of her hens
And the ale together;

1. This rowdy poem—whose heroine really did keep an alehouse in Surrey—recounts Elinour's brewing practices ("tunning") and the social life in her establishment.
2. *Second Section* (Latin).
3. Go to the dais—i.e., take the best place.

45 And saith, "Gossip,° come hither,   *friend*
 This ale shall be thicker,
 And flower° the more quicker;   *froth*
 For I may tell you,
 I learned it of a Jew,
50 When I began to brew,
 And I have found it true;
 Drink now while it is new;
 And ye may it brook,[4]
 It shall make you look
55 Younger than ye be,
 Years two or three,
 For ye may prove it by me.
 Behold," she said, "and see
 How bright I am of ble!°   *complexion*
60 Ich° am not cast away,   *I*
 That can my husband say,
 When we kiss and play
 In lust and in liking;
 He calleth me his whiting,[5]
65 His mulling and his miting,
 His nobs° and his cony,°   *dear / bunny*
 His sweeting and his honey,
 With, 'Bas,° my pretty bonny,   *kiss*
 Thou art worth good° and money!'   *goods*
70 Thus make I my falyre fonny,° *make my fellow foolish*
 Till that he dream and dronny,°   *laze*
 For after all our sport,
 Then will he rout° and snort;   *snore*
 Then sweetly together we lie
75 As two pigs in a sty."
  To cease meseemeth best,
 And of this tale to rest,
 And for to leave this letter,°   *text, subject*
 Because it is no better,
80 And because it is no sweeter;
 We will no farther rhyme
 Of it at this time,
 But we will turn plain
 Where we left again.[6]

1517?   ca. 1545

---

4. If you can tolerate it.
5. A small white fish—here a term of endearment, like "mulling" (meaning unclear) and "miting" (mite).
6. I.e., go back to where we left off.

SIR THOMAS MORE
1478–1535

S ir Thomas More is one of the most brilliant, compelling, and disturbing figures of the English Renaissance. He has been the hero of people who, given the chance, would (and on occasion did) tear each other apart: the Catholic Church made him a saint; leading Communists celebrated his book *Utopia* as a forerunner of their plan to abolish private property; and middle-class liberals have admired his vision of free public education, careers open to talents, and freedom of thought. But at the same time each of these groups has been deeply troubled by aspects of More's life and writings: the Catholic bishops of sixteenth-century Spain and Portugal placed *Utopia* on their list of prohibited books; Karl Marx reserved his most-bitter scorn for those impractical socialists he branded as "utopian"; and liberals have noticed uneasily that More embraced the idea of the forced labor camp.

More was born in London, the son of a prominent lawyer. As a boy he served as a page in the grand household of the archbishop of Canterbury, John Morton, who was also King Henry VII's lord chancellor. It is reported that at Christmastime, when wandering actors would perform plays at the archbishop's palace, young More would step in among the players and improvise a part for himself. This early talent for improvisation characterized More throughout his life, as did a lingering sense that he was never quite at home in any of the parts he played. (In the famous portrait of More by Hans Holbein the Younger—included in the color insert in this volume— More may well have been wearing a hair shirt under his rich robe of office.)

He studied at Oxford and at the Inns of Court, but he did not automatically follow in his father's footsteps. He was torn between a career as a lawyer, with its promise of wealth and access to power, and a life of religious devotion. For some four years, according to one of his early biographers, he lived as a layman among the ascetic monks in London's Charterhouse, but deciding that he wanted to marry, he turned toward a secular career in public affairs. Still, amid his law practice, his position as undersheriff of London, his participation in Parliament and on the king's council, his service in diplomatic and commercial negotiations, and ultimately his three tumultuous years as lord chancellor, More constantly showed signs of reserving some part of himself for other realms. One of those realms was his growing family, to whom he was a devoted and loving father, but he himself spoke of his familial concerns as a kind of business that took him away from the life of the mind. Shortly after his law studies, he gave a series of public lectures on Saint Augustine's monumental work *The City of God*, and theological and moral arguments continued to fascinate him until his death. He also had a passion for Greek and Latin literature, a passion he shared with his close friend Desiderius Erasmus of Rotterdam (ca. 1466–1536), the greatest humanist scholar of the Northern Renaissance.

Erasmus and More shared not only the profound classical learning that lay at the heart of the humanist movement but also an ardent Christian piety, a suspicion of scholastic hair-splitting, a delight in rhetoric, a taste for the ancient satirist Lucian, and a lively interest in experimental, unsettling wit. For Erasmus this interest bore fruit in his most enduring work, *The Praise of Folly* (1511), which he composed as a guest in More's London house and dedicated to him. For More, the love of playful, subversive wit culminated in *Utopia*, which he began in 1515 while in the Netherlands on a diplomatic mission for Henry VIII and completed the next year. Both works, written in Latin and quickly circulated among humanists throughout Europe, are daring intellectual games that call into question the period's most cherished assumptions.

Utopia displays the strong influence of Plato's *Republic*, with its radically communalistic reimagining of society, but it was also shaped by more contemporary influences: monastic communities, which forbade private property and required everyone to labor; emerging market societies, with their emphasis on education and social mobility over hereditary privilege, and their dislike of the old warrior aristocracy; the recurrent outcries of peasant rebels demanding a more just distribution of wealth; and, explicitly, Amerigo Vespucci's published accounts of his voyages to the newly discovered lands across the Atlantic Ocean. Those voyages disclosed a whole world organized on principles utterly unlike those that governed European societies, a world seemingly free of the inequality, economic exploitation, dynastic squabbles, and legal chicanery that More observed everywhere around him.

Vespucci's letters, part sober reportage, part wild fantasy, helped More imagine an alternative to the world he inhabited. Book II of *Utopia* (the part of the work More composed first) describes in detail the laws and customs of a country that bears some striking physical resemblances to England. But, in other ways, how unlike England it is! The abolition of money and private property has prevented any neurotic attachment to goods and status, and the parasitic classes—nobles, lawyers, idle priests, rapacious soldiers—have been eliminated. In Utopia, a well-ordered political democracy, education is free and universal. Instead of the misery of oppressed peasants, there are prosperous collective farms. Instead of stench and suffering in crowded, crooked streets, there are gleaming, rational cities, with free hospitals and child care. Since everyone works, no one is overburdened; and there is ample time for all citizens to pursue the arts of peace and the pleasures of the mind and the body.

The picture of England in Book I of *Utopia*—beggars in the streets, convicted petty thieves hanging from the gibbets, hungry farmers displaced from lands fenced off for more profitable sheep-rearing, cynical flatterers encouraging the king to embark on imperialistic wars—makes the sharpest contrast imaginable with the ordered and peaceable state described in Book II. Yet Book I is not, or not directly, a call for revolutionary social reform. It is, rather, a meditation, in the form of a dialogue, on the question of whether intellectuals should involve themselves in politics. The two speakers in the dialogue are a traveler named Raphael Hythloday and someone named Thomas More, who closely resembles but perhaps should not be identified precisely with the real More. More argues that Hythloday, with his extraordinary learning, experience, and high principles, should offer his services as a councillor to one of the great monarchs of Europe. Hythloday counters that kings, who only desire flattery from their councillors, would never dream of adopting the radical policies, such as the abandonment of warfare and the abolition of private property, which alone might lead to a good society. In the dialogue, Hythloday is the aloof idealist, unwilling to dirty his hands in a pointless cause; More is the sincere pragmatist, prepared to compromise with the system and seek to change it from within rather than give up on any possibility of action. In Book I, the debate between Hythloday and More has no clear winner; but not long after completing *Utopia*, the real Thomas More entered the council of Henry VIII.

Book II, Hythloday's narrative of his visit to Utopia, is also in some sense a dialogue, a complex, often ambiguous meditation on the nature of the ideal commonwealth. The dialogue form not only allows the actual Thomas More some rhetorical cover for caustic critiques in both books of the social policy of his own country but also encourages the reader to register the disturbing underside of More's island commonwealth: Utopia is a society that rests upon slavery, including enslavement for social deviance. There is no variety in dress or housing or cityscape, and no privacy. Citizens are encouraged to value pleasure, but they are constantly monitored, lest their pursuit of pleasure pass the strict bounds set by "nature" or "reason." There are constitutional guarantees of freedom of thought and toleration of religious diversity, but people who fail to believe in divine providence and the afterlife are regarded as subhuman and, accordingly, not treated as citizens. The Utopians officially despise war, but they nevertheless appear to fight a good many of them. It is very difficult to gauge More's attitude toward his imaginary commonwealth; perhaps he himself could not have said with any absolute certainty what it was.

If there is deep ambivalence in More's attitude toward Utopia, there is no comparable ambivalence in the other great work he wrote at approximately the same time, *The History of King Richard III*. In More's influential account, Richard III, the last Yorkist king, was an unmitigated monster, twisted in mind and body, subtle, hypocritical, and murderous. This account, obviously appealing to the Tudors, whose dynasty was founded upon Richard's overthrow, was incorporated verbatim into several sixteenth-century chronicles and so came down to Shakespeare, whose *Richard III* (ca. 1592) fixed the portrait of Richard as a deformed, homicidal tyrant.

More wrote *Utopia* in Latin, for an international audience of humanist intellectuals; he wrote *Richard III*, which he left unfinished, in both Latin and English versions. The English text, in prose of great energy and suppleness, suggests that he was, in this highly charged vernacular account of the recent past, thinking of a different readership, more national in scope and interests. In his subsequent works, he continued to address both audiences on the matters that most concerned him, but he never repeated the mode of either playful speculation or historical narrative. Instead he focused on theology, moral philosophy, and religious controversy, and though his wit and irony are everywhere evident in these writings, they are yoked to the service of an increasingly desperate struggle.

The struggle was against Lutheranism, which began to make inroads into England precisely during the period of More's rise to great power. More, an ardent Catholic, hated the central tenets of the Protestant Reformation and fought its adherents with every means at his disposal, including book burnings, imprisonment, and execution. As Henry VIII's confidant and, finally, lord chancellor (1529–32), he played for a time a significant role in the war on heresy, but he resigned his high office when the king, seeking a divorce in order to marry Anne Boleyn, broke with the Roman Catholic Church. When More was required to take the oath for the Act of Succession, acknowledging that the rightful claim to the throne would lie with Henry's children by Anne, and to state his approval of the Act of Supremacy, affirming that the king rather than the pope was the supreme head of the Church in England, he declined. He attempted to remain silent, but the king treated his silence as a refusal and deemed this refusal to be treason. Against the pleadings of his family, More maintained his silence, choosing, as he put it, "to die the king's good servant, but God's first." In 1535 he was beheaded. Four hundred years later he was canonized by the Catholic Church as Saint Thomas More.*

---

* For an excerpt from More's *History of King Richard III*, see the supplemental ebook.

Utopia[1]

CONCERNING THE BEST
STATE OF A COMMONWEALTH
AND THE NEW ISLAND
OF UTOPIA

A Truly Golden Handbook
No Less Beneficial Than Entertaining
by the Most Distinguished and Eloquent Author
THOMAS MORE
Citizen and Undersheriff[2] of the Famous City
of London

Thomas More to Peter Giles,[3] Greetings

My very dear Peter Giles, I am almost ashamed to be sending you after nearly a year this little book about the Utopian commonwealth, which I'm sure you expected in less than six weeks. For, as you were well aware, I faced no problem in finding my materials, and had no reason to ponder the arrangement of them. All I had to do was repeat what you and I together heard Raphael[4] describe. There was no occasion, either, for labor over the style, since what he said, being extempore and informal, couldn't be couched in fancy terms. And besides, as you know, he's a man not so well versed in Latin as in Greek; so that my language would be nearer the truth, the closer it approached to his casual simplicity. Truth in fact is the only quality at which I should have aimed, or did aim, in writing this book.

I confess, friend Peter, that having all these materials ready to hand left hardly anything at all for me to do. Otherwise, thinking through a topic like this from scratch and disposing it in proper order might have demanded no little time and work even if a man were not entirely deficient in talent and learning. And then if the matter had to be set forth with eloquence, not just factually, there's no way I could have done that, however hard I worked, for however long a time. But now when I was relieved of all these problems, over which I could have sweated forever, there was nothing for me to do but simply write down what I had heard. Well, little as it was, that task was rendered almost impossible by my many other obligations. Most of my day is given to the law—pleading some cases, hearing others, compromising

1. More coined the word "Utopia" from Greek *ou* ("not")+*topos* ("place"): "Noplace"; perhaps with a pun on *eu*+*topos*, "Happy" or "Fortunate" Place. The book was written in Latin and published—elaborately titled, as below—on the European continent under the supervision of More's friend the great Dutch humanist Desiderius Erasmus (ca. 1466–1536). This translation is by Robert M. Adams, as published in the Norton Critical Edition of *Utopia* (3rd ed., 2011), with revisions by George M. Logan.
2. As an undersheriff, More's principal duty was to serve as a judge in the Sheriff's Court, a city court that heard a wide variety of cases.
3. Giles (ca. 1486–1533) was both a humanistic scholar and a practical man of affairs, city clerk of Antwerp. Erasmus had recommended him and More to each other, and they met in Antwerp in the summer of 1515 (see below, pp. 575–76); *Utopia* seems to have originated in conversations between them. In the first edition of the book, this letter is called its Preface.
4. I.e., the fictitious character Raphael Hythloday. His given name associates him with the archangel Raphael, traditionally a guide and healer.

others, and deciding still others. I have to visit this man because of his official position and that man because of his business; and so almost the whole day is devoted to other people's business and the rest to my own; and then for myself—that is, my studies—there's nothing left.

For when I get home, I have to talk with my wife, chatter with my children, and consult with the servants. All these matters I consider part of my business, since they have to be done, unless a man wants to be a stranger in his own house. Besides, you are bound to bear yourself as agreeably as you can toward those whom nature or chance or your own choice has made the companions of your life. But of course you mustn't spoil them with your familiarity, or by overindulgence turn the servants into your masters. And so, amid these concerns, the day, the month, and the year slip away.

What time do I find to write, then? especially since I still have taken no account of sleeping or even of eating, to which many people devote as much time as to sleep itself, which consumes almost half of our lives.[5] My own time is only what I steal from sleeping and eating. It isn't very much, but it's something, and so I've finally been able to finish *Utopia*, even though belatedly, and I'm sending it to you now. I hope, my dear Peter, that you'll read it over and let me know if you find anything that I've overlooked. Though I'm not really afraid of having forgotten anything important—I wish my judgment and learning were up to my memory, which isn't half bad—still, I don't feel so sure of it that I would swear I've missed nothing.

For my servant John Clement[6] has raised a great doubt in my mind. As you know, he was there with us, for I always want him to be present at conversations where there's profit to be gained. (And one of these days I expect we'll get a fine crop of learning from this young sprout, who's already made excellent progress in Greek as well as Latin.) Anyhow, as I recall matters, Hythloday said the bridge over the Anyder at Amaurot[7] was five hundred yards long; but my John says that is two hundred yards too much—that in fact the river is not more than three hundred yards wide there. So I beg you, consult your memory. If your recollection agrees with his, I'll yield to the two of you, and confess myself mistaken. But if you don't recall the point, I'll follow my own memory and keep my present figure. For, as I've taken particular pains to avoid having anything false in the book, so, if anything is in doubt, I'd rather say something untrue than tell a lie. In short, I'd rather be honest than clever.

But the whole matter can easily be cleared up if you'll ask Raphael about it—either face to face or else by letter. And I'm afraid you must do this anyway, because of another problem that has cropped up—whether through my fault, or yours, or Raphael's, I'm not sure. For it didn't occur to us to ask, nor to him to say, in what area of the New World Utopia is to be found. I wouldn't have missed hearing about this for a sizable sum of money, for I'm quite ashamed not to know even the name of the ocean where this island

---

5. More's 16th-century biographer Thomas Stapleton says he slept four or five hours a night, rising at 2 A.M.
6. Clement (d. 1572) had entered More's household by 1514, as servant and pupil. He later became a respected physician.

7. From Greek: "made dark or dim." "Hythloday": its first root is surely Greek *hythlos*, "nonsense"; the second part is probably from *daiein*, "to distribute"—hence, together, "nonsense-peddler." "Anyder": waterless (also from Greek).

lies about which I've written so much. Besides, there are various people here, and one in particular, a devout man and a professor of theology, who very much wants to go to Utopia. His motive is not by any means idle curiosity, a hankering after new sights, but rather a desire to foster and further the growth of our religion, which has made such a happy start there. To do this properly, he has decided to arrange to be sent there by the pope, and even to be named bishop to the Utopians. He feels no particular scruples about applying for this post, for he considers it a holy ambition, arising not from motives of glory or gain, but simply from religious zeal.[8]

Therefore I beg you, my dear Peter, to get in touch with Hythloday—in person if you can, or by letters if he's gone—and make sure that my work contains nothing false and omits nothing true. It would probably be just as well to show him the book itself. If I've made a mistake, there's nobody better qualified to correct me; but even he cannot do it, unless he reads over my book. Besides, you will be able to discover in this way whether he's pleased or annoyed that I have written the book. If he has decided to write out his own story himself, he may not want me to do so; and I should be sorry, too, if, in publicizing the Utopian commonwealth, I had robbed him and his story of the flower of novelty.

But to tell the truth, I'm still of two minds as to whether I should publish the book at all. For the tastes of mortals are so various, the tempers of some are so severe, their minds so ungrateful, their judgments so foolish, that there seems no point in publishing something, even if it's intended for their advantage, that they will receive only with contempt and ingratitude. Better simply to follow one's own natural inclinations, lead a merry life, and ignore the vexing problems of publication. Most people know nothing of learning; many despise it. The clod rejects as too difficult whatever isn't cloddish. The pedant dismisses as mere trifling anything that isn't stuffed with obsolete words. Some readers approve only of ancient authors; many men like only their own writing. Here's a man so solemn he won't allow a shadow of levity, and there's one so insipid of taste that he can't endure the salt of a little wit. Some dullards dread satire as a man bitten by a rabid dog dreads water;[9] some are so changeable that they like one thing when they're seated and another when they're standing.

These people lounge around the taverns, and as they swill their ale pass judgment on the intelligence of writers. With complete assurance they condemn every author by his writings, just as they think best, plucking each one, as it were, by the beard. But they themselves remain safe and, as the proverb has it, out of harm's way. No use trying to lay hold of them; they're shaved so close, there's not so much as a hair of their heads to catch them by.

Finally, some people are so ungrateful that even though they're delighted with a work, they don't like the author any better because of it. They are like rude guests who, after they have stuffed themselves with a splendid dinner, go off, carrying their full bellies homeward without a word of thanks to the host who invited them. A fine task, providing at your own

8. Tradition has it that this zealous theologian was Rowland Phillips, warden of Merton College, Oxford. But there is no real support for the identification, and the passage may be wholly fabricated.

9. A late-stage symptom of rabies, which gives the disease its other name, hydrophobia.

expense a banquet for men of such finicky palates and such various tastes, who will remember and reward you with such thanks!

At any rate, my dear Peter, will you take up with Hythloday the points I spoke of? After I've heard from him, I'll take a fresh look at the whole matter. But since I've already taken the pains to write up the subject, it's too late to be wise. In the matter of publication, I hope we can have Hythloday's approval; after that, I'll follow the advice of my friends—and especially yours. Farewell, my dear Peter Giles. My regards to your excellent wife. Love me as you have always done; I am more fond of you than ever.

THE BEST STATE OF A COMMONWEALTH
A DISCOURSE BY THE EXTRAORDINARY
RAPHAEL HYTHLODAY
AS RECORDED BY THE NOTED THOMAS MORE
CITIZEN AND UNDERSHERIFF OF LONDON
THE FAMOUS CITY OF GREAT BRITAIN

Book I

The most invincible king of England, Henry, the eighth of that name, a prince adorned with the royal virtues beyond any other, had recently some differences of no slight import with Charles, the most serene prince of Castille,[1] and sent me into Flanders as his spokesman to discuss and settle them. I was companion and associate to that incomparable man Cuthbert Tunstall,[2] whom the king has recently created master of the rolls, to everyone's great satisfaction. I will say nothing in praise of this man, not because I fear the judgment of a friend might be questioned, but because his integrity and learning are greater than I can describe and too well known everywhere to need my commendation—unless I would, according to the proverb, "light up the sun with a lantern."

Those appointed by the prince to deal with us, all excellent men, met us at Bruges by prearrangement. Their head and leader was the mayor of Bruges, a most distinguished person. But their main speaker and guiding spirit was Georgius de Theimseke, the provost of Cassel, a man eloquent by nature as well as by training, very learned in the law, and most skillful in diplomatic affairs through his ability and long practice. After we had met several times, certain points remained on which we could not come to agreement; so they adjourned the meetings and went to Brussels for some days to learn their prince's pleasure.

Meanwhile, since my business required it, I went to Antwerp.[3] Of those who visited me while I was there, no one was more welcome than Peter Giles.

1. Later (1519), as Charles V, he became the Holy Roman Emperor. By 1515 he had already (at age fifteen) inherited the Low Countries, and he was soon to become king of Spain. The matters in dispute between him and Henry VIII were certain Dutch import duties.
2. An admired scholar and influential cleric, Tunstall (1474–1559) was appointed ambassador to Brussels in May 1515 and a year later became master of the rolls (principal clerk of the Chancery Court).
3. Antwerp and Brussels are about equidistant (sixty miles) from Bruges.

He was a native of Antwerp, a man of high reputation, already appointed to a good position and worthy of the very best: I hardly know whether the young man is more distinguished in learning or in character. Apart from being cultured, virtuous, and courteous to all, with his intimates he is so open-hearted, affectionate, loyal, and sincere that you would be hard-pressed to find anywhere a man comparable to him in all the points of friendship. No one is more modest or more frank; none better combines simplicity with wisdom. His conversation is so pleasant, and so witty without malice, that the ardent desire I felt to see again my native country, my wife, and my children (from whom I had been separated more than four months) was much eased by his agreeable company and delightful talk.

One day after I had heard mass at Nôtre Dame, the most beautiful and most popular church in Antwerp, I was about to return to my quarters when I happened to see him talking with a stranger, a man of quite advanced years. The stranger had a sunburned face, a long beard, and a cloak hanging loosely from his shoulders; from his appearance and dress, I took him to be a ship's captain. When Peter saw me, he approached and greeted me. As I was about to return his greeting, he drew me aside, and, indicating the stranger, said, "Do you see that fellow? I was just on the point of bringing him to you."

"He would have been very welcome on your behalf," I answered.

"And on his own too, if you knew him," said Peter, "for there is no mortal alive today can tell you so much about unknown peoples and lands; and I know that you're always greedy for such information."

"In that case," said I, "my guess wasn't a bad one, for at first glance I supposed he was a skipper."

"Then you're far off the mark," he replied, "for his sailing has not been like that of Palinurus, but more that of Ulysses, or rather of Plato.[4] This man, who is named Raphael—his family name is Hythloday—knows a good deal of Latin, and is particularly learned in Greek. He studied Greek more than Latin because his main interest is philosophy, and in that field he found that the Romans have left us nothing very valuable except certain works of Seneca and Cicero.[5] Being eager to see the world, he left to his brothers the patrimony to which he was entitled at home (he is a native of Portugal) and took service with Amerigo Vespucci.[6] He was Vespucci's constant companion on the last three of his four voyages, accounts of which are now common reading everywhere; but on the last voyage, he did not return home with the commander. After much persuasion and expostulation he got Amerigo's permission to be one of the twenty-four men who were left in a fort at the farthest point of the last voyage.[7] Being marooned in this way was altogether agreeable to him, as he was more anxious to pursue his travels than afraid of death. He would often say, 'The man who has no grave is covered by the sky,'

---

4. Palinurus—Aeneas's pilot, who dozed over his steering oar and fell overboard (*Aeneid* 5.831ff).—is an exemplar of the careless traveler; Ulysses, of the person who learns from traveling; and Plato (who made trips to Sicily and Egypt), of the person who travels to learn.

5. The great orator Cicero (106–43 B.C.E.), though not a philosopher, in his writings rehearsed at length the views of the various philosophical schools. Seneca (ca. 4 B.C.E.—65 C.E.) was the foremost Roman Stoic philosopher.

6. The Florentine explorer was sponsored first by the king of Spain and later by the king of Portugal and was reputed to have made four trips to the New World, starting in 1497. Accounts of his voyages published in the opening years of the 16th century were widely circulated and made his exploits more famous than the more substantial explorations of Columbus and Cabot.

7. Reputedly at Cape Frio, east of present-day Rio de Janeiro.

and 'The road to heaven is the same length from all places.'[8] Yet this frame of mind would have cost him dear, if God had not been gracious to him. After Vespucci's departure, he traveled through many countries with five companions from the garrison. At last, by strange good fortune, he got, via Ceylon, to Calicut, where he opportunely found some Portuguese ships; and so, beyond anyone's expectation, he returned to his own country."[9]

When Peter had told me this, I thanked him for his great kindness in wishing to introduce me to a man whose conversation he hoped I would enjoy, and then I turned to Raphael. After we had greeted each other and exchanged the usual civilities of strangers upon their first meeting, we all went off to my house. There in the garden we sat down on a bench covered with turf, to talk together.

He told us that when Vespucci sailed away, he and his companions who had stayed behind in the fort often met with the people of the countryside, and by ingratiating speeches gradually won their friendship. Before long they came to dwell with them safely and even affectionately. The prince (I have forgotten his name and that of his country) also gave them his favor, furnishing Raphael and his five companions not only with ample provisions but with means for traveling—rafts when they went by water, wagons when they went by land. In addition, he sent with them a most trusty guide, who was to conduct them to other princes to whom he heartily recommended them. After many days' journey, he said, they came to towns and cities, and to commonwealths that were both very populous and not badly governed.

To be sure, under the equator and as far on both sides of the line as the sun moves, there lie vast empty deserts, scorched with perpetual heat. The whole region is desolate and squalid, grim and uncultivated, inhabited by wild beasts, serpents, and also by men no less wild and dangerous than the beasts themselves. But as you go on, conditions gradually grow milder. The sun is less fierce, the earth greener, the creatures less savage. At last you reach people, cities, and towns which not only trade among themselves and with their neighbors but even carry on commerce by sea and land with remote countries. After that, he said, they were able to visit different lands in every direction, for he and his companions were welcome as passengers aboard any ship about to make a journey.

The first vessels they saw were flat-bottomed, he said, with sails made of stitched papyrus-reeds or wicker, or elsewhere of leather. Farther on, they found ships with pointed keels and canvas sails, in every respect like our own.[1] The seamen were not unskilled in managing wind and water; but they were most grateful to him, Raphael said, for showing them the use of the compass, of which they had been ignorant. For that reason, they had formerly sailed with great timidity, and only in summer. Now they have such trust in the compass that they no longer fear winter at all, and tend to be overconfident rather than cautious. There is some danger that through their imprudence this device, which they thought would be so advantageous to them, may become the cause of much mischief.

8. Both these dicta have classical sources: the epic poet Lucan (Seneca's nephew), *Pharsalia* 7.819; and Cicero, *Tusculan Disputations* 1.43.104.
9. Thus becoming the first circumnavigator of the globe. (Magellan's men completed the trip in 1522.) Calicut is a seaport on the west coast of India.
1. As a matter of fact, the South American natives, when they traveled by water, used canoes made from hollowed logs. In general, More's depiction is fanciful.

It would take too long to repeat all that Raphael told us he had observed in each place, nor would it make altogether for our present purpose. Perhaps on another occasion we shall tell more about the things that are most profitable, especially the wise and sensible institutions that he observed among the civilized nations. We asked him many eager questions about such things, and he answered us willingly enough. We made no inquiries, however, about monsters, for nothing is less new or strange than they are. Scyllas, ravenous Celaenos, man-eating Lestrygonians,[2] and that sort of monstrosity you can hardly avoid, but well and wisely trained citizens you will hardly find anywhere. While he told us of many ill-considered usages in these new-found nations, he also described quite a few other customs from which our own cities, nations, races, and kingdoms might take example in order to correct their errors. These I shall discuss in another place, as I said. Now I intend to relate only what he told us about the customs and institutions of the Utopians,[3] first recounting the conversation that led him to speak of that commonwealth. Raphael had been talking very sagely about the faulty arrangements and also the wise institutions found in that hemisphere and this (many of both sorts in each), speaking as shrewdly about the manners and governments of each place he had visited as though he had lived there all his life. Peter was amazed.

"My dear Raphael," he said, "I'm surprised that you don't enter some king's service; for I don't know of a single prince who wouldn't be eager to employ you. Your learning and your knowledge of various countries and peoples would entertain him, while your advice and your supply of examples would be very helpful in the council chamber. Thus you might advance your own interests and be useful at the same time to all your relatives and friends."

"I am not much concerned about my relatives and friends," he replied, "because I consider that I have already done my duty by them. While still young and healthy, I distributed among my relatives and friends the possessions that most men do not part with till they are old and sick (and then only reluctantly, because they can no longer keep them). I think they should be content with this gift of mine, and not expect that for their sake I should enslave myself to any king whatever."

"Well said," Peter replied; "but I do not mean that you should be in servitude to any king, only in his service."

"The difference is only a matter of one syllable," said Raphael.

"All right," said Peter, "but whatever you call it, I do not see any other way in which you can be so useful to your friends or to the general public, in addition to making yourself happier."

"Happier indeed!" exclaimed Raphael. "Would a way of life so absolutely repellent to my spirit make my life happier? As it is now, I live as I please, and I fancy very few courtiers, however splendid, can say that. As a matter of fact, there are so many men soliciting favors from the powerful that it will be no great loss if they have to do without me and a couple of others like me."

---

2. Scylla and the Lestrygonians were Homeric bogeys: the former, a six-headed sea monster (*Odyssey* 12.73ff.); the latter, giant cannibals (*Odyssey* 10.76ff.). Celaeno, one of the Harpies (birds with women's faces), appears in the *Aeneid* (3.209ff.).

3. As J. H. Hexter argues (*More's "Utopia": The Biography of an Idea* [1952], pp. 18–21), it is almost certain that at this point More opened a seam in the original version of *Utopia*—which evidently included only the account of the Utopian commonwealth (now Book II) and the opening pages of what is now Book I—to insert the additions that constitute the remainder of Book I.

Then I said, "It is clear, my dear Raphael, that you seek neither wealth nor power, and indeed I value and revere a man of such a disposition as much as I do the mightiest persons in the world. Yet I think if you would devote your time and energy to public affairs, you would do a thing worthy of a generous and philosophical nature, even if you did not much like it. You could best perform such a service by joining the council of some great prince and inciting him to just and noble actions (as I'm sure you would): for a people's welfare or misery flows in a stream from their prince, as from a never-failing spring. Your learning is so full, even if it weren't combined with experience, and your experience is so great, even apart from your learning, that you would be an extraordinary counselor to any king in the world."

"You are twice mistaken, my dear More," he replied, "first in me and then in the situation itself. I don't have the capacity you ascribe to me, and if I had it in the highest degree, the public would still not be any better off if I exchanged my contemplative leisure for this kind of action. In the first place, most princes apply themselves to the arts of war, in which I have neither ability nor interest, instead of to the good arts of peace. They are generally more set on acquiring new kingdoms by hook or by crook than on governing well those they already have. Moreover, the counselors of kings are all so wise already that they need no advice from anyone else (or at least that's the way they see it). At the same time, they approve and even flatter the most absurd statements of favorites through whose influence they seek to stand well with the prince. It is only natural, of course, that each man should think his own opinions best: the crow loves his fledgling, and the ape his cub.

"Now in a court composed of people who envy everyone else and admire only themselves, if a man should suggest something he had read of in other ages or seen in practice elsewhere, the other counselors would think their reputation for wisdom was endangered and they would look like simpletons, unless they could find fault with his proposal. If all else failed, they would take refuge in some remark like this: 'The way we're doing it was good enough for our ancestors, and I only hope we're as wise as they were.' And with this deep thought they would take their seats, as though they had said the last word on the subject—implying, of course, that it would be a very dangerous matter if anyone were found to be wiser in any point than his ancestors were. As a matter of fact, we have no misgivings about neglecting the best examples they have left us; but if something better is proposed, we eagerly seize upon the excuse of reverence for times past and cling to it desperately. Such proud, obstinate, ridiculous judgments I have encountered many times, and once even in England."

"What!" I said. "Were you ever in my country?"

"Yes," he answered, "I spent several months there. It was not long after the revolt of the Cornishmen against the king had been put down, with the miserable slaughter of the rebels.[4] During my stay I was deeply beholden to the reverend father John Cardinal Morton,[5] archbishop of Canterbury, and in

---

4. Angered by the greedy taxation of Henry VII, an army of Cornishmen marched on London in 1497 but were defeated at the Battle of Blackheath.

5. Morton (1420–1500) was a distinguished prelate, statesman, and administrator. More's father, following a custom of the age, sent his son to serve as a page for two years (1490–92) in the cardinal's household; the seventy-year-old Morton is said to have been so impressed with the twelve-year-old More that he arranged for his education at Oxford.

addition at that time lord chancellor of England. He was a man, my dear Peter (for More knows about him, and can tell what I'm going to say), as much respected for his wisdom and virtue as for his authority. He was of medium height, not bent over despite his years; his looks inspired respect rather than fear. In conversation, he was not forbidding, though serious and grave. When suitors came to him on business, he liked to test their spirit and presence of mind by speaking to them sharply, though not rudely. He liked to uncover these qualities, which were those of his own nature, as long as they were not carried to the point of effrontery; and he thought such men were best qualified to carry on business. His speech was polished and pointed; his knowledge of the law was great; he had an incomparable understanding and a prodigious memory, for he had improved extraordinary natural abilities by study and practice. At the time when I was in England, the king relied heavily on his advice, and he seemed the chief support of the nation as a whole. He had been taken from school to court when scarcely more than a boy, had devoted all his life to important business, and had acquired from weathering violent changes of fortune and many great perils a supply of practical wisdom, which is not soon lost when so purchased.

"One day when I was dining with him, there was present a layman, learned in the laws of your country, who for some reason took occasion to praise the rigid execution of justice then being practiced upon thieves. They were being executed everywhere, he said, with as many as twenty at a time being hanged on a single gallows.[6] And then he declared that he could not understand how so many thieves sprang up everywhere, when so few of them escaped hanging. I ventured to speak freely before the cardinal, and said, 'There is no need to wonder: this way of punishing thieves goes beyond the call of justice, and is not, in any case, for the public good. The penalty is too harsh in itself, yet it isn't an effective deterrent. Simple theft[7] is not so great a crime that it ought to cost a man his life, yet no punishment however severe can withhold those from robbery who have no other way to eat. In this matter not only you in England but a good part of the world seem to imitate bad schoolmasters, who would rather whip their pupils than teach them. Severe and terrible punishments are enacted against theft, when it would be much better to enable every man to earn his own living, instead of being driven to the awful necessity of stealing and then dying for it.'

"'Oh, we've taken care of that,' said the fellow. 'There are the trades and there is farming, by which men may make a living unless they choose deliberately to be rogues.'

"'Oh no you don't,' I said, 'you won't get out of it that way. We may disregard for the moment the cripples who come home from foreign and civil wars, as lately from the Cornish battle and before that from your wars with France. These men, who have lost limbs in the service of king and country, are too badly crippled to follow their old trades, and too old to learn new ones. But since wars occur only from time to time, let us, I say, disregard these men, and consider what happens every day. There are a great many noblemen who live idly like drones off the labor of others, their tenants

---

6. Later in the 16th century, Holinshed's *Chronicles* recorded that 72,000 thieves and vagabonds were hanged in the reign of Henry VIII alone.

7. Theft is "simple" when not accompanied by violence or intimidation.

whom they bleed white by constantly raising their rents. (This is the only instance of their tightfistedness, because they are prodigal in everything else, ready to spend their way to the poorhouse.) These noblemen drag around with them a great train of idle servants,[8] who have never learned any trade by which they could earn a living. As soon as their master dies, or they themselves fall ill, they are promptly turned out of doors, for lords would rather support idlers than invalids, and the son is often unable to maintain as big a household as his father had, at least at first. Those who are turned off soon set about starving, unless they set about stealing. What else can they do? Then when a wandering life has left their health impaired and their clothes threadbare, when their faces look pinched and their garments tattered, men of rank will not care to engage them. And country people dare not do so, for they don't have to be told that one who has been raised softly to idle pleasures, who has been used to swaggering about with sword and buckler, is likely to look down on the whole neighborhood and despise everybody else as beneath him. Such a man can't be put to work with spade and mattock; he will not serve a poor man faithfully for scant wages and sparse diet.'

" 'But we ought to encourage these men in particular,' said the lawyer. 'In case of war the strength and power of our army depend on them, because they have a bolder and nobler spirit than workmen and farmers have.'

" 'You may as well say that thieves should be encouraged for the sake of wars,' I answered, 'since you will never lack for thieves as long as you have men like these. In fact thieves don't make bad soldiers, and soldiers turn out to be pretty good robbers—so nearly are these two ways of life related. But the custom of keeping too many retainers is not peculiar to this nation; it is common to almost all of them. France suffers from an even more grievous plague. Even in peacetime—if you can call it peace—the whole country is crowded with foreign mercenaries, imported on the same principle that you've given for your noblemen keeping idle servants.[9] Wise fools think that the public safety depends on having ready a strong army, preferably of veteran soldiers. They think inexperienced men are not reliable, and they sometimes hunt out pretexts for war, just so they may have trained soldiers and experienced cutthroats—or, as Sallust neatly puts it, that "hand and spirit may not grow dull through lack of practice."[1] But France has learned to her cost how pernicious it is to feed such beasts. The examples of the Romans, the Carthaginians, the Syrians,[2] and many other peoples show the same thing; for not only their governments but their fields and even their cities were ruined more than once by their own standing armies. Besides, this preparedness is unnecessary: not even the French soldiers, practiced in arms from their cradles, can boast of having often got the best of your raw recruits.[3] I shall say no more on this point, lest I seem to flatter present

---

8. Some of these were household servants; others were the last vestiges of the private armies by which, under feudalism, every lord was followed.
9. Charles VII of France (reigned 1422–61) had tried to establish a national army, but his successors reverted to mercenaries, mostly Swiss infantrymen.
1. Paraphrasing the *Catiline* (16.3) of the Roman historian Sallust (86–35 B.C.E.).
2. The Romans and Carthaginians both had to

fight servile wars against gladiators and mercenaries. The victimizers of the Syrians that Hythloday has in mind are probably the Mamelukes, a military caste of foreign extraction that ruled, from the 13th century to the early 16th, a state that included much of the Middle East.
3. Past English victories over the French included Crécy (1346), Poitiers (1356), and Henry V's triumph at Agincourt (1415).

company. At any rate, neither your town workmen nor your rough farm laborers—except for those whose physiques aren't suited for strength or boldness, or whose spirits have been cowed by inability to feed their families—seem to be much afraid of fighting the idle attendants of noblemen. So you need not fear that retainers, once strong and vigorous (for that's the only sort noblemen deign to corrupt), but now soft and flabby because of their idle, effeminate life, would be weakened if they were taught practical crafts to earn their living, and trained to manly labor. Anyway, I cannot think it's in the public interest to maintain for the emergency of war such a vast multitude of people who trouble and disturb the peace. You never have war unless you choose it, and peace is always more to be considered than war. Yet this is not the only circumstance that makes thieving necessary. There is another one, which, I believe, applies more especially to you Englishmen.'

"'What is that?' asked the cardinal.

"'Your sheep,' I replied, 'that used to be so meek and eat so little. Now they have become so greedy and fierce that they devour human beings themselves, as I hear.[4] They devastate and depopulate fields, houses, and towns. For in whatever parts of the land the sheep yield the softest and most expensive wool, there the nobility and gentry, yes, and even some abbots—holy men—are not content with the old rents that the land yielded to their predecessors. Living in idleness and luxury, without doing any good to society, no longer satisfies them; they have to do positive harm. For they leave no land free for the plow: they enclose every acre for pasture; they destroy houses and abolish towns, keeping only the churches, and those for sheep-barns. And as if enough of your land were not already wasted on woods and game-preserves, these worthy men turn all human habitations and cultivated fields back to wilderness. Thus one greedy, insatiable glutton, a frightful plague to his native country, may enclose many thousand acres of land within a single hedge. The tenants are dismissed; some are stripped of their belongings by trickery or brute force, or, wearied by constant harassment, are driven to sell them. By hook or by crook these miserable people—men, women, husbands, wives, orphans, widows, parents with little children, whole families (poor but numerous, since farming requires many hands)—are forced to move out. They leave the only homes familiar to them, and they can find no place to go. Since they cannot afford to wait for a buyer, they sell for a pittance all their household goods, which would not bring much in any case. When that little money is gone (and it's soon spent in wandering from place to place), what remains for them but to steal, and so be hanged—justly, you'd say!—or to wander and beg? And yet if they go tramping, they are jailed as idle vagrants. They would be glad to work, but they can find no one who will hire them. There is no need for farm labor, in which they have been trained, when there is no land left to be planted. One herdsman or shepherd can look after a flock of beasts large enough to stock an area that would require many hands if it were plowed and harvested.

---

4. This vivid image introduces Hythloday's treatment of the social dislocation brought about by "enclosure"—the gradual amalgamation and fencing, over a period extending from the 12th century to the 19th, of the open fields of the feudal system: one incentive to the practice was the increasing profitability of the wool trade.

" 'This enclosing has had the effect of raising the price of food in many places. In addition, the price of raw wool has risen so much that poor people who used to make cloth are no longer able to buy it, and so great numbers are forced from work to idleness. One reason is that after the enlarging of the pasture-land, a murrain killed a great number of sheep—as though God were punishing greed by sending a plague upon the animals, which in justice should have fallen on the owners! But even if the number of sheep should increase greatly, their price will not fall a penny. The reason is that the wool trade, though it can't be called a monopoly, because it isn't in the hands of one single person, is concentrated in few hands (an oligopoly, you might say), and these so rich that the owners are never pressed to sell until they have a mind to, and that is only when they can get their price.

" 'For the same reason other kinds of livestock also are priced exorbitantly, the more so because with so many farmhouses being pulled down, and farming in a state of decay, there are not enough people to look after the breeding of animals. These rich men will not breed other animals as they do lambs, but buy them lean and cheap, fatten them in their own pastures, and then sell them at a high price. I don't think the full impact of this bad system has yet been felt. We know these dealers raise prices where the fattened animals are sold. But when, over a period of time, they keep buying beasts from other localities faster than they can be bred, then as the supply gradually diminishes where they are purchased, a severe shortage is bound to ensue. So your island, which seemed especially fortunate in this matter, will be ruined by the crass avarice of a few. For the high food prices cause everyone to dismiss as many retainers as he can from his household; and what, I ask, can these men do, but rob or beg? And a man of courage is more likely to steal than to cringe.

" 'To make this hideous poverty and scarcity worse, they exist side by side with wanton luxury.[5] Not only the servants of noblemen, but tradespeople, even some farmers, and people of every social rank are given to ostentatious dress and gluttonous greed. Look at the eating houses, the bawdy houses, and those other places just as bad, the wine bars and alehouses. Look at all the crooked games of chance, dice, cards, backgammon, tennis, bowling, and quoits, in which money slips away so fast. Don't all these lead their habitués straight to robbery? Banish these blights, make those who have ruined farmhouses and villages restore them, or hand them over to someone who will rebuild. Restrict the right of the rich to buy up anything and everything, and then to exercise a kind of monopoly. Let fewer people be brought up in idleness. Let agriculture be restored and the wool manufacture revived as an honest trade, so there will be useful work for the whole crowd of those now idle—whether those whom poverty has already made into thieves, or those whom vagabondage and habits of lazy service are converting, just as surely, into the robbers of the future.

" 'If you do not find a cure for these evils, it is futile to boast of your justice in punishing theft. Your policy may look superficially like justice, but in

---

5. Luxurious living was not, in fact, characteristic of the reign of the parsimonious Henry VII (when Hythloday is supposed to be addressing Cardinal Morton). More is projecting onto the earlier period, perhaps unconsciously, a kind of extravagant display that began in 1509 with the accession of Henry VIII.

reality it is neither just nor practical. If you allow young folk to be abominably brought up and their characters corrupted, little by little, from childhood; and if then you punish them as grownups for committing crimes to which their early training has inclined them, what else is this, I ask, but first making them thieves and then punishing them for it?'

"As I was speaking thus, the lawyer had made ready his answer, choosing the usual style of disputants who are better at summing up than at replying, and who like to show off their memory. So he said to me, 'You have talked very well for a stranger, but you have heard about more things than you have been able to understand correctly. I will make the matter clear to you in a few words. First, I will summarize what you have said; then I will show how you have been misled by ignorance of our customs; finally, I will demolish all your arguments and reduce them to rubble. And so to begin where I promised, on four points you seemed to me—'

"'Hold your tongue,' said the cardinal, 'for you won't be finished in a few words, if this is the way you start. We will spare you the trouble of answering now, and reserve the pleasure of your reply till our next meeting, which will be tomorrow, if your affairs and Raphael's permit it. Meanwhile, my dear Raphael, I am eager to hear why you think theft should not be punished with death, or what other punishment you think would be more in the public interest. For I'm sure even you don't think it should go unpunished entirely. Even as it is, the fear of death does not restrain evildoers; once they were sure of their lives, as you propose, what force or fear could restrain them? They would look on a lighter penalty as an open invitation to commit more crimes—it would be like offering them a reward.'

"'It seems to me, most kind and reverend father,' I said, 'that it's altogether unjust to take someone's life for taking money. Nothing in the world that fortune can bestow is equal in value to a human life. If they say the thief suffers not for the money, but for violation of justice and transgression of laws, then this extreme justice should really be called extreme injury.[6] We ought not to approve of these fierce Manlian edicts[7] that invoke the sword for the smallest violations. Neither should we accept the Stoic view that considers all crimes equal,[8] as if there were no difference between killing a man and taking a coin from him. If equity means anything, there is no proportion or relation at all between these two crimes. God has said, "Thou shalt not kill"; shall we kill so readily for the theft of a bit of small change? Perhaps it will be argued that God's commandment against killing does not apply where human law allows it. But then what prevents men from making other laws in the same way—perhaps even laws legalizing rape, adultery, and perjury? God has taken from each person the right not only to kill another, but even to kill himself. If mutual consent to human laws on manslaughter entitles men freely to exempt their agents from divine law and allows them to kill those condemned by human decrees where God has given no precedent, what is this but preferring the law of man to the law of God? The result will be that in every situation men will decide for themselves how far it suits

6. Echoing the classical adage *summum ius, summa iniuria*, long cited in discussions of equity.
7. Manlian edicts (like those imposed by the Roman consul Titus Manlius in the 4th century

B.C.E.) are proverbially strict. Manlius executed his own son for disobeying one of them.
8. This view was actually maintained by some of the ancient Stoic philosophers.

them to observe the laws of God. The law of Moses was harsh and severe, as for an enslaved and stubborn people, but it punished theft with a fine, not death.[9] Let us not think that in his new law of mercy, where he rules us with the tenderness of a father, God has given us greater license to be cruel to one another.

"'These are the reasons why I think it is wrong to put thieves to death. But surely everybody knows how absurd and even harmful to the public welfare it is to punish theft and murder alike. If theft carries the same penalty as murder, the thief will be encouraged to kill the victim whom otherwise he would only have robbed. When the punishment is the same, murder is safer, since one conceals both crimes by killing the witness. Thus while we try to terrify thieves with extreme cruelty, we really invite them to kill the innocent.

"'As for the usual question of what more suitable punishment can be found, in my judgment it would be much easier to find a better one than a worse. Why should we question the value of the punishments long used by the Romans, who were most expert in the arts of government? They condemned those convicted of heinous crimes to work, shackled, for life, in stone quarries and mines. But of all the alternatives, I prefer the method which I observed in my Persian travels, among the people commonly called the Polylerites.[1] They are a sizable nation, not badly governed, free and subject only to their own laws, except that they pay annual tribute to the Persian king. Living far from the sea, they are nearly surrounded by mountains. Being contented with the products of their own land, which is by no means unfruitful, they do not visit other nations, nor are they much visited. According to their ancient customs, they do not try to enlarge their boundaries, and easily protect themselves behind their mountains by paying tribute to their overlord. Thus they have no wars and live in a comfortable rather than a showy manner, more contented than renowned or glorious. Indeed, I think they are hardly known by name to anyone but their next-door neighbors.

"'In their land, whoever is found guilty of theft must make restitution to the owner, not (as elsewhere) to the prince; they think the prince has no more right to the stolen goods than the thief. If the stolen property has disappeared, its value is repaid from the thief's possessions. Whatever remains of those is handed over to his wife and children, while the thief himself is sentenced to hard labor.

"'Unless their crimes were compounded with atrocities, thieves are neither imprisoned nor shackled, but go freely and unconstrained about their work on public projects. If they shirk and do their jobs slackly, they are not chained, but they are whipped. If they work hard, they are treated without any indignities, except that at night after roll call they are locked up in their dormitories. Apart from constant work, they undergo no discomfort in living. As they work for the public good, they are decently fed out of the public stores, though arrangements vary from place to place. In some districts they are supported by alms. Unreliable as this support may seem, the Polylerites are so compassionate that no way is found more rewarding. In other places, public revenues are set aside for their support, or a special tax is levied on

---

9. The Mosaic law is that spelled out in the first verses of Exodus 22. It provides various penalties for theft, but nowhere death. This is contrasted with the "new law" of Christ, under which England is supposed to be operating.
1. From Greek: "the People of Much Nonsense."

every individual for their use; and sometimes they do not do public work, but anyone in need of workmen can go to the market and hire some of them by the day at a set rate, a little less than that for free men. If they are lazy, it is lawful to whip them. Thus they never lack for work, and each one of them brings a little profit into the public treasury beyond the cost of his keep.

"'They are all dressed in clothes of the same distinctive color. Their hair is not shaved but trimmed close about the ears,[2] and the tip of one ear is cut off. Their friends are allowed to give them food, drink, or clothing, as long as it is of the proper color; but to give them money is death, both to the giver and to the taker. It is just as serious a crime for any free man to take money from them for any reason whatever; and it is also a capital crime for any of these slaves (as the condemned are called) to carry weapons. In each district of the country they are required to wear a special badge. It is a capital crime to throw away the badge, to go beyond one's own district, or to talk with a slave of another district. Plotting escape is no more secure than escape itself: it is death for any other slave to know of a plot to escape, and slavery for a free man. On the other hand, there are rewards for informers— money for a free man, freedom for a slave, and for both of them pardon and amnesty. Thus it can never be safer for them to persist in an illicit scheme than to renounce it.

"'Such are their laws and policies in this matter. It is clear how mild and practical they are, for the aim of the punishment is to destroy vices and save men. The criminals are treated so that they become good of necessity, and for the rest of their lives they atone for the wrong they have done before. There is so little danger of relapse that travelers going from one part of the country to another think slaves the most reliable guides, changing them at the boundary of each district. The slaves have no means of committing robbery, since they are unarmed, and any money in their possession is evidence of a crime. If caught, they would be punished, and there is no hope of escape anywhere. Since every bit of a slave's clothing is unlike the usual clothing of the country, how could a slave escape, unless he fled naked? Even then his cropped ear would give him away. Might not the slaves form a conspiracy against the government? Perhaps. But the slaves of one district could hardly expect to succeed unless they first involved in their plot the slave-gangs of many other districts. And that is impossible, since they are not allowed to meet or talk together or even to greet one another. No one would risk a plot when they all know joining is so dangerous to the participant and betrayal so profitable to the informer. Besides, no one is quite without hope of gaining his freedom eventually if he accepts his punishment in the spirit of obedience and patience, and gives promise of future good conduct. Indeed, every year some are pardoned as a reward for their submissive behavior.'

"When I had finished this account, I added that I saw no reason why this system could not be adopted even in England, and with much greater advan-

---

2. At this point in the text, the early editions have a marginal gloss—in translation, "Yet nowadays the servants of noblemen think such a haircut quite handsome." This is one of a series of some 200 glosses, which were supplied by Peter Giles after Erasmus shared More's manuscript with him. The glosses range in length from a single word to a full sentence and provide a valuable record of the response to *Utopia* (especially to Book II, where they are heavily concentrated) by a particularly well-positioned member of the humanist audience for it. The present edition includes a selection of the more pungent glosses, as footnotes.

tage than the 'justice' which my legal antagonist had praised so highly. But the lawyer replied that such a system could never be established in England without putting the commonwealth in serious peril. And so saying, he shook his head, made a wry face, and fell silent. And all the company sided with him.

"Then the cardinal remarked, 'It is not easy to guess whether this scheme would work well or not, since nobody has yet tried it out. But perhaps when the death sentence has been passed on a thief, the king might reprieve him for a time without right of sanctuary,[3] and thus see how the plan worked. If it turned out well, then he might establish it by law; if not, he could execute immediate punishment on the man formerly condemned. This would be neither less nor more unjust than if the condemned man had been put to death at once, and the experiment would involve no risk. I think vagabonds too might be treated this way, for though we have passed many laws against them, they have had no real effect as yet.'

"When the cardinal had concluded, they all began praising enthusiastically ideas which they had received with contempt when I suggested them; and they particularly liked the idea about vagabonds, because it was the cardinal's addition.

"I don't know whether it is worthwhile telling what followed, because it was silly, but I'll tell it anyhow, for there's no harm in it, and it bears on our subject. There was a hanger-on standing around, who was so good at playing the fool that you could hardly tell him from the real thing. He was constantly making jokes, but so awkwardly that we laughed more at him than at them; yet sometimes a rather clever thing came out, confirming the old proverb that a man who throws the dice often will sooner or later make a lucky cast. One of the company happened to say that in my speech I had taken care of the thieves, and the cardinal had taken care of the vagabonds, so now all that was left to do was to take care of the poor whom sickness or old age had reduced to poverty and kept from earning a living.

"'Leave that to me,' said the fool, 'and I'll set it right at once. These are people I'm eager to get out of my sight, having been so often vexed with them and their woeful complaints. No matter how pitifully they beg for money, they've never whined a single penny out of my pocket. They can't win with me: either I don't want to give them anything, or I haven't anything to give them. Now they're getting wise; they know me so well, they don't waste their breath, but let me pass without a word or a hope—no more, by heaven, than if I were a priest. But I would make a law sending all these beggars to Benedictine monasteries, where the men could become lay brothers,[4] as they're called, and the women could be nuns.'

"The cardinal smiled and passed it off as a joke; the rest took it seriously. But a certain friar, a theologian, took such pleasure in this jest at the expense of priests and monks that he too began to make merry, though generally he was grave to the point of sourness. 'Even so, you will not get rid of the beggars,' he began, 'unless you take care of us friars[5] too.'

---

3. In earlier days almost any criminal could take sanctuary in any church and be safe from the law. By More's time the privilege had been considerably abridged.
4. Men who lived and worked in monasteries (mostly performing menial tasks) but who were not admitted to clerical orders.
5. Members of a mendicant (begging) order, as opposed to monks, who live, and labor, in a cloister.

"'You have been taken care of already,' retorted the fool. 'The cardinal provided for you splendidly when he said vagabonds should be arrested and put to work, for you friars are the greatest vagabonds of all.'

"When the company, watching the cardinal closely, saw that he admitted this jest like the other, they all took it up with vigor—except for the friar. He, as you can easily imagine, was stung by the vinegar,[6] and flew into such a rage that he could not keep from abusing the fool. He called him a knave, a slanderer, a sneak, and a 'son of perdition,'[7] quoting the meanwhile terrible denunciations from Holy Scripture. Now the joker began to jest in earnest, for he was clearly on his own ground.

"'Don't get angry, good friar,' he said, 'for it is written, "In your patience possess ye your souls."'[8]

"In reply, the friar said, and I quote his very words, 'I am not angry, you gallows-bird, or at least I do not sin, for the psalmist says, "Be ye angry, and sin not."'[9]

"At this point the cardinal gently cautioned the friar to calm down, but he answered: 'No, my lord, I speak only from righteous zeal, as I ought to. For holy men have had great zeal. That is why Scripture says, "the zeal of thine house hath eaten me up,"[1] and we sing in church, "those who mocked Elisha as he went up to the house of God, felt the zeal of the baldhead,"[2] just as this mocker, this rascal, this guttersnipe may very well feel it.'

"'Perhaps you mean well,' said the cardinal, 'but you would act in a holier, and certainly in a wiser way, if you didn't set your wit against a fool's wit and try to spar with a buffoon.'

"'No, my lord,' he replied, 'I would not act more wisely. For Solomon himself, the wisest of men, said, "Answer a fool according to his folly,"[3] and that's what I'm doing now. I am showing him the pit into which he will fall if he does not take care. For if the many mockers of Elisha, who was only one bald man, felt the effects of his zeal, how much more effect shall be felt by a single mocker of many friars, who include a great many baldheads! And besides, we have a papal bull,[4] by which all who mock us are excommunicated.'

"When the cardinal saw there was no end to the matter, he nodded to the fool to leave, and turned the conversation to another subject. Soon after, he rose from table, and, going to hear petitioners, dismissed us.

"Look, my dear More, what a long story I have inflicted on you. I would be quite ashamed, if you had not yourself asked for it, and seemed to listen as if you did not want any part to be left out. Though I ought to have related this conversation more concisely, I did feel bound to recount it, so you might see how those who rejected what I said at first approved of it immediately afterward, when they saw the cardinal did not disapprove. In fact they went so far in their flattery that they indulged and almost took seriously ideas

6. Alluding to a phrase in Horace's *Satires* 1.7.32: *italo perfusus aceto*, "soaked in Italian vinegar."
7. John 17.12; 2 Thessalonians 2.3.
8. Luke 21.19.
9. Psalms 4.4. The Vulgate Bible translates as *Irascimini* ("Be angry") the Hebrew word that is rendered as "Stand in awe" in the King James Version.
1. Psalms 69.9.
2. Some children mocked Elisha, son of Elijah the

prophet, for his baldness; but he called two bears out of the woods, and they tore the bad children to pieces (2 Kings 23–24). The friar quotes a hymn that was based on this cautionary tale.
3. Proverbs 26.5. But compare the previous verse: "Answer not a fool according to his folly, lest thou also be like unto him."
4. A formal papal document, named after the seal (Latin *bulla*) that authenticated it.

that he tolerated only as the jesting of a fool. From this episode you can see how little courtiers would value me or my advice."

To this I answered, "You have given me great pleasure, my dear Raphael, for everything you've said has been both wise and witty. As you spoke, I seemed to be a child and in my own native land once more, through the pleasant recollection of that cardinal in whose court I was brought up as a lad. Dear as you are to me on other accounts, you cannot imagine how much dearer you are because you honor his memory so highly. Still, my friend Raphael, I don't give up my former opinion: I think if you could overcome your aversion to court life, your advice to a prince would be of the greatest advantage to the public welfare. This, after all, is the chief duty of every good man, including you. Your friend Plato thinks that commonwealths will become happy only when philosophers become kings or kings become philosophers.[5] No wonder we are so far from happiness, when philosophers do not condescend even to assist kings with their counsels."

"They are not so ungracious," Raphael replied, "but that they would gladly do it; in fact, they have already done it in a great many published books, if the rulers would only read their good advice. But doubtless Plato was right in foreseeing that unless kings became philosophical themselves, they would never take the advice of real philosophers, drenched as they are and infected with false values from boyhood on. Plato certainly had this experience with Dionysius of Syracuse.[6] If I proposed wise laws to some king, and tried to root out of his soul the seeds of evil and corruption, don't you suppose I would be either banished forthwith, or treated with scorn?

"Imagine, if you will, that I am at the court of the king of France.[7] Suppose I were sitting in his royal council, meeting in secret session with the king himself presiding, and all the cleverest councillors were hard at work devising a set of crafty machinations by which the king might keep hold of Milan, recover Naples, which has proved so slippery;[8] then overthrow the Venetians and subdue all Italy; next add Flanders, Brabant, and the whole of Burgundy to his realm, besides some other nations he has in mind to invade. One man urges him to make an alliance with the Venetians for just as long as the king finds it convenient—perhaps to develop a common strategy with them, and even allow them some of the loot, which can be recovered later when things work out according to plan. While one recommends hiring German mercenaries, his neighbor proposes paying the Swiss to stay neutral.[9] A fourth voice suggests soothing the offended divinity of the emperor with an offering of gold.[1] Still another, who is of a different mind, thinks a settlement should be made with the king of Aragon, and that, to cement the

---

5. Plato, *Republic* 5.473.

6. Plato is reported to have made three visits to Syracuse (in Sicily), where his attempts to reform the tyrant Dionysius the Elder, and later his son Dionysius the Younger, were notoriously unsuccessful.

7. At the time of writing, Francis I; at the time of Hythloday's supposed visit to England, either Charles VIII (d. 1498) or Louis XII (d. 1515). All three were would-be imperialists with hereditary claims to Milan and Naples, and all three bogged down in the intricacies of Italian political intrigue.

8. A marginal gloss at this point says, "Indirectly he discourages the French from seizing Italy." France gained Milan in 1499, lost it in 1512, and regained it at the Battle of Marignano in September 1515. Naples was won in 1495, lost in 1496, won again in 1501, and lost again in 1504. But, as Hythloday goes on to suggest, French territorial ambitions in the period extended almost limitlessly.

9. Among foot soldiers for hire, the Swiss ranked first, the Germans second.

1. Maximilian of Austria, Holy Roman Emperor, had grandiose schemes (he even dreamed of being pope) but little money. He was always accessible to a bribe.

peace, he should be allowed to take Navarre from its proper ruler.[2] Meanwhile, someone suggests snaring the prince of Castile into a marriage alliance—a first step would be to buy up some nobles of his court with secret pensions.[3]

"The hardest problem of all is what to do about England. They all agree that peace should be made, and that the alliance, which is weak at best, should be strengthened as much as possible; but while the English are being treated as friends, they should also be suspected as enemies. And so the Scots must be kept in constant readiness, poised to attack the English in case they stir ever so little.[4] Also a banished nobleman with some pretensions to the English throne must be secretly encouraged (there are treaties against doing it openly), and in this way pressure can be brought to bear on the English king, and a ruler kept in check who can't really be trusted.[5]

"Now in a meeting like this one, where so much is at stake, where so many brilliant men are competing to think up intricate strategies of war, what if an insignificant fellow like me were to get up and advise going on another tack entirely? Suppose I said the king should leave Italy alone and stay at home, because the single kingdom of France all by itself is almost too much for one man to govern well, and the king should not dream of adding others to it? Then imagine I told about the decrees of the Achorians,[6] who live off the island of Utopia toward the southeast. Long ago, these people went to war to gain another realm for their king, who had inherited an ancient claim to it through marriage. When they had conquered it, they soon saw that keeping it was going to be as hard as getting it had been. The seeds of war were constantly sprouting, their new subjects were continually rebelling or being attacked by foreign invaders, the Achorians had to be constantly at war for them or against them, and they saw no hope of ever being able to disband their army. In the meantime, they were being heavily taxed, money flowed out of their kingdom, their blood was being shed for the advantage of others, and peace was no closer than it had ever been. The war corrupted their own citizens by encouraging lust for robbery and murder; and the laws fell into contempt because their king, distracted with the cares of two kingdoms, could give neither one his proper attention.

"When they saw that the list of these evils was endless, the Achorians took counsel together and very courteously offered their king his choice of keeping whichever of the two kingdoms he preferred, because he couldn't rule them both. They were too numerous a people, they said, to be ruled by half a king; and they added that a man would not even hire a muledriver, if he had to divide his services with somebody else. The worthy king was thus obliged to be content with his own realm and give his new one to a friend, who before long was driven out.

---

2. Navarre was a small independent enclave astride the Pyrenees, long disputed between Spain and France.
3. The future emperor Charles V was a great matrimonial and diplomatic catch. (Before he was twenty, he had been engaged ten times.) The question of a French marriage that would unite the two greatest Continental and Catholic powers was continually in the air.

4. The Scots, as traditional enemies of England, were traditional allies of France.
5. The French had in fact supported various pretenders to the English throne—most recently, Richard de la Pole, the inheritor of the Yorkist claim.
6. The name arises from Greek *a* ("without") and *chora* ("place"): "the People without a Country."

"Finally, suppose I told the French king's council that all this warmongering, by which so many different nations were kept in turmoil as a result of one man's connivings, would exhaust his treasury and demoralize his people, and yet in the end come to nothing, through some mishap or other.[7] And therefore he should look after his ancestral kingdom, improve it as much as he could, cultivate it in every conceivable way. He should love his people and be loved by them; he should live among them, govern them kindly, and let other kingdoms alone, since his own is big enough, if not too big, for him. How do you think, my dear More, the other councillors would take this speech of mine?"

"Not very well, I'm sure," said I.

"Well, let's go on," he said. "Suppose the councillors of some other king are discussing various schemes for raising money to fill his treasury. One man recommends increasing the value of money when the king pays his debts and devaluing it when he collects his revenues.[8] Thus he can discharge a huge debt with a small payment, and collect a large sum when only a small one is due him. Another suggests a make-believe war, so that money can be raised under pretext of carrying it on; then, when the money is in, he can conclude a ceremonious peace treaty—which the deluded common people will attribute to the piety of their prince and his careful compassion for the lives of his subjects.[9] Another councillor calls to mind some old motheaten laws, antiquated by long disuse, which no one remembers being made and consequently everyone has transgressed. By imposing fines for breaking these laws, the king will get great sums of money, as well as credit for upholding law and order, since the whole procedure can be made to look like justice.[1] Another recommendation is that he forbid under particularly heavy fines a lot of practices that are contrary to the public interest; afterward, he can dispense with his own rules for large sums of money. Thus he pleases the people and makes a double profit, one from the heavy fines imposed on lawbreakers, and the other from selling dispensations. Meanwhile he seems careful of his people's welfare, since it is plain he will not allow private citizens to do anything contrary to the public interest, except for a huge price.

"Another councillor proposes that he work on the judges so that they will decide every case in favor of the king. They should be summoned to court often, and invited to debate his affairs in the royal presence. However unjust his claims, one or another of the judges, whether from love of contradiction, or desire to seem original, or simply to serve his own interest, will be bound to find some way of twisting the law in the king's favor. If the judges can be brought to differ, then the clearest matter in the world will be obscured, and the truth itself brought into question. The king is given leverage to interpret the law as he will, and everyone else will acquiesce from shame or fear. The judges will have no hesitation about supporting the

7. Francis I lost Milan in 1520 (that is, four years after More wrote this passage) and, in a catastrophic effort to regain it in 1522, was defeated and taken prisoner by Charles V.

8. Both Henry VII and (after *Utopia* was written) Henry VIII fiddled with the English currency in ways like those suggested here.

9. Something like this happened in 1492, when Henry VII not only pretended war with France on behalf of Brittany and levied taxes for the war (which was hardly fought) but collected a bribe from Charles VIII for not fighting it.

1. This had been common practice under Henry VII, whose ministers Empson and Dudley scratched up many forgotten laws for strictly mercenary purposes.

royal interest, for there are always plenty of pretexts for giving judgment in favor of the king. Either equity is on his side, or the letter of the law happens to make for him, or the words of the law can be twisted into obscurity—or, if all else fails, he can appeal above the law to the royal prerogative, which is a never-failing argument with judges who know their 'duty.'

"Then all the councillors agree with the famous maxim of Crassus: a king can never have too much gold, because he must maintain an army.[2] Further, that a king, even if he wants to, can do no wrong, for all property belongs to the king, and so do his subjects themselves; a man owns nothing but what the king, in his goodness, sees fit to leave him. The king should in fact leave his subjects as little as possible, because his own safety depends on keeping them from growing insolent with wealth and freedom. For riches and liberty make people less patient to endure harsh and unjust commands, whereas meager poverty blunts their spirits, makes them docile, and grinds out of the oppressed the lofty spirit of rebellion.

"Now at this point, suppose I were to get up again and declare that all these counsels are both dishonorable and ruinous to the king? Suppose I said his honor and his safety alike rest on the people's resources rather than his own? Suppose I said that the people choose a king for their own sake, not for his, so that by his efforts and troubles they may live in comfort and safety? This is why, I would say, it is the king's duty to take more care of his people's welfare than of his own, just as it is the duty of a shepherd who cares about his job to feed his sheep rather than himself.[3]

"They are absolutely wrong when they say that the people's poverty safeguards public peace—experience shows the contrary. Where will you find more squabbling than among beggars? Who is more eager for revolution than the man who is most discontented with his present position? Who is more reckless about creating disorder than the man who knows he has nothing to lose and thinks he may have something to gain? If a king is so hated or despised by his subjects that he can rule them only by mistreatment, plundering, confiscation, and pauperization of his people, then he'd do much better to abdicate his throne—for under these circumstances, though he keeps the name of authority, he loses all the majesty of a king. A king has no dignity when he exercises authority over beggars, only when he rules over prosperous and happy subjects. This was certainly what that noble and lofty spirit Fabricius meant when he said he would rather be a ruler of rich men than be rich himself.[4]

"A solitary ruler who enjoys a life of pleasure and self-indulgence while all about him are grieving and groaning is acting like a jailer, not a king. Just as an incompetent doctor can cure his patient of one disease only by throwing him into another, so it's an incompetent king who can rule his

---

2. Adapted from Cicero, *On Moral Obligation* 1.8.25. Crassus was a rich Roman who joined with Pompey and Caesar to form the First Triumvirate, which dominated Rome from 60 B.C.E. to Crassus's death seven years later. Legend has it that he died when a Parthian general, after defeating and capturing Crassus at the Battle of Carrhae, disproved his maxim by pouring molten gold down his throat.

3. This metaphor is one of the great commonplaces. Ezekiel 34.2 reads: "Woe be to the shepherds of Israel that do feed themselves! should not the shepherds feed the flocks?"

4. Gaius Fabricius Luscinus, who took part in the wars against Pyrrhus, king of Epirus (280–275 B.C.E.); the saying attributed to him here was actually coined by his colleague Manius Curius Dentatus, but it is quite in his spirit.

people only by depriving them of all life's pleasures. Such a king openly confesses that he does not know how to rule free men.

"A king of this stamp should correct his own sloth or arrogance, because these are the vices that cause people to hate or despise him. Let him live on his own income without wronging others, and limit his spending to his income. Let him curb crime, and by wise training of his subjects keep them from misbehavior, instead of letting it breed and then punishing it. Let him not suddenly revive antiquated laws, especially if they have been long forgotten and never missed. And let him never take money as a fine when a judge would regard an ordinary subject as a low fraud for claiming it.

"Suppose I should then describe for them the law of the Macarians,[5] a people who also live not far from Utopia? On the day that their king first assumes office, he must take an oath confirmed by solemn ceremonies that he will never have in his treasury at any one time more than a thousand pounds in gold, or its equivalent in silver. They say this law was made by an excellent king, who cared more for his country's prosperity than for his own wealth; he established it as a barrier against any king heaping up so much money as to impoverish his people.[6] He thought this sum would enable the king to put down rebellions or repel hostile invasions, but would not tempt him into aggressive adventures. His law was aimed chiefly at keeping the king in check, but he also wanted to ensure an ample supply of money for the daily business transactions of the citizens. Besides, a king who has to distribute all his excess money to the people will not be much disposed to seek out opportunities for extortion. Such a king will be both a terror to evildoers and beloved by the good.—Now, don't you suppose if I set such ideas before men strongly inclined to the contrary, they would turn deaf ears to me?"

"Stone deaf, indeed, there's no doubt about it," I said, "and no wonder! To tell you the truth, I don't think you should offer advice or thrust on people ideas of this sort, that you know will not be listened to. What good can it do? When your listeners are already prepossessed against you and firmly convinced of opposite opinions, how can you win over their minds with such out-of-the-way speeches? This academic philosophy is quite agreeable in the private conversation of close friends, but in the councils of kings, where grave matters are being authoritatively decided, there is no place for it."

"That is just what I was saying," Raphael replied. "There is no place for philosophy in the councils of kings."

"Yes, there is," I said, "but not for this school philosophy which supposes that every topic is suitable for every occasion. There is another philosophy that is better suited for political action, that takes its cue, adapts itself to the drama in hand, and acts its part neatly and appropriately. This is the philosophy for you to use. Otherwise, when a comedy of Plautus is being played, and the household slaves are cracking trivial jokes together, you propose to come on stage in the garb of a philosopher and repeat Seneca's speech to Nero from the *Octavia*.[7] Wouldn't it be better to take a silent role than to say

5. From Greek *makarios*, "blessed," "happy."
6. Once again More glances at the previous English monarch, Henry VII, who died the richest prince in Christendom and probably the most hated. He combined unscrupulous greed with skinflint stinginess.

7. Most of the plays of the Roman comic dramatist Plautus (ca. 250–184 B.C.E.) involve low intrigue: needy young men, expensive prostitutes, senile moneybags, and clever slaves, in predictable combinations. The tragedy *Octavia*, involving Seneca as a character and long

something wholly inappropriate, and thus turn the play into a tragicomedy? You pervert and ruin a play when you add irrelevant speeches, even if they are better than the original. So go through with the drama in hand as best you can, and don't spoil it all simply because you happen to think of a play by someone else that would be better.

"That's how things go in the commonwealth, and in the councils of princes. If you cannot pluck up bad ideas by the root, if you cannot cure long-standing evils as completely as you would like, you must not therefore abandon the commonwealth. Don't give up the ship in a storm because you cannot hold back the winds. And don't force strange ideas on people who you know have set their minds on a different course from yours. You must strive to influence policy indirectly, handle the situation tactfully, and thus what you cannot turn to good, you may at least make as little bad as possible. For it is impossible to make everything good unless you make all men good, and that I don't expect to see for a long time to come."

"The only result of this," he answered, "will be that while I try to cure others of madness, I'll be raving along with them myself. If I am to speak the truth, I will simply have to talk in the way I have described. For all I know, it may be the business of a philosopher to tell lies, but it certainly isn't mine. Though my advice may be repugnant and irksome to the king's councillors, I don't see why they should consider it eccentric to the point of folly. What if I told them the kind of thing that Plato advocates in his republic, or that the Utopians actually practice in theirs? However superior those institutions might be (and as a matter of fact they are), yet here they would seem inappropriate, because private property is the rule here, and there all things are held in common.

"People who have made up their minds to rush headlong down the opposite road are never pleased with someone who calls them back and tells them they are on the wrong course. But, apart from that, what did I say that could not and should not be said anywhere and everywhere? If we dismiss as out of the question and absurd everything which the perverse customs of men have made to seem alien to us, we shall have to set aside most of the commandments of Christ, even in a community of Christians. Yet he forbade us to dissemble them, and even ordered that what he had whispered to his disciples should be preached openly from the housetops.[8] Most of his teachings differ more radically from the common customs of mankind than my discourse did. But preachers, like the crafty fellows they are, have found that people would rather not change their lives to conform to Christ's rule, and so, just as you suggest, they have accommodated his teaching to the way people live, as if it were a leaden yardstick.[9] At least in that manner they can get the two things to correspond in some way or other. The only real thing they accomplish that I can see is to make people feel more secure about doing evil.

"And this is all that I could accomplish in the councils of princes. For either I would have different ideas from the others, and that would come to

---

supposed to have been written by him, is full of high seriousness. In the speech More refers to (lines 440–592), Seneca lectures Nero on the abuses of power.

8. Matthew 10.27; Luke 12.3.

9. A flexible measuring rod of lead was particu-

larly useful in the ancient building style known as the "Lesbian" mode, because of the great number of curved moldings. Aristotle in *Nicomachean Ethics* 5.10.7 uses it as a metaphor for adaptable moral standards.

the same thing as having no ideas at all, or else I would agree with them, and that, as Mitio says in Terence, would merely confirm them in their madness.[1] When you say I should 'influence policy indirectly,' I simply don't know what you mean; remember, you said I should try hard to handle the situation tactfully, and what can't be made good I should try to make as little bad as possible. In a council, there is no way to dissemble, no way to shut your eyes to things. You must openly approve the worst proposals, and consent to the most vicious policies. A man who went along only halfheartedly even with the worst decisions would immediately get himself a name as a spy and perhaps a traitor. How can one individual do any good when he is surrounded by colleagues who would more readily corrupt the best of men than do any reforming of themselves? Either they will seduce you by their evil ways or, if you keep yourself honest and innocent, you will be made a screen for the knavery and folly of others. Influencing policy indirectly! You wouldn't have a chance.

"This is why Plato in a very fine comparison declares that wise men are right in keeping clear of public business.[2] They see the people swarming through the streets and getting soaked with rain, and they cannot persuade them to go indoors and get out of the wet. They know if they go out themselves, they can do no good but only get drenched with the rest. So they stay indoors and are content to keep at least themselves dry, since they cannot remedy the folly of others.

"But as a matter of fact, my dear More, to tell you what I really think, as long as you have private property, and as long as money is the measure of all things, it is scarcely ever possible for a commonwealth to be just or happy. For justice cannot exist where all the best things in life are held by the worst people; nor can anyone be happy where property is limited to a few, since even those few are always uneasy, and the many are utterly wretched.

"So I reflect on the wonderfully wise and sacred institutions of the Utopians, who are so well governed with so few laws. Among them virtue has its reward, yet everything is shared equally, and everyone lives in plenty. I contrast them with the many other nations, which are constantly passing new ordinances and yet can never order their affairs satisfactorily. In these other nations, whatever a man can get he calls his own private property; but all the mass of laws old and new don't enable him to secure his own, or defend it, or even distinguish it from someone else's property—as is shown by innumerable and interminable lawsuits, fresh ones every day. When I consider all these things, I become more sympathetic to Plato and do not wonder that he declined to make laws for any people who refused to share their goods equally.[3] Wisest of men, he saw easily that the one and only road to the welfare of all lies through the absolute equality of goods. I doubt whether such equality can ever be achieved where property belongs to individuals. However abundant goods may be, when everyone tries to get as much as he can for his own exclusive use, a handful of men end up sharing the whole pile,

1. The allusion is to a comedy—*The Brothers* (lines 145–47)—by the Roman playwright Terence (ca. 190–159 B.C.E.).
2. *Republic* 6.496.
3. Diogenes Laertius (3rd century C.E.) reports that the Arcadians and Thebans united to build a great city, and asked Plato to be its legislator. He made communism a condition of his going there, and when the inhabitants would not consent, declined the offer (*Lives of Eminent Philosophers* 3.23).

and the rest are left in poverty. The result generally is two sorts of people whose fortunes ought to be interchanged: the rich are rapacious, wicked, and useless, while the poor are unassuming, modest men who work hard, more for the benefit of the public than of themselves.

"Thus I am wholly convinced that unless private property is entirely done away with, there can be no fair or just distribution of goods, nor can the business of mortals be happily conducted. As long as private property remains, by far the largest and the best part of the human race will be oppressed by a heavy and inescapable burden of cares and anxieties. This load, I admit, may be lightened to some extent, but I maintain it cannot be entirely removed. Laws might be made that no one should own more than a certain amount of land or receive more than a certain income. Or laws might be passed to prevent the prince from becoming too powerful and the populace too unruly. It might be made unlawful for public offices to be solicited, or put up for sale, or made burdensome for the officeholder by great expense. Otherwise, officials are tempted to get their money back by fraud or extortion, and only rich men can afford to accept positions which ought to be held by the wise. Laws of this sort, I agree, may have as much effect as poultices continually applied to sick bodies that are past cure. The social evils I mentioned may be alleviated and their effects mitigated for a while, but so long as private property remains, there is no hope at all of effecting a cure and restoring society to good health. While you try to cure one part, you aggravate the disease in other parts. Suppressing one symptom causes another to break out, since you cannot give something to one person without taking it away from someone else."[4]

"But I don't see it that way," I replied. "It seems to me that people cannot possibly live well where all things are in common. How can there be plenty of commodities where every man stops working? The hope of gain will not spur him on; he will rely on others, and become lazy. If men are driven by need, and yet cannot legally protect what they have gained, what can follow but continual bloodshed and turmoil, especially when respect for magistrates and their authority has been lost? I for one cannot conceive of authority existing among men who are equal to one another in every respect."[5]

"I'm not surprised," said Raphael, "that you think of it this way, since you have no idea, or only a false idea, of such a commonwealth. But you should have been with me in Utopia, and seen with your own eyes their manners and customs as I did—for I lived there more than five years, and would never have left, if it had not been to make that new world known to others. If you had seen them, you would frankly confess that you had never seen a people well governed anywhere but there."

"You will have a hard time persuading me," said Peter Giles, "that people in that new land are better governed than in the world we know. Our minds are not inferior to theirs, and our governments, I believe, are older. Long experience has helped us develop many conveniences of life, and by good luck we have discovered many other things which human ingenuity could never have hit upon."

---

4. Plato also employs the metaphor of societal disease, and of the statesman as physician (*Republic* 4.425E–426A; *Statesman* 279E–298E; Epistle 7, 330C–331A).

5. These objections to communism derive from the critique of the *Republic* in Aristotle's *Politics* 2.1–2.

"As for the relative ages of the governments," Raphael replied, "you might judge more accurately if you had read their histories. If we believe these records, they had cities before there were even people here. What ingenuity has discovered or chance hit upon could have turned up just as well in one place as the other. For the rest, I believe that even if we surpass them in natural intelligence, they leave us far behind in their diligence and zeal to learn.

"According to their chronicles, they had heard nothing of ultra-equatorials (that's their name for us) until we arrived, except that once, some twelve hundred years ago, a ship which a storm had blown toward Utopia was wrecked on their island. Some Romans and Egyptians were cast ashore, and never departed. Now note how the Utopians profited, through their diligence, from this one chance event. They learned every single useful art of the Roman empire either directly from their guests or indirectly from hints and surmises on which they based their own investigations. What benefits from the mere fact that on a single occasion some Europeans landed there! If a similar accident has hitherto brought anyone here from their land, the incident has been completely forgotten, as it will perhaps be forgotten in time to come that I was ever in their country. From one such accident they made themselves masters of all our useful inventions, but I suspect it will be a long time before we accept any of their institutions which are better than ours. This willingness to learn is, I think, the really important reason for their being better governed and living more happily than we do, though we are not inferior to them in brains or resources."

"Then let me implore you, my dear Raphael," said I, "to describe that island to us. Do not try to be brief, but explain in order everything relating to their land, their rivers, towns, people, manners, institutions, laws—everything, in short, that you think we would like to know. And you can take it for granted that we want to know everything that we don't know yet."

"There's nothing I'd rather do," he replied, "for these things are fresh in my mind. But it will take quite some time."

"In that case," I said, "let's first go to lunch. Afterward, we shall have all the time we want."

"Agreed," he said. So we went in and had lunch. Then we came back to the same spot, and sat down on the bench. I ordered my servants to take care that no one should interrupt us. Peter Giles and I urged Raphael to keep his promise. When he saw that we were attentive and eager to hear him, he sat silent and thoughtful a moment, and then began as follows.

Book II

[THE GEOGRAPHY OF UTOPIA][1]

The island of the Utopians is two hundred miles across in the middle part, where it is widest, and is nowhere much narrower than this except toward the two ends, where it gradually tapers. These ends, drawn toward one

---

1. The early editions of *Utopia* include, in Book II, eight section headings. These help in locating the treatment of particular topics in Hythloday's rather sprawling discourse, but since in several instances the headings identify only the *initial* topic of a section, they can also be misleading. In the present edition, they are supplemented by additional headings, enclosed in brackets to identify them as editorial insertions.

UTOPIAE INSVLAE TABVLA.

Woodcut map of Utopia, by Ambrosius Holbein (brother of the more famous Hans Holbein the Younger). This map appeared in the two 1518 editions.

another as if in a five-hundred-mile circle, make the island crescent-shaped, like a new moon.[2] Between the horns of the crescent, which are about eleven miles apart, the sea enters and spreads into a broad bay. Being sheltered from the wind by the surrounding land, the bay is never rough, but quiet and smooth instead, like a big lake. Thus nearly the whole inner coast is one great harbor, across which ships pass in every direction, to the great advantage of the people. What with shallows on one side and rocks on the

2. The island is similar to England in size, though not at all in shape.

other, the entrance into the bay is perilous. Near the middle of the channel, there is one rock that rises above the water, and so presents no danger in itself; on top of it a tower has been built, and there a garrison is kept. Since the other rocks lie underwater, they are very dangerous to navigation. The channels are known only to the Utopians, so hardly any strangers enter the bay without one of their pilots; and even they themselves could not enter safely if they did not direct their course by some landmarks on the coast. If these landmarks were shifted about, the Utopians could easily lure to destruction an enemy fleet coming against them, however big it was.

On the outer side of the island there are likewise occasional harbors; but the coast is rugged by nature, and so well fortified that a few defenders could beat off the attack of a strong force. They say (and the appearance of the place confirms this) that their land was not always an island. But Utopus, who conquered the country and gave it his name (it had previously been called Abraxa),[3] and who brought its rude and uncouth inhabitants to such a high level of culture and humanity that they now excel in that regard almost every other people, also changed its geography. After winning the victory at his first landing, he cut a channel fifteen miles wide where their land joined the continent, and caused the sea to flow around the country. He put not only the natives to work at this task, but all his own soldiers too, so that the vanquished would not think the labor a disgrace. With the work divided among so many hands, the project was finished quickly, and the neighboring peoples, who at first had laughed at his folly, were struck with wonder and terror at his success.

There are fifty-four cities on the island, all spacious and magnificent, identical in language, customs, institutions, and laws. So far as the location permits, all of them are built on the same plan and have the same appearance. The nearest are twenty-four miles apart, and the farthest are not so remote that a person cannot go on foot from one to the other in a day.

Once a year each city sends three of its old and experienced citizens to Amaurot to consider affairs of common interest to the island. Amaurot lies at the navel of the land, so to speak, and is convenient to every other district, so it acts as a capital. Every city has enough ground assigned to it so that at least twelve miles of farm land are available in every direction, though where the cities are farther apart, they have much more land.[4] No city wants to enlarge its boundaries,[5] for the inhabitants consider themselves good tenants rather than landlords. At proper intervals all over the countryside they have built houses and furnished them with farm equipment. These houses are inhabited by citizens who come to the country by turns. No rural household has fewer than forty men and women in it, besides two slaves bound to the land. A master and mistress, serious and mature persons, are in charge of each household. Over every thirty households is placed a single phylarch.[6] Each year twenty persons from each household move back to the city, after

---

3. The Greek Gnostic Basilides (2nd century C.E.) postulated 365 heavens and called the highest of them Abraxas. The Greek letters that constitute the word have numerical equivalents summing to 365, but what it actually *means* is unknown.

4. Each consisting of a central metropolis and the surrounding countryside, the Utopian cities recall the ancient Greek city-states.

5. The marginal gloss at this point: "But today this is the curse of all countries." Although Utopia exists in the present, the glosses repeatedly refer to it as if it belonged to the distant past, like classical Greece and Rome.

6. From Greek *phylarchos*, "ruler of a tribe."

completing a two-year stint in the country. In their place, twenty others are sent out from town, to learn farm work from those who have already been in the country for a year and are therefore better skilled in farming. They, in turn, will teach those who come the following year. If all were equally unskilled in farm work, and new to it, they might harm the crops out of ignorance. This custom of alternating farm workers is the usual procedure, so that no one will have to do such hard work unwillingly for more than two years; but many of them, who take a natural pleasure in farm life, are allowed to stay longer.

The farm workers till the soil, feed the animals, hew wood, and take it to the city by land or by water, as is more convenient. They breed an enormous number of chickens by a marvelous method. The farmers, not hens, hatch the eggs, by keeping them in a warm place at an even temperature. As soon as they come out of the shell, the chicks recognize the humans, follow them around, and are devoted to them instead of to their mothers.

They raise very few horses, and those full of mettle, which they keep only to exercise the young people in the art of horsemanship.[7] For all the work of plowing and hauling they use oxen, which they agree are inferior to horses over the short haul, but which can hold out longer under heavy burdens, are less subject to disease (as they suppose), and can be kept with less cost and trouble. Moreover, when oxen are too old for work, they can be used for meat.

Grain they use only to make bread.[8] They drink wine, apple or pear cider, or simple water, which they sometimes boil with honey or licorice, of which they have an abundance. Although they know very well, down to the last detail, how much food each city and its surrounding district will consume, they produce much more grain and cattle than they need for themselves, and share the surplus with their neighbors. Whatever goods the folk in the country need which cannot be produced there, they request of the town magistrates, and since there is nothing to be paid or exchanged, they get what they want without any trouble. They generally go to town once a month in any case, for the feast day. When harvest time approaches, the phylarchs in the country notify the town magistrates how many hands will be needed. Crews of harvesters come just when they're wanted, and in one day of good weather they can usually get in the whole crop.

THEIR CITIES, ESPECIALLY AMAUROT

If you know one of their cities, you know them all, for they're exactly alike, except where geography itself makes a difference. So I'll describe one of them, and no matter which. But what one rather than Amaurot, the most worthy of all?—since its eminence is acknowledged by the other cities, which send representatives to the annual meeting there; besides which, I know it best, because I lived there for five full years.

Well, then, Amaurot lies up against a gently sloping hill; the town is almost square in shape. From a little below the crest of the hill, it runs down about two miles to the river Anyder, and then spreads out along the river bank for a

---

7. In fact, horses were long extinct in the New World before Europeans imported them.

8. I.e., they don't, like the English, use it to make beer and ale.

somewhat greater distance. The Anyder rises from a small spring about eighty miles above Amaurot, but other streams flow into it, two of them being pretty big, so that, as it runs past Amaurot, the river has grown to a width of five hundred yards. It continues to grow even larger until at last, sixty miles farther along, it is lost in the ocean. In all this stretch between the sea and the city, and also for some miles above the city, the river is tidal, ebbing and flowing every six hours with a swift current.[9] When the tide comes in, it fills the whole Anyder with salt water for about thirty miles, driving the fresh water back. Even above that, for several miles farther, the water is brackish; but a little higher up, as it runs past the city, the water is always fresh, and when the tide ebbs, the river runs clean and sweet all the way to the sea.

The two banks of the river at Amaurot are linked by a bridge, built not on wooden piles but on remarkable stone arches. It is placed at the upper end of the city, farthest removed from the sea, so that ships can sail along the entire length of the city quays without obstruction. There is also another stream, not particularly large, but very gentle and pleasant, which gushes from the hill on which the city is situated, flows down through the center of town, and into the Anyder. The inhabitants have walled around the source of this river, which takes its rise a little outside the town, and joined it to the town proper so that if they should be attacked, the enemy would not be able to cut off the stream or divert or poison it. Water from the stream is carried by tile piping into various sections of the lower town. Where the terrain makes this impractical, they collect rain water in cisterns, which serve just as well.

The town is surrounded by a thick, high wall, with many towers and bastions. On three sides it is also surrounded by a dry ditch, broad and deep and filled with thorn hedges; on its fourth side the river itself serves as a moat. The streets are conveniently laid out for use by vehicles and for protection from the wind. Their buildings are by no means shabby; unbroken rows of houses face each other across the streets along the whole block. The streets are twenty feet wide.[1] Behind each row of houses—at the center of every block and extending the full length of the street—there are large gardens.

Every house has a door to the street and another to the garden. The doors, which are made with two leaves, open easily and swing shut automatically, letting anyone enter who wants to—so there is nothing private anywhere. Every ten years, they change houses by lot. The Utopians are very fond of these gardens of theirs. They raise vines, fruits, herbs, and flowers, so well cared for and flourishing that I have never seen any gardens more productive or elegant than theirs. They keep interested in gardening, partly because they delight in it, and also because of the competition between different blocks, which challenge one another to produce the best gardens. Certainly you will not easily find anything else in the whole city more useful or more pleasant to the citizens. And this gives reason to think that the founder of the city paid particular attention to the siting of these gardens.

They say that in the beginning the whole city was planned by Utopus himself, but that he left to posterity matters of adornment and improvement

9. Many of the details of Amaurot—its situation on a tidal river, its stone bridge (below), though not the location of that bridge—are reminiscent of London.
1. Lavish, by 16th-century standards.

such as could not be perfected in one man's lifetime. Their records began 1,760 years ago with the conquest of the island, have been diligently compiled, and are carefully preserved. From these it appears that the first houses were low, like cabins or peasant huts, built out of any sort of timber, with mud-plastered walls and pointed roofs thatched with straw. But now their houses are all three stories high and handsomely constructed; the fronts are faced with fieldstone, quarried rock, or brick, over rubble construction. The roofs are flat, and are covered with a kind of plaster that is cheap but fireproof, and more weather-resistant even than lead.[2] Glass (which is plentiful there) is used in windows to keep out the weather;[3] and they also use thin linen cloth treated with oil or gum so that it lets in more light and keeps out more wind.

THEIR OFFICIALS

Once a year, every group of thirty households elects an official, formerly called the syphogrant,[4] but now called the phylarch. Over every group of ten syphogrants with their households there is another official, once called the tranibor but now known as the head phylarch. All the syphogrants, two hundred in number, elect the governor. They take an oath to choose the man they think best qualified; and then by secret ballot they elect the governor from among four men nominated by the people of the four sections of the city. The governor holds office for life, unless he is suspected of aiming at a tyranny. Though the tranibors are elected annually, they are not changed for light or casual reasons. All their other officials hold office for a single year only.

The tranibors meet to consult with the governor every other day, and more often if necessary: they discuss affairs of state, and settle any disputes between private parties (there are very few), acting as quickly as possible.[5] The tranibors always invite two syphogrants to the senate chamber, different ones every day. There is a rule that no decision can be made on a matter of public business unless it has been discussed in the senate on three separate days. It is a capital offense to make plans about public business outside of the senate or the popular assembly. The purpose of these rules, they say, is to prevent the governor and the tranibors from conspiring together to alter the government and enslave the people. Therefore all matters which are considered important are first laid before the assembly of the syphogrants. They talk the matter over with the households they represent, debate it with one another, then report their recommendation to the senate. Sometimes a question is brought before the general council of the whole island.

The senate also has a standing rule never to discuss a matter on the day when it is first introduced; all new business is deferred to the next meeting.[6] They do this so that a man will not blurt out the first thought that occurs to

---

2. Used in More's time to roof important buildings.

3. During More's day in England window glass was not common; oiled cloth and lattices of wicker or wood were more frequent.

4. The word appears to be constructed from Greek *sophos* ("wise")—or perhaps *sypheos* ("of the sty")—plus *gerontes* ("old men"). For "tranibor" (below), the etymology seems to be *traneis* or

tranos ("clear," "plain," "distinct") plus *boros* ("devouring," "gluttonous"). There is no explanation of why Hythloday consistently uses the "older" form of the titles.

5. Marginal gloss: "A quick ending to disputes, which now are endlessly and deliberately prolonged."

6. Gloss: "Would that the same rule prevailed in our modern councils."

him, and then devote all his energies to defending those foolish impulses, instead of considering impartially the public good. They know that some men would rather jeopardize the general welfare than admit to having been heedless and shortsighted—so perverse and preposterous is their sense of pride. They should have had enough foresight at the beginning to speak with prudence rather than haste.

THEIR OCCUPATIONS

Agriculture is the one occupation at which everyone works, men and women alike, with no exceptions. They are trained in it from childhood, partly in the schools, where they learn theory, and partly through field trips to nearby farms, which make something like a game of practical instruction. On these trips they not only watch the work being done, but frequently pitch in and get a workout by doing the jobs themselves.

Besides farm work (which, as I said, everybody performs), each person is taught a particular trade of his own, such as wool-working, linen-making, masonry, metal-work, or carpentry. There is no other craft that is practiced by any considerable number of them.[7] Throughout the island people wear, and throughout their lives always wear, the same style of clothing, except for the distinction between the sexes, and between married and unmarried persons. Their clothing is attractive, does not hamper bodily movement, and serves for warm as well as cold weather; what is more, each household makes its own.

Every person (and this includes women as well as men) learns a second trade, besides agriculture. As the weaker sex, women practice the lighter crafts, such as working in wool or linen; the heavier jobs are assigned to the men. As a rule, the son is trained to his father's craft, for which most feel a natural inclination. But if anyone is attracted to another occupation, he is transferred by adoption into a family practicing the trade he prefers. Both his father and the authorities make sure that he is assigned to a grave and responsible householder. After someone has learned one trade, if he wants to learn another he gets the same permission. When he has learned both, he pursues whichever he likes better, unless the city needs one more than the other.

The chief and almost the only business of the syphogrants is to manage matters so that no one sits around in idleness, and assure that everyone works hard at his trade. But no one has to exhaust himself with endless toil from early morning to late at night, as if he were a beast of burden. Such wretchedness, really worse than slavery, is the common lot of workmen almost everywhere except Utopia.[8] Of the day's twenty-four hours, the Utopians devote only six to work. They work three hours before noon, when they go to lunch. After lunch they rest for a couple of hours, then go to work for another three hours. Then they have supper, and at eight o'clock (counting the first hour after noon as one) they go to bed, and sleep eight hours.

---

7. Would not considerable numbers also be employed making such things as pottery, harnesses, bread, and books, as well as in mining and the merchant marine? Presumably all the professionals—doctors, for example—are drawn from the class of scholars (see p. 605).

8. In England, for example, a law of 1514–15 required workmen to be present at the workplace from daybreak to nightfall in fall and winter and from 5 A.M. to between 7 and 8 P.M. in spring and summer. (There were breaks for meals and, in summer, for a brief afternoon nap.)

The other hours of the day, when they are not working, eating, or sleeping, are left to each person's individual discretion, provided that free time is not wasted in roistering or sloth but used properly in some chosen occupation. Generally these periods are devoted to intellectual activity. For they have an established custom of giving daily public lectures before dawn;[9] attendance at these lectures is required only of those who have been specially chosen to devote themselves to learning, but a great many other people, both men and women, choose voluntarily to attend. Depending on their interests, some go to one lecture, some to another. But if anyone would rather devote his spare time to his trade, as many do who don't care for the intellectual life, this is not discouraged; in fact, such persons are commended as especially useful to the commonwealth.

After supper, they devote an hour to recreation, in their gardens in summer, or during winter in the common halls where they have their meals. There they either play music or amuse themselves with conversation. They know nothing about gambling with dice, or other such foolish and ruinous games.[1] They do play two games not unlike chess. One is a battle of numbers, in which one number captures another. The other is a game in which the vices fight a battle against the virtues. The game is ingeniously set up to show how the vices oppose one another, yet combine against the virtues; then, what vices oppose what virtues, how they try to assault them openly or undermine them insidiously; how the defenses of the virtues can break the strength of the vices or skillfully elude their plots; and finally, by what means one side or the other gains the victory.[2]

But in all this, you may get a wrong impression, if we don't go back and consider one point more carefully. Because they allot only six hours to work, you might think the necessities of life would be in scant supply. This is far from the case. Their working hours are ample to provide not only enough but more than enough of the necessities and even the conveniences of life. You will easily appreciate this if you consider how large a part of the population in other countries exists without doing any work at all. In the first place, hardly any of the women, who are a full half of the population, work;[3] or, if they do, then as a rule their husbands lie snoring in bed. Then there is a great lazy gang of priests and so-called religious.[4] Add to them all the rich, especially the landlords, who are commonly called gentlemen and nobles. Include with them their retainers, that mob of swaggering bullies. Finally, reckon in with these the sturdy and lusty beggars who go about feigning some disease as an excuse for their idleness. You will certainly find that the things which satisfy our needs are produced by far fewer hands than you had supposed.

And now consider how few of those who do work are doing really essential things. For where money is the standard of everything, many vain, superfluous trades are bound to be carried on simply to satisfy luxury and

---

9. Renaissance universities got under way early: first lecture was between 5 and 7 A.M.
1. Marginal gloss: "But now dicing is the sport of princes."
2. Moral games of this general character were popular with Renaissance educators.
3. A strange statement, since in More's time most women selected, prepared, and cooked the family food; did the family laundry; performed a thousand other routine tasks of domestic drudgery; and were responsible for taking care of the children. In Utopia, too, they are responsible for at least some of these duties—cooking, childcare—in addition to practicing a craft and taking their turn at farmwork.
4. I.e., members of the various religious orders.

licentiousness. Suppose the multitude of those who now work were limited to a few trades, and set to producing just those commodities that nature really requires. They would be bound to produce so much that prices would drop and the workmen would be unable to gain a living. But suppose again that all the workers in useless trades were put to useful ones, and that all the idlers (who now guzzle twice as much as the workingmen who make what they consume) were assigned to productive tasks—well, you can easily see how little time would be enough and more than enough to produce all the goods that human needs and conveniences require—yes, and human pleasure too, as long as it's true and natural pleasure.

The experience of Utopia makes this perfectly apparent. In each city and its surrounding countryside barely five hundred of those men and women whose age and strength make them fit for work are exempted from it.[5] Among these are the syphogrants, who by law are free not to work; yet they don't take advantage of the privilege, preferring to set a good example to their fellow citizens. Some others are permanently exempted from work so that they may devote themselves to study, but only on the recommendation of the priests[6] and through a secret vote of the syphogrants. If any of these scholars disappoints their hopes, he becomes a workman again. On the other hand, it happens from time to time that a craftsman devotes his leisure so earnestly to study, and makes such progress as a result, that he is relieved of manual labor and promoted to the class of learned men. From this class of scholars are chosen ambassadors, priests, tranibors, and the governor himself, who used to be called Barzanes, but in their modern tongue is known as Ademus.[7] Since almost all the rest of the population is neither idle nor occupied in useless trades, it is easy to see why they produce so much in so short a working day.

Apart from all this, in several of the necessary crafts their way of life requires less total labor than does that of people elsewhere. In other countries, building and repairing houses requires the constant work of many men, because what a father has built, his thriftless heir lets fall into ruin; and then his successor has to repair, at great expense, what could easily have been maintained at a very small charge. Further, when a man has built a splendid house at vast cost, someone else may think he has finer taste, let the first house fall to ruin, and then build another one somewhere else for just as much money. But among the Utopians, where everything has been well ordered and the commonwealth properly established, building a brand-new home on a new site is a rare event. They are not only quick to repair damage, but foresighted in preventing it. The result is that their buildings last for a very long time with minimal repairs; and the carpenters and masons sometimes have so little to do that they are set to hewing timber and cutting stone in case some future need for it should arise.

---

5. I.e., are exempted from manual labor. As Hythloday proceeds to explain, in each city those exempted include the 200 syphogrants and the class of scholars, from which is chosen the other exempted individuals: the twenty tranibors, the governor, ambassadors, and the thirteen (p. 638, below) priests.

6. Who are in charge of the education of children (p. 639).
7. Marginal gloss: "Only the learned hold public office." "Ademus": from Greek for "Without People." "Barzanes": "Son of Zeus" (Hebrew—*bar*—plus Greek).

Consider, too, how little labor their clothing requires. Their work clothes are unpretentious garments made of leather, which last seven years. When they go out in public, they cover these rough working-clothes with a cloak. Throughout the entire island, these cloaks are of the same color, which is that of natural wool.[8] As a result, they not only need less wool than people in other countries, but what they do need is less expensive. Even so, they use linen cloth most, because it requires least labor. They like linen cloth to be white and wool cloth to be clean; but they put no price on fineness of texture. Elsewhere a man may not be satisfied with four or five woolen cloaks of different colors and as many silk shirts; or if he's a clotheshorse, even ten are not enough. But there everyone is content with a single cloak, and generally wears it for two years. There is no reason at all why he should want any others, for if he had them, he would not be better protected against the cold, nor would he appear in any way better dressed.

Since there is an abundance of everything, as a result of everyone working at useful trades and the trades requiring less work, they sometimes assemble great numbers of people to work on the roads, if any of them need repairing. And when there is no need even for this sort of work, then the officials very often proclaim a shorter workday, since they never force their citizens to perform useless labor. The chief aim of their constitution is that, whenever public needs permit, all citizens should be free to withdraw as much time as possible from the service of the body and devote themselves to the freedom and culture of the mind. For in that, they think, is the real happiness of life.

SOCIAL RELATIONS

Now I must explain how the citizens behave toward one another, the nature of their social relations, and how they distribute their goods within the society.

Each city, then, consists of households, the households consisting generally of blood-relations. When the women grow up and are married, they move into their husbands' households. On the other hand, male children and after them grandchildren remain in the family, and are subject to the oldest member, unless his mind has started to fail, in which case the next oldest takes his place. To keep the cities from becoming too large or too small, they take care that there should be no more than six thousand households in each (exclusive of the surrounding countryside), each family containing between ten and sixteen adults.[9] They do not, of course, try to regulate the number of minor children in a family. The limit on adults is easily observed by transferring individuals from a household with too many into a household with not enough. Likewise if a city has too many people, the extra persons serve to make up a shortage of population in other cities. And if the population throughout the entire island exceeds the quota, they enroll citizens out of

8. In a letter to Erasmus of ca. December 4, 1516, More identifies this garment as the habit of a Franciscan friar.
9. If an average household includes thirteen adults, and there are 6,000 households per city (not counting those on the surrounding farms), then there are about 78,000 adults per city; allowing for children and slaves, the total population must be well in excess of 100,000, making every Utopian city larger than all but the greatest European cities of the time. Whether More actually made these calculations (or whether there is really much point in making them) is another matter.

every city and plant a colony under their own laws on the mainland near them, wherever the natives have plenty of unoccupied and uncultivated land. Those natives who want to live with the Utopian settlers are taken in. When such a merger occurs, the two peoples gradually and easily blend together, sharing the same way of life and customs, much to the advantage of both. For by their policies the Utopians make the land yield an abundance for all, though previously it had seemed too poor and barren even to support the natives. But if the natives will not join in living under their laws, the Utopians drive them out of the land they claim for themselves, and if they resist make war on them. They think it is perfectly justifiable to make war on people who leave their land idle and waste, yet forbid the use of it to others who, by the law of nature, ought to be supported from it.

If for any reason one of their cities shrinks so sharply in population that it cannot be made up from other cities without bringing them too under proper strength, the numbers are restored by bringing people back from the colonies. This has happened only twice, they say, in their whole history, both times as a result of a frightful plague. They would rather that their colonies disappeared than that any of the cities on their island should get too small.

But to return to their manner of living. The oldest of every household, as I said, is the ruler. Wives are subject to their husbands, children to their parents, and generally the younger to their elders.[1] Every city is divided into four equal districts, and in the middle of each district is a market for all kinds of commodities. Whatever each household produces is brought here and stored in warehouses, each kind of goods in its own place. Here the head of each household looks for what he or his family needs, and carries off what he wants without any sort of payment or compensation. Why should anything be refused him? There is plenty of everything, and no reason to fear that anyone will claim more than he needs. Why would anyone be suspected of asking for more than is needed, when everyone knows there will never be any shortage? Fear of want, no doubt, makes every living creature greedy and rapacious—and, in addition, man develops these qualities out of sheer pride, pride which glories in getting ahead of others by a superfluous display of possessions. But this kind of vice has no place whatever in the Utopian way of life.

Next to the marketplace of which I just spoke are the food markets, where people bring all sorts of vegetables, fruit, and bread. Fish, meat, and poultry are also brought there from designated places outside the city, where running water can carry away all the blood and refuse. Bondsmen do the slaughtering and cleaning in these places: citizens are not allowed to do such work. The Utopians feel that slaughtering our fellow creatures gradually destroys the sense of compassion, which is the finest sentiment of which our human nature is capable. Besides, they don't allow anything dirty or filthy to be brought into the city, lest the air become tainted by putrefaction and thus infectious.

---

1. Utopian women enjoy considerably more equality with men than did their 16th-century European counterparts, but Utopian social relations as a whole exhibit the same patriarchal structure that had always been prevalent in Europe and was sanctioned in classical and biblical texts (e.g., Aristotle, *Politics* 1.5.1–2; Ephesians 5.22–6.4) as well as in many later ones.

Each block has its own spacious halls, equally distant from one another, and each known by a special name. In these halls live the syphogrants. Thirty families are assigned to each hall, to take their meals in common[2]— fifteen live on one side of the hall, fifteen on the other. The stewards of all the halls meet at a fixed time in the market and get food according to the number of persons for whom each is responsible.

But first consideration goes to the sick, who are cared for in public hospitals. Every city has four of these, built at the city limits, slightly outside the walls, and spacious enough to appear like little towns. The hospitals are large for two reasons: so that the sick, however numerous they may be, will not be packed closely and uncomfortably together, and also so that those who have a contagious disease, such as might pass from one to the other, may be isolated. The hospitals are well ordered and supplied with everything needed to cure the patients, who are nursed with tender and watchful care. Highly skilled physicians are in constant attendance. Consequently, though nobody is sent there against his will, there is hardly anyone in the city who would not rather be treated for an illness at the hospital than at home.

When the hospital steward has received the food prescribed for the sick by their doctors, the best of the remainder is fairly divided among the halls according to the number in each, except that special regard is paid to the governor, the high priest, and the tranibors, as well as to ambassadors and foreigners, if there are any. In fact, foreigners are very few; but when they do come, they have certain furnished houses assigned to them.

At the hours of lunch and supper, a brazen trumpet summons the entire syphogranty to assemble in their hall, except for those who are bedridden in the hospitals or at home. After the halls have been served with their quotas of food, nothing prevents an individual from taking food home from the marketplace. They realize that no one would do this without good reason. For while it is not forbidden to eat at home, no one does it willingly, because it is not thought proper; and besides, it would be stupid to take the trouble of preparing a worse meal at home when there is an elegant and sumptuous one near at hand in the hall.

In this hall, slaves do all the particularly dirty and heavy work. But planning the meal, as well as preparing and cooking the food, is carried out by the women alone, with each family taking its turn. Depending on their number, they sit down at three or more tables. The men sit with their backs to the wall, the women on the outside, so that if a woman has a sudden qualm or pain, such as occasionally happens during pregnancy, she may get up without disturbing the others and go off to the nurses.

A separate dining room is assigned to the nurses and infants, with a plentiful supply of cradles, clean water, and a warm fire. Thus the nurses may lay the infants down, or remove their swaddling clothes and let them refresh themselves by playing freely before the fire. Each child is nursed by its own mother, unless death or illness prevents. When that happens, the wives of the syphogrants quickly find a nurse. The problem is not difficult. Any

2. The institution of the common messes has precedents in ancient Sparta and in the designs for an ideal commonwealth by Plato (*Republic* 3.416E) and Aristotle (*Politics* 7.10.10). It has also been a feature of other communities with a utopian bent—for example, the Israeli kibbutzim.

woman who can, gladly volunteers for the job, since everyone applauds her kindness and the child itself regards its nurse as its natural mother.

Children under the age of five sit together in the nursery. All other minors, both boys and girls up to the age of marriage, either wait on table or, if not old and strong enough for that, stand by in absolute silence. Both groups eat whatever is handed to them by those sitting at the table, and have no other set time for their meals.

The syphogrant with his wife sits at the middle of the first table, in the highest part of the dining hall. This is the place of greatest honor, and from this table, which is placed crosswise to the others, the whole gathering can be seen. Two of the eldest sit with them, for they always sit in groups of four; if there is a church in the district, the priest and his wife sit with the syphogrant, so as to preside.[3] On both sides of them sit younger people, next to them older people again, and so through the hall: those of about the same age sit together, yet are mingled with others of a different age. The reason for this, as they explain it, is that the dignity of the aged, and the respect due them, may restrain the younger people from improper freedom of words and gestures, since nothing said or done at table can pass unnoticed by the old, who are present on every side.

Dishes of food are not served down the tables in order from top to bottom, but all the old persons, who are seated in conspicuous places, are served with the best food; and then equal shares are given to the rest. The old people, as they feel inclined, give their neighbors a share of those delicacies which are not plentiful enough to be served to everyone. Thus due respect is paid to seniority, yet everyone enjoys some of the benefits.

They begin every lunch and supper with some reading on a moral topic,[4] but keep it brief lest it become a bore. Taking that as an occasion, the elders introduce proper topics of conversation, which they try not to make gloomy or dull. They never monopolize the conversation with long monologues, but are eager to hear what the young people say. In fact, they deliberately draw them out, in order to discover the natural temper and quality of each one's mind, as revealed in the freedom of mealtime talk.

Their lunches are light, their suppers rather more elaborate, because lunch is followed by work, supper by rest and a night's sleep, which they think particularly helpful to good digestion. No evening meal passes without music, and the dessert course is never scanted; during the meal, they burn incense and scatter perfume, omitting nothing which will make the occasion festive. For they are somewhat inclined to think that no kind of pleasure is forbidden, provided harm does not come of it.

This is the pattern of life in the city; but in the country, where they are farther removed from neighbors, they all eat in their own homes. No family lacks for food, since, after all, whatever the city-dwellers eat comes originally from those in the country.

---

3. Marginal gloss: "Priest before prince. But now even bishops act as servants to royalty."
4. Humanists were fond of this social custom, the origins of which were part monastic, part classical.

THE TRAVELS [AND TRADE] OF THE UTOPIANS

Anyone who wants to visit friends in another city, or simply to see the place itself, can easily obtain permission from his syphogrant and tranibor, unless for some special reason he is needed at home. They travel together in groups, taking a letter from the governor granting leave to travel and fixing a day of return. They are given a wagon and a public slave to drive the oxen and look after them, but unless women are in the company they dispense with the wagon as an unnecessary bother. Wherever they go, though they take nothing with them, they never lack for anything, because they are at home everywhere. If they stay more than a day in one place, each one practices his trade there, and is kindly received by his fellow artisans.

Anyone who takes upon himself to leave his district without permission, and is caught without the governor's letter, is treated with contempt, brought back as a runaway, and severely punished. If he is bold enough to try it a second time, he is made a slave. Anyone who wants to stroll about and explore the extent of his own district is not prevented, provided he first obtains his father's permission and his wife's consent. But wherever he goes in the countryside, he gets no food until he has completed either a morning's or an afternoon's stint of work. On these terms, he may go where he pleases within his own district, yet be just as useful to the city as if he were at home.

So you see there is no chance to loaf or any pretext for evading work; there are no wine bars or alehouses or brothels, no chances for corruption, no hiding places, no spots for secret meetings. Because they live in the full view of all, they are bound to be either working at their usual trades or enjoying their leisure in a respectable way. Such customs must necessarily result in plenty of life's good things, and since they share everything equally, it follows that no one can ever be reduced to poverty or forced to beg.

In the senate at Amaurot (to which, as I said before, three representatives come every year from each city), they survey the island to find out where there are shortages and surpluses, and promptly satisfy one district's shortage with another's surplus. These are outright gifts; those who give receive nothing in return from those to whom they give. Though they give freely to one city, asking nothing in return, they get freely from another to which they gave nothing; and thus the whole island is like a single family.

After they have accumulated enough for themselves—and this they consider to be a full two-years' store, because next year's crop is always uncertain—then they export their surpluses to other countries: great quantities of grain, honey, wool, flax, timber, scarlet and purple dyestuffs, hides, wax, tallow, and leather, as well as livestock. One-seventh of their cargo they give freely to the poor of the importing country, and the rest they sell at moderate prices. In exchange they receive not only such goods as they lack at home (in fact, about the only important thing they lack is iron) but immense quantities of silver and gold. They have been carrying on trade for a long time now, and have accumulated a greater supply of the precious metals than you would believe possible. As a result, they now care very little whether they sell for cash or on credit, and most payments to them actually take the form of promissory notes. However, in all such transactions, they never trust individuals but insist that the foreign city become officially responsible. When the day of payment comes, the city collects the money due from private debtors, puts it into the treasury, and enjoys the use of it till the Utopians claim payment. Most of it, in fact, is never claimed. The Utopians think it hardly right to take what they don't need away from people who do need it. But if they need to lend some part of the money to another nation, then they call it in—as they do also when they must wage war. This is the only reason that they keep such an immense treasure at home, as a protection against extreme peril or sudden emergency. They use it above all to hire, at extravagant rates of pay, foreign mercenaries, whom they would much rather risk in battle than their own citizens. They know very well that for large enough sums of money many of the enemy's soldiers can themselves be bought off or set at odds with one another, either secretly or openly.[5]

[THEIR ATTITUDE TO GOLD AND SILVER]

For this reason, therefore, they have accumulated a vast treasure; but they do not keep it like a treasure. I'm really quite ashamed to tell you how they do keep it, because you probably won't believe me. I would not have believed it myself if someone had just told me about it; but I was there, and saw it with my own eyes. It is a general rule that the more different anything is from what people are used to, the harder it is to accept. But, considering that all their other customs are so unlike ours, a sensible judge will perhaps not be surprised that they treat gold and silver quite differently from the way we do. After all, they never do use money among themselves, but keep it only for a contingency which may or may not actually arise. So in the meanwhile they take care that no one shall overvalue gold and silver, of which money is made, beyond what the metals themselves deserve. Anyone can see, for example, that iron is far superior to either; men could not live without iron, by heaven, any more than without fire or water. But Nature granted to gold and silver no function with which we cannot easily dispense. Human folly has made them precious because they are rare. In contrast, Nature, like a most indulgent mother, has placed the best things out in the open, like air, water, and the earth itself; but vain and unprofitable things she has hidden away in remote places.

If in Utopia gold and silver were kept locked up in some tower, foolish heads among the common people might concoct a story that the governor and senate were out to cheat ordinary folk and get some advantage for themselves. They might indeed put the gold and silver into plate-ware and such handiwork, but then in case of necessity the people would not want to give up such articles, on which they had begun to fix their hearts, only to melt them down for soldiers' pay. To avoid all these inconveniences, they thought of a plan which conforms with their institutions as clearly as it contrasts with our own. Unless one has actually seen it working, their plan may seem incredible, because we prize gold so highly and are so careful about protecting it. While they eat from pottery dishes and drink from glass cups, well made but inexpensive, their chamber pots and all their humblest vessels, for use in the common halls and even in private homes, are made of gold and silver.[6] The chains and heavy fetters of slaves are also made of these metals.

5. Marginal gloss: "Better to avoid war by bribery or guile than to wage it with great loss of human blood."

6. Marginal gloss: "O magnificent scorn for gold!" Vespucci had reported Native Americans' indifference to gold and gems.

Finally, criminals who are to bear the mark of some disgraceful act are forced to wear golden rings in their ears and on their fingers, golden chains around their necks, and even golden headbands. Thus they hold gold and silver up to scorn in every conceivable way. As a result, if they had to part with their entire supply of these metals, which other nations give up with as much agony as if they were being disemboweled, the Utopians would feel it no more than the loss of a penny.

They pick up pearls by the seashore, and diamonds and garnets from certain cliffs, but never go out of set purpose to look for them. If they happen to find some, they polish them and give them to the children, who, when they are small, feel proud and pleased with such gaudy decorations. But after, when they grow a bit older, and notice that only babies like such toys, they lay them aside. Their parents don't have to say anything; the children simply put these trifles away out of shame, just as our children when they grow up put away their marbles, baubles, and dolls.

These customs so different from those of other people produce quite different attitudes: this never became clearer to me than it did in the case of the Anemolian[7] ambassadors, who came to Amaurot while I was there. Because they came to discuss important business, the national council had assembled ahead of time, three citizens from each city. The ambassadors from nearby nations, who had visited Utopia before and knew something of their customs, understood that fine clothing was not respected in that land, silk was despised, and gold a badge of contempt; therefore they always came in the very plainest of their clothes. But the Anemolians, who lived farther off and had had fewer dealings with the Utopians, had heard only that they all dressed alike and very simply; so they took for granted that their hosts had nothing to wear that they didn't put on. Being themselves rather more proud than wise, they decided to dress as resplendently as the very gods, and dazzle the eyes of the poor Utopians by the glitter of their garb.

Consequently the three ambassadors made a grand entry with a suite of a hundred attendants, all in clothing of many colors, and most in silk. Being noblemen at home, the ambassadors were arrayed in cloth of gold, with heavy gold chains on their necks, gold earrings, gold rings on their fingers, and sparkling strings of pearls and gems on their caps. In fact, they were decked out in all the articles which in Utopia are used to punish slaves, shame wrongdoers, or entertain infants. It was a sight to see how they strutted when they compared their finery with the dress of the Utopians, who had poured out into the streets to see them pass. But it was just as funny to see how wide they fell of the mark, and how far they were from getting the consideration they wanted and expected. Except for a very few Utopians who for some special reason had visited foreign countries, all the onlookers considered this pomp and splendor a mark of disgrace. They therefore bowed to the humblest of the party as lords, and took the ambassadors, because of their golden chains, to be slaves, passing them by without any reverence at all. You might have seen children, who had themselves thrown away their

---

7. From Greek *anemolios*, "windy." The story of the Anemolian ambassadors owes much to "Nigrinus," a dialogue by the Syrian satirist Lucian (2nd century C.E.) in which a rich Roman makes a fool of himself by stalking around Athens in a purple robe. More and Erasmus had published a volume of Latin translations of Lucian (who wrote in Greek) in 1506.

pearls and gems, nudge their mothers when they saw the ambassadors' jeweled caps, and say:

"Look at that big lummox, mother, who's still wearing pearls and jewels as if he were a little boy!"

But the mother, in all seriousness, would answer:

"Hush, son, I think he is one of the ambassadors' fools."

Others found fault with the golden chains as useless, because they were so flimsy any slave could break them, and so loose that he could easily shake them off and run away whenever he wanted, footloose and fancy-free. But after the ambassadors had spent a couple of days among the Utopians, they saw the immense amounts of gold which were as thoroughly despised there as they were prized at home. They saw too that more gold and silver went into making the chains and fetters of a single runaway slave than into costuming all three of them. Somewhat ashamed and crestfallen, they put away all the finery in which they had strutted so arrogantly, especially after they had talked with the Utopians enough to learn their customs and opinions.

[THEIR PHILOSOPHY]

The Utopians marvel that any mortal can take pleasure in the dubious sparkle of a little jewel or bright gemstone, when he has a star, or the sun itself, to look at. They are amazed at the foolishness of any man who considers himself a nobler fellow because he wears clothing of specially fine wool. No matter how delicate the thread, they say, a sheep wore it once, and still was nothing but a sheep.[8] They are surprised that gold, a useless commodity in itself, is everywhere valued so highly that man himself, who for his own purposes conferred this value on it, is considered far less valuable than the gold. They do not understand why a dunderhead with no more brains than a post, and who is as depraved as he is foolish, should command a great many wise and good men simply because he happens to have a great pile of gold. Yet if this master should lose his money to the lowest rascal in his household (as can happen by chance, or through some legal trick—for the law can produce reversals as violent as Fortune herself), he would promptly become the servant of his servant, as if he were personally attached to the coins, and a mere appendage to them.[9] Even more than this, the Utopians are appalled at those people who practically worship a rich man, though they neither owe him anything nor are obligated to him in any way. What impresses them is simply that the man is rich. Yet all the while they know he is so mean and grasping that as long as he lives not a single penny out of that great mound of money will ever come their way.

These and the like attitudes the Utopians have picked up partly from their upbringing, since the institutions of their commonwealth are completely opposed to such folly, and partly from instruction and their reading of good books. For though not many people in each city are excused from labor and assigned to scholarship full-time (these are persons who from childhood have given evidence of excellent character, unusual intelligence, and devotion to learning), every child gets an introduction to good literature, and throughout

8. Echoing Lucian's "Demonax" (sect. 41).
9. Alongside this passage and obviously applying to several sentences in it, a marginal gloss proclaims, "How much wiser are the Utopians than the ruck of Christians!"

their lives a large part of the people, men and women alike, spend their leisure time in reading.

They study all the branches of learning in their native tongue, which is not deficient in terminology or unpleasant in sound, and adapts itself as well as any to the expression of thought. Just about the same language is spoken throughout that entire area of the world, though elsewhere it is corrupted to various degrees.

Before we came there, the Utopians had never so much as heard about a single one of those philosophers[1] whose names are so celebrated in our part of the world. Yet in music, dialectic, arithmetic, and geometry they have found out just about the same things as our great men of the past. But while they equal the ancients in almost all subjects, they are far from matching the inventions of our modern logicians.[2] In fact they have not discovered even one of those elaborate rules about restrictions, amplifications, and suppositions which our own young men study in the Litle Logicbook.[3] They are so far from being able to speculate on "second intentions" that not one of them was able to see "man-in-general,"[4] though I pointed straight at him with my finger, and he is, as you well know, bigger than any giant, maybe even a colossus. On the other hand, they have learned to plot expertly the courses of the stars and the movements of the heavenly bodies. They have devised a number of different instruments by which they compute with the greatest exactness the course and position of the sun, the moon, and the other stars that are visible in their area of the sky. As for the conjunctions and oppositions of the planets, and that whole deceitful business of divination by the stars, they have never so much as dreamed of it.[5] From long experience in observation, they are able to forecast rains, winds, and other changes in the weather. But as to the causes of the weather, of the tides in the sea and its saltiness, and the origins and nature of the heavens and the earth, they have various opinions. They agree with our ancient philosophers on some matters, but on others, just as the ancients disagreed with one another, so the Utopians differ from all the ancients and yet reach no consensus among themselves.

In matters of moral philosophy, they carry on the same arguments as we do. They inquire into the nature of the good, distinguishing goods of the body from goods of the mind and external goods.[6] They ask whether the name of "good" may be applied to all three, or applies only to goods of the mind. They discuss virtue and pleasure, but their chief concern is what to think of human happiness, and whether it consists of one thing or of more. On this point, they seem overly inclined to the view of those who think that all or most human happiness consists of pleasure.[7] And what is more surpris-

---

1. As the next sentence indicates, the idea of "philosophy" here is the old, broad one that encompasses learning in general (the sense that survives in the title Doctor of Philosophy).
2. The Scholastic philosophers, constantly deprecated by humanists.
3. Probably the Parva logicalia, a textbook of logic by Peter of Spain, later Pope John XXI (d. 1277).
4. Man conceived of as a "universal." "Second intentions": in Scholastic discourse, purely abstract conceptions, derived from "first intentions" (the direct apprehensions of things). The

sentence is typical of the way humanists liked to ridicule, in the name of common sense, the Scholastics' abstractions.
5. Marginal gloss: "Yet these astrologers are revered by Christians to this day."
6. This threefold classification of goods is associated especially with Aristotle (Nicomachean Ethics 1.8.2, Politics 7.1.3–4).
7. I.e., the Utopians' primary affinity in moral philosophy is with the hedonistic school founded by Epicurus (341–271 B.C.E.). Cf. Vespucci on the Native Americans: "I deem their manner of life to

ing, they seek support for this comfortable opinion from their religion, which is serious and strict, indeed almost stern and forbidding. For they never discuss happiness without joining to their philosophic rationalism certain principles drawn from religion. Without these religious principles, they think that reason by itself is weak and defective in its efforts to investigate true happiness.

Their religious principles are of this nature: that the soul of man is immortal, and by God's goodness born for happiness; that after this life, rewards are appointed for our virtues and good deeds, punishments for our sins. Though these are indeed religious beliefs, they think that reason leads us to believe and accept them. And they add unhesitatingly that if these beliefs were rejected, no one would be so stupid as not to feel that he should seek pleasure, regardless of right and wrong. His only care would be to keep a lesser pleasure from standing in the way of a greater one, and to avoid pleasures that are inevitably followed by pain.[8] They think you would have to be actually crazy to pursue harsh and painful virtue, give up the pleasures of life, and suffer pain from which you can expect no advantage. For if there is no reward after death, you have no compensation for having passed your entire existence without pleasure, that is, miserably.

To be sure, they believe happiness is found, not in every kind of pleasure, but only in good and honest pleasure. Virtue itself, they say, draws our nature to this kind of pleasure, as to the supreme good. There is an opposed school which declares that virtue is itself happiness.[9]

They define virtue as living according to nature; and God, they say, created us to that end. When an individual obeys the dictates of reason in choosing one thing and avoiding another, he is following nature. Now the first rule of reason is to love and venerate the Divine Majesty to whom we owe our existence and our capacity for happiness. The second rule of nature is to lead a life as free of anxiety and as full of joy as possible, and to help all one's fellow men toward that end. The most hard-faced eulogist of virtue and the grimmest enemy of pleasure, while they invite us to toil and sleepless nights and self-laceration, still admonish us to relieve the poverty and misfortune of others as best we can. It is especially praiseworthy, they tell us, when we provide for our fellow creatures' comfort and welfare. Nothing is more humane (and humanity is the virtue most proper to human beings) than to relieve the misery of others and, by removing all sadness from their lives, restore them to enjoyment, that is, pleasure. Well, if this is the case, why doesn't nature equally invite us to do the same thing for ourselves? Either a joyful life (that is, one of pleasure) is a good thing, or it isn't. If it isn't, then you should not help anyone to it—indeed, you ought to take it away from everyone you can, as being harmful and deadly to them. But if such a life is good, and if we are supposed, indeed obliged, to help others to it, why shouldn't we first of all seek it for ourselves, to whom we owe no less charity

---

be Epicurean." Contrary to popular opinion, however, Epicurus himself did not mean, by the pursuit of pleasure, mere undiscriminating sensual indulgence: like the Utopians, he placed primary emphasis on the pleasures of a virtuous, rational life.

8. These rules for choosing among pleasures are attributed to Epicurus (Diogenes Laertius, *Lives of Eminent Philosophers* 10.129).

9. This is the position of the Stoics, who asserted that virtue constitutes happiness whether or not it leads to pleasure. The definition of *virtue* as "living according to nature" (below) is also Stoic.

than to anyone else? When nature prompts you to be kind to your neighbors, she does not mean that you should be cruel and merciless to yourself.[1] Thus they say that nature herself prescribes for us a joyous life, in other words, pleasure, as the goal of our actions; and living according to her prescriptions is to be defined as virtue. But as nature bids mortals to make one another's lives merrier, to the extent that they can, so she warns us constantly not to seek our own advantage in ways that cause misfortune to our fellows. And the reason for this is an excellent one; for no one is placed so far above the rest that he is nature's sole concern: she cherishes alike all those living beings to whom she has granted the same form.

Consequently, the Utopians maintain that one should not only abide by private agreements but also obey all those public laws which control the distribution of vital goods, such as are the very substance of pleasure. Any such laws, provided they have been properly promulgated by a good king, or ratified by a people free of force and fraud, should be observed; and as long as they are observed, to pursue your own interests is prudent; to pursue the public interest as well is pious; but to pursue your own pleasure by depriving others of theirs is unjust. On the other hand, deliberately to decrease one's own pleasure in order to augment that of others is a work of humanity and benevolence which never fails to reward the doer over and above his sacrifice. You may be repaid for your kindness; and in any case you are conscious of having done a good deed. Your mind draws more joy from recalling the affection and good will of those whom you have benefited than your body would have drawn pleasure from the things you gave up. Finally, they believe (as religion easily persuades a well-disposed mind to believe) that God will recompense us, for surrendering a brief and transitory pleasure here, with immense and neverending joy in heaven. And so they conclude, after carefully considering and weighing the matter, that all our actions and the virtues exercised within them look toward pleasure and happiness as their ultimate end.

By pleasure they understand every state or movement of body or mind in which we find delight in accordance with the behests of nature. They are right in adding that the desire must accord with nature. By simply following our senses and right reason[2] we may discover what is pleasant by nature: it is a delight that does not injure others, that does not preclude a greater pleasure, and that is not followed by pain. But a pleasure which is against nature, and which men call "delightful" only by the emptiest of fictions (as if one could change the real nature of things just by changing their names), does not, they hold, really make for happiness; in fact, they say it often precludes happiness. And the reason is that men whose minds are filled with false ideas of pleasure have no room left for true and genuine delight. As a matter of fact, there are a great many things which have no genuine sweetness in them but are for the most part actually bitter, yet which, through the perverse enticements of evil desires, are considered very great pleasures, and even included among the supreme goals of life.

---

1. Marginal gloss: "But now some people cultivate pain as if it were the essence of religion, rather than incidental to performance of a pious duty or the result of natural necessity—and thus to be borne, not pursued."

2. The power, thought to have been implanted by God in all humankind, to apprehend truth and moral law; conscience.

Among the devotees of this false pleasure, they include those whom I mentioned before, the people who think themselves finer fellows because they wear finer clothes. These people are twice mistaken: first in thinking their clothes better than anyone else's, and then in thinking themselves better because of their clothes. As far as a garment's usefulness goes, what does it matter if it was woven of fine thread or coarse? Yet they act as if they were set apart by Nature herself, rather than their own fantasies; they strut about, and put on airs. Because they have a fancy suit, they think themselves entitled to honors they would never have expected if they were dressed in homespun, and they grow indignant if someone passes them by without showing special respect.

It is the same kind of absurdity to be pleased by empty, ceremonial honors. What true and natural pleasure can you get from someone's bent knee or bared head? Will the creaks in your own knees be eased thereby, or the madness in your head? The phantom of false pleasure is illustrated by others who run mad with delight over their own blue blood, plume themselves on their nobility, and applaud themselves for all their rich ancestors (the only ancestors that count nowadays), and especially for all their ancient family estates. Even if they don't have the shred of an estate themselves, or if they've squandered every penny of their inheritance, they don't consider themselves a bit less noble.

In the same class the Utopians put those people I described before who are mad for jewelry and gems, and think themselves divinely happy if they find a good specimen, especially of the sort that happens to be fashionable in their country at the time—for stones vary in value from one market to another. The collector will not make an offer for a stone till it's taken out of its gold setting, and even then he will not buy unless the dealer guarantees and gives security that it is a true and genuine stone. What he fears is that his eyes will be deceived by a counterfeit. But if you consider the matter, why should a counterfeit give any less pleasure, when your eyes cannot distinguish it from a real gem? Both should be of equal value to you—as they would be, in fact, to a blind man.[3]

What about those who pile up money not because they want to do anything with the heap, but so they can sit and look at it? Is that true pleasure they experience, or aren't they simply cheated by a show of pleasure? Or what of those with the opposite vice, who hide away gold they will never use and perhaps never even see again? In their anxiety to hold onto it, they actually lose it. For what else happens when you deprive yourself, and perhaps other people too, of a chance to use your gold, by burying it in the ground? And yet when you've hidden your treasure away, you exult over it as if your mind were now free to rejoice. Suppose someone stole it, and you died ten years later, knowing nothing of the theft. During all those ten years, what did it matter whether the money was stolen or not? In either case, it was equally useless to you.

To these false and foolish pleasures they add gambling, which they have heard about, though they've never tried it, as well as hunting and hawking. What pleasure can there be, they wonder, in throwing dice on a table? If

3. In *The Praise of Folly*, Erasmus tells a story about More giving his young wife some false gems, which he passed off as being real and highly valuable.

there were any pleasure in the action, wouldn't doing it over and over again quickly make one tired of it? What pleasure can there be in listening to the barking and yelping of dogs—isn't that rather a disgusting noise? Is there any more pleasure felt when a dog chases a hare than when a dog chases a dog? If what you like is fast running, there's plenty of that in both cases; they're just about the same. But if what you really want is slaughter, if you want to see a living creature torn apart under your eyes—you ought to feel nothing but pity when you see the little hare fleeing from the hound, the weak creature tormented by the stronger, the fearful and timid beast brutalized by the savage one, the harmless hare killed by the cruel dog. The Utopians, who regard this whole activity of hunting as unworthy of free men, have assigned it accordingly, to their butchers, who, as I said before, are all slaves.[4] In their eyes, hunting is the lowest thing even butchers can do. In the slaughterhouse, their work is more useful and honest, since there they kill animals only from necessity; but the hunter seeks merely his own pleasure from the killing and mutilating of some poor little creature. Even in beasts, taking such relish in the sight of death reveals, in the Utopians' opinion, a cruel disposition, or else one that has become so through the constant practice of such brutal pleasures.

Common opinion considers these activities, and countless others like them, to be pleasures; but the Utopians say flatly they have nothing at all to do with real pleasure, since there's nothing naturally pleasant about them. They often please the senses, and in this they are like pleasure, but that does not alter their basic nature. The enjoyment doesn't arise from the experience itself, but only from the perverse habits of the mob, as a result of which they mistake the bitter for the sweet, just as pregnant women, whose taste has been turned awry, sometimes think pitch and tallow taste sweeter than honey. A person's taste may be similarly depraved by disease or by custom, but that does not change the nature of pleasure, or of anything else.

They distinguish several different classes of true pleasure, some being pleasures of the mind and others pleasures of the body. Those of the mind are knowledge and the delight which rises from contemplating the truth, also the gratification of looking back on a well-spent life and the unquestioning hope of happiness to come.

Pleasures of the body they also divide into two classes. The first is that which fills the senses with immediate delight. Sometimes this happens when bodily organs that have been weakened by natural heat are restored with food and drink; sometimes it happens when we eliminate some excess in the body, as when we move our bowels, generate children, or relieve an itch somewhere by rubbing or scratching it. Now and then pleasure arises, not from restoring a deficiency or discharging an excess, but from something that excites our senses with a hidden but unmistakable force, and attracts them to itself. Such is the power of music.

The second kind of bodily pleasure they describe as nothing but the calm and harmonious state of the body, its state of health when undisturbed by any disorder. Health itself, when not oppressed by pain, gives pleasure, without any external excitement at all. Even though it appeals less directly to the

4. Marginal gloss: "Yet today this is the chosen art of our court-divinities."

senses than the gross gratifications of eating and drinking, many consider this to be the greatest pleasure of all. Most of the Utopians regard it as the foundation and basis of all the pleasures, since by itself alone it can make life peaceful and desirable, whereas without it there is no possibility of any other pleasure. Mere absence of pain, without positive health, they regard as insensibility, not pleasure.

Some have maintained that a stable and tranquil state of health is not really a pleasure, on the grounds that the presence of health cannot be felt except through some external stimulus.[5] The Utopians (who have considered the matter thoroughly) long ago rejected this opinion. On the contrary, they nearly all agree that health is crucial to pleasure. Since pain is inherent in disease, they argue, and pain is the bitter enemy of pleasure, just as disease is the enemy of health, then pleasure must be inherent in quiet good health. You may say pain is not the disease itself, simply an accompanying effect; but they argue that that makes no difference, since the effect is the same either way. For whether health is itself a pleasure or is merely the cause of pleasure (as fire is the cause of heat), the fact remains that those who have stable health must also have pleasure.

When we eat, they say, what happens is that health, which was starting to fade, takes food as its ally in the fight against hunger. While our health gains strength, the simple process of returning vigor gives us pleasure and refreshment. If our health feels delight in the struggle, will it not rejoice when the victory has been won? When at last it is restored to its original strength, which was its aim all through the conflict, will it at once become insensible, and fail to recognize and embrace its own good? The idea that health cannot be felt they consider completely wrong. Every man who's awake, they say, feels that he's in good health—unless he isn't. Is anyone so torpid and dull that he won't admit health is delightfully agreeable to him? And what is delight except pleasure under another name?

Of all the different pleasures, they seek primarily those of the mind, and prize them most highly. The foremost mental pleasure, they believe, arises from the practice of the virtues and the consciousness of a good life. Among the pleasures of the body, they give the first place to health. As for eating and drinking and other delights of that sort, they consider them desirable, but only for the sake of health. They are not pleasant in themselves, but only as ways to withstand the insidious attacks of sickness. A wise man would rather escape sickness altogether than have a good cure for it; he would rather prevent pain than find a palliative for it. And so it would be better not to need this kind of pleasure at all than to be assuaged by it.

Anyone who thinks happiness consists of this sort of pleasure must confess that his ideal life would be one spent in an endless round of hunger, thirst, and itching, followed by eating, drinking, scratching, and rubbing. Who can fail to see that such an existence is not only disgusting but miserable? These pleasures are certainly the lowest of all, as they are the most adulterate— for they never occur except in connection with the pains that are their contraries. Hunger, for example, is linked to the pleasure of eating, and far from equally, since the pain is sharper and lasts longer; it precedes the pleasure,

5. This is, especially, the position of Plato, e.g., *Republic* 9.583C–585A.

and ends only when the pleasure ends with it. So the Utopians think pleasures of this sort should not be much valued, except insofar as they are necessary to life. Yet they enjoy these pleasures too, and acknowledge gratefully the kindness of Mother Nature, who coaxes her children with allurements and cajolery to do what in any case they must do from necessity. How wretched life would be if the daily diseases of hunger and thirst had to be overcome by bitter potions and drugs, like some other diseases that afflict us less often!

Beauty, strength, and agility, as special and pleasant gifts of nature, they joyfully accept. The pleasures of sound, sight, and smell they also pursue as the special seasonings of life, recognizing that nature intended these delights to be the particular province of man. No other kind of animal admires the shape and loveliness of the universe, or enjoys odors, except in the way of searching for food, or distinguishes harmonious from dissonant sounds. But in all their pleasures, the Utopians observe this rule, that the lesser pleasure must not interfere with the greater, and that no pleasure shall carry pain with it as a consequence. If a pleasure is dishonorable, they think it will inevitably lead to pain.

Moreover, they think it is crazy for a man to despise beauty of form, to impair his own strength, to grind his energy down to lethargy, to exhaust his body with fasts, to ruin his health, and to scorn all other natural delights, unless by so doing he can better serve the welfare of others or the public good. Then indeed he may expect a greater reward from God. But otherwise for a man to inflict pain on himself does no one any good. He gains, perhaps, the empty and shadowy reputation of virtue; and no doubt he hardens himself against fantastic adversities which may never occur. But such a person the Utopians consider absolutely crazy—cruel to himself, as well as most ungrateful to Nature—as if, to avoid being in her debt, he rejects all her gifts.

This is the way they think about virtue and pleasure. Human reason, they believe, can attain to no surer conclusions than these, unless a revelation from heaven should inspire men with holier notions. In all this, I have no time now to consider whether they are right or wrong, and don't feel obliged to do so. I have undertaken only to describe their principles, not to defend them. But of this I am sure, that whatever you think of their ideas, there is not a more excellent people or a happier commonwealth anywhere in the whole world.

In body they are nimble and lively, and stronger than you would expect from their stature, though they're by no means tiny. Their soil is not very fertile, nor their climate of the best, but they protect themselves against the weather by temperate living, and improve their soil by industry, so that nowhere do grain and cattle flourish more plentifully, nowhere are people more vigorous, and liable to fewer diseases. There you can see not only that they do all the things farmers usually do to improve poor soil by hard work and technical knowledge, but you can see a forest which they uprooted with their own hands and moved to another site. They did this not so much for the sake of better growth but to make transport easier, by having wood closer to the sea, the rivers, or the cities themselves. For grain is easier than wood to carry by land over a long distance.

[THEIR DELIGHT IN LEARNING]

The people in general are easygoing, cheerful, clever, and like their leisure. When they must, they can stand heavy labor, but otherwise they are not very fond of it. In intellectual pursuits, they are tireless. When they heard from us about the literature and learning of the Greeks (for we thought there was nothing in Latin, except the historians and poets, that they would value), it was wonderful to behold how eagerly they sought to be instructed in Greek. We therefore began to study a little of it with them, at first more to avoid seeming lazy than out of any expectation that they would profit by it. But after a short trial, their diligence convinced us that our efforts would not be wasted. They picked up the forms of the letters so easily, pronounced the language so aptly, memorized it so quickly, and began to recite so accurately that it seemed like a miracle. Most of our pupils were established scholars, of course, picked for their unusual ability and mature minds; and they studied with us, not just of their own free will, but at the command of the senate.[6] Thus in less than three years they had perfect control of the language and could read the best authors fluently, unless the text was corrupt. I have a feeling they picked up Greek more easily because it was somewhat related to their own tongue. Though their language resembles Persian in most respects, I suspect their race descends from the Greeks, because their language retains some vestiges of Greek in the names of cities and in official titles.

Before leaving on the fourth voyage, I placed on board, instead of merchandise, a good-sized packet of books; for I had resolved not to return at all rather than come home soon. Thus they received from me most of Plato's works and more of Aristotle's, as well as Theophrastus's book *On Plants*, though the latter, I'm sorry to say, was somewhat mutilated.[7] During the voyage I carelessly left it lying around, a monkey got hold of it, and from sheer mischief ripped out a few pages here and there and tore them up. Of the grammarians they have only Lascaris, for I did not take Theodorus with me, nor any dictionary except that of Hesychius; and they have Dioscorides.[8] They are very fond of Plutarch's writings, and delighted with the witty persiflage of Lucian.[9] Among the poets they have Aristophanes, Homer, and Euripides, together with Sophocles in the small typeface of the Aldine edition.[1] Of the historians they possess Thucydides and Herodotus, as well as Herodian.[2]

As for medical books, a comrade of mine named Tricius Apinatus brought with him some small treatises by Hippocrates, and the *Microtechne* of

---

6. Marginal gloss: "But now clods and blockheads are assigned to learning, while the best minds are corrupted by pleasures."

7. Theophrastus, Aristotle's pupil, was studied in the Renaissance not as a quaint curiosity but because his views were still current in botany.

8. Dioscorides (1st century C.E.) wrote a treatise on drugs and herbs that was printed in 1499. The Renaissance scholars Constantine Lascaris and Theodore of Gaza wrote grammars of Greek. The Greek dictionary of Hesychius of Alexandria (5th century C.E.) was published in 1514.

9. The Syrian-born ironist who was admired, translated, and imitated by both More and Erasmus (see n. 7, p. 612). The writings of Plutarch

(ca. 46–ca. 120 C.E.) referred to presumably include his *Moral Essays* as well as his *Parallel Lives* of eminent Greeks and Romans.

1. The first printed edition of Sophocles was that of Aldus Manutius in 1502. The house of Aldus, established in Venice toward the end of the 15th century, was not only the first establishment to print Greek texts in Greek type but was responsible for some of the best-designed books in the history of the art.

2. Thucydides and Herodotus (both 5th century B.C.E.) are the preeminent Greek historians. Herodian (ca. 175–250 C.E.) wrote a history of the Roman emperors of the 2nd and 3rd centuries.

a b c d e f g h i k l m n o p q r s t u x y

ⓞⒶⒸⓄⒼⒸⒼⒸⒶⓌⒺⒶ⅃⅃Γ⌐⅃⊡⊟⊟Ⓔ⊡

TETRASTICHON VERNACVLA VTO-
PIENSIVM LINGVA.

Vtopos   ha   Boccas   peula   chama.

polta   chamaan

Bargol   he   maglomi   baccan

foma   gymnofophaon

Agrama   gymnofophon   labarem

bacha   bodamilomin

Voluala   barchin   heman   la

lauoluola   dramme   pagloni.

HORVM VERSVVM AD VERBVM HAEC
EST SENTENTIA.

Vtopus me dux ex non infula fecit infulam.
Vna ego terrarum omnium abſcʒ philoſophia.
Ciuitatem philoſophicam expreſſi mortalibus.
Libenter impartio mea, non grauatim accipio meliora.

b 3

This sample of the Utopian language, which first appeared in the earliest edition of More's book (1516), reveals affinities with Greek and Latin and has enough internal consistency to suggest that it was worked out with care (evidently by Peter Giles). The stilted Latin quatrain at the end, which purports to be a literal translation, can itself be translated as follows: "Me, once a peninsula, Utopus the king made an island. / Alone among all nations, and without complex abstractions, / I set before men's eyes the philosophical city. / What I give is free; what is better I am not slow to take from others."

Galen.[3] They were delighted to have these books. Even though there's hardly a country in the world that needs doctors less, medicine is nowhere held in greater honor: they consider it one of the finest and most useful parts of philosophy. They think that when, with the help of philosophy, they explore the secrets of nature they are gratifying not only themselves but the author and maker of nature. They suppose that, like other artists, he created this beautiful mechanism of the world to be admired—and by whom, if not by man, who is alone in being able to appreciate so great a thing? Therefore he is bound to prefer a careful observer and sensitive admirer of his work before one who, like a brute beast, looks on the grand spectacle with a stupid and blockish mind.

Once stimulated by learning, the minds of the Utopians are wonderfully quick to seek out those various arts which make life more agreeable. Two inventions, to be sure, they owe to us: the art of printing and the manufacture of paper. At least they owe these arts partly to us, though partly to their own ingenuity. While we were showing them the Aldine editions of various works, we talked about papermaking and how letters are printed, though without going into detail, for none of us had had any practical experience of either skill. But with great sharpness of mind they immediately grasped the basic principles. While previously they had written only on vellum, bark, and papyrus, they now undertook to make paper and to print with type. Their first attempts were not altogether successful, but with practice they soon mastered both arts. They became so proficient that, if they had texts of the Greek authors, they would soon have no lack of volumes; but as they have no more than those I mentioned, they have contented themselves with reprinting each in thousands of copies.

Any sightseer coming to their land who has some special intellectual gift, or who has traveled widely and seen many countries, is sure of a warm welcome, for they love to hear what is happening throughout the world. This is why we were received so kindly. Few merchants, however, go there to trade. What could they import except iron—or else gold and silver, which everyone would rather bring home than send abroad? As for the export trade, the Utopians prefer to do their own transportation, rather than invite strangers to do it. By carrying their own cargos they are able to learn more about foreign countries on all sides, and keep up their skill in navigation.

SLAVES[4]

The only prisoners of war the Utopians enslave are those captured in wars they fight themselves. The children of slaves are not automatically enslaved,[5]

3. Hippocrates (5th century B.C.E.) and Galen (2nd century C.E.) were the most influential Greek medical writers. The *Microtechne* is a medieval summary of Galen's ideas. The name Tricius Apinatus (like Hythloday) is a learned joke: in classical Italy, Trica and Apina were extinct towns whose names, taken together, were proverbial for trifling, worthless things.
4. The institution of slavery—with prisoners of war (civilians as well as combatants) as a major source of the slaves—was ubiquitous in the ancient world, including the Greek and Roman civilizations that Utopia resembles in various

ways. In Europe, slavery declined in the Middle Ages, being replaced as a source of labor by feudal serfdom, in which individuals were bound to the land rather than to a particular owner. Chattel slavery, however, revived strongly in the European colonies in the New World: the enslavement of Native Americans began with the earliest settlements, in the 1490s, and the first African slaves were imported in 1502.
5. This fact sharply distinguishes Utopian slavery from both classical and early modern slavery and medieval serfdom.

nor are slaves obtained from foreign countries. Their slaves are either their own citizens, enslaved for some heinous offense, or else foreigners who were condemned to death in their own land. Most are of the latter sort. Sometimes the Utopians buy them at a very modest rate, more often they ask for them, get them for nothing, and bring them home in considerable numbers. Both kinds of slaves are kept constantly at work, and are always fettered. But the Utopians deal with their own people more harshly than with the others, feeling that their crimes are worse and deserve stricter punishment because they had an excellent education and the best of moral training, yet still couldn't be restrained from wrongdoing. A third class of slaves consists of hardworking penniless drudges from other nations who voluntarily choose to become slaves in Utopia. Such people are treated well, almost as well as citizens, except that they are given a little extra work, on the score that they're used to it. If one of them wants to leave, which seldom happens, no obstacles are put in his way, nor is he sent off emptyhanded.

[SUICIDE AND EUTHANASIA]

As I said before, the sick are carefully tended, and nothing is neglected in the way of medicine or diet which might cure them. Everything possible is done to mitigate the pain of those who are suffering from incurable diseases; and visitors do their best to console them by sitting and talking with them. But if the disease is not only incurable but excruciatingly and constantly painful, then the priests and public officials come and urge the invalid not to endure such agony any longer. They remind him that he is now unfit for any of life's duties, a burden to himself and to others; he has really outlived his own death. They tell him he should not let the disease prey on him any longer, but now that life is simply torture, he should not hesitate to die but should rely on hope for something better. Since life has become a mere prison cell, where he is bitterly tormented, he should free himself, or let others free him, from the rack of living. This would be a wise act, they say, since for him death would put an end not to pleasure but to agony. In addition, he would be obeying the advice of the priests, who are the interpreters of God's will; which ensures that it would be a holy and pious act.[6]

Those who have been persuaded by these arguments either starve themselves to death or, having been put to sleep, are freed from life without any sensation of dying. But they never force this step on a man against his will; nor, if he decides against it, do they lessen their care of him. Under these circumstances, when death is advised by the authorities, they consider self-destruction honorable. But the suicide, who takes his own life without the approval of priests and senate, they consider unworthy either of earth or fire, and throw his body, unburied and disgraced, into a bog.

[MARRIAGE AND DIVORCE]

Women do not marry till they are eighteen, nor men till they are twenty-two. Premarital intercourse, if discovered and proved, brings severe punishment

---

6. In ancient Rome, suicide was regarded as an honorable way out of deep personal or political difficulties, but neither suicide nor euthanasia has ever been acceptable in Catholic Christianity. Cf. Hythloday's earlier reference to God's prohibition of suicide (p. 584).

on both man and woman, and the guilty parties are forbidden to marry during their whole lives, unless the governor by his pardon remits the sentence. In addition both the father and mother of the household where the offense occurred suffer public disgrace for having been remiss in their duty. The reason they punish this offense so severely is that they suppose few people would join in married love—with confinement to a single partner, and all the petty annoyances that married life involves—unless they were strictly restrained from a life of promiscuity.

In choosing marriage partners, they solemnly and seriously follow a custom which seemed to us foolish and absurd in the extreme. Whether she is a widow or a virgin, the woman is shown naked to the suitor by a responsible and respectable matron; and similarly, some respectable man presents the suitor naked to the woman.[7] We laughed at this custom and called it absurd; but they were just as amazed at the folly of all other peoples. When men go to buy a colt, where they are risking only a little money, they are so suspicious that, though the beast is almost bare, they won't close the deal until the saddle and blanket have been taken off, lest there be a hidden sore underneath. Yet in the choice of a mate, which may cause either delight or disgust for the rest of their lives, people are completely careless. They leave all the rest of her body covered up with clothes and estimate the attractiveness of a woman from a mere handsbreadth of her person, the face, which is all they can see. And so they marry, running great risk of bitter discord, if something in either's person should offend the other. Not all people are so wise as to concern themselves solely with character; and even the wise appreciate physical beauty, as a supplement to the virtues of the mind. There's no question but that deformity may lurk under clothing, serious enough to make a man hate his wife when it's too late to be separated from her. If some disfiguring accident occurs after marriage, each person must bear his own fate; but beforehand everyone should be legally protected from deception.

There is extra reason for them to be careful, because in that part of the world they are the only people who practice monogamy. Their marriages are seldom terminated except by death, though they do allow divorce for adultery or for intolerably offensive behavior. A husband or wife who is the aggrieved party in such a divorce is granted permission by the senate to remarry, but the guilty party is considered disreputable and is permanently forbidden to take another mate.[8] They absolutely forbid a husband to put away his wife against her will and without any fault on her part, just because of some bodily misfortune; they think it cruel that a person should be abandoned when most in need of comfort; and they add that old age, since it not only entails disease but is actually a disease itself, needs more than a precarious fidelity.

It happens occasionally that a married couple cannot get along, and have both found other persons with whom they hope to live more harmoniously. After getting the approval of the senate, they may then separate by mutual consent and contract new marriages. But such divorces are allowed only after the senators and their wives have carefully investigated the case. They allow divorce only very reluctantly, because they know that husbands and

---

7. Marginal gloss: "Not very modest, but not so imprudent, either."
8. In Europe, the Catholic Church allowed sepa- ration in cases of adultery but did not allow even the aggrieved party to remarry.

wives will find it hard to settle down together if each has in mind that a new marriage is easily available.

They punish adulterers with the strictest form of slavery. If both parties were married, they are both divorced, and the injured parties may marry one another, if they want, or someone else. But if one of the injured parties continues to love such an undeserving spouse, the marriage may go on, providing the innocent person chooses to share in the labor to which the slave is condemned. And sometimes it happens that the repentance of the guilty and the devotion of the innocent party move the governor to pity, so that he restores both to freedom. But a second conviction of adultery is punished by death.

[PUNISHMENTS AND REWARDS; CUSTOMS AND LAWS]

No other crimes carry fixed penalties; the senate sets specific penalties for each particular misdeed, as it is considered atrocious or venial. Husbands chastise their wives, and parents their children, unless the offense is so serious that public punishment is called for. Generally, the gravest crimes are punished by slavery, for they think this deters offenders just as much as getting rid of them by immediate capital punishment, and is more beneficial to the commonwealth. In addition, slaves contribute more by their labor than by their death, and they are permanent and visible reminders that crime does not pay. If the slaves rebel against their condition, then, like savage beasts which neither bars nor chains can tame, they are finally put to death. But if they are patient, they are not left altogether without hope. When subdued by long hardships, if they show by their behavior that they regret the crime more than the punishment, their slavery is lightened or remitted altogether, sometimes by the governor's pardon, sometimes by popular vote.

Attempted seduction is subject to the same penalty as seduction itself. They think that a crime clearly and deliberately attempted is as bad as one committed, and that failure should not confer advantages on a criminal who did all he could to succeed.

They are very fond of fools, and think it contemptible to insult them.[9] There is no prohibition against enjoying their foolishness, and they even regard this as beneficial to the fools. If anyone is so serious and solemn that the foolish behavior and comic patter of a clown do not amuse him, they don't entrust him with the care of such a person, for fear that a man who gets not only no use from a fool but not even any amusement—a fool's only gift— will not treat him kindly.

To mock a person for being deformed or crippled is considered ugly and disfiguring, not to the victim but to the mocker, who stupidly reproaches the cripple for something he cannot help.

They think it a sign of a weak and sluggish character to neglect one's natural beauty, but they consider cosmetics a detestable affectation. From experience they have learned that no physical beauty recommends a wife to her husband so effectually as goodness and respect. Though some men are captured by beauty alone, none are held except by virtue and compliance.

---

9. More's household included a fool, Henry Patenson.

As they deter people from crime by penalties, so they incite them to virtue by public honors. They set up in the marketplace statues of distinguished men who have served their country well, thinking thereby to preserve the memory of their good deeds and to spur on the citizens to emulate the glory of their ancestors.

Any man who campaigns for a public office is disqualified for all of them. They live together harmoniously, and the public officials are never arrogant or unapproachable. Instead, they are called "fathers," and that is the way they behave. Because the officials never extort respect from the people against their will, the people respect them spontaneously, as they should. Not even the governor is distinguished from his fellow citizens by a robe or crown; he is known only by a sheaf of grain he carries, just as the high priest is distinguished by a wax candle borne before him.[1]

They have very few laws, and their training is such that they need no more. The chief fault they find with other nations is that, even with infinite volumes of laws and interpretations, they cannot manage their affairs properly. They think it completely unjust to bind people by a set of laws that are too many to be read and too obscure for anyone to understand. As for lawyers, a class of men whose trade it is to manipulate cases and multiply quibbles, they exclude them entirely.[2] They think it is better for each man to plead his own case, and say the same thing to the judge that he would tell his lawyer. This makes for less ambiguity, and readier access to the truth. A man speaks his mind without tricky instructions from a lawyer, and the judge examines each point carefully, taking pains to protect simple folk against the false accusations of the crafty. It is hard to find this kind of plain dealing in other countries, where they have such a multitude of incomprehensibly intricate laws. But in Utopia everyone is a legal expert. For the laws are very few, as I said, and they consider the most obvious interpretation of any law to be the fairest. As they see things, all laws are promulgated for the single purpose of teaching every man his duty. Subtle interpretations teach very few, since hardly anybody is able to understand them, whereas the more simple and apparent sense of the law is open to everyone. If laws are not clear, they are useless; for simpleminded men (and most men are of this sort, and need to be told where their duty lies), there might as well be no laws at all as laws which can be interpreted only by devious minds after endless disputes. The dull common man cannot understand this legal chicanery, and couldn't even if he studied it his whole life, since he has to earn a living in the meantime.

[FOREIGN RELATIONS]

Some of the Utopians' free and independent neighbors (many of whom were previously liberated by them from tyranny), having learned to admire Utopian virtues, have made a practice of asking the Utopians to supply magistrates for them. Some of these magistrates serve one year, others five. When their service is over, they bring them home with honor and praise, and take back new ones to their country. These peoples seem to have settled on an

---

1. Grain and candle evidently symbolize the special function of each ruler: to ensure prosperity and to provide spiritual vision.

2. Marginal gloss: "The useless crowd of lawyers." More was, of course, one himself.

excellent scheme to safeguard the commonwealth. Since the welfare or ruin of a commonwealth depends on the character of its officials, where could they make a more prudent choice than among Utopians, who cannot be tempted by money? For money is useless to them when they go home, as they soon must, and they can have no partisan or factional feelings, since they are strangers in the city over which they rule. Wherever they take root in men's minds, these two evils, greed and faction, are the destruction of all justice—and justice is the strongest bond of any society. The Utopians call these people who have borrowed magistrates from them their *allies*; others whom they have benefited they call simply *friends*.

While other nations are constantly making treaties, breaking them, and renewing them, the Utopians never make any treaties at all. If nature, they say, doesn't bind man adequately to his fellow man, will an alliance do so? If a man scorns nature herself, is there any reason to think he will care about mere words? They are confirmed in this view by the fact that in that part of the world, treaties and alliances between kings are not generally observed with much good faith.

In Europe, of course, the dignity of treaties is everywhere kept sacred and inviolable, especially in those regions where the Christian religion prevails. This is partly because the kings are all so just and virtuous, partly also because of the reverence and fear that everyone feels toward the popes.[3] Just as the popes themselves never promise anything which they do not most conscientiously perform, so they command all other princes to abide by their promises in every way. If someone declines to do so, they compel him to obey by means of pastoral censure and sharp reproof. The popes rightly declare that it would be particularly disgraceful if people who are specifically called "the faithful" acted in bad faith.

But in that new world, which is as distant from ours in customs and way of life as in the distance the equator puts between us, nobody trusts treaties. The greater the formalities, the more numerous and solemn the oaths, the sooner the treaty will be broken. The rulers will easily find some defect in the wording of it, which often enough they deliberately inserted themselves. No treaty can be made so strong and explicit that a government will not be able to worm out of it, breaking in the process both the treaty and its own word. If such craft, deceit, and fraud were practiced in private contracts, the politicians would raise a great outcry against both parties, calling them sacrilegious and worthy of the gallows. Yet the very same politicians think themselves clever fellows when they give this sort of advice to kings. As a consequence, people are apt to think that justice is a humble, plebeian virtue, far beneath the majesty of kings. Or else they conclude that there are two kinds of justice, one which is only for the common herd, a lowly justice that creeps along the ground, hedged in everywhere and encumbered with chains; and the other, which is the justice of princes, much more free and majestic, so that it can do anything it wants and nothing it doesn't want.

This royal practice of keeping treaties badly there is, I suppose, the reason the Utopians don't make any; doubtless if they lived here in Europe they would change their minds. However, they think it a bad idea to make trea-

---

3. In fact the crowned heads of Europe and the popes alike were ruthless and casual violators of treaties.

ties at all, even if they are faithfully observed. A treaty implies that people who are separated by some natural obstacle as slight as a hill or a brook are joined by no bond of nature; it assumes that they are born rivals and enemies, and are right in aiming to destroy one another except insofar as a treaty restrains them. Moreover, they see that treaties do not really promote friendship; for both parties still retain the right to prey upon one another to whatever extent incautious drafting has left the treaty without sufficient provisions against it. The Utopians think, on the other hand, that no one should be considered an enemy who has done you no harm, that the fellowship of nature is as good as a treaty, and that men are united more firmly by good will than by pacts, by their hearts than by their words.

MILITARY PRACTICES

They despise war as an activity fit only for beasts, yet practiced more by man than by any other creature. Unlike almost every other people in the world, they think nothing so inglorious as the glory won in battle. Yet on certain fixed days, men and women alike carry on vigorous military training, so they will be fit to fight should the need arise. But they go to war only for good reasons: to protect their own land, to protect their friends from an invading army, or to liberate an oppressed people from tyranny and servitude. Out of human sympathy, they not only protect their friends from present danger but sometimes avenge previous injuries; they do this, however, only if they themselves have previously been consulted, have approved the cause, and have demanded restitution in vain. Then and only then they think themselves free to declare war. They take this final step not only when their friends have been plundered but also, and even more fiercely, when their friends' merchants have been subjected to extortion in another country, either on the pretext of laws unjust in themselves or through the perversion of good laws.

This and no other was the cause of the war which the Utopians waged a little before our time on behalf of the Nephelogetes against the Alaopolitans.[4] Under pretext of right, a wrong (as they saw it) had been inflicted on some Nephelogete traders residing among the Alaopolitans. Whatever the rights and wrongs of the quarrel, it developed into a fierce war, into which, apart from the hostile forces of the two parties themselves, the neighboring nations poured their efforts and resources. Some prosperous nations were ruined completely, others badly shaken. One trouble led to another, and in the end the Alaopolitans were crushed and reduced to slavery (since the Utopians weren't involved on their own account) by the Nephelogetes—a people who, before the war, had not been remotely comparable in power to their rivals.

So severely do the Utopians punish wrong done to their friends, even in matters of mere money; but they are not so strict in enforcing their own rights. When they are cheated out of their goods, so long as no bodily harm is done, their anger goes no further than cutting off trade relations with that nation till restitution is made. The reason is not that they care more for their allies' citizens than for their own, but simply this: when the merchants

---

4. "People Born from the Clouds" versus "Citizens of a Country without People."

of their friends are cheated, it is their own property that is lost, but when the Utopians lose something, it comes from the common stock, and is bound to be in plentiful supply at home; otherwise they wouldn't have been exporting it. Hence no one individual even notices the loss. So small an injury, which affects neither the life nor the livelihood of any of their own people, they consider it cruel to avenge by the deaths of many soldiers. On the other hand, if one of their own is maimed or killed anywhere, whether by a government or by a private citizen, they first send envoys to look into the circumstances; then they demand that the guilty persons be surrendered; and if that demand is refused, they are not to be put off, but at once declare war. If the guilty persons are surrendered, their punishment is death or slavery.

The Utopians are not only troubled but ashamed when their forces gain a bloody victory, thinking it folly to pay too high a price even for the best goods. But if they overcome the enemy by skill and cunning, they exult mightily, celebrate a public triumph, and raise a monument as for a hard-won victory. They think they have really acted with manly virtue when they have won a victory such as no animal except man could have won—a victory achieved by strength of understanding. Bears, lions, boars, wolves, dogs, and other wild beasts fight with their bodies, they say; and most of them are superior to us in strength and ferocity; but we outdo them all in shrewdness and rationality.

The only thing they aim at, in going to war, is to secure what would have prevented the declaration of war, if the enemy had conceded it beforehand. Or if they cannot get that, they try to take such bitter revenge on those who have provoked them that they will be afraid ever to do it again. These are their chief aims, which they try to achieve quickly, yet in such a way as to avoid danger rather than to win fame and glory.

As soon as war is declared, therefore, they have their secret agents simultaneously post many placards, each marked with their official seal, in the most conspicuous places throughout the enemy territory. In these proclamations they promise immense rewards to anyone who will kill the enemy's king. They offer smaller but still very substantial sums for killing any of a list of other individuals whom they name. These are the persons whom they regard as most responsible, after the king, for plotting aggression against them. The reward for an assassin is doubled for anyone who succeeds in bringing in one of the proscribed men alive. The same reward, plus a guarantee of personal safety, is offered to any one of the proscribed men who turns against his comrades. As a result, the enemies of the Utopians quickly come to suspect everyone, particularly one another; and the many perils of their situation lead to panic. They know perfectly well that many of them, including their princes, have been betrayed by those in whom they placed complete trust—so effective are bribes as an incitement to crime. Knowing this, the Utopians are lavish in their promises of bounty. Being well aware of the risks their agents must run, they make sure that the payments are in proportion to the peril; thus they not only offer, but actually deliver, enormous sums of gold, as well as large landed estates in very secure locations on the territory of their friends.

Everywhere else in the world, this process of bidding for and buying the life of an enemy is condemned as the cruel villainy of a degenerate mind; but the Utopians consider it good policy, both wise and merciful. In the first place, it enables them to win tremendous wars without fighting any actual battles; and in the second place it enables them, by the sacrifice of a few guilty men, to spare the lives of many innocent persons who would have died in battle, some on their side, some on the enemy's. They pity the mass of the enemy's soldiers almost as much as their own citizens, for they know common people do not go to war of their own accord, but are driven to it by the madness of princes.

If assassination does not work, they sow the seeds of dissension in enemy ranks by inciting the prince's brother or some other member of the nobility to scheme for the crown. If internal discord dies down, they try to rouse up neighboring peoples against the enemy by reviving forgotten claims to dominion, of which kings always have an ample supply.

When they promise their resources to help in a war, they send money very freely, but commit their own citizens only sparingly. They hold their own people dear, and value them so highly that they would not willingly exchange one of their citizens for an enemy's prince. Since they keep their gold and silver for the purpose of war alone, they spend it without hesitation; after all, they will continue to live just as well even if they expend the whole sum. Besides the wealth they have at home, they have a vast treasure abroad, since, as I said before, many nations owe them money. So they hire mercenary soldiers from all sides, especially the Zapoletes.[5]

These people live five hundred miles to the east of Utopia, and are rude, rough, and fierce. The forests and mountains where they are bred are the kind of country they like: tough and rugged. They are a hard race, capable of standing heat, cold, and drudgery, unacquainted with any luxuries, careless of what houses they live in or what they wear; they don't till the fields but raise cattle instead. Most of them survive by hunting and stealing. These people are born for battle and are always eager for a fight; they seek one out at every opportunity. Leaving their own country in great numbers, they offer themselves for cheap hire to anyone in need of warriors. The only art they know for earning a living is the art of taking life.

They fight with great courage and incorruptible loyalty for the people who pay them, but they will not bind themselves to serve for any fixed period of time. If someone, even the enemy, offers them more money tomorrow, they will take his side; and day after tomorrow, if a trifle more is offered to bring them back, they'll return to their first employers. Hardly a war is fought in which a good number of them are not engaged on both sides. It happens every day that men who are united by ties of blood and have served together in friendship, but who are now separated into opposing armies, meet in battle. Forgetful of kinship and comradeship alike, they furiously run one another through, driven to mutual destruction for no other reason than that they were hired for paltry pay by opposing princes. They care so much about money that they can easily be induced to change sides for an increase of only a penny a day. They have picked up the habit of avarice, but none of the profit; for what they earn by shedding blood, they quickly squander on debauchery of the most squalid sort.

Because the Utopians give higher pay than anyone else, these people are ready to serve them against any enemy whatever. And the Utopians, who seek

---

5. "Busy sellers." The Zapoletes resemble the Swiss, who produced the best and most feared mercenaries of Europe (a remnant still survives as the Swiss Guard in the Vatican).

out the best possible men for proper uses, hire these, the worst possible men, for improper uses. When the situation requires, they thrust the Zapoletes into the positions of greatest danger by offering them immense rewards. Most of them never come back to collect their pay, but the Utopians faithfully pay off those who do survive, to encourage them to try it again. As for how many Zapoletes get killed, the Utopians never worry about that, for they think they would deserve very well of all mankind if they could exterminate from the face of the earth that entire disgusting and vicious race.

Besides the Zapoletes, they employ as auxiliaries the soldiers of the people for whom they have taken up arms, and then squadrons of their other friends. Last, they add their own citizens, including some man of known bravery to command the entire army. In addition, they appoint two substitutes for him, who hold no rank as long as he is safe. But if the commander is captured or killed, the first of these two substitutes becomes his successor, and in case of a mishap to him, the other. Thus, though the accidents of war cannot be foreseen, they make sure that the whole army will not be disorganized through the loss of their leader.

In each city, soldiers are chosen from those who have volunteered. No one is forced to fight abroad against his will, because they think a man who is naturally fearful will act weakly at best, and may even spread panic among his comrades. But if their own country is invaded, they call everyone to arms, posting the fearful (as long as they are physically fit) on shipboard among braver men, or here and there along fortifications, where there is no place to run away. Thus shame at failing their countrymen, desperation at the immediate presence of the enemy, and the impossibility of flight often combine to overcome their fear, and they make a virtue out of sheer necessity.

Just as no man is forced into a foreign war against his will, so women are allowed to accompany their men on military service if they want to—not only not forbidden, but encouraged and praised for doing so. Each goes with her husband to the front, and stands shoulder to shoulder with him in the line of battle; in addition, they place around a man his children and blood- or marriage-relations, so that those who by nature have most reason to help one another may be closest at hand for mutual aid. It is a matter of great reproach for either partner to come home without the other, or for a son to return after losing a parent. The result is that if the enemy stands his ground, the hand-to-hand fighting is apt to be long and bitter, ending only when everyone is dead.

As I observed, they take every precaution to avoid having to fight in person, so long as they can bring the war to an end with mercenaries. But when they are forced to take part in battle, they are as bold in the struggle as they were prudent in avoiding it while they could. In the first charge they are not fierce, but gradually as the fighting goes on they grow more determined, putting up a steady, stubborn resistance. Their spirit is so strong that they will die rather than yield ground. They are certain that everyone at home will be provided for, and they have no worries about the future of their families (and that sort of worry often daunts the boldest courage); so their spirit is exalted and unconquerable. Their skill in the arts of war gives them extra confidence; also from childhood they have been trained in sound principles of conduct (which their education and the good institutions of their commonwealth reinforce); and that too adds to their courage. They don't hold life so cheap that they throw it away recklessly, nor so dear as to grasp it avidly at the price of shame, when duty bids them give it up.

At the height of the battle, a band of the bravest young men, who have taken a special oath, devote themselves to seeking out the opposing general. They attack him directly, they lay secret traps for him, they hit at him from near and far. A long and continuous supply of fresh men keep up the assault as the exhausted drop out. In the end, they rarely fail to kill or capture him, unless he takes to flight.

When they win a battle, it never ends in a massacre, for they would much rather take prisoners than cut throats. They never pursue fugitives without keeping one line of their army drawn up under the colors. They are so careful of this that if they win the victory, with this last reserve force (supposing the rest of their army has been beaten), they would rather let the enemy army escape than pursue fugitives with their own ranks in disorder. They remember what has happened more than once to themselves: that when the enemy seemed to have the best of the day, had routed the main Utopian force and, exulting in their victory, had scattered to pursue the fugitives, a few Utopians held in reserve and watching their opportunity have suddenly attacked the dispersed and scattered enemy at the very moment when he felt safe and had lowered his guard. Thereby they changed the fortune of the day, snatched certain victory out of the enemy's hands, and, though conquered themselves, conquered their conquerors.

It is not easy to say whether they are more crafty in laying ambushes or more cautious in avoiding those laid for them. Sometimes they seem to be on the point of breaking and running when that is the last thing they have in mind; but when they really are ready to retreat, you would never guess it. If they are outnumbered, or if the terrain is unsuitable, they shift their ground silently by night or slip away from the enemy by some stratagem. Or if they have to withdraw by day, they do so gradually, and in such good order that they are as dangerous to attack then as if they were advancing. They fortify their camps very carefully with a deep, broad ditch all around them, the earth being thrown inward to make a wall; the work is done not by workmen but by the soldiers themselves with their own hands. The whole army pitches in, except for an armed guard posted around the rampart to prevent a surprise attack. With so many hands at work, they complete great fortifications, enclosing wide areas with unbelievable speed.

The armor they wear is strong enough to protect them from blows, but does not prevent easy movement of the body; in fact, it doesn't interfere even with their swimming, and part of their military training consists of swimming in armor. For long-range fighting they use arrows, which they fire with great force and accuracy, and from horseback as well as on foot. At close quarters they use not swords but battle-axes, which because of their sharp edge and great weight are lethal weapons, whether used in slashing or thrusting. They are very skillful in inventing machines of war, but conceal them with the greatest care, since if they were made known before they were needed, they might be more ridiculous than useful. Their first consideration in designing them is to make them easy to move and aim.[6]

---

6. The military devices of the Utopians represent a patchwork of notions from the common knowledge of the day. Their camps are fortified like Roman ones. Their reliance on archery links them with the

When the Utopians make a truce with the enemy, they observe it religiously, and will not break it even if provoked. They do not ravage the enemy's territory or burn his crops; indeed, so far as possible, they avoid any trampling of the fields by men or horses, thinking they may need the grain themselves later on. Unless he is a spy, they injure no unarmed man. When cities are surrendered to them, they keep them intact; even when they have stormed a place, they do not plunder it, but put to death the men who prevented surrender, enslave the other defenders, and do no harm to the civilians. If they find any inhabitants who recommended surrender, they give them a share in the property of the condemned, and present their auxiliaries with the rest; for the Utopians themselves never take any booty.

After a war is ended, they collect the cost of it, not from the allies for whose sake they undertook it, but from the conquered. They take as indemnity not only money, which they set aside to finance future wars, but also landed estates, from which they may enjoy forever a substantial annual income. They now have revenues of this sort in many different countries, acquired little by little in various ways, till it now amounts to over seven hundred thousand ducats a year.[7] As managers of these estates, they send abroad some of their own citizens to serve as collectors of revenue. Though they live on the properties in grand style and conduct themselves like great lords, plenty of income is still left over to be put in the public treasury, unless they choose to give the conquered nation credit. They often do the latter, until they happen to need the money, and even then it's rare for them to call in the entire debt. Some of the estates are given, as I've already described, to those who have risked great dangers on their behalf.

If any prince takes up arms and prepares to invade their land, they immediately attack him in full force outside their own borders. They are most reluctant to wage war on their own soil, and no necessity could ever compel them to admit foreign auxiliaries onto their island.

THE RELIGIONS OF THE UTOPIANS

There are different forms of religion throughout the island, and even in individual cities. Some worship as a god the sun, others the moon, and still others one of the planets. There are some who worship a man of past ages who was conspicuous either for virtue or glory; they consider him not only a god but the supreme god. The vast majority, however, and these by far the wisest, believe nothing of the sort: they believe in a single power, unknown, eternal, infinite, inexplicable, beyond the grasp of the human mind, and diffused throughout the universe, not physically, but in influence. Him they call their parent, and to him alone they attribute the origin, increase, progress, changes, and ends of all things; they do not offer divine honors to any other.

English, whose archers had played key roles in the famous victories over the French at Crécy and Agincourt—though the Utopians' skill in shooting arrows from horseback recalls the ancient Parthians and Scythians. Their "machines" are presumably like Roman dart hurlers, battering rams, and stone throwers, but the emphasis on their portability probably reflects contemporary experience with cannon, which were extremely hard to drag over the muddy roads of the time.

7. Gold coins of this name were minted by several European states. Four ducats of Venice, Burgundy, or Hungary were roughly equivalent to an English pound, and the pound itself was worth several hundred times its value today. The point is that the Utopians' annual income from the estates is huge.

Though the other sects of the Utopians differ from this main group in various particular doctrines, they agree with them in this single head, that there is one supreme power, the maker and ruler of the universe, whom they all call in their native language Mithra.[8] Different people define him differently, and each supposes the object of his worship is that one and only nature to whose divine majesty, by the consensus of all nations, the creation of all things is attributed. But gradually they are coming to forsake this mixture of superstitions, and to unite in that one religion which seems more reasonable than any of the others. And there is no doubt that the other religions would have disappeared long ago, had not various unlucky accidents that befell certain Utopians who were thinking about changing their religion been interpreted, out of fear, as signs of divine anger, not chance, as if the deity who was being abandoned were avenging an insult against himself.

But after they had heard from us the name of Christ, and learned of his teachings, his life, his miracles, and the no less marvelous constancy of the many martyrs whose blood, freely shed, has drawn many nations far and near into the Christian fellowship, you would not believe how eagerly they assented to it, either through the mysterious inspiration of God, or because Christianity seemed very like the religion already prevailing among them. But I think they were also much influenced by the fact that Christ approved a communal way of life for his disciples, and that among the truest communities of Christians the practice still prevails.[9] Whatever the reason, no small number of them chose to join our communion, and received the holy water of baptism. By that time, two of our group had died, and among us four survivors there was, I am sorry to say, no priest; so, though they received the other sacraments, they still lack those which in our religion can be administered only by priests.[1] They do, however, understand what these are, and earnestly desire them. In fact, they dispute vigorously whether a man chosen from among themselves could legitimately assume the functions of a priest without the dispatch of a Christian bishop. Though they seemed on the point of selecting such a person, they had not yet done so when I left.

Those who have not accepted Christianity make no effort to restrain others from it, nor do they criticize new converts to it. While I was there, only one of the Christians was interfered with. As soon as he was baptized, he took upon himself to preach the Christian religion publicly, with more zeal than discretion. We warned him not to do so, but he soon worked himself up to a pitch where he not only set our religion above the rest but condemned all others as profane in themselves, leading their impious and sacrilegious followers to the hell-flames they richly deserved. After he had been going on in this style for a long time, they arrested him. He was tried on a charge, not of despising their religion, but of creating a public disorder, convicted, and sentenced to exile. For it is one of their oldest rules that no man's religion, as such, shall be held against him.

---

8. In ancient Persian religion, Mithra (or Mithras) was the spirit of light.
9. The communist practice of the early Christians is described in Acts 2.44–45 and 4.32–35. Many monastic and ascetic orders still made a practice of abolishing private property for their members.
1. Of the seven Catholic sacraments, only baptism and matrimony can be conferred by laymen. Priests are created by ordination by a bishop (cf. below).

Utopus had heard that before his arrival the inhabitants were continually quarreling over religious matters. In fact, he found it was easy to conquer the country because the different sects were too busy fighting one another to oppose him. As soon as he had gained the victory, therefore, he decreed that everyone could cultivate the religion of his choice, and strenuously proselytize for it too, provided he did so quietly, modestly, rationally, and without bitterness toward others. If persuasion failed, no one was allowed to resort to abuse or violence. Anyone who fights wantonly about religion is punished by exile or enslavement.

Utopus laid down these rules not simply for the sake of peace, which he saw was in danger of being destroyed by constant quarrels and implacable hatreds, but also for the sake of religion itself. In matters of religion, he was not at all quick to dogmatize, because he suspected that God perhaps likes diverse and manifold forms of worship and has therefore deliberately inspired different people with different views. On the other hand, he was quite sure that it was arrogant folly for anyone to enforce conformity with his own beliefs on everyone else by means of threats or violence.[2] He supposed that if one religion is really true and the rest false, the true one will sooner or later emerge and prevail by its own natural strength, provided only that men consider the matter reasonably and moderately. But if they try to decide these matters by fighting and rioting, since the worst men are always the most headstrong, the best and holiest religion in the world will be crowded out by blind superstitions, like grain choked out of a field by thorns and briars. So he left the whole matter open, allowing each individual to choose what he would believe. The only exception he made was a solemn and strict law against any person who should sink so far below the dignity of human nature as to think that the soul perishes with the body, or that the universe is ruled by mere chance rather than divine providence.

Thus the Utopians all believe that after this life vices are to be punished and virtue rewarded; and they consider that anyone who denies this proposition is not even one of the human race, since he has degraded the sublimity of his own soul to the base level of a beast's wretched body. Still less will they count him as one of their citizens, since he would openly despise all the laws and customs of society, if not prevented by fear. Who can doubt that a man who has nothing to fear but the law, and no hope of life beyond the grave, will do anything he can to evade his country's laws by craft or break them by violence, in order to gratify his own private greed? Therefore a person who holds such views is offered no honors, entrusted with no offices, and given no public responsibility; he is universally regarded as low and torpid. Yet they do not afflict him with punishments, because they are persuaded that no one can choose to believe by a mere act of the will. They do not compel him by threats to dissemble his views, nor do they tolerate in the matter any deceit or lying, which they detest as next door to deliberate

---

2. This was not the attitude More took a decade after *Utopia*, when, the Reformation schism having begun, he was involved in the prosecution of Protestant heretics, sometimes to the death. In the *Dialogue Concerning Heresies* (1529), he wrote that "if it were now doubtful and ambiguous whether the church of Christ were in the right rule of doctrine or not, then were it very necessary to give them all good audience that could and would anything dispute on either party for it or against it, to the end that if we were now in a wrong way, we might leave it and walk in some better." Utopia was in this hypothetical situation; England, in More's view, was not.

malice. The man may not argue with the common people in behalf of his opinion; but in the presence of the priests and other important persons, in private, they not only permit but encourage it. For they are confident that in the end his madness will yield to reason.

There are some others, in fact no small number of them, who err in the opposite direction, in supposing that animals too have immortal souls,[3] though not comparable to ours in excellence, nor destined to equal felicity. These people are not thought to be evil, their opinion is not thought to be wholly unreasonable, and so they are not interfered with.

Almost all the Utopians are absolutely convinced that human bliss after death will be enormous; thus they lament every individual's sickness, but mourn over a death only if the person was torn from life anxiously and unwillingly. Such behavior they take to be a very bad sign, as if the soul, despairing and conscious of guilt, dreaded death through a secret premonition of punishments to come. Besides, they suppose God can hardly be well pleased with the coming of one who, when he is summoned, does not come gladly but is dragged off reluctantly and against his will. Such a death fills the onlookers with horror, and they carry the corpse out to burial in melancholy silence. There, after begging God to have mercy on his spirit and to pardon his infirmities, they commit his body to the earth. But when someone dies blithely and full of good hope, they do not mourn for him but carry the body cheerfully away, singing and commending the dead man's soul to God. They cremate him in a spirit more of reverence than of grief, and erect a column on which the dead man's honors are inscribed. After they have returned home, they talk of his character and deeds, and no part of his life is mentioned more frequently or more gladly than his joyful death.

They think that recollecting the dead person's goodness helps the living to behave virtuously and is also the most acceptable form of honor to the dead. For they think that dead people are actually present among us, and hear what we say about them, though through the dullness of human sight they are invisible to our eyes. Given their state of bliss, the dead must be able to travel freely where they please, and it would be unkind of them to cast off every desire of revisiting their friends, to whom they had been bound by mutual affection and charity during their lives. Like all other good things, they think that after death charity is increased rather than decreased in good men; and thus they believe the dead come frequently among the living, to observe their words and actions. Hence they go about their business the more confidently because of their trust in such protectors; and the belief that their forefathers are physically present keeps them from any secret dishonorable deed.

Fortune-telling and other vain forms of superstitious divination, such as other peoples take very seriously, they have no part of and consider ridiculous. But they venerate miracles which occur without the help of nature, considering them direct and visible manifestations of the divine power. Indeed, they report that miracles have frequently occurred in their country. Sometimes in great and dangerous crises they pray publicly for a miracle, which they then anticipate with great confidence, and obtain.

3. These Utopians resemble the ancient Pythagoreans, who, as a facet of their doctrine of the transmigration of souls, conceded them to animals.

They think that the contemplation of nature, and the sense of reverence arising from it, are acts of worship to God. There are some people, however, and not just a few of them, who from religious motives reject learning and pursue no studies; but none of them is the least bit idle. Constant dedication to the offices of charity, these people think, will increase their chances of happiness after death; and so they are always busy in the service of others. Some tend the sick; others repair roads, clean ditches, rebuild bridges, dig turf, sand, or stones; still others fell trees and cut them up, and transport wood, grain, or other commodities into the cities by wagon. They work for private citizens as well as for the public, and work even harder than slaves. They undertake with cheery good will any task that is so rough, hard, and dirty that most people refuse to tackle it because of the toil, boredom, and frustration involved. While constantly engaged in heavy labor themselves, they secure leisure for others, and yet they claim no credit for it. They do not criticize the way other people live, nor do they boast of their own doings. The more they put themselves in the position of slaves, the more highly they are honored by everyone.

These people are of two sects. The first are celibates who abstain not only from sex but also from eating meat, and some of them from any sort of animal food whatever. They reject all the pleasures of this life as harmful, and look forward only to the joys of the life to come, which they hope to deserve by hard labor and all-night vigils. As they hope to attain it soon, they are cheerful and active in the here and now. The other kind are just as fond of hard work, but prefer to marry. They don't despise the comforts of marriage, but think that, as their duty to nature requires work, so their duty to their country requires them to beget children. They avoid no pleasure unless it interferes with their labor, and gladly eat meat, precisely because they think it makes them stronger for any sort of heavy work. The Utopians regard the second sort as more sensible, but the first sort as holier. If they claimed to prefer celibacy to marriage, and a hard life to a comfortable one, on grounds of reason alone, the Utopians would think them absurd. But since these men claim to be motivated by religion, the Utopians respect and revere them. There is no subject on which they are warier of jumping to conclusions than in this matter of religion. These then are the men whom in their own language they call Buthrescas, a term which may be translated as "the especially religious."

Their priests are of great holiness, and therefore very few. In each city, there are no more than thirteen, one for each church. In case of war, seven of them go out with the army, and seven substitutes are appointed to fill their places for the time being. When the regular priests come back, the substitutes return to their former posts—that is, they serve as assistants to the high priest, until one of the regular thirteen dies, and then one of them succeeds to his position. The high priest is, of course, in authority over all the others. Priests are elected, just like all other officials, by secret popular vote, in order to avoid partisan feeling. After election they are ordained by the college of priests.

They preside over divine worship, attend to religious matters, and act as censors of public morality. For a man to be summoned before them and scolded for not living an honorable life is considered a great disgrace. As the duty of the priests is simply to counsel and advise, so correcting and punishing offenders is the duty of the governor and the other officials, though the priests do exclude from divine service persons whom they find to be extraordinarily wicked. Hardly any punishment is more dreaded than this; the excommunicate incurs great disgrace, and is tortured by the fear of damnation. Not even his body is safe for long, for unless he quickly convinces the priests of his repentance he will be seized and punished by the senate for impiety.

The priests are entrusted with teaching the children and young people.[4] Instruction in morality and virtue is considered just as important as the accumulation of learning. From the very first they try to instill in the pupils' minds, while they are still young and tender, principles which will be useful to preserve the commonwealth. What is planted in the minds of children lives on in the minds of adults, and is of great value in strengthening the commonwealth: the decline of society can always be traced to vices which arise from wrong attitudes.

Women are not debarred from the priesthood, but only a widow of advanced years is ever chosen, and it doesn't happen often. The wives of the male priests are the very finest women in the whole country.

No official in Utopia is more honored than the priest. Even if one of them commits a crime, he is not brought into a court of law, but left to God and his own conscience. They think it is wrong to lay human hands on a man, however guilty, who has been specially consecrated to God as a holy offering, so to speak. This custom is the easier for them to observe because their priests are very few and very carefully chosen. Besides, it rarely happens that a man selected for his goodness and raised to high dignities wholly because of his moral character will fall into corruption and vice. And even if such a thing should happen, human nature being as changeable as it is, no great harm is to be feared, because the priests are so few and have no power beyond that which derives from their good reputation. In fact, the reason for having so few priests is to prevent the order, which the Utopians now esteem so highly, from being cheapened by numbers.[5] Besides, they think it would be hard to find many men qualified for a dignity for which merely ordinary virtues are not sufficient.

Their priests are esteemed no less highly abroad than at home, which can be seen from the following fact: Whenever their armies join in battle, the Utopian priests are to be found, a little removed from the fray but not far, wearing their sacred vestments and down on their knees. With hands raised to heaven, they pray first of all for peace, and then for victory to their own side, but without much bloodshed on either hand.[6] Should their side be victorious, they rush among the combatants and restrain the rage of their own men against the enemy. If any of the enemy see these priests and call to them, it is enough to save their lives; to touch the flowing robes of a priest will save all their property from confiscation. This custom has brought them such veneration among all peoples, and given them such genuine authority, that they have saved the Utopians from the rage of the enemy as often as

---

4. Presumably the priests only *supervise* the teaching: there are only thirteen of them per city, whereas each city is home to thousands of children.

5. Marginal gloss: "But what a crowd of them we have!"
6. Gloss: "O priests far holier than our own!"

they have protected the enemy from Utopians. Instances of this are well known. Sometimes when the Utopian line has buckled, when the field was lost, and the enemy was rushing in to kill and plunder, the priests have intervened to stop the carnage and separate the armies, and an equitable peace has been concluded. There was never anywhere a tribe so fierce, cruel, and barbarous as not to hold their persons sacrosanct and inviolable.

The Utopians celebrate the first and last days of every month, and likewise of each year, as feast days. They divide the year into months which they measure by the orbit of the moon, just as they measure the year itself by the course of the sun. In their language, the first days are known as the Cynemerns and the last days as the Trapemerns, which is to say "First-feasts" and "Last-feasts."[7] Their churches are beautifully constructed, finely adorned, and large enough to hold a great many people. This is a necessity, since churches are so few. Their interiors are all rather dark, not from architectural ignorance but from deliberate policy; for the priests think that in bright light the congregation's thoughts will go wandering, whereas a dim light tends to concentrate the mind and encourage devotion.

Though there are various religions in Utopia, all of them, even the most diverse, agree in the main point, which is worship of the divine nature; they are like travelers going to one destination by different roads. So nothing is seen or heard in the churches that does not square with all the creeds. If any sect has a special rite of its own, that is celebrated in a private house; the public service is ordered by a ritual which in no way derogates from any of the private services. Therefore in the churches no image of the gods is to be seen, so that each person may be free to form his own image of God according to his own religion, in any shape he pleases. They do not invoke God by any name except Mithra. Whatever the nature of the divine majesty may be, they all agree to refer to it by that single word, and their prayers are so phrased as to accommodate the beliefs of all the different sects.

On the evening of the "Last-feast" they meet in their churches, and while still fasting they thank God for their prosperity during that month or year which is just ending. Next day, which is "First-feast," they all flock to the churches in the morning, to pray for prosperity and happiness in the month or year which is just beginning. On the day of "Last-feast," in the home before they go to church, wives kneel before their husbands and children before their parents, to confess their various sins of commission or of negligence and beg forgiveness for their offenses. Thus if any cloud of anger or resentment has arisen in the family, it is dispersed, and they can attend divine services with clear and untroubled minds—for they consider it sacrilege to worship with a rankling conscience. If they are conscious of hatred or anger toward anyone, they do not take part in divine services till they have been reconciled and have cleansed their hearts, for fear of some swift and terrible punishment.

As they enter the church, they separate, men going to the right side and women to the left.[8] Then they take their seats so that the males of each household are placed in front of the head of that household, while the women-

---

7. "Cynemerns" actually means, in Greek, "dog-days" (or perhaps "starting-days"); "Trapemerns," "turning-days."

8. Separation of the sexes in church had been customary since the early Christian centuries.

folk are directly in front of the mother of the family. In this way they ensure that everyone's behavior in public is supervised by the same person whose authority and discipline direct him at home. They take great care that the young are everywhere placed in the company of their elders. For if children were trusted to the care of other children, they might spend in childish foolery the time they should devote to developing a religious fear of the gods, which is the greatest and almost the only incitement to virtue.

They do not slaughter animals in their sacrifices, and do not think that a merciful God, who gave life to all creatures precisely so that they might live, will be gratified with the shedding of blood. They burn incense, scatter perfumes, and display a great number of candles—not that they think these practices profit the divine nature in any way, any more than human prayers do; but they like this harmless kind of worship. They feel that sweet smells, lights, and other such rituals elevate the mind and lift it with a livelier devotion toward the adoration of God.

When they go to church, the people all wear white. The priest wears robes of various colors, wonderful for their workmanship and decoration, though not of materials as costly as one would suppose. The robes have no gold embroidery nor any precious stones, but are decorated with the feathers of different birds so skillfully woven together that the value of the handiwork far exceeds the cost of the most precious materials.[9] Also, certain symbolic mysteries are hidden in the patterning of the feathers on the robes, the meaning of which is carefully handed down among the priests. These messages serve to remind them of God's benefits toward them, and consequently of the devotion they owe to God, as well as of their duty to one another.

As the priest in his robes appears from the vestibule, the people all fall to the ground in reverence. The stillness is so complete that the scene strikes one with awe, as if a divinity were actually present. After remaining in this posture for some time, they rise at a signal from the priest. Then they sing hymns to the accompaniment of musical instruments, most of them quite different in shape from those in our part of the world. Many of them produce sweeter tones than ours, but others are not even comparable. In one respect, however, they are beyond doubt far ahead of us, because all their music, both vocal and instrumental, renders and expresses natural feelings and perfectly matches the sound to the subject. Whether the words of the hymn are supplicatory, cheerful, troubled, mournful, or angry, the music represents the meaning through the contour of the melody so admirably that it penetrates and inspires the minds of the ardent hearers. Finally, the priest and the people together recite certain fixed forms of prayer, so composed that what they all repeat in unison each individual can apply to himself.

In these prayers, the worshipers acknowledge God to be the creator and ruler of the universe and the author of all good things. They thank God for benefits received, and particularly for the divine favor which placed them in the happiest of commonwealths and inspired them with religious ideas which they hope are the truest. If they are wrong in this, and if there is some sort of society or religion more acceptable to God, they pray that he will, in his goodness, reveal it to them, for they are ready to follow wherever he

---

9. Perhaps related to Vespucci's observation that the Native Americans' wealth "consists of feathers of many-hued birds . . . and of many other things to which we attach no value."

leads. But if their form of society is the best and their religion the truest, then they pray that God will keep them steadfast, and bring other mortals to the same way of life and the same religious faith—unless, indeed, there is something in this variety of religions which delights his inscrutable will.

Then they pray that after an easy death God will receive each of them to himself, how soon or how late it is not for them to say. But if God's divine majesty so please, they ask to be brought to him soon, even by the hardest possible death, rather than be kept away from him longer, even by the most fortunate of earthly lives. When this prayer has been said, they prostrate themselves on the ground again; then after a little while they rise and go to lunch. The rest of the day they pass in games and military training.

Now I have described to you as accurately as I could the structure of that commonwealth which I consider not only the best but indeed the only one that can rightfully claim that name. In other places men talk very liberally of the commonwealth, but what they mean is simply their own wealth; in Utopia, where there is no private business, everyone zealously pursues the public business. And in both places people are right to act as they do. For among us, even though the commonwealth may flourish, there are very few who do not know that unless they make separate provision for themselves, they may perfectly well die of hunger. Bitter necessity, then, forces them to think that they must look out for themselves rather than for others, that is, for the people. But in Utopia, where everything belongs to everybody, no one need fear that, so long as the public warehouses are filled, anyone will ever lack for anything he needs. For the distribution of goods is not niggardly; in Utopia no one is poor, there are no beggars, and though no one owns anything, everyone is rich.

For what can be greater riches than to live joyfully and peacefully, free from all anxieties, and without worries about making a living? No man is bothered by his wife's querulous entreaties about money, no man fears poverty for his son, or struggles to scrape up a dowry for his daughter. Everyone can feel secure of his own livelihood and happiness, and of his whole family's as well: wife, sons, grandsons, great-grandsons, great-great-grandsons, and that whole long line of descendants that gentlefolk are so fond of contemplating. Indeed, even those who once worked but can no longer do so are cared for just as well as those who are still working.

Now here I'd like to see anyone try to compare this equity of the Utopians with the so-called justice that prevails among other peoples—among whom let me perish if I can discover the slightest scrap of justice or fairness. What kind of justice is it when a nobleman or a goldsmith or a moneylender, or someone else who makes his living by doing either nothing at all or something completely useless to the commonwealth, gets to live a life of luxury and grandeur, while in the meantime a laborer, a carter, a carpenter, or a farmer works so hard and so constantly that even a beast of burden could scarcely endure it? Although this work of theirs is so necessary that no commonwealth could survive a year without it, they earn so meager a living and lead such miserable lives that beasts of burden would really seem to be better off. Beasts do not have to work every minute, and their food is not much worse; in fact they like it better. And besides, they do not have to worry about their future. But workingmen not only have to sweat and suffer without present reward, but agonize over the prospect of a penniless old age. Their daily wage is inadequate even for their present needs, so there is no possible chance of their saving toward the future.

Now isn't this an unjust and ungrateful commonwealth? It lavishes rich rewards on so-called gentry, goldsmiths, and the rest of that crew, who don't work at all or are mere parasites, purveyors of empty pleasures. And yet it makes no provision whatever for the welfare of farmers and colliers, laborers, carters, and carpenters, without whom the commonwealth would simply cease to exist. After society has taken the labor of their best years, when they are worn out by age and sickness and utter destitution, then the thankless commonwealth, forgetting all their sleepless nights and great services, throws them out to die a miserable death. What is worse, the rich constantly try to grind out of the poor part of their meager wages, not only by private swindling but by public laws. Before, it appeared to be unjust that people who deserve most from the commonwealth should receive least; but now, by promulgating law, they have palmed injustice off as "legal." When I run over in my mind the various commonwealths flourishing today, so help me God, I can see in them nothing but a conspiracy of the rich, who are fattening up their own interests under the name and title of the commonwealth.[1] They invent ways and means to hang onto whatever they have acquired by sharp practice, and then they scheme to oppress the poor by buying up their toil and labor as cheaply as possible. These devices become law as soon as the rich, speaking for the commonwealth—which, of course, includes the poor as well—say they must be observed.

And yet, when these insatiably greedy and evil men have divided among themselves all the goods which would have sufficed for the entire people, how far they remain from the happiness of the Utopian republic, which has abolished not only money but with it greed! What a mass of trouble was cut away by that one step! What a multitude of crimes was pulled up by the roots! Everyone knows that if money were abolished, fraud, theft, robbery, quarrels, brawls, altercations, seditions, murders, treasons, poisonings, and a whole set of crimes which are avenged but not prevented by the hangman would at once die out. If money disappeared, so would fear, anxiety, worry, toil, and sleepless nights. Even poverty, the one condition which seems more than anything else to need money for its relief, would die away if money were entirely abolished.

Consider, if you will, this example. Take a barren year of failed harvests, when many thousands of people have been carried off by famine. If at the end of the scarcity the barns of the rich were searched, I dare say positively that enough grain would be found in them to have kept all those who died of starvation and disease from even realizing that a shortage ever existed—if only it had been divided among them. So easily might people get the necessities of life if that cursed money, that marvelous invention which is supposed to provide access to them, were not in fact the only barrier to our getting what we need to live. Even the rich, I'm sure, understand this. They must

---

1. Marginal gloss: "Reader, note well!" In the text at this point, More may be alluding to the judgment of St. Augustine in *The City of God* 4.4: "Take away justice, and what are kingdoms but great robber-bands?" As a young man, More had given a series of public lectures on Augustine's book.

know that it's better to have enough of what we really need than an abundance of superfluities, much better to escape from our many present troubles than to be burdened with great masses of wealth. And in fact I have no doubt that every man's perception of where his true interest lies, along with the authority of Christ our Savior (whose wisdom could not fail to recognize the best, and whose goodness would not fail to counsel it), would long ago have brought the whole world to adopt Utopian laws, if it were not for one single monster, the prime plague and begetter of all others—I mean Pride.

Pride measures her advantages not by what she has but by what others lack. Pride would not condescend even to be made a goddess, if there were no wretches for her to sneer at and domineer over. Her good fortune is dazzling only by contrast with the miseries of others, her riches are valuable only as they torment and tantalize the poverty of others. Pride is a serpent from hell that twines itself around the hearts of men; and it acts like a suckfish[2] in holding them back from choosing a better way of life.

Pride is too deeply fixed in human nature to be easily plucked out. So I am glad that the Utopians at least have been lucky enough to achieve this commonwealth, which I wish all mankind would imitate. The institutions they have adopted have made their community most happy, and, as far as anyone can tell, capable of lasting forever. Now that they have rooted up the seeds of ambition and faction at home, along with most other vices, they are in no danger from internal strife, which alone has been the ruin of many cities that seemed secure. As long as they preserve harmony at home, and keep their institutions healthy, the Utopians can never be overcome or even shaken by all the envious princes of neighboring countries, who have often attempted their ruin, but always in vain.

When Raphael had finished his story, I was left thinking that not a few of the customs and laws he had described as existing among the Utopians were quite absurd. These included their methods of waging war, their religious practices, as well as other customs of theirs, but my chief objection was to the basis of their whole system, that is, their communal living and their moneyless economy. This one thing alone takes away all the nobility, magnificence, splendor, and majesty which (in the popular view) are the true ornaments and glory of any commonwealth. But I saw Raphael was tired with talking, and I was not sure he could take contradiction in these matters, particularly when I remembered what he had said about certain people who were afraid they might not appear wise unless they found out something to criticize in the ideas of others. So with praise for the Utopian way of life and his account of it, I took him by the hand and led him in to supper. But first I said that we would find some other time for thinking of these matters more deeply, and for talking them over in more detail. And I still hope such an opportunity will present itself someday.

Meanwhile, though he is a man of unquestionable learning, and highly experienced in the ways of the world, I cannot agree with everything he

2. The suckfish (remora) has a suction plate atop its head, by which it attaches itself to the underbelly of larger fishes or the hulls of ships. Impressed by the tenacity of its grip, the ancients fabled that it could stop ships in their courses.

said. Yet I freely confess there are very many things in the Utopian commonwealth that in our own societies I would wish rather than expect to see.

1515–16   1516

Thomas More to His Friend Peter Giles, Warmest Greetings[1]

My dear Peter, I was absolutely delighted with the judgment of that very sharp fellow you recall, who posed this dilemma about my *Utopia*: if the story is put forward as fact, he said, then I see a number of absurdities in it; but if it's fiction, then it seems to me that in various respects More's usual good judgment is at fault. I suspect this fellow of being learned, and I see that he's a friend; but whoever he is, I'm much obliged to him. By this frank opinion of his, he has pleased me more than anyone else since the book was published.

For in the first place, either out of fondness for me or for the work itself, he seems to have borne up under the burden of reading the book all the way through—and that not perfunctorily or hastily, the way priests read the divine office—those, at least, who read it at all.[2] No, he read slowly and attentively, noting all the particular points. Then, having singled out certain matters for criticism, and not very many, as a matter of fact, he gives careful and considered approval to the rest. And finally, in the very expressions he uses to criticize me, he implies higher praises than some of those who have put all their energies into compliment. It's easy to see what a high opinion he has of me, when he expresses disappointment over reading something imperfect or inexact—whereas I don't expect, in treating so many different matters, to be able to say more than a few things which aren't totally ridiculous.

Still, I'd like to be just as frank with him as he was with me; and, in fact, I don't see why he should think himself so acute (so "sharp-sighted," as the Greeks would say) just because he's discovered some absurdities in the institutions of Utopia, or caught me putting forth some half-baked ideas about the constitution of a republic. Aren't there any absurdities elsewhere in the world? And did any one of the philosophers who've offered a pattern of a society, a ruler, or even a private household set down everything so well that nothing ought to be changed? Actually, if it weren't for the great respect I retain for certain highly distinguished names, I could easily produce from each of them a number of notions which I can hardly doubt would be universally condemned as absurd.

But when he wonders whether *Utopia* is fact or fiction, then I find *his* judgment, in turn, sorely at fault. I do not deny that if I'd decided to write about a commonwealth, and a tale of this sort had occurred to me, I might have spread a little fiction, like so much honey, over the truth, to make it more acceptable. But I would certainly have tempered the fiction a little, so

---

1. This second letter of More to Giles appeared only in the second edition of *Utopia* (Paris, 1517), where it immediately follows Book II. The letter praises a supposedly perspicacious critique of *Utopia* by a "very sharp fellow," whose identity is unknown—if indeed More didn't simply invent him.

2. Priests read the "divine office"—the daily round of prescribed prayers to be recited at set hours—with varying degrees of enthusiasm, according to More.

that, while it deceived the common folk, I gave hints to the more learned which would enable them to see what I was about. So, if I'd done nothing but give special names to the governor, the river, the city, and the island, which hinted to the learned that the island was nowhere, the city a phantom, the river waterless, and that the governor had no people,[3] that would not have been hard to do, and would have been far more clever than what I actually did. Unless I had a historian's devotion to fact, I am not so stupid as to have used those barbarous and senseless names of Utopia, Anyder, Amaurot, and Ademus.

Still, my dear Giles, I see some people are so suspicious that what we simple-minded and credulous fellows have written down of Hythloday's account can hardly find any credence at all with these circumspect and sagacious persons. I'm afraid my personal reputation, as well as my authority as a historian, may be threatened by their skepticism; so it's a good thing that I can defend myself by saying, as Terence's Mysis says about Glycerium's boy, to confirm his legitimacy, "Praise be to God there were some free women present at his birth."[4] And so it was a good thing for me that Raphael told his story not just to you and me, but to a great many perfectly respectable and serious-minded men. Whether he told them more things, and more important things, I don't know; but I'm sure he told them no fewer and no less important things than he told us.

Well, if these doubters won't believe such witnesses, let them consult Hythloday himself, for he is still alive. I heard only recently from some travelers coming out of Portugal that on the first of last March he was as healthy and vigorous a man as he ever was. Let them get the truth from him—dig it out of him with questions, if they want. I only want them to understand that I'm responsible for my own work, and my own work alone, not for anyone else's credibility.

Farewell, my dearest Peter, to you, your charming wife, and your clever little girl—to all, my wife sends her very best wishes.

1517

---

3. This is of course precisely what the names do mean.

4. *The Lady of Andros*, lines 770–71.

SIR THOMAS WYATT THE ELDER
1503–1542

Thomas Wyatt made his career in the shifting, dangerous currents of Renaissance courts, and court culture, with its power struggles, sexual intrigues, and sophisticated tastes, shaped his remarkable achievements as a poet. Educated at St. John's College, Cambridge, Wyatt entered the service of Henry VIII, becoming clerk of the king's jewels, a member of diplomatic missions to France and the Low Countries, and, in 1537–39, ambassador to Spain at the court of the Holy Roman Emperor, Charles V. The years he spent abroad as a diplomat had a significant impact upon his writing, most obvious in his translations and imitations of poems by the Italian Renaissance writers Serafino, Aretino, Sannazaro, Alamanni, and, above all, Petrarch. Diplomacy, with its veiled threats, rhetorical manipulation, and cynical role-playing, may have had a more indirect impact as well, reinforcing the lessons in self-presentation and self-concealment that Wyatt would have received at the English court.

Life in the orbit of the ruthless, unpredictable Henry VIII was competitive and risky. When, in the late 1530s, Wyatt wrote to his son of the "thousand dangers and hazards, enmities, hatreds, prisonments, despites, and indignations" he had faced, he was not exaggerating. He probably came closest to the executioner's axe when in 1536 he was imprisoned in the Tower of London along with several others accused of having committed adultery with the queen, Anne Boleyn. As his poem "Who list his wealth and ease retain" suggests, Wyatt may have watched from his cell the execution of the queen and her alleged lovers; but he himself was spared, as he was spared a few years later, when he was again imprisoned in the Tower on charges of high treason brought by his enemies at court. His death, at the age of thirty-nine, came from a fever.

It is not surprising, given his career, that many of Wyatt's poems, including his satires and his psalm translations, express an intense longing for "steadfastness" and an escape from the corruption, anxiety, and duplicity of the court. The praise, in his verse epistle to John Poins, of a quiet retired life in the country and the harsh condemnation of courtly hypocrisy derive from his own experience. But of course the eloquent celebration of simplicity and truthfulness can itself be a cunning strategy. Wyatt was a master of the game of poetic self-display. Again and again he represents himself as a plain-speaking and steadfast man, betrayed by the "doubleness" of a fickle mistress or the instability of fortune. At this distance it is impossible to know how much this account corresponds to reality, but we can admire, as Wyatt's contemporaries did, the rhetorical deftness of the performance.

In a move with momentous consequences for English poetry, Wyatt introduced into English the sonnet, a fourteen-line poem in iambic pentameter with a complex, intertwining rhyme scheme. For the most part, he took his subject matter from Petrarch's sonnets, but his rhyme schemes make a significant departure. Petrarch's sonnets consist of an "octave," rhyming *abba abba*, followed, after a turn (*volta*) in the sense, by a "sestet" with various rhyme schemes (such as *cd cd cd* and *cde cde*) that have in common their avoidance of a rhyming couplet at the end. Wyatt employs the Petrarchan octave, but his most common sestet scheme is *cddc ee*: the Petrarchan sonnet was already beginning to change into the characteristic "English" structure for the sonnet, three quatrains and a closing couplet.

In his freest translations of Petrarchan sonnets, such as "Whoso list to hunt," Wyatt tends to turn the idealizing of the woman into disillusionment and complaint. For the lover in Petrarch's poems, love is a transcendent experience, extending beyond the boundaries of life itself; for the lover in Wyatt's poems, it is all too transient, and embittering. The tone of bitterness carries over to many poems less closely linked to Italian and French models, poems with short stanzas and refrains that associate them with the native English song tradition. Some of Wyatt's songs, to be sure, strike a note of jaunty independence, often tinged with misogyny; but melancholy complaint is rarely very distant. Perhaps the poem that most brilliantly captures his blend of passion, anger, cynicism, longing, and pain is "They flee from me."

Though Wyatt's representations of women are often cynical, it is clear that aristocratic women played a key role in the reception and preservation of his poetry. Women were not excluded from the courtly game of lyric-making. The Devonshire Manuscript, one of the chief sources for Wyatt's poetry, contains a number of poems that were probably by women, many more transcribed by female hands, and some male-authored poems written in a female voice, as well as any number of misogynist verses, by Wyatt and others.

Wyatt never published a collection of his own poems, and very little of his verse appeared in print during his lifetime. In 1557 (fifteen years after his death), the printer Richard Tottel included 97 poems attributed to Wyatt among the 271 poems in his miscellany, *Songs and Sonnets*. Wyatt was not primarily concerned with regularity of accent and smoothness of rhythm. By the time Tottel's collection was published, Wyatt's deliberately rough, vigorous, and expressive metrical practice was felt to be crude, and Tottel (or perhaps some intermediary) smoothed out the versification. We reprint "They flee from me" both in Tottel's "improved" version and in the version found in the Egerton Manuscript, which contains poems in Wyatt's own hand and corrections he made to scribal copies of his poems. Unlike the Egerton Manuscript (E. MS.), the Devonshire Manuscript (D. MS.) was not apparently in the poet's possession, but some of its texts seem earlier than Egerton's, and it furnishes additional poems, as do the Blage Manuscript (B. MS.) and the Arundel Manuscript (A. MS.).

In the following selections we have indicated the manuscript from which each of the poems derives and divided the poems into three generic groups: sonnets, other lyrics, and finally a satire. Within each of the first two groups, the poems are printed in the order in which they appear in the manuscripts. There is no reason to think that this is a chronological ordering.*

The long love that in my thought doth harbor[1]

The long love that in my thought doth harbor,
And in mine heart doth keep his residence,
Into my face presseth with bold pretense
And therein campeth, spreading his banner.[2]
5 She that me learneth° to love and suffer   teaches me
And will that my trust and lust's negligence[3]
Be reined by reason, shame, and reverence,
With his hardiness taketh displeasure.
Wherewithal° unto the heart's forest he fleeth,   because of which
10 Leaving his enterprise with pain and cry,
And there him hideth, and not appeareth.
What may I do, when my master feareth,
But in the field with him to live and die?
For good is the life ending faithfully.

E. MS.

---

* For the Italian originals of the Petrarchan sonnets translated in our selection, as well as additional poems by Wyatt, see the supplemental ebook. For a broad grouping of 16th-century love poems, see below, "Renaissance Love and Desire" (pp. 1000ff.).
1. Wyatt's version of poem 140 of Petrarch's *Rime sparse* (Scattered rhymes); his younger friend the earl of Surrey also translated it (p. 663).
2. I.e., the speaker's blush. The first four lines of this sonnet introduce the "conceit" (elaborately sustained metaphor) of Love as a warrior who, "with bold pretense" (i.e., making bold claim), flaunts his presence by means of the "banner." Elaborate metaphors of this kind are common in Petrarchan (and Elizabethan) love poetry, and often, as in this instance, an entire sonnet will turn on a single conceit.
3. I.e., my open and careless revelation of my love.

Petrarch, Rima 140

A MODERN PROSE TRANSLATION[4]

Love, who lives and reigns in my thought and keeps his principal seat in my heart, sometimes comes forth all in armor into my forehead, there camps, and there sets up his banner.

She who teaches us to love and to be patient, and wishes my great desire, my kindled hope, to be reined in by reason, shame, and reverence, at our boldness is angry within herself.

Wherefore Love flees terrified to my heart, abandoning his every enterprise, and weeps and trembles; there he hides and no more appears outside.

What can I do, when my lord is afraid, except stay with him until the last hour? For he makes a good end who dies loving well.

Whoso list to hunt[5]

Whoso list° to hunt, I know where is an hind,°   cares / female deer
But as for me, alas, I may no more.
The vain travail° hath wearied me so sore,°   labor / sorely, seriously
I am of them that farthest cometh behind.
5 Yet may I, by no means, my wearied mind
Draw from the deer, but as she fleeth afore,
Fainting I follow. I leave off, therefore,
Since in a net I seek to hold the wind.
Who list her hunt, I put him out of doubt,°   assure him
10 As well as I, may spend his time in vain.
And graven with diamonds in letters plain
There is written, her fair neck round about,
"*Noli me tangere*, for Caesar's I am,
And wild for to hold, though I seem tame."

E. MS.

Petrarch, Rima 190

A MODERN PROSE TRANSLATION

A white doe on the green grass appeared to me, with two golden horns, between two rivers, in the shade of a laurel, when the sun was rising in the unripe season.

---

4. This and the prose translations of Rime 190, 134, and 189 are by Robert K. Durling.
5. An adaptation of Petrarch's Rima 190, perhaps influenced by commentators on Petrarch, who said that *Noli me tangere quia Caesaris sum* ("Touch me not, for I am Caesar's") was inscribed on the collars of Caesar's hinds, which were then set free and were presumably safe from hunters. Wyatt's sonnet is usually supposed to refer to Anne Boleyn, in whom Henry VIII became interested in 1526.

Her look was so sweet and proud that to follow her I left every task, like the miser who as he seeks treasure sweetens his trouble with delight.

"Let no one touch me," she bore written with diamonds and topazes around her lovely neck. "It has pleased my Caesar to make me free."

And the sun had already turned at midday; my eyes were tired by looking but not sated, when I fell into the water, and she disappeared.

Farewell, Love

Farewell, Love, and all thy laws forever,
Thy baited hooks shall tangle me no more;
Senec and Plato call me from thy lore,
To perfect wealth my wit for to endeavor.[6]
5 In blind error when I did persever,
Thy sharp repulse, that pricketh aye° so sore,   *always*
Hath taught me to set in trifles no store,°   *value*
And 'scape forth since liberty is lever.°   *more pleasing, dearer*
Therefore farewell, go trouble younger hearts,
10 And in me claim no more authority;
With idle youth go use thy property,[7]
And thereon spend thy many brittle darts.°   *arrows*
For hitherto though I have lost all my time,
Me lusteth° no longer rotten boughs to climb.   *I care*

E. MS.

I find no peace[8]

I find no peace, and all my war is done,
I fear and hope, I burn and freeze like ice,
I fly above the wind, yet can I not arise,
And naught I have, and all the world I seize on.
5 That° looseth nor locketh holdeth me in prison,   *that which*
And holdeth me not, yet can I 'scape nowise;
Nor letteth me live nor die at my devise,°   *my own will*
And yet of death it giveth me occasion.
Without eyen° I see, and without tongue I plain;[9]   *eyes*

6. I.e., "Senec" (Seneca, the Roman moral philosopher and tragedian) and Plato call him to educate his mind ("wit") to perfect well-being ("wealth").

7. Do what you characteristically do.
8. Translated from Petrarch's Rima 134.
9. Complain; lament.

10   I desire to perish, and yet I ask health;
I love another, and thus I hate myself;
I feed me in sorrow, and laugh in all my pain.
Likewise displeaseth me both death and life,
And my delight is causer of this strife.

E. MS.

Petrarch, Rima 134

A MODERN PROSE TRANSLATION

Peace I do not find, and I have no wish to make war; and I fear and hope, and burn and am of ice; and I fly above the heavens and lie on the ground; and I grasp nothing and embrace all the world.

One has me in prison who neither opens nor locks, neither keeps me for his own nor unties the bonds; and Love does not kill and does not unchain me, he neither wishes me alive nor frees me from the tangle.

I see without eyes, and I have no tongue and yet cry out; and I wish to perish and I ask for help; and I hate myself and love another.

I feed on pain, weeping I laugh; equally displeasing to me are death and life. In this state am I, Lady, on account of you.

My galley[1]

My galley charged° with forgetfulness[2]	*freighted*
Thorough° sharp seas, in winter nights doth pass	*through*
'Tween rock and rock; and eke° mine enemy, alas,	*also*
That is my lord, steereth with cruelness;	
5 And every oar a thought in readiness,	
As though that death were light in such a case.[3]	
An endless wind doth tear the sail apace°	*swiftly*
Of forced sighs and trusty fearfulness.°	*fear to trust*
A rain of tears, a cloud of dark disdain,	
10 Hath done the wearied cords great hinderance;	
Wreathed° with error and eke with ignorance.	*twisted*
The stars be hid that led me to this pain.	
Drowned is reason that should me consort,°	*accompany*
And I remain despairing of the port.	

E. MS.

---

1. Translated from Petrarch's Rima 189. For Edmund Spenser's adaptation of the same poem, see p. 986.

2. I.e., obliviousness of everything except love.
3. As though my destruction would not matter much.

Petrarch, Rima 189

A MODERN PROSE TRANSLATION

My ship laden with forgetfulness passes through a harsh sea, at midnight, in winter, between Scylla and Charybdis,[4] and at the tiller sits my lord, rather my enemy;

each oar is manned by a ready, cruel thought that seems to scorn the tempest and the end; a wet, changeless wind of sighs, hopes, and desires breaks the sail;

a rain of weeping, a mist of disdain wet and loosen the already weary ropes, made of error twisted up with ignorance.

My two usual sweet stars are hidden; dead among the waves are reason and skill; so that I begin to despair of the port.

Divers doth use

Divers doth use,[5] as I have heard and know,
When that to change their ladies do begin,
To mourn and wail, and never for to lin,°   *cease*
Hoping thereby to pease° their painful woe.   *appease, relieve*
5 And some there be, that when it chanceth so
That women change and hate where love hath been,
They call them false and think with words to win
The hearts of them which otherwhere doth grow.
But as for me, though that by chance indeed
10 Change hath outworn the favor that I had,
I will not wail, lament, nor yet be sad,
Nor call her false that falsely did me feed,
But let it pass, and think it is of kind°   *nature*
That often° change doth please a woman's mind.   *frequent*

D. MS.

What vaileth truth?[6]

What vaileth° truth? or by it to take pain,   *avails*
To strive by steadfastness for to attain.
To be just and true and flee from doubleness;

---

4. The monster and the whirlpool that threaten Odysseus's ship on either side of the Straits of Messina, in *Odyssey* 12.
5. Are accustomed. "Divers": the adjective ("various," "sundry"), not the noun; i.e., various other men.
6. A rondeau: a difficult French verse form in which the unrhymed refrain "rounds" back to the opening words, and the rest of the poem uses only two rhyme sounds.

Sithens all° alike, where ruleth craftiness,   *since exactly*
5 Rewarded is both false and plain?
Soonest he speedeth° that most can feign;   *succeeds*
True-meaning heart is had in disdain.
Against deceit and doubleness,
    What vaileth truth?

10 Deceived is he by crafty train°   *treachery*
That meaneth no guile and doth remain
Within the trap without redress.°   *remedy*
But for° to love, lo, such a mistress,   *except*
Whose cruelty nothing can refrain,°   *restrain*
15   What vaileth truth?

                                             E. MS.

Madam, withouten many words

Madam, withouten many words,
Once,° I am sure, ye will or no.   *sometime*
And if ye will, then leave your bordes,°   *jests*
And use your wit° and show it so.   *mind*

5 And with a beck ye shall me call.
And if of one that burneth alway
Ye have any pity at all,
Answer him fair with yea or nay.

If it be yea, I shall be fain.°   *glad*
10 If it be nay, friends as before.
Ye shall another man obtain,
And I mine own and yours no more.

                                             E. MS.

They flee from me

They flee from me, that sometime did me seek
With naked foot stalking° in my chamber.   *walking softly*
I have seen them gentle, tame, and meek
That now are wild and do not remember
5 That sometime they put themself in danger
To take bread at my hand; and now they range,
Busily seeking with a continual change.

Thanked be fortune it hath been otherwise
Twenty times better; but once in special,
10 In thin array, after a pleasant guise,

When her loose gown from her shoulders did fall,
And she me caught in her arms long and small,°   *slender*
Therewithal° sweetly did me kiss   *with that*
And softly said, "Dear heart, how like you this?"

15 It was no dream, I lay broad waking.
But all is turned, thorough° my gentleness,   *through*
Into a strange fashion of forsaking;
And I have leave to go, of her goodness,
And she also to use newfangleness.°   *fickleness*
20 But since that I so kindely[7] am served,
I fain would° know what she hath deserved.   *would like to*

E. MS.

The Lover Showeth How He Is Forsaken of Such as He Sometime Enjoyed

[THEY FLEE FROM ME]

They flee from me, that sometime did me seek
With naked foot stalking within my chamber.
Once have I seen them gentle, tame, and meek
That now are wild and do not once remember
5 That sometime they have put themselves in danger
To take bread at my hand; and now they range,
Busily seeking in continual change.

Thankèd be fortune, it hath been otherwise
Twenty times better; but once especial,
10 In thin array, after a pleasant guise,
When her loose gown did from her shoulders fall,
And she me caught in her arms long and small,
And therewithal so sweetly did me kiss
And softly said, "Dear heart, how like you this?"

15 It was no dream, for I lay broad awaking.
But all is turned now, through my gentleness,
Into a bitter fashion of forsaking;
And I have leave to go, of her goodness,
And she also to use newfangleness.
20 But since that I unkindly so am served,
How like you this? What hath she now deserved?

TOTTEL, 1557

7. Naturally (from *kind*: "nature," but with an ironic suggestion of the modern meaning of "kindly"). In Wyatt's spelling, the word should presumably be pronounced as three syllables.

My lute, awake!

My lute, awake! Perform the last
Labor that thou and I shall waste,
And end that I have now begun:
For when this song is sung and past,
5   My lute be still, for I have done.

As to be heard where ear is none,
As lead to grave in marble stone,[8]
My song may pierce her heart as soon.
Should we then sigh or sing or moan?
10   No, no, my lute, for I have done.

The rocks do not so cruelly
Repulse the waves continually
As she my suit and affectiön.
So that I am past remedy,
15   Whereby my lute and I have done.

Proud of the spoil that thou hast got
Of simple hearts, thorough° Love's shot,   *through*
By whom, unkind, thou hast them won,
Think not he hath his bow forgot,
20   Although my lute and I have done.

Vengeance shall fall on thy disdain
That makest but game on earnest pain.
Think not alone under the sun
Unquit° to cause thy lovers plain,°   *unrevenged / to complain*
25   Although my lute and I have done.

Perchance thee lie[9] withered and old
The winter nights that are so cold,
Plaining in vain unto the moon.
Thy wishes then dare not be told.
30   Care then who list,° for I have done.   *likes*

And then may chance thee to repent
The time that thou hast lost and spent
To cause thy lovers sigh and swoon.
Then shalt thou know beauty but lent,
35   And wish and want as I have done.

Now cease, my lute. This is the last
Labor that thou and I shall waste,
And ended is that we begun.

---

8. I.e., when sound may be heard with no ear to   hard marble.
hear it or when soft lead is able to carve ("grave")   9. Perhaps it may befall you to lie.

Now is this song both sung and past;
40   My lute be still, for I have done.

E. MS.

Forget not yet

Forget not yet the tried intent
Of such a truth° as I have meant,   *fidelity*
My great travail so gladly spent,
    Forget not yet.

5 Forget not yet when first began
The weary life ye know since when,
The suit,° the service[1] none tell can,   *pursuit, wooing*
    Forget not yet.

Forget not yet the great essays,°   *trials*
10 The cruel wrong, the scornful ways,
The painful patience in denays,°   *denials, refusals*
    Forget not yet.

Forget not yet, forget not this,
How long ago hath been and is
15 The mind that never meant amiss,
    Forget not yet.

Forget not then thine own approved,
The which so long hath thee so loved,
Whose steadfast faith yet never moved,
20   Forget not this.

D. MS.

Blame not my lute

Blame not my lute, for he must sound
Of this or that as liketh° me: *pleases*
For lack of wit° the lute is bound   *intelligence*
To give such tunes as pleaseth me.
5 Though my songs be somewhat strange,
And speaks such words as touch thy change,°   *unfaithfulness*
    Blame not my lute.

My lute, alas, doth not offend,
Though that perforce° he must agree   *of necessity*

---

1. Actions of a lover, often called the lady's "servant."

10 To sound such tunes as I intend
To sing to them that heareth me.
Then though my songs be somewhat plain,
And toucheth some that use to feign,[2]
    Blame not my lute.

15 My lute and strings may not deny,
But as I strike they must obey:
Break not them then so wrongfully,
But wreak° thyself some wiser way.   *avenge*
And though the songs which I indite°   *write*
20 Do quit thy change[3] with rightful spite,
    Blame not my lute.

Spite asketh° spite, and changing change,   *calls for*
And falsèd faith must needs be known;
The fault so great, the case so strange,
25 Of right it must abroad be blown.
Then since that by thine own desert
My songs do tell how true thou art,
    Blame not my lute.

Blame but thyself, that hast misdone
30 And well deservèd to have blame;
Change thou thy way so evil begun,
And then my lute shall sound that same.
But if till then my fingers play
By thy desert their wonted° way,   *accustomed*
35   Blame not my lute.

Farewell, unknown, for though thou break
My strings in spite with great disdain,
Yet have I found out for thy sake
Strings for to string my lute again.
40 And if perchance this foolish rhyme
Do make thee blush at any time,
    Blame not my lute.

                          D. MS.

Stand whoso list[4]

Stand whoso list° upon the slipper° top   *cares to / slippery*
Of court's estates,° and let me here rejoice   *high positions*
And use me quiet without let or stop,[5]

---

2. And comment on some who are accustomed
to dissemble.
3. Requite your unfaithfulness.
4. A translation of Seneca, *Thyestes*, lines 391–
403. For a literal translation of this famous passage, and other verse translations of it, see the
supplemental ebook.
5. Comport myself quietly without hindrance or
impediment.

Unknown in court, that hath such brackish[6] joys.
5 In hidden place so let my days forth pass
That when my years be done withouten noise,
I may die aged after the common trace.°   way
For him death grippeth right hard by the crop°   throat
That is much known of other, and of himself, alas,
10 Doth die unknown, dazed, with dreadful° face.   fearful

A. MS.

Who list his wealth and ease retain[7]

Who list° his wealth° and ease retain,   desires / well-being
Himself let him unknown contain.[8]
Press not too fast in at that gate
Where the return stands by disdain:
5 For sure, *circa regna tonat.*[9]

The high mountains are blasted oft
When the low valley is mild and soft.
Fortune with Health stands at debate.[1]
The fall is grievous from aloft.
10 And sure, *circa regna tonat.*

These bloody days have broken my heart.
My lust,° my youth did then depart,   pleasure
And blind desire of estate.°   status
Who hastes to climb seeks to revert.°   fall back
15 Of truth, *circa regna tonat.*

The Bell Tower showed me such sight
That in my head sticks day and night.
There did I learn out of a grate,°   barred window
For all favor, glory, or might,[2]
20 That yet *circa regna tonat.*

By proof,° I say, there did I learn: experience
Wit helpeth not defense to yerne,
Of innocence to plead or prate.[3]
Bear low, therefore, give God the stern,[4]
25 For sure, *circa regna tonat.*

B. MS.

6. Spoiled by mixture, as of seawater with fresh.
7. This poem was almost certainly written at the time of Wyatt's imprisonment in 1536, during which he witnessed from the Bell Tower the execution of Anne Boleyn.
8. I.e., let him keep himself unknown.
9. "He [i.e., Jupiter] thunders around thrones" (Seneca, *Phaedra*, line 1140). The first two stanzas of Wyatt's poem paraphrase lines from that

play. "The return stands by disdain": i.e., "you will be disdained as you make your (forced) exit."
1. I.e., fortune and well-being are always at odds.
2. I.e., whatever one's favor, glory, or might.
3. I.e., intelligence does not help one earn ("yerne") a defense, [nor does it help] to plead or prattle about one's innocence.
4. Let God do the steering. "Bear low": be humble.

Mine own John Poins[5]

    Mine own John Poins, since ye delight to know
    The cause why that homeward I me draw
    (And flee the press of courts, whereso they go,
    Rather than to live thrall under the awe
5   Of lordly looks) wrapped within my cloak,
    To will and lust° learning to set a law;   *desire*
    It is not for because I scorn or mock
    The power of them to whom Fortune hath lent
    Charge over us, of right to strike the stroke.[6]
10 But true it is that I have always meant
    Less to esteem them than the common sort,
    Of outward things that judge in their intent,
    Without regard what doth inward resort.
    I grant sometime that of glory the fire
15 Doth touch my heart; me list not to report
    Blame by honor, and honor to desire.[7]
    But how may I this honor now attain,
    That cannot dye the color black a liar?[8]
    My Poins, I cannot frame my tune to feign,
20 To cloak the truth for praise, without desert,
    Of them that list° all vice for to retain.   *desire*
    I cannot honor them that sets their part
    With Venus and Bacchus all their life long,[9]
    Nor hold my peace of° them although I smart.   *concerning*
25 I cannot crouch nor kneel nor do so great a wrong
    To worship them like God on earth alone
    That are as wolves these sely° lambs among.   *innocent*
    I cannot with my words complain and moan
    And suffer naught,° nor smart without complaint, *wickedness*
30 Nor turn the word that from my mouth is gone;
    I cannot speak and look like a saint,
    Use wiles for wit° and make deceit a pleasure,   *wisdom*
    And call craft° counsel, for profit still to paint;° *craftiness / deceive*
    I cannot wrest the law to fill the coffer,
35 With innocent blood to feed myself fat,
    And do most hurt where most help I offer.
    I am not he that can allow° the state°   *approve / exaltation*
    Of high Caesar and damn Cato[1] to die,
    That with his death did 'scape out of the gate

---

5. Poins was a friend of Wyatt's. This verse epistle of informal satire is based on the tenth satire of the Italian Luigi Alamanni but is personalized and Anglicized in detail by Wyatt. It was apparently written during his banishment from court, in 1536. Lines 1–52 of the poem are missing from the authoritative Egerton Manuscript and are here supplied from the Devonshire Manuscript.
6. I.e., my retirement from court is not because I scorn the powerful, or their prerogatives of rule and punishment. But I esteem them less than do the "common sort" of people, who judge by externals only (lines 10–13).
7. I.e., I do not wish to attack honor or to call dishonorable desire honorable.
8. I.e., cannot pretend that black is not black.
9. I.e., I cannot honor those who devote their lives to Venus (goddess of love) and Bacchus (god of drinking).
1. Cato the Younger, the famous Roman patriot who committed suicide rather than submit to Caesar.

40　From Caesar's hands, if Livy[2] do not lie,
　　And would not live where liberty was lost,
　　So did his heart the common weal apply.[3]
　　I am not he such eloquence to boast
　　To make the crow singing as the swan,
45　Nor call the lion of coward beasts the most,
　　That cannot take a mouse as the cat can;
　　And he that dieth for hunger of the gold,
　　Call him Alexander,[4] and say that Pan
　　Passeth° Apollo in music many fold;[5]　　　　　　　　　　*surpasses*
50　Praise Sir Thopas for a noble tale,
　　And scorn the story that the Knight told;[6]
　　Praise him for counsel that is drunk of ale;
　　Grin when he laugheth that beareth all the sway,°　　　*power*
　　Frown when he frowneth, and groan when he is pale;
55　On other's lust° to hang both night and day—　　　　　*wishes*
　　None of these points would ever frame in me;°　　　　*appeal to me*
　　My wit° is naught:° I cannot learn the way;　　　*intellect / worthless*
　　And much the less of things that greater be,
　　That asken help of colors of device°　　　　　　　　*tricks of rhetoric*
60　To join the mean with each extremity:
　　With the nearest virtue to cloak alway the vice,
　　And, as to purpose likewise it shall fall,[7]
　　To press the virtue that it may not rise;
　　As drunkenness, good fellowship to call;
65　The friendly foe, with his double face,
　　Say he is gentle and courteous therewithal;°　　　　　*besides*
　　And say that favel° hath a goodly grace　　　　　　　*flattery*
　　In eloquence; and cruelty to name
　　Zeal of justice, and change in time and place;[8]
70　And he that suffereth offense° without blame,　　　*allows offenses*
　　Call him pitiful,° and him true and plain　　　　*compassionate*
　　That raileth reckless° to every man's shame;　　　　*recklessly*
　　Say he is rude° that cannot lie and feign,　　　　*uneducated*
　　The lecher a lover, and tyranny
75　To be the right of a prince's reign.
　　I cannot, I: no, no, it will not be.
　　This is the cause that I could never yet
　　Hang on their sleeves that weigh, as thou mayst see,
　　A chip of chance more than a pound of wit.
80　This maketh me at home to hunt and hawk
　　And in foul weather at my book to sit;
　　In frost and snow then with my bow to stalk.
　　No man doth mark° whereso I ride or go.　　　　　　　*note*
　　In lusty leas° at liberty I walk,　　　　　　　　　　*pleasant fields*

2. Titus Livius (59 B.C.E.–17 C.E.), the great Roman historian.
3. So much did he devote himself to the common good.
4. Compare him to Alexander the Great with his towering ambition.
5. According to classical mythology, the music of the nature god Pan was far inferior to that of Apollo, patron of music and art.
6. The silly tale of Sir Thopas, in *The Canterbury Tales*, is told by Chaucer himself, until the Host forces him to stop. *The Knight's Tale* is the most courtly and dignified of the tales.
7. I.e., as will also be opportune.
8. I.e., to miscall cruelty zeal for justice, and to rationalize it by appeals to altered circumstances.

85 And of these news I feel nor weal nor woe,
Save that a clog doth hang yet at my heel.[9]
No force° for that, for it is ordered so   *no matter*
That I may leap both hedge and dike full well.
I am not now in France, to judge the wine,
90 With sav'ry sauce the delicates° to feel;   *delicacies*
Nor yet in Spain, where one must him incline,
Rather than to be, outwardly to seem.
I meddle not with wits that be so fine;
Nor Flanders' cheer[1] letteth° not my sight to deem   *hinders*
95 Of black and white, nor taketh my wit away
With beastliness they, beasts, do so esteem.
Nor am I not where Christ is given in prey
For money, poison, and treason—at Rome[2]
A common practice, usèd night and day.
100 But here I am in Kent and Christendom,
Among the Muses, where I read and rhyme;
Where if thou list, my Poins, for to come,
Thou shalt be judge how I do spend my time.

D. MS., E. MS.

9. "I feel neither happiness nor unhappiness about current political affairs, except that a 'clog' (i.e., his confinement on parole to his estate) keeps me from traveling far." Note that "news" is a plural in Elizabethan English.
1. I.e., the drinking for which, in the 16th cen-
tury, Flemings were notorious.
2. In *Tottel's Miscellany*, published in the reign of the Catholic Queen Mary, these lines were altered as follows: "where *truth* is given in prey / For money, poison, and treason—*of some*."

HENRY HOWARD, EARL OF SURREY
1517–1547

The axe that decapitated Surrey at the age of thirty had been hanging over his head for much of his life. In the court of Henry VIII, it was dangerous to be a potential claimant to the throne, and Surrey was descended from kings on both sides of his family. He was brought up at Windsor Castle as the close companion of Henry VIII's illegitimate son, the duke of Richmond, who married Surrey's sister. As the eldest son of the duke of Norfolk, the chief bulwark of the old Catholic aristocracy against the rising tide of "new men" and the reformed religion, Surrey was the heir not only to the Howard family's great wealth but also to their immense pride, their sense at once of noble privilege and of obligation. Like his father and grandfather, he was a brave and able soldier, serving in Henry VIII's French wars as "Lieutenant General of the King on Sea and Land." He was also repeatedly imprisoned for rash behavior, on one occasion for striking a courtier, on another for wandering through the streets of London breaking the windows of sleeping townspeople. In 1541 Surrey used his family connections—his first cousin, Catherine Howard, was queen—to secure the release from the Tower of his close friend the poet Thomas

Wyatt, who had been accused of treason. But a year later, Catherine Howard was executed for adultery, like Anne Boleyn before her. Power returned to the rival family of the former queen Jane Seymour, who had died in childbirth giving a son and heir to the aging Henry VIII. Surrey's situation was already precarious, and his vocal opposition to the Seymours, with their strong Protestant leanings, sealed his fate. Convicted of treason, he had the grim distinction of being Henry's last victim.

Poets and critics of the later sixteenth century, fascinated by Surrey's noble rank and his tragic fate, routinely praised him as one of the very greatest English poets. The full title of Tottel's influential miscellany, published in 1557 (ten years after Surrey's death), is *Songs and Sonnets Written by the Right Honorable Lord Henry Howard Late Earl of Surrey and Other.* The principal "other" here is his older friend Wyatt, with whose poetry Surrey's is closely linked. Poets who circulated their verse in manuscript in a courtly milieu, the two shared a passion for French and Italian poetry, especially for Petrarch's sonnets. Surrey established a form for these that was used by Shakespeare and that has become known as the English sonnet: three quatrains and a couplet, all in iambic pentameter and rhyming *abab cdcd efef gg*. Even more significant, he was the first English poet to publish in blank verse—unrhymed iambic pentameter—a verse form so popular in the succeeding centuries that it has come to seem almost indigenous to the language. The work in which he used his "strange meter," as the publisher called it, was a translation of part of Virgil's *Aeneid.* Managing the five-stress line with exceptional skill, Surrey initiated the rhythmic fluency that distinguishes so many Elizabethan lyrics. It is striking that his two great literary innovations, the English sonnet and blank verse, should emerge in the same period that saw radical upheavals in traditional religious and social life. It is possible that he was drawn to Virgil's epic because it offered a model of continuity in the face of disaster. Aeneas cannot prevent the fall of Troy, but he goes on to establish a new world without abandoning his old values.

As a conventional love poet Surrey is not very convincing: in 1593 Thomas Nashe wrote sardonically that Surrey "was more in love with his own curious forming fancy" than with this mistress's face. His verse comes alive when he writes about his deep male friendships ("So cruel prison" and the moving epitaph he published on Wyatt), or imagines himself as a woman longing for her absent man ("O happy dames"), or employs his new sonnet form in a savage attack on the "womanish delight" of an unmanly king ("Th'Assyrians' king").

Our selections from Surrey are divided into three groups: sonnets; lyric and reflective poems; classical translations.*

The soote season[1]

> The soote° season, that bud and bloom forth brings,   *sweet, fragrant*
> With green hath clad the hill and eke° the vale.   *also*
> The nightingale with feathers new she sings;
> The turtle to her make° hath told her tale.   *turtledove to her mate*
> 5 Summer is come, for every spray now springs.
> The hart hath hung his old head on the pale;°   *fence, paling*
> The buck in brake° his winter coat he flings;   *thicket*
> The fishes float with new repairèd scale;

---

* For additional lyrics by Surrey, as well as two other excerpts from his partial translation of Virgil's *Aeneid* and the Italian originals of the Petrarchan sonnets translated here, see the supplemental ebook.

1. This poem is a free adaptation of Petrarch's Rima 310, one of the sonnets written after the death of the poet's beloved.

The adder all her slough° away she slings; *cast-off skin*
10   The swift swallow pursueth the fliès small;
The busy bee her honey now she mings.° *mingles*
Winter is worn, that was the flowers' bale.° *harm*
And thus I see among these pleasant things,
Each care decays, and yet my sorrow springs.

1557

Petrarch, Rima 310

A MODERN PROSE TRANSLATION[1]

Zephyrus[2] returns and leads back the fine weather and the flowers and the grass, his sweet family, and chattering Procne and weeping Philomena, and Spring, all white and vermilion;

the meadows laugh and the sky becomes clear again, Jupiter is gladdened looking at his daughter, the air and the waters and the earth are full of love, every animal takes counsel again to love.

But to me, alas, come back heavier sighs, which she draws from my deepest heart, she who carried off to Heaven the keys to it;

and the singing of little birds, and the flowering of meadows, and virtuous gentle gestures in beautiful ladies are a wilderness and cruel, savage beasts.

Love, that doth reign and live within my thought[1]

Love, that doth reign and live within my thought,
And built his seat within my captive breast,
Clad in the arms wherein with me he fought,
Oft in my face he doth his banner rest.
5   But she that taught me love and suffer pain,
My doubtful hope and eke° my hot desire *also*
With shamefast° look to shadow and refrain,° *modest / restrain*
Her smiling grace converteth straight to ire.
And coward Love then to the heart apace° *at once*
10   Taketh his flight, where he doth lurk and plain,° *complain*
His purpose lost, and dare not show his face.
For my lord's guilt thus faultless bide° I pain, *endure*
Yet from my lord shall not my foot remove:
Sweet is the death that taketh end by love.

1557

1. This and the prose translation of Rima 164 are by Robert K. Durling.
2. Zephyrus is the west wind; Procne and Philomena (below), the swallow and the nightingale; Jupiter and his daughter Venus are here the plan-

ets, in favorable astrological relation.
1. Cf. Surrey's version of Petrarch's Rima 140 with Wyatt's translation of the same original (pp. 648–49; with a modern prose translation).

Alas! so all things now do hold their peace[1]

Alas! so all things now do hold their peace,
Heaven and earth disturbèd in no thing.
The beasts, the air, the birds their song do cease;
The nightès chare[2] the stars about doth bring;
5 Calm is the sea, the waves work less and less.
So am not I, whom love, alas, doth wring,
Bringing before my face the great increase
Of my desires, whereat I weep and sing,
In joy and woe, as in a doubtful ease:
10 For my sweet thoughts sometime do pleasure bring,
But by and by° the cause of my disease[3]   *immediately*
Gives me a pang that inwardly doth sting,
When that I think what grief it is, again,
To live, and lack the thing should rid my pain.

1557

Petrarch, Rima 164

A MODERN PROSE TRANSLATION

Now that the heavens and the earth and the wind are silent, and
sleep reins in the beasts and the birds, Night drives her starry car
about, and in its bed the sea lies without a wave,

I am awake, I think, I burn, I weep; and she who destroys me is
always before me, to my sweet pain: war is my state, full of sorrow
and suffering, and only thinking of her do I have any peace.

Thus from one clear living fountain alone spring the sweet and the
bitter on which I feed; one hand alone heals me and pierces me.

And that my suffering may not reach an end, a thousand times a
day I die and a thousand am born, so distant am I from health.

Th'Assyrians' king,[1] in peace with foul desire

Th'Assyrians' king, in peace with foul desire
And filthy lust that stained his regal heart,
In war, that should set princely hearts afire,
Vanquished did yield for want° of martial art.   *lack*
5 The dint of swords from° kisses seemèd strange,   *after*
And harder than his lady's side, his targe;°   *shield*

---

1. Adapted from Petrarch's Rima 164.
2. From Italian *carro* (the Great Bear).
3. Dis-ease, i.e., discomfort.

1. The legendary Sardanapalus was often cited
as an example of degenerate kingship. Surrey's
poem may allude to Henry VIII.

From glutton feasts to soldier's fare, a change,
His helmet, far above a garland's charge.[2]
Who scace° the name of manhood did retain,   *scarcely*
10   Drenchèd in sloth and womanish delight,
Feeble of sprite,° unpatient° of pain,   *spirit / impatient*
When he had lost his honor and his right
(Proud, time of wealth; in storms, appalled with dread),
Murdered himself, to show some manful deed.[3]

                                                      1557

So cruel prison how could betide[1]

So cruel prison how could betide,[2] alas,
As proud Windsor, where I in lust° and joy   *pleasure*
With a king's son my childish° years did pass   *youthful*
In greater feast than Priam's sons of Troy?[3]

5   Where each sweet place returns a taste full sour:
The large green courts, where we were wont to hove,°   *linger*
With eyes cast up unto the Maidens' Tower,
And easy sighs, such as folk draw in love.

The stately sales,° the ladies bright of hue,   *halls*
10   The dances short, long tales of great delight,
With words and looks that tigers could but rue,[4]
Where each of us did plead the other's right.

The palm play° where, dispoilèd° for the game,   *handball / stripped*
With dazed eyes oft we by gleams of love
15   Have missed the ball and got sight of our dame,
To bait° her eyes, which kept the leads[5] above.   *attract, as in fishing*

The graveled ground, with sleeves° tied on the helm,   *ladies' favors*
On foaming horse, with swords and friendly hearts,
With cheer° as though the one should overwhelm,   *countenance*
20   Where we have fought and chasèd oft with darts.°   *spears*

With silver drops the meads yet spread[6] for ruth,°   *pity*
In active games of nimbleness and strength,
Where we did strain, trailèd by swarms of youth,
Our tender limbs that yet shot up in length.

---

2. I.e., a far heavier burden than a garland.
3. Sardanapalus committed suicide by casting himself into a fire in which he had first burned up his treasure. Line 13: i.e., he was arrogant in good times but overcome with dread in times of trouble.
1. In the summer of 1537 Surrey was imprisoned at Windsor Castle for striking another courtier. The poem recalls his boyhood stay

there (1530–32) with Henry Fitzroy, illegitimate son of Henry VIII.
2. I.e., how could there happen to be.
3. Priam, king of Troy in the *Iliad*, had fifty sons.
4. Take pity on, despite tigers' legendary fierceness.
5. Who was on the lead-covered roof.
6. I.e., when the dew, like tears, was still on the meadows.

25   The secret groves which oft we made resound
     Of pleasant plaint and of our ladies' praise,
     Recording soft what grace° each one had found,   *favor*
     What hope of speed,° what dread of long delays.   *success*

     The wild forest, the clothèd holts° with green,   *wooded hills*
30   With reins availed° and swift ybreathèd horse,   *slackened*
     With cry of hounds and merry blasts° between,   *i.e., of the horn*
     Where we did chase the fearful hart a force.[7]

     The void° walls eke° that harbored us each night,   *empty / also*
     Wherewith, alas, revive within my breast
35   The sweet accord, such sleeps as yet delight,
     The pleasant dreams, the quiet bed of rest,

     The secret thoughts imparted with such trust,
     The wanton° talk, the divers change of play,   *playful*
     The friendship sworn, each promise kept so just,
40   Wherewith we passed the winter nights away.

     And with this thought, the blood forsakes my face,
     The tears berain my cheeks of deadly hue,
     The which as soon as sobbing sighs, alas,
     Upsuppèd have, thus I my plaint renew:

45   "O place of bliss, renewer of my woes,
     Give me accompt,° where is my noble fere,[8]   *account*
     Whom in thy walls thou didst each night enclose,
     To other lief,° but unto me most dear."   *dear*

     Each stone, alas, that doth my sorrow rue,°   *pity*
50   Returns thereto a hollow sound of plaint.
     Thus I alone, where all my freedom grew,
     In prison pine with bondage and restraint.

     And with remembrance of the greater grief
     To banish the less, I find my chief relief.

1537   1557

Wyatt resteth here, that quick could never rest

     Wyatt resteth here, that quick° could never rest,   *alive*
     Whose heavenly gifts, increasèd by disdain[1]
     And virtue, sank the deeper in his breast:
     Such profit he by envy could obtain.

7. I.e., to run it down.
8. Companion. Henry Fitzroy had died the year
before, aged seventeen.

1. Hostility (equivalent to "envy" in line 4). I.e.,
he could turn hostility toward him to his advantage.

5   A head where wisdom mysteries° did frame,   *subtle meanings*
Whose hammers beat still in that lively brain
As on a stith,° where that some work of fame   *anvil*
Was daily wrought to turn to Britain's gain.

A visage stern and mild, where both did grow
10 Vice to contemn,° in virtue to rejoice;   *despise*
Amid great storms whom grace assurèd so
To live upright and smile at fortune's choice.

A hand that taught what might be said in rhyme,
That reft° Chaucer the glory of his wit—[2]   *bereft*
15 A mark the which, unperfited° for time,   *unperfected*
Some may approach, but never none shall hit.

A tongue that served in foreign realms his king;
Whose courteous talk to virtue did inflame
Each noble heart: a worthy guide to bring
20 Our English youth by travail° unto fame.   *labor*

An eye whose judgment none affect° could blind,   *no partiality*
Friends to allure and foes to reconcile,
Whose piercing look did represent a mind
With virtue fraught, reposèd, void of guile.

25 A heart where dread yet never so impressed
To hide the thought that might the truth advance;
In neither fortune loft nor yet repressed[3]
To swell in wealth° or yield unto mischance.   *well-being*

A valiant corpse[4] where force and beauty met,
30 Happy°—alas, too happy, but° for foes;   *fortunate / if not*
Lived and ran the race that Nature set,
Of manhood's shape, where she the mold did lose.[5]

But to the heavens that simple° soul is fled,   *innocent*
Which left, with such as covet Christ to know,
35 Witness of faith[6] that never shall be dead,
Sent for our health,° but not receivèd so.   *welfare*

Thus for our guilt, this jewel have we lost;
The earth his bones, the heavens possess his ghost.°   *spirit*

1542   1542

---

2. Genius. I.e., Wyatt (supposedly) replaced Chaucer as England's greatest poet.
3. I.e., neither overly elated by good fortune nor downcast by bad.
4. Body (not, as now, a dead one).

5. A conventional praise—that Nature, in creating someone, made a masterpiece and then lost the pattern.
6. I.e., which left with Christians ("such as covet Christ to know") a testimony of faith.

O happy dames, that may embrace[1]

O happy dames,° that may embrace   *wives*
The fruit of your delight,
Help to bewail the woeful case
And eke° the heavy plight   *also*
5   Of me, that wonted° to rejoice   *was accustomed*
The fortune of my pleasant choice:
Good ladies, help to fill my mourning voice.

In ship, freight° with rememberance   *loaded*
Of thoughts and pleasures past,
10 He sails that hath in governance
My life while it will last;
With scalding sighs, for lack of gale,
Futhering his hope, that is his sail,
Toward me, the sweet port of his avail.°   *destination*

15 Alas, how oft in dreams I see
Those eyes that were my food,
Which sometime so delighted me,
That yet they do me good;
Wherewith I wake with his return,
20 Whose absent flame did make me burn:
But when I find the lack, Lord how I mourn!

When other lovers in arms across°   *embracing*
Rejoice their chief delight,
Drowned in tears to mourn my loss
25 I stand the bitter night
In my window, where I may see
Before the winds how the clouds flee.
Lo, what a mariner love hath made me!

And in green waves when the salt flood
30 Doth rise by rage of wind,
A thousand fancies in that mood
Assail my restless mind.
Alas, now drencheth° my sweet foe,[2]   *drowns*
That with the spoil° of my heart did go   *plunder, booty*
35 And left me; but, alas, why did he so?

And when the seas wax calm again,
To chase from me annoy,°   *distress*
My doubtful hope doth cause me plain,°   *to complain*

---

1. The speaker is a woman. The poem was probably written for Surrey's wife, from whom he
was separated while on military duty in France

in the 1540s.
2. A conventional expression for a loved one,
going back to medieval love poetry.

So dread cuts off my joy.
40 Thus is my wealth° mingled with woe,   *happiness*
And of each thought a doubt doth grow:
Now he comes! Will he come? Alas, no, no!

1557

Martial, the things for to attain[1]

Martial, the things for to attain
The happy life be these, I find:
The riches left, not got with pain;
The fruitful ground, the quiet mind;

5 The equal friend; no grudge nor strife;
No charge° of rule, nor governance;   *burden*
Without disease the healthy life;
The household of continuance;°   *long duration*

The mean diet, no delicate fare;
10 Wisdom joined with simplicity;
The night dischargèd of all care,
Where wine may bear no sovereignty;

The chaste wife, wise, without debate;°   *strife*
Such sleeps as may beguile° the night;   *charm away*
15 Contented with thine own estate;
Neither wish death nor fear his might.

1547

From The Fourth Book of Virgil[1]

[DIDO IN LOVE]

Unhappy Dido burns, and in her rage°   *passion*
Throughout the town she wand'reth up and down,
Like to the stricken hind with shaft[2] in Crete
Throughout the woods, which chasing with his darts°   *arrows*
90 Aloof,° the shepherd smiteth at unwares°   *at a distance / without warning*
And leaves unwist° in her the thirling° head,   *unknown / piercing*
That through the groves and launds° glides in her flight;   *glades*
Amid whose side the mortal° arrow sticks.   *deadly*

---

1. A translation of an epigram (10.47) by the Roman poet Martial (ca. 40–104 C.E.). The theme, a glorification of "the mean estate" (the modest, moderate life), is very common in literature of this period.

1. Surrey translated Books 2 and 4 of Virgil's *Aeneid.* In this excerpt, Dido, the widowed queen of Carthage, suffers the pangs of undeclared love for her guest Aeneas.
2. I.e., like a deer shot with an arrow.

Aeneas now about the walls she leads,
95 The town prepared and Carthage wealth to show.
Off'ring to speak, amid her voice, she whists.°   *falls silent*
And when the day gan fail, new feasts she makes;
The Troys'° travails to hear anew she lists,°   *Trojans' / wants*
Enragèd all,° and stareth in his face   *wholly impassioned*
100 That tells the tale. And when they were all gone,
And the dim moon doth eft° withhold the light,   *again*
And sliding stars provokèd unto sleep,
Alone she mourns within her palace void,
And sets her down on her forsaken bed;
105 And absent him she hears, when he is gone,
And seeth eke.° Oft in her lap she holds   *also*
Ascanius,[3] trapped by his father's form,
So to beguile the love° cannot be told.   *the love that*

1554

---

3. Aeneas's son; Dido is captivated ("trapped") by the boy's likeness to his father.

Faith in Conflict

When, in the late 1520s, the Catholic authorities of England tried to burn all copies of William Tyndale's English translation of the New Testament, they were attempting to stop the spread of what they viewed as a dangerous new plague of heresies. The plague was the Protestant Reformation, a movement opposed to crucial aspects of both the belief system and the institutional structure of Roman Catholicism.

The movement had been launched by the German theologian Martin Luther, who in 1517 challenged the authority of the pope and attacked several key doctrines of the Catholic Church. According to Luther, the Church, with its elaborate hierarchical structure centered in Rome, its rich monasteries and convents, and its enormous political influence, had become a hopelessly corrupt conspiracy of venal priests who manipulated popular superstitions to enrich themselves and amass worldly power. Luther began by vehemently attacking the sale of indulgences—certificates promising the remission of punishments to be suffered in the afterlife by souls sent to Purgatory to expiate their sins before being allowed into heaven. Purgatory, he argued, had no foundation in Scripture, which in his view was the only legitimate source of religious truth (*sola scriptura*). Christians would be saved not by scrupulously following the ritual practices fostered by the Catholic Church— observing fast days, reciting the ancient Latin prayers, endowing chantries to say prayers for the dead, invoking the protection of individual saints, and so on—but by faith and faith alone (*sola fide*).

This challenge spread and gathered force, especially in northern Europe, where major leaders like the French theologian Calvin (who, after his break with Catholicism, established a theocracy in Geneva) transformed religious institutions and elaborated various and sometimes conflicting doctrinal principles. Calvin, whose thought came to be particularly influential in England, emphasized the obligation of governments to implement God's will in the world. He advanced too the doctrine of predestination, by which, as he put it, "God adopts some to hope of life and sentences others to eternal death." God's "secret election" of the saved troubled Calvin, but his study of the Scriptures had led him to conclude that "only a small number, out of an incalculable multitude, should obtain salvation." It might seem that such a conclusion would lead to passivity or even despair, but for Calvin predestination was a mystery bound up with faith, confidence, and an active engagement in the fashioning of a Christian community.

The Reformation had a direct and powerful impact on those realms where it gained control. Monasteries were sacked, their possessions seized by princes or sold off to the highest bidder; monks and nuns, expelled from their cloisters, were encouraged to break their vows of chastity and find spouses, as Luther and his wife, a former nun, had done. In the great cathedrals and in hundreds of smaller churches and chapels, the elaborate altarpieces, bejeweled crucifixes, crystal reliquaries holding the bones of saints, venerated statues, and paintings were attacked as "idols" and often defaced or destroyed. Protestant congregations continued, for the most part, to celebrate the most sacred Christian ritual, the Eucharist, or Lord's Supper, but they did so in a profoundly different spirit from the Catholic Church, more as commemoration than as miracle, and the service was conducted not in the old liturgical Latin but in the vernacular.

The Reformation was at first vigorously resisted in England. Protestant writings were seized by officials of the Church and the state and burned. Protestants who made their views known were persecuted—driven to flee the country or arrested, put on trial, and burned at the stake. But the situation changed drastically after Henry decided to seek a divorce from his first wife, Catherine of Aragon, in order to marry Anne Boleyn. When the Roman Catholic Church, under pressure from Catherine's powerful family, refused to grant the divorce, Henry defied papal authority, declared himself head of the Church in England, seized the wealth of the monasteries, and unleashed Protestant energies, including fierce bursts of iconoclasm. On most doctrinal questions, however, Henry remained an orthodox Catholic, and in the latter part of his reign, his clerical authorities renewed the persecution of Protestants.

The turn toward the Reformation was more decisive in the reign (1547–53) of Henry's heir, Edward VI; and the attempt by Edward's successor, Mary (daughter of Catherine of Aragon), to reimpose Roman Catholicism as the national religion came to an end with her death in 1558. The long reign of Henry's daughter by Anne Boleyn, Elizabeth I (1558–1603), firmly established Protestantism as the faith of the Church of England. Reformation doctrine shaped the vernacular liturgy eloquently formulated in the officially sanctioned *Book of Common Prayer* and was reinforced in the series of homilies, or sermons, that ministers were commanded to deliver to their parishioners.

The Reformation did not spread quickly or easily among the mass of the English population. Like Henry VIII himself, most English people in the decades after the break with Rome were far from being full-fledged Protestants. Emotional attachment to the traditional religion ran deep, as did resentment of an aggressively intolerant Protestant officialdom. From the 1530s to the end of the century, a few individuals, including Thomas More and the Jesuit Robert Southwell, were prepared to die for the old faith. Many more, though still a small minority, stubbornly rejected the new orthodoxy, absenting themselves from Protestant worship; these recusants, as they were known, were subjected to fines and sometimes worse punishments. A much greater number conformed in public but remained largely untouched by Protestant doctrine.

Though Protestantism and Catholicism were exposed, under different regimes, to brutal persecution, both faiths proved impossible to eradicate. In large part this tenacity arose from the passionate, often suicidal heroism of men and women who felt that their soul's salvation depended upon the precise character of their Christianity and who consequently embraced martyrdom rather than repudiate their beliefs. It arose too from a mid-fifteenth-century technological innovation that made it extremely difficult to suppress unwelcome ideas: the printing press. Early Protestants quickly grasped that with a few clandestine presses they could defy the Catholic authorities and flood the country with their texts. "How many printing presses there be in the world," wrote the Protestant polemicist and martyrologist John Foxe, "so many blockhouses there be against the high castle" of the pope in Rome, "so that either the pope must abolish knowledge and printing or printing at length will root him out." By the century's end, it was the Catholics, as well as the more radical Protestants—known as Puritans—who were using the clandestine press to propagate their beliefs in the face of official persecution.*

---

* For additional texts and images related to conflicts of faith in sixteenth-century England, see "Dissent, Doubt, and Spiritual Violence in the Reformation" in the supplemental ebook.

THE ENGLISH BIBLE

Protestant insistence that true belief must be based on the Holy Scriptures alone made the translation and dissemination of the Bible in English and other vernacular languages a matter of utmost urgency. Prior to the Reformation, the Roman Catholic Church had not always and everywhere opposed vernacular translations of the Bible, but it generally preferred that the populace encounter the Scriptures through the interpretations of its priests, trained to read the Latin translation known as the Vulgate. In times of great conflict this preference for clerical mediation hardened into outright prohibition of vernacular translation and into persecution and book burning. It was in the face of fierce opposition that zealous Protestants all over Europe set out to put the Bible into the hands of the laity. A remarkable translation of the New Testament by an English Lutheran named William Tyndale was printed on the Continent and smuggled into England in 1525; Tyndale's translation of the Pentateuch, the first five books of the Hebrew Bible, followed in 1530. Many copies of these translations were seized and destroyed, as was the translator himself, but the printing press made it extremely difficult for authorities to eradicate books for which there was a passionate demand.

Tyndale's translation was completed by an associate, Miles Coverdale, whose rendering of the Psalms proved to be particularly influential. Their joint labor was the basis for the Great Bible (1539), a copy of which was ordered to be placed in every church in the kingdom. Four years later, as Henry VIII sought to halt the tide of reform, a law was passed forbidding women, craftsmen, servants, and laborers from reading the Bible either in public or in private. Yet nothing could be done at this stage to take the Scriptures out of the hands of the populace. Though there would be further opposition in years to come—innumerable Bibles were printed under Edward VI, only to be burned during the reign of his sister Mary—the English Bible was a force that could not be suppressed, and it became, in its various forms, the single most important book of the sixteenth century.

Marian persecution was indirectly responsible for what would become the most scholarly Protestant English Bible, the translation known as the Geneva Bible, prepared, with extensive, learned, and often fiercely polemical marginal notes, by English exiles in Calvin's Geneva and widely diffused in England after Elizabeth came to the throne. In addition, Elizabethan church authorities ordered a careful revision of the Great Bible, and this version, known as the Bishops' Bible, was the one read in the churches. The success of the Geneva Bible in particular prompted those Elizabethan Catholics who now in turn found themselves in exile to bring out a vernacular translation of their own, the Douay-Rheims version, in order to counter the Protestant readings and glosses.

After Elizabeth's death, in 1603, King James I and his bishops ordered that a revised translation of the entire Bible be undertaken by a group of forty-seven scholars. The result, published in 1611, was the Authorized Version, more popularly known as the King James Bible.

In the passage selected here, 1 Corinthians 13, Tyndale's use of the word "love," echoed by the Geneva Bible, is set against the Catholic "charity." The latter term gestures toward the religious doctrine of "works," against the Protestant insistence on salvation by faith alone. It is a sign of the conservative, moderate Protestantism of the King James version that it too opts for "charity."

1 Corinthians 13[1]

From *Tyndale's Translation*

Though I spake with the tongues of men and angels, and yet had no love, I were even as sounding brass: or as a tinkling cymbal. And though I could prophesy, and understood all secrets, and all knowledge: yea, if I had all faith, so that I could move mountains out of their places, and yet had no love, I were nothing. And though I bestowed all my goods to feed the poor, and though I gave my body even that I burned, and yet had no love, it profiteth me nothing.

Love suffereth long, and is courteous. Love envieth not. Love doth not forwardly,[2] swelleth not, dealeth not dishonestly, seeketh not her own, is not provoked to anger, thinketh not evil, rejoiceth not in iniquity: but rejoiceth in the truth, suffereth all things, believeth all things, hopeth all things, endureth in all things. Though that prophesying fail, other[3] tongues shall cease, or knowledge vanish away, yet love falleth never away.

For our knowledge is unperfect and our prophesying is unperfect. But when that which is perfect is come, then that which is unperfect shall be done away. When I was a child, I spake as a child, I understood as a child, I imagined as a child. But as soon as I was a man, I put away childishness. Now we see in a glass, even in a dark[4] speaking: but then shall we see face to face. Now I know unperfectly: but then shall I know even as I am known. Now abideth faith, hope, and love, even these three: but the chief of these is love.

1525, 1535

From *The Geneva Bible*

Though I speak with the tongues of men and Angels, and have not love, I am as sounding brass, or a tinkling cymbal. And though I had the gift of prophecy, and knew all secrets and all knowledge, yea, if I had all faith, so that I could remove mountains, and had not love, I were nothing. And though I feed the poor with all my goods, and though I give my body, that I be burned, and have not love, it profiteth me nothing. Love suffereth long: it is bountiful: love envieth not: love doth not boast itself: it is not puffed up: It disdaineth not: it seeketh not her own things: it is not provoked to anger: it thinketh not evil: It rejoiceth not in iniquity, but rejoiceth in the truth: It suffereth all things: it believeth all things: it hopeth all things: it endureth all things. Love doth never fall away, though that prophesyings be abolished, or the tongues cease, or knowledge vanish away. For we know in part, and we prophesy in part. But when that which is perfect is come, then that which is in part shall be abolished. When I was a child, I spake as a child, I understood as a child, I thought as a child: but when I became a man, I put away childish things. For now we see through a glass darkly:[5] but

---

1. For two additional sets of passages from 16th-century English Bibles (Psalm 23, Isaiah 53.3–6), see the supplemental ebook.
2. Perversely, evilly.
3. Or.

4. Obscure, unclear. "Glass": mirror. The metaphor of indirect and imperfect sight seems to derive from Plato's Allegory of the Cave (*Republic* 7).
5. By means of a mirror, obscurely.

then shall we see face to face. Now I know in part: but then shall I know even as I am known. And now abideth faith, hope, and love, even these three: but the chiefest of these is love.

1560, 1602

From *The Douay-Rheims Version*

If I speak with the tongues of men and of Angels, and have not charity,[6] I am become as sounding brass, or a tinkling cymbal. And if I should have prophecy,

A page from the Geneva Bible, with commentary; 1583 edition. The Geneva Bible includes elaborate marginal notes, often with a sharply Protestant inflection. Some Elizabethan Catholics may have detected such a perspective in the note's anticipation of a redeemed state "where we shal neither nede scholes nor teachers."

---

6. From Latin *caritas*, love; but also carrying the modern sense.

and knew all mysteries, and all knowledge, and if I should have all faith so that I could remove mountains, and have not charity, I am nothing. And if I should distribute all my goods to be meat[7] for the poor, and if I should deliver my body so that I burn, and have not charity, it doth profit me nothing.

Charity is patient, is benign: charity envieth not, dealeth not perversely: is not puffed up, is not ambitious, seeketh not her own, is not provoked to anger, thinketh not evil: rejoiceth not upon iniquity, but rejoiceth with the truth: suffereth all things, believeth all things, hopeth all things, beareth all things. Charity never falleth away: whether prophecies shall be made void, or tongues shall cease, or knowledge shall be destroyed. For in part we know, and in part we prophesy. But when that shall come that is perfect, that shall be made void that is in part. When I was a little one, I spake as a little one, I understood as a little one, I thought as a little one. But when I was made a man, I did away the things that belonged to a little one. We see now by a glass in a dark sort: but then face to face. Now I know in part: but then I shall know as also I am known. And now there remain faith, hope, charity, these three, but the greater of these is charity.

1582

From *The Authorized (King James) Version*

Though I speak with the tongues of men and of angels, and have not charity, I am become as sounding brass, or a tinkling cymbal. And though I have the gift of prophecy, and understand all mysteries, and all knowledge; and though I have all faith, so that I could remove mountains, and have no charity, I am nothing. And though I bestow all my goods to feed the poor, and though I give my body to be burned, and have not charity, it profiteth me nothing. Charity suffereth long, and is kind; charity envieth not; charity vaunteth not itself, is not puffed up, doth not behave itself unseemly, seeketh not her own, is not easily provoked, thinketh no evil; rejoiceth not in iniquity, but rejoiceth in the truth; beareth all things, believeth all things, hopeth all things, endureth all things. Charity never faileth: but whether there be prophecies, they shall fail; whether there be tongues, they shall cease; whether there be knowledge, it shall vanish away. For we know in part, and we prophesy in part. But when that which is perfect is come, then that which is in part shall be done away. When I was a child, I spake as a child, I understood as a child, I thought as a child: but when I became a man, I put away childish things. For now we see through a glass, darkly; but then face to face: now I know in part; but then shall I know even as also I am known. And now abideth faith, hope, charity, these three; but the greatest of these is charity.

1611

---

7. Food (in general).

WILLIAM TYNDALE

Educated at Oxford, William Tyndale (ca. 1490–1536) became a lecturer at Cambridge, where he was associated with a group of humanist scholars who met regularly at the White Horse Inn. Having become convinced that salvation depended upon direct access to the word of God, he sought support to undertake a translation of the Bible into English, but English church authorities, concerned about the spread of heresies, blocked this project. In 1524 Tyndale went to Germany, where with the financial assistance of wealthy London merchants, he completed a translation of the New Testament the following year.* Deeply influenced by the writings of Martin Luther and other reformers, he also wrote a series of doctrinal and polemical works, such as *The Obedience of a Christian Man* (1528), that eloquently express the Protestant hope of salvation through faith alone and reject the principles and practices of Roman Catholicism. Because of their vitriolic assaults upon the Catholic Church, Protestants like Tyndale were often accused of fomenting rebellion. *The Obedience of a Christian Man* attempts to answer the charge by insisting upon the subject's absolute secular obligation to obey the king. At Anne Boleyn's urging, Henry VIII read it and is reported to have remarked that "this is a book for me and for all kings to read." Notwithstanding this supposed endorsement, English Catholic authorities during Henry's reign managed to lure Tyndale into a trap and had him executed in Vilvorde, Flanders.

From The Obedience of a Christian Man

[THE FORGIVENESS OF SINS]

* * * For sin we through fragility never so oft, yet as soon as we repent and come into the right way again, and unto the testament[1] which God hath made in Christ's blood, our sins vanish away as smoke in the wind, and as darkness at the coming of light; or as thou castest a little blood, or milk, into the main sea: insomuch that whosoever goeth about to make satisfaction for his sins to God-ward,[2] saying in his heart, This much have I sinned, this much will I do again; or this-wise will I live to make amends withal; or this will I do, to get heaven withal; the same is an infidel, faithless, and damned in his deed-doing, and hath lost his part in Christ's blood; because he is disobedient unto God's testament, and setteth up another of his own imagination, unto which he will compel God to obey. If we love God, we have a commandment to love our neighbor also, as saith John in his epistle;[3] and if we have offended him, to make him amends; or if we have not wherewith, to ask him forgiveness, and to do and suffer all things for his sake, to win him

---

* For the preface to Tyndale's 1530 translation of the first five books of the Old Testament, see "Dissent, Doubt, and Spiritual Violence in the Reformation," in the supplemental ebook.
1. Covenant. "Fragility": frailty, moral weakness.
2. I.e., in his relationship to God.

3. "If a man say, I love God, and hateth his brother, he is a liar: for he that loveth not his brother whom he hath seen, how can he love God whom he hath not seen? And this commandment have we from him, That he who loveth God love his brother also" (1 John 4.20–21).

to God, and to nourish peace and unity. But to God-ward Christ is an everlasting satisfaction, and ever sufficient.[4]

[SCRIPTURAL INTERPRETATION]

Thou shalt understand, therefore, that the Scripture hath but one sense, which is the literal sense. And that literal sense is the root and ground of all, and the anchor that never faileth, whereunto if thou cleave, thou canst never err or go out of the way. And if thou leave the literal sense, thou canst not but go out of the way. Neverthelater,[5] the Scripture useth proverbs, similitudes, riddles, or allegories, as all other speeches do; but that which the proverb, similitude, riddle, or allegory signifieth, is ever the literal sense, which thou must seek out diligently: as in the English we borrow words and sentences of one thing, and apply them unto another, and give them new significations. We say, "Let the sea swell and rise as high as he will, yet hath God appointed how far he shall go": meaning that the tyrants shall not do what they would, but that only which God hath appointed them to do. "Look ere thou leap": whose literal sense is, "Do nothing suddenly, or without advisement." "Cut not the bough that thou standest upon": whose literal sense is, "Oppress not the commons"; and is borrowed of hewers. When a thing speedeth[6] not well, we borrow speech, and say, "The bishop hath blessed it"; because that nothing speedeth well that they meddle withal. If the porridge be burned too, or the meat over-roasted, we say, "The bishop hath put his foot in the pot," or "The bishop hath played the cook"; because the bishops burn whom they lust,[7] and whosoever displeaseth them. "He is a pontifical fellow"; that is, proud and stately. "He is popish"; that is, superstitious and faithless.

* * *

Beyond all this, when we have found out the literal sense of the Scripture by the process of the text, or by a like text of another place, then go we, and as the Scripture borroweth similitudes of worldly things, even so we again borrow similitudes or allegories of the Scripture, and apply them to our purposes; which allegories are no sense of the Scripture, but free things besides the Scripture, and altogether in the liberty of the Spirit. * * * This allegory proveth nothing, neither can do. For it is not the Scripture, but an ensample[8] or a similitude borrowed of the Scripture, to declare a text or a conclusion of the Scripture more expressly, and to root it and grave[9] it in the heart. For a similitude, or an ensample, doth print a thing much deeper in the wits of a man than doth a plain speaking, and leaveth behind him as it were a sting to prick him forward, and to awake him withal. Moreover, if I could not prove with an open[1] text that which the allegory doth express, then were the allegory a thing to be jested at, and of no greater value than a tale of Robin Hood.

1527, 1528

---

4. To the ecclesiastical commissioners who examined Tyndale's works in 1530, this passage was clearly heretical. One of the commissioners, Sir Thomas More, lambasted it as constituting an encouragement to sin, since it made obtaining forgiveness seem such an easy matter.

5. Nevertheless.
6. Succeeds, prospers.
7. Whomever they please.
8. Example.
9. Engrave.
1. Plain, clear.

THOMAS MORE

s early as 1521, when he became Henry VIII's "theological councillor," Thomas More had played an important role in the official campaign against Luther. Initially writing as the king's surrogate in doctrinal polemics conducted in Latin, by 1529, when he became lord chancellor of England, More had become deeply immersed in the anti-Protestant campaign in his own right. His extremely energetic contributions included written attacks; in English, on Tyndale's Bible translations and other prohibited books, and extended to active persecution of those defined as heretics. "I find that breed of men absolutely loathsome," More wrote to his friend Erasmus; "I want to be as hateful to them as anyone can possibly be." If More was willing to kill in defense of the Christian consensus in which he fervently believed, he also proved himself willing in the end to die for his belief.

More had two principal quarrels with Lutheranism: (1) he objected to Luther's denial that Christians could contribute toward their own salvation through their good works; and (2) he objected to Luther's account of biblical interpretation. For Luther, Scripture preceded and ideally determined the form of the Church; for More, the Church preceded and determined the interpretation of Scripture.

In *A Dialogue Concerning Heresies* (1529), More broaches both issues. Departing from the head-on, vituperative attacks of his Latin works, More here adopts a different approach: his interlocutor in the *Dialogue* is a young man on friendly terms with More, but infatuated with Protestant ideas. More's aim seems less to attack Luther directly than, by using wit and cajolery as well as dialectic, to dissuade English men and women from embracing Protestantism.

The selection printed here tackles the fundamental issues of biblical interpretation. Who decides on the meaning of Scripture: the Church or individual readers? More's interlocutor is in no doubt: Scripture is for the most part entirely plain; individual readers have no trouble interpreting it. More strongly counters such simple faith in the plain and literal sense. Everything, he argues (in a passage playing with the consonance of "goose" and "gloss"), requires a commentary. Even to compare one text with another is to gloss it. If commentary is always necessary, then some stable ground for establishing authority over that commentary also becomes necessary. For More that ground is the Catholic Church, whose authority is established by the many centuries of its continued existence and by the consensus of the Church's Councils. More casts the young Lutheran's position as that of a single opinionated reader perversely resisting the "common faith" of Christendom.

From A Dialogue Concerning Heresies

From *Book 1, Chapter 28*: * * * *proving the authority of the old interpreters and the infallible authority of the Church* * * *

"* * * in somewhat, ye say, ye will believe the Church, but not in all. In anything beside Scripture ye will not, nor in the interpretation of Scripture ye will not; and so, where ye said that ye believe the Church in somewhat, in very deed ye believe the Church in right nought. For wherein will ye believe it, if ye believe it not in the interpretation of Scripture? For as touching the text, ye believe the Scripture self, and not the Church."

"Methinketh," quod[1] he, "the text is good enough and plain enough, needing no gloss[2] if it be well considered, and every part compared with other."

"Hard it were," quod I, "to find anything so plain that it should need no gloss at all."

"In faith," quod he, "they make a gloss to some texts that be as plain as it is that twice two make four."

"Why," quod I, "needeth that no gloss at all?"

"I trow[3] so," quod he. "Or else the devil is on it."

"Iwis,"[4] quod I, "and yet though ye would believe one that would tell you that twice two ganders made always four geese, yet ye would be advised[5] ere ye believed him that would tell you that twice two geese made always four ganders. For therein might ye be deceived. And him would ye not believe at all, that would tell you that twice two geese would always make four horse."

"Tut," quod he, "this is a merry[6] matter. They must be all the twice twain always of one kind. But geese and horse be of diverse."

"Well," quod I, "then every man that is neither goose nor horse seeth that there is one gloss yet.[7] But now," quod I, "the geese and the ganders be both of one kind, and yet twice two geese make not always four ganders."

"A sweet matter," quod he. "Ye wot[8] what I mean well enough."

"I think I do," quod I. "But I think if ye bring it forth it will make another gloss to your text, as plain as your text is; and[9] ye will in all Holy Scripture have no gloss at all. And yet will ye have collation made of one text with another, and show how they may be agreed together[1]—as though all that were no gloss."

"Yea," quod he, "but would you that we should believe the Church if it set a gloss that will in no wise[2] agree with the text, but that it appeareth plainly that the text, well considered, saith clean the contrary?"

"To whom doth that appear," quod I, "so plainly, when it appeareth one to you, and to the whole Church another?"

"Yet if I see it so," quod he, "though holy doctors and all the whole Church would tell me the contrary, methinketh I were no more bounden to believe them all, that the Scripture meaneth as they take it, than if they would all tell me that a thing were white which I see myself is black."

"Of late," quod I, "ye would believe the Church in something. And now not only ye would believe it in nothing, but also whereas God would the Church should be your judge, ye would now be judge over the Church. And ye will by your wit[3] be judge whether the Church, in the understanding of Holy Scripture that God hath written to His Church, do judge aright or err. As for your white and black, never shall it be that ye shall see the thing black that all other shall see white. But ye may be sure that if all other see it white, and ye take it for black, your eyen[4] be sore deceived. For the Church will not, I think, agree to call it other than it seemeth to them. And

---

1. Quoth, said.
2. Interpretation, commentary.
3. Believe.
4. Certainly.
5. Warned.
6. Frivolous.
7. Still.

8. Know.
9. Whereas.
1. Reconciled.
2. Way.
3. Intellect.
4. Eyes.

much marvel were it, if ye should in Holy Scripture see better than the old holy doctors and Christ's whole Church."

* * *

1528–29   1529

JOHN CALVIN

B orn to middle-class parents in Picardy, France, and trained as a lawyer, Calvin (1509–1564) was steeped in the Greek and Latin learning associated with Renaissance humanism. He acquired as well a knowledge of Hebrew, so that he was powerfully equipped to respond to the call, from Erasmus and others, for a study of the Bible in its original languages. Drawn increasingly toward Protestantism, Calvin left Catholic France for Switzerland, where he eventually became the dominant figure in Geneva, establishing a stern theocratic rule. Through his voluminous writings, he also became the principal theologian of the Protestant Reformation, exercising immense influence in England as well as on the Continent. His major work, revised in successive Latin and French editions and widely translated, is *The Institution of Christian Religion*. The passage selected here is from Calvin's famous, troubling account of the doctrine of predestination, according to which God has determined before the foundation of the world whom he will save and whom he will damn, regardless of the merits or defects of these individuals. The good deeds that a virtuous person does in life are a sign of divine election, not a means to secure it. The translation, closely adhering to the Latin original, is by Thomas Norton (1532–1584), a lawyer and member of Parliament and, with Thomas Sackville, the author of the earliest English tragedy in blank verse, *Gorboduc*—first performed in the same year (1561) that Norton's translation of Calvin appeared.

From The Institution of Christian Religion, written in Latin by Master John Calvin, and translated into English according to the author's last edition

From *Book 3, Chapter 21*
Of the eternal election, whereby God hath predestinate some to salvation, and other some to destruction

But now whereas the covenant of life is not equally preached to all men, and with them to whom it is preached it doth not either equally or continually find like place, in this diversity the wondrous depth of the judgment of God appeareth. For neither is it any doubt but that this diversity also serveth the free choice of God's eternal election.[1] If it be evident that it is wrought by the will of God that salvation is freely offered to some, and

---

1. Choice—i.e., of whom to save.

other some are debarred from coming to it, here by and by[2] arise great and hard questions which cannot otherwise be discussed than if the godly minds have that certainly stablished which they ought to hold[3] concerning election and predestination. This is (as many think) a cumbersome[4] question: because they think nothing to be less reasonable than of the common multitude of men some to be foreordained to salvation, other some to destruction. But how they wrongfully encumber themselves shall afterward be evident by the framing of the matter together.[5] Beside that in the very same darkness which maketh men afraid, not only the profitableness of this doctrine but also the most sweet fruit showeth forth itself. We shall never be clearly persuaded, as we ought to be, that our salvation floweth out of the fountain of the free mercy of God, till his eternal election be known to us, which by this comparison brightly setteth forth the grace of God, that he doth not without difference adopt all into the hope of salvation, but giveth to some that which he denieth to other. How much the ignorance of this principle diminisheth of the glory of God, how much it withdraweth from true humility, it is plain to see.

*　*　*

They which shut the gates, that none may be bold to come to the tasting of this doctrine, do no less wrong to men than to God: because neither shall any other thing suffice to humble us as we ought to be, neither shall we otherwise feel from our heart how much we are bound to God. Neither yet is there any otherwhere the upholding stay of sound affiance,[6] as Christ himself teacheth, which to deliver us from all fear, and to make us unvanquishable among so many dangers, ambushes, and deadly battles, promiseth that whatsoever he hath received of[7] his Father to keep shall be safe.[8] Whereof we gather that they shall with continual trembling be miserable, whosoever they be that know not themselves to be the proper possession of God; and therefore that they do very ill provide both for themselves and for all the faithful, which, in being blind at these three profits which we have touched,[9] would wish the whole foundation of our salvation to be quite taken from among us. Moreover, hereby the Church appeareth unto us, which otherwise (as Bernard rightly teacheth)[1] were not possible to be found nor to be known among creatures, because both ways in marvelous wise[2] it lieth hidden: within the bosom of blessed predestination, and within the mass of miserable damnation.

But ere I enter into the matter itself, I must beforehand in two sorts speak to two sorts of men.[3] That the entreating[4] of predestination, whereas of itself it is somewhat cumbersome, is made very doubtful, yea, and dangerous, the curiousness of men is the cause: which can by no stops be refrained

---

2. Immediately.
3. Believe. "Stablished": established.
4. Troublesome.
5. I.e., from the following discussion.
6. Trust, faith. "Bound": obliged. "Stay": support.
7. From.
8. "My sheep hear my voice, and I know them, and they follow me: And I give unto them eternal life; and they shall never perish, neither shall any man pluck them out of my hand. My Father, which gave them me, is greater than all; and no man is

able to pluck them out of my Father's hand" (John 10.27–29).
9. I.e., God's free mercy, God's glory, and our true humility.
1. St. Bernard of Clairvaux (1090–1153), in his *Sermons on the Song of Songs*.
2. In a marvelous fashion.
3. I must first speak in two different ways about two sorts of men.
4. Treating, discussing.

from wandering into forbidden compasses,[5] and climbing up on high; which, if it may, will leave to God no secret which it will not search and turn over. Into this boldness and importunacy[6] forasmuch as we commonly see many to run headlong, and among those some that are otherwise not evil men, here is fit occasion to warn them what is in this behalf[7] the due measure of their duty. First, therefore, let them remember that when they inquire upon predestination, they pierce into the secret closets[8] of the wisdom of God: whereinto if any man too carelessly and boldly break in, he shall both not attain wherewith to satisfy his curiousness, and he shall enter into a maze whereof he shall find no way to get out again. For neither is it meet[9] that man should freely search those things which God hath willed to be hidden in himself, and to turn over from very eternity the height of wisdom,[1] which he willed to be honored and not to be conceived, that by it also he mought[2] be marvelous unto us. Those secrets of his will which he hath determined to be opened unto us, he hath disclosed in his Word: and he hath determined, so far as he foresaw to pertain to us and to be profitable for us.[3]

* * *

There be other which, when they have a will to remedy this evil,[4] do command all mention of predestination to be in a manner buried: at the least they teach men to flee from every manner of questioning thereof as from a rock. Although the moderation of these men be herein worthily to be praised, that they judge that mysteries should be tasted of with such sobriety, yet because they descend too much beneath the mean,[5] they little prevail with the wit[6] of man, which doth not lightly suffer itself to be restrained. Therefore, that in this behalf also we may keep a right end,[7] we must return to the Word of the Lord, in which we have a sure rule of understanding. For the Scripture is the school of the Holy Ghost, in which as nothing is left out which is both necessary and profitable to be known, so nothing is taught but that which is behoveful[8] to learn. Whatsoever therefore is uttered in the Scripture concerning predestination, we must beware that we debar not the faithful from it, lest we should seem either enviously to defraud them of the benefit of their God or to blame and accuse the Holy Ghost, who hath published those things which it is in any wise[9] profitable to be suppressed.

* * *

That, therefore, which the Scripture clearly showeth, we say that God by eternal and unchangeable counsel hath once appointed whom in time to come he would take to salvation, and on the other side whom he would condemn to destruction. This counsel as touching the elect, we say to be

---

5. Places.
6. Pertinacity, stubborn persistence.
7. In this regard.
8. Inner chambers.
9. Fitting.
1. And to search out from eternity itself the sublimest wisdom.
2. Might. "Conceived": understood.
3. I.e., God has let us know, in the Scriptures, as much about these matters as he foresaw would

be useful for us to know.
4. I.e., the audacious attempt to learn more about predestination than Scripture teaches.
5. I.e., fall short of the appropriate middle ground ("mean").
6. Intellect.
7. Keep within proper bounds.
8. Useful, advantageous.
9. In any way.

grounded upon his free mercy, without any respect of the worthiness of man: but whom he appointeth to damnation, to them by his judgment (which is indeed just and irreprehensible but also incomprehensible) the entry of life is foreclosed. Now in the elect we set vocation to be the testimony of election; and then justification[1] to be another sign of the manifest showing of it, till they come to glory, wherein is the fulfilling of it. But as by vocation and election God marketh his elect, so by shutting out the reprobate either from the knowledge of his name or from the sanctification of his spirit, he doth as it were by these marks open what judgment abideth[2] for them. * * *

1561

1. The state of being justified—i.e., freed from the penalty of sin and accounted righteous by God. The underlying Scriptural text for this passage is Romans 8.30: "whom he did predestinate, them he also called: and whom he called, them he also justified: and whom he justified, them he also glorified." "Vocation": a calling—a predisposition to the religious life. "Testimony": evidence.
2. Waits. "Open": reveal.

ANNE ASKEW

In the 1540s, Henry VIII sought to return the English Church to a basically Catholic doctrinal position, and Protestants were subjected to persecution. The outspoken Protestant Anne Askew (1521–1546) was called in for questioning in 1545; the next year, she was tortured and burned at the stake. Askew's accounts of her two examinations were smuggled out of England and published in Germany (1546–47) by the reformer John Bale. The texts were later incorporated into John Foxe's *Acts and Monuments* (1563).*

The theological controversies over the Eucharist, for which Askew and her companions along with many other Protestants and Catholics were willing to lay down their lives, require some explanation. Catholic doctrine held that sacraments properly performed were independent of the spiritual condition either of the priest or of the worshipper. Hence, for example, if the formula of consecration of the bread and wine was correctly spoken by a properly ordained priest, the miraculous transubstantiation of the Host into the body and blood of Christ would occur, whether or not the priest or the communicant was in a state of grace. Indeed, some Catholic theologians argued, since the bread had objectively been transformed into the body of God, even a mouse, nibbling on a consecrated host, would be receiving Christ's flesh. Protestants argued that the efficacy of certain key religious sacraments, including the Lord's Supper, depended on the spiritual state of the minister and the congregant. An evil priest, in such a conception, would not only be damning himself (as Catholics also believed) but would be turning the Lord's Supper into the Devil's Supper.

* For "A Ballad of Anne Askew" (possibly by Askew herself), see "Dissent, Doubt, and Spiritual Violence in the Reformation" in the supplemental ebook.

From The First Examination of Anne Askew

To satisfy your expectation, good people (sayeth she), this was my first examination in the year of our Lord 1545, and in the month of March. First, Christopher Dare examined me at Saddlers' Hall,[1] being one of the quest,[2] and asked if I did not believe that the sacrament hanging over the altar[3] was the very body of Christ really. Then I demanded this question of him: wherefore Saint Stephen was stoned to death.[4] And he said he could not tell. Then I answered that no more would I assoil[5] his vain question.

Secondly, he said that there was a woman which did testify that I should read[6] how God was not in temples made with hands. Then I showed him the seventh and the seventeenth chapters of the Acts of the Apostles, what Stephen and Paul had said therein.[7] Whereupon he asked me how I took those sentences. I answered that I would not throw pearls among swine,[8] for acorns were good enough.

Thirdly, he asked me wherefore I said that I had rather to read five lines in the Bible than to hear five masses in the temple. I confessed that I said no less. Not for the dispraise of either the Epistle or Gospel, but because the one did greatly edify me and the other[9] nothing at all. As Saint Paul doth witness in the fourteenth chapter of his first Epistle to the Corinthians, whereas he doth say: "If the trumpet giveth an uncertain sound, who will prepare himself to the battle?"

Fourthly, he laid unto my charge that I should say: "If an ill[1] priest ministered, it was the Devil and not God." My answer was that I never spake such thing. But this was my saying: "That whatsoever he were which ministered unto me, his ill conditions could not hurt my faith, but in spirit I received nevertheless the body and blood of Christ." He asked me what I said concerning confession. I answered him my meaning, which was as Saint James sayeth, that every man ought to knowledge[2] his faults to other, and the one to pray for the other.

Sixthly, he asked me what I said to the king's book.[3] And I answered him that I could say nothing to it, because I never saw it.

Seventhly, he asked me if I had the spirit of God in me. I answered if I had not, I was but reprobate or cast away. Then he said he had sent for a priest to examine me, which was there at hand. The priest asked me what I said to the sacrament of the altar.[4] And required much to know therein my meaning. But I desired him again to hold me excused concerning that matter. None other answer would I make him, because I perceived him a papist.[5]

---

1. Belonging to the guild of saddle-makers.
2. Inquest.
3. The holy wafers were sometimes held in a hanging vessel in the shape of a dove, symbolizing the Holy Ghost.
4. Stephen was martyred in Jerusalem after proclaiming that God "dwelleth not in temples made with hands" and accusing the priests of the temple of resisting the Holy Ghost and persecuting the prophets (Acts 7.48–60). "Demanded": asked.
5. Resolve.
6. Would teach.
7. Acts 17.24 repeats the assertion of Acts 7 that God does not dwell in temples built by human hands.

8. Matthew 7.6. "Took those sentences": interpreted those pronouncements.
9. "The one . . . the other": i.e., the Bible . . . the mass.
1. Wicked.
2. Acknowledge. James 5.16.
3. *A Necessary Doctrine and Erudition for Any Christian Man* (1543), with a preface by the king, sought to put a brake on reformers' "sinister understanding of Scripture, presumption, arrogancy, carnal liberty, and contention," by affirming a number of basically Catholic positions.
4. The Eucharist.
5. Follower of the pope—i.e., Roman Catholic.

Eighthly, he asked me if I did not think that private masses did help souls departed.[6] And [I] said it was great idolatry to believe more in them than in the death which Christ died for us. Then they had me thence unto my lord mayor and he examined me, as they had before, and I answered him directly in all things as I answered the quest afore. Besides this, my lord mayor laid one thing unto my charge which was never spoken of[7] me but of them. And that was whether a mouse eating the host received God or no. This question did I never ask, but indeed they asked it of me, whereunto I made them no answer, but smiled. Then the bishop's chancellor rebuked me and said that I was much to blame for uttering the Scriptures. For Saint Paul (he said) forbade women to speak or to talk of the word of God. I answered him that I knew Paul's meaning as well as he, which is, 1 Corinthians 14, that a woman ought not to speak in the congregation by the way of teaching. And then I asked him how many women he had seen go into the pulpit and preach? He said he never saw none. Then I said he ought to find no fault in poor women, except[8] they had offended the law. Then my lord mayor commanded me to ward. I asked him if sureties[9] would not serve me, and he made me short answer, that he would take none.

Then was I had to the Counter,[1] and there remained eleven days, no friend admitted to speak with me. But in the meantime there was a priest sent to me which said that he was commanded of the bishop to examine me and to give me good counsel, which he did not. But first he asked me for what cause I was put in the Counter. And I told him I could not tell. Then he said it was great pity that I should be there without cause, and concluded that he was very sorry for me.

Secondly, he said it was told him that I should deny the sacrament of the altar. And I answered him again that, that[2] I had said, I had said. Thirdly, he asked me if I were shriven.[3] I told him, so that I might have one of these three, that is to say, Doctor Crome, Sir William, or Huntingdon,[4] I was contented, because I knew them to be men of wisdom. "As for you or any other I will not dispraise, because I know ye not."

Then he said, "I would not have you think but that I or another that shall be brought you shall be as honest as they. For if we were not, ye may be sure, the king would not suffer us to preach."

Then I answered by the saying of Solomon, "By communing with the wise, I may learn wisdom: But by talking with a fool, I shall take scathe"[5] (Proverbs 1).

Fourthly, he asked me, if the host should fall and a beast did eat it, whether the beast did receive God or no. I answered, "Seeing ye have taken the pains to ask this question, I desire you also to assoil it yourself. For I will not do it, because I perceive ye come to tempt me." And he said it was against the order of schools that he which asked the question should answer it. I told him I was but a woman and knew not the course of schools.[6] Fifthly, he asked me if I

---

6. By shortening their time in Purgatory.
7. By.
8. Unless.
9. Guarantors of good behavior. "Ward": imprisonment.
1. A London prison.

2. What.
3. Absolved after confessing to a priest.
4. Reformist preachers. "So": if.
5. Injury.
6. Rules governing Catholic theological debates; scholastic procedures.

intended to receive the sacrament at Easter or no. I answered that else I were no Christian woman, and that I did rejoice that the time was so near at hand. And then he departed thence with many fair words.

* * *

In the meanwhile he commanded his archdeacon to common[7] with me, who said unto me, "Mistress, wherefore are ye accused and thus troubled here before the bishop?"

To whom I answered again and said, "Sir, ask, I pray you, my accusers, for I know not as yet."

Then took he my book out of my hand and said, "Such books as this hath brought you to the trouble you are in. Beware," sayeth he, "beware, for he that made this book and was the author thereof was an heretic, I warrant you, and burnt in Smithfield."[8]

Then I asked him if he were certain and sure that it was true that[9] he had spoken. And he said he knew well the book was of John Frith's making.[1] Then I asked him if he were not ashamed for to judge of the book before he saw it within, or yet knew the truth thereof. I said also that such unadvised and hasty judgment is token apparent of a very slender wit.[2] Then I opened the book and showed it to him. He said he thought it had been another, for he could find no fault therein. Then I desired him no more to be so unadvisedly rash and swift in judgment, till he thoroughly knew the truth; and so he departed from me. * * *

1546–47, 1563

7. Converse.
8. Smithfield Market, just outside the London city walls, was a site of public executions until the 17th century.
9. What.
1. The reformer John Frith was executed in 1533. *A Book Made by John Frith, Prisoner in the*

Tower of London, Answering unto Master More's Letter . . . Concerning the Sacrament of the Body and Blood of Christ, published in that year, was reissued in revised form in 1546, a few weeks before Askew was executed.
2. Shallow mind.

JOHN FOXE

John Foxe's career at Oxford University, where he had become a fellow of Magdalen College, was interrupted when his Puritan convictions led him to protest energetically against some college rules and practices. Foxe (1516–1587) then served as tutor to the children of various noble families, but when Mary became queen in 1553 and Protestants were once again persecuted, he fled to the Continent. His great book was already under way: the first version (Strasbourg, 1554) was in Latin and dealt with the persecutions suffered by the early reformers, particularly Wycliffe and John Hus. But the book grew and grew as Foxe received from England accounts of the hideous tortures and persecutions being inflicted on the Protestants there. When Elizabeth came to the throne in 1558, Foxe returned at once to England, and there he translated his Latin volume, adding to it hundreds of stories of the Marian martyrs (many based on eyewitness testimony, some on hearsay and rumor). The English edition was first published in 1563; often called "Foxe's Book of Martyrs," its title was *Acts and Monuments of these latter and perilous days, touching matters of the church, wherein are comprehended and described the great persecution and horrible troubles that have been wrought and practiced by the Romish prelates from the year of Our Lord a thousand to the time now present.*

Foxe saw life as an apocalyptic struggle between good and evil, Christ and Antichrist. Immediately and enormously popular, his book is a compendium of memoirs, stories, personal letters, court records, and the like, rendering the words, acts, and sufferings of some hundreds of martyrs in graphic—if often fictionalized—detail. The final version of the book (1583) is massive—more than six thousand folio pages, containing four million words. Apart from fanning the flames of anti-Catholic feeling, Foxe had an immense influence on English nationalism. His stories, from the medieval crypto-Protestants burned for heresy to the Protestant martyrs who passed through the fiery trials of the Marian persecutions, portrayed England as the land of a new chosen people, destined to lead the way toward the kingdom of God on earth. Foxe's second edition (1570) was placed, by government order, in churches throughout England.[*]

From Acts and Monuments

[THE DEATH OF ANNE ASKEW]

Hitherto we have entreated of[1] this good woman; now it remaineth that we touch somewhat as touching her end and martyrdom. She being born of such stock and kindred that she might have lived in great wealth and prosperity, if she would rather have followed the world than Christ, but now she was so tormented, that she could neither live long in so great distress, neither yet by the adversaries be suffered[2] to die in secret. Wherefore the day of her execution was appointed, and she brought into Smithfield[3] in a chair, because she could not go on her feet, by means[4] of her great torments. When she was brought unto the stake she was tied by the middle with a chain that held up her body. When all things were thus prepared to the fire, the king's letters of pardon were brought, whereby to offer her safeguard of her life if she would recant, which she would neither receive neither[5] yet vouchsafe once to look upon. Shaxton[6] also was there present, who, openly that day recanting his opinions, went about with a long oration to cause her also to turn, against whom she stoutly resisted. Thus she being troubled so many manner of ways, and having passed through so many torments, having now ended the long course of her agonies, being compassed in with flames of fire, as a blessed sacrifice unto God, she slept in the Lord, in anno[7] 1546, leaving behind her a singular example of Christian constancy for all men to follow.

1563

---

[*] For Foxe's account of the execution of Lady Jane Grey, see below, p. 735. For his account of the burning of Nicholas Ridley (bishop of London) and Hugh Latimer (former bishop of Worcester), see the supplemental ebook.
1. Treated, discussed.
2. Allowed.
3. See above, p. 687, n. 8.
4. Because.
5. Nor.
6. Nicholas Shaxton, formerly bishop of Salisbury.
7. The year.

L. Receive my spirit.

The burning of Thomas Cranmer, from Foxe's *Acts and Monuments*. Cranmer, archbishop of Canterbury, was arrested, tried for treason, and burned at the stake in front of Balliol College, Oxford, on March 21, 1556. Here he stretches his right hand into the fire, since that hand had been responsible for writing (or at least signing) a recantation of his Protestant faith, an apostasy that he repudiated just before his execution. The image also shows Cranmer crying out, "Lord, receive my spirit," traditionally said to be part of the dying words of the first Christian martyr, St. Stephen.

BOOK OF COMMON PRAYER

The Protestant attack on Catholic rituals and the demand for worship in the vernacular led during the reign of Edward VI to the preparation of an English liturgical book, authorized to be the official and only text for public worship in England. Initiated by the Act of Uniformity in 1549, the work's principal architect was Thomas Cranmer (1489–1556). Cranmer, the archbishop of Canterbury, was at first careful to translate and shape the old Latin liturgy into a moderate, occasionally ambiguous compromise between Catholic and Protestant positions. His thorough revision in 1552 put the *Book of Common Prayer* much more decisively into the Protestant camp. Banned by the Catholic Mary Tudor, during whose reign Cranmer was executed, the *Book of Common Prayer* was restored, with small revisions, by Elizabeth, and has remained the basis of Anglican worship ever since. Cranmer was, among his other accomplishments, a brilliant prose stylist, and the cadences of his book have had a profound influence on the English language. The selection, part of the marriage service, is from the version used during the reign of Elizabeth.

From The Book of Common Prayer and Administration of the Sacraments and Other Rites and Ceremonies in the Church of England

From *The Form of Solemnization of Matrimony*

* * * At the day appointed for solemnization of matrimony, the persons to be married shall come into the body of the church with their friends and neighbors. And there the priest shall thus say:

Dearly beloved friends, we are gathered together here in the sight of God, and in the face of his congregation, to join together this man and this woman in holy matrimony, which is an honorable estate,[1] instituted of God in paradise, in the time of man's innocency, signifying unto us the mystical union that is betwixt Christ and his church:[2] which holy estate Christ adorned and beautified with his presence and first miracle that he wrought in Cana of Galilee,[3] and is commended of Saint Paul to be honorable among all men,[4] and therefore is not to be enterprised[5] nor taken in hand unadvisedly, lightly, or wantonly, to satisfy men's carnal lusts and appetites, like brute beasts that have no understanding; but reverently, discreetly, advisedly, soberly, and in the fear of God, duly considering the causes for the which matrimony was ordained. One was, the procreation of children, to be brought up in the fear and nurture of the Lord, and praise of God. Secondly, it was ordained for a remedy against sin, and to avoid fornication, that such persons as have not the gift of continency might marry, and keep themselves undefiled members of Christ's body.[6] Thirdly, for the mutual society, help, and comfort that the one ought to have of the other, both in prosperity and adversity: into the which holy estate these two persons present come now to be joined. Therefore if any man can show any just cause why they may not lawfully be joined together, let him now speak, or else hereafter forever hold his peace.

And also speaking to the persons that shall be married, he shall say:

I require and charge you (as you will answer at the dreadful day of judgment, when the secrets of all hearts shall be disclosed) that if either of you do know any impediment why ye may not be lawfully joined together in matrimony, that ye confess it. For be ye well assured, that so many as be coupled together otherwise than God's word doth allow are not joined together by God, neither is their matrimony lawful.

At which day of marriage, if any man do allege and declare any impediment why they may not be coupled together in matrimony by God's law or the laws of this realm; and will be bound, and sufficient sureties with

---

1. State, condition.
2. Cf. Ephesians 5.31–32: "For this cause shall a man leave his father and mother, and shall be joined unto his wife, and they two shall be one flesh. This is a great mystery: but I speak concerning Christ and the church."

3. He changed water into wine (John 2.1–11).
4. "Marriage is honorable in all, and the bed undefiled: but whoremongers and adulterers God will judge" (Hebrews 13.4).
5. Undertaken.
6. The church.

him, to the parties, or else put in a caution,[7] to the full value of such charges as the persons to be married doth sustain, to prove his allegation: then the solemnization must be deferred unto such time as the truth be tried. If no impediment be alleged, then shall the curate[8] say unto the man,

N.[9] Wilt thou have this woman to thy wedded wife, to live together after God's ordinance in the holy estate of matrimony? Wilt thou love her, comfort her, honor and keep her, in sickness and in health? And forsaking all other, keep thee only to her, so long as you both shall live?

The man shall answer,
I will.
Then shall the priest say to the woman,

N. Wilt thou have this man to thy wedded husband, to live together after God's ordinance in the holy estate of matrimony? Wilt thou obey him and serve him, love, honor, and keep him, in sickness and in health, and forsaking all other, keep thee only unto him, so long as you both shall live?

The woman shall answer,
I will.
Then shall the minister say,

Who giveth this woman to be married unto this man?

And the minister receiving the woman at her father or friend's hands, shall cause the man to take the woman by the right hand, and so either to give their troth[1] to other. The man first saying:

I N. take thee N. to my wedded wife, to have and to hold from this day forward, for better, for worse, for richer, for poorer, in sickness and in health, to love and to cherish, till death us depart,[2] according to God's holy ordinance: and thereto I plight thee my troth.

Then shall they loose their hands, and the woman taking again the man by the right hand shall say:

I N. take thee N. to my wedded husband, to have and to hold from this day forward, for better, for worse, for richer, for poorer, in sickness and in health, to love, cherish, and to obey, till death us depart, according to God's holy ordinance: and thereto I give thee my troth.

Then shall they again loose their hands, and the man shall give unto the woman a ring, laying the same upon the book with the accustomed duty[3] to the priest and clerk. And the priest taking the ring, shall deliver it unto the man, to put it upon the fourth finger of the woman's left hand. And the man taught by the priest shall say:

---

7. Surety.
8. A clergyman who has charge of a parish.
9. Name—i.e., the minister inserts the man's given name here.

1. Truth—i.e., pledge.
2. Part.
3. Payment. "Book": Bible.

With this ring I thee wed: with my body I thee worship: and with all my worldly goods I thee endow. In the name of the Father, and of the Son, and of the Holy Ghost. Amen.

Then the man leaving the ring upon the fourth finger of the woman's left hand, the minister shall say:

O eternal God, creator and preserver of all mankind, giver of all spiritual grace, the author of everlasting life: send thy blessing upon these thy servants, this man and this woman, whom we bless in thy name; that as Isaac and Rebecca lived faithfully together,[4] so these persons may surely perform and keep the vow and covenant betwixt them made, whereof this ring given and received is a token and pledge, and may ever remain in perfect love and peace together, and live according unto thy laws: through Jesus Christ our Lord. Amen.

Then shall the priest join their right hands together, and say:

Those whom God hath joined together, let no man put asunder.[5]

Then shall the minister speak unto the people:

Forasmuch as N. and N. have consented together in holy wedlock, and have witnessed the same before God and this company, and thereto have given and pledged their troth, either to other, and have declared the same by giving and receiving of a ring, and by joining of hands: I pronounce that they be man and wife together. In the name of the Father, and of the Son, and of the Holy Ghost. Amen.

And the minister shall add this blessing:

God the Father, God the Son, God the Holy Ghost, bless, preserve, and keep you: the Lord mercifully with his favor look upon you, and so fill you with all spiritual benediction and grace that you may so live together in this life that in the world to come you may have life everlasting. Amen.

1559

---

4. In Genesis 24–27.　　　　5. From Mark 10.9.

BOOK OF HOMILIES

The first Protestant archbishop of Canterbury, Thomas Cranmer, was responsible in 1547 for the publication of the *Book of Homilies*. Hoping to curb the influence of "ignorant preachers" and fearing the spread of unauthorized beliefs, Cranmer brought together twelve sermons that were, by royal and ecclesiastical decree, to be read over and over, in the order in which they were set forth, in parish churches throughout the realm. The *Homilies*, revised and reissued during the reign of Elizabeth, are political as well as religious documents. As the "Homily Against Disobedience" (added in 1570 in the aftermath of a Catholic uprising the preceding year) amply demonstrates, the intention was to teach the English people "to honor

God and to serve their king with all humility and subjection, and godly and honestly to behave themselves toward all men." Artfully crafted and tirelessly reiterated, these sermons would have been familiar to almost everyone in the latter half of the sixteenth century.*

From An Homily Against Disobedience and Willful Rebellion

* * * How horrible a sin against God and man rebellion is cannot possibly be expressed according unto the greatness thereof. For he that nameth rebellion nameth not a singular, or one only sin, as is theft, robbery, murder, and suchlike, but he nameth the whole puddle and sink[1] of all sins against God and man, against his prince, his country, his countrymen, his parents, his children, his kinfolks, his friends, and against all men universally: all sins, I say, against God and all men heaped together nameth he that nameth rebellion. For concerning the offense of God's majesty, who seeth not that rebellion riseth first by contempt of God and of his holy ordinances and laws, wherein he so straitly[2] commandeth obedience, forbiddeth disobedience and rebellion?[3] And besides the dishonor done by rebels unto God's holy name by their breaking of the oath made to their prince with the attestation of God's name and calling of his majesty to witness, who heareth not the horrible oaths and blasphemies of God's holy name that are used daily amongst rebels, that is either amongst them or heareth the truth of their behavior? Who knoweth not that rebels do not only themselves leave all works necessary to be done upon workdays undone, whiles they accomplish their abominable work of rebellion, and do compel others that would gladly be well occupied to do the same, but also how rebels do not only leave the sabbath day of the Lord unsanctified, the temple and church of the Lord unresorted unto, but also do by their works of wickedness most horribly profane and pollute the sabbath day, serving Satan, and by doing of his work making it the devil's day instead of the Lord's day? Besides that they compel good men that would gladly serve the Lord assembling in his temple and church upon his day, as becometh the Lord's servants, to assemble and meet armed in the field to resist the fury[4] of such rebels. Yea, and many rebels, lest they should leave any part of God's commandments in the first table of his law[5] unbroken or any sin against God undone, do make rebellion for the maintenance of their images and idols, and of their idolatry committed or to be committed by them, and, in despite of God, cut and tear in sunder his Holy Word, and tread it under their feet, as of late ye know was done.[6]

---

* For extracts from another of the homilies, "An Exhortation Concerning Good Order and Obedience to Rulers and Magistrates," see the supplemental ebook.

1. Cesspool.

2. Strictly.

3. Romans 13.1–2: "Let every soul be subject unto the higher powers. For there is no power but of God: the powers that be are ordained of God. Whosoever therefore resisteth the power, resisteth the ordinance of God: and they that resist shall receive to themselves damnation."

4. Violence.

5. The first of the two "tables" (tablets) of stone on which God wrote the Ten Commandments (Deuteronomy 5.22): those on the first table specify our obligations to God, those on the second (below) our obligations to one another.

6. These enormities were purportedly perpetrated by the Catholic rebels who, in the winter of 1569, rose in the north of England against Queen Elizabeth and in support of her Catholic cousin, Mary, Queen of Scots (who had been imprisoned in England since May 1568).

As concerning the second table of God's law, and all sins that may be committed against man, who seeth not that they be all contained in rebellion? For first, the rebels do not only dishonor their prince, the parent of their country, but also do dishonor and shame their natural parents, if they have any, do shame their kindred and friends, disherit[7] and undo forever their children and heirs. Thefts, robberies, and murders, which of all sins are most loathed of most men, are in no men so much, nor so perniciously and mischievously, as in rebels. For the most arrant thieves and cruelest murderers that ever were, so long as they refrain from rebellion, as they are not many in number, so spreadeth their wickedness and damnation unto a few: they spoil[8] but a few, they shed the blood but of few in comparison. But rebels are the cause of infinite robberies and murders of great multitudes, and of those also whom they should defend from the spoil and violence of other; and, as rebels are many in number, so doth their wickedness and damnation spread itself unto many. And if whoredom and adultery amongst such persons as are agreeable to such wickedness are (as they indeed be) most damnable, what are the forcible oppressions[9] of matrons and men's wives, and the violating and deflowering of virgins and maids, which are most rife with rebels; how horrible and damnable, think you, are they? Now, besides that rebels, by breach of their faith given and oath made to their prince, be guilty of most damnable perjury, it is wondrous to see what false colors and feigned causes, by slanderous lies made upon their prince and the counselers, rebels will devise to cloak their rebellion withal, which is the worst and most damnable of all false-witness-bearing that may be possible. For what should I speak of coveting or desiring of other men's wives, houses, lands, goods, and servants in rebels, who by their wills would leave unto no man anything of his own?

Thus you see that all God's laws are by rebels violated and broken, and that all sins possible to be committed against God or man be contained in rebellion: which sins, if a man list[1] to name by the accustomed names of the seven capital or deadly sins, as pride, envy, wrath, covetousness, sloth, gluttony, and lechery, he shall find them all in rebellion, and amongst rebels. For first, as ambition and desire to be aloft, which is the property of pride, stirreth up many men's minds to rebellion, so cometh it of a luciferian pride and presumption that a few rebellious subjects should set themselves up against the majesty of their prince, against the wisdom of the counselors, against the power and force of all nobility, and the faithful subjects and people of the whole realm. As for envy, wrath, murder, and desire of blood, and covetousness of other men's goods, lands, and livings, they are the inseparable accidents of all rebels, and peculiar properties[2] that do usually stir up wicked men unto rebellion. Now such as by riotousness, gluttony, drunkenness, excess of apparel, and unthrifty[3] games have wasted their own goods unthriftily, the same are most apt unto and most desirous of rebellion, whereby they trust to come by other men's goods unlawfully and violently. And where other

---

7. Disinherit.
8. Despoil, plunder.
9. Rapes.
1. Wants.

2. Distinctive characteristics. "Inseparable accidents": unavoidable accompaniments.
3. Dissolute.

gluttons and drunkards take too much of such meats and drinks as are served to tables, rebels waste and consume in short space all corn in barns, fields, or elsewhere, whole graners,[4] whole storehouses, whole cellars, devour whole flocks of sheep, whole droves of oxen and kine.[5] And as rebels that are married, leaving their own wives at home, do most ungraciously, so much more do unmarried men than any stallions or horses, being now by rebellion set at liberty from correction of laws which bridled them before, which abuse by force other men's wives and daughters, and ravish virgins and maidens most shamefully, abominably, and damnably. Thus all sins, by all names that sins may be named, and by all means that all sins may be committed and wrought, do all wholly upon heaps follow rebellion, and are to be found all together amongst rebels.

1570

4. Granaries. "Corn": grain.   5. Cattle.

RICHARD HOOKER

Out of the long and bitter controversy over the government of the church in sixteenth-century England emerged one literary masterpiece. It is a work in eight books called *Of the Laws of Ecclesiastical Polity* (that is, the governmental system of the church). The author was the Oxford-educated Richard Hooker (1554–1600), a scholar and minister. In 1585 Hooker was master of the Temple (in modern terms, dean of a law school); one of his subordinates was a Puritan intellectual named Walter Travers. Between them a contentious debate developed on the burning question of how the church should be governed. The Puritan view was that no organization or authority in the church was valid unless it was based clearly and specifically on the Bible; the whole hierarchical system of the English Church, with its deacons, priests, bishops, and archbishops, was accordingly wrong, along with its liturgy and most of its rituals. The position Hooker undertook to defend was that the Scriptures, or divine revelation, are not the only guide given to Christians for organizing and administering the church. Another guide is the law of nature, also divinely given, which can be discerned by the use of human reason.

In the book that grew out of his controversy with Travers, Hooker explained how the law of nature affords principles that justify the existing organization and practices of the English Church. Book 1 of *Ecclesiastical Polity* deals with law in general and the several kinds of law; it pictures the entire universe, and also human society, as founded on reason and operating under various natural and divine laws. Book 2 deals with the nature, authority, and adequacy of Scripture. Books 3 to 5 explain and defend the rites, ceremonies, worship, and government of the English Church. Books 6, 7, and 8 deal with various embodiments of authority, legitimate and illegitimate—elders, bishops, kings, and popes.

Hooker was a close and effective reasoner; avoiding the fiery invective or impassioned rhetoric that characterized most disputants of his time, he wrote in a calm, reasonable, and judicious manner. His defense of existing ecclesiastical practices went back to fundamental principles, to a philosophy of nature and our place in it, to the subordination of the individual to a larger community and to God. It is this worldview, set forth in what is perhaps the period's most sonorous and quietly elegant prose, that makes *Ecclesiastical Polity* of enduring interest.*

From Of the Laws of Ecclesiastical Polity

From *Book 1, Chapter 3*

[ON THE SEVERAL KINDS OF LAW, AND ON THE NATURAL LAW]

I am not ignorant that by law eternal the learned for the most part do understand the order, not which God hath eternally purposed himself in all his works to observe, but rather that which with himself he hath set down as expedient to be kept by all his creatures, according to the several[1] conditions wherewith he hath indued them. They who thus are accustomed to speak apply the name of *Law* unto that only rule of working which superior authority imposeth; whereas we, somewhat more enlarging the sense thereof, term any kind of rule or canon whereby actions are framed a law. Now that law, which as it is laid up in the bosom of God they call *eternal*, receiveth according unto the different kinds of things which are subject unto it different and sundry kinds of names. That part of it which ordereth natural agents, we call usually *nature's* law; that which angels do clearly behold, and without any swerving observe, is a law *celestial* and heavenly; the law of *reason* that which bindeth creatures reasonable in this world, and with which by reason they may most plainly perceive themselves bound; that which bindeth them, and is not known but by special revelation from God, *divine* law; *human* law, that which, out of the law either of reason or of God, men probably[2] gathering to be expedient, they make it a law. All things, therefore, which are as they ought to be, are conformed unto *this second law eternal*, and even those things which to this *eternal* law are not conformable are notwithstanding in some sort ordered by *the first eternal law*. For what good or evil is there under the sun, what action correspondent to or repugnant unto the law which God hath imposed upon his creatures, but in or upon it God doth work according to the law which himself hath eternally purposed to keep, that is to say, the *first law eternal?* So that a twofold law eternal being thus made, it is not hard to conceive how they both take place in all things. Wherefore to come to the law of nature, albeit thereby we sometimes mean that manner of working which God hath set for each created thing to keep, yet forasmuch as those things are termed most properly natural agents, which keep the law of their kind unwittingly, as the heavens and elements of the world, which can do no otherwise than they do, and forasmuch as we give unto intellectual natures the name of voluntary agents, that so we may distinguish them from the other, expedient it will be that we sever[3] the law of nature observed by the one from that which the other is tied unto. Touching the former, their strict keeping of

---

* For several additional excerpts from *Ecclesiastical Polity*, see the supplemental ebook.
1. Different.
2. Plausibly.
3. Distinguish.

one tenure statute[4] and law is spoken of by all, but hath in it more than men have as yet attained to know, or perhaps ever shall attain, seeing the travail of wading herein is given of God to the sons of men, that perceiving how much the least thing in the world hath in it more than the wisest are able to reach unto, they may by this means learn humility. Moses in describing the work of creation attributeth speech unto God: "God said, Let there be light, Let there be a firmament; Let the waters under the heaven be gathered together into one place; Let the earth bring forth; Let there be lights in the firmament of heaven."[5] Was this only the intent of Moses, to signify the greatness of God's power by the easiness of his accomplishing such effects without travail, pain, or labor? Surely it seemeth that Moses had herein besides this a further purpose: namely, first to teach that God did not work as a necessary, but a voluntary, agent, intending beforehand and decreeing with himself that which did outwardly proceed from him; secondly, to show that God did then institute a law natural to be observed by creatures, and therefore according to the manner of laws, the institution thereof is described as being established by solemn injunction. His commanding those things to be which are, and to be in such sort as they are, to keep that tenure and course which they do, importeth[6] the establishment of nature's law. This world's first creation, and the preservation since of things created, what is it but only so far forth a manifestation by execution, what the eternal law of God is concerning things natural? And as it cometh to pass in a kingdom rightly ordered, that after a law is once published, it presently takes effect far and wide, all states[7] framing themselves thereunto; even so let us think it fareth in the natural course of the world: since the time that God did first proclaim the edicts of his law upon it, heaven and earth have hearkened unto his voice, and their labor hath been to do his will. He made a law for the rain. He gave his decree unto the sea, that the waters should not pass his commandment.[8]

Now if Nature should intermit her course and leave altogether, though it were but for a while, the observation of her own laws; if those principal and mother elements of the world, whereof all things in this lower world are made, should lose the qualities which now they have; if the frame of that heavenly arch erected over our heads should loosen and dissolve itself; if celestial spheres should forget their wonted motions and by irregular volubility[9] turn themselves any way as it might happen; if the prince of the lights of heaven, which now as a giant doth run his unwearied course, should as it were through a languishing faintness begin to stand and to rest himself; if the moon should wander from her beaten way, the times and seasons of the year blend themselves by disordered and confused mixture, the winds breathe out their last gasp, the clouds yield no rain, the earth be defeated of heavenly influence, the fruits of the earth pine away as children at the withered breasts of their mother no longer able to yield them relief, what would

---

4. Decree establishing the domains of the various creatures and the conditions of service by which they hold these domains.
5. Genesis 1.3, 6, 9, 11, 14. In this period, Moses was generally assumed to be the author of the Book of Genesis.
6. Signifies, implies.
7. Classes. "Presently": immediately.
8. Proverbs 8.29.
9. Revolution, rotation. "Wonted": accustomed.

become of man himself, whom these things now do all serve? See we not plainly that obedience of creatures unto the law of nature is the stay[1] of the whole world? Notwithstanding with nature it cometh sometimes to pass as with art. Let Phidias[2] have rude and obstinate stuff to carve, though his art do that[3] it should, his work will lack that beauty which otherwise in fitter matter it might have had. He that striketh an instrument with skill may cause notwithstanding a very unpleasant sound, if the string whereon he striketh chance to be uncapable of harmony. In the matter whereof natural things consist, that of Theophrastus taketh place:[4] "much of it is oftentimes such as will by no means yield to receive that impression which were best and most perfect." Which defect in the matter of things natural, they who gave themselves unto the contemplation of nature among the heathen observed often; but the true original cause thereof divine malediction,[5] laid for the sin of man upon those creatures which God had made for the use of man. This, being an article of that saving truth which God hath revealed unto his church, was above the reach of their[6] merely natural capacity and understanding. But howsoever these swervings are now and then incident into the course of nature, nevertheless so constantly the laws of nature are by natural agents observed, that no man denieth but those things which nature worketh are wrought either always or for the most part after one and the same manner. * * *

1593

1. Mainstay, support.
2. The greatest of ancient Greek sculptors (5th century B.C.E.).
3. What.
4. I.e., "that remark of Theophrastus carries weight." Theophrastus was a Greek writer of the 3rd century B.C.E., a follower of Aristotle and inventor of the species of essay called the "character," which portrayed a type of person in concise form.
5. God's curse in Eden, which fell not only on sinful humankind but on the earth as well.
6. I.e., the ancient pagans'.

ROBERT SOUTHWELL

Robert Southwell (1561–1595), the younger son of a prominent Roman Catholic family, went to the English seminary for Catholics at Douai, France, in his youth, then to Rome, where he entered the Society of Jesus (the Jesuits). In 1586 he returned to England to minister to English Catholics. His mission was a dangerous one, because of laws that proscribed Roman Catholic worship and banished priests; in 1592 he was apprehended, imprisoned, tortured, and, three years later, executed as a traitor in the usual grisly manner—by being hanged, disemboweled, and then beheaded. Southwell wrote a good deal of religious prose and verse; the most famous of his lyrics is "The Burning Babe." Ben Jonson told his friend William Drummond of Hawthornden that if he had written "The Burning Babe" he would have been content to destroy many of his own poems.

The Burning Babe

As I in hoary winter's night stood shivering in the snow,
Surprised I was with sudden heat which made my heart to glow;
And lifting up a fearful eye to view what fire was near,
A pretty babe all burning bright did in the air appear;
5   Who, scorchèd with excessive heat, such floods of tears did shed
As though his floods should quench his flames which with his tears
        were fed.
"Alas," quoth he, "but newly born in fiery heats I fry,[1]
Yet none approach to warm their hearts or feel my fire but I!
My faultless breast the furnace is, the fuel wounding thorns,
10 Love is the fire, and sighs the smoke, the ashes shame and scorns;
The fuel justice layeth on, and mercy blows the coals,
The metal in this furnace wrought are men's defilèd souls,
For which, as now on fire I am to work them to their good,
So will I melt into a bath to wash them in my blood."
15 With this he vanished out of sight and swiftly shrunk away,
And straight[2] I callèd unto mind that it was Christmas day.

1602

1. Burn.   2. Straightway, immediately.

ROGER ASCHAM
1515–1568

When she heard of the death of her former tutor and Latin Secretary, Queen Elizabeth is said to have exclaimed, "I would rather have cast ten thousand pounds in the sea than parted from my Ascham." Educated at St. John's College, Cambridge, one of the great centers of humanism in England, Ascham passionately believed in the study of the Greek and Latin classics, not merely for erudition and aesthetic pleasure but for guidance in moral values and in political activity. He corresponded widely in Latin with learned men on the Continent, but eager to influence his countrymen, whether they read Latin or not, he wrote several important books in English, including *Toxophilus*, a dialogue in praise of archery with the traditional English longbow, and *A Report and Discourse of the State of Germany*, based on his experience as secretary to the English ambassador there in 1550–53. His most famous work in English was *The Schoolmaster*, published two years after his death.

The Schoolmaster eloquently opposes the widespread use of corporal punishment in schools. Instilling a love of learning, rather than a fear of physical pain, inspires young children to excel in their studies. Ascham advocates "double translation" as the most effective way of acquiring a sound Latin style: students would translate a passage from Latin to English and then, without consulting the Latin original, translate the English back into Latin. The approach thus downplays rote learning of the rules of grammar and emphasizes instead a sense of style.

In the hands of a pedant, Ascham's method (which included discouraging students from speaking Latin, for fear that everyday life would corrupt the linguistic purity of classical antiquity) could, like so many other educational reforms, harden into a rigid frame into which individuals are hammered. But his ultimate goal was not a sterile miming but an ethical and aesthetic fashioning of the self. Deeply fearing what he called the "divorce between the tongue and the heart," he believed that education should teach a person to conjoin language and values in the achievement of what *The Schoolmaster* calls "decorum." Ascham's most despairing vision of a society without this moral decorum comes in his account of a brief trip to Italy, which he viewed as an evil seductress, luring unwitting Englishmen away from their ethical and religious values.*

From The Schoolmaster

From *The First Book for the Youth*

[TEACHING LATIN]

There is a way, touched in the first book of Cicero *De oratore,*[1] which, wisely brought into schools, truly taught, and constantly used, would not only take wholly away this butcherly fear in making of Latins[2] but would also, with ease and pleasure and in short time, as I know by good experience, work a true choice and placing of words, a right ordering of sentences, an easy understanding of the tongue, a readiness to speak, a facility to write, a true judgment both of his own and other men's doings, what tongue soever he doth use.

The way is this. After the three concordances[3] learned, as I touched before, let the master read unto him the epistles of Cicero gathered together and chosen out by Sturmius[4] for the capacity of children.

First, let him teach the child, cheerfully and plainly, the cause and matter of the letter; then, let him construe it into English so oft as the child may easily carry away the understanding of it; lastly, parse[5] it over perfectly. This done thus, let the child, by and by,[6] both construe and parse it over again so that it may appear that the child doubteth in nothing that his master taught him before. After this, the child must take a paper book and, sitting in some place where no man shall prompt him, by himself, let him translate into English his former lesson. Then, showing it to his master, let the master take from him his Latin book, and, pausing an hour at the least, then let the child translate his own English into Latin again in another paper book. When the child bringeth it turned into Latin, the master must compare it with Tully's[7] book and lay them both together, and where the child doth well,

---

* Another excerpt from *The Schoolmaster*—on Ascham's last conversation with Lady Jane Grey— is found on p. 728. For an excerpt from Ascham's *Toxophilus*, see the supplemental ebook.
1. Cicero's *On the Orator* consists of three parts, or books.
2. In Latin composition.
3. Agreement of noun and adjective, verb and noun, relative with antecedent.
4. Johannes Sturm (1507–1589), German scholar and educator.
5. Give a grammatical analysis.
6. Immediately.
7. Common English name for Marcus Tullius Cicero.

either in choosing or true placing of Tully's words, let the master praise him and say, "Here ye do well." For I assure you, there is no such whetstone to sharpen a good wit and encourage a will to learning as is praise.

But if the child miss, either in forgetting a word, or in changing a good with a worse, or misordering the sentence, I would not have the master either frown or chide with him, if the child have done his diligence and used no truantship therein. For I know by good experience that a child shall take more profit of two faults gently warned of than of four things rightly hit. For then the master shall have good occasion to say unto him:

> N[omen],[8] Tully would have used such a word, not this; Tully would have placed this word here, not there; would have used this case, this number, this person, this degree, this gender; he would have used this mood, this tense, this simple rather than this compound; this adverb here, not there; he would have ended the sentence with this verb, not with that noun or participle, etc.

In these few lines I have wrapped up the most tedious part of grammar and also the ground of almost all the rules that are so busily taught by the master, and so hardly learned by the scholar, in all common schools, which after this sort[9] the master shall teach without all error, and the scholar shall learn without great pain, the master being led by so sure a guide, and the scholar being brought into so plain and easy a way. And therefore we do not contemn rules, but we gladly teach rules, and teach them more plainly, sensibly, and orderly than they be commonly taught in common schools. For when the master shall compare Tully's book with his scholar's translation, let the master, at the first, lead and teach his scholar to join the rules of his grammar book with the examples of his present lesson, until the scholar by himself be able to fetch out of his grammar every rule for every example, so as the grammar book be ever in the scholar's hand and also used of him, as a dictionary, for every present use. This is a lively and perfect way of teaching of rules, where the common way, used in common schools, to read the grammar alone by itself, is tedious for the master, hard for the scholar, cold and uncomfortable to them both.

Let your scholar be never afraid to ask you any doubt,[1] but use discreetly the best allurements ye can to encourage him to the same, lest his overmuch fearing of you drive him to seek some misorderly shift,[2] as to seek to be helped by some other book, or to be prompted by some other scholar, and so go about to beguile you much, and himself more.

[THE ITALIANATE ENGLISHMAN]

* * * But I am afraid that overmany of our travelers into Italy do not eschew the way to Circe's court but go[3] and ride and run and fly thither; they make great haste to come to her; they make great suit to serve her; yea, I could point out some with my finger that never had[4] gone out of England but only

---

8. Name (Latin). The teacher will substitute the child's name.
9. Method. "So hardly": with such difficulty.
1. Question.
2. Subterfuge.

3. Walk. Circe was an enchantress in Homer's *Odyssey* who changed men into swine and other animals.
4. Would never have.

to serve Circe in Italy. Vanity and vice and any license to ill-living in England was counted stale and rude unto them. And so, being mules and horses before they went, returned very[5] swine and asses home again; yet everywhere very foxes with subtle and busy heads and, where they may, very wolves with cruel malicious hearts. A marvelous monster which for filthiness of living, for dullness to learning himself, for wiliness in dealing with others, for malice in hurting without cause, should carry at once in one body the belly of a swine, the head of an ass, the brain of a fox, the womb of a wolf. If you think we judge amiss and write too sore against you, hear what the Italian saith of the Englishman, what the master reporteth of the scholar, who uttereth plainly what is taught by him and what is learned by you, saying, *Inglese italianato è un diavolo incarnato*; that is to say, "You remain men in shape and fashion but become devils in life and condition." This is not the opinion of one, for some private spite, but the judgment of all in a common proverb which riseth of that learning and those manners which you gather in Italy—a good schoolhouse of wholesome doctrine, and worthy masters of commendable scholars, where the master had rather defame himself for his teaching than not shame his scholar for his learning: a good nature of the master, and fair conditions of the scholars. And now choose you, you Italian Englishmen, whether you will be angry with us for calling you monsters, or with the Italians for calling you devils, or else with your own selves, that take so much pains and go so far to make yourselves both. If some yet do not well understand what is an Englishman Italianated, I will plainly tell him: he that by living and traveling in Italy bringeth home into England out of Italy the religion, the learning, the policy, the experience, the manners[6] of Italy. That is to say, for religion, papistry or worse; for learning, less, commonly, than they carried out with them; for policy, a factious heart, a discoursing head, a mind to meddle in all men's matters; for experience, plenty of new mischiefs never known in England before; for manners, variety of vanities and change of filthy living. These be the enchantments of Circe brought out of Italy to mar men's manners in England: much by example of ill life but more by precepts of fond[7] books, of late translated out of Italian into English, sold in every shop in London, commended by honest titles the sooner to corrupt honest manners, dedicated overboldly to virtuous and honorable personages, the easilier to beguile simple and innocent wits. It is pity that those which have authority and charge to allow and disallow books to be printed be no more circumspect herein than they are. Ten sermons at Paul's Cross[8] do not so much good for moving men to true doctrine as one of those books do harm with enticing men to ill-living. Yea, I say farther, those books tend not so much to corrupt honest living as they do to subvert true religion. More papists be made by your merry books of Italy than by your earnest books of Louvain.[9] And because our great physicians do wink at the matter and make no count of this sore, I, though not admitted one of their fellowship, yet having been many years a prentice to

5. True.
6. Morals. "Policy": trickery, deceit.
7. Foolish.
8. An outdoor pulpit near St. Paul's Cathedral

where important and eloquent ministers preached.
9. Town in Belgium noted in the 16th century for its Catholic university, especially the theological faculty.

God's true religion, and trust to continue a poor journeyman therein all days of my life, for the duty I owe and love I bear both to true doctrine and honest living, though I have no authority to amend the sore myself, yet I will declare my good will to discover the sore to others.

St. Paul saith that sects and ill opinions be the works of the flesh and fruits of sin.[1] This is spoken no more truly for the doctrine than sensibly for the reason. And why? For ill-doings breed ill-thinkings, and of corrupted manners spring perverted judgments. And how? There be in man two special things: man's will, man's mind. Where will inclineth to goodness the mind is bent to truth; where will is carried from goodness to vanity the mind is soon drawn from truth to false opinion. And so the readiest way to entangle the mind with false doctrine is first to entice the will to wanton living. Therefore, when the busy and open papists abroad could not by their contentious books turn men in England fast enough from truth and right judgment in doctrine, then the subtle and secret papists at home procured bawdy books to be translated out of the Italian tongue, whereby overmany young wills and wits, allured to wantonness, do now boldly contemn all severe books that sound to[2] honesty and godliness. In our forefathers' time, when papistry as a standing pool covered and overflowed all England, few books were read in our tongue, saving certain books of chivalry, as they said, for pastime and pleasure, which, as some say, were made in monasteries by idle monks or wanton canons; as one for example, *Morte Darthur*,[3] the whole pleasure of which book standeth in two special points—in open manslaughter and bold bawdry; in which book those be counted the noblest knights that do kill most men without any quarrel and commit foulest adulteries by subtlest shifts:[4] as Sir Lancelot with the wife of King Arthur his master, Sir Tristram with the wife of King Mark his uncle, Sir Lamorak with the wife of King Lot that was his own aunt. This is good stuff for wise men to laugh at or honest men to take pleasure at. Yet I know when God's Bible was banished the court and *Morte Darthur* received into the prince's chamber.[5] * * *

1570

---

1. In Galatians 5.19–21.
2. Treat of. "Severe": serious.
3. Sir Thomas Malory's collection of Arthurian romances.
4. Stratagems.
5. Referring to the prohibition of the Protestant translations of the Bible during the reign of the Catholic Queen Mary I (1553–58).

SIR THOMAS HOBY
1530–1566

One of the great and influential books of the Renaissance was *Il Cortegiano* (The Courtier), published in 1528 in Italian by Count Baldassare Castiglione (1478–1529) and soon translated into all the major European languages. The English translation, by the humanist and diplomat Sir Thomas Hoby, was not published until 1561 but had been written earlier, probably during the reign of Queen Mary (1553–58), when Hoby lived abroad as a Protestant exile.

Castiglione's book describes, by means of four fictitious dialogues—on successive evenings, among actual men and women living at the court of the duke of Urbino in the years 1504–08—the qualities of the ideal courtier. Supreme among these qualities is grace, the mysterious attribute which renders a person's speech and actions not merely impressive or accomplished but persuasive, touching, and beautiful. Though a few people are born with grace, most learn to have it by the mastery of certain techniques. In a famous passage, one of *The Courtier's* speakers, Count Lodovico Canossa, defines the most important of these techniques as *sprezzatura* or, as Hoby translates it, "recklessness." *Sprezzatura* is in fact close to the opposite of recklessness, as we ordinarily understand the term; it is a device for manipulating appearances and masking all the tedious memorizing of lines and secret rehearsals that underlie successful social performances. There is a paradox here, still evident in many social settings: success requires the painstaking mastery of complex codes of behavior, yet there is no surer recipe for failure than to be seen (like Malvolio in *Twelfth Night*) to be trying too hard.

The most famous passage in *The Courtier* is Peter Bembo's elegant restatement, Christianized and heterosexualized, of an ideal of love that ultimately derives from Plato's *Symposium*. Bembo declares that love is not the mere gratification of the senses but is the yearning of the soul after beauty, which is finally identical with the eternal good. Love properly understood is, therefore, a kind of ladder by which the soul progresses from lower to higher things. As he pursues his theme, Bembo becomes more and more enraptured and ends with a vision of the soul ravished by heavenly beauty, purged of the flesh, and admitted to the feast of the angels. One of the spirited ladies in the court, Emilia Pia, plucks his garment and gently reminds him that he has a body.*

From Castiglione's *The Courtier*

From *Book I, Sections 25–26*

[GRACE]

"* * * Perhaps I am able to tell you what a perfect Courtier ought to be, but not to teach you how ye should do to be one. Notwithstanding, to fulfill your request in what I am able, although it be (in manner) in a proverb that

---

* Additional excerpts from Bembo's discourse can be found in the supplemental ebook.

Grace[1] *is not to be learned*, I say unto you, whoso mindeth to be gracious or to have a good grace in the exercises of the body (presupposing first that he be not of nature unapt) ought to begin betimes, and to learn his principles of cunning[2] men. The which thing how necessary a matter Philip, king of Macedonia,[3] thought it, a man may gather in that his will was that Aristotle, so famous a philosopher, and perhaps the greatest that ever hath been in the world, should be the man that should instruct Alexander, his son, in the first principles of letters. And of men whom we know nowadays, mark how well and with what a good grace Sir Galeazzo Sanseverino, master of the horse to the French king, doth all exercises of the body; and that because, besides the natural disposition of person that is in him, he hath applied all his study to learn of cunning men, and to have continually excellent men about him, and, of every one, to choose the best of that they have skill in. For as in wrestling, in vaulting, and in learning to handle sundry kind of weapons he hath taken for his guide our Master Peter Mount, who (as you know) is the true and only master of all artificial[4] force and sleight, so in riding, in jousting, and in every other feat, he hath always had before his eyes the most perfectest that hath been known to be in those professions.

"He therefore that will be a good scholar, beside the practicing of good things, must evermore set all his diligence to be like his master, and, if it were possible, change himself into him. And when he hath had some entry,[5] it profiteth him much to behold sundry men of that profession; and, governing himself with that good judgment that must always be his guide, go about to pick out, sometime of one and sometime of another, sundry matters. And even as the bee in the green meadows flieth always about the grass choosing out flowers, so shall our Courtier steal this grace from them that to his seeming have it, and from each one that parcel[6] that shall be most worthy praise. And not do as a friend of ours whom you all know, that thought he resembled much King Ferdinand the Younger, of Aragon, and regarded not to resemble him in any other point but in the often lifting up his head, wrying, therewithal,[7] a part of his mouth, the which custom the king had gotten by infirmity. And many such there are that think they do much, so they resemble a great man in somewhat, and take many times the thing in him that worst becometh him.

"But I, imagining with myself often times how this grace cometh, leaving apart such as have it from above, find one rule that is most general which in this part (methink) taketh place[8] in all things belonging to a man, in word or deed, above all other. And that is to eschew as much as a man may, and as a sharp and dangerous rock, *Affectation* or curiosity,[9] and, to speak a new word, to use in everything a certain *Recklessness*, to cover art[1] withal, and seem whatsoever he doth and sayeth to do it without pain, and, as it were, not

---

1. *Grace* had a wide range of meanings for Elizabethans, and many puns were made on the word. It refers especially to a natural, easy manner, and also to that favor of God that can be neither earned nor deserved. "In manner": in the manner of; almost.
2. Knowing. "Betimes": early.
3. Philip II (ca. 382–336 B.C.E.), the father of Alexander the Great.
4. Artful, skillful.

5. Introduction.
6. Aspect. "To his seeming": in his opinion.
7. Twisting awry, moreover.
8. Precedence.
9. Overfastidiousness.
1. Artifice. "Recklessness": care-lessness; i.e., nonchalance. The Italian word—whose sense Hoby's translation does not clearly convey—is *sprezzatura*: a natural, easy grace.

minding[2] it. And of this do I believe grace is much derived, for in rare matters and well brought to pass every man knoweth the hardness of them, so that a readiness therein maketh great wonder. And contrariwise to use force and, as they say, to hale by the hair, giveth a great disgrace and maketh everything, how great soever it be, to be little esteemed. Therefore that may be said to be a very[3] art that appeareth not to be art; neither ought a man to put more diligence in anything than in covering it, for in case it be open, it loseth credit clean, and maketh a man little set by.[4] And I remember that I have read in my days that there were some most excellent orators which among other their cares enforced themselves to make every man believe that they had no sight[5] in letters, and dissembling their cunning, made semblant[6] their orations to be made very simply, and rather as nature and truth made them than study and art, the which if it had been openly known would have put a doubt in the people's mind, for fear lest he beguiled them. You may see then how to show art and such bent[7] study taketh away the grace of everything. * * *"

From *Book 4, Sections 49–73*

[THE LADDER OF LOVE]

Then the Lord Gaspar:[8] "I remember," quoth he, "that these lords yester-night, reasoning of the Courtier's qualities, did allow him to be a lover; and in making rehearsal[9] of as much as hitherto hath been spoken, a man may pick out a conclusion that the Courtier which with his worthiness and credit must incline his prince to virtue[1] must in manner of necessity be aged, for knowledge cometh very seldom-time before years, and specially in matters that be learned with experience. I cannot see, when he is well drawn[2] in years, how it will stand well with him to be a lover, considering, as it hath been said the other night, love frameth not with[3] old men, and the tricks that in young men be gallantness, courtesy, and preciseness[4] so acceptable to women, in them are mere follies and fondness[5] to be laughed at, and purchase him that useth them hatred of women and mocks of others. Therefore, in case this your Aristotle, an old Courtier, were a lover and practiced the feats that young lovers do, as some that we have seen in our days, I fear me he would forget to teach his prince; and peradventure boys would mock him behind his back, and women would have none other delight in him but to make him a jesting-stock."

Then said the Lord Octavian:[6] "Since all the other qualities appointed to the Courtier are meet[7] for him, although he be old, methink we should not then bar him from this happiness to love."

---

2. Noticing.
3. True.
4. Lightly regarded. "Clean": entirely.
5. Skill, insight.
6. Pretended.
7. Assiduous.
8. Gaspar Pallavicino, whose attitude in the dialogue is usually that of the misogynist.
9. Reviewing.
1. The courtier's role in counseling his prince

had been discussed in the preceding part of Book 4.
2. Advanced.
3. Is not suitable to.
4. Excessive neatness.
5. Foolishness. "In them": i.e., in old men.
6. Ottaviano Fregoso, a soldier, later doge of Genoa.
7. Suitable.

"Nay rather," quoth the Lord Gaspar, "to take this love from him is a perfection over and above, and a making him to live happily out of misery and wretchedness."

* * *

Then M. Peter[8] after a while's silence, somewhat settling himself as though he should entreat upon a weighty matter, said thus: "My lords, to show that old men may love not only without slander, but otherwhile[9] more happily than young men, I must be enforced to make a little discourse to declare what love is, and wherein consisteth the happiness that lovers may have. Therefore I beseech you give the hearing with needfulness, for I hope to make you understand that it were not unfitting for any man here to be a lover, in case he were fifteen or twenty years elder than M. Morello."[1]

And here, after they had laughed awhile, M. Peter proceeded: "I say, therefore, that according as it is defined of the wise men of old time, love is nothing else but a certain coveting to enjoy beauty;[2] and forsomuch as coveting longeth for nothing but for things known, it is requisite that knowledge go evermore before coveting, which of his own nature willeth the good, but of himself is blind and knoweth it not. Therefore hath nature so ordained that to every virtue[3] of knowledge there is annexed a virtue of longing. And because in our soul there be three manner ways to know, namely, by sense, reason, and understanding:[4] of sense ariseth appetite or longing, which is common to us with brute beasts; of reason ariseth election or choice, which is proper[5] to man; of understanding, by the which man may be partner with angels, ariseth will. Even as therefore the sense knoweth not but sensible matters and that which may be felt, so the appetite or coveting only desireth the same; and even as the understanding is bent but to behold things that may be understood, so is that will only fed with spiritual goods. Man of nature endowed with reason, placed, as it were, in the middle between these two extremities, may, through his choice inclining to sense or reaching to understanding, come nigh to the coveting sometime of the one, sometime of the other part. In these sorts therefore may beauty be coveted; the general name whereof may be applied to all things, either natural or artificial, that are framed in good proportion and due temper,[6] as their nature beareth. But speaking of the beauty that we mean, which is only it that appeareth in bodies, and especially in the face of man, and moveth this fervent coveting which we call love, we will term it an influence of the heavenly bountifulness, the which for all it stretcheth over all things that be created (like the light of the sun), yet when it findeth out a face well proportioned, and framed with a certain lively agreement of several colors, and set forth with lights and shadows, and with an orderly distance and limits of lines, thereinto it distilleth itself and appeareth most well favored, and decketh out and lighteneth the subject where it shineth with a marvelous grace and

8. Pietro Bembo (1470–1547), poet, Platonist, grammarian, and historian, later a cardinal. He undertakes to prove that it is suitable for an older courtier to be (in a special sense) a lover.
9. Sometimes.
1. Morello da Ortona, a courtier and musician. "In case": even if.
2. The definition derives from Plato's *Symposium*.
3. Power.
4. Direct intellectual apprehension, without need of reasoning. "Manner": kinds of.
5. Distinctive.
6. The right mixture or combination of elements. Bembo's definition of beauty, as of love, derives from Plato.

glistering,[7] like the sunbeams that strike against beautiful plate of fine gold wrought and set with precious jewels, so that it draweth unto it men's eyes with pleasure, and piercing through them imprinteth himself in the soul, and with an unwonted sweetness all to-stirreth[8] her and delighteth, and setting her on fire maketh her to covet him.

* * *

"Do you believe, M. Morello," quoth then Count Lewis,[9] that beauty is always so good a thing as M. Peter Bembo speaketh of?"

"Not I, in good sooth," answered M. Morello. "But I remember rather that I have seen many beautiful women of a most ill inclination, cruel and spiteful, and it seemeth that, in a manner, it happeneth always so, for beauty maketh them proud, and pride, cruel."

Count Lewis said, smiling: "To you perhaps they seem cruel, because they content you not with it that you would have. But cause M. Peter Bembo to teach you in what sort old men ought to covet beauty, and what to seek at their ladies' hands, and what to content themselves withal; and in not passing out of these bounds ye shall see that they shall be neither proud nor cruel, and will satisfy you with what you shall require."

M. Morello seemed then somewhat out of patience, and said: "I will not know the thing that toucheth[1] me not. But cause you to be taught how the young men ought to covet this beauty that are not so fresh and lusty as old men be."

Here Sir Frederick,[2] to pacify M. Morello and to break their talk, would not suffer Count Lewis to make answer, but interrupting him said: "Perhaps M. Morello is not altogether out of the way in saying that beauty is not always good, for the beauty of women is many times cause of infinite evils in the world—hatred, war, mortality, and destruction, whereof the razing of Troy[3] can be a good witness; and beautiful women for the most part be either proud and cruel, as is said, or unchaste; but M. Morello would find no fault with that. There be also many wicked men that have the comeliness of a beautiful countenance, and it seemeth that nature hath so shaped them because they may be the readier to deceive, and that this amiable look were like a bait that covereth the hook."

Then M. Peter Bembo: "Believe not," quoth he, "but[4] beauty is always good."

Here Count Lewis, because he would return again to his former purpose, interrupted him and said: "Since M. Morello passeth[5] not to understand that which is so necessary for him, teach it me, and show me how old men may come by this happiness of love, for I will not care to be counted old, so it may profit me."

M. Peter Bembo laughed, and said: "First will I take the error out of these gentlemen's mind, and afterward will I satisfy you also." So beginning

---

7. Glittering, sparkling.
8. Moves violently. In this passage, "it" and "him" refer to beauty, "her" to the soul.
9. Lodovico Canossa, who had earlier discoursed on grace.
1. Concerns.
2. Federico Fregoso, later archbishop of Salerno.

3. The destruction of Troy by the Greeks, celebrated in Homer's *Iliad*, was caused by the Trojan Paris's abduction of Helen, the most beautiful woman in the world.
4. I.e., anything but that.
5. Cares.

afresh: "My Lords," quoth he, "I would not that with speaking ill of beauty, which is a holy thing, any of us as profane and wicked should purchase him the wrath of God. Therefore, to give M. Morello and Sir Frederick warning, that they lose not their sight, as Stesichorus did—a pain most meet[6] for whoso dispraiseth beauty—I say that beauty cometh of God and is like a circle, the goodness whereof is the center. And therefore, as there can be no circle without a center, no more can beauty be without goodness. Whereupon doth very seldom an ill[7] soul dwell in a beautiful body. And therefore is the outward beauty a true sign of the inward goodness, and in bodies this comeliness is imprinted, more and less, as it were, for a mark of the soul, whereby she is outwardly known; as in trees, in which the beauty of the buds giveth a testimony of the goodness of the fruit. And the very same happeneth in bodies, as it is seen that palmisters by the visage know many times the conditions and otherwhile the thoughts of men. And, which is more, in beasts also a man may discern by the face the quality of the courage,[8] which in the body declareth itself as much as it can. Judge you how plainly in the face of a lion, a horse, and an eagle, a man shall discern anger, fierceness, and stoutness; in lambs and doves, simpleness and very innocency; the crafty subtlety in foxes and wolves; and the like, in a manner, in all other living creatures. The foul,[9] therefore, for the most part be also evil, and the beautiful good. Therefore it may be said that beauty is a face pleasant, merry, comely, and to be desired for goodness; and foulness a face dark, uglesome,[1] unpleasant, and to be shunned for ill. And in case you will consider all things, you shall find that whatsoever is good and profitable hath also evermore the comeliness of beauty. Behold the state of this great engine of the world,[2] which God created for the health and preservation of everything that was made: the heaven round beset with so many heavenly lights; and in the middle the earth environed with the elements and upheld with the very weight of itself; the sun, that compassing about giveth light to the whole, and in winter season draweth to the lowermost sign,[3] afterward by little and little climbeth again to the other part; the moon, that of him taketh her light, according as she draweth nigh or goeth farther from him; and the other five stars[4] that diversely keep the very same course. These things among themselves have such force by the knitting together of an order so necessarily framed that, with altering them any one jot, they should all be loosed and the world would decay. They have also such beauty and comeliness that all the wits men have cannot imagine a more beautiful matter.

"Think now of the shape of man, which may be called a little world, in whom every parcel of his body is seen to be necessarily framed by art and not by hap,[5] and then the form altogether most beautiful, so that it were a hard matter to judge whether the members (as the eyes, the nose, the mouth, the ears, the arms, the breast, and in like manner the other parts) give either more profit to the countenance and the rest of the body, or comeliness. The

---

6. Fitting. Stesichorus: "a notable poet which lost his sight for writing against Helena, and recanting, had his sight restored him again" [Hoby's note].
7. Evil.
8. Heart. "Palmisters": fortune-tellers.
9. Ugly.

1. Horribly ugly (apparently first used by Hoby).
2. Mechanism of the universe.
3. Of the zodiac. "Compassing about": revolving.
4. I.e., the five other planets then known: Mercury, Venus, Mars, Jupiter, and Saturn.
5. By skill rather than by chance.

like may be said of all other living creatures. Behold the feathers of fowls, the leaves and boughs of trees, which be given them of nature to keep them in their being, and yet have they withal a very great sightliness. Leave nature, and come to art. What thing is so necessary in sailing vessels as the forepart, the sides, the main yards, the mast, the sails, the stern, oars, anchors, and tacklings? All these things notwithstanding are so well-favored in the eye that unto whoso beholdeth them they seem to have been found out as well for pleasure as for profit. Pillars and great beams uphold high buildings and palaces, and yet are they no less pleasureful unto the eyes of the beholders than profitable to the buildings. When men began first to build, in the middle of temples and houses they reared the ridge of the roof, not to make the works to have a better show, but because the water might the more commodiously avoid[6] on both sides; yet unto profit there was forthwith adjoined a fair sightliness, so that if, under the sky where there falleth neither hail nor rain, a man should build a temple without a reared ridge, it is to be thought that it could have neither a sightly show nor any beauty. Besides other things, therefore, it giveth a great praise to the world in saying that it is beautiful. It is praised in saying the beautiful heaven, beautiful earth, beautiful sea, beautiful rivers, beautiful woods, trees, gardens, beautiful cities, beautiful churches, houses, armies. In conclusion, this comely and holy beauty is a wondrous setting out of everything. And it may be said that good and beautiful be after a sort one self[7] thing, especially in the bodies of men; of the beauty whereof the nighest cause, I suppose, is the beauty of the soul; the which, as a partner of the right and heavenly beauty, maketh sightly and beautiful whatever she toucheth, and most of all if the body where she dwelleth be not of so vile a matter that she cannot imprint in it her property. Therefore beauty is the true monument and spoil[8] of the victory of the soul, when she with heavenly influence beareth rule over material and gross nature, and with her light overcometh the darkness of the body. It is not, then, to be spoken that beauty maketh women proud or cruel, although it seem so to M. Morello. Neither yet ought beautiful women to bear the blame of that hatred, mortality, and destruction which the unbridled appetites of men are the cause of. I will not now deny but it is possible also to find in the world beautiful women unchaste; yet not because beauty inclineth them to unchaste living, for it rather plucketh them from it, and leadeth them into the way of virtuous conditions, through the affinity that beauty hath with goodness; but otherwhile ill bringing-up, the continual provocations of lovers' tokens,[9] poverty, hope, deceits, fear, and a thousand other matters overcome the steadfastness, yea, of beautiful and good women; and for these and like causes may also beautiful men become wicked."

Then said the Lord Cesar:[1] "In case the Lord Gaspar's saying be true of yesternight, there is no doubt but the fair women be more chaste than the foul."

"And what was my saying?" quoth the Lord Gaspar.

The Lord Cesar answered: "If I do well bear in mind, your saying was that the women that are sued to always refuse to satisfy him that sueth to them,

---

6. Escape.
7. Same.
8. Reward, trophy. "Property": attribute, quality.

9. Gifts. "Otherwhile": sometimes.
1. Cesar Gonzaga, cousin of Castiglione.

but those that are not sued to, sue to others. There is no doubt but the beautiful women have always more suitors, and be more instantly laid at[2] in love, than the foul. Therefore the beautiful always deny, and consequently be more chaste than the foul, which, not being sued to, sue unto others."

M. Peter Bembo laughed, and said: "This argument cannot be answered to."

Afterward he proceeded: "It chanceth also, oftentimes, that as the other senses, so the sight is deceived and judgeth a face beautiful which indeed is not beautiful. And because in the eyes and in the whole countenance of some woman a man beholdeth otherwhile a certain lavish wantonness painted, with dishonest flickerings,[3] many, whom that manner delighteth because it promiseth them an easiness to come by the thing that they covet, call it beauty; but indeed it is a cloaked un-shamefastness,[4] unworthy of so honorable and holy a name."

M. Peter Bembo held his peace, but those lords still were earnest upon him to speak somewhat more of this love and of the way to enjoy beauty aright, and at the last, "Methink," quoth he, "I have showed plainly enough that old men may love more happily than young, which was my drift;[5] therefore it belongeth not to me to enter any farther."

Count Lewis answered: "You have better declared the unluckiness of young men than the happiness of old men, whom you have not as yet taught what way they must follow in this love of theirs; only you have said that they must suffer themselves to be guided by reason, and the opinion of many is that it is unpossible for love to stand with reason."

Bembo notwithstanding sought to make an end of reasoning, but the duchess[6] desired him to say on, and he began thus afresh: "Too unlucky were the nature of man, if our soul, in which this so fervent coveting may lightly[7] arise, should be driven to nourish it with that only which is common to her with beasts, and could not turn it to the other noble part,[8] which is proper to her. Therefore, since it is so your pleasure, I will not refuse to reason upon this noble matter. And because I know myself unworthy to talk of the most holy mysteries of Love, I beseech him to lead my thought and my tongue so that I may show this excellent Courtier how to love contrary to the wonted[9] manner of the common ignorant sort; and even as from my childhood I have dedicated all my whole life unto him, so also now that my words may be answerable to the same intent, and to the praise of him. I say, therefore, that since the nature of man in youthful age is so much inclined to sense, it may be granted the Courtier, while he is young, to love sensually; but in case afterward also, in his riper years, he chance to be set on fire with this coveting of love, he ought to be good and circumspect, and heedful that he beguile not himself to be led willfully into the wretchedness that in young men deserveth more to be pitied than blamed, and contrariwise in old men more to be blamed than pitied. Therefore when an amiable counte-

2. Persistently urged.
3. Hints of lewdness.
4. Immodesty.
5. Purpose. In a passage omitted above, Bembo had argued that old men, whose senses have cooled, find it easier than young men to be guided in love by reason and can therefore more easily avoid the miseries that, he argues, inevitably follow from sensual love.
6. Elisabetta Gonzaga, duchess of Urbino, the presiding figure in the life of the court and in these dialogues.
7. Easily, readily.
8. I.e., reason.
9. Accustomed.

nance of a beautiful woman cometh in his sight, that is accompanied with noble conditions and honest[1] behaviors, so that, as one practiced in love, he wotteth well that his hue[2] hath an agreement with hers, as soon as he is aware that his eyes snatch that image and carry it to the heart, and that the soul beginneth to behold it with pleasure, and feeleth within herself the influence that stirreth her and by little and little setteth her in heat, and that those lively spirits[3] that twinkle out through the eyes put continually fresh nourishment to the fire, he ought in this beginning to seek a speedy remedy and to raise up reason, and with her to fence the fortress of his heart, and to shut in such wise the passages against sense and appetites that they may enter neither with force nor subtle practice.[4] Thus, if the flame be quenched, the jeopardy is also quenched. But in case it continue or increase, then must the Courtier determine, when he perceiveth he is taken, to shun throughly[5] all filthiness of common love, and so enter into the holy way of love with the guide of reason, and first consider that the body where that beauty shineth is not the fountain from whence beauty springeth, but rather because beauty is bodiless and, as we have said, an heavenly shining beam, she loseth much of her honor when she is coupled with that vile subject[6] and full of corruption: because the less she is partner thereof, the more perfect she is, and, clean sundered from it, is most perfect. And as a man heareth not with his mouth, nor smelleth with his ears, no more can he also in any manner wise enjoy beauty, nor satisfy the desire that she stirreth up in our minds, with feeling, but with the sense unto whom beauty is the very butt to level at,[7] namely, the virtue[8] of seeing. Let him lay aside, therefore, the blind judgment of the sense, and enjoy with his eyes the brightness, the comeliness, the loving sparkles, laughters, gestures, and all the other pleasant furnitures of beauty, especially with hearing the sweetness of her voice, the tunableness[9] of her words, the melody of her singing and playing on instruments (in case the woman beloved be a musician); and so shall he with most dainty food feed the soul through the means of these two senses which have little bodily substance in them and be the ministers of reason, without entering farther toward the body with coveting unto any longing otherwise than honest. Afterward, let him obey, please, and honor with all reverence his woman, and reckon her more dear to him than his own life, and prefer all her commodities[1] and pleasures before his own, and love no less in her the beauty of the mind than of the body. Therefore let him have a care not to suffer her to run into any error, but with lessons and good exhortations seek always to frame her to modesty, to temperance, to true honesty, and so to work that there may never take place in her other than pure thoughts and far wide from all filthiness of vices. And thus in sowing of virtue in the garden of that mind, he shall also gather the fruits of most beautiful conditions, and savor them with a marvelous good relish. And this shall be the right engendering and imprinting of beauty in beauty, the which some hold opinion to be the end[2] of love. In this manner shall our Courtier

1. Virtuous (as also several times in the following pages). "Conditions": personal qualities.
2. Aspect. "Wotteth": knows.
3. Vital, animating powers. Cf. p. 714, n. 4.
4. Treachery. "In such wise": in such a way.
5. Thoroughly.

6. I.e., the body.
7. Target to aim at.
8. Power.
9. Musical quality. "Furnitures": ornaments.
1. Conveniences.
2. Goal.

be most acceptable to his lady, and she will always show herself toward him tractable, lowly,[3] and sweet in language, and as willing to please him as to be beloved of him; and the wills of them both shall be most honest and agreeable, and they consequently shall be most happy."

Here M. Morello: "The engendering," quoth he, "of beauty in beauty aright were the engendering of a beautiful child in a beautiful woman; and I would think it a more manifest token a great deal that she loved her lover, if she pleased him with this than with the sweetness of language that you speak of."

M. Peter Bembo laughed, and said: "You must not, M. Morello, pass your bounds. I may tell you it is not a small token that a woman loveth when she giveth unto her lover her beauty, which is so precious a matter; and by the ways that be a passage to the soul (that is to say, the sight and the hearing) sendeth the looks of her eyes, the image of her countenance, and the voice of her words, that pierce into the lover's heart and give a witness of her love."

M. Morello said: "Looks and words may be, and oftentimes are, false witnesses. Therefore whoso hath not a better pledge of love, in my judgment he is in an ill assurance. And surely I looked[4] still that you would have made this woman of yours somewhat more courteous and free toward the Courtier than my Lord Julian hath made his; but meseemeth ye be both of the property[5] of those judges that, to appear wise, give sentence against their own."

Bembo said: "I am well pleased to have this woman much more courteous toward my Courtier not young than the Lord Julian's is to the young; and that with good reason, because mine coveteth but honest matters, and therefore may the woman grant him them all without blame. But my Lord Julian's woman, that is not so assured of the modesty of the young man, ought to grant him the honest matters only, and deny him the dishonest. Therefore more happy is mine, that hath granted him whatsoever he requireth, than the other, that hath part granted and part denied. And because[6] you may moreover the better understand that reasonable love is more happy than sensual, I say unto you that selfsame things in sensual ought to be denied otherwhile, and in reasonable granted; because in the one they be honest, and in the other dishonest. Therefore the woman, to please her good lover, besides the granting him merry countenances, familiar and secret talk, jesting, dallying, hand-in-hand, may also lawfully and without blame come to kissing, which in sensual love, according to the Lord Julian's rules, is not lawful. For since a kiss is a knitting together both of body and soul, it is to be feared lest the sensual lover will be more inclined to the part of the body than of the soul; but the reasonable lover wotteth well that although the mouth be a parcel[7] of the body, yet is it an issue for the words that be the interpreters of the soul, and for the inward breath, which is also called the soul; and therefore hath a delight to join his mouth with the woman's beloved with a kiss, not to stir him to any unhonest desire, but because he feeleth that that bond is the opening of an entry to the souls, which, drawn with a coveting the one of the other, pour themselves by turn the one into the other's body,

---

3. Modest.
4. Expected.
5. Nature. "Lord Julian": Giuliano de' Medici, younger son of Lorenzo the Magnificent. In Book 3, discussing the ideal courtier's female

counterpart, he expresses the opinions alluded to here.
6. So that.
7. Part.

and be so mingled together that each of them hath two souls, and one alone, so framed of them both, ruleth, in a manner, two bodies. Whereupon a kiss may be said to be rather a coupling together of the soul than of the body, because it hath such force in her that it draweth her unto it, and, as it were, separateth her from the body. For this do all chaste lovers covet a kiss as a coupling of souls together. And therefore Plato,[8] the divine lover, saith that in kissing his soul came as far as his lips to depart out of the body. And because the separating of the soul from the matters of the sense, and the thorough coupling of her with matters of understanding, may be betokened by a kiss, Solomon saith[9] in his heavenly book of ballads, 'Oh that he would kiss me with a kiss of his mouth,' to express the desire he had that his soul might be ravished through heavenly love to the beholding of heavenly beauty in such manner that, coupling herself inwardly with it, she might forsake the body."

They stood all hearkening heedfully to Bembo's reasoning, and after he had stayed[1] a while and saw that none spake, he said: "Since you have made me to begin to show our not-young Courtier this happy love, I will lead him yet somewhat farther forwards; because to stand still at this stay were somewhat perilous for him, considering, as we have oftentimes said, the soul is most inclined to the senses, and for all[2] reason with discourse chooseth well, and knoweth that beauty not to spring of the body, and therefore setteth a bridle to the unhonest desires, yet to behold it always in that body doth oftentimes corrupt the right judgment. And where no other inconvenience ensueth upon it, one's absence from the wight[3] beloved carrieth a great passion with it; because the influence of that beauty when it is present giveth a wondrous delight to the lover and, setting his heart on fire, quickeneth and melteth certain virtues in a trance and congealed in the soul, the which, nourished with the heat of love, flow about and go bubbling nigh the heart, and thrust out through the eyes those spirits which be most fine vapors made of the purest and clearest part of the blood, which receive the image of beauty[4] and deck it with a thousand sundry furnitures. Whereupon the soul taketh a delight, and with a certain wonder is aghast, and yet enjoyeth she it, and, as it were, astonied[5] together with the pleasure, feeleth the fear and reverence that men accustomably have toward holy matters, and thinketh herself to be in paradise. The lover, therefore, that considereth only the beauty in the body loseth this treasure and happiness as soon as the woman beloved with her departure leaveth the eyes without their brightness, and consequently the soul as a widow without her joy. For since beauty is far off, that influence of love setteth not the heart on fire, as it did in presence. Whereupon the pores be dried up and withered, and yet doth the remembrance of beauty somewhat stir those virtues of the soul in such wise that they seek to scatter abroad the spirits, and they, finding the ways closed up, have no issue, and still they seek to get out, and so with those shootings enclosed prick the soul and torment her bitterly, as young children when in

---

8. Plato's discussion of love in *The Symposium*.
9. Song of Solomon 1.2. "Betokened": symbolized.
1. Paused.
2. "For all": although.
3. Person.

4. Love "melts" certain elements ("virtues") that were before "congealed," releasing the vital blood "spirits" that take in the image of beauty through the eyes.
5. Stunned.

their tender gums they begin to breed teeth. And hence come the tears, sighs, vexations, and torments of lovers; because the soul is always in affliction and travail and, in a manner, waxeth wood,[6] until the beloved beauty cometh before her once again, and then she is immediately pacified and taketh breath, and, throughly bent to it, is nourished with most dainty food, and by her will would never depart from so sweet a sight. To avoid, therefore, the torment of this absence, and to enjoy beauty without passion, the Courtier by the help of reason must full and wholly call back again the coveting of the body to beauty alone, and, in what he can, behold it in itself simple and pure, and frame it within his imagination sundered from all matter, and so make it friendly and loving to his soul, and there enjoy it, and have it with him day and night, in every time and place, without mistrust ever to lose it; keeping always fast in mind that the body is a most diverse[7] thing from beauty, and not only not increaseth but diminisheth the perfection of it. In this wise shall our not-young Courtier be out of all bitterness and wretchedness that young men feel, in a manner continually, as jealousies, suspicions, disdains, angers, desperations, and certain rages full of madness, whereby many times they be led into so great error that some do not only beat the women whom they love, but rid themselves out of their life. He shall do no wrong to the husband, father, brethren, or kinsfolk of the woman beloved. He shall not bring her in slander. He shall not be in case with[8] much ado otherwhile to refrain his eyes and tongue from discovering his desires to others. He shall not take thought[9] at departure or in absence, because he shall evermore carry his precious treasure about with him shut fast within his heart. And besides, through the virtue of imagination, he shall fashion within himself that beauty much more fair than it is indeed. But among these commodities the lover shall find another yet far greater, in case he will take this love for a stair, as it were, to climb up to another far higher than it. The which he shall bring to pass, if he will go and consider with himself what a strait bond it is to be always in the trouble to behold the beauty of one body alone. And therefore, to come out of this so narrow a room, he shall gather in his thought by little and little so many ornaments that, meddling[1] all beauties together, he shall make a universal concept, and bring the multitude of them to the unity of one alone, that is generally spread over all the nature of man. And thus shall he behold no more the particular beauty of one woman, but an universal, that decketh out all bodies. Whereupon, being made dim with this greater light, he shall not pass upon[2] the lesser, and, burning in a more excellent flame, he shall little esteem it that[3] he set great store by at the first. This stair of love, though it be very noble and such as few arrive at it, yet is it not in this sort to be called perfect, forsomuch as where the imagination is of force to make conveyance, and hath no knowledge but through those beginnings that the senses help her withal, she is not clean purged from gross darkness; and therefore, though she do consider that universal beauty in sunder and in itself alone, yet doth she not well and clearly discern it, nor without some doubtfulness, by reason of the

6. Mad, crazy.
7. Very different.
8. In the situation of having.
9. Be distressed.

1. Mingling. "Room": space.
2. Concern himself with.
3. I.e., the thing that.

agreement that the fancies have with the body. Wherefore such as come to this love are like young birds almost flush,[4] which for all they flutter a little their tender wings, yet dare they not stray far from the nest, nor commit themselves to the wind and open weather. When our Courtier, therefore, shall be come to this point, although he may be called a good and happy lover, in respect of them that be drowned in the misery of sensual love, yet will I not have him to set his heart at rest, but boldly proceed farther, following the highway, after his guide[5] that leadeth him to the point of true happiness. And thus, instead of going out of his wit[6] with thought, as he must do that will consider the bodily beauty, he may come into his wit to behold the beauty that is seen with the eyes of the mind, which then begin to be sharp and through-seeing when the eyes of the body lose the flower of their sightliness.

"Therefore the soul, rid of vices, purged with the studies of true philosophy, occupied in spiritual, and exercised in matters of understanding, turning her to the beholding of her own substance, as it were raised out of a most deep sleep, openeth the eyes that all men have and few occupy,[7] and seeth in herself a shining beam of that light which is the true image of the angel-like beauty partened[8] with her, whereof she also partneth with the body a feeble shadow; therefore, waxed blind about earthly matters, is made most quick of sight about heavenly. And otherwhile, when the stirring virtues of the body are withdrawn alone through earnest beholding, either[9] fast bound through sleep, when she is not hindered by them, she feeleth a certain privy[1] smell of the right angel-like beauty, and, ravished with the shining of that light, beginneth to be inflamed, and so greedily followeth after, that in a manner she waxeth drunken and beside herself, for coveting to couple herself with it, having found, to her weening,[2] the footsteps of God, in the beholding of whom, as in her happy end, she seeketh to settle herself. And therefore, burning in this most happy flame, she ariseth to the noblest part of her, which is the understanding, and there, no more shadowed with the dark night of earthly matters, seeth the heavenly beauty; but yet doth she not for all that enjoy it altogether perfectly, because she beholdeth it only in her particular understanding, which cannot conceive the passing[3] great universal beauty; whereupon, not throughly satisfied with this benefit, love giveth unto the soul a greater happiness. For like as through the particular beauty of one body he guideth her to the universal beauty of all bodies, even so in the last degree of perfection through particular understanding he guideth her to the universal understanding. Thus the soul kindled in the most holy fire of heavenly love fleeth to couple herself with the nature of angels, and not only clean forsaketh sense, but hath no more need of the discourse of reason, for, being changed into an angel, she understandeth all things that may be understood; and without any veil or cloud she seeth the main sea of the pure heavenly beauty, and receiveth it into her, and enjoyeth that sovereign happiness that cannot be comprehended of the senses. Since, therefore, the beauties which we daily see with these our dim eyes in bodies

4. Fledged, fit to fly.
5. I.e., reason.
6. Mind, intellect.
7. Use.
8. Shared.

9. Or. "Otherwhile": sometimes.
1. Intimate.
2. Thinking, opinion.
3. Surpassing. "Particular": individual.

subject to corruption, that nevertheless be nothing else but dreams and most thin shadows of beauty, seem unto us so well favored and comely that oftentimes they kindle in us a most burning fire, and with such delight that we reckon no happiness may be compared to it that we feel otherwhile through the only look[4] which the beloved countenance of a woman casteth at us; what happy wonder, what blessed abashment, may we reckon that to be that taketh the souls which come to have a sight of the heavenly beauty? What sweet flame, what sweet incense, may a man believe that to be which ariseth of the fountain of the sovereign and right beauty? Which is the origin of all other beauty, which never increaseth nor diminisheth, always beautiful, and of itself, as well on the one part as on the other, most simple, only like itself, and partner of none other, but in such wise beautiful that all other beautiful things be beautiful because they be partners of the beauty of it.

"This is the beauty unseparable from the high bounty which with her voice calleth and draweth to her all things; and not only to the endowed with understanding giveth understanding, to the reasonable reason, to the sensual sense and appetite to live, but also partaketh with plants and stones, as a print of herself, stirring, and the natural provocation of their properties.[5] So much, therefore, is this love greater and happier than others, as the cause that stirreth it is more excellent. And therefore, as common fire trieth gold and maketh it fine, so this most holy fire in souls destroyeth and consumeth whatsoever is mortal in them, and relieveth and maketh beautiful the heavenly part, which at the first by reason of the sense was dead and buried in them. This is the great fire in the which, the poets write, that Hercules was burned on the top of the mountain Oeta,[6] and, through that consuming with fire, after his death was holy and immortal. This is the fiery bush of Moses;[7] the divided tongues of fire;[8] the inflamed chariot of Elias;[9] which doubleth grace and happiness in their souls that be worthy to see it, when they forsake this earthly baseness and flee up into heaven. Let us, therefore, bend all our force and thoughts of soul to this most holy light, which showeth us the way which leadeth to heaven; and after it, putting off the affections we were clad withal at our coming down, let us climb up the stairs which at the lowermost step have the shadow of sensual beauty, to the high mansion place where the heavenly, amiable, and right beauty dwelleth, which lieth hid in the innermost secrets of God, lest unhallowed eyes should come to the sight of it; and there shall we find a most happy end for our desires, true rest for our travails, certain remedy for miseries, a most healthful medicine for sickness, a most sure haven in the troublesome storms of the tempestuous sea of this life.

"What tongue mortal is there then, Oh most holy Love, that can sufficiently praise thy worthiness? Thou most beautiful, most good, most wise,

---

4. Through the look alone.

5. I.e., motion ("stirring") and, as we would say, their natural instincts.

6. "A mountain between Thessalia and Macedonia where is the sepulcher of Hercules" [Hoby's note].

7. "And the angel of the Lord appeared unto ... [Moses] in a flame of fire out of the midst of a bush; and he looked, and, behold, the bush burned with fire, and the bush was not consumed" (Exodus 3.2).

8. "And there appeared unto ... [the Apostles] cloven tongues like as to fire, and it sat upon each of them. And they were all filled with the Holy Ghost, and began to speak with other tongues, as the Spirit gave them utterance" (Acts 2.3–4).

9. The prophet Elijah. "And it came to pass, as they still went on, and talked, that, behold, there appeared a chariot of fire, and horses of fire, and parted them both asunder: and Elijah went up by a whirlwind into heaven" (2 Kings 2.11).

art derived of the unity of heavenly beauty, goodness, and wisdom, and therein dost thou abide, and unto it through it, as in a circle, turnest about. Thou the most sweet bond of the world, a mean betwixt heavenly and earthly things, with a bountiful temper bendest the high virtues[1] to the government of the lower, and turning back the minds of mortal men to their beginning, couplest them with it. Thou with agreement bringest the elements in one, and stirrest nature to bring forth that which ariseth and is born for the succession of the life.[2] Thou bringest severed matters into one, to the unperfect givest perfection, to the unlike likeness, to enmity amity, to the earth fruits, to the sea calmness, to the heaven lively light. Thou art the father of true pleasures, of grace, peace, lowliness, and goodwill, enemy to rude wildness and sluggishness—to be short, the beginning and end of all goodness. And forsomuch as thou delightest to dwell in the flower of beautiful bodies and beautiful souls, I suppose that thy abiding-place is now here among us, and from above otherwhile showest thyself a little to the eyes and minds of them that be worthy to see thee. Therefore vouchsafe, Lord, to hearken to our prayers, pour thyself into our hearts, and with the brightness of thy most holy fire lighten our darkness, and, like a trusty guide in this blind maze, show us the right way; reform the falsehood of the senses, and after long wandering in vanity give us the right and sound joy. Make us to smell those spiritual savors that relieve the virtues of the understanding, and to hear the heavenly harmony so tunable that no discord of passion take place any more in us. Make us drunken with the bottomless fountain of contentation that always doth delight and never giveth fill, and that giveth a smack[3] of the right bliss unto whoso drinketh of the running and clear water thereof. Purge with the shining beams of thy light our eyes from misty ignorance, that they may no more set by[4] mortal beauty, and well perceive that the things which at the first they thought themselves to see be not indeed, and those that they saw not, to be in effect. Accept our souls that be offered unto thee for a sacrifice. Burn them in the lively flame that wasteth[5] all gross filthiness, that after they be clean sundered from the body they may be coupled with an everlasting and most sweet bond to the heavenly beauty. And we, severed from ourselves, may be changed like right lovers into the beloved, and, after we be drawn from the earth, admitted to the feast of the angels, where, fed with immortal ambrosia and nectar,[6] in the end we may die a most happy and lively death, as in times past died the fathers of old time, whose souls with most fervent zeal of beholding, thou didst hale from the body and coupledst them with God."

When Bembo had hitherto spoken with such vehemency that a man would have thought him, as it were, ravished and beside himself, he stood still without once moving, holding his eyes toward heaven as astonied; when the Lady Emilia,[7] which together with the rest gave most diligent ear to this talk, took him by the plait of his garment and plucking him a little, said: "Take heed, M. Peter, that these thoughts make not your soul also to forsake the body."

---

1. Powers.
2. I.e., for the perpetuation of life.
3. Taste.
4. Set store by.
5. Consumes.

6. The food and drink of the gods in classical mythology.
7. Emilia Pia, a widow living at court, the faithful companion of the duchess Elisabetta and the mistress of ceremonies of the discussions.

"Madam," answered M. Peter, "it should not be the first miracle that love hath wrought in me."

Then the Duchess and all the rest began afresh to be instant[8] upon M. Bembo that he would proceed once more in his talk, and everyone thought he felt in his mind, as it were, a certain sparkle of that godly love that pricked him, and they all coveted to hear farther; but M. Bembo: "My Lords," quoth he, "I have spoken what the holy fury of love hath, unsought for, indited[9] to me; now that, it seemeth, he inspireth me no more, I wot not what to say. And I think verily that Love will not have his secrets discovered any farther, nor that the Courtier should pass the degree that his pleasure is I should show him, and therefore it is not perhaps lawful to speak any more in this matter."

"Surely," quoth the Duchess, "if the not-young Courtier be such a one that he can follow this way which you have showed him, of right he ought to be satisfied with so great a happiness, and not to envy the younger."

Then the Lord Cesar Gonzaga: "The way," quoth he, "that leadeth to this happiness is so steep, in my mind, that I believe it will be much ado to get to it."

The Lord Gaspar said: "I believe it be hard to get up for men, but unpossible for women."

The Lady Emilia laughed, and said: "If you fall so often to offend us, I promise you you shall be no more forgiven."

The Lord Gaspar answered: "It is no offense to you in saying that women's souls be not so purged from passions as men's be, nor accustomed in beholdings,[1] as M. Peter hath said is necessary for them to be that will taste of the heavenly love. Therefore it is not read that ever woman hath had this grace; but many men have had it, as Plato, Socrates, Plotinus,[2] and many other, and a number of our holy fathers, as Saint Francis, in whom a fervent spirit of love imprinted the most holy seal of the five wounds.[3] And nothing but the virtue[4] of love could hale up Saint Paul the Apostle to the sight of those secrets which is not lawful for man to speak of; nor show Saint Stephen the heavens open."[5]

Here answered the Lord Julian: "In this point men shall nothing pass women, for Socrates himself doth confess that all the mysteries of love which he knew were oped unto him by a woman, which was Diotima.[6] And the angel that with the fire of love imprinted the five wounds in Saint Francis hath also made some women worthy of the same print in our age. You must remember, moreover, that Saint Mary Magdalen[7] had many faults forgiven her, because she loved much; and perhaps with no less grace than Saint Paul she many times through angelic love haled up to the third heaven. And

8. Insistent.
9. Dictated. "Fury": frenzy; enthusiasm of one possessed as by a god.
1. Contemplations.
2. Plotinus (205–270 C.E.) was the founder of the Neoplatonic philosophical school of late antiquity—the tradition revived by Bembo and, especially, his predecessor the great Florentine philosopher Marsilio Ficino (1433–1499).
3. St. Francis of Assisi (1182–1226) is supposed to have received the stigmata, marking on his body the five wounds of Jesus on the Cross.
4. Power.

5. Before being stoned to death, St. Stephen, the first Christian martyr, said, "Behold, I see the heavens opened, and the Son of man standing on the right hand of God" (Acts 7.56). St. Paul's vision of the "third heaven" is in 2 Corinthians 12.2–4.
6. In Plato's *Symposium,* Socrates claims that a wise woman, Diotima, taught him his philosophy of love. "Oped": opened, disclosed.
7. Magdalen, traditionally though baselessly regarded as a converted prostitute, became one of Jesus' most faithful followers.

many other, as I showed you yesterday more at large, that for love of the name of Christ have not passed upon[8] life, nor feared torments, nor any other kind of death how terrible and cruel ever it were. And they were not, as M. Peter will have his Courtier to be, aged, but soft and tender maidens, and in the age when he saith that sensual love ought to be borne withal[9] in men."

The Lord Gaspar began to prepare himself to speak, but the Duchess: "Of this," quoth she, "let M. Peter be judge, and the matter shall stand to his verdict, whether women be not as meet for heavenly love as men. But because the plead[1] between you may happen be too long, it shall not be amiss to defer it until tomorrow."

"Nay, tonight," quoth the Lord Cesar Gonzaga.

"And how can it be tonight?" quoth the Duchess.

The Lord Cesar answered: "Because it is day already," and showed her the light that began to enter in at the clefts of the windows. Then every man arose upon his feet with much wonder, because they had not thought that the reasonings had lasted longer than the accustomed wont, saving only that they were begun much later, and with their pleasantness had deceived so the lords' minds that they wist[2] not of the going away of the hours. And not one of them felt any heaviness of sleep in his eyes, the which often happeneth when a man is up after his accustomed hour to go to bed. When the windows then were opened on the side of the palace that hath his prospect toward the high top of Mount Catri, they saw already risen in the east a fair morning like unto the color of roses, and all stars voided,[3] saving only the sweet governess of the heaven, Venus, which keepeth the bounds of the night and the day, from which appeared to blow a sweet blast that, filling the air with a biting cold, began to quicken the tunable notes of the pretty birds among the hushing woods of the hills at hand. Whereupon they all, taking their leave with reverence of the Duchess, departed toward their lodgings without torch, the light of the day sufficing.

And as they were now passing out at the great chamber door, the Lord General[4] turned him to the Duchess and said: "Madam, to take up the variance between the Lord Gaspar and the Lord Julian, we will assemble this night with the judge sooner than we did yesterday."

The Lady Emilia answered: "Upon condition that in case my Lord Gaspar will accuse women, and give them, as his wont is, some false report, he will also put us in surety to stand to trial:[5] for I reckon him a wavering starter."[6]

1561

---

8. Cared for.
9. Put up with.
1. Controversy. "Meet": fitted.
2. Knew.
3. Vanished.
4. Francesco Maria della Rovere, nephew and adopted heir of the duke.
5. I.e., he must give us some pawn ("surety") to guarantee that he will answer the charge of falsely accusing women. "Wont": habit.
6. I.e., one who is likely to "start"—suddenly desert his post.

Women in Power

Tudor England was a patriarchal and in many respects intensely misogynistic society, one that took for granted the subordination of women in public, private, economic, and spiritual life. The relatively few dissenting voices were vastly outnumbered by those of writers who cited alleged scriptural, medical, moral, historical, and philosophical "proofs" of male superiority. Women were tirelessly urged to be chaste, silent, and obedient, and these urgings could be enforced. Husbands perceived to be dominated by their wives were on occasion publicly ridiculed, and women perceived to be scolds could be brutally punished with a "brank"—a metal cage for the head with a built-in gag. Yet from 1553 to 1603 England had five uninterrupted decades of female rule. How much did this unprecedented experience affect gender relations in the society? The answer would seem to be, precious little.

To be sure, even the most belligerent misogynists had to acknowledge the commanding authority of the women on top. But these powerful female rulers were generally perceived as anomalies; and none of them showed a personal interest in improving the general lot of women in their society. Their principal focus, understandably, was not sisterhood but survival. And the path to survival in the sixteenth century, for women as for men, was blood-soaked. Two of the figures introduced in this section, Mary Tudor and Elizabeth, signed the death warrants of the two others, Jane Grey and Mary Stuart. In addition, Mary Tudor probably came close to having her half-sister, Elizabeth, executed, and Mary Stuart plotted Elizabeth's assassination.

In certain respects women were if anything more disadvantaged at the end of the Tudor era than they had been half a century earlier. Before the Reformation, some learned and ambitious women found within convents scope for both literary expression and the exercise of authority. With the dissolution of the monasteries under Henry VIII, that option was closed, and the strong Protestant emphasis on marriage further harrowed for women the possibilities of an independent life. At the same time that Protestantism had the effect of restricting the scope of women's authority, however, its insistence on Scripture as the crucial guide to faith sharply increased the emphasis on literacy, which contributed to a gradual rise in the number of women readers and writers. Moreover, if male chauvinism and misogyny were as ubiquitous as ever, condemnations of the female sex could not under Elizabeth be quite so sweeping or absolute as in previous times. When the prominent humanist Sir Thomas Smith considered how he should describe his country's social order, he declared that "we do reject women, as those whom nature hath made to keep home and to nourish their family and children, and not to meddle with matters abroad, nor to bear office in a city or commonwealth." Then, with a kind of nervous glance over his shoulder, he made an exception of those few in whom "the blood is respected, not the age nor the sex": for example, the queen.

Even at the top, however, women could not easily escape being defined by their marital status, sexual behavior, and reproductive potential. Such was the case for Jane Grey, matched to Guildford Dudley as a move in a reckless political game; for Mary Tudor, with her marriage to a foreign king and her phantom pregnancies; and for Mary Stuart, with her string of disastrous marriages and reputed sexual liaisons. Imagining how the careers of these contemporary women must have appeared to the eyes of Elizabeth helps explain her choice to remain unwed.

MARY I (MARY TUDOR)

Mary Tudor (1516–1558) was the only surviving child of Henry VIII's first wife, Catherine of Aragon. The king saw his daughter as a useful bargaining chip in international diplomacy—at the age of six she was engaged to be married to her cousin Charles V, the Holy Roman Emperor and England's chief ally against France—but balked at the thought of leaving his kingdom to a female heir. Blaming Catherine for failing to produce a son, he determined to seek a divorce. The pope's refusal to grant it precipitated the Protestant Reformation in England.

In the years immediately following the royal divorce and the break with Rome, Mary had good reason to believe that her life was in danger. When she refused to take the Oaths of Succession and Supremacy (affirming, respectively, the invalidity of her parents' marriage and her father's supreme authority over the English Church), Henry came close to having her arrested for treason. At length, her own Catholic councillors prevailed on her to sign the oaths rather than lose her life. Sparing her no humiliation, the Privy Council insisted that she add a postscript acknowledging that Henry VIII's marriage to her mother had been "incestuous and unlawful," thus effectively declaring herself a bastard. In his will, however, Henry VIII left Mary second in line for the throne, after her younger half-brother, Edward.

Harassed for harboring priests and attending Mass during Edward's reign, Mary very nearly did not survive the attempt, at its end, to establish as successor the Protestant Jane Grey. But when, somewhat surprisingly, Protestants as well as Catholic's rallied firmly to Mary's cause, she ascended the throne, and Jane Grey and her supporters went to the scaffold. The early eagerness of Protestants to accept Henry VIII's legitimate heir as their queen, regardless of her religion, diminished sharply when it became clear that Mary intended to marry a foreign ruler, Philip II of Spain. (Eleven years her junior, Philip was the son of her childhood fiancé, Charles V.) Sir Thomas Wyatt, son of the poet of the same name, led an uprising in January 1554 to prevent the match. Urged to flee, Mary instead went to the Guildhall in London and made a forceful speech that garnered popular support.

Wyatt's rebellion was subdued, but there would never thereafter be real peace between Mary and her subjects. Her determination to restore the Catholic religion was probably welcomed by the majority, but there was no hope of avoiding confrontation with committed Protestants, and Mary did not attempt to avoid it. Between the beginning of 1555 and the end of her reign in 1558, she had 283 Protestants, from famous bishops to village zealots, executed for heresy. The immediate popular response of horror and resentment, which would soon solidify into the lurid historical legend of "Bloody Mary," had less to do with the number of executions than with the nature of the charge and with the grisly method employed. In reality both Henry VIII and Elizabeth executed many more people in the course of their reigns than did Mary. But Henry and Elizabeth, who were disposed to treat religious dissent as treason, typically had their victims executed as traitors, that is, hanged or beheaded. The pious Mary attempted to stamp out heresy and had *her* victims burned at the stake.

Impelled to marry for political reasons, Mary seemed to fall genuinely in love with her husband, who, however, did not reciprocate her feelings. On two occasions in her reign, she believed and announced herself to be with child, but both were phantom pregnancies. The melancholy from which she had always suffered intensified in the later years of her reign, when she grappled with bitter disappointments: many of her subjects incorrigibly heretical, her husband aloof and usually absent, her body apparently incapable of child-bearing. In 1558 Mary died, leaving the throne to her

Protestant half-sister. The two royal half-sisters are buried in a single tomb in Westminster Abbey.

Letter to Henry VIII

To the King's Most Gracious Highness, my father:[1]

Most humbly prostrate before the feet of Your Most Excellent Majesty, your most humble, faithful, and obedient subject, which hath so extremely offended Your Most Gracious Highness that my heavy and fearful heart dare not presume to call you father, ne[2] Your Majesty hath any cause by my deserts, saving the benignity of your most blessed nature doth surmount all evils, offenses, and trespasses, and is ever merciful and ready to accept the penitent calling for grace in any convenient time. Having received this Thursday at night certain letters from Mr. Secretary,[3] as well advising me to make my humble submission immediately to yourself, which because I durst not without your gracious license presume to do before, I lately sent unto him, as signifying that your most merciful heart and fatherly pity had granted me your blessing, with condition that I should persevere in that I had commenced and begun, and that I should not eftsoons[4] offend Your Majesty by the denial or refusal of any such articles and commandments as it may please Your Highness to address unto me for the perfect trial of mine heart and inward affection. For the perfect declaration of the bottom of my heart and stomach,[5] first, I knowledge[6] myself to have most unkindly and unnaturally offended Your Most Excellent Highness, in that I have not submitted myself to your most just and virtuous laws, and for mine offense therein, which I must confess were in me a thousandfold more grievous than they could be in any other living creature, I put myself wholly and entirely to your gracious mercy; at whose hands I cannot receive that punishment for the same[7] that I have deserved. Secondly, to open my heart to Your Grace in these things which I have hitherto refused to condescend[8] unto, and have now written with mine own hand, sending the same to Your Highness herewith; I shall never beseech Your Grace to have pity and compassion of me, if ever you shall perceive that I shall privily or apertly[9] vary or alter from one piece of that I have written and subscribed, or refuse to confirm, ratify, or declare the same where Your Majesty shall appoint me. Thirdly, as I have and

---

1. After the execution of Anne Boleyn on May 19, 1536, Mary thought that she would quickly be restored to her father's favor. Henry, though, persisted in the demand that he had been making of her for several years: that she acknowledge in writing his supremacy over the English Church, as well as the invalidity of his marriage to her mother. In the weeks following Anne's beheading, Mary's continuing refusal to comply with this demand infuriated Henry to the point that he threatened her (not for the first time) with death. Finally, lambasted by Henry's secretary and principal adviser Thomas Cromwell, who had supported her until the king's rage made him fear for his own safety, and urged to submit even by her Spanish allies, Mary yielded, signing the prescribed articles on a Thursday night in June (either the 15th or the 22nd), and writing her father this supplicatory letter (which may have been drafted by Cromwell).
2. Nor.
3. Cromwell.
4. Again.
5. The stomach, like the heart, often designated the inward seat of thought and feeling.
6. Acknowledge.
7. I.e., for my offense.
8. Consent.
9. Secretly or openly.

shall, knowing your excellent learning, virtue, wisdom, and knowledge, put my soul into your direction, and, by the same, hath and will, in all things, from henceforth direct my conscience, so my body I do wholly commit to your mercy and fatherly pity; desiring no state, no condition, nor no manner degree of living, but such as Your Grace shall appoint unto me; knowledging and confessing that my state cannot be so vile as either the extremity of justice would appoint unto me, or as mine offenses have required and deserved. And whatsoever Your Grace shall command me to do, touching any of these points, either for things past, present, or to come, I shall as gladly do the same, as Your Majesty can command me. Most humbly therefore, beseeching your mercy, most gracious sovereign lord and benign father, to have pity and compassion of your miserable and sorrowful child, and with the abundance of your inestimable goodness so to overcome my iniquity towards God, Your Grace, and your whole realm, as I may feel some sensible[1] token of reconciliation, which, God is my judge, I only desire, without other respect.[2] To Whom I shall daily pray for the preservation of Your Highness, with the Queen's Grace,[3] and that it may please Him to send you issue. From Hunsdon, this Thursday, at 11 of the clock at night.

Your Grace's most humble and
obedient daughter and handmaid,
Mary

1536   1830

From An Ambassadorial Dispatch to the Holy Roman Emperor, Charles V: The Coronation of Mary I[1]

Your Highness's own cousin,[2] Queen Mary, now wears the crown of this kingdom. She was crowned on the first day of this month,[3] with the pomp and ceremonies customary here, which are far grander than elsewhere, as I shall briefly show; and according to the rites of the old religion.[4] On the eve of her coronation-day, the queen was removed from the Tower and castle of London to Westminster Palace, where the sovereigns of England are by custom wont to reside in London. She was accompanied by the earls, lords, gentlemen, ambassadors, and officers, all dressed in rich garments. The queen was carried in an open litter covered with brocade. Two coaches followed her: the Lady Elizabeth and the Lady of Cleves[5] rode in one; some of the ladies of the court in the other. The streets were hung with tapestries and strewn with grass and flowers; and many triumphal arches were erected along her way. The next day, coronation-day, the queen went from the Hall

---

1. Evident. "As": so that.
2. Regard.
3. Jane Seymour, whom Henry had married on May 30 (eleven days after the execution of Anne Boleyn).
1. Translated from Spanish, in *Calendar of State Papers, Spanish*, vol. 5, pt. 1.
2. Mary and Charles were first cousins.

3. October 1553.
4. I.e., Catholicism.
5. Anne of Cleves, the German noblewoman who had been Henry VIII's fourth wife, was the only one of the six still alive in 1553. Henry had had the marriage annulled after seven months, but Anne had remained in England. "The Lady Elizabeth" is Mary's half-sister, the future Elizabeth I.

of Parliament and Justice to the church,[6] in procession with the bishops and priests in full canonical dress, the streets being again covered with flowers and decked with stuffs.[7] She mounted a scaffolding that was erected at the church for this purpose, and showed herself to the people. The queen's coronation was proclaimed to them and the question asked of them if they were willing to accept her as their queen. All answered: Yes; and the ordinary ceremonies were then gone through, the queen making an offering of silver and silken stuffs. The bishop of Winchester, who officiated, gave her the scepter and the orb, fastened on the spurs, and girt her with the sword; he received the oath, and she was twice anointed and crowned with three crowns. The ceremonies lasted from ten in the morning till five o'clock in the afternoon. She was carried from the church to the Parliament Hall, where a banquet was prepared. The queen sat on a stone chair covered with brocade,[8] which they say was carried off from Scotland in sign of a victory, and was once used by the kings of Scotland at their crowning; she rested her feet upon two of her ladies, which is also a part of the prescribed ceremonial, and ate thus. She was served by the earls and lords, Knights of the Order[9] and officers, each one performing his own special office. The meats[1] were carried by the Knights of the Bath. These knights are made by the kings on the eve of their coronation and at no other time; and their rank is inferior to the other order. The queen instituted twenty fresh ones. They are called Knights of the Bath because they plunge naked into a bath with the king and kiss his shoulder. The queen being a woman, the ceremony was performed for her by the earl of Arundel, her great master of the household. The earl marshal and the lord steward[2] directed the ceremonies mounted on horseback in the great hall. When the banquet was over, an armed knight rode in upon a Spanish horse and flung down his glove,[3] while one of the kings-of-arms[4] challenged anyone who opposed the queen's rights to pick up the glove and fight the champion in single combat. The queen gave him a gold cup, as it is usual to do. Meanwhile the earls, vassals, and councillors paid homage to her, kissing her on the shoulder; and the ceremonies came to an end without any of the interruptions or troubles that were feared on the part of the Lutherans, who would rejoice in upsetting the queen's reign. They were feared especially because of the Lady Elizabeth, who does not feel sincerely the oath she took at the coronation; she has had intelligence with the king of France, which has been discovered.[5] A remedy is to be sought at the convocation of the estates,[6] which is to take place on the fifth of this month: Elizabeth is to be declared a bastard, having been born during the lifetime of Queen Catherine, mother of the queen. The affairs of the

6. I.e., from Westminster Hall to Westminster Abbey.
7. Pieces of cloth.
8. The coronation throne—not itself stone, but having the Stone of Scone (taken from Scotland by Edward I in 1292) encased in its seat.
9. The Order of the Garter.
1. Food in general (not just animal flesh).
2. The earl of Arundel was both the lord steward and the lord great master of the household. The earl marshal was the duke of Norfolk.
3. I.e., threw down the gauntlet. The challenge

by the "king's champion" (a hereditary office) was a part of the coronation ritual until 1821.
4. The title of the three chief heralds of the College of Arms.
5. There is, at least now, no evidence of Elizabeth's conniving with the French king. "Intelligence": communication.
6. I.e., Parliament. Statutes declaring both Mary and Elizabeth illegitimate were already in place; Parliament nullified those pertaining to Mary, but left unrepealed the ones concerning Elizabeth.

kingdom are unsettled because the vassals and people are prone to scandal, and seekers after novelties; they are strange and troublesome folk.

* * *

1553   1916

The Oration of Queen Mary in the Guildhall, on the First of February, 1554[1]

I am come unto you in mine own person, to tell you that which already you see and know; that is, how traitorously and rebelliously a number of Kentish-men have assembled themselves against both us and you. Their pretense (as they said at the first) was for a marriage determined for us: to the which, and to all the articles thereof, ye have been made privy. But since,[2] we have caused certain of our Privy Council to go again unto them, and to demand the cause of this their rebellion: and it appeared then unto our said council that the matter of the marriage seemed to be but a Spanish cloak to cover their pretended purpose against our religion; for that they arrogantly and traitorously demanded to have the governance of our person, the keeping of the Tower,[3] and the placing of our councillors.

Now, loving subjects, what I am, ye right well know. I am your queen, to whom at my coronation, when I was wedded to the realm and laws of the same (the spousal ring whereof I have on my finger, which never hitherto was, nor hereafter shall be, left off), you promised your allegiance and obedience unto me. And that I am the right and true inheritor of the crown of this realm of England, I take all Christendom to witness. My father, as ye all know, possessed the same regal state, which now rightly is descended unto me: and to him always ye showed yourselves most faithful and loving subjects; and therefore I doubt not, but ye will show yourselves likewise to me, and that ye will not suffer a vile traitor to have the order and governance of our person, and to occupy our estate,[4] especially being so vile a traitor as Wyatt is; who most certainly, as he hath abused mine ignorant subjects which be on his side, so doth he intend and purpose the destruction of you, and spoil[5] of your goods. And this I say to you, on the word of a prince: I cannot tell how naturally the mother loveth the child, for I was never the mother of any; but certainly, if a prince and governor may as naturally and earnestly love her subjects, as the mother doth the child, then assure yourselves that I, being your lady and mistress, do as earnestly and as tenderly

---

1. When, in the early months of Mary's reign, it became clear that she intended to marry the heir to the Spanish throne (the future Philip II, son of her cousin Charles V), discontent broke into insurrection. In late January 1554, a sizable army led by the Kentishman Sir Thomas Wyatt II began an advance on London. In the crisis, Mary went to the Guildhall and made this rousing speech to the assembled Londoners. They rallied to her side, and when Wyatt reached the city he found

an unreceptive populace. The uprising collapsed, and he and other rebel leaders were executed. The version of Mary's speech given here was printed, with grudging admiration, by the Protestant martyrologist John Foxe, in his *Acts and Monuments* (see above, p. 687).
2. Subsequently.
3. I.e., the Tower of London. "For that": because.
4. Position.
5. Despoliation, pillage.

love and favor you. And I, thus loving you, cannot but think that ye as heartily and faithfully love me; and then I doubt not but we shall give these rebels a short and speedy overthrow.

As concerning the marriage, ye shall understand that I enterprised not the doing thereof without advice, and that by the advice of all our Privy Council, who so considered and weighed the great commodities[6] that might ensue thereof, that they not only thought it very honorable, but also expedient, both for the wealth[7] of our realm and also of all you our subjects. And as touching myself, I assure you, I am not so bent to my will, neither[8] so precise nor affectionate,[9] that either for mine own pleasure I would choose where I lust,[1] or that I am so desirous as needs[2] I would have one. For God, I thank him, to whom be the praise therefore, I have hitherto lived a virgin, and doubt nothing[3] but with God's grace am able so to live still. But if, as my progenitors have done before, it might please God that I might leave some fruit of my body behind me to be your governor, I trust ye would not only rejoice thereat, but also I know it would be to your great comfort. And certainly, if I either did think or know that this marriage were to the hurt of any of you my commons, or to the impeachment[4] of any part or parcel of the royal state of this realm of England, I would never consent thereunto, neither would I ever marry while I lived. And on the word of a queen I promise you that if it shall not probably[5] appear to all the nobility and commons in the high court of Parliament that this marriage shall be for the high benefit and commodity of the whole realm, then I will abstain from marriage while I live.

And now, good subjects, pluck up your hearts, and like true men stand fast against these rebels, both our enemies and yours, and fear them not; for I assure you, I fear them nothing at all. And I will leave with you my Lord Howard and my lord treasurer,[6] who shall be assistants with the mayor for your defense.

1554   1563

6. Benefits.
7. Well-being.
8. Nor.
9. "Precise nor affectionate": fastidious nor willful.
1. Where I please.
2. "As needs": that it is necessary. "Desirous":
full of desire.
3. Not at all.
4. Injury; discrediting.
5. Plausibly.
6. Sir William Paulet, marquis of Winchester. "My Lord Howard": William Howard, earl of Warwick.

LADY JANE GREY

Jane Grey (1537–1554) was unlucky in her parents, the duke and duchess of Suffolk. They were, by her own account, impossible to please, subjecting her to taunts, threats, and physical abuse whenever she made a minor error in performance or deportment. Much worse for Jane, her mother was a granddaughter of Henry VII with a distant but plausible claim to the English throne. This fact, more than any action of her own, determined the course of Jane's life and death.

In 1553 England was ruled in name by the boy-king Edward VI, but in reality by John Dudley, duke of Northumberland, who as protector (regent) stood at the head of an aggressively Protestant regime. With Edward's health in decline and his Catholic half-sister Mary next in line to the throne, Protestant nobles feared for their future and for England's. For Northumberland, Jane Grey's bloodline offered an elegant solution. Aged fifteen, Lady Jane was married to Northumberland's son, Guildford Dudley. Within six weeks of the marriage, Edward VI was dead, and the Privy Council, pressured by Northumberland, had denounced Mary Tudor as a bastard and declared Jane Grey queen of England (her mother having instantly abdicated in her favor).

Jane's reign lasted a mere nine days, July 9–18. For the first seventy-two hours, there seemed some hope of the coup's success; even the hostile ambassadors of Catholic powers were ready to hail Jane as queen. But the nobility and the common people, Protestant as well as Catholic, soon rallied to Mary's cause: respect for the rights of inheritance seems to have outweighed religious partisanship. Within weeks Northumberland was defeated, arrested, and executed. Jane, who had briefly reigned from the Tower of London, was now made prisoner there. The victorious Mary initially had no intention of executing Jane or her young husband, who, she recognized, had been no more than pawns in their parents' political games. But in January 1554 the duke of Suffolk joined in an ill-fated rebellion intended to reinstate his daughter on the throne. Mary's councillors convinced her that Jane would pose a danger as long as she remained alive. On the morning of February 12, 1554, Jane watched from a Tower window as her husband, Guildford, went to his public execution; within an hour she too had been beheaded, privately, on Tower Green.

Jane Grey was never really a woman in power. Her ability to command her own destiny, let alone that of others, was hardly greater when she was queen of England than when she was prisoner in the Tower. Yet it is clear from her writings and the testimony of others that Jane possessed a firm, even fiery will. In her brief stint as queen, she shocked her controllers by refusing to allow Guildford to take the title of king and rule jointly with her, and again by insisting that Northumberland, rather than her father, Suffolk, should lead her forces against Mary. Her will was harnessed to a militant and unshakable Protestantism; from an early age she mocked Catholic beliefs. In the Tower, where a politic conversion to Catholicism might well have saved her life, she instead wrote a violent and soon public letter to her one-time tutor Thomas Harding, who had converted, lambasting him as a "seed of Satan." Yet far from being a narrow bigot, Jane was, though dead at sixteen, among the most learned women of her century; she had mastered Latin and Greek and was a student of Hebrew. She rivaled Elizabeth in intellectual brilliance and—to her fatal cost—exceeded her greatly in religious fervor.

From Roger Ascham's *Schoolmaster*[1]

[A TALK WITH LADY JANE]

* * * One example whether love or fear doth work more in a child for virtue and learning I will gladly report; which may be heard with some pleasure and followed with more profit. Before I went into Germany,[2] I came to Broadgate in Leicestershire to take my leave of that noble Lady Jane Grey, to

---

1. On Ascham—the preeminent humanist educational theorist of mid-16th-century England— see above, p. 699.
2. In 1550, as secretary of the English ambassador to the emperor Charles V. So Lady Jane was thirteen at the time of the conversation Ascham recounts.

whom I was exceeding much beholding. Her parents, the duke and the duchess, with all the household, gentlemen and gentlewomen, were hunting in the park. I found her in her chamber reading *Phaedon Platonis*[3] in Greek, and that with as much delight as some gentleman would read a merry tale in Boccaccio.[4] After salutation and duty done, with some other talk, I asked her why she would lose[5] such pastime in the park. Smiling she answered me, "Iwis,[6] all their sport in the park is but a shadow to that pleasure that I find in Plato. Alas, good folk, they never felt what true pleasure meant." "And how came you, madam," quoth I, "to this deep knowledge of pleasure, and what did chiefly allure you unto it, seeing not many women, but very few men, have attained thereunto?" "I will tell you," quoth she, "and tell you a truth which perchance ye will marvel at. One of the greatest benefits that ever God gave me is that he sent me so sharp and severe parents and so gentle a schoolmaster. For when I am in presence either of father or mother, whether I speak, keep silence, sit, stand, or go,[7] eat, drink, be merry or sad, be sewing, playing, dancing, or doing anything else, I must do it, as it were, in such weight, measure, and number even so perfectly as God made the world, or else I am so sharply taunted, so cruelly threatened, yea, presently sometimes, with pinches, nips, and bobs,[8] and other ways which I will not name for the honor I bear them,[9] so without measure misordered, that I think myself in hell till time come that I must go to Master Aylmer,[1] who teacheth me so gently, so pleasantly, with such fair allurements to learning, that I think all the time nothing whilst I am with him. And when I am called from him, I fall on weeping, because whatsoever I do else but learning is full of grief, trouble, fear, and whole misliking unto me. And thus my book hath been so much my pleasure, and bringeth daily to me more pleasure and more, that in respect of it all other pleasures in very deed be but trifles and troubles unto me." I remember this talk gladly, both because it is so worthy of memory and because also it was the last talk that ever I had, and the last time that ever I saw, that noble and worthy lady.

1570

3. Plato's dialogue *Phaedo*.
4. Boccaccio's *Decameron* (1348–53), a collection of one hundred "merry," sometimes licentious, tales, not translated into English in Ascham's time.
5. Miss, forgo.
6. Truly.
7. Walk.
8. Raps, blows. "Presently": on the spot.

9. Her parents.
1. John Aylmer (1521–1594). As a schoolboy he attracted the notice of Henry Grey, marquis of Dorset, later duke of Suffolk, who provided for his education. After graduating from Cambridge in 1541 he became chaplain to Dorset and tutor to his children. Queen Elizabeth made him bishop of London in 1577.

From A Letter of the Lady Jane to M. H., late chaplain to the duke of Suffolk her father, and then fallen from the truth of God's most Holy Word[1]

So oft as I call to mind the dreadful and fearful saying of God, "That he which layeth hold upon the plough, and looketh back, is not meet for the kingdom of heaven,"[2] and, on the other side, the comfortable[3] words of our Savior Christ to all those that, forsaking themselves, do follow him, I cannot but marvel at thee, and lament thy case, which seemed sometime to be the lively member of Christ, but now the deformed imp[4] of the devil; sometime the beautiful temple of God, but now the stinking and filthy kennel of Satan; sometime the unspotted spouse of Christ, but now the unshamefaced paramour of Antichrist; sometime my faithful brother, but now a stranger and apostate; sometime a stout Christian soldier, but now a cowardly runaway. Yea, when I consider these things, I cannot but speak to thee, and cry out upon thee, thou seed of Satan, and not of Judah,[5] whom the devil hath deceived, the world hath beguiled, and the desire of life subverted, and made thee of a Christian an infidel. Wherefore hast thou taken the testament of the Lord in thy mouth? Wherefore hast thou preached the law and the will of God to others? Wherefore hast thou instructed others to be strong in Christ, when thou thyself dost now so shamefully shrink, and so horribly abuse the testament and law of the Lord? when thou thyself preachest not to steal, yet most abominably stealest, not from men but from God, and, committing most heinous sacrilege, robbest Christ thy Lord of his right members, thy body and thy soul, and choosest rather to live miserably with shame to the world, than to die and gloriously with honor reign with Christ, in whom even in death is life? Why dost thou now show thyself most weak, when indeed thou oughtest to be most strong? The strength of a fort is unknown before the assault: but thou yieldest thy hold before any battery be made.

O wretched and unhappy man, what art thou, but dust and ashes? and wilt thou resist thy maker that fashioned thee and framed thee? Wilt thou now forsake Him that called thee from the custom gathering among the Romish Antichristians,[6] to be an ambassador and messenger of his eternal word? He that first framed thee, and since thy first creation and birth preserved thee, nourished, and kept thee, yea, and inspired thee with the spirit of knowledge (I cannot say of grace), shall he not now possess thee? Darest thou deliver up thyself to another, being not thine own, but his? How canst thou, having knowledge, or how darest thou neglect the law of the Lord and follow the vain traditions of men, and whereas thou hast been a public professor of his name, become now a defacer of his glory? Wilt thou refuse the true God, and worship the invention of man, the golden calf, the whore of

---

1. Taken from the second edition (1570) of John Foxe's *Acts and Monuments*. (See above, p. 687.) In a subsequent edition, "M. H." is identified as "Master Harding"—the eminent theologian Thomas Harding, who was one of Lady Jane's tutors. Like many other English clergymen, Harding had renounced his Protestantism after Mary I made clear her determination to restore Catholicism. Jane wrote to him from her prison in the Tower.

2. Luke 9.62. "Meet": fit.
3. Comforting.
4. Offshoot.
5. Patriarch of the biblical kingdom of the Hebrews.
6. In the late 1540s, Harding had studied in Catholic Italy.

Lady Jane Grey. Dating from the 1590s and by an unknown artist, this oil painting on oak panel has been claimed to represent Jane Grey, though the claim has been contested. Scratched lines across the painting suggest that the work might have been the victim of an iconoclastic attack.

Babylon,[7] the Romish religion, the abominable idol, the most wicked Mass? Wilt thou torment again, rend and tear the most precious body of our Savior Christ, with thy bodily and fleshly teeth?[8] Wilt thou take upon thee to offer up any sacrifice unto God for our sins, considering that Christ offered up himself, as Paul saith, upon the cross, a lively sacrifice once for all? Can neither the punishment of the Israelites (which, for their idolatry, they so oft received), nor the terrible threatenings of the prophets, nor the curses of God's own mouth, fear thee to honor any other god than him? Dost thou so regard Him that spared not his dear and only son for thee, so diminishing, yea, utterly extinguishing his glory, that thou wilt attribute the praise and honor due unto him to the idols, "which have mouths and speak not, eyes and see not, ears and hear not";[9] which shall perish with them that made them?

* * *

7. Revelation 17–19. Protestants often identified her with the Church of Rome. "The golden calf": the idol fashioned by the Israelites while Moses was on Mt. Sinai receiving the Ten Commandments (Exodus 32).
8. Alluding to the bitter controversy over transubstantiation: Catholic doctrine holds that although the bread and wine of the Eucharist retain their normal appearance, they are miraculously transformed into the actual body and blood of Christ; Protestants believe that the identification is symbolic rather than substantive.
9. Psalm 115.

Return, return again into Christ's war, and, as becometh a faithful warrior, put on that armor that St. Paul teacheth to be most necessary for a Christian man.[1] And above all things take to you the shield of faith, and be you provoked by Christ's own example to withstand the devil, to forsake the world, and to become a true and faithful member of his mystical body, who spared not his own body for our sins.

Throw down yourself with the fear of his threatened vengeance for this so great and heinous an offense of apostasy; and comfort yourself, on the other part, with the mercy, blood, and promise of him that is ready to turn unto you whensoever you turn unto him. Disdain not to come again with the lost son,[2] seeing you have so wandered with him. Be not ashamed to turn again with him from the swill of strangers[3] to the delicates of your most benign and loving Father, acknowledging that you have sinned against heaven and earth: against heaven, by staining the glorious name of God and causing his most sincere and pure word to be evil-spoken-of through you; against earth, by offending so many of your weak brethren, to whom you have been a stumbling-block through your sudden sliding. Be not abashed to come home again with Mary, and weep bitterly with Peter,[4] not only with shedding the tears of your bodily eyes, but also pouring out the streams of your heart—to wash away, out of the sight of God, the filth and mire of your offensive fall. Be not abashed to say with the publican, "Lord be merciful unto me a sinner."[5]

Last of all, let the lively remembrance of the last day[6] be always before your eyes, remembering the terror that such shall be in at that time, with the runagates[7] and fugitives from Christ, which, setting more by the world than by heaven, more by their life than by him that gave them life, did shrink, yea did clean fall away, from him that forsook not them; and, contrariwise, the inestimable joys prepared for them that, fearing no peril nor dreading death, have manfully fought and victoriously triumphed over all power of darkness, over hell, death, and damnation, through their most redoubted[8] captain, Christ, who now stretcheth out his arms to receive you, ready to fall upon your neck and kiss you, and, last of all, to feast you with the dainties and delicates of his own precious blood: which undoubtedly, if it might stand with his determinate purpose, he would not let[9] to shed again, rather than you should be lost. To whom, with the Father and the Holy Ghost, be all honor, praise, and glory everlasting. Amen.

> Be constant, be constant; fear not for pain:
> Christ hath redeemed thee, and heaven is thy gain.

1553–54   1563

---

1. Ephesians 6.11–18.
2. The Prodigal Son (Luke 15.10–32).
3. The Prodigal journeyed into a "far country," where, having "wasted his substance with riotous living," he "would fain have filled his belly with the husks that the swine did eat."
4. After thrice denying Christ, Peter wept bitterly for his apostasy (Matthew 26.75; Luke 22.62). "Mary": Christ's follower Mary Magdalene, long regarded (though without substantive basis in the

Gospels) as a repentant sinner.
5. Luke 18.13. "Publican": in Christ's parable of the Pharisee and the publican (tax collector—agent of the hated Roman occupiers), the latter humbles himself before God and is forgiven.
6. Judgment Day.
7. Runaways—apostates.
8. Reverenced; dreaded.
9. Hesitate.

A Letter of the Lady Jane, Sent unto her Father[1]

Father, although it hath pleased God to hasten my death by you, by whom my life should rather have been lengthened; yet can I so patiently take it, as I yield God more hearty thanks for shortening my woeful days than if all the world had been given into my possession, with life lengthened at my own will. And albeit I am well assured of your impatient dolors, redoubled manifold ways, both in bewailing your own woe and especially, as I hear, my unfortunate state, yet, my dear father (if I may without offense rejoice in my own mishaps), meseems in this I may account myself blessed, that washing my hands with the innocency of my fact,[2] my guiltless blood may cry before the Lord, Mercy, mercy to the innocent! And yet, though I must needs acknowledge that, being constrained and, as you wot well enough, continually assayed,[3] in taking upon me I seemed to consent,[4] and therein grievously offended the queen and her laws: yet do I assuredly trust that this mine offense towards God is so much the less in that, being in so royal estate as I was, mine enforced honor never agreed with mine innocent heart. And thus, good father, I have opened unto you the state wherein I presently stand; whose death at hand, although to you perhaps it may seen right woeful, to me there is nothing that can be more welcome than from this vale of misery to aspire to that heavenly throne of all joy and pleasure with Christ our savior. In whose steadfast faith (if it may be lawful for the daughter so to write to the father) the Lord that hitherto hath strengthened you so continue you that at the last we may meet in heaven with the Father, the Son, and the Holy Ghost.[5]

1554   1563

A Prayer of the Lady Jane[1]

O Lord, thou God and Father of my life, hear me, poor and desolate woman, which flieth unto thee only, in all troubles and miseries. Thou, O Lord, art the only defender and deliverer of those that put their trust in thee: and therefore I, being defiled with sin, encumbered with affliction, unquieted with troubles, wrapped in cares, overwhelmed with miseries, vexed with temptations, and grievously tormented with the long imprisonment of this vile mass of clay, my sinful body, do come unto thee, O merciful Savior,

---

1. Written shortly before her execution. Lady Jane's father, the duke of Suffolk, had been pardoned by Mary I for his involvement in the attempt to put Jane on the throne following the death of Edward VI; Jane herself, though remaining in custody, also had good hopes of being pardoned. But when Suffolk joined in the insurrection of January 1554 against Mary, the queen decided that both must die. Suffolk was executed eleven days after his daughter, on February 23.
2. Actions. Jane had had to be coerced to accept the crown in July 1553, and was in no way involved in the later uprising.
3. Assailed—browbeaten. "Wot": know.
4. I.e., though I accepted the crown only under intense pressure, nonetheless, by accepting it at all I apparently consented to Mary's displacement.
5. As Foxe noted, this final sentence amounts to an admonition that Suffolk not renounce his Protestantism.
1. Also written shortly before her death.

craving thy mercy and help, without the which so little hope of deliverance is left that I may utterly despair of any liberty.

Albeit it is expedient, that, seeing our life standeth upon trying,[2] we should be visited sometime with some adversity, whereby we might both be tried whether we be of thy flock or no, and also know thee and ourselves the better, yet thou, that saidst thou wouldst not suffer us to be tempted above our power,[3] be merciful unto me now, a miserable wretch, I beseech thee; which with Solomon[4] do cry unto thee, humbly desiring thee that I may neither be too much puffed up with prosperity, neither too much pressed down with adversity, lest I, being too full, should deny thee, my God, or being too low brought, should despair and blaspheme thee, my Lord and Savior.

O merciful God, consider my misery, best known unto thee; and be thou now unto me a strong tower of defense, I humbly require[5] thee. Suffer me not to be tempted above my power, but either be thou a deliverer unto me out of this great misery, either[6] else give me grace patiently to bear thy heavy hand and sharp correction. It was thy right hand that delivered the people of Israel out of the hands of Pharaoh, which for the space of four hundred years did oppress them and keep them in bondage. Let it, therefore, likewise seem good to thy fatherly goodness to deliver me, sorrowful wretch (for whom thy son Christ shed his precious blood on the cross), out of this miserable captivity and bondage wherein I am now.

How long wilt thou be absent? forever? O Lord, hast thou forgotten to be gracious, and hast thou shut up thy loving-kindness in displeasure? Wilt thou be no more entreated? Is thy mercy clean gone forever, and thy promise come utterly to an end for evermore?[7] Why dost thou make so long tarrying? Shall I despair of thy mercy, O God? Far be that from me. I am thy workmanship, created in Christ Jesu: give me grace, therefore, to tarry thy leisure, and patiently to bear thy works; assuredly knowing that as thou canst, so thou wilt deliver me when it shall please thee, nothing doubting or mistrusting thy goodness towards me; for thou knowest better what is good for me than I do: therefore do with me in all things what thou wilt, and plague me what way thou wilt. Only in the meantime, arm me, I beseech thee, with thy armor,[8] that I may stand fast, my loins being girded about with verity, having on the breastplate of righteousness and shod with the shoes prepared by the gospel of peace; above all things, taking to me the shield of faith, wherewith I may be able to quench all the fiery darts of the wicked, and taking the helmet of salvation and the sword of the spirit, which is thy most holy Word: praying always with all manner of prayer and supplication, that I may refer myself wholly to thy will, abiding thy pleasure and comforting myself in those troubles that it shall please thee to send me; seeing such troubles be profitable for me, and seeing I am assuredly persuaded that it cannot be but well, all that thou doest.

---

2. Trial.
3. 1 Corinthians 10.13.
4. Proverbs 30.7–9.
5. Ask.

6. Or.
7. Psalm 77.8.
8. The allegorical armor of Ephesians 6.11–18. The ensuing passage closely echoes these verses.

Hear me, O merciful Father, for His sake whom thou wouldst should be a sacrifice for my sins: to whom with thee and the Holy Ghost, be all honor and glory. Amen.

1554   1563

A Second Letter to Her Father[1]

The Lord comfort your grace, and that in his Word, wherein all creatures only are to be comforted. And though it hath pleased God to take away two of your children,[2] yet think not, I most humbly beseech your grace, that you have lost them, but trust that we, by losing this mortal life, have won an immortal life. And I for my part, as I have honored your grace in this life, will pray for you in another life. Your grace's humble daughter,

Jane Dudley

1554   1850

From Foxe's *Acts and Monuments*[1]

The Words and Behavior of the Lady Jane upon the Scaffold

These are the words that the Lady Jane spake upon the scaffold, at the hour of her death. First, when she mounted upon the scaffold, she said to the people standing thereabout, "Good people, I am come hither to die, and by a law I am condemned to the same. The fact[2] against the queen's highness was unlawful, and the consenting thereunto by me; but, touching the procurement and desire thereof by me, or on my behalf, I do wash my hands thereof in innocency before God and the face of you, good Christian people, this day." And therewith she wrung her hands, wherein she had her book.[3] Then said she, "I pray you all, good Christian people, to bear me witness that I die a true Christian woman, and that I do look to be saved by no other mean but only by the mercy of God,[4] in the blood of his only Son Jesus Christ; and I confess that when I did know the word of God I neglected the same, loved myself and the world; and therefore this plague and punishment is happily and worthily happened unto me for my sins; and yet I thank God of his goodness that he hath thus given me a time and respite to repent. And now, good people, while I am alive, I pray you assist me with your prayers."[5] And then, kneeling down, she turned her to Feckenham,[6] saying, "Shall I

---

1. Lady Jane inscribed this farewell message in a prayer book, now in the British Library.
2. I.e., his daughter and son-in-law.
1. On the Protestant martyrologist John Foxe (1516–1587), see above, p. 687.
2. Act.
3. Prayer book.
4. Asserting the Protestant doctrine of salvation by faith alone.
5. Implicitly challenging the Catholic doctrine

of the efficacy of prayers for the *dead*.
6. John de Feckenham, Queen Mary's confessor, who at her behest had tried unsuccessfully, in Lady Jane's last days, to convert her to Catholicism. A gifted and tolerant man, Feckenham was later put in charge of Mary's project of restoring the Benedictine monastery of Westminster Abbey, where he thus became the last abbot.

say this psalm?" And he said, "Yea." Then said she the psalm of *Miserere mei Deus*[7] in English, in most devout manner, throughout to the end; and then she stood up, and gave her maiden, Mistress Ellen, her gloves and handkerchief, and her book to Master Brydges.[8] And then she untied her gown, and the hangman pressed upon her to help her off with it;[9] but she, desiring him to let her alone, turned towards her two gentlewomen, who helped her off therewith, and also with her frau's paste[1] and neckerchief, giving her a fair handkerchief to knit about her eyes.

Then the hangman kneeled down and asked her forgiveness, whom she forgave most willingly. Then he willed her to stand upon the straw;[2] which doing, she saw the block. Then she said, "I pray you, dispatch me quickly." Then she kneeled down, saying, "Will you take it off before I lay me down?" And the hangman said, "No, madam." Then tied she the kerchief about her eyes, and feeling for the block she said, "What shall I do? Where is it? Where is it?" One of the standers-by guiding her thereunto, she laid her head down upon the block, and then stretched forth her body and said, "Lord, into thy hands I commend my spirit";[3] and so finished her life, in the year of our Lord God 1554, the twelfth day of February.

1563

7. Psalm 51: "Have mercy upon me, O God."
8. Sir John Brydges, lieutenant of the Tower.
9. The victim's adornments were part of the executioner's fee.
1. A type of elaborate headdress worn by married women.
2. Strewn about the execution block to soak up some of the blood.
3. Echoing Christ's dying words, Luke 23.46.

MARY, QUEEN OF SCOTS

Mary Stuart (1542–1587) was born on December 8, and within a week, following the death of her father, King James V, she had inherited the throne of Scotland. She has always been remembered as the "Queen of Scots," though she spent very few years in Scotland, never spoke its language as easily as French, and was forced to abdicate at the age of twenty-four.

Determined to foil the ambitions of Henry VIII, who sought to force a union between England and Scotland by having Mary married to his own son, Edward, Mary's guardians sent her at the age of five to the court of France, where she would be brought up. At age fifteen she married Francis, the French dauphin, who became king in 1559. A year later, Francis II died, and at the age of eighteen Mary returned to her own kingdom, Scotland, a land she could barely remember. As a Catholic woman coming to rule over a patriarchal society in which militant Protestantism was gathering force, Mary could hardly hope for a unanimously warm welcome. Her own subsequent decisions destroyed whatever chance she may have had of enjoying a peaceful reign. In 1565 she married her vain and erratic cousin, Henry Stewart, Lord Darnley, with whom she was soon deeply unhappy. In 1566 Darnley was implicated in the murder of Mary's secretary, David Rizzio, who was rumored to be her lover. In 1567 Darnley was murdered in turn, certainly with the connivance of the powerful James Hepburn, earl of Bothwell. Soon Mary was married to Bothwell, though her own will in the matter remains unclear. The scandal of this marriage alienated many of her supporters and helped provoke an uprising of the Scottish nobility. Mary was imprisoned at Lochleven Castle and forced to abdicate in favor of her one-year-old son, James. Though she escaped, she failed to rally the Scottish people to her side, and in 1568 she fled across the border into England, where she appealed for help from her cousin Elizabeth.

The arrival on English soil of the twenty-five-year-old Queen of Scots was not welcome news to the Protestant queen and her wary advisers. As a descendant of Henry VII with a good claim to the English throne, Mary was seen to be a dangerous and destabilizing presence. She was immediately taken prisoner and remained so until her execution at the age of forty-four. She was tried in England in 1568–69 on the charge of murdering her second husband. At this point her Scottish accuser produced the notorious Casket Letters, which had supposedly been discovered in a silver casket seized from an associate of Bothwell's. The casket, it was said, contained eight letters and twelve sonnets, all in French, testifying (if they are authentic) to an adulterous relationship with Bothwell and, more ambiguously, to Mary's involvement in the murder of Darnley. Mary herself was not permitted to inspect the letters, which were withdrawn shortly after being displayed in court and subsequently disappeared, though not before translations of them had been made into English and Scots. The result of the trial was inconclusive; Elizabeth declared that nothing had been proven which would make her "conceive an evil opinion of her good sister"; yet she continued to keep Mary prisoner, moving her from one place of confinement to another for the next nineteen years.

Mary quickly became the focus for the aspirations of discontented Catholics at home and abroad. She conspired with these adherents by means of secret messages, written in ciphers or in invisible ink on white taffeta, smuggled in and out of her prison hidden in such things as beer barrels. The conspiracies were monitored, and to some extent even engineered, by Elizabeth's spymaster, Francis Walsingham, who was setting a trap for the Queen of Scots and English Catholics generally. In 1586 Mary was found to be in communication with a young Englishman named Anthony Babington, who was plotting to assassinate Elizabeth and place Mary on the throne. Babington and his coconspirators were drawn and quartered, their heads displayed on Tower Bridge. Though she insisted that, as the sovereign queen of another country, she could not be charged with treason against England's queen, Mary was convicted as a traitor and sentenced to death. Elizabeth vacillated for some time over carrying out the sentence, worrying about the reaction abroad and about the precedent involved in executing a monarch. Eventually she was prevailed upon to sign the death warrant, and Mary was beheaded on February 8, 1587. A week later, Elizabeth wrote to the orphaned James VI of Scotland, lamenting the "miserable accident, which far contrary to my meaning hath befallen."*

Many of the words that seem to speak to us most eloquently of Mary's self and circumstances are not in fact her own. Throughout her life, Mary encountered no shortage of people—some who were admirers and others deadly foes—who were eager to seize control of her voice. The controversy over the Casket Letters thus crystallizes the more general problem of locating the "real" Mary Stuart. It will probably never be possible to prove with certainty whether the letters are products of Mary's own hand or cunning forgeries designed to incriminate her, and indeed it is this impossibility that lends them much of their fascination, opening them up for the endless play of interpretation. Yet if the interpretation of the Casket Letters has become a kind of intellectual game, it began as a matter of life or death. If Mary

---

* For further information on relations between England and Scotland in the 16th century, see, in the supplemental ebook, "Island Nations," which includes a portrait of Mary (with the excerpt from Robert Wedderburn).

was in one respect a text with many authors, she was also a singular woman inhabiting a body that, on the orders of another woman, was at last cut in two.

From Casket Letter Number 2[1]

* * * This day I have wrought[2] till two of the clock upon this bracelet, to put the key in the cleft[3] of it, which is tied with two laces. I have had so little time that it is very ill,[4] but I will make a fairer; and in the meantime take heed that none of those that be here do see it: for all the world would know it, for I have made it in haste in their presence. I go to my tedious talk.[5] You make me dissemble so much that I am afraid thereof with horror; and you make me almost to play the part of a traitor. Remember that if it were not for obeying you, I had rather be dead;[6] my heart bleedeth for it. To be short, he will not come[7] but with condition that I shall promise to be with him as heretofore at bed and board,[8] and that I shall forsake him no more; and upon my word[9] he will do whatsoever I will, and will come, but he hath prayed me to tarry till after tomorrow. * * * But now, to make him trust me, I must feign something unto him; and therefore when he desired me to promise that when he should be whole[1] we should make but one bed, I told him (feigning to believe his fair promises) [that if he][2] did not change his mind between this time and that, I was contented, so as[3] he would say nothing thereof: for (to tell it between us two) the lords wished no ill to him,[4] but did fear lest (considering the threatenings which he made in case we did agree together) he would make them feel the small account[5] they have made of him, and that he would persuade me to pursue some of them; and for this respect should be in jealousy if at one instant,[6] without their knowledge, I did break a game made to the contrary in their presence.[7] And he said unto me, very pleasant and merry, "Think you that they do the more esteem you therefore? But I am glad that you talk to me of the lords. I hear[8] that you desire now that we shall live a happy life—for if it were otherwise, it could not be but greater inconvenience should happen to us both than you think. But I will do now whatsoever you will have me do, and will love all those that you shall love, so as you make them to love me also. For, so as they seek not my life, I love them all equally."

1. The English translation was made shortly after the French originals of the Casket Letters were produced at Mary's first trial in England (1568–69).
2. Worked.
3. I.e., lock.
4. Badly made.
5. I.e., with Darnley. He was lying ill (probably from syphilis, though smallpox was given out as the cause) at Glasgow; Mary had joined him there.
6. I.e., than play the traitor.
7. I.e., to Craigmillar Castle, outside Edinburgh. "To be short": in short.
8. I.e., to live again with him as husband and wife.

9. I.e., if I give my word to do this.
1. Well.
2. The manuscript of the English translation has a tear at this point; the missing words have been inferred from the contemporary Scottish translation.
3. Provided that.
4. Darnley—weak, arrogant, and vicious—had many bitter enemies among the other Scottish lords.
5. Make them suffer for the low estimate.
6. Suddenly. "Respect": reason.
7. At their urging, Mary had authorized a confederacy of nobles to find a way for her to divorce Darnley. "Game": undertaking.
8. I.e., I am convinced.

Thereupon I have willed this bearer to tell you many pretty[9] things; for I have too much to write, and it is late, and I trust him, upon your word. To be short, he[1] will go anywhere upon my word. Alas! and I never deceived anybody; but I remit[2] myself wholly to your will. And send me word what I shall do, and whatever happen to me, I will obey you. Think also if you will not find some invention more secret, by physic,[3] for he is to take physic at Craigmillar, and the baths also, and shall not come forth of[4] long time. To be short, for that that[5] I can learn, he hath great suspicion, and yet nevertheless trusteth upon my word, but not to tell me as yet anything. Howbeit, if you will that I shall *avow*[6] him, I will know all of him; but I shall never be willing[7] to beguile one who putteth his trust in me. Nevertheless, you may do all.[8] And do not esteem me the less therefore, for you are the cause thereof; for, for my own revenge, I would not do it.

He giveth me certain charges[9] (and those strong) of that that I fear: even to say that his faults be published, but there be that commit some secret faults and fear not to have them spoken of so loudly, and that there is speech of great and small. And even touching the Lady Reres,[1] he said, "God grant that she serve you to your honor," and that men may not think, nor he neither, that mine own power was not in myself,[2] seeing I did refuse his offers. To conclude, for a surety he mistrusteth us of that that you know,[3] and for his life. But in the end, after I had spoken two or three good words to him, he was very merry and glad. I have not seen him this night, for ending[4] your bracelet; but I can find no clasps for it. It is ready thereunto,[5] and yet I fear lest it should bring you ill hap, or that it should be known if you were hurt.[6] Send me word whether you will have it, and more money,[7] and when I shall return, and how far I may speak. * * *

He hath sent to me, and prayeth me to see him rise tomorrow in the morning early. To be short, this bearer shall declare unto you the rest; and if I shall learn anything, I will make every night a memorial[8] thereof. He shall tell you the cause of my stay.[9] Burn this letter, for it is too dangerous; neither is there anything well said in it, for I think upon nothing but upon grief if you be at Edinburgh.[1]

Now if to please you, my dear life, I spare neither honor, conscience, nor hazard, nor greatness, take it in good part, and not according to the

9. Small(er). "This bearer": the bearer of the letter.
1. I.e., Darnley.
2. Submit.
3. Medicine (i.e., a poisoned drink). "Invention": contrivance. If Mary wrote this sentence, it shows her complicit in the plot to murder Darnley (who was in fact strangled—and the house he was occupying at Kirk O'Field, just outside Edinburgh, blown up—on the night of February 9–10, 1567).
4. For a.
5. As far as.
6. Assure him by taking a vow. "Howbeit": however.
7. I.e., without reluctance.
8. I.e., you may command me in all things.
9. Admonitions: the idea seems to be that Darnley hinted that he might reveal Mary's secrets.

1. Who was acting as wet nurse to Mary's son, James (later James VI of Scotland and, in 1603, James I of England).
2. I.e., that I was not acting of my own will.
3. The thing that you know about. "For a surety": for certain.
4. Because I was finishing.
5. Apart from that.
6. Recognized if you were wounded (and thus powerless to conceal the bracelet). "Ill hap": misfortune.
7. I.e., whether you want more money.
8. Memorandum.
9. Delay.
1. The Scottish translation makes this clause the beginning of a new sentence, which says, in effect, "If you are in Edinburgh when you receive this, send me word soon."

interpretation of your false brother-in-law,[2] to whom I pray you give no credit against the most faithful lover that ever you had, or shall have.

See not also her whose feigned tears you ought not more to regard than the true travails which I endure to deserve her place, for obtaining of which, against my own nature I do betray those that could let[3] me. God forgive me, and give you, my only friend,[4] the good luck and prosperity that your humble and faithful lover doth wish unto you: who hopeth shortly to be another thing unto you, for the reward of my pains. I have not made[5] one word, and it is very late, although I should never be weary in writing to you, yet will I end, after kissing of your hands. Excuse my evil[6] writing, and read it over twice. Excuse also that [I scribbled,[7] for I had yesternight no paper, when I took the paper of a memorial.[8] . . . Remember your friend, and write unto her, and often. Love me al[ways, as I shall do you].[9]

1567   1571

A Letter to Elizabeth I, May 17, 1568[1]

Madam my good sister,[2] I believe you are not ignorant how long certain of my subjects, whom from the least of my kingdom I have raised to be the first, have taken upon themselves to involve me in trouble, and to do what it appears they had in view from the first. You know how they purposed to seize me and the late king my husband, from which attempt it pleased God to protect us, and to permit us to expel them from the country, where, at your request, I again afterwards received them; though, on their return, they committed another crime, that of holding me a prisoner, and killing in my presence a servant of mine, I being at the time in a state of pregnancy.[3] It again pleased God that I should save myself from their hands; and, as above said, I not only pardoned them, but even received them into favor. They, however, not yet satisfied with so many acts of kindness, have, on the contrary, in spite of their promises, devised, favored, subscribed to, and aided in a crime[4] for the purpose of charging it falsely upon me, as I hope fully to make you understand. They have, under this pretence, arrayed themselves

---

2. Presumably the brother of Bothwell's wife, Jean Gordon—who is presumably the person referred to in the following sentence.
3. Prevent.
4. Lover.
5. Possibly "reade"—in which case the meaning is "I have not read over a word."
6. Poor.
7. Words torn off the English manuscript here; reading inferred from the Scottish translation.
8. She apologizes for having had to use paper already used for memoranda.
9. Again words torn from the English manuscript are inferred from the Scottish translation. The latter continues with what seem to be the memoranda—to herself or perhaps to the bearer of the letter—mentioned above: "Remember zow [you] of the purpois of the Lady Reres. Of the Inglismen. Of his mother. Of the Erle of Argyle. Of the Erle Bothwell. Of the ludgeing [lodging]

in Edinburgh."

1. This letter (translated from the French by Agnes Strickland) was written just after Mary, in flight from her Scottish enemies, made her fateful crossing into England. Its account of her troubles is, though not exaggerated, inevitably one-sided. In 1565, Mary's ill-advised marriage to her cousin Lord Darnley had upset the power structure of the nation's factious and violent nobility. A group of nobles rebelled against her, led by Mary's illegitimate half-brother James Stewart, earl of Moray, who had previously been her key supporter and adviser.
2. Fellow queen.
3. The servant was David Rizzio, Mary's secretary and confidant. At the time of his murder, Mary was six months pregnant with her only child, the future King James VI. She omits the fact that Darnley was involved in the murder.
4. The murder of Darnley.

against me, accusing me of being ill-advised, and pretending a desire of seeing me delivered from bad counsels, in order to point out to me the things that required reformation. I, feeling myself innocent, and desirous to avoid the shedding of blood, placed myself in their hands, wishing to reform what was amiss.[5] They immediately seized and imprisoned me. When I upbraided them with a breach of their promise, and requested to be informed why I was thus treated, they all absented themselves. I demanded to be heard in council, which was refused me. In short, they have kept me without any servants, except two women, a cook, and a surgeon; and they have threatened to kill me, if I did not sign an abdication of my crown, which the fear of immediate death caused me to do,[6] as I have since proved before the whole of the nobility, of which I hope to afford you evidence.

After this, they again laid hold of me in parliament, without saying why, and without hearing me; forbidding, at the same time, every advocate to plead for me; and, compelling the rest to acquiesce in their unjust usurpation of my rights, they have robbed me of everything I had in the world, not permitting me either to write or to speak, in order that I might not contradict their false inventions.

At last, it pleased God to deliver me,[7] when they thought of putting me to death, that they might make more sure of their power, though I repeatedly offered to answer any thing they had to say to me, and to join them in the punishment of those who should be guilty of any crime. In short, it pleased God to deliver me, to the great content of all my subjects, except Moray, Morton, the Humes, Glencairn, Mar, and Sempill, to whom, after that my whole nobility was come from all parts, I sent to say that, notwithstanding their ingratitude and unjust cruelty employed against me, I was willing to invite them to return to their duty, and to offer them security of their lives and estates, and to hold a parliament for the purpose of reforming every thing. I sent twice. They seized and imprisoned my messengers, and made proclamation, declaring traitors all those who should assist me, and guilty of that odious crime. I demanded that they should name one of them, and I would give him up, and begged them, at the same time, to deliver to me such as should be named to them. They seized upon my officer and my proclamation. I sent to demand a safe-conduct for my Lord Boyd, in order to treat of an accommodation, not wishing, as far as I might be concerned, for any effusion of blood. They refused, saying that those who had not been true to their regent and to my son, whom they denominate king, should leave me and put themselves at their disposal, a thing at which the whole nobility were greatly offended.

Seeing, therefore, that they were only a few individuals, and that my nobility were more attached to me than ever, I was in hope that, in course of time, and under your favor, they would be gradually reduced; and, seeing that they said they would either retake me or all die, I proceeded toward Dumbarton,[8]

---

5. Unhappy about the elevation of Bothwell to the position of Mary's consort (she had married him three months after Darnley's murder, in which he was well known to have been the principal conspirator), the nobles brought an army against the royal couple in June 1567. With their own forces melting away, Bothwell escaped, and Mary surrendered herself to the nobles.

6. In late July. Her infant son was then crowned king on July 29, in a Protestant church. Moray became regent.
7. Mary escaped from captivity on May 2, 1568.
8. In the west of Scotland. The royal army passed near Glasgow, in a deliberate attempt to draw Moray's army, which was smaller, into battle.

passing at the distance of two miles from them, my nobility accompanying me, marching in order of battle between them and me; which they seeing, sallied forth, and came to cut off my way and take me. My people seeing this, and moved by that extreme malice of my enemies, with a view to check their progress, encountered them without order, so that, though they were twice their number, their sudden advance caused them so great a disadvantage that God permitted them to be discomfited, and several killed and taken; some of them were cruelly put to death when taken on their retreat. The pursuit was immediately interrupted, in order to take me on my way to Dumbarton; they stationed people in every direction, either to kill or take me. But God through his infinite goodness has preserved me, and I escaped to my Lord Herries's,[9] who, as well as other gentlemen, have come with me into your country,[1] being assured that, hearing the cruelty of my enemies, and how they have treated me, you will, conformably to your kind disposition and the confidence I have in you, not only receive me for the safety of my life but also aid and assist me in my just quarrel; and I shall solicit other princes to do the same. I entreat you to send to fetch me as soon as you possibly can,[2] for I am in a pitiable condition, not only for a queen, but for a gentlewoman; for I have nothing in the world but what I had on my person when I made my escape, traveling across the country the first day, and not having since ever ventured to proceed except in the night, as I hope to declare before you, if it pleases you to have pity, as I trust you will, upon my extreme misfortune; of which I will forbear complaining, in order not to importune you, and pray to God that he may give to you a happy state of health and long life, and to me patience, and that consolation which I expect to receive from you, to whom I present my humble commendations. From Workington, the 17th of May.

> Your most faithful and affectionate good
> sister, and cousin, and escaped prisoner,
> Mary R.[3]

1568   1844

From Narrative of the Execution of the Queen of Scots. In a Letter to the Right Honorable Sir William Cecil[1]

It may please your lordship to be advertised[2] that, according as your honor gave me in command, I have here set down in writing the true order and manner of the execution of the Lady Mary, late queen of Scots, the 8th of February last, in the great hall within the castle of Fotheringhay,[3] together

---

9. Herries was a magnate of southwestern Scotland, which remained strongly Catholic.
1. Crossing the Solway Firth in a fishing boat, Mary and twenty supporters landed in the Cumberland port of Workington on May 16, 1568.
2. Elizabeth never granted Mary an audience; two days after arriving in England, she was conducted to Carlisle Castle, where her nineteen years of English captivity began.
3. A royal signature: "R."="Regina" (Latin for "Queen").

1. Elizabeth's lord high treasurer and principal minister. The author of the letter (of which there are various versions extant) was Robert Wingfield, Cecil's nephew, sent by him to report on the execution.
2. Informed.
3. In Northamptonshire. Mary had been moved to Fotheringhay in September 1586 and was there tried and convicted of treason against Elizabeth (though she was not Elizabeth's subject).

with relation of all such speeches and actions spoken and done by the said queen or any others, and all other circumstances and proceedings concerning the same, from and after the delivery of the said Scottish queen to Thomas Andrews, Esquire, high sheriff for Her Majesty's county of Northampton, unto the end of the said execution: as followeth.

It being certified the 6th of February last to the said queen, by the right honorable the earl of Kent, the earl of Shrewsbury, and also by Sir Amyas Paulet and Sir Drue Drury, her governors,[4] that she was to prepare herself to die the 8th of February next, she seemed not [to] be in any terror, for aught that appeared by any her outward gesture or behavior (other than marveling she should die), but rather with smiling cheer and pleasing countenance digested and accepted the said admonition of preparation to her (as she said) unexpected execution, saying that her death should be welcome unto her, seeing Her Majesty was so resolved, and that that soul were too too far unworthy the fruition of joys of heaven forever, whose body would not in this world be content to endure the stroke of the executioner for a moment. And that spoken, she wept bitterly and became silent.

The said 8th day of February being come, and time and place appointed for the execution, the said queen, being of stature tall, of body corpulent, round-shouldered, her face fat and broad, double-chinned, and hazel-eyed, her borrowed hair auburn, her attire was this. On her head she had a dressing of lawn edged with bone lace,[5] a pomander chain[6] and an *Angus Dei* about her neck,[7] a crucifix in her hand, a pair of beads at her girdle,[8] with a silver cross at the end of them. A veil of lawn fastened to her caul,[9] bowed out with wire and edged round about with bone lace. Her gown was of black satin painted, with a train and long sleeves to the ground, set with acorn buttons of jet trimmed with pearl, and short sleeves of satin black cut,[1] with a pair of sleeves of purple velvet whole under them. Her kirtle[2] whole, of figured black satin, and her petticoat skirts of crimson velvet, her shoes of Spanish leather with the rough side outward, a pair of green silk garters, her nether stockings[3] worsted colored watchet,[4] clocked[5] with silver, and edged on the tops with silver, and next her leg a pair of jersey[6] hose, white, etc. Thus apparelled, she departed her chamber, and willingly bended her steps towards the place of execution.

As the commissioners and divers other knights were meeting the queen coming forth, one of her servants, called Melvin,[7] kneeling on his knees to his queen and mistress, wringing his hands and shedding tears, used these words unto her: "Ah, Madam, unhappy me: what man on earth was ever before the messenger of so important sorrow and heaviness as I shall be,

4. Keepers. The earls of Kent and Shrewsbury were sent by the royal council to oversee the execution. Paulet had been Mary's principal custodian since January 1585; Drury joined him in his charge in November 1586.

5. A kind of lace originally knitted with bobbins made of bone. "Lawn": fine linen.

6. Pomander is a mixture of aromatic substances; a small bag of it was sometimes suspended from a necklace.

7. A medallion bearing the figure of a lamb: an emblem of Christ. From *"Agnus Dei"* ("Lamb of God"), a part of the Mass beginning with those words.

8. Belt. "Beads": rosary beads.

9. Close-fitting cap.

1. Slashed, to reveal the contrasting-colored sleeves beneath.

2. Outer petticoat.

3. "Nether stockings" means simply "stockings." ("Nether" = "of the legs.")

4. Light blue.

5. Embroidered.

6. Worsted.

7. Sir Andrew Melville.

when I report that my good and gracious queen and mistress is beheaded in England?" This said, tears prevented him of further speaking. Whereupon the said queen, pouring forth her dying tears, thus answered him: "My good servant, cease to lament, for thou hast cause rather to joy than to mourn. For now shalt thou see Mary Stuart's troubles receive their long-expected end and determination. For know (said she), good servant, all the world is but vanity, and subject still to more sorrow than a whole ocean of tears can bewail. But I pray thee (said she), carry this message from me, that I die a true woman to my religion, and like a true queen of Scotland and France. But God forgive them (said she) that have long desired my end and thirsted for my blood, as the hart doth for the water brooks. Oh God (said she), thou that art the author of truth, and truth itself, knowest the inward chamber of my thought, how that I was ever willing that England and Scotland should be united together. Well (said she), commend me to my son, and tell him that I have not done anything prejudicial to the state and kingdom of Scotland"; and so resolving[8] herself again into tears, said, "Good Melvin, farewell"; and with weeping eyes and her cheeks all besprinkled with tears as they were, kissed him, saying once again, "Farewell, good Melvin, and pray for thy mistress and queen."

And then she turned herself unto the lords, and told them she had certain requests to make unto them. One was, for certain money to be paid to Curle, her servant. Sir Amyas Paulet, knowing of that money, answered to this effect, "it should." Next, that her poor servants might have that with quietness[9] which she had given them by her will, and that they might be favorably entreated,[1] and to send them safely into their countries. "To this (said she) I conjure[2] you." Last, that it would please the lords to permit her poor distressed servants to be present about her at her death, that their eyes and hearts may see and witness how patiently their queen and mistress would endure her execution, and so make relation, when they came into their country, that she died a true constant Catholic to her religion. Then the earl of Kent did answer thus: "Madam, that which you have desired cannot conveniently be granted. For if it should, it were to be feared lest some of them, with speeches or other behavior, would both be grievous to Your Grace and troublesome and unpleasing to us and our company, whereof we have had some experience. For if such an access might be allowed, they would not stick to put some superstitious trumpery in practice, and if it were but dipping their handkerchiefs in Your Grace's blood, whereof it were very unmeet[3] for us to give allowance."

"My lord," said the queen of Scots, "I will give my word, although it be but dead, that they shall not deserve any blame in any the actions you have named. But alas, poor souls, it would do them good to bid their mistress farewell; and I hope your mistress" (meaning the queen), "being a maiden queen, will vouchsafe in regard of[4] womanhood that I shall have some of my own people about me at my death: and I know Her Majesty hath not given

8. Dissolving.
9. Without contestation.
1. Treated.

2. Earnestly entreat.
3. Unfitting.
4. For the sake of.

you any such strait[5] charge or commission but that you might grant me a request of far greater courtesy than this is, if I were a woman of far meaner calling[6] than the queen of Scots." And then, perceiving that she could not obtain her request without some difficulty, burst out into tears, saying, "I am cousin to your queen, and descended from the blood royal of Henry the Seventh, and a married queen of France, and an anointed queen of Scotland." Then, upon great consultation had betwixt the two earls and the others in commission, it was granted to her what she instantly[7] before earnestly entreated, and desired her to make choice of six of her best-beloved men and women. Then of her men she chose Melvin, her apothecary, her surgeon, and one old man more;[8] and of her women, those two which did lie in her chamber. Then, with an unappalled countenance, without any terror of the place, the persons, or the preparations, she came out of the entry into the hall, stepped up to the scaffold, being two foot high and twelve foot broad, with rails round about, hanged and covered with black, with a low stool, long fair cushion, and a block covered also with black. The stool brought her, she sat down. The earl of Kent stood on the right hand, the earl of Shrewsbury on the other, other knights and gentlemen stood about the rails. The commission for her execution was read (after silence made) by Mr. Beale, clerk of the council;[9] which done, the people with a loud voice said, "God save the Queen!" During the reading of this commission, the said queen was very silent, listening unto it with so careless a regard as if it had not concerned her at all, nay, rather with so merry and cheerful a countenance as if it had been a pardon from Her Majesty for her life; and withal[1] used such a strangeness in her words as if she had not known any of the assembly, nor had been anything seen[2] in the English tongue.

Then Mr. Doctor Fletcher, dean of Peterborough,[3] standing directly before her without[4] the rails, bending his body with great reverence, uttered the exhortation following:

"Madam, the Queen's Most Excellent Majesty (whom God preserve long to reign over us), having (notwithstanding this preparation for the execution of justice justly to be done upon you for your many trespasses against her sacred person, state, and government) a tender care over your soul, which presently departing out of your body must either be separated in the true faith in Christ or perish forever, doth for Jesus Christ offer unto you the comfortable[5] promises of God, wherein I beseech Your Grace, even in the bowels of Jesus Christ,[6] to consider these three things:

"First, your state past, and transitory glory;

"Secondly, your condition present, of death;

"Thirdly, your estate to come, either in everlasting happiness or perpetual infelicity.

---

5. Strict.
6. Far lower station.
7. Importunely.
8. Her aged porter, Didier.
9. I.e., the royal council.
1. As well.
2. At all fluent.

3. I.e., of the Anglican cathedral there.
4. Outside.
5. Comforting, reassuring.
6. "In the bowels of Jesus Christ": in the name of Christ's pity. The bowels were regarded as the seat of pity and compassion.

"For the first, let me speak to Your Grace with David the King: Forget, Madam, yourself, and your own people, and your father's house; forget your natural birth, your regal and princely dignity: so shall the King of Kings have pleasure in your spiritual beauty, etc.[7]

"Madam, even now, Madam, doth God Almighty open you a door into a heavenly kingdom; shut not therefore this passage by the hardening of your heart, and grieve not the Spirit of God, which may seal your hope to a day of redemption."

The queen three or four times said unto him, "Mr. Dean, trouble not yourself nor me: for know that I am settled in the ancient Catholic and Roman religion, and in defense thereof, by God's grace, I mind to spend my blood."

Then said Mr. Dean, "Madam, change your opinion, and repent you of your former wickedness. Settle your faith only upon this ground, that in Christ Jesus you hope to be saved." She answered again and again, with great earnestness, "Good Mr. Dean, trouble yourself not anymore about this matter, for I was born in this religion, have lived in this religion, and am resolved to die in this religion."

Then the earls, when they saw how far uncomfortable[8] she was to hear Mr. Dean's good exhortation, said, "Madam, we will pray for Your Grace with Mr. Dean, that you may have your mind lightened with the true knowledge of God and his word."

"My lords," answered the queen, "if you will pray with me, I will even from my heart thank you, and think myself greatly favored by you; but to join in prayer with you in your manner, who are not of one[9] religion with me, it were a sin, and I will not."

Then the lords called Mr. Dean again, and bade him say on, or what he thought good else. The dean kneeled and prayed. * * *[1]

All the assembly, save the queen and her servants, said the prayer after Mr. Dean as he spake it, during which prayer the queen sat upon her stool, having her *Agnus Dei*, crucifix, beads, and an office[2] in Latin. Thus furnished with superstitious trumpery, not regarding what Mr. Dean said, she began very fastly[3] with tears and a loud voice to pray in Latin, and in the midst of her prayers, with overmuch weeping and mourning, slipped off her stool, and kneeling presently said diverse other Latin prayers. Then she rose, and kneeled down again, praying in English for Christ's afflicted church, an end of her troubles, for her son, and for the Queen's Majesty, to God for forgiveness of the sins of them in this island: she forgave her enemies with all her heart, that had long sought her blood. This done, she desired all saints to make intercession for her to the Savior of the World, Jesus Christ. Then she began to kiss her crucifix and to cross herself, saying these words: "Even as thy arms, oh Jesu Christ, were spread here upon the cross, so receive me into the arms of mercy." Then the two executioners kneeled down unto her, desiring her to forgive them her death. She answered, "I forgive you with all

---

7. The dean paraphrases Psalm 45.10–11, a passage addressed to the bride of a king: "forget also thine own people, and thy father's house; So shall the king greatly desire thy beauty. . . ."
8. Unwilling.
9. The same.

1. The dean prays at considerable length, beseeching God to wash away Mary's "blindness and ignorance of heavenly things."
2. Prayer book.
3. Steadfastly.

my heart. For I hope this death shall give an end to all my troubles." They, with her two women helping, began to disrobe her, and then she laid the crucifix upon the stool. One of the executioners took from her neck the *Agnus Dei*, and she laid hold of it, saying she would give it to one of her women, and, withal, told the executioner that he should have money for it.[4] Then they took off her chain. She made herself unready[5] with a kind of gladness, and, smiling, putting on a pair of sleeves with her own hands, which the two executioners before had rudely[6] put off, and with such speed as if she had longed to be gone out of the world.

During the disrobing of this queen, she never altered her countenance, but smiling said she never had such grooms before to make her unready, nor ever did put off her clothes before such a company. At length, unattired and unapparelled to her petticoat and kirtle, the two women burst out into a great and pitiful shrieking, crying, and lamentation, crossed themselves, and prayed in Latin. The queen turned towards them: "Ne criez vous; j'ai promis pour vous";[7] and so crossed and kissed them, and bade them pray for her.

Then with a smiling countenance she turned to her menservants, Melvin and the rest, crossed them, bade them fare well, and pray for her to the last.

One of the women having a Corpus Christi cloth,[8] lapped[9] it up three-corner-wise and kissed it, and put it over the face of her queen, and pinned it fast upon the caul of her head. Then the two women departed. The queen kneeled down upon the cushion resolutely, and without any token of fear of death, said aloud in Latin the Psalm *"In te, Domine, confido."*[1] Then, groping for the block, she laid down her head, putting her chain over her back with both her hands, which, holding there still,[2] had been cut off, had they not been espied.

Then she laid herself upon the block most quietly, and stretching out her arms and legs cried out: *"In manus tuas, Domine, commendo spiritum meum,"*[3] three or four times.

At last, while one of the executioners held her straitly[4] with one of his hands, the other gave two strokes with an axe before he did cut off her head, and yet left a little gristle behind.

She made very small noise, no part stirred from the place where she lay. The executioners lifted up the head, and bade God save the Queen. Then her dressing of lawn fell from her head,[5] which appeared as gray as if she had been threescore and ten years old,[6] polled[7] very short. Her face much altered, her lips stirred up and down almost a quarter of an hour after her head was cut off. Then said Mr. Dean: "So perish all the Queen's enemies!" The earl of

4. A condemned person's adornments were normally perquisites of the executioner.
5. Undressed.
6. Roughly.
7. "Don't make an outcry; I promised you wouldn't."
8. The veil (also known as the "pyx cloth") that covered the vessel holding the consecrated Host of the Communion. "Corpus Christi": Latin for "the body of Christ."
9. Folded.

1. Psalm 10 (Vulgate), 11 (King James): "In the Lord put I my trust."
2. I.e., if her hands had remained there.
3. Luke 13.46: "Father, into thy hands I commend my spirit": the words of Christ on the cross.
4. Tightly.
5. That is, her headcovering and auburn wig came off in the executioner's hand.
6. She was actually forty-four.
7. Cut.

The execution of Mary, Queen of Scots. Though this watercolor image was not painted until some years after Mary's execution, it reflects eyewitness accounts. The minister depicted is likely Dr. Richard Fletcher, dean of Peterborough, who was so nervous that he stammered, and never actually delivered his sermon because he was interrupted by Mary herself. Mary wears a Corpus Christi cloth around her head as a blindfold. On the stool beside her is a prayer book, and in her hands a crucifix. Her gentlewomen stand weeping to the left of the scaffold, which is covered in black cloth. On the far left of the image is a bonfire, for burning any cloth or other items with Mary's blood on them, so that they could not serve as Catholic relics after her death.

Kent came to the dead body, and with a loud voice said, "Such end happen to all the Queen's and Gospel's enemies." One of the executioners, plucking off her garters, espied her little dog, which was crept under her clothes, which would not be gotten forth but with force, and afterwards would not depart from the dead corpse, but came and laid between her head and shoulders: a thing much noted. The dog, imbrued in her blood, was carried away and washed, as all things else were that had any blood, save those things which were burned. The executioners were sent away with money for their fees, not having any one thing that belonged unto her. Afterwards everyone was commanded forth of the hall, saving[8] the sheriff and his men, who carried her up into a great chamber made ready for the surgeons to embalm her; and there she was embalmed.

And thus I hope (my very good lord) I have certifieth Your Honor of all actions, matters, and circumstances as did proceed from her or any other at her death: wherein I dare promise unto your good lordship (if not in some better or worse words than were spoken I am somewhat mistaken), in matter I have not in any whit offended.[9] Howbeit,[1] I will not so justify my duty

---

8. Except. "Forth of": out of.
9. I.e., though I may not have gotten the speeches word-for-word, I promise that my account is completely accurate in substance.
1. However.

herein but that[2] many things might well have been omitted, as not worthy noting. Yet because it is your lordship's fault to desire to know all, and so I have certified all, it is an offense pardonable. So, resting at Your Honor's further commandment, I take my leave this 11th of February, 1587.

> Your Honor's in all humble service to command,
> R. W.

1587   1843

2. I.e., I will concede that.

ELIZABETH I

Elizabeth I (1533–1603), queen of England from 1558 to her death, set her mark indelibly on the age that has come to bear her name. Endowed with intelligence, courage, cunning, and a talent for self-display, she managed to survive and flourish in a world that would easily have crushed a weaker person. Her birth was a disappointment to her father, Henry VIII, who had hoped for a male heir to the throne, and her prospects were further dimmed when her mother, Anne Boleyn, was executed a few years later on charges of adultery and treason. At six years old, observers noted, Elizabeth had as much gravity as if she had been forty.

Under distinguished tutors, including the Protestant humanist Roger Ascham, the young princess received a rigorous education, with training in classical and modern languages, history, rhetoric, theology, and moral philosophy. Her own religious orientation was also Protestant, which put her in great danger during the reign of her Catholic older half-sister, Mary. Imprisoned in the Tower of London, interrogated and constantly spied upon, Elizabeth steadfastly professed innocence, loyalty, and a pious abhorrence of heresy. Upon Mary's death, she ascended the throne and quickly made clear that the official religion of the land would be Protestantism.

When she came to the throne, at twenty-five, speculation about a suitable match, already widespread, intensified. It remained for decades at a fever pitch, for the stakes were high. If Elizabeth died childless, the Tudor line would come to an end. The nearest heir was her cousin Mary, Queen of Scots, a Catholic whose claim was supported by France and by the papacy, and whose penchant for sexual and political intrigue soon confirmed the worst fears of English Protestants. The obvious way to avert the nightmare was for Elizabeth to marry and produce an heir, and the pressure upon her to do so was intense.

More than the royal succession hinged on the question of the queen's marriage; Elizabeth's perceived eligibility was a vital factor in the complex machinations of international diplomacy. A dynastic marriage between the queen of England and a foreign ruler could forge an alliance sufficient to alter the balance of power in Europe. The English court hosted a steady stream of ambassadors from kings and princelings eager to win the hand of the royal maiden, and Elizabeth played her romantic part with exemplary skill, sighing and spinning the negotiations out for months and even years. Most probably, she never meant to marry any of her numerous foreign (and domestic) suitors. Such a decisive act would have meant the end of her independence, as well as the end of the marriage game by which she played one power off against another. One day she would seem to be on the verge of accepting a proposal; the next, she would vow never to forsake her virginity. "She is a princess," the French ambassador remarked, "who can act any part she pleases." Ultimately she refused all offers and declared repeatedly that she was wedded to her country.

In the face of deep skepticism about the ability of any woman to rule, Elizabeth strategically blended imperiousness with an elaborate cult of love. Quickly making it clear that she would not be a figurehead, she gathered around her an able group of advisers, but she held firmly to the reins of power, subtly manipulating factional disputes, conducting diplomacy, and negotiating with an often contentious Parliament. Her courtiers and advisers, on their knees, approached the queen, glittering in jewels and gorgeous gowns, and addressed her in extravagant terms that conjoined romantic passion and religious veneration. Artists and poets celebrated her in mythological guise—as Diana, the chaste goddess of the moon; Astraea, the goddess of justice; Gloriana, the queen of the fairies. Though she could suddenly veer, whenever she chose, toward bluntness and anger, Elizabeth often contrived to transform the language of politics into the language of love. "We all loved her," her godson John Harington wrote with a touch of irony, "for she said she loved us."

Throughout her life, Elizabeth took pride in her command of languages (she spoke fluent French and Italian and read Latin and Greek) and in her felicity of expression. Her own writing includes carefully crafted letters and speeches on several state occasions; a number of prayers; prose and verse translations, including works of Horace, Seneca, Plutarch, Boethius, Calvin, and the French Protestant Queen Margaret of Navarre; and a few original poems. The original poems known to be hers deal with actual events in her life. They show her to be an exceptionally agile, poised, and self-conscious writer, a gifted role-player fully in control of the rhetorical as well as political situation in which she found herself. The texts printed here, occasionally altered in light of variant versions, are from *Elizabeth I: Collected Works*, ed. Leah Marcus, Janel Mueller, and Mary Beth Rose (2000).[*]

Verses Written with a Diamond

In her imprisonment at Woodstock, these verses she wrote with her diamond in a glass window:[1]

> Much suspected by[2] me,
> Nothing proved can be.
> > *Quod*[3] Elizabeth the prisoner

1554–55   1563

[*] See the supplemental ebook for an additional letter from Elizabeth—to Henry III of France, furiously objecting to his intervention on behalf of Mary, Queen of Scots. For a painting of the queen in procession, see the color insert in this volume.

1. This is the heading given to the verses in John Foxe's *Acts and Monuments*. After the insurrection of January 1554 against Mary I, Elizabeth was imprisoned in the Tower of London. Extensive interrogation and investigation yielded against her no firm evidence of treason, but she was transferred to the royal manor at Woodstock in Oxfordshire, and held there in close custody for a year.

2. About.

3. Quoth, said.

From The Passage of Our Most Dread Sovereign Lady Queen Elizabeth through the City of London to Westminster on the Day before Her Coronation[1]

* * * Her grace, by holding up her hands and merry countenance to such as stood far off, and most tender and gentle language to those that stood nigh to her grace, did declare herself no less thankfully to receive her people's goodwill than they lovingly offered it unto her. To all that wished her grace well she gave hearty thanks, and to such as bade God save her grace she said again,[2] God save them all, and thanked them with all her heart. So that on either side there was nothing but gladness, nothing but prayer, nothing but comfort. The queen's majesty rejoiced marvelously to see it so exceedingly showed toward her grace which all good princes have ever desired: I mean, so earnest love of subjects, so evidently declared even to her grace's own person being carried in the midst of them. The people, again, were wonderfully ravished with welcoming answers and gestures of their princess, like to the which they had before tried at her first coming to the Tower from Hatfield.[3] This her grace's loving behavior, preconceived in the people's heads, upon these considerations was thoroughly confirmed, and indeed implanted a wonderful hope in them touching her worthy government in the rest of her reign. For in all her passage she did not only show her most gracious love toward the people in general, but also privately. If the baser personages had either offered her grace any flowers or such like as a signification of their goodwill, or moved to her any suit, she most gently, to the common rejoicing of all the lookers-on and private comfort of the party, stayed her chariot[4] and heard their requests. So that if a man should say well, he could not better term the City of London that time than a stage wherein was showed the wonderful spectacle of a noble-hearted princess toward her most loving people and the people's exceeding comfort in beholding so worthy a sovereign and hearing so princelike a voice. * * *

Out at the windows and penthouses of every house did hang a number of rich and costly banners and streamers, till her grace came to the upper end of Cheap.[5] And there, by appointment, the right worshipful Master Ranulph Cholmley, recorder[6] of the City, presented to the queen's majesty a purse of crimson satin richly wrought with gold, wherein the City gave unto the queen's majesty a thousand marks[7] in gold, as Master Recorder did declare briefly unto the queen's majesty, whose words tended to this end: that the lord mayor, his brethren, and commonality of the City, to declare their

---

1. By Richard Mulcaster (ca. 1530–1611), who became a well-known authority on the education of children. Elizabeth had succeeded to the throne upon the death of Mary I on November 17, 1558, but her coronation did not take place until January 15, 1559. By long-established custom, the ceremonies began the day before the coronation itself, with the ruler being conducted across the city in procession from the Tower of London to Westminster. See the account of Mary's coronation procession, p. 724 above.
2. I.e., said in reply.
3. Elizabeth had set out from the royal manor at Hatfield (in Hertfordshire) to London on November 23.
4. Wearing a robe made of gold and silver cloth, trimmed with ermine, and overlaid with gold lace, Elizabeth rode in a litter trimmed to the ground with gold damask.
5. Also known as Cheapside or Westcheap: the chief market street in London. (The name derives from the Old English word for "market.")
6. Senior law officer.
7. The mark was valued at two-thirds of a pound sterling; and the pound was worth far more than at present—so this was a very large gift.

gladness and goodwill towards the queen's majesty, did present her grace with that gold, desiring her grace to continue their good and gracious queen and not to esteem the value of the gift, but the mind of the givers. The queen's majesty with both her hands took the purse and answered to him again marvelous pithily, and so pithily that the standers-by, as they embraced entirely her gracious answer, so they marveled at the couching thereof, which was in words, truly reported these:

> I thank my lord mayor, his brethren, and you all. And whereas your request is that I should continue your good lady and queen, be ye ensured that I will be as good unto you as ever queen was to her people. No will in me can lack, neither do I trust shall there lack any power. And persuade yourselves that for the safety and quietness of you all I will not spare, if need be, to spend my blood. God thank you all.

Which answer of so noble an hearted princess, if it moved a marvelous shout and rejoicing, it is nothing to be marveled at, since both the heartiness thereof was so wonderful, and the words so jointly[8] knit.

But because princes be set in their seat by God's appointing and therefore they must first and chiefly tender[9] the glory of Him from whom their glory issueth, it is to be noted in her grace that forsomuch as God hath so wonderfully placed her in the seat of government over this realm, she in all doings doth show herself most mindful of His goodness and mercy showed unto her. And amongst all other, two principal signs thereof were noted in this passage. First in the Tower, where her grace, before she entered her chariot, lifted up her eyes to heaven and said:

> O Lord, almighty and everlasting God, I give Thee most hearty thanks that Thou hast been so merciful unto me as to spare me to behold this joyful day. And I acknowledge that Thou hast dealt as wonderfully and as mercifully with me as Thou didst with Thy true and faithful servant Daniel, Thy prophet, whom Thou deliveredst out of the den from the cruelty of the greedy and raging lions.[1] Even so was I overwhelmed and only by Thee delivered. To Thee (therefore) only be thanks, honor, and praise forever, amen.

The second was the receiving of the Bible at the Little Conduit[2] in Cheap. For when her grace had learned that the Bible in English[3] should there be offered, she thanked the City therefor, promised the reading thereof most diligently, and incontinent[4] commanded that it should be brought. At the receipt whereof, how reverently did she with both her hands take it, kiss it, and lay it upon her breast, to the great comfort of the lookers-on! God will undoubtedly preserve so worthy a prince, which at His honor so reverently taketh her beginning. For this saying is true and written in the book of truth: he that first seeketh the kingdom of God shall have all other things cast unto him.[5]

---

8. Concordantly.
9. Have regard to.
1. Daniel 6.16–23.
2. The smaller of two lead pipe water conduits situated at the west end of Cheap Street.

3. In contrast to the Latin Bibles of the restored Catholicism of Mary's reign.
4. Immediately.
5. Matthew 6.33.

Now, therefore, all English hearts and her natural people must needs praise God's mercy, which hath sent them so worthy a prince, and pray for her grace's long continuance amongst us.

1559   1559

Speech to the House of Commons, January 28, 1563[1]

Williams,[2] I have heard by you the common request of my Commons, which I may well term (methinketh) the whole realm, because they give, as I have heard, in all these matters of Parliament their common consent to such as be here assembled. The weight and greatness of this matter might cause in me, being a woman wanting both wit[3] and memory, some fear to speak and bashfulness besides, a thing appropriate to my sex. But yet the princely seat and kingly throne wherein God (though unworthy) hath constituted me, maketh these two causes to seem little in mine eyes, though grievous perhaps to your ears, and boldeneth me to say somewhat in this matter, which I mean only to touch but not presently to answer. For this so great a demand[4] needeth both great and grave advice. I read of a philosopher whose deeds upon this occasion I remember better than his name[5] who always when he was required to give answer in any hard question of school points would rehearse over his alphabet before he would proceed to any further answer therein, not for that he could not presently have answered, but have his wit the riper and better sharpened to answer the matter withal.[6] If he, a common man, but[7] in matters of school took such delay the better to show his eloquent tale, great cause may justly move me in this, so great a matter touching the benefits of this realm and the safety of you all, to defer mine answer till some other time, wherein I assure you the consideration of my own safety (although I thank you for the great care that you seem to have thereof) shall be little in comparison of that great regard that I mean to have of the safety and surety of you all. And although God of late seemed to touch me rather like one that He chastised than one that He punished, and though death possessed almost every joint of me,[8] so as I wished then that the feeble thread of life, which lasted (methought) all too long, might by Clotho's hand[9] have quietly been cut off, yet desired I not then life (as I have some witnesses here) so much for mine own safety, as for yours. For I know that in exchanging of this reign I should have enjoyed a better reign where residence is perpetual.

---

1. Since a secure royal succession depended on Elizabeth's marrying and producing an heir, Parliament had been concerned about her single state from the beginning of her reign. The Commons raised the matter with her (not for the first time) in January 1563; the speech printed here is a later, written version of her extemporaneous response.
2. Thomas Williams, speaker of the Parliament.
3. Intellect.
4. Question.

5. According to the *Moral Essays* of Plutarch (ca. 46–ca. 120 C.E.), the philosopher was Athenodorus.
6. By that means.
7. Merely.
8. Elizabeth had nearly died of smallpox the past October.
9. Clotho is one of the three Fates of classical mythology, who spin and eventually cut the thread of each individual life.

There needs no boding of my bane.[1] I know now as well as I did before that I am mortal. I know also that I must seek to discharge myself of that great burden that God hath laid upon me; for of them to whom much is committed, much is required.[2] Think not that I, that in other matters have had convenient[3] care of you all, will in this matter touching the safety of myself and you all be careless. For I know that this matter toucheth me much nearer than it doth you all, who if the worst happen can lose but your bodies. But if I take not that convenient care that it behoveth me to have therein, I hazard to lose both body and soul. And though I am determined in this so great and weighty a matter to defer mine answer till some other time because I will not in so deep a matter wade with so shallow a wit, yet have I thought good to use these few words, as well to show you that I am neither careless nor unmindful of your safety in this case, as I trust you likewise do not forget that by me you were delivered whilst you were hanging on the bough ready to fall into the mud—yea, to be drowned in the dung; neither[4] yet the promise which you have here made concerning your duties and due obedience, wherewith, I assure you, I mean to charge[5] you, as, further, to let you understand that I neither mislike any of your requests herein, nor the great care that you seem to have of the surety and safety of yourselves in this matter.

Lastly, because I will discharge[6] some restless heads in whose brains the needless hammers beat with vain judgment that I should mislike this their petition, I say that of the matter and sum thereof I like and allow very well. As to the circumstances, if any be, I mean upon further advice further to answer. And so I assure you all that though after my death you may have many stepdames, yet shall you never have any a more mother than I mean to be unto you all.

1563   1921

From A Speech to a Joint Delegation of Lords and Commons, November 5, 1566[1]

* * * Was I not born in the realm? Were my parents born in any foreign country? Is there any cause I should alienate myself from being careful over this country? Is not my kingdom here? Whom have I oppressed? Whom have I enriched to others' harm? What turmoil have I made in this commonwealth, that I should be suspected to have no regard to the same? How have

1. "Boding of my bane": prognosticating of my death.
2. Luke 12.48.
3. Befitting.
4. Nor. "Mud . . . dung": harsh characterizations of the Roman Catholicism that Mary I had been restoring to England.
5. Exhort.
6. Disabuse.
1. The birth on June 19, 1566, of a son—James— to Mary, Queen of Scots, imparted new urgency

to the concern about Elizabeth's unmarried state. Mary was Elizabeth's second cousin and, in the absence of any child of Elizabeth's own, had a strong claim to be her heir; Mary's male child would have an even stronger one. On November 5, a delegation of sixty members of the Lords and Commons met with Elizabeth, to urge her to marry and also to establish formally the line of succession. After the meeting, a member of the delegation wrote down Elizabeth's impromptu response.

I governed since my reign? I will be tried by envy itself.[2] I need not to use many words, for my deeds do try me.

Well, the matter whereof they[3] would have made their petition, as I am informed, consisteth in two points: in my marriage and in the limitation of the succession of the crown, wherein my marriage was first placed as for manner[4] sake. I did send them answer by my Council I would marry, although of mine own disposition I was not inclined thereunto. But that was not accepted nor credited, although spoken by their prince. And yet I used so many words that I could say no more. And were it not now I had spoken those words, I would never speak them again. I will never break the word of a prince spoken in public place, for my honor[5] sake. And therefore I say again I will marry as soon as I can conveniently, if God take not him away with whom I mind to marry, or myself, or else some other great let[6] happen. I can say no more except[7] the party were present. And I hope to have children; otherwise I would never marry. A strange order of petitioners, that will make a request and cannot be otherwise ascertained[8] but by the prince's word, and yet will not believe it when it is spoken! But they, I think, that moveth the same will be as ready to mislike him with whom I shall marry as they are now to move it, and then it will appear they nothing meant it. I thought they would have been rather ready to have given me thanks than to have made any new request for the same. There hath been some that have, ere this, said unto me they never required more than that they might once hear me say I would marry. Well, there was never so great a treason but might be covered under as fair a pretense.

The second point was the limitation of the succession of the crown, wherein was nothing said for my safety, but only for themselves. A strange thing that the foot should direct the head in so weighty a cause, which cause hath been so diligently weighed by us for that[9] it toucheth us more than them. I am sure there was not one of them that ever was a second person,[1] as I have been, and have tasted of the practices against my sister, who I would to God were alive again. I had great occasions to hearken to their motions,[2] of whom some of them are of the Common House. But when friends fall out truth doth appear, according to the old proverb, and were it not for my honor, their knavery should be known. There were occasions in me at that time: I stood in danger of my life, my sister was so incensed against me. I did differ from her in religion and I was sought for divers ways; and so shall never be my successor.

I have conferred before this time with those that are well learned and have asked their opinions touching the limitation of succession, who have been silent—not that by their silence after lawlike manner[3] they have seemed to assent to it, but that indeed they could not tell what to say, considering the great peril to the realm and most danger to myself. But now the matter

2. I.e., envy itself could not fault my governance.
3. Parliament, which had planned to submit a written petition to the queen.
4. Manners'.
5. Honor's.
6. Hindrance. At the time, there were negotiations for a possible match with Archduke Charles of Austria.
7. Unless.

8. Assured.
9. Because.
1. Next in line to the throne, as Elizabeth had been under her half-sister, Mary I.
2. "To hearken to their motions": to pay heed to their doings.
3. "After lawlike manner": in accordance with the legal maxim (that silence implies consent).

must needs go trimly and pleasantly, when the bowl runneth all on the one side.[4] And alas, not one amongst them all would answer for us, but all their speeches was for the surety[5] of their country. They would have twelve or fourteen limited in succession, and the mo the better. And those shall be of such uprightness and so divine as in them shall be divinity itself. Kings were wont to honor philosophers, but if I had such[6] I would honor them as angels, that should have such piety in them that they would not seek where they are the second to be the first, and where the third to be the second, and so forth.

It is said I am no divine.[7] Indeed, I studied nothing else but divinity till I came to the crown, and then I gave myself to the study of that which was meet[8] for government, and am not ignorant of stories wherein appeareth what hath fallen out for ambition of kingdoms, as in Spain, Naples, Portingal,[9] and at home. And what cocking[1] hath been between the father and the son for the same! You would have a limitation of succession. Truly if reason did not subdue will in me, I would cause you to deal in it, so pleasant a thing it should be unto me. But I stay[2] it for your benefit; for if you should have liberty to treat of it, there be so many competitors—some kinsfolk, some servants, and some tenants; some would speak for their master, and some for their mistress, and every man for his friend—that it would be an occasion of a greater charge than a subsidy.[3] And if my will did not yield to reason, it should be that thing I would gladly desire, to see you deal in it.

Well, there hath been error—I say not errors, for there were too many in the proceeding in this matter. But we will not judge that these attempts were done of any hatred to our person, but even for lack of good foresight. I do not marvel though *Domini Doctores*[4] with you, my lords, did so use themselves therein, since after my brother's[5] death they openly preached and set forth that my sister and I were bastards.[6] Well, I wish not the death of any man, but only this I desire: that they which have been the practitioners herein may before their deaths repent the same and show some open confession of their faults, whereby the scabbed[7] sheep may be known from the whole. As for my own part, I care not for death, for all men are mortal; and though I be a woman, yet I have as good a courage answerable to my place as ever my father had. I am your anointed queen. I will never be by violence constrained to do anything. I thank God I am indeed endued with such qualities that if I were turned out of the realm in my petticoat, I were able to live in any place of Christendom.

* * *

1566   1949

4. A metaphorical extension of the preceding clause: in the game of bowls, the ball has a flat place: rolled unskillfully, it wobbles, bounces, and prematurely stops; rolled well ("all on the one side"), it runs smoothly.
5. Security.
6. I.e., such virtuous potential successors. "Mo": more.
7. Theologian.
8. Relevant to. Elizabeth's claim that before ascending the throne she studied nothing but theology is an exaggeration, but it is true that she had devoted much effort to the subject, as evidenced by her translations of several religious works.
9. Portugal. "Fallen out for": happened as a result of.
1. Cockfighting: strife, contention.
2. Stop.
3. I.e., it would cost more than a tax. (Subsidies were tax levies granted to the sovereign to meet special expenses.)
4. The Doctors of the Lord: her derisive Latin term for the bishops who had supported the petition in the House of Lords.
5. Edward VI's.
6. Presumably in support of the claim of Lady Jane Grey to the throne. (See p. 727 above.)
7. Infected with scab (the skin disease also known as scabies).

From A Letter to Mary, Queen of Scots, February 24, 1567[1]

Madame:

My ears have been so deafened and my understanding so grieved and my heart so affrighted to hear the dreadful news of the abominable murder of your mad husband and my killed cousin[2] that I scarcely yet have the wits to write about it. And inasmuch as my nature compels me to take his death in the extreme, he being so close in blood, so it is that I will boldly tell you what I think of it. I cannot dissemble that I am more sorrowful for you than for him. O madame, I would not do the office of faithful cousin or affectionate friend if I studied rather to please your ears than employed myself in preserving your honor. However, I will not at all dissemble what most people are talking about: which is that you will look through your fingers at[3] the revenging of this deed, and that you do not take measures that touch those who have done as you wished, as if the thing had been entrusted in a way that the murderers felt assurance in doing it.[4] Among the thoughts in my heart I beseech you to want no such thought to stick at this point. Through all the dealings of the world I never was in such miserable haste to lodge and have in my heart such a miserable opinion of any prince as this would cause me do. Much less will I have such of her to whom I wish as much good as my heart is able to imagine or as you were able a short while ago to wish. However, I exhort you, I counsel you, and I beseech you to take this thing so much to heart that you will not fear to touch even him whom you have nearest to you[5] if the thing touches him, and that no persuasion will prevent you from making an example out of this to the world: that you are both a noble princess and a loyal wife. I do not write so vehemently out of doubt that I have, but out of the affection that I bear you in particular. For I am not ignorant that you have no wiser counselors than myself. Thus it is that, when I remember that our Lord had one Judas out of twelve, and I assure myself that there could be no one more loyal than myself, I offer you my affection in place of this prudence.

* * *

1567   1900

---

1. Written after news reached Elizabeth of the murder of Henry Stuart, Lord Darnley, the arrogant and erratic Scottish nobleman whom Mary had ill-advisedly married in 1565.
2. Darnley, like Mary, was Elizabeth's second cousin and a potential claimant to the throne of England.
3. Wink at.

4. Since Mary and Darnley had been estranged, there were immediately rumors that she had been complicit in his murder.
5. Evidently an allusion to James Hepburn, earl of Bothwell, whom Mary married (under much-disputed circumstances) three months after Darnley's death, although Bothwell was known to have been one of the chief conspirators in the murder.

The doubt of future foes[1]

The doubt° of future foes exiles my present joy,   *fear*
And wit° me warns to shun such snares as threatens mine   *intelligence*
   annoy.[2]
For falsehood now doth flow, and subjects' faith doth ebb,[3]
Which should not be, if reason ruled or wisdom weaved the web.
5 But clouds of toys untried do cloak aspiring minds,
Which turns to rain of late repent, by course of changèd winds.[4]
The top of hope supposed, the root of rue° shall be,   *regret*
And fruitless all their grafted guile, as shortly you shall see.[5]
Their dazzled eyes with pride, which great ambition blinds,
10 Shall be unsealed° by worthy wights° whose foresight   *opened / men*
   falsehood finds.
The daughter of debate,[6] that discord aye° doth sow,   *continually*
Shall reap no gain where former rule[7] still° peace hath taught   *stable*
   to grow.
No foreign banished wight shall anchor in this port:
Our realm brooks no seditious sects—let them elsewhere resort.
15 My rusty sword through rest[8] shall first his edge employ
To poll their tops[9] who seek such change or gape for future joy.
        Vivat Regina[1]

ca. 1571   1589

On Monsieur's Departure[1]

I grieve and dare not show my discontent,
I love and yet am forced to seem to hate,
I do, yet dare not say I ever meant,
I seem stark mute but inwardly do prate.°   *chatter*
5   I am and not, I freeze and yet am burned,
    Since from myself another self I turned.

My care is like my shadow in the sun,
Follows me flying, flies when I pursue it,
Stands and lies by me, doth what I have done.[2]

1. The poem concerns Mary, Queen of Scots, who in 1568 sought refuge in England from her rebellious subjects.
2. I.e., threaten to do me harm ("annoy").
3. I.e., the tide of faith (loyalty) is ebbing, yielding to the rising tide of falsehood.
4. Clouds of tricks ("toys") not yet tested or detected hide the "aspiring minds" of ambitious foes, but those clouds will turn at last into rains of repentance.
5. The deception ("guile") grafted into them will not bear fruit.
6. Strife. Mary Stuart also was sometimes called "Mother of Debate," because she was constantly

the focus of conspiracies and plots.
7. "Former rule": either the reign of Henry VIII or that of Edward VI, which established the Reformation in England.
8. Sword rusty from disuse.
9. Strike off their heads.
1. Long live the queen.
1. The heading, present in a 17th-century manuscript, identifies the occasion of this poem as the breaking off of marriage negotiations between Elizabeth and the French duke of Anjou, in 1582.
2. Does everything I do.

10   His too familiar care[3] doth make me rue° it.   *regret*
       No means I find to rid him from my breast,
       Till by the end of things it be suppressed.

       Some gentler passion slide into my mind,
       For I am soft and made of melting snow;
15   Or be more cruel, love, and so be kind.
       Let me or° float or sink, be high or low.   *either*
       Or let me live with some more sweet content,
       Or die and so forget what love e'er° meant.   *ever*

ca. 1582   1823

A Letter to Robert Dudley, Earl of Leicester, February 10, 1586[1]

How contemptuously we conceive ourselves to have been used by you, you shall by this bearer[2] understand: whom we have expressly sent unto you to charge you withal. We could never have imagined (had we not seen it fall out[3] in experience) that a man raised up by ourself and extraordinarily favored by us, above any other subject of this land, would have in so contemptible a sort broken our commandment in a cause that so greatly toucheth us in honor. Whereof although you have showed yourself to make but little account in so most undutiful a sort, you may not therefore think that we have so little care of the reparation thereof as we mind to pass so great a wrong in silence unredressed. And therefore our express pleasure and commandment is that, all delays and excuses laid apart, you do presently upon the duty of your allegiance obey and fulfill whatsoever the bearer hereof shall direct you to do in our name.[4] Whereof fail you not, as you will answer the contrary at your uttermost peril.

1586   1935

---

3. I.e., my own care, which he caused.
1. Leicester (ca. 1532–1588) had been the queen's greatest favorite from the beginning of her reign, and was for a time her suitor and possibly lover. Sent to the Netherlands to assist the revolt of the Dutch Protestants against Spanish rule, however, he incurred her rage by accepting, without her permission, the offer of the Dutch to make him their absolute governor. They had been without a leader since the assassination of William of Orange, in 1584, and had offered Elizabeth her-

self the sovereignty of the United Provinces (which she declined) the preceding summer.
2. Sir Thomas Heneage, one of Elizabeth's most trusted courtiers.
3. Happen.
4. Heneage was instructed to direct Leicester to resign the governorship immediately. Though it was several months before Leicester did so, Elizabeth was by April already addressing him fondly again.

A Letter to Sir Amyas Paulet, August 1586[1]

Amyas, my most careful and faithful servant,

God reward thee treblefold in the double for thy most troublesome charge[2] so well discharged. If you knew, my Amyas, how kindly, besides dutifully, my careful[3] heart accepts your double labors and faithful actions, your wise orders and safe regards performed in so dangerous and crafty[4] a charge, it would ease your troubles' travail and rejoice your heart. In which I charge you to carry this most nighest thought: that I cannot balance in any weight of my judgment the value that I prize you at. And suppose no treasure to countervail[5] such a faith, and condemn me in that behalf which I never committed if I reward not such deserts. Yea, let me lack when I have most need if I acknowledge not such a merit with a reward *non omnibus datum*.[6]

But let your wicked mistress know how, with hearty sorrow, her vile deserts compels these orders; and bid her, from me, ask God forgiveness for her treacherous dealing towards the saver of her life many years, to the intolerable peril of her own.[7] And yet not content with so many forgivenesses, must fall again so horribly, far passing a woman's thought, much more a princess', instead of excusing, whereof not one can serve, it being so plainly confessed by the actors[8] of my guiltless death. Let repentance take place; and let not the fiend possess her so as her best part be lost, which I pray with hands lifted up to Him that may both save and spill,[9] with my loving adieu and prayer for thy long life.

> Your most assured and loving sovereign in heart,
> by good desert induced, *Elizabeth Regina.*

1586   1854

A Letter to King James VI of Scotland, February 14, 1587

My dear brother,[1]

I would you knew though not felt the extreme dolor that overwhelms my mind for that miserable accident,[2] which far contrary to my meaning hath befallen. I have now sent this kinsman of mine,[3] whom ere now it hath

---

1. Paulet was the keeper of Mary, Queen of Scots. In 1586 a number of her supporters, led by Anthony Babington, plotted to murder Elizabeth and place Mary on the throne. The plot was discovered, and the plotters were executed in September. Mary, who had been complicit with them, was placed under stricter confinement, and then tried for treason.

Elizabeth's letter to Paulet circulated widely in manuscript: to her contemporaries, it was evidently the single best-known of the queen's letters.
2. Duty, responsibility.
3. Full of care.
4. Requiring skill.
5. To be equal in value to.
6. Not given to all.

7. I.e., Elizabeth's own life.
8. I.e., the conspirators.
9. Destroy.
1. Fellow ruler.
2. I.e., the execution, six days before, of James's mother, Mary, Queen of Scots. In the aftermath of the Babington plot, Elizabeth decided to have Mary tried and convicted of treason—legally an outrageous charge, since she was not a subject of England. Mary was sentenced to death, and Elizabeth, after much vacillation, signed the warrant for her execution. Once the sentence had been carried out, however, the queen went to great lengths to exculpate herself, even in her own mind, from responsibility for her cousin's death.
3. Sir Robert Carey, related to Elizabeth on her mother's side.

pleased you to favor, to instruct you truly of that which is too irksome for my pen to tell you. I beseech you that—as God and many more know—how innocent I am in this case, so you will believe me that if I had bid aught I would have bid by it.[4] I am not so base minded that fear of any living creature or prince should make me afraid to do that[5] were just or, done, to deny the same. I am not of so base a lineage nor carry so vile a mind; but as not to disguise fits most a king, so will I never dissemble my actions but cause them show even as I meant them. Thus assuring yourself of me that, as I know this was deserved, yet if I had meant it I would never lay it on others' shoulders, no more will I not damnify[6] myself that thought it not. The circumstance it may please you to have of this bearer. And for your part, think you have not in the world a more loving kinswoman nor a more dear friend than myself, nor any that will watch more carefully to preserve you and your estate.[7] And who shall otherwise persuade you, judge them more partial to others than you. And thus in haste, I leave to trouble you, beseeching God to send you a long reign. The 14 of February, 1587.

> Your most assured, loving sister and cousin,
> *Elizabeth R.*

1587   1834

Verse Exchange between Elizabeth and Sir Walter Ralegh[1]

[RALEGH TO ELIZABETH]

Fortune hath taken away my love,
My life's joy and my soul's heaven above.
Fortune hath taken thee away, my princess,
My world's joy and my true fantasy's mistress.

5   Fortune hath taken thee away from me;
Fortune hath taken all by taking thee.
Dead to all joys, I only live to woe:
So is Fortune become my fantasy's foe.

In vain, my eyes, in vain ye waste your tears;
10   In vain, my sights,[2] the smoke of my despairs,
In vain you search the earth and heaven above.
In vain you search, for Fortune keeps my love.

Then will I leave my love in Fortune's hand;
Then will I leave my love in worldlings' band,[3]
15   And only love the sorrows due to me—
Sorrow, henceforth, that shall my princess be—

---

4. I.e., if I had commanded her death, I would have abided by my decision. ("Bid" is a form of the past participle of both "bid" and "bide.")
5. I.e., the thing that.
6. Wrong.
7. Position.
1. This exchange, which exemplifies the poetic banter that sometimes passed between the queen and her favorites, took place about 1587, when Ralegh believed that the rapid rise of the earl of Essex in Elizabeth's favor entailed a diminution of his own standing with her.
2. Sighs?
3. Bond.

And only joy that Fortune conquers kings.
Fortune, that rules the earth and earthly things,
Hath taken my love in spite of virtue's might:
20 So blind a goddess did never virtue right.

With wisdom's eyes had but blind Fortune seen,
Then had my love, my love forever been.
But love, farewell—though Fortune conquer thee,
No fortune base nor frail shall alter me.

[ELIZABETH TO RALEGH]

Ah, silly Pug,[4] wert thou so sore afraid?
Mourn not, my Wat,[5] nor be thou so dismayed.
It passeth fickle Fortune's power and skill
To force my heart to think thee any ill.
5 No Fortune base, thou sayest, shall alter thee?
And may so blind a witch so conquer me?
No, no, my Pug, though Fortune were not blind,
Assure thyself she could not rule my mind.
Fortune, I know, sometimes doth conquer kings,
10 And rules and reigns on earth and earthly things,
But never think Fortune can bear the sway
If virtue watch, and will her not obey.
Ne chose I thee by fickle Fortune's rede,[6]
Ne she shall force me alter with such speed
15 But if to try this mistress' jest with thee.[7]
Pull up thy heart, suppress thy brackish tears,
Torment thee not, but put away thy fears.
Dead to all joys and living unto woe,
Slain quite by her that ne'er gave wise men blow,
20 Revive again and live without all dread,
The less afraid, the better thou shalt speed.[8]

ca. 1587   ca. 1600?

Speech to the Troops at Tilbury[1]

My loving people, I have been persuaded by some that are careful of[2] my
safety, to take heed how I committed myself to armed multitudes, for fear of
treachery. But I tell you that I would not desire to live to distrust my faithful
and loving people. Let tyrants fear! I have so behaved myself that, under

---

4. An endearment, which Elizabeth used as her
pet name for Ralegh.
5. Short for Walter.
6. Decision. "Ne": nor.
7. Since "thee" has nothing to rhyme with, and
since the line is hard to construe, it seems likely
that there is a line missing before or after this
one. "But if": unless I do it.
8. Succeed.

1. Delivered by Elizabeth on August 9, 1588, to
the land forces assembled at Tilbury (in Essex) to
repel the anticipated invasion of the Spanish
Armada, a fleet of warships sent by Philip II. The
Armada was defeated at sea and never reached
England, a miraculous deliverance and sign of
God's special favor to Elizabeth and to England,
in the general view.
2. Anxious about.

God, I have placed my chiefest strength and safeguard in the loyal hearts and goodwill of my subjects. Wherefore I am come among you at this time but for my recreation and pleasure, being resolved in the midst and heat of the battle to live and die amongst you all,[3] to lay down for my God and for my kingdom and for my people mine honor and my blood even in the dust. I know I have the body but of a weak and feeble woman; but I have the heart and stomach of a king, and of a king of England too[4]—and take foul scorn that Parma[5] or any prince of Europe should dare to invade the borders of my realm. To the which, rather than any dishonor shall grow by me, I myself will venter[6] my royal blood; I myself will be your general, judge, and rewarder of your virtue in the field. I know that already for your forwardness you have deserved rewards and crowns,[7] and I assure you in the word of a prince you shall not fail of them. In the meantime, my lieutenant general[8] shall be in my stead, than whom never prince commanded a more noble or worthy subject; not doubting but by your concord in the camp and valor in the field, and your obedience to myself and my general, we shall shortly have a famous victory over these enemies of my God and of my kingdom.

1588   1654

The "Golden Speech"

The "Golden Speech"   A speech to Elizabeth's last Parliament, delivered November 30, 1601, and here given as recorded by one of the members. The designation "Golden Speech" stems from the headnote to a version of the speech printed near the end of the Puritan interregnum (1659?): "This speech ought to be set in letters of gold, that as well the majesty, prudence, and virtue of this royal queen might in general most exquisitely appear, as also that her religious love and tender respect which she particularly and constantly did bear to her Parliament in unfeigned sincerity might (to the shame and perpetual disgrace and infamy of some of her successors) be nobly and truly vindicated."

The royal prerogatives included the right to grant or sell "letters patent," which gave the recipient monopoly control of some branch of commerce. (Sir Walter Ralegh, for example, was given the exclusive right, for a period of thirty years, to license all taverns.) Discontent with the monopolies—which had resulted in higher prices for a wide range of commodities, including such basic ones as salt and starch—came to a head in the Parliament of 1601. Under parliamentary pressure (and in return for a subsidy granted to her treasury), Elizabeth agreed to revoke some of the most obnoxious patents and to allow the courts to rule freely on charges brought against the holders of others. She invited members of Parliament who wished to offer

---

3. In another version of the speech (based, like this one, on an auditor's memory), the sentence up to this point reads: "And therefore I am come amongst you, as you see at this time, not for my recreation and disport, but being resolved in the midst and heat of the battle to live or die amongst you all."
4. An allusion to the concept of the king's (or queen's) two bodies, the one natural and mortal, the other an ideal and enduring political construct. "Stomach": valor.
5. Alessandro Farnese, duke of Parma, allied with the king of Spain and expected to join with him in the invasion of England.
6. Venture, risk.
7. The crown was an English coin. "Forwardness": eagerness.
8. The earl of Leicester led the English troops. Elizabeth's great and powerful favorite, he died just a month later.

thanks for this largesse to come to her in a body, and on November 30 received about 150 of them at Whitehall Palace. After effusive remarks by the speaker of the House of Commons (Sir John Croke), the queen responded more or less as recorded here. (Elizabeth revised the speech for publication; and none of the surviving versions of it—which differ considerably—was printed earlier than about 1628.)

The "Golden Speech"[1]

Mr. Speaker, we have heard your declaration and perceive your care of our estate,[2] by falling into the consideration of a grateful acknowledgment of such benefits as you have received; and that your coming is to present thanks unto us, which I accept with no less joy than your loves can have desire to offer such a present.

I do assure you that there is no prince that loveth his subjects better, or whose love can countervail[3] our loves. There is no jewel, be it of never so rich a price, which I set before this jewel—I mean your loves. For I do more esteem it than any treasure or riches: for that we know how to prize, but love and thanks I count unvaluable.[4] And though God hath raised me high, yet this I count the glory of my crown, that I have reigned with your loves. This makes me that I do not so much rejoice that God hath made me to be a queen, as to be a queen over so thankful a people. Therefore I have cause to wish nothing more than to content the subjects, and that is a duty which I owe. Neither do I desire to live longer days than that I may see your prosperity, and that is my only desire. And as I am that person that still,[5] yet under God, hath delivered you, so I trust, by the almighty power of God, that I shall be His instrument to preserve you from envy, peril, dishonor, shame, tyranny, and oppression, partly by means of your intended helps, which we take very acceptable because it manifesteth the largeness of your loves and loyalties unto your sovereign.

Of myself I must say this: I never was any greedy, scraping grasper, nor a strait, fast-holding prince, nor yet a waster. My heart was never set on worldly goods, but only for my subjects' good. What you bestow on me, I will not hoard it up, but receive it to bestow on you again. Yea, my own properties I account yours to be expended for your good, and your eyes shall see the bestowing of all for your good. Therefore render unto them from me, I beseech you, Mr. Speaker, such thanks as you imagine my heart yieldeth but my tongue cannot express.

Mr. Speaker, I would wish you and the rest to stand up, for I shall yet trouble you with longer speech.[6]

Mr. Speaker, you give me thanks, but I doubt[7] me that I have more cause to thank you all than you me; and I charge you to thank them of the Lower

1. We print only the words of the queen, omitting various interpolations, as well as opening remarks by the speaker of the Parliament.
2. Rank, position.
3. Match.

4. Invaluable.
5. Continually.
6. Up to this point, the assemblage had been kneeling.
7. Fear.

House[8] from me. For had I not received a knowledge from you, I might have fallen into the lapse of an error only for lack of true information.

Since I was queen yet did I never put my pen to any grant but that upon pretext and semblance made unto me, it was both good and beneficial to the subject in general, though a private profit to some of my ancient servants who had deserved well. But the contrary being found by experience, I am exceedingly beholding to such subjects as would move the same at the first.[9] And I am not so simple to suppose but that there be some of the Lower House whom these grievances never touched; and for them I think they speak out of zeal to their countries[1] and not out of spleen or malevolent affection, as being parties grieved. And I take it exceedingly gratefully from them, because it gives us to know that no respects or interests had moved them other than the minds they bear to suffer[2] no diminution of our honor and our subjects' love unto us, the zeal of which affection, tending to ease my people and knit their hearts unto me, I embrace with a princely care.

For above all earthly treasures I esteem my people's love, more than which I desire not to merit. That my grants should be grievous to my people and oppressions to be privileged under color[3] of our patents, our kingly dignity shall not suffer it. Yea, when I heard it I could give no rest unto my thoughts until I had reformed it.[4] Shall they (think you) escape unpunished that have thus oppressed you and have been respectless of their duty and regardless of our honor? No, no, Mr. Speaker, I assure you were it not more for conscience' sake than for any glory or increase of love that I desire, these errors, troubles, vexations, and oppressions done by these varlets and low persons (not worthy the name of subjects) should not escape without condign punishment. But I perceive they dealt with me like physicians who, ministering a drug, make it more acceptable by giving it a good aromatical savor; or when they give pills, do gild them all over.

I have ever used[5] to set the Last Judgment Day before my eyes and so to rule as I shall be judged, to answer before a higher Judge. To whose judgment seat I do appeal that never thought was cherished in my heart that tended not unto my people's good. And now if my kingly bounties have been abused and my grants turned to the hurts of my people, contrary to my will and meaning, or if any in authority under me have neglected or perverted what I have committed to them, I hope God will not lay their culps[6] and offenses to my charge. Who, though there were danger in repealing our grants, yet what danger would I not rather incur for your good than I would suffer them still to continue?

I know the title of a king is a glorious title, but assure yourself that the shining glory of princely authority hath not so dazzled the eyes of our understanding but that we well know and remember that we also are to yield an account of our actions before the great Judge. To be a king and wear a crown is more glorious to them that see it than it is pleasant to them that bear it.

---

8. The House of Commons.
9. I.e., those members of the House of Commons who had raised the issue of monopolies in previous sessions.
1. Their constituents.
2. Permit. "Minds": intentions.
3. Pretext.

4. In fact Elizabeth was extremely slow to respond to the grievances, which had, for example, previously been raised in the Parliament of 1597.
5. Been accustomed.
6. Sins.

For myself, I was never so much enticed with the glorious name of a king or royal authority of a queen as delighted that God hath made me His instrument to maintain His truth and glory, and to defend this kingdom (as I said) from peril, dishonor, tyranny, and oppression.

There will never queen sit in my seat with more zeal to my country, care to my subjects, and that will sooner with willingness venture her life for your good and safety, than myself. For it is not my desire to live nor reign longer than my life and reign shall be for your good. And though you have had and may have many princes more mighty and wise sitting in this seat, yet you never had or shall have any that will be more careful and loving.

Shall I ascribe anything to myself and my sexly[7] weakness? I were not worthy to live then, and of all most unworthy of the mercies I have had from God, who hath ever yet given me a heart which yet never feared any foreign or home enemy. I speak it to give God the praise as a testimony before you, and not to attribute anything unto myself. For I, O Lord, what am I, whom practices and perils past should not fear?[8] O, what can I do, that I should speak for any glory? God forbid!

This, Mr. Speaker, I pray you deliver unto the House, to whom heartily recommend me. And so I commit you all to your best fortunes and further counsels. And I pray you, Mr. Comptroller, Mr. Secretary,[9] and you of my council, that before these gentlemen depart into their countries,[1] you bring them all to kiss my hand.

1601   1601 (in a summary version)

7. Characteristic of my sex. "Ascribe": attribute.
8. Frighten. "Practices": treacherous schemes.
9. William Knollys, earl of Banbury, and Robert

Cecil, earl of Salisbury.
1. Districts.

EDMUND SPENSER
1552?–1599

Edmund Spenser set out, consciously and deliberately, to become the great English poet of his age. In a culture in which most accomplished poetry was written by those who were, or at least professed to be, principally interested in something else—advancement at court, diplomacy, statecraft, or the church—Spenser's ambition was altogether remarkable, and it is still more remarkable that he succeeded in reaching his goal. Unlike such poets as Wyatt, Surrey, and Sidney, born to privilege and social distinction, Spenser was born to parents of modest means and station, in London, probably in 1552. He nonetheless received an impressive education, first at the Merchant Taylors' School, under its demanding headmaster, the humanist Richard Mulcaster, then at Pembroke College, Cambridge, where he was enrolled as a "sizar," or poor (meaning impoverished) scholar. At Cambridge, which harbored many Puritans, Spenser started as a poet by translating some poems for a volume of anti-Catholic propaganda. He also began his friendship with Gabriel Harvey, an eccentric Cambridge don, humanist, and pamphleteer. Their correspondence shows that they shared a passionate and patriotic interest in the reformation of English verse. In a 1580 letter to Harvey, Spenser demanded, "Why a God's name may not we, as else the Greeks, have the kingdom of our own language?"

After receiving the B.A. degree in 1573 and the M.A. in 1576, Spenser served as personal secretary and aide to several prominent men, including the earl of Leicester, the queen's principal favorite. During his employment in Leicester's household he came to know Sir Philip Sidney and Sir Edward Dyer, courtiers who sought to promote a new English poetry. Spenser's contribution to the movement was *The Shepheardes Calender,* published in 1579 and dedicated to Sidney.

In *The Shepheardes Calender* Spenser used a deliberately archaic language, partly in homage to Chaucer, whose work he praised as a "well of English undefiled," and partly to achieve a rustic effect, in keeping with the feigned simplicity of pastoral poetry's shepherd singers. Sidney did not entirely approve, and another contemporary, Ben Jonson, growled that Spenser "writ no language." In the eighteenth century, Samuel Johnson described the language of *The Shepheardes Calender* as "studied barbarity." Johnson's characterization is, in a way, quite accurate, for Spenser was attempting to conjure up a native English style to which he could wed the classical mode of the pastoral. Moreover, since pastoral was traditionally viewed as the prelude in a great national poet's career to more ambitious undertakings, Spenser was also in effect announcing his extravagant ambition.

Spenser was a prolific and daring experimenter: the poems of *The Shepheardes Calender* use no fewer than thirteen different metrical schemes. In his later poems, he went on to make further innovations: the best-known of these are the special rhyme scheme of the Spenserian sonnet; the remarkably beautiful adaptation of the Italian *canzone* forms for the *Epithalamion* and *Prothalamion;* and the nine-line, or "Spenserian," stanza of *The Faerie Queene*, with its hexameter (six-stress) line at the end. Spenser is sometimes called the "poet's poet," because so many later English poets learned the art of versification from him. In the nineteenth century alone his influence may be seen in Shelley's *Revolt of Islam*, Byron's *Childe Harold's Pilgrimage*, Keats's *Eve of St. Agnes*, and Tennyson's "The Lotos-Eaters."

The year after the publication of *The Shepheardes Calender,* Spenser went to Ireland as secretary and aide to Lord Grey of Wilton, lord deputy of Ireland. Although he tried continually to obtain appointments in England and to secure the patronage of the queen, he spent the rest of his career in Ireland, holding various minor government posts and hence participating actively in the English struggle against those who resisted colonial domination. The grim realities of that struggle—massacre, the burning of miserable hovels and of crops with the deliberate intention of starving the inhabitants, the forced relocation of whole communities, the manipulation of treason charges so as to facilitate the seizure of lands, the endless repetition of acts of military "justice" calculated to intimidate and break the spirit—may be glimpsed in distorted and on occasion direct form throughout Spenser's writings, along with dreamlike depictions of the beauty of the Irish landscape. Those writings include an anonymously published political tract, *A View of the Present State of Ireland*, which was unusual in its time both for its genuine fascination with Irish culture and for the ruthlessness of the policies it recommended.

Spenser's attitudes toward Ireland and his conduct there raise difficult questions concerning the relationship between literature and colonialism. Are the harsh policies of the *View* echoed, allegorically, in *The Faerie Queene?* What does it mean to admire a poet who might, by modern standards, be judged a war criminal (as his master, Lord Grey, was judged to be, even by notoriously brutal Elizabethan standards)? Does Spenser use his Irish vantage point to launch daring criticisms of Queen Elizabeth and the English form of government? In addition to sharpening racial chauvinism, the experience of Ireland seems to have given English settlers a new perspective on events back home. As one of Spenser's contemporaries remarked, words that would be considered treasonous in England were common table talk among the Irish settlers.

Spenser was rewarded for his efforts in Ireland with a castle and 3,028 acres of expropriated land at Kilcolman, in the province of Munster. There he was visited by another colonist and poet, the powerful and well-connected Sir Walter Ralegh, to whom Spenser showed the great chivalric epic on which he was at work. With Ralegh's influential backing, Spenser traveled to England and published, in 1590, the first three books of *The Faerie Queene*, which made a strong bid for the queen's favor and patronage. He was rewarded with a handsome pension of fifty pounds a year for life, though the queen's principal councillor, Lord Burghley, is said to have complained that it was a lot for a song. Soon after, Spenser published a volume of poems called *Complaints*; a pastoral called *Colin Clouts Come Home Againe* (1595), commenting on the courtiers and ladies at the center of English court life at the time of his 1590 visit; his sonnet cycle, *Amoretti*; and two wedding poems, *Epithalamion* and *Prothalamion*. The six-book *Faerie Queene* was published in 1596, with some revisions in the first part and a changed ending to Book 3 to provide a bridge to the added books; the two so-called Mutability Cantos and two stanzas of a third—perhaps part of an intended seventh book—appeared posthumously, in the edition of 1609.

In 1598 there was an uprising in Munster, and rebels burned down the house in which Spenser lived. The poet fled with his wife; their newborn baby is said to have died in the flames. Spenser was sent to England with messages from the besieged English garrison. He died on January 13, 1599, and was buried near his beloved Chaucer in what is now called the Poets' Corner of Westminster Abbey.

Spenser cannot be put into neatly labeled categories. His work is steeped in Renaissance Neoplatonism but is also earthy and practical. He is a lover and celebrator of physical beauty yet also a profound analyst of good and evil in all their perplexing shapes and complexities. Strongly influenced by Puritanism in his early days, he remained a thoroughgoing Protestant all his life, and portrayed the Roman Catholic Church as a demonic villain in *The Faerie Queene*; yet his understanding of faith and of sin owes much to Catholic thinkers. He is a poet of sensuous images yet also something of an iconoclast, deeply suspicious of the power of images (material and verbal) to turn into idols. He is an idealist, drawn to courtesy, gentleness, and exquisite moral refinement, yet also a celebrant of English nationalism, empire, and martial power. He is the author of the most memorable literary idealization of Elizabeth I, yet he fills his poem with coded criticisms of the queen. He is in some ways a backward-looking poet, who paid homage to Chaucer, used archaic language, and compared his own age unfavorably with the feudal past. Yet as a British epic poet and poet-prophet, he points forward to the poetry of the Romantics and especially Milton—who himself paid homage to the "sage and serious" Spenser as "a better teacher than Scotus or Aquinas."

Because it was a deliberate choice on Spenser's part that his language should seem antique, his poetry is always printed in the original spelling and punctuation; a few of the most confusing punctuation marks have, however, been altered in the present text. Spenser also spells words variably, in such a way as to suggest rhymes to the eye or to suggest etymologies (often incorrect ones). This inconsistency in his spelling is typical of his time; in the sixteenth century, people varied even the spelling of their own names.*

---

* For additional writings by Spenser—"Aprill" from *The Shepheardes Calender*, four more sonnets from the *Amoretti* (nos. 15, 35, 59, 70), "A Hymne in Honour of Beautie," and, from *The Faerie Queene*, the Cave of Mammon canto from Book 2, extensive excerpts from Book 3, and the Mutabilitie Cantos—see the supplemental ebook. For excerpts from *A View of the Present State of Ireland* and a portrait of Spenser, see "Island Nations" in the ebook.

The Shepheardes Calender

Pastoral poetry—with its odd idea of shepherds among their flocks piping on their flutes and singing beautiful songs of love, sadness, and complaint—was an influential classical form whose most famous practitioners were the Alexandrian poet Theocritus (third century B.C.E.) and the Roman poet Virgil (first century B.C.E.). The singers of the pastoral, or eclogue, were depicted as simple rustics who inhabited a world in which human beings and nature lived in harmony, but the form was always essentially urban, and Spenser, a Londoner, was self-consciously assuming a highly conventional literary role. That role enabled him both to lay claim to the prestige of classical poetry and to insist upon his native Englishness, an insistence that is signaled by the deliberately archaic, pseudo-Chaucerian language. The rustic mask also allowed Spenser, in certain of the eclogues, to make sharply satirical comments on controversial religious and political issues of his day, such as Elizabeth's suppression of Puritan clergy in the Church of England, and to reflect on his own marginal position.

The twelve eclogues of *The Shepheardes Calender* are titled for the months of the year. Each is prefaced by an illustrative woodcut representing the characters and theme of the poem and picturing, in the clouds above, the sign of the zodiac for that month, and each is accompanied by a commentary ascribed to "E. K.," who also wrote an introductory epistle to the work as a whole. "E. K.," who has not been identified but must have been someone close to Spenser (or, in the opinion of some, Spenser himself), trumpets the arrival of a "new poet" whose skills are conspicuously displayed in the sequence of poems. "October" deals with the place of poetry and the responsibility of the poet in the world, an important theme throughout the *Calender* and in much of Spenser's work.

From The Shepheardes Calender

To His Booke

Goe little booke:[1] thy selfe present,
As child whose parent is unkent:°   *unknown*
To him that is the president°   *pattern*
Of noblesse and of chevalree,
5   And if that Envie barke at thee,
As sure it will, for succoure° flee   *aid*
    Under the shadow of his wing,[2]
And askèd, who thee forth did bring,
A shepheards swaine° saye did thee sing,   *boy*
10   All as his straying flocke he fedde:
And when his honor has thee redde,°   *seen*
Crave pardon for my hardyhedde.°   *boldness*
    But if that any aske thy name,
Say thou wert base° begot with blame: *lowly*
15   For thy° thereof thou takest shame.   *therefore*
And when thou art past jeopardee,
Come tell me, what was sayd of mee:
And I will send more after thee.
           IMMERITO.°   *unworthy*

---

1. A deliberate echo of Chaucer's line "Go litel bok, go litel myn tragedye" (*Troilus and Criseyde* 5.1786).

2. I.e., the protective sponsorship of Sir Philip Sidney, to whom this poem dedicates the book.

October[3]

Aegloga decima[4]

ARGUMENT

In Cuddie[5] is set out the perfecte paterne of a Poete, which finding no main-tenaunce of his state and studies, complayneth of the comtempte of Poetrie, and the causes thereof: Specially having bene in all ages, and even amongst the most barbarous alwayes of singular accounpt[6] and honor, and being in-dede so worthy and commendable an arte: or rather no arte, but a divine gift and heavenly instinct not to bee gotten by laboure and learning, but adorned with both: and poured into the witte by a certaine *enthousiasmos* and celes-tiall inspiration, as the Author hereof els where at large discourseth, in his booke called the English Poete,[7] which booke being lately come to my hands, I mynde[8] also by Gods grace upon further advisement to publish.

PIERS   CUDDIE

Cuddie, for shame hold up thy heavye head,
And let us cast with what delight to chace,

3. When *The Shepheardes Calender* was published, in 1579, each of the twelve eclogues was followed by a commentary (called a "Glosse") by the mysterious "E. K.," which contained explications of difficult or archaic words, together with learned discussions of—and disagreements with—Spenser's ideas, imagery, and poetics. Designed to appear authoritative, the commentaries in fact often serve to complicate the process of interpretation. In order to give the reader some sense of them, we have included several of the individual notes from the "October" Glosse. For the complete Glosse, see the edition of "October" in the supplemental ebook.
4. Tenth Eclogue. An eclogue ("aeglogue") is a short pastoral poem in the form of a dialogue or soliloquy. Spenser's spelling is based on a false etymology (aix, "goat"+logos, "speech"), signifying, according to E. K., "Goteheards tales." For this eclogue, E. K. identifies as sources Theocritus's *Idyl* 16, which reproves the tyrant Hiero of

Syracuse for his neglect of poets, and also Baptista Spagnuoli (1448–1516), called Mantuan (the fifth eclogue). The illustration portrays Cuddie (left) holding a pipe and crowned with a laurel wreath (emblems of a poet). He talks with his fellow shepherd, Piers, in a pastoral landscape, with the court in the background. The astrological sign for October, Scorpio, is at the top of the picture.
5. E. K. queries "whether by Cuddie be specified the authour selfe, or some other," noting that in "August" he was introduced as singing a song "of Colins making. So that some doubt, that the persons be different." It may be that Cuddie and Piers present different aspects of Spenser the poet.
6. Esteem.
7. *The English Poete* is evidently a lost work by Spenser. *"Enthousiasmos"*: inspiration. The Greek word originally meant "possessed by a god."
8. Intend.

And weary thys long lingring Phoebus race.[9]
Whilome thou wont[1] the shepheards laddes to leade,
5   In rymes, in ridles, and in bydding base:[2]
Now they in thee, and thou in sleepe art dead.

CUDDIE

Piers, I have pypèd erst° so long with payne,°   *up to now / care*
That all mine Oten reedes[3] bene rent° and wore: *torn*
And my poore Muse hath spent her sparèd° store,   *saved up*
10 Yet little good hath got, and much lesse gayne.
Such pleasaunce makes the Grashopper so poore,
And ligge so layd,[4] when Winter doth her straine.°   *constrain*

The dapper° ditties, that I wont devise,   *pretty*
To feede youthes fancie, and the flocking fry,[5]
15 Delighten much: what I the bett for thy?[6]
They han° the pleasure, I a sclender prise.   *have*
I beate the bush, the byrds to them doe flye:
What good thereof to Cuddie can arise?

PIERS

Cuddie, the prayse is better, then° the price,   *than*
20 The glory eke° much greater then the gayne: *also*
O what an honor is it, to restraine
The lust° of lawlesse youth with good advice:[7]   *desires*
Or pricke° them forth with pleasaunce of thy vaine°   *spur / talent*
Whereto thou list° their traynèd° willes entice.   *desire / ensnared*

25 Soone as thou gynst° to sette thy notes in frame,   *begin*
O how the rurall routes° to thee doe cleave: *crowds*
Seemeth thou dost their soule of sence bereave,[8]
All as the shepheard, that did fetch his dame
From Plutoes balefull bowre withouten leave:
30 His musicks might the hellish hound did tame.[9]

CUDDIE

So praysen babes the Peacoks spotted traine,
And wondren at bright Argus blazing eye:[1]

9. I.e., let us see how we may pass this long day pleasantly.
1. Formerly you were accustomed.
2. A popular game; here, perhaps a poetry contest.
3. The shepherd's pipe, symbol of pastoral poetry.
4. I.e., lie so subdued. The reference is to the fable of the industrious ant who laid up supplies for winter, and the carefree grasshopper who did not.
5. "A bold Metaphor, forced from the spawning fishes. For the multitude of young fish be called the frye" [E. K.]. "Wont": am accustomed to.
6. I.e., how am I the better for that?
7. E. K. compares these lines with *The Laws* 1, in which Plato declares "that the first invention of Poetry was of very vertuous intent."

8. I.e., hypnotize them. E. K. cites Plato and Pythagoras for the theory that the mind is made of "a certaine harmonie and musicall nombers," and gives several examples of music's irresistible power over the emotions.
9. In classical mythology, the three-headed dog Cerberus guards the entrance to Hades. But he let pass Orpheus, "of whom is sayd, that by his excellent skil in Musick and Poetry, he recovered his wife Eurydice from hell" [E. K.]; that is, from "Plutoes balefull bowre."
1. E. K. alludes to the myth of Argus of the hundred eyes, who, set by Juno to guard Io, Jupiter's current paramour, was lulled asleep by Mercury's music and then killed. Juno placed his eyes in the tail of her bird, the peacock, whose splendor elicits the praises even of "babes."

But who rewards him ere° the more for thy?°   *at all / therefore*
Or feedes him once the fuller by a graine?
35 Sike° prayse is smoke, that sheddeth° in the skye, *such / is dispersed*
Sike words bene wynd, and wasten soone in vayne.

PIERS

Abandon then the base and viler clowne,°   *rustic*
Lyft up thy selfe out of the lowly dust:
And sing of bloody Mars, of wars, of giusts.°   *jousts*
40 Turne thee to those, that weld° the awful° crowne, *bear / awesome*
To doubted° Knights, whose woundlesse[2] armour rusts, *dreaded*
And helmes unbruzèd waxen° dayly browne.   *grow*

There may thy Muse display her fluttryng wing,
And stretch her selfe at large from East to West:[3]
45 Whither thou list° in fayre Elisa rest,   *choose*
Or if thee please in bigger notes to sing,
Advaunce° the worthy whome shee loveth best,   *extol*
That first the white beare to the stake did bring.[4]

And when the stubborne stroke of stronger stounds,° *efforts*
50 Has somewhat slackt[5] the tenor of thy string:
Of love and lustihead tho° mayst thou sing,   *pleasure then*
And carrol lowde, and leade the Myllers rownde,[6]
All° were Elisa one of thilke same ring.[7]   *although*
So mought our Cuddies name to Heaven sownde.

CUDDIE

55 Indeede the Romish Tityrus,[8] I heare,
Through his Mecaenas left his Oaten reede,
Whereon he earst° had taught his flocks to feede,   *formerly*
And laboured lands to yield the timely eare,
And eft° did sing of warres and deadly drede,° *afterward / danger*
60 So as the Heavens did quake his verse to here.[9]

But ah Mecaenas is yclad in claye,
And great Augustus long ygoe is dead:
And all the worthies liggen° wrapt in leade,   *lie*

2. "Unwounded in warre, doe rust through long peace" [E. K.].
3. E. K. explains this "poeticall metaphore" as indicating the heroic subjects available to Cuddie if he wishes to "showe his skill in matter of more dignitie, then [i.e., than] is the homely Aeglogue." These include "our most gratious soveraign, whom (as before) he calleth Elisa," and also the "noble and valiaunt men" who deserve his praise and have been his patrons.
4. "He meaneth (as I guesse) the most honorable and renowmed the Erle of Leycester" [E. K.]. Leicester's device was the bear and ragged staff.
5. "That is when thou chaungest thy verse from stately discourse, to matter of more pleasaunce and delight" [E. K.].
6. "A kind of daunce" [E. K.].
7. A "company of dauncers" [E. K.].
8. "Wel knowen to be Virgile, who by Mecaenas means was brought into the favour of the Emperor Augustus, and by him moved to write in loftier kinde, then he erst had doen" [E. K.]. Maecenas ("Mecaenas") was Virgil's patron.
9. "In these three verses are the three severall workes of Virgile intended. For in teaching his flocks to feede, is meant his Aeglogues. In labouring of lands, is hys Georgiques. In singing of wars and deadly dreade, is his divine Aeneis figured" [E. K.]. The *Georgics* ("Georgiques") is Virgil's idealizing poem about farm life.

That matter made for Poets on to play:
65 For ever, who in derring doe were dreade,°   *held in awe*
The loftie verse of hem° was lovèd aye.[1]   *them*

But after vertue gan for age to stoupe,
And mighty manhode brought a bedde of° ease:[2]   *to bed by*
The vaunting Poets found nought worth a pease,°   *pea*
70 To put in preace° among the learned troupe.   *present for competition*
Tho° gan the streames of flowing wittes to cease,   *then*
And sonnebright honour pend in shamefull coupe.[3]

And if that any buddes of Poesie,
Yet of the old stocke gan to shoote agayne:
75 Or° it mens follies mote° be forst to fayne,°   *either / must / feign*
And rolle with rest in rymes of rybaudrye:°   *ribaldry*
Or as it sprong, it wither must agayne:
Tom Piper makes us better melodie.[4]

PIERS

O pierlesse Poesye, where is then thy place?
80 If nor in Princes pallace thou doe sitt:
(And yet is Princes pallace the most fitt)
Ne brest of baser birth[5] doth thee embrace.
Then make thee winges of thine aspyring wit,°   *mind*
And, whence thou camst, flye backe to heaven apace.

CUDDIE

85 Ah Percy it is all to° weake and wanne,   *too*
So high to sore,° and make so large a flight: *soar*
Her peecèd pyneons bene not so in plight,
For Colin fittes such famous flight to scanne:[6]
He, were he not with love so ill bedight,°   *afflicted*
90 Would mount as high, and sing as soote° as Swanne.[7]   *sweet*

PIERS

Ah fon,° for love does teach him climbe so hie,   *fool*
And lyftes him up out of the loathsome myre:
Such immortall mirrhor,[8] as he doth admire,
Would rayse ones mynd above the starry skie.

---

1. "He sheweth the cause, why Poetes were wont be had in such honor of noble men; that is, that by them their worthines and valor shold through theyr famous Posies be commended to al posterities" [E. K.]. "In derring doe": "In manhoode and chevalrie" [E. K.].
2. "He sheweth the cause of contempt of Poetry to be idlenesse and basenesse of mynd" [E. K.].
3. Coop, cage. I.e., poets found nothing worthy to write of, and the spirit of heroic achievement (sun-bright honor) found expression neither in deeds nor in song.
4. "An Ironicall Sarcasmus, spoken in derision

of these rude wits, whych make more account of a ryming rybaud, then of skill grounded upon learning and judgment" [E. K.].
5. "The meaner sort of men" [E. K.].
6. Cuddie explains that the imperfect, patched wings ("peecèd pyneons") of his own poetic powers are not in condition, but that it is proper for ("fittes") Colin to attempt ("scanne") such a high poetic flight.
7. "It is sayd of the learned that the swan a little before hir death, singeth most pleasantly" [E. K.].
8. "Beauty, which is an excellent object of Poeticall spirites" [E. K.].

95 And cause a caytive corage[9] to aspire,
  For lofty love doth loath a lowly eye.

CUDDIE

 All otherwise the state of Poet stands,
 For lordly love is such a Tyranne fell:°   *fierce*
 That where he rules, all power he doth expell.
100 The vaunted verse a vacant head demaundes,
  Ne wont with crabbèd care the Muses dwell:
  Unwisely weaves, that takes two webbes in hand.[1]

 Who ever casts° to compasse° weightye prise,   *tries / attain*
 And thinks to throwe out thondring words of threate:
105 Let powre in lavish cups and thriftie bitts of meate,
  For Bacchus fruite is frend to Phoebus wise.[2]
  And when with Wine the braine begins to sweate,
  The nombers° flowe as fast as spring doth ryse.   *verses*

 Thou kenst° not Percie howe the ryme should rage. *knowest*
110 O if my temples were distaind° with wine,   *stained*
  And girt in girlonds of wild Yvie[3] twine,
  How I could reare the Muse on stately stage,
  And teache her tread aloft in buskin fine,
  With queint Bellona[4] in her equipage.° *equipment; retinue*

115 But ah my corage cooles ere it be warme,
  For thy,° content us in thys humble shade: *therefore*
  Where no such troublous tydes° han us assayde,° *times / assaulted*
  Here we our slender pipes may safely charme.[5]

PIERS

 And when my Gates shall han their bellies layd:[6]
120 *Cuddie* shall have a Kidde to store his farme.

Cuddies Embleme

Agitante calescimus illo &c.[7]

9. "A base and abject minde" [E. K.].
1. I.e., the Muses are not accustomed ("wont") to dwell with those afflicted by love ("crabbèd care"); he is an unwise weaver who takes two pieces of cloth ("webbes") in hand at once.
2. I.e., let him pour lavish drink but take only a little food, for wine ("Bacchus fruite") promotes poetry ("Phoebus"—Apollo—is god of poetry).
3. Worn by followers of Bacchus. "He seemeth here to be ravished with a Poetical furie. For (if one rightly mark) the numbers rise so ful, and the verse groweth so big, that it seemeth he hath forgot the meanenesse of shepheards state and stile" [E. K.].
4. "Strange Bellona; the goddesse of battaile, that

is Pallas" [E. K.]. Pallas Athena, the Greek goddess of wisdom, is not normally identified with Bellona, the Roman goddess of war. "Buskin": a boot worn by the actors in classical tragedies—hence, a symbol for tragedy.
5. "Temper and order" [E.K.].
6. I.e., when my goats bear their young.
7. The Latin line, of which Spenser gives the first three words, is from Ovid's *Fasti* 6.5: "There is a god within us; it is from his stirring that we feel warm." E. K. comments, "Hereby is meant, as also in the whole course of this Aeglogue, that Poetry is a divine instinct and unnatural rage passing the reache of comen reason."

The Faerie Queene   In a letter to Sir Walter Ralegh, appended to the first, 1590, edition of *The Faerie Queene*, Spenser describes his exuberant, multifaceted poem as an allegory—an extended metaphor or "dark conceit"—and invites us to interpret the characters and adventures in its several books in terms of the particular virtues and vices they enact or come to embody. Thus the Redcrosse Knight in Book 1 is the knight of Holiness (and also St. George, the patron saint of England); Sir Guyon in Book 2 is the knight of Temperance; the female knight Britomart in Book 3 is the knight of Chastity (chastity here meaning chaste love leading to marriage). The heroes of Books 4, 5, and 6 represent Friendship, Justice, and Courtesy. The poem's general end, Spenser writes, is "to fashion a gentleman or noble person in vertuous and gentle discipline," and the individual moral qualities, taken together, constitute the ideal human being.

However, Spenser's allegory is not as simple as the letter to Ralegh might suggest, and the fashioning of identity proves to be anything but straightforward. Far from being the static embodiments of abstract moral precepts, the knights have a surprisingly complex, altogether human relation to their allegorical identities, identities into which they grow only through painful trial and error in the course of their adventures. These adventures repeatedly take the form of mortal combat with sworn enemies—hence the Redcrosse Knight of Holiness smites the "Saracen" (that is, Muslim) Sansfoy (literally, "without faith")—but the enemies are revealed more often than not to be weirdly dissociated aspects of the knights themselves: when he encounters Sansfoy, Redcrosse has just been faithless to his lady, Una, and his most dangerous enemy ultimately proves to be his own despair. Accordingly, the meaning of the various characters, episodes, and places is richly complex, revealed to us (and to the characters themselves) only by degrees.

The complexity is heightened by the inclusion, in addition to the moral allegory, of a historical allegory to which Spenser calls attention, in the letter to Ralegh, by observing that both the Faerie Queene and Belphoebe are personifications of Queen Elizabeth. (In fact, they are only two among many oblique representations of Elizabeth in the poem, some of them far from complimentary.) Throughout the poem there is a dense network of allusions to events, issues, and particular persons in England and Ireland—for example, the queen, her rival Mary, Queen of Scots, the Spanish Armada, the English Reformation, the controversies over religious images, and the bitter colonial struggles against Irish rebellion. Some of Spenser's characters are identified by conventional symbols and attributes that would have been obvious to readers of his time. For example, they would know immediately that a woman who wears a miter and scarlet clothes and dwells near the river Tiber represents (in one sense at least) the Roman Catholic Church, which had often been identified by Protestant preachers with the Whore of Babylon in the Book of Revelation. Marginal notes jotted in early copies of *The Faerie Queene* suggest, however, that there was no consensus among Spenser's contemporaries about the precise historical referents of others of the poem's myriad figures. (Sir Walter Ralegh's wife, Bess, for example, seems to have identified many of the virtuous female characters as allegorical representations of herself.) Spenser's poem may be enjoyed as a fascinating story with multiple meanings, a story that works on several levels at once and continually eludes the full and definitive allegorical explanation it constantly promises to deliver.

The poem is also an epic. In moving from *The Shepheardes Calender* to *The Faerie Queene* Spenser deliberately fashioned himself after the great Roman poet Virgil, who began his poetic career with pastoral poetry and moved on to his epic poem, the *Aeneid*. Spenser was acutely conscious that poets elsewhere in Europe, such as Ariosto and Tasso in Italy, and Camoens in Portugal, had already produced works modeled on Virgil's, in celebration of their respective nations. In weaving together classical and medieval sources, drawing on pictorial traditions, and adapting whole episodes from Ariosto and Tasso, he was providing his country with the epic it had hitherto lacked. Like Virgil, Spenser is deeply concerned with the dangerous struggles and painful renunciations required to achieve the highest values of human civilization. The heroic deeds of Spenser's brave knights are the achievements of individual aristocratic men and women, not the triumphs of armies or communities united in serving a common purpose, not even the triumph of the virtually invisible royal court of Gloriana, the Faerie Queene. Yet, taken together, the disjointed adventures of these solitary warriors constitute in Spenser's fervent vision the glory of Britain, the collective memory of its heroic past and the promise of a still more glorious future. And if the Faerie Queene herself is consigned to the margins of the poem that bears her name, she nonetheless is the symbolic embodiment of a shared national destiny, a destiny that reaches beyond mere political success to participate in the ultimate, millennial triumph of good over evil.

If *The Faerie Queene* is thus an epic celebration of Queen Elizabeth, the Protestant faith, and the English nation, it is also a chivalric romance, full of jousting knights and damsels in distress, dragons, witches, enchanted trees, wicked magicians, giants, dark caves, shining castles, and "paynims" (with French names). A clear, pleasant stream may be dangerous to drink from because to do so produces loss of strength. A pious hermit may prove to be a cunningly disguised villain. Houses, castles, and gardens are often places of education and challenge or of especially dense allegorical significance, as if they possess special, half-hidden keys to the meaning of the books in which they appear. As a romance, Spenser's poem is designed to produce wonder, to enthrall its readers with sprawling plots, marvelous adventures, heroic characters, ravishing descriptions, and esoteric mysteries.

In addition to enthralling readers, the poem habitually entraps, misleads, and deludes them. Like Spenser's protagonists, readers are constantly in danger of mistaking hypocritical evil for good, or cunningly disguised foulness for true beauty. *The Faerie Queene* demands vigilance from readers, and many passages must be reread in light of what follows after. In some sections, such as the dialogue between Redcrosse and Despaire (Book 1, canto 9), the repeated use of pronouns instead of proper names can lead to confusion as to who is speaking; the effect is intentional, for the promptings of evil are not always easy to disentangle from the voice of conscience.

The whole of *The Faerie Queene* is written in a remarkable nine-line stanza of closely interlocking rhymes (*ababbcbcc*), the first eight lines with five stresses each (iambic pentameter) and the final line with six stresses (iambic hexameter, or Alexandrine). The stanza gives the work a certain formal regularity, but the various books are composed on quite different structural principles. Book 1 is almost entirely self-contained; it has been called a miniature epic in itself, centering on the adventures of one principal hero, Redcrosse, who at length achieves the quest he undertakes at Una's behest: killing the dragon who has imprisoned her parents and thereby winning her as his bride. The spiritual allegory is similarly self-contained; it presents the Christian struggling heroically against many evils and temptations—doctrinal error, hypocrisy, the Seven Deadly Sins, and despair—to some of which he succumbs before finally emerging triumphant. It shows him separated from the one true faith and, aided by interventions of divine grace, at length reunited with it. Then it treats his purgation from sin, his education in the House of Holinesse, and his final salvation. By contrast, the structure of Book 3 is more romancelike, with its multiplicity of principal characters (who present, allegorically, several varieties of chaste and unchaste love), its interwoven stories, its heightened attention to women, and its conspicuous lack of closure.

To some degree a lack of closure characterizes all of *The Faerie Queene*, including the more self-contained of the six finished books, and it is fitting that there survives the fragment of another book, the cantos of Mutabilitie, in which Spenser broods on the tension in nature between systematic order and ceaseless change. The poem as a whole is built around principles that pull tautly against one another: a commitment to a life of constant struggle and a profound longing for rest; a celebration of human heroism and a perception of ineradicable human sinfulness; a vision of evil as a terrifyingly potent force and a vision of evil as mere emptiness and filth; a faith in the supreme value of visionary art and a recurrent suspicion that art is dangerously allied to graven images and deception. That Spenser's knights never quite reach the havens they seek may reflect irresolvable tensions to which we owe much of the power and beauty of this great, unfinished work.

From The Faerie Queene

A Letter of the Authors[1]

EXPOUNDING HIS WHOLE INTENTION IN THE COURSE OF THIS WORKE: WHICH FOR THAT IT GIVETH GREAT LIGHT TO THE READER, FOR THE BETTER UNDERSTANDING IS HEREUNTO ANNEXED

To the Right noble, and Valorous, Sir Walter Raleigh knight, Lo. Wardein of the Stanneryes,[2] and her Majesties liefetenaunt of the County of Cornewayll

Sir knowing how doubtfully all Allegories may be construed, and this booke of mine, which I have entituled the *Faery Queene*, being a continued Allegory, or darke conceit,[3] I have thought good as well for avoyding of gealous opinions and misconstructions, as also for your better light in reading thereof, (being so by you commanded,) to discover unto you the general intention and meaning, which in the whole course thereof I have fashioned, without expressing of any particular purposes or by-accidents[4] therein occasioned. The generall end therefore of all the booke is to fashion a gentleman or noble person in vertuous and gentle[5] discipline: Which for that I conceived shoulde be most plausible and pleasing, being coloured with an historicall fiction, the which the most part of men delight to read, rather for variety of matter, then for profite of the ensample:[6] I chose the historye of King Arthure, as most fitte for the excellency of his person, being made famous by many mens former workes, and also furthest from the daunger of envy, and suspition of present time.[7] In which I have followed all the antique Poets historicall,[8] first

---

1. The Letter was appended—not prefixed—to the 1590 edition of the poem. (It was omitted from the 1596 edition.) We follow the common practice of printing it as a "preface" to the work.
2. I.e., the mining districts of Cornwall and Devon. "Lo.": Lord.
3. Obscure or difficult poetic figure.

4. Secondary matters.
5. Pertaining to a gentleman. "Fashion": (1) to represent; (2) to educate.
6. Example. "Then": than.
7. I.e., free from current political controversy.
8. I.e., epic.

Homere, who in the Persons of Agamemnon and Ulysses hath ensampled a good governour and a vertuous man, the one in his *Ilias*, the other in his *Odysseis*: then Virgil, whose like intention was to doe in the person of Aeneas: after him Ariosto comprised them both in his Orlando: and lately Tasso dissevered them againe, and formed both parts in two persons, namely that part which they in Philosophy call Ethice, or vertues of a private man, coloured in his Rinaldo: The other named Politice in his Godfredo.[9] By ensample of which excellente Poets, I labour to pourtraict in Arthure, before he was king, the image of a brave knight, perfected in the twelve private morall vertues, as Aristotle hath devised,[1] the which is the purpose of these first twelve bookes: which if I finde to be well accepted, I may be perhaps encouraged, to frame the other part of pollitcke vertues in his person, after that hee came to be king. To some I know this Methode will seeme displeasaunt, which had rather have good discipline[2] delivered plainly in way of precepts, or sermoned at large, as they use, then thus clowdily enwrapped in Allegoricall devises. But such, me seeme, should be satisfide with the use of these dayes, seeing all things accounted by their showes, and nothing esteemed of, that is not delightfull and pleasing to commune sence.[3] For this cause is Xenophon preferred before Plato, for that the one in the exquisite depth of his judgment, formed a Commune welth such as it should be, but the other in the person of Cyrus and the Persians fashioned a governement such as might best be:[4] So much more profitable and gratious is doctrine by ensample, then by rule. So have I laboured to doe in the person of Arthure: whome I conceive after his long education by Timon, to whom he was by Merlin delivered to be brought up, so soone as he was borne of the Lady Igrayne, to have seene in a dream or vision the Faery Queen, with whose excellent beauty ravished, he awaking resolved to seeke her out, and so being by Merlin armed, and by Timon throughly[5] instructed, he went to seeke her forth in Faerye land. In that Faery Queene I meane glory in my generall intention, but in my particular I conceive the most excellent and glorious person of our soveraine the Queene, and her kingdome in Faery land. And yet in some places els, I doe otherwise shadow[6] her. For considering she beareth two persons, the one of a most royall Queene or Empresse, the other of a most vertuous and beautifull Lady, this latter part in some places I doe express in Belphoebe, fashioning her name according to your owne excellent conceipt of Cynthia,[7] (Phoebe and Cynthia being both names of Diana.) So in the person of Prince Arthure I sette forth magnificence in particular, which vertue for that (according to Aristotle and the rest) it is the perfection of all

---

9. Torquato Tasso (1544–1595) published his chivalric romance *Rinaldo* in 1562 and completed the epic *Gerusalemme liberata* (centered on the heroic figure of Count Godfredo) in 1575. Lodovico Ariosto (1474–1533) was author of the epic romance *Orlando furioso*, first published in 1516.
1. Though Aristotle distinguished between private and public virtues, he did not devise lists of twelve of each. Spenser was in fact relying on more modern philosophers—his friend Lodowick Bryskett and the Italian Alessandro Piccolomini. That

Spenser contemplated (as he proceeds to indicate) a poem four times as long as the six books we now have rather staggers the imagination.
2. Teaching.
3. The notions of the many. "Showes": appearances.
4. The allusion is to Plato's *Republic* and Xenophon's *Cyropaedia*.
5. Thoroughly.
6. Picture, portray.
7. Ralegh's poem *The Ocean to Cynthia* praised Queen Elizabeth.

the rest,[8] and conteineth in it them all, therefore in the whole course I mention the deedes of Arthure applyable to that vertue, which I write of in that booke. But of the xii. other vertues, I make xii. other knights the patrones, for the more variety of the history. Of which these three bookes contayn three, The first of the knight of the Redcrosse, in whome I expresse Holynes: The seconde of Sir Guyon, in whome I sette forth Temperaunce: The third of Britomartis a Lady knight, in whome I picture Chastity. But because the beginning of the whole worke seemeth abrupte and as depending upon other antecedents, it needs that ye know the occasion of these three knights severall adventures. For the Methode of a Poet historical is not such, as of an Historiographer.[9] For an Historiographer discourseth of affayres orderly as they were donne, accounting as well the times as the actions, but a Poet thrusteth into the middest, even where it most concerneth him, and there recoursing to the thinges forepaste,[1] and divining of thinges to come, maketh a pleasing Analysis of all. The beginning therefore of my history, if it were to be told by an Historiographer, should be the twelfth booke, which is the last, where I devise that the Faery Queene kept her Annuall feaste xii. dayes, uppon which xii. severall dayes, the occasions of the xii. severall adventures hapned, which being undertaken by xii. severall knights, are in these xii books severally handled and discoursed. The first was this. In the beginning of the feaste, there presented him selfe a tall clownishe[2] younge man, who falling before the Queen of Faeries desired a boone (as the manner then was) which during that feast she might not refuse: which was that hee might have the atchievement of any adventure, which during that feaste should happen: that being graunted, he rested him on the floore, unfitte through his rusticity for a better place. Soone after entred a faire Ladye in mourning weedes, riding on a white Asse, with a dwarfe behind her leading a warlike steed, that bore the Armes of a knight, and his speare in the dwarfes hand. Shee falling before the Queene of Faeries, complayned that her father and mother an ancient King and Queene, had bene by an huge dragon many years shut up in a brasen Castle, who thence suffred them not to yssew:[3] and therefore besought the Faery Queene to assygne her some one of her knights to take on him that exployt. Presently[4] that clownish person upstarting, desired that adventure: whereat the Queene much wondering, and the Lady much gainesaying, yet he earnestly importuned his desire. In the end the Lady told him that unlesse that armour which she brought, would serve him (that is the armour of a Christian man specified by Saint Paul v. Ephes.[5]) that he could not succeed in that enterprise, which being forthwith put upon him with dewe furnitures[6] thereunto, he seemed the goodliest man in

---

8. For Aristotle, magnanimity ("magnificence" in Spenser)—greatness of soul—is the ultimate virtue.

9. Historian.

1. Past. "Thrusteth into the middest": referring to the critical dictum that epic should begin, as the Roman poet Horace said, *in medias res*—"in the middle of things" (*Art of Poetry*, lines 147–48).

2. Rustic-looking.

3. Come forth.

4. Immediately.

5. Ephesians 6.11, "Put on the whole armor of God, that ye may be able to stand against the wiles of the devil." The parts (verses 14 to 17) are loins girt about with truth, breastplate of righteousness, feet shod with the gospel of peace, shield of faith "wherewith ye shall be able to quench all the fiery darts of the wicked," helmet of salvation, and "sword of the Spirit, which is the word of God."

6. Suitable equipment.

al that company, and was well liked of the Lady. And eftesoones[7] taking on him knighthood, and mounting on that straunge Courser, he went forth with her on that adventure: where beginneth the first booke, vz.

A gentle knight was pricking on the playne. &c.

The second day ther came in a Palmer[8] bearing an Infant with bloody hands, whose Parents he complained to have bene slayn by an Enchaunteresse called Acrasia: and therfore craved of the Faery Queene, to appoint him some knight, to performe that adventure, which being assigned to Sir Guyon, he presently went forth with that same Palmer: which is the beginning of the second booke and the whole subject thereof. The third day there came in, a Groome who complained before the Faery Queene, that a vile Enchaunter called Busirane had in hand a most faire Lady called Amoretta, whom he kept in most grievous torment, because she would not yield him the pleasure of her body. Whereupon Sir Scudamour the lover of that Lady presently tooke on him that adventure. But being unable to performe it by reason of the hard Enchauntments, after long sorrow, in the end met with Britomartis, who succoured him, and reskewed his love.

But by occasion hereof, many other adventures are intermedled, but rather as Accidents, then intendments.[9] As the love of Britomart, the overthrow of Marinell, the misery of Florimell, the vertuousnes of Belphoebe, the lasciviousnes of Hellenora, and many the like.

Thus much Sir, I have briefly overronne[1] to direct your understanding to the wel-head of the History, that from thence gathering the whole intention of the conceit,[2] ye may as in a handfull gripe al the discourse, which otherwise may happily[3] seeme tedious and confused. So humbly craving the continuaunce of your honorable favour towards me, and th' eternall establishment of your happines, I humbly take leave.

23. January, 1589[4]
Yours most humbly affectionate.
ED. SPENSER.

---

7. Forthwith.
8. Pilgrim.
9. I.e., there are episodes that are not part of these principal stories.
1. Run through, summarized.

2. Conception.
3. Perhaps.
4. The date is actually 1590, because until England adopted the Gregorian calendar in 1752, the new year began on March 25.

The First Booke of The Faerie Queene

Contayning
The Legende of the
Knight of the Red Crosse, or
Of Holinesse

1

Lo I the man, whose Muse whilome did maske,
  As time her taught, in lowly Shepheards weeds,[1]
  Am now enforst a far unfitter taske,
  For trumpets sterne to chaunge mine Oaten reeds,[2]
  And sing of Knights and Ladies gentle° deeds;   *noble*
  Whose prayses having slept in silence long,[3]
  Me, all too meane,° the sacred Muse areeds°   *low / counsels*
  To blazon° broad emongst her learned throng: *proclaim*
Fierce warres and faithfull loves shall moralize[4] my song.

2

Helpe then, O holy Virgin chiefe of nine,[5]
  Thy weaker° Novice to performe thy will,   *too weak*
  Lay forth out of thine everlasting scryne°   *a chest for papers*
  The antique rolles, which there lye hidden still,
  Of Faerie knights and fairest Tanaquill,°   *i.e., Gloriana*
  Whom that most noble Briton Prince[6] so long
  Sought through the world, and suffered so much ill,
  That I must rue° his undeserved wrong: *pity*
O helpe thou my weake wit, and sharpen my dull tong.

3

And thou most dreaded impe° of highest Jove,   *offspring*
  Faire Venus sonne,° that with thy cruell dart   *Cupid*
  At that good knight so cunningly didst rove,°   *shoot*
  That glorious fire it kindled in his hart,
  Lay now thy deadly Heben° bow apart,   *ebony*
  And with thy mother milde come to mine ayde:
  Come both, and with you bring triumphant Mart,[7]
  In loves and gentle jollities arrayd,
After his murdrous spoiles and bloudy rage allayd.

4

And with them eke,° O Goddesse heavenly bright,   *also*
  Mirrour of grace and Majestie divine,

---

1. Garb. The poet appeared before ("whilome") as a writer of humble pastoral (i.e., *The Shepheardes Calender*). These lines are imitated from the verses prefixed to Renaissance editions of Virgil's *Aeneid*.
2. To write heroic poetry, of which the trumpet is a symbol, instead of pastoral poetry symbolized by the humble shepherd's pipe ("Oaten reeds").
3. This and the preceding line are imitated from the opening of Ariosto's *Orlando furioso*.
4. Provide subjects for moralizing.
5. Scholars have debated whether the reference is to Clio, the Muse of history, or to Calliope, the Muse of epic.
6. I.e., Arthur, named in canto 9, stanza 6.
7. Mars, god of war and lover of Venus.

Great Lady of the greatest Isle, whose light
Like Phoebus lampe throughout the world doth shine,
Shed thy faire beames into my feeble eyne,°   *eyes*
And raise my thoughts too humble and too vile,°   *lowly*
To thinke of that true glorious type[8] of thine,
The argument° of mine afflicted stile:°   *subject / humble work*
The which to heare, vouchsafe, O dearest dred° a-while.   *object of awe*

Canto 1

The Patron of true Holinesse,
Foule Errour doth defeate:
Hypocrisie him to entrappe,
Doth to his home entreate.

1

A Gentle Knight was pricking° on the plaine,   *spurring*
Ycladd[9] in mightie armes and silver shielde,
Wherein old dints of deepe wounds did remaine,
The cruell markes of many a bloudy fielde;
Yet armes till that time did he never wield:
His angry steede did chide his foming bitt,
As much disdayning to the curbe to yield:
Full jolly° knight he seemd, and faire did sitt,   *gallant*
As one for knightly giusts° and fierce encounters fitt.   *jousts, tourneys*

2

But on his brest a bloudie Crosse he bore,
The deare remembrance of his dying Lord,
For whose sweete sake that glorious badge he wore,
And dead as living ever him adored:[1]
Upon his shield the like was also scored,°   *incised*
For soveraine[2] hope, which in his helpe he had:
Right faithfull true[3] he was in deede and word,
But of his cheere[4] did seeme too solemne sad;°   *grave*
Yet nothing did he dread, but ever was ydrad.°   *dreaded, feared*

3

Upon a great adventure he was bond,
That greatest Gloriana to him gave,
That greatest Glorious Queene of Faerie Lond,
To winne him worship,° and her grace to have,   *honor*

8. I.e., Gloriana is the "type" (prefiguration) of
Queen Elizabeth.
9. Imitating Chaucerian English, Spenser sometimes uses the prefix *y* as the sign of a past participle.
1. A compressed reference to Revelation 1.18:
"I am he that liveth, and was dead; and, behold, I

am alive for evermore."
2. Having greatest power (often applied to medical remedies).
3. Compare Revelation 19.11: "And I saw heaven
opened; and behold a white horse; and he that
sat upon him was called Faithful and True."
4. Facial expression; mood.

Which of all earthly things he most did crave;
And ever as he rode, his hart did earne°   *yearn*
To prove his puissance° in battell brave   *might*
Upon his foe, and his new force to learne;
Upon his foe, a Dragon horrible and stearne.

4

A lovely Ladie rode him faire beside,
Upon a lowly Asse more white then° snow,   *than*
Yet she much whiter, but the same did hide
Under a vele, that wimpled° was full low,   *lying in folds*
And over all a blacke stole she did throw,
As one that inly mournd: so was she sad,
And heavie sat upon her palfrey slow:
Seemèd in heart some hidden care she had,
And by her in a line° a milke white lambe she lad.   *on a leash*

5

So pure an innocent, as that same lambe,
She was in life and every vertuous lore,
And by descent from Royall lynage came
Of ancient Kings and Queenes, that had of yore
Their scepters stretcht from East to Westerne shore,
And all the world in their subjection held;
Till that infernall feend with foule uprore
Forwasted° all their land, and them expeld: *laid waste*
Whom to avenge, she had this Knight from far compeld.°   *summoned*

6

Behind her farre away a Dwarfe did lag,
That lasie seemd in being ever last,
Or wearièd with bearing of her bag
Of needments at his backe. Thus as they past,
The day with cloudes was suddeine overcast,
And angry Jove an hideous storme of raine
Did poure into his Lemans[5] lap so fast,
That every wight° to shrowd° it did constrain,   *creature / take shelter*
And this faire couple eke° to shroud themselves were fain.° *also / eager*

7

Enforst to seeke some covert nigh at hand,
A shadie grove not far away they spide,
That promist ayde the tempest to withstand:
Whose loftie trees yclad with sommers pride,
Did spred so broad, that heavens light did hide,
Not perceable° with power of any starre: *penetrable*

5. His lover's, i.e., the earth's.

And all within were pathes and alleies wide,
  With footing worne, and leading inward farre:
Faire harbour that them seemes; so in they entred arre.

8

And foorth they passe, with pleasure forward led,
  Joying to heare the birdes sweete harmony,
  Which therein shrouded from the tempest dred,°   *fearful*
  Seemd in their song to scorne the cruell sky.
  Much can° they prayse the trees, so straight and hy,   *did*
  The sayling Pine, the Cedar proud and tall,
  The vine-prop Elme, the Poplar never dry,
  The builder Oake, sole king of forrests all,
The Aspine good for staves, the Cypresse funerall.°   *funereal*

9

The Laurell, meed° of mightie Conquerours   *reward*
  And Poets sage, the Firre that weepeth still,[6]
  The Willow worne of forlorne Paramours,
  The Eugh° obedient to the benders will,   *yew*
  The Birch for shaftes, the Sallow° for the mill,   *willow*
  The Mirrhe sweete bleeding in the bitter wound,
  The warlike Beech, the Ash for nothing ill,
  The fruitfull Olive, and the Platane° round,   *plane-tree*
The carver Holme,[7] the Maple seeldom inward sound.

10

Led with delight, they thus beguile the way,
  Untill the blustring storme is overblowne;
  When weening° to returne, whence they did stray,   *thinking*
  They cannot finde that path, which first was showne,
  But wander too and fro in wayes unknowne,
  Furthest from end then, when they neerest weene,
  That makes them doubt, their wits be not their owne:
  So many pathes, so many turnings seene,
That which of them to take, in diverse doubt they been.

11

At last resolving forward still to fare,
  Till that some end they finde or° in or out,   *either*
  That path they take, that beaten seemed most bare,
  And like to lead the labyrinth about°   *out of*
  Which when by tract they hunted had throughout,
  At length it brought them to a hollow cave,
  Amid the thickest woods. The Champion stout

---

6. I.e., exudes resin continuously. Spenser in these stanzas imitates Chaucer's catalog of trees in the *Parliament of Fowls*; the convention goes back to Ovid.

7. Holly or holm-oak, both suitable for carving.

Eftsoones° dismounted from his courser brave,   *at once*
And to the Dwarfe a while his needlesse spere[8] he gave.

12

"Be well aware,"° quoth then that Ladie milde,   *watchful*
  "Least suddaine mischiefe° ye too rash provoke: *misfortune*
  The danger hid, the place unknowne and wilde,
  Breedes dreadfull doubts: Oft fire is without smoke,
  And perill without show: therefore your stroke
  Sir knight with-hold, till further triall made."
  "Ah Ladie," said he, "shame were to revoke°   *draw back*
  The forward footing for° an hidden shade: *because of*
Vertue gives her selfe light, through darkenesse for to wade."

13

"Yea but," quoth she, "the perill of this place
  I better wot then° you, though now too late   *know than*
  To wish you backe returne with foule disgrace,
  Yet wisedome warnes, whilest foot is in the gate,
  To stay the stepe, ere forcèd to retrate.
  This is the wandring wood, this Errours den,
  A monster vile, whom God and man does hate:
  Therefore I read° beware." "Fly fly," quoth then   *advise*
The fearefull Dwarfe: "this is no place for living men."

14

But full of fire and greedy hardiment,°   *boldness*
  The youthfull knight could not for ought° be staide,   *anything*
  But forth unto the darksome hole he went,
  And lookèd in: his glistring° armor made   *shining*
  A litle glooming light, much like a shade,
  By which he saw the ugly monster plaine,
  Halfe like a serpent horribly displaide,
  But th' other halfe did womans shape retaine,
Most lothsom, filthie, foule, and full of vile disdaine.°[9]   *loathsomeness*

15

And as she lay upon the durtie ground,
  Her huge long taile her den all overspred,
  Yet was in knots and many boughtes° upwound,   *coils*
  Pointed with mortall sting. Of her there bred
  A thousand yong ones, which she dayly fed,
  Sucking upon her poisonous dugs, eachone
  Of sundry shapes, yet all ill favorèd:
  Soone as that uncouth° light upon them shone,   *unfamiliar*
Into her mouth they crept, and suddain all were gone.

---

8. "Needlesse" because the spear is used only on horseback. "By tract" (line 5): by following the track.

9. The description echoes both classical and biblical monsters (cf. Revelation 9.7–10).

16

Their dam upstart, out of her den efrraide,°   *alarmed*
  And rushèd forth, hurling her hideous taile
  About her cursèd head, whose folds displaid°   *extended*
  Were stretcht now forth at length without entraile.°   *coiling*
  She lookt about, and seeing one in mayle
  Armèd to point,° sought backe to turne againe; *i.e., completely*
  For light she hated as the deadly bale,°   *injury*
  Ay wont° in desert darknesse to remain, *ever accustomed*
Where plaine none might her see, nor she see any plaine.

17

Which when the valiant Elfe[1] perceived, he lept
  As Lyon fierce upon the flying pray,
  And with his trenchand° blade her boldly kept   *cutting*
  From turning backe, and forcèd her to stay:
  Therewith enraged she loudly gan to bray,
  And turning fierce, her speckled taile advaunst;
  Threatning her angry sting, him to dismay:°   *defeat*
  Who nought aghast, his mightie hand enhaunst:° *lifted up*
The stroke down from her head unto her shoulder glaunst.

18

Much daunted with that dint,° her sence was dazd,   *blow*
  Yet kindling rage, her selfe she gathered round,
  And all attonce her beastly body raizd
  With doubled forces high above the ground:
  Tho° wrapping up her wrethèd sterne arownd,   *then*
  Lept fierce upon his shield, and her huge traine° *tail*
  All suddenly about his body wound,
  That hand or foot to stirre he strove in vaine:
God helpe the man so wrapt in Errours endlesse traine.

19

His Lady sad to see his sore constraint,
  Cride out, "Now now Sir knight, shew what ye bee,
  Add faith unto your force, and be not faint:
  Strangle her, else she sure will strangle thee."
  That when he heard, in great perplexitie,[2]
  His gall did grate[3] for griefe° and high disdaine, *wrath*
  And knitting all his force got one hand free,
  Wherewith he grypt her gorge° with so great paine, *throat*
That soone to loose her wicked bands did her constraine.

---

1. I.e., knight of Faerie Land.
2. In both the usual sense and the sense of "entangled condition."

3. I.e., his gallbladder (considered the seat of anger) was violently disturbed.

20

Therewith she spewd out of her filthy maw
  A floud of poyson horrible and blacke,
  Full of great lumpes of flesh and gobbets raw,
  Which stunck so vildly, that it forst him slacke
  His grasping hold, and from her turne him backe:
  Her vomit full of bookes and papers was,[4]
  With loathly frogs and toades, which eyes did lacke,
  And creeping sought way in the weedy gras:
Her filthy parbreake° all the place defilèd has.[5]   *vomit*

21

As when old father Nilus gins to swell
  With timely° pride above the Aegyptian vale,   *in season*
  His fattie° waves do fertile slime outwell,   *rich*
  And overflow each plaine and lowly dale:
  But when his later spring gins to avale,°   *subside*
  Huge heapes of mudd he leaves, wherein there breed
  Ten thousand kindes of creatures, partly male
  And partly female of his fruitfull seed;
Such ugly monstrous shapes elswhere may no man reed.°   *see*

22

The same so sore annoyed° has the knight,   *injuriously affected*
  That welnigh chokèd with the deadly stinke,
  His forces faile, ne° can no longer fight.   *nor*
  Whose corage when the feend perceived to shrinke,
  She pourèd forth out of her hellish sinke[6]
  Her fruitfull cursèd spawne of serpents small,
  Deformèd monsters, fowle, and blacke as inke,
  Which swarming all about his legs did crall,
And him encombred sore, but could not hurt at all.

23

As gentle Shepheard in sweete even-tide,
  When ruddy Phoebus gins to welke° in west,   *sink*
  High on an hill, his flocke to vewen wide,
  Markes° which do byte their hasty supper best;   *observes*
  A cloud of combrous° gnattes do him molest,   *encumbering*
  All striving to infixe their feeble stings,
  That from their noyance he no where can rest,
  But with his clownish° hands their tender wings   *rustic*
He brusheth oft, and oft doth mar their murmurings.

---

4. Alluding (at one level) to books and pamphlets of Catholic propaganda, notably attacks on Queen Elizabeth.
5. Revelation 16.13: "And I saw three unclean spirits like frogs come out of the mouth of the dragon, and out of the mouth of the beast, and out of the mouth of the false prophet."
6. Cesspool (i.e., her womb or organ of excretion).

24

Thus ill bestedd,° and fearful more of shame,   *situated*
 Then of the certaine perill he stood in,
 Halfe furious unto his foe he came,
 Resolved in minde all suddenly to win,
 Or soone to lose, before he once would lin;°   *cease*
 And strooke at her with more then manly force,
 That from her body full of filthie sin
 He raft° her hatefull head without remorse;   *cut away*
A streame of cole black bloud forth gushèd from her corse.

25

Her scattred brood, soone as their Parent deare
 They saw so rudely° falling to the ground, *with great force*
 Groning full deadly, all with troublous feare,
 Gathred themselves about her body round,
 Weening° their wonted entrance to have found *thinking*
 At her wide mouth: but being there withstood
 They flockèd all about her bleeding wound,
 And suckèd up their dying mothers blood,
Making her death their life, and eke° her hurt their good. *also*

26

That detestable sight him much amazde,°   *stunned*
 To see th'unkindly Impes° of heaven accurst, *unnatural offspring*
 Devoure their dam; on whom while so he gazd,
 Having all satisfide their bloudy thurst,
 Their bellies swolne he saw with fulnesse burst,
 And bowels gushing forth: well worthy end
 Of such as drunke her life, the which them nurst;
 Now needeth him no lenger° labour spend,   *longer*
His foes have slaine themselves, with whom he should contend.

27

His Ladie seeing all, that chaunst, from farre
 Approcht in hast to greet° his victorie,   *congratulate*
 And said, "Faire knight, borne under happy starre,
 Who see your vanquisht foes before you lye;
 Well worthy be you of that Armorie,°   *armor*
 Wherein ye have great glory wonne this day,
 And prooved your strength on a strong enimie,
 Your first adventure: many such I pray,
And henceforth ever wish, that like succeed it may."

28

Then mounted he upon his Steede againe,
 And with the Lady backward sought to wend;° *go*
 That path he kept, which beaten was most plaine,

Ne ever would to any by-way bend,
    But still did follow one unto the end,
    The which at last out of the wood them brought.
    So forward on his way (with God to frend)°   *with God as friend*
    He passèd forth, and new adventure sought;
Long way he travelèd, before he heard of ought.°   *aught, anything*

29

At length they chaunst to meet upon the way
    An agèd Sire, in long blacke weedes yclad,[7]
    His feete all bare, his beard all hoarie gray,
    And by his belt his booke he hanging had;
    Sober he seemde, and very sagely sad,°   *grave*
    And to the ground his eyes were lowly bent,
    Simple in shew,° and voyde of malice bad,   *show*
    And all the way he prayèd, as he went,
And often knockt his brest, as one that did repent.

30

He faire the knight saluted, louting° low,   *bowing*
    Who faire him quited,° as that courteous was: *responded*
    And after askèd him, if he did know
    Of straunge adventures, which abroad did pas.
    "Ah my deare Sonne," quoth he, "how should, alas,
    Silly° old man, that lives in hidden cell,   *simple*
    Bidding his beades° all day for his trespas,   *saying his prayers*
    Tydings of warre and worldly trouble tell?
With holy father sits not with such things to mell.[8]

31

"But if of daunger which hereby doth dwell,
    And homebred evill ye desire to heare,
    Of a straunge man I can you tidings tell,
    That wasteth all this countrey farre and neare."
    "Of such," said he, "I chiefly do inquere,
    And shall you well reward to shew the place,
    In which that wicked wight his dayes doth weare.°   *spend*
    For to all knighthood it is foule disgrace,
That such a cursèd creature lives so long a space."

32

"Far hence," quoth he, "in wastfull° wildernesse   *desolate*
    His dwelling is, by which no living wight°   *creature*
    May ever passe, but thorough° great distresse."   *through*
    "Now," sayd the Lady, "draweth toward night,
    And well I wote, that of your later° fight   *recent*

---

7. Dressed in long black garments.
8. I.e., it is not fitting for a holy hermit to meddle ("mell") with such things.

Ye all forwearied be: for what so strong,
But wanting° rest will also want of might?   *lacking*
The Sunne that measures heaven all day long,
At night doth baite° his steedes the Ocean waves emong.   *feed; refresh*

33

"Then with the Sunne take Sir, your timely rest,
And with new day new worke at once begin:
Untroubled night they say gives counsell best."
"Right well Sir knight ye have advisèd bin,"
Quoth then that agèd man; "the way to win
Is wisely to advise:° now day is spent;   *take thought*
Therefore with me ye may take up your In°   *lodging*
For this same night." The knight was well content.
So with that godly father to his home they went.

34

A little lowly Hermitage it was,
Downe in a dale, hard by° a forests side,   *close to*
Far from resort of people, that did pas
In travell to and froe: a little wyde°   *apart*
There was an holy Chappell edifyde,°   *built*
Wherein the Hermite dewly wont° to say   *was accustomed*
His holy things° each morne and eventyde: *prayers*
Thereby a Christall streame did gently play,
Which from a sacred fountaine wellèd forth alway.

35

Arrivèd there, the little house they fill,
Ne looke for entertainement,° where none was: *elegant provision*
Rest is their feast, and all things at their will;
The noblest mind the best contentment has.
With faire discourse the evening so they pas:
For that old man of pleasing wordes had store,
And well could file° his tongue as smooth as glas;   *polish*
He told of Saintes and Popes, and evermore
He strowd an *Ave-Mary*[9] after and before.

36

The drouping Night thus creepeth on them fast,
And the sad humour° loading their eye liddes,   *heavy moisture*
As messenger of Morpheus[1] on them cast
Sweet slombring deaw, the which to sleepe them biddes.
Unto their lodgings then his guestes he riddes:°   *leads*
Where when all drownd in deadly sleepe° he findes,   *sleep like death*
He to his study goes, and there amiddes

---

9. "Hail Mary"—that is, a Catholic prayer.
1. Here (as often) Morpheus, the classical god of

dreams, is conflated with his father, Somnus, god
of sleep.

His Magick bookes and artes of sundry kindes,
He seekes out mighty charmes, to trouble sleepy mindes.

37

Then choosing out few wordes most horrible
    (Let none them read), thereof did verses frame,
    With which and other spelles like terrible,
    He bade awake blacke Plutoes griesly Dame,[2]
    And cursèd heaven, and spake reprochfull shame
    Of highest God, the Lord of life and light;
    A bold bad man, that dared to call by name
    Great Gorgon,[3] Prince of darknesse and dead night,
At which Cocytus quakes, and Styx is put to flight.

38

And forth he cald out of deepe darknesse dred
    Legions of Sprights,° the which like little flyes[4]   *spirits*
    Fluttring about his ever damnèd hed,
    A-waite whereto their service he applyes,
    To aide his friends, or fray° his enimies: *frighten*
    Of those he chose out two, the falsest twoo,
    And fittest for to forge true-seeming lyes;
    The one of them he gave a message too,
The other by him selfe staide other worke to doo.

39

He making speedy way through spersèd° ayre,   *dispersed*
    And through the world of waters wide and deepe,
    To Morpheus house doth hastily repaire.
    Amid the bowels of the earth full steepe,
    And low, where dawning day doth never peepe,
    His dwelling is; there Tethys° his wet bed   *the wife of Ocean*
    Doth ever wash, and Cynthia[5] still° doth steepe   *continually*
    In silver deaw his ever-drouping hed,
Whiles sad° Night over him her mantle black doth spred.   *sober*

40

Whose double gates he findeth lockèd fast,
    The one faire framed of burnisht Yvory,
    The other all with silver overcast;
    And wakefull dogges before them farre do lye,
    Watching to banish Care their enimy,
    Who oft is wont° to trouble gentle Sleepe.   *accustomed*
    By them the Sprite doth passe in quietly,

2. Proserpine, as patron of witchcraft.
3. Demogorgon, in some myths the progenitor of all the gods, so powerful that the mention of his name causes hell's rivers (Styx and Cocytus) to tremble.
4. The simile associates him with Beelzebub ("Lord of Flies"), the name given to "the prince of the devils."
5. Diana, as goddess of the moon.

And unto Morpheus comes, whom drownèd deepe
In drowsie fit he findes: of nothing he takes keepe.°   *notice*

41

And more, to lulle him in his slumber soft,
    A trickling streame from high rocke tumbling downe
    And ever-drizling raine upon the loft,°   *aloft, above*
    Mixt with a murmuring winde, much like the sowne°   *sound*
    Of swarming Bees, did cast him in a swowne:°   *swoon*
    No other noyse, nor peoples troublous cryes,
    As still° are wont t'annoy the wallèd towne,   *always*
    Might there be heard: but carelesse° Quiet lyes,   *free from care*
Wrapt in eternall silence farre from enemyes.[6]

42

The messenger approching to him spake,
    But his wast° wordes returnd to him in vaine: *wasted*
    So sound he slept, that nought mought° him awake.   *might*
    Then rudely he him thrust, and pusht with paine,°   *effort*
    Whereat he gan to stretch: but he againe
    Shooke him so hard, that forcèd him to speake.
    As one then in a dreame, whose dryer braine[7]
    Is tost with troubled sights and fancies° weake,   *fantasies*
He mumbled soft, but would not all his silence breake.

43

The Sprite then gan more boldly him to wake,
    And threatned unto him the dreaded name
    Of Hecate:° whereat he gan to quake,   *queen of Hades*
    And lifting up his lumpish° head, with blame   *heavy*
    Halfe angry askèd him, for what° he came.   *why*
    "Hither," quoth he, "me Archimago[8] sent,
    He that the stubborne Sprites can wisely tame,
    He bids thee to him send for his intent
A fit false dreame, that can delude the sleepers sent."°   *senses*

44

The God obayde, and calling forth straight way
    A diverse° dreame out of his prison darke,   *diverting, distracting*
    Delivered it to him, and downe did lay
    His heavie head, devoide of carefull carke,°   *anxious concerns*
    Whose sences all were straight benumbd and starke.[9]
    He backe returning by the Yvorie dore,[1]

---

6. Spenser is imitating descriptions of the caves of Morpheus in Chaucer (*Book of the Duchess*, lines 153–77) and of Somnus in Ovid (*Metamorphoses* 11.592–632).
7. According to the old physiology, elderly people and other light sleepers had too little moisture in the brain.
8. The name can be construed as meaning both "archmagician" and "architect of images."
9. Immediately ("straight") benumbed and paralyzed.
1. According to Homer (*Odyssey* 19.562–67) and Virgil (*Aeneid* 6.893–96), false dreams come through Sleep's ivory gate, true dreams through his gate of horn.

Remounted up as light as chearefull Larke,
And on his litle winges the dreame he bore
In hast unto his Lord, where he him left afore.

45

Who all this while with charmes and hidden artes,
Had made a Lady of that other Spright,
And framed of liquid ayre her tender partes
So lively,° and so like in all mens sight,   *lifelike*
That weaker° sence it could have ravisht quight: *too weak*
The maker selfe for all his wondrous witt,
Was nigh beguilèd° with so goodly sight: *deceived*
Her all in white he clad, and over it
Cast a blacke stole, most like to seeme for Una[2] fit.° *fitting*

46

Now when that ydle dreame was to him brought
Unto that Elfin knight he bad him fly,
Where he slept soundly void of evill thought
And with false shewes abuse his fantasy,° *imagination*
In sort as° he him schoolèd privily: *in the way that*
And that new creature borne without her dew,° *unnaturally*
Full of the makers guile, with usage sly
He taught to imitate that Lady trew,
Whose semblance she did carrie under feignèd hew.° *form*

47

Thus well instructed, to their worke they hast
And comming where the knight in slomber lay
The one upon his hardy head him plast,° *placed*
And made him dreame of loves and lustfull play,
That nigh his manly hart did melt away,
Bathèd in wanton blis and wicked joy:
Then seemèd him his Lady by him lay,
And to him playnd,° how that false wingèd boy° *complained / Cupid*
Her chast hart had subdewd, to learne Dame pleasures toy.° *lustful play*

48

And she her selfe of beautie soveraigne Queene,
Faire Venus seemde unto his bed to bring
Her, whom he waking evermore did weene° *think*
To be the chastest flowre, that ay° did spring *ever*
On earthly braunch, the daughter of a king,
Now a loose Leman° to vile service bound: *paramour*
And eke° the Graces seemèd all to sing, *also*

---

2. Her name means "one, unity." Elizabethan readers would know the Latin phrase *Una Vera Fides* ("one true faith") and also the proverb "Truth is one."

> *Hymen iô Hymen*, dauncing all around,
> Whilst freshest Flora her with Yvie girlond crownd.[3]

49

In this great passion of unwonted° lust,   *unaccustomed*
  Or wonted feare of doing ought amis,
  He started up, as seeming to mistrust°   *suspect*
  Some secret ill, or hidden foe of his:
  Lo there before his face his Lady is,
  Under blake stole hyding her bayted hooke,
  And as halfe blushing offred him to kis,
  With gentle blandishment and lovely° looke,   *loving*
Most like that virgin true, which for her knight him took.

50

All cleane dismayd to see so uncouth° sight,   *strange; unseemly*
  And halfe enragèd at her shamelesse guise,
  He thought have slaine her in his fierce despight:°   *indignation*
  But hasty heat tempring with sufferance° wise,   *patience*
  He stayde his hand, and gan himselfe advise
  To prove his sense, and tempt° her faignèd truth.   *test*
  Wringing her hands in wemens pitteous wise,
  Tho can° she weepe, to stirre up gentle ruth,°   *then did / pity*
Both for her noble bloud, and for her tender youth.

51

And said, "Ah Sir, my liege Lord and my love,
  Shall I accuse the hidden cruell fate,
  And mightie causes wrought in heaven above,
  Or the blind God, that doth me thus amate,°   *dismay*
  For° hopèd love to winne me certaine hate?   *instead of*
  Yet thus perforce° he bids me do, or die.   *forcibly*
  Die is my dew:[4] yet rew° my wretched state   *pity*
  You, whom my hard avenging destinie
Hath made judge of my life or death indifferently.°   *impartially*

52

"Your owne deare sake forst me at first to leave
  My Fathers kingdome," There she stopt with teares;
  Her swollen hart her speach seemd to bereave,
  And then againe begun, "My weaker yeares
  Captived to fortune and frayle worldly feares,
  Fly to your faith for succour and sure ayde:
  Let me not dye in languor° and long teares.   *sorrow*

---

3. The Three Graces of classical mythology were personifications of grace and beauty; here they sing a call to the pleasures of the marriage bed (Hymen was god of marriage). In the March eclogue of *The Shepheardes Calender*, E. K. glossed Flora as "the Goddesse of flowres, but indede (as saith Tacitus) a famous harlot."
4. I.e., I deserve to die.

"Why Dame," quoth he, "what hath ye thus dismayd?
What frayes° ye, that were wont to comfort me affrayd?"   *frightens*

53

"Love of your selfe," she said, "and deare° constraint   *dire*
   Lets me not sleepe, but wast the wearie night
   In secret anguish and unpittied plaint,
   Whiles you in carelesse sleepe are drownèd quight."
   Her doubtfull words made that redoubted[5] knight
   Suspect her truth: yet since no'untruth he knew,
   Her fawning love with foule disdainefull spight
   He would not shend,° but said, "Deare dame I rew,   *reject*
That for my sake unknowne such griefe unto you grew.

54

"Assure your selfe, it fell not all to ground;
   For all so deare as life is to my hart,
   I deeme your love, and hold me to you bound;
   Ne let vaine feares procure your needlesse smart,°   *pain*
   Where cause is none, but to your rest depart."
   Not all content, yet seemd she to appease°   *cease*
   Her mournefull plaintes, beguilèd of her art,°   *foiled in her cunning*
   And fed with words, that could not chuse° but please,   *choose*
So slyding softly forth, she turnd° as to her ease.   *returned*

55

Long after lay he musing at her mood,
   Much grieved to thinke that gentle Dame so light,°   *frivolous; wanton*
   For whose defence he was to shed his blood.
   At last dull wearinesse of former fight
   Having yrockt a sleepe his irkesome spright,
   That troublous dreame gan freshly tosse his braine,
   With bowres and beds, and Ladies deare delight:
   But when he saw his labour all was vaine,
With that misformèd spright[6] he backe returnd againe.

Canto 2

*The guilefull great Enchaunter parts
The Redcrosse Knight from Truth:
Into whose stead faire falshood steps,
And workes him wofull ruth.°*   *mischief*

1

By this the Northerne wagoner had set
   His seven fold teame behind the stedfast starre,[7]

---

5. Dreaded, but also "doubting again." "Doubtfull": fearful; also questionable, arousing doubt.
6. I.e., with the spirit impersonating Una.

7. I.e., by this time the Big Dipper had set, behind
the North Star.

That was in Ocean waves yet never wet,
But firme is fixt, and sendeth light from farre
To all, that in the wide deepe wandring arre:
And chearefull Chaunticlere with his note shrill
Had warnèd once, that Phoebus fiery carre[8]
In hast was climbing up the Easterne hill,
Full envious that night so long his roome° did fill.   place

2

When those accursèd messengers of hell,
    That feigning dreame, and that faire-forgèd Spright
    Came to their wicked maister, and gan tell
    Their bootelesse° paines, and ill succeeding night: useless
    Who all in rage to see his skilfull might
    Deluded so, gan threaten hellish paine
    And sad Proserpines wrath, them to affright.
    But when he saw his threatning was but vaine,
He cast about, and searcht his balefull° bookes againe.   deadly

3

Eftsoones° he tooke that miscreated faire,   immediately
    And that false other Spright, on whom he spred
    A seeming body of the subtile° aire,   rarefied
    Like a young Squire, in loves and lusty-hed
    His wanton dayes that ever loosely led,
    Without regard of armes and dreaded fight:
    Those two he tooke, and in a secret bed,
    Covered with darknesse and misdeeming° night,   misleading
Them both together laid, to joy in vaine delight.

4

Forthwith he runnes with feignèd faithfull hast
    Unto his guest, who after troublous sights
    And dreames, gan now to take more sound repast,°   rest
    Whom suddenly he wakes with fearefull frights,
    As one aghast with feends or damnèd sprights,
    And to him cals, "Rise rise unhappy Swaine,°   youth; rustic
    That here wex° old in sleepe, whiles wicked wights   grow
    Have knit themselves in Venus shamefull chaine;
Come see, where your false Lady doth her honour staine."

5

All in amaze he suddenly up start
    With sword in hand, and with the old man went;
    Who soone him brought into a secret part,
    Where that false couple were full closely ment°   mingled
    In wanton lust and lewd embracèment:

---

8. Chariot of the sun god, Phoebus Apollo. "Chaunticlere": Chanticleer—generic name for a rooster.

Which when he saw, he burnt with gealous fire,
 The eye of reason was with rage yblent,°   *blinded*
 And would have slaine them in his furious ire,
But hardly° was restreinèd of° that agèd sire.   *with difficulty / by*

6

Returning to his bed in torment great,
 And bitter anguish of his guiltie sight,
 He could not rest, but did his stout heart eat,
 And wast his inward gall with deepe despight,°   *malice*
 Yrkesome° of life, and too long lingring night.   *tired*
 At last faire Hesperus[9] in highest skie
 Had spent his lampe, and brought forth dawning light,
 Then up he rose, and clad him hastily;
The Dwarfe him brought his steed: so both away do fly.

7

Now when the rosy-fingred Morning faire,
 Weary of aged Tithones[1] saffron bed,
 Had spred her purple robe through deawy aire,
 And the high hils Titan° discoverèd,°   *the sun / revealed*
 The royall virgin shooke off drowsy-hed,
 And rising forth out of her baser° bowre,   *too lowly*
 Lookt for her knight, who far away was fled,
 And for her Dwarfe, that wont° to wait each houre: *was accustomed*
Then gan she waile and weepe, to see that woefull stowre.° *affliction*

8

And after him she rode with so much speede
 As her slow beast could make; but all in vaine:
 For him so far had borne his light-foot steede,
 Prickèd with wrath and fiery fierce disdaine,°   *indignation*
 That him to follow was but fruitlesse paine;
 Yet she her weary limbes would never rest,
 But every hill and dale, each wood and plaine
 Did search, sore grievèd in her gentle brest,
He so ungently left her, whom she lovèd best.

9

But subtill° Archimago, when his guests   *cunning*
 He saw divided into double parts,
 And Una wandring in woods and forrests,
 Th' end of his drift,° he praisd his divelish arts   *plot*
 That had such might over true meaning harts;
 Yet rests not so, but other meanes doth make,
 How he may worke unto her further smarts:°   *pains*

9. The morning star.
1. Tithonus is the husband of Aurora, goddess of the dawn.

For her he hated as the hissing snake,
And in her many troubles did most pleasure take.

10

He then devisde himselfe how to disguise;
    For by his mightie science° he could take   *knowledge*
    As many formes and shapes in seeming wise,°   *in appearance*
    As ever Proteus[2] to himselfe could make:
    Sometime a fowle, sometime a fish in lake,
    Now like a foxe, now like a dragon fell,°   *fierce*
    That of himselfe he oft for feare would quake,
    And oft would flie away. O who can tell
The hidden power of herbes, and might of Magicke spell?

11

But now seemde best, the person to put on
    Of that good knight, his late beguilèd guest:
    In mighty armes he was yclad anon,
    And silver shield: upon his coward brest
    A bloudy crosse, and on his craven crest
    A bounch of haires discolourd diversly:°   *variously colored*
    Full jolly° knight he seemde, and well addrest,° *gallant / armed*
    And when he sate upon his courser free,°   *high-spirited*
Saint George himself ye would have deemèd him to be.

12

But he the knight, whose semblaunt° he did beare,   *likeness*
    The true Saint George was wandred far away,
    Still flying from° his thoughts and gealous feare; *because of*
    Will was his guide, and griefe led him astray.
    At last him chaunst to meete upon the way
    A faithlesse Sarazin[3] all armed to point,°   *completely*
    In whose great shield was writ with letters gay
    Sans foy:[4] full large of limbe and every joint
He was, and carèd not for God or man a point.°   *at all*

13

He had a faire companion of his way,
    A goodly Lady clad in scarlot red,
    Purfled° with gold and pearle of rich assay,[5]   *decorated*
    And like a Persian mitre on her hed
    She wore, with crownes and owches° garnishèd,   *brooches*
    The which her lavish lovers to her gave;[6]

---

2. A sea god who could change his shape at will (*Odyssey* 4.398–424).
3. Saracen, i.e., a Muslim, especially the foes of the Christian knights in the Crusades to the Holy Land; sometimes used generically of any "pagan."
4. Without faith, faithless (French).
5. Proven of rich value.
6. The lady's garb associates her with the biblical

Whore of Babylon (Revelation 17.3–4): "And I saw a woman sit upon a scarlet colored beast, full of names of blasphemy, having seven heads and ten horns. And the woman was arrayed in purple and scarlet color, and decked with gold and precious stones and pearls, having a golden cup in her hand full of abominations and filthiness of her fornication."

Her wanton° palfrey all was overspred   *unruly*
    With tinsell trappings, woven like a wave,
Whose bridle rung with golden bels and bosses brave.°   *handsome studs*

14

With faire disport° and courting dalliaunce   *diversion*
    She intertainde her lover all the way:
    But when she saw the knight his speare advaunce,
    She soone left off her mirth and wanton play,
    And bad her knight addresse him to the fray:
    His foe was nigh at hand. He prickt with pride
    And hope to winne his Ladies heart that day,
    Forth spurrèd fast: adowne his coursers side
The red bloud trickling staind the way, as he did ride.

15

The knight of the Redcrosse when him he spide,
    Spurring so hote with rage dispiteous,°   *cruel*
    Gan fairely couch° his speare, and towards ride: *lower*
    Soone meete they both, both fell° and furious,   *fierce*
    That daunted° with their forces hideous,   *dazed*
    Their steeds do stagger, and amazèd° stand,   *stunned*
    And eke° themselves too rudely rigorous,°   *also / violent*
    Astonied° with the stroke of their owne hand,   *stunned*
Do backe rebut,° and each to other yeeldeth land.   *recoil*

16

As when two rams stird with ambitious pride,
    Fight for the rule of the rich fleecèd flocke,
    Their hornèd fronts so fierce on either side
    Do meete, that with the terrour of the shocke
    Astonied both, stand sencelesse as a blocke,
    Forgetfull of the hanging° victory: *in the balance*
    So stood these twaine, unmovèd as a rocke,
    Both staring fierce, and holding idely
The broken reliques of their former cruelty.

17

The Sarazin sore daunted with the buffe
    Snatcheth his sword, and fiercely to him flies;
    Who well it wards, and quyteth° cuff with cuff: *requites, repays*
    Each others equall puissaunce envies,°   *power seeks to rival*
    And through their iron sides with cruell spies°   *looks*
    Does seeke to perce: repining courage yields
    No foote to foe. The flashing fier flies
    As from a forge out of their burning shields,
And streames of purple bloud new dies the verdant fields.

18

"Curse on that Crosse," quoth then the Sarazin,
  "That keepes thy body from the bitter fit;°   *death pangs*
  Dead long ygoe I wote° thou haddest bin,   *know*
  Had not that charme from thee forwarnèd° it: *prevented*
  But yet I warne thee now assurèd° sitt,   *securely*
  And hide thy head." Therewith upon his crest
  With rigour° so outrageöus he smitt,   *violence*
  That a large share it hewd out of the rest,
And glauncing downe his shield, from blame him fairely blest.[7]

19

Who thereat wondrous wroth, the sleeping spark
  Of native vertue° gan eftsoones° revive,   *strength / again*
  And at his haughtie helmet making mark,°   *taking aim*
  So hugely° stroke, that it the steele did rive,   *mightily*
  And cleft his head. He tumbling downe alive,
  With bloudy mouth his mother earth did kis,
  Greeting his grave: his grudging° ghost did strive   *complaining*
  With the fraile flesh; at last it flitted is,
Whither the soules do fly of men, that live amis.

20

The Lady when she saw her champion fall,
  Like the old ruines of a broken towre,
  Staid not to waile his woefull funerall,°   *death*
  But from him fled away with all her powre;
  Who after her as hastily gan scowre,°   *scurry*
  Bidding the Dwarfe with him to bring away
  The Sarazins shield, signe of the conqueroure.
  Her soone he overtooke, and bad to stay,
For present cause was none of dread her to dismay.

21

She turning backe with ruefull° countenaunce,   *pitiable*
  Cride, "Mercy mercy Sir vouchsafe to show
  On silly° Dame, subject to hard mischaunce,   *helpless*
  And to your mighty will." Her humblesse low
  In so ritch weedes° and seeming glorious show, *clothes*
  Did much emmove his stout heroicke heart,
  And said, "Deare dame, your suddein overthrow
  Much rueth° me; but now put feare apart,   *grieves*
And tell, both who ye be, and who that tooke your part."

22

Melting in teares, then gan she thus lament;
  "The wretched woman, whom unhappy howre

7. Preserved him from harm.

Hath now made thrall° to your commandèment,   *slave*
Before that angry heavens list to lowre,°   *chose to frown*
And fortune false betraide me to your powre,
Was (O what now availeth that I was!)
Borne the sole daughter of an Emperour,
He that the wide West under his rule has,
And high hath set his throne, where Tiberis doth pas.[8]

23

"He in the first flowre of my freshest age,
Betrothèd me unto the onely haire°   *heir*
Of a most mighty king, most rich and sage;[9]
Was never Prince so faithfull and so faire,
Was never Prince so meeke and debonaire;°   *gracious*
But ere my hopèd day of spousall shone,
My dearest Lord fell from high honours staire,
Into the hands of his accursèd fone,°   *foes*
And cruelly was slaine, that shall I ever mone.

24

"His blessèd body spoild of lively breath,
Was afterward, I know not how, convaid°   *carried away*
And fro° me hid: of whose most innocent death   *from*
When tidings came to me unhappy maid,
O how great sorrow my sad soule assaid.°   *afflicted*
Then forth I went his woefull corse to find,
And many yeares throughout the world I straid,
A virgin widow, whose deepe wounded mind
With love, long time did languish as the striken hind.°   *deer*

25

"At last it chauncèd this proud Sarazin
To meete me wandring, who perforce° me led   *by violence*
With him away, but yet could never win
The fort, that Ladies hold in soveraigne dread.°   *utmost reverence*
There lies he now with foule dishonour dead,
Who whiles he livde, was callèd proud Sans foy,
The eldest of three brethren, all three bred
Of one bad sire, whose youngest is Sans joy,
And twixt them both was borne the bloudy bold Sans loy.[1]

26

"In this sad plight, friendlesse, unfortunate,
Now miserable I Fidessa° dwell,   *Faithful*

---

8. The Tiber River runs through Rome. The lady is hence associated with the Catholic Church. Her father, she says, is ruler of the west—but Una's father had the rule of both east *and* west (canto 1, stanza 5); historically, the true church once embraced east and west.
9. The lady claims to have been betrothed to Christ, bridegroom of the Church (Matthew 9.15).
1. Without law—lawless.

Craving of you in pitty of my state,
To do none° ill, if please ye not do well."   no
He in great passion all this while did dwell,°   continue
More busying his quicke eyes, her face to view,
Then his dull eares, to heare what she did tell;
And said, "Faire Lady hart of flint would rew
The undeservèd woes and sorrowes, which ye shew.

27

"Henceforth in safe assuraunce may ye rest,
Having both found a new friend you to aid,
And lost an old foe, that did you molest:
Better new friend than an old foe is° said."   it is
With chaunge of cheare° the seeming simple maid   countenance
Let fall her eyen, as shamefast° to the earth,   as if modestly
And yeelding soft, in that she nought gain-said,°   objected
So forth they rode, he feining° seemely merth,   simulating
And she coy lookes: so dainty they say maketh derth.²

28

Long time they thus together traveilèd,
Till weary of their way, they came at last,
Where grew two goodly trees, that faire did spred
Their armes abroad, with gray mosse overcast,
And their greene leaves trembling with every blast,°   breeze
Made a calme shadow far in compasse round:
The fearefull Shepheard often there aghast
Under them never sat, ne wont° there sound   nor was accustomed to
His mery oaten pipe, but shund th'unlucky ground.

29

But this good knight soone as he them can° spie,   did
For the coole shade him thither hastly got:
For golden Phoebus now ymounted hie,
From fiery wheeles of his faire chariot
Hurlèd his beame so scorching cruell hot,
That living creature mote° it not abide;   might
And his new Lady it endurèd not.
There they alight, in hope themselves to hide
From the fierce heat, and rest their weary limbs a tide.°   time

30

Faire seemely pleasaunce° each to other makes,   courtesy
With goodly purposes° there as they sit: courteous conversation
And in his falsèd° fancy he her takes   deceived
To be the fairest wight° that livèd yit;   creature
Which to expresse, he bends° his gentle wit,°   applies / mind

2. Proverbial: what's dear is rare; here, coyness creates unsatisfied desire.

And thinking of those braunches greene to frame
A girlond for her dainty forehead fit,
He pluckt a bough; out of whose rift there came
Small drops of gory bloud, that trickled downe the same.

31

Therewith a piteous yelling voyce was heard,
  Crying, "O spare with guilty hands to teare
  My tender sides in this rough rynd embard,°   *imprisoned*
  But fly, ah fly far hence away, for feare
  Least° to you hap, that happened to me heare,   *lest*
  And to this wretched Lady, my deare love,
  O too deare love, love bought with death too deare."
  Astond° he stood, and up his haire did hove,°   *stunned / rise*
And with that suddein horror could no member move.

32

At last whenas the dreadfull passiön
  Was overpast, and manhood well awake,
  Yet musing at the straunge occasiön,
  And doubting much his sence, he thus bespake;
  "What voyce of damnèd Ghost from Limbo[3] lake,
  Or guilefull spright wandring in empty aire,
  Both which fraile men do oftentimes mistake,°   *mislead*
  Sends to my doubtfull eares these speaches rare,°   *strange*
And ruefull plaints, me bidding guiltlesse bloud to spare?"

33

Then groning deepe, "Nor° damnèd Ghost," quoth he,   *neither*
  "Nor guilefull sprite to thee these wordes doth speake,
  But once a man Fradubio,[4] now a tree,
  Wretched man, wretched tree; whose nature weake,
  A cruell witch her cursèd will to wreake,
  Hath thus transformed, and plast in open plaines,
  Where Boreas° doth blow full bitter bleake,   *the north wind*
  And scorching Sunne does dry my secret vaines:
For though a tree I seeme, yet cold and heat me paines."

34

"Say on Fradubio then, or° man, or tree,"   *whether*
  Quoth then the knight, "by whose mischievous arts
  Art thou misshapèd thus, as now I see?
  He oft finds med'cine, who his griefe imparts;°   *expresses*
  But double griefs afflict concealing harts,
  As raging flames who striveth to suppresse."
  "The author then," said he, "of all my smarts,

---

3. A region of hell, traditionally the abode of the unbaptized.
4. *Fra* (Italian "in" or "brother") + *dubbio* ("doubt").

The motif of a man imprisoned in a tree derives from Virgil (*Aeneid* 3.27–42) and is used by Ariosto (*Orlando furioso* 6.26–53).

Is one Duessa[5] a false sorceresse,
That many errant° knights hath brought to wretchednesse.　*wandering*

35

"In prime of youthly yeares, when corage hot
　The fire of love and joy of chevalree
　First kindled in my brest, it was my lot
　To love this gentle Lady, whom ye see,
　Now not a Lady, but a seeming tree;
　With whom as once I rode accompanyde,
　Me chauncèd of a knight encountred bee,
　That had a like faire Lady by his syde,
Like a faire Lady, but did fowle Duessa hyde.

36

"Whose forgèd beauty he did take in hand,°　*he maintained*
　All other Dames to have exceeded farre,
　I in defence of mine did likewise stand,
　Mine, that did then shine as the Morning starre:
　So both to battell fierce arraungèd arre,
　In which his harder fortune was to fall
　Under my speare: such is the dye° of warre:　*hazard*
　His Lady left as a prise martiäll,°　*spoil of battle*
Did yield her comely person, to be at my call.

37

"So doubly loved of Ladies unlike° faire,　*diversely*
　Th'one seeming such, the other such indeede,
　One day in doubt I cast° for to compare,　*determined*
　Whether° in beauties glorie did exceede;　*which one (of two)*
　A Rosy girlond was the victors meede:°　*reward*
　Both seemde to win, and both seemde won to bee,
　So hard the discord was to be agreede.
　Fraelissa[6] was as faire, as faire mote bee,
And ever false Duessa seemde as faire as shee.

38

"The wicked witch now seeing all this while
　The doubtfull ballaunce equally to sway,
　What not by right, she cast to win by guile,
　And by her hellish science° raisd streight way　*magic*
　A foggy mist, that overcast the day,
　And a dull blast, that breathing on her face,
　Dimmed her former beauties shining ray,
　And with foule ugly forme did her disgrace:
Then was she faire alone, when none was faire in place.[7]

---

5. *Duessa* means "double being." *Due* (Italian "two") + *esse* (Latin "being").

6. Frailty (Italian *Fralezza*).
7. When nobody else was fair. "She": Duessa.

39

"Then cride she out, 'Fye, fye, deformèd wight,
 Whose borrowed beautie now appeareth plaine
 To have before bewitchèd all mens sight;
 O leave her soone, or let her soone be slaine.'
 Her lothly visage viewing with disdaine,
 Eftsoones° I thought her such, as she me told,   *presently*
 And would have kild her; but with faignèd paine,
 The false witch did my wrathfull hand withhold;
So left her, where she now is turnd to treën mould.°   *the form of a tree*

40

"Thens forth I tooke Duessa for my Dame,
 And in the witch unweeting° joyd long time,   *unknowingly*
 Ne ever wist,° but that she was the same,   *knew*
 Till on a day (that day is every Prime,[8]
 When Witches wont° do penance for their crime) *are accustomed to*
 I chaunst to see her in her proper hew,°   *in her own shape*
 Bathing her selfe in origane and thyme:[9]
 A filthy foule old woman I did vew,
That ever to have toucht her, I did deadly rew.°   *regret*

41

"Her neather partes misshapen, monstruous,
 Were hidd in water, that I could not see,
 But they did seeme more foule and hideous,
 Then° womans shape man would beleeve to bee.   *than*
 Thens forth from her most beastly companie
 I gan refraine, in minde to slip away,
 Soone as appeard safe opportunitie:
 For danger great, if not assured decay°   *destruction*
I saw before mine eyes, if I were knowne to stray.

42

"The divelish hag by chaunges of my cheare°   *demeanor*
 Perceived my thought, and drownd in sleepie night,
 With wicked herbes and ointments did besmeare
 My bodie all, through charmes and magicke might,
 That all my senses were bereavèd quight:°   *quite*
 Then brought she me into this desert waste,
 And by my wretched lovers side me pight,°   *planted*
 Where now enclosd in wooden wals full faste,[1]
Banisht from living wights, our wearie dayes we waste."

---

8. Spring; or the first appearance of the new moon.
9. Oregano and thyme were used to cure scabs and itching.
1. I.e., imprisoned within the trees.

43

"But how long time," said then the Elfin knight,
   "Are you in this misformèd house to dwell?"
"We may not chaunge," quoth he, "this evil plight,
Till we be bathèd in a living well;[2]
That is the terme prescribèd by the spell."
"O how," said he, "mote° I that well out find,   *might*
That may restore you to your wonted well?"°   *well-being*
"Time and suffisèd fates to former kynd
Shall us restore,[3] none else from hence may us unbynd."

44

The false Duessa, now Fidessa hight,°   *called*
   Heard how in vaine Fradubio did lament,
And knew well all was true. But the good knight
Full of sad feare and ghastly dreriment,°   *gloom*
When all this speech the living tree had spent,
The bleeding bough did thrust into the ground,
That from the bloud he might be innocent,
And with fresh clay did close the wooden wound:
Then turning to his Lady, dead with feare her found.

45

Her seeming dead he found with feignèd feare,
   As all unweeting of that well she knew,[4]
And paynd himselfe with busie care to reare
Her out of carelesse° swowne. Her eylids blew   *unconscious*
And dimmèd sight with pale and deadly hew° *deathlike appearance*
At last she up gan lift: with trembling cheare
Her up he tooke, too simple and too trew,
And oft her kist. At length all passèd feare,[5]
He set her on her steede, and forward forth did beare.

Canto 3

Forsaken Truth long seekes her love,
*   And makes the Lyon mylde,*
Marres° blind Devotions mart,° and fals   *spoils / trade*
*   In hand of leachour° vylde.*   *lecher*

I

Nought is there under heav'ns wide hollownesse,°   *concavity*
   That moves more deare compassiön of mind,
Then beautie brought t'unworthy° wretchednesse   *undeserved*

---

2. With allusion to John 4.14, the "well of water springing up into everlasting life."
3. I.e., time and the satisfaction of the fates alone can restore us to our former human nature.

4. I.e., pretending ignorance of what she knew well.
5. I.e., having overcome all fear.

Through envies snares or fortunes freakes° unkind: *sudden changes*
I, whether lately through her brightnesse blind,
Or through alleageance and fast fealtie,
Which I do owe unto all woman kind,
Feele my heart perst° with so great agonie,   *pierced*
When such I see, that all for pittie I could die.

2

And now it is empassionèd° so deepe,   *moved*
  For fairest Unas sake, of whom I sing,
  That my fraile eyes these lines with teares do steepe,
  To thinke how she through guilefull handeling,°   *treatment*
  Though true as touch,° though daughter of a king,   *touchstone*
  Though faire as ever living wight was faire,
  Though nor in word nor deede ill meriting,
  Is from her knight divorcèd° in despaire   *separated*
And her due loves derived° to that vile witches share.   *diverted*

3

Yet she most faithfull Ladie all this while
  Forsaken, wofull, solitarie mayd
  Farre from all peoples prease,° as in exile,   *press, crowd*
  In wildernesse and wastfull° deserts strayd,   *desolate*
  To seeke her knight; who subtilly betrayd
  Through that late vision, which th'Enchaunter wrought,
  Had her abandond. She of nought affrayd,
  Through woods and wastnesse° wide him daily sought;   *wilderness*
Yet wishèd tydings none° of him unto her brought.   *no one*

4

One day nigh wearie of the yrkesome way,
  From her unhastie° beast she did alight,   *slow*
  And on the grasse her daintie limbes did lay
  In secret shadow,° farre from all mens sight: *shade*
  From her faire head her fillet she undight,[6]
  And laid her stole aside. Her angels face
  As the great eye of heaven shynèd bright,
  And made a sunshine in the shadie place;
Did never mortall eye behold such heavenly grace.

5

It fortunèd° out of the thickest wood   *chanced*
  A ramping° Lyon rushèd suddainly,   *raging*
  Hunting full greedie after salvage blood;°   *wild game*
  Soone as the royall virgin he did spy,
  With gaping mouth at her ran greedily,
  To have attonce° devoured her tender corse;°   *at once / body*

6. She took off her headband.

But to the pray when as he drew more ny,
   His bloudie rage asswagèd with remorse,
And with the sight amazd, forgat his furious forse.

6

In stead thereof he kist her wearie feet,
   And lickt her lilly hands with fawning tong,
   As° he her wrongèd innocence did weet.°   *as if / understand*
   O how can beautie maister the most strong,
   And simple truth subdue avenging wrong?
   Whose yeelded pride and proud submissiön,
   Still dreading death, when she had markèd long,
   Her hart gan melt in great compassiön,
And drizling teares did shed for pure affectiön.

7

"The Lyon Lord of everie beast in field,"
   Quoth she, "his princely puissance° doth abate,   *power*
   And mightie proud to humble weake does yield,
   Forgetfull of the hungry rage, which late
   Him prickt, in pittie of my sad estate:°   *condition*
   But he my Lyon, and my noble Lord,
   How does he find in cruell hart to hate
   Her that him loved, and ever most adord,
As the God of my life? why hath he me abhord?"

8

Redounding° teares did choke th'end of her plaint,   *overflowing*
   Which softly ecchoed from the neighbour wood;
   And sad to see her sorrowfull constraint°   *affliction*
   The kingly beast upon her gazing stood;
   With pittie calmd, downe fell his angry mood.
   At last in close hart shutting up her paine,
   Arose the virgin borne of heavenly brood,°   *parentage*
   And to her snowy Palfrey got againe,
To seeke her strayèd Champion, if she might attaine.°   *overtake*

9

The Lyon would not leave her desolate,
   But with her went along, as a strong gard
   Of her chast person, and a faithfull mate
   Of her sad troubles and misfortunes hard:
   Still° when she slept, he kept both watch and ward,   *always*
   And when she wakt, he waited diligent,
   With humble service to her will prepard:
   From her faire eyes he tooke commaundèment,
And ever by her lookes conceivèd her intent.

10

Long she thus traveilèd through deserts wyde,
   By which she thought her wandring knight shold pas,
   Yet never shew° of living wight espyde;   *show*
   Till that at length she found the troden gras,
   In which the tract° of peoples footing was,   *track*
   Under the steepe foot of a mountaine hore;°   *gray*
   The same she followes, till at last she has
   A damzell spyde slow footing her before,[7]
That on her shoulders sad° a pot of water bore.   *heavy*

11

To whom approching she to her gan call,
   To weet,° if dwelling place were nigh at hand;   *know*
   But the rude° wench her answered nought at all, *impolite; ignorant*
   She could not heare, nor speake, nor understand;[8]
   Till seeing by her side the Lyon stand,
   With suddaine feare her pitcher downe she threw,
   And fled away: for never in that land
   Face of faire Ladie she before did vew,
And that dread Lyons looke her cast in deadly° hew. *deathlike*

12

Full fast she fled, ne ever lookt behynd,
   As if her life upon the wager lay,°   *were at stake*
   And home she came, whereas her mother blynd
   Sate in eternall night: nought could she say,
   But suddaine catching hold, did her dismay
   With quaking hands, and other signes of feare:
   Who full of ghastly fright and cold affray,°   *terror*
   Gan shut the dore. By this arrivèd there
Dame Una, wearie Dame, and entrance did requere.° *request*

13

Which when none yeelded, her unruly Page
   With his rude° clawes the wicket° open rent,   *rough / door*
   And let her in; where of his cruell rage
   Nigh dead with feare, and faint astonishment,[9]
   She found them both in darkesome corner pent;° *huddled*
   Where that old woman day and night did pray
   Upon her beades° devoutly penitent;   *rosary*
   Nine hundred *Pater nosters* every day,
And thrise nine hundred *Aves* she was wont to say.[1]

---

7. I.e., walking slowly ahead of her.
8. Cf. Mark 4.11–12: "unto them that are without, all these things are done in parables: That seeing they may see, and not perceive; and hearing they may hear, and not understand."
9. I.e., fainting with amazement.
1. Her prayers are the Lord's Prayer ("Our Father") and the Hail Mary.

14

And to augment her painefull pennance more,
   Thrise every weeke in ashes she did sit,
   And next her wrinkled skin rough sackcloth wore,[2]
   And thrise three times did fast from any bit:°   *food*
   But now for feare her beads she did forget.
   Whose needlesse dread for to remove away,
   Faire Una framèd words and count'nance fit:
   Which hardly° doen, at length she gan them pray,   *with difficulty*
That in their cotage small, that night she rest her may.[3]

15

The day is spent, and commeth drowsie night,
   When every creature shrowded is in sleepe;
   Sad Una downe her laies in wearie plight,
   And at her feet the Lyon watch doth keepe:
   In stead of rest, she does lament, and weepe
   For the late° losse of her deare lovèd knight,   *recent*
   And sighes, and grones, and evermore does steepe
   Her tender brest in bitter teares all night,
All night she thinks too long, and often lookes for light.

16

Now when Aldeboran was mounted hie
   Above the shynie Cassiopeias chaire,[4]
   And all in deadly sleepe did drownèd lie,
   One knockèd at the dore, and in would fare;°   *come*
   He knockèd fast,° and often curst, and sware,   *insistently*
   That readie entrance was not at his call:
   For on his backe a heavy load he bare
   Of nightly stelths and pillage severall,[5]
Which he had got abroad by purchase° criminall.   *acquisition*

17

He was to weete° a stout and sturdie thiefe,   *in fact*
   Wont to robbe Churches of their ornaments,
   And poore mens boxes[6] of their due reliefe,
   Which given was to them for good intents;
   The holy Saints of their rich vestiments
   He did disrobe, when all men carelesse slept,
   And spoild the Priests of their habiliments,°   *vestments*
   Whiles none the holy things in safety kept;
Then he by cunning sleights in at the window crept.

---

2. Sackcloth and ashes are symbols of penitence.
3. I.e., that she might rest herself.
4. The star Aldebaran, in the constellation Taurus, mounts over the constellation Cassiopeia.

5. I.e., he carried the booty gained from nightly thefts and various kinds of pillage.
6. A box for alms for the poor.

18

And all that he by right or wrong could find,
 Unto this house he brought, and did bestow
 Upon the daughter of this woman blind,
 Abessa daughter of Corceca[7] slow,
 With whom he whoredome usd, that few did know,
 And fed her fat with feast of offerings,
 And plentie, which in all the land did grow;
 Ne sparèd he to give her gold and rings:
And now he to her brought part of his stolen things.

19

Thus long the dore with rage and threats he bet,°   *beat*
 Yet of those fearefull women none durst rize,
 The Lyon frayèd them, him in to let:[8]
 He would no longer stay him to advize,°   *consider*
 But open breakes the dore in furious wize,
 And entring is; when that disdainfull° beast   *indignant*
 Encountring fierce, him suddaine doth surprize,
 And seizing° cruell clawes on trembling brest,   *fastening*
Under his Lordly foot him proudly hath supprest.

20

Him booteth not resist,[9] nor succour° call,   *help*
 His bleeding hart is in the vengers hand,
 Who streight° him rent in thousand peeces small,   *immediately*
 And quite dismembred hath: the thirstie land
 Drunke up his life; his corse left on the strand.°   *ground*
 His fearefull friends weare out the wofull night,
 Ne dare to weepe, nor seeme to understand
 The heavie hap,° which on them is alight,°   *lot / fallen*
Affraid, least to themselves the like mishappen might.[1]

21

Now when broad day the world discovered° has,   *revealed*
 Up Una rose, up rose the Lyon eke,°   *also*
 And on their former journey forward pas,
 In wayes unknowne, her wandring knight to seeke,
 With paines farre passing that long wandring Greeke,
 That for his love refusèd deitie;[2]
 Such were the labours of this Lady meeke,
 Still seeking him, that from her still did flie,
Then furthest from her hope, when most she weenèd nie.°   *believed near*

---

7. *Corceca* means "blind heart." Abessa's name comes from "abbess," also *ab+esse* (Latin): "from being," i.e., without substance.
8. I.e., neither of the women dared rise to let him in because the lion terrified ("frayed") them.

9. It does him no good to resist.
1. I.e., lest the same thing might happen amiss ("mishappen") to them.
2. Odysseus, who rejected immortality and the love of the nymph Calypso for his wife, Penelope.

22

Soone as she parted thence, the fearefull twaine,
  That blind old woman and her daughter deare
  Came forth, and finding Kirkrapine° there slaine,   *church robber*
  For anguish great they gan to rend their heare,
  And beat their brests, and naked flesh to teare.
  And when they both had wept and wayld their fill,
  Then forth they ranne like two amazèd deare,
  Halfe mad through malice, and revenging will,°   *desire of revenge*
To follow her, that was the causer of their ill.

23

Whom overtaking, they gan loudly bray,
  With hollow howling, and lamenting cry,
  Shamefully at her rayling all the way,
  And her accusing of dishonesty,°   *unchastity*
  That was the flowre of faith and chastity;
  And still amidst her rayling, she[3] did pray,
  That plagues, and mischiefs, and long misery
  Might fall on her, and follow all the way,
And that in endlesse error° she might ever stray.   *wandering*

24

But when she saw her prayers nought prevaile,
  She backe returnèd with some labour lost;
  And in the way as she did weepe and waile
  A knight her met in mighty armes embost,°   *encased*
  Yet knight was not for all his bragging bost,°   *boast*
  But subtill Archimag, that Una sought
  By traynes° into new troubles to have tost: *tricks*
  Of that old woman tydings he besought,
If that of such a Ladie she could tellen ought.[4]

25

Therewith she gan her passion to renew,
  And cry, and curse, and raile, and rend her heare,°   *hair*
  Saying, that harlot she too lately knew,
  That causd her shed so many a bitter teare,
  And so forth told the story of her feare:
  Much seemèd he to mone her haplesse chaunce,
  And after for that Ladie did inquere;
  Which being taught, he forward gan advaunce
His fair enchaunted steed, and eke his charmèd launce.

---

3. Corceca. (Abessa cannot speak.)
4. I.e., if she could tell anything ("ought") about such a lady.

26

Ere long he came, where Una traveild slow,
   And that wilde Champion wayting° her besyde: *attending*
   Whom seeing such, for dread he durst not show
   Himselfe too nigh at hand, but turnèd wyde
   Unto an hill; from whence when she him spyde,
   By his like seeming shield, her knight by name
   She weend it was, and towards him gan ryde:
   Approching nigh, she wist° it was the same,   *believed*
And with faire fearefull humblesse° towards him shee came. *humility*

27

And weeping said, "Ah my long lackèd Lord,
   Where have ye bene thus long out of my sight?
   Much fearèd I to have bene quite abhord,
   Or ought° have done, that ye displeasen might,   *aught*
   That should as death unto my deare hart light:[5]
   For since mine eye your joyous sight did mis,
   My chearefull day is turnd to chearelesse night,
   And eke my night of death the shadow is;
But welcome now my light, and shining lampe of blis."

28

He thereto meeting[6] said, "My dearest Dame,
   Farre be it from your thought, and fro my will,
   To thinke that knighthood I so much should shame,
   As you to leave, that have me lovèd still,
   And chose in Faery court of meere° goodwill,   *pure*
   Where noblest knights were to be found on earth:
   The earth shall sooner leave her kindly° skill   *natural*
   To bring forth fruit, and make eternall derth,°   *desert*
Then I leave you, my liefe,° yborne of heavenly berth. *beloved*

29

"And sooth to say, why I left you so long,
   Was for to seeke adventure in strange place,
   Where Archimago said a felon strong
   To many knights did daily worke disgrace;
   But knight he now shall never more deface:°   *discredit*
   Good cause of mine excuse; that mote° ye please   *may*
   Well to accept, and evermore embrace
   My faithfull service, that by land and seas
Have vowd you to defend, now then your plaint appease."° *cease*

5. I.e., be as a deathblow to my loving heart. ("Deare" can also mean *heavy, sore.*)
6. Answering in like manner.

30

His lovely° words her seemd due recompence　　　　　*loving*
　　Of all her passèd paines: one loving howre
　　For many yeares of sorrow can dispence:°　　　　*make amends*
　　A dram of sweet is worth a pound of sowre:
　　She has forgot, how many a wofull stowre°　　　　*trouble*
　　For him she late endured; she speakes no more
　　Of past: true is, that true love hath no powre
To looken backe; his eyes be fixt before.
Before her stands her knight, for whom she toyld so sore.

31

Much like, as when the beaten marinere,
　　That long hath wandred in the Ocean wide,
　　Oft soust° in swelling Tethys[7] saltish teare,　　　　*soaked*
　　And long time having tand his tawney hide
　　With blustring breath of heaven, that none can bide,
　　And scorching flames of fierce Orions hound,[8]
　　Soone as the port from farre he has espide,
　　His chearefull whistle merrily doth sound,
And Nereus crownes with cups;[9] his mates him pledg° around.　　*toast*

32

Such joy made Una, when her knight she found;
　　And eke th'enchaunter joyous seemd no lesse,
　　Then the glad marchant, that does vew from ground
　　His ship farre come from watrie wildernesse,
　　He hurles out vowes, and Neptune oft doth blesse:
　　So forth they past, and all the way they spent
　　Discoursing of her dreadfull late distresse,
　　In which he askt her, what the Lyon ment:
Who told her all that fell in journey as she went.[1]

33

They had not ridden farre, when they might see
　　One pricking° towards them with hastie heat,　　　　*spurring*
　　Full strongly armd, and on a courser free,°　　　　*eager to charge*
　　That through his fiercenesse fomèd all with sweat,
　　And the sharpe yron° did for anger eat,　　　　*bit*
　　When his hot ryder spurd his chauffèd° side;　　　　*chafed, heated*
　　His looke was sterne, and seemèd still to threat
　　Cruell revenge, which he in hart did hyde,
And on his shield Sans loy in bloudie lines was dyde.

---

7. The wife of Ocean; here, the ocean itself.
8. Sirius, the dog star, symbolizing hot weather (the dog days).
9. Nereus, a benevolent sea god, to whom the mariner in gratitude makes libations.
1. I.e., she told all that had befallen her on her journey.

34

When nigh he drew unto this gentle payre
    And saw the Red-crosse, which the knight did beare,
    He burnt in fire, and gan eftsoones° prepare   *immediately*
    Himselfe to battell with his couchèd° speare.   *leveled*
    Loth was that other, and did faint° through feare,   *lose heart*
    To taste th'untryed dint° of deadly steele;   *blow*
    But yet his Lady did so well him cheare,
    That hope of new good hap he gan to feele;
So bent his speare, and spurnd[2] his horse with yron heele.

35

But that proud Paynim° forward came so fierce,   *pagan*
    And full of wrath, that with his sharp-head speare
    Through vainely crossèd shield[3] he quite did pierce,
    And had his staggering steede not shrunke for feare,
    Through shield and bodie eke he should him beare:°   *thrust*
    Yet so great was the puissance° of his push,   *force*
    That from his saddle quite he did him beare:
    He tombling rudely° downe to ground did rush,   *violently*
And from his gorèd wound a well of bloud did gush.

36

Dismounting lightly from his loftie steed,
    He to him lept, in mind to reave° his life,   *take*
    And proudly said, "Lo there the worthie meed°   *recompense*
    Of him, that slew Sansfoy with bloudie knife;
    Henceforth his ghost freed from repining strife,
    In peace may passen over Lethe[4] lake,
    When mourning altars purgd° with enemies life,   *cleansed*
    The blacke infernall Furies[5] doen aslake:°   *appease*
Life from Sansfoy thou tookst, Sansloy shall from thee take."

37

Therewith in haste his helmet gan unlace,
    Till Una cride, "O hold that heavie hand,
    Deare Sir, what ever that thou be in place:°   *whoever you are*
    Enough is, that thy foe doth vanquisht stand
    Now at thy mercy: Mercie not withstand:
    For he is one the truest knight alive,[6]
    Though conquered now he lie on lowly land,°   *i.e., low on the ground*
    And whilest him fortune favourd, faire did thrive
In bloudie field: therefore of life him not deprive."

2. Spurred. "Bent": lowered.
3. The cross on Archimago's shield was false and did not give him the protection the Redcrosse knight received in his fight with Sansfoy (see canto 2, stanza 18).
4. The river of forgetfulness in Hades (but Styx—the river at hell's entrance—would seem more appropriate here: see canto 5, stanza 10).
5. Spirits of discord and revenge.
6. I.e., do not withhold mercy, for he is the one truest knight.

38

Her piteous words might° not abate his rage,   *could*
   But rudely rending up his helmet, would
   Have slaine him straight: but when he sees his age,
   And hoarie head of Archimago old,
   His hastie hand he doth amazèd hold,
   And halfe ashamèd, wondred at the sight:
   For the old man well knew he, though untold,[7]
   In charmes and magicke to have wondrous might,
Ne ever wont° in field, ne in round lists[8] to fight.   *accustomed*

39

And said, "Why Archimago, lucklesse syre,
   What doe I see? what hard mishap is this,
   That hath thee hither brought to taste mine yre?
   Or thine the fault, or mine the error is,
   In stead of foe to wound my friend amis?"
   He answered nought, but in a traunce still lay,
   And on those guilefull dazèd eyes of his
   The cloud of death did sit. Which doen away,°   *when the swoon passed*
He left him lying so, ne would no lenger stay.

40

But to the virgin comes, who all this while
   Amasèd stands, her selfe so mockt° to see   *deceived*
   By him, who has the guerdon° of his guile,   *reward*
   For so misfeigning her true knight to bee:
   Yet is she now in more perplexitie,°   *trouble*
   Left in the hand of that same Paynim bold,
   From whom her booteth not° at all to flie;   *is of no use*
   Who by her cleanly° garment catching hold,   *pure*
Her from her Palfrey pluckt, her visage to behold.

41

But her fierce servant full of kingly awe°   *awesomeness*
   And high disdaine,° whenas his soveraine Dame   *indignation*
   So rudely handled by her foe he sawe,
   With gaping jawes full greedy at him came,
   And ramping° on his shield, did weene° the same   *rearing / intend*
   Have reft away with his sharpe rending clawes:
   But he was stout, and lust did now inflame
   His corage more, that from his griping pawes
He hath his shield redeemed,° and foorth his swerd he drawes.   *recovered*

7. I.e., without needing to be told.   8. Enclosures for fighting tournaments.

42

O then too weake and feeble was the forse
   Of salvage beast, his puissance to withstand:
   For he was strong, and of so mightie corse,°   *body*
   As ever wielded speare in warlike hand,
   And feates of armes did wisely° understand.   *skillfully*
   Eftsoones he percèd through his chaufèd chest
   With thrilling point of deadly yron brand,⁹
   And launcht° his Lordly hart: with death opprest   *pierced*
He roared aloud, whiles life forsooke his stubborne brest.

43

Who now is left to keepe the forlorne maid
   From raging spoile° of lawlesse victors will?   *plunder*
   Her faithfull gard removed, her hope dismaid,
   Her selfe a yeelded pray to save or spill.°   *destroy*
   He now Lord of the field, his pride to fill,
   With foule reproches, and disdainfull spight
   Her vildly entertaines, and will or nill,
   Beares her away upon his courser light:¹
Her prayers nought prevaile; his rage is more of might.

44

And all the way, with great lamenting paine,
   And piteous plaints she filleth his dull° eares,   *deaf*
   That stony hart could riven have in twaine,
   And all the way she wets with flowing teares:
   But he enraged with rancor, nothing heares.
   Her servile beast° yet would not leave her so,   *the palfrey*
   But followes her farre off, ne ought° he feares,   *aught, anything*
   To be partaker of her wandring woe,
More mild in beastly kind,° then that her beastly foe.   *nature*

Canto 4

*To sinfull house of Pride, Duessa
   guides the faithfull knight,
Where brothers death to wreak° Sansjoy   avenge
   doth chalenge him to fight.*

1

Young knight, what ever that dost armes professe,
   And through long labours huntest after fame,
   Beware of fraud, beware of ficklenesse,
   In choice, and change of thy deare lovèd Dame,

---

9. I.e., he pierced through the lion's angry ("chaufèd") chest with the penetrating ("thrilling") point of his sword.

1. I.e., he treats her basely ("vildly") and willingly or not bears her away quickly ("light") on his horse.

Least thou of her beleeve too lightly blame,[2]
And rash misweening° doe thy hart remove: *misjudgment*
For unto knight there is no greater shame,
Then lightnesse and inconstancie in love;
That doth this Redcrosse knights ensample° plainly prove. *example*

2

Who after that he had faire Una lorne,°   *forsaken*
Through light misdeeming° of her loialtie,   *misjudging*
And false Duessa in her sted had borne,° *taken as companion*
Called Fidess', and so supposd to bee;
Long with her traveild, till at last they see
A goodly building, bravely garnishèd,°   *adorned*
The house of mightie Prince it seemd to bee:
And towards it a broad high way[3] that led,
All bare through peoples feet, which thither traveilèd.

3

Great troupes of people traveild thitherward
Both day and night, of each degree and place,°   *rank*
But few returnèd, having scapèd hard,° *with difficulty*
With balefull° beggerie, or foule disgrace,   *wretched*
Which ever after in most wretched case,
Like loathsome lazars,° by the hedges lay.   *lepers*
Thither Duessa bad him bend his pace:° *direct his steps*
For she is wearie of the toilesome way,
And also nigh consumèd is the lingring day.

4

A stately Pallace built of squarèd bricke,
Which cunningly was without morter laid,
Whose wals were high, but nothing strong, nor thick,
And golden foile° all over them displaid,   *thin layer of gold*
That purest skye with brightnesse they dismaid:°   *outdid*
High lifted up were many loftie towres,
And goodly galleries farre over laid,°   *placed above*
Full of faire windowes, and delightfull bowres;
And on the top a Diall told the timely howres.[4]

5

It was a goodly heape° for to behould,   *building*
And spake the praises of the workmans wit;°   *skill*
But full great pittie, that so faire a mould°   *structure*
Did on so weake foundation ever sit:
For on a sandie hill,[5] that still did flit,°   *shift*

---

2. Lest you too readily believe accusations about her.
3. "Broad is the way that leadeth to destruction" (Matthew 7.13).

4. A sundial measured the hours of the day.
5. Matthew 7.26–27: "A foolish man . . . built his house upon the sand: And the rain descended, and the floods came, and the winds blew, and

And fall away, it mounted was full hie,
That every breath of heaven shakèd it:
And all the hinder parts, that few could spie,
Were ruinous and old, but painted cunningly.

6

Arrivèd there they passèd in forth right;
For still° to all the gates stood open wide,   *always*
Yet charge of them was to a Porter hight°   *committed*
Cald Malvenù,[6] who entrance none denide:
Thence to the hall, which was on every side
With rich array and costly arras dight:[7]
Infinite sorts of people did abide
There waiting long, to win the wishèd sight
Of her, that was the Lady of that Pallace bright.

7

By them they passe, all gazing on them round,
And to the Presence[8] mount; whose glorious vew
Their frayle amazèd senses did confound:
In living Princes court none ever knew
Such endlesse richesse, and so sumptuous shew;°   *show*
Ne° Persia selfe, the nourse of pompous pride   *nor*
Like ever saw. And there a noble crew
Of Lordes and Ladies stood on every side,
Which with their presence faire, the place much beautifide.

8

High above all a cloth of State° was spred,   *canopy*
And a rich throne, as bright as sunny day,
On which there sate most brave embellishèd°   *handsomely clad*
With royall robes and gorgeous array,
A mayden Queene, that shone as Titans° ray,   *the sun's*
In glistring gold, and peerelesse pretious stone:
Yet her bright blazing beautie did assay°   *attempt*
To dim the brightnesse of her glorious throne,
As envying her selfe, that too exceeding shone.

9

Exceeding shone, like Phoebus fairest childe,
That did presume° his fathers firie wayne,°   *usurp / chariot*
And flaming mouthes of steedes unwonted° wilde   *unusually*
Through highest heaven with weaker° hand to rayne;   *too weak*
Proud of such glory and advancement vaine,
While flashing beames do daze his feeble eyen,

---

beat upon that house; and it fell; and great was
the fall of it."
6. "Unwelcome." In courtly love allegories, the
porter is often called Bienvenu or Bel-accueil

("welcome").
7. Decorated with costly wall hangings.
8. Presence chamber, where a sovereign receives
guests.

He leaves the welkin° way most beaten plaine,   *heavenly*
  And rapt° with whirling wheeles, inflames the skyen,   *carried away*
With fire not made to burne, but fairely for to shyne.[9]

10

So proud she shynèd in her Princely state,
  Looking to heaven; for earth she did disdayne,
  And sitting high; for lowly° she did hate: *lowliness*
  Lo underneath her scornefull feete, was layne
  A dreadfull Dragon with an hideous trayne,°   *tail*
  And in her hand she held a mirrhour bright,[1]
  Wherein her face she often vewèd fayne,°   *with pleasure*
  And in her selfe-loved semblance tooke delight;
For she was wondrous faire, as any living wight.

11

Of griesly° Pluto she the daughter was,   *horrid*
  And sad Proserpina the Queene of hell;
  Yet did she thinke her pearelesse worth to pas°   *surpass*
  That parentage, with pride so did she swell,
  And thundring Jove, that high in heaven doth dwell,
  And wield° the world, she claymèd for her syre,   *govern*
  Or if that any else did Jove excell:
  For to the highest she did still aspyre,
Or if ought° higher were then that, did it desyre.   *anything*

12

And proud Lucifera men did her call,
  That made her selfe a Queene, and crownd to be,
  Yet rightfull kingdome she had none at all,
  Ne heritage of native soveraintie,
  But did usurpe with wrong and tyrannie
  Upon the scepter, which she now did hold:
  Ne ruld her Realmes with lawes, but pollicie,°   *political cunning*
  And strong advizement of six wisards old,
That with their counsels bad her kingdome did uphold.

13

Soone as the Elfin knight in presence came,
  And false Duessa seeming Lady faire,
  A gentle Husher,° Vanitie by name   *usher*
  Made rowme, and passage for them did prepaire:
  So goodly° brought them to the lowest staire   *graciously*
  Of her high throne, where they on humble knee
  Making obeyssance,° did the cause declare,   *submission*

---

9. Phaëthon tried to drive the chariot of his father, Phoebus, the sun god, but set the skies on fire and fell.

1. Pride and figures associated with her in Renaissance literature and art often hold a mirror, emblematic of self-love.

Why they were come, her royall state to see,
To prove° the wide report of her great Majestee.   *verify*

14

With loftie eyes, halfe loth to looke so low,
    She thankèd them in her disdainefull wise,°   *manner*
Ne other grace vouchsafèd them to show
Of Princesse worthy, scarse them bad° arise.   *bade*
    Her Lordes and Ladies all this while devise°   *make ready*
    Themselves to setten forth to straungers sight:
    Some frounce° their curlèd haire in courtly guise,   *frizzle*
    Some prancke° their ruffes, and others trimly dight°   *pleat / arrange*
Their gay attire: each others greater pride does spight.[2]

15

Goodly they all that knight do entertaine,
    Right glad with him to have increast their crew:
But to Duess' each one himselfe did paine
All kindnesse and faire courtesie to shew;
    For in that court whylome° her well they knew: *formerly*
    Yet the stout Faerie mongst the middest° crowd   *thickest*
    Thought all their glorie vaine in knightly vew,
    And that great Princesse too exceeding prowd,
That to strange° knight no better countenance° allowd.   *stranger / favor*

16

Suddein upriseth from her stately place
    The royall Dame, and for her coche doth call:
All hurtlen° forth and she with Princely pace,   *rush*
As faire Aurora in her purple pall,[3]
    Out of the East the dawning day doth call:
    So forth she comes: her brightnesse brode° doth blaze;   *abroad*
    The heapes of people thronging in the hall,
    Do ride° each other, upon her to gaze: *climb up on*
Her glorious glitterand° light doth all mens eyes amaze.   *glittering*

17

So forth she comes, and to her coche does clyme,
    Adornèd all with gold, and girlonds gay,
That seemd as fresh as Flora° in her prime,   *the goddess of flowers*
And strove to match, in royall rich array,
    Great Junos golden chaire,° the which they say   *chariot*
    The Gods stand gazing on, when she does ride
    To Joves high house through heavens bras-pavèd way
    Drawne of faire Pecocks, that excell in pride,
And full of Argus eyes their tailes dispredden wide.[4]

---

2. Each despises the others' greater pride.
3. Goddess of dawn, in her crimson robe ("purple pall").

4. Peacocks, with their tails outspread ("dispredden wide"), are a symbol of pride. The hundred-eyed monster Argus was set by Juno to watch Io,

18

But this was drawne of six unequall beasts,
   On which her six sage Counsellours did ryde,
   Taught to obay their bestiall beheasts,°   *bidding*
   With like conditions to their kinds applyde:[5]
   Of which the first, that all the rest did guyde,
   Was sluggish Idlenesse the nourse of sin;
   Upon a slouthfull Asse he chose to ryde,
   Arayd in habit blacke, and amis thin,[6]
Like to an holy Monck, the service to begin.

19

And in his hand his Portesse° still he bare,   *breviary, prayerbook*
   That much was worne, but therein little red,
   For of devotion he had little care,
   Still drownd in sleepe, and most of his dayes ded;
   Scarse could he once uphold his heavie hed,
   To looken, whether it were night or day:
   May seeme the wayne° was very evill led,   *chariot*
   When such an one had guiding of the way,
That knew not, whether right he went, or else astray.

20

From worldly cares himselfe he did esloyne,°   *withdraw*
   And greatly shunnèd manly exercise,
   From every worke he chalengèd essoyne,°   *claimed exemption*
   For contemplation sake: yet otherwise,
   His life he led in lawlesse riotise;°   *riotous conduct*
   By which he grew to grievous malady;
   For in his lustlesse° limbs through evill guise°   *feeble / living*
   A shaking fever raignd continually:
Such one was Idlenesse, first of this company.

21

And by his side rode loathsome Gluttony,
   Deformèd creature, on a filthie swyne,
   His belly was up-blowne with luxury,°   *indulgence*
   And eke° with fatnesse swollen were his eyne,°   *also / eyes*
   And like a Crane his necke was long and fyne,[7]
   With which he swallowd up excessive feast,
   For want whereof poore people oft did pyne;°   *starve*

---

one of Jupiter's loves. When Mercury killed Argus, his eyes were put in the peacock's tail feathers.

5. I.e., each bestial rider gave commands to his beast appropriate to its particular nature: the beasts and riders are suited to each other. This procession of the Seven Deadly Sins—of which Pride is queen—had a long tradition in medieval art and literature (see also Marlowe, *Dr. Faustus*,

scene 5, lines 272–328).

6. Idleness wears the gown ("habit") and hood or amice ("amis") of a monk. Traditionally, Idleness led the procession of the deadly sins.

7. The crane is a common symbol of gluttony because its long and thin ("fyne") neck allows extended pleasure in swallowing.

And all the way, most like a brutish beast,
He spuèd up his gorge,[8] that° all did him deteast.   *so that*

22

In greene vine leaves he was right fitly clad;
　For other clothes he could not weare for heat,
　And on his head an yvie girland had,[9]
　From under which fast trickled downe the sweat:
　Still as he rode, he somewhat° still did eat,   *something*
　And in his hand did beare a bouzing° can,   *drinking*
　Of which he supt so oft, that on his seat
　His dronken corse° he scarse upholden can,   *body*
In shape and life more like a monster, then° a man.   *than*

23

Unfit he was for any worldly thing,
　And eke unhable once° to stirre or go,°   *at all / walk*
　Not meet° to be of counsell to a king,   *fit*
　Whose mind in meat and drinke was drownèd so,
　That from his friend he seldome knew his fo:
　Full of diseases was his carcas blew,
　And a dry dropsie through his flesh did flow,
　Which by misdiet daily greater grew:
Such one was Gluttony, the second of that crew.

24

And next° to him rode lustfull Lechery,   *just after*
　Upon a bearded Goat,[1] whose rugged° haire,   *shaggy*
　And whally° eyes (the signe of gelosy,°)   *glaring / jealousy*
　Was like the person selfe, whom he did beare:
　Who rough, and blacke, and filthy did appeare,
　Unseemely man to please faire Ladies eye;
　Yet he of Ladies oft was lovèd deare,
　When fairer faces were bid standen by:°   *away*
O who does know the bent of womens fantasy?°   *caprice, whim*

25

In a greene gowne he clothèd was full faire,
　Which underneath did hide his filthinesse,
　And in his hand a burning hart he bare,
　Full of vaine follies, and new fangleness:°   *fickleness*
　For he was false, and fraught with ficklenesse,
　And learnèd had to love with secret lookes,
　And well could daunce, and sing with ruefulnesse,°   *pathos*
　And fortunes tell, and read in loving bookes,[2]
And thousand other wayes, to bait his fleshly hookes.

---

8. Vomited up what he had swallowed.
9. He resembles the drunken satyr Silenus, foster father of Bacchus, god of wine; ivy is sacred
to Bacchus.

1. Traditional symbol of lust.
2. Either manuals on the art of love (e.g., Ovid's
Ars Amatoria) or more ordinary erotica.

26

Inconstant man, that lovèd all he saw,
  And lusted after all, that he did love,
  Ne would his looser life be tide to law,
  But joyd weake wemens hearts to tempt and prove°   *try*
  If from their loyall loves he might them move;
  Which lewdnesse fild him with reprochfull paine
  Of that fowle evill, which all men reprove,°   *i.e., syphilis*
  That rots the marrow, and consumes the braine:
Such one was Lecherie, the third of all this traine.

27

And greedy Avarice by him did ride,
  Upon a Camell loaden all with gold;[3]
  Two iron coffers hong on either side,
  With precious mettall full, as they might hold,
  And in his lap an heape of coine he told;°   *counted*
  For of his wicked pelfe° his God he made,   *money*
  And unto hell him selfe for money sold;
  Accursèd usurie was all his trade,
And right and wrong ylike in equall ballaunce waide.[4]

28

His life was nigh unto deaths doore yplast,
  And thread-bare cote, and cobled° shoes he ware,   *roughly mended*
  Ne scarse good morsell all his life did tast,
  But both from backe and belly still did spare,
  To fill his bags, and richesse to compare;°   *acquire*
  Yet chylde ne° kinsman living had he none   *nor*
  To leave them to; but thorough° daily care   *through*
  To get, and nightly feare to lose his owne,
He led a wretched life unto him selfe unknowne.

29

Most wretched wight, whom nothing might suffise,
  Whose greedy lust° did lacke in greatest store,°   *desire / plenty*
  Whose need had end, but no end covetise,
  Whose wealth was want, whose plenty made him pore,
  Who had enough, yet wishèd ever more;
  A vile disease, and eke in foote and hand
  A grievous gout tormented him full sore,
  That well he could not touch, nor go,° nor stand: *walk*
Such one was Avarice, the fourth of this faire band.

3. The camel as a symbol of avarice is based on Matthew 19.24: "It is easier for a camel to go through the eye of a needle, than for a rich man to enter into the kingdom of God." 4. I.e., he made no distinction between right and wrong.

30

And next to him malicious Envie rode,
 Upon a ravenous wolfe, and still° did chaw   *continually*
 Betweene his cankred° teeth a venemous tode, *infected*
 That all the poison ran about his chaw;°   *jaw*
 But inwardly he chawèd his owne maw°   *entrails*
 At neighbours wealth, that made him ever sad;
 For death it was, when any good he saw,
 And wept, that cause of weeping none he had,
But when he heard of harme, he wexèd° wondrous glad. *waxed, grew*

31

All in a kirtle of discolourd say[5]
 He clothèd was, ypainted full of eyes;
 And in his bosome secretly there lay
 An hatefull Snake,[6] the which his taile uptyes
 In many folds, and mortall sting implyes.° *enfolds*
 Still as he rode, he gnasht his teeth, to see
 Those heapes of gold with griple Covetyse,° *grasping Avarice*
 And grudgèd at the great felicitie
Of proud Lucifera, and his owne companie.

32

He hated all good workes and vertuous deeds,
 And him no lesse, that any like did use,°   *perform*
 And who with gracious bread the hungry feeds,
 His almes for want of faith he doth accuse;[7]
 So every good to bad he doth abuse:°   *twist*
 And eke the verse of famous Poets witt
 He does backebite, and spightfull poison spues
 From leprous mouth on all, that ever writt:
Such one vile Envie was, that fifte in row did sitt.

33

And him beside rides fierce revenging Wrath,
 Upon a Lion, loth for to be led;
 And in his hand a burning brond° he hath, *sword*
 The which he brandisheth about his hed;
 His eyes did hurle forth sparkles fiery red,
 And starèd sterne on all, that him beheld,
 As ashes pale of hew and seeming ded;
 And on his dagger still° his hand he held, *always*
Trembling through hasty rage, when choler° in him sweld. *anger*

---

5. Robe or gown of many-colored cloth.
6. Traditional attribute of envy.
7. Envy perversely discounts others' good works by attributing them to a selfish motive: the desire to compensate (in God's eyes) for lack of faith.

34

His ruffin° raiment all was staind with blood,   *disorderly*
 Which he had spilt, and all to rags yrent,°   *torn*
 Through unadvisèd rashnesse woxen wood,° *grown insane*
 For of his hands he had no governement,°   *control*
 Ne cared for° bloud in his avengement: *minded*
 But when the furious fit was overpast,
 His cruell facts° he often would repent;   *actions*
 Yet wilfull man he never would forecast,
How many mischieves should ensue his heedlesse hast.[8]

35

Full many mischiefes follow cruell Wrath;
 Abhorrèd bloudshed, and tumultuous strife,
 Unmanly murder, and unthrifty scath,[9]
 Bitter despight,° with rancours rusty knife,   *malice*
 And fretting griefe the enemy of life;
 All these, and many evils moe° haunt ire,° *more / anger*
 The swelling Splene,[1] and Frenzy raging rife,
 The shaking Palsey, and Saint Fraunces fire:[2]
Such one was Wrath, the last of this ungoldly tire.° *train*

36

And after all, upon the wagon beame
 Rode Sathan,° with a smarting whip in hand,   *Satan*
 With which he forward lasht the laesie teme,
 So oft as Slowth° still in the mire did stand. *Idleness*
 Huge routs° of people did about them band,   *crowds*
 Showting for joy, and still before their way
 A foggy mist had covered all the land;
 And underneath their feet, all scattered lay
Dead sculs and bones of men, whose life had gone astray.

37

So forth they marchen in this goodly sort,°   *company*
 To take the solace° of the open aire,   *pleasure*
 And in fresh flowring fields themselves to sport;
 Emongst the rest rode that false Lady faire,
 The fowle Duessa, next unto the chaire
 Of proud Lucifera, as one of the traine:
 But that good knight would not so nigh repaire,° *approach*
 Him selfe estraunging from their joyaunce° vaine, *festivity*
Whose fellowship seemd far unfit for warlike swaine.

---

8. I.e., he never would foresee ("forecast") the calamities his careless haste caused.
9. I.e., inhuman murder and destructive harm.
1. In Renaissance physiology, the spleen was regarded as the seat of ill-humor.
2. Presumably St. Anthony's fire: erysipelas, or the flaming itch; appropriate to Wrath.

38

So having solacèd themselves a space
  With pleasaunce of the breathing° fields yfed,   *emitting fragrance*
  They backe returnèd to the Princely Place;
  Whereas an errant knight in armes ycled,°   *clad*
  And heathnish shield, wherein with letters red
  Was writ Sans joy, they new arrivèd find:
  Enflamed with fury and fiers hardy-hed,°   *hardihood*
  He seemd in hart to harbour thoughts unkind,
And nourish bloudy vengeaunce in his bitter mind.

39

Who when the shamèd shield³ of slaine Sans foy
  He spied with that same Faery champions page,°   *i.e., the dwarf*
  Bewraying° him, that did of late destroy   *revealing*
  His eldest brother, burning all with rage
  He to him leapt, and that same envious gage°   *envied prize*
  Of victors glory from him snatcht away:
  But th'Elfin knight, which ought that warlike wage,⁴
  Disdaind to loose the meed he wonne in fray,°   *battle*
And him rencountring° fierce, reskewd the noble pray.   *encountering*

40

Therewith they gan to hurtlen° greedily,   *rush together*
  Redoubted battaile ready to darrayne,°   *contest*
  And clash their shields, and shake their swords on hy,
  That with their sturre° they troubled all the traine;   *tumult*
  Till that great Queene upon eternall paine
  Of high displeasure, that ensewen° might,   *ensue*
  Commaunded them their fury to refraine,
  And if that either to that shield had right,
In equall lists⁵ they should the morrow next it fight.

41

"Ah dearest Dame," quoth then the Paynim° bold,   *pagan*
  "Pardon the errour of enragèd wight,°   *creature; man*
  Whom great griefe made forget the raines to hold
  Of reasons rule, to see this recreant° knight,   *cowardly*
  No knight, but treachour° full of false despight°   *traitor / disdain*
  And shamefull treason, who through guile° hath slayn   *deceit*
  The prowest° knight, that ever field did fight,   *bravest*
  Even stout Sans foy (O who can then refrayn?)
Whose shield he beares renverst, the more to heape disdayn.

---

3. Carrying a shield upside down, with the heraldic arms reversed, was a great insult (see stanza 41, line 9).

4. The knight (Redcrosse) who owned ("ought") that spoil of war ("warlike wage").
5. I.e., in impartial formal combat.

42

"And to augment the glorie of his guile,
  His° dearest love the faire Fidessa loe   *i.e., Sansfoy's*
  Is there possessèd of⁶ the traytour vile,
  Who reapes the harvest sowen by his foe,
  Sowen in bloudy field, and bought with woe:
  That° brothers hand shall dearely well requight   *that act*
  So be, O Queene, you equall favour showe."⁷
  Him litle answerd th'angry Elfin knight:
He never meant with words, but swords to plead his right.

43

But threw his gauntlet as a sacred pledge,
  His cause in combat the next day to try:
  So been they parted both, with harts on edge,
  To be avenged each on his enimy.
  That night they pas in joy and jollity,
  Feasting and courting both in bowre and hall;⁸
  For Steward was excessive Gluttonie,
  That of his plenty pourèd forth to all;
Which doen,° the Chamberlain⁹ Slowth did to rest them call.   *done*

44

Now whenas darkesome night had all displayd
  Her coleblacke curtein over brightest skye,
  The warlike youthes on dayntie° couches layd,   *fine*
  Did chace away sweet sleepe from sluggish eye,
  To muse on meanes of hopèd victory.
  But whenas Morpheus¹ had with leaden mace
  Arrested all that courtly company,
  Up-rose Duessa from her resting place,
And to the Paynims lodging comes with silent pace.

45

Whom broad awake she finds, in troublous fit,°   *troubled mood*
  Forecasting, how his foe he might annoy,°   *injure*
  And him amoves° with speaches seeming fit: *arouses*
  "Ah deare Sans joy, next dearest to Sans foy,
  Cause of my new griefe, cause of my new joy,
  Joyous, to see his ymage in mine eye,
  And greeved, to thinke how foe did him destroy,
  That was the flowre of grace and chevalrye;
Lo his Fidessa to thy secret faith I flye."

6. Possessed by (i.e., sexually).
7. I.e., if, O Queen, you show impartiality ("equall favour").
8. I.e., feasting in hall, courting in bowers (inner apartments, bedrooms).

9. The court attendant in charge of the bed-chambers,
1. Here, the god of sleep (cf. canto 1, stanza 36, and note).

46

With gentle wordes he can° her fairely° greet,   *did / courteously*
    And bad say on the secret of her hart.
    Then sighing soft, "I learne that litle sweet
    Oft tempred is," quoth she, "with muchell° smart: *much*
    For since my brest was launcht with lovely dart[2]
    Of deare Sansfoy, I never joyèd howre,
    But in eternall woes my weaker° hart   *too weak*
    Have wasted, loving him with all my powre,
And for his sake have felt full many an heavie stowre.°   *grief*

47

"At last when perils all I weenèd past,
    And hoped to reape the crop of all my care,
    Into new woes unweeting° I was cast,   *unknowing*
    By this false faytor,° who unworthy ware°   *imposter / wore*
    His worthy shield, whom he with guilefull snare
    Entrappèd slew, and brought to shamefull grave.
    Me silly° maid away with him he bare,   *helpless*
    And ever since hath kept in darksome cave,
For that I would not yeeld, that° to Sans foy I gave.   *what*

48

"But since faire Sunne hath sperst° that lowring clowd,   *dispersed*
    And to my loathèd life now shewes some light,
    Under your beames I will me safely shrowd,°   *take shelter*
    From dreaded storme of his disdainfull spight:
    To you th'inheritance belongs by right
    Of brothers prayse, to you eke longs° his love.   *belongs*
    Let not his love, let not his restlesse spright°   *ghost*
    Be unrevenged, that calles to you above
From wandring Stygian[3] shores, where it doth endlesse move."

49

Thereto said he, "Faire Dame be nought dismaid
    For sorrowes past; their griefe is with them gone:
    Ne yet of present perill be affraid;
    For needlesse feare did never vantage° none,   *aid*
    And helplesse hap it booteth not to mone.[4]
    Dead is Sans-foy, his vitall° paines are past,   *living*
    Though greevèd ghost for vengeance deepe do grone:
    He lives, that shall him pay his dewties° last,   *rites*
And guiltie Elfin bloud shall sacrifice in hast."

---

2. I.e., since my breast was pierced with the arrow of love.
3. I.e., from wandering on the banks of the river Styx, in Hades.
4. I.e., it does not help to moan over that which is beyond help ("helplesse hap").

50

"O but I feare the fickle freakes,"° quoth shee,   *unpredictable tricks*
   "Of fortune false, and oddes of armes[5] in field."
   "Why dame," quoth he, "what oddes can ever bee,
   Where both do fight alike, to win or yield?"
   "Yea but," quoth she, "he beares a charmèd shield,
   And eke enchaunted armes, that none can perce,
   Ne none can wound the man, that does them wield."
   "Charmd or enchaunted," answerd he then ferce,°   *fiercely*
"I no whit reck,[6] ne you the like need to reherce.°   *recount*

51

"But faire Fidessa, sithens° fortunes guile,   *since*
   Or enimies powre hath now captivèd you,
   Returne from whence ye came, and rest a while
   Till morrow next, that I the Elfe subdew,
   And with Sans-foyes dead dowry you endew."[7]
   "Ay me, that is a double death," she said,
   "With proud foes sight my sorrow to renew:
   Where ever yet I be, my secrete aid
Shall follow you." So passing forth she him obaid.

Canto 5

The faithfull knight in equall field
subdewes his faithlesse foe,
Whom false Duessa saves, and for
his cure to hell does goe.

1

The noble hart, that harbours vertuous thought,
   And is with child of° glorious great intent,   *pregnant with*
   Can never rest, untill it forth have brought
   Th'eternall brood of glorie excellent:[8]
   Such restlesse passion did all night torment
   The flaming corage° of that Faery knight,   *heart; mind*
   Devizing, how that doughtie° turnament   *worthy*
   With greatest honour he atchieven might;
Still did he wake, and still did watch for dawning light.

2

At last the golden Orientall gate
   Of greatest heaven gan to open faire,
   And Phoebus[9] fresh, as bridegrome to his mate,

5. Advantage of superior arms.
6. I do not care at all.
7. I.e., endow you with the legacy of the dead Sansfoy.
8. That good must be manifested in action, not in mere intent, is an important Renaissance commonplace.
9. I.e., the sun. Cf. Psalm 19.4–5: "In them hath he sat a Tabernacle for the sun, Which is as a bridegroom coming out of his chamber."

Came dauncing forth, shaking his deawie haire:
And hurld his glistring beames through gloomy aire.
Which when the wakeful Elfe perceived, streight way
He started up, and did him selfe prepaire,
In sun-bright armes, and battailous° array: *warlike*
For with that Pagan proud he combat will that day.

3

And forth he comes into the commune hall,
   Where earely waite him many a gazing eye,
   To weet° what end to straunger knights may fall.°   *learn / befall*
   There many Minstrales maken melody,
   To drive away the dull melancholy,
   And many Bardes, that to the trembling chord
   Can tune their timely° voyces cunningly,   *measured*
   And many Chroniclers, that can record
Old loves, and warres for ladies doen° by many a Lord.[1]   *done*

4

Soone after comes the cruell Sarazin,°   *Saracen*
   In woven maile all armèd warily,
   And sternly lookes at him, who not a pin
   Does care for looke of living creatures eye.
   They bring them wines of Greece and Araby,
   And daintie spices fetcht from furthest Ynd,°   *India*
   To kindle heat of courage privily:°   *within*
   And in the wine a solemne oth they bynd
T'observe the sacred lawes of armes, that are assynd.

5

At last forth comes that far renowmèd Queene,
   With royall pomp and Princely majestie;
   She is ybrought unto a palèd° greene,   *fenced*
   And placèd under stately canapee,°   *canopy*
   The warlike feates of both those knights to see.
   On th'other side in all mens open vew
   Duessa placèd is, and on a tree
Sans-foy his shield is hangd with bloudy hew:
Both those the lawrell girlonds[2] to the victor dew.

6

A shrilling trompet sownded from on hye,
   And unto battaill bad° them selves addresse: *bade*
   Their shining shieldes about their wrestes° they tye,   *wrists*
   And burning blades about their heads do blesse,°   *brandish*
   The instruments of wrath and heavinesse:°   *rage*

1. Minstrels play the music on their instruments, bards sing the words, chroniclers—historians, epic poets—write of love and war.

2. Laurel wreaths were awarded to the victor of a joust.

With greedy force each other doth assayle,
And strike so fiercely, that they do impresse
Deepe dinted furrowes in the battred mayle;
The yron walles to ward their blowes are weake and fraile.[3]

7

The Sarazin was stout,° and wondrous strong,   *bold*
And heapèd blowes like yron hammers great:
For after bloud and vengeance he did long.
The knight was fiers,° and full of youthly heat: *high-spirited*
And doubled strokes, like dreaded thunders threat:
For all for prayse and honour he did fight.
Both stricken strike, and beaten both do beat,
That from their shields forth flyeth firie light,
And helmets hewen deepe, shew marks of eithers might.

8

So th'one for wrong, the other strives for right:
As when a Gryfon[4] seizèd° of his pray,   *in possession*
A Dragon fiers encountreth in his flight,
Through widest ayre making his ydle° way,   *casual*
That would his rightfull ravine° rend away: *plunder*
With hideous horrour both together smight,
And souce° so sore, that they the heavens affray:°   *strike / startle*
The wise Southsayer° seeing so sad sight,   *soothsayer*
Th'amazèd vulgar tels of warres and mortall fight.

9

So th'one for wrong, the other strives for right,
And each to deadly shame would drive his foe:
The cruell steele so greedily doth bight
In tender flesh, that streames of bloud down flow,
With which the armes, that earst° so bright did show,   *at first*
Into a pure vermillion now are dyde:
Great ruth° in all the gazers harts did grow,   *pity*
Seeing the gorèd woundes to gape so wyde,
That victory they dare not wish to either side.

10

At last the Paynim chaunst to cast his eye,
His suddein° eye, flaming with wrathfull fyre,   *darting*
Upon his brothers shield, which hong thereby:
Therewith redoubled was his raging yre,°   *anger*
And said, "Ah wretched sonne of wofull syre,
Doest thou sit wayling by black Stygian lake
Whilest here thy shield is hangd for victors hyre,°   *reward*

3. I.e., their armor is too frail to withstand such blows.
4. A legendary monster, half-eagle, half-lion.

And sluggish german[5] doest thy forces slake,°   *slacken*
To after-send his foe, that him may overtake?

11

"Goe caytive° Elfe, him quickly overtake,   *servile*
  And soone redeeme from his long wandring woe;
  Goe guiltie ghost, to him my message make,
  That I his shield have quit° from dying foe."   *rescued*
  Therewith upon his crest he stroke him so,
  That twise he reelèd, readie twise to fall;
  End of the doubtfull battell deemèd tho
  The lookers on,[6] and lowd to him gan call
The false Duessa, "Thine the shield, and I, and all."

12

Soone as the Faerie heard his Ladie speake,
  Out of his swowning dreame he gan awake,
  And quickning° faith, that earst was woxen weake,   *life-restoring*
  The creeping deadly cold away did shake:
  Tho moved with wrath, and shame, and Ladies sake,°   *regard*
  Of all attonce he cast° avengd to bee,   *determined*
  And with so'exceeding furie at him strake,
  That forcèd him to stoupe upon his knee;
Had he not stoupèd so, he should have cloven bee.

13

And to him said, "Goe now proud Miscreant,°   *misbeliever*
  Thy selfe thy message doe° to german deare,   *give*
  Alone he wandring thee too long doth want:
  Goe say, his foe thy shield with his doth beare."
  Therewith his heavie hand he high gan reare,
  Him to have slaine; when loe a darkesome clowd
  Upon him fell: he no where doth appeare,
  But vanisht is. The Elfe him cals alowd,
But answer none receives: the darknes him does shrowd.[7]

14

In haste Duessa from her place arose,
  And to him running said, "O prowest° knight,   *bravest*
  That ever Ladie to her love did chose,
  Let now abate the terror of your might,
  And quench the flame of furious despight,°   *anger*
  And bloudie vengeance; lo th'infernall powres
  Covering your foe with cloud of deadly night,

---

5. Kinsman; here, brother.
6. I.e., the onlookers then ("tho") thought this would end the battle, heretofore in doubt ("doubt-full").

7. The device of a god rescuing a hero in danger by hiding him in a cloud has parallels in *Iliad* 3.380, *Aeneid* 5.810–12, and *Gerusalemme liberata* 7.44–45.

Have borne him hence to Plutoes balefull bowres.°   *i.e., Hades*
The conquest yours, I yours, the shield, and glory yours."

15

Not all so satisfide, with greedie eye
 He sought all round about, his thirstie blade
 To bath in bloud of faithlesse enemy;
 Who all that while lay hid in secret shade:
 He standes amazèd, how he thence should fade.
 At last the trumpets Triumph sound on hie,
 And running Heralds humble homage made,
 Greeting him goodly° with new victorie,   *respectfully*
And to him brought the shield, the cause of enmitie.

16

Wherewith he goeth to that soveraine Queene,
 And falling her before on lowly knee,
 To her makes present of his service seene;°   *proved*
 Which she accepts, with thankes, and goodly gree,° *favor*
 Greatly advauncing° his gay chevalree.   *extolling*
 So marcheth home, and by her takes the knight,
 Whom all the people follow with great glee,
 Shouting, and clapping all their hands on hight,° *aloud*
That all the aire it fils, and flyes to heaven bright.

17

Home is he brought, and laid in sumptuous bed:
 Where many skilfull leaches° him abide,° *doctors / attend*
 To salve° his hurts, that yet still freshly bled. *anoint*
 In wine and oyle they wash his woundès wide,
 And softly can embalme° on every side. *carefully did anoint*
 And all the while, most heavenly melody
 About the bed sweet musicke did divide,° *descanted*
 Him to beguile of° griefe and agony: *divert from*
And all the while Duessa wept full bitterly.

18

As when a wearie traveller that strayes
 By muddy shore of broad seven-mouthèd Nile,
 Unweeting of the perillous wandring wayes,
 Doth meet a cruell craftie Crocodile,
 Which in false griefe hyding his harmefull guile,
 Doth weepe full sore, and sheddeth tender teares:[8]
 The foolish man, that pitties all this while
 His mournefull plight, is swallowed up unwares,° *unexpectedly*
Forgetfull of his owne, that mindes anothers cares.

8. Medieval bestiaries popularized the legend of the hypocritical crocodile's tears.

19

So wept Duessa untill eventide,
　　That shyning lampes in Joves high house were light:[9]
　　Then forth she rose, ne lenger° would abide, longer
　　But comes unto the place, where th'Hethen knight
　　In slombring swownd nigh voyd of vitall spright,[1]
　　Lay covered with inchaunted cloud all day:
　　Whom when she found, as she him left in plight,[2]
　　To wayle his woefull case she would not stay,
But to the easterne coast of heaven makes speedy way.

20

Where griesly° Night, with visage deadly sad, grim, horrible
　　That Phoebus chearefull face durst never vew,
　　And in a foule blacke pitchie mantle clad,
　　She findes forth comming from her darkesome mew,° den
　　Where she all day did hide her hated hew.° shape; color
　　Before the dore her yron charet stood,
　　Alreadie harnessèd for journey new;
　　And cole blacke steedes yborne of hellish brood,
That on their rustie bits did champ, as° they were wood.° as if / mad

21

Who when she saw Duessa sunny bright,
　　Adorned with gold and jewels shining cleare,° brightly
　　She greatly grew amazèd at the sight,
　　And th'unacquainted° light began to feare: unfamiliar
　　For never did such brightnesse there appeare,
　　And would have backe retyred to her cave,
　　Untill the witches speech she gan to heare,
　　Saying, "Yet O thou dreaded Dame, I crave
Abide,° till I have told the message, which I have." stay

22

She stayd, and foorth Duessa gan proceede,
　　"O thou most auncient Grandmother of all,[3]
　　More old then Jove, whom thou at first didst breede,
　　Or that great house of Gods caelestiall,
　　Which wast begot in Daemogorgons hall,
　　And sawst the secrets of the world unmade,° before it was made
　　Why suffredst thou thy Nephewes° deare to fall grandsons
　　With Elfin sword, most shamefully betrade?
Lo where the stout Sansjoy doth sleepe in deadly shade.

9. I.e., when ("that") the stars came out.
1. Nearly ("nigh") devoid of life.
2. I.e., in the same desperate state in which she
had left him.

3. By tradition, Night was eldest of the gods, existing before the world was formed and the Olympian
gods were begotten in the hall of Demogorgon
(Chaos).

23

"And him before, I saw with bitter eyes
   The bold Sansfoy shrinke underneath his speare;
   And now the pray of fowles in field he lyes,
   Nor wayld of friends, nor laid on groning beare,[4]
   That whylome° was to me too dearely deare.   *formerly*
   O what of Gods then boots it° to be borne,   *is it worth*
   If old Aveugles sonnes so evill heare?[5]
   Or who shall not great Nightès children scorne,
When two of three her Nephews are so fowle forlorne?°   *wretchedly lost*

24

"Up then, up dreary Dame, of darknesse Queene,
   Go gather up the reliques° of thy race,   *remnants*
   Or else goe them avenge, and let be seene,
   That dreaded Night in brightest day hath place,
   And can the children of faire light deface."°   *destroy*
   Her feeling speeches some compassion moved
   In hart, and chaunge in that great mothers face:
   Yet pittie in her hart was never proved°   *known*
Till then: for evermore she hated, never loved.

25

And said, "Deare daughter rightly may I rew
   The fall of famous children borne of mee,
   And good successes, which their foes ensew:°   *attend*
   But who can turne the streame of destinee,
   Or breake the chayne of strong necessitee,
   Which fast is tyde to Joves eternall seat?[6]
   The sonnes of Day he favoureth, I see,
   And by my ruines thinkes to make them great:
To make one great by others losse, is bad excheat.°   *exchange*

26

"Yet shall they not escape so freely all;
   For some shall pay the price of others guilt:
   And he the man that made Sansfoy to fall,
   Shall with his owne bloud price° that he hath spilt.   *pay for*
   But what art thou, that telst of Nephews kilt?"
   "I that do seeme not I, Duessa am,"
   Quoth she, "how ever now in garments gilt,
   And gorgeous gold arayd I to thee came:
Duessa I, the daughter of Deceipt and Shame."

4. Bier attended by mourners (thus "groning").
5. I.e., are so badly thought of. "Aveugle": "blind."
He is the son of Night and father of Sansfoy, Sansjoy, and Sansloy.

6. The golden chain that binds the entire universe; the image goes back as far as Homer (*Iliad* 8.18–27).

27

Then bowing downe her agèd backe, she kist
  The wicked witch, saying; "In that faire face
  The false resemblance of Deceipt, I wist°   *knew*
  Did closely° lurke; yet so true-seeming grace   *secretly*
  It carried, that I scarse in darkesome place
  Could it discerne, though I the mother bee
  Of falshood, and root of Duessaes race.
  O welcome child, whom I have longd to see,
And now have seene unwares.° Lo now I go with thee."   *unexpectedly*

28

Then to her yron wagon she betakes,
  And with her beares the fowle welfavourd witch:
  Through mirkesome° aire her readie way she makes.   *murky; dense*
  Her twyfold° Teme, of which two blacke as pitch,   *twofold*
  And two were browne, yet each to each unlich,°   *unlike*
  Did softly swim away, ne ever stampe,
  Unlesse she chaunst their stubborne mouths to twitch;
  Then foming tarre,° their bridles they would champe, *black froth*
And trampling the fine element,° would fiercely rampe.° *the air / rear up*

29

So well they sped, that they be come at length
  Unto the place, whereas the Paynim lay,
  Devoid of outward sense, and native strength,
  Coverd with charmèd cloud from vew of day,
  And sight of men, since his late° luckelesse fray.   *recent*
  His cruell wounds with cruddy° bloud congealed,   *clotted*
  They binden up so wisely,° as they may,   *skillfully*
  And handle softly, till they can be healed:
So lay him in her charet, close in night concealed.

30

And all the while she stood upon the ground,
  The wakefull dogs did never cease to bay,
  As giving warning of th'unwonted° sound,   *unusual*
  With which her yron wheeles did them affray,
  And her darke griesly° looke them much dismay;   *horrid*
  The messenger of death, the ghastly Owle
  With drearie shriekes did also her bewray;°   *reveal*
  And hungry Wolves continually did howle,
At her abhorrèd face, so filthy and so fowle.

31

Thence turning backe in silence soft they stole,
  And brought the heavie corse with easie pace

To yawning gulfe of deepe Avernus hole.[7]
By that same hole an entrance darke and bace
With smoake and sulphure hiding all the place,
Descends to hell: there creature never past,
That backe returnèd without heavenly grace;
But dreadfull Furies, which their chaines have brast,°   *burst*
And damnèd sprights sent forth to make ill° men aghast.   *evil*

32

By that same way the direfull dames doe drive
Their mournefull charet, fild° with rusty blood,   *defiled*
And downe to Plutoes house are come bilive:°   *quickly; alive*
Which passing through, on every side them stood
The trembling ghosts with sad amazèd mood,
Chattring their yron teeth, and staring wide
With stonie eyes; and all the hellish brood
Of feends infernall flockt on every side,
To gaze on earthly wight, that with the Night durst ride.

33

They pas the bitter waves of Acheron,
Where many soules sit wailing woefully,
And come to fiery flood of Phlegeton,[8]
Whereas the damnèd ghosts in torments fry,
And with sharpe shrilling shriekes doe bootlesse° cry,   *without avail*
Cursing high Jove, the which them thither sent.
The house of endlesse paine is built thereby,
In which ten thousand sorts of punishment
The cursèd creatures doe eternally torment.

34

Before the threshold dreadfull Cerberus[9]
His three deformèd heads did lay along,°   *at full length*
Curlèd with thousand adders venemous,
And lillèd° forth his bloudie flaming tong: *lolled*
At them he gan to reare his bristles strong,
And felly gnarre,° untill dayes enemy   *savagely snarl*
Did him appease; then downe his taile he hong
And suffered them to passen quietly:
For she in hell and heaven had power equally.

35

There was Ixion turnèd on a wheele,
For daring tempt the Queene of heaven to sin;
And Sisyphus an huge round stone did reele°   *roll*
Against an hill, ne° might from labour lin;°   *nor / cease*

7. In classical mythology Avernus is hell, where Pluto (stanza 32) reigns.
8. Acheron and Phlegeton are rivers in hell.

9. The three-headed dog that guards hell. Stanzas 31–35 recall Aeneas's descent into hell (Virgil, *Aeneid* 6.200, 239–40).

There thirstie Tantalus hong by the chin;
And Tityus fed a vulture on his maw;°   *liver*
Typhoeus joynts were strechèd on a gin,°   *rack*
Theseus condemned to endlesse slouth° by law,   *sloth*
And fifty sisters water in leake vessels draw.[1]

36

They all beholding worldly° wights in place,°   *mortal / there*
  Leave off their worke, unmindfull of their smart,°   *pain*
  To gaze on them; who forth by them doe pace,
  Till they be come unto the furthest part:
  Where was a Cave ywrought by wondrous art,
  Deepe, darke, uneasie,° dolefull, comfortlesse,   *lacking ease*
  In which sad Aesculapius° farre a part   *the god of medicine*
  Emprisond was in chaines remedilesse,°   *beyond any remedy*
For that Hippolytus rent corse° he did redresse.°   *body / cure*

37

Hippolytus a jolly° huntsman was,   *gallant*
  That wont° in charet chace the foming Bore;   *used to*
  He all his Peeres in beautie did surpas,
  But Ladies love as losse of time forbore:
  His wanton stepdame[2] lovèd him the more,
  But when she saw her offred sweets refused
  Her love she turnd to hate, and him before
  His father fierce of treason false accused,
And with her gealous° termes his open eares abused.   *arousing jealousy*

38

Who all in rage his Sea-god syre° besought,   *Poseidon (Neptune)*
  Some cursèd vengeance on his sonne to cast:
  From surging gulf two monsters straight° were brought, *immediately*
  With dread whereof his chasing steedes aghast,
  Both charet swift and huntsman overcast.
  His goodly corps on ragged cliffs yrent,°   *torn*
  Was quite dismembred, and his members chast
  Scattered on every mountaine, as he went,
That of Hippolytus was left no moniment.[3]

39

His cruell stepdame seeing what was donne,
  Her wicked dayes with wretched knife did end,
  In death avowing th'innocence of her sonne.

---

1. Ixion was being punished for attempting to seduce Juno; Sisyphus, for refusing to pray to the gods; Tantalus, for stealing the gods' nectar; Tityus, for his attempted assault on Apollo's mother, Leto; the monster Typhoeus, for creating destructive winds; Theseus, for stealing Persephone from Hades; and the fifty daughters of King Danaus, for having killed their husbands on their wedding night. Tantalus stood chin-deep in water that receded whenever he tried to drink—hence he is "thirstie." Ovid, Virgil, and Homer are Spenser's sources here.
2. Phaedra, the wife of his father, Theseus.
3. I.e., no trace of identity.

Which hearing his rash Syre, began to rend
His haire, and hastie tongue, that did offend:
Tho° gathering up the relicks of his smart[4]   *then*
By Dianes meanes, who was Hippolyts frend,
Them brought to Aesculape, that by his art
Did heale them all againe, and joynèd every part.

40

Such wondrous science in mans wit to raine
When Jove avizd,° that could the dead revive,   *discovered*
And fates expirèd[5] could renew againe,
Of endlesse life he might him not deprive,
But unto hell did thrust him downe alive,
With flashing thunderbolt ywounded sore:
Where long remaining, he did alwaies strive
Himselfe with salves to health for to restore,
And slake the heavenly fire, that raged evermore.

41

There auncient Night arriving, did alight
From her nigh wearie waine,[6] and in her armes
To Aesculapius brought the wounded knight:
Whom having softly disarayd of armes,
Tho gan to him discover° all his harmes,   *reveal*
Beseeching him with prayer, and with praise,
If either salves, or oyles, or herbes, or charmes
A fordonne° wight from dore of death mote raise,   *undone*
He would at her request prolong her nephews daies.

42

"Ah Dame," quoth he, "thou temptest me in vaine,
To dare the thing, which daily yet I rew,
And the old cause of my continued paine
With like attempt to like end to renew.
Is not enough, that thrust from heaven dew[7]
Here endlesse penance for one fault I pay,
But that redoubled crime with vengeance new
Thou biddest me to eeke?° Can Night defray°   *increase / appease*
The wrath of thundring Jove, that rules both night and day?"

43

"Not so," quoth she; "but sith° that heavens king   *since*
From hope of heaven hath thee excluded quight,
Why fearest thou, that canst not hope for thing,°   *anything*
And fearest not, that more thee hurten might,
Now in the powre of everlasting Night?

---

4. I.e., his son's remains, which caused his grief.
5. The completed term of life as fixed by the Fates.
6. I.e., the horses of Night's chariot ("waine") are nearly exhausted.
7. The proper ("dew") place for a god.

Goe to then, O thou farre renowmèd sonne
  Of great Apollo, shew thy famous might
  In medicine, that else° hath to thee wonne   *already*
Great paines, and greater praise, both never to be donne."°   *ended*

44

Her words prevaild: And then the learnèd leach°   *doctor*
  His cunning hand gan to his wounds to lay,
  And all things else, the which his art did teach:
  Which having seene, from thence arose away
  The mother of dread darknesse, and let stay
  Aveugles sonne there in the leaches cure,°   *care*
  And backe returning tooke her wonted° way,   *accustomed*
  To runne her timely race,° whilst Phoebus pure   *her nightly journey*
In westerne waves his wearie wagon did recure.°   *refresh*

45

The false Duessa leaving noyous° Night,   *harmful*
  Returnd to stately pallace of dame Pride;
  Where when she came, she found the Faery knight
  Departed thence, albe° his woundès wide   *although*
  Not throughly heald, unreadie were to ride.
  Good cause he had to hasten thence away;
  For on a day his wary Dwarfe had spide,
  Where in a dongeon deepe huge numbers lay
Of caytive° wretched thrals,° that waylèd night and day.   *captive / slaves*

46

A ruefull sight, as could be seene with eie;
  Of whom he learnèd had in secret wise
  The hidden cause of their captivitie,
  How mortgaging their lives to Covetise,
  Through wastfull° Pride, and wanton Riotise,   *causing desolation*
  They were by law of that proud Tyrannesse[8]
  Provokt with Wrath, and Envies false surmise,
  Condemnèd to that Dongeon mercilesse,
Where they should live in woe, and die in wretchednesse.

47

There was that great proud king of Babylon[9]
  That would compell all nations to adore,
  And him as onely God to call upon,
  Till through celestiall doome° throwne out of dore,   *judgment*
  Into an Oxe he was transformed of yore:
  There also was king Croesus,[1] that enhaunst°   *exalted*
  His heart too high through his great riches store;

---

8. Lucifera. The noble sinners named in stanzas 47–50 exemplify a theme common in Renaissance morality, the fall of princes.

9. Nebuchadnezzar (Daniel 3–4).
1. King of Lydia, famous for his riches.

And proud Antiochus,[2] the which advaunst
His cursèd hand gainst God, and on his altars daunst.°   *danced*

48

And them long time before, great Nimrod was,
   That first the world with sword and fire warrayd;°   *ravaged*
   And after him old Ninus[3] farre did pas°   *surpass*
   In princely pompe, of° all the world obayd;   *by*
   There also was that mightie Monarch layd
   Low under all, yet above all in pride,
   That name of native° syre did fowle upbrayd,   *natural*
   And would as Ammons sonne be magnifide,
Till scornd of God and man a shamefull death he dide.[4]

49

All these together in one heape were throwne,
   Like carkases of beasts in butchers stall.
   And in another corner wide° were strowne   *lying apart*
   The antique ruines of the Romaines fall:
   Great Romulus the Grandsyre of them all,
   Proud Tarquin, and too lordly Lentulus,
   Stout Scipio, and stubborne Hanniball,
   Ambitious Sylla, and sterne Marius,
High Caesar, great Pompey, and fierce Antonius.[5]

50

Amongst these mighty men were wemen mixt,
   Proud wemen, vaine, forgetfull of their yoke:°   *duty*
   The bold Semiramis,° whose sides transfixt   *wife of Ninus*
   With sonnes owne blade, her fowle reproches spoke;
   Faire Sthenoboea,[6] that her selfe did choke
   With wilfull cord, for wanting° of her will;   *lacking*
   High minded Cleopatra, that with stroke
   Of Aspes sting her selfe did stoutly kill:
And thousands moe the like, that did that dongeon fill.

51

Besides the endlesse routs° of wretched thralles,   *crowds*
   Which thither were assembled day by day,
   From all the world after their wofull falles,

---

2. King of Syria, who desecrated the Jewish temple of Jerusalem (1 Maccabees 1.20–24).
3. In classical mythology, Ninus was founder of Nineveh, archetype of the wicked city (see the Book of Jonah). Nimrod, identified as the first tyrant, caused the Tower of Babel to be built in defiance of God (Genesis 10.9–10, 11.1–9).
4. The reference is to Alexander the Great, whose "shamefull death" came ten days after he fell ill at a drinking party. The son of Philip II of Macedon, Alexander was occasionally worshipped as the son of Jupiter Ammon.
5. Romulus was the founder of Rome; Tarquin, a Roman tyrant; Lentulus, a conspirator with Catiline to overthrow the Republic; Scipio, a. Roman general, conqueror of Carthage; Hannibal, a Carthaginian general; Sulla, a Roman civil war general; Marius, Sulla's rival. The figures in the final line are Julius Caesar, Pompey the Great, and Mark Antony.
6. Queen of King Proteus of Argos; she lusted after her brother-in-law Bellerophon.

Through wicked pride, and wasted wealthes decay.
But most of all, which in that Dongeon lay
Fell from high Princes courts, or Ladies bowres,
Where they in idle pompe, or wanton play,
Consumèd had their goods, and thriftlesse howres,
And lastly throwne themselves into these heavy stowres.°   *disasters*

52

Whose case wheneas the carefull° Dwarfe had tould,   *wary*
And made ensample of their mournefull sight
Unto his maister, he no lenger would
There dwell in perill of like painefull plight,
But early rose, and ere that dawning light
Discovered had the world to heaven wyde,
He by a privie Posterne° tooke his flight,   *secret back door*
That of no envious eyes he mote be spyde:
For doubtlesse death ensewd, if any him descryde.°   *descried, observed*

53

Scarse could he footing find in that fowle way,
For many corses, like a great Lay-stall°   *burial place; rubbish heap*
Of murdred men which therein strowèd lay,
Without remorse, or decent funerall:
Which all through that great Princesse pride did fall
And came to shamefull end. And them beside
Forth ryding underneath the castell wall,
A donghill of dead carkases he spide,
The dreadfull spectacle of that sad house of Pride.[7]

Canto 6

From lawlesse lust by wondrous grace
fayre Una is releast:
Whom salvage° nation does adore,   *wild; of the woods*
and learnes her wise beheast.°   *bidding*

1

As when a ship, that flyes faire under saile,
An hidden rocke escapèd hath unwares,°   *unexpectedly*
That lay in waite her wrack for to bewaile,[8]
The Marriner yet halfe amazèd stares
At perill past, and yet in doubt ne dares
To joy at his foole-happie oversight:°   *lucky ignorance*
So doubly is distrest twixt joy and cares
The dreadlesse° courage of this Elfin knight,   *fearless*
Having escapt so sad ensamples in his sight.

7. Named in the argument of canto 4, but in the poem itself, only now, after we have been shown what the name means.

8. I.e., cause the shipwreck and thereby cause it to be bewailed.

2

Yet sad he was that his too hastie speed
   The faire Duess' had forst him leave behind;
   And yet more sad, that Una his deare dreed°   *object of reverence*
   Her truth had staind with treason so unkind;°   *unnatural*
   Yet crime in her could never creature find,
   But for his love, and for her owne selfe sake,
   She wandred had from one to other Ynd,[9]
   Him for to seeke, ne ever would forsake,
Till her unwares the fierce Sansloy did overtake.

3

Who after Archimagoes fowle defeat,
   Led her away into a forrest wilde,
   And turning wrathfull fire to lustfull heat,
   With beastly sin thought her to have defilde,
   And made the vassall of his pleasures vilde.°   *vile*
   Yet first he cast by treatie,° and by traynes,°   *persuasion / tricks*
   Her to perswade, that stubborne fort to yilde:
   For greater conquest of hard love he gaynes,
That workes it to his will, then° he that it constraines.°   *than / forces*

4

With fawning wordes he courted her a while,
   And looking lovely,° and oft sighing sore,   *lovingly*
   Her constant hart did tempt with diverse guile:
   But wordes, and lookes, and sighes she did abhore,
   As rocke of Diamond stedfast evermore.[1]
   Yet for to feed his fyrie lustfull eye,
   He snatcht the vele, that hong her face before;
   Then gan her beautie shine, as brightest skye,
And burnt his beastly hart t'efforce° her chastitye.   *violate*

5

So when he saw his flatt'ring arts to fayle,
   And subtile engines bet from batteree,[2]
   With greedy force he gan the fort assayle,
   Whereof he weend° possessèd soone to bee,   *thought*
   And win rich spoile of ransackt chastetee.
   Ah heavens, that do this hideous act behold,
   And heavenly virgin thus outragèd see,
   How can ye vengeance just so long withhold,
And hurle not flashing flames upon that Paynim bold?

9. I.e., she would have wandered from the East to the West Indies.
1. The diamond, because of its hardness, was an emblem of fidelity.
2. I.e., beaten ("bet") from their fruitless assault ("batteree") on her unmovable virtue.

6

The pitteous maiden carefull° comfortlesse, *full of cares*
 Does throw out thrilling° shriekes, and shrieking cryes, *piercing*
 The last vaine helpe of womens great distresse,
 And with loud plaints importuneth the skyes,
 That molten starres do drop like weeping eyes;
 And Phoebus flying so most shamefull sight,
 His blushing face in foggy cloud implyes,° *buries*
 And hides for shame. What wit of mortall wight
Can now devise to quit a thrall° from such a plight? *release a captive*

7

Eternall providence exceeding° thought, *transcending*
 Where none appeares can make her selfe a way:
 A wondrous way it for this Lady wrought,
 From Lyons clawes to pluck the gripèd° pray. *grasped*
 Her shrill outcryes and shriekes so loud did bray,
 That all the woodes and forestes did resownd;
 A troupe of Faunes and Satyres³ far away
 Within the wood were dauncing in a rownd,
Whiles old Sylvanus slept in shady arber sownd.

8

Who when they heard that pitteous strainèd voice,
 In hast forsooke their rurall meriment,
 And ran towards the far rebownded° noyce, *re-echoed*
 To weet,° what wight so loudly did lament. *learn*
 Unto the place they come incontinent:° *immediately*
 Whom when the raging Sarazin espide,
 A rude, misshapen, monstrous rablement,
 Whose like he never saw, he durst not bide,
But got his ready steed, and fast away gan ride.

9

The wyld woodgods arrivèd in the place,
 There find the virgin dolefull desolate,
 With ruffled rayments, and faire blubbred° face, *flooded with tears*
 As her outrageous foe had left her late,
 And trembling yet through feare of former hate;
 All stand amazèd at so uncouth° sight, *strange*
 And gin to pittie her unhappie state,
 All stand astonied° at her beautie bright, *stupified*
In their rude° eyes unworthie° of so wofull plight. *rustic / undeserving*

3. Woodland deities with men's bodies above the waist and goats' bodies below, noted for their sensuality. Sylvanus, Roman god of the woods, is traditionally associated with fauns.

10

She more amazed, in double dread doth dwell;
   And every tender part for feare does shake:
   As when a greedie Wolfe through hunger fell°   *fierce*
   A seely° Lambe farre from the flocke does take,   *innocent*
   Of whom he meanes his bloudie feast to make,
   A Lyon spyes fast running towards him,
   The innocent pray in hast he does forsake,
   Which quit° from death yet quakes in every lim   *rescued*
With chaunge of feare, to see the Lyon looke so grim.°   *savage*

11

Such fearefull fit assaid° her trembling hart,   *assailed*
   Ne word to speake, ne joynt to move she had:
   The salvage nation feele her secret smart,
   And read her sorrow in her count'nance sad;
   Their frowning forheads with rough hornes yclad,
   And rusticke horror° all a side doe lay,   *roughness*
   And gently grenning, shew a semblance glad
   To comfort her, and feare to put away,
Their backward bent knees teach her humbly to obay.[4]

12

The doubtfull Damzell dare not yet commit
   Her single person to their barbarous truth,[5]
   But still twixt feare and hope amazd does sit,
   Late learnd° what harme to hastie trust ensu'th: *taught*
   They in compassion of her tender youth,
   And wonder of her beautie soveraine,°   *supreme*
   Are wonne with pitty and unwonted ruth,°   *unaccustomed pity*
   And all prostrate upon the lowly plaine,
Do kisse her feete, and fawne on her with count'nance faine.°   *glad*

13

Their harts she ghesseth by their humble guise,°   *appearance*
   And yieldes her to extremitie of time;[6]
   So from the ground she fearelesse doth arise,
   And walketh forth without suspect° of crime: *suspicion*
   They all as glad, as birdes of joyous Prime,°   *springtime*
   Thence lead her forth, about her dauncing round,
   Shouting, and singing all a shepheards ryme,
   And with greene braunches strowing all the ground,
Do worship her, as Queene, with olive girlond cround.

4. I.e., teach their knees, bent backward like a goat's, to obey her.
5. I.e., her solitary self to their wild allegiance ("barbarous truth").
6. I.e., necessity of the time.

14

And all the way their merry pipes they sound,
  That all the woods with doubled Eccho ring,
  And with their hornèd feet do weare the ground,
  Leaping like wanton kids in pleasant Spring.
  So towards old Sylvanus they her bring;
  Who with the noyse awakèd, commeth out,
  To weet the cause, his weake steps governing,
  And agèd limbs on Cypresse stadle° stout,   *staff*
And with an yvie twyne his wast is girt about.

15

Far off he wonders, what them makes so glad,
  Or Bacchus merry fruit they did invent,[7]
  Or Cybeles franticke rites[8] have made them mad;
  They drawing nigh, unto their God present
  That flowre of faith and beautie excellent.
  The God himselfe vewing that mirrhour rare,
  Stood long amazd, and burnt in his intent;[9]
  His owne faire Dryope now he thinkes not faire,
And Pholoe fowle, when her to this he doth compaire.[1]

16

The woodborne people fall before her flat,
  And worship her as Goddesse of the wood;
  And old Sylvanus selfe bethinkès not,° what   *cannot decide*
  To thinke of wight so faire, but gazing stood,
  In doubt to deeme her borne of earthly brood;
  Sometimes Dame Venus selfe he seemes to see,
  But Venus never had so sober mood;
  Sometimes Diana he her takes to bee,
But misseth bow, and shaftes, and buskins° to her knee.   *soft boots*

17

By vew of her he ginneth to revive
  His ancient love, and dearest Cyparisse,[2]
  And calles to mind his pourtraiture alive,[3]
  How faire he was, and yet not faire to° this,   *compared to*
  And how he slew with glauncing dart amisse
  A gentle Hynd, the which the lovely boy
  Did love as life, above all worldly blisse;
  For griefe whereof the lad n'ould° after joy,   *would not*
But pynd away in anguish and selfe-wild annoy.°   *self-willed suffering*

7. I.e., whether ("or") they did find ("invent") wine grapes.
8. Orgiastic dances in worship of Cybele, goddess of the powers of nature.
9. Glowed with intense concentration. Una is a "mirrhour rare" in the sense that she is a paragon, a perfect reflection of heavenly faith and beauty.

1. Dryope and Pholoe were nymphs loved by Faunus and Pan; for Spenser, the names *Faunus, Pan,* and *Sylvanus* were apparently interchangeable.
2. A fair youth, beloved of Sylvanus, turned into a cypress tree.
3. I.e., his appearance when alive.

18

The wooddy Nymphes, faire Hamadryades[4]
  Her to behold do thither runne apace,
  And all the troupe of light-foot Naiades,°   *water nymphs*
  Flocke all about to see her lovely face:
  But when they vewèd have her heavenly grace,
  They envie her in their malitious mind,
  And fly away for feare of fowle disgrace:
  But all the Satyres scorne their woody kind,°   *woodborn race*
And henceforth nothing faire, but her on earth they find.

19

Glad of such lucke, the luckelesse lucky maid,
  Did her content to please their feeble eyes,
  And long time with that salvage people staid,
  To gather breath in many miseries.
  During which time her gentle wit she plyes,
  To teach them truth, which worshipt her in vaine,
  And made her th'Image of Idolatryes;[5]
  But when their bootlesse° zeale she did restraine   *useless*
From her own worship, they her Asse would worship fayn.°   *willingly*

20

It fortunèd a noble warlike knight
  By just occasion to that forrest came,
  To seeke his kindred, and the lignage right,°   *true*
  From whence he took his well deservèd name:
  He had in armes abroad wonne muchell° fame,   *great*
  And fild far landes with glorie of his might,
  Plaine, faithfull, true, and enimy of shame,
  And ever loved to fight for Ladies right,
But in vaine glorious frayes° he litle did delight.   *frays, fights*

21

A Satyres sonne yborne in forrest wyld,
  By straunge adventure as it did betyde,°   *happen*
  And there begotten of a Lady myld,
  Faire Thyamis the daughter of Labryde,
  That was in sacred bands of wedlocke tyde
  To Therion,[6] a loose unruly swayne;
  Who had more joy to raunge the forrest wyde,
  And chase the salvage beast with busie payne,°   *painstaking care*
Then serve his Ladies love, and wast° in pleasures vayne.   *live idly*

---

4. Spirits of trees, whose lives ended when the tree they inhabited died.
5. The idol of their idolatries.

6. The name means "wild beast." "Thyamis": passion. "Labryde": turbulence.

22

The forlorne mayd did with loves longing burne,
  And could not lacke° her lovers company,   *be without*
  But to the wood she goes, to serve her turne,
  And seeke her spouse, that from her still° does fly,   *always*
  And followes other game and venery:[7]
  A Satyre chaunst her wandring for to find,
  And kindling coles of lust in brutish eye,
  The loyall links of wedlocke did unbind,
And made her person thrall unto his beastly kind.

23

So long in secret cabin there he held
  Her captive to his sensuall desire,
  Till that with timely° fruit her belly sweld,   *ripening*
  And bore a boy unto that salvage sire:
  Then home he suffred her for to retire,°   *return*
  For ransome leaving him the late borne childe;
  Whom till to ryper yeares he gan aspire,°   *grow up*
  He noursled° up in life and manners wilde,   *reared*
Emongst wild beasts and woods, from lawes of men exilde.

24

For all he taught the tender ymp,° was but   *child*
  To banish cowardize and bastard° feare;   *base*
  His trembling hand he would him force to put
  Upon the Lyon and the rugged Beare,
  And from the she Beares teats her whelps to teare;
  And eke° wyld roring Buls he would him make   *also*
  To tame, and ryde their backes not made to beare;
  And the Robuckes[8] in flight to overtake,
That every beast for feare of him did fly and quake.

25

Thereby so fearelesse, and so fell° he grew,   *fierce*
  That his owne sire and maister of his guise°   *teacher of his behavior*
  Did often tremble at his horrid vew,°   *rough appearance*
  And oft for dread of hurt would him advise,
  The angry beasts not rashly to despise,
  Nor too much to provoke; for he would learne°   *teach*
  The Lyon stoup to him in lowly wise,
  (A lesson hard) and make the Libbard° sterne   *leopard*
Leave roaring, when in rage he for revenge did earne.°   *yearn*

26

And for to make his powre approvèd° more,   *demonstrated*
  Wyld beasts in yron yokes he would compell;

7. The word means both hunting and sexual play.   8. A species of deer noted for its speed.

The spotted Panther, and the tuskèd Bore,
The Pardale° swift, and the Tigre cruell;   *female leopard*
The Antelope, and Wolfe both fierce and fell;°   *savage*
And them constraine in equall teme[9] to draw.
Such joy he had, their stubborne harts to quell,
And sturdie courage tame with dreadfull aw,
That his beheast they fearèd, as a tyrans law.

27

His loving mother came upon a day
Unto the woods, to see her little sonne;
And chaunst unwares° to meet him in the way,   *unexpectedly*
After his sportes, and cruell pastime donne,
When after him a Lyonesse did runne,
That roaring all with rage, did lowd requere°   *demand*
Her children deare, whom he away had wonne:°   *seized*
The Lyon whelpes she saw how he did beare,
And lull in rugged armes, withouten childish feare.

28

The fearefull Dame all quakèd at the sight,
And turning backe, gan fast to fly away,
Untill with love revokt° from vaine affright,   *recalled*
She hardly° yet perswaded was to stay,   *with difficulty*
And then to him these womanish words gan say;
"Ah Satyrane, my dearling, and my joy,
For love of me leave off this dreadfull play;
To dally thus with death, is no fit toy,
Go find some other play-fellowes, mine own sweet boy."

29

In these and like delights of bloudy game
He traynèd was, till ryper yeares he raught,°   *reached*
And there abode, whilst any beast of name
Walkt in that forest, whom he had not taught
To feare his force: and then his courage haught°   *high*
Desird of forreine foemen to be knowne;
And far abroad for straunge adventures sought:
In which his might was never overthrowne,
But through all Faery lond his famous worth was blown.°   *spread*

30

Yet evermore it was his manner faire,
After long labours and adventures spent,
Unto those native woods for to repaire,°   *return*
To see his sire and ofspring° auncient.   *origin*
And now he thither came for like intent;

---

9. Side by side, yoked together in a team.

Where he unwares the fairest Una found,
Straunge Lady, in so straunge habiliment,°   *attire*
Teaching the Satyres, which her sat around,
Trew sacred lore, which from her sweet lips did redound.°   *flow*

31

He wondred at her wisedome heavenly rare,
  Whose like in womens wit he never knew;
  And when her curteous deeds he did compare,
  Gan her admire, and her sad sorrowes rew,°   *pity*
  Blaming of Fortune, which such troubles threw,
  And joyd to make proofe of her crueltie
  On gentle Dame, so hurtlesse,° and so trew: *harmless*
  Thenceforth he kept her goodly company,
And learnd her discipline° of faith and veritie.   *teachings*

32

But she all vowd° unto the Redcrosse knight,   *entirely promised*
  His wandring perill closely° did lament,   *secretly*
  Ne in this new acquaintaunce could delight,
  But her deare° heart with anguish did torment,   *loving*
  And all her wit in secret counsels spent,
  How to escape. At last in privie wise°   *privately*
  To Satyrane she shewèd her intent;
  Who glad to gain such favour, gan devise,
How with that pensive Maid he best might thence arise.°   *depart*

33

So on a day when Satyres all were gone,
  To do their service to Sylvanus old,
  The gentle virgin left behind alone
  He led away with courage stout and bold.
  Too late it was, to Satyres to be told,
  Or ever hope recover her againe:
  In vaine he seekes that having cannot hold.
  So fast he carried her with carefull paine,°   *painstaking care*
That they the woods are past, and come now to the plaine.

34

The better part now of the lingring day,
  They traveild had, when as they farre espide
  A wearie wight forwandring° by the way,   *wandering far and wide*
  And towards him they gan in hast to ride,
  To weet of newes, that did abroad betide,
  Or tydings of her knight of the Redcrosse.
  But he them spying, gan to turne aside,
  For feare as seemd, or for some feignèd losse;°   *pretended harm*
More greedy they of newes, fast towards him do crosse.

35

A silly° man, in simple weedes forworne,°   *simple / worn out*
   And soild with dust of the long drièd way;
   His sandales were with toilesome travell torne,
   And face all tand with scorching sunny ray,
   As° he had traveild many a sommers day,   *as if*
   Through boyling sands of Arabie and Ynde;°   *India*
   And in his hand a Jacobs staffe,° to stay   *pilgrim's staff*
   His wearie limbes upon: and eke behind,
His scrip° did hang, in which his needments he did bind.   *bag*

36

The knight approching nigh, of him inquerd
   Tydings of warre, and of adventures new;
   But warres, nor new adventures none he herd.
   Then Una gan to aske, if ought° he knew,   *aught, anything*
   Or heard abroad of that her champion trew,
   That in his armour bare a croslet° red.   *small cross*
   "Aye me, Deare dame," quoth he, "well may I rew
   To tell the sad sight, which mine eies have red:°   *beheld*
These eyes did see that knight both living and eke ded."

37

That cruell word her tender hart so thrild,°   *pierced*
   That suddein cold did runne through every vaine,
   And stony horrour all her sences fild
   With dying fit,° that downe she fell for paine.   *deathlike swoon*
   The knight her lightly° rearèd up againe,   *quickly*
   And comforted with curteous kind reliefe:
   Then wonne from death, she bad him tellen plaine
   The further processe° of her hidden griefe;   *account*
The lesser pangs can beare, who hath endured the chiefe.

38

Then gan the Pilgrim thus, "I chaunst this day,
   This fatall day, that shall I ever rew,°   *rue, regret*
   To see two knights in travell on my way
   (A sory° sight) arraunged° in battell new,   *grievous / drawn up*
   Both breathing vengeaunce, both of wrathfull hew:
   My fearefull flesh did tremble at their strife,
   To see their blades so greedily imbrew,[1]
   That drunke with bloud, yet thristed after life:
What more? the Redcrosse knight was slaine with Paynim knife."

39

"Ah dearest Lord," quoth she, "how might that bee,
   And he the stoutest knight, that ever wonne?"°   *lived*

1. Soak themselves in blood.

"Ah dearest dame," quoth he, "how might I see
The thing, that might not be, and yet was donne?"
"Where is," said Satyrane, "that Paynims sonne,
That him of life, and us of joy hath reft?"
"Not far away," quoth he, "he hence doth wonne°   *stay*
Foreby° a fountaine, where I late him left   *close by*
Washing his bloudy wounds, that through° the steele were cleft."   *by*

40

Therewith the knight thence marchèd forth in hast,
  Whiles Una with huge heavinesse° opprest,   *grief*
  Could not for sorrow follow him so fast;
  And soone he came, as he the place had ghest,
  Whereas that Pagan proud him selfe did rest,
  In secret shadow by a fountaine side:
  Even he it was, that earst° would have supprest°   *before / violated*
  Faire Una: whom when Satyrane espide,
With fowle reprochfull words he boldly him defide.

41

And said, "Arise thou cursèd Miscreaunt,°   *infidel*
  That hast with knightlesse guile and trecherous train[2]
  Faire knighthood fowly shamed, and doest vaunt
  That good knight of the Redcrosse to have slain:
  Arise, and with like treason now maintain°   *defend*
  Thy guilty wrong, or else thee guilty yield."
  The Sarazin this hearing, rose amain,°   *at once*
  And catching up in hast his three square° shield,   *triangular*
And shining helmet, soone him buckled to the field.

42

And drawing nigh him said, "Ah misborne Elfe,[3]
  In evill houre thy foes thee hither sent,
  Anothers wrongs to wreake upon thy selfe:
  Yet ill thou blamest me, for having blent°   *stained*
  My name with guile and traiterous intent;
  That Redcrosse knight, perdie,° I never slew,   *by God (pardieu)*
  But had he beene, where earst his armes were lent,
  Th'enchaunter vaine his errour should not rew:
But thou his errour shalt, I hope now proven trew."[4]

43

Therewith they gan, both furious and fell,°   *fierce*
  To thunder blowes, and fiersly to assaile
  Each other bent° his enimy to quell,°   *determined / kill*

2. Deceit. "Knightlesse": unknightly.
3. Base-born knight of Faerie Land ("Elfe").
4. I.e., had Redcrosse been wearing his arms, the enchanter Archimago would not have to regret his error in fighting me. But you will now repeat that error and that regret.

That with their force they perst° both plate and maile,   *pierced*
And made wide furrowes in their fleshes fraile,
That it would pitty° any living eie.   *bring pity to*
Large floods of bloud adowne their sides did raile:°   *flow*
But floods of bloud could not them satisfie:
Both hungred after death: both chose to win, or die.

44

So long they fight, and fell revenge pursue,
    That fainting° each, themselves to breathen let,   *weakening*
    And oft refreshèd, battell oft renue:
    As when two Bores with rancling malice met,
    Their gory sides fresh bleeding fiercely fret,°   *tear*
    Til breathlesse both them selves aside retire,
    Where foming wrath, their cruell tuskes they whet,
    And trample th'earth, the whiles they may respire;
Then backe to fight againe, new breathèd and entire.°   *fresh*

45

So fiersly, when these knights had breathèd once,
    They gan to fight returne, increasing more
    Their puissant° force, and cruell rage attonce,   *mighty*
    With heapèd strokes more hugely, then before,
    That with their drerie° wounds and bloudy gore   *gory*
    They both deformèd,° scarsely could be known.   *disfigured*
    By this sad Una fraught° with anguish sore,   *burdened*
    Led with their noise, which through the aire was thrown,
Arrived, where they in erth their fruitles bloud had sown.

46

Whom all so soone as that proud Sarazin
    Espide, he gan revive the memory
    Of his lewd lusts, and late attempted sin,
    And left the doubtfull° battell hastily,   *undecided*
    To catch her, newly offred to his eie:
    But Satyrane with strokes him turning, staid,
    And sternely bad him other businesse plie,
    Then° hunt the steps of pure unspotted Maid: *than*
Wherewith he all enraged, these bitter speaches said.

47

"O foolish faeries sonne, what furie mad
    Hath thee incenst, to hast thy dolefull fate?
    Were it not better, I that Lady had,
    Then that thou hadst repented it too late?
    Most sencelesse man he, that himselfe doth hate,
    To love another. Lo then for thine ayd
    Here take thy lovers token on thy pate."
So they to fight; the whiles the royall Mayd
Fled farre away, of that proud Paynim sore afrayd.

48

But that false Pilgrim, which that leasing° told,   *lie*
 Being in deed old Archimage, did stay
 In secret shadow, all this to behold,
 And much rejoycèd in their bloudy fray:
 But when he saw the Damsell passe away
 He left his stond,° and her pursewd apace, *place*
 In hope to bring her to her last decay.° *i.e., her death*
 But for to tell her lamentable cace,
And eke° this battels end, will need another place.[5] *also*

Canto 7

The Redcrosse knight is captive made
 By Gyaunt proud opprest,°   *overwhelmed*
Prince Arthur meets with Una great-
 ly with those newes distrest.

1

What man so wise, what earthly wit so ware,° *wary*
 As to descry° the crafty cunning traine,° *perceive / guile*
 By which deceipt doth maske in visour° faire, *a mask*
 And cast her colours dyèd deepe in graine,[6]
 To seeme like Truth, whose shape she well can faine,
 And fitting gestures to her purpose frame,
 The guiltlesse man with guile to entertaine?° *engage*
 Great maistresse of her art was that false Dame,
The false Duessa, clokèd with Fidessaes name.

2

Who when returning from the drery Night,
 She fownd not in that perilous house of Pryde,
 Where she had left, the noble Redcrosse knight,
 Her hopèd pray, she would no lenger bide,
 But forth she went, to seeke him far and wide.
 Ere long she fownd, whereas° he wearie sate, *where*
 To rest him selfe, foreby° a fountaine side, *beside*
 Disarmèd all of yron-coted Plate,
And by his side his steed the grassy forage ate.

3

He feedes upon the cooling shade, and bayes° *bathes*
 His sweatie forehead in the breathing wind,
 Which through the trembling leaves full gently playes
 Wherein the cherefull birds of sundry kind
 Do chaunt sweet musick, to delight his mind:

---

5. In fact Spenser never tells how the battle ended. But Satyrane reappears in Book 3.

6. I.e., Deceit disposes her colors, thoroughly dyed, so as to seem like Truth.

The Witch approaching gan him fairely° greet,   *courteously*
And with reproch of carelesnesse° unkind   *indifference*
Upbrayd, for leaving her in place unmeet,°   *unfitting*
With fowle words tempring° faire, soure gall with hony sweet.   *mingling*

4

Unkindnesse past, they gan of solace treat,°   *pleasure speak*
  And bathe in pleasaunce of the joyous shade,
  Which shielded them against the boyling heat,
  And with greene boughes decking a gloomy glade,
  About the fountaine like a girlond made;
  Whose bubbling wave did ever freshly well,
  Ne ever would through fervent° sommer fade:°   *hot / dry up*
  The sacred Nymph, which therein wont° to dwell,   *was accustomed*
Was out of Dianes favour, as it then befell.

5

The cause was this: one day when Phoebe[7] fayre
  With all her band was following the chace,°   *hunt*
  This Nymph, quite tyred with heat of scorching ayre
  Sat downe to rest in middest of the race:
  The goddesse wroth gan fowly her disgrace,
  And bad the waters, which from her did flow,
  Be such as she her selfe was then in place.°   *there*
  Thenceforth her waters waxèd dull and slow,
And all that drunke thereof, did faint and feeble grow.

6

Hereof this gentle knight unweeting° was,   *ignorant*
  And lying downe upon the sandie graile,°   *gravel*
  Drunke of the streame, as cleare as cristall glas;
  Eftsoones° his manly forces gan to faile,   *immediately*
  And mightie strong was turnd to feeble fraile.
  His chaunged powres at first themselves not felt,
  Till crudled° cold his corage° gan assaile,   *congealing / vigor*
  And chearefull° bloud in faintnesse chill did melt,   *lively*
Which like a fever fit through all his body swelt.°   *raged*

7

Yet goodly court he made still to his Dame,
  Pourd out in loosnesse[8] on the grassy grownd,
  Both carelesse of his health, and of his fame:°   *reputation*
  Till at the last he heard a dreadfull sownd,
  Which through the wood loud bellowing, did rebownd,
  That all the earth for terrour seemed to shake,
  And trees did tremble. Th'Elfe therewith astownd,°   *amazed*

---

7. I.e., Diana, goddess of the moon and of chastity.

8. Spread out in lewdness ("loosnesse"); sexually expended.

Upstarted lightly° from his looser make,[9]　　　　　　　　　*quickly*
And his unready weapons gan in hand to take.

8

But ere he could his armour on him dight,
　Or get his shield, his monstrous enimy
　With sturdie steps came stalking in his sight,
　An hideous Geant horrible and hye,
　That with his talnesse seemd to threat the skye,
　The ground eke° gronèd under him for dreed;°　　　*also / dread*
　His living like saw never living eye,
　Ne durst behold: his stature did exceed
The hight of three the tallest sonnes of mortall seed.

9

The greatest Earth his uncouth° mother was,　　　　*vile; strange*
　And blustring Aeolus his boasted sire,[1]
　Who with his breath, which through the world doth pas,
　Her hollow womb did secretly inspire,°　　　　　*breathe into*
　And fild her hidden caves with stormie yre,°　　　*ire, anger*
　That she conceived; and trebling the dew time,
　In which the wombes of women do expire,°　　　　*bring forth*
　Brought forth this monstrous masse of earthly slime,
Puft up with emptie wind, and fild with sinfull crime.

10

So growen great through arrogant delight
　Of th'high descent, whereof he was yborne,
　And through presumption of his matchlesse might,
　All other powres and knighthood he did scorne.
　Such now he marcheth to this man forlorne,°　　　*abandoned*
　And left to losse:° his stalking steps are stayde°　*destruction / supported*
　Upon a snaggy Oke,[2] which he had torne
　Out of his mothers bowelles, and it made
His mortall° mace, wherewith his foemen he dismayde.[3]　*death-dealing*

11

That when the knight he spide, he gan advance
　With huge force and insupportable mayne,°　　　*irresistible power*
　And towardes him with dreadfull fury praunce;°　*strut*
　Who haplesse, and eke hopelesse, all in vaine
　Did to him pace, sad battaile to darrayne,°　　*engage*
　Disarmd, disgrast, and inwardly dismayde,
　And eke so faint in every joynt and vaine,
　Through that fraile° fountaine, which him feeble made,　*enfeebling*
That scarsely could he weeld his bootlesse° single blade.　*useless*

---

9. Too licentious ("looser") companion.
1. Aeolus was keeper of the winds. The giant's descent from Earth and Wind links him to earthquakes.

2. I.e., he uses as walking stick a knotty ("snaggy") oak tree.
3. In its usual sense, but also "dis-made, dissolved."

12

The Geaunt strooke so maynly° mercilesse,   *mightily*
  That could have overthrowne a stony towre,
  And were not heavenly grace, that him did blesse,
  He had beene pouldred° all, as thin as flowre: *powdered*
  But he was wary of that deadly stowre,°   *peril*
  And lightly° lept from underneath the blow: *quickly*
  Yet so exceeding was the villeins powre,
  That with the wind it did him overthrow,
And all his sences stound,° that still he lay full low.   *stunned*

13

As when that divelish yron Engin° wrought   *i.e., cannon*
  In deepest Hell, and framd by Furies skill,
  With windy Nitre and quick Sulphur fraught,[4]
  And ramd with bullet round, ordaind to kill,
  Conceiveth fire, the heavens it doth fill
  With thundring noyse, and all the ayre doth choke,
  That none can breath, nor see, nor heare at will,
  Through smouldry cloud of duskish stincking smoke,
That th'onely breath him daunts,[5] who hath escapt the stroke.

14

So daunted when the Geaunt saw the knight,
  His heavie hand he heavèd up on hye,
  And him to dust thought to have battred quight,
  Untill Duessa loud to him gan crye;
  "O great Orgoglio,[6] greatest under skye,
  O hold thy mortall hand for Ladies sake,
  Hold for my sake, and do him not to dye,°   *do not cause him to die*
  But vanquisht thine eternall bondslave make,
And me thy worthy meed unto thy Leman take."[7]

15

He hearkned, and did stay° from further harmes,   *refrain*
  To gayne so goodly guerdon,° as she spake: *reward*
  So willingly she came into his armes,
  Who her as willingly to grace° did take,   *favor*
  And was possessèd of his new found make.°   *mate*
  Then up he tooke the slombred° sencelesse corse,   *unconscious*
  And ere he could out of his swowne awake,
  Him to his castle brought with hastie forse,
And in a Dongeon deepe him threw without remorse.

---

4. Filled ("fraught") with gunpowder ("Nitre" and "Sulphur").

5. I.e., so that the blast or smell alone ("onely") overcomes him.

6. Italian: pride, haughtiness, disdain.

7. I.e., take me, your worthy reward, as your mistress.

16

From that day forth Duessa was his deare,
    And highly honourd in his haughtie eye,
    He gave her gold and purple pall° to weare,   *crimson robe of royalty*
    And triple crowne set on her head full hye,[8]
    And her endowd with royall majestye:
    Then for to make her dreaded more of men,
    And peoples harts with awfull terrour tye,°   *bind*
    A monstrous beast ybred in filthy fen
He chose, which he had kept long time in darksome den.

17

Such one it was, as that renowmèd Snake
    Which great Alcides in Stremona slew,
    Long fostred in the filth of Lerna lake,[9]
    Whose many heads out budding ever new,
    Did breed° him endlesse labour to subdew: *cause*
    But this same Monster much more ugly was;
    For seven great heads out of his body grew,
    An yron brest, and backe of scaly bras,
And all embrewd° in bloud, his eyes did shine as glas.   *stained*

18

His tayle was stretchèd out in wondrous length,
    That to the house of heavenly gods it raught,°   *reached*
    And with extorted powre, and borrowed strength,
    The ever-burning lamps° from thence it brought,   *stars*
    And prowdly threw to ground, as things of nought;
    And underneath his filthy feet did tread
    The sacred things, and holy heasts foretaught.[1]
    Upon this dreadfull Beast with sevenfold head
He set the false Duessa, for more aw and dread.

19

The wofull Dwarfe, which saw his maisters fall,
    Whiles he had keeping of his grasing steed,
    And valiant knight become a caytive° thrall,   *captive*
    When all was past, tooke up his forlorne weed,°   *abandoned garment*
    His mightie armour, missing most at need;
    His silver shield, now idle maisterlesse;
    His poynant° speare, that many made to bleed,   *sharp*
    The ruefull moniments° of heavinesse,°   *memorials / grief*
And with them all departes, to tell his great distresse.

---

8. Duessa is attired like the Whore of Babylon in Revelation 17.3–4; the triple crown is that of the papacy (see canto 2, stanzas 13 and 22).
9. The nine-headed Lernean hydra slain by Hercules (Alcides). Orgoglio's seven-headed monster recalls the red dragon of Revelation: "behold a great red dragon, having seven heads and ten horns, and seven crowns upon his heads. And his tail drew the third part of the stars of heaven, and did cast them to the earth . . . [he is] that old serpent, called the Devil, and Satan, which deceiveth the whole world" (12.3–14.9). Many Protestants associated the Beast with the Roman Church.
1. Doctrines ("holy heasts") previously taught.

20

He had not travaild long, when on the way
  He wofull Ladie, wofull Una met,
  Fast flying from the Paynims greedy pray,°   *clutch*
  Whilest Satyrane him from pursuit did let:°   *prevent*
  Who when her eyes she on the Dwarfe had set,
  And saw the signes, that deadly tydings spake,
  She fell to ground for sorrowfull regret,°   *grief*
  And lively breath her sad brest did forsake,
Yet might her pitteous hart be seene to pant and quake.

21

The messenger of so unhappie newes
  Would faine° have dyde: dead was his hart within,   *gladly*
  Yet outwardly some little comfort shewes:
  At last recovering hart, he does begin
  To rub her temples, and to chaufe her chin,
  And every tender part does tosse and turne:
  So hardly he the flitted life does win,
  Unto her native prison to retourne:[2]
Then gins her grievèd ghost° thus to lament and mourne.   *spirit*

22

"Ye dreary instruments of dolefull sight,
  That doe this deadly spectacle behold,
  Why do ye lenger° feed on loathèd light,   *longer*
  Or liking find to gaze on earthly mould,[3]
  Sith° cruell fates the carefull° threeds unfould,   *since / intricate*
  The which my life and love together tyde?
  Now let the stony dart of senselesse cold°   *i.e., death*
  Perce to my hart, and pas through every side,
And let eternall night so sad sight fro me hide.

23

"O lightsome day, the lampe of highest Jove,
  First made by him,[4] mens wandring wayes to guyde,
  When darknesse he in deepest dongeon drove,
  Henceforth thy hated face for ever hyde,
  And shut up heavens windowes shyning wyde:
  For earthly sight can nought but sorrow breed,
  And late° repentance, which shall long abyde.   *too late*
  Mine eyes no more on vanitie shall feed,
But seelèd up with death, shall have their deadly meed."°   *reward of death*

---

2. I.e., with such difficulty ("so hardly") he persuades ("does win") the life back to her body ("native prison").
3. I.e., or find it pleasure to gaze on earthly forms ("mould").
4. An allusion to Genesis 1.3: "And God said, Let there be light: and there was light."

24

Then downe againe she fell unto the ground;
    But he her quickly rearèd up againe:
    Thrise did she sinke adowne in deadly swownd,
    And thrise he her revived with busie paine:°   *care*
    At last when life recovered had the raine,°   *rule*
    And over-wrestled his strong enemie,
    With foltring° tong, and trembling every vaine,   *faltering*
    "Tell on," quoth she, "the wofull Tragedie,
The which these reliques° sad present unto mine eie.   *remains*

25

"Tempestuous fortune hath spent all her spight,
    And thrilling° sorrow throwne his utmost dart;   *piercing*
    Thy sad tongue cannot tell more heavy plight,
    Then that I feele, and harbour in mine hart:
    Who hath endured the whole, can beare each part.
    If death it be, it is not the first wound,
    That launchèd° hath my brest with bleeding smart.   *pierced*
    Begin, and end the bitter balefull stound;°   *time (of sorrow)*
If lesse, then that° I feare, more favour I have found."   *than what*

26

Then gan the Dwarfe the whole discourse° declare,   *story*
    The subtill traines° of Archimago old;   *wiles*
    The wanton loves of false Fidessa faire,
    Bought with the bloud of vanquisht Paynim bold:
    The wretched payre transformed to treen mould;°   *shape of a tree*
    The house of Pride, and perils round about;
    The combat, which he with Sansjoy did hould;
    The lucklesse conflict with the Gyant stout,
Wherein captived, of life or death he stood in doubt.

27

She heard with patience all unto the end,
    And strove to maister sorrowfull assay,°   *affliction*
    Which greater grew, the more she did contend,
    And almost rent her tender hart in tway;°   *two*
    And love fresh coles unto her fire did lay:
    For greater love, the greater is the losse.
    Was never Ladie lovèd dearer day,[5]
    Then she did love the knight of the Redcrosse;
For whose deare sake so many troubles her did tosse.

28

At last when fervent sorrow slakèd was,
    She up arose, resolving him to find

---

5. I.e., there was never a lady who loved life ("day") more dearly than she loved Redcrosse.

Alive or dead: and forward forth doth pas,
All° as the Dwarfe the way to her assynd:°   *just / showed*
And evermore in constant carefull° mind   *full of care, sorrowful*
She fed her wound with fresh renewèd bale;°   *anguish*
Long tost with stormes, and bet° with bitter wind,   *beaten*
High over hils, and low adowne the dale,
She wandred many a wood, and measurd many a vale.

29

At last she chauncèd by good hap to meet
A goodly knight, faire marching by the way
Together with his Squire, arayèd meet:°   *properly*
His glitterand° armour shinèd farre away,   *glittering*
Like glauncing° light of Phoebus brightest ray;   *flashing*
From top to toe no place appearèd bare,
That deadly dint° of steele endanger may: *stroke*
Athwart his brest a bauldrick[6] brave° he ware,   *splendid*
That shynd, like twinkling stars, with stons most pretious rare.

30

And in the midst thereof one pretious stone
Of wondrous worth, and eke of wondrous mights,°   *powers*
Shapt like a Ladies head, exceeding shone,
Like Hesperus° emongst the lesser lights,°   *evening star / stars*
And strove for to amaze the weaker sights;
Thereby his mortall blade full comely hong
In yvory sheath, ycarved with curious slights;°   *designs*
Whose hilts were burnisht gold, and handle strong
Of mother pearle, and buckled with a golden tong.°   *pin*

31

His haughtie helmet, horrid° all with gold,   *bristling*
Both glorious brightnesse, and great terrour bred;
For all the crest a Dragon did enfold
With greedie pawes, and over all did spred
His golden wings: his dreadfull hideous hed
Close couchèd on the bever,° seemed to throw   *visor*
From flaming mouth bright sparkles fierie red,
That suddeine horror to faint harts did show;
And scaly tayle was stretcht adowne his backe full low.

32

Upon the top of all his loftie crest,°   *top of helmet*
A bunch of haires discolourd° diversly,   *dyed*
With sprincled pearle, and gold full richly drest,
Did shake, and seemed to daunce for jollity,
Like to an Almond tree ymounted hye

6. Sash worn over the shoulder to support the sword.

On top of greene Selinis[7] all alone,
  With blossomes brave bedeckèd daintily;
  Whose tender locks do tremble every one
At every little breath, that under heaven is blowne.

33

His warlike shield all closely covered was,
  Ne might of mortall eye be ever seene;
  Not made of steele, nor of enduring bras,
  Such earthly mettals soone consumèd bene:
  But all of Diamond perfect pure and cleene°   *clear*
  It framèd was, one massie entire mould,[8]
  Hewen out of Adamant rocke with engines° keene,   *tools*
  That point of speare it never percen could,
Ne dint° of direfull sword divide the substance would.   *blow*

34

The same to wight° he never wont disclose,   *creature*
  But° when as monsters huge he would dismay,   *except*
  Or daunt unequall armies of his foes,
  Or when the flying heavens he would affray;[9]
  For so exceeding shone his glistring ray,
  That Phoebus golden face it did attaint,°   *make dim*
  As when a cloud his beames doth over-lay;
  And silver Cynthia° wexèd pale and faint,   *the moon*
As when her face is staynd with magicke arts constraint.[1]

35

No magicke arts hereof had any might,
  Nor bloudie wordes of bold Enchaunters call,
  But all that was not such, as seemd in sight,
  Before that shield did fade, and suddeine fall:
  And when him list° the raskall routes° appall,   *wanted to / unruly mobs*
  Men into stones therewith he could transmew,°   *change*
  And stones to dust, and dust to nought at all;
  And when him list the prouder lookes subdew,
He would them gazing blind, or turne to other hew.°   *form*

36

Ne let it seeme, that credence this exceedes,
  For he that made the same, was knowne right well
  To have done much more admirable° deedes.   *marvelous*
  It Merlin was, which whylome° did excell   *formerly*
  All living wightes in might of magicke spell:
  Both shield, and sword, and armour all he wrought

---

7. Town associated with the palm awarded to victors (Virgil, *Aeneid* 3.705).
8. The shield was made of one solid piece of diamond, unflawed, unpierceable, translucent.

9. I.e., when he would frighten ("affray") the revolving constellations.
1. Magicians were said to be able to cause an eclipse of the moon.

For this young Prince,[2] when first to armes he fell;°   *came*
But when he dyde, the Faerie Queene it brought
To Faerie lond, where yet it may be seene, if sought.

37

A gentle° youth, his dearely lovèd Squire   *noble*
  His speare of heben° wood behind him bare,   *ebony*
  Whose harmefull head, thrice heated in the fire,
  Had riven many a brest with pikehead° square;   *spearhead*
  A goodly person, and could menage° faire   *control*
  His stubborne steed with curbèd canon bit,[3]
  Who under him did trample as the aire,
  And chauft,° that any on his backe should sit;   *fretted*
The yron rowels° into frothy fome he bit.   *ends of the bit*

38

When as this knight nigh to the Ladie drew,
  With lovely court° he gan her entertaine;   *kind courtesy*
  But when he heard her answers loth, he knew
  Some secret sorrow did her heart distraine:°   *afflict*
  Which to allay, and calme her storming paine,
  Faire feeling words he wisely gan display,°   *pour forth*
  And for her humour fitting purpose faine,[4]
  To tempt° the cause it selfe for to bewray;°   *invite / reveal*
Wherewith emmoved, these bleeding words she gan to say.

39

"What worlds delight, or joy of living speach
  Can heart, so plunged in sea of sorrowes deepe,
  And heapèd with so huge misfortunes, reach?
  The carefull° cold beginneth for to creepe,   *afflicting*
  And in my heart his yron arrow steepe,
  Soone as I thinke upon my bitter bale:°   *grief*
  Such helplesse harmes yts better hidden keepe,
  Then rip up° griefe, where it may not availe,   *than lay open*
My last left comfort is, my woes to weepe and waile."

40

"Ah Ladie deare," quoth then the gentle knight,
  "Well may I weene,° your griefe is wondrous great;   *suppose*
  For wondrous great griefe groneth in my spright,°   *spirit*
  Whiles thus I heare you of your sorrowes treat.
  But wofull Ladie let me you intrete,
  For to unfold the anguish of your hart:
  Mishaps are maistred by advice discrete,

2. The reference to Merlin indicates that the prince is Arthur (who had been mentioned in the canto's prefatory quatrain). In the *Letter to Ralegh*, he is identified with "magnificence," understood as the perfection of all the virtues and containing them all.
3. "Canon bit": a smooth, round bit.
4. I.e., suited his manner to her mood.

And counsell mittigates the greatest smart;
Found never helpe, who never would his hurts impart."[5]

41

"O but," quoth she, "great griefe will not be tould,
   And can more easily be thought, then said."
"Right so"; quoth he, "but he, that never would,
   Could never: will to might gives greatest aid."[6]
"But grief," quoth she, "does greater grow displaid,°   *when revealed*
   If then it find not helpe, and breedes despaire."
"Despaire breedes not," quoth he, "where faith is staid."°   *firm*
"No faith so fast," quoth she, "but flesh does paire."°   *impair*
"Flesh may empaire," quoth he, "but reason can repaire."

42

His goodly reason, and well guided speach
   So deepe did settle in her gratious thought,
   That her perswaded to disclose the breach,°   *wound*
   Which love and fortune in her heart had wrought,
   And said; "Faire Sir, I hope good hap hath brought
   You to inquire the secrets of my griefe,
   Or° that your wisedome will direct my thought,   *either*
   Or that your prowesse can me yield reliefe:
Then heare the storie sad, which I shall tell you briefe.

43

"The forlorne° Maiden, whom your eyes have seene   *forsaken*
   The laughing stocke of fortunes mockeries,
   Am th'only daughter of a King and Queene,
   Whose parents deare, whilest equall destinies
   Did runne about,[7] and their felicities
   The favourable heavens did not envy,
   Did spread their rule through all the territories,
   Which Phison and Euphrates floweth by,
And Gehons golden waves doe wash continually.[8]

44

"Till that their cruell cursèd enemy,
   An huge great Dragon horrible in sight,
   Bred in the loathly lakes of Tartary,°   *Tartarus (hell)*
   With murdrous ravine,° and devouring might   *destruction*
   Their kingdome spoild,° and countrey wasted quight: *plundered*
   Themselves, for feare into his jawes to fall,
   He forst to castle strong to take their flight,

---

5. I.e., he never found help who would not tell
his sorrows.
6. I.e., he that fails to will something cannot do
it: willing gives the greatest help to one's power
("might").

7. I.e., while the impartial fates ran their course.
8. Phison, Euphrates, and Gehon, along with
the Tigris, were the rivers of the Garden of Eden
(Genesis 2.11–14).

Where fast embard° in mightie brasen wall,   *imprisoned*
He has them now foure yeres besiegd to make them thrall.

45

"Full many knights adventurous and stout
  Have enterprizd that Monster to subdew;
  From every coast° that heaven walks about,   *land*
  Have thither come the noble Martiall crew,
  That famous hard atchievements still pursew,
  Yet never any could that girlond win,
  But all still shronke,° and still he greater grew: *quailed*
All they for want of faith, or guilt of sin,
The pitteous pray of his fierce crueltie have bin.

46

"At last yledd° with farre reported praise,   *led*
  Which flying fame throughout the world had spread,
  Of doughtie° knights, whom Faery land did raise,   *brave*
  That noble order hight° of Maidenhed,[9]   *called*
  Forthwith to court of Gloriane I sped,
  Of Gloriane great Queene of glory bright,
  Whose kingdomes seat Cleopolis[1] is red,°   *named*
  There to obtaine some such redoubted knight,
That Parents deare from tyrants powre deliver might.

47

"It was my chance (my chance was faire and good)
  There for to find a fresh unprovèd° knight,   *untried*
  Whose manly hands imbrewed in guiltie blood
  Had never bene,[2] ne ever by his might
  Had throwne to ground the unregarded° right: *unrespected*
  Yet of his prowesse proofe he since hath made
  (I witnesse am) in many a cruell fight;
  The groning ghosts of many one dismaide°   *defeated*
Have felt the bitter dint of his avenging blade.

48

"And ye the forlorne reliques of his powre,
  His byting sword, and his devouring speare,
  Which have endurèd many a dreadfull stowre,°   *conflict*
  Can speake his prowesse, that did earst° you beare,   *before*
  And well could rule: now he hath left you heare,
  To be the record of his ruefull losse,
  And of my dolefull disaventurous deare:°   *sad unfortunate dear one*
  O heavie record of the good Redcrosse,
Where have you left your Lord, that could so well you tosse?°   *handle*

---

9. The type or analogue of the Order of the Garter. Its emblem shows St. George killing the dragon, and its star is the Red Cross.

1. Cleopolis means "famous city."
2. I.e., his strong hands had never been guiltily stained ("imbrewed") with blood.

49

"Well hopèd I, and faire beginnings had,
   That he my captive langour should redeeme,[3]
   Till all unweeting,° an Enchaunter bad   *unknowing*
   His sence abusd, and made him to misdeeme°   *misjudge*
   My loyalty, not such as it did seeme;
   That rather death desire, then such despight.[4]
   Be judge ye heavens, that all things right esteeme,°   *judge rightly*
   How I him loved, and love with all my might,
So thought I eke of him, and thinke I thought aright.

50

"Thenceforth me desolate he quite forsooke,
   To wander, where wilde fortune would me lead,
   And other bywaies he himselfe betooke,
   Where never foot of living wight did tread,
   That brought not backe the balefull body dead;°   *i.e., who was not killed*
   In which him chauncèd false Duessa meete,
   Mine onely foe, mine onely deadly dread,[5]
   Who with her witchcraft and misseeming° sweete,   *false appearance*
Inveigled him to follow her desires unmeete.°   *improper*

51

"At last by subtill sleights she him betraid
   Unto his foe, a Gyant huge and tall,
   Who him disarmèd, dissolute,° dismaid,   *enfeebled*
   Unwares surprisèd and with mightie mall°   *club*
   The monster mercilesse him made to fall,
   Whose fall did never foe before behold;
   And now in darkesome dungeon, wretched thrall,
   Remedilesse, for aie[6] he doth him hold;
This is my cause of griefe, more great, then may be told."

52

Ere she had ended all, she gan to faint:°   *grow weak; lose heart*
   But he her comforted and faire bespake,
   "Certès,° Madame, ye have great cause of plaint,   *certainly*
   That stoutest heart, I weene, could cause to quake.
   But be of cheare, and comfort to you take:
   For till I have acquit° your captive knight,   *freed*
   Assure your selfe, I will you not forsake."
   His chearefull words revived her chearelesse spright,
So forth they went, the Dwarfe them guiding ever right.

---

3. I.e., relieve my state, captive to sadness.
4. I.e., I, who prefer death to such treachery ("despight").
5. I.e., the only object of my mortal fear.
6. I.e., forever ("for aie") without hope of rescue ("remedilesse").

Canto 8

Faire virgin to redeeme her deare
brings Arthur to the fight:
Who slayes the Gyant, wounds the beast,
and strips Duessa quight.

1

Ay me, how many perils doe enfold
  The righteous man, to make him daily fall?
  Were not, that heavenly grace doth him uphold,
  And stedfast truth acquite° him out of all.   *deliver*
  Her love is firme, her care continuall,
  So oft as he through his owne foolish pride,
  Or weaknesse is to sinfull bands° made thrall: *bonds*
  Else should this Redcrosse knight in bands have dyde,
For whose deliverance she this Prince doth thither guide.

2

They sadly traveild thus, untill they came
  Nigh to a castle builded strong and hie:
  Then cryde the Dwarfe, "lo yonder is the same,
  In which my Lord my liege doth lucklesse lie,
  Thrall to that Gyants hatefull tyrannie:
  Therefore, deare Sir, your mightie powres assay."°   *put to trial*
  The noble knight alighted by and by°   *immediately*
  From loftie steede, and bad the Ladie stay,
To see what end of fight should him befall that day.

3

So with the Squire, th'admirer of his might,
  He marchèd forth towards that castle wall;
  Whose gates he found fast shut, ne living wight
  To ward° the same, nor answere commers call.   *guard*
  Then tooke that Squire an horne of bugle° small,   *wild ox*
  Which hong adowne his side in twisted gold,
  And tassels gay. Wyde wonders over all°   *everywhere*
  Of that same hornes great vertues° weren told,[7]   *powers*
Which had approvèd° bene in uses manifold.   *demonstrated*

4

Was never wight, that heard that shrilling sound,
  But trembling feare did feele in every vaine;
  Three miles it might be easie heard around,
  And Ecchoes three answered it selfe againe:
  No false enchauntment, nor deceiptfull traine°   *snare*
  Might once abide the terror of that blast,

---

7. "Wyde wonders" (marvelous tales) told of the horn connect it with the horn of the legendary French hero Roland and the ram's horn of Joshua, with which he razed the walls of Jericho (Joshua 6.5).

But presently° was voide and wholly vaine: *at once*
 No gate so strong, no locke so firme and fast,
But with that percing noise flew open quite, or brast.° *burst*

5

The same before the Geants gate he blew,
 That all the castle quakèd from the ground,
 And every dore of freewill open flew.
 The Gyant selfe dismaièd with that sownd,
 Where he with his Duessa dalliance° fownd,   *amorous play*
 In hast came rushing forth from inner bowre,
 With staring° countenance sterne, as one astownd, *glaring*
 And staggering steps, to weet, what suddein stowre° *disturbance*
Had wrought that horror strange, and dared his dreaded powre.

6

And after him the proud Duessa came,
 High mounted on her manyheaded beast,
 And every head with fyrie tongue did flame,
 And every head was crownèd on his creast,
 And bloudie mouthèd with late cruell feast.
 That when the knight beheld, his mightie shild
 Upon his manly arme he soone addrest,°   *made ready*
 And at him fiercely flew, with courage fild,
And eger greedinesse° through every member thrild. *eagerness for battle*

7

Therewith the Gyant buckled him to fight,
 Inflamed with scornefull wrath and high disdaine,° *indignation*
 And lifting up his dreadfull club on hight,
 All armed with ragged snubbes° and knottie graine, *snags*
 Him thought at first encounter to have slaine.
 But wise and warie was that noble Pere,°   *peer*
 And lightly leaping from so monstrous maine,° *force*
 Did faire° avoide the violence him nere;   *quite*
It booted nought, to thinke, such thunderbolts to beare.[8]

8

Ne shame he thought to shunne so hideous might:
 The idle° stroke, enforcing furious way,   *useless*
 Missing the marke of his misaymèd sight
 Did fall to ground, and with his° heavie sway° *its / force*
 So deepely dinted in the driven clay,
 That three yardes deepe a furrow up did throw:
 The sad earth wounded with so sore assay,° *assault*
 Did grone full grievous underneath the blow,
And trembling with strange feare, did like an earthquake show.

8. I.e., it was useless to think of withstanding such blows.

9

As when almightie Jove in wrathfull mood,
    To wreake° the guilt of mortall sins is bent,°   *punish / disposed*
    Hurles forth his thundring dart with deadly food,°   *hatred (feud)*
    Enroll in flames, and smouldring dreriment,°   *smothering darkness*
    Through riven cloudes and molten firmament;
    The fierce threeforkèd engin° making way,   *weapon*
    Both loftie towres and highest trees hath rent,
    And all that might his angrie passage stay,
And shooting in the earth, casts up a mount of clay.

10

His boystrous° club, so buried in the ground,   *massive*
    He could not rearen up againe so light,°   *easily*
    But that the knight him at avantage found,
    And whiles he strove his combred clubbe to quight[9]
    Out of the earth, with blade all burning bright
    He smote off his left arme, which like a blocke
    Did fall to ground, deprived of native might;
    Large streames of bloud out of the trunckèd stocke°   *truncated stump*
Forth gushèd, like fresh water streame from riven rocke.[1]

11

Dismaièd with so desperate deadly wound,
    And eke° impatient of unwonted paine,[2]   *also*
    He loudly brayd with beastly yelling sound,
    That all the fields rebellowèd againe;
    As great a noyse, as when in Cymbrian[3] plaine
    An heard of Bulles, whom kindly° rage doth sting,   *natural*
    Do for the milkie mothers want complaine,[4]
    And fill the fields with troublous bellowing,
The neighbour woods around with hollow murmur ring.

12

That when his deare Duessa heard, and saw
    The evill stownd, that daungerd her estate,[5]
    Unto his aide she hastily did draw
    Her dreadfull beast, who swolne with bloud of late
    Came ramping° forth with proud presumpteous gate,°   *rearing / gait*
    And threatned all his heads like flaming brands.°   *torches*
    But him the Squire made quickly to retrate,
    Encountring fierce with single° sword in hand,   *only*
And twixt him and his Lord did like a bulwarke stand.

---

9. Strove to release his encumbered club.
1. Cf. Exodus 17.6, where Moses smites the rock and water flows forth.
2. I.e., unable to bear ("impatient of") this unfamiliar ("unwonted") pain.
3. Jutland, once called the Cimbric peninsula.
4. I.e., mourn the cows' absence.
5. I.e., the peril ("stownd") that endangered her state.

13

The proud Duessa full of wrathfull spight,
  And fierce disdaine, to be affronted so,
  Enforst her purple° beast with all her might   *scarlet*
  That stop° out of the way to overthroe,   *obstacle*
  Scorning the let° of so unequall foe: *hindrance*
  But nathemore° would that courageous swayne   *never the more*
  To her yeeld passage, gainst his Lord to goe,
  But with outrageous° strokes did him restraine,   *exceedingly fierce*
And with his bodie bard the way atwixt them twaine.

14

Then tooke the angrie witch her golden cup,
  Which still° she bore, replete with magick artes;[6]   *always*
  Death and despeyre did many thereof sup,
  And secret poyson through their inner parts,
  Th'eternall bale° of heavie wounded harts;   *woe*
  Which after charmes and some enchauntments said,
  She lightly sprinkled on his weaker° parts;   *too weak*
  Therewith his sturdie courage soone was quayd,°   *quelled*
And all his senses were with suddeine dread dismayd.

15

So downe he fell before the cruell beast,
  Who on his necke his bloudie clawes did seize,
  That life nigh crusht out of his panting brest:
  No powre he had to stirre, nor will to rize.
  That when the carefull° knight gan well avise,°   *watchful / observe*
  He lightly° left the foe, with whom he fought,   *quickly*
  And to the beast gan turne his enterprise;
  For wondrous anguish in his hart it wrought,
To see his lovèd Squire into such thraldome° brought.   *slavery*

16

And high advauncing° his bloud-thirstie blade,   *lifting up*
  Stroke one of those deformèd heads so sore,[7]
  That of his puissance° proud ensample made;   *strength*
  His monstrous scalpe° downe to his teeth it tore   *skull*
  And that misformèd shape mis-shapèd more:
  A sea of bloud gusht from the gaping wound,
  That her gay garments staynd with filthy gore,
  And overflowèd all the field around;
That over shoes in bloud he waded on the ground.

---

6. Alludes to the golden cup of the woman in Revelation, which is "full of abominations and filthiness of her fornications" (17.4); the chalice of the Roman Church; and the cup of Circe, the sorceress who turned men into beasts (in *Odyssey* 10).
7. "I saw one of . . . [the beast's] heads as it were wounded to death" (Revelation 13.3).

17

Thereat he roarèd for exceeding paine,
  That to have heard, great horror would have bred,°   *produced*
  And scourging th'emptie ayre with his long traine,°   *tail*
  Through great impatience of his grievèd hed[8]
  His gorgeous ryder from her loftie sted°   *place*
  Would have cast downe, and trod in durtie myre,
  Had not the Gyant soone her succourèd;
  Who all enraged with smart° and franticke yre,°   *pain / anger*
Came hurtling in full fierce, and forst the knight retyre.

18

The force, which wont° in two to be disperst,   *used*
  In one alone left hand[9] he now unites,
  Which is through rage more strong then both were erst;°   *before*
  With which his hideous club aloft he dites,°   *raises*
  And at his foe with furious rigour° smites,   *violence*
  That strongest Oake might seeme to overthrow:
  The stroke upon his shield so heavie lites,
  That to the ground it doubleth him full low:
What mortall wight could ever beare so monstrous blow?

19

And in his fall his shield, that covered was,
  Did loose his vele° by chaunce, and open flew: *its covering*
  The light whereof, that heavens light did pas,°   *surpass*
  Such blazing brightnesse through the aier threw,
  That eye mote not the same endure to vew.
  Which when the Gyaunt spyde with staring eye,
  He downe let fall his arme, and soft withdrew
  His weapon huge, that heavèd was on hye
For to have slaine the man, that on the ground did lye.

20

And eke the fruitfull-headed° beast, amazed   *many-headed*
  At flashing beames of that sunshiny shield,
  Became starke blind, and all his senses dazed,
  That downe he tumbled on the durtie field,
  And seemed himselfe as conquerèd to yield.
  Whom when his maistresse proud perceived to fall,
  Whiles yet his feeble feet for faintnesse reeld,
  Unto the Gyant loudly she gan call,
"O helpe Orgoglio, helpe, or else we perish all."

8. I.e., through inability to endure ("impatience") his afflicted ("grievèd") head.   9. I.e., in the one hand left to him.

21

At her so pitteous cry was much amooved
    Her champion stout, and for to ayde his frend,°   *lover*
    Againe his wonted° angry weapon prooved:°   *usual / tried*
    But all in vaine: for he has read his end
    In that bright shield, and all their forces spend
    Themselves in vaine: for since that glauncing° sight,   *flashing*
    He hath no powre to hurt, nor to defend;
    As where th'Almighties lightning brond° does light,   *firebrand*
It dimmes the dazèd eyen, and daunts the senses quight.

22

Whom when the Prince, to battell new addrest,
    And threatning high his dreadfull stroke did see,
    His sparkling blade about his head he blest,°   *brandished*
    And smote off quite his right leg by the knee,
    That downe he tombled; as an agèd tree,
    High growing on the top of rocky clift,
    Whose hartstrings with keene steele nigh hewen be,
    The mightie trunck halfe rent, with ragged rift°   *split*
Doth roll adowne the rocks, and fall with fearefull drift.°   *impact*

23

Or as a Castle rearèd high and round,
    By subtile engins and malitious slight[1]
    Is underminèd from the lowest ground,
    And her foundation forst,° and feebled quight,   *shattered*
    At last downe falles, and with her heapèd hight
    Her hastie ruine does more heavie make,
    And yields it selfe unto the victours might;
    Such was this Gyaunts fall, that seemed to shake
The stedfast globe of earth, as° it for feare did quake.   *as if*

24

The knight then lightly° leaping to the pray,   *quickly*
    With mortall steele him smot againe so sore,
    That headlesse his unweldy bodie lay,
    All wallowd in his owne fowle bloudy gore,
    Which flowèd from his wounds in wondrous store.°   *abundance*
    But soone as breath out of his breast did pas,
    That huge great body, which the Gyaunt bore,
    Was vanisht quite, and of that monstrous mas
Was nothing left, but like an emptie bladder was.

---

1. Clever machines of war ("engins") and evil strategy.

25

Whose grievous fall, when false Duessa spide,
   Her golden cup she cast unto the ground,
   And crownèd mitre[2] rudely° threw aside;   *violently*
   Such percing griefe her stubborne hart did wound,
   That she could not endure that dolefull stound,°   *sorrow*
   But leaving all behind her, fled away:
   The light-foot Squire her quickly turned around,
   And by hard meanes enforcing her to stay,
So brought unto his Lord, as his deservèd pray.

26

The royall Virgin, which beheld from farre,
   In pensive° plight, and sad perplexitie,   *anxious*
   The whole achievement of this doubtfull warre,[3]
   Came running fast to greet his victorie,
   With sober gladnesse, and myld modestie,
   And with sweet joyous cheare° him thus bespake;   *countenance*
   "Faire braunch of noblesse, flowre of chevalrie,
   That with your worth the world amazèd make,
How shall I quite° the paines, ye suffer for my sake?   *requite*

27

"And you° fresh bud of vertue springing fast,   *i.e., the Squire*
   Whom these sad eyes saw nigh unto deaths dore,
   What hath poore Virgin for such perill past,
   Wherewith you to reward? Accept therefore
   My simple selfe, and service evermore;
   And he that high does sit, and all things see
   With equall° eyes, their merites to restore,°   *impartial / reward*
   Behold what ye this day have done for mee,
And what I cannot quite, requite with usuree.°   *interest*

28

"But sith° the heavens, and your faire handeling°   *since / conduct*
   Have made you maister of the field this day,
   Your fortune maister eke with governing,[4]
   And well begun end all so well, I pray,
   Ne let that wicked woman scape away;
   For she it is, that did my Lord bethrall,
   My dearest Lord, and deepe in dongeon lay,
   Where he his better dayes hath wasted all.[5]
O heare, how piteous he to you for ayd does call."

2. An allusion to the pope's triple tiara.
3. I.e., the final outcome, which had been in doubt, of this battle.
4. Secure your good fortune also by prudent man-
agement.
5. I.e., he has consumed ("wasted") there his best days.

29

Forthwith he gave in charge unto his Squire,
  That scarlot whore to keepen carefully;
  Whiles he himselfe with greedie° great desire   *eager*
  Into the Castle entred forcibly,
  Where living creature none he did espye;
  Then gan he lowdly through the house to call:
  But no man cared to answere to his crye.
  There raignd a solemne silence over all,
Nor voice was heard, nor wight was seene in bowre or hall.

30

At last with creeping crooked pace forth came
  An old old man, with beard as white as snow,
  That on a staffe his feeble steps did frame,°   *support*
  And guide his wearie gate° both too and fro: *gait*
  For his eye sight him failèd long ygo,
  And on his arme a bounch of keyes he bore,
  The which unusèd, rust did overgrow:
  Those were the keyes of every inner dore,
But he could not them use, but kept them still in store.

31

But very uncouth° sight was to behold,   *strange*
  How he did fashion his untoward° pace,   *awkward*
  For as he forward mooved his footing old,
  So backward still was turned his wrincled face,
  Unlike to men, who ever as they trace,°   *walk*
  Both feet and face one way are wont to lead.
  This was the auncient keeper of that place,
  And foster father of the Gyant dead;
His name Ignaro° did his nature right aread.°   *Ignorance / declare*

32

His reverend haires and holy gravitie
  The knight much honord, as beseemèd well,°   *seemed proper*
  And gently° askt, where all the people bee,   *courteously*
  Which in that stately building wont to dwell.
  Who answerd him full soft, he could not tell.
  Againe he askt, where that same knight was layd,
  Whom great Orgoglio with his puissaunce fell
  Had made his caytive° thrall; againe he sayde,   *captive*
He could not tell: ne ever other answere made.

33

Then askèd he, which way he in might pas:
  He could not tell, againe he answerèd.
  Thereat the curteous knight displeasèd was,

And said, "Old sire, it seemes thou hast not red°   *recognized*
How ill it sits with° that same silver hed   *suits*
In vaine to mocke, or mockt in vaine to bee:
But if thou be, as thou art pourtrahèd
With natures pen, in ages grave degree,
Aread° in graver wise, what I demaund° of thee."   *answer / ask*

34

His answere likewise was, he could not tell.
  Whose sencelesse speach, and doted° ignorance   *foolish*
  When as the noble Prince had markèd well,
  He ghest his nature by his countenance,
  And calmd his wrath with goodly temperance.
  Then to him stepping, from his arme did reach
  Those keyes, and made himselfe free enterance.
  Each dore he opened without any breach;°   *forcing*
There was no barre to stop, nor foe him to empeach.°   *hinder*

35

There all within full rich arayd he found,
  With royal arras° and resplendent gold,   *tapestry*
  And did with store of every thing abound,
  That greatest Princes presence° might behold.   *person*
  But all the floore (too filthy to be told)
  With bloud of guiltlesse babes, and innocents trew,[6]
  Which there were slaine, as sheepe out of the fold,
  Defilèd was, that dreadfull was to vew,
And sacred ashes over it was strowèd new.

36

And there beside of marble stone was built
  An Altare, carved with cunning imagery,[7]
  On which true Christians bloud was often spilt,
  And holy Martyrs often doen to dye,°   *put to death*
  With cruell malice and strong tyranny:
  Whose blessed sprites from underneath the stone
  To God for vengeance cryde continually,[8]
  And with great griefe were often heard to grone,
That hardest heart would bleede, to heare their piteous mone.

37

Through every rowme he sought, and every bowr,
  But no where could he find that wofull thrall:
  At last he came unto an yron doore,

---

6. Probably alluding to Herod's massacre of the Innocents (Matthew 2.16), who were traditionally viewed as the first martyrs for Christ.
7. Skillfully wrought images.
8. "And when he had opened the fifth seal, I saw under the altar the souls of them that were slain for the word of God, and for the testimony which they held: And they cried with a loud voice, saying, How long, O Lord, holy and true, dost thou not judge and avenge our blood on them that dwell on the earth?" (Revelation 6.9–10).

That fast was lockt, but key found not at all
Emongst that bounch, to open it withall;
But in the same a little grate was pight,°   *placed*
Through which he sent his voyce, and lowd did call
With all his powre, to weet,° if living wight   *learn*
Were housèd therewithin, whom he enlargen° might.   *set free*

38

Therewith an hollow, dreary, murmuring voyce
These piteous plaints and dolours° did resound;   *laments*
"O who is that, which brings me happy choyce
Of death,[9] that here lye dying every stound,°   *moment*
Yet live perforce in balefull° darkenesse bound?   *evil*
For now three Moones have changèd thrice their hew,° *shape*
And have beene thrice hid underneath the ground,
Since I the heavens chearefull face did vew,
O welcome thou, that doest of death bring tydings trew."

39

Which when that Champion heard, with percing point
Of pitty deare° his hart was thrillèd° sore,   *extreme / pierced*
And trembling horrour ran through every joynt,
For ruth of gentle knight so fowle forlore:°   *grievously lost*
Which shaking off, he rent that yron dore,
With furious force, and indignation fell;°   *fierce*
Where entred in, his foot could find no flore,
But all a deepe descent, as darke as hell,
That breathèd ever forth a filthie banefull smell.

40

But neither darkenesse fowle, nor filthy bands,°   *bonds*
Nor noyous° smell his purpose could withhold,   *noxious*
(Entire affection hateth nicer° hands)   *too fastidious*
But that with constant zeale, and courage bold,
After long paines and labours manifold,
He found the meanes that Prisoner up to reare;
Whose feeble thighes, unhable to uphold
His pinèd° corse, him scarse to light could beare,   *wasted*
A ruefull spectacle of deathe and ghastly drere.°   *sorrow, wretchedness*

41

His sad dull eyes deepe sunck in hollow pits,
Could not endure th'unwonted° sunne to view;   *unaccustomed*
His bare thin cheekes for want of better bits,°   *food*
And empty sides deceivèd° of their dew,   *cheated*
Could make a stony hart his hap to rew;°   *to pity his lot*
His rawbone armes, whose mighty brawnèd bowrs° *brawny muscles*

9. I.e., the chance or right to choose death.

Were wont to rive steele plates, and helmets hew,
Were cleane consumed, and all his vitall powres
Decayd, and all his flesh shronk up like withered flowres.

42

Whom when his Lady saw, to him she ran
With hasty joy: to see him made her glad,
And sad to view his visage pale and wan,
Who earst° in flowres of freshest youth was clad.   *formerly*
Tho° when her well of teares she wasted° had,   *then / expended*
She said, "Ah dearest Lord, what evill starre
On you hath fround, and pourd his influence bad,
That of your selfe ye thus berobbèd arre,
And this misseeming hew° your manly looks doth marre?   *unseemly*
                                                                  appearance

43

"But welcome now my Lord, in wele or woe,
Whose presence I have lackt to long a day;
And fie on Fortune mine avowèd foe,
Whose wrathfull wreakes° them selves do now alay.   *punishments*
And for these wrongs shall treble penaunce pay
Of treble good: good growes of evils priefe."[1]
The chearelesse man, whom sorrow did dismay,°   *unnerve*
Had no delight to treaten° of his griefe;   *speak*
His long endurèd famine needed more reliefe.

44

"Faire Lady," then said that victorious knight,°   *i.e., Arthur*
"The things, that grievous were to do, or beare,
Them to renew,° I wote,° breeds no delight;   *recall / know*
Best musicke breeds delight in loathing eare:
But th'onely good, that growes of passèd feare,
Is to be wise, and ware° of like agein.   *wary*
This dayes ensample hath this lesson deare
Deepe written in my heart with yron pen,
That blisse may not abide in state of mortall men.

45

"Henceforth sir knight, take to you wonted strength,
And maister these mishaps with patient might;
Loe where your foe lyes stretcht in monstrous length,
And loe that wicked woman in your sight,
The roote of all your care, and wretched plight,
Now in your powre, to let her live, or dye."
"To do her dye," quoth Una, "were despight,[2]

---

1. I.e., Fortune will now make amends for his
wrongs with triple benefits, as good comes from
evils endured ("priefe").
2. I.e., to cause her to die would be spiteful.

> And shame t'avenge so weake an enimy;
> But spoile° her of her scarlot robe, and let her fly."   *despoil, strip*

46

> So as she bad, that witch they disaraid,
> And robd of royall robes, and purple pall,°   *scarlet cloak*
> And ornaments that richly were displaid;
> Ne sparèd they to strip her naked all.
> Then when they had despoild her tire° and call,°   *robe / caul, headdress*
> Such as she was, their eyes might her behold,
> That her misshapèd parts did them appall,
> A loathly, wrinckled hag, ill favoured, old,
> Whose secret filth good manners biddeth not be told.

47

> Her craftie head was altogether bald,
> And as in hate of honorable eld,°   *age*
> Was overgrowne with scurfe° and filthy scald;[3]   *scabs*
> Her teeth out of her rotten gummes were feld,°   *fallen*
> And her sowre breath abhominably smeld;
> Her drièd dugs,° like bladders lacking wind,   *breasts*
> Hong downe, and filthy matter from them weld;°   *welled*
> Her wrizled° skin as rough, as maple rind,   *wrinkled*
> So scabby was, that would have loathd° all womankind.   *revolted*

48

> Her neather parts, the shame of all her kind,°   *i.e., womankind*
> My chaster° Muse for shame doth blush to write;   *too chaste*
> But at her rompe she growing had behind
> A foxes taile, with dong all fowly dight;°   *covered*
> And eke her feete most monstrous were in sight;
> For one of them was like an Eagles claw,
> With griping talaunts armd to greedy fight,
> The other like a Beares uneven° paw: *rough*
> More ugly shape yet never living creature saw.[4]

49

> Which when the knights beheld, amazd they were,
> And wondred at so fowle deformèd wight.
> "Such then," said Una, "as she seemeth here,
> Such is the face of falshood, such the sight
> Of fowle Duessa, when her borrowed light
> Is laid away, and counterfesaunce° knowne."   *deceit*
> Thus when they had the witch disrobèd quight,
> And all her filthy feature° open showne,   *form*
> They let her goe at will, and wander wayes unknowne.

3. A scabby disease of the scalp.
4. The passage alludes to Revelation 17.16: "these shall hate the whore, and shall make her desolate and naked." Foxes were emblems of cunning; eagles and bears, of rapacity, cruelty, and brutality.

50

She flying fast from heavens hated face,
    And from the world that her discovered° wide,   *exposed to view*
    Fled to the wastfull° wildernesse apace,   *desolate*
    From living eyes her open shame to hide,
    And lurkt in rocks and caves long unespide.
    But that faire crew° of knights, and Una faire   *company*
    Did in that castle afterwards abide,
    To rest them selves, and weary powres repaire,
Where store they found of all, that dainty° was and rare.   *precious*

Canto 9

His loves and lignage° Arthur tells: *lineage*
   The knights knit friendly bands:°   *bonds*
   Sir Trevisan flies from Despayre,
   Whom Redcrosse knight withstands.

1

O goodly golden chaine,[5] wherewith yfere°   *together*
    The vertues linkèd are in lovely wize:°   *manner*
    And noble minds of yore allyèd were,
    In brave poursuit of chevalrous emprize,°   *adventure*
    That none did others safety despize,°   *disregard*
    Nor aid envy° to him, in need that stands,   *begrudge*
    But friendly each did others prayse devize
How to advaunce with favourable hands,
As this good Prince redeemd the Redcrosse knight from bands.

2

Who when their powres, empaird through labour long,
    With dew repast° they had recurèd° well,   *rest / restored*
    And that weake captive wight now wexèd° strong,   *waxed, grown*
    Them list° no lenger there at leasure dwell,   *they cared*
    But forward fare, as their adventures fell,
    But ere they parted, Una faire besought
    That straunger knight his name and nation tell;
    Least° so great good, as he for her had wrought,   *lest*
Should die unknown, and buried be in thanklesse thought.

3

"Faire virgin," said the Prince, "ye me require
    A thing without the compas of° my wit: *beyond the reach of*
    For both the lignage and the certain Sire,
    From which I sprong, from me are hidden yit.
    For all so soone as life did me admit

---

5. The golden chain of love or concord that binds the world and the human race together (cf. canto 5, stanza 25, and note).

Into this world, and shewèd heavens light,
From mothers pap I taken was unfit:°   *i.e., not yet weaned*
And streight delivered to a Faery knight,
To be upbrought in gentle thewes° and martiall might.   *manners*

4

"Unto old Timon[6] he me brought bylive,°   *immediately*
Old Timon, who in youthly yeares hath beene
In warlike feates th'expertest man alive,
And is the wisest now on earth I weene;
His dwelling is low in a valley greene,
Under the foot of Rauran mossy hore,°   *gray*
From whence the river Dee as silver cleene°   *pure*
His tombling billowes rolls with gentle rore:[7]
There all my dayes he traind me up in vertuous lore.

5

"Thither the great Magicien Merlin came,
As was his use,° ofttimes to visit me: *custom*
For he had charge my discipline° to frame,   *education*
And Tutours nouriture° to oversee.   *tutor's upbringing*
Him oft and oft I askt in privitie,
Of what loines and what lignage I did spring:
Whose aunswere bad me still assurèd bee,
That I was sonne and heire unto a king,
As time in her just terme° the truth to light should bring."   *due course*

6

"Well worthy impe,"° said then the Lady gent,°   *offspring / gentle*
"And Pupill fit for such a Tutours hand.
But what adventure, or what high intent
Hath brought you hither into Faery land,
Aread° Prince Arthur,[8] crowne of Martiall band?"   *declare*
"Full hard it is," quoth he, "to read° aright   *discern*
The course of heavenly cause, or understand
The secret meaning of th'eternall might,
That rules mens wayes, and rules the thoughts of living wight.

7

"For whither he through fatall deepe foresight,[9]
Me hither sent, for cause to me unghest,
Or that fresh bleeding wound, which day and night
Whilome° doth rancle in my riven brest,   *all the while*
With forcèd fury following his behest,°   *its command*

---

6. The name means "honor."
7. The hill Rauran is in Wales; the river Dee also flows in, and forms part of the boundary of, Wales. The Tudors (Queen Elizabeth's family) were originally Welsh, and the legends of Arthur had their beginnings in the Celtic mythology of early Wales.

8. Arthur had been named in the quatrains that precede cantos 7 and 8, but not previously in the body of the text.
9. I.e., whether he (God, "th'eternall might") sent me here through foresight ordained by fate ("fatall").

Me hither brought by wayes yet never found,
You to have helpt I hold my selfe yet blest."
"Ah curteous knight," quoth she, "what secret wound
Could ever find,° to grieve the gentlest hart on ground?"   *succeed*

8

"Deare Dame," quoth he, "you sleeping sparkes awake,
    Which troubled once, into huge flames will grow,
    Ne ever will their fervent fury slake
    Till living moysture into smoke do flow,
    And wasted° life do lye in ashes low.   *consumed*
    Yet sithens° silence lesseneth not my fire,   *since*
    But told it flames, and hidden it does glow,
    I will revele, what ye so much desire:
Ah Love, lay downe thy bow, the whiles I may respire.°   *take breath*

9

"It was in freshest flowre of youthly yeares,
    When courage first does creepe in manly chest,
    Then first the coale of kindly° heat appeares   *natural*
    To kindle love in every living brest;
    But me had warnd old Timons wise behest,
    Those creeping flames by reason to subdew,
    Before their rage grew to so great unrest,
    As miserable lovers use° to rew,   *are accustomed*
Which still wex° old in woe, whiles woe still wexeth new.   *grow*

10

"That idle name of love, and lovers life,
    As° losse of time, and vertues enimy   *as being*
    I ever scornd, and joyd to stirre up strife,
    In middest of their mournfull Tragedy,
    Ay° wont to laugh, when them I heard to cry,   *always*
    And blow the fire, which them to ashes brent:°   *burned*
    Their God himselfe, grieved at my libertie,
    Shot many a dart at me with fiers intent,
But I them warded all with wary government.[1]

11

"But all in vaine: no fort can be so strong,
    Ne fleshly brest can armèd be so sound,
    But will at last be wonne with battrie° long,   *siege*
    Or unawares at disavantage found;
    Nothing is sure, that growes on earthly ground:
    And who most trustes in arme of fleshly might,
    And boasts, in beauties chaine not to be bound,

---

1. I.e., self-control. The descriptions here of Cupid's archery and of the siege of the castle of chastity (in the next stanza) have many echoes from the medieval courtly love tradition.

Doth soonest fall in disaventrous° fight,   *disastrous*
And yeeldes his caytive° neck to victours most° despight.   *captive / greatest*

12

"Ensample make of him your haplesse joy,°   *i.e., Redcrosse*
  And of my selfe now mated,° as ye see;   *overcome*
  Whose prouder° vaunt that proud avenging boy   *too proud*
  Did soone pluck downe, and curbd my libertie.
  For on a day prickt° forth with jollitie   *spurred*
  Of looser° life, and heat of hardiment,°   *too loose / boldness*
  Raunging the forest wide on courser free,
  The fields, the floods, the heavens with one consent
Did seeme to laugh on me, and favour mine intent.

13

"For-wearied° with my sports, I did alight   *utterly wearied*
  From loftie steed, and downe to sleepe me layd;
  The verdant° gras my couch did goodly dight,°   *green / make*
  And pillow was my helmet faire displayd:
  Whiles every sence the humour sweet embayd,[2]
  And slombring soft my hart did steale away,
  Me seemèd, by my side a royall Mayd
  Her daintie limbes full softly down did lay:
So faire a creature yet saw never sunny day.

14

"Most goodly glee° and lovely blandishment°   *entertainment / compliment*
  She to me made, and bad me love her deare,
  For dearely sure her love was to me bent,
  As when just time expirèd[3] should appeare.
  But whether dreames delude, or true it were,
  Was never hart so ravisht with delight,
  Ne living man like words did ever heare,
  As she to me delivered all that night;
And at her parting said, She Queene of Faeries hight.[4]

15

"When I awoke, and found her place devoyd,°   *empty*
  And nought but pressèd gras, where she had lyen,
  I sorrowed all so much, as earst° I joyd,   *previously*
  And washèd all her place with watry eyen.
  From that day forth I loved that face divine;
  From that day forth I cast° in carefull° mind,   *resolved / care-filled*
  To seeke her out with labour, and long tyne,°   *hardship*

2. I.e., while the dew ("humour") of sleep pervaded ("embayd") every sense.
3. A fitting length of time having passed.
4. Was called. In the background are many folk-tales and ballads of a hero bewitched by a fairy. Spenser's Letter to Ralegh identifies Gloriana allegorically with glory and with Queen Elizabeth.

And never vowd° to rest, till her I find,   *vowed never*
Nine monethes I seeke in vaine yet ni'll° that vow unbind."   *will not*

16

Thus as he spake, his visage wexèd pale,
    And chaunge of hew great passion did bewray;°   *reveal*
    Yet still he strove to cloke his inward bale,°   *grief*
    And hide the smoke, that did his fire display,
    Till gentle Una thus to him gan say;
    "O happy Queene of Faeries, that hast found
    Mongst many, one that with his prowesse may
    Defend thine honour, and thy foes confound:
True Loves are often sown, but seldom grow on ground."

17

"Thine, O then," said the gentle Redcrosse knight,
    "Next to that Ladies love shalbe the place,
    O fairest virgin, full of heavenly light,
    Whose wondrous faith, exceeding earthly race,
    Was firmest fixt in mine extremest case.°   *plight*
    And you, my Lord, the Patrone° of my life,   *protector*
    Of that great Queene may well gaine worthy grace:
    For onely worthy you through prowes priefe°   *demonstration of prowess*
Yf living man mote° worthy be, to be her liefe."°   *may / love*

18

So diversly discoursing of their loves,
    The golden Sunne his glistring° head gan shew,   *glittering*
    And sad remembraunce now the Prince amoves,
    With fresh desire his voyage to pursew:
    Als° Una earnd° her traveill to renew.   *also / yearned*
    Then those two knights, fast friendship for to bynd,
    And love establish each to other trew,
    Gave goodly gifts, the signes of gratefull mynd,
And eke as pledges firme, right hands together joynd.

19

Prince Arthur gave a boxe of Diamond sure,°   *true*
    Embowd° with gold and gorgeous ornament,   *bound*
    Wherein were closd few drops of liquor pure,
    Of wondrous worth, and vertue° excellent,   *power*
    That any wound could heale incontinent:°   *immediately*
    Which to requite, the Redcrosse knight him gave
    A booke, wherein his Saveours testament
    Was writ with golden letters rich and brave;°   *splendid*
A worke of wondrous grace, and able soules to save.

20

Thus beene they parted, Arthur on his way
 To seeke his love, and th'other for to fight
 With Unas foe, that all her realme did pray.°   *prey on*
 But she now weighing the decayèd plight,
 And shrunken synewes of her chosen knight,
 Would not a while her forward course pursew,
 Ne bring him forth in face of dreadfull fight,
 Till he recovered had his former hew:°   *appearance*
For him to be yet weake and wearie well she knew.

21

So as they traveild, lo they gan espy
 An armèd knight towards them gallop fast,
 That seemèd from some fearèd foe to fly,
 Or other griesly thing, that him agast.°   *terrified*
 Still° as he fled, his eye was backward cast,   *continually*
 As if his feare still followed him behind;
 Als flew his steed, as he his bands had brast,°   *broken*
 And with his wingèd heeles did tread the wind,
As he had beene a fole of Pegasus his kind.[5]

22

Nigh as he drew, they might perceive his head
 To be unarmd, and curld uncombèd heares
 Upstaring° stiffe, dismayd with uncouth° dread; *bristling / strange*
 Nor drop of bloud in all his face appeares
 Nor life in limbe: and to increase his feares,
 In fowle reproch° of knighthoods faire degree,° *disgrace / condition*
 About his neck an hempen rope he weares,
 That with his glistring armes does ill agree;
But he of rope or armes has now no memoree.

23

The Redcrosse knight toward him crossèd fast,
 To weet,° what mister° wight was so dismayd: *learn / kind of*
 There him he finds all sencelesse and aghast,
 That of him selfe he seemd to be afrayd;
 Whom hardly° he from flying forward stayd,   *with difficulty*
 Till he these wordes to him deliver might;
 "Sir knight, aread° who hath ye thus arayd,   *declare*
 And eke from whom make ye this hasty flight:
For never knight I saw in such misseeming° plight."   *unseemly*

5. I.e., as if he had been a foal of a horse like Pegasus, the flying horse of classical mythology.

24

He answerd nought at all, but adding new
    Feare to his first amazmment, staring wide
    With stony eyes, and hartlesse hollow hew,[6]
    Astonisht stood, as one that had aspide
    Infernall furies, with their chaines untide.
    Him yet againe, and yet againe bespake
    The gentle knight; who nought to him replide,
    But trembling every joynt did inly quake,
And foltring tongue at last these words seemd forth to shake.

25

"For Gods deare love, Sir knight, do me not stay;
    For loe he comes, he comes fast after mee."
    Eft° looking backe would faine have runne away;   *again*
    But he him forst to stay, and tellen free
    The secret cause of his perplexitie:°   *distress*
    Yet nathemore° by his bold hartie speach,   *not at all*
    Could his bloud-frosen hart emboldned bee,
    But through his boldnesse rather feare did reach,
Yet forst, at last he made through silence suddein breach.

26

"And am I now in safetie sure," quoth he,
    "From him, that would have forcèd me to dye?
    And is the point of death now turnd fro mee,
    That I may tell this haplesse history?"°   *story of misfortune*
    "Feare nought:" quoth he, "no daunger now is nye."
    "Then shall I you recount a ruefull cace,"°   *pitiable event*
    Said he, "the which with this unlucky eye
    I late beheld, and had not greater grace
Me reft° from it, had bene partaker of the place.[7]   *carried*

27

"I lately chaunst (Would I had never chaunst)
    With a faire knight to keepen companee,
    Sir Terwin[8] hight,° that well himselfe advaunst   *named*
    In all affaires, and was both bold and free,
    But not so happie as mote happie bee:
    He loved, as was his lot, a Ladie gent,°   *gentle*
    That him againe° loved in the least degree: *in return*
    For she was proud, and of too high intent,°   *mind*
And joyd to see her lover languish and lament.

---

6. I.e., with blanched, bloodless countenance.
7. I.e., shared the same fate.

8. His name may connote weariness or fatigue ("terwyn").

28

"From whom returning sad and comfortlesse,°   *desolate*
  As on the way together we did fare,
  We met that villen (God from him me blesse°)   *defend*
  That cursèd wight, from whom I scapt whyleare,°   *a while before*
  A man of hell, that cals himselfe Despaire;[9]
  Who first us greets, and after faire areedes°   *tells*
  Of tydings strange, and of adventures rare:
  So creeping close, as Snake in hidden weedes,
Inquireth of our states, and of our knightly deedes.

29

"Which when he knew, and felt our feeble harts
  Embost° with bale,° and bitter byting griefe,   *exhausted / sorrow*
  Which love had launchèd° with his deadly darts,   *pierced*
  With wounding words and termes of foule repriefe,°   *insult, scorn*
  He pluckt from us all hope of due reliefe,
  That earst° us held in love of lingring life;   *formerly*
  Then hopelesse hartlesse, gan the cunning thiefe
  Perswade us die, to stint° all further strife: *end*
To me he lent this rope, to him a rustie° knife.   *i.e., bloodstained*

30

"With which sad instrument of hastie death,
  That wofull lover, loathing lenger° light,   *longer*
  A wide way made to let forth living breath.
  But I more fearefull, or more luckie wight,
  Dismayd with that deformèd dismall sight,
  Fled fast away, halfe dead with dying feare:°   *fear of death*
  Ne yet assur'd of life by you, Sir knight,
  Whose like infirmitie like chaunce may beare:
But God you never let his charmèd speeches heare."[1]

31

"How may a man," said he, "with idle speach
  Be wonne, to spoyle° the Castle of his health?"   *destroy*
  "I wote," quoth he, "whom triall° late did teach,   *experience*
  That like would not[2] for all this worldes wealth:
  His subtill tongue, like dropping honny, mealt'th°   *melts*
  Into the hart, and searcheth every vaine,
  That ere one be aware, by secret stealth
  His powre is reft, and weaknesse doth remaine.
O never Sir desire to try° his guilefull traine."°   *test / treachery*

9. Despair is the ultimate Christian sin, denying the possibility of divine mercy and grace.
1. I.e., may God never let you hear his mesmer-izing ("charmèd") speeches.
2. I.e., would not do the like again.

32

"Certès,"° said he, "hence shall I never rest,   *surely*
  Till I that treachours art have heard and tride;
  And you Sir knight, whose name mote° I request,   *might*
  Of grace° do me unto his cabin° guide."   *favor / cave*
  "I that hight° Trevisan,"[3] quoth he, "will ride   *am called*
  Against my liking backe, to doe you grace:°   *a favor*
  But nor for gold nor glee[4] will I abide
  By you, when ye arrive in that same place;
For lever° had I die, then° see his deadly face."   *rather / than*

33

Ere long they come, where that same wicked wight
  His dwelling has, low in an hollow cave,
  Farre underneath a craggie clift ypight,°   *placed*
  Darke, dolefull, drearie, like a greedie grave,
  That still° for carrion carcases doth crave: *continually*
  On top whereof aye° dwelt the ghastly Owle,[5]   *ever*
  Shrieking his balefull note, which ever drave
  Farre from that haunt all other chearefull fowle;
And all about it wandring ghostes did waile and howle.

34

And all about old stockes° and stubs of trees,   *stumps*
  Whereon nor fruit, nor leafe was ever seene,
  Did hang upon the ragged rocky knees;°   *crags*
  On which had many wretches hangèd beene,
  Whose carcases were scattered on the greene,
  And throwne about the cliffs. Arrivèd there,
  That bare-head knight for dread and dolefull teene,°   *grief*
  Would faine° have fled, ne durst approachen neare,   *gladly*
But th' other forst him stay, and comforted in feare.

35

That darkesome cave they enter, where they find
  That cursèd man, low sitting on the ground,
  Musing full sadly in his sullein° mind;   *morose*
  His griesie° lockes, long growen, and unbound,   *gray*
  Disordred hong about his shoulders round,
  And hid his face; through which his hollow eyne
  Lookt deadly dull, and starèd as astound;°   *as if stunned*
  His raw-bone cheekes through penurie and pine,°   *starvation*
Were shronke into his jawes, as° he did never dine.   *as if*

---

3. The meaning is uncertain, but may be "flight" or "dread."
4. Beauty; i.e., not for anything in the world.
5. Traditionally a messenger of death.

36

His garment nought but many ragged clouts,°   *scraps*
  With thornes together pind and patchèd was,
  The which his naked sides he wrapt abouts;
  And him beside there lay upon the gras
  A drearie corse,° whose life away did pas,   *bloody corpse*
  All wallowd in his owne yet luke-warme blood,
  That from his wound yet wellèd fresh alas;
  In which a rustie knife fast fixèd stood,
And made an open passage for the gushing flood.

37

Which piteous spectacle, approving° trew   *confirming*
  The wofull tale that Trevisan had told,
  When as the gentle Redcrosse knight did vew,
  With firie zeale he burnt in courage bold,
  Him to avenge, before his bloud were cold,
  And to the villein said, "Thou agèd damnèd wight,
  The author of this fact,° we here behold,   *deed*
  What justice can but judge against thee right,
With thine owne bloud to price° his bloud, here shed in sight?" *pay for*

38

"What franticke fit," quoth he, "hath thus distraught
  Thee, foolish man, so rash a doome° to give?   *judgment*
  What justice ever other judgement taught,
  But he should die, who merites not to live?
  None else to death this man despayring drive,°   *drove*
  But his owne guiltie mind deserving death.
  Is then unjust to each his due to give?
  Or let him die, that loatheth living breath?
Or let him die at ease, that liveth here uneath?°   *in hardship*

39

"Who travels by the wearie wandring way,
  To come unto his wishèd home in haste,
  And meetes a flood, that doth his passage stay,
  Is not great grace to helpe him over past,
  Or free his feet, that in the myre sticke fast?
  Most envious man, that grieves at neighbours good,
  And fond,° that joyest in the woe thou hast,   *foolish*
  Why wilt not let him passe, that long hath stood
Upon the banke, yet wilt thy selfe not passe the flood?

40

"He there does now enjoy eternall rest
  And happie ease, which thou doest want and crave,
  And further from it daily wanderest:
  What if some litle paine the passage have,

That makes fraile flesh to feare the bitter wave?
Is not short paine well borne, that brings long ease,
And layes the soule to sleepe in quiet grave?
Sleepe after toyle, port after stormie seas,
Ease after warre, death after life does greatly please."[6]

41

The knight much wondred at his suddeine wit,°   *quick intelligence*
And said, "The terme of life is limited,
Ne may a man prolong, nor shorten it;
The souldier may not move from watchfull sted,[7]
Nor leave his stand, untill his Captaine bed."°   *commands*
"Who life did limit by almightie doome,"
Quoth he, "knowes best the termes establishèd;
And he, that points the Centonell his roome,°   *station*
Doth license him depart at sound of morning droome.[8]

42

"Is not his deed, what ever thing is donne,
In heaven and earth? did not he all create
To die againe? all ends that was begonne.
Their times in his eternall booke of fate
Are written sure, and have their certaine° date.   *fixed*
Who then can strive with strong necessitie,
That holds the world in his still chaunging state,
Or shunne the death ordaynd by destinie?
When houre of death is come, let none aske whence, nor why.

43

"The lenger° life, I wote° the greater sin,   *longer / know*
The greater sin, the greater punishment:
All those great battels, which thou boasts to win,
Through strife, and bloud-shed, and avengement,
Now praysd, hereafter deare° thou shalt repent: *bitterly*
For life must life, and bloud must bloud repay.[9]
Is not enough thy evill life forespent?
For he, that once hath missèd the right way,
The further he doth goe, the further he doth stray.

44

"Then do no further goe, no further stray,
But here lie downe, and to thy rest betake,
Th'ill to prevent, that life ensewen may.[1]
For what hath life, that may it lovèd make,

---

6. Despaire's arguments on behalf of suicide as against a painful life are derived, like those of Hamlet in his third soliloquy (*Hamlet* 3.1.58–90), principally from Seneca, Marcus Aurelius, other ancient Stoics, and Old Testament statements on divine justice.
7. The sentry post assigned him.
8. Drum, with a pun on *doom*.
9. An echo of Genesis 9.6: "Whoso sheddeth man's blood, by man shall his blood be shed."
1. I.e., to prevent the evil that will ensue in the rest of your life.

And gives not rather cause it to forsake?
   Feare, sicknesse, age, losse, labour, sorrow, strife,
   Paine, hunger, cold, that makes the hart to quake;
   And ever fickle fortune rageth rife,
All which, and thousands mo° do make a loathsome life.   *more*

45

"Thou wretched man, of death hast greatest need,
   If in true ballance thou wilt weigh thy state:
   For never knight, that darèd warlike deede,
   More lucklesse disaventures° did amate:°   *mishaps / daunt*
   Witnesse the dongeon deepe, wherein of late
   Thy life shut up, for death so oft did call;
   And though good lucke prolongèd hath thy date,°   *span of life*
   Yet death then, would the like mishaps forestall,
Into the which hereafter thou maiest happen fall.°   *happen to fall*

46

"Why then doest thou, O man of sin, desire
   To draw thy dayes forth to their last degree?
   Is not the measure of thy sinfull hire°   *service to sin*
   High heapèd up with huge iniquitie,
   Against the day of wrath,° to burden thee?   *Judgment Day*
   Is not enough that to this Ladie milde
   Thou falsèd° hast thy faith with perjurie,°   *betrayed / oath-breaking*
   And sold thy selfe to serve Duessa vilde,°   *vile*
With whom in all abuse thou hast thy selfe defilde?

47

"Is not he just, that all this doth behold
   From highest heaven, and beares an equall° eye?   *impartial*
   Shall he thy sins up in his knowledge fold,
   And guiltie be of thine impietie?
   Is not his law, Let every sinner die:[2]
   Die shall all flesh? what then must needs be donne,
   Is it not better to doe willinglie,
   Then linger, till the glasse° be all out ronne?   *hourglass*
Death is the end of woes: die soone, O faeries sonne."

48

The knight was much enmovèd with his speach,
   That as a swords point through his hart did perse,
   And in his conscience made a secret breach,°   *wound*
   Well knowing true all, that he did reherse,°   *recount*
   And to his fresh remembrance did reverse°   *bring back*
   The ugly vew of his deformèd crimes,

---

2. Despaire cites only half of the Scripture verse: "The wages of sin is death; but the gift of God is eternal life through Jesus Christ our Lord" (Romans 6.23).

That all his manly powres it did disperse,
 As he were charmèd with inchaunted rimes,
That oftentimes he quakt, and fainted° oftentimes.   *lost heart*

49

In which amazement, when the Miscreant°   *misbeliever*
 Perceivèd him to waver weake and fraile,
 Whiles trembling horror did his conscience dant,°   *daunt*
 And hellish anguish° did his soule assaile,   *i.e., fear of hell*
 To drive him to despaire, and quite to quaile,°   *be dismayed*
 He shewed him painted in a table° plaine,   *picture*
 The damnèd ghosts, that doe in torments waile,
 And thousand feends that doe them endlesse paine
With fire and brimstone, which for ever shall remaine.

50

The sight whereof so throughly him dismaid,
 That nought but death before his eyes he saw,
 And ever burning wrath before him laid,
 By righteous sentence of th'Almighties law:
 Then gan the villein him to overcraw,°   *exult over*
 And brought unto him swords, ropes, poison, fire,
 And all that might him to perdition draw;
 And bad him choose, what death he would desire:
For death was due to him, that had provokt Gods ire.

51

But when as none of them he saw him take,
 He to him raught° a dagger sharpe and keene,   *reached*
 And gave it him in hand: his hand did quake,
 And tremble like a leafe of Aspin greene,
 And troubled bloud through his pale face was seene
 To come, and goe with tydings from the hart,
 As it a running messenger had beene.
 At last resolved to worke his finall smart,°   *pain*
He lifted up his hand, that backe againe did start.

52

Which when as Una saw, through every vaine
 The crudled° cold ran to her well of life,°   *congealing / heart*
 As in a swowne: but soone relived° againe,   *revived*
 Out of his hand she snatcht the cursèd knife,
 And threw it to the ground, enragèd rife,°   *deeply*
 And to him said, "Fie, fie, faint harted knight,
 What meanest thou by this reprochfull° strife? *deserving reproach*
 Is this the battell, which thou vauntst to fight
With the fire-mouthèd Dragon, horrible and bright?

53

"Come, come away, fraile, feeble, fleshly wight,
 Ne let vaine words bewitch thy manly hart,
 Ne divelish thoughts dismay thy constant spright.°   *spirit*
 In heavenly mercies hast thou not a part?
 Why shouldst thou then despeire, that chosen[3] art?
 Where justice growes, there grows eke° greater grace,   *also*
 The which doth quench the brond° of hellish smart,   *firebrand*
 And that accurst hand-writing[4] doth deface.°   *blot out*
Arise, Sir knight arise, and leave this cursèd place."

54

So up he rose, and thence amounted° streight.   *mounted his horse*
 Which when the carle° beheld, and saw his guest   *churl*
 Would safe depart, for° all his subtill sleight,   *in spite of*
 He chose an halter° from among the rest,   *noose*
 And with it hung himselfe, unbid° unblest.   *unprayed for*
 But death he could not worke himselfe thereby;
 For thousand times he so himselfe had drest,°   *made ready*
 Yet nathelesse it could not doe° him die,   *make*
Till he should die his last, that is eternally.

Canto 10

Her faithfull knight faire Una brings
 to house of Holinesse,
Where he is taught repentance, and
 the way to heavenly blesse.°   *bliss*

I

What man is he, that boasts of fleshly might,
 And vaine assurance of mortality,°   *mortal life*
 Which all so soone, as it doth come to fight,
 Against spirituall foes, yeelds by and by,°   *immediately*
 Or from the field most cowardly doth fly?
 Ne let the man ascribe it to his skill,
 That thorough° grace hath gainèd victory.   *through*
 If any strength we have, it is to ill,
But all the good is Gods, both power and eke° will.[5]   *also*

---

3. Cf. 2 Thessalonians 2.13: "God hath from the beginning chosen you to salvation through sanctification of the Spirit and belief of the truth." This is one of several similar passages in the epistles of St. Paul that form the basis of the theological doctrine of predestination.
4. An echo of Colossians 2.14: "Blotting out the handwriting of ordinances [i.e., the Old Testament Law] that was against us, which was contrary to us, and took it out of the way, nailing it to his cross."
5. "For by grace are ye saved through faith; and that not of yourselves: it is the gift of God: Not of works, lest any man should boast" (Ephesians 2.8–9); "it is God which worketh in you both to will and to do of his good pleasure" (Philippians 2.13).

2

By that, which lately hapned, Una saw,
  That this her knight was feeble, and too faint;
  And all his sinews woxen weake and raw,°   *unready*
  Through long enprisonment, and hard constraint,°   *affliction*
  Which he endurèd in his late restraint,
  That yet he was unfit for bloudie fight:
  Therefore to cherish him with diets daint,°   *choice*
  She cast° to bring him, where he chearen° might, *resolved / be cheered*
Till he recovered had his° late decayèd plight.   *i.e., from his*

3

There was an auntient house not farre away,
  Renowmd throughout the world for sacred lore,
  And pure unspotted life: so well they say
  It governd was, and guided evermore,
  Through wisedome of a matrone grave and hore;°   *hoar, venerable*
  Whose onely joy was to relieve the needes
  Of wretched soules, and helpe the helpelesse pore:
  All night she spent in bidding of her bedes,°   *saying prayers*
And all the day in doing good and godly deedes.

4

Dame Caelia° men did her call, as thought   *Heavenly*
  From heaven to come, or thither to arise,
  The mother of three daughters, well upbrought
  In goodly thewes,° and godly exercise:°   *habits / deeds*
  The eldest two most sober, chast, and wise,
  Fidelia and Speranza virgins were,
  Though spousd,° yet wanting° wedlocks solemnize; *betrothed / lacking*
  But faire Charissa to a lovely fere°   *loving mate*
Was linckèd, and by him had many pledges dere.[6]

5

Arrivèd there, the dore they find fast lockt;
  For it was warely watchèd night and day,
  For feare of many foes: but when they knockt,
  The Porter opened unto them streight way:
  He was an agèd syre, all hory gray,
  With lookes full lowly cast, and gate° full slow,   *gait*
  Wont° on a staffe his feeble steps to stay,   *accustomed*
  Hight Humilta.° They passe in stouping low;   *called Humility*
For streight and narrow was the way, which he did show.[7]

---

6. I.e., many children. The daughters' names mean "faith," "hope," and "charity"; cf. the three Saracens: Sansfoy, Sansjoy, and Sansloy. This canto draws heavily on scriptural references, especially 1 Corinthians 13.13: "And now abideth faith, hope, charity, these three; but the greatest of these is charity." Many aspects of the House of Holiness oppose their counterparts in the House of Pride (canto 4). "Solemnize": solemnization.
7. Alluding to Matthew 7.13–14: see the note to stanza 10 below.

6

Each goodly thing is hardest to begin,
But entred in a spacious court they see,
Both plaine, and pleasant to be walkèd in,
Where them does meete a francklin[8] faire and free,
And entertaines with comely courteous glee,
His name was Zele,° that him right well became,   *zeal*
For in his speeches and behaviour hee
Did labour lively to expresse the same,
And gladly did them guide, till to the Hall they came.

7

There fairely them receives a gentle Squire,
Of milde demeanure, and rare courtesie,
Right cleanly clad in comely sad° attire;   *sober*
In word and deede that shewed great modestie,
And knew his good° to all of each degree,   *proper respect*
Hight Reverence. He them with speeches meet°   *fitting*
Does faire entreat; no courting nicetie,[9]
But simple true, and eke unfainèd sweet,
As might become a Squire so great persons to greet.

8

And afterwards them to his Dame he leades,
That agèd Dame, the Ladie of the place:
Who all this while was busie at her beades:
Which doen, she up arose with seemely grace,
And toward them full matronely[1] did pace.
Where when that fairest Una she beheld,
Whom well she knew to spring from heavenly race,
Her hart with joy unwonted inly sweld,°   *swelled*
As feeling wondrous comfort in her weaker eld.°   *too weak age*

9

And her embracing said, "O happie earth,
Whereon thy innocent feet doe ever tread,
Most vertuous virgin borne of heavenly berth,
That to redeeme thy woefull parents head,
From tyrans rage, and ever-dying dread,°   *constant fear of death*
Hast wandred through the world now long a day°   *many a long day*
Yet ceasest not thy wearie soles to lead,
What grace hath thee now hither brought this way?
Or doen thy feeble feet unweeting° hither stray?   *unwittingly*

---

8. Freeholder, landowner.
9. He treats them courteously ("faire"); no courtly
affectation ("nicetie").

1. Like a matron, i.e., a woman in charge of an
establishment.

10

"Strange thing it is an errant° knight to see   *wandering*
  Here in this place, or any other wight,
  That hither turnes his steps. So few there bee,
  That chose the narrow path, or seeke the right:
  All keepe the broad high way, and take delight
  With many rather for to go astray,
  And be partakers of their evill plight,
  Then with a few to walke the rightest way;[2]
O foolish men, why haste ye to your owne decay?"

11

"Thy selfe to see, and tyred limbs to rest,
  O matrone sage," quoth she, "I hither came,
  And this good knight his way with me addrest,°   *directed*
  Led with thy prayses and broad-blazèd fame,
  That up to heaven is blowne."[3] The auncient Dame
  Him goodly greeted in her modest guise,
  And entertaynd them both, as best became,
  With all the court'sies,° that she could devise,   *courtesies*
Ne wanted ought,° to shew her bounteous or wise.   *nor lacked anything*

12

Thus as they gan of sundry things devise,°   *talk*
  Loe two most goodly virgins came in place,
  Ylinkèd arme in arme in lovely wise,°   *loving fashion*
  With countenance demure, and modest grace,
  They numbred even steps and equall pace:
  Of which the eldest, that Fidelia hight,
  Like sunny beames threw from her Christall face,
  That could have dazd° the rash beholders sight,   *dazzled*
And round about her head did shine like heavens light.

13

She was araièd° all in lilly white,   *arrayed*
  And in her right hand bore a cup of gold,
  With wine and water fild up to the hight,
  In which a Serpent[4] did himselfe enfold,
  That horrour made to all, that did behold;
  But she no whit did chaunge her constant mood:°   *expression*
  And in her other hand she fast did hold

---

2. An echo of Matthew 7.13–14: "Broad is the way that leadeth to destruction, and many there be which go in thereat: . . . strait is the gate and narrow is the way, which leadeth unto life, and few there be that find it."
3. I.e., your praises and fame are widely celebrated

("blazèd"), reaching ("blowne") up to heaven.
4. The cup of wine and water signifies the sacrament of Communion; the serpent is a symbol of the crucified Christ (of whom the serpent lifted up by Moses, Numbers 21.9, is a recognized "type" or prefiguration).

A booke, that was both signd and seald with blood,
Wherein darke° things were writ, hard to be understood.[5]   *obscure*

14

Her younger sister, that Speranza hight,
　Was clad in blew, that her beseemèd well;
　Not all so chearefull seemèd she of sight,°   *in appearance*
　As was her sister; whether dread° did dwell,   *fear*
　Or anguish in her hart, is hard to tell:
　Upon her arme a silver anchor[6] lay,
　Whereon she leanèd ever, as befell:°   *as was fitting*
　And ever up to heaven, as she did pray,
Her stedfast eyes were bent, ne swarvèd other way.

15

They seeing Una, towards her gan wend,°   *walk*
　Who them encounters° with like courtesie;   *meets*
　Many kind speeches they betwene them spend,
　And greatly joy each other well to see:
　Then to the knight with shamefast° modestie   *humble*
　They turne themselves, at Unas meeke request,
　And him salute with well beseeming glee;°   *appropriate joy*
　Who faire them quites,° as him beseemèd best,   *requites*
And goodly gan discourse of many a noble gest.°   *deed*

16

Then Una thus; "But she your sister deare,
　The deare Charissa where is she become?°   *gone to*
　Or wants° she health, or busie is elsewhere?"   *is lacking*
　"Ah no," said they, "but forth she may not come:
　For she of late is lightned of her wombe,
　And hath encreast the world with one sonne more,[7]
　That her to see should be but troublesome."
　"Indeede," quoth she, "that should her trouble sore,
But thankt be God, that her encrease so evermore."[8]

17

Then said the agèd Caelia, "Deare dame,
　And you good Sir, I wote° that of your toyle,   *know*
　And labours long, through which ye hither came,
　Ye both forwearied° be: therefore a whyle   *utterly weary*
　I read° you rest, and to your bowres recoyle."[9]   *counsel*
　Then callèd she a Groome, that forth him led
　Into a goodly lodge, and gan despoile°   *disrobe*

5. The book is the New Testament. See 2 Peter 3.16: "in which [i.e., in the epistles of the apostle Paul] are some things hard to be understood."
6. The iconographic symbol of hope.
7. Charity, the fruitful virtue, is often depicted as a mother with many children.
8. I.e., God be thanked, who continually increases her thus.
9. Retire to your rooms.

Of puissant armes, and laid in easie° bed;   *comfortable*
His name was meeke Obedience rightfully arèd.°   *understood*

18

Now when their wearie limbes with kindly° rest,   *natural*
    And bodies were refresht with due repast,°   *repose*
    Faire Una gan Fidelia faire request,
    To have her knight into her schoolehouse plaste,
    That of her heavenly learning he might taste,
    And heare the wisedome of her words divine.
    She graunted, and that knight so much agraste,°   *favored*
    That she him taught celestiall discipline,°   *instruction*
And opened his dull eyes, that light mote in them shine.

19

And that her sacred Booke, with bloud° ywrit,   *i.e., the blood of Christ*
    That none could read, except she did them teach,
    She unto him disclosèd every whit,
    And heavenly documents° thereout did preach,   *doctrines*
    That weaker wit° of man could never reach,   *too weak mind*
    Of God, of grace, of justice, of free will,
    That wonder was to heare her goodly speach:
    For she was able, with her words to kill,
And raise againe to life the hart, that she did thrill.°   *pierce*

20

And when she list° poure out her larger spright,°   *chose to / greater power*
    She would commaund the hastie Sunne to stay,
    Or backward turne his course from heavens hight;
    Sometimes great hostes of men she could dismay,
    Dry-shod to passe, she parts the flouds in tway;
    And eke huge mountaines from their native seat
    She would commaund, themselves to beare away,
    And throw in raging sea with roaring threat.
Almightie God her gave such powre, and puissance great.[1]

21

The faithfull knight now grew in litle space,°   *time*
    By hearing her, and by her sisters lore,
    To such perfection of all heavenly grace,
    That wretched world he gan for to abhore,[2]
    And mortall life gan loath, as thing forelore,°   *doomed*
    Greeved with remembrance of his wicked wayes,
    And prickt with anguish of his sinnes so sore,

---

1. Joshua made the sun stand still (Joshua 10.12); Hezekiah made it turn backward (2 Kings 20.10); with 300 men Gideon was victorious over the Midianite hosts (Judges 7.7); Moses led the Israelites through the parted waters of the Red Sea (Exodus 14.21–31); faith, said Christ, can move mountains (Matthew 21.21). All these are miracles of faith.
2. I.e., he began to abhor the world.

That he desirde to end his wretched dayes:
So much the dart of sinfull guilt the soule dismayes.

22

But wise Speranza gave him comfort sweet,
    And taught him how to take assurèd hold
    Upon her silver anchor, as was meet;
    Else had his sinnes so great, and manifold
    Made him forget all that Fidelia told.
    In this distressèd doubtfull° agonie,   *fearful*
    When him his dearest Una did behold,
    Disdeining life, desiring leave to die,
She found her selfe assayld with great perplexitie.°   *distress*

23

And came to Caelia to declare her smart,°   *pain*
    Who well acquainted with that commune° plight,   *common*
    Which sinfull horror° workes in wounded hart,   *horror of sin*
    Her wisely comforted all that she might,
    With goodly counsell and advisement right;
    And streightway sent with carefull diligence,
    To fetch a Leach,° the which had great insight   *doctor*
    In that disease of grievèd° consciënce,   *distressed*
And well could cure the same; His name was Patience.

24

Who comming to that soule-diseasèd knight,
    Could hardly° him intreat, to tell his griefe: *with difficulty*
    Which knowne, and all that noyd° his heavie spright   *troubled*
    Well searcht,° eftsoones° he gan apply reliefe   *probed / immediately*
    Of salves and med'cines, which had passing priefe,[3]
    And thereto added words of wondrous might:
    By which to ease he him recurèd briefe,°   *restored quickly*
    And much asswaged the passion° of his plight,   *suffering*
That he his paine endured, as seeming now more light.

25

But yet the cause and root of all his ill,
    Inward corruption, and infected sin,[4]
    Not purged nor heald, behind remainèd still,
    And festring sore did rankle yet within,
    Close° creeping twixt the marrow and the skin.   *secretly*
    Which to extirpe,° he laid him privily   *extirpate*
    Downe in a darkesome lowly place farre in,
    Whereas° he meant his corrosives to apply,   *where*
And with streight° diet tame his stubborne malady.   *strict*

---

3. Which had extraordinary power.   4. Apparently, the effects of original sin.

26

In ashes and sackcloth he did array
   His daintie corse,° proud humors[5] to abate,   *handsome body*
   And dieted with fasting every day,
   The swelling of his wounds to mitigate,
   And made him pray both earely and eke late:
   And ever as superfluous flesh did rot
   Amendment readie still at hand did wayt,
   To pluck it out with pincers firie whot,°   *hot*
That soone in him was left no one corrupted jot.

27

And bitter Penance with an yron whip,
   Was wont him once to disple° every day: *discipline*
   And sharpe Remorse his hart did pricke and nip,
   That drops of bloud thence like a well did play;
   And sad Repentance usèd to embay°   *bathe*
   His bodie in salt water smarting sore,
   The filthy blots of sinne to wash away.[6]
   So in short space they did to health restore
The man that would not live, but earst° lay at deathes dore.   *formerly*

28

In which his torment often was so great,
   That like a Lyon he would cry and rore,
   And rend his flesh, and his owne synewes eat.
   His own deare Una hearing evermore
   His ruefull shriekes and gronings, often tore
   Her guiltlesse garments, and her golden heare,
   For pitty of his paine and anguish sore;
   Yet all with patience wisely she did beare;
For well she wist, his crime could else be never cleare.°   *cleansed*

29

Whom thus recovered by wise Patience,
   And trew Repentance they to Una brought:
   Who joyous of his curèd conscience,
   Him dearely kist, and fairely° eke besought   *courteously*
   Himselfe to chearish,° and consuming thought   *cheer; cherish*
   To put away out of his carefull° brest.   *care-full*
   By this° Charissa, late° in child-bed brought,   *by this time / recently*
   Was woxen° strong, and left her fruitfull nest;   *grown*
To her faire Una brought this unacquainted guest.

---

5. The "humors" (bodily fluids) that conduce to pride. In Renaissance physiology, the proportions of the various fluids determine one's temperament. "Ashes and sackcloth": symbols of penitence.

6. "Wash me throughly from mine iniquity, and cleanse me from my sin" (Psalms 51.2).

30

She was a woman in her freshest age,
    Of wondrous beauty, and of bountie° rare,   *goodness*
    With goodly grace and comely personage,°   *appearance*
    That was on earth not easie to compare;°   *rival*
    Full of great love, but Cupids wanton snare
    As hell she hated, chast in worke and will;
    Her necke and breasts were ever open bare,
    That ay° thereof her babes might sucke their fill;   *ever*
The rest was all in yellow robes arayèd still.[7]

31

A multitude of babes about her hong,
    Playing their sports, that joyd her to behold,
    Whom still she fed, whiles they were weake and young,
    But thrust them forth° still, as they wexèd old: *i.e., weaned them*
    And on her head she wore a tyre° of gold,   *headdress*
    Adornd with gemmes and owches° wondrous faire,   *jewels*
    Whose passing° price uneath° was to be told; *surpassing / scarcely*
    And by her side there sate a gentle paire
Of turtle doves,[8] she sitting in an yvorie chaire.

32

The knight and Una entring, faire her greet,
    And bid her joy of that her happie brood;
    Who them requites with court'sies seeming meet,°   *appropriate*
    And entertaines with friendly chearefull mood.
    Then Una her besought, to be so good,
    As in her vertuous rules to schoole her knight,
    Now after all his torment well withstood,
    In that sad° house of Penaunce, where his spright   *solemn*
Had past° the paines of hell, and long enduring night. *passed through*

33

She was right joyous of her just request,
    And taking by the hand that Faeries sonne,
    Gan him instruct in every good behest,°   *command*
    Of love, and righteousness, and well to donne,°   *i.e., right action*
    And wrath, and hatred warely° to shonne,   *warily*
    That drew on men Gods hatred, and his wrath,
    And many soules in dolours° had fordonne:°   *misery / destroyed*
    In which when him she well instructed hath,
From thence to heaven she teacheth him the ready° path.   *direct*

7. Always. Her yellow (saffron) robe is the color of marriage, fertility, and maternity. Her chaste, fruitful love (Christian *agape*) is opposed to "Cupid's wanton snare" (*eros*).

8. Emblem of true love and faithful marriage.

34

Wherein his weaker° wandring steps to guide,   *too weak*
  An auncient matrone she to her does call,
  Whose sober lookes her wisedome well descride:°   *made known*
  Her name was Mercie, well knowne over all,
  To be both gratious, and eke liberall:
  To whom the carefull charge of him she gave,
  To lead aright, that he should never fall
  In all his wayes through this wide worldès wave,°   *expanse*
That Mercy in the end his righteous soule might save.

35

The godly Matrone by the hand him beares°   *leads*
  Forth from her° presence, by a narrow way,   *i.e., Charissa's*
  Scattred with bushy thornes, and ragged breares,°   *briers*
  Which still before him she removed away,
  That nothing might his ready passage stay:
  And ever when his feet encombred were,
  Or gan to shrinke, or from the right to stray,
  She held him fast, and firmely did upbeare,
As carefull Nourse her child from falling oft does reare.

36

Eftsoones unto an holy Hospitall,°   *hospice*
  That was fore° by the way, she did him bring,   *close*
  In which seven Bead-men° that had vowèd all   *men of prayer*
  Their life to service of high heavens king
  Did spend their dayes in doing godly thing:
  Their gates to all were open evermore,
  That by the wearie way were traveiling,
  And one sate wayting ever them before,
To call in commers-by, that needy were and pore.[9]

37

The first of them that eldest was, and best,°   *chiefest*
  Of all the house had charge and governement,
  As Guardian and Steward of the rest:
  His office° was to give entertainement   *duty*
  And lodging, unto all that came, and went:
  Not unto such, as could him feast againe,°   *in return*
  And double quite,° for that he on them spent,   *repay*
  But such, as want of harbour° did constraine:° *shelter / afflict*
Those for Gods sake his dewty was to entertaine.

---

9. I.e., one beadsman sat in front of the gates, to call in needy wayfarers.

38

The second was as Almner[1] of the place,
    His office was, the hungry for to feed,
    And thristy give to drinke, a worke of grace:
    He feard not once him selfe to be in need,
    Ne cared to hoord for those, whom he did breede:°   *i.e., his children*
    The grace of God he layd up still in store,
    Which as a stocke° he left unto his seede;°   *resource / children*
    He had enough, what need him care for more?
And had he lesse, yet some he would give to the pore.

39

The third had of their wardrobe custodie,
    In which were not rich tyres,° nor garments gay,   *attire*
    The plumes of pride, and wings of vanitie,
    But clothes meet to keepe keene could° away,   *cold*
    And naked nature seemely° to aray;   *decently*
    With which bare wretched wights he dayly clad,
    The images of God in earthly clay;
    And if that no spare clothes to give he had,
His owne coate he would cut, and it distribute glad.

40

The fourth appointed by his office was,
    Poore prisoners to relieve with gratious ayd,
    And captives to redeeme with price of bras,°   *payment of money*
    From Turkes and Sarazins, which them had stayd;°   *held captive*
    And though they faultie were, yet well he wayd,
    That God to us forgiveth every howre
    Much more then that, why° they in bands° were layd,   *for which / bonds*
    And he that harrowd hell[2] with heavie stowre,°   *assault*
The faultie° soules from thence brought to his heavenly bowre.   *sinful*

41

The fift had charge sicke persons to attend,
    And comfort those, in point of death which lay;
    For them most needeth comfort in the end,
    When sin, and hell, and death do most dismay
    The feeble soule departing hence away.
    All is but lost, that living we bestow,°   *store up*
    If not well ended at our dying day.
    O man have mind of that last bitter throw;°   *throes of death*
For as the tree does fall, so lyes it ever low.[3]

---

1. An almoner distributed charity (*alms*) to the poor.
2. Christ, who journeyed to hell to deliver those good people who lived before his time, according to a story popular in the Middle Ages. It originated in the apocryphal gospel of Nicodemus (cf. *Piers Plowman*, Passus 18).
3. "In the place where the tree falleth, there it shall be" (Ecclesiastes 11.3).

42

The sixt had charge of them now being dead,
    In seemely sort their corses to engrave,°   *bodies to bury*
    And deck with dainty flowres their bridall bed,
    That to their heavenly spouse° both sweet and brave° *i.e., Christ / fair*
    They might appeare, when he their soules shall save.
    The wondrous workemanship of Gods owne mould,[4]
    Whose face he made, all beasts to feare, and gave
    All in his hand,[5] even dead we honour should.
Ah dearest God me graunt, I dead be not defould.°   *defiled*

43

The seventh now after death and buriall done,
    Had charge the tender Orphans of the dead
    And widowes ayd, least° they should be undone: *lest*
    In face of judgement° he their right would plead, *i.e., in court*
    Ne ought° the powre of mighty men did dread   *nor at all*
    In their defence, nor would for gold or fee°   *bribe*
    Be wonne their rightfull causes downe to tread:
    And when they stood in most necessitee,
He did supply their want, and gave them ever free.[6]

44

There when the Elfin knight arrivèd was,
    The first and chiefest of the seven, whose care
    Was guests to welcome, towardes him did pas:
    Where seeing Mercie, that his steps up bare,°   *supported*
    And alwayes led, to her with reverence rare
    He humbly louted° in meeke lowlinesse,   *bowed*
    And seemely welcome for her did prepare:
    For of their order she was Patronesse,
Albe° Charissa were their chiefest founderesse.   *although*

45

There she awhile him stayes, him selfe to rest,
    That to the rest more able he might bee:
    During which time, in every good behest°   *command*
    And godly worke of Almes and charitee
    She him instructed with great industree;
    Shortly therein so perfect he became,
    That from the first unto the last degree,
    His mortall life he learnèd had to frame
In holy righteousnesse, without rebuke or blame.

4. The human body is God's own image ("mould") and a "mould" of God's making (see Genesis 1.26–30, 2.7).
5. "And the fear of you and the dread of you shall be upon every beast of the earth, and upon every fowl of the air, upon all that moveth upon the earth, and upon all the fishes of the sea; into your hand are they delivered" (Genesis 9.2).
6. Always freely. The seven beadsmen here correspond to, and perform, the seven works of charity, or corporal mercy: lodging the homeless, feeding the hungry, clothing the naked, redeeming the captive, comforting the sick, burying the dead, and succoring the orphan.

46

Thence forward by that painfull way they pas,
    Forth to an hill, that was both steepe and hy;
    On top whereof a sacred chappell was,
    And eke a litle Hermitage thereby,
    Wherein an agèd holy man did lye,°   *live*
    That day and night said his devotïon,
    Ne other worldly busines did apply;[7]
    His name was heavenly Contemplation;
Of God and goodnesse was his meditation.

47

Great grace that old man to him given had;
    For God he often saw from heavens hight,
    All° were his earthly eyen both blunt° and bad,   *although / dim*
    And through great age had lost their kindly° sight,   *natural*
    Yet wondrous quick and persant° was his spright,°   *piercing / spirit*
    As Eagles eye, that can behold the Sunne:
    That hill they scale with all their powre and might,
    That his frayle thighes nigh wearie and fordonne°   *exhausted*
Gan faile, but by her helpe the top at last he wonne.

48

There they do finde that godly agèd Sire,
    With snowy lockes adowne his shoulders shed,
    As hoarie frost with spangles doth attire
    The mossy braunches of an Oke halfe ded.
    Each bone might through his body well be red,°   *seen*
    And every sinew seene through° his long fast: *because of*
    For nought he cared his carcas long unfed;
    His mind was full of spirituall repast,
And pyned° his flesh, to keepe his body low° and chast.   *starved / weak*

49

Who when these two approching he aspide,
    At their first presence grew agrievèd sore,[8]
    That forst him lay his heavenly thoughts aside;
    And had he not that Dame respected more,°   *greatly*
    Whom highly he did reverence and adore,
    He would not once have movèd for the knight.
    They him saluted standing far afore;°   *away*
    Who well them greeting, humbly did requight,°   *respond*
And askèd, to what end they clomb° that tedious height.   *had climbed*

50

    "What end," quoth she, "should cause us take such paine,
    But that same end, which every living wight

---

7. I.e., he did not attend to any worldly activities.   8. I.e., he was at first sorely grieved at their arrival.

Should make his marke,° high heaven to attaine?   *goal*
Is not from hence the way, that leadeth right
To that most glorious house, that glistreth bright
With burning starres, and everliving fire,
Whereof the keyes are to thy hand behight°   *entrusted*
By wise Fidelia? she doth thee require,
To shew it to this knight, according° his desire."   *granting*

51

"Thrise happy man," said then the father grave,
   "Whose staggering steps thy° steady hand doth lead,   *i.e., Mercy's*
   And shewes the way, his sinfull soule to save.
   Who better can the way to heaven aread°   *direct*
   Then thou thy selfe, that was both borne and bred
   In heavenly throne, where thousand Angels shine?
   Thou doest the prayers of the righteous sead°   *seed*
   Present before the majestie divine,
And his avenging wrath to clemencie incline.

52

"Yet since thou bidst, thy pleasure shalbe donne.
   Then come thou man of earth,⁹ and see the way,
   That never yet was seene of Faeries sonne,
   That never leads the traveiler astray,
   But after labours long, and sad delay,
   Brings them to joyous rest and endlesse blis.
   But first thou must a season fast and pray,
   Till from her bands the spright assoilèd° is,   *spirit released*
And have her strength recured° from fraile infirmitis."   *recovered*

53

That done, he leads him to the highest Mount;
   Such one, as that same mighty man of God,
   That bloud-red billowes like a wallèd front
   On either side disparted° with his rod,   *parted asunder*
   Till that his army dry-foot through them yod,°   *went*
   Dwelt fortie dayes upon; where writ in stone
   With bloudy letters by the hand of God,
   The bitter doome of death and balefull mone¹
He did receive, whiles flashing fire about him shone.

54

Or like that sacred hill, whose head full hie,
   Adornd with fruitfull Olives all arownd,

---

9. An allusion to humankind's formation from the dust of the earth (Genesis 2.7) and also to the knight's name (see below, stanza 66 and note).
1. I.e., the Ten Commandments ("bloudy let-ters") carried with them the judgment ("doome") of death and pain (causing sorrowful moans—"balefull mone").

Is, as it were for endlesse memory
  Of that deare Lord, who oft thereon was fownd,
  For ever with a flowring girlond crownd:
  Or like that pleasaunt Mount, that is for ay
  Through famous Poets verse each where° renownd,   *everywhere*
  On which the thrise three learned Ladies play
Their heavenly notes, and make full many a lovely lay.[2]

55

From thence, far off he unto him did shew
  A litle path, that was both steepe and long,
  Which to a goodly Citie led his vew;
  Whose wals and towres were builded high and strong
  Of perle and precious stone, that earthly tong
  Cannot describe, nor wit of man can tell;
  Too high a ditty° for my simple song;   *subject*
  The Citie of the great king hight° it well,   *is called*
Wherein eternall peace and happinesse doth dwell.

56

As he thereon stood gazing, he might° see   *could*
  The blessed Angels to and fro descend
  From highest heaven, in gladsome companee,
  And with great joy into that Citie wend,
  As commonly° as friend does with his frend.[3]   *familiarly*
  Whereat he wondred much, and gan enquere,
  What stately building durst so high extend
  Her loftie towres unto the starry sphere,
And what unknowen nation there empeopled were.

57

"Faire knight," quoth he, "Hierusalem that is,
  The new Hierusalem, that God has built
  For those to dwell in, that are chosen his,
  His chosen people purged from sinfull guilt,
  With pretious bloud, which cruelly was spilt
  On cursèd tree, of that unspotted lam,[4]
  That for the sinnes of all the world was kilt:
  Now are they Saints all in that Citie sam,°   *together*
More deare unto their God, then younglings to their dam."[5]

---

2. Song. The mountain is successively compared to Mount Sinai, where Moses, after parting the "bloud-red billowes" of the Red Sea, received the tablets of the Ten Commandments; to the Mount of Olives, associated with Christ; and to Mount Parnassus, where the Nine Muses of art and poetry dwelt.
3. Cf. Jacob's ladder, which "reached to heaven; and behold the angels of God ascending and descending on it" (Genesis 28.12).
4. Christ (the lamb of God), whose death on the cross ("cursèd tree") purged the guilt of sin from those "chosen his."
5. The New Jerusalem is described in Revelation 21–22; "the nations of them which are saved shall walk in the light of it" (21.24).

58

"Till now," said then the knight, "I weenèd well,
    That great Cleopolis,[6] where I have beene,
    In which that fairest Faerie Queene doth dwell,
    The fairest Citie was, that might be seene;
    And that bright towre all built of christall cleene,°   *clear*
    Panthea,[7] seemd the brightest thing, that was:
    But now by proofe° all otherwise I weene;   *experience*
    For this great Citie that[8] does far surpas,
And this bright Angels towre quite dims that towre of glas."

59

"Most trew," then said the holy agèd man;
    "Yet is Cleopolis for earthly frame,°   *structure*
    The fairest peece,° that eye beholden can: *masterpiece*
    And well beseemes° all knights of noble name,   *becomes*
    That covet in th'immortall booke of fame
    To be eternizèd, that same to haunt,°   *frequent*
    And doen their service to that soveraigne Dame,
    That glorie does to them for guerdon° graunt: *reward*
For she is heavenly borne, and heaven may justly vaunt.[9]

60

"And thou faire ymp,° sprong out from English race,   *youth*
    How ever now accompted° Elfins sonne,   *accounted*
    Well worthy doest thy service for her grace,°   *favor*
    To aide a virgin desolate foredonne.°   *undone*
    But when thou famous victorie hast wonne,
    And high emongst all knights hast hong thy shield,
    Thenceforth the suit° of earthly conquest shonne,   *pursuit*
    And wash thy hands from guilt of bloudy field:
For bloud can nought but sin, and wars but sorrowes yield.

61

"Then seeke this path, that I to thee presage,°   *show prophetically*
    Which after all to heaven shall thee send;
    Then peaceably thy painefull° pilgrimage   *laborious*
    To yonder same Hierusalem do bend,
    Where is for thee ordaind a blessèd end:
    For thou emongst those Saints, whom thou doest see,
    Shalt be a Saint, and thine owne nations frend
    And Patrone: thou Saint George shalt callèd bee,
Saint George of mery England, the signe of victoree."[1]

---

6. "City of Fame"; in the historical allegory, London or Westminster.
7. Reminiscent of the temple of glass in Chaucer's *House of Fame*; perhaps intended to allude to Westminster Abbey as pantheon of the English great.

8. I.e., the New Jerusalem far surpasses Cleopolis ("that").
9. I.e., may justly boast ("vaunt") that heaven is her home.
1. Spenser's conception of St. George, patron saint of England, draws on the *Legenda Aurea*

62

"Unworthy wretch," quoth he, "of so great grace,
  How dare I thinke such glory to attaine?"
"These that have it attaind, were in like cace,"
Quoth he, "as wretched, and lived in like paine."
  "But deeds of armes must I at last be faine,°   *content (to leave)*
  And Ladies love to leave so dearely bought?"
  "What need of armes, where peace doth ay° remaine,"   *ever*
  Said he, "and battailes none are to be fought?
As for loose° loves are° vaine, and vanish into nought."   *wanton / i.e., they are*

63

"O let me not," quoth he, "then turne againe
  Backe to the world, whose joyes so fruitlesse are;
  But let me here for aye in peace remaine,
  Or streight way on that last long voyage fare,
  That nothing may my present hope empare."°   *impair*
  "That may not be," said he, "ne maist thou yit
  Forgo that royall maides bequeathèd care,°   *charge*
  Who did her cause into thy hand commit,
Till from her cursèd foe thou have her freely quit."°   *released*

64

"Then shall I soone," quoth he, "so God me grace,
  Abet° that virgins cause disconsolate,   *maintain*
  And shortly backe returne unto this place
  To walke this way in Pilgrims poore estate.
  But now aread,° old father, why of late   *declare*
  Didst thou behight° me borne of English blood,   *call*
  Whom all a Faeries sonne doen nominate?"°   *name*
  "That word shall I," said he, "avouchen° good,   *prove*
Sith° to thee is unknowne the cradle of thy brood.   *since*

65

"For well I wote,° thou springst from ancient race   *know*
  Of Saxon kings, that have with mightie hand
  And many bloudie battailes fought in place°   *there*
  High reard their royall throne in Britane land,
  And vanquisht them,° unable to withstand: *i.e., the ancient Britons*
  From thence a Faerie thee unweeting reft,°   *secretly stole*
  There as thou slepst in tender swadling band,
  And her base Elfin brood° there for thee left.   *offspring*
Such men do Chaungelings call, so chaungd by Faeries theft.

(*The Golden Legend*—a medieval manual of ecclesiastical lore, translated into English by William Caxton in 1487) and on pictures, tapestries, pageants, and folklore.

66

"Thence she thee brought into this Faerie lond,
 And in an heapèd furrow did thee hyde,
 Where thee a Ploughman all unweeting° fond,   *unknowing*
 As he his toylesome teme° that way did guyde,   *team of oxen*
 And brought thee up in ploughmans state to byde,
 Whereof Georgos he thee gave to name;[2]
 Till prickt° with courage, and thy forces pryde,   *spurred*
 To Faery court thou cam'st to seeke for fame,
And prove thy puissaunt° armes, as seemes thee best became."[3]   *powerful*

67

"O holy Sire," quoth he, "how shall I quight°   *repay*
 The many favours I with thee have found,
 That hast my name and nation red° aright,   *declared*
 And taught the way that does to heaven bound?"°   *go*
 This said, adowne he lookèd to the ground,
 To have returnd, but dazèd° were his eyne,   *dazzled*
 Through passing° brightnesse, which did quite confound   *surpassing*
 His feeble sence, and too exceeding shyne.
So darke are earthly things compard to things divine.

68

At last whenas himselfe he gan to find,°   *recover*
 To Una back he cast him to retire;
 Who him awaited still with pensive° mind.   *anxious*
 Great thankes and goodly meed° to that good syre,   *gift*
 He thence departing gave for his paines hyre.°   *reward*
 So came to Una, who him joyd to see,
 And after litle rest, gan him desire,
 Of her adventure mindfull for to bee.
So leave they take of Caelia, and her daughters three.

Canto 11

The knight with that old Dragon fights
two dayes incessantly:
The third him overthrowes, and gayns
most glorious victory.

1

High time now gan it wex° for Una faire,   *grow*
 To thinke of those her captive Parents deare,
 And their forwasted kingdome to repaire:[4]
 Whereto whenas they now approachèd neare,
 With hartie° words her knight she gan to cheare,   *bold*

2. I.e., as a name. *Georgos* is Greek for "farmer" (cf. Virgil's *Georgics*, on farming).
3. As best suited you.
4. I.e., to restore their kingdom, laid waste (by the dragon).

And in her modest manner thus bespake;
  "Deare knight, as deare, as ever knight was deare,
  That all these sorrowes suffer for my sake,
High heaven behold the tedious toyle, ye for me take.

2

"Now are we come unto my native soyle,
  And to the place, where all our perils dwell;
  Here haunts that feend, and does his dayly spoyle,
  Therefore henceforth be at your keeping well,°   *be well on your guard*
  And ever ready for your foeman fell.
  The sparke of noble courage now awake,
  And strive your excellent selfe to excell;
  That shall ye evermore renowmèd make,
Above all knights on earth, that batteill undertake."

3

And pointing forth, "lo yonder is," said she,
  "The brasen towre in which my parents deare
  For dread of that huge feend emprisond be,
  Whom I from far see on the walles appeare,
  Whose sight my feeble soule doth greatly cheare:
  And on the top of all I do espye
  The watchman wayting tydings glad to heare,
  That O my parents might I happily
Unto you bring, to ease you of your misery."

4

With that they heard a roaring hideous sound,
  That all the ayre with terrour fillèd wide,
  And seemd uneath° to shake the stedfast ground.   *almost*
  Eftsoones° that dreadfull Dragon they espide,   *immediately*
  Where stretcht he lay upon the sunny side
  Of a great hill, himselfe like a great hill.
  But all so soone, as he from far descride
  Those glistring armes, that heaven with light did fill,
He rousd himselfe full blith,° and hastned them untill.°   *joyfully / toward*

5

Then bad° the knight his Lady yede° aloofe,   *bade / go*
  And to an hill her selfe withdraw aside,
  From whence she might behold that battailles proof°   *outcome*
  And eke° be safe from daunger far descryde:°   *also / observed from afar*
  She him obayd, and turnd a little wyde.°   *aside*
  Now O thou sacred Muse, most learnèd Dame,
  Faire ympe° of Phoebus, and his agèd bride,[5]   *child*
  The Nourse of time, and everlasting fame,
That warlike hands ennoblest with immortall name;

---

5. I.e., Mnemosyne (memory), mother of the Muses.

6

O gently come into my feeble brest,
   Come gently, but not with that mighty rage,
   Wherewith the martiall troupes thou doest infest,°   *arouse*
   And harts of great Heroes doest enrage,
   That nought their kindled courage may aswage,
   Soone as thy dreadfull trompe° begins to sownd;   *trumpet*
   The God of warre with his fiers equipage
   Thou doest awake, sleepe never he so sownd,
And scarèd nations doest with horrour sterne astown.°   *appall*

7

Faire Goddesse lay that furious fit° aside,   *strain*
   Till I of warres and bloudy Mars do sing,[6]
   And Briton fields with Sarazin° bloud bedyde,°   *Saracen / dyed*
   Twixt that great faery Queene and Paynim° king,   *pagan*
   That with their horrour heaven and earth did ring,
   A worke of labour long, and endlesse prayse:
   But now a while let downe that haughtie string,
   And to my tunes thy second tenor rayse,[7]
That I this man of God his godly armes may blaze.°   *proclaim*

8

By this the dreadfull Beast drew nigh to hand,
   Halfe flying, and halfe footing° in his hast,   *walking*
   That with his largenesse measurèd much land,
   And made wide shadow under his huge wast;°   *girth*
   As mountaine doth the valley overcast.
   Approching nigh, he rearèd high afore
   His body monstrous, horrible, and vast,
   Which to increase his wondrous greatnesse more,
Was swolne with wrath, and poyson, and with bloudy gore.

9

And over, all with brasen scales was armd,
   Like plated coate of steele, so couchèd neare,°   *placed so closely*
   That nought mote perce,[8] ne might his corse° be harmd   *body*
   With dint of sword, nor push of pointed speare;
   Which as an Eagle, seeing pray appeare,
   His aery Plumes doth rouze,° full rudely dight,°   *shake / ruggedly arrayed*
   So shakèd he, that horrour was to heare,
   For as the clashing of an Armour bright,
Such noyse his rouzèd scales did send unto the knight.

---

6. Perhaps a reference to a projected but unwritten book of *The Faerie Queene*.
7. The "haughtie" (high-pitched) mode would be

appropriate to a large-scale epic war; the "second tenor" (lower in pitch) to this present battle.
8. Nothing might pierce.

10

His flaggy° wings when forth he did display,   *drooping*
  Were like two sayles, in which the hollow wynd
  Is gathered full, and worketh speedy way:
  And eke the pennes, that did his pineons bynd,
  Were like mayne-yards, with flying canvas lynd,[9]
  With which whenas him list° the ayre to beat,   *he chose*
  And there by force unwonted° passage find,   *unaccustomed*
  The cloudes before him fled for terrour great,
And all the heavens stood still amazèd with his threat.

11

His huge long tayle wound up in hundred foldes,
  Does overspred his long bras-scaly backe,
  Whose wreathèd boughts° when ever he unfoldes,   *coils*
  And thicke entangled knots adown does slacke,
  Bespotted as with shields° of red and blacke,   *scales*
  It sweepeth all the land behind him farre,
  And of three furlongs[1] does but litle lacke;
  And at the point two stings in-fixèd arre,
Both deadly sharpe, that sharpest steele exceeden farre.

12

But stings and sharpest steele did far exceed°   *i.e., were far exceeded by*
  The sharpnesse of his cruell rending clawes;
  Dead was it sure, as sure as death in deed,°   *in its effect*
  What ever thing does touch his ravenous pawes,
  Or what within his reach he ever drawes.
  But his most hideous head my toung to tell
  Does tremble: for his deepe devouring jawes
  Wide gapèd, like the griesly° mouth of hell,   *horrid*
Through which into his darke abisse all ravin° fell.   *prey; booty*

13

And that° more wondrous was, in either jaw   *what*
  Three ranckes of yron teeth enraungèd were,
  In which yet trickling bloud and gobbets raw°   *chunks of unswallowed food*
  Of late° devourèd bodies did appeare,   *recently*
  That sight thereof bred cold congealèd feare:
  Which to increase, and all at once to kill,
  A cloud of smoothering smoke and sulphur seare°   *burning*
  Out of his stinking gorge° forth steemèd still,   *maw*
That all the ayre about with smoke and stench did fill.

---

9. I.e., the ribs of his wings were like the massive   affixed.
spars (main yards) to which a ship's mainsail is   1. I.e., three-eighths of a mile.

14

His blazing eyes, like two bright shining shields,
  Did burne with wrath, and sparkled living fyre;
  As two broad Beacons, set in open fields,
  Send forth their flames farre off to every shyre,°   *shire*
  And warning give, that enemies conspyre,
  With fire and sword the region to invade;
  So flamed his eyne° with rage and rancorous yre:°   *eyes / ire, anger*
  But farre within, as in a hollow glade,
Those glaring lampes were set, that made a dreadfull shade.

15

So dreadfully he towards him did pas,
  Forelifting up aloft his speckled brest,
  And often bounding on the brusèd gras,
  As for great joyance of his newcome guest.
  Eftsoones he gan advance his haughtie crest,
  As chauffèd° Bore his bristles doth upreare,   *angry*
  And shoke his scales to battell readie drest;°   *prepared*
  That made the Redcrosse knight nigh quake for feare,
As bidding bold defiance to his foeman neare.

16

The knight gan fairely couch° his steadie speare,   *level*
  And fiercely ran at him with rigorous° might: *violent*
  The pointed steele arriving rudely° theare,   *roughly*
  His harder hide would neither perce, nor bight,
  But glauncing by forth passèd forward right;
  Yet sore amovèd with so puissant push,
  The wrathfull beast about him turnèd light,°   *quickly*
  And him so rudely passing by, did brush
With his long tayle, that horse and man to ground did rush.

17

Both horse and man up lightly rose againe,
  And fresh encounter towards him addrest:
  But th'idle stroke yet backe recoyld in vaine,
  And found no place his° deadly point to rest.   *its*
  Exceeding rage enflamed the furious beast,
  To be avengèd of so great despight;°   *outrage*
  For never felt his imperceable brest
  So wondrous force, from hand of living wight;
Yet had he provèd° the powre of many a puissant knight.   *tested*

18

Then with his waving wings displayèd wyde,
  Himselfe up high he lifted from the ground,
  And with strong flight did forcibly divide
  The yielding aire, which nigh° too feeble found   *nearly*

Her flitting° partes, and element unsound,°   *moving / weak*
To beare so great a weight: he cutting way
With his broad sayles, about him soarèd round:
At last low stouping with unweldie sway,°   *ponderous force*
Snatcht up both horse and man, to beare them quite away.

19

Long he them bore above the subject plaine,°   *i.e., the ground below*
   So farre as Ewghen° bow a shaft may send,   *yewen, of yew*
   Till struggling strong did him at last constraine,
   To let them downe before his flightès end:
   As hagard° hauke presuming to contend   *untamed*
   With hardie fowle, above his hable might,°   *able power*
   His wearie pounces° all in vaine doth spend,   *claws*
   To trusse° the pray too heavie for his flight;   *seize*
Which comming downe to ground, does free it selfe by fight.

20

He so disseizèd of his gryping grosse,[2]
   The knight his thrilant° speare againe assayd   *piercing*
   In his bras-plated body to embosse,°   *plunge*
   And three mens strength unto the stroke he layd;
   Wherewith the stiffe beame quakèd, as affrayd,
   And glauncing from his scaly necke, did glyde
   Close under his left wing, then broad displayd.
   The percing steele there wrought a wound full wyde,
That with the uncouth° smart the Monster lowdly cryde.   *unfamiliar*

21

He cryde, as raging seas are wont° to rore,   *accustomed*
   When wintry storme his wrathfull wreck° does threat,   *ruin*
   The rolling billowes beat the ragged shore,
   As° they the earth would shoulder from her seat,   *as if*
   And greedie gulfe° does gape, as he would eat   *i.e., the sea*
   His neighbour element° in his revenge: *i.e., earth*
   Then gin the blustring brethren° boldly threat,   *the winds*
   To move the world from off his stedfast henge,°   *axis*
And boystrous battell make, each other to avenge.

22

The steely head stucke fast still in his flesh,
   Till with his cruell clawes he snatcht the wood,
   And quite a sunder broke. Forth flowèd fresh
   A gushing river of blacke goarie° blood,   *clotted*
   That drownèd all the land, whereon he stood;
   The stream thereof would drive a water-mill.
   Trebly augmented was his furious mood

2. Freed from his formidable grip.

With bitter sense of his deepe rooted ill,°   injury
That flames of fire he threw forth from his large nosethrill.°   nostril

23

His hideous tayle then hurlèd he about,
  And therewith all enwrapt the nimble thyes°   thighs
  Of his froth-fomy steed, whose courage stout
  Striving to loose the knot, that fast him tyes,
  Himselfe in streighter° bandes too rash implyes,[3]   tighter
  That to the ground he is perforce° constraynd   of necessity
  To throw his rider: who can° quickly ryse   did
  From off the earth, with durty bloud distaynd,°   defiled
For that reprochfull fall right fowly he disdaynd.°   resented

24

And fiercely tooke his trenchand° blade in hand,   sharp
  With which he stroke so furious and so fell,°   fiercely
  That nothing seemd the puissance could withstand:
  Upon his crest the hardned yron fell,
  But his more hardned crest was armd so well,
  That deeper dint therein it would not make;[4]
  Yet so extremely did the buffe° him quell,°   blow / dismay
  That from thenceforth he shund the like to take,
But when he saw them come, he did them still forsake.°   avoid

25

The knight was wrath to see his stroke beguyld,°   foiled
  And smote againe with more outrageous might;
  But backe againe the sparckling steele recoyld,
  And left not any marke, where it did light;
  As if in Adamant rocke it had bene pight.°   struck against
  The beast impatient of his smarting wound,
  And of so fierce and forcible despight,°   powerful injury
  Thought with his wings to stye° above the ground;   mount
But his late wounded wing unserviceable found.

26

Then full of griefe and anguish vehement,
  He lowdly brayd, that like was never heard,
  And from his wide devouring oven sent
  A flake of fire, that flashing in his beard,
  Him all amazd, and almost made affeard;
  The scorching flame sore swingèd° all his face,   singed
  And through his armour all his bodie seard,
  That he could not endure so cruell cace,°   plight
But thought his armes to leave, and helmet to unlace.

---

3. I.e., too quickly entangles.   4. I.e., it could not make a deep gash there.

27

Not that great Champion of the antique world,
   Whom famous Poetes verse so much doth vaunt,
   And hath for twelve huge labours high extold,
   So many furies and sharpe fits did haunt,
   When him the poysoned garment did enchaunt
   With Centaures bloud, and bloudie verses charmed,
   As did this knight twelve thousand dolours° daunt,   *pains*
   Whom fyrie steele now burnt, that earst° him armed,   *formerly*
That erst him goodly armed, now most of all him harmed.[5]

28

Faint, wearie, sore, emboylèd, grievèd, brent°   *burned*
   With heat, toyle, wounds, armes, smart, and inward fire
   That never man such mischiefes° did torment;   *misfortunes*
   Death better were, death did he oft desire,
   But death will never come, when needes require.
   Whom so dismayd when that his foe beheld,
   He cast to suffer° him no more respire,°   *allow / live*
   But gan his sturdie sterne° about to weld,°   *tail / lash*
And him so strongly stroke, that to the ground him feld.

29

It fortunèd (as faire it then befell)
   Behind his backe unweeting,° where he stood,   *unnoticed*
   Of auncient time there was a springing well,
   From which fast trickled forth a silver flood,
   Full of great vertues,° and for med'cine good.   *powers*
   Whylome,° before that cursèd Dragon got   *formerly*
   That happie land, and all with innocent blood
   Defyld those sacred waves, it rightly hot°   *was called*
The Well of Life,[6] ne yet his vertues had forgot.

30

For unto life the dead it could restore,
   And guilt of sinfull crimes cleane wash away,
   Those that with sicknesse were infected sore,
   It could recure, and agèd long decay
   Renew, as one were borne that very day.
   Both Silo this, and Jordan did excell,
   And th'English Bath, and eke the german Spau,

---

5. Redcrosse's fire baptism is compared with the burning shirt of Nessus, which killed Hercules, "that great Champion of the antique world" (line 1). His "twelve huge labours" are paralleled to the knight's "twelve thousand dolours."
6. An allusion to Revelation 22.1–2: "And he showed me a pure river of water of life, clear as crystal, proceeding out of the throne of God, and of the Lamb. In the midst of the street of it, and on either side of the river, was the tree of life which bare twelve manner of fruits and yielded her fruit every month: and the leaves of the tree were for the healing of the nations."

Ne can Cephise, nor Hebrus match this well:
Into the same the knight backe overthrowen, fell.[7]

31

Now gan the golden Phoebus for to steepe
  His fierie face in billowes of the west,
  And his faint steedes watred in Ocean deepe,
  Whiles from their journall° labours they did rest,   *daily*
  When that infernall Monster, having kest°   *cast*
  His wearie foe into that living well,
  Can° high advaunce his broad discoloured brest,   *did*
  Above his wonted pitch,° with countenance fell,°   *height / sinister*
And clapt his yron wings, as victor he did dwell.°   *remain*

32

Which when his pensive° Ladie saw from farre,   *anxious*
  Great woe and sorrow did her soule assay,°   *assail*
  As weening° that the sad end of the warre,   *thinking*
  And gan to highest God entirely° pray,   *earnestly*
  That feared chaunce° from her to turne away;   *fate*
  With folded hands and knees full lowly bent
  All night she watcht, ne once adowne would lay
  Her daintie limbs in her sad dreriment,°   *dismal condition*
But praying still did wake, and waking did lament.

33

The morrow next gan early to appeare,
  That° Titan° rose to runne his daily race;   *when / the sun god*
  But early ere the morrow next gan reare
  Out of the sea faire Titans deawy face,
  Up rose the gentle virgin from her place,
  And looked all about, if she might spy
  Her loved knight to move° his manly pace: *i.e., moving*
  For she had great doubt of his safety,
Since late she saw him fall before his enemy.

34

At last she saw, where he upstarted brave
  Out of the well, wherein he drenched lay;
  As Eagle fresh out of the Ocean wave,
  Where he hath left his plumes all hoary gray,
  And deckt himselfe with feathers youthly gay,
  Like Eyas hauke° up mounts unto the skies,   *unfledged hawk*
  His newly budded pineons to assay,

7. The Well of Life, with its powers of renewal, is successively compared with waters of the Bible, of England and Europe, and of classical antiquity. In the pool of Siloam ("Silo"), a blind man was cured by Christ (John 9.7); water of the river Jordan cured Naaman of leprosy (2 Kings 5.14) and Christ was baptized therein (Matthew 3.16). "Bath" and "Spau" (Spa) were famed for their medicinal waters. "Cephise" and "Hebrus" in Greece were rivers noted for purifying and healing powers.

And marveiles at himselfe, still as he flies:
So new this new-borne knight to battell new did rise.

35

Whom when the damnèd feend so fresh did spy,
  No wonder if he wondred at the sight,
  And doubted, whether his late enemy
  It were, or other new supplièd knight.
  He, now to prove° his late renewèd might,   *try*
  High brandishing his bright deaw-burning blade,
  Upon his crested scalpe so sore did smite,
  That to the scull a yawning wound it made:
The deadly dint° his dullèd senses all dismaid.   *blow*

36

I wote° not, whether the revenging steele   *know*
  Were hardnèd with that holy water dew,
  Wherein he fell, or sharper edge did feele,
  Or his baptizèd hands now greater° grew;   *stronger*
  Or other secret vertue° did ensew;   *power*
  Else never could the force of fleshly arme,
  Ne molten mettall in his bloud embrew:°   *plunge*
  For till that stownd° could never wight him harme,   *moment*
By subtilty, nor slight,° nor might, nor mighty charme.   *trickery*

37

The cruell wound enragèd him so sore,
  That loud he yellèd for exceeding paine;
  As hundred ramping° Lyons seemed to rore,   *rearing*
  Whom ravenous hunger did thereto constraine:
  Then gan he tosse aloft his stretchèd traine,°   *tail*
  And therewith scourge the buxome° aire so sore,   *yielding*
  That to his force to yeelden it was faine;°   *obliged*
  Ne ought his sturdie strokes might stand afore,[8]
That high trees overthrew, and rocks in peeces tore.

38

The same advauncing high above his head,
  With sharpe intended° sting so rude° him smot,   *extended / roughly*
  That to the earth him drove, as stricken dead,
  Ne living wight would have him life behot:[9]
  The mortall sting his angry needle shot
  Quite through his shield, and in his shoulder seasd,
  Where fast it stucke, ne would there out be got:
  The griefe° thereof him wondrous sore diseasd,°   *pain / afflicted*
Ne might his ranckling paine with patience be appeasd.

8. I.e., neither could anything ("ought") stand before his violent ("sturdie") strokes.

9. Promised. I.e., no one would have thought he could survive the blow.

39

But yet more mindfull of his honour deare,
    Then° of the grievous smart, which him did wring,°   *than / torment*
    From loathèd soile he can° him lightly reare,   *did*
    And strove to loose the farre infixèd sting:
    Which when in vaine he tryde with struggeling,
    Inflamed with wrath, his raging blade he heft,°   *heaved*
    And strooke so strongly, that the knotty string
    Of his huge taile he quite a sunder cleft,
Five joynts thereof he hewd, and but the stump him left.

40

Hart cannot thinke, what outrage,° and what cryes,   *violent clamor*
    With foule enfouldred[1] smoake and flashing fire,
    The hell-bred beast threw forth unto the skyes,
    That all was coverèd with darknesse dire:
    Then fraught° with rancour, and engorgèd° ire,   *filled / swollen*
    He cast at once him to avenge for all,
    And gathering up himselfe out of the mire,
    With his uneven wings did fiercely fall
Upon his sunne-bright shield, and gript it fast withall.

41

Much was the man encombred with his hold,
    In feare to lose his weapon in his paw,
    Ne wist° yet, how his talents° to unfold;   *knew / talons*
    Nor harder was from Cerberus[2] greedie jaw
    To plucke a bone, then from his cruell claw
    To reave° by strength the gripèd gage° away: *seize / prize*
    Thrise he assayd° it from his foot to draw,   *tried*
    And thrise in vaine to draw it did assay,
It booted nought to thinke, to robbe him of his pray.

42

Tho° when he saw no power might prevaile,   *then*
    His trustie sword he cald to his last aid,
    Wherewith he fiercely did his foe assaile,
    And double blowes about him stoutly laid,
    That glauncing fire out of the yron plaid;
    As sparckles from the Andvile° use to fly,   *anvil*
    When heavie hammers on the wedge are swaid;°   *struck*
    Therewith at last he forst him to unty°   *loosen*
One of his grasping feete, him to defend thereby.

43

The other foot, fast fixèd on his shield,
    Whenas no strength, nor stroks mote° him constraine   *might*

---

1. Black as a thundercloud.   2. The dog that guards the mouth of Hades.

To loose, ne yet the warlike pledge to yield,
He smot thereat with all his might and maine,
That nought so wondrous puissance might sustaine;
Upon the joynt the lucky steele did light,
And made such way, that hewd it quite in twaine;
The paw yet missèd not his minisht° might,   *lessened*
But hong still on the shield, as it at first was pight.°   *placed*

44

For griefe° thereof, and divelish despight,   *pain*
From his infernall fournace forth he threw
Huge flames, that dimmèd all the heavens light,
Enrold in duskish smoke and brimstone blew;
As burning Aetna from his boyling stew°   *cauldron*
Doth belch out flames, and rockes in peeces broke,
And ragged ribs of mountaines molten new
Enwrapt in coleblacke clouds and filthy smoke,
That all the land with stench, and heaven with horror choke.

45

The heate whereof, and harmefull pestilence
So sore him noyd,° that forst him to retire   *troubled*
A little backward for his best defence,
To save his bodie from the scorching fire,
Which he from hellish entrailes did expire.°   *breathe out*
It chaunst (eternall God that chaunce did guide)
As he recoylèd backward, in the mire
His nigh forwearied° feeble feet did slide,   *exhausted*
And downe he fell, with dread of shame sore terrifide.

46

There grew a goodly tree him faire beside,
Loaden with fruit and apples rosie red,
As they in pure vermilion had beene dide,
Whereof great vertues over all were red:°   *everywhere were told*
For happie life to all, which thereon fed,
And life eke everlasting did befall:
Great God it planted in that blessed sted°   *place*
With his almightie hand, and did it call
The Tree of Life, the crime of our first fathers fall.[3]

47

In all the world like was not to be found,
Save in that soile, where all good things did grow,

3. Genesis 2.9 describes the Tree of Life and also the Tree of Knowledge of Good and Evil, both of which God planted in the Garden of Eden. The "crime of our first fathers fall" is that Adam, in eating of the second and being banished from Eden, separated himself—and (according to Christian doctrine) his descendants—from the first. The Tree of Life appears again in the New Jerusalem (Revelation 22.2).

And freely sprong out of the fruitfull ground,
As incorrupted Nature did them sow,
Till that dread Dragon all did overthrow.
Another like faire tree eke grew thereby,
Whereof who so did eat, eftsoones did know
Both good and ill: O mornefull memory:
That tree through one mans fault hath doen us all to dy.° *i.e., killed us*

48

From that first tree forth flowd, as from a well,
 A trickling streame of Balme, most soveraine° *powerful for cures*
 And daintie deare,° which on the ground still fell, *precious*
 And overflowèd all the fertill plaine,
 As it had deawèd bene with timely° raine: *seasonable*
 Life and long health that gratious° ointment gave, *full of grace*
 And deadly woundes could heale, and reare° againe *raise*
 The senselesse corse appointed° for the grave. *made ready*
Into that same he fell: which did from death him save.[4]

49

For nigh thereto the ever damnèd beast
 Durst not approch, for he was deadly made,° *i.e., a child of death*
 And all that life preservèd, did detest:
 Yet he it oft adventured° to invade. *attempted*
 By this the drouping day-light gan to fade,
 And yeeld his roome° to sad succeeding night, *its place*
 Who with her sable mantle gan to shade
 The face of earth, and wayes of living wight,
And high her burning torch set up in heaven bright.

50

When gentle Una saw the second fall
 Of her deare knight, who wearie of long fight,
 And faint through losse of bloud, moved not at all,
 But lay as in a dreame of deepe delight,
 Besmeard with pretious Balme, whose vertuous might
 Did heale his wounds, and scorching heat alay,[5]
 Againe she stricken was with sore affright,
 And for his safetie gan devoutly pray;
And watch the noyous° night, and wait for joyous day. *noxious*

51

The joyous day gan early to appeare,
 And faire Aurora from the deawy bed
 Of agèd Tithone gan her selfe to reare,[6]

---

4. The healing balm flowing from the Tree of Life is understood to be Christ's blood, shed to redeem humankind from eternal damnation.
5. Cf. Revelation 2.7, 11: "To him that overcometh will I give to eat of the tree of life" and "He cometh shall not be hurt of the second death" (i.e., the eternal death, of the soul).
6. Aurora is goddess of the dawn, Tithonus her husband ("agèd" because he was granted everlasting life without everlasting youth).

With rosie cheekes, for shame as blushing red;
 Her golden lockes for haste were loosely shed
 About her eares, when Una her did marke
 Clymbe to her charet, all with flowers spred,
 From heaven high to chase the chearelesse darke;
With merry note her loud salutes the mounting larke.

52

Then freshly up arose the doughtie° knight,   *valiant*
 All healèd of his hurts and woundès wide,
 And did himselfe to battell readie dight;°   *prepare*
 Whose early foe awaiting him beside
 To have devourd, so soone as day he spyde,
 When now he saw himselfe so freshly reare,
 As if late fight had nought him damnifyde,°   *injured*
 He woxe° dismayd, and gan his fate to feare;   *grew*
Nathlesse° with wonted rage he him advauncèd neare. *nevertheless*

53

And in his first encounter, gaping wide,
 He thought attonce him to have swallowed quight,
 And rusht upon him with outragious pride;
 Who him r'encountring fierce, as hauke in flight,
 Perforce rebutted° backe. The weapon bright   *drove*
 Taking advantage of his open jaw,
 Ran through his mouth with so importune° might,   *violent*
 That deepe emperst his darksome hollow maw,
And back retyrd,[7] his life bloud forth with all did draw.

54

So downe he fell, and forth his life did breath,
 That vanisht into smoke and cloudès swift;
 So downe he fell, that th'earth him underneath
 Did grone, as feeble so great load to lift;
 So downe he fell, as an huge rockie clift,
 Whose false° foundation waves have washt away,   *insecure*
 With dreadfull poyse° is from the mayneland rift,° *falling weight / split*
 And rolling downe, great Neptune doth dismay;
So downe he fell, and like an heapèd mountaine lay.

55

The knight himselfe even trembled at his fall,
 So huge and horrible a masse it seemed;
 And his deare Ladie, that beheld it all,
 Durst not approch for dread, which she misdeemed,° *misjudged*
 But yet at last, when as the direfull feend
 She saw not stirre, off-shaking vaine affright,
 She nigher drew, and saw that joyous end:

7. I.e., on being drawn back.

Then God she praysd, and thankt her faithfull knight,
That had atchiev'd so great a conquest by his might.

Canto 12

Faire Una to the Redcrosse knight
betrouthèd is with joy:
Though false Duessa it to barre
her false sleights doe imploy.

1

Behold I see the haven nigh at hand,
  To which I meane my wearie course to bend;
  Vere the maine shete, and beare up with the land,[8]
  The which afore is fairely to be kend,°   recognized
  And seemeth safe from stormes, that may offend;
  There this faire virgin wearie of her way
  Must landed be, now at her journeyes end:
  There eke° my feeble barke° a while may stay,   also / ship
Till merry° wind and weather call her thence away.   favorable

2

Scarsely had Phoebus in the glooming East°   i.e., dawn
  Yet harnessèd his firie-footed teeme,
  Ne reard above the earth his flaming creast,°   crest
  When the last deadly smoke aloft did steeme,
  That signe of last outbreathèd life did seeme
  Unto the watchman on the castle wall;
  Who thereby dead that balefull° Beast did deeme,   evil
  And to his Lord and Ladie lowd gan call,
To tell, how he had seene the Dragons fatall fall.

3

Uprose with hastie joy, and feeble speed
  That agèd Sire, the Lord of all that land,
  And lookèd forth, to weet,° if true indeede   know
  Those tydings were, as he did understand,
  Which whenas true by tryall he out fond,
  He bad° to open wyde his brazen gate,   bade
  Which long time had bene shut, and out of hond°   straightway
  Proclaymèd joy and peace through all his state;
For dead now was their foe, which them forrayèd late.[9]

4

Then gan triumphant Trompets sound on hie,
  That sent to heaven the ecchoed report

---

8. Release the mainsail line and sail toward the
land. The nautical metaphor echoes many classical authors and Chaucer's *Troilus and Criseyde*
(2.1–7).
9. Had recently ravaged.

Of their new joy, and happie victorie
  Gainst him, that had them long opprest with tort,°   *wrong*
  And fast imprisonèd in siegèd fort.
  Then all the people, as in solemne feast,
  To him assembled with one full consort,°   *all together*
  Rejoycing at the fall of that great beast,
From whose eternall bondage now they were releast.

5

Forth came that auncient Lord and agèd Queene,
  Arayd in antique robes downe to the ground,
  And sad habiliments right well beseene;[1]
  A noble crew about them waited round
  Of sage and sober Peres,° all gravely gownd;   *peers*
  Whom farre before did march a goodly band
  Of tall young men, all hable armes to sownd,[2]
  But now they laurell braunches bore in hand;
Glad signe of victorie and peace in all their land.

6

Unto that doughtie Conquerour they came,
  And him before themselves prostrating low,
  Their Lord and Patrone° loud did him proclame,   *defender*
  And at his feet their laurell boughes did throw.
  Soone after them all dauncing on a row
  The comely virgins came, with girlands dight,°   *adorned*
  As fresh as flowres in medow greene do grow,
  When morning deaw upon their leaves doth light:
And in their hands sweet Timbrels° all upheld on hight.   *tambourines*

7

And them before, the fry° of children young   *crowd*
  Their wanton° sports and childish mirth did play,   *playful*
  And to the Maydens sounding tymbrels sung
  In well attunèd notes, a joyous lay,°   *song*
  And made delightfull musicke all the way,
  Untill they came, where that faire virgin stood;
  As faire Diana° in fresh sommers day   *goddess of the hunt*
  Beholds her Nymphes, enraunged° in shadie wood,   *ranged*
Some wrestle, some do run, some bathe in christall flood.

8

So she beheld those maydens meriment
  With chearefull vew; who when to her they came,
  Themselves to ground with gratious humblesse° bent,   *humility*
  And her adored by honorable name,°   *with titles of honor*
  Lifting to heaven her everlasting fame:

---

1. I.e., sober, appropriate ("right well beseene")   2. Able to fight with weapons.
attire.

Then on her head they set a girland greene,
And crownèd her twixt earnest and twixt game:°   *i.e., half in fun*
Who in her selfe-resemblance well beseene,[3]
Did seeme such, as she was, a goodly maiden Queene.

9

And after all, the raskall many° ran,   *rabble throng*
   Heapèd together in rude rablement,°   *confusion*
   To see the face of that victorious man:
   Whom all admirèd,° as from heaven sent,   *wondered at*
   And gazd upon with gaping wonderment.
   But when they came, where that dead Dragon lay,
   Stretcht on the ground in monstrous large extent,
   The sight with idle° feare did them dismay,   *baseless*
Ne durst approch him nigh, to touch, or once assay.°   *venture to*

10

Some feard, and fled; some feard and well it faynd;°   *concealed*
   One that would wiser seeme, then all the rest,
   Warnd him not touch, for yet perhaps remaynd
   Some lingring life within his hollow brest,
   Or in his wombe might lurke some hidden nest
   Of many Dragonets,° his fruitfull seed;   *young dragons*
   Another said, that in his eyes did rest
   Yet sparckling fire, and bad thereof take heed;
Another said, he saw him move his eyes indeed.

11

One mother, when as her foolehardie chyld
   Did come too neare, and with his talants° play,   *talons*
   Halfe dead through feare, her litle babe revyld,°   *scolded*
   And to her gossips° gan in counsell° say;   *women friends / private*
   "How can I tell, but that his talants may
   Yet scratch my sonne, or rend his tender hand?"
   So diversly themselves in vaine they fray;°   *frighten*
   Whiles some more bold, to measure him nigh stand,
To prove° how many acres he did spread of land.   *determine*

12

Thus flockèd all the folke him round about,
   The whiles that hoarie° king, with all his traine,   *gray-haired*
   Being arrivèd, where that champion stout
   After his foes defeasance° did remaine,   *defeat*
   Him goodly greetes, and faire does entertaine,
   With princely gifts of yvorie and gold,
   And thousand thankes him yeelds for all his paine.
   Then when his daughter deare he does behold,
Her dearely doth imbrace, and kisseth manifold.°   *many times*

---

3. I.e., looking appropriately like herself.

13

And after to his Pallace he them brings,
   With shaumes, and trompets, and with Clarions[4] sweet;
   And all the way the joyous people sings,
   And with their garments strowes the pavèd street:
   Whence mounting up, they find purveyance° meet   *provisions*
   Of all, that royall Princes court became,°   *suited*
   And all the floore was underneath their feet
   Bespred with costly scarlot of great name,°   *i.e., famous scarlet cloth*
On which they lowly sit, and fitting purpose frame.[5]

14

What needs me tell their feast and goodly guize,°   *behavior*
   In which was nothing riotous nor vaine?
   What needs of daintie dishes to devize,°   *talk*
   Of comely° services, or courtly trayne?°   *becoming / assembly*
   My narrow leaves cannot in them containe
   The large discourse° of royall Princes state.   *i.e., full description*
   Yet was their manner then but bare and plaine:
   For th'antique world excesse and pride did hate;
Such proud luxurious pompe is swollen up but late.°   *just recently*

15

Then when with meates and drinkes of every kinde
   Their fervent appetites they quenchèd had,
   That auncient Lord gan fit occasion finde,
   Of straunge adventures, and of perils sad,°   *grave*
   Which in his travell him befallen had,
   For to demaund° of his renowmèd guest: *inquire*
   Who then with utt'rance grave, and count'nance sad,
   From point to point, as is before exprest,
Discourst his voyage long, according° his request.   *granting*

16

Great pleasure mixt with pittifull° regard,   *sympathetic*
   That godly King and Queene did passionate,°   *i.e., feel and express*
   Whiles they his pittifull° adventures heard,   *deserving pity*
   That oft they did lament his lucklesse state,
   And often blame the too importune° fate,   *severe*
   That heapd on him so many wrathfull wreakes:°   *vengeful injuries*
   For never gentle knight, as he of late,
   So tossèd was in fortunes cruell freakes;°   *whims*
And all the while salt teares bedeawd the hearers cheaks.

---

4. Trumpet calls. "Shaumes": the shawm was the medieval and Renaissance predecessor of the oboe.
5. Make seemly conversation.

17

Then said that royall Pere in sober wise:
  "Deare Sonne, great beene the evils, which ye bore
  From first to last in your late enterprise,
  That I note,° whether prayse, or pitty more: *know not*
  For never living man, I weene,° so sore   *think*
  In sea of deadly daungers was distrest;
  But since now safe ye seisèd° have the shore,   *reached*
  And well arrivèd are (high God be blest),
Let us devize° of ease and everlasting rest."   *think*

18

"Ah dearest Lord," said then that doughty knight,
  "Of ease or rest I may not yet devize;
  For by the faith, which I to armes have plight,°   *pledged*
  I bounden am streight° after this emprize,°   *immediately / enterprise*
  As that your daughter can ye well advize,
  Backe to returne to that great Faerie Queene,
  And her to serve six yeares in warlike wize,
  Gainst that proud Paynim king, that workes her teene:°   *sorrow*
Therefore I ought° crave pardon, till I there have beene."[6]   *must*

19

"Unhappie falles that hard necessitie,"
  Quoth he, "the troubler of my happie peace,
  And vowèd foe of my felicitie;
  Ne° I against the same can justly preace:°   *nor / press, contend*
  But since that band° ye cannot now release,   *obligation*
  Nor doen undo (for vowes may not be vaine),[7]
  Soone as the terme of those six yeares shall cease,
  Ye then shall hither backe returne againe,
The marriage to accomplish vowd betwixt you twain.

20

"Which for my part I covet to performe,
  In sort as° through the world I did proclame,   *even as*
  That who so kild that monster most deforme,°   *hideous*
  And him in hardy battaile overcame,
  Should have mine onely daughter to his Dame,°   *wife*
  And of my kingdome heire apparaunt bee:
  Therefore since now to thee perteines° the same,   *belongs*
  By dew desert of noble chevalree,
Both daughter and eke kingdome, lo I yield to thee."

---

6. The final Christian triumph, the marriage of Christ and the true Church, will be achieved only at the end of time. Meanwhile, the struggle against evil (and the Roman Church) continues.
7. I.e., you cannot undo what is done ("doen"), for vows may not be (made) vain.

21

Then forth he callèd that his daughter faire,
  The fairest Un' his onely daughter deare,
  His onely daughter, and his onely heyre;
  Who forth proceeding with sad° sober cheare,°   *grave / countenance*
  As bright as doth the morning starre appeare
  Out of the East, with flaming lockes bedight,°   *bedecked*
  To tell that dawning day is drawing neare,
  And to the world does bring long wishèd light;
So faire and fresh that Lady shewd her selfe in sight.

22

So faire and fresh, as freshest flowre in May;
  For she had layd her mournefull stole aside,
  And widow-like sad wimple° throwne away,   *veil*
  Wherewith her heavenly beautie she did hide,
  Whiles on her wearie journey she did ride;
  And on her now a garment she did weare,
  All lilly white, withoutten spot, or pride,°   *ornament*
  That seemed like silke and silver woven neare,°   *tightly*
But neither silke nor silver therein did appeare.[8]

23

The blazing brightnesse of her beauties beame,
  And glorious light of her sunshyny face[9]
  To tell, were as to strive against the streame.
  My ragged rimes are all too rude and bace,
  Her heavenly lineaments for to enchace.°   *adorn*
  Ne wonder; for her owne deare lovèd knight,
  All° were she dayly with himselfe in place,   *although*
  Did wonder much at her celestiall sight:
Oft had he seene her faire, but never so faire dight.°   *arrayed*

24

So fairely dight, when she in presence came,
  She to her Sire made humble reverence,
  And bowèd low, that her right well became,
  And added grace unto her excellence:
  Who with great wisdome, and grave eloquence
  Thus gan to say. But eare° he thus had said,   *ere*
  With flying speede, and seeming great pretence,°   *purpose*
  Came running in, much like a man dismaid,
A Messenger with letters, which his message said.

---

8. "The marriage of the Lamb is come, and his wife hath made herself ready. And to her was granted that she should be arrayed in fine linen, clean and white: for the fine linen is the righteousness of saints" (Revelation 19.7–8).
9. Revelation 21.9, 11 describes the New Jerusalem as "the bride, the Lamb's wife . . . her light was like unto a stone most precious."

25

All in the open hall amazèd stood,
 At suddeinnesse of that unwarie° sight,   *unexpected*
 And wondred at his breathlesse hastie mood.
 But he for nought would stay his passage right°   *direct*
 Till fast° before the king he did alight;   *close*
 Where falling flat, great humblesse he did make,
 And kist the ground, whereon his foot was pight;°   *placed*
 Then to his hands that writ° he did betake,° *document / deliver*
Which he disclosing, red thus, as the paper spake.

26

"To thee, most mighty king of Eden faire,
 Her greeting sends in these sad lines addrest,
 The wofull daughter, and forsaken heire
 Of that great Emperour of all the West;
 And bids thee be advizèd for the best,
 Ere thou thy daughter linck in holy band
 Of wedlocke to that new unknowen guest:
 For he already plighted his right hand
Unto another love, and to another land.

27

"To me sad mayd, or rather widow sad,
 He was affiauncèd long time before,
 And sacred pledges he both gave, and had,
 False erraunt knight, infamous, and forswore:
 Witnesse the burning Altars, which° he swore,   *by which*
 And guiltie heavens of° his bold perjury, *i.e., and heavens polluted by*
 Which though he hath polluted oft of yore,
 Yet I to them for judgement just do fly,
And them conjure° t'avenge this shamefull injury.   *implore*

28

"Therefore since mine he is, or° free or bond,°   *whether / bound*
 Or false or trew, or living or else dead,
 Withhold, O soveraine Prince, your hasty hond
 From knitting league with him, I you aread;°   *advise*
 Ne wene° my right with strength adowne to tread, *think*
 Through weakenesse of my widowhed, or woe:
 For truth is strong, her rightfull cause to plead,
 And shall find friends, if need requireth soe,
So bids thee well to fare, Thy neither friend, nor foe, Fidessa."

29

When he these bitter byting words had red,
 The tydings straunge did him abashèd make,
 That still he sate long time astonishèd
 As in great muse,° ne word to creature spake.   *amazement*

At last his solemne silence thus he brake,
  With doubtfull eyes fast fixèd on his guest:
  "Redoubted° knight, that for mine onely sake[1]   *honored*
  Thy life and honour late adventurest,
Let nought be hid from me, that ought to be exprest.

30

"What meane these bloudy vowes, and idle threats,
  Throwne out from womanish impatient mind?
  What heavens? what altars? what enragèd heates
  Here heapèd up with termes of love unkind,°   *unnatural*
  My conscience cleare with guilty bands° would bind?   *bonds of guilt*
  High God be witnesse, that I guiltlesse ame.
  But if your selfe, Sir knight, ye faultie° find,   *guilty*
  Or wrappèd be in loves of former Dame,
With crime do not it cover, but disclose the same."

31

To whom the Redcrosse knight this answere sent,
  "My Lord, my King, be nought hereat dismayd,
  Till well ye wote by grave intendiment,°   *serious investigation*
  What woman, and wherefore doth me upbrayd
  With breach of love, and loyalty betrayd.
  It was in my mishaps, as hitherward
  I lately traveild, that unwares I strayd
  Out of my way, through perils straunge and hard;
That day should faile me, ere I had them all declard.

32

"There did I find, or rather I was found
  Of this false woman, that Fidessa hight,°   *is called*
  Fidessa hight the falsest Dame on ground,
  Most false Duessa, royall richly dight,
  That easie was t'invegle weaker° sight: *deceive too weak*
  Who by her wicked arts, and wylie skill,
  Too false and strong for earthly skill or might,
  Unwares me wrought unto her wicked will,
And to my foe betrayd, when least I fearèd ill."

33

Then steppèd forth the goodly royall Mayd,
  And on the ground her selfe prostrating low,
  With sober countenaunce thus to him sayd:
  "O pardon me, my soveraigne Lord, to show
  The secret treasons, which of late I know
  To have bene wroght by that false sorceresse.
  She onely she it is, that earst° did throw   *formerly*

1. For my sake alone.

This gentle knight into so great distresse,
That death him did awaite in dayly wretchednesse.

34

"And now it seemes, that she subornèd hath
  This craftie messenger with letters vaine,
  To worke new woe and improvided scath,°   *unexpected harm*
  By breaking of the band° betwixt us twaine;   *bond*
  Wherein she usèd hath the practicke paine°   *treacherous skill*
  Of this false footman, clokt with simplenesse,
  Whom if ye please for to discover plaine,
  Ye shall him Archimago find, I ghesse,
The falsest man alive; who tries° shall find no lesse."   *investigates*

35

The king was greatly movèd at her speach,
  And all with suddein indignation fraight,°   *filled*
  Bad° on that Messenger rude hands to reach.   *bade*
  Eftsoones° the Gard, which on his state did wait,   *immediately*
  Attacht° that faitor° false, and bound him strait: *arrested / impostor*
  Who seeming sorely chauffèd° at his band,   *angered*
  As chainèd Beare, whom cruell dogs do bait,
  With idle force did faine them to withstand,
And often semblaunce made to scape out of their hand.

36

But they him layd full low in dungeon deepe,
  And bound him hand and foote with yron chains.
  And with continuall watch did warely° keepe;   *vigilantly*
  Who then would thinke, that by his subtile trains°   *tricks*
  He could escape fowle death or deadly paines?[2]
  Thus when that Princes wrath was pacifide,
  He gan renew the late forbidden banes,[3]
  And to the knight his daughter deare he tyde,
With sacred rites and vowes for ever to abyde.

37

His owne two hands the holy knots did knit,
  That none but death for ever can devide;
  His owne two hands, for such a turne° most fit,   *act*
  The housling° fire did kindle and provide,   *sacramental*
  And holy water thereon sprinckled wide;[4]
  At which the bushy Teade° a groome did light,   *nuptial torch*
  And sacred lampe in secret chamber hide,

2. "And he laid hold on the dragon, that old serpent, which is the Devil, and Satan, and bound him a thousand years, And cast him into the bottomless pit, and shut him up, and set a seal upon him, that he should deceive the nations no more, till the thousand years should be fulfilled: and after that he must be loosed a little season" (Revelation 20.2–3).

3. Banns, i.e., announcements of marriage.

4. Marriages in ancient times were solemnized with sacramental fire and water.

Where it should not be quenchèd day nor night,
For feare of evill fates, but burnen ever bright.

38

Then gan they sprinckle all the posts with wine,
    And made great feast to solemnize that day;
    They all perfumde with frankencense divine,
    And precious odours fetcht from far away,
    That all the house did sweat with great aray:
    And all the while sweete Musicke did apply
    Her curious° skill, the warbling notes to play,   *intricate*
    To drive away the dull Melancholy;
The whiles one sung a song of love and jollity.

39

During the which there was an heavenly noise
    Heard sound through all the Pallace pleasantly,
    Like as it had bene many an Angels voice,
    Singing before th'eternall majesty,
    In their trinall triplicities[5] on hye;
    Yet wist° no creature, whence that heavenly sweet°   *knew / delight*
    Proceeded, yet each one felt secretly°   *inwardly*
    Himselfe thereby reft of his sences meet,°   *proper*
And ravishèd with rare impression in his sprite.[6]

40

Great joy was made that day of young and old,
    And solemne feast proclaimd throughout the land,
    That their exceeding merth may not be told:
    Suffice it heare by signes to understand
    The usuall joyes at knitting of loves band.
    Thrise happy man the knight himselfe did hold,
    Possessèd of his Ladies hart and hand,
    And ever, when his eye did her behold,
His heart did seeme to melt in pleasures manifold.

41

Her joyous presence and sweet company
    In full content he there did long enjoy,
    Ne wicked envie, ne vile gealosy
    His deare delights were able to annoy:
    Yet swimming in that sea of blisfull joy,
    He nought forgot, how he whilome° had sworne,   *formerly*
    In case he could that monstrous beast destroy,

5. The "trinall triplicities" are the nine angelic orders, divided into three groups of three, the whole hierarchy corresponding to the nine spheres of the universe. The music heard in this stanza is the music of the spheres, not audible on earth since the Fall.

6. Spirit. "Let us be glad and rejoice, and give honor to him: for the marriage of the Lamb is come" (Revelation 19.7). In Revelation, the marriage of Christ and the New Jerusalem signals the general redemption.

Unto his Faerie Queene backe to returne:
The which he shortly did, and Una left to mourne.

42

Now strike your sailes ye jolly Mariners,
  For we be come unto a quiet rode,°   *harbor*
  Where we must land some of our passengers,
  And light this wearie vessell of her lode.
  Here she a while may make her safe abode,
  Till she repairèd have her tackles spent,°   *worn out*
  And wants supplide. And then againe abroad
  On the long voyage whereto she is bent:
Well may she speede and fairely finish her intent.

From The Second Booke of The Faerie Queene

Contayning
The Legend of Sir Guyon,
or
Of Temperaunce

Summary   In Book 2, Sir Guyon represents and becomes the virtue of Temperance, which requires moderation, self-control, and sometimes abstinence in regard to anger, sex, greed, ambition, and the whole spectrum of passions, desires, pleasures, and material goods. In his climactic adventure, he visits and destroys the Bower of Bliss of the witch Acrasia.

From *Canto 12*

[THE BOWER OF BLISS][1]

42

Thence passing forth, they[2] shortly do arrive,
  Whereas the Bowre of Blisse was situate;
  A place pickt out by choice of best alive,°   *the best living artisans*
  That natures worke by art can imitate:
  In which what ever in this worldly state
  Is sweet, and pleasing unto living sense,
  Or that may dayntiest fantasie aggrate,°   *please, satisfy*
  Was pourèd forth with plentifull dispence,°   *liberality*
And made there to abound with lavish affluence.

---

1. The Bower of Bliss, perhaps the most famous of Spenser's symbolic places, has been variously interpreted. Some critics emphasize its aspects of sterility and artifice; others, its seductive and threatening eroticism and idolatry akin to that associated, in Spenser's time, with the New World and Ireland.

2. I.e., Guyon and a character called the Palmer, who is his guide throughout Book 2 (and who is usually thought to represent reason). Pilgrims to the Holy Land were called palmers in token of the palm leaves they often brought back.

43

Goodly it was enclosèd round about,
  Aswell their entred guests to keepe within,
  As those unruly beasts to hold without;[3]
  Yet was the fence thereof but weake and thin;
  Nought feard their force, that fortilage° to win,[4]   *fortress*
  But wisedomes powre, and temperaunces might,
  By which the mightiest things efforcèd bin:°   *are compelled*
  And eke° the gate was wrought of substaunce light,   *also*
Rather for pleasure, then° for battery or fight.   *than*

44

Yt framèd° was of precious yvory,   *made*
  That seemd a worke of admirable wit;°   *marvelous skill*
  And therein all the famous history
  Of Jason and Medaea was ywrit;
  Her mighty charmes, her furious loving fit,
  His goodly conquest of the golden fleece,
  His falsèd° faith, and love too lightly flit,°   *violated / altering*
  The wondred° Argo, which in venturous peece[5]   *admired*
First through the Euxine seas bore all the flowr of Greece.[6]

45

Ye might° have seene the frothy billowes fry°   *could / foam*
  Under the ship, as thorough° them she went,   *through*
  That seemd the waves were into yvory,
  Or yvory into the waves were sent;
  And other where the snowy substaunce sprent°   *sprinkled*
  With vermell,° like the boyes bloud therein shed,[7]   *vermilion*
  A piteous spectacle did represent,
  And otherwhiles° with gold besprinkelèd;   *elsewhere*
Yt seemd th'enchaunted flame, which did Creüsa wed.[8]

46

All this, and more might in that goodly gate
  Be red; that ever open stood to all,
  Which thither came: but in the Porch there sate
  A comely personage of stature tall,
  And semblaunce° pleasing, more then naturall,   *appearance*
  That travellers to him seemd to entize;
  His looser° garment to the ground did fall,   *too loose*

---

3. Just outside the Bower, Guyon and the Palmer had encountered "many beasts, that roard outrageously, / As if that hungers point, or Venus sting / Had them enraged" (stanza 39). The Palmer had used the magical power of his staff to turn their aggression into cringing fear.
4. I.e., it was not at all feared that the physical force of the beasts could breach that fortress.
5. I.e., adventurous vessel.
6. Jason, in his ship the *Argo*, sought the Golden Fleece of the king of Colchis; the sorceress Medea, the king's daughter, fell in love with him and used "her mighty charmes" to help him obtain it.
7. The blood of Absyrtus, Medea's younger brother, whose body she cut into pieces and scattered to delay her father's pursuit.
8. Jason later deserted Medea for Creüsa. In revenge, Medea gave her a dress that burst into flame when she put it on; the flame consumed and thus "wed" her.

And flew about his heeles in wanton wize,
Not fit for speedy pace, or manly exercize.

47

They in that place him Genius° did call: *presiding spirit*
  Not that celestiall powre, to whom the care
  Of life, and generatiön of all
  That lives, pertaines in charge particulare,[9]
  Who wondrous things concerning our welfare,
  And strange phantomes doth let us oft forsee,
  And oft of secret ill bids us beware:
  That is our Selfe,[1] whom though we do not see,
Yet each doth in him selfe it well perceive to bee.

48

Therefore a God him sage Antiquity
  Did wisely make,[2] and good Agdistes call:
  But this same[3] was to that quite contrary,
  The foe of life, that good envyes° to all,   *grudges*
  That secretly doth us procure° to fall,   *cause*
  Through guilefull semblaunts,° which he makes us see. *illusions*
  He of this Gardin had the governall,°   *management*
  And Pleasures porter was devizd° to bee,   *appointed*
Holding a staffe in hand for more formalitee.

49

With diverse flowres he daintily was deckt,
  And strowèd round about, and by his side
  A mighty Mazer bowle[4] of wine was set,
  As if it had to him bene sacrifide;°   *consecrated*
  Wherewith all new-come guests he gratifide:
  So did he eke Sir Guyon passing by:
  But he his idle curtesie defide,
  And overthrew his bowle disdainfully;
And broke his staffe, with which he charmèd semblants sly.[5]

50

Thus being entred, they behold around
  A large and spacious plaine, on every side
  Strowed with pleasauns,° whose faire grassy ground *pleasure-grounds*
  Mantled with greene, and goodly beautifide
  With all the ornaments of Floraes° pride,   *goddess of flowers*
  Wherewith her mother Art, as halfe in scorne

---

9. I.e., not Agdistes (see next stanza), the god of generation. The true Agdistes appears in the Garden of Adonis canto of Book 3 (canto 6, stanzas 31–33).
1. I.e., the *daemon*, or indwelling divine power, that directs the course of our lives.
2. I.e., the wise ancients were right to declare

this power a god.
3. I.e., the Genius of the Bower.
4. A drinking cup of maple.
5. Raised deceitful apparitions. The rod and bowl are traditional emblems of enchantment (cf. Duessa's cup, Book 1, canto 8, stanza 14).

Of niggard° Nature, like a pompous bride   *stingy*
    Did decke her, and too lavishly adorne,
When forth from virgin bowre she comes in th'early morne.

51

Thereto the Heavens alwayes Joviall,[6]
    Lookt on them lovely,° still° in stedfast state,   *lovingly / always*
    Ne° suffred storme nor frost on them to fall,   *nor*
    Their tender buds or leaves to violate,
    Nor scorching heat, nor cold intemperate
    T'afflict the creatures, which therein did dwell,
    But the milde aire with season moderate
    Gently attempred, and disposd so well,
That still it breathèd forth sweet spirit° and holesome smell.   *breath*

52

More sweet and holesome, then° the pleasaunt hill   *than*
    Of Rhodope, on which the Nimphe, that bore
    A gyaunt babe, her selfe for griefe did kill;
    Or the Thessalian Tempe, where of yore
    Faire Daphne Phoebus hart with love did gore;
    Or Ida, where the Gods lov'd to repaire,°   *resort*
    When ever they their heavenly bowres forlore;°   *deserted*
    Or sweet Parnasse, the haunt of Muses faire;[7]
Or Eden selfe, if ought° with Eden mote compaire.   *aught, anything*

53

Much wondred Guyon at the faire aspect
    Of that sweet place, yet suffred no delight
    To sincke into his sence, nor mind affect,
    But passèd forth, and lookt still forward right,°   *straight ahead*
    Bridling his will, and maistering his might:
    Till that he came unto another gate,
    No gate, but like one, being goodly dight°   *arrayed*
    With boughes and braunches, which did broad dilate° *spread out*
Their clasping armes, in wanton wreathings intricate.

54

So fashionèd a Porch with rare device,°   *design*
    Archt over head with an embracing vine,
    Whose bounches hanging downe, seemed to entice
    All passers by, to tast their lushious wine,
    And did themselves into their hands incline,
    As freely offering to be gatherèd:

---

6. Serene and beneficent, as influenced by the planet Jupiter.
7. The nymph Rhodope, who had a "gyaunt babe," Athos, by Neptune, was turned into a mountain. Daphne, another nymph, charmed Apollo so much that he pursued her until she prayed for aid and was turned into a laurel tree. Mount Ida was the scene of the rape of Ganymede by Jupiter, the judgment of Paris, and the gods' vantage point for viewing the Trojan War. Mount Parnassus is the home of the Muses.

Some deepe empurpled as the Hyacine,[8]
Some as the Rubine,° laughing sweetly red,   *ruby*
Some like faire Emeraudes, not yet well ripenèd.

55

And them amongst, some were of burnisht gold,
So made by art, to beautifie the rest,
Which did themselves emongst the leaves enfold,
As lurking from the vew of covetous guest,
That the weake bowes,° with so rich load opprest,   *boughs*
Did bowe adowne, as over-burdenèd.
Under that Porch a comely dame did rest,
Clad in faire weedes,° but fowle disorderèd,   *garments*
And garments loose, that seemd unmeet for womanhed.[9]

56

In her left hand a Cup of gold she held,
And with her right the riper° fruit did reach,   *overripe*
Whose sappy liquor, that with fulnesse sweld,
Into her cup she scruzd,° with daintie breach°   *squeezed / crushing*
Of her fine fingers, without fowle empeach,°   *injury*
That so faire wine-presse made the wine more sweet:
Thereof she usd to give to drinke to each,
Whom passing by she happenèd to meet:
It was her guise,° all Straungers goodly so to greet.   *custom*

57

So she to Guyon offred it to tast;
Who taking it out of her tender hond,
The cup to ground did violently cast,
That all in peeces it was broken fond,°   *found*
And with the liquor stainèd all the lond:°   *land*
Whereat Excesse exceedingly was wroth,
Yet no'te° the same amend, ne yet withstond,   *knew not how to*
But suffered° him to passe, all° were she loth;   *allowed / although*
Who nought regarding her displeasure forward goth.

58

There the most daintie Paradise on ground,
It selfe doth offer to his sober eye,
In which all pleasures plenteously abound,
And none does others happinesse envye:
The painted° flowres, the trees upshooting hye,   *brightly colored*
The dales for shade, the hilles for breathing space,
The trembling groves, the Christall° running by;   *clear stream*
And that, which all faire workes doth most aggrace,°   *add grace to*
The art, which all that wrought, appearèd in no place.

8. The hyacinth or jacinth, a sapphire-colored   9. Unfitting for womanhood.
stone.

59

One would have thought (so cunningly, the rude,
   And scornèd parts were mingled with the fine)
   That nature had for wantonesse ensude°   *playfulness imitated*
   Art, and that Art at nature did repine;°   *complain*
   So striving each th'other to undermine,
   Each did the others worke more beautifie;
   So diff'ring both in willes, agreed in fine:°   *in the end*
   So all agreed through sweete diversitie,
This Gardin to adorne with all varietie.

60

And in the midst of all, a fountaine stood,
   Of richest substaunce, that on earth might bee,
   So pure and shiny, that the silver flood
   Through every channell running one might see;
   Most goodly it with curious imageree
   Was over-wrought, and shapes of naked boyes,
   Of which some seemd with lively jollitee,
   To fly about, playing their wanton toyes,°   *sports*
Whilest others did them selves embay° in liquid joyes.   *bathe*

61

And over all, of purest gold was spred,
   A trayle of yvie in his native hew:
   For the rich mettall was so colourèd,
   That wight, who did not well avis'd° it vew,   *carefully*
   Would surely deeme it to be yvie trew:
   Low his lascivious armes adown did creepe,
   That themselves dipping in the silver dew,
   Their fleecy flowres they tenderly did steepe,
Which° drops of Christall seemd for wantones to weepe. *on which*

62

Infinit streames continually did well
   Out of this fountaine, sweet and faire to see,
   The which into an ample laver° fell,   *basin*
   And shortly grew to so great quantitie,
   That like a little lake it seemd to bee;
   Whose depth exceeded not three cubits[1] hight,
   That through the waves one might the bottom see,
   All pav'd beneath with Jaspar shining bright,
That seemd the fountaine in that sea did sayle upright.

63

And all the margent° round about was set,   *border*
   With shady Laurell trees, thence to defend°   *ward off*

---

1. A cubit is about twenty inches (thus the depth is no more than five feet).

The sunny beames, which on the billowes bet,°   beat
And those which therein bathèd, mote offend.°   harm
As Guyon hapned by the same to wend,
Two naked Damzelles he therein espyde,
Which therein bathing, seemèd to contend,
And wrestle wantonly, ne car'd to hyde,
Their dainty parts from vew of any, which them eyde.

64

Sometimes the one would lift the other quight
  Above the waters, and then downe againe
  Her plong,° as over maisterèd by might,   plunge
  Where both awhile would coverèd remaine,
  And each the other from to rise° restraine;   rising
  The whiles their snowy limbes, as through a vele,
  So through the Christall waves appearèd plaine:
  Then suddeinly both would themselves unhele,°   uncover
And th'amarous sweet spoiles° to greedy eyes revele.   booty, plunder

65

As that faire Starre, the messenger of morne,[2]
  His deawy face out of the sea doth reare:
  Or as the Cyprian goddess,[3] newly borne
  Of th'Oceans fruitfull froth,° did first appeare: foam
  Such seemèd they, and so their yellow heare
  Christalline humour° droppèd downe apace.   clear water
  Whom such when Guyon saw, he drew him neare,
  And somewhat gan relent his earnest pace,
His stubborne brest gan secret pleasaunce to embrace.

66

The wanton Maidens him espying, stood
  Gazing a while at his unwonted guise;°   unaccustomed behavior
  Then th'one her selfe low duckèd in the flood,
  Abasht, that her a straunger did avise:°   see
  But th'other rather higher did arise,
  And her two lilly paps aloft displayd,
  And all, that might his melting hart entise
  To her delights, she unto him bewrayed:°   revealed
The rest hid underneath, him more desirous made.

67

With that, the other likewise up arose,
  And her faire lockes, which formerly were bownd
  Up in one knot, she low adowne did lose:°   loosen

2. Unless "his" in the next line is to be taken as neuter, it implies that the reference is not to Venus but to Phosphorus (or Heophorus), the minor male divinity sometimes identified with the morning star.
3. Venus, one of whose principal shrines was on the island of Cyprus.

Which flowing long and thick, her cloth'd arownd,
  And th'yvorie in golden mantle gownd:
  So that faire spectacle from him was reft,°   *taken*
  Yet that, which reft it, no lesse faire was fownd:
  So hid in lockes and waves from lookers theft,
Nought but her lovely face she for his looking left.

68

Withall she laughèd, and she blusht withall,
  That blushing to her laughter gave more grace,
  And laughter to her blushing, as did fall:
  Now when they spide the knight to slacke his pace,
  Them to behold, and in his sparkling face
  The secret signes of kindled lust appeare,
  Their wanton meriments they did encreace,
  And to him beckned, to approch more neare,
And shewd him many sights, that courage cold could reare.[4]

69

On which when gazing him the Palmer saw,
  He much rebukt those wandring eyes of his,
  And counseld well, him forward thence did draw.
  Now are they come nigh to the Bowre of blis
  Of her fond° favorites so nam'd amis: *enamored; foolish*
  When thus the Palmer; "Now Sir, well avise;°   *take care*
  For here the end of all our travell° is: *travel; travail*
  Here wonnes° Acrasia, whom we must surprise,   *dwells*
Else she will slip away, and all our drift despise."° *plan set at nought*

70

Eftsoones° they heard a most melodious sound,   *immediately*
  Of all that mote delight a daintie eare,
  Such as attonce might not on living ground,
  Save in this Paradise, be heard elswhere:
  Right hard it was, for wight,° which did it heare,   *person*
  To read,° what manner musicke that mote bee: *discern*
  For all that pleasing is to living eare,
  Was there consorted in one harmonee,
Birdes, voyces, instruments, windes, waters, all agree.

71

The joyous birdes shrouded in chearefull shade,
  Their notes unto the voyce attempred° sweet;   *attuned*
  Th'Angelicall soft trembling voyces made
  To th'instruments divine respondence meet:°   *fitting*
  The silver sounding instruments did meet°   *join*
  With the base murmure of the waters fall:

4. That could arouse sexual desire ("courage") when cold.

The waters fall with difference discreet,°   *distinct variation*
Now soft, now loud, unto the wind did call:
The gentle warbling wind low answerèd to all.

72

There, whence that Musick seemèd heard to bee,
  Was the faire Witch her selfe[5] now solacing,°   *taking pleasure*
  With a new Lover, whom through sorceree
  And witchcraft, she from farre did thither bring:
  There she had him now layd a slombering,
  In secret shade, after long wanton joyes:
  Whilst round about them pleasauntly did sing
  Many faire Ladies, and lascivious boyes,
That ever mixt their song with light licentious toyes.°   *amorous play*

73

And all that while, right over him she hong,
  With her false° eyes fast fixèd in his sight,   *deceitful*
  As seeking medicine, whence she was stong,°   *stung*
  Or greedily depasturing° delight: *feeding on*
  And oft inclining downe with kisses light,
  For feare of waking him, his lips bedewd,
  And through his humid eyes did sucke his spright,°   *spirit*
  Quite molten into lust and pleasure lewd;
Wherewith she sighèd soft, as if his case she rewd.°   *pitied*

74

The whiles some one did chaunt this lovely lay:[6]
  "Ah see, who so faire thing doest faine° to see,   *delight*
  In springing flowre the image of thy day;
  Ah see the Virgin Rose, how sweetly shee
  Doth first peepe forth with bashfull modestee,
  That fairer seemes, the lesse ye see her may;
  Lo see soone after, how more bold and free
  Her barèd bosome she doth broad display;
Loe see soone after, how she fades, and falles away.

75

"So passeth, in the passing of a day,
  Of mortall life the leafe, the bud, the flowre,
  Ne more doth flourish after first decay,
  That earst° was sought to decke both bed and bowre,   *formerly*

---

5. Acrasia—whose name means both "intemperance" and "incontinence"—bears many resemblances to the classical Circe (in *Odyssey* 10 as well as the more witchlike and seductive figure in Ovid's *Metamorphoses* 14) and also to the enchantresses of Italian romance who derive from Circe: Acratia in Trissino's *L'Italia liberata* and Armida in Tasso's *Gerusalemme liberata*.

Much of the description in this scene is imitated from Tasso's account of the garden of Armida.
6. The song ("lay") of stanzas 74 and 75 imitates that in *Gerusalemme liberata* 16.14–15; this is a classic statement of the *carpe florem* (or *carpe diem*) theme—pick the flower of youth before it fades.

Of many a Ladie, and many a Paramowre:°   *lover*
Gather therefore the Rose, whilest yet is prime,°   *(its) springtime*
For soone comes age, that will her pride deflowre:
Gather the Rose of love, whilest yet is time,
Whilest loving thou mayst lovèd be with equal crime."

76

He ceast, and then gan all the quire of birdes
  Their diverse notes t'attune unto his lay,
  As in approvance of his pleasing words.
  The constant paire[7] heard all, that he did say,
  Yet swarvèd not, but kept their forward way,
  Through many covert groves, and thickets close,
  In which they creeping did at last display°   *discover*
  That wanton Ladie, with her lover lose,°   *loose, wanton*
Whose sleepie head she in her lap did soft dispose.

77

Upon a bed of Roses she was layd,
  As faint through heat, or dight to° pleasant sin,   *ready for*
  And was arayd, or rather disarayd,
  All in a vele of silke and silver thin,
  That hid no whit her alablaster skin,
  But rather shewd more white, if more might bee:
  More subtile web Arachne° cannot spin,   *the spider*
  Nor the fine nets, which oft we woven see
Of scorchèd deaw, do not in th'aire more lightly flee.°   *float*

78

Her snowy brest was bare to readie spoyle
  Of hungry eies, which n'ote° therewith be fild,   *could not*
  And yet through languor of her late sweet toyle,
  Few drops, more cleare then Nectar, forth distild,
  That like pure Orient perles[8] adowne it trild,°   *trickled*
  And her faire eyes sweet smyling in delight,
  Moystened their fierie beames, with which she thrild°   *pierced*
  Fraile harts, yet quenchèd° not; like starry light *quenched; killed*
Which sparckling on the silent waves, does seeme more bright.

79

The young man sleeping by her, seemd to bee
  Some goodly swayne of honorable place,°   *rank*
  That certès° it great pittie was to see   *certainly*
  Him his nobilitie so foule deface;°   *disgrace*
  A sweet regard,° and amiable grace,   *demeanor*
  Mixèd with manly sternnesse did appeare
  Yet sleeping, in his well proportioned face,

---

7. I.e., Guyon and the Palmer.   8. Lustrous pearls of the East.

And on his tender lips the downy heare
Did now but freshly spring, and silken blossomes beare.

80

His warlike armes, the idle instruments
   Of sleeping praise,° were hong upon a tree,   *worthiness*
   And his brave° shield, full of old moniments,°   *splendid / marks of honor*
   Was fowly ra'st,° that none the signes might see;   *erased*
   Ne for them, ne for honour carèd hee,
   Ne ought,° that did to his advauncement tend,   *aught, anything*
   But in lewd loves, and wastfull luxuree,°   *licentiousness*
   His dayes, his goods, his bodie he did spend:
O horrible enchantment, that him so did blend.°   *blind*

81

The noble Elfe,[9] and carefull Palmer drew
   So nigh them, minding nought, but° lustfull game,   *heedful only of*
   That suddein forth they on them rusht, and threw
   A subtile net, which onely for the same
   The skilfull Palmer formally° did frame.[1]   *expressly*
   So held them under fast, the whiles the rest
   Fled all away from feare of fowler shame.
   The faire Enchauntresse, so unwares opprest,°   *surprised*
Tryde all her arts, and all her sleights, thence out to wrest.

82

And eke° her lover strove: but all in vaine;   *also*
   For that same net so cunningly was wound,
   That neither guile, nor force might it distraine.°   *tear*
   They tooke them both, and both them strongly bound
   In captive bandes,° which there they readie found: *bonds*
   But her in chaines of adamant[2] he tyde;
   For nothing else might keepe her safe and sound;
   But Verdant° (so he hight°) he soone untyde,   *Green / was called*
And counsell sage in steed° thereof to him applyde.   *instead*

83

But all those pleasant bowres and Pallace brave,°   *splendid*
   Guyon broke downe, with rigour pittilesse;
   Ne ought their goodly workmanship might save
   Them from the tempest of his wrathfulnesse,
   But that their blisse he turn'd to balefulnesse:°   *distress*
   Their groves he feld, their gardins did deface,
   Their arbers spoyle, their Cabinets° suppresse,   *bowers*
   Their banket° houses burne, their buildings race,°   *banquet / raze*
And of the fairest late,° now made the fowlest place.   *lately*

9. Knight of Faerie Land, here, Guyon.
1. The episode recalls the capture of Venus and her lover Mars in a net cunningly set around his marriage bed by Venus's husband, Vulcan, the blacksmith god (*Odyssey* 8.272–84).
2. Steel or some other extremely hard substance.

84

Then led they her away, and eke that knight
  They with them led, both sorrowfull and sad:
  The way they came, the same retourn'd they right,
  Till they arrivèd, where they lately had
  Charm'd those wild-beasts, that rag'd with furie mad.[3]
  Which now awaking, fierce at them gan fly,
  As in their mistresse reskew, whom they lad;°   *led*
  But them the Palmer soone did pacify.
Then Guyon askt, what meant those beastes, which there did ly.

85

Said he, "These seeming beasts are men indeed,
  Whom this Enchauntresse hath transformèd thus,
  Whylome° her lovers, which her lusts did feed,   *formerly*
  Now turnèd into figures hideous,
  According to their mindes like monstruous."[4]
  "Sad end," quoth he, "of life intemperate,
  And mournefull meed° of joyes delicious: *reward*
  But Palmer, if it mote thee so aggrate,°   *please*
Let them returnèd be unto their former state."

86

Streight way he with his vertuous° staffe them strooke,   *powerful*
  And streight of beasts they comely men became;
  Yet being men they did unmanly looke,
  And starèd ghastly, some for inward shame,
  And some for wrath, to see their captive Dame:
  But one aboye the rest in speciall,
  That had an hog beene late, hight° Grille[5] by name,   *called*
  Repinèd° greatly, and did him miscall,°   *complained / revile*
That had from hoggish forme him brought to naturall.

87

Said Guyon, "See the mind of beastly man,
  That hath so soone forgot the excellence
  Of his creation, when he life began,
  That now he chooseth, with vile difference,°   *preference*
  To be a beast, and lacke intelligence."
  To whom the Palmer thus, "The donghill kind
  Delights in filth and foule incontinence:
  Let Grill be Grill, and have his hoggish mind,
But let us hence depart, whilest wether serves and wind."

3. See above, stanza 43, note 3.
4. Even as their own minds were similarly monstrous. Circe changed Odysseus's companions into animals, but Odysseus had a charm to release them.

5. According to one of Plutarch's dialogues, a man named Gryllus ("fierce," "cruel"), having been changed into a hog by Circe, refused to be restored to human form by Odysseus.

From The Third Booke of The Faerie Queene

Containing
The Legend of Britomartis,[1]
or
Of Chastitie

Summary The third book of *The Faerie Queene* is a multifaceted exploration of the virtue of chastity, which is, for Spenser, closely bound up with the power of love. The principal character is the lady knight Britomart, on a quest to find her destined beloved, the knight Artegall. Her adventures are braided together with those of many others, including the twins Belphoebe and Amoret, whose miraculous conception and birth is related at the opening of canto 6. The infant Belphoebe is adopted by the goddess Diana; Amoret is taken up by the goddess Venus and brought to the Garden of Adonis, Spenser's most remarkable allegorical vision of erotic union and procreation.

From *Canto 6*

[THE GARDEN OF ADONIS]

The birth of faire Belphoebe and
Of Amoret is told.
The Gardins of Adonis fraught
With pleasures manifold.

1

Well may I weene,° faire Ladies, all this while	*suppose*
Ye wonder, how this noble Damozell°	*i.e., Belphoebe*
So great perfections did in her compile,°	*gather together*
Sith° that in salvage° forests she did dwell,	*since / wild*
So farre from court and royall Citadell,	
The great schoolmistresse of all curtesy:	
Seemeth that such wild woods should far expell	
All civill° usage and gentility,	*polite*
And gentle sprite deforme with rude rusticity.	

2

But to this faire Belphoebe in her berth	
The heavens so favourable were and free,°	*generous*
Looking with myld aspect upon the earth,	
In th'Horoscope of her nativitee,	
That all the gifts of grace and chastitee	
On her they pourèd forth of plenteous horne;[2]	

---

1. The heroine's name comes from the pseudo-Virgilian poem *Ciris* (lines 295–305), where Britomartis is a goddess associated with Diana, the chaste goddess of the moon. For Spenser, her name suggests the (false) etymology *Brito* ("Brit-oness") + *Mart* ("Mars," god of war).
2. Horn of plenty, cornucopia. The planets were in favorable relationship ("myld aspect") at her birth; the combination of Jupiter ("Jove") and Venus was thought to be especially fortunate.

Jove laught on Venus from his soveraigne see,° *throne*
   And Phoebus with faire beames did her adorne,
And all the Graces rockt her cradle being borne.

3

Her berth was of the wombe of Morning dew,[3]
   And her conception of the joyous Prime,° *springtime*
   And all her whole creation did her shew
   Pure and unspotted from all loathly crime,
   That is ingenerate in fleshly slime.[4]
   So was this virgin borne, so was she bred,° *nourished*
   So was she traynèd up from time to time,° *at all times*
   In all chast vertue, and true bounti-hed° *goodness*
Till to her dew perfection she was ripenèd.

4

Her mother was the faire Chrysogonee,
   The daughter of Amphisa,[5] who by race
   A Faerie was, yborne of high degree,
   She bore Belphoebe, she bore in like cace
   Faire Amoretta in the second place:
   These two were twinnes, and twixt them two did share
   The heritage of all celestiall grace.
   That all the rest it seem'd they robbèd bare
Of bountie,° and of beautie, and all vertues rare. *goodness*

5

It were a goodly storie, to declare,
   By what straunge accident° faire Chrysogone *happening*
   Conceived these infants, and how them she bare,
   In this wild forrest wandring all alone,
   After she had nine moneths fulfild and gone:
   For not as other wemens commune brood,
   They were enwombèd in the sacred throne
   Of her chaste bodie, nor with commune food,
As other wemens babes, they suckèd vitall blood.

6

But wondrously they were begot, and bred
   Through influence of th'heavens fruitfull ray,[6]
   As it in antique bookes is mentionèd.
   It was upon a Sommers shynie day,

---

3. An echo of Psalm 110.3 (Book of Common Prayer): "The dew of thy birth is of the womb of the morning," taken to refer to the conception and birth of Christ.
4. Like Christ or the Virgin, she is said to be free of original sin, which is innate ("ingenerate") in human flesh.

5. "Of double nature" (Greek). "Chrysogonee": "golden-born" (Greek), alluding to the myth of Danaë, who conceived when Jove visited her as a golden shower.
6. I.e., an emanation from the heavens—continuing the analogue to the Virgin's miraculous conception of Christ.

When Titan[7] faire his beamès did display,
In a fresh fountaine, farre from all mens vew,
She bathed her brest, the boyling heat t'allay;
She bathed with roses red, and violets blew,
And all the sweetest flowres, that in the forrest grew.

7

Till faint through irkesome° wearinesse, adowne   *burdensome*
Upon the grassie ground her selfe she layd
To sleepe, the whiles a gentle slombring swowne°   *deep sleep*
Upon her fell all naked bare displayd;
The sunne-beames bright upon her body playd,
Being through former bathing mollifide,°   *softened*
And pierst into her wombe, where they embayd°   *steeped*
With so sweet sence° and secret power unspide,   *sensation*
That in her pregnant flesh they shortly fructifide.°   *bore fruit*

8

Miraculous may seeme to him, that reades
So straunge ensample of conceptiön;
But reason teacheth that the fruitfull seades
Of all things living, through impression
Of the sunbeames in moyst complexion,
Doe life conceive and quickned are by kynd:°   *nature*
So after Nilus° inundation,   *the Nile's*
Infinite shapes of creatures men do fynd,
Informèd in° the mud, on which the Sunne hath shynd.[8]   *formed within*

9

Great father he of generation
Is rightly cald, th'author of life and light;
And his faire sister for creation
Ministreth matter fit, which tempred right
With heate and humour,° breedes the living wight.[9]   *bodily fluid*
So sprong these twinnes in wombe of Chrysogone,
Yet wist° she nought thereof, but sore affright,°   *knew / afraid*
Wondred to see her belly so upblone,
Which still increast, till she her terme had full outgone.

10

Whereof conceiving shame and foule disgrace,
Albe° her guiltlesse consciënce her cleard,   *albeit*
She fled into the wildernesse a space,°   *for a time*
Till that unweeldy burden she had reard,°   *brought forth*
And shund dishonor, which as death she feard:

---

7. The sun; the first Greek sun god, Helios, was descended from the Titans.
8. The theory that life was spontaneously generated by the sun's influence on the moist earth is drawn from Ovid and Lucretius.

9. Creature. The moon (the sun's "sister") is thought to furnish ("ministreth") matter for the creation of life through its control of mortal bodies, especially women's.

Where wearie of long travell,[1] downe to rest
    Her selfe she set, and comfortably cheard;[2]
    There a sad° cloud of sleepe her overkest,°   *heavy / overcast*
And seizèd every sense with sorrow sore opprest.

11

It fortunèd,° faire Venus having lost   *chanced*
    Her little sonne, the wingèd god of love,
    Who for some light° displeasure, which him crost,°   *trivial / thwarted*
    Was from her fled, as flit as ayerie Dove,[3]
    And left her blisfull bowre of joy above,
    (So from her often he had fled away,
    When she for ought° him sharpely did reprove,   *aught, anything*
    And wandred in the world in strange aray,
Disguiz'd in thousand shapes, that none might him bewray.°) *discover*

12

Him for to seeke, she left her heavenly hous,
    The house of goodly formes and faire aspects,[4]
    Whence all the world derives the glorious
    Features of beautie, and all shapes select,°   *choice*
    With which high God his workmanship hath deckt;°   *adorned*
    And searchèd every way, through which his wings
    Had borne him, or° his tract° she mote° detect: *ere / track / might*
    She promist kisses sweet, and sweeter things
Unto the man, that of him tydings to her brings.

13

First she him sought in Court, where most he used
    Whylome° to haunt,° but there she found him not;   *formerly / resort*
    But many there she found, which sore accused
    His falsehood, and with foule infamous blot
    His cruell deedes and wicked wyles did spot:°   *vilify*
    Ladies and Lords she every where mote heare
    Complayning, how with his empoysned shot
    Their wofull harts he wounded had whyleare,°   *a while before*
And so had left them languishing twixt hope and feare.

14

She then the Cities sought from gate to gate,
    And every one did aske, did he him see;
    And every one her answerd, that too late
    He had him seene, and felt the crueltie
    Of his sharpe darts and whot artillerie;°   *hot weapons*
    And every one threw forth reproches rife
    Of his mischievous deedes, and said, That hee

---

1. Also "travail": labor—i.e., that of childbirth.
2. I.e., weary of her long travels she sat down to rest and was cheered by that comfort.
3. Venus's bird. Venus's search for the lost Cupid is based on a Greek poem by Moschus (2nd century B.C.E.), often imitated in the Renaissance.
4. Astrological aspects of the planet Venus.

Was the disturber of all civill life,
The enimy of peace, and author of all strife.

15

Then in the countrey she abroad him sought,
    And in the rurall cottages inquired,
    Where also many plaints to her were brought,
    How he their heedlesse harts with love had fyred,
    And his false venim through their veines inspyred;°   *breathed*
    And eke° the gentle shepheard swaynes,° which sat   *also / lovers*
    Keeping their fleecie flockes, as they were hyred,
    She sweetly heard complaine, both how and what
Her sonne had to them doen; yet she did smile thereat.

16

But when in none of all these she him got,
    She gan avize,° where else he mote him hyde: *consider*
    At last she her bethought, that she had not
    Yet sought the salvage° woods and forrests wyde,   *wild*
    In which full many lovely Nymphes abyde,
    Mongst whom might be, that he did closely lye,
    Or that the love of some of them him tyde:°   *bound*
    For thy° she thither cast° her course t'apply,   *therefore / resolved*
To search the secret haunts of Dianes company.

17

Shortly unto the wastefull° woods she came,   *desolate*
    Whereas she found the Goddesse with her crew,
    After late chace of their embrewèd° game,   *bloodstained*
    Sitting beside a fountaine in a rew,°   *row*
    Some of them washing with the liquid dew
    From off their dainty limbes the dustie sweat,
    And soyle which did deforme their lively hew;
    Others lay shaded from the scorching heat;
The rest upon her person gave attendance great.[5]

18

She having hong upon a bough on high
    Her bow and painted quiver, had unlaste°   *unlaced*
    Her silver buskins° from her nimble thigh,   *boots*
    And her lancke loynes° ungirt, and brests unbraste,   *slender waist*
    After her heat the breathing cold to taste;
    Her golden lockes, that late in tresses bright
    Embreaded were for hindring of her haste,[6]
    Now loose about her shoulders hong undight,°   *unbound*
And were with sweet Ambrosia° all besprinckled light.   *perfume*

---

5. This episode alludes to the myth of Actaeon, who angered the huntress goddess Diana by surprising her in her bath; she transformed him into a stag and he was torn apart by his own hounds.
6. I.e., her golden locks were braided ("embreaded"), lest they should hinder her swiftness.

19

Soone as she Venus saw behind her backe,
   She was ashamed to be so loose surprized,
   And woxe° halfe wroth against her damzels slacke,   *waxed, grew*
   That had not her thereof before avized,[7]
   But suffred her so carelesly disguized°   *undressed*
   Be overtaken. Soone her garments loose
   Upgath'ring, in her bosome she comprized,°   *drew together*
   Well as she might, and to the Goddesse rose,
Whiles all her Nymphes did like a girlond her enclose.

20

Goodly° she gan faire Cytherea[8] greet,   *courteously*
   And shortly askèd her, what cause her brought
   Into that wildernesse for her unmeet,°   *unsuitable*
   From her sweete bowres, and beds with pleasures fraught:
   That suddein change she strange adventure° thought.   *chance*
   To whom halfe weeping, she thus answerèd,
   That she her dearest sonne Cupido sought,
   Who in his frowardnesse° from her was fled;   *stubbornness*
That she repented sore, to have him angerèd.

21

Thereat Diana gan to smile, in scorne
   Of her vaine plaint, and to her scoffing sayd;
   "Great pittie sure, that ye be so forlorne°   *bereft*
   Of your gay sonne, that gives ye so good ayd
   To your disports: ill mote ye bene apayd."[9]
   But she was more engrievèd, and replide;
   "Faire sister, ill beseemes it to upbrayd
   A dolefull heart with so disdainfull pride;
The like that mine, may be your paine another tide.°   *time*

22

"As you in woods and wanton wildernesse
   Your glory set, to chace the salvage beasts,
   So my delight is all in joyfulnesse,
   In beds, in bowres, in banckets,° and in feasts: *banquets*
   And ill becomes you with your loftie creasts,°   *helmets*
   To scorne the joy, that Jove is glad to seeke;
   We both are bound to follow heavens beheasts,
   And tend our charges° with obeisance meeke: *duties*
Spare, gentle sister, with reproch my paine to eeke.°   *augment*

7. I.e., she was half-angered at her nymphs, who were remiss in not warning her (of Venus's presence).
8. Venus, so named in allusion to her emergence from the sea near the island of Cythera.
9. I.e., your son aids you in your bad sports; may you be repaid in kind by this ill trick he plays on you.

23

"And tell me, if that ye my sonne have heard,
　To lurk emongst your Nymphes in secret wize;
　Or keepe their cabins:° much I am affeard,　　　　　　　*caves*
　Least° he like one of them him selfe disguize,　　　　　　*lest*
　And turne his arrowes to their exercize:[1]
　So may he long himselfe full easie hide:
　For he is faire and fresh in face and guize,
　As any Nymph (let not it be envyde.°)"　　　　　　*begrudged*
So saying every Nymph full narrowly she eyde.

24

But Phoebe° therewith sore was angerèd,　　　*another name for Diana*
　And sharply said; "Goe Dame, goe seeke your boy,
　Where you him lately left, in Mars his bed;[2]
　He comes not here, we scorne his foolish joy,
　Ne lend we leisure to his idle toy:°　　　　　　*game*
　But if I catch him in this company,
　By Stygian lake I vow, whose sad annoy°　　　*grievous affliction*
　The Gods doe dread,[3] he dearely shall abye:°　　　*suffer*
Ile clip his wanton wings, that he no more shall fly."

25

Whom when as Venus saw so sore displeased,
　She inly sory was, and gan relent,°　　　　　　*soften*
　What she had said: so her she soone appeased,
　With sugred words and gentle blandishment,[4]
　Which as a fountaine from her sweet lips went,
　And wellèd goodly forth, that in short space
　She was well pleasd, and forth her damzels sent,
　Through all the woods, to search from place to place,
If any tract° of him or tydings they mote trace.　　　*track*

26

To search the God of love, her Nymphes she sent
　Throughout the wandring forrest every where:
　And after them her selfe eke° with her went　　　　*also*
　To seeke the fugitive, both farre and nere.
　So long they sought, till they arrivèd were
　In that same shadie covert, whereas lay
　Faire Crysogone in slombry traunce whilere:°　　*a while before*
　Who in her sleepe (a wondrous thing to say)
Unwares had borne two babes, as faire as springing° day.　　*dawning*

---

1. I.e., he may shoot his arrows disguised as one
of Diana's hunting nymphs (also, he may shoot at
them, causing them to fall in love).
2. Referring to Venus's love affair with Mars.

3. An oath sworn on the river Styx even the gods
feared to break.
4. In making peace with her opposite, Venus here
enacts one of her traditional roles, Concord.

27

Unwares she them conceived, unwares she bore:
　　She bore withouten paine, that° she conceived　　　*what*
　　Withouten pleasure: ne her need° implore　　*nor did she need to*
　　Lucinaes[5] aide: which when they both perceived,
　　They were through wonder nigh of sense bereaved,
　　And gazing each on other, nought bespake:
　　At last they both agreed, her seeming grieved°　　*oppressed (with sleep)*
　　Out of her heavy swowne not to awake,
But from her loving side the tender babes to take.

28

Up they them tooke, each one a babe uptooke,
　　And with them carried, to be fosterèd;
　　Dame Phoebe to a Nymph her babe betooke,°　　*gave in charge*
　　To be upbrought in perfect Maydenhed,°　　*virginity*
　　And of her selfe her name Belphoebe red:°　　*called*
　　But Venus hers thence farre away convayd,
　　To be upbrought in goodly womanhed,
　　And in her litle loves stead, which was strayd,
Her Amoretta[6] cald, to comfort her dismayd.

29

She brought her to her joyous Paradize,
　　Where most she wonnes,° when she on earth does dwel.　　*dwells*
　　So faire a place, as Nature can devize:
　　Whether in Paphos, or Cytheron hill,
　　Or it in Gnidus be, I wote not well;[7]
　　But well I wote° by tryall,° that this same　　*know / experience*
　　All other pleasant places doth excell,
　　And callèd is by her lost lovers name,
The Gardin of Adonis,[8] farre renowmd by fame.

30

In that same Gardin all the goodly flowres,
　　Wherewith dame Nature doth her beautifie,
　　And decks the girlonds° of her paramoures,°　　*garlands / lovers*
　　Are fetcht: there is the first seminarie°　　*seedbed*
　　Of all things, that are borne to live and die,
　　According to their kindes. Long worke it were,
　　Here to account° the endlesse progenie　　*recount*
　　Of all the weedes,° that bud and blossome there;　　*plants*
But so much as doth need, must needs be counted° here.　　*recounted*

---

5. "Lucina" is another name for Juno (or sometimes Diana) as goddess of childbirth.
6. Because she takes the place of Cupid (Amor),
she is named Amoretta, "a little love."

7. These are all shrines of Venus.
8. The beautiful young hunter Adonis, passionately loved by Venus, was, in the standard version
of the myth, killed by a boar.

31

It sited° was in fruitfull soyle of old,   *placed*
  And girt in with two walles on either side;
  The one of yron, the other of bright gold,
  That none might thorough breake, nor over-stride:
  And double gates it had, which opened wide,
  By which both in and out men moten° pas;   *might*
  Th'one faire and fresh, the other old and dride:
  Old Genius[9] the porter of them was,
Old Genius, the which a double nature has.

32

He letteth in, he letteth out to wend,°   *go*
  All that to come into the world desire;
  A thousand thousand naked babes attend
  About him day and night, which doe require,
  That he with fleshly weedes would them attire:[1]
  Such as him list,° such as eternall fate   *as he chooses*
  Ordainèd hath, he clothes with sinfull mire,°   *earth*
  And sendeth forth to live in mortall state,
Till they againe returne backe by the hinder gate.

33

After that they againe returnèd beene,
  They in that Gardin planted be againe;
  And grow afresh, as° they had never seene   *as if*
  Fleshly corruptiön, nor mortall paine.
  Some thousand yeares so doen they there remaine;
  And then of him are clad with other hew,°   *form*
  Or sent into the chaungefull world againe,
  Till thither they returne, where first they grew:
So like a wheele around they runne from old to new.[2]

34

Ne° needs there Gardiner to set, or sow,   *neither*
  To plant or prune: for of their owne accord
  All things, as they created were, doe grow,
  And yet remember well the mightie word,
  Which first was spoken by th'Almightie lord,
  That bad them to increase and multiply:[3]
  Ne° doe they need with water of the ford,°   *nor / stream*
  Or of the clouds to moysten their roots dry;
For in themselves eternall moisture they imply.°   *contain*

---

9. God of generation and so of the natural processes birth and death. The Garden of Adonis is a myth of Spenser's devising.

1. I.e., the souls in their preexistent state ("naked babes") request to be clothed with flesh.

2. The original source for Spenser's myth of cyclic generation and reincarnation is Plato's *Republic* 10 (the myth of Er).

3. "And God said unto them, Be fruitful, and multiply, and replenish the earth" (Genesis 1.28).

35

Infinite shapes of creatures there are bred,
    And uncouth° formes, which none yet ever knew,   *strange*
    And every sort is in a sundry° bed   *separate*
    Set by it selfe, and ranckt in comely rew:°   *row*
    Some fit for reasonable soules t'indew,[4]
    Some made for beasts, some made for birds to weare,
    And all the fruitfull spawne of fishes hew°   *shape*
    In endlesse rancks along enraungèd were,
That seem'd the Oceän could not containe them there.

36

Daily they grow, and daily forth are sent
    Into the world, it to replenish more;
    Yet is the stocke not lessenèd, nor spent,
    But still remaines in everlasting store,°   *abundance*
    As it at first created was of yore.
    For in the wide wombe of the world there lyes,
    In hatefull darkenesse and in deepe horrore,
    An huge eternall Chaos, which supplyes
The substances of natures fruitfull progenyes.

37

All things from thence doe their first being fetch,
    And borrow matter, whereof they are made,
    Which when as forme and feature it does ketch,°   *take*
    Becomes a bodie, and doth then invade°   *enter*
    The state of life, out of the griesly° shade.   *ghastly*
    That substance° is eterne, and bideth so,   *matter*
    Ne when the life decayes, and forme does fade,
    Doth it consume,° and into nothing go,   *is it destroyed*
But chaungèd is, and often altred to and fro.

38

The substance is not chaunged, nor alterèd,
    But th'only forme° and outward fashiön;   *except only the form*
    For every substance is conditionèd
    To change her hew,° and sundry formes to don,   *appearance*
    Meet° for her temper and complexion: *suited*
    For formes are variable and decay,
    By course of kind,° and by occasion;   *nature*
    And that faire flowre of beautie fades away,
As doth the lilly fresh before the sunny ray.

---

4. I.e., some of these shapes are fit for humans to assume. An echo of 1 Corinthians 15.39: "All flesh is not the same flesh: but there is one kind of flesh of men, another flesh of beasts, another of fishes, and another of birds."

39

Great enimy to it, and to all the rest,
  That in the Gardin of Adonis springs,
  Is wicked Time, who with his scyth addrest,°   *armed*
Does mow the flowring herbes and goodly things,
And all their glory to the ground downe flings,
Where they doe wither, and are fowly mard:°   *marred*
He flyes about, and with his flaggy° wings   *drooping*
  Beates downe both leaves and buds without regard,
Ne ever pittie may relent° his malice hard.   *soften*

40

Yet pittie often did the gods relent,
  To see so faire things mard, and spoylèd quight:°   *quite*
  And their great mother Venus did lament
The losse of her deare brood, her deare delight;
Her hart was pierst with pittie at the sight,
When walking through the Gardin, them she spyde,
Yet no'te° she find redresse for such despight.°   *could not / wrong*
  For all that lives, is subject to that law:
All things decay in time, and to their end do draw.

41

But were it not, that Time their troubler is,
  All that in this delightfull Gardin growes,
  Should happie be, and have immortall blis:
For here all plentie, and all pleasure flowes,
And sweet love gentle fits° emongst them throwes,   *i.e., fits of passion*
Without fell° rancor, or fond° gealosie;   *fierce / foolish*
Franckly each paramour his leman knowes,[5]
  Each bird his mate, ne any does envie
Their goodly meriment, and gay felicitie.

42

There is continuall spring, and harvest there[6]
  Continuall, both meeting at one time:
  For both the boughes doe laughing blossomes beare,
And with fresh colours decke the wanton Prime,°   *spring*
And eke attonce the heavy trees they clime,
Which seeme to labour under their fruits lode:
The whiles the joyous birdes make their pastime
  Emongst the shadie leaves, their sweet abode,
And their true loves without suspition° tell abrode.   *fear*

---

5. Openly each lover has intercourse with ("knowes") his mistress.
6. The coincidence of spring and autumn is char-acteristic of unfallen nature in Eden; other fea-tures of this description are drawn from a common literary topic, the *locus amoenus* (pleasant place).

43

Right in the middest of that Paradise,
  There stood a stately Mount, on whose round top
  A gloomy° grove of mirtle trees[7] did rise,   *dark, shady*
  Whose shadie boughes sharpe steele did never lop,
  Nor wicked beasts their tender buds did crop,
  But like a girlond compassèd the hight,
  And from their fruitfull sides sweet gum did drop,
  That all the ground with precious deaw bedight,
Threw forth most dainty odours, and most sweet delight.

44

And in the thickest covert of that shade,
  There was a pleasant arbour, not by art,
  But of the trees owne inclination° made,   *inclining*
  Which knitting their rancke° braunches part to part,   *dense*
  With wanton yvie twyne entrayld athwart,[8]
  And Eglantine, and Caprifole° emong,   *honeysuckle*
  Fashiond above within their inmost part,
  That nether Phoebus beams could through them throng,°   *press*
Nor Aeolus° sharp blast could worke them any wrong.   *god of winds*

45

And all about grew every sort° of flowre,   *species*
  To which sad lovers were transformd of yore;
  Fresh Hyacinthus, Phoebus paramoure,
  And dearest love,[9]
  Foolish Narcisse, that likes the watry shore,
  Sad Amaranthus, made a flowre but late,°   *only recently*
  Sad Amaranthus, in whose purple gore
  Me seemes I see Amintas wretched fate,
To whom sweet Poets verse hath given endlesse date.[1]

46

There wont° faire Venus often to enjoy   *was accustomed*
  Her deare Adonis joyous company,
  And reape sweet pleasure of the wanton boy;
  There yet, some say, in secret he does ly,
  Lappèd in flowres and pretious spycery,°   *spices*
  By her hid from the world, and from the skill°   *knowledge*
  Of Stygian Gods,[2] which doe her love envy;

---

7. Myrtle ("mirtle") trees were sacred to Venus. "Mount": with allusion to the *mons veneris*.
8. I.e., with luxuriant ivy entwined among them.
9. This quatrain is damaged—in rhyme pattern as well as in the truncated fourth line.
1. The purple Amaranthus is a symbol of immortality; the Greek name means "unfading." By one poetic account, Amintas died for the love of Phillis and was transformed into the Amaranthus. Hyacinth and Narcissus were also transformed into flowers and thereby eternized.
2. Gods of the underworld (e.g., Pluto, Hecate, the Furies, Charon), who have a claim on Adonis, since in the usual formulation of the myth he was killed by the boar.

But she her selfe, when ever that she will,
Possesseth° him, and of his sweetnesse takes her fill. *i.e., sexually*

47

And sooth° it seemes they say: for he may° not *truth / can*
    For ever die, and ever buried bee
    In balefull night, where all things are forgot;
    All° be he subject to mortalitie, *although*
    Yet is eterne in mutabilitie,
    And by succession made perpetuall,
    Transformèd oft, and chaungèd diverslie:
    For him the Father of all formes they call;[3]
Therefore needs mote° he live, that living gives to all. *must*

48

There now he liveth in eternall blis,
    Joying° his goddesse, and of her enjoyd: *enjoying*
    Ne feareth he henceforth that foe of his,
    Which with his cruell tuske him deadly cloyd:° *gored*
    For that wilde Bore, the which him once annoyd,° *injured*
    She firmely hath emprisonèd for ay,
    That her sweet love his malice mote° avoyd, *might*
    In a strong rocky Cave, which is they say,
Hewen underneath that Mount, that none him losen° may. *set free*

49

There now he lives in everlasting joy,
    With many of the Gods in company,
    Which thither haunt,° and with the wingèd boy *frequent*
    Sporting himselfe in safe felicity:
    Who when he[4] hath with spoiles° and cruelty *plundering*
    Ransackt the world, and in the wofull harts
    Of many wretches set his triumphes hye,
    Thither resorts, and laying his sad darts° *arrows*
Aside, with faire Adonis playes his wanton parts.

50

And his true love faire Psyche with him playes,[5]
    Faire Psyche to him lately reconcyld,
    After long troubles and unmeet upbrayes,° *upbraidings, scoldings*
    With which his mother Venus her revyld,° *reviled*
    And eke himselfe her cruelly exyld:
    But now in stedfast love and happy state
    She with him lives, and hath him borne a chyld,

3. Adonis imposes successive forms on enduring substance and thereby brings living creatures into being.
4. Cupid, now restored to Venus.
5. "Playes" suggests, as well, sexual play. Cupid abandoned Psyche when she disobeyed his com-mand not to look on his face; she became his bride, and immortal, after enduring many severe trials imposed by Venus. The myth was often read as an allegory of the soul's trials in this life before it gains heaven.

Pleasure, that doth both gods and men aggrate,°   *gratify*
Pleasure, the daughter of Cupid and Psyche late.°   *recently born*

51

Hither great Venus brought this infant faire,
  The younger daughter of Chrysogonee,
  And unto Psyche with great trust and care
  Committed her, yfosterèd to bee,
  And trainèd up in true feminitee:°   *womanliness*
  Who no lesse carefully her tenderèd,°   *cared for*
  Then her owne daughter Pleasure, to whom shee
  Made her companion, and her lessonèd
In all the lore of love, and goodly womanhead.

52

In which when she to perfect ripenesse grew,
  Of grace and beautie noble Paragone,
  She brought her forth into the worldès vew,
  To be th'ensample of true love alone,
  And Lodestarre° of all chaste affectiöne,   *guiding star*
  To all faire Ladies, that doe live on ground.
  To Faery court she came, where many one
  Admyrd her goodly haveour,° and found   *demeanor*
His feeble hart wide launched° with loves cruell wound.   *pierced*

53

But she to none of them her love did cast,
  Save to the noble knight Sir Scudamore,[6]
  To whom her loving hart she linkèd fast
  In faithfull love, t'abide for evermore,
  And for his dearest sake endurèd sore,
  Sore trouble of an hainous enimy;
  Who her would forcèd have to have forlore°   *forsaken*
  Her former love, and stedfast loyalty,
As ye may elsewhere read that ruefull history.[7]

*   *   *

Cantos 7–10 *Summary*   Cantos 7 and 8 focus especially on the adventures of the beautiful maiden Florimell, who, always in flight from threatening males, narrowly escapes a series of disasters. Cantos 9 and 10 tell the story of the aged and fanatically jealous miser Malbecco, his lusty young wife, Hellenore, her elopement with the knight Paridell, Malbecco's fruitless pursuit of them, and his eventual transformation into the allegorical figure of Jealousy.

---

6. See canto 11, stanza 7, and note.
7. The final, transitional stanza of the canto is omitted.

Canto 11

Britomart chaceth Ollyphant,
findes Scudamour distrest:
Assayes° the house of Busyrane,   *assails*
where Loves spoyles° are exprest.°   *plunders / displayed*

1

O Hatefull hellish Snake,° what furie furst   *i.e., jealousy*
　　Brought thee from balefull house of Proserpine,[8]
　　Where in her bosome she thee long had nurst,
　　And fostred up with bitter milke of tine,°   *anguish*
　　Fowle Gealosie, that turnest love divine
　　To joylesse dread, and mak'st the loving hart
　　With hatefull thoughts to languish and to pine,
　　And feed it selfe with selfe-consuming smart?
Of all the passions in the mind thou vilest art.

2

O let him far be banishèd away,
　　And in his stead let Love for ever dwell,
　　Sweet Love, that doth his golden wings embay°   *steep*
　　In blessèd Nectar,° and pure Pleasures well,   *the drink of the gods*
　　Untroubled of° vile feare, or bitter fell.°   *by / gall, rancor*
　　And ye faire Ladies, that your kingdomes make
　　In th'harts of men, them governe wisely well,
　　And of faire Britomart ensample take,
That was as trew in love, as Turtle to her make.[9]

3

Who with Sir Satyrane, as earst ye red,[1]
　　Forth ryding from Malbeccoes hostlesse° hous,   *inhospitable*
　　Far off aspyde a young man, the which fled
　　From an huge Geaunt, that with hideous
　　And hatefull outrage long him chacèd thus;
　　It was that Ollyphant, the brother deare
　　Of that Argante vile and vitious,°   *vicious*
　　From whom the Squire of Dames was reft whylere;°   *formerly*
This all as bad as she, and worse, if worse ought° were.[2]   *anything*

4

For as the sister did in feminine
　　And filthy lust exceede all woman kind,

---

8. Queen of Hades and consort of Pluto. The snake is an attribute of Envy, to which Jealousy is related; also the hair of the vengeful deities, the Furies, is made up of snakes.
9. The turtledove was a common symbol of matrimonial love and fidelity.
1. I.e., as the reader saw earlier (in the first stanza of canto 10). Satyrane had first appeared in Book 1, canto 6, stanzas 20–48.
2. Ollyphant and Argante, brother and sister giants, lived in incest and practiced many other sexual evils. Satyrane rescued the exceptionally promiscuous Squire of Dames from Argante in Book 3, canto 7, stanzas 37–38.

So he surpassèd his sex masculine,
    In beastly use that I did ever find;
    Whom when as Britomart beheld behind
    The fearefull boy so greedily pursew,
    She was emmovèd in her noble mind,
    T'employ her puissaunce° to his reskew,   *power*
And prickèd° fiercely forward, where she him did vew.   *spurred*

5

Ne was Sir Satyrane her far behinde,
    But with like fiercenesse did ensew° the chace: *follow*
    Whom when the Gyaunt saw, he soone resinde°   *resigned*
    His former suit, and from them fled apace;
    They after both, and boldly bad him bace,°   *challenged him*
    And each did strive the other to out-goe,
    But he them both outran a wondrous space,
    For he was long, and swift as any Roe,°   *female deer*
And now made better speed, t'escape his fearèd foe.

6

It was not Satyrane, whom he did feare,
    But Britomart the flowre of chastity;
    For he the powre of chast hands might not beare,
    But always did their dread encounter fly:
    And now so fast his feet he did apply,°   *direct*
    That he has gotten to a forrest neare,
    Where he is shrowded in security.
    The wood they enter, and search every where,
They searchèd diversely,° so both divided were.   *in different directions*

7

Faire Britomart so long him followèd,
    That she at last came to a fountaine sheare,°   *clear*
    By which there lay a knight all wallowèd°   *lying prostrate*
    Upon the grassy ground, and by him neare
    His haberjeon,° his helmet, and his speare;   *coat of mail*
    A little off, his shield was rudely throwne,
    On which the wingèd boy° in colours cleare   *Cupid*
    Depeincted° was, full easie to be knowne,   *depicted*
And he thereby, where ever it in field was showne.[3]

8

His face upon the ground did groveling° ly,   *prone*
    As if he had bene slombring in the shade,
    That the brave Mayd would not for courtesy,
    Out of his quiet slomber him abrade,°   *arouse*
    Nor seeme too suddeinly him to invade:°   *intrude on*

---

3. The knight's shield implies that he is the Sir Scudamore (Italian *scudo* + *amore*: "shield of love") mentioned in the prefatory quatrain.

Still° as she stood, she heard with grievous throb   *ever*
    Him grone, as if his hart were peeces made,
    And with most painefull pangs to sigh and sob,
That pitty did the Virgins hart of patience rob.

9

At last forth breaking into bitter plaintes
    He said, "O soveraigne Lord that sit'st on hye,
    And raignst in blis emongst thy blessèd Saintes,
    How suffrest thou such shamefull cruelty,
    So long unwreakèd° of thine enimy?   *unrevenged*
    Or hast thou, Lord, of good mens cause no heed?
    Or doth thy justice sleepe, and silent ly?
    What booteth° then the good and righteous deed,   *what is the use of*
If goodnesse find no grace, nor righteousnesse no meed?°   *reward*

10

"If good find grace, and righteousnesse reward,
    Why then is Amoret in caytive band,°   *captive bond*
    Sith° that more bounteous° creature never fared   *since / virtuous*
    On foot, upon the face of living land?
    Or if that heavenly justice may withstand
    The wrongfull outrage of unrighteous men,
    Why then is Busirane[4] with wicked hand
    Suffred,° these seven monethes day in secret den   *permitted*
My Lady and my love so cruelly to pen?

11

"My Lady and my love is cruelly pend
    In dolefull darkenesse from the vew of day,
    Whilest deadly torments do her chast brest rend,
    And the sharpe steele doth rive° her hart in tway,°   *cut / two*
    All for° she Scudamore will not denay.°   *because / deny*
    Yet thou vile man, vile Scudamore art sound,
    Ne° canst her ayde, ne° canst her foe dismay;°   *neither / nor / defeat*
    Unworthy wretch to tread upon the ground,
For whom so faire a Lady feeles so sore a wound."

12

There an huge heape of singulfes° did oppresse   *sobs*
    His strugling soule, and swelling throbs empeach°   *hinder*
    His foltring toung with pangs of drerinesse,°   *anguish*
    Choking the remnant of his plaintife speach,
    As if his dayes were come to their last reach.
    Which when she heard, and saw the ghastly fit,
    Threatning into his life to make a breach,

---

4. His name associates him with Busiris, an Egyptian king famous for his cruelty and identified with the Pharaoh of Exodus; hence he is a symbol of tyranny.

Both with great ruth° and terrour she was smit,   *pity*
Fearing least° from her cage the wearie soule would flit. *lest*

13

Tho° stooping downe she him amovèd° light;   *then / touched*
 Who therewith somewhat starting, up gan looke,
 And seeing him behind a straunger knight,
 Whereas no living creature he mistooke,°   *thought to be*
 With great indignaunce he that sight forsooke,
 And downe againe himselfe disdainefully
 Abjecting, th'earth with his faire forhead strooke:
 Which the bold Virgin seeing, gan apply
Fit medcine to his griefe, and spake thus courtesly.

14

"Ah gentle knight, whose deepe conceivèd griefe
 Well seemes t'exceede the powre of patiënce,
 Yet if that heavenly grace some good reliefe
 You send, submit you to high providence,
 And ever in your noble hart prepense,°   *consider before*
 That all the sorrow in the world is lesse,
 Then vertues might, and values° confidence, *valor's*
 For who nill° bide the burden of distresse, *will not*
Must not here thinke to live: for life is wretchednesse.

15

"Therefore, faire Sir, do comfort to you take,
 And freely read,° what wicked felon so   *tell*
 Hath outraged you, and thrald° your gentle make.° *enslaved / beloved*
 Perhaps this hand may helpe to ease your woe,
 And wreake° your sorrow on your cruell foe, *revenge*
 At least it faire endevour will apply."
 Those feeling wordes so neare the quicke° did goe, *heart*
 That up his head he rearèd easily,°   *readily*
And leaning on his elbow, these few wordes let fly.

16

"What boots it plaine, that cannot be redrest,[5]
 And sow vaine sorrow in a fruitlesse eare,
 Sith powre of hand, nor skill of learnèd brest,
 Ne worldly price cannot redeeme my deare,
 Out of her thraldome° and continuall feare? *slavery*
 For he the tyraunt, which her hath in ward° *in his power*
 By strong enchauntments and blacke Magicke leare,° *lore*
 Hath in a dungeon deepe her close embard,
And many dreadfull feends hath pointed° to her gard. *appointed*

---

5. What is the use of complaining for what cannot be helped?

17

"There he tormenteth her most terribly,
 And day and night afflicts with mortall paine,
 Because to yield him love she doth deny,
 Once to me yold,° not to be yold againe:[6]   *yielded*
 But yet by torture he would her constraine
 Love to conceive in her disdainfull brest;
 Till so she do, she must in doole° remaine,   *dole, pain*
 Ne may by living meanes be thence relest:
What boots it then to plaine, that cannot be redrest?"

18

With this sad hersall° of his heavy stresse,° *rehearsal, tale / affliction*
 The warlike Damzell was empassiond sore,
 And said, "Sir knight, your cause is nothing lesse,
 Then° is your sorrow, certès if not more;[7]   *than*
 For nothing so much pitty doth implore,
 As gentle Ladies helplesse misery.
 But yet, if please ye listen to my lore,°   *teaching*
 I will with proofe of last extremity,[8]
Deliver her fro thence, or with her for you dy."

19

"Ah gentlest° knight alive," said Scudamore,   *noblest*
 "What huge heroicke magnanimity[9]
 Dwels in thy bounteous brest? what couldst thou more,
 If she were thine, and thou as now am I?
 O spare thy happy dayes, and them apply
 To better boot,° but let me dye, that ought;   *use*
 More is more losse: one is enough to dy."
 "Life is not lost," said she, "for which is bought
Endlesse renowm, that more then death is to be sought."

20

Thus she at length perswaded him to rise,
 And with her wend,° to see what new successe   *go*
 Mote° him befall upon new enterprise;   *might*
 His armes, which he had vowed to disprofesse,° *renounce*
 She gathered up and did about him dresse,°   *array*
 And his forwandred° steed unto him got: *wandered away*
 So forth they both yfere° make their progresse, *together*
 And march not past the mountenaunce of a shot,
Till they arrived, whereas their purpose they did plot.[1]

---

6. Scudamore's courtship and winning of Amoret as his love was recounted in canto 4, stanza 10.
7. I.e., certainly ("certès") your cause is worthy of your great sorrow, or even more.
8. I.e., at the extreme peril of my life.

9. Nobility of mind, which produces the highest virtues and the greatest deeds.
1. I.e., they went no farther than the distance of a bow shot before they arrived at the place they purposed to go.

21

There they dismounting, drew their weapons bold
   And stoutly° came unto the Castle gate;   *bravely*
   Whereas no gate they found, them to withhold,
   Nor ward° to wait at morne and evening late,   *guard*
   But in the Porch, that did them sore amate,°   *dismay*
   A flaming fire, ymixt with smouldry smoke,
   And stinking Sulphure, that with griesly° hate   *horrid*
   And dreadfull horrour did all entraunce choke,
Enforcèd them their forward footing to revoke.°   *draw back*

22

Greatly thereat was Britomart dismayd,
   Ne in that stownd wist,[2] how her selfe to beare;
   For daunger vaine it were, to have assayd°   *attempted*
   That cruell element, which all things feare,
   Ne none can suffer to approchen neare:
   And turning backe to Scudamour, thus sayd;
   "What monstrous enmity provoke° we heare,   *challenge*
   Foolhardy as th'Earthes children, the which made
Battell against the Gods?[3] so we a God invade.

23

"Daunger without discretion to attempt,
   Inglorious and beastlike is: therefore Sir knight,
   Aread° what course of you is safest dempt,°   *declare / deemed*
   And how we with our foe may come to fight."
   "This is," quoth he, "the dolorous despight,°   *evil*
   Which earst° to you I playnd:° for neither may *earlier / complained of*
   This fire be quencht by any wit or might,
   Ne yet by any meanes remov'd away,
So mighty be th'enchauntments, which the same do stay.°   *maintain*

24

"What is there else, but cease these fruitlesse paines,
   And leave me to my former languishing?
   Faire Amoret must dwell in wicked chaines,
   And Scudamore here dye with sorrowing."
   "Perdy° not so," said she, "for shamefull thing   *truly*
   It were t'abandon noble chevisaunce,° *chivalric enterprise*
   For shew of perill, without venturing:
   Rather let try extremities of chaunce,
Then enterprisèd prayse for dread to disavaunce."[4]

2. I.e., nor in that trouble ("stownd") did she know ("wist") what to do.
3. I.e., we are like the Titans who dared to do battle against the Olympian gods.

4. I.e., it is better to chance extreme danger than retreat from praiseworthy enterprises because of fear.

25

Therewith resolv'd to prove her utmost might,
   Her ample shield she threw before her face,
   And her swords point directing forward right,
   Assayld the flame, the which eftsoones° gave place,   *immediately*
   And did it selfe divide with equall space,°   *equally on both sides*
   That through she passèd; as a thunder bolt
   Perceth the yielding ayre, and doth displace
   The soring clouds into sad showres ymolt;°   *melted*
So to her yold° the flames, and did their force revolt.° *yielded / turn back*

26

Whom whenas Scudamour saw past the fire,
   Safe and untoucht, he likewise gan assay,°   *attempt*
   With greedy will, and envious desire,
   And bad° the stubborne flames to yield him way: *bade*
   But cruell Mulciber° would not obay   *god of fire*
   His threatfull pride, but did the more augment
   His mighty rage, and with imperious sway°   *power*
   Him forst (maulgre)° his fiercenesse to relent,° *nevertheless / give way*
And backe retire, all scorcht and pitifully brent.

27

With huge impatience he inly swelt,°   *inwardly burned*
   More for great sorrow, that he could not pas,
   Then for the burning torment, which he felt,
   That with fell woodnesse he effiercèd was,[5]
   And wilfully him throwing on the gras,
   Did beat and bounse° his head and brest full sore;   *thump*
   The whiles the Championesse now entred has
   The utmost° rowme, and past the formest° dore *outermost / foremost*
The utmost rowme, abounding with all precious store.°   *goods*

28

For round about, the wals yclothèd were
   With goodly arras° of great majesty,   *tapestries*
   Woven with gold and silke so close and nere,°   *tight*
   That the rich metall lurkèd privily,°   *secretly*
   As faining° to be hid from envious eye;   *enjoying*
   Yet here, and there, and every where unwares°   *unexpectedly*
   It shewd it selfe, and shone unwillingly;
   Like a discolourd° Snake, whose hidden snares   *multicolored*
Through the greene gras his long bright burnisht backe declares.

29

And in those Tapets° weren fashionèd   *tapestries*
   Many faire pourtraicts, and many a faire feate,

5. I.e., he was maddened with fierce fury.

And all of love, and all of lusty-hed,
As seemèd by their semblaunt did entreat;[6]
And eke° all Cupids warres they did repeate,°   *also / recount*
And cruell battels, which he whilome° fought   *formerly*
Gainst all the Gods, to make his empire great;
Besides the huge massacres, which he wrought
On mighty kings and kesars,° into thraldome brought.   *caesars*

30

Therein was writ,° how often thundring Jove   *woven*
  Had felt the point of his hart-percing dart,
  And leaving heavens kingdome, here did rove
  In straunge disguize, to slake his scalding smart;
  Now like a Ram, faire Helle to pervart,
  Now like a Bull, Europa to withdraw:[7]
  Ah, how the fearefull Ladies tender hart
  Did lively° seeme to tremble, when she saw   *lifelike*
The huge seas under her t'obay her servaunts° law.   *lover's*

31

Soone after that into a golden showre
  Him selfe he chaunged faire Danaë to vew,
  And through the roofe of her strong brasen towre
  Did raine into her lap an hony dew,[8]
  The whiles her foolish garde, that little knew
  Of such deceipt, kept th'yron dore fast bard,
  And watcht, that none should enter nor issew;°   *go out*
  Vaine was the watch, and bootlesse° all the ward,   *useless*
Whenas the God to golden hew him selfe transfard.[9]

32

Then was he turnd into a snowy Swan,
  To win faire Leda to his lovely° trade:[1]   *loving*
  O wondrous skill, and sweet wit° of the man,   *ingenuity*
  That her in daffadillies sleeping made,
  From scorching heat her daintie limbes to shade:
  Whiles the proud Bird ruffing° his fethers wyde,   *ruffling*
  And brushing° his faire brest, did her invade;   *preening*
  She slept, yet twixt her eyelids closely° spyde,   *secretly*
How towards her he rusht, and smilèd at his pryde.°   *sexual desire*

33

Then shewd it, how the Thebane Semelee
  Deceived of gealous Juno, did require

---

6. I.e., the pictures ("pourtraicts") seemed, by their appearance ("semblaunt"), to treat entirely of deeds of love and merriment ("lusty-hed").
7. A golden ram (not specifically identified in legend as Jove) came to carry away ("pervart") Helle from the fury of her stepmother, Ino; Jove assumed the shape of a bull to seduce Europa and carried her over the seas.
8. In another part of the tapestry ("soone after") Jove is shown as a shower of gold, impregnating Danaë.
9. Transmuted himself into golden form.
1. Jove became a swan to seduce Leda.

To see him in his soveraigne majestee,
Armd with his thunderbolts and lightning fire,
Whence dearely she with death bought her desire.[2]
But faire Alcmena better match did make,
Joying his love in likenesse more entire;
Three nights in one, they say, that for her sake
He then did put, her pleasures lenger° to partake.[3]   *longer*

34

Twise was he seene in soaring Eagles shape,
    And with wide wings to beat the buxome° ayre,   *yielding*
    Once, when he with Asterie did scape,
    Againe, when as the Trojane boy so faire
    He snatcht from Ida hill, and with him bare:[4]
Wondrous delight it was, there to behould,
    How the rude Shepheards after him did stare,
    Trembling through feare, least° down he fallen should,   *lest*
And often to him calling, to take surer hould.

35

In Satyres shape Antiopa he snatcht:
    And like a fire, when he Aegin' assayd:
    A shepheard, when Mnemosyne he catcht:
    And like a Serpent to the Thracian mayd.[5]
    Whiles thus on earth great Jove these pageaunts° playd,   *tricks*
The wingèd boy did thrust into° his throne,   *usurped*
    And scoffing, thus unto his mother sayd,
    "Lo now the heavens obey to me alone,
And take me for their Jove, while Jove to earth is gone."

36

And thou, faire Phoebus, in thy colours bright
    Wast there enwoven, and the sad distresse,
    In which that boy thee plongèd, for despight,
    That thou bewrayedst° his mothers wantonnesse,   *revealed*
    When she with Mars was meynt° in joyfulnesse: *mingled, joined*
For thy° he thrild° thee with a leaden dart,   *therefore / pierced*
    To love faire Daphne, which thee lovèd lesse:[6]
    Lesse she thee loved, then° was thy just desart,   *than*
Yet was thy love her death, and her death was thy smart.°   *pain*

2. Juno tricked Semele into having Jove visit her in all his power; she was burned to death by lightning and thunderbolts.
3. Jove visited Alcmena in the likeness of her husband, Amphitryon, and made that one night the length of three.
4. Asterie changed herself into a quail to avoid Jove's advances, but he captured her as an eagle; in that form he also snatched Ganymede, who became cupbearer to the gods.

5. Jove came as a satyr to Antiope; in fire to Aegina; as a shepherd to Mnemosyne, goddess of memory (who bore the Nine Muses); and as a serpent to Proserpina, "the Thracian mayd."
6. Two stories are combined: Apollo's punishment for revealing Venus's adultery with Mars was "the sad distresse" of doting on Leucothoe; later he chased Daphne, who escaped by metamorphosis into a laurel tree. Cupid's lead-tipped arrows produce unhappiness in love.

37

So lovedst thou the lusty° Hyacinct,	*handsome*
So lovedst thou the faire Coronis deare:	
Yet both are of° thy haplesse hand extinct,	*by*
Yet both in flowres do live, and love thee beare,	
The one a Paunce, the other a sweet breare:[7]	
For griefe whereof, ye mote have lively° seene	*lifelike*
The God himselfe rending his golden heare,	
And breaking quite his gyrlond° ever greene,	*garland*
With other signes of sorrow and impatient teene.°	*grief*

38

Both for those two, and for his owne deare sonne,	
The sonne of Climene he did repent,	
Who bold to guide the charet of the Sunne,	
Himselfe in thousand peeces fondly rent,[8]	
And all the world with flashing fier brent;	
So like, that all the walles did seeme to flame.	
Yet cruell Cupid, not herewith content,	
Forst him eftsoones° to follow other game,	*soon after*
And love a Shepheards daughter for his dearest Dame.	

39

He lovèd Isse for his dearest Dame,	
And for her sake her cattell fed a while,	
And for her sake a cowheard vile° became,	*lowly*
The servant of Admetus cowheard vile,	
Whiles that from heaven he sufferèd exile.[9]	
Long were to tell each other lovely fit,°	*amorous passion*
Now like a Lyon, hunting after spoile,	
Now like a Stag, now like a faulcon flit:°	*fleet*
All which, in that faire arras was most lively writ.	

40

Next unto him was Neptune[1] picturèd,	
In his divine resemblance wondrous lyke:	
His face was rugged, and his hoarie° hed	*gray*
Droppèd with brackish° deaw; his three-forkt Pyke	*salty*
He stearnly shooke, and therewith fierce did stryke	
The raging billowes, that on every syde	
They trembling stood, and made a long broad dyke,°	*trench*

---

7. Apollo accidentally killed his lover Hyacinth at a game of quoits, and transformed him into a flower ("paunce," pansy); he killed Coronis out of jealousy, but her transformation to a sweetbriar seems to be Spenser's invention.
8. Foolishly tore apart. Phaëthon, son of Apollo and Climene, extracted permission to drive the chariot of the Sun through the heavens; unable to control the horses, he killed himself and almost burned up the world.
9. Two stories are combined: Apollo disguising himself as a shepherd to gain Isse, and serving Admetus, king of Pheres in Thessaly, as a cowherd.
1. Neptune, god of the sea, is here portrayed with his trident ("three-forkt Pyke") and riding in a chariot ("charet") drawn by a team of four sea horses ("Hippodames").

That his swift charet might have passage wyde,
Which foure great Hippodames did draw in temewise tyde.°   *harnessed*

41

His sea-horses did seeme to snort amayne,°   *violently*
   And from their nosethrilles° blow the brynie streame,   *nostrils*
   That made the sparckling waves to smoke agayne,
   And flame with gold, but the white fomy creame,
   Did shine with silver, and shoot forth his beame.
   The God himselfe did pensive seeme and sad,
   And hong adowne his head, as° he did dreame: *as if*
   For privy° love his brest empiercèd had,   *secret*
Ne ought but deare Bisaltis[2] ay° could make him glad.   *ever*

42

He lovèd eke° Iphimedia deare,   *also*
   And Aeolus faire daughter Arne hight,°   *called*
   For whom he turnd him selfe into a Steare,°   *steer*
   And fed on fodder, to beguile° her sight.   *deceive*
   Also to win Deucalions daughter bright,°   *beautiful*
   He turnd him selfe into a Dolphin fayre;[3]
   And like a wingèd horse he tooke his flight,
   To snaky-locke Medusa to repayre,°   *resort*
On whom he got faire Pegasus, that flitteth in the ayre.[4]

43

Next Saturne was, (but who would ever weene,°   *think*
   That sullein Saturne ever weend° to love?   *was minded*
   Yet love is sullein,° and Saturnlike seene,   *melancholy*
   As he did for Erigone it prove,)
   That to a Centaure did him selfe transmove.
   So prooved it eke that gracious° God of wine,   *graceful*
   When for to compasse° Philliras hard love,   *gain*
   He turnd himselfe into a fruitfull vine,
And into her faire bosome made his grapes decline.[5]

44

Long were to tell the amorous assayes,°   *assaults*
   And gentle pangues, with which he° makèd meeke   *i.e., Cupid*
   The mighty Mars, to learne his wanton playes:
   How oft for Venus, and how often eek°   *also*
   For many other Nymphes he sore did shreek,
   With womanish teares, and with unwarlike smarts,°   *pains*

2. In Greek myth it was Bisaltes's daughter Theophane who made Neptune happy: he made love to her in the form of a ram.
3. Neptune came to Iphimedia as a flowing river, to Arne as a steer, and to Deucalion's daughter Melantho as a dolphin.
4. Neptune's ravishment of Medusa in Minerva's temple caused her hair to be turned into snakes; she gave birth to the winged horse, Pegasus.
5. Hang down. Saturn, associated with melancholy, is not usually portrayed as a lover. Spenser here transposes two myths: Saturn loved Philyra ("Philliras") not Erigone, from which union came the centaur Chiron; Bacchus ("God of wine") tricked Erigone with a false bunch of grapes.

Privily° moystening his horrid° cheek.   *secretly / bristly*
There was he painted full of burning darts,°   *arrows*
And many wide woundes launchèd° through his inner parts.   *torn*

45

Ne did he spare (so cruell was the Elfe)
  His owne deare mother, (ah why should he so?)
  Ne did he spare sometime to pricke himselfe,
  That he might tast the sweet consuming woe,
  Which he had wrought to many others moe.°   *more*
  But to declare the mournfull Tragedyes,
  And spoiles,° wherewith he all the ground did strow,   *plunder*
  More eath° to number, with how many eyes   *easy*
High heaven beholds sad lovers nightly theeveryes.[6]

46

Kings Queenes, Lords Ladies, Knights and Damzels gent°   *gentle*
  Were heaped together with the vulgar sort,
  And mingled with the raskall rablement,°   *rabble, masses*
  Without respect of person or of port,°   *position*
  To shew Dan° Cupids powre and great effort:°   *master / strength*
  And round about a border was entrayld,°   *woven*
  Of broken bowes and arrowes shivered° short,   *splintered*
  And a long bloudy river through them rayld,°   *flowed*
So lively and so like, that living sence it fayld.[7]

47

And at the upper end of that faire rowme,
  There was an Altar built of pretious stone,
  Of passing° valew, and of great renowme,   *surpassing*
  On which there stood an Image all alone,
  Of massy° gold, which with his owne light shone;   *solid*
  And wings it had with sundry colours dight,°   *adorned*
  More sundry colours, then the proud Pavone°   *peacock*
  Beares in his boasted fan, or Iris° bright,   *goddess of the rainbow*
When her discolourd[8] bow she spreds through heaven bright.

48

Blindfold he was, and in his cruell fist
  A mortall° bow and arrowes keene did hold,   *deadly*
  With which he shot at randon, when him list,°   *when it pleased him*
  Some headed with sad lead, some with pure gold;[9]
  (Ah man beware, how thou those darts behold)
  A wounded Dragon[1] under him did ly,
  Whose hideous tayle his left foot did enfold,

6. I.e., it would be easier to number the stars ("eyes") that watch lovers' nightly exploits ("theeveryes"; i.e., thieveries) than the tragedies caused by love.
7. I.e., so animated and so lifelike that it deceived ("fayld") the senses of those looking on.

8. Multicolored.
9. Cupid, by tradition blindfolded, shoots at random ("randon"). His leaden arrows cause unhappiness in love; his golden arrows, happiness.
1. The dragon is traditionally a guard, symbolic of vigilance.

And with a shaft was shot through either eye,
That no man forth might draw, ne no man remedye.

49

And underneath his feet was written thus,
   Unto the Victor of the Gods this bee:
   And all the people in that ample hous
   Did to that image bow their humble knee,
   And oft committed fowle Idolatree.
   That wondrous sight faire Britomart amazed,
   Ne seeing could her wonder satisfie,
   But ever more and more upon it gazed,
The whiles the passing° brightnes her fraile sences dazed.   *surpassing*

50

Tho° as she backward° cast her busie eye,   *then / i.e., behind the statue*
   To search each secret of that goodly sted,°   *place*
   Over the dore thus written she did spye
   Be bold: she oft and oft it over-red,
   Yet could not find what sence it figurèd:
   But what so were therein or° writ or ment,   *either*
   She was no whit thereby discouragèd
From prosecuting of her first intent,
But forward with bold steps into the next roome went.

51

Much fairer, then° the former, was that roome,   *than*
   And richlier by many partes arayd:[2]
   For not with arras made in painefull° loome,   *painstaking*
   But with pure gold it all was overlayd,
   Wrought with wilde Antickes,[3] which their follies playd,
   In the rich metall, as° they living were: *as if*
   A thousand monstrous formes therein were made,
   Such as false love doth oft upon him weare,
For love in thousand monstrous formes doth oft appeare.

52

And all about, the glistring° walles were hong   *glittering*
   With warlike spoiles, and with victorious prayes,°   *prizes*
   Of mighty Conquerours and Captaines strong,
   Which were whilome° captivèd in their dayes   *formerly*
   To cruell love, and wrought their owne decayes:
   Their swerds and speres were broke, and hauberques[4] rent;
   And their proud girlonds of tryumphant bayes[5]
   Troden in dust with fury insolent,
To shew the victors might and mercilesse intent.

---

2. I.e., much ("by many partes") more richly
decorated ("arayd").
3. Grotesque statues.

4. Coats of mail. "Swerds": swords.
5. Wreaths of laurel ("bayes") were traditionally
awarded to great military conquerors.

53

The warlike Mayde beholding earnestly
    The goodly ordinance° of this rich place,   *ordnance, military supplies*
    Did greatly wonder, ne could satisfie
    Her greedy eyes with gazing a long space,
    But more she mervaild that no footings trace,°   *trace of footprints*
    Nor wight appear'd, but wastefull° emptinesse,   *uninhabited*
    And solemne silence over all that place:
    Straunge thing it seem'd, that none was to possesse
So rich purveyance,° ne them keepe with carefulnesse.   *furnishings*

54

And as she lookt about, she did behold,
    How over that same dore was likewise writ,
    Be bold, be bold, and every where *Be bold,*
    That much she muz'd, yet could not cónstrue it
    By any ridling skill, or commune wit.°   *common sense*
    At last she spyde at that roomes upper end,
    Another yron dore, on which was writ,
    Be not too bold; whereto though she did bend
Her earnest mind, yet wist not what it might intend.°   *mean*

55

Thus she there waited untill eventyde,
    Yet living creature none she saw appeare:
    And now sad° shadowes gan the world to hyde,   *somber*
    From mortall vew, and wrap in darkenesse dreare;
    Yet nould° she d'off her weary armes, for feare   *would not*
    Of secret daunger, ne let sleepe oppresse
    Her heavy eyes with natures burdein deare,
    But drew her selfe aside in sickernesse,°   *safety*
And her welpointed weapons did about her dresse.[6]

Canto 12

The maske[7] of Cupid, and th'enchaunted
    Chamber are displayd,
Whence Britomart redeemes faire
    Amoret, through charmes decayd.°   *wasted away*

1

Tho° when as chearelesse Night ycovered had   *then*
    Faire heaven with an universall cloud,

---

6. Her well-appointed (and/or sharp) weapons she drew ("did dresse") about her.
7. This episode resembles a court masque (elaborate dramatic presentation) with allegorical personages and emblematic clothing and props. It is also a "Triumph" (ceremonial victory parade) of Cupid, who is preceded and followed by the allegorical qualities that attend on his reign and who displays Amoret as the spoils of his victory, the victim of the attitudes toward love which he promotes.

That every wight dismayd with darknesse sad,°   *sober*
In silence and in sleepe themselves did shroud,
She heard a shrilling Trompet sound aloud,
Signe of nigh° battell, or got° victory;   *approaching / achieved*
Nought therewith daunted was her courage proud,
But rather stird to cruell° enmity,   *fierce*
Expecting° ever, when some foe she might descry.°   *waiting / perceive*

2

With that, an hideous storme of winde arose,
   With dreadfull thunder and lightning atwixt,
   And an earth-quake, as if it streight° would lose° *immediately / loosen*
   The worlds foundations from his centre fixt;
   A direfull stench of smoke and sulphure mixt
   Ensewd, whose noyance° fild the fearefull sted,° *annoyance / place*
   From the fourth houre of night untill the sixt;[8]
   Yet the bold Britonesse was nought ydred,
Though much emmoved, but stedfast still perseverèd.

3

All suddenly a stormy whirlwind blew
   Throughout the house, that clappèd° every dore, *slammed*
   With which that yron wicket° open flew, *door*
   As° it with mightie levers had bene tore: *as if*
   And forth issewd, as on the ready flore
   Of some Theatre, a grave personage,
   That in his hand a branch of laurell bore,
   With comely haveour° and count'nance sage, *pleasing bearing*
Yclad in costly garments, fit for tragicke Stage.

4

Proceeding to the midst, he still did stand,
   As if in mind he somewhat had to say,
   And to the vulgar° beckning with his hand, *groundlings*
   In signe of silence, as to heare a play,
   By lively actiöns he gan bewray° *reveal*
   Some argument of matter passionèd;
   Which doen, he backe retyrèd soft away,
   And passing by, his name discoverèd,° *revealed*
Ease, on his robe in golden letters cypherèd.[9]

5

The noble Mayd, still standing all this vewd,
   And merveild at his strange intendiment;° *purpose*
   With that a joyous fellowship issewd

8. Night begins at 6 P.M., so these effects take place from 10 P.M. to midnight, when the masque begins.
9. I.e., by pantomime he indicates that the subject ("argument") of the masque concerns passion. The part of presenter is taken by Ease, suggesting that it predisposes to lechery. Similarly, Idleness leads the procession of the Seven Deadly Sins (Book 1, canto 4, stanzas 18–20).

Of Minstrals, making goodly meriment,
With wanton Bardes, and Rymers impudent,
All which together sung full chearefully
A lay° of loves delight, with sweet concent:°   *song / harmony*
After whom marcht a jolly company,
In manner of a maske, enrangèd orderly.[1]

6

The whiles a most delirious harmony,
 In full straunge notes was sweetly heard to sound,
 That the rare sweetnesse of the melody
 The feeble senses wholly did confound,
 And the fraile soule in deepe delight nigh dround:
 And when it ceast, shrill trompets loud did bray,
 That their report° did farre away rebound,   *echo*
 And when they ceast, it gan againe to play,
The whiles the maskers marchèd forth in trim aray.

7

The first was Fancy,[2] like a lovely boy,
 Of rare aspect, and beautie without peare;°   *peer, equal*
 Matchable either to that ympe of Troy,[3]
 Whom Jove did love, and chose his cup to beare,
 Or that same daintie lad, which was so deare
 To great Alcides,[4] that when as he dyde,
 He wailèd womanlike with many a teare,
 And every wood, and every valley wyde
He fild with Hylas name; the Nymphes eke° Hylas cryde. *also*

8

His garment neither was of silke nor say,°   *fine wool*
 But painted plumes, in goodly order dight,°   *placed*
 Like as the sunburnt Indians° do aray   *Native Americans*
 Their tawney bodies, in their proudest plight:° *attire*
 As those same plumes, so seemd he vaine and light,
 That by his gate° might easily appeare;   *gait*
 For still° he far'd as dauncing in delight,   *ever*
 And in his hand a windy° fan did beare,   *causing wind*
That in the idle aire he mov'd still here and there.

9

And him beside marcht amorous Desyre,
 Who seemd of riper yeares, then th'other Swayne,° *lover*
 Yet was that other swayne this elders syre,
 And gave him being, commune to them twaine:

1. As here, most masques had twelve masquers, forming six couples. The love song at the processional is performed by musicians ("Minstrals") and poets of varying quality ("Bardes" and "Rymers").
2. The mind's power to produce images that are often misleading or false.
3. Ganymede, as in canto 11, stanza 34.
4. Hercules, whose beloved Hylas was drowned.

His garment was disguisèd very vaine,[5]
    And his embrodered Bonet sat awry;
    Twixt both his hands few sparkes he close did straine,°   *clasp*
    Which still he blew, and kindled busily,
That soone they life conceiv'd, and forth in flames did fly.

10

Next after him went Doubt, who was yclad
    In a discolour'd° cote, of straunge disguyse,   *multicolored*
    That at his backe a brode Capuccio had,
    And sleeves dependant Albanese-wyse:[6]
    He lookt askew with his mistrustfull eyes,
    And nicely° trode, as° thornes lay in his way,   *cautiously / as if*
    Or that the flore to shrinke he did avyse,
    And on a broken reed he still did stay
His feeble steps, which shrunke, when hard theron he lay.[7]

11

With him went Daunger, clothed in ragged weed,°   *garment*
    Made of Beares skin, that him more dreadfull made;
    Yet his owne face was dreadfull, ne did need,
    Straunge horrour, to deforme his griesly shade;
    A net in th'one hand, and a rustie blade[8]
    In th'other was, this Mischiefe, that Mishap;
    With th'one his foes he threatned to invade,°   *attack*
    With th'other he his friends ment to enwrap:
For whom he could not kill, he practizd° to entrap.   *plotted*

12

Next him was Feare, all arm'd from top to toe,
    Yet thought himselfe not safe enough thereby,
    But feard each shadow moving to and fro,
    And his owne armes when glittering he did spy,
    Or clashing heard, he fast away did fly,
    As ashes pale of hew, and wingyheeld;[9]
    And evermore on Daunger fixt his eye,
    Gainst whom he alwaies bent° a brasen shield,   *turned*
Which his right hand unarmèd fearefully did wield.

13

With him went Hope in rancke, a handsome Mayd,
    Of chearefull looke and lovely to behold;

---

5. I.e., Desire seems older than Fancy, but Fancy is in fact his father; he was dressed fantastically ("disguisèd very vaine").
6. Hanging down in Albanian (i.e., Scottish: Albany is a dukedom in Scotland) fashion—as in academic gowns. His hood ("Capuccio") resembles that of a Capuchin monk.
7. I.e., he trod with great precision and care ("nicely") as if thorns lay in his path or as if he perceived ("did avyse") the floor to give way ("shrinke"). His cane was a broken reed, which collapsed ("shrunke") when he leaned on it.
8. Danger's face was terrifying, needing nothing external ("straunge") to further deform his horrid ("griesly") appearance. His net and bloodstained ("rustie") knife indicate the kinds of perils he signifies.
9. I.e., he was pale as ashes and fled as if his heels had wings.

In silken samite° she was light arayd,   *a rich silk*
And her faire lockes were woven up in gold;
She alway smyld, and in her hand did hold
An holy water Sprinckle,[1] dipt in deowe,°   *water (dew)*
With which she sprinckled favours manifold,
On whom she list,° and did great liking sheowe,   *pleased*
Great liking unto many, but true love to feowe.°   *few*

14

And after them Dissemblance, and Suspect[2]
   Marcht in one rancke, yet an unequall paire:
   For she was gentle, and of milde aspect,
   Courteous to all, and seeming debonaire,°   *gracious*
   Goodly adornèd, and exceeding faire:
   Yet was that all but painted, and purloynd,°   *stolen*
   And her bright° browes were deckt with borrowed haire: *lovely*
   Her deedes were forgèd, and her words false coynd,
And alwaies in her hand two clewes° of silke she twynd.   *balls*

15

But he was foule, ill favourèd, and grim,
   Under his eyebrowes looking still askaunce;°   *sideways*
   And ever as Dissemblance laught on him,
   He lowrd° on her with daungerous° eyeglaunce;   *scowled / threatening*
   Shewing his nature in his countenance;
   His rolling eyes did never rest in place,
   But walkt° each where, for feare of hid mischaunce,   *moved*
   Holding a lattice° still before his face,   *screen*
Through which he still did peepe, as forward he did pace.

16

Next him went Griefe, and Fury matcht yfere;°   *together*
   Griefe all in sable sorrowfully clad,
   Downe hanging his dull head, with heavy chere,°   *countenance*
   Yet inly being more, then° seeming sad: *than*
   A paire of Pincers in his hand he had,
   With which he pinchèd people to the hart,
   That from thenceforth a wretchèd life they lad,°   *led*
   In wilfull languor° and consuming smart,°   *pining / pain*
Dying each day with inward wounds of dolours dart.°   *grief's arrow*

17

But Fury was full ill appareilèd
   In rags, that naked nigh° she did appeare,   *nearly*
   With ghastly lookes and dreadfull drerihed;°   *wretchedness*
   For from her backe her garments she did teare,
   And from her head oft rent her snarlèd heare:
   In her right hand a firebrand she did tosse°   *brandish*

---

1. Aspergillum, a brush to sprinkle holy water.   2. Dissimulation and Suspicion.

About her head, still roming here and there;
   As a dismayèd° Deare in chace embost,°   *panic-stricken / hard-pressed*
Forgetfull of his safety, hath his right way lost.

18

After them went Displeasure and Pleasance,
   He looking lompish° and full sullein sad,°   *dejected / morose*
   And hanging downe his heavy countenance;
   She chearefull fresh and full of joyance glad,
   As if no sorrow she ne felt ne drad;°   *feared*
   That evill matchèd paire they seemd to bee:
   An angry Waspe th'one in a viall had,
   Th'other in hers an hony-lady Bee;[3]
Thus marchèd these six couples forth in faire degree.°   *order*

19

After all these there marcht a most faire Dame,
   Led of two grysie° villeins, th'one Despight,   *grim*
   The other clepèd° Cruelty by name:[4]   *called*
   She dolefull Lady, like a dreary Spright,°   *spirit*
   Cald by strong charmes out of eternall night,
   Had deathes owne image figurd in her face,
   Full of sad signes, fearefull to living sight;
   Yet in that horror shewd a seemely grace,
And with her feeble feet did move a comely pace.

20

Her brest all naked, as net° ivory,   *pure*
   Without adorne° of gold or silver bright,   *adornment*
   Wherewith the Craftesman wonts it beautify,[5]
   Of her dew honour was despoylèd quight,
   And a wide wound therein (O ruefull sight)
   Entrenchèd deepe with knife accursèd keene,
   Yet freshly bleeding forth her fainting spright,
   (The worke of cruell hand) was to be seene,
That dyde in sanguine° red her skin all snowy cleene.   *bloody*

21

At that wide orifice her trembling hart
   Was drawne forth, and in silver basin layd,
   Quite through transfixèd with a deadly dart,
   And in her bloud yet steeming fresh embayd:°   *steeped*
   And those two villeins, which her steps upstayd,
   When her weake feete could scarcely her sustaine,
   And fading vitall powers gan to fade,

---

3. Honeybee or honey-laden bee.
4. Typical attributes of the lady in the world of courtly love and love sonnets: her "cruelty" causes her to reject her lover with scorn ("despight").
5. I.e., without the jewels that usually beautify her breast.

Her forward still with torture did constraine,
And evermore encreasèd her consuming paine.

22

Next after her the wingèd God himselfe°   *Cupid*
  Came riding on a Lion ravenous,
  Taught to obay the menage° of that Elfe,   *horsemanship*
  That man and beast with powre imperious
  Subdeweth to his kingdome tyrannous:
  His blindfold eyes he bad° a while unbind,   *bade*
  That his proud spoyle of that same dolorous
  Faire Dame he might behold in perfect kind;°   *clearly*
Which seene, he much rejoyced in his cruell mind.

23

Of which full proud, himselfe up rearing hye,
  He lookèd round about with sterne disdaine;
  And did survay his goodly company:
  And marshalling the evill ordered traine,°   *retinue*
  With that the darts which his right hand did straine,° *clasp*
  Full dreadfully he shooke that all did quake,
  And clapt on hie his coulourd wingès twaine,
  That all his many° it affraide did make: *company*
Tho blinding° him againe, his way he forth did take. *then blindfolding*

24

Behinde him was Reproch, Repentance, Shame;
  Reproch the first, Shame next, Repent behind:
  Repentance feeble, sorrowfull, and lame:
  Reproch despightfull, carelesse,[6] and unkind;
  Shame most ill favour, bestiall, and blind:
  Shame lowrd,° Repentance sigh'd, Reproch did scould; *scowled*
  Reproch sharpe stings, Repentance whips entwind,
  Shame burning brond-yrons° in her hand did hold: *branding irons*
All three to each unlike, yet all made in one mould.

25

And after them a rude confusèd rout°   *crowd*
  Of persons flockt, whose names is hard to read:° *distinguish*
  Emongst them was sterne Strife, and Anger stout,° *fierce*
  Unquiet Care, and fond° Unthriftihead,   *foolish*
  Lewd° Losse of Time, and Sorrow seeming dead,   *base*
  Inconstant Chaunge, and false Disloyaltie,
  Consuming Riotise,° and guilty Dread   *debauchery*
  Of heavenly vengeance, faint Infirmitie,
Vile Povertie, and lastly Death with infamie.

6. I.e., full of scorn, careless of where his attacks fall.

26

There were full many moe° like maladies,   *more*
   Whose names and natures I note readen well;°   *I cannot well interpret*
   So many moe, as there be phantasies
   In wavering wemens wit, that none can tell,°   *count*
   Or paines in love, or punishments in hell;
   All which disguizèd marcht in masking wise,
   About the chamber with that Damozell,
   And then returnèd, having marchèd thrise,
Into the inner roome, from whence they first did rise.

27

So soone as they were in, the dore streight way
   Fast lockèd, driven with that stormy blast,
   Which first it opened; and bore all away.
   Then the brave Maid, which all this while was plast°   *placed*
   In secret shade, and saw both first and last,
   Issewèd° forth, and went unto the dore,   *came*
   To enter in, but found it lockèd fast:
   It vaine she thought with rigorous uprore°   *violent force*
For to efforce, when charmes had closèd it afore.

28

Where force might not availe, there sleights and art
   She cast° to use, both fit for hard emprize;°   *resolved / enterprise*
   For thy° from that same roome not to depart   *therefore*
   Till morrow next, she did her selfe avize,°   *counsel*
   When that same Maske againe should forth arize.
   The morrow next appeard with joyous cheare,
   Calling men to their daily exercize,
   Then she, as morrow fresh, her selfe did reare
Out of her secret stand,° that day for to out weare.   *standing place*

29

All that day she outwore in wandering,
   And gazing on that Chambers ornament,
   Till that againe the second evening
   Her covered with her sable vestiment,
   Wherewith the worlds faire beautie she hath blent:°   *obscured*
   Then when the second watch[7] was almost past,
   That brasen dore flew open, and in went
   Bold Britomart, as she had late forecast,°   *planned*
Neither of idle shewes, nor of false charmes aghast.°   *terrified*

30

So soone as she was entred, round about
   She cast her eies, to see what was become

---

7. From 9 P.M. to midnight.

Of all those persons, which she saw without:
But lo, they streight° were vanisht all and some,   *immediately*
Ne living wight she saw in all that roome,
Save that same woefull Ladie, both whose hands
Were bounden fast, that did her ill become,
And her small wast girt round with yron bands,
Unto a brasen pillour, by the which she stands.

31

And her before the vile Enchaunter sate,
Figuring straunge characters of his art,
With living bloud he those characters wrate,°   *wrote*
Dreadfully dropping from her dying hart,
Seeming transfixèd with a cruell dart,
And all perforce° to make her him to love.   *by force*
Ah who can love the worker of her smart?
A thousand charmes he formerly did prove;°   *try*
Yet thousand charmes could not her stedfast heart remove.

32

Soone as that virgin knight he saw in place,
His wicked bookes in hast he overthrew,
Not caring his long labours to deface,[8]
And fiercely ronning to that Lady trew,
A murdrous knife out of his pocket drew,
The which he thought, for villeinous despight,°   *cruelty*
In her tormented bodie to embrew:°   *plunge*
But the stout° Damzell to him leaping light,   *fierce*
His cursèd hand withheld, and maisterèd his might.

33

From her, to whom his fury first he ment,°   *directed*
The wicked weapon rashly° he did wrest,°   *suddenly / turned*
And turning to her selfe his fell intent,
Unwares° it strooke into her snowie chest,   *without warning*
That little drops empurpled her faire brest.
Exceeding wroth therewith the virgin grew,
Albe° the wound were nothing deepe imprest,   *although*
And fiercely forth her mortall blade she drew,
To give him the reward for such vile outrage dew.

34

So mightily she smote him, that to ground
He fell halfe dead; next stroke him should have slaine,
Had not the Lady, which by him stood bound,
Dernely° unto her callèd to abstaine,   *dismally*
From doing him to dy. For else her paine
Should be remedilesse, sith° none but hee,   *since*

8. I.e., he did not care if he ruined the spells he had labored over.

Which wrought it, could the same recure° againe.　　　　*heal*
Therewith she stayd her hand, loth stayd to bee;
For life she him envyde,° and long'd revenge to see.　　*begrudged*

35

And to him said, "Thou wicked man, whose meed°　　　　*reward*
　For so huge mischiefe, and vile villany
Is death, or if that ought° do death exceed,　　　　*aught, anything*
　Be sure, that nought may save thee from to dy,
　But if that thou this Dame doe presently
Restore unto her health, and former state;[9]
　This doe and live, else die undoubtedly."
He glad of life, that lookt for death but late,°　　　　*just recently*
Did yield himselfe right willing to prolong his date.°　*term of life*

36

And rising up, gan streight to overlooke°　　　　*look over*
　Those cursèd leaves, his charmes backe to reverse;
Full dreadfull things out of that balefull booke
　He red, and measured many a sad verse,[1]
　That horror gan the virgins hart to perse,°　　　　*pierce*
And her faire locks up starèd° stiffe on end,　　　　*stood*
　Hearing him those same bloudy lines reherse;°　　　*say over again*
　And all the while he red, she did extend
Her sword high over him if ought he did offend.

37

Anon she gan perceive the house to quake,
　And all the dores to rattel round about;
Yet all that did not her dismaièd make,
　Nor slacke her threatfull hand for daungers dout,[2]
　But still with stedfast eye and courage stout
Abode,° to weet° what end would come of all.　　　*waited / learn*
　At last that mightie chaine, which round about
　Her tender waste was wound, adowne gan fall,
And that great brasen pillour broke in peeces small.

38

The cruell steele, which thrild° her dying hart,　　　*pierced*
　Fell softly forth, as of his owne accord,
And the wyde wound, which lately did dispart°　　　*divide*
　Her bleeding brest, and riven bowels gor'd,
　Was closèd up, as it had not bene bor'd,
And every part to safety full sound,
　As she were never hurt, was soone° restor'd:　　　*immediately*

---

9. I.e., you deserve death or, if possible, something worse than death, and nothing will save you from death ("to dy") unless ("But if") you immediately ("presently") restore this lady.

1. I.e., he pronounced in proper meter many distressing verses (incantations).
2. I.e., nor relax her threatening hand for fear of danger.

Tho° when she felt her selfe to be unbound,   *then*
And perfect hole, prostrate she fell unto the ground.

39

Before Faire Britomart, she fell prostrate,
   Saying, "Ah noble knight what worthy meed°   *reward*
   Can wretched Lady, quit° from wofull state,   *released*
   Yield you in liew of° this your gratious deed?   *in return for*
   Your vertue selfe her owne reward shall breed,
   Even immortall praise, and glory wyde,
   Which I your vassall, by your prowesse freed,
   Shall through the world make to be notifyde,
And goodly well advaunce, that goodly well was tryde."[3]

40

But *Britomart* uprearing her from ground,
   Said, "Gentle Dame, reward enough I weene°   *think*
   For many labours more, then° I have found,   *than*
   This, that in safety now I have you seene,
   And meane° of your deliverance have beene: *means*
   Henceforth faire Lady comfort to you take,
   And put away remembrance of late teene;°   *pain*
   In stead thereof know, that your loving Make,° *mate*
Hath no lesse griefe endurèd for your gentle sake."

41

She much was cheard to heare him mentiönd,
   Whom of all living wights she lovèd best.
   Then laid the noble Championesse strong hond
   Upon th'enchaunter, which had her distrest
   So sore, and with foule outrages opprest:
   With that great chaine, wherewith not long ygo
   He bound that pitteous Lady prisoner, now relest,° *released*
   Himselfe she bound, more worthy to be so,
And captive with her led to wretchednesse and wo.

42

Returning backe, those goodly roomes, which erst° *before*
   She saw so rich and royally arayd,
   Now vanisht utterly, and cleane subverst°   *overturned*
   She found, and all their glory quite decayd,°   *destroyed*
   That sight of such a chaunge her much dismayd.
   Thence forth descending to that perlous° Porch, *perilous*
   Those dreadfull flames she also found delayd,° *allayed*
   And quenchèd quite, like a consumèd torch,
That erst° all enters wont so cruelly to scorch. *previously*

---

3. I.e., as your vassal I will make known ("notifyde") throughout the world and extol ("advaunce") your virtue, which was so fully tested ("tryde").

43

More easie issew now, then entrance late
 She found: for now that fainèd° dreadfull flame,   *feigned*
 Which chokt the porch of that enchaunted gate,
 And passage bard to all, that thither came,
 Was vanisht quite, as it were not the same,
 And gave her leave at pleasure forth to passe.
 Th'Enchaunter selfe, which all that fraud did frame,
 To have efforst° the love of that faire lasse,   *enforced*
Seeing his worke now wasted deepe engrievèd was.

44

But when the victoresse arrivèd there,
 Where late she left the pensife° Scudamore,   *sad; anxious*
 With her owne trusty Squire,[4] both full of feare,
 Neither of them she found where she them lore:°   *left*
 Thereat her noble hart was stonisht sore;
 But most faire Amoret, whose gentle spright
 Now gan to feede on hope, which she before
 Conceivèd had, to see her owne deare knight,
Being thereof beguyld was fild with new affright.

45

But he sad man, when he had long in drede
 Awayted there for Britomarts returne,
 Yet saw her not nor signe of her good speed,°   *success*
 His expectation to despaire did turne,
 Misdeeming[5] sure that her those flames did burne;
 And therefore gan advize° with her old Squire,   *consult*
 Who her deare nourslings losse no lesse did mourne,
 Thence to depart for further aide t'enquire:
Where let them wend at will, whilest here I doe respire.[6]

                  1590, 1596

---

4. Her nurse, Glauce, is her squire.
5. Mistakenly thinking.
6. Take a breath, rest from my labors. In the 1590 edition, Book 3, and the poem, ended with the happy reunion of Scudamour and Amoret in a passionate embrace:

> Lightly he clipt her twixt his armès twaine,
> And streightly did embrace her body bright,
> Her body, late the prison of sad paine,
> Now the sweet lodge of love and deare
>   delight:

> But she faire Lady overcommen quight
> Of huge affection, did in pleasure melt,
> And in sweete ravishment pourd out her
> spright:
> No word they spake, nor earthly thing they
> felt,
> But like two senceles stocks in long
> embracement dwelt.

But in the 1596 edition Spenser made a bridge to his three added books by replacing the earlier ending with stanzas 43–45, as given here.

Amoretti *and* Epithalamion In the early 1590s the widowed Spenser wooed and won Elizabeth Boyle, whom he married in Ireland in 1594. The next year he published a small volume that included the sonnet sequence *Amoretti* ("little loves" or "little cupids") and the *Epithalamion*. Several of the sonnets explicitly address an "Elizabeth," and the volume's subtitle, "Written not long since," suggests that these poems, taken together, are a portrait of Spenser's recent courtship and marriage. It was unusual to write sonnets about a happy and successful love; traditionally, the sonneteer's love was for someone painfully inaccessible. Spenser rehearses some of the conventional motifs of frustration and longing, but his cycle of polished, eloquent poems leads toward joyous possession. Thus, for example, in sonnet 67 ("Lyke as a huntsman after weary chace"), he transforms a Petrarchan lament into a vision of unexpected fulfillment.*

Spenser's great celebration of this fulfillment is the *Epithalamion*. A learned poet, he was acutely conscious that he was writing within a tradition: an epithalamion is a wedding song whose Greek name conveys that it was sung on the threshold of the bridal chamber. The genre, which goes back at least as far as Sappho (ca. 612 B.C.E.), was widely practiced by the Roman poets, particularly Catullus, and imitated in the Renaissance. Its elements typically include an invocation of the Muses, followed by a celebratory description of the procession of the bride, the religious rites, the singing and dancing at the wedding party, the preparations for the wedding night, and the sexual consummation of the marriage.

In long, flowing stanzas, Spenser follows these conventions closely, adapting them with exquisite delicacy to his small-town Irish setting and native folklore. But his first stanza announces a major innovation: "So I unto myselfe alone will sing." Traditionally, the poet of an epithalamion was an admiring observer, a kind of master of ceremonies; by combining the roles of poet and bridegroom, Spenser transforms a genial social performance into a passionate lyric utterance. Equally remarkable innovations are the complex stanza form, for which no direct model has been discovered, and the still more complex overall structure. That structure is a triumph of symbolic patterning; the more scholars have studied it, the more elaborate the order they seem to have uncovered. This subtle and rich poetic structure conjures up not only a single day of celebration but also, beyond this particular event, an orderly, harmonious universe, with a hidden pattern of coherence and regularity. If the *Epithalamion* goes to remarkable lengths to affirm this pattern, it is perhaps because it also registers so insistently all that threatens the enduring happiness of wedded love and indeed of human life itself. The greatest threat is the force over which the poem exercises its greatest power: time.

From Amoretti

Sonnet 1

Happy ye leaves[1] when as those lilly hands,
    Which hold my life in their dead doing° might,   *killing*
    Shall handle you and hold in loves soft bands,°   *bonds*
    Lyke captives trembling at the victors sight.
5 And happy lines, on which with starry light,
    Those lamping° eyes will deigne sometimes to look   *flashing*
    And read the sorrowes of my dying spright,°   *spirit*

---

* For a broad grouping of other 16th-century love poems, see below, "Renaissance Love and Desire" (pp. 1000ff.).
1. I.e., of the book: pages.

Written with teares in harts close° bleeding book.   *secret*
And happy rymes bath'd in the sacred brooke
10 Of Helicon[2] whence she derivèd is,
When ye behold that Angels blessèd looke,
My soules long lackèd foode, my heavens blis.
Leaves, lines, and rymes, seeke her to please alone,
Whom if ye please, I care for other none.

Sonnet 34[3]

Lyke as a ship that through the Ocean wyde,
 By conduct of some star doth make her way,
 Whenas a storme hath dimd her trusty guyde,
 Out of her course doth wander far astray:
5 So I whose star, that wont° with her bright ray *was accustomed*
 Me to direct, with cloudes is overcast,
 Doe wander now in darknesse and dismay,
 Through hidden perils round about me plast.°   *placed*
Yet hope I well, that when this storme is past
10 My Helice[4] the lodestar° of my lyfe   *guiding star*
 Will shine again, and looke on me at last,
 With lovely light to cleare my cloudy grief.
Till then I wander carefull° comfortlesse,   *full of cares*
 In secret sorow and sad pensivenesse.

Sonnet 37

What guyle is this, that those her golden tresses,
 She doth attyre under a net of gold:
 And with sly° skill so cunningly them dresses,   *clever*
 That which is gold or heare,° may scarse be told? *hair*
5 Is it that mens frayle eyes, which gaze too bold,
 She may entangle in that golden snare:
 And being caught may craftily enfold
 Theyr weaker harts, which are not wel aware?
Take heed therefore, myne eyes, how ye doe stare
10 Henceforth too rashly on that guilefull net,
 In which if ever ye entrappèd are,
 Out of her bands ye by no means shall get.
Fondnesse° it were for any being free,   *foolishness*
 To covet fetters, though they golden bee.

Sonnet 54

Of this worlds Theatre in which we stay,
 My love like the Spectator ydly sits
 Beholding me that all the pageants° play,   *dramatic scenes*

---

2. The "sacred brooke" is Hippocrene, which flows from Mount Helicon, the mountain sacred to the Muses.
3. An adaptation of Petrarch's Rima 189 (translated by Sir Thomas Wyatt, pp. 651–52, where a modern prose translation can also be found).
4. A name for the Big Dipper (after the nymph who, in classical mythology, was transformed into it).

Disguysing diversly my troubled wits.
5 Sometimes I joy when glad occasion fits,
　　And mask in myrth lyke to a Comedy:
　　Soone after when my joy to sorrow flits,
　　I waile and make my woes a Tragedy.
Yet she beholding me with constant° eye,　　　　　　*unmoved*
10 　　Delights not in my merth nor rues my smart:°　　*pities my hurt*
　　But when I laugh she mocks, and when I cry
　　She laughes and hardens evermore her hart.
What then can move her? if nor merth nor mone,°　　　*moan*
　　She is no woman, but a sencelesse stone.

Sonnet 64[5]

Comming to kisse her lyps (such grace I found)
　　Me seemd I smelt a gardin of sweet flowres
　　That dainty odours from them threw around,
　　For damzels fit to decke their lovers bowres.
5 Her lips did smell lyke unto Gillyflowers,°　　　　*carnations*
　　Her ruddy cheeks lyke unto Roses red;
　　Her snowy browes lyke budded Bellamoures,[6]
　　Her lovely eyes like Pincks but newly spred,
Her goodly bosome lyke a Strawberry bed,
10 　　Her neck lyke to a bounch of Cullambynes;
　　Her brest lyke lillyes, ere theyr leaves be shed,
　　Her nipples lyke yong blossomd Jessemynes.°　　　*jasmines*
Such fragrant flowres doe give most odorous smell,
　　But her sweet odour did them all excell.

Sonnet 65

The doubt which ye misdeeme,° fayre love, is vaine,　　*misconceive*
　　That fondly° feare to loose your liberty,　　　　　*foolishly*
　　When loosing one, two liberties ye gayne,
　　And make him bond° that bondage earst° dyd fly.　*bound / formerly*
5 Sweet be the bands, the which true love doth tye,
　　Without constraynt or dread of any ill:
　　The gentle birde feels no captivity
　　Within her cage, but singes and feeds her fill.
There pride dare not approch, nor discord spill°　　　*destroy*
10 　　The league twixt them, that loyal love hath bound;
　　But simple truth and mutuall good will
　　Seekes with sweet peace to salve each others wound.
There fayth° doth fearlesse dwell in brasen towre,　　*fidelity*
　　And spotlesse pleasure builds her sacred bowre.

5. Much of the imagery of this sonnet is imitated from the Song of Solomon 4.10–16.

6. Unidentified flower, evidently white.

Sonnet 67[7]

Lyke as a huntsman after weary chace,
  Seeing the game from him escapt away,
  Sits downe to rest him in some shady place,
  With panting hounds beguilèd° of their pray: *deluded*
5 So after long pursuit and vaine assay,°   *attempt*
  When I all weary had the chace forsooke,
  The gentle deare returnd the selfe-same way,
  Thinking to quench her thirst at the next° brooke.   *nearby*
There she beholding me with mylder looke,
10   Sought not to fly, but fearelesse still did bide:
  Till I in hand her yet halfe trembling tooke,
  And with her owne goodwill hir fyrmely tyde.
Strange thing me seemd to see a beast so wyld,
  So goodly wonne with her owne will beguyld.

Sonnet 68

Most glorious Lord of lyfe, that on this day,°   *i.e., Easter*
  Didst make thy triumph over death and sin:
  And having harrowd hell,[8] didst bring away
  Captivity thence captive us to win:
5 This joyous day, deare Lord, with joy begin,
  And grant that we for whom thou diddest dye
  Being with thy deare blood clene washt from sin,
  May live for ever in felicity.
And that thy love we weighing worthily,
10   May likewise love thee for the same againe:
  And for thy sake that all lyke deare didst buy,[9]
  With love may one another entertayne.°   *sustain*
So let us love, deare love, lyke as we ought,
  Love is the lesson which the Lord us taught.[1]

Sonnet 74

Most happy letters fram'd by skilfull trade,°   *practice*
  With which that happy name° was first desynd: *i.e., Elizabeth*
  The which three times thrise happy hath me made,
  With guifts of body, fortune and of mind.
5 The first my being to me gave by kind,°   *nature*
  From mothers womb deriv'd by dew descent,
  The second is my sovereigne Queene most kind,
  That honour and large richesse to me lent.°   *bestowed*
The third my love, my lives last ornament,

---

7. An imitation of Petrarch's Rima 190, but with a very different ending. Cf. Sir Thomas Wyatt's adaptation ("Whoso list to hunt") of the same sonnet, and the prose translation of the Petrarchan original appended to it: pp. 649–50.
8. In the apocryphal Gospel of Nicodemus, Christ descended into hell and led out into Paradise the righteous who had lived before his time. "Captivity thence captive" (line 4) is a biblical phrase, as in Judges 5.12 and Ephesians 4.8.
9. I.e., Christ bought all people at the same great cost.
1. Cf. John 15.12: "This is my commandment, That ye love one another, as I have loved you."

10   By whom my spirit out of dust was raysed:
      To speake her prayse and glory excellent,
      Of all alive most worthy to be praysed.
Ye three Elizabeths for ever live,
      That three such graces did unto me give.

Sonnet 75

One day I wrote her name upon the strand,°   *shore*
      But came the waves and washèd it away:
      Agayne I wrote it with a second hand,
      But came the tyde, and made my paynes his pray.°   *prey*
5   "Vayne man," sayd she, "that doest in vaine assay,°   *attempt*
      A mortall thing so to immortalize,
      For I my selve shall lyke to this decay,
      And eek° my name bee wypèd out lykewize."   *also*
"Not so," quod° I, "let baser things devize°   *quoth / contrive*
10   To dy in dust, but you shall live by fame:
      My verse your vertues rare shall eternize,
      And in the heavens wryte your glorious name.
Where whenas death shall all the world subdew,
      Our love shall live, and later life renew."

Sonnet 79

Men call you fayre, and you doe credit° it,   *believe*
      For that your selfe ye dayly such doe see:
      But the trew fayre,° that is the gentle wit,°   *beauty / intelligence*
      And vertuous mind, is much more praysd of me.
5   For all the rest, how ever fayre it be,
      Shall turne to nought and loose that glorious hew:°   *form*
      But onely that is permanent and free
      From frayle corruption, that doth flesh ensew.°   *outlast*
That is true beautie: that doth argue° you   *prove*
10   To be divine and borne of heavenly seed:
      Deriv'd from that fayre Spirit,° from whom al true   *i.e., God*
      And perfect beauty did at first proceed.
He onely fayre, and what he fayre hath made:
      All other fayre, lyke flowres, untymely fade.

1595

Epithalamion

Ye learnèd sisters which have oftentimes
Beene to me ayding, others to adorne:[1]
Whom ye thought worthy of your gracefull rymes,
That even the greatest did not greatly scorne
5   To heare theyr names sung in your simple layes,°   *songs*
But joyèd in theyr prayse.
And when ye list° your owne mishaps to mourne,   *chose*
Which death, or love, or fortunes wreck did rayse,
Your string could soone to sadder tenor° turne,   *mood*
10   And teach the woods and waters to lament
Your dolefull dreriment.°   *sorrow*
Now lay those sorrowfull complaints aside,
And having all your heads with girland crownd,
Helpe me mine owne loves prayses to resound,
15   Ne° let the same of° any be envide: *nor / by*
So Orpheus did for his owne bride,[2]
So I unto my selfe alone will sing,
The woods shall to me answer and my eccho ring.

Early before the worlds light giving lampe,
20   His golden beame upon the hils doth spred,
Having disperst the nights unchearefull dampe,
Doe ye awake, and with fresh lustyhed°   *vigor*
Go to the bowre° of my belovèd love,   *bedchamber*
My truest turtle dove,
25   Bid her awake; for Hymen[3] is awake,
And long since ready forth his maske to move,
With his bright Tead[4] that flames with many a flake,°   *spark*
And many a bachelor to waite on him,
In theyr fresh garments trim.
30   Bid her awake therefore and soone her dight,°   *dress*
For lo the wishèd day is come at last,
That shall for al the paynes and sorrowes past,
Pay to her usury° of long delight: *interest*
And whylest she doth her dight,
35   Doe ye to her of joy and solace° sing,   *pleasure*
That all the woods may answer and your Eccho ring.

Bring with you all the Nymphes that you can heare°   *can hear you*
Both of the rivers and the forrests greene:
And of the sea that neighbours to her neare,
40   Al with gay girlands goodly wel beseene.°   *beautified*
And let them also with them bring in hand,
Another gay girland

---

1. To write poems in praise of others. The "learnèd sisters" are the Muses.
2. Orpheus, archetype of the poet in classical
antiquity, was famous for his love for his wife,
Eurydice.

3. The god of marriage, who leads a "maske" or
procession at weddings.
4. A ceremonial torch, associated with marriages
since classical times.

For my fayre love of lillyes and of roses,
Bound truelove wize° with a blew silke riband.   *i.e., in a love knot*
45 And let them make great store° of bridale poses,°   *abundance / posies*
And let them eeke° bring store of other flowers   *also*
To deck the bridale bowers.
And let the ground whereas° her foot shall tread,   *where*
For feare the stones her tender foot should wrong
50 Be strewed with fragrant flowers all along,
And diapred lyke the discolorèd mead.[5]
Which done, doe at her chamber dore awayt,
For she will waken strayt,°   *straightway*
The whiles doe ye this song unto her sing,
55 The woods shall to you answer and your Eccho ring.

Ye Nymphes of Mulla[6] which with careful heed,
The silver scaly trouts doe tend full well,
And greedy pikes which use° therein to feed,   *are accustomed*
(Those trouts and pikes all others doo excell)
60 And ye likewise which keepe the rushy lake,
Where none doo fishes take,
Bynd up the locks the which hang scatterd light,
And in his waters which your mirror make,
Behold your faces as the christall bright,
65 That when you come whereas° my love doth lie,   *where*
No blemish she may spie.
And eke ye lightfoot mayds which keepe the deere,
That on the hoary mountayne use to towre,[7]
And the wylde wolves which seeke them to devoure,
70 With your steele darts° doo chace from comming neer,   *spears*
Be also present heere,
To helpe to decke her and to help to sing,
That all the woods may answer and your eccho ring.

Wake now my love, awake; for it is time,
75 The Rosy Morne long since left Tithones bed,[8]
All ready to her silver coche° to clyme,   *coach*
And Phoebus° gins to shew his glorious hed.   *the sun god*
Hark how the cheerefull birds do chaunt theyr laies
And carroll of loves praise.
80 The merry Larke hir mattins° sings aloft,   *morning prayers*
The thrush replyes, the Mavis descant playes,
The Ouzell shrills, the Ruddock warbles soft,[9]
So goodly all agree with sweet consent,
To this dayes merriment.

5. Ornamented like the many-colored meadow.
6. A river near Spenser's home in Ireland.
7. A falconry term meaning to occupy heights. "The deere": all wild animals, kept by the woodland nymphs.
8. See Song of Solomon 2.10–13: "Rise up, my love, my fair one, and come away. For, lo, the winter is past, the rain is over and gone; the flowers appear on the earth; the time of the singing of birds is come." In classical myth, Tithonus is the aged husband of Aurora, the dawn.
9. The "Mavis" is the song thrush; the "Ouzell," the blackbird (which sings in England); and the "Ruddock," the European robin. The birds' concert is a convention of medieval love poetry. "Descant": a melody or counterpoint written above a musical theme—a soprano obbligato.

85 Ah my deere love why doe ye sleepe thus long,
　When meeter° were that ye should now awake,   *more fitting*
　T'awayt the comming of your joyous make,°   *mate*
　And hearken to the birds lovelearnèd song,
　The deawy leaves among.
90 For they of joy and pleasance to you sing,
　That all the woods them answer and theyr eccho ring.

　My love is now awake out of her dreame,
　And her fayre eyes like stars that dimmèd were
　With darksome cloud, now shew° theyr goodly beams   *show*
95 More bright then° Hesperus° his head doth rere.   *than / evening star*
　Come now ye damzels, daughters of delight,
　Helpe quickly her to dight,°   *attire*
　But first come ye fayre houres which were begot
　In Joves sweet paradice, of Day and Night,
100 Which doe the seasons of the yeare allot,
　And al that ever in this world is fayre
　Doe make and still° repayre.   *continuously*
　And ye three handmayds of the Cyprian Queene,[1]
　The which doe still adorne her beauties pride,
105 Helpe to addorne my beautifullest bride:
　And as ye her array, still throw betweene°   *at intervals*
　Some graces to be seene,
　And as ye use° to Venus, to her sing,   *are accustomed*
　The whiles the woods shal answer and your eccho ring.

110 Now is my love all ready forth to come,
　Let all the virgins therefore well awayt,
　And ye fresh boyes that tend upon her groome
　Prepare your selves; for he is comming strayt.°   *straightway*
　Set all your things in seemely good aray°   *order*
115 Fit for so joyfull day,
　The joyfulst day that ever sunne did see.
　Faire Sun, shew forth thy favourable ray,
　And let thy lifull° heat not fervent° be   *life-giving / hot*
　For feare of burning her sunshyny face,
120 Her beauty to disgrace.°   *mar*
　O fayrest Phoebus, father of the Muse,[2]
　If ever I did honour thee aright,
　Or sing the thing, that mote° thy mind delight,   *might*
　Doe not thy servants simple boone° refuse,   *request*
125 But let this day let this one day be myne,
　Let all the rest be thine.
　Then I thy soverayne prayses loud wil sing,
　That all the woods shal answer and theyr eccho ring.

　Harke how the Minstrels gin° to shrill aloud   *begin*
130 Their merry Musick that resounds from far,

---

1. The Graces attending on Venus ("Cyprian Queene"), representing brightness, joy, and bloom.
2. Phoebus Apollo, god of the sun, was also god of music and poetry, but he was not normally regarded as the father of the Nine Muses (Zeus was).

The pipe, the tabor,° and the trembling Croud,[3]   *small drum*
That well agree withouten breach or jar.°   *discord*
But most of all the Damzels doe delite,
When they their tymbrels° smyte,   *tambourines*
135 And thereunto doe daunce and carrol sweet,
That all the sences they doe ravish quite,
The whyles the boyes run up and downe the street,
Crying aloud with strong confusèd noyce,
As if it were one voyce.
140 *Hymen iô Hymen, Hymen*[4] they do shout,
That even to the heavens theyr shouting shrill
Doth reach, and all the firmament doth fill,
To which the people standing all about,
As in approvance doe thereto applaud
145 And loud advaunce her laud,°   *praise*
And evermore they *Hymen Hymen* sing,
That all the woods them answer and theyr eccho ring.

Loe where she comes along with portly° pace,   *stately*
Lyke Phoebe from her chamber of the East,
150 Arysing forth to run her mighty race,[5]
Clad all in white, that seemes° a virgin best.   *beseems, suits*
So well it her beseems that ye would weene°   *think*
Some angell she had beene.
Her long loose yellow locks lyke golden wyre,
155 Sprinckled with perle, and perling° flowres a tweene,   *winding*
Doe lyke a golden mantle her attyre,
And being crownèd with a girland greene,
Seeme lyke some mayden Queene.
Her modest eyes abashèd to behold
160 So many gazers, as on her do stare,
Upon the lowly ground affixèd are.
Ne dare lift up her countenance too bold,
But blush to heare her prayses sung so loud,
So farre from being proud.
165 Nathlesse doe ye still loud her prayses sing,
That all the woods may answer and your eccho ring.

Tell me ye merchants daughters did ye see
So fayre a creature in your towne before,
So sweet, so lovely, and so mild as she,
170 Adornd with beautyes grace and vertues store,
Her goodly eyes lyke Saphyres shining bright,
Her forehead yvory white,
Her cheekes lyke apples which the sun hath rudded,°   *made red*
Her lips lyke cherryes charming men to byte,
175 Her brest like to a bowle of creame uncrudded,°   *uncurdled*
Her paps° lyke lyllies budded,   *breasts*

3. Primitive fiddle. Spenser here designates Irish, not classical, instruments and music for the classical masque or ballet.
4. The name of the classical god of marriage, used as a conventional exclamation at weddings in ancient Greece.
5. Phoebe is the moon, a virgin like the bride; the reference to her anticipates the night.

Her snowie necke lyke to a marble towre,
And all her body like a pallace fayre,
Ascending uppe with many a stately stayre,
180   To honors seat and chastities sweet bowre.[6]
Why stand ye still ye virgins in amaze,
Upon her so to gaze,
Whiles ye forget your former lay to sing,
To which the woods did answer and your eccho ring.

185   But if ye saw that which no eyes can see,
The inward beauty of her lively spright,°   *living spirit, soul*
Garnisht with heavenly guifts of high degree,
Much more then would ye wonder at that sight,
And stand astonisht lyke to those which red°   *saw*
190   Medusaes mazeful hed.[7]
There dwels sweet love and constant chastity,
Unspotted fayth° and comely womanhood,   *fidelity*
Regard of honour and mild modesty,
There vertue raynes as Queene in royal throne,
195   And giveth lawes alone.
The which the base° affections doe obay,   *lower*
And yeeld theyr services unto her will,
Ne thought of thing uncomely ever may
Thereto approch to tempt her mind to ill.
200   Had ye once seene these her celestial threasures,
And unrevealèd pleasures,
Then would ye wonder and her prayses sing,
That all the woods should answer and your Echo ring.

Open the temple gates unto my love,
205   Open them wide that she may enter in,[8]
And all the postes adorne as doth behove,[9]
And all the pillours deck with girlands trim,
For to recyve this Saynt with honour dew,
That commeth in to you.
210   With trembling steps and humble reverence,
She commeth in, before th'almighties vew,
Of her ye virgins learne obedience,
When so ye come into those holy places,
To humble your proud faces:
215   Bring her up to th'high altar, that she may
The sacred ceremonies there partake,
The which do endless matrimony make,
And let the roring Organs loudly play
The praises of the Lord in lively notes,
220   The whiles with hollow throates

---

6. The head, where the higher faculties are. The catalog of qualities is a convention in love poetry (cf. Song of Solomon 4–8).
7. Medusa, one of the Gorgons, had serpents instead of hair (hence a "mazeful hed"): the effect on beholders was to turn them to stone.

8. Cf. Psalm 24.7: "Lift up your heads, O ye gates; and be ye lift up, ye everlasting doors; and the King of glory shall come in."
9. As is proper. The doorposts were trimmed for weddings in classical times, and the custom was often referred to in classical and later love poetry.

The Choristers the joyous Antheme sing,
That all the woods may answere and theyr eccho ring.

Behold whiles she before the altar stands
Hearing the holy priest that to her speakes
225 And blesseth her with his two happy hands,
How the red roses flush up in her cheekes,
And the pure snow with goodly vermill° stayne,   *vermilion*
Like crimsin dyde in grayne,°   *fast color*
That even th'Angels which continually,
230 About the sacred Altare doe remaine,
Forget their service and about her fly,
Ofte peeping in her face that seemes more fayre,
The more they on it stare.
But her sad° eyes still° fastened on the ground,   *serious / ever*
235 Are governèd with goodly modesty,
That suffers° not one looke to glaunce awry,   *permits*
Which may let in a little thought unsownd.
Why blush ye love to give to me your hand,
The pledge of all our band?°   *bond, tie*
240 Sing ye sweet Angels, Alleluya sing,
That all the woods may answere and your eccho ring.

Now al is done; bring home the bride againe,
Bring home the triumph of our victory,
Bring home with you the glory of her gaine,[1]
245 With joyance bring her and with jollity.
Never had man more joyfull day then this,
Whom heaven would heape with blis.
Make feast therefore now all this live long day,
This day for ever to me holy is,
250 Poure out the wine without restraint or stay,
Poure not by cups, but by the belly° full,   *wineskin*
Poure out to all that wull,°   *want it*
And sprinkle all the postes and wals with wine,
That they may sweat, and drunken be withall.
255 Crowne ye God Bacchus° with a coronall,°   *god of wine / garland*
And Hymen also crowne with wreathes of vine,
And let the Graces daunce unto the rest;
For they can doo it best:
The whiles the maydens doe theyr carroll sing,
260 To which the woods shall answer and theyr eccho ring.

Ring ye the bels, ye young men of the towne,
And leave your wonted° labors for this day: *usual*
This day is holy; doe ye write it downe,
That ye for ever it remember may.
265 This day the sunne is in his chiefest hight,
With Barnaby the bright,[2]

1. I.e., the glory of gaining her.
2. St. Barnabas's Day, at the time of the summer solstice.

From whence declining daily by degrees,
He somewhat loseth of his heat and light,
When once the Crab[3] behind his back he sees.
270 But for this time it ill ordainèd was,
To chose the longest day in all the yeare,
And shortest night, when longest fitter weare:
Yet never day so long, but late° would passe.   *at last*
Ring ye the bels, to make it weare away,
275 And bonefiers° make all day,   *bonfires*
And daunce about them, and about them sing:
That all the woods may answer, and your eccho ring.

Ah when will this long weary day have end,
And lende me leave to come unto my love?
280 How slowly do the houres theyr numbers spend?
How slowly does sad Time his feathers move?
Hast° thee O fayrest Planet to thy home   *haste*
Within the Westerne fome:
Thy tyred steedes long since have need of rest.[4]
285 Long though it be, at last I see it gloome,°   *begin to darken*
And the bright evening star with golden creast°   *crest*
Appeare out of the East.
Fayre childe of beauty, glorious lampe of love
That all the host of heaven in rankes doost lead,
290 And guydest lovers through the nightès dread,
How chearefully thou lookest from above,
And seemst to laugh atweene thy twinkling light
As joying in the sight
Of these glad many which for joy doe sing,
295 That all the woods them answer and theyr echo ring.

Now ceasse ye damsels your delights forepast;
Enough is it, that all the day was youres:
Now day is doen, and night is nighing fast:
Now bring the Bryde into the brydall boures.
300 Now night is come, now soone her disaray,°   *undress*
And in her bed her lay;
Lay her in lillies and in violets,
And silken courteins over her display,°   *spread*
And odourd° sheetes, and Arras° coverlets.   *perfumed / tapestry*
305 Behold how goodly my faire love does ly
In proud humility;
Like unto Maia,[5] when as Jove her tooke,
In Tempe,[6] lying on the flowry gras,
Twixt sleepe and wake, after she weary was,
310 With bathing in the Acidalian brooke.[7]

---

3. The constellation Cancer between Gemini and Leo. The sun, passing through the zodiac, leaves the Crab behind toward the end of July.
4. The sun's chariot completes its daily course in the western sea.
5. The eldest and most beautiful of the seven daughters of Atlas. (They were stellified as the Pleiades.) Jove fathered Mercury on her.
6. The Vale of Tempe in Thessaly (not, however, traditionally the site of Jove's encounter with Maia).
7. The Acidalian brook is associated with Venus.

Now it is night, ye damsels may be gon,
And leave my love alone,
And leave likewise your former lay to sing:
The woods no more shall answere, nor your echo ring.

315 Now welcome night, thou night so long expected,
That long daies labour doest at last defray,°   *pay for*
And all my cares, which cruell love collected,
Hast sumd in one, and cancellèd for aye:°   *forever*
Spread thy broad wing over my love and me,
320 That no man may us see,
And in thy sable mantle us enwrap,
From feare of perrill and foule horror free.
Let no false treason seeke us to entrap,
Nor any dread disquiet once annoy°   *interfere with*
325 The safety of our joy:
But let the night be calme and quietsome,
Without tempestuous storms or sad afray:°   *fear*
Lyke as when Jove with fayre Alcmena[8] lay,
When he begot the great Tirynthian groome:
330 Or lyke as when he with thy selfe[9] did lie,
And begot Majesty.
And let the mayds and yongmen cease to sing:
Ne let the woods them answer, nor theyr Eccho ring.

Let no lamenting cryes, nor dolefull teares,
335 Be heard all night within nor yet without:
Ne let false whispers, breeding hidden feares,
Breake gentle sleepe with misconceivèd dout.°   *fear*
Let no deluding dreames, nor dreadful sights
Make sudden sad affrights;
340 Ne let housefyres, nor lightnings helpelesse harmes,
Ne let the Pouke,[1] nor other evill sprights,
Ne let mischivous witches with theyr charmes,
Ne let hob Goblins, names whose sence we see not,
Fray° us with things that be not.   *terrify*
345 Let not the shriech Oule, nor the Storke be heard:
Nor the night Raven that still° deadly yels,[2]   *always*
Nor damnèd ghosts cald up with mighty spels,
Nor griesly° vultures make us once affeard: *horrid*
Ne let th'unpleasant Quyre of Frogs still croking
350 Make us to wish theyr choking.
Let none of these theyr drery accents sing;
Ne let the woods them answer, nor theyr eccho ring.

But let stil Silence trew night watches keepe,
That sacred peace may in assurance rayne,

---

8. The mother of Hercules ("the great Tirynthian groome"). Jove made that first night last as
long as three.
9. Night. This is Spenser's own myth.
1. Puck, Robin Goodfellow—here more powerful

and evil than Shakespeare made him in *A Midsummer Night's Dream.*
2. The owl and the night raven were birds of ill
omen; the stork, in Chaucer's *Parliament of Fowls,*
is called an avenger of adultery.

355 And tymely Sleep, when it is tyme to sleepe,
May poure his limbs forth on your pleasant playne,
The whiles an hundred little wingèd loves,°   *cupids (or amoretti)*
Like divers fethered doves,
Shall fly and flutter round about your bed,
360 And in the secret darke, that none reproves,
Their prety stealthes shal worke, and snares shal spread
To filch away sweet snatches of delight,
Conceald through covert night.
Ye sonnes of Venus, play your sports at will,
365 For greedy pleasure, carelesse of your toyes,°   *amorous dallying*
Thinks more upon her paradise of joyes,
Then° what ye do, albe it° good or ill.   *than / albeit, although*
All night therefore attend your merry play,
For it will soone be day:
370 Now none doth hinder you, that say or sing,
Ne will the woods now answer, nor your Eccho ring.

Who is the same, which at my window peepes?
Or whose is that faire face, that shines so bright,
Is it not Cinthia,[3] she that never sleepes,
375 But walkes about high heaven al the night?
O fayrest goddesse, do thou not envy
My love with me to spy:
For thou likewise didst love, though now unthought,° *not thought of*
And for a fleece of woll,° which privily,   *wool*
380 The Latmian shephard[4] once unto thee brought,
His pleasures with thee wrought.
Therefore to us be favorable now;
And sith° of wemens labours thou hast charge,[5]   *since*
And generation goodly dost enlarge,
385 Encline thy will t'effect our wishfull vow,
And the chast wombe informe° with timely seed,   *give life to*
That may our comfort breed:
Till which we cease our hopefull hap° to sing, *fortune we hope for*
Ne let the woods us answer, nor our Eccho ring.

390 And thou great Juno, which with awful° might   *awesome*
The lawes of wedlock still dost patronize,°   *watch over*
And the religion° of the faith first plight° *sanctity / pledged*
With sacred rites hast taught to solemnize:
And eeke° for comfort often callèd art   *also*
395 Of women in their smart,°   *(labor) pains*
Eternally bind thou this lovely band,°   *bond*
And all thy blessings unto us impart.
And thou glad Genius,[6] in whose gentle hand,
The bridale bowre and geniall bed remaine,

---

3. Cynthia (or Diana) is goddess of the moon.
4. Endymion, beloved of the moon. The "fleece of woll," however, comes from another story—that of Pan's enticement of the moon.
5. Diana is, as Lucina, patroness of births. The

"labours" are, of course, those of childbirth.
6. God of generation and birth. In the next line, "geniall"—having both the usual sense and the sense of "generative"—puns on his name.

400 Without blemish or staine,
And the sweet pleasures of theyr loves delight
With secret ayde doest succour° and supply,   *help*
Till they bring forth the fruitfull progeny,
Send us the timely fruit of this same night.
405 And thou fayre Hebe,[7] and thou Hymen free,
Grant that it may so be.
Til which we cease your further prayse to sing,
Ne any woods shall answer, nor your Eccho ring.

And ye high heavens, the temple of the gods,
410 In which a thousand torches flaming bright
Doe burne, that to us wretched earthly clods,
In dreadful darknesse lend desirèd light;
And all ye powers which in the same remayne,
More then we men can fayne,°   *imagine*
415 Poure out your blessing on us plentiously,
And happy influence upon us raine,
That we may raise a large posterity,
Which from the earth, which they may long possesse,
With lasting happinesse,
420 Up to your haughty° pallaces may mount,   *lofty*
And for the guerdon° of theyr glorious merit   *reward*
May heavenly tabernacles there inherit,
Of blessèd Saints for to increase the count.
So let us rest, sweet love, in hope of this,
425 And cease till then our tymely joyes to sing,
The woods no more us answer, nor our eccho ring.

Song made in lieu of many ornaments,
With which my love should duly have bene dect,°   *adorned*
Which cutting off through hasty accidents,
430 Ye would not stay your dew time to expect,°   *await*
But promist both to recompens,
Be unto her a goodly ornament,
And for short time an endlesse moniment.[8]

1595

---

7. Goddess of youth and freedom.
8. The envoy (brief final stanza addressed to the poem itself) is traditionally apologetic in tone: the poem is offered as a substitute for presents ("orna-ments") that did not arrive in time for the wedding. But this elaborate poem is itself a "goodly orna-ment," for it stands as a timeless monument of art to the passing day that it celebrates.

Renaissance Love and Desire

"No one can advise or help you—no one," Rainer Maria Rilke wrote to a young poet in February 1903: "There is only one thing you should do. Go into yourself. Find the reason that commands you to write; see whether it has spread its roots into the very depths of your heart; confess to yourself whether you would have to die if you were forbidden to write. This most of all: ask yourself in the most silent hour of your night: *must* I write?" For Rilke, the authentic poet must experience, alone and indifferent to the judgment of others, an absolute imperative in whose grip he or she must then write "as if no one had ever tried before." Since the goal is to create something unique and individual, it is best to avoid those forms in which glorious traditions already exist. Therefore, Rilke warned the aspiring poet, "Don't write love poems."

Some young men and women of the sixteenth century may have asked themselves the same core question, "*Must* I write?" And in one of the age's most famous poems, the first of Sir Philip Sidney's *Astrophil and Stella* sonnets, the muse tells the perplexed poet, "Look in thy heart and write." But there are very great differences between the twentieth-century injunctions and those that typified Renaissance poetry. Renaissance poets would never aspire to write "as if no one had ever tried before"; they actively embraced rather than avoided the established forms; and they particularly favored love poems.

The ability to write poems was part of a larger cultural competence, akin to knowing how to move gracefully, how to carry a tune, how to speak eloquently. Men and women were expected to have some facility in making and reciting verses—not everyone, of course, but a much larger cohort than we have come to expect in our own world. The Tudor monarchs and their glittering courtiers, sober bureaucrats, hard-working law students, fashionable ladies, country gentlemen, parsons and parsons' wives, soldiers, saints, schoolchildren and schoolmasters—all tried their hands at making metaphors, counting syllables, shaping words into pleasing patterns.

The true testing ground in Tudor culture was not individual but social: poems were objects embedded in a thoroughly rhetorical world. Their creators thought of themselves as performing such acts as praising and blaming, inviting, commemorating, excusing, persuading, warning, insulting, lamenting, and—if possible—seducing. And all of these acts, along with ample opportunity for self-display, were present in heightened form in love poetry. Yet at the same time there was that impulse toward revealing—or, if need be, persuasively simulating the revelation of—the secret domains of the heart.

The single most powerful influence on Renaissance love poetry was the fourteenth-century Italian writer Petrarch (Francesco Petrarca, 1304–1374), who supplied a perfect model for poetry both as virtuoso rhetorical display and as intensely personal expression. No poet was ever more aware of the achievements of his contemporaries and predecessors, or more dazzlingly able to assimilate, fuse, and often surpass what was best in them; yet at the same time no poet was ever more able to write love poetry that seemed to come directly or solely from the deepest recesses of a suffering individual heart. Composed over a period of four decades, Petrarch's *Rime sparse* (Scattered Rhymes) consisted of a loosely unified sequence of 366 poems, 317 of them sonnets. Blending elements of classical Roman poetry with medieval courtly traditions, he created a representation, unprecedented in intensity and psychological nuance, of his unrequited passion for a young woman named Laura and for all she came to symbolize for him: the first of the *rime*—written retrospectively, after he had been working on the sequence, off and on, for some twenty years—tells us that in reading the poems we will learn, as he himself has painfully learned, that *"whatever the world loves is a brief dream."*

Petrarch's passion for Laura continued long after her untimely death and was at once a transcendent experience and a state of spiritual paralysis, an ecstatic joy and a torment of self-blame and self-justification. His sonnets tirelessly, even obsessively, tease out the lover's emotional states, figuring his passion as a ravishment, a deadly wound, a hunt, a form of bondage, or a storm at sea, and depicting his beloved as a master, a mortal enemy, a sun, a bejeweled idol, a flower, a milk-white deer, a star, the epitome of all virtue or the source of all pain. These and other metaphors are deployed most often in an elegant fourteen-line rhymed form that enables the poet to hold each one up for careful attention, elaboration, and interrogation while at the same time conveying emotional force.

Petrarch was celebrated in his lifetime as a scholar and as a Latin poet, but the fame of his Italian love poems did not spread across Europe until after his death, and it was only in the early sixteenth century, with brilliant translations and adaptations by Thomas Wyatt and others at the court of Henry VIII, that the *Rime sparse* began to shape English poetry. Its influence was at its height in the 1590s, during the sonnet craze initiated by Sidney's *Astrophil and Stella*. Petrarch's characteristic yoking of opposites, as a way to describe the experience of love, is directly imitated in Henry Constable's "To live in hell, and heaven to behold"; his characteristic depiction of the lover's solitude and melancholy is mirrored in Samuel Daniel's "If this be love, to draw a weary breath." When at the beginning of *Romeo and Juliet* Shakespeare wishes to depict the conventional pangs of love—before the tragedy takes a drastic turn toward the radically *un*conventional—he gives his hero the familiar oxymoronic lament of the Petrarchan lover: "Feather of lead, bright smoke, cold fire, sick health" (1.1.173).

Parody of the conventional descriptions of a sonneteer's mistress. The illustration literalizes the conceits of many sonnets: the woman's breasts are globes, her lips are red coral, her teeth are pearls, her cheeks are roses and lilies, her eyes are suns loosing arrows of desire, her eyebrows are bows, and her hairnets are hearts. Cupid sits in her brow. From *The Extravagant Shepherd; or, The History of the Shepherd Lysis,* by Charles Sorel. The work was translated into English by John Davies of Kidwelly, 1654.

But the very familiarity of what Sidney's Astrophil called "poor Petrarch's long-deceasèd woes" posed a problem for English Renaissance poets: though they understood themselves to be the heirs of a powerful poetic achievement, they needed to make it seem that they were not merely following in the wake of the great Italian, or of anyone else. Strategies for doing so included the direct repudiation, most famously exemplified in Shakespeare's "My mistress' eyes are nothing like the sun," and the mockery expressed in Sir John Davies's "Mine eye, mine ear, my will, my wit, my heart." But there were many other, less direct means of achieving distance from Petrarch and hence of creating the impression of a distinct, individual voice.

As Shakespeare does in many of his sonnets, Richard Barnfield produces an effect of surprise by redirecting the Petrarchan conventions of praise—"A lovely creature, brighter than the day"—to a man. Michael Drayton pushes the trope of the lady's cruelty to a wildly sadistic extreme ("As in some countries far remote from hence"): his mistress becomes a surgeon participating in a fiendish ritual of torture. Thomas Campion takes the conventional description of the lady's face as a garden "Where roses and white lilies grow" and introduces into it an unexpected note, the voice of a street vender crying "Cherry ripe!" In another of the Campion poems gathered here ("I care not for these ladies"), the lover jauntily rejects the whole cult of pining after an inaccessible, high-born mistress and opts instead for a "nut-brown lass" who "never will say no."

Petrarch was a powerful force in shaping structures of thought and feeling and in provoking various strategies of resistance, but he was by no means the only influence on sixteenth-century English love poetry. Working within a relatively restricted range of themes—the experience of intense sexual desire (or its waning), the allure of beauty (or its fading), the fear of betrayal, the hopeless urge to stop time or, alternatively, to "seize the day," and the dream of gaining immortality through poetry—English writers explored a range of ways to express themselves and call attention to their particular eloquence. Though, in order to emphasize the collective nature of the period's poetic achievement, the poets here are presented as a group, the reader can sense each of them individually jostling for attention: Thomas, Lord Vaux, grimly renouncing love (in lines Shakespeare recalled in *Hamlet*); Edward de Vere, earl of Oxford, staging a bitterly cynical conversation with Desire; George Gascoigne writing a lul-

Cupid and his victims. In this image, entitled "The force of love," Cupid shoots an arrow into the bosom of a woman with the bow in his right hand (while her beloved looks on) and cradles the torch of love in his left arm. From *Hecatomgraphie*, by Gilles Corrozet, 1540.

laby to his penis; Thomas Lodge urging his readers to "Pluck the fruit and taste the pleasure"; Michael Drayton imagining his mistress as a crone with hair "Like grizzled moss upon some agèd tree"; Barnabe Barnes wishing himself transformed into wine trickling down his lover's throat; Richard Linche frankly celebrating carnal desire.

It is against the background of a widespread cultural competence and shared conventions that each of these writers of love poems attempted to distinguish himself. What seems to have mattered to them was not an escape from convention at all costs but rather the achievement of grace within formal structures. Hence they tended to opt for highly disciplined forms like the sonnet and then to contrive to give those forms a startling effect of naturalness: "Since there's no help, come, let us kiss and part," begins one of Michael Drayton's characteristically agile sonnets. "Nay, I have done, you get no more of me." In the introductory poem to his sonnet sequence *Idea*, Drayton declares that his "verse is the true image of my mind, / Ever in motion, still desiring change." The ability to capture change and the distinctness of a personal voice within the tight constraints of formal meter and rhyme scheme— like someone who dances with a joyous natural energy inside a very small room—is one of the hallmarks of sixteenth-century love poetry.

The Poets*

Thomas Vaux, second Baron Vaux (1509–1556). Born into a noble family and married at fourteen, Vaux was by the age of twenty a member of Parliament and a figure familiar in the court of Henry VIII, where his poetry was linked with that of Wyatt and Surrey. But probably because as a Catholic he was unhappy with the king's divorce and the turn toward Protestantism, he retired from public life while still in his twenties, withdrawing to his country estates.

George Gascoigne (1534/5?–1577). The son of a respectable country gentleman, Gascoigne lived a turbulent life. Having squandered his inheritance in an attempt to cut a figure at court, he failed both as a lawyer and as a soldier and was perennially in search of occupation and patronage. Serving as part of this search, his writing, which included courtly entertainments, plays, literary criticism, moral tracts, a hunting treatise, military reportage, and a brilliant work of prose fiction, as well as many poems, won him considerable esteem. But the esteem was not unmixed— some of his work was criticized as obscene—and Gascoigne seems to have died, as he lived, in financial straits.

Edward de Vere, seventeenth earl of Oxford (1550–1604). The only son of an immensely wealthy aristocrat, de Vere succeeded to the earldom at the age of twelve and became the ward of William Cecil, Queen Elizabeth's principal counselor. The young man was grossly indulged: when at the age of seventeen, while practicing his fencing, he ran through an unarmed bystander, the coroner's jury, in the pocket of de Vere's powerful guardian, ruled that the victim had committed suicide by spitting himself on the sword. Much of de Vere's subsequent life followed in the same pattern of recklessness and indulgence, but he wrote, and was widely acclaimed for, both plays (none of which has survived) and lyric poems. Having dissipated an enormous fortune, he died shortly after the accession of James I.

---

* For additional poems by several of the writers in this unit—Campion, Daniel, Davies, Drayton, Gascoigne, and Greville—see the supplemental ebook.

Fulke Greville, Lord Brooke (1554–1628). The wealthy Greville was educated at Cambridge, traveled widely on the Continent, served in Parliament, and was a generally successful courtier, under Elizabeth I, James I, and Charles I. Never married, he wrote some conventionally heterosexual love poetry, but his most passionate expressions of love were for his friend Sir Philip Sidney, whose death in 1586 he never ceased to mourn. In addition to a number of somberly powerful, brooding short poems, Greville wrote long philosophical verse treatises, several politically charged closet dramas, and a moving biography of Sidney. The end of Greville's life was grimly in keeping with his pessimism: he was fatally stabbed by a longtime servant who then killed himself.

Thomas Lodge (1558–1625). London-born Lodge was educated at Oxford, studied law, and eventually became a physician. He sailed in 1591 on a disastrous voyage to the New World, which he was fortunate to survive. In a career complicated by his lifelong Catholicism at a time of persecution, he tried his hand at writing poems, literary and moral tracts, plays, translations, and prose fictions (one of which became the source of Shakespeare's *As You Like It*).

Henry Constable (1562–1613). Constable was the second English poet, after Sidney, to publish a sonnet sequence. He also wrote many theological tracts. Born to a wealthy Protestant family, he converted to Catholicism, giving up his inheritance and putting himself at risk in attempts to convert King James and to argue for the toleration of Catholics.

Samuel Daniel (1562/3–1619). Daniel was for a time a member of the circle of Mary Sidney, countess of Pembroke, and he later held offices in the household of James I's queen, Anne of Denmark. A prolific, deeply thoughtful writer, he produced tragedies, court masques, a historical epic, a celebrated prose history of England, a defense of rhyme, several fine verse epistles, a verse dialogue on the purpose of writing poetry, a popular "complaint" poem in which the ghost of a king's mistress laments her fate, and one of the best Elizabethan sonnet sequences, *Delia*.

Michael Drayton (1563–1631). The son of a Warwickshire butcher or tanner, Drayton had a long and productive career as a professional writer. He collaborated on plays, wrote scriptural paraphrases, pastorals, "complaints," satires, odes, verse epistles, and historical poems, including an epic. His masterpiece is *Poly-Olbion*, a nearly fifteen-thousand-line historical-geographical poem celebrating all the counties of England and Wales. He contributed as well to the period's vogue for sonnets, publishing a sequence of fifty-one sonnets called *Idea's Mirror* (1594) that, following substantial revision, he republished as *Idea*.

Thomas Campion (1567–1620). After three years at Cambridge, Campion studied law before finally settling on medicine; he also became a composer, a writer of court masques, and a poet. Much of his poetry was in Latin, and he had an abiding interest in the possibility of applying the classical principles of quantitative versification to English. His most memorable achievements arose from the fact that he was both poet and composer: his aim, he wrote, was "to couple my words and notes lovingly together."

Sir John Davies (1569–1626). Davies attended Oxford before studying law in London, where, in his rambunctious twenties—at one point he was disbarred, for assaulting a friend and fellow lawyer—he wrote most or all of his best poems. They include the lengthy philosophical poem *Nosce teipsum* (Know Thyself) and *Orchestra, or a Poem of Dancing*, along with lyrics, scandalous satiric epigrams, and the parodic "gulling sonnets." Subsequently he went on to a major legal and political career, especially in Ireland, where he held important judicial appointments.

Barnabe Barnes (1571–1609). The son of the bishop of Durham, Barnes, who studied at Oxford, lived on his inheritance and had no settled profession. He published a play, a prose tract, and two collections of sonnets. Known for his fascination with all things Italian, he was accused of attempting to kill someone—in the Italian manner, it was said—with a poisoned lemon. He was arrested, but the charge did not lead to conviction.

Richard Barnfield (1574–1620). The eldest son in a family of landed gentry, Barnfield was educated at Oxford. In 1594 and 1595, he published two collections of pastoral verse, *The Affectionate Shepherd, Containing the Complaint of Daphnis for the Love of Ganymede* and *Cynthia, with Certain Sonnets*. Both collections, which earned admiring attention, have overt homoerotic themes. After publishing one further work, in 1598, Barnfield fell silent for the rest of his life. For reasons that remain unknown, he was disinherited by his father.

Richard Linche. Little is known about Linche, a poet and translator. He is thought to be the "R. L." who was the author of a collection of sonnets, *Diella*, published in 1596.

THOMAS, LORD VAUX

The Aged Lover Renounceth Love[1]

I loathe that° I did love,   *that which*
  In youth that I thought sweet;
As time requires, for my behoof°   *behoof (use)*
  Methinks they are not meet.°   *suitable*

5 My lusts they do me leave,
  My fancies all be fled,
And tract° of time begins to weave   *passage*
  Gray hairs upon my head.

For Age with stealing steps
10   Hath clawed me with his crutch,[2]
And lusty Life away she leaps
  As there had been none such.

My Muse doth not delight
  Me as she did before;
15 My hand and pen are not in plight,°   *good condition*
  As they have been of yore.

---

1. Three stanzas of this extremely popular poem are artfully misquoted by the first grave digger in *Hamlet* (5.1.57 ff.); two centuries later, Goethe, in Part 2 of *Faust*, has grave-digging spirits of the dead recite a German paraphrase of stanzas 1 and 3.

2. Sometimes (as in *Hamlet*) emended to "clutch," in which case "clawed" means "gripped."

For Reason me denies
    This youthly idle rhyme;
And day by day to me she cries,
20   "Leave off these toys° in time."   *trifles*

The wrinkles in my brow,
    The furrows in my face,
Say limping age will lodge him now
    Where youth must give° him place.   *yield*

25 The harbinger° of Death,   *herald*
    To me I see him ride:
The cough, the cold, the gasping breath
    Doth bid me to provide

A pickaxe and a spade,
30   And eke° a shrouding sheet,   *also*
A house of clay for to be made
    For such a guest most meet.

Methinks I hear the clerk°   *cleric (here, sexton)*
    That knolls the careful knell,³
35 And bids me leave my woeful work,
    Ere Nature me compel.⁴

My keepers knit the knot
    That youth did laugh to scorn,
Of me that clean° shall be forgot   *utterly*
40   As° I had not been born.   *as if*

Thus must I Youth give up,
    Whose badge I long did wear;
To them I yield the wanton cup,
    That better may it bear.

45 Lo, here the barèd skull,
    By whose bald sign I know
That stooping Age away shall pull
    Which° youthful years did sow.   *that which*

For Beauty with her band°   *bond*
50   These crooked cares hath wrought,
And shippèd me into the land
    From whence I first was brought.

And ye that bide behind,
    Have ye none other trust:°   *expectation*

---

3. Who tolls the slow, sorrowful ("care-full")
bell-ringing that announces a death.

4. Before nature—that is, death—forces me to
do so.

55   As ye of clay were cast by Kind,°   *formed by Nature*
    So shall ye waste to dust.

1557

GEORGE GASCOIGNE

And if I did, what then?[1]

"And if I did, what then?
Are you aggrieved therefore?
The sea hath fish for every man,
And what would you have more?"

5   Thus did my mistress once
    Amaze° my mind with doubt,   *stupefy; perplex*
    And popped a question, for the nonce,°   *on purpose; expressly*
    To beat my brains about.

    Whereto I thus replied,
10   "Each fisherman can wish
    That all the sea at every tide
    Were his alone to fish.

    "And so did I (in vain);
    But since it may not be,
15   Let such° fish there as find the gain,   *such men*
    And leave the loss for me.

    "And with such luck and loss,
    I will content myself,
    Till tides of turning time may toss
20   Such fishers on the shelf.°   *to one side*

    "And when they stick on sands,
    That every man may see,
    Then will I laugh and clap my hands,
    As they do now at me."

1573

1. This poem appears just at the end of Gascoigne's evidently autobiographical novella, *The Adventures of Master F. J.* (which mixes prose and verse throughout); it is occasioned by a conversation between F. J. and his mistress, the wife of his host in Italy. F. J. accuses her of betraying him with her male secretary, "and she . . . denied it, until at last being still urged with such evident tokens [i.e., clear proofs] as he alleged, she gave him this bone to gnaw upon: And if I did so (quoth she), what then? Whereunto F. J. made none answer, but departed. . . . And when he was in place solitary, he compiled these following [verses], for a final end of the matter."

The Lullaby of a Lover

Sing lullaby, as women do,
Wherewith they bring their babes to rest,
And lullaby can I sing too,
As womanly as can the best.
5   With lullaby they still the child,
And if I be not much beguiled,°   *deceived*
Full many wanton° babes have I,   *unruly (but with sexual overtone)*
Which must be stilled with lullaby.

First, lullaby my youthful years,
10   It is now time to go to bed,
For crooked age and hoary hairs
Have won the haven° within my head.   *come to harbor*
With lullaby then, youth, be still,
With lullaby content thy will,[1]
15   Since courage quails and comes behind,
Go sleep, and so beguile thy mind.

Next, lullaby my gazing eyes,
Which wonted were° to glance apace:° *were accustomed / unhesitatingly*
For every glass° may now suffice   *mirror*
20   To show the furrows in my face.
With lullaby then wink° awhile,   *close your eyes*
With lullaby your looks beguile.
Let no fair face nor beauty bright
Entice you eft° with vain delight.   *again*

25   And lullaby my wanton will,
Let reason's rule now rein thy thought,
Since all too late I find by skill°   *experience*
How dear I have thy fancies bought.
With lullaby now take thine ease,
30   With lullaby thy doubts appease.
For trust to this, if thou be still,
My body shall obey thy will.

Eke° lullaby my loving boy,   *also*
My little Robin,° take thy rest.   *i.e., his penis*
35   Since age is cold and nothing coy,° *not at all lascivious*
Keep close thy coin, for so is best.
With lullaby be thou content,
With lullaby thy lusts relent.°   *relinquish*
Let others pay which hath mo° pence;   *more*
40   Thou art too poor for such expense.[2]

1. With an overtone from the common 16th-century sense of "will" as "sexual desire." "Courage" (line 15): vigor, but *also* sexual desire.
2. Punning on "expense" as ejaculation: cf.

Shakespeare, Sonnet 129, line 1 (below, p. 1182). Each ejaculation was thought to shorten life by a day—a cost that, Gascoigne suggests, old age cannot afford.

Thus lullaby, my youth, mine eyes,
My will, my ware,° and all that was.   *genitals*
I can no mo delays devise,
But welcome pain, let pleasure pass.
45   With lullaby now take your leave,
With lullaby your dreams deceive,
And when you³ rise with waking eye,
Remember then this lullaby.

Ever or never.

1573, 1575

3. I.e., youth, eyes, will, and ware in the first lines of the stanza: despite the lullaby, they won't sleep long.

EDWARD DE VERE, EARL OF OXFORD

The lively lark stretched forth her wing

The lively lark stretched forth her wing,
The messenger of morning bright,
And with her cheerful voice did sing
The day's approach, discharging night,
5   When that Aurora, blushing red,
Descried the guilt of Thetis' bed.¹

I went abroad to take the air,
And in the meads° I met a knight,   *meadows*
Clad in carnation color fair.
10   I did salute this gentle wight;
Of him I did his name inquire.
He sighed and said, "I am Desire."

Desire I did desire to stay;
A while with him I craved to talk.
15   The courteous knight said me no nay,
But hand in hand with me did walk.
Then of Desire I asked again
What thing did please, and what did pain.

He smiled, and thus he answered then:
20   "Desire can have no greater pain
Than for to see another man
That° he desireth, to obtain;   *the thing that*

1. Aurora, goddess of the dawn, reddens at seeing that the sun, Phoebus, has once again spent the night in the bed of the sea goddess Thetis (here, as often, identified with the ocean).

Nor greater joy can be than this,
Than to enjoy that° others miss."   *what*

1576

FULKE GREVILLE, LORD BROOKE

From Caelica

61[1]

Caelica, while you do swear you love me best,
And ever lovèd only me,
I feel that all powers are oppressed
By love, and love by Destiny.

5   For as the child in swaddling-bands,[2]
When it doth see the nurse come nigh,
With smiles and crows doth lift the hands,
Yet still° must in the cradle lie: *nevertheless*
     So in the boat of fate I row,
10   And looking to you, from you go.[3]

When I see in thy once-belovèd brows
The heavy marks of constant love,
I call to mind my broken vows,
And childlike to the nurse would move;[4]

15   But love is of the phoenix-kind,[5]
And burns itself in self-made fire,
To breed still new birds in the mind,
From ashes of the old desire:
     And hath his wings from constancy,
20   As mountains called of moving be.[6]

Then, Caelica, lose not heart-eloquence:
Love understands not "Come again";
Who changes in her own defense,
Needs not cry to the deaf in vain.

---

1. Like many other sonnet sequences (beginning with the first one, Petrarch's), *Caelica* includes some poems that aren't sonnets. "Caelica": heavenly.
2. "Clothes consisting of narrow lengths of bandage wrapped round a new-born infant's limbs to prevent free movement" (*OED*).
3. In a rowboat, the rower faces the stern.
4. I.e., my guilt makes me wish, childishly, that I could love you again.

5. Only one of this mythical Arabian bird existed at a time: after 500 years of life, it immolated itself on a funeral pyre, and a new phoenix rose from the ashes.
6. "His wings are called constant although rarely still, just as mountains are sometimes called 'Moving' mountains although their landslides are very occasional; *i.e.* such epithets are earned by the rarity of the phenomena they ascribe to their subject" (Greville's editor Geoffrey Bullough).

25 Love is no true-made looking glass,
    Which perfect yields the shape we bring;
    It ugly shows us all that was,[7]
    And flatters every future thing:
        When Phoebus' beams no more appear,
30   'Tis darker that the day was here.[8]

    Change, I confess, it is a hateful power,
    To them that all at once must think;[9]
    Yet Nature made both sweet and sour,
    She gave the eye a lid to wink.

35 And though the youth that are estranged
    From mother's lap to other skies,
    Do think that Nature there is changed,
    Because at home their knowledge lies;
        Yet shall they see, who far have gone,
40   That pleasure speaks more tongues than one.

    The leaves fall off, when sap goes to the root,°   *i.e., in winter*
    The warmth[1] doth clothe the bough again;
    But to the dead tree what doth boot°   *what good is*
    The silly man's manuring pain?°   *care in cultivating*

45 Unkindness may piece up° again,   *make up*
    But kindness either changed or dead,
    Self-pity may in fools complain.[2]
    Put thou thy horns on others' head:[3]
        For constant faith is made a drudge,
50   But when requiting love is judge.[4]

69

    When all this All doth pass from age to age,
    And revolution in a circle turn,[5]
    Then heavenly justice doth appear like rage,
    The caves do roar, the very seas do burn,
5   Glory grows dark, the sun becomes a night,
        And makes this great world feel a greater might.

    When Love doth change his seat from heart to heart,
    And worth about the wheel of Fortune goes,
    Grace is diseased, desert seems overthwart,°   *thwarted; obstructed*

---

7. I.e., it makes our past loves look ugly in retrospect.
8. I.e., after the sun has set, the night seems darker because the day was bright.
9. "To those who regard past, present, and future as all one" (Bullough).
1. Yet the warm weather (in spring).
2. "Only fools will complain in self-pity, of a changed or dead affection" (Bullough).
3. I.e., the proper response to being cuckolded (given "horns") is to cuckold someone else.
4. Except when given justice by reciprocated love.
5. Referring to the ancient theory of the Great Year, in which the completion of an entire revolution of the universe ("this All") marks the transition, with cataclysmic events, from one epoch ("age") to the next. For a modern version, cf. Yeats, "The Second Coming" and "Two Songs from a Play."

10 Vows are forlorn,° and truth doth credit° lose,   *abandoned / credence*
   Chance then gives law, Desire must be wise,
   And look more ways than one, or lose her eyes.

   My age of joy is past, of woe begun,
   Absence my presence is, strangeness my grace,[6]
15 With them that walk against me, is my sun:
   The wheel is turned, I hold° the lowest place.   *occupy*
   What can be good to me since my love is,
   To do me harm, content to do amiss?

ca. 1580–1600   1633

6. Instead of favor ("grace"), I now find aloofness ("strangeness").

THOMAS LODGE

Pluck the fruit and taste the pleasure[1]

   Pluck the fruit and taste the pleasure,
     Youthful lordings,° of delight,   *gentlemen*
   Whilst occasion gives you seizure,[2]
     Feed your fancies and your sight:
5   After death when you are gone,
     Joy and pleasure is there none.

   Here on earth no thing is stable,
     Fortune's changes well are known,
   Whilst as youth doth then enable,
10   Let your seeds of joy be sown:
     After death when you are gone,
     Joy and pleasure is there none.

   Feast it freely with your lovers,
     Blithe and wanton sweets do fade,
15 Whilst that lovely Cupid hovers
     Round about this lovely shade:
     Sport it freely one to one,
     After death is pleasure none.

   Now the pleasant spring allureth,
20   And both place and time invites:
   Out alas,[3] what heart endureth

1. One of several poems interspersed in Lodge's romance *The Famous, True, and Historical Life of Robert, Second Duke of Normandy.*

2. While you have the opportunity to seize it.

3. "Out" simply intensifies "alas."

To disclaim° his sweet delights?   *renounce; relinquish*
After death when we are gone,
Joy and pleasure is there none.

1591

HENRY CONSTABLE

From Diana[1]

Decade 6, Sonnet 2

To live in hell, and heaven to behold,
To welcome life and die a living death,
To sweat with heat and yet be freezing cold,
To grasp at stars and lie the earth beneath;
5   To tread a maze that never shall have end,
To burn in sighs and starve[2] in daily tears,
To climb a hill and never to descend,
Giants to kill, and quake at childish fears;
To pine for food, and watch° th' Hesperian tree,[3]   *watch over*
10   To thirst for drink, and nectar still to draw,[4]
To live accursed, whom men hold blest to be,
And weep those wrongs which never creature saw:°   *experienced*
If this be love, if love in these be founded,
My heart is love, for these in it are grounded.°   *firmly fixed*

1594?

---

1. The very name that Constable gives his beloved—Diana, the chaste hunter goddess of classical mythology—suggests how little chance he (like the smitten narrators of other sonnet sequences, beginning with Petrarch) has of success. This particular sonnet, however, is found only in the second, 1594(?) edition of Constable's sequence and may not be by him at all: there is no manuscript copy linking the poem to Constable, and the title page of the edition describes it as containing "The excellent conceitful Sonnets of H. C. Augmented with divers Quatorzains [14-line poems] of honorable and learned personages." Whoever wrote the poem, it represents a durably popular kind of paradoxical sonnet ultimately traceable to Petrarch's Rima 134 (above, p. 651), and is based directly on a sonnet by the 16th-century French poet Philippe Desportes: *Diane* 1.29.

2. Die slowly (not necessarily of hunger).

3. In Greek mythology, this tree, which bore golden apples, was guarded by the Hesperides (daughters, according to some, of Atlas) and the dragon Ladon. Its fruit would not actually be of any use as food.

4. And always to drink nectar (in classical myth, the delicious, immortality-conferring drink of the gods).

SAMUEL DANIEL

From Delia

9[1]

    If this be love, to draw a weary breath,
    Paint on floods, till the shore, cry to the air,[2]
    With downward looks still° reading on the earth   *always*
    The sad memorials of my love's despair;
5   If this be love, to war against my soul,
    Lie down to wail, rise up to sigh and grieve me,
    The never-resting stone of care to roll,[3]
    Still to complain my griefs, and none relieve me;
     If this be love, to clothe me with dark thoughts,
    Haunting untrodden paths to wail apart,
10   My pleasures, horror; music, tragic notes,
    Tears in my eyes and sorrow at my heart;
      If this be love, to live a living death—
      Oh then love I, and draw this weary breath.

32

    But love whilst that thou may'st be loved again,°   *in return*
    Now whilst thy May hath filled thy lap with flowers;
    Now whilst thy beauty bears° without a stain;   *endures*
    Now use thy summer smiles ere winter lours.
5   And whilst thou spread'st unto the rising sun,
    The fairest flower that ever saw the light,
    Now joy thy time before thy sweet be done,
    And Delia, think thy morning must have night,
     And that thy brightness sets at length to west,
10 When thou wilt close up that which now thou showest:
    And think the same becomes° thy fading best,   *suits*
    Which then shall hide it most, and cover lowest.
      Men do not weigh° the stalk for that it was,   *value*
      When once they find her flower, her glory pass.

33

    When men shall find thy flower, thy glory, pass,
    And thou, with careful° brow sitting alone,   *full of care; sorrowful*

1. Like the sonnet by Constable, this one is adapted from Desportes, *Diane* 1.29. "Delia": in classical mythology, one of the epithets of the goddess Diana, deriving from her birthplace, the island of Delos. In giving the name to the woman he celebrates, Daniel follows the Roman love poet Tibullus (ca. 55–19 B.C.E.).

2. A series of pointless activities: painting on water, tilling the seashore, . . .

3. The line—like the poem's entire list of pointless, unending labors—alludes to the myth of Sisyphus, who, having offended the gods, is punished in the Underworld by having to roll a large stone to the top of a hill—a task he can never complete, because just as the stone nears the summit, it always slips from his grasp and rolls to the bottom again.

Receivèd hast this message from thy glass,°   *looking glass*
That tells thee truth, and says that all is gone,
5   Fresh shalt thou see in me the wounds thou madest,
Though spent thy flame, in me the heat remaining:
I that have loved thee thus before thou fadest,
My faith shall wax,° when thou art in thy waning.   *fidelity shall increase*
    The world shall find this miracle in me,
10   That fire can burn when all the matter's spent;
Then, what my faith hath been thyself shall see,
And that thou wast unkind thou may'st repent.
       Thou may'st repent that thou hast scorned my tears,
       When winter snows upon thy golden hairs.

1592

MICHAEL DRAYTON

From Idea

To the Reader of These Sonnets

Into these loves° who but° for passion looks,   *i.e., love poems / only*
At this first sight here let him lay them by
And seek elsewhere, in turning other books
Which better may his labor satisfy.
5   No farfetched sigh shall ever wound my breast,
Love from mine eye a tear shall never wring,
Nor in *Ah me's* my whining sonnets dressed;
A libertine, fantasticly¹ I sing.
My verse is the true image of my mind,
10   Ever in motion, still° desiring change;   *always*
And as thus to variety inclined,
So in all humors° sportively I range;   *manners; fancies*
    My muse is rightly of the English strain,
    That cannot long one fashion entertain.

1599, 1619

6

How many paltry, foolish, painted things,
That now in coaches trouble every street,
Shall be forgotten, whom no poet sings,
Ere they be well wrapped in their winding sheet?°   *shroud*
5   Where° I to thee eternity shall give,   *whereas*
When nothing else remaineth of these days;
And queens hereafter shall be glad to live

---

1. Capriciously. "Libertine": one who follows his (or her) own inclinations.

Upon the alms of thy superfluous praise.
Virgins and matrons, reading these my rhymes,
10 Shall be so much delighted with thy story
That they shall grieve they lived not in these times,
To have seen thee, their sex's only glory:
    So shalt thou fly above the vulgar° throng,   *common*
    Still to survive in my immortal song.

                                                  1619

8

There's nothing grieves me but that° age should haste,   *but the possibility that*
That° in my days I may not see thee old;   *with the result that*
That where those two clear, sparkling eyes are placed,
Only two loopholes then I might behold;
5 That lovely archèd, ivory, polished brow
Defaced with wrinkles that I might but see;
Thy dainty hair, so curled and crispèd now,
Like grizzled moss upon some agèd tree;
Thy cheek, now flush with roses, sunk and lean;
10 Thy lips, with age as any wafer thin;
Thy pearly teeth out of thy head so clean,°   *entirely*
That when thou feed'st, thy nose shall touch thy chin.
    These lines that now thou scorn'st, which should delight thee,
    Then would I make thee read, but to despite° thee.   *spite*

                                                  1619

50

As in some countries far remote from hence,
The wretched creature destinèd to die,
Having the judgment due to his offense,
By surgeons begg'd their art° on him to try,   *skill*
5 Which° on the living work without remorse,   *who*
First make incision on each mast'ring vein,°   *major blood vessel*
Then stanch the bleeding, then transpierce the corse,°   *pierce through the body*
And with their balms recure° the wounds again,   *heal*
Then poison, and with physic° him restore,   *medical treatment*
10 Not that they fear the hopeless man to kill,
But their experience to increase the more:
Ev'n so my mistress works upon my ill,°   *illness (i.e., love's pangs)*
    By curing me and killing me each hour
    Only to show her beauty's sov'reign power.

                                                  1605

61

Since there's no help, come, let us kiss and part.
Nay, I have done, you get no more of me,
And I am glad, yea glad with all my heart

That thus so cleanly I myself can free.
5   Shake hands forever, cancel all our vows,
And when we meet at any time again,
Be it not seen in either of our brows
That we one jot of former love retain.
Now at the last gasp of love's latest breath,
10   When, his pulse failing, Passion speechless lies,
When Faith° is kneeling by his bed of death,   *faithfulness*
And Innocence is closing up his eyes;
   Now if thou would'st, when all have given him over,°   *given up on him*
   From death to life thou might'st him yet recover.

1619

THOMAS CAMPION

My sweetest Lesbia[1]

My sweetest Lesbia, let us live and love,
And though the sager sort our deeds reprove,
Let us not weigh° them: heav'n's great lamps do dive   *heed*
Into their west, and straight° again revive,   *at once*
5   But soon as once set is our little light,
Then must we sleep one ever-during° night.   *everlasting*

If all would lead their lives in love like me,
Then bloody swords and armor should not be;
No drum nor trumpet peaceful sleeps should move,°   *disturb*
10   Unless alarm° came from the camp of love.   *the call to arms*
But fools do live, and waste their little light,
And seek with pain their ever-during night.

When timely death my life and fortune ends,
Let not my hearse° be vexed with mourning friends,   *bier*
15   But let all lovers, rich in triumph, come
And with sweet pastimes grace my happy tomb;
And Lesbia, close up thou my little light,
And crown with love my ever-during night.

1601

1. Imitated and partly translated from a poem by Catullus (87–ca. 54 B.C.E.), the Latin lyric poet who often celebrated the charms of Lesbia in his verses. This and the three lyrics that follow appeared, with musical settings, in *A Book of Airs*, which contains Campion's first work as a composer.

I care not for these ladies

I care not for these ladies
That must be wooed and prayed;
Give me kind Amaryllis,
The wanton country² maid.
5   Nature art° disdaineth;   *artifice*
Her beauty is her own.
    Her when we court and kiss,
    She cries "Forsooth,° let go!"   *Truly!*
    But when we come where comfort is,
10   She never will say no.

If I love Amaryllis,
She gives me fruit and flowers;
But if we love these ladies,
We must give golden showers.
15   Give them gold that sell love,
Give me the nut-brown° lass   *i.e., sun-tanned*
    Who when we court and kiss,
    She cries "Forsooth, let go!"
    But when we come where comfort is,
20   She never will say no.

These ladies must have pillows,
And beds by strangers wrought.°   *i.e., imported*
Give me a bower of willows,
Of moss and leaves unbought,
25   And fresh Amaryllis,
With milk and honey fed,
    Who when we court and kiss,
    She cries "Forsooth, let go!"
    But when we come where comfort is,
30   She never will say no.

1601

When to her lute Corinna sings

When to her lute Corinna³ sings,
Her voice revives the leaden° strings,   *i.e., heavy*
And doth in highest notes appear
As any challenged° echo clear;   *aroused*

---

2. Probably with an obscene pun. "Amaryllis": in classical and later pastoral poetry, a conventional name for a shepherdess.
3. Like Amaryllis (preceding note), a classical name: (1) a female Greek poet (whose work sur-vives only in fragments); (2) Ovid's pseudonymous—and probably fictitious—mistress in his collection of erotic poems, the *Amores*. "Lute": a stringed instrument somewhat like a guitar.

5   But when she doth of mourning speak,
     Ev'n with her sighs the strings do break.

     And as her lute doth live or die,
     Led by her passion, so must I:
     For when of pleasure she doth sing,
10 My thoughts enjoy a sudden spring;
     But if she doth of sorrow speak,
     Ev'n from my heart the strings do break.

1601

When thou must home to shades of underground

When thou must home to shades of underground,[4]
And there arrived, a new admirèd guest,
The beauteous spirits do engirt° thee round,   *gird, encircle*
White Iope, blithe Helen,[5] and the rest,
5 To hear the stories of thy finished love
From that smooth tongue whose music hell can move,

Then wilt thou speak of banqueting delights,
Of masques[6] and revels which sweet youth did make,
Of tourneys and great challenges of knights,
10 And all these triumphs[7] for thy beauty's sake:
When thou hast told these honors done to thee,
Then tell, O tell, how thou didst murther me.

1601

Never love unless you can

Never love unless you can
Bear with all the faults of man:
Men sometimes will jealous be,
Though but little cause they see,
5   And hang the head, as discontent,
     And speak what straight° they will repent.   *immediately*

Men that but one saint adore
Make a show of love to more:
Beauty must be scorned in none,
10 Though but truly served in one;

4. The classical abode of the dead, Hades.
5. Helen of Troy. "Iope": another famously beautiful woman of classical mythology. In a passage that Campion has in mind here, the Roman love poet Propertius (ca. 50–after 16 B.C.E.) includes Iope in a list (2.28.49–56) of lovely women now among the dead.
6. See the Literary Terminology appendix in this volume.
7. Public festivities—especially, jousting tournaments.

For what is courtship but disguise?
True hearts may have dissembling eyes.

Men when their affairs° require   *business*
Must a while themselves retire:°   *withdraw*
15 Sometimes hunt, and sometimes hawk,
And not ever sit and talk.
    If these and suchlike you can bear,
    Then like, and love, and never fear.

ca. 1617

There is a garden in her face

There is a garden in her face,
Where roses and white lilies grow;
    A heav'nly paradise is that place,
Wherein all pleasant fruits do flow.[8]
5   There cherries grow, which none may buy
    Till "Cherry ripe!"[9] themselves do cry.

Those cherries fairly do enclose
Of orient° pearl a double row;   *lustrous; precious*
    Which when her lovely laughter shows,
10 They look like rosebuds filled with snow.
    Yet them nor° peer nor prince can buy,   *neither*
    Till "Cherry ripe!" themselves do cry.

Her eyes like angels watch° them still;   *guard*
Her brows like bended bows do stand,
15   Threatening with piercing frowns to kill
All that attempt with eye or hand
    Those sacred cherries to come nigh,
    Till "Cherry ripe!" themselves do cry.

ca. 1617

---

8. Abound—as in the biblical Promised Land, "flowing with milk and honey" (Exodus 3.8).

9. A familiar cry of London street vendors.

SIR JOHN DAVIES

From Gulling Sonnets[1]

5

Mine eye, mine ear, my will, my wit,° my heart,   *mind*
Did see, did hear, did like, discern, did love,
Her face, her speech, her fashion, judgment, art,° *skill*
Which did charm, please, delight, confound, and move.
5 Then fancy, humor,° love, conceit,° and thought *whim / opinion*
Did so draw, force, entice, persuade, devise,
That she was won, moved, carried, compassed, wrought,
To think me kind, true, comely, valiant, wise.
That heaven, earth, hell, my folly, and her pride
10 Did work, contrive, labor, conspire, and swear
To make me scorned, vile, cast off, base, defied
With her my love, light, my life, my dear:
So that my heart, my wit, will, ear, and eye
Doth grieve, lament, sorrow, despair, and die.

ca. 1599   1873

1. In late 16th-century English slang, a "gull" is either a credulous, easily duped person (whence, in the 19th century, the adjective "gullible") or a deception perpetrated *on* such a person. The particular fraudulent practices that Davies's nine *Gulling Sonnets* satirize are those of uninspired writers who pass off as poetry sonnets constructed by the mechanical application of endlessly exploited conventions of Petrarchan poetry. In the fifth sonnet, the object of mockery is "correlative verse," which became extremely popular in the century's closing decades.

BARNABE BARNES

From Parthenophil and Parthenope[1]

63

Jove for Europa's love took shape of bull,
 And for Callisto played Diana's part;
 And in a golden shower he fillèd full
 The lap of Danaë,[2] with celestial art.°   *skill*
5 Would I were changed but to my mistress' gloves,
 That those white lovely fingers I might hide,

1. In Greek mythology, Parthenope was one of the Sirens, who lured seafarers to destruction by their irresistible singing. "Parthenophil" means "lover of Parthenope."
2. Jupiter raped Danaë by changing himself into a shower of gold, which she spread her lap to catch; he abducted Europa by taking the form of a beautiful swimming bull and inveigling her to mount him; he overcame the nymph Callisto's chastity by disguising himself as her mistress, the virgin goddess Diana.

That I might kiss those hands which mine heart loves;
  Or else that chain of pearl (her neck's vain pride)
Made proud with her neck's veins, that I might fold
10   About that lovely neck, and her paps° tickle;   *breasts*
  Or her to compass° like a belt of gold;   *encircle, embrace*
Or that sweet wine which down her throat doth trickle,
  To kiss her lips and lie next at her heart,
  Run through her veins, and pass by° pleasure's part.   *via*

1593

RICHARD BARNFIELD

From Cynthia[1]

9

Diana (on a time) walking the wood
  To sport herself, of her fair train forlorn,[2]
  Chanced for to prick her foot against a thorn,
And from thence issued out a stream of blood.
5 No sooner she was vanished out of sight,
    But love's fair queen° came there away by chance,   *Venus*
    And having of this hap° a glimm'ring glance, *accident, happenstance*
  She put the blood into a crystal° bright.   *vessel of crystal*
When being now come unto Mount Rhodope,[3]
10   With her fair hands she forms a shape of snow,
    And blends it with this blood; from whence doth grow
A lovely creature, brighter than the day.
    And being christened in fair Paphos'[4] shrine,
    She called him Ganymede,[5] as all divine.

11

Sighing, and sadly sitting by my love,
  He asked the cause of my heart's sorrowing,
  Conjuring me by heaven's eternal king
To tell the cause which me so much did move.
5 Compelled (quoth I), to thee will I confess
    Love is the cause, and only love it is
    That doth deprive me of my heavenly bliss;
Love is the pain that doth my heart oppress.
    And what is she (quoth he) whom thou dost love?

1. Cynthia, or Diana, was the chaste hunter goddess, and moon goddess, of classical mythology. Cynthia is also the name of the mistress in the erotic elegies of the Roman poet Propertius.
2. Left without her fair retinue (of wood nymphs).
3. In frigid Thrace, and associated with Diana.

4. A city in Cyprus, sacred to Venus.
5. A Trojan boy, said to be the most beautiful of mortals. Enamored of him, Zeus brought Ganymede away to Olympus, where he was deified and became cupbearer to the gods.

10   Look in this glass° (quoth I), there shalt thou see   *mirror*
     The perfect form of my felicity.
When, thinking that it would strange magic prove,°   *show*
     He opened it: and taking off the cover,
     He straight perceived himself to be my lover.

1595

RICHARD LINCHE

From Diella

33

The last so sweet, so balmy, so delicious,
     Lips, breath, and tongue, which I delight to drink on;
The first so fair, so bright, so purely precious,
     Brow, eyes, and cheeks, which still I joy to think on.
5   But much more joy to gaze and aye° to look on   *ever*
     Those lily rounds° which ceaseless hold their moving,   *i.e., breasts*
From where my prisoned eyes would ne'er be gone,
     Which to such beauties are exceeding loving.
O that I might but press their dainty swelling
10   And thence depart to which° must now be hidden,   *that which*
And which my crimson verse abstains from telling,
     Because by chaste ears I am so forbidden:
There in the crystal-pavèd vale of pleasure
Lies locked up a world of richest treasure.

1596

SIR WALTER RALEGH
1552–1618

The brilliant and versatile Sir Walter Ralegh was a soldier, courtier, philosopher, explorer and colonist, student of science, historian, and poet. Born to West Country gentry of modest means, Ralegh amassed great wealth thanks to his position at court, leading him to be denounced by some as an upstart and hated by others as a rapacious monopolist. He fought ruthlessly in Ireland and Cádiz, directed the colonization of Virginia, introduced the potato to Ireland and tobacco to Europe, brought Spenser from Ireland to the English court, conducted scientific experiments, led expeditions to Guiana in an unsuccessful effort to find gold, and wrote several reports urging England to challenge Spanish dominance in the New World. He was known for his violent temper, his dramatic sense of life, his extravagant dress, his skepticism in religious matters, his bitter hatred of Spain, and his great favor with Queen Elizabeth, interrupted in 1592 when he seduced, and then married, one of her ladies-in-waiting. His long poem to the queen, *The Ocean to Cynthia*, remains in manuscript fragments, one of more than five hundred lines. His best-known shorter poems include the reply to Marlowe's "Passionate Shepherd" and "The Lie," an attack on social classes and institutions which itself provoked many replies. His active resistance to printing his poems—in one case he forced a printer to recall a volume and paste a slip of paper over his initials—makes it very difficult to put the copies that circulated in manuscript in any reliable chronological order.

King James suspected Ralegh of opposing his succession and threw him into the Tower of London in 1603 on trumped-up charges of treason; there he remained for the rest of his life save for an ill-fated last voyage to Guiana in 1617, which again failed to discover gold. In prison he wrote his long, unfinished *History of the World*, which begins with the Creation, emphasizes the providential punishment of evil princes, and projects a treatment of English history—although not of recent events, because, he declared, he who follows truth too closely at the heels might get kicked in the teeth. The work was to have been dedicated to Henry, prince of Wales, Ralegh's most powerful friend and supporter, who declared, "Only my father would keep such a bird in a cage." But Henry died in 1612, and Ralegh broke off his narrative at 168 B.C.E. Six years later James, bowing to Spanish pressure, had Ralegh executed on the old treason charge.*

The Nymph's Reply to the Shepherd[1]

If all the world and love were young,
And truth in every shepherd's tongue,
These pretty pleasures might me move
To live with thee and be thy love.

5 Time drives the flocks from field to fold
When rivers rage and rocks grow cold,
And Philomel° becometh dumb;   *the nightingale*
The rest complains of cares to come.

The flowers do fade, and wanton fields
10 To wayward winter reckoning yields;°   *renders an account*
A honey tongue, a heart of gall,
Is fancy's spring, but sorrow's fall.

Thy gowns, thy shoes, thy beds of roses,
Thy cap, thy kirtle,° and thy posies°   *dress / bouquets*
15 Soon break, soon wither, soon forgotten—
In folly ripe, in reason rotten.

* See the supplemental ebook for Ralegh's poem beginning "As you came from the holy land of Walsinghame" and for excerpts from his account of the battle between the *Revenge* and a Spanish fleet.
1. Cf. Marlowe, "The Passionate Shepherd to His Love," p. 1126.

Thy belt of straw and ivy buds,
Thy coral clasps and amber studs,
All these in me no means can move
20   To come to thee and be thy love.

But could youth last and love still breed,
Had joys no date° nor age no need,   *ending*
Then these delights my mind might move
To live with thee and be thy love.

1600

What is our life?

What is our life? a play of passion;
Our mirth the music of division;[1]
Our mothers' wombs the tiring-houses[2] be
Where we are dressed for this short comedy.
5   Heaven the judicious sharp spectator is
That sits and marks still who doth act amiss;
Our graves that hide us from the searching sun
Are like drawn curtains when the play is done.
Thus march we, playing, to our latest rest,
10   Only we die in earnest—that's no jest.

1612

[Sir Walter Ralegh to His Son][1]

Three things there be that prosper up apace
And flourish, whilst they grow asunder far,
But on a day, they meet all in one place,
And when they meet, they one another mar;
5   And they be these: the wood, the weed,° the wag.   *i.e., hemp*
The wood is that which makes the gallow tree;
The weed is that which strings the hangman's bag;[2]
The wag, my pretty knave, betokeneth° thee.   *signifies*
Mark well, dear boy, whilst these assemble not,
10   Green springs the tree, hemp grows, the wag is wild,
But when they meet, it makes the timber rot,
It frets the halter,° and it chokes the child.   *tightens the noose*
    Then bless thee, and beware, and let us pray
    We part not with thee at this meeting day.

ca. 1600

---

1. A rapid melodic passage; or the music between the acts of a play.
2. Dressing rooms in an Elizabethan theater.
1. The sonnet has this title in one of the manuscripts in which it appears.
2. I.e., when woven into rope, the hemp secures the hangman's hood ("bag") to the condemned person's neck.

The Lie

Go, soul, the body's guest,
　　Upon a thankless errand;
Fear not to touch° the best;　　　　　　　*speak of; censure*
　　The truth shall be thy warrant.
5　Go, since I needs must die,
　　And give the world the lie.[1]

Say to the court, it glows
　　And shines like rotten wood;°　　　　*i.e., with phosphorescence*
Say to the church, it shows
10　What's good, and doth no good.
If church and court reply,
　　Then give them both the lie.

Tell potentates they live
　　Acting by others' action;
15　Not loved unless they give,
　　Not strong but by a faction.
If potentates reply,
　　Give potentates the lie.

Tell men of high condition,
20　That manage the estate,°　　　　　　　*state*
Their purpose is ambition,
　　Their practice only hate.
And if they once reply,
　　Then give them all the lie.

25　Tell them that brave it° most,　　　　*live ostentatiously*
　　They beg for more by spending,
Who, in their greatest cost,
　　Seek nothing but commending.°　　　*i.e., others' approval*
And if they make reply,
30　Then give them all the lie.

Tell zeal it wants° devotion;　　　　　　*lacks*
　　Tell love it is but lust;
Tell time it is but motion;
　　Tell flesh it is but dust.
35　And wish them not reply,
　　For thou must give the lie.

Tell age it daily wasteth;°　　　　　　　*decays*
　　Tell honor how it alters;
Tell beauty how she blasteth;°　　　　　*withers away*
40　Tell favor how it falters.

1. "Give the lie": accuse of lying.

And as they shall reply,
   Give every one the lie.

Tell wit° how much it wrangles   *intellect*
   In tickle points of niceness;°   *in trivial distinctions*
45 Tell wisdom she entangles
   Herself in overwiseness.
And when they do reply,
   Straight give them both the lie.

Tell physic° of her boldness;°   *medicine / presumption*
50   Tell skill it is pretension;
Tell charity of coldness;
   Tell law it is contention.
And as they do reply,
   So give them still the lie.

55 Tell fortune of her blindness;
   Tell nature of decay;
Tell friendship of unkindness;
   Tell justice of delay.
And if they will reply,
60   Then give them all the lie.

Tell arts they have no soundness,
   But vary by esteeming;[2]
Tell schools[3] they want profoundness,
   And stand too much on seeming.
65 If arts and schools reply,
   Give arts and schools the lie.

Tell faith° it's fled the city;   *faithfulness, fidelity*
   Tell how the country erreth;
Tell manhood shakes off pity;
70   Tell virtue least preferreth.°   *advances*
And if they do reply,
   Spare not to give the lie.

So when thou hast, as I
   Commanded thee, done blabbing,°   *revealing secrets*
75 Although to give the lie
   Deserves no less than stabbing,
Stab at thee he that will,
   No stab thy soul can kill.

ca. 1592   1608

---

2. I.e., seem good or bad according to different tastes or judgments. The "arts" are the Seven Liberal Arts, basis of the academic curriculum.
3. The various philosophical traditions.

Farewell, false love

Farewell, false love, the oracle° of lies,   *i.e., authoritative source*
A mortal foe and enemy to rest;
An envious boy, from whom all cares arise,
A bastard vile, a beast with rage possessed;
5   A way of error, a temple full of treason,
In all effects contrary unto reason.

A poisoned serpent covered all with flowers,
Mother of sighs and murtherer° of repose,   *murderer*
A sea of sorrows from whence are drawn such showers
10   As moisture lends to every grief that grows;
A school of guile, a net of deep deceit,
A gilded hook that holds a poisoned bait.

A fortress foiled° which reason did defend,   *overthrown*
A siren song, a fever of the mind,
15   A maze wherein affection finds no end,
A raging cloud that runs before the wind,
A substance like the shadow of the sun,
A goal of grief for which the wisest run.

A quenchless fire, a nurse of trembling fear,
20   A path that leads to peril and mishap;
A true retreat of sorrow and despair,
An idle boy that sleeps in pleasure's lap,
A deep distrust of that which certain seems,
A hope of that which reason doubtful deems.

25   Sith° then thy trains° my younger years betrayed,   *since / tricks*
And for my faith° ingratitude I find,   *faithfulness*
And sith repentance hath my wrongs bewrayed°   *revealed*
Whose course was ever contrary to kind°—   *nature*
False love, desire, and beauty frail, adieu!
30   Dead is the root whence all these fancies grew.

1588

Methought I saw the grave where Laura lay[1]

Methought I saw the grave where Laura lay,
Within that temple where the vestal° flame   *celebrating virginity*
Was wont° to burn; and passing by that way   *accustomed*
To see that buried dust of living fame,

---

1. A commendatory sonnet to the first three books of *The Faerie Queene*, by Ralegh's friend Spenser. Laura was the lady celebrated in the sonnets of Petrarch (1304–1374).

5   Whose tomb fair Love and fairer Virtue kept,
    All suddenly I saw the Fairy Queen;
    At whose approach the soul of Petrarch wept,
    And from thenceforth those graces° were not seen,   *i.e., Love and Virtue*
    For they this Queen attended; in whose stead
10 Oblivion laid him down on Laura's hearse.°   *grave*
    Hereat the hardest stones were seen to bleed,
    And groans of buried ghosts the heavens did pierce;
      Where Homer's sprite[2] did tremble all for grief,
    And cursed th' access° of that celestial thief.[3]   *accession*

1590

Nature, that washed her hands in milk

Nature, that washed her hands in milk,
    And had forgot to dry them,
Instead of earth took snow and silk,
    At Love's request to try them,
5 If she a mistress could compose
To please Love's fancy out of those.

Her eyes he would should be of light,
    A violet breath, and lips of jelly;
Her hair not black, nor overbright,
10   And of the softest down her belly;
As for her inside he'd have it
Only of wantonness° and wit.   *playfulness*

At Love's entreaty such a one
    Nature made, but with her beauty
15 She hath framed a heart of stone;
    So as Love, by ill destiny,
Must die for her whom Nature gave him,
Because her darling would not save him.

But Time (which Nature doth despise,
20   And rudely gives her love the lie,
Makes Hope a fool, and Sorrow wise)
    His hands do neither wash nor dry;
But being made of steel and rust,
Turns snow and silk and milk to dust.

25 The light, the belly, lips, and breath,
    He dims, discolors, and destroys;

---

2. The spirit of Homer. Ralegh is giving extravagant praise to Spenser's poem as an epic, the type of poem Homer wrote.

3. The queen, stealing Laura's fame, or Spenser, stealing Homer's.

With those he feeds but fills not death,
 Which sometimes were the food of joys.
Yea, Time doth dull each lively wit,
30 And dries all wantonness with it.

Oh, cruel Time! which takes in trust
 Our youth, our joys, and all we have,
And pays us but with age and dust;
 Who in the dark and silent grave
35 When we have wandered all our ways
Shuts up the story of our days.

          1902

[The Author's Epitaph, Made by Himself][1]

Even such is time, which takes in trust
Our youth, our joys, and all we have,
And pays us but with age and dust;
Who in the dark and silent grave,
5 When we have wandered all our ways,
Shuts up the story of our days:
And from which earth, and grave, and dust
The Lord shall raise me up, I trust.

          1628

From The discovery of the large, rich, and beautiful Empire of Guiana, with a relation of the great and golden city of Manoa (which the Spaniards call El Dorado)[*][1]

* * * When we were come to the tops of the first hills of the plains adjoining to the river, we beheld that wonderful breach of waters which ran down Caroni:[2] and might from that mountain see the river how it ran in three parts, above twenty miles off, and there appeared some ten or twelve overfalls in sight, every one as high over the other as a church tower, which fell with that

---

* For other 16th-century narratives of exploration and a general introduction to this genre, see, in the supplemental ebook, "The Wider World."
1. The final stanza of the preceding poem, recast as a farewell to life. The 17th-century story, which may be true, was that Ralegh inscribed the poem in his Bible the night before his execution.
1. Ralegh had reports from several Spaniards of the unexplored Indian kingdom of Guiana ("Land of Waters"; now a part of Venezuela). Lying between the Orinoco and Amazon rivers, the

kingdom supposedly included the city the Spaniards called El Dorado—The Golden City. Ralegh led an expedition to Guiana in 1595, and the following year published an account of it, which was reprinted in 1598–1600 in Richard Hakluyt's massive collection *The Principal Navigations, Voyages, Traffics, and Discoveries of the English Nation.*
2. The Caroni River is a tributary of the Orinoco. Intrigued by reports of its waterfalls and the country above them, Ralegh led a small group to explore the region.

fury, that the rebound of water made it seem as if it had been all covered over with a great shower of rain: and in some places we took it at the first for a smoke that had risen over some great town. For mine own part, I was well persuaded from thence to have returned, being a very ill footman,[3] but the rest were all so desirous to go near the said strange thunder of waters as they drew me on by little and little till we came into the next valley, where we might better discern the same. I never saw a more beautiful country nor more lively prospects,[4] hills so raised here and there over the valleys, the river winding into divers branches, the plains adjoining without bush or stubble, all fair green grass, the ground of hard sand easy to march on either for horse or foot, the deer crossing in every path, the birds towards the evening singing on every tree with a thousand several[5] tunes, cranes and herons of white, crimson, and carnation perching in the river's side, the air fresh with a gentle easterly wind, and every stone that we stooped to take up promised either gold or silver by his complexion.

* * *

I will promise these things that follow, which I know to be true. Those that are desirous to discover and to see many nations may be satisfied within this river,[6] which bringeth forth so many arms and branches leading to several countries and provinces, above 2000 miles east and west, and 800 miles south and north, and of these, the most either rich in gold or in other merchandises. The common soldier shall here fight for gold, and pay himself, instead of pence, with plates of half a foot broad, whereas he breaketh his bones in other wars for provant[7] and penury. Those commanders and chieftains that shoot at honor and abundance shall find there more rich and beautiful cities, more temples adorned with golden images, more sepulchers filled with treasure, than either Cortez found in Mexico, or Pizarro in Peru: and the shining glory of this conquest will eclipse all those so far extended beams of the Spanish nation. There is no country which yieldeth more pleasure to the inhabitants, either for those common delights of hunting, hawking, fishing, fowling, or the rest, than Guiana doth.
* * * Both for health, good air, pleasure, and riches I am resolved it cannot be equalled by any region either in the east or west. Moreover, the country is so healthful, as of an hundred persons and more (which lay without shift most sluttishly,[8] and were every day almost melted with heat in rowing and marching, and suddenly wet again with great showers, and did eat of all sorts of corrupt fruits, and made meals of fresh fish without seasoning, of tortugas, of lagartos[9] or crocodiles, and of all sorts good and bad, without either order or measure, and besides lodged in the open air every night) we lost not any one, nor had one ill disposed to my knowledge, nor found any calentura, or other of those pestilent diseases which dwell in all hot regions, and so near the equinoctial line.[1]

3. Poor walker.
4. "Lively prospects": striking vistas.
5. Different.
6. The Orinoco.
7. Rations. "Plates": plate-metal.

8. Who idled without initiative most carelessly.
9. Alligators. "Without seasoning": i.e., as preservative. "Tortugas": tortoises.
1. Equator. "Calentura": a tropical disease that causes hallucinations.

Where there is store[2] of gold, it is in effect needless to remember other commodities for trade: but it hath, towards the south part of the river, great quantities of brazil-wood, and diverse berries that dye a most perfect crimson and carnation. * * * All places yield abundance of cotton, of silk, of balsam, and of those kinds most excellent and never known in Europe, of all sorts of gums, of Indian pepper: and what else the countries may afford within the land, we know not, neither had we time to abide the trial,[3] and search. The soil besides is so excellent and so full of rivers, as it will carry sugar, ginger, and all those other commodities which the West Indies have.

The navigation is short, for it may be sailed with an ordinary wind in six weeks, and in the like time back again.

* * *

Guiana is a country that hath yet her maidenhead, never sacked, turned, nor wrought,[4] the face of the earth hath not been torn, nor the virtue and salt of the soil spent by manurance,[5] the graves have not been opened for gold, the mines not broken with sledges,[6] nor their images pulled down out of their temples. It hath never been entered by any army of strength, and never conquered or possessed by any Christian prince. It is besides so defensible, that if two forts be builded in one of the provinces which I have seen, the flood[7] setteth in so near the bank, where the channel also lieth, that no ship can pass up but within a pike's length[8] of the artillery, first of the one, and afterwards of the other. * * *

* * * Guiana hath but one entrance by the sea (if it hath that) for any vessels of burden: so as whosoever shall first possess it, it shall be found unaccessible for any enemy, except he come in wherries,[9] barges, or canoes, or else in flat-bottomed boats, and if he do offer to enter it in that manner, the woods are so thick two hundred miles together upon the rivers of such entrance, as a mouse cannot sit in a boat unhit from the bank. By land it is more impossible to approach, for it hath the strongest situation of any region under the sun, and is so environed with impassable mountains on every side, as it is impossible to victual[1] any company in the passage: which hath been well proved by the Spanish nation, who since the conquest of Peru have never left five years free from attempting this empire, or discovering some way into it, and yet of three and twenty several gentlemen, knights, and noblemen there was never any that knew which way to lead an army by land, or to conduct ships by sea, anything near the said country. Orellana, of whom the river of Amazones taketh name, was the first, and Don Antonio de Berreo[2] (whom we displanted) the last: and I doubt much, whether he himself or any of his yet know the best way into the said empire.

* * *

---

2. Abundance.
3. To wait to find out.
4. Quarried or mined. "Turned": tilled.
5. I.e., the fertility of the soil has not been exhausted by cultivation ("manurance").
6. Sledgehammers.
7. Tide.

8. The pike was a long-shafted infantry weapon.
9. Rowboats.
1. Provision.
2. One of Ralegh's informants, a captured Spanish officer at Trinidad. Francisco de Orellana (ca. 1490–ca. 1546), a Spanish soldier, was the first explorer of the Amazon.

The West Indies were first offered Her Majesty's grandfather[3] by Columbus, a stranger, in whom there might be doubt[4] of deceit, and besides it was then thought incredible that there were such and so many lands and regions never written of before. This empire is made known to Her Majesty by her own vassal, and by him that oweth to her more duty than an ordinary subject, so that it shall ill sort with the many graces and benefits which I have received, to abuse Her Highness, either with fables or imaginations. The country is already discovered, many nations won to Her Majesty's love and obedience, and those Spaniards which have latest and longest labored about the conquest, beaten out, discouraged and disgraced, which among these nations were thought invincible. Her Majesty may in this enterprise employ all those soldiers and gentlemen that are younger brethren, and all captains and chieftains that want employment, and the charge[5] will be only the first setting out in victualing and arming them: for after the first or second year I doubt not but to see in London a contractation house[6] of more receipt for Guiana, than there is now in Seville for the West Indies.

And I am resolved that if there were but a small army afoot in Guiana, marching towards Manoa the chief city of Inca, he[7] would yield to Her Majesty by composition[8] so many hundred thousand pounds yearly, as should both defend all enemies abroad and defray all expenses at home, and that he would besides pay a garrison of three or four thousand soldiers very royally to defend him against other nations. * * * For whatsoever prince shall possess it shall be greatest, and if the king of Spain enjoy it, he will become unresistible. Her Majesty hereby shall confirm and strengthen the opinions of all nations as touching[9] her great and princely actions. * * *

To speak more at this time, I fear would be but troublesome: I trust in God, this being true, will suffice, and that he which is King of all Kings and Lord of Lords will put it into her heart which is Lady of Ladies to possess it; if not, I will judge those men worthy to be kings thereof, that by her grace and leave will undertake it of themselves.[1]

1596, 1599

From The History of the World

[CONCLUSION: ON DEATH]

It is * * * Death alone that can suddenly make man to know himself. He tells the proud and insolent that they are but abjects,[1] and humbles them at the instant; makes them cry, complain, and repent; yea, even to hate their forepassed happiness. He takes the account[2] of the rich, and proves him a beggar,

---

3. Henry VII. In 1488 Bartholomew Columbus petitioned Henry to sponsor his brother Christopher in an attempt to find a new route to the (East) Indies, by sailing west. The king declined, so Christopher sought the sponsorship of Queen Isabella of Spain.
4. Fear.
5. Cost. "Younger brethren": likely recruits because without patrimony. "Want": lack.
6. Place for receiving the goods contracted to be sent back to the investors who would finance the

Guiana expedition.
7. The Inca, the supposed ruler of Guiana and its chief city, Manoa. "Resolved": convinced.
8. Treaty.
9. Concerning.
1. Despite all Ralegh's enticements and admonitions, Queen Elizabeth declined to support his proposal for the conquest of Guiana.
1. Castoffs.
2. Estimate, measure.

a naked beggar, which hath interest in nothing but in the gravel that fills his mouth. He holds a glass[3] before the eyes of the most beautiful, and makes them see therein their deformity and rottenness, and they acknowledge it.

O eloquent, just, and mighty Death! Whom none could advise, thou hast persuaded; what none hath dared, thou hast done; and whom all the world hath flattered, thou only hast cast out of the world and despised; thou hast drawn together all the far-stretched greatness, all the pride, cruelty, and ambition of man, and covered it all over with these two narrow words: *Hic jacet!*[4]

1614

---

3. Mirror.
4. Latin for "Here lies," often carved on tombstones.

JOHN LYLY
1554–1606

John Lyly was the grandson of William Lily, the author of the standard Latin grammar that every English schoolboy studied. After receiving the M.A. degree at Oxford, Lyly went to London, where his prose romance *Euphues* (1578) was an instant success. Subsequently, he wrote several elegant, sophisticated plays acted at court by the children's companies, and served several terms as a member of Parliament, though his hopes of obtaining a lucrative court appointment, such as Master of the Revels, were disappointed.

The title *Euphues*, taken from the name of that book's hero, is Greek for "of good natural parts, graceful, witty"; the subtitle, *Anatomy of Wit*, means something like "analysis of the mental faculties." The plot of the work involves a young man who leaves university for the carnal temptations of the city, falls in love, betrays his best friend, is in turn betrayed, repents, and thereafter ladles out great quantities of moral wisdom. But the story of the repentant prodigal is distinctly secondary to the prose style, which has come to be known as Euphuism. It has two features: an elaborately patterned sentence structure based on comparison and antithesis, and a wealth of ornament including proverbs, incidents from history and poetry, and fanciful similes drawn from contemporary science, classical texts, or the author's own imagination. Euphuism became a rage for a while, especially at court, though it was criticized by Sidney, parodied by Shakespeare, and mocked by Thomas Nashe and Ben Jonson. The style may have been particularly popular among court women; the publisher of Lyly's *Six Court Comedies,* in 1632, informed his readers that "all our ladies were then his [Euphues's or Lyly's] scholars, and the beauty in court who could not parley Euphuism was as little regarded as she which now there speaks not French." Although it did not last, this highly self-conscious, overwrought style is an example of the Elizabethans' fascination with ornate language and artifice.*

---

* For an additional passage from *Euphues*, and Lyly's sonnet "Cupid and my Campaspe played," see the supplemental ebook.

From Euphues: The Anatomy of Wit

[EUPHUES INTRODUCED]

There dwelt in Athens a young gentleman of great patrimony, and of so comely a personage, that it was doubted[1] whether he were more bound to Nature for the lineaments of his person, or to Fortune for the increase of his possessions. But Nature impatient of comparisons, and as it were disdaining a companion or copartner in her working, added to this comeliness of his body such a sharp capacity of mind, that not only she proved Fortune counterfeit, but was half of that opinion that she herself was only current.[2] This young gallant, of more wit[3] than wealth, and yet of more wealth than wisdom, seeing himself inferior to none in pleasant conceits,[4] thought himself superior to all in honest conditions, insomuch that he deemed himself so apt to all things, that he gave himself almost to nothing, but practicing of those things commonly which are incident to these sharp wits, fine phrases, smooth quipping, merry taunting, using jesting without mean,[5] and abusing mirth without measure. As therefore the sweetest rose hath his prickle, the finest velvet his brack,[6] the fairest flower his bran,[7] so the sharpest wit hath his wanton will, and the holiest head his wicked way. And true it is that some men write and most men believe, that in all perfect shapes, a blemish bringeth rather a liking every way to the eyes, than a loathing any way to the mind. Venus had her mole in her cheek which made her more amiable: Helen[8] her scar on her chin which Paris called *cos amoris*, the whetstone of love. Aristippus his wart, Lycurgus[9] his wen: So likewise in the disposition of the mind, either virtue is over-shadowed with some vice, or vice overcast with some virtue. Alexander valiant in war, yet given to wine. Tully eloquent in his glozes, yet vainglorious: Solomon wise, yet too too wanton: David holy but yet an homicide:[1] none more witty than Euphues, yet at the first none more wicked. The freshest colors soonest fade, the teenest[2] razor soonest turneth his edge, the finest cloth is soonest eaten with moths, and the cambric sooner stained than the coarse canvas: which appeared well in this Euphues, whose wit being like wax apt to receive any impression, and having the bridle in his own hands, either to use the rein or the spur, disdaining counsel, leaving his country, loathing his old acquaintance, thought either by wit to obtain some conquest, or by shame to abide[3] some conflict, and leaving the rule of reason, rashly ran unto destruction. Who preferring fancy before friends, and his present humor[4] before honor to come, laid reason in water being too salt for his taste, and followed unbridled affection, most pleasant for his tooth.[5] When parents have more care how to

---

1. Doubtful, uncertain.
2. Genuine.
3. Intellect.
4. Witty expressions.
5. Moderation.
6. Break, flaw.
7. Husk.
8. The Greek queen whom Paris abducted to Troy: the most beautiful woman in the world.
9. Lycurgus was a Spartan lawmaker. Aristippus was a disciple of Socrates and traditionally the founder of the Cyrenaic school of philosophy, which taught that life's goal is pleasure.

1. The biblical King David loved Bathsheba and had her husband, Uriah, killed so he could marry her. Alexander the Great killed his friend Clitus in a drunken brawl. Tully (Marcus Tullius Cicero) was the great Roman orator, famous for his "glozes" (flattering speeches). Solomon, David's son, was famous both for his wisdom and for his many wives.
2. Keenest.
3. Stand firm in.
4. Whimsy.
5. Taste. "Affection": passion.

leave their children wealthy than wise, and are more desirous to have them maintain the name than the nature of a gentleman; when they put gold into the hands of youth, where they should put a rod under their girdle,[6] when instead of awe they make them past grace, and leave them rich executors of goods, and poor executors of godliness, then is it no marvel that the son, being left rich by his father's will, become retchless by his own will.[7]

It hath been an old-said saw,[8] and not of less truth than antiquity, that wit is the better if it be the dearer bought: as in the sequel of this history shall most manifestly appear. It happened this young imp[9] to arrive at Naples (a place of more pleasure than profit, and yet of more profit than piety), the very walls and windows whereof shewed it rather to be the Tabernacle of Venus than the Temple of Vesta.[1]

There was all things necessary and in readiness that might either allure the mind to lust or entice the heart to folly, a court more meet[2] for an atheist than for one of Athens, for Ovid than for Aristotle, for a graceless lover than for a godly liver: more fitter for Paris than Hector, and meeter for Flora than Diana.[3]

Here my youth (whether for weariness he could not, or for wantonness would not, go any further) determined to make his abode: whereby it is evidently seen that the fleetest fish swalloweth the delicatest bait, that the highest soaring hawk traineth[4] to the lure, and that the wittiest sconce[5] is inveigled with the sudden view or alluring vanities.

Here he wanted[6] no companions which courted him continually with sundry kinds of devices, whereby they might either soak[7] his purse to reap commodity, or soothe his person to win credit, for he had guests and companions of all sorts.

There frequented to this lodging and mansion house as well the spider to suck poison of his fine wit as the bee to gather honey, as well the drone as the dove, the fox as the lamb, as well Damocles[8] to betray him as Damon[9] to be true to him: yet he behaved himself so warily, that he singled his game[1] wisely. He could easily discern Apollo's music from Pan his pipe,[2] and Venus's beauty from Juno's bravery,[3] and the faith of Laelius[4] from the flattery of Aristippus, he welcomed all but trusted none, he was merry but yet so wary that neither the flatterer could take advantage to entrap him in his talk nor the wisest any assurance of his friendship: who being demanded of[5] one what countryman he was, he answered, "What countryman am I not? If I be

---

6. I.e., whip them. ("Girdle": belt.)

7. Appetite, the opposite of reason. "Retchless": reckless.

8. Saying, proverb.

9. Novice. "Sequel of this history": rest of this story.

1. Symbolizing chastity, in contrast to Venus.

2. Fitting.

3. Diana was the goddess of chastity. Ovid was famous for his love poems, Aristotle for his profound philosophical works. Paris was the lover of Helen, in contrast to his brother Hector, a great Trojan soldier. Flora was a fertility goddess whose annual celebrations were noted for lasciviousness.

4. Is attracted to.

5. Head, brain.

6. Lacked.

7. Drain.

8. Famous as a flatterer of Dionysius, who gave him a gorgeous banquet but made him sit with a sword suspended over his head by a single hair, to show how dangerous eminence is.

9. Famous in classical legend as the friend of Pythias, so loyal to him that he offered to be executed in his place.

1. Separated his target animal from the herd—that is, made distinctions.

2. In classical myth, Apollo's music was much superior to that which the wood-god Pan produced on his pipes.

3. Splendid attire.

4. Laelius was famous as the faithful friend of Scipio Africanus the Younger.

5. Asked by.

in Crete, I can lie, if in Greece I can shift, if in Italy I can court it:[6] if thou ask whose son I am also, I ask thee whose son I am not. I can carouse with Alexander, abstain with Romulus, eat with the Epicure, fast with the Stoic, sleep with Endymion, watch with Chrysippus,"[7] using these speeches and other like. An old gentleman in Naples seeing his pregnant wit,[8] his eloquent tongue somewhat taunting, yet with delight, his mirth without measure yet not without wit, his sayings vainglorious yet pithy, began to bewail his nurture and to muse at his nature, being incensed against the one as most pernicious, and enflamed with the other as most precious: for he well knew that so rare a wit would in time either breed an intolerable trouble or bring an incomparable treasure to the common weal:[9] at the one he greatly pitied, at the other he rejoiced.

1578

6. Inhabitants of the island of Crete early had a reputation as liars. Lyly is elaborating or inventing when he says that the Greeks "shift" (practice or live by deceit) and that the Italians "court it" (behave in a courtly manner).

7. Chrysippus was a celebrated Stoic philosopher, so devoted to study that he would "watch" (stay up all night) with his books. Romulus was the legendary founder and first king of Rome. Exposed as an infant with his twin brother, Remus, he was

rescued and suckled by a she-wolf and became a symbol of abstinence. The followers of Epicurus (Epicureans) were thought to care for nothing but pleasure; the austere Stoics venerated duty. Endymion was a youth in Greek legend renowned for his beauty and his eternal sleep on Mount Latmus, where the moon goddess fell in love with him.

8. Fertile mind.

9. Commonwealth.

SIR PHILIP SIDNEY
1554–1586

Sir Philip Sidney's face was "spoiled with pimples," Ben Jonson remarked in 1619, wryly distancing himself from the virtual Sidney cult that had arisen in the years after his death. Knight, soldier, poet, friend, and patron, Sidney seemed to the Elizabethans to embody all the traits of character and personality they admired: he was Castiglione's perfect courtier come to life. When he was killed in battle in the Low Countries at the age of thirty-two, fighting for the Protestant cause against the hated Spanish, all England mourned. Stories, possibly apocryphal, began immediately to circulate about his gallantry on the battlefield—grievously wounded, he gave his water to a dying foot soldier with the words "Thy necessity is yet greater than mine"—and about his astonishing self-composure as he himself lay dying: suffering from his putrifying, gangrenous wound, Sidney composed a song and had it sung by his deathbed. When his corpse was brought back to England for burial, the spectacular funeral procession, one of the most elaborate ever staged, almost bankrupted his father-in-law, Francis Walsingham, the wealthy head of Queen Elizabeth's secret service.

Philip Sidney's father was Sir Henry Sidney, thrice lord deputy (governor) of Ireland, and his mother was a sister of Robert Dudley, earl of Leicester, the most spectacular and powerful of all the queen's favorites. He entered Shrewsbury School in 1564, at the age of ten, on the same day as Fulke Greville, who became his lifelong friend and his biographer. Greville wrote of Sidney, "though I lived with him and knew him from a child, yet I never knew him other than a man—with such staidness of mind, lovely and familiar gravity, as carried grace and reverence above greater years." He attended Oxford but left without taking a degree and completed his education by extended travels on the Continent. There he met many of the most important people of the time, from kings and queens to philosophers, theologians, and poets. In France he witnessed the Massacre of St. Bartholomew's Day, which began in Paris on August 24, 1572, and raged through France for more than a month, as Catholic mobs incited by Queen Catherine de Médicis slaughtered perhaps 50,000 Huguenots (French Protestants). This experience undoubtedly strengthened Sidney's ardent Protestantism, which had been inculcated by his family background and education. In an intense correspondence with his mentor, the Burgundian humanist Hubert Languet, he brooded on how he could help to save Europe from what he viewed as the Roman Catholic menace.

Languet and his associates clearly hoped that this brilliant and wonderfully well-connected young Englishman would be able to steer royal policy toward active intervention in Europe's wars of religion. Yet when he returned to England, Sidney found the direct path to heroic action blocked by the caution and hard-nosed realism of Queen Elizabeth and her principal advisers. Though she sent him on some diplomatic missions, the queen clearly regarded the zealous young man with considerable skepticism. As a prominent courtier with literary interests, Sidney actively encouraged authors such as Edward Dyer, Greville, and, most important, Edmund Spenser, who dedicated *The Shepheardes Calender* to him as "the president [chief exemplar] of noblesse and of chevalree." But he clearly longed to be something more than an influential patron of letters. In 1580 his Protestant convictions led him publicly to oppose Queen Elizabeth's projected marriage to the Catholic duke of Anjou. The queen, who hated interference with her diplomatic maneuvers, angrily dismissed Sidney from the court.

He retired to Wilton, the estate of his beloved and learned sister, Mary Herbert, countess of Pembroke, and there he wrote a long, elaborate epic romance in prose, called *Arcadia*. Sidney's claim, made with studied nonchalance, that the work was casually tossed off for his sister's private entertainment is belied by its considerable literary, political, and moral ambitions, qualities that were reinforced and intensified in the extensive revisions he began to make to it in 1582. Our selection is from this revised version, termed by scholars the *New Arcadia*.

In addition to *Arcadia*, which inspired many imitations, including the *Urania* of Sidney's niece, Lady Mary Wroth, two other influential works by Sidney have had still more lasting importance. One of these, *The Defense of Poesy*, is the major work of literary criticism produced in the English Renaissance. In this long essay Sidney eloquently defends poetry (his term for all imaginative literature) against its attackers and, in the process, greatly exalts the role of the poet, the freedom of the imagination, and the moral value of fiction. Perhaps Sidney's finest literary achievement is *Astrophil and Stella* (Starlover and Star), the first of the great Elizabethan sonnet cycles. The principal focus of these sonnets is not a sequence of events or an unfolding relationship. Rather, they explore the lover's state of mind and soul, the contradictory impulses, intense desires, and frustrations that haunt him.

In his guise as a Petrarchan sonneteer, Sidney repeatedly insists that the thought of his beloved drives all more mundane matters from his mind. Yet a number of the sonnets betray a continuing preoccupation with matters of politics and foreign policy. Neither love nor literature could distract Sidney for long from what he took to be his destined role. In 1585 he tried to join Sir Francis Drake's West Indian expedition but was prevented by the queen; instead, she appointed him governor of Flushing in the Netherlands, where as a volunteer and knight-errant he engaged in several vicious skirmishes in the war against Spain. At Zutphen on September 13, 1586, leading a charge against great odds, Sidney was wounded in the thigh, shortly after he had thrown away his thigh armor in an ill-fated chivalric gesture. He died after lingering for twenty-six days.

Sidney called poetry his "unelected vocation," and in keeping with the norms of his class, he did not publish any of his major literary works himself. His ambition, continually thwarted, was to be a man of action whose deeds would affect his country's destiny. Yet he was the author of the most ambitious work of prose fiction, the most important piece of literary criticism, and the most influential sonnet cycle of the Elizabethan Age.[*]

The Countess of Pembroke's Arcadia   Sidney wrote his epic romance in two forms which scholars have dubbed the *Old Arcadia* and the *New Arcadia*. Shortly after the *Old Arcadia* was completed, in five "books," Sidney began to recast and greatly expand it, but broke off in mid-sentence and left the revision unfinished. This revised fragment, almost three books, is known as the *New Arcadia*; it was published posthumously, in 1590. In 1593 Sidney's sister, the countess of Pembroke, herself a gifted writer, made some small changes to the *New Arcadia* and the last two books of the *Old*, stitched them together, and published them as a single text. (The complete *Old Arcadia*, as Sidney had left it in manuscript, was not rediscovered and published until the twentieth century.) Both Sidney's original version and his revision are full of oracles, princes in disguise, mistaken identity, melodramatic incidents, and tangled love situations, but the *New Arcadia* has a much more labyrinthine, interwoven plot, as well as a more consistently elevated tone of moral and heroic high seriousness. Some episodes are of political interest, and Sidney clearly put into the work more of his serious thought on statecraft (the responsibilities of a king or queen, the evils of rebellion, and the duties of ministers, judges, and advisers of state) than his description of the *Arcadia* as mere entertainment suggests. Many poems—pastoral eclogues and songs—are interspersed throughout the narrative; they represent Sidney's experiments with diverse lyric kinds and verse forms.

Prior to the chapter reprinted below, Pyrocles, prince of Macedon, has fallen in love with Philoclea, daughter of Basilius and Gynecia, the king and queen of Arcadia. To gain entrance to the royal household, he has disguised himself as a woman, the Amazon Zelmane. To his dismay, though, both Basilius and Gynecia (who sees through his disguise) have fallen in love with him.

From The Second Book of the Countess of Pembroke's Arcadia

Chapter 1

In these pastoral pastimes[1] a great number of days were sent to follow their flying predecessors, while the cup of poison[2] (which was deeply tasted of this noble company) had left no sinew of theirs without mortally searching into it; yet never manifesting his venomous work, till once that the night (parting away angry that she could distill no more sleep into the eyes of lovers) had no sooner given place to the breaking out of the morning light and

---

[*] For additional writings by Sidney—another sonnet from *Astrophil and Stella* (64), four poems from *Certain Sonnets*, and more excerpts from *Arcadia*—see the supplemental ebook.

1. The reference is to the elaborate entertainment, featuring a series of pastoral songs, that had concluded Book 1.
2. I.e., love.

the sun bestowed his beams upon the tops of the mountains, but that the woeful Gynecia (to whom rest was no ease) had left her loathed lodging and gotten herself into the solitary places those deserts[3] were full of, going up and down with such unquiet motions as a grieved and hopeless mind is wont to bring forth. There appeared unto the eyes of her judgment the evils she was like to run into, with ugly infamy waiting upon them: she felt the terrors of her own conscience; she was guilty of a long exercised virtue which made this vice the fuller of deformity. The uttermost of the good she could aspire unto was a mortal wound to her vexed spirits; and lastly, no small part of her evils was that she was wise to see her evils. Insomuch that, having a great while thrown her countenance ghastly about her[4] (as if she had called all the powers of the world to be witness of her wretched estate), at length casting up her watery eyes to heaven:

"O sun," said she, "whose unspotted light directs the steps of mortal mankind, art thou not ashamed to impart the clearness of thy presence to such a dust-creeping worm as I am? O you heavens, which continually keep the course allotted unto you, can none of your influences prevail so much upon the miserable Gynecia as to make her preserve a course so long embraced by her? O deserts, deserts, how fit a guest am I for you, since my heart can people you with wild ravenous beasts, which in you are wanting! O virtue, where dost thou hide thyself? What hideous thing is this which doth eclipse thee? Or is it true that thou wert never but a vain name and no essential thing, which hast thus left thy professed servant when she had most need of thy lovely presence? O imperfect proportion of reason, which can too much foresee and too little prevent! Alas, alas," said she, "if there were but one hope for all my pains or but one excuse for all my faultiness! But wretch that I am, my torment is beyond all succor, and my evil-deserving doth exceed my evil fortune. For nothing else did my husband take this strange resolution to live so solitarily, for nothing else have the winds delivered this strange guest to my country, for nothing else have the destinies reserved my life to this time, but that only I, most wretched I, should become a plague to myself and a shame to womankind. Yet if my desire, how unjust soever it be, might take effect, though a thousand deaths followed it and every death were followed with a thousand shames, yet should not my sepulcher receive me without some contentment. But alas, though sure I am that Zelmane is such as can answer my love, yet as sure I am that this disguising must needs come for some foretaken conceit.[5] And then, wretched Gynecia, where canst thou find any small ground-plot for hope to dwell upon? No, no, it is Philoclea his heart is set upon; it is my daughter I have borne to supplant me. But if it be so, the life I have given thee, ungrateful Philoclea, I will sooner with these hands bereave thee of than my birth[6] shall glory she hath bereaved me of my desires. In shame there is no comfort but to be beyond all bounds of shame."

Having spoken thus, she began to make a piteous war with her fair hair, when she might hear not far from her an extremely doleful voice, but so suppressed with a kind of whispering note that she could not conceive the words distinctly. But as a lamentable tune is the sweetest music to a woeful mind,

---

3. Uninhabited regions. In consequence of an oracle, Basilius has taken the royal family to live in "a certain forest which he calleth his desert."
4. "Thrown . . . her": looked about her in a fright-

ful manner.
5. With some prior purpose.
6. Offspring.

she drew thither near-away[7] in hope to find some companion of her misery; and as she paced on she was stopped with a number of trees so thickly placed together that she was afraid she should, with rushing through, stop the speech of the lamentable party which she was so desirous to understand. And therefore sitting her down as softly as she could (for she was now in distance to hear) she might first perceive a lute excellently well played upon, and then the same doleful voice accompanying it with these verses:

> In vain, mine eyes, you labor to amend
>   With flowing tears your fault of hasty sight;
> Since to my heart her shape you so did send,
>   That her I see, though you did lose your light.
>
> In vain, my heart, now you with sight are burned,
>   With sighs you seek to cool your hot desire;
> Since sighs, into mine inward furnace turned,
>   For bellows serve to kindle more the fire.
>
> Reason in vain, now you have lost my heart,
>   My head you seek, as to your strongest fort;
> Since there mine eyes have played so false a part,
>   That to your strength your foes have sure resort.
>   Then since in vain I find were all my strife,
>   To this strange death I vainly yield my life.

The ending of the song served but for a beginning of new plaints, as if the mind, oppressed with too heavy a burden of cares, was fain to discharge itself of all sides and, as it were, paint out the hideousness of the pain in all sorts of colors. For the woeful person (as if the lute had evil[8] joined with the voice) threw it to the ground with suchlike words:

"Alas, poor lute, how much art thou deceived to think that in my miseries thou could'st ease my woes, as in my careless[9] times thou wast wont to please my fancies! The time is changed, my lute, the time is changed; and no more did my joyful mind then receive everything to a joyful consideration than my careful[1] mind now makes each thing taste like the bitter juice of care. The evil is inward, my lute, the evil is inward; which all thou dost doth serve but to make me think more freely of, and the more I think, the more cause I find of thinking, but less of hoping. And alas, what is then thy harmony but the sweetmeats of sorrow? The discord of my thoughts, my lute, doth ill agree to the concord of thy strings; therefore be not ashamed to leave thy master, since he is not afraid to forsake himself."

And thus much spoken, instead of a conclusion was closed up with so hearty a groaning that Gynecia could not refrain to show herself, thinking such griefs could serve fitly for nothing but her own fortune. But as she came into the little arbor of this sorrowful music, her eyes met with the eyes of Zelmane, which was the party that thus had indicted herself of misery, so that either of them remained confused with a sudden astonishment, Zelmane fearing lest she had heard some part of those complaints which she had risen up that morning early of purpose to breathe out in secret to

---

7. Near to it.
8. Badly.
9. Carefree.
1. Full of care.

herself. But Gynecia a great while stood still with a kind of dull amazement, looking steadfastly upon her. At length returning to some use of herself, she began to ask Zelmane what cause carried her so early abroad. But, as if the opening of her mouth to Zelmane had opened some great floodgate of sorrow whereof her heart could not abide the violent issue, she sank to the ground with her hands over her face, crying vehemently, "Zelmane, help me, O Zelmane have pity on me!"

Zelmane ran to her, marveling what sudden sickness had thus possessed her; and beginning to ask her the cause of her pain and offering her service to be employed by her, Gynecia opening her eyes wildly upon her, pricked with the flames of love and the torments of her own conscience, "O Zelmane, Zelmane," said she, "dost thou offer me physic,[2] which art my only poison? Or wilt thou do me service, which hast already brought me into eternal slavery?"

Zelmane then knowing well at what mark she shot, yet loth to enter into it, "Most excellent lady," said she, "you were best retire yourself into your lodging, that you the better may pass this sudden fit."

"Retire myself?" said Gynecia, "If I had retired myself into myself when thou (to me unfortunate guest) camest to draw me from myself, blessed had I been, and no need had I had of this counsel. But now, alas, I am forced to fly to thee for succor whom I accuse of all my hurt, and make thee judge of my cause, who art the only author of my mischief."

Zelmane the more astonished, the more she understood her, "Madam," said she, "whereof do you accuse me that I will not clear myself? Or wherein may I stead[3] you that you may not command me?"

"Alas!" answered Gynecia, "What shall I say more? Take pity of me, O Zelmane, but not as Zelmane, and disguise not with me in words, as I know thou dost in apparel."

Zelmane was much troubled with that word, finding herself brought to this strait. But as she was thinking what to answer her, they might see old Basilius pass hard by them without ever seeing them, complaining likewise of love very freshly, and ending his complaint with this song, love having renewed both his invention and voice:

> Let not old age disgrace my high desire,
>   O heavenly soul in human shape contained:
> Old wood inflamed doth yield the bravest fire,
>   When younger doth in smoke his virtue[4] spend.
>
> Ne let white hairs which on my face do grow
>   Seem to your eyes of a disgraceful hue,
> Since whiteness doth present the sweetest show,[5]
>   Which makes all eyes do homage unto you.
>
> Old age is wise and full of constant truth;
>   Old age well stayed from ranging humor[6] lives;
> Old age hath known whatever was in youth;

2. Medicine.
3. Be of use to.
4. Power. "Bravest": most splendid.

5. Appearance.
6. Caprice. "Stayed": settled.

> Old age o'ercome, the greater honor gives.
> And to old age since you yourself aspire,
> Let not old age disgrace my high desire.

Which being done, he looked very curiously[7] upon himself, sometimes fetching a little skip as if he had said his strength had not yet forsaken him.

But Zelmane, having in this time gotten some leisure to think for an answer, looking upon Gynecia as if she thought she did her some wrong, "Madam," said she, "I am not acquainted with those words of disguising; neither is it the profession of an Amazon; neither are you a party with whom it is to be used. If my service may please you, employ it, so long as you do me no wrong in misjudging of me."

"Alas, Zelmane," said Gynecia, "I perceive you know full little how piercing the eyes are of a true lover. There is no one beam of those thoughts you have planted in me but is able to discern a greater cloud than you do go in. Seek not to conceal yourself further from me, nor force not the passion of love into violent extremities."

Now was Zelmane brought to an exigent,[8] when the king, turning his eyes that way through the trees, perceived his wife and mistress together; so that framing the most lovely[9] countenance he could, he came straightway towards them, and at the first word, thanking his wife for having entertained Zelmane, desired her she would now return into the lodge, because he had certain matters of estate[1] to impart to the Lady Zelmane. The queen, being nothing troubled with jealousy in that point, obeyed the king's commandment, full of raging agonies, and determinately bent[2] that as she would seek all loving means to win Zelmane, so she would stir up terrible tragedies rather than fail of her intent. And so went she from them to the lodge-ward;[3] with such a battle in her thoughts and so deadly an overthrow given to her best resolutions that even her body (where the field was fought) was oppressed withal, making a languishing sickness wait upon the triumph of passion,[4] which the more it prevailed in her, the more it made her jealousy watchful both over her daughter and Zelmane, having ever one of them entrusted to her own eyes.[5]

But as soon as Basilius was rid of his wife's presence, falling down on his knees, "O lady," said he, "which hast only had the power to stir up again those flames which had so long lain dead in me, see in me the power of your beauty, which can make old age come to ask counsel of youth, and a prince unconquered to become a slave to a stranger. And when you see that power of yours, love that at least in me, since it is yours, although of me you see nothing to be loved."

"Worthy prince," answered Zelmane, taking him up from his kneeling, "both your manner and your speech are so strange unto me as I know not how to answer it better than with silence."

"If silence please you," said the king, "it shall never displease me, since my heart is wholly pledged to obey you. Otherwise, if you would vouchsafe mine ears such happiness as to hear you, they shall convey your words to such a mind which is with the humblest degree of reverence to receive them."

---

7. Carefully, attentively.
8. Crisis.
9. Loving. "Mistress": i.e., the woman who rules his heart.
1. State.

2. Resolutely determined.
3. Toward the lodge.
4. Attend upon passion's victory procession.
5. Always having one of them in her sight.

"I disdain not to speak to you, mighty prince," said Zelmane, "but I disdain to speak to any matter which may bring my honor into question."

And therewith, with a brave counterfeited scorn she departed from the king, leaving him not so sorry for his short answer as proud in himself that he had broken[6] the matter. And thus did the king, feeding his mind with those thoughts, pass great time in writing verses and making more of himself than he was wont to do, that, with a little help, he would have grown into a pretty kind of dotage.

But Zelmane, being rid of this loving but little loved company, "Alas," said she, "poor Pyrocles, was there ever one but I that had received wrong and could blame nobody, that having more than I desire, am still in want of that I would?[7] Truly, love, I must needs say thus much on thy behalf: thou hast employed my love there where all love is deserved, and for recompense hast sent me more love than ever I desired. But what wilt thou do, Pyrocles? Which way canst thou find to rid thee of thy intricate troubles? To her whom I would be known to, I live in darkness; and to her am revealed from whom I would be most secret. What shift[8] shall I find against the diligent love of Basilius? What shield against the violent passions of Gynecia? And if that be done, yet how am I the nearer to quench the fire that consumes me? Well, well, sweet Philoclea, my whole confidence must be builded in thy divine spirit, which cannot be ignorant of the cruel wound I have received by you."

1578–83   1593

The Defense of Poesy

In 1579 Sidney found himself the unwilling dedicatee of a small book entitled *The School of Abuse*. Its author, the playwright-turned-moralist Stephen Gosson, attacked poets and actors from a narrowly Puritan perspective that called into question the morality of any fiction-making. Sidney may have shared in the author's militant Protestantism, but he took a very different, more sympathetic and more complex view of the poet's art. He did not specifically answer Gosson's polemic, but he must have had it in mind when he composed, perhaps in the same year, a major piece of critical prose that was published after his death under two titles, *The Defense of Poesy* and *An Apology for Poetry*. Probably written in the winter of 1579–80 though not published until 1595, *The Defense of Poesy* is an eloquent argument for the dignity, social efficacy, and moral value of imaginative literature in verse or prose.

Sidney gives this argument the underlying form of a classical oration, as if he were a lawyer in ancient Rome defending his client against defamatory accusations. The great masters of rhetoric, Cicero and Quintilian, prescribed a set structure for such orations, and, as our footnotes indicate in detail, Sidney adapts his defense to this structure.

Sidney responds to old charges against poetic fictions—charges of irresponsibility and unreality—that had been revived in his own time most strenuously by Puritan moralists. In a graceful, if strikingly paradoxical, rhetorical performance, the *Defense* argues both that the poet, liberated from the world, is free to range "within the zodiac of his own wit" and that poetry actively intervenes in the world and transforms it for the better. After a slyly self-deprecating introduction, Sidney points out the antiquity of poetry, its prestige in the biblical and classical worlds, and its universality; also, he

---

6. Broached.
7. Of the thing I desire.

8. Evasion, stratagem.

cites the names given to poets—*vates*, or "prophet," by the Romans and *poietes*, or "maker," by the Greeks—as evidence of their ancient dignity. But he bases his defense essentially on the special status of the poetic imagination. While all arts, from astronomy to music to medicine, depend ultimately on nature as their object, poetry, he claims, is uniquely free: "Only the poet, disdaining to be tied to any such subjection, lifted up with the vigor of his own invention, doth grow in effect another nature."

This freedom, Sidney argues, enables the poet to present virtues and vices in a livelier and more affecting way than nature does, teaching, delighting, and moving the reader at the same time. The poet is superior to both the philosopher and the historian, because he is more concrete than the one and more universal than the other. The *Defense* also refutes Plato's charge that poets are liars, by arguing that the poet "nothing affirms, and therefore never lieth," and it denies as well the Platonic claim that poetry arouses base desires. Tragedy, for example, "openeth the greatest wounds," in Sidney's account, "and showeth forth the ulcers that are covered with tissue," thereby making "kings fear to be tyrants." Surveying the English literary scene of his own century, Sidney finds little to praise except for Surrey's lyrics, the moralizing verse narratives of the popular mid-century collection *A Mirror for Magistrates*, and Spenser's *Shepheardes Calender*; the drama he faults for "mingling kings and clowns" and for unrealistic distortions of time and space. (The great, sprawling plays of Marlowe and Shakespeare, plays that triumphantly violated many of Sidney's cherished principles, lay just ahead.) The *Defense* ends with a mock conjuration and a playful curse, reminders of the magical power of poetry, a power that lurks beneath both Sidney's idealism and his didacticism.

The Defense of Poesy

[THE LESSONS OF HORSEMANSHIP]

When the right virtuous Edward Wotton and I were at the Emperor's court together,[1] we gave ourselves to learn horsemanship of John Pietro Pugliano, one that with great commendation had the place of an esquire[2] in his stable. And he, according to the fertileness of the Italian wit, did not only afford us the demonstration of his practice, but sought to enrich our minds with the contemplations therein which he thought most precious. But with none I remember mine ears were at that time more laden, than when (either angered with slow payment, or moved with our learner-like admiration) he exercised his speech in the praise of his faculty.[3] He said soldiers were the noblest estate of mankind, and horsemen the noblest of soldiers. He said they were the masters of war and ornaments of peace, speedy goers and strong abiders, triumphers both in camps and courts. Nay, to so unbelieved a point he proceeded, as that no earthly thing bred such wonder to a prince as to be a good horseman—skill of government was but a *pedanteria*[4] in comparison. Then would he add certain praises, by telling what a peerless beast the horse was, the only serviceable courtier without flattery, the beast

---

1. Sidney and Edward Wotton (1548–1626), an English courtier and diplomat, became good friends at the court of Maximilian II (the Holy Roman Emperor) in Vienna in 1574–75. "Right virtuous": most virtuous.
 Wittily shaping his defense of literature as a judicial oration (a trial lawyer's speech) according to the pattern laid down in classical and Renaissance rhetorical theory, Sidney opens with an

exordium: a brief section designed to put the audience into a receptive frame of mind and, especially, to make it well-disposed toward the speaker.
2. Equerry, an officer in charge of the horses and stables of a noble house.
3. Profession.
4. Pedantry, narrow and overly detailed knowledge, of use only to schoolmasters. "Prince": ruler.

of most beauty, faithfulness, courage, and such more, that if I had not been a piece of a logician[5] before I came to him, I think he would have persuaded me to have wished myself a horse.[6] But thus much at least with his no few words he drave into me, that self-love is better than any gilding[7] to make that seem gorgeous wherein ourselves be parties. Wherein, if Pugliano's strong affection[8] and weak arguments will not satisfy you, I will give you a nearer example of myself, who (I know not by what mischance) in these my not old years and idlest times having slipped into the title of a poet, am provoked to say something unto you in the defense of that my unelected vocation, which if I handle with more good will than good reasons, bear with me, since the scholar is to be pardoned that followeth the steps of his master.[9] And yet I must say that, as I have more just cause to make a pitiful defense of poor poetry, which from almost the highest estimation of learning is fallen to be the laughingstock of children, so have I need to bring some more available[1] proofs: since the former[2] is by no man barred of his deserved credit, the silly[3] latter hath had even the names of philosophers used to the defacing of it, with great danger of civil war among the Muses.

[POETRY'S HISTORICAL IMPORTANCE]

And first, truly, to all them that, professing learning, inveigh against poetry may justly be objected that they go very near to ungratefulness, to seek to deface that which, in the noblest nations and languages that are known, hath been the first light-giver to ignorance, and first nurse, whose milk by little and little enabled them to feed afterwards of tougher knowledges.[4] And will they now play the hedgehog that, being received into the den, drave out his host? Or rather the vipers, that with their birth kill their parents?[5]

Let learned Greece in any of his manifold sciences be able to show me one book before Musaeus, Homer, and Hesiod, all three nothing else but poets.[6] Nay, let any history be brought that can say any writers were there before them, if they were not men of the same skill, as Orpheus, Linus,[7] and some other are named, who, having been the first of that country that made pens deliverers of their knowledge to the posterity, may justly challenge to be called their fathers in learning: for not only in time they had this priority (although in itself antiquity be venerable) but went before them, as causes to draw with their charming sweetness the wild untamed wits to an admiration of knowledge. So, as Amphion was said to move stones with his poetry to build Thebes,[8] and Orpheus to be listened to by beasts, indeed, stony and

---

5. I.e., if I had not had some skill in logic.
6. With an allusion to the root meaning of Sidney's given name, from Greek *phil* + *hippos*, "horse-lover."
7. With a pun on "gelding." "Drave": drove.
8. Feeling; partiality.
9. I.e., Pugliano.
1. Effective. "Pitiful": compassionate.
2. I.e., horsemanship.
3. Weak, poor.
4. In a judicial oration, the second section is the *narratio*: a brief overview of the facts of the case. Sidney substitutes a short history of poetry and an investigation of its essential nature as inferred from the etymology of Latin and Greek words for "poet."

5. According to an ancient tradition, vipers eat their way out of their mother's womb, killing her. The ungrateful hedgehog is from a pseudo-Aesopic fable. The idea that poets were the earliest teachers descends from classical antiquity.
6. Musaeus was a mythical Greek poet, thought to have preceded Homer and Hesiod (both ca. 8th century B.C.E.). He was conflated with a much later (5th century C.E.) poet of the same name who wrote a brief epic on Hero and Leander (cf. below, p. 1107). "Sciences": branches of knowledge.
7. In Greek myth, Linus was the teacher of Orpheus, the archetypal poet and musician.
8. Usually the mythological Amphion is said to have accomplished this feat with the music of his harp.

beastly people; so among the Romans were Livius Andronicus and Ennius.[9] So in the Italian language the first that made it aspire to be a treasure-house of science were the poets Dante, Boccaccio, and Petrarch. So in our English were Gower and Chaucer,[1] after whom, encouraged and delighted with their excellent fore-going, others have followed, to beautify our mother tongue, as well in the same kind as in other arts.

This did so notably show itself, that the philosophers of Greece durst not a long time appear to the world but under the masks of poets. So Thales, Empedocles, and Parmenides sang their natural philosophy in verses; so did Pythagoras and Phocylides their moral counsels; so did Tyrtaeus in war matters, and Solon in matters of policy:[2] or rather they, being poets, did exercise their delightful vein in those points of highest knowledge, which before them lay hid to the world. For that wise Solon was directly a poet it is manifest, having written in verse the notable fable of the Atlantic Island, which was continued by Plato.[3] And truly even Plato whosoever well considereth shall find that in the body of his work, though the inside and strength were philosophy, the skin, as it were, and beauty depended most of poetry: for all standeth upon[4] dialogues, wherein he feigneth many honest burgesses of Athens to speak of such matters that, if they had been set on the rack, they would never have confessed them, besides his poetical describing the circumstances of their meetings, as the well ordering of a banquet, the delicacy of a walk, with interlacing mere tales, as Gyges' ring[5] and others, which who knoweth not to be flowers of poetry did never walk into Apollo's garden.[6]

And even historiographers (although their lips sound of things done, and verity be written in their foreheads) have been glad to borrow both fashion[7] and, perchance, weight of the poets. So Herodotus entitled his history by the name of the nine Muses; and both he and all the rest that followed him either stale[8] or usurped of poetry their passionate describing of passions, the many particularities of battles, which no man could affirm; or, if that be denied me, long orations put in the mouths of great kings and captains, which it is certain they never pronounced.[9]

So that truly neither philosopher nor historiographer could at the first have entered into the gates of popular judgments if they had not taken a great passport of poetry, which in all nations at this day where learning flourisheth not, is plain to be seen; in all which they have some feeling of poetry.

9. Livius (3rd century B.C.E.), a Greek writer taken to Rome as a prisoner of war, was credited with having there become the first poet to write in Latin. Ennius (239–169 B.C.E.) authored a verse history of Rome.

1. Evidently Sidney thought the late 14th-century poets Chaucer and John Gower the earliest English writers worth mentioning—corresponding, in English literary culture, to the great Italian writers Dante (ca. 1265–1321), Petrarch (1304–1374), and Boccaccio (1313–1375).

2. Thales and the others Sidney lists here were legendary wise men of early Greece (7th–5th centuries B.C.E.), to whom various surviving fragments of verse were attributed. The first five were associated with science ("natural philosophy") or moral philosophy. Tyrtaeus's poetry inspired the Spartans to martial exploits; Solon was the great political reformer of early Athens.

3. Plato wrote about the sunken continent Atlan-

tis in his dialogue *Timaeus*; Solon's poem on the subject is lost.

4. Is constructed on; depends on.

5. *Republic* 2.359–60 relates the shepherd Gyges's descent to the Underworld and his theft there of a ring that conferred invisibility. Sidney's argument is that Plato's dialogues rely on poetry, because they include fictional elements. Cf. his later assertion that "feigning"—fiction—is a defining element of poetry: p. 1052.

6. Apollo is the Greek god of poetry (among other things).

7. Form. "Historiographers": writers of history.

8. Stole. Herodotus (5th century B.C.E.) was the first great Greek historian. After his own time, his *Histories* were divided into nine books named for the nine Muses.

9. Fictitious accounts of battles and speeches were conventional in classical historiography and Renaissance humanists' histories emulating it.

In Turkey, besides their law-giving divines, they have no other writers but poets.[1] In our neighbor country Ireland, where truly learning goes very bare, yet are their poets held in a devout reverence. Even among the most barbarous and simple Indians, where no writing is, yet have they their poets who make and sing songs, which they call *areytos*,[2] both of their ancestors' deeds and praises of their gods: a sufficient probability that, if ever learning come among them, it must be by having their hard dull wits softened and sharpened with the sweet delights of poetry—for until they find a pleasure in the exercises of the mind, great promises of much knowledge will little persuade them that know not the fruits of knowledge. In Wales, the true remnant of the ancient Britons, as there are good authorities to show the long time they had poets, which they called bards, so through all the conquests of Romans, Saxons, Danes, and Normans, some of whom did seek to ruin all memory of learning from among them, yet do their poets even to this day last; so as it is not more notable in soon beginning than in long continuing.

[THE POET AS PROPHET AND CREATOR]

But since the authors of most of our sciences were the Romans, and before them the Greeks, let us a little stand upon their authorities, but even so far as to see what names they have given unto this now scorned skill.

Among the Romans a poet was called *vates*, which is as much as a diviner, foreseer, or prophet, as by his conjoined words *vaticinium* and *vaticinari*[3] is manifest: so heavenly a title did that excellent people bestow upon this heart-ravishing knowledge. And so far were they carried into the admiration thereof, that they thought in the chanceable hitting upon any such verses great foretokens of their following fortunes were placed. Whereupon grew the word of *Sortes Virgilianae*,[4] when by sudden opening Virgil's book they lighted upon any verse of his making, whereof the histories of the emperors' lives are full: as of Albinus,[5] the governor of our island, who in his childhood met with this verse

> Arma amens capio nec sat rationis in armis[6]

and in his age performed it. Which, although it were a very vain and godless superstition, as also it was to think spirits were commanded by such verses—whereupon this word charms, derived of *carmina*,[7] cometh—so yet serveth it to show the great reverence those wits were held in; and altogether not without ground, since both the oracles of Delphos and Sibylla's prophecies[8] were wholly delivered in verses. For that same exquisite observing of number and measure in the words, and that high flying liberty of conceit[9] proper to the poet, did seem to have some divine force in it.

---

1. In the Ottoman Empire in Sidney's time, poetry was more highly developed than prose, but it is a great exaggeration to say the Turks had no writers other than their poets and their "law-giving divines" (the *mufti*).
2. Poems (accompanied by music and dancing) of the indigenous Haitians, celebrating ancestral valor.
3. "Prophecy" and "to prophesy."
4. Virgilian lots; i.e., accepting as prophecy a line of Virgil chosen by random ("changeable") opening of the *Aeneid*.

5. Roman governor of Britain, declared emperor by his troops in 193 C.E. but defeated and killed four years later.
6. Frantic, I take up arms, yet there is little purpose in arms (*Aeneid* 2.314).
7. Songs, poems.
8. The Pythia (priestess) at Delphi in Greece proclaimed Apollo's oracles; "Sibylla" (Sibyl) was a general name given to various prophetesses in Greek and Roman culture. "Wits": talented people (i.e., the poets).
9. Imaginative conception.

And may not I presume a little further, to show the reasonableness of this word *vates*, and say that the holy David's[1] Psalms are a divine poem? If I do, I shall not do it without the testimony of great learned men, both ancient and modern. But even the name of Psalms will speak for me, which being interpreted, is nothing but songs; then that it is fully written in meter, as all learned Hebricians agree, although the rules be not yet fully found;[2] lastly and principally, his handling his prophecy, which is merely[3] poetical: for what else is the awaking his musical instruments, the often and free changing of persons, his notable *prosopopoeias*,[4] when he maketh you, as it were, see God coming in His majesty, his telling of the beasts' joyfulness and hills leaping, but a heavenly poesy, wherein almost[5] he showeth himself a passionate lover of that unspeakable and everlasting beauty to be seen by the eyes of the mind, only cleared by faith? But truly now having named him, I fear me I seem to profane that holy name, applying it to poetry, which is among us thrown down to so ridiculous an estimation. But they that with quiet judgments will look a little deeper into it, shall find the end and working of it such as, being rightly applied, deserveth not to be scourged out of the Church of God.

But now let us see how the Greeks named it, and how they deemed of it. The Greeks called him a "poet," which name hath, as the most excellent, gone through other languages. It cometh of this word *poiein*, which is, to make: wherein, I know not whether by luck or wisdom, we Englishmen have met with the Greeks in calling him a maker:[6] which name, how high and incomparable a title it is, I had rather were known by marking the scope of other sciences than by any partial[7] allegation.

There is no art delivered to mankind that hath not the works of nature for his principal object, without which they[8] could not consist, and on which they so depend, as they become actors and players, as it were, of what nature will have set forth. So doth the astronomer look upon the stars, and, by that he seeth, set down what order nature hath taken therein. So doth the geometrician and arithmetician in their diverse sorts of quantities. So doth the musician in times tell you which by nature agree,[9] which not. The natural philosopher thereon hath his name, and the moral philosopher standeth upon[1] the natural virtues, vices, or passions of man; and follow nature (saith he) therein, and thou shalt not err. The lawyer saith what men have determined; the historian what men have done. The grammarian speaketh only of the rules of speech; and the rhetorician and logician, considering what in nature will soonest prove and persuade, thereon give artificial rules, which still are compassed within the circle of a question according to the proposed matter.[2] The physician weigheth[3] the nature of man's body, and the nature of

1. The biblical King David, commonly identified in the Renaissance as author of the Book of Psalms in its entirety.
2. Many Renaissance scholars who knew some Hebrew ("Hebricians") thought the Psalms were written in verse forms approximating classical Greek and Latin meters.
3. Entirely.
4. Personifications. "Changing of persons": shifts in narrative perspective, between first- and third-person expressions.
5. Indeed. "Poesy": art of making poetry.
6. A common word for *poet* in 16th-century England. "Met with": agreed with.
7. Biased. "Marking": noting.
8. The several arts. The following argument owes much to the *Poetics* (1561) of the Renaissance Italian theorist Julius Caesar Scaliger.
9. Which rhythms are naturally consonant.
1. Takes as subject matter. "Natural philosopher": scientist. "Thereon": i.e., from nature.
2. The rules of those arts ("artificial rules") are always limited in their application to questions pertaining to the subject at hand.
3. Considers.

things helpful or hurtful unto it. And the metaphysic, though it be in the second and abstract notions, and therefore be counted supernatural,[4] yet doth he indeed build upon the depth of nature. Only the poet, disdaining to be tied to any such subjection, lifted up with the vigor of his own invention, doth grow in effect another nature, in making things either better than nature bringeth forth, or, quite anew, forms such as never were in nature, as the Heroes, Demigods, Cyclops, Chimeras, Furies,[5] and suchlike: so as he goeth hand in hand with nature, not enclosed within the narrow warrant of her gifts, but freely ranging only within the zodiac of his own wit.[6] Nature never set forth the earth in so rich tapestry as divers poets have done; neither with so pleasant rivers, fruitful trees, sweet-smelling flowers, nor whatsoever else may make the too much loved earth more lovely. Her world is brazen, the poets only deliver a golden.[7]

But let those things alone, and go to man—for whom as the other things are, so it seemeth in him her uttermost cunning is employed—and know whether she have brought forth so true a lover as Theagenes, so constant a friend as Pylades, so valiant a man as Orlando, so right a prince as Xenophon's Cyrus,[8] so excellent a man every way as Virgil's Aeneas. Neither let this be jestingly conceived, because the works of the one be essential, the other in imitation or fiction;[9] for any understanding knoweth the skill of each artificer standeth in that *idea* or fore-conceit[1] of the work, and not in the work itself. And that the poet hath that *idea* is manifest, by delivering them forth in such excellency as he had imagined them. Which delivering forth also is not wholly imaginative, as we are wont[2] to say by them that build castles in the air; but so far substantially it worketh, not only to make a Cyrus, which had been but a particular excellency as nature might have done, but to bestow a Cyrus upon the world to make many Cyruses, if they will learn aright why and how that maker made him.

Neither let it be deemed too saucy a comparison to balance the highest point of man's wit with the efficacy of nature; but rather give right honor to the heavenly Maker of that maker, who having made man to His own likeness, set him beyond and over all the works of that second nature:[3] which in nothing he showeth so much as in poetry, when with the force of a divine breath he bringeth things forth surpassing her doings—with no small arguments to the incredulous of that first accursed fall of Adam, since our erected wit maketh us know what perfection is, and yet our infected will[4] keepeth us from reaching unto it. But these arguments will by few be understood, and by fewer granted. This much (I hope) will be given me, that the Greeks with some probability of reason gave him[5] the name above all names of learning.

4. Outside the physical world—entirely mental. "Metaphysic": metaphysician.
5. Avenging deities who punish crimes both in this world and after death. "Heroes": in the Greek sense, part human, part divine. "Cyclops": one-eyed giants (the correct plural is "Cyclopes") in Homer's *Odyssey*. "Chimeras": fire-breathing monsters with lion's head, goat's body, and serpent's tail.
6. Intellect.
7. A reference to the classical tradition of "The Four Ages of Man," the idea that the world has declined from the first and perfect Golden Age, through the Silver, Brass (or Bronze), and Iron ages. "Her": Nature's.

8. Cyrus the Great of Persia, exemplary hero of Xenophon's prose romance, the *Cyropaedia* (4th century B.C.E.); Theagenes, hero of Heliodorus's Greek romance, *Aethiopica* (3rd or 4th century C.E.); Pylades, friend of the Greek hero Orestes; Orlando, hero especially of Ariosto's *Orlando furioso* (1516).
9. The works of nature are real ("essential"); those of the poet are fiction.
1. Imaginative plan; conception.
2. Accustomed. "Imaginative": fanciful.
3. Physical nature.
4. Will corrupted in the Fall by original sin. "The incredulous": skeptics.
5. I.e., poesy.

Now let us go to a more ordinary opening[6] of him, that the truth may be the more palpable: and so I hope, though we get not so unmatched a praise as the etymology of his names will grant, yet his very description, which no man will deny, shall not justly be barred from a principal commendation.

[DEFINITION AND CLASSIFICATION OF POETRY]

Poesy therefore is an art of imitation, for so Aristotle termeth it in the word *mimesis*[7]—that is to say, a representing, counterfeiting, or figuring forth—to speak metaphorically, a speaking picture—with this end, to teach and delight.[8]

Of this have been three general kinds. The chief, both in antiquity and excellency, were they that did imitate the unconceivable excellencies of God. Such were David in his Psalms; Solomon in his Song of Songs, in his Ecclesiastes, and Proverbs; Moses and Deborah in their Hymns; and the writer of Job: which, beside other, the learned Emanuel Tremellius and Franciscus Junius[9] do entitle the poetical part of the Scripture. Against these none will speak that hath the Holy Ghost in due holy reverence. (In this kind, though in a full wrong divinity, were Orpheus, Amphion, Homer in his Hymns,[1] and many other, both Greeks and Romans.) And this poesy must be used by whosoever will follow St. James's counsel in singing psalms when they are merry;[2] and I know is used with the fruit of comfort by some, when, in sorrowful pangs of their death-bringing sins, they find the consolation of the never-leaving goodness.

The second kind is of them that deal with matters philosophical, either moral, as Tyrtaeus, Phocylides, Cato;[3] or natural, as Lucretius and Virgil's *Georgics;* or astronomical, as Manilius and Pontanus; or historical, as Lucan:[4] which who mislike, the fault is in their judgment quite out of taste, and not in the sweet food of sweetly uttered knowledge.

But because this second sort is wrapped within the fold of the proposed subject, and takes not the course of his own invention, whether they properly be poets or no let grammarians dispute, and go to the third, indeed right[5] poets, of whom chiefly this question ariseth: betwixt whom and these second

---

6. Analysis or explanation.

7. *Poetics* 1.2. The third part of a judicial oration is the *propositio*—as Thomas Elyot explains it in *The Art of Rhetoric* (1553), "a pithy sentence, comprehending in a small room the sum of the whole matter." This is followed by the *divisio*, in which the subject is divided into its parts and the orator clarifies which of these are in dispute.

8. The primary authorities for the commonplace notions that a poem is a "speaking picture" and that the end of poetry is "to teach and delight" are, respectively, Plutarch (ca. 46–ca. 120 C.E.), especially in *How to Study Poetry* 17–18, and Horace (65–8 B.C.E.), *Art of Poetry*, lines 343–44. The compounded definition, and the threefold classification of poets that follows, stem from Scaliger.

9. Two scholars who published a Protestant Latin translation of the Bible, in 1579. "Moses and Deborah in their Hymns": see Exodus 15.1–18, Deuteronomy 32.1–44; Judges 5.

1. The "Homeric Hymns" are a collection of ancient Greek poems addressed to various gods and formerly attributed to Homer. Similarly,

Orpheus (the archetypal poet of Greek mythology) was thought to be the author of a group of poems that expound the beliefs of a Greek mystery-religion. The lyre-playing of Amphion (a son of Zeus) moved stones to form themselves into the walls of Thebes.

2. "Is any merry? Let him sing psalms" (James 5.13).

3. The Roman Marcus Cato was the author of *Disticha de moribus*, an immensely popular collection, in verse and prose, of moral maxims. Tyrtaeus and Phocylides are among the Greek poets Sidney has previously mentioned.

4. Lucan wrote *De bello civili* (On the Civil War; also known as the *Pharsalia*), an epic poem on the struggle between Caesar and Pompey. Lucretius wrote a philosophical poem, *De rerum natura* (On the Nature of Things). Virgil's *Georgics* exalts the life and work of the farmer. Manilius wrote a long poem entitled *Astronomica*. The 15th-century Italian writer Pontanus—the only post-classical poet in this list—was the author of another celebrated astronomical poem, *Urania*.

5. Justly entitled to the name.

is such a kind of difference as betwixt the meaner[6] sort of painters, who counterfeit only such faces as are set before them, and the more excellent, who having no law but wit, bestow that in colors upon you which is fittest for the eye to see: as the constant though lamenting look of Lucretia, when she punished in herself another's fault,[7] wherein he painteth not Lucretia, whom he never saw, but painteth the outward beauty of such a virtue. For these third[8] be they which most properly do imitate to teach and delight, and to imitate borrow nothing of what is, hath been, or shall be; but range, only reined with learned discretion, into the divine consideration of what may be and should be. These be they that, as the first and most noble sort may justly be termed *vates,* so these are waited on in the excellentest languages and best understandings with the fore-described name of poets. For these indeed do merely[9] make to imitate, and imitate both to delight and teach; and delight, to move men to take that goodness in hand, which without delight they would fly as from a stranger; and teach, to make them know that goodness where-unto they are moved—which being the noblest scope to which ever any learning was directed, yet want[1] there not idle tongues to bark at them.

These be subdivided into sundry more special denominations. The most notable be the heroic,[2] lyric, tragic, comic, satiric, iambic, elegiac,[3] pastoral, and certain others, some of these being termed according to the matter they deal with, some by the sorts of verses they liked best to write in; for indeed the greatest part of poets have appareled their poetical inventions in that numbrous[4] kind of writing which is called verse—indeed but appareled, verse being but an ornament and no cause to poetry, since there have been many most excellent poets that never versified, and now swarm many versi-fiers that need never answer to the name of poets. For Xenophon, who did imitate so excellently as to give us *effigiem iusti imperii,* the portraiture of a just empire, under the name of Cyrus (as Cicero saith of him), made therein an absolute heroical poem. So did Heliodorus in his sugared invention of that picture of love in Theagenes and Chariclea; and yet both these wrote in prose: which I speak to show that it is not rhyming and versing that maketh a poet—no more than a long gown maketh an advocate,[5] who though he pleaded in armor should be an advocate and no soldier. But it is that feigning notable images of virtues, vices, or what else, with that delightful teaching, which must be the right describing note[6] to know a poet by; although indeed the senate of poets hath chosen verse as their fittest raiment, meaning, as in matter they passed all in all,[7] so in manner to go beyond them: not speaking (table-talk fashion or like men in a dream) words as they chanceably fall from the mouth, but peising[8] each syllable of each word by just proportion according to the dignity of the subject.

---

6. Lower.
7. A notable exemplar of chastity and honor, the Roman matron Lucretia committed suicide after being raped by the son of King Tarquinius Superbus. "Wit": creative imagination.
8. I.e., the right poets.
9. Only. "Waited on . . . with": distinguished by.
1. Lack. "Scope": aim.
2. Epic.
3. Two genres are named after their Greek and

Latin verse forms: *iambic,* associated with directly vituperative poetry (as distinguished from the irony of satire); *elegiac:* poetry written in the "ele-giac couplet," which was used especially for reflec-tive, lamenting, or erotic poetry.
4. I.e., in numbers, poetic meters.
5. Lawyer.
6. The true distinguishing characteristics.
7. All others, in all respects.
8. Weighing.

[POETRY VERSUS PHILOSOPHY AND HISTORY]

Now therefore it shall not be amiss first to weigh this latter sort of poetry by his works, and then by his parts; and if in neither of these anatomies he be condemnable, I hope we shall obtain a more favorable sentence.[9]

This purifying of wit—this enriching of memory, enabling of judgment, and enlarging of conceit[1]—which commonly we call learning, under what name soever it come forth, or to what immediate end soever it be directed, the final end is to lead and draw us to as high a perfection as our degenerate souls, made worse by their clayey lodgings, can be capable of.

This, according to the inclination of the man, bred many-formed[2] impressions. For some that thought this felicity principally to be gotten by knowledge, and no knowledge to be so high or heavenly as acquaintance with the stars, gave themselves to astronomy; others, persuading themselves to be demigods if they knew the causes of things, became natural and supernatural philosophers; some an admirable delight drew to music; and some the certainty of demonstration to the mathematics. But all, one and other, having this scope: to know, and by knowledge to lift up the mind from the dungeon of the body to the enjoying his own divine essence.

But when by the balance of experience it was found that the astronomer, looking to the stars, might fall in a ditch,[3] that the inquiring philosopher might be blind in himself, and the mathematician might draw forth a straight line with a crooked heart, then lo, did proof, the overruler of opinions, make manifest that all these are but serving sciences, which, as they have each a private end in themselves, so yet are they all directed to the highest end of the mistress-knowledge, by the Greeks called *architectonike*,[4] which stands (as I think) in the knowledge of a man's self, in the ethic and politic consideration, with the end of well-doing and not of well-knowing only—even as the saddler's next[5] end is to make a good saddle, but his further end to serve a nobler faculty, which is horsemanship, so the horseman's to soldiery, and the soldier not only to have the skill, but to perform the practice of a soldier. So that, the ending end of all earthly learning being virtuous action, those skills that most serve to bring forth that have a most just title to be princes over all the rest.

Wherein, if we can, show we the poet's nobleness, by setting him before his other competitors. Among whom as principal challengers step forth the moral philosophers, whom, methinketh, I see coming towards me with a sullen gravity, as though they could not abide vice by daylight, rudely clothed for to witness outwardly their contempt of outward things, with books in their hands against glory, whereto they set their names, sophistically[6] speaking against subtlety, and angry with any man in whom they see the foul fault of anger. These men casting largess as they go, of definitions, divisions, and distinctions,[7] with a scornful interrogative do soberly ask whether it be

---

9. Judgment. "Works": effects. "Anatomies": analyses. Here Sidney moves to the central and longest part of the judicial oration, the *confirmatio* or *examinatio*, in which the speaker develops the arguments in support of his (or her) position.
1. Conceptual power. "Wit": intellect; understanding. "Enabling": strengthening.
2. Manifold. "Inclination": natural disposition.

3. As Plato (*Theatatus* 174) reported of the philosopher and astronomer Thales.
4. The "chief art," to which all others are subordinate. The term is Aristotle's (*Ethics* 1.1). "Private": particular.
5. Nearest.
6. Subtly.
7. I.e., bountiful gifts of scholastic terms and arguments.

possible to find any path so ready to lead a man to virtue as that which teacheth what virtue is; and teach it not only by delivering forth his very being, his causes and effects, but also by making known his enemy, vice, which must be destroyed, and his cumbersome[8] servant, passion, which must be mastered; by showing the generalities that containeth it, and the specialities that are derived from it; lastly, by plain setting down how it extendeth itself out of the limits of a man's own little world to the government of families and maintaining of public societies.

The historian scarcely giveth leisure to the moralist to say so much, but that he, laden with old mouse-eaten records, authorizing himself[9] (for the most part) upon other histories, whose greatest authorities are built upon the notable foundation of hearsay; having much ado to accord differing writers and to pick truth out of their partiality;[1] better acquainted with a thousand years ago than with the present age, and yet better knowing how this world goeth than how his own wit runneth; curious for antiquities and inquisitive of novelties; a wonder to young folks and a tyrant in table talk, denieth, in a great chafe,[2] that any man for teaching of virtue and virtuous actions is comparable to him. "I am *testis temporum, lux veritatis, vita memoriae, magistra vitae, nuntia vetustatis.*[3] "The philosopher," saith he, "teacheth a disputative virtue, but I do an active. His virtue is excellent in the dangerless Academy of Plato, but mine showeth forth her honorable face in the battles of Marathon, Pharsalia, Poitiers, and Agincourt.[4] He teacheth virtue by certain abstract considerations, but I only bid you follow the footing of them that have gone before you. Old-aged experience goeth beyond the fine-witted philosopher, but I give the experience of many ages. Lastly, if he make the songbook, I put the learner's hand to the lute; and if he be the guide, I am the light." Then would he allege you innumerable examples, confirming story by stories, how much the wisest senators and princes have been directed by the credit of history, as Brutus, Alphonsus of Aragon,[5] and who not, if need be? At length the long line of their disputation maketh a point[6] in this, that the one giveth the precept, and the other[7] the example.

Now whom shall we find (since the question standeth for the highest form in the school of learning) to be moderator?[8] Truly, as me seemeth, the poet; and if not a moderator, even the man that ought to carry the title from them both, and much more from all other serving sciences. Therefore compare we the poet with the historian and with the moral philosopher; and if he go beyond them both, no other human skill can match him. For as for the divine, with all reverence it is ever to be excepted, not only for having his scope as far beyond any of these as eternity exceedeth a moment, but even for passing[9] each of these in themselves. And for the lawyer, though *Ius*[1] be the daughter

---

8. Obstructive; troublesome.
9. Basing his authority.
1. Bias. "Accord": reconcile.
2. Temper.
3. "I am the witness of times, the light of truth, the life of memory, the teacher of life, the messenger of antiquity" (Cicero, *De oratore* 2.9.36).
4. At Poitiers (1356) and Agincourt (1415), the English defeated the French; at Marathon, the Greeks defeated the Persians (490 B.C.E.); at Pharsalia, Caesar defeated Pompey (48 B.C.E.).
5. Alfonso V of Aragon (1396–1458) carried the histories of Livy and Caesar into battle with him.

Marcus Brutus was inspired to rise up against Caesar by the history of his great republican ancestor, Junius Brutus, who expelled the Tarquin kings.
6. Comes to a full stop.
7. The historian. "The one": the philosopher.
8. Judge, arbitrator. Sidney images the rival claims of philosophy and history as a formal academic disputation—a standard exercise at the time—engaging the top class ("highest form") in the "school of learning."
9. Surpassing. "The divine": the theologian.
1. Law (Latin).

of Justice, and justice the chief of virtues, yet because he seeketh to make men good rather *formidine poenae* than *virtutis amore;*[2] or, to say righter, doth not endeavor to make men good, but that their evil hurt not others; having no care, so he be a good citizen, how bad a man he be: therefore as our wickedness maketh him[3] necessary, and necessity maketh him honorable, so is he not in the deepest truth to stand in rank with these who all endeavor to take naughtiness away and plant goodness even in the secretest cabinet[4] of our souls. And these four are all that any way deal in that consideration of men's manners,[5] which being the supreme knowledge, they that best breed it deserve the best commendation.

The philosopher, therefore, and the historian are they which would win the goal, the one by precept, the other by example. But both, not having both, do both halt.[6] For the philosopher, setting down with thorny arguments the bare rule, is so hard of utterance and so misty to be conceived, that one that hath no other guide but him shall wade in him till he be old before he shall find sufficient cause to be honest.[7] For his knowledge standeth so upon the abstract and general, that happy[8] is that man who may understand him, and more happy that can apply what he doth understand. On the other side, the historian, wanting[9] the precept, is so tied, not to what should be but to what is, to the particular truth of things and not to the general reason of things, that his example draweth no necessary consequence, and therefore a less fruitful doctrine.

Now doth the peerless poet perform both: for whatsoever the philosopher saith should be done, he giveth a perfect picture of it in someone by whom he presupposeth it was done, so as he coupleth the general notion with the particular example. A perfect picture I say, for he yieldeth to the powers of the mind an image of that whereof the philosopher bestoweth but a wordish description, which doth neither strike, pierce, nor possess the sight of the soul so much as that other doth. For as in outward things, to a man that had never seen an elephant or a rhinoceros, who should tell him most exquisitely[1] all their shapes, color, bigness, and particular marks, or of a gorgeous palace the architecture, with declaring the full beauties, might well make the hearer able to repeat, as it were by rote, all he had heard, yet should never satisfy his inward conceit[2] with being witness to itself of a true lively knowledge; but the same man, as soon as he might see those beasts well painted, or that house well in model, should straightways grow, without need of any description, to a judicial[3] comprehending of them: so no doubt the philosopher with his learned definitions—be it of virtue, vices, matters of public policy or private government[4]—replenisheth the memory with many infallible grounds of wisdom, which, notwithstanding, lie dark before the imaginative and judging power, if they be not illuminated or figured forth[5] by the speaking picture of poesy.

---

2. Through fear of punishment than love of virtue. The distinction is from Horace, *Epistles* 1.16.52–53.
3. I.e., the lawyer. "These" (below): moral philosopher, historian, and poet.
4. Most private chamber. "Naughtiness": wickedness.
5. Moral conduct.
6. Limp (having, after all, only one leg each).

7. Virtuous.
8. Fortunate.
9. Not having.
1. Discriminatingly.
2. Conception.
3. Judicious.
4. "Private government": individual conduct (as opposed to "public policy").
5. Given form or shape.

Tully[6] taketh much pains, and many times not without poetical helps, to make us know the force love of our country hath in us. Let us but hear old Anchises speaking in the midst of Troy's flames, or see Ulysses in the fullness of all Calypso's delights bewail his absence from barren and beggarly Ithaca.[7] Anger, the Stoics said, was a short madness:[8] let but Sophocles bring you Ajax on a stage, killing or whipping sheep and oxen, thinking them the army of Greeks,[9] with their chieftains Agamemnon and Menelaus, and tell me if you have not a more familiar insight into anger than finding in the schoolmen his *genus* and difference.[1] See whether wisdom and temperance in Ulysses and Diomedes, valor in Achilles, friendship in Nisus and Euryalus,[2] even to an ignorant man carry not an apparent shining;[3] and, contrarily, the remorse of conscience in Oedipus, the soon repenting pride in Agamemnon, the self-devouring cruelty in his father Atreus, the violence of ambition in the two Theban brothers, the sour-sweetness of revenge in Medea;[4] and, to fall lower, the Terentian Gnatho and our Chaucer's Pandar[5] so expressed that we now use their names to signify their trades: and finally, all virtues, vices, and passions so in their own natural seats laid to the view, that we seem not to hear of them, but clearly to see through them.

But even in the most excellent determination of goodness, what philosopher's counsel can so readily direct a prince, as the feigned Cyrus in Xenophon; or a virtuous man in all fortunes, as Aeneas in Virgil; or a whole commonwealth, as the way of Sir Thomas More's *Utopia?* I say the way, because where Sir Thomas More erred, it was the fault of the man and not of the poet, for that way of patterning a commonwealth was most absolute,[6] though he perchance hath not so absolutely performed it. For the question is, whether the feigned image of poetry or the regular instruction of philosophy hath the more force in teaching: wherein if the philosophers have more rightly showed themselves philosophers than the poets have attained to the high top of their profession, as in truth

> Mediocribus esse poetis,
> Non dii, non homines, non concessere columnae;[7]

it is, I say again, not the fault of the art, but that by few men that art can be accomplished.

Certainly, even our Savior Christ could as well have given the moral commonplaces of uncharitableness and humbleness as the divine narration of

---

6. A common English name for Cicero (Marcus Tullius Cicero).

7. All the charms of the lovely nymph Calypso, and the promise of immortality with her, could not make Odysseus forget his home on the Greek isle of Ithaca (*Odyssey* 5.149–224). Anchises, the father of Aeneas, laments his destroyed homeland in *Aeneid* 2.638–49.

8. The formulation is Horace's (*Epistles* 1.2.62).

9. In fact, Sophocles's *Ajax* does not portray its protagonist's mad actions on the stage but has them reported by Menelaus (lines 1052–61).

1. In the logic of the Scholastic philosophers ("schoolmen"), "differences" are the attributes that distinguish among the species in a genus.

2. All are figures in the story of the Trojan War, as recounted in the *Iliad* and, for the faithful friends Nisus and Euryalus, the *Aeneid* (9.176–449).

3. An evident splendor.

4. All are figures from Greek and Roman tragedy. "The two Theban brothers": Eteocles and Polynices, twin sons of Oedipus, who killed each other in battle. (For Atreus—the father of Agamemnon, leader of the Greeks against Troy—see below, p. 1058, n. 8.)

5. The common noun "pander" derives from Pandarus, the go-between in Chaucer's *Troilus and Criseyde*; similarly, "Gnatho"—a figure in the *Eunuch* of the Roman comic dramatist Terence—became a type-name for a fawning parasite.

6. Perfect. Sidney approves of More's casting a work of political philosophy as an account of a voyage to a fictional country, but he does not want to be thought of as endorsing all features of the Utopian commonwealth (especially, one surmises, its communism).

7. "That poets be middling, neither gods, nor men, nor booksellers ever allowed" (Horace, *Art of Poetry* 372–73).

Dives and Lazarus; or of disobedience and mercy, as that heavenly discourse of the lost child and the gracious father;[8] but that His through-searching wisdom knew the estate[9] of Dives burning in hell, and of Lazarus in Abraham's bosom, would more constantly (as it were) inhabit both the memory and judgment. Truly, for myself, meseems I see before mine eyes the lost child's disdainful prodigality, turned to envy a swine's dinner: which by the learned divines are thought not historical acts,[1] but instructing parables.

For conclusion, I say the philosopher teacheth, but he teacheth obscurely, so as the learned only can understand him, that is to say, he teacheth them that are already taught; but the poet is the food for the tenderest stomachs, the poet is indeed the right popular philosopher, whereof Aesop's tales give good proof: whose pretty allegories, stealing under the formal[2] tales of beasts, make many, more beastly than beasts, begin to hear the sound of virtue from these dumb speakers.

But now may it be alleged that if this imagining of matters be so fit for the imagination, then must the historian needs surpass, who bringeth you images of true matters; such as indeed were done, and not such as fantastically or falsely may be suggested to have been done. Truly, Aristotle himself, in his discourse of poesy, plainly determineth this question, saying that poetry is *philosophoteron* and *spoudaioteron*, that is to say, it is more philosophical and more studiously serious than history.[3] His reason is, because poesy dealeth with *katholou*, that is to say, with the universal consideration, and the history with *kathekaston*, the particular: now, saith he, the universal weighs what is fit to be said or done, either in likelihood or necessity (which the poesy considereth in his imposed names), and the particular only marks whether Alcibiades did, or suffered, this or that.[4] Thus far Aristotle: which reason of his (as all his) is most full of reason. For indeed, if the question were whether it were better to have a particular act truly or falsely set down, there is no doubt which is to be chosen, no more than whether you had rather have Vespasian's[5] picture right as he was, or, at the painter's pleasure, nothing resembling. But if the question be for your own use and learning, whether it be better to have it set down as it should be, or as it was, then certainly is more doctrinable the feigned Cyrus in Xenophon than the true Cyrus in Justin, and the feigned Aeneas in Virgil than the right Aeneas in Dares Phrygius:[6] as to a lady that desired to fashion her countenance to the best grace, a painter should more benefit her to portrait a most sweet face, writing Canidia upon it, than to paint Canidia as she was, who, Horace sweareth, was full ill-favored.[7]

---

8. The Prodigal Son (Luke 15.11–32); for the parable of the rich Dives and the beggar Lazarus, see Luke 16.19–31.
9. Condition.
1. Records.
2. I.e., in the form of.
3. *Poetics* 9.
4. Alcibiades, an Athenian politician and disciple of Socrates, died in 404 B.C.E.—twenty years before Aristotle's birth. Sidney's summary of Aristotle's passage is accurate, with the important exception that he imposes the notion that Aristotelian universals have a morally prescriptive

force, weighing "what is *fit* to be said or done." Aristotle says only that "by a universal statement I mean one as to what such or such a kind of man will probably or necessarily say or do."
5. Vespasian was emperor of Rome 69–79 C.E.
6. Mentioned in the *Iliad*, Dares Phrygius was the supposed author of an eyewitness account of the Trojan War. Justin was a Roman historian of the 2nd or 3rd century C.E. who wrote an abridgment of a now-lost universal history by one Trogus. "Doctrinable": instructive.
7. For the lost looks of the witch Canidia, see Horace, *Epodes* 5.

If the poet do his part aright, he will show you in Tantalus, Atreus,[8] and suchlike, nothing that is not to be shunned; in Cyrus, Aeneas, Ulysses, each thing to be followed; where the historian, bound to tell things as things were, cannot be liberal (without he will be poetical) of a perfect pattern, but, as in Alexander or Scipio himself,[9] show doings, some to be liked, some to be misliked. And then how will you discern what to follow but by your own discretion, which you had without reading Quintus Curtius? And whereas a man may say, though in universal consideration of doctrine the poet prevaileth, yet that the history,[1] in his saying such a thing was done, doth warrant a man more in that he shall follow[2]—the answer is manifest: that, if he stand upon that was (as if he should argue, because it rained yesterday, therefore it should rain today), then indeed hath it some advantage to a gross conceit;[3] but if he know an example only informs a conjectured likelihood, and so go by reason,[4] the poet doth so far exceed him[5] as he is to frame his example to that which is most reasonable (be it in warlike, politic, or private matters), where the historian in his bare "was" hath many times that which we call fortune to overrule the best wisdom. Many times he must tell events whereof he can yield no cause; or, if he do, it must be poetically.

For that a feigned example hath as much force to teach as a true example (for as for to move, it is clear, since the feigned may be tuned to the highest key of passion), let us take one example wherein an historian and a poet did concur. Herodotus and Justin do both testify that Zopyrus, King Darius' faithful servant, seeing his master long resisted by the rebellious Babylonians, feigned himself in extreme disgrace of his king: for verifying of which, he caused his own nose and ears to be cut off, and so flying to the Babylonians was received, and for his known valor so sure credited, that he did find means to deliver them over to Darius.[6] Much like matter doth Livy record of Tarquinius and his son. Xenophon excellently feigneth such another stratagem performed by Abradatas in Cyrus' behalf. Now would I fain know, if occasion be presented unto you to serve your prince by such an honest dissimulation, why you do not as well learn it of Xenophon's fiction as of the other's verity; and truly so much the better, as you shall save your nose by the bargain: for Abradatas did not counterfeit so far. So then the best of the historian is subject to the poet; for whatsoever action, or faction, whatsoever counsel, policy, or war stratagem the historian is bound to recite, that may the poet (if he list)[7] with his imitation make his own, beautifying it both for further teaching and more delighting, as it please him: having all, from Dante's heaven to his hell, under the authority of his pen.

8. Figures from Greek mythology. In one version of his story, Tantalus served up his son at a banquet for the gods; similarly, his grandson Atreus served his brother's children to him.

9. Alexander the Great was often represented—for example, by the Roman historian Quintus Curtius (below)—as having been corrupted by power; and even Scipio Africanus—the conqueror of Hannibal and one of the most unreservedly admired Romans—was, in his later years, accused of political misconduct. "Cannot be liberal . . . of": is not at liberty to give.

1. The historian. "Doctrine": instruction.

2. I.e., provides more reliable assurance as to what course one should follow.

3. I.e., to a person of undiscriminating intelligence.

4. I.e., if a person is sufficiently sophisticated to understand that reason is a better guide than example.

5. I.e., the historian.

6. Darius I was king of Persia 521–486 B.C.E. The story of his faithful servant Zopyrus was told in Herodotus's *Histories* 3.153–60 and repeated in Justin's *Histories* 1.10. Somewhat similar stories (see below) are recounted by the Roman historian Livy (concerning the last of the Tarquin kings and his son) in *From the Foundation of the City* 1.53–54 and in Xenophon's *Cyropaedia* 6.1.38–44, 6.3.14–20 (though about Cyrus and one Araspas—not, as Sidney has it, Abradatas).

7. Likes.

Which if I be asked what poets have done so, as I might well name some, so yet say I, and say again, I speak of the art, and not of the artificer.

Now, to that which commonly is attributed to the praise of history, in respect of the notable learning is got by marking the success,[8] as though therein a man should see virtue exalted and vice punished—truly that commendation is particular to poetry, and far off from history. For indeed poetry ever sets virtue so out in her best colors, making Fortune her well-waiting handmaid, that one must needs be enamored of her. Well may you see Ulysses in a storm,[9] and in other hard plights; but they are but exercises of patience and magnanimity, to make them shine the more in the near-following prosperity. And of the contrary part, if evil men come to the stage, they ever go out (as the tragedy writer[1] answered to one that misliked the show of such persons) so manacled as they little animate folks to follow them. But the history, being captived to the truth of a foolish world, is many times a terror[2] from well-doing, and an encouragement to unbridled wickedness. For see we not valiant Miltiades rot in his fetters? The just Phocion and the accomplished Socrates put to death like traitors? The cruel Severus live prosperously? The excellent Severus miserably murdered? Sulla and Marius dying in their beds? Pompey and Cicero[3] slain then when they would have thought exile a happiness? See we not virtuous Cato driven to kill himself,[4] and rebel Caesar so advanced that his name yet, after 1600 years, lasteth in the highest honor? And mark but even Caesar's own words of the aforenamed Sulla (who in that only did honestly, to put down his dishonest tyranny), *literas nescivit*, as if want of learning caused him to do well.[5] He meant it not by poetry, which, not content with earthly plagues, deviseth new punishments in hell for tyrants, nor yet by philosophy, which teacheth *occidendos esse*;[6] but no doubt by skill in history, for that indeed can afford you Cypselus, Periander, Phalaris, Dionysius,[7] and I know not how many more of the same kennel, that speed[8] well enough in their abominable injustice of usurpation.

I conclude, therefore, that he[9] excelleth history, not only in furnishing the mind with knowledge, but in setting it forward to that which deserveth to be called and accounted good: which setting forward, and moving to well-doing, indeed setteth the laurel crown upon the poets as victorious, not only of the historian, but over the philosopher, howsoever in teaching it may be questionable.[1]

For suppose it be granted (that which I suppose with great reason may be denied) that the philosopher, in respect of his methodical proceeding, doth

---

8. Outcome.
9. In *Odyssey* 5.291ff.
1. Euripides (as reported by Plutarch, *How to Study Poetry* 4).
2. I. e., a deterrent.
3. The great orator, killed at Mark Antony's command. Miltiades, Athenian general and architect of victory at Marathon over the Persians, later imprisoned by the Athenians. Phocion, Athenian general and statesman executed for treason because he opposed ill-advised opposition to Athens' Macedonian conquerors. "Cruel Severus": Emperor Lucius Septimius Severus, noted for ruthlessness. "Excellent Severus": Emperor Alexander Severus, a reformer slain by his troops. Sulla and Marius, political rivals who brought unrest and destruction to Rome for two decades.

Pompey: Pompey the Great, defeated by Caesar at Pharsalia and slain in Egypt.
4. Cato the Younger committed suicide after his party failed to defeat Caesar.
5. When Sulla resigned ("put down") his dictatorship, Caesar joked that he was illiterate (*literas nescivit*), since he left the *dictatura* (which means both "dictatorship" and "dictation") to others. "By" (below): with reference to.
6. "They [tyrants] must be killed."
7. Four famous tyrants of the classical world: the first two were from Corinth; Phalaris, Agrigentum; Dionysus the Elder, Syracuse.
8. Succeed.
9. I.e., poetry.
1. Arguable.

teach more perfectly than the poet, yet do I think that no man is so much *philophilosophos*[2] as to compare the philosopher in moving with the poet. And that moving is of a higher degree than teaching, it may by this appear, that it is well nigh both the cause and effect of teaching. For who will be taught, if he be not moved with desire to be taught? And what so much good doth that teaching bring forth (I speak still of moral doctrine) as that it moveth one to do that which it doth teach? For, as Aristotle saith, it is not *gnosis* but *praxis*[3] must be the fruit. And how *praxis* cannot be, without being moved to practice, it is no hard matter to consider.

The philosopher showeth you the way, he informeth you of the particularities, as well of the tediousness of the way, as of the pleasant lodging you shall have when your journey is ended, as of the many by-turnings that may divert you from your way. But this is to no man but to him that will read him, and read him with attentive studious painfulness;[4] which constant desire whosoever hath in him, hath already passed half the hardness of the way, and therefore is beholding to the philosopher but for the other half. Nay truly, learned men have learnedly thought that where once reason hath so much overmastered passion as that the mind hath a free desire to do well, the inward light each mind hath in itself is as good as a philosopher's book; since in nature[5] we know it is well to do well, and what is well, and what is evil, although not in the words of art which philosophers bestow upon us; for out of natural conceit[6] the philosophers drew it. But to be moved to do that which we know, or to be moved with desire to know, *hoc opus, hic labor est.*[7]

Now therein of all sciences (I speak still of human,[8] and according to the human conceit) is our poet the monarch. For he doth not only show the way, but giveth so sweet a prospect into the way, as will entice any man to enter into it. Nay, he doth, as if your journey should lie through a fair vineyard, at the first give you a cluster of grapes, that full of that taste, you may long to pass further. He beginneth not with obscure definitions, which must blur the margin with interpretations and load the memory with doubtfulness; but he cometh to you with words set in delightful proportion, either accompanied with, or prepared for, the well enchanting skill of music; and with a tale forsooth he cometh unto you, with a tale which holdeth children from play, and old men from the chimney corner. And, pretending no more, doth intend the winning of the mind from wickedness to virtue—even as the child is often brought to take most wholesome things by hiding them in such other as have a pleasant taste, which, if one should begin to tell them the nature of *aloes* or *rhabarbarum*[9] they should receive, would sooner take their physic at their ears than at their mouth.[1] So is it in men (most of which are childish in the best things, till they be cradled in their graves): glad will they be to hear the tales of Hercules, Achilles, Cyrus, Aeneas; and, hearing them, must needs hear the right description of wisdom, valor, and justice; which, if they had been barely, that is to say philosophically, set out, they would swear they be brought to school again.

---

2. A lover of philosophers.
3. Not knowing but doing (*Ethics* 1.3).
4. Painstaking effort.
5. Considering that by nature.
6. Natural understanding, as opposed to the philosophers' special vocabulary ("words of art").
7. This is the task, this is the work to be done

(Virgil, *Aeneid* 6.129).
8. As opposed to divine. "Sciences": branches of learning.
9. Two bitter purgatives: aloe and rhubarb.
1. I.e., would rather have their ears boxed than take the medicine.

That imitation whereof poetry is hath the most conveniency[2] to nature of all other, insomuch that, as Aristotle saith, those things which in themselves are horrible, as cruel battles, unnatural monsters, are made in poetical imitation delightful.[3] Truly, I have known men that even with reading *Amadis de Gaule*[4] (which God knoweth wanteth much of a perfect poesy) have found their hearts moved to the exercise of courtesy, liberality, and especially courage. Who readeth Aeneas carrying old Anchises on his back, that wisheth not it were his fortune to perform so excellent an act? Whom doth not these words of Turnus move, the tale of Turnus having planted his image in the imagination,

> Fugientem haec terra videbit?
> Usque adeone mori miserum est?[5]

Where the philosophers, as they scorn to delight, so much they be content little to move—saving wrangling whether *virtus*[6] be the chief or the only good, whether the contemplative or the active life do excell—which Plato and Boethius well knew, and therefore made Mistress Philosophy very often borrow the masking raiment of poesy.[7] For even those hard-hearted evil men who think virtue a school name, and know no other good but *indulgere genio*,[8] and therefore despise the austere admonitions of the philosopher, and feel not the inward reason they stand upon, yet will be content to be delighted—which is all the good-fellow poet seemeth to promise—and so steal[9] to see the form of goodness (which seen they cannot but love) ere themselves be aware, as if they took a medicine of cherries.

Infinite proofs of the strange effects of this poetical invention might be alleged; only two shall serve, which are so often remembered as I think all men know them. The one of Menenius Agrippa,[1] who, when the whole people of Rome had resolutely divided themselves from the senate, with apparent show of utter ruin, though he were (for that time) an excellent orator, came not among them upon trust of figurative speeches or cunning insinuations, and much less with far-fet maxims of philosophy, which (especially if they were Platonic) they must have learned geometry before they could well have conceived;[2] but forsooth he behaves himself like a homely and familiar poet. He telleth them a tale, that there was a time when all the parts of the body made a mutinous conspiracy against the belly, which they thought devoured the fruits of each other's labor; they concluded they would let so unprofitable a spender starve. In the end, to be short (for the tale is notorious, and as notorious that it was a tale), with punishing the belly they plagued themselves. This applied by him wrought such effect in the people,

2. Congruity; suitability.
3. *Poetics* 4.
4. A chivalric romance of Spanish origin, which became extremely popular in a French translation.
5. *Aeneid* 12.645–46: "Shall this land see Turnus in flight? Is it so bad a thing to die?" The Italian king Turnus is Aeneas's worthy rival, killed by the epic hero in the poem's closing lines. Aeneas carries his father, Anchises, away from burning Troy in 2.705 ff.
6. Virtue. "Saving": except. The (satiric) point is that wrangling over standard philosophical questions is unlikely to move anyone other than the wrangling philosophers themselves.

7. For Plato's use of "poetry" (that is, fiction), see above, p. 1047. The *Consolation of Philosophy* of Boethius (476–524 C.E.) is cast as a dialogue between himself and Lady Philosophy, and alternates prose and verse.
8. "To follow one's natural inclination."
9. I.e., come accidentally.
1. Roman consul in 503 B.C.E. The story of his parable was first related by Livy, *From the Foundation of the City* 2.32.
2. A medieval tradition held that over the door of Plato's Academy was written: "No man untaught in geometry should enter." "Far-fet": farfetched.

as I never read that only words brought forth but then[3] so sudden and so good an alteration; for upon reasonable conditions a perfect reconcilement ensued. The other is of Nathan the prophet, who, when the holy David had so far forsaken God as to confirm adultery with murder,[4] when he was to do the tenderest office of a friend in laying his own shame before his eyes, sent by God to call again so chosen a servant, how doth he it but by telling of a man whose beloved lamb was ungratefully[5] taken from his bosom? The application most divinely true, but the discourse itself feigned; which made David (I speak of the second and instrumental cause)[6] as in a glass see his own filthiness, as that heavenly psalm of mercy[7] well testifieth.

By these, therefore, examples and reasons, I think it may be manifest that the poet, with that same hand of delight, doth draw the mind more effectually than any other art doth. And so a conclusion[8] not unfitly ensue: that, as virtue is the most excellent resting place for all worldly learning to make his end of, so poetry, being the most familiar[9] to teach it, and most princely to move towards it, in the most excellent work is the most excellent workman.

[THE POETIC KINDS]

But I am content not only to decipher him[1] by his works (although works, in commendation or dispraise, must ever hold a high authority), but more narrowly will examine his parts; so that (as in a man) though all together may carry a presence full of majesty and beauty, perchance in some one defectous piece[2] we may find blemish.

Now in his parts, kinds, or species (as you list[3] to term them), it is to be noted that some poesies have coupled together two or three kinds, as the tragical and comical, whereupon is risen the tragi-comical. Some, in the manner, have mingled prose and verse, as Sannazzaro and Boethius.[4] Some have mingled matters heroical and pastoral. But that cometh all to one in this question, for, if severed they be good, the conjunction cannot be hurtful. Therefore, perchance forgetting some and leaving some as needless to be remembered, it shall not be amiss in a word to cite the special kinds, to see what faults may be found in the right use of them.

Is it then the Pastoral poem which is misliked? (For perchance where the hedge is lowest[5] they will soonest leap over.) Is the poor pipe[6] disdained, which sometime out of Meliboeus' mouth can show the misery of people under hard lords or ravening soldiers, and again, by Tityrus, what blessedness is derived to them that lie lowest from the goodness of them that sit highest;[7] sometimes, under the pretty tales of wolves and sheep, can include the whole considerations of wrong-doing and patience; sometimes show that conten-

---

3. "But then": except on that occasion. "Only words": words alone.
4. By killing the husband of his mistress, Bathsheba. For the deed, and Nathan's rebuke, see 2 Samuel 11–12.
5. Cruelly.
6. The *first* cause was God's intention to bring David to repentance.
7. Psalm 51, in which David pleads for God's mercy. "Glass": mirror.
8. I.e., to the argument weighing poetry by its "works" (cf. above, p. 1053).
9. Congenial, suitable. "End": aim, objective.
1. I.e., poetry.

2. Defective part.
3. May choose.
4. Like Boethius's *Consolation of Philosophy* (above, p. 1061, n. 7), Jacopo Sannazaro's pastoral romance *Arcadia* (1502), which greatly influenced Sidney's own *Arcadia*, mixed prose and verse.
5. Pastoral was considered the humblest kind of poetry, written in the lowest style.
6. The shepherd's oaten flute, symbol of pastoral poetry.
7. In Virgil's first eclogue, Meliboeus laments the seizure of his land, while Tityrus rejoices that his lands were protected by the emperor.

tions for trifles can get but a trifling victory: where perchance a man may see that even Alexander and Darius, when they strave who should be cock of this world's dunghill, the benefit they got was that the after-livers may say

> Haec memini et victum frustra contendere Thirsin:
> Ex illo Corydon, Corydon est tempore nobis.[8]

Or is it the lamenting Elegiac; which in a kind heart would move rather pity than blame; who bewails with the great philosopher Heraclitus[9] the weakness of mankind and the wretchedness of the world; who surely is to be praised, either for compassionate accompanying just causes of lamentations or for rightly painting out how weak be the passions of woefulness?[1] Is it the bitter but wholesome Iambic[2] who rubs the galled mind, in making shame the trumpet of villainy, with bold and open crying out against naughtiness? Or the Satiric, who

> Omne vafer vitium ridenti tangit amico;[3]

who sportingly never leaveth till he make a man laugh at folly, and at length ashamed, to laugh at himself, which he cannot avoid without avoiding the folly; who, while

> circum praecordia ludit,[4]

giveth us to feel how many headaches a passionate life bringeth us to; how, when all is done,

> Est Ulubris, animus si nos non deficit aequus?[5]

No, perchance it is the Comic, whom naughty play-makers and stage-keepers have justly made odious. To the arguments of abuse I will answer after. Only this much now is to be said, that the comedy is an imitation of the common errors of our life, which he representeth in the most ridiculous and scornful sort that may be, so as it is impossible that any beholder can be content to be such a one. Now, as in geometry the oblique must be known as well as the right, and in arithmetic the odd as well as the even, so in the actions of our life who seeth not the filthiness of evil wanteth[6] a great foil to perceive the beauty of virtue. This doth the comedy handle so in our private and domestical matters as with hearing it we get as it were an experience what is to be looked for of a niggardly Demea, of a crafty Davus, of a flattering Gnatho, of a vainglorious Thraso;[7] and not only to know what effects are to be expected, but to know who be such, by the signifying badge given them by the comedian.[8] And little reason hath any man to say that men

---

8. "This I remember, and how Thyrsis, vanquished, strove in vain. / From that day it is Corydon, Corydon with us" (Virgil, *Eclogue* 7.69–70). I.e., the great victory of Alexander the Great over Darius of Persia comes to the same thing as Corydon's victory over Thyrsis in a singing contest.
9. Ancient Greek philosopher who wept at human folly. "Who": i.e., which.
1. Sidney restricts the elegiac to lamentations; classical poets used elegiac meter for this purpose but also in poems treating love and other topics.
2. Iambic trimeter was first used by Greek poets for direct attacks (as opposed to the wit and ironic indirection that mark satire).
3. Persius (*Satires* 1.116) on the satire of Horace, who "probes every fault while making his friends

laugh." "Naughtiness": wickedness.
4. "He plays with the very vitals [of his target]" (Persius, *Satires* 1.117).
5. "It is at Ulubrae, if a well-balanced mind does not fail us" (an adaptation of Horace, *Epistles* 1.11.30). Ulubrae was a proverbially uninspiring town surrounded by marshes.
6. Is lacking. "Who": whoever.
7. Type characters in the Roman comedies of Terence (195–159 B.C.E.), respectively, the harsh father, clever servant, parasite, and braggart. Terence and Plautus (251–184 B.C.E.) were the chief classical models for comedy for the Renaissance. "Niggardly": stingy.
8. Writer of comedies. "Signifying badge": i.e., stereotypical features of looks, dress, or behavior.

learn the evil by seeing it so set out, since, as I said before, there is no man living but, by the force truth hath in nature, no sooner seeth these men play their parts, but wisheth them *in pistrinum*;[9] although perchance the sack of his own faults lie so hidden behind his back that he seeth not himself dance the same measure;[1] whereto yet nothing can more open his eyes than to find his own actions contemptibly set forth.

So that the right use of comedy will (I think) by nobody be blamed; and much less of the high and excellent Tragedy, that openeth the greatest wounds, and showeth forth the ulcers that are covered with tissue;[2] that maketh kings fear to be tyrants, and tyrants manifest their tyrannical humors; that, with stirring the affects of admiration[3] and commiseration, teacheth the uncertainty of this world, and upon how weak foundations gilden roofs are builded; that maketh us know

> Qui sceptra saevus duro imperio regit
> Timet timentes; metus in auctorem redit.[4]

But how much it can move, Plutarch yieldeth a notable testimony of the abominable tyrant Alexander Pheraeus,[5] from whose eyes a tragedy, well made and represented, drew abundance of tears, who without all pity had murdered infinite numbers, and some of his own blood: so as he, that was not ashamed to make matters for tragedies, yet could not resist the sweet violence of a tragedy. And if it wrought no further good in him, it was that he, in despite of himself, withdrew himself from hearkening to that which might mollify his hardened heart. But it is not the tragedy they do mislike; for it were too absurd to cast out so excellent a representation of whatsoever is most worthy to be learned.

Is it the Lyric[6] that most displeaseth, who with his tuned lyre and well-accorded voice giveth praise, the reward of virtue, to virtuous acts; who gives moral precepts, and natural problems;[7] who sometimes raiseth up his voice to the height of the heavens, in singing the lauds[8] of the immortal God? Certainly, I must confess my own barbarousness, I never heard the old song of Percy and Douglas[9] that I found not my heart moved more than with a trumpet; and yet is it sung but by some blind crowder,[1] with no rougher voice than rude style; which, being so evil appareled in the dust and cobwebs of that uncivil age, what would it work trimmed in the gorgeous eloquence of Pindar?[2] In Hungary I have seen it the manner at all feasts, and other such meetings, to have songs of their ancestors' valor, which that right soldierlike nation think one of the chiefest kindlers of brave courage. The incomparable Lacedemonians[3] did not only carry that kind of music ever

---

9. Mill used for punishment of Roman slaves.
1. In a fable of Aesop, a sack filled with one's own faults is carried (out of sight) on the back, while one filled with the faults of others is carried in front.
2. Rich fabrics.
3. Awe. "Humors": natures or dispositions, as thought to be influenced by the balance of four chief bodily fluids, or humors—blood, phlegm, choler, and bile. "Affects": feelings.
4. "He who rules his people with a harsh government / Fears those who fear him; the fear returns upon its author" (Seneca, *Oedipus*, lines 705–6).
5. Plutarch records that this cruel tyrant wept at the sufferings of Hecuba and Andromache in

Euripides' *Trojan Women*. Ashamed to be seen weeping, he abruptly left the theater.
6. Here defined as poetry concerned chiefly with praise, and sung (originally) to musical accompaniment.
7. Discussions of problems of natural philosophy (the study of nature).
8. Praises.
9. "The Ballad of Chevy Chase."
1. Fiddler.
2. The odes of Pindar (518–after 446 B.C.E.), the most exalted lyric poetry of Greece, celebrated victors in athletic games. "That uncivil age": the Middle Ages.
3. Spartans, incomparable in fighting.

with them to the field, but even at home, as such songs were made, so were they all content to be singers of them—when the lusty men were to tell what they did, the old men what they had done, and the young what they would do. And where a man may say that Pindar many times praiseth highly victories of small moment, matters rather of sport than virtue; as it may be answered, it was the fault of the poet, and not of the poetry, so indeed the chief fault was in the time and custom of the Greeks, who set those toys at so high a price that Philip of Macedon reckoned a horserace won at Olympus among his three fearful felicities.[4] But as the unimitable Pindar often did, so is that kind most capable and most fit to awake the thoughts from the sleep of idleness to embrace honorable enterprises.

There rests the Heroical[5]—whose very name (I think) should daunt all backbiters: for by what conceit[6] can a tongue be directed to speak evil of that which draweth with him no less champions than Achilles, Cyrus, Aeneas, Turnus, Tydeus, and Rinaldo?[7]—who doth not only teach and move to a truth, but teacheth and moveth to the most high and excellent truth; who maketh magnanimity and justice shine through all misty fearfulness and foggy desires; who, if the saying of Plato and Tully be true, that who could see virtue would be wonderfully ravished with the love of her beauty—this man[8] sets her out to make her more lovely in her holiday apparel, to the eye of any that will deign not to disdain until they understand. But if anything be already said in the defense of sweet poetry, all concurreth to the maintaining the heroical, which is not only a kind, but the best and most accomplished kind of poetry. For, as the image of each action stirreth and instructeth the mind, so the lofty image of such worthies most inflameth the mind with desire to be worthy, and informs with counsel how to be worthy. Only let Aeneas be worn in the tablet of your memory, how he governeth himself in the ruin of his country; in the preserving his old father, and carrying away his religious ceremonies;[9] in obeying God's commandment to leave Dido, though not only all passionate kindness, but even the human consideration of virtuous gratefulness, would have craved other of him; how in storms, how in sports, how in war, how in peace, how a fugitive, how victorious, how besieged, how besieging, how to strangers, how to allies, how to enemies, how to his own; lastly, how in his inward self, and how in his outward government—and I think, in a mind not prejudiced with a prejudicating humor, he will be found in excellency fruitful, yea, even as Horace saith,

> melius Chrysippo et Crantore.[1]

But truly I imagine it falleth out with these poet-whippers, as with some good women, who often are sick, but in faith they cannot tell where; so the name of poetry is odious to them, but neither his cause nor effects, neither

---

4. Plutarch records that Philip received three awesome tidings in one day: that his general was victorious in battle, that his wife had borne a son, and that his horse had won a race at Olympia (not, as Sidney mistakenly says, Olympus). "Toys": trifles.
5. I.e., epic. "Rests": remains.
6. Conception.
7. In the Renaissance Italian Ariosto's *Orlando furioso* and his compatriot Tasso's *Gerusalemme liberata*. "Tydeus": in the Roman poet Statius's epic, *Thebaid*.

8. I.e., the epic poet.
9. Sacred objects, household gods. After fleeing Troy, Aeneas and his men stayed for a time in Carthage, whose queen, Dido (below), became Aeneas's lover. She killed herself when Aeneas (at Jupiter's command) sailed away to accomplish his fate, the founding of the Roman empire.
1. In *Epistles* 1.2.4, Horace praises Homer as a "better [teacher] than Chrysippus [a great Stoic philosopher] and Crantor [a commentator on Plato]." "Humor": disposition.

the sum that contains him, nor the particularities descending from him, give any fast[2] handle to their carping dispraise.

Since then poetry is of all human learning the most ancient and of most fatherly antiquity, as from whence other learnings have taken their beginnings; since it is so universal that no learned nation doth despise it, nor barbarous nation is without it; since both Roman and Greek gave such divine names unto it, the one of prophesying, the other of making, and that indeed that name of making is fit for him, considering that where all other arts retain themselves within their subject, and receive, as it were, their being from it, the poet only bringeth his own stuff, and doth not learn a conceit out of a matter, but maketh matter for a conceit; since neither his description nor end containing any evil, the thing described cannot be evil; since his effects be so good as to teach goodness and to delight the learners; since therein (namely in moral doctrine, the chief of all knowledges) he doth not only far pass the historian but, for instructing, is well nigh comparable to the philosopher, for moving leaves him behind him; since the Holy Scripture (wherein there is no uncleanness) hath whole parts in it poetical, and that even our Savior Christ vouchsafed to use the flowers of it; since all his kinds are not only in their united forms but in their severed dissections fully commendable; I think (and think I think rightly) the laurel crown appointed for triumphant captains doth worthily (of all other learnings) honor the poet's triumph.

[ANSWERS TO CHARGES AGAINST POETRY]

But because we have ears as well as tongues, and that the lightest reasons that may be will seem to weigh greatly, if nothing be put in the counterbalance, let us hear and, as well as we can, ponder what objections be made against this art, which may be worthy either of yielding or answering.[3]

First, truly I note not only in these *misomousoi*, poet-haters, but in all that kind of people who seek a praise by dispraising others, that they do prodigally spend a great many wandering words in quips and scoffs, carping and taunting at each thing which, by stirring the spleen,[4] may stay the brain from a through-beholding the worthiness of the subject. Those kind of objections, as they are full of a very idle easiness,[5] since there is nothing of so sacred a majesty but that an itching tongue may rub itself upon it, so deserve they no other answer but, instead of laughing at the jest, to laugh at the jester. We know a playing wit can praise the discretion of an ass, the comfortableness of being in debt, and the jolly commodities of being sick of the plague.[6] So of the contrary side, if we will turn Ovid's verse

Ut lateat virtus proximitate mali,[7]

that good lie hid in nearness of the evil, Agrippa will be as merry in showing the vanity of science[8] as Erasmus was in the commending of folly. Neither shall any man or matter escape some touch of these smiling railers.

---

2. Firm.
3. The sixth part of a judicial oration is the *refutatio*, which, as Thomas Wilson's *Art of Rhetoric* says, is (or attempts to be) "a dissolving or wiping away of all such reasons as make against us."
4. Regarded as the seat of laughter.
5. An empty glibness. "Through-beholding": thorough consideration.

6. Sidney gives several examples of the subjects of mock encomia popular in the classical world and among Renaissance humanists; the greatest of these encomia is Erasmus's *Praise of Folly* (below).
7. *Art of Love* 2.662 (translated just below).
8. Referring to the German scholar Cornelius Agrippa's *Of the Uncertainty and Vanity of the Sciences and the Arts* (1530).

But for Erasmus and Agrippa, they had another foundation than the superficial part would promise. Marry,[9] these other pleasant faultfinders, who will correct the verb before they understand the noun, and confute others' knowledge before they confirm their own—I would have them only remember that scoffing cometh not of wisdom. So as the best title in true English they get with their merriments is to be called good fools; for so have our grave forefathers ever termed that humorous kind of jesters.

But that which giveth greatest scope to their scorning humor is rhyming and versing. It is already said[1] (and, as I think, truly said), it is not rhyming and versing that maketh poesy. One may be a poet without versing, and a versifier without poetry. But yet, presuppose it were inseparable (as indeed it seemeth Scaliger judgeth),[2] truly it were an inseparable commendation. For if *oratio* next to *ratio*, speech next to reason, be the greatest gift bestowed upon mortality,[3] that cannot be praiseless which doth most polish that blessing of speech; which considers each word, not only (as a man may say) by his most forcible quality, but by his best measured quantity,[4] carrying even in themselves a harmony—without,[5] perchance, number, measure, order, proportion be in our time grown odious. But lay aside the just praise it hath, by being the only fit speech for music (music, I say, the most divine striker of the senses), thus much is undoubtedly true, that if reading be foolish without remembering, memory being the only treasure of knowledge,[6] those words which are fittest for memory are likewise most convenient for knowledge. Now, that verse far exceedeth prose in the knitting up of memory, the reason is manifest: the words (besides their delight, which hath a great affinity to memory) being so set as one cannot be lost but the whole work fails; which accusing itself, calleth the remembrance back to itself, and so most strongly confirmeth it. Besides, one word so, as it were, begetting another, as, be it in rhyme or measured verse, by the former a man shall have a near guess to the follower. Lastly, even they that have taught the art of memory have showed nothing so apt for it as a certain room divided into many places well and thoroughly known.[7] Now, that hath the verse in effect perfectly, every word having his natural seat, which seat must needs make the word remembered. But what needeth more, in a thing so known to all men? Who is it that ever was a scholar that doth not carry away some verses of Virgil, Horace, or Cato,[8] which in his youth he learned, and even to his old age serve him for hourly lessons? But the fitness it hath for memory is notably proved by all delivery of arts: wherein for the most part, from grammar to logic, mathematics, physic, and the rest, the rules chiefly necessary to be borne away are compiled in verses.[9] So that, verse being in itself sweet and orderly, and being best for memory, the only handle of knowledge, it must be in jest that any man can speak against it.

9. Interjection expressing surprise or indignation. It is a euphemistic variant of "Mary" (the Virgin).
1. Above, p. 1052. "Humor": disposition.
2. *Poetics* 1.2. (For Scaliger, see above, p. 1049, n. 8.)
3. I.e., reason and speech are the primary distinguishing characteristics of human beings (a commonplace originating in the classical era).
4. I.e., by its accent ("quality") and its duration ("quantity").
5. Unless.
6. Proverbial.

7. Standard systems for memorization involved associating the items to be remembered with particular features of imagined rooms.
8. Referring to the *Distichs of Cato*, which had for centuries been an immensely popular school text of moral advice, most of it embodied in distichs (verse couplets).
9. This pedagogical practice—which still survives in bits and pieces such as alphabet songs—was widespread in the Middle Ages and Renaissance. "Physic": medicine.

Now then go we to the most important imputations laid to the poor poets.[1] For aught I can yet learn, they are these. First, that there being many other more fruitful knowledges, a man might better spend his time in them than in this. Secondly, that it is the mother of lies. Thirdly, that it is the nurse of abuse, infecting us with many pestilent desires; with a siren's sweetness drawing the mind to the serpent's tail of sinful fancies (and herein, especially, comedies give the largest field to ear,[2] as Chaucer saith); how, both in other nations and in ours, before poets did soften us, we were full of courage, given to martial exercises, the pillars of manlike liberty, and not lulled asleep in shady idleness with poets' pastimes. And lastly, and chiefly, they cry out with open mouth as if they had overshot Robin Hood, that Plato banished them out of his commonwealth.[3] Truly, this is much, if there be much truth in it.

First, to the first.[4] That a man might better spend his time, is a reason indeed; but it doth (as they say) but *petere principium*.[5] For if it be as I affirm, that no learning is so good as that which teacheth and moveth to virtue; and that none can both teach and move thereto so much as poetry: then is the conclusion manifest that ink and paper cannot be to a more profitable purpose employed. And certainly, though a man should grant their first assumption, it should follow (methinks) very unwillingly, that good is not good because better is better. But I still and utterly deny that there is sprung out of earth a more fruitful knowledge.

To the second, therefore, that they should be the principal liars, I will answer paradoxically, but truly, I think truly, that of all writers under the sun the poet is the least liar, and, though he would, as a poet can scarcely be a liar. The astronomer, with his cousin the geometrician, can hardly escape,[6] when they take upon them to measure the height of the stars. How often, think you, do the physicians lie, when they aver things good for sicknesses, which afterwards send Charon a great number of souls drowned in a potion[7] before they come to his ferry? And no less of the rest which take upon them to affirm. Now, for the poet, he nothing affirms, and therefore never lieth. For, as I take it, to lie is to affirm that to be true which is false. So as the other artists,[8] and especially the historian, affirming many things, can, in the cloudy knowledge of mankind, hardly escape from many lies. But the poet (as I said before) never affirmeth. The poet never maketh any circles[9] about your imagination, to conjure you to believe for true what he writes. He citeth not authorities of other histories, but even for his entry[1] calleth the sweet Muses to inspire into him a good invention; in truth, not laboring to tell you what is or is not, but what should or should not be. And therefore, though he recount things not true, yet because he telleth them not for true,

---

1. All four of these major charges against poetry are traceable to classical antiquity and continued, in Sidney's time, to be principal items of the stock in trade of imaginative literature's detractors; and many of the points Sidney makes in rebuttal had been made by its previous defenders.
2. To plow ("Knight's Tale," line 28).
3. Plato argued that most sorts of poets would be banished from an ideal commonwealth, because they stir up unworthy emotions and because their imitations are far removed from truth (*Republic* 10.595–608).

4. First objection.
5. Beg the question—i.e., simply *presuppose* a conclusion on the matter in question.
6. I.e., can hardly avoid lying. "Though he would": even if he wished to.
7. I.e., killed by medicine. "Charon": in classical myth, the ferryman who takes the souls of the dead to the River Styx.
8. Practitioners of the liberal arts.
9. As a magician does in conjuring spirits.
1. In his opening lines.

he lieth not—without we will say that Nathan lied in his speech before-alleged to David:[2] which as a wicked man durst scarce say, so think I none so simple would say that Aesop lied in the tales of his beasts; for who thinks that Aesop wrote it for actually true were well worthy to have his name chronicled among the beasts he writeth of. What child is there, that, coming to a play, and seeing *Thebes* written in great letters upon an old door,[3] doth believe that it is Thebes? If then a man can arrive to that child's age to know that the poets' persons and doings are but pictures what should be, and not stories what have been, they will never give the lie to[4] things not affirmatively but allegorically and figuratively written. And therefore, as in history, looking for truth, they may go away full fraught with falsehood, so in poesy, looking but for fiction, they shall use the narration but as an imaginative ground-plot of a profitable invention.[5] But hereto is replied, that the poets give names to men they write of, which argueth a conceit of an actual truth, and so, not being true, proves a falsehood. And doth the lawyer lie, then, when under the names of *John-a-stiles* and *John-a-nokes*[6] he puts his case? But that is easily answered. Their naming of men is but to make their picture the more lively, and not to build any history: painting men, they cannot leave men nameless. We see we cannot play at chess but that we must give names to our chessmen; and yet, methinks, he were a very partial champion of truth that would say we lied for giving a piece of wood the reverend title of a bishop. The poet nameth Cyrus or Aeneas no other way than to show what men of their fames, fortunes, and estates should do.

Their third is, how much it abuseth men's wit,[7] training it to wanton sinfulness and lustful love: for indeed that is the principal, if not only, abuse I can hear alleged. They say, the comedies rather teach than reprehend amorous conceits. They say the lyric is larded with passionate sonnets; the elegiac weeps the want of his mistress; and that even to the heroical, Cupid hath ambitiously climbed.[8] Alas, Love, I would thou couldst as well defend thyself as thou canst offend others. I would those on whom thou dost attend could either put thee away, or yield good reason why they keep thee. But grant love of beauty to be a beastly fault (although it be very hard, since only man, and no beast, hath that gift to discern beauty); grant that lovely name of Love to deserve all hateful reproaches (although even some of my masters the philosophers spent a good deal of their lamp-oil in setting forth the excellency of it);[9] grant, I say, whatsoever they will have granted, that not only love, but lust, but vanity, but (if they list) scurrility, possesseth many leaves of the poets' books; yet think I, when this is granted, they will find their sentence may with good manners put the last words foremost, and not say that poetry abuseth man's wit, but that man's wit abuseth poetry.

For I will not deny but that man's wit may make poesy, which should be *eikastiké* (which some learned have defined: figuring forth good things), to be

---

2. For Nathan's parable, see above, p. 1062. "Without": unless.

3. Thebes is the setting of several classical tragedies.

4. Accuse of lying.

5. I.e., readers will find that poetry's fictions are actually the foundation ("ground-plot") on which are erected "profitable invention[s]"—that is (as above), verbal "pictures [of] what should be."

6. John (who lives) at the stile and John (who lives) at the oak: fictitious names—equivalent to our John and Jane Doe—used in legal proceedings.

7. Mind.

8. I.e., epic is infused with eroticism, as in the Italian romance epics—and in Sidney's own contribution to that genre, *Arcadia*. "Want": lack.

9. Plato, for one, in the *Symposium* and the *Phaedrus*.

phantastiké[1] (which doth, contrariwise, infect the fancy with unworthy objects), as the painter, that should give to the eye either some excellent perspective or some fine picture, fit for building or fortification, or containing in it some notable example (as Abraham sacrificing his son Isaac, Judith killing Holofernes, David fighting with Goliath),[2] may leave those, and please an ill-pleased eye with wanton shows of better hidden matters.[3] But what, shall the abuse of a thing make the right use odious? Nay truly, though I yield that poesy may not only be abused, but that being abused, by the reason of his sweet charming force, it can do more hurt than any other army of words: yet shall it be so far from concluding that the abuse should give reproach to the abused, that, contrariwise, it is a good reason that whatsoever, being abused, doth most harm, being rightly used (and upon the right use each thing conceiveth his title), doth most good. Do we not see the skill of physic, the best rampire[4] to our often-assaulted bodies, being abused, teach poison, the most violent destroyer? Doth not knowledge of law, whose end is to even and right all things, being abused, grow the crooked fosterer of horrible injuries? Doth not (to go to the highest) God's word abused breed heresy, and His name abused become blasphemy? Truly, a needle cannot do much hurt, and as truly (with leave of ladies be it spoken), it cannot do much good: with a sword thou mayst kill thy father, and with a sword thou mayst defend thy prince and country. So that, as in their calling poets fathers of lies they said nothing, so in this their argument of abuse they prove the commendation.

They allege herewith, that before poets began to be in price[5] our nation had set their hearts' delight upon action, and not imagination: rather doing things worthy to be written, than writing things fit to be done. What that before-time was, I think scarcely Sphinx can tell, since no memory is so ancient that hath not the precedent of poetry. And certain it is that, in our plainest homeliness, yet never was the Albion[6] nation without poetry. Marry, this argument, though it be leveled against poetry, yet is it indeed a chainshot[7] against all learning, or bookishness, as they commonly term it. Of such mind were certain Goths, of whom it is written that, having in the spoil of a famous city taken a fair library, one hangman (belike fit to execute the fruits of their wits), who had murdered a great number of bodies, would have set fire in it: no, said another very gravely, take heed what you do, for while they are busy about these toys, we shall with more leisure conquer their countries.[8] This indeed is the ordinary doctrine of ignorance, and many words sometimes I have heard spent in it. But because this reason is generally against all learning as well as poetry, or rather, all learning but poetry; because it were too large a digression to handle it, or at least too

---

1. Plato's distinction, *Sophist* 236: *eikastiké*: making likenesses; *phantastiké*: making fantasies.
2. Abraham and Isaac: Genesis 21–22; David and Goliath: 1 Samuel 17. The story of the Israelite Judith decapitating the Assyrian general Holofernes while he lay in a drunken stupor is in Chapters 10–13 of the Book of Judith—a book included in the Roman Catholic and Eastern Orthodox versions of the Old Testament but excluded from the Jewish version and relegated to the Apocrypha by Protestants.
3. Matters better to remain hidden. "Ill-pleased eye": eye pleased by evil sights.
4. Rampart; defense. "Conceiveth his title":

receives its justification.
5. Honor, esteem.
6. Ancient name for Britain.
7. Two cannon balls linked by a chain, to do maximum damage.
8. This story of the Goths (a Germanic tribe)—relating to their sack of Athens in 267 C.E.—derives from the continuation of the *Roman History* of Dio Cassius. Sidney's near-contemporary Montaigne also records the story, in "Of Pedantry" (*Essays* 1.25)—though he deploys it in *support* of the view that book learning and martial prowess are inversely related. "Hangman": here used as a term of general abuse, equivalent to "villain."

superfluous (since it is manifest that all government of action is to be gotten by knowledge, and knowledge best by gathering many knowledges, which is reading), I only, with Horace, to him that is of that opinion

> jubeo stultum esse libenter;[9]

for as for poetry itself, it is the freest from this objection.

For poetry is the companion of camps. I dare undertake, Orlando Furioso[1] or honest King Arthur will never displease a soldier; but the quiddity of *ens* and *prima materia* will hardly agree with a corslet;[2] and therefore, as I said in the beginning, even Turks and Tartars are delighted with poets. Homer, a Greek, flourished before Greece flourished. And if to a slight conjecture a conjecture may be opposed, truly it may seem, that as by him their learned men took almost their first light of knowledge, so their active men received their first motions of courage. Only Alexander's example[3] may serve, who by Plutarch is accounted of such virtue that Fortune was not his guide but his footstool; whose acts speak for him, though[4] Plutarch did not: indeed the phoenix of warlike princes. This Alexander left his schoolmaster, living Aristotle, behind him, but took dead Homer with him.[5] He put the philosopher Callisthenes to death for his seeming philosophical, indeed mutinous, stubbornness, but the chief thing he was ever heard to wish for was that Homer had been alive.[6] He well found he received more bravery of mind by the pattern of Achilles than by hearing the definition of fortitude. And therefore, if Cato misliked Fulvius for carrying Ennius with him to the field,[7] it may be answered that, if Cato misliked it, the noble Fulvius liked it, or else he had not done it; for it was not the excellent Cato Uticensis[8] (whose authority I would much more have reverenced), but it was the former, in truth a bitter punisher of faults (but else a man that had never well sacrificed to the Graces:[9] he misliked and cried out against all Greek learning, and yet, being eighty years old, began to learn it, belike fearing that Pluto[1] understood not Latin). Indeed, the Roman laws allowed no person to be carried to the wars but he that was in the soldiers' roll; and therefore, though Cato misliked his unmustered person, he misliked not his work.[2] And if he had, Scipio Nasica, judged by common consent the best Roman,[3] loved him. Both the other

9. "I bid him be a fool as much as he likes" (adapting *Satires* 1.1.63).
1. See above, p. 1050 and n. 8. "Camps": i.e., military encampments.
2. Body armor. "The quiddity of *ens* and *prima materia*": the essential nature of "being" and "first matter"—terms in Scholastic philosophy.
3. I.e., the example of Alexander the Great alone. Plutarch's estimate of him (below) is in his *Lives* and, in his *Moral Essays*, the two tracts *On the Fortune or the Virtue of Alexander*. "Motions": promptings.
4. Even if.
5. Plutarch, *Life of Alexander* 8, says Alexander (who had Aristotle as his tutor) took the *Iliad* with him everywhere.
6. Plutarch, *How a Man may Become Aware of His Progress in Virtue* 16. Callisthenes, Aristotle's relative, and both a philosopher and a historian, accompanied Alexander on his expedition to India.
7. The Roman general Fulvius took the poet Ennius (above, p. 1047, n. 9) with him on a military expedition to Greece. The stern moralist Cato

the Elder (234–149 B.C.E.) disapproved. The story was often repeated by poetry's detractors.
8. Cato of Utica (great-grandson of Cato the Elder), hugely admired as the epitome of Roman Stoic virtue.
9. I.e., he was not a cultured person. (The three Graces were sister deities who personified grace and beauty.) "Else": otherwise.
1. God of the Underworld (whither Cato, at 80, was soon bound). To undermine the authority of this prestigious enemy of poetry, Sidney does not scruple to employ *argumentum ad hominem* and mockery (as also with Plato, below). The story of Cato's late acquisition of Greek is from Plutarch's *Life* (2).
2. A different explanation for Cato's objection to Ennius's accompanying Fulvius: it was against Roman law for an "unmustered" person (i.e., one not formally enrolled as a soldier) to go on a military mission. But one cannot logically draw from that fact the conclusion that Cato did not dislike Ennius's poetry.
3. The Roman Senate so judged him, in 204 B.C.E. (Livy, *From the Foundation of the City* 29.14).

Scipio brothers, who had by their virtues no less surnames than of Asia and Afric,[4] so loved him that they caused his body to be buried in their sepulture. So as Cato's authority, being but against his person, and that answered with so far greater than himself, is herein of no validity.

But now indeed my burden is great; now Plato's name is laid upon me, whom, I must confess, of all philosophers I have ever esteemed most worthy of reverence, and with good reason: since of all philosophers he is the most poetical.[5] Yet if he will defile the fountain out of which his flowing streams have proceeded, let us boldly examine with what reasons he did it. First, truly, a man might maliciously object that Plato, being a philosopher, was a natural enemy of poets. For indeed, after the philosophers had picked out of the sweet mysteries of poetry the right discerning true points of knowledge, they forthwith putting it in method, and making a school-art of that which the poets did only teach by a divine delightfulness, beginning to spurn at their guides, like ungrateful prentices,[6] were not content to set up shops for themselves, but sought by all means to discredit their masters; which by the force of delight being barred them, the less they could overthrow them, the more they hated them. For indeed, they found for Homer seven cities strave who should have him for their citizen; where many cities banished philosophers as not fit members to live among them.[7] For only repeating certain of Euripides' verses, many Athenians had their lives saved of the Syracusans, where the Athenians themselves thought many philosophers unworthy to live.[8] Certain poets, as Simonides and Pindar, had so prevailed with Hiero the First that of a tyrant they made him a just king; where Plato could do so little with Dionysius that he himself of a philosopher was made a slave.[9] But who should do thus, I confess, should requite the objections made against poets with like cavilations[1] against philosophers; as likewise one should do that should bid one read *Phaedrus* or *Symposium* in Plato, or the discourse of love in Plutarch, and see whether any poet do authorize abominable filthiness, as they do.[2] Again, a man might ask out of what commonwealth Plato did banish them: in sooth, thence where he himself alloweth community of women[3]—so as belike this banishment grew not for effeminate wantonness, since little should poetical sonnets be hurtful, when a man might have what woman he listed.[4] But I honor philosophical instructions, and bless the wits which bred them: so as they be not abused, which is likewise stretched to poetry.

4. Scipio Africanus (granted that cognomen as conqueror of Hannibal) and Scipio Asiaticus (conqueror of the Seleucid emperor Antiochus III, in Asia Minor). Cousins (not brothers) of Scipio Nasica, both were patrons of Ennius.

5. See above, p. 1047.

6. Apprentices.

7. Among the several philosophers banished from their native cities were Empedocles and Protagoras. Cicero's oration on behalf of the poet Archias (8.19) is one of the sources for the claim that seven cities competed for Homer.

8. Whatever the Athenians may have "thought," the only philosopher they are known to have executed was Socrates (though the sophist Prodicus of Ceos was sometimes said to have been executed with him). Plutarch's *Life of Nicias* (29) says that many members of an Athenian army defeated by the army of Syracuse were afterward spared because of the Sicilians' love for the writings of the Athenians' compatriot Euripides.

9. Plato visited the Syracusan tyrant Dionysius I, but fell out with him and, according to legend, was through his contrivances sold into slavery (from which he was rescued by friends). By contrast, the poets Simonides (556–468 B.C.E.) and Pindar enjoyed the patronage of Dionysius's predecessor Hiero I, whose court was a center of art and literature.

1. Faultfinding. "Who should do thus": anyone who would argue in this (ad hominem) fashion—as Sidney has, of course, just done (and proceeds to do again, just below).

2. Parts of Plato's dialogues *Phaedrus* and *Symposium*, and of Plutarch's dialogue *On Love*, exalt male homosexual love.

3. In *Republic* 5, Plato has Socrates argue that the ruling class in his ideal commonwealth would share all things, including women, communally.

4. Pleased.

St. Paul himself (who yet, for the credit of poets, twice citeth poets, and one of them by the name of "their prophet") setteth a watchword upon philosophy[5]— indeed upon the abuse. So doth Plato upon the abuse, not upon poetry. Plato found fault that the poets of his time filled the world with wrong opinions of the gods, making light tales of that unspotted essence, and therefore would not have the youth depraved with such opinions.[6] Herein may much be said. Let this suffice: the poets did not induce such opinions, but did imitate those opinions already induced. For all the Greek stories can well testify that the very religion of that time stood upon many and many-fashioned gods, not taught so by the poets, but followed according to their nature of imitation. Who list may read in Plutarch the discourses of Isis and Osiris, of the cause why oracles ceased, of the divine providence,[7] and see whether the theology of that nation stood not upon such dreams, which the poets indeed superstitiously observed— and truly (since they had not the light of Christ) did much better in it than the philosophers, who, shaking off superstition, brought in atheism. Plato, therefore (whose authority I had much rather justly construe than unjustly resist), meant not in general of poets, in those words of which Julius Scaliger saith *Qua authoritate barbari quidam atque hispidi abuti velint ad poetas e republica exigendos*,[8] but only meant to drive out those wrong opinions of the Deity (whereof now, without further law,[9] Christianity hath taken away all the hurtful belief) perchance (as he thought) nourished by the then esteemed poets. And a man need go no further than to Plato himself to know his meaning: who, in his dialogue called *Ion*, giveth high and rightly divine commendation unto poetry.[1] So as Plato, banishing the abuse, not the thing; not banishing it, but giving due honor unto it, shall be our patron, and not our adversary. For indeed I had much rather (since truly I may do it) show their mistaking of Plato (under whose lion's skin they would make an ass-like braying against poesy)[2] than go about to overthrow his authority; whom the wiser a man is, the more just cause he shall find to have in admiration; especially since he attributeth unto poesy more than myself do,[3] namely, to be a very inspiring of a divine force, far above man's wit, as in the forenamed dialogue is apparent.

Of the other side, who would show the honors have been by the best sort of judgments granted them, a whole sea of examples would present themselves: Alexanders, Caesars, Scipios, all favorers of poets; Laelius, called the Roman Socrates, himself a poet, so as part of *Heautontimorumenos* in Terence was supposed to be made by him;[4] and even the Greek Socrates, whom Apollo confirmed to be the only wise man, is said to have spent part of his

---

5. A word of warning against philosophy (in Colossians 2.8). "Their prophet": see Titus 1.12. Paul's other citation of poets comes in Acts 17.28.
6. This is Plato's objection to poetry in *Republic* 2, and Sidney answers it well. But he entirely ignores the far more profound objection in 10.595–608, where Plato argues that artistic mimesis in general is at the "third remove" (597) from the true nature of things (being an imitation of the physical world, which is itself a poor imitation of the realm of the Platonic Forms) and that poetry in particular "has no serious value or claim to truth" (608).
7. Sidney gives English versions of the titles of three of Plutarch's *Moral Essays*.
8. "Which authority certain barbarians and uncivilized persons seek to misuse in order to have poets banned from the state" (*Poetics* 1.2).

9. Without further ado.
1. In the *Ion*, Plato argues that poets are divinely inspired. The argument is now regarded as ironic, but in Sidney's day it was taken seriously.
2. Referring to Aesop's fable of the ass masquerading as a lion.
3. Cf. above, pp. 1048–49, where Sidney, departing from the main trend of 16th-century poetics, avoids claiming that any poetry other than that of the Bible is divinely inspired.
4. Gaius Laelius (2nd century B.C.E.) was an orator and intellectual much admired by Cicero, who compared him to Socrates and noted that many people ascribed the plays of Terence in whole or in part to him. In the prologues to *Heauton timorumenos* (The Self-Tormentor) and *The Brothers*, Terence himself hints at his debts to Laelius.

old time in putting Aesop's fables into verses.[5] And therefore, full evil should it become his scholar Plato to put such words in his master's mouth against poets. But what need more? Aristotle writes the Art of Poesy; and why, if it should not be written? Plutarch teacheth the use to be gathered of them; and how, if they should not be read? And who reads Plutarch's either history or philosophy shall find he trimmeth both their garments with guards[6] of poesy. But I list not to defend poesy with the help of his underling historiography. Let it suffice to have showed it is a fit soil for praise to dwell upon; and what dispraise may be set upon it is either easily overcome or transformed into just commendation.

So that, since the excellencies of it may be so easily and so justly confirmed, and the low-creeping objections so soon trodden down: it not being an art of lies, but of true doctrine;[7] not of effeminateness, but of notable stirring of courage; not of abusing man's wit, but of strengthening man's wit; not banished, but honored by Plato: let us rather plant more laurels for to engarland the poets' heads (which honor of being laureate, whereas besides them only triumphant captains were, is a sufficient authority to show the price they ought to be held in) than suffer the ill-savored breath of such wrong-speakers once to blow upon the clear springs of poesy.

[POETRY IN ENGLAND]

But since I have run so long a career[8] in this matter, methinks, before I give my pen a full stop, it shall be but a little more lost time to inquire why England, the mother of excellent minds, should be grown so hard a stepmother to poets, who certainly in wit[9] ought to pass all other, since all only proceedeth from their wit, being indeed makers of themselves, not takers of others.[1] How can I but exclaim

Musa, mihi causas memora, quo numine laeso?[2]

Sweet poesy, that hath anciently had kings, emperors, senators, great captains, such as, besides a thousand others, David, Adrian, Sophocles, Germanicus, not only to favor poets, but to be poets;[3] and of our nearer times can present for her patrons a Robert, king of Sicily, the great King Francis of France, King James of Scotland; such cardinals as Bembus and Bibbiena; such famous preachers and teachers as Beza and Melanchthon; so learned philosophers as Fracastorius and Scaliger; so great orators as Pontanus and Muretus; so piercing wits as George Buchanan;[4] so grave counsellors as,

---

5. According to Plato, *Phaedo* 60, and Plutarch, *How to Study Poetry* 16. Apollo confirmed Socrates to be the wisest of men through his oracle at Delphi.

6. Ornamental borders. "Plutarch's either history or philosophy": i.e., either Plutarch's *Parallel Lives* (of notable Greeks and Romans) or his *Moral Essays*.

7. Teaching.

8. Course.

9. Intellect.

1. Rhetorical theory allowed for a *digressio* following the *refutatio*, and Sidney's lengthy digression—on the very pertinent topic of why English poetry is, in his time, in such poor repute—has itself the form of an oration, comprising a narration, proposition (see below: "the very true cause of our wanting estimation is

want of desert": we lack esteem because we don't *deserve* it), division (into "matter" and "words"), and confirmation.

2. The beginning of the invocation of the *Aeneid* (1.8): "Tell me, O Muse, the cause: by what offense to the deity . . . ?"

3. Four military leaders who wrote poetry: the biblical King David; the Roman emperor Hadrian; the tragedian Sophocles (who in 440 B.C.E. was appointed a general for Athens in its war against Samos); Germanicus (15 B.C.E.–19 C.E.), commander of the Roman troops against the Germans.

4. *Kings*: Robert II of Anjou; Francis I; probably James I. *Cardinals*: Pietro Bembo (who figures in Castiglione's *Courtier*, above, pp. 704, 707ff.) and Bernardo Dovizi, cardinal of Bibbiena, in Italy. *Preachers*: Théodore de Bèze and Philip Melan-

beside many, but before all, that Hôpital of France, than whom (I think) that realm never brought forth a more accomplished judgment, more firmly builded upon virtue: I say these, with numbers of others, not only to read others' poesies, but to poetize for others' reading—that poesy, thus embraced in all other places, should only find in our time a hard welcome in England, I think the very earth lamenteth it, and therefore decketh our soil with fewer laurels than it was accustomed.[5] For heretofore poets have in England also flourished, and, which is to be noted, even in those times when the trumpet of Mars did sound loudest.[6] And now that an overfaint quietness should seem to strew the house for poets, they are almost in as good reputation as the mountebanks at Venice.[7] Truly even that, as of the one side it giveth great praise to poesy, which like Venus (but to better purpose) had rather be troubled in the net with Mars than enjoy the homely quiet of Vulcan:[8] so serves it for a piece of a reason why they are less grateful[9] to idle England, which now can scarce endure the pain of a pen.

Upon this necessarily followeth that base men with servile wits undertake it, who think it enough if they can be rewarded of the printer. And so as Epaminondas is said with the honor of his virtue to have made an office, by his exercising it, which before was contemptible, to become highly respected;[1] so these men, no more but setting their names to it, by their own disgracefulness disgrace the most graceful poesy. For now, as if all the Muses were got with child to bring forth bastard poets, without any commission they do post over the banks of Helicon,[2] till they make the readers more weary than post-horses; while in the meantime they

Queis meliore luto finxit praecordia Titan[3]

are better content to suppress the outflowings of their wit than, by publishing them, to be accounted knights of the same order. But I that, before ever I durst aspire unto the dignity, am admitted into the company of the paper-blurrers, do find the very true cause of our wanting estimation is want of desert—taking upon us to be poets in despite of Pallas.[4]

Now, wherein we want desert were a thankworthy labor to express; but if I knew, I should have mended myself. But I, as I never desired the title, so have I neglected the means to come by it. Only, overmastered by some thoughts, I yielded an inky tribute unto them. Marry, they that delight in poesy itself

---

chthon, both professors of Greek who became important Protestant reformers. *Philosophers:* Girolamo Fracastorio, author of medical and scientific works (some of them in verse); Scaliger: see above, p. 1049, n. 8. *Orators:* Giovanni Pontano, diplomat and writer; Marc-Antoine Muret, humanist scholar and poet. Also: Buchanan: eminent Scottish humanist and Latin poet; Michel de l'Hôpital (below), chancellor of France.
5. I.e., England now has fewer poets (whose success is traditionally rewarded with a laurel crown) than in the past.
6. I.e., when England had its most notable wars.
7. Venice's notorious quick-tongued hucksters of quack medicines and other trifles. For a wonderful simulation, see Ben Jonson's *Volpone* 2.2 (below, pp. 1443–1539). "Strew the house": i.e., prepare a welcome, by strewing fresh rushes (a standard floor covering).
8. Venus was caught in adultery with Mars by her

husband, the blacksmith god Vulcan, who concealed a net under the bed and then hoisted the amorous couple into the air *in flagrante delicto* (*Odyssey* 8.266–366).
9. Agreeable.
1. The Theban general Epaminondas (d. 362 B.C.E.) conferred dignity on the office of telearch (chief street cleaner).
2. Like many others, Sidney confuses Mt. Helicon (sacred to the Muses) with Hippocrene—a fountain on it said to have been created by the hoof of Pegasus, the winged horse of poetic flight. "Post": ride fast.
3. "Whose hearts the Titan [Prometheus] has made of better clay" (Juvenal, *Satires* 14.35). "Post-horses": used in relay by postal couriers or kept for hire, thus often ridden to exhaustion.
4. I.e., without wisdom (of which Pallas Athena is goddess). "Wanting estimation": lacking esteem.

should seek to know what they do, and how they do; and especially look themselves in an unflattering glass of reason, if they be inclinable unto it. For poesy must not be drawn by the ears; it must be gently led, or rather it must lead—which was partly the cause that made the ancient-learned affirm it was a divine gift, and no human skill: since all other knowledges lie ready for any that hath strength of wit. A poet no industry can make, if his own genius be not carried into it; and therefore it is an old proverb, *orator fit, poeta nascitur.*[5]

Yet confess I always that as the fertilest ground must be manured, so must the highest-flying wit have a Daedalus[6] to guide him. That Daedalus, they say, both in this and in other, hath three wings to bear itself up into the air of due commendation: that is, art, imitation, and exercise.[7] But these, neither artificial rules nor imitative patterns, we much cumber ourselves withal. Exercise indeed we do, but that very forebackwardly: for where we should exercise to know, we exercise as having known; and so is our brain delivered of much matter which never was begotten by knowledge. For there being two principal parts, matter to be expressed by words and words to express the matter, in neither we use art or imitation rightly. Our matter is *quodlibet* indeed, though wrongly performing Ovid's verse,

Quicquid conabor dicere, versus erit;[8]

never marshaling it into any assured rank, that almost the readers cannot tell where to find themselves.

Chaucer, undoubtedly, did excellently in his *Troilus and Criseyde;* of whom, truly, I know not whether to marvel more, either that he in that misty time could see so clearly, or that we in this clear age go so stumblingly after him. Yet had he great wants,[9] fit to be forgiven in so reverent an antiquity. I account the *Mirror of Magistrates* meetly[1] furnished of beautiful parts, and in the earl of Surrey's lyrics many things tasting of a noble birth, and worthy of a noble mind. The *Shepherds' Calendar*[2] hath much poetry in his eclogues, indeed worthy the reading, if I be not deceived. (That same framing of his style to an old rustic language I dare not allow, since neither Theocritus in Greek, Virgil in Latin, nor Sannazzaro in Italian did affect it.[3]) Besides these I do not remember to have seen but few (to speak boldly) printed that have poetical sinews in them; for proof whereof, let but most of the verses be put in prose, and then ask the meaning, and it will be found that one verse did but beget another, without ordering at the first what should be at the last; which becomes a confused mass of words, with a tingling[4] sound of rhyme, barely accompanied with reason.

Our tragedies and comedies (not without cause cried out against), observing rules neither of honest civility nor skillful poetry—excepting *Gorboduc*[5]

---

5. An orator is made; a poet is born.
6. In classical mythology, a great artificer, who invented wings of wax for himself and his son, Icarus. Ignoring his father's instructions, Icarus flew too close to the sun, melted his wings, and fell into the sea. "Manured": cultivated.
7. The tripartite prescription for mastery advocated especially in rhetorical theory.
8. "Whatever I try to say will turn to verse" (Ovid, *Tristia* 4.10.26). "*Quodlibet*": what you will.
9. Deficiencies.
1. Properly. *The Mirror for Magistrates* (first edition 1559) was a large collection of poems on

the downfall of princes and other notables.
2. Spenser's first major work (1579), a set of pastoral poems ("eclogues") dedicated to Sidney. See above, p. 769; for Surrey, see p. 661.
3. I.e., none of the great models for pastoral poetry offered a precedent for Spenser's archaic diction. This is, however, not strictly true of Theocritus and Virgil.
4. Tinkling.
5. Senecan tragedy by Thomas Sackville and Thomas Norton (1561): the earliest English tragedy written in blank verse. "Honest civility": decency.

(again, I say, of those that I have seen), which notwithstanding as it is full of stately speeches and well-sounding phrases, climbing to the height of Seneca's style,[6] and as full of notable morality, which it doth most delightfully teach, and so obtain the very end of poesy, yet in truth it is very defectuous in the circumstances, which grieveth me, because it might not remain as an exact model of all tragedies. For it is faulty both in place and time, the two necessary companions of all corporal actions. For where the stage should always represent but one place, and the uttermost time presupposed in it should be, both by Aristotle's precept and common reason, but one day, there is both many days, and many places, inartificially[7] imagined.

But if it be so in *Gorboduc*, how much more in all the rest, where you shall have Asia of the one side and Afric of the other, and so many other underkingdoms that the player, when he cometh in, must ever begin with telling where he is, or else the tale will not be conceived? Now you shall have three ladies walk to gather flowers: and then we must believe the stage to be a garden. By and by we hear news of shipwreck in the same place: and then we are to blame if we accept it not for a rock. Upon the back of that comes out a hideous monster with fire and smoke: and then the miserable beholders are bound to take it for a cave. While in the meantime two armies fly in, represented with four swords and bucklers: and then what hard heart will not receive it for a pitched field?[8]

Now, of time they are much more liberal: for ordinary it is that two young princes fall in love; after many traverses,[9] she is got with child, delivered of a fair boy; he is lost, groweth a man, falls in love, and is ready to get another child; and all this in two hours' space: which, how absurd it is in sense, even sense may imagine, and art hath taught, and all ancient examples justified— and at this day, the ordinary players in Italy will not err in. Yet will some bring in an example of *Eunuchus* in Terence, that containeth matter of two days,[1] yet far short of twenty years. True it is, and so was it to be played in two days, and so fitted to the time it set forth. And though Plautus have in one place done amiss,[2] let us hit with him, and not miss with him.

But they will say: How then shall we set forth a story which containeth both many places and many times? And do they not know that a tragedy is tied to the laws of poesy, and not of history; not bound to follow the story, but having liberty either to feign a quite new matter or to frame the history to the most tragical conveniency? Again, many things may be told which cannot be showed, if they know the difference betwixt reporting and representing. As, for example, I may speak (though I am here) of Peru, and in speech digress from that to the description of Calicut; but in action I cannot represent it without Pacolet's horse;[3] and so was the manner the ancients took, by some *Nuntius*[4] to recount things done in former time or other place. Lastly, if they

---

6. The highly declamatory and relentlessly moralizing Roman tragedies of Seneca (ca. 4 B.C.E.— 65 C.E.) were models of the grand tragic style in the Renaissance.
7. Inartistically. Sidney here voices the Renaissance commonplace (erroneously derived from Aristotle's *Poetics*) that tragedies should observe the "three unities": of time (one day), place (one locale), and action (one plot). Aristotle insisted only on unity of action (though he does observe that most tragedies take place within a 24-hour span: *Poetics* 5).

8. Battle. "Bucklers": shields.
9. Difficulties, mishaps.
1. In point of fact, the action of Terence's *Eunuch* takes place in a single day. Sidney is probably confusing it with another of Terence's plays, *The Self-Tormentor*.
2. Plautus's *Captives* does not fulfill the unity of time.
3. A flying horse in the French romance *Valentine and Orson* (1489). "Calicut": a seaport on the southwest coast of India.
4. Messenger.

will represent a history, they must not (as Horace saith) begin *ab ovo*;[5] but they must come to the principal point of that one action which they will represent.

By example this will be best expressed. I have a story of young Polydorus,[6] delivered for safety's sake, with great riches, by his father Priam to Polymnestor, king of Thrace, in the Trojan war time; he, after some years, hearing the overthrow of Priam, for to make the treasure his own, murdereth the child; the body of the child is taken up by Hecuba;[7] she, the same day, findeth a sleight[8] to be revenged most cruelly of the tyrant. Where now would one of our tragedy writers begin, but with the delivery of the child? Then should he sail over into Thrace, and so spend I know not how many years, and travel numbers of places. But where doth Euripides? Even with the finding of the body, leaving the rest to be told by the spirit of Polydorus. This need no further to be enlarged; the dullest wit may conceive it.

But besides these gross absurdities, how all their plays be neither right tragedies nor right comedies, mingling kings and clowns, not because the matter so carrieth it, but thrust in the clown by head and shoulders to play a part in majestical matters with neither decency nor discretion,[9] so as neither the admiration and commiseration, nor the right sportfulness,[1] is by their mongrel tragi-comedy obtained. I know Apuleius[2] did somewhat so, but that is a thing recounted with space of time, not represented in one moment; and I know the ancients have one or two examples of tragi-comedies, as Plautus hath *Amphitruo*;[3] but, if we mark them well, we shall find that they never, or very daintily, match hornpipes[4] and funerals. So falleth it out that, having indeed no right comedy, in that comical part of our tragedy, we have nothing but scurrility, unworthy of any chaste ears, or some extreme show of doltishness, indeed fit to lift up a loud laughter, and nothing else: where the whole tract of a comedy should be full of delight, as the tragedy should be still maintained in a well-raised admiration.

But our comedians think there is no delight without laughter; which is very wrong, for though laughter may come with delight, yet cometh it not of delight, as though delight should be the cause of laughter; but well may one thing breed both together. Nay, rather in themselves they have, as it were, a kind of contrariety: for delight we scarcely do but in things that have a conveniency[5] to ourselves or to the general nature; laughter almost ever cometh of things most disproportioned to ourselves and nature. Delight hath a joy in it, either permanent or present. Laughter hath only a scornful tickling.

For example, we are ravished with delight to see a fair woman, and yet are far from being moved to laughter; we laugh at deformed creatures, wherein certainly we cannot delight. We delight in good chances, we laugh at mischances: we delight to hear the happiness of our friends, or country, at which he were worthy to be laughed at that would laugh; we shall, contrarily, laugh sometimes to find a matter quite mistaken and go down the hill against the

---

5. From the beginning; literally, from the egg (*Art of Poetry*, line 147).
6. In Euripides' *Hecuba*.
7. Priam and Hecuba were king and queen of Troy.
8. Trick, contrivance.
9. Sidney regards English tragicomedy as violating the rhetorical precept of *decorum*. But earlier (p. 1062) he had, in principle, approved of mixed genres. "Decency": appropriateness.

1. Effect proper to comedy, as "admiration and commiseration" are proper to tragedy.
2. Roman author of *The Golden Ass*, a satirical romance (2nd century C.E.).
3. *Amphitruo* is tragicomic only in that it contains gods and heroes; otherwise it is pure comedy.
4. Merry tunes for country dances. "Mark them well": inspect them carefully. "Daintily": reluctantly.
5. Agreement, correspondence.

bias[6] in the mouth of some such men—as for the respect of them one shall be heartily sorry, he cannot choose but laugh, and so is rather pained than delighted with laughter.

Yet deny I not but that they may go well together. For as in Alexander's picture well set out we delight without laughter, and in twenty mad antics we laugh without delight; so in Hercules, painted with his great beard and furious countenance, in a woman's attire, spinning at Omphale's command-ment,[7] it breedeth both delight and laughter: for the representing of so strange a power in love procureth delight, and the scornfulness of the action stirreth laughter. But I speak to this purpose, that all the end of the comical part be not upon such scornful matters as stir laughter only, but, mixed with it, that delightful teaching which is the end of poesy. And the great fault even in that point of laughter, and forbidden plainly by Aristotle,[8] is that they stir laughter in sinful things, which are rather execrable than ridicu-lous, or in miserable, which are rather to be pitied than scorned. For what is it to make folks gape at a wretched beggar and a beggarly clown; or, against law of hospitality, to jest at strangers, because they speak not English so well as we do? What do we learn, since it is certain

> Nil habet infelix paupertas durius in se,
> Quam quod ridiculos homines facit?[9]

But rather, a busy loving courtier and a heartless threatening Thraso; a self-wise-seeming schoolmaster; an awry-transformed traveler. These, if we saw walk in stage names, which we play naturally,[1] therein were delightful laugh-ter, and teaching delightfulness—as in the other, the tragedies of Buchanan[2] do justly bring forth a divine admiration.

But I have lavished out too many words of this play matter. I do it because, as they are excelling parts of poesy, so is there none so much used in England, and none can be more pitifully abused; which, like an unmannerly daughter showing a bad education, causeth her mother Poesy's honesty[3] to be called in question.

Other sort of poetry almost have we none, but that lyrical kind of songs and sonnets: which, Lord, if He gave us so good minds, how well it might be employed, and with how heavenly fruit, both private and public, in singing the praises of the immortal beauty: the immortal goodness of that God who giveth us hands to write and wits to conceive; of which we might well want words, but never matter; of which we could turn our eyes to nothing, but we should ever have new-budding occasions. But truly many of such writings as come under the banner of unresistible love, if I were a mistress, would never persuade me they were in love: so coldly they apply fiery speeches, as men that had rather read lovers' writings—and so caught up certain swell-ing phrases which hang together like a man that once told my father that the wind was at northwest and by south, because he would be sure to name winds enough—than that in truth they feel those passions, which easily (as

6. End in unexpected disaster, as when in the game of bowls a slope deflects the ball from its course, or "bias."
7. Hercules, infatuated with Omphale, queen of Lydia, submitted to be dressed as her female slave and to spin wool.
8. In *Poetics* 5.

9. "Unfortunate poverty has in itself no thing harder to bear than that it makes men ridiculous" (Juvenal, *Satires* 3.152–53).
1. In real life. "Thraso": see above, p. 1063.
2. George Buchanan (1506–1582), influential Scottish humanist and poet.
3. Virtue.

I think) may be bewrayed by that same forcibleness or *energia*[4] (as the Greeks call it) of the writer. But let this be a sufficient though short note, that we miss the right use of the material point[5] of poesy.

Now, for the outside of it, which is words, or (as I may term it) diction, it is even well worse. So is that honey-flowing matron Eloquence apparelled, or rather disguised, in a courtesan-like painted affectation: one time, with so far-fet words that may seem monsters but must seem strangers to any poor Englishman; another time, with coursing of a letter, as if they were bound to follow the method of a dictionary; another time, with figures and flowers extremely winter-starved.[6] But I would this fault were only peculiar to versifiers, and had not as large possession among prose-printers; and (which is to be marveled) among many scholars; and (which is to be pitied) among some preachers. Truly I could wish, if at least I might be so bold to wish a thing beyond the reach of my capacity, the diligent imitators of Tully and Demosthenes (most worthy to be imitated) did not so much keep Nizolian paper-books of their figures and phrases,[7] as by attentive translation (as it were) devour them whole, and make them wholly theirs: for now they cast sugar and spice upon every dish that is served to the table—like those Indians, not content to wear earrings at the fit and natural place of the ears, but they will thrust jewels through their nose and lips, because they will be sure to be fine.[8] Tully, when he was to drive out Catiline, as it were with a thunderbolt of eloquence, often used the figure of repetition, as *Vivit. Vivit? Imo in senatum venit, etc.*[9] Indeed, inflamed with a well-grounded rage, he would have his words (as it were) double out of his mouth, and so do that artificially which we see men in choler[1] do naturally. And we, having noted the grace of those words, hale them in sometimes to a familiar epistle, when it were too too much choler to be choleric. How well store of *similiter cadences* doth sound with the gravity of the pulpit,[2] I would but invoke Demosthenes' soul to tell, who with a rare daintiness[3] useth them. Truly they have made me think of the sophister that with too much subtlety would prove two eggs three, and though he might be counted a sophister, had none for his labor.[4] So these men bringing in such a kind of eloquence, well may they obtain an opinion of a seeming finesse,[5] but persuade few—which should be the end of their finesse. Now for similitudes, in certain printed discourses, I think all herbarists, all stories of beasts, fowls, and fishes are rifled up, that they come in multitudes to wait upon any of our conceits; which certainly is as

4. A rhetorical term, glossed by Sidney as he introduces it. "Bewrayed": manifested.
5. I.e., the (subject) matter.
6. Sidney criticizes three abuses: exotic ("far-fet": far-fetched) borrowings from other languages; excessive alliteration ("coursing of a letter"); and sterile ("winter-starved") figurative language.
7. Commonplace books of phrases from classical rhetoricians (among whom Cicero—"Tully"—and Demosthenes were supreme), named after the Italian scholar Marius Nizolius, who in 1535 had published *Thesaurus Ciceronianus*. In place of the slavish imitation that was all too common, Sidney advocates (below) true *absorption* of the great classical models ("attentive translation": studious transference, appropriation) and imitation with discretion.
8. Sidney had read or heard about New World indigenes whose piercings seemed "unnatural" to

him (that is, different from European practices).
9. In Cicero's famous first oration against the Roman senator Catiline—who had attempted a coup against the Republic—he marvels that Catiline still "lives. Lives? Even comes into the Senate."
1. Anger. "Artificially": through art.
2. Again Sidney expresses disapproval of the affectations of elaborate rhetoric—in this case, the excessive use ("store": abundance) of similar endings ("*similiter cadences*")—including similar rhythms, or rhyme—at the ends of successive phrases.
3. Good taste.
4. A familiar story of a logic chopper ("sophister") who proved two eggs to be three—here is one, and there are two, and one and two make three—and who for his pains was awarded the third egg.
5. Good taste.

absurd a surfeit to the ears as is possible.[6] For the force of a similitude not being to prove anything to a contrary disputer, but only to explain to a willing hearer, when that is done, the rest is a most tedious prattling, rather over-swaying the memory from the purpose whereto they were applied, than any whit informing the judgment, already either satisfied or by similitudes not to be satisfied. For my part, I do not doubt, when Antonius and Crassus, the great forefathers of Cicero in eloquence, the one (as Cicero testifieth of them)[7] pretended not to know art, the other not to set by it, because with a plain sensibleness they might win credit[8] of popular ears (which credit is the nearest step to persuasion, which persuasion is the chief mark[9] of oratory), I do not doubt (I say) but that they used these knacks very sparingly; which who doth generally use, any man may see doth dance to his own music, and so be noted by the audience more careful to speak curiously[1] than to speak truly. Undoubtedly (at least to my opinion undoubtedly), I have found in divers smally learned courtiers a more sound style than in some professors of learning; of which I can guess no other cause, but that the courtier, following that which by practice he findeth fittest to nature, therein (though he know it not) doth according to art, though not by art: where the other, using art to show art, and not to hide art[2] (as in these cases he should do), flieth from nature, and indeed abuseth art.

But what? Methinks I deserve to be pounded[3] for straying from poetry to oratory. But both have such an affinity in the wordish consideration,[4] that I think this digression will make my meaning receive the fuller understanding: which is not to take upon me to teach poets how they should do, but only, finding myself sick among the rest, to show some one or two spots of the common infection grown among the most part of writers, that, acknowledging ourselves somewhat awry, we may bend to the right use both of matter and manner: whereto our language giveth us great occasion, being indeed capable of any excellent exercising of it. I know some will say it is a mingled language.[5] And why not so much the better, taking the best of both the other? Another will say it wanteth grammar. Nay truly, it hath that praise, that it wants not grammar:[6] for grammar it might have, but it needs it not, being so easy in itself, and so void of those cumbersome differences of cases, genders, moods, and tenses, which I think was a piece of the Tower of Babylon's curse,[7] that a man should be put to school to learn his mother tongue. But for the uttering sweetly and properly the conceits of the mind (which is the end of speech), that hath it equally with any other tongue in the world; and is particularly happy in compositions[8] of two or three words together, near the

---

6. Sidney mocks the "euphuistic" style associated with John Lyly's popular romance *Euphues* (1578; above, p. 1034), whose affectations included an abundance of similes drawn from (often false) natural history. "Conceits": conceptions—here perhaps also with the sense of elaborate sustained comparisons.
7. *On the Orator* 2.1. Lucius Crassus (d. 91 B.C.E.) and Marcus Antonius (d. 87 B.C.E.—the grandfather of Cleopatra's Marc Antony) are speakers in this dialogue and are lauded by Cicero in the prefaces to the second and third of its three books.
8. Credence, trust.
9. Aim.
1. Elaborately.
2. Alluding to the proverb "It is art to hide art."

3. Impounded, like a stray animal.
4. In matters of diction.
5. Mingling, especially, words from French and Latin with those of Anglo-Saxon origin.
6. "Wanteth grammar . . . wants not grammar": lacks grammar . . . does not require grammar. English, of course, has grammar. But its grammar was not, at the time, elaborately systematized and studied, like Greek and Latin grammar.
7. Elizabethans identified Babel—where, according to Genesis 11.1–9, God stymied human overreaching by instituting a confounding variety of languages—with Babylon.
8. Compounds. (Sidney's use of them is one of the most distinctive and attractive features of his style.) "Happy": fortunate.

Greek, far beyond the Latin, which is one of the greatest beauties can be in a language.

Now of versifying there are two sorts, the one ancient, the other modern: the ancient marked the quantity of each syllable, and according to that framed his verse; the modern, observing only number[9] (with some regard of the accent), the chief life of it standeth in that like sounding of the words, which we call rhyme. Whether of these be the more excellent, would bear many speeches: the ancient (no doubt) more fit for music, both words and time observing quantity, and more fit lively to express diverse passions, by the low or lofty sound of the well-weighed syllable; the latter likewise, with his rhyme, striketh a certain music to the ear, and, in fine, since it doth delight, though by another way, it obtains the same purpose: there being in either sweetness, and wanting[1] in neither majesty. Truly the English, before any vulgar[2] language I know, is fit for both sorts. For, for the ancient, the Italian is so full of vowels that it must ever be cumbered with elisions; the Dutch[3] so, of the other side, with consonants, that they cannot yield the sweet sliding, fit for a verse; the French in his whole language hath not one word that hath his accent in the last syllable saving two, called *antepenultima*; and little more hath the Spanish, and therefore very gracelessly may they use dactyls. The English is subject to none of these defects. Now for the rhyme,[4] though we do not observe quantity, yet we observe the accent very precisely, which other languages either cannot do, or will not do so absolutely. That *caesura*, or breathing place in the midst of the verse, neither Italian nor Spanish have, the French and we never almost fail of. Lastly, even the very rhyme itself, the Italian cannot put it in the last syllable, by the French named the masculine rhyme, but still[5] in the next to the last, which the French call the female, or the next before that, which the Italians term *sdrucciola*. The example of the former is *buono: suono*, of the *sdrucciola* is *femina: semina*. The French, of the other side, hath both the male, as *bon: son*, and the female, as *plaise: taise*, but the *sdrucciola* he hath not: where the English hath all three, as *due: true, father: rather, motion: potion*[6]—with much more which might be said, but that already I find the triflingness of this discourse is much too much enlarged.

[CONCLUSION]

So that since the ever-praiseworthy Poesy is full of virtue-breeding delightfulness, and void of no gift that ought to be in the noble name of learning;[7] since the blames laid against it are either false or feeble; since the cause why it is not esteemed in England is the fault of poet-apes,[8] not poets; since, lastly, our tongue is most fit to honor poesy, and to be honored by poesy;

9. Classical "quantity" meant the length or duration of syllables. Moderns simply count the "number" of syllables.

1. Lacking. "In fine": in conclusion.

2. Vernacular.

3. The term referred to the languages both of the Low Countries and of Germany.

4. I.e., rhymed verse as opposed to "ancient" (i.e., quantitative) verse. "Dactyls": see (as for *caesura*, below) the "Literary Terminology" appendix to this volume. Because of the accent patterns in French and Spanish, those languages cannot make good use of this poetic foot.

5. Always.

6. Pronounced with three syllables, accented on the first.

7. This final paragraph constitutes the *peroratio* of Sidney's judicial oration: though it includes a brief recapitulation of arguments, the main function of the peroration is, like that of the exordium, to work on the audience's feelings, leaving it well-disposed toward the speaker and the speaker's client.

8. False poets, who mimic ("ape") the real ones.

I conjure you all that have had the evil luck to read this ink-wasting toy of mine, even in the name of the nine Muses, no more to scorn the sacred mysteries of poesy; no more to laugh at the name of poets, as though they were next inheritors to fools; no more to jest at the reverent title of a rhymer; but to believe, with Aristotle, that they were the ancient treasurers of the Grecians' divinity; to believe, with Bembus, that they were first bringers-in of all civility; to believe, with Scaliger, that no philosopher's precepts can sooner make you an honest man than the reading of Virgil; to believe, with Clauserus, the translator of Cornutus, that it pleased the heavenly Deity, by Hesiod[9] and Homer, under the veil of fables, to give us all knowledge, logic, rhetoric, philosophy natural and moral, and *quid non?*;[1] to believe, with me, that there are many mysteries contained in poetry, which of purpose were written darkly, lest by profane wits it should be abused; to believe, with Landino,[2] that they are so beloved of the gods that whatsoever they write proceeds of a divine fury; lastly, to believe themselves, when they tell you they will make you immortal by their verses. Thus doing, your name shall flourish in the printers' shops; thus doing, you shall be of kin to many a poetical preface; thus doing, you shall be most fair, most rich, most wise, most all, you shall dwell upon superlatives; thus doing, though you be *libertino patre natus*, you shall suddenly grow *Herculea proles*,[3]

Si quid mea carmina possunt;[4]

thus doing, your soul shall be placed with Dante's Beatrice, or Virgil's Anchises.[5] But if (fie of such a but) you be born so near the dull-making cataract of Nilus that you cannot hear the planet-like[6] music of poetry; if you have so earth-creeping a mind that it cannot lift itself up to look to the sky of poetry, or rather, by a certain rustical disdain, will become such a mome as to be a Momus[7] of poetry; then, though I will not wish unto you the ass's ears of Midas,[8] nor to be driven by a poet's verses, as Bubonax[9] was, to hang himself, nor to be rhymed to death, as is said to be done in Ireland;[1] yet thus much curse I must send you, in the behalf of all poets, that while you live, you live in love, and never get favor for lacking skill of a sonnet;[2] and, when you die, your memory die from the earth for want of an epitaph.

ca. 1579   1595

---

9. Early Greek poet whose *Theogony* recounts myths of the birth and warfare of the gods and the origin of the world. "Aristotle": cf. *Metaphysics* 3.4.12. "Bembus": above, p. 1074 and n. 4. "Scaliger": above, p. 1049, n. 8. "Clauserus": Conrad Clauser, a German scholar who translated a Greek treatise by Cornutus, a Stoic pedagogue of Nero's time.

1. "What not?"

2. Christoforo Landino, Florentine humanist who developed this argument in his edition of Dante's *Divine Comedy* (1481). "Divine fury" (below): divinely inspired frenzy.

3. "Offspring of Hercules." "*Libertino patre natus*": "born of a freed-slave father" (Horace, *Satires* 1.6.6).

4. "If my songs are of any avail" (*Aeneid* 9.446).

5. I.e., in Paradise with Dante's beloved or in the Elysian Fields with Aeneas's honored father.

6. Resembling the music of the spheres, most beautiful of all music. According to Cicero (*Dream of Scipio* 5), the noise of the waterfalls in the upper Nile deafened those who lived nearby.

7. God of ridicule, son of Night; hence, a critic. "Mome": dunce.

8. He was given ass's ears because he preferred Pan's music to Apollo's (Ovid, *Metamorphoses* 11.146–79).

9. Bupalus, an ancient Greek sculptor who, according to an apocryphal story, hanged himself when his works were satirized by the poet Hipponax. Sidney fuses the two names.

1. Irish bards were thought to be able to cause death with their rhymed charms.

2. Because you are unable to write a sonnet.

Astrophil and Stella   Sidney was a jealous protector of his privacy. "I assure you before God," he had written once in an angry letter to his father's private secretary, Molyneux, "that if ever I know you do so much as read any letter I write to my father, without his commandment or my consent, I will thrust my dagger into you. And trust to it, for I speak it in earnest." Yet in *Astrophil and Stella* he seems to hold up a mirror to every nuance of his emotional being. For its original coterie audience, Sidney's sonnet sequence must have been an elaborate game of literary masks, psychological risk-taking, and open secrets. The loosely linked succession of 108 sonnets and eleven songs, with its dazzling display of technical virtuosity, provides tantalizing glimpses of identifiable characters and, still more, a sustained and remarkably intimate portrait of the poet's inner life.

Much biographical speculation has centered on Sidney's ambiguous relationship with Penelope Devereux, the supposed original of Stella. A marriage between the two had been proposed in 1576 and was talked about for some years, but in 1581 she married Lord Robert Rich, and two years later Sidney also married. (At their high social rank, marriages were negotiated in the interests of the powerful families involved, not of the individuals.) Some of the sonnets contain sly puns on the name *Rich*, and it seems likely that there are autobiographical elements in the shadowy narrative sketched by the work. At the same time, however, the "plot" of the sequence, full of trials, setbacks, much suffering on the part of the lover and occasional encouragement on the part of the lady, is highly conventional, derived from Petrarch and his many Italian, French, and Spanish imitators.

Poets in this tradition undertook to produce an anatomy of love, displaying its shifting and often contradictory states: hope and despair, tenderness and bitterness, exultation and modesty, bodily desire and spiritual transcendence. Petrarch had deployed a series of ingenious metaphors to describe these states, but by Sidney's time the metaphors—love as a freezing fire, the beloved's glance as an arrow striking the lover's heart, and so forth—had through endless repetition become familiar and predictable, less a revelation than a role. Sidney, in the role of Astrophil, protests that he uses no standard conventional phrases, that his verse is original and comes from his heart. This protest is itself conventional, and yet Sidney manages to infuse his sonnets with an extraordinary vigor and freshness. Certain of the sonnets have, within their narrow fourteen-line bounds, the force of the drama: "Fly, fly, my friends, I have my death-wound, fly" or "What, have I thus betrayed my liberty?" Others, in their grappling with insistent desire, have the probing, psychological resonance of private confession: "With what sharp checks I in myself am shent" or "Who will in fairest book of Nature know." Still others ask crucial questions about the whole project of self-representation: "Stella oft sees the very face of woe." Virtually all of them manifest the exceptional *energia*—forcibleness—that Sidney, in *The Defense of Poesy*, says is the key ingredient of good love poetry.*

From Astrophil and Stella

1[1]

> Loving in truth, and fain° in verse my love to show,   desirous
> That the dear She might take some pleasure of my pain,
> Pleasure might cause her read, reading might make her know,

---

* For a broad grouping of other 16th-century love poems, see above, "Renaissance Love and Desire" (pp. 1000 ff.).

1. One of six sonnets in the sequence written in hexameters.

Knowledge might pity win, and pity grace obtain,
5 I sought fit words to paint the blackest face of woe,
Studying inventions fine, her wits to entertain,
Oft turning others' leaves, to see if thence would flow
Some fresh and fruitful showers upon my sunburned brain.
    But words came halting forth, wanting Invention's stay;[2]
10 Invention, Nature's child, fled step-dame Study's blows,
And others' feet still° seemed but strangers in my way.   *continually*
Thus great with child to speak, and helpless in my throes,
    Biting my truant pen, beating myself for spite,
    "Fool," said my Muse to me, "look in thy heart and write."

2

Not at first sight, nor with a dribbèd[3] shot
    Love gave the wound, which while I breathe will bleed,
    But known worth did in mine[4] of time proceed,
Till by degrees it had full conquest got.
5 I saw and liked, I liked but lovèd not,
    I loved, but straight did not[5] what Love decreed;
    At length to Love's decrees, I, forced, agreed,
Yet with repining° at so partial° lot.   *complaining / unfair*
    Now even that footstep of lost liberty
10 Is gone, and now like slave-born Muscovite,[6]
I call it praise to suffer tyranny;
    And now employ the remnant of my wit°   *mind*
    To make myself believe that all is well,
    While with a feeling skill I paint my hell.

5

It is most true that eyes are formed to serve
    The inward light,° and that the heavenly part   *i.e., reason, understanding*
Ought to be king, from whose rules who do swerve,
    Rebels to Nature, strive for their own smart.°   *pain*
5   It is most true, what we call Cupid's dart
An image is, which for ourselves we carve;
And, fools, adore in temple of our heart,
Till that good god make church and churchman starve.[7]
    True, that true beauty virtue is indeed,
10 Whereof this beauty can be but a shade,°   *shadow*
Which elements with mortal mixture[8] breed;
    True, that on earth we are but pilgrims made,

2. I.e., lacking the support of Invention, his words moved haltingly.
3. Ineffectual or at random.
4. Tunnel dug to undermine a besieged fortress.
5. Did not immediately do.
6. Inhabitant of Muscovy, Russian principality ruled from Moscow; 16th-century travel books describe Muscovites as contented slaves.
7. Die (not necessarily of hunger). The concessions made in the argument are to Neoplatonic and Christian doctrines opposed to romantic love. Neoplatonic theory held that physical beauty is only a shadow of inner virtue, which is at one with the true, transcendent, and immortal Idea of Beauty. For a highly influential exposition of this theory, see the excerpts from Book 4 of Castiglione's *The Courtier*, pp. 706ff.
8. Physical beauty is a mixture of the four elements (earth, air, water, and fire) and is therefore mortal.

And should in soul up to our country move:
True, and yet true that I must *Stella* love.

6

Some lovers speak, when they their muses entertain,
Of hopes begot by fear, of wot° not what desires,   know
Of force of heavenly beams infusing hellish pain,
Of living deaths, dear wounds, fair storms, and freezing fires.[9]
5   Some one his song in Jove and Jove's strange tales attires,
Bordered with bulls and swans, powdered with golden rain;[1]
Another humbler wit to shepherd's pipe retires,
Yet hiding royal blood full oft in rural vein.[2]
      To some a sweetest plaint a sweetest style affords,[3]
10   While tears pour out his ink, and sighs breathe out his words,
His paper pale Despair, and Pain his pen doth move.
      I can speak what I feel, and feel as much as they,
      But think that all the map of my state I display,
When trembling voice brings forth that I do Stella love.

7

When Nature made her chief work, Stella's eyes,
In color black why wrapped she beams so bright?
Would she in beamy° black, like painter wise,   radiant
Frame daintiest luster, mixed of shades and light?
5   Or did she else that sober hue devise,
In object° best to knit and strength° our sight,   with purpose / strengthen
Lest if no veil those brave° gleams did disguise,   splendid
They sun-like should more dazzle than delight?
      Or would she her miraculous power show,
10   That whereas black seems beauty's contrary,
She even in black doth make all beauties flow?
      Both so and thus: she, minding° Love should be   remembering
      Placed ever there, gave him this mourning weed,°   funeral garb
To honor all their deaths, who for her bleed.

9

Queen Virtue's court, which some call Stella's face,
      Prepared by Nature's chiefest furniture,[4]
      Hath his front° built of alablaster° pure;   *i.e., Stella's forehead / alabaster*
Gold is the covering of that stately place.
5   The door, by which sometimes comes forth her grace,
      Red porphir[5] is, which lock of pearl makes sure;
      Whose porches rich (which name of cheeks endure),

---

9. Conventional Petrarchan oxymorons.
1. Jove courted Europa in the shape of a bull;
Leda, as a swan; and Danaë, as a golden shower.
For "Bordered," the emendation "Broadred"
(embroidered) has been proposed.
2. I.e., in pastoral allegory. By convention, a
pastoral poet pipes his songs on an oaten or reed

pipe.
3. Parodying the overuse of the word *sweet* in
love complaints, with allusion to the very musical
dolce stil nuovo (sweet new style) associated with
Dante and his Italian contemporaries.
4. The best materials Nature furnishes.
5. Porphyry, an ornamental red or purple stone.

Marble mixed red and white do interlace.
    The windows now through which this heavenly guest
10 Looks o'er the world, and can find nothing such
Which dare claim from those lights the name of best,
Of touch[6] they are that without touch doth touch,
    Which Cupid's self from Beauty's mine did draw:
    Of touch they are, and poor I am their straw.

10

Reason, in faith thou art well served, that still
Wouldst brabbling° be with sense and love in me: *quarreling*
I rather wished thee climb the Muses' hill,[7]
Or reach the fruit of Nature's choicest tree,[8]
5   Or seek heaven's course, or heaven's inside to see.
Why shouldst thou toil our thorny soil to till?
Leave sense, and those which sense's objects be;
Deal thou with powers of thoughts, leave love to will.
    But thou wouldst needs fight both with love and sense,
10 With sword of wit,° giving wounds of dispraise,   *intellect*
Till downright blows did foil thy cunning fence:°   *swordplay*
For soon as they strake° thee with Stella's rays,   *struck*
    Reason thou kneel'dst, and offeredst straight° to prove   *straightway*
    By reason good, good reason her to love.

15

You that do search for every purling° spring   *murmuring*
    Which from the ribs of old Parnassus[9] flows,
    And every flower,[1] not sweet perhaps, which grows
Near therabout, into your poesy[2] wring;
5   You that do dictionary's method bring
    Into your rhymes, running in rattling rows;
    You that poor Petrarch's long-deceasèd woes
With new-born sighs and denizened wit° do sing: *naturalized ingenuity*
    You take wrong ways, those far-fet° helps be such   *far-fetched*
10   As do bewray a want of inward touch,[3]
And sure at length stolen goods do come to light.
    But if (both for your love and skill) your name
    You seek to nurse at fullest breasts of Fame,
Stella behold, and then begin to indite.°   *compose, write*

16

In nature apt to like when I did see
    Beauties, which were of many carats fine,

---

6. Glossy black stone (lignite or jet) able to attract
light bodies such as straw by static electricity.
7. Mount Helicon in Greece, sacred to the Nine
Muses—a symbol of poetic inspiration.
8. The Tree of Knowledge.

9. Mountain near Delphi in Greece, sacred to
the Muses.
1. Also, poetic figures ("flowers of rhetoric").
2. Also, a nosegay (posy).
3. Reveal a lack of innate talent.

My boiling sprites° did thither soon incline,   *spirits*
And, Love, I thought that I was full of thee:
5   But finding not those restless flames in me,
    Which others said did make their souls to pine,
    I thought those babes of some pin's hurt did whine,
By my love judging what love's pain might be.
    But while I thus with this young lion[4] played,
10 Mine eyes (shall I say cursed or blessed) beheld
Stella; now she is named, need more be said?
In her sight I a lesson new have spelled:
    I now have learned love right, and learned even so,
    As who by being poisoned doth poison know.

18

With what sharp checks° I in myself am shent,°   *rebukes / shamed*
    When into Reason's audit I do go,
    And by just counts myself a bankrout° know   *bankrupt*
Of all those goods, which heaven to me hath lent:
5   Unable quite to pay even Nature's rent,
    Which unto it by birthright I do owe;
    And which is worse, no good excuse can show,
But that my wealth I have most idly spent.
    My youth doth waste, my knowledge brings forth toys,[5]
10 My wit° doth strive those passions to defend,   *intellect*
Which for reward spoil it with vain annoys.°   *troubles*
I see my course to lose myself doth bend:°   *turn*
    I see and yet no greater sorrow take,
    Than that I lose no more for Stella's sake.

20

Fly, fly, my friends, I have my death-wound, fly;
    See there that boy, that murth'ring° boy, I say,   *murdering*
Who like a thief hid in dark bush doth lie
Till bloody bullet get him wrongful prey.
5   So tyran° he no fitter place could spy,   *tyrant*
Nor so fair level° in so secret stay,°   *aim / stopping place*
As that sweet black° which veils the heav'nly eye;   *i.e., pupil*
There himself with his shot he close° doth lay.   *secretly*
    Poor passenger,° pass now thereby I did,   *passerby*
10 And stayed, pleased with the prospect of the place,
While that black hue from me the bad guest hid:
But straight I saw motions of lightning grace,
    And then descried° the glist'ring° of his dart;°   *saw / glittering / arrow*
    But ere I could fly thence, it pierced my heart.

---

4. In a popular fable, a shepherd raised a lion cub that, while young, was a pet for his children but when grown destroyed all his flocks.
5. Trifles; i.e., these poems.

21

Your words, my friend (right healthful caustics),[6] blame
   My young mind marred, whom Love doth windlass° so,   *ensnare*
   That mine own writings like bad servants show
My wits quick in vain thoughts, in virtue lame;
5 That Plato I read for nought, but if° he tame   *unless*
   Such coltish gyres,[7] that to my birth I owe
   Nobler desires, least° else that friendly foe,   *lest*
Great Expectation, wear a train of shame.
   For since mad March great promise made of me,
10 If now the May of my years much decline,
What can be hoped my harvest time will be?
Sure you say well; your wisdom's golden mine
   Dig deep with learning's spade; now tell me this:
   Hath this world ought° so fair as Stella is?   *aught, anything*

27

Because I oft, in dark abstracted guise,
   Seem most alone in greatest company,
   With dearth of words, or answers quite awry,
To them that would make speech of speech arise,
5 They deem, and of their doom° the rumor flies,   *judgment*
   That poison foul of bubbling pride doth lie
   So in my swelling breast that only I°   *that I do nothing but*
Fawn on myself, and others do despise.
   Yet pride, I think, doth not my soul possess,
10 Which looks too oft in his unflatt'ring glass;°   *mirror*
But one worse fault, ambition, I confess,
That makes me oft my best friends overpass,°   *pass by, ignore*
   Unseen, unheard, while thought to highest place
   Bends all his powers, even unto Stella's grace.°   *beauty, elegance; favor*

28

You that with allegory's curious frame°   *intricate contrivance*
   Of others' children changelings use° to make,   *are accustomed*
   With me those pains for God's sake do not take:
I list not° dig so deep for brazen fame.   *I don't care to*
5 When I say Stella, I do mean the same
   Princess of beauty for whose only sake
   The reins of love I love, though never slake,°   *slack*
And joy therein, though nations count it shame.
   I beg no subject to use eloquence,[8]
10 Nor in hid ways to guide philosophy;

---

6. Caustic substances for burning away diseased tissue.
7. Wild circles, like those of a young horse; there is a probable reference to Plato's story of the char-ioteer Reason reining in the horses of Passion (*Phaedrus* 254).
8. I.e., I don't ask for a topic simply as an excuse to display my rhetorical skills.

Look at my hands for no such quintessence,[9]
But know that I in pure simplicity
    Breathe out the flames which burn within my heart,
    Love only reading unto me this art.

31

With how sad steps, O Moon, thou climb'st the skies,
    How silently, and with how wan a face!
    What, may it be that even in heavenly place
That busy archer° his sharp arrows tries?   *Cupid*
5 Sure, if that long-with-love-acquainted eyes
    Can judge of love, thou feel'st a lover's case;
    I read it in thy looks: thy languished grace,
To me that feel the like, thy state descries.°   *reveals*
    Then even of fellowship, O Moon, tell me,
10 Is constant love deemed there but want of wit?°   *lack of intelligence*
Are beauties there as proud as here they be?
Do they above love to be loved, and yet
    Those lovers scorn whom that love doth possess?
    Do they call virtue there ungratefulness?[1]

33[2]

I might (unhappy word), O me, I might,
And then would not, or could not, see my bliss:
Till now, wrapped in a most infernal night,
I find how heav'nly day, wretch, I did miss.
5   Heart, rent° thyself, thou dost thyself but right: *rend, tear*
No lovely Paris made thy Helen his;[3]
No force, no fraud robbed thee of thy delight;
Nor Fortune of thy fortune author is;
    But to myself myself did give the blow,
10 While too much wit° (forsooth) so troubled me,   *cleverness*
That I respects for both our sakes must show:[4]
And yet could not by rising morn foresee
    How fair a day was near. O punished eyes,
    That I had been more foolish, or more wise!

34

Come, let me write. "And to what end?" To ease
    A burdened heart. "How can words ease, which are
    The glasses° of thy daily vexing care?"   *mirrors*
Oft cruel fights well pictured forth do please.

9. The mysterious "fifth element" of matter (supplementary to earth, air, fire, and water), which alchemists labored to extract.
1. I.e., is the lady's ingratitude considered virtue in heaven (as here)? Also, is the lover's virtue (fidelity) considered distasteful in heaven (as here)?
2. The sonnet seems to allude to the abortive scheme to betroth Sidney to Penelope Devereux in 1576, when she was thirteen, he twenty-one.
3. I.e., Astrophil did not lose Stella to a more attractive rival, as Menelaus lost Helen of Troy to Paris.
4. I.e., he thought he was acting in the best interests of both. "Forsooth": truly.

5   "Art° not ashamed to publish thy disease?"   *are you*
     Nay, that may breed my fame, it is so rare.
     "But will not wise men think thy words fond ware?"°   *foolish trinkets*
Then be they close,⁵ and so none shall displease.
     "What idler thing, than speak and not be hard?"°   *heard*
10 What harder thing than smart,° and not to speak?   *feel pain*
Peace, foolish wit;° with wit my wit is marred.   *reason; intellect*
Thus while I write I doubt° to write, and wreak°   *hesitate; fear / avenge*
     My harms on Ink's poor loss: perhaps some find
     Stella's great powers, that so confuse my mind.

37

My mouth doth water, and my breast doth swell,
     My tongue doth itch, my thoughts in labor be:
     Listen then, lordings, with good ear to me,
For of my life I must a riddle tell.
5   Towards Aurora's court a nymph doth dwell,⁶
     Rich in all beauties which man's eye can see,
     Beauties so far from reach of words, that we
Abase her praise, saying she doth excel:
     Rich in the treasure of deserved renown,
10 Rich in the riches of a royal heart,
Rich in those gifts which give th' eternal crown;
     Who though most rich in these and every part
         Which make the patents⁷ of true worldly bliss,
         Hath no misfortune, but that Rich she is.

39

Come, Sleep, O Sleep, the certain knot of peace,
The baiting place⁸ of wit,° the balm of woe,   *mind*
The poor man's wealth, the prisoner's release,
Th' indifferent° judge between the high and low;   *impartial*
5   With shield of proof⁹ shield me from out the prease°   *press, throng*
Of those fierce darts Despair at me doth throw:
O make in me those civil wars to cease;
I will good tribute pay if thou do so.
     Take thou of me smooth pillows, sweetest bed,
10 A chamber deaf to noise and blind to light,
A rosy garland, and a weary head:¹
And if these things, as being thine by right,
     Move not thy heavy grace, thou shalt in me
     Livelier° than elsewhere Stella's image see.   *more lifelike*

5. Let them (my words) be kept private.
6. Aurora (the dawn) has her court in the east; Penelope Devereux Rich, the original of Stella, dwells in Essex, one of the eastern counties. Sidney puns on her married name throughout this sonnet.

7. Grants, titles to possession.
8. Resting place on a journey.
9. Proven strength.
1. The offer of gifts to Morpheus, god of sleep, is a poetic convention. A likely source is Chaucer's *Book of the Duchess*, lines 240–69.

41

Having this day my horse, my hand, my lance
   Guided so well that I obtained the prize,
   Both by the judgment of the English eyes
And of some sent from that sweet enemy France;[2]

5 Horsemen my skill in horsemanship advance;[3]
   Townfolks my strength; a daintier° judge applies   *more discerning*
   His praise to sleight,[4] which from good use° doth rise;   *experience*
Some lucky wits impute it but to chance;
   Others, because of both sides I do take
10 My blood from them who did excel in this,[5]
Think Nature me a man of arms did make.
   How far they shoot awry! The true cause is,
   Stella looked on, and from her heavenly face
Sent forth the beams which made so fair my race.[6]

45

Stella oft sees the very face of woe
   Painted in my beclouded stormy face,
   But cannot skill to° pity my disgrace,°   *is unable to / misfortune*
Not though thereof the cause herself she know.[7]
5 Yet hearing late a fable which did show,
   Of lovers never known, a grievous case,
   Pity thereof gate° in her breast such place   *got*
That, from that sea derived, tears' spring did flow.
   Alas, if fancy,° drawn by imaged things,   *fantasy*
10 Though false, yet with free scope more grace° doth breed   *favor*
Than servant's wrack, where new doubts honor brings,[8]
   Then think, my dear, that you in me do read
   Of lover's ruin some sad tragedy:
I am not I; pity the tale of me.

47

What, have I thus betrayed my liberty?
   Can those black beams such burning marks° engrave   *brands of slavery*
   In my free side? or am I born a slave,
Whose neck becomes° such yoke of tyranny?   *is suited to*
5 Or want I sense to feel my misery?
   Or sprite,° disdain of such disdain to have?   *spirit*
   Who for long faith, though daily help I crave,
May get no alms but scorn of beggary.[9]

---

2. Sidney took part in several jousting tournaments between 1579 and 1585 with French spectators present, but the one in May 1581 was devised specifically to entertain French commissioners.
3. I.e., put forward as the reason for my triumph.
4. Skill, dexterity.
5. Sidney's father and grandfather and his maternal uncles, the earls of Leicester and Warwick,

were frequent participants in tournaments.
6. Course in a tournament.
7. I.e., even though she knows she herself is the cause of it.
8. I.e., than the ruin of her lover ("servant"), caused by the new scruples ("doubts") her honor brings up.
9. I.e., scorn for [my] begging.

Virtue awake! Beauty but beauty is;
10   I may, I must, I can, I will, I do
Leave following that which it is gain to miss.
Let her go. Soft, but here she comes. Go to,[1]
    Unkind, I love you not. O me, that eye
    Doth make my heart give to my tongue the lie.°   *contradict my tongue*

49

I on my horse, and Love on me doth try
    Our horsemanships, while by strange work I prove
    A horseman to my horse, a horse to Love;
And now man's wrongs in me, poor beast, descry.°   *discover*
5   The reins wherewith my rider doth me tie
    Are humbled thoughts, which bit of reverence move,
    Curbed in with fear, but with gilt boss° above   *gold stud*
Of hope, which makes it seem fair to the eye.
    The wand° is will; thou, Fancy, saddle art,[2]   *whip*
10 Girt fast by Memory; and while I spur
My horse, he spurs with sharp desire my heart;
    He sits me fast,° however I do stir,   *tightly*
    And now hath made me to his hand so right
    That in the manage[3] myself takes delight.

52

A strife is grown between Virtue and Love,
    While each pretends° that Stella must be his: *claims*
    Her eyes, her lips, her all, saith Love, do this,
Since they do wear his badge,[4] most firmly prove.
5   But Virtue thus that title doth disprove:
    That Stella (O dear name) that Stella is
    That virtuous soul, sure heir of heavenly bliss;
Not this fair outside, which our hearts doth move.
    And therefore, though her beauty and her grace
10 Be Love's indeed, in Stella's self he may
By no pretence claim any manner° place.   *kind of*
Well, Love, since this demur° our suit[5] doth stay,°   *objection / stop*
    Let Virtue have that Stella's self; yet thus,
    That Virtue but° that body grant to us.   *only*

53

In martial sports I had my cunning° tried,   *skill*
    And yet to break more staves° did me address;   *lances*
    While with the people's shouts, I must confess,
Youth, luck, and praise even filled my veins with pride.
5   When Cupid having me his slave descried°   *discerned*

---

1. An emphatic expression, like "I tell you."
2. I.e., you, Fancy (imagination), are the saddle.
3. Training or handling of a horse.

4. Device or livery worn to identify someone's (here, Cupid's) servants.
5. "Courtship," in addition to the legal meaning.

In Mars's livery,[6] prancing in the press,°   *throng*
"What now, Sir Fool," said he, "I would no less;[7]
Look here, I say." I looked, and Stella spied,
Who hard by° made a window send forth light.   *nearby*
10 My heart then quaked, then dazzled were mine eyes,
One hand forgot to rule,° th' other to fight.   *govern the horse*
Nor trumpets' sound I heard, nor friendly cries;
My foe came on, and beat the air for me,[8]
Till that her blush taught me my shame to see.

54

Because I breathe not love to every one,
Nor do not use set colors for to wear,[9]
Nor nourish special locks of vowèd hair,[1]
Nor give each speech a full point[2] of a groan,
5 The courtly nymphs, acquainted with the moan
Of them who in their lips Love's standard° bear,   *ensign*
"What, he?" say they of me, "now I dare swear
He cannot love; no, no, let him alone!"
And think so still, so[3] Stella know my mind.
10 Profess indeed I do not Cupid's art;
But you, fair maids, at length this true shall find,
That his right badge[4] is but worn in the heart:
Dumb swans, not chatt'ring pies,° do lovers prove;[5]   *magpies*
They love indeed, who quake to say they love.

56

Fie, school of Patience, fie, your lesson is
Far far too long to learn it without book:°   *i.e., by memory*
What, a whole week without one piece of look,[6]
And think I should not your large precepts miss?°   *forget*
5 When I might read those letters fair of bliss,
Which in her face teach virtue, I could brook°   *bear*
Somewhat thy leaden counsels, which I took
As of a friend that meant not much amiss.
But now that I, alas, do want° her sight,   *lack*
10 What, dost thou think that I can ever take
In thy cold stuff a phlegmatic° delight?   *sluggish*
No, Patience, if thou wilt my good, then make
Her come and hear with patience my desire,
And then with patience bid me bear my fire.

---

6. Cf. sonnet 52, lines 1–4, and note. Dressed in armor for the tournament, Astrophil is wearing the "livery" of Mars, god of war.
7. I.e., I want no less [service from you].
8. Struck the empty air instead of me.
9. Am not accustomed to wear colors associated with a particular woman.

1. I.e., lovelocks: long, flowing locks characteristic of amorous courtiers.
2. Final punctuation, period.
3. Go on thinking so, provided only that.
4. True badge, livery.
5. Prove to be (true) lovers.
6. Without the briefest glimpse of her.

61

Oft with true sighs, oft with uncallèd tears,
Now with slow words, now with dumb eloquence
I Stella's eyes assail, invade her ears;
But this at last is her sweet-breathed defense:
5   That who indeed infelt affection bears,
So captives to his saint both soul and sense
That, wholly hers, all selfness° he forbears;   *concern with self*
Thence his desires he learns, his life's course thence.
    Now since her chaste mind hates this love in me,
10   With chastened mind I straight must shew° that she   *show*
Shall quickly me from what she hates remove.
    O Doctor[7] Cupid, thou for me reply,
    Driven else° to grant by angel's sophistry   *otherwise*
That I love not, without I leave to love.°   *unless I stop loving*

69

O joy, too high for my low style to show,
    O bliss, fit for a nobler state than me!
    Envy, put out thine eyes, least° thou do see   *lest*
What oceans of delight in me do flow.
5   My friend, that oft saw through all masks my woe,
    Come, come, and let me pour myself on thee:
    Gone is the winter of my misery;
My spring appears; O see what here doth grow.
    For Stella hath, with words where faith doth shine,
10   Of her high heart given me the monarchy:
I, I, O I may say that she is mine.
    And though she give but thus conditionly
    This realm of bliss, while virtuous course I take,
    No kings be crowned but° they some covenants[8] make.   *unless*

71

Who will in fairest book of Nature know
    How Virtue may best lodged in beauty be,
    Let him but learn of Love to read in thee,
Stella, those fair lines, which true goodness show.
5   There shall he find all vices' overthrow,
    Not by rude force, but sweetest sovereignty
    Of reason, from whose light those night-birds[9] fly;
That inward sun in thine eyes shineth so.
    And not content to be Perfection's heir
10   Thyself, dost strive all minds that way to move,
Who mark° in thee what is in thee most fair.[1]   *perceive*

7. In the sense of eminently learned scholar.
8. Solemn coronation oaths taken by English monarchs, promising to protect the laws and the people.
9. The owl, for example, was an emblem of various vices.
1. I.e., her virtue, which is fairer even than her beauty.

So while thy beauty draws the heart to love,
    As fast° thy Virtue bends that love to good;   *at the same rate*
    "But, ah," Desire still cries, "give me some food."

72

Desire, though thou my old companion art,
    And oft so clings to my pure Love that I
    One from the other scarcely can descry,°   *distinguish*
While each doth blow the fire of my heart,
5 Now from thy fellowship I needs must part:
    Venus is taught with Dian's wings to fly;[2]
    I must no more in thy sweet passions lie;
Virtue's gold now must head my Cupid's dart.
    Service and honor, wonder with delight,
10 Fear to offend, will worthy to appear,[3]
    Care shining in mine eyes, faith in my sprite:°   *spirit*
These things are left me by my only dear.
    But thou, Desire, because thou wouldst have all,
    Now banished art. But yet alas how shall?

74

I never drank of Aganippe well,
    Nor ever did in shade of Tempe[4] sit;
    And Muses scorn with vulgar° brains to dwell;   *common*
Poor layman I, for sacred rites unfit.
5 Some do I hear of poets' fury° tell,   *inspiration*
    But God wot,° wot not what they mean by it;   *knows*
    And this I swear by blackest brook of hell,[5]
I am no pick-purse of another's wit.
    How falls it then that with so smooth an ease
10 My thoughts I speak, and what I speak doth flow
In verse, and that my verse best wits doth please?
    Guess we the cause. "What, is it thus?" Fie no.
    "Or so?" Much less. "How then?" Sure thus it is:
    My lips are sweet, inspired with Stella's kiss.[6]

81

O kiss, which dost those ruddy gems impart,
    Or° gems, or fruits of new-found Paradise,   *either*
Breathing all bliss and sweet'ning to the heart,
    Teaching dumb lips a nobler exercise!
5   O kiss, which souls, even souls, together ties

---

2. Diana, goddess of the moon and patron of chastity; Venus, goddess of beauty and love, mother of Cupid.
3. The phrase can mean either "the wish to appear worthy" or "desire that is worthy to appear [i.e., not shameful]."
4. Valley beside Mount Olympus, sacred to

Apollo, the god of poetry. "Aganippe well": fountain at the foot of Mount Helicon in Greece, sacred to the Muses.
5. The most binding of all oaths were those sworn by the River Styx.
6. A kiss he stole from Stella when he caught her napping (Song 2).

By links of Love, and only Nature's art,
How fain° would I paint thee to all men's eyes,   *gladly*
Or of thy gifts at least shade out° some part.   *sketch*
    But she forbids, with blushing words she says
10   She builds her fame on higher-seated praise.
But my heart burns, I cannot silent be.
    Then since (dear life) you fain would have me peace,[7]
    And I, mad with delight, want wit[8] to cease,
Stop you my mouth with still still kissing me.

Fourth Song[9]

    Only joy, now here you are,
    Fit to hear and ease my care;
    Let my whispering voice obtain
    Sweet reward for sharpest pain:
5   Take me to thee, and thee to me.
    "No, no, no, no, my dear, let be."

    Night hath closed all in her cloak,
    Twinkling stars love-thoughts provoke,
    Danger hence good care doth keep,
10   Jealousy itself doth sleep:
    Take me to thee, and thee to me.
    "No, no, no, no, my dear, let be."

    Better place no wit can find,
    Cupid's yoke to loose or bind;
15   These sweet flowers on fine bed, too,
    Us in their best language woo:
    Take me to thee, and thee to me.
    "No, no, no, no, my dear, let be."

    This small light the moon bestows
20   Serves thy beams but to disclose,
    So to raise my hap° more high;   *good fortune*
    Fear not else, none can us spy:
    Take me to thee, and thee to me.
    "No, no, no, no, my dear, let be."

25   That you heard was but a mouse,
    Dumb sleep holdeth all the house;
    Yet asleep methinks they say,
    "Young folks, take time while you may."
    Take me to thee, and thee to me.
30   "No, no, no, no, my dear, let be."

    Niggard° Time threats, if we miss   *stingy*
    This large offer of our bliss,

---

7. You want me to be silent.
8. Lack the mental faculties.
9. Like Petrarch, Sidney intersperses songs (eleven of them, in various verse forms) in his sequence. Some of them incorporate Stella's voice. This song appears between sonnets 85 and 86.

Long stay° ere he grant the same;   *wait*
Sweet, then, while each thing doth frame,°   *serve*
35 Take me to thee, and thee to me.
"No, no, no, no, my dear, let be."

Your fair mother is abed,
Candles out, and curtains spread;
She thinks you do letters write:
40 Write, but first let me indite:°   *dictate*
Take me to thee, and thee to me.
"No, no, no, no, my dear, let be."

Sweet, alas, why strive you thus?
Concord better fitteth us.
45 Leave to Mars the force of hands;
Your power in your beauty stands:
Take me to thee, and thee to me.
"No, no, no, no, my dear, let be."

Woe to me, and do you swear
50 Me to hate? But I forbear.°   *desist*
Cursèd be my destines° all,   *fates*
That brought me so high to fall:
Soon with my death I will please thee.
"No, no, no, no, my dear, let be."

87

When I was forced from Stella ever dear,
Stella, food of my thoughts, heart of my heart,
Stella, whose eyes make all my tempests clear,
By iron laws of duty to depart,
5   Alas, I found that she with me did smart:°   *suffer*
I saw that tears did in her eyes appear;
I saw that sighs her sweetest lips did part,
And her sad words my sadded sense did hear.
   For me, I wept to see pearls scattered so,
10   I sighed her sighs, and wailèd for her woe,
Yet swam in joy, such love in her was seen.
   Thus while th' effect most bitter was to me,
   And nothing than the cause more sweet could be,
I had been° vexed, if vexed I had not been.   *i.e., would have been*

89[1]

Now that of absence the most irksome night
   With darkest shade doth overcome my day,
   Since Stella's eyes, wont° to give me my day,   *accustomed*
Leaving my hemisphere, leave me in night,

---

1. A sonnet with only two rhyme words, *night* and *day*.

5 Each day seems long, and longs for long-stayed° night,   *long-delayed*
       The night, as tedious, woos th' approach of day;
       Tired with the dusty toils of busy day,
   Languished with horrors of the silent night,
   Suffering the evils both of the day and night,
10   While no night is more dark than is my day,
   Nor no day hath less quiet than my night,
       With such bad mixture of my night and day
   That, living thus in blackest winter night,
       I feel the flames of hottest summer day.

91

   Stella, while now by Honor's cruel might
       I am from° you, light of my life, mis-led,   *away from*
       And that fair you, my sun, thus overspread
   With absence' veil, I live in Sorrow's night,
5 If this dark place yet shew,° like candlelight,   *show*
       Some beauty's piece,[2] as amber-colored head,
       Milk hands, rose cheeks, or lips more sweet, more red,
   Or seeing jets,[3] black, but in blackness bright,
       They please I do confess, they please mine eyes:
10 But why? because of you they models be;
   Models such be wood-globes of glist'ring° skies.[4]   *glittering*
   Dear, therefore be not jealous over me,
       If you hear that they seem my heart to move:
       Not them, O no, but you in them I love.

94

   Grief, find the words; for thou hast made my brain
       So dark with misty vapors which arise
       From out thy heavy mold,° that in-bent° eyes   *earth / inward-turned*
   Can scarce discern the shape of mine own pain.
5 Do thou, then (for thou canst), do thou complain
       For[5] my poor soul, which now that sickness tries°   *experiences*
       Which even to sense, sense of itself denies,[6]
   Though harbingers[7] of Death lodge there his train.
       Or if thy love of plaint° yet mine forbears,[8]   *complaint, lamentation*
10 As of a caitiff worthy so to die,
   Yet wail thyself,° and wail with causeful° tears,   *for yourself / well-founded*
   That though in wretchedness thy life doth lie,
   Yet grow'st more wretched than thy nature bears,
   By being placed in such a wretch as I.

2. Some beauties in other women.
3. "Seeing jets": i.e., jet-black eyes.
4. Wooden globes of the heavens, with painted constellations and planets.
5. "Complain For": lament on behalf of.
6. I.e., his soul, sick unto death, is incapable of expression, cut off from the use of the senses.
7. Those sent in advance to find lodgings for a royal retinue ("train").
8. Nonetheless declines to make mine.

Eleventh Song[9]

"Who is it that this dark night
Underneath my window plaineth?"[1]
It is one who from thy sight
Being (ah) exiled, disdaineth
5   Every other, vulgar° light.   *common*

"Why, alas, and are you he?
Be not yet those fancies changèd?"
Dear, when you find change in me,
Though from me you be estrangèd,
10   Let my change to ruin be.

"Well, in absence this will die;
Leave° to see, and leave to wonder."   *cease*
Absence sure will help, if I
Can learn how myself to sunder
15   From what in my heart doth lie.

"But time will these thoughts remove:
Time doth work what no man knoweth."
Time doth as the subject prove;[2]
With time still° th' affection groweth   *ever*
20   In the faithful turtledove.

"What if you new beauties see;
Will not they stir new affection?"
I will think they pictures be,
Image-like of saint's perfection,
25   Poorly counterfeiting thee.

"But your reason's purest light,
Bids you leave such minds to nourish."[3]
Dear, do reason no such spite:
Never doth thy beauty flourish
30   More than in my reason's sight.

"But the wrongs love bears will make
Love at length leave undertaking."
No, the more fools it do shake,
In a ground of so firm making,
35   Deeper still they drive the stake.

"Peace, I think that some give ear:
Come no more, lest I get anger."[4]
Bliss, I will my bliss forbear,

---

9. This last song, a dialogue between Astrophil and Stella, is located between sonnets 104 and 105.
1. Complains (in song) of his love woes.
2. Things change in time according to their natures.
3. Stop indulging such thoughts.
4. The meaning is either "incur anger" or, perhaps, "become angry"—in any case, a threat designed to make Astrophil go away.

Fearing, sweet, you to endanger,
40　But my soul shall harbor there.

"Well, begone, begone I say,
Lest that Argus'[5] eyes perceive you."
O unjustest Fortune's sway,°   *power*
Which can make me thus to leave you,
45　And from louts to run away.

106

O absent presence, Stella is not here;
　False flattering Hope, that with so fair a face
　Bare me in hand,° that in this orphan place   *deceived me*
Stella, I say my Stella, should appear.
5　What say'st thou now? Where is that dainty cheer°   *countenance; food*
　Thou told'st mine eyes should help their famished case?
　But thou art gone, now that self-felt disgrace
Dost make me most to wish thy comfort near.
　But here I do store° of fair ladies meet,   *abundance*
10　Who may with charm of conversation sweet
Make in my heavy mold° new thoughts to grow: *earth*
　Sure they prevail as much with me, as he
　That bade his friend, but then new-maimed, to be
Merry with him, and not think of his woe.

108[6]

When Sorrow (using mine own fire's might)
　Melts down his lead into my boiling breast,
　Through that dark furnace to my heart oppressed
There shines a joy from thee, my only light;
5　But soon as thought of thee breeds my delight,
　And my young soul flutters to thee, his nest,
　Most rude Despair, my daily unbidden guest,
Clips straight° my wings, straight wraps me in his night,   *immediately*
　And makes me then bow down my head and say,
10　"Ah, what doth Phoebus'° gold that wretch avail,   *god of the sun*
Whom iron doors do keep from use of day?"
So strangely (alas) thy works in me prevail,
　That in my woes for thee thou art my joy,
　And in my joys for thee my only annoy.°   *trouble, pain*

1582?   1591, 1598

---

5. The hundred-eyed monster set by Juno to guard Io, a mistress of Jupiter whom Juno had transformed into a cow.

6. In many sonnet sequences, as here, the final poem brings no resolution.

MARY (SIDNEY) HERBERT, COUNTESS OF PEMBROKE
1562–1621

When her brother, the celebrated courtier and author Philip Sidney, died, in 1586, Mary Sidney, the countess of Pembroke, became the custodian not only of his writings but also of his last name. Though her marriage in 1577 to Henry Herbert, the second earl of Pembroke, represented a great social advance for her family—her offspring would no longer be members of the gentry but rather would be among the nation's tiny hereditary nobility—yet throughout her life the countess of Pembroke held onto her identity as a Sidney.

She had good reason to do so. The Sidneys were celebrated for their generous support of poets, clergymen, alchemists, naturalists, scientists, and musicians. The Pembroke country estate, Wilton, quickly became a gathering place for thinkers who enjoyed the countess's patronage and shared her staunch Protestant convictions and her literary interests. Books, pamphlets, and scores of poems were dedicated to her in the 1590s and thereafter, as well as to her brother Robert (whose country house, Penshurst, is praised in a well-known poem by Ben Jonson). Nicholas Breton and Samuel Daniel in particular benefited from her support, as did her niece, goddaughter, and frequent companion, Mary Wroth.

In one of the dedicatory poems to *Salve Deus Rex Judaeorum*, Aemilia Lanyer praises Mary Sidney not only for her generosity toward poets but also for those "works that are more deep and more profound." These include her translation of Robert Garnier's neoclassical French tragedy *Antonius* and a translation of the religious tract *A Discourse of Life and Death* by the French Protestant Philippe de Mornay. Her translation of Petrarch's *Triumph of Death* was the first in English to maintain the original *terza rima* (a particularly challenging rhyme scheme for an English versifier). Although translation was considered an especially appropriate genre for women to work in, it is a mistake to assume that Mary Sidney's efforts as a poet are merely derivative: Elizabethans understood that translation offered the opportunity not only for the display of linguistic and technical skills but also for the indirect expression of personal and political concerns. Mary Sidney also expressed these concerns more directly: among her original poems was a powerful elegy for her brother Philip and a short pastoral entertainment for Queen Elizabeth.

Mary Sidney was best known for having prepared a composite edition of Philip Sidney's *Arcadia* and for contributing the larger number (107) of the verse translations of the 150 biblical psalms that her brother had begun. Her very free renderings re-create the psalms as English poems, using an amazing variety of stanzaic and metrical patterns and some strikingly effective images. Widely circulated in manuscript, this influential collection was an important bridge between the many metrical paraphrases of psalms in this period and the works of the great religious lyric poets of the seventeenth century, especially George Herbert. Donne's poem *Upon the Translation of the Psalms by Sir Philip Sidney and the Countess of Pembroke His Sister* testifies to that importance: "They tell us *why*, and teach us *how* to sing."*

---

* For Mary Sidney's elegy on Sir Philip Sidney, her translation of Psalm 58, her "Dialogue between two shepherds," and the King James Bible version of the psalms printed here, see the supplemental ebook.

Psalm 52

Tyrant, why swell'st thou thus,
    Of mischief vaunting?
Since help from God to us
    Is never wanting.

5 Lewd° lies thy tongue contrives,   *vile*
    Loud lies it soundeth;
Sharper than sharpest knives
    With lies it woundeth.

Falsehood thy wit° approves,   *mind*
10   All truth rejected:
Thy will all vices loves,
    Virtue neglected.

Not words from cursèd thee,
    But gulfs° are pourèd;   *abysses, yawning chasms*
15 Gulfs wherein daily be
    Good men devourèd.

Think'st thou to bear it° so?   *bear it off, triumph*
    God shall displace thee;
God shall thee overthrow,
20   Crush thee, deface° thee.   *destroy*

The just shall fearing see
    These fearful chances,
And laughing shoot at thee
    With scornful glances.

25 Lo, lo, the wretched wight,°   *creature*
    Who, God disdaining,
His mischief made his might,
    His guard his gaining.°   *riches*

I as an olive tree
30   Still green shall flourish:
God's house the soil shall be
    My roots to nourish.

My trust on his true love
    Truly attending,
35 Shall never thence remove,
    Never see ending.

Thee will I honor still,
    Lord, for this justice;
There fix my hopes I will
40   Where thy saints' trust is.

Thy saints trust in thy name,
 Therein they joy them:
  Protected by the same,
  Nought° can annoy° them.   *nothing / harm*

ca. 1595   1823

Psalm 139

O Lord, in me there lieth nought
 But to thy search revealèd lies:
  For when I sit
  Thou markest it;°   *you note it*
5 No less thou notest when I rise;
Yea, closest closet° of my thought   *most secret private chamber*
 Hath open windows to thine eyes.

Thou walkest with me when I walk;
 When to my bed for rest I go,
10 I find thee there,
  And everywhere:
Not youngest thought in me doth grow,
No, not one word I cast° to talk   *resolve*
 But yet unuttered thou dost know.

15 If forth I march, thou goest before,
 If back I turn, thou com'st behind:
  So forth nor back
  Thy guard I lack,
Nay, on me too thy hand I find.
20 Well I thy wisdom may adore,
 But never reach with earthy mind.

To shun thy notice, leave thine eye,
 O whither might I take my way?
  To starry sphere?
25 Thy throne is there.
To dead men's undelightsome stay?°   *place*
There is thy walk, and there to lie
 Unknown° in vain I should assay.°   *(to thee) / attempt*

O sun, whom light nor flight can match,
30 Suppose thy lightful flightful wings
  Thou lend to me,
  And I could flee
As far as thee the ev'ning brings:
Even led to west he would me catch,
35 Nor should I lurk° with western things.   *hide*

Do thou thy best, O secret night,
  In sable veil to cover me:
    Thy sable veil
    Shall vainly fail;
40 With day unmasked my night shall be,
For night is day and darkness light,
  O father of all lights, to thee.

Each inmost piece in me is thine:
  While yet I in my mother dwelt,
45   All that me clad
    From thee I had.
Thou in my frame° hast strangely dealt: *form*
Needs in my praise thy works must shine,
  So inly them my thoughts have felt.

50 Thou, how my back was beam-wise laid,
  And raft'ring of my ribs, dost know;
    Know'st every point
    Of bone and joint,
How to this whole these parts did grow,
55 In brave° embroid'ry fair arrayed,   *splendid*
  Though wrought in shop both dark and low.

Nay, fashionless, ere form I took,
  Thy all and more beholding eye
    My shapeless shape
60   Could not escape:
All these, with times appointed by,[1]
Ere one had being, in the book
  Of thy foresight enrolled did lie.

My God, how I these studies prize,
65 That do thy hidden workings show!
    Whose sum is such
    No sum so much:
Nay, summed as° sand they sumless grow.   *like*
I lie to sleep, from sleep I rise,
70 Yet still° in thought with thee I go.   *always*

My God, if thou but one[2] wouldst kill,
  Then straight would leave my further chase[3]
    This cursèd brood
    Inured to blood,
75 Whose graceless taunts at thy disgrace
Have aimèd oft, and hating still
  Would with proud lies thy truth outface.°   *defy*

---

1. With appropriate times indicated (for each step of the work of creation).
2. Only one (wicked man).
3. Then immediately [the wicked] would stop pursuing me.

Hate not I them, who thee do hate?
Thine, Lord, I will the censure be.[4]
80   Detest I not
The cankered knot
Whom I against thee banded see?
O Lord, thou know'st in highest rate
I hate them all as foes to me.

85 Search me, my God, and prove my heart,
Examine me, and try° my thought;   test
And mark in me
If ought° there be   aught, anything
That hath with cause their anger wrought.
90 If not (as not) my life's each part,
Lord, safely guide from danger brought.

ca. 1595   1823

4. I.e., I leave it to you to censure them.

CHRISTOPHER MARLOWE
1564–1593

The son of a Canterbury shoemaker, Christopher Marlowe was born two months before William Shakespeare. In 1580 he went to Corpus Christi College, Cambridge, on a scholarship that was ordinarily awarded to students preparing for the ministry. He held the scholarship for the maximum time, six years, but did not take holy orders. Instead, he began to write plays. When he applied for his Master of Arts degree in 1587, the university was about to deny it to him on the ground that he intended to go abroad to join the dissident English Catholics at Rheims. But the Privy Council intervened and requested that because Marlowe had done the queen "good service" he be granted his degree at the next commencement. "It is not Her Majesty's pleasure," the government officials added, "that anyone employed as he had been in matters touching the benefit of his country should be defamed by those that are ignorant in the affairs he went about." Although much sensational information about Marlowe has been discovered in modern times, we are still largely "ignorant in the affairs he went about." The likeliest possibility is that he served as a spy or an agent provocateur against English Catholics who were conspiring to overthrow the Protestant regime.

Before he left Cambridge, Marlowe had written his tremendously successful play *Tamburlaine* and perhaps also, in collaboration with his younger Cambridge contemporary Thomas Nashe, the tragedy of *Dido, Queen of Carthage*. *Tamburlaine* dramatizes the exploits of a fourteenth-century Mongol warrior who rose from humble origins to conquer a huge territory that extended from the Black Sea to Delhi. In some sixteenth-century chronicles, Tamburlaine is represented as God's scourge, the instrument of divine wrath. In Marlowe's play there are few if any glimpses of a transcendent design. His hero is the vehicle for the expression of boundless energy and ambition, the impulse to strive ceaselessly for absolute dominance. Tamburlaine's conquests are achieved not only by force of arms but also by his extraordinary mastery of language, his "high astounding terms." The English theater audience had never before heard such resonant, immensely energetic blank verse. The great period of Elizabethan drama was launched by what Ben Jonson called "Marlowe's mighty line."

From the time of his first theatrical success, when he was twenty-three, Marlowe had only six years to live. They were not calm years. In 1589 he was involved in a brawl with one William Bradley, in which the poet Thomas Watson intervened and killed Bradley. Both poets were jailed, but Watson got off on a plea of self-defense, and Marlowe was released. In 1591 Marlowe was living in London with the playwright Thomas Kyd, who later, under torture, gave information to the Privy Council accusing him of atheism and treason. On May 30, 1593, an informer named Richard Baines submitted a note to the Council which, on the evidence of Marlowe's own alleged utterances, branded him with atheism, sedition, and homosexuality. Four days later, at an inn in the London suburb of Deptford, Marlowe was killed by a dagger thrust, purportedly in an argument over the bill. Modern scholars have discovered that the murderer and the others present in the room at the inn had connections to the world of spies, double agents, and swindlers to which Marlowe himself was in some way linked. Those who were arrested in connection with the murder were briefly held and then quietly released.

On the bare surface, Marlowe's tragic vision seems for the most part religiously and socially conventional. Tamburlaine at last suffers divine retribution and death at the end of the sequel, *Tamburlaine Part II*; the central character of *The Jew of Malta* is a monstrous anti-Semitic caricature; *Doctor Faustus* and *Edward II* (which treats the tragic fate of a homosexual king) demonstrate the destruction that awaits those who rebel against God or violate the official moral order. Yet there is a force at work in these plays that relentlessly questions and undermines conventional morality. The crime for which Tamburlaine is apparently struck down is the burning of the Muslim Koran; the Jew of Malta turns out to be, if anything, less ruthless and hypocritical than his Christian counterparts; and Edward II's life of homoerotic indulgence seems innocent in comparison with the cynical and violent dealings of the corrupt rebels who turn against him. In a way that goes far beyond the demands of moral instruction, Marlowe seems to revel in the depiction of flamboyant transgression, physical abjection, and brutal punishment. Whether as a radical pursuit of absolute liberty or as an expression of sheer destructive negativity, Marlowe's plays, written in the turbulent years before his murder at the age of twenty-nine, have continued to fascinate and disturb readers and audiences.

Hero and Leander

Marlowe's mythological erotic poem is a free and original treatment of a classic tale about two ill-fated lovers. The story derives from a version by the Alexandrian poet Musaeus (ca. fifth century C.E.), but in its blend of poignancy and irony *Hero and Leander* is closer to that of the Roman poet Ovid, who briefly recounts the story in two epistles of his *Heroides* and who refers to it in one of his *Elegies,* which Marlowe translated.

Hero and Leander is a rich and elusive poem: it is comic, erotic, decorative, cruel; now swiftly narrative, now digressive; playful and yet, in a light way, philosophical. The characters are evidently not intended to be consistent or psychologically credible; they inhabit a world of fancy, of strange contrasts between innocence and the wild riot of amorous intrigues among the gods that is Ovid's subject matter. Hero is paradoxically a nun vowed to chastity and a devotee of Venus, the love goddess; Leander is both a sharp, sophisticated seducer and a sexual innocent. The deadpan asides, with their irony, hyperbole, and cynicism mingling with exuberant delight in the body's instinctual freedom, heighten the poem's elusiveness, its cunning evasion of all fixed categories.

Hero and Leander cannot be precisely dated. Marlowe's translations of Ovid, to which *Hero and Leander* is closely related in spirit, are generally thought to be work of the later 1580s. But, alternatively, Marlowe may have been participating in a vogue for brief erotic epics (epyllia, as they are sometimes called) that dates from the early 1590s, when Shakespeare composed his contribution to the genre, *Venus and Adonis*. *Hero and Leander* was entered in the Stationers' Register (a list of forthcoming titles) on September 28, 1593, four months after the poet's death, but the earliest known edition was not published until 1598.

Marlowe left his poem unfinished; George Chapman, the playwright and translator of Homer, undertook to complete it. Chapman's moralizing, weightily philosophical continuation, which divides the poem into "sestiads" (named after Sestos, where Hero lived), was published shortly after Marlowe's fragment. The work is printed here without Chapman's additions.

Hero and Leander

> On Hellespont, guilty of true-loves'° blood,   *sweethearts'*
> In view and opposite, two cities stood,
> Sea-borderers, disjoined by Neptune's might;
> The one Abydos, the other Sestos hight.°   *called*
> 5 At Sestos Hero dwelt; Hero the fair,
> Whom young Apollo courted for her hair,
> And offered as a dower his burning throne,
> Where she should sit for men to gaze upon.
> The outside of her garments were of lawn,[1]
> 10 The lining purple silk, with gilt stars drawn;
> Her wide sleeves green, and bordered with a grove
> Where Venus in her naked glory strove
> To please the careless and disdainful eyes
> Of proud Adonis, that before her lies;[2]
> 15 Her kirtle° blue, whereon was many a stain,   *long dress*
> Made with the blood of wretched lovers slain.[3]
> Upon her head she ware a myrtle wreath,
> From whence her veil reached to the ground beneath.
> Her veil was artificial flowers and leaves,
> 20 Whose workmanship both man and beast deceives;
> Many would praise the sweet smell as she passed,
> When 'twas the odor which her breath forth cast;
> And there for honey, bees have sought in vain,
> And, beat from thence, have lighted there again.
> 25 About her neck hung chains of pebble-stone,
> Which, lightened° by her neck, like diamonds shone.   *illuminated*
> She ware no gloves, for neither sun nor wind

1. A kind of fine linen or thin cambric.
2. Venus's love for the young hunter Adonis and his death in a boar hunt are recounted by Ovid, and by Shakespeare in *Venus and Adonis*.

3. The extravagant claim is made that many "wretched lovers" had committed suicide at her feet because Hero would not have them.

Would burn or parch her hands, but to her mind°   *as she wished*
Or° warm or cool them, for they took delight   *either*
30 To play upon those hands, they were so white.
Buskins° of shells all silvered usèd she,   *boots*
And branched with blushing coral to the knee,
Where sparrows perched, of hollow pearl and gold,
Such as the world would wonder to behold;
35 Those with sweet water oft her handmaid fills,
Which, as she went,° would chirrup through the bills.   *walked*
Some say, for her the fairest Cupid pined,
And looking in her face, was strooken blind.
But this is true: so like was one the other,
40 As he imagined Hero was his mother;°   *i.e., Venus*
And oftentimes into her bosom flew,
About her naked neck his bare arms threw,
And laid his childish head upon her breast,
And with still° panting rocked, there took his rest.   *continual*
45 So lovely fair was Hero, Venus' nun,[4]
As Nature wept, thinking she was undone,
Because she took more from her than she left
And of such wondrous beauty her bereft;
Therefore, in sign her° treasure suffered wrack,°   *i.e., Nature's / destruction*
50 Since Hero's time hath half the world been black.
Amorous Leander, beautiful and young
(Whose tragedy divine Musaeus[5] sung),
Dwelt at Abydos; since him dwelt there none
For whom succeeding times make greater moan.
55 His dangling tresses that were never shorn,
Had they been cut and unto Colchos borne,
Would have allured the vent'rous youth of Greece[6]
To hazard more than for the Golden Fleece.
Fair Cynthia° wished his arms might be her sphere;°   *the moon / orbit*
60 Grief makes her pale, because she moves not there.
His body was as straight as Circe's wand;[7]
Jove might have sipped out nectar from his hand.
Even as delicious meat is to the taste,
So was his neck in touching, and surpassed
65 The white of Pelops' shoulder.[8] I could tell ye
How smooth his breast was, and how white his belly,
And whose immortal fingers did imprint
That heavenly path, with many a curious dint,°   *exquisite indentation*
That runs along his back; but my rude° pen   *crude*
70 Can hardly blazon forth the loves of men,
Much less of powerful gods; let it suffice

---

4. The connotations of these two words are contradictory. Hero is a maiden in attendance at the temple of Venus, who is, of course, the goddess of physical love.
5. The author of the Greek poem on which *Hero and Leander* is remotely based. Though he lived in late antiquity (ca. 5th century C.E.), he was sometimes confused with a legendary early Musaeus, supposed son of Orpheus—hence Marlowe calls him "divine."
6. "Colchos": the country in Asia where the Argonauts ("the ven'trous youth of Greece") found the Golden Fleece.
7. The wand with which Circe, in the *Odyssey*, turned men into beasts.
8. Pelops, according to Ovid, had a shoulder of ivory.

That my slack° muse sings of Leander's eyes,　　　　　　　*dull*
Those orient° cheeks and lips, exceeding his　　　　　　　*shining*
That leapt into the water for a kiss
75　Of his own shadow,° and despising many,　　　　　　　*reflection*
Died ere he could enjoy the love of any.[9]
Had wild Hippolytus[1] Leander seen,
Enamored of his beauty had he been;
His presence made the rudest peasant melt,
80　That in the vast uplandish country dwelt;
The barbarous Thracian soldier, moved with nought,
Was moved with him, and for his favor sought.
Some swore he was a maid in man's attire,
For in his looks were all that men desire:
85　A pleasant smiling cheek, a speaking° eye,　　　　　　　*expressive*
A brow for love to banquet royally;
And such as knew he was a man, would say,
"Leander, thou art made for amorous play;
Why art thou not in love, and loved of° all?　　　　　　　*by*
90　Though thou be fair, yet be not thine own thrall."°　　　*captive*
　　The men of wealthy Sestos every year,
For his sake whom their goddess held so dear,
Rose-cheeked Adonis, kept a solemn feast.
Thither resorted many a wandering guest
95　To meet their loves; such as had none at all
Came lovers home from this great festival;
For every street, like to a firmament,
Glistered° with breathing stars, who, where they went,　　*glittered*
Frighted the melancholy earth, which deemed
100　Eternal heaven to burn, for so it seemed
As if another Phaëton[2] had got
The guidance of the sun's rich chariot.
But far above the loveliest, Hero shined,
And stole away th' enchanted gazer's mind;
105　For like sea nymphs' inveigling harmony,
So was her beauty to the standers by.
Nor that night-wandering pale and watery star°　　　　　*the moon*
(When yawning dragons draw her thirling car°　　　　　*chariot*
From Latmos' mount[3] up to the gloomy sky,
110　Where, crowned with blazing light and majesty,
She proudly sits) more over-rules° the flood°　　　　*rules over / tide*
Than she the hearts of those that near her stood.
Even as when gaudy nymphs pursue the chase,°　　　　　*hunt*
Wretched Ixion's shaggy-footed race,[4]
115　Incensed with savage heat, gallop amain
From steep pine-bearing mountains to the plain,
So ran the people forth to gaze upon her,

9. An allusion to Narcissus.
1. Like Adonis, he preferred hunting to love.
2. A son of the sun god, he drove his father's chariot erratically across the sky and almost burned up the world.
3. Latmos was the mountain where the moon vis-

ited her lover, Endymion. "Thirling": flying like a spear.
4. The centaurs, fathered by Ixion on a cloud. For his presumption in loving Juno, Ixion was chained to a wheel, hence "wretched."

And all that viewed her were enamored on her.
And as in fury of a dreadful fight,
120 Their fellows being slain or put to flight,
Poor soldiers stand with fear of death dead-strooken,
So at her presence all, surprised and tooken,
Await the sentence of her scornful eyes;
He whom she favors lives, the other dies.
125 There might you see one sigh, another rage,
And some, their violent passions to assuage,
Compile sharp satires; but alas, too late,
For faithful love will never turn to hate.
And many, seeing great princes were denied,
130 Pined as they went, and thinking on her, died.
On this feast day, oh, cursèd day and hour!
Went Hero thorough° Sestos, from her tower   *through*
To Venus' temple, where unhappily,
As after chanced, they did each other spy.
135 So fair a church as this had Venus none;
The walls were of discolored° jasper stone,   *many-colored*
Wherein was Proteus[5] carved, and o'erhead
A lively° vine of green sea-agate spread,   *lifelike*
Where, by one hand, light-headed Bacchus[6] hung,
140 And with the other, wine from grapes out-wrung.
Of crystal shining fair the pavement was;
The town of Sestos called it Venus' glass;°   *looking glass*
There might° you see the gods in sundry shapes,   *could*
Committing heady° riots, incest, rapes: *passionate; violent*
145 For know that underneath this radiant floor
Was Danaë's statue in a brazen tower,
Jove slyly stealing from his sister's[7] bed
To dally with Idalian Ganymed,
And for his love Europa bellowing loud,[8]
150 And tumbling with the rainbow in a cloud;[9]
Blood-quaffing Mars heaving the iron net
Which limping Vulcan and his Cyclops set;[1]
Love kindling fire to burn such towns as Troy;
Sylvanus weeping for the lovely boy[2]
155 That now is turned into a cypress tree,
Under whose shade the wood-gods love to be.
And in the midst a silver altar stood;
There Hero sacrificing turtles'[3] blood,
Vailed° to the ground, veiling her eyelids close,   *bowed down*
160 And modestly they opened as she rose;
Thence flew love's arrow with the golden head,[4]

---

5. A sea god, who could change his shape at will.
6. God of wine and revelry.
7. Juno's; she was Jove's wife. Danaë, imprisoned in a tower, was visited by Jove in the form of a shower of gold.
8. To abduct Europa, Jove took the form of a bull. "Ganymed": a beautiful youth whom Jove kidnapped from Mount Ida, hence "Idalian."
9. Jove as Jupiter Pluvius, god of rain, frolicking with Iris, goddess of the rainbow. But no such tryst is found in classical mythology.
1. Vulcan used a net to trap Venus (his wife) and Mars, "blood-quaffing" god of war, in the act of love. "Cyclops": probably plural; members of this one-eyed race worked as Vulcan's assistants.
2. Cyparissus, beloved of the wood god Sylvanus.
3. Turtledoves, symbolic of constancy in love.
4. The "golden head" of some of Cupid's arrows produced love; he had others, of lead, that produced dislike.

And thus Leander was enamorèd.
Stone still he stood, and evermore he gazed,
Till with the fire that from his countenance blazed,
165 Relenting Hero's gentle heart was strook;
Such force and virtue° hath an amorous look.   *power*
    It lies not in our power to love or hate,
For will in us is overruled by fate.
When two are stripped, long ere the course° begin   *race*
170 We wish that one should lose, the other win;
And one especially do we affect°   *fancy*
Of two gold ingots, like in each respect.
The reason no man knows, let it suffice,
What we behold is censured° by our eyes.   *judged*
175 Where both deliberate, the love is slight;
Who ever loved, that loved not at first sight?[5]
    He kneeled, but unto her devoutly prayed.
Chaste Hero to herself thus softly said,
"Were I the saint he worships, I would hear him,"
180 And as she spake those words, came somewhat near him.
He started up; she blushed as one ashamed,
Wherewith Leander much more was inflamed.
He touched her hand; in touching it she trembled:
Love deeply grounded hardly° is dissembled.   *with difficulty*
185 These lovers parlèd° by the touch of hands;   *spoke*
True love is mute, and oft amazèd stands.
Thus while dumb signs their yielding hearts entangled,
The air with sparks of living fire was spangled,
And Night, deep drenched in misty Acheron,[6]
190 Heaved up her head, and half the world upon
Breathed darkness forth. (Dark night is Cupid's day.)
And now begins Leander to display
Love's holy fire, with words, with sighs and tears,
Which like sweet music entered Hero's ears,
195 And yet at every word she turned aside
And always cut him off as he replied.
At last, like to a bold sharp sophister,[7]
With cheerful hope thus he accosted° her: *addressed*
    "Fair creature, let me speak without offense;
200 I would my rude° words had the influence   *rough*
To lead thy thoughts as thy fair looks do mine;
Then shouldst thou be his prisoner, who is thine.
Be not unkind and fair—misshapen stuff°   *persons*
Are of behavior boisterous and rough.
205 O shun me not, but hear me ere you go;
God knows I cannot force° love, as you do.   *compel*
My words shall be as spotless as my youth,
Full of simplicity and naked truth.
This sacrifice, whose sweet perfume descending
210 From Venus' altar to your footsteps bending,°   *turning*

5. Shakespeare quotes this famous line in *As You Like It* (3.5.83).
6. One of the rivers of Hades.

7. Sophist, person skilled in arguments, especially specious ones.

Doth testify that you exceed her far
To whom you offer and whose nun you are.
Why should you worship her? Her you surpass
As much as sparkling diamonds flaring° glass.   *glaring*
215 A diamond set in lead his worth retains;
A heavenly nymph, beloved of human swains,°   *youths*
Receives no blemish but ofttimes more grace;
Which makes me hope, although I am but base—
Base in respect of° thee, divine and pure—   *in comparison with*
220 Dutiful service may thy love procure;
And I in duty will excel all other,
As thou in beauty dost exceed Love's mother.°   *Venus*
Nor heaven, nor thou, were made to gaze upon;
As heaven preserves all things, so save thou one.
225 A stately builded ship, well rigged and tall,
The ocean maketh more majestical:
Why vowest thou then to live in Sestos here,
Who on Love's seas more glorious wouldst appear?
Like untuned golden strings all women are,
230 Which, long time lie untouched, will harshly jar.[8]
Vessels of brass, oft handled, brightly shine;
What difference betwixt the richest mine°   *ore*
And basest mold,° but use? for both not used   *earth*
Are of like worth. Then treasure is abused
235 When misers keep it; being put to loan,
In time it will return us two for one.
Rich robes themselves and others do adorn;
Neither themselves nor others, if not worn.
Who builds a palace and rams up the gate
240 Shall see it ruinous and desolate.
Ah, simple Hero, learn thyself to cherish;
Lone women, like to empty houses, perish.
Less sins the poor rich man that starves himself
In heaping up a mass of drossy pelf,°   *wealth*
245 Than such as you: his golden earth remains,
Which after his decease some other gains.
But this fair gem, sweet in the loss alone,
When you fleet hence can be bequeathed to none.
Or if it could, down from th' enameled° sky   *many-colored*
250 All heaven would come to claim this legacy,
And with intestine° broils the world destroy   *internal, civil*
And quite confound Nature's sweet harmony.
Well therefore by the gods decreed it is,
We human creatures should enjoy that bliss.
255 One is no number;[9] maids are nothing then
Without the sweet society of men.
Wilt thou live single still? One shalt thou be,
Though never-singling Hymen[1] couple thee.
Wild savages, that drink of running springs,

---

8. I.e., instruments not played will be out of tune and harsh.
9. A traditional concept, going back to Aristotle.

1. God of marriage. "Never-singling": i.e., one who never separates, but always joins.

260 Think water far excels all earthly things;
But they that daily taste neat° wine despise it.   undiluted
Virginity, albeit° some highly prize it,   although
Compared with marriage, had you tried them both,
Differs as much as wine and water doth.
265 Base bullion for the stamp's sake[2] we allow:°   approve
Even so for men's impression do we you;
By which alone, our reverend fathers[3] say,
Women receive perfection every way.
This idol which you term Virginity,
270 Is neither essence,° subject to the eye,   something real
No, nor to any one exterior sense,
Nor hath it any place of residence,
Nor is 't of earth or mold° celestial,   form
Or capable of any form at all.
275 Of that which hath no being do not boast:
Things that are not at all are never lost.
Men foolishly do call it virtuous:
What virtue is it that is born with us?[4]
Much less can honor be ascribed thereto:
280 Honor is purchased by the deeds we do.
Believe me, Hero, honor is not won
Until some honorable deed be done.
Seek you for chastity, immortal fame,
And know that some have wronged Diana's name?[5]
285 Whose name is it, if she be false or not,
So she be fair, but some vile tongues will blot?
But you are fair, aye me! so wondrous fair,
So young, so gentle, and so debonair,°   gracious
As Greece will think, if thus you live alone,
290 Some one or other keeps you as his own.
Then, Hero, hate me not, nor from me fly
To follow swiftly-blasting° infamy.   -blighting
Perhaps thy sacred priesthood makes thee loath.
Tell me, to whom madest thou that heedless oath?"
295 "To Venus," answered she, and as she spake,
Forth from those two tralucent cisterns° brake   i.e., translucent eyes
A stream of liquid pearl, which down her face
Made milk-white paths whereon the gods might trace°   go
To Jove's high court. He thus replied: "The rites
300 In which Love's beauteous empress most delights
Are banquets, Doric music,[6] midnight revel,
Plays, masques, and all that stern age counteth evil.
Thee as a holy idiot doth she scorn;
For thou, in vowing chastity, hast sworn
305 To rob her name and honor, and thereby

---

2. For the impression that makes metal ("bullion") into a coin.
3. Ancient philosophers, like Aristotle.
4. I.e., a virtue is not a virtue unless it is
acquired.
5. I.e., no fame for chastity is secure. Even Diana,

goddess of chastity, has been slandered.
6. A solemn, military mode. Leander would more
appropriately have said "Lydian" (as in Milton's
"L'Allegro," line 136); Lydian music was soft and
sensual.

Commit'st a sin far worse than perjury—
Even sacrilege against her Deity,
Through regular and formal purity.
To expiate which sin, kiss and shake hands;
310 Such sacrifice as this Venus demands."
    Thereat she smiled and did deny him so
As, put° thereby, yet might he hope for mo.°   *put off / more*
Which makes him quickly reinforce his speech
And her in humble manner thus beseech:
315   "Though neither gods nor men may thee deserve,
Yet for her sake whom you have vowed to serve,
Abandon fruitless, cold Virginity,
The gentle Queen of Love's sole enemy.
Then shall you most resemble Venus' nun,
320 When Venus' sweet rites are performed and done.
Flint-breasted Pallas[7] joys in single life,
But Pallas and your mistress are at strife.
Love, Hero, then, and be not tyrannous,
But heal the heart that thou hast wounded thus,
325 Nor stain thy youthful years with avarice;[8]
Fair fools delight to be accounted nice.°   *shy, reluctant*
The richest corn° dies, if it be not reaped;   *grain*
Beauty alone is lost, too warily kept."
    These arguments he used, and many more,
330 Wherewith she yielded, that was won before.
Hero's looks yielded, but her words made war:
Women are won when they begin to jar.°   *dispute*
Thus, having swallowed Cupid's golden hook,
The more she strived, the deeper was she strook.
335 Yet, evilly° feigning anger, strove she still   *badly*
And would be thought to grant against her will.
So having paused a while, at last she said:
"Who taught thee rhetoric to deceive a maid?
Aye me, such words as these should I abhor,
340 And yet I like them for the orator."
    With that, Leander stooped to have embraced her,
But from his spreading arms away she cast her,
And thus bespake him: "Gentle youth, forbear
To touch the sacred garments which I wear.
345   "Upon a rock, and underneath a hill,
Far from the town, where all is whist° and still,   *silent*
Save that the sea, playing on yellow sand,
Sends forth a rattling murmur to the land,
Whose sound allures the golden Morpheus[9]
350 In silence of the night to visit us,
My turret stands, and there, God knows, I play
With Venus' swans and sparrows[1] all the day.
A dwarfish beldame° bears me company,   *old hag*

7. Athena, a rival goddess, usually portrayed in armor.
8. I.e., by hoarding the treasure of her beauty.
9. God of sleep. "Golden slumbers" was a common expression.
1. Venus was often portrayed in a chariot drawn by swans, and sparrows were associated with her because of their traditionally reputed lechery.

That hops about the chamber where I lie
355 And spends the night, that might be better spent,
In vain discourse and apish° merriment.   *silly*
Come thither." As she spake this, her tongue tripped,
For unawares "Come thither" from her slipped;
And suddenly her former color changed
360 And here and there her eyes through anger ranged.
And like a planet, moving several° ways,[2]   *different*
At one self° instant, she, poor soul, assays,°   *one and the same / tries*
Loving, not to love at all, and every part
Strove to resist the motions of her heart;
365 And hands so pure, so innocent, nay, such
As might have made heaven stoop to have a touch,
Did she uphold to Venus, and again
Vowed spotless chastity, but all in vain.
Cupid beat down her prayers with his wings;
370 Her vows above the empty air he flings.
All deep enraged, his sinewy° bow he bent,   *strong*
And shot a shaft that burning from him went,
Wherewith she, strooken, looked so dolefully
As made Love sigh to see his tyranny.
375 And as she wept, her tears to pearl he turned,
And wound them on his arm, and for her mourned.
Then towards the palace of the Destinies,°   *the Fates*
Laden with languishment and grief, he flies,
And to those stern nymphs humbly made request
380 Both might enjoy each other and be blessed.
But with a ghastly dreadful countenance,
Threatening a thousand deaths at every glance,
They answered Love, nor would vouchsafe° so much   *grant*
As one poor word, their hate to him was such.
385 Harken a while, and I will tell you why:
Heaven's wingèd herald, Jove-born Mercury,
The selfsame day that he asleep had laid
Enchanted Argus,[3] spied a country maid
Whose careless hair, instead of pearl t' adorn it,
390 Glistered with dew, as one that seemed to scorn it;[4]
Her breath as fragrant as the morning rose,
Her mind pure, and her tongue untaught to glose.°   *deceive*
Yet proud she was, for lofty pride that dwells
In towered courts is oft in shepherds' cells,°   *huts*
395 And too-too well the fair vermilion knew,
And silver tincture of her cheeks, that drew
The love of every swain. On her, this god
Enamored was, and with his snaky rod[5]
Did charm her nimble feet and made her stay;
400 The while upon a hillock down he lay,

2. In Ptolemaic astronomy each planet moved in
its own orbit or sphere but was also carried along
in the motion of the surrounding spheres.
3. Mercury (or Hermes), the messenger god with
winged feet, put to sleep Argus, the hundred-eyed
monster whom Juno had placed as a guard over Io,
with whom her husband, Jupiter, was in love. The
myth that follows is Marlowe's invention.
4. I.e., pearl or other jewelry.
5. The caduceus (now the symbol of medicine).

And sweetly on his pipe began to play,
And with smooth speech, her fancy to assay,°   *test*
Till in his twining arms he locked her fast,
And then he wooed with kisses, and at last,
405   As shepherds do, her on the ground he laid,
And tumbling in the grass, he often strayed
Beyond the bounds of shame, in being bold
To eye those parts which no eye should behold;
And, like an insolent commanding lover,
410   Boasting his parentage, would needs discover
The way to new Elysium; but she,
Whose only dower was her chastity,
Having striven in vain, was now about to cry
And crave the help of shepherds that were nigh.
415   Herewith he stayed his fury,° and began   *passion*
To give her leave to rise. Away she ran;
After went Mercury, who used such cunning
As she, to hear his tale, left off her running.
Maids are not won by brutish force and might,
420   But speeches full of pleasure and delight.
And knowing Hermes courted her, was glad
That she such loveliness and beauty had
As could provoke his liking, yet was mute,
And neither would deny nor grant his suit.
425   Still vowed he love; she, wanting° no excuse   *lacking*
To feed him with delays, as women use,°   *as women usually do*
Or thirsting after immortality
(All women are ambitious naturally),
Imposed upon her lover such a task
430   As he ought not perform, nor yet she ask.
A draft of flowing nectar she requested,
Wherewith the king of gods and men is feasted.
He, ready to accomplish what she willed,
Stole some from Hebe (Hebe Jove's cup filled)
435   And gave it to his simple rustic love,
Which being known (as what is hid from Jove?)
He inly stormed and waxed more furious
Than for the fire filched by Prometheus,
And thrusts him down from heaven. He, wandering here,
440   In mournful terms,° with sad and heavy cheer,°   *condition / countenance*
Complained to Cupid. Cupid, for his sake,
To be revenged on Jove did undertake;
And those on whom heaven, earth, and hell relies
(I mean the adamantine[6] Destinies)
445   He wounds with love and forced them equally
To dote upon deceitful Mercury.
They offered him the deadly fatal knife
That shears the slender threads of human life;[7]

6. Of extreme hardness (so called because the
Destinies'—or Fates'—decrees were irrevocable).
7. According to classical mythology, the Fates

spun and cut the thread that measures each
life.

At his fair feathered feet the engines° laid   *contrivances*
450   Which th' earth from ugly Chaos' den upweighed.[8]
These he regarded not, but did entreat
That Jove, usurper of his father's seat,
Might presently° be banished into hell   *immediately*
And agèd Saturn in Olympus dwell.
455   They granted what he craved,° and once again   *requested*
Saturn and Ops began their golden reign.
Murder, rape, war, lust, and treachery
Were with Jove closed in Stygian empery.°   *realm*
But long this blessèd time continued not;
460   As soon as he his wishèd purpose got,
He, reckless of his promise, did despise
The love of th' everlasting Destinies.
They seeing it, both Love and him abhorred,
And Jupiter unto his place restored.[9]
465   And but that Learning, in despite of Fate,
Will mount aloft and enter heaven gate,
And to the seat of Jove itself advance,
Hermes had slept in hell with Ignorance.
Yet as a punishment they added this,
470   That he and Poverty should always kiss.[1]
And to this day is every scholar poor;
Gross gold from them runs headlong to the boor.°   *ignorant clod*
Likewise the angry sisters, thus deluded,
To venge themselves on Hermes, have concluded
475   That Midas' brood[2] shall sit in Honor's chair,
To which the Muses' sons are only heir.
And fruitful wits° that inaspiring[3] are   *minds*
Shall discontent run into regions far;
And few great lords in virtuous deeds shall joy,
480   But be surprised with° every garish toy,°   *captivated by / trifle*
And still° enrich the lofty servile clown,°   *ever / ignorant person*
Who, with encroaching guile, keeps learning down.
Then muse not° Cupid's suit no better sped,   *i.e., don't be surprised*
Seeing in their loves the Fates were injurèd.
485   By this, sad Hero, with love unacquainted,
Viewing Leander's face, fell down and fainted.
He kissed her and breathed life into her lips,

8. The Fates also controlled the supports that had held up ("upweighed") the earth since it arose out of Chaos, the yawning abyss from which all things came.

9. The story in lines 451–64 may be summarized as follows: Mercury scorns the gifts offered by the Fates but asks instead that Jove be dethroned (Jove had overthrown his father, Saturn, who ruled heaven during the Golden Age). Mercury persuades the Fates to reverse this revolution, so Saturn and his wife, Ops, return to Olympus and Jove is thrust down into "Stygian empery" (line 458), or Hades. During the Golden Age there was no murder, rape, war, lust, or treachery; these came in with Jove, so when he is sent to Hades they go with him. But this second Golden Age

did not last long, because once he got what he wanted, Mercury forgot the Destinies and they restored Jove.

1. Mercury, the god of learning, would have slept in hell with Ignorance were it not that Learning is so divine that it always mounts up, even to heaven, the "seat of Jove." But it was not beyond the Fates' power to make Learning and Poverty go together, which they decreed in revenge for Mercury's neglect.

2. The rich, because everything Midas touched turned to gold; also the stupid, because Midas, judging a musical contest between Apollo and Pan, preferred the latter, against all sensible opinion.

3. Not ambitious for riches or power.

Wherewith, as one displeased, away she trips.
Yet as she went, full often looked behind,
490   And many poor excuses did she find
To linger by the way, and once she stayed
And would have turned again, but was afraid
In offering parley to be counted light.°   *immodest*
So on she goes, and in her idle flight
495   Her painted fan of curlèd plumes let fall,
Thinking to train° Leander therewithal.   *entice*
He, being a novice, knew not what she meant,
But stayed, and after her a letter sent,
Which joyful Hero answered in such sort
500   As he had hope to scale the beauteous fort
Wherein the liberal Graces[4] locked their wealth,
And therefore to her tower he got by stealth.
Wide open stood the door; he need not climb,
And she herself before the pointed° time   *appointed*
505   Had spread the board,° with roses strewed the room,   *set the table*
And oft looked out, and mused° he did not come.   *wondered*
At last he came; O who can tell the greeting
These greedy lovers had at their first meeting?
He asked, she gave, and nothing was denied;
510   Both to each other quickly were affied.°   *engaged*
Look how° their hands, so were their hearts united, *just as*
And what he did, she willingly requited.
(Sweet are the kisses, the embracements sweet,
When like desires and affections meet,
515   For from the earth to heaven is Cupid raised,
Where fancy is in equal balance peised.°)   *weighed*
Yet she this rashness suddenly repented
And turned aside and to herself lamented,
As if her name and honor had been wronged
520   By being possessed of him for whom she longed.
Ay, and she wished, albeit not from her heart,
That he would leave her turret and depart.
The mirthful god of amorous pleasure smiled
To see how he this captive nymph beguiled,°   *deceived*
525   For hitherto he did but fan the fire
And kept it down that it might mount the higher.
Now waxed she jealous° lest his love abated,   *possessively fearful*
Fearing her own thoughts made her to be hated.
Therefore unto him hastily she goes
530   And, like light Salmacis,[5] her body throws
Upon his bosom where, with yielding eyes,
She offers up herself a sacrifice
To slake his anger, if he were displeased.
O what god would not therewith be appeased?
535   Like Aesop's cock,[6] this jewel he enjoyed,

---

4. Three goddesses, embodying aspects of beauty.
5. An amorous nymph in Ovid's *Metamorphoses*.
6. In Aesop's fable, a cock, scratching in the barn-yard, uncovers a jewel but prefers a barley corn to it.

And as a brother with his sister toyed,
Supposing nothing else was to be done,
Now he her favor and good will had won.
But know you not that creatures wanting sense°   *lacking intelligence*
540 By nature have a mutual appetence,[7]
And wanting organs to advance a step,
Moved by love's force, unto each other leap?
Much more in subjects having intellect
Some hidden influence breeds like effect.
545 Albeit Leander, rude° in love and raw,   *untutored*
Long dallying with Hero, nothing saw
That might delight him more, yet he suspected
Some amorous rites or other were neglected.
Therefore unto his body, hers he clung;
550 She, fearing on the rushes[8] to be flung,
Strived with redoubled strength; the more she strived,
The more a gentle, pleasing heat revived,
Which taught him all that elder lovers know.
And now the same gan so to scorch and glow,
555 As, in plain terms, yet cunningly,° he craved° it.   *skillfully / asked for*
(Love always makes those eloquent that have it.)
She, with a kind of granting, put him by it,
And, ever as he thought himself most nigh it,
Like to the tree of Tantalus,[9] she fled,
560 And, seeming lavish, saved her maidenhead.
Ne'er king more sought to keep his diadem
Than Hero this inestimable gem.
Above our life we love a steadfast friend;
Yet, when a token of great worth we send,
565 We often kiss it, often look thereon,
And stay the messenger that would be gone.
No marvel then, though Hero would not yield
So soon to part from that she dearly held.
Jewels being lost are found again, this never;
570 'Tis lost but once, and once lost, lost forever.
    Now had the Morn espied her lover's steeds,[1]
Whereat she starts, puts on her purple weeds,°   *clothes*
And, red for anger that he stayed so long,
All headlong throws herself the clouds among.
575 And now Leander, fearing to be missed,
Embraced her suddenly, took leave, and kissed;
Long was he taking leave, and loath to go,
And kissed again, as lovers use° to do.   *are accustomed*
Sad Hero wrung him by the hand and wept,
580 Saying, "Let your vows and promises be kept."
Then, standing at the door, she turned about,
As loath to see Leander going out.
And now the sun that through th' horizon peeps,

---

7. Attraction, as iron to a magnet.
8. Reeds used as carpeting in Elizabethan homes.
9. Tantalus was punished in Hades by constantly

reaching for fruit from a tree that eluded him and
by trying to drink water that also escaped him.
1. The horses that pull the chariot of the sun.

As pitying these lovers, downward creeps,
585 So that in silence of the cloudy night,
Though it was morning, did he take his flight.
But what the secret trusty night concealed,
Leander's amorous habit° soon revealed.   *dress*
With Cupid's myrtle[2] was his bonnet° crowned;   *hat*
590 About his arms the purple riband° wound   *ribbon*
Wherewith she wreathed her largely spreading hair;
Nor could the youth abstain but he must wear
The sacred ring wherewith she was endowed
When first religious chastity she vowed;
595 Which made his love through Sestos to be known,
And thence unto Abydos sooner blown
Than he could sail, for incorporeal Fame,
Whose weight consists in nothing but her name,
Is swifter than the wind, whose tardy plumes
600 Are reeking water and dull earthly fumes.[3]
Home when he came, he seemed not to be there,
But like exilèd air thrust from his sphere,
Set in a foreign place, and straight from thence,
Alcides-like,[4] by mighty violence
605 He would have chased away the swelling main°   *sea*
That him from her unjustly did detain.
Like as the sun in a diameter[5]
Fires and inflames objects removèd far,
And heateth kindly, shining lat'rally,[6]
610 So beauty sweetly quickens° when 'tis nigh,   *gives life*
But being separated and removed,
Burns where it cherished, murders where it loved.
Therefore, even as an index to a book,
So to his mind was young Leander's look.
615 O none but gods have power their love to hide:
Affection by the count'nance is descried.°   *revealed*
The light of hidden fire itself discovers,
And love that is concealed betrays° poor lovers.   *gives away*
His secret flame apparently° was seen;   *openly*
620 Leander's father knew where he had been,
And for the same mildly rebuked his son,
Thinking to quench the sparkles new begun.
But love, resisted once, grows passionate,
And nothing more than counsel lovers hate.
625 For as a hot, proud horse highly disdains
To have his head controlled, but breaks the reins,
Spits forth the ringled° bit, and with his hooves   *with rings at the ends*
Checks° the submissive ground; so he that loves,   *stamps*
The more he is restrained, the worse he fares.

---

2. A plant sacred to Venus or Cupid, symbolic of
love.
3. I.e., are mist and smoke.
4. Like Hercules, with brute force. ("Alcides" is a
patronymic of Hercules, deriving from his step-
grandfather, Alcaeus.)

5. I.e., shining straight down at noon.
6. I.e., when it is lower in the sky. The idea is
that the sun, paradoxically, causes harm only
when it appears to be farthest away (at the zenith).
Beauty, Marlowe goes on to claim, works the
same way.

630 What is it now but mad Leander dares?[7]
"O Hero, Hero!" thus he cried full oft,
And then he got him to a rock aloft,
Where, having spied her tower, long stared he on 't
And prayed the narrow toiling Hellespont
635 To part in twain, that he might come and go;
But still the rising billows answered "No!"
With that he stripped him to the ivory skin,
And crying, "Love, I come!" leapt lively in.
Whereat the sapphire-visaged god° grew proud,[8]   *Neptune, god of the sea*
640 And made his capering Triton[9] sound aloud;
Imagining that Ganimed,[1] displeased,
Had left the heavens, therefore on him seized.
Leander strived; the waves about him wound
And pulled him to the bottom, where the ground
645 Was strewed with pearl, and in low coral groves
Sweet singing mermaids sported with their loves
On heaps of heavy gold and took great pleasure
To spurn in careless sort° the shipwreck treasure;   *manner*
For here the stately azure palace stood
650 Where kingly Neptune and his train° abode.   *attendants*
The lusty god embraced him, called him love,
And swore he never should return to Jove.
But when he knew it was not Ganimed,
For under water he was almost dead,
655 He heaved him up, and looking on his face,
Beat down the bold waves with his triple mace,[2]
Which mounted up, intending to have kissed him,
And fell in drops like tears because they missed him.
Leander being up, began to swim,
660 And, looking back, saw Neptune follow him;
Whereat aghast, the poor soul gan to cry,
"O let me visit Hero ere I die!"
The god put Helle's bracelet[3] on his arm,
And swore the sea should never do him harm.
665 He clapped his plump cheeks, with his tresses played,
And, smiling wantonly, his love bewrayed.°   *revealed*
He watched his arms, and as they opened wide,
At every stroke betwixt them he would slide
And steal a kiss, and then run out and dance
670 And, as he turned, cast many a lustful glance
And throw him gaudy toys to please his eye,
And dive into the water and there pry
Upon his breast, his thighs, and every limb,
And up again and close beside him swim,
675 And talk of love. Leander made reply,

7. I.e., what is there now Leander dares not do?
8. The primary sense is probably "became sexually aroused."
9. A subordinate sea god who blew on a conch shell.
1. Ganymede, a beautiful boy taken by Jove to be his cupbearer.

2. The three-pronged fork carried by Neptune.
3. Helle was the daughter of King Athamas of Thebes. To escape a cruel stepmother, she fled on a winged, golden-fleeced ram but fell off into the Hellespont, which was named for her. Marlowe apparently invented the detail of the bracelet.

"You are deceived; I am no woman, I."
Thereat smiled Neptune, and then told a tale
How that a shepherd, sitting in a vale,
Played with a boy so lovely fair and kind,
680 As for his love both earth and heaven pined;
That of the cooling river durst not drink,
Lest water nymphs should pull him from the brink;
And when he sported in the fragrant lawns,
Goat-footed satyrs and up-staring fawns[4]
685 Would steal him thence. Ere half this tale was done
"Ay me!" Leander cried, "th' enamored sun
That now should shine on Thetis' glassy bower[5]
Descends upon my radiant Hero's tower.
O that these tardy arms of mine were wings!"
690 And as he spake, upon the waves he springs.
Neptune was angry that he gave no ear,
And in his heart revenging malice bare.
He flung at him his mace, but as it went
He called it in, for love made him repent.
695 The mace returning back, his own hand hit,
As meaning to be venged for darting it.
When this fresh bleeding wound Leander viewed,
His color went and came, as if he rued°   regretted
The grief° which Neptune felt. In gentle breasts   pain
700 Relenting thoughts, remorse, and pity rests;
And who have hard hearts and obdurate minds
But vicious, harebrained, and illit'rate hinds?°   rustics
The god, seeing him with pity to be moved,
Thereon concluded that he was beloved.
705 (Love is too full of faith, too credulous,
With folly and false hope deluding us.)
Wherefore Leander's fancy to surprise,°   i.e., to capture his love
To the rich ocean for gifts he flies.
'Tis wisdom to give much; a gift prevails
710 When deep persuading oratory fails.
By this° Leander, being near the land,   by this time
Cast down his weary feet and felt the sand.
Breathless albeit he were, he rested not
Till to the solitary tower he got,
715 And knocked and called; at which celestial noise
The longing heart of Hero much more joys
Than nymphs and shepherds when the timbrel° rings,   tambourine
Or crooked[6] dolphin when the sailor sings.
She stayed not for her robes, but straight arose
720 And, drunk with gladness, to the door she goes;
Where, seeing a naked man, she screeched for fear
(Such sights as this to tender maids are rare)
And ran into the dark herself to hide.

---

4. Woodland spirits, who prophesied by looking
up to the heavens.
5. I.e., the sea; Thetis was a sea nymph, mother
of the hero Achilles.

6. "Crooked" because of the undulating path of
the dolphin in the water. The musician Arion
was saved from drowning by a dolphin charmed
by his music.

Rich jewels in the dark are soonest spied.
725 Unto her was he led, or rather drawn
By those white limbs which sparkled through the lawn.°   *fine linen*
The nearer that he came, the more she fled,
And, seeking refuge, slipped into her bed.
Whereon Leander sitting, thus began,
730 Through numbing cold, all feeble, faint, and wan:
    "If not for love, yet, love, for pity's sake
Me in thy bed and maiden bosom take;
At least vouchsafe° these arms some little room,   *grant*
Who, hoping to embrace thee, cheerly° swum.   *gladly*
735 This head was beat with many a churlish billow,
And therefore let it rest upon thy pillow."
Herewith affrighted Hero shrunk away
And in her lukewarm place Leander lay;
Whose lively heat, like fire from heaven fet,°   *fetched*
740 Would animate gross clay, and higher set
The drooping thoughts of base declining souls
Than dreary° Mars° carousing nectar bowls.   *bloody / god of war*
His hands he cast upon her like a snare;
She, overcome with shame and sallow fear,
745 Like chaste Diana when Actaeon[7] spied her,
Being suddenly betrayed, dived down to hide her,
And as her silver body downward went,
With both her hands she made the bed a tent,
And in her own mind thought herself secure,
750 O'ercast with dim and darksome coverture.
And now she lets him whisper in her ear,
Flatter, entreat, promise, protest, and swear;
Yet ever as he greedily assayed°   *tried*
To touch those dainties, she the Harpy[8] played,
755 And every limb did, as a soldier stout,
Defend the fort and keep the foeman out.
For though the rising ivory mount he scaled,
Which is with azure circling lines empaled,°   *surrounded*
Much like a globe (a globe may I term this,
760 By which love sails to regions full of bliss),
Yet there with Sisyphus[9] he toiled in vain,
Till gentle parley did the truce obtain.[1]
Wherein Leander on her quivering breast,
Breathless spoke something, and sighed out the rest;
765 Which so prevailed, as he, with small ado,
Enclosed her in his arms and kissed her, too.

---

7. A hunter who happened on Diana bathing. She turned him into a stag, and he was killed by his own hounds.
8. A monster, half-bird, half-woman, who snatches away banquets in Virgil's *Aeneid* and Shakespeare's *Tempest*.
9. Condemned in Hades endlessly to roll a stone uphill.
1. In both the authoritative early printings of the poem (1598), the lines here numbered 775–84 follow at this point (that is, they precede the lines

here numbered 763–74). Like almost all modern editors, though, we have adopted the rearrangement first made in 1910 by Tucker Brooke, in his edition of Marlowe's *Works*. The original order, Brooke thought, did not make good sense; he hypothesized that two sheets of Marlowe's manuscript had been accidentally reversed by the time (five years after his death) the poem was printed. Students may, though, want to read the passage both ways and make up their own minds as to which order is preferable.

And every kiss to her was as a charm,
And to Leander as a fresh alarm,°   *call to battle*
So that the truce was broke, and she, alas,
770 Poor silly° maiden, at his mercy was.   *innocent*
Love is not full of pity, as men say,
But deaf and cruel, where he means to prey.
Even as a bird which in our hands we wring
Forth plungeth and oft flutters with her wing,
775 She trembling strove; this strife of hers, like that
Which made the world,[2] another world begat
Of unknown joy. Treason was in her thought,
And cunningly to yield herself she sought.
Seeming not won, yet won she was, at length.
780 (In such wars women use but half their strength.)
Leander now, like Theban Hercules,
Entered the orchard of th' Hesperides,
Whose fruit none rightly can describe but he
That pulls or shakes it from the golden tree.[3]
785 And now she wished this night were never done,
And sighed to think upon th' approaching sun,
For much it grieved her that the bright daylight
Should know the pleasure of this blessèd night,
And them like Mars and Erycine[4] displayed,
790 Both in each other's arms chained as they laid.
Again she knew not how to frame her look
Or speak to him who in a moment took
That which so long so charily° she kept;   *carefully*
And fain° by stealth away she would have crept   *gladly*
795 And to some corner secretly have gone,
Leaving Leander in the bed alone.
But as her naked feet were whipping out,
He on the sudden clinged her so about
That mermaid-like unto the floor she slid:
800 One half appeared, the other half was hid.
Thus near the bed she blushing stood upright;
And from her countenance behold ye might
A kind of twilight break, which through the hair,
As from an orient° cloud, glims° here and there,   *bright / gleams*
805 And round about the chamber this false morn
Brought forth the day before the day was born.
So Hero's ruddy cheek Hero betrayed,
And her all naked to his sight displayed,
Whence his admiring eyes more pleasure took
810 Than Dis[5] on heaps of gold fixing his look.
By this Apollo's golden harp began
To sound forth music to the Ocean,

---

2. The Greek philosopher Empedocles held that creation was the result of love and strife acting in opposition to each other and alternately ruling the universe.
3. One of Hercules' labors was to get the golden apples of the Hesperides, guarded by a dragon.
Hercules was born in Thebes.
4. A name for Venus, who was caught in bed with Mars by her husband, Vulcan, who enmeshed them in a fine chain net.
5. Pluto, god of the underworld and of wealth.

Which watchful Hesperus[6] no sooner heard
But he the day's bright-bearing car prepared,
815 And ran before, as harbinger of light,
And with his flaring beams mocked ugly Night
Till she, o'ercome with anguish, shame, and rage,
Danged° down to hell her loathsome carriage.   *hurled*
        Desunt nonnulla.°   *something is lacking*

1598

The Passionate Shepherd to His Love[1]

Come live with me and be my love,
And we will all the pleasures prove°   *test, experience*
That valleys, groves, hills, and fields,
Woods, or steepy mountain yields.

5 And we will sit upon the rocks,
Seeing the shepherds feed their flocks,
By shallow rivers to whose falls
Melodious birds sing madrigals.

And I will make thee beds of roses
10 And a thousand fragrant posies,°   *bouquets (also of poems)*
A cap of flowers, and a kirtle°   *dress*
Embroidered all with leaves of myrtle;

A gown made of the finest wool
Which from our pretty lambs we pull;
15 Fair linèd slippers for the cold,
With buckles of the purest gold;

A belt of straw and ivy buds,
With coral clasps and amber studs:
And if these pleasures may thee move,
20 Come live with me, and be my love.

The shepherd swains shall dance and sing
For thy delight each May morning:
If these delights thy mind may move,
Then live with me and be my love.

1599, 1600

---

6. The evening star; one would expect Lucifer, the morning star.
1. This pastoral lyric of invitation is one of the most famous of Elizabethan songs, and a few lines from it are sung in Shakespeare's *Merry Wives of Windsor.* Many poets have written replies to it, the best known of which is by Sir Walter Ralegh (p. 1024).

Doctor Faustus

Marlowe's major dramas, *Tamburlaine*, *The Jew of Malta*, and *Doctor Faustus*, all portray heroes who passionately seek power—the power of rule, the power of money, and the power of knowledge, respectively. Each of the heroes is an overreacher, striving to get beyond the conventional boundaries established to contain the human will.

Unlike Tamburlaine, whose aim and goal is "the sweet fruition of an earthly crown," or Barabas, the Jew of Malta, who lusts for "infinite riches in a little room," Faustus seeks the mastery and voluptuous pleasure that come from forbidden knowledge. To achieve his goal Faustus must make—or chooses to make—a bargain with Lucifer. This is an old folklore motif, but it would have been taken seriously in a time when belief in the reality of devils was almost universal. The story's power over its original audience is vividly suggested by the numerous accounts of uncanny events at performances of the play: strange noises in the theater or extra devils who suddenly appeared among the actors on stage, causing panic.

In the opening soliloquy, Marlowe's Faustus bids farewell to each of his studies—logic, medicine, law, and divinity—as something he has used up. He turns instead to black magic, but the devil exacts a fearful price in exchange: the eternal damnation of Faustus's soul. Faustus aspires to be more than a man: "A sound magician is a mighty god," he declares. His fall is caused by the same pride and ambition that caused the fall of the angels in heaven and of humankind in the Garden of Eden. But it is characteristic of Marlowe that he makes this aspiration nonetheless magnificent.

The immediate source of the play is a German narrative called, in its English translation, *The History of the Damnable Life and Deserved Death of Doctor John Faustus*. That source supplies Marlowe's drama with the scenes of horseplay and low practical joking that contrast so markedly with the passages of huge ambition. It is quite possible that these comic scenes are the work of a collaborator; but no other Elizabethan could have written the first scene (with its brilliant representation of the insatiable aspiring mind of the hero), the ecstatic address to Helen of Troy, or the searing scene of Faustus's last hour. And though compared with these celebrated passages the comic scenes often seem crude, they too contribute to the overarching vision of Faustus's fate: the half-trivial, half-daring exploits, the alternating states of bliss and despair, the questions that are not answered and the answers that bring no real satisfaction, the heroic wanderings that lead nowhere.

Marlowe's play exists in two very different forms: the A text (1604) and the much longer B text (1616), which probably incorporates additions by other hands and which has also been revised to conform to the severe censorship statutes of 1606. We use Roma Gill's edition, based on the A text. Following the play are parallel versions of a key scene that will enable the reader to compare the two texts.*

---

* For additional scenes from the B texts and a host of texts and images related to the play, its author, and 16th-century conceptions of sorcery, see "The Magician, the Heretic, and the Playwright" in the supplemental ebook.

The Tragical History of Doctor Faustus

DRAMATIS PERSONAE[1]

CHORUS
DR. JOHN FAUSTUS
WAGNER, *his servant, a student*
VALDES ⎱ *his friends, magicians*
CORNELIUS ⎰
BELZEBUB
OLD MAN
CLOWN
ROBIN ⎱ *ostlers at an inn*
RAFE ⎰
VINTNER
HORSE-COURSER
THE POPE
THE CARDINAL OF LORRAINE
CHARLES V, EMPEROR OF
  GERMANY
A KNIGHT *at the* EMPEROR's *court*
DUKE OF VANHOLT
DUCHESS OF VANHOLT

THREE SCHOLARS
GOOD ANGEL
EVIL ANGEL
MEPHASTOPHILIS
LUCIFER
Spirits presenting
THE SEVEN DEADLY SINS
  PRIDE
  COVETOUSNESS
  WRATH
  ENVY
  GLUTTONY
  SLOTH
  LECHERY
ALEXANDER THE GREAT *and his*
  PARAMOUR
HELEN OF TROY

ATTENDANTS, FRIARS, *and* DEVILS

Prologue

[*Enter* CHORUS.][2]

CHORUS   Not marching now in fields of Thrasimene,
    Where Mars[3] did mate° the Carthaginians,   *join with*
    Nor sporting in the dalliance of love,
    In courts of kings where state° is overturned,   *political power*
5   Nor in the pomp of proud audacious deeds,
    Intends our Muse to vaunt his heavenly verse:
    Only this (Gentlemen) we must perform,
    The form of Faustus' fortunes good or bad.
    To patient judgments we appeal our plaud,°   *applause*
10   And speak for Faustus in his infancy:
    Now is he born, his parents base of stock,
    In Germany, within a town called Rhodes;
    Of riper years to Wittenberg[4] he went,
    Whereas° his kinsmen chiefly brought him up.   *where*
15   So soon he profits in divinity,°   *theology*
    The fruitful plot of scholarism graced,
    That shortly he was graced with doctor's name,[5]

---

1. There is no list of characters in the A text. The one here is an editorial construction.
2. A single actor who recited a prologue to an act or a whole play, and occasionally delivered an epilogue.
3. God of war. The battle of Lake Trasimene (217 B.C.E.) was one of the Carthaginian leader Hannibal's great victories.

4. The famous university where Martin Luther studied, as did Shakespeare's Hamlet and Horatio. "Rhodes": Roda, or Stadtroda, in Germany.
5. The lines play on two senses of *graced*: he so (1) adorned the place ("plot") of scholarship— i.e., the university—that shortly he was (2) honored with a doctor's degree.

Excelling all whose sweet delight disputes[6]
In heavenly matters of theology.

20 Till, swollen with cunning,° of a self-conceit,   *knowledge*
His waxen wings did mount above his reach,
And melting heavens conspired his overthrow.[7]
For falling to a devilish exercise,
And glutted more with learning's golden gifts,

25 He surfeits upon cursed necromancy:°   *black magic*
Nothing so sweet as magic is to him,
Which he prefers before his chiefest bliss.[8]
And this the man[9] that in his study sits.   [*Exit.*]

SCENE 1

[*Enter* FAUSTUS *in his study.*]

FAUSTUS   Settle thy studies, Faustus, and begin
To sound the depth of that thou wilt profess:
Having commenced, be a divine in show,[1]
Yet level° at the end of every art,   *aim*

5 And live and die in Aristotle's works.
Sweet *Analytics*, 'tis thou hast ravished me.
Bene disserere est finis logices.[2]
Is to dispute well logic's chiefest end?
Affords this art no greater miracle?

10 Then read no more, thou hast attained the end;
A greater subject fitteth Faustus' wit.°   *intellect*
Bid *on kai me on* farewell;[3] Galen come:
Seeing, *ubi desinit philosophus, ibi incipit medicus.*[4]
Be a physician, Faustus, heap up gold,

15 And be eternized for some wondrous cure.
Summum bonum medicinae sanitas:[5]
The end of physic° is our body's health.   *medicine*
Why Faustus, hast thou not attained that end?
Is not thy common talk found aphorisms?[6]

20 Are not thy bills° hung up as monuments,   *prescriptions*
Whereby whole cities have escaped the plague,
And thousand desperate maladies been eased?
Yet art thou still but Faustus, and a man.
Couldst thou make men to live eternally,

25 Or, being dead, raise them to life again,

---

6. Referring to formal disputations, academic exercises that occupied the place now held by examinations.
7. In Greek myth, Icarus flew too near the sun on wings of feathers and wax made by his father, Daedalus; the wax melted, and he fell into the sea and drowned.
8. The salvation of his soul.
9. Apparently a cue for the Chorus to draw aside the curtain to the enclosed space at the rear of the stage.
1. In external appearance. "Commenced": grad-

uated, i.e., received the doctor's degree.
2. "To carry on a disputation well is the end [or purpose] of logic" (Latin). *Analytics:* the title of two treatises on logic by Aristotle.
3. The Greek phrase means "being and not being"; i.e., philosophy.
4. "Where the philosopher leaves off the physician begins" (Latin). Galen: the supreme ancient authority on medicine (2nd century C.E.).
5. The Latin is translated in the following line.
6. I.e., generally accepted wisdom.

Then this profession were to be esteemed.
Physic farewell! Where is Justinian?[7]
Si una eademque res legatur duobus,
Alter rem alter valorem rei, etc.[8]
30 A pretty case of paltry legacies.
Exhereditare filium non potest pater nisi . . . [9]
Such is the subject of the Institute
And universal Body of the Law:
This study fits a mercenary drudge
35 Who aims at nothing but external trash!
Too servile and illiberal for me.
When all is done, divinity is best.
Jerome's Bible,[1] Faustus, view it well:
Stipendium peccati mors est:[2] ha! *Stipendium, etc.*
40 The reward of sin is death? That's hard.
Si pecasse negamus, fallimur, et nulla est in nobis veritas:[3]
If we say that we have no sin,
We deceive ourselves, and there's no truth in us.
Why then belike° we must sin,   in all likelihood
45 And so consequently die.
Ay, we must die an everlasting death.
What doctrine call you this? *Che sarà, sarà:*
What will be, shall be? Divinity, adieu!
These metaphysics° of magicians   occult lore
50 And necromantic books are heavenly!
Lines, circles, schemes, letters, and characters!
Ay, these are those that Faustus most desires.
O what a world of profit and delight,
Of power, of honor, of omnipotence
55 Is promised to the studious artisan![4]
All things that move between the quiet° poles   unmoving
Shall be at my command: emperors and kings
Are but obeyed in their several° provinces,   separate
Nor can they raise the wind, or rend the clouds;
60 But his dominion that exceeds in this
Stretcheth as far as doth the mind of man:
A sound magician is a mighty god.
Here, Faustus, try thy brains to gain a deity.
        [*Enter* WAGNER.]
Wagner, commend me to my dearest friends,
65 The German Valdes and Cornelius,

---

7. Roman emperor and authority on law (483–565 C.E.). The Latin passages that follow paraphrase Justinian's *Institutiones*, a manual included in his *Corpus Iuris* (Body of the Law: cf. below, lines 32–33).
8. "If something is bequeathed to two persons, one shall have the thing itself, the other something of equal value."
9. "A father cannot disinherit his son unless . . ."

1. The Latin translation, or "Vulgate," of St. Jerome (ca. 340–420 C.E.).
2. Romans 6.23. But Faustus reads only part of the Scripture verse: "For the wages of sin is death; but the gift of God is eternal life through Jesus Christ our Lord."
3. I John 1.8 (translated in the following two lines).
4. A practitioner of an art; here, necromancy.

Request them earnestly to visit me.
WAGNER   I will, sir.   [*Exit.*]
FAUSTUS   Their conference will be a greater help to me
    Than all my labors, plod I ne'er so fast.
        [*Enter the* GOOD ANGEL *and the* EVIL ANGEL.]
70 GOOD ANGEL   O Faustus, lay that damnèd book aside,
    And gaze not on it, lest it tempt thy soul
    And heap God's heavy wrath upon thy head:
    Read, read the Scriptures; that is blasphemy.
  EVIL ANGEL   Go forward, Faustus, in that famous art,
75   Wherein all nature's treasury is contained:
    Be thou on earth as Jove[5] is in the sky,
    Lord and commander of these elements.   [*Exeunt.*]
  FAUSTUS   How am I glutted with conceit° of this!   *filled with the idea*
    Shall I make spirits fetch me what I please,
80   Resolve me of all ambiguities,
    Perform what desperate enterprise I will?
    I'll have them fly to India for gold,
    Ransack the ocean for orient pearl,[6]
    And search all corners of the new-found world
85   For pleasant fruits and princely delicates.
    I'll have them read me strange philosophy,
    And tell the secrets of all foreign kings;
    I'll have them wall all Germany with brass,
    And make swift Rhine circle fair Wittenberg;[7]
90   I'll have them fill the public schools[8] with silk,
    Wherewith the students shall be bravely° clad.   *splendidly*
    I'll levy soldiers with the coin they bring,
    And chase the Prince of Parma[9] from our land,
    And reign sole king of all our provinces.
95   Yea, stranger engines for the brunt of war
    Than was the fiery keel at Antwerp's bridge,[1]
    I'll make my servile spirits to invent.
    Come German Valdes and Cornelius,
    And make me blest with your sage conference.
        [*Enter* VALDES *and* CORNELIUS.]
100 Valdes, sweet Valdes, and Cornelius,
    Know that your words have won me at the last
    To practise magic and concealèd arts;
    Yet not your words only, but mine own fantasy,°   *imagination*
    That will receive no object[2] for my head,
105   But ruminates on necromantic skill.

---

5. God—a common substitution in Elizabethan drama.
6. Pearl of orient—the especially lustrous pearl from the seas around India.
7. Wittenberg is in fact on the Elbe River.
8. The university lecture rooms.
9. The duke of Parma was the Spanish governor-general of the Low Countries, 1579–92.
1. A reference to the burning ship sent by the Protestant Netherlanders in 1585 against the barrier on the river Scheldt that Parma had built as a part of the blockade of Antwerp.
2. That will pay no attention to physical reality.

Philosophy is odious and obscure,
Both law and physic are for petty wits;
Divinity is basest of the three,
Unpleasant, harsh, contemptible, and vile.
110 'Tis magic, magic that hath ravished me.
Then, gentle friends, aid me in this attempt,
And I, that have with concise syllogisms
Graveled° the pastors of the German church   confounded
And made the flowering pride of Wittenberg
115 Swarm to my problems[3] as the infernal spirits
On sweet Musaeus when he came to hell,
Will be as cunning as Agrippa was,
Whose shadows made all Europe honor him.[4]

VALDES   Faustus, these books, thy wit,° and our experience   intellect
120 Shall make all nations to canonize us.
As Indian Moors[5] obey their Spanish lords,
So shall the spirits of every element
Be always serviceable to us three.
Like lions shall they guard us when we please,
125 Like Almaine rutters° with their horsemen's staves,   German horsemen
Or Lapland giants trotting by our sides;
Sometimes like women, or unwedded maids,
Shadowing° more beauty in their airy brows   harboring
Than in the white breasts of the Queen of Love.
130 From Venice shall they drag huge argosies,°   merchant ships
And from America the golden fleece
That yearly stuffs old Philip's treasury,[6]
If learnèd Faustus will be resolute.

FAUSTUS   Valdes, as resolute am I in this
135 As thou to live, therefore object it not.[7]

CORNELIUS   The miracles that magic will perform
Will make thee vow to study nothing else.
He that is grounded in astrology,
Enriched with tongues,° well seen° in minerals,   languages / expert
140 Hath all the principles magic doth require:
Then doubt not, Faustus, but to be renowned
And more frequented° for this mystery°   visited / craft
Than heretofore the Delphian oracle.[8]
The spirits tell me they can dry the sea,
145 And fetch the treasure of all foreign wrecks,
Ay, all the wealth that our forefathers hid

---

3. Questions posed for public academic disputation.
4. Cornelius Agrippa, German author of *The Vanity and Uncertainty of Arts and Sciences* (1530), was popularly believed to have had the power of calling up the "shadows" or shades of the dead. Musaeus was a legendary singer, supposed son of Orpheus; it was, however, Orpheus who charmed the denizens of hell with his music.
5. Dark-skinned Native Americans. ("India" in the period could refer to either the East Indies or the West Indies.)
6. Comparing the treasures Phillip II of Spain received from the Americas to the Golden Fleece taken, in Greek mythology, from Colchis by Jason and the Argonauts. (Evidently the Venetian argosies put Marlowe in mind of Jason's ship, the *Argo*.)
7. I.e., do not make an issue of my resolve.
8. The oracle of Apollo at Delphi in Greece.

Within the massy° entrails of the earth.   *massive*
Then tell me, Faustus, what shall we three want?°   *lack*
FAUSTUS   Nothing, Cornelius. O this cheers my soul!
150   Come, show me some demonstrations magical,
That I may conjure in some lusty° grove,   *pleasant*
And have these joys in full possessiön.
VALDES   Then haste thee to some solitary grove,
And bear wise Bacon's and Abanus'⁹ works,
155   The Hebrew Psalter, and New Testament;
And whatsoever else is requisite
We will inform thee ere our conference cease.
CORNELIUS   Valdes, first let him know the words of art,¹
And then, all other ceremonies learned,
160   Faustus may try his cunning by himself.
VALDES   First I'll instruct thee in the rudiments,
And then wilt thou be perfecter° than I.   *more accomplished*
FAUSTUS   Then come and dine with me, and after meat
We'll canvass every quiddity° thereof: *essential feature*
165   For ere I sleep, I'll try what I can do.
This night I'll conjure,° though° I die therefore.   *call up spirits / even if*
                                                                            [*Exeunt.*]

SCENE 2

[*Enter two* SCHOLARS.]
1 SCHOLAR   I wonder what's become of Faustus, that was wont to
make our schools ring with *sic probo*.²
2 SCHOLAR   That shall we know; for see, here comes his boy.³
[*Enter* WAGNER.]
1 SCHOLAR   How now, sirra,⁴ where's thy master?
5   WAGNER   God in heaven knows.
2 SCHOLAR   Why, dost not thou know?
WAGNER   Yes I know, but that follows not.
1 SCHOLAR   Go to,⁵ sirra, leave your jesting, and tell us where he is.
WAGNER   That follows not necessary by force of argument, that you,
10   being licentiates,⁶ should stand upon't; therefore acknowledge
your error, and be attentive.
2 SCHOLAR   Why, didst thou not say thou knew'st?
WAGNER   Have you any witness on't?
1 SCHOLAR   Yes, sirra, I heard you.
15   WAGNER   Ask my fellow if I be a thief.⁷
2 SCHOLAR   Well, you will not tell us.
WAGNER   Yes sir, I will tell you; yet if you were not dunces you would
never ask me such a question. For is not he *corpus naturale*? And is

9. Roger Bacon, the 13th-century friar and scientist popularly thought to be a magician, and
Pietro d'Abano, 13th-century alchemist.
1. I.e., the technical terms.
2. Thus I prove; a phrase in scholastic disputation.
3. In this case, a poor student acting as a servant

to earn his living.
4. A variant of "sir," used condescendingly.
5. Come on!
6. Graduate students.
7. I.e., the testimony of your companion ("fellow")
is worth no more than one thief's testimony for
another.

not that *mobile*?[8] Then wherefore should you ask me such a ques-
20   tion? But that I am by nature phlegmatic,[9] slow to wrath and prone
to lechery—to love I would say—it were not for you to come within
forty foot of the place of execution,[1] although I do not doubt to see
you both hanged the next sessions. Thus having triumphed over
you, I will set my countenance like a precisian,[2] and begin to speak
20   thus: Truly, my dear brethren, my master is within at dinner with
Valdes and Cornelius, as this wine, if it could speak, it would
inform your worships. And so the Lord bless you, preserve you, and
keep you, my dear brethren, my dear brethren.   [*Exit.*]

1 SCHOLAR   Nay then, I fear he is fallen into that damned art, for
30   which they two are infamous through the world.

2 SCHOLAR   Were he a stranger, and not allied to me, yet should I
grieve for him. But come, let us go and inform the rector,[3] and see
if he by his grave counsel can reclaim him.

1 SCHOLAR   O but I fear me nothing can reclaim him.

35   2 SCHOLAR   Yet let us try what we can do.   [*Exeunt.*]

SCENE 3

[*Enter* FAUSTUS *to conjure.*]

FAUSTUS   Now that the gloomy shadow of the earth,
Longing to view Orion's drizzling look,[4]
Leaps from th'antarctic world unto the sky,
And dims the welkin° with her pitchy breath,   sky
5   Faustus, begin thine incantations,
And try if devils will obey thy hest,°   command
Seeing thou hast prayed and sacrificed to them.
Within this circle[5] is Jehovah's name,
Forward and backward anagrammatized;
10   Th'bbreviated names of holy saints,
Figures of every adjunct to the heavens,
And characters of signs and erring stars,[6]
By which the spirits are enforced to rise.
Then fear not Faustus, but be resolute,
15   And try the uttermost magic can perform.
Sint mihi dei Acherontis propitii! Valeat numen triplex Jehovae!
Ignei, aerii, aquatici, terreni spiritus salvete! Orientis princeps, Bel-
zebub inferni ardentis monarcha, et Demogorgon, propitiamus vos
ut appareat et surgat Mephastophilis. Quid tu moraris? Per Jehovam,

---

8. *Corpus naturale et mobile* ("matter natural and movable") was a scholastic definition of the subject matter of physics. Wagner is here parodying the language of learning at the university.
9. Dominated by the phlegm, one of the four humors (bodily fluids) whose relative proportions were thought to determine a person's physical and psychological qualities.
1. I.e., if I were not slow to anger, it would be fatally dangerous for you to come near me.
2. Puritan. The rest of his speech is in the style of the Puritans. "Sessions": sittings of a court.

3. The head of a German university.
4. The constellation Orion appears at the beginning of winter. The phrase is a reminiscence of Virgil.
5. The magic circle drawn on the ground, within which the magician would be safe from the spirits he conjured.
6. The moving planets. "Adjunct": heavenly body, thought to be joined to the solid firmament of the sky. "Characters of signs": signs of the zodiac and the planets.

20 *Gehennam, et consecratam aquam quam nunc spargo, signumque*
crucis quod nunc facio, et per vota nostra, ipse nunc surgat nobis
dicatus Mephastophilis.[7]

    [*Enter a* DEVIL.]

I charge thee to return and change thy shape,
Thou art too ugly to attend on me;

25 Go and return an old Franciscan friar,
That holy shape becomes a devil best.   [*Exit* DEVIL.]
I see there's virtue° in my heavenly words!   *power*
Who would not be proficient in this art?
How pliant is this Mephastophilis,

30 Full of obedience and humility,
Such is the force of magic and my spells.
Now Faustus, thou art conjurer laureate°   *preeminent*
That canst command great Mephastophilis.
Quin redis, Mephastophilis, fratris imagine![8]

    [*Enter* MEPHASTOPHILIS.]

35 MEPHASTOPHILIS   Now Faustus, what would'st thou have me do?
FAUSTUS   I charge thee wait upon me whilst I live,
To do whatever Faustus shall command,
Be it to make the moon drop from her sphere,
Or the ocean to overwhelm the world.

40 MEPHASTOPHILIS   I am a servant to great Lucifer,
And may not follow thee without his leave;
No more than he commands must we perform.
FAUSTUS   Did not he charge thee to appear to me?
MEPHASTOPHILIS   No, I came now hither of mine own accord.

45 FAUSTUS   Did not my conjuring speeches raise thee? Speak!
MEPHASTOPHILIS   That was the cause, but yet *per accidens,*[9]
For when we hear one rack[1] the name of God,
Abjure° the Scriptures, and his savior Christ,   *repudiate*
We fly in hope to get his glorious soul;

50 Nor will we come unless he use such means
Whereby he is in danger to be damned:
Therefore the shortest cut for conjuring
Is stoutly to abjure the Trinity,
And pray devoutly to the prince of hell.

55 FAUSTUS   So Faustus hath already done, and holds this principle:
There is no chief but only Belzebub,
To whom Faustus doth dedicate himself.
This word damnation terrifies not him,

7. Faustus's Latin conjures the devils: "May the gods of the lower regions favor me! Farewell to the Trinity! Hail, spirits of fire, air, water, and earth! Prince of the East, Belzebub, monarch of burning hell, and Demogorgon, we pray to you that Mephastophilis may appear and rise. What are you waiting for? By Jehovah, Gehenna, and the holy water that I now sprinkle, and the sign of the cross that I now make, and by our vows, may Mephastophilis himself now rise to serve us." "Beelzebub" ("Lord of Flies"): an ancient Phoenician deity; in Matthew 12.24, he is called "the prince of the devils." "Demogorgon": in Renaissance versions of classical mythology, a mysterious primeval god.
8. "Return, Mephastophilis, in the shape of a friar."
9. The immediate, not ultimate, cause.
1. Torture (here, by anagrammatizing).

For he confounds hell in Elysium:
60   His ghost be with the old philosophers.[2]
But leaving these vain trifles of men's souls,
Tell me, what is that Lucifer thy lord?
MEPHASTOPHILIS   Arch-regent and commander of all spirits.
FAUSTUS   Was not that Lucifer an angel once?
65 MEPHASTOPHILIS   Yes Faustus, and most dearly loved of God.
FAUSTUS   How comes it then that he is prince of devils?
MEPHASTOPHILIS   O, by aspiring pride and insolence,
For which God threw him from the face of heaven.
FAUSTUS   And what are you that live with Lucifer?
70 MEPHASTOPHILIS   Unhappy spirits that fell with Lucifer,
Conspired against our God with Lucifer,
And are forever damned with Lucifer.
FAUSTUS   Where are you damned?
MEPHASTOPHILIS   In hell.
75 FAUSTUS   How comes it then that thou art out of hell?
MEPHASTOPHILIS   Why this is hell, nor am I out of it.
Think'st thou that I, who saw the face of God,
And tasted the eternal joys of heaven,
Am not tormented with ten thousand hells
80 In being deprived of everlasting bliss?[3]
O Faustus, leave these frivolous demands,°   *questions*
Which strike a terror to my fainting soul.
FAUSTUS   What, is great Mephastophilis so passionate
For being deprivèd of the joys of heaven?
85 Learn thou of Faustus manly fortitude,
And scorn those joys thou never shalt possess.
Go bear these tidings to great Lucifer:
Seeing Faustus hath incurred eternal death
By desp'rate thoughts against Jove's deity,
90 Say he surrenders up to him his soul,
So° he will spare him four and twenty years,   *on condition that*
Letting him live in all voluptuousness,
Having thee ever to attend on me,
To give me whatsoever I shall ask,
95 To tell me whatsoever I demand,
To slay mine enemies and aid my friends,
And always be obedient to my will.
Go, and return to mighty Lucifer,
And meet me in my study at midnight
100 And then resolve me of thy master's mind.[4]
MEPHASTOPHILIS   I will, Faustus.   [*Exit.*]
FAUSTUS   Had I as many souls as there be stars,
I'd give them all for Mephastophilis.

2. Faustus considers hell to be the Elysium of
the classical philosophers, not the Christian hell
of torment.
3. This is the punishment of loss of God's presence, which is supposed to be the greatest torment of hell.
4. I.e., give me his decision.

By him I'll be great emperor of the world,
105 And make a bridge through the moving air
To pass the ocean with a band of men;
I'll join the hills that bind the Afric shore,
And make that land continent to° Spain,   connected to
And both contributory to my crown.
110 The emperor[5] shall not live but by my leave,
Nor any potentate of Germany.
Now that I have obtained what I desire,
I'll live in speculation° of this art   contemplation
Till Mephastophilis return again.   [*Exit.*]

SCENE 4

[*Enter* WAGNER *and the* CLOWN.[6]]

WAGNER   Sirra boy, come hither.

CLOWN   How, boy? Zounds, boy! I hope you have seen many boys
with such pickadevants as I have. Boy, quotha![7]

WAGNER   Tell me, sirra, hast thou any comings in?[8]

5 CLOWN   Ay, and goings out too; you may see else.[9]

WAGNER   Alas poor slave, see how poverty jesteth in his nakedness!
The villain is bare, and out of service,[1] and so hungry that I know
he would give his soul to the devil for a shoulder of mutton, though
it were blood raw.

10 CLOWN   How, my soul to the devil for a shoulder of mutton though
'twere blood raw? Not so good, friend; by'rlady,[2] I had need have it
well roasted, and good sauce to it, if I pay so dear.

WAGNER   Well, wilt thou serve me, and I'll make thee go like *qui mihi
discipulus?*[3]

15 CLOWN   How, in verse?

WAGNER   No, sirra; in beaten silk and stavesacre.[4]

CLOWN   How, how, knavesacre?[5] Ay, I thought that was all the land
his father left him! Do ye hear, I would be sorry to rob you of your
living.

20 WAGNER   Sirra, I say in stavesacre.

CLOWN   Oho, oho, stavesacre! Why then belike, if I were your man,
I should be full of vermin.

WAGNER   So thou shalt, whether thou be'st with me or no. But sirra,
leave your jesting, and bind yourself presently unto me for seven
25 years, or I'll turn all the lice about thee into familiars,[6] and they
shall tear thee in pieces.

---

5. The Holy Roman Emperor.
6. Not a court jester (as in some of Shakespeare's plays) but an older stock character, a rustic buffoon.
7. Says he. The point of the clown's retort is that he is a man and wears a beard. "Zounds": an oath, meaning "God's wounds." "Pickadevants": small, pointed beards.
8. Income, but the clown then puns on the literal meaning.
9. I.e., if you don't believe me.

1. Out of a job.
2. An oath: "by Our Lady."
3. "You who are my pupil" (the opening phrase of a poem on how students should behave, from Lily's *Latin Grammar*, ca. 1509). Wagner means "like a proper servant of a learned man."
4. A preparation from delphinium seeds, used for killing vermin.
5. Wordplay, here and below.
6. Familiar spirits, demons. "Bind yourself": i.e., as apprentice. "Presently": immediately.

CLOWN   Do you hear, sir? You may save that labor: they are too familiar with me already—zounds, they are as bold with my flesh as if
they had paid for my meat and drink.

30   WAGNER   Well, do you hear, sirra? Hold, take these guilders.[7]

CLOWN   Gridirons; what be they?

WAGNER   Why, French crowns.[8]

CLOWN   'Mass, but for the name of French crowns a man were as
good have as many English counters![9] And what should I do with
35   these?

WAGNER   Why, now, sirra, thou art at an hour's warning whensoever
or wheresoever the devil shall fetch thee.

CLOWN   No, no, here take your gridirons again.

WAGNER   Truly I'll none of them.

40   CLOWN   Truly but you shall.

WAGNER   Bear witness I gave them him.

CLOWN   Bear witness I give them you again.

WAGNER   Well, I will cause two devils presently to fetch thee away.
Baliol[1] and Belcher!

45   CLOWN   Let your Baliol and your Belcher come here, and I'll knock[2]
them, they were never so knocked since they were devils! Say I
should kill one of them, what would folks say? "Do ye see yonder
tall fellow in the round slop?[3] He has killed the devil!" So I should
be called "Killdevil" all the parish over.

[*Enter two* DEVILS, *and the* CLOWN *runs up and down crying.*]

50   WAGNER   Baliol and Belcher, spirits, away!   [*Exeunt* DEVILS.]

CLOWN   What, are they gone? A vengeance on them! They have vile
long nails. There was a he devil and a she devil. I'll tell you how you
shall know them: all he devils has horns,[4] and all she devils has
clefts and cloven feet.

55   WAGNER   Well, sirra, follow me.

CLOWN   But do you hear? If I should serve you, would you teach me
to raise up Banios and Belcheos?

WAGNER   I will teach thee to turn thyself to anything, to a dog, or a
cat, or a mouse, or a rat, or anything.

60   CLOWN   How! A Christian fellow to a dog or a cat, a mouse or a rat?
No, no, sir, if you turn me into anything, let it be in the likeness of
a little pretty frisking flea, that I may be here, and there, and everywhere. O I'll tickle the pretty wenches' plackets! I'll be amongst
them, i'faith.[5]

65   WAGNER   Well, sirra, come.

CLOWN   But do you hear, Wagner . . . ?

WAGNER   How? Baliol and Belcher!

CLOWN   O Lord I pray, sir, let Banio and Belcher go sleep.

7. Coins. "Hold": here.
8. French crowns, legal tender in England at
this period, were easily counterfeited.
9. Worthless tokens. "'Mass": by the Mass.
1. Probably a corruption of Belial.
2. Beat.

3. Baggy pants. "Tall": fine.
4. Traditional mark both of devils and of cuckolded husbands.
5. In faith. "Plackets": slits in garments—but with
an obvious sexual allusion.

WAGNER   Villain, call me Master Wagner; and let thy left eye be dia-
70   metarily fixed upon my right heel, with *quasi vestigias nostras insis-*
        tere.[6]   [*Exit.*]

CLOWN   God forgive me, he speaks Dutch fustian![7] Well, I'll follow
        him, I'll serve him; that's flat.   [*Exit.*]

SCENE 5

[*Enter* FAUSTUS *in his study.*]

FAUSTUS   Now Faustus, must thou needs be damned,
        And canst thou not be saved.
        What boots° it then to think of God or heaven?   *avails*
        Away with such vain fancies, and despair,
5   Despair in God, and trust in Belzebub.
        Now go not backward: no, Faustus, be resolute;
        Why waverest thou? O, something soundeth in mine ears:
        "Abjure this magic, turn to God again."
        Ay, and Faustus will turn to God again.
10   To God? He loves thee not:
        The god thou servest is thine own appetite,
        Wherein is fixed the love of Belzebub.
        To him I'll build an altar and a church,
        And offer lukewarm blood of newborn babes.
        [*Enter* GOOD ANGEL *and* EVIL.]
15 GOOD ANGEL   Sweet Faustus, leave that execrable° art.   *accursed*
    FAUSTUS   Contrition, prayer, repentance: what of them?
    GOOD ANGEL   O they are means to bring thee unto heaven.
    EVIL ANGEL   Rather illusions, fruits of lunacy,
        That makes men foolish that do trust them most.
20 GOOD ANGEL   Sweet Faustus, think of heaven, and heavenly things.
    EVIL ANGEL   No, Faustus, think of honor and of wealth.   [*Exeunt.*]
    FAUSTUS   Of wealth!
        Why, the signory° of Emden[8] shall be mine,   *lordship*
        When Mephastophilis shall stand by me.
25   What god can hurt thee, Faustus? Thou art safe,
        Cast no more doubts. Come, Mephastophilis,
        And bring glad tidings from great Lucifer.
        Is't not midnight? Come, Mephastophilis:
        Veni, veni, Mephastophile![9]
        [*Enter* MEPHASTOPHILIS.]
30   Now tell, what says Lucifer thy lord?
    MEPHASTOPHILIS   That I shall wait on Faustus whilst he lives,
        So° he will buy my service with his soul.   *provided that*
    FAUSTUS   Already Faustus hath hazarded that for thee.
    MEPHASTOPHILIS   But Faustus, thou must bequeath it solemnly,
35   And write a deed of gift with thine own blood,

6. A pedantic way of saying "Follow my footsteps." "Diametarily": diametrically.
7. Gibberish.

8. A wealthy German trade center.
9. "Come, come, Mephastophilis!"

For that security° craves great Lucifer.　　　　　　　　*guarantee*
If thou deny it, I will back to hell.
FAUSTUS　Stay, Mephastophilis, and tell me,
What good will my soul do thy lord?

40　MEPHASTOPHILIS　Enlarge his kingdom.
FAUSTUS　Is that the reason he tempts us thus?
MEPHASTOPHILIS　*Solamen miseris socios habuisse doloris.*[1]
FAUSTUS　Have you any pain that tortures others?
MEPHASTOPHILIS　As great as have the human souls of men.

45　But tell me Faustus, shall I have thy soul?
And I will be thy slave and wait on thee,
And give thee more than thou hast wit to ask.
FAUSTUS　Ay Mephastophilis, I give it thee.
MEPHASTOPHILIS　Then stab thine arm courageously,

50　And bind thy soul, that at some certain day
Great Lucifer may claim it as his own,
And then be thou as great as Lucifer.
FAUSTUS　Lo Mephastophilis, for love of thee,
I cut my arm, and with my proper° blood　　　　　　　*own*

55　Assure my soul to be great Lucifer's,
Chief lord and regent of perpetual night.
View here the blood that trickles from mine arm,
And let it be propitious for my wish.
MEPHASTOPHILIS　But Faustus, thou must write it

60　In manner of a deed of gift.
FAUSTUS　Ay, so I will; but, Mephastophilis,
My blood congeals and I can write no more.
MEPHASTOPHILIS　I'll fetch thee fire to dissolve it straight.　　*[Exit.]*
FAUSTUS　What might the staying of my blood portend?

65　Is it unwilling I should write this bill?°　　　　　　　*contract*
Why streams it not, that I may write afresh:
"Faustus gives to thee his soul"? Ah, there it stayed!
Why should'st thou not? Is not thy soul thine own?
Then write again: "Faustus gives to thee his soul."
　　　[Enter MEPHASTOPHILIS *with a chafer° of coals.]*　　*a portable grate*

70　MEPHASTOPHILIS　Here's fire, come Faustus, set it on.
FAUSTUS　So, now the blood begins to clear again.
Now will I make an end immediately.
MEPHASTOPHILIS　O what will not I do to obtain his soul!
FAUSTUS　*Consummatum est,*[2] this bill is ended,

75　And Faustus hath bequeathed his soul to Lucifer.
But what is this inscription on mine arm?
Homo fuge.° Whither should I fly?　　　　　　　　*"O man, fly"*
If unto God, he'll throw me down to hell.
My senses are deceived, here's nothing writ;

80　I see it plain, here in this place is writ,
Homo fuge! Yet shall not Faustus fly.

---

1. "Misery loves company."
2. "It is finished": a blasphemy, because these are the words of Christ on the Cross (John 19.30).

MEPHASTOPHILIS   I'll fetch him somewhat to delight his mind. [*Exit.*]
　　　[*Enter with* DEVILS, *giving crowns and rich apparel to* FAUSTUS,
　　　and dance, and then depart.]
FAUSTUS   Speak, Mephastophilis, what means this show?
MEPHASTOPHILIS   Nothing, Faustus, but to delight thy mind withal,
85　　And to show thee what magic can perform.
FAUSTUS   But may I raise up spirits when I please?
MEPHASTOPHILIS   Ay, Faustus, and do greater things than these.
FAUSTUS   Then there's enough for a thousand souls!
　　Here, Mephastophilis, receive this scroll,
90　　A deed of gift of body and of soul:
　　But yet conditionally, that thou perform
　　All articles prescribed between us both.
MEPHASTOPHILIS   Faustus, I swear by hell and Lucifer
　　To effect all promises between us made.
95　FAUSTUS   Then hear me read them. On these conditions following:
　　First, that Faustus may be a spirit[3] *in form and substance.*
　　Secondly, that Mephastophilis shall be his servant, and at his
　　command.
　　Thirdly, that Mephastophilis shall do for him, and bring him whatso-
100　　*ever.*
　　Fourthly, that he shall be in his chamber or house invisible.
　　Lastly, that he shall appear to the said John Faustus at all times, in
　　what form or shape soever he please.
　　I, John Faustus of Wittenberg, doctor, by these presents,[4] *do give*
105　　*both body and soul to Lucifer, Prince of the East, and his minister*
　　Mephastophilis; and furthermore grant unto them that, four and
　　twenty years being expired, the articles above-written inviolate, full
　　power to fetch or carry the said John Faustus, body and soul, flesh,
　　blood, or goods, into their habitation wheresoever.
110　　　　　　　　　　　　　　　　　*By me John Faustus.*
MEPHASTOPHILIS   Speak, Faustus: do you deliver this as your deed?
FAUSTUS   Ay, take it; and the devil give thee good on't.
MEPHASTOPHILIS   Now, Faustus, ask what thou wilt.
FAUSTUS   First will I question with thee about hell:
115　　Tell me, where is the place that men call hell?
MEPHASTOPHILIS   Under the heavens.
FAUSTUS   Ay, but whereabouts?
MEPHASTOPHILIS   Within the bowels of these elements,
　　Where we are tortured and remain for ever.
120　　Hell hath no limits, nor is circumscribed
　　In one self place; for where we are is hell,
　　And where hell is, there must we ever be.
　　And to conclude, when all the world dissolves,
　　And every creature shall be purified,
125　　All places shall be hell that is not heaven.
FAUSTUS   Come, I think hell's a fable.

3. I.e., have the supernatural powers of a spirit.　　4. Legal articles.

MEPHASTOPHILIS Ay, think so still, till experience change thy mind.

FAUSTUS Why? think'st thou then that Faustus shall be damned?

MEPHASTOPHILIS Ay, of necessity, for here's the scroll
130   Wherein thou hast given thy soul to Lucifer.

FAUSTUS Ay, and body too; but what of that?
Think'st thou that Faustus is so fond° to imagine   *foolish*
That after this life there is any pain?
Tush, these are trifles and mere old wives' tales.

MEPHASTOPHILIS But Faustus, I am an instance to prove the
135   contrary:
For I am damned, and am now in hell.

FAUSTUS How, now in hell? Nay, and this be hell, I'll willingly be
damned here! What? walking, disputing, etc. . . . . But leaving off
this, let me have a wife, the fairest maid in Germany, for I am
140   wanton and lascivious, and cannot live without a wife.

MEPHASTOPHILIS How, a wife? I prithee Faustus, talk not of a wife.[5]

FAUSTUS Nay sweet Mephastophilis, fetch me one, for I will have
one.

MEPHASTOPHILIS Well, thou wilt have one; sit there till I come.
145   I'll fetch thee a wife in the devil's name.   [*Exit.*]
      [*Enter with a* DEVIL *dressed like a woman, with fireworks.*]

MEPHASTOPHILIS Tell, Faustus, how dost thou like thy wife?

FAUSTUS A plague on her for a hot whore!

MEPHASTOPHILIS Tut, Faustus, marriage is but a ceremonial toy;
If thou lovest me, think no more of it.
150   I'll cull thee out the fairest courtesans
And bring them every morning to thy bed:
She whom thine eye shall like, thy heart shall have,
Be she as chaste as was Penelope,
As wise as Saba,[6] or as beautiful
155   As was bright Lucifer before his fall.
Hold, take this book, peruse it thoroughly:
The iterating° of these lines brings gold;   *repeating*
The framing° of this circle on the ground   *drawing*
Brings whirlwinds, tempests, thunder and lightning.
160   Pronounce this thrice devoutly to thyself,
And men in armor shall appear to thee,
Ready to execute what thou desirest.

FAUSTUS Thanks, Mephastophilis, yet fain would I have a book
wherein I might behold all spells and incantations, that I might
165   raise up spirits when I please.

MEPHASTOPHILIS Here they are in this book.   [*There turn to them.*]

FAUSTUS Now would I have a book where I might see all characters
and planets of the heavens, that I might know their motions and
dispositions.[7]

---

5. Mephastophilis cannot produce a wife for Faustus because marriage is a sacrament.
6. The queen of Sheba, who tested Solomon's wisdom with "hard questions" (1 Kings 10). "Penelope": the wife of Ulysses, famed for chastity and fidelity.
7. Relationships to other planets. "Characters": occult symbols.

170 MEPHASTOPHILIS   Here they are too.   [*Turn to them.*]
   FAUSTUS   Nay, let me have one book more, and then I have done,
       wherein I might see all plants, herbs, and trees that grow upon the
       earth.
   MEPHASTOPHILIS   Here they be.
175 FAUSTUS   O thou art deceived!
   MEPHASTOPHILIS   Tut, I warrant[8] thee.   [*Turn to them.*]
   FAUSTUS   When I behold the heavens, then I repent,
       And curse thee, wicked Mephastophilis,
       Because thou hast deprived me of those joys.
180 MEPHASTOPHILIS   Why Faustus,
       Think'st thou that heaven is such a glorious thing?
       I tell thee 'tis not half so fair as thou,
       Or any man that breathes on earth.
   FAUSTUS   How prov'st thou that?
185 MEPHASTOPHILIS   It was made for man, therefore is man more excellent.
   FAUSTUS   If it were made for man, 'twas made for me:
       I will renounce this magic, and repent.
           [*Enter* GOOD ANGEL *and* EVIL ANGEL.]
   GOOD ANGEL   Faustus, repent, yet° God will pity thee.   *still*
   EVIL ANGEL   Thou art a spirit,° God cannot pity thee.   *evil spirit, devil*
190 FAUSTUS   Who buzzeth in mine ears I am a spirit?
       Be I a devil, yet God may pity me.
       Ay, God will pity me if I repent.
   EVIL ANGEL   Ay, but Faustus never shall repent.   [*Exeunt.*]
   FAUSTUS   My heart's so hardened I cannot repent!
195   Scarce can I name salvation, faith, or heaven,
       But fearful echoes thunders in mine ears,
       "Faustus, thou are damned"; then swords and knives,
       Poison, guns, halters,° and envenomed steel   *hangman's nooses*
       Are laid before me to dispatch myself:
200   And long ere this I should have slain myself,
       Had not sweet pleasure conquered deep despair.
       Have I not made blind Homer sing to me
       Of Alexander's[9] love, and Oenon's death?
       And hath not he that built the walls of Thebes
205   With ravishing sound of his melodious harp,[1]
       Made music with my Mephastophilis?
       Why should I die then, or basely despair?
       I am resolved! Faustus shall ne'er repent.
       Come, Mephastophilis, let us dispute again,
210   And argue of divine astrology.
       Tell me, are there many heavens above the moon?
       Are all celestial bodies but one globe,

---

8. Assure.
9. Alexander is another name for Paris, the lover
of Oenone; later he deserted her and abducted
Helen, causing the Trojan War. Oenone refused
to heal the wounds Paris received in battle,

and when he died of them, she killed herself in
remorse.
1. The legendary musician Amphion, whose
harp caused stones, of themselves, to form the
walls of Thebes.

As is the substance of this centric earth?[2]

MEPHASTOPHILIS As are the elements, such are the spheres,
215   Mutually folded in each other's orb.
        And, Faustus, all jointly move upon one axletree
        Whose terminè° is termed the world's wide pole,   *end*
        Nor are the names of Saturn, Mars, or Jupiter
        Feigned, but are erring stars.[3]
220 FAUSTUS But tell me, have they all one motion, both *situ et tempore?*[4]

MEPHASTOPHILIS All jointly move from east to west in four-and-
        twenty hours upon the poles of the world, but differ in their
        motion upon the poles of the zodiac.[5]

FAUSTUS Tush, these slender trifles Wagner can decide!
225   Hath Mephastophilis no greater skill?
        Who knows not the double motion of the planets?
        The first is finished in a natural day, the second thus: as Saturn in
        thirty years; Jupiter in twelve; Mars in four; the Sun, Venus, and
        Mercury in a year; the Moon in twenty-eight days. Tush, these are
230   freshmen's suppositions. But tell me, hath every sphere a domin-
        ion or *intelligentia?*[6]

MEPHASTOPHILIS Ay.

FAUSTUS How many heavens or spheres are there?

MEPHASTOPHILIS Nine: the seven planets, the firmament, and the
235   empyreal heaven.[7]

FAUSTUS Well, resolve me then in this question: why have we not
        conjunctions, oppositions,[8] aspects, eclipses, all at one time, but
        in some years we have more, in some less?

MEPHASTOPHILIS *Per inaequalem motum respectu totius.*[9]
240 FAUSTUS Well, I am answered. Tell me who made the world?

MEPHASTOPHILIS I will not.

FAUSTUS Sweet Mephastophilis, tell me.

MEPHASTOPHILIS Move° me not, for I will not tell thee.   *urge*

FAUSTUS Villain, have I not bound thee to tell me anything?
245 MEPHASTOPHILIS Ay, that is not against our kingdom; but this is.
        Think thou on hell, Faustus, for thou art damned.

FAUSTUS Think, Faustus, upon God, that made the world.

MEPHASTOPHILIS Remember this.   [*Exit.*]

FAUSTUS Ay, go accursèd spirit, to ugly hell,
250   'Tis thou hast damned distressèd Faustus' soul:
        Is't not too late?

---

2. Faustus asks whether all the apparently different heavenly bodies form really "one globe" like
the earth. Mephastophilis answers that like the
elements, which are separate but combined, the
heavenly bodies are separate but their spheres
are enfolded and they move on one axletree.
3. It is appropriate to give individual names to
Saturn, Mars, Jupiter, and the other planets—
which are called wandering, or "erring" stars. The
fixed stars were in the eighth sphere (the firmament, or crystalline sphere).
4. "In position and in time."
5. The common axletree on which all the spheres

revolve.
6. An angel, or intelligence, thought to be the
source of motion in each sphere.
7. The ninth sphere was the immovable empyrean.
8. "Oppositions": when two planets are most
remote from each other. "Conjunctions": the
apparent joinings of two planets. These are two
of the planetary "aspects" (relative positions)
that figure in astrology.
9. "Because of their unequal movements in
respect of the whole."

[*Enter* GOOD ANGEL *and* EVIL.]

EVIL ANGEL   Too late.

GOOD ANGEL   Never too late, if Faustus will repent.

EVIL ANGEL   If thou repent, devils shall tear thee in pieces.

255 GOOD ANGEL   Repent, and they shall never raze° thy skin.   *graze*

[*Exeunt.*]

FAUSTUS   Ah Christ my Savior! seek to save

Distressèd Faustus' soul!

[*Enter* LUCIFER, BELZEBUB, *and* MEPHASTOPHILIS.]

LUCIFER   Christ cannot save thy soul, for he is just.

There's none but I have interest in the same.

260 FAUSTUS   O who art thou that look'st so terrible?

LUCIFER   I am Lucifer, and this is my companion prince in hell.

FAUSTUS   O Faustus, they are come to fetch away thy soul!

LUCIFER   We come to tell thee thou dost injure us.

Thou talk'st of Christ, contrary to thy promise.

265 Thou should'st not think of God; think of the devil,

And his dam[1] too.

FAUSTUS   Nor will I henceforth: pardon me in this,

And Faustus vows never to look to heaven,

Never to name God, or to pray to him,

270 To burn his Scriptures, slay his ministers,

And make my spirits pull his churches down.

LUCIFER   Do so, and we will highly gratify thee. Faustus, we are
come from hell to show thee some pastime; sit down, and thou
shalt see all the Seven Deadly Sins[2] appear in their proper shapes.

275 FAUSTUS   That sight will be as pleasing unto me as Paradise was to
Adam, the first day of his creation.

LUCIFER   Talk not of Paradise, nor creation, but mark this show;
talk of the devil and nothing else. Come away.

[*Enter the* SEVEN DEADLY SINS.]

Now Faustus, examine them of their several names and disposi-
280 tions.

FAUSTUS   What art thou, the first?

PRIDE   I am Pride: I disdain to have any parents. I am like to Ovid's
flea, I can creep into every corner of a wench: sometimes like a
periwig,[3] I sit upon her brow; or like a fan of feathers, I kiss her lips.
285 Indeed I do—what do I not! But fie, what a scent is here? I'll not
speak another word, except the ground were perfumed and covered
with cloth of arras.[4]

FAUSTUS   What art thou, the second?

COVETOUSNESS   I am Covetousness, begotten of an old churl in an
290 old leathern bag; and might I have my wish, I would desire that this

---

1. Mother. "The devil and his dam" was a common colloquial expression.
2. Pride, avarice, lust, anger, gluttony, envy, and
sloth, called deadly because they lead to spirtual
death. All other sins are said to grow out of them
(cf. the procession of the Seven Deadly Sins in
Spenser's *The Faerie Queene*, Book 1, canto 4,

stanzas 16–37).
3. Wig. "Ovid's flea": a salacious medieval poem
"Carmen de Pulice" (Song of the Flea) was attributed to Ovid.
4. Arras in Flanders exported fine cloth used
for tapestry hangings. "Scent": stink. "Except":
unless.

house, and all the people in it, were turned to gold, that I might lock you up in my good chest. O my sweet gold!

FAUSTUS   What art thou, the third?

WRATH   I am Wrath. I had neither father nor mother: I leaped out of a lion's mouth when I was scarce half an hour old, and ever since I have run up and down the world with this case of rapiers, wounding myself when I had nobody to fight withal. I was born in hell— and look to it, for some of you shall be my father.

FAUSTUS   What art thou, the fourth?

ENVY   I am Envy, begotten of a chimney-sweeper and an oyster-wife. I cannot read, and therefore wish all books were burnt; I am lean with seeing others eat—O that there would come a famine through all the world, that all might die, and I live alone; then thou should'st see how fat I would be! But must thou sit and I stand? Come down, with a vengeance!

FAUSTUS   Away, envious rascal! What art thou, the fifth?

GLUTTONY   Who, I sir? I am Gluttony. My parents are all dead, and the devil a penny they have left me but a bare pension, and that is thirty meals a day and ten bevers[5]—a small trifle to suffice nature. O, I come of a royal parentage: my grandfather was a gammon[6] of bacon, my grandmother a hogshead of claret wine; my godfathers were these: Peter Pickled-Herring, and Martin Martlemas-Beef.[7] O but my godmother! She was a jolly gentlewoman, and well-beloved in every good town and city; her name was Mistress Margery March-Beer.[8] Now, Faustus, thou hast heard all my progeny;[9] wilt thou bid me to supper?

FAUSTUS   No, I'll see thee hanged; thou wilt eat up all my victuals.

GLUTTONY   Then the devil choke thee!

FAUSTUS   Choke thyself, Glutton. What art thou, the sixth?

SLOTH   I am Sloth; I was begotten on a sunny bank, where I have lain ever since—and you have done me great injury to bring me from thence. Let me be carried thither again by Gluttony and Lechery. I'll not speak another word for a king's ransom.

FAUSTUS   What are you, Mistress Minx, the seventh and last?

LECHERY   Who, I sir? I am one that loves an inch of raw mutton better than an ell of fried stockfish;[1] and the first letter of my name begins with Lechery.

LUCIFER   Away! To hell, to hell!   [Exeunt the SINS.]
Now Faustus, how dost thou like this?

FAUSTUS   O this feeds my soul!

LUCIFER   Tut, Faustus, in hell is all manner of delight.

FAUSTUS   O might I see hell, and return again, how happy were I then!

---

5. Snacks.
6. The lower side of pork, including the leg.
7. Meat, salted to preserve it during the winter, was prepared around Martinmas (November 11).
8. A rich ale, made in March.

9. Lineage.
1. Dried cod. "Mutton": frequently a bawdy term in Elizabethan English; here, the penis. "Ell": forty-five inches.

LUCIFER   Thou shalt; I will send for thee at midnight. In meantime,
335   take this book, peruse it thoroughly, and thou shalt turn thyself
        into what shape thou wilt.

FAUSTUS   Great thanks, mighty Lucifer; this will I keep as chary[2] as
        my life.

LUCIFER   Farewell, Faustus; and think on the devil.

340   FAUSTUS   Farewell, great Lucifer; come, Mephastophilis.

                                    [*Exeunt* OMNES.]

SCENE 6

[Enter ROBIN *the ostler[3] with a book in his hand.]*

ROBIN   O this is admirable! here I ha' stolen one of Doctor Faustus'
        conjuring books, and i'faith I mean to search some circles[4] for my
        own use: now will I make all the maidens in our parish dance at
        my pleasure stark naked before me, and so by that means I shall
5   see more than ere I felt or saw yet.

        [Enter RAFE *calling* ROBIN.*]*

RAFE   Robin, prithee come away, there's a gentleman tarries to have
        his horse, and he would have his things rubbed and made clean.
        He keeps such a chafing[5] with my mistress about it, and she has
        sent me to look thee out. Prithee, come away.

10   ROBIN   Keep out, keep out; or else you are blown up, you are dis-
        membered, Rafe. Keep out, for I am about a roaring[6] piece of work.

RAFE   Come, what dost thou with that same book? Thou canst not
        read!

ROBIN   Yes, my master and mistress shall find that I can read—he
15   for his forehead,[7] she for her private study. She's born to bear with
        me,[8] or else my art fails.

RAFE   Why Robin, what book is that?

ROBIN   What book? Why the most intolerable[9] book for conjuring
        that ere was invented by any brimstone devil.

20   RAFE   Canst thou conjure with it?

ROBIN   I can do all these things easily with it: first, I can make thee
        drunk with 'ipocrase[1] at any tavern in Europe for nothing, that's
        one of my conjuring works.

RAFE   Our master parson says that's nothing.

25   ROBIN   True, Rafe! And more, Rafe, if thou hast any mind to Nan
        Spit, our kitchen maid, then turn her and wind her to thy own
        use, as often as thou wilt, and at midnight.

RAFE   O brave Robin! Shall I have Nan Spit, and to mine own use?
        On that condition I'll feed thy devil with horsebread as long as he
30   lives, of free cost.[2]

---

2. Carefully.
3. Hostler, stablehand.
4. Magicians' circles, but with a sexual innuendo.
5. Scolding. "Tarries": is waiting.
6. Dangerous.
7. That is, Robin intends to give his master

horns—cuckold him.
8. I.e., bear his weight, or bear him a child.
9. Irresistible.
1. Robin's pronunciation of *hippocras*, a spiced wine.
2. Free of charge. "Horsebread": fodder.

ROBIN No more, sweet Rafe; let's go and make clean our boots which lie foul upon our hands, and then to our conjuring in the devil's name.   [*Exeunt.*]

CHORUS 2

[*Enter* WAGNER *solus.*]

WAGNER   Learned Faustus,
　　To know the secrets of astronomy
　　Graven in the book of Jove's high firmament,
　　Did mount himself to scale Olympus'[3] top.
5　　Being seated in a chariot burning bright,
　　Drawn by the strength of yokèd dragons' necks.
　　He now is gone to prove cosmography,[4]
　　And, as I guess, will first arrive at Rome
　　To see the pope, and manner of his court,
10　　And take some part of holy Peter's feast,[5]
　　That to this day is highly solemnized.   [*Exit* WAGNER.]

SCENE 7

[*Enter* FAUSTUS *and* MEPHASTOPHILIS.]

FAUSTUS   Having now, my good Mephastophilis,
　　Passed with delight the stately town of Trier,[6]
　　Environed round with airy mountain tops,
　　With walls of flint, and deep entrenchèd lakes,°   moats
5　　Not to be won by any conquering prince;
　　From Paris next, coasting° the realm of France,   traversing
　　We saw the river Main fall into Rhine,
　　Whose banks are set with groves of fruitful vines;
　　Then up to Naples, rich Campania,
10　　With buildings fair and gorgeous to the eye,
　　The streets straight forth, and paved with finest brick,
　　Quarters the town in four equivalents;
　　There saw we learned Maro's[7] golden tomb,
　　The way° he cut, an English mile in length,   tunnel
15　　Thorough° a rock of stone in one night's space.   through
　　From thence to Venice, Padua, and the rest,
　　In midst of which a sumptuous temple° stands   St. Mark's in Venice
　　That threats the stars with her aspiring top.
　　Thus hitherto hath Faustus spent his time.
20　　But tell me now, what resting place is this?
　　Hast thou, as erst° I did command,   earlier
　　Conducted me within the walls of Rome?

MEPHASTOPHILIS   Faustus, I have; and because we will not be unprovided, I have taken up his holiness' privy chamber[8] for our use.

---

3. The home of the gods in Greek mythology.
4. To test the accuracy of maps.
5. St. Peter's feast is June 29.
6. Treves (in Prussia).
7. Virgil's. In medieval legend the Roman poet

Virgil was considered a magician whose powers produced a tunnel on the promontory of Posilippo at Naples, near his tomb.
8. Private quarters.

25 FAUSTUS   I hope his holiness will bid us welcome.

MEPHASTOPHILIS   Tut, 'tis no matter, man, we'll be bold with his good
cheer.[9]
And now, my Faustus, that thou may'st perceive
What Rome containeth to delight thee with,
30 Know that this city stands upon seven hills
That underprop the groundwork of the same;
Just through the midst runs flowing Tiber's stream,
With winding banks, that cut it in two parts;
Over the which four stately bridges lean,
35 That makes safe passage to each part of Rome.
Upon the bridge called Ponte Angelo
Erected is a castle passing[1] strong,
Within whose walls such store of ordnance are
And double cannons, framed of carvèd brass,
40 As match the days within one complete year—
Besides the gates and high pyramides°   obelisks
Which Julius Caesar brought from Africa.

FAUSTUS   Now by the kingdoms of infernal rule,
Of Styx, Acheron, and the fiery lake
45 Of ever-burning Phlegethon,[2] I swear
That I do long to see the monuments
And situation of bright-splendent Rome.
Come therefore, let's away.

MEPHASTOPHILIS   Nay, Faustus, stay. I know you'd fain see the pope,
50 And take some part of holy Peter's feast,
Where thou shalt see a troop of bald-pate friars,
Whose *summum bonum*[3] is in belly-cheer.

FAUSTUS   Well, I am content to compass[4] then some sport,
And by their folly make us merriment.
55 Then charm me that I may be invisible, to do what I please
unseen of any whilst I stay in Rome.

MEPHASTOPHILIS [*casts a spell on him*].   So Faustus, now do what
thou wilt, thou shalt not be discerned.
[*Sound a sennet;*[5] *enter the* POPE *and the* CARDINAL OF LORRAINE
to the banquet, with FRIARS *attending.*]

POPE   My lord of Lorraine, will't please you draw near?

60 FAUSTUS   Fall to; and the devil choke you and[6] you spare.

POPE   How now, who's that which spake? Friars, look about.

1 FRIAR   Here's nobody, if it like[7] your holiness.

POPE   My lord, here is a dainty dish was sent to me from the bishop
of Milan.

65 FAUSTUS   I thank you, sir.   [*Snatch it.*]

---

9. Entertainment.
1. Surpassingly. Actually the castle is on the
bank, not the bridge.
2. Classical names for rivers of the underworld.
3. The greatest good; often refers to God.

4. Take part in.
5. A set of notes on the trumpet or cornet.
6. If. "Fall to": start eating.
7. Please.

POPE   How now, who's that which snatched the meat from me? Will no man look? My lord, this dish was sent me from the cardinal of Florence.

FAUSTUS   You say true? I'll have't.   [*Snatch it.*]

70   POPE   What, again! My lord, I'll drink to your grace.

FAUSTUS   I'll pledge[8] your grace.   [*Snatch the cup.*]

LORRAINE   My lord, it may be some ghost newly crept out of purgatory come to beg a pardon of your holiness.

POPE   It may be so; friars, prepare a dirge[9] to lay the fury of this ghost.

75   Once again my lord, fall to.   [*The* POPE *crosseth himself.*]

FAUSTUS   What, are you crossing of your self? Well, use that trick no more, I would advise you.
        [*Cross again.*]

FAUSTUS   Well, there's the second time; aware[1] the third! I give you fair warning.
        [*Cross again, and* FAUSTUS *hits him a box of the ear, and they all run away.*]

80   Come on, Mephastophilis, what shall we do?

MEPHASTOPHILIS   Nay, I know not; we shall be cursed with bell, book, and candle.[2]

FAUSTUS   How! Bell, book, and candle; candle, book, and bell, Forward and backward, to curse Faustus to hell.

85   Anon you shall hear a hog grunt, a calf bleat, and an ass bray, Because it is St. Peter's holy day.
        [*Enter all the* FRIARS *to sing the Dirge.*]

1 FRIAR   Come brethren, let's about our business with good devotion.
        [*Sing this.*]
        Cursed be he that stole away His Holiness' meat from the table.
          Maledicat Dominus.[3]

90   Cursed be he that struck His Holiness a blow on the face.
          Maledicat Dominus.
        Cursed be he that took Friar Sandelo a blow on the pate.
          Maledicat Dominus.
        Cursed be he that disturbeth our holy dirge.

95   *Maledicat Dominus.*
        Cursed be he that took away His Holiness' wine.
          Maledicat dominus.
          Et omnes sancti.[4] Amen.
        [*Beat the* FRIARS, *and fling fireworks among them, and so Exeunt.*]

SCENE 8

[*Enter* ROBIN *and* RAFE *with a silver goblet.*]

ROBIN   Come, Rafe, did not I tell thee we were forever made by this Doctor Faustus' book? *Ecce signum!*[5] Here's a simple purchase for horsekeepers: our horses shall eat no hay as long as this lasts.

8. Toast.
9. A requiem mass. But what actually follows is a litany of curses.
1. Beware.
2. The traditional paraphernalia for cursing and excommunication.
3. "May the Lord curse him."
4. "And all the saints (also curse him)."
5. "Behold the proof."

[*Enter the* VINTNER.]

RAFE But Robin, here comes the vintner.

5 ROBIN Hush, I'll gull him supernaturally![6] Drawer, I hope all is paid; God be with you. Come, Rafe.

VINTNER Soft, sir, a word with you. I must yet have a goblet paid from you ere you go.

ROBIN I, a goblet, Rafe? I, a goblet? I scorn you: and you are but a
10 etc.[7] . . . I, a goblet? Search me.

VINTNER I mean so, sir, with your favor.   [*Searches* ROBIN.]

ROBIN How say you now?

VINTNER I must say somewhat to your fellow; you, sir!

RAFE Me, sir? Me, sir? Search your fill. Now sir, you may be ashamed
15 to burden honest men with a matter of truth.

VINTNER [*searches* RAFE] Well, t'one of you hath this goblet about you.

ROBIN You lie, drawer; 'tis afore me. Sirra you, I'll teach ye to impeach[8] honest men: [*to* RAFE] stand by. [*to the* VINTNER] I'll scour
20 you for a goblet—stand aside, you were best—I charge you in the name of Belzebub—look to the goblet, Rafe!

VINTNER What mean you, sirra?

ROBIN I'll tell you what I mean: [*he reads*] *Sanctobulorum Periphrasticon*—nay, I'll tickle you, vintner—look to the goblet,
25 Rafe—*Polypragmos Belseborams framanto pacostiphos tostis Mephastophilis, etc.* . . . [9]

[*Enter* MEPHASTOPHILIS: *sets squibs*[1] *at their backs: they run about.*]

VINTNER *O nomine Domine!*[2] What mean'st thou, Robin? Thou hast no goblet.

RAFE *Peccatum peccatorum!*[3] Here's thy goblet, good vintner.

30 ROBIN *Misericordia pro nobis!*[4] What shall I do? Good devil, forgive me now, and I'll never rob thy library more.

[*Enter to them* MEPHASTOPHILIS.]

MEPHASTOPHILIS Vanish, villains, th'one like an ape, another like a bear, the third an ass, for doing this enterprise.   [*Exit* VINTNER.]
Monarch of hell, under whose black survey
35 Great potentates do kneel with awful fear;
Upon whose altars thousand souls do lie;
How am I vexèd with these villains' charms!
From Constantinople am I hither come,
Only for pleasure of these damnèd slaves.

40 ROBIN How, from Constantinople? You have had a great journey! Will you take sixpence in your purse to pay for your supper, and be gone?

---

6. Wine-drawer. "Gull": trick.
7. The actor might ad lib abuse at this point.
8. Accuse.
9. Dog-Latin, as Robin attempts to conjure from Faustus's book.
1. Firecrackers. Evidently Mephastophilis is on stage only long enough to set off the firecrackers

and is not seen by Robin, Rafe, or the vintner. He then reenters at line 32.
2. "In the name of the Lord"; the Latin invocations are used in swearing.
3. "Sin of sins!"
4. "Have mercy on us!"

MEPHASTOPHILIS   Well, villains, for your presumption, I transform
    thee into an ape, and thee into a dog; and so begone!   [*Exit.*]

45 ROBIN   How, into an ape? That's brave: I'll have fine sport with the
    boys; I'll get nuts and apples enow.[5]

RAFE   And I must be a dog.

ROBIN   I'faith, thy head will never be out of the potage[6] pot.
                                           [*Exeunt.*]

CHORUS 3

[*Enter* CHORUS.[7]]

CHORUS   When Faustus had with pleasure ta'en the view
    Of rarest things, and royal courts of kings,
    He stayed his course, and so returnèd home;
    Where such as bare his absence but with grief—
5   I mean his friends and nearest companions—
    Did gratulate his safety with kind words.
    And in their conference of what befell,
    Touching his journey through the world and air,
    They put forth questions of astrology,
10 Which Faustus answered with such learnèd skill
    As they admired and wondered at his wit.
    Now is his fame spread forth in every land:
    Amongst the rest the emperor is one,
    Carolus the Fifth,[8] at whose palace now
15 Faustus is feasted 'mongst his noblemen.
    What there he did in trial° of his art   *demonstration*
    I leave untold: your eyes shall see performed.   [*Exit.*]

SCENE 9

[*Enter* EMPEROR, FAUSTUS, *and a* KNIGHT, *with Attendants.*]

EMPEROR   Master Doctor Faustus, I have heard strange report of thy
    knowledge in the black art, how that none in my empire, nor in the
    whole world, can compare with thee for the rare effects of magic.
    They say thou hast a familiar spirit, by whom thou canst accom-
5 plish what thou list! This therefore is my request: that thou let me
    see some proof of thy skill, that mine eyes may be witnesses to con-
    firm what mine ears have heard reported. And here I swear to thee,
    by the honor of mine imperial crown, that whatever thou dost, thou
    shalt be in no ways prejudiced or endamaged.

10 KNIGHT [*aside*]   I'faith, he looks much like a conjuror.

FAUSTUS   My gracious sovereign, though I must confess myself far
    inferior to the report men have published, and nothing answerable
    to[9] the honor of your imperial majesty, yet for that love and duty
    binds me thereunto, I am content to do whatsoever your majesty
15 shall command me.

---

5. Enough. "Brave": splendid.
6. Porridge.
7. I.e., Wagner.

8. The Holy Roman Emperor Charles V (reigned
1519–56).
9. Not at all deserving of.

EMPEROR   Then Doctor Faustus, mark what I shall say. As I was
    sometime solitary set within my closet,[1] sundry thoughts arose
    about the honor of mine ancestors—how they had won by prowess
    such exploits, got such riches, subdued so many kingdoms, as we
20   that do succeed, or they that shall hereafter possess our throne,
    shall (I fear me) never attain to that degree of high renown and
    great authority. Amongst which kings is Alexander the Great,[2]
    chief spectacle of the world's pre-eminence:
    The bright shining of whose glorious acts
25   Lightens the world with his reflecting beams;
    As when I hear but motion° made of him,   *mention*
    It grieves my soul I never saw the man.
    If therefore thou, by cunning of thine art,
    Canst raise this man from hollow vaults below,
30   Where lies entombed this famous conqueror,
    And bring with him his beauteous paramour,[3]
    Both in their right shapes, gesture, and attire
    They used to wear during their time of life,
    Thou shalt both satisfy my just desire
35   And give me cause to praise thee whilst I live.
FAUSTUS   My gracious lord, I am ready to accomplish your request,
    so far forth as by art and power of my spirit I am able to perform.
KNIGHT [*aside*]   I'faith, that's just nothing at all.
FAUSTUS   But, if it like your grace, it is not in my ability to present
40   before your eyes the true substantial bodies of those two deceased
    princes, which long since are consumed to dust.
KNIGHT [*aside*]   Ay, marry,[4] master doctor, now there's a sign of
    grace in you, when you will confess the truth.
FAUSTUS   But such spirits as can lively resemble Alexander and his
45   paramour shall appear before your grace, in that manner that they
    best lived in, in their most flourishing estate: which I doubt not
    shall sufficiently content your imperial majesty.
EMPEROR   Go to, master doctor, let me see them presently.[5]
KNIGHT   Do you hear, master doctor? You bring Alexander and his
50   paramour before the emperor!
FAUSTUS   How then, sir?
KNIGHT   I'faith, that's as true as Diana turned me to a stag.
FAUSTUS   No sir; but when Actaeon died, he left the horns[6] for you!
    Mephastophilis, begone   [*Exit* MEPHASTOPHILIS.]
55 KNIGHT   Nay, and[7] you go to conjuring I'll be gone.   [*Exit* KNIGHT.]
FAUSTUS   I'll meet with you anon[8] for interrupting me so. Here they
    are, my gracious lord.

1. Private chamber.
2. The emperor traces his ancestry to the world
conqueror (356–323 B.C.E.).
3. Probably Roxana, Alexander's wife.
4. To be sure.
5. Immediately. "Estate": condition.
6. Horns were traditionally a sign of the cuck-

olded husband (cf. Scene 6, lines 14–15).
"Actaeon": the hunter of classical legend who happened to see the goddess Diana bathing. For punishment he was changed into a stag; he was then
chased and killed by his own hounds.
7. If.
8. Shortly. "Meet with": be revenged on.

[*Enter* MEPHASTOPHILIS *with* ALEXANDER *and his* PARAMOUR.]

EMPEROR Master doctor, I heard this lady, while she lived, had a wart or mole in her neck; how shall I know whether it be so or no?

60 FAUSTUS Your highness may boldly go and see.

[*The* EMPEROR *examines the lady's neck.*]

EMPEROR Sure, these are no spirits, but the true substantial bodies of those two deceased princes.

[*Exit* ALEXANDER (*and his* PARAMOUR).]

FAUSTUS Will't please your highness now to send for the knight that was so pleasant with me here of late?

65 EMPEROR One of you call him forth.

[*Enter the* KNIGHT *with a pair of horns on his head.*]

How now, sir knight? Why, I had thought thou hadst been a bachelor, but now I see thou hast a wife that not only gives thee horns but makes thee wear them! Feel on thy head.

KNIGHT Thou damnèd wretch and execrable° dog, detestable
70 Bred in the concave of some monstrous rock,
How dar'st thou thus abuse a gentleman?
Villain, I say, undo what thou hast done.

FAUSTUS O not so fast, sir, there's no haste but good. Are you remembered[9] how you crossed me in my conference with the
75 emperor? I think I have met with you for it.

EMPEROR Good master doctor, at my entreaty release him; he hath done penance sufficient.

FAUSTUS My gracious lord, not so much for the injury he offered me here in your presence, as to delight you with some mirth, hath Faus-
80 tus worthily requited this injurious knight; which being all I desire, I am content to release him of his horns. And, sir knight, hereafter speak well of scholars: Mephastophilis, transform him straight.[1] Now, my good lord, having done my duty, I humbly take my leave.

EMPEROR Farewell, master doctor; yet ere you go, expect from me a
85 bounteous reward.

[*Exit* EMPEROR (*and his* ATTENDANTS).]

FAUSTUS Now, Mephastophilis, the restless course
That time doth run with calm and silent foot,
Shortening my days and thread of vital life,
Calls for the payment of my latest years;
90 Therefore, sweet Mephastophilis, let us make haste to Wittenberg.

MEPHASTOPHILIS What, will you go on horseback or on foot?

FAUSTUS Nay, till I am past this fair and pleasant green, I'll walk on foot.

SCENE 10

[*Enter a* HORSE-COURSER.[2]]

HORSE-COURSER I have been all this day seeking one Master Fustian: 'Mass,[3] see where he is! God save you, master doctor.

---

9. Have you forgotten. "No haste but good": a proverb: no point hurrying, unless it's to good effect.
1. Immediately.

2. Horse trader, traditionally a sharp bargainer or cheat.
3. By the Mass. "Fustian": the horse-courser's comic mistake for Faustus's name.

FAUSTUS   What, horse-courser: you are well met.

HORSE-COURSER   Do you hear, sir; I have brought you forty dollars[4]
5   for your horse.

FAUSTUS   I cannot sell him so: if thou lik'st him for fifty, take him.

HORSE-COURSER   Alas sir, I have no more. I pray you speak for me.

MEPHASTOPHILIS   I pray you let him have him; he is an honest fellow, and he has a great charge[5]—neither wife nor child.

10   FAUSTUS   Well, come, give me your money; my boy will deliver him
to you. But I must tell you one thing before you have him: ride him
not into the water at any hand.[6]

HORSE-COURSER   Why sir, will he not drink of all waters?

FAUSTUS   O yes, he will drink of all waters, but ride him not into the
15   water. Ride him over hedge or ditch, or where thou wilt, but not
into the water.

HORSE-COURSER   Well sir. Now am I made man forever: I'll not
leave my horse for forty! If he had but the quality of hey ding ding,
hey ding ding,[7] I'd make a brave living on him! He has a buttock
20   as slick as an eel. Well, God b'y,[8] sir; your boy will deliver him me.
But hark ye sir, if my horse be sick, or ill at ease, if I bring his
water[9] to you, you'll tell me what it is?

[*Exit* HORSE-COURSER.]

FAUSTUS   Away, you villain! What, dost think I am a horse-doctor?
What art thou, Faustus, but a man condemned to die?
25   Thy fatal time° doth draw to final end.   *time allotted by fate*
Despair doth drive distrust unto my thoughts.
Confound these passions with a quiet sleep:
Tush, Christ did call the thief upon the cross.[1]
Then rest thee, Faustus, quiet in conceit.°   *in mind*

[*Sleep in his chair.*]

[*Enter* HORSE-COURSER *all wet, crying.*]

30   HORSE-COURSER   Alas, alas, Doctor Fustian, quotha? 'Mass, Doctor
Lopus[2] was never such a doctor! H'as given me a purgation, h'as
purged me of forty dollars! I shall never see them more. But yet,
like an ass as I was, I would not be ruled by him; for he bade me
I should ride him into no water. Now I, thinking my horse had had
35   some rare quality that he would not have had me known of, I, like
a vent'rous youth, rid him into the deep pond at the town's end.
I was no sooner in the middle of the pond, but my horse vanished
away, and I sat upon a bottle[3] of hay, never so near drowning in
my life! But I'll seek out my doctor, and have my forty dollars
40   again, or I'll make it the dearest[4] horse. O, yonder is his snipper-
snapper! Do you hear, you hey-pass,[5] where's your master?

---

4. Common German coins.
5. Burden.
6. On any account.
7. I.e., he wishes his horse were a stallion, not a
gelding, so he could put him to stud.
8. Good-bye (contracted from "God be with
you").
9. Urine.
1. In Luke 23.39–43 one of the two thieves crucified with Jesus is promised paradise. "Tush": a

scoffing exclamation.
2. In February 1594 Roderigo Lopez, the queen's
personal physician, was executed for plotting to
poison her. Obviously Marlowe, who died in 1593,
did not write the line. "Quotha": he said.
3. Bundle. "Vent'rous": adventurous.
4. Most expensive.
5. A conjurer's phrase. "Snipper-snapper": insignificant youth, whipper-snapper.

MEPHASTOPHILIS   Why, sir, what would you? You cannot speak with him.

HORSE-COURSER   But I will speak with him.

45 MEPHASTOPHILIS   Why, he's fast asleep; come some other time.

HORSE-COURSER   I'll speak with him now, or I'll break his glasswindows[6] about his ears.

MEPHASTOPHILIS   I tell thee, he has not slept this eight nights.

HORSE-COURSER   And he have not slept this eight weeks I'll speak
50   with him.

MEPHASTOPHILIS   See where he is, fast asleep.

HORSE-COURSER   Ay, this is he; God save ye, master doctor, master doctor, master Doctor Fustian, forty dollars, forty dollars for a bottle of hay!

55 MEPHASTOPHILIS   Why, thou seest he hears thee not.

HORSE-COURSER   So ho ho; so ho ho.[7] [Halloo in his ear.] No, will you not wake? I'll make you wake ere I go. [Pull him by the leg, and pull it away.] Alas, I am undone! What shall I do?

FAUSTUS   O my leg, my leg! Help, Mephastophilis! Call the officers!
60   My leg, my leg!

MEPHASTOPHILIS   Come villain, to the constable.

HORSE-COURSER   O Lord, sir! Let me go, and I'll give you forty dollars more.

MEPHASTOPHILIS   Where be they?

65 HORSE-COURSER   I have none about me: come to my ostry[8] and I'll give them you.

MEPHASTOPHILIS   Begone quickly!

    [HORSE-COURSER runs away.]

FAUSTUS   What, is he gone? Farewell he: Faustus has his leg again, and the horse-courser—I take it—a bottle of hay for his labor!
70   Well, this trick shall cost him forty dollars more.

    [Enter WAGNER.]

How now, Wagner, what's the news with thee?

WAGNER   Sir, the duke of Vanholt doth earnestly entreat your company.

FAUSTUS   The duke of Vanholt! An honorable gentleman, to whom
75   I must be no niggard of my cunning.[9] Come, Mephastophilis, let's away to him.   [Exeunt.]

SCENE 11

[FAUSTUS and MEPHASTOPHILIS return to the stage. Enter to them the DUKE and the DUCHESS; the DUKE speaks.]

DUKE   Believe me, master doctor, this merriment hath much pleased me.

FAUSTUS   My gracious lord, I am glad it contents you so well: but it may be, madam, you take no delight in this; I have heard that

---

6. Spectacles.
7. The huntsman's cry, when he sights the quarry.
8. Hostelry, inn.
9. I.e., must generously display my skill.

great-bellied[1] women do long for some dainties or other—what is
it, madam? Tell me, and you shall have it.

DUCHESS   Thanks, good master doctor; and for I see your courteous
intent to pleasure me, I will not hide from you the thing my heart
desires. And were it now summer, as it is January and the dead of
winter, I would desire no better meat than a dish of ripe grapes.

FAUSTUS   Alas madam, that's nothing! Mephastophilis, begone! [*Exit*
MEPHASTOPHILIS.] Were it a greater thing than this, so it would
content you, you should have it. [*Enter* MEPHASTOPHILIS *with the
grapes.*] Here they be, madam; will't please you taste on them?

DUKE   Believe me, master doctor, this makes me wonder above the
rest: that being in the dead time of winter, and in the month of
January, how you should come by these grapes?

FAUSTUS   If it like your grace, the year is divided into two circles over
the whole world, that when it is here winter with us, in the contrary
circle it is summer with them, as in India, Saba,[2] and farther countries in the east; and by means of a swift spirit that I have, I had
them brought hither, as ye see. How do you like them, madam;
be they good?

DUCHESS   Believe me, master doctor, they be the best grapes that ere
I tasted in my life before.

FAUSTUS   I am glad they content you so, madam.

DUKE   Come, madam, let us in, where you must well reward this
learned man for the great kindness he hath showed to you.

DUCHESS   And so I will, my lord; and whilst I live, rest beholding for
this courtesy.

FAUSTUS   I humbly thank your grace.

DUKE   Come, master doctor, follow us, and receive your reward.

[*Exeunt*]

CHORUS 4

[*Enter* WAGNER *solus.*]

WAGNER   I think my master means to die shortly,
For he hath given to me all his goods.
And yet methinks, if that death were near,
He would not banquet, and carouse, and swill
Amongst the students, as even now he doth,
Who are at supper with such belly-cheer°   gluttony
As Wagner ne'er beheld in all his life.
See where they come: belike the feast is ended.   [*Exit.*]

SCENE 12

[*Enter* FAUSTUS (*and* MEPHASTOPHILIS), *with two or three*
SCHOLARS.]

1 SCHOLAR   Master Doctor Faustus, since our conference about
fair ladies, which was the beautifulest in all the world, we have

---

1. Pregnant.
2. The biblical kingdom of Sheba, in southwestern Arabia. "Like": please.

determined with ourselves that Helen of Greece was the admira-
blest lady that ever lived. Therefore, master doctor, if you will do
us that favor as to let us see that peerless dame of Greece, whom
all the world admires for majesty, we should think ourselves much
beholding unto you.

FAUSTUS Gentlemen, for that I know your friendship is unfeigned,
And Faustus' custom is not to deny
The just requests of those that wish him well,
You shall behold that peerless dame of Greece,
No otherways for pomp and majesty
Than when Sir Paris crossed the seas with her
And brought the spoils to rich Dardania.°   Troy
Be silent then, for danger is in words.
    [*Music sounds, and* HELEN *passeth over the stage.*]
2 SCHOLAR   Too simple is my wit to tell her praise,
Whom all the world admires for majesty.
3 SCHOLAR   No marvel though the angry Greeks pursued
With ten years' war the rape° of such a queen,   *abduction*
Whose heavenly beauty passeth all compare.
1 SCHOLAR   Since we have seen the pride of Nature's works
And only paragon of excellence,
Let us depart; and for this glorious deed
Happy and blest be Faustus evermore.
FAUSTUS Gentlemen, farewell; the same I wish to you.
                                        [*Exeunt* SCHOLARS.]
        [*Enter an* OLD MAN.]
OLD MAN   Ah Doctor Faustus, that I might prevail
To guide thy steps unto the way of life,
By which sweet path thou may'st attain the goal
That shall conduct thee to celestial rest.
Break heart, drop blood, and mingle it with tears,
Tears falling from repentant heaviness°   *grief*
Of thy most vile and loathsome filthiness,
The stench whereof corrupts the inward soul
With such flagitious° crimes of heinous sins,   *villainous*
As no commiseration may expel
But mercy, Faustus, of thy savior sweet,
Whose blood alone must wash away thy guilt.
FAUSTUS Where art thou, Faustus? Wretch, what hast thou done!
Damned art thou, Faustus, damned; despair and die!
Hell calls for right, and with a roaring voice
Says, "Faustus, come: thine hour is come!"
    [MEPHASTOPHILIS *gives him a dagger.*]
And Faustus will come to do thee right.
OLD MAN   Ah stay, good Faustus, stay thy desperate steps!
I see an angel hovers o'er thy head
And with a vial full of precious grace
Offers to pour the same into thy soul!
Then call for mercy, and avoid despair.
FAUSTUS Ah my sweet friend, I feel thy words

To comfort my distressèd soul;
50 Leave me awhile to ponder on my sins.
OLD MAN   I go, sweet Faustus; but with heavy cheer,°   *heavy heart*
Fearing the ruin of thy hopeless soul.   [*Exit.*]
FAUSTUS   Accursèd Faustus, where is mercy now?
I do repent, and yet I do despair:
55 Hell strives with grace for conquest in my breast!
What shall I do to shun the snares of death?
MEPHASTOPHILIS   Thou traitor, Faustus: I arrest thy soul
For disobedience to my sovereign lord.
Revolt,[3] or I'll in piecemeal tear thy flesh.
60 FAUSTUS   Sweet Mephastophilis, entreat thy lord
To pardon my unjust presumptiön;
And with my blood again I will confirm
My former vow I made to Lucifer.
MEPHASTOPHILIS   Do it then quickly, with unfeignèd heart,
65 Lest greater danger do attend thy drift.°   *intent*
FAUSTUS   Torment, sweet friend, that base and crooked age°   *aged man*
That durst° dissuade me from thy Lucifer,   *dared to*
With greatest torments that our hell affords.
MEPHASTOPHILIS   His faith is great, I cannot touch his soul,
70 But what I may afflict his body with
I will attempt—which is but little worth.
FAUSTUS   One thing, good servant, let me crave of thee,
To glut the longing of my heart's desire:
That I might have unto° my paramour   *for*
75 That heavenly Helen which I saw of late,
Whose sweet embracings may extinguish clean
These thoughts that do dissuade me from my vow,
And keep mine oath I made to Lucifer.
MEPHASTOPHILIS   Faustus, this, or what else thou shalt desire,
80 Shall be performed in twinkling of an eye.
       [*Enter* HELEN.]
FAUSTUS   Was this the face that launched a thousand ships,
And burnt the topless[4] towers of Ilium?°   *Troy*
Sweet Helen, make me immortal with a kiss:
Her lips sucks forth my soul, see where it flies!
85 Come Helen, come, give me my soul again.
Here will I dwell, for heaven be in these lips,
And all is dross that is not Helena!
       [*Enter* OLD MAN.]
I will be Paris, and for love of thee,
Instead of Troy shall Wittenberg be sacked;
90 And I will combat with weak Menelaus,°   *Helen's husband*
And wear thy colors on my plumèd crest;
Yea, I will wound Achilles in the heel,[5]

---

3. Turn back (to your allegiance to Lucifer).   5. Achilles could be wounded only in his heel—
4. Immeasurably high; matchless.   where he was shot by Paris.

And then return to Helen for a kiss.
O thou art fairer than the evening air
95 Clad in the beauty of a thousand stars,
Brighter art thou than flaming Jupiter
When he appeared to hapless Semele;[6]
More lovely than the monarch of the sky
In wanton Arethusa's azured arms;[7]
100 And none but thou shalt be my paramour.

[*Exeunt* (FAUSTUS *and* HELEN).]

OLD MAN   Accursèd Faustus, miserable man,
That from thy soul exclud'st the grace of heaven
And fliest the throne of His tribunal seat!
[*Enter the* DEVILS.]
Satan begins to sift me with his pride,[8]
105 As in this furnace God shall try my faith.
My faith, vile hell, shall triumph over thee!
Ambitious fiends, see how the heavens smiles
At your repulse, and laughs your state° to scorn.   royal power
Hence hell, for hence I fly unto my God.

[*Exeunt.*]

SCENE 13

[*Enter* FAUSTUS *with the* SCHOLARS.]
FAUSTUS   Ah gentlemen!
1 SCHOLAR   What ails Faustus?
FAUSTUS   Ah my sweet chamber-fellow, had I lived with thee, then
had I lived still;[9] but now I die eternally. Look, comes he not, comes
5   he not?
2 SCHOLAR   What means Faustus?
3 SCHOLAR   Belike he is grown into some sickness by being over-
solitary.
1 SCHOLAR   If it be so, we'll have physicians to cure him; 'tis but a
10   surfeit:[1] never fear, man.
FAUSTUS   A surfeit of deadly sin, that hath damned both body and
soul.
2 SCHOLAR   Yet Faustus, look up to heaven; remember God's mercies are infinite.
15 FAUSTUS   But Faustus' offense can ne'er be pardoned! The serpent
that tempted Eve may be saved, but not Faustus. Ah gentlemen,
hear me with patience, and tremble not at my speeches, though
my heart pants and quivers to remember that I have been a student here these thirty years—O would I had never seen Witten-
20   berg, never read book—and what wonders I have done, all
Wittenberg can witness—yea, all the world; for which Faustus

---

6. A Theban girl, loved by Jupiter and destroyed
by the fire of his lightning when he appeared to
her in his full splendor.
7. Arethusa was the nymph of a fountain, as well
as the fountain itself; she excited the passion of

the river god Alpheus, who was by some accounts
related to the sun.
8. To test me with his strength.
9. Always.
1. Indigestion caused by overeating.

hath lost both Germany and the world—yea, heaven itself—
heaven, the seat of God, the throne of the blessed, the kingdom of
joy; and must remain in hell forever—hell, ah, hell forever! Sweet
25   friends, what shall become of Faustus, being in hell forever?

3 SCHOLAR   Yet Faustus, call on God.

FAUSTUS   On God, whom Faustus hath abjured? On God, whom
Faustus hath blasphemed? Ah, my God—I would weep, but the
devil draws in my tears! Gush forth blood, instead of tears—yea,
30   life and soul! O, he stays my tongue! I would lift up my hands, but
see, they hold them, they hold them!

ALL   Who, Faustus?

FAUSTUS   Lucifer and Mephastophilis! Ah gentlemen, I gave them
my soul for my cunning.

35 ALL   God forbid!

FAUSTUS   God forbade it indeed, but Faustus hath done it: for the
vain pleasure of four-and-twenty years hath Faustus lost eternal
joy and felicity. I writ them a bill[2] with mine own blood, the date
is expired, the time will come, and he will fetch me.

40 1 SCHOLAR   Why did not Faustus tell us of this before, that divines
might have prayed for thee?

FAUSTUS   Oft have I thought to have done so, but the devil threatened to tear me in pieces if I named God, to fetch both body and
soul if I once gave ear to divinity; and now 'tis too late. Gentlemen,
45   away, lest you perish with me!

2 SCHOLAR   O what shall we do to save Faustus?

3 SCHOLAR   God will strengthen me. I will stay with Faustus.

1 SCHOLAR   Tempt not God, sweet friend, but let us into the next
room, and there pray for him.

50 FAUSTUS   Ay, pray for me, pray for me; and what noise soever ye
hear, come not unto me, for nothing can rescue me.

2 SCHOLAR   Pray thou, and we will pray, that God may have mercy
upon thee.

FAUSTUS   Gentlemen, farewell. If I live till morning, I'll visit you; if
55   not, Faustus is gone to hell.

ALL   Faustus, farewell.   [*Exeunt* SCHOLARS.]
        [*The clock strikes eleven.*]

FAUSTUS   Ah Faustus,
  Now hast thou but one bare hour to live,
  And then thou must be damned perpetually.
60   Stand still, you ever-moving spheres of heaven,
  That time may cease, and midnight never come.
  Fair Nature's eye, rise, rise again, and make
  Perpetual day, or let this hour be but
  A year, a month, a week, a natural day,
65   That Faustus may repent and save his soul.
  O lente, lente currite noctis equi![3]

2. Document.
3. "Slowly, slowly run, O horses of the night"; adapted from a line in Ovid's *Amores*.

The stars move still, time runs, the clock will strike,
The devil will come, and Faustus must be damned.
O I'll leap up to my God! Who pulls me down?
70   See, see where Christ's blood streams in the firmament!°   sky
One drop would save my soul, half a drop: ah my Christ—
Ah, rend not my heart for naming of my Christ;
Yet will I call on him—O spare me, Lucifer!
Where is it now? 'Tis gone: and see where God
75   Stretcheth out his arm, and bends his ireful brows!
Mountains and hills, come, come and fall on me,
And hide me from the heavy wrath of God.
No, no?
Then will I headlong run into the earth:
80   Earth, gape! O no, it will not harbor me.
You stars that reigned at my nativity,
Whose influence hath allotted death and hell,
Now draw up Faustus like a foggy mist
Into the entrails of yon laboring cloud,
85   That when you vomit forth into the air
My limbs may issue from your smoky mouths,
So that my soul may but ascend to heaven.[4]
        [*The watch strikes.*]
Ah, half the hour is past: 'twill all be past anon.°   shortly
O God, if thou wilt not have mercy on my soul,
90   Yet for Christ's sake, whose blood hath ransomed me,
Impose some end to my incessant pain:
Let Faustus live in hell a thousand years,
A hundred thousand, and at last be saved.
O no end is limited to damnèd souls!
95   Why wert thou not a creature wanting° soul?   lacking
Or why is this immortal that thou hast?
Ah, Pythagoras' *metempsychosis*[5]—were that true,
This soul should fly from me, and I be changed
Unto some brutish beast:
100   All beasts are happy, for when they die,
Their souls are soon dissolved in elements;
But mine must live still° to be plagued in hell.   always
Cursed be the parents that engendered me!
No, Faustus, curse thy self, curse Lucifer,
105   That hath deprived thee of the joys of heaven.
        [*The clock striketh twelve.*]
O it strikes, it strikes! Now body, turn to air,
Or Lucifer will bear thee quick° to hell.   alive
        [*Thunder and lightning.*]
O soul, be changed into little water drops
And fall into the ocean, ne'er be found.

---

4. Faustus wants to be drawn up into a cloud, which would compact his body into a thunderbolt so that his soul, thus purified, might ascend to heaven.
5. Pythagoras's doctrine of the transmigration of souls.

110 My God, my God, look not so fierce on me!
    [Enter DEVILS.*]*
Adders and serpents, let me breathe awhile!
Ugly hell gape not! Come not, Lucifer!
I'll burn my books—ah, Mephastophilis!
    [Exeunt with him.]

Epilogue

    [Enter CHORUS.*]*
Cut is the branch that might have grown full straight,
And burnèd is Apollo's laurel bough,[6]
That sometime grew within this learnèd man.
Faustus is gone! Regard his hellish fall,
5 Whose fiendful fortune° may exhort the wise   *devilish fate*
Only to wonder at[7] unlawful things:
Whose deepness doth entice such forward wits°   *aspiring minds*
To practice more than heavenly power permits.
    [Exit.]

    Terminat hora diem, terminat author opus.[8]

        1604, 1616

---

6. The laurel crown of Apollo symbolizes (among other things) learning and wisdom.
7. Be content simply to observe with awe.

8. "The hour ends the day, the author ends his work"; this motto was probably added by the printer.

The Two Texts of *Doctor Faustus*   The following excerpts enable readers to compare a sample passage (from Scene 12) of the A text (1604) with the corresponding passage of the B text (1616). (On the two texts, see above, p. 1127.) Here the differences in tone and content in the two versions of the Old Man's speech may signal different attitudes toward the finality of Faustus's damnation.

For additional parallel passages from the A and B texts, see "The Magician, the Heretic, and the Playwright" in the supplemental ebook.

Doctor Faustus, A Text

[*Enter an* OLD MAN.]

OLD MAN   Ah Doctor Faustus, that I might prevail
    To guide thy steps unto the way of life,
    By which sweet path thou may'st attain the goal
    That shall conduct thee to celestial rest.
5   Break heart, drop blood, and mingle it with tears,
    Tears falling from repentant heaviness°   *grief*
    Of thy most vile and loathsome filthiness,
    The stench whereof corrupts the inward soul
    With such flagitious° crimes of heinous sins   *villainous*
10   As no commiseration may expel
    But mercy, Faustus, of thy savior sweet,
    Whose blood alone must wash away thy guilt.
FAUSTUS   Where art thou, Faustus? Wretch, what hast thou done!
    Damned art thou, Faustus, damned; despair and die!
15   Hell calls for right, and with a roaring voice
    Says, "Faustus, come: thine hour is come!"
    [MEPHASTOPHILIS *gives him a dagger.*]
    And Faustus will come to do thee right.
OLD MAN   Ah stay, good Faustus, stay thy desperate steps!
    I see an angel hovers o'er thy head
20   And with a vial full of precious grace
    Offers to pour the same into thy soul!
    Then call for mercy, and avoid despair.
FAUSTUS   Ah my sweet friend, I feel thy words
    To comfort my distressèd soul;
25   Leave me awhile to ponder on my sins.
OLD MAN   I go, sweet Faustus; but with heavy cheer,°   *heavy heart*
    Fearing the ruin of thy hopeless soul.   [*Exit.*]
FAUSTUS   Accursèd Faustus, where is mercy now?
    I do repent, and yet I do despair:
30   Hell strives with grace for conquest in my breast!
    What shall I do to shun the snares of death?
MEPHASTOPHILIS   Thou traitor, Faustus: I arrest thy soul
    For disobedience to my sovereign lord.
    Revolt,[1] or I'll in piecemeal tear thy flesh.

---

1. Turn back (to your allegiance to Lucifer).

Doctor Faustus, B Text

[*Enter an* OLD MAN.]

OLD MAN   O gentle Faustus, leave this damnèd art,
This magic that will charm thy soul to hell
And quite bereave thee of salvatiön.
Though thou hast now offended like a man,
5   Do not persèver° in it like a devil.   *persevere*
Yet, yet, thou hast an amiable° soul,   *worthy of (divine) love*
If sin by custom grow not into nature.
Then, Faustus, will repentance come too late;
Then thou art banished from the sight of heaven.
10   No mortal can express the pains of hell.
It may be this my exhortatiön
Seems harsh and all unpleasant; let it not,
For, gentle son, I speak it not in wrath
Or envy of° thee, but in tender love   *ill will toward*
15   And pity of thy future misery.
And so have hope that this my kind rebuke,
Checking° thy body, may amend thy soul.   *rebuking*
FAUSTUS   Where art thou, Faustus? Wretch, what hast thou done?
Hell claims his right, and with a roaring voice
20   Says, "Faustus, come; thine hour is almost come";
And Faustus now will come to do thee right.
[MEPHOSTOPHILIS *gives him a dagger.*]
OLD MAN   O stay, good Faustus, stay thy desperate steps.
I see an angel hover o'er thy head,
And with a vial full of precious grace
25   Offers to pour the same into thy soul.
Then call for mercy and avoid despair.
FAUSTUS   O friend, I feel thy words
To comfort my distressèd soul.
Leave me a while to ponder on my sins.
30   OLD MAN   Faustus, I leave thee, but with grief of heart,
Fearing the enemy of thy hapless soul.   [*Exit.*]
FAUSTUS   Accursèd Faustus, wretch, what hast thou done?
I do repent, and yet I do despair.
Hell strives with grace for conquest in my breast.
35   What shall I do to shun the snares of death?
MEPHOSTOPHILIS   Thou traitor, Faustus, I arrest thy soul
For disobedience to my sovereign lord.
Revolt,[1] or I'll in piecemeal tear thy flesh.

1. Turn back (to your allegiance to Lucifer).

WILLIAM SHAKESPEARE
1564–1616

William Shakespeare was born in the small market town of Stratford-on-Avon in April (probably April 23) 1564. His father, a successful glovemaker, landowner, moneylender, and dealer in agricultural commodities, was elected to several important posts in local government but later suffered financial and social reverses, possibly as a result of adherence to the Catholic faith. Shakespeare almost certainly attended the free Stratford grammar school, where he would have acquired a reasonably impressive education, including a respectable knowledge of Latin, but he did not proceed to Oxford or Cambridge. There are legends about Shakespeare's youth but no documented facts. Some scholars are tempted to associate him with "William Shakeshafte," a young actor attached to a recusant Catholic circle in Lancashire around 1581; one of Shakespeare's former Stratford schoolmasters belonged to this circle. But the first unambiguous record we have of his life after his christening is that of his marriage, in 1582, at age eighteen, to Anne Hathaway, eight years his senior. A daughter, Susanna, was born six months later, in 1583, and twins, Hamnet and Judith, in 1585. We possess no information about his activities for the next seven years, but by 1592 he was in London as an actor and apparently already well known as a playwright, for a rival dramatist, Robert Greene, refers to him resentfully in *A Groatsworth of Wit* as "an upstart crow, beautified with our feathers."

At this time, there were several companies of professional actors in London and in the provinces. What links Shakespeare had with one or more of them before 1592 is conjectural, but we do know of his long and fruitful connection, established by 1594, with the most successful troupe, the Lord Chamberlain's Men, who later, when James I came to the throne, became the King's Men. Shakespeare not only acted with this company but eventually became a leading shareholder and the principal playwright. Then as now, making a living in the professional theater was not easy: competition among the repertory companies was stiff, civic officials and religious moralists regarded playacting as a sinful, time-wasting nuisance and tried to ban it altogether, government officials exercised censorship over the contents of the plays, and periodic outbreaks of bubonic plague led to temporary closing of the London theaters. But Shakespeare's company, which included some of the most famous actors of the day, nonetheless thrived and in 1599 began to perform in the Globe, a fine, open-air theater that the company built for itself on the south bank of the Thames. The company also performed frequently at court and, after 1608, at Blackfriars, an indoor London theater. Already by 1597 Shakespeare had so prospered that he was able to purchase New Place, a handsome house in Stratford; he could now call himself a gentleman, as his father had (probably with the financial assistance of his successful playwright son) been granted a coat of arms the previous year. Shakespeare's wife and daughters (his son, Hamnet, having died in 1596) resided in Stratford, while the playwright, living in rented rooms in London, pursued his career. Shortly after writing *The Tempest* (ca. 1611), he retired from direct involvement in the theater and returned to Stratford. In March 1616, he signed his will; he died a month later, leaving the bulk of his estate to his daughter Susanna. To his wife of thirty-four years, he left "my second best bed."

Shakespeare began his career as a playwright, probably in the early 1590s, by writing comedies and history plays. The earliest of these histories, generally based on accounts of English kings written by Raphael Holinshed and other sixteenth-century chroniclers, seem theatrically vital but crude, as does an early attempt at

Sketch of the Swan Theater. This drawing by Arend van Buchell (ca. 1596), based on the observations of Johannes De Witt, shows features of the public playhouse in Shakespeare's time. Resembling the courtyard of an Elizabethan inn, the Swan had three galleries for the audience, and probably additional room for audience members in the gallery at the back of the stage, above the tiring-house (dressing-room). The stage itself had two doors for players' entrances and exits, and the roof over the stage was supported by pillars. The flag flying from the roof signals that a play is to be performed that day, and a trumpeter announces the beginning of the performance (though the sketch shows a performance already under way). De Witt labeled parts of the sketch using Latin names derived from the Roman theater.

tragedy, *Titus Andronicus*. But Shakespeare quickly moved on to create by the later 1590s a sequence of profoundly searching and ambitious history plays—*Richard II*, the first and second parts of *Henry IV*, and *Henry V*—which together explore the death throes of feudal England and the birth of the modern nation-state ruled by a charismatic monarch. In the same years he wrote a succession of romantic comedies (*The Merchant of Venice, The Merry Wives of Windsor, Much Ado About Nothing, As You Like It, Twelfth Night*) whose poetic richness and emotional complexity remain unmatched.

Twelfth Night was probably written in the same year as *Hamlet* (ca. 1601), which initiated an outpouring of great tragic dramas: *Othello, King Lear, Macbeth, Antony and Cleopatra*, and *Coriolanus*. These plays, written from 1601 to 1607, seem to mark a major shift in sensibility, an existential and metaphysical darkening that many readers think must have originated in personal anguish. Whatever the truth of this speculation—and we have no direct, personal testimony either to support or to undermine it—there appears to have occurred in the same period a shift as well in Shakespeare's comic sensibility. The comedies written between 1601 and 1604, *Troilus and Cressida, All's Well That Ends Well*, and *Measure for Measure*, are suffi- ciently different from the earlier comedies—more biting in tone, more uneasy with comic conventions, more ruthlessly questioning of the values of the characters and the resolutions of the plots—to have led some modern scholars to classify them as "problem plays" or "dark comedies." Another group of plays, among the last that Shakespeare wrote, seem similarly to define a distinct category. *Pericles, Cymbe- line, The Winter's Tale*, and *The Tempest*, written between 1608 and 1611, when Shakespeare had developed a remarkably fluid, dream-like sense of plot and a poetic style that could veer, apparently effortlessly, from the tortured to the ineffa- bly sweet, are now commonly known as the "romances." These plays share an inter- est in the moral and emotional life less of the adolescents who dominate the earlier comedies than of their parents. The "romances" are deeply concerned with patterns of loss and recovery, suffering and redemption, despair and renewal. They have seemed to many critics to constitute a self-conscious conclusion to a career that opened with histories and comedies and passed through the dark and tormented tragedies.

Shakespeare himself apparently had no interest in preserving for posterity the sum of his writings, let alone in clarifying the chronology of his works or in specify- ing which plays he wrote alone and which with collaborators. He wrote plays for performance by his company, and his scripts existed in his own handwritten manu- scripts or in scribal copies, in playhouse prompt books, and probably in pirated texts based on shorthand reports of a performance or on reconstructions from memory by an actor or a spectator. None of these manuscript versions has survived. Eighteen of his plays were published during his lifetime in the small-format, inexpensive books called quartos; to these were added eighteen other plays, never before printed, in the large, expensive folio volume of *Mr. William Shakespeares Comedies, Histories, & Tragedies* (1623), published seven years after his death. This First Folio, edited by two of his friends and fellow actors, John Heminges and Henry Condell, is prefaced by a poem of Ben Jonson's, in which Shakespeare is hailed, presciently, as "not of an age, but for all time."

That Shakespeare is "for all time" does not mean that he did not also belong to his own age. It is possible to see where Shakespeare adapted the techniques of his contemporaries and where, crucially, he differed from them. Shakespeare rarely invented the plots of his dramas, preferring to work, often quite closely, with stories he found ready-made in histories, novellas, narrative poems, or other plays. The reli- gious mystery plays and the allegorical morality plays still popular during his child- hood taught him that dramas worth seeing must get at something central to the human condition, that they should embody as well as narrate the crucial actions, and that they could reach not only a coterie of the educated elite but also the great mass of ordinary people. From these and other theatrical models, Shakespeare learned how to construct plays around the struggle for the soul of a protagonist, how to create theatrically compelling and subversive figures of wickedness, and how to focus attention on his characters' psychological, moral, and spiritual lives, as well as on their outward behavior.

The authors of the morality plays thought that they could enhance the broad impact they sought to achieve by stripping their characters of all incidental distinguishing traits and getting to their essences. They believed that their audiences would thereby not be distracted by the irrelevant details of individual identities. Shakespeare grasped that the spectacle of human destiny was in fact vastly more compelling when it was attached not to generalized abstractions but to particular people, people whom he realized with an unprecedented intensity of individuation: not Youth but Viola, not Everyman but Lear. No other writer of his time was able to create and enter into the interior worlds of so many characters, conveying again and again a sense of unique and irreducible selfhood. In the plays of Shakespeare's brilliant contemporary Marlowe, the protagonist overwhelms virtually all of the other characters; in Shakespeare, by contrast, even relatively minor characters—Maria in *Twelfth Night*, for example, or the fool in *King Lear*—make astonishingly powerful claims on the audience's attention. The Romantic critic William Hazlitt observed that Shakespeare had the power to multiply himself marvelously. His plays convey the sense of an inexhaustible imaginative generosity.

Shakespeare was singularly alert to the fantastic vitality of the English language. His immense vocabulary bears witness to an uncanny ability to absorb terms from a wide range of pursuits and to transform them into intimate registers of thought and feeling. He had a seemingly boundless capacity to generate metaphors, and he was virtually addicted to wordplay. Double-meanings, verbal echoes, and submerged associations ripple through every passage, deepening the reader's enjoyment and understanding, though sometimes at the expense of a single clear sense. The eighteenth-century critic Samuel Johnson complained with some justice that the quibble, the pun, was "the fatal Cleopatra for which Shakespeare lost the world and was content to lose it." For the power that continually discharges itself throughout his plays and poems, at once constituting and unsettling everything it touches, is the polymorphous power of language.

Anachronism is rarely a concern for Shakespeare. His ancient Romans throw their caps into the air and use Christian oaths: to this extent he pulled everything he touched into his contemporary existence. But at the same time he was not a social realist; other writers in this period are better at conveying the precise details of the daily lives of shoemakers, alchemists, and judges. The settings of his plays—"Illyria" in *Twelfth Night*, for example, or ancient Britain in *King Lear*—were for Shakespeare not realistic representations of particular historical times and places but rather imaginative displacements into alternative worlds that remain strangely familiar.

Though on occasion he depicts ghosts, demons, and other supernatural figures, the universe Shakespeare conjures up seems resolutely human-centered and secular: the torments and joys that most deeply matter are found in this world, not in the next. Attempts to claim him for one or another religious system have proven unconvincing, as have attempts to assign him a specific political label. Activists and ideologues of all political stripes have viewed him as an ally: he has been admiringly quoted by kings and by revolutionaries, by fascists, liberal democrats, socialists, republicans, and communists. At once an agent of civility and an agent of subversion, Shakespeare seems to have been able to view society simultaneously as an insider and as an outsider. His plays can be interpreted and performed—with deep conviction and compelling power—in utterly contradictory ways. The centuries-long accumulation of these interpretations and performances, far from exhausting

Shakespeare's aesthetic appeal, seems only to have enhanced its perennial freshness.*

Sonnets In Elizabethan England aristocratic patronage, with the money, protection, and prestige it alone could provide, was probably a professional writer's most important asset. This patronage, or at least Shakespeare's quest for it, is most visible in his dedication, in 1593 and 1594, of his narrative poems, *Venus and Adonis* and *The Rape of Lucrece*, to the wealthy young nobleman Henry Wriothesley, earl of Southampton. What return the poet got for his exquisite offerings is unknown. We do know that among wits and gallants the narrative poems won Shakespeare a fine reputation as an immensely stylish and accomplished poet. This reputation was enhanced as well by manuscript circulation of his sonnets, which were mentioned admiringly in print more than ten years before they were published, in 1609 (apparently without his personal supervision and perhaps without his consent).

Shakespeare's sonnets are quite unlike the other sonnet sequences of his day, notably in his almost unprecedented choice of a beautiful young man (rather than a lady) as the principal object of praise, love, and idealizing devotion and in his portrait of a dark, sensuous, and sexually promiscuous mistress (rather than the usual chaste and aloof blond beauty). Nor are the moods confined to what the Renaissance thought were those of the despairing Petrarchan lover: they include delight, pride, melancholy, shame, disgust, and fear. Shakespeare's sequence suggests a story, although the details are vague, and there is even doubt whether the sonnets as published are in an order established by the poet himself. Certain motifs are evident: an introductory series (1 to 17) celebrates the beauty of a young man and urges him to marry and beget children who will bear his image. The subsequent long sequence (18 to 126), passionately focused on the beloved young man, develops as a dominant motif the transience and destructive power of time, countered only by the force of love and the permanence of poetry. The remaining sonnets focus chiefly on the so-called Dark Lady as an alluring but degrading object of desire. Some sonnets (like 144) intimate a love triangle involving the speaker, the male friend, and the woman; others take note of a rival poet (sometimes identified as George Chapman or Christopher Marlowe). The biographical background of the sonnets has inspired a mountain of speculation, but very little of it has any factual support.

Though there are many variations, Shakespeare's most frequent rhyme scheme in the sonnets is *abab cdcd efef gg*. This so-called Shakespearean pattern often (though not always) calls attention to three distinct quatrains (each of which may develop a separate metaphor), followed by a closing couplet that may either confirm or pull sharply against what has gone before. Startling shifts in direction may occur in lines other than the closing ones; consider, for example, the twists and turns in the opening lines of sonnet 138: "When my love swears that she is made of truth, / I do believe her, though I know she lies." Shakespeare's sonnets as a whole are strikingly intense, conveying a sense of high psychological and moral stakes. They are also remarkably dense, written with a daunting energy, concentration, and compression. Often the main idea of the poem may be grasped quickly, but the precise movement of thought and feeling, the links among the shifting images, the syntax, tone, and rhetorical structure prove immensely challenging. These are poems that famously reward rereading.†

---

* For additional writings by Shakespeare—including the full text of *The First Part of King Henry IV*, Ulysses' speech on degree from *Troilus and Cressida*, a collection of songs from the plays, five additional sonnets (nos. 56, 104, 118, 121, 124), and the philosophical poem "The Phoenix and the Turtle"—see the supplemental ebook. See the color insert in this volume for the "Chandos" portrait of Shakespeare and a portrait of Henry Wriothesley, third earl of Southampton and the dedicatee of Shakespeare's two narrative poems and, possibly, of his *Sonnets*.

† For a broad grouping of other 16th-century love poems, see above, "Renaissance Love and Desire" (pp. 1000 ff.).

Sonnets

To the Only Begetter of
These Ensuing Sonnets
Mr. W. H. All Happiness
and That Eternity
Promised
By
Our Ever-Living Poet
Wisheth
The Well-Wishing
Adventurer in
Setting Forth
T. T.[1]

1

From fairest creatures we desire increase,
That thereby beauty's rose might never die,
But as the riper should by time decease,
His tender heir might bear his memory;
5   But thou, contracted[2] to thine own bright eyes,
Feed'st thy light's flame with self-substantial[3] fuel,
Making a famine where abundance lies,
Thyself thy foe, to thy sweet self too cruel.
Thou that art now the world's fresh ornament
10 And only[4] herald to the gaudy spring,
Within thine own bud buriest thy content[5]
And, tender churl,[6] mak'st waste in niggarding.°   hoarding
     Pity the world, or else this glutton be,
     To eat the world's due, by the grave and thee.[7]

3

Look in thy glass° and tell the face thou viewest   mirror
Now is the time that face should form another,
Whose fresh repair° if now thou not renewest,   state
Thou dost beguile° the world, unbless some mother.   cheat
5   For where is she so fair whose uneared° womb   unplowed
Disdains the tillage of thy husbandry?
Or who is he so fond° will be the tomb   foolish

---

1. This odd dedication bears the initials of the publisher, Thomas Thorpe. The W. H. addressed here may or may not be the male friend addressed in sonnets 1 to 126. Leading candidates for that role are Henry Wriothesley, earl of Southampton, the dedicatee of *Venus and Adonis* (1593) and *The Rape of Lucrece* (1594), and William Herbert, earl of Pembroke, a dedicatee of the First Folio. But there is no hard evidence to support these or other suggested identifications of the male friend or of the so-called Dark Lady; these sonnet personages may or may not have had real-life counterparts.

Since all the sonnets save two were first pub-lished in 1609, we do not repeat the date after each one. Numbers 138 and 144 were first pub-lished in 1599, in a verse miscellany called *The Passionate Pilgrim.*
2. Betrothed; also, withdrawn into.
3. Of your own substance.
4. Principal, with overtones of single, solitary.
5. What you contain (potential for fatherhood), also what would content you (marriage and father-hood).
6. Gentle boor (an oxymoron).
7. "This . . . thee": be a glutton by causing what is owed to the world (your posterity) to be con-sumed by the grave and within yourself.

Of his self-love, to stop posterity?
Thou art thy mother's glass, and she in thee
10　Calls back the lovely April of her prime;
So thou through windows of thine age shalt see,
Despite of wrinkles, this thy golden time.
　　But if thou live rememb'red not to be,[8]
　　Die single, and thine image dies with thee.

12

When I do count the clock that tells the time
And see the brave° day sunk in hideous night, 　　　　　　*splendid*
When I behold the violet past prime
And sable curls all silvered o'er with white,
5　When lofty trees I see barren of leaves,
Which erst° from heat did canopy the herd 　　　　　　*formerly*
And summer's green all girded up in sheaves
Borne on the bier with white and bristly beard:
Then of thy beauty do I question make° 　　　　　　*speculate*
10　That thou among the wastes of time must go,
Since sweets and beauties do themselves forsake,
And die as fast as they see others grow,
　　And nothing 'gainst Time's scythe can make defense
　　Save breed,° to brave° him when he takes thee hence. 　　*offspring / defy*

15

When I consider every thing that grows
Holds° in perfection but a little moment; 　　　　　　*remains*
That this huge stage presenteth nought but shows
Whereon the stars in secret influence comment;[9]
5　When I perceive that men as plants increase,
Cheered and checked[1] even by the selfsame sky,
Vaunt[2] in their youthful sap, at height decrease,
And wear their brave state out of memory;[3]
Then the conceit° of this inconstant stay 　　　　　　*conception*
10　Sets you most rich in youth before my sight,
Where wasteful Time debateth[4] with Decay
To change your day of youth to sullied° night, 　　　　*soiled, blackened*
　　And all in war with Time for love of you,
　　As he takes from you, I ingraft[5] you new.

18

Shall I compare thee to a summer's day?
Thou art more lovely and more temperate:
Rough winds do shake the darling buds of May,
And summer's lease hath all too short a date;
5　Sometime too hot the eye of heaven shines,

---

8. But if you live to be forgotten.
9. The stars secretly affect human actions.
"Shows": (1) appearances, (2) performances.
1. Encouraged and reproached or stopped.
2. Exult, display themselves.

3. Wear their showy splendor out and are forgotten.
4. (1)Fights, (2) joins forces.
5. Renew by grafting; implant beauty again (by my verse).

And often is his gold complexion dimmed;
And every fair from fair sometime declines,
By chance or nature's changing course untrimmed.[6]
But thy eternal summer shall not fade,
10 Nor lose possession of that fair thou ow'st;°   *ownest*
Nor shall death brag thou wander'st in his shade,
When in eternal lines to time thou grow'st:°   *are grafted*
    So long as men can breathe or eyes can see,
    So long lives this,[7] and this gives life to thee.

19

Devouring Time, blunt thou the lion's paws,
And make the earth devour her own sweet brood;
Pluck the keen teeth from the fierce tiger's jaws,
And burn the long-lived phoenix in her blood;[8]
5 Make glad and sorry seasons as thou fleet'st,
And do whate'er thou wilt, swift-footed Time,
To the wide world and all her fading sweets,
But I forbid thee one most heinous crime:
O carve not with thy hours my love's fair brow,
10 Nor draw no lines there with thine antique[9] pen;
Him in thy course untainted[1] do allow,
For beauty's pattern to succeeding men.
    Yet do thy worst, old Time: despite thy wrong,
    My love shall in my verse ever live young.

20

A woman's face with Nature's own hand painted[2]
Hast thou, the master mistress of my passion;[3]
A woman's gentle heart but not acquainted
With shifting change as is false women's fashion;
5 An eye more bright than theirs, less false in rolling,°   *roving*
Gilding the object whereupon it gazeth;
A man in hue all hues[4] in his controlling,
Which steals men's eyes and women's souls amazeth.
And for a woman wert thou first created,
10 Till Nature as she wrought thee fell a-doting,[5]
And by addition me of thee defeated,
By adding one thing to my purpose nothing.
    But since she pricked[6] thee out for women's pleasure,
    Mine be thy love, and thy love's use[7] their treasure.

6. Stripped of gay apparel.
7. I.e., the poem. The boast of immortality for one's verse was a convention going back to the Greek and Roman classics.
8. In full vigor of life (a hunting term). The phoenix was a mythical bird that lived five hundred years, then died in flames to rise again from its ashes.
9. (1) Old, (2) fantastic (antic).
1. (1) Undefiled, (2) untouched by a weapon (a term from jousting).

2. I.e., not made up with cosmetics.
3. (1) Strong feeling, (2) poem.
4. "Hue" probably means appearance or form. In the first edition, "hues" is spelled *"Hews,"* which some have taken as indicating a pun on a proper name. It has also been suggested that "man in" is a copyist's or compositor's misreading of "maiden."
5. (1) Crazy, (2) infatuated.
6. Marked, with obvious sexual pun.
7. (1) Sexual enjoyment, (2) interest (as in usury).

23

As an unperfect actor on the stage
Who with his fear is put besides° his part,   *forgets*
Or some fierce thing replete with too much rage
Whose strength's abundance weakens his own heart,
5   So I, for fear of trust,° forget to say   *lack of confidence*
The perfect ceremony of love's rite,[8]
And in mine own love's strength seem to decay,
O'er-charged° with burden of mine own love's might.   *overweighed*
O let my books be then the eloquence
10 And dumb presagers° of my speaking breast,   *mute presenters*
Who plead for love, and look for recompense
More than that tongue that more hath more expressed.[9]
    O learn to read what silent love hath writ;
    To hear with eyes belongs to love's fine wit.°   *intelligence*

29

When, in disgrace° with Fortune and men's eyes,   *disfavor*
I all alone beweep my outcast state,
And trouble deaf heaven with my bootless° cries,   *futile*
And look upon myself and curse my fate,
5   Wishing me like to one more rich in hope,
Featured like him, like him with friends possessed,[1]
Desiring this man's art° and that man's scope,°   *skill / ability*
With what I most enjoy contented least;
Yet in these thoughts myself almost despising,
10 Haply I think on thee, and then my state[2]
(Like to the lark at break of day arising
From sullen earth) sings hymns at heaven's gate;
    For thy sweet love remembered such wealth brings
    That then I scorn to change my state with kings.

30

When to the sessions[3] of sweet silent thought
I summon up remembrance of things past,
I sigh the lack of many a thing I sought,
And with old woes new wail° my dear time's waste: *bewail anew*
5   Then can I drown an eye (unused to flow)
For precious friends hid in death's dateless° night,   *endless*
And weep afresh love's long since canceled woe,
And moan th' expense° of many a vanished sight: *loss*
Then can I grieve at grievances foregone,°   *former*
10 And heavily from woe to woe tell° o'er   *count*
The sad account of fore-bemoanèd moan,
Which I new pay as if not paid before.

8. The first edition has "right," suggesting love's
due as well as love's ritual ("rite").
9. More than that (rival) speaker who has more
often said more.
1. I.e., I wish I had one man's looks, another man's
friends.
2. Condition, state of mind; but in line 14 there
is a pun on *state* meaning chair of state, throne.
3. Sittings of court. "Summon up" (next line) continues the metaphor.

But if the while I think on thee, dear friend,
All losses are restored and sorrows end.

33

Full many a glorious morning have I seen
Flatter the mountain tops with sovereign eye,°   *sunlight*
Kissing with golden face the meadows green,
Gilding pale streams with heavenly alchemy;
5 Anon° permit the basest° clouds to ride   *(but) soon / darkest*
With ugly rack° on his celestial face,   *cloudy mask*
And from the forlorn world his visage hide,
Stealing unseen to west with this disgrace.
Even so my sun one early morn did shine
10 With all triumphant splendor on my brow;
But out, alack,° he was but one hour mine;   *alas*
The region° cloud hath masked him from me now.   *high*
    Yet him for this my love no whit disdaineth:
    Suns of the world may stain° when heaven's sun staineth.   *darken*

35

No more be grieved at that which thou hast done:
Roses have thorns, and silver fountains mud.
Clouds and eclipses stain° both moon and sun,   *dim*
And loathsome canker° lives in sweetest bud.   *rose worm*
5 All men make faults, and even I in this,
Authorizing thy trespass with compare,°   *comparisons*
Myself corrupting, salving thy amiss,°   *palliating your offense*
Excusing thy sins more than thy sins are;
For to thy sensual fault I bring in sense°—   *i.e., reason*
10 Thy adverse party is thy advocate—
And 'gainst myself a lawful plea commence.
Such civil war is in my love and hate
    That I an accessory needs must be
    To that sweet thief which sourly robs from me.

55

Not marble nor the gilded monuments
Of princes shall outlive this powerful rhyme;
But you shall shine more bright in these contents
Than unswept stone, besmeared with sluttish time.[4]
5 When wasteful war shall statues overturn,
And broils° root out the work of masonry,   *battles*
Nor Mars his° sword nor war's quick fire shall burn   *neither Mars's*
The living record of your memory.
'Gainst death and all-oblivious enmity[5]
10 Shall you pace forth; your praise shall still find room
Even in the eyes of all posterity

---

4. I.e., than in a stone tomb or effigy that time   enly.
wears away and covers with dust. "Sluttish": slov-   5. The enmity of oblivion, of being forgotten.

That wear this world out to the ending doom.°   *Judgment Day*
  So, till the judgment that yourself arise,[6]
  You live in this, and dwell in lovers' eyes.

60

Like as the waves make towards the pebbled shore,
So do our minutes hasten to their end;
Each changing place with that which goes before,
In sequent toil all forwards do contend.[7]
5 Nativity, once in the main° of light,   *broad expanse*
Crawls to maturity, wherewith being crowned,
Crooked° eclipses 'gainst his glory fight,   *pernicious*
And Time that gave doth now his gift confound.
Time doth transfix the flourish set on youth,
10 And delves the parallels[8] in beauty's brow,
Feeds on the rarities of nature's truth,
And nothing stands but for his scythe to mow.
    And yet to times in hope° my verse shall stand,   *future times*
    Praising thy worth, despite his cruel hand.

62

Sin of self-love possesseth all mine eye,
And all my soul, and all my every part;
And for this sin there is no remedy,
It is so grounded inward in my heart.
5 Methinks no face so gracious° is as mine,   *pleasing*
No shape so true,° no truth of such account,   *perfect*
And for myself mine own worth do define
As° I all other° in all worths surmount.   *as if / others*
But when my glass° shows me myself indeed,   *mirror*
10 Beated and chapped with tanned antiquity,
Mine own self-love quite contrary° I read;   *differently*
Self so self-loving were iniquity.
    'Tis thee, my self,° that for° myself I praise,   *you, my other self / as*
    Painting my age with beauty of thy days.

65

Since[9] brass, nor stone, nor earth, nor boundless sea,
But sad mortality o'ersways their power,
How with this rage° shall beauty hold a plea,   *destructive power*
Whose action is no stronger than a flower?
5 O how shall summer's honey breath hold out
Against the wrackful° siege of batt'ring days,   *destructive*
When rocks impregnable are not so stout,
Nor gates of steel so strong, but Time decays?
O fearful meditation! Where, alack,

---

6. Until you rise from the dead on Judgment Day.
7. Toiling and following each other, all struggle
to move forward.
8. Digs the parallel furrows (wrinkles). "Trans-

fix the flourish": destroy the embellishment. To
"flourish" is also to blossom.
9. I.e., since there is neither.

10   Shall Time's best jewel from Time's chest[1] he hid?
     Or what strong hand can hold his swift foot back?
     Or who his spoil° of beauty can forbid?   *ravaging*
       O none, unless this miracle have might,
       That in black ink my love may still shine bright.

71

     No longer mourn for me when I am dead
     Than you shall hear the surly sullen bell[2]
     Give warning to the world that I am fled
     From this vile world, with vilest worms to dwell.
5   Nay, if you read this line, remember not
     The hand that writ it; for I love you so,
     That I in your sweet thoughts would be forgot,
     If thinking on me then should make you woe.
     O, if, I say, you look upon this verse
10   When I perhaps compounded am with clay,
     Do not so much as my poor name rehearse,°   *repeat*
     But let your love even with my life decay;
       Lest the wise world should look into your moan,
       And mock you with me after I am gone.

73

     That time of year thou may'st in me behold
     When yellow leaves, or none, or few, do hang
     Upon those boughs which shake against the cold,
     Bare ruined choirs,[3] where late° the sweet birds sang.   *lately*
5   In me thou seest the twilight of such day
     As after sunset fadeth in the west;
     Which by and by black night doth take away,
     Death's second self that seals up all in rest.
     In me thou seest the glowing of such fire
10   That on the ashes of his youth doth lie,
     As the deathbed whereon it must expire,
     Consumed with that which it was nourished by.[4]
       This thou perceiv'st, which makes thy love more strong,
       To love that well, which thou must leave ere long.

74

     But be contented; when that fell[5] arrest
     Without all bail shall carry me away,
     My life hath in this line some interest,[6]
     Which for memorial still° with thee shall stay.   *always*
5   When thou reviewest this, thou dost review

---

1. I.e., from being coffered up by Time.
2. The bell was tolled to announce the death of a member of the parish—one stroke for each year of his or her life.
3. The part of a church where divine service was sung.

4. Choked by the ashes of that which once nourished its flame.
5. Cruel. Hamlet says, "this fell sergeant / Death is strict in his arrest" (5.2.278–79).
6. Share, participation. "In this line": i.e., in this poetry.

The very part was° consecrate to thee.   *which was*
The earth can have but earth, which is his due;
My spirit is thine, the better part of me.
So then thou hast but lost the dregs of life,
10 The prey of worms, my body being dead,
The coward conquest of a wretch's knife,[7]
Too base of° thee to be rememberèd.   *by*
  The worth of that is that which it contains,[8]
  And that is this, and this with thee remains.

80

O, how I faint° when I of you do write,   *get discouraged*
Knowing a better spirit[9] doth use your name,
And in the praise thereof spends all his might,
To make me tongue-tied, speaking of your fame!
5 But since your worth, wide as the ocean is,
The humble as° the proudest sail doth bear,   *as well as*
My saucy bark,° inferior far to his,   *impudent boat*
On your broad main° doth willfully° appear. *waters / boldly*
Your shallowest help will hold me up afloat
10 Whilst he upon your soundless° deep doth ride; *bottomless*
Or, being wrecked, I am a worthless boat,
He of tall building[1] and of goodly pride.°   *magnificence*
  Then if he thrive and I be cast away,
  The worst was this: my love was my decay.

85

My tongue-tied muse in manners holds her still° *tactfully says nothing*
While comments of° your praise, richly compiled, *commentaries in*
Reserve thy character° with golden quill *hoard up your features*
And precious phrase by all the muses filed.°   *polished*
5 I think good thoughts whilst other° write good words, *others*
And like unlettered clerk still cry "Amen"
To every hymn[2] that able spirit affords°   *offers*
In polished form of well-refinèd pen.
Hearing you praised I say "'Tis so, 'tis true,"
10 And to the most° of praise add something more;   *highest*
But that is in my thought,° whose love to you, *i.e., is unspoken*
Though words come hindmost, holds his rank before.° *before all others*
  Then others for the breath of words respect,°   *regard*
  Me for my dumb thoughts, speaking in effect.°   *in reality*

87

Farewell: thou art too dear[3] for my possessing,
And like enough thou know'st thy estimate.°   *value*

---

7. Death's weapon (like Time's scythe).
8. I.e., the only value of the body is that it contains the spirit.
9. A rival poet. See the headnote.
1. Tall, strong build.

2. "Like . . . hymn": like an illiterate parish clerk reflexively approve ("cry 'Amen'" after) every poem ("hymn") of praise.
3. (1) Expensive, (2) beloved.

The charter° of thy worth gives thee releasing;[4]   *deed; contract for property*
My bonds in thee are all determinate.°   *expired*
5 For how do I hold thee but by thy granting,
And for that riches where is my deserving?
The cause of this fair gift in me is wanting,°   *absent*
And so my patent° back again is swerving.[5]   *title*
Thy self thou gav'st, thy own worth then not knowing,
10 Or me, to whom thou gav'st it, else mistaking;°   *i.e., overestimating*
So thy great gift, upon misprision growing,°   *based on error*
Comes home again, on better judgment making.[6]
    Thus have I had thee as a dream doth flatter:
    In sleep a king, but waking no such matter.

93

So shall I live supposing thou art true,
Like a deceivèd husband; so love's face°   *appearance*
May still seem love to me, though altered new—
Thy looks with me, thy heart in other place.
5 For there can live no hatred in thine eye;
Therefore in that I cannot know thy change.
In many's looks the false heart's history
Is writ in moods and frowns and wrinkles strange:[7]
But heaven in thy creation did decree
10 That in thy face sweet love should ever dwell;
Whate'er thy thoughts or thy heart's workings be,
Thy looks should nothing thence but sweetness tell.
    How like Eve's apple doth thy beauty grow°   *become*
    If thy sweet virtue answer not thy show![8]

94

They that have power to hurt and will do none,
That do not do the thing they most do show,[9]
Who, moving others, are themselves as stone,
Unmovèd, cold, and to temptation slow;
5 They rightly do inherit heaven's graces
And husband nature's riches from expense;[1]
They are the lords and owners of their faces,
Others but stewards of their excellence.
The summer's flower is to the summer sweet,
10 Though to itself it only live and die,[2]
But if that flower with base infection meet,
The basest weed outbraves° his dignity: *surpasses*
    For sweetest things turn sourest by their deeds;
    Lilies that fester smell far worse than weeds.

4. Releases you (from love's bonds).
5. I.e., reverting to you.
6. I.e., when you realize your error.
7. Unaccustomed. "Moods": moody expressions.
8. Does not correspond to your appearance.

9. Seem to do, or seem capable of doing.
1. I.e., they do not squander nature's gifts.
2. Even if it lives and dies in apparent isolation (unpollinated).

97

How like a winter hath my absence been
From thee, the pleasure of the fleeting year!
What freezings have I felt, what dark days seen!
What old December's bareness everywhere!
5   And yet this time removed[3] was summer's time,
The teeming autumn, big with rich increase,
Bearing the wanton burthen of the prime,[4]
Like widowed wombs after their lords' decease.
Yet this abundant issue° seemed to me   *outgrowth*
10 But hope of orphans and unfathered fruit;
For summer and his pleasures wait° on thee,   *attend*
And, thou away, the very birds are mute;
   Or, if they sing, 'tis with so dull a cheer°   *such a dismal mood*
   That leaves look pale, dreading the winter's near.

98

From you have I been absent in the spring,
When proud-pied[5] April, dressed in all his trim,
Hath put a spirit of youth in everything,
5   That heavy Saturn° laughed and leapt with him.   *god of melancholy*
Yet nor° the lays° of birds, nor the sweet smell   *neither / songs*
Of different flowers in odor and in hue
Could make me any summer's story tell,
Or from their proud lap pluck them where they grew;
Nor did I wonder at° the lily's white,   *admire*
10 Nor praise the deep vermilion in the rose;
They were but sweet, but figures° of delight,   *merely emblems*
Drawn after you, you pattern of all those.
   Yet seemed it winter still, and, you away,
   As with your shadow I with these did play.

105

Let not my love be called idolatry,
Nor my belovèd as an idol show,
Since all alike my songs and praises be
To one, of one, still° such, and ever so.   *continually*
5   Kind is my love today, tomorrow kind,
Still constant in a wondrous excellence.
Therefore my verse, to constancy confined,
One thing expressing, leaves out difference.°   *variety*
"Fair, kind, and true" is all my argument,°   *theme*
10 "Fair, kind, and true" varying to other words,
And in this change is my invention spent,[6]
Three themes in one, which wonderous scope affords.

---

3. I.e., when I was absent.
4. Spring, which has engendered the lavish crop ("wanton burthen") that autumn is now left to bear.

5. Magnificent in many colors.
6. And in varying the words alone my inventiveness is expended.

Fair, kind, and true have often lived alone,°   *separately*
Which three till now never kept seat° in one.   *dwelt permanently*

106

When in the chronicle of wasted° time   *past*
I see descriptions of the fairest wights,°   *persons*
And beauty making beautiful old rhyme
In praise of ladies dead and lovely knights,
5   Then, in the blazon[7] of sweet beauty's best,
Of hand, of foot, of lip, of eye, of brow,
I see their antique pen would have expressed
Even such a beauty as you master now.
So all their praises are but prophecies
10 Of this our time, all you prefiguring;
And, for they looked but with divining eyes,[8]
They had not skill enough your worth to sing:
    For we, which now behold these present days,
    Have eyes to wonder, but lack tongues to praise.

107

Not mine own fears, nor the prophetic soul
Of the wide world dreaming on things to come,[9]
Can yet the lease of my true love control,
Supposed as forfeit to a confined doom.[1]
5   The mortal moon hath her eclipse endured,
And the sad augurs mock their own presage;[2]
Incertainties now crown themselves assured,
And peace[3] proclaims olives of endless age.
Now with the drops of this most balmy time
10 My love looks fresh, and death to me subscribes,°   *submits*
Since, spite of him, I'll live in this poor rhyme,
While he insults o'er dull and speechless tribes:
    And thou in this shalt find thy monument,
    When tyrants' crests and tombs of brass are spent.°   *wasted away*

110

Alas, 'tis true I have gone here and there
And made myself a motley° to the view,   *fool, jester*
Gored[4] mine own thoughts, sold cheap what is most dear,
Made old offenses of affections° new.   *passions*

---

7. Catalog of excellencies.
8. Because ("for") they were able only ("but") to foresee prophetically.
9. This sonnet refers to contemporary events and the prophecies, common in Elizabethan almanacs, of disaster.
1. I.e., can yet put an end to my love, which I thought doomed to early forfeiture.
2. The "mortal moon" is probably Queen Elizabeth; her "eclipse" could be either her death (March 1603) or, perhaps, her "climacteric" year, her sixty-third (thought meaningful because the

product of two "significant" numbers, 7 and 9), which ended in September 1596. The sober astrologers ("sad augurs") now ridicule their own predictions ("presage") of catastrophe, because they turned out to be false.
3. Perhaps referring to the peace treaty signed with Spain by Elizabeth's successor, James I, or, if the sonnet refers to the time of Elizabeth's climacteric, to an earlier treaty between England and France.
4. Wounded, pierced.

5   Most true it is that I have looked on truth°   *fidelity*
     Askance and strangely;⁵ but, by all above,
     These blenches° gave my heart another youth,   *turnings aside*
     And worse essays⁶ proved thee my best of love.
     Now all is done, have what shall have no end:
10   Mine appetite I never more will grind°   *whet*
     On newer proof,° to try° an older friend,   *experiences / test*
     A god in love, to whom I am confined.
        Then give me welcome, next my heaven the best,⁷
        Even to thy pure and most most loving breast.

116

     Let me not to the marriage of true minds
     Admit impediments;⁸ love is not love
     Which alters when it alteration finds,
     Or bends with the remover to remove:
5   O, no, it is an ever-fixèd mark,⁹
     That looks on tempests and is never shaken;
     It is the star to every wand'ring bark,
     Whose worth's unknown, although his height¹ be taken.
     Love's not Time's fool,° though rosy lips and cheeks   *plaything*
10   Within his² bending sickle's compass come;
     Love alters not with his brief hours and weeks,
     But bears it out even to the edge of doom.°   *brink of Judgment Day*
        If this be error and upon me proved,
        I never writ, nor no man ever loved.

126

     O thou, my lovely boy, who in thy power
     Dost hold Time's fickle glass,³ his sickle, hour;°   *hourglass*
     Who hast by waning grown and therein show'st°   *i.e., in contrast*
     Thy lovers withering as thy sweet self grow'st;
5   If Nature (sovereign mistress over wrack°)   *destruction*
     As thou goest onwards still will pluck thee back,
     She keeps thee to this purpose, that her skill
     May Time disgrace and wretched minutes kill.
     Yet fear her, O thou minion° of her pleasure,   *darling*
10   She may detain, but not still° keep, her treasure!   *always*
        Her audit° (though delayed) answered must be,   *accounting*
        And her quietus° is to render° thee.   *settlement / surrender*

---

5. Obliquely or asquint, and coldly (like a stranger).
6. Trials of worse relationships.
7. I.e., the next best thing to the Christian heaven.
8. From the Anglican marriage service: "If either of you do know any impediment why ye may not be lawfully joined together . . ."

9. Seamark, such as a lighthouse or a beacon.
1. The star's value is incalculable, although its altitude may be known and used for navigation.
2. Time's (as also in line 11).
3. Mirror, fickle because as the subject ages, the mirror reflects a changed image.

127

In the old age black was not counted fair,[4]
Or, if it were, it bore not beauty's name;
But now is black beauty's successive heir,[5]
And beauty slandered with a bastard shame:°   *declared illegitimate*
5   For since each hand hath put on nature's power,
Fairing the foul with art's false borrowed face,°   *i.e., with cosmetics*
Sweet beauty hath no name, no holy bower,[6]
But is profaned, if not lives in disgrace.
Therefore my mistress' brows are raven black,
10 Her eyes so suited,° and they mourners seem   *i.e., also black*
At° such who, not born fair, no beauty lack,[7]   *for*
Sland'ring creation with a false esteem:
  Yet so they mourn, becoming of° their woe,   *gracing*
  That every tongue says beauty should look so.

128

How oft when thou, my music, music play'st
Upon that blessèd wood[8] whose motion sounds
With thy sweet fingers when thou gently sway'st°   *governest*
The wiry concord that mine ear confounds,[9]
5   Do I envỳ those jacks[1] that nimble leap
To kiss the tender inward of thy hand,
Whilst my poor lips, which should that harvest reap,
At the wood's boldness by thee blushing stand.
To be so tickled they would change their state
10 And situation[2] with those dancing chips,
O'er whom thy fingers walk with gentle gait,
Making dead wood more blessed than living lips.
  Since saucy jacks[3] so happy are in this,
  Give them thy fingers, me thy lips to kiss.

129

Th' expense of spirit in a waste of shame
Is lust in action;[4] and till action, lust
Is perjured, murd'rous, bloody, full of blame,
Savage, extreme, rude,° cruel, not to trust;   *brutal*
5   Enjoyed no sooner but despisèd straight;°   *immediately*
Past reason hunted, and no sooner had,
Past reason hated as a swallowed bait
On purpose laid to make the taker mad:

4. Beautiful, equated with blond hair and coloring. "Old": former. "Black": dark hair and coloring, equated with ugliness.
5. Heir in line of succession.
6. Shrine. The next line suggests that natural (unpainted) beauty is now discredited.
7. I.e., nevertheless possess the appearance of beauty.
8. Keys of the spinet or virginal.
9. The harmony from the strings that overcomes my ear with delight.

1. The keys (actually, "jacks" are the plectra that pluck the strings when activated by the keys).
2. Physical location. "State": place in the order of things.
3. With a quibble on the sense "impertinent fellows."
4. The word order here is inverted and slightly obscures the meaning. Lust, when put into action, expends "spirit" (life, vitality; also semen) in a "waste" (desert; also with a pun on *waist*) of shame.

Mad in pursuit, and in possession so;
10 Had, having, and in quest to have, extreme;
A bliss in proof,[5] and proved, a very° woe;   *true*
Before, a joy proposed; behind, a dream.
    All this the world well knows; yet none knows well
    To shun the heaven that leads men to this hell.

130

My mistress' eyes are nothing like the sun;[6]
Coral is far more red than her lips' red;
If snow be white, why then her breasts are dun;
If hairs be wires, black wires grow on her head.
5 I have seen roses damasked,° red and white,   *dappled*
But no such roses see I in her cheeks;
And in some perfumes is there more delight
Than in the breath that from my mistress reeks.[7]
I love to hear her speak, yet well I know
10 That music hath a far more pleasing sound;
I grant I never saw a goddess go;°   *walk*
My mistress, when she walks, treads on the ground.
    And yet, by heaven, I think my love as rare°   *admirable; extraordinary*
    As any she belied° with false compare.   *misrepresented*

135

Whoever hath her wish, thou hast thy *Will*,[8]
And *Will* to boot, and *Will* in overplus;
More than enough am I that vex thee still,°   *always*
To thy sweet will making addition thus.
5 Wilt thou, whose will is large and spacious,
Not once vouchsafe° to hide my will in thine?   *consent*
Shall will in others seem right gracious,
And in° my will no fair acceptance shine?   *in the case of*
The sea, all water, yet receives rain still,
10 And in abundance addeth to his store,°   *plenty*
So thou being rich in *Will* add to thy *Will*
One will of mine to make thy large *Will* more.
    Let no unkind, no fair beseechers kill;[9]
    Think all but one, and me in that one *Will*.

138

When my love swears that she is made of truth,
I do believe her, though I know she lies,[1]

---

5. A bliss during the experience.
6. An anti-Petrarchan sonnet. All of the details commonly attributed by other Elizabethan sonneteers to their ladies (for example, in Spenser's *Amoretti* 64, p. 987) are here denied to the poet's mistress. For a visual parody of Petrarchan metaphors, see p. 1001.
7. Not with our pejorative sense, but simply "emanates."

8. (1) Wishes, (2) carnal desire, (3) the male and female sexual organs, (4) one or more lovers—evidently including Shakespeare—named Will. This is one of several sonnets punning on the word.
9. I.e., do not kill with unkindness any of your wooers.
1. With the obvious sexual pun (as also in lines 13–14). "Made of truth": (1) is utterly honest, (2) is faithful.

That she might think me some untutored youth,
Unlearnèd in the world's false subtleties.
5   Thus vainly thinking that she thinks me young,
Although she knows my days are past the best,[2]
Simply° I credit her false-speaking tongue: *like a simpleton*
On both sides thus is simple truth suppressed.
But wherefore says she not she is unjust?°   *unfaithful*
10 And wherefore say not I that I am old?
Oh, love's best habit° is in seeming trust,   *clothing, guise*
And age in love loves not to have years told.°   *counted*
    Therefore I lie with her and she with me,
    And in our faults by lies we flattered be.

144

Two loves I have of comfort and despair,[3]
Which like two spirits do suggest me still:°   *tempt me constantly*
The better angel is a man right fair,
The worser spirit a woman colored ill.°   *dark*
5   To win me soon to hell, my female evil
Tempteth my better angel from my side,
And would corrupt my saint to be a devil,
Wooing his purity with her foul pride.[4]
And whether that my angel be turned fiend
10 Suspect I may, yet not directly tell;
But being both from me, both to each[5] friend,
I guess one angel in another's hell.
    Yet this shall I ne'er know, but live in doubt,
    Till my bad angel fire my good one out.[6]

146

Poor soul, the center of my sinful earth,
Lord of[7] these rebel powers that thee array,[8]
Why dost thou pine within and suffer dearth,
Painting thy outward walls so costly gay?
5   Why so large cost, having so short a lease,
Dost thou upon thy fading mansion spend?
Shall worms, inheritors of this excess,
Eat up thy charge?[9] Is this thy body's end?°   *destiny; purpose*
Then, soul, live thou upon thy servant's loss,
10 And let that pine to aggravate thy store;[1]
Buy terms divine in selling hours of dross;[2]
Within be fed, without be rich no more.

---

2. Shakespeare was thirty-five or younger when he wrote this sonnet (it first appeared in *The Passionate Pilgrim*, 1599).
3. I have two beloveds, one bringing me comfort and the other despair.
4. (1) Vanity, (2) sexuality.
5. Each other. "From": away from.
6. I.e., until she infects him with venereal disease.
7. "Lord of": an emendation. The 1609 edition repeats the last three words of line 1. Other suggestions are "Thrall to," "Starved by," "Pressed by," and leaving the repetition but dropping "that thee" in line 2.
8. The rebellious body that clothes you.
9. (1) Your expense, (2) the thing you were responsible for (i.e., the body).
1. Let "that" (i.e., the body) deteriorate to increase ("aggravate") the soul's riches ("thy store").
2. Rubbish. "Terms": long periods.

So shalt thou feed on death, that feeds on men,
And death once dead, there's no more dying then.

147

My love is as a fever, longing still°   continually
For that which longer nurseth[3] the disease,
Feeding on that which doth preserve the ill,°   maintain the illness
Th' uncertain sickly appetite[4] to please.
5   My reason, the physician to my love,
Angry that his prescriptions are not kept,
Hath left me, and I desperate now approve
Desire is death, which physic did except.[5]
Past cure I am, now reason is past care,[6]
10 And frantic mad with evermore unrest;
My thoughts and my discourse as madmen's are,
At random from the truth, vainly expressed:[7]
    For I have sworn thee fair, and thought thee bright,
    Who art as black as hell, as dark as night.

152

In loving thee thou know'st I am forsworn,[8]
But thou art twice forsworn to me love swearing:
In act thy bed-vow° broke, and new faith torn   to husband (or lover)
In vowing new hate after new love bearing.[9]
5   But why of two oaths' breach do I accuse thee
When I break twenty? I am perjured most,
For all my vows are oaths but to misuse° thee,   deceive; misrepresent
And all my honest faith in thee is lost.
For I have sworn deep oaths of thy deep kindness,
10 Oaths of thy love, thy truth, thy constancy,
And to enlighten thee gave eyes to blindness,[1]
Or made them swear against the thing they see.
    For I have sworn thee fair—more perjured eye°   (punning on "I")
    To swear against the truth so foul a lie.

                                                              1609

---

3. (1) Nourishes, (2) takes care of.
4. (1) Desire for food, (2) lust.
5. I.e., I learn by experience that desire, which rejected reason's medicine, is death.
6. I.e., medical care (of me). The line is a version of the proverb "past cure, past care."
7. Wide of the mark and senselessly uttered.

8. I.e., am breaking loving vows to another.
9. The object of the "new faith" followed by "new hate" could be either the speaker's young friend or the speaker himself.
1. And to make you fair (or give you insight), I looked blindly on your failings (or pretended to see what I couldn't).

Twelfth Night

Twelfth Night   Women did not perform on the English public stage during Shakespeare's lifetime; all the great women's roles in Elizabethan and Jacobean plays, from Juliet and Lady Macbeth to the Duchess of Malfi, were written to be performed by trained adolescent boys. These boy actors were evidently extraordinarily skillful, and the audiences were sufficiently immersed in the conventions both of theater and of social life in general to accept gesture, makeup, and above all dress as a convincing representation of femininity. *Twelfth Night, or What You Will*, written for Shakespeare's all-male company, plays brilliantly with these conventions. The comedy depends upon an actor's ability to transform himself, through costume, voice, and gesture, into a young noblewoman, Viola, who transforms herself, through costume, voice, and gesture, into a young man, Cesario. The play's delicious complications follow from the emotional tangles that these transformations engender, unsettling fixed categories of sexual identity and social class and allowing characters to explore emotional territory that a culture officially hostile to same-sex desire and cross-class marriage would ordinarily have ruled out of bounds. In *Twelfth Night* conventional expectations repeatedly give way to a different mode of perceiving the world.

Shakespeare wrote *Twelfth Night* around 1601. He had already written such comedies as *A Midsummer Night's Dream, Much Ado About Nothing*, and *As You Like It*, with their playful, subtly ironic investigations of the ways in which heterosexual couples are produced out of the murkier crosscurrents of male and female friendships; as interesting, perhaps, he had probably just recently completed *Hamlet*, with its unprecedented exploration of mourning, betrayal, antic humor, and tragic isolation. *Twelfth Night* would prove to be, in the view of many critics, both the most nearly perfect and in some sense the last of the great festive comedies. Shakespeare returned to comedy later in his career but always with more insistent overtones of bitterness, loss, and grief. There are dark notes in *Twelfth Night* as well—the countess Olivia is in mourning for her brother, Viola thinks that her brother too is dead, Antonio believes that he has been betrayed by the man he loves, Duke Orsino threatens to kill Cesario—but these notes are swept up in a giddy, carnivalesque dance of illusion, disguise, folly, and clowning.

The complex tonal shifts of Shakespeare's comedy are conveyed in part by the pervasive music and in part by the constant oscillation between blank verse and prose. Generally, the characters in the main, romantic plot speak in the more elevated, aristocratic, and dignified register of verse, while the comic subplot proceeds in prose. Yet these formal distinctions between serious and comic, high and low, are frequently undermined, as when the wronged steward Malvolio in his final speech addresses Olivia in dignified verse, or when the mercurial Viola shifts with the greatest ease between verse and prose.

The play's subtitle, *What You Will*, underscores the celebratory spirit associated with Twelfth Night, the Feast of the Epiphany (January 6), that in Elizabethan England marked the culminating night of the traditional Christmas revels. In the time-honored festivities associated with the midwinter season, a rigidly hierarchical social order that ordinarily demanded deference, sobriety, and strict obedience to authority temporarily gave way to raucous rituals of inversion: young boys were crowned for a day as bishops and carried through the streets in mock religious processions, abstemiousness was toppled by bouts of heavy drinking and feasting, and the spirit of parody, folly, and misrule reigned briefly in places normally reserved for stern-faced moralists and sober judges. The fact that these festivities were associated with Christian holidays—the Epiphany marked the visit of the Three Kings to Bethlehem to worship the Christ child—did not altogether obscure the continuities with pagan winter rituals such as the Roman Saturnalia, with its comparably explosive release from everyday discipline into a disorderly realm of belly laughter and belly cheer. Puritans emphasized these continuities in launching a fierce attack on the Elizabethan festive calendar and its whole ethos, just as they attacked the theater for what they saw as its links with paganism, idleness, and sexual license.

Elizabethan and Jacobean authorities in the church and the state had their own concerns about idleness and subversion, but they generally protected and patronized both festive ritual and theater on the ground that these provided a valuable release from tensions that might otherwise prove dangerous. Sobriety, piety, and discipline were no doubt admirable virtues, but most human beings were not saints. "Dost thou think because thou art virtuous," the drunken Sir Toby asks the censorious Malvolio, "there shall be no more cakes and ale?" (2.3.106–07).

Fittingly, the earliest firm record of a performance of *Twelfth Night*, as noted in the diary of John Manningham, was "at our feast" in the Middle Temple (one of London's law schools) in February 1602. Manningham noted cannily the comedy's resemblance to Shakespeare's earlier play on twins, *The Comedy of Errors*, as well as to the Roman playwright Plautus's *Menaechmi* and to an early-sixteenth-century Italian comedy, *Gl'Ingannati* (The Deceived). Shakespeare also drew upon an English story, Barnabe Riche's tale of *Apollonius and Silla* in *Riche His Farewell to the Military Profession* (1581), which was in turn based on French and Italian sources. There is, however, little precedent, in Riche or in any of the other known sources, for the aspect of *Twelfth Night* that Manningham found particularly memorable and that has continued to delight audiences: the gulling of Malvolio.

Malvolio (in Italian, "ill will") is explicitly linked to those among Shakespeare's contemporaries most hostile to the theater and to such holidays as Twelfth Night: "Sometimes," says the Lady Olivia's gentlewoman Maria, "he is a kind of puritan" (2.3.129). Shakespeare does not hide the cruelty of the treatment to which Malvolio is subjected—"He hath been most notoriously abused" (5.1.374), says Olivia—nor does he shrink from showing the audience other disagreeable qualities in Olivia's kinsman Sir Toby Belch and his companions. But while the close of the comedy seems to embrace these failings in a tolerant, amused aristocratic recognition of human folly, it can find no place for Malvolio's blend of puritanism and social climbing.

Malvolio is scapegoated for indulging in a fantasy that colors several of the key relationships in *Twelfth Night:* the fantasy of winning the favor, and ultimately the hand, of the noble and wealthy aristocrats who reign over the social world of the play. The beautiful heiress Olivia, mistress of a great house, is a glittering prize that lures not only Malvolio but also the foolish Sir Andrew and the elegant, imperious Duke Orsino. In falling in love with the duke's graceful messenger (and, as she thinks she has done, in marrying him), Olivia seems to have made precisely the kind of match that had fueled Malvolio's social-climbing imagination. As it turns out, the match is not between unequals: "Be not amazed," the duke tells her when she realizes that she has married someone she scarcely knows. "Right noble is his blood" (5.1.262). The

Robert Armin (from the title page of his comedy, *The History of the Two Maids of More-Clacke* [1609]) was the leading comic actor in Shakespeare's company after 1600. He played both Feste in *Twelfth Night* and the Fool in *King Lear.*

social order then has not been overturned: as in a carnival, when the disguises are removed, the revelers resume their "proper," socially and sexually approved positions.

Yet there is something irreducibly odd about the marriages with which *Twelfth Night* ends. Sir Toby has married the lady's maid Maria as a reward for devising the plot against Malvolio. Olivia has entered into a "contract of eternal bond of love" (5.1.153) with someone whose actual identity is revealed to her only after the marriage is sealed. The strangeness of the bond between virtual strangers is matched by the strangeness of Orsino's instantaneous decision to marry Cesario—as soon as "he" can become Viola by changing into women's clothes. Shakespeare conspicuously chooses not to stage this return to conventionality.

Part of the quirky delight of the play's conclusion depends upon the resilient hopefulness of its central character, Viola, a hopefulness that is linked to her improvisatory boldness, eloquent tongue, and keen wit. These qualities link her to the fool Feste, who does not have a major part in the comedy's plot, but who occupies a place at its imaginative center. Viola seems to acknowledge this place in paying handsome tribute to Feste's intelligence: "This fellow is wise enough to play the fool, / And to do that well craves a kind of wit" (3.1.59–60). His wit often takes the form of a perverse literalism that slyly calls attention to the play's repeated confounding of such simple binaries as male and female, outside and inside, role and reality. Feste is irresponsible, vulnerable, and dependent, but he also understands, as he teasingly shows Olivia, that it is foolish to bewail forever a loss that cannot be recovered. And he understands that it is important to take such pleasures as life offers and not to wait: "In delay there lies no plenty," he sings, "Then come kiss me, sweet and twenty. / Youth's a stuff will not endure" (2.3.48–50). There is in this wonderful song, as in all of his jests, a current of sadness. Feste knows, as the refrain of the last of his songs puts it, that "the rain it raineth every day" (5.1.387). His counsel is for "present mirth" and "present laughter" (2.3.46). This is, of course, the advice of a fool. But do the Malvolios of the world have anything wiser to suggest?

Twelfth Night, or What You Will

THE PERSONS OF THE PLAY

ORSINO, duke of Illyria
VALENTINE ⎱
CURIO ⎰ attending on Orsino
FIRST OFFICER
SECOND OFFICER
VIOLA, a lady, later disguised as
   Cesario
A CAPTAIN
SEBASTIAN, Viola's twin brother
ANTONIO, another sea-captain
OLIVIA, a countess

MARIA, Olivia's waiting-gentlewoman
SIR TOBY Belch, Olivia's kinsman
SIR ANDREW Aguecheek, companion of
   Sir Toby
MALVOLIO, Olivia's steward
FABIAN, a member of Olivia's
   household
FESTE the clown, Olivia's jester
A PRIEST
A SERVANT of Olivia
Musicians, sailors, lords, attendants

1.1

Enter ORSINO, *Duke of Illyria,* CURIO, *and other lords, with musicians playing*

ORSINO   If music be the food of love, play on.
   Give me excess of it, that, surfeiting,

1.1 Location: Illyria, Greek and Roman name for the eastern Adriatic coast; probably not suggesting a real country to Shakespeare's audience.

The appetite may sicken and so die.
That strain again! It had a dying fall.°   *cadence*
5 O, it came o'er my ear like the sweet sound
That breathes upon a bank of violets,
Stealing and giving odor. Enough; no more.
'Tis not so sweet now as it was before.
O spirit of love, how quick and fresh° art thou, *lively and eager*
10 That, notwithstanding thy capacity,
Receiveth as the sea,° naught enters there, *receives without limit*
Of what validity° and pitch° soe'er, *value / height; excellence*
But falls into abatement° and low price *lesser value*
Even in a minute. So full of shapes is fancy
15 That it alone is high fantastical.° *uniquely imaginative*
CURIO Will you go hunt, my lord?
ORSINO   What, Curio?
CURIO   The hart.
ORSINO Why, so I do, the noblest that I have.[1]
O, when mine eyes did see Olivia first,
Methought she purged the air of pestilence.[2]
20 That instant was I turned into a hart,
And my desires, like fell° and cruel hounds, *savage*
E'er since pursue me.[3]
  Enter VALENTINE
     How now, what news from her?
VALENTINE So please my lord, I might° not be admitted, *could*
But from her handmaid do return this answer:
25 The element itself, till seven years' heat,[4]
Shall not behold her face at ample° view, *full*
But like a cloistress° she will veilèd walk, *nun*
And water once a day her chamber round
With eye-offending brine°—all this to season *stinging tears*
30 A brother's dead love,[5] which she would keep fresh
And lasting in her sad remembrance.
ORSINO O, she that hath a heart of that fine° frame *exquisitely made*
To pay this debt of love but to a brother,
How will she love when the rich golden shaft[6]
35 Hath killed the flock of all affections else° *other emotions*
That live in her; when liver, brain, and heart,[7]
These sovereign thrones, are all supplied, and filled
Her sweet perfections[8] with one self° king! *one and the same*
Away before me to sweet beds of flowers!
40 Love thoughts lie rich when canopied with bowers.
      Exeunt

1. Orsino plays on "hart/heart."
2. Plague and other illnesses were thought to be caused by bad air.
3. Alluding to the classical myth of Actaeon, who was turned into a stag and hunted by his own hounds for having seen the goddess Diana naked.
4. The sky itself for seven hot summers.

5. I.e., all this to preserve (by the salt of the tears) the love of a dead brother.
6. Of Cupid's golden-tipped arrow, which caused desire.
7. In Elizabethan psychology, the seats of passion, intellect, and feeling.
8. And her sweet perfections have been filled.

1.2

Enter VIOLA, A CAPTAIN, *and sailors*

VIOLA[1]   What country, friends, is this?

CAPTAIN   This is Illyria, lady.

VIOLA   And what should I do in Illyria?
My brother he is in Elysium.[2]
Perchance° he is not drowned. What think you, sailors?   *perhaps*

5   CAPTAIN   It is perchance° that you yourself were saved.   *by chance*

VIOLA   O my poor brother! And so perchance may he be.

CAPTAIN   True, madam. And to comfort you with chance,[3]
Assure yourself, after our ship did split,
When you and those poor number saved with you

10   Hung on our driving boat,[4] I saw your brother,
Most provident in peril, bind himself—
Courage and hope both teaching him the practice—
To a strong mast that lived° upon the sea,   *remained afloat*
Where, like Arion[5] on the dolphin's back,

15   I saw him hold acquaintance with the waves
So long as I could see.

VIOLA [*giving him money*]   For saying so, there's gold.
Mine own escape unfoldeth to° my hope,   *encourages*
Whereto thy speech serves for authority,°   *support*
The like of him.[6] Know'st thou this country?

20   CAPTAIN   Ay, madam, well, for I was bred and born
Not three hours' travel from this very place.

VIOLA   Who governs here?

CAPTAIN   A noble duke, in nature as in name.

VIOLA   What is his name?

25   CAPTAIN   Orsino.

VIOLA   Orsino. I have heard my father name him.
He was a bachelor then.

CAPTAIN   And so is now, or was so very late;°   *lately*
For but a month ago I went from hence,

30   And then 'twas fresh in murmur°—as, you know,   *newly rumored*
What great ones do the less will prattle of—
That he did seek the love of fair Olivia.

VIOLA   What's she?

CAPTAIN   A virtuous maid, the daughter of a count

35   That died some twelvemonth since, then leaving her
In the protection of his son, her brother,
Who shortly also died, for whose dear love,
They say, she hath abjured° the sight   *renounced*
And company of men.

1.2 Location: The coast of Illyria.
1. Viola is not named in the dialogue until 5.1.239.
2. The heaven of classical mythology.
3. With what may have happened.
4. The ship's boat. "Driving": being driven by the wind.
5. A legendary Greek musician who, in order to save himself from being murdered on a voyage, jumped overboard and was carried to land by a dolphin.
6. I.e., that he too has survived.

VIOLA   O, that I served that lady,
40   And might not be delivered° to the world   *revealed*
      Till I had made mine own occasion mellow,°   *ripe (to be revealed)*
      What my estate° is.   *social rank*
CAPTAIN   That were hard to compass,°   *achieve*
      Because she will admit no kind of suit,°   *petition*
      No, not the Duke's.
45   VIOLA   There is a fair behavior[7] in thee, captain,
      And though that nature with a beauteous wall
      Doth oft close in pollution, yet of thee
      I will believe thou hast a mind that suits
      With this thy fair and outward character.[8]
50   I prithee°—and I'll pay thee bounteously—   *pray thee*
      Conceal me what I am, and be my aid
      For such disguise as haply shall become
      The form of my intent.[9] I'll serve this duke.
      Thou shalt present me as an eunuch[1] to him.
55   It may be worth thy pains, for I can sing
      And speak to him in many sorts of music
      That will allow° me very worth his service.   *prove*
      What else may hap, to time I will commit.
      Only shape thou thy silence to my wit.°   *imagination; plan*
60   CAPTAIN   Be you his eunuch, and your mute[2] I'll be.
      When my tongue blabs, then let mine eyes not see.
      VIOLA   I thank thee. Lead me on.   *Exeunt*

1.3

Enter SIR TOBY [*Belch*] *and* MARIA

SIR TOBY   What a plague means my niece to take the death
      of her brother thus? I am sure care's an enemy to life.
MARIA   By my troth, Sir Toby, you must come in earlier o'
      nights. Your cousin,[1] my lady, takes great exceptions to
5   your ill hours.
SIR TOBY   Why, let her except before excepted![2]
MARIA   Ay, but you must confine yourself within the mod-
      est° limits of order.   *moderate*
SIR TOBY   Confine? I'll confine myself no finer[3] than I am.
10   These clothes are good enough to drink in, and so be
      these boots too. An° they be not, let them hang them-   *if*
      selves in their own straps!

7. Outward appearance; conduct.
8. Appearance (suggesting moral qualities).
9. That perhaps may be fitting to my purpose. "Form": shape.
1. Castrati (hence, "eunuchs") were prized as male sopranos; the disguise would have explained Viola's feminine voice. Viola (or perhaps Shakespeare) seems to have changed plans: she presents herself instead as a young page.
2. In Turkish harems, eunuchs served as guards

and were assisted by "mutes" (usually servants whose tongues had been cut out).
1.3 Location: The Countess Olivia's house.
1. Term used generally of kinsfolk. "Troth": faith.
2. Playing on the legal jargon *exceptis excipiendis*, "with the previous stated exceptions." Sir Toby refuses to take Olivia's displeasure seriously.
3. Suggesting both "a refined manner of dress" and "narrowly" (referring to his girth).

MARIA   That quaffing and drinking will undo you. I heard
my lady talk of it yesterday, and of a foolish knight that
15   you brought in one night here to be her wooer.
SIR TOBY   Who, Sir Andrew Aguecheek?
MARIA   Ay, he.
SIR TOBY   He's as tall a man as any's[4] in Illyria.
MARIA   What's that to th' purpose?
20   SIR TOBY   Why, he has three thousand ducats a year!
MARIA   Ay, but he'll have but a year in all these ducats.[5]
He's a very° fool and a prodigal.   *an absolute*
SIR TOBY   Fie that you'll say so! He plays o' th' viol-de-
gamboys,[6] and speaks three or four languages word for
25   word without book,° and hath all the good gifts of nature.   *from memory*
MARIA   He hath indeed, almost natural,[7] for besides that
he's a fool, he's a great quarreler, and but that he hath
the gift of a coward to allay the gust° he hath in quarrel-   *gusto*
ing, 'tis thought among the prudent he would quickly
30   have the gift of a grave.
SIR TOBY   By this hand, they are scoundrels and substrac-
tors[8] that say so of him. Who are they?
MARIA   They that add, moreover, he's drunk nightly in
your company.
35   SIR TOBY   With drinking healths to my niece. I'll drink to
her as long as there is a passage in my throat and drink
in Illyria. He's a coward and a coistrel° that will not drink   *horse groom; lout*
to my niece till his brains turn o' th' toe like a parish top.
What, wench! *Castiliano vulgo*,[9] for here comes Sir Andrew
40   Agueface.
        Enter SIR ANDREW [*Aguecheck*]
SIR ANDREW   Sir Toby Belch! How now, Sir Toby Belch?
SIR TOBY   Sweet Sir Andrew!
SIR ANDREW [*to* MARIA]   Bless you, fair shrew.[1]
MARIA   And you too, sir.
45   SIR TOBY   Accost, Sir Andrew, accost![2]
SIR ANDREW   What's that?
SIR TOBY   My niece's chambermaid.[3]
SIR ANDREW   Good Mistress Accost, I desire better
acquaintance.
50   MARIA   My name is Mary, sir.
SIR ANDREW   Good Mistress Mary Accost—

---

4. Any (man who) is. "Tall": brave; worthy. (Maria
takes it in the modern sense of height.)
6. A facetious corruption of "viola da gamba," a
bass viol held between the knees.
7. Idiots and fools were called "naturals."
8. Corruption of "detractors." (In reply, Maria
puns on "substract" as "subtract.")
9. Variously interpreted, but may mean "Speak of
the devil," since Castilians were considered devilish, and *vulgo* refers to the common tongue.

"Parish top": parishes kept large tops that were
spun by whipping them, for the parishioners'
amusement and exercise.
1. Andrew possibly confuses "shrew" (ill-tempered
woman) with "mouse," an endearment.
2. Address (her); originally a naval term meaning "go alongside; greet."
3. Lady-in-waiting; not a menial servant, but a
gentlewoman in attendance on a great lady.

SIR TOBY   You mistake, knight. "Accost" is front° her, board   confront
her, woo her, assail[4] her.

SIR ANDREW   By my troth, I would not undertake[5] her in
55   this company.° Is that the meaning of "accost"?   i.e., the audience

MARIA   Fare you well, gentlemen. [*begins to exit*]

SIR TOBY   An thou let part so,[6] Sir Andrew, would thou
mightst never draw sword again.

SIR ANDREW   An you part so, mistress, I would I might
60   never draw sword again. Fair lady, do you think you have
fools in hand?°   to deal with

MARIA   Sir, I have not you by th' hand.

SIR ANDREW   Marry, but you shall have, and here's my
hand.

65   MARIA [*taking his hand*]   Now, sir, thought is free.[7] I pray
you, bring your hand to th' butt'ry bar[8] and let it drink.

SIR ANDREW   Wherefore, sweetheart? What's your metaphor?

MARIA   It's dry,[9] sir.

70   SIR ANDREW   Why, I think so. I am not such an ass but I
can keep my hand dry.[1] But what's your jest?

MARIA   A dry jest,[2] sir.

SIR ANDREW   Are you full of them?

MARIA   Ay, sir, I have them at my fingers' ends.[3] Marry,
75   now I let go your hand, I am barren.°   *Exit*   empty of jokes

SIR TOBY   O knight, thou lack'st a cup of canary![4] When
did I see thee so put down?[5]

SIR ANDREW   Never in your life, I think, unless you see
canary put me down. Methinks sometimes I have no
80   more wit than a Christian[6] or an ordinary man has. But
I am a great eater of beef,[7] and I believe that does harm
to my wit.

SIR TOBY   No question.

SIR ANDREW   An I thought that, I'd forswear it. I'll ride
85   home tomorrow, Sir Toby.

SIR TOBY   *Pourquoi,*° my dear knight?   why

SIR ANDREW   What is "*pourquoi*"? Do, or not do? I would I
had bestowed that time in the tongues[8] that I have in
fencing, dancing, and bear-baiting. O, had I but followed
90   the arts!

SIR TOBY   Then hadst thou° had an excellent head of hair.   you would have

---

4. Greet (also nautical). "Board": speak to; tackle.
5. Take her on (with sexual implication).
6. If you let her go without protest or without bidding her farewell.
7. The customary retort to "Do you think I am a fool?" "Marry": indeed (originally, the name of the Virgin Mary used as an oath).
8. Ledge on the half-door to a buttery or a wine cellar, on which drinks were served.
9. Thirsty; but a dry hand was also thought to be a sign of impotence.
1. Alluding to the proverb "Even fools have

enough wit to come in out of the rain."
2. A stupid joke (referring to Andrew's stupidity); an ironic quip; a joke about dryness.
3. Always ready; or "by th' hand" (line 62).
4. A sweet wine, like sherry, originally from the Canary Islands.
5. Defeated in repartee; "put down" with drink.
6. i.e., an average man.
7. Contemporary medicine held that beef dulled the intellect ("wit").
8. Foreign languages; Toby takes him to mean "curling tongs."

SIR ANDREW   Why, would that have mended° my hair?   *improved*

SIR TOBY   Past question, for thou seest it will not curl by
nature.[9]

95   SIR ANDREW   But it becomes me well enough, does't not?

SIR TOBY   Excellent! It hangs like flax on a distaff,[1] and I
hope to see a housewife[2] take thee between her legs and
spin it off.[3]

SIR ANDREW   Faith, I'll home tomorrow, Sir Toby. Your
100   niece will not be seen, or if she be, it's four to one she'll
none of me. The Count himself here hard by woos her.

SIR TOBY   She'll none o' th' Count. She'll not match above
her degree,° neither in estate,[4] years, nor wit. I have heard   *social rank*
her swear't. Tut, there's life in't,[5] man.

105   SIR ANDREW   I'll stay a month longer. I am a fellow o' th'
strangest mind i' th' world. I delight in masques and revels sometimes altogether.

SIR TOBY   Art thou good at these kickshawses,[6] knight?

SIR ANDREW   As any man in Illyria, whatsoever he be,
110   under the degree of my betters; and yet I will not compare with an old man.[7]

SIR TOBY   What is thy excellence in a galliard,[8] knight?

SIR ANDREW   Faith, I can cut a caper.[9]

SIR TOBY   And I can cut the mutton to't.

115   SIR ANDREW   And I think I have the back-trick[1] simply as
strong as any man in Illyria.

SIR TOBY   Wherefore are these things hid? Wherefore have
these gifts a curtain[2] before 'em? Are they like to take
dust, like Mistress Mall's[3] picture? Why dost thou not go
120   to church in a galliard and come home in a coranto?[4]
My very walk should be a jig. I would not so much as
make water but in a cinquepace.[5] What dost thou mean?
Is it a world to hide virtues in? I did think, by the excellent constitution of thy leg, it was formed under the star
125   of a galliard.[6]

SIR ANDREW   Ay, 'tis strong, and it does indifferent° well in   *moderately*
a flame-colored stock.° Shall we set about some revels?   *stocking*

SIR TOBY   What shall we do else? Were we not born under
Taurus?[7]

---

9. To contrast with Andrew's "arts" (line 90).
1. In spinning, flax would hang in long, thin, yellowish strings on the "distaff," a pole held between
the knees.
2. Housewives spun flax; the pronunciation, "hus-
wife," also suggests the meaning "prostitute."
3. Make him bald (as a result of venereal disease).
4. Status; possessions.
5. Proverbial: "While there's life, there's hope."
6. Trifles; trivialities (from the French *quelque
chose*).
7. Expert (perhaps a backhanded compliment).
8. A lively, complex dance, including the caper.
9. Leap. (Toby puns on the pickled flower buds
used in a sauce of mutton.)

1. Probably a dance movement, a kick of the foot
behind the body (also suggesting sexual prowess,
with later reference to "mutton" as "prostitute").
2. Used to protect paintings from dust.
3. Like "Moll[y]," "Mall" was a nickname for
"Mary."
4. An even more rapid dance than the galliard.
5. Galliard, or, more properly, the steps joining
the figures of the dance; punning on "sink," as in
"sewer."
6. Astrological influences favorable to dancing.
7. The astrological sign of the bull was usually
thought to govern the neck and throat (appropriate to heavy drinkers).

130   SIR ANDREW   Taurus? That's sides and heart.

      SIR TOBY   No, sir, it is legs and thighs. Let me see thee caper.

          [SIR ANDREW *dances*]

      Ha, higher! Ha, ha, excellent.   *Exeunt*

1.4

     Enter VALENTINE, *and* VIOLA *in man's attire* [*as Cesario*]

  VALENTINE   If the Duke continue these favors towards
    you, Cesario, you are like to be much advanced. He hath
    known you but three days, and already you are no
    stranger.

5   VIOLA   You either fear his humor° or my negligence, that   *moodiness*
    you call in question the continuance of his love. Is he
    inconstant, sir, in his favors?

  VALENTINE   No, believe me.

  VIOLA   I thank you. Here comes the Count.

     Enter ORSINO, CURIO, *and attendants*

10   ORSINO   Who saw Cesario, ho?

  VIOLA   On your attendance,° my lord, here.   *waiting at your service*

  ORSINO [*to* CURIO *and Attendants*]   Stand you a while
    aloof.° [*to* VIOLA] Cesario,   *aside*
    Thou know'st no less but all.° I have unclasped   *than everything*
    To thee the book even of my secret soul.

15   Therefore, good youth, address thy gait° unto her.   *go*
    Be not denied access, stand at her doors
    And tell them, there thy fixèd foot shall grow°   *take root*
    Till thou have audience.

  VIOLA   Sure, my noble lord,
    If she be so abandoned to her sorrow

20   As it is spoke, she never will admit me.

  ORSINO   Be clamorous and leap all civil bounds[1]
    Rather than make unprofited° return.   *unsuccessful*

  VIOLA   Say I do speak with her, my lord, what then?

  ORSINO   O, then unfold the passion of my love.

25   Surprise[2] her with discourse of my dear° faith.   *heartfelt*
    It shall become thee well to act my woes—
    She will attend it better in thy youth
    Than in a nuncio's° of more grave aspect.°   *messenger's / appearance*

  VIOLA   I think not so, my lord.

  ORSINO   Dear lad, believe it;

30   For they shall yet° belie thy happy years   *thus far*
    That say thou art a man. Diana's lip
    Is not more smooth and rubious,° thy small pipe°   *ruby red / voice*
    Is as the maiden's organ, shrill and sound,[3]
    And all is semblative° a woman's part.   *like*

35   I know thy constellation[4] is right apt

1.4 Location: Orsino's palace.
1. All constraints of polite behavior.
2. Capture by unexpected attack.

3. High-pitched and uncracked.
4. Nature and abilities (as supposedly determined by the stars).

For this affair. [*to* CURIO *and attendants*] Some four or
   five attend him,
All, if you will, for I myself am best
When least in company. [*to* VIOLA] Prosper well in this
And thou shalt live as freely as thy lord,
To call his fortunes thine.

40 VIOLA   I'll do my best
     To woo your lady. [*aside*] Yet a barful strife![5]
     Whoe'er I woo, myself would be his wife.   *Exeunt*

1.5

     Enter MARIA *and* [FESTE,[1] *the*] *clown*

  MARIA   Nay, either tell me where thou hast been or I will
     not open my lips so wide as a bristle may enter in° way of   *by*
     thy excuse. My lady will hang thee for thy absence.

  FESTE   Let her hang me. He that is well hanged in this
5   world needs to fear no colors.[2]

  MARIA   Make that good.°   *explain that*

  FESTE   He shall see none to fear.

  MARIA   A good Lenten[3] answer. I can tell thee where that
     saying was born, of "I fear no colors."

10 FESTE   Where, good Mistress Mary?

  MARIA   In the wars;[4] and that may you be bold to say in
     your foolery.

  FESTE   Well, God give them wisdom that have it, and
     those that are fools, let them use their talents.[5]

15 MARIA   Yet you will be hanged for being so long absent, or
     to be turned away[6]—is not that as good as a hanging to
     you?

  FESTE   Many a good hanging prevents a bad marriage,[7]
     and, for turning away, let summer bear it out.°   *make it endurable*

20 MARIA   You are resolute, then?

  FESTE   Not so, neither, but I am resolved on two points.°   *matters; laces*

  MARIA   That if one break, the other will hold, or, if both
     break, your gaskins° fall.   *wide breeches*

  FESTE   Apt, in good faith, very apt. Well, go thy way. If Sir
25   Toby would leave drinking, thou wert as witty a piece of
     Eve's flesh[8] as any in Illyria.

  MARIA   Peace, you rogue. No more o' that. Here comes my
     lady. Make your excuse wisely, you were best.°   [*Exit*] *you had better*

---

5. An undertaking full of impediments.
1.5 Location: Olivia's house.
1. The name is used only once, at 2.4.11.
2. Proverbial for "fear nothing." "Colors": worldly
deceptions, with puns on "collars" as "hangman's
nooses" and "cholers" as "anger."
3. Thin or meager (like Lenten fare).
4. "Colors" in line 9 refers to military flags.
5. Alluding to the parable of the talents, Matthew
25. The comic implication is that a fool should

strive to increase his measure of folly. Since "fool"
and "fowl" had similar pronunciations, there may
also be a play on "talents/talons."
6. Dismissed; also, perhaps, turned off or hanged.
7. Proverbial. "Hanging": execution; sexual prowess.
8. Woman. Feste may imply both that Maria and
Toby would make a good match and that Maria is
as witty as Toby is sober.

Enter Lady OLIVIA *with* MALVOLIO *[and attendants]*

FESTE *[aside]* Wit,[9] an't° be thy will, put me into good   *if it*
fooling! Those wits that think they have thee do very oft
prove fools, and I that am sure I lack thee may pass for a
wise man. For what says Quinapalus?[1] "Better a witty
Fool than a foolish wit." God bless thee, lady.

OLIVIA *[to attendants]* Take the fool away.

FESTE Do you not hear, fellows? Take away the lady.

OLIVIA Go to, you're a dry[2] fool. I'll no more of you.
Besides, you grow dishonest.°   *unreliable*

FESTE Two faults, madonna,° that drink and good counsel   *my lady*
will amend. For give the dry fool drink, then is the fool
not dry. Bid the dishonest man mend° himself: if he   *reform*
mend, he is no longer dishonest; if he cannot, let the
botcher° mend him. Anything that's mended is but   *tailor; cobbler*
patched; virtue that transgresses is but patched with sin,
and sin that amends is but patched with virtue. If that
this simple syllogism will serve, so; if it will not, what
remedy? As there is no true cuckold but calamity, so
beauty's a flower.[3] The lady bade take away the fool.
Therefore, I say again, take her away.

OLIVIA Sir, I bade them take away you.

FESTE Misprision[4] in the highest degree! Lady, *cucullus
non facit monachum.*[5] That's as much to say as, I wear
not motley[6] in my brain. Good madonna, give me leave
to prove you a fool.

OLIVIA Can you do it?

FESTE Dexteriously,° good madonna.   *dexterously*

OLIVIA Make your proof.

FESTE I must catechize[7] you for it, madonna. Good my
mouse of virtue,° answer me.   *my good virtuous mouse*

OLIVIA Well, sir, for want of other idleness,° I'll bide° your   *pastime / await*
proof.

FESTE Good madonna, why mournest thou?

OLIVIA Good fool, for my brother's death.

FESTE I think his soul is in hell, madonna.

OLIVIA I know his soul is in heaven, fool.

FESTE The more fool, madonna, to mourn for your brother's soul, being in heaven. Take away the fool, gentlemen.

OLIVIA What think you of this fool, Malvolio? Doth he
not mend?[8]

---

9. Intelligence, which is often contrasted with
will.
1. Feste frequently invents his own authorities.
2. Dull, but Feste interprets as "thirsty." "Go to":
an expression of impatience.
3. In taking her vow (1.2.38–39), Olivia has
wedded herself to calamity but must be unfaithful, or let pass her moment of beauty.

4. Misapprehension; wrongful arrest.
5. The cowl does not make the monk (a Latin
proverb).
6. The multicolored costume of a fool.
7. Question (as in catechism, which tests the
orthodoxy of belief).
8. Improve, but Malvolio takes "mend" to mean
"grow more foolish."

70 MALVOLIO Yes, and shall do till the pangs of death shake
     him. Infirmity,° that decays the wise, doth ever make   *(old) age*
     the better fool.⁹

FESTE God send you, sir, a speedy infirmity, for the better
     increasing your folly! Sir Toby will be sworn that I am no
75   fox, but he will not pass his word for twopence that you
     are no fool.

OLIVIA How say you to that, Malvolio?

MALVOLIO I marvel your ladyship takes delight in such a
     barren rascal. I saw him put down¹ the other day with an
80   ordinary fool that has no more brain than a stone. Look
     you now, he's out of his guard° already. Unless you laugh   *defenseless*
     and minister occasion² to him, he is gagged. I protest I
     take these wise men that crow so at these set° kind of   *artificial*
     fools no better than the fools' zanies.°   *"straight men"*

85 OLIVIA O, you are sick of° self-love, Malvolio, and taste   *with*
     with a distempered³ appetite. To be generous, guiltless,
     and of free° disposition is to take those things for bird-   *magnanimous*
     bolts⁴ that you deem cannon bullets. There is no slander
     in an allowed fool, though he do nothing but rail; nor no
90   railing in a known discreet man, though he do nothing
     but reprove.

FESTE Now Mercury indue thee with leasing,⁵ for thou
     speakest well of fools.

         Enter MARIA

MARIA Madam, there is at the gate a young gentleman
95   much desires to speak with you.

OLIVIA From the Count Orsino, is it?

MARIA I know not, madam. 'Tis a fair young man, and
     well attended.

OLIVIA Who of my people hold him in delay?

100 MARIA Sir Toby, madam, your kinsman.

OLIVIA Fetch him off, I pray you. He speaks nothing but
     madman.° Fie on him! [MARIA *exits.*] Go you, Malvolio.   *madman's talk*
     If it be a suit from the Count, I am sick, or not at home;
     what you will, to dismiss it. [*Malvolio exits.*] Now you see,
105 sir, how your fooling grows old,° and people dislike it.   *stale*

FESTE Thou hast spoke for us, madonna, as if thy eldest
     son should be a fool, whose skull Jove cram with brains,
     for—here he comes—one of thy kin has a most weak *pia
     mater.*⁶

         Enter SIR TOBY

110 OLIVIA By mine honor, half-drunk. What is he at the
     gate, cousin?°   *kinsman*

SIR TOBY A gentleman.

---

9. Make the fool more foolish.
1. Defeated in repartee.
2. And give opportunity.
3. Unbalanced; sick.

4. Blunt arrows for shooting birds.
5. May Mercury, the god of deception, endow
you with the talent of tactful lying.
6. Brain; or literally, the membrane enclosing it.

OLIVIA A gentleman? What gentleman?

SIR TOBY 'Tis a gentleman here. [*He belches.*] A plague o'
115 these pickle herring!—How now, sot?° *fool, drunkard*

FESTE Good Sir Toby.

OLIVIA Cousin, cousin, how have you come so early by
this lethargy?

SIR TOBY Lechery? I defy lechery. There's one° at the gate. *someone*

120 OLIVIA Ay, marry, what is he?

SIR TOBY Let him be the devil an° he will, I care not. Give *if*
me faith,[7] say I. Well, it's all one.° *Exit* *it doesn't matter*

OLIVIA What's a drunken man like, fool?

FESTE Like a drowned man, a fool, and a madman. One
125 draught above heat[8] makes him a fool, the second mads
him, and a third drowns him.

OLIVIA Go thou and seek the coroner and let him sit o'° *hold an inquest for*
my coz,° for he's in the third degree of drink: he's *cousin; uncle*
drowned. Go look after him.

130 FESTE He is but mad yet, madonna, and the fool shall
look to the madman. [*Exit*]

    Enter MALVOLIO

MALVOLIO Madam, yond young fellow swears he will
speak with you. I told him you were sick; he takes on
him to understand so much, and therefore[9] comes to
135 speak with you. I told him you were asleep; he seems to
have a foreknowledge of that too, and therefore comes
to speak with you. What is to be said to him, lady? He's
fortified against any denial.

OLIVIA Tell him he shall not speak with me.

140 MALVOLIO He's been told so, and he says he'll stand at
your door like a sheriff's post[1] and be the supporter to a
bench, but he'll speak with you.

OLIVIA What kind o' man is he?

MALVOLIO Why, of mankind.° *like any other*

145 OLIVIA What manner of man?

MALVOLIO Of very ill manner. He'll speak with you, will
you or no.

OLIVIA Of what personage° and years is he? *appearance*

MALVOLIO Not yet old enough for a man, nor young
150 enough for a boy—as a squash is before 'tis a peascod,
or a codling when 'tis almost an apple. 'Tis with him in
standing water,[2] between boy and man. He is very well-
favored,° and he speaks very shrewishly.[3] One would *handsome*
think his mother's milk were scarce out of him.

155 OLIVIA Let him approach. Call in my gentlewoman.

MALVOLIO Gentlewoman, my lady calls. *Exit*

---

7. To defy the devil by faith alone.
8. One drink ("draught") beyond the quantity
necessary to warm him.
9. For that very reason.
1. A decorative post set before a sheriff's door,

as a sign of authority.
2. At the turn of the tide. "Squash": an undeveloped pea pod. "Codling": an unripe apple.
3. Sharply.

Enter MARIA

OLIVIA   Give me my veil. Come, throw it o'er my face.
We'll once more hear Orsino's embassy.

Enter VIOLA [*as Cesario*]

VIOLA   The honorable lady of the house, which is she?

160 OLIVIA   Speak to me. I shall answer for her. Your will?

VIOLA   Most radiant, exquisite, and unmatchable beauty—
I pray you, tell me if this be the lady of the house, for I
never saw her. I would be loath to cast away° my speech,   *waste*
for, besides that it is excellently well penned, I have taken

165 great pains to con° it. Good beauties, let me sustain° no   *memorize / suffer*
scorn. I am very comptible,° even to the least sinister   *sensitive*
usage.[4]

OLIVIA   Whence came you, sir?

VIOLA   I can say little more than I have studied,[5] and that

170 question's out of my part. Good gentle one, give me
modest° assurance if you be the lady of the house, that   *adequate*
I may proceed in my speech.

OLIVIA   Are you a comedian?°   *an actor*

VIOLA   No, my profound heart.[6] And yet, by the very fangs

175 of malice, I swear I am not that° I play. Are you the lady   *what*
of the house?

OLIVIA   If I do not usurp[7] myself, I am.

VIOLA   Most certain, if you are she, you do usurp yourself,
for what is yours to bestow is not yours to reserve. But

180 this is from my commission.[8] I will on with my speech in
your praise and then show you the heart of my message.

OLIVIA   Come to what is important in't, I forgive you° the   *excuse you from*
praise.

VIOLA   Alas, I took great pains to study it, and 'tis poetical.

185 OLIVIA   It is the more like to be feigned. I pray you, keep it
in. I heard you were saucy° at my gates, and allowed   *impertinent*
your approach rather to wonder at you than to hear you.
If you be not mad, be gone. If you have reason,° be brief.   *any sanity*
'Tis not that time of moon with me to make one in so

190 skipping a dialogue.[9]

MARIA   Will you hoist sail, sir? Here lies your way.

VIOLA   No, good swabber, I am to hull[1] here a little longer.
—Some mollification for your giant,[2] sweet lady. Tell me
your mind, I am a messenger.[3]

195 OLIVIA   Sure you have some hideous matter to deliver,
when the courtesy of it is so fearful. Speak your office.[4]

---

4. To the slightest discourteous treatment.
5. Learned by heart (a theatrical term).
6. My most wise lady; upon my soul.
7. Counterfeit; misappropriate.
8. Beyond my instructions.
9. I am not lunatic enough to take part in so
flighty a conversation. (Lunacy was thought to be
influenced by the phases of the moon.)

1. To lie unanchored with lowered sails.
2. Mythical giants guarded ladies; here, also
mocking Maria's diminutive size. "Some . . . for":
please pacify.
3. From Orsino; Olivia pretends she understands
her to mean a king's messenger, or a messenger-at-
arms, employed on important state affairs.
4. Business. "Courtesy": introduction.

VIOLA   It alone concerns your ear. I bring no overture° of   *declaration*
war, no taxation of homage.[5] I hold the olive[6] in my hand.
My words are as full of peace as matter.°   *meaning*

200   OLIVIA   Yet you began rudely. What are you? What would
you?

VIOLA   The rudeness that hath appeared in me have I
learned from my entertainment.° What I am and what I   *reception*
would are as secret as maidenhead:° to your ears, divin-   *virginity*

205   ity; to any other's, profanation.

OLIVIA   [*to* MARIA *and attendants*]   Give us the place alone.
We will hear this divinity.° [MARIA *and attendants exit.*]   *religious discourse*
Now, sir, what is your text?[7]

VIOLA   Most sweet lady—

210   OLIVIA   A comfortable° doctrine, and much may be said of   *comforting*
it. Where lies your text?

VIOLA   In Orsino's bosom.

OLIVIA   In his bosom? In what chapter of his bosom?

VIOLA   To answer by the method,° in the first of his heart.   *in the same style*

215   OLIVIA   O, I have read it; it is heresy. Have you no more to
say?

VIOLA   Good madam, let me see your face.

OLIVIA   Have you any commission from your lord to negotiate with my face? You are now out of° your text. But we   *straying from*

220   will draw the curtain and show you the picture. [*She
removes her veil.*] Look you, sir, such a one I was this present.[8] Is't not well done?

VIOLA   Excellently done, if God did all.[9]

OLIVIA   'Tis in grain,° sir; 'twill endure wind and weather.   *the dye is fast*

225   VIOLA   'Tis beauty truly blent,[1] whose red and white
Nature's own sweet and cunning° hand laid on.   *skillful*
Lady, you are the cruel'st she° alive   *woman*
If you will lead these graces to the grave
And leave the world no copy.[2]

230   OLIVIA   O, sir, I will not be so hard-hearted! I will give
out divers schedules° of my beauty. It shall be invento-   *inventories*
ried and every particle and utensil labeled[3] to my will:
as, *item*, two lips, indifferent° red; *item*, two gray eyes,   *moderate*
with lids[4] to them; *item*, one neck, one chin, and so

235   forth.   Were you sent hither to praise° me?   *appraise; flatter*

VIOLA   I see you what you are. You are too proud.
But if° you were the devil, you are fair.   *even if*
My lord and master loves you. O, such love

---

5. Demand for dues paid to a superior.
6. Olive branch (as a symbol of peace).
7. Quotation (as a theme of a sermon, in keeping
with "divinity," "doctrine," "heresy," etc.).
8. Portraits usually gave the year of painting.
"This present" was a term used to date letters.
9. If it is natural (without the use of cosmetics).
1. Blended, or mixed (of paints). Shakespeare
uses the same metaphor in sonnet 20, lines 1–2.

As Cesario, Viola is playing with established conventions of poetic courtship.
2. Viola means "child"; Olivia takes her to mean
"list" or "inventory."
3. Every single part and article added as a codi-
cil (parodying the legal language of a last will
and testament).
4. Eyelids, but also punning on "pot lids" (punning on "utensil" as a household implement).

Could be but recompensed though⁵ you were crowned
The nonpareil of beauty.°   *an unequaled beauty*

240 OLIVIA   How does he love me?

VIOLA   With adorations, fertile° tears,   *ever-flowing*
With groans that thunder love, with sighs of fire.

OLIVIA   Your lord does know my mind. I cannot love him.
Yet I suppose him virtuous, know him noble,

245 Of great estate,° of fresh and stainless youth;   *high status*
In voices⁶ well divulged,° free,° learned, and valiant,   *spoken of / generous*
And in dimension and the shape of nature⁷
A gracious person. But yet I cannot love him.
He might have took his answer long ago.

250 VIOLA   If I did love you in° my master's flame,°   *with / passion*
With such a suff'ring, such a deadly° life,   *deathlike*
In your denial I would find no sense,
I would not understand it.

OLIVIA   Why, what would you?

VIOLA   Make me a willow⁸ cabin at your gate

255 And call upon my soul° within the house,   *i.e., Olivia*
Write loyal cantons of contemnèd° love   *songs of rejected*
And sing them loud even in the dead of night,
Hallow⁹ your name to the reverberate° hills   *echoing*
And make the babbling gossip of the air¹

260 Cry out "Olivia!" O, you should not rest
Between the elements of air and earth
But° you should pity me.   *unless*

OLIVIA   You might do much.
What is your parentage?

265 VIOLA   Above my fortunes, yet my state° is well.   *social status*
I am a gentleman.

OLIVIA   Get you to your lord.
I cannot love him. Let him send no more—
Unless perchance° you come to me again   *perhaps*
To tell me how he takes it. Fare you well.

270 I thank you for your pains. Spend this for me.
[*She offers money.*]

VIOLA   I am no fee'd post,° lady. Keep your purse.   *hired messenger*
My master, not myself, lacks recompense.
Love make his heart of flint that you shall love.²
And let your fervor, like my master's, be

275 Placed in contempt. Farewell, fair cruelty.   *Exit*

OLIVIA   "What is your parentage?"
"Above my fortunes, yet my state is well.
I am a gentleman." I'll be sworn thou art.
Thy tongue, thy face, thy limbs, actions, and spirit

---

5. Would have to be requited even if.
6. In the general opinion.
7. "Dimension" and "shape of nature" are synonymous, meaning "bodily form."
8. Traditional symbol of rejected love.
9. Shout; or perhaps "hallow," as in "bless."

1. For the love of Narcissus, the nymph Echo wasted away to a mere voice, only able to repeat whatever she heard spoken.
2. May love make the heart of the man you love as hard as flint.

280 Do give thee fivefold blazon.[3] Not too fast! Soft,° soft—   *wait*
Unless the master were the man.[4] How now?
Even so quickly may one catch the plague?
Methinks I feel this youth's perfections
With an invisible and subtle stealth
285 To creep in at mine eyes. Well, let it be.—
What ho, Malvolio!

        Enter MALVOLIO

MALVOLIO   Here, madam, at your service.
OLIVIA   Run after that same peevish messenger,
  The County's° man. He left this ring behind him,   *Count's*
  Would I° or not. Tell him I'll none of it.   *whether I wished it*
290 Desire him not to flatter with° his lord,   *encourage*
  Nor hold him up with hopes. I am not for him.
  If that the youth will come this way tomorrow,
  I'll give him reasons for't. Hie thee,° Malvolio.   *hurry*
MALVOLIO   Madam, I will.   *Exit*
295 OLIVIA   I do I know not what, and fear to find
  Mine eye too great a flatterer for my mind.[5]
  Fate, show thy force. Ourselves we do not owe.°   *own*
  What is decreed must be, and be this so.

              [Exit at another door]

2.1

      Enter ANTONIO *and* SEBASTIAN

ANTONIO   Will you stay no longer? Nor will° you not that I   *wish*
go with you?
SEBASTIAN   By your patience, no. My stars shine darkly[1]
over me. The malignancy of my fate[2] might perhaps
5 distemper° yours. Therefore I shall crave of you your   *infect*
leave that I may bear my evils alone. It were a bad recompense for your love to lay any of them on you.
ANTONIO   Let me yet know of you whither you are bound.
SEBASTIAN   No, sooth,° sir. My determinate° voyage is   *truly / destined*
10 mere extravagancy.° But I perceive in you so excellent a   *idle wandering*
touch of modesty° that you will not extort from me what   *politeness*
I am willing to keep in. Therefore it charges me in manners[3] the rather to express° myself. You must know of me,   *reveal*
then, Antonio, my name is Sebastian, which I called
15 Roderigo. My father was that Sebastian of Messaline[4]
whom I know you have heard of. He left behind him
myself and a sister, both born in an° hour. If the heavens   *within the same*
had been pleased, would we had so ended! But you, sir,

---

3. Formal description of a gentleman's coat of
arms.
4. If Orsino were Cesario ("man": servant).
5. I.e., my eye (through which love has entered
my heart) has seduced my reason.
2.1 Location: Near the coast of Illyria.

1. Forebodingly; unfavorably.
2. Evil influence of the stars; "malignancy" also
signifies a deadly disease.
3. Therefore courtesy requires.
4. Possibly Messina, Sicily.

altered that, for some hour before you took me from the
20   breach° of the sea was my sister drowned.   surf
ANTONIO   Alas the day!
SEBASTIAN   A lady, sir, though it was said she much
resembled me, was yet of many accounted beautiful. But
though I could not with such estimable° wonder overfar   appreciative
25   believe that, yet thus far I will boldly publish° her: she   proclaim
bore a mind that envy° could not but call fair. She is   malice
drowned already, sir, with salt water, though I seem to
drown her remembrance again with more.
ANTONIO   Pardon me, sir, your bad entertainment.[5]
30   SEBASTIAN   O good Antonio, forgive me your trouble.
ANTONIO   If you will not murder me[6] for my love, let me
be your servant.
SEBASTIAN   If you will not undo what you have done—that
is, kill him whom you have recovered°—desire it not. Fare   rescued
35   ye well at once. My bosom is full of kindness,° and I am   tender emotion
yet° so near the manners of my mother[7] that, upon the   still
least occasion more, mine eyes will tell tales of me.° I am   betray my feelings
bound to the Count Orsino's court. Farewell.   Exit
ANTONIO   The gentleness° of all the gods go with thee!   favor
40   I have many enemies in Orsino's court,
Else° would I very shortly see thee there.   otherwise
But come what may, I do adore thee so
That danger shall seem sport, and I will go.   Exit

2.2

Enter VIOLA *and* MALVOLIO, *at several° doors*   separate
MALVOLIO   Were not you even° now with the Countess   just
Olivia?
VIOLA   Even now, sir. On° a moderate pace I have since   at
arrived but hither.°   come only this far
5   MALVOLIO   She returns this ring to you, sir. You might
have saved me my pains to have taken° it away yourself.   by taking
She adds, moreover, that you should put your lord into a
desperate assurance° she will none of him. And one thing   hopeless certainty
more, that you be never so hardy° to come again in his   bold
10   affairs, unless it be to report your lord's taking of this.[1]
Receive it so.
VIOLA   She took the ring of me.[2] I'll none of it.
MALVOLIO   Come, sir, you peevishly threw it to her, and
her will is it should be so returned.
                    [*He throws down the ring.*]
15   If it be worth stooping for, there it lies, in your eye;° if   sight
not, be it his that finds it.   Exit

5. Your poor reception; your inhospitality.
6. I.e., murder him by insisting that they part.
7. I.e., so near woman's readiness to weep.
2.2 Location: Between Olivia's house and Orsino's palace.
1. Reception of this (rejection).
2. Viola pretends to believe Olivia's story. "Of":
from.

VIOLA I left no ring with her. What means this lady?

[*She picks up the ring.*]

Fortune forbid my outside° have not charmed her!   *appearance*
She made good view of° me, indeed so much   *looked carefully at*
20 That sure methought her eyes had lost° her tongue,   *made her lose*
For she did speak in starts distractedly.
She loves me, sure! The cunning of her passion
Invites me in° this churlish messenger.   *by means of*
None of my lord's ring? Why, he sent her none!
25 I am the man.[3] If it be so, as 'tis,
Poor lady, she were better love a dream.
Disguise, I see thou art a wickedness
Wherein the pregnant enemy[4] does much.
How easy is it for the proper false[5]
30 In women's waxen hearts to set their forms![6]
Alas, our frailty is the cause, not we,
For such as we are made of, such we be.[7]
How will this fadge?° My master loves her dearly,   *turn out*
And I, poor monster,[8] fond° as much on him,   *dote*
35 And she, mistaken, seems to dote on me.
What will become of this? As I am man,
My state is desperate° for my master's love.   *hopeless*
As I am woman (now, alas the day!),
What thriftless° sighs shall poor Olivia breathe!   *unprofitable*
40 O Time, thou must untangle this, not I.
It is too hard a knot for me t' untie.   [*Exit*]

2.3

Enter SIR TOBY *and* SIR ANDREW

SIR TOBY Approach, Sir Andrew. Not to be abed after
midnight is to be up betimes,° and "*diluculo surgere*,"[1]   *early*
thou knowest.

SIR ANDREW Nay, by my troth,° I know not. But I know to   *faith*
5 be up late is to be up late.

SIR TOBY A false conclusion. I hate it as an unfilled can.°   *tankard*
To be up after midnight and to go to bed then, is early, so
that to go to bed after midnight is to go to bed betimes.
Does not our lives consist of the four elements?[2]

10 SIR ANDREW Faith, so they say, but I think it rather consists
of eating and drinking.

SIR TOBY Thou'rt a scholar. Let us therefore eat and
drink. Marian, I say, a stoup° of wine!   *two-pint tankard*

Enter [FESTE, *the*] *clown*

SIR ANDREW Here comes the fool, i' faith.

3. I.e., the man with whom she has fallen in
love.
4. The devil. "Pregnant": teeming with ideas.
5. Handsome, but deceitful (men).
6. To impress their images on women's affections (as a seal stamps its image in wax).
7. For being made of frail flesh, we are frail.

8. Since she is both man and woman.
2.3 Location: Olivia's house.
1. Part of a Latin proverb, meaning "to rise at
dawn (is most healthy)."
2. The four elements, thought to make up all
matter, were earth, air, fire, and water.

15 FESTE   How now, my hearts? Did you never see the picture
of "We Three"?[3]

SIR TOBY   Welcome, ass. Now let's have a catch.[4]

SIR ANDREW   By my troth, the fool has an excellent breast.°   *singing voice*
I had rather than forty shillings I had such a leg,° and so   *(for dancing)*
20 sweet a breath to sing, as the fool has.—In sooth, thou
wast in very gracious fooling last night when thou spokest of Pigrogromitus, of the Vapians passing the equinoctial of Queubus.[5] 'Twas very good, i' faith. I sent thee
sixpence for thy leman.° Hadst it?   *sweetheart*

25 FESTE   I did impeticos thy gratillity,[6] for Malvolio's nose is
no whipstock, my lady has a white hand, and the Myrmidons are no bottle-ale houses.[7]

SIR ANDREW   Excellent! Why, this is the best fooling, when
all is done. Now, a song.

30 SIR TOBY [*to* FESTE]   Come on, there is sixpence for you.
Let's have a song.

SIR ANDREW [*to* FESTE]   There's a testril[8] of me, too. If one
knight give a—[9]

FESTE   Would you have a love song or a song of good life?

35 SIR TOBY   A love song, a love song.

SIR ANDREW   Ay, ay, I care not for good life.

FESTE *sings*
O mistress mine, where are you roaming?
O, stay and hear! Your truelove's coming,
    That can sing both high and low.
40 Trip° no further, pretty sweeting.   *go*
Journeys end in lovers meeting,
    Every wise man's son doth know.[1]

SIR ANDREW   Excellent good, i' faith.

SIR TOBY   Good, good.

45 FESTE   What is love? 'Tis not hereafter.
Present mirth hath present laughter.
    What's to come is still° unsure.   *always*
In delay there lies no plenty,
Then come kiss me, sweet and twenty.°   *twenty-times sweet*
50   Youth's a stuff will not endure.

SIR ANDREW   A mellifluous voice, as I am true knight.

SIR TOBY   A contagious breath.[2]

SIR ANDREW   Very sweet and contagious, i' faith.

---

3. A trick picture portraying two fools' or asses'
heads, the third being the viewer.
4. Round: a simple song for several voices.
5. "Pigrogromitus . . . Queubus": Feste's mock
learning. "Equinoctial": equator of the astronomical heavens.
6. Comic jargon for "impocket (or impetticoat)
your gratuity."
7. Perhaps it is the sheer inscrutability of Feste's
foolery that so impresses Sir Andrew (line 28).
"Whipstock": handle of a whip. "Myrmidons": in
the *Iliad*, Achilles's warriors. "Bottle-ale houses":

cheap taverns.
8. Sir Andrew's version of "tester" (sixpence).
9. In the First Folio, "give a" appears at the end
of a justified line; an omission is possible.
1. The words of the song are not certainly Shakespeare's; they fit the tune of an instrumental piece
printed in Thomas Morley's *First Book of Consort
Lessons* (1599). "Wise man's son": wise men were
thought to have foolish sons.
2. Catchy voice; with a play on "disease-causing
air."

SIR TOBY To hear by the nose, it is dulcet in contagion.[3]
But shall we make the welkin° dance indeed? Shall we *sky*
rouse the night owl in a catch that will draw three souls
out of one weaver?[4] Shall we do that?

SIR ANDREW An° you love me, let's do't. I am dog° at a catch. *if / clever*

FESTE By'r Lady, sir, and some dogs will catch well.

SIR ANDREW Most certain. Let our catch be "Thou Knave."

FESTE "Hold thy peace, thou knave,"[5] knight? I shall be
constrained in't to call thee "knave," knight.

SIR ANDREW 'Tis not the first time I have constrained one
to call me "knave." Begin, Fool. It begins "Hold thy peace."

FESTE I shall never begin if I hold my peace.

SIR ANDREW Good, i' faith. Come, begin. [*They sing the catch.*]
    Enter MARIA

MARIA What a caterwauling do you keep here! If my lady
have not called up her steward Malvolio and bid him turn
you out of doors, never trust me.

SIR TOBY My lady's a Cathayan,[6] we are politicians,° Mal- *schemers*
volio's a Peg-a'-Ramsey,[7] and [*sings*] "Three merry men be
we." Am not I consanguineous?[8] Am I not of her blood?
Tillyvally!° "Lady"! [*sings*] "There dwelt a man in Baby- *fiddlesticks*
lon, lady, lady."[9]

FESTE Beshrew° me, the knight's in admirable fooling. *curse*

SIR ANDREW Ay, he does well enough if he be disposed,
and so do I, too. He does it with a better grace, but I do
it more natural.[1]

SIR TOBY [*sings*] "O' the twelfth day of December"[2]—

MARIA For the love o' God, peace!
    Enter MALVOLIO

MALVOLIO My masters, are you mad? Or what are you?
Have you no wit,° manners, nor honesty° but to gabble *sense / decency*
like tinkers at this time of night? Do ye make an alehouse
of my lady's house, that you squeak out your coziers'° *cobblers'*
catches without any mitigation or remorse[3] of voice? Is
there no respect of place, persons, nor time in you?

SIR TOBY We did keep time, sir, in our catches. Sneck up!° *go hang yourself*

MALVOLIO Sir Toby, I must be round° with you. My lady *plainspoken*
bade me tell you that, though she harbors you as her
kinsman, she's nothing allied to your disorders. If you
can separate yourself and your misdemeanors, you are
welcome to the house; if not, an it would please you to
take leave of her, she is very willing to bid you farewell.

---

3. If one could hear through the nose, the sound would be sweetly ("dulcet") infectious.
4. Weavers were traditionally addicted to psalm singing, so to move them with popular catches would be a great triumph. Music was said to be able to draw the soul from the body.
5. The words of the catch are "Hold thy peace, I prithee hold thy peace, thou knave." Each singer repeatedly calls the others knaves and tells them to stop singing.
6. Chinese; but also ethnocentric slang for "trickster" or "cheat."

7. Name of a dance and popular song; here, used contemptuously.
8. A blood relative (of Olivia's). "Three . . . we": refrain of a popular song.
9. The opening and refrain of a popular song.
1. Effortlessly; but, unconsciously playing on the sense of *natural* as "fool" or "idiot."
2. Snatch of a ballad; or possibly a drunken version of "twelfth day of Christmas," that is, Twelfth Night.
3. Without any abating or softening.

SIR TOBY [*sings*] "Farewell, dear heart, since I must needs
be gone."[4]
95 MARIA Nay, good Sir Toby.
FESTE "His eyes do show his days are almost done."
MALVOLIO Is't even so?
SIR TOBY "But I will never die."
FESTE "Sir Toby, there you lie."
100 MALVOLIO This is much credit to you.
SIR TOBY "Shall I bid him go?"
FESTE "What an if° you do?" *an if = if*
SIR TOBY "Shall I bid him go, and spare not?"
FESTE "O no, no, no, no, you dare not."
105 SIR TOBY Out o' tune, sir? Ye lie. Art any more than a
steward? Dost thou think because thou art virtuous
there shall be no more cakes and ale?[5]
FESTE Yes, by Saint Anne, and ginger[6] shall be hot i' th'
mouth, too.
110 SIR TOBY Thou'rt i' th' right.—Go, sir, rub your chain
with crumbs.[7]—A stoup of wine, Maria!
MALVOLIO Mistress Mary, if you prized my lady's favor at
anything more than contempt, you would not give
means for this uncivil rule.° She shall know of it, by this *behavior*
115 hand. *Exit*[8]
MARIA Go shake your ears!° *(like an ass)*
SIR ANDREW 'Twere as good a deed as to drink when a
man's a-hungry, to challenge him the field° and then to *to a duel*
break promise with him and make a fool of him.
120 SIR TOBY Do't, knight. I'll write thee a challenge. Or I'll
deliver thy indignation to him by word of mouth.
MARIA Sweet Sir Toby, be patient for tonight. Since the
youth of the Count's was today with my lady, she is much
out of quiet. For Monsieur Malvolio, let me alone with
125 him.° If I do not gull him into a nayword[9] and make him *leave him to me*
a common recreation,° do not think I have wit enough to *sport, jest*
lie straight in my bed. I know I can do it.
SIR TOBY Possess° us, possess us, tell us something of him. *inform*
MARIA Marry, sir, sometimes he is a kind of puritan.[1]
130 SIR ANDREW O, if I thought that, I'd beat him like a dog!
SIR TOBY What, for being a puritan? Thy exquisite° rea- *ingenious*
son, dear knight?
SIR ANDREW I have no exquisite reason for't, but I have
reason good enough.
135 MARIA The devil a puritan that he is, or anything constantly but a time-pleaser;° an affectioned[2] ass that cons *boot licker*

4. Part of another song that Sir Toby and Feste adapt for the occasion.
5. Traditionally associated with church festivals and therefore disliked by Puritans.
6. Used to spice ale. Saint Anne was the mother of the Virgin; the oath would be offensive to Puritans, who attacked her cult.
7. Clean your steward's chain; mind your own business.
8. Feste plays no further part in this scene. This is the suggested exit for him too.
9. If I do not trick ("gull") him into a byword (for "dupe").
1. Could mean "morally strict and censorious," as well as "a follower of the Puritan religious faith."
2. Affected.

state without book and utters it by great swaths;[3] the
best persuaded of himself,[4] so crammed, as he thinks,
with excellencies, that it is his grounds of faith° that all   *his creed*
140   that look on him love him. And on that vice in him will
my revenge find notable cause to work.

SIR TOBY   What wilt thou do?

MARIA   I will drop in his way some obscure epistles of
love, wherein by the color of his beard, the shape of his
145   leg, the manner of his gait, the expressure° of his eye,   *expression*
forehead, and complexion, he shall find himself most
feelingly personated.° I can write very like my lady your   *represented*
niece; on a forgotten matter, we can hardly make distinc-
tion of our hands.°   *handwriting*

150 SIR TOBY   Excellent! I smell a device.

SIR ANDREW   I have't in my nose, too.

SIR TOBY   He shall think, by the letters that thou wilt
drop, that they come from my niece, and that she's in
love with him.

155 MARIA   My purpose is indeed a horse of that color.

SIR ANDREW   And your horse now would make him an ass.

MARIA   Ass° I doubt not.   *(punning on "as")*

SIR ANDREW   O, 'twill be admirable!

MARIA   Sport royal, I warrant you. I know my physic° will   *medicine*
160   work with him. I will plant you two, and let the fool
make a third, where he shall find the letter. Observe
his construction° of it. For this night, to bed, and dream   *interpretation*
on the event.° Farewell.   *Exit*   *outcome*

SIR TOBY   Good night, Penthesilea.[5]

165 SIR ANDREW   Before me,[6] she's a good wench.

SIR TOBY   She's a beagle true bred, and one that adores
me. What o' that?

SIR ANDREW   I was adored once, too.

SIR TOBY   Let's to bed, knight. Thou hadst need send for
170   more money.

SIR ANDREW   If I cannot recover° your niece, I am a foul   *win*
way out.°   *out of money*

SIR TOBY   Send for money, knight. If thou hast her not i'
th' end, call me "Cut."[7]

175 SIR ANDREW   If I do not, never trust me, take it how you
will.

SIR TOBY   Come, come, I'll go burn some sack.[8] 'Tis too
late to go to bed now. Come, knight; come, knight.

                                     Exeunt

---

3. Memorizes dignified and high-flown language
and utters it in great sweeps (like hay falling
under a scythe).
4. Having the highest opinion of himself.
5. Queen of the Amazons (a joke about Maria's
small size).
6. On my soul (a mild oath).
7. A dock-tailed horse; also, slang for "gelding"
or for "female genitals."
8. I'll go warm and spice some Spanish wine.

2.4

Enter ORSINO, VIOLA, CURIO, *and others*

ORSINO   Give me some music. Now good morrow,° friends.   morning
　　Now good Cesario, but° that piece of song,   just
　　That old and antique° song we heard last night.   quaint
　　Methought it did relieve my passion° much,   suffering
5　More than light airs and recollected° terms   studied; artificial
　　Of these most brisk and giddy-pacèd times.
　　Come, but one verse.
CURIO   He is not here, so please your lordship, that should
　　sing it.
10 ORSINO   Who was it?
CURIO   Feste the jester, my lord, a fool that the Lady Oliv-
　　ia's father took much delight in. He is about the house.
ORSINO   Seek him out, and play the tune the while.

　　　　　　　　　　　　　　　　　　　　[*Exit* CURIO]

　　Music plays.
　　[*To* VIOLA] Come hither, boy. If ever thou shalt love,
15　In the sweet pangs of it remember me,
　　For such as I am, all true lovers are,
　　Unstaid° and skittish in all motions° else   unstable / emotions
　　Save° in the constant image of the creature   except
　　That is beloved. How dost thou like this tune?
20 VIOLA   It gives a very echo to the seat
　　Where love is throned.[1]
ORSINO　　　　　　　　Thou dost speak masterly.°   expertly
　　My life upon't, young though thou art, thine eye
　　Hath stayed upon some favor° that it loves.   face
　　Hath it not, boy?
VIOLA　　　　　　A little, by your favor.°   leave; face
ORSINO   What kind of woman is't?
25 VIOLA　　　　　　　　　　Of your complexion.
ORSINO   She is not worth thee, then. What years, i' faith?
VIOLA   About your years, my lord.
ORSINO   Too old, by heaven. Let still° the woman take   always
　　An elder than herself. So wears° she to him;   adapts
30　So sways she level[2] in her husband's heart.
　　For, boy, however we do praise ourselves,
　　Our fancies° are more giddy and unfirm,   affections
　　More longing, wavering, sooner lost and worn,°   exhausted
　　Than women's are.
VIOLA　　　　　　I think° it well, my lord.   believe
35 ORSINO   Then let thy love be younger than thyself,
　　Or thy affection cannot hold the bent.[3]
　　For women are as roses, whose fair flower,
　　Being once displayed,° doth fall that very hour.   opened

2.4 Location: Orsino's palace.
1. I.e., it reflects back to the heart.
2. So does she balance (influence and affection).

3. Cannot remain at full stretch (like the taut-
ness of a bowstring).

VIOLA   And so they are. Alas, that they are so,
40   To die even° when they to perfection grow!   *just*
          Enter CURIO *and* [FESTE, *the*] *clown*
ORSINO   O, fellow, come, the song we had last night.—
          Mark it, Cesario. It is old and plain;
          The spinsters° and the knitters in the sun   *spinners*
          And the free° maids that weave their thread with bones[4]   *carefree*
45   Do use to chant it. It is silly sooth,°   *simple truth*
          And dallies with° the innocence of love   *lingers lovingly on*
          Like the old age.°   *i.e., the Golden Age*
FESTE   Are you ready, sir?
ORSINO   Ay, prithee, sing.
          Music
50   FESTE [*sings*] Come away,° come away, death,   *come hither*
                    And in sad cypress[5] let me be laid.
                Fly away, fly away, breath,
                    I am slain by a fair cruel maid.
                My shroud of white, stuck all with yew,°   *yew sprigs*
55   O prepare it.
                My part of death, no one so true
                    Did share it.[6]

                Not a flower, not a flower sweet
                    On my black coffin let there be strewn;
60   Not a friend, not a friend greet
                    My poor corpse, where my bones shall be thrown.
                A thousand thousand sighs to save,
                    Lay me, O, where
                Sad true lover never find my grave,
65   To weep there.
ORSINO [*giving money*]   There's for thy pains.
FESTE   No pains, sir. I take pleasure in singing, sir.
ORSINO   I'll pay thy pleasure, then.
FESTE   Truly, sir, and pleasure will be paid,° one time or   *paid for*
70   another.
ORSINO   Give me now leave° to leave° thee.   *permission / dismiss*
FESTE   Now the melancholy god[7] protect thee, and the
          tailor make thy doublet of changeable taffeta,[8] for thy
          mind is a very opal.[9] I would have men of such constancy
75   put to sea, that their business might be everything and
          their intent° everywhere, for that's it that always makes   *destination*
          a good voyage of nothing.[1] Farewell.   *Exit*
ORSINO   Let all the rest give place.°   *withdraw*
          [*Exeunt all but* ORSINO *and* VIOLA]
                    Once more, Cesario,

---

4. Spools made from bone on which lace (called "bone lace") was woven.
5. Cypress-wood coffin. Like yews, cypresses were emblematic of mourning.
6. I.e., no one has died so true to love as I.
7. Saturn (thought to control the melancholic).
8. Shot silk, whose color changes with the angle

of vision. "Doublet": a close-fitting jacket.
9. An iridescent gemstone that changes color depending on the angle from which it is seen.
1. I.e., this fickle lack of direction can make a voyage in the notoriously changeful sea carefree and consonant with one's desires.

Get thee to yond same sovereign° cruelty.   *supreme*
80 Tell her my love, more noble than the world,
Prizes not quantity of dirty lands.
The parts° that fortune hath bestowed upon her,   *possessions*
Tell her, I hold as giddily[2] as fortune.
But 'tis that miracle and queen of gems
85 That nature pranks° her in attracts my soul.   *adorns*
VIOLA But if she cannot love you, sir—
ORSINO I cannot be so answered.
VIOLA   Sooth,° but you must.   *in truth*
Say that some lady, as perhaps there is,
Hath for your love as great a pang of heart
90 As you have for Olivia. You cannot love her;
You tell her so. Must she not then be answered?
ORSINO There is no woman's sides
Can bide° the beating of so strong a passion   *withstand*
As love doth give my heart; no woman's heart
95 So big, to hold so much; they lack retention.°   *constancy*
Alas, their love may be called appetite,
No motion° of the liver, but the palate,[3]   *impulse*
That suffer surfeit, cloyment,° and revolt;°   *satiety / revulsion*
But mine is all as hungry as the sea,
100 And can digest as much. Make no compare
Between that love a woman can bear me
And that I owe° Olivia.   *have for*
VIOLA Ay, but I know—
ORSINO What dost thou know?
105 VIOLA Too well what love women to men may owe.
In faith, they are as true of heart as we.
My father had a daughter loved a man
As it might be, perhaps, were I a woman,
I should your lordship.
ORSINO   And what's her history?
110 VIOLA A blank, my lord. She never told her love,
But let concealment, like a worm i' th' bud,
Feed on her damask[4] cheek. She pined in thought,
And with a green and yellow° melancholy   *pale and sallow*
She sat like Patience on a monument,[5]
115 Smiling at grief. Was not this love indeed?
We men may say more, swear more, but indeed
Our shows are more than will;[6] for still° we prove   *always*
Much in our vows but little in our love.
ORSINO But died thy sister of her love, my boy?
120 VIOLA I am all the daughters of my father's house,
And all the brothers, too—and yet I know not.
Sir, shall I to this lady?

---

2. Lightly (fortune being fickle).
3. Appetite, like the palate, is easily sated and thus lacks the emotional depth and complexity of real love, whose seat is the liver.
4. Pink and white, like a damask rose.
5. A memorial statue symbolizing patience.
6. Our displays of love are greater than our actual feelings.

ORSINO   Ay, that's the theme.
To her in haste. Give her this jewel. Say
My love can give no place, bide no denay.[7]

                           Exeunt [*severally*]

2.5

Enter SIR TOBY, SIR ANDREW, *and* FABIAN

SIR TOBY   Come thy ways,° Signior Fabian.   *come along*

FABIAN   Nay, I'll come. If I lose a scruple° of this sport, let   *miss a scrap*
me be boiled to death with melancholy.[1]

SIR TOBY   Wouldst thou not be glad to have the niggardly°   *stingy*
5   rascally sheep-biter[2] come by some notable shame?

FABIAN   I would exult, man. You know he brought me out
o' favor with my lady about a bearbaiting[3] here.

SIR TOBY   To anger him, we'll have the bear again, and we
will fool° him black and blue, shall we not, Sir Andrew?   *mock*

10   SIR ANDREW   An° we do not, it is pity of our lives.   *if*

Enter MARIA [*with a letter*]

SIR TOBY   Here comes the little villain.—How now, my metal
of India?[4]

MARIA   Get ye all three into the boxtree.° Malvolio's com-   *hedge of boxwood*
ing down this walk. He has been yonder i' the sun prac-

15   ticing behavior to his own shadow this half hour. Observe
him, for the love of mockery, for I know this letter will
make a contemplative° idiot of him. Close,° in the name   *vacuous / hide*
of jesting! [*The men hide.*] Lie thou there, [*putting down
the letter*] for here comes the trout that must be caught

20   with tickling.[5]   *Exit*

Enter MALVOLIO

MALVOLIO   'Tis but fortune, all is fortune. Maria once told
me she° did affect° me, and I have heard herself come   *Olivia / care for*
thus near, that should she fancy,° it should be one of my   *fall in love*
complexion. Besides, she uses me with a more exalted

25   respect than anyone else that follows her. What should I
think on't?

SIR TOBY   Here's an overweening° rogue.   *presumptuous*

FABIAN   O, peace! Contemplation makes a rare turkey-
cock[6] of him. How he jets° under his advanced° plumes!   *struts / raised*

30   SIR ANDREW   'Slight,[7] I could so beat the rogue!

SIR TOBY   Peace, I say.

MALVOLIO   To be Count Malvolio!

SIR TOBY   Ah, rogue!

---

7. My love cannot be bated, nor tolerate refusal.
2.5 Location: Olivia's garden.
1. Melancholy was a cold humor; "boiled" puns
on "bile," the surplus of which produced melancholy.
2. Literally, a dog that attacks sheep; here, a
malicious sneak.
3. Puritans disapproved of blood sports like

bearbaiting.
4. A woman worth her weight in gold.
5. Flattery; trout can supposedly be caught by
stroking them under the gills.
6. Proverbially proud; they display their feathers
like peacocks.
7. By God's light (an oath).

SIR ANDREW Pistol° him, pistol him!   *shoot*

35 SIR TOBY Peace, peace!

MALVOLIO There is example° for't. The Lady of the Strachy   *precedent*
married the yeoman of the wardrobe.[8]

SIR ANDREW Fie on him, Jezebel![9]

FABIAN O, peace, now he's deeply in. Look how imagina-

40 tion blows him.°   *puffs him up*

MALVOLIO Having been three months married to her, sit-
ting in my state°—   *chair of state*

SIR TOBY O, for a stone-bow,[1] to hit him in the eye!

MALVOLIO Calling my officers about me, in my branched[2]

45 velvet gown, having come from a daybed,° where I have   *couch*
left Olivia sleeping—

SIR TOBY Fire and brimstone!

FABIAN O, peace, peace!

MALVOLIO And then to have the humor of state;[3] and

50 after a demure travel of regard,[4] telling them I know my
place, as I would they should do theirs, to ask for my
kinsman Toby—

SIR TOBY Bolts and shackles!

FABIAN O, peace, peace, peace! Now, now.

55 MALVOLIO Seven of my people, with an obedient start,
make° out for him. I frown the while, and perchance wind   *go*
up my watch, or play with my[5]—some rich jewel. Toby
approaches; curtsies° there to me—   *bows*

SIR TOBY Shall this fellow live?

60 FABIAN Though our silence be drawn from us with cars,[6]
yet peace.

MALVOLIO I extend my hand to him thus, quenching my
familiar smile with an austere regard° of control—   *look*

SIR TOBY And does not Toby take° you a blow o' the lips   *give*

65 then?

MALVOLIO Saying "Cousin Toby, my fortunes, having cast
me on your niece, give me this prerogative of speech"—

SIR TOBY What, what?

MALVOLIO "You must amend your drunkenness."

70 SIR TOBY Out, scab!

FABIAN Nay, patience, or we break the sinews of our plot.

MALVOLIO "Besides, you waste the treasure of your time
with a foolish knight"—

SIR ANDREW That's me, I warrant you.

75 MALVOLIO "One Sir Andrew."

---

8. Perhaps an allusion to a noblewoman who had married her manservant, but there is no certain identification. "Yeoman of the wardrobe": keeper of clothes and linen.
9. Biblical allusion to the proud wife of Ahab, king of Israel.
1. Catapult, or crossbow for stones.
2. Embroidered with branch patterns. "Officers": household attendants.

3. To adopt the grand air of exalted greatness.
4. After casting my eyes gravely about the room.
5. Evidently touching his steward's chain. Malvolio momentarily forgets that he will have abandoned his chain. "My watch": watches were an expensive luxury at this time.
6. A prisoner might be tied to two carts or chariots ("cars") and pulled by horses in opposite directions to extort information.

SIR ANDREW   I knew 'twas I, for many do call me fool.

MALVOLIO [*seeing the letter*]   What employment° have we   business
here?

FABIAN   Now is the woodcock near the gin.[7]

80   SIR TOBY   O, peace, and the spirit of humors intimate[8]
reading aloud to him.

MALVOLIO [*taking up the letter*]   By my life, this is my lady's
hand. These be her very *c*'s, her *u*'s, and her *t*'s,[9] and thus
makes she her great *P*'s. It is in contempt of° question   beyond

85   her hand.

SIR ANDREW   Her *c*'s, her *u*'s, and her *t*'s? Why that?

MALVOLIO [*reads*]   "To the unknown beloved, this, and my
good wishes."—Her very phrases! By your leave, wax.[1]
Soft.° And the impressure her Lucrece,[2] with which she   wait

90   uses to seal°—'tis my lady! [*He opens the letter.*] To whom   habitually seals
should this be?

FABIAN   This wins him, liver and all.

MALVOLIO [*reads*]   "Jove knows I love,
            But who?

95   Lips, do not move;
                No man must know."

"No man must know." What follows? The numbers altered.°   meter changed
"No man must know." If this should be thee, Malvolio!

SIR TOBY   Marry, hang thee, brock![3]

100 MALVOLIO [*reads*]   "I may command where I adore,
                But silence, like a Lucrece knife,[4]
                    With bloodless stroke my heart doth gore;
                    M.O.A.I. doth sway my life."

FABIAN   A fustian° riddle!   bombastic

105 SIR TOBY   Excellent wench, say I.

MALVOLIO   "M.O.A.I. doth sway my life." Nay, but first let
me see, let me see, let me see.

FABIAN   What dish o' poison has she dressed° him!   prepared

SIR TOBY   And with what wing the staniel checks at it![5]

110 MALVOLIO   "I may command where I adore." Why, she may
command me; I serve her, she is my lady. Why, this is
evident to any formal capacity.[6] There is no obstruction
in this. And the end—what should that alphabetical posi-
tion° portend? If I could make that resemble something   arrangement

115 in me! Softly! "M.O.A.I."—

SIR TOBY   O, ay,[7] make up that.—He is now at a cold scent.

---

7. Snare. The woodcock is a proverbially foolish bird.
8. And may a capricious impulse suggest.
9. Malvolio unwittingly spells out "cut," slang for female genitals; the meaning is compounded by "great *P*'s." In fact, these letters do not appear on the outside of the letter.
1. He addresses himself to the sealing wax.
2. The figure of Lucrece, Roman model of chas-

tity, is the device ("impressure") imprinted on the seal.
3. Badger (proverbially stinking).
4. After being raped, Lucretia stabbed herself to death.
5. And with what alacrity the sparrow hawk goes after it.
6. Normal intelligence.
7. Playing on "O.I."

as though

FABIAN   Sowter will cry upon't for all this, though° it be as
     rank as a fox.[8]

MALVOLIO   "M"—Malvolio. "M"—why, that begins my name!

120 FABIAN   Did not I say he would work it out? The cur is
     excellent at faults.[9]

MALVOLIO   "M." But then there is no consonancy in the
     sequel.[1] That suffers under probation.[2] "A" should follow,
     but "O" does.

125 FABIAN   And "O"[3] shall end, I hope.

SIR TOBY   Ay, or I'll cudgel him and make him cry "O."

MALVOLIO   And then "I" comes behind.

FABIAN   Ay, an you had any eye behind you, you might
     see more detraction° at your heels than fortunes before   *defamation*
130 you.

MALVOLIO   "M.O.A.I." This simulation° is not as the former,   *disguise; riddle*
     and yet to crush° this a little, it would bow° to me, for *force / yield; point*
     every one of these letters are in my name. Soft, here fol-
     lows prose. [*He reads.*] "If this fall into thy hand, revolve.°   *consider*
135 In my stars° I am above thee, but be not afraid of greatness.   *fortunes*
     Some are born great, some achieve greatness, and some
     have greatness thrust upon 'em. Thy fates open their
     hands.° Let thy blood and spirit embrace them. And, to   *bestow gifts*
     inure° thyself to what thou art like° to be, cast thy humble *accustom / likely*
140 slough[4] and appear fresh. Be opposite° with a kinsman,   *contrary*
     surly with servants. Let thy tongue tang arguments of
     state.[5] Put thyself into the trick of singularity.[6] She thus
     advises thee that sighs for thee. Remember who com-
     mended thy yellow stockings and wished to see thee ever
145 cross-gartered.[7] I say, remember. Go to,[8] thou art made, if
     thou desirest to be so. If not, let me see thee a steward still,
     the fellow of servants, and not worthy to touch Fortune's
     fingers. Farewell. She that would alter services[9] with thee.
                    The Fortunate-Unhappy."

150 Daylight and champaign discovers[1] not more! This is
     open.° I will be proud, I will read politic° authors, I will   *clear / political*
     baffle[2] Sir Toby, I will wash off gross acquaintance, I will
     be point-device the very man.[3] I do not now fool myself,
     to let imagination jade° me; for every reason excites to   *trick*
155 this, that my lady loves me. She did commend my yellow

8. "Sowter" (the name of a hound), having lost
the scent, will start to bay loudly as he picks up
the new, rank (stinking) smell of the fox.
9. At picking up a scent after it is momentarily
lost. A "fault" is a "cold scent" (line 116).
1. There is no consistency in what follows.
2. That weakens upon being put to the test.
3. As in the hangman's noose; the last letter of
Malvolio's name; or "O" as a lamentation.
4. A snake's old skin, which peels away.
5. Let your tongue ring out arguments of statecraft or politics.

6. Cultivate eccentricity.
7. An antiquated way of adjusting a garter—
going once below the knee, crossing behind it,
and knotting above the knee at the side.
8. An emphatic expression, like "I tell you."
9. Change places (of servant and mistress or
master).
1. Open countryside reveals.
2. Term used to describe the formal unmaking
of a knight; hence, "disgrace."
3. I will be in every detail the identical man
(described in the letter).

stockings of late, she did praise my leg being cross-
gartered, and in this she manifests herself to my love and,
with a kind of injunction, drives me to these habits° of her   *clothes*
liking. I thank my stars, I am happy. I will be strange,°   *aloof*
160 stout,° in yellow stockings, and cross-gartered, even with   *proud*
the swiftness of putting on. Jove and my stars be praised!
Here is yet a postscript. [*He reads.*] "Thou canst not
choose but know who I am. If thou entertainest° my love,   *accept*
let it appear in thy smiling; thy smiles become thee well.
165 Therefore in my presence still° smile, dear my sweet, I   *constantly*
prithee." Jove, I thank thee. I will smile, I will do every-
thing that thou wilt have me.   *Exit*
FABIAN   I will not give my part of this sport for a pension
of thousands to be paid from the Sophy.°   *shah of Persia*
170 SIR TOBY   I could marry this wench for this device.
SIR ANDREW   So could I, too.
SIR TOBY   And ask no other dowry with her but such
another jest.
SIR ANDREW   Nor I neither.
         Enter MARIA
175 FABIAN   Here comes my noble gull-catcher.°   *trickster*
SIR TOBY   Wilt thou set thy foot o' my neck?
SIR ANDREW   Or o' mine either?
SIR TOBY   Shall I play° my freedom at tray-trip[4] and   *wager*
become thy bondslave?
180 SIR ANDREW   I' faith, or I either?
SIR TOBY   Why, thou hast put him in such a dream that
when the image° of it leaves him he must run mad.   *illusion*
MARIA   Nay, but say true, does it work upon him?
SIR TOBY   Like aqua vitae° with a midwife.   *spirits, liquor*
185 MARIA   If you will then see the fruits of the sport, mark
his first approach before my lady. He will come to her in
yellow stockings, and 'tis a color she abhors, and cross-
gartered, a fashion she detests; and he will smile upon
her, which will now be so unsuitable to her disposition,
190 being addicted to a melancholy as she is, that it cannot
but turn him into a notable contempt.[5] If you will see it,
follow me.
SIR TOBY   To the gates of Tartar,° thou most excellent dev-   *hell*
il of wit!
195 SIR ANDREW   I'll make one,° too.   *Exeunt*   *go along*

---

4. A game of dice in which the winner throws a   5. A notorious object of contempt.
three ("tray" is from the Spanish *tres*).

3.1

Enter VIOLA *and* [FESTE, *the*] *clown* [, *with pipe and tabor*][1]

VIOLA   Save° thee, friend, and thy music. Dost thou live   *God save*
  by thy tabor?

FESTE   No, sir, I live by° the church.   *near*

VIOLA   Art thou a churchman?

5 FESTE   No such matter, sir. I do live by[2] the church, for I
  do live at my house, and my house doth stand by the
  church.

VIOLA   So thou mayst say the king lies by[3] a beggar if a
  beggar dwell near him, or the church stands° by thy tabor   *is maintained*
10 if thy tabor stand by the church.

FESTE   You have said, sir. To see this age! A sentence° is   *saying*
  but a chev'ril° glove to a good wit. How quickly the wrong   *kidskin*
  side may be turned outward!

VIOLA   Nay, that's certain. They that dally nicely° with   *play subtly*
15 words may quickly make them wanton.[4]

FESTE   I would therefore my sister had had no name, sir.

VIOLA   Why, man?

FESTE   Why, sir, her name's a word, and to dally with that
  word might make my sister wanton. But, indeed, words
20 are very rascals since bonds disgraced them.[5]

VIOLA   Thy reason, man?

FESTE   Troth, sir, I can yield you none without words, and
  words are grown so false I am loath to prove reason with
  them.

25 VIOLA   I warrant thou art a merry fellow and carest for
  nothing.

FESTE   Not so, sir. I do care for something. But in my conscience, sir, I do not care for you. If that be to care for
  nothing, sir, I would it would make you invisible.

30 VIOLA   Art not thou the Lady Olivia's fool?

FESTE   No indeed, sir. The Lady Olivia has no folly. She
  will keep no fool, sir, till she be married, and fools are as
  like husbands as pilchards[6] are to herrings: the husband's
  the bigger. I am indeed not her fool but her corrupter of
35 words.

VIOLA   I saw thee late° at the Count Orsino's.   *lately*

FESTE   Foolery, sir, does walk about the orb[7] like the sun;
  it shines everywhere. I would be sorry, sir, but the fool
  should be as oft with your master as with my mistress.[8] I
40 think I saw your wisdom[9] there.

3.1 Location: Olivia's garden.

1. The dialogue demands only a tabor, but jest-ers commonly played a pipe with one hand while tapping a tabor (small drum, hanging from the neck) with the other.

2. I do earn my keep with.

3. Lives near; punning on "goes to bed with."

4. Equivocal; Viola puns on the sense "unchaste."

5. Since legal contracts replaced a man's word of honor. ("Bonds" plays on "sworn statements" and "fetters," betokening criminality.)

6. Small fish similar to herring.

7. World; the sun was still believed to circle the earth.

8. Unless ("but") Feste should visit his foolery upon others, but also unless Orsino should be called "fool" as often as Olivia.

9. A mocking title for Cesario.

VIOLA   Nay, an thou pass upon[1] me, I'll no more with thee.
Hold, there's expenses for thee. [*giving a coin*]

FESTE   Now Jove in his next commodity° of hair send thee   shipment
a beard!

45   VIOLA   By my troth I'll tell thee, I am almost sick for one,[2]
[*aside*] though I would not have it grow on *my* chin.—Is
thy lady within?

FESTE   Would not a pair of these have bred,[3] sir?

VIOLA   Yes, being kept together and put to use.[4]

50   FESTE   I would play Lord Pandarus[5] of Phrygia, sir, to bring
a Cressida to this Troilus.

VIOLA   I understand you, sir. 'Tis well begged. [*giving
another coin*]

FESTE   The matter I hope is not great, sir, begging but a
55   beggar: Cressida was a beggar.[6] My lady is within, sir. I
will conster° to them whence you come. Who you are and   explain
what you would are out of my welkin—I might say "ele-
ment," but the word is overworn.[7]   *Exit*

VIOLA   This fellow is wise enough to play the fool,
60   And to do that well craves a kind of wit.°   intelligence
He must observe their mood on whom he jests,
The quality of persons, and the time,
And, like the haggard, check at every feather
That comes before his eye.[8] This is a practice°   skill
65   As full of labor as a wise man's art,
For folly that he wisely shows is fit,[9]
But wise men, folly-fall'n,° quite taint[1] their wit.   fallen into folly
Enter SIR TOBY *and* SIR ANDREW

SIR TOBY   Save you, gentleman.

VIOLA   And you, sir.

70   SIR ANDREW   *Dieu vous garde, monsieur.*[2]

VIOLA   *Et vous aussi. Votre serviteur!*[3]

SIR ANDREW   I hope, sir, you are, and I am yours.

SIR TOBY   Will you encounter[4] the house? My niece is
desirous you should enter, if your trade be to her.

75   VIOLA   I am bound to° your niece, sir; I mean, she is the   for
list° of my voyage.   destination

SIR TOBY   Taste° your legs, sir; put them to motion.   try

1. If you express an opinion of; if you joke about.
2. Almost eager for a beard; almost pining for a
man (Orsino).
3. Would not a pair of coins such as these have
multiplied (with possible pun on "be enough to
buy bread").
4. Invested to produce interest.
5. Go-between or "pander," since Feste needs a
"mate" for his coin(s). Shakespeare dramatizes
the story in *Troilus and Cressida.*
6. In asking for the "mate" to his Troilus coin,
Feste draws on a version of the story of Troilus
and Cressida in which Cressida became a leprous
beggar.

7. "Welkin" (sky or air) is synonymous with one
meaning of "element," used in what Feste regards
as the overworn phrase "out of my element."
8. I.e., as a wild hawk ("haggard") must be sensitive to its prey's disposition.
9. For folly that he skillfully displays is proper.
1. Discredit; spoil.
2. God protect you, sir (French).
3. And you also, (I am) your servant. (Sir Andrew's
awkward reply demonstrates that his French is
limited.)
4. Pedantry for "enter" (Toby mocks Viola's
courtly language).

VIOLA My legs do better understand° me, sir, than I under-   *stand under*
  stand what you mean by bidding me taste my legs.
80 SIR TOBY I mean, to go, sir, to enter.
VIOLA I will answer you with gait and entrance.
  Enter OLIVIA, *and* [MARIA, *her*] *gentlewoman.*
  But we are prevented.° Most excellent accomplished lady,   *anticipated*
  the heavens rain odors on you!
SIR ANDREW [*to* SIR TOBY] That youth's a rare° courtier.   *an excellent*
85 "Rain odors," well.°   *well put*
VIOLA My matter hath no voice,° lady, but to your own   *must not be spoken*
  most pregnant° and vouchsafed° ear.   *receptive / proffered*
SIR ANDREW [*to* SIR TOBY] "Odors," "pregnant," and
  "vouchsafed." I'll get 'em all three all ready.[5]
90 OLIVIA Let the garden door be shut, and leave me to my
  hearing.   [*Exeunt* SIR TOBY, SIR ANDREW, *and* MARIA]
  Give me your hand, sir.
VIOLA My duty, madam, and most humble service.
OLIVIA What is your name?
95 VIOLA Cesario is your servant's name, fair princess.
OLIVIA My servant, sir? 'Twas never merry world[6]
  Since lowly feigning° was called compliment.   *pretended humility*
  You're servant to the Count Orsino, youth.
VIOLA And he is yours, and his must needs be yours.
100 Your servant's servant is *your* servant, madam.
OLIVIA For° him, I think not on him. For his thoughts,   *as for*
  Would they were blanks rather than filled with me.
VIOLA Madam, I come to whet your gentle thoughts
  On his behalf.
OLIVIA   O, by your leave,[7] I pray you.
105 I bade you never speak again of him;
  But would you undertake another suit,
  I had rather hear you to solicit that
  Than music from the spheres.[8]
VIOLA   Dear lady—
OLIVIA Give me leave, beseech you. I did send,
110 After the last enchantment you did here,
  A ring in chase of you. So did I abuse°   *deceive; dishonor*
  Myself, my servant, and, I fear me, you.°   *and, as I fear, you*
  Under your hard construction[9] must I sit,
  To force° that on you in a shameful cunning   *for forcing*
115 Which you knew none of yours. What might you think?
  Have you not set mine honor at the stake,
  And baited it with all th' unmuzzled thoughts[1]
  That tyrannous heart can think? To one of your receiving°   *perception*

---

5. I.e., to commit to memory for later use.
6. The proverbial "Things have never been the same."
7. Permit me to interrupt (polite expression).
8. Exquisite music thought to be made by the planets as they moved, but inaudible to mortal ears.
9. Your unfavorable interpretation (of my behavior).
1. As bears that were tied up at the stake and baited with dogs.

Enough is shown. A cypress,[2] not a bosom,
120　　Hides my heart. So let me hear you speak.
VIOLA　　I pity you.
OLIVIA　　　　　That's a degree to° love.　　　　　*toward*
VIOLA　　No, not a grize,° for 'tis a vulgar proof°　　　*step / common experience*
　　That very oft we pity enemies.
OLIVIA　　Why then methinks 'tis time to smile again.[3]
125　　O world, how apt° the poor are to be proud!　　　*ready*
　　If one should be a prey, how much the better
　　To fall before the lion than the wolf.[4]

　　　　　Clock strikes.

　　The clock upbraids° me with the waste of time.　　　*reproaches*
　　Be not afraid, good youth, I will not have you.
130　　And yet when wit and youth is come to harvest,
　　Your wife is like to reap a proper° man.　　　*handsome; worthy*
　　There lies your way, due west.
VIOLA　　　　　　　　　　　Then westward ho![5]
　　Grace and good disposition° attend your ladyship.　　　*peace of mind*
　　You'll nothing, madam, to my lord by me?
135　　OLIVIA　　Stay. I prithee, tell me what thou[6] think'st of me.
VIOLA　　That you do think you are not what you are.[7]
OLIVIA　　If I think so, I think the same of you.[8]
VIOLA　　Then think you right. I am not what I am.
OLIVIA　　I would you were as I would have you be.
140　　VIOLA　　Would it be better, madam, than I am?
　　I wish it might, for now I am your fool.[9]
OLIVIA　　*[aside]*　O, what a deal of scorn looks beautiful
　　In the contempt and anger of his lip!
　　A murd'rous guilt shows not itself more soon
145　　Than love that would seem hid. Love's night is noon.—[1]
　　Cesario, by the roses of the spring,
　　By maidhood, honor, truth, and everything,
　　I love thee so, that, maugre° all thy pride,　　　*despite*
　　Nor° wit nor reason can my passion hide.　　　*neither*
150　　Do not extort thy reasons from this clause,
　　For that° I woo, thou therefore hast no cause;[2]　　　*that because*
　　But rather reason thus with reason fetter:[3]
　　Love sought is good, but given unsought is better.
VIOLA　　By innocence I swear, and by my youth,
155　　I have one heart, one bosom, and one truth,

2. Veil of transparent silken gauze; the cypress tree was also emblematic of mourning.
3. Time to discard love's melancholy.
4. I.e., if I had to fall prey to love, it would have been better to succumb to the noble Orsino than to the hardhearted Cesario.
5. Thames watermen's cry to attract London passengers for the court at Westminster.
6. Olivia changes from "you" to the familiar "thou."
7. That you think you are in love with a man, but you are mistaken.

8. Olivia may think that Cesario has suggested that she is mad; or she may imply that she thinks that Cesario, despite his subordinate position, is noble.
9. You have made a fool of me.
1. Love, though attempting secrecy, still shines out as bright as day.
2. Do not take the position that just because I woo you, you are under no obligation to reciprocate.
3. But instead constrain your reasoning with this argument.

And that no woman has, nor never none
Shall mistress be of it, save I alone.
And so adieu, good madam. Nevermore
Will I my master's tears to you deplore.°   *lament*
160 OLIVIA   Yet come again, for thou perhaps mayst move
That heart, which now abhors, to like his love.

Exeunt [severally]

3.2

Enter SIR TOBY, SIR ANDREW, *and* FABIAN

SIR ANDREW   No, faith, I'll not stay a jot longer.

SIR TOBY   Thy reason, dear venom,° give thy reason.   *venomous one*

FABIAN   You must needs yield your reason, Sir Andrew.

SIR ANDREW   Marry, I saw your niece do more favors to
5   the Count's servingman than ever she bestowed upon me.
I saw't i' th' orchard.°   *garden*

SIR TOBY   Did she see thee the while,° old boy? Tell me that.   *meanwhile*

SIR ANDREW   As plain as I see you now.

FABIAN   This was a great argument° of love in her toward   *proof*
10   you.

SIR ANDREW   'Slight,° will you make an ass o' me?   *by God's light*

FABIAN   I will prove it legitimate, sir, upon the oaths of
judgment and reason.

SIR TOBY   And they have been grand-jurymen[1] since before
15   Noah was a sailor.

FABIAN   She did show favor to the youth in your sight only
to exasperate you, to awake your dormouse° valor, to put   *meek, timid*
fire in your heart and brimstone in your liver. You should
then have accosted her, and with some excellent jests,
20   fire-new from the mint,° you should have banged the   *newly minted*
youth into dumbness. This was looked for at your hand,
and this was balked.° The double gilt[2] of this opportunity   *neglected*
you let time wash off, and you are now sailed into the
north of my lady's opinion,[3] where you will hang like an
25   icicle on a Dutchman's[4] beard, unless you do redeem it
by some laudable attempt either of valor or policy.°   *cunning*

SIR ANDREW   An't° be any way, it must be with valor, for   *if it*
policy I hate. I had as lief° be a Brownist as a politician.[5]   *as soon*

SIR TOBY   Why then, build me thy fortunes upon the basis
30   of valor. Challenge me° the Count's youth to fight with   *for me*
him. Hurt him in eleven places. My niece shall take note
of it, and assure thyself, there is no love-broker in the
world can more prevail in man's commendation with
woman than report of valor.

3.2 Location: Olivia's house.
1. Grand-jurymen were supposed to be good judges of evidence.
2. Twice gilded, and as such, Sir Andrew's "golden opportunity" to prove both love and valor.
3. Into Olivia's cold disfavor.
4. Perhaps an allusion to William Barentz, who led an expedition to the Arctic in 1596–97.
5. Schemer. A Brownist was a member of the Puritan sect founded in 1581 by Robert Browne.

35 FABIAN There is no way but this, Sir Andrew.

SIR ANDREW Will either of you bear me a challenge to him?

SIR TOBY Go, write it in a martial hand. Be curst° and brief.   *sharp*
It is no matter how witty, so it be eloquent and full of
invention. Taunt him with the license of ink.[6] If thou
40 "thou'st"[7] him some thrice, it shall not be amiss, and as
many lies[8] as will lie in thy sheet of paper, although the
sheet were big enough for the bed of Ware[9] in England,
set 'em down. Go, about it. Let there be gall[1] enough in
thy ink, though thou write with a goose-pen,[2] no matter.
45 About it.

SIR ANDREW Where shall I find you?

SIR TOBY We'll call thee at the cubiculo.° Go.   *little chamber*

Exit SIR ANDREW

FABIAN This is a dear manikin° to you, Sir Toby.   *puppet*

SIR TOBY I have been dear° to him, lad, some two thousand   *costly*
50 strong, or so.

FABIAN We shall have a rare letter from him. But you'll not
deliver't?

SIR TOBY Never trust me, then. And by all means stir on
the youth to an answer. I think oxen and wainropes[3]
55 cannot hale° them together. For Andrew, if he were opened   *drag*
and you find so much blood in his liver[4] as will clog° the   *weigh down*
foot of a flea, I'll eat the rest of th' anatomy.°   *cadaver*

FABIAN And his opposite,° the youth, bears in his visage   *adversary*
no great presage of cruelty.

Enter MARIA

60 SIR TOBY Look where the youngest wren of nine[5] comes.

MARIA If you desire the spleen,° and will laugh yourselves   *a laughing fit*
into stitches, follow me. Yond gull° Malvolio is turned hea-   *dupe*
then, a very renegado;[6] for there is no Christian that
means to be saved by believing rightly can ever believe
65 such impossible passages of grossness.[7] He's in yellow
stockings.

SIR TOBY And cross-gartered?

MARIA Most villainously,° like a pedant[8] that keeps a   *abominably*
school i' th' church.[9] I have dogged him like his murderer.
70 He does obey every point of the letter that I dropped to
betray him. He does smile his face into more lines than
is in the new map with the augmentation of the Indies.[1]

---

6. I.e., with the freedom taken in writing but not risked in conversation. "Invention": imagination; untruth.
7. Call him "thou" (an insult, to a stranger).
8. Accusations of lying.
9. Famous Elizabethan bedstead, nearly eleven feet square, now in the Victoria and Albert Museum, London.
1. (1) Oak gall, an ingredient in ink; (2) bitterness or rancor.
2. Quill made of a goose feather. (The goose was proverbially cowardly and foolish.)
3. Wagon ropes pulled by oxen.

4. Supposed to be the source of blood, which engendered courage.
5. The smallest of small birds; the smallest wren in a family of nine.
6. Renegade (Spanish); a Christian converted to Islam.
7. Such patent absurdities (in the letter).
8. Teacher.
9. Because no schoolroom is available in a small rustic community.
1. Possibly refers to a map published in 1599 showing the East Indies more fully than in earlier maps and crisscrossed by many rhumb lines.

You have not seen such a thing as 'tis. I can hardly forbear
hurling things at him. I know my lady will strike him. If
75 she do, he'll smile and take't for a great favor.
SIR TOBY Come, bring us, bring us where he is.   *Exeunt*

                              3.3

          Enter SEBASTIAN *and* ANTONIO
SEBASTIAN   I would not by my will have troubled you,
     But, since you make your pleasure of your pains,
     I will no further chide you.
ANTONIO   I could not stay behind you. My desire,
5   More sharp than filèd steel, did spur me forth;
     And not all° love to see you—though so much   only
     As might have drawn one to a longer voyage—
     But jealousy° what might befall your travel,   apprehension
     Being skill-less in° these parts, which to a stranger,   unfamiliar to
10   Unguided and unfriended, often prove
     Rough and unhospitable. My willing love,
     The rather° by these arguments of fear,   more willingly
     Set forth in your pursuit.
SEBASTIAN   My kind Antonio,
     I can no other answer make but thanks,
15   And thanks, and ever [thanks; and] oft° good turns   very often
     Are shuffled off° with such uncurrent[1] pay.   shrugged off
     But were my worth, as is my conscience,° firm,   sense of indebtedness
     You should find better dealing. What's to do?
     Shall we go see the relics° of this town?   sights
20   ANTONIO   Tomorrow, sir. Best first go see your lodging.
SEBASTIAN   I am not weary, and 'tis long to night.
     I pray you let us satisfy our eyes
     With the memorials and the things of fame
     That do renown this city.
ANTONIO   Would you'd pardon me.
25   I do not without danger walk these streets.
     Once in a sea fight 'gainst the Count his° galleys   i.e., the Count's
     I did some service, of such note indeed
     That were I ta'en° here it would scarce be answered.[2]   captured
SEBASTIAN   Belike° you slew great number of his people?   perhaps
30   ANTONIO   Th' offense is not of such a bloody nature,
     Albeit° the quality° of the time and quarrel   although / circumstances
     Might well have given us bloody argument.°   cause for bloodshed
     It might have since been answered in repaying
     What we took from them, which, for traffic's° sake,   trade's
35   Most of our city did. Only myself stood out,
     For which if I be latchèd° in this place,   caught
     I shall pay dear.

3.3 Location: A street scene.
1. Out of currency; worthless. The interpolation
in the preceding line conjecturally fills out its

deficient sense and meter.
2. It would be difficult for me to make reparation (and thus my life would be in danger).

SEBASTIAN   Do not then walk too open.

ANTONIO   It doth not fit me. Hold, sir, here's my purse.
In the south suburbs at the Elephant°   *name of an inn*
40   Is best to lodge. I will bespeak our diet°   *order our meals*
Whiles you beguile° the time and feed your knowledge   *pass*
With viewing of the town. There shall you have me.

SEBASTIAN   Why I your purse?

ANTONIO   Haply° your eye shall light upon some toy°   *perhaps / trifle*
45   You have desire to purchase, and your store,°   *resources*
I think, is not for idle markets,³ sir.

SEBASTIAN   I'll be your purse-bearer and leave you
For an hour.

ANTONIO   To th' Elephant.

SEBASTIAN   I do remember.

Exeunt [severally]

3.4

Enter OLIVIA *and* MARIA

OLIVIA *[aside]*   I have sent after him. He says he'll come.
How shall I feast him? What bestow of° him?   *on*
For youth is bought more oft than begged or borrowed.¹
I speak too loud.—
5   *[To* MARIA*]*   Where's Malvolio? He is sad° and civil°   *sober / respectful*
And suits well for a servant with my fortunes.
Where is Malvolio?

MARIA   He's coming, madam, but in very strange manner.
He is sure possessed,° madam.   *(by the devil); insane*

10   OLIVIA   Why, what's the matter? Does he rave?

MARIA   No, madam, he does nothing but smile. Your ladyship were best to have some guard about you if he come,
for sure the man is tainted in's wits.

OLIVIA   Go call him hither.   *[Exit* MARIA*]*
I am as mad as he,
15   If sad and merry madness equal be.

*Enter [*MARIA *with]* MALVOLIO *[cross-gartered and
wearing yellow stockings]*

How now, Malvolio?

MALVOLIO   Sweet lady, ho, ho!

OLIVIA   Smil'st thou? I sent for thee upon a sad occasion.°   *a serious matter*

MALVOLIO   Sad, lady? I could be sad. This does make some
20   obstruction in the blood, this cross-gartering, but what
of that? If it please the eye of one, it is with me as the
very true sonnet° is: "Please one, and please all."²   *song*

OLIVIA   Why, how dost thou, man? What is the matter with
thee?

---

3. Not large enough to spend on luxuries.
3.4 Location: The garden of Olivia's house.
1. "Better to buy than to beg or borrow" was

proverbial.
2. If I please one, I please all I care to please
(words of a popular bawdy ballad).

25 MALVOLIO Not black in my mind, though yellow[3] in my
legs. It did come to his hands, and commands shall be
executed. I think we do know the sweet Roman hand.°   *italic calligraphy*

OLIVIA Wilt thou go to bed,[4] Malvolio?

MALVOLIO [*kissing his hand*] To bed? "Ay, sweetheart,
30 and I'll come to thee."[5]

OLIVIA God comfort thee! Why dost thou smile so, and kiss
thy hand so oft?

MARIA How do you, Malvolio?

MALVOLIO At your request? Yes, nightingales answer daws![6]

35 MARIA Why appear you with this ridiculous boldness
before my lady?

MALVOLIO "Be not afraid of greatness." 'Twas well writ.

OLIVIA What meanest thou by that, Malvolio?

MALVOLIO "Some are born great"—

40 OLIVIA Ha?

MALVOLIO "Some achieve greatness"—

OLIVIA What sayst thou?

MALVOLIO "And some have greatness thrust upon them."

OLIVIA Heaven restore thee!

45 MALVOLIO "Remember who commended thy yellow stockings"—

OLIVIA Thy yellow stockings?

MALVOLIO "And wished to see thee cross-gartered."

OLIVIA Cross-gartered?

50 MALVOLIO "Go to, thou art made, if thou desirest to be
so"—

OLIVIA Am I made?

MALVOLIO "If not, let me see thee a servant still."

OLIVIA Why, this is very midsummer° madness!   *the height of*
      Enter a SERVANT

55 SERVANT Madam, the young gentleman of the Count
Orsino's is returned. I could hardly entreat him back.
He attends your ladyship's pleasure.

OLIVIA I'll come to him.   [*Exit* SERVANT]
Good Maria, let this fellow be looked to. Where's my
60 cousin Toby? Let some of my people have a special care
of him. I would not have him miscarry° for the half of my   *come to harm*
dowry.

      [*Exeunt* OLIVIA *and* MARIA, *severally*]

MALVOLIO O ho, do you come near° me now? No worse   *appreciate*
man than Sir Toby to look to me. This concurs directly
65 with the letter. She sends him on purpose that I may
appear stubborn to him, for she incites me to that in the

---

3. Black and yellow biles indicated choleric and
melancholic dispositions, respectively. "Black and
yellow" was the name of a popular song; to "wear
yellow hose" was to be jealous.
4. In order to cure his madness with sleep.

5. A line from a popular song.
6. Shall I deign to reply to you? Yes, since even
the nightingale sings in response to the crowing
of the jackdaw.

letter: "Cast thy humble slough," says she. "Be opposite
with a kinsman, surly with servants; let thy tongue tang
with arguments of state; put thyself into the trick of sin-
70 gularity," and consequently° sets down the manner how: *subsequently*
as, a sad face, a reverend carriage, a slow tongue, in the
habit of some sir of note,° and so forth. I have limed[7] her,   *gentleman*
but it is Jove's doing, and Jove make me thankful! And
when she went away now, "Let this fellow be looked to."
75 "Fellow."[8] Not "Malvolio," nor after my degree, but "fellow." Why, everything adheres together, that no dram of a
scruple, no scruple of a scruple,[9] no obstacle, no incredulous or unsafe circumstance—what can be said? Nothing that can be can come between me and the full
80 prospect of my hopes. Well, Jove, not I, is the doer of
this, and he is to be thanked.
           Enter SIR TOBY, FABIAN, *and* MARIA
SIR TOBY   Which way is he, in the name of sanctity? If all
     the devils of hell be drawn in little,[1] and Legion[2] himself
     possessed him, yet I'll speak to him.
85 FABIAN   Here he is, here he is.—How is't with you, sir?
     How is't with you, man?
MALVOLIO   Go off, I discard you. Let me enjoy my private.°   *privacy*
     Go off.
MARIA [*to* SIR TOBY]   Lo, how hollow° the fiend speaks   *resonantly*
90   within him! Did not I tell you? Sir Toby, my lady prays
     you to have a care of him.
MALVOLIO   Aha, does she so?
SIR TOBY   Go to, go to! Peace, peace. We must deal gently
     with him. Let me alone.°—How do you, Malvolio? How   *leave him to me*
95   is't with you? What, man, defy° the devil! Consider, he's   *renounce*
     an enemy to mankind.
MALVOLIO   Do you know what you say?
MARIA   La° you, an you speak ill of the devil, how he takes   *look*
     it at heart! Pray God he be not bewitched!
100 FABIAN   Carry his water to th' wise woman.[3]
MARIA   Marry, and it shall be done tomorrow morning if I
     live. My lady would not lose him for more than I'll say.
MALVOLIO   How now, mistress?
MARIA   O Lord!
105 SIR TOBY   Prithee, hold thy peace. This is not the way. Do
     you not see you move° him? Let me alone with him.   *anger*
FABIAN   No way but gentleness, gently, gently. The fiend is
     rough° and will not be roughly used.   *violent*

---

7. Birds were caught by smearing sticky birdlime
on branches.
8. Malvolio takes the word to mean "companion."
9. Both phrases mean "no scrap of a doubt."
"Dram": one-eighth of a fluid ounce. "Scruple":
one-third of a dram.
1. Be contracted into a small space (punning on
"painted in miniature").

2. Alluding to a scene of exorcism in Mark 5.8–
9: "For he [Jesus] said unto him, Come out of the
man, thou unclean spirit. And he asked him,
What is thy name? And he answered saying, My
name is Legion: for we are many."
3. Local healer, "good witch." "Water": urine (for
medical diagnosis).

SIR TOBY   Why, how now, my bawcock? How dost thou, chuck?[4]

MALVOLIO   Sir!

SIR TOBY   Ay, biddy,° come with me.—What, man, 'tis not for gravity to play at cherry-pit[5] with Satan. Hang him, foul collier![6]   *hen*

MARIA   Get him to say his prayers, good Sir Toby; get him to pray.

MALVOLIO   My prayers, minx?°   *impertinent girl*

MARIA   No, I warrant you, he will not hear of godliness.

MALVOLIO   Go hang yourselves all! You are idle,° shallow things. I am not of your element.° You shall know more hereafter.   *foolish* · *social sphere*   *Exit*

SIR TOBY   Is't possible?

FABIAN   If this were played upon a stage now, I could condemn it as an improbable fiction.

SIR TOBY   His very genius° hath taken the infection of the device,° man.   *spirit* · *trick*

MARIA   Nay, pursue him now, lest the device take air and taint.[7]

FABIAN   Why, we shall make him mad indeed.

MARIA   The house will be the quieter.

SIR TOBY   Come, we'll have him in a dark room and bound.[8] My niece is already in the belief that he's mad. We may carry it thus,[9] for our pleasure and his penance, till our very pastime, tired out of breath, prompt us to have mercy on him, at which time we will bring the device to the bar[1] and crown thee for a finder of madmen.[2] But see, but see!

Enter SIR ANDREW

FABIAN   More matter for a May morning.[3]

SIR ANDREW   [*presenting a paper*]   Here's the challenge. Read it. I warrant there's vinegar and pepper in't.

FABIAN   Is't so saucy?

SIR ANDREW   Ay, is't? I warrant him. Do but read.

SIR TOBY   Give me. [*He reads.*] "Youth, whatsoever thou art, thou art but a scurvy fellow."

FABIAN   Good, and valiant.

SIR TOBY,   "Wonder not, nor admire° not in thy mind, why I do call thee so, for I will show thee no reason for't."   *marvel*

FABIAN   A good note, that keeps you from the blow of the law.[4]

4. A term of endearment, perhaps from *chick, chicken.* "Bawcock": fine fellow (from the French *beau coq,* "fine bird").
5. A children's game in which cherry stones were thrown into a hole. "For gravity": i.e., for a man of dignity.
6. Dirty coalman (the devil was supposed to be black).
7. Spoil (like leftover food) by exposure to air; become known (and thus ruined).
8. Customary treatments for madness.
9. Continue the pretense.
1. Into the open court (to be judged).
2. I.e., one of a jury "finding," or declaring, a man to be mad.
3. More pastime fit for a holiday.
4. That protects you from a charge of a breach of peace.

SIR TOBY   "Thou comest to the Lady Olivia, and in my sight
150   she uses thee kindly. But thou liest in thy throat;° that is   *deeply*
       not the matter I challenge thee for."
FABIAN   Very brief, and to exceeding good sense—
       less.[5]
SIR TOBY   "I will waylay thee going home, where if it be thy
155   chance to kill me"—
FABIAN   Good.
SIR TOBY   "Thou killest me like a rogue and a villain."
FABIAN   Still you keep o' th' windy side[6] of the law. Good.
SIR TOBY   "Fare thee well, and God have mercy upon one
160   of our souls. He may have mercy upon mine, but my hope
       is better,[7] and so look to thyself. Thy friend, as thou
       usest him, and thy sworn enemy,

                                   Andrew Aguecheek."
       If this letter move° him not, his legs cannot. I'll give't him.   *provoke*
165 MARIA   You may have very fit occasion for't. He is now in
       some commerce° with my lady, and will by and by depart.   *conversation*
SIR TOBY   Go, Sir Andrew. Scout me° for him at the corner   *look out*
       of the orchard like a bum-baily.[8] So soon as ever thou
       seest him, draw, and as thou drawest, swear horrible, for
170   it comes to pass oft that a terrible oath, with a swaggering
       accent sharply twanged off, gives manhood more appro-
       bation° than ever proof° itself would have earned him.   *credit / trial*
       Away!
SIR ANDREW   Nay, let me alone for swearing.[9]   *Exit*
175 SIR TOBY   Now will not I deliver his letter, for the behavior
       of the young gentleman gives him out to be of good
       capacity and breeding;[1] his employment between his
       lord and my niece confirms no less. Therefore, this let-
       ter, being so excellently ignorant, will breed no terror in
180   the youth. He will find it comes from a clodpoll.° But,   *blockhead*
       sir, I will deliver his challenge by word of mouth, set
       upon Aguecheek a notable report of valor, and drive
       the gentleman—as I know his youth will aptly receive
       it[2]—into a most hideous opinion of his rage, skill, fury,
185   and impetuosity. This will so fright them both that they
       will kill one another by the look, like cockatrices.[3]
            Enter OLIVIA *and* VIOLA
FABIAN   Here he comes with your niece. Give them way°   *stand aside*
       till he take leave, and presently after him.
SIR TOBY   I will meditate the while upon some horrid mes-
190   sage for a challenge.
            [*Exeunt* SIR TOBY, FABIAN, *and* MARIA]

5. The Folio's "sence-lesse" appears to use the
hyphen to signal an aside.
6. Downwind of the law—on the safe side of it.
7. Andrew means he expects to survive, but he
ineptly implies that he expects to be damned.
8. Petty sheriff's officer employed to arrest debtors.

9. Have no doubts as to my swearing ability.
1. Upbringing. "Capacity": ability.
2. As I know his inexperience will readily believe
the report.
3. Basilisks: mythical creatures supposed to kill
at a glance.

OLIVIA   I have said too much unto a heart of stone
And laid mine honor too unchary° on't.   *carelessly*
There's something in me that reproves my fault,
But such a headstrong potent fault it is
195   That it but mocks reproof.
VIOLA   With the same 'havior that your passion bears[4]
Goes on my master's griefs.
OLIVIA   Here, wear this jewel[5] for me. 'Tis my picture.
Refuse it not, it hath no tongue to vex you.
200   And I beseech you come again tomorrow.
What shall you ask of me that I'll deny,
That honor, saved, may upon asking give?[6]
VIOLA   Nothing but this: your true love for my master.
OLIVIA   How with mine honor may I give him that
Which I have given to you?
205   VIOLA   I will acquit you.[7]
OLIVIA   Well, come again tomorrow. Fare thee well.
A fiend like thee might bear my soul to hell.   [*Exit*]
           Enter [SIR] TOBY *and* FABIAN
SIR TOBY   Gentleman, God save thee.
VIOLA   And you, sir.
210   SIR TOBY   That defense thou hast, betake thee to't. Of what
nature the wrongs are thou hast done him, I know not,
but thy intercepter, full of despite,° bloody as the hunter,   *defiance*
attends° thee at the orchard end. Dismount thy tuck,[8] be   *awaits*
yare° in thy preparation, for thy assailant is quick, skillful,   *prompt*
215   and deadly.
VIOLA   You mistake, sir, I am sure no man hath any quarrel
to me. My remembrance° is very free and clear from any   *memory*
image of offense done to any man.
SIR TOBY   You'll find it otherwise, I assure you. Therefore,
220   if you hold your life at any price, betake you to your guard,
for your opposite° hath in him what youth, strength, skill,   *opponent*
and wrath can furnish man withal.
VIOLA   I pray you, sir, what is he?
SIR TOBY   He is knight dubbed with unhatched[9] rapier and
225   on carpet consideration,[1] but he is a devil in private
brawl. Souls and bodies hath he divorced three, and his
incensement at this moment is so implacable that satisfaction can be none but by pangs of death and sepulcher.
"Hob, nob"[2] is his word;° "give't or take't."   *motto*
230   VIOLA   I will return again into the house and desire some
conduct° of the lady. I am no fighter. I have heard of some   *escort*
kind of men that put quarrels purposely on others, to
taste° their valor. Belike this is a man of that quirk.   *test*

---

4. Behavior that characterizes your lovesickness.
5. Jeweled ornament, here a brooch or a locket
with Olivia's picture.
6. That honor may grant without compromising
itself.
7. I will release you from your promise.

8. Draw your rapier.
9. Unhacked, or undented, never used in battle.
1. A "carpet knight" obtained his title through
connections at court rather than valor on the
battlefield.
2. Have or have not ("all or nothing").

SIR TOBY   Sir, no. His indignation derives itself out of a very
235   competent° injury. Therefore get you on and give him his   *sufficient*
        desire. Back you shall not to the house, unless you under-
        take that° with me which with as much safety you might   *i.e., a duel*
        answer him. Therefore on, or strip your sword stark
        naked, for meddle° you must, that's certain, or forswear   *engage in a duel*
240   to wear iron about you.[3]

VIOLA   This is as uncivil as strange. I beseech you, do me
        this courteous office, as to know of° the knight what my   *ascertain from*
        offense to him is. It is something of my negligence, noth-
        ing of my purpose.

245   SIR TOBY   I will do so.—Signior Fabian, stay you by this
        gentleman till my return.   *Exit*

VIOLA   Pray you, sir, do you know of this matter?

FABIAN   I know the knight is incensed against you even to
        a mortal arbitrement,° but nothing of the circumstance   *deadly duel*
250   more.

VIOLA   I beseech you, what manner of man is he?

FABIAN   Nothing of that wonderful promise, to read him by
        his form,[4] as you are like to find him in the proof° of his   *experience*
        valor. He is indeed, sir, the most skillful, bloody, and fatal
255   opposite° that you could possibly have found in any part   *opponent*
        of Illyria. Will you° walk towards him, I will make your   *if you will*
        peace with him if I can.

VIOLA   I shall be much bound to you for't. I am one that
        had rather go with Sir Priest[5] than Sir Knight, I care not
260   who knows so much of my mettle.°   *Exeunt*   *disposition*
                Enter SIR TOBY *and* SIR ANDREW

SIR TOBY   Why, man, he's a very devil. I have not seen such
        a virago.[6] I had a pass° with him, rapier, scabbard, and   *fencing bout*
        all, and he gives me the stuck-in[7] with such a mortal
        motion that it is inevitable; and on the answer,° he pays   *return hit*
265   you as surely as your feet hits the ground they step on.
        They say he has been fencer to the Sophy.°   *shah of Persia*

SIR ANDREW   Pox on't! I'll not meddle with him.

SIR TOBY   Ay, but he will not now be pacified. Fabian can
        scarce hold him yonder.

270   SIR ANDREW   Plague on't! An° I thought he had been val-   *if*
        iant and so cunning in fence, I'd have seen him damned
        ere I'd have challenged him. Let him let the matter slip,
        and I'll give him my horse, gray Capilet.

SIR TOBY   I'll make the motion.° Stand here, make a good   *offer*
275   show on't. This shall end without the perdition of souls.°   *loss of lives*
        [*aside*] Marry, I'll ride your horse as well as I ride you.
                Enter FABIAN *and* VIOLA

---

3. Or forfeit your right to wear a sword.
4. I.e., from his outward appearance, you cannot perceive him to be as remarkable.
5. Priests were often addressed as "sir."

6. Woman warrior (suggesting great ferocity with
a feminine appearance).
7. Thrust (from the Italian *stoccata*).

[*aside to* FABIAN] I have his horse to take up° the quarrel. I   *settle*
have persuaded him the youth's a devil.

FABIAN [*aside to* SIR TOBY] He is as horribly conceited[8] of
280   him, and pants and looks pale as if a bear were at his heels.

SIR TOBY [*to* VIOLA] There's no remedy, sir; he will fight
with you for's oath' sake. Marry, he hath better bethought
him of his quarrel, and he finds that now scarce to be
worth talking of. Therefore, draw for the supportance of
285   his vow. He protests he will not hurt you.

VIOLA [*aside*] Pray God defend me. A little thing would
make me tell them how much I lack of a man.

FABIAN [*to* SIR ANDREW] Give ground if you see him furious.

SIR TOBY Come, Sir Andrew, there's no remedy. The gen-
290   tleman will, for his honor's sake, have one bout with
you. He cannot by the duello° avoid it. But he has prom-   *code of dueling*
ised me, as he is a gentleman and a soldier, he will not
hurt you. Come on, to't.

SIR ANDREW [*drawing his sword*] Pray God he keep his oath.
295 VIOLA [*drawing his sword*] I do assure you, 'tis against my
will.

      Enter ANTONIO

ANTONIO [*to* SIR ANDREW] Put up your sword. If this
    young gentleman
Have done offense, I take the fault on me.
If you offend him, I for him defy you.

SIR TOBY You, sir? Why, what are you?
300 ANTONIO [*drawing his sword*] One, sir, that for his love dares
    yet do more
Than you have heard him brag to you he will.

SIR TOBY [*drawing his sword*] Nay, if you be an under-
taker,[9] I am for you.

      Enter OFFICERS

FABIAN O, good Sir Toby, hold. Here come the officers.
305 SIR TOBY [*to* ANTONIO] I'll be with you anon.

VIOLA [*to* SIR ANDREW] Pray, sir, put your sword up, if you
please.

SIR ANDREW Marry, will I, sir. And for that° I promised you,   *as for that*
I'll be as good as my word. He will bear you easily, and
310   reins well.

      [SIR ANDREW *and* VIOLA *put up their swords.*]

FIRST OFFICER This is the man. Do thy office.

SECOND OFFICER Antonio, I arrest thee at the suit of
Count Orsino.

ANTONIO You do mistake me, sir.

FIRST OFFICER No, sir, no jot. I know your favor° well,   *face*
315   Though now you have no sea-cap on your head.—
Take him away. He knows I know him well.

ANTONIO I must obey. [*to* VIOLA] This comes with seeking you.

---

8. He has as terrifying an idea.
9. One who would take upon himself a task (here, a challenge).

But there's no remedy. I shall answer° it.   *answer for*
What will you do, now my necessity
320   Makes me to ask you for my purse? It grieves me
Much more for what I cannot do for you
Than what befalls myself. You stand amazed,
But be of comfort.
SECOND OFFICER   Come, sir, away.
ANTONIO [*to* VIOLA]   I must entreat of you some of that money.
325   VIOLA   What money, sir?
For the fair kindness you have showed me here,
And part° being prompted by your present trouble,   *in part*
Out of my lean and low ability
I'll lend you something. My having is not much.
330   I'll make division of my present° with you.   *ready money*
Hold, there's half my coffer. [*offering him money*]
ANTONIO   Will you deny me now?
Is't possible that my deserts to you
Can lack persuasion?[1] Do not tempt my misery,
Lest that it make me so unsound° a man   *morally weak*
335   As to upbraid you with those kindnesses
That I have done for you.
VIOLA   I know of none,
Nor know I you by voice or any feature.
I hate ingratitude more in a man
Than lying, vainness, babbling drunkenness,
340   Or any taint of vice whose strong corruption
Inhabits our frail blood—
ANTONIO   O heavens themselves!
SECOND OFFICER   Come, sir, I pray you go.
ANTONIO   Let me speak a little. This youth that you see here
I snatched one half out of the jaws of death,
345   Relieved him with such sanctity° of love,   *great devotion*
And to his image,[2] which methought did promise
Most venerable worth,[3] did I devotion.
FIRST OFFICER   What's that to us? The time goes by. Away!
ANTONIO   But O, how vile an idol proves this god!
350   Thou hast, Sebastian, done good feature° shame.   *physical beauty*
In nature there's no blemish but the mind;
None can be called deformed but the unkind.
Virtue is beauty, but the beauteous evil
Are empty trunks o'er-flourished[4] by the devil.
355   FIRST OFFICER   The man grows mad. Away with him.—
Come, come, sir.
ANTONIO   Lead me on.   *Exit* [*with* OFFICERS]
VIOLA [*aside*]   Methinks his words do from such passion fly
That he believes himself; so do not I.[5]

---

1. Is it possible my past kindness can fail to persuade you?
2. Appearance (with a play on "religious icon").
3. Was worthy of veneration.

4. Chests decorated with carving or painting;
beautified bodies.
5. I.e., I do not entirely believe the passionate
hope (for my brother's rescue) that is arising in me.

Prove true, imagination, O, prove true,
360   That I, dear brother, be now ta'en for you!
SIR TOBY   Come hither, knight; come hither, Fabian. We'll
   whisper o'er a couplet or two of most sage saws.°   *sayings, maxims*
   [SIR TOBY, FABIAN, *and* SIR ANDREW *move aside.*]
VIOLA   He named Sebastian. I my brother know
   Yet living in my glass.° Even such and so   *mirror*
365   In favor° was my brother, and he went   *appearance*
   Still° in this fashion, color, ornament,   *always*
   For him I imitate. O, if it prove,
   Tempests are kind, and salt waves fresh in love!   *Exit*
SIR TOBY   A very dishonest,° paltry boy, and more a coward   *dishonorable*
370   than a hare. His dishonesty appears in leaving his friend
   here in necessity, and denying him; and for his coward-
   ship, ask Fabian.
FABIAN   A coward, a most devout coward, religious in it.
SIR ANDREW   'Slid,° I'll after him again and beat him.   *by God's eyelid*
375 SIR TOBY   Do, cuff him soundly, but never draw thy sword.
SIR ANDREW   An I do not—   [*Exit*]
FABIAN   Come, let's see the event.°   *outcome*
SIR TOBY   I dare lay any money 'twill be nothing yet.°   *after all*
                                             Exeunt

4.1

Enter SEBASTIAN *and* [FESTE, *the*] *clown*
FESTE   Will you° make me believe that I am not sent for   *are you trying to*
   you?
SEBASTIAN   Go to, go to, thou art a foolish fellow.
   Let me be clear° of thee.   *rid*
5 FESTE   Well held out,° i' faith. No, I do not know you, nor   *kept up*
   I am not sent to you by my lady to bid you come speak
   with her, nor your name is not Master Cesario, nor this
   is not my nose neither. Nothing that is so is so.
SEBASTIAN   I prithee, vent° thy folly somewhere else.   *utter; excrete*
10   Thou know'st not me.
FESTE   Vent my folly? He has heard that word of some
   great man and now applies it to a fool. Vent my folly? I
   am afraid this great lubber° the world will prove a cock-   *lout*
   ney.[1] I prithee now, ungird thy strangeness[2] and tell me
15   what I shall vent to my lady. Shall I vent to her that thou
   art coming?
SEBASTIAN   I prithee, foolish Greek,° depart from me.   *buffoon*
   There's money for thee. If you tarry longer,
   I shall give worse payment.
20 FESTE   By my troth, thou hast an open hand. These wise
   men that give fools money get themselves a good report—°   *reputation*
   after fourteen years' purchase.[3]

4.1 Location: Near Olivia's house.
1. A pampered child.
2. I.e., stop pretending not to know me. (Feste

mocks Sebastian's affected language.)
3. I.e., at a high price. The purchase price of
land was normally twelve times its annual rent.

Enter SIR ANDREW, SIR TOBY, *and* FABIAN

SIR ANDREW [*to* SEBASTIAN]   Now, sir, have I met you again?
[*striking him*] There's for you.

25 SEBASTIAN [*returning the blow*]   Why, there's for thee, and
there, and there.—Are all the people mad?

SIR TOBY   Hold, sir, or I'll throw your dagger o'er the house.

FESTE [*aside*]   This will I tell my lady straight.° I would   straightway
not be in some of your coats for twopence.   [*Exit*]

30 SIR TOBY [*seizing Sebastian*]   Come on, sir, hold!

SIR ANDREW   Nay, let him alone. I'll go another way to work
with him. I'll have an action of battery[4] against him, if
there be any law in Illyria. Though I struck him first,
yet it's no matter for that.

35 SEBASTIAN [*to* SIR TOBY]   Let go thy hand!

SIR TOBY   Come, sir, I will not let you go. Come, my young
soldier, put up your iron. You are well fleshed.[5] Come on.

SEBASTIAN   I will be free from thee.
[*He pulls free and draws his sword.*]
                                 What wouldst thou now?
If thou dar'st tempt me further, draw thy sword.

40 SIR TOBY   What, what? Nay, then, I must have an ounce or
two of this malapert° blood from you.   impudent
[*He draws his sword.*]
          Enter OLIVIA

OLIVIA   Hold, Toby! On thy life I charge thee, hold!

SIR TOBY   Madam.

OLIVIA   Will it be ever thus? Ungracious wretch,
45 Fit for the mountains and the barbarous caves,
Where manners ne'er were preached! Out of my sight!—
Be not offended, dear Cesario.—
Rudesby,° be gone!   ruffian
          [*Exeunt* SIR TOBY, SIR ANDREW, *and* FABIAN]
                    I prithee, gentle friend,
Let thy fair wisdom, not thy passion, sway
50 In this uncivil and unjust extent°   assault
Against thy peace. Go with me to my house,
And hear thou there how many fruitless pranks
This ruffian hath botched up,° that thou thereby   clumsily contrived
Mayst smile at this. Thou shalt not choose but go.
55 Do not deny. Beshrew° his soul for me!   curse
He started one poor heart of mine, in thee.[6]

SEBASTIAN [*aside*]   What relish° is in this? How runs the   task; meaning
stream?
Or° I am mad, or else this is a dream.   either
Let fancy° still my sense in Lethe[7] steep;   imagination
60 If it be thus to dream, still° let me sleep!   ever

---

4. Lawsuit for assault.
5. Experienced in combat. Hunting hounds were
said to be "fleshed" after being fed part of their
first kill.
6. By attacking Sebastian, Sir Toby frightened

Olivia, who has exchanged hearts with Sebastian. "Started": an allusion to hunting, creating a
pun on "hart/heart."
7. The mythical river of oblivion.

OLIVIA   Nay, come, I prithee. Would thou'dst be ruled by me!
SEBASTIAN   Madam, I will.
OLIVIA   O, say so, and so be!   *Exeunt*

4.2

Enter MARIA *and* [FESTE, *the*] *clown*

MARIA   Nay, I prithee, put on this gown and this beard;
make him believe thou art Sir Topas[1] the curate. Do it
quickly. I'll call Sir Toby the whilst.°   [*Exit*]   *in the meantime*

FESTE   Well, I'll put it on, and I will dissemble[2] myself in't,
5   and I would I were the first that ever dissembled in such
a gown. [*He puts on gown and beard.*] I am not tall enough
to become the function well,[3] nor lean enough to be
thought a good student, but to be said[4] an honest man
and a good housekeeper° goes as fairly as[5] to say a   *host*
10   careful man and a great scholar. The competitors° enter.   *associates*

Enter SIR TOBY [*and* MARIA]

SIR TOBY   Jove bless thee, Master Parson.

FESTE   *Bonos dies,*[6] Sir Toby; for, as the old hermit of
Prague, that never saw pen and ink, very wittily° said to   *intelligently*
a niece of King Gorboduc,[7] "That that is, is," so I, being
15   Master Parson, am Master Parson; for what is "that" but
"that" and "is" but "is"?

SIR TOBY   To him, Sir Topas.

FESTE [*disguising his voice*]   What ho, I say! Peace in this
prison!

20   SIR TOBY   The knave counterfeits well. A good knave.

MALVOLIO *within*

MALVOLIO   Who calls there?

FESTE   Sir Topas the curate, who comes to visit Malvolio
the lunatic.

MALVOLIO   Sir Topas, Sir Topas, good Sir Topas, go to my
25   lady—

FESTE   Out, hyperbolical fiend![8] How vexest thou this man!
Talkest thou nothing but of ladies?

SIR TOBY [*aside*]   Well said, Master Parson.

MALVOLIO   Sir Topas, never was man thus wronged. Good
30   Sir Topas, do not think I am mad. They have laid me here
in hideous darkness—

FESTE   Fie, thou dishonest Satan! I call thee by the most
modest° terms, for I am one of those gentle ones that will   *mildest*
use the devil himself with courtesy. Sayst thou that
35   house° is dark?   *room*

4.2 Location: Olivia's house, where Malvolio
will be found (offstage) "in a dark room and
bound" (3.4.131).
1. The comical hero of Chaucer's *Tale of Sir
Thopas*. Also alluding to the topaz stone, which
was thought to have special curative qualities for
insanity.
2. Disguise; with subsequent play on "lie."
3. Grace the priestly office. "Tall": stout, rather

than of great height.
4. Reputed. "A good student": i.e., a student of
divinity.
5. Sounds as well as.
6. Good day (false Latin).
7. Legendary British king. "Old hermit of
Prague": probably an invented authority.
8. Feste treats Malvolio as a man possessed by
vehement ("hyperbolical") evil spirits.

MALVOLIO As hell, Sir Topas.

FESTE Why, it hath bay windows transparent as barricadoes, and the clerestories[9] toward the south-north are as
lustrous as ebony;[1] and yet complainest thou of obstruc-
40 tion?

MALVOLIO I am not mad, Sir Topas. I say to you this house
is dark.

FESTE Madman, thou errest. I say there is no darkness but
ignorance, in which thou art more puzzled than the Egyp-
45 tians in their fog.[2]

MALVOLIO I say this house is as dark as ignorance, though
ignorance were as dark as hell. And I say there was never
man thus abused. I am no more mad than you are. Make
the trial of it in any constant question.° *logical discussion*

50 FESTE What is the opinion of Pythagoras[3] concerning
wildfowl?

MALVOLIA That the soul of our grandam might haply° *perhaps*
inhabit a bird.

FESTE What thinkest thou of his opinion?

55 MALVOLIO I think nobly of the soul, and no way approve
his opinion.

FESTE Fare thee well. Remain thou still in darkness. Thou
shalt hold th' opinion of Pythagoras ere I will allow of thy
wits,° and fear to kill a woodcock[4] lest thou dispossess *certify your sanity*
60 the soul of thy grandam. Fare thee well.

MALVOLIO Sir Topas, Sir Topas!

SIR TOBY My most exquisite Sir Topas!

FESTE Nay, I am for all waters.[5]

MARIA Thou mightst have done this without thy beard and
65 gown. He sees thee not.

SIR TOBY To him in thine own voice, and bring me word
how thou findest him. I would we were well rid of this
knavery. If he may be conveniently delivered, I would he
were, for I am now so far in offense with my niece that I
70 cannot pursue with any safety this sport to the upshot.
Come by and by to my chamber.

[*Exeunt* SIR TOBY *and* MARIA]

FESTE [*sings*][6] "Hey, Robin, jolly Robin,
Tell me how thy lady *does*."

MALVOLIO Fool!

75 FESTE [*sings*] "My lady is unkind, perdy."[7]

MALVOLIO Fool!

FESTE "Alas, why is she so?"

---

9. Upper windows, usually in a church or great
hall. "Barricadoes": barricades (subsequent paradoxes are equivalent to "as clear as mud").
1. A dense and naturally dull black wood.
2. One of the plagues of Egypt was a "black darkness" lasting for three days (Exodus 10.21–23).
3. The ancient Greek philosopher held that the
same soul could successively inhabit different

creatures.
4. A traditionally stupid bird.
5. I am able to turn my hand to anything.
6. Feste's song, which makes Malvolio aware of
his presence, is traditional. There is a version by
Sir Thomas Wyatt.
7. A corruption of the French *pardieu,* "by God."

MALVOLIO Fool, I say!

FESTE "She loves another"—

Who calls, ha?

80 MALVOLIO Good fool, as ever thou wilt deserve well at my
hand, help me to a candle, and pen, ink, and paper. As I
am a gentleman, I will live to be thankful to thee for't.

FESTE Master Malvolio?

MALVOLIO Ay, good fool.

85 FESTE Alas, sir, how fell you besides° your five wits?[8]   out of

MALVOLIO Fool, there was never man so notoriously°   outrageously
abused. I am as well in my wits, fool, as thou art.

FESTE But as well? Then you are mad indeed, if you be no
better in your wits than a fool.

90 MALVOLIO They have here propertied me,[9] keep me in
darkness, send ministers to me—asses!—and do all they
can to face me[1] out of my wits.

FESTE Advise you° what you say. The minister is here.   be careful
[as Sir Topas] Malvolio, Malvolio, thy wits the heavens
95 restore. Endeavor thyself to sleep and leave thy vain
bibble-babble.

MALVOLIO Sir Topas!

FESTE [as Sir Topas] Maintain no words with him, good
fellow. [as fool] Who, I, sir? Not I, sir. God buy you,° good   God be with you
100 Sir Topas. [as Sir Topas] Marry, amen. [as fool] I will, sir,
I will.

MALVOLIO Fool! Fool! Fool, I say!

FESTE Alas, sir, be patient. What say you, sir? I am shent°   scolded
for speaking to you.

105 MALVOLIO Good fool, help me to some light and some
paper. I tell thee, I am as well in my wits as any man in
Illyria.

FESTE Welladay° that you were, sir!   alas

MALVOLIO By this hand, I am. Good fool, some ink, paper,
110 and light; and convey what I will set down to my lady. It
shall advantage thee more than ever the bearing of letter
did.

FESTE I will help you to't. But tell me true, are you not
mad indeed, or do you but counterfeit?

115 MALVOLIO Believe me, I am not. I tell thee true.

FESTE Nay, I'll ne'er believe a madman till I see his brains.
I will fetch you light and paper and ink.

MALVOLIO Fool, I'll requite it in the highest degree. I
prithee, be gone.

120 FESTE [sings] I am gone, sir,
And anon, sir,
I'll be with you again,
In a trice,

8. Usually regarded as common sense, fantasy,   9. Treated me as a piece of property.
memory, judgment, and imagination.   1. Brazenly construe me as.

Like to the old Vice,[2]
125   Your need to sustain.
Who with dagger of lath,
In his rage and his wrath,
      Cries "aha!" to the devil;
Like a mad lad,
130   "Pare thy nails, dad!
      Adieu, goodman[3] devil."   *Exit*

4.3

Enter SEBASTIAN

SEBASTIAN   This is the air; that is the glorious sun.
This pearl she gave me, I do feel't and see't.
And though 'tis wonder that enwraps me thus,
Yet 'tis not madness. Where's Antonio, then?
5   I could not find him at the Elephant.
Yet there he was;° and there I found this credit,°   *had been / report*
That he did range the town to seek me out.
His counsel now might do me golden service.
For though my soul disputes well with my sense[1]
10   That this may be some error, but no madness,
Yet doth this accident and flood of fortune
So far exceed all instance,° all discourse,°   *precedent / reasoning*
That I am ready to distrust mine eyes
And wrangle with my reason that persuades me
15   To any other trust° but that I am mad—   *belief*
Or else the lady's mad. Yet if 'twere so,
She could not sway° her house, command her followers,   *rule*
Take and give back affairs and their dispatch[2]
With such a smooth, discreet, and stable bearing
20   As I perceive she does. There's something in't
That is deceivable.° But here the lady comes.   *deceptive*

Enter OLIVIA *and* PRIEST

OLIVIA   Blame not this haste of mine. If you mean well,
Now go with me and with this holy man
Into the chantry by.° There, before him   *nearby chapel*
25   And underneath that consecrated roof,
Plight me the full assurance of your faith,[3]
That my most jealous and too doubtful soul
May live at peace. He shall conceal it
Whiles° you are willing it shall come to note,   *until*
30   What° time we will our celebration keep   *at which*
According to my birth.° What do you say?   *rank*

SEBASTIAN   I'll follow this good man and go with you

---

2. A stock comic figure in the old morality plays;
he often carried a wooden dagger.
3. Yeoman; a title given to one not of gentle
birth, hence a parting insult to Malvolio.
4.3 Location: Near Olivia's house.

1. For though my reason and my sense both concur.
2. Undertake business, and ensure that it is carried out.
3. Enter into the solemn contract of betrothal.

And, having sworn truth, ever will be true.

OLIVIA Then lead the way, good father, and heavens so shine

35 That they may fairly note[4] this act of mine. *Exeunt*

5.1

Enter [FESTE, *the*] *clown and* FABIAN

FABIAN Now, as thou lovest me, let me see his letter.

FESTE Good Master Fabian, grant me another request.

FABIAN Anything.

FESTE Do not desire to see this letter.

5 FABIAN This is to give a dog and in recompense desire my
dog again.[1]

Enter ORSINO, VIOLA, CURIO, *and lords*

ORSINO Belong you to the Lady Olivia, friends?

FESTE Ay, sir, we are some of her trappings.° ornaments

ORSINO I know thee well. How dost thou, my good fellow?

10 FESTE Truly, sir, the better for my foes and the worse for
my friends.

ORSINO Just the contrary: the better for thy friends.

FESTE No, sir, the worse.

ORSINO How can that be?

15 FESTE Marry, sir, they praise me and make an ass of me.
Now my foes tell me plainly I am an ass; so that by my
foes, sir, I profit in the knowledge of myself, and by my
friends I am abused.° So that, conclusions to be as kisses, deceived
if your four negatives make your two affirmatives,[2] why

20 then the worse for my friends and the better for my foes.

ORSINO Why, this is excellent.

FESTE By my troth, sir, no—though it please you to be
one of my friends.

ORSINO [*giving a coin*] Thou shalt not be the worse for

25 me; there's gold.

FESTE But° that it would be double-dealing,[3] sir, I would except for the fact
you could make it another.

ORSINO O, you give me ill counsel.

FESTE Put your grace in your pocket,[4] sir, for this once,

30 and let your flesh and blood obey it.[5]

ORSINO Well, I will be so much a sinner to° be a double- as to
dealer. [*giving a coin*] There's another.

FESTE *Primo, secundo, tertio*[6] is a good play,° and the old game
saying is, the third pays for all.[7] The triplex,° sir, is a triple time (music)

---

4. Look favorably upon.
5.1 Location: Before Olivia's house.
1. Perhaps a reference to an anecdote, recorded
in John Manningham's diary, in which Queen
Elizabeth requested a dog, and the donor, when
granted a wish in return, asked for the dog back.
2. As in grammar a double negative can make an
affirmative (and therefore four negatives can
make two affirmatives), so when a coy girl is asked
for a kiss, her four refusals can be construed as
"yes, yes."

3. (1) A duplicity; (2) a double donation.
4. Set aside (pocket up) your virtue; also (with a
play on the customary form of address for a duke,
"your grace"), reach into your pocket and grace
me with another coin.
5. Let your normal human instincts (as opposed
to grace) follow the "ill counsel" (line 28).
6. First, second, third (Latin): perhaps an allusion to a dice throw or a child's game.
7. Third time lucky (proverbial).

35 good tripping measure, or the bells of Saint Bennet,[8] sir,
may put you in mind—one, two, three.

ORSINO   You can fool no more money out of me at this
throw.° If you will let your lady know I am here to speak   throw of the dice
with her, and bring her along with you, it may awake my
40 bounty° further.   generosity

FESTE   Marry, sir, lullaby to your bounty till I come again.
I go, sir, but I would not have you to think that my desire
of having is the sin of covetousness. But, as you say, sir, let
your bounty take a nap. I will awake it anon.   *Exit*

        Enter ANTONIO *and* OFFICERS

45 VIOLA   Here comes the man, sir, that did rescue me.

ORSINO   That face of his I do remember well.
Yet when I saw it last, it was besmeared
As black as Vulcan[9] in the smoke of war.
A baubling° vessel was he captain of,   trifling
50 For shallow draft and bulk unprizable,[1]
With which such scatheful° grapple did he make   destructive
With the most noble bottom° of our fleet   ship
That very envy° and the tongue of loss°   even enmity / the losers
Cried fame and honor on him.—What's the matter?

55 FIRST OFFICER   Orsino, this is that Antonio
That took the *Phoenix* and her freight from Candy,[2]
And this is he that did the *Tiger* board
When your young nephew Titus lost his leg.
Here in the streets, desperate of shame and state,[3]
60 In private brabble° did we apprehend him.   brawl

VIOLA   He did me kindness, sir, drew on my side,[4]
But in conclusion put strange speech upon° me.   spoke strangely to
I know not what 'twas but distraction.°   if not insanity

ORSINO   Notable° pirate, thou salt-water thief,   notorious
65 What foolish boldness brought thee to their mercies
Whom thou, in terms so bloody and so dear,°   dire
Hast made thine enemies?

ANTONIO   Orsino, noble sir,
Be pleased that I shake off these names you give me.
Antonio never yet was thief or pirate,
70 Though, I confess, on base° and ground enough,   foundation
Orsino's enemy. A witchcraft drew me hither.
That most ingrateful boy there by your side
From the rude sea's enraged and foamy mouth
Did I redeem; a wrack past hope he was.
75 His life I gave him and did thereto add
My love, without retention° or restraint,   reservation

---

8. A London church, across the Thames from the
Globe theater, was known as St. Bennet Hithe.
9. Blacksmith god of the Romans.
1. Of no value because of its small size. "Draft":
water displaced by a vessel.

2. Candia, capital of Crete.
3. Recklessly oblivious of the danger to his honor
and his position (as a free man and public enemy).
4. Drew his sword in my defense.

All his in dedication. For his sake
Did I expose myself, pure° for his love,   *only*
Into the danger of this adverse° town;   *hostile*
80 Drew to defend him when he was beset;
Where, being apprehended, his false cunning—
Not meaning to partake with me in danger—
Taught him to face me out of his acquaintance[5]
And grew a twenty years' removèd thing
85 While one would wink;[6] denied me mine own purse,
Which I had recommended° to his use   *consigned*
Not half an hour before.

VIOLA   How can this be?

ORSINO [*to Antonio*]   When came he to this town?

90 ANTONIO   Today, my lord; and for three months before,
No int'rim, not a minute's vacancy,°   *interval*
Both day and night did we keep company.

Enter OLIVIA *and attendants*

ORSINO   Here comes the Countess. Now heaven walks on earth!—
But for thee, fellow: fellow, thy words are madness.
95 Three months this youth hath tended upon me—
But more of that anon. [*to an* OFFICER] Take him aside.

OLIVIA   What would my lord, but that he may not have,[7]
Wherein Olivia may seem serviceable?—
Cesario, you do not keep promise with me.

100 VIOLA   Madam?

ORSINO   Gracious Olivia—

OLIVIA   What do you say, Cesario?—Good my lord—

VIOLA   My lord would speak; my duty hushes me.

OLIVIA   If it be aught° to the old tune, my lord,   *anything*
105 It is as fat and fulsome° to mine ear   *gross and offensive*
As howling after music.

ORSINO   Still so cruel?

OLIVIA   Still so constant, lord.

ORSINO   What, to perverseness? You, uncivil lady,
110 To whose ingrate and unauspicious° altars   *unfavorable*
My soul the faithful'st off'rings hath breathed out
That e'er devotion tendered—what shall I do?

OLIVIA   Even what it please my lord that shall become° him.   *be fitting for*

ORSINO   Why should I not, had I the heart to do it,
115 Like to th' Egyptian thief at point of death,
Kill what I love?[8]—a savage jealousy
That sometime savors nobly.° But hear me this: *of nobility*
Since you to non-regardance° cast my faith,   *oblivion*
And that I partly know the instrument

---

5. To brazenly deny my acquaintance.
6. I.e., in the wink of an eye, pretended we had
been estranged for twenty years.
7. Except that which he may not have (my love).
8. In Heliodorus's *Ethiopica*, a Greek prose

romance translated into English in 1569 and popular in Shakespeare's day, the Egyptian robber chief Thyamis tries to kill his captive Chariclea, whom he loves, when he is in danger from a rival band.

120   That screws° me from my true place in your favor,   *wrenches*
    Live you the marble-breasted tyrant still.
    But this your minion,° whom I know you love,   *darling*
    And whom, by heaven I swear, I tender° dearly,   *regard*
    Him will I tear out of that cruel eye
125   Where he sits crownèd in his master's spite—[9]
    Come, boy, with me. My thoughts are ripe in mischief.
    I'll sacrifice the lamb that I do love
    To spite a raven's heart within a dove.
VIOLA   And I, most jocund,° apt,° and willingly,   *cheerfully / ready*
130   To do you rest a thousand deaths would die.
OLIVIA   Where goes Cesario?
VIOLA   After him I love
    More than I love these eyes, more than my life,
    More by all mores[1] than e'er I shall love wife.
    If I do feign, you witnesses above,
135   Punish my life for tainting of my love.
OLIVIA   Ay me, detested! How am I beguiled!°   *deceived*
VIOLA   Who does beguile you? Who does do you wrong?
OLIVIA   Hast thou forgot thyself? Is it so long?
    Call forth the holy father.   *[Exit an attendant]*
ORSINO *[to* VIOLA*]*   Come, away!
140 OLIVIA   Whither, my lord?—Cesario, husband, stay.
ORSINO   Husband?
OLIVIA   Ay, husband. Can he that deny?
ORSINO   Her husband, sirrah?[2]
VIOLA   No, my lord, not I.
OLIVIA   Alas, it is the baseness of thy fear
    That makes thee strangle thy propriety.[3]
145   Fear not, Cesario. Take thy fortunes up.
    Be that thou know'st thou art, and then thou art
    As great as that° thou fear'st.   *him whom*
       Enter PRIEST
                  O, welcome, father.
    Father, I charge thee by thy reverence
    Here to unfold—though lately we intended
150   To keep in darkness what occasion° now   *necessity*
    Reveals before 'tis ripe—what thou dost know
    Hath newly passed between this youth and me.
PRIEST   A contract of eternal bond of love,
    Confirmed by mutual joinder° of your hands,   *joining*
155   Attested by the holy close° of lips,   *meeting*
    Strengthened by interchangement of your rings,
    And all the ceremony of this compact
    Sealed in my function,[4] by my testimony;
    Since when, my watch hath told me, toward my grave

---

9. To the mortification of his master.
1. More beyond all comparison.
2. Contemptuous form of address to an inferior.

3. That makes you deny your identity (as my husband).
4. Ratified by priestly authority.

160   I have traveled but two hours.
ORSINO [to VIOLA]   O thou dissembling cub! What wilt thou be
    When time hath sowed a grizzle on thy case?[5]
    Or will not else° thy craft° so quickly grow   *otherwise / craftiness*
    That thine own trip shall be thine overthrow?[6]
165   Farewell, and take her, but direct thy feet
    Where thou and I henceforth may never meet.
VIOLA   My lord, I do protest—
OLIVIA   O, do not swear.
    Hold little° faith, though thou hast too much fear.   *preserve some*
        Enter SIR ANDREW
SIR ANDREW   For the love of God, a surgeon! Send one
170   presently° to Sir Toby.   *immediately*
OLIVIA   What's the matter?
SIR ANDREW   He's broke° my head across, and has given Sir   *cut*
    Toby a bloody coxcomb[7] too. For the love of God, your
    help! I had rather than forty pound I were at home.
175 OLIVIA   Who has done this, Sir Andrew?
SIR ANDREW   The Count's gentleman, one Cesario. We
    took him for a coward, but he's the very devil incardi-
    nate.[8]
ORSINO   My gentleman Cesario?
180 SIR ANDREW   'Od's lifelings,° here he is!—You broke my   *by God's little lives*
    head for nothing, and that that I did, I was set on to do't by
    Sir Toby.
VIOLA   Why do you speak to me? I never hurt you.
    You drew your sword upon me without cause,
185   But I bespake you fair[9] and hurt you not.
SIR ANDREW   If a bloody coxcomb be a hurt, you have
    hurt me. I think you set nothing by° a bloody coxcomb.   *think nothing of*
        Enter SIR TOBY *and* [FESTE, *the*] *clown*
    Here comes Sir Toby halting.° You shall hear more. But   *limping*
    if° he had not been in drink, he would have tickled°   *if only / chastised*
                                                              in other ways
190   you othergates° than he did.
ORSINO   How now, gentleman? How is't with you?
SIR TOBY   That's all one.° He's hurt me, and there's th'   *no matter*
    end on't. [to FESTE]   Sot,° didst see Dick Surgeon,   *fool; drunkard*
    sot?
195 FESTE   O, he's drunk, Sir Toby, an hour agone. His eyes
    were set[1] at eight i 'th' morning.
SIR TOBY   Then he's a rogue and a passy-measures pavan.[2]
    I hate a drunken rogue.
OLIVIA   Away with him! Who hath made this havoc with
200   them?

5. A gray hair ("grizzle") on your hide (sustaining the metaphor of "cub").
6. That your attempt to trip someone else will be
the cause of your downfall.
7. Head; also, a fool's cap, which resembles the
crest of a cock.
8. Sir Andrew's blunder for "incarnate" (in the

flesh).
9. But I spoke courteously to you.
1. Closed (as the sun sets).
2. A variety of the slow dance known as "pavane"
(from the Italian *passemezzo pavana*). Sir Toby
may think its swaying movements suggest drunkenness.

SIR ANDREW I'll help you, Sir Toby, because we'll be
dressed[3] together.

SIR TOBY Will *you* help?—an ass-head, and a coxcomb,° and   *fool*
a knave, a thin-faced knave, a gull?°   *dupe*

205   OLIVIA Get him to bed, and let his hurt be looked to.
>   [*Exeunt* SIR TOBY, SIR ANDREW, FESTE, *and* FABIAN]
>   *Enter* SEBASTIAN

SEBASTIAN I am sorry, madam, I have hurt your kinsman,
But, had it been the brother of my blood,
I must have done no less with wit and safety.[4]
You throw a strange regard upon me,° and by that   *regard me strangely*
210   I do perceive it hath offended you.
Pardon me, sweet one, even for the vows
We made each other but so late ago.

ORSINO One face, one voice, one habit, and two persons!
A natural perspective,[5] that is and is not!

215   SEBASTIAN Antonio, O, my dear Antonio!
How have the hours racked and tortured me
Since I have lost thee!

ANTONIO Sebastian are you?

SEBASTIAN Fear'st thou° that, Antonio?   *do you doubt*

220   ANTONIO How have you made division of yourself?
An apple cleft in two is not more twin
Than these two creatures. Which is Sebastian?

OLIVIA Most wonderful!°   *full of wonder*

SEBASTIAN [*looking at* VIOLA] Do I stand there? I never had a
brother,
225   Nor can there be that deity° in my nature   *divine power*
Of here and everywhere.° I had a sister,   *of omnipresence*
Whom the blind waves and surges have devoured.
Of charity,° what kin are you to me?   *please*
What countryman? What name? What parentage?

230   VIOLA Of Messaline. Sebastian was my father.
Such a Sebastian was my brother, too.
So went he suited° to his watery tomb.   *in appearance; clad*
If spirits can assume both form and suit,
You come to fright us.

SEBASTIAN   A spirit I am indeed,
235   But am in that dimension grossly clad
Which from the womb I did participate.[6]
Were you a woman, as the rest goes even,°   *the rest suggests*
I should my tears let fall upon your cheek
And say "Thrice welcome, drownèd Viola."

240   VIOLA My father had a mole upon his brow.

SEBASTIAN And so had mine.

VIOLA And died that day when Viola from her birth

---

3. We'll have our wounds dressed.
4. With any sense of my welfare.
5. An optical illusion produced by nature (rather than by a mirror).
6. I.e., I am clad, like all mortals, in the flesh in which I was born.

Had numbered thirteen years.
SEBASTIAN   O, that record is lively[7] in my soul!
245   He finishèd indeed his mortal act
That day that made my sister thirteen years.
VIOLA   If nothing lets° to make us happy both   *hinders*
But this my masculine usurped attire,
Do not embrace me till each circumstance
250   Of place, time, fortune, do cohere and jump°   *agree*
That I am Viola; which to confirm,
I'll bring you to a captain in this town,
Where lie my maiden weeds;° by whose gentle help   *clothes*
I was preserved to serve this noble count.
255   All the occurrence of my fortune since
Hath been between this lady and this lord.
SEBASTIAN [*to* OLIVIA]   So comes it, lady, you have been mistook.
But nature to her bias drew in that.[8]
You would have been contracted° to a maid.   *betrothed*
260   Nor are you therein, by my life, deceived:
You are betrothed both to a maid and man.[9]
ORSINO [*to* OLIVIA]   Be not amazed; right noble is his blood.
If this be so, as yet the glass seems true,[1]
I shall have share in this most happy wrack.—
265   Boy, thou hast said to me a thousand times
Thou never shouldst love woman like to me.
VIOLA   And all those sayings will I overswear°   *swear again*
And all those swearings keep as true in soul
As doth that orbèd continent[2] the fire
That severs day from night.
270   ORSINO   Give me thy hand,
And let me see thee in thy woman's weeds.
VIOLA   The captain that did bring me first on shore
Hath my maid's garments. He, upon some action,°   *legal charge*
Is now in durance° at Malvolio's suit,   *prison*
275   A gentleman and follower of my lady's.
OLIVIA   He shall enlarge° him. Fetch Malvolio hither.   *release*
And yet, alas, now I remember me,
They say, poor gentleman, he's much distract.°   *crazed*
     Enter [FESTE, *the*] *clown with a letter, and* FABIAN
A most extracting° frenzy of mine own   *distracting*
280   From my remembrance clearly banished his.
How does he, sirrah?
FESTE   Truly, madam, he holds Beelzebub at the stave's
end[3] as well as a man in his case may do. He's here writ
a letter to you. I should have given't you today morning.

---

7. The memory of that is vivid.
8. But nature followed her inclination. (The
image is from the game of bowls, which sometimes used a ball with an off-center weight that
caused it to curve away from a straight course.)
9. I.e., a man who is a virgin.

1. The "natural perspective" (line 214) continues to seem real.
2. Referring to either the sun or the sphere within
which the sun was thought to be fixed.
3. He holds the devil (who threatens to possess
him) at a distance (proverbial).

285   But as a madman's epistles are no gospels,[4] so it skills°   *matters*
          not much when they are delivered.

      OLIVIA   Open't and read it.

      FESTE   Look then to be well edified, when the fool deliv-
          ers° the madman. [*He reads.*] "By the Lord, madam"—   *speaks the words of*

290   OLIVIA   How now, art thou mad?

      FESTE   No, madam, I do but read madness. An your lady-
          ship will have it as it ought to be, you must allow *vox.*[5]

      OLIVIA   Prithee, read i' thy right wits.

      FESTE   So I do, madonna. But to read his right wits[6] is
295   to read thus. Therefore, perpend,° my princess, and give   *pay attention*
          ear.

      OLIVIA [*giving letter to Fabian*]   Read it you, sirrah.

      FABIAN "By the Lord, madam, you wrong me, and the
          world shall know it. Though you have put me into
300   darkness and given your drunken cousin rule over me, yet
          have I the benefit of my senses as well as your Ladyship. I
          have your own letter that induced me to the semblance I
          put on, with the which I doubt not but to do myself much
          right or you much shame. Think of me as you please. I
305   leave my duty a little unthought of and speak out of my
          injury.[7]

                                    The madly-used Malvolio."

      OLIVIA   Did he write this?

      FESTE   Ay, madam.

310   ORSINO   This savors not much of distraction.°   *insanity*

      OLIVIA   See him delivered,° Fabian. Bring him hither.   *released*

                              [*Exit* FABIAN]

      My lord, so please you, these things further thought on,
      To think me as well a sister as a wife,[8]
      One day shall crown th' alliance[9] on't, so please you,
315   Here at my house, and at my proper cost.°   *own expense*

      ORSINO   Madam, I am most apt° t' embrace your offer.   *ready*
      [*to* VIOLA] Your master quits° you; and for your service   *releases*
          done him,
      So much against the mettle° of your sex,   *disposition*
      So far beneath your soft and tender breeding,
320   And since you called me "master" for so long,
      Here is my hand. You shall from this time be
      Your master's mistress.

      OLIVIA [*to* VIOLA]

                      A sister! You are she.

          Enter MALVOLIO [*and* FABIAN]

      ORSINO   Is this the madman?

      OLIVIA   Ay, my lord, this same.—

---

4. Gospel truths. "Epistles": letters (playing on
the sense of apostolic accounts of Christ in the
New Testament).
5. The appropriate voice (Latin).
6. To accurately represent his mental state.

7. I neglect the formality I owe you as your servant and speak as an injured person.
8. To think as well of me as a sister-in-law as you
would have thought of me as a wife.
9. The impending double-marriage ceremony.

How now, Malvolio?

MALVOLIO   Madam, you have done me wrong,
Notorious wrong.

325 OLIVIA   Have I, Malvolio? No.

MALVOLIA [*handing her a paper*] Lady, you have. Pray
    you peruse that letter.
You must not now deny it is your hand.°   *handwriting*
Write from° it if you can, in hand or phrase,   *differently from*
Or say 'tis not your seal, not your invention.°   *composition*
330 You can say none of this. Well, grant it then,
And tell me, in the modesty of honor,[1]
Why you have given me such clear lights° of favor?   *signs*
Bade me come smiling and cross-gartered to you,
To put on yellow stockings, and to frown
335 Upon Sir Toby and the lighter° people?   *lesser*
And, acting° this in an obedient hope,   *upon doing*
Why have you suffered° me to be imprisoned,   *allowed*
Kept in a dark house, visited by the priest,
And made the most notorious geck° and gull   *fool*
340 That e'er invention° played on? Tell me why.   *trickery*

OLIVIA   Alas, Malvolio, this is not my writing,
Though I confess much like the character.°   *handwriting*
But out of question, 'tis Maria's hand.
And now I do bethink me, it was she
345 First told me thou wast mad; then cam'st° in smiling,   *you came*
And in such forms which here were presupposed°   *previously suggested*
Upon thee in the letter. Prithee, be content.
This practice hath most shrewdly passed[2] upon thee.
But when we know the grounds and authors of it,
350 Thou shalt be both the plaintiff and the judge
Of thine own cause.

FABIAN   Good madam, hear me speak,
And let no quarrel nor no brawl to come
Taint the condition of this present hour,
Which I have wondered at. In hope it shall not,
355 Most freely I confess myself and Toby
Set this device against Malvolio here,
Upon° some stubborn and uncourteous parts°   *because / behavior*
We had conceived against him.[3] Maria writ
The letter, at Sir Toby's great importance,°   *importunity, insistence*
360 In recompense whereof he hath married her.
How with a sportful malice it was followed°   *followed through*
May rather pluck on° laughter than revenge,   *incite*
If that the injuries be justly weighed
That have on both sides passed.

OLIVIA [*to* MALVOLIO]   Alas, poor fool, how have they
365   baffled° thee!   *disgraced*

---

1. Tell me with the propriety that becomes a noblewoman.
2. This trick has most mischievously played.
3. To which we took exception.

FESTE   Why, "Some are born great, some achieve greatness, and some have greatness thrown upon them." I was
one, sir, in this interlude,° one Sir Topas, sir, but that's   *comedy*
all one. "By the Lord, fool, I am not mad"—but, do you
370   remember "Madam, why laugh you at such a barren rascal; an you smile not, he's gagged"? And thus the whirli-
gig° of time brings in his revenges.   *spinning top*
MALVOLIO   I'll be revenged on the whole pack of you!
                                              [*Exit*]
OLIVIA   He hath been most notoriously abused.
375   ORSINO   Pursue him and entreat him to a peace.
                                    [*Exit one or more*]
He hath not told us of the captain yet.
When that is known, and golden time convents,°   *summons; is convenient*
A solemn combination shall be made
Of our dear souls. Meantime, sweet sister,
380   We will not part from hence.° Cesario, come—   *(Olivia's house)*
For so you shall be while you are a man.
But when in other habits° you are seen,   *attire*
Orsino's mistress, and his fancy's° queen.   *love's; imagination's*
                              Exeunt [*all but* FESTE]
FESTE *sings*   When that I was and a little tiny boy,
385   With hey, ho, the wind and the rain,
                 A foolish thing was but a toy,
                      For the rain it raineth every day.

                 But when I came to man's estate,
                     With hey, ho, the wind and the rain,
390   'Gainst knaves and thieves men shut their gate,
                      For the rain it raineth every day.

                 But when I came, alas, to wive,
                     With hey, ho, the wind and the rain,
                 By swaggering° could I never thrive,   *bullying*
395   For the rain it raineth every day.

                 But when I came unto my beds,
                     With hey, ho, the wind and the rain,
                 With tosspots° still had drunken heads,   *drunkards*
                      For the rain it raineth every day.

400   A great while ago the world begun,
                     With hey, ho, the wind and the rain,
                 But that's all one, our play is done,
                      And we'll strive to please you every day.
                                              Exit

ca. 1601   1623

King Lear

The story of King Lear and his three daughters had often been told, in chronicles, poems, and sermons as well as on stage, when Shakespeare undertook to make it the subject of a tragedy. The play, performed at court in December 1605, was probably written and first performed somewhat earlier, though not before 1603, since it contains allusions to a florid piece of anti-Catholic propaganda published that year, Samuel Harsnett's *Declaration of Egregious Popish Impostures*. Thus scholars generally assign Shakespeare's composition of *King Lear* to 1604–05, shortly after *Othello* (ca. 1603–04) and before *Macbeth* (ca. 1606): an astounding succession of tragic masterpieces.

When *King Lear* was first performed, it may have struck contemporaries as strangely timely in the wake of a lawsuit that had occurred in late 1603. The two elder daughters of a doddering gentleman named Sir Brian Annesley attempted to get him legally certified as insane, thereby enabling themselves to take over his estate, while his youngest daughter vehemently protested on her father's behalf. The youngest daughter's name happened to be Cordell, a name uncannily close to that of Lear's youngest daughter, Cordelia, who tries to save her father from the malevolent designs of her older sisters.

The Annesley case directs our own attention to the ordinary family tensions and fears around which *King Lear*, for all its wildness, violence, and strangeness, is constructed. Though the Lear story has the mythic quality of a folktale (specifically, it resembles both the tale of Cinderella and the tale of a daughter who falls into disfavor for telling her father she loves him as much as salt), it was recounted in Shakespeare's time both as a piece of authentic British history from the very ancient past (ca. 800 B.C.E.) and as a warning to contemporary fathers not to put too much trust in the flattery of their children. In some versions of the story, including Shakespeare's, the warning centers on a decision to retire.

Retirement has come to seem a routine event, but in the patriarchal culture of Tudor and Stuart England, where the old demanded the public deference of the young, it was generally shunned. When, through illness or extreme old age, it became unavoidable, retirement put a severe strain on the politics and psychology of deference by driving a wedge between status—what Lear at society's pinnacle calls "The name, and all the additions to a king" (1.1.137)—and power. In both the state and the family, the strain could be somewhat eased by transferring power to the eldest legitimate male successor, but as the families of both the legendary Lear and the real Brian Annesley show, such a successor did not always exist. In the absence of a male heir, the aged Lear, determined to "shake all cares and business" from himself and confer them on "younger strengths," attempts to divide his kingdom among his daughters so that, as he puts it, "future strife / May be prevented now" (1.1.38–44). But this attempt, centered on a public love test, is a disastrous failure, since it leads him to banish the one child who truly loves him.

Shakespeare contrives to show that the problem with which his characters are grappling does not simply result from the absence of a son and heir. In his most brilliant and complex use of a double plot, he intertwines the story of Lear and his three daughters with the story of Gloucester and his two sons, a story he adapted from an episode in Philip Sidney's prose romance, *Arcadia*. Gloucester has a legitimate heir, his elder son, Edgar, as well as an illegitimate son, Edmund, and in this family the tragic conflict originates not in an unusual manner of transferring property from one generation to another but rather in the reverse: Edmund seethes with murderous resentment at the disadvantage entirely customary for someone in his position, both as a younger son and as what was called a "base," or "natural," child.

But why does Lear, who has, as the play begins, already drawn up the map equitably dividing the kingdom, stage the love test? In Shakespeare's principal source, an anonymous play called *The True Chronicle History of King Leir* (published in 1605 but dating from 1594 or earlier), there is a gratifyingly clear answer. Leir's strong-willed daughter Cordella has vowed that she will marry only a man whom she herself loves; Leir wishes her to marry the man he chooses for his own dynastic purposes. He stages the love test, anticipating that in competing with her sisters, Cordella will declare that she loves her father best, at which point Leir will demand that she prove her love by marrying the suitor of his choice. The stratagem backfires, but its purpose is clear.

By stripping his character of a comparable motive, Shakespeare makes Lear's act seem stranger, at once more arbitrary and more rooted in deep psychological needs. His Lear is a man who has determined to retire from power but who cannot endure dependence. Unwilling to lose his identity as an absolute authority both in the state and in the family, he arranges a public ritual—"Which of you shall we say doth love us most?" (1.1.50)—whose aim seems to be to allay his own anxiety by arousing it in his children. But Cordelia refuses to perform: "What shall Cordelia speak? Love, and be silent" (1.1.61). When she says "Nothing," a word that echoes darkly throughout the play, Lear hears what he most dreads: emptiness, loss of respect, the extinction of identity. And when, under further interrogation, she declares that she loves her father "according to my bond" (1.1.93), Lear understands these words too to be the equivalent of "nothing."

As Cordelia's subsequent actions demonstrate, his youngest daughter's bond is in reality a sustaining, generous love; but it is a love that ultimately leads to her death. Here Shakespeare makes an even more startling departure not only from *The True Chronicle History of King Leir* but from all his known sources. The earliest of these, the account in Geoffrey of Monmouth's twelfth-century *Historia Regum Britanniae*, sets the pattern repeated in John Higgins's version in *A Mirror for Magistrates* (1574 ed.), William Warner's *Albion's England* (1586), Raphael Holinshed's *Chronicles* (1587), and Edmund Spenser's *Faerie Queene* (1590: 2.10.27–32): the aged Lear is overthrown by his wicked daughters and their husbands, but he is restored to the throne by the army of his good daughter's husband, the king of France. The story then is one of loss and restoration: Lear resumes his reign, and then "made ripe for death" by old age, as Spenser puts it, he dies and is succeeded by Cordelia. The conclusion is not unequivocally happy: in all of the known chronicles, Cordelia rules worthily for several years and then, after being deposed and imprisoned by her nephews, in despair commits suicide. But Shakespeare's ending is unprecedented in its tragic devastation. When in Act 5 Lear suddenly enters with the lifeless body of Cordelia in his arms, the original audience, secure in the expectation of a very different resolution, must have been doubly shocked, a shock cruelly reinforced when the signs that she might be reviving—"This feather stirs; she lives!" (5.3.265)—all prove false. Lear apparently dies in the grip of the illusion that he detects some breath on his daughter's lips, but we know that Cordelia will, as he says a moment earlier, "come no more, / Never, never, never, never, never!" (5.3.307–08).

Those five reiterated words, the bleakest pentameter line Shakespeare ever wrote, are the climax of an extraordinary poetics of despair that is set in motion when Lear disinherits Cordelia and when Gloucester credits Edmund's lies about Edgar. *King Lear* has seemed to many modern readers and audiences the greatest of Shakespeare's tragedies precisely because of its anguished look into the heart of darkness, but its vision of suffering and evil has not always commanded unequivocal admiration. In the eighteenth century, Samuel Johnson wrote that "I was many years ago so shocked by Cordelia's death that I know not whether I ever endured to read again the last scenes of the play till I undertook to revise them as an editor." Johnson's contemporaries preferred a revision of Shakespeare's tragedy undertaken in 1681 by Nahum Tate. Finding the play, he writes, "a Heap of Jewels, unstrung, and unpolished," Tate proceeded to restring them in order to save Cordelia's life and to produce the unambiguous triumph of the forces of good, culminating in the joyous marriage of Cordelia and Edgar.

Only in the nineteenth century was Shakespeare's deeply pessimistic ending—the old generation dead or dying, the survivors shaken to the core, the ruling families all broken, with no impending marriage to promise renewal—generally restored to theatrical performance and the tragedy's immense power fully acknowledged. Even passionate admirers of *King Lear*, however, continued to express deep uneasiness, questioning whether the tragedy was suitable for the stage. Charles Lamb, for example, concluded flatly that "Lear is essentially impossible to be represented on stage." "To see Lear acted," Lamb wrote, "to see an old man tottering about the stage with a walking stick, turned out of doors by his daughters in a rainy night, has nothing in it but what is painful and disgusting." In such a view, *King Lear* could be staged successfully only in the imagination, where, freed from the limits of the human body, it could assume its true, stupendous proportions and enable the reader to grasp its ultimate spiritual meaning.

A succession of brilliant stage performances and, more recently, films has not only belied the view that *King Lear* is unactable but also underscored the crucial importance in the play of the body. If Shakespeare explores the extremes of the mind's anguish and the soul's devotion, he never forgets that his characters have bodies as well, bodies that have needs, cravings, and terrible vulnerabilities. When in this tragedy characters fall from high station, they plunge unprotected into a world of violent storms, murderous cruelty, and physical horror. The old king wanders raging on the heath, through a wild night of thunder and rain. Disguised as Poor Tom, a mad beggar possessed by demons, Gloucester's son Edgar enacts a life of utmost degradation. Gloucester's fate is even more terrible: betrayed by his son Edmund, he is seized in his own house by Lear's reptilian daughter Regan and her husband, Cornwall, tied to a chair, brutally interrogated, blinded, and then thrust bleeding out of doors.

The body in *King Lear* is a site not only of abject misery, nausea, and pain but also of care and a nascent moral awareness. In the midst of his mad ravings, Lear turns to the shivering Fool and asks, "Art cold?" (3.2.68). The question anticipates his recognition a few moments later that there is more suffering in the world than his own. Such signs of goodness and empathy, as simple as offering one's hand to someone who is frightened, do not outweigh the harshness of the physical world of the play, let alone cancel out the vicious cruelty of certain of its inhabitants, but they do qualify its moral bleakness. For a time evil seems to flourish unchecked in the world of the play, but the wicked do not ultimately triumph, and, in the midst of their anguish, humiliation, and pain, Lear and Gloucester achieve flashes of insight.

The tragedy is not only that the intervals of moral resolution, mental lucidity, and spiritual calm are so brief, continually giving way to feverish grief and rage, but also that the modest human understandings, moving in their simplicity, cost such an enormous amount of pain. Edgar saves his father from despair but also in some sense breaks his father's heart. Cordelia's steadfast honesty, her refusal to flatter the father she loves, is admirable but has disastrous consequences, and her attempt to save Lear leads only to her own death. For a sublime moment, Lear actually *sees* his daughter, understands her separateness, acknowledges her existence:

> Do not laugh at me;
> For, as I am a man, I think this lady
> To be my child Cordelia. (4.7.69–71)

But it has taken the destruction of virtually his whole world to reach this recognition.

An apocalyptic dream of last judgment and redemption hovers over the entire tragedy, but it is a dream forever deferred. At the sight of the howling Lear with the dead Cordelia in his arms, the bystanders can only ask a succession of stunned questions. Lear's own question seems the most terrible and the most important:

> Why should a dog, a horse, a rat, have life,
> And thou no breath at all? (5.3.306–07)

It is a sign of *King Lear's* astonishing freedom from orthodoxy that it refuses to offer any of the conventional answers to this question, answers that serve largely to conceal or deflect the mourner's anguish.

King Lear first appeared in print in a quarto published in 1608 entitled *The History of King Lear*; a substantially different text, entitled *The Tragedy of King Lear* and grouped with the other tragedies, was printed in the 1623 Folio. From the eighteenth century, when the difference between the two texts was first noted, editors, assuming that they were imperfect versions of the identical play, customarily conflated them, blending together the approximately one hundred folio lines not printed in the quarto with the approximately three hundred quarto lines not printed in the folio, and selecting as best they could among the hundreds of particular alternative readings. But there is a growing scholarly consensus that the 1608 text of *Lear* represents the play as Shakespeare first wrote it and that the 1623 text represents a substantial revision. In order to make available as much of both texts as possible within the space constraints of this anthology, we here present a conflated version. For samples in which readers can compare in detail *The History of King Lear* and *The Tragedy of King Lear,* see the supplemental ebook. Readers who wish to pursue this comparison further may consult the *Norton Shakespeare*, where the two texts are printed in their entirety on facing pages.

King Lear

THE PERSONS OF THE PLAY

LEAR, king of Britain
GONERIL, Lear's eldest daughter
Duke of ALBANY, her husband
REGAN, Lear's second daughter
Duke of CORNWALL, her husband
CORDELIA, Lear's youngest daughter
King of FRANCE ⎤ suitors of
Duke of BURGUNDY ⎦ Cordelia
Earl of KENT, later disguised as Caius
Earl of GLOUCESTER
EDGAR, elder son of Gloucester, later
   disguised as Tom o' Bedlam

EDMUND, bastard son of Gloucester
OLD MAN, Gloucester's tenant
CURAN, Gloucester's retainer
Lear's FOOL
OSWALD, Goneril's steward
A DOCTOR
A CAPTAIN
A GENTLEMAN
A HERALD
SERVANTS to Cornwall
Knights, officers, messengers,
   soldiers, attendants

1.1

Enter KENT, GLOUCESTER,[1] *and* EDMUND

KENT   I thought the king had more affected° the Duke of   *favored*
Albany° than Cornwall.   *Scotland*

1.1 Location: King Lear's court.   1. Pronounced "Gloster."

GLOUCESTER It did always seem so to us; but now, in the
    division of the kingdom, it appears not° which of the   *is not clear*
5   dukes he values most; for equalities° are so weighed,° that   *shares / equal*
    curiosity in neither can make choice of either's moiety[2]
KENT Is not this your son, my lord?
GLOUCESTER His breeding,° sir, hath been at my charge.[3]   *upbringing*
    I have so often blushed to acknowledge him, that now I
10   am brazed° to it.   *hardened*
KENT I cannot conceive° you.   *comprehend*
GLOUCESTER Sir, this young fellow's mother could;[4]
    whereupon she grew round-wombed, and had, indeed,
    sir, a son for her cradle ere she had a husband for her
15   bed. Do you smell a fault?[5]
KENT I cannot wish the fault undone, the issue° of it being   *offspring; result*
    so proper.°   *handsome; right*
GLOUCESTER But I have, sir, a son by order of law,° some   *legitimate*
    year elder than this, who yet is no dearer in my account.°   *estimation*
20   Though this knave° came something saucily[6] into the   *scamp, fellow*
    world before he was sent for, yet was his mother fair;
    there was good sport at his making, and the whoreson°   *rogue; bastard*
    must be acknowledged. Do you know this noble gentle-
    man, Edmund?
25 EDMUND No, my lord.
GLOUCESTER My lord of Kent. Remember him hereafter as
    my honorable friend.
EDMUND My services to your lordship.
KENT I must love you, and sue° to know you better.   *ask*
30 EDMUND Sir, I shall study deserving.°   *shall learn to deserve*
GLOUCESTER He hath been out° nine years, and away he   *away, abroad*
    shall again. (*Sound a sennet*°) The king is coming.   *fanfare of trumpets*
        Enter one bearing a coronet, then King LEAR, CORN-
        WALL, ALBANY, GONERIL, REGAN, CORDELIA, *and*
        attendants
LEAR Attend the lords of France and Burgundy, Gloucester.
GLOUCESTER I shall, my liege.°   *feudal superior*
        Exeunt GLOUCESTER *and* EDMUND
35 LEAR Meantime we° shall express our darker° purpose.   *("royal" we) / secret*
    Give me the map there. Know° that we have divided   *be informed*
    In three our kingdom; and 'tis our fast° intent   *steadfast*
    To shake all cares and business from our age,
    Conferring them on younger strengths, while we
40   Unburthened crawl toward death. Our son° of Cornwall,   *son-in-law*
    And you, our no less loving son of Albany,

---

2. That careful scrutiny ("curiosity") of both parts cannot determine which portion ("moiety") is preferable.
3. My responsibility; at my cost.
4. Could conceive—punning on biological conception.
5. Sin, wrongdoing; female genitals.
6. Somewhat rudely; somewhat shamefully.

We have this hour a constant will to publish[7]
Our daughters' several dowers,° that future strife *individual dowries*
May be prevented now. The princes, France and
 Burgundy,
45 Great rivals in our youngest daughter's love,
Long in our court have made their amorous sojourn,
And here are to be answered. Tell me, my daughters—
Since now we will divest us, both of rule,
Interest° of territory, cares of state— *legal title*
50 Which of you shall we say doth love us most?
That° we our largest bounty° may extend *so that / generosity*
Where nature doth with merit challenge.[8] Goneril,
Our eldest-born, speak first.
GONERIL Sir, I love you more than words can wield° the *convey*
 matter;
55 Dearer than eye-sight, space,° and liberty; *freedom of movement*
Beyond what can be valued, rich or rare;
No less than life, with grace, health, beauty, honor;
As much as child e'er loved, or father found;
A love that makes breath° poor, and speech unable; *language*
60 Beyond all manner of so much° I love you. *beyond all comparison*
CORDELIA (*aside*) What shall Cordelia speak? Love, and
 be silent.
LEAR Of all these bounds, even from this line to this,
With shadowy forests and with champains riched,° *plains enriched*
With plenteous rivers and wide-skirted meads,° *broad meadows*
65 We make thee lady:° to thine and Albany's issue° *mistress / children, heirs*
Be this perpetual. What says our second daughter,
Our dearest Regan, wife to Cornwall? Speak.
REGAN Sir, I am made
Of the self-same metal° that my sister is, *spirit; substance*
70 And prize me at her worth.° In my true heart *believe myself her equal*
I find she names my very deed of love;
Only she comes too short, that° I profess *in that*
Myself an enemy to all other joys,
Which the most precious square of sense possesses,[9]
75 And find I am alone felicitate° *am only made happy*
In your dear highness' love.
CORDELIA (*aside*)   Then poor Cordelia!
And yet not so; since, I am sure, my love's
More ponderous° than my tongue. *weighty*
LEAR To thee and thine, hereditary ever
80 Remain this ample third of our fair kingdom;
No less in space, validity,° and pleasure, *value*
Than that conferred on Goneril. Now, our joy,
Although our last and least;° to whose young love *youngest; smallest*

---

7. A fixed determination to announce publicly.
8. I.e., to the one whose natural love and good

deeds mutually enhance each other.
9. That the body can enjoy.

The vines of France and milk of Burgundy
85 Strive to be interessed,° what can you say to draw — *given access to*
A third more opulent than your sisters? Speak.
CORDELIA Nothing, my lord.
LEAR Nothing?
CORDELIA Nothing.
90 LEAR Nothing will come of nothing, speak again.
CORDELIA Unhappy that I am, I cannot heave
My heart into my mouth. I love your majesty
According to my bond;° nor more nor less. — *filial duty*
LEAR How, how, Cordelia! mend your speech a little,
Lest it may mar your fortunes.
95 CORDELIA   Good my lord,
You have begot me, bred° me, loved me; I — *raised*
Return those duties back as are right fit,
Obey you, love you, and most honor you.
Why have my sisters husbands, if they say
100 They love you all?° Haply,° when I shall wed, — *exclusively / perhaps*
That lord whose hand must take my plight° shall carry — *vow; condition*
Half my love with him, half my care and duty.
Sure, I shall never marry like my sisters,
To love my father all.
105 LEAR But goes thy heart with this?
CORDELIA Ay, good my lord.
LEAR So young, and so untender?
CORDELIA So young, my lord, and true.° — *honest; faithful*
LEAR Let it be so! Thy truth, then, be thy dower!
110 For, by the sacred radiance of the sun,
The mysteries of Hecate,[1] and the night;
By all the operation of the orbs
From whom we do exist and cease to be;[2]
Here I disclaim all my paternal care,
115 Propinquity° and property of blood,° — *closeness / kinship*
And as a stranger to my heart and me
Hold thee, from this,° for ever. The barbarous Scythian,[3] — *this time*
Or he that makes his generation messes[4]
To gorge his appetite, shall to my bosom
120 Be as well neighbored, pitied, and relieved,° — *assisted in trouble*
As thou my sometime° daughter. — *former*
KENT   Good my liege—
LEAR Peace, Kent!
Come not between the dragon and his wrath.
I loved her most, and thought to set my rest[5]

1. Classical goddess of the moon and patron of witchcraft.
2. Referring to the belief that the movements of stars and planets ("orbs") corresponded to physical and spiritual motions in a person and thus controlled his or her fate.
3. Notoriously savage Crimean nomads of classical antiquity.
4. I.e., he who makes meals of his parents or his children.
5. To secure my repose; to stake my all, as in the card game known as primero.

125 On her kind nursery.° Hence, and avoid my sight!   *care*
So be my grave my peace,[6] as here I give
Her father's heart from her! Call France; who stirs?[7]
Call Burgundy. Cornwall and Albany,
With my two daughters' dowers digest° this third: *incorporate*
130 Let pride, which she calls plainness,° marry her.   *directness*
I do invest you jointly with my power,
Pre-eminence, and all the large effects°   *outward shows, trappings*
That troop with° majesty. Ourself, by monthly course,   *accompany*
With reservation° of an hundred knights,   *legal right to retain*
135 By you to be sustained, shall our abode
Make with you by due turns. Only we still retain
The name, and all the additions° to a king;   *prerogatives*
The sway,° revenue, execution of the rest,   *power*
Beloved sons, be yours; which to confirm,
This coronet[8] part betwixt you.
140 KENT   Royal Lear,
Whom I have ever honored as my king,
Loved as my father, as my master followed,
As my great patron thought on in my prayers—
LEAR   The bow is bent and drawn, make from° the shaft.   *get clear of*
145 KENT   Let it fall° rather, though the fork° invade   *strike home / arrowhead*
The region of my heart: be Kent unmannerly,
When Lear is mad. What wilt thou do, old man?
Think'st thou that duty shall have dread to speak,
When power to flattery bows? To plainness° honor's   *plain speaking*
  bound,
150 When majesty stoops to folly. Reverse thy doom,°   *revoke your sentence*
And, in thy best consideration, check°   *halt*
This hideous rashness. Answer my life my judgment,[9]
Thy youngest daughter does not love thee least;
Nor are those empty-hearted whose low sounds
Reverb no hollowness.°   *echo no insincerity*
155 LEAR   Kent, on thy life, no more.
KENT   My life I never held but as a pawn°   *chess piece; stake*
To wage° against thy enemies; nor fear to lose it,   *wager; war*
Thy safety being the motive.
LEAR   Out of my sight!
KENT   See better, Lear; and let me still° remain   *always*
160 The true blank° of thine eye.   *precise bull's-eye*
LEAR   Now, by Apollo—
KENT   Now, by Apollo, king,
Thou swear'st thy gods in vain.[1]
LEAR   O, vassal! miscreant!°   *villain; unbeliever*
  Laying his hand on his sword

---

6. So may I rest in peace.
7. Does nobody stir? An order, with the force of "Get moving."
8. Cordelia's crown, symbol of the endowment she has lost.
9. I'll stake my life on my opinion.
1. You invoke your gods falsely and without effect. Lear's blindness and misdirected imprecations are particularly inapt for Apollo, god of the sun and of archery.

ALBANY
CORNWALL } Dear sir, forbear.

KENT   Do;

165 Kill thy physician, and the fee bestow
Upon thy foul disease.[2] Revoke thy doom;
Or, whilst I can vent clamor from my throat,
I'll tell thee thou dost evil.

LEAR   Hear me, recreant!°   *traitor*
On thine allegiance, hear me!

170 Since thou hast sought to make us break our vow,
Which we durst never yet, and with strained° pride   *overblown*
To come between our sentence and our power,
Which nor our nature nor our place[3] can bear,
Our potency made good,° take thy reward.   *demonstrated*

175 Five days we do allot thee, for provision
To shield thee from diseases° of the world;   *dis-eases, discomforts*
And on the sixth to turn thy hated back
Upon our kingdom: if, on the tenth day following,
Thy banished trunk° be found in our dominions,   *body*

180 The moment is thy death. Away! by Jupiter,
This shall not be revoked.

KENT   Fare thee well, king. Sith° thus thou wilt appear,   *since*
Freedom lives hence, and banishment is here.
(*To* CORDELIA) The gods to their dear shelter take thee, maid,

185 That justly think'st, and hast most rightly said!
(*To* REGAN *and* GONERIL) And your large speeches may
    your deeds approve,[4]
That good effects may spring from words of love.
Thus Kent, O princes, bids you all adieu;
He'll shape his old course in a country new.   *Exit*

    Flourish.° Re-enter GLOUCESTER, *with* FRANCE,   *fanfare of trumpets*
    BURGUNDY, *and attendants*

190 GLOUCESTER   Here's France and Burgundy, my noble lord.

LEAR   My lord of Burgundy,
We first address towards you, who with this king
Hath rivaled for our daughter. What, in the least,
Will you require in present dower with her,
Or cease your quest of love?

195 BURGUNDY   Most royal majesty,
I crave no more than what your highness offered,
Nor will you tender° less.   *offer*

LEAR   Right noble Burgundy,
When she was dear to us, we did hold her so;
But now her price is fallen. Sir, there she stands;

200 If aught° within that little seeming substance,[5]   *anything*
Or all of it, with our displeasure pieced,°   *joined*

---

2. You would not only kill the doctor but hand
his fee over to the disease.
3. Which neither my temperament nor my royal
position.

4. And let your actions live up to your fine words.
5. I.e., one who appears more substantial than
she is; one who will not pretend.

And nothing more, may fitly like° your grace,   *please*
She's there, and she is yours.
BURGUNDY   I know no answer.
LEAR   Will you, with those infirmities she owes,°   *owns*
205   Unfriended, new-adopted to our hate,
Dowered with our curse, and strangered° with our oath,   *estranged*
Take her, or leave her?
BURGUNDY   Pardon me, royal sir;
Election makes not up on such conditions.[6]
LEAR   Then leave her, sir; for, by the power that made me,
210   I tell you° all her wealth. (*To* FRANCE) For° you,   *inform you of / as for*
    great king,
I would not from your love make such a stray°   *stray so far*
To° match you where I hate; therefore beseech you   *as to*
To avert your liking° a more worthier way   *to turn your affections*
Than on a wretch whom nature is ashamed
Almost to acknowledge hers.
215 FRANCE   This is most strange,
That she, whom even but now was your best object,
The argument° of your praise, balm of your age,   *theme*
Most best, most dearest, should in this trice° of time   *moment*
Commit a thing so monstrous, to dismantle°   *as to strip off, disrobe*
220   So many folds of favor. Sure, her offense
Must be of such unnatural degree,
That monsters it,° or your fore-vouched affection   *makes it monstrous*
Fall'n into taint;[7] which to believe of her,
Must be a faith that reason without miracle
Could never plant in me.
225 CORDELIA   I yet beseech your majesty—
If for I want° that glib and oily art,   *because I lack*
To speak and purpose not°—since what I well intend,   *and not intend*
I'll do't before I speak—that you make known
It is no vicious blot, murder, or foulness,
230   No unchaste action, or dishonored step,
That hath deprived me of your grace and favor;
But even for want of that for which I am richer,
A still-soliciting° eye, and such a tongue   *an always-begging*
As I am glad I have not, though not to have it
Hath lost me in your liking.
235 LEAR   Better thou
Hadst not been born than not to have pleased me better.
FRANCE   Is it but this—a tardiness in nature
Which often leaves the history unspoke
That it intends to do?[8] My lord of Burgundy,
240   What say you to the lady? Love's not love
When it is mingled with regards° that stands   *considerations*

---

6. A choice cannot be made under those terms.
7. I.e., or else the love you earlier swore for Cordelia must be regarded with suspicion. "Or" may also mean "before," in which case the phrase would mean "before the love you once proclaimed could have decayed."
8. A natural reserve that inhibits voicing one's intentions.

Aloof from th' entire point. Will you have her?
She is herself a dowry.
BURGUNDY   Royal Lear,
   Give but that portion which yourself proposed,
245   And here I take Cordelia by the hand,
   Duchess of Burgundy.
LEAR   Nothing! I have sworn; I am firm.
BURGUNDY   I am sorry, then, you have so lost a father
   That you must lose a husband.
CORDELIA   Peace be with Burgundy!
250   Since that respects of fortune are his love,
   I shall not be his wife.
FRANCE   Fairest Cordelia, that art most rich, being poor;
   Most choice, forsaken; and most loved, despised!
   Thee and thy virtues here I seize upon:
255   Be it lawful I take up what's cast away.
   Gods, gods! 'tis strange that from their cold'st neglect
   My love should kindle to inflamed respect.°   ardent regard
   Thy dowerless daughter, king, thrown to my chance,
   Is queen of us, of ours, and our fair France.
260   Not all the dukes of waterish° Burgundy   irrigated, watery; weak
   Can buy this unprized° precious maid of me.   unappreciated
   Bid them farewell, Cordelia, though unkind;°   though they are unkind
   Thou losest here,° a better where° to find.   this place / place
LEAR   Thou hast her, France; let her be thine; for we
265   Have no such daughter, nor shall ever see
   That face of hers again. Therefore be gone
   Without our grace, our love, our benison.°   blessing
   Come, noble Burgundy.
        Flourish. Exeunt all but FRANCE, GONERIL, REGAN, *and*
        CORDELIA
FRANCE   Bid farewell to your sisters.
270   CORDELIA   The jewels of our father, with washed eyes
   Cordelia leaves you. I know you what you are,
   And like a sister am most loath to call
   Your faults as they are named.° Love well our father.   are properly called
   To your professed bosoms° I commit him;   publicly proclaimed love
275   But yet, alas, stood I° within his grace,   if I stood
   I would prefer° him to a better place.   promote; recommend
   So, farewell to you both.
REGAN   Prescribe not us our duties.
GONERIL   Let your study
   Be to content your lord, who hath received you
280   At fortune's alms.⁹ You have obedience scanted,°   stinted on
   And well are worth the want that you have wanted.¹
CORDELIA   Time shall unfold what pleated cunning hides:

9. As a charitable gift from Dame Fortune.
1. And you deserve to get no more love (from
your husband) than you have given (to your
father). "Want" plays on its alternative meanings
of "lack" and "desire."

Who cover faults, at last shame them derides.[2]
Well may you prosper!

FRANCE   Come, my fair Cordelia.

Exeunt FRANCE *and* CORDELIA

285 GONERIL   Sister, it is not a little I have to say of what most
nearly appertains to us both. I think our father will hence
tonight.

REGAN   That's most certain, and with you; next month with
us.

290 GONERIL   You see how full of changes° his age is; the obser- | *fickleness*
vation we have made of it hath not been little:[3] he always
loved our sister most; and with what poor judgment he
hath now cast her off appears too grossly.° | *blatantly*

REGAN   'Tis the infirmity of his age; yet he hath ever but
295 slenderly known himself.

GONERIL   The best and soundest of his time hath been but
rash;[4] then° must we look to receive from his age, not | *therefore*
alone the imperfections of long-engraffed condition,° but | *deep-rooted habit*
therewithal the unruly waywardness that infirm and chol-
300 eric° years bring with them. | *prone to anger*

REGAN   Such unconstant starts[5] are we like° to have from | *likely*
him as this of Kent's banishment.

GONERIL   There is further compliment° of leave-taking | *ceremony*
between France and him. Pray you, let's hit° together: if | *join; strike*
305 our father carry authority with such dispositions[6] as he
bears, this last surrender° of his will but offend° us. | *abdication / harm*

REGAN   We shall further think on 't.

GONERIL   We must do something, and i' the heat.° *Exeunt* | *while the iron is*
hot

1.2

Enter EDMUND *, with a letter*

EDMUND   Thou, nature, art my goddess; to thy law
My services are bound.[1] Wherefore° should I | *why*
Stand in the plague of custom,[2] and permit
The curiosity° of nations to deprive me, | *legal fine points*
5 For that° I am some twelve or fourteen moonshines° | *because / months*
Lag of° a brother? Why bastard? wherefore base? | *younger than*
When my dimensions are as well compact,° | *composed*
My mind as generous° and my shape as true,° | *noble / well-formed*
As honest° madam's issue? Why brand they us | *married; chaste*
10 With base? with baseness? bastardy? base, base?
Who, in the lusty stealth of nature, take

---

2. Those who hide their faults will in the end be
put to shame.
3. We have observed it more than a little.
4. Even in the prime of his life he was impetuous.
5. Such impulsive outbursts.
6. Frame of mind.
1.2 Location: The earl of Gloucester's house.

1. Edmund declares the raw force of unsocialized
and unregulated existence, as opposed to human
law, to be his ruler; ironically, "nature" also means
"natural filial affection." A "natural" was another
word for "bastard" (illegitimate child).
2. I.e., submit to the imposition of inheritance law.

More composition and fierce quality[3]
Than doth, within a dull, stale, tired bed,
Go to creating a whole tribe of fops,°   *fools*
15 Got° 'tween asleep and wake? Well, then,   *begotten*
Legitimate Edgar, I must have your land.
Our father's love is to° the bastard Edmund   *as much to*
As to the legitimate. Fine word—"legitimate"!
Well, my legitimate, if this letter speed,°   *succeed*
20 And my invention° thrive, Edmund the base   *plot*
Shall top° the legitimate. I grow; I prosper.   *overcome; usurp*
Now, gods, stand up for bastards!

      Enter GLOUCESTER

GLOUCESTER   Kent banished thus? and France in choler
  parted?°   *in anger departed*
And the king gone tonight?° subscribed° his power?   *last night / limited*
25 Confirmed to exhibition?[4] All this done
Upon the gad?° Edmund, how now! what news?   *spur of the moment*

EDMUND   So please your lordship, none.

      Putting up the letter

GLOUCESTER   Why so earnestly seek you to put up that
letter?

30 EDMUND   I know no news, my lord.

GLOUCESTER   What paper were you reading?

EDMUND   Nothing, my lord.

GLOUCESTER   No? What needed, then, that terrible dis-
patch° of it into your pocket? The quality of nothing hath   *frightened haste*
35 not such need to hide itself. Let's see. Come, if it be
nothing, I shall not need spectacles.

EDMUND   I beseech you, sir, pardon me. It is a letter from
my brother, that I have not all o'er-read; and for so much
as I have perused, I find it not fit for your o'er-looking.

40 GLOUCESTER   Give me the letter, sir.

EDMUND   I shall offend, either to detain or give it. The contents, as in part I understand them, are to blame.

GLOUCESTER   Let's see, let's see.

EDMUND   I hope, for my brother's justification, he wrote
45 this but as an essay or taste[5] of my virtue.

GLOUCESTER (*reads*) "This policy and reverence of age
makes the world bitter to the best of our times;[6] keeps
our fortunes from us till our oldness cannot relish them.
I begin to find an idle and fond° bondage in the   *useless and foolish*
50 oppression of aged tyranny; who sways, not as it hath
power, but as it is suffered.[7] Come to me, that of this I
may speak more. If our father would sleep till I waked

3. Engendering a bastard, by virtue of its illicit-
ness and furtiveness, entails heightened sexual
energy, in Edmund's view, and hence produces
more well-formed, vigorous offspring.
4. Established as mere show; relegated to pension.
5. Simply as a proof or test. Both terms derive

from metallurgy.
6. The established primacy of the elderly embit-
ters us at the prime of our lives. "Policy": statecraft; craftiness; established order.
7. Which rules not because it is powerful but
because it is permitted to ("suffered").

him, you should enjoy half his revenue for ever, and live
the beloved of your brother, Edgar."

55 Hum—conspiracy!—"Sleep till I waked him—you
should enjoy half his revenue"—My son Edgar! Had he a
hand to write this? a heart and brain to breed it in?—
When came this to you? who brought it?

EDMUND   It was not brought me, my lord; there's the cun-
60 ning of it; I found it thrown in at the casement° of my   *window*
closet.°   *private room*

GLOUCESTER   You know the character° to be your   *handwriting*
brother's?

EDMUND   If the matter° were good, my lord, I durst swear it   *content*
65 were his; but, in respect of that, I would fain° think it   *gladly*
were not.

GLOUCESTER   It is his.

EDMUND   It is his hand, my lord; but I hope his heart is not
in the contents.

70 GLOUCESTER   Hath he never heretofore sounded you° in   *sounded you out*
this business?

EDMUND   Never, my lord. But I have heard him oft main-
tain it to be fit that, sons at perfect age,° and fathers   *at maturity*
declining, the father should be as ward[8] to the son, and
75 the son manage his revenue.

GLOUCESTER   O villain, villain! His very opinion in the letter! Abhorred villain! Unnatural, detested, brutish villain!
worse than brutish! Go, sirrah,[9] seek him. I'll apprehend
him. Abominable villain! Where is he?

80 EDMUND   I do not well know, my lord. If it shall please you
to suspend your indignation against my brother till
you can derive from him better testimony of his intent,
you shall run a certain° course; where,° if you violently   *reliable / whereas*
proceed against him, mistaking his purpose, it would
85 make a great gap in your own honor and shake in pieces
the heart of his obedience. I dare pawn down° my life for   *I dare stake*
him that he hath wrote this to feel° my affection to your   *feel out*
honor, and to no further pretense of danger.[1]

GLOUCESTER   Think you so?

90 EDMUND   If your honor judge it meet,° I will place you   *appropriate*
where you shall hear us confer of this, and by an auricular
assurance have your satisfaction; and that without any
further delay than this very evening.

GLOUCESTER   He cannot be such a monster—

95 EDMUND   Nor is not, sure.

GLOUCESTER   To his father, that so tenderly and entirely
loves him. Heaven and earth! Edmund, seek him out;
wind me into him,[2] I pray you; frame° the business after   *arrange*

---

8. An underage child who was legally dependent, often orphaned.
9. A form of address used with children or social
inferiors.

1. No further intention to do harm.
2. Worm your way into his confidence (with
"me" as an intensifier); worm your way into his
confidence for me ("me" as a term of respect).

your own wisdom. I would unstate myself, to be in a due
resolution.[3]

EDMUND I will seek him, sir, presently;° convey° the busi- *at once / carry out*
ness as I shall find means, and acquaint you withal.° *therewith*

GLOUCESTER These late° eclipses in the sun and moon por- *recent*
tend no good to us.[4] Though the wisdom of nature
can reason it thus and thus, yet nature finds itself
scourged by the sequent effects.[5] Love cools, friendship
falls off, brothers divide; in cities, mutinies; in countries,
discord; in palaces, treason; and the bond cracked 'twixt
son and father. This villain of mine comes under the prediction; there's son against father. The king falls from
bias of nature;[6] there's father against child. We have seen
the best of our time. Machinations, hollowness,° treach- *insincerity*
ery, and all ruinous disorders, follow us disquietly to our
graves. Find out this villain, Edmund; it shall lose thee
nothing; do it carefully. And the noble and true-hearted
Kent banished! his offense, honesty! 'Tis strange. *Exit*

EDMUND This is the excellent foppery° of the world, that, *foolishness*
when we are sick in fortune, often the surfeit[7] of our own
behavior, we make guilty of[8] our disasters the sun, the
moon, and the stars; as if we were villains by necessity;
fools by heavenly compulsion; knaves, thieves, and treach-
ers,° by spherical predominance;[9] drunkards, liars, and *traitors*
adulterers, by an enforced obedience of planetary influ-
ence; and all that we are evil in, by a divine thrusting on.° *imposition*
An admirable° evasion of whore-master man, to lay his *amazing*
goatish disposition to the charge of a star![1] My father
compounded° with my mother under the dragon's tail, *coupled*
and my nativity was under Ursa Major,[2] so that it follows
I am rough and lecherous. Fut!° I should have been that *by Christ's foot*
I am, had the maidenliest star in the firmament twinkled
on my bastardizing. Edgar—

Enter EDGAR

and pat° he comes like the catastrophe° of the old comedy. *on cue / resolution*
My cue is villainous melancholy, with a sigh like Tom o'
Bedlam.[3] O, these eclipses do portend these divisions!
Fa, sol, la, mi.[4]

3. I would give up everything to have my doubts
resolved.
4. Lunar and solar eclipses that were seen in London about a year before the play's first recorded
performance would have added spice to this
superstitious belief in the role of heavenly bodies
as augurs of misfortune.
5. Though natural science may explain the
eclipses this way or that, nature (like family bonds)
suffers in the effects that follow.
6. The king deviates from his natural inclination.
In the game of bowls, the "bias" (course) is the
eccentric path taken by the weighted ball when
thrown.
7. Sickness caused by intemperance.
8. We hold responsible for.

9. By the ascendancy of a particular planet. In
the pre-Copernican cosmology, the planets
revolved about the earth on crystalline spheres.
1. I.e., to hold a star responsible for his lustful
desires.
2. Constellations: "dragon's tail"=Draco; "Ursa
Major"=Great Bear.
3. The usual name for lunatic beggars; "Bethlehem," shortened to "Bedlam," was the name of
the oldest and best-known London madhouse.
4. In the musical notation of Shakespeare's
time, Edmund's sequence of tones spans an augmented fourth (F to B), an interval regarded
then as now as especially dissonant; it was sometimes referred to as "the devil in music." "Divisions": social fractures; melodic embellishments.

EDGAR   How now, brother Edmund? What serious contemplation are you in?

EDMUND   I am thinking, brother, of a prediction I read this other day, what should follow these eclipses.

140   EDGAR   Do you busy yourself about that?

EDMUND   I promise you, the effects he writes of succeed° unhappily; as of unnaturalness between the child and the parent; death, dearth, dissolutions of ancient amities; divisions in state, menaces and maledictions against king
145   and nobles; needless diffidences,° banishment of friends, dissipation of cohorts,° nuptial breaches, and I know not what.   °follow

°baseless suspicions
°scattering of forces

EDGAR   How long have you been a sectary astronomical?°   °devotee of astrology

EDMUND   Come, come! When saw you my father last?

150   EDGAR   Why, the night gone by.

EDMUND   Spake you with him?

EDGAR   Ay, two hours together.

EDMUND   Parted you in good terms? Found you no displeasure in him by word or countenance?°   °appearance; demeanor

155   EDGAR   None at all.

EDMUND   Bethink yourself wherein you may have offended him; and at my entreaty forbear° his presence till some little time hath qualified° the heat of his displeasure; which at this instant so rageth in him, that with
160   the mischief of your person it would scarcely allay.[5]   °avoid

°mollified

EDGAR   Some villain hath done me wrong.

EDMUND   That's my fear. I pray you, have a continent forbearance° till the speed of his rage goes slower; and, as I say, retire with me to my lodging, from whence I will fitly°
165   bring you to hear my lord speak. Pray ye, go! There's my key. If you do stir abroad, go armed.   °restrained absence

°when suitable

EDGAR   Armed, brother?

EDMUND   Brother, I advise you to the best. Go armed. I am no honest man if there be any good meaning towards
170   you. I have told you what I have seen and heard; but faintly, nothing like the image and horror of it. Pray you, away!

EDGAR   Shall I hear from you anon?

EDMUND   I do serve you in this business.   *Exit* EDGAR
175   A credulous father, and a brother noble,
Whose nature is so far from doing harms,
That he suspects none; on whose foolish honesty
My practices° ride easy! I see the business.[6]
Let me, if not by birth, have lands by wit:°   °plots

°intelligence
180   All with me's meet that I can fashion fit.[7]   *Exit*

---

5. Even harming you bodily would hardly relieve his anger; alternatively, with the irritant of your presence, it (Gloucester's anger) would not be abated.

6. It is now clear to me what needs to be done.
7. Anything is fine by me as long as I can make it serve my purpose. "Meet": justifiable; appropriate.

1.3

Enter GONERIL, *and* OSWALD, *her steward*

GONERIL   Did my father strike my gentleman for chiding
of his fool?

OSWALD   Yes, madam.

GONERIL   By day and night he wrongs me; every hour
5 He flashes into one gross crime° or other,   *offense*
That sets us all at odds. I'll not endure it.
His knights grow riotous, and himself upbraids° us   *scolds*
On every trifle. When he returns from hunting,
I will not speak with him. Say I am sick.
10 If you come slack of former services,[1]
You shall do well; the fault of it I'll answer.°   *answer for*

OSWALD   He's coming, madam; I hear him.
Horns within°   *hunting horns offstage*

GONERIL   Put on what weary negligence you please,
You and your fellows.° I'd have it come to question.   *i.e., the other servants*
15 If he dislike it, let him to our sister,
Whose mind and mine, I know, in that are one,
Not to be overruled. Idle° old man,   *foolish*
That still would manage those authorities
That he hath given away! Now, by my life,
20 Old fools are babes again, and must be used
With checks as flatteries, when they are seen abused.[2]
Remember what I tell you.

OSWALD   Well, madam.

GONERIL   And let his knights have colder looks among you.
What grows of it, no matter; advise your fellows so.
25 I would breed from hence occasions, and I shall,
That I may speak.[3] I'll write straight° to my sister,   *straightway*
To hold my very° course. Prepare for dinner.   *Exeunt*   *exact*

1.4

Enter KENT, *disguised*

KENT   If but as well[1] I other accents borrow,
That can my speech defuse,° my good intent   *disguise*
May carry through itself to that full issue°   *result*
For which I razed my likeness.[2] Now, banished Kent,
5 If thou canst serve where thou dost stand condemned,
So may it come,° thy master, whom thou lovest,   *come to pass*
Shall find thee full of labors.°   *helpful; keen*
Horns within.° Enter LEAR, *knights, and attendants*   *offstage*

1.3 Location: The duke of Albany's castle.
1. If you offer him less service (and respect)
than before.
2. When foolish old men act like children,
rebukes are the kindest treatment when kind
treatment is abused.

3. I wish to foster situations, and I shall, in
which to speak my mind.
1.4 Location: As before.
1. As well as disguising my appearance.
2. Disguised my appearance; shaved off my
beard (with a pun on "razor").

LEAR   Let me not stay° a jot for dinner; go get it ready.   *wait*

                              Exit an attendant

    How now! What° art thou?   *who*

10 KENT   A man, sir.

    LEAR   What dost thou profess?[3] What wouldst thou with
    us?

    KENT   I do profess to be no less than I seem; to serve him
    truly that will put me in trust; to love him that is honest;

15 to converse° with him that is wise and says little; to fear   *associate*
    judgment; to fight when I cannot choose;° and to eat no   *when I must*
    fish.[4]

    LEAR   What art thou?

    KENT   A very honest-hearted fellow, and as poor as the

20 king.

    LEAR   If thou be as poor for a subject as he is for a king,
    thou art poor enough. What wouldst thou?

    KENT   Service.

    LEAR   Who wouldst thou serve?

25 KENT   You.

    LEAR   Dost thou know me, fellow?

    KENT   No, sir; but you have that in your countenance
    which I would fain° call master.   *gladly*

    LEAR   What's that?

30 KENT   Authority.

    LEAR   What services canst thou do?

    KENT   I can keep honest counsel,° ride, run, mar a curious   *keep secrets*
    tale in telling it, and deliver a plain message bluntly. That
    which ordinary men are fit for, I am qualified in; and the

35 best of me is diligence.

    LEAR   How old art thou?

    KENT   Not so young, sir, to love a woman for singing, nor
    so old to dote on her for anything. I have years on my
    back forty-eight.

40 LEAR   Follow me; thou shalt serve me. If I like thee no
    worse after dinner, I will not part from thee yet. Dinner,
    ho dinner! Where's my knave? my fool? Go you, and call
    my fool hither.   *Exit an attendant*

                              Enter OSWALD

    You, you, sirrah, where's my daughter?

45 OSWALD   So please you—   *Exit*

    LEAR   What says the fellow there? Call the clotpoll° back.   *blockhead*
    (*Exit a* KNIGHT) Where's my fool, ho? I think the world's
    asleep.

                              Re-enter KNIGHT

    How now! where's that mongrel?

---

3. What is your job (profession)? Kent, in reply,
uses "profess" punningly to mean "claim."
4. And not to be a Catholic or penitent (Catholics were obliged to eat fish on specified occasions, and as penance); alternatively, to be a
manly man, a meat eater.

KNIGHT   He says, my lord, your daughter is not well.

LEAR   Why came not the slave back to me when I called
him?

KNIGHT   Sir, he answered me in the roundest° manner, he   *bluntest; rudest*
would not.

LEAR   He would not!

KNIGHT   My lord, I know not what the matter is; but, to my
judgment, your highness is not entertained with that ceremonious affection as you were wont.° There's a great   *accustomed to*
abatement of kindness appears as well in the general
dependants° as in the duke himself also and your daugh-   *servants*
ter.

LEAR   Ha! sayest thou so?

KNIGHT   I beseech you pardon me, my lord, if I be mistaken; for my duty cannot be silent when I think your
highness wronged.

LEAR   Thou but rememberest° me of mine own concep-   *remind*
tion.° I have perceived a most faint neglect of late; which   *perception*
I have rather blamed as mine own jealous curiosity⁵ than
as a very pretense° and purpose of unkindness. I   *a true intention*
will look further into 't. But where's my fool? I have not
seen him this two days.

KNIGHT   Since my young lady's going into France, sir, the
fool hath much pined away.

LEAR   No more of that; I have noted it well. Go you and
tell my daughter I would speak with her.   *Exit* KNIGHT
Go you, call hither my fool.   *Exit an attendant*
     Re-enter OSWALD
O, you sir, you! Come you hither, sir. Who am I, sir?

OSWALD   My lady's father.

LEAR   "My lady's father"! My lord's knave! You whoreson
dog! you slave! you cur!

OSWALD   I am none of these, my lord; I beseech your pardon.

LEAR   Do you bandy° looks with me, you rascal? (*Striking*   *give and take*
him)

OSWALD   I'll not be struck, my lord.

KENT   Nor tripped neither, you base foot-ball player.⁶
     Tripping up his heels

LEAR   I thank thee, fellow; thou servest me, and I'll love
thee.

KENT   Come, sir, arise, away! I'll teach you differences.°   *(of rank)*
Away, away! If you will measure your lubber's length
again,⁷ tarry; but away! Go to! Have you wisdom? so.
     Pushes OSWALD *out*

---

5. Paranoid concern with niceties.
6. Foot-ball was a rough street game played by
the poor.

7. If you will be stretched out by me again. "Lubber": clumsy oaf.

LEAR Now, my friendly knave, I thank thee: there's earnest
    of° thy service. (*Giving* KENT *money*)   *downpayment for*
    Enter FOOL

FOOL Let me hire him too. Here's my coxcomb.°   *fool's cap*
    Offering KENT *his cap*

LEAR How now, my pretty knave! How dost thou?

95 FOOL Sirrah, you were best take my coxcomb.

KENT Why, fool?

FOOL Why, for taking one's part that's out of favor. Nay,
    an thou canst not smile as the wind sits, thou'lt catch
    cold shortly.[8] There, take my coxcomb! Why, this fellow
100   has banished two on's daughters,[9] and did the third a
    blessing against his will. If thou follow him, thou must
    needs wear my coxcomb. How now, nuncle!° Would I had   *(mine) uncle*
    two coxcombs and two daughters!

LEAR Why, my boy?

105 FOOL If I gave them all my living,° I'd keep my coxcombs   *goods*
    myself.[1] There's mine; beg another of thy daughters.

LEAR Take heed, sirrah; the whip.

FOOL Truth's a dog must to° kennel; he must be whipped   *go to*
    out, when Lady the brach[2] may stand by the fire and
110   stink.

LEAR A pestilent gall° to me!   *annoyance; bitterness*

FOOL Sirrah, I'll teach thee a speech.

LEAR Do.

FOOL Mark it, nuncle:

115   Have more than thou showest,
           Speak less than thou knowest,
           Lend less than thou owest,°   *own*
           Ride more than thou goest,°   *walk*
           Learn° more than thou trowest,°   *hear / believe*
120   Set less than thou throwest,[3]
           Leave thy drink and thy whore,
           And keep in-a-door,
           And thou shalt have more
           Than two tens to a score.[4]

125 KENT This is nothing, fool.

FOOL Then 'tis like the breath° of an unfeed° lawyer; you   *speech / unpaid*
    gave me nothing for 't. Can you make no use of nothing,
    nuncle?

LEAR Why, no, boy; nothing can be made out of nothing.

130 FOOL (*to* KENT) Prithee, tell him, so much the rent of his
    land comes to.[5] He will not believe a fool.

---

8. I.e., if you can't keep in with those in power,
you will soon find yourself left out in the cold.
9. By abdicating, Lear has in effect prevented
his daughters from any longer being his subjects,
just as if he had banished them.
1. I.e., I'd be twice as much a fool.
2. Lady the bitch. Pet dogs were often called
"Lady" such-and-such. The allusion is to Regan

and Goneril, who are now being preferred to
truthful Cordelia.
3. Don't gamble everything on a single cast of
the dice.
4. And there will be more than two tens in your
twenty; that is, you will become richer.
5. Remind him that no land means no rent; with
a pun on "rent" meaning "torn, divided."

LEAR A bitter fool!

FOOL Dost thou know the difference, my boy, between a
    bitter fool and a sweet fool?

135 LEAR No, lad; teach me.

FOOL   That lord that counseled thee
             To give away thy land,
          Come place him here by me,
            Do thou for him stand:°   *represent him*

140   The sweet and bitter fool
             Will presently appear;
          The one in motley[6] here,
            The other found out there.

LEAR Dost thou call me fool, boy?

145 FOOL All thy other titles thou hast given away; that thou
    wast born with.

KENT This is not altogether fool,° my lord.   *foolish; folly*

FOOL No, faith, lords and great men will not let me; if I
    had a monopoly out, they would have part on 't: and ladies
150   too, they will not let me have all fool to myself; they'll be
    snatching. Give me an egg, nuncle, and I'll give thee two
    crowns.

LEAR What two crowns shall they be?

FOOL Why, after I have cut the egg i' the middle, and eat
155   up the meat,° the two crowns of the egg. When thou clov-   *edible part*
    est° thy crown i' the middle, and gavest away both parts,   *cleaved*
    thou borest° thy ass on thy back o'er the dirt.[7] Thou hadst   *you carried*
    little wit° in thy bald crown, when thou gavest thy golden   *sense*
    one away. If I speak like myself° in this, let him be   *(like a fool)*
160   whipped that first finds it so.[8]
        Singing
          Fools had ne'er less grace in a year;
            For wise men are grown foppish,[9]
          They know not how their wits to wear,
            Their manners are so apish.°   *stupid; imitative*

165 LEAR When were you wont° to be so full of songs, sirrah?   *accustomed*

FOOL I have used° it, nuncle, ever since thou madest thy   *practiced*
    daughters thy mother; for when thou gavest them the rod,
    and put'st down thine own breeches,
        Singing
          Then they for sudden joy did weep,
170   And I for sorrow sung,
          That such a king should play bo-peep,°   *a child's game*
            And go the fools among.
    Prithee, nuncle, keep a schoolmaster that can teach thy
    fool to lie. I would fain° learn to lie.   *gladly*

---

6. Multicolored dress of a court jester.
7. In a fable of Aesop, a man carried his ass instead of riding it, thereby reversing the order of nature.
8. I.e., who first discovers for himself that this is true; colloquially, who deserves to be whipped as a fool.
9. Professional fools have gone out of favor ("grace") since wise men have lately outdone them in idiocy.

175 LEAR An° you lie, sirrah, we'll have you whipped. *if*

FOOL I marvel what kin° thou and thy daughters are. *how alike*
They'll have me whipped for speaking true, thou'lt have
me whipped for lying; and sometimes I am whipped for
holding my peace. I had rather be any kind o' thing than

180 a fool; and yet I would not be thee, nuncle; thou hast
pared thy wit o' both sides, and left nothing i' the middle.
Here comes one o' the parings.

Enter GONERIL

LEAR How now, daughter! What makes that frontlet[1] on?
Methinks you are too much of late i' the frown.

185 FOOL Thou wast a pretty fellow when thou hadst no need
to care for her frowning; now thou art an O without a
figure.[2] I am better than thou art now; I am a fool, thou
art nothing. [*To* GONERIL] Yes, forsooth,° I will hold my *indeed*
tongue; so your face bids me, though you say nothing.

190 Mum, mum,
He that keeps nor crust nor crumb,
Weary of all, shall want° some. *lack, be in need of*
(*Pointing to* LEAR) That's a shealed peascod.° *empty pea pod*

GONERIL Not only, sir, this your all-licensed° fool, *unrestrained*
195 But other of your insolent retinue
Do hourly carp and quarrel, breaking forth
In rank° and not-to-be-endured riots. Sir, *foul; spreading*
I had thought, by making this well known unto you,
To have found a safe° redress; but now grow fearful, *sure*
200 By what yourself too late° have spoke and done, *recently*
That you protect this course, and put it on° *encourage it*
By your allowance; which if you should, the fault
Would not 'scape censure, nor the redresses sleep,
Which, in the tender of a wholesome weal,
205 Might in their working do you that offense,
Which else were shame, that then necessity
Will call discreet proceeding.[3]

FOOL For, you know, nuncle,
The hedge-sparrow fed the cuckoo[4] so long,
210 That it had it° head bit off by it young.° *its / (the young cuckoo)*
So, out went the candle, and we were left darkling.° *in the dark*

LEAR Are you our daughter?

GONERIL Come, sir.
I would you would make use of that good wisdom
215 Whereof I know you are fraught,° and put away *full*
These dispositions,° that of late transform you *moods, attitudes*
From what you rightly are.

1. Band worn on the forehead; here, a metaphor for "frown."
2. A zero without a preceding digit; nothing.
3. I.e., if you do approve (of your attendants' behavior), you will not escape criticism, nor will it be without retribution, which for the common good will cause you pain. While this would otherwise be improper, it will be seen as a prudent ("discreet") action under the circumstances. "Tender of": concern for. "Weal": state, commonwealth. "Then necessity": the demands of the time.
4. The cuckoo lays its eggs in other birds' nests.

FOOL   May not an ass know when the cart draws the horse?
   Whoop, Jug!⁵ I love thee.
220   LEAR   Doth any here know me? This is not Lear.
   Doth Lear walk thus? speak thus? Where are his eyes?
   Either his notion° weakens, his discernings   *intellect*
   Are lethargied—Ha! waking?° 'Tis not so.   *am I awake*
   Who is it that can tell me who I am?
225   FOOL   Lear's shadow.
   LEAR   I would° learn that; for, by the marks° of sovereignty,   *wish to / evidence*
   knowledge, and reason, I should be false persuaded I had
   daughters.
   FOOL   Which° they will make an obedient father.   *whom*
230   LEAR   Your name, fair gentlewoman?
   GONERIL   This admiration,° sir, is much o' the savor   *excessive amazement*
   Of other your new pranks. I do beseech you
   To understand my purposes aright.
   As you are old and reverend,° you should be wise.   *to be respected*
235   Here do you keep a hundred knights and squires;
   Men so disordered,° so deboshed° and bold,   *disorderly / debauched*
   That this our court, infected with their manners,
   Shows° like a riotous inn. Epicurism° and lust   *appears / gluttony*
   Make it more like a tavern or a brothel
240   Than a graced° palace. The shame itself doth speak   *an honored*
   For instant remedy; be then desired
   By her, that else° will take the thing she begs,   *otherwise*
   A little to disquantity your train;°   *to reduce your retinue*
   And the remainder that shall still depend,°   *be retained*
245   To be such men as may besort° your age,   *befit*
   And know themselves° and you.   *know their place*
   LEAR   Darkness and devils!
   Saddle my horses! call my train together!
   Degenerate bastard! I'll not trouble thee.
   Yet° have I left a daughter.   *still*
250   GONERIL   You strike my people, and your disordered rabble
   Make servants of their betters.
         Enter ALBANY
   LEAR   Woe that° too late repents!—(*To* ALBANY)   *woe to him who*
   O, sir, are you come?
   Is it your will? Speak, sir. Prepare my horses!
255   Ingratitude, thou marble-hearted fiend,
   More hideous when thou show'st thee in a child
   Than the sea-monster!
   ALBANY   Pray, sir, be patient.
   LEAR (*to* GONERIL)   Detested kite!° thou liest: *carrion-eating hawk*
   My train are men of choice and rarest parts,°   *qualities*
260   That all particulars of duty know
   And in the most exact regard support
   The worships of° their name. O most small fault,   *honors accorded*

5. Nickname for "Joan"; sobriquet for a whore.

How ugly didst thou in Cordelia show!
That, like an engine, wrench'd my frame of nature
265   From the fixed place;[6] drew from my heart all love,
And added to the gall. O Lear, Lear, Lear!
Beat at this gate, that let thy folly in, (*striking his head*)
And thy dear° judgment out! Go, go, my people.   *precious*

ALBANY   My lord, I am guiltless, as I am ignorant
Of what hath moved you.

270 LEAR   It may be so, my lord.
Hear, Nature, hear! dear goddess, hear!
Suspend thy purpose, if thou didst intend
To make this creature fruitful!
Into her womb convey sterility!
275   Dry up in her the organs of increase;
And from her derogate° body never spring   *debased*
A babe to honor her! If she must teem,°   *breed*
Create her child of spleen,° that it may live   *malice*
And be a thwart, disnatured° torment to her!   *a perverse unnatural*
280   Let it stamp wrinkles in her brow of youth;
With cadent° tears fret° channels in her cheeks;   *flowing / carve*
Turn all her mother's pains and benefits°   *cares and kind actions*
To laughter and contempt, that she may feel
How sharper than a serpent's tooth it is
285   To have a thankless child! Away, away!   *Exit*

ALBANY   Now, gods that we adore, whereof comes this?

GONERIL   Never afflict yourself to know the cause;
But let his disposition° have that scope   *inclination*
That dotage gives it.

        Re-enter LEAR

290 LEAR   What, fifty of my followers at a clap?
Within a fortnight?[7]

ALBANY   What's the matter, sir?

LEAR   I'll tell thee. (*To* GONERIL) Life and death! I am ashamed
That thou hast power to shake my manhood thus;
That these hot tears, which break from me perforce,°   *against my will*
295   Should make thee worth them. Blasts and fogs upon thee!
The untented woundings° of a father's curse   *the undressed wounds*
Pierce every sense about thee! Old fond° eyes,   *foolish*
Beweep° this cause again, I'll pluck ye out,   *if you weep over*
And cast you, with the waters that you lose,
300   To temper° clay. Yea, is it come to this?   *soften*
Let it be so. Yet have I left a daughter,
Who, I am sure, is kind and comfortable.°   *comforting*
When she shall hear this of thee, with her nails
She'll flay thy wolvish visage. Thou shalt find

---

6. As a machine (or lever) dislocated my natural affections from their proper foundations.
7. Evidently Goneril has already given orders that fully half of Lear's retinue is to be dismissed. See lines 241–43 above.

305 That I'll resume the shape which thou dost think
I have cast off for ever; thou shalt, I warrant thee.
Exeunt LEAR, KENT, *and attendants*
GONERIL   Do you mark that, my lord?
ALBANY   I cannot be so partial,° Goneril,   *biased*
To° the great love I bear you—   *because of*
310 GONERIL   Pray you, content.° What, Oswald, ho! (*To the*   *be quiet*
FOOL) You sir, more knave than fool, after your master!
FOOL   Nuncle Lear, nuncle Lear, tarry and take the fool
with thee.
             A fox, when one has caught her,
315   And such a daughter,
             Should sure° to the slaughter,   *surely be sent*
             If my cap would buy a halter:°   *collar; noose*
             So the fool follows after.   *Exit*
GONERIL   This man hath had good counsel!—a hundred knights?
320 'Tis politic° and safe to let him keep   *prudent*
At point° a hundred knights? Yes, that on every dream,   *armed*
Each buzz,° each fancy, each complaint, dislike,   *rumor*
He may enguard° his dotage with their powers,   *protect*
And hold our lives in mercy. Oswald, I say!
ALBANY   Well, you may fear too far.
325 GONERIL   Safer than trust too far:
Let me still° take away the harms I fear,   *always*
Not° fear still to be taken. I know his heart.   *rather than*
What he hath uttered I have writ my sister.
If she sustain him and his hundred knights,
When I have showed the unfitness—
             Re-enter OSWALD
330   How now, Oswald!
What, have you writ that letter to my sister?
OSWALD   Yes, madam.
GONERIL   Take you some company, and away to horse!
Inform her full of my particular fear,
335 And thereto add such reasons of your own
As may compact° it more. Get you gone,   *compound*
And hasten your return.   *Exit* OSWALD
             No, no, my lord,
This milky gentleness and course of yours
340 Though I condemn not, yet, under pardon,°   *begging your pardon*
You are much more attaxed° for want of wisdom   *taken to task, censured*
Than praised for harmful mildness.
ALBANY   How far your eyes may pierce° I cannot tell: *foresee*
Striving to better, oft we mar what's well.
345 GONERIL   Nay, then—
ALBANY   Well, well; the event.°   *Exeunt*   *time will tell*

1.5

Enter LEAR, KENT, *and* FOOL

LEAR   Go you before° to Gloucester[1] with these letters.   *on ahead*
Acquaint my daughter no further with any thing you
know than comes from her demand out of the letter.[2] If
your diligence be not speedy, I shall be there afore you.

5   KENT   I will not sleep, my lord, till I have delivered your
letter.   *Exit*

FOOL   If a man's brains were in 's heels, were't not in danger of kibes?°   *chilblains*

LEAR   Ay, boy.

10   FOOL   Then, I prithee, be merry; thy wit shall ne'er go
slipshod.[3]

LEAR   Ha, ha, ha!

FOOL   Shalt° see thy other daughter will use thee kindly;   *thou shalt*
for though she's as like this as a crab's[4] like an apple, yet

15   I can tell what I can tell.

LEAR   Why, what canst thou tell, my boy?

FOOL   She will taste as like this as a crab does to a crab.
Thou canst tell why one's nose stands i' the middle
on's° face?   *of one's*

20   LEAR   No.

FOOL   Why, to keep one's eyes of either side's° nose, that   *of his*
what a man cannot smell out, 'a° may spy into.   *he*

LEAR   I did her° wrong—   *(Cordelia)*

FOOL   Canst tell how an oyster makes his shell?

25   LEAR   No.

FOOL   Nor I neither; but I can tell why a snail has a house.

LEAR   Why?

FOOL   Why, to put his head in; not to give it away to his
daughters, and leave his horns without a case.[5]

30   LEAR   I will forget my nature.[6] So kind a father! Be my
horses ready?

FOOL   Thy asses° are gone about 'em. The reason why the   *(servants)*
seven stars° are no more than seven is a pretty reason.   *the Pleiades*

LEAR   Because they are not eight?

35   FOOL   Yes, indeed. Thou wouldst make a good fool.

LEAR   To take 't again perforce![7] Monster ingratitude!

FOOL   If thou wert my fool, nuncle, I'd have thee beaten
for being old before thy time.

1.5 Location: Before Albany's castle.
1. To the city of Gloucester.
2. Other than such questions as are prompted
by the letter.
3. Literally, your brains will not wear slippers
(to warm feet that are afflicted with chilblains);
feet of any intelligence would not walk toward
Regan.
4. Crab apple, sour apple.

5. Protective covering for his head or concealment for his horns (horns were the conventional
sign of a cuckold). The Fool reflects the cynical
view, common in the period, that all married
men are inevitably cuckolded.
6. Lose my fatherly feelings.
7. To take it back by force. Lear may refer to
Goneril's treachery, or he may be contemplating
resuming his authority.

LEAR   How's that?

40 FOOL   Thou shouldst not have been old till thou hadst been wise.

LEAR   O, let me not be mad, not mad, sweet heaven!
      Keep me in temper;° I would not be mad!   *sane*
         Enter GENTLEMAN
      How now! Are the horses ready?

GENTLEMAN   Ready, my lord.

45 LEAR   Come, boy.

FOOL   She that's a maid now, and laughs at my departure,
      Shall not be a maid long, unless things be cut shorter.[8]

                                    Exeunt

2.1

        Enter EDMUND *and* CURAN *meeting*

EDMUND   Save° thee, Curan.   *God save*

CURAN   And you, sir. I have been with your father, and
      given him notice that the Duke of Cornwall and Regan
      his duchess will be here with him this night.

5 EDMUND   How comes that?

CURAN   Nay, I know not. You have heard of the news
      abroad—I mean the whispered ones, for they are yet but
      ear-bussing arguments?[1]

EDMUND   Not I. Pray you, what are they?

10 CURAN   Have you heard of no likely wars toward,° 'twixt   *impending*
      the Dukes of Cornwall and Albany?

EDMUND   Not a word.

CURAN   You may do,° then, in time. Fare you well, sir.   *do so*

                                      Exit

EDMUND   The duke be here tonight? The better! best!

15 This weaves itself perforce° into my business.   *i.e., of its own accord*
      My father hath set guard to take my brother;
      And I have one thing, of a queasy question,
      Which I must act.[2] Briefness and fortune, work!°   *be with me*
      Brother, a word! Descend! Brother, I say!
        Enter EDGAR

20 My father watches. O sir, fly this place!
      Intelligence is given where you are hid.
      You have now the good advantage of the night.
      Have you not spoken 'gainst the Duke of Cornwall?
      He's coming hither; now, i' the night, i' the haste,

25 And Regan with him: have you nothing said
      Upon his party° 'gainst the Duke of Albany?   *on his (Cornwall's) side*
      Advise yourself.°   *consider carefully*

EDGAR   I am sure on't,° not a word.   *of it*

---

8. A girl who would laugh at my leaving would be
so foolish that she could not remain a virgin for
long; "things" refers both to the unfolding event
and to penises.

2.1 Location: Gloucester's castle.
1. Barely whispered affairs. "Bussing": kissing.
2. There is one thing, of a ticklish sort, that I
must do.

EDMUND I hear my father coming. Pardon me!
In cunning I must draw my sword upon you:
30 Draw; seem to defend yourself; now quit you° well.   *acquit yourself*
Yield! Come before my father. Light, ho, here!
Fly, brother. Torches, torches! So farewell.   *Exit* EDGAR
Some blood drawn on me would beget opinion°   *produce the impression*
    (*wounds his arm*)
Of my more fierce endeavor. I have seen drunkards
35 Do more than this in sport. Father, father!
Stop, stop! No help?

    Enter GLOUCESTER, *and servants with torches*

GLOUCESTER Now, Edmund, where's the villain?
EDMUND Here stood he in the dark, his sharp sword out,
Mumbling of wicked charms, conjuring the moon
To stand° auspicious mistress—   *to act as his*
40 GLOUCESTER   But where is he?
EDMUND Look, sir, I bleed.
GLOUCESTER   Where is the villain, Edmund?
EDMUND Fled this way, sir. When by no means he could—
GLOUCESTER Pursue him, ho! Go after.

      Exeunt some servants

By no means what?
45 EDMUND Persuade me to the murder of your lordship;
But that° I told him, the revenging gods   *in response to that*
'Gainst parricides did all their thunders bend;
Spoke, with how manifold and strong a bond
The child was bound to the father; sir, in fine,°   *finally*
50 Seeing how loathly opposite° I stood   *opposed*
To his unnatural purpose, in fell° motion,   *deadly*
With his prepared sword, he charges home°   *strikes to the heart of*
My unprovided° body, lanched° mine arm: *unprotected / wounded*
But when he saw my best alarumed spirits,
55 Bold in the quarrel's right,[3] roused to the encounter,
Or whether gasted° by the noise I made,   *frightened*
Full suddenly he fled.
GLOUCESTER   Let him fly far.
Not in this land shall he remain uncaught;
And found—dispatch.° The noble duke my master,   *and once found—killed*
60 My worthy arch° and patron, comes tonight: *lord*
By his authority I will proclaim it,
That he which finds him shall deserve our thanks,
Bringing the murderous caitiff° to the stake;[4]   *wretch*
He that conceals him, death.
65 EDMUND When I dissuaded him from his intent,
And found him pight° to do it, with curst° speech   *resolved / bitter*
I threatened to discover° him. He replied,   *expose*

---

3. I.e., that I was fully roused to action, made brave by righteousness.

4. Treachery and rebellion were crimes for which one could be burned.

"Thou unpossessing bastard! dost thou think
If I would stand against thee, would the reposal°   *placing*
70 Of any trust, virtue, or worth in thee
Make thy words faithed?° No. What I should deny—   *believed*
As this I would; ay, though thou didst produce
My very character⁵—I'd turn it all
To⁶ thy suggestion, plot, and damnèd practice:°   *scheming*
75 And thou must make a dullard of the world,
If they not thought the profits of my death
Were very pregnant° and potential spurs°   *full / powerful temptations*
To make thee seek it."⁷
  GLOUCESTER   Strong° and fast'ned° villain!   *flagrant / incorrigible*
Would he deny his letter? I never got° him.   *begot*
     Tucket° within   *flourish of trumpets*
80 Hark, the duke's trumpets! I know not why he comes.
All ports° I'll bar; the villain shall not 'scape;   *seaports; exits*
The duke must grant me that. Besides, his picture⁸
I will send far and near, that all the kingdom
May have due note of him; and of my land,
85 Loyal and natural° boy, I'll work the means   *loving; illegitimate*
To make thee capable.°   *legally able to inherit*
     Enter CORNWALL, REGAN, *and attendants*
  CORNWALL   How now, my noble friend! Since I came hither
(Which I can call but now), I have heard strange news.
  REGAN   If it be true, all vengeance comes too short
90 Which can pursue the offender. How dost, my lord?
  GLOUCESTER   O, madam, my old heart is cracked, is cracked!
  REGAN   What, did my father's godson seek your life?
He whom my father named? Your Edgar?
  GLOUCESTER   O, lady, lady, shame would have it hid!
95   REGAN   Was he not companion with the riotous knights
That tend° upon my father?   *attend*
  GLOUCESTER   I know not, madam. 'Tis too bad, too bad!
  EDMUND   Yes, madam, he was of that consort.°   *company*
  REGAN   No marvel, then, though° he were ill affected.°   *that / ill-disposed*
100 'Tis they have put him on° the old man's death,   *have urged him to seek*
To have th' expense° and waste of his revenues.   *use*
I have this present evening from my sister
Been well informed of them; and with such cautions
That if they come to sojourn at my house,
I'll not be there.
105   CORNWALL   Nor I, assure thee, Regan.
Edmund, I hear that you have shown your father
A child-like office.°   *filial service*

---

5. Handwriting; but also, a true summary of my character.
6. I'd blame it all on.
7. And do you think the world so stupid that it could not see the benefit you would get from my death (and thus a motive for plotting to kill me)?
8. Likenesses of outlaws were drawn up, printed, and publicly displayed, sometimes with an offer of reward, as in "Wanted" posters.

EDMUND   'Twas my duty, sir.

GLOUCESTER   He did bewray his practice,[9] and received
  This hurt you see, striving to apprehend him.

CORNWALL   Is he pursued?

110   GLOUCESTER   Ay, my good lord.

CORNWALL   If he be taken, he shall never more
  Be feared of doing harm. Make your own purpose,
  How in my strength you please.[1] For you, Edmund,
  Whose virtue and obedience doth this instant

115   So much commend itself, you shall be ours.
  Natures of such deep trust we shall much need;
  You we first seize on.

EDMUND   I shall serve you, sir,
  Truly, however else.°   *if nothing else*

GLOUCESTER [*to* CORNWALL] For him I thank your grace.

CORNWALL   You know not why we came to visit you—

120   REGAN   Thus out of season, threading dark-eyed night.
  Occasions, noble Gloucester, of some poise,°   *weight*
  Wherein we must have use of your advice:
  Our father he hath writ, so hath our sister,
  Of differences,° which I best thought it fit   *quarrels*

125   To answer from° our home. The several° messengers   *away from / various*
  From hence attend° dispatch. Our good old friend,   *await*
  Lay comforts to your bosom, and bestow
  Your needful° counsel to our business,   *badly needed*
  Which craves the instant use.[2]

GLOUCESTER   I serve you, madam.

130   Your graces are right welcome.   *Exeunt*

2.2

    Enter KENT *and* OSWALD, *severally*°   *separately*

OSWALD   Good dawning to thee, friend. Art° of this house?   *are you a servant*

KENT   Ay.

OSWALD   Where may we set our horses?

KENT   I' the mire.

5   OSWALD   Prithee, if thou lovest me,° tell me.   *if you will be so kind*

KENT   I love thee not.

OSWALD   Why, then, I care not for thee.

KENT   If I had thee in Lipsbury pinfold,[1] I would make
  thee care for me.

10   OSWALD   Why dost thou use° me thus? I know thee not.   *treat*

KENT   Fellow, I know thee.

OSWALD   What dost thou know me for?°   *i.e, to be*

---

9. Reveal his (Edgar's) plot.
1. Devise your plots making use of my forces and authority as you see fit.
2. Which requires immediate attention.
2.2 Location: Before Gloucester's house.

1. If I had you in the enclosure of my mouth (gripped in my teeth). Lipsbury is probably an invented place-name. "Pinfold": pen, animal enclosure.

KENT   A knave; a rascal; an eater of broken meats;° a base,   *scraps*
     proud, shallow, beggarly, three-suited, hundred-pound,
15   filthy, worsted-stocking knave;[2] a lily-livered,° action-   *cowardly*
     taking knave; a whoreson, glass-gazing,° superserviceable,   *mirror-gazing*
     finical° rogue; one-trunk-inheriting[3] slave; one that   *finicky, fastidious*
     wouldst be a bawd in way of good service,[4] and art noth-
     ing but the composition° of a knave, beggar, coward, pan-   *combination*
20   dar, and the son and heir of a mongrel bitch; one whom I
     will beat into clamorous whining, if thou deniest the least
     syllable of thy addition.[5]
OSWALD   Why, what a monstrous fellow art thou, thus to
     rail on one that is neither known of° thee nor knows thee!   *by*
25 KENT   What a brazen-faced varlet° art thou, to deny thou   *rascal*
     knowest me! Is it two days ago since I tripped up thy
     heels, and beat thee before the king? Draw, you rogue!
     For, though it be night, yet the moon shines. I'll make a
     sop of the moonshine[6] of you. Draw, you whoreson cul-
30   lionly barber-monger,[7] draw!
          Drawing his sword
OSWALD   Away! I have nothing to do with thee.
KENT   Draw, you rascal! You come with letters against the
     king, and take Vanity the puppet's part against the roy-
     alty of her father.[8] Draw, you rogue, or I'll so carbonado[9]
35   your shanks! Draw, you rascal! Come your ways!°   *come forward*
OSWALD   Help, ho! murther! help!
KENT   Strike, you slave! Stand, rogue! Stand, you neat°   *elegant; foppish*
     slave! Strike! [*Beating him*]
OSWALD   Help, ho! murther! murther!
          Enter EDMUND *with his rapier drawn,* CORNWALL,
          REGAN, GLOUCESTER, *and servants*
40 EDMUND   How now! What's the matter?
          Parts them
KENT   With you, goodman° boy, an° you please! Come, I'll   *i.e., lowborn / if*
     flesh ye![1] Come, on, young master!
GLOUCESTER   Weapons! arms! What's the matter here?
CORNWALL   Keep peace, upon your lives!
45   He dies that strikes again. What is the matter?
REGAN   The messengers from our sister and the king.
CORNWALL   What is your difference? Speak.

---

2. Oswald is being called a poor imitation of a
gentleman. Servants were permitted three suits a
year; one hundred pounds was the minimum
qualification for the purchase of one of King
James's knighthoods; a gentleman would wear
silk, not "worsted" (of thick woolen material),
stockings.
3. Owning only what would fill one trunk.
"Action-taking": litigious, one who would rather
use the law than his fists. "Superserviceable":
overly officious, or too ready to serve.
4. One who would be a pimp if called upon.
5. Of the descriptions Kent has just applied to

him. "Addition": title (used ironically).
6. Kent proposes so to skewer and pierce Oswald
that his body might soak up moonlight. "Sop":
piece of bread to be steeped or dunked in soup.
7. Despicable frequenter of hairdressers. A "cul-
lion" is a testicle.
8. And support Goneril, here depicted as a
dressed-up doll whose pride is contrasted with
Lear's kingliness.
9. Slash or score as one would the surface of meat
in preparation for broiling.
1. I'll blood you (as a hunting dog); I'll initiate
you into fighting.

OSWALD   I am scarce in breath, my lord.

KENT   No marvel, you have so bestirred your valor. You
50   cowardly rascal, nature disclaims° in thee; a tailor made   *disowns her part*
thee.

CORNWALL   Thou art a strange fellow. A tailor[2] make a man?

KENT   Ay, a tailor, sir. A stone-cutter or a painter could
not have made him so ill,° though he had been but two   *so badly*
55   hours at the trade.

CORNWALL   Speak yet, how grew your quarrel?

OSWALD   This ancient ruffian, sir, whose life I have spared
at suit of° his gray beard—   *on account of*

KENT   Thou whoreson zed![3] thou unnecessary letter! My
60   lord, if you will give me leave, I will tread this unbolted°   *unsifted, coarse*
villain into mortar and daub the walls of a jakes° with   *privy, toilet*
him. Spare my gray beard, you wagtail?[4]

CORNWALL   Peace, sirrah!
You beastly knave, know you no reverence?°   *respect*

65   KENT   Yes, sir, but anger hath a privilege.

CORNWALL   Why art thou angry?

KENT   That such a slave as this should wear a sword,
Who wears no honesty. Such smiling rogues as these,
Like rats, oft bite the holy cords[5] a-twain
70   Which are too intrinse° t' unloose; smooth° every passion   *intricate / flatter*
That in the natures of their lords rebel;
Bring oil to fire, snow to their colder moods;
Renege,° affirm, and turn their halcyon beaks[6]   *deny*
With every gale and vary° of their masters,   *mood*
75   Knowing nought, like dogs, but following.
A plague upon your epileptic° visage!   *distorted, grimacing*
Smile you° my speeches, as° I were a fool?   *do you smile at / as if*
Goose, if I had you upon Sarum plain
I'ld drive ye cackling home to Camelot.[7]

80   CORNWALL   What, art thou mad, old fellow?

GLOUCESTER   How fell you out?° Say that.   *came you to disagree*

KENT   No contraries° hold more antipathy   *opposites*
Than I and such a knave.

CORNWALL   Why dost thou call him knave? What's his offense?

85   KENT   His countenance likes° me not.   *pleases*

CORNWALL   No more, perchance,° does mine, nor his, nor hers.   *perhaps*

KENT   Sir, 'tis my occupation to be plain.
I have seen better faces in my time
Than stands on any shoulder that I see
90   Before me at this instant.

---

2. Tailors, considered effeminate, were stock objects of mockery.
3. The letter Z (zed) was considered superfluous and was omitted from many dictionaries.
4. A common English bird that takes its name from the up-and-down flicking of its tail; this, and its characteristic hopping from foot to foot, causes it to appear nervous.
5. Bonds of kinship, affection, marriage, or rank.

6. It was believed that the kingfisher (in Greek, *halcyon*) could be used as a weather vane when dead: if the bird were suspended by a thread, its beak would turn whatever way the wind blew.
7. Comparing him to a cackling goose, Kent tells Oswald that if he had him on Salisbury Plain, he would drive him all the way to Camelot, legendary home of King Arthur.

CORNWALL   This is some fellow
Who, having been praised for bluntness, doth affect
A saucy roughness, and constrains the garb
Quite from his nature.[8] He cannot flatter, he,
An honest mind and plain, he must speak truth!

95   An they will take it, so; if not, he's plain.[9]
These kind of knaves I know, which in this plainness
Harbor more craft and more corrupter ends
Than twenty silly ducking observants
That stretch their duties nicely.[1]

100 KENT   Sir, in good sooth, in sincere verity,
Under the allowance of your great aspect,[2]
Whose influence, like the wreath of radiant fire
On flickering Phoebus' front—°   *the sun god's forehead*

CORNWALL   What mean'st by this?

KENT   To go out of my dialect,[3] which you discommend so
105   much. I know, sir, I am no flatterer. He that beguiled
you in a plain accent was a plain knave; which for my
part I will not be, though I should win your displeasure
to entreat me to 't.[4]

CORNWALL   What was the offense you gave him?

110 OSWALD   I never gave him any:
It pleased the king his master very late°   *lately*
To strike at me, upon his misconstruction,°   *misunderstanding (me)*
When he, conjunct,° and flattering his displeasure,   *in league with*
Tripped me behind; being down, insulted,° railed,   *I being down, he insulted*

115   And put upon him such a deal of man,
That worthied him,[5] got praises of the king
For him attempting who was self-subdued;[6]
And, in the fleshment° of this dread exploit,   *excitement; flush*
Drew on me here again.

KENT   None of these rogues and cowards
120   But Ajax is their fool.[7]

CORNWALL   Fetch forth the stocks!
You stubborn miscreant knave, you reverent° braggart,   *old; revered*
We'll teach you—

KENT   Sir, I am too old to learn.
Call not your stocks for me. I serve the king;

---

8. I.e., and assumes the appearance though it is untrue to his real self. Alternatively (with "his" meaning "its"), and distorts the true shape of plainness from what it naturally is (by turning it into disrespect).

9. If they will accept (Kent's attitude), well and good; if not, he is a plainspoken man (and does not care).

1. Than twenty obsequious attendants who constantly bow idiotically and who perform their functions with excessive diligence ("nicely").

2. With the permission of your great countenance. "Aspect" also refers to the astrological position of a planet; Kent's bombastic language here raises Cornwall to the mock-heroic proportions of a heavenly body.

3. Normal mode of speech.

4. The person who tried to hoodwink you with plain speaking was, indeed, a pure knave—something I won't be, even if you were to beg me to be one (a plain knave, or flatterer).

5. And put on such a show of manliness that he was thought a worthy fellow.

6. For attacking a man who had already yielded.

7. I.e., by their own account, such rogues and cowards are always vastly superior to Ajax (next to Achilles, the mightiest of the Greeks in the *Iliad*).

On whose employment I was sent to you:
125 You shall do small respect, show too bold malice
Against the grace° and person° of my master,   *majesty / personal honor*
Stocking° his messenger.   *by stocking*
CORNWALL Fetch forth the stocks! As I have life and honor,
There shall he sit till noon.
130 REGAN Till noon? Till night, my lord, and all night too!
KENT Why, madam, if I were your father's dog,
You should not use me so.
REGAN   Sir, being° his knave, I will.   *since you are*
CORNWALL This is a fellow of the self-same color°   *character*
Our sister° speaks of. Come, bring away the stocks!   *sister-in-law*
    Stocks brought out
135 GLOUCESTER Let me beseech your grace not to do so.
His fault is much, and the good king his master
Will check° him for't. Your purposed° low correction   *reprimand / intended*
Is such as basest and contemned'st wretches
For pilferings and most common trespasses
140 Are punished with: the king must take it ill,
That he, so slightly valued in his messenger,
Should have him thus restrained.
CORNWALL   I'll answer° that.   *be responsible for*
REGAN My sister may receive it much more worse,
To have her gentleman abused, assaulted,
145 For following° her affairs. Put in his legs.   *carrying out*
    KENT *is put in the stocks*
Come, my good lord, away.
    Exeunt all but GLOUCESTER *and* KENT
GLOUCESTER I am sorry for thee, friend: 'tis the duke's pleasure,
Whose disposition, all the world well knows,
Will not be rubbed° nor stopped: I'll entreat for thee.   *obstructed*
150 KENT Pray do not, sir. I have watched° and traveled hard;   *gone without sleep*
Some time I shall sleep out, the rest I'll whistle.
A good man's fortune may grow out at heels:[8]
Give° you good morrow!   *God give*
GLOUCESTER The duke's to blame in this; 'twill be ill-taken.
    Exit
155 KENT Good king, that must approve° the common saw,°   *prove / saying*
Thou out of heaven's benediction comest
To the warm sun![9]
Approach, thou beacon[1] to this under globe,
That by thy comfortable beams I may
160 Peruse this letter! Nothing almost sees miracles
But misery.[2] I know 'tis from Cordelia,

---

8. The fortunes of even good men sometimes wear thin.
9. You come from the blessing of heaven into the heat of the sun (go from good to bad).
1. It is arguable whether Kent here refers to the sun or to the moon.
2. Only those suffering misery are granted miracles; any comfort seems miraculous to those who are miserable.

Who hath most fortunately been informed
Of my obscurèd° course; (*reads*) "and shall find time   *hidden, disguised*
From this enormous state,° seeking to give   *awful state of affairs*
165 Losses their remedies." All weary and o'er-watched,°   *too long awake*
Take vantage,° heavy eyes, not to behold   *the opportunity*
This shameful lodging.
Fortune, good night; smile once more; turn thy wheel![3]

2.3

Enter EDGAR
EDGAR   I heard myself proclaimed;°   *declared an outlaw*
And by the happy° hollow of a tree   *opportune*
Escaped the hunt. No port° is free; no place,   *seaport; exit*
That guard, and most unusual vigilance,
5 Does not attend my taking.° Whiles° I may 'scape,   *await my capture / until*
I will preserve myself; and am bethought°   *resolved*
To take the basest and most poorest shape
That ever penury, in contempt of° man,   *for*
Brought near to beast. My face I'll grime with filth,
10 Blanket my loins, elf[1] all my hair in knots,
And with presented° nakedness outface   *exposed*
The winds and persecutions of the sky.
The country gives me proof and precedent
Of Bedlam° beggars, who, with roaring voices,   *i.e., mad*
15 Strike° in their numbed and mortified° bare arms   *stick / deadened*
Pins, wooden pricks, nails, sprigs of rosemary;
And with this horrible object,° from low farms,   *spectacle*
Poor pelting° villages, sheep-cotes, and mills,   *paltry, contemptible*
Sometime with lunatic bans,° sometime with prayers,   *curses*
20 Enforce their charity. Poor Turlygod![2] poor Tom!
That's something yet! Edgar I nothing am.[3]   *Exit*

2.4

Enter LEAR, FOOL, *and* GENTLEMAN
LEAR   'Tis strange that they should so depart from home,
And not send back my messenger.
GENTLEMAN   As I learned,
The night before there was no purpose in them°   *they had no intention*
Of this remove.°   *change of residence*
KENT   Hail to thee, noble master!
5 LEAR   Ha!
Makest thou this shame thy pastime?
KENT   No, my lord.

---

3. The goddess Fortune was traditionally depicted with a wheel to signify her mutability and caprice. She was believed to take pleasure in arbitrarily lowering those at the top of her wheel and raising those at the bottom.
2.3 Location: As before.

1. Tangle the hair into "elf locks," supposed to be a favorite trick of malicious elves.
2. A word of unknown origin.
3. Edgar, I am nothing; I am no longer Edgar.
2.4 Location: As before.

FOOL Ha, ha! he wears cruel garters.[1] Horses are tied by
the heads, dogs and bears by the neck, monkeys by the
loins, and men by the legs. When a man's over-lusty at

10 legs,[2] then he wears wooden nether-stocks.° *knee socks*

LEAR What's° he that hath so much thy place° mistook *who's / position*
To set thee here?

KENT   It is both he and she;
Your son° and daughter. *son-in-law*

LEAR No.

15 KENT Yes.

LEAR No, I say.

KENT I say, yea.

LEAR No, no, they would not!

KENT Yes, yes, they have!

20 LEAR By Jupiter, I swear, no!

KENT By Juno,[3] I swear, aye!

LEAR   They durst not do 't;
They would not, could not do 't. 'Tis worse than murder,
To do upon respect[4] such violent outrage.
Resolve° me, with all modest° haste, which way *inform / reasonable*

25 Thou mightst deserve, or they impose, this usage,
Coming from us.

KENT   My lord, when at their home
I did commend° your highness' letters to them, *deliver*
Ere I was risen from the place that showed
My duty kneeling, came there a reeking post,° *steaming post-rider*

30 Stewed in his haste, half breathless, panting forth
From Goneril his mistress, salutations;
Delivered letters, spite of intermission,[5]
Which presently° they read; on whose contènts, *immediately*
They summoned up their meiny,° straight° took horse; *retinue / straightway*

35 Commanded me to follow, and attend
The leisure of their answer, gave me cold looks,
And meeting here the other messenger,
Whose welcome, I perceived, had poisoned mine—
Being the very° fellow that of late *same*

40 Displayed so saucily° against your highness— *acted so insolently*
Having more man° than wit° about me, drew. *courage / sense*
He raised the house with loud and coward cries.
Your son and daughter found this trespass worth° *deserving of*
The shame which here it suffers.

45 FOOL Winter's not gone yet, if the wild-geese fly that way.[6]
Fathers that wear rags

---

1. Worsted garters, punning on "crewel," a thin
yarn. The Fool is actually referring to the stocks
in which Kent's feet are held.
2. When a man's liable to run away.
3. Queen of the Roman gods and wife of Jupiter,
with whom she constantly quarreled.

4. To do to one who deserves respect.
5. Regardless of interrupting me; despite the
interruptions in his account (as he gasped for
breath).
6. That is, things will get worse before they get
better.

        Do make their children blind;[7]
        But fathers that bear bags
        Shall see their children kind.
50   Fortune, that arrant° whore,   *downright*
        Ne'er turns the key° to the poor.   *opens the door*
But, for all this, thou shalt have as many dolors[8] for thy
daughters as thou canst tell° in a year.   *count*

LEAR   O, how this mother° swells up toward my heart!   *hysteria*
55 *Hysterica passio*, down, thou climbing sorrow,[9]
    Thy element's° below! Where is this daughter?   *natural place is*

KENT   With the earl, sir, here within.

LEAR   Follow me not; stay
here.   *Exit*

GENTLEMAN   Made you no more offenses but what you
speak of?
60 KENT   None. How chance the king comes with so small a
train?

FOOL   An° thou hadst been set i' the stocks for that ques-   *if*
tion, thou hadst well deserved it.

KENT   Why, fool?

65 FOOL   We'll set thee to school to an ant, to teach thee
there's no laboring i' the winter.[1] All that follow their
noses are led by their eyes but blind men, and there's not
a nose among twenty but can smell him that's stinking.[2]
Let go thy hold when a great wheel runs down a hill,[3]
70 lest it break thy neck with following it; but the great one
that goes up the hill, let him draw thee after. When a
wise man gives thee better counsel, give me mine again.
I would have none but knaves follow it, since a fool gives
it.
75   That sir which serves and seeks for gain,
            And follows but for form,
         Will pack° when it begins to rain,   *pack up and go*
            And leave thee in the storm.
         But I will tarry; the fool will stay,
80   And let the wise man fly.
         The knave turns fool that runs away;[4]
            The fool no knave, perdy.°   *by God (from French pardieu)*

KENT   Where learned you this, fool?

FOOL   Not i' the stocks, fool.
      Re-enter LEAR, *with* GLOUCESTER

---

7. I.e., blind to their father's needs.

8. Pains, sorrows; punning on "dollar," the English term for the German "thaler," a large silver coin.

9. *Hysterica passio* (a Latin expression originating in the Greek *steiros*, "suffering in the womb") was an inflammation of the senses. In Renaissance medicine, vapors from the abdomen were thought to rise up through the body, and in women, the uterus itself to wander around.

1. Ants, proverbially prudent, know they cannot work in winter. Implicitly, a wise person should know better than to look for sustenance to an old man who has fallen on wintry times.

2. I.e., stinking as his fortunes decay.

3. A great wheel is a figure for Lear and of Fortune's wheel itself, which has swung downward.

4. The scoundrel who runs away is the real fool.

85   LEAR   Deny to speak with me? They are sick? They are weary?
      They have traveled all the night? Mere fetches;°   *ruses, pretexts*
      The images of revolt and flying off.[5]
      Fetch me a better answer.
  GLOUCESTER   My dear lord,
      You know the fiery quality° of the duke;   *disposition*
90   How unremovable and fixed he is
      In his own course.
  LEAR   Vengeance! plague! death! confusion!°   *destruction*
      Fiery? what quality? Why, Gloucester, Gloucester,
      I'd speak with the Duke of Cornwall and his wife.
95   GLOUCESTER   Well, my good lord, I have informed them so.
  LEAR   Informed them! Dost thou understand me, man?
  GLOUCESTER   Ay, my good lord.
  LEAR   The king would speak with Cornwall; the dear father
      Would with his daughter speak, commands her service.
100   Are they informed of this? My breath and blood!
      Fiery? the fiery duke? Tell the hot duke that—
      No, but not yet. May be he is not well.
      Infirmity doth still° neglect all office°   *always / obligation*
      Whereto our health is bound; we are not ourselves
105   When nature, being oppressed, commands the mind
      To suffer with the body. I'll forbear;
      And am fallen out with my more headier will,[6]
      To take° the indisposed and sickly fit   *mistake*
      For the sound man. Death on my state![7] Wherefore°   *why*
        looking on KENT
110   Should he sit here? This act persuades me
      That this remotion° of the duke and her   *remoteness, aloofness*
      Is practice° only. Give me my servant forth.°   *trickery / i.e., release Kent*
      Go tell the duke and 's wife I'd speak with them,
      Now, presently!° Bid them come forth and hear me   *at once*
115   Or at their chamber-door I'll beat the drum
      Till it cry sleep to death.[8]
  GLOUCESTER   I would have all well betwixt you.   *Exit*
  LEAR   O me, my heart, my rising heart! but, down!
  FOOL   Cry to it, nuncle, as the cockney° did to the eels   *Londoner*
120   when she put 'em i' the paste° alive; she knapped 'em o'   *pie, pastry*
      the coxcombs° with a stick, and cried "Down, wantons,°   *heads / rogues*
      down!" 'Twas her brother that, in pure kindness to his
      horse, buttered his hay.[9]
        Enter CORNWALL, REGAN, GLOUCESTER, *and servants*
  LEAR   Good morrow to you both.

---

5. Signs of revolt and of desertion or insurrection.
6. And disagree with my (earlier) more rash intention.
7. May my royal authority end (an oath).

8. Till the noise kills sleep.
9. Like that of his sister (who wanted to make eel pie without killing the eels), his kindness was misplaced. Lear's earlier kindness to his daughters was equally foolish.

CORNWALL   Hail to your grace!
　　　　　KENT is set at liberty
125 REGAN   I am glad to see your highness.
LEAR   Regan, I think you are; I know what reason
　　I have to think so. If thou shouldst not be glad,
　　I would divorce me from thy mother's tomb,
　　Sepulchring° an adultress. (*To* KENT) O, are you free?　*because it entombed*
130 　Some other time for that. Belovèd Regan,
　　Thy sister's naught.° O Regan, she hath tied　　　　*wicked; nothing*
　　Sharp-toothed unkindness, like a vulture, here!
　　　　　Points to his heart
　　I can scarce speak to thee; thou'lt not believe
　　With how depraved a quality—O Regan!
135 REGAN   I pray you, sir, take patience. I have hope
　　You less know how to value her desert
　　Than she to scant her duty.[1]
LEAR   Say, how is that?
REGAN   I cannot think my sister in the least
　　Would fail her obligation. If, sir, perchance
140 　She have restrained the riots of your followers,
　　'Tis on such ground, and to such wholesome end,
　　As clears her from all blame.
LEAR   My curses on her!
REGAN   O, sir, you are old;
　　Nature° in you stands on the very verge　　　　　*life*
145 　Of her confine.° You should be ruled and led　　*of its limit*
　　By some discretion,° that discerns your state　*discreet person*
　　Better than you yourself. Therefore, I pray you,
　　That to our sister you do make return;
　　Say you have wronged her, sir.
LEAR   Ask her forgiveness?
150 　Do you but mark how this becomes the house:[2]
　　"Dear daughter, I confess that I am old; (*kneeling*)
　　Age° is unnecessary. On my knees I beg　　　　*old age*
　　That you'll vouchsafe me raiment,° bed, and food."　*grant me clothing*
REGAN   Good sir, no more! These are unsightly tricks.
　　Return you to my sister.
155 LEAR (*rising*)   Never, Regan!
　　She hath abated° me of half my train;　　　　　*deprived*
　　Looked black upon me; struck me with her tongue
　　Most serpent-like, upon the very heart.
　　All° the stored vengeances of heaven fall　　　　*let all*
160 　On her ingrateful top!° Strike her young bones,　　*head*
　　You taking° airs, with lameness!　　　　*infectious, malignant*
CORNWALL   Fie, sir, fie!

---

1. I expect that you are worse at valuing her deservings than she is at neglecting her duty. The double negative here ("less," "scant") is acceptable Jacobean usage.
2. Do you see how appropriate this is among members of a family (spoken ironically)?

LEAR   You nimble lightnings, dart your blinding flames
    Into her scornful eyes! Infect her beauty,
    You fen-sucked fogs, drawn by the powerful sun,[3]
165   To fall and blast her pride!
REGAN   O the blest gods! so will you wish on me,
    When the rash mood is on.
LEAR   No, Regan, thou shalt never have my curse.
    Thy tender-hafted[4] nature shall not give
170   Thee o'er to harshness. Her eyes are fierce; but thine
    Do comfort and not burn. 'Tis not in thee
    To grudge my pleasures, to cut off my train,
    To bandy hasty words, to scant my sizes,°   *reduce my allowances*
    And in conclusion to oppose the bolt°   *to lock the door*
175   Against my coming in. Thou better know'st
    The offices° of nature, bond of childhood,   *duties*
    Effects° of courtesy, dues of gratitude;   *actions*
    Thy half o' the kingdom hast thou not forgot,
    Wherein I thee endowed.
REGAN   Good sir, to the purpose.°   *get to the point*
LEAR   Who put my man i' the stocks?
    Tucket within
180 CORNWALL   What trumpet's that?
REGAN   I know't, my sister's. This approves° her letter,   *confirms*
    That she would soon be here.
    Enter OSWALD
                Is your lady come?
LEAR   This is a slave, whose easy-borrowed pride[5]
    Dwells in the fickle grace of her he follows.
    Out varlet,° from my sight!   *wretch*
185 CORNWALL   What means your grace?
LEAR   Who stocked my servant? Regan, I have good hope
    Thou didst not know on 't.°   *of it*
    Enter GONERIL
              Who comes here? O heavens,
    If you do love old men, if your sweet sway
    Allow obedience, if yourselves are old,
190   Make it your cause! Send down, and take my part!
    (*To* GONERIL) Art not ashamed to look upon this beard?
    O Regan, wilt thou take her by the hand?
GONERIL   Why not by the hand, sir? How have I offended?
    All's not offense that indiscretion finds
    And dotage terms so.
195 LEAR   O sides,[6] you are too tough!
    Will you yet hold? How came my man i' the stocks?
CORNWALL   I set him there, sir; but his own disorders°   *disorderly behavior*
    Deserved much less advancement.[7]

---

3. The sun was thought to suck poisonous vapors from marshy ground.
4. Tenderly placed; firmly set in a tender disposition (as a knife blade into its haft).
5. Unmerited and unpaid-for arrogance; "pride" may also refer to Oswald's fine clothing received for his services to Goneril.
6. Chest, where Lear's heart is swelling with emotion.
7. Deserved far worse treatment.

LEAR   You! did you?

REGAN   I pray you, father, being weak, seem so.°   *behave so*

200   If, till the expiration of your month,

       You will return and sojourn with my sister,

       Dismissing half your train, come then to me.

       I am now from home, and out of that provision

       Which shall be needful for your entertainment.

205   LEAR   Return to her, and fifty men dismissed?

       No, rather I abjure° all roofs, and choose   *renounce*

       To be a comrade with the wolf and owl,

       To wage against the enmity o' the air

       Necessity's sharp pinch![8] Return with her?

210   Why, the hot-blooded France, that dowerless took

       Our youngest born, I could as well be brought

       To knee° his throne, and, squire-like, pension beg   *kneel to*

       To keep base life afoot. Return with her?

       Persuade me rather to be slave and sumpter°   *pack horse*

       To this detested groom. (*Pointing at* OSWALD)

215   GONERIL   At your choice, sir.

     LEAR   I prithee, daughter, do not make me mad.

       I will not trouble thee, my child; farewell.

       We'll no more meet, no more see one another.

       But yet thou art my flesh, my blood, my daughter;

220   Or rather a disease that's in my flesh,

       Which I must needs call mine. Thou art a boil,

       A plague-sore, an embossed carbuncle,°   *a swollen tumor*

       In my corrupted blood. But I'll not chide thee;

       Let shame come when it will, I do not call° it.   *call upon*

225   I do not bid the Thunder-bearer° shoot,   *i.e., Jove*

       Nor tell tales of thee to high-judging Jove.

       Mend when thou canst; be better at thy leisure.

       I can be patient, I can stay with Regan,

       I and my hundred knights.

     REGAN   Not altogether so.

230   I looked not for° you yet, nor am provided   *I did not expect*

       For your fit welcome. Give ear, sir, to my sister;

       For those that mingle reason with your passion[9]

       Must be content to think you old, and so—

       But she knows what she does.

     LEAR   Is this well° spoken?   *earnestly*

235   REGAN   I dare avouch° it, sir. What, fifty followers?   *vouch for*

       Is it not well? What should you need of more?

       Yea, or so many, sith° that both charge° and danger *since / expense*

       Speak 'gainst so great a number? How, in one house,

       Should many people, under two commands,

240   Hold amity? 'Tis hard; almost impossible.

---

8. I.e., to counter, like predators, the harshness of the elements with the hardness brought on by the stress or pressure of necessity.

9. For those who temper your passionate argument with their own calm reasoning.

GONERIL   Why might not you, my lord, receive attendance
　　　From those that she calls servants, or from mine?

REGAN   Why not, my lord? If then they chanced to slack° you,   *neglect*
　　　We could control them. If you will come to me—

245　　For now I spy a danger—I entreat you
　　　To bring but five-and-twenty. To no more
　　　Will I give place or notice.°   *acknowledgment*

LEAR   I gave you all—

REGAN   　　　　　　　　　And in good time° you gave it.   *it was about time*

LEAR   Made you my guardians, my depositaries;°   *trustees*

250　　But kept a reservation° to be followed   *reserved a right*
　　　With such a number. What, must I come to you
　　　With five-and-twenty, Regan? Said you so?

REGAN   And speak't again, my lord; no more with me.

LEAR   Those wicked creatures yet do look well-favored,°   *attractive*

255　　When others are more wicked; not being the worst
　　　Stands in some rank of praise.[1] (*To* GONERIL) I'll go with thee:
　　　Thy fifty yet doth double five-and-twenty,
　　　And thou art twice her love.

GONERIL   　　　　　　　　Hear me, my lord.
　　　What need you five-and-twenty, ten, or five,

260　　To follow in a house where twice so many
　　　Have a command to tend you?

REGAN   　　　　　　　　　What need one?

LEAR   O, reason not the need! Our basest beggars
　　　Are in the poorest thing superfluous.[2]
　　　Allow not° nature more than nature needs,   *if you don't allow*

265　　Man's life's as cheap as beast's. Thou art a lady;
　　　If only to go warm were gorgeous,
　　　Why, nature needs not what thou gorgeous wear'st,
　　　Which scarcely keeps thee warm.[3] But, for true need—
　　　You heavens, give me that patience,° patience I need!   *endurance*

270　　You see me here, you gods, a poor old man,
　　　As full of grief as age; wretched in both!
　　　If it be you that stirs these daughters' hearts
　　　Against their father, fool me not so much
　　　To bear it tamely;[4] touch me with noble anger,

275　　And let not women's weapons, water-drops,
　　　Stain my man's cheeks! No, you unnatural hags,
　　　I will have such revenges on you both,
　　　That all the world shall—I will do such things—
　　　What they are, yet I know not; but they shall be

280　　The terrors of the earth! You think I'll weep;
　　　No, I'll not weep.

---

1. Deserves some degree ("rank") of praise.
2. Even the lowliest beggars have something more than the barest minimum.
3. If gorgeousness in clothes is measured by the warmth they provide, your elaborate clothes are superfluous, for they barely cover your body.
4. Do not make me so foolish as to accept it meekly.

I have full cause of weeping, but this heart
Shall break into a hundred thousand flaws°   *fragments*
Or ere° I'll weep. O fool, I shall go mad!   *before ever*
      Exeunt LEAR, GLOUCESTER, KENT, *and* FOOL
        Storm and tempest

285 CORNWALL   Let us withdraw; 'twill be a storm.
    REGAN   This house is little; the old man and his people
      Cannot be well bestowed.°   *lodged*
    GONERIL   'Tis his own blame; hath put himself from° rest,   *deprived himself of*
      And must needs taste his folly.
290 REGAN   For his particular,° I'll receive him gladly,   *single self*
      But not one follower.
    GONERIL   So am I purposed.
    Where is my lord of Gloucester?
    CORNWALL   Followed the old man forth. He is returned.
      Re-enter GLOUCESTER
    GLOUCESTER   The king is in high rage.
    CORNWALL   Whither is he going?
295 GLOUCESTER   He calls to horse, but will° I know not whither.   *will go*
    CORNWALL   'Tis best to give him way; he leads himself.
    GONERIL   My lord, entreat him by no means to stay.
    GLOUCESTER   Alack, the night comes on, and the bleak winds
      Do sorely ruffle.° For many miles about   *bluster*
      There's scarce a bush.
300 REGAN   O, sir, to willful men,
    The injuries that they themselves procure
    Must be their schoolmasters. Shut up your doors.
    He is attended with a desperate° train;   *violent*
    And what they may incense° him to, being apt   *incite*
305 To have his ear abused,° wisdom bids fear.   *deceived*
    CORNWALL   Shut up your doors, my lord; 'tis a wild night.
    My Regan counsels well. Come out o' the storm.
                  Exeunt

3.1

    Storm still. Enter KENT *and a* GENTLEMAN, *at several°*   *different*
    doors
  KENT   Who's there, besides foul weather?
  GENTLEMAN   One minded like the weather, most unquietly.
  KENT   I know you. Where's the king?
  GENTLEMAN   Contending with the fretful elements;
5   Bids the wind blow the earth into the sea,
    Or swell the curlèd waters 'bove the main,°   *mainland*
    That things might change or cease; tears his white hair,
    Which the impetuous blasts, with eyeless rage,
    Catch in their fury, and make nothing of;

3.1 Location: Bare, open country.

10 Strives in his little world of man to out-scorn
The to-and-fro-conflicting wind and rain.
This night, wherein the cub-drawn bear would couch,[1]
The lion and the belly-pinchèd wolf
Keep their fur dry, unbonneted° he runs,   *hatless; uncrowned*
And bids what will take all.

15 KENT   But who is with him?
GENTLEMAN   None but the fool, who labors to out-jest
His heart-struck injuries.[2]
KENT   Sir, I do know you;
And dare, upon the warrant of my note,[3]
Commend a dear° thing to you. There is division,   *entrust a crucial*
20 Although as yet the face of it be covered
With mutual cunning, 'twixt Albany and Cornwall;
Who have—as who have not, that their great stars
Throned and set high?[4]—servants, who seem no less,° *who appear as such*
Which are to France the spies and speculations°   *observers*
25 Intelligent of[5] our state. What hath been seen,
Either in snuffs and packings° of the dukes,   *quarrels and plots*
Or the hard rein° which both of them have borne   *treatment*
Against the old kind king; or something deeper,
Whereof perchance these are but furnishings;°   *pretexts*
30 But, true it is, from France there comes a power°   *army*
Into this scattered kingdom; who already,
Wise in° our negligence, have secret feet   *aware of*
In some of our best ports, and are at point°   *ready*
To show their open banner. Now to you:
35 If on my credit you dare build° so far   *if you trust me*
To make your speed to Dover, you shall find
Some that will thank you, making just° report   *accurate*
Of how unnatural and bemadding° sorrow   *maddening*
The king hath cause to plain.°   *complain*
40 I am a gentleman of blood° and breeding;   *good family*
And, from some knowledge and assurance, offer
This office° to you.   *role; duty*
GENTLEMAN   I will talk further with you.
KENT   No, do not.
For confirmation that I am much more
45 Than my out-wall,° open this purse, and take   *outward appearance*
What it contains. If you shall see Cordelia—
As fear not but you shall—show her this ring,
And she will tell you who your fellow° is   *(Kent himself)*
That yet you do not know. Fie on this storm!

1. In which even the bear, though starving, having been sucked dry ("drawn") by its cub, would
not go out to forage.
2. "To out-jest": to relieve with laughter; to exor-
cise through ridicule. "Heart-struck injuries":
injuries (from the betrayal of his paternal love)
that penetrated to the heart.
3. On the basis of my skill (at judging people).
4. I.e., as has everybody who has been favored
by destiny.
5. Supplying intelligence about; well informed of.

50   I will go seek the king.

    GENTLEMAN   Give me your hand. Have you no more to say?

    KENT   Few words, but, to effect,° more than all yet;   *in importance*

      That, when we have found the king—in which your pain

      That way, I'll this[6]—he that first lights on him

55   Holla the other.

                           Exeunt severally

3.2

    Enter LEAR *and* FOOL. *Storm still*

    LEAR   Blow, winds, and crack your cheeks! rage! blow!

      You cataracts and hurricanoes,[1] spout

      Till you have drenched our steeples, drowned the cocks!°   *weather vanes*

      You sulphurous and thought-executing fires,[2]

5   Vaunt-couriers° to oak-cleaving thunderbolts,   *forerunners*

      Singe my white head! And thou, all-shaking thunder,

      Smite flat the thick rotundity o' the world!

      Crack Nature's molds, all germens° spill at once,   *seeds*

      That make ingrateful man!

10   FOOL   O nuncle, court holy-water[3] in a dry house is better

      than this rain-water out o' door. Good nuncle, in, and

      ask thy daughters' blessing! Here's a night pities neither

      wise man nor fool.

    LEAR   Rumble thy bellyful! Spit, fire! spout, rain!

15   Nor° rain, wind, thunder, fire, are my daughters: *neither*

      I tax° not you, you elements, with unkindness;   *blame*

      I never gave you kingdom, called you children,

      You owe me no subscription.° Then let fall   *obedience, allegiance*

      Your horrible pleasure. Here I stand, your slave,

20   A poor, infirm, weak, and despised old man.

      But yet I call you servile ministers,°   *agents*

      That have with two pernicious daughters joined

      Your high engendered battles° 'gainst a head   *heaven-bred forces*

      So old and white as this. O! O! 'tis foul!

25   FOOL   He that has a house to put 's head in has a good

      headpiece.°   *hat; brain*

                 The cod-piece that will house

                   Before the head has any,

                 The head and he shall louse;

30   So beggars marry many.[4]

              The man that makes his toe

               What he his heart should make

---

6. In which effort you will go that way and I this.

3.2 Location: As before.

1. Waterspouts (water from both sky and sea). "Cataracts": floodgates of the heavens.

2. Lightning that strikes as swiftly as thought.

3. Sprinkled blessings of a courtier; flattery.

4. Whoever finds his penis a lodging before providing shelter for his head will end up in lice-infested poverty and live in married beggary. A codpiece was a pouch-like covering for the male genitals, often conspicuous, particularly in the costume of a fool.

                    Shall of a corn cry woe,
                    And turn his sleep to wake.[5]
35   For there was never yet fair woman but she made mouths
            in a glass.[6]
            LEAR   No, I will be the pattern of all patience; I will say
            nothing.
                    Enter KENT
            KENT   Who's there?
40   FOOL   Marry, here's grace and a cod-piece; that's a wise
            man and a fool.[7]
            KENT   Alas, sir, are you here? Things that love night
            Love not such nights as these; the wrathful skies
            Gallow° the very wanderers of the dark,°   *frighten / nightwalking spirits*
45   And make them keep° their caves. Since I was man,   *keep inside*
            Such sheets of fire, such bursts of horrid thunder,
            Such groans of roaring wind and rain, I never
            Remember to have heard. Man's nature cannot carry°   *bear*
            The affliction nor the fear.
            LEAR   Let the great gods,
50   That keep this dreadful pother° o'er our heads,   *commotion*
            Find out their enemies now. Tremble, thou wretch,
            That hast within thee undivulgèd crimes,
            Unwhipped of° justice. Hide thee, thou bloody hand;   *unpunished by*
            Thou perjured, and thou simular° of virtue   *simulator, pretender*
55   That art incestuous. Caitiff,° to pieces shake,   *wretch*
            That under covert and convenient seeming°   *fitting hypocrisy*
            Hast practiced on° man's life. Close° pent-up guilts   *against / secret*
            Rive° your concealing continents,° and cry   *split open / coverings*
            These dreadful summoners grace.[8] I am a man
            More sinned against than sinning.
60   KENT   Alack, bare-headed?
            Gracious my lord, hard by° here is a hovel;   *close by*
            Some friendship will it lend you 'gainst the tempest.
            Repose you there, while I to this hard house—
            More harder than the stones whereof 'tis raised,
65   Which[9] even but now, demanding after° you,   *inquiring about*
            Denied me to come in—return, and force
            Their scanted° courtesy.   *niggardly*
            LEAR   My wits begin to turn.
            Come on, my boy. How dost, my boy? Art cold?
            I am cold myself. Where is this straw, my fellow?
70   The art° of our necessities is strange,   *skill; alchemy*
            That can make vile things precious. Come, your hovel.

---

5. I.e., the man who values an inferior part of his
body over the part that is truly valuable (as Lear
valued Goneril and Regan over Cordelia) will suffer from and lose sleep over that inferior part.
6. She practiced making pretty faces in a mirror.
7. The supposedly wise King is symbolized by
royal grace, the Fool by his codpiece (here, slang

for "penis"). The Fool speaks ironically: the King,
as he has pointed out, is now the foolish one.
"Marry": by the Virgin Mary (a mild oath).
8. And pray for mercy from these elements that
bring you to justice.
9. I.e., the occupants of the house.

Poor fool and knave, I have one part in my heart
That's sorry yet for thee.

FOOL (*singing*)[1]

    He that has and° a little tiny wit°—   *even / sense*
75   With hey, ho, the wind and the rain—
    Must make content with his fortunes fit,
    Though the rain it raineth every day.

LEAR   True, boy. Come, bring us to this hovel.

                  Exeunt LEAR *and* KENT

FOOL   This is a brave° night to cool a courtesan.[2]   *splendid*
80 I'll speak a prophecy ere I go:[3]

    When priests are more in word than matter;°   *real virtue*
    When brewers mar their malt with water;
    When nobles are their tailors' tutors;[4]
    No heretics burned, but wenches' suitors,[5]
85   When every case in law is right;°   *just*
    No squire in debt, nor no poor knight;
    When slanders do not live in tongues,
    Nor cutpurses° come not to throngs;   *pickpockets*
    When usurers tell their gold i' the field,[6]
90   And bawds and whores do churches build;
    Then shall the realm of Albion°   *Britain*
    Come to great confusion.°   *decay*
    Then comes the time, who lives to see 't,
    That going° shall be used° with feet.   *walking / practiced*
95 This prophecy Merlin shall make; for I live before his
time.[7]   *Exit*

3.3

Enter GLOUCESTER *and* EDMUND

GLOUCESTER   Alack, alack, Edmund, I like not this unnatural dealing. When I desired their leave that I might pity°   *relieve*
him, they took from me the use of mine own house;
charged me, on pain of their perpetual displeasure, nei-
5 ther to speak of him, entreat for him, nor any way sustain
him.

EDMUND   Most savage and unnatural!

GLOUCESTER   Go to;° say you nothing. There's a division   *(an expletive)*
betwixt the dukes, and a worse matter than that. I have
10 received a letter this night; 'tis dangerous to be spoken;
I have locked the letter in my closet.° These injuries the   *private chamber*
king now bears will be revenged home;° there's part of a   *to the hilt*

---

1. The following song is an adaptation of that sung by Feste at the end of *Twelfth Night*.
2. To cool even the hot lusts of a prostitute.
3. What follows is a parody of the pseudo-Chaucerian "Merlin's Prophecy" from George Puttenham's *The Art of English Poesy* (1589).
4. When noblemen follow fashion more closely than their tailors do.

5. When the only heretics burned are lovers, who burn from venereal disease.
6. When usurers can count their profits openly (because they have no shady dealings to hide).
7. Merlin was the great wizard at the legendary court of King Arthur. Lear's Britain is set in an even more distant past.
3.3 Location: At Gloucester's castle.

power already footed;[1] we must incline to[2] the king. I will
seek him, and privily° relieve him. Go you and maintain   *secretly, privately*
15   talk with the duke, that my charity be not of° him per-   *by*
ceived. If he ask for me, I am ill, and gone to bed. Though
I die for it, as no less is threatened me, the king my old
master must be relieved. There is some strange thing
toward,° Edmund; pray you, be careful.   *Exit*   *coming*
20   EDMUND   This courtesy, forbid[3] thee, shall the duke
Instantly know, and of that letter too.
This seems a fair deserving,[4] and must draw me
That which my father loses—no less than all.
The younger rises when the old doth fall.   *Exit*

3.4

Enter LEAR, KENT, *and* FOOL
KENT   Here is the place, my lord; good my lord, enter:
The tyranny of the open night's too rough
For nature° to endure.   *i.e., human weakness*
Storm still
LEAR   Let me alone.
KENT   Good my lord, enter here.
5   LEAR   Wilt break my heart?
KENT   I had rather break mine own. Good my lord, enter.
LEAR   Thou think'st 'tis much that this contentious storm
Invades us to the skin. So 'tis to thee;
But where the greater malady is fixed,°   *rooted*
10   The lesser is scarce felt. Thou'dst shun a bear;
But if thy flight lay toward the raging sea,
Thou'dst meet the bear i' the mouth. When the mind's free,° *unburdened*
The body's delicate.° The tempest in my mind   *sensitive*
Doth from my senses take all feeling else
15   Save° what beats there. Filial ingratitude!   *except*
Is it not as° this mouth should tear this hand   *as if*
For lifting food to 't? But I will punish home.°   *thoroughly*
No, I will weep no more. In such a night
To shut me out! Pour on; I will endure.
20   In such a night as this! O Regan, Goneril!
Your old kind father, whose frank heart gave all—
O, that way madness lies; let me shun that;
No more of that.
KENT   Good my lord, enter here.
LEAR   Prithee, go in thyself; seek thine own ease:
25   This tempest will not give me leave to° ponder   *allow me to*
On things would hurt me more. But I'll go in.
(*To the* FOOL) In, boy; go first. You houseless poverty°—   *poor*

---

1. Part of an army already landed.
2. We must take the side of.
3. Forbidden. "Courtesy": act of kindness.

4. This seems an action that deserves to be
rewarded.
3.4 Location: Open country, before a cattle shed.

Nay, get thee in. I'll pray, and then I'll sleep.
          FOOL goes in
Poor naked wretches, whereso'er you are,

30 That bide° the pelting of this pitiless storm,   *endure; dwell in*
How shall your houseless heads and unfed sides,°   *starved ribs*
Your looped and windowed[1] raggedness, defend you
From seasons such as these? O, I have ta'en
Too little care of this! Take physic, pomp;[2]

35 Expose thyself to feel what wretches feel,
That thou mayst shake the superflux[3] to them,
And show the heavens more just.
EDGAR (*within*)   Fathom and half,[4] fathom and half!
Poor Tom!
          The FOOL runs out from the hovel

40 FOOL   Come not in here, nuncle, here's a spirit.
Help me, help me!
KENT   Give me thy hand. Who's there?
FOOL   A spirit, a spirit! He says his name's Poor Tom.
KENT   What art thou that dost grumble there i' the straw?

45 Come forth.
          Enter EDGAR disguised as a madman
EDGAR   Away! the foul fiend follows me!
Through the sharp hawthorn blows the cold wind.[5]
Humh! go to thy cold bed, and warm thee.[6]
LEAR   Hast thou given all to thy two daughters? And art

50 thou come to this?
EDGAR   Who gives any thing to Poor Tom? whom the foul
fiend hath led through fire and through flame, through
ford and whirlpool, o'er bog and quagmire; that hath
laid knives under his pillow and halters° in his pew; set   *nooses*

55 ratsbane° by his porridge;[7] made him proud of heart, to   *rat poison*
ride on a bay trotting-horse over four-inched bridges,[8] to
course° his own shadow for° a traitor. Bless thy five wits![9]   *hunt / as*
Tom's a-cold—O, do, de, do de, do de. Bless thee from
whirlwinds, star-blasting, and taking![1] Do Poor Tom

60 some charity, whom the foul fiend vexes: there could I
have him now—and there—and there again, and there.[2]
          Storm still

---

1. I.e., full of holes and vents; "windowed" could also refer to cloth worn through to semitransparency, like the oilcloth window "panes" of the poor.
2. Cure yourself, pompous person.
3. Superfluity; bodily discharge, suggested by "physic" (which also has the meaning of "purgative") in line 34.
4. Nine feet: a sailor's cry when taking soundings to gauge the depth of water.
5. Perhaps a fragment from a ballad.
6. This expression is also used by the drunken beggar Christopher Sly in Shakespeare's *The Taming of the Shrew*, Induction 1.

7. These are all means by which the foul fiend tempts Tom to commit suicide.
8. Impossibly narrow, and probably suicidal to attempt without diabolical help.
9. The five wits were common wit, imagination, fantasy, estimation, and memory (from medieval and Renaissance cognitive theory).
1. Infection; bewitchment. "Whirlwinds," "star-blasting": malign astrological influences capable of causing sickness or death.
2. As Edgar speaks this sentence, he might kill vermin on his body, as if they were devils.

LEAR   What, has his daughters brought him to this pass?
Couldst thou save nothing? Didst thou give them all?

FOOL   Nay, he reserved a blanket, else we had been all
65   shamed.

LEAR   Now, all the plagues that in the pendulous° air   *overhanging; portentous*
Hang fated o'er men's faults light on thy daughters!

KENT   He hath no daughters, sir.

LEAR   Death, traitor! nothing could have subdued nature
70   To such a lowness but his unkind daughters.
Is it the fashion that discarded fathers
Should have thus little mercy on their flesh?
Judicious punishment! 'twas this flesh begot
Those pelican[3] daughters.

75   EDGAR   Pillicock sat on Pillicock-hill.
Halloo, halloo, loo, loo![4]

FOOL   This cold night will turn us all to fools and madmen.

EDGAR   Take heed o' the foul fiend; obey thy parents; keep
thy word justly; swear not; commit not with man's sworn
80   spouse; set not thy sweet heart on proud array.[5] Tom's
a-cold.

LEAR   What hast thou been?

EDGAR   A serving-man, proud in heart and mind; that
curled my hair; wore gloves in my cap;[6] served the lust of
85   my mistress' heart, and did the act of darkness with her;
swore as many oaths as I spake words, and broke them
in the sweet face of heaven: one that slept in the contriving of lust, and waked to do it. Wine loved I deeply, dice
dearly; and in woman out-paramoured the Turk.[7] False
90   of heart, light of ear,°   bloody of hand; hog in sloth, fox in   *rumor-hungry*
stealth, wolf in greediness, dog in madness, lion in prey.
Let not the creaking of shoes[8] nor the rustling of silks
betray thy poor heart to woman. Keep thy foot[9] out of
brothels, thy hand out of plackets,[1] thy pen from lenders'
95   books, and defy°   the foul fiend. Still through the haw-   *renounce*
thorn blows the cold wind: Says suum, mun, ha, no,
nonny. Dolphin my boy, my boy, sessa! let him trot by.[2]
      Storm still

LEAR   Why, thou wert better in thy grave than to answer°   *encounter*
with thy uncovered body this extremity of the skies.° Is   *violent weather*
100   man no more than this? Consider him well. Thou owest

---

3. I.e., greedy. Young pelicans were reputed to
feed on blood from the wounds they made in
their mother's breast; in some versions, they first
killed their father.
4. A fragment of an old rhyme, followed by hunting cries or a ballad refrain; "Pillicock" was both a
term of endearment and a euphemism for "penis."
5. These are fragments from the Ten Commandments.
6. Favors from his mistress. In Petrarchan
poetry, wooers are "servants" to their ladies.

7. And had more women than the sultan had in
his harem.
8. Creaking shoes were a fashionable affectation.
9. Punning on the French *foutre* ("fuck").
1. Slits in skirts or petticoats.
2. These phrases are probably snatches from
songs and proverbs. "Dolphin" is an imagined animal or devil or the heir to the French throne
("dauphin," which Shakespeare usually Anglicized), or all three.

the worm no silk, the beast no hide, the sheep no wool,
the cat[3] no perfume. Ha! here's three on's° are sophisti-   *of us*
cated! Thou art the thing itself; unaccommodated[4] man
is no more but such a poor, bare, forked animal as thou
105 art. Off, off, you lendings!° come unbutton here.   *borrowed clothes*
   Tearing off his clothes

FOOL Prithee, nuncle, be contented; 'tis a naughty° night   *foul*
to swim in. Now a little fire in a wild° field were like an   *barren; lustful*
old lecher's heart; a small spark, all the rest on's° body   *of his*
cold. Look, here comes a walking fire.
   Enter GLOUCESTER, *with a* TORCH

110 EDGAR This is the foul fiend Flibbertigibbet.[5] He
begins at curfew,° and walks till the first cock.° He   *9:00 P.M. / midnight*
gives the web and the pin,° squinies[6] the eye, and   *cataract*
makes the harelip; mildews the white° wheat, and hurts   *near-ripe*
the poor creature of earth.
115   St. Withold footed thrice the old;[7]
   He met the night-mare[8] and her nine-fold;°   *nine familiars, demons*
   Bid her alight,
   And her troth plight,°   *and give her word*
   And, aroint thee,° witch, aroint thee!   *begone*

120 KENT How fares your grace?

LEAR What's° he?   *who's*

KENT Who's there? What is't you seek?

GLOUCESTER What are you there? Your names?

EDGAR Poor Tom, that eats the swimming frog, the toad,
125 the tadpole, the wall-newt and the water;° that in the fury   *water newt*
of his heart, when the foul fiend rages, eats cow-dung
for sallets;° swallows the old rat and the ditch-dog;[9] drinks   *savories*
the green mantle° of the standing-pool; who is whipped   *scum*
from tithing° to tithing, and stock-punished,° and impris-   *parish / put in stocks*
130 oned; who hath had three suits to his back, six shirts to
his body, horse to ride, and weapon to wear;
   But mice and rats, and such small deer,[1]
   Have been Tom's food for seven long year.
Beware my follower. Peace, Smulkin;° peace, thou fiend!   *a Harsnett devil*

135 GLOUCESTER What, hath your grace no better company?

EDGAR The prince of darkness is a gentleman. Modo he's
call'd, and Mahu.[2]

GLOUCESTER Our flesh and blood is grown so vile, my lord,
That it doth hate what gets° it.   *begets*

140 EDGAR Poor Tom's a-cold.

---

3. Civet cat, in Shakespeare's time the major
source of musk for perfume.
4. Naked; without the trappings of civilization.
5. A devil drawn from folk beliefs, but famous for
his prominent place in Samuel Harsnett's *Declara-*
tion of Egregious Popish Impostures (1603); the frequent borrowings from Harsnett in *King Lear* set
the earliest possible composition date for the play.
6. Makes cross-eyed.
7. St. Withold traversed the hilly countryside

three times. "Old": wold, uplands.
8. A demon (not necessarily in the shape of a
horse).
9. A dog found dead in a ditch.
1. Animals. These verses are adapted from a
romance popular in Shakespeare's time, *Bevis of*
Hampton.
2. Modo and Mahu, more Harsnett devils, were
commanding generals of the hellish troops.

GLOUCESTER   Go in with me. My duty cannot suffer°   *permit me*
    To obey in all your daughters' hard commands:
    Though their injunction be to bar my doors
    And let this tyrannous night take hold upon you,
145   Yet have I ventured to come seek you out
    And bring you where both fire and food is ready.
LEAR   First let me talk with this philosopher.
    What is the cause of thunder?
KENT   Good my lord, take his offer; go into the house.
150 LEAR   I'll take a word with this same learned Theban.°   *i.e., Greek sage*
    What is your study?°   *field of expertise*
EDGAR   How to prevent the fiend, and to kill vermin.
LEAR   Let me ask you one word in private.
KENT   Importune° him once more to go, my lord;   *beg*
    His wits begin to unsettle.
155 GLOUCESTER   Canst thou blame him?
       Storm still
    His daughters seek his death; ah, that good Kent!
    He said it would be thus, poor banished man!
    Thou say'st the king grows mad; I'll tell thee, friend,
    I am almost mad myself. I had a son,
160   Now outlawed° from my blood. He sought my life   *disowned*
    But lately, very late.° I loved him, friend;   *recently*
    No father his son dearer. True to tell thee,
    The grief hath crazed my wits. What a night's this!
    I do beseech your grace—
LEAR   O, cry you mercy,° sir.   *beg your pardon*
165 Noble philosopher, your company.
EDGAR   Tom's a-cold.
GLOUCESTER   In, fellow, there, into the hovel; keep thee
    warm.
LEAR   Come, let's in all.
KENT   This way, my lord.
LEAR   With him!
170 I will keep still° with my philosopher.   *stay*
KENT   Good my lord, soothe° him; let him take the fellow.   *humor*
GLOUCESTER   Take him you on.°   *on ahead*
KENT   Sirrah, come on; go along with us.
LEAR   Come, good Athenian.
175 GLOUCESTER   No words, no words: hush.
EDGAR   Child Roland[3] to the dark tower came,
    His word° was still° "Fie, foh, and fum,   *motto / always*
    I smell the blood of a British[4] man."   *Exeunt*

---

3. Roland is the famous hero of the Charlemagne cycle of legends. "Child": an aspirant to knighthood. In the nineteenth century, Robert Browning built a notable poem from this line.

4. "An Englishman" usually appears in this rhyme from the cycle of tales of which "Jack and the Beanstalk" is the best-known. The alteration befits Lear's ancient Britain.

3.5

Enter CORNWALL *and* EDMUND

CORNWALL   I will have my revenge ere I depart his house.

EDMUND   How, my lord, I may be censured,° that nature°   *judged / kinship*
thus gives way to loyalty, something fears me[1] to think
of.

CORNWALL   I now perceive, it was not altogether your

5   brother's evil disposition made him seek his° death; but   *(Gloucester's)*
a provoking merit, set a-work by a reprovable badness in
himself.[2]

EDMUND   How malicious is my fortune, that I must repent
to be just! This is the letter he spoke of, which approves

10   him an intelligent party to the advantages of France.[3] O
heavens! that this treason were not, or not I the detector!

CORNWALL   Go with me to the duchess.

EDMUND   If the matter of this paper be certain, you have
mighty business in hand.

15   CORNWALL   True or false, it hath made thee Earl of
Gloucester. Seek out where thy father is, that he may be
ready for our apprehension.°   *arrest*

EDMUND (*aside*)   If I find him comforting the king, it will
stuff his° suspicion more fully.—I will persèver in my   *(Cornwall's)*

20   course of loyalty, though the conflict be sore between
that and my blood.°   *filial duty*

CORNWALL   I will lay trust upon thee, and thou shalt find
a dearer father in my love.   *Exeunt*

3.6

Enter GLOUCESTER, LEAR, KENT, FOOL, *and* EDGAR

GLOUCESTER   Here is better than the open air; take it
thankfully. I will piece° out the comfort with what addi-   *pad*
tion I can; I will not be long from you.

KENT   All the power of his wits have given sway to his

5   impatience:[1] the gods° reward your kindness!   *may the gods*
Exit GLOUCESTER

EDGAR   Frateretto° calls me; and tells me Nero is an   *a Harsnett devil*
angler in the lake of darkness.[2] Pray, innocent, and
beware the foul fiend.

FOOL   Prithee, nuncle, tell me whether a madman be a

10   gentleman or a yeoman?[3]

LEAR   A king, a king!

3.5 Location: At Gloucester's castle.
1. I am somewhat afraid.
2. I.e., Gloucester's own wickedness deservedly
triggered the blameworthy evil in Edgar.
3. Which proves him a spy and informer in the
aid of France.
3.6 Location: Within an outbuilding of Gloucester's.

1. Rage; inability to bear more suffering.
2. In Chaucer's *Monk's Tale*, the infamously cruel
Roman emperor Nero is found fishing in hell.
3. A free landowner but not a member of the
gentry, lacking official family arms and the distinctions they confer. Shakespeare seems to have
procured a coat of arms for his father in 1596.

FOOL   No, he's a yeoman that has a gentleman to his son;
for he's a mad yeoman that sees his son a gentleman
before him.

15   LEAR   To have a thousand with red burning spits
Come hissing in upon 'em—

EDGAR   The foul fiend bites my back.

FOOL   He's mad that trusts in the tameness of a wolf, a
horse's health, a boy's love, or a whore's oath.

20   LEAR   It shall be done; I will arraign° them straight.°   *prosecute / immediately*
(*To* EDGAR) Come, sit thou here, most learned justicer;°   *judge*
(*to the* FOOL) Thou, sapient° sir, sit here. Now, you she   *wise*
foxes!

EDGAR   Look, where he stands and glares! Wantest thou
25   eyes° at trial, madam?   *do you lack observers*
          Come o'er the bourn,° Bessy, to me[4]—   *small stream*

FOOL   Her boat hath a leak,[5]
          And she must not speak
          Why she dares not come over to thee.

30   EDGAR   The foul fiend haunts poor Tom in the voice of a
nightingale. Hopdance° cries in Tom's belly for two   *a demon*
white° herring. Croak° not, black angel; I have no food   *fresh / growl*
for thee.

KENT   How do you, sir? Stand you not so amazed:
35   Will you lie down and rest upon the cushions?

LEAR   I'll see their trial first. Bring in the evidence.
(*To* EDGAR) Thou robed man of justice, take thy place;
(*to the* FOOL) And thou, his yoke-fellow of equity,°   *partner of law*
Bench° by his side. (*To* KENT) You are o' the commission,°   *sit / judiciary*
40   Sit you too.

EDGAR   Let us deal justly.
          Sleepest or wakest thou, jolly shepherd?
          Thy sheep be in the corn;°   *grain*
          And for one blast of thy minikin° mouth,   *dainty*
45   Thy sheep shall take no harm.
Purr! the cat[6] is gray.

LEAR   Arraign her first; 'tis Goneril. I here take my oath
before this honorable assembly, she kicked the poor king
her father.

50   FOOL   Come hither, mistress. Is your name Goneril?

LEAR   She cannot deny it.

FOOL   Cry you mercy, I took you for a joint-stool.[7]

LEAR   And here's another, whose warped looks proclaim
What store° her heart is made on.° Stop her there!   *material / of*
55   Arms, arms, sword, fire! Corruption in the place!
False justicer, why hast thou let her 'scape?

---

4. From an old song.
5. She has venereal disease; punning on "boat"
as body and "burn" as genital discomfort.
6. Purr the cat is another devil; such devils in

the shape of cats were the familiars of witches.
7. "I beg your pardon, I mistook you for a stool."
Here the part of Goneril is actually being played
by a stool.

EDGAR   Bless thy five wits!

KENT   O pity! Sir, where is the patience now,
   That you so oft have boasted to retain?

60   EDGAR (*aside*)   My tears begin to take his part so much,
   They'll mar my counterfeiting.

LEAR   The little dogs and all,°   *even the little dogs*
   Tray, Blanch, and Sweetheart, see, they bark at me.

EDGAR   Tom will throw his head at° them. Avaunt,°   *will threaten (?) / begone*
65   you curs!

               Be thy mouth or° black or white,   *either*
               Tooth that poisons° if it bite;   *gives rabies*
               Mastiff, greyhound, mongrel grim,
               Hound or spaniel, brach° or lym,°   *bitch / bloodhound*
70   Or bobtail tike or trundle-tail,[8]
               Tom will make them weep and wail:
               For, with throwing thus my head,
               Dogs leap the hatch,[9] and all are fled.

   Do de, de, de. Sessa![1] Come, march to wakes° and fairs   *parish festivals*
75   and market-towns. Poor Tom, thy horn is dry.[2]

LEAR   Then let them anatomize° Regan; see what breeds   *dissect*
   about her heart. Is there any cause in nature that makes
   these hard hearts? (*To* EDGAR) You, sir, I entertain° for   *retain*
   one of my hundred; I do not like the fashion of your gar-
80   ments. You will say they are Persian;° but let them be   *oriental; splendid*
   changed.

KENT   Now, good my lord, lie there and rest awhile.

LEAR   Make no noise, make no noise; draw the curtains.°   *bed curtains*
   So, so, so. We'll go to supper i' the morning.

85   FOOL   And I'll go to bed at noon.

          [*Re-enter* GLOUCESTER]

GLOUCESTER   Come hither, friend. Where is the king my master?

KENT   Here, sir; but trouble him not; his wits are gone.

GLOUCESTER   Good friend, I prithee, take him in thy arms;
   I have o'erheard a plot of death upon° him: *against*
90   There is a litter ready; lay him in 't
   And drive° towards Dover, friend, where thou shalt meet   *hurry*
   Both welcome and protection. Take up thy master.
   If thou shouldst dally half an hour, his life,
   With thine, and all that offer to defend him,
95   Stand in assured loss.° Take up, take up!   *are certainly doomed*
   And follow me, that will to some provision
   Give thee quick conduct.[3]

KENT   Oppressèd nature sleeps:
   This rest might yet have balmed° thy broken sinews,°   *soothed / nerves*

---

8. Short-tailed mongrel or long-tailed.
9. Dogs leap over the lower half of a divided door.
1. Apparently nonsense, although "Sessa" may be
a version of the French *cessez* ("stop" or "hush").
2. A begging formula that refers to the horn ves-

sel that vagabonds carried for drink; the covert
sense is that Edgar has run out of Bedlamite
inspiration.
3. Who will quickly guide you to some supplies.

Which, if convenience will not allow,
100 Stand in hard cure.° (*To the* FOOL) Come, help to   *will be hard to cure*
     bear thy master:
Thou must not stay behind.
GLOUCESTER   Come come, away.
             Exeunt all but EDGAR
EDGAR   When we our betters see bearing our° woes,   *our same*
We scarcely think our miseries our foes.
Who alone suffers suffers most i' the mind,
105 Leaving free° things and happy shows° behind: *carefree / scenes*
But then the mind much sufferance doth o'erskip
When grief hath mates, and bearing° fellowship.   *pain, suffering*
How light and portable° my pain seems now,   *supportable*
When that which makes me bend, makes the king bow;
110 He° childed as I fathered! Tom, away!   *he is*
Mark the high noises,° and thyself bewray°   *important rumors / reveal*
When false opinion, whose wrong thought defiles thee,
In thy just proof repeals and reconciles thee.[4]
What° will hap° more tonight, safe 'scape the king!   *whatever / chance*
115 Lurk, lurk.   *Exit*

3.7

     Enter CORNWALL, REGAN, GONERIL, EDMUND, *and servants*
CORNWALL (*to* GONERIL)   Post° speedily to my lord your   *ride*
husband; show him this letter. The army of France is
landed. Seek out the villain Gloucester.
             Exeunt some of the servants
REGAN   Hang him instantly.
5 GONERIL   Pluck out his eyes.
CORNWALL   Leave him to my displeasure. Edmund, keep
you our sister° company. The revenges we are bound[1] to   *sister-in-law*
take upon your traitorous father are not fit for your
beholding. Advise the duke, where you are going, to a
10 most festinate preparation.[2] We are bound° to the like.   *committed*
Our posts° shall be swift and intelligent[3] betwixt us.   *messengers*
Farewell, dear sister: farewell, my lord of Gloucester.
     Enter OSWALD
How now! Where's the king?
OSWALD   My lord of Gloucester hath conveyed him hence.
15 Some five or six and thirty of his° knights,   *(Lear's)*
Hot questrists° after him, met him at gate;   *searchers*
Who, with some other of the lord's° dependants,   *(Gloucester's)*
Are gone with him towards Dover; where they boast
To have well-armed friends.

4. When true evidence pardons you and reconciles you (with your father).
3.7 Location: At Gloucester's castle.
1. Bound by duty.

2. I.e., when you reach Albany, tell the duke to
prepare quickly.
3. Well-informed.

CORNWALL   Get horses for your mistress.
20   GONERIL   Farewell, sweet lord, and sister.
CORNWALL   Edmund, farewell.
                         Exeunt GONERIL, EDMUND, *and* OSWALD
Go seek the traitor Gloucester,
Pinion him° like a thief, bring him before us.   *tie his arms*
                         Exeunt other servants
Though well we may not pass° upon his life   *pass sentence*
25   Without the form° of justice, yet our power   *official proceedings*
Shall do a courtesy⁴ to our wrath, which men
May blame, but not control. Who's there? the traitor?
       Enter GLOUCESTER, *brought in by two or three*
REGAN   Ingrateful fox! 'tis he.
CORNWALL   Bind fast his corky° arms.   *withered*
30   GLOUCESTER   What mean your graces? Good my friends,
       consider
You are my guests. Do me no foul play, friends.
CORNWALL   Bind him, I say.
       Servants bind him
REGAN   Hard, hard. O filthy traitor!
GLOUCESTER   Unmerciful lady as you are, I'm none.
CORNWALL   To this chair bind him. Villain, thou shalt find—
                         REGAN *plucks his beard°*   *(an extreme insult)*
35   GLOUCESTER   By the kind gods, 'tis most ignobly done
To pluck me by the beard.
REGAN   So white,° and such a traitor!   *white-haired; venerable*
GLOUCESTER   Naughty° lady,   *wicked*
These hairs, which thou dost ravish from my chin,
Will quicken,° and accuse thee. I am your host.   *come alive*
40   With robbers' hands my hospitable favors°   *features*
You should not ruffle° thus. What will you do?   *snatch at*
CORNWALL   Come, sir, what letters had you late° from France?   *lately*
REGAN   Be simple answered,° for we know the truth.   *answer straightforwardly*
CORNWALL   And what confederacy have you with the traitors
45   Late footed° in the kingdom?   *landed*
REGAN   To whose hands have you sent the lunatic king?
Speak.
GLOUCESTER   I have a letter guessingly set down,⁵
Which came from one that's of a neutral heart,
And not from one opposed.
CORNWALL   Cunning.
50   REGAN   And false.
CORNWALL   Where hast thou sent the king?
GLOUCESTER   To Dover.

---

4. Shall allow a courtesy, or indulgence; shall   5. Written without confirmation; speculative.
bow to.

REGAN   Wherefore° to Dover? Wast thou not charged° at   *why / commanded*
55   peril—
CORNWALL   Wherefore to Dover? Let him first answer that.
GLOUCESTER   I am tied to the stake, and I must stand the course.[6]
REGAN   Wherefore to Dover?
GLOUCESTER   Because I would not see thy cruel nails
60   Pluck out his poor old eyes; nor thy fierce sister
   In his anointed[7] flesh stick boarish fangs.
   The sea, with such a storm as his bare head
   In hell-black night endured, would have buoyed° up   *risen*
   And quenched the stellèd° fires.   *stars'*
65   Yet, poor old heart, he holp° the heavens to rage.   *helped*
   If wolves had at thy gate howled that dern° time,   *dreary; dreadful*
   Thou shouldst have said "Good porter, turn the key."°   *(to open the door)*
   All cruels else subscribed.[8] But I shall see
   The wingèd vengeance[9] overtake such children.
70 CORNWALL   See 't shalt thou never. Fellows,° hold the chair.   *servants*
   Upon these eyes of thine I'll set my foot.
GLOUCESTER   He that will think° to live till he be old,   *whoever hopes*
   Give me some help! O cruel! O ye gods!
REGAN   One side will mock another.° The other too!   *the other*
CORNWALL   If you see vengeance—
75 FIRST SERVANT   Hold your hand, my lord:
   I have served you ever since I was a child;
   But better service have I never done you
   Than now to bid you hold.
REGAN   How now, you dog!
80 FIRST SERVANT   If you did wear a beard upon your chin,
   I'd shake it on this quarrel.[1]
REGAN   What do you mean?°   *intend*
CORNWALL   My villain!°   *servant; villain*
FIRST SERVANT   Why, then, come on, and take the chance of anger.[2]
85 REGAN   Give me thy sword. A peasant stand up thus!
        CORNWALL is wounded.
      Takes a sword, and runs at him behind
FIRST SERVANT   O, I am slain! My lord, you have one eye left
   To see some mischief° on him. O!   *Dies*   *injury*
CORNWALL   Lest it see more, prevent it. Out, vile jelly!
   Where is thy luster now?
90 GLOUCESTER   All dark and comfortless. Where's my son Edmund?
   Edmund, enkindle all the sparks of nature,[3]
   To quit° this horrid act.   *requite, avenge*

---

6. An image from bearbaiting—in which a bear, sometimes blinded, on a short tether had to fight off the assault of dogs.
7. Consecrated with holy oils (as part of a king's coronation).
8. All other cruel creatures yielded to compassion.
9. Swift or heaven-sent revenge; either an angel of God or the Furies, who were flying executors

of divine vengeance in classical myth.
1. I'd pluck it over this point; I'd issue a challenge.
2. Take the risk of fighting when angry; take the fortune of one who is governed by his anger.
3. All the warmth of filial love; all the anger that your father has received such treatment.

REGAN   Out, treacherous villain!
  Thou call'st on him that hates thee. It was he
  That made the overture° of thy treasons to us;   *revelation*
95 Who is too good to pity thee.
GLOUCESTER   O my follies! Then Edgar was abused.°   *slandered*
  Kind gods, forgive me that, and prosper him!
REGAN   Go thrust him out at gates, and let him smell
  His way to Dover.   *Exit one with* GLOUCESTER
100 How is't, my lord? how look you?°   *how do you feel*
CORNWALL   I have received a hurt. Follow me, lady;
  Turn out that eyeless villain. Throw this slave
  Upon the dunghill. Regan, I bleed apace.
  Untimely comes this hurt. Give me your arm.
                         Exit CORNWALL *led by* REGAN
105 SECOND SERVANT   I'll never care what wickedness I do,
  If this man come to good.[4]
THIRD SERVANT   If she live long,
  And in the end meet the old° course of death,   *usual*
  Women will all turn monsters.
SECOND SERVANT   Let's follow the old earl, and get the Bedlam°   *madman*
110 To lead him where he would. His roguish madness
  Allows itself to anything.
THIRD SERVANT   Go thou; I'll fetch some flax and whites of eggs
  To apply to his bleeding face. Now, heaven help him!
                         Exeunt severally

4.1

    Enter EDGAR
EDGAR   Yet better thus, and known to be contemned°   *despised*
  Than still° contemned and flattered. To be worst,   *always*
  The lowest and most dejected thing of fortune,
  Stands still in esperance, lives not in fear.[1]
5 The lamentable change is from the best;
  The worst returns to laughter.[2] Welcome, then,
  Thou unsubstantial air that I embrace!
  The wretch that thou hast blown unto the worst
  Owes nothing° to thy blasts. But who comes here?   *(because he can't pay)*
    Enter GLOUCESTER, *led by an* OLD MAN
10 My father, parti-eyed?[3] World, world, O world!
  But that thy strange mutations make us hate thee,
  Life would not yield to age.[4]

---

4. I.e., because this may be a sign that evil goes unpunished.
4.1 Location: Open country.
1. Remains in hope ("esperance") because there is no fear of falling further.
2. The change to be lamented is one that alters the best of circumstances; the worst luck can only improve.
3. Multicolored like a fool's costume (red with blood under white dressings).
4. If there were no strange reversals of fortune to make the world hateful, we would not consent to aging and death.

OLD MAN O my good lord, I have been your tenant, and
your father's tenant, these fourscore years.

15 GLOUCESTER Away, get thee away! Good friend, be gone.
Thy comforts° can do me no good at all;   *assistance*
Thee they may hurt.

OLD MAN Alack, sir, you cannot see your way.

GLOUCESTER I have no way,° and therefore want no eyes;   *path*
20 I stumbled when I saw. Full oft 'tis seen,
Our means secure us, and our mere defects
Prove our commodities.5 O dear son Edgar,
The food° of thy abusèd° father's wrath!   *fuel; prey / despised*
Might I but live to see thee in° my touch,   *through*
I'd say I had eyes again!

25 OLD MAN   How now! Who's there?

EDGAR (*aside*) O gods! Who is't can say "I am at the worst"?
I am worse than e'er I was.

OLD MAN   'Tis poor mad Tom.

EDGAR (*aside*) And worse I may be yet: the worst is not
So long as we can say "This is the worst."

OLD MAN Fellow, where goest?

30 GLOUCESTER   Is it a beggar-man?

OLD MAN Madman and beggar too.

GLOUCESTER He has some reason, else° he could not beg.   *otherwise*
I' the last night's storm I such a fellow saw;
Which made me think a man a worm. My son
35 Came then into my mind, and yet my mind
Was then scarce friends with him. I have heard more since.
As flies to wanton° boys are we to the gods;   *playful; careless*
They kill us for their sport.

EDGAR (*aside*)   How should this be?
Bad is the trade that must play fool to sorrow,6
40 Angering itself and others.—Bless thee, master!

GLOUCESTER Is that the naked fellow?

OLD MAN   Ay, my lord.

GLOUCESTER Then, prithee, get thee gone. If, for my sake,
Thou wilt o'ertake us, hence a mile or twain,
I' the way toward Dover, do it for ancient love;7
45 And bring some covering for this naked soul,
Who I'll entreat to lead me.

OLD MAN   Alack, sir, he is mad.

GLOUCESTER 'Tis the times' plague, when8 madmen lead the blind.
Do as I bid thee, or rather do thy pleasure;
Above the rest,° be gone.   *most important*
50 OLD MAN I'll bring him the best 'parel° that I have,   *apparel*
Come on 't what will.   *Exit*

---

5. Our wealth makes us overconfident, and our
utter deprivation proves to be beneficial.
6. It is a bad business to have to play the fool in
the face of sorrow.

7. For the sake of our long and loyal relationship
(as master and servant).
8. The time is truly sick when.

GLOUCESTER   Sirrah, naked fellow—

EDGAR   Poor Tom's a-cold. (*Aside*) I cannot daub it further.[9]

GLOUCESTER   Come hither, fellow.

55 EDGAR (*aside*)   And yet I must.—Bless thy sweet eyes, they bleed.

GLOUCESTER   Know'st thou the way to Dover?

EDGAR   Both stile and gate, horse-way and foot-path. Poor
   Tom hath been scared out of his good wits. Bless thee,
   good man's son, from the foul fiend! Five fiends have
60   been in Poor Tom at once; of lust, as Obidicut; Hobbidi-
   dance, prince of dumbness; Mahu, of stealing; Modo, of
   murder; Flibbertigibbet, of mopping and mowing,° who   *making faces*
   since possesses chambermaids and waiting-women. So,
   bless thee, master!

65 GLOUCESTER   Here, take this purse, thou whom the heavens' plagues
   Have humbled to all strokes.° That I am wretched   *to accept all blows*
   Makes thee the happier. Heavens, deal so still!°   *always*
   Let the superfluous and lust-dieted man,[1]
   That slaves your ordinance,[2] that will not see
70   Because he doth not feel, feel your power quickly;
   So distribution should undo excess,
   And each man have enough. Dost thou know Dover?

EDGAR   Ay, master.

GLOUCESTER   There is a cliff, whose high and bending° head   *overhanging*
75   Looks fearfully in the confinèd deep.[3]
   Bring me but to the very brim of it,
   And I'll repair the misery thou dost bear
   With something rich about me. From that place
   I shall no leading need.

EDGAR   Give me thy arm.
80   Poor Tom shall lead thee.   *Exeunt*

4.2

Enter GONERIL *and* EDMUND

GONERIL   Welcome, my lord. I marvel our mild husband
   Not° met us on the way.   *has not*

   Enter OSWALD

                        Now where's your master?

OSWALD   Madam, within, but never man so changed.
   I told him of the army that was landed;
5   He smiled at it. I told him you were coming;
   His answer was "The worse." Of Gloucester's treachery,
   And of the loyal service of his son,
   When I informed him, then he called me sot,°   *fool*
   And told me I had turned the wrong side out.[1]

---

9. I cannot continue the charade. "Daub": plaster; i.e., mask.
1. Let the overprosperous man who indulges his appetite.
2. Makes your law subject to him.

3. Looks fearsomely into the straits below.
4.2 Location: Before Albany's castle.
1. I had reversed things (by mistaking loyalty for treachery).

10 What most he should dislike seems pleasant to him;
What like, offensive.
GONERIL (*to* EDMUND)   Then shall you go no further.
It is the cowish° terror of his spirit,   cowardly
That dares not undertake. He'll not feel wrongs
Which tie him to an answer.[2] Our wishes on the way
15 May prove effects.[3] Back, Edmund, to my brother;°   brother-in-law
Hasten his musters° and conduct his powers.°   call-up of troops / armies
I must change arms at home, and give the distaff[4]
Into my husband's hands. This trusty servant
Shall pass between us. Ere long you are like° to hear,   likely
20 If you dare venture in your own behalf,
A mistress's° command. Wear this; spare speech;   (playing on "lover's")
     (*giving a favor*)
Decline your head. This kiss, if it durst speak,
Would stretch thy spirits up into the air.
Conceive,° and fare thee well.   understand my meaning
EDMUND   Yours in° the ranks of death.   even in
25 GONERIL   My most dear Gloucester!
                                              Exit EDMUND
O, the difference of man and man!
To thee a woman's services are due:
My fool usurps my body.[5]
OSWALD   Madam, here comes my lord.   *Exit*
     Enter ALBANY
GONERIL   I have been worth the whistling.[6]
ALBANY   O Goneril!
30 You are not worth the dust which the rude wind
Blows in your face. I fear your disposition.
That nature which contemns° it origin   despises its
Cannot be bordered certain° in itself.   be defended securely
She that herself will sliver and disbranch°   split
35 From her material sap, perforce must wither
And come to deadly use.[7]
GONERIL   No more; the text is foolish.
ALBANY   Wisdom and goodness to the vile seem vile;
Filths savor but themselves. What have you done?
40 Tigers, not daughters, what have you performed?
A father, and a gracious agèd man,
Whose reverence even the head-lugged° bear would   dragged by the head
     lick,
Most barbarous, most degenerate, have you madded.
Could my good brother° suffer you to do it?   brother-in-law

---

2. He'll ignore insults that should provoke him
to retaliate.
3. May be put into action.
4. A device used in spinning and thus emblematic of the female role.
5. My idiot husband presumes to possess me.
6. I.e., at one time, you would have come to wel-

come me home; referring to the proverb "It is a
poor dog that is not worth the whistling."
7. Be destroyed; be used for burning. The allusion is probably biblical: "But that which beareth
thorns and briers is reproved, and is near unto
cursing; whose end is to be burned" (Hebrews
6.8).

45 A man, a prince, by him so benefited!
If that the heavens do not their visible spirits
Send quickly down to tame these vild° offenses,   *vile*
It will come,
Humanity must perforce° prey on itself,   *inevitably*
Like monsters of the deep.
50 GONERIL   Milk-livered° man!   *cowardly*
That bear'st a cheek for blows, a head for wrongs;[8]
Who hast not in thy brows an eye discerning
Thine honor from thy suffering;[9] that not know'st
Fools do those villains pity who are punished
55 Ere they have done their mischief. Where's thy drum?°   *(to muster troops)*
France spreads his banners in our noiseless° land,   *peaceful*
With plumèd helm thy state begins to threat;
Whiles thou, a moral° fool, sit'st still and criest   *moralizing*
"Alack, why does he so?"
ALBANY   See thyself, devil!
60 Proper deformity shows not in the fiend
So horrid as in woman.[1]
GONERIL   O vain° fool!   *useless*
ALBANY   Thou changèd and self-covered[2] thing, for shame,
Be-monster not thy feature. Were't my fitness°   *if it were appropriate*
To let these hands obey my blood,
65 They are apt enough to dislocate and tear
Thy flesh and bones. Howe'er° thou art a fiend,   *although*
A woman's shape doth shield thee.
GONERIL   Marry, your manhood! mew![3]
       Enter a MESSENGER
ALBANY   What news?
70 MESSENGER   O, my good lord, the Duke of Cornwall's dead;
Slain by his servant, going to put out
The other eye of Gloucester.
ALBANY   Gloucester's eyes?
MESSENGER   A servant that he bred, thrilled with remorse,°   *pierced by pity*
Opposed against the act, bending° his sword   *directing*
75 To° his great master; who, thereat enraged,   *against*
Flew on him, and amongst them felled him dead;
But not without that harmful stroke, which since
Hath plucked him after.[4]
ALBANY   This shows you are above,
You justicers,° that these our nether crimes[5]   *judges*

---

8. Fit for abuse; ready for cuckold's horns.
9. That can distinguish between an insult to your honor and something you should patiently endure.
1. Deformity (of morals) is appropriate in the devil and so less horrid than in woman (from whom virtue is expected). Albany may hold a mirror in front of Goneril, since Jacobean women sometimes wore small mirrors attached to their dresses.
2. Altered and with your true (womanly) self concealed.
3. A derisive catcall. "Marry": By the Virgin Mary.
4. Has sent him to follow his servant into death.
5. Lower crimes, and so committed on earth, but also suggesting that the deeds smack of the netherworld of hell.

80 So speedily can venge! But, O poor Gloucester!
　 Lost he his other eye?
MESSENGER　　　　　　　Both, both, my lord.
　 This letter, madam, craves a speedy answer;
　 'Tis from your sister.
GONERIL (*aside*)　　　 One way I like this well;[6]
　 But being° a widow, and my Gloucester with her,　　　　*her being*
85 May all the building in my fancy pluck
　 Upon my hateful life.[7] Another way,
　 The news is not so tart.°—I'll read, and answer.　*Exit*　*bitter*
ALBANY　Where was his son when they did take his eyes?
MESSENGER　Come with my lady hither.
ALBANY　　　　　　　　　　　　He is not here.
90 MESSENGER　No, my good lord; I met him back° again.　　*returning*
ALBANY　Knows he the wickedness?
MESSENGER　Ay, my good lord; 'twas he informed against him;
　 And quit the house on purpose, that their punishment
　 Might have the freer course.
ALBANY　　　　　　　　　　 Gloucester, I live
95 To thank thee for the love thou show'dst the king,
　 And to revenge thine eyes. Come hither, friend.
　 Tell me what more thou know'st.　　　　　*Exeunt*

4.3

　　　Enter KENT *and a* GENTLEMAN
KENT　Why the King of France is so suddenly gone back
　 know you the reason?
GENTLEMAN　Something he left imperfect° in the state,　　*unsettled*
　 which since his coming forth is thought of;° which　　*remembered*
5 imports° to the kingdom so much fear and danger, that　　*portends*
　 his personal return was most required and necessary.
KENT　Who hath he left behind him general?
GENTLEMAN　The Marshall of France, Monsieur LaFar.
KENT　Did your letters pierce the queen to any demon-
10 stration of grief?
GENTLEMAN　Ay, sir. She took them, in my presence;
　 And now and then an ample tear trilled° down　　　　*rolled*
　 Her delicate cheek. It seemed she was a queen
　 Over her passion, who,° most rebel-like,　　　　　　*which*
　 Sought to be king o'er her.
15 KENT　　　　　　　　　 O, then it moved her.
GENTLEMAN　Not to a rage. Patience and sorrow strove
　 Who should express her goodliest.[1] You have seen
　 Sunshine and rain at once: her smiles and tears
　 Were like a° better way. Those happy smilets,　　*were similar in a*

---

6. Because a political rival has been eliminated.
7. May pull down all of my built-up fantasies and thus make my life hateful.

4.3 Location: Near the French camp at Dover.
1. Which should better express her feelings.

20 That played on her ripe lip, seemed not to know
What guests were in her eyes, which parted thence,
As pearls from diamonds dropped. In brief,
Sorrow would be a rarity° most beloved,   *gem*
If all could so become it.[2]

KENT   Made she no verbal question?

25 GENTLEMAN   'Faith, once or twice she heaved the name of "father"
Pantingly forth, as if it pressed her heart;
Cried "Sisters! sisters! Shame of ladies! sisters!
Kent! father! sisters! What, i' the storm? i' the night?
Let pity not be believed!"[3] There she shook

30 The holy water from her heavenly eyes,
And clamor moistened.[4] Then away she started,°   *sprang*
To deal with grief alone.

KENT   It is the stars,
The stars above us, govern our conditions;
Else one self mate and make[5] could not beget

35 Such different issues.° You spoke not with her since?   *offspring*

GENTLEMAN   No.

KENT   Was this before the king returned?

GENTLEMAN   No, since.

KENT   Well, sir, the poor distressed Lear's i' the town;
Who sometime, in his better tune,° remembers   *state of mind*

40 What we are come about, and by no means
Will yield° to see his daughter.   *consent*

GENTLEMAN   Why, good sir?

KENT   A sovereign shame so elbows° him; his own unkindness,   *prods, nudges*
That stripped her from his benediction, turned her
To foreign casualties,° gave her dear rights   *risks*

45 To his dog-hearted daughters, these things sting
His mind so venomously that burning shame
Detains him from Cordelia.

GENTLEMAN   Alack, poor gentleman!

KENT   Of Albany's and Cornwall's powers° you heard not?   *armies*

GENTLEMAN   'Tis so, they are afoot.

50 KENT   Well, sir, I'll bring you to our master Lear,
And leave you to attend him. Some dear cause°   *some important reason*
Will in concealment wrap me up awhile;
When I am known aright, you shall not grieve°   *repent*
Lending me this acquaintance.° I pray you, go   *news*
Along with me.   *Exeunt*

---

2. If everyone wore it so beautifully.   4. And moistened her anguish (with tears).
3. Never believe in pity; compassion cannot exist.   5. Or else the same pair of spouses.

4.4

Enter, with drum and colors, CORDELIA, DOCTOR, *and soldiers*

CORDELIA   Alack, 'tis he! Why, he was met even now
  As mad as the vexed sea; singing aloud;
  Crowned with rank fumiter and furrow-weeds,[1]
  With hor-docks, hemlock, nettles, cuckoo-flowers,
5 Darnel, and all the idle° weeds that grow   *useless*
  In our sustaining corn.° A century° send forth;   *grain / battalion (100 men)*
  Search every acre in the high-grown field,
  And bring him to our eye.   *Exit an officer*
  What can man's wisdom
10 In the restoring° his bereaved sense?   *do to restore*
  He that helps him, take all my outward° worth.   *material*
DOCTOR   There is means, madam.
  Our foster-nurse of nature[2] is repose,
  The which he lacks. That to provoke in him,
15 Are many simples operative,[3] whose power
  Will close the eye of anguish.
CORDELIA   All blest secrets,
  All you unpublished virtues° of the earth,   *obscure healing plants*
  Spring with my tears! be aidant and remediate°   *healing and remedial*
  In the good man's distress! Seek, seek for him,
20 Lest his ungoverned rage dissolve the life
  That wants° the means to lead it.   *lacks*
          Enter a MESSENGER
MESSENGER   News, madam;
  The British powers° are marching hitherward.   *armies*
CORDELIA   'Tis known before; our preparation stands
  In expectation of them. O dear father,
25 It is thy business that I go about;[4]
  Therefore great France
  My mourning and importuned° tears hath pitied.   *importunate; solicitous*
  No blown° ambition doth our arms incite,   *inflated*
  But love, dear love, and our aged father's right.
30 Soon may I hear and see him!   *Exeunt*

4.5

Enter REGAN *and* OSWALD

REGAN   But are my brother's powers° set forth?   *(Albany's forces)*
OSWALD   Ay, madam.

4.4 Location: The French camp at Dover.
1. Fumiter was used against brain sickness. Furrow-weeds, like the other weeds in the following lines, grow in the furrows of plowed fields.
2. That which comforts and nourishes human nature.
3. To induce that ("repose") in him, there are many effective medicinal herbs.
4. The line echoes Christ's explanation of his mission in Luke 2.49: "I must be about my Father's business."
4.5 Location: At Gloucester's castle.

REGAN   Himself in person there?

OSWALD   Madam, with much ado.°   *trouble*
  Your sister is the better soldier.

5 REGAN   Lord Edmund spake not with your lord at home?

OSWALD   No, madam.

REGAN   What might import° my sister's letter to him?   *mean*

OSWALD   I know not, lady.

REGAN   Faith, he is posted° hence on serious matter.   *hurried*
10   It was great ignorance, Gloucester's eyes being out,
  To let him live. Where he arrives he moves
  All hearts against us. Edmund, I think, is gone,
  In pity of his misery,° to dispatch   *(ironic)*
  His nighted° life; moreover, to descry°   *darkened / investigate*
15   The strength o' the enemy.

OSWALD   I must needs after° him, madam, with my letter.   *go after*

REGAN   Our troops set forth tomorrow. Stay with us;
  The ways are dangerous.

OSWALD   I may not, madam:
  My lady charged° my duty in this business.   *commanded*

20 REGAN   Why should she write to Edmund? Might not you
  Transport her purposes by word? Belike,°   *perhaps*
  Something—I know not what. I'll love° thee much: *reward*
  Let me unseal the letter.

OSWALD   Madam, I had rather—

REGAN   I know your lady does not love her husband;
25   I am sure of that; and at her late° being here   *recently*
  She gave strange oeillades° and most speaking looks   *amorous glances*
  To noble Edmund. I know you are of her bosom.°   *in her confidence*

OSWALD   I, madam?

REGAN   I speak in understanding;° y'are, I know't.   *with certainty*
30   Therefore I do advise you, take this note:°   *take note of this*
  My lord is dead; Edmund and I have talked;
  And more convenient° is he for my hand   *appropriate*
  Than for your lady's. You may gather° more.   *infer*
  If you do find him, pray you, give him this;[1]
35   And when your mistress hears thus much from you,
  I pray, desire her call her wisdom to her.[2]
  So, fare you well.
  If you do chance to hear of that blind traitor,
  Preferment falls on him that cuts him off.°   *cuts his life short*
40 OSWALD   Would I could meet him, madam! I should show
  What party I do follow.

REGAN   Fare thee well.   *Exeunt*

1. This information, but possibly another letter   2. Tell her to come to her senses.
or token.

4.6

Enter GLOUCESTER, *and* EDGAR *dressed like a peasant*

GLOUCESTER   When shall we come to the top of that same°   *agreed-upon*
    hill?
EDGAR   You do climb up it now. Look how we labor.
GLOUCESTER   Methinks the ground is even.
EDGAR   Horrible steep.
    Hark, do you hear the sea?
GLOUCESTER   No, truly.
5   EDGAR   Why, then, your other senses grow imperfect
    By your eyes' anguish.
GLOUCESTER   So may it be, indeed.
    Methinks thy voice is altered, and thou speakest
    In better phrase and matter° than thou didst.   *sense*
EDGAR   Y'are much deceived. In nothing am I changed
    But in my garments.
10 GLOUCESTER   Methinks y'are better spoken.
EDGAR   Come on, sir; here's the place. Stand still. How fearful
    And dizzy 'tis, to cast one's eyes so low!
    The crows and choughs° that wing the midway air   *jackdaws*
    Show° scarce so gross° as beetles. Halfway down   *appear / big*
15   Hangs one that gathers sampire,[1] dreadful trade!
    Methinks he seems no bigger than his head.
    The fishermen, that walk upon the beach,
    Appear like mice; and yond tall anchoring bark,°   *ship*
    Diminished to her cock;° her cock, a buoy   *dinghy*
20   Almost too small for sight. The murmuring surge,
    That on the unnumbered° idle pebble chafes,   *innumerable*
    Cannot be heard so high. I'll look no more,
    Lest my brain turn, and the° deficient sight   *my*
    Topple° down headlong.   *topple me*
GLOUCESTER   Set me where you stand.
25 EDGAR   Give me your hand. You are now within a foot
    Of th' extreme verge. For all beneath the moon
    Would I not leap upright.[2]
GLOUCESTER   Let go my hand.
    Here, friend, 's another purse; in it a jewel
    Well worth a poor man's taking. Fairies and gods
30   Prosper it[3] with thee! Go thou farther off;
    Bid me farewell, and let me hear thee going.
EDGAR   Now fare you well, good sir.
GLOUCESTER   With all my heart.
EDGAR *(aside)*   Why I do trifle thus with his despair
    Is done to cure it.
GLOUCESTER *(kneeling)*   O you mighty gods!

4.6 Location: Near Dover.
1. Samphire: a plant that grows on rocks by the
sea; used in making pickles.
2. I would not jump up and down (for fear of losing my balance).
3. Make it increase. Fairies were sometimes held
to hoard and multiply treasure.

35 This world I do renounce, and, in your sights,
Shake patiently my great affliction off.
If I could bear it longer, and not fall
To quarrel° with your great opposeless wills,   *into conflict*
My snuff and loathèd part of nature[4] should
40 Burn itself out. If Edgar live, O, bless him!
Now, fellow, fare thee well.

He falls forward and swoons

EDGAR   Gone, sir; farewell.—
And yet I know not how conceit may rob
The treasury of life, when life itself
Yields to the theft.[5] Had he been where he thought,
45 By this° had thought been past. Alive or dead?   *now*
Ho, you sir! friend! Hear you, sir? speak!
Thus might he pass° indeed. Yet he revives.   *pass away*
What are you, sir?

GLOUCESTER   Away, and let me die.

EDGAR   Hadst thou been aught° but gossamer, feathers, air,   *anything*
50 So many fathom down precipitating,°   *plunging*
Thou'dst shivered° like an egg; but thou dost breathe;   *shattered*
Hast heavy substance; bleed'st not; speak'st; art sound.
Ten masts at each° make not the altitude   *end to end*
Which thou hast perpendicularly fell.
55 Thy life's a miracle. Speak yet again.

GLOUCESTER   But have I fallen, or no?

EDGAR   From the dread summit of this chalky bourn.[6]
Look up a-height; the shrill-gorged° lark so far   *shrill-throated*
Cannot be seen or heard. Do but look up.

60 GLOUCESTER   Alack, I have no eyes.
Is wretchedness deprived° that benefit,   *deprived of*
To end itself by death? 'Twas yet some comfort,
When misery could beguile° the tyrant's rage   *cheat*
And frustrate his proud will.

EDGAR   Give me your arm.
65 Up—so. How is 't? Feel you your legs? You stand.

GLOUCESTER   Too well, too well.

EDGAR   This is above all strangeness.
Upon the crown o' the cliff, what thing was that
Which parted from you?

GLOUCESTER   A poor unfortunate beggar.

EDGAR   As I stood here below, methought his eyes
70 Were two full moons; he had a thousand noses,
Horns whelked° and waved like the enridgèd sea: *twisted*
It was some fiend. Therefore, thou happy father,°   *lucky old man*
Think that the clearest° gods, who make them honors   *purest; most illustrious*

---

4. The scorched and hateful remnant of my life-time. "Snuff": end of a candle wick.
5. Edgar worries that the imagined scenario ("conceit") he has invented may be enough to kill

his father, particularly as Gloucester wishes for ("yields to") his own death.
6. The white chalk cliffs of Dover, which make a boundary ("bourn") between land and sea.

Of men's impossibilities,[7] have preserved thee.

75 GLOUCESTER   I do remember now. Henceforth I'll bear
Affliction till it do cry out itself
"Enough, enough," and die. That thing you speak of,
I took it for a man; often 'twould say
"The fiend, the fiend"—he led me to that place.

80 EDGAR   Bear free and patient thoughts. But who comes here?

Enter LEAR, *fantastically dressed with wild flowers*

The safer sense will ne'er accommodate
His master thus.[8]

LEAR   No, they cannot touch me for coining;[9] I am the king
himself.

85 EDGAR   O thou side-piercing sight!

LEAR   Nature's above art in that respect.[1] There's your
press-money.[2] That fellow handles his bow like a crow-
keeper.[3] Draw me a clothier's yard.[4] Look, look, a mouse!
Peace, peace; this piece of toasted cheese will do't.°   *(lure the mouse)*
90 There's my gauntlet; I'll prove it on a giant.[5] Bring up the
brown bills.[6] O, well flown, bird!° i' the clout,° i' the clout.   *arrow / bull's-eye*
Hewgh! Give the word.°   *password*

EDGAR   Sweet marjoram.[7]

LEAR   Pass.

95 GLOUCESTER   I know that voice.

LEAR   Ha! Goneril, with a white beard! They flattered me
like a dog;° and told me I had white hairs in my beard ere   *fawningly*
the black ones were there.[8] To say "aye" and "no" to everything that I said!—"Aye" and "no" too was no good divin-
100 ity.[9] When the rain came to wet me once, and the wind
to make me chatter; when the thunder would not peace
at my bidding; there I found° 'em, there I smelt 'em out.   *understood*
Go to, they are not men o' their words! They told me I
was everything. 'Tis a lie, I am not ague-proof.°   *immune to illness*

105 GLOUCESTER   The trick° of that voice I do well remember.   *peculiarity*
Is't not the king?

LEAR   Aye, every inch a king!
When I do stare, see how the subject quakes.
I pardon that man's life. What was thy cause?°   *crime*
Adultery?
110 Thou shalt not die. Die for adultery? No.
The wren goes to't, and the small gilded fly

---

7. Who attain honor for themselves by performing deeds impossible to men.
8. A sane mind would never allow its possessor
to dress up this way.
9. Cannot equal me (or, perhaps, censure me),
because minting money was the prerogative of the
king.
1. My true feelings will always outvalue others'
hypocrisy; my natural supremacy surpasses any
attempt to create a false new reign. This image
may also be based on coining (see preceding note).
2. Fee paid to a soldier impressed, or forced, into
the army.
3. A person hired as a scarecrow, and thus unfit

for anything else.
4. Draw the bowstring the full length of the
arrow (a standard English arrow was a cloth
yard—thirty-seven inches—long).
5. I'll defend my stand even against a giant. To
throw down an armored glove ("gauntlet") was to
issue a challenge.
6. Brown painted pikes; or, the soldiers carrying
them.
7. Used medicinally against madness.
8. I.e., told me I had wisdom before age.
9. I.e., poor theology (because insincere); from
James 5.12, "Let your yea be yea; nay, nay."

Does lecher in my sight.
Let copulation thrive; for Gloucester's bastard son
Was kinder to his father than my daughters
115 Got 'tween the lawful sheets. To't luxury,° pell-mell!   lechery
For I lack soldiers. Behold yond simpering dame,
Whose face between her forks presages snow;[1]
That minces° virtue, and does shake the head   affects
To hear of° pleasure's name;   even of
120 The fitchew, nor the soilèd horse,[2] goes to't
With a more riotous appetite.
Down from the waist they are Centaurs,[3]
Though women all above.
But° to the girdle° do the gods inherit.°   only / waist / own
125 Beneath is all the fiends'; there's hell,[4] there's darkness,
There's the sulphurous pit, burning, scalding,
Stench, consumption! Fie, fie fie! pah! pah!
Give me an ounce of civet,[5] good apothecary,
To sweeten my imagination.
130 There's money for thee.
GLOUCESTER   O, let me kiss that hand!
LEAR   Let me wipe it first; it smells of mortality.
GLOUCESTER   O ruined piece° of nature! This great world   masterpiece
Shall so wear out to nought.[6] Dost thou know me?
135 LEAR   I remember thine eyes well enough. Dost thou
squiny° at me? No, do thy worst, blind Cupid; I'll not love.   squint
Read thou this challenge; mark but the penning of it.
GLOUCESTER   Were all the letters suns, I could not see one.
EDGAR (aside)   I would not take° this from report. It is,   believe
140 And my heart breaks at it.
LEAR   Read.
GLOUCESTER   What, with the case° of eyes?   socket
LEAR   O, ho, are you there with me?[7] No eyes in your head,
nor no money in your purse? Your eyes are in a heavy
145 case,[8] your purse in a light. Yet you see how this world
goes.
GLOUCESTER   I see it feelingly.°   by touch; painfully
LEAR   What, art mad? A man may see how this world goes
with no eyes. Look with thine ears. See how yond justice
150 rails upon yond simple° thief. Hark, in thine ear. Change   lowly; innocent
places and, handy-dandy,[9] which is the justice, which is
the thief? Thou hast seen a farmer's dog bark at a beggar?

1. Whose expression implies cold chastity. "Face" refers to the area between her legs ("forks"), as well as to her literal facial expression as framed by the aristocratic lady's starched headpiece, also called a "fork."
2. Neither the polecat nor a horse full of fresh grass.
3. Lecherous mythological creatures that have a human body to the waist and the legs and torso of a horse below.
4. Shakespeare's frequent term for female genitals.
5. Exotic perfume derived from the sex glands of the civet cat.
6. Shall decay to nothing in the same way. In Renaissance philosophy, humans were perfectly analogous to the cosmos, standing for the whole in miniature.
7. Is that what you are telling me?
8. In a sad condition; playing on "case" as "sockets."
9. Pick a hand, as in a child's game.

GLOUCESTER   Aye, sir.

LEAR   And the creature° run from the cur? There thou   *wretch*
155   mightst behold the great image of authority: a dog's
obeyed in office.
Thou rascal beadle,[1] hold° thy bloody hand!   *restrain*
Why dost thou lash that whore? Strip thine own back;
Thou hotly lusts to use her in that kind°   *way*
160   For which thou whipp'st her. The usurer hangs the cozener.[2]
Through tattered clothes small vices do appear;
Robes and furred gowns hide all. Plate° sin with gold,   *armor; gild*
And the strong lance of justice hurtless° breaks;   *harmlessly*
Arm it in rags, a pigmy's straw does pierce it.
165   None does offend, none, I say, none; I'll able° 'em;   *authorize*
Take that of me, my friend, who have the power
To seal the accuser's lips. Get thee glass eyes,
And, like a scurvy politician,[3] seem
To see the things thou dost not. Now, now, now, now!
170   Pull off my boots. Harder, harder! So.

EDGAR   O, matter and impertinency° mixed!   *sense and nonsense*
Reason in madness!

LEAR   If thou wilt weep my fortunes, take my eyes.
I know thee well enough; thy name is Gloucester:
175   Thou must be patient. We came crying hither;
Thou knows't, the first time that we smell the air,
We wail and cry. I will preach to thee. Mark.°   *give heed*
     LEAR *takes off his crown of weeds and flowers*[4]

GLOUCESTER   Alack, alack the day!

LEAR   When we are born, we cry that we are come
180   To this great stage of fools. This'° a good block;[5]   *this is*
It were a delicate° stratagem, to shoe   *subtle*
A troop of horse with felt.[6] I'll put't in proof;°   *to the test*
And when I have stol'n upon these sons-in-law,
Then, kill, kill, kill, kill, kill, kill!
     Enter a GENTLEMAN, *with attendants*

185   GENTLEMAN   O, here he is; lay hand upon him. Sir,
Your most dear daughter—

LEAR   No rescue? What, a prisoner? I am even
The natural fool[7] of fortune. Use° me well;   *treat*
You shall have ransom. Let me have surgeons;
I am cut to the brains.

190   GENTLEMAN   You shall have anything.

---

1. The parish officer responsible for whippings.
2. The ruinous moneylender, prosperous enough to be made a judge, convicts the ordinary cheat.
3. A vile schemer. In early modern England, "politician" meant an ambitious, even Machiavellian, upstart.
4. Like a preacher removing his hat in the pulpit.
5. Stage (often called "scaffold" and hence linked to executioner's block); block used to shape a felt hat (such as the hat removed by a preacher before a sermon); mounting block (such as the stump or stock Lear may have sat on to remove his boots).
6. Hat material, to muffle the sound of the approaching cavalry.
7. Born plaything; playing on "natural" as "mentally deficient."

LEAR No seconds?° all myself?   *supporters*
  Why, this would make a man a man of salt,[8]
  To use his eyes for garden water-pots,
  Aye, and laying° autumn's dust.   *settling*

GENTLEMAN   Good sir—

195 LEAR I will die bravely,[9] like a smug° bridegroom. What!   *an elegant*
  I will be jovial. Come, come; I am a king,
  My masters, know you that?

GENTLEMAN You are a royal one, and we obey you.

LEAR Then there's life° in't. Nay, if you get it, you shall get   *hope*
200 it with running. Sa, sa, sa, sa.[1]

(Exit running; attendants follow)

GENTLEMAN A sight most pitiful in the meanest wretch,
  Past speaking of in a king! Thou hast one daughter
  Who redeems nature from the general curse
  Which twain have brought her to.[2]

EDGAR Hail, gentle° sir.   *noble*

205 GENTLEMAN   Sir, speed you.° What's your will?   *God speed you*

EDGAR Do you hear aught, sir, of a battle toward?°   *coming*

GENTLEMAN Most sure and vulgar.° Everyone hears that,   *commonly known*
  Which° can distinguish sound.   *who*

EDGAR   But, by your favor,
  How near's the other army?

210 GENTLEMAN Near and on speedy foot. The main descry°   *appearance*
  Stands on the hourly thought.°   *is expected forthwith*

EDGAR I thank you, sir. That's all.

GENTLEMAN Though that the queen on° special cause° is   *for / reason*
  here,
  Her army is moved on.

EDGAR   I thank you, sir.

Exit GENTLEMAN

215 GLOUCESTER You ever-gentle gods, take my breath from me;
  Let not my worser spirt[3] tempt me again
  To die before you please!

EDGAR   Well pray you, father.[4]

GLOUCESTER Now, good sir, what are you?

EDGAR A most poor man, made tame to fortune's blows;
220   Who, by the art of known and feeling° sorrows,   *profound*
  Am pregnant to° good pity. Give me your hand,   *disposed to feel*
  I'll lead you to some biding.°   *resting place*

GLOUCESTER   Hearty thanks.
  The bounty and the benison of heaven
  To boot, and boot![5]

---

8. A man reduced to nothing but the salt his tears deposit.
9. With courage; showily. "Die" plays on the Renaissance sense of "have an orgasm."
1. A cry to encourage dogs in the hunt.
2. I.e., who restores proper meaning and order to a universe plagued by the crimes of the other two daughters; alluding to the fall of humankind and nature caused by the sin of Adam and Eve.
3. Wicked inclination; bad angel.
4. A term of respect for an elderly man.
5. In addition to my thanks, and may it bring you some worldly reward.

Enter OSWALD

225 OSWALD   A proclaimed prize!⁶ Most happy!°   *lucky*
    That eyeless head of thine was first framed° flesh   *made of*
    To raise my fortunes. Thou old unhappy traitor,
    Briefly thyself remember.⁷ The sword is out
    That must destroy thee.
GLOUCESTER   Now let thy friendly hand
    Put strength enough to't.
        EDGAR *interposes*
230 OSWALD   Wherefore, bold peasant,
    Darest thou support a published° traitor? Hence,   *proclaimed*
    Lest that the infection° of his fortune take   *(deathly) sickness*
    Like° hold on thee. Let go his arm.   *the same*
EDGAR   Chill⁸ not let go, zir, without vurther 'casion.°   *further occasion*
235 OSWALD   Let go, slave, or thou diest!
EDGAR   Good gentleman, go your gait,° and let poor volk   *walk on*
    pass. An chud ha'° bin zwaggered out of my life, 'twould   *if I could have*
    not ha' bin zo long as 'tis by a vortnight. Nay, come not
    near th'old man; keep out, che vor ye, or ise try whether
240   your costard or my ballow be the harder.⁹ Chill be plain
    with you.
OSWALD   Out, dunghill!
EDGAR   Chill pick your teeth, zir. Come! No matter vor
    your foins.°   *sword thrusts*
      They fight, and EDGAR *knocks him down*
245 OSWALD   Slave, thou hast slain me. Villain, take my purse.
    If ever thou wilt° thrive, bury my body;   *you wish to*
    And give the letters which thou find'st about me
    To Edmund earl of Gloucester. Seek him out
    Upon° the British party. O, untimely death!   *within*
250   Death!   *He dies*
EDGAR   I know thee well: a serviceable° villain,   *an officious*
    As duteous to the vices of thy mistress
    As badness would desire.
GLOUCESTER   What, is he dead?
EDGAR   Sit you down, father; rest you.
255   Let's see his pockets; the letters that he speaks of
    May be my friends. He's dead; I am only sorry
    He had no other death'sman.° Let us see.   *executioner*
    Leave,° gentle wax;¹ and manners, blame us not.   *by your leave*
    To know our enemies' minds, we'd rip their hearts;
260   Their° papers, is more lawful.   *to rip their*
    (*Reads*) "Let our reciprocal vows be remembered. You
    have many opportunities to cut him off. If your will want°   *lacks*

---

6. A wanted man, with a bounty on his life.
7. Recollect and pray forgiveness for your sins.
8. I will; dialect from Somerset was a stage convention for peasant dialogue.
9. I warn you, or I shall test whether your head or my cudgel is harder. "Costard": a kind of apple.
1. The wax seal on the letter.

not, time and place will be fruitfully offered. There is
nothing done,° if he return the conqueror. Then am I the   *accomplished*
265   prisoner, and his bed my jail; from the loathed warmth
whereof deliver me, and supply° the place for your labor.[2]   *fill*
             Your—wife, so I would say—
               Affectionate servant,
                  Goneril."

270   O undistinguished space of woman's will![3]
A plot upon her virtuous husband's life;
And the exchange° my brother! Here, in the sands,   *substitute*
Thee I'll rake up,° the post unsanctified°   *cover up / unholy messenger*
Of murderous lechers; and in the mature time°   *when the time is ripe*
275   With this ungracious° paper strike the sight   *ungodly*
Of the death-practiced duke.[4] For him 'tis well
That of thy death and business I can tell.
GLOUCESTER   The king is mad. How stiff is my vile sense,[5]
That I stand up, and have ingenious feeling[6]
280   Of my huge sorrows! Better I were distract;°   *mad*
So should my thoughts be severed from my griefs,
And woes by wrong° imaginations lose   *false*
The knowledge of themselves.
      Drum afar off
EDGAR   Give me your hand.
Far off, methinks, I hear the beaten drum.
285   Come, father, I'll bestow° you with a friend.   *Exeunt*   *lodge*

4.7

Enter CORDELIA, KENT, DOCTOR, *and a* GENTLEMAN
CORDELIA   O thou good Kent, how shall I live and work,
To match thy goodness? My life will be too short,
And every measure° fail me.   *attempt*
KENT   To be acknowledged, madam, is o'erpaid.°   *is more than enough*
5   All my reports go[1] with the modest truth;
Nor more, nor clipped, but so.[2]
CORDELIA   Be better suited.°   *attired*
These weeds° are memories of those worser hours.   *clothes*
I prithee, put them off.
KENT   Pardon me, dear madam;
Yet to be known shortens my made intent.[3]
10   My boon I make it,[4] that you know° me not   *acknowledge*
Till time and I think meet.°   *suitable*

2. As a reward for your endeavors; for sexual exertion.
3. Limitless extent of woman's willfulness. As with "hell" in line 125, "will" might also refer to a woman's genitals.
4. Of the duke whose death is plotted.
5. How obstinate is my unwanted power of reason.

6. That I remain upright and firm in my sanity and have rational perceptions.
4.7 Location: The French camp at Dover.
1. May all accounts of me agree.
2. Not greater or less, but exactly the modest amount I deserve.
3. Revealing myself now would abort my designs.
4. The reward I beg is.

CORDELIA   Then be't so, my good lord. (*To the* DOCTOR)
    How does the king?
DOCTOR   Madam, sleeps still.
CORDELIA   O you kind gods,
15   Cure this great breach in his absènd nature!
    The untuned and jarring senses, O, wind up[5]
    Of this child-changed[6] father!
DOCTOR   So please your majesty
    That we may wake the king? He hath slept long.
CORDELIA   Be governed by your knowledge, and proceed
20   I' the sway° of your own will. Is he arrayed?°   *by the authority / clothed*
    Enter LEAR *in a chair carried by servants*
GENTLEMAN   Aye, madam. In the heaviness of his sleep
    We put fresh garments on him.
DOCTOR   Be by, good madam, when we do awake him;
    I doubt not of his temperance.°   *calmness*
CORDELIA   Very well.
    Music
25 DOCTOR   Please you, draw near. Louder the music there!
CORDELIA   O my dear father! Restoration hang
    Thy medicine on my lips; and let this kiss
    Repair those violent harms that my two sisters
    Have in thy reverence° made!   *aged dignity*
KENT   Kind and dear princess!
30 CORDELIA   Had you not° been their father, these white   *even if you had not*
    flakes°   *locks of hair*
    Had challenged° pity of them. Was this a face   *would have provoked*
    To be opposed against the warring winds?
    To stand against the deep dread-bolted thunder?
    In the most terrible and nimble stroke
35   Of quick, cross lightning? to watch°—poor perdu![7]— *to stand guard*
    With this thin helm?° Mine enemy's dog,   *helmet (of hair)*
    Though he had bit me, should have stood that night
    Against my fire; and wast thou fain,° poor father,   *glad*
    To hovel thee with swine, and rogues forlorn,
40   In short° and musty straw? Alack, alack!   *scant; broken*
    'Tis wonder that thy life and wits at once
    Had not concluded all.° He wakes; speak to him.   *altogether*
DOCTOR   Madam, do you; 'tis fittest.
CORDELIA   How does my royal lord? How fares your majesty?
45 LEAR   You do me wrong to take me out o' the grave.
    Thou art a soul in bliss; but I am bound
    Upon a wheel of fire, that mine own tears
    Do scald like molten lead.[8]
CORDELIA   Sir, do you know me?

---

5. Reorder his confused and delirious mind. The image is of tightening the strings of a lute.
6. Changed by his children; changed into a child; playing on a musical key-change.
7. Lost one; in military terminology, a danger-ously exposed sentry.
8. Lear puts himself in either hell or purgatory, both places of such punishment in medieval accounts.

LEAR   You are a spirit, I know. When did you die?

50 CORDELIA   Still, still, far wide!°   *unbalanced*

DOCTOR   He's scarce awake. Let him alone awhile.

LEAR   Where have I been? Where am I? Fair daylight?
    I am mightily abused.° I should e'en die with pity,   *wronged; deceived*
    To see another thus. I know not what to say.

55   I will not swear these are my hands. Let's see.
    I feel this pin prick. Would I were assured
    Of my condition!

CORDELIA   O, look upon me, sir,
    And hold your hands in benediction o'er me:
    No, sir, you must not kneel.

60 LEAR   Pray, do not mock me.
    I am a very foolish fond° old man,   *silly*
    Fourscore and upward, not an hour more nor less;
    And, to deal plainly,
    I fear I am not in my perfect mind.

65   Methinks I should know you, and know this man;
    Yet I am doubtful; for I am mainly° ignorant   *entirely*
    What place this is; and all the skill I have
    Remembers not these garments; nor I know not
    Where I did lodge last night. Do not laugh at me;

70   For, as I am a man, I think this lady
    To be my child Cordelia.

CORDELIA   And so I am, I am.

LEAR   Be your tears wet?[9] Yes, faith. I pray, weep not.
    If you have poison for me, I will drink it.
    I know you do not love me; for your sisters

75   Have, as I do remember, done me wrong.
    You have some cause, they have not.

CORDELIA   No cause, no cause.

LEAR   Am I in France?

KENT   In your own kingdom, sir.

LEAR   Do not abuse° me.   *deceive; mock*

DOCTOR   Be comforted, good madam. The great rage,

80   You see, is killed in him; and yet it is danger
    To make him even o'er° the time he has lost.   *go over*
    Desire him to go in. Trouble him no more
    Till further settling.°   *until his mind eases*

CORDELIA   Will't please your highness walk?

LEAR   You must bear with me:

85   Pray you now, forget and forgive. I am old and foolish.

                Exeunt all but KENT *and* GENTLEMAN

GENTLEMAN   Holds it true, sir, that the Duke of Cornwall
    was so slain?

KENT   Most certain, sir.

GENTLEMAN   Who is conductor° of his people?   *commander*

90 KENT   As 'tis said, the bastard son of Gloucester.

9. Are your tears real? Is this really happening?

GENTLEMAN   They say Edgar, his banished son, is with the
 Earl of Kent in Germany.
KENT   Report° is changeable. 'Tis time to look about.°   *rumor / prepare defenses*
 The powers of the kingdom approach apace.
95 GENTLEMAN   The arbitrement° is like to be bloody. Fare   *encounter*
 you well, sir.   *Exit*
KENT   My point and period[1] will be throughly° wrought,   *thoroughly*
 Or° well or ill, as this day's battle's fought.   *Exit*   *for*

5.1

Enter, with drum and colors, EDMUND, REGAN, *gentle-*
men, and soldiers

EDMUND   Know° of the duke if his last purpose hold,[1]   *inquire*
 Or whether since he is advised by aught[2]
 To change the course. He's full of alteration°   *indecision*
 And self-reproving. Bring his constant pleasure.°   *his settled intent*
                                  Exit one or more
5 REGAN   Our sister's man° is certainly miscarried.[3]   *servant*
EDMUND   'Tis to be doubted,° madam.   *feared*
REGAN   Now, sweet lord,
 You know the goodness I intend upon you.
 Tell me—but truly—but then speak the truth,
 Do you not love my sister?
EDMUND   In honored° love.   *honorable*
10 REGAN   But have you never found my brother's way
 To the forfended[4] place?
EDMUND   That thought abuses° you.   *deceives*
REGAN   I am doubtful° that you have been conjunct°   *I fear / complicit*
 And bosomed with° her, as far as we call hers.[5]   *enamored of*
EDMUND   No, by mine honor, madam.
15 REGAN   I never shall endure her. Dear my lord,
 Be not familiar° with her.   *intimate*
EDMUND   Fear° me not.   *doubt*
 She and the duke her husband!
        Enter, with drum and colors, ALBANY, GONERIL, *and*
        soldiers
GONERIL *(aside)*   I had rather lose the battle than that sister
 Should loosen° him and me.   *disunite*
20 ALBANY   Our very loving sister, well be-met.
 Sir, this I hear: the king is come to his daughter,
 With others whom the rigor° of our state°   *harshness / government*
 Forced to cry out. Where I could not be honest,°   *honorable*
 I never yet was valiant. For this business,
25 It toucheth° us, as France invades our land,   *concerns*

---

1. The purpose and end of my life; literally, the full stop.
5.1 Location: The British camp near Dover.
1. If his previous intention (to wage war) remains firm.

2. Since then anything has persuaded him.
3. Has surely come to grief by some accident.
4. Forbidden (to Edmund, because it is adulterous).
5. In total intimacy; all the way.

Not bolds the king, with others, whom, I fear,
Most just and heavy causes make oppose.[6]
EDMUND   Sir, you speak nobly.
REGAN   Why is this reasoned?[7]
GONERIL   Combine together 'gainst the enemy;
30   For these domestic and particular broils°   *minor quarrels*
Are not the question here.
ALBANY   Let's then determine
With the ancient° of war on our proceeding.   *experienced officer*
EDMUND   I shall attend you presently° at your tent.   *in a moment*
REGAN   Sister, you'll go with us?[8]
35   GONERIL   No.
REGAN   'Tis most convenient;° pray you, go with us.   *suitable*
GONERIL   *(aside)*   O, ho, I know the riddle.°—I will go.   *disguised meaning*
          As they are going out, enter EDGAR *disguised*
EDGAR   If e'er your grace had speech with man so poor,
Hear me one word.
ALBANY   I'll overtake you. Speak.
          Exeunt all but ALBANY *and* EDGAR
40   EDGAR   Before you fight the battle, ope this letter.
If you have victory, let the trumpet sound
For him that brought it. Wretched though I seem,
I can produce a champion that will prove°   *defend*
What is avouched° there. If you miscarry,°   *maintained / perish*
45   Your business of the world hath so an end,
And machination° ceases. Fortune love you!   *plotting*
ALBANY   Stay till I have read the letter.
EDGAR   I was forbid it.
When time shall serve, let but the herald cry,
And I'll appear again.
50   ALBANY   Why, fare thee well. I will o'erlook thy paper.
          Exit EDGAR
          Re-enter EDMUND
EDMUND   The enemy's in view; draw up your powers.°   *troops*
Here is the guess° of their true strength and forces   *estimate*
By diligent discovery;° but your haste   *spying*
Is now urged on you.
ALBANY   We will greet the time.[9]   *Exit*
55   EDMUND   To both these sisters have I sworn my love;
Each jealous° of the other, as the stung   *suspicious*
Are of the adder. Which of them shall I take?
Both? one? or neither? Neither can be enjoyed,
If both remain alive. To take the widow
60   Exasperates, makes mad her sister Goneril;

6. This is of concern to us because France lands on our soil, not because it emboldens the king and others, who, I am afraid, have been provoked for good and solid reasons.
7. What is the point of this kind of speech?
8. Regan wants Goneril to go with Albany and her, rather than with Edmund.
9. We will be ready to meet the occasion.

And hardly° shall I carry out my side,°   *with difficulty / plan*
Her husband being alive. Now then we'll use
His countenance[1] for the battle; which being done,
Let her who would be rid of him devise
65   His speedy taking off. As for the mercy
Which he intends to Lear and to Cordelia,
The battle done, and they within our power,
Shall° never see his pardon; for my state°   *they shall / condition*
Stands on° me to defend, not to debate.   *Exit*   *obliges*

5.2

Alarum within.[1] Enter, with drum and colors, LEAR,
CORDELIA, *and soldiers, over the stage; and exeunt*
Enter EDGAR *and* GLOUCESTER

EDGAR   Here, father,[2] take the shadow of this tree
For your good host;° pray that the right may thrive: *shelter*
If ever I return to you again,
I'll bring you comfort.
GLOUCESTER   Grace go with you, sir!

Exit EDGAR

Alarum and retreat° within. Re-enter EDGAR   *trumpet signal*
5   EDGAR   Away, old man! give me thy hand! away!
King Lear hath lost, he and his daughter ta'en.
Give me thy hand! come on!
GLOUCESTER   No farther, sir; a man may rot even° here.   *right*
EDGAR   What, in ill thoughts again? Men must endure
10   Their going hence, even as their coming hither;
Ripeness is all.[3] Come on!
GLOUCESTER   And that's true, too.   *Exeunt*

5.3

Enter, in conquest, with drum and colors, EDMUND;
LEAR *and* CORDELIA, *prisoners;* CAPTAIN, *soldiers, &c.*

EDMUND   Some officers take them away. Good guard,
Until their greater pleasures[1] first be known
That are to censure° them.   *judge*
CORDELIA   We are not the first
Who, with best meaning,° have incurred the worst.   *intention*
5   For thee, oppressèd king, am I cast down;°   *(into unhappiness)*
Myself could else out-frown false Fortune's frown.[2]
Shall we not see these daughters and these sisters?

---

1. Authority or backing; also suggesting "face,"
to be used like a mask for Edmund's ambition.
5.2 Location: The rest of the play takes place
near the battlefield.
1. Trumpet call to battle (backstage).
2. See note to 4.6.217.
3. I.e., to await the destined time is the most
important thing, as fruit falls only when ripe

(playing on Gloucester's "rot," line 8); readiness
for death is our only duty (compare *Hamlet*
5.2.160, "The readiness is all").
5.3
1. Guard them well until the desires of those
greater persons.
2. Otherwise, I could be defiant in the face of
bad fortune.

LEAR   No, no, no, no! Come, let's away to prison.
    We two alone will sing like birds i' the cage.
10   When thou dost ask me blessing, I'll kneel down,
    And ask of thee forgiveness. So we'll live,
    And pray, and sing, and tell old tales, and laugh
    At gilded butterflies,[3] and hear poor rogues
    Talk of court news; and we'll talk with them too,
15   Who loses and who wins; who's in, and who's out;
    And take upon 's the mystery of things,
    As if we were God's spies; and we'll wear out,°   *outlast*
    In a walled prison, packs and sects of great ones,
    That ebb and flow by the moon.[4]

EDMUND   Take them away.

20 LEAR   Upon such sacrifices,[5] my Cordelia,
    The gods themselves throw incense. Have I caught thee?
    He that parts us shall bring a brand from heaven
    And fire us hence like foxes.[6] Wipe thine eyes;
    The good-years shall devour them, flesh and fell,[7]
25   Ere they shall make us weep! We'll see 'em starved first.
    Come.   *Exeunt* LEAR *and* CORDELIA *guarded*

EDMUND   Come hither, captain; hark.
    Take thou this note (*giving a paper*). Go follow them to prison:
    One step I have advanced° thee. If thou dost   *promoted*
30   As this instructs thee, thou dost make thy way
    To noble fortunes. Know thou this, that men
    Are as the time is. To be tender-minded
    Does not become a sword.° Thy great employment   *befit a swordsman*
    Will not bear question.° Either say thou'lt do't,   *discussion*
    Or thrive by other means.

35 CAPTAIN   I'll do't, my lord.

EDMUND   About it; and write happy when thou hast done.[8]
    Mark, I say, instantly; and carry it° so   *carry it out*
    As I have set it down.

CAPTAIN   I cannot draw a cart, nor eat dried oats;°   *(like a horse)*
40   If it be a man's work, I'll do it.   *Exit*
        Flourish. Enter ALBANY, GONERIL, REGAN, *another* CAP-
        TAIN, *and soldiers*

ALBANY   Sir, you have showed today your valiant strain,°   *qualities; birth*
    And fortune led you well. You have the captives
    That were the opposites° of this day's strife.   *opponents*
    I do require them of you, so to use° them   *treat*
45   As we shall find their merits and our safety

---

3. I.e., gaudy and ephemeral courtiers; trivial matters.
4. Followers, and factions of important people whose positions at court vary as the tide.
5. Upon such sacrifices as we are, or as you have made.
6. I.e., must have divine aid to do so. The image is of using a torch to smoke foxes out of their holes, or, in the case of Lear and Cordelia, prison cells.
7. Meat and skin; entirely. The precise meaning of "good-years" has not been explained; it may signify simply the passage of time or may suggest some ominous, destructive power.
8. Go to it, and call yourself happy when you are done.

May equally determine.

EDMUND   Sir, I thought it fit
To send the old and miserable king
To some retention° and appointed guard;   confinement
Whose° age has charms in it, whose title more,   (Lear's)
50   To pluck the common bosom[9] on his side
And turn our impressed lances° in our eyes   conscripted lancers
Which[1] do command them. With him I sent the queen;
My reason all the same; and they are ready
Tomorrow, or at further space,° t'appear   at a future point
55   Where you shall hold your session.° At this time   court of judgment
We sweat and bleed; the friend hath lost his friend;
And the best quarrels, in the heat, are cursed
By those that feel their sharpness.[2]
The question of Cordelia and her father
Requires a fitter place.
60   ALBANY   Sir, by your patience,
I hold you but a subject of° this war,   in waging
Not as a brother.°   an equal
REGAN   That's as we list° to grace him.   like
Methinks our pleasure might have been demanded[3]
Ere you had spoken so far. He led our powers;°   armies
65   Bore the commission of my place and person;
The which immediacy° may well stand up   close connection
And call itself your brother.
GONERIL   Not so hot!°   not so fast
In his own grace° he doth exalt himself   merit
More than in your addition.[4]
REGAN   In my rights,
70   By me invested, he compeers° the best.   equals
GONERIL   That were the most,[5] if he should husband you.
REGAN   Jesters do oft prove prophets.
GONERIL   Holla, holla!
That eye that told you so looked but a-squint.[6]
REGAN   Lady, I am not well; else I should answer
75   From a full-flowing stomach.° General,   anger
Take thou my soldiers, prisoners, patrimony:
Dispose of them, of me; the walls° are thine.   fortress of my heart
Witness the world, that I create thee here
My lord and master.
GONERIL   Mean you to enjoy him?
80   ALBANY   The let-alone° lies not in your good will.   veto
EDMUND   Nor in thine, lord.
ALBANY   Half-blooded° fellow, yes.   bastard

---

9. To garner the affection of the populace.
1. In the eyes of us who.
2. And in the heat of battle, even the most just wars are cursed by those who must suffer the fighting.
3. I think you should have inquired into my

wishes.
4. In the honors you confer upon him.
5. That investiture would be complete.
6. Only looked sideways. "Looking asquint" was a proverbial effect of jealousy, because of the tendency to look suspiciously at potential rivals.

REGAN (*to* EDMUND)   Let the drum strike,[7] and prove my title thine.

ALBANY   Stay yet; hear reason. Edmund, I arrest thee

On capital treason; and, in thine attaint,[8]

85   This gilded serpent (*pointing to* GONERIL). For your
    claim, fair sister,°   sister-in-law

I bar it in the interest of my wife;

'Tis she is sub-contracted to this lord,

And I, her husband, contradict your banns.°   announced intent to marry

If you will marry, make your loves to me.

My lady is bespoke.

90   GONERIL   An interlude!°   a farce

ALBANY   Thou art armed, Gloucester. Let the trumpet sound.

If none appear to prove upon thy head

Thy heinous, manifest, and many treasons,

There is my pledge (*throwing down a glove*); I'll prove it
    on thy heart,

95   Ere I taste bread, thou art in nothing less°   in no way less guilty

Than I have proclaimed thee.

REGAN   Sick, O, sick!

GONERIL (*aside*)   If not, I'll ne'er trust medicine.°   poison (euphemistic)

EDMUND   There's my exchange (*throwing down a glove*).

What° in the world he is   whoever

That names me traitor, villain-like he lies.

100 Call by thy trumpet. He that dares approach,

On him, on you, who not? I will maintain

My truth and honor firmly.

ALBANY   A herald, ho!

EDMUND   A herald, ho, a herald!

ALBANY   Trust to thy single virtue;° for thy soldiers,   your unassisted power

105 All levied in my name, have in my name

Took their discharge.

REGAN   My sickness grows upon me.

ALBANY   She is not well; convey her to my tent.

Exit REGAN, *led*

Enter a HERALD

Come hither, herald—Let the trumpet sound—

And read out this.

CAPTAIN   Sound, trumpet! (*A trumpet sounds*)

110 HERALD (*reads*)   "If any man of quality or degree within the
    lists of the army will maintain upon Edmund, supposed
    Earl of Gloucester, that he is a manifold traitor, let him
    appear by the third sound of the trumpet. He is bold in
    his defense."

115 EDMUND   Sound!

(*First trumpet*)

Again!

(*Second trumpet*)

---

7. Perhaps to announce the betrothal or a challenge.

8. And in order to accuse you; and as one who
shares your corruption or crime.

Again!
(*Third trumpet*)
Trumpet answers within
Enter EDGAR, *at the third sound, armed, with a trumpet*
before him

ALBANY Ask him his purposes, why he appears
Upon this call o' the trumpet.

HERALD   What° are you?   *who*
120   Your name, your quality?° and why you answer   *degree, rank*
This present summons?

EDGAR   Know, my name is lost;
By treason's tooth bare-gnawn and canker-bit.°   *worm-eaten*
Yet am I noble as the adversary
I come to cope.°   *to encounter*

ALBANY   Which is that adversary?

125   EDGAR What's he that speaks for Edmund Earl of Gloucester?

EDMUND   Himself. What say'st thou to him?

EDGAR   Draw thy sword,
That,° if my speech offend a noble heart,   *so that*
Thy arm may do thee justice. Here is mine.
Behold, it is the privilege of mine honors,
130   My oath, and my profession. I protest,
Maugre° thy strength, youth, place, and eminence,   *despite*
Despite thy victor sword and fire-new° fortune,   *newly minted*
Thy valor and thy heart,° thou art a traitor;   *courage*
False to thy gods, thy brother, and thy father;
135   Conspirant 'gainst this high-illustrious prince;
And, from the extremest upward° of thy head   *top*
To the descent° and dust below thy foot,   *lowest part; sole*
A most toad-spotted[9] traitor. Say thou "No,"°   *if you say no*
This sword, this arm, and my best spirits, are bent°   *ready*
140   To prove upon thy heart, whereto I speak,
Thou liest.

EDMUND   In wisdom I should ask thy name;
But since thy outside looks so fair and warlike
And that thy tongue some say of breeding° breathes,   *good upbringing*
What safe and nicely I might well delay
145   By rule of knighthood, I disdain and spurn.[1]
Back do I toss these treasons to thy head;
With the hell-hated° lie o'erwhelm thy heart;   *hated as much as hell*
Which, for° they yet glance by and scarcely bruise,   *since*
This sword of mine shall give them instant way°   *access*
150   Where they shall rest for ever. Trumpets, speak!
Alarums. They fight, EDMUND *falls*

ALBANY   Save° him, save him!   *spare*

GONERIL   This is practice,° Gloucester: *trickery*
By the law of arms thou wast not bound to answer

---

9. Venomous, like a toad; spotted with disgrace.
1. I.e., and since your speech may suggest high

birth, I will not stick safely and meticulously to
the rules of knighthood by refusing to fight you.

An unknown opposite.° Thou art not vanquished, *opponent*
But cozened and beguiled.° *cheated and deceived*
ALBANY   Shut your mouth, dame,
155 Or with this paper shall I stople° it. *plug*
Thou worse than any name, read thine own evil.
No tearing, lady! I perceive you know it.
        Gives the letter to EDMUND
GONERIL   Say, if I do, the laws are mine, not thine.
Who can arraign° me for 't? *prosecute*
ALBANY   Most monstrous! O!
Know'st thou this paper?
160 GONERIL   Ask me not what I know.   *Exit*
ALBANY   Go after her: she's desperate; govern° her. *restrain*
EDMUND   What you have charged me with, that have I done;
And more, much more; the time will bring it out.
'Tis past, and so am I. But what art thou
165 That hast this fortune on me?[2] If thou'rt noble,
I do forgive thee.
EDGAR   Let's exchange charity.° *forgiveness*
I am no less in blood than thou art, Edmund;
If more, the more thou hast wronged me.
My name is Edgar, and thy father's son.
170 The gods are just, and of our pleasant vices
Make instruments to plague us.
The dark and vicious place where thee he got° *begot*
Cost him his eyes.
EDMUND   Thou hast spoken right, 'tis true;
The wheel° is come full circle! I am here.[3] *Fortune's wheel*
175 ALBANY   Methought thy very gait did prophesy
A royal nobleness. I must embrace thee.
Let sorrow split my heart, if ever I
Did hate thee or thy father!
EDGAR   Worthy prince. I know't.
ALBANY   Where have you hid yourself?
180 How have you known the miseries of your father?
EDGAR   By nursing them, my lord. List° a brief tale; *listen to*
And when 'tis told, O, that my heart would burst!
The bloody proclamation to escape,[4]
That followed me so near—O, our lives' sweetness!
185 That we the pain of death would hourly die
Rather than die at once![5]—taught me to shift
Into a madman's rags; to assume a semblance
That very° dogs disdained; and in this habit° *even / guise*
Met I my father with his bleeding rings,° *sockets*
190 Their precious stones new lost; became his guide,
Led him, begged for him, saved him from despair;

2. Who have this good fortune at my expense.
3. Back at the lowest point.
4. In order to escape the sentence of death.

5. How sweet must life be that we prefer the constant pain of dying to death itself.

Never—O fault!—revealed myself unto him
Until some half-hour past, when I was armed:
Not sure, though hoping, of this good success,°   *conclusion*
195   I asked his blessing, and from first to last
Told him my pilgrimage. But his flawed° heart—   *cracked*
Alack, too weak the conflict to support!—
'Twixt two extremes of passion, joy and grief,
Burst smilingly.

EDMUND   This speech of yours hath moved me,
200   And shall perchance do good; but speak you on;
You look as you had something more to say.

ALBANY   If there be more, more woeful, hold it in;
For I am almost ready to dissolve,°   *melt into tears*
Hearing of this.

EDGAR   This would have seemed a period°   *conclusion*
205   To such as love not sorrow; but another
To amplify° too much would make much more,   *enlarge, extend*
And top extremity.
Whilst I was big in clamor° came there in a man,   *lamenting loudly*
Who, having seen me in my worst estate,
210   Shunned my abhorred society; but then, finding
Who 'twas that so endured, with his strong arms
He fastened on my neck, and bellowed out
As he'd burst heaven; threw him on my father;
Told the most piteous tale of Lear and him°   *himself*
215   That ever ear received; which in recounting
His grief grew puissant,° and the strings of life   *powerful*
Began to crack. Twice then the trumpets sounded,
And there I left him tranced.

ALBANY   But who was this?

EDGAR   Kent, sir, the banished Kent; who in disguise
220   Followed his enemy king,[6] and did him service
Improper° for a slave.   *unfit even*

Enter a GENTLEMAN, *with a bloody knife*

GENTLEMAN   Help, help, O, help!

EDGAR   What kind of help?

ALBANY   Speak, man.

EDGAR   What means that bloody knife?

GENTLEMAN   'Tis hot, it smokes,
It came even from the heart of—O, she's dead!
225   ALBANY   Who dead? speak, man.

GENTLEMAN   Your lady, sir, your lady! and her sister
By her is poisoned; she hath confessed it.

EDMUND   I was contracted to them both. All three
Now marry° in an instant.   *unite (in death)*

Enter KENT

EDGAR   Here comes Kent.
230   ALBANY   Produce their bodies, be they alive or dead:

---

6. "Enemy"—that is, hostile—because Lear had previously banished him.

This judgment of the heavens, that makes us tremble,
Touches us not with pity.   *Exit* GENTLEMAN
                      O, is this he?
The time will not allow the compliment
Which very manners urges.[7]

KENT   I am come

235   To bid my king and master aye° good night.   *forever*
    Is he not here?

ALBANY   Great thing of° us forgot!   *by*
    Speak, Edmund, where's the king? and where's Cordelia?
    See'st thou this object,° Kent?   *spectacle*
       The bodies of GONERIL *and* REGAN *are brought in*

KENT   Alack, why thus?

EDMUND   Yet° Edmund was beloved.   *despite all*

240   The one the other poisoned for my sake,
    And after slew herself.

ALBANY   Even so. Cover their faces.

EDMUND   I pant for life. Some good I mean to do,
    Despite of mine own nature. Quickly send,

245   Be brief° in it, to the castle; for my writ°   *speedy / order for execution*
    Is on the life of Lear and on Cordelia:
    Nay, send in time.

ALBANY   Run, run, O, run!

EDGAR   To who, my lord? Who hath the office?° Send   *commission*
    Thy token of reprieve.

250   EDMUND   Well thought on. Take my sword,
    Give it the° captain.   *to the*

ALBANY   Haste thee for thy life.   *Exit* EDGAR

EDMUND   He hath commission from thy wife and me
    To hang Cordelia in the prison, and
    To lay the blame upon her own despair,

255   That she fordid herself.[8]

ALBANY   The gods defend her! Bear him hence awhile.
                         EDMUND *is borne off*
      Re-enter LEAR, *with* CORDELIA *dead in his arms;* EDGAR,
      CAPTAIN, *and others following*

LEAR   Howl, howl, howl, howl! O, you are men of stones:
    Had I your tongues and eyes, I'd use them so
    That heaven's vault should crack. She's gone forever!

260   I know when one is dead, and when one lives;
    She's dead as earth. Lend me a looking-glass;
    If that her breath will mist or stain the stone,[9]
    Why, then she lives.

KENT   Is this the promised end?[1]

EDGAR   Or image of that horror?

ALBANY   Fall, and cease![2]

7. The ceremony that barest custom demands.
8. Destroyed herself. In most of Shakespeare's
source texts for the play, Cordelia does in fact kill
herself, but only after reigning for some years.
9. Mica, or stone polished to a mirror finish.

1. Doomsday; expected end of the play. In no version of the story previous to Shakespeare's does
Cordelia die at this point.
2. Let the world collapse and end.

265 LEAR   This feather stirs; she lives! If it be so,
     It is a chance which does redeem all sorrows
     That ever I have felt.
KENT (*kneeling*)[3]   O my good master!
LEAR   Prithee, away.
EDGAR   'Tis noble Kent, your friend.
LEAR   A plague upon you, murderers, traitors all!
270   I might have saved her; now she's gone for ever!
     Cordelia, Cordelia! stay a little. Ha!
     What is't thou say'st? Her voice was ever soft,
     Gentle, and low, an excellent thing in woman.
     I killed the slave that was a-hanging thee.
CAPTAIN   'Tis true, my lords, he did.
275 LEAR   Did I not, fellow?
     I have seen the day, with my good biting falchion°   *light sword*
     I would have made them skip: I am old now,
     And these same crosses spoil me.[4] Who are you?
     Mine eyes are not o' the best. I'll tell you straight.°   *recognize you soon*
280 KENT   If fortune brag of two she loved and hated,
     One of them we behold.[5]
LEAR   This is a dull sight.[6] Are you not Kent?
KENT   The same,
     Your servant Kent. Where is your servant Caius?°   *(Kent's pseudonym)*
LEAR   He's a good fellow, I can tell you that;
285   He'll strike, and quickly too. He's dead and rotten.
KENT   No, my good lord; I am the very man—
LEAR   I'll see that straight.[7]
KENT   That, from your first of difference and decay,[8]
     Have followed your sad steps.
LEAR   You are welcome hither.
290 KENT   Nor no man else.[9] All's cheerless, dark, and deadly.°   *deathly*
     Your eldest daughters have fordone° themselves,   *destroyed*
     And desperately° are dead.   *in despair*
LEAR   Aye, so I think.
ALBANY   He knows not what he says; and vain° it is   *in vain*
     That we present us to him.
EDGAR   Very bootless.°   *futile*
     Enter a CAPTAIN
CAPTAIN   Edmund is dead, my lord.
295 ALBANY   That's but a trifle here.
     You lords and noble friends, know our intent.
     What comfort to this great decay° may come   *ruin, destruction*

3. Lear probably kneels over Cordelia's body during most of the scene, and Kent kneels here partly
in submission, partly to catch Lear's attention.
4. And these recent adversities have weakened
me; and these parries I could once match would
now destroy me.
5. If there were only two supreme examples in
the world of Fortune's ability to raise up and cast
down, Lear would be one; alternatively, we are

each of us one (Lear and Kent are here looking
at each other).
6. This is a sad sight; my vision is failing.
7. I'll attend to that shortly; I'll comprehend that
in a moment.
8. Who from the beginning of your alteration and
deterioration.
9. No, neither I nor anyone else is welcome—that
is, this is not a welcoming sight.

Shall be applied. For us, we will resign,
During the life of this old majesty,
300 To him our absolute power; (*to* EDGAR *and* KENT) you, to
your rights;
With boot,° and such addition as your honors   *good measure*
Have more than merited. All friends shall taste
The wages of their virtue, and all foes
The cup of their deserving. O, see, see!
305 LEAR   And my poor fool[1] is hanged! No, no, no life!
Why should a dog, a horse, a rat, have life,
And thou no breath at all? Thou'lt come no more,
Never, never, never, never, never!
Pray you, undo this button. Thank you, sir.
310 Do you see this? Look on her, look, her lips,
Look there, look there!   *Dies*
EDGAR   He faints! My lord, my lord!
KENT   Break, heart; I prithee,° break!   *pray you*
EDGAR   Look up, my lord.
KENT   Vex not his ghost.[2] O, let him pass! He hates him much
That would upon the rack[3] of this tough world
Stretch him out longer.
315 EDGAR   He is gone, indeed.
KENT   The wonder is, he hath endured so long.
He but usurped his life.[4]
ALBANY   Bear them from hence. Our present business
Is general woe. (*To* KENT *and* EDGAR) Friends of my
soul, you twain
320 Rule in this realm, and the gored° state sustain.   *wounded; bloody*
KENT   I have a journey, sir, shortly to go;
My master calls me, I must not say no.
EDGAR   The weight of this sad time we must obey;
Speak what we feel, not what we ought to say.
325 The oldest hath borne most; we that are young
Shall never see so much, nor live so long.
                      Exeunt, with dead march[5]

1604–05   1608, 1623

---

1. A term of endearment, here used for Cordelia.
2. Do not disturb his departing soul.
3. Instrument of torture, used to stretch its victims.
4. From death, which already had a claim on it.
5. March for a funeral procession.

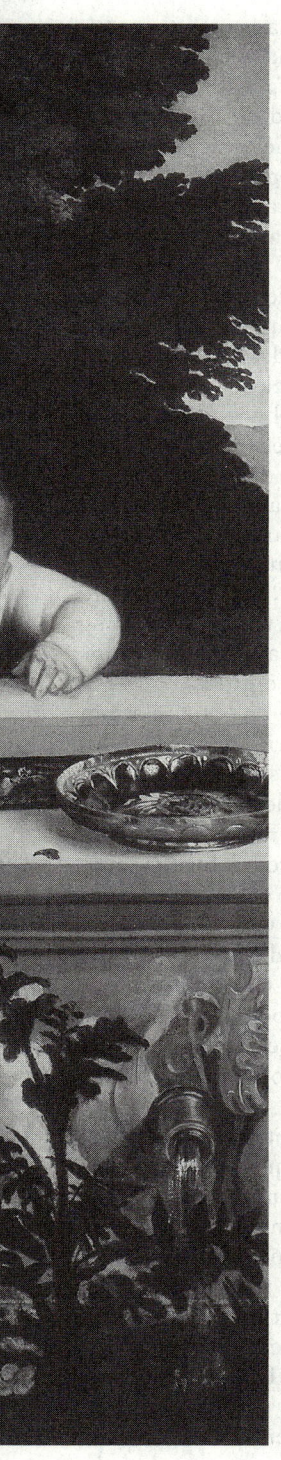

The Early
Seventeenth
Century
1603–1660

1603: Death of Elizabeth I; accession of James I, first Stuart king of England
1605: The Gunpowder Plot, a failed effort by Catholic extremists to blow up Parliament and the king
1607: Establishment of first permanent English colony in the New World at Jamestown, Virginia
1625: Death of James I; accession of Charles I
1642: Outbreak of civil war; theaters closed
1649: Execution of Charles I; beginning of Commonwealth and Protectorate, known inclusively as the Interregnum (1649–60)
1660: End of the Protectorate; restoration of Charles II

Queen Elizabeth died on March 24, 1603, after ruling England for more than four decades. The Virgin Queen had not, of course, produced a child to inherit her throne, but her kinsman, the thirty-six-year-old James Stuart, James VI of Scotland, succeeded her as James I without the violence that many had feared. Many welcomed the accession of a man in the prime of life, supposing that he would prove more decisive than his notoriously vacillating predecessor. Worries over the succession, which had plagued the reigns of the Tudor monarchs since Henry VIII, could finally subside: James already had several children with his queen, Anne of Denmark. Writers and scholars jubilantly noted that their new

Sacred and Profane Love (detail), ca. 1515, Titian. For more information about this image, see the color insert in this volume.

ruler had literary inclinations. He was the author of treatises on government and witchcraft, and some youthful efforts at poetry.

Nonetheless, there were grounds for disquiet. James had come to maturity in Scotland, in the seventeenth century a foreign land with a different church, different customs, and different institutions of government. Two of his books, *The True Law of Free Monarchies* (1598) and *Basilikon Doron* (1599), expounded authoritarian theories of kingship: James's views seemed incompatible with the English tradition of "mixed" government, in which power was shared by the monarch, the House of Lords, and the House of Commons. As Thomas Howard wrote in 1611, while Elizabeth "did talk of her subjects' love and good affection," James "talketh of his subjects' fear and subjection." James liked to imagine himself as a modern version of the wise, peace-loving Roman Augustus Caesar, who autocratically governed a vast empire. The Romans had deified their emperors, and while the Christian James could not expect the same, he insisted on his closeness to divinity. Kings, he believed, derived their powers from God rather than from the people. As God's specially chosen delegate, surely he deserved his subjects' reverent, unconditional obedience.

Yet unlike the charismatic Elizabeth, James was personally unprepossessing. One contemporary, Anthony Weldon, provides a barbed description: "His tongue too large for his mouth, which ever made him speak full in the mouth, and drink very uncomely as if eating his drink . . . he never washed his hands . . . his walk was ever circular, his fingers ever in that walk fiddling about his codpiece." Unsurprisingly, James did not always inspire in his subjects the deferential awe to which he thought himself entitled.

The relationship between the monarch and his people and the relationship between England and Scotland would be sources of friction throughout James's reign. James had hoped to unify his domains as a single nation, "the empire of Britain." But the two realms' legal and ecclesiastical systems proved difficult to reconcile, and the English Parliament, traditionally a sporadically convened advisory body to the monarch, offered robustly xenophobic opposition. The failure of unification was only one of several clashes with the English Parliament, especially with the House of Commons, which had authority over taxation. After James died in 1625 and his son, Charles I, succeeded him, tensions persisted and intensified. Charles, indeed, attempted to rule without summoning Parliament at all between 1629 and 1638. By 1642 England was up in arms, in a civil war between the king's forces and armies loyal to the House of Commons. The conflict ended with Charles's defeat and beheading in 1649.

Although in the early 1650s the monarchy as an institution seemed as dead as the man who had last worn the crown, an adequate replacement proved difficult to devise. Executive power devolved upon a "Lord Protector," Oliver Cromwell, former general of the parliamentary forces, who wielded power nearly as autocratically as Charles had done. Yet without an institutionally sanctioned method of transferring power upon Cromwell's death in 1658, the attempt to fashion a commonwealth without a hereditary monarch eventually failed. In 1660 Parliament invited the eldest son of the old king home from exile. He succeeded to the throne as King Charles II.

As James's accession marks the beginning of "the early seventeenth century," his grandson's marks the end. Literary periods often fail to correlate neatly with the reigns of monarchs, and the period 1603–60 can seem especially arbitrary. Many of the most important cultural trends in seventeenth-century Europe neither began nor ended in these years but were in the process of unfolding slowly, over several centuries. The Protestant Reformation of the sixteenth century was still ongoing in the seventeenth, and still producing turmoil. The printing press, invented in the fifteenth century, made books ever more widely available, contributing to an expansion of literacy and to a changed conception of authorship. Although the English economy remained primarily agrarian, its manufacturing and trade sectors were expanding rapidly. England was beginning to establish itself as a colonial power and as a leading maritime nation. From 1550 on, London grew explosively as a center of population, trade, and literary endeavor. All these important developments got under way before James came to the throne, and many of them would continue after the 1714 death of James's great-granddaughter Queen Anne, the last of the Stuarts to reign in England.

From a literary point of view, 1603 can seem a particularly capricious dividing line because at the accession of James I so many writers happened to be in midcareer. The professional lives of William Shakespeare, Ben Jonson, John Donne, Francis Bacon, Walter Ralegh, and many less important writers—Thomas Dekker, George Chapman, Samuel Daniel, Michael Drayton, and Thomas Heywood, for instance—straddle the reigns of Elizabeth and James. The Restoration of Charles II, with which this section ends, is likewise a more significant political than literary milestone: John Milton completed *Paradise Lost* and wrote two other major poems in the 1660s. Nonetheless, recognizing the years 1603–60 as a period sharpens our awareness of some important political, intellectual, cultural, and stylistic currents that bear directly upon literary production. It helps focus attention too upon the seismic shift in national consciousness that, in 1649, could permit the formal trial, conviction, and execution of an anointed king at the hands of his former subjects.

STATE AND CHURCH, 1603–40

In James's reign, the most pressing difficulties were apparently financial, but money troubles were merely symptoms of deeper quandaries about the proper relationship between the king and the people. Compared to James's native Scotland, England seemed a prosperous nation, but James was less wealthy than he believed. Except in times of war, the Crown was supposed to fund the government not through regular taxation but through its own extensive land revenues and by exchanging Crown prerogatives, such as the collection of taxes on luxury imports, in return for money or services. Yet the Crown's independent income had declined throughout the sixteenth century as inflation eroded the value of land rents. Meanwhile, innovations in military technology and shipbuilding dramatically increased the expense of port security and other defenses, a traditional Crown responsibility. Elizabeth had responded to straitened finances with parsimony, transferring much of the expense of her court, for instance, onto wealthy subjects, whom she visited for extended periods on her annual "progresses." She kept a tight lid on honorific titles too, creating new knights or peers very rarely, even though the years of her reign saw considerable upward social mobility. In consequence, by 1603 there was considerable pent-up pressure both for "honors" and for more tangible rewards for government officials. As soon as James came to power, he was immediately besieged with supplicants.

James responded with what seemed to him appropriate royal munificence, knighting and ennobling many of his courtiers and endowing them with opulent gifts. His expenses were unavoidably higher than Elizabeth's, because he had to maintain not only his own household, but also separate establishments for his queen and for the heir apparent, Prince Henry. Yet he quickly became notorious for his financial heedlessness. Compared to Elizabeth's, his court was disorderly and wasteful, marked by hard drinking, gluttonous feasting, and a craze for hunting. "It is not possible for a king of England . . . to be rich or safe, but by frugality," warned James's lord treasurer, Robert Cecil, but James seemed unable to restrain himself. Soon he was deep in debt and unable to convince Parliament to bankroll him by raising taxes.

The king's financial difficulties set his authoritarian assertions about the monarch's supremacy at odds with Parliament's control over taxation. How were his prerogatives as a ruler to coexist with the rights of his subjects? Particularly disturbing to many was James's tendency to bestow high offices upon favorites apparently chosen for good looks rather than for good judgment. James's openly romantic attachment first to Robert Carr, Earl of Somerset, and then to George Villiers, Duke of Buckingham, gave rise to widespread rumors of homosexuality at court. The period had complex attitudes toward same-sex relationships; on the one hand, "sodomy" was a capital crime (though it was very rarely prosecuted); on the other hand, passionately intense male friendship, sometimes suffused with eroticism, constituted an important cultural ideal. In James's case, at least, contemporaries considered his susceptibility to lovely, expensive youths more a political than a moral calamity. For his critics, it crystallized what was wrong with unlimited royal power: the ease with which a king could confuse his own whim with a divine mandate.

Despite James's ungainly demeanor, his frictions with Parliament, and his chronic problems of self-management, he was politically astute. Often, like Elizabeth, he succeeded not through decisiveness but through canny inaction. Cautious by temperament, he characterized himself as a peacemaker and, for many years, successfully kept England out of the religious wars raging on the Continent. His 1604 peace treaty with England's old enemy, Spain, made the Atlantic safe for English ships, a prerequisite for the colonization of the New World and for regular long-distance trading expeditions into the Mediterranean and down the African coast into the Indian Ocean. During James's reign the first permanent English settlements were established in North America, first at Jamestown, then in Bermuda, at Plymouth, and in the Caribbean. In 1611 the East India Company established England's first foothold in India. Even when expeditions ended disastrously, as did Henry Hudson's 1611 attempt to find the Northwest Passage and Walter Ralegh's 1617 expedition to Guiana, they often asserted territorial claims that England would exploit in later decades.

Although the Crown's deliberate attempts to manage the economy were often misguided, its frequent inattention or refusal to interfere had the unintentional effect of stimulating growth. Early seventeenth-century entrepreneurs undertook a wide variety of schemes for industrial or agricultural improvement. Some ventures were almost as loony as Sir Politic Would-be's ridiculous moneymaking notions in Ben Jonson's *Volpone* (1606), but others were serious, profitable enterprises. In the south, domestic industries began manufacturing goods like pins and light woolens that had previously been imported. In the north, newly developed coal mines provided fuel for England's growing cities. In the east, landowners drained wetlands, producing more arable land to feed England's rapidly growing population. These endeavors gave rise to a new respect for the practical arts, a faith in technology as a means of improving human life, and a conviction that the future might be better than the past: all important influences upon the scientific theories of Francis Bacon and his seventeenth-century followers. Economic growth in this period owed more to the initiative of individuals and small groups than to government policy, a factor that encouraged a reevaluation of the role of self-interest, the profit motive, and the role of business contracts in the betterment of the community. This reevaluation was a prerequisite for the secular, contractual political theories proposed by Thomas Hobbes and John Locke later in the seventeenth century.

On the vexations faced by the Church of England, James was likewise often most successful when he was least activist. Since religion cemented sociopolitical order, it seemed necessary to English rulers that all of their subjects belong to a single church. Yet how could they do so when the Reformation had discredited many familiar religious practices and had bred disagreement over many theological issues? Sixteenth- and seventeenth-century English people argued over many religious topics. How should public worship be conducted, and what sorts of qualifications should ministers possess? How should Scripture be understood? How should people pray? What did the sacrament of Communion mean? What happened to people's souls after they died? Elizabeth's government had needed to devise a common religious practice when actual consensus was impossible. Sensibly, it sought a middle ground between traditional and reformed views. Everyone was legally required to attend Church of England services, and the form of the services themselves was mandated in the Elizabethan Book of Common Prayer. Yet the Book of Common Prayer deliberately avoided addressing abstruse theological controversies. The language of the English church service was carefully chosen to be open to several interpretations and acceptable to both Protestant- and Catholic-leaning subjects.

The Elizabethan compromise effectively tamed many of the Reformation's divisive energies and proved acceptable to the majority of Elizabeth's subjects. To staunch Catholics on one side and ardent Protestants on the other, however, the Elizabethan church seemed to have sacrificed truth to political expediency. Catholics wanted to return England to the Roman fold; while some of them were loyal subjects of the queen, others advocated invasion by a foreign Catholic power. Meanwhile the Puritans, as they were disparagingly called, pressed for more thoroughgoing reformation in doctrine, ritual, and church government, urging the elimination of "popish" elements from worship services and "idolatrous" religious images from churches. Some, the Presbyterians, wanted to separate lay and clerical power in the national church, so that church leaders would be appointed by other ministers, not by secular authorities. Others, the separatists, advocated abandoning a national church in favor of small congregations of the "elect."

The resistance of religious minorities to Elizabeth's established church opened them to state persecution. In the 1580s and 1590s, Catholic priests and the laypeople who harbored them were executed for treason, and radical Protestants for heresy. Both groups greeted James's accession enthusiastically; his mother had been the Catholic Mary, Queen of Scots, while his upbringing had been in the strict Reformed tradition of the Scottish Presbyterian Kirk.

James began his reign with a conference at Hampton Court, one of his palaces, at which advocates of a variety of religious views could openly debate them. Yet the Puritans failed to persuade him to make any substantive reforms. Practically speaking, the Puritan belief that congregations should choose their leaders diminished the monarch's power by stripping him of authority over ecclesiastical appointments. More generally, allowing people to choose their leaders in any sphere of life threatened to subvert the entire system of deference and hierarchy upon which the institution of monarchy itself seemed to rest. "No bishop, no king," James famously remarked.

Nor did Catholics fare well in the new reign. Initially inclined to lift Elizabeth's sanctions against them, James hesitated when he realized how entrenched was the opposition to toleration. Then, in 1605, a small group of disaffected Catholics packed a cellar adjacent to the Houses of Parliament with gunpowder, intending to detonate it on the day that the king formally opened Parliament, with Prince Henry, the Houses of Lords and Commons, and the leading justices in attendance. The conspirators were arrested before they could effect their plan. If the "Gunpowder Plot" had succeeded, it would have eliminated much of England's ruling class in a single tremendous explosion, leaving the land vulnerable to invasion by a foreign, Catholic

The Execution of the Gunpowder Plot Conspirators. This engraving by the Dutch artist Crispijn van de Passe shows the execution of the Gunpowder Conspirators for treason in January 1606. The punishment for treason was deliberately "cruel and unusual": the traitor was sentenced to be dragged through town on a wicker hurdle "at horse's tail," hanged but cut down while still conscious, and then castrated, disemboweled, beheaded, and his body cut into four pieces and parboiled. Though the punishment was often commuted to simple beheading or hanging, in the case of the Gunpowder Conspirators it was carried out in its entirety. On the left, the condemned men are taken to the place of execution. In the middle, the heart of one of the conspirators is being torn out, to be thrown into the fire. On the right, the heads of the conspirators are mounted on poles for display.

power. Not surprisingly, the Gunpowder Plot dramatically heightened anti-Catholic paranoia in England, and its apparently miraculous revelation was widely seen as a sign of God's care for England's Protestant governors.

By and large, then, James's ecclesiastical policies continued along the lines laid down by Elizabeth. By appointing bishops of varying doctrinal views, he restrained any single faction from controlling church policy. The most important religious event of James's reign was a newly commissioned translation of the Bible. First published in 1611, it was a typically moderating document. A much more graceful rendering than its predecessor, the Geneva version produced by Puritan expatriates in the 1550s, the King James Bible immediately became the standard English Scripture. Its impressive rhythms and memorable phrasing would influence writers for centuries. On the one hand, the new translation contributed to the Protestant aim of making the Bible widely available to every reader in the vernacular. On the other hand, unlike the Geneva Bible, the King James Version translated controversial and ambiguous passages in ways that bolstered conservative preferences for a ceremonial church and for a hierarchically organized church government.

James's moderation was not universally popular. Some Protestants yearned for a more confrontational policy toward Catholic powers, particularly toward Spain, England's old enemy. In the first decade of James's reign, this party clustered around James's eldest son and heir apparent, Prince Henry, who cultivated a militantly Protestant persona. When Henry died of typhoid fever in 1612, those who favored his policies were forced to seek avenues of power outside the royal court. By the 1620s, the House of Commons was developing a vigorous sense of its own independence, debating policy agendas often quite at odds with the Crown's and openly attempting to use its power to approve taxation as a means of exacting concessions from the king.

James's second son, Prince Charles, came to the throne upon James's death in 1625. Unlike his father, Charles was not a theorist of royal absolutism, but he acted on that principle with an inflexibility that his father had never been able to muster. By 1629 he had dissolved Parliament three times in frustration with its recalcitrance, and he then began more than a decade of "personal rule" without Parliament. Charles was more prudent in some respects than his father had been—he not only restrained the costs of his own court, but paid off his father's staggering debts by the early 1630s. Throughout his reign, he conscientiously applied himself to the business of government. Yet his refusal to involve powerful individuals and factions in the workings of the state inevitably alienated them, even while it cut him off dangerously from important channels of information about the reactions of his people. Money was a constant problem, too. Even a relatively frugal king required some funds for ambitious government initiatives; but without parliamentary approval, any taxes Charles imposed were widely perceived as illegal. As a result, even wise policies, such as Charles's effort to build up the English navy, spawned misgivings among many of his subjects.

Religious conflicts intensified. Charles's queen, the French princess Henrietta Maria, supported an entourage of Roman Catholic priests, protected English Catholics, and encouraged several noblewomen in her court to convert to the Catholic faith. While Charles remained a staunch member of the Church of England, he loved visual splendor and majestic ceremony in all aspects of life, spiritual and otherwise—proclivities that led his Puritan subjects to suspect him of popish sympathies. Charles's profound attachment to his wife, so different from James's neglect of Anne, only deepened their qualms. Like many fellow Puritans, Lucy Hutchinson blamed the entire debacle of Charles's reign on his wife's influence.

Charles's appointment of William Laud as archbishop of Canterbury, the ecclesiastical head of the English Church, further alienated Puritans. Laud subscribed to a theology that most Puritans rejected. As followers of the sixteenth-century reformer John Calvin, Puritans held that salvation depended upon faith in Christ, not "works." Works were meaningless because the deeds of sinful human beings could not be sanctified in the absence of faith; moreover, the Fall had so thoroughly corrupted human beings that they could not muster this faith without the help of God's grace. God chose (or refused) to extend grace to particular individuals on grounds that human beings were incapable of comprehending, and his decision had been made from eternity, before the individuals concerned were even born. In other words, Puritans believed, God predestined people to be saved or damned, and Christ's redemptive sacrifice was designed only for the saved group, the "elect." Laud, by contrast, advocated the Arminian doctrine that through Christ, God made redemption freely available to all human beings. Individuals could choose whether or not to respond to God's grace, and they could work actively toward their salvation by acts of charity, ritual devotion, and generosity to the church.

Although Laud's theology appears more generously inclusive than the Calvinist alternative, his ecclesiastical policies were uncompromising. Stripping many Puritan ministers of their posts, Laud aligned the doctrine and ceremonies of the English church with Roman Catholicism, which like Arminianism held works in high regard. In an ambitious project of church renovation, Laud installed religious paintings and images in churches; he thought they promoted reverence in worshippers, but the Puritans believed they encouraged idolatry. He rebuilt and resituated altars, making them more ornate and prominent: another change that dismayed Puritans, since it implied that the Eucharist rather than the sermon was the central element of a worship service. In the 1630s thousands of Puritans departed for the New England colonies, but many more remained at home, deeply discontented.

As the 1630s drew to a close, Archbishop Laud and Charles attempted to impose a version of the English liturgy and episcopal organization upon Presbyterian Scotland. Unlike his father, Charles had little acquaintance with his northern realm, and he drastically underestimated the difficulties involved. The Scots objected both on nationalist and on religious grounds, and they were not shy about expressing their objections: the bishop of Brechin, obliged to conduct divine service in the prescribed English style, mounted the pulpit armed with two pistols against his unruly congregation, while his wife, stationed on the floor below, backed him up with a blunderbuss. In the conflict that followed, the Bishops' Wars of 1639 and 1640, Charles's forces met with abject defeat. Exacerbating the situation, Laud was simultaneously insisting upon greater conformity within the English church. Riots in the London streets and the Scots' occupation of several northern English cities forced Charles to call the so-called Long Parliament, which would soon be managing a revolution.

LITERATURE AND CULTURE, 1603–40

Old Ideas and New

In the first part of the seventeenth century, exciting new scientific theories were in the air, but the older ways of thinking about the nature of things had not yet been superseded. Writers such as John Donne, Robert Burton, and Ben Jonson often invoked an inherited body of concepts even though they were aware that those concepts were being questioned or displaced. The Ptolemaic universe, with its fixed earth and circling sun, moon, planets, and stars, was a rich source of poetic imagery. So were the four elements—fire, earth, water, and air—that together were thought to comprise all matter, and the four bodily humors—choler, blood, phlegm, and black bile—which were supposed to determine a person's temperament and to cause physical and mental disease when out of balance. Late Elizabethans and Jacobeans (so called from *Jacobus*, Latin for James) considered themselves especially prone to melancholy, an ailment of scholars and thinkers stemming from an excess of black bile. Shakespeare's Hamlet is melancholic, as is Bosola in John Webster's *Duchess of Malfi* and Milton's title figure in "Il Penseroso" ("the serious-minded one"). In his panoramic *Anatomy of Melancholy*, Burton argued that melancholy was universal.

Key concepts of the inherited system of knowledge were analogy and order. Donne was especially fond of drawing parallels between the macrocosm, or "big world," and the microcosm, or "little world," of the individual human being. Also widespread were versions of the "chain of being" that linked and ordered various kinds of beings in hierarchies. The order of nature, for instance, put God above angels, angels above human beings, human beings above animals, animals above plants, plants above rocks. The social order installed the king over his nobles, nobles over the gentry, gentry over yeomen, yeomen over common laborers. The order of the family set husband above wife, parents above children, master and mistress above servants, the elderly above the young. Each level had its peculiar function, and each was connected to those above and beneath in a tight network of obligation and dependency. Items that occupied similar positions in different hierarchies were related by analogy: thus a monarch was like God, and he was also like a father, the head of the family, or like a lion, most majestic of beasts, or like the sun, the most excellent of heavenly bodies. A medieval or Renaissance poet who calls a king a sun or a lion, then, imagines himself not to be forging a metaphor in his own creative imagination, but to be describing something like an obvious fact of nature. Many Jacobean tragedies, Shakespeare's *King Lear* perhaps most comprehensively, depict the catastrophes that ensue when these hierarchies rupture, and both the social order and the natural order disintegrate.

Yet this conceptual system was itself beginning to crumble. Francis Bacon advocated rooting out of the mind all the intellectual predilections that had made the old ideas so attractive: love of ingenious correlations, reverence for tradition, and a priori assumptions about what was possible in nature. Instead, he argued, groups of collaborators ought to design controlled experiments to find the truths of nature by empirical means. Even as Bacon was promoting his views in *The Advancement of Learning, Novum Organum,*

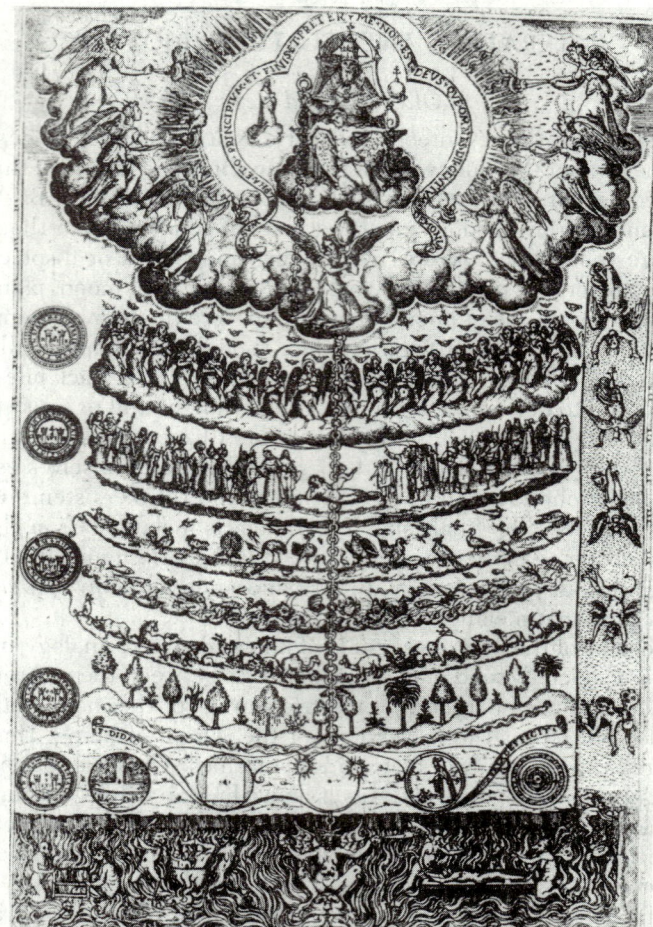

The Great Chain of Being. This illustration of the "Great Chain of Being" shows the hierarchy of the universe according to Christian orthodoxy. God is at the top of the diagram surrounded by angels, with the blessed souls in heaven sitting on clouds just beneath; below them is the layer of humans, with Eve emerging from Adam's rib in the center; below that are layers of birds, fish, and beasts; below that is a layer of plants upon the earth. All these layers are connected by a chain running down the middle, imagined as connecting all of God's creation. At the bottom, detached from the Great Chain, are Satan and his rebel angels, who can be seen falling from heaven into hell in the right margin.

and *The New Atlantis*, actual experiments and discoveries were calling the old verities into question. From the far-flung territories England was beginning to colonize or to trade with, collectors brought animal, plant, and ethnological novelties, many of which were hard to subsume under old categories of understanding. William Harvey's discovery that blood circulated in the body shook received views on the function of blood, casting doubt on the theory of the humors. Galileo's telescope provided evidence confirming Copernican astronomical theory, which dislodged the earth from its stable central position in the cosmos and, in defiance of all ordinary observation, set it whirling around the sun. Galileo found evidence as well of change in the heavens, which were supposed to be perfect and incorruptible above the level of the moon. Donne, like other writers of his age, responded with a mixture of excitement and anxiety to such novel ideas as these:

> And new philosophy calls all in doubt:
> The element of fire is quite put out;
> The sun is lost, and the earth, and no man's wit
> Can well direct him where to look for it.

Several decades later, however, Milton embraced the new science, proudly recalling a visit during his European tour to "the famous Galileo, grown old, a prisoner to the Inquisition for thinking in astronomy otherwise than the Franciscan and Dominican licensers thought." In *Paradise Lost*, he would make complex poetic use of the astronomical controversy, considering how, and how far, humans should pursue scientific knowledge.

Patrons, Printers, and Acting Companies

The social institutions, customs, and practices that had supported and regulated writers in Tudor times changed only gradually before 1640. As it had under Elizabeth, the church promoted writing of several kinds: devotional treatises; guides to meditation; controversial tracts; "cases of conscience," which work out difficult moral issues in complex situations; and especially sermons. Since everyone was required to attend church, everyone heard sermons at least once and often twice on Sunday, as well as on religious or national holidays. The essence of a sermon, Protestants agreed, was the careful exposition of Scripture, and its purpose was to instruct and to move. Yet styles varied; while some preachers, like Donne, strove to enthrall their congregations with all the resources of artful rhetoric, others, especially many Puritans, sought an undecorated style that would display God's word in its own splendor. Printing made it easy to circulate many copies of sermons, blurring the line between oral delivery and written text and enhancing the role of printers and booksellers in disseminating God's word.

Many writers of the period depended in one way or another upon literary patronage. A Jacobean or Caroline aristocrat, like his medieval forebears, was expected to reward dependents in return for services and homage. Indeed, his status was gauged partly on the size of his entourage (that is one reason why in *King Lear* the hero experiences his daughters' attempts to dismiss his retainers as so intensely humiliating). In the early seventeenth century, although commercial relationships were rapidly replacing feudal ones, patronage pervaded all walks of life: governing relationships between landlords and tenants, masters and servants, kings and courtiers. Writers were assimilated into this system partly because their works reflected well on the patron, and partly because their all-around intelligence made them useful members of a great man's household. Important patrons of the time included the royal family—especially Queen Anne, who sponsored the court masques, and Prince Henry—the members of the intermarried Sidney/ Herbert family, and the Countess of Bedford, Queen Anne's confidante.

Because the patronage relationship often took the form of an exchange of favors rather than a simple financial transaction, its terms were very variable and are difficult to recover with any precision at this historical remove. A poet might dedicate a poem or a work to a patron in the expectation of a simple cash payment. But a patron might provide a wide range of other benefits: a place to live; employment as a secretary, tutor, or household servant; or gifts of clothing (textiles were valuable commodities). Donne, for instance, received inexpensive lodging from the Drury family, for whom he wrote the *Anniversaries*; a suit of clerical attire from Lucy Russell, Countess of Bedford, when he took orders in the Church of England; and advancement in the church from King James. Ben Jonson lived for several years at the country estates of Lord Aubigny and of Robert Sidney, in whose honor he wrote "To Penshurst"; he received a regular salary from the king in return for writing court masques; and he served as chaperone to Sir Walter Ralegh's son on a Continental tour. Aemilia Lanyer apparently resided for some time in the household of Margaret Clifford, Countess of Cumberland. Andrew Marvell lived for two years with Thomas Fairfax, tutored his daughter and wrote "Upon Appleton House" for him. All these quite different relationships and forms of remuneration fall under the rubric of patronage.

The patronage system required the poets involved to hone their skills at eulogizing their patrons. Jonson's epigrams and many of Lanyer's dedicatory poems evoke communities of virtuous poets and patrons joined by bonds of mutual respect and affection. Like the line between sycophantic flattery and truthful depiction, the line between patronage and friendship could be a thin one. Literary manuscripts circulated among circles of acquaintances and supporters, many of whom were, at least occasionally, writers as well as readers. Jonson esteemed Mary Wroth both as a fellow poet and as a member of the Sidney family to whom he owed so much. Donne became part of a coterie around Queen Anne's closest confidante, Lucy Russell, Countess of Bedford, who was also an important patron for Ben Jonson, Michael Drayton, and Samuel Daniel. The countess evidently wrote poems herself, although only one attributed to her has apparently survived.

Presenting a poem to a patron, or circulating it among the group of literary people who surrounded the patron, did not require printing it. In early-seventeenth-century England, the reading public for sophisticated literary works was tiny and concentrated in a few social settings: the royal court, the universities, and the Inns of Court or law schools. In these circumstances, manuscript circulation could be an effective way of reaching one's audience. So a great deal of writing remained in manuscript in early-seventeenth-century England. The collected works of many important writers of the period—most notably John Donne, George Herbert, William Shakespeare, and Andrew Marvell—appeared in print only posthumously, in editions produced by friends or admirers. Other writers, like Robert Herrick, collected and printed their own works long after they were written and (probably) circulated in manuscript. In consequence, it is often difficult to date accurately the composition of a seventeenth-century poem. In addition, when authors do not participate in the printing of their own works, editorial problems multiply—when, for instance, the printed version of a poem is inconsistent with a surviving manuscript copy.

Nonetheless, the printing of all kinds of literary works was becoming more common. Writers such as Francis Bacon or Robert Burton, who hoped to reach large numbers of readers with whom they were not acquainted, usually arranged for the printing of their texts soon after they were composed. The sense that the printing of lyric poetry, in particular, was a bit vulgar began to fade when the famous Ben Jonson collected his own works in a grand folio edition.

Until 1640 the Stuart kings kept in place the strict controls over print publication originally instituted by Henry VIII, in response to the ideological threat posed by the Reformation. King Henry had given the members of London's Stationer's Company a monopoly on all printing; in return for their privilege, they were supposed to submit texts to prepublication censorship. In the latter part of the sixteenth century, presses associated with the universities at Oxford and Cambridge would begin operation as well, but they were largely concerned with scholarly and theological books. As a result, with a very few exceptions (such as George Herbert's *The Temple*, published by Cambridge University Press), almost all printed literary texts were produced in London. Most of them were sold there as well, in the booksellers' stalls set up outside St. Paul's Cathedral.

The licensing system located not only primary responsibility for a printed work, but its ownership, with the printer rather than with the author. Printers typically paid writers a onetime fee for the use of their work, but the payment was scanty, and the authors of popular texts realized no royalties from the many copies sold. As a result, no one could make a living as a writer in the early seventeenth century by producing best sellers. The first writer formally to arrange for royalties was apparently John Milton, who received five pounds up front for *Paradise Lost*, and another five pounds and two hundred copies at the end of each of the first three impressions. Still, legal ownership of and control over a printed work remained with the printer: authorial copyright would not become a reality until the early eighteenth century.

In monetary terms, a more promising outlet for writers was the commercial theater, which provided the first literary market in English history. Profitable and popular acting companies, established successfully in London in Elizabeth's time, continued to play a very important cultural role under James and Charles. Because the acting companies staged a large number of different plays and paid for them at a predictable, if not generous, rate, they enabled a few hardworking writers to support themselves as full-time professionals. One of them, Thomas Dekker, commented bemusedly on the novelty of being paid for the mere products of one's imagination: "the theater," he wrote, "is your poet's Royal Exchange upon which their muses—that are now turned to merchants—meeting, barter away that light commodity of words." In James's reign, Shakespeare was at the height of his powers: *Othello, King Lear, Macbeth, Antony and Cleopatra, The Winter's Tale, The Tempest*, and other important plays were first staged during these years. So were Jonson's major comedies: *Volpone, Epicene, The Alchemist*, and *Bartholomew Fair*. The most important new playwright was John Webster, whose dark tragedies *The White Devil* and *The Duchess of Malfi* combined gothic horror with stunningly beautiful poetry.

Just as printers were legally the owners of the texts they printed, so theater companies, not playwrights, were the owners of the texts they performed. Typically, companies guarded their scripts closely, permitting them to be printed only in times of financial distress or when they were so old that printing them seemed unlikely to reduce the paying audience. As a result, many Jacobean and Caroline plays are lost to us or available only in corrupt or posthumous versions. For contemporaries, though, a play was "published" not by being printed but by being performed. Aware of the dangerous potential of plays in arousing the sentiments of large crowds of onlookers, the Stuarts, like the Tudors before them, instituted tight controls over dramatic performances. Acting companies, like printers, were obliged to submit works to the censor before public presentation.

Authors, printers, and acting companies who flouted the censorships laws were subject to imprisonment, fines, or even bodily mutilation. Queen Elizabeth cut off the hand of a man who disagreed in print with her marriage plans, King Charles the ears of a man who inveighed against court masques. Jonson and his collaborators found themselves in prison for ridiculing King James's broad Scots accent in one of their comedies. The effects of censorship on writers' output were therefore far reaching across literary genres. Since overt criticism or satire of the great was so dangerous, political writing was apt to be oblique and allegorical. Writers often employed animal fables, tales of distant lands, or long-past historical events to comment upon contemporary issues.

While the commercial theaters were profitable businesses that made most of their money from paying audiences, several factors combined to bring writing for the theater closer to the Stuart court than it had been in Elizabeth's time. The Elizabethan theater companies had been officially associated with noblemen who guaranteed their legitimacy (in contrast to unsponsored traveling players, who were subject to punishment as vagrants). Early in his reign, James brought the major theater companies under royal auspices. Shakespeare's company, the most successful of the day, became the King's Men: it performed not only all of Shakespeare's plays but also *Volpone* and *The Duchess of Malfi*. Queen Anne, Prince Henry, Prince Charles, and Princess Elizabeth sponsored other companies of actors. Royal patronage, which brought with it tangible rewards and regular court performances, naturally encouraged the theater companies to pay more attention to courtly taste. Shakespeare's *Macbeth* put onstage Scots history and witches, two of James's own interests; in *King Lear*, the hero's disastrous division of his kingdom may reflect controversies over the proposed union of Scotland and England. In the first four decades of the seventeenth century, court-affiliated theater companies such as the King's Men increasingly cultivated audiences markedly more affluent than the audiences they had sought in the 1580s and 1590s, performing in intimate, expensive indoor theaters instead of, or as well as, in the cheap popular amphitheaters. *The Duchess of Malfi*, for instance, was probably written with the King's Men's indoor theater at Blackfriars in mind, because several scenes depend for their effect upon a control over lighting that is impossible outdoors. Partly because the commercial theaters seemed increasingly to cater to the affluent and courtly elements of society, they attracted the ire of the king's opponents when civil war broke out in the 1640s.

Jacobean Writers and Genres

The era saw important changes in poetic fashion. Some major Elizabethan genres fell out of favor—long allegorical or mythological narratives, sonnet sequences, and pastoral poems. The norm was coming to be short, concentrated, often witty poems. Poets and prose writers alike often preferred the jagged rhythms of colloquial speech to the elaborate ornamentation and near-musical orchestration of sound that many Elizabethans had sought. The major poets of these years, Jonson, Donne, and Herbert, led this shift and also promoted a variety of "new" genres: love elegy and satire after the classical models of Ovid and Horace, epigram, verse epistle, meditative religious lyric, and country-house poem. Although these poets differed enormously from one another, all three exercised an important influence on the poets of the next generation.

A native Londoner, Jonson first distinguished himself as an acute observer of urban manners in a series of early, controversial satiric plays. Although he wrote two of his most moving poems to his dead children, Jonson focused rather rarely on the dynamics of the family relationships that so profoundly concerned his contemporary Shakespeare. When generational and dynastic matters do figure in his poetry, as they do at the end of "To Penshurst," they seem part of the agrarian, feudal order that Jonson may have romanticized but that he suspected was rapidly disappearing. By and large, Jonson interested himself in relationships that seemed to be negotiated by the participants, often in a bustling urban or courtly world in which blood kinship no longer decisively determined one's social place. Jonson's poems of praise celebrate and exemplify classical and humanist ideals of friendship: like-minded men and women elect to join in a community that fosters wisdom, generosity, civic responsibility, and mutual respect. In the plays and satiric poems, Jonson stages the violation of those values with such riotous comprehensiveness that the very survival of such ideals seem endangered: the plays swarm with voracious swindlers and their eager victims, social climbers both adroit and inept, and a dizzying assortment of morons and misfits. In many of Jonson's plays, rogues or wits collude to victimize others; their stormy, self-interested alliances, apparently so different from the virtuous friendships of the poems of praise, in fact resemble them in one respect: they are connections entered into by choice, not by law, inheritance, or custom.

Throughout his life, Jonson earned his living entirely from his writing, composing plays for the public theater while also attracting patronage as a poet and a writer of court masques. His acute awareness of his audience was partly, then, a sheerly practical matter. Yet Jonson's yearning for recognition ran far beyond any desire for material reward. A gifted poet, Jonson argued, was a society's proper judge and teacher, and he could only be effective if his audience understood and respected the poet's exalted role. Jonson set out unabashedly to create that audience and to monumentalize himself as a great English author. In 1616 he took the unusual step, for his time, of collecting his poems, plays, and masques in an elegant folio volume.

Jonson's influence upon the next generation of writers, and through them into the Restoration and the eighteenth century, was an effect both of his poetic mastery of his chosen modes and of his powerful personal example. Jonson mentored a group of younger poets, known as the Tribe, or Sons, of Ben, meeting regularly with some of them in the Apollo Room of the Devil Tavern in London. Many of the royalist, or Cavalier, poets—Robert Herrick, Thomas Carew, Richard Lovelace, Sir John Suckling, Edmund Waller, Henry Vaughan in his secular verse—proudly acknowledged their relationship to Jonson or gave some evidence of it in their verse. Most of them absorbed too Jonson's attitude toward print and in later decades supervised the publication of their own poems.

Donne, like Jonson, spent most of his life in or near London, often in the company of other writers and intellectuals—indeed, in the company of many of the same writers and intellectuals, since the two men were friends and shared some of the same patrons. Yet, unlike Jonson's, most of Donne's poetry concerns itself not with a crowded social panorama, but with a dyad—with the relationship between the speaker and one single other being, a woman or God—that in its intensity blots out the claims of lesser relationships. Love for Donne encompasses an astonishing range of emotional experiences, from the lusty impatience of "To His Mistress Going to Bed" to the cheerful promiscuity of "The Indifferent"; to the mysterious platonic telepathy of "Air and Angels," from the vengeful wit of "The Apparition" to the postcoital tranquility of "The Good Morrow." While for Jonson the shared meal among friends often becomes an emblem of communion, for Donne sexual consummation has something of the same highly charged symbolic character, a moment in which the isolated individual can, however temporarily, escape the boundaries of selfhood in union with another:

> The phoenix riddle hath more with
> By us: we two being one, are it.
> So, to one neutral thing both sexes fit.

In the religious poems, where Donne both yearns for a physical relationship with God and knows it is impossible, he does not abandon his characteristic bodily metaphors. The doctrine of the Incarnation—God's taking material form in the person of Jesus Christ—and the doctrine of the bodily resurrection of the dead at the Last Day are Christian teachings that fascinate Donne, to which he returns again and again in his poems, sermons, and devotional writings. While sexual and religious love had long shared a common vocabulary, Donne delights in making that overlap seem new and shocking. He likens conjoined lovers to saints; demands to be raped by God; speculates, after his wife's death, that God killed her because He was jealous of Donne's divided loyalty; imagines Christ encouraging his Bride, the church, to "open" herself to as many men as possible.

Throughout Donne's life, his faith, like his intellect, was anything but quiet. Born into a family of devout Roman Catholics just as the persecution of Catholics was intensifying in Elizabethan England, Donne eventually became a member of the Church of England. If "Satire 3" is any indication, the conversion was attended by profound doubts and existential crisis. Donne's restless mind can lead him in surprising and sometimes unorthodox directions. At the same time, overwhelmed with a sense of his own unworthiness, he courts God's punishment, demanding to be spat upon, flogged, burnt, broken down, in the expectation that suffering at God's hand will restore him to grace and favor.

In both style and content, Donne's poems were addressed to a select few rather than to the public at large. His style is demanding, characterized by learned terms, audaciously far-fetched analogies, and an intellectually sophisticated play of ironies. Even Donne's sermons, attended by large crowds, share the knotty difficulty of the poems, and something too of their quality of intimate address. Donne circulated his poems in manuscript and largely avoided print publication (most of his poems were printed after his death in 1631). By some critics Donne has been regarded as the founder of a Metaphysical school of poetry. We find echoes of Donne's style in many later poets: in Thomas Carew, who praised Donne as a "monarch of wit," George Herbert, Richard Crashaw, John Cleveland, Sir John Suckling, Abraham Cowley, and Andrew Marvell.

Herbert, the younger son of a wealthy, cultivated, and well-connected family, seemed destined in early adulthood for a brilliant career as a diplomat or government servant. Yet he turned his back on worldly greatness to be ordained a priest in the Church of England. Moreover, eschewing a highly visible career as an urban preacher, he spent the remaining years of his short life ministering to the tiny rural parish of Bemerton. Herbert's poetry is shot through with the difficulty and joy of this renunciation, with all it entailed for him. Literary ambition—pride in one's independent creativity—appears to Herbert a temptation that must be resisted, whether it takes the form of Jonson's openly competitive aspiration for literary preeminence or Donne's brilliantly ironic self-displaying performances. Instead, Herbert seeks other models for poetic agency: the secretary taking dictation from a master, the musician playing in harmonious consort with others, the member of a church congregation who speaks with and for a community.

Herbert destroyed his secular verse in English and he turned his volume of religious verse over to a friend only on his deathbed, desiring him to print it if he thought it would be useful to "some dejected poor soul," but otherwise to burn it. The 177 lyrics contained in that volume, *The Temple*, display a complex religious sensibility and great artistic subtlety in an amazing variety of stanza forms. Herbert was the major influence on the next generation of religious lyric poets and was explicitly recognized as such by Henry Vaughan and Richard Crashaw.

The Jacobean period saw the emergence of what would become a major prose genre, the familiar essay. The works of the French inventor of the form, Michel de Montaigne, appeared in English translation in 1603, influencing Shakespeare as well as such later writers as Sir Thomas Browne. Yet the first essays in English, the work of Francis Bacon, attorney general under Elizabeth and eventually lord chancellor under James, bear little resemblance to Montaigne's intimate, tentative, conversational pieces. Bacon's essays present pithy, sententious, sometimes provocative claims in a tone of cool objectivity, tempering moral counsel with an awareness of the importance of prudence and expediency in practical affairs. In *Novum Organum* Bacon adapts his deliberately discontinuous mode of exposition to outline a new scientific method, holding out the tantalizing prospect of eventual mastery over the natural world and boldly articulating the ways in which science might improve the human condition. In his fictional Utopia, described in *The New Atlantis*, Bacon imagines a society that realizes his dream of carefully orchestrated collaborative research, so different from the erratic, uncoordinated efforts of alchemists and amateurs in his own day. Bacon's philosophically revolutionary approach to the natural world profoundly impacted scientifically minded people over the next several generations. His writings influenced the materialist philosophy of his erstwhile secretary, Thomas Hobbes, encouraged Oliver Cromwell to attempt a large-scale overhaul of the university curriculum during the 1650s, and inspired the formation of the Royal Society, an organization of experimental scientists, after the Restoration.

The reigns of the first two Stuart kings mark the entry of Englishwomen, in some numbers, into authorship and publication. Most female writers of the period were from the nobility or gentry; all were much better educated than most women of the period, many of whom remained illiterate. In 1611 Aemilia Lanyer was the first Englishwoman to publish a substantial volume of original poems. It contained poetic dedications, a long poem on Christ's passion, and a country-house poem, all defending women's interests and importance. In 1613 Elizabeth Cary, Lady Falkland, was the first Englishwoman to publish a tragedy, *Mariam*, a closet drama that probes the situation of a queen subjected to her husband's domestic and political tyranny. In 1617 Rachel Speght, the first female polemicist who can be securely identified, published a defense of her sex in response to a notorious attack upon "Lewd, Idle, Froward, and Unconstant Women"; she was also the author of a long dream-vision poem. Lady Mary Wroth, niece of Sir Philip Sidney and the Countess of Pembroke, wrote a long prose romance, *Urania* (1612), which presents a range of women's experiences as lovers, rulers, counselors, scholars, storytellers, poets, and seers. Her Petrarchan sonnet sequence *Pamphilia to Amphilanthus*, published with *Urania*, gives poetic voice to the female in love.

THE CAROLINE ERA, 1625–40

When King Charles came to the throne in 1625, "the fools and bawds, mimics and catamites of the former court grew out of fashion," as the Puritan Lucy Hutchinson recalled. The changed style of the court directly affected the arts and literature of the Caroline period (so called after *Carolus*, Latin for Charles). Charles and his queen, Henrietta Maria, were art collectors on a large scale and patrons of such painters as Peter Paul Rubens and Sir Anthony Van Dyke; the latter portrayed Charles as a heroic figure of knightly romance, mounted on a splendid stallion. The conjunction of chivalric virtue and divine beauty or love, symbolized in the union of the royal couple, was the dominant theme of Caroline court masques, which were even more extravagantly hyperbolic than their Jacobean predecessors. Even as Henrietta Maria encouraged an artistic and literary cult of platonic love, several courtier-poets, such as Carew and Suckling, wrote playful, sophisticated love lyrics that both alluded to this fashion and sometimes urged a more licentiously physical alternative.

The religious tensions between the Caroline court's Laudian church and the Puritan opposition produced something of a culture war. In 1633 Charles reissued the *Book of Sports*, originally published by his father in 1618, prescribing traditional holiday festivities and Sunday sports in every parish. Like his father, he saw these recreations as the rural, downscale equivalent of the court masque: harmless, healthy diversions for people who otherwise spent most of their waking hours hard at work. Puritans regarded masques and rustic dances alike as occasions for sin, the Maypole as a vestige of pagan phallus worship, and Sunday sports as a profanation of the Sabbath. In 1632 William Prynne staked out the most extreme Puritan position, publishing a tirade of over one thousand pages against stage plays,

King Charles at Prayer. This frontispiece from *Eikon Basilike* represents the praying king as a Christlike martyr surrounded by allegorical representations of virtue under trial. The left background shows a rock besieged by waves in a storm, surmounted with a Latin caption reading "unmoved I triumph." The left foreground displays palm trees with weights hung to their branches, which was supposed to make them grow more vigorously; the Latin caption reads "Virtue grows under burdens." A shaft of light pierces the stormclouds to illuminate Charles's head, with the caption "More clear out of the shadows." Wearing his coronation robes, Charles is nonetheless shown turning away from this turmoil, having cast aside an earthly crown, labeled "Vanity," to grasp a crown of thorns, labeled "Grace." Set before him is a "treatise of Christ" and a Bible reading "In Your Words, My Hope." Charles is receiving a vision from heaven of the immortal crown, "blessed and eternal," with which his supporters believed God would reward him.

court masques, Maypoles, Laudian church rituals, stained-glass windows, mixed dancing, and other outrages, all of which he associated with licentiousness, effeminacy, and the seduction of popish idolatry. For this cultural critique, Prynne was stripped of his academic degrees, ejected from the legal profession, set in the pillory, sentenced to life imprisonment, and had his books burned and his ears cut off. The severity of the punishments indicates the perceived danger of the book and the inextricability of literary and cultural affairs from politics.

Milton's astonishingly virtuosic early poems also respond to the tensions of the 1630s. Milton repudiated both courtly aesthetics and also Prynne's wholesale prohibitions, developing reformed versions of pastoral, masque, and hymn. In "On the Morning of Christ's Nativity," the birth of Christ coincides with a casting out of idols and a flight of false gods, stanzas that suggest contemporary Puritan resistance to Archbishop Laud's policies. Milton's magnificent funeral elegy "Lycidas" firmly rejects the poetic career of the Cavalier poet, who disregards high artistic ambition to "sport with Amaryllis in the shade / Or with the tangles of Neaera's hair." The poem also vehemently denounces the establishment clergy, ignorant and greedy "blind mouths" who rob their flocks of spiritual nourishment.

THE REVOLUTIONARY ERA, 1640–60

Early in the morning on January 30, 1649, Charles Stuart, the dethroned king Charles I, set off across St. James Park for his execution, surrounded by a heavy guard. He wore two shirts because the weather was frigid, and he did not want to look as if he were shivering with fear to the thousands who had gathered to watch him be beheaded. The black-draped scaffold had been erected just outside James I's elegant Banqueting House, inside of which so many court masques, in earlier decades, had celebrated the might of the Stuart monarchs and assured them of their people's love and gratitude. To those who could not attend, newsbooks provided eyewitness accounts of the dramatic events of the execution, as they had of Charles's trial the week before. Andrew Marvell also memorably describes the execution scene in "An Horatian Ode."

The execution of Charles I was understood at the time, and is still seen by many historians today, as a watershed event in English history. How did it come to pass? Historians do not agree over what caused "the English revolution," or, as it is alternatively called, the English civil war. One group argues that long-term changes in English society and the English economy led to rising social tensions and eventually to violent conflict. New capitalist modes of production in agriculture, industry, and trade were often incompatible with older feudal norms. The gentry, an affluent, highly educated class below the nobility but above the artisans, mechanics, and yeomen, played an increasingly important part in national affairs, as did the rich merchants in London; but the traditional social hierarchies failed to grant them the economic, political, and religious freedoms they believed they deserved. Another group of historians, the "revisionists," emphasize instead short-term and avoidable causes of the war—unlucky chances, personal idiosyncrasies, and poor decisions made by a small group of individuals.

Whatever caused the outbreak of hostilities, there is no doubt that the twenty-year period between 1640 and 1660 saw the emergence of concepts central to bourgeois liberal thought for centuries to come: religious toleration, separation of church and state, freedom from press censorship, and popular sovereignty. These concepts developed out of bitter disputes centering on three fundamental questions: What is the ultimate source of political power? What kind of church government is laid down in Scripture, and therefore ought to be settled in England? What should be the relation between the church and the state? The theories that evolved in response to these questions contained the seeds of much that is familiar in modern thought, mixed with much that is forbiddingly alien. It is vital to recognize that the participants in the disputes were not haphazardly attempting to predict the shape of modern liberalism, but were responding powerfully to the most important problems of their day. The need to find right answers seemed particularly urgent for the Millenarians among them, who, interpreting the upheavals of the time through the lens of the apocalyptic Book of Revelation, believed that their day was very near to being the last day of all.

When the so-called Long Parliament convened in 1640, it did not plan to execute a monarch or even to start a war. It did, however, want to secure its rights in the face of King Charles's perceived absolutist tendencies. Refusing merely to approve taxes and go home, as Charles would have wished, Parliament insisted that it could remain in session until its members agreed to disband. Then it set about abolishing extralegal taxes and courts, reining in the bishops' powers, and arresting (and eventually trying and executing) the king's ministers, the Earl of Strafford and Archbishop Laud. The collapse of effective royal government meant that the machinery of press censorship, which had been a Crown responsibility, no longer restrained the printing of explicit commentary on contemporary affairs of state. As Parliament debated, therefore, presses poured forth a flood of treatises arguing vociferously on all sides of the questions about church and state, creating a lively public forum for political discussion where none had existed before. The suspension of censorship permitted the development of weekly newsbooks that reported, and editorialized on, current domestic events from varying political and religious perspectives.

As the rift widened between Parliament and the king in 1641, Charles sought to arrest five members of Parliament for treason, and Londoners rose in arms against him. The king fled to York, while the queen escaped to the Continent. Negotiations for compromise broke down over the issues that would derail them at every future stage: control of the army and the church. On July 12, 1642, Parliament voted to raise an army, and on August 22 the king stood before a force of two thousand horse and foot at Nottingham, unfurled his royal standard, and summoned his liege men to his aid. Civil war had begun. Regions of the country, cities, towns, social classes, and even families found themselves painfully divided. The king set up court and an alternative parliament in Oxford, to which many in the House of Lords and some in the House of Commons transferred their allegiance.

In the First Civil War (1642–46), Parliament and the Presbyterian clergy that supported it had limited aims. They hoped to secure the rights of the House of Commons, to limit the king's power over the army and the church—but not to depose him—and to settle Presbyterianism as the national established church. As Puritan armies moved through the country, fighting at Edgehill, Marston Moor, Naseby, and elsewhere, they also undertook a crusade to stamp out idolatry in English churches, smashing religious images and stained-glass windows and lopping off the heads of statues as an earlier generation had done at the time of the English Reformation. Their ravages are still visible in English churches and cathedrals.

The Puritans were not, however, a homogeneous group, as the 1643 Toleration Controversy revealed. The Presbyterians wanted a national Presbyterian church, with dissenters punished and silenced as before. But Congregationalists, Independents, Baptists, and other separatists opposed a national church and pressed for some measure of toleration, for themselves at least. The religious radical Roger Williams, just returned from New England, argued that Christ mandated the complete separation of church and state and the civic toleration of all religions, even Roman Catholics, Jews, and Muslims. Yet to most people, the civil war itself seemed to confirm that people of different faiths could not coexist peacefully. Thus even as sects continued to proliferate—Seekers, Finders, Antinomians, Fifth Monarchists, Quakers, Muggletonians, Ranters—even the most broad-minded of the age often attempted to draw a line between what was acceptable and what was not. Predictably, their lines failed to coincide. In *Areopagitica* (1644), John Milton argues vigorously against press censorship and for toleration of most Protestants—but for him, Catholics are beyond the pale. Robert Herrick and Sir Thomas Browne regarded Catholic rites, and even some pagan ones, indulgently but could not stomach Puritan zeal.

In 1648, after a period of negotiation and a brief Second Civil War, the king's army was definitively defeated. His supporters were captured or fled into exile, losing position and property. Yet Charles, imprisoned on the Isle of Wight, remained a threat. He was a natural rallying point for those disillusioned by parliamentary rule—many people disliked Parliament's legal but heavy taxes even more than they had the king's illegal but lighter ones. Charles repeatedly attempted to escape and was accused of trying to open the realm to a foreign invasion. Some powerful leaders of the victorious New Model Army took drastic action. They expelled royalists and Presbyterians, who still wanted to come to an accommodation with the king, from the House of Commons and abolished the House of Lords. With consensus assured by the purgation of dissenting viewpoints, the army brought the king to trial for high treason in the Great Hall of Westminster.

After the king's execution, the Rump Parliament, the part of the House of Commons that had survived the purge, immediately established a new government "in the way of a republic, without king or House of Lords." The new state was extremely fragile. Royalists and Presbyterians fiercely resented their exclusion from power and pronounced the execution of the king a sacrilege. The Rump Parliament and the army were at odds, with the army rank and file arguing that voting rights ought not be restricted to men of property. The Levelers, led by John Lilburne, called for suffrage for all adult males. An associated but more radical group, called the Diggers or True Levelers, pushed for economic reforms to match the political ones. Their spokesman, Gerrard Winstanley, wrote eloquent manifestos developing a Christian communist program. Meanwhile, Millenarians and Fifth Monarchists wanted political power vested in the regenerate "saints" in prepara-

Cromwell. This depiction of Oliver Cromwell, published in 1658, shows him in armor, surrounded by emblems symbolizing his military prowess, civic authority, piety, and divine favor.

tion for the thousand-year reign of Christ on earth foretold in the biblical Book of Revelation. Quakers defied both state and church authority by refusing to take oaths and by preaching incendiary sermons in open marketplaces. Most alarming of all, out of proportion to their scant numbers, were the Ranters, who believed that because God dwelt in them none of their acts could be sinful. Notorious for sexual license and for public nudity, they got their name from their deliberate blaspheming and their penchant for rambling prophecy. In addition to internal disarray, the new state faced serious external threats. After Charles I's execution, the Scots and the Irish—who had not been consulted about the trial—immediately proclaimed his eldest son, Prince Charles, the new king. The prince, exiled on the Continent, was attempting to enlist the support of a major European power for an invasion.

The formidable Oliver Cromwell, now undisputed leader of the army, crushed external threats, suppressing rebellions in Ireland and Scotland. The Irish war was especially bloody, as Cromwell's army massacred the Catholic natives in a frenzy of religious hatred. When trade rivalries erupted with the Dutch over control of shipping lanes in the North Sea and the English Channel, the new republic was again victorious. Yet the domestic situation remained unstable. Given popular disaffection and the unresolved disputes between Parliament and the army, the republic's leaders dared not call new elections. In 1653 power effectively devolved upon Cromwell, who was sworn in as Lord Protector for life under England's first written constitution. Many property owners considered Cromwell the only hope for stability, while others, including Milton, saw him as a champion of religious liberty. Although persecution of Quakers and Ranters continued, Cromwell sometimes intervened to mitigate the lot of the Quakers. He also began a program to readmit Jews to England, partly in the interests of trade but also to open the way for their conversion, supposedly a precursor of the Last Day as prophesied in the Book of Revelation.

The problem of succession remained unresolved, however. When Oliver Cromwell died in 1658, his son, Richard, was appointed in his place, but he had inherited none of his father's leadership qualities. In 1660 General George Monck succeeded in calling elections for a new "full and free" parliament, open to supporters of the monarchy as well as of the republic. The new Parliament immediately recalled the exiled prince, officially proclaiming him King Charles II on May 8, 1660. The period that followed, therefore, is called the Restoration: it saw the restoration of the monarchy and with it the royal court, the established Church of England, and the professional theater.

Over the next few years, the new regime executed some of the regicides that had participated in Charles I's trial and execution and harshly repressed radical Protestants (the Baptist John Bunyan wrote *Pilgrim's Progress* in prison). Yet Charles II, who came to the throne at Parliament's invitation, could not lay claim to absolute power as his father had done. After his accession, Parliament retained its legislative supremacy and complete power over taxation, and exercised some control over the king's choice of counselors. It assembled by its own authority, not by the king's mandate. During the Restoration years, the journalistic commentary and political debates that had first flourished in the 1640s remained forceful and open, and the first modern political parties developed out of what had been the royalist and republican factions in the civil war. In London and in other cities, the merchant classes, filled with dissenters, retained their powerful economic leverage. Although the English revolution was apparently dismantled in 1660, its long-term effects profoundly changed English institutions and English society.

LITERATURE AND CULTURE, 1640–60

The English civil war was disastrous for the English theater. One of Parliament's first acts after hostilities began in 1642 was to abolish public plays and sports, as "too commonly expressing lascivious mirth and levity." Some drama continued to be written and published, but performances were rare and would-be theatrical entrepreneurs had to exploit loopholes in the prohibitions by describing their works as "operas" or presenting their productions in semiprivate circumstances.

As the king's government collapsed, the patronage relationships centered upon the court likewise disintegrated. Many leading poets were staunch royalists, or Cavaliers, who suffered considerably in the war years. Robert Herrick lost his position; Richard Lovelace was imprisoned; Margaret Cavendish went into exile. With their usual networks of manuscript circulation disrupted, many royalist writers printed their verse. Volumes of poetry by Thomas Carew, John Denham, Richard Lovelace, and Robert Herrick appeared in the 1640s. Their poems, some dating from the 1620s or 1630s, celebrate the courtly ideal "of the good life: good food, plenty of wine, good verse, hospitality, and high-spirited loyalty, especially to the king. One characteristic genre is the elegant love lyric, often with a carpe diem theme. In Herrick's case especially, apparent ease and frivolity masks a frankly political subtext. The Puritans excoriated May Day celebrations, harvest-home festivities, and other time-honored holidays and "sports" as unscriptural, idolatrous, or frankly pagan. For Herrick, they sustained a community that strove neither for ascetic perfection nor for equality among social classes, but that knew the value of pleasure in cementing social harmony and that incorporated everyone—rich and poor, unlettered and learned—as the established church had traditionally tried to do.

During the 1640s and 1650s, as they faced defeat, the Cavaliers wrote movingly of the relationship between love and honor, of fidelity under duress, of like-minded friends sustaining one another in a hostile environment. They presented themselves as amateurs, writing verse in the midst of a life devoted to more important matters: war, love, the king's service, the endurance of loss. Rejecting the radical Protestant emphasis on the "inner light," which they considered merely a pretext for presumptuousness and violence, the Cavalier poets often cultivated a deliberately unidiosyncratic, even self-deprecating poetic persona. Thus the poems of Richard Lovelace memorably express sentiments that he represents not as the unique insights of an isolated genius, but as principles easily grasped by all honorable men. When in "The Vine" Herrick relates a wet dream, he not only laughs at himself but at those who mistake their own fantasies for divine inspiration.

During the 1650s, royalists wrote lyric poems in places far removed from the hostile centers of parliamentary power. In Wales, Henry Vaughan wrote religious verse expressing his intense longing for past eras of innocence and for the perfection of heaven or the millennium. Also in Wales, Katherine Philips wrote and circulated in manuscript poems that celebrate female friends in terms normally reserved for male friendships. The publication of her poems after the Restoration brought Philips some celebrity as "the Matchless Orinda." Richard Crashaw, an exile in Paris and Rome and a convert to Roman Catholicism, wrote lush religious poetry that attempted to reveal the spiritual by stimulating the senses. Margaret Cavendish, also in exile, with the queen in Paris, published two collections of lyrics when she returned to England in 1653; after the Restoration she published several dramas and a remarkable Utopian romance, *The Blazing World*.

Several prose works by royalist sympathizers have become classics in their respective genres. Thomas Hobbes, the most important English philosopher of the period, another exile in Paris, developed his materialist philosophy and psychology there and, in *Leviathan* (1651), his unflinching defense of absolute sovereignty based on a theory of social contract. Some royalist writing seems to have little to do with the contemporary scene, but in fact carries a political charge. In *Religio Medici* (1642–43), Sir Thomas Browne presents himself as a genial, speculative doctor who loves ritual and ceremony not for complicated theological reasons, but because they move him emotionally. While he can sympathize with all Christians, even Roman Catholics, and while he recognizes in himself many idiosyncratic views, he willingly submits his judgment to the Church of England, in sharp contrast to Puritans bent on ridding the church of its errors. Izaak Walton's treatise on fishing, *The Complete Angler* (1653), presents a dialogue between Walton's persona, Piscator the angler, and Venator the hunter. Piscator, speaking like many Cavalier poets for the values of warmheartedness, charity, and inclusiveness, converts the busy, warlike Venator, a figure for the Puritan, to the tranquil and contemplative pursuit of fishing.

The revolutionary era gave new impetus to women's writing. The circumstances of war placed women in novel, occasionally dangerous situations, giving them unusual events to describe and prompting self-discovery. The autobiographies of royalists Lady Anne Halkett and Margaret Cavendish, Duchess of Newcastle, published after the Restoration, report their experiences and their sometimes daring activities during those trying days. Lucy Hutchinson's memoir of her husband, Colonel John Hutchinson, first published in 1806, narrates much of the history of the times from a republican point of view. Leveler women offered petitions and manifestos in support of their cause and of their imprisoned husbands. The widespread belief that the Holy Spirit was moving in unexpected ways encouraged a number of female prophets: Anna Trapnel, Mary Cary, and Lady Eleanor Davies. Their published prophecies often carried a strong political critique of Charles or of Cromwell. Quaker women came into their own as preachers and sometimes as writers of tracts, authorized by the Quaker belief in the spiritual equality of women and men, and by the conviction that all persons should testify to whatever the inner light communicates to them. Many of their memoirs, such as Dorothy Waugh's "Relation," were originally published both to call attention to their sufferings and to inspire other Quakers to similar feats of moral fortitude.

While most writers during this period were royalists, two of the best, Andrew Marvell and John Milton, sided with the republic. Marvell wrote most of the poems for which he is still remembered while at Nunappleton in the early 1650s, tutoring the daughter of the retired parliamentary general Thomas Fairfax; in 1657 he joined his friend Milton in the office of Cromwell's Latin Secretariat. In Marvell's love poems and pastorals, older convictions about ordered harmony give way to wittily unresolved or unresolvable oppositions, some playful, some painful. Marvell's conflictual worldview seems unmistakably the product of the unsettled civil war decades. In his country-house poem "Upon Appleton House," even agricultural practices associated with regular changes of the season, like the flooding of fallow fields, become emblems of unpredictability, reversal, and category confusion. In other poems Marvell eschews an authoritative poetic persona in favor of speakers that seem limited or even a bit unbalanced: a mower who argues for the values of pastoral with disconcerting belligerence, a nymph who seems to exemplify virginal innocence but also immature self-absorption and possibly unconscious sexual perversity. Marvell's finest political poem, "An Horatian Ode upon Cromwell's Return from Ireland," celebrates Cromwell's providential victories even while inviting sympathy for the executed king and warning about the potential dangers of Cromwell's meteoric rise to power.

A promising, prolific young poet in the 1630s, Milton committed himself to the English republic as soon as the conflict between the king and Parliament began to take shape. His loyalty to the revolution remained unwavering despite his disillusion when it failed to realize his ideals: religious toleration for all Protestants and the free circulation of ideas without prior censorship. First as a self-appointed adviser to the state, then as its official defender, he addressed the great issues at stake in the 1640s and the 1650s. In a series of treatises he argued for church disestablishment and for the removal of bishops, for a republican government based on natural law and popular sovereignty, for the right of the people to dismiss from office and even execute their rulers, and, most controversial even to his usual allies, in favor of divorce on the grounds of incompatibility. Milton was a Puritan, but both his theological heterodoxies and his poetic vision mark him as a distinctly unusual one.

During his years as a political polemicist, Milton also wrote several sonnets, revising that small, love-centered genre to accommodate large private and public topics: a Catholic massacre of proto-Protestants in the foothills of Italy, the agonizing questions posed by his blindness, various threats to intellectual and religious liberty. In 1645 he published his collected English and Latin poems as a counterstatement to the royalist volumes of the 1640s. Yet his most ambitious poetry remained to be written. Milton probably wrote some part of *Paradise Lost* in the late 1650s and completed it after the Restoration, encompassing in it all he had thought, read, and experienced of tyranny, political controversy, evil, deception, love, and the need for companionship. This cosmic blank-verse epic assimilates and critiques the epic tradition and Milton's entire intellectual and literary heritage, classical and Christian. Yet it centers not on martial heroes but on a domestic couple who must discover how to live a good life day by day, in Eden and later in the fallen world, amid intense emotional pressures and the seductions of evil.

Seventeenth-century poetry, prose, and drama retains its hold on readers because so much of it is so very good, fusing intellectual power, emotional passion, and extraordinary linguistic artfulness. Poetry in this period ranges over an astonishing variety of topics and modes: highly erotic celebrations of sexual desire, passionate declarations of faith and doubt, lavishly embroidered paeans to friends and benefactors, tough-minded assessments of social and political institutions. English dramatists were at the height of their powers, situating characters of unprecedented complexity in plays sometimes remorselessly satiric, sometimes achingly moving. In these years English prose becomes a highly flexible instrument, suited to informal essays, scientific treatises, religious meditation, political polemic, biography and autobiography, and journalistic reportage. Literary forms evolve for the exquisitely modulated representation of the self: dramatic monologues, memoirs, spiritual autobiographies, sermons in which the preacher takes himself for an example. Finally, we have in Milton an epic poet who assumed the role of inspired prophet, envisioning a world created by God but shaped by human choice and imagination.

The Early Seventeenth Century

TEXTS	CONTEXTS
1603 James I, *Basilikon Doron* reissued	**1603** Death of Elizabeth I; accession of James I. Plague
1604 William Shakespeare, *Othello*	
1605 Shakespeare, *King Lear*. Ben Jonson, *The Masque of Blackness*. Francis Bacon, *The Advancement of Learning*	**1605** Gunpowder Plot, failed effort by Roman Catholic extremists to blow up Parliament
1606 Jonson, *Volpone*. Shakespeare, *Macbeth*	
	1607 Founding of Jamestown colony in Virginia
1609 Shakespeare, *Sonnets*	**1609** Galileo begins observing the heavens with a telescope
1611 "King James" Bible (Authorized Version). Shakespeare, *The Tempest*. John Donne, *The First Anniversary*. Aemilia Lanyer, *Salve Deus Rex Judaeorum*	
1612 Donne, *The Second Anniversary*	**1612** Death of Prince Henry
1613 Elizabeth Cary, *The Tragedy of Mariam*	
1614 John Webster, *The Duchess of Malfi*	
1616 Jonson, *Works*. James I, *Works*	**1616** Death of Shakespeare
	1618 Beginning of the Thirty Years War
	1619 First African slaves in North America exchanged by Dutch frigate for food and supplies at Jamestown
1620 Bacon, *Novum Organum*	**1620** Pilgrims land at Plymouth
1621 Mary Wroth, *The Countess of Montgomery's Urania* and *Pamphilia to Amphilanthus*. Robert Burton, *The Anatomy of Melancholy*	**1621** Donne appointed dean of St. Paul's Cathedral
1623 Shakespeare, First Folio	
1625 Bacon, *Essays*	**1625** Death of James I; accession of Charles I; Charles I marries Henrietta Maria
	1629 Charles I dissolves Parliament
1633 Donne, *Poems*. George Herbert, *The Temple*	**1633** Galileo forced by the Inquisition to recant the Copernican theory
1637 John Milton, "Lycidas"	
1640 Thomas Carew, *Poems*	**1640** Long Parliament called (1640–53). Archbishop Laud impeached
1642 Thomas Browne, *Religio Medici*. Milton, *The Reason of Church Government*	**1642** First Civil War begins (1642–46). Parliament closes the theaters
1643 Milton, *The Doctrine and Discipline of Divorce*	**1643** Accession of Louis XIV of France
1644 Milton, *Areopagitica*	

TEXTS	CONTEXTS
1645 Milton, *Poems*. Edmund Waller, *Poems*	**1645** Archbishop Laud executed. Royalists defeated at Naseby
1648 Robert Herrick, *Hesperides* and *Noble Numbers*	**1648** Second Civil War. "Pride's Purge" of Parliament
1649 Milton, *The Tenure of Kings and Magistrates* and *Eikonoklastes*	**1649** Trial and execution of Charles I. Republic declared. Milton becomes Latin Secretary (1649–59)
1650 Henry Vaughan, *Silex Scintillans* (Part II, 1655)	
1651 Thomas Hobbes, *Leviathan*. Andrew Marvell, "Upon Appleton House" (unpublished)	
	1652 Anglo-Dutch War (1652–54)
	1653 Cromwell made Lord Protector
	1658 Death of Cromwell; his son Richard made Protector
1660 Milton, *Ready and Easy Way to Establish a Free Commonwealth*	**1660** Restoration of Charles II to throne. Royal Society founded
	1662 Charles II marries Catherine of Braganza
	1665 The Great Plague
1666 Margaret Cavendish, *The Blazing World*	**1666** The Great Fire
1667 Milton, *Paradise Lost* (in ten books). Katherine Philips, *Collected Poems*. John Dryden, *Annus Mirabilis*	
1671 Milton, *Paradise Regained* and *Samson Agonistes*	
1674 Milton, *Paradise Lost* (in twelve books)	**1674** Death of Milton
1681 Marvell, *Poems*, published posthumously	

JOHN DONNE
1572–1631

Lovers' eyeballs threaded on a string. A god who assaults the human heart with a battering ram. A teardrop that encompasses and drowns the world. John Donne's poems abound with startling images, some of them exalting and others grotesque. With his strange and playful intelligence, expressed in puns, paradoxes, and the elaborately sustained metaphors known as "conceits," Donne has enthralled and sometimes enraged readers from his day to our own. The tired clichés of love poetry—cheeks like roses, hearts pierced by the arrows of love—emerge reinvigorated and radically transformed, demanding from the reader an unprecedented level of mental alertness and engagement. Donne prided himself on his wit and displayed it not only in his conceits but in his grasp of learned discourses ranging from theology to alchemy, from cosmology to law. Yet for all their ostentatious intellectuality Donne's poems never give the impression of being academic exercises. Rather, they are intense dramatic monologues in which the speaker's ideas and feelings shift and evolve from one line to the next. Donne's prosody is equally dramatic, its jagged rhythms capturing the effect of speech (and eliciting from his classically minded contemporary Ben Jonson the gruff observation that "Donne, for not keeping of accent deserved hanging").

Donne began life as an outsider, and in some respects remained one until death. He was born in London in 1572 into a devout Roman Catholic household. The family was prosperous, but, as the poet later remarked, none had suffered more heavily for its loyalty to the Catholic Church: "I have been ever kept awake in a meditation of martyrdom." Donne was distantly related to the great Catholic humanist and martyr Sir Thomas More. Two of Donne's uncles, Jesuit priests, were forced to flee the realm; Donne's brother Henry, arrested for harboring a priest, died in prison of the plague. As a Catholic in Protestant England, growing up in decades when anti-Roman feeling reached new heights, Donne could not expect any kind of public career, nor could he receive a university degree (he left Oxford without one and studied law for a time at the Inns of Court). What he could reasonably expect instead was prejudice, official harassment, and crippling financial penalties. He chose not to live under such conditions. At some point in the 1590s, having returned to London after travels abroad, and having devoted some years to studying theological issues, Donne converted to the English church.

The poems that belong with certainty to this period of his life—the five satires and most of the elegies—reveal a man both fascinated by and keenly critical of English society. Four of the satires treat commonplace Elizabethan topics—foppish and obsequious courtiers, bad poets, corrupt lawyers and a corrupt court—but are unique both in their visceral revulsion and in their intellectual excitement. Donne uses striking images of pestilence, vomit, excrement, and pox to create a unique satiric world, busy, vibrant, and corrupt, in which his dramatic speakers have only to step outside the door to be inundated by all the fools and knaves in Christendom. By contrast, the third satire treats the quest for true religion—the question that preoccupied him above all others in these years—in terms that are serious, passionately witty, and deeply felt. Donne argues that honest doubting search is better than the facile acceptance of any religious tradition, epitomizing that point brilliantly in the image of Truth on a craggy hill, very difficult to climb. Society's values are of no help whatsoever to the individual seeker—none will escape the final judgment by pleading that "A Harry, or a Martin taught [them] this." In the love elegies Donne seems intent on making up for his social powerlessness through witty representations of mastery in the bedroom and of adventurous travel. In "Elegy 16" he imagines his speaker embarking on a journey "O'er the white Alps" and with mingled tenderness and condescension argues down a naive mistress's proposal to accompany him. In "Elegy 19," his fondling of a naked lover becomes in a famous conceit the equivalent of exploration in America. Donne's interest in satire and elegy—classical Roman genres, which he helped introduce to English verse—is itself significant. He wrote in English, but he reached out to other traditions.

If Donne's conversion to the Church of England promised him security, social acceptance, and the possibility of a public career, that promise was soon to be cruelly withdrawn. In 1596–97 he participated in the Earl of Essex's military expeditions against Catholic Spain in Cádiz and the Azores (the experience prompted two remarkable descriptive poems of life at sea, "The Storm" and "The Calm") and upon his return became secretary to Sir Thomas Egerton, Lord Keeper of the Great Seal. This should have been the beginning of a successful public career. But his secret marriage in 1601 to Egerton's seventeen-year-old niece Ann More enraged Donne's employer and the bride's wealthy father; Donne was briefly imprisoned and dismissed from service. The poet was reduced to a retired country life beset by financial insecurity and a rapidly increasing family; Ann bore twelve children (not counting miscarriages) by the time she died at age thirty-three. At one point, Donne wrote despairingly that while the death of a child would mean one less mouth to feed, he could not afford the burial expenses. In this bleak period, he wrote but dared not publish *Biathanatos*, a paradoxical defense of suicide.

As his family grew, Donne made every effort to reinstate himself in the favor of the great. To win the approval of James I, he penned *Pseudo-Martyr* (1610), defending the king's insistence that Catholics take the Oath of Allegiance. This set an irrevocable public stamp on his renunciation of Catholicism, and Donne followed up with a witty satire on the Jesuits, *Ignatius His Conclave* (1611). In the same period he was producing a steady stream of occasional poems for friends and patrons such as Somerset (the king's favorite), the Countess of Bedford, and Magdalen Herbert, and for small coteries of courtiers and ladies. Like most gentlemen of his era, Donne saw poetry as a polite accomplishment rather than as a trade or vocation, and in consequence he circulated his poems in manuscript but left most of them uncollected and unpublished. In 1611 and 1612, however, he published the first and second *Anniversaries* on the death of the daughter of his patron Sir Robert Drury.

For some years King James had urged an ecclesiastical career on Donne, denying him any other means of advancement. In 1615 Donne finally consented, overcoming his sense of unworthiness and the pull of other ambitions. He was ordained in the Church of England and entered upon a distinguished career as court preacher, reader in divinity at Lincoln's Inn, and dean of St. Paul's. Donne's metaphorical style, bold erudition, and dramatic wit established him as a great preacher in an age that appreciated learned sermons powerfully delivered. Some 160 of his sermons survive, preached to monarchs and courtiers, lawyers and London magistrates, city merchants and trading companies. As a distinguished clergyman in the Church of England, Donne had traveled an immense distance from the religion of his childhood and the adventurous life of his twenties. Yet in his sermons and late poems we find the same brilliant and idiosyncratic mind at work, refashioning his profane conceits to serve a new and higher purpose. In "Expostulation 19" he praises God as the greatest of literary stylists: "a figurative, a metaphorical God," imagining God as a conceit-maker like himself. In poems, meditations, and sermons, Donne came increasingly to be engaged in anxious contemplation of his own mortality. In "Hymn to God My God, in My Sickness," Donne imagines himself spread out on his deathbed like a map showing the route to the next world. Only a few days before his death he preached "Death's Duel," a terrifying analysis of all life as a decline toward death and dissolution, which contemporaries termed his own funeral sermon. On his deathbed, according to his contemporary biographer Izaak Walton, Donne had a portrait made of himself in his shroud and meditated on it daily. Meditations upon skulls as emblems of mortality were common in the period, but nothing is more characteristic of Donne than to find a way to meditate on his own skull.

Given the shape of Donne's career, it is no surprise that his poems and prose works display an astonishing variety of attitudes, viewpoints, and feelings on the great subjects of love and religion. Yet this variety cannot be fully explained in biographical terms. The poet's own attempt to distinguish between Jack Donne, the young rake, and Dr. Donne, the grave and religious dean of St. Paul's, is (perhaps intentionally) misleading. We do not know the time and circumstances for most of Donne's verses, but it is clear that many of his finest religious poems predate his ordination, and it is possible that he continued to add to the love poems known as his "songs and sonnets" after he entered the church. Theological language abounds in his love poetry, and daringly erotic images in his religious verse.

Donne's "songs and sonnets" have been the cornerstone of his reputation almost since their publication in 1633. The title *Songs and Sonnets* associates them with the popular miscellanies of love poems and sonnet sequences in the Petrarchan tradition, but they directly challenge the popular Petrarchan sonnet sequences of the 1590s. The collection contains only one formal sonnet, the "songs" are not notably lyrical, and Donne draws upon and transforms a whole range of literary traditions concerned with love. Like Petrarch, Donne can present himself as the despairing lover of an unattainable lady ("The Funeral"); like Ovid he can be lighthearted, witty, cynical, and frankly lustful ("The Flea," "The Indifferent"); like the Neoplatonists, he espouses a theory of transcendent love, but he breaks from them with his insistence in many poems on the union of physical and spiritual love. What binds these poems together and grants them enduring power is their compelling immediacy. The speaker is always in the throes of intense emotion, and that emotion is not static but constantly shifting with the turns of the poet's thought. Donne seems supremely present in these poems, standing behind their various speakers. Where Petrarchan poets exhaustively catalogue their beloved's physical features (though in highly conventional terms), Donne's speakers tell us little or nothing about the loved woman, or about the male friends imagined as the audience for many poems. Donne's repeated insistence that the private world of lovers is superior to the wider public world, or that it somehow contains all of that world, is understandable in light of the many disappointments of his career. Yet this was also a poet who threw himself headlong into life, love, and sexuality, and later into the very visible role of court and city preacher.

Donne was long grouped with Herbert, Vaughan, Crashaw, Marvell, Traherne, and Cowley under the heading of "Metaphysical poets." The expression was first employed by critics like Samuel Johnson and William Hazlitt, who found the intricate conceits and self-conscious learning of these poets incompatible with poetic beauty and sincerity. Early in the twentieth century, T. S. Eliot sought to restore their reputation, attributing to them a unity of thought and feeling that had since their time been lost. There was, however, no formal "school" of Metaphysical poetry, and the characteristics ascribed to it by later critics pertain chiefly to Donne. Like Ben Jonson, John Donne immensely influenced the succeeding generation, but he remains a singularity.

From Songs and Sonnets[1]

The Flea[2]

Mark but this flea, and mark in this,
How little that which thou deniest me is;
Me it sucked first, and now sucks thee,
And in this flea our two bloods mingled be;
5 Thou know'st that this cannot be said
A sin, or shame, or loss of maidenhead,°   *virginity*
  Yet this enjoys before it woo,
    And pampered° swells with one blood made of two,[3]   *overfed*
  And this, alas, is more than we would do.

10 Oh stay, three lives in one flea spare,
Where we almost, nay more than married are.
This flea is you and I, and this
Our marriage bed and marriage temple is;
Though parents grudge, and you, we are met,
15 And cloistered[4] in these living walls of jet.°   *black*
  Though use° make you apt to kill me,[5]   *habit*
    Let not to that, self-murder added be,
  And sacrilege, three sins in killing three.

Cruel and sudden, hast thou since
20 Purpled thy nail in blood of innocence?
Wherein could this flea guilty be,
Except in that drop which it sucked from thee?
Yet thou triumph'st, and say'st that thou
Find'st not thy self nor me the weaker now;
25 'Tis true; then learn how false fears be:
  Just so much honor, when thou yield'st to me,
  Will waste, as this flea's death took life from thee.

1633

The Good-Morrow°   *morning greeting*

I wonder, by my troth,° what thou and I   *good faith*
Did, till we loved? Were we not weaned till then,

1. Donne's love poems were written over nearly two decades, beginning around 1595; they were not published in Donne's lifetime but circulated widely in manuscript. The title *Songs and Sonnets* was supplied in the second edition (1635), which grouped the poems by kind, but neither this arrangement nor the more haphazard organization of the first edition (1633) is Donne's own. In Donne's time the term "sonnet" often meant simply "love lyric," and in fact there is only one formal sonnet in this collection. For the poems we present we follow the 1635 edition, beginning with the extremely popular poem "The Flea."
2. This insect afforded a popular erotic theme for poets all over Europe, deriving from a pseudo-Ovidian medieval poem in which a lover envies the flea for the liberties it takes with his mistress's body.
3. The swelling suggests pregnancy.
4. As in a convent or monastery.
5. By denying me sexual gratification.

But sucked on country pleasures, childishly?
Or snorted° we in the seven sleepers' den?[1]   snored
5   'Twas so; but° this, all pleasures fancies be.   except for
If ever any beauty I did see,
Which I desired, and got, 'twas but a dream of thee.

And now good morrow to our waking souls,
Which watch not one another out of fear;
10 For love all love of other sights controls,
And makes one little room an everywhere.
Let sea-discoverers to new worlds have gone,
Let maps to others, worlds on worlds have shown:
Let us possess one world;[2] each hath one, and is one.

15 My face in thine eye, thine in mine appears,
And true plain hearts do in the faces rest;
Where can we find two better hemispheres,
Without sharp North, without declining West?
Whatever dies was not mixed equally;[3]
20 If our two loves be one, or thou and I
Love so alike that none do slacken, none can die.

                                                    1633

Song

Go and catch a falling star,
    Get with child a mandrake root,[1]
Tell me where all past years are,
    Or who cleft the Devil's foot,
5   Teach me to hear mermaids° singing,   sirens
Or to keep off envy's stinging,
        And find
        What wind
Serves to advance an honest mind.

10 If thou beest born to strange sights,
    Things invisible to see,
Ride ten thousand days and nights,
    Till age snow white hairs on thee,
Thou, when thou return'st, wilt tell me
15 All strange wonders that befell thee,
        And swear
        No where
Lives a woman true, and fair.

1. Cave in Ephesus where, according to legend, seven Christian youths hid from pagan persecutors and slept for 187 years.
2. "Our world" in many manuscripts.
3. Scholastic philosophy taught that when the elements were imperfectly mixed ("not mixed equally"), matter was mutable and mortal; con-versely, when the elements were perfectly mixed, matter was immutable and hence immortal.
1. The mandrake root, or mandragora, is forked like the lower part of the human body. It was thought to shriek when pulled from the ground and to kill all humans who heard it; it was also (paradoxically) thought to help women conceive.

If thou find'st one, let me know,
20   Such a pilgrimage were sweet;
Yet do not, I would not go,
    Though at next door we might meet;
Though she were true when you met her,
And last till you write your letter,
25   Yet she
        Will be
False, ere I come, to two, or three.

1633

The Undertaking

I have done one braver° thing   *more glorious*
    Than all the Worthies[1] did,
And yet a braver thence doth spring,
    Which is, to keep that hid.

5   It were but madness now t' impart
    The skill of specular stone,[2]
When he which can have learned the art
    To cut it, can find none.

So, if I now should utter this,
10   Others (because no more
Such stuff to work upon, there is)
    Would love but as before.

But he who loveliness within
    Hath found, all outward loathes,
15 For he who color loves, and skin,
    Loves but their oldest clothes.

If, as I have, you also do
    Virtue attired in woman see,
And dare love that, and say so too,
20   And forget the He and She;

And if this love, though placèd so,
    From profane men you hide,
Which will no faith on this bestow,
    Or, if they do, deride;

1. According to medieval legend, the Nine Worthies, or supreme heroes of history, included three Jews (Joshua, David, Judas Maccabaeus), three pagans (Hector, Alexander, Julius Caesar), and three Christians (Arthur, Charlemagne, Godfrey of Boulogne).

2. A transparent or translucent material, reputed to have been used in antiquity for windows, but no longer known. Great skill was needed to cut it.

25 Then you have done a braver thing
      Than all the Worthies did;
    And a braver thence will spring,
      Which is, to keep that hid.

1633

The Sun Rising

      Busy old fool, unruly sun,
        Why dost thou thus
    Through windows and through curtains call on us?
    Must to thy motions lovers' seasons run?
5   Saucy pedantic wretch, go chide
        Late schoolboys and sour prentices,
      Go tell court huntsmen that the king will ride,[1]
      Call country ants to harvest offices;[2]
    Love, all alike, no season knows nor clime,
10 Nor hours, days, months, which are the rags of time.

      Thy beams, so reverend and strong
        Why shouldst thou think?
    I could eclipse and cloud them with a wink,
    But that I would not lose her sight so long;
15   If her eyes have not blinded thine,
        Look, and tomorrow late, tell me,
      Whether both th' Indias of spice and mine[3]
      Be where thou leftst them, or lie here with me.
    Ask for those kings whom thou saw'st yesterday,
20 And thou shalt hear, All here in one bed lay.

      She is all states,° and all princes I,   *nations*
        Nothing else is.
    Princes do but play us; compared to this,
    All honor's mimic, all wealth alchemy.
25   Thou, sun, art half as happy as we,
        In that the world's contracted thus;
      Thine age asks ease, and since thy duties be
      To warm the world, that's done in warming us.
    Shine here to us, and thou art everywhere;
30 This bed thy center is, these walls thy sphere.[4]

1633

---

1. King James was very fond of hunting.
2. Autumn chores. "Country ants": farm drudges.
3. The India of "spice" is the East Indies; that of "mine" (gold), the West Indies.

4. According to the old Ptolemaic astronomy, the earth was the center of the sun's orbit, and the sun's motion was contained within its sphere.

The Indifferent

I can love both fair and brown,[1]
Her whom abundance melts, and her whom want betrays,
Her who loves loneness best, and her who masks and plays,
Her whom the country formed, and whom the town,
5 Her who believes, and her who tries,°   *tests*
Her who still° weeps with spongy eyes,   *always*
And her who is dry cork, and never cries;
I can love her, and her, and you, and you,
I can love any, so she be not true.

10 Will no other vice content you?
Will it not serve your turn to do as did your mothers?
Or have you all old vices spent, and now would find out others?
Or doth a fear that men are true torment you?
O we are not, be not you so;
15 Let me, and do you, twenty know.
Rob me, but bind me not, and let me go.
Must I, who came to travail thorough[2] you,
Grow your fixed subject, because you are true?

Venus heard me sigh this song,
20 And by love's sweetest part, variety, she swore,
She heard not this till now; and that it should be so no more.
She went, examined, and returned ere long,
And said, Alas, some two or three
Poor heretics in love there be,
25 Which think to 'stablish dangerous constancy.
But I have told them, Since you will be true,
You shall be true to them who are false to you.

1633

The Canonization[1]

For God's sake hold your tongue, and let me love,
 Or chide my palsy, or my gout,
My five gray hairs, or ruined fortune, flout,
 With wealth your state, your mind with arts improve,
5 Take you a course, get you a place,[2]
  Observe His Honor, or His Grace,[3]
Or the king's real, or his stampèd face[4]
  Contemplate; what you will, approve,°   *try, test*
  So you will let me love.

---

1. Both blonde and brunette.
2. Through. "Travail": grief.
1. The poem plays off against the Roman Catholic process of determining that certain persons are saints, proper objects of veneration and prayer.

2. An appointment, at court or elsewhere. "Take you a course": follow some career.
3. Pay court to some lord or bishop.
4. On coins; "real" (royal) refers also to a particular Spanish coin.

10   Alas, alas, who's injured by my love?
        What merchant's ships have my sighs drowned?
    Who says my tears have overflowed his ground?
        When did my colds a forward° spring remove?[5]   *early*
        When did the heats which my veins fill
15   Add one man to the plaguy bill?[6]
    Soldiers find wars, and lawyers find out still
        Litigious men, which quarrels move,
        Though she and I do love.

    Call us what you will, we are made such by love;
20   Call her one, me another fly,
    We're tapers too, and at our own cost die,[7]
        And we in us find the eagle and the dove.
        The phoenix riddle hath more wit
        By us: we two being one, are it.[8]
25   So, to one neutral thing both sexes fit.
        We die and rise the same, and prove
        Mysterious by this love.

    We can die by it, if not live by love,
        And if unfit for tombs and hearse
30   Our legend be, it will be fit for verse;
        And if no piece of chronicle we prove,
        We'll build in sonnets pretty rooms;[9]
        As well a well-wrought urn becomes°   *befits*
    The greatest ashes, as half-acre tombs,
35   And by these hymns,[1] all shall approve°   *confirm*
        Us canonized for love:

    And thus invoke us: You whom reverend love
        Made one another's hermitage;
    You, to whom love was peace, that now is rage;
40   Who did the whole world's soul contract,[2] and drove
        Into the glasses of your eyes
        (So made such mirrors, and such spies,°   *spyglasses, telescopes*
    That they did all to you epitomize)
        Countries, towns, courts:[3] Beg from above
45   A pattern of your love!

1633

---

5. Petrarchan lovers traditionally sigh, weep, and are frozen because of their mistresses' neglect.

6. Deaths from the plague, which raged in summer, were recorded by parish in weekly lists.

7. Flies were emblems of transience and lustfulness; tapers (candles) attract flies to their death and also consume themselves. "Die" in the punning terminology of the period means to experience orgasm, and there was a superstition that intercourse shortened life.

8. The eagle signifies strength and vision; the dove, meekness and mercy. The phoenix was a mythic Arabian bird, only one of which existed at any one time. After living five hundred years, it was consumed by fire, then rose triumphantly from its ashes a new bird. Thus it was a symbol of immortality and sometimes associated with Christ. "Eagle" and "dove" are also alchemical terms for processes leading to the rise of "phoenix," a stage in the transmutation of metals to gold.

9. "Rooms" (punning on the Italian meaning of "stanza") will contain their exploits, as prose chronicle histories contain great deeds done in the world.

1. The lover's own poems.

2. An alternative meaning is "extract."

3. "Countries, towns, courts" are objects of the verb "drove." The notion is that eyes both see and reflect the outside world, and so can contain all of it.

Song

Sweetest love, I do not go,
   For weariness of thee,
Nor in hope the world can show
   A fitter love for me;
5   But since that I
Must die at last, 'tis best,
To use myself in jest
    Thus by feigned deaths° to die.   *i.e., absences*

Yesternight the sun went hence
10   And yet is here today,
He hath no desire nor sense,
   Nor half so short a way:
    Then fear not me,
But believe that I shall make
15 Speedier journeys, since I take
    More wings and spurs than he.

O how feeble is man's power,
   That if good fortune fall,°   *happen*
Cannot add another hour,
20 Nor a lost hour recall!
    But come bad chance,
And we join to'it our strength,
And we teach it art and length,
    Itself o'er us to'advance.

25 When thou sigh'st, thou sigh'st not wind,
   But sigh'st my soul away,
When thou weep'st, unkindly[1] kind,
   My life's blood doth decay.
    It cannot be
30 That thou lov'st me, as thou say'st,
If in thine my life thou waste,
    Thou art the best of me.

Let not thy divining° heart   *prophetic*
   Forethink me any ill,
35 Destiny may take thy part,
   And may thy fears fulfill;
    But think that we
Are but turned aside to sleep;
They who one another keep
40   Alive, ne'er parted be.

1633

---

1. Also carries the meaning "unnaturally."

Air and Angels

Twice or thrice had I loved thee,
Before I knew thy face or name;
So in a voice, so in a shapeless flame,
Angels affect us oft, and worshipped be;
5   Still° when, to where thou wert, I came,   *always*
Some lovely glorious nothing[1] I did see.
    But since my soul, whose child love is,
Takes limbs of flesh, and else could nothing do,[2]
    More subtle° than the parent is   *rarefied*
10 Love must not be, but take a body too;
    And therefore what thou wert, and who,
      I bid love ask, and now
That it assume thy body I allow,
And fix itself in thy lip, eye, and brow.
15 Whilst thus to ballast love I thought,
    And so more steadily to have gone,
With wares which would sink° admiration,   *overwhelm*
I saw I had love's pinnace° overfraught;°   *small boat / overloaded*
    Every thy hair for love to work upon
20 Is much too much, some fitter must be sought;
    For, nor in nothing, nor in things
Extreme and scatt'ring° bright, can love inhere.   *dazzling*
    Then as an angel, face and wings
Of air, not pure as it, yet pure doth wear,[3]
25   So thy love may be my love's sphere;[4]
      Just such disparity
As is 'twixt air and angels' purity,
'Twixt women's love and men's will ever be.

1633

Break of Day[1]

'Tis true, 'tis day; what though it be?
O wilt thou therefore rise from me?
Why should we rise because 'tis light?
Did we lie down because 'twas night?
5 Love, which in spite of darkness brought us hither,
Should in despite of light keep us together.

---

1. Spiritual beauty, the true object of love in Neoplatonic philosophy.
2. My soul could not function unless it were in a body.
3. It was commonly believed that angels, when they appeared to humans, assumed a body of air which, though pure, was less so than the angel's spiritual essence.

4. Each sphere in the cosmos was thought to be governed by an angel (an intelligence).
1. An aubade, or song of the lovers' parting at dawn, this poem is unusual for Donne in having a female speaker. The poem was given a musical setting and published in 1622, in William Corkine's *Second Book of Ayers*.

Light hath no tongue, but is all eye;
If it could speak as well as spy,
This were the worst that it could say,
10 That being well, I fain° would stay,　　　　　　　　　*gladly*
And that I loved my heart and honor so
That I would not from him, that had them, go.

Must business thee from hence remove?
O, that's the worst disease of love.
15 The poor, the foul, the false, love can
Admit, but not the busied man.
He which hath business, and makes love, doth do
Such wrong, as when a married man doth woo.

1622, 1633

A Valediction:[1] Of Weeping

Let me pour forth
My tears before thy face whilst I stay here,
For thy face coins them, and thy stamp° they bear,　　　　*image*
And by this mintage they are something worth,
5　　For thus they be
　　Pregnant of thee;
Fruits of much grief they are, emblems° of more—　　　*symbols*
When a tear falls, that thou falls which it bore,
So thou and I are nothing then, when on a diverse° shore.　*different*

10　　On a round ball
A workman that hath copies by can lay
An Europe, Afric, and an Asia,
And quickly make that, which was nothing, all;[2]
　　So doth each tear
15　　Which thee doth wear,[3]
A globe, yea world, by that impression grow,
Till thy tears mixed with mine do overflow
This world; by waters sent from thee, my heaven dissolvèd so.

O more than moon,
20　Draw not up seas to drown me in thy sphere;[4]
Weep me not dead in thine arms, but forbear
To teach the sea what it may do too soon.
　　Let not the wind
　　Example find
25　To do me more harm than it purposeth;

---

1. A farewell poem, one of four so titled in the *Songs and Sonnets.* Another is "A Valediction: Forbidding Mourning," p. 1385.
2. I.e., on a blank globe one can place maps of the continents and so convert "nothing" into the whole world ("all").
3. Which bears your image.
4. A star or planet with more power of attraction than the moon might not only affect tides but draw the very seas unto itself.

Since thou and I sigh one another's breath,
Whoe'er sighs most is cruelest, and hastes the other's death.

1633

Love's Alchemy

Some that have deeper digged love's mine than I,
Say where his centric° happiness doth lie: *central*
    I have loved, and got, and told,
But should I love, get, tell, till I were old,
5   I should not find that hidden mystery;
    O, 'tis imposture all:
And as no chemic° yet the elixir[1] got,   *alchemist*
    But glorifies his pregnant pot[2]
    If by the way to him befall
10 Some odoriferous thing, or medicinal;
    So lovers dream a rich and long delight,
    But get a winter-seeming summer's night.[3]

Our ease, our thrift, our honor, and our day,
Shall we for this vain bubble's shadow pay?
15   Ends love in this, that my man°   *servant*
Can be as happy as I can, if he can
Endure the short scorn of a bridegroom's play?
    That loving wretch that swears
'Tis not the bodies marry, but the minds,
20   Which he in her angelic finds,
    Would swear as justly that he hears,
In that day's rude hoarse minstrelsy, the spheres.[4]
    Hope not for mind in women; at their best
    Sweetness and wit, they are but mummy, possessed.[5]

1633

A Nocturnal upon Saint Lucy's Day, Being the Shortest Day[1]

'Tis the year's midnight and it is the day's,
Lucy's, who scarce seven hours herself unmasks;

---

1. A magic medicine sought by alchemists and reputed to heal all ills.
2. A fertile (and womb-shaped) retort, calling up the common analogy between producing the elixir of life and human generation.
3. A night cold as in winter and short as in summer.
4. The perfect harmony of the planets, moving in concentric crystalline "spheres," is contrasted with the boisterous serenade of pots, pans, and trumpets performed on the wedding night.

5. The syntax of the last two lines is unclear, and they are punctuated differently in various copies. The 1633 edition reads: "at their best, / Sweetnesse, and wit they'are, but, *mummy*, possesst." Many modern editors punctuate as we do here. "Mummy" suggests a corpselike body, without mind or spirit.
1. The nocturne, or night office of the Roman Catholic Church, is a service held in the primitive church at midnight. St. Lucy's Day fell on December 13 according to the old calendar still in use in

The sun is spent, and now his flasks[2]
Send forth light squibs,° no constant rays.   *small fireworks*
5   The world's whole sap is sunk;
The general balm th' hydroptic[3] earth hath drunk,
Whither, as to the bed's feet, life is shrunk,
Dead and interred; yet all these seem to laugh,
Compared with me, who am their epitaph.

10 Study me, then, you who shall lovers be
At the next world, that is, at the next spring;
    For I am every dead thing
    In whom love wrought new alchemy.
    For his art did express°   *extract*
15 A quintessence[4] even from nothingness,
From dull privations and lean emptiness.
He ruined me, and I am re-begot
Of absence, darkness, death: things which are not.

All others from all things draw all that's good,
20 Life, soul, form, spirit, whence they being have;
    I, by love's limbeck,[5] am the grave
    Of all that's nothing. Oft a flood
       Have we two wept, and so
Drowned the whole world, us two; oft did we grow
25 To be two chaoses when we did show
Care to aught° else; and often absences   *anything*
Withdrew our souls, and made us carcasses.

But I am by her death (which word wrongs her)
Of the first nothing the elixir grown;[6]
30   Were I a man, that I were one
       I needs must know; I should prefer,
          If I were any beast,
Some ends, some means; yea plants, yea stones detest
And love.[7] All, all some properties invest.
35 If I an ordinary nothing were,
As shadow, a light and body must be here.

But I am none; nor will my sun renew.
You lovers, for whose sake the lesser sun
    At this time to the Goat[8] is run
40   To fetch new lust and give it you,

England at the time, and its vigil (the previous day and night) was the winter solstice, the shortest day of the year. At this time of the year, the sun rises after 8 A.M. in the latitude of London and sets well before 4 P.M.
2. The stars are "flasks," thought to store up light from the sun.
3. Dropsical, thus insatiably thirsty. "General balm": the supposedly life-preserving essence of all things.
4. The reputed fifth essence, a celestial element beyond the mundane four elements (earth, water,

air, fire), thought to be latent in all things and to be a universal cure. Alchemists sought to extract it.
5. Alembic; a vessel used in distilling.
6. I.e., the quintessence of that absolute nothingness that existed before the creation.
7. Beasts have intentions; plants and even stones (like lodestones) have attractions and antipathies.
8. The sign of Capricorn, which the sun enters at the winter solstice; the goat is an emblem of sexual vigor.

Enjoy your summer all.
Since she enjoys her long night's festival,
Let me prepare towards her, and let me call
This hour her vigil and her eve, since this
45 Both the year's and the day's deep midnight is.

1633

The Bait[1]

Come live with me and be my love,
And we will some new pleasures prove,°   *try*
Of golden sands and crystal brooks,
With silken lines and silver hooks.

5 There will the river whispering run,
Warmed by thine eyes more than the sun.
And there the enamored fish will stay,
Begging themselves they may betray.

When thou wilt swim in that live bath,
10 Each fish, which every channel hath,
Will amorously to thee swim,
Gladder to catch thee, than thou him.

If thou, to be so seen, beest loath,
By sun or moon, thou darkenest both;
15 And if myself have leave to see,
I need not their light, having thee.

Let others freeze with angling reeds,
And cut their legs with shells and weeds,
Or treacherously poor fish beset
20 With strangling snare or windowy net.

Let coarse bold hands from slimy nest
The bedded fish in banks outwrest,
Or curious traitors, sleave-silk flies,[2]
Bewitch poor fishes' wandering eyes.

25 For thee, thou need'st no such deceit,
For thou thyself art thine own bait;
That fish that is not catched thereby,
Alas, is wiser far than I.

1633

---

1. This poem is Donne's response to Marlowe's "Passionate Shepherd to His Love," p. 1126. Another of the many responses was Ralegh's "The Nymph's Reply to the Shepherd," p. 1024.
2. Flies made of unraveled silk. "Curious": exquisitely made.

The Apparition

When by thy scorn, O murderess, I am dead,
And that thou thinkst thee free
From all solicitation from me,
Then shall my ghost come to thy bed,
5   And thee, feigned vestal,[1] in worse arms shall see;
Then thy sick taper will begin to wink,°   *flicker*
And he whose thou art then, being tired before,
Will, if thou stir, or pinch to wake him, think
    Thou call'st for more,
10 And in false sleep will from thee shrink,
And then, poor aspen wretch,[2] neglected thou
Bathed in a cold quicksilver sweat[3] wilt lie
    A verier° ghost than I;   *truer*
What I will say, I will not tell thee now,
15 Lest that preserve thee; and since my love is spent,
I had rather thou shouldst painfully repent,
Than by my threatenings rest still innocent.

1633

A Valediction: Forbidding Mourning[1]

As virtuous men pass mildly away,
    And whisper to their souls to go,
Whilst some of their sad friends do say
    The breath goes now, and some say, No;

5   So let us melt, and make no noise,
    No tear-floods, nor sigh-tempests move;
'Twere profanation° of our joys   *desecration*
    To tell the laity our love.

Moving of th' earth brings harms and fears,
10   Men reckon what it did and meant;
But trepidation of the spheres,
    Though greater far, is innocent.[2]

---

1. Virgins consecrated to the Roman goddess Vesta.
2. Aspen leaves flutter in the slightest breeze.
3. Sweating in terror; quicksilver (mercury) was a stock prescription for venereal disease, and sweating was part of the cure.
1. For "valediction" see p. 1381, n. 1. Izaak Walton speculated that this poem was addressed to

Donne's wife on the occasion of his trip to the Continent in 1611, but there is no proof of that.
2. Earthquakes cause damage and were thought to be portentous. "Trepidation" (in the Ptolemaic cosmology) is an oscillation of the ninth or crystalline sphere imparted to all the inner spheres. Though a much more violent motion than an earthquake, it is neither destructive nor sinister.

Dull sublunary[3] lovers' love
    (Whose soul is sense) cannot admit
15 Absence, because it doth remove
    Those things which elemented° it.   *composed*

But we, by a love so much refined
    That ourselves know not what it is,
Inter-assurèd of the mind,
20   Care less, eyes, lips, and hands to miss.

Our two souls therefore, which are one,
    Though I must go, endure not yet
A breach, but an expansion,
    Like gold to airy thinness beat.

25 If they be two, they are two so
    As stiff twin compasses[4] are two;
Thy soul, the fixed foot, makes no show
    To move, but doth, if th' other do.

And though it in the center sit,
30   Yet when the other far doth roam,
It leans and hearkens after it,
    And grows erect, as that comes home.

Such wilt thou be to me, who must,
    Like th' other foot, obliquely run;
35 Thy firmness makes my circle just,
    And makes me end where I begun.

1633

The Ecstasy[1]

Where, like a pillow on a bed,
    A pregnant bank swelled up to rest
The violet's reclining head,
    Sat we two, one another's best.

5 Our hands were firmly cemented
    With a fast balm° which thence did spring,   *perspiration*
Our eye-beams[2] twisted, and did thread
    Our eyes upon one double string;

So to intergraft our hands, as yet
10   Was all our means to make us one,

3. Beneath the moon, therefore earthly, sensual, and subject to change.
4. The two legs of a geometer's or draftsman's compass.
1. From *ekstasis* (Greek), a movement of the soul outside of the body.
2. Invisible shafts of light, thought of as going out of the eyes and thereby enabling one to see things.

And pictures in our eyes[3] to get°   *beget*
 Was all our propagation.

As 'twixt two equal armies Fate
 Suspends uncertain victory,
15 Our souls (which to advance their state
 Were gone out) hung 'twixt her and me;

And whilst our souls negotiate there,
 We like sepulchral statues lay;
All day the same our postures were,
20 And we said nothing all the day.

If any, so by love refined
 That he soul's language understood,
And by good love were grown all mind,
 Within convenient distance stood,

25 He (though he knew not which soul spake,
 Because both meant, both spake the same)
Might thence a new concoction[4] take,
 And part far purer than he came.

This ecstasy doth unperplex,
30 We said, and tell us what we love;
We see by this it was not sex;
 We see we saw not what did move;°   *motivate us*

But as all several° souls contain   *separate*
 Mixture of things, they know not what,
35 Love these mixed souls doth mix again,
 And makes both one, each this and that.

A single violet transplant,
 The strength, the color, and the size
(All which before was poor and scant)
40 Redoubles still,° and multiplies.   *continually*

When love with one another so
 Interinanimates two souls,
That abler soul, which thence doth flow,
 Defects of loneliness controls.

45 We then, who are this new soul, know
 Of what we are composed and made,
For th' atomies° of which we grow   *components*
 Are souls, whom no change can invade.

But O alas, so long, so far
50 Our bodies why do we forbear?

---

3. Reflections of each in the other's eyes, often called "making babies."

4. In the alchemical sense of sublimation or purification.

They are ours, though they are not we; we are
　　The intelligences, they the sphere.[5]

We owe them thanks because they thus
　　Did us to us at first convey,
55　Yielded their forces, sense, to us,
　　Nor are dross to us, but allay.[6]

On man heaven's influence works not so
　　But that it first imprints the air:[7]
So soul into the soul may flow,
60　　Though it to body first repair.° 　　　　　　　　　　*go*

As our blood labors to beget
　　Spirits[8] as like souls as it can,
Because such fingers need° to knit 　　　　　　　*are needed*
　　That subtle knot which makes us man,

65　So must pure lovers' souls descend
　　T' affections, and to faculties
Which sense may reach and apprehend;
　　Else a great prince in prison lies.

To our bodies turn we then, that so
70　　Weak men on love revealed may look;
Love's mysteries[9] in souls do grow,
　　But yet the body is his book.

And if some lover, such as we,
　　Have heard this dialogue of one,[1]
75　Let him still mark° us; he shall see 　　　　　*observe*
　　Small change when we are to bodies gone.

　　　　　　　　　　　　　　　　　　1633

The Funeral

Whoever comes to shroud me, do not harm
　　Nor question much
That subtle wreath of hair which crowns my arm;
The mystery, the sign you must not touch,
5　　　For 'tis my outward soul,
Viceroy to that, which then to heaven being gone,

---

5. In Ptolemaic astronomy, each planet, set in a transparent "sphere" that revolved and so carried it around the earth, was inhabited by a controlling angelic "intelligence."
6. "Dross" is an impurity that weakens metal; "allay" (alloy) strengthens it.
7. Astrological influences were thought to work on people through the medium of the surrounding air.

8. Subtle substances thought to be produced by the blood to serve as intermediaries between body and soul.
9. The implied comparison is with God's mysteries, which are revealed and may be read in the book of Nature and the book of Scripture.
1. "Dialogue of one" because "both meant, both spake the same" (line 26).

Will leave this to control,
And keep these limbs, her[1] provinces, from dissolution.

10 For if the sinewy thread[2] my brain lets fall
    Through every part
Can tie those parts and make me one of all,
These hairs which upward grew, and strength and art
    Have from a better brain,
Can better do it; except° she meant that I   *unless*
15   By this should know my pain,
As prisoners then are manacled, when they're condemned to die.

Whate'er she meant by it, bury it with me,
    For since I am
Love's martyr, it might breed idolatry,
20 If into others' hands these relics[3] came:
    As 'twas humility
To afford to it all that a soul can do,
    So 'tis some bravery,
That since you would save[4] none of me, I bury some of you.

                            1633

The Blossom

Little think'st thou, poor flower,
    Whom I have watched six or seven days,
And seen thy birth, and seen what every hour
Gave to thy growth, thee to this height to raise,
5 And now dost laugh and triumph on this bough,
    Little think'st thou
That it will freeze anon, and that I shall
Tomorrow find thee fall'n, or not at all.

Little think'st thou, poor heart,
10   That labor'st yet to nestle thee,
And think'st by hovering here to get a part
In a forbidden or forbidding tree,[1]
And hop'st her stiffness by long siege to bow,
    Little think'st thou
15 That thou tomorrow, ere that sun doth wake,
Must with this sun and me a journey take.

But thou, which lov'st to be
    Subtle to plague thyself, wilt say,

---

1. The soul's, but also the mistress's (cf. "she," line 14).
2. The nervous system.
3. Body parts or other objects belonging to a saint, venerated by Roman Catholics.
4. All the early printed texts read "have" (which carries sexual connotations), while many manuscripts read "save."
1. The fruit of this tree is "forbidden" (presumably because the woman is married) or "forbidding" (because she is unwilling).

Alas, if you must go, what's that to me?
20　Here lies my business, and here I will stay:
You go to friends whose love and means present
　　　Various content°　　　　　　　　　　*satisfactions*
To your eyes, ears, and tongue, and every part.
If then your body go, what need you a heart?

25　Well, then, stay here; but know,
　　When thou hast stayed and done thy most,
A naked thinking heart that makes no show
Is to a woman but a kind of ghost.
How shall she know my heart; or, having none,
30　　　Know thee for one?
Practice may make her know some other part,
But take my word, she doth not know a heart.

Meet me at London, then,
　　Twenty days hence, and thou shalt see
35　Me fresher and more fat° by being with men　　*prosperous*
Than if I had stayed still with her and thee.
For God's sake, if you can, be you so too:
　　　I would give you
There to another friend, whom we shall find
40　As glad to have my body as my mind.

　　　　　　　　　　　　　　　　　　　　　　1633

The Relic

When my grave is broke up again
Some second guest to entertain
(For graves have learned that woman-head°　　*female trait*
To be to more than one a bed),[1]
5　　　And he that digs it spies
A bracelet of bright hair about the bone,
　　Will he not let us alone,
And think that there a loving couple lies,
Who thought that this device might be some way
10　To make their souls, at the last busy day,°　　*Judgment Day*
Meet at this grave, and make a little stay?

If this fall° in a time, or land,　　　　　　　　*happen*
Where mis-devotion[2] doth command,
Then he that digs us up will bring
15　Us to the bishop and the king,
　　To make us relics; then
Thou shalt be a Mary Magdalen, and I

---

1. Graves were often used to inter successive corpses, the bones of previous occupants being deposited in charnel houses.

2. False devotion, superstition, i.e., Roman Catholicism.

A something else thereby;
All women shall adore us, and some men;
20 And since at such times, miracles are sought,
I would have that age by this paper taught
What miracles we harmless lovers wrought.

First, we loved well and faithfully,
Yet knew not what we loved, nor why,
25 Difference of sex no more we knew,
Than our guardian angels do;
Coming and going, we
Perchance might kiss, but not between those meals;[3]
Our hands ne'er touched the seals°   *sexual organs*
30 Which nature, injured by late law, sets free:[4]
These miracles we did: but now, alas,
All measure and all language I should pass,
Should I tell what a miracle she was.

1633

A Lecture upon the Shadow

Stand still, and I will read to thee
A lecture, Love, in love's philosophy.
These three hours that we have spent
Walking here, two shadows went
5 Along with us, which we ourselves produced;
But, now the sun is just above our head,
We do those shadows tread
And to brave° clearness all things are reduced.   *splendid*
So, whilst our infant loves did grow,
10 Disguises did and shadows flow
From us and our care;° but now, 'tis not so.   *caution*

That love hath not attained the high'st degree
Which is still diligent lest others see.

Except° our loves at this noon stay,   *unless*
15 We shall new shadows make the other way.
As the first were made to blind
Others, these which come behind
Will work upon ourselves, and blind our eyes.
If our loves faint and westwardly decline,
20 To me thou falsely thine
And I to thee mine actions shall disguise.
The morning shadows wear away,
But these grow longer all the day,
But, oh, love's day is short if love decay.

3. The kisses of salutation and parting.
4. Human law forbids the free love permitted by nature. "Late": recent (comparatively speaking).

25   Love is a growing or full constant light,
       And his first minute after noon is night.

                                                 1635

Elegy[1] 16. On His Mistress

    By our first strange and fatal interview,
    By all desires which thereof did ensue,
    By our long starving hopes, by that remorse°   *pity*
    Which my words' masculine persuasive force
5   Begot in thee, and by the memory
    Of hurts which spies and rivals threatened me,
    I calmly beg; but by thy father's wrath,
    By all pains which want and divorcement hath,
    I conjure thee; and all the oaths which I
10   And thou have sworn to seal joint constancy
    Here I unswear and overswear them thus:
    Thou shalt not love by ways so dangerous.
    Temper, oh fair love, love's impetuous rage;
    Be my true mistress still, not my feigned page.[2]
15   I'll go, and, by thy kind leave, leave behind
    Thee, only worthy to nurse in my mind
    Thirst to come back. Oh, if thou die before,
    My soul from other lands to thee shall soar.
    Thy (else almighty) beauty cannot move
20   Rage from the seas, nor thy love teach them love,
    Nor tame wild Boreas' harshness.[3] Thou hast read
    How roughly he in pieces shiv01rèd
    Fair Orithea, whom he swore he loved.
    Fall ill or good, 'tis madness to have proved°   *sought out*
25   Dangers unurged; feed on this flattery,
    That absent lovers one in th' other be.
    Dissemble nothing, not a boy, nor change
    Thy body's habit,° nor mind's; be not strange   *clothing*
    To thyself only; all will spy in thy face
30   A blushing womanly discovering grace.
    Richly clothed apes are called apes, and as soon
    Eclipsed as bright we call the moon the moon.
    Men of France, changeable chameleons,
    Spitals° of diseases, shops of fashions,   *hospitals*
35   Love's fuelers[4] and the rightest company

1. In Latin poetry, an elegy is a discursive or reflective poem written in "elegiacs" (unrhymed couplets of alternating dactylic hexameters and pentameters). This meter was used for funeral laments and especially for love poetry. The most famous classical elegist was the Roman poet Ovid; his *Amores*, a collection of witty and sensual love poems, deeply influenced Donne's erotic poetry.

2. The speaker's mistress wanted to accompany him abroad, disguised as a page boy. Such escapades occasionally took place in real life; in 1605, Elizabeth Southwell, disguised as a page, went abroad with Sir Robert Dudley.

3. God of the north wind; in *Metamorphoses* 6 Ovid describes the wild force with which Boreas abducted Orithea.

4. Providers of aphrodisiacs.

Of players which upon the world's stage be,
Will quickly know thee, and know thee; and alas!⁵
Th' indifferent° Italian, as we pass   *bisexual*
His warm land, well content to think thee page,
40 Will hunt thee with such lust and hideous rage
As Lot's fair guests were vexed.⁶ But none of these
Nor spongy, hydroptic⁷ Dutch shall thee displease
If thou stay here. O stay here, for, for thee,
England is only a worthy gallery
45 To walk in expectation, till from thence
Our greatest king call thee to his presence.⁸
When I am gone, dream me some happiness,
Nor let thy looks our long-hid love confess;
Nor praise nor dispraise me, bless nor curse
50 Openly love's force, nor in bed fright thy nurse
With midnight's startings, crying out "Oh, oh!
Nurse, oh my love is slain, I saw him go
O'er the white Alps alone; I saw him, I,
Assailed, fight, taken, stabbed, bleed, fall, and die."
55 Augur me better chance, except dread Jove
Think it enough for me t' have had thy love.

1635

Elegy 19. To His Mistress Going to Bed

Come, Madam, come, all rest my powers defy,
Until I labor, I in labor lie.¹
The foe ofttimes having the foe in sight,
Is tired with standing though he never fight.
5 Off with that girdle,° like heaven's zone° glistering,   *belt / zodiac*
But a far fairer world encompassing.
Unpin that spangled breastplate² which you wear
That th' eyes of busy fools may be stopped there.
Unlace yourself, for that harmonious chime
10 Tells me from you that now it is bed-time.
Off with that happy busk,° which I envy,   *bodice*
That still° can be and still can stand so nigh.   *always*
Your gown going off, such beauteous state reveals
As when from flowery meads th' hill's shadow steals.
15 Off with that wiry coronet and show
The hairy diadem which on you doth grow;
Now off with those shoes, and then safely tread

---

5. May pun on "a lass." "Know": in the sexual sense.
6. The inhabitants of Sodom tried to rape two angels who visited Lot in the guise of men to warn of the city's impending destruction (Genesis 19.1–11).
7. Dropsical, thus insatiably thirsty.
8. Throne rooms commonly had antechambers (galleries) where visitors waited until the monarch was ready to see them.
1. "Labor" in the dual sense of "get to work (sexually)" and "distress."
2. The stomacher, an ornamental, often jeweled, covering for the chest, worn under the lacing of the bodice.

In this love's hallowed temple, this soft bed.
In such white robes, heaven's angels used to be
20   Received by men; thou, angel, bring'st with thee
A heaven like Mahomet's paradise;[3] and though
Ill spirits walk in white, we easily know
By this these angels from an evil sprite,
Those set our hairs, but these our flesh upright.
25   License my roving hands, and let them go
Before, behind, between, above, below.
O my America! my new-found-land,
My kingdom, safeliest when with one man manned,
My mine of precious stones, my empery,°   *empire*
30   How blest am I in this discovering thee!
To enter in these bonds is to be free;
There where my hand is set, my seal shall be.[4]
    Full nakedness! All joys are due to thee.
As souls unbodied, bodies unclothed must be,
35   To taste whole joys. Gems which you women use
Are like Atalanta's balls,[5] cast in men's views,
That when a fool's eye lighteth on a gem,
His earthly soul may covet theirs, not them.
Like pictures, or like books' gay coverings, made
40   For laymen, are all women thus arrayed;
Themselves are mystic books, which only we
(Whom their imputed grace will dignify)
Must see revealed.[6] Then since that I may know,
As liberally as to a midwife show
45   Thyself: cast all, yea, this white linen hence,
Here is no penance, much less innocence.[7]
    To teach thee, I am naked first; why then
What need'st thou have more covering than a man?

                                                            1669

Satire 3   In satire the author holds a subject up to ridicule. Like his elegies, Donne's five verse satires were written in his twenties and are in the forefront of an effort in the 1590s (by Donne, Ben Jonson, Joseph Hall, and John Marston) to naturalize those classical forms in England. While elements of satire figure in many different kinds of literature, the great models for formal verse satire were the Roman poets Horace and Juvenal, the former for an urbanely witty style, the latter for an indignant or angry manner. While Donne's other satires call on these models, his third satire more nearly resembles those of a third Roman satirist, Persius, known

---

3. A place of sensual pleasure, thought to be populated by seductive houris for the delectation of the faithful.
4. The jokes mingle law with sex: where he has signed a document (placed his hand) he will now place his seal; and in the bonds of her arms he will find freedom.
5. Atalanta, running a race against her suitor Hippomenes, was beaten when he dropped golden apples ("balls") for her to pick up. Donne reverses the story.

6. By granting favors to their lovers, women impute to them grace that they don't deserve, as God, in Calvinist doctrine, imputes grace to undeserving sinners. Laymen can only look at the covers of mystic books (clothed women), but "we" elect can read them (see women naked).
7. Some manuscripts read: "There is no penance due to innocence." White garments would be appropriate either for the innocent virgin or for the sinner doing formal penance.

for an abstruse style and moralizing manner. This work is a strenuous discussion of an acute theological problem, for the age and for Donne himself: How may one discover the true Christian church among so many claimants to that role? At the time Donne wrote "Satire 3," he was in the process of leaving the Roman Catholic Church of his heritage for the Church of England.

Satire 3

Kind pity chokes my spleen;[1] brave° scorn forbids   *defiant*
Those tears to issue which swell my eyelids;
I must not laugh, nor weep° sins, and be wise: *lament*
Can railing then cure these worn maladies?
5 Is not our mistress, fair Religion,
As worthy of all our souls' devotion
As virtue was to the first blinded age?[2]
Are not heaven's joys as valiant to assuage
Lusts, as earth's honor was to them?° Alas,   *pagans*
10 As we do them in means, shall they surpass
Us in the end, and shall thy father's spirit
Meet blind philosophers in heaven, whose merit
Of strict life may be imputed faith,[3] and hear
Thee, whom he taught so easy ways and near
15 To follow, damned? O, if thou dar'st, fear this;
This fear great courage and high valor is.
Dar'st thou aid mutinous Dutch,[4] and dar'st thou lay
Thee in ships, wooden sepulchers, a prey
To leaders' rage, to storms, to shot, to dearth?°   *famine*
20 Dar'st thou dive seas and dungeons° of the earth?   *mines, caves*
Hast thou courageous fire to thaw the ice
Of frozen north discoveries?[5] And thrice
Colder than salamanders, like divine
Children in the oven,[6] fires of Spain and the line,
25 Whose countries limbecks to our bodies be,
Canst thou for gain bear?[7] And must every he
Which cries not "Goddess!" to thy mistress, draw,°   *fight a duel*
Or eat thy poisonous words? Courage of straw!
O desperate coward, wilt thou seem bold, and
30 To thy foes and His° (who made thee to stand   *God's*
Sentinel in his world's garrison) thus yield,
And for forbidden wars leave th' appointed field?[8]

---

1. The seat of bile, hence scorn and ridicule.
2. The age of paganism, blind to Christianity but capable of natural morality ("virtue").
3. Donne's formulation wittily turns on its head the key concept of Protestant theology—that salvation is to be achieved only by imputing Christ's merits to Christians through faith—by suggesting that virtuous pagans might be saved by imputing faith to them on the basis of their moral life.
4. English volunteers took frequent part with the Dutch in their wars against Spain. Donne himself had sailed in two raiding expeditions against the Spanish.

5. Many explorers tried to find a northwest passage to the Pacific.
6. In the biblical story (Daniel 3), Shadrach, Meshach, and Abednego were rescued from a fiery furnace. The salamander (a lizardlike creature) was thought to be so cold-blooded that it could live in fire.
7. The object of "bear" is "fires of Spain and the line"—inquisitorial and equatorial heats, which roast people as chemists heat materials in "limbecks" (alembics, or vessels for distilling).
8. Of moral struggle.

Know thy foes: The foul Devil (whom thou
Strivest to please) for hate, not love, would allow
35 Thee fain° his whole realm to be quit;° and as   *gladly / to satisfy you*
The world's all parts wither away and pass,[9]
So the world's self, thy other loved foe, is
In her decrepit wane, and thou, loving this,
Dost love a withered and worn strumpet; last,
40 Flesh (itself's death) and joys which flesh can taste
Thou lovest; and thy fair goodly soul, which doth
Give this flesh power to taste joy, thou dost loathe.
Seek true religion. O, where? Mirreus,[1]
Thinking her unhoused here, and fled from us,
45 Seeks her at Rome; there, because he doth know
That she was there a thousand years ago.
He loves her rags so, as we here obey
The statecloth[2] where the prince sat yesterday.
Crantz to such brave loves will not be enthralled,
50 But loves her only, who at Geneva is called
Religion—plain, simple, sullen, young,
Contemptuous, yet unhandsome; as among
Lecherous humors,° there is one that judges   *temperaments*
No wenches wholesome but coarse country drudges.
55 Graius stays still at home here, and because
Some preachers, vile ambitious bawds, and laws
Still new, like fashions, bid him think that she
Which dwells with us is only perfect, he
Embraceth her whom his godfathers will
60 Tender to him, being tender, as wards still
Take such wives as their guardians offer, or
Pay values.[3] Careless Phrygius doth abhor
All, because all cannot be good, as one
Knowing some women whores, dares marry none.
65 Graccus loves all as one, and thinks that so
As women do in divers countries go
In divers habits,° yet are still one kind,   *styles of clothing*
So doth, so is religion; and this blind-
ness too much light breeds;[4] but unmoved thou
70 Of force° must one, and forced but one allow;   *necessity*
And the right; ask thy father which is she,
Let him ask his; though truth and falsehood be
Near twins, yet truth a little elder is;
Be busy to seek her, believe me this,
75 He's not of none, nor worst, that seeks the best.[5]
To adore, or scorn an image, or protest,

9. The common belief that the world was growing old and becoming decrepit.
1. The satiric types in this passage represent
different creeds: "Mirreus" is a Roman Catholic;
"Crantz," an austere Calvinist Presbyterian of
Geneva; "Graius" a Church of England Erastian
who believes in any religion sponsored by the
state; "Phrygius," a skeptic; and "Graccus," a complete relativist.
2. The royal canopy, a symbol of kingly power.

3. If minors in care of a guardian (in wardship)
rejected the wives offered ("tendered") to them
they had to pay fines ("values").
4. I.e., Graccus considers the differences between
religions merely incidental, like womens' clothes,
but his apparently tolerant, "enlightened" attitude
is itself a form of blindness.
5. The person who seeks the best church is neither an unbeliever nor the worst sort of believer.

May all be bad; doubt wisely; in strange way
To stand inquiring right, is not to stray;
To sleep, or run wrong, is. On a huge hill,
80 Cragged and steep, Truth stands, and he that will
Reach her, about must, and about must go,
And what the hill's suddenness resists, win so;
Yet strive so, that before age, death's twilight,
Thy soul rest, for none can work in that night.[6]
85 To will° implies delay, therefore now do.   *intend a future act*
Hard deeds, the body's pains; hard knowledge too
The mind's endeavors reach,° and mysteries   *achieve*
Are like the sun, dazzling, yet plain to all eyes.
Keep the truth which thou hast found; men do not stand
90 In so ill case here, that God hath with his hand
Signed kings' blank charters to kill whom they hate,
Nor are they vicars, but hangmen to fate.[7]
Fool and wretch, wilt thou let thy soul be tied
To man's laws, by which she shall not be tried
95 At the last day? O, will it then boot° thee   *profit*
To say a Philip, or a Gregory,
A Harry, or a Martin taught thee this?[8]
Is not this excuse for mere° contraries   *complete*
Equally strong? Cannot both sides say so?
100 That thou mayest rightly obey power, her bounds know;
Those passed, her nature and name is changed; to be
Then humble to her is idolatry.
As streams are, power is; those blest flowers that dwell
At the rough stream's calm head, thrive and prove well,
105 But having left their roots, and themselves given
To the stream's tyrannous rage, alas, are driven
Through mills, and rocks, and woods, and at last, almost
Consumed in going, in the sea are lost:
So perish souls, which more choose men's unjust
110 Power from God claimed, than God himself to trust.

1633

Sappho to Philaenis[1]

Where is that holy fire, which verse is said
 To have? Is that enchanting force decayed?
Verse, that draws° Nature's works, from° Nature's law, *copies / according to*
 Thee, her best work, to her work[2] cannot draw.

---

6. Echoes John 9.4, "the night cometh, when no man can work."
7. Kings are not God's vicars on earth, with license ("blank charters") to persecute or kill whomever they wish on grounds of religion.
8. "Philip" is Philip II of Spain, "Gregory" is Pope Gregory XIII or XIV, "Harry" is England's Henry VIII, and "Martin" is Martin Luther.
1. A heroic epistle, modeled on Ovid's *Heroi-*

des, erotic poems set forth as letters between famous lovers and often with female speakers. Sappho was a famous woman poet of Lesbos (b. 612 B.C.E.). Her poems to her several female lovers made "lesbian" a term for same-sex love between women.
2. I.e., you are not drawn to sexual intimacy ("Nature's work") by poetry, which imitates nature's works.

5   Have my tears quenched my old poetic fire;
     Why quenched they not as well, that of desire?
Thoughts, my mind's creatures, often are with thee,
     But I, their maker, want their liberty.
Only thine image in my heart doth sit,
10   But that is wax, and fires environ it.
My fires have driven, thine have drawn it hence;
     And I am robbed of picture, heart, and sense.
Dwells with me still mine irksome memory,
     Which both to keep and lose, grieves equally.
15   That tells me how fair thou art: thou art so fair,
     As gods, when gods to thee I do compare,
Are graced thereby;[3] and to make blind men see,
     What things gods are, I say they are like to thee.
For, if we justly call each silly° man   *ordinary*
20   A little world,[4] what shall we call thee then?
Thou art not soft, and clear, and straight, and fair,
     As down, as stars, cedars, and lilies are,
But thy right hand, and cheek, and eye, only
     Are like thy other hand, and cheek, and eye.
25   Such was my Phao[5] awhile, but shall be never,
     As thou wast, art, and, oh, mayst thou be ever.
Here lovers swear in their idolatry,
     That I am such; but grief discolors me.
And yet I grieve the less, lest grief remove
30 My beauty, and make me unworthy of thy love.
Plays some soft boy with thee, oh there wants yet
     A mutual feeling which should sweeten it.
His chin, a thorny hairy unevenness
     Doth threaten, and some daily change possess.
35 Thy body is a natural paradise,
     In whose self, unmanured,° all pleasure lies,   *untilled, unfertilized*
Nor needs perfection,[6] why shouldst thou then
     Admit the tillage of a harsh rough man?
Men leave behind them that which their sin shows,
40   And are as thieves traced, which rob when it snows.
But of our dalliance no more signs there are,
     Than fishes leave in streams, or birds in air.
And between us all sweetness may be had;
     All, all that Nature yields, or Art can add.
45 My two lips, eyes, thighs, differ from thy two,
     But so, as thine from one another do;
And, oh, no more; the likeness being such,
     Why should they not alike in all parts touch?
Hand to strange hand, lip to lip none denies;
50   Why should they breast to breast, or thighs to thighs?
Likeness begets such strange self-flattery,

---

3. I.e., when I compare you to gods it is they who are exalted by the comparison.
4. The traditional belief that man is a microcosm containing in himself everything that is in the entire world, the macrocosm.
5. Sappho was said to have loved a handsome youth named Phaon.
6. A woman was said to receive "perfection" only when she married and had sex with her husband.

That touching myself, all seems done to thee.
Myself I embrace, and mine own hands I kiss,
    And amorously thank myself for this.
55 Me, in my glass,° I call thee; but alas,   *mirror*
    When I would kiss, tears dim mine eyes, and glass.
O cure this loving madness, and restore
    Me to me; thee, my half,[7] my all, my more.
So may thy cheeks' red outwear scarlet dye,[8]
60   And their white, whiteness of the galaxy,°   *the milky way*
So may thy mighty, amazing beauty move
    Envy in all women, and in all men, love,
And so be change, and sickness, far from thee,
    As thou by coming near, keep'st them from me.

                                                                    1633

An Anatomy of the World: The First Anniversary

Donne composed and published this poem in 1611 to mark the first anniversary of the death of Elizabeth Drury, fifteen-year-old daughter of his patron and friend Sir Robert Drury. On the actual occasion of her death he composed a "Funeral Elegy," and on the second anniversary he wrote a companion poem to this one, titled *The Progress of the Soul: The Second Anniversary*, publishing all three poems together in 1612. This is not a poem about personal grief: responding to criticism of his wildly hyperbolic praises of Elizabeth, Donne commented that he had never met the young woman but intended rather to describe "the idea of a woman, and not as she was." Nor is this merely a poem to please a patron, though Donne obviously hoped to do that. Rather, as the full title indicates, Donne took the occasion of Elizabeth's untimely death to analyze (the term "anatomy" evokes both a rigorous logical analysis and a medical dissection in an anatomy theater) the corruption, decay, and disintegration of the world in all its aspects, due ultimately to the Fall of humankind. Here, the death of the young virgin Elizabeth epitomizes that loss and all its dire effects; in *The Second Anniversary* her death figures the soul's progress to heavenly glory. The marginal glosses on the left-hand side are by Donne, added in 1612.

An Anatomy of the World: The First Anniversary

The entry into the work.

When that rich soul which to her heaven is gone,
Whom all they celebrate who know they have one
    (For who is sure he hath a soul, unless
    It see, and judge, and follow worthiness,
    And by deeds praise it? He who doth not this,   5
    May lodge an inmate soul, but 'tis not his);
When that queen ended here her progress time,[1]
And, as to her standing house,[2] to heaven did climb,
    Where, loath to make the saints attend° her long,   *await*
    She's now a part both of the choir and song,   10

---

7. Some manuscripts read "heart."
8. Sappho promises that her verse will preserve her lover's beauty and its fame.
1. "That queen" is the soul of Elizabeth Drury,

implicitly compared to Queen Elizabeth, who liked to go on "progresses," formal visits from one country house to another.
2. I.e., her royal palace or permanent residence.

This world in that great earthquake languishèd;
For in a common bath of tears it bled,
Which drew the strongest vital spirits[3] out:
But succored° then with a perplexèd doubt,   *comforted*
Whether the world did lose or gain in this   15
(Because since now no other way there is
But goodness to see her, whom all would see,
All must endeavor to be good as she),
This great consumption° to a fever turned, *wasting disease*
And so the world had fits; it joyed, it mourned. 20
And as men think that agues physic are,[4]
And the ague being spent, give over care,
So thou, sick world, mistak'st thyself to be
Well, when, alas, thou art in a lethargy.° *in a near-death coma*
Her death did wound and tame thee then, and then 25
Thou might'st have better spared the sun, or man;
That wound was deep, but 'tis more misery
That thou hast lost thy sense and memory.
'Twas heavy° then to hear thy voice of moan, *sad, depressing*
But this is worse, that thou art speechless grown. 30
Thou hast forgot thy name thou hadst; thou wast
Nothing but she, and her thou hast o'erpast.° *outlined*
For as a child kept from the font,° until *baptismal font*
A prince, expected long, come to fulfill
The ceremonies, thou unnamed had'st laid, 35
Had not her coming, thee her palace made:[5]
Her name defined thee, gave thee form and frame,
And thou forget'st to celebrate thy name.
 Some months she hath been dead (but being dead,
Measures of times are all determinèd),° *ceased*
But long she hath been away, long, long, yet none
Offers to tell us who it is that's gone.
But as in states doubtful of future heirs,
When sickness without remedy impairs
The present prince, they're loath it should be said 45
The prince doth languish, or the prince is dead:
So mankind, feeling now a general thaw,° *melting, disintegration*
A strong example gone, equal to law,
The cèment which did faithfully compact
And glue all virtues, now resolved,° and slacked, *dissolved*
Thought it some blasphemy to say she was dead,
Or that our weakness was discoverèd° *disclosed*
In that confession; therefore spoke no more
Than tongues, the soul being gone, the loss deplore.
But though it be too late to succor thee, 55
Sick world, yea, dead, yea, putrefied, since she,
Thy intrinsic balm[6] and thy preservative,

---

3. "Vital spirits" of the blood were mysterious agents supposed to link soul with body.
4. "Ague" is chills and fever. "Physic": medicine. Some people think the fever stage of the disease is itself a cure.

5. The sick world is still being addressed; until it was made her palace, the world was a nameless nothing.
6. A medicine that preserved one in perfect health forever.

Can never be renewed, thou never live,
I (since no man can make thee live) will try
What we may gain by thy anatomy.[7]   60
Her death hath taught us dearly that thou art
Corrupt and mortal in thy purest part.
    Let no man say, the world itself being dead,
'Tis labor lost to have discovered
The world's infirmities, since there is none   65
Alive to study this dissection;

What life the world hath still.   For there's a kind of world remaining still,
Though she which did inanimate and fill
The world be gone, yet in this last long night,
Her ghost doth walk; that is, a glimmering light,   70
A faint weak love of virtue and of good
Reflects from her on them which understood
Her worth; and though she have shut in all day,
The twilight of her memory doth stay;
Which, from the carcass of the old world free,   75
Creates a new world; and new creatures be
Produced:[8] the matter and the stuff of this,
Her virtue, and the form our practice is;
And though to be thus elemented,° arm   *constituted*
These creatures, from home-born intrinsic harm   80
(For all assumed° unto this dignity   *raised*
So many weedless Paradises be,
Which of themselves produce no venomous sin,
Except some foreign serpent bring it in),
Yet, because outward storms the strongest break,   85
And strength itself by confidence grows weak,
This new world may be safer, being told

The sickness of the world.   The dangers and diseases of the old:
For with due temper men do then forgo
Or covet things, when they their true worth know.   90

Impossibility of health   There is no health; physicians say that we
At best enjoy but a neutrality.
And can there be worse sickness than to know
That we are never well, nor can be so?
We are born ruinous;° poor mothers cry   *falling into ruin*
That children come not right, nor orderly,
Except they headlong come and fall upon
An ominous precipitation.[9]
How witty's° ruin! How importunate   *ingenious is*
Upon mankind! It labored to frustrate   100
Even God's purpose; and made woman, sent
For man's relief, cause of his languishment.
They were to good ends, and they are so still,
But accessory, and principal in ill.[1]

---

7. I.e., by dissecting and analyzing the world's corpse.
8. The sun was thought to have power to breed new life out of carcasses and mud.
9. "We do not make account that a child comes right, except it come with the head forward, and

thereby prefigure that headlong falling into calamities which it must suffer after" (Donne, *Sermons*, ed. Potter and Simpson, 4.333).
1. Women are only helpers in good but leaders in evil. "That first marriage" (line 105): Adam and Eve's.

For that first marriage was our funeral: 105
One woman at one blow then killed us all,
And singly, one by one, they kill us now.
We do delightfully ourselves allow
To that consumption; and profusely blind,
We kill ourselves to propagate our kind.[2]   110
    And yet we do not that; we are not men:
There is not now that mankind which was then
When as the sun and man did seem to strive

Shortness of life. (Joint tenants[3] of the world) who should survive;
When stag and raven and the long-lived tree,   115
Compared with man, died in minority;[4]
When, if a slow-paced star had stolen away
From the observer's marking, he might stay
Two or three hundred years to see it again,
And then make up his observation plain;   120
When, as the age was long, the size was great;
Man's growth confessed and recompensed the meat;[5]
So spacious and large, that every soul
Did a fair kingdom and large realm control;
And when the very stature, thus erect,   125
Did that soul a good way towards heaven direct.
Where is this mankind now? Who lives to age
Fit to be made Methusalem his page?
Alas, we scarce live long enough to try
Whether a new-made clock run right, or lie.   130
Old grandsires talk of yesterday with sorrow,
And for our children we reserve tomorrow.
So short is life that every peasant strives,
In a torn house, or field, to have three lives.[6]
    And as in lasting, so in length is man   135

Smallness of stature. Contracted to an inch, who was a span;[7]
For had a man at first in forests strayed,
Or shipwrecked in the sea, one would have laid
A wager that an elephant or whale
That met him would not hastily assail   140
A thing so equal to him: now, alas,
The fairies and the pygmies well may pass
As credible; mankind decays so soon,
We're scarce our fathers' shadows cast at noon.
Only death adds to our length:[8] nor are we grown   145
In stature to be men, till we are none.
But this were light,° did our less volume hold   *a trifle*
All the old text, or had we changed to gold

2. Popular superstition had it that every act of sex shortened one's life by a day.
3. Joint owners. The survivor would enjoy sole ownership.
4. Stags, ravens, and oak trees were thought to live particularly long, but compared with early humans, they died in youth.
5. Early humans were thought to have eaten better than modern humans, lived longer, and grown to greater stature. Methuselah ("Methusalem," below) is said to have lived 969 years (Genesis 5.27).
6. Leases of farmland were often made for "three lives," i.e., through the longest-lived of three designated persons.
7. I.e., the distance from the tip of the thumb to the tip of the little finger, about nine inches.
8. The corpse of a person was said to measure a little more than his or her height when alive.

Their silver; or disposed into less glass
Spirits of virtue,[9] which then scattered was.   150
But 'tis not so: we're not retired, but damped;[1]
And as our bodies, so our minds are cramped:
'Tis shrinking, not close weaving, that hath thus
In mind and body both bedwarfèd us.
We seem ambitious, God's whole work to undo;   155
Of nothing He made us, and we strive, too,
To bring ourselves to nothing back; and we
Do what we can to do it so soon as He.
With new diseases[2] on ourselves we war,
And with new physic,[3] a worse engine° far.   *contrivance*
    Thus man, this world's vice-emperor, in whom
All faculties, all graces are at home—
And if in other creatures they appear,
They're but man's ministers and legates there,
To work on their rebellions, and reduce   165
Them to civility, and to man's use—
This man, whom God did woo, and loath to attend°   *wait*
Till man came up, did down to man descend,
This man, so great, that all that is, is his,
Oh what a trifle, and poor thing he is!   170
If man were anything, he's nothing now:
Help, or at least some time to waste, allow°   *one might give*
To his other wants, yet when he did depart°   *part*
With her whom we lament, he lost his heart.
    She, of whom th' ancients seemed to prophesy   175
When they called virtues by the name of *she*;[4]
She in whom virtue was so much refined
That for allay° unto so pure a mind   *alloy*
She took the weaker sex, she that could drive
The poisonous tincture, and the stain of Eve,   180
Out of her thoughts and deeds, and purify
All, by a true religious alchemy;
She, she is dead; she's dead: when thou knowest this,
Thou knowest how poor a trifling thing man is.
And learn'st thus much by our anatomy,   185
The heart being perished, no part can be free.
And that except thou feed (not banquet)[5] on
The supernatural food, religion,
Thy better growth grows witherèd and scant,
Be more than man, or thou'rt less than an ant.   190
    Then, as mankind, so is the world's whole frame
Quite out of joint, almost created lame:
For, before God had made up all the rest,
Corruption entered and depraved the best.

---

9. I.e., distilled virtue, which would fit into a smaller bottle. "Virtue" includes the sense of "power" as well as that of "goodness."
1. I.e., not compressed but shrunk.
2. I.e., influenza, and especially syphilis.
3. New medications—said to be far worse than the diseases they ostensibly combated.
4. The virtues are all represented in Latin by feminine nouns and portrayed as female figures.
5. Taste, nibble. A banquet usually contained desserts and delicacies.

It seized the angels,[6] and then first of all   195
The world did in her cradle take a fall,
And turned her brains, and took a general maim,
Wronging each joint of th' universal frame.
The noblest part, man, felt it first; and then
Decay of nature in Both beasts and plants, cursed in the curse of man.[7]   200
other parts.
So did the world from the first hour decay,
That evening was beginning of the day,[8]
And now the springs and summers which we see
Like sons of women after fifty be.[9]
And new philosophy calls all in doubt: 205
The element of fire is quite put out;[1]
The sun is lost, and the earth, and no man's wit°   *intellect*
Can well direct him where to look for it.
And freely men confess that this world's spent,°   *exhausted*
When in the planets and the firmament°   *sky*
They seek so many new;[2] they see that this
Is crumbled out again to his atomies.°   *atoms*
'Tis all in pieces, all coherence gone;
All just supply, and all relation:
Prince, subject; father, son,[3] are things forgot,   215
For every man alone thinks he hath got
To be° a phoenix, and that there can be   *has become*
None of that kind of which he is, but he.[4]
    This is the world's condition now, and now
She that should all parts to reunion bow,   220
She that had all magnetic force alone,
To draw and fasten sundered parts in one;
She whom wise nature had invented then
When she observed that every sort of men
Did in their voyage in this world's sea stray,   225
And needed a new compass for their way;
She that was best, and first original
Of all fair copies, and the general
Steward to Fate;[5] she whose rich eyes and breast
Gilt the West Indies, and perfumed the East;[6]   230
Whose having breathed in this world did bestow
Spice on those isles, and bade them still smell so,
And that rich Indie which doth gold inter
Is but as single money,° coined from her;   *small change*
She to whom this world must itself refer   235

6. The angels who fell from heaven with Satan and became demons. As purely intellectual beings, angels are the world's "brains" (line 197).
7. For a similar account of the way humankind's fall corrupted the physical universe, see *Paradise Lost* 10.706ff.
8. The world's day began with the darkness of sin.
9. Women giving birth after the age of fifty were thought to produce feeble or defective children.
1. The Polish astronomer Copernicus in the 16th century and the Italian Galileo in the 17th argued a "new philosophy," that the sun, not the earth, was the center of the cosmos. This theory also contradicted the notion that a realm of fire surrounded the earth beyond the air.
2. Galileo's first accounts of his telescope observations were published in 1610, intensifying speculations as to whether there were other inhabited worlds.
3. I.e., all traditional relationships.
4. Legend had it that there was only one phoenix on earth at any one time.
5. Fate or Providence disposes all things, but she was their "Steward," dispensing what has been decreed.
6. The West Indies were a source of gold, the East Indies a source of spices and perfumes.

As suburbs, or the microcosm of her,
She, she is dead; she's dead: when thou know'st this,
Thou know'st how lame a cripple this world is.
And learn'st thus much by our anatomy,
That this world's general sickness doth not lie   240
In any humor,[7] or one certain part;
But, as thou sawest it rotten at the heart,
Thou seest a hectic° fever hath got hold   *consumptive*
Of the whole substance, not to be controlled,
And that thou hast but one way not to admit   245
The world's infection, to be none of it.
For the world's subtlest immaterial parts
Feel this consuming wound, and age's darts.
For the world's beauty is decayed, or gone,
Deformity of parts.   Beauty, that's color and proportion.   250
We think the heavens enjoy their spherical
Their round proportion embracing all,[8]
But yet their various and perplexed° course,   *tangled, involuted*
Observed in divers ages doth enforce
Men to find out° so many eccentric parts,   *invent* 255
Such divers downright lines, such overthwarts,
As disproportion that pure form.[9] It tears
The firmament in eight and forty shires[1]
And in those constellations there arise
New stars, and old do vanish from our eyes,[2]   260
As though heaven suffered earthquakes, peace or war,
When new towns rise, and old demolished are.
They have impaled° within a zodiac[3]   *enclosed, imprisoned*
The freeborn sun, and keep twelve signs awake
To watch his steps, the Goat and Crab[4] control,   265
And fright him back, who else to either pole
(Did not those tropics fetter him) might run:
For his course is not round, nor can the sun
Perfect a circle, or maintain his way
One inch direct, but where he rose today   270
He comes no more,[5] but with a cozening° line,   *deceptive*
Steals by that point, and so is serpentine.

---

7. The four bodily "humors"—blood, phlegm, bile, choler—were thought to combine to make up a temperament; when they are out of balance a person is ill. So with the world.
8. The heavenly spheres' "course" was traditionally supposed to be "spherical," "round," but deviations and irregular motions ("eccentric parts," line 255) had long been recognized in the Ptolemaic system, and elliptical movements were posited by recent astronomers like Kepler.
9. Plato wrote that the heavenly bodies moved in perfect circles, (a "pure form"). The "disproportion" of that form is marked in astronomical charts, with vertical ("downright") lines that crisscross horizontal lines ("overthwarts").
1. In the Ptolemaic system, the stars were divided into forty-eight constellations.
2. The traditional understanding was that the heavens are not subject to change. The modern astronomers Kepler and Brahe discovered "new stars" and Galileo's *Siderius Nuncius* (1610) revealed the discovery of four satellites of Jupiter and innumerable fixed stars. Other stars were observed to disappear.
3. A great circle of twelve star-groups (Aquarius, Pisces, Cancer, Capricorn, etc.) through which the sun passes in its supposed annual movement from west to east and north to south.
4. The Tropic of Capricorn (the "Goat") marks the sun's winter solstice and the Tropic of Cancer (the "Crab") its summer solstice, the points farthest north and south in its apparent annual journey.
5. The sun's path crosses the equator at a point slightly farther on each year, deviating from a circular path in a "serpentine" motion.

And seeming weary with his reeling thus,
He means to sleep, being now fall'n nearer us.[6]
So, of the stars which boast that they do run   275
In circle still, none ends where he begun.
All their proportion's lame, it sinks, it swells,
For of meridians, and parallels,[7]
Man hath weaved out a net, and this net thrown
Upon the heavens, and now they are his own.   280
Loth to go up the hill,[8] or labor thus
To go to heaven, we make heaven come to us.
We spur, we rein the stars, and to their race
They're diversely content t'obey our pace.
But keeps the earth her round proportion still?   285
Doth not a Tenerife,[9] or higher hill
Rise so high like a rock, that one might think
The floating moon would shipwreck there, and sink?
Seas are so deep, that whales being struck° today,   *harpooned*
Perchance tomorrow, scarce at middle way   290
Of their wished journey's end, the bottom, die.
And men, to sound depths, so much line untie
As one might think that there would rise
At end thereof, one of th'Antipodes.[1]
If under all, a vault infernal[2] be,   295
(Which sure is spacious,° except that we   *three syllables*
Invent another torment, that there must
Millions into a strait° hot room be thrust)   *narrow*
Then solidness, and roundness have no place.
Are these but warts, and pock-holes in the face   300
Of the earth? Think so. But yet confess, in this,
The world's proportion° disfigured is,   *four syllables*

Disorder in the
world. That those two legs whereon it doth rely,
Reward and punishment, are bent awry.°   *out of shape*
And oh! It can no more be questioned°   *three syllables* 305
That beauty's best, proportion, is dead,
Since even grief itself, which now alone
Is left us, is without proportion.
She by whose lines proportion should be
Examined, measure of all symmetry,   310
Whom had that Ancient[3] seen, who thought souls made
Of harmony, he would at next have said
That harmony was she, and thence infer
That souls were but resultances° from her   *emanations*
And did from her into our bodies go   315

As to our eyes, the forms from objects flow.[4]
She, who if those great Doctors truly said
That th'Ark to man's proportions was made,[5]
Had been a type for that, as that might be
A type of her in this, that contrary   320
Both elements and passions lived at peace
In her, who caused all civil wars to cease.
She, after whom, what form soe'er we see
Is discord, and rude incongruity.
She, she is dead, she's dead, when thou know'st this   325
Thou know'st how vile a monster this world is,
And learn'st thus much by our Anatomy,
That here is nothing to enamour thee;
And that, not onely faults in inward parts,
Corruptions in our brains, or in our hearts,   330
Poisoning the fountains whence our actions spring
Endanger us, but that if everything
Be not done fitly'nd in proportion
To satisfy wise and good lookers on
(Since most men be such as most think they be)   335
They're loathsome too, by this deformity,
For good, and well,° must in our actions meet: *seemly, decorous*
Wicked is not much worse than indiscreet.
But beauty's other second element,
Color, and luster now, is as neer spent   340
And had the world his just proportion,
Were it a ring still, yet the stone is gone.
As a compassionate turquoise which doth tell
By looking pale, the wearer is not well,[6]
As gold falls sick being stung with mercury[7]   345
All the world's parts of such complexion be.
When nature was most busie, the first week,[8]
Swaddling the newborn earth, God seemed to like
That she should sport herself sometimes, and play
To mingle, and vary colors every day.   350
And then, as though she could not make enow°   *enough*
Himself his various° rainbow did allow.   *multicolored*
Sight is the noblest sense of any one,
Yet sight hath only color to feed on,
And color is decayed: summer's robe grows   355
Dusky, and like an oft-dyed garment shows.
Our blushing red, which used in cheeks to spread,
Is inward sunk, and only our souls are red.[9]
Perchance the world might have recovered,

---

4. A theory ascribed to Aristotle held that objects emit rays that imprint the forms of those objects upon our eyes and mind.
5. Both Ambrose and Augustine held that Noah's Ark was built to the proportions of the human body, so "she" can be said to be a type of the Ark, and the Ark (in regard to the harmony of the animals it contained) a type of her.
6. The turquoise was believed to gain or lose luster reflecting the wearer's state of health.
7. An amalgam of gold and mercury is lighter in color, and of much less value, than pure gold.
8. The six days of creation described in Genesis 1, when the earth was clothed ("swaddled," like a newborn) with all forms of life.
9. Blushing red indicates innocence; souls are red with sin and guilt.

If she, whom we lament had not been dead. 360
But she, in whom all white, and red, and blue[1]
(Beauty's ingredients) voluntary grew,
As in an unvexed Paradise;° from whom   *unfallen Eden*
Did all things verdure,° and their luster come,   *grow green*
Whose composition was miraculous, 365
Being all color, all diaphanous
(For air and fire but thick gross bodies were,[2]
And liveliest stones but drowsy and pale to her,)
She, she is dead, she's dead: when thou know'st this,
Thou know'st how wan a ghost this our world is, 370
And learn'st thus much by our anatomy,
That it should more affright, than pleasure thee.
And that, since all faire color then did sink,
Tis now but wicked vanity to think
To color vicious deeds with good pretence, 375
Or with bought colors to elude° men's sense,   *deceive*

Weakness in the want of correspondence of heaven and earth.

Nor in ought more this world's decay appears,
Than that her influence the heav'n forbears,
Or that the elements do not feel this.
The father, or the mother, barren is.[3] 380
The clouds conceive not rain, or do not pour
In the due birth-time down their balmy[4] shower.
Th'air doth not motherly sit on the earth,
To hatch her seasons, and give all things birth,
Spring-times were common cradles, but are tombs, 385
And false conceptions° fill the general womb.   *abortions,*
Th'air shows such meteors,[5] as none can see,   *monsters*
Not only what they mean, but what they be.
Earth such new worms, as would have troubled much
Th'Egyptian mages to have made more such.[6] 390
What artist° now dares boast that he can bring   *alchemist or*
Heaven hither, or constellate[7] anything   *astrologer*
So as the influence of those stars may be
Imprisoned in an herb, or charm, or tree,
And do by touch all which those stars could do? 395
The art is lost, and correspondence[8] too.
For heaven gives little, and the earth takes less,
And man least knows their trade, and purposes.
If this commerce twixt heaven and earth were not
Embarred,° and all this traffic quite forgot,   *stopped, blocked* 400
She, for whose loss we have lamented thus,
Would work more fully and pow'rfully on us.
Since herbs and roots by dying, lose not all,

---

1. White symbolizes innocence, red, love, and blue, truth.
2. Air and fire were thought to be the lightest and purest of the four elements.
3. Either the stars and planets (the Father) withhold their influence or the earth's elements (the Mother) are not receptive, making for barrenness.
4. Balm was thought to preserve and heal.

5. Especially comets, thought to portend disaster.
6. Egyptian magicians ("mages") turned their rods into serpents ("worms"), Exodus 7.10–12.
7. Bring the stars together, or judge when their conjunction is favorable.
8. The close link between heaven and earth, so that the powers of the various heavenly bodies are contained ("imprisoned") in particular herbs or stones, which can cure by "touch."

But they, yea ashes too, are medicinal,[9]
Death could not quench her virtue[1] so, but that   405
It would be (if not followed) wondered at:
And all the world would be one dying swan,[2]
To sing her funeral praise, and vanish then.
But as some serpents' poison hurteth not,
Except it be from the live serpent shot,[3]   410
So doth her virtue need her here, to fit
That unto us; she working more than it.
But she, in whom, to such maturity
Virtue was grown, past growth, that it must die,
She from whose influence all impressions came,   415
But, by receivers' impotencies, lame,
Who, though she could not transubstantiate°   *change the*
All states to gold, yet gilded every state,   *substance of*
So that some princes have some temperance,
Some counselors some purpose to advance   420
The common profit; and some people have
Some stay,° no more than kings should give, to crave;   *restraint*
Some women have some taciturnity,
Some nunneries, some grains of chastity.
She, that thus much, and much more could do,   425
But that our age was iron, and rusty too,[4]
She, she is dead, she's dead: when thou know'st this
Thou know'st how dry a cinder this world is.
And learn'st thus much by our Anatomy,
That 'tis in vain to dew, or mollify°   *soften*   430
It with thy tears, or sweat, or blood: no thing
Is worth our travail, grief, or perishing,
But those rich joys, which did possess her heart,
Of which she's now partaker, and a part.

Conclusion.   But as in cutting up a man that's dead,   435
The body will not last out to have read
On every part, and therefore men direct
Their speech to parts that are of most effect;
So the world's carcass would not last, if I
Were punctual° in this Anatomy.   *detailed, point by point*   440
Nor smells it well to hearers, if one tell
Them their disease, who fain would think they're well.
Here therefore be the end: And, blessed maid,
Of whom is meant whatever hath been said,
Or shall be spoken well by any tongue,   445
Whose name refines coarse lines, and makes prose song,
Accept this tribute, and his first year's rent,
Who till his dark short taper's° end be spent,   *candle*

9. Healing power was thought to remain in certain dead herbs and roots, as well as in their ashes after burning.
1. Power, goodness.
2. Swans were believed to sing just once, before their deaths.
3. The allusion conflates the poison with which the first serpent (Satan) infected humankind, with the curative power against snakebite pos-

sessed by the serpent of brass that Moses raised up to cure the Israelites (Numbers 21.6–9)—identified by Christian biblical commentators as a type of Christ.
4. The present is the last of the legendary four ages—gold, silver, bronze, and iron—through which history was said to pass, each marking a decline.

As oft as thy feast° sees this widowed earth,   *saint's feastday*
Will yearly celebrate thy second birth,   450
That is, thy death. For though the soul of man
Be got when man is made, 'tis born but then
When man doth die. Our body's as the womb,
And as a midwife death directs it home.
And you her creatures, whom she works upon   455
And have your last, and best concoction°   *purification (in*
From her example, and her virtue, if you   *alchemy)*
In reverence to her, do think it due
That no one should her praises thus rehearse,
As matter fit for chronicle, not verse,[5]   460
Vouchsafe to call to mind, that God did make
A last, and lasting'st piece, a song.[6] He spake
To Moses, to deliver unto all
That song: because He knew they would let fall
The Law, the Prophets, and the History,[7]   465
But keep the song still in their memory.
Such an opinion (in due measure) made
Me this great office boldly to invade.
Nor could incomprehensibleness deter
Me from thus trying to imprison her.   470
Which when I saw that a strict grave could do,
I saw not why verse might not do so too.
Verse hath a middle nature: heaven keeps souls,
The grave keeps bodies, verse the fame enrolls.

1611

From Holy Sonnets[1]

1

Thou hast made me, and shall thy work decay?
Repair me now, for now mine end doth haste;
I run to death, and death meets me as fast,
And all my pleasures are like yesterday.
5   I dare not move my dim eyes any way,
Despair behind, and death before doth cast
Such terror, and my feeble flesh doth waste
By sin in it, which it towards hell doth weigh.°   *incline, weigh down*
Only thou art above, and when towards thee

---

5. "Chronicle" history is the appropriate genre for recording the great events of rulers and kingdoms; verse can treat themes of love and other private matters. Cf. Donne's "Canonization," lines 31–34.
6. The Mosaic song in Deuteronomy 32.1–43 celebrating God's mercy to the Israelites, and threat of vengeance against them if they abandon him.
7. The books of the Hebrew Bible were often divided into these three categories.

1. Donne wrote a variety of religious poems (called "Divine Poems"), including a group of nineteen "Holy sonnets" that reflect his interest in Jesuit and Protestant meditative procedures. He probably began writing them about 1609, a decade or so after leaving the Catholic Church. Our selections follow the traditional numbering established in Sir Herbert Grierson's influential edition, since for most of these sonnets we cannot tell when they were written or in what order they were intended to appear.

10   By thy leave I can look, I rise again;
      But our old subtle foe so tempteth me
      That not one hour myself I can sustain.
      Thy grace may wing° me to prevent° his art,   *give wings to / forestall*
      And thou like adamant° draw mine iron heart.   *magnetic lodestone*

                                                         1635

5

      I am a little world[2] made cunningly
      Of elements, and an angelic sprite;°   *spirit, soul*
      But black sin hath betrayed to endless night
      My world's both parts, and O, both parts must die.
5   You which beyond that heaven which was most high
      Have found new spheres, and of new lands can write,[3]
      Pour new seas in mine eyes, that so I might
      Drown my world with my weeping earnestly,
      Or wash it if it must be drowned no more.[4]
10 But O, it must be burnt! Alas, the fire
      Of lust and envy have burnt it heretofore,
      And made it fouler; let their flames retire,
      And burn me, O Lord, with a fiery zeal
      Of thee and thy house, which doth in eating heal.[5]

                                                           1635

7

      At the round earth's imagined corners,[6] blow
      Your trumpets, angels; and arise, arise
      From death, you numberless infinities
      Of souls, and to your scattered bodies go:
5   All whom the flood did, and fire[7] shall, o'erthrow,
      All whom war, dearth,° age, agues,° tyrannies,   *famine / fevers*
      Despair, law, chance hath slain, and you whose eyes
      Shall behold God, and never taste death's woe.[8]
      But let them sleep, Lord, and me mourn a space;
10 For, if above all these, my sins abound,
      'Tis late to ask abundance of thy grace
      When we are there. Here on this lowly ground,
      Teach me how to repent; for that's as good
      As if thou hadst sealed my pardon with thy blood.

                                                           1633

2. The traditional idea of the human being as microcosm (a "little world"), containing in miniature all the features of the macrocosm, or great world.
3. Astronomers, especially Galileo, and explorers.
4. God promised Noah (Genesis 9.11) never to flood the earth again.
5. See Psalm 69.9: "For the zeal of thine house hath eaten me up." These lines refer to three kinds of flame—those of the Last Judgment, those of lust and envy, and those of zeal, which alone save.
6. Cf. Revelation 7.1: "I saw four angels standing on the four corners of the earth."
7. Noah's flood, and the universal conflagration at the end of the world (Revelation 6.11).
8. Those who will be alive at the Second Coming (cf. Luke 9.27).

9

If poisonous minerals, and if that tree[9]
Whose fruit threw death on else-immortal us,
If lecherous goats, if serpents envious[1]
Cannot be damned, alas! why should I be?
5   Why should intent or reason, born in me,
Make sins, else equal, in me more heinous?
And, mercy being easy and glorious
To God, in his stern wrath why threatens he?
But who am I that dare dispute with thee
10   O God? Oh, of thine only worthy blood
And my tears, make a heavenly Lethean[2] flood,
And drown in it my sin's black memory.
That thou remember them some claim as debt;
I think it mercy if thou wilt forget.[3]

1633

10

Death, be not proud, though some have callèd thee
Mighty and dreadful, for thou art not so;
For those whom thou think'st thou dost overthrow
Die not, poor Death, nor yet canst thou kill me.
5   From rest and sleep, which but thy pictures be,
Much pleasure; then from thee much more must flow,
And soonest our best men with thee do go,
Rest of their bones, and soul's delivery.[4]
Thou art slave to fate, chance, kings, and desperate men,
10   And dost with poison, war, and sickness dwell,
And poppy° or charms can make us sleep as well   *opium*
And better than thy stroke; why swell'st° thou then?   *puff with pride*
One short sleep past, we wake eternally
And death shall be no more; Death, thou shalt die.[5]

1633

11

Spit in my face ye Jews, and pierce my side,
Buffet, and scoff,° scourge, and crucify me,   *scoff at*
For I have sinned, and sinned, and only he,
Who could do no iniquity, hath died:
5   But by my death cannot be satisfied°   *atoned for*

---

9. The Tree of Knowledge of Good and Evil, whose fruit was forbidden to Adam and Eve in Eden.
1. Traits commonly associated with these creatures.
2. In classical mythology, the waters of the river Lethe in the underworld caused total forgetfulness.

3. Cf. Jeremiah 31.34: "I will forgive their iniquity, and I will remember their sins no more."
4. I.e., to find rest for their bones and freedom ("delivery") for their souls.
5. Cf. 1 Corinthians 15.26: "The last enemy that shall be destroyed is death."

My sins, which pass the Jews' impiety:
They killed once an inglorious° man, but I   *obscure*
Crucify him daily,[6] being now glorified.
Oh let me then, his strange love still admire:°   *wonder at*
10   Kings pardon, but he bore our punishment.[7]
And Jacob came clothed in vile harsh attire
But to supplant, and with gainful intent:[8]
God clothed himself in vile man's flesh, that so
He might be weak enough to suffer woe.

                                                                          1633

13

What if this present were the world's last night?
Mark in my heart, O soul, where thou dost dwell,
The picture of Christ crucified, and tell
Whether that countenance can thee affright.
5   Tears in his eyes quench the amazing light,
Blood fills his frowns, which from his pierced head fell;
And can that tongue adjudge thee unto hell
Which prayed forgiveness for his foes' fierce spite?
No, no; but as in my idolatry
10   I said to all my profane° mistresses,   *secular*
Beauty of pity, foulness only is
A sign of rigor:[9] so I say to thee,
To wicked spirits are horrid shapes assigned,
This beauteous form assures a piteous mind.

                                                                          1633

14

Batter my heart, three-personed God; for you
As yet but knock, breathe, shine, and seek to mend;
That I may rise and stand, o'erthrow me, and bend
Your force to break, blow, burn, and make me new.
5   I, like an usurped town, to another due,
Labor to admit you, but O, to no end;
Reason, your viceroy[1] in me, me should defend,
But is captived, and proves weak or untrue.
Yet dearly I love you, and would be loved fain,°   *gladly*
10   But am betrothed[2] unto your enemy.
Divorce me, untie or break that knot again;

---

6. Cf. Hebrews 6.6: "they [sinners] crucify to themselves the Son of God afresh."
7. Kings may pardon crimes, but the King of Kings, Christ, bore the punishment due to our sins.
8. Jacob disguised himself in goatskins to gain from his blind father the blessing belonging to the firstborn son, his brother Esau (Genesis 27.1–36).

9. In Neoplatonic theory, beautiful features are the sign of a compassionate mind, while ugliness signifies the contrary.
1. The governor in your stead.
2. Humanity's relationship with God has been described in terms of marriage and adultery from the time of the Hebrew prophets.

Take me to you, imprison me, for I,
Except° you enthrall me, never shall be free,   *unless*
Nor ever chaste, except you ravish[3] me.

    1633

17

Since she whom I loved hath paid her last debt[4]
To Nature, and to hers, and my good is dead,
And her soul early into heaven ravishèd,
Wholly on heavenly things my mind is set.
5   Here the admiring her my mind did whet
To seek thee, God; so streams do show the head;°   *source*
But though I have found thee, and thou my thirst hast fed,
A holy thirsty dropsy° melts me yet.   *immoderate thirst*
But why should I beg more love, whenas thou
10   Dost woo my soul, for hers offering all thine:
And dost not only fear lest I allow
My love to saints and angels, things divine,
But in thy tender jealousy dost doubt°   *fear*
Lest the world, flesh, yea, devil put thee out.

    1899

18

Show me, dear Christ, thy spouse[5] so bright and clear.
What! is it she which on the other shore
Goes richly painted? or which, robbed and tore,
Laments and mourns in Germany and here?[6]
5   Sleeps she a thousand, then peeps up one year?
Is she self-truth, and errs? now new, now outwore?
Doth she, and did she, and shall she evermore
On one, on seven, or on no hill appear?[7]
Dwells she with us, or like adventuring knights
10   First travel we to seek, and then make love?
Betray, kind husband, thy spouse to our sights,
And let mine amorous soul court thy mild dove,
Who is most true and pleasing to thee then
When she is embraced and open to most men.[8]

    1899

3. Rape, also overwhelm with wonder. "Enthrall": enslave, also enchant.

4. Donne's wife died in 1617 at the age of thirty-three, having just given birth to her twelfth child. This very personal sonnet and the following two survive in a single manuscript discovered only in 1892.

5. The church is commonly called the bride of Christ. Cf. Revelation 19.7–8: "The marriage of the Lamb is come, and his wife hath made herself ready. / And to her was granted that she should be arrayed in fine linen, clean and white."

6. I.e., the painted woman (the Church of Rome) or the ravished virgin (the Lutheran and Calvinist churches in Germany and England).

7. The church on one hill is probably Solomon's temple on Mount Moriah; that on seven hills is the Church of Rome; that on no hill is the Presbyterian church of Geneva.

8. The final lines wittily rework, with startling sexual associations, Song of Solomon 5.2: "Open to me, my sister, my love, my dove, my undefiled." That biblical book was often interpreted as the song of love between Christ and the church.

19

Oh, to vex me, contraries meet in one:
Inconstancy unnaturally hath begot
A constant habit; that when I would not
I change in vows, and in devotion.
5   As humorous° is my contrition   *subject to whim*
As my profane love, and as soon forgot:
As riddlingly distempered, cold and hot,⁹
As praying, as mute, as infinite, as none.
I durst not view heaven yesterday; and today
10   In prayers and flattering speeches I court God:
Tomorrow I quake with true fear of his rod.
So my devout fits come and go away
Like a fantastic ague:¹ save° that here   *except*
Those are my best days, when I shake with fear.

1899

Good Friday, 1613. Riding Westward

Let man's soul be a sphere, and then, in this,
The intelligence that moves, devotion is,¹
And as the other spheres, by being grown
Subject to foreign motions, lose their own,
5   And being by others hurried every day,
Scarce in a year their natural form² obey;
Pleasure or business, so, our souls admit
For° their first mover, and are whirled by it.   *instead of*
Hence is 't, that I am carried towards the West
10   This day, when my soul's form bends toward the East.
There I should see a Sun³ by rising, set,
And by that setting endless day beget:
But that Christ on this cross did rise and fall,
Sin had eternally benighted all.
15   Yet dare I almost be glad I do not see
That spectacle, of too much weight for me.
Who sees God's face, that is self-life, must die;⁴
What a death were it then to see God die?
It made his own lieutenant,° Nature, shrink;   *deputy*
20   It made his footstool crack, and the sun wink.⁵

9. Arising from the unbalanced humors, inexplicably changeable.
1. A fever, attended with paroxysms of hot and cold and trembling fits. "Fantastic": capricious, extravagant.
1. As angelic intelligences guide the celestial spheres, so devotion is or should be the guiding principle of the soul.
2. Their true moving principle or intelligence. The orbit of the celestial spheres was thought to be governed by an unmoving outermost sphere, the primum mobile, or first mover (line 8), but sometimes outside influences ("foreign motions," line 4) deflected the spheres from their correct orbits.
3. The "sun" / "Son" pun was an ancient one. Christ the Son of God "set" when he rose on the Cross, and that setting (death) gave rise to the Christian era and the promise of immortality.
4. God told Moses, "Thou canst not see my face, for there shall no man see me, and live" (Exodus 33.20).
5. An earthquake and eclipse supposedly accompanied the Crucifixion (Matthew 27.45, 51). Cf. Isaiah 66.1: "Thus saith the Lord, The heaven is my throne, and the earth is my footstool."

Could I behold those hands which span the poles,
And tune[6] all spheres at once, pierced with those holes?
Could I behold that endless height which is
Zenith to us, and t'our antipodes,[7]
25 Humbled below us? Or that blood which is
The seat° of all our souls, if not of his,   *dwelling place*
Make dirt of dust, or that flesh which was worn
By God for his apparel, ragg'd and torn?
If on these things I durst not look, durst I
30 Upon his miserable mother cast mine eye,
Who was God's partner here, and furnished thus
Half of that sacrifice which ransomed us?
Though these things, as I ride, be from° mine eye,   *away from*
They are present yet unto my memory,
35 For that looks towards them; and thou look'st towards me,
O Savior, as thou hang'st upon the tree.
I turn my back to thee but to receive
Corrections,[8] till thy mercies bid thee leave.°   *cease*
O think me worth thine anger; punish me;
40 Burn off my rusts and my deformity;
Restore thine image so much, by thy grace,
That thou may'st know me, and I'll turn my face.

1633

A Hymn to Christ, at the Author's Last Going into Germany[1]

In what torn ship soever I embark,
That ship shall be my emblem of thy ark;°   *Noah's ark*
What sea soever swallow me, that flood
Shall be to me an emblem of thy blood;
5 Though thou with clouds of anger do disguise
Thy face, yet through that mask I know those eyes,
    Which, though they turn away sometimes, they never will despise.

I sacrifice this island° unto thee,   *England*
And all whom I loved there, and who loved me;
10 When I have put our seas twixt them and me,
Put thou thy sea[2] betwixt my sins and thee.
As the tree's sap doth seek the root below
In winter, in my winter now I go
    Where none but thee, th' eternal root of true love, I may know.

15 Nor thou nor thy religion dost control°   *censure, restrain*
The amorousness of an harmonious soul,

---

6. Some manuscripts read "turn."
7. God is at once the highest point for us and for our "antipodes," those who live on the opposite side of the earth.
8. Suggests a flogging.
1. Donne went to Germany in 1619 as chaplain to the Earl of Doncaster. The mission was a diplomatic one, to the king and queen of Bohemia, King James's son-in-law and daughter, who at that time were mainstays of the Protestant cause on the Continent.
2. Sea of Christ's blood.

But thou wouldst have that love thyself; as thou
Art jealous, Lord, so I am jealous now.
Thou lov'st not, till from loving more[3] thou free
20 My soul; whoever gives, takes liberty;
　　Oh, if thou car'st not whom I love, alas, thou lov'st not me.

Seal then this bill of my divorce to all
On whom those fainter beams of love did fall;
Marry those loves which in youth scattered be
25 On fame, wit, hopes (false mistresses) to thee.
Churches are best for prayer that have least light:
To see God only, I go out of sight,
　　And to 'scape stormy days, I choose an everlasting night.

1633

Hymn to God My God, in My Sickness[1]

Since I am coming to that holy room
　　Where, with thy choir of saints for evermore,
I shall be made thy music; as I come
　　I tune the instrument here at the door,
5　　And what I must do then, think now before.[2]

Whilst my physicians by their love are grown
　　Cosmographers, and I their map, who lie
Flat on this bed, that by them may be shown
　　That this is my southwest discovery[3]
10　　*Per fretum febris,*[4] by these straits to die,

I joy, that in these straits, I see my West;
　　For, though their currents yield return to none,
What shall my West hurt me? As West and East
　　In all flat maps (and I am one) are one,[5]
15　　So death doth touch the resurrection.

Is the Pacific Sea my home? Or are
　　The Eastern riches?° Is Jerusalem?　　　　　*Cathay, China*
Anyan,[6] and Magellan, and Gibraltar,
　　All straits, and none but straits, are ways to them,
20　　Whether where Japhet dwelt, or Cham, or Shem.[7]

3. From loving any other thing.
1. Though Izaak Walton, Donne's friend and biographer, assigns this poem to the last days of his life, it was probably written during another illness, in December 1623.
2. This and the previous poem are less hymns (songs of praise) than meditations preparing (tuning the instrument) for such hymns.
3. South is the region of heat, west the region of sunset and death.
4. Through the straits of fever, with a pun on straits as sufferings, rigors, and a geographical reference to the Strait of Magellan.
5. If a flat map is pasted on a round globe, west and east meet.
6. Anian, a strait on the west coast of America, shown on early maps as separating America from Asia.
7. The three sons of Noah by whom the world was repopulated after the Flood (Genesis 10). The descendants of Japhet were thought to inhabit Europe; those of Cham (Ham), Africa; and those of Shem, Asia.

We think that Paradise and Calvary,
   Christ's cross and Adam's tree, stood in one place;
Look, Lord and find both Adams[8] met in me;
   As the first Adam's sweat surrounds my face,
25   May the last Adam's blood my soul embrace.

So, in his purple wrapped,[9] receive me, Lord;
   By these his thorns° give me his other crown;   *crown of thorns*
And, as to others' souls I preached thy word,
   Be this my text, my sermon to mine own:
30   Therefore that he may raise the Lord throws down.

                        1635

A Hymn to God the Father[1]

Wilt thou forgive that sin where I begun,
   Which is my sin, though it were done before?[2]
Wilt thou forgive that sin through which I run,
   And do run still, though still I do deplore?
5   When thou hast done,[3] thou hast not done,
     For I have more.

Wilt thou forgive that sin by which I have won
   Others to sin? and made my sin their door?
Wilt thou forgive that sin which I did shun
10   A year or two, but wallowed in a score?
     When thou hast done, thou hast not done,
     For I have more.

I have a sin of fear, that when I have spun
   My last thread, I shall perish on the shore;
15   Swear by thy self, that at my death thy Son
   Shall shine as he shines now and heretofore;
     And, having done that, thou hast done,
     I fear[4] no more.

                        1633

8. Adam and Christ. Legend had it that Christ's cross was erected on the spot, or at least in the region, where the tree forbidden to Adam in Eden had stood.

9. In his blood, also in his kingly robes.

1. This hymn was used as a congregational hymn. Walton tells us that Donne wrote it during his illness of 1623, had it set to music, and was delighted to hear it performed (as it frequently was) by the choir of St. Paul's Cathedral.

2. I.e., he inherits the original sin of Adam and Eve.

3. In the refrains, Donne puns on his own name and may pun on his wife's maiden name, Ann More.

4. Some manuscripts read "have."

From Devotions upon Emergent Occasions[1]

Meditation 4

Medicusque vocatur.
The physician is sent for.[2]

It is too little to call man a little world; except God, man is a diminutive to nothing.[3] Man consists of more pieces, more parts, than the world; than the world doth, nay, than the world is. And if those pieces were extended and stretched out in man as they are in the world, man would be the giant and the world the dwarf; the world but the map, and the man the world. If all the veins in our bodies were extended to rivers, and all the sinews to veins of mines, and all the muscles that lie upon one another to hills, and all the bones to quarries of stones, and all the other pieces to the proportion of those which correspond to them in the world, the air would be too little for this orb of man to move in, the firmament would be but enough for this star. For as the whole world hath nothing to which something in man doth not answer,[4] so hath man many pieces of which the whole world hath no representation. Enlarge this meditation upon this great world, man, so far as to consider the immensity of the creatures this world produces. Our creatures are our thoughts, creatures that are born giants, that reach from east to west, from earth to heaven, that do not only bestride all the sea and land, but span the sun and firmament at once: my thoughts reach all, comprehend all.

Inexplicable mystery! I their creator am in a close prison, in a sick bed, anywhere, and any one of my creatures, my thoughts, is with the sun, and beyond the sun, overtakes the sun, and overgoes the sun in one pace, one step, everywhere. And then as the other world produces serpents and vipers, malignant and venomous creatures, and worms and caterpillars, that endeavor to devour that world which produces them, and monsters compiled and complicated[5] of divers parents and kinds, so this world, our selves, produces all these in us, in producing diseases and sicknesses of all those sorts; venomous and infectious diseases, feeding and consuming diseases, and manifold and entangled diseases made up of many several ones. And can the other world name so many venomous, so many consuming, so many monstrous creatures, as we can diseases of all these kinds? O miserable abundance, O beggarly riches! How much do we lack of having remedies for every disease, when as yet we have not names for them?

---

1. Donne's *Devotions* were composed in the aftermath of his serious illness in the winter of 1623, though Donne characteristically writes as if the events of the illness were happening as he describes them. The *Devotions* recount in twenty-three sections the stages ("emergent occasions") of the illness and recovery: the term associates the exercise with a popular kind of Protestant meditation on the occasions that daily life presents to us. Each section contains a "meditation upon our human condition," an "expostulation and debatement with God," and a prayer to God. The book was published almost immediately, offering its meditation on an intensely personal experience as exemplary for others.

2. Donne's Latin epigraphs are followed by his English translations, often quite free.

3. This meditation is based on the notion that each human being is a microcosm, a little world, analogous in every respect to the macrocosm, or great world. But in playing with this notion, Donne paradoxically reverses it.

4. Correspond.

5. Mixed.

But we have a Hercules against these giants, these monsters: that is the physician. He musters up all the forces of the other world to succor this, all nature to relieve man. We have the physician but we are not the physician. Here we shrink in our proportion, sink in our dignity in respect of very mean creatures who are physicians to themselves. The hart that is pursued and wounded, they say, knows an herb which, being eaten, throws off the arrow: a strange kind of vomit.[6] The dog that pursues it, though he be subject to sickness, even proverbially knows his grass that recovers him. And it may be true that the drugger is as near to man as to other creatures; it may be that obvious and present simples,[7] easy to be had, would cure him; but the apothecary is not so near him, nor the physician so near him, as they two are to other creatures.[8] Man hath not that innate instinct to apply these natural medicines to his present danger, as those inferior creatures have. He is not his own apothecary, his own physician, as they are. Call back therefore thy meditation again, and bring it down.[9] What's become of man's great extent and proportion, when himself shrinks himself and consumes himself to a handful of dust? What's become of his soaring thoughts, his compassing thoughts, when himself brings himself to the ignorance, to the thoughtlessness, of the grave? His diseases are his own, but the physician is not; he hath them at home, but he must send for the physician.

Meditation 17

Nunc lento sonitu dicunt, morieris.
Now this bell tolling softly for another, says to me,
Thou must die.

Perchance he for whom this bell[1] tolls may be so ill as that he knows not it tolls for him; and perchance I may think myself so much better than I am, as that they who are about me and see my state may have caused it to toll for me, and I know not that. The church is catholic, universal, so are all her actions; all that she does belongs to all. When she baptizes a child, that action concerns me; for that child is thereby connected to that head which is my head too, and ingrafted into that body[2] whereof I am a member. And when she buries a man, that action concerns me: all mankind is of one author and is one volume; when one man dies, one chapter is not torn out of the book, but translated[3] into a better language; and every chapter must be so translated. God employs several translators; some pieces are translated by age, some by sickness, some by war, some by justice; but God's hand is in every translation, and his hand shall bind up all our scattered leaves again for that library where every book shall lie open to one another. As therefore the bell that rings to a sermon calls not upon the preacher only, but upon the congregation to come, so this bell calls us all; but how much more me, who am brought so near the door by this sickness. There was a contention

---

6. Deer supposedly expelled arrows wounding them by eating the herb dittany.
7. Medicinal plants.
8. One who administers drugs might do this for man as well as for other creatures, but one who sells drugs ("the apothecary") and the physician do not know how to prescribe for man as well as for other creatures.
9. I.e., apply it to the present situation.
1. The "passing bell" for the dying.
2. The church.
3. Punning on the literal sense, "carried across."

as far as a suit[4] (in which piety and dignity, religion and estimation,[5] were mingled) which of the religious orders should ring to prayers first in the morning; and it was determined that they should ring first that rose earliest. If we understand aright the dignity of this bell that tolls for our evening prayer, we would be glad to make it ours by rising early, in that application, that it might be ours as well as his whose indeed it is. The bell doth toll for him that thinks it doth; and though it intermit again, yet from that minute that that occasion wrought upon him, he is united to God. Who casts not up his eye to the sun when it rises? But who takes off his eye from a comet when that breaks out? Who bends not his ear to any bell which upon any occasion rings? But who can remove it from that bell which is passing a piece of himself out of this world? No man is an island, entire of itself; every man is a piece of the continent, a part of the main.[6] If a clod be washed away by the sea, Europe is the less, as well as if a promontory were, as well as if a manor of thy friend's or of thine own were. Any man's death diminishes me, because I am involved in mankind; and therefore never send to know for whom the bell tolls; it tolls for thee.[7] Neither can we call this a begging of misery or a borrowing of misery, as though we were not miserable enough of ourselves but must fetch in more from the next house, in taking upon us the misery of our neighbors. Truly it were an excusable covetousness if we did; for affliction is a treasure, and scarce any man hath enough of it. No man hath affliction enough that is not matured and ripened by it, and made fit for God by that affliction. If a man carry treasure in bullion, or in a wedge of gold, and have none coined into current moneys, his treasure will not defray[8] him as he travels. Tribulation is treasure in the nature of it, but it is not current money in the use of it, except we get nearer and nearer our home, heaven, by it. Another man may be sick too, and sick to death, and this affliction may lie in his bowels as gold in a mine and be of no use to him; but this bell that tells me of his affliction digs out and applies that gold to me, if by this consideration of another's danger I take mine own into contemplation and so secure myself by making my recourse to my God, who is our only security.

From *Expostulation 19*

[THE LANGUAGE OF GOD]

My God, my God, thou art a direct God, may I not say a literal God, a God that wouldst be understood literally and according to the plain sense of all that thou sayest. But thou art also (Lord, I intend it to thy glory, and let no profane misinterpreter abuse it to thy diminution), thou art a figurative, a metaphorical God too: a God in whose words there is such a height of figures, such voyages, such peregrinations to fetch remote and precious metaphors, such extensions, such spreadings, such curtains of allegories, such third heavens of hyperboles, so harmonious elocutions, so retired and so reserved expressions, so commanding persuasions, so persuading commandments, such sinews even in thy milk and such things in thy words, as

---

4. Controversy that went as far as a lawsuit.
5. Self-esteem.
6. Mainland.

7. This phrase gave Hemingway the title for his novel *For Whom the Bell Tolls*.
8. Meet his expenses.

all profane[9] authors seem of the seed of the serpent that creeps; thou art the dove that flies. Oh, what words but thine can express the inexpressible texture and composition of thy word; in which, to one man, that argument that binds his faith to believe that to be the word of God is the reverent simplicity of the word, and to another, the majesty of the word; and in which two men, equally pious, may meet, and one wonder that all should not understand it, and the other as much that any man should. So, Lord, thou givest us the same earth to labor on and to lie in; a house and a grave of the same earth; so, Lord, thou givest us the same word for our satisfaction and for our inquisition,[1] for our instruction and for our admiration too. For there are places that thy servants Jerome and Augustine would scarce believe (when they grew warm by mutual letters) of one another that they understood them, and yet both Jerome and Augustine call upon persons whom they knew to be far weaker than they thought one another (old women and young maids) to read thy Scriptures, without confining them to these or those places.[2]

Neither art thou thus a figurative, a metaphorical God, in thy word only, but in thy works too. The style of thy works, the phrase of thine actions, is metaphorical. The institution of thy whole worship in the old law was a continual allegory; types and figures[3] overspread all, and figures flowed into figures, and poured themselves out into further figures. Circumcision carried a figure of baptism,[4] and baptism carries a figure of that purity which we shall have in perfection in the New Jerusalem. Neither didst thou speak and work in this language only in the time of the prophets; but since thou spokest in thy son it is so too. How often, how much more often, doth thy son call himself a way and a light and a gate and a vine and bread than the son of God or of man? How much oftener doth he exhibit a metaphorical Christ than a real, a literal? This hath occasioned thine ancient servants, whose delight it was to write after thy copy,[5] to proceed the same way in their expositions of the Scriptures, and in their composing both of public liturgies and of private prayers to thee, to make their accesses to thee in such a kind of language as thou wast pleased to speak to them, in a figurative, in a metaphorical language; in which manner I am bold to call the comfort which I receive now in this sickness, in the indication of the concoction[6] and maturity thereof, in certain clouds[7] and residences[8] which the physicians observe, a discovering of land from sea after a long and tempestuous voyage. * * *

1623   1624

---

9. Secular.
1. Investigation.
2. Saints Jerome and Augustine did in fact differ over the proper way of interpreting the Bible, yet they both encouraged its use by the unlearned.
3. Anticipations or prefigurations, especially persons and events in the Hebrew Bible that were read as prefiguring Christ, or some aspect of the New Testament or of Christian practice. For a

beautiful poem exemplifying this process, see Herbert, "The Bunch of Grapes" (p. 1718).
4. Both circumcision and baptism are rites of admission to a religious community.
5. Text.
6. Ripening.
7. Cloudy urine.
8. Residues.

From Death's Duel[1]

[Donne's last sermon, on Psalm 68.20: "And unto God the Lord belong the issues[2] of Death"—i.e., from death.]

* * * First, then, we consider this *exitus mortis*, to be *liberatio à morte*, that with God, the Lord are the issues of death, and therefore in all our deaths, and the deadly calamities of this life, we may justly hope of a good issue from him; and all our periods and transitions in this life, are so many passages from death to death. Our very birth and entrance into this life is *exitus à morte*, an issue from death, for in our mother's womb we are dead so, as that we do not know we live, not so much as we do in our sleep, neither is there any grave so close, or so putrid a prison, as the womb would be unto us, if we stayed in it beyond our time, or died there before our time. In the grave the worms do not kill us, we breed and feed, and then kill the worms which we ourselves produced. In the womb the dead child kills the mother that conceived it, and is a murderer, nay a parricide, even after it is dead. And if we be not dead so in the womb, so as that being dead, we kill her that gave us our first life, our life of vegetation,[3] yet we are dead so, as David's idols are dead. In the womb we have eyes and see not, ears and hear not.[4] There in the womb we are fitted for works of darkness, all the while deprived of light: And there in the womb we are taught cruelty, by being fed with blood, and may be damned, though we be never born. * * *

But then this *exitus à morte* is but *introitus in mortem*, this issue, this deliverance from that death, the death of the womb, is an entrance, a delivering over to another death, the manifold deaths of this world. We have a winding-sheet[5] in our mother's womb, which grows with us from our conception, and we come into the world wound up in that winding-sheet, for we come to seek a grave. * * *

Now this which is so singularly peculiar to him [Christ], that his flesh should not see corruption, at his second coming, his coming to Judgment, shall extend to all then alive, their flesh shall not see corruption. . . . But for us that die now and sleep in the state of the dead, we must all pass this posthume death, this death after death, nay this death after burial, this dissolution after dissolution, this death of corruption and putrefaction, of vermiculation and incineration, of dissolution and dispersion in and from the grave. When those bodies that have been the children of royal parents, and the parents of royal children, must say with Job, to corruption, thou art

---

1. The printed version of this sermon (1632) has the subtitle "A Consolation to the Soul, against the dying life, and living death of the body." Donne's friend and executor Henry King (later bishop of Chichester) supplied the further information that the sermon was delivered at Whitehall, before King Charles, that it was delivered only a few days before Donne's death, and that it was fitly styled "the author's own funeral sermon." Donne was a powerful and popular preacher, and this sermon was especially moving according to the testimony of many auditors, including Izaak Walton (see his account of Donne on his deathbed, pp. 1426–28). Besides the personal drama of the preacher himself visibly ill and perhaps dying,

the audience must have responded to the almost unbearably graphic analysis of the forms of death and decay—a theme that often preoccupied Donne. As in his poems, the language is personal, rich in learning and curious lore, dazzling in verbal ingenuity and metaphor. As in the *Devotions*, the sentences are long, sinuous, and elaborate. Typically, he uses a number of Latin phrases, but almost always translates or paraphrases them immediately.
2. Passages out.
3. I.e., of growth.
4. Paraphrases Psalm 115.5–6.
5. The placenta.

my father, and to the worm, thou art my mother and my sister.[6] Miserable riddle, when the same worm must be my mother, and my sister, and myself. Miserable incest, when I must be married to my mother and my sister, beget, and bear that worm which is all that miserable penury; when my mouth shall be filled with dust, and the worm shall feed, and feed sweetly upon me,[7] when the ambitious man shall have no satisfaction, if the poorest alive tread upon him, nor the poorest receive any contentment in being made equal to princes, for they shall be equal but in dust. One dies at his full strength, being wholly at ease and in quiet, and another dies in the bitterness of his soul, and never eats with pleasure, but they lie down alike in the dust, and the worm covers them.[8] The worm covers them in Job, and in Isaiah, it covers them and is spread under them, the worm is spread under thee, and the worm covers thee.[9] There's the mats and the carpets that lie under, and there's the state and the canopy,[1] that hangs over the greatest of the sons of men. Even those bodies that were the temple of the Holy Ghost, come to this dilapidation, to ruin, to rubbish, to dust: even the Israel of the Lord, and Jacob himself hath no other specification, no other denomination, but that *vermis Jacob*, thou worm of Jacob.[2] Truly the consideration of this posthume death, this death after burial, that after God (with whom are the issues of death) hath delivered me from the death of the womb, by bringing me into the world, and from the manifold deaths of the world, by laying me in the grave, I must die again in an incineration of this flesh, and in a dispersion of that dust. * * *

There we leave you in that blessed dependency, to hang upon him that hangs upon the Cross, there bathe in his tears, there suck at his wounds, and lie down in peace in his grave, till he vouchsafe you a resurrection, and an ascension into that Kingdom, which he hath purchased for you, with the inestimable price of his incorruptible blood. Amen.

1632

6. Paraphrases Job 17.14.
7. Echoes Job 24.20.
8. Echoes Job 21.23–26.
9. Echoes Isaiah 14.11.

1. Cloth of state, a canopy erected over a king's throne.
2. That epithet is used in Isaiah 41.14.

IZAAK WALTON
1593–1683

Walton's *Life of Donne*, first published in 1640 as a biographical introduction to Donne's collected sermons, was the most artistic and accurate English biography to date. Walton drew on his personal knowledge of and friendship with Donne in his later years, talked with others who knew him, and looked over his poems, letters, and papers; but he enlivens his narrative with anecdotes that are often questionably accurate, and he quotes conversations that he could not have heard. While Walton made an effort to research his facts, his is not a scholarly biography, written in accord with the canons of evidence that have evolved since Walton's time. Rather, it is shaped by the models of life-writing admired in the seventeenth century: Plutarch's *Lives of the Noble Grecians and Romans* portraying subjects as examples of virtue and vice; and hagiography or saints' lives, exemplified by Augustine's autobiographical *Confessions* (ca. 400) and by Foxe's *Book of Martyrs*. Walton explicitly reads Donne's life against that of St. Augustine: rakish in youth and saintly in age. The influence of hagiography is especially evident in the passage below, on Donne's remarkable preparations for death. It is no accident that this biography, published as religious tensions were growing acute and civil war loomed, represented Donne as a "saint" of Anglicanism. The other lives Walton wrote—of George Herbert, Richard Hooker, Henry Wotton, and Bishop Robert Sanderson—presented them as exemplary Anglican worthies to the triumphant Anglican church after the Restoration.

A prosperous merchant in the clothing trade, Walton lived for several years in the parish of St. Dunstans in the west, where Donne was vicar. He was a staunch royalist, credited with smuggling one of Prince Charles's jewels out of the country, but

Donne in His Shroud. Shortly before his death in 1631, Donne posed in the shroud in which he would be buried. The resulting painting, reproduced in the 1633 edition of Donne's collected poetry as the engraving shown here, served as a model for the stone effigy of Donne in St. Paul's Cathedral.

his life was otherwise unremarkable, save for his wildly popular book on fishing, *The Complete Angler* (1653). Written during the Cromwellian ascendancy, this series of dialogues between a fisherman and a hunter (and briefly a falconer) creates for Walton a fascinating surrogate self, Piscator, the angler. Setting the representative values of fishermen—moderation, peacefulness, generosity, thankfulness, contemplation—over against the contrasting values assigned to hunters and falconers, Walton makes "angling" stand in for the ceremonious, peaceful, ordered life of royalist Anglicans, now so violently disrupted. As a stylist Walton writes prose that is easy and colloquial but graceful and polished.

From The Life of Dr. John Donne[1]

[DONNE ON HIS DEATHBED]

It is observed that a desire of glory or commendation is rooted in the very nature of man; and that those of the severest and most mortified[2] lives, though they may become so humble as to banish self-flattery, and such weeds as naturally grow there; yet they have not been able to kill this desire of glory, but that like our radical heat,[3] it will both live and die with us; and many think it should do so; and we want not sacred examples to justify the desire of having our memory to outlive our lives; which I mention, because Dr. Donne, by the persuasion of Dr. Fox,[4] easily yielded at this very time to have a monument made for him; but Dr. Fox undertook not to persuade him how, or what monument it should be; that was left to Dr. Donne himself.

A monument being resolved upon, Dr. Donne sent for a carver to make for him in wood the figure of an urn, giving him directions for the compass and height of it; and to bring with it a board, of the just[5] height of his body. These being got, then without delay a choice painter was got to be in readiness to draw his picture, which was taken as followeth. Several charcoal fires being first made in his large study, he brought with him into that place his winding-sheet in his hand, and having put off all his clothes, had this sheet put on him, and so tied with knots at his head and feet, and his hands so placed, as dead bodies are usually fitted to be shrouded and put into their coffin or grave. Upon this urn he thus stood with his eyes shut and with so much of the sheet turned aside as might show his lean, pale, and deathlike face, which was purposely turned toward the east, from whence he expected the second coming of his and our savior Jesus. In this posture he was drawn at his just height; and when the picture was fully finished, he caused it to be set by his bedside, where it continued and became his hourly object till his death, and was then given to his dearest friend and executor Dr. Henry King,[6] then chief residentiary of St. Paul's, who caused him to be thus carved in one entire piece of white marble, as it now stands in that church;[7] and by Dr. Donne's own appointment, these words were to be affixed to it as his epitaph:

---

1. See Donne's sermon, "Death's Duel" (pp. 1423–24), preached on February 25, 1631; he died on March 31 and was buried in St. Paul's on April 3.
2. Self-denying.
3. Bodily warmth.
4. His physician, Dr. Simeon Fox.

5. Exact.
6. Poet, canon ("residentiary") of St. Paul's, and later bishop of Chichester. "Object": of meditation.
7. The statue on Donne's tomb, executed by the well-known sculptor Nicholas Stone, survived the great fire and may still be seen in St. Paul's.

JOHANNES DONNE
Sac. Theol. Profess.

Post varia studia quibus ab annis tenerrimis
fideliter, nec infeliciter incubuit,
instinctu et impulsu Sp. Sancti, monitu
et hortatu

REGIS JACOBI, *ordines sacros*
amplexus, anno sui Jesu, 1614, et suae aetatis 42,
decanatu huius ecclesiae indutus 27
Novembris, 1621,

exutus morte ultimo die Martii, 1631,
hic licet in occiduo cinere aspicit eum
cuius nomen est Oriens.[8]

And now, having brought him through the many labyrinths and perplexities of a various life, even to the gates of death and the grave, my desire is he may rest till I have told my reader that I have seen many pictures of him in several habits and at several ages and in several postures; and I now mention this because I have seen one picture of him, drawn by a curious[9] hand, at his age of eighteen, with his sword and what other adornments might then suit with the present fashions of youth and the giddy gaieties of that age;[1] and his motto then was—

How much shall I be changed,
Before I am changed!

And if that young and his now dying picture were at this time set together, every beholder might say, "Lord! how much is Dr. Donne already changed, before he is changed!" And the view of them might give my reader occasion to ask himself with some amazement, "Lord! how much may I also, that am now in health, be changed before I am changed; before this vile, this changeable body shall put off mortality!" and therefore to prepare for it. But this is not writ so much for my reader's memento[2] as to tell him that Dr. Donne would often in his private discourses, and often publicly in his sermons, mention the many changes both of his body and mind; especially of his mind from a vertiginous giddiness; and would as often say, "his great and most blessed change was from a temporal to a spiritual employment"; in which he was so happy, that he accounted the former part of his life to be lost; and the beginning of it to be from his first entering into sacred orders and serving his most merciful God at his altar.

8. "John Donne, Professor of Sacred Theology. After various studies, which he plied from his tenderest youth faithfully and not unsuccessfully, moved by the instinct and impulse of the Holy Spirit and the admonition and encouragement of King James, he took holy orders in the year of his Jesus 1614 and the year of his age forty-two. On the 27th of November 1621, he was invested as dean of this church, and divested by death, the last day of March 1631. Here in the decline of ashes he looks to One whose name is the Rising Sun."

9. Skillful. "Habits": garbs.

1. The picture is reproduced as the frontispiece to the second edition (1635) of Donne's *Poems.* It bears the Spanish motto *Antes muerto que mudado* (Rather dead than changed, i.e., constant until death), which Walton mistranslates below.

2. Memento mori, remembrance of death.

Upon Monday after the drawing this picture, he took his last leave of his beloved study; and being sensible of his hourly decay, retired himself to his bedchamber; and that week sent at several[3] times for many of his most considerable friends, with whom he took a solemn and deliberate farewell, commending to their considerations some sentences useful for the regulation of their lives; and then dismissed them, as good Jacob did his sons, with a spiritual benediction. The Sunday following, he appointed his servants, that if there were any business yet undone that concerned him or themselves, it should be prepared against Saturday next; for after that day he would not mix his thoughts with anything that concerned this world; nor ever did; but, as Job, so he "waited for the appointed day of his dissolution."[4]

And now he was so happy as to have nothing to do but to die, to do which he stood in need of no longer time; for he had studied it long and to so happy a perfection that in a former sickness he called God to witness, "he was that minute ready to deliver his soul into his hands, if that minute God would determine his dissolution."[5] In that sickness he begged of God the constancy to be preserved in that estate forever; and his patient expectation to have his immortal soul disrobed from her garment of mortality makes me confident he now had a modest assurance that his prayers were then heard and his petition granted. He lay fifteen days earnestly expecting his hourly change; and in the last hour of his last day, as his body melted away and vapored into spirit, his soul having, I verily believe, some revelation of the beatifical vision, he said, "I were miserable if I might not die"; and after those words, closed many periods of his faint breath by saying often, "Thy kingdom come, thy will be done." His speech, which had long been his ready and faithful servant, left him not till the last minute of his life, and then forsook him, not to serve another master (for who speaks like him), but died before him; for that it was then become useless to him that now conversed with God on earth as angels are said to do in heaven, only by thoughts and looks. Being speechless, and seeing heaven by that illumination by which he saw it, he did, as St. Stephen, "look steadfastly into it, till he saw the Son of Man standing at the right hand of God his Father";[6] and being satisfied with this blessed sight, as his soul ascended and his last breath departed from him, he closed his own eyes; and then disposed his hands and body into such a posture as required not the least alteration by those that came to shroud him.

Thus variable, thus virtuous was the life; thus excellent, thus exemplary was the death of this memorable man.

He was buried in that place of St. Paul's Church which he had appointed for that use some years before his death; and by which he passed daily to pay his public devotions to almighty God (who was then served twice a day by a public form of prayer and praises in that place): but he was not buried privately, though he desired it; for, beside an unnumbered number of others, many persons of nobility, and of eminency for learning, who did love and honor him in his life, did show it at his death by a voluntary and sad attendance of his body to the grave, where nothing was so remarkable as a public sorrow.

To which place of his burial some mournful friends repaired, and, as Alexander the Great did to the grave of the famous Achilles,[7] so they strewed

3. Separate.
4. Job 14.14.
5. Walton paraphrases from Donne's *Devotions*

upon Emergent Occasions, Prayer 23.
6. Acts 7.55.
7. Plutarch, "Alexander," sec. 15.

his with an abundance of curious and costly flowers; which course they (who were never yet known) continued morning and evening for many days, not ceasing till the stones that were taken up in that church to give his body admission into the cold earth (now his bed of rest) were again by the mason's art so leveled and firmed as they had been formerly, and his place of burial undistinguishable to common view.

The next day after his burial, some unknown friend, some one of the many lovers and admirers of his virtue and learning, wrote this epitaph with a coal on the wall over his grave:

> Reader! I am to let thee know,
> Donne's body only lies below;
> For, could the grave his soul comprise,
> Earth would be richer than the skies!

Nor was this all the honor done to his reverend ashes; for, as there be some persons that will not receive a reward for that for which God accounts himself a debtor, persons that dare trust God with their charity and without a witness; so there was by some grateful unknown friend that thought Dr. Donne's memory ought to be perpetuated, an hundred marks sent to his two faithful friends and executors,[8] towards the making of his monument. It was not for many years known by whom; but after the death of Dr. Fox, it was known that it was he that sent it; and he lived to see as lively a representation of his dead friend as marble can express: a statue indeed so like Dr. Donne, that (as his friend Sir Henry Wotton hath expressed himself) "it seems to breathe faintly, and posterity shall look upon it as a kind of artificial miracle."

He was of stature moderately tall; of a straight and equally proportioned body, to which all his words and actions gave an unexpressible addition of comeliness.

The melancholy and pleasant humor were in him so contempered that each gave advantage to the other, and made his company one of the delights of mankind.

His fancy was unimitably high, equaled only by his great wit;[9] both being made useful by a commanding judgment.

His aspect was cheerful, and such as gave a silent testimony of a clear knowing soul, and of a conscience at peace with itself.

His melting eye showed that he had a soft heart, full of noble compassion; of too brave a soul to offer injuries and too much a Christian not to pardon them in others.

He did much contemplate (especially after he entered into his sacred calling) the mercies of almighty God, the immortality of the soul, and the joys of heaven; and would often say, in a kind of sacred ecstasy, "Blessed be God that he is God, only and divinely like himself."

He was by nature highly passionate, but more apt to reluct at[1] the excesses of it. A great lover of the offices of humanity, and of so merciful a spirit that he never beheld the miseries of mankind without pity and relief.

He was earnest and unwearied in the search of knowledge, with which his vigorous soul is now satisfied, and employed in a continual praise of that God

---

8. Henry King and Dr. John Monfort.
9. Mental acuity. "Fancy": imagination.

1. Struggle against.

that first breathed it into his active body: that body, which once was a temple of the Holy Ghost and is now become a small quantity of Christian dust:

But I shall see it reanimated.

Feb. 15, 1640

I.W.

1640, 1675

AEMILIA LANYER
1569–1645

Aemilia Lanyer was the first Englishwoman to publish a substantial volume of original poems and the first to make an overt bid for patronage. She was daughter to an Italian family of court musicians who came to England in the reign of Henry VIII; they may have been Christianized Jews or, alternatively, Protestants forced to flee Catholic persecution in their native land. Some information about Lanyer's life has come down to us from the notebooks of the astrologer and fortune-teller Simon Forman, whom Lanyer consulted in 1597. Educated in the aristocratic household of the Countess of Kent, in her late teens and early twenties Lanyer was the mistress of Queen Elizabeth's lord chamberlain, Henry Carey, Lord Hunsdon. The wealthy Hunsdon, forty-five years her senior, was a notable patron of the arts— Shakespeare's company performed under his auspices in the 1590s—and he maintained his mistress in luxury. Yet when she became pregnant by Hunsdon at age twenty-three, she was married off to Alfonso Lanyer, one of another family of gentleman musicians attached to the courts of Elizabeth I and James I. Lanyer's fortunes declined after her marriage. Lanyer's poetry suggests that she resided for some time in the bookish and cultivated household of Margaret Clifford, Countess of Cumberland, and Margaret's young daughter Anne. Lanyer reports receiving there encouragement in learning, piety, and poetry, as well as, perhaps, some support in the unusual venture of offering her poems for publication. Yet her efforts to find some niche at the Jacobean court came to nothing.

Lanyer's single volume of poems, *Salve Deus Rex Judaeorum* (1611) has a decided feminist thrust. A series of dedicatory poems to former and would-be patronesses praises them as a community of contemporary good women. The title poem, a meditation on Christ's Passion that at times invites comparison with Donne and Crashaw, contrasts the good women in the Passion story with the weak, evil men portrayed there. It also incorporates a defense of Eve and all women. That defense and Lanyer's prose epistle, "To the Virtuous Reader," are spirited contributions to the so-called *querelle des femmes*, or "debate about women," a massive body of writings in several genres and languages: some examples include Chaucer's Wife of Bath's Prologue and Tale, Shakespeare's *Taming of the Shrew*, Joseph Swetnam's attack on "lewd, idle, froward, and unconstant women" and Rachel Speght's reply. The final poem in Lanyer's volume, "The Description of Cookham," celebrates in elegiac mode the Crown estate occasionally occupied by the Countess of Cumberland, portraying it as an Edenic paradise of women, now lost. The poem may or may not have been written before Ben Jonson's "To Penshurst"—commonly thought to have inaugurated the "country-house" genre in English literature—but Lanyer's poem can claim priority in publication. The poems' different conceptions of the role of women in the ideal social order make an instructive comparison.

From Salve Deus Rex Judaeorum[1]

To the Doubtful Reader[2]

Gentle Reader, if thou desire to be resolved, why I give this title, *Salve Deus Rex Judaeorum*, know for certain, that it was delivered unto me in sleep many years before I had any intent to write in this manner, and was quite out of my memory, until I had written the Passion of Christ, when immediately it came into my remembrance, what I had dreamed long before. And thinking it a significant token[3] that I was appointed to perform this work, I gave the very same words I received in sleep as the fittest title I could devise for this book.

To the Queen's Most Excellent Majesty[4]

Renowned empress, and Great Britain's queen,
Most gracious mother of succeeding kings;
Vouchsafe° to view that which is seldom seen,   *be willing*
A woman's writing of divinest things:
5   Read it fair queen, though it defective be,
Your excellence can grace both it and me.

*   *   *

Behold, great queen, fair Eve's apology,°   *defense*
Which I have writ in honor of your sex,
75   And do refer unto your majesty
To judge if it agree not with the text:[5]
And if it do, why are poor women blamed,
Or by more faulty men so much defamed.

*   *   *

My weak distempered brain and feeble spirits,
140   Which all unlearned have adventured, this
To write of Christ, and of his sacred merits,
Desiring that this book her° hands may kiss: *the queen's*
And though I be unworthy of that grace,
Yet let her blessed thoughts this book embrace.

1. "Hail God, King of the Jews," a variant of the inscription affixed to Christ's cross.
2. Lanyer placed this explanation at the end of her volume, not the beginning, as a further authorizing gesture. Invoking the familiar genre of the dream vision, she lays claim to poetic, even divine, inspiration. "Doubtful": doubting.
3. Sign.
4. The first of eight poems addressed to court ladies whom Lanyer sought to attract as patrons; such poems commonly preface literary works by male courtier-poets, though usually not in such numbers. These poems are followed by a prose address to her actual patron, the Countess of Cumberland, and then by the prose epistle included here, "To the Virtuous Reader." This first poem addresses Anne of Denmark, James I's queen, patron of writers such as Ben Jonson and Samuel Daniel, and mother of Prince Henry, Princess Elizabeth, and the future Charles I.
5. The biblical text (Genesis 1–3).

145 And pardon me, fair queen, though I presume
To do that which so many better can;
Not that I learning to myself assume,
Or that I would compare with any man:
　　But as they are scholars, and by art do write,
150 　So Nature yields my soul a sad° delight.　　　　*solemn, serious*

And since all arts at first from Nature came,
That goodly creature, mother of perfection
Whom Jove's[6] almighty hand at first did frame,
Taking both her and hers[7] in his protection:
155 　Why should not she now grace my barren muse,
　And in a woman all defects excuse.

So peerless princess humbly I desire,
That your great wisdom would vouchsafe t'omit°　　　　*overlook*
All faults; and pardon if my spirits retire,
160 Leaving° to aim at what they cannot hit:　　　　*declining*
　To write your worth, which no pen can express,
　Were but t'eclipse your fame, and make it less.[8]

To the Virtuous Reader

Often have I heard, that it is the property of some women, not only to emulate the virtues and perfections of the rest, but also by all their powers of ill speaking, to eclipse the brightness of their deserved fame: now contrary to their custom, which men I hope unjustly lay to their charge, I have written this small volume, or little book, for the general use of all virtuous ladies and gentlewomen of this kingdom; and in commendation of some particular persons of our own sex, such as for the most part, are so well known to myself, and others, that I dare undertake Fame dares not to call any better. And this have I done, to make known to the world, that all women deserve not to be blamed though some forgetting they are women themselves, and in danger to be condemned by the words of their own mouths, fall into so great an error, as to speak unadvisedly against the rest of their sex; which if it be true, I am persuaded they can show their own imperfection in nothing more: and therefore could wish (for their own ease, modesties, and credit) they would refer such points of folly, to be practiced by evil-disposed men, who forgetting they were born of women, nourished of women, and that if it were not by the means of women, they would be quite extinguished out of the world, and a final end of them all, do like vipers deface the wombs wherein they were bred, only to give way and utterance to their want of discretion and goodness. Such as these, were they that dishonored Christ's his apostles and prophets, putting them to shameful deaths. Therefore we are not to regard any imputations, that they undeservedly lay upon us, no otherwise than to make use of them to our own benefits, as spur to virtue, making us fly all occasions that

6. God as creator of Nature.
7. Nature and those (especially women) under Nature's protection.
8. As her poetry of praise cannot possibly do

justice to the queen, she abandons an attempt that would obscure rather than promote the queen's fame.

may color their unjust speeches to pass current. Especially considering that they have tempted even the patience of God himself, who gave power to wise and virtuous women, to bring down their pride and arrogancy. As was cruel Cesarus by the discreet counsel of noble Deborah, judge and prophetess of Israel: and resolution of Jael wife of Heber the Kenite:[9] wicked Haman, by the divine prayers and prudent proceedings of beautiful Hester:[1] blasphemous Holofernes, by the invincible courage, rare wisdom, and confident carriage of Judith: and the unjust Judges, by the innocency of chaste Susanna:[2] with infinite others, which for brevity sake I will omit. As also in respect it pleased our lord and savior Jesus Christ, without the assistance of man, being free from original and all other sins, from the time of his conception, till the hour of his death, to be begotten of a woman, born of a woman, nourished of a woman, obedient to a woman; and that he healed women, pardoned women, comforted women: yea, even when he was in his greatest agony and bloody sweat, going to be crucified, and also in the last hour of his death, took care to dispose of a woman:[3] after his resurrection, appeared first to a woman, sent a woman[4] to declare his most glorious resurrection to the rest of his disciples. Many other examples I could allege of divers faithful and virtuous women, who have in all ages not only been confessors but also endured most cruel martyrdom for their faith in Jesus Christ. All which is sufficient to enforce all good Christians and honorable-minded men to speak reverently of our sex, and especially of all virtuous and good women. To the modest censures of both which, I refer these my imperfect endeavors, knowing that according to their own excellent dispositions they will rather cherish, nourish, and increase the least spark of virtue where they find it, by their favorable and best interpretations, than quench it by wrong constructions. To whom I wish all increase of virtue, and desire their best opinions.

Eve's Apology in Defense of Women[5]

Now Pontius Pilate is to judge the cause°   *case*
Of faultless Jesus, who before him stands,
Who neither hath offended prince, nor laws,
Although he now be brought in woeful bands.
5   O noble governor, make thou yet a pause,

---

9. Sisera (Canaanite leader, hence "Cesarus,"i.e., "Caesar") was a Canaanite military commander (12th century B.C.E.) routed in battle by the Israelites under the leadership of the prophetess Deborah. Sisera was subsequently killed by the Kenite woman Jael, who enticed him to her tent and then drove a tent spike through his temples while he slept (Judges 4).
1. Esther, the Jewish wife (5th century B.C.E.) of the Persian King Ahasuerus (Xerxes I), who by her wit and courage subverted the plot of the king's minister, Haman, to annihilate the Jews (Esther 1–7).
2. Jewish wife and example of chastity (6th century B.C.E.). She was falsely accused of adultery by two Jewish elders, in revenge for refusing their sexual advances, and condemned to death. The wise judge Daniel saved her by uncovering the elders' perjury (Apocrypha, Book of Susanna).

Judith in the 5th century B.C.E. delivered her Judean countrymen from the Assyrians by captivating their leader, Holofernes, with her charms and then decapitating him while he was drunk (Apocrypha, Book of Judith).
3. Christ asked his apostle John to care for his mother Mary (John 19.25–27). "Dispose of": provide for.
4. Mary Magdalen (John 20.1–18).
5. Lanyer supplies the title for this subsection of the *Salve Deus* on her title page. Eve is not, however, the speaker; rather, the narrator presents Eve's "Apology" (defense of her actions), which is also a defense of all women. She does so by means of an apostrophe (impassioned address) to Pilate, the Roman official who authorized the crucifixion of Jesus. Lanyer makes Pilate and Adam representatives of the male gender, whereas Eve and Pilate's wife represent womankind.

Do not in innocent blood inbrue° thy hands;   *stain*
But hear the words of thy most worthy wife,
Who sends to thee, to beg her Savior's life.[6]

Let barb'rous cruelty far depart from thee,
10 And in true justice take affliction's part;
Open thine eyes, that thou the truth may'st see.
Do not the thing that goes against thy heart,
Condemn not him that must thy Savior be;
But view his holy life, his good desert.
15 Let not us women glory in men's fall,[7]
Who had power given to overrule us all.

Till now your indiscretion sets us free.
And makes our former fault much less appear;
Our mother Eve, who tasted of the tree,
20 Giving to Adam what she held most dear,
Was simply good, and had no power to see;[8]
The after-coming harm did not appear:
    The subtle serpent that our sex betrayed
    Before our fall so sure a plot had laid.

25 That undiscerning ignorance perceived
No guile or craft that was by him intended;
For had she known of what we were bereaved,[9]
To his request she had not condescended.°   *consented*
But she, poor soul, by cunning was deceived;
30 No hurt therein her harmless heart intended:
    For she alleged° God's word, which he° denies,   *asserted / serpent*
    That they should die, but even as gods be wise.

But surely Adam cannot be excused;
Her fault though great, yet he was most to blame;
35 What weakness offered, strength might have refused,
Being lord of all, the greater was his shame.
Although the serpent's craft had her abused,
God's holy word ought all his actions frame,°   *determine*
    For he was lord and king of all the earth,
40   Before poor Eve had either life or breath,

Who being framed° by God's eternal hand   *fashioned*
The perfectest man that ever breathed on earth;
And from God's mouth received that strait° command,   *strict*
The breach whereof he knew was present death;

---

6. Pilate's wife wrote her husband a letter urging Pilate to spare Jesus, about whom she had a warning dream (Matthew 27.19).
7. The fall of Adam, and the prospective fall of Pilate.
8. In Eden, Eve ate the forbidden fruit first, at the serpent's bidding. Genesis commentary usually emphasized Eve's full knowledge that God had forbidden them on pain of death and banishment from Eden to eat the fruit of the Tree of Knowledge of Good and Evil. Her action was usually ascribed to intemperance, pride, and ambition.
9. Deprived, specifically of eternal life. In Genesis 3, Eve was enticed by the serpent to eat the forbidden fruit; she in turn enticed her husband. God expelled them from Eden, condemning Adam to hard labor, Eve to pain in childbirth and subjection to her husband, and both to suffering and death.

45 Yea, having power to rule both sea and land,
Yet with one apple won to lose that breath[1]
    Which God had breathed in his beauteous face,
    Bringing us all in danger and disgrace.

And then to lay the fault on Patience' back,
50 That we (poor women) must endure it all.
We know right well he did discretion lack,
Being not persuaded thereunto at all.
If Eve did err, it was for knowledge sake;
The fruit being fair persuaded him to fall:
55   No subtle serpent's falsehood did betray him;
    If he would eat it, who had power to stay° him?   *prevent*

Not Eve, whose fault was only too much love,
Which made her give this present to her dear,
That what she tasted he likewise might prove,°   *experience*
60 Whereby his knowledge might become more clear;
He never sought her weakness to reprove
With those sharp words which he of God did hear;
    Yet men will boast of knowledge, which he took
    From Eve's fair hand, as from a learned book.

65 If any evil did in her remain,
Being made of him,[2] he was the ground of all.
If one of many worlds[3] could lay a stain
Upon our sex, and work so great a fall
To wretched man by Satan's subtle train,[4]
70 What will so foul a fault amongst you all?
    Her weakness did the serpent's words obey,
    But you in malice God's dear Son betray,

Whom, if unjustly you condemn to die,
Her sin was small to what you do commit;
75 All mortal sins[5] that do for vengeance cry
Are not to be compared unto it.
If many worlds would altogether try
By all their sins the wrath of God to get,
    This sin of yours surmounts them all as far
80   As doth the sun another little star.[6]

Then let us have our liberty again,
And challenge° to yourselves no sovereignty.   *claim*
You came not in the world without our pain,
Make that a bar against your cruelty;
85 Your fault being greater, why should you disdain
Our being your equals, free from tyranny?

---

1. The breath of life, which would have been eternal.
2. Genesis 2.21–22 reports God's creation of Eve from Adam's rib.
3. May allude to the commonplace that man is a little world, applying it here to woman.

4. Tradition identifies Satan with the serpent, although that identification is not made in Genesis.
5. Sins punishable by damnation.
6. In the Ptolemaic system, the sun was larger than the other planets and the fixed stars.

> If one weak woman simply did offend,
> This sin of yours hath no excuse nor end,
>
> To which, poor souls, we never gave consent.
> 90 Witness, thy wife, O Pilate, speaks for all,
> Who did but dream, and yet a message sent
> That thou shouldest have nothing to do at all
> With that just man° which, if thy heart relent,   *Christ*
> Why wilt thou be a reprobate° with Saul[7]   *damned*
> 95 To seek the death of him that is so good,
> For thy soul's health to shed his dearest blood?

1611

The Description of Cookham[1]

> Farewell, sweet Cookham, where I first obtained
> Grace[2] from that grace where perfect grace remained;
> And where the muses gave their full consent,
> I should have power the virtuous to content;
> 5 Where princely palace willed me to indite,°   *write*
> The sacred story of the soul's delight.[3]
> Farewell, sweet place, where virtue then did rest,
> And all delights did harbor in her breast;
> Never shall my sad eyes again behold
> 10 Those pleasures which my thoughts did then unfold.
> Yet you, great lady, mistress of that place,
> From whose desires did spring this work of grace;
> Vouchsafe° to think upon those pleasures past,   *be willing*
> As fleeting worldly joys that could not last,
> 15 Or, as dim shadows of celestial pleasures,
> Which are desired above all earthly treasures.
> Oh how, methought, against° you thither came,   *in preparation for*
> Each part did seem some new delight to frame!
> The house received all ornaments to grace it,
> 20 And would endure no foulness to deface it.
> And walks put on their summer liveries,[4]
> And all things else did hold like similes:[5]
> The trees with leaves, with fruits, with flowers clad,
> Embraced each other, seeming to be glad,

7. King of Israel who sought the death of God's annointed prophet-king, David. The parallel is with Pilate, who sought Christ's death.
1. The poem was written in honor of Margaret Clifford, Countess of Cumberland, and celebrates a royal estate leased to her brother, at which the countess occasionally resided. The poem should be compared with Jonson's "To Penshurst" (pp. 1546–48). Lanyer's poem is based on a familiar classical topic, the "farewell to a place," which had its most famous development in Virgil's *Eclogue* 1. Lanyer makes extensive use of the common pastoral motif of nature's active sympathy with and response to human emotion—which later came to be called the "pathetic fallacy."
2. Here, both God's grace and the favor of Her Grace, the Countess of Cumberland. Lanyer attributes both her religious conversion and her vocation as poet to a period of residence at Cookham in the countess's household. We do not know how long or under what circumstances Lanyer resided there.
3. Apparently a reference to the countess as her patron, commissioning her Passion poem.
4. Distinctive garments worn by persons in the service of great families, to indicate whose servants they were.
5. Behaved in similar fashion.

25 Turning themselves to beauteous canopies,
   To shade the bright sun from your brighter eyes;
   The crystal streams with silver spangles graced,
   While by the glorious sun they were embraced;
   The little birds in chirping notes did sing,
30 To entertain both you and that sweet spring.
   And Philomela[6] with her sundry lays,
   Both you and that delightful place did praise.
   Oh how me thought each plant, each flower, each tree
   Set forth their beauties then to welcome thee!
35 The very hills right humbly did descend,
   When you to tread on them did intend.
   And as you set your feet, they still did rise,
   Glad that they could receive so rich a prize.
   The gentle winds did take delight to be
40 Among those woods that were so graced by thee,
   And in sad murmur uttered pleasing sound,
   That pleasure in that place might more abound.
   The swelling banks delivered all their pride
   When such a phoenix[7] once they had espied.
45 Each arbor, bank, each seat, each stately tree,
   Thought themselves honored in supporting thee.
   The pretty birds would oft come to attend thee,
   Yet fly away for fear they should offend thee;
   The little creatures in the burrow by
50 Would come abroad to sport them in your eye,
   Yet fearful of the bow in your fair hand,
   Would run away when you did make a stand.
   Now let me come unto that stately tree,
   Wherein such goodly prospects you did see;
55 That oak that did in height his fellows pass,
   As much as lofty trees, low growing grass,
   Much like a comely cedar straight and tall,
   Whose beauteous stature far exceeded all.
   How often did you visit this fair tree,
60 Which seeming joyful in receiving thee,
   Would like a palm tree spread his arms abroad,
   Desirous that you there should make abode;
   Whose fair green leaves much like a comely veil,
   Defended Phoebus° when he would assail;   *resisted the sun*
65 Whose pleasing boughs did yield a cool fresh air,
   Joying° his happiness when you were there.   *enjoying*
   Where being seated, you might plainly see
   Hills, vales, and woods, as if on bended knee
   They had appeared, your honor to salute,
70 Or to prefer some strange unlooked-for suit;[8]

---

6. In myth, Philomela was raped by her brother-in-law Tereus, who also tore out her tongue; the gods transformed her into a nightingale. Here the bird's song is joyous but later mournful (line 189), associating her own woes with those of Cookham at the women's departure.
7. Mythical bird that lived alone of its kind for five hundred years, then was consumed in flame and reborn from its own ashes; metaphorically, a person of rare excellence. "All their pride": fish (cf. "To Penshurst," lines 31–36).
8. To urge some unexpected petition, as to a monarch.

All interlaced with brooks and crystal springs,
A prospect fit to please the eyes of kings.
And thirteen shires appeared all in your sight,
Europe could not afford much more delight.
75 What was there then but gave you all content,
While you the time in meditation spent
Of their Creator's power, which there you saw,
In all his creatures held a perfect law;
And in their beauties did you plain descry°   perceive
80 His beauty, wisdom, grace, love, majesty.
In these sweet woods how often did you walk,
With Christ and his apostles there to talk;
Placing his holy writ in some fair tree
To meditate what you therein did see.
85 With Moses you did mount his holy hill
To know his pleasure, and perform his will.[9]
With lowly David you did often sing
His holy hymns to heaven's eternal King.[1]
And in sweet music did your soul delight
90 To sound his praises, morning, noon, and night.
With blessed Joseph you did often feed
Your pined brethren, when they stood in need.[2]
And that sweet lady sprung from Clifford's race,
Of noble Bedford's blood, fair stem of grace,[3]
95 To honorable Dorset now espoused,[4]
In whose fair breast true virtue then was housed,
Oh what delight did my weak spirits find
In those pure parts° of her well framéd mind.   qualities
And yet it grieves me that I cannot be
100 Near unto her, whose virtues did agree
With those fair ornaments of outward beauty,
Which did enforce from all both love and duty.
Unconstant Fortune, thou art most to blame,
Who casts us down into so low a frame
105 Where our great friends we cannot daily see,
So great a difference is there in degree.[5]
Many are placéd in those orbs of state,
Parters[6] in honor, so ordained by Fate,
Nearer in show, yet farther off in love,
110 In which, the lowest always are above.[7]
But whither am I carried in conceit,°   thought, fancy

9. You sought out and followed God's law, like
Moses, who received the Ten Commandments
on Mount Sinai.
1. You often sang David's psalms.
2. Like Joseph, who fed the starving Israelites in
Egypt, you fed the hungry.
3. Main line of the family tree. Anne Clifford,
only surviving child of the seaman-adventurer
George Clifford, third Earl of Cumberland, and
the countess, a Russell (of "Bedford's blood").
4. Anne Clifford was married to Richard Sackville, third Earl of Dorset, on February 25, 1609;
the reference helps date Lanyer's poem.
5. These lines and lines 117–25 probably exag-
gerate Lanyer's former familiarity with Anne Clifford.
6. Separators, i.e., the various honorific ranks
("orbs of state") act to separate person from person.
7. An egalitarian sentiment playing on the Christian notion that in spiritual things—love and
charity—the poor and lowly surpass the great
ones.

My wit too weak to conster° of the great.   *construe*
Why not? Although we are but born of earth,
We may behold the heavens, despising death;
115   And loving heaven that is so far above,
May in the end vouchsafe us entire love.[8]
Therefore sweet memory do thou retain
Those pleasures past, which will not turn again:
Remember beauteous Dorset's[9] former sports,
120   So far from being touched by ill reports,
Wherein myself did always bear a part,
While reverend love presented my true heart.
Those recreations let me bear in mind,
Which her sweet youth and noble thoughts did find,
125   Whereof deprived, I evermore must grieve,
Hating blind Fortune, careless to relieve.
And you sweet Cookham, whom these ladies leave,
I now must tell the grief you did conceive
At their departure, when they went away,
130   How everything retained a sad dismay.
Nay long before, when once an inkling came,
Methought each thing did unto sorrow frame:
The trees that were so glorious in our view,
Forsook both flowers and fruit, when once they knew
135   Of your depart, their very leaves did wither,
Changing their colors as they grew together.
But when they saw this had no power to stay you,
They often wept, though, speechless, could not pray you,
Letting their tears in your fair bosoms fall,
140   As if they said, Why will ye leave us all?
This being vain, they cast their leaves away
Hoping that pity would have made you stay:
Their frozen tops, like age's hoary hairs,
Shows their disasters, languishing in fears.
145   A swarthy riveled rind° all over spread,   *bark*
Their dying bodies half alive, half dead.
But your occasions called you so away[1]
That nothing there had power to make you stay.
Yet did I see a noble grateful mind
150   Requiting each according to their kind,
Forgetting not to turn and take your leave
Of these sad creatures, powerless to receive
Your favor, when with grief you did depart,
Placing their former pleasures in your heart,
155   Giving great charge to noble memory
There to preserve their love continually.
But specially the love of that fair tree,
That first and last you did vouchsafe to see,
In which it pleased you oft to take the air

---

8. I.e., we (lowly) may also love God and enjoy God's love, and hence are equal to anyone.
9. As was common, Anne Clifford is here referred to by her husband's title.

1. After her husband's death (1605) Margaret Clifford chiefly resided in her dower properties in the north; Anne Clifford was married in 1609.

160 With noble Dorset, then a virgin fair,
  Where many a learned book was read and scanned,
  To this fair tree, taking me by the hand,
  You did repeat the pleasures which had passed,
  Seeming to grieve they could no longer last.
165 And with a chaste, yet loving kiss took leave,
  Of which sweet kiss I did it soon bereave,°   *soon take from it*
  Scorning a senseless creature should possess
  So rare a favor, so great happiness.
  No other kiss it could receive from me,
170 For fear to give back what it took of thee,
  So I ungrateful creature did deceive it
  Of that which you in love vouchsafed to leave it.
  And though it oft had given me much content,
  Yet this great wrong I never could repent;
175 But of the happiest made it most forlorn,
  To show that nothing's free from Fortune's scorn,
  While all the rest with this most beauteous tree
  Made their sad comfort sorrow's harmony.
  The flowers that on the banks and walks did grow,
180 Crept in the ground, the grass did weep for woe.
  The winds and waters seemed to chide together
  Because you went away they knew not whither;
  And those sweet brooks that ran so fair and clear,
  With grief and trouble wrinkled did appear.
185 Those pretty birds that wonted° were to sing,   *accustomed*
  Now neither sing, nor chirp, nor use their wing,
  But with their tender feet on some bare spray,
  Warble forth sorrow, and their own dismay.
  Fair Philomela leaves her mournful ditty,
190 Drowned in deep sleep, yet can procure no pity.
  Each arbor, bank, each seat, each stately tree
  Looks bare and desolate now for want of thee,
  Turning green tresses into frosty gray,
  While in cold grief they wither all away.
195 The sun grew weak, his beams no comfort gave,
  While all green things did make the earth their grave.
  Each briar, each bramble, when you went away
  Caught fast your clothes, thinking to make you stay;
  Delightful Echo wonted to reply
200 To our last words, did now for sorrow die;
  The house cast off each garment that might grace it,
  Putting on dust and cobwebs to deface it.
  All desolation then there did appear,
  When you were going whom they held so dear.
205 This last farewell to Cookham here I give,
  When I am dead thy name in this may live,
  Wherein I have performed her noble hest°   *commission*
  Whose virtues lodge in my unworthy breast,
  And ever shall, so long as life remains,
210 Tying my life to her by those rich chains.°   *her virtues*

BEN JONSON
1572–1637

I n 1616 Ben Jonson published his *Works*, to the derision of those astounded to see mere plays and poems collected under the same title the king gave to his political treatises. Many of Jonson's contemporaries shied away from publication, either because, like Donne, they wrote for small coterie audiences or because, like Shakespeare, they wrote for theater companies that preferred not to let go of the scripts. Jonson knew and admired both Donne and Shakespeare and more than any Jacobean belonged to both of their very different worlds, but in publishing his *Works* he laid claim to higher literary status. He had risen from humble beginnings to become England's unofficial poet laureate, with a pension from the king and honorary degrees from both Oxford and Cambridge. If he was not the first professional author in England, he was the first to invest that role with dignity and respectability. His published *Works*, over which he labored with painstaking care, testify to an extraordinary feat of self-transformation.

Jonson's early life was tough and turbulent. The posthumous son of a London clergyman, he was educated at Westminster School under the great antiquarian scholar William Camden. There he developed his love of classical learning, but lacking the resources to continue his education, Jonson was forced to turn to his stepfather's trade of bricklaying, a life he "could not endure." He escaped by joining the English forces in Flanders, where, as he later boasted, he killed a man in single combat before the eyes of two armies. Back in London, his attempt to make a living as an actor and playwright almost ended in early disaster. He was imprisoned in 1597 for collaborating with Thomas Nashe on the scandalous play *The Isle of Dogs* (now lost), and shortly after his release he killed one of his fellow actors in a duel. Jonson escaped the gallows by pleading benefit of clergy (a medieval privilege exempting felons who could read Latin from the death penalty). His learning had saved his life, but he emerged from captivity branded on the thumb, and with another mark against him as well. Under the influence of a priest imprisoned with him, he had converted to Catholicism. Jonson was now more than ever a marginal figure, distrusted by the society that he satirized brilliantly in his early plays.

Jonson's fortunes improved with the accession of James I, though not at once. In 1603 he was called before the Privy Council to answer charges of "popery and treason" found in his play *Sejanus*. Little more than a year later he was in jail again for his part in the play *Eastward Ho*, which openly mocked the king's Scots accent and propensity for selling knighthoods. Yet Jonson was now on the way to establishing himself at the new court. In 1605 he received the commission to organize the Twelfth Night entertainment, or masque; eventually he would produce twenty-four masques for the court, most of them in collaboration with the architect and scene designer Inigo Jones. In the same years that he was writing the masques he produced his greatest works for the public theater. His first successful play, *Every Man in His Humor* (1598), had inaugurated the so-called comedy of humors, which ridicules the eccentricities or passions of the characters, thought to be caused by physiological imbalance. He capitalized on this success with the comedies *Volpone* (1606), *Epicene* (1609), *The Alchemist* (1610), and *Bartholomew Fair* (1614). Jonson preserved the detached, satiric perspective of an outsider, but he was rising in society and making accommodations where necessary. In 1605, when suspicion fell upon him as a Catholic following the exposure of the Gunpowder Plot, he showed

Jonson's 1616 *Works*. This title page makes a strong claim for the
importance of Jonson's literary achievement and for the significance
of English drama in general. The columned portico suggests Jonson's
connection to the classical tradition, and the figures within it
represent his mastery of various genres; they represent, clockwise
from the top, Tragicomedy, Pastoral, Comedy, Tragedy, and Satire.
Underneath Tragedy is a cart of the sort medieval traveling players
would have used; underneath Comedy is an ancient Greek amphitheater. Centered just beneath Tragicomedy is a depiction of the English
public theaters for which Jonson wrote many of his plays.

his loyalty by agreeing to serve as a spy for the Privy Council. Five years later he
would return to the Church of England.

Although he rose to a position of eminent respectability, Jonson retained a quarrelsome spirit all his life. Much of his best work emerged out of fierce tensions with
collaborators and contemporaries. At the turn of the century he became embroiled
in the so-called War of the Theaters, in which he satirized and was satirized by his

fellow playwrights John Marston and Thomas Dekker. Later, his long partnership with Inigo Jones was marked by ever more bitter rivalry over the relative importance of words and scenery in the masques. Jonson also poured invective on the theater audiences when they failed, in his view, to appreciate his plays. The failure of his play *The New Inn* elicited his "Ode to Himself" (1629), a disgusted farewell to the "loathed stage." Yet even after a stroke in 1629 left him partially paralyzed and confined to his home, Jonson continued to write, and was at work on a new play when he died in 1637.

In spite of his antagonistic nature, Jonson had a great capacity for friendship. His friends included Shakespeare, Donne, Francis Bacon, and John Selden. In later years he gathered about himself a group of admiring younger men known as the "Sons of Ben," whose numbers included Robert Herrick, Thomas Carew, and Sir John Suckling. He was a fascinating and inexhaustible conversationalist, as recorded by his friend William Drummond of Hawthornden, who carefully noted down Jonson's remarks on a wide variety of subjects, ranging from his fellow poets to his sexual predilections. Jonson also moved easily among the great of the land. His patrons included Lady Mary Wroth and other members of the Sidney and Herbert families. In "To Penshurst," a celebration of Robert Sidney's country estate, Jonson offers an ideal image of a social order in which a virtuous patriarchal governor offers ready hospitality to guests of all stations, from poets to kings.

"To Penshurst," together with Aemilia Lanyer's "Description of Cookham," inaugurated the small genre of the "country-house poem" in England. Jonson tried his hand, usually with success, at a wide range of poetic genres, including epitaph and epigram, love and funeral elegy, verse satire and verse letter, song and ode. More often than not he looked back to classical precedents. From the Roman poets Horace and Martial he derived not only generic models but an ideal vision of the artist and society against which he measured himself and the court he served. In many poems he adopted the persona of a witty, keenly perceptive, and scrupulously honest judge of men and women. The classical values Jonson most admired are enumerated in "Inviting a Friend to Supper," which describes a dinner party characterized by moderation, civility, graciousness, and pleasure that delights without enslaving—all contrasting sharply with the excess and licentiousness that marked the banquets and entertainments of imperial Rome and Stuart England. Yet the poet who produced this image of moderation was a man of immense appetites, which found expression in his art as well as in his life. His best works seethe with an almost uncontrollable imaginative energy and lust for abundance. Even his profound classical learning manifests this impulse. The notes and references to learned authorities that spill across the margins of his *Works* can be seen as the literary equivalent of food and drink piled high on the poet's table. Years of hardship had taught Jonson to seek his feasts in his imagination, and he could make the most mundane object the basis for flights of high fancy. As he told Drummond, he once "consumed a whole night in lying looking to his great toe, about which he had seen Tartars and Turks, Romans and Carthaginians fight in his imagination." In Drummond's view, Jonson was "oppressed with fantasy." Perhaps it was so—but Jonson's capacity for fantasy also produced a wide variety of plays, masques, and poems, in styles ranging from witty comedy to delicate lyricism.

Volpone

This dark satire on human rapacity is set in Venice, but its true target is the city of London, or the city that, Jonson feared, London was about to become. It is a place devoted to commerce and mired in corruption, populated by greedy fools and conniving rascals. Like Shakespeare, Donne, and Thomas More before him, Jonson was deeply disturbed by the rise of a protocapitalist economic order

Fox Handling Masks. This woodcut from Andrea Alciato's *Emblemata* depicts the traditional association between foxes and deceptive human role-playing, a connection central to *Volpone.*

that seemed to emphasize competition and the acquisition of material goods over reciprocal goodwill and mutual obligation. On the other hand, Jonson was also fascinated by the entrepreneurial potential liberated by the new economic order. His protagonists, Volpone and Mosca, may be morally bankrupt, but they are also the most intelligent, adaptable characters in the play. Moreover, although Jonson was a strong advocate for the educational and morally improving potential of the theater—his theater in particular—the talents of his main characters are essentially those of theatrical performance and improvisation. In fact, as Jonson was well aware, he was himself deeply implicated in what he satirized. The low-born, unscrupulous, brilliantly inventive Mosca, a flattering aristocratic hanger-on who aspires to high status himself, at times seems to be the author's evil twin. Perhaps his very resemblances to Jonson required Jonson so energetically to repudiate his motives and punish his presumption at the end of the play.

Volpone combines elements from several sources. The classical satirist Lucian provided the theme of the rich old man playing with moneygrubbing scoundrels who hope to inherit his wealth. Roman comedy provided prototypes for some characters: the wily parasite, the unscrupulous lawyer, the avaricious dotard, the voluble woman. Some scenes, such as that in which Volpone disguised as a mountebank woos Celia at her window, are drawn from the Italian commedia dell'arte. Jonson draws as well upon ancient and medieval beast fables: stories about the crafty antihero Reynard the fox, as well as a fable about a fox that plays dead in order to catch greedy birds. But *Volpone* is much more than the sum of its borrowings. It is a work of enormous comic energy, full of black humor, which holds its loathsome characters up for appalled but gleeful inspection.

Volpone was first performed by the King's Men (Shakespeare's company) in the spring of 1606, at the Globe Theater. (See the illustration, in the appendices to this volume, of a contemporary popular theater constructed on similar lines.) The Globe seated some two thousand persons—aristocrats and prosperous citizens in the tiered galleries, lower-class "groundlings" in the pit in the front of the stage. The play was also performed to great applause before learned audiences at Oxford and Cambridge, to whom Jonson dedicated the printed edition of *Volpone*. It was first published in quarto form in 1607 and republished with a few changes in the 1616 *Works*, the basis for the present text.

1 4 4 5

Volpone

or
The Fox

THE PERSONS OF THE PLAY[1]

VOLPONE, *a magnifico*°		*Venetian nobleman*
MOSCA, *his parasite*°		*hanger-on*
NANO, *a dwarf*		
ANDROGYNO, *a hermaphrodite*		
CASTRONE, *an eunuch*		
VOLTORE, *an advocate*°		*lawyer*
CORBACCIO, *an old gentleman*		
BONARIO, *a young gentleman* [CORBACCIO's son]		
CORVINO, *a merchant*		
CELIA, *the merchant's wife*		
Servitore, a SERVANT [*to* CORVINO]		
[*Sir*] POLITIC *Would-be, a knight*		
Fine Madame [LADY] WOULD-BE, *the knight's wife*		
[*Two*] WOMEN [*servants to* LADY WOULD-BE]		
PEREGRINE, *a gentleman traveler*		
AVOCATORI,° *four magistrates*		*public prosecutors*
Notario [NOTARY], *the register*°		*court recorder*
COMMENDATORI,° *officers*		*court deputies*
[*Other court officials, litter-bearers*]		
Mercatori, three MERCHANTS		
Grege [*members of a* CROWD]		

SCENE. *Venice*

The Argument[1]

V	olpone, childless, rich, feigns sick, despairs,°		*is despaired of*
O	ffers his state° to hopes of several heirs,		*estate*
L	ies languishing; his parasite receives		
P	resents of all, assures, deludes, then weaves		
O	ther cross-plots, which ope themselves,° are told.°		*unfold / exposed*
N	ew tricks for safety are sought; they thrive—when, bold,		
E	ach tempts th'other again, and all are sold.°		*betrayed*

Prologue

Now, luck yet send us, and a little wit
Will serve to make our play hit

The Persons of the Play
1. Many of the characters have allegorically apt names. "Volpone" is defined in John Florio's 1598 Italian-English dictionary as "an old fox . . . a sneaking, lurking, wily deceiver." "Mosca" means "fly." "Nano" means "dwarf." "Voltore" means "vulture." "Corbaccio" means "raven." "Bonario" is derived from *bono*, meaning "good." "Corvino"

means "crow." "Celia" means "heaven." "Politic" means "worldly-wise" or "temporizing." "Peregrine" means "traveler" or "small hawk." In many performances the symbolism of the animal names is reinforced by costuming.
The Argument
1. Plot summary. Jonson imitates the acrostic "arguments" of the Latin playwright Plautus.

According to the palates of the season.°   *fashionable taste*
Here is rhyme not empty of reason.
5 This we were bid to credit° from our poet,   *asked to believe*
Whose true scope,° if you would know it,   *aim*
In all his poems still hath been this measure,
To mix profit with your pleasure;[1]
And not as some—whose throats their envy failing°— *not fully expressing*
10 Cry hoarsely, "all he writes is railing,"°   *personal insult*
And when his plays come forth think they can flout them
With saying he was a year about them.[2]
To these there needs no lie° but this his creature,° *denial / creation*
Which was, two months since, no feature;°   *nonexistent*
15 And, though he dares give them° five lives to mend it, *his detractors*
'Tis known five weeks fully penned it
From his own hand, without a coadjutor,°   *collaborator*
Novice, journeyman,° or tutor.   *apprentice*
Yet thus much I can give you, as a token
20 Of his play's worth: no eggs are broken,
Nor quaking custards with fierce teeth affrighted,[3]
Wherewith your rout° are so delighted;   *mob*
Nor hales he in a gull,° old ends° reciting,   *fool / saws*
To stop gaps in his loose writing,
25 With such a deal of monstrous and forced action
As might make Bethlehem a faction.[4]
Nor made he his play for jests stol'n from each table,° *plagiarized jokes*
But makes jests to fit his fable,
And so presents quick° comedy, refined   *lively*
30 As best critics have designed.
The laws of time, place, persons he observeth;[5]
From no needful rule he swerveth.
All gall and copperas[6] from his ink he draineth;
Only a little salt[7] remaineth
35 Wherewith he'll rub your cheeks, till, red with laughter,
They shall look fresh a week after.

Prologue
1. Rule, as laid down by Horace, that the poet ought both to please his audience and teach it something useful.
2. Thomas Dekker ridiculed the slow pace at which Jonson produced new work in *Satiromastix, or The Untrussing of the Humorous Poet* (1602), and John Marston did the same in *The Dutch Courtesan* (1605).
3. The satirist John Marston, in a line Jonson had previously ridiculed, boasted: "let custards [cowards] quake, my rage must freely run." Huge custards were a staple feature of city feasts.
4. As might win approval from lunatics (who inhabited Bethlehem hospital in London).
5. He observes the unities of time and place and the consistency of character.
6. Ferrous sulfate, like gall a corrosive substance used in ink.
7. A traditional metaphor for satiric wit.

Act 1

SCENE 1. VOLPONE's *house*.

[*Enter*] VOLPONE [*and*] MOSCA.[1]

VOLPONE   Good morning to the day, and, next, my gold!
  Open the shrine that I may see my saint.
                     [*Mosca reveals the treasure.*][2]
  Hail the world's soul,° and mine! More glad than is   *animating principle*
  The teeming earth to see the longed-for sun
5 Peep through the horns of the celestial Ram[3]
  Am I to view thy splendor darkening his,°   *outshining the sun's*
  That, lying here amongst my other hoards,
  Show'st like a flame by night, or like the day
  Struck out of chaos, when all darkness fled
10 Unto the center.° O thou son of Sol[4]—   *center of the earth*
  But brighter than thy father—let me kiss
  With adoration thee and every relic
  Of sacred treasure in this blessèd room.
  Well did wise poets by thy glorious name
15 Title that age which they would have the best,[5]
  Thou being the best of things, and far transcending
  All style of joy in children, parents, friends,
  Or any other waking dream on earth.
  Thy looks when they to Venus did ascribe,
20 They should have giv'n her twenty thousand Cupids,[6]
  Such are thy beauties and our loves.° Dear saint,   *our love of thee*
  Riches, the dumb god, that giv'st all men tongues,
  That canst do naught and yet mak'st men do all things,
  The price of souls; even hell, with thee to boot,°   *in the bargain*
25 Is made worth heaven! Thou art virtue, fame,
  Honor, and all things else. Who° can get thee,   *Whoever*
  He shall be noble, valiant, honest, wise—
MOSCA   And what he will, sir. Riches are in fortune
  A greater good than wisdom is in nature.
30 VOLPONE   True, my belovèd Mosca. Yet I glory
  More in the cunning purchase° of my wealth   *acquisition*
  Than in the glad possession, since I gain
  No common way. I use no trade, no venture;°   *risky commerce*
  I wound no earth with plowshares; fat no beasts
35 To feed the shambles;° have no mills for iron,   *slaughterhouse*
  Oil, corn, or men, to grind 'em into powder;

1.1
1. Alternatively, the play may begin with Volpone rising from his onstage bed.
2. The treasure is probably hidden behind a curtain in the alcove at the back of the stage.
3. Aries, the constellation ascendant in early spring.
4. Alchemists believed gold to have issued from the sun ("Sol"). Volpone blasphemously applies this metaphor to God's creation of the world in Genesis.
5. The mythical Golden Age (when, ironically, gold was not yet in use) was influentially described by Ovid in *The Metamorphoses*.
6. In Latin poetry, Venus was commonly described as *aurea*, meaning "golden." The throng of Cupids Volpone imagines around her suggests gold's irresistible, and for him highly sexual, appeal.

I blow no subtle[7] glass; expose no ships
To threat'nings of the furrow-facèd sea;
I turn° no moneys in the public bank,   *exchange*
Nor usure° private—   *lend money at interest*

40 MOSCA   No, sir, nor devour
Soft prodigals. You shall ha' some will swallow
A melting° heir as glibly as your Dutch   *financially dwindling*
Will pills° of butter, and ne'er purge for't;[8]   *morsels*
Tear forth the fathers of poor families

45 Out of their beds and coffin them alive
In some kind, clasping° prison, where their bones *manacling*
May be forthcoming° when the flesh is rotten. *protruding; carted away*
But your sweet nature doth abhor these courses;
You loathe the widow's or the orphan's tears

50 Should wash your pavements, or their piteous cries
Ring in your roofs and beat the air for vengeance.
VOLPONE Right, Mosca, I do loathe it.
MOSCA   And besides, sir,
You are not like the thresher that doth stand
With a huge flail, watching a heap of corn,

55 And, hungry, dares not taste the smallest grain,
But feeds on mallows° and such bitter herbs; *unpalatable weeds*
Nor like the merchant who hath filled his vaults
With Romagnia and rich Candian wines,
Yet drinks the lees of Lombard's vinegar.[9]

60 You will not lie in straw whilst moths and worms
Feed on your sumptuous hangings° and soft beds. *bed curtains*
You know the use of riches, and dare give now
From that bright heap to me, your poor observer,° *follower*
Or to your dwarf, or your hermaphrodite,

65 Your eunuch, or what other household° trifle *menial*
Your pleasure allows maint'nance°— *You're pleased to support*
VOLPONE [*giving money*] Hold thee, Mosca,
Take of my hand; thou strik'st on truth in all,
And they are envious term° thee parasite. *who term*
Call forth my dwarf, my eunuch, and my fool,
And let 'em make me sport. [*Exit* MOSCA.]

70   What should I do
But cocker up my genius,° and live free *indulge my appetite*
To all delights my fortune calls me to?
I have no wife, no parent, child, ally
To give my substance to, but whom I make° *he whom I designate*

75 Must be my heir, and this makes men observe° me. *flatter*
This draws new clients° daily to my house, *petitioners*
Women and men of every sex and age,

---

7. (1) Delicate; (2) artful. (Venice was and is renowned for its art glass.)
8. Never use a remedy for gastric distress. (The Dutch were notoriously fond of butter.)

9. Romagnia and rich Candian wines are expensive wines from Greece and Crete. The lees of Lombard's vinegar are the dregs of cheap Italian wine.

That bring me presents, send me plate,° coin, jewels,   *gold or silver plate*
With hope that when I die—which they expect
80   Each greedy minute—it shall then return
Tenfold upon them; whilst some, covetous
Above the rest, seek to engross° me whole,   *swallow; monopolize*
And counterwork,° the one unto the other,   *compete; undermine*
Contend in gifts as they would seem in love;
85   All which I suffer, playing with their hopes,
And am content to coin 'em into profit,
And look upon their kindness and take more,
And look on that, still bearing them in hand,°   *leading them on*
Letting the cherry knock against their lips,
90   And draw it by their mouths and back again.¹—
How now!

SCENE 2. *The scene continues.*

[*Enter*] MOSCA, NANO, ANDROGYNO, [*and*] CASTRONE.

NANO   Now, room for fresh gamesters,° who do will
         you to know   *entertainers*
They do bring you neither play nor university show,¹
And therefore do entreat you that whatsoever they rehearse
May not fare a whit the worse for the false pace of the verse.²
5   If you wonder at this, you will wonder more ere we pass,
For know here [*indicating* ANDROGYNO] is enclosed the soul
         of Pythagoras,³
That juggler° divine, as hereafter shall follow;   *trickster*
Which soul (fast and loose, sir) came first from Apollo,
And was breathed into Aethalides,⁴ Mercurius his° son,   *Mercury's*
10   Where it had the gift to remember all that ever was done.
From thence it fled forth and made quick transmigration
To goldilocked Euphorbus,⁵ who was killed in good fashion
At the siege of old Troy, by the cuckold of Sparta.⁶
Hermotimus⁷ was next—I find it in my *charta*°—   *record*
15   To whom it did pass, where no sooner it was missing
But with one Pyrrhus of Delos° it learned to go   *another philosopher*
         a-fishing;
And thence did it enter the Sophist of Greece.°   *Pythagoras*
From Pythagore she went into a beautiful piece°   *slut*

1. In the game of chop-cherry, one player dangles a cherry in front of another, who tries to bite it.
1.2
1. University students performed classical plays or their imitations to hone their abilities in Latin oratory.
2. The four-stress meter of the skit Nano, Androgyno, and Castrone here perform was common in medieval drama but old-fashioned by Jonson's time.
3. Ancient Greek philosopher, mathematician, and music theorist who believed in the transmigration of souls and in the mystical properties of geometrical relationships (especially triangles [triangles = trigon]). His followers observed strict dietary restrictions and took five-year vows of silence. His thigh was rumored to be made of gold. Jonson adapts much of the career of Pythagoras's soul from *The Dialogue of the Cobbler and the Cock*, by the Greek satirist Lucian.
4. The herald of the Greek Argonauts and son of the god Mercury, who inherited his father's divine gift of memory. Thus, unlike other souls, which forget their previous lives, Aethalides' soul can recall its transmigrations.
5. Trojan youth who injured Achilles' beloved friend, Patroclus, in the *Iliad*.
6. Menelaus, the Spartan king whose wife, Helen, was stolen by the Trojan prince Paris.
7. Greek philosopher of about 500 B.C.E.

Hight° Aspasia the meretrix;[8] and the next toss of her   *named*

20   Was again of a whore; she became a philosopher,

Crates the Cynic,[9] as itself doth relate it.

Since,° kings, knights, and beggars, knaves, lords, and fools   *since then*

    gat° it,   *received*

Besides ox and ass, camel, mule, goat, and brock,°   *badger*

In all which it hath spoke as in the cobbler's cock.[1]

25   But I come not here to discourse of that matter,

Or his one, two, or three, or his great oath, "By quater,"[2]

His musics, his trigon, his golden thigh,°   *see n. 3, p. 1449*

Or his telling how elements° shift; but I   *earth, air, fire, water*

Would ask how of late thou hast suffered translation,°   *metamorphosis*

30   And shifted thy coat in these days of reformation?°   *religious change*

ANDROGYNO   Like one of the reformed, a fool,[3] as you see,

Counting all old doctrine heresy.

NANO   But not on thine own forbid meats hast thou ventured?

ANDROGYNO   On fish, when first a Carthusian I entered.[4]

35 NANO   Why, then thy dogmatical silence° hath left thee?   *vow of silence*

ANDROGYNO   Of that an obstreperous lawyer bereft me.

NANO   Oh, wonderful change! When Sir Lawyer forsook thee,

For Pythagore's sake, what body then took thee?

ANDROGYNO   A good dull mule.

NANO   And how, by that means,

40   Thou wert brought to allow of the eating of beans?

ANDROGYNO   Yes.

NANO   But from the mule into whom didst thou pass?

ANDROGYNO   Into a very strange beast, by some writers called

    an ass;

By others a precise, pure, illuminate brother[5]

45   Of those devour flesh and sometimes one another,°   *prey on each other*

And will drop you forth a libel° or a sanctified lie   *polemic*

Betwixt every spoonful of a Nativity pie.[6]

NANO   Now quit thee, for heaven, of that profane nation,°   *sect*

And gently report thy next transmigration.

ANDROGYNO   To the same that I am.°   *what I am now*

50 NANO   A creature of delight?

And—what is more than a fool—an hermaphrodite?

Now pray thee, sweet soul, in all thy variation°   *of all your shapes*

Which body wouldst thou choose to take up thy station?

ANDROGYNO   Troth, this I am in, even here would I tarry.

55 NANO   'Cause here the delight of each sex thou canst vary?

---

8. Whore. Aspasia was the mistress of the Athenian statesman Pericles.

9. Student of Diogenes, founder of the Cynic philosophy.

1. The speaker in Lucian's dialogue (see note 3 above).

2. A quater is an equilateral triangle the sides of which are evenly divisible by four.

3. The "reformed" are Protestants in general, but more specifically the Puritan wing of the Church of England. Jonson was a Catholic when he wrote *Volpone*.

4. Pythagoreans abstained from fish, but Carthusians, an order of Catholic monks, ate fish on fast days.

5. Puritan who claimed immediate, visionary knowledge of religious truth. Puritans did not observe the traditional fasting days (hence "devour flesh" in the following line).

6. Puritans substituted the term "Nativity" for "Christmas," to avoid reference to the Mass.

ANDROGYNO   Alas, those pleasures be stale and forsaken.
   No, 'tis your fool wherewith I am so taken,
   The only one creature that I can call blessèd,
   For all other forms I have proved° most distressèd.   *found to be*
60 NANO   Spoke true, as thou wert in Pythagoras still.
   This learnèd opinion we celebrate will,
   Fellow eunuch, as behooves us, with all our wit and art,
   To dignify that° whereof ourselves are so great and special a part.   *folly*
VOLPONE [*applauding*]   Now, very, very pretty! Mosca, this
   Was thy invention?
65 MOSCA   If it please my patron,
   Not else.
VOLPONE   It doth, good Mosca.
MOSCA   Then it was, sir.

SONG

NANO *and* CASTRONE [*sing*]
      Fools, they are the only nation°   *group*
      Worth men's envy or admiration,
      Free from care or sorrow-taking,
70   Selves° and others merry making;   *Themselves*
      All they speak or do is sterling.
      Your fool, he is your great man's dearling,
      And your lady's sport and pleasure;
      Tongue and bauble° are his treasure.   *fool's staff; penis*
75   E'en his face begetteth laughter,
      And he speaks truth free from slaughter.°   *with impunity*
      He's the grace of every feast,
      And sometimes the chiefest guest,
      Hath his trencher° and his stool,   *platter*
80   When wit waits upon the fool.
        Oh, who would not be
        He, he, he?   *One knocks without.*
VOLPONE   Who's that? Away!
               [*Exeunt* NANO *and* CASTRONE.]
          Look, Mosca.
MOSCA   Fool, begone!
               [*Exit* ANDROGYNO.]
   'Tis Signor Voltore, the advocate;
   I know him by his knock.
85 VOLPONE   Fetch me my gown,
   My furs, and nightcaps; say my couch is changing,[7]
   And let him entertain himself awhile
   Without i'th'gallery.   [*Exit* MOSCA.]
         Now, now, my clients
   Begin their visitation! Vulture, kite,
90 Raven, and gorcrow,° all my birds of prey   *carrion crow*
   That think me turning carcass, now they come.

---

7. My bedsheets are being changed.

I am not for 'em° yet.   *ready to die*
   [*Enter* MOSCA.]
               How now? The news?

MOSCA   A piece of plate,° sir.   *gold platter*
VOLPONE   Of what bigness?
MOSCA   Huge,
   Massy, and antique, with your name inscribed
   And arms° engraven.   *coat of arms*
95 VOLPONE   Good! And not a fox
   Stretched on the earth, with fine delusive sleights°   *deceptive tricks*
   Mocking a gaping crow?[8] Ha, Mosca?
MOSCA [*laughing*]   Sharp, sir.
VOLPONE   Give me my furs. Why dost thou laugh so, man?
MOSCA   I cannot choose, sir, when I apprehend
100 What thoughts he has, without,° now, as he walks: *outside*
   That this might be the last gift he should° give;   *would have to*
   That this would fetch you;° if you died today   *bring you around*
   And gave him all, what he should be tomorrow;
   What large return would come of all his ventures;
105 How he should worshipped be and reverenced;
   Ride with his furs and footcloths,[9] waited on
   By herds of fools and clients; have clear way
   Made for his mule, as lettered° as himself;   *educated*
   Be called the great and learnèd advocate;
110 And then concludes there's naught impossible.
VOLPONE   Yes, to be learnèd, Mosca.
MOSCA   Oh, no, rich
   Implies it.° Hood an ass with reverend purple,[1]   *wealth implies learning*
   So you can hide his two ambitious° ears,   *aspiring; upraised*
   And he shall pass for a cathedral doctor.°   *Doctor of Divinity*
115 VOLPONE   My caps, my caps, good Mosca. Fetch him in.
MOSCA   Stay, sir, your ointment for your eyes.
         [MOSCA *helps* VOLPONE *with his disguise.*]
VOLPONE   That's true.
   Dispatch, dispatch! I long to have possession
   Of my new present.
MOSCA   That, and thousands more
   I hope to see you lord of.
VOLPONE   Thanks, kind Mosca.
120 MOSCA   And that, when I am lost in blended dust,
   And hundred such as I am in succession—
VOLPONE   Nay, that were too much, Mosca.
MOSCA   —you shall live
   Still, to delude these Harpies.[2]
VOLPONE   Loving Mosca!
   'Tis well. My pillow now, and let him enter.
        [*Exit* MOSCA. VOLPONE *lies down.*]

---

8. In one of Aesop's *Fables*, the fox tricks the
crow into dropping its cheese.
9. Ornamental cloths for the back of a horse.
1. Doctors of Divinity wore purple academic

hoods.
2. Mythological ravenous monsters with wom-
en's heads and the bodies and claws of birds.

125   Now, my feigned cough, my phthisic,° and my gout,   *consumption; asthma*
    My apoplexy, palsy, and catarrhs,°   *mucus discharges*
    Help with your forcèd functions this my posture,°   *imposture*
    Wherein this three year I have milked their hopes.
    He comes, I hear him. [*Coughing*] Uh, uh, uh, uh! Oh—

SCENE 3. *The scene continues.*

    [*Enter*] VOLTORE [*with a platter, ushered by*] MOSCA.
MOSCA [*to* VOLTORE]   You still are what you were, sir.
    Only you,
    Of all the rest, are he commands° his love;   *the one who possesses*
    And you do wisely to preserve it thus
    With early visitation and kind notes°   *tokens*
5   Of your good meaning to° him, which, I know,   *intentions toward*
    Cannot but come most grateful. [*Loudly, to* VOLPONE]
    Patron, sir!
    Here's Signor Voltore is come—
VOLPONE [*weakly*]   What say you?
MOSCA   Sir, Signor Voltore is come this morning
    To visit you.
VOLPONE   I thank him.
MOSCA   And hath brought
10   A piece of antique plate bought of Saint Mark,[1]
    With which he here presents you.
VOLPONE   He is welcome.
    Pray him to come more often.
MOSCA   Yes.
VOLTORE [*straining to hear*]   What says he?
MOSCA   He thanks you, and desires you see him often.
VOLPONE   Mosca.
MOSCA   My patron?
VOLPONE [*groping*]   Bring him near. Where is he?
    I long to feel his hand.
15   MOSCA [*guiding* VOLPONE's *hands toward the platter*]   The plate is here, sir.
VOLTORE   How fare you, sir?
VOLPONE   I thank you, Signor Voltore.
    Where is the plate? Mine eyes are bad.
VOLTORE [*relinquishing the platter*]   I'm sorry
    To see you still thus weak.
MOSCA [*aside*]   That he is not weaker.
VOLPONE   You are too munificent.
VOLTORE   No, sir, would to heaven
20   I could as well give health to you as that plate.
VOLPONE   You give, sir, what you can. I thank you. Your love
    Hath taste in° this, and shall not be unanswered.   *is suggested by*
    I pray you see me often.
VOLTORE   Yes, I shall, sir.

1.3
1. Goldsmiths kept shop in the square of Saint Mark's Basilica.

VOLPONE Be not far from me.

MOSCA [*aside to* VOLTORE]   Do you observe that, sir?

25 VOLPONE Hearken unto me still. It will concern you.

MOSCA [*aside to* VOLTORE] You are a happy man, sir. Know your good.

VOLPONE I cannot now last long—

MOSCA (*aside to* VOLTORE)   You are his heir, sir.

VOLTORE (*aside to* MOSCA) Am I?

VOLPONE   I feel me going, uh, uh, uh, uh!

I am sailing to my port, uh, uh, uh, uh!

30 And I am glad I am so near my haven.

[*He pretends to lapse into unconsciousness.*]

MOSCA Alas, kind gentleman! Well, we must all go—

VOLTORE But Mosca—

MOSCA   Age will conquer.

VOLTORE   Pray thee, hear me.

Am I inscribed his heir for certain?

MOSCA   Are you?

I do beseech you, sir, you will vouchsafe

35 To write me i'your family.[2] All my hopes

Depend upon Your Worship. I am lost

Except° the rising sun do shine on me.   unless

VOLTORE It shall both shine and warm thee, Mosca.

MOSCA   Sir,

I am a man that have not done your love

40 All the worst offices:° here I wear your keys,   services

See all your coffers and your caskets locked,

Keep the poor inventory of your jewels,

Your plate, and moneys, am your steward, sir,

Husband your goods here.

VOLTORE   But am I sole heir?

45 MOSCA Without a partner, sir, confirmed this morning;

The wax° is warm yet, and the ink scarce dry   of the seal

Upon the parchment.

VOLTORE   Happy, happy me!

By what good chance, sweet Mosca?

MOSCA   Your desert, sir;

I know no second cause.

VOLTORE   Thy modesty

50 Is loath to know it.° Well, we shall requite it.   admit your role

MOSCA He ever liked your course, sir; that first took him.

I oft have heard him say how he admired

Men of your large[3] profession, that could speak

To every cause, and things mere contraries,°   utterly contradictory

55 Till they were hoarse again, yet all be law;

That with most quick agility could turn

And re-turn, make knots and undo them,

Give forkèd° counsel, take provoking gold   ambiguous

2. Employ me in your household (after Volpone's death).

3. Expansive, liberal (with the suggestion of "unscrupulous").

On either hand, and put it up:[4] these men,
60 He knew, would thrive with their humility.°   *obsequiousness*
And for his part, he thought he should be blessed
To have his heir of such a suffering° spirit,   *long-suffering*
So wise, so grave, of so perplexed° a tongue,   *bewildering*
And loud withal,° that would not wag nor scarce   *besides*
65 Lie still without a fee, when every word
Your Worship but lets fall is a *cecchine!*°   *Another knocks.*   *gold coin*
Who's that? One knocks; I would not have you seen, sir.
And yet—pretend you came and went in haste;
I'll fashion an excuse. And, gentle sir,
70 When you do come to swim in golden lard,
Up to the arms in honey, that your chin
Is born up stiff with fatness of the flood,
Think on your vassal; but° remember me.   *only*
I ha' not been your worst of clients.
VOLTORE   Mosca—
75 MOSCA   When will you have your inventory brought, sir?
Or see a copy of the will? [*More knocking.*] Anon!°—   *Just a minute!*
I'll bring 'em to you, sir. Away, begone,
Put business i'your face.[5]   [*Exit* VOLTORE.]
VOLPONE   Excellent, Mosca!
Come hither, let me kiss thee.
MOSCA   Keep you still, sir.
Here is Corbaccio.
80 VOLPONE   Set the plate away.
The vulture's gone, and the old raven's come.

SCENE 4. *The scene continues.*

MOSCA [*to* VOLPONE]   Betake you to your silence and your sleep;
                              [*He puts up the plate.*]
Stand there and multiply.°—Now shall we see   *beget more booty*
A wretch who is indeed more impotent
Than this° can feign to be, yet hopes to hop   *Volpone*
Over his grave.
         [*Enter*] CORBACCIO.
5   Signor Corbaccio!
You're very welcome, sir.
CORBACCIO   How does your patron?
MOSCA   Troth, as he did, sir: no amends.
CORBACCIO   What? Mends he?
MOSCA   No, sir, he is rather worse.
CORBACCIO   That's well. Where is he?
MOSCA   Upon his couch, sir, newly fall'n asleep.
CORBACCIO   Does he sleep well?
10 MOSCA   No wink, sir, all this night,

---

4. Take a bribe from each party to a suit and pocket it.   5. Look as if you were here on business.

Nor yesterday, but slumbers.° *dozes fitfully*
CORBACCIO Good! He should take
Some counsel of physicians. I have brought him
An opiate here, from mine own doctor—
MOSCA He will not hear of drugs.
CORBACCIO Why, I myself
15 Stood by while't was made, saw all th'ingredients,
And know it cannot but most gently work.
My life for his, 'tis but to make him sleep.
VOLPONE [*aside*] Ay, his last sleep, if he would take it.
MOSCA Sir,
He has no faith in physic.° *medicine*
CORBACCIO 'Say you? 'Say you?
20 MOSCA He has no faith in physic. He does think
Most of your doctors[1] are the greater danger
And worse disease t'escape. I often have
Heard him protest that your physician
Should never be his heir.
CORBACCIO Not I his heir?
MOSCA Not your physician, sir.
25 CORBACCIO Oh, no, no, no,
I do not mean it.
MOSCA No, sir, nor their fees
He cannot brook.° He says they flay° a man *tolerate / skin*
Before they kill him.
CORBACCIO Right, I do conceive° you. *understand*
MOSCA And then, they do it by experiment,[2]
30 For which the law not only doth absolve 'em,
But gives them great reward; and he is loath
To hire his death so.
CORBACCIO It is true, they kill
With as much license as a judge.
MOSCA Nay, more:
For he° but kills, sir, where the law condemns, *the judge*
And these° can kill him,° too. *the doctors / the judge*
35 CORBACCIO Ay, or me
Or any man. How does his apoplex?° *apoplexy, stroke*
Is that strong on him still?
MOSCA Most violent.[3]
His speech is broken and his eyes are set,° *fixed*
His face drawn longer than 'twas wont—
CORBACCIO How? How?
Stronger than he was wont?
40 MOSCA No, sir: his face
Drawn longer than 'twas wont.

1.4
1. Not Corbaccio's doctors, but doctors generally. (Also in line 23.)
2. By testing possible remedies on their patients.

3. In the following lines, Mosca attributes to
Volpone a wide variety of symptoms that were,
even occurring singly, considered sure signs of
impending death.

CORBACCIO   Oh, good.

MOSCA   His mouth
Is ever gaping, and his eyelids hang.

CORBACCIO   Good.

MOSCA A freezing numbness stiffens all his joints,
And makes the color of his flesh like lead.

CORBACCIO   'Tis good.

MOSCA His pulse beats slow and dull.

45 CORBACCIO   Good symptoms still.

MOSCA And from his brain—

CORBACCIO   Ha? How? Not from his brain?

MOSCA Yes, sir, and from his brain—

CORBACCIO   I conceive you, good.

MOSCA   —Flows a cold sweat with a continual rheum°   *mucus discharge*
Forth the resolvèd° corners of his eyes.   *watery; limp*

50 CORBACCIO Is't possible? Yet I am better, ha!
How does he with the swimming of his head?

MOSCA Oh, sir, 'tis past the scotomy;[4] he now
Hath lost his feeling, and hath left to snort;°   *stopped snoring*
You hardly can perceive him that he breathes.

55 CORBACCIO Excellent, excellent. Sure I shall outlast him!
This makes me young again a score of years.

MOSCA I was a-coming for you, sir,

CORBACCIO   Has he made his will?
What has he giv'n me?

MOSCA   No, sir.

CORBACCIO   Nothing? Ha?

MOSCA He has not made his will, sir.

CORBACCIO   Oh, oh, oh.

60 What then did Voltore, the lawyer, here?

MOSCA He smelt a carcass, sir, when he but heard
My master was about his testament°—   *making his will*
As I did urge him to it, for your good—

CORBACCIO He came unto him, did he? I thought so.

65 MOSCA Yes, and presented him this piece of plate.

CORBACCIO To be his heir?

MOSCA   I do not know, sir.

CORBACCIO   True,
I know it too.

MOSCA *[aside]* By your own scale,° sir.   *scale of values*

CORBACCIO *[showing a bag of gold]* Well,
I shall prevent° him yet. See, Mosca, look,   *forestall*
Here I have brought a bag of bright *cecchines*,
Will quite weigh down his plate.

70 MOSCA   Yea, marry, sir!
This is true physic, this your sacred medicine;
No talk of opiates to° this great elixir.[5]   *compared to*

---

4. Dizziness, accompanied by partial blindness.
5. In alchemy, a liquid thought to be capable of prolonging life indefinitely or changing base metal into gold.

CORBACCIO   'Tis *aurum palpabile*, if not *potabile*.[6]

MOSCA   It shall be ministered to him in his bowl?

CORBACCIO   Ay, do, do, do.

75 MOSCA   Most blessed cordial!°   heart medicine
This will recover him.

CORBACCIO   Yes, do, do, do.

MOSCA   I think it were not best, sir.

CORBACCIO   What?

MOSCA   To recover him.

CORBACCIO   Oh, no, no, no; by no means.

MOSCA   Why, sir, this
Will work some strange effect, if he but feel it.

80 CORBACCIO   'Tis true, therefore forbear, I'll take my venture.°   investment
Give me 't again.   [*He snatches for the bag.*]

MOSCA [*keeping it out of his reach*]   At no hand.° Pardon me,   By no means
You shall not do yourself that wrong, sir. I
Will so advise you, you shall have it all.

CORBACCIO   How?

MOSCA   All, sir, 'tis your right, your own; no man

85 Can claim a part. 'Tis yours without a rival,
Decreed by destiny.

CORBACCIO   How? How, good Mosca?

MOSCA   I'll tell you, sir. This fit he shall recover—

CORBACCIO   I do conceive you.

MOSCA   —and, on first advantage°   opportunity
Of his gained sense, will I re-importune him

90 Unto the making of his testament,
And show him this.

CORBACCIO   Good, good.

MOSCA   'Tis better yet,
If you will hear, sir.

CORBACCIO   Yes, with all my heart.

MOSCA   Now, would I counsel you, make home with speed;
There frame a will, whereto you shall inscribe
My master your sole heir.

95 CORBACCIO   And disinherit
My son?

MOSCA   Oh, sir, the better, for that color°   appearance, fiction
Shall make it much more taking.°   plausible; attractive

CORBACCIO   Oh, but color?°   it's only a ruse?

MOSCA   This will, sir, you shall send it unto me.
Now, when I come to enforce°—as I will do—   urge

100 Your cares, your watchings, and your many prayers,
Your more than many gifts, your this day's present,
And last produce your will, where—without thought
Or least regard unto your proper issue,°   own offspring
A son so brave° and highly meriting—   splendid

---

6. It is gold that can be felt, if not drunk. (Latin.) Dissolved gold was used as a medicine.

105 The stream of your diverted love hath thrown you
Upon my master, and made him your heir,
He cannot be so stupid or stone dead
But out of conscience and mere gratitude—
CORBACCIO He must pronounce me his?
MOSCA   'Tis true.
CORBACCIO   This plot
Did I think on before.
110 MOSCA   I do believe it.
CORBACCIO Do you not believe it?
MOSCA   Yes, sir.
CORBACCIO   Mine own project.
MOSCA Which when he hath done, sir—
CORBACCIO   Published me his heir?
MOSCA And you so certain to survive him—
CORBACCIO   Ay.
MOSCA Being so lusty a man—
CORBACCIO   'Tis true.
MOSCA   Yes, sir—
115 CORBACCIO I thought on that too. See how he° should be   *Mosca*
The very organ to express my thoughts!
MOSCA You have not only done yourself a good—
CORBACCIO But multiplied it on my son?
MOSCA   'Tis right, sir.
CORBACCIO Still my invention.
MOSCA   'Las, sir, heaven knows,
120 It hath been all my study, all my care,
(I e'en grow gray withal) how to work things—
CORBACCIO I do conceive, sweet Mosca.
MOSCA   You are he
For whom I labor here.
CORBACCIO   Ay, do, do, do.
I'll straight about it.   [CORBACCIO *starts to leave.*]
MOSCA   Rook go with you,[7] raven!
CORBACCIO I know thee honest.
MOSCA   You do lie, sir—
125 CORBACCIO   And—
MOSCA Your knowledge is no better than your ears, sir.
CORBACCIO I do not doubt to be a father to thee.
MOSCA Nor I to gull my brother of his blessing.[8]
CORBACCIO I may ha' my youth restored to me, why not?
MOSCA Your Worship is a precious ass—
130 CORBACCIO   What say'st thou?
MOSCA I do desire Your Worship to make haste, sir.

7. May you be swindled ("rooked"). Playing on "rook" meaning "crow," "raven." This speech and Mosca's following lines, through line 130, could be considered asides since Corbaccio cannot hear them; but they need not be delivered sotto voce.
8. If Corbaccio were Mosca's father, then Bonario would be his brother. A reference to Genesis 25, in which Jacob tricks his elder brother, Esau, into resigning his birthright, and Genesis 27, in which Jacob tricks their dying father, Isaac, into giving him the paternal blessing and property.

CORBACCIO 'Tis done, 'tis done, I go.   [*Exit.*]
VOLPONE [*leaping from the bed*]   Oh, I shall burst!
   Let out my sides,° let out my sides—   *Loosen my clothes*
MOSCA   Contain
   Your flux of laughter, sir. You know this hope
135 Is such a bait it covers any hook.
VOLPONE Oh, but thy working and thy placing it!
   I cannot hold;° good rascal, let me kiss thee.   *contain my delight*
   I never knew thee in so rare a humor.°   *so excellently witty*
MOSCA Alas, sir, I but do as I am taught:
140 Follow your grave instructions, give 'em words,
   Pour oil into their ears,° and send them hence.   *Flatter them*
VOLPONE 'Tis true, 'tis true. What a rare punishment
   Is avarice to itself!⁹
MOSCA   Ay, with our help, sir.
VOLPONE So many cares, so many maladies,
145 So many fears attending on old age,
   Yea, death so often called on,° as no wish   *invoked*
   Can be more frequent with 'em, their limbs faint,
   Their senses dull, their seeing, hearing, going,°   *ability to walk*
   All dead before them; yea, their very teeth,
150 Their instruments of eating, failing them—
   Yet this is reckoned life! Nay, here was one
   Is now gone home that wishes to live longer!
   Feels not his gout nor palsy, feigns himself
   Younger by scores of years, flatters his age
155 With confident belying it,¹ hopes he may
   With charms, like Aeson,² have his youth restored,
   And with these thoughts so battens,° as if fate   *gluts himself*
   Would be as easily cheated on as he,
   And all turns air!°   *Another knocks.*   *is illusory*
   Who's that there, now? A third?
160 MOSCA Close,° to your couch again. I hear his voice.   *Hide yourself*
   It is Corvino, our spruce° merchant.   *dapper*
VOLPONE [*lying down again*]   Dead.°   *I'll play dead*
MOSCA Another bout, sir, with your eyes.
                   [*He applies ointment.*]
                   Who's there?

SCENE 5. *The scene continues.*

   [*Enter*] CORVINO.
   Signor Corvino! Come° most wished for! Oh,   *You come*
   How happy were you if you knew it now!
CORVINO Why? What? Wherein?
MOSCA   The tardy hour is come, sir.

---

9. Quoting the Stoic philosopher Seneca's *Moral Epistles*, no. 115.
1. Deceives himself, and attempts to deceive others, about his age by vigorously refusing to admit the truth.
2. Father of the Greek hero Jason; his youth was restored by Medea, his sorceress daughter-in-law.

CORVINO He is not dead?

MOSCA   Not dead, sir, but as good;
  He knows no man.

CORVINO   How shall I do, then?

5 MOSCA   Why, sir?

CORVINO I have brought him here a pearl.

MOSCA   Perhaps he has
  So much remembrance left as to know you, sir;
  He still calls on you; nothing but your name
  Is in his mouth. Is your pearl orient,[1] sir?

10 CORVINO Venice was never owner of the like.

VOLPONE [weakly] Signor Corvino—

MOSCA   Hark.

VOLPONE   —Signor Corvino—

MOSCA He calls you. Step and give it him.—He's here, sir,
  And he has brought you a rich pearl.

CORVINO [to VOLPONE]   How do you, sir?
  [To MOSCA] Tell him it doubles the twelfth carat.[2]
                    [He gives VOLPONE the pearl.]

MOSCA [to CORVINO]   Sir,
15 He cannot understand. His hearing's gone;
  And yet it comforts him to see you—

CORVINO   Say
  I have a diamond for him too.

MOSCA   Best show't, sir.
  Put it into his hand; 'tis only there
  He apprehends; he has his feeling yet.
                    [CORVINO gives VOLPONE the diamond.]
  See how he grasps it!

20 CORVINO   'Las, good gentleman!
  How pitiful the sight is!

MOSCA   Tut, forget, sir.
  The weeping of an heir should still° be laughter   always
  Under a visor.°   mask

CORVINO   Why, am I his heir?

MOSCA Sir, I am sworn; I may not show the will
25 Till he be dead. But here has been Corbaccio,
  Here has been Voltore, here were others too,
  I cannot number 'em they were so many,
  All gaping here for legacies; but I,
  Taking the vantage° of his naming you—   opportunity
30 "Signor Corvino! Signor Corvino!"—took
  Paper and pen and ink, and there I asked him
  Whom he would have his heir? "Corvino." Who
  Should be executor? "Corvino." And
  To any question he was silent to,

1.5
1. Especially brilliant. (The most beautiful
pearls came from the Indian Ocean.)
2. In the seventeenth century, a carat was
between 1/144 and 1/150 of an ounce. A twenty-
four-carat pearl was therefore very large, weighing roughly 1/6 of an ounce.

35 I still interpreted the nods he made
Through weakness for consent, and sent home th'others,
Nothing bequeathed them but to cry and curse.

CORVINO Oh, my dear Mosca! (*They embrace*.) Does he not
perceive us?

MOSCA No more than a blind harper.[3] He knows no man,
40 No face of friend, nor name of any servant,
Who 'twas that fed him last or gave him drink;
Not those he hath begotten or brought up
Can he remember.

CORVINO   Has he children?

MOSCA   Bastards,[4]
Some dozen or more, that he begot on beggars,
45 Gypsies and Jews and blackmoors,° when he was drunk.   black Africans
Knew you not that, sir? 'Tis the common fable.°   rumor
The dwarf, the fool, the eunuch are all his;
He's the true father of his family
In all save° me, but he has given 'em nothing.   except

50 CORVINO That's well, that's well. Art sure he does not
hear us?

MOSCA Sure, sir? Why, look you, credit your own sense.°   believe your senses
[*Shouting at* VOLPONE] The pox° approach and add to   syphilis
your diseases
If it would send you hence the sooner, sir.
For your incontinence, it hath deserved it
55 Throughly° and throughly, and the plague to boot.   thoroughly
[*To* CORVINO] You may come near, sir. [*Shouting at* VOLPONE *again*]
Would you would once close
Those filthy eyes of yours, that flow with slime
Like two frog-pits,° and those same hanging cheeks,   mud puddles
Covered with hide instead of skin—nay, help, sir—
60 That look like frozen dishclouts° set on end!   dishrags

CORVINO [*shouting at* VOLPONE] Or like an old smoked wall on
which the rain
Ran down in streaks!

MOSCA   Excellent, sir! Speak out;
You may be louder yet; a culverin°   firearm
Dischargèd in his ear would hardly bore it.

65 CORVINO [*shouting*] His nose is like a common sewer, still°   continually
running.

MOSCA 'Tis good! And what his mouth?

CORVINO [*shouting*]   A very draught!°   cesspool

MOSCA Oh, stop it up—

CORVINO   By no means.

MOSCA   Pray you let me.
Faith, I could stifle him rarely with a pillow
As well as any woman that should keep° him.   take care of

CORVINO Do as you will, but I'll be gone.

3. Harp players were often blind.
4. By law, ordinarily barred from the line of inheritance.

70 MOSCA   Be so;
   It is your presence makes him last so long.
   CORVINO   I pray you, use no violence.
   MOSCA   No, sir? Why?
   Why should you be thus scrupulous? Pray you, sir.
   CORVINO   Nay, at your discretion.
   MOSCA   Well, good sir, begone.
75 CORVINO   I will not trouble him now to take my pearl?
   MOSCA   Pooh! Nor your diamond. What a needless care
   Is this afflicts you? Is not all here yours?
   Am not I here, whom you have made your creature?
   That owe my being to you?
   CORVINO   Grateful Mosca!
80 Thou art my friend, my fellow, my companion,
   My partner, and shalt share in all my fortunes.
   MOSCA   Excepting one.
   CORVINO   What's that?
   MOSCA   Your gallant° wife, sir.   splendid
                                      [_Exit_ CORVINO.]
   Now is he gone. We had no other means
   To shoot him hence but this.
   VOLPONE   My divine Mosca!
   Thou hast today outgone thyself.   _Another knocks._
85   Who's there?
   I will be troubled with no more. Prepare
   Me music, dances, banquets, all delights.
   The Turk[5] is not more sensual in his pleasures
   Than will Volpone.   [_Exit_ MOSCA.]
                     Let me see, a pearl?
90 A diamond? Plate? _Cecchines?_ Good morning's purchase.°   haul
   Why, this is better than rob churches, yet,
   Or fat by eating, once a month, a man.°   _i.e., taking monthly interest_
           [_Enter_ MOSCA.]
   Who is't?
   MOSCA   The beauteous Lady Would-be, sir,
   Wife to the English knight, Sir Politic Would-be—
95 This is the style, sir, is directed me[6]—
   Hath sent to know how you have slept tonight,°   last night
   And if you would be visited.
   VOLPONE   Not now.
   Some three hours hence—
   MOSCA   I told the squire° so much.   messenger
   VOLPONE   When I am high with mirth and wine: then, then.
100 'Fore heaven, I wonder at the desperate° valor   reckless
   Of the bold English, that they dare let loose
   Their wives to all encounters![7]

5. Stereotyped as given to decadent luxuries.
6. This is the mode of address I've been told to use.
7. Married Englishwomen were reputed to enjoy more personal freedom than their southern European counterparts; Venetian wives in particular were much restricted, though Celia's situation is obviously extreme (see below, lines 118–26).

MOSCA Sir, this knight
Had not his name for nothing. He is politic,°   *canny*
And knows, howe'er his wife affect strange° airs,   *foreign; bizarre*
105 She hath not yet the face[8] to be dishonest.°   *unchaste*
But had she Signor Corvino's wife's face—
VOLPONE Has she so rare a face?
MOSCA Oh, sir, the wonder,
The blazing star[9] of Italy! A wench
O'the first year!° A beauty ripe as harvest!   *unflawed and in her prime*
110 Whose skin is whiter than a swan, all over,
Than silver, snow, or lilies! A soft lip,
Would° tempt you to eternity of kissing!   *That would*
And flesh that melteth in the touch to blood![1]
Bright as your gold, and lovely as your gold!
VOLPONE Why had not I known this before?
115 MOSCA Alas, sir,
Myself but yesterday discovered it.
VOLPONE How might I see her?
MOSCA Oh, not possible.
She's kept as warily as is your gold:
Never does come abroad,° never takes air   *outside*
120 But at a window. All her looks are sweet
As the first° grapes or cherries, and are watched   *of the season*
As near° as they are.   *closely*
VOLPONE I must see her—
MOSCA Sir,
There is a guard of ten spies thick upon her—
All his whole household—each of which is set
125 Upon his fellow, and have all their charge
When he goes out; when he comes in, examined.[2]
VOLPONE I will go see her, though but at her window.
MOSCA In some disguise, then.
VOLPONE That is true. I must
Maintain mine own shape still the same.[3] We'll think.
                    [*Exeunt.*]

Act 2

SCENE 1. *Saint Mark's Square.*

[*Enter*] POLITIC WOULD-BE [*and*] PEREGRINE.
POLITIC Sir, to a wise man all the world's his soil.[1]
It is not Italy, nor France, nor Europe
That must bound me if my fates call me forth.
Yet I protest it is no salt° desire   *inordinate*

---

8. (1) Beauty; (2) shamelessness.
9. Comet. (Rare and beautiful.)
1. (1) Blushes; (2) sexual responsiveness. (Mosca is evidently conjecturing here.)
2. Each member of the household spies on all the others; each gets his instructions when Corvino departs and is interrogated when he returns.
3. I must, in my own person, continue to pretend to be near death.
2.1
1. Proverbial, like most of Sir Pol's "original" advice. "Soil": native land.

5   Of seeing countries, shifting a religion,[2]
   Nor any disaffection to the state
   Where I was bred—and unto which I owe
   My dearest plots°—hath brought me out;° much less   *projects / abroad*
   That idle, antique, stale, gray-headed project
10   Of knowing men's minds and manners with Ulysses;[3]
   But a peculiar humor° of my wife's   *whim*
   Laid for this height° of Venice, to observe,   *latitude*
   To quote,° to learn the language, and so forth.—   *jot things down*
   I hope you travel, sir, with license?[4]

PEREGRINE   Yes.

15 POLITIC   I dare the safelier converse. How long, sir,
   Since you left England?

PEREGRINE   Seven weeks.

POLITIC   So lately!
   You ha' not been with my Lord Ambassador?

PEREGRINE   Not yet, sir.

POLITIC   Pray you, what news, sir, vents our climate?[5]
   I heard last night a most strange thing reported
20   By some of my lord's° followers, and I long   *the ambassador's*
   To hear how't will be seconded.°   *confirmed*

PEREGRINE   What was't, sir?

POLITIC   Marry, sir, of a raven that should build°   *reportedly built*
   In a ship royal of the King's.

PEREGRINE *[aside]*   This fellow,
   Does he gull° me, trow?° Or is gulled?—Your name, sir?   *trick / do you*

POLITIC   My name is Politic Would-be.   *suppose?*

25 PEREGRINE *[aside]*   Oh, that speaks° him.— *characterizes*
   A knight, sir?

POLITIC   A poor knight, sir.[6]

PEREGRINE   Your lady
   Lies° here in Venice for intelligence°   *stays / news*
   Of tires° and fashions and behavior   *apparel*
   Among the courtesans?[7] The fine Lady Would-be?

30 POLITIC   Yes, sir, the spider and the bee ofttimes
   Suck from one flower.

PEREGRINE   Good Sir Politic,
   I cry you mercy!° I have heard much of you.   *beg your pardon*
   'Tis true, sir, of your raven.

POLITIC   On your knowledge?

PEREGRINE   Yes, and your lion's whelping in the Tower.[8]

POLITIC   Another whelp!

---

2. Throughout the 16th and 17th centuries, members of religious minorities throughout Europe sought refuge in lands more hospitable to their faiths.
3. The hero of the *Odyssey*, an archetype of the wise traveler.
4. A passport. (English people could not travel abroad without permission.)
5. Comes from our part of the world?

6. In the first decade of the 17th century, King James I raised badly needed money by selling knighthoods to many whose birth, attainments, or wealth would not have previously merited a title.
7. Venice was famous for its elegant prostitutes.
8. A lioness kept at the Tower of London gave birth in 1604 and 1605.

PEREGRINE   Another, sir.

35 POLITIC   Now, heaven!
What prodigies° be these? The fires at Berwick!   *strange occurrences*
And the new star!⁹ These things concurring,° strange!   *happening together*
And full of omen! Saw you those meteors?

PEREGRINE   I did, sir.

POLITIC   Fearful! Pray you sir, confirm me:

40 Were there three porpoises seen above the bridge,¹
As they give out?°   *people report*

PEREGRINE   Six, and a sturgeon, sir.

POLITIC   I am astonished!

PEREGRINE   Nay, sir, be not so.
I'll tell you a greater prodigy than these—

POLITIC   What should these things portend!

PEREGRINE   The very day—

45 Let me be sure—that I put forth from London,
There was a whale discovered in the river
As high° as Woolwich,² that had waited there—   *far upstream*
Few know how many months—for the subversion
Of the Stode Fleet.³

POLITIC   Is't possible? Believe it,

50 'Twas either sent from Spain or the Archdukes.⁴
Spinola's⁵ whale, upon my life, my credit!°   *honor*
Will they not leave these projects? Worthy sir,
Some other news.

PEREGRINE   Faith, Stone the fool is dead;
And they do lack a tavern-fool extremely.

POLITIC   Is Mas' Stone dead?⁶

55 PEREGRINE   He's dead, sir. Why, I hope
You thought him not immortal? [*Aside*] Oh, this knight,
Were he well known, would be a precious thing
To fit our English stage. He that should write
But such a fellow should be thought to feign
Extremely, if not maliciously.

60 POLITIC   Stone dead!

PEREGRINE   Dead. Lord, how deeply, sir, you apprehend it!
He was no kinsman to you?

POLITIC   That° I know of.   *Not that*
Well, that same fellow was an unknown fool.⁷

---

9. The fires at Berwick were aurora borealis visible above Berwick, Northumberland, in 1605, said to resemble battling armies. The new star, a supernova, was described by the astronomer Johannes Kepler in 1604.
1. A porpoise was found upstream of London Bridge in the Thames River the January before *Volpone* was first performed.
2. A town on the Thames, a bit to the east of London.
3. The English merchant adventurers' ships, which were harboring at Stade, in the mouth of the Elbe River.
4. The Archduke Albert of Austria and his wife,

Isabella, the Infanta of Spain, ruled the Netherlands in the name of Spain.
5. Ambrosio de Spinola was general of the Spanish army in the Netherlands.
6. "Mas'" means "master," a term of address for boys and fools. Stone, King James's outspoken court jester, was a well-known urban character. He was whipped the year before *Volpone*'s first performance for slandering the Lord Admiral. Politic is evidently unaware of the play on words in "Stone dead."
7. The person who said this was not commonly recognized as a spy; he used foolery as his cover.

PEREGRINE	And yet you knew him, it seems?	
POLITIC	I did so. Sir,	
65	I knew him one of the most dangerous heads	
Living within the state, and so I held° him.	*considered*
PEREGRINE	Indeed, sir?	
POLITIC	While he lived, in action,°	*subversive activities*
He has received weekly intelligence,	
Upon my knowledge, out of the Low Countries,	
70	For all parts of the world, in cabbages,°	*a Dutch import*
And those dispensed again to ambassadors	
In oranges, muskmelons, apricots,	
Lemons, pome-citrons,° and suchlike—sometimes	*grapefruitlike fruits*
In Colchester oysters, and your Selsey cockles.[8]	
PEREGRINE	You make me wonder!	
75	POLITIC	Sir, upon my knowledge.
Nay, I have observed him at your public ordinary°	*tavern*
Take his advertisement° from a traveler—	*information*
A concealed statesman—in a trencher° of meat,	*wooden plate*
And instantly before the meal was done	
Convey an answer in a toothpick.[9]	
80	PEREGRINE	Strange!
How could this be, sir?	
POLITIC	Why, the meat was cut
So like his character,° and so laid as he	*code letters*
Must easily read the cipher.	
PEREGRINE	I have heard
He could not read, sir.	
POLITIC	So 'twas given out,
85	In polity,° by those that did employ him.	*craftily*
But he could read, and had your languages,°	*knew foreign languages*
And to't° as sound a noddle°—	*in addition / head*
PEREGRINE	I have heard, sir,
That your baboons were spies, and that they were	
A kind of subtle nation near to China.	
90	POLITIC	Ay, ay, your *Mamuluchi*.[1] Faith, they had
Their hand in a French plot or two, but they	
Were so extremely given to women as	
They made discovery of° all. Yet I	*They revealed*
Had my advices° here, on Wednesday last,	*information*
95	From one of their own coat;° they were returned,	*kind*
Made their relations,° as the fashion is,	*reports*
And now stand fair° for fresh employment.	*ready*
PEREGRINE [*aside*]	Heart,
This Sir Pol will be° ignorant of nothing.	*admit to being*
[*To* POLITIC] It seems, sir, you know all?	
POLITIC	Not all, sir. But

8. Expensive delicacies, unlikely tavern fare.
9. Presumably by inserting a tiny note into a toothpick hollowed out for espionage use.

1. Mamluks, a class of warriors originally from Asia Minor, who ruled Egypt from 1250 to 1517.

100 I have some general notions; I do love
     To note and to observe. Though I live out,°   *abroad*
     Free from the active torrent, yet I'd mark
     The currents and the passages of things
     For mine own private use, and know the ebbs
     And flows of state.
105 PEREGRINE   Believe it, sir, I hold
     Myself in no small tie unto my fortunes°   *much obliged to my luck*
     For casting me thus luckily upon you,
     Whose knowledge—if your bounty equal it—
     May do me great assistance in instruction
110 For my behavior and my bearing, which
     Is yet so rude and raw—
     POLITIC   Why, came you forth
     Empty of rules for travel?
     PEREGRINE   Faith, I had
     Some common ones from out that vulgar grammar,[2]
     Which he that cried° Italian to me taught me.   *taught orally*
115 POLITIC   Why, this it is that spoils all our brave bloods,°   *fine young men*
     Trusting our hopeful° gentry unto pedants,   *promising*
     Fellows of outside and mere bark.[3] You seem
     To be a gentleman of ingenuous race°—   *honorable family*
     I not profess it,° but my fate hath been   *don't declare it openly*
120 To be where I have been consulted with
     In this high kind,° touching some great men's sons,   *important matter*
     Persons of blood° and honor—   *noble birth*
     PEREGRINE   Who be these, sir?

SCENE 2. *The scene continues.*

[*Enter*] MOSCA [*and*] NANO [*disguised as a mountebank's assistants*].
MOSCA   Under that window, there't must be. The same.
                    [MOSCA *and* NANO *set up a platform.*]
POLITIC   Fellows to mount a bank!° Did your instructor   *platform*
     In the dear tongues[1] never discourse to you
     Of the Italian mountebanks?
PEREGRINE   Yes, sir.
POLITIC   Why,
     Here shall you see one.
5 PEREGRINE   They are quacksalvers,
     Fellows that live by venting° oils and drugs.   *selling*
POLITIC   Was that the character he gave you of them?
PEREGRINE   As I remember.
POLITIC   Pity his ignorance.
     They are the only knowing men of Europe!
10 Great general scholars, excellent physicians,
     Most admired statesmen, professed favorites

2. Modern language textbook, which sometimes
included travelers' tips.
3. Superficial accomplishments.

2.2
1. Italian was called the "cara lingua," a phrase
Sir Politic translates.

And cabinet counselors° to the greatest princes!   *close advisers*
The only languaged° men of all the world!   *most eloquent*
PEREGRINE   And I have heard they are most lewd° impostors,   *ignorant*
15   Made all of terms° and shreds, no less beliers   *jargon*
Of great men's favors than their own vile med'cines,
Which they will utter° upon monstrous oaths,   *advertise for sale*
Selling that drug for twopence ere they part
Which they have valued at twelve crowns° before.   *silver or gold coins*
20 POLITIC   Sir, calumnies are answered best with silence.
Yourself shall judge. [*To* MOSCA *and* NANO] Who is it mounts, my friends?
MOSCA   Scoto of Mantua,[2] sir.
POLITIC   Is't he? [*To* PEREGRINE] Nay, then,
I'll proudly promise, sir, you shall behold
Another man than has been fancied° to you.   *presented in imagination*
25 I wonder yet that he should mount his bank
Here in this nook, that has been wont t'appear
In face of° the piazza! Here he comes.   *Facing*
    [*Enter*] VOLPONE [*disguised as a mountebank, followed
    by*] *a crowd.*
VOLPONE [*to* NANO]   Mount, zany.°   *clown; performer*
    [VOLPONE *and* NANO *climb onto the platform.*]
CROWD   Follow, follow, follow, follow, follow!
30 POLITIC   See how the people follow him! He's a man
May write ten thousand crowns in bank here. Note,
Mark but his gesture. I do use° to observe   *make it my practice*
The state° he keeps, in getting up.   *stateliness*
PEREGRINE   'Tis worth it, sir.
VOLPONE   Most noble gentlemen and my worthy patrons, it
35 may seem strange that I, your Scoto Mantuano, who was
ever wont to fix my bank in face of the public piazza near
the shelter of the portico to the *procuratia*,[3] should now,
after eight months' absence from this illustrious city of
Venice, humbly retire myself into an obscure nook of the
40 piazza.
POLITIC [*to* PEREGRINE]   Did not I now object the same?°   *ask the same*
PEREGRINE   Peace, sir.   *question*
VOLPONE   Let me tell you: I am not, as your Lombard prov-
erb saith, cold on my feet,° or content to part with my com-   *in desperate*
modities at a cheaper rate than I accustomed; look not for   *straits*
45 it. Nor that the calumnious reports of that impudent detrac-
tor and shame to our profession (Alessandro Buttone,°   *a rival*
I mean) who gave out in public I was condemned a   *mountebank*
'*sforzato*° to the galleys for poisoning the Cardinal   *prisoner*
Bembo's—cook,[4] hath at all attached,° much less dejected   *stuck to*
50 me. No, no, worthy gentlemen. To tell you true, I cannot

---

2. An Italian juggler and magician who visited England and performed before Elizabeth I in the 1570s.
3. Arcade on the north side of the Piazza di San Marco.

4. Pietro Bembo (1470–1547) was a famous humanist, featured as a speaker in Castiglione's *Courtier* (1528). "Cook" is a teasing substitution for "whore."

endure to see the rabble of these ground *ciarlitani*,[5] that
spread their cloaks on the pavement as if they meant to
do feats of activity° and then come in lamely with their   *acrobatics*
moldy tales out of Boccaccio, like stale Tabarine,[6] the
55   fabulist: some of them discoursing their travels and of
their tedious captivity in the Turks' galleys, when indeed,
were the truth known, they were the Christians' galleys,
where very temperately they ate bread and drunk water as
a wholesome penance, enjoined them by their confessors,
for base pilferies.

60   POLITIC [*to* PEREGRINE]   Note but his bearing and contempt
of these.

VOLPONE   These turdy-facy-nasty-paty-lousy-fartical rogues,
with one poor groatsworth° of unprepared antimony,[7]   *fourpenceworth*
finely wrapped up in several *scartoccios*,° are able very well   *paper envelopes*
65   to kill their twenty a week, and play;° yet these meager   *as if it were a*
starved spirits, who have half stopped the organs of their   *game*
minds with earthy oppilations,° want° not their favorers   *obstructions / lack*
among your shriveled, salad-eating artisans, who are over-
joyed that they may have their ha'p'orth° of physic; though   *halfpennyworth*
70   it purge 'em into another world, 't makes no matter.

POLITIC   Excellent! Ha' you heard better language, sir?

VOLPONE   Well, let 'em go.° And, gentlemen, honorable   *say no more*
gentlemen, know that for this time, our bank, being thus   *about them*
removed from the clamors of the *canaglia*,° shall be the   *mob*
75   scene of pleasure and delight. For I have nothing to sell,
little or nothing to sell.

POLITIC   I told you, sir, his end.

PEREGRINE   You did so, sir.

VOLPONE   I protest, I and my six servants are not able to
80   make of this precious liquor so fast as it is fetched away
from my lodging by gentlemen of your city, strangers of the
terra firma,[8] worshipful merchants, ay, and senators too,
who ever since my arrival have detained me to their uses by
their splendidous liberalities. And worthily. For what avails
your rich man to have his magazines° stuffed with *mosc-*   *storehouses*
85   *adelli*,° or of° the purest grape, when his physicians pre-   *wine / wine of*
scribe him (on pain of death) to drink nothing but water
cocted° with anise seeds? Oh, health, health! The blessing   *boiled*
of the rich! The riches of the poor! Who can buy thee at
too dear a rate, since there is no enjoying this world with-
90   out thee? Be not then so sparing of your purses, honorable
gentlemen, as to abridge the natural course of life—

PEREGRINE   You see his end?

POLITIC   Ay, is't not good?

---

5. Charlatans too poor to afford a "bank," or
platform. "Activity" (following): acrobatics.
6. Boccaccio's *Decameron* is a storehouse of tales.
Tabarine was a member of an Italian comic troupe
that played in France and perhaps in England.
7. White metal used as an emetic and poison.
8. Mainland territory of Venice.

VOLPONE   For when a humid flux° or catarrh, by the muta-   *runny discharge*
bility of air, falls from your head into an arm or shoulder
95   or any other part, take you a ducat or your *cecchine* of
gold and apply to the place affected; see what good effect
it can work. No, no, 'tis this blessed *unguento,*° this rare   *ointment*
extraction, that hath only power to disperse all malignant
humors that proceed either of hot, cold, moist, or windy
causes[9]—

PEREGRINE   I would he had put in "dry," too.

100 POLITIC   Pray you, observe.

VOLPONE   To fortify the most indigest and crude° stomach,   *upset*
ay, were it of one that, through extreme weakness, vomited blood, applying only a warm napkin to the place after
the unction and fricace;° for the *vertigine*° in the head   *massage /*
105   putting but a drop into your nostrils, likewise behind the   *dizziness*
ears, a most sovereign° and approved remedy; the *mal*   *potent*
caduco, cramps, convulsions, paralyses, epilepsies, *tremor*
cordia, retired nerves, ill vapors of the spleen, stoppings of
the liver, the stone, the strangury, *hernia ventosa, iliaca*
110   *passio*; stops a *dysenteria* immediately; easeth the torsion
of the small guts; and cures *melancholia hypochondriaca,*[1]
being taken and applied according to my printed receipt.°   *direction*
(*Pointing to his bill and his glass*).° For this is the physician,   *paper and flagon*
this the medicine; this counsels, this cures; this gives the
115   direction, this works the effect; and in sum, both together
may be termed an abstract of the theoric and practic in the
Aesculapian[2] art. 'Twill cost you eight crowns. And, Zan
Fritatta,[3] pray thee sing a verse extempore in honor of it.

POLITIC   How do you like him, sir?

PEREGRINE   Most strangely, I!

POLITIC   Is not his language rare?°   *unrivaled*

120 PEREGRINE   But° alchemy   *except for*
I never heard the like, or Broughton's books.[4]

SONG

NANO [*sings*]   Had old Hippocrates or Galen,[5]
That to their books put med'cines all in,
But known this secret, they had never
125   (Of which they will be guilty ever)
Been murderers of so much paper,°   *written so much*

9. Renaissance medicine was based on the theory of the humors, four bodily fluids whose balance within the body determined both physical and mental health. Their qualities, in various combinations, were hot, cold, moist, and dry; hence Peregrine's comment in the next line.
1. Volpone's list of diseases includes *"mal caduco,"* epilepsy; *"tremor cordia,"* palpitations; "retired nerves," withered sinews; "ill vapors of the spleen," short temper; "stone," kidney stones; "strangury," painful urination; *"hernia ventosa,"* a hernia containing air; *"iliaca passio,"* intestinal cramps; *"dysenteria,"* diarrhea; "torsion of the small guts,"

spasmodic bowel pain; and *"melancholia hypo-chondriaca,"* depression.
2. Medical. Aesculapius was the classical god of medicine.
3. Italian dialect for "Jack Omelet," the name of the zany (see line 28), here referring to Nano.
4. Hugh Broughton was a Puritan rabbinical scholar who wrote impenetrable treatises on scriptural matters.
5. Greek physicians (ca. 460–377 B.C.E. and 129–ca. 199 C.E., respectively) who developed the theory of humors.

Or wasted many a hurtless taper;°   *candle (working at night)*
No Indian drug had e'er been famed,
Tobacco, sassafras[6] not named,
130   Ne° yet of *guacum*[7] one small stick, sir,   *Nor*
Nor Raymond Lully's great elixir.
Ne had been known the Danish Gonswart
Or Paracelsus with his long sword.[8]

PEREGRINE   All this yet will not do; eight crowns is high.

135   VOLPONE [*to* NANO]   No more.—Gentlemen, if I had but
time to discourse to you the miraculous effects of this my
oil, surnamed *oglio del Scoto,* with the countless catalogue
of those I have cured of th'aforesaid and many more diseases, the patents and privileges of all the princes and
140   commonwealths of Christendom, or but the depositions of
those that appeared on my part before the signory of the
Sanitá,[9] and most learned College of Physicians, where I
was authorized, upon notice taken of the admirable virtues
of my medicaments and mine own excellency in matter
145   of rare and unknown secrets, not only to disperse them
publicly in this famous city but in all the territories that
happily joy under the government of the most pious and
magnificent states of Italy. But may some other gallant fellow say, "Oh, there be divers that make profession° to have   *that claim*
150   as good and as experimented receipts as yours." Indeed,
very many have assayed like apes in imitation of that which
is really and essentially in me, to make of° this oil; bestowed   *some of*
great cost in furnaces, stills, alembics,[1] continual fires, and
preparation of the ingredients (as indeed there goes to it
155   six hundred several simples,° besides some quantity of   *different ingredients / to*
human fat for the conglutination,° which we buy of the   *glue it together*
anatomists); but, when these practitioners come to the last
decoction,° blow, blow, puff, puff, and all flies *in fumo.*°   *boiling down / up in smoke*
Ha, ha, ha! Poor wretches! I rather pity their folly and
160   indiscretion° than their loss of time and money; for those   *lack of discernment*
may be recovered by industry, but to be a fool born is a
disease incurable. For myself, I always from my youth have
endeavored to get the rarest secrets and book° them, either   *record*
in exchange or for money; I spared nor° cost nor labor   *neither*
165   where anything was worthy to be learned. And, gentlemen,
honorable gentlemen, I will undertake, by virtue of chemical art, out of the honorable hat that covers your head to
extract the four elements—that is to say, the fire, air, water,
and earth—and return you your felt° without burn or stain.   *felt hat*
170   For, whilst others have been at the balloo° I have been at   *Venetian ball game*

---

6. New World plants, used medicinally.
7. The bark of a tropical tree, used medicinally.
8. Raymond Lully was a medieval astrologer rumored to have discovered the elixir of life. "Dan-ish Gonswart" has not been positively identified.

Paracelsus was an early 16th-century alchemist who developed an alternative to Galenic medicine; he carried his medicines in his sword pommel.
9. Venetian medical licensing board.
1. Vessels for purifying liquids.

my book, and am now past the craggy paths of study and
come to the flow'ry plains of honor and reputation.

POLITIC   I do assure you, sir, that is his aim.

VOLPONE   But to our price.

PEREGRINE   And that withal,° Sir Pol.   as well

175 VOLPONE   You all know, honorable gentlemen, I never valued this *ampulla*, or vial, at less than eight crowns, but for
this time I am content to be deprived of it for six; six
crowns is the price, and less, in courtesy, I know you cannot offer me. Take it or leave it howsoever, both it and I am

180 at your service. I ask you not as the value of the thing, for
then I should demand° of you a thousand crowns; so the   ask
Cardinals Montalto, Fernese, the great Duke of Tuscany,
my gossip,° with divers other princes, have given me. But   buddy
I despise money. Only to show my affection to you, honor-

185 able gentlemen, and your illustrious state here, I have
neglected the messages of these princes, mine own offices,°   duties
framed° my journey hither only to present you with the   devised
fruits of my travels. [*To* NANO *and* MOSCA] Tune your voices
once more to the touch of your instruments, and give the

190 honorable assembly some delightful recreation.

PEREGRINE   What monstrous and most painful circum-
stance°   beating around the bush
Is here, to get some three or four *gazets!*°   small Venetian coins
Some threepence, i'th'whole, for that 'twill come to.

SONG

[*During the song,* CELIA *appears at her window, above.*]

NANO [*sings*]°   You that would last long, list to my song,   accompanied

195   Make no more coil,° but buy of this oil.   by Mosca / fuss
                 Would you be ever fair and young?
                 Stout of teeth and strong of tongue?
                 Tart° of palate? Quick of ear?   Keen
                 Sharp of sight? Of nostril clear?

200   Moist of hand² and light of foot?
                 Or (I will come nearer to't)°   get to the point
                 Would you live free from all diseases,
                 Do the act your mistress pleases,
                 Yet fright all aches° from your bones?   venereal disease

205   Here's a med'cine for the nones.°   occasion

VOLPONE   Well, I am in a humor at this time to make a present of the small quantity my coffer contains: to the rich in
courtesy, and to the poor for God's sake.° Wherefore, now   charity
mark; I asked you six crowns, and six crowns at other

210 times you have paid me. You shall not give me six crowns,
nor five, nor four, nor three, nor two, nor one, nor half a
ducat, no, nor a *moccenigo.*° Six—pence it will cost you, or   worth ninepence

---

2. Associated with youth and sexual vigor.

six hundred pound—expect no lower price, for by the banner of my front,° I will not bate a *bagatine*,[3] that I will °displayed on my
215 have only a pledge of your loves, to carry something from °"bank"
amongst you to show I am not contemned° by you. There- °scorned
fore now, toss your handkerchiefs cheerfully, cheerfully,
and be advertised° that the first heroic spirit that deigns to °notified
grace me with a handkerchief, I will give it a little remem-
220 brance of something beside, shall please° it better than if I °which will please
had presented it with a double *pistolet*.[4]
PEREGRINE   Will you be that heroic spark,° Sir Pol? °gallant

CELIA *at the window throws down her handkerchief*
[*with a coin tied inside it*].

Oh, see! The window has prevented you.° °beaten you to it
VOLPONE   Lady, I kiss your bounty, and, for this timely grace
225 you have done your poor Scoto of Mantua, I will return
you, over and above my oil, a secret of that high and inestimable nature shall° make you forever enamored on that °which will
minute wherein your eye first descended on so mean,° yet °lowly
not altogether to be despised, an object. Here is a powder
230 concealed in this paper of which, if I should speak to the
worth, nine thousand volumes were but as one page, that
page as a line, that line as a word—so short is this pilgrimage of man, which some call life, to° the expressing of it. °compared to
Would I reflect on the price, why, the whole world were but
235 as an empire, that empire as a province, that province as a
bank, that bank as a private purse, to the purchase of it. I
will only tell you it is the powder that made Venus a goddess, given her by Apollo,[5] that kept her perpetually young,
cleared her wrinkles, firmed her gums, filled° her skin, °filled out
240 colored her hair; from her derived to Helen, and at the
sack of Troy unfortunately lost; till now in this our age it
was as happily° recovered by a studious antiquary out of °fortunately
some ruins of Asia, who sent a moiety° of it to the court °part
of France (but much sophisticated)° wherewith the ladies °adulterated
245 there now color their hair. The rest, at this present, remains
with me, extracted to a quintessence,° so that wherever °refined
it but touches, in youth it perpetually preserves, in age °concentrate
restores the complexion; seats your teeth, did° they dance °even if
like virginal jacks,[6] firm as a wall; makes them white as
250 ivory that were black as—

SCENE 3. *The scene continues.*

[*Enter*] CORVINO. *He beats away the mountebank, etc.*
CORVINO   Spite o'the devil, and my shame! Come down here,
Come down! No house but mine to make your scene?° °stage set
Signor Flaminio, will you down, sir? Down!

---

3. I won't reduce the price by even a tiny coin.
4. Spanish gold coin worth about one English pound.
5. In his capacity as the god of health.

6. The virginal is a type of harpsichord; its "jacks" are quills that pluck strings when the keys are played, but the term was also sometimes used for the keys.

What, is my wife your Franciscina, sir?[1]
No windows on the whole piazza here
To make your properties° but mine? But mine?   *stage props*
Heart! Ere tomorrow I shall be new christened
And called the *pantalone di besogniosi*[2]
About the town.   [*Exeunt* VOLPONE, NANO, *and* MOSCA,
           followed by CORVINO *and the crowd.*]

PEREGRINE   What should this mean, Sir Pol?
POLITIC   Some trick of state, believe it. I will home.
PEREGRINE   It may be some design on you.
POLITIC   I know not.
  I'll stand upon my guard.
PEREGRINE   It is your best,° sir.   *best course of action*
POLITIC   This three weeks, all my advices, all my letters,
  They have been intercepted,
PEREGRINE   Indeed, sir?
  Best have a care.
POLITIC   Nay, so I will.   [*Exit.*]
PEREGRINE   This knight,
  I may not lose him,° for my mirth, till night.   [*Exit.*] *I won't leave him*

SCENE 4. VOLPONE's *house.*

[*Enter*] VOLPONE [*and*] MOSCA.
VOLPONE   Oh, I am wounded!
MOSCA   Where, sir?
VOLPONE   Not without;°   *externally*
  Those blows were nothing; I could bear them ever,
  But angry Cupid, bolting° from her° eyes,   *shooting darts / Celia's*
  Hath shot himself into me like a flame,
  Where now he flings about his burning heat,
  As in a furnace an ambitious° fire   *rising*
  Whose vent is stopped. The fight is all within me.
  I cannot live except thou help me, Mosca;
  My liver[1] melts, and I, without the hope
  Of some soft air from her refreshing breath,
  Am but a heap of cinders.
MOSCA   'Las, good sir!
  Would you had never seen her.
VOLPONE   Nay, would thou
  Hadst never told me of her.
MOSCA   Sir, 'tis true;
  I do confess I was unfortunate,
  And you unhappy; but I'm bound in conscience

2.3
1. Corvino imagines the scene in terms of a stock episode from the Italian commedia dell'arte, in which the young lover, conventionally named Flaminio after the famous actor Flaminio Scala, seduces Franciscina, the easygoing serving wench.
2. The *pantalone* is another stock figure in the commedia dell'arte, a decrepit old man suspicious of his desirable young wife. *Di besogniosi* is his jocular surname, meaning "descended from poor people."
2.4
1. Supposed to be the seat of lust.

No less than duty to effect my best
To your release of torment, and I will, sir.
VOLPONE   Dear Mosca, shall I hope?
MOSCA   Sir, more than dear,
  I will not bid you to despair of aught
  Within a human compass.°   *that's humanly possible*
20 VOLPONE   Oh, there spoke
  My better angel. Mosca, take my keys.
  Gold, plate, and jewels, all's at thy devotion;°   *disposal*
  Employ them how thou wilt; nay, coin me too,[2]
  So° thou in this but crown my longings. Mosca?   *provided that*
MOSCA   Use but your patience.
VOLPONE   So I have.[3]
25 MOSCA   I doubt not
  To bring success to your desires.
VOLPONE   Nay, then,
  I not repent me of my late disguise.
MOSCA   If you can horn him,[4] sir, you need not.
VOLPONE   True;
  Besides, I never meant him for my heir.
30 Is not the color o'my beard and eyebrows[5]
  To make me known?
MOSCA   No jot.
VOLPONE   I did it well.
MOSCA   So well, would I could follow you in mine
  With half the happiness!° And yet I would   *success*
  Escape your epilogue.°   *the beating*
VOLPONE   But were they gulled°   *fooled*
  With a belief that I was Scoto?
35 MOSCA   Sir,
  Scoto himself could hardly have distinguished!
  I have not time to flatter you now. We'll part,
  And, as I prosper, so applaud my art.   [*Exeunt.*]

SCENE 5. CORVINO'S *house.*

  [*Enter*] CORVINO [*and*] CELIA.
CORVINO   Death of mine honor, with the city's fool?
  A juggling, tooth-drawing,[1] prating° mountebank?   *chattering*
  And at a public window? Where, whilst he
  With his strained action° and his dole of faces[2]   *overacting*
5 To his drug lecture draws your itching ears,
  A crew of old, unmarried, noted lechers
  Stood leering up like satyrs;° and you smile   *lustful goat-men*
  Most graciously! And fan your favors forth

---

2. Use my coins as well. (But also with the implication "make coins out of me," i.e., "turn my body
into money.")
3. Punning on the original meaning of "patience,"
"enduring blows."
4. Cuckold him. (The husbands of adulterous

wives were traditionally supposed to sprout horns.)
5. Red, because he is a fox.
2.5
1. Mountebanks, like barbers, performed dental
work.
2. Small repertory of facial expressions.

To give your hot spectators satisfaction!
10 What, was your mountebank their call? Their whistle?[3]
Or were you enamored on his copper rings?
His saffron jewel with the toadstone° in't?   agatelike stone
Or his embroidered suit with the cope-stitch,°   gaudy needlework
Made of a hearse-cloth? Or his old tilt-feather?[4]
15 Or his starched beard? Well! You shall have him, yes.
He shall come home and minister unto you
The fricace for the mother.[5] Or, let me see,
I think you'd rather mount?[6] Would you not mount?
Why, if you'll mount, you may; yes truly, you may—
20 And so you may be seen down to th'foot.
Get you a cittern, Lady Vanity,[7]
And be a dealer with the virtuous man;
Make one.[8] I'll but protest° myself a cuckold   proclaim
And save your dowry.[9] I am a Dutchman, I!
25 For if you thought me an Italian,
You would be damned ere you did this, you whore.[1]
Thou'dst tremble to imagine that the murder
Of father, mother, brother, all thy race,
Should follow as the subject of my justice!
CELIA   Good sir, have patience!
30 CORVINO [drawing a weapon]   What couldst thou propose
Less to thyself° than, in this heat of wrath   as your punishment
And stung with my dishonor, I should strike
This steel unto thee, with as many stabs
As thou wert gazed upon with goatish° eyes?   lustful
35 CELIA   Alas, sir, be appeased! I could not think
My being at the window should more now
Move your impatience than at other times.
CORVINO   No? Not to seek and entertain a parley°   have a conversation
With a known knave? Before a multitude?
40 You were an actor with your handkerchief!
Which he most sweetly kissed in the receipt,
And might, no doubt, return it with a letter,
And 'point the place where you might meet—your sister's,
Your mother's, or your aunt's might serve the turn.°   occasion; sexual act
45 CELIA   Why, dear sir, when do I make these excuses?
Or ever stir abroad but to the church?
And that, so seldom—
CORVINO   Well, it shall be less;
And thy restraint before was liberty

---

3. Used to lure trained falcons.
4. The feather from a tilting (jousting) helmet.
A hearse-cloth is a heavy cloth for draping over a coffin.
5. Womb massage; with obvious sexual innuendo. "The mother" was a term for the uterus, but also for a variety of ailments, from cramps to depression, that were supposed to originate there.
6. (1) Climb up on the mountebank's stage yourself; (2) take the top sexual position.

7. Allegorical character of a morality play representing pride and worldly pleasure. A cittern is a guitarlike instrument that conventionally was played by whores.
8. Join up with him. (With sexual innuendo.)
9. The husbands of proven adultresses could divorce them and keep their dowry.
1. The Dutch were proverbially phlegmatic, in contrast to Italians, who were stereotypically impetuous and vengeful.

To what I now decree: and therefore, mark me.

50   [*Pointing to the window*] First, I will have this bawdy light dammed up,
And, till't be done, some two or three yards off
I'll chalk a line, o'er which if thou but chance
To set thy desp'rate foot, more hell, more horror,
More wild, remorseless rage shall seize on thee
55 Than on a conjurer that had heedless left
His circle's safety ere his devil was laid.[2]
Then here's a lock which I will hang upon thee.

                         [*He shows a chastity belt.*]

And now I think on't, I will keep thee backwards;[3]
Thy lodging shall be backwards, thy walks backwards,
60 Thy prospect°—all be backwards; and no pleasure   *view (see n. 3)*
That thou shalt know but backwards. Nay, since you force
My honest nature, know it is your own
Being too open makes me use you thus,
Since you will not contain your subtle° nostrils   *delicate; crafty*
65 In a sweet° room, but they must snuff the air   *sweet-smelling*
Of rank and sweaty passengers°—   *Knock within.*   *passersby*
                       One knocks.

Away, and be not seen, pain of thy life!
Not look toward the window. If thou dost—

                    [CELIA *begins to exit.*]

Nay stay, hear this—let me not prosper, whore,
70 But I will make thee an anatomy,[4]
Dissect thee mine own self, and read a lecture
Upon thee to the city, and in public.
Away!   [*Exit* CELIA.]
     Who's there?
     [*Enter*] Servitore [*a* SERVANT].
SERVANT   'Tis Signor Mosca, sir.

SCENE 6. *The scene continues.*

CORVINO   Let him come in.   [*Exit* SERVANT.]
               His master's dead! There's yet
Some good to help the bad.
     [*Enter*] MOSCA.
               My Mosca, welcome!
I guess your news.
MOSCA   I fear you cannot, sir.
CORVINO   Is't not his death?
MOSCA   Rather the contrary.
CORVINO   Not his recovery?
MOSCA   Yes, sir.
5 CORVINO   I am cursed,

---

2. Conjurers protected themselves from the devils who served them by staying inside a magical circle.
3. In the back part of the house, lacking a view out onto the piazza; but with the suggestion of anal intercourse, supposedly favored by Italians.
4. Use you for anatomical research. (In the early modern period, physicians obtained the bodies of executed criminals upon which to perform dissections, often before large crowds.)

I am bewitched! My crosses° meet to vex me!   *misfortunes*
How? How? How? How?
MOSCA   Why, sir, with Scoto's oil.
  Corbaccio and Voltore brought of it
  Whilst I was busy in an inner room—
10 CORVINO   Death! That damned mountebank! But for the law,
  Now, I could kill the rascal. 'T cannot be
  His oil should have that virtue. Ha' not I
  Known him a common rogue, come fiddling in
  To th'*osteria*° with a tumbling whore,   *tavern (Italian)*
15 And, when he has done all his forced tricks, been glad
  Of a poor spoonful of dead wine with flies in't?
  It cannot be. All his ingredients
  Are a sheep's gall, a roasted bitch's marrow,
  Some few sod° earwigs, pounded caterpillars,   *boiled*
20 A little capon's grease, and fasting spittle:[1]
  I know 'em to a dram.°   *tiny amount*
MOSCA   I know not, sir,
  But some on't there they poured into his ears,
  Some in his nostrils, and recovered him,
  Applying but the fricace.°   *massage*
CORVINO   Pox o'that fricace!
25 MOSCA And since, to seem the more officious°   *zealous*
  And flatt'ring of his health, there they have had—
  At extreme fees—the College of Physicians
  Consulting on him how they might restore him;
  Where one would have a cataplasm[2] of spices,
30 Another a flayed ape clapped to his breast,
  A third would ha' it a dog, a fourth an oil
  With wildcats' skins. At last, they all resolved
  That to preserve him was no other means
  But some young woman must be straight sought out,
35 Lusty and full of juice, to sleep by him;
  And to this service—most unhappily
  And most unwillingly—am I now employed,
  Which here I thought to preacquaint you with,
  For your advice, since it concerns you most,
40 Because I would not do that thing might cross
  Your ends,[3] on whom I have my whole dependence, sir.
  Yet if I do it not, they may delate[4]
  My slackness to my patron, work me out
  Of his opinion;° and there all your hopes,   *favor*
45 Ventures, or whatsoever, are all frustrate.
  I do but tell you, sir. Besides, they are all

2.6
1. Saliva of a fasting person. (Scoto cannot afford anything to eat.)
2. Poultice. (The substances described in the following lines were believed to work by absorbing the patient's infection, which bodes ill for the young woman prescribed for Volpone in lines 34–35.)
3. Do anything that might frustrate your purposes.
4. Report. (A legal term for making an accusation.)

Now striving who shall first present him. Therefore,
I could entreat you briefly, conclude somewhat;° *decide something*
Prevent 'em if you can.

CORVINO   Death to my hopes!

50 This is my villainous fortune! Best to hire
Some common courtesan.

MOSCA   Ay, I thought on that, sir.
But they are all so subtle,° full of art,° *cunning / deceit*
And age again° doting and flexible, *old people moreover*
So as—I cannot tell—we may perchance
Light on a quean° may cheat us all. *whore (who)*

55 CORVINO   'Tis true.

MOSCA No, no; it must be one that has no tricks, sir,
Some simple thing, a creature made unto° it; *suited to; forced into*
Some wench you may command. Ha' you no kinswoman?
Godso°—think, think, think, think, think, think, think, sir. *an oath*

60 One o'the doctors offered there his daughter.

CORVINO How!

MOSCA   Yes, Signor Lupo,° the physician. *Wolf (Italian)*

CORVINO   His daughter?

MOSCA And a virgin, sir. Why, alas,
He knows the state of's body, what it is,
That naught can warm his blood, sir, but a fever,

65 Nor any incantation raise his spirit.° *vigor; semen*
A long forgetfulness hath seized that part.° *his penis*
Besides, sir, who shall know it? Some one or two—

CORVINO I pray thee give me leave.° [*He walks apart.*] If *give me a minute*
any man
But I had had this luck—The thing in 'tself,

70 I know, is nothing.—Wherefore should not I
As well command my blood and my affections
As this dull doctor? In the point of honor
The cases are all one, of wife and daughter.

MOSCA [*aside*] I hear him coming.° *coming around*

CORVINO [*aside*]   She shall do't. 'Tis done.

75 'Slight,° if this doctor, who is not engaged, *by God's light (an oath)*
Unless 't be for his counsel (which is nothing),⁵
Offer his daughter, what should I, that am
So deeply in? I will prevent him. Wretch!
Covetous wretch!—Mosca, I have determined.

MOSCA How, sir?

80 CORVINO   We'll make all sure. The party you wot° *know (a circumlo-*
of   *cution)*
Shall be mine own wife, Mosca.

MOSCA   Sir, the thing
(But that I would not seem to counsel you)
I should have motioned° to you at the first. *proposed*
And, make your count,° you have cut all their throats. *rest assured*

---

5. Who is not financially involved, except for whatever slight fee he could expect for his advice.

85 Why, 'tis directly taking a possession!⁶
    And in his next fit we may let him go.
    'Tis but to pull the pillow from his head
    And he is throttled; 't had been done before,
    But for your scrupulous doubts,
    CORVINO   Ay, a plague on't!
90 My conscience fools my wit.° Well, I'll be brief,   *common sense*
    And so be thou, lest they should be before us.
    Go home, prepare him, tell him with what zeal
    And willingness I do it; swear it was
    On the first hearing (as thou mayst do, truly)
    Mine own free motion.°   *initiative*
95 MOSCA   Sir, I warrant you,
    I'll so possess° him with it that the rest   *impress*
    Of his starved clients shall be banished all,
    And only you received. But come not, sir,
    Until I send, for I have something else
100 To ripen for your good; you must not know't.
    CORVINO   But do not you forget to send, now.
    MOSCA   Fear not.
                                                    [*Exit.*]

SCENE 7. *The scene continues.*

CORVINO   Where are you, wife? My Celia? Wife?
        [*Enter*] CELIA [*weeping.*]
                                          What, blubbering?
    Come, dry those tears. I think thou thought'st me in earnest?
    Ha! By this light, I talked so but to try° thee.   *test*
    Methinks the lightness° of the occasion   *triviality*
5   Should ha' confirmed thee.¹ Come, I am not jealous.
    CELIA   No?
    CORVINO
              Faith, I am not, I, nor never² was;
    It is a poor, unprofitable humor.
    Do not I know if women have a will
    They'll do 'gainst all the watches° o'the world?   *despite the vigilance*
10 And that the fiercest spies are tamed with gold?
    Tut, I am confident in thee, thou shalt see't;
    And see, I'll give thee cause too, to believe it.
    Come, kiss me. Go and make thee ready straight
    In all thy best attire, thy choicest jewels;
15 Put 'em all on, and, with 'em thy best looks.
    We are invited to a solemn feast
    At old Volpone's, where it shall appear
    How far I am free from jealousy or fear.   [*Exeunt.*]

6. A legal term for the heir's formal assumption of
inherited property.
2.7
1. Convinced you that I was not serious.

2. Double negatives are grammatical in Jacobean English.

Act 3

SCENE 1. *The piazza.*

[*Enter*] MOSCA.

MOSCA   I fear I shall begin to grow in love
With my dear self and my most prosp'rous parts,°   *talents*
They do so spring and burgeon.° I can feel   *swell; thrive*
A whimsy° i'my blood. I know not how,   *giddiness*
5   Success hath made me wanton. I could skip
Out of my skin now like a subtle snake,
I am so limber. Oh, your parasite
Is a most precious thing, dropped from above,°   *sent from heaven*
Not bred 'mongst clods and clodpolls here on earth.
10   I muse the mystery was not made a science,
It is so liberally professed!¹ Almost
All the wise world is little else in nature
But parasites or subparasites. And yet
I mean not those that have your bare town-art,²
15   To know who's fit to feed 'em; have no house,
No family, no care, and therefore mold
Tales for men's ears,° to bait° that sense; or get   *tell juicy rumors / entice*
Kitchen-invention, and some stale receipts°   *recipes*
To please the belly and the groin;° nor those,   *as aphrodisiacs*
20   With their court-dog tricks, that can fawn and fleer,°   *smile insincerely*
Make their revenue out of legs and faces,
Echo my lord, and lick away a moth;³
But your fine, elegant rascal, that can rise
And stoop almost together, like an arrow,
25   Shoot through the air as nimbly as a star,°   *meteor*
Turn short as doth a swallow, and be here
And there and here and yonder all at once,
Present to any humor, all occasion,⁴
And change a visor° swifter than a thought!   *mask; expression*
30   This is the creature had the art born with him,
Toils not to learn it, but doth practice it
Out of most excellent nature, and such sparks
Are the true parasites, others but their zanies.°   *clownish imitators*

SCENE 2. *The scene continues.*

[*Enter*] BONARIO.

[*Aside*] Who's this? Bonario? Old Corbaccio's son?
The person I was bound° to seek.—Fair sir,   *on my way*
You are happ'ly met.

3.1
1. I wonder why the craft was not made a subject for academic study, it is so frequently practiced! (Punning on the "liberal professions.")
2. Crude skills of ingratiation, sufficient only for getting free meals in taverns.

3. Make a living from bows and sycophantic looks, repeat anything a nobleman says, and fawn over him, fussing over every detail of his appearance.
4. Ready to respond to any mood or opportunity.

BONARIO   That cannot be by thee.

MOSCA   Why, sir?

BONARIO   Nay, pray thee know thy way and leave me.

5   I would be loath to interchange discourse

With such a mate° as thou art.   *fellow (contemptuous)*

MOSCA   Courteous sir,

Scorn not my poverty.

BONARIO   Not I, by heaven,

But thou shalt give me leave to hate thy baseness.

MOSCA   Baseness?

BONARIO   Ay. Answer me, is not thy sloth

10   Sufficient argument? Thy flattery?

Thy means of feeding?

MOSCA   Heaven, be good to me!

These imputations are too common, sir,

And eas'ly stuck on virtue when she's poor.

You are unequal° to me, and howe'er   *superior; unfair*

15   Your sentence° may be righteous, yet you are not,   *verdict*

That, ere you know me, thus proceed in censure.

Saint Mark bear witness 'gainst you, 'tis inhuman.   [*He weeps.*]

BONARIO [*aside*]   What? Does he weep? The sign is soft and good.

I do repent me that I was so harsh.

20   MOSCA   'Tis true that, swayed by strong necessity,

I am enforced to eat my careful bread

With too much obsequy;° 'tis true, beside,   *obsequiousness*

That I am fain° to spin mine own poor raiment   *obliged*

Out of my mere observance,° being not born   *deferential service*

25   To a free fortune. But that I have done

Base offices in rending friends asunder,

Dividing families, betraying counsels,

Whispering false lies, or mining° men with praises,   *undermining*

Trained° their credulity with perjuries,   *lured on*

30   Corrupted chastity, or am in love

With mine own tender ease, but would not rather

Prove° the most rugged and laborious course   *undergo*

That might redeem my present estimation,[1]

Let me here perish in all hope of goodness.

35   BONARIO [*aside*]   This cannot be a personated passion!—

I was to blame, so to mistake thy nature;

Pray thee forgive me, and speak out thy business.

MOSCA   Sir, it concerns you; and though I may seem

At first to make a main° offense in manners   *great*

40   And in my gratitude unto my master,

Yet for the pure love which I bear all right

And hatred of the wrong, I must reveal it.

This very hour your father is in purpose

To disinherit you—

BONARIO   How!

3.2
1. That might improve your current appraisal of me.

MOSCA   And thrust you forth
45   As a mere stranger to his blood. 'Tis true, sir.
      The work no way engageth° me but as   *concerns*
      I claim an interest in the general state
      Of goodness and true virtue, which I hear
      T'abound in you, and for which mere respect,°   *for which reason alone*
50   Without a second aim, sir, I have done it.
BONARIO   This tale hath lost thee much of the late° trust   *recent*
      Thou hadst with me. It is impossible.
      I know not how to lend it any thought°   *believe that*
      My father should be so unnatural.
55 MOSCA   It is a confidence that well becomes
      Your piety;° and formed, no doubt, it is   *filial loyalty*
      From your own simple innocence, which makes
      Your wrong more monstrous and abhorred. But, sir,
      I now will tell you more. This very minute
60   It is or will be doing; and if you
      Shall be but pleased to go with me, I'll bring you,
      I dare not say where you shall see, but where
      Your ear shall be a witness of the deed:
      Hear yourself written bastard, and professed
      The common issue of the earth.[2]
65 BONARIO   I'm mazed!
MOSCA   Sir, if I do it not, draw your just sword
      And score your vengeance on my front° and face;   *brow*
      Mark me your villain. You have too much wrong,
      And I do suffer for you, sir. My heart
      Weeps blood in anguish—
70 BONARIO   Lead. I follow thee.   [*Exeunt.*]

SCENE 3. VOLPONE'S *house.*

[*Enter*] VOLPONE, NANO, ANDROGYNO, [*and*] CASTRONE.

VOLPONE   Mosca stays long, methinks. Bring forth your sports
      And help to make the wretched time more sweet.
NANO   Dwarf, fool, and eunuch, well met here we be.
      A question it were now, whether° of us three,   *which*
5   Being all the known delicates° of a rich man,   *playthings*
      In pleasing him, claim the precedency can?
CASTRONE   I claim for myself.
ANDROGYNO   And so doth the fool.
NANO   'Tis foolish indeed; let me set you both to school.
      First, for your dwarf: he's little and witty,
10   And everything, as it is little, is pretty;
      Else why do men say to a creature of my shape,
      So soon as they see him, "It's a pretty little ape"?
      And why a pretty ape? But for pleasing imitation

---

2. A bastard was called *filius terrae,* "son of the earth."

Of greater men's action in a ridiculous fashion.
15 Beside, this feat° body of mine doth not crave   *neat, trim*
Half the meat, drink, and cloth one of your bulks will have.
Admit your fool's face be the mother of laughter,
Yet for his brain, it must always come after;°   *be lesser*
And though that do feed him,° it's a pitiful case,[1]   *earns his keep*
20 His body is beholding° to such a bad face.   *One knocks.*   *beholden*
VOLPONE   Who's there? My couch. [*He lies down.*] Away,
    look, Nano, see!
Give me my caps, first—go, inquire.
           [*Exeunt* NANO, ANDROGYNO, *and* CASTRONE.]
                                    Now, Cupid
Send° it be Mosca, and with fair return!°   *grant / good results*
           [*Enter* NANO.]
NANO   It is the beauteous Madam—
VOLPONE   Would-be—is it?
NANO   The same
25 VOLPONE   Now, torment on me! Squire her in,
For she will enter or dwell here forever.
Nay, quickly, that my fit were past!   [*Exit* NANO.]
                                    I fear
A second hell, too, that my loathing this
Will quite expel my appetite to the other.°   *Celia*
30 Would she were taking, now, her tedious leave.
Lord, how it threats me what I am to suffer!

SCENE 4. *The scene continues.*

       [*Enter*] LADY [WOULD-BE *and*] NANO.
LADY WOULD-BE [*to* NANO]   I thank you, good sir. Pray you signify
Unto your patron I am here.[1] [*Regarding herself in a mirror*] This
    band°   *ruff*
Shows not my neck enough. I trouble you, sir.
Let me request you, bid one of my women
Come hither to me.   [*Exit* NANO.]
5   In good faith, I am dressed
Most favorably today!° It is no matter;   *sarcastic*
'Tis well enough.
       [*Enter* NANO *and* FIRST] WOMAN.
                    Look, see, these petulant things!°   *her women; her curls*
How they have done this!
VOLPONE [*aside*]   I do feel the fever
Ent'ring in at mine ears. Oh, for a charm
To fright it hence!
10 LADY WOULD-BE [*to* FIRST WOMAN]   Come nearer. Is this curl
In his° right place? Or this? Why is this higher   *its*
Than all the rest? You ha' not washed your eyes yet?

3.3
1. With a pun on "container."
3.4
1. Much of Lady Would-be's dialogue in the fol-   lowing scene is adapted from Libanius of Antioch's
On Talkative Women.

Or do they not stand even° i'your head?   *level*
Where's your fellow? Call her.   [*Exit* FIRST WOMAN.]

NANO [*aside*]   Now Saint Mark

15   Deliver us! Anon she'll beat her women
Because her nose is red.
[*Enter* FIRST *and* SECOND WOMEN.]

LADY WOULD-BE   I pray you, view
This tire,° forsooth. Are all things apt or no?   *headdress*

SECOND WOMAN   One hair a little here sticks out, forsooth.

LADY WOULD-BE   Does 't so, forsooth? [*To* FIRST WOMAN] And
where was your dear sight

20   When it did so, forsooth? What now? Bird-eyed?°   *startled (?); asquint (?)*
[*To* SECOND WOMAN]
And you, too? Pray you both approach and mend it.
                    [*They tend to her.*]
Now, by that light,° I muse you're not ashamed!   *i.e., by heaven*
I, that have preached these things so oft unto you,
Read you the principles, argued all the grounds,

25   Disputed every fitness, every grace,
Called you to counsel of so frequent dressings—

NANO (*aside*)   More carefully than of your fame° or honor.   *reputation*

LADY WOULD-BE   Made you acquainted what an ample dowry
The knowledge of these things would be unto you,

30   Able alone to get you noble husbands
At your return,° and you thus to neglect it?   *to England*
Besides, you seeing what a curious° nation   *fastidious*
Th'Italians are, what will they say of me?
"The English lady cannot dress herself."

35   Here's a fine imputation to our country!
Well, go your ways, and stay i'the next room.
This fucus° was too coarse, too; it's no matter.   *makeup*
[*To* NANO] Good sir, you'll give 'em entertainment?°   *look after them*
              [*Exeunt* NANO *and* WOMEN.]

VOLPONE [*aside*]   The storm comes toward me.

LADY WOULD-BE [*approaching the bed*]   How does my Volp?

40 VOLPONE   Troubled with noise. I cannot sleep; I dreamt
That a strange Fury entered now my house,
And with the dreadful tempest of her breath
Did cleave my roof asunder.

LADY WOULD-BE   Believe me, and I
Had the most fearful dream, could I remember't—

45 VOLPONE [*aside*]   Out on° my fate! I ha' giv'n her the occasion   *curses on*
How to torment me: she will tell me hers.

LADY WOULD-BE   Methought the golden mediocrity,°   *golden mean*
Polite and delicate—

VOLPONE   Oh, if you do love me,
No more! I sweat and suffer at the mention

50   Of any dream. Feel how I tremble yet.

LADY WOULD-BE   Alas, good soul! The passion of the heart.°   *heartburn*
Seed pearl were good now, boiled with syrup of apples,

Tincture of gold and coral, citron pills,
Your elecampane° root, myrobalans[2]—   *perennial herb*

55 VOLPONE [*aside*]   Ay me, I have ta'en a grasshopper by the wing!
LADY WOULD-BE   Burnt silk and amber; you have muscadel
Good i'the house—
VOLPONE   You will not drink and part?
LADY WOULD-BE   No, fear not that. I doubt we shall not get
Some English saffron—half a dram would serve—

60 Your sixteen cloves, a little musk, dried mints,
Bugloss,° and barley-meal—   *an herb*
VOLPONE [*aside*]   She's in again.
Before I feigned diseases; now I have one.
LADY WOULD-BE   And these applied with a right scarlet cloth—
VOLPONE [*aside*]   Another flood of words! A very torrent!
LADY WOULD-BE   Shall I, sir, make you a poultice?

65 VOLPONE   No, no, no.
I'm very well; you need prescribe no more.
LADY WOULD-BE   I have a little studied physic, but now
I'm all for music, save i'the forenoons
An hour or two for painting. I would have

70 A lady indeed t' have all letters and arts,
Be able to discourse, to write, to paint,
But principal, as Plato holds,° your music   *in* The Republic
(And so does wise Pythagoras, I take it)
Is your true rapture, when there is concent°   *harmony*

75 In face, in voice, and clothes, and is indeed
Our sex's chiefest ornament.
VOLPONE   The poet°   *Sophocles, in* Ajax
As old in time as Plato, and as knowing,
Says that your highest female grace is silence.
LADY WOULD-BE   Which o' your poets? Petrarch? Or Tasso? Or Dante?

80 Guarini? Ariosto? Aretine?
Cieco di Hadria?[3] I have read them all.
VOLPONE [*aside*]   Is everything a cause to my destruction?
LADY WOULD-BE [*searching her garments*]   I think I ha' two or three of 'em
about me.
VOLPONE [*aside*]   The sun, the sea will sooner both stand still

85 Than her eternal tongue! Nothing can scape it.
LADY WOULD-BE   Here's *Pastor Fido*[4]—
VOLPONE [*aside*]   Profess obstinate silence,
That's now my safest.
LADY WOULD-BE   All our English writers,
I mean such as are happy in th'Italian,
Will deign to steal out of this author mainly,

90 Almost as much as from Montaignié°   *French essayist*
He has so modern and facile° a vein,   *graceful*

---

2. Dried tropical fruits.
3. Lady Would-be juxtaposes major Italian writers with the minor di Hadria and the obscene Aretino.
4. A pastoral by Giovanni Guarini, translated into English in 1602.

Fitting the time, and catching the court ear.
Your Petrarch is more passionate, yet he,
In days of sonneting, trusted 'em with much.[5]
95   Dante is hard, and few can understand him.
But for a desperate° wit, there's Aretine!   *outrageous*
Only his pictures are a little obscene[6]—
You mark me not?

VOLPONE   Alas, my mind's perturbed.

LADY WOULD-BE   Why, in such cases we must cure ourselves,
Make use of our philosophy—

100 VOLPONE   Ay me!

LADY WOULD-BE   And, as we find our passions do rebel,
Encounter 'em with reason, or divert 'em
By giving scope unto some other humor
Of lesser danger—as in politic bodies°   *political councils*
105   There's nothing more doth overwhelm the judgment
And clouds the understanding than too much
Settling and fixing and (as 'twere) subsiding°   *alchemical jargon*
Upon one object. For the incorporating
Of these same outward things into that part
110   Which we call mental leaves some certain feces°   *dregs*
That stop the organs and, as Plato says,
Assassinates our knowledge.

VOLPONE [*aside*]   Now, the spirit
Of patience help me!

LADY WOULD-BE   Come, in faith, I must
Visit you more o'days and make you well.
Laugh and be lusty.°   *merry*
115 VOLPONE [*aside*]   My good angel save me!

LADY WOULD-BE   There was but one sole man in all the world
With whom I e'er could sympathize, and he
Would lie you° often three, four hours together   *lie*
To hear me speak, and be sometime so rapt
120   As he would answer me quite from the purpose,
Like you—and you are like him, just. I'll discourse—
An't° be but only, sir, to bring you asleep—   *if it*
How we did spend our time and loves together
For some six years.

VOLPONE   Oh, oh, oh, oh, oh, oh!

125 LADY WOULD-BE   For we were *coaetani*° and brought up—   *the same age*
VOLPONE [*aside*]   Some power, some fate, some fortune rescue me!

SCENE 5. *The scene continues.*

[*Enter*] MOSCA.

MOSCA   God save you, madam.

LADY WOULD-BE   Good sir.

---

5. When sonnet writing was popular, gave poets plenty to imitate.
6. The libertine poems of Aretine (Pietro Aret-
ine 1492–1556) were published with pornographic illustrations by Giulio Romano.

VOLPONE [*aside to* MOSCA]   Mosca? Welcome,
    Welcome to my redemption.
MOSCA [*to* VOLPONE]   Why, sir?
VOLPONE [*aside to* MOSCA]   Oh,
    Rid me of this my torture quickly, there,
    My madam with the everlasting voice!
5   The bells in time of pestilence ne'er made
    Like noise, or were in that perpetual motion;[1]
    The cockpit° comes not near it. All my house   *cockfighting arena*
    But now steamed like a bath with her thick breath.
    A lawyer could not have been heard, nor scarce
10   Another woman, such a hail of words
    She has let fall. For hell's sake, rid her hence.
MOSCA [*aside to* VOLPONE]   Has she presented?°   *given a gift*
VOLPONE [*aside to* MOSCA]   Oh, I do not care.
    I'll take her absence upon any price,
    With any loss.
MOSCA   Madam—
LADY WOULD-BE   I ha' brought your patron
    A toy,° a cap here, of mine own work—   *trifle; embroidered piece*
15 MOSCA [*taking it from her*]   'Tis well.
    I had forgot to tell you, I saw your knight
    Where you'd little think it—
LADY WOULD-BE   Where?
MOSCA   Marry,
    Where yet, if you make haste, you may apprehend him,
    Rowing upon the water in a gondole
20   With the most cunning courtesan of Venice.
LADY WOULD-BE   Is't true?
MOSCA   Pursue 'em, and believe your eyes.
    Leave me to make your gift.   [*Exit* LADY WOULD-BE.]
         I knew 'twould take.°   *do the trick*
    For lightly,° they that use themselves most license   *commonly*
    Are still° most jealous.   *always*
VOLPONE   Mosca, hearty thanks
25   For thy quick fiction and delivery of me.
    Now, to my hopes, what say'st thou?
        [*Enter* LADY WOULD-BE.]
LADY WOULD-BE   But do you hear, sir?
VOLPONE [*aside*]   Again! I fear a paroxysm.°   *relapse*
LADY WOULD-BE   Which way
    Rowed they together?
MOSCA   Toward the Rialto.°   *commercial district*
LADY WOULD-BE   I pray you, lend me your dwarf.
MOSCA   I pray you, take him.
        [*Exit* LADY WOULD-BE.]

3.5
1. Church bells marked the deaths of parishioners; in times of plague they therefore rang almost constantly.

30   Your hopes, sir, are like happy blossoms: fair,
And promise timely fruit if you will stay
But the maturing. Keep you at your couch.
Corbaccio will arrive straight with the will;
When he is gone I'll tell you more.   [*Exit.*]

VOLPONE   My blood,

35   My spirits are returned. I am alive;
And like your wanton° gamester at primero,[2]   *reckless; lustful*
Whose thought had whispered to him, not go° less,   *don't gamble*
Methinks I lie, and draw—for an encounter.[3]
    [*He gets into bed and closes the bed curtains.*]

SCENE 6. *The scene continues.*

    [*Enter*] MOSCA [*and*] BONARIO. [MOSCA *shows* BONARIO
    to a hiding place.]

MOSCA   Sir, here concealed you may hear all. But pray you
Have patience, sir. (*One knocks.*) The same's your father knocks.
I am compelled to leave you.

BONARIO   Do so. Yet
Cannot my thought imagine this a truth.
    [*He conceals himself.*]

SCENE 7. *The scene continues.*

    [*Enter*] CORVINO [*and*] CELIA. MOSCA [*crosses the stage
    to intercept them*].

MOSCA   Death on me! You are come too soon. What meant you?
Did not I say I would send?

CORVINO   Yes, but I feared
You might forget it, and then they prevent us.

MOSCA [*aside*]   Prevent? Did e'er man haste so for his horns?°   *cuckold's horns*

5   A courtier would not ply it so for a place.[1]
    [*To* CORVINO] Well, now there's no helping it, stay here;
I'll presently return.   [*He crosses the stage to* BONARIO.]

CORVINO   Where are you, Celia?
You know not wherefore I have brought you hither?

CELIA   Not well, except you told me.

CORVINO   Now I will.
Hark hither.   [CORVINO *and* CELIA *talk apart.*]

10 MOSCA (*to* BONARIO)   Sir, your father hath sent word
It will be half an hour ere he come;
And therefore, if you please to walk the while
Into that gallery, at the upper end
There are some books to entertain the time;

15   And I'll take care no man shall come unto you, sir.

BONARIO   Yes, I will stay there. [*aside*] I do doubt this fellow.
                [*He retires.*]

---

2. A card game.
3. (1) Winning play in primero; (2) sexual act.

3.7
1. Work so hard for a position at court.

MOSCA   There, he is far enough; he can hear nothing.
   And for° his father, I can keep him off.   *as for*
     [MOSCA *joins* VOLPONE *and opens his bed curtains.*]
  CORVINO [*to* CELIA]   Nay, now, there is no starting back, and therefore
20   Resolve upon it; I have so decreed.
   It must be done. Nor would I move't° afore,   *suggest it*
   Because I would avoid all shifts° and tricks   *evasions*
   That might deny me.
CELIA   Sir, let me beseech you,
   Affect° not these strange trials. If you doubt   *undertake*
25   My chastity, why, lock me up forever;
   Make me the heir of darkness. Let me live
   Where I may please° your fears, if not your trust.   *satisfy*
  CORVINO   Believe it, I have no such humor, I.
   All that I speak, I mean; yet I am not mad,
30   Not horn-mad,° see you? Go to, show yourself   *crazy with jealousy*
   Obedient, and a wife.
CELIA   O heaven!
CORVINO   I say it,
   Do so.
CELIA   Was this the train?°   *scheme*
CORVINO   I have told you reasons:
   What the physicians have set down; how much
   It may concern me; what my engagements are;
35   My means, and the necessity of those means
   For my recovery. Wherefore, if you be
   Loyal and mine, be won, respect my venture.°   *support my endeavor*
  CELIA   Before your honor?
CORVINO   Honor? Tut, a breath.
   There's no such thing in nature; a mere term
40   Invented to awe fools. What is my gold
   The worse for touching? Clothes for being looked on?
   Why, this's no more. An old, decrepit wretch,
   That has no sense,° no sinew; takes his meat   *sensory perception*
   With others' fingers; only knows to gape
45   When you do scald his gums; a voice, a shadow.
   And what can this man hurt you?
CELIA   Lord! What spirit
   Is this hath entered him?
CORVINO   And for your fame,°   *reputation*
   That's such a jig;° as if I would go tell it,   *joke*
   Cry° it on the piazza! Who shall know it   *advertise*
50   But he that cannot speak it,° and this fellow°   *Volpone / Mosca*
   Whose lips are i'my pocket, save yourself?
   If you'll proclaim't, you may. I know no other
   Should come to know it.
CELIA   Are heaven and saints then nothing?
   Will they be blind or stupid?
CORVINO   How?°   *What's this?*
CELIA   Good sir,

55   Be jealous still, emulate them, and think
        What hate they burn with toward every sin.
    CORVINO   I grant you, if I thought it were a sin
        I would not urge you. Should I offer this
        To some young Frenchman, or hot Tuscan blood
60   That had read Aretine, conned° all his prints,   *learned by heart*
        Knew every quirk within lust's labyrinth,
        And were professed critic° in lechery,   *connoisseur*
        And I would look upon him and applaud him,
        This were a sin. But here 'tis contrary,
65   A pious work, mere charity, for physic,
        And honest polity° to assure mine own.   *prudence*
    CELIA   O heaven! Canst thou suffer such a change?
    VOLPONE [*aside to* MOSCA]   Thou art mine honor, Mosca, and my pride,
        My joy, my tickling, my delight! Go, bring 'em.
    MOSCA [*to* CORVINO]   Please you draw near, sir.
70   CORVINO [*dragging* CELIA *toward* VOLPONE]   Come on, what—
        You will not be rebellious? By that light—
    MOSCA [*to* VOLPONE]   Sir, Signor Corvino here is come to see you.
    VOLPONE   Oh!
    MOSCA   And, hearing of the consultation had
        So lately for your health, is come to offer,
        Or rather, sir, to prostitute—
75   CORVINO   Thanks, sweet Mosca.
    MOSCA   Freely, unasked or unentreated—
    CORVINO   Well.
    MOSCA   As the true, fervent instance of his love,
        His own most fair and proper wife, the beauty
        Only of price° in Venice—   *beyond comparison*
    CORVINO   'Tis well urged.
80   MOSCA   To be your comfortress and to preserve you.
    VOLPONE   Alas, I am past already! Pray you, thank him
        For his good care and promptness. But for° that,   *as for*
        'Tis a vain labor e'en to fight 'gainst heaven,
        Applying fire to a stone (uh! uh! uh! uh!),
85   Making a dead leaf grow again. I take
        His wishes gently, though; and you may tell him
        What I have done for him. Marry, my state is hopeless!
        Will him to pray for me, and t' use his fortune
        With reverence when he comes to't.
    MOSCA [*to* CORVINO]   Do you hear, sir?
        Go to him with your wife.
90   CORVINO [*to* CELIA]   Heart of my father!°   *an oath*
        Wilt thou persist thus? Come, I pray thee, come.
        Thou see'st 'tis nothing. [*He threatens to strike her.*] Celia! By this hand,
        I shall grow violent. Come, do't, I say.
    CELIA   Sir, kill me, rather. I will take down poison,
        Eat burning coals, do anything—
95   CORVINO   Be damned!
        Heart! I will drag thee hence, home, by the hair,

Cry thee a strumpet through the streets, rip up
Thy mouth unto thine ears, and slit thy nose
Like a raw rochet!°—Do not tempt me. Come,   *a fish, the red gurnard*
100   Yield! I am loath—Death!° I will buy some slave   *God's death! (an oath)*
Whom I will kill,[2] and bind thee to him alive,
And at my window hang you forth, devising
Some monstrous crime, which I in capital letters
Will eat into thy flesh with *aquafortis*°   *nitric acid*
105   And burning cor'sives° on this stubborn breast.   *corrosives*
Now, by the blood thou hast incensed, I'll do't.
CELIA   Sir, what you please, you may; I am your martyr.
CORVINO   Be not thus obstinate. I ha' not deserved it.
Think who it is entreats you. Pray thee, sweet!
110   Good faith, thou shalt have jewels, gowns, attires,
What° thou wilt think and ask. Do but go kiss him.   *whatever*
Or touch him but. For my sake. At my suit.
This once. No? Not? I shall remember this.
Will you disgrace me thus? Do you thirst my undoing?
MOSCA   Nay, gentle lady, be advised.
115   CORVINO   No, no.
She has watched her time.[3] God's precious,[4] this is scurvy;
'Tis very scurvy, and you are—
MOSCA   Nay, good, sir.
CORVINO   An arrant locust,° by heaven, a locust. Whore,   *destroyer*
Crocodile,[5] that hast thy tears prepared,
Expecting° how thou'lt bid 'em flow!   *anticipating*
120   MOSCA   Nay, pray you, sir,
She will consider.
CELIA   Would my life would serve
To satisfy—
CORVINO   'Sdeath, if she would but speak to him
And save my reputation, 'twere somewhat—
But spitefully to effect my utter ruin!
125   MOSCA   Ay, now you've put your fortune in her hands.
Why, i'faith, it is her modesty; I must quit° her.   *absolve*
If you were absent she would be more coming,°   *compliant*
I know it, and dare undertake for her.
What woman can before her husband? Pray you,
Let us depart and leave her here.
130   CORVINO   Sweet Celia,
Thou mayst redeem all yet; I'll say no more.
If not, esteem yourself as lost.—Nay, stay there.
              [*Exeunt* CORVINO *and* MOSCA.]
CELIA   O God and his good angels! Whither, whither
Is shame fled human breasts, that with such ease

---

2. In the following lines, Corvino elaborates luridly upon the fate that the notorious rapist Tarquin promised the chaste Roman matron Lucretia if she did not capitulate; unlike Celia, Lucretia yielded to threats.

3. Waited for her chance (to ruin me).
4. God's precious blood. (An oath.)
5. Which was supposed to weep while preying upon its victims.

135 Men dare put off your° honors and their own? *God's and the angels'*
Is that which ever was a cause of life° *sex and wedlock*
Now placed beneath the basest circumstance,° *lowest of concerns*
And modesty an exile made for money?

He [VOLPONE] *leaps off from his couch.*

VOLPONE   Ay, in Corvino, and such earth-fed minds
140 That never tasted the true heav'n of love.
Assure thee, Celia, he that would sell thee
Only for hope of gain, and that uncertain,
He would have sold his part of paradise
For ready money, had he met a copeman.° *buyer*
145 Why art thou mazed to see me thus revived?
Rather applaud thy beauty's miracle;
'Tis thy great work, that hath, not now alone° *not only just now*
But sundry times raised me in several shapes,
And but this morning like a mountebank
150 To see thee at thy window. Ay, before
I would have left my practice° for thy love, *scheming*
In varying figures I would have contended
With the blue Proteus or the hornèd flood.[6]
Now art thou welcome.

CELIA   Sir!

VOLPONE   Nay, fly me not,
155 Nor let thy false imagination
That I was bedrid make thee think I am so.
Thou shalt not find it. I am now as fresh,
As hot, as high, and in as jovial plight° *robust condition*
As when—in that so celebrated scene,
160 At recitation of our comedy
For entertainment of the great Valois[7]—
I acted young Antinoüs,[8] and attracted
The eyes and ears of all the ladies present,
T'admire each graceful gesture, note, and footing.° *dance step*

SONG

165 [*He sings.*]   Come, my Celia, let us prove,[9]
While we can, the sports of love.
Time will not be ours forever;
He at length our good will sever.
Spend not then his gifts in vain.
170 Suns that set may rise again,
But if once we lose this light
'Tis with us perpetual night.
Why should we defer our joys?

---

6. Proteus is a shape-changing sea god with whom Menelaus wrestles in the *Odyssey*. The "hornèd flood" is the river god Achelous, defeated by Hercules despite changing into an ox.
7. Henry of Valois, Duke of Anjou, and later King Henry III of France (1574–89), was sumptuously entertained at Venice in 1574. His sexual taste for men was widely remarked.
8. The beautiful homosexual favorite of the Roman emperor Hadrian.
9. Try out. (The song is an adaptation of the Roman poet Catullus's fifth ode.)

Fame and rumor are but toys.°   *trifles*
175 Cannot we delude the eyes
Of a few poor household spies?
Or his° easier ears beguile,   *Corvino's*
Thus removèd by our wile?
'Tis no sin love's fruits to steal,
180 But the sweet thefts to reveal.
To be taken,° to be seen,   *caught*
These have crimes accounted been.

CELIA   Some serene° blast me, or dire lightning strike   *poisonous mist*
This my offending face!

VOLPONE   Why droops my Celia?
185 Thou hast in place of a base husband found
A worthy lover. Use thy fortune well,
With secrecy and pleasure. See, behold
What thou art queen of, not in expectation,°   *merely in hope*
As I feed others, but possessed and crowned.

                    [*He reveals his treasures.*]

190 See here a rope of pearl, and each more orient°   *brilliant*
Than that the brave Egyptian queen caroused;[1]
Dissolve and drink 'em. See, a carbuncle[2]
May put out both the eyes of our Saint Mark;[3]
A diamond would have bought Lollia Paulina[4]
195 When she came in like starlight, hid with jewels
That were the spoils of provinces. Take these,
And wear, and lose 'em; yet remains an earring
To purchase them again, and this whole state.
A gem but worth a private patrimony
200 Is nothing; we will eat such at a meal.
The heads of parrots, tongues of nightingales,
The brains of peacocks and of ostriches
Shall be our food, and, could we get the phoenix,[5]
Though nature lost her kind,° she were our dish.   *it became extinct*

205 CELIA   Good sir, these things might move a mind affected
With such delights; but I, whose innocence
Is all I can think wealthy° or worth th'enjoying,   *valuable*
And which once lost, I have naught to lose beyond it,
Cannot be taken with these sensual baits.
If you have conscience—

210 VOLPONE   'Tis the beggar's virtue.
If thou hast wisdom, hear me, Celia.
Thy baths shall be the juice of July flowers,°   *clove pinks*
Spirit° of roses, and of violets,   *extract*
The milk of unicorns, and panthers' breath[6]

---

1. Cleopatra dissolved and drank a pearl during a banquet with her lover, Marc Antony. "Brave": magnificent.
2. Ruby, thought to emit light.
3. Patron saint of Venice, whose statue stood in the basilica.
4. Third wife of the Roman emperor Caligula.
5. Mythical bird, of which it was supposed that only one existed at a time; it died in flames and was reborn from its own ashes.
6. Panthers were believed to use their sweet-smelling breath to lure prey.

215 Gathered in bags, and mixed with Cretan wines.
Our drink shall be preparèd gold and amber,
Which we will take until my roof whirl round
With the vertigo; and my dwarf shall dance,
My eunuch sing, my fool make up the antic,[7]
220 Whilst we, in changèd shapes, act Ovid's tales:
Thou like Europa now and I like Jove,
Then I like Mars and thou like Erycine,[8]
So of the rest, till we have quite run through
And wearied all the fables of the gods.
225 Then will I have thee in more modern forms,
Attirèd like some sprightly dame of France,
Brave Tuscan lady, or proud Spanish beauty;
Sometimes unto the Persian Sophy's° wife,   *Shah of Persia's*
Or the Grand Signor's° mistress; and for change,   *Sultan of Turkey's*
230 To one of our most artful courtesans,
Or some quick° Negro, or cold Russian.   *energetic*
And I will meet thee in as many shapes,
Where we may so transfuse° our wand'ring souls   *pour into each other*
Out at our lips, and score up sums of pleasures,
235 [*He sings.*]   That the curious shall not know
How to tell° them as they flow;   *count*
And the envious, when they find
What their number is, be pined.°   *tormented*
CELIA   If you have ears that will be pierced, or eyes
240 That can be opened, a heart may be touched,
Or any part that yet sounds man[9] about you;
If you have touch of holy saints or heaven,
Do me the grace to let me scape. If not,
Be bountiful and kill me. You do know
245 I am a creature hither ill betrayed
By one whose shame I would forget it were.
If you will deign me neither of these graces,
Yet feed your wrath, sir, rather than your lust—
It is a vice comes nearer manliness—
250 And punish that unhappy crime of nature
Which you miscall my beauty. Flay my face
Or poison it with ointments for seducing
Your blood to this rebellion.° Rub these hands   *sexual mutiny*
With what may cause an eating leprosy
255 E'en to my bones and marrow—anything
That may disfavor me,° save in my honor—   *make me ugly*
And I will kneel to you, pray for you, pay down
A thousand hourly vows, sir, for your health,
Report and think you virtuous—
VOLPONE   Think me cold,

---

7. Grotesque dance or pageant.
8. Ovid's *Metamorphoses* retells the pagan myths of transformation. Jove, king of the gods, became a bull to seduce the lovely Europa. The adulterous couple Mars, god of war, and Erycine (Venus), goddess of sexual love, were caught in a net by Vulcan, her husband.
9. That has a hint of manliness.

260 Frozen, and impotent, and so report me?
That I had Nestor's[1] hernia, thou wouldst think.
I do degenerate, and abuse my nation[2]
To play with opportunity thus long.
I should have done the act and then have parleyed.
Yield, or I'll force thee.

CELIA   O just God!

265 VOLPONE [*seizing* CELIA]   In vain—

      He [BONARIO] *leaps out from where* MOSCA *had placed him.*

BONARIO   Forbear, foul ravisher, libidinous swine!
Free the forced lady or thou diest, impostor.
But that I am loath to snatch thy punishment
Out of the hand of justice, thou shouldst yet

270 Be made the timely sacrifice of vengeance
Before this altar and this dross,° thy idol.—   *the treasure*
Lady, let's quit the place. It is the den
Of villainy. Fear naught; you have a guard;
And he° ere long shall meet his just reward.   *Volpone*

                [*Exeunt* BONARIO *and* CELIA.]

275 VOLPONE   Fall on me, roof, and bury me in ruin!
Become my grave, that wert my shelter! Oh!
I am unmasked, unspirited, undone,
Betrayed to beggary, to infamy—

      SCENE 8. *The scene continues.*

    [*Enter*] MOSCA [*bloody*].[1]

MOSCA   Where shall I run, most wretched shame of men,
To beat out my unlucky brains?

VOLPONE   Here, here.
What! Dost thou bleed?

MOSCA   Oh, that his well-driv'n sword
Had been so courteous to have cleft me down

5 Unto the navel, ere I lived to see
My life, my hopes, my spirits, my patron, all
Thus desperately engagèd° by my error!   *placed at risk*

VOLPONE   Woe on thy fortune!

MOSCA   And my follies, sir.

VOLPONE   Th'hast made me miserable.

MOSCA   And myself, sir.

10 Who would have thought he would have hearkened° so?   *eavesdropped*

VOLPONE   What shall we do?

MOSCA   I know not. If my heart
Could expiate the mischance, I'd pluck it out.
Will you be pleased to hang me, or cut my throat?

---

1. Nestor was the oldest of the Greek leaders in the Trojan War.
2. I fall away from my ancestors' virtues and abuse the Italian reputation for virility.
3.8
1. Bonario apparently remembered Mosca's invi-

tation, in 3.2.66–68, to punish him if he turns out to be lying: "draw your just sword / And score your vengeance on my front and face; / Mark me your villain."

And I'll requite you, sir. Let's die like Romans,
Since we have lived like Grecians.[2]   *They knock without.*

15 VOLPONE   Hark, who's there?
I hear some footing: officers, the *Saffi,*°   *arresting officers*
Come to apprehend us! I do feel the brand
Hissing already at my forehead; now
Mine ears are boring.[3]

MOSCA   To your couch, sir; you
20 Make that place good, however.[4]   [VOLPONE *gets into bed.*]
                                        Guilty men
Suspect° what they deserve still.°   [*He opens the door.*]   *dread / always*
                                        Signor Corbaccio!

SCENE 9. *The scene continues.*

[*Enter*] CORBACCIO [*and converses with*] MOSCA;
VOLTORE [*enters unnoticed by them*].

CORBACCIO   Why, how now, Mosca!
MOSCA   Oh, undone, amazed, sir.
Your son—I know not by what accident—
Acquainted with your purpose to my patron
Touching° your will and making him your heir,   *concerning*
5 Entered our house with violence, his sword drawn,
Sought for you, called you wretch, unnatural,
Vowed he would kill you.
CORBACCIO   Me?
MOSCA   Yes, and my patron.
CORBACCIO   This act shall disinherit him indeed.
Here is the will.
MOSCA [*taking it from him*]   'Tis well, sir.
CORBACCIO   Right and well.
Be you as careful now for me.
10 MOSCA   My life, sir,
Is not more tendered;° I am only yours.   *cherished*
CORBACCIO   How does he? Will he die shortly, think'st thou?
MOSCA   I fear
He'll outlast May.
CORBACCIO   Today?
MOSCA   No, last out May, sir.
CORBACCIO   Couldst thou not gi' him a dram?°   *dose (of poison)*
MOSCA   Oh, by no means, sir.
CORBACCIO   Nay, I'll not bid you.
15 VOLTORE [*aside*]   This is a knave, I see.
        [VOLTORE *comes forward to speak privately with* MOSCA.]
MOSCA [*aside*]   How, Signor Voltore! Did he hear me?
VOLTORE   Parasite!
MOSCA   Who's that? Oh, sir, most timely welcome—

---

2. Romans often committed suicide in adversity;
Greeks were thought to be pleasure-loving.
3. Branding was a common criminal punishment;
ear-boring is described as an Italian torture in
Thomas Nashe's *Unfortunate Traveler* (1594).
4. (1) Defend that place, whatever happens; (2)
maintain your invalid's role at all costs, since that
role suits you.

VOLTORE   Scarce°   *only just in time*

    To the discovery of your tricks, I fear.

    You are his only? And mine also? Are you not?

MOSCA   Who, I, sir?   [*They speak out of* CORBACCIO's *hearing.*]

20   VOLTORE   You, sir. What device° is this   *ruse*

    About a will?

MOSCA   A plot for you, sir.

VOLTORE   Come,

    Put not your foists° upon me. I shall scent 'em.   *tricks; stenches*

MOSCA   Did you not hear it?

VOLTORE   Yes, I hear Corbaccio

    Hath made your patron there his heir.

MOSCA   'Tis true,

25   By my device, drawn to it by my plot,

    With hope—

VOLTORE   Your patron should reciprocate?

    And you have promised?

MOSCA   For your good I did, sir.

    Nay, more, I told his son, brought, hid him here

    Where he might hear his father pass the deed,

30   Being persuaded to it by this thought, sir,

    That the unnaturalness, first, of the act,

    And then, his father's oft disclaiming in° him   *disowning*

    (Which I did mean t' help on) would sure enrage him

    To do some violence upon his parent,

35   On which the law should take sufficient hold,

    And you be stated° in a double hope.   *installed*

    Truth be my comfort and my conscience,

    My only aim was to dig you a fortune

    Out of these two old rotten sepulchres—

VOLTORE   I cry thee mercy, Mosca.

40   MOSCA   Worth your patience

    And your great merit, sir. And see the change!

VOLTORE   Why? What success?°   *outcome*

MOSCA   Most hapless!° You must help,   *unfortunate*

    sir.

    Whilst we expected th'old raven, in comes

    Corvino's wife, sent hither by her husband—

VOLTORE   What, with a present?

45   MOSCA   No, sir, on visitation—

    I'll tell you how, anon—and, staying long,

    The youth, he grows impatient, rushes forth,

    Seizeth the lady, wounds me, makes her swear—

    Or he would murder her, that was his vow—

50   T'affirm my patron to have done her rape,   *unlikely*

    Which how unlike° it is, you see! And hence,

    With that pretext, he's gone t'accuse his father,

    Defame my patron, defeat you—

VOLTORE   Where's her husband?

    Let him be sent for straight.

MOSCA   Sir, I'll go fetch him.
VOLTORE   Bring him to the *Scrutineo.*°   *Venetian law court*
55   MOSCA   Sir, I will.
VOLTORE   This must be stopped.
MOSCA   Oh, you do nobly, sir.
Alas, 'twas labored all, sir, for your good;
Nor was there want of counsel° in the plot.   *lack of wisdom*
But fortune can at any time o'erthrow
60   The projects of a hundred learnèd clerks,° sir.   *scholars*
CORBACCIO [*striving to hear*]   What's that?
VOLTORE [*to* CORBACCIO]   Will't please you, sir, to go along?
                    [*Exeunt* CORBACCIO *and* VOLTORE.]
MOSCA   Patron, go in and pray for our success.
VOLPONE [*rising*]   Need makes devotion. Heaven your labor bless!

Act 4

SCENE 1. *The piazza.*

[*Enter*] POLITIC [*and*] PEREGRINE.
POLITIC   I told you, sir, it° was a plot. You see   *the mountebank episode*
What observation is! You mentioned me
For° some instructions; I will tell you, sir,   *as one who could give*
Since we are met here, in this height° of Venice,   *latitude*
5   Some few particulars I have set down
Only for this meridian, fit to be known
Of your crude° traveler, and they are these.   *inexperienced*
I will not touch, sir, at your phrase or clothes,
For they are old.[1]
PEREGRINE   Sir, I have better.
POLITIC   Pardon,
I meant as they are themes.°   *topics for advice*
10   PEREGRINE   Oh; sir, proceed.
I'll slander° you no more of wit, good sir.   *accuse*
POLITIC   First, for your garb,[2] it must be grave and serious,
Very reserved and locked;° not° tell a secret   *guarded / do not*
On any terms, not to your father; scarce
15   A fable[3] but with caution. Make sure choice
Both of your company and discourse. Beware
You never speak a truth—
PEREGRINE   How!
POLITIC   Not to strangers,°   *foreigners*
For those be they you must converse with most;
Others° I would not know, sir, but at distance,   *fellow countrymen*
20   So as I still might be a saver[4] in 'em.

4.1
1. I will not discuss those familiar ("old") topics:
the language one ought to use or the clothes one
ought to wear. In the next line, in an attempt at a
joke, Peregrine deliberately misconstrues "your
clothes" to refer to his own apparel, but Politic
does not get it.

2. As for a traveler's bearing.
3. An apparently trivial story subject to political
allegorization.
4. So that I might not be imposed upon. ("Be
a saver" is a gambling term, meaning "to escape
loss.")

You shall have tricks else passed upon you hourly.
And then, for your religion, profess none,
But wonder at the diversity of all,
And, for your part, protest, were there no other
25 But simply the laws o'th'land, you could content you.
Nick Machiavel and Monsieur Bodin both
Were of this mind.[5] Then must you learn the use
And handling of your silver fork° at meals,   *an Italian novelty*
The metal° of your glass—these are main matters   *composition*
30 With your Italian—and to know the hour
When you must eat your melons and your figs.
PEREGRINE   Is that a point of state,° too?   *statecraft*
POLITIC   Here it is.
For your Venetian, if he see a man
Preposterous in the least, he has° him straight;   *sees through*
35 He has, he strips° him. I'll acquaint you, sir.   *ridicules; defrauds*
I now have lived here—'tis some fourteen months;
Within the first week of my landing here,
All took me for a citizen of Venice,
I knew the forms so well—
PEREGRINE [*aside*]   And nothing else.
40 POLITIC   I had read Contarine,[6] took me a house,
Dealt with my Jews[7] to furnish it with movables°—   *household goods*
Well, if I could but find one man, one man
To mine own heart, whom I durst trust, I would—
PEREGRINE   What? What, sir?
POLITIC   Make him rich, make him a fortune.
45 He should not think° again. I would command it.   *have to think*
PEREGRINE   As how?
POLITIC   With certain projects° that I   *entrepreneurial schemes*
have—
Which I may not discover.°   *reveal*
PEREGRINE [*aside*]   If I had
But one° to wager with, I would lay odds, now,   *Someone*
He tells me instantly.
POLITIC   One is—and that
50 I care not greatly who knows—to serve the state
Of Venice with red herrings for three years,
And at a certain rate, from Rotterdam,[8]
Where I have correspondence. [*He shows* PEREGRINE *a paper.*]
There's a letter
Sent me from one o'th'States,° and to that purpose;   *Dutch provinces*
55 He cannot write his name, but that's his mark.
PEREGRINE [*examining the paper*]   He is a chandler?[9]

5. Political theorists Niccolò Machiavelli (1469–1527) and Jean Bodin (1530–1596) argued that religious zeal was often politically inexpedient or divisive; as a result both were popularly thought to be atheists.
6. An English translation of Gasparo Contarini's important book, *The Commonwealth and Government of Venice*, was published in 1599.
7. The usual Jews. (In Venice Jews served as moneylenders and pawnbrokers.)
8. Venice, on the Adriatic Sea, had little need to import pickled fish from afar.
9. Candlemaker. (Evidently the paper is grease-stained.)

POLITIC   No, a cheesemonger.

There are some other° too, with whom I treat°   *others / deal*
About the same negotiation;
And I will undertake it, for 'tis thus

60   I'll do't with ease; I've cast it all.° Your hoy[1]   *figured it all out*
Carries but three men in her and a boy,
And she shall make me three returns° a year.   *round trips*
So if there come but one of three, I save;°   *break even*
If two, I can defalk.° But this is, now,   *pay off loans*
If my main project fail.

65   PEREGRINE   Then you have others?

POLITIC   I should be loath to draw° the subtle air   *breathe*
Of such a place without my thousand aims.
I'll not dissemble, sir: where'er I come,
I love to be considerative;° and 'tis true   *analytic*

70   I have at my free hours thought upon
Some certain goods° unto the state of Venice,   *benefits*
Which I do call my cautions,° and, sir, which   *precautions*
I mean, in hope of pension,° to propound   *financial reward*
To the Great Council, then unto the Forty,

75   So to the Ten.[2] My means° are made already—   *contacts*

PEREGRINE   By whom?

POLITIC   Sir, one that though his place b'obscure,
Yet he can sway and they will hear him. He's
A *commendatore.*

PEREGRINE   What, a common sergeant?

POLITIC   Sir, such as they are put it in their mouths

80   What they should say, sometimes, as well as greater.[3]
I think I have my notes to show you—

                         [*He searches in his garments.*]

PEREGRINE   Good, sir.

POLITIC   But you shall swear unto me on your gentry°   *gentleman's honor*
Not to anticipate—

PEREGRINE   I, sir?

POLITIC   Nor reveal
A circumstance—My paper is not with me.

PEREGRINE   Oh, but you can remember, sir.

85   POLITIC   My first is
Concerning tinderboxes.° You must know   *for lighting fires*
No family is here without its box.
Now, sir, it being so portable a thing,
Put case° that you or I were ill affected°   *suppose / disposed*

90   Unto the state; sir, with it in our pockets
Might not I go into the Arsenale?[4]
Of you? Come out again? And none the wiser?

---

1. Small vessel, not suitable for long voyages. Sir Pol's scheme is thus obviously impractical.
2. The Great Council was a large legislative group made up of wealthy Venetians; the Councils of Forty were much smaller groups that oversaw judicial affairs; the Council of Ten consisted of the elected Doge and his cabinet.
3. Common men, as well as those of higher status, may sometimes make suggestions to the government.
4. Shipyard where Venice built and repaired its naval vessels.

PEREGRINE   Except yourself, sir.

POLITIC   Go to,° then. I therefore   *impatient expression*
 Advertise to° the state how fit it were   *warn*
95 That none but such as were known patriots,
 Sound lovers of their country, should be suffered
 T'enjoy them° in their houses, and even those   *tinderboxes*
 Sealed° at some office, and at such a bigness   *licensed; sealed shut*
 As might not lurk in pockets.

PEREGRINE   Admirable!

100 POLITIC   My next is, how t'inquire and be resolved°   *satisfied*
 By present° demonstration whether a ship   *immediate*
 Newly arrived from Syria, or from
 Any suspected part of all the Levant,°   *Middle East*
 Be guilty of the plague. And where they use°   *are accustomed*
105 To lie out° forty, fifty days sometimes   *at anchor*
 About the Lazaretto,[5] for their trial,
 I'll save that charge and loss unto the merchant,
 And in an hour clear the doubt.

PEREGRINE   Indeed, sir?

POLITIC   Or—I will lose my labor.

PEREGRINE   My faith, that's much.

110 POLITIC   Nay, sir, conceive° me. 'Twill cost me in onions[6]   *understand*
 Some thirty livres°—   *French coins*

PEREGRINE   Which is one pound sterling.

POLITIC   Beside my waterworks. For this I do, sir.
 First I bring in your ship° 'twixt two brick walls—   *a ship in question*
 But those the state shall venture.° On the one   *pay for*
115 I strain° me a fair tarpaulin, and in that   *stretch*
 I stick my onions cut in halves; the other
 Is full of loopholes out at which I thrust
 The noses of my bellows, and those bellows
 I keep with° waterworks in perpetual motion[7]—   *by means of*
120 Which is the easiest matter of a hundred.°   *as easy as can be*
 Now, sir, your onion, which doth naturally
 Attract th'infection, and your bellows, blowing
 The air upon him,° will show instantly   *it (the onion)*
 By his changed color if there be contagion,
125 Or else remain as fair as at the first.
 Now 'tis known, 'tis nothing.°   *there's nothing to it*

PEREGRINE   You are right, sir.

POLITIC   I would I had my note.

    [He searches again in his garments.]

PEREGRINE   Faith, so would I;
 But, you ha' done well for once, sir.

POLITIC   Were I false,°   *traitorous*
 Or would be made so, I could show you reasons

---

5. Quarantine hospital on an outlying island.
6. Onions were popularly supposed to absorb plague infection.
7. Perpetual-motion machines were popular attractions in early modern England, but Jonson regarded them contemptuously. Since Venice is in flat marshland, there are no waterfalls to harness there, as Sir Pol proposes.

130 How I could sell this state now to the Turk,[8]
Spite of their galleys° or their—   *warships*

PEREGRINE   Pray you, Sir Pol.

POLITIC   I have 'em° not about me.   *the notes*

PEREGRINE   That I feared.
They are there, sir? [*He indicates a book* POLITIC *is holding.*]

POLITIC   No, this is my diary,
Wherein I note my actions of the day.[9]

135 PEREGRINE   Pray you, let's see, sir. What is here? [*Reading*]
"*Notandum,*°   *Be it noted*
A rat had gnawn my spur leathers;° notwithstanding   *laces*
I put on new and did go forth, but first
I threw three beans over the threshold.° *Item,*   *for good luck*
I went and bought two toothpicks, whereof one

140 I burst immediately in a discourse
With a Dutch merchant, 'bout *ragion' del stato.*°   *political expediency*
From him I went, and paid a *moccinigo*°   *small coin*
For piecing° my silk stockings; by the way   *mending*
I cheapened sprats,[1] and at Saint Mark's I urined."
Faith, these are politic notes!

145 POLITIC   Sir, I do slip°   *let pass*
No action of my life thus but I quote° it.   *without noting*

PEREGRINE   Believe me, it is wise!

POLITIC   Nay, sir, read forth.

SCENE 2. *The scene continues.*

[*Enter*] LADY [WOULD-BE], NANO, [*and the two*] WOMEN.
[*They do not see* POLITIC *and* PEREGRINE *at first.*]

LADY WOULD-BE   Where should this loose knight be, trow?°   *do you suppose?*
Sure he's housed.°   *in a brothel*

NANO   Why, then he's fast.°   *fast-moving; secure*

LADY WOULD-BE   Ay, he plays both° with me.   *both fast and loose*
I pray you, stay. This heat will do more harm
To my complexion than his heart is worth.

5 I do not care to hinder, but to take° him.   *catch*
[*She rubs her cheeks.*]
How it° comes off!   *the makeup*

FIRST WOMAN [*pointing*]   My master's yonder.

LADY WOULD-BE   Where?

FIRST WOMAN   With a young gentleman.

LADY WOULD-BE   That same's the party,
In man's apparel![1] [*To* NANO] Pray you, sir, jog my knight.
I will be tender to his reputation,
However he demerit.°   *deserves blame*

---

8. The Ottoman Turks, southeast of Venice along
the Adriatic Sea, were maritime and religious
rivals and a long-standing military threat.
9. Many Renaissance travel writers recommended that travelers keep a written record of
their journeys.
1. Bargained over some small fish.
4.2
1. Lady Would-be believes that Peregrine is the
whore Mosca mentioned, in transvestite attire.

POLITIC [*seeing her*]   My lady!

10 PEREGRINE   Where?

POLITIC   'Tis she indeed, sir; you shall know her. She is,
     Were she not mine,[2] a lady of that merit
     For fashion and behavior; and for beauty
     I durst compare—

PEREGRINE   It seems you are not jealous,
     That dare commend her.

15 POLITIC   Nay, and for discourse—

PEREGRINE   Being your wife, she cannot miss° that.   lack (sarcastic)

POLITIC [*introducing* PEREGRINE]   Madam,
     Here is a gentleman; pray you use him fairly.
     He seems a youth, but he is—

LADY WOULD-BE   None?

POLITIC   Yes, one
     Has° put his face as soon° into the world—   who has / so young

LADY WOULD-BE   You mean, as early? But today

20 POLITIC   How's this!

LADY WOULD-BE   Why, in this habit,° sir; you apprehend° me.   apparel /
     Well, Master Would-be, this doth not become you;   understand
     I had thought the odor, sir, of your good name
     Had been more precious to you, that you would not

25 Have done this dire massacre on your honor—
     One of your gravity and rank besides!
     But knights, I see, care little for the oath
     They make to ladies, chiefly their own ladies.

POLITIC   Now, by my spurs—the symbol of my knighthood—

30 PEREGRINE (*aside*)   Lord, how his brain is humbled[3] for an oath!

POLITIC   —I reach° you not.   comprehend

LADY WOULD-BE   Right, sir, your polity°   cunning
     May bear° it through thus. [*To* PEREGRINE] Sir, a word with you.   bluff
     I would be loath to contest publicly
     With any gentlewoman, or to seem

35 Froward° or violent; as *The Courtier*[4] says,   bad-tempered
     It comes too near rusticity° in a lady,   ill breeding
     Which I would shun by all means. And however
     I may deserve from Master Would-be, yet
     T' have one fair gentlewoman° thus be made   i.e., Peregrine

40 Th'unkind instrument to wrong another,
     And one she knows not, ay, and to persevere,
     In my poor judgment is not warranted
     From being a solecism° in our sex,   impropriety
     If not in manners.

PEREGRINE   How is this?

POLITIC   Sweet madam,
     Come nearer to your aim.°   speak more clearly

2. Even though I, her husband, say so.
3. Literally, "brought down" to his feet—where
spurs, the appurtenances of a knight, are worn.

4. Baldassare Castiglione's famous handbook of
gentility.

45   LADY WOULD-BE   Marry, and will, sir.
      Since you provoke me with your impudence
      And laughter of your light land-siren[5] here,
      Your Sporus,[6] your hermaphrodite—
  PEREGRINE   What's here?
      Poetic fury and historic storms![7]
50   POLITIC   The gentleman, believe it, is of worth,
      And of our nation.
  LADY WOULD-BE   Ay, your Whitefriars° nation!   *London brothel district*
      Come, I blush for you, Master Would-be, I,
      And am ashamed you should ha' no more forehead°   *shame*
      Than thus to be the patron, or Saint George,[8]
55   To a lewd harlot, a base fricatrice,°   *whore*
      A female devil in a male outside.
  POLITIC [*to* PEREGRINE]   Nay,
      An° you be such a one, I must bid adieu   *If*
      To your delights. The case appears too liquid.[9]
                       [POLITIC *starts to leave.*]
  LADY WOULD-BE   Ay, you may carry't clear, with your state-
      face!°   *dignified expression*
60   But for your carnival concupiscence,°   *lecherous strumpet*
      Who here is fled for liberty of conscience°   *licentious conduct*
      From furious persecution of the marshal,[1]
      Her will I disc'ple.°   *discipline*
         [*Exit* POLITIC, LADY POLITIC *accosts* PEREGRINE.]
  PEREGRINE   This is fine, i'faith!
      And do you use this° often? Is this part   *act this way*
65   Of your wit's exercise, 'gainst you have occasion?[2]
      Madam—
  LADY WOULD-BE   Go to,° sir.   *impatient expression*
  PEREGRINE   Do you hear me, lady?
      Why, if your knight have set you to beg shirts,[3]
      Or to invite me home, you might have done it
      A nearer° way by far.   *more direct*
  LADY WOULD-BE   This cannot work you
      Out of my snare.
70   PEREGRINE   Why, am I in it, then?
      Indeed, your husband told me you were fair,
      And so you are; only your nose inclines—
      That side that's next the sun—to the queen-apple.[4]
  LADY WOULD-BE   This cannot be endured by any patience.

---

5. The Sirens were mythical sea creatures who lured sailors to their deaths by sitting on dangerous rocks and singing irresistibly. (Lady Would-be refers to Peregrine.)
6. A eunuch whom the emperor Nero dressed in drag and married.
7. Peregrine notes that even Lady Would-be's tantrums include literary allusions.
8. Patron saint of England, often pictured rescuing a damsel from a dragon.
9. Obvious. (Politic has become convinced that his wife is right in believing that Peregrine is a transvestite whore.)
1. Official charged with punishing prostitutes. Lady Would-be thinks that Peregrine has dressed as a man to flee prosecution.
2. To keep it ready for when it is really needed?
3. Peregrine pretends to believe that Lady Would-be is tearing off her shirt in order to give it to her husband. Probably she is just trying to prevent his leaving.
4. A bright red apple. See 3.4.15–16, where we learn that Lady Would-be is sensitive about her red nose.

SCENE 3. *The scene continues.*

[*Enter*] MOSCA.

MOSCA   What's the matter, madam?

LADY WOULD-BE   If the Senate°   *Venetian government*
Right not my quest° in this, I will protest 'em   *petition*
To all the world no aristocracy.

MOSCA   What is the injury, lady?

LADY WOULD-BE   Why, the callet°   *prostitute*
5   You told me of, here I have ta'en disguised.

MOSCA   Who, this? What means Your Ladyship? The creature
I mentioned to you is apprehended now
Before the Senate. You shall see her—

LADY WOULD-BE   Where?

MOSCA   I'll bring you to her. This young gentleman,
10   I saw him land this morning at the port.

LADY WOULD-BE   Is't possible! How has my judgment wandered!
[*Releasing* PEREGRINE] Sir, I must, blushing, say to you I have erred,
And plead your pardon.

PEREGRINE   What, more changes yet?

LADY WOULD-BE   I hope you ha' not the malice to remember
15   A gentlewoman's passion. If you stay
In Venice here, please you to use me,[1] sir—

MOSCA   Will you go, madam?

LADY WOULD-BE   Pray you, sir, use me. In faith,
The more you see me, the more I shall conceive
You have forgot our quarrel.

[*Exeunt* MOSCA, LADY WOULD-BE, NANO, *and* WOMEN.]

PEREGRINE   This is rare!
20   Sir Politic Would-be? No, Sir Politic Bawd,
To bring me thus acquainted with his wife!
Well, wise Sir Pol, since you have practiced thus
Upon my freshmanship,[2] I'll try your salt-head,
What proof° it is against a counterplot.   [*Exit.*]   *how invulnerable*

SCENE 4. *The Scrutineo, or Court of Law, in the
Doge's palace.*

[*Enter*] VOLTORE, CORBACCIO, CORVINO, [*and*] MOSCA.

VOLTORE   Well, now you know the carriage° of the business,   *management*
Your constancy is all that is required
Unto the safety of it.

MOSCA   Is the lie
Safely conveyed° amongst us? Is that sure?   *agreed upon*
Knows every man his burden?°   *refrain, tune*

4.3
1. Make use of my services. (With a sexual innuendo continued in "The more you see me, the more I shall conceive" [line 18], where "conceive" means both "understand" and "conceive a child.")
2. Taken advantage of my inexperience. (Pere-

grine apparently believes that Sir Pol has deliberately involved him in a humiliating setup. "Salt-head," following, plays on both "salt" meaning "seasoned," "old," and "salt" meaning "lecherous."

CORVINO   Yes.

5   MOSCA   Then shrink not.

CORVINO [*aside to* MOSCA]   But knows the advocate the truth?

MOSCA [*aside to* CORVINO]   Oh, sir,
   By no means. I devised a formal° tale   elaborate
   That salved your reputation. But be valiant, sir.

CORVINO   I fear no one but him,° that this his pleading   Voltore
   Should make him stand for a co-heir—

10 MOSCA   Co-halter![1]
   Hang him, we will but use his tongue, his noise,
   As we do Croaker's,° here.   Corbaccio's

CORVINO   Ay, what shall he do?

MOSCA   When we ha' done, you mean?

CORVINO   Yes.

MOSCA   Why, we'll think—
   Sell him for *mummia*;[2] he's half dust already.

15 ([*Aside*] *to* VOLTORE) Do not you smile to see this buffalo,[3]
   How he doth sport it with his head? [*To himself*] I should,
   If all were well and past. ([*Aside*] *to* CORBACCIO) Sir, only you
   Are he that shall enjoy the crop° of all,   harvest
   And these not know for whom they toil.

CORBACCIO   Ay, peace!

20 MOSCA ([*aside*] *to* CORVINO)   But you shall eat it. [*To himself*]
         Much!° (*then to* VOLTORE *again*) Worshipful sir,   Sure you will!
   Mercury[4] sit upon your thund'ring tongue,
   Or the French Hercules, and make your language
   As conquering as his club,[5] to beat along,
   As with a tempest, flat, our adversaries!
   [*Aside to* CORVINO] But much more yours,° sir.   your adversaries

25 VOLTORE   Here they come. Ha' done.°   shut up

MOSCA   I have another witness° if you need, sir,   Lady Would-be
   I can produce.

VOLTORE   Who is it?

MOSCA   Sir, I have her.

SCENE 5. *The scene continues.*

[*Enter*] *four* AVOCATORI, BONARIO, CELIA. *Notario*
[NOTORY], COMMENDATORI° [*and other court officials*].   law court deputies

FIRST AVOCATORE   The like of this the Senate never heard of.

SECOND AVOCATORE   'Twill come most strange to them when we report it.

FOURTH AVOCATORE   The gentlewoman has been ever held
   Of unreprovèd name.

THIRD AVOCATORE   So, the young man.

5   FOURTH AVOCATORE   The more unnatural part that of his father.

4.4
1. Playing on "halter," a hangman's noose, to suggest that both Corbaccio and Voltore are being duped.
2. Powdered embalmed corpse, used medicinally.
3. Corvino, with his cuckold's horns.

4. May the god of rhetoric (and thieves).
5. After his tenth labor, according to some legendary accounts, Hercules, aged by now but powerfully eloquent, fathered the Celts in Gaul, or France. He was traditionally pictured with a club.

SECOND AVOCATORE   More of the husband.

FIRST AVOCATORE   I not know to give
His act a name, it is so monstrous!

FOURTH AVOCATORE   But the impostor,° he is a thing created   *Volpone*
T'exceed example!°   *precedent*

FIRST AVOCATORE   And all aftertimes!°   *later eras*

10   SECOND AVOCATORE   I never heard a true voluptuary
Described but him.

THIRD AVOCATORE   Appear yet those were cited?

NOTARY   All but the old magnifico, Volpone.

FIRST AVOCATORE   Why is not he here?

MOSCA   Please Your Fatherhoods,
Here is his advocate. Himself's so weak,
So feeble—

FOURTH AVOCATORE   What are you?

15   BONARIO   His parasite,
His knave, his pander! I beseech the court
He may be forced to come, that your grave eyes
May bear strong witness of his strange impostures.

VOLTORE   Upon my faith and credit with your virtues,
20   He is not able to endure the air.

SECOND AVOCATORE   Bring him, however.

THIRD AVOCATORE   We will see him.

FOURTH AVOCATORE   Fetch him.
                           [*Exit officers.*]

VOLTORE   Your Fatherhoods' fit pleasures be obeyed,
But sure the sight will rather move your pities
Than indignation. May it please the court,
25   In the meantime he may be heard in me.
I know this place most void of prejudice,
And therefore crave it, since we have no reason
To fear our truth should hurt our cause.

THIRD AVOCATORE   Speak free.

VOLTORE   Then know, most honored fathers, I must now
30   Discover° to your strangely abusèd ears   *reveal*
The most prodigious and most frontless° piece   *shameless*
Of solid° impudence and treachery   *complete*
That ever vicious nature yet brought forth
To shame the state of Venice. [*Indicating* CELIA] This lewd woman,
35   That wants° no artificial looks or tears   *who lacks*
To help the visor° she has now put on,   *(weeping) mask*
Hath long been known a close° adulteress   *secret; intimate*
To that lascivious youth there [*indicating* BONARIO]; not suspected,
I say, but known, and taken in the act
40   With him; and by this man, the easy° husband,   *lenient*
Pardoned; whose timeless° bounty makes him now *unseasonable; endless*
Stand here, the most unhappy, innocent person
That ever man's own goodness made accused.[1]

4.5
1. That ever had his own goodness turned against him.

For these, not knowing how to owe° a gift   *acknowledge*
45   Of that dear grace but° with their shame, being placed   *other than*
     So above all powers of their gratitude,[2]
     Began to hate the benefit, and in place
     Of thanks devise t'extirp° the memory   *to extirpate, wipe out*
     Of such an act. Wherein I pray Your Fatherhoods
50   To observe the malice, yea, the rage of creatures
     Discovered in their evils, and what heart°   *audacity*
     Such take even from their crimes. But that anon
     Will more appear. This gentleman, the father,
        [*indicating* CORBACCIO]
     Hearing of this foul fact,° with many others   *deed*
55   Which daily struck at his too tender ears,
     And grieved in nothing more than that he could not
     Preserve himself a parent—his son's ills°   *evil deeds*
     Growing to that strange flood—at last decreed
     To disinherit him.
   FIRST AVOCATORE   These be strange turns!
60   SECOND AVOCATORE   The young man's fame° was ever fair   *reputation*
     and honest.
   VOLTORE   So much more full of danger is his vice,
     That can beguile so under shade of virtue.
     But, as I said, my honored sires, his father
     Having this settled purpose, by what means
65   To him° betrayed we know not, and this day   *Bonario*
     Appointed for the deed, that parricide—
     I cannot style him better°—by confederacy   *give him a better name*
     Preparing this his paramour to be there,
     Entered Volpone's house—who was the man,
70   Your Fatherhoods must understand, designed
     For the inheritance—there sought his father.
     But with what purpose sought he him, my lords?
     I tremble to pronounce it, that a son
     Unto a father, and to such a father,
75   Should have so foul, felonious intent:
     It was to murder him. When, being prevented
     By his more happy° absence, what then did he?   *Corbaccio's fortunate*
     Not check his wicked thoughts; no, now new deeds—
     Mischief doth ever end where it begins[3]—
80   An act of horror, fathers! He dragged forth
     The agèd gentleman, that had there lain bedrid
     Three years and more, out of his innocent couch;
     Naked upon the floor there left him; wounded
     His servant in the face, and with this strumpet,
85   The stale° to his forged practice,° who was glad   *decoy / plot*
     To be so active—I shall here desire
     Your Fatherhoods to note but my collections°   *deductions*

---

2. Since the rare value of Corvino's forgiveness   3. Wickedness is always persistent.
was so far beyond their powers of gratitude.

As most remarkable—thought at once to stop

His father's ends,° discredit his free choice   *aims*

90   In the old gentleman,° redeem themselves   *Volpone*

By laying infamy upon this man°   *Corvino*

To whom with blushing they should owe their lives.

FIRST AVOCATORE   What proofs have you of this?

BONARIO   Most honored fathers,

I humbly crave there be no credit given

To this man's mercenary tongue.

95   SECOND AVOCATORE   Forbear.

BONARIO   His soul moves in his fee.

THIRD AVOCATORE   Oh, sir!

BONARIO   This fellow,

For six sols° more, would plead against his Maker.   *halfpennies*

FIRST AVOCATORE   You do forget yourself.

VOLTORE   Nay, nay, grave fathers,

Let him have scope. Can any man imagine

100   That he will spare 's° accuser, that would not   *spare his*

Have spared his parent?

FIRST AVOCATORE   Well, produce your proofs.

CELIA   I would I could forget I were a creature!°   *living being*

VOLTORE [*calling a witness*]   Signor Corbaccio!

FOURTH AVOCATORE   What is he?

VOLTORE   The father.

SECOND AVOCATORE   Has he had an oath?

NOTARY   Yes.

CORBACCIO   What must I do now?

NOTARY   Your testimony's craved.

105   CORBACCIO [*mis-hearing*]   Speak to the knave?

I'll ha' my mouth first stopped with earth! My heart

Abhors his knowledge;° I disclaim in° him.   *knowing him / disavow*

FIRST AVOCATORE   But for what cause?

CORBACCIO   The mere portent of nature.[4]

He is an utter stranger to my loins.

BONARIO   Have they made you to this?

CORBACCIO   I will not hear thee,

110   Monster of men, swine, goat, wolf, parricide!

Speak not, thou viper.

BONARIO   Sir, I will sit down,

And rather wish my innocence should suffer

Than I resist the authority of a father.

VOLTORE [*calling a witness*]   Signor Corvino!

SECOND AVOCATORE   This is strange!

115   FIRST AVOCATORE   Who's this?

NOTARY   The husband.

FOURTH AVOCATORE   Is he sworn?

NOTARY   He is.

THIRD AVOCATORE   Speak, then.

---

4. A completely monstrous birth. (A deformed child was often considered to be a portent, or evil omen.)

CORVINO   This woman, please Your Fatherhoods, is a whore
  Of most hot exercise, more than a partridge,[5]
  Upon record°—   *as is well attested*
FIRST AVOCATORE   No more.
CORVINO   Neighs like a jennet.°   *mare (in heat)*
NOTARY   Preserve the honor of the court.
120 CORVINO   I shall,
  And modesty of your most reverend ears.
  And yet I hope that I may say these eyes
  Have seen her glued unto that piece of cedar,
  That fine well-timbered gallant;[6] and that here
125 [*Pointing to his forehead*] The letters may be read, thorough the horn,[7]
  That make the story perfect.°   *complete*
MOSCA [*aside to* CORVINO]   Excellent, sir!
CORVINO [*aside to* MOSCA]   There is no shame in this, now, is there?
MOSCA [*aside to* CORVINO]   None.
CORVINO [*to the court*]   Or if I said I hoped that she were
    onward°   *well on her way*
  To her damnation, if there be a hell
130 Greater than whore and woman—a good Catholic
  May make the doubt°—   *may wonder*
THIRD AVOCATORE   His grief hath made him frantic.
FIRST AVOCATORE   Remove him hence.   *She* [CELIA] *swoons.*
SECOND AVOCATORE   Look to the woman!
CORVINO [*taunting her*]   Rare!
  Prettily feigned! Again!
FOURTH AVOCATORE   Stand from about her.
FIRST AVOCATORE   Give her the air.
THIRD AVOCATORE [*to* MOSCA]   What can you say?
MOSCA   My wound,
135 May't please Your Wisdoms, speaks for me, received
  In aid of my good patron when he° missed   *Bonario*
  His sought-for father, when that well-taught dame
  Had her cue given her to cry out a rape.
BONARIO   Oh, most laid° impudence! Fathers—   *premeditated*
THIRD AVOCATORE   Sir, be silent.
140 You had your hearing free,° so must they theirs.   *uninterrupted*
SECOND AVOCATORE   I do begin to doubt th'imposture here.
FOURTH AVOCATORE   This woman has too many moods.
VOLTORE   Grave fathers,
  She is a creature of a most professed
  And prostituted lewdness.
CORVINO   Most impetuous!
  Unsatisfied,° grave fathers!   *insatiable*
145 VOLTORE   May her feignings

---

5. A bird capable of numerous consecutive sexual acts and so a byword for lechery.
6. Corvino sarcastically compliments Bonario as a strapping fellow to whom Celia no doubt wishes to cling. The cedars of the Middle East are tall and stately.
7. Children learned to read the alphabet from pages protected by transparent sheets of horn. (With an allusion to the cuckold's horn.)

Not take° Your Wisdoms! But° this day she baited   *take in / only*
A stranger, a grave knight, with her loose eyes
And more lascivious kisses. This man° saw 'em   *Mosca*
Together on the water in a gondola.

150 MOSCA   Here is the lady herself that saw 'em too,
Without;° who then had in the open streets   *waiting outside*
Pursued them, but for saving her knight's honor.

FIRST AVOCATORE   Produce that lady.

SECOND AVOCATORE   Let her come.
                              [*Exit* MOSCA.]

FOURTH AVOCATORE   These things,
They strike with wonder!

THIRD AVOCATORE   I am turned a stone!

SCENE 6. *The scene continues.*

[*Enter*] MOSCA [*and*] LADY [WOULD-BE].

MOSCA   Be resolute, madam.

LADY WOULD-BE   Ay, this same is she.
[*To* CELIA] Out, thou chameleon° harlot! Now thine   *deceitfully changeable*
    eyes
Vie tears with the hyena.[1] Dar'st thou look
Upon my wrongèd face? [*To the* AVOCATORI] I cry° your pardons.   *beg*
5 I fear I have forgettingly transgressed
Against the dignity of the court—

SECOND AVOCATORE   No, madam.

LADY WOULD-BE   And been exorbitant°—   *excessive*

SECOND AVOCATORE   You have not, lady.

FOURTH AVOCATORE   These proofs are strong.

LADY WOULD-BE   Surely, I had no purpose
To scandalize your honors, or my sex's.

THIRD AVOCATORE   We do believe it.

10 LADY WOULD-BE   Surely, you may believe it.

SECOND AVOCATORE   Madam, we do.

LADY WOULD-BE   Indeed, you may. My breeding
Is not so coarse—

FOURTH AVOCATORE   We know it.

LADY WOULD-BE   —to offend
With pertinacy°—   *stubborn resolution*

THIRD AVOCATORE   Lady—

LADY WOULD-BE   —such a presence;
No, surely.

FIRST AVOCATORE   We well think it.

LADY WOULD-BE   You may think it.

FIRST AVOCATORE [*to the other* AVOCATORI]   Let her o'ercome.°   *have the last*
15 [*To* CELIA *and* BONARIO] What witnesses have you   *word*
To make good your report?

BONARIO   Our consciences.

4.6
1. A symbol of treachery, the hyena was supposed to be able to change its sex and the color of its eyes at will and to imitate human voices.

CELIA   And heaven, that never fails the innocent.

FOURTH AVOCATORE   These are no testimonies.

BONARIO   Not in your courts,
Where multitude and clamor overcomes.

FIRST AVOCATORE   Nay, then, you do wax insolent.

> VOLPONE *is brought in* [*on a litter*], *as impotent.*°   disabled
> [LADY WOULD-BE *embraces him.*]°   *see 5.2.97*

20 VOLTORE   Here, here
The testimony comes that will convince
And put to utter dumbness their bold tongues.
See here, grave fathers, here's the ravisher,
The rider on men's wives, the great impostor,
25 The grand voluptuary! Do you not think
These limbs should affect venery?[2] Or these eyes
Covet a concubine? Pray you, mark these hands:
Are they not fit to stroke a lady's breasts?
Perhaps he doth dissemble?

BONARIO   So he does.

VOLTORE   Would you ha' him tortured?

30 BONARIO   I would have him proved.[3]

VOLTORE   Best try him, then, with goads or burning irons;
Put him to the strappado.[4] I have heard
The rack[5] hath cured the gout; faith, give it him
And help him of a malady; be courteous.
35 I'll undertake, before these honored fathers,
He shall have yet as many left° diseases   *remaining*
As she has known adulterers, or thou strumpets.
O my most equal° hearers, if these deeds,   *impartial*
Acts of this bold and most exorbitant strain,
40 May pass with sufferance,° what one citizen   *be permitted*
But owes the forfeit of his life, yea, fame
To him that dares traduce him?[6] Which of you
Are safe, my honored fathers? I would ask,
With leave of Your grave Fatherhoods, if their plot
45 Have any face or color like to truth?
Or if unto the dullest nostril here
It smell not rank and most abhorrèd slander?
I crave your care of this good gentleman,
Whose life is much endangered by their fable;
50 And as for them, I will conclude with this:
That vicious persons, when they are hot, and fleshed[7]
In impious acts, their constancy° abounds.   *resoluteness*
Damned deeds are done with greatest confidence.

FIRST AVOCATORE   Take 'em to custody, and sever them.

---

2. Delight in sexual activity.
3. Tested for impotence, a regular court procedure in some divorce and rape cases. (Torture was another method sometimes used to extract confessions.)
4. Torture in which the victim's arms were tied behind his back; he was then hoisted up by the wrists and dropped.
5. Torture instrument that stretched the victim to the point of dislocating his joints.
6. What citizen is there whose life and reputation might not be forfeit to a slanderer?
7. Excited by the taste of blood, like hunting hounds.

55 SECOND AVOCATORE 'Tis pity two such prodigies° should live.   *monsters*
               [*Exeunt* CELIA *and* BONARIO, *guarded.*]
FIRST AVOCATORE   Let the old gentleman be returned with care.
   I'm sorry our credulity wronged him.
               [*Exeunt litter-bearers with* VOLPONE.]
FOURTH AVOCATORE   These are two creatures!°   *monsters*
THIRD AVOCATORE   I have an earthquake in me!
SECOND AVOCATORE   Their shame, even in their cradles, fled their faces.
60 FOURTH AVOCATORE [*to* VOLTORE]   You've done a worthy service to the
   state, sir,
   In their discovery.
FIRST AVOCATORE   You shall hear ere night
   What punishment the court decrees upon 'em.
VOLTORE   We thank Your Fatherhoods.
            [*Exeunt* AVOCATORI, NOTARY, COMMENDATORI.]
   [*To* MOSCA]   How like you it?
MOSCA   Rare!
   I'd ha' your tongue, sir, tipped with gold for this;
65   I'd ha' you be the heir to the whole city;
   The earth I'd have want men ere you want living.°   *lack income*
   They're bound to erect your statue in Saint Mark's.—
   Signor Corvino, I would have you go
   And show yourself,[8] that you have conquered
CORVINO   Yes.
70 MOSCA [*aside to* CORVINO]   It was much better that you should profess
   Yourself a cuckold thus, than that the other[9]
   Should have been proved.
CORVINO   Nay, I considered that.
   Now it is her fault.
MOSCA   Then it had been yours.
CORVINO   True. I do doubt this advocate still.
MOSCA   I'faith,
75   You need not; I dare ease you of that care.
CORVINO   I trust thee, Mosca.
MOSCA   As your own soul, sir.
             [*Exit* CORVINO.]
CORBACCIO   Mosca!
MOSCA   Now for your business, sir.
CORBACCIO   How? Ha' you business?
MOSCA   Yes, yours, sir.
CORBACCIO   Oh, none else?
MOSCA   None else, not I.
CORBACCIO   Be careful, then.
MOSCA   Rest you with both your eyes,° sir.   *rest assured*
CORBACCIO   Dispatch it.[1]
MOSCA   Instantly.
80 CORBACCIO   And look that all

---

8. Appear in public. (To indicate that he is not ashamed of having admitted to being a cuckold.)
9. The attempt to prostitute Celia to Volpone.

1. I.e., Hurry to make Volpone's will, since Corbaccio has already delivered on his half of the promise.

Whatever be put in: jewels, plate, moneys,
Household stuff, bedding, curtains.
MOSCA   Curtain rings, sir.
Only the advocate's fee must be deducted.
CORBACCIO   I'll pay him, now; you'll be too prodigal.
MOSCA   Sir, I must tender° it.   *present*
85   CORBACCIO   Two *cecchines* is well?
MOSCA   No, six, sir.
CORBACCIO   'Tis too much.
MOSCA   He talked a great while,
You must consider that, sir.
CORBACCIO [*giving money*]   Well, there's three—
MOSCA   I'll give it him.
CORBACCIO   Do so, and [*he tips* MOSCA] there's for thee.
                                        [*Exit* CORBACCIO.]
MOSCA [*aside*]   Bountiful bones! What horrid strange offense
90   Did he commit 'gainst nature in his youth
Worthy this age?[2] [*To* VOLTORE] You see, sir, how I work
Unto your ends; take you no notice.°   *leave it to me*
VOLTORE   No,
I'll leave you.
MOSCA   All is yours,   [*Exit* VOLTORE.]
                      [*aside*] the devil and all,
Good advocate! [*To* LADY WOULD-BE] Madam, I'll bring you home.
LADY WOULD-BE   No, I'll go see your patron.
95   MOSCA   That you shall not.
I'll tell you why. My purpose is to urge
My patron to reform° his will; and, for   *revise*
The zeal you've shown today, whereas before
You were but third or fourth, you shall be now
100   Put in the first, which would appear as begged
If you were present. Therefore—
LADY WOULD-BE   You shall sway me.
                                        [*Exeunt.*]

Act 5

SCENE 1. VOLPONE'S *house.*

[*Enter*] VOLPONE [*attended*].
VOLPONE   Well, I am here, and all this brunt° is past.   *crisis*
I ne'er was in dislike with my disguise
Till this fled° moment; here 'twas good, in private,   *past*
But, in your public—*cavé*° whilst I breathe.   *watch out*
5   Fore God, my left leg 'gan to have the cramp,
And I apprehended straight° some power had struck me   *thought at once*
With a dead palsy.° Well, I must be merry   *paralysis*
And shake it off. A many of these fears
Would put me into some villainous disease,

2. To deserve this old age.

10 Should they come thick upon me. I'll prevent 'em.
Give me a bowl of lusty wine to fright
This humor from my heart.[1]—Hum, hum, hum! *He drinks.*
'Tis almost gone already; I shall conquer,°   *overcome my fears*
Any device, now, of rare ingenious knavery,
15 That would possess me with a violent laughter,
Would make me up° again. So, so, so, so. *Drinks again.*   *restore me*
This heat is life; 'tis blood by this time. [*Calling*] Mosca!

SCENE 2. *The scene continues.*

[*Enter*] MOSCA.

MOSCA How now, sir? Does the day look clear again?
Are we recovered and wrought out of error
Into our way, to see our path before us?
Is our trade free once more?
VOLPONE   Exquisite Mosca!
MOSCA Was it not carried learnedly?
5 VOLPONE   And stoutly.°   *resolutely*
Good wits are greatest in extremities.
MOSCA It were a folly beyond thought to trust
Any grand act unto a cowardly spirit.
You are not taken with it enough, methinks?
10 VOLPONE Oh, more than if I had enjoyed the wench!
The pleasure of all womankind's not like it.
MOSCA Why, now you speak, sir. We must here be fixed;
Here we must rest. This is our masterpiece.
We cannot think to go beyond this.
VOLPONE   True,
Th'hast played thy prize,[1] my precious Mosca.
15 MOSCA   Nay, sir,
To gull° the court—   *hoodwink*
VOLPONE   And quite divert the torrent
Upon the innocent.
MOSCA   Yes, and to make
So rare a music out of discords[2]—
VOLPONE   Right.
That yet to me's the strangest, how th'ast borne it!°   *brought it off*
20 That these,° being so divided 'mongst themselves,   *these men*
Should not scent° somewhat, or° in me or thee,   *suspect / either*
Or doubt their own side.°   *position*
MOSCA   True, they will not see't.
Too much light blinds 'em, I think. Each of 'em
Is so possessed and stuffed with his own hopes
25 That anything unto the contrary,
Never so true or never so apparent,

5.1
1. Wine was supposed to convert quickly to blood
(see line 17), thus giving courage to the drinker.
5.2
1. Professional fencers "played the prize," i.e.,

competed for purses and titles, in virtuoso displays of swordsmanship.
2. To bring harmony out of various discordant elements was thought to be the highest achievement of art.

Never so palpable, they will resist it—
VOLPONE   Like a temptation of the devil.
MOSCA   Right, sir.
Merchants may talk of trade, and your great signors
30   Of land that yields well; but if Italy
Have any glebe° more fruitful than these fellows,   soil
I am deceived. Did not your advocate rare?°   do brilliantly
VOLPONE   Oh!—"My most honored fathers, my grave fathers,
Under correction of Your Fatherhoods,
35   What face of truth is here? If these strange deeds
May pass, most honored fathers"—I had much ado
To forbear laughing.
MOSCA   'T seemed to me you sweat,° sir.   sweated (with fear)
VOLPONE   In troth, I did a little.
MOSCA   But confess, sir,
Were you not daunted?
VOLPONE   In good faith, I was
40   A little in a mist,° but not dejected;°   uncertain / overwhelmed
Never but still myself.
MOSCA   I think° it, sir.   believe
Now, so truth help me, I must needs say this, sir,
And out of conscience for your advocate:
He's taken pains, in faith, sir, and deserved,
45   In my poor judgment—I speak it under favor,°   with your permission
Not to contrary° you, sir—very richly—   contradict
Well—to be cozened.°   cheated
VOLPONE   Troth, and I think so too,
By that° I heard him° in the latter end.   what / him say
MOSCA   Oh, but before, sir! Had you heard him first
50   Draw it to certain heads, then aggravate,[3]
Then use his vehement figures°—I looked still   figures of speech
When he would shift[4] a shirt; and doing this
Out of pure love, no hope of gain—
VOLPONE   'Tis right.
I cannot answer° him, Mosca, as I would,   repay
55   Not yet; but for thy sake, at thy entreaty
I will begin ev'n now to vex 'em all,
This very instant.
MOSCA   Good, sir.
VOLPONE   Call the dwarf
And eunuch forth.
MOSCA [calling]   Castrone, Nano!
        [Enter] NANO [and] CASTRONE.
NANO   Here.
VOLPONE   Shall we have a jig, now?
MOSCA   What you please, sir.
VOLPONE   [to CASTRONE and NANO]   Go,

3. Arrange his material under various headings, then bring charges.

4. Change (because his efforts made him sweat).

60 Straight give out about the streets, you two,
That I am dead. Do it with constancy,°   *conviction*
Sadly, do you hear? Impute it to the grief
Of this late slander.   [*Exeunt* CASTRONE *and* NANO.]

MOSCA   What do you mean, sir?

VOLPONE   Oh,
I shall have instantly my vulture, crow,
65 Raven come flying hither on the news
To peck for carrion, my she-wolf° and all,   *Lady Would-be*
Greedy and full of expectation—

MOSCA   And then to have it ravished from their mouths?

VOLPONE   'Tis true. I will ha' thee put on a gown[5]
70 And take upon thee as° thou wert mine heir;   *act as though*
Show 'em a will. Open that chest and reach
Forth one of those that has the blanks.° I'll straight   *blank spaces*
Put in thy name.

MOSCA [*fetching a blank will*]   It will be rare, sir.

VOLPONE   Ay,
When they e'en gape, and find themselves deluded—

MOSCA   Yes.

75 VOLPONE   And thou use them scurvily. Dispatch,
Get on thy gown.

            [VOLPONE *signs the will* MOSCA *has given him.*
                  MOSCA *puts on a mourning garment.*]

MOSCA   But, what, sir, if they ask
After the body?

VOLPONE   Say it was corrupted.

MOSCA   I'll say it stunk, sir, and was fain° t'have it   *I was obliged*
Coffined up instantly and sent away.

80 VOLPONE   Anything; what thou wilt. Hold, here's my will.
Get thee a cap, a count-book, pen and ink,
Papers afore thee; sit as thou wert taking
An inventory of parcels.° I'll get up   *items*
Behind the curtain on a stool, and hearken;
85 Sometime peep over, see how they do look,
With what degrees their blood doth leave their faces.
Oh, 'twill afford me a rare meal of laughter!

MOSCA   Your advocate will turn stark dull° upon it.   *gloomy*

VOLPONE   It will take off his oratory's edge.

90 MOSCA   But your *clarissimo*,° old round-back, he   *aristocrat (Corbaccio)*
Will crump you° like a hog-louse with the touch.   *curl up on you*

VOLPONE   And what Corvino?

MOSCA   Oh, sir, look for him
Tomorrow morning with a rope and a dagger[6]
To visit all the streets; he must run mad.

---

5. This must be the long black gown ordinarily worn by chief mourners, not the *clarissimo*'s (aristocrat's) garment, which Mosca dons later in the scene and which constitutes a different kind of insult to Voltore, Corbaccio, and Corvino.

6. Traditional equipment of suicidal madmen, borne by the allegorical figure of Despair in Spenser's *Faerie Queene* 1.9, and by the revenger Hieronimo in *The Spanish Tragedy*.

95 My lady, too, that came into the court
To bear false witness for Your Worship—

VOLPONE   Yes,
And kissed me 'fore the fathers, when my face
Flowed all with oils.°   *see 4.6.20.1–2*

MOSCA   And sweat, sir. Why, your gold
Is such another° med'cine, it dries up   *so effective a*
100 All those offensive savors! It transforms
The most deformèd, and restores 'em lovely,
As 'twere the strange poetical girdle.[7] Jove
Could not invent t'himself a shroud more subtle
To pass Acrisius' guards.[8] It is the thing
105 Makes all the world her grace, her youth, her beauty.

VOLPONE   I think she loves me.

MOSCA   Who? The lady, sir?
She's jealous of you.[9]

VOLPONE   Dost thou say so?

                              [*Knocking offstage.*]

MOSCA   Hark,
There's some already.

VOLPONE   Look.

MOSCA   [*peeping out the door*] It is the vulture.
He has the quickest scent.

VOLPONE   I'll to my place,
Thou to thy posture.°   *pose*

MOSCA   I am set.

110 VOLPONE   But, Mosca,
Play the artificer° now; torture 'em rarely.   *artist*

                              [VOLPONE *conceals himself.*]

SCENE 3. *The scene continues.*

            [*Enter*] VOLTORE.

VOLTORE   How now, my Mosca?

MOSCA [*pretending not to notice him, and reading from an
      inventory*]   "Turkey carpets,° nine"—   *Oriental rugs*

VOLTORE   Taking an inventory? That is well.

MOSCA   "Two suits of bedding, tissue"[1]—

VOLTORE   Where's the will?
Let me read that the while.°   *while you're busy*

      [*Enter*] CORBACCIO [*on a litter*].

CORBACCIO [*to the litter-beaters*]   So, set me down
And get you home.   [*Exeunt litter-bearers.*]

5 VOLTORE   Is he come now to trouble us?

MOSCA   "Of cloth-of-gold,[2] two more"—

---

7. The girdle of Venus, the goddess of love, made
its wearer irresistible.
8. King Acrisius shut his daughter Danaë in a
tower, but the god Jove came to her in a shower
of gold.
9. (1) Devoted to you; (2) covetous of your
wealth.

5.3
1. Sets of bedcovers and hangings, made of
cloth with gold or silver threads interwoven. The
fancy textiles Mosca mentions in this scene were
extremely expensive to produce in the days
before automation.
2. Cloth made of gold threads.

CORBACCIO   Is it done, Mosca?
MOSCA   "Of several velvets,° eight"—   *separate velvet hangings*
VOLTORE [*aside*]   I like his care.
CORBACCIO [*to* MOSCA]   Dost thou not hear?
       [*Enter*] CORVINO.
CORVINO   Ha! Is the hour come, Mosca?
             VOLPONE *peeps from behind a traverse.°*   *curtain*
VOLPONE [*aside*]   Ay, now they muster.°   *assemble*
CORVINO   What does the advocate here?
   Or this Corbaccio?
CORBACCIO   What do these here?
       [*Enter*] LADY [WOULD-BE].
10   LADY WOULD-BE   Mosca,
   Is his thread spun?[3]
MOSCA   "Eight chests of linen"—
VOLPONE [*aside*]   Oh,
   My fine Dame Would-be, too!
CORVINO   Mosca, the will,
   That I may show it these, and rid 'em hence.
MOSCA   "Six chests of diaper, four of damask"[4]—there.
     [*He gives them the will.*]
CORBACCIO   Is that the will?
MOSCA   "Down beds and bolsters"—
15   VOLPONE [*aside*]   Rare!
   Be busy still. Now they begin to flutter;
   They never think of me. Look, see, see, see!
   How their swift eyes run over the long deed
   Unto the name, and to the legacies,
   What is bequeathed them there—
20   MOSCA   "Ten suits of hangings"°—   *sets of*
VOLPONE [*aside*]   Ay, i' their garters,[5] Mosca. Now their hopes   *tapestries*
   Are at the gasp.°   *last gasp*
VOLTORE   Mosca the heir!
CORBACCIO   What's that?
VOLPONE [*aside*]   My advocate is dumb. Look to my merchant;
   He has heard of some strange storm, a ship is lost,
25   He faints. My lady will swoon. Old glazen-eyes,[6]
   He hath not reached his despair yet.
CORBACCIO   All these
   Are out of hope; I'm sure the man.
CORVINO   But, Mosca—
MOSCA   "Two cabinets"—
CORVINO   Is this in earnest?
MOSCA   "One
   Of ebony"—

---

3. Is he dead? (In Greek mythology, the Fates spin out the thread of a human being's life and cut it at the time of death.)
4. Two kinds of costly textile with interwoven motifs. Diaper was linen with a diamond pattern; damask could be linen or silk with floral or other designs.
5. "Go hang yourself in your own garters" was a common phrase of ridicule.
6. Corbaccio wears spectacles (see also line 63 below).

CORVINO   Or do you but delude me?

30 MOSCA   "The other, mother-of-pearl"—I am very busy.
    Good faith, it is a fortune thrown upon me—
    "Item, one salt° of agate"—not my seeking.   *saltcellar*

LADY WOULD-BE   Do you hear, sir?

MOSCA   "A perfumed box"—pray you, forbear;
    You see I am troubled°—"made of an onyx"—   *busy*

LADY WOULD-BE   How!

35 MOSCA   Tomorrow or next day I shall be at leisure
    To talk with you all.

CORVINO   Is this my large hope's issue?°   *outcome*

LADY WOULD-BE   Sir, I must have a fairer answer.

MOSCA   Madam!
    Marry, and shall: pray you, fairly° quit my house.   *positively*
    Nay, raise no tempest with your looks, but hark you,

40   Remember what Your Ladyship offered me°   *implicitly, sexual favors*
    To put you in° an heir; go to, think on't,   *your name in as*
    And what you said e'en your best madams did
    For maintenance,° and why not you? Enough.   *financial support*
    Go home and use the poor Sir Pol, your knight, well,

45   For fear I tell some riddles.° Go, be melancholic.   *secrets*
                  [*Exit* LADY WOULD-BE.]

VOLPONE [*aside*]   Oh, my fine devil!

CORVINO   Mosca, pray you a word.

MOSCA   Lord! Will not you take your dispatch hence yet?
    Methinks of all you should have been th'example.°   *led the way*
    Why should you stay here? With what thought? What promise?

50   Hear you, do not you know I know you an ass?
    And that you would most fain have been a wittol°   *willing cuckold*
    If fortune would have let you? That you are
    A declared cuckold, on good terms?° This pearl,   *in good standing*
    You'll say, was yours? Right. This diamond?

55   I'll not deny't, but thank you. Much here else?
    It may be so. Why, think that these good works
    May help to hide your bad. I'll not betray you.
    Although you be but extraordinary°   *in name only*
    And have it° only in title, it sufficeth.   *the name of cuckold*

60   Go home. Be melancholic too, or mad.   [*Exit* CORVINO.]

VOLPONE [*aside*]   Rare, Mosca! How his villainy becomes him!

VOLTORE [*aside*]   Certain he doth delude all these for me.

CORBACCIO [*finally making out the will*]   Mosca the heir?

VOLPONE [*aside*]   Oh, his four eyes have found it!

CORBACCIO   I'm cozened, cheated by a parasite-slave!
    Harlot,[7] th'ast gulled me.

65 MOSCA   Yes, sir. Stop your mouth,
    Or I shall draw the only tooth is left.
    Are not you he, that filthy covetous wretch
    With the three legs,° that here, in hope of prey,   *including his cane*

---

7. A word used of wicked men as well as women.

Have, any time this three year, snuffed about
70　With your most grov'ling nose, and would have hired
Me to the pois'ning of my patron? Sir?
Are not you he that have today in court
Professed the disinheriting of your son?
Perjured yourself? Go home, and die, and stink.
75　If you but croak a syllable, all comes out.
Away and call your porters. Go, go stink!　　　　　[*Exit* CORBACCIO.]
VOLPONE [*aside*]　Excellent varlet!°　　　　　　　　　　*servant; rascal*
VOLTORE　　　　　　　　　　Now, my faithful Mosca,
I find thy constancy—
MOSCA　　　　　　　　Sir?
VOLTORE　　　　　　　　　　Sincere.
MOSCA　　　　　　　　　　　　"A table
Of porphyry"—I mar'l° you'll be thus troublesome.　　　　*marvel*
VOLTORE　Nay, leave off now, they are gone.
80　MOSCA　　　　　　　　　　　　Why, who are you?
What? Who did send for you? Oh, cry you mercy,°　　　*beg your pardon*
Reverend sir! Good faith, I am grieved for you,
That any chance of mine should thus defeat
Your—I must needs say—most deserving travails.
85　But I protest, sir, it was cast upon me,
And I could almost wish to be without it,
But that the will o'th'dead must be observed.
Marry, my joy is that you need it not;
You have a gift, sir—thank your education—
90　Will never let you want, while there are men
And malice to breed causes.° Would I had　　　　　　*lawsuits*
But half the like, for all my fortune, sir!
If I have any suits—as I do hope,
Things being so easy and direct,[8] I shall not—
95　I will make bold with your obstreperous° aid,　　　　*vociferous*
Conceive me, for your fee,[9] sir. In meantime
You, that have so much law, I know, ha' the conscience
Not to be covetous of what is mine.
Good sir, I thank you for my plate;° 'twill help　　　*see 1.3.1–20*
100　To set up a young man.° Good faith, you look　　　*set up my household*
As you were costive;° best go home and purge, sir.　　　　[*Exit* VOLTORE.]
VOLPONE [*coming from behind the traverse*]　Bid him eat
lettuce° well. My witty mischief,　　　　　　　　*used as a laxative*
Let me embrace thee! [*He hugs* MOSCA.] Oh, that I could now
Transform thee to a Venus!° Mosca, go,　　　　*for Volpone's sexual use*
105　Straight take my habit of *clarissimo*[1]
And walk the streets; be seen, torment 'em more.
We must pursue as well as plot. Who would

---

8. The situation being so straightforward.
9. It being understood that I will pay you, of course.
1. Aristocrat. (By obeying this order, Mosca vio-

lates the sumptuary laws that restricted the wearing of distinctive high-status garments, such as the *clarissimo*'s robe, to persons of the appropriate rank.)

Have lost° this feast?   *missed*
MOSCA   I doubt° it will lose them.°   *fear / as dupes*
VOLPONE   Oh, my recovery shall recover all.²
110   That I could now but think on some disguise
To meet 'em in, and ask 'em questions.
How I would vex 'em still at every turn!
MOSCA   Sir, I can fit you.
VOLPONE   Canst thou?
MOSCA   Yes, I know
One o'the *commendatori*, sir, so like you,
115   Him will I straight make drunk, and bring you his habit.
VOLPONE   A rare disguise, and answering thy brain!°   *suiting your wit*
Oh, I will be a sharp disease unto 'em.
MOSCA   Sir, you must look for curses—
VOLPONE   Till they burst!
The fox fares ever best when he is curst.°   [*Exeunt.*]   *proverbial wisdom*

SCENE 4. *The* WOULD-BES' *house.*

[*Enter*] PEREGRINE [*in disguise, and*] *three* MERCATORI
[MERCHANTS].

PEREGRINE   Am I enough disguised?
FIRST MERCHANT   I warrant you.
PEREGRINE   All my ambition is to fright him only.
SECOND MERCHANT   If you could ship him away, 'twere excellent.
THIRD MERCHANT   To Zante, or to Aleppo?¹
PEREGRINE   Yes, and ha' his
5   Adventures put i'th'book of voyages,²
And his gulled° story registered for truth?   *erroneous*
Well, gentlemen, when I am in awhile,
And that you think us warm in our discourse,
Know° your approaches.   *make*
FIRST MERCHANT   Trust it to our care.
                                        [*Exeunt* MERCHANTS.]
        [PEREGRINE *knocks. A*] WOMAN [*servant answers the*
        door].
10   PEREGRINE   Save you, fair lady. Is Sir Pol within?
WOMAN   I do not know, sir.
PEREGRINE   Pray you, say unto him
Here is a merchant upon earnest business
Desires to speak with him.
WOMAN   I will see, sir.
PEREGRINE   Pray you.
                                        [*Exit* WOMAN.]
I see the family is all female here.
        [*Enter* WOMAN.]

2. Volpone believes that by "undoing" his death, he will be able to resuscitate his scam.
5.4
1. Zante is an island off Greece under Venetian control; Aleppo, a big trading center, is in Syria.

2. An enlarged edition of Richard Hakluyt's *Principal Navigations, Voyages, Traffics, and Discoveries of the English Nation* was published in 1598–1600.

15 WOMAN   He says, sir, he has weighty affairs of state
          That now require him whole;° some other time   *demand all his attention*
          You may possess° him.   *gain audience with*
    PEREGRINE   Pray you say again,
          If those require him whole, these will exact him°   *force him out*
          Whereof I bring him tidings.   [*Exit* WOMAN.]
                                    What might be
20   His grave affair of state, now? How to make
          Bolognian sausages here in Venice, sparing
          One o'th'ingredients?
                    [*Enter* WOMAN.]
    WOMAN   Sir, he says he knows
          By your word "tidings" that you are no statesman,[3]
          And therefore wills you stay.°   *wishes you to wait*
    PEREGRINE   Sweet, pray you return° him   *reply to*
25   I have not read so many proclamations
          And studied them for words as he has done,
          But—here he deigns to come.
                    [*Enter*] POLITIC.
                                          [*Exit* WOMAN.]
    POLITIC   Sir, I must crave
          Your courteous pardon. There hath chanced today
          Unkind disaster 'twixt my lady and me,
30   And I was penning my apology
          To give her satisfaction, as you came now.
    PEREGRINE   Sir, I am grieved I bring you worse disaster.
          The gentleman you met at th'port today,
          That told you he was newly arrived—
    POLITIC   Ay, was
          A fugitive punk?°   *prostitute*
35 PEREGRINE   No, sir, a spy set on you;
          And he has made relation to the Senate
          That you professed to him to have a plot
          To sell the state of Venice to the Turk.°   *see 4.1.128–30*
    POLITIC   Oh, me!
    PEREGRINE   For which warrants are signed by this time
40   To apprehend you, and to search your study
          For papers—
    POLITIC   Alas, sir, I have none but notes
          Drawn out of playbooks°—   *printed plays*
    PEREGRINE   All the better, sir.
    POLITIC   And some essays. What shall I do?
    PEREGRINE   Sir, best
          Convey yourself into a sugar-chest;
45   Or, if you could lie round, a frail were rare,[4]
          And I could send you aboard.
    POLITIC   Sir, I but talked so,

---

3. Government agent. (Sir Politic believes that a   4. If you could curl up, a fruit basket would be
spy would use the word "intelligence.")   excellent.

For discourse sake merely.°   *They knock without.*   *Just to be conversing*

PEREGRINE   Hark, they are there!

POLITIC   I am a wretch, a wretch!

PEREGRINE   What will you do, sir?

    Ha' you ne'er a currant-butt° to leap into?   *casket for currants*

50   They'll put you to the rack; you must be sudden.

POLITIC   Sir, I have an engine°—   *contrivance*

THIRD MERCHANT [*without*]   Sir Politic Would-be!

SECOND MERCHANT [*without*]   Where is he?

POLITIC   That I have thought upon

    beforetime.

PEREGRINE   What is it?

POLITIC   I shall ne'er endure the torture!

    Marry, it is, sir, of a tortoiseshell, [*producing the shell*]

55   Fitted for these extremities. Pray you sir, help me.

    Here I have a place, sir, to put back my legs—

    Please you to lay it on, sir—with this cap

    And my black gloves. I'll lie, sir, like a tortoise

    Till they are gone.

PEREGRINE   [*laying the shell on* POLITIC's *back*]   And call you this an

    engine?

60   POLITIC   Mine own device—good sir, bid my wife's women

    To burn my papers.   [*Exit* PEREGRINE.]

       They [*the* MERCHANTS] *rush in.*

FIRST MERCHANT   Where's he hid?

THIRD MERCHANT   We must

    And will, sure, find him.

SECOND MERCHANT   Which is his study?

      [*Enter* PEREGRINE.]

FIRST MERCHANT   What

    Are you, sir?

PEREGRINE   I'm a merchant, that came here

    To look upon this tortoise.

THIRD MERCHANT   How?

FIRST MERCHANT   Saint Mark!

    What beast is this?

PEREGRINE   It is a fish.

65   SECOND MERCHANT [*to* POLITIC]   Come out here!

PEREGRINE   Nay, you may strike him, sir, and tread upon him.

    He'll bear a cart.

FIRST MERCHANT   What, to run over him?

PEREGRINE   Yes.

THIRD MERCHANT   Let's jump upon him.

SECOND MERCHANT   Can he not go?°   *walk*

PEREGRINE   He creeps, sir.

FIRST MERCHANT [*poking* POLITIC]   Let's see him creep.

PEREGRINE   No, good sir, you

    will hurt him.

70   SECOND MERCHANT   Heart! I'll see him creep, or prick his guts.

THIRD MERCHANT [*to* POLITIC]   Come out here!

PEREGRINE   [*aside to* POLITIC]   Pray you, sir, creep a little.
                                                                   [POLITIC *creeps.*]
FIRST MERCHANT   Forth!
SECOND MERCHANT   Yet further.
PEREGRINE [*aside to* POLITIC]   Good sir, creep.
SECOND MERCHANT   We'll see his legs.
                   They pull off the shell and discover° him.   expose
THIRD MERCHANT   Godso, he has garters!
FIRST MERCHANT   Ay, and gloves!
SECOND MERCHANT   Is this
   Your fearful tortoise?
PEREGRINE [*revealing himself*]   Now, Sir Pol, we are even.
75   For your next project I shall be prepared.
   I am sorry for the funeral of your notes, sir.
FIRST MERCHANT   'Twere a rare motion to be seen in Fleet Street![5]
SECOND MERCHANT   Ay, i'the term.
FIRST MERCHANT   Or Smithfield, in the fair.[6]
THIRD MERCHANT   Methinks 'tis but a melancholic sight!
80   PEREGRINE   Farewell, most politic tortoise.
                   [*Exeunt* PEREGRINE *and* MERCHANTS.]
         [*Enter* WOMAN.]
POLITIC   Where's my lady?
   Knows she of this?
WOMAN   I know not, sir.
POLITIC   Inquire.
                                        [*Exit* WOMAN.]
   Oh, I shall be the fable of all feasts,°   talk of the town
   The freight of the *gazetti*, ship boys' tale,[7]
   And, which is worst, even talk for ordinaries.°   taverns
         [*Enter* WOMAN.]
85   WOMAN   My lady's come most melancholic home,
   And says, sir, she will straight to sea for physic.
POLITIC   And I, to shun this place and clime forever,
   Creeping with house on back, and think it well
   To shrink my poor head in my politic shell.   [*Exeunt.*]

                   SCENE 5. VOLPONE's *house.*

         [*Enter*] VOLPONE [*and*] MOSCA, *the first in the habit of a*
         commendatore, the other, of a clarissimo.°   see 5.3.104–15
VOLPONE   Am I then like him?
MOSCA   Oh, sir, you are he.
   No man can sever° you.   distinguish
VOLPONE   Good.
MOSCA   But what am I?
VOLPONE   'Fore heav'n, a brave° *clarissimo*; thou becom'st it!   splendid

---

5. Puppet shows, called "motions," were frequently performed on London's Fleet Street, adjacent to the Inns of Court, where attorneys were
trained and cases were argued during the three
law terms.

6. Smithfield, just northwest of London, was the
site every August of Bartholomew Fair; puppet
shows were a prime entertainment there.
7. Topic of the newspapers and the gossip of
boys serving on board ships.

Pity thou wert not born one.

MOSCA   If I hold
My made one, 'twill be well.

5   VOLPONE   I'll go and see
What news, first, at the court.

MOSCA   Do so.   [*Exit* VOLPONE.]
                       My fox
Is out on° his hole,[1] and ere he shall reenter   *of*
I'll make him languish in his borrowed case,°   *disguise*
Except he come to composition° with me.   *unless he makes a deal*
[*Calling*] Androgyno, Castrone, Nano!
          [*Enter* ANDROGYNO, CASTRONE, *and* NANO.]

10   ALL   Here.

MOSCA   Go recreate yourselves abroad;° go sport.   *outside*
       [*Exeunt* ANDROGYNO, CASTRONE, *and* NANO.]
So, now I have the keys, and am possessed.°   *in possession*
Since he will needs be dead afore his time,
I'll bury him or gain by him. I am his heir,

15   And so will keep me° till he share at least.   *remain*
To cozen him of all were but a cheat
Well placed; no man would construe it a sin.
Let his sport pay for't.° This is called the Fox Trap. [*Exit.*]   *for itself*

SCENE 6. *A street in Venice.*

     [*Enter*] CORBACCIO [*and*] CORVINO.

CORBACCIO   They say the court is set.°   *in session*

CORVINO   We must maintain
Our first tale good, for both our reputations.

CORBACCIO   Why, mine's no tale; my son would there have killed me.

CORVINO   That's true; I had forgot. [*Aside*] Mine is, I am sure.—
But for your will, sir.

5   CORBACCIO   Ay, I'll come upon him
For that hereafter, now his patron's dead.
       [*Enter*] VOLPONE [*disguised*].

VOLPONE   Signor Corvino! And Corbaccio! Sir,
Much joy unto you.

CORVINO   Of what?

VOLPONE   The sudden good
Dropped down upon you—

CORBACCIO   Where?

VOLPONE   And none knows how—
From old Volpone, sir.

10   CORBACCIO   Out, arrant knave!

VOLPONE   Let not your too much wealth, sir, make you furious.°   *insane*

CORBACCIO   Away, thou varlet!

VOLPONE   Why, sir?

CORBACCIO   Dost thou mock me?

5.5
1. Alluding to the children's game, fox-in-the-hole.

VOLPONE You mock the world, sir.[1] Did you not change° wills?   *exchange*
CORBACCIO Out, harlot!
VOLPONE [*to* CORVINO] Oh, belike you are the man,
15 Signor Corvino? Faith, you carry it° well;   *carry it off*
You grow not mad withal. I love your spirit.
You are not overleavened° with your fortune.   *too puffed up*
You should ha' some would swell now like a wine-vat
With such an autumn.° Did he gi' you all, sir?   *harvest*
CORVINO Avoid,° you rascal!   *Go away*
20 VOLPONE   Troth, your wife has shown
Herself a very° woman. But you are well;   *typical*
You need not care; you have a good estate
To bear it out, sir, better by this chance—
Except Corbaccio have a share?
CORBACCIO   Hence, varlet!
25 VOLPONE You will not be aknown,[2] sir; why, 'tis wise.
Thus do all gamesters at all games dissemble.
No man will seem to win.°   *admit he's winning*
        [*Exeunt* CORBACCIO *and* CORVINO.]
                    Here comes my vulture,
Heaving his beak up i'the air and snuffing.

SCENE 7. *The scene continues.*

[*Enter*] VOLTORE.
VOLTORE [*to himself*] Outstripped thus by a parasite? A slave
Would run on errands, and make legs° for crumbs?   *curtsies*
Well, what I'll do—
VOLPONE   The court stays for° Your Worship.   *awaits*
I e'en rejoice, sir, at Your Worship's happiness,
5 And that it fell into so learnèd hands
That understand the fingering[1]—
VOLTORE   What do you mean?
VOLPONE I mean to be a suitor to Your Worship
For the small tenement, out of reparations[2]—
That at the end of your long row of houses
10 By the *piscaria*.° It was in Volpone's time,   *fish market*
Your predecessor, ere he grew diseased,
A handsome, pretty, customed° bawdy house   *much-patronized*
As any was in Venice—none dispraised[3]—
But fell with him; his body and that house
Decayed together.
15 VOLTORE   Come, sir, leave your prating.°   *chattering*
VOLPONE Why, if Your Worship give me but your hand,
That I may ha' the refusal,° I have done.   *right of first refusal*

5.6
1. Volpone pretends to believe that Corbaccio is misleading people by refusing to admit to his good fortune.
2. You prefer not to be recognized (as heir).

5.7
1. That understand how to handle money.
2. For the rental house in bad repair.
3. Not to disparage the others.

'Tis a mere toy to you, sir, candle-rents,[4]
As Your learned Worship knows—

VOLTORE   What do I know?

20   VOLPONE   Marry, no end of your wealth, sir, God decrease° it.   *instead of*

VOLTORE   Mistaking knave! What, mock'st thou my misfortune?   *"increase"*

VOLPONE   His° blessing on your heart, sir! Would 'twere more.   *God's*

                                [*Exit* VOLTORE.]

Now, to my first[5] again, at the next corner.

SCENE 8. *The scene continues.*

[*Enter*] CORBACCIO [*and*] CORVINO. [*Enter*] MOSCA,
passant° [*over the stage in* clarissimo's *attire, and exit*].   *passing*

CORBACCIO   See, in our habit! See the impudent varlet!

CORVINO   That I could shoot mine eyes at him, like gunstones!°   *cannonballs*

VOLPONE   But, is this true, sir, of the parasite?

CORBACCIO   Again t'afflict us? Monster!

VOLPONE   In good faith, sir,

5   I'm heartily grieved a beard of your grave length°   *so wise an old man*

Should be so overreached. I never brooked°   *could stand*

That parasite's hair; methought his nose should cozen.°   *he had a cheating nose*

There still° was somewhat in his look did promise.   *always*

The bane° of a *clarissimo*.   *ruin*

CORBACCIO   Knave—

VOLPONE [*to* CORVINO]   Methinks

10   Yet you that are so traded° i'the world,   *experienced*

A witty merchant, the fine bird Corvino,

That have such moral emblems[1] on your name,

Should not have sung your shame and dropped your cheese,

To let the fox laugh at your emptiness.[2]

15   CORVINO   Sirrah, you think the privilege of the place,[3]

And your red saucy cap, that seems to me

Nailed to your jolt-head with those two *cecchines*,[4]

Can warrant° your abuses. Come you hither.   *sanction*

You shall perceive, sir, I dare beat you. Approach!

20   VOLPONE   No haste, sir, I do know your valor well,

Since you durst publish° what you are, sir.   *make public*

                       [VOLPONE *makes as if to leave.*]

CORVINO   Tarry!

I'd speak with you.

VOLPONE   Sir, sir, another time—

CORVINO   Nay, now.

VOLPONE   Oh, God, sir! I were a wise man

Would stand° the fury of a distracted cuckold.   *to withstand*

      MOSCA [*enters and*] *walks by 'em.*

CORBACCIO   What! Come again?

---

4. (1) Revenue from deteriorating property; (2) "pin money," money for incidentals.
5. The ones I was taunting earlier, Corvino and Corbaccio.
5.8

1. Mottoes accompanying symbolic engravings.
2. As in Aesop's fable; see 1.2.95–97 and note.
3. Violence was forbidden near the court.
4. The *commendatore's* cap is decorated with gold buttons.

25 VOLPONE [*aside to* MOSCA]   Upon 'em, Mosca; save me.
CORBACCIO   The air's infected where he breathes.
CORVINO   Let's fly him.
     [*Exeunt* CORVINO *and* CORBACCIO.]
VOLPONE   Excellent basilisk![5] Turn upon the vulture.

SCENE 9. *The scene continues.*

     [*Enter*] VOLTORE.
VOLTORE [*to Mosca*]   Well, flesh fly, it is summer with you now;
   Your winter will come on.
MOSCA   Good advocate,
   Pray thee not rail, nor threaten out of place° thus;   *unsuitably*
   Thou'lt make a solecism,° as madam says.   *see 4.2.43*
5   Get you a biggin[1] more; your brain breaks loose.
VOLTORE   Well, sir.   [*Exit* MOSCA.]
VOLPONE   Would you ha' me beat the insolent slave?
   Throw dirt upon his first good clothes?
VOLTORE   This same°   *the disguised Volpone*
   Is doubtless some familiar!°   *attendant devil*
VOLPONE   Sir, the court,
   In troth, stays for you. I am mad° a mule   *furious that*
10   That never read Justinian[2] should get up
   And ride an advocate. Had you no quirk°   *trick*
   To avoid gullage,° sir, by such a creature?   *deception*
   I hope you do but jest; he has not done't.
   This's but confederacy to blind the rest.°   *Corvino and Corbaccio*
   You are the heir?
15 VOLTORE   A strange, officious,
   Troublesome knave! Thou dost torment me.
VOLPONE   I know—
   It cannot be, sir, that you should be cozened;
   'Tis not within the wit of man to do it.
   You are so wise, so prudent, and 'tis fit
20   That wealth and wisdom still should go together.
                                             [*Exeunt.*]

SCENE 10. *The law court.*

     [*Enter*] *four* AVOCATORI, NOTARIO [NOTARY], COMMEN-
     DATORI, BONARIO [*and*] CELIA [*under guard*], COR-
     BACCIO, [*and*] CORVINO.
FIRST AVOCATORE   Are all the parties here?
NOTARY   All but the advocate.
SECOND AVOCATORE   And here he comes.
FIRST AVOCATORE   Then bring 'em forth to sentence.
     [*Enter*] VOLTORE, [*and*] VOLPONE [*still disguised as a*
     commendatore].

5. A legendary monster whose breath and glance   2. The Roman law, codified under Emperor Jus-
were deadly.   tinian and still influential on the Continent.
5.9   Lawyers traditionally rode mules to the courts;
1. A larger skullcap (worn by lawyers).   here the image is comically inverted.

VOLTORE   O my most honored fathers, let your mercy
  Once win upon° your justice, to forgive—   *prevail over*
  I am distracted—
VOLPONE (*aside*)   What will he do now?
5 VOLTORE   Oh,
  I know not which t'address myself to first,
  Whether Your Fatherhoods or these innocents°—   *Celia and Bonario*
CORVINO [*aside*]   Will he betray himself?
VOLTORE   Whom equally
  I have abused, out of most covetous ends—
CORVINO [*aside to* CORBACCIO]   The man is mad!
CORBACCIO   What's that?
10 CORVINO
                                    He is possessed.
VOLTORE   For which, now struck in conscience, here I prostrate
  Myself at your offended feet for pardon.
                                    [*He throws himself down.*]

FIRST AND SECOND AVOCATORI   Arise!
CELIA   O heav'n, how just thou art!
VOLPONE [*aside*]   I'm caught
  I' mine own noose—
CORVINO [*aside to* CORBACCIO]   Be constant, sir; naught now
  Can help but impudence.   [VOLTORE *rises.*]
FIRST AVOCATORE [*to* VOLTORE]   Speak forward.°   *continue*
15 COMMENDATORI [*to the courtroom*]   Silence!
VOLTORE   It is not passion° in me, reverend fathers,   *madness*
  But only conscience, conscience, my good sires,
  That makes me now tell truth. That parasite,
  That knave hath been the instrument of all.
SECOND AVOCATORE   Where is that knave? Fetch him.
VOLPONE [*as commendatore*]   I go.   [*Exit.*]
20 CORVINO   Grave fathers,
  This man's distracted; he confessed it now;°   *just now*
  For, hoping to be old Volpone's heir,
  Who now is dead—
THIRD AVOCATORE   How?
SECOND AVOCATORE   Is Volpone dead?
CORVINO   Dead since,° grave fathers—   *since his appearance here*
BONARIO   O sure vengeance!
FIRST AVOCATORE   Stay.
  Then he was no deceiver?
25 VOLTORE   Oh, no, none.
  The parasite, grave fathers.
CORVINO   He does speak
  Out of mere envy, 'cause the servant's made
  The thing he gaped° for. Please Your Fatherhoods,   *Voltore yearned*
  This is the truth; though I'll not justify
30 The other,° but he may be somedeal° faulty.   *Mosca / somewhat*
VOLTORE   Ay, to your hopes as well as mine, Corvino;
  But I'll use modesty.° Pleaseth Your Wisdoms   *self-control*

To view these certain notes, and but confer° them. °*compare*
As I hope favor, they shall speak clear truth.
  [*He gives documents to the* AVOCATORI.]

CORVINO The devil has entered him!

35 BONARIO   Or bides in you.

FOURTH AVOCATORE We have done ill, by a public officer
To send for him, if he be heir.

SECOND AVOCATORE   For whom?

FOURTH AVOCATORE Him that they call the parasite.

THIRD AVOCATORE   'Tis true;
He is a man of great estate now left.° °*bequeathed to him*

40 FOURTH AVOCATORE [*to* NOTARY.] Go you and learn his name,
  and say the court
Entreats his presence here but to the clearing
Of some few doubts.   [*Exit* NOTARY.]

SECOND AVOCATORE This same's a labyrinth!

FIRST AVOCATORE [*to* CORVINO] Stand you unto° your first
  report?   °*Do you stand by*

CORVINO   My state,°   °*estate*
My life, my fame°—   °*reputation*

BONARIO   Where is't?[1]

CORVINO   —are at the stake.

FIRST AVOCATORE [*to* CORBACCIO] Is yours so too?

45 CORBACCIO   The advocate's a knave,
And has a forkèd tongue—

SECOND AVOCATORE   Speak to the point.

CORBACCIO So is the parasite, too.

FIRST AVOCATORE   This is confusion.

VOLTORE I do beseech Your Fatherhoods, read but those.

CORVINO And credit nothing the false spirit hath writ.

50 It cannot be but he is possessed, grave fathers.
  [*The* AVOCATORI *examine* VOLTORE'S *papers.*]

SCENE 11. *A street.*[1]

[*Enter*] VOLPONE [*on a separate part of the stage*].

VOLPONE To make a snare for mine own neck! And run
My head into it willfully! With laughter!
When I had newly scaped, was free and clear!
Out of mere wantonness!° Oh, the dull devil   °*caprice*

5 Was in this brain of mine when I devised it,
And Mosca gave it second. He must now
Help to sear up° this vein, or we bleed dead.   °*cauterize*
  [*Enter*] NANO, ANDROGYNO, [*and*] CASTRONE.
How now, who let you loose? Whither go you now?
What, to buy gingerbread? Or to drown kitlings?°   °*kittens*

5.10
1. Implying that Corvino has nothing of worth to lose.
5.11

1. The courtroom characters remain visible onstage, perhaps in silent tableau, while Volpone is understood to be outside.

10 NANO Sir, Master Mosca called us out of doors,
And bid us all go play, and took the keys.
ANDROGYNO   Yes.
VOLPONE Did Master Mosca take the keys? Why, so!
I am farther in.° These are my fine conceits!°   *in trouble / notions*
I must be merry, with a mischief to me!
15 What a vile wretch was I, that could not bear
My fortune soberly! I must ha' my crotchets°   *perverse whims*
And my conundrums! Well, go you and seek him.
His meaning may be truer than my fear.²
Bid him he straight come to me, to the court.
20 Thither will I, and, if't be possible,
Unscrew° my advocate upon° new hopes.   *dissuade / by means of*
When I provoked him, then I lost myself.
                    [*Exeunt* VOLPONE *and his entourage.*
                    The AVOCATORI *and parties to the*
                    courtroom proceedings remain onstage.]

SCENE 12. *The courtroom.*

FIRST AVOCATORE [*with* VOLTORE's *notes*]   These things can ne'er be
        reconciled. He here
Professeth that the gentleman° was wronged,   *Bonario*
And that the gentlewoman was brought thither,
Forced by her husband, and there left.
VOLTORE   Most true.
CELIA How ready is heav'n to those that pray!
5 FIRST AVOCATORE   But that
Volpone would have ravished her, he holds
Utterly false, knowing his impotence.
CORVINO Grave fathers, he is possessed; again I say,
Possessed. Nay, if there be possession
And obsession, he has both.
10 THIRD AVOCATORE   Here comes our officer.
            [*Enter* VOLPONE, *still disguised.*]
VOLPONE The parasite will straight be here, grave fathers.
FOURTH AVOCATORE You might invent some other name, sir varlet.
THIRD AVOCATORE Did not the notary meet him?
VOLPONE   Not that I know.
FOURTH AVOCATORE His coming will clear all.
SECOND AVOCATORE   Yet it is misty.
VOLTORE May't please Your Fatherhoods—
15 VOLPONE (*whispers* [*to*] *the advocate*)   Sir, the parasite
Willed me to tell you that his master lives,
That you are still the man, your hopes the same;
And this was only a jest—
VOLTORE [*aside to* VOLPONE] How?
VOLPONE [*aside to* VOLTORE]   Sir, to try
If you were firm, and how you stood affected.°   *how loyal you were*

2. Mosca's intentions may be truer (more loyal) than my fear is true (accurate).

VOLTORE   Art sure he lives?

VOLPONE   Do I live,° sir?   *he's as alive as I am*

20 VOLTORE   Oh, me!

I was too violent.

VOLPONE   Sir, you may redeem it.

They said you were possessed; fall down, and seem so.

I'll help to make it good.   VOLTORE *falls.*

                    [*Aloud*] God bless the man!

[*Aside to* VOLTORE] Stop your wind hard, and swell.¹ [*Aloud*]

      See, see, see, see!

25 He vomits crooked pins! His eyes are set

Like a dead hare's hung in a poulter's² shop!

His mouth's running away!° [*To* CORVINO] Do you see,   *twitching*
      signor?   *spasmodically*

Now 'tis in his belly.

CORVINO   Ay, the devil!

VOLPONE   Now in his throat.

CORVINO   Ay, I perceive it plain.

30 VOLPONE   'Twill out, 'twill out! Stand clear. See where it flies,

In shape of a blue toad with a bat's wings!

[*To* CORBACCIO] Do not you see it, sir?

CORBACCIO   What? I think I do.

CORVINO   'Tis too manifest.

VOLPONE   Look! He comes t' himself!

VOLTORE   Where am I?

VOLPONE   Take good heart; the worst is past, sir.

You are dispossessed.

35 FIRST AVOCATORE   What accident° is this?   *unforeseen event*

SECOND AVOCATORE   Sudden, and full of wonder!

THIRD AVOCATORE   If he were

Possessed, as it appears, all this° is nothing.   *Voltore's written statement*

CORVINO   He has been often subject to these fits.

FIRST AVOCATORE   Show him that writing. [*To* VOLTORE] Do
      you know it, sir?

40 VOLPONE [*aside to* VOLTORE]   Deny it, sir; forswear it; know it not.

VOLTORE   Yes, I do know it well, it is my hand;

But all that it contains is false.

BONARIO   Oh, practice!°   *deception*

SECOND AVOCATORE   What maze is this!

FIRST AVOCATORE   Is he not guilty, then,

Whom you there name the parasite?

VOLTORE   Grave fathers,

45 No more than his good patron, old Volpone.

FOURTH AVOCATORE   Why, he is dead!

VOLTORE   Oh, no, my honored fathers.

He lives—

5.12

1. The details of Voltore's dispossession in the following lines resemble the fake exorcisms described in Samuel Harsnett's lively exposé, *A*

Discovery of the Fraudulent Practices of John Darrell (1599). "Stop your wind": hold your breath.
2. Seller of poultry and small game.

FIRST AVOCATORE   How! Lives?
VOLTORE   Lives.
SECOND AVOCATORE   This is subtler yet!
THIRD AVOCATORE [*to* VOLTORE]   You said he was dead?
VOLTORE   Never.
THIRD AVOCATORE [*to* CORVINO]   You said so?
CORVINO   I heard so.
FOURTH AVOCATORE   Here comes the gentleman; make him way.
         [*Enter* MOSCA.]

50   THIRD AVOCATORE   A stool!
FOURTH AVOCATORE [*aside*]   A proper° man! And, were Volpone   *handsome*
      dead,
      A fit match for my daughter.
THIRD AVOCATORE   Give him way.
VOLPONE [*aside to* MOSCA]   Mosca, I was almost lost; the advocate
      Had betrayed all; but now it is recovered.
      All's o'the hinge° again. Say I am living.   *running smoothly*
55   MOSCA [*aloud*]   What busy° knave is this? Most reverend   *troublesome*
      fathers,
      I sooner had attended your grave pleasures,
      But that my order for the funeral
      Of my dear patron did require me—
VOLPONE (*aside*)   Mosca!
MOSCA   Whom I intend to bury like a gentleman.
VOLPONE [*aside*]   Ay, quick,° and cozen me of all.[3]   *alive*
60   SECOND AVOCATORE   Still stranger!
      More intricate!
FIRST AVOCATORE   And come about° again!   *reversing direction*
FOURTH AVOCATORE [*aside*]   It is a match; my daughter is bestowed.
MOSCA [*aside to* VOLPONE]   Will you gi' me half?
VOLPONE [*aside to* MOSCA]   First, I'll be hanged.
MOSCA [*aside to* VOLPONE]
                                              I know
      Your voice is good. Cry not so loud.
FIRST AVOCATORE   Demand°   *question*
65   The advocate. [*To* VOLTORE] Sir, did not you affirm
      Volpone was alive?
VOLPONE   Yes, and he is;
      This gent'man told me so. (*Aside to* MOSCA) Thou shalt have half.
MOSCA   Whose drunkard is this same? Speak, some that know him;
      I never saw his face. (*Aside to* VOLPONE) I cannot now
      Afford it you so cheap.
VOLPONE (*aside to* MOSCA)   No?
70   FIRST AVOCATORE [*to* VOLTORE]   What say you?
VOLTORE   The officer told me.
VOLPONE   I did, grave fathers,
      And will maintain he lives with mine own life,
      And that this creature° told me. (*Aside*) I was born   *Mosca*

3. Volpone sees that Mosca's pious pretense of burying the "dead" Volpone will mean an end to all of
Volpone's hopes; he'll be cheated out of everything.

With all good stars my enemies.

MOSCA   Most grave fathers,

75   If such an insolence as this must pass°   *be permitted*
     Upon me, I am silent. 'Twas not this
     For which you sent, I hope.

SECOND AVOCATORE [*pointing to* VOLPONE]   Take him away.

VOLPONE (*aside to* MOSCA)   Mosca!

THIRD AVOCATORE   Let him be whipped.

VOLPONE (*aside to* MOSCA)   Wilt thou betray me?
     Cozen me?

THIRD AVOCATORE   And taught to bear himself
     Toward a person of his° rank.   *Mosca's*

80   FOURTH AVOCATORE   Away!
                                    [*Officers seize* VOLPONE.]

MOSCA   I humbly thank Your Fatherhoods.

VOLPONE   Soft, soft. [*Aside*] Whipped?
     And lose all that I have? If I confess,
     It cannot be much more.

FOURTH AVOCATORE [*to* MOSCA]   Sir, are you married?

VOLPONE [*aside*]   They'll be allied° anon; I must be resolute.   *linked by marriage*
     The fox shall here uncase.°   *He puts off his disguise.*   *reveal himself*

MOSCA (*aside*)   Patron!

85   VOLPONE   Nay, now
     My ruins shall not come alone. Your match
     I'll hinder sure; my substance shall not glue you
     Nor screw you into a family.

MOSCA (*aside*)   Why, patron!

VOLPONE   I am Volpone, and [*pointing to* MOSCA] this is my knave;

90   [*Pointing to* VOLTORE] This his own knave; [*pointing to* CORBACCIO]
     this, avarice's fool;
     [*Pointing to* CORVINO] This, a chimera° of wittol,   *monstrous combination*
     fool, and knave;
     And, reverend fathers, since we all can hope
     Naught but a sentence, let's not now despair it.°   *be disappointed (ironic)*
     You hear me brief.°   *That's all I have to say*

CORVINO   May it please Your Fatherhoods—

COMMENDATORE[4]   Silence!

95   FIRST AVOCATORE   The knot is now undone by miracle!

SECOND AVOCATORE   Nothing can be more clear.

THIRD AVOCATORE   Or can more prove
     These innocent.

FIRST AVOCATORE   Give 'em their liberty.
                          [BONARIO *and* CELIA *are released.*]

BONARIO   Heaven could not long let such gross crimes be hid.

SECOND AVOCATORE   If this be held the highway to get riches,
     May I be poor!

100 THIRD AVOCATORE   This's not the gain, but torment.

FIRST AVOCATORE   These possess wealth as sick men possess fevers,

---

4. Not Volpone, of course, but one of the genuine Commendatori. They are probably the officers who
strip Mosca at line 103.

Which trulier may be said to possess them.

SECOND AVOCATORE   Disrobe that parasite.

[MOSCA *is stripped of his clarissimo's robe.*]

CORVINO [*and*] MOSCA   Most honored fathers!

FIRST AVOCATORE   Can you plead aught to stay the course of justice?
  If you can, speak.

CORVINO [*and*] VOLTORE   We beg favor—

105 CELIA   And mercy.

FIRST AVOCATORE [*to* CELIA]   You hurt your innocence, suing°   pleading
  for the guilty.

  [*To the others*] Stand forth; and, first, the parasite. You appear
  T'have been the chiefest minister,° if not plotter,   agent
  In all these lewd° impostures, and now, lastly,   vile, obscene
110 Have with your impudence abused the court
  And habit° of a gentleman of Venice,   garb
  Being a fellow of no birth or blood;
  For which our sentence is, first thou be whipped,
  Then live perpetual prisoner in our galleys.

VOLPONE   I thank you for him.

115 MOSCA   Bane to° thy wolfish nature!   curses on

FIRST AVOCATORE   Deliver him to the *saffi*.° [MOSCA *is placed*   bailiffs
  under guard.] Thou, Volpone,
  By blood and rank a gentleman, canst not fall
  Under like censure;° but our judgment on thee   the same sentence
  Is that thy substance° all be straight confiscate   wealth
120 To the hospital of the *Incurabili*;[5]
  And since the most was gotten by imposture,
  By feigning lame, gout, palsy, and such diseases,
  Thou art to lie in prison, cramped with irons,
  Till thou be'st sick and lame indeed.—Remove him.

            [VOLPONE *is placed under guard.*]

125 VOLPONE   This is called mortifying[6] of a fox.

FIRST AVOCATORE   Thou, Voltore, to take away the scandal
  Thou hast giv'n all worthy men of thy profession,
  Art banished from their fellowship and our state.°   Venice

            [VOLTORE *is placed under guard.*]

  Corbaccio—bring him near.—We here possess
130 Thy son of all thy state,° and confine thee   estate
  To the monastery of San' Spirito,°   the Holy Spirit
  Where, since thou knew'st not how to live well here,
  Thou shalt be learned° to die well.   taught

CORBACCIO   Ha! What said he?

COMMENDATORE   You shall know anon,° sir.   soon enough

            [CORBACCIO *is placed under guard.*]

FIRST AVOCATORE   Thou, Corvino, shalt
135 Be straight embarked from thine own house and rowed

---

5. The Hospital of the Incurables was founded in Venice in 1522 to care for people terminally ill with syphilis.

6. (1) Hanging of meat to make it tender; (2) disciplining spiritually; (3) killing. (Volpone's sentence is almost certain to bring about his death.)

Bound about Venice, through the Grand Canal,
Wearing a cap with fair° long ass's ears   *handsome; clearly visible*
Instead of horns, and so to mount, a paper
Pinned on thy breast, to the *berlino*[7]—

CORVINO   Yes,
140   And have mine eyes beat out with stinking fish,
Bruised fruit, and rotten eggs—'Tis well. I'm glad
I shall not see my shame yet.

FIRST AVOCATORE   And to expiate
Thy wrongs done to thy wife, thou art to send her
Home to her father with her dowry trebled.[8]
And these are all your judgments—

145   ALL   Honored fathers!

FIRST AVOCATORE   Which may not be revoked. Now you begin,
When crimes are done and past and to be punished,
To think what your crimes are.—Away with them!

        [MOSCA, VOLPONE, VOLTORE, CORBACCIO, *and* CORVINO
               retire to the back of the stage, guarded.][9]

Let all that see these vices thus rewarded
150   Take heart,° and love to study 'em. Mischiefs feed   *take them to heart*
Like beasts, till they be fat, and then they bleed.
                    [*The* AVOCATORI *step back.*]

          [VOLPONE *comes forward.*]

VOLPONE   The seasoning of a play is the applause
Now, though the fox be punished by the laws,
He yet doth hope there is no suff'ring due
155   Nor any fact° which he hath done 'gainst you.   *crime*
If there be, censure him; here he, doubtful,° stands.   *apprehensive*
If not, fare jovially, and clap your hands.   [*Exeunt.*]

performed 1606   *published* 1616

From Epigrams[1]

To My Book

It will be looked for, book, when some but see
Thy title, *Epigrams*, and named of me,

---

7. Pillory. Versions of such shaming punishments were commonly imposed for sexual and marital infractions. The offender typically had to wear a placard specifying his crimes; hence the paper pinned on Corvino's breast.

8. The judges grant Celia "separation from bed and board." Such legal separations could be permitted to the innocent party in a case of adultery or, as here, to a victim of gross spousal abuse. Because legal separation entailed the finding of serious fault, the guilty spouse could also, as here, be forced to pay financial damages. Legal separation did not bring with it, however, the right of remarriage for either party.

9. Alternatively, the prisoners, and later the Avocatori and the others, could exit, and Volpone could return to speak the epilogue. The advantage of the staging preferred here is that almost all the players are onstage to receive the audience's applause.

1. Epigrams are commonly thought of as brief, witty, incisive poems of personal invective, often with a surprise turn at the end. But Jonson uses the word in a more liberal sense. His "Epigrams," a separate section in his collected *Works* of 1616, include not only sharp, satiric poems but many complimentary ones to friends and patrons, as well as memorial epitaphs and a verse letter, "Inviting a Friend to Supper."

Thou should'st be bold, licentious, full of gall,
    Wormwood° and sulphur, sharp and toothed[2] withal,   *bitter-tasting plant*
5 Become a petulant thing, hurl ink and wit
    As madmen stones, not caring whom they hit.
Deceive their malice who could wish it so,
    And by thy wiser temper let men know
Thou art not covetous of least self-fame
10   Made from the hazard of another's shame[3]—
Much less with lewd, profane, and beastly phrase
    To catch the world's loose laughter or vain gaze.
He that departs° with his own honesty   *parts*
    For vulgar praise, doth it too dearly buy.

                           1616

On Something, That Walks Somewhere

At court I met it, in clothes brave° enough   *fine*
    To be a courtier, and looks grave enough
To seem a statesman: as I near it came,
    It made me a great face. I asked the name.
5 "A lord," it cried, "buried in flesh and blood,
    And such from whom let no man hope least good,
For I will do none; and as little ill,
    For I will dare none." Good lord, walk dead still.

                           1616

To William Camden[1]

Camden, most reverend head, to whom I owe
    All that I am in arts, all that I know
(How nothing's that!), to whom my country owes
    The great renown and name wherewith she goes;[2]
5 Than thee the age sees not that thing more grave,
    More high, more holy, that she more would crave.
What name, what skill, what faith hast thou in things!
    What sight in searching the most antique springs!
What weight and what authority in thy speech!
10   Man scarce can make that doubt, but[3] thou canst teach.
Pardon free truth and let thy modesty,
    Which conquers all, be once o'ercome by thee.

---

2. The distinction between toothed (biting) and
toothless (general) satires was a commonplace.
3. Here, as often elsewhere, Jonson echoes the
greatest Roman epigrammatist, Martial.
1. Camden, a distinguished scholar and antiquary, had been Jonson's teacher at Westminster

School.
2. Camden's studies of his native land in *Britannia* (1586) and *Remains of a Greater Work Concerning Britain* (1605) ran to several editions and
were translated abroad.
3. One hardly needs wonder whether.

Many of thine° this better could than I;   *your pupils*
But for° their powers, accept my piety.   *in place of*

1616

On My First Daughter[1]

Here lies, to each her parents' ruth,°   *grief*
Mary, the daughter of their youth;
Yet all heaven's gifts being heaven's due,
It makes the father less to rue.°   *regret*
5 At six months' end she parted hence
With safety of her innocence;
Whose soul heaven's queen,° whose name she bears,   *Mary*
In comfort of her mother's tears,
Hath placed amongst her virgin-train:
10 Where, while that severed doth remain,
This grave partakes the fleshly birth;°   *the body*
Which cover lightly, gentle earth![2]

1616

To John Donne

Donne, the delight of Phoebus° and each Muse,   *god of poetry*
Who, to thy one, all other brains refuse;[1]
Whose every work, of thy most early wit,
Came forth example[2] and remains so yet;
5 Longer a-knowing than most wits do live,
And which no affection praise enough can give.
To it[3] thy language, letters, arts, best life,
Which might with half mankind maintain a strife.
All which I meant to praise, and yet I would,
10 But leave, because I cannot as I should.

1616

On Giles and Joan

Who says that Giles and Joan at discord be?
   Th' observing neighbors no such mood can see.
Indeed, poor Giles repents he married ever,
   But that his Joan doth too. And Giles would never
5 By his free will be in Joan's company;
   No more would Joan he should. Giles riseth early,

---

1. Probably written in the late 1590s, in Jonson's
Roman Catholic period (ca. 1598–1610).
2. A common sentiment in Latin epitaphs.
1. I.e., the muses shower their favors exclusively

on you.
2. A pattern for others to imitate.
3. In addition to your wit.

And having got him out of doors is glad;
 The like is Joan. But turning home is sad,
And so is Joan. Ofttimes, when Giles doth find
10 Harsh sights at home, Giles wisheth he were blind:
All this doth Joan. Or that his long-yearned[1] life
 Were quite outspun. The like wish hath his wife.
The children that he keeps Giles swears are none
 Of his begetting; and so swears his Joan.
15 In all affections° she concurreth still.   *desires*
 If now, with man and wife, to will and nill°   *not will*
The self-same things a note of concord be,
 I know no couple better can agree.

             1616

On My First Son

Farewell, thou child of my right hand,[1] and joy;
My sin was too much hope of thee, loved boy.
Seven years thou wert lent to me, and I thee pay,
Exacted by thy fate, on the just day.
5 O could I lose all father now! For why
Will man lament the state he should envy,
To have so soon 'scaped world's and flesh's rage,
And, if no other misery, yet age?
Rest in soft peace, and asked, say, "Here doth lie
10 Ben Jonson his best piece of poetry."[2]
For whose sake henceforth all his vows be such
As what he loves may never like too much.[3]

             1616

On Lucy, Countess of Bedford[1]

This morning, timely rapt with holy fire,
I thought to form unto my zealous muse,
What kind of creature I could most desire,
To honor, serve, and love; as poets use.[2]
5 I meant to make her fair, and free, and wise,
Of greatest blood, and yet more good than great;
I meant the day-star° should not brighter rise,   *the sun*

1. Spun from long skeins of yarn.
1. A literal translation of the Hebrew name "Benjamin," which implies the meaning "dexterous" or "fortunate." The boy was born in 1596 and died on his birthday in 1603.
2. Poet and father are both "makers," Jonson's favorite term for the poet.
3. The obscure grammar of the last lines allows for various readings; "like" may carry the sense of "please."

1. Lucy Russell, Countess of Bedford, was a famous patroness of the age, to whom Jonson, Donne, and many other poets addressed poems of compliment.
2. This elegant epigram of praise plays off against the Pygmalion story, in which the sculptor molds a statue of his ideal woman and she then comes to life.

Nor lend like influence[3] from his lucent seat.
I meant she should be courteous, facile,° sweet, *affable*
10 Hating that solemn vice of greatness, pride;
I meant each softest virtue, there should meet,
Fit in that softer bosom to reside.
Only a learnèd, and a manly soul
I purposed her; that should, with even powers,
15 The rock, the spindle, and the shears[4] control
Of destiny, and spin her own free hours.
Such when I meant to feign, and wished to see,
My muse bad, *Bedford* write, and that was she.

1616

To Lucy, Countess of Bedford, with Mr. Donne's Satires[1]

Lucy, you brightness[2] of our sphere, who are
Life of the Muses' day, their morning star!
If works, not th' authors, their own grace should look,° *have regard to*
Whose poems would not wish to be your book?
5 But these, desired by you, the maker's ends
Crown with their own. Rare poems ask rare friends.
Yet satires, since the most of mankind be
Their unavoided° subject, fewest see: *inevitable*
For none e'er took that pleasure in sin's sense,° *experience*
10 But, when they heard it taxed, took more offense.
They then that, living where the matter is bred,[3]
Dare for these poems yet both ask and read
And like them too, must needfully, though few,
Be of the best: and 'mongst those, best are you;
15 Lucy, you brightness of our sphere, who are
The Muses' evening, as their morning star.[4]

1616

To Sir Thomas Roe[1]

Thou hast begun well, Roe, which stand° well too, *continue*
And I know nothing more thou hast to do.

---

3. Stars were supposed to emit an ethereal fluid, or "influence," that affected the affairs of mortals, for good or ill.
4. Emblems of the three Fates: Clotho spun the thread of life, Lachesis decided its length, and Atropos cut the thread to end life.
1. With this poem, Jonson offered a manuscript collection of Donne's satires (see pp. 1394–97), such as commonly passed from hand to hand in court circles.

2. Lucy's name derives from the Latin *lux*, meaning "light."
3. I.e., at court.
4. The planet Venus is called Lucifer ("light-bearing") when it appears before sunrise, Hesperus when it appears after sunset.
1. Knighted in 1605, Roe was sent as ambassador to the Great Mogul in 1614. His collection of coins and of Greek and Oriental manuscripts is in the Bodleian Library.

He that is round° within himself, and straight,   *honest*
Need seek no other strength, no other height;
5   Fortune upon him breaks herself, if ill,
And what should hurt his virtue makes it still.°   *constant*
That thou at once, then, nobly may'st defend
With thine own course the judgment of thy friend,
Be always to thy gathered self the same,
10 And study conscience, more than thou wouldst fame.
Though both be good, the latter yet is worst,
And ever is ill got without the first.

1616

Inviting a Friend to Supper

Tonight, grave sir, both my poor house and I
    Do equally desire your company:
Not that we think us worthy such a guest,
    But that your worth will dignify our feast
5   With those that come; whose grace may make that seem
    Something, which else could hope for no esteem.
It is the fair acceptance, sir, creates
    The entertainment perfect: not the cates.°   *food*
Yet shall you have, to rectify your palate,
10   An olive, capers, or some better salad
Ushering the mutton; with a short-legged hen,
    If we can get her, full of eggs, and then
Lemons and wine for sauce; to° these, a coney°   *besides / rabbit*
    Is not to be despaired of for our money;
15 And though fowl now be scarce, yet there are clerks,°   *scholars*
    The sky not falling, think we may have larks.
I'll tell you of more, and lie, so you will come:
    Of partridge, pheasant, woodcock, of which some
May yet be there; and godwit if we can,
20   Knot, rail, and ruff, too.[1] Howsoe'er, my man°   *servant*
Shall read a piece of Virgil, Tacitus,
    Livy, or of some better book to us,
Of which we'll speak our minds amidst our meat;°   *food (of any kind)*
    And I'll profess° no verses to repeat: *promise*
25 To this,° if aught appear which I not know of,   *on this point*
    That will the pastry, not my paper, show of.[2]
Digestive cheese and fruit there sure will be;
    But that which most doth take my muse and me
Is a pure cup of rich canary wine,
30   Which is the Mermaid's now, but shall be mine;
Of which, had Horace or Anacreon[3] tasted,

---

1. All these are edible birds.
2. Paper-lined pans were used to keep pies from sticking; the writing sometimes rubbed off on the piecrust.
3. Horace and Anacreon (one in Latin, the other in Greek) wrote many poems in praise of wine. The Mermaid tavern was a favorite haunt of the poets; sweet wine from the Canary Islands was popular in England.

Their lives, as do their lines, till now had lasted.
Tobacco, nectar, or the Thespian spring
    Are all but Luther's beer to this I sing.[4]
35 Of this we will sup free but moderately,
    And we will have no Pooly or Parrot[5] by;
Nor shall our cups make any guilty men,
    But at our parting we will be as when
We innocently met. No simple word
40   That shall be uttered at our mirthful board
Shall make us sad next morning, or affright
    The liberty that we'll enjoy tonight.

                                  1616

On Gut

Gut eats all day, and lechers all the night,
    So all his meat he tasteth over twice;
And striving so to double his delight,
    He makes himself a thoroughfare of vice.
5 Thus in his belly can he change a sin:
    Lust it comes out, that gluttony went in.

                                    1616

Epitaph on S. P., a Child of Queen Elizabeth's Chapel[1]

Weep with me, all you that read
    This little story;
And know for whom a tear you shed,
    Death's self is sorry.
5 'Twas a child that so did thrive
    In grace and feature,
As Heaven and Nature seemed to strive
    Which owned the creature.
Years he numbered scarce thirteen
10   When Fates turned cruel,
Yet three filled zodiacs had he been
    The stage's jewel;[2]
And did act (what now we moan)
    Old men so duly,°   *aptly*
15 As, sooth,° the Parcae° thought him one,   *in truth / Fates*
    He played so truly.

---

4. Tobacco was an expensive New World novelty in Jonson's time. Nectar is the drink of the gods. The Thespian spring, on Mount Helicon, is a legendary source of poetic inspiration. Compared with canary, these intoxicants are no better than inferior German beer.
5. Pooly and Parrot were government spies. As a

Roman Catholic, Jonson had reason to be wary of undercover agents.
1. Salomon Pavy, a boy actor in the troupe known as the Children of Queen Elizabeth's Chapel, who had appeared in several of Jonson's plays; he died in 1602.
2. He had been on the stage for three seasons.

So, by error, to his fate
   They all consented;
But, viewing him since (alas, too late),
20   They have repented,
And have sought (to give new birth)
   In baths[3] to steep him;
But, being so much too good for earth,
   Heaven vows to keep him.

1616

FROM THE FOREST[1]

To Penshurst[2]

Thou art not, Penshurst, built to envious show,
   Of touch[3] or marble; nor canst boast a row
Of polished pillars, or a roof of gold;
   Thou hast no lantern° whereof tales are told,   *cupola*
5 Or stair, or courts; but stand'st an ancient pile,°   *edifice*
   And, these grudged at,[4] art reverenced the while.
Thou joy'st in better marks, of soil, of air,
   Of wood, of water; therein thou art fair.
Thou hast thy walks for health, as well as sport;
10   Thy mount, to which the dryads° do resort,   *wood nymphs*
Where Pan and Bacchus their high feasts have made,
   Beneath the broad beech and the chestnut shade;
That taller tree, which of a nut was set
   At his great birth where all the Muses met.[5]
15 There in the writhèd bark are cut the names
   Of many a sylvan,° taken with his flames;   *countryman*
And thence the ruddy satyrs oft provoke
   The lighter fauns[6] to reach thy Lady's Oak.[7]
Thy copse° too, named of Gamage[8] thou hast there,   *little woods*
20   That never fails to serve thee seasoned deer
When thou wouldst feast or exercise thy friends.
   The lower land, that to the river bends,
Thy sheep, thy bullocks, kine,° and calves do feed;   *cattle*
   The middle grounds thy mares and horses breed.
25 Each bank doth yield thee conies;° and the tops,° *rabbits / high ground*

3. Perhaps such magic baths as that of Medea, which restored Jason's father to his first youth (Ovid, *Metamorphoses* 7).

1. In the 1616 *Works*, Jonson grouped some of his nonepigrammatic poems under the heading "The Forest," a translation of the term *Sylvae*, meaning a poetic miscellany. "To Penshurst" and the two following poems are from that group.

2. Penshurst, in Kent, was the estate of Robert Sidney, Viscount Lisle (later, Earl of Leicester), a younger brother of the poet Sir Philip Sidney. Along with Lanyer's "The Description of Cookham" (pp. 1436–40), this poem inaugurated

the small genre of English "country-house" poems, which includes Marvell's *Upon Appleton House* (pp. 1811–33).

3. Touchstone, an expensive black basalt.

4. More pretentious houses attract envy.

5. Sir Philip Sidney was born at Penshurst.

6. Satyrs and fauns were woodland spirits. Satyrs had the bodies of men and the legs (and horns) of goats. "Provoke": challenge to a race.

7. Named after a lady of the house who went into labor under its branches.

8. Lady Barbara (Gamage) Sidney, wife of Sir Robert.

Fertile of wood, Ashore and Sidney's copse,
To crown thy open table, doth provide
The purpled pheasant with the speckled side;
The painted partridge lies in every field,
30 And for thy mess° is willing to be killed.   *table*
And if the high-swollen Medway[9] fail thy dish,
Thou hast thy ponds, that pay thee tribute fish:
Fat agèd carps that run into thy net,
And pikes, now weary their own kind to eat,
35 As loath the second draft or cast to stay,
Officiously° at first themselves betray;   *dutifully*
Bright eels that emulate them, and leap on land
Before the fisher, or into his hand.
Then hath thy orchard fruit, thy garden flowers,
40 Fresh as the air, and new as are the hours.
The early cherry, with the later plum,
Fig, grape, and quince, each in his time doth come;
The blushing apricot and woolly peach
Hang on thy walls, that every child may reach.
45 And though thy walls be of the country stone,
They're reared with no man's ruin, no man's groan;
There's none that dwell about them wish them down;
But all come in, the farmer and the clown,°   *peasant*
And no one empty-handed, to salute
50 Thy lord and lady, though they have no suit.°   *request to make*
Some bring a capon, some a rural cake,
Some nuts, some apples; some that think they make
The better cheeses bring them, or else send
By their ripe daughters, whom they would commend
55 This way to husbands, and whose baskets bear
An emblem of themselves in plum or pear.
But what can this (more than express their love)
Add to thy free provisions, far above
The need of such? whose liberal board doth flow
60 With all that hospitality doth know;
Where comes no guest but is allowed to eat,
Without his fear, and of thy lord's own meat;°   *food*
Where the same beer and bread, and selfsame wine,
That is his lordship's shall be also mine,[1]
65 And I not fain to sit (as some this day
At great men's tables), and yet dine away.
Here no man tells° my cups; nor, standing by,   *counts*
A waiter doth my gluttony envy,°   *resent*
But gives me what I call, and lets me eat;
70 He knows below° he shall find plenty of meat.   *in the servants' quarters*
Thy tables hoard not up for the next day;
Nor, when I take my lodging, need I pray
For fire, or lights, or livery;° all is there,   *provisions*
As if thou then wert mine, or I reigned here:

---

9. The local river.
1. Different courses might be served to different

guests, depending on their social status. The
lord would have the best food.

75　There's nothing I can wish, for which I stay.°　　　　　　　*wait*
　　　That found King James when, hunting late this way
　　With his brave son, the Prince,[2] they saw thy fires
　　　Shine bright on every hearth, as the desires
　　Of thy Penates° had been set on flame　　　　*Roman household gods*
80　　To entertain them; or the country came
　　With all their zeal to warm their welcome here.
　　　What (great I will not say, but) sudden cheer
　　Didst thou then make 'em! And what praise was heaped
　　　On thy good lady then, who therein reaped
85　The just reward of her high housewifery;
　　　To have her linen, plate, and all things nigh,
　　When she was far; and not a room but dressed
　　　As if it had expected such a guest!
　　These, Penshurst, are thy praise, and yet not all.
90　　Thy lady's noble, fruitful, chaste withal.
　　His children thy great lord may call his own,
　　　A fortune in this age but rarely known.
　　They are, and have been, taught religion; thence
　　　Their gentler spirits have sucked innocence.
95　Each morn and even they are taught to pray,
　　　With the whole household, and may, every day,
　　Read in their virtuous parents' noble parts°　　　　　*attributes*
　　　The mysteries of manners,° arms, and arts.　　　*moral behavior*
　　Now, Penshurst, they that will proportion° thee　　　*compare*
100　　With other edifices, when they see
　　Those proud, ambitious heaps, and nothing else,
　　　May say, their lords have built, but thy lord dwells.

　　　　　　　　　　　　　　　　　　　　　　1616

Song: To Celia[1]

　　　Drink to me only with thine eyes,
　　　　And I will pledge with mine;
　　　Or leave a kiss but in the cup,
　　　　And I'll not look for wine.
5　　The thirst that from the soul doth rise
　　　　Doth ask a drink divine:
　　　But might I of Jove's nectar sup,
　　　　I would not change for thine.
　　　I sent thee late a rosy wreath,
10　　　Not so much honoring thee,
　　　As giving it a hope that there
　　　　It could not withered be.
　　　But thou thereon didst only breathe,
　　　　And sent'st it back to me;

2. Prince Henry, the heir apparent, who died in November 1612.
1. These famous lines translate a patchwork of five separate prose passages by Philostratus, a Greek sophist (3rd century c.e.). The music that has made it a barroom favorite is by an anonymous 18th-century composer.

15 Since when it grows and smells, I swear,
    Not of itself, but thee.

                                                  1616

To Heaven

Good and great God, can I not think of thee
    But it must straight° my melancholy be?   *immediately*
Is it interpreted in me disease
    That, laden with my sins, I seek for ease?
5 Oh, be thou witness, that the reins[1] dost know
    And hearts of all, if I be sad for show,
And judge me after, if I dare pretend
    To aught but grace, or aim at other end.
As thou art all, so be thou all to me,
10   First, midst, and last, converted° one and three, *interchanging*
My faith, my hope, my love; and in this state,
    My judge, my witness, and my advocate.
Where have I been this while exiled from thee,
    And whither rapt,° now thou but stoop'st to me?   *carried off*
15 Dwell, dwell here still:° Oh, being everywhere,   *always*
    How can I doubt to find thee ever here?
I know my state, both full of shame and scorn,
    Conceived in sin and unto labor born,
Standing with fear, and must with horror fall,
20   And destined unto judgment after all.
I feel my griefs too, and there scarce is ground
    Upon my flesh to inflict another wound.
Yet dare I not complain or wish for death
    With holy Paul,[2] lest it be thought the breath
25 Of discontent; or that these prayers be
    For weariness of life, not love of thee.

                                                  1616

From UNDERWOOD[1]

From A Celebration of Charis in Ten Lyric Pieces[2]

4. Her Triumph[3]

See the chariot at hand here of Love,
    Wherein my lady rideth!

1. Literally, kidneys, but also the seat of the affections, with a glance at Psalm 7.9: "the righteous God trieth the hearts and reins."
2. "Who shall deliver me from the body of this death?" (Romans 7.24).
1. Preparing a second edition of his *Works* (published posthumously in 1640–41), Jonson added a third section of poems, "Underwood," "out of the analogy they hold to *The Forest* in my former book."
2. The Greek word *charis*, from which Jonson's lady takes her name, means "grace" or "loveliness."
3. Following Petrarch, many Renaissance poets used the figure of the triumphal procession to celebrate a person or concept—time, chastity, fame, etc. Metrically, this poem is highly complex.

Each that draws is a swan or a dove,[4]
   And well the car Love guideth.
5 As she goes, all hearts do duty
      Unto her beauty;
And enamored do wish, so they might
      But enjoy such a sight,
That they still° were to run by her side,   *always*
10 Through swords, through seas, whither she would ride.

Do but look on her eyes, they do light
   All that Love's world compriseth!
Do but look on her hair, it is bright
   As Love's star° when it riseth!   *Venus, the morning star*
15 Do but mark,° her forehead's smoother   *observe*
      Than words that soothe her!
And from her archèd brows, such a grace
      Sheds itself through the face,
As alone there triumphs to the life
20 All the gain, all the good, of the elements' strife.[5]

Have you seen but a bright lily grow,
   Before rude hands have touched it?
Have you marked but the fall o' the snow,
   Before the soil hath smutched it?
25 Have you felt the wool o' the beaver,
      Or swan's down ever?
Or have smelt o' the bud o' the briar,
      Or the nard[6] i' the fire?
Or have tasted the bag o' the bee?
30 O so white! O so soft! O so sweet is she!

1640–41

A Sonnet, to the Noble Lady, the Lady Mary Wroth[1]

I that have been a lover, and could show it,
   Though not in these,° in rhymes not wholly dumb,   *in sonnets*
   Since I exscribe° your sonnets, am become   *copy out*
A better lover, and much better poet.
5 Nor is my muse, or I, ashamed to owe it
   To those true numerous graces; whereof some
   But charm the senses, others overcome
Both brains and hearts; and mine now best do know it:

---

4. Venus's birds.
5. The four elements—earth, water, air, fire—
were thought to be in perpetual conflict.
6. Spikenard, an aromatic ointment.
1. Mary Wroth, author of the sonnet sequence
Pamphilia to Amphilanthus (pp. 1566–71) and the
romance *The Countess of Montgomery's Urania*
(pp. 1562–66), was the daughter of Robert Sidney
and his wife, Barbara Gamage, of Penshurst, the

niece of Sir Philip Sidney and the Countess of
Pembroke; she was the wife of Sir Robert Wroth,
whose country estate Jonson also praised in "The
Forest." The poem exhibits how poems were
exchanged within a coterie, though Jonson also
writes as a client to a patron. This is Jonson's only
sonnet, used here to pay tribute to Wroth's
sequence, and notably to its erotic power.

For in your verse all Cupid's armory,
10   His flames, his shafts, his quiver, and his bow,
His very eyes are yours to overthrow.
But then his mother's° sweets you so apply,   *Venus's*
Her joys, her smiles, her loves, as readers take
For Venus' ceston,[2] every line you make.

          1640–41

My Picture Left in Scotland[1]

I now think Love is rather deaf than blind,
    For else it could not be
        That she
Whom I adore so much should so slight me
5   And cast my love behind;
I'm sure my language to her was as sweet,
      And every close° did meet   *cadence*
      In sentence° of as subtle feet,°   *wise sayings / rhythm*
      As hath the youngest he
10   That sits in shadow of Apollo's tree.[2]

O, but my conscious fears
    That fly my thoughts between,
    Tell me that she hath seen
    My hundreds of gray hairs,
15   Told° seven and forty years,   *counted*
Read so much waist[3] as she cannot embrace
My mountain belly and my rocky face;
And all these through her eyes have stopped her ears.

1619   1640–41

The Ode on Cary and Morison

The ode, originally a classical form, is a lyric poem in an elevated style, celebrating a lofty theme, a noble personage, or a grand occasion. The Greek poet Pindar wrote many odes for winners of the Olympic games, known as "Great Odes" because of their exalted subject and style. Later, the Roman poet Horace wrote more restrained poems that came to be known as "Lesser Odes." Jonson's Cary-Morison ode comes closer than any other in the language to the lofty style and manner of Pindar, while his "To Penshurst" is in the Horatian style, as is, later, Marvell's "Horatian Ode upon Cromwell's Return from Ireland."

Pindar's odes were designed to be sung by a chorus and often followed a three-part scheme: the chorus moved in one direction while chanting the strophe, reversed direction for the antistrophe, and stood still for the epode. Jonson imitates

2. Venus's girdle or belt, which had aphrodisia-cal powers; it aroused passion in all beholders.
1. After his walking tour of Scotland in 1618–19, Jonson sent a manuscript version of this poem to William Drummond, with whom he had stayed. The woman of the poem may or may not be a real person.
2. Bay laurel, the tree associated with Apollo, god of poetry.
3. With a pun on "waste," meaning "untillable ground."

this pattern with his triple division of "turn," "counterturn," and "stand"—the terms more or less literally translated from the original Greek. His turns and counterturns rhyme in couplets, with line lengths varying in all stanzas according to a uniform scheme; the twelve-line stands follow a more complex but equally strict design. He imitates Pindar also in his moral generalizations and lofty but impersonal praise of the two noble friends. Later in the century, under the influence of Abraham Cowley and under a misapprehension about Pindar's style, odes became more extravagant, more vehement in tone, and more irregular in form.

To the Immortal Memory and Friendship of That Noble Pair, Sir Lucius Cary and Sir H. Morison[1]

The Turn

Brave infant of Saguntum,[2] clear°   *explain*
Thy coming forth in that great year
When the prodigious Hannibal did crown
His rage, with razing your immortal town.
5 Thou, looking then about
Ere thou wert half got out,
Wise child, didst hastily return
And mad'st thy mother's womb thine urn.° *burial vessel*
How summed° a circle[3] didst thou leave mankind *complete*
10 Of deepest lore, could we the center find!

The Counterturn

Did wiser nature draw thee back
From out the horror of that sack,
Where shame, faith, honor, and regard of right
Lay trampled on?—the deeds of death and night
15 Urged, hurried forth, and hurled
Upon th' affrighted world?
Sword, fire, and famine, with fell° fury met, *fierce*
And all on utmost ruin set:
As, could they but life's miseries foresee,
20 No doubt all infants would return like thee.

The Stand

For what is life if measured by the space,
Not by the act?
Or maskèd man, if valued by his face,
Above his fact?°   *deeds*
25 Here's one outlived his peers

---

1. Henry Morison died in 1629 at the age of twenty. His good friend Lucius Cary (son of Elizabeth Cary, the author of *Mariam*) became the second Viscount Falkland. He was known for his learning, and he died fighting for King Charles in the first years of the civil war.

2. Pliny the Elder, a Roman writer, tells the story of an infant born while Saguntc, in Spain, was being assaulted by Hannibal; he dived back into his mother's womb (setting a record for brevity of life) and was buried there.

3. Emblem of perfection.

And told forth fourscore years:
He vexèd time, and busied the whole state,
Troubled both foes and friends,
But ever to no ends:
30   What did this stirrer but die late?[4]
How well at twenty had he fall'n or stood!
For three of his four score, he did no good.

The Turn

He[5] entered well, by virtuous parts,°   *qualities*
Got up and thrived with honest arts:
35   He purchased friends and fame and honors then,
And had his noble name advanced with men;
But, weary of that flight,
He stooped in all men's sight
To sordid flatteries, acts of strife,
40   And sunk in that dead sea of life
So deep, as he did then death's waters sup;
But that the cork of title buoyed him up.

The Counterturn

Alas, but Morison fell young;—
He never fell, thou fall'st,[6] my tongue.
45   He stood, a soldier, to the last right end,
A perfect patriot and a noble friend,
But most a virtuous son.
All offices° were done   *duties of life*
By him, so ample, full, and round
50   In weight, in measure, number, sound,
As, though his age imperfect might appear,
His life was of humanity the sphere.

The Stand

Go now, and tell out° days summed up with fears,   *count*
And make them years;
55   Produce thy mass of miseries on the stage
To swell thine age;
Repeat of things a throng,
To show thou hast been long,
Not lived; for life doth her great actions spell,°   *tell over*
60   By what was done and wrought
In season, and so brought
To light: her measures are, how well
Each syllab'e° answered, and was formed how fair;   *syllable*
These make the lines of life, and that's her air.[7]

4. Punning on "dilate," meaning "talk endlessly."
5. I.e., another man.
6. Slip, with a latent pun on Latin *fallo*, "to make a mistake."

7. Life is a poem set to music; life's "measures" are its metrical patterns as well as the standards by which it is judged.

The Turn

65 It is not growing like a tree
In bulk, doth make man better be,
Or standing long an oak, three hundred year,
To fall a log at last, dry, bald, and sere:°   *withered*
A lily of a day
70 Is fairer far in May,
Although it fall and die that night;
It was the plant and flower of light.
In small proportions we just beauties see,
And in short measures life may perfect be.

The Counterturn

75 Call, noble Lucius, then for wine,
And let thy looks with gladness shine:
Accept this garland,[8] plant it on thy head,
And think, nay, know, thy Morison's not dead.
He leaped the present age,
80 Possessed with holy rage,°   *inspiration*
To see that bright eternal day,
Of which we priests and poets say
Such truths as we expect for happy men,
And there he lives with memory: and Ben

The Stand

85 Jonson, who sung this of him ere he went
Himself to rest,
Or taste a part of that full joy he meant
To have expressed
In this bright asterism:°   *constellation*
90 Where it were friendship's schism
(Were not his Lucius long with us to tarry)
To separate these twi-
Lights, the Dioscuri,[9]
And keep the one half from his Harry.
95 But fate doth so alternate the design,
Whilst that in heaven, this light on earth must shine.

The Turn

And shine as you exalted are,
Two names of friendship, but one star,
Of hearts the union. And those not by chance
100 Made, or indentured,° or leased out t' advance   *contracted for*
The profits for a time.

---

8. Celebratory wreath; i.e., this poem.
9. The mythical Greek twins, Castor and Pollux, the Dioscuri, were said to have exchanged places regularly, after Castor's death, between earth and the underworld. They are the principal stars of the constellation Gemini (the twins).

No pleasures vain did chime
Of rhymes or riots at your feasts,
Orgies of drink, or feigned protests;
105 But simple love of greatness and of good
That knits brave minds and manners, more than blood.

The Counterturn

This made you first to know the why
You liked, then after to apply
That liking; and approach so one the tother,°   *other*
110 Till either grew a portion of the other;
Each stylèd° by his end,   *called*
The copy of his friend.
You lived to be the great surnames
And titles by which all made claims
115 Unto the virtue: nothing perfect done,
But as a Cary or a Morison.

The Stand

And such a force the fair example had,
As they that saw
The good and durst not practice it, were glad
120 That such a law
Was left yet to mankind;
Where they might read and find
Friendship in deed was written, not in words.
And with the heart, not pen,
125 Of two so early° men,   *youthful*
Whose lives her rolls were, and records,
Who, ere the first down bloomèd on the chin
Had sowed these fruits, and got the harvest in.

1629   1640–41

Queen and Huntress[1]

Queen and huntress, chaste and fair,
Now the sun is laid to sleep,
Seated in thy silver chair,
State in wonted° manner keep;   *accustomed*
5 Hesperus entreats thy light,
Goddess excellently bright.

---

1. Also from *Cynthia's Revels* (4.3), this song is sung by Hesperus, the evening star, to Cynthia, or Diana, goddess of chastity and the moon—with whom Queen Elizabeth was constantly compared.

Earth, let not thy envious shade
Dare itself to interpose;[2]
Cynthia's shining orb was made
10   Heaven to clear, when day did close.
Bless us then with wishèd sight,
Goddess excellently bright.

Lay thy bow of pearl apart,
And thy crystal-shining quiver;
15   Give unto the flying hart
Space to breathe, how short soever.
Thou that mak'st a day of night,
Goddess excellently bright.

1600

To the Memory of My Beloved, The Author,
Mr. William Shakespeare, and What He Hath Left Us[1]

To draw no envy, Shakespeare, on thy name,
  Am I thus ample° to thy book and fame,   *copious*
While I confess thy writings to be such
  As neither man nor muse can praise too much.
5   'Tis true, and all men's suffrage.° But these ways   *admission*
  Were not the paths I meant unto thy praise;
For silliest° ignorance on these may light,   *simplest*
  Which, when it sounds at best, but echoes right;
Or blind affection, which doth ne'er advance
10   The truth, but gropes, and urgeth all by chance;
Or crafty malice might pretend this praise,
  And think to ruin where it seemed to raise.
These are as° some infamous bawd or whore   *as though*
  Should praise a matron. What could hurt her more?
15 But thou art proof against them, and, indeed,
  Above th' ill fortune of them, or the need.
I therefore will begin. Soul of the age!
  The applause! Delight! The wonder of our stage!
My Shakespeare, rise; I will not lodge thee by
20   Chaucer or Spenser, or bid Beaumont lie
A little further to make thee a room:[2]
  Thou art a monument without a tomb,
And art alive still while thy book doth live,
  And we have wits to read and praise to give.
25 That I not mix thee so, my brain excuses,
  I mean with great, but disproportioned° Muses;   *not comparable*
For, if I thought my judgment were of years,
  I should commit thee surely with thy peers,
And tell how far thou didst our Lyly outshine,

2. Eclipses were thought to portend evil.
1. This poem was prefixed to the first folio of
Shakespeare's plays (1623).

2. Chaucer, Spenser, and Francis Beaumont were
buried in Westminster Abbey; Shakespeare, in
Stratford.

30   Or sporting Kyd, or Marlowe's mighty line.[3]
   And though thou hadst small Latin and less Greek,[4]
    From thence to honor thee I would not seek°   *lack*
   For names, but call forth thund'ring Aeschylus,
    Euripides, and Sophocles to us,
35   Pacuvius, Accius, him of Cordova dead,[5]
    To life again, to hear thy buskin° tread   *symbol of tragedy*
   And shake a stage; or, when thy socks° were on,   *symbol of comedy*
    Leave thee alone for the comparison
   Of all that insolent Greece or haughty Rome
40   Sent forth, or since did from their ashes come.
   Triumph, my Britain; thou hast one to show
    To whom all scenes° of Europe homage owe.   *stages*
   He was not of an age, but for all time!
    And all the Muses still were in their prime
45   When like Apollo° he came forth to warm   *god of poetry*
    Our ears, or like a Mercury° to charm.   *god of eloquence*
   Nature herself was proud of his designs,
    And joyed to wear the dressing of his lines,
   Which were so richly spun, and woven so fit,
50   As, since, she will vouchsafe° no other wit: *grant*
   The merry Greek, tart Aristophanes,
    Neat Terence, witty Plautus[6] now not please,
   But antiquated and deserted lie,
    As they were not of Nature's family.
55   Yet must I not give nature all; thy art,
    My gentle Shakespeare, must enjoy a part.
   For though the poet's matter° nature be,   *subject matter*
    His art doth give the fashion;° and that he   *form, style*
   Who casts° to write a living line must sweat   *undertakes*
60   (Such as thine are) and strike the second heat
   Upon the Muses' anvil; turn the same,
    And himself with it, that he thinks to frame,
   Or for° the laurel he may gain a scorn;   *instead of*
    For a good poet's made as well as born,
65   And such wert thou. Look how the father's face
    Lives in his issue;° even so the race   *offspring*
   Of Shakespeare's mind and manners brightly shines
    In his well-turnèd and true-filèd lines,
   In each of which he seems to shake a lance,[7]
70   As brandished at the eyes of ignorance.
   Sweet swan of Avon, what a sight it were
    To see thee in our waters yet appear,
   And make those flights upon the banks of Thames
    That so did take Eliza and our James![8]

---

3. John Lyly, Thomas Kyd, and Christopher Marlowe were Elizabethan dramatists contemporary or nearly contemporary with Shakespeare.
4. Shakespeare's Latin was pretty good, but Jonson is judging by the standard of his own remarkable scholarship.
5. Marcus Pacuvius, Lucius Accius (2nd century B.C.E.), and "him of Cordova," Seneca the Younger (1st century C.E.), were Latin tragedians. Seneca's tragedies had a large influence on Elizabethan revenge tragedy.
6. Aristophanes, an ancient Greek satirist and writer of comedy; Terence and Plautus (2nd and 3rd centuries B.C.E.), Roman writers of comedy.
7. Pun on Shake-speare.
8. Queen Elizabeth and King James.

75 But stay; I see thee in the hemisphere
 Advanced and made a constellation there![9]
Shine forth, thou star of poets, and with rage
 Or influence[1] chide or cheer the drooping stage,
Which, since thy flight from hence, hath mourned like night,
80 And despairs day, but for thy volume's light.

                1623

Ode to Himself[1]

 Come, leave the loathèd stage,
 And the more loathsome age,
Where pride and impudence, in faction knit,
 Usurp the chair of wit,
5 Indicting and arraigning every day
  Something they call a play.
 Let their fastidious, vain
 Commission of the brain
Run on and rage, sweat, censure, and condemn:
10 They were not made for thee, less thou for them.

 Say that thou pour'st them wheat,
 And they will acorns eat;
'Twere simple° fury still thyself to waste   *foolish*
 On such as have no taste!
15 To offer them a surfeit of pure bread,
  Whose appetites are dead!
 No, give them grains their fill,
 Husks, draff to drink, and swill:[2]
If they love lees,° and leave the lusty wine,   *dregs*
20 Envy them not; their palate's with the swine.

 No doubt some moldy tale
 Like *Pericles*,[3] and stale
As the shrieve's° crusts, and nasty as his fish—   *sheriff's*
 Scraps, out of every dish
25 Thrown forth and raked into the common tub,[4]
  May keep up the play club:
 There, sweepings do as well
 As the best-ordered meal;
For who the relish of these guests will fit
30 Needs set them but the alms basket of wit.

9. Heroes and demigods were typically exalted after death to a place among the stars.
1. "Rage" and "influence" describe the supposed effects of the planets on earthly affairs. "Rage" also implies poetic inspiration.
1. The failure of Jonson's play *The New Inn* (1629) inspired this assault on criticism and the public taste. For Carew's affectionate, mocking rebuke, see pp. 1771–73.
2. All three items are food for pigs.
3. Shakespeare's play, at least in part (printed 1609).
4. The basket outside the jail to receive food for prisoners was called the sheriff's tub.

And much good do 't you then:
    Brave plush and velvet men
Can feed on orts;° and, safe in your stage clothes,[5]   *scraps*
    Dare quit,° upon your oaths,   *acquit*
35 The stagers and the stage-wrights[6] too, your peers,
    Of larding your large ears
    With their foul comic socks,°   *symbols of comedy*
    Wrought upon twenty blocks;[7]
Which, if they're torn, and turned, and patched enough,
40 The gamesters° share your guilt,[8] and you their stuff.   *gamblers*

    Leave things so prostitute
    And take th' Alcaic lute;
Or thine own Horace, or Anacreon's lyre;
    Warm thee by Pindar's fire:[9]
45 And though thy nerves° be shrunk, and blood be cold,   *sinews*
    Ere years have made thee old,
    Strike that disdainful heat
    Throughout, to their defeat,
As curious fools, and envious of thy strain,
50 May, blushing, swear no palsy's in thy brain.[1]

    But when they hear thee sing
    The glories of thy king,
His zeal to God and his just awe o'er men,
    They may, blood-shaken then,
55 Feel such a flesh-quake to possess their powers
    As they shall cry, "Like ours,
    In sound of peace or wars,
    No harp e'er hit the stars
In tuning forth the acts of his sweet reign,
60 And raising Charles his chariot 'bove his Wain."[2]

1629   1631, 1640–41

---

5. Actors often wore on the stage clothes cast off by the gentry; these parasites wear clothes cast off by actors.
6. Playwrights. "Stagers": actors.
7. A pun: molds/blockheads.
8. A pun: guilt/gilt.
9. Alcaeus (ca. 600 B.C.E.), Horace, Anacreon,

and Pindar were among the greatest lyric poets in ancient Greece and Rome.
1. By 1629 Jonson was partially paralyzed.
2. Jonson's poetry will elevate the chariot of Charles I (symbol of his royal power) above Charles's Wain (Wagon)—the seven bright stars of Ursa Major.

MARY WROTH
1587–1651?

Lady Mary Wroth was the most prolific, self-conscious, and impressive female author of the Jacobean era. Her published work (1621) includes two firsts for an Englishwoman: a 558-page romance, *The Countess of Montgomery's Urania*, which includes more than fifty poems, and appended to it a Petrarchan lyric sequence that had circulated some years in manuscript, 103 sonnets and elegant songs titled *Pamphilia to Amphilanthus*. Wroth left unpublished a very long but unfinished continuation of the *Urania* and a pastoral drama, *Love's Victory*, also a first for an Englishwoman. Her achievement was fostered by her strong sense of identity as a Sidney, heir to the literary talent and cultural role of her famous uncle Sir Philip Sidney, her famous aunt Mary Sidney Herbert, Countess of Pembroke, who may have served as mentor to her; and her father Robert Sidney, Viscount Lisle, author of a recently discovered sonnet sequence. But she used that heritage transgressively to replace heroes with heroines in genres employed by the male Sidney authors—notably Philip Sidney's *Astrophil and Stella* and *The Countess of Pembroke's Arcadia*—transforming their gender politics and exploring the poetics and situation of women writers.

As Robert Sidney's eldest daughter, she lived and was educated at Penshurst, the Sidney country house celebrated by Ben Jonson, and was often at her aunt's "little college" at Wilton. She was married (incompatibly) at age seventeen to Sir Robert Wroth of Durrance and Loughton Manor, whose office it was to facilitate the king's hunting; and she was patron to several poets, including Jonson. He celebrated her in two epigrams and in a verse letter honoring her husband, dedicated his great comedy *The Alchemist* to her, and claimed in his only sonnet (p. 1550) that the artistry and erotic power of her sonnets had made him "a better lover, and much better poet." After her husband's death she carried on a long-standing love affair with her married first cousin, William Herbert, Earl of Pembroke, himself a poet, a powerful courtier, and a patron of the theater and of literature. That relationship produced two children and occasioned some scandal.

The significant names in the title of Wroth's Petrarchan sequence, *Pamphilia* ("all-loving") *to Amphilanthus* ("lover of two"), are from characters in her romance who at times shadow Wroth and her lover Pembroke. The Petrarchan lyric sequence had long served as the major genre for analyzing a male lover's passions, frustrations, and fantasies (and sometimes his career anxieties). So although the sonnet sequence was becoming passé by Wroth's time, it was an obvious choice for a woman poet undertaking the construction of subjectivity in a female lover-speaker. Wroth does not, however, simply reverse roles. Pamphilia addresses very few sonnets to Amphilanthus and seldom assumes the Petrarchan lover's position of abject servitude to a cruel beloved. Instead, she proclaims subjection to Cupid, usually identified with the force of her own desire. This radical revision identifies female desire as the source and center of the love relationship and celebrates the woman lover-poet's movement from the bondage of chaotic passion to the freedom of self-chosen constancy.

Wroth's romance, *Urania*, breaks the romance convention of a plot centered on courtship, portraying instead married heroines and their love relationships, both inside and outside of marriage. It is in part an idealizing fantasy: the principal characters are queens, kings, and emperors, with the power and comparative freedom such positions allow. However, the landscape is not Arcadia or Fairyland but wartorn Europe and Asia. The romance fantasy, with Spenserian symbolic places and knights

Lady Mary Wroth, with archlute (artist unknown). The image represents Mary Wroth in a conventional pose and role, holding the archlute, which indicates that she has been educated in the graceful arts that an aristocratic woman was expected to know. But the massive archlute, emblem of song-making, also points to her Sidney heritage—as niece of the poets Sir Philip Sidney and the Countess of Pembroke, and as daughter of Sir Robert Sidney of Penshurst, also a poet—and to her own unconventional role as female poet.

fighting evil tyrants and monsters, only partially overlays a rigidly patriarchal Jacobean world rife with rape, incest, arranged or forced marriages, jealous husbands, tortured women, and endangered children. Those perils, affecting all women from shepherdesses to queens, are rendered in large part through the numerous stories interpolated in romance fashion within the principal plots. The male heroes are courageous fighters and attractive lovers, but all are flawed by inconstancy. For Wroth, true heroism consists of integrity in love despite social constraints and psychological pressures. A few women are heroic in this sense: Pamphilia, the good queen and pattern of constancy; Urania, the wise counselor who wins self-knowledge and makes wise choices in love; and Veralinda, who weds her true lover after great trials. Almost all Wroth's female characters define themselves through storytelling and making poems. The women compose twice as many of the poems as the men do. Pamphilia, Wroth's surrogate, is singled out as a poet by vocation, both by the number of her poems and by their recognized excellence.

Many contemporaries assumed that the *Urania* was a scandalous roman à clef, alluding not only to Sidney-Pembroke-Wroth affairs but to notable personages of the Jacobean court. A public outcry from one of them, Lord Edward Denny, elicited a spirited satiric response from Wroth. Although she suggested to the king's minister Buckingham that she withdraw the work from circulation, there is no evidence that she actually did so. The uproar, however, may have discouraged her from publishing part 2 of the romance and her pastoral drama.

From The Countess of Montgomery's Urania[1]

From *The First Book*

When the spring began to appear like the welcome messenger of summer, one sweet (and in that more sweet) morning, after Aurora[2] had called all careful eyes to attend the day, forth came the fair shepherdess Urania[3] (fair indeed; yet that far too mean a title for her, who for beauty deserved the highest style[4] could be given by best-knowing judgments). Into the mead[5] she came, where usually she drove her flocks to feed, whose leaping and wantonness showed they were proud of such a guide: but she, whose sad thoughts led her to another manner of spending her time, made her soon leave them, and follow her late-begun custom; which was (while they delighted themselves) to sit under some shade, bewailing her misfortune; while they fed, to feed upon her own sorrow and tears, which at this time she began again to summon, sitting down under the shade of a well-spread beech; the ground (then blest) and the tree, with full and fine-leaved branches, growing proud to bear and shadow such perfections. But she regarding nothing, in comparison of her woe, thus proceeded in her grief: "Alas Urania," said she (the true servant to misfortune), "of any misery that can befall woman, is not this the most and greatest which thou art fallen into? Can there be any near the unhappiness of being ignorant, and that in the highest kind, not being certain of mine own estate or birth? Why was I not still continued in the belief I was, as I appear, a shepherdess, and daughter to a shepherd? My ambition then went no higher than this estate, now flies it to a knowledge; then was I contented, now perplexed. O ignorance, can thy dullness yet procure so sharp a pain? and that such a thought as makes me now aspire unto knowledge? How did I joy in this poor life, being quiet! blessed in the love of those I took for parents, but now by them I know the contrary, and by that knowledge, now to know myself. Miserable Urania, worse art thou now than these thy lambs; for they know their dams, while thou dost live unknown of any." By this were others come into that mead with their flocks: but she, esteeming her sorrowing thoughts her best and choicest company, left that place, taking a little path which brought her to the further side of the plain, to the foot of the rocks, speaking as she went these lines, her eyes fixed upon the ground, her very soul turned into mourning.

> Unseen, unknown, I here alone complain
> To rocks, to hills, to meadows, and to springs,

1. Wroth's title echoes *The Countess of Pembroke's Arcadia*, the romance written by her uncle Sir Philip Sidney. The countess of Montgomery was Susan (Vere) Herbert, Wroth's close friend and the sister-in-law of her lover, William Herbert. The opening of *Urania* is meant to be compared to (and contrasted with) the opening of the *Arcadia*, in which two shepherds lament the absence of their beloved, the mysterious shepherdess Urania.
2. The Greek goddess of the dawn.
3. The name has multiple associations: the Muse of astronomy, the Muse of Christian poetry, a surname for Aphrodite (Venus) designating heavenly beauty. It was also an honorific commonly bestowed on Wroth's aunt, Mary Sidney, Countess of Pembroke. In Wroth's romance, Urania is a foundling adopted by shepherds but actually the daughter of the king of Naples: after losing one lover and gaining another, she marries, becomes a matriarch, and is throughout (as in this episode) a counselor of others.
4. Title.
5. Meadow.

Which can no help return to ease my pain,
  But back my sorrows the sad Echo[6] brings.
5   Thus still increasing are my woes to me,
  Doubly resounded by that moanful voice,
Which seems to second me in misery,
  And answer gives like friend of mine own choice.
Thus only she doth my companion prove,
10   The others silently do offer ease.
But those that grieve, a grieving note do love;
  Pleasures to dying eyes bring but disease:
And such am I, who daily ending live,
  Wailing a state which can no comfort give.

In this passion she went on, till she came to the foot of a great rock, she
thinking of nothing less than ease, sought how she might ascend it; hoping
there to pass away her time more peaceably with loneliness, though not to
find least respite from her sorrow, which so dearly she did value, as by no
means she would impart it to any. The way was hard, though by some windings making the ascent pleasing. Having attained the top, she saw under
some hollow trees the entry into the rock: she fearing nothing but the continuance of her ignorance, went in; where she found a pretty room, as if that
stony place had yet in pity, given leave for such perfections to come into the
heart as chiefest, and most beloved place, because most loving. The place was
not unlike the ancient (or the descriptions of ancient) hermitages, instead of
hangings, covered and lined with ivy, disdaining aught else should come
there, that being in such perfection. This richness in Nature's plenty made
her stay to behold it, and almost grudge the pleasant fullness of content that
place might have, if sensible, while she must know to taste of torments. As she
was thus in passion mixed with pain, throwing her eyes as wildly as timorous
lovers do for fear of discovery, she perceived a little light, and such a one, as a
chink doth oft discover to our sights. She curious to see what this was, with
her delicate hands put the natural ornament aside, discerning a little door,
which she putting from her, passed through it into another room, like the
first in all proportion; but in the midst there was a square stone, like to a
pretty table, and on it a wax candle burning; and by that a paper,[7] which had
suffered itself patiently to receive the discovering of so much of it, as presented this sonnet (as it seemed newly written) to her sight.

Here all alone in silence might I mourn:
  But how can silence be where sorrows flow?
Sighs with complaints have poorer pains outworn;
  But broken hearts can only true grief show.
5   Drops of my dearest blood shall let Love know
  Such tears for her I shed, yet still do burn,
As no spring can quench least part of my woe,
  Till this live earth, again to earth do turn.
Hateful all thought of comfort is to me,

---

6. In classical mythology Echo was a wood nymph who pined away in unrequited love for the hand-some Narcissus until only her voice remained (Ovid, *Metamorphoses* 3).

7. The episode alludes to an episode in Sidney's *Old Arcadia* in which one of the heroines, Cleoph-ila, enters a darkened cave illuminated by a single candle and finds a poem on top of a stone table.

10   Despised day, let me still night possess;
        Let me all torments feel in their excess,
            And but this light allow my state to see.
        Which still doth waste, and wasting as this light,
        Are my sad days unto eternal night.

"Alas Urania!" sighed she. "How well do these words, this place, and all agree with thy fortune? Sure, poor soul, thou wert here appointed to spend thy days, and these rooms ordained to keep thy tortures in; none being assuredly so matchlessly unfortunate."

Turning from the table, she discerned in the room a bed of boughs, and on it a man lying, deprived of outward sense, as she thought, and of life, as she at first did fear, which struck her into a great amazement: yet having a brave spirit, though shadowed under a mean habit,[8] she stepped unto him, whom she found not dead, but laid upon his back, his head a little to her wards,[9] his arms folded on his breast, hair long, and beard disordered, manifesting all care;[1] but care itself had left him: curiousness thus far afforded him, as to be perfectly discerned the most exact piece of misery; apparel he had suitable to the habitation, which was a long gray[2] robe. This grieveful spectacle did much amaze the sweet and tender-hearted shepherdess; especially, when she perceived (as she might by the help of the candle) the tears which distilled from his eyes; who seeming the image of death, yet had this sign of worldly sorrow, the drops falling in that abundance, as if there were a kind strife among them, to rid their master first of that burdenous[3] carriage; or else meaning to make a flood, and so drown their woeful patient in his own sorrow, who yet lay still, but then fetching a deep groan from the profoundest part of his soul, he said:

"Miserable Perissus,[4] canst thou thus live, knowing she that gave thee life is gone? Gone, O me! and with her all my joy departed. Wilt thou (unblessed creature) lie here complaining for her death, and know she died for thee? Let truth and shame make thee do something worthy of such a love, ending thy days like thyself, and one fit to be her servant. But that I must not do: then thus remain and foster storms, still to torment thy wretched soul withall, since all are little, and too too little for such a loss. O dear Limena,[5] loving Limena, worthy Limena, and more rare, constant Limena: perfections delicately feigned to be in women were verified in thee, was such worthiness framed only to be wondered at by the best, but given as a prey to base and unworthy jealousy? When were all worthy parts joined in one, but in thee my best Limena? Yet all these grown subject to a creature ignorant of all but ill; like unto a fool, who in a dark cave, that hath but one way to get out, having a candle, but not the understanding what good it doth him, puts it out: this ignorant wretch not being able to comprehend thy virtues, did so by thee in thy murder, putting out the world's light, and men's admiration: Limena, Limena, O my Limena."

With that he fell from complaining into such a passion, as weeping and crying were never in so woeful a perfection, as now in him; which brought as deserved a compassion from the excellent shepherdess, who already had her

---

8. Lowly garment.
9. Toward her.
1. Trouble.
2. Gray is typically associated with mourning

and despair.
3. Burdensome.
4. Perissus: "Lost one."
5. Woman of home or threshold.

heart so tempered with grief, as that it was apt to take any impression that it would come to seal withal. Yet taking a brave courage to her, she stepped unto him, kneeling down by his side, and gently pulling him by the arm, she thus spoke.

"Sir," said she, "having heard some part of your sorrows, they have not only made me truly pity you, but wonder at you; since if you have lost so great a treasure, you should not lie thus leaving her and your love unrevenged, suffering her murderers to live, while you lie here complaining; and if such perfections be dead in her, why make you not the phoenix[6] of your deeds live again, as to new life raised out of the revenge you should take on them? Then were her end satisfied, and you deservedly accounted worthy of her favor, if she were so worthy as you say."

"If she were, O God," cried out Perissus, "what devilish spirit art thou, that thus dost come to torture me? But now I see you are a woman; and therefore not much to be marked, and less resisted: but if you know charity, I pray now practice it, and leave me who am afflicted sufficiently without your company; or if you will stay, discourse not to me."

"Neither of these will I do," said she.

"If you be then," said he, "some Fury[7] of purpose sent to vex me, use your force to the uttermost in martyring me; for never was there a fitter subject, then the heart of poor Perissus is."

"I am no Fury," replied the divine Urania, "nor hither come to trouble you, but by accident lighted on this place; my cruel hap being such, as only the like can give me content, while the solitariness of this like cave might give me quiet, though not ease. Seeking for such a one, I happened hither; and this is the true cause of my being here, though now I would use it to a better end if I might: Wherefore favor me with the knowledge of your grief; which heard, it may be I shall give you some counsel, and comfort in your sorrow."

"Cursed may I be," cried he, "if ever I take comfort, having such cause of mourning: but because you are, or seem to be afflicted, I will not refuse to satisfy your demand, but tell you the saddest story that ever was rehearsed by dying man to living woman, and such a one, as I fear will fasten too much sadness in you; yet should I deny it, I were to blame, being so well known to these senseless places; as were they sensible of sorrow, they would condole, or else amazed at such cruelty stand dumb as they do, to find that man should be so inhuman."

* * *

SONG[8]

Love what art thou? A vain thought
In our minds by fancy wrought.
Idle smiles did thee beget,
While fond wishes made the net
5   Which so many fools have caught.

---

6. Mythical bird said to live five hundred years, then expire in flames, out of which a new phoenix arose. Only one phoenix existed at a time.
7. Goddess of vengeance.

8. This song, one of a group of eclogues that marks the conclusion of Book 1 of the *Urania*, is sung to a shepherdess by a shepherd, "being, as it seemed, fallen out with Love."

Love what art thou? Light and fair,
Fresh as morning, clear as th' air.
But too soon thy evening change
Makes thy worth with coldness range;
10 Still thy joy is mixed with care.

Love what art thou? A sweet flower
Once full blown,° dead in an hour.   *in full bloom*
Dust in wind as staid remains
As thy pleasure or our gains,
15 If thy humor° change, to lour.°   *whim / frown*

Love what art thou? Childish, vain,
Firm as bubbles made by rain,
Wantonness thy greatest pride.
These foul faults thy virtues hide—
20 But babes can no staidness gain.

Love what art thou? Causeless cursed,
Yet alas these not the worst:
Much more of thee may be said.
But thy law I once obeyed,
25 Therefore say no more at first.

1621

From Pamphilia to Amphilanthus[1]

1

When night's black mantle could most darkness prove,
And sleep, death's image, did my senses hire
From knowledge of myself, then thoughts did move
Swifter than those most swiftness need require.
5 In sleep, a chariot drawn by winged desire
I saw, where sat bright Venus, Queen of Love,
And at her feet, her son,° still adding fire   *Cupid*
To burning hearts, which she did hold above.
But one heart flaming more than all the rest
10 The goddess held, and put it to my breast.
"Dear son, now shut,"[2] said she: "thus must we win."
He her obeyed, and martyred my poor heart.

---

1. Pamphilia ("all-loving") is the protagonist of *Urania*. Her unfaithful beloved's name means "lover of two." These characters are first cousins, like Mary Wroth and William Herbert; their names adumbrate the main theme of both the romance and the appended sonnet sequence, constancy in the face of unfaithfulness. *Pamphilia to Amphilanthus* is broken into several separately numbered series (the first of which includes forty-eight sonnets, with songs inserted after every sixth sonnet except the last). In Josephine A. Roberts's edition of Wroth's poetry, the poems are numbered consecutively throughout the work; we have adopted this convenient renumbering.
2. I.e., shut the burning heart into Pamphilia's breast.

I, waking, hoped as dreams it would depart:
Yet since, O me, a lover I have been.

16

Am I thus conquered? Have I lost the powers
    That to withstand, which joys to ruin me?[3]
    Must I be still while it my strength devours,
    And captive leads me prisoner, bound, unfree?
5 Love first shall leave men's fancies to them free,[4]
    Desire shall quench Love's flames, spring hate sweet showers,
    Love shall loose all his darts, have sight, and see
    His shame, and wishings hinder happy hours.
Why should we not Love's purblind° charms resist?   *completely blind*
10   Must we be servile, doing what he list?°   *what pleases him*
    No, seek some host to harbor thee: I fly
Thy babish tricks, and freedom do profess.
    But O my hurt makes my lost heart confess
    I love, and must: So farewell liberty.

25

Like to the Indians scorched with the sun,
    The sun which they do as their god adore,
    So am I used by Love, for evermore°   *the more*
    I worship him, less favors have I won.
5 Better are they who thus to blackness run,
    And so can only whiteness' want deplore:
    Than I, who pale and white am with grief's store,
    Nor can have hope, but to see hopes undone.
Besides their sacrifice received in sight
10   Of their chose Saint, mine hid as worthless rite,
    Grant me to see where I my offerings give;
Then let me wear the mark of Cupid's might
    In heart, as they in skin of Phoebus° light,   *the sun god*
    Not ceasing offerings to Love while I live.

28

SONG[5]

Sweetest love, return again,
    Make not too long stay:
Killing mirth and forcing pain,
    Sorrow leading way.
5   Let us not thus parted be:
    Love and absence ne'er agree.

3. I.e., have I lost the power to withstand love ("That"), which takes pleasure in ruining me?
4. I.e., this and the other impossibilities that fol-low will occur before I surrender to love.
5. The poem seems to revise one of Donne's songs: "Sweetest love, I do not go," p. 1379.

But since you must needs depart,
    And me hapless leave,
In your journey take my heart,
10   Which will not deceive.
Yours it is, to you it flies,
Joying in those lovèd eyes.

So in part we shall not part,
    Though we absent be:
15 Time, nor place, nor greatest smart
    Shall my bands make free.
Tied I am, yet think it gain:
In such knots I feel no pain.

But can I live, having lost
20   Chiefest part of me?
Heart is fled, and sight is crossed,
    These my fortunes be.
Yet dear heart go, soon return:
As good there as here to burn.

39

Take heed mine eyes, how you your looks do cast
  Lest they betray my heart's most secret thought,
  Be true unto yourselves, for nothing's bought
  More dear than doubt which brings a lover's fast.[6]
5 Catch you all watching eyes, ere they be past,
  Or take yours fixed where your best love hath sought
  The pride of your desires; let them be taught
  Their faults for shame, they could no truer last.
Then look, and look with joy for conquest won
10 Of those that searched your hurt in double kind;[7]
  So you kept safe, let them themselves look blind,
  Watch, gaze, and mark till they to madness run,
While you, mine eyes enjoy full sight of love
Contented that such happinesses move.

40

False hope which feeds but to destroy, and spill[8]
  What it first breeds; unnatural to the birth
  Of thine own womb; conceiving but to kill,
  And plenty gives to make the greater dearth,[9]
5 So tyrants do who falsely ruling earth
  Outwardly grace them,[1] and with profits fill,

---

6. Lack of nourishment for love, due to jealousy ("doubt").
7. Those who spy and pry with their two eyes, to discover my secret love.
8. Kill. The image is of miscarriage or infanti-cide.
9. Gives abundance only to make scarcity more painful afterward.
1. I.e., those whom they mean to destroy (see next line).

Advance those who appointed are to death,
  To make their greater fall to please their will.
Thus shadow° they their wicked vile intent,   *conceal*
10   Coloring evil with a show of good
  While in fair shows their malice so is spent;[2]
  Hope kills the heart, and tyrants shed the blood.
For hope deluding brings us to the pride
Of our desires the farther down to slide.

64

Love like a juggler comes to play his prize,°   *perform skillfully*
  And all minds draw his wonders to admire,
  To see how cunningly he, wanting eyes,[3]
  Can yet deceive the best sight of desire.
5   The wanton child how he can feign his fire
  So prettily, as none sees his disguise!
  How finely do his tricks; while we fools hire
  The badge and office of his tyrannies.[4]
For in the end such juggling he doth make,
10   As he our hearts instead of eyes doth take;
  For men can only by their sleights abuse
The sight with nimble and delightful skill;
  But if he play, his gain is our lost will.
  Yet child-like we cannot his sports refuse.

68

My pain, still smothered in my grievèd breast,
  Seeks for some ease, yet cannot passage find
  To be discharged of this unwelcome guest:
  When most I strive, most fast his burdens bind,
5   Like to a ship on Goodwin's[5] cast by wind,
  The more she strives, more deep in sand is pressed,
  Till she be lost; so am I, in this kind,°   *manner*
  Sunk, and devoured, and swallowed by unrest,
Lost, shipwrecked, spoiled, debarred of smallest hope,
10   Nothing of pleasure left; save thoughts have scope,
  Which wander may. Go then, my thoughts, and cry
"Hope's perished, love tempest-beaten, joy lost:
  Killing despair hath all these blessings crossed."
  Yet faith still cries, "love will not falsify."

---

2. Expended, employed. "Shows": appearances.
3. Cupid, the god of Love, was represented as a blind child.
4. Seek, at our own cost, the external tokens and ceremonies of tyrannical Love.
5. Goodwin Sands, a line of shoals at the entrance to the Strait of Dover.

74

SONG

Love a child is ever crying,
    Please him, and he straight is flying;
    Give him, he the more is craving,
    Never satisfied with having.

5   His desires have no measure,
    Endless folly is his treasure;
    What he promiseth he breaketh:
    Trust not one word that he speaketh.

He vows nothing but false matter,
10   And to cozen° you he'll flatter.   *cheat*
    Let him gain the hand,° he'll leave you,   *the upper hand*
    And still glory to deceive you.

He will triumph in your wailing,
    And yet cause be of your failing:
15   These his virtues are, and slighter
    Are his gifts, his favors lighter.

Feathers are as firm in staying,
    Wolves no fiercer in their preying.
    As a child then leave him crying,
20   Nor seek him, so given to flying.

From *A Crown of Sonnets Dedicated to Love*[6]

77

In this strange labyrinth how shall I turn?
    Ways° are on all sides, while the way I miss: *paths*
    If to the right hand, there in love I burn;
    Let me go forward, therein danger is;
5   If to the left, suspicion hinders bliss,
    Let me° turn back, shame cries I ought return,   *if I*
    Nor faint though crosses[7] with my fortunes kiss;
    Stand still is harder, although sure to mourn.[8]
  Then let me take the right- or left-hand way;
10   Go forward, or stand still, or back retire;

---

6. The "crown" is a difficult poetic form (originally Italian and usually known by its Italian name, *corona*) in which the last line of each poem serves as the first line of the next, until a circle is completed by the last line of the final poem, which is the same as the first line of the first one. The number of poems varies from seven to (as in Wroth's *corona*) fourteen.
  In contrast to the errant-child Cupid of the preceding part of the sequence, Love in this series is a mature and just monarch, whose true service ennobles lovers. The crown is in part a recantation of the harsh judgment of love earlier in the sequence. But Pamphilia relapses into melancholy afterward.
7. Troubles, adversity. "Faint": lose heart.
8. I.e., certain to make me mourn.

I must these doubts endure without allay°   abatement
Or help, but travail find for my best hire.[9]
Yet that which most my troubled sense doth move
Is to leave all, and take the thread of love.[1]

103

My muse now happy, lay thyself to rest,
   Sleep in the quiet of a faithful love,
   Write you no more, but let these fancies move
   Some other hearts, wake not to new unrest.
5   But if you study, be those thoughts addressed
   To truth, which shall eternal goodness prove;
   Enjoying of true joy, the most, and best,
   The endless gain which never will remove.
Leave the discourse of Venus and her son
10   To young beginners,[2] and their brains inspire
   With stories of great love, and from that fire
   Get heat to write the fortunes they have won.
And thus leave off, what's past shows you can love,
Now let your constancy your honor prove.[3]

1621

9. I.e., I find travail (with a pun on "travel," the spelling in the 1621 edition) is my only reward.
1. Ariadne gave Theseus a thread to follow so as to find his way out of the Labyrinth, after killing the Minotaur at its center.
2. In Neoplatonic love philosophy, "beginners" in love are attracted to physical beauty and sensory delights, while more advanced lovers love virtue

and spiritual beauty. Writing love sonnets is traditionally the business of young lovers.
3. In a symbolic episode in the *Urania*, Pamphilia embodies the virtue of Constancy; she accepts the keys to the Throne of Love, "at which instant Constancy vanished as metamorphosing herself into her breast" (1.1.141).

JOHN WEBSTER
1580?–1625?

John Webster's fame rests on two remarkable tragedies, both set in Roman Catholic Italy and both evoking the common Jacobean stereotype of that land as a place of sophisticated corruption. Both have at their center bold heroines who choose for themselves in love and refuse to submit to male authority. *The White Devil*, first performed in 1608, is based on events that took place in Italy in 1581–85; in this play Vittoria Corombona defies a courtroom full of corrupt magistrates who convict her of adultery and murder. *The Duchess of Malfi*, first performed in 1614 and published in 1623, is based on an Italian novella. In this play, the spirited ruler of Malfi secretly marries her steward for love, defying her brothers, a duke and a cardinal, who demand that she remain a widow. Their dark motives include greed for her fortune, overweening pride in their noble blood, and incestuous desire. The play weds sublime poetry and gothic horror in the devious machinations set in motion against the duchess by her brothers' melancholy spy Bosola, in the macabre mental and physical torments to which they subject her, and in the final scenes in which the stage is littered with the slaughtered bodies of all the principal characters.

Webster was the son of a London tailor and a member of the Merchant Tailors' Company, but we know little else about him. He wrote a tragicomedy, *The Devil's Law Case* (1621), and collaborated on several plays with contemporary playwrights, among them Thomas Dekker in *Westward Ho* (1607) and John Marston in *The Malcontent* (1604). Of all the Stuart dramatists, Webster is the one who comes closest to Shakespeare in his power of tragic utterance and his flashes of poetic brilliance.

The Duchess of Malfi

Dramatis Personae

FERDINAND, *Duke of Calabria*
THE CARDINAL, *his brother*
ANTONIO BOLOGNA, *steward of the household to the* DUCHESS
DELIO, *his friend*
DANIEL DE BOSOLA, *gentleman of the horse to the* DUCHESS
CASTRUCCIO, *an old lord*
MARQUIS OF PESCARA
COUNT MALATESTE
SILVIO, *a lord, of Milan*
RODERIGO ⎤ *gentlemen attending*
GRISOLAN ⎦ *on the* DUCHESS

DOCTOR
Several MADMEN, PILGRIMS, EXECUTIONERS, OFFICERS, ATTENDANTS &c.
THE DUCHESS OF MALFI, *sister of* FERDINAND *and the* CARDINAL
CARIOLA, *her woman*
JULIA, CASTRUCCIO'S *wife, and the* CARDINAL'S *mistress*
OLD LADY, LADIES, *and* CHILDREN

SCENE. *Amalfi, Rome, Loreto, and Milan*

Act 1

SCENE 1. *Amalfi; a hall in the* DUCHESS's *palace.*

[*Enter* ANTONIO *and* DELIO.]

DELIO   You are welcome to your country, dear Antonio;
   You have been long in France, and you return
   A very formal Frenchman in your habit.[1]
   How do you like the French court?
ANTONIO   I admire it:
5   In seeking to reduce both state and people
   To a fixed order, their judicious king
   Begins at home; quits° first his royal palace   °rids
   Of flattering sycophants, of dissolute
   And infamous persons—which he sweetly terms

1.1
1. An absolute Frenchman in your dress.

His Master's masterpiece, the work of heaven[2]—
Considering duly that a prince's court
Is like a common fountain, whence should flow
Pure silver drops in general, but if 't chance
Some cursed example poison 't near the head,
Death and diseases through the whole land spread.
And what is 't makes this blessed government
But a most provident council, who dare freely
Inform him the corruption of the times?
Though some o' th' court hold it presumption
To instruct princes what they ought to do,
It is a noble duty to inform them
What they ought to foresee.—Here comes Bosola,
The only court-gall;[3] yet I observe his railing
Is not for simple love of piety.
Indeed, he rails at those things which he wants;
Would be as lecherous, covetous, or proud,
Bloody, or envious, as any man,
If he had means to be so. Here's the cardinal.
    [*Enter the* CARDINAL *and* BOSOLA.]

BOSOLA   I do haunt you still.

CARDINAL   So.

BOSOLA   I have done you better service than to be slighted thus. Miserable age, where the only reward of doing well is the doing of it!

CARDINAL   You enforce your merit too much.

BOSOLA   I fell into the galleys[4] in your service; where, for two years together, I wore two towels instead of a shirt, with a knot on the shoulder, after the fashion of a Roman mantle. Slighted thus? I will thrive some way. Blackbirds fatten best in hard weather; why not I in these dog days?[5]

CARDINAL   Would you could become honest!

BOSOLA   With all your divinity do but direct me the way to it. I have known many travel far for it, and yet return as arrant knaves as they went forth, because they carried themselves always along with them. [*Exit* CARDINAL.] Are you gone? Some fellows, they say, are possessed with the devil, but this great fellow were able to possess the greatest devil, and make him worse.

ANTONIO   He hath denied thee some suit?

BOSOLA   He and his brother are like plum trees that grow crooked over standing pools;[6] they are rich and o'erladen with fruit, but none but crows, pies,[7] and caterpillars feed on them. Could I be one of their flattering panders, I would hang on their ears like a horse leech till I were full and then drop off. I pray, leave me. Who would rely upon these miserable dependencies, in expectation to be advanced tomorrow? What creature ever fed worse than hoping Tantalus?[8] Nor ever died any

---

2. Alludes to Christ ridding the temple of moneychangers (John 2.13–22).
3. One who frets the court, but with the overtone of a disease, a blight.
4. Forced labor at the oar of a Mediterranean galley was the last penalty this side of torture and execution, and was likely to be a death sentence.

5. The hot, sultry season of midsummer.
6. Stagnant waters.
7. Magpies, birds of evil omen like blackbirds.
8. Tantalus, in classical mythology, was "tantalized" by the constant presence of delectable food and drink that, though he was desperate, he could never reach.

man more fearfully than he that hoped for a pardon. There are rewards for hawks and dogs when they have done us service; but for a soldier that hazards his limbs in a battle, nothing but a kind of geometry is his last supportation.[9]

DELIO Geometry?

BOSOLA Aye, to hang in a fair pair of slings, take his latter swing in the world upon an honorable pair of crutches, from hospital to hospital.[1] Fare ye well, sir: and yet do not you scorn us; for places in the court are but like beds in the hospital, where this man's head lies at that man's foot, and so lower and lower.   [Exit.]

DELIO I knew this fellow seven years[2] in the galleys
For a notorious murder; and 'twas thought
The cardinal suborned it. He was released
By the French general, Gaston de Foix,
When he recovered Naples.[3]

ANTONIO   'Tis great pity
He should be thus neglected; I have heard
He's very valiant. This foul melancholy
Will poison all his goodness; for, I'll tell you,
If too immoderate sleep be truly said
To be an inward rust unto the soul,
It then doth follow want of action
Breeds all black malcontents; and their close rearing,
Like moths in cloth, do hurt for want of wearing.[4]

SCENE 2. *The scene continues.*

[*Enter* CASTRUCCIO, SILVIO, RODERIGO, *and* GRISOLAN.]

DELIO The presence° 'gins to fill: you promised me   *audience hall*
To make me the partaker of the natures
Of some of your great courtiers.

ANTONIO   The Lord Cardinal's,
And other strangers' that are now in court?
I shall. Here comes the great Calabrian duke.

[*Enter* FERDINAND *and* ATTENDANTS.]

FERDINAND Who took the ring oftenest?[1]

SILVIO Antonio Bologna, my lord.

FERDINAND Our sister duchess' great master of her household? Give him the jewel. When shall we leave this sportive action, and fall to action indeed?

CASTRUCCIO Methinks, my lord, you should not desire to go to war in person.

FERDINAND Now for some gravity. Why, my lord?

CASTRUCCIO It is fitting a soldier arise to be a prince, but not necessary a prince descend to be a captain.

---

9. Support.
1. In the 17th century, a place of last resort for the indigent dying.
2. In speaking to the cardinal himself (line 34), Bosola had mentioned only two years.
3. Gaston de Foix, French commander, was active in Italy during the early 1500s; hence, the time of the tragedy is about a hundred years before Webster wrote. Ferdinand and the cardi-

nal are Spaniards established in Italy, like the infamous house of Borgia.
4. I.e., enforced idleness breeds discontent, as moths breed in unused clothing.
1.2
1. A common game around court, used in training for tournaments, involved catching a hanging ring on the tip of a lance. But some of Webster's audience would have caught a sexual analogy.

15 FERDINAND   No?

CASTRUCCIO   No, my lord, he were far better do it by a deputy.

FERDINAND   Why should he not as well sleep or eat by a deputy? This might take idle, offensive, and base office from him, whereas the other deprives him of honor.

20 CASTRUCCIO   Believe my experience, that realm is never long in quiet where the ruler is a soldier.

FERDINAND   Thou told'st me thy wife could not endure fighting.

CASTRUCCIO   True, my lord.

FERDINAND   And of a jest she broke of a captain she met full of wounds. I
25 have forgot it.

CASTRUCCIO   She told him, my lord, he was a pitiful fellow, to lie, like the children of Israel, all in tents.[2]

FERDINAND   Why, there's a wit were able to undo all the chirurgeons[3] o' the city; for although gallants should quarrel and had drawn their weapons
30 and were ready to go to it, yet her persuasions would make them put up.

CASTRUCCIO   That she would, my lord.

FERDINAND   How do you like my Spanish gennet?[4]

RODERIGO   He is all fire.

FERDINAND   I am of Pliny's opinion, I think he was begot by the wind; he
35 runs as if he were ballassed[5] with quicksilver.

SILVIO   True, my lord, he reels from the tilt often.[6]

RODERIGO and GRISOLAN   Ha, ha, ha!

FERDINAND   Why do you laugh? Methinks, you that are courtiers should be my touchwood, take fire when I give fire; that is, laugh but when I
40 laugh, were the subject never so witty.

CASTRUCCIO   True, my lord, I myself have heard a very good jest, and have scorned to seem to have so silly a wit as to understand it.

FERDINAND   But I can laugh at your fool, my lord.

CASTRUCCIO   He cannot speak, you know, but he makes faces: my lady
45 cannot abide him.

FERDINAND   No?

CASTRUCCIO   Nor endure to be in merry company, for she says too much laughing and too much company fills her too full of the wrinkle.

FERDINAND   I would, then, have a mathematical instrument made for her
50 face, that she might not laugh out of compass.[7] I shall shortly visit you at Milan, Lord Silvio.

SILVIO   Your grace shall arrive most welcome.

FERDINAND   You are a good horseman, Antonio. You have excellent riders in France. What do you think of good horsemanship?

55 ANTONIO   Nobly, my lord: as out of the Grecian horse issued many famous princes,[8] so out of brave horsemanship arise the first sparks of growing resolution that raise the mind to noble action.

FERDINAND   You have bespoke it worthily.

---

2. Lint bandages were called "tents."

3. Surgeons.

4. Sometimes "jennet": a small Spanish horse of Arabian stock.

5. Ballasted. Pliny in his *Natural History* tells about some Spanish horses generated by a swift wind (8.67).

6. Veers away from the target, undesirable in a war horse.

7. Excessively; with a pun on the draftsman's compass.

8. The Trojan horse, in which the Greek warriors hid, to overrun Troy.

SILVIO Your brother, the Lord Cardinal, and sister duchess.
    [*Reenter* CARDINAL, *with* DUCHESS, CARIOLA, *and* JULIA.]
CARDINAL Are the galleys come about?
60 GRISOLAN   They are, my lord.
FERDINAND Here's the Lord Silvio, is come to take his leave.
DELIO [*Aside to* ANTONIO] Now, sir, your promise. What's that Cardinal?
    I mean his temper? They say he's a brave fellow,
    Will play[9] his five thousand crowns at tennis, dance,
65   Court ladies, and one that hath fought single combats.
ANTONIO Some such flashes superficially hang on him for form; but
    observe his inward character: he is a melancholy churchman; the spring
    in his face is nothing but the engendering of toads; where he is jealous of
    any man, he lays worse plots for them than ever was imposed on Hercu-
70   les,[1] for he strews in his way flatterers, panders, intelligencers,[2] atheists,
    and a thousand such political monsters. He should have been Pope; but
    instead of coming to it by the primitive decency of the church, he did
    bestow bribes so largely and so impudently as if he would have carried it
    away without heaven's knowledge. Some good he hath done—
75 DELIO You have given too much of him. What's his brother?
ANTONIO The duke there? A most perverse and turbulent nature.
    What appears in him mirth is merely outside;
    If he laugh heartily, it is to laugh
    All honesty out of fashion.
DELIO   Twins?
80 ANTONIO   In quality.
    He speaks with others' tongues, and hears men's suits
    With others' ears; will seem to sleep o' th' bench
    Only to entrap offenders in their answers;
    Dooms men to death by information;°   *testimony of spies*
    Rewards by hearsay.°   *random report*
85 DELIO   Then the law to him
    Is like a foul black cobweb to a spider:
    He makes of it his dwelling and a prison
    To entangle those shall feed him.
ANTONIO   Most true:
    He ne'er pays debts unless they be shrewd turns,°   *hurtful acts*
90   And those he will confess that he doth owe.
    Last, for his brother there, the Cardinal,
    They that do flatter him most say oracles
    Hang at his lips; and verily I believe them,
    For the devil speaks in them.
95   But for their sister, the right noble duchess,
    You never fixed your eye on three fair medals
    Cast in one figure, of so different temper.
    For her discourse, it is so full of rapture,
    You only will begin then to be sorry

---

9. Wager. "Brave": fine; ostentatious.
1. Hercules' uncle, King Eurystheus, sent him on twelve suicide missions to get rid of him, but Her-

cules performed all these "labors" successfully.
2. Spies, "political" schemers.

100 When she doth end her speech, and wish, in wonder,
    She held it less vainglory° to talk much,   *excessive pride*
    Than your penance to hear her: whilst she speaks,
    She throws upon a man so sweet a look,
    That it were able to raise one to a galliard°   *gay and lively dance*
105 That lay in a dead palsy, and to dote
    On that sweet countenance; but in that look
    There speaketh so divine a continence
    As cuts off all lascivious and vain hope.
    Her days are practiced in such noble virtue
110 That sure her nights, nay, more, her very sleeps,
    Are more in heaven than other ladies' shrifts.°   *confessions*
    Let all sweet ladies break their flattering glasses,°   *mirrors*
    And dress themselves in her.

DELIO   Fie, Antonio,
    You play the wire-drawer[3] with her commendations.

115 ANTONIO   I'll case° the picture up only thus much;   *frame*
    All her particular worth grows to this sum:
    She stains° the time past, lights the time to come.   *darkens*

CARDINAL   You must attend my lady in the gallery,
    Some half an hour hence.

ANTONIO   I shall.   [*Exeunt* ANTONIO *and* DELIO.]

FERDINAND   Sister, I have a suit to you.

120 DUCHESS   To me, sir?

FERDINAND   A gentleman here, Daniel de Bosola,
    One that was in the galleys—

DUCHESS   Yes, I know him.

FERDINAND   A worthy fellow he is. Pray, let me entreat for
    The provisorship of your horse.[4]

DUCHESS   Your knowledge of him
    Commends him and prefers him.

125 FERDINAND   Call him hither.   [*Exit* ATTENDANT.]
    We are now upon° parting. Good Lord Silvio,   *at the point of*
    Do us commend to all our noble friends
    At the leaguer.°   *camp*

SILVIO   Sir, I shall.

DUCHESS   You are for Milan?

SILVIO   I am.

DUCHESS   Bring the caroches. We'll bring you down to the haven.[5]
                       [*Exeunt all but* FERDINAND *and the* CARDINAL.]

130 CARDINAL   Be sure you entertain° that Bosola   *hire*
    For your intelligence:° I would not be seen in 't;   *spy*
    And therefore many times I have slighted him
    When he did court our furtherance, as this morning.

FERDINAND   Antonio, the great master of her household,
    Had been far fitter.

135 CARDINAL   You are deceived in him:

---

3. Draw out her praises excessively.   sor of your horse.
4. Let me beg (for him) the position of supervi-   5. Harbor. "Caroches": carriages.

His nature is too honest for such business.
He comes: I'll leave you. [*Exit.*]
    [*Reenter* BOSOLA.]
BOSOLA   I was lured to you.
FERDINAND   My brother here the cardinal could never
     Abide you.
BOSOLA   Never since he was in my debt.

140   FERDINAND   Maybe some oblique character° in your face   *crooked feature*
     Made him suspect you.
BOSOLA   Doth he study physiognomy?
     There's no more credit to be given to th' face
     Than to a sick man's urine, which some call
     The physician's whore, because she cozens° him.   *tricks*
     He did suspect me wrongfully.

145   FERDINAND   For that
     You must give great men leave to take their times.
     Distrust doth cause us seldom be deceived:
     You see, the oft shaking of the cedar tree
     Fastens it more at root.
BOSOLA   Yet, take heed;

150   For to suspect a friend unworthily
     Instructs him the next° way to suspect you,   *nearest*
     And prompts him to deceive you.
FERDINAND [*giving him money*]   There's gold.
BOSOLA   So:
     What follows? Never rained such showers as these
     Without thunderbolts i' th' tail of them.

155   Whose throat must I cut?
FERDINAND   Your inclination to shed blood rides post°   *hurries*
     Before my occasion to use you. I give you that
     To live i' th' court here, and observe the duchess;
     To note all the particulars of her 'havior,

160   What suitors do solicit her for marriage,
     And whom she best affects. She's a young widow:
     I would not have her marry again.
BOSOLA   No, sir?
FERDINAND   Do not you ask the reason, but be satisfied
     I say I would not.
BOSOLA   It seems you would create me
     One of your familiars.°   *diabolical spirits*

165   FERDINAND   Familiar? What's that?
BOSOLA   Why, a very quaint invisible devil in flesh,
     An intelligencer.°   *spy*
FERDINAND   Such a kind of thriving thing
     I would wish thee, and ere long thou may'st arrive
     At a higher place by 't.
BOSOLA   Take your devils,

170   Which hell calls angels;[6] these cursed gifts would make

6. Gold coins, marked with the image of the archangel Michael.

You a corrupter, me an impudent traitor;
And should I take these, they'd take me to hell.

FERDINAND   Sir, I'll take nothing from you that I have given:
There is a place that I procured for you
175   This morning, the provisorship o' th' horse;
Have you heard on 't?

BOSOLA   No.

FERDINAND   'Tis yours. Is 't not worth thanks?

BOSOLA   I would have you curse yourself now, that your bounty,
Which makes men truly noble, e'er should make me
A villain. Oh, that to avoid ingratitude
180   For the good deed you have done me, I must do
All the ill man can invent! Thus the devil
Candies all sins o'er; and what heaven terms vile,
That names he complimental.°   *gracious*

FERDINAND   Be yourself;
Keep your old garb of melancholy; 'twill express
185   You envy those that stand above your reach,
Yet strive not to come near 'em: this will gain
Access to private lodgings, where yourself
May, like a politic dormouse—

BOSOLA   As I have seen some
Feed in a lord's dish, half asleep, not seeming
190   To listen to any talk; and yet these rogues
Have cut his throat in a dream. What's my place?
The provisorship o' th' horse? Say, then, my corruption
Grew out of horse dung. I am your creature.

FERDINAND   Away!

BOSOLA   Let good men, for good deeds, covet good fame,
195   Since place and riches oft are bribes of shame:
Sometimes the devil doth preach.   [*Exit.*]

SCENE 3. *The scene continues.*

[*Enter* DUCHESS, CARDINAL, *and* CARIOLA.]

CARDINAL   We are to part from you, and your own discretion
Must now be your director.

FERDINAND   You are a widow:
You know already what man is; and therefore
Let not youth, high promotion, eloquence—
5   CARDINAL   No, nor any thing without the addition, honor,
Sway your high blood.

FERDINAND   Marry! They are most luxurious°   *lecherous*
Will wed twice.

CARDINAL   Oh, fie!

FERDINAND   Their livers are more spotted
Than Laban's sheep.[1]

1.3
1. In Genesis 30.31–33, Laban promises to Jacob any speckled lambs born while Jacob is herding
Laban's sheep; the liver as seat of the passions was thought to be diseased when spotted.

DUCHESS   Diamonds are of most value,
They say, that have passed through most jewelers' hands.

FERDINAND   Whores by that rule are precious.

10 DUCHESS   Will you hear me?
I'll never marry.

CARDINAL   So most widows say;
But commonly that motion° lasts no longer   *impulse*
Than the turning of an hourglass; the funeral sermon
And it end both together.

FERDINAND   Now hear me:

15 You live in a rank pasture, here, i' th' court;
There is a kind of honeydew[2] that's deadly;
'Twill poison your fame° look to 't; be not cunning;   *reputation*
For they whose faces do belie their hearts
Are witches ere they arrive at twenty years,
Aye, and give the devil suck.

20 DUCHESS   This is terrible good counsel.

FERDINAND   Hypocrisy is woven of a fine small thread,
Subtler than Vulcan's engine:[3] yet, believe 't,
Your darkest actions, nay, your privatest thoughts,
Will come to light.

CARDINAL   You may flatter yourself,

25 And take your own choice; privately be married
Under the eaves of night—

FERDINAND   Think 't the best voyage
That e'er you made; like the irregular crab,
Which, though 't goes backward, thinks that it goes right
Because it goes its own way; but observe,

30 Such weddings may more properly be said
To be executed than celebrated.

CARDINAL   The marriage night
Is the entrance into some prison.

FERDINAND   And those joys,
Those lustful pleasures, are like heavy sleeps
Which do forerun man's mischief.

CARDINAL   Fare you well.

35 Wisdom begins at the end: remember it.   [*Exit.*]

DUCHESS   I think this speech between you both was studied,
It came so roundly° off.   *glibly*

FERDINAND   You are my sister;
This was my father's poniard,° do you see?   *dagger*
I'd be loath to see 't look rusty, 'cause 'twas his.

40 I would have you to give o'er these chargeable° revels: *expensive*
A visor[4] and a mask are whispering rooms
That were ne'er built for goodness—fare ye well—
And women like that part which, like the lamprey,[5]

---

2. A sweet, sticky substance left on plants by aphids.
3. The net in which Vulcan, Venus's husband, caught her misbehaving with Mars.
4. A half-mask, worn by ladies at carnivals, theaters, and other dubious resorts.
5. Lamprey eels have a cartilaginous, not a bony, skeleton.

Hath never a bone in 't.

DUCHESS   Fie, sir!

FERDINAND   Nay,

45   I mean the tongue; variety of courtship.
     What cannot a neat knave with a smooth tale
     Make a woman believe? Farewell, lusty widow.   [*Exit.*]

DUCHESS   Shall this move me? If all my royal kindred
     Lay in my way unto this marriage,

50   I'd make them my low footsteps; and even now,
     Even in this hate, as men in some great battles,
     By apprehending danger, have achieved
     Almost impossible actions (I have heard soldiers say so),
     So I through frights and threatenings will assay°   *attempt*

55   This dangerous venture. Let old wives report
     I winked and chose a husband. Cariola,
     To thy known secrecy I have given up
     More than my life—my fame.

CARIOLA   Both shall be safe,
     For I'll conceal this secret from the world

60   As warily as those that trade in poison
     Keep poison from their children.

DUCHESS   Thy protestation
     Is ingenious° and hearty:° I believe it.   *ingenuous / sincere*
     Is Antonio come?

CARIOLA   He attends you.

DUCHESS   Good dear soul,
     Leave me, but place thyself behind the arras,[6]

65   Where thou mayst overhear us. Wish me good speed,
     For I am going into a wilderness
     Where I shall find nor path nor friendly clue
     To be my guide.   [CARIOLA *goes behind the arras.*]
         [*Enter* ANTONIO]
         I sent for you: sit down;
     Take pen and ink, and write. Are you ready?

ANTONIO   Yes.

DUCHESS   What did I say?

70 ANTONIO   That I should write somewhat.

DUCHESS   Oh, I remember:
     After these triumphs° and this large expense,   *tournaments*
     It's fit, like thrifty husbands,[7] we inquire
     What's laid up for tomorrow.

ANTONIO   So please your beauteous excellence.

75 DUCHESS   Beauteous?
     Indeed, I thank you: I look young for your sake;
     You have ta'en my cares upon you.

ANTONIO   I'll fetch your grace

---

6. Tapestries were often hung in Renaissance palaces to moderate the chill of the bare walls.
7. Though used here in its original sense of one who preserves and safeguards property, the word shows where the duchess's thoughts are tending.

The particulars of your revenue and expense.

DUCHESS   Oh, you are an upright treasurer: but you mistook;
80   For when I said I meant to make inquiry
        What's laid up for tomorrow, I did mean
        What's laid up yonder for me.

ANTONIO   Where?

DUCHESS   In heaven.
        I am making my will (as 'tis fit princes should,
        In perfect memory), and I pray sir, tell me,
85   Were not one better make it smiling thus
        Than in deep groans and terrible ghastly looks,
        As if the gifts we parted with procured°   *brought on*
        That violent distraction?

ANTONIO   Oh, much better.

DUCHESS   If I had a husband now, this care were quit:
90   But I intend to make you overseer.
        What good deed shall we first remember? Say.

ANTONIO   Begin with that first good deed begun i' th' world
        After man's creation, the sacrament of marriage:
        I'd have you first provide for a good husband;
        Give him all.

DUCHESS   All?

95 ANTONIO   Yes, your excellent self.

DUCHESS   In a winding-sheet?

ANTONIO   In a couple.

DUCHESS   Saint Winfred, that were a strange will![8]

ANTONIO   'Twere stranger if there were no will in you
        To marry again.

DUCHESS   What do you think of marriage?

100 ANTONIO   I take 't, as those that deny purgatory;
        It locally° contains or heaven or hell;   *within itself*
        There's no third place in 't.

DUCHESS   How do you affect it?°   *feel about it*

ANTONIO   My banishment,° feeding my melancholy,   *solitary condition*
        Would often reason thus—

DUCHESS   Pray, let's hear it.

105 ANTONIO   Say a man never marry, nor have children,
        What takes that from him? Only the bare name
        Of being a father, or the weak delight
        To see the little wanton ride a-cock-horse
        Upon a painted stick, or hear him chatter
        Like a taught starling.

110 DUCHESS   Fie, fie, what's all this?
        One of your eyes is bloodshot; use my ring to 't,
        They say 'tis very sovereign.[9] 'Twas my wedding ring,
        And I did vow never to part with it

---

8. Saint Winifred, Welsh virgin and martyr, is an
odd saint for the Duchess of Malfi to swear on.
"In a couple": i.e., of sheets—but with a play on
"coupling."
9. Healing, but with an overtone implying royal
power.

But to my second husband.

ANTONIO   You have parted with it now.

DUCHESS   Yes, to help your eyesight.

ANTONIO   You have made me stark blind.

115   DUCHESS   How?

ANTONIO   There is a saucy and ambitious devil
Is dancing in this circle.[1]

DUCHESS   Remove him.

ANTONIO   How?

DUCHESS   There needs small conjuration, when your finger
May do it: thus; is it fit?   [*She puts the ring upon his finger; he kneels.*]

ANTONIO   What said you?

DUCHESS   Sir,

120   This goodly roof of yours[2] is too low built;
I cannot stand upright in 't nor discourse,
Without I raise it higher: raise yourself;
Or, if you please, my hand to help you: so. [*Raises him.*]

ANTONIO   Ambition, madam, is a great man's madness,

125   That is not kept in chains and close-pent rooms,
But in fair lightsome lodgings, and is girt
With the wild noise of prattling visitants,
Which makes it lunatic beyond all cure.
Conceive not I am so stupid but I aim

130   Whereto your favors tend; but he's a fool
That, being a-cold, would thrust his hands i' th' fire
To warm them.

DUCHESS   So, now the ground's broke,
You may discover what a wealthy mine
I make you lord of.

ANTONIO   O my unworthiness!

135   DUCHESS   You were ill to sell° yourself: *evaluate*
This darkening of your worth is not like that
Which tradesmen use i' th' city; their false lights
Are to rid bad wares off:[3] and I must tell you,
If you will know where breathes a complete man

140   (I speak it without flattery), turn your eyes,
And progress through yourself.

ANTONIO   Were there nor heaven
Nor hell, I should be honest: I have long served virtue,
And ne'er ta'en wages of her.

DUCHESS   Now she pays it.
The misery of us that are born great!

145   We are forced to woo, because none dare woo us;
And as a tyrant doubles° with his words   *speaks ambiguously*
And fearfully equivocates, so we
Are forced to express our violent passions

---

1. To conjure up a devil, the necromancer first
draws a charmed circle on the ground—like the
duchess's ring.

2. His head as he kneels.
3. Tradesmen in the city display their goods in a
poor light so the defects won't be seen.

In riddles and in dreams, and leave the path
150 Of simple virtue, which was never made
To seem the thing it is not. Go, go brag
You have left me heartless;° mine is in your bosom: *without a heart*
I hope 'twill multiply love there. You do tremble:
Make not your heart so dead a piece of flesh,
155 To fear more than to love me. Sir, be confident:
What is 't distracts you? This is flesh and blood, sir;
'Tis not the figure cut in alabaster
Kneels at my husband's tomb. Awake, awake, man!
I do here put off all vain ceremony,
160 And only do appear to you a young widow
That claims you for her husband, and, like a widow,
I use but half a blush in 't.

ANTONIO   Truth speak for me,
I will remain the constant sanctuary
Of your good name.

DUCHESS   I thank you, gentle love:
165 And 'cause° you shall not come to me in debt,   *so that*
Being now my steward, here upon your lips
I sign your *Quietus est.*[4] This you should have begged now;
I have seen children oft eat sweetmeats thus,
As fearful to devour them too soon.

ANTONIO   But for your brothers?

170 DUCHESS   Do not think of them.
All discord without this circumference[5]
Is only to be pitied, and not feared;
Yet, should they know it, time will easily
Scatter the tempest.

ANTONIO   These words should be mine,
175 And all the parts you have spoke, if some part of it
Would not have savored flattery.

DUCHESS   Kneel.

                              [CARIOLA *comes from behind the arras.*]

ANTONIO   Ha!

DUCHESS   Be not amazed; this woman's of my counsel:
I have heard lawyers say, a contract in a chamber
Per verba de presenti[6] is absolute marriage.   [*She and* ANTONIO *kneel.*]
180 Bless, heaven, this sacred gordian,° which let violence   *knot*
Never untwine!

ANTONIO   And may our sweet affections, like the spheres,
Be still° in motion!   *constantly*

DUCHESS   Quickening,° and make   *giving life*
The like soft music![7]

185 ANTONIO   That we may imitate the loving palms,

---

4. The legal formula for marking a bill "paid" or "acquitted."
5. Outside this room, or their embrace.
6. "By words in the present tense" (i.e., not a betrothal or promise for the future). In canon law, the agreement of two parties to consider themselves married is valid with or without priest, ceremony, or witness.
7. Like the supposed music of the spheres.

Best emblem of a peaceful marriage, that ne'er
Bore fruit, divided!
DUCHESS   What can the church force more?
ANTONIO   That fortune may not know an accident,
Either of joy or sorrow, to divide
Our fixèd wishes!
190   DUCHESS   How can the church bind faster?°   *tighter*
We now are man and wife, and 'tis the church
That must but echo this. Maid, stand apart:[8]
I now am blind.
ANTONIO   What's your conceit° in this?   *idea*
DUCHESS   I would have you lead your fortune by the hand
195   Unto your marriage bed
(You speak in me this, for we now are one);
We'll only lie, and talk together, and plot
To appease my humorous° kindred; and if you please,   *choleric*
Like the old tale in *Alexander and Lodowick,*
200   Lay a naked sword between us, keep us chaste.[9]
Oh, let me shroud my blushes in your bosom,
Since 'tis the treasury of all my secrets!   [*Exeunt* DUCHESS *and* ANTONIO.]
CARIOLA   Whether the spirit of greatness or of woman
Reign most in her, I know not; but it shows
205   A fearful madness: I owe her much of pity.   [*Exit.*]

Act 2

SCENE 1. *The scene continues.*

[*Enter* BOSOLA *and* CASTRUCCIO.]
BOSOLA   You say you would fain be taken for an eminent courtier?
CASTRUCCIO   'Tis the very main of my ambition.
BOSOLA   Let me see: you have a reasonable good face for 't already, and
your nightcap expresses your ears sufficient largely. I would have you
5   learn to twirl the strings of your band[1] with a good grace, and in a set
speech, at th' end of every sentence, to hum three or four times, or blow
your nose till it smart again, to recover your memory. When you come to
be a president[2] in criminal causes, if you smile upon a prisoner, hang
him, but if you frown upon him and threaten him, let him be sure to
10   'scape the gallows.
CASTRUCCIO   I would be a very merry president.
BOSOLA   Do not sup o' nights; 'twill beget you an admirable wit.
CASTRUCCIO   Rather it would make me have a good stomach[3] to quarrel;
for they say, your roaring boys[4] eat meat seldom, and that makes them

---

8. The phrase is addressed to Cariola as the duchess shuts her eyes and rejects all support.
9. Alexander and Lodowick were look-alike friends in an old ballad. For purely virtuous reasons, one slept with the wife of the other, but with the precaution indicated.

2.1
1. The elaborate ruff of the day had strings attached to it.
2. Presiding magistrate.
3. Disposition.
4. London town bullies.

15   so valiant. But how shall I know whether the people take me for an emi-
     nent fellow?

BOSOLA   I will teach a trick to know it: give out you lie a-dying, and if you
     hear the common people curse you, be sure you are taken for one of the
     prime nightcaps.[5]

          [*Enter an* OLD LADY.]

20   You come from painting now?

OLD LADY   From what?

BOSOLA   Why, from your scurvy face-physic. To behold thee not painted
     inclines somewhat near a miracle; these in thy face here were deep ruts
     and foul sloughs the last progress.[6] There was a lady in France that,
25   having had the smallpox, flayed the skin off her face to make it more
     level; and whereas before she looked like a nutmeg grater, after she
     resembled an abortive hedgehog.

OLD LADY   Do you call this painting?

BOSOLA   No, no, but you call it careening of an old morphewed lady, to
30   make her disembogue again: there's rough-cast phrase to your plastic.[7]

OLD LADY   It seems you are well acquainted with my closet.

BOSOLA   One would suspect it for a shop of witchcraft, to find in it the fat of
     serpents, spawn of snakes, Jews' spittle, and their young children's ordure;
     and all these for the face. I would sooner eat a dead pigeon taken from the
35   soles of the feet of one sick of the plague than kiss one of you fasting.[8]
     Here are two of you, whose sin of your youth is the very patrimony of the
     physician; makes him renew his footcloth with the spring, and change his
     high-prized courtesan with the fall of the leaf.[9] I do wonder you do not
     loathe yourselves. Observe my meditation now:

40   What thing is in this outward form of man
     To be beloved? We account it ominous,
     If nature do produce a colt, or lamb,
     A fawn, or goat, in any limb resembling
     A man, and fly from 't as a prodigy:°   *evil omen*
45   Man stands amazed to see his deformity
     In any other creature but himself.
     But in our own flesh, though we bear diseases
     Which have their true names only ta'en from beasts—
     As the most ulcerous wolf and swinish measle[1]—
50   Though we are eaten up of lice and worms,
     And though continually we bear about us
     A rotten and dead body, we delight
     To hide it in rich tissue: all our fear,
     Nay, all our terror, is lest our physician

---

5. Lawyers (who wore a white coif or skullcap;
cf. line 4, above).
6. A progress was a formal royal journey of state.
7. Scraping ("careening") of an old, scaly ("morphewed") ship ("lady") to fit her for the ocean
("making her disembogue") again. All these metaphors are applied to the model ("plastic") of the
lady's condition as "rough-cast," a mixture of lime
and gravel, is troweled over a base.
8. Centuries of traditional invective about wom-
en's cosmetic practices lie behind this speech.

Freshly killed pigeons were applied to the feet of
plague victims to draw off the infection; fasting
was supposed to cause bad breath.
9. The physician grows rich on those who have
outworn their youth; every spring he buys a new
harness for his horse and every fall a new mistress
for himself.
1. "Wolf": cancer or lupus; "measle": an infection of swine, sometimes confused with human
measles.

55   Should put us in the ground to be made sweet—
      Your wife's gone to Rome: you two couple, and get you
      To the wells at Lucca to recover your aches.[2]
                                    [*Exeunt* CASTRUCCIO *and* OLD LADY.]
      I have other work on foot. I observe our duchess
      Is sick a-days: she pukes, her stomach seethes,
60   The fins of her eyelids look most teeming blue,
      She wanes i' th' cheek, and waxes fat i' th' flank,
      And contrary to our Italian fashion,
      Wears a loose-bodied gown: there's somewhat in 't.
      I have a trick may chance discover it,
65   A pretty one; I have bought some apricots,
      The first our spring yields.
                          [*Enter* ANTONIO *and* DELIO, *talking apart.*]
DELIO   And so long since married?
      You amaze me.
ANTONIO   Let me seal your lips forever:
      For, did I think that anything but th' air
      Could carry these words from you, I should wish
70   You had no breath at all.   [*turning to* BOSOLA]
      Now, sir, in your contemplation? You are studying to become a great
      wise fellow?
BOSOLA   Oh, sir, the opinion of wisdom is a foul tetter[3] that runs all over
      a man's body. If simplicity[4] direct us to have no evil, it directs us to a
75   happy being, for the subtlest folly proceeds from the subtlest wisdom.
      Let me be simply honest.
ANTONIO   I do understand your inside.
BOSOLA   Do you so?
ANTONIO   Because you would not seem to appear to th' world
      Puffed up with your preferment, you continue
80   This out-of-fashion melancholy. Leave it, leave it.
BOSOLA   Give me leave to be honest in any phrase, in any compliment what-
      soever. Shall I confess myself to you? I look no higher than I can reach:
      they are the gods that must ride on winged horses. A lawyer's mule of a
      slow pace will both suit my disposition and business; for, mark me, when a
85   man's mind rides faster than his horse can gallop, they quickly both tire.
ANTONIO   You would look up to heaven, but I think
      The devil, that rules i' th' air, stands in your light.
BOSOLA   Oh, sir, you are lord of the ascendant,[5] chief man with the duchess;
      a duke was your cousin-german removed.[6] Say you were lineally descended
90   from King Pepin,[7] or he himself, what of this? Search the heads of the
      greatest rivers in the world, you shall find them but bubbles of water. Some
      would think the souls of princes were brought forth by some more weighty
      cause than those of meaner persons: they are deceived, there's the same
      hand to them; the like passions sway them; the same reason that makes a

---

2. The wells at Lucca are the mineral springs at
nearby Montecatini, renowned as a place to "take
the cure." Aches are a symptom of syphilis.
3. Skin disease.
4. Foolishness.

5. In astrology, the predominating influence,
controlling destiny.
6. First cousin once removed.
7. Father of Charlemagne, hence source of a
great dynasty.

95   vicar go to law for a tithe-pig[8] and undo his neighbors, makes them spoil a
  whole province, and batter down goodly cities with the cannon.
    [*Enter* DUCHESS *and* LADIES.]
DUCHESS   Your arm, Antonio; do I not grow fat?
  I am exceeding short-winded. Bosola,
  I would have you, sir, provide for me a litter,
100   Such a one as the Duchess of Florence rode in.
BOSOLA   The duchess used one when she was great with child.
DUCHESS   I think she did. Come hither, mend my ruff;
  Here, when? Thou art such a tedious° lady, and   *clumsy*
  Thy breath smells of lemon peels;[9] would thou hadst done;
105   Shall I swoon under thy fingers? I am
  So troubled with the mother![1]
BOSOLA [*aside*]   I fear too much.
DUCHESS   I have heard you say that the French courtiers
  Wear their hats on 'fore the king.
ANTONIO   I have seen it.
DUCHESS   In the presence?
ANTONIO   Yes.
110 DUCHESS   Why should not we bring up that fashion? 'Tis
  Ceremony more than duty that consists
  In the removing of a piece of felt.
  Be you the example to the rest o' th' court;
  Put on your hat first.
ANTONIO   You must pardon me.
115   I have seen, in colder countries than in France,
  Nobles stand bare to th' prince, and the distinction
  Methought showed reverently.
BOSOLA   I have a present for your grace.
DUCHESS   For me, sir?
BOSOLA   Apricots, madam.
DUCHESS   O, sir, where are they?
  I have heard of none to-year.
120 BOSOLA [*aside*]   Good: her color rises.
DUCHESS   Indeed, I thank you: they are wondrous fair ones.
  What an unskillful fellow is our gardener!
  We shall have none this month.
BOSOLA   Will not your grace pare them?
125 DUCHESS   No. They taste of musk, methinks; indeed they do.
BOSOLA   I know not: yet I wish your grace had pared 'em.
DUCHESS   Why?
BOSOLA   I forgot to tell you, the knave gardener,
  Only to raise his profit by them the sooner,
  Did ripen them in horse dung.[2]
DUCHESS   O, you jest.
  You shall judge: pray taste one.

---

8. A parson was entitled to a tenth ("tithe") of his parishioners' annual profit and was often paid in crops or livestock, but was thought mean if he sued for a petty sum.

9. Lemon peels, chewed to sweeten the breath.
1. Heartburn, but with a second meaning not lost on Bosola.
2. Which grows warm as it decomposes.

130 ANTONIO   Indeed, madam,
    I do not love the fruit.
    DUCHESS   Sir, you are loath
    To rob us of our dainties: 'tis a delicate fruit;
    They say they are restorative.
    BOSOLA   'Tis a pretty art,
    This grafting.
    DUCHESS   'Tis so; a bettering of nature.
135 BOSOLA   To make a pippin grow upon a crab,°   *crab apple*
    A damson on a blackthorn. [*aside*] How greedily she eats them!
    A whirlwind strike off these bawd farthingales![3]
    For, but for that and the loose-bodied gown,
    I should have discovered apparently°   *certainly*
140   The young springal° cutting a caper in her belly.   *fellow*
    DUCHESS   I thank you, Bosola. They were right good ones,
    If they do not make me sick.
    ANTONIO   How now, madam?
    DUCHESS   This green fruit and my stomach are not friends;
    How they swell me!
    BOSOLA [*aside*]   Nay, you are too much swelled already.
    DUCHESS   Oh, I am in an extreme cold sweat!
145 BOSOLA   I am very sorry.
    DUCHESS   Lights to my chamber! O good Antonio,
    I fear I am undone!
    DELIO   Lights there, lights!
             [*Exeunt* DUCHESS *and* LADIES. *Exit, on the other side,* BOSOLA.]
    ANTONIO   O my most trusty Delio, we are lost!
    I fear she's fall'n in labor; and there's left
    No time for her remove.
150 DELIO   Have you prepared
    Those ladies to attend her? And procured
    That politic° safe conveyance for the midwife   *secret*
    Your duchess plotted?
    ANTONIO   I have.
    DELIO   Make use, then, of this forced occasion:
155   Give out that Bosola hath poisoned her
    With these apricots; that will give some color
    For her keeping close.
    ANTONIO   Fie, fie, the physicians
    Will then flock to her.
    DELIO   For that you may pretend
    She'll use some prepared antidote of her own,
160   Lest the physicians should re-poison her.
    ANTONIO   I am lost in amazement:° I know not what   *confusion*
    to think on 't.   [*Exeunt.*]

---

3. Early hoopskirts, capable of concealing the figure.

SCENE 2. *The scene continues.*

[*Enter* BOSOLA.]

BOSOLA So, so, there's no question but her tetchiness[1] and most vultur-
ous eating of the apricots are apparent signs of breeding.

[*Enter an* OLD LADY.]

Now?

OLD LADY I am in haste, sir.

5   BOSOLA There was a young waiting woman had a monstrous desire to see
the glasshouse[2]—

OLD LADY Nay, pray let me go.

BOSOLA And it was only to know what strange instrument it was should
swell up a glass to the fashion of a woman's belly.

10   OLD LADY I will hear no more of the glasshouse. You are still[3] abusing
women!

BOSOLA Who, I? No; only by the way now and then mention your frailties.
The orange tree bears ripe and green fruit and blossoms all together;
and some of you give entertainment for pure love, but more for more pre-

15   cious reward. The lusty spring smells well, but drooping autumn tastes
well. If we have the same golden showers that rained in the time of Jupiter the thunderer, you have the same Danaës still,[4] to hold up their laps
to receive them. Didst thou never study the mathematics?

OLD LADY What's that, sir?

20   BOSOLA Why, to know the trick how to make a many lines meet in one
center. Go, go, give your foster daughters good counsel: tell them that
the devil takes delight to hang at a woman's girdle, like a false rusty
watch, that she cannot discern how the time passes.   [*Exit* OLD LADY.]

[*Enter* ANTONIO, DELIO, RODERIGO, *and* GRISOLAN.]

ANTONIO Shut up the courtgates.

RODERIGO   Why, sir? What's the danger?

25   ANTONIO Shut up the posterns presently,[5] and call
All the officers o' th' court.

GRISOLAN   I shall instantly.   [*Exit.*]

ANTONIO Who keeps the key o' th' park gate?

RODERIGO   Forobosco.

ANTONIO Let him bring 't presently.

[*Reenter* GRISOLAN *with* SERVANTS.]

1 SERVANT O, gentlemen o' the court, the foulest treason!

30   BOSOLA [*aside*] If that these apricots should be poisoned now,
Without my knowledge!

1 SERVANT   There was taken even now
A Switzer° in the duchess' bedchamber—   *Swiss guard*

2 SERVANT   A Switzer?

1 SERVANT With a pistol in his great codpiece.[6]

BOSOLA   Ha, ha, ha!

2.2
1. Irritability.
2. Where bottles were blown, near the theater in
Blackfriars.
3. Always.

4. Jupiter's success in wooing Danaë in a shower
of gold traditionally illustrated female venality.
5. At once. "Posterns": outer gates.
6. An outsize flap worn on the front of men's
trunk hose.

1 SERVANT   The codpiece was the case for 't.

2 SERVANT   There was

35   A cunning traitor: who would have searched his codpiece?

1 SERVANT   True, if he had kept out of the ladies' chambers.
   And all the molds of his buttons were leaden bullets.

2 SERVANT   O wicked cannibal!
   A firelock° in 's codpiece!   *pistol*

1 SERVANT   'Twas a French plot,
   Upon my life.

40   2 SERVANT   To see what the devil can do!

ANTONIO   Are all the officers here?

SERVANTS   We are.

ANTONIO   Gentlemen,
   We have lost much plate[7] you know, and but this evening
   Jewels, to the value of four thousand ducats,
   Are missing in the duchess' cabinet.
   Are the gates shut?

SERVANT   Yes.

45   ANTONIO   'Tis the duchess' pleasure
   Each officer be locked into his chamber
   Till the sun-rising; and to send the keys
   Of all their chests and of their outward doors
   Into her bedchamber. She is very sick.

RODERIGO   At her pleasure.

50   ANTONIO   She entreats you take 't not ill:
   The innocent shall be the more approved by it.

BOSOLA   Gentlemen o' th' wood-yard, where's your Switzer now?

1 SERVANT   By this hand, 'twas credibly reported by one o' th' black guard.[8]

                       [*Exeunt all except* ANTONIO *and* DELIO.]

DELIO   How fares it with the duchess?

ANTONIO   She's exposed

55   Unto the worst of torture, pain, and fear.

DELIO   Speak to her all happy comfort.

ANTONIO   How I do play the fool with mine own danger!
   You are this night, dear friend, to post to Rome;
   My life lies in your service.

DELIO   Do not doubt me.

60   ANTONIO   Oh, 'tis far from me, and yet fear presents me
   Somewhat that looks like danger.

DELIO   Believe it,
   'Tis but the shadow of your fear, no more;
   How superstitiously we mind our evils!
   The throwing down salt, or crossing of a hare,

65   Bleeding at nose, the stumbling of a horse,
   Or singing of a cricket, are of power
   To daunt whole man° in us. Sir, fare you well: *all courage*
   I wish you all the joys of a blessed father:

---

7. Massive gold and silver dishes, a frequent
form of wealth in the days before banks.

8. Kitchen scullions. The "wood-yard" is a source
of firewood for kitchen and fireplaces.

And, for my faith, lay this unto your breast,
70 Old friends, like old swords, still are trusted best.   [*Exit.*]
        [*Enter* CARIOLA.]
CARIOLA   Sir, you are the happy father of a son:
    Your wife commends him to you.
ANTONIO   Blessed comfort!
    For heaven's sake tend her well: I'll presently
    Go set a figure for 's nativity.[9]   [*Exeunt.*]

SCENE 3. *The scene continues.*

        [*Enter* BOSOLA, *with a dark lantern.*]
BOSOLA   Sure I did hear a woman shriek: list, ha!
    And the sound came, if I received it right,
    From the duchess' lodgings. There's some stratagem
    In the confining all our courtiers
5   To their several° wards: I must have part of it;   separate
    My intelligence will freeze else.[1] List, again!
    It may be 'twas the melancholy bird,
    Best friend of silence and of solitariness,
    The owl, that screamed so. Ha! Antonio?
        [*Enter* ANTONIO *with a candle, his sword drawn.*]
10 ANTONIO   I heard some noise. Who's there? What art thou? Speak.
BOSOLA   Antonio? Put not your face nor body
    To such a forced expression of fear.
    I am Bosola, your friend.
ANTONIO   Bosola!
    [*aside*] This mole does undermine me.—Heard you not
    A noise even now?
BOSOLA   From whence?
15 ANTONIO   From the duchess' lodging.
BOSOLA   Not I. Did you?
ANTONIO   I did, or else I dreamed.
BOSOLA   Let's walk towards it.
ANTONIO   No, it may be 'twas
    But the rising of the wind.
BOSOLA   Very likely.
    Methinks 'tis very cold, and yet you sweat:
    You look wildly.
20 ANTONIO   I have been setting a figure[2]
    For the duchess' jewels.
BOSOLA   Ah, and how falls your question?
    Do you find it radical?°   significant
ANTONIO   What's that to you?
    'Tis rather to be questioned what design,
    When all men were commanded to their lodgings,
    Makes you a nightwalker.

9. Cast his horoscope right away.   2. Establishing the loss involved. But Bosola
2.3   takes the expression astrologically, as if Antonio
1. All my news will be cold otherwise.   were casting a horoscope.

25 BOSOLA   In sooth, I'll tell you:
  Now all the court's asleep, I thought the devil
  Had least to do here; I came to say my prayers;
  And if it do offend you I do so,
  You are a fine courtier.
  ANTONIO [aside]   This fellow will undo me.
30 You gave the duchess apricots today:
  Pray heaven they were not poisoned!
  BOSOLA   Poisoned? A Spanish fig[3]
  For the imputation!
  ANTONIO   Traitors are ever confident
  Till they are discovered. There were jewels stolen, too;
  In my conceit,° none are to be suspected   opinion
  More than yourself.
35 BOSOLA   You are a false steward.
  ANTONIO Saucy slave, I'll pull thee up by the roots.
  BOSOLA May be the ruin will crush you to pieces.
  ANTONIO You are an impudent snake indeed, sir:
  Are you scarce warm, and do you show your sting?
  You libel well, sir.
40 BOSOLA   No, sir: copy it out,
  And I will set my hand to 't.[4]
  ANTONIO [aside]   My nose bleeds.
  One that were superstitious would count
  This ominous, when it merely comes by chance:
  Two letters, that are wrought here for my name,[5]
45 Are drowned in blood!
  Mere accident.—For you, sir, I'll take order
  I' th' morn you shall be safe.° [aside] 'Tis that must color   under guard
  Her lying-in°—Sir, this door you pass not: giving birth
  I do not hold it fit that you come near
50 The duchess' lodgings, till you have quit° yourself.   cleared
  [aside] The great are like the base, nay, they are the same,
  When they seek shameful ways to avoid shame.   [Exit.]
  BOSOLA Antonio hereabout did drop a paper:
  Some of your help, false friend: [opening his lantern] Oh, here it is.
55 What's here? A child's nativity calculated?   [reads]
  "The duchess was delivered of a son, 'tween the hours twelve and one in
  the night, Anno Dom. 1504,"—that's this year—"decimo nono
  Decembris,"[6]—that's this night—"taken according to the meridian of
  Malfi"—that's our duchess: happy discovery! "The lord of the first house
60 being combust[7] in the ascendant, signifies short life; and Mars being in
  a human sign, joined to the tail of the Dragon, in the eighth house, doth
  threaten a violent death. Caetera non scrutantur."[8]
  Why, now 'tis most apparent: this precise° fellow   officious

---

3. An obscene gesture, which Bosola doubtless makes onstage.
4. Bosola denies the charge, not by denying malignancy, but by offering to publish it.
5. Embroidered on the handkerchief.
6. December 19.

7. Burnt up; i.e., the ruling planet is close to the sun.
8. "The rest is not examined"—i.e., the horoscope is incomplete. Mars and the Dragon are sinister signs, even separately; fatal together.

Is the duchess' bawd:° I have it to my wish!   *procurer*
65   This is a parcel of intelligency
Our courtiers were cased up for: it needs must follow
That I must be committed on pretense
Of poisoning her; which I'll endure, and laugh at.
If one could find the father now! But that
70   Time will discover. Old Castruccio
I' th' morning posts to Rome: by him I'll send
A letter that shall make her brothers' galls
O'erflow their livers. This was a thrifty° way.   *shrewd*
Though lust do mask in ne'er so strange disguise,
75   She's oft found witty, but is never wise.   [*Exit.*]

SCENE 4. *The palace of the* CARDINAL *at Rome.*

[*Enter* CARDINAL *and* JULIA.]

CARDINAL   Sit. Thou art my best of wishes. Prithee, tell me
What trick didst thou invent to come to Rome
Without thy husband.
JULIA   Why, my lord, I told him
I came to visit an old anchorite°   *hermit*
Here for devotion.
5   CARDINAL   Thou are a witty false one—
I mean, to him.
JULIA   You have prevailed with me
Beyond my strongest thoughts! I would not now
Find you inconstant.
CARDINAL   Do not put thyself
To such a voluntary torture, which proceeds
Out of your own guilt.
JULIA   How, my lord?
10   CARDINAL   You fear
My constancy, because you have approved°   *experienced*
Those giddy and wild turnings in yourself.
JULIA   Did you e'er find them?
CARDINAL   Sooth, generally for women;
A man might strive to make glass malleable,
Ere he should make them fixed.
15   JULIA   So, my lord.
CARDINAL   We had need go borrow that fantastic glass
Invented by Galileo the Florentine[1]
To view another spacious world i' th' moon,
And look to find a constant woman there.
JULIA   This is very well, my lord.
20   CARDINAL   Why do you weep?
Are tears your justification? The selfsame tears
Will fall into your husband's bosom, lady,

2.4
1. In 1504, Galileo's telescope was more than one hundred years in the future, but the reference was topical for Webster's audience.

With a loud protestation that you love him
Above the world. Come, I'll love you wisely,
25 That's jealously, since I am very certain
You cannot make me cuckold.

JULIA   I'll go home
To my husband.

CARDINAL   You may thank me, lady,
I have taken you off your melancholy perch,
Bore you upon my fist, and showed you game,
30 And let you fly at it.[2] I pray thee, kiss me.
When thou wast with thy husband, thou wast watched
Like a tame elephant: still you are to thank me:
Thou hadst only kisses from him and high feeding;
But what delight was that? 'Twas just like one
35 That hath a little fingering on the lute,
Yet cannot tune it: still you are to thank me.

JULIA   You told me of a piteous wound i' th' heart
And a sick liver, when you wooed me first,
And spake like one in physic.[3]   [*A knock is heard.*]

CARDINAL   Who's that?
40 Rest firm,° for my affection to thee,   *be assured*
Lightning moves slow to 't.°   *by comparison*
      [*Enter* SERVANT.]

SERVANT   Madam, a gentleman,
That's come post from Malfi, desires to see you.

CARDINAL   Let him enter. I'll withdraw.   [*Exit.*]

SERVANT   He says
Your husband, old Castruccio, is come to Rome,
45 Most pitifully tired with riding post.[4]   [*Exit.*]
      [*Enter* DELIO.]

JULIA   Signor Delio! [*aside*]—'tis one of my old suitors.

DELIO   I was bold to come and see you.

JULIA   Sir, you are welcome.

DELIO   Do you lie° here?   *lodge*

JULIA   Sure, your own experience
Will satisfy you no: our Roman prelates
Do not keep lodging for ladies.

50 DELIO   Very well.
I have brought you no commendations from your husband,
For I know none by him.

JULIA   I hear he's come to Rome.

DELIO   I never knew man and beast, of a horse and a knight,
So weary of each other: if he had had a good back,
55 He would have undertook to have borne his horse,
His breech was so pitifully sore.

JULIA   Your laughter
Is my pity.

---

2. The cardinal speaks of himself as a falconer training a bird (Julia).
3. Like a person under a doctor's care.

4. When riding post, one changed horses at regular intervals without stopping to rest oneself.

DELIO   Lady, I know not whether
You want money, but I have brought you some.

JULIA   From my husband?

DELIO   No, from mine own allowance.

60   JULIA   I must hear the condition, ere I be bound to take it.

DELIO   Look on 't, 'tis gold: hath it not a fine color?

JULIA   I have a bird more beautiful.

DELIO   Try the sound on 't.

JULIA   A lute string far exceeds it:
It hath no smell, like cassia or civet;

65   Nor is it physical,° though some fond° doctors   *medicinal / foolish*
Persuade us seethe 't in cullises:° I'll tell you,   *broth*
This is a creature bred by—
        [*Reenter* SERVANT.]

SERVANT   Your husband's come,
Hath delivered a letter to the Duke of Calabria
That, to my thinking, hath put him out of his wits.   [*Exit.*]

70   JULIA   Sir, you hear:
Pray, let me know your business and your suit
As briefly as can be.

DELIO   With good speed: I would wish you,
At such time as you are nonresident
With your husband, my mistress.

75   JULIA   Sir, I'll go ask my husband if I shall,
And straight return your answer.   [*Exit.*]

DELIO   Very fine!
Is this her wit, or honesty,° that speaks thus?   *chastity*
I heard one say the duke was highly moved
With a letter sent from Malfi. I do fear

80   Antonio is betrayed: how fearfully
Shows his ambition now! Unfortunate fortune!
They pass through whirlpools, and deep woes do shun,
Who the event weigh ere the action's done.[5]   [*Exit.*]

SCENE 5. *The scene continues.*

[*Enter* CARDINAL, *and* FERDINAND *with a letter.*]

FERDINAND   I have this night digged up a mandrake.[1]

CARDINAL   Say you?

FERDINAND   And I am grown mad with 't.

CARDINAL   What's the prodigy?° *fearful wonder*

FERDINAND   Read there—a sister damned: she's loose i' th' hilts;[2]
Grown a notorious strumpet.

CARDINAL   Speak lower.

FERDINAND   Lower?

5   Rogues do not whisper 't now, but seek to publish 't
(As servants do the bounty of their lords)

---

5. I.e., who judge of actions before seeing their final consequences.
2.5

1. A fabulous root, violently aphrodisiac but also deadly poison. Both aspects apply to Ferdinand.
2. I.e., promiscuous.

Aloud; and with a covetous searching eye,
To mark who note them. O, confusion seize her!
She hath had most cunning bawds to serve her turn,
10 And more secure conveyances for lust
Than towns of garrison for service.°   *receiving supplies*

CARDINAL   Is 't possible?
Can this be certain?

FERDINAND   Rhubarb, oh, for rhubarb
To purge this choler![3] Here's the cursèd day
To prompt my memory, and here 't shall stick
15 Till of her bleeding heart I make a sponge
To wipe it out.

CARDINAL   Why do you make yourself
So wild a tempest?

FERDINAND   Would I could be one,
That I might toss her palace 'bout her ears,
Root up her goodly forests, blast her meads,°   *meadows*
20 And lay her general territory as waste
As she hath done her honors.

CARDINAL   Shall our blood,
The royal blood of Aragon and Castile,
Be thus attainted?

FERDINAND   Apply desperate physic:°   *medicine*
We must not now use balsamum,° but fire,°   *balm / cautery*
25 The smarting cupping glass[4] for that's the mean
To purge infected blood, such blood as hers.
There is a kind of pity in mine eye,
I'll give it to my handkercher; and now 'tis here,
I'll bequeath this to her bastard.

CARDINAL   What to do?

30 FERDINAND   Why, to make soft lint for his mother's wounds,
When I have hewed her to pieces.

CARDINAL   Cursèd creature!
Unequal nature, to place women's hearts
So far upon the left side![5]

FERDINAND   Foolish men,
That e'er will trust their honor in a bark
35 Made of so slight weak bulrush as is woman,
Apt every minute to sink it!

CARDINAL   Thus ignorance, when it hath purchased honor,
It cannot wield it.

FERDINAND   Methinks I see her laughing—
Excellent hyena! Talk to me somewhat, quickly,
40 Or my imagination will carry me
To see her in the shameful act of sin.

CARDINAL   With whom?

FERDINAND   Haply° with some strong-thighed bargeman,   *perhaps*

---

3. Rhubarb, as a laxative, was thought curative
of the high pressures of hot rage.
4. By which people were bled.

5. The left is the sinister side, associated with
bad luck, deceit, and passion.

Or one o' th' wood-yard that can quoit the sledge°   *throw the hammer*
45 Or toss the bar,[6] or else some lovely squire
That carries coal up to her privy lodgings.
CARDINAL   You fly beyond your reason.
FERDINAND   Go to, mistress!
'Tis not your whore's milk that shall quench my wild fire,
But your whore's blood.
50 CARDINAL   How idly shows this rage, which carries you,
As men conveyed by witches through the air,
On violent whirlwinds! This intemperate noise
Fitly resembles deaf men's shrill discourse,
Who talk aloud,° thinking all other men   *loudly*
To have their imperfection.
55 FERDINAND   Have not you
My palsy?
CARDINAL   Yes, I can be angry, but
Without this rupture: there is not in nature
A thing that makes man so deformed, so beastly,
As doth intemperate anger. Chide yourself.
60 You have divers men who never yet expressed
Their strong desire of rest but by unrest,
By vexing of themselves. Come, put yourself
In tune.
FERDINAND   So; I will only study to seem
The thing I am not. I could kill her now,
65 In you, or in myself; for I do think
It is some sin in us heaven doth revenge
By her.
CARDINAL   Are you stark mad?
FERDINAND   I would have their bodies
Burnt in a coal pit with the ventage° stopped,   *chimney*
That their cursed smoke might not ascend to heaven;
70 Or dip the sheets they lie in in pitch or sulphur,
Wrap them in 't, and then light them like a match;
Or else to boil their bastard to a cullis,°   *broth*
And give 't his lecherous father to renew°   *repair*
The sin of his back.[7]
CARDINAL   I'll leave you.
FERDINAND   Nay, I have done.
75 I am confident, had I been damned in hell,
And should have heard of this, it would have put me
Into a cold sweat. In, in; I'll go sleep.
Till I know who leaps my sister, I'll not stir:
That known, I'll find scorpions to string my whips,[8]
80 And fix her in a general eclipse.   [*Exeunt.*]

---

6. Gross tests of strength.
7. As Atreus did to Thyestes in Greek legend. "The sin of his back": sexual capacity.
8. Tipping the thongs of a whip with "scorpions"

(tips of jagged steel or lead that sting and bite the flesh) is an old metaphor for aggravated punishment.

Act 3

SCENE 1. *Amalfi.*

[*Enter* ANTONIO *and* DELIO.]

ANTONIO   Our noble friend, my most belovèd Delio!
    Oh, you have been a stranger long at court;
    Came you along with the Lord Ferdinand?

DELIO   I did, sir. And how fares your noble duchess?

5 ANTONIO   Right fortunately well: she's an excellent
    Feeder of pedigrees; since you last saw her,
    She hath had two children more, a son and daughter.

DELIO   Methinks 'twas yesterday: let me but wink,
    And not behold your face, which to mine eye

10   Is somewhat leaner, verily I should dream
    It were within this half-hour.

ANTONIO   You have not been in law, friend Delio,
    Nor in prison, nor a suitor at the court,
    Nor begged the reversion of some great man's place,

15   Nor troubled with an old wife, which doth make
    Your time so insensibly° hasten.   *imperceptibly*

DELIO   Pray, sir, tell me,
    Hath not this news arrived yet to the ear
    Of the Lord Cardinal?

ANTONIO   I fear it hath:
    The Lord Ferdinand, that's newly come to court,
    Doth bear himself right dangerously.

20 DELIO   Pray, why?

ANTONIO   He is so quiet that he seems to sleep
    The tempest out, as dormice do in winter.
    Those houses that are haunted are most still
    Till the devil be up.

DELIO   What say the common people?

25 ANTONIO   The common rabble do directly say
    She is a strumpet.

DELIO   And your graver heads,
    Which would be politic,° what censure° they?   *statesmanlike / opine*

ANTONIO   They do observe I grow to infinite purchase
    The left-hand way,[1] and all suppose the duchess

30   Would amend it, if she could; for, say they,
    Great princes, though they grudge their officers
    Should have such large and unconfinèd means
    To get wealth under them, will not complain,
    Lest thereby they should make them odious

35   Unto the people; for other obligation
    Of love or marriage between her and me
    They never dream of.

3.1
1. I.e., they think I am getting rich dishonestly.

DELIO   The Lord Ferdinand
   Is going to bed.
      [Enter DUCHESS, FERDINAND, *and* BOSOLA.]
FERDINAND   I'll instantly to bed,
   For I am weary.—I am to bespeak
   A husband for you.
40 DUCHESS   For me, sir? Pray, who is 't?
   FERDINAND   The great Count Malateste.
   DUCHESS   Fie upon him!
   A count? He's a mere stick of sugar candy;
   You may look quite through him. When I choose
   A husband, I will marry for your honor.
45 FERDINAND   You shall do well in 't.—How is 't, worthy Antonio?
   DUCHESS   But, sir, I am to have private conference with you
   About a scandalous report is spread
   Touching mine honor.
   FERDINAND   Let me be ever deaf to 't:
   One of Pasquil's paper bullets,[2] court-calumny,
50 A pestilent air, which princes' palaces
   Are seldom purged of. Yet, say that it were true,
   I pour it in your bosom, my fixed love
   Would strongly excuse, extenuate, nay, deny
   Faults, were they apparent in you. Go, be safe
   In your own innocency.
55 DUCHESS *[aside]*   O blessèd comfort!
   This deadly air is purged.
           [Exeunt DUCHESS, ANTONIO, *and* DELIO.]
   FERDINAND   Her guilt treads on
   Hot-burning coulters.[3] Now, Bosola,
   How thrives our intelligence?°   *detective work*
   BOSOLA   Sir, uncertainly:
   'Tis rumored she hath had three bastards, but
   By whom, we may go read i' th' stars.
60 FERDINAND   Why, some
   Hold opinion all things are written there.
   BOSOLA   Yes, if we could find spectacles to read them.
   I do suspect there hath been some sorcery
   Used on the duchess.
   FERDINAND   Sorcery? To what purpose?
65 BOSOLA   To make her dote on some desertless fellow
   She shames to acknowledge.
   FERDINAND   Can your faith give way
   To think there's power in potions or in charms,
   To make us love whether we will or no?
   BOSOLA   Most certainly.
70 FERDINAND   Away! These are mere gulleries,° horrid things,   *deceits*

---

2. Anonymous satires were traditionally pasted on the statue of Pasquillo, or Pasquino, near Piazza Navona in Rome, and attributed to his authorship.

3. Medieval chastity inquests customarily required the questioned lady to walk barefoot over red-hot plowshares ("coulters").

Invented by some cheating mountebanks[4]
To abuse us. Do you think that herbs or charms
Can force the will? Some trials have been made
In this foolish practice, but the ingredients
75 Were lenitive° poisons, such as are of force   slow-working
To make the patient mad; and straight the witch
Swears by equivocation they are in love.
The witchcraft lies in her rank° blood. This night   wanton
I will force confession from her. You told me
80 You had got, within these two days, a false° key   unauthorized
Into her bedchamber.
BOSOLA   I have.
FERDINAND   As I would wish.
BOSOLA   What do you intend to do?
FERDINAND   Can you guess?
BOSOLA   No.
FERDINAND   Do not ask, then:
He that can compass° me, and know my drifts,°   comprehend / purposes
85 May say he hath put a girdle 'bout the world,
And sounded all her quicksands.
BOSOLA   I do not
Think so.
FERDINAND   What do you think, then, pray?
BOSOLA   That you
Are your own chronicle too much, and grossly
Flatter yourself.
FERDINAND   Give me thy hand; I thank thee:
90 I ne'er gave pension but to flatterers,
Till I entertained° thee. Farewell.   employed
That friend a great man's ruin strongly checks,
Who rails into his belief all his defects.   [Exeunt.]

SCENE 2. *The bedchamber of the* DUCHESS.

[*Enter* DUCHESS, ANTONIO, *and* CARIOLA.]
DUCHESS   Bring me the casket hither, and the glass.
You get no lodging here tonight, my lord.
ANTONIO   Indeed, I must persuade one.
DUCHESS   Very good:
I hope in time 'twill grow into a custom,
5 That noblemen shall come with cap and knee
To purchase a night's lodging of their wives.
ANTONIO   I must lie here.
DUCHESS   Must! You are a lord of misrule.[1]
ANTONIO   Indeed, my rule is only in the night.
DUCHESS   To what use will you put me?
ANTONIO   We'll sleep together.
10 DUCHESS   Alas, what pleasure can two lovers find in sleep?

---

4. A mixture of street entertainer and patent
medicine salesman.

3.2
1. The mock-monarch of a carnival festival.

CARIOLA   My lord, I lie with her often, and I know
    She'll much disquiet you.
ANTONIO   See, you are complained of.
CARIOLA   For she's the sprawling'st bedfellow.
ANTONIO   I shall like her
    The better for that.
CARIOLA   Sir, shall I ask you a question?
ANTONIO   I pray thee, Cariola.
15 CARIOLA   Wherefore still,° when you lie   *always*
    with my lady,
    Do you rise so early?
ANTONIO   Laboring men
    Count the clock oftenest, Cariola,
    Are glad when their task's ended.
DUCHESS   I'll stop your mouth.   [*Kisses him.*]
ANTONIO   Nay, that's but one; Venus had two soft doves
20 To draw her chariot; I must have another—   [*She kisses him again.*]
    When wilt thou marry, Cariola?
CARIOLA   Never, my lord.
ANTONIO   Oh, fie upon this single life! Forgo it.
    We read how Daphne, for her peevish flight,
    Became a fruitless bay tree; Syrinx turned
25 To the pale empty reed; Anaxarete
    Was frozen into marble: whereas those
    Which married, or proved kind unto their friends,
    Were by a gracious influence trans-shaped
    Into the olive, pomegranate, mulberry,
30 Became flowers, precious stones, or eminent stars.[2]
CARIOLA   This is a vain poetry, but I pray you tell me,
    If there were proposed me, wisdom, riches, and beauty,
    In three several young men, which should I choose?
ANTONIO   'Tis a hard question: this was Paris' case,
35 And he was blind in 't, and there was great cause;
    For how was 't possible he could judge right,
    Having three amorous goddesses in view,
    And they stark naked? 'Twas a motion[3]
    Were able to benight the apprehension
40 Of the severest counselor of Europe.
    Now I look on both your faces so well formed,
    It puts me in mind of a question I would ask.
CARIOLA   What is 't?
ANTONIO   I do wonder why hard-favored ladies,
    For the most part, keep worse-favored waiting women
45 To attend them, and cannot endure fair ones.

---

2. The olive was created by Athena; the mulberry
gained its color from the blood of Pyramus and
Thisbe; the pomegranate seems to have no particular mythological origin. Most of the other stories
of ladies being transformed for complying, or not
complying, with the solicitations of a god are from
Ovid's *Metamorphoses*.
3. Spectacle. Paris had to choose among Hera,
Athena, and Aphrodite, goddesses of regal power,
wisdom, and love; his selecting the third led to the
Trojan War.

DUCHESS   Oh, that's soon answered.
Did you ever in your life know an ill painter
Desire to have his dwelling next door to the shop
Of an excellent picture-maker? 'Twould disgrace
50   His face-making, and undo him. I prithee,
When were we so merry?—My hair tangles.
ANTONIO   Pray thee, Cariola, let's steal forth the room,
And let her talk to herself: I have divers times
Served her the like, when she hath chafed extremely.
55   I love to see her angry. Softly, Cariola.   [*Exeunt* ANTONIO *and* CARIOLA.]
DUCHESS   Doth not the color of my hair 'gin to change?
When I wax gray, I shall have all the court
Powder their hair with arras,[4] to be like me.
You have cause to love me; I entered you into my heart
60   Before you would vouchsafe to call for the keys.
        [*Enter* FERDINAND *behind.*]
We shall one day have my brothers take you napping;
Methinks his presence, being now in court,
Should make you keep your own bed; but you'll say
Love mixed with fear is sweetest. I'll assure you,
65   You shall get no more children till my brothers
Consent to be your gossips.[5] Have you lost your tongue?
                        [*She turns and sees* FERDINAND.]
'Tis welcome:
For know, whether I am doomed to live or die,
I can do both like a prince.
FERDINAND   Die, then, quickly!   [*Giving her a poniard.*]
70   Virtue, where art thou hid? What hideous thing
Is it that doth eclipse thee?
DUCHESS   Pray, sir, hear me.
FERDINAND   Or is it true thou art but a bare name,
And no essential° thing?   *actual*
DUCHESS   Sir—
FERDINAND   Do not speak.
DUCHESS   No, sir: I will plant my soul in mine ears, to hear you.
75   FERDINAND   O most imperfect light of human reason,
That mak'st us so unhappy to foresee
What we can least prevent! Pursue thy wishes,
And glory in them: there's in shame no comfort
But to be past all bounds and sense of shame.
DUCHESS   I pray, sir, hear me. I am married.
80   FERDINAND   So!
DUCHESS   Haply,° not to your liking: but for that,   *perhaps*
Alas, your shears do come untimely now
To clip the bird's wings that's already flown!
Will you see my husband?

4. Orris root, used in powdered form to make   5. Sponsors in baptism.
hair artificially gray.

FERDINAND   Yes, if I could change
Eyes with a basilisk.[6]

85 DUCHESS   Sure, you came hither
By his confederacy.

FERDINAND   The howling of a wolf
Is music to thee, screech owl: prithee, peace.
Whate'er thou art that hast enjoyed my sister,
For I am sure thou hear'st me, for thine own sake

90 Let me not know thee. I came hither prepared
To work thy discovery; yet am now persuaded
It would beget such violent effects
As would damn us both. I would not for ten millions
I had beheld thee: therefore use all means

95 I never may have knowledge of thy name;
Enjoy thy lust still, and a wretched life,
On that condition. And for thee, vile woman,
If thou do wish thy lecher may grow old
In thy embracements, I would have thee build

100 Such a room for him as our anchorites
To holier use inhabit. Let not the sun
Shine on him till he's dead; let dogs and monkeys
Only converse with him, and such dumb things
To whom nature denies use to sound his name;

105 Do not keep a paraquito,° lest she learn it;   *parrot*
If thou do love him, cut out thine own tongue,
Lest it bewray° him.   *betray*

DUCHESS   Why might not I marry?
I have not gone about in this to create
Any new world or custom.

FERDINAND   Thou art undone;

110 And thou hast ta'en that massy sheet of lead
That hid thy husband's bones, and folded it
About my heart.

DUCHESS   Mine bleeds for 't.

FERDINAND   Thine? Thy heart?
What should I name 't unless a hollow bullet
Filled with unquenchable wildfire?

DUCHESS   You are in this

115 Too strict, and were you not my princely brother,
I would say, too willful. My reputation
Is safe.

FERDINAND   Dost thou know what reputation is?
I'll tell thee—to small purpose, since the instruction
Comes now too late.

120 Upon a time, Reputation, Love, and Death
Would travel o'er the world; and it was concluded
That they should part, and take three several ways.
Death told them, they should find him in great battles,

---

6. Monster that was fabled to kill with a glance.

Or cities plagued with plagues. Love gives them counsel
125 To inquire for him 'mongst unambitious shepherds,
Where dowries were not talked of, and sometimes
'Mongst quiet kindred that had nothing left
By their dead parents. "Stay," quoth Reputation,
"Do not forsake me; for it is my nature,
130 If once I part from any man I meet,
I am never found again." And so for you:
You have shook hands° with Reputation,   *parted*
And made him invisible. So, fare you well.
I will never see you more.
DUCHESS   Why should only I,
135 Of all the other princes of the world,
Be cased up, like a holy relic? I have youth
And a little beauty.
FERDINAND   So you have some virgins
That are witches. I will never see thee more.   [*Exit.*]
     [*Enter* ANTONIO *with a pistol, and* CARIOLA.]
DUCHESS   You saw this apparition?
ANTONIO   Yes. We are
140 Betrayed. How came he hither? I should turn
This to thee, for that.   [*Pointing the pistol at* CARIOLA.]
CARIOLA   Pray, sir, do; and when
That you have cleft my heart, you shall read there
Mine innocence.
DUCHESS   That gallery gave him entrance.
ANTONIO   I would this terrible thing would come again,
145 That, standing on my guard, I might relate
My warrantable[7] love.   [*She shows the poniard.*]
          Ha! What means this?
DUCHESS   He left this with me.
ANTONIO   And it seems did wish
You would use it on yourself.
DUCHESS   His action seemed
To intend so much.
ANTONIO   This hath a handle to 't
150 As well as a point: turn it towards him, and
So fasten the keen edge in his rank gall.   [*Knocking within.*]
How now! Who knocks? More earthquakes?
DUCHESS   I stand
As if a mine beneath my feet were ready
To be blown up.
CARIOLA   'Tis Bosola.
DUCHESS   Away!
155 O misery! Methinks unjust actions
Should wear these masks and curtains, and not we.
You must instantly part hence: I have fashioned it already.
            [*Exit* ANTONIO.]

7. Legitimate, defensible.

[*Enter* BOSOLA.]

BOSOLA The duke your brother is ta'en up in a whirlwind,
Hath took horse, and 's rid post to Rome.

DUCHESS   So late?

160 BOSOLA He told me, as he mounted into th' saddle,
You were undone.

DUCHESS   Indeed, I am very near it.

BOSOLA What's the matter?

DUCHESS Antonio, the master of our household,
Hath dealt so falsely with me in 's accounts:

165 My brother stood engaged with me for money
Ta'en up of certain Neapolitan Jews,
And Antonio lets the bonds be forfeit.[8]

BOSOLA Strange!—[*aside*] This is cunning.

DUCHESS   And hereupon
My brother's bills at Naples are protested
Against.[9]—Call up our officers.

170 BOSOLA   I shall.   [*Exit.*]

    [*Reenter* ANTONIO.]

DUCHESS The place that you must fly to is Ancona:[1]
Hire a house there; I'll send after you
My treasure and my jewels. Our weak safety
Runs upon enginous wheels: short syllables

175 Must stand for periods.[2] I must now accuse you
Of such a feignèd crime as Tasso calls
Magnanima menzogna, a noble lie,
'Cause it must shield our honors. Hark! They are coming.

    [*Reenter* BOSOLA *and* OFFICERS.]

ANTONIO Will your grace hear me?

180 DUCHESS I have got well by you; you have yielded me
A million of loss: I am like to inherit
The people's curses for your stewardship.
You had the trick in audit time to be sick,
Till I had signed your *quietus;*° and that cured you   receipt

185 Without help of a doctor.—Gentlemen,
I would have this man be an example to you all;
So shall you hold my favor; I pray, let him;°   release him
For he's done that, alas, you would not think of,
And, because I intend to be rid of him,

190 I mean not to publish. [*to* ANTONIO] Use your fortune elsewhere.

ANTONIO I am strongly armed to brook my overthrow;
As commonly men bear with a hard year,
I will not blame the cause on 't; but do think
The necessity of my malevolent star

---

8. I.e., my brother stood security for some money
I borrowed from Neapolitan moneylenders; now
Antonio has let them call on the duke for payment.
9. I.e., Duke Ferdinand's checks have bounced.
1. On the Adriatic coast of Italy, across the peninsula from Amalfi and well to the north.

2. Full sentences. "Enginous": delicately balanced, as in clockwork. The allusion to Tasso
(next line) is literally accurate (*Jerusalem Delivered* 2.22) but anachronistic, since Tasso's poem
was not published until 1574.

195 Procures this, not her humor. Oh, the inconstant
And rotten ground of service! You may see,
'Tis even like him that in a winter night
Takes a long slumber o'er a dying fire,
As loath to part from 't; yet parts thence as cold
200 As when he first sat down.

DUCHESS   We do confiscate,
Towards the satisfying of your accounts,
All that you have.

ANTONIO   I am yours, and 'tis very fit
All mine should be so.

DUCHESS   So, sir, you have your pass.°   passport

ANTONIO   You may see, gentlemen, what 'tis to serve
205 A prince with body and soul.   [Exit.]

BOSOLA   Here's an example for extortion: what moisture is drawn out of the
sea, when foul weather comes, pours down, and runs into the sea again.

DUCHESS   I would know what are your opinions of this Antonio.

SECOND OFFICER   He could not abide to see a pig's head gaping: I thought
210 your grace would find him a Jew.[3]

THIRD OFFICER   I would you had been his officer, for your own sake.

FOURTH OFFICER   You would have had more money.

FIRST OFFICER   He stopped his ears with black wool, and to those came to
him for money said he was thick of hearing.

215 SECOND OFFICER   Some said he was an hermaphrodite, for he could not
abide a woman.

FOURTH OFFICER   How scurvy proud he would look when the treasury was
full! Well, let him go!

FIRST OFFICER   Yes, and the chippings of the buttery fly after him, to scour
220 his gold chain![4]

DUCHESS   Leave us. [Exeunt OFFICERS.] What do you think of these?

BOSOLA   That these are rogues that in 's prosperity, but to have waited on his
fortune, could have wished his dirty stirrup riveted through their noses,
and followed after 's mule, like a bear in a ring; would have prostituted their
225 daughters to his lust; made their firstborn intelligencers;[5] thought none
happy but such as were born under his blessed planet, and wore his livery:
and do these lice drop off now? Well, never look to have the like again:[6]
he hath left a sort of flattering rogues behind him; their doom must follow. Princes pay flatterers in their own money: flatterers dissemble their
230 vices, and they dissemble their lies; that's justice. Alas, poor gentleman!

DUCHESS   Poor? He hath amply filled his coffers.

BOSOLA   Sure, he was too honest. Pluto, the god of riches, when he 's sent
by Jupiter to any man, he goes limping, to signify that wealth that comes
on God's name comes slowly; but when he's sent on the devil's errand, he
235 rides post and comes in by scuttles. Let me show you what a most unval-
ued[7] jewel you have in a wanton humor thrown away, to bless the man

---

3. Jews were identified by their antipathy to pork,
but the assumptions here are deliberately ridiculous.
4. A gold chain was the steward's traditional
badge of office. Bread crumbs (the "chippings of

the buttery") were used to polish gold and silver
plate.
5. Spies.
6. I.e., a servant as good as he was.
7. Invaluable. "By scuttles": in haste.

shall[8] find him. He was an excellent courtier and most faithful; a soldier
that thought it as beastly to know his own value too little as devilish to
acknowledge it too much. Both his virtue and form deserved a far better
fortune: his discourse rather delighted to judge itself than show itself; his
breast was filled with all perfection, and yet it seemed a private whispering-
room, it made so little noise of 't.

DUCHESS But he was basely descended.

BOSOLA Will you make yourself a mercenary herald, rather to examine
men's pedigrees than virtues? You shall want[9] him: for know, an honest
statesman to a prince is like a cedar planted by a spring; the spring bathes
the tree's root, the grateful tree rewards it with his shadow: you have not
done so. I would sooner swim to the Bermoothes[1] on two politicians' rotten bladders, tied together with an intelligencer's heartstring, than depend
on so changeable a prince's favor. Fare thee well, Antonio! Since the malice of the world would needs down with thee, it cannot be said yet that any
ill happened unto thee, considering thy fall was accompanied with virtue.

DUCHESS Oh, you render me excellent music!

BOSOLA   Say you?

DUCHESS This good one that you speak of is my husband.

BOSOLA Do I not dream? Can this ambitious age
Have so much goodness in 't as to prefer
A man merely for worth, without these shadows
Of wealth and painted honors? Possible?

DUCHESS I have had three children by him.

BOSOLA   Fortunate lady!
For you have made your private nuptial bed
The humble and fair seminary° of peace.   seedbed
No question but many an unbeneficed scholar[2]
Shall pray for you for this deed, and rejoice
That some preferment in the world can yet
Arise from merit. The virgins of your land
That have no dowries shall hope your example
Will raise them to rich husbands. Should you want
Soldiers, 'twould make the very Turks and Moors
Turn Christians, and serve you for this act.
Last, the neglected poets of your time,
In honor of this trophy of a man,
Raised by that curious° engine, your white hand,   exquisite
Shall thank you, in your grave, for 't; and make that
More reverend than all the cabinets
Of living princes.[3] For Antonio,
His fame shall likewise flow from many a pen,
When heralds shall want coats to sell to men.[4]

8. Who shall.
9. Miss.
1. The Bermudas, unknown at the time of the
action, but very topical a hundred years later,
when the play was written.
2. A scholar without an official appointment.

3. She will be more honored in her grave than
living princes in their courts. "Cabinets": council
chambers.
4. The Heralds' College (an English royal corporation) carried on a brisk trade in coats of arms.

DUCHESS As I taste comfort in this friendly speech,
  So would I find concealment.
280 BOSOLA Oh, the secret of my prince,
  Which I will wear on th' inside of my heart!
DUCHESS You shall take charge of all my coin and jewels,
  And follow him; for he retires himself
  To Ancona.
BOSOLA   So.
DUCHESS   Whither, within few days,
  I mean to follow thee.
285 BOSOLA   Let me think:
  I would wish your grace to feign a pilgrimage
  To our Lady of Loreto,[5] scarce seven leagues
  From fair Ancona; so may you depart
  Your country with more honor, and your flight
290   Will seem a princely progress,° retaining   *state journey*
  Your usual train about you.
DUCHESS   Sir, your direction
  Shall lead me by the hand.
CARIOLA   In my opinion,
  She were better progress to the baths at Lucca,
  Or go visit the Spa in Germany;
295   For, if you will believe me, I do not like
  This jesting with religion, this feigned
  Pilgrimage.
DUCHESS   Thou art a superstitious fool.
  Prepare us instantly for our departure.
  Past sorrows, let us moderately lament them;
300   For those to come, seek wisely to prevent them.
                          [Exit DUCHESS, with CARIOLA.]
BOSOLA A politician° is the devil's quilted anvil;   *crafty intriguer*
  He fashions all sins on him, and the blows
  Are never heard: he may work in a lady's chamber,
  As here for proof. What rests° but I reveal   *remains*
305   All to my lord? Oh, this base quality
  Of intelligencer! Why, every quality° i' th' world   *profession*
  Prefers° but gain or commendation: *offers*
  Now for this act I am certain to be raised,
  And men that paint weeds to the life are praised.   *[Exit.]*

SCENE 3. *Rome.*

[*Enter* CARDINAL, FERDINAND, MALATESTE, PESCARA, SILVIO, DELIO.]
CARDINAL Must we turn soldier, then?
MALATESTE   The Emperor,[1]
  Hearing your worth that way, ere you attained
  This reverend garment, joins you in commission

---

5. The shrine of the Virgin at Loreto was famous throughout Europe.

3.3
1. The Spanish emperor, Charles V.

With the right fortunate soldier the Marquis of Pescara,
And the famous Lannoy.

5 CARDINAL He that had the honor
Of taking the French king prisoner?[2]
MALATESTE The same.
Here's a plot drawn for a new fortification
At Naples. [*They talk apart.*]
FERDINAND This great Count Malateste, I perceive,
Hath got employment?
DELIO No employment, my lord;
10 A marginal note in the muster book, that he is
A voluntary lord.
FERDINAND He's no soldier?
DELIO He has worn gunpowder in 's hollow tooth for the toothache.[3]
SILVIO He comes to the leaguer° with a full intent   *siege*
To eat fresh beef and garlic, means to stay
15 Till the scent be gone, and straight return to court.
DELIO He hath read all the late service[4] as the city chronicle relates it,
and keeps two painters going, only to express battles in model.
SILVIO Then he'll fight by the book.
DELIO By the almanac, I think, to choose good days and shun the critical.
20 That's his mistress' scarf.
SILVIO Yes, he protests he would do much for that taffeta.
DELIO I think he would run away from a battle, to save it from taking[5]
prisoner.
SILVIO He is horribly afraid gunpowder will spoil the perfume on 't.
25 DELIO I saw a Dutchman break his pate once for calling him pot-gun;[6]
he made his head have a bore in 't like a musket.
SILVIO I would he had made a touchhole to 't. He is indeed a guarded
sumpter cloth,[7] only for the remove of the court.
[*Enter* BOSOLA *and speaks to* FERDINAND *and the* CARDINAL.]
PESCARA Bosola arrived? What should be the business?
30 Some falling out amongst the cardinals.
These factions amongst great men, they are like
Foxes; when their heads are divided,
They carry fire in their tails, and all the country
About them goes to wrack for 't.[8]
SILVIO What's that Bosola?
35 DELIO I knew him in Padua—a fantastical scholar, like such who study
to know how many knots were in Hercules' club, of what color Achilles'
beard was, or whether Hector were not troubled with the toothache.
He hath studied himself half blear-eyed to know the true symmetry of

---

2. Charles de Lannoy, Belgian by origin, did indeed capture Francis I at Pavia in 1525, about two decades after the date of the play's supposed action. "Pescara": also a commander at Pavia.
3. Saltpeter was sometimes used to relieve a toothache. "Leaguer" (next line): gathering of the armies.
4. Recent military operations.
5. Being taken.

6. Popgun.
7. Decorated saddlecloth used only when the court is changing its residence; i.e., he's only for show. "Touchhole": where the match was applied to set off a cannon.
8. Samson once tied some foxes together by the tail and set them afire to burn down the fields of the Philistines (Judges 15).

Caesar's nose by a shoeing-horn; and this he did to gain the name of a
40   speculative[9] man.
PESCARA   Mark Prince Ferdinand:
  A very salamander lives in 's eye,
  To mock the eager violence of fire.[1]
SILVIO   That Cardinal hath made more bad faces with his oppression
45   than ever Michelangelo[2] made good ones: he lifts up 's nose, like a foul
  porpoise before a storm.
PESCARA   The Lord Ferdinand laughs.
DELIO   Like a deadly cannon that lightens ere it smokes.
PESCARA   These are your true pangs of death,
50   The pangs of life, that struggle with great statesmen.
DELIO   In such a deformed silence witches whisper
  Their charms.
CARDINAL   Doth she make religion her riding hood
  To keep her from the sun and tempest?
FERDINAND   That,
  That damns her. Methinks her fault and beauty,
55   Blended together, show like leprosy,
  The whiter, the fouler. I make it a question
  Whether her beggarly brats were ever christened.
CARDINAL   I will instantly solicit the state of Ancona
  To have them banished.
FERDINAND   You are for Loreto?
60   I shall not be at your ceremony; fare you well.
  Write to the Duke of Malfi, my young nephew
  She had by her first husband, and acquaint him
  With 's mother's honesty.
BOSOLA   I will.
FERDINAND   Antonio!
  A slave that only smelled of ink and counters,
65   And never in 's life looked like a gentleman,
  But in the audit time. Go, go presently,°   *at once*
  Draw me out an hundred and fifty of our horse,°   *cavalry*
  And meet me at the fort-bridge.[3]   [*Exeunt.*]

SCENE 4. *The shrine of Our Lady of Loreto.*

[*Enter* TWO PILGRIMS.]
FIRST PILGRIM   I have not seen a goodlier shrine than this;
  Yet I have visited many.
SECOND PILGRIM   The Cardinal of Aragon
  Is this day to resign his cardinal's hat:
  His sister duchess likewise is arrived
5   To pay her vow of pilgrimage. I expect

9. Profound, given to abstruse thoughts. Intense
and especially fantastical scholarship was
thought to be a cause of melancholy—Bosola's
temperament—caused by an imbalance of black
bile.
1. The salamander was supposed to be so cold
and wet of constitution that it could live in fire.
2. Michelangelo Buonarroti (1475–1564), the
great Florentine painter and sculptor. Another
anachronism.
3. Drawbridge.

A noble ceremony.

FIRST PILGRIM   No question. They come.

> [*Here the ceremony of the* CARDINAL's *installment in the habit of a soldier: performed in delivering up his cross, hat, robes, and ring at the shrine, and investing him with sword, helmet, shield, and spurs; then* ANTONIO, *the* DUCHESS, *and their children, having presented themselves at the shrine, are, by a form of banishment in dumb show expressed towards them by the* CARDINAL *and the state of Ancona, banished: during all which ceremony, this ditty is sung, to very solemn music, by divers churchmen.*][1]

Arms and honors deck thy story,
To thy fame's eternal glory!
Adverse fortune ever fly thee;
10 No disastrous fate come nigh thee!

I alone will sing thy praises,
Whom to honor virtue raises;
And thy study, that divine is,
Bent to martial discipline is.
15 Lay aside all those robes lie by thee;
Crown thy arts with arms, they'll beautify thee.

O worthy of worthiest name, adorned in this manner,
Lead bravely thy forces on under war's warlike banner!
Oh, mayst thou prove fortunate in all martial courses!
20 Guide thou still by skill in arts and forces!
Victory attend thee nigh, whilst fame sings loud thy powers;
Triumphant conquest crown thy head, and blessings pour down showers!

> [*Exeunt all except the* TWO PILGRIMS.]

FIRST PILGRIM   Here's a strange turn of state! Who would have thought
So great a lady would have matched herself
25 Unto so mean a person? Yet the cardinal
Bears himself much too cruel.

SECOND PILGRIM   They are banished.

FIRST PILGRIM   But I would ask what power hath this state
Of Ancona to determine[2] of a free prince?

SECOND PILGRIM   They are a free state, sir, and her brother showed
30 How that the pope, fore-hearing of her looseness,
Hath seized into the protection of the church
The dukedom which she held as dowager.[3]

FIRST PILGRIM   But by what justice?

SECOND PILGRIM   Sure, I think by none,
Only her brother's instigation.

35 FIRST PILGRIM   What was it with such violence he took
Off from her finger?

SECOND PILGRIM   'Twas her wedding ring,

3.4
1. This song is not very suitable to the scene, and Webster, in the edition of 1623, denied writing it.

2. Pass judgment on.
3. As widow to her first husband, the Duke of Malfi.

Which he vowed shortly he would sacrifice
To his revenge.
FIRST PILGRIM   Alas, Antonio!
    If that a man be thrust into a well,
40   No matter who sets hands to 't, his own weight
    Will bring him sooner to th' bottom. Come, let's hence.
    Fortune makes this conclusion general,
    All things do help th' unhappy man to fall.   [*Exeunt.*]

SCENE 5. *Near Loreto.*

[*Enter* DUCHESS, ANTONIO, CHILDREN, CARIOLA, *and* SERVANTS.]
DUCHESS   Banished Ancona!
ANTONIO   Yes, you see what power
    Lightens° in great men's breath.   *flashes out*
DUCHESS   Is all our train
    Shrunk to this poor remainder?
ANTONIO   These poor men,
    Which have got little in your service, vow
5   To take your fortune, but your wiser buntings,[1]
    Now they are fledged, are gone.   They have done wisely.
DUCHESS
    This puts me in mind of death: physicians thus,
    With their hands full of money, use° to give o'er   *are accustomed*
    Their patients.
ANTONIO   Right° the fashion of the world: *exactly*
10   From decayed fortunes every flatterer shrinks;
    Men cease to build where the foundation sinks.
DUCHESS   I had a very strange dream tonight.°   *last night*
ANTONIO   What was 't?
DUCHESS   Methought I wore my coronet of state,
    And on a sudden all the diamonds
    Were changed to pearls.
15 ANTONIO   My interpretation
    Is, you'll weep shortly, for to me the pearls
    Do signify your tears.
DUCHESS   The birds that live
    I' th' field on the wild benefit of nature
    Live happier than we; for they may choose their mates,
20   And carol their sweet pleasures to the spring.
    [*Enter* BOSOLA *with a letter.*]
BOSOLA   You are happily o'erta'en.
DUCHESS   From my brother?
BOSOLA   Yes, from the Lord Ferdinand your brother
    All love and safety.
DUCHESS   Thou dost blanch° mischief,   *whitewash*
    Wouldst make it white. See, see, like to calm weather
25   At sea before a tempest, false hearts speak fair

3.5
1. Migratory birds. "Take": accept.

To those they intend most mischief. [*reads*]
"Send Antonio to me; I want his head in a business."
A politic equivocation!
He doth not want your counsel, but your head;
30 That is, he cannot sleep till you be dead.
And here's another pitfall that's strewed o'er
With roses: mark it, 'tis a cunning one:
"I stand engaged for your husband for several debts at Naples: let not
that trouble him; I had rather have his heart than his money."
And I believe so too.
35 BOSOLA What do you believe?
DUCHESS That he so much distrusts my husband's love,
He will by no means believe his heart is with him
Until he see it: the devil is not cunning
Enough to circumvent us in riddles.
40 BOSOLA Will you reject that noble and free league
Of amity and love which I present you?
DUCHESS Their league is like that of some politic° kings, *crafty*
Only to make themselves of strength and power
To be our after-ruin: tell them so.
BOSOLA And what from you?
45 ANTONIO Thus tell him: I will not come.
BOSOLA And what of this? [*Pointing to the letter.*]
ANTONIO My brothers have dispersed
Bloodhounds abroad; which till I hear are muzzled,
No truce, though hatched with ne'er such politic skill,
Is safe, that hangs upon our enemies' will.
I'll not come at° them. *to*
50 BOSOLA This proclaims your breeding:
Every small thing draws a base mind to fear,
As the adamant° draws iron. Fare you well, sir; *lodestone*
You shall shortly hear from 's. [*Exit.*]
DUCHESS I suspect some ambush;
Therefore, by all my love I do conjure you
55 To take your eldest son, and fly towards Milan.
Let us not venture all this poor remainder
In one unlucky bottom.²
ANTONIO You counsel safely.
Best of my life, farewell. Since we must part,
Heaven hath a hand in 't, but no otherwise
60 Than as some curious artist takes in sunder
A clock or watch, when it is out of frame,³
To bring 't in better order.
DUCHESS I know not which is best,
To see you dead, or part with you. Farewell, boy:
65 Thou art happy that thou hast not understanding
To know thy misery; for all our wit

2. The metaphor is mercantile: let's not load all our cargo in one ship ("bottom").

3. Not working. "Curious artist": clever craftsman.

And reading brings us to a truer sense
Of sorrow. In the eternal church,° sir,   *heavenly society*
I do hope we shall not part thus.

ANTONIO   Oh, be of comfort!

70   Make patience a noble fortitude,
And think not how unkindly we are used:
Man, like to cassia, is proved best being bruised.[4]

DUCHESS   Must I, like to a slave-born Russian,
Account it praise to suffer tyranny?

75   And yet, O heaven, thy heavy hand is in 't!
I have seen my little boy oft scourge his top,[5]
And compared myself to 't: naught made me e'er
Go right but heaven's scourge stick.

ANTONIO   Do not weep:
Heaven fashioned us of nothing, and we strive

80   To bring ourselves to nothing. Farewell, Cariola,
And thy sweet armful. If I do never see thee more,
Be a good mother to your little ones,
And save them from the tiger. Fare you well.

DUCHESS   Let me look upon you once more, for that speech

85   Came from a dying father. Your kiss is colder
Than that I have seen an holy anchorite°   *hermit*
Give to a dead man's skull.

ANTONIO   My heart is turned to a heavy lump of lead,
With which I sound[6] my danger. Fare you well.

                              [*Exeunt* ANTONIO *and his son.*]

90   DUCHESS   My laurel is all withered.

CARIOLA   Look, madam, what a troop of armèd men
Make toward us.

DUCHESS   Oh, they are very welcome:
When Fortune's wheel[7] is overcharged with princes,
The weight makes it move swift: I would have my ruin
Be sudden.

          [*Enter* BOSOLA *vizarded,° with a guard.*]   *masked*

95   I am your adventure,[8] am I not?

BOSOLA   You are. You must see your husband no more.

DUCHESS   What devil art thou that counterfeits heaven's thunder?

BOSOLA   Is that terrible? I would have you tell me whether
Is that note worse that frights the silly birds

100   Out of the corn,° or that which doth allure them   *grain*
To the nets? You have hearkened to the last too much.

DUCHESS   Oh, misery! Like to a rusty o'ercharged cannon,
Shall I never fly in pieces?—Come, to what prison?

BOSOLA   To none.

DUCHESS   Whither, then?

---

4. Cinnamon bark ("cassia") is most aromatic
(virtuous) when pressed.
5. Children used to make tops spin by whipping
them.
6. Plumb the depths of.

7. The wheel of fortune is an ancient emblem of
mutability; people have their fixed positions on it
and rise or fall as it turns.
8. The object of your journey.

BOSOLA   To your palace.
DUCHESS   I have heard
105   That Charon's boat serves to convey all o'er
      The dismal lake,[9] but brings none back again.
BOSOLA   Your brothers mean you safety and pity.
DUCHESS   Pity!
      With such a pity men preserve alive
      Pheasants and quails, when they are not fat enough
110   To be eaten.
BOSOLA   These are your children?
DUCHESS   Yes.
BOSOLA   Can they prattle?
DUCHESS   No.
      But I intend, since they were born accursed,
      Curses shall be their first language.
BOSOLA   Fie, madam!
      Forget this base, low fellow—
DUCHESS   Were I a man,
115   I'd beat that counterfeit face° into thy other.   *mask*
BOSOLA   One of no birth.[1]
DUCHESS   Say that he was born mean,
      Man is most happy when 's own actions
      Be arguments and examples of his virtue.
BOSOLA   A barren, beggarly virtue!
120   DUCHESS   I prithee, who is greatest? Can you tell?
      Sad tales befit my woe: I'll tell you one.
      A salmon, as she swam unto the sea,
      Met with a dogfish, who encounters her
      With this rough language: "Why art thou so bold
125   To mix thyself with our high state of floods,
      Being no eminent courtier, but one
      That for the calmest and fresh time o' th' year
      Dost live in shallow rivers, rank'st thyself
      With silly° smelts and shrimps? And darest thou   *simple*
130   Pass by our dog-ship without reverence?"
      "Oh!" quoth the salmon, "sister, be at peace:
      Thank Jupiter we both have passed the net!
      Our value never can be truly known,
      Till in the fisher's basket we be shown:
135   I' th' market then my price may be the higher,
      Even when I am nearest to the cook and fire."
      So to great men the moral may be stretchèd:
      Men oft are valued high, when they're most wretched.
      But come, whither you please. I am armed 'gainst misery;
140   Bent to all sways of the oppressor's will:
      There's no deep valley but near some great hill.   [*Exeunt.*]

---

9. In classical mythology, Charon transports the   1. Of low rank by birth.
souls of the dead across the river Styx to Hades.

Act 4

SCENE 1. *Amalfi.*

[*Enter* FERDINAND *and* BOSOLA.]

FERDINAND   How doth our sister duchess bear herself
  In her imprisonment?

BOSOLA   Nobly. I'll describe her.
  She's sad as one long used to 't, and she seems
  Rather to welcome the end of misery

5   Than shun it; a behavior so noble
  As gives a majesty to adversity:
  You may discern the shape of loveliness
  More perfect in her tears than in her smiles;
  She will muse four hours together; and her silence,

10   Methinks, expresseth more than if she spake.

FERDINAND   Her melancholy seems to be fortified
  With a strange disdain.

BOSOLA   'Tis so; and this restraint,
  Like English mastiffs that grow fierce with tying,
  Makes her too passionately apprehend
  Those pleasures she's kept from.

15 FERDINAND   Curse upon her!
  I will no longer study in the book
  Of another's heart. Inform her what I told you.   [*Exit.*]
     [*Enter* DUCHESS.]

BOSOLA   All comfort to your grace!

DUCHESS   I will have none.
  Pray thee, why dost thou wrap thy poisoned pills

20   In gold and sugar?

BOSOLA   Your elder brother, the Lord Ferdinand,
  Is come to visit you, and sends you word,
  'Cause once he rashly made a solemn vow
  Never to see you more, he comes i' th' night,

25   And prays you gently neither torch nor taper
  Shine in your chamber. He will kiss your hand
  And reconcile himself, but for his vow
  He dares not see you.

DUCHESS   At his pleasure.
  Take hence the lights: he's come.
     [*Enter* FERDINAND.]

FERDINAND   Where are you?

30 DUCHESS   Here, sir.

FERDINAND   This darkness suits you well.

DUCHESS   I would ask your pardon.

FERDINAND   You have it;
  For I account it the honorabl'st revenge,
  Where I may kill, to pardon. Where are your cubs?

DUCHESS   Whom?

35 FERDINAND   Call them your children;

For though our national law distinguish bastards
From true legitimate issue, compassionate nature
Makes them all equal.

DUCHESS   Do you visit me for this?
You violate a sacrament o' th' church
Shall make you howl in hell for 't.

40 FERDINAND   It had been well
Could you have lived thus always; for, indeed,
You were too much i' th' light[1]—but no more—
I come to seal my peace with you. Here's a hand

                                        [*Gives her a dead man's hand.*]

To which you have vowed much love; the ring upon 't
You gave.

45 DUCHESS   I affectionately kiss it.

FERDINAND   Pray, do, and bury the print of it in your heart.
I will leave this ring with you for a lovetoken,
And the hand as sure as the ring; and do not doubt
But you shall have the heart, too. When you need a friend,
50 Send it to him that owed° it; you shall see   owned
Whether he can aid you.

DUCHESS   You are very cold;
I fear you are not well after your travel.
Ha! Lights! Oh, horrible!

FERDINAND   Let her have lights enough.   [*Exit.*]

DUCHESS   What witchcraft doth he practice, that he hath left
55 A dead man's hand here?

          [*Here is discovered, behind a traverse,[2] the artificial figures of Antonio
          and his children, appearing as if they were dead.*]

BOSOLA   Look you, here's the piece from which 'twas ta'en.
He doth present you this sad spectacle,
That, now you know directly they are dead,
Hereafter you may wisely cease to grieve
60 For that which cannot be recovered.

DUCHESS   There is not between heaven and earth one wish
I stay for after this: it wastes[3] me more
Than were 't my picture, fashioned out of wax,
Stuck with a magical needle, and then buried
65 In some foul dunghill; and yond's an excellent property[4]
For a tyrant, which I would account mercy.

BOSOLA   What's that?

DUCHESS   If they would bind me to that lifeless trunk
And let me freeze to death.

BOSOLA   Come, you must live.

DUCHESS   That's the greatest torture souls feel in hell,
70 In hell: that they must live, and cannot die.
Portia,[5] I'll new-kindle thy coals again,

4.1
1. Punning on "light," wanton.
2. Curtain.
3. Consumes, as by secret disease; witches were supposed to be able to "waste" their enemies by

making wax images and tormenting them as indicated below.
4. Appropriate act.
5. Portia, the wife of Brutus, committed suicide by swallowing hot coals.

And revive the rare and almost dead example
Of a loving wife.
BOSOLA   Oh, fie! Despair? Remember
You are a Christian.
DUCHESS   The church enjoins fasting:
I'll starve myself to death.
75 BOSOLA   Leave this vain sorrow.
Things being at the worst begin to mend: the bee
When he hath shot his sting into your hand, may then
Play with your eyelid.
DUCHESS   Good comfortable fellow,
Persuade a wretch that's broke upon the wheel[6]
80 To have all his bones new set; entreat him live
To be executed again. Who must dispatch me?
I account this world a tedious theater,
For I do play a part in 't 'gainst my will.
BOSOLA Come, be of comfort; I will save your life.
DUCHESS   Indeed,
85 I have not leisure to tend so small a business.
BOSOLA Now, by my life, I pity you.
DUCHESS   Thou art a fool, then,
To waste thy pity on a thing so wretched
As cannot pity itself. I am full of daggers.
Puff, let me blow these vipers from me.
        [Enter SERVANT.]
What are you?
90 SERVANT   One that wishes you long life.
DUCHESS I would thou wert hanged for the horrible curse
Thou hast given me. I shall shortly grow one
Of the miracles of pity. I'll go pray—
No, I'll go curse.
BOSOLA   Oh, fie!
DUCHESS   I could curse the stars—
95 BOSOLA Oh, fearful!
DUCHESS And those three smiling seasons of the year
Into a Russian winter,[7] nay, the world
To its first chaos.
BOSOLA   Look you, the stars shine still.
DUCHESS Oh, but you must
100 Remember, my curse hath a great way to go.
Plagues, that make lanes through largest families,
Consume them!
BOSOLA   Fie, lady!
DUCHESS   Let them, like tyrants,
Never be remembered but for the ill they have done;
Let all the zealous prayers of mortified
Churchmen forget them!

6. Instrument of torture for stretching the body.
7. A Russian winter would last all year long.

105   BOSOLA   Oh, uncharitable!

DUCHESS   Let Heaven a little while cease crowning martyrs
    To punish them!
    Go, howl them this, and say, I long to bleed:
    It is some mercy when men kill with speed.

                      [*Exeunt* DUCHESS *and* SERVANT.]

          [*Reenter* FERDINAND.]

110   FERDINAND   Excellent, as I would wish; she's plagued
        in art:°   *by a cunning device*
    These presentations are but framed in wax
    By the curious master in that quality,
    Vincentio Lauriola,[8] and she takes them
    For true substantial bodies.

  BOSOLA   Why do you do this?

  FERDINAND   To bring her to despair.

115   BOSOLA   'Faith, end here,
    And go no farther in your cruelty.
    Send her a penitential garment to put on
    Next to her delicate skin, and furnish her
    With beads and prayer books.

  FERDINAND   Damn her! That body of hers,

120   While that my blood ran pure in 't, was more worth
    Than that which thou wouldst comfort, called a soul.
    I will send her masques of common courtesans,
    Have her meat° served up by bawds and ruffians,   *food (of any kind)*
    And, 'cause she'll needs be mad, I am resolved
125   To remove forth the common hospital°   *asylum*
    All the mad-folk, and place them near her lodging;
    There let them practice together, sing and dance,
    And act their gambols to the full o' th' moon:
    If she can sleep the better for it, let her.
130   Your work is almost ended.

  BOSOLA   Must I see her again?

  FERDINAND   Yes.

  BOSOLA   Never.

  FERDINAND   You must.

  BOSOLA   Never in mine own shape;
    That's forfeited by my intelligence°   *betrayal*
    And this last cruel lie. When you send me next,
    The business shall be comfort.

135   FERDINAND   Very likely.
    Thy pity is nothing of kin to thee.[9] Antonio
    Lurks about Milan: thou shalt shortly thither
    To feed a fire as great as my revenge,
    Which ne'er will slack till it have spent his fuel.
140   Intemperate agues[1] make physicians cruel.   [*Exeunt.*]

---

8. The art of wax modeling was common enough, but the name of the artist seems to be imaginary.

9. I.e., pity doesn't suit you very well.

1. Fevers that cannot be controlled.

The Middle Ages (to ca. 1485)

Scepter, from the Sutton Hoo Treasure, ca. 625 C.E.

Discovered in 1939, among other items (jewelry, pottery, fragments of a helmet and shield), in a funeral ship buried in a mound near the coast of East Anglia, the scepter—probably a symbol of royal authority—consists of a massive ceremonial whetstone carved with faces and attached to a ring of twisted bronze wires mounted by an intricately carved stag. The treasure suggests the one laden on Scyld's funeral ship in *Beowulf* (lines 26–52; p. 42) and the material world imagined throughout the poem; the scepter evokes the "gold standard . . . / high above [the king's] head." THE BRITISH MUSEUM, LONDON, UK / BRIDGEMAN ART LIBRARY.

Annunciation to the Shepherds; the Magi before Herod, ca. 1150

Stories of the Nativity figure prominently both in the mystery plays and in medieval Psalters such as this one. The Latin text on the angels' scrolls is from Luke 2.11: "Natus est nobis hodie salvator qui est Christus Dominus in civitate David" (Unto us is born in the city of David a savior who is Christ the Lord). Herod's scroll gives his instructions to the Magi from Matthew 2.8: "ite et interrogate diligenter de puero" (go and inquire diligently about the child). The caption above each image is in French. THE BRITISH LIBRARY, COTTON NERO C. IV, FOLIO 11.

Noah urging his wife to board the ark, ca. 1290

Noah's trouble getting his wife to board the ark was a popular subject in medieval drama and art (See Chaucer, *The Miller's Tale,* lines 430–35; pp. 273–74). In this illustration from a Psalter, Noah admonishes his wife with his left hand and grabs her wrist with the right, urging her to come aboard. Concealed, riding piggyback on the wife, a winged devil comes along as a stowaway. Below, he exits through the hull among drowned bodies on the seafloor. Other manuscripts show the serpent plugging the hole with his tail. THE PIERPONT MORGAN LIBRARY / ART RESOURCE, NY.

Plowing, the Luttrell Psalter, ca. 1330

The Psalter made for Sir Geoffrey Luttrell is sumptuously illustrated with idealized depictions of family, servants, workers, animals, and their activities (plowing, sowing, harvesting,
feasting, playing) on the lord's estate; it is also elaborately decorated with foliage and
grotesques. The Plowman here is a symbolic figure of order like Chaucer's Plowman (p. 256)
and Langland's Piers Plowman (p. 373). The image echoes line 6 of the Psalm above: "Si
dicebam motus est pes meus, misericordia tua, domine, adiuvabat me" (If I said: My foot is
moved: thy mercy, Lord, helped me); "pes" (foot) anticipates the plow foot that moves the soil.
THE BRITISH LIBRARY, FOLIO 170R FROM THE LUTTRELL PSALTER, MS ADDITIONAL 42130.

The Wilton Diptych,
Flemish school,
1395–96

Richard II commissioned this double-panel painting, both pious and political, not long before his deposition. In it he is portrayed as a boy, perhaps ten years old, the age at which he became king. Two English kings, St. Edmund and St. Edward "the Confessor," and John the Baptist, Richard's patron saint, present the young king to the Virgin and Child, who are surrounded by angels. The Christ Child blesses the red-cross standard of St. George (the patron saint of England), about to be given into the kneeling king's open hands. Richard's robe and the angels' sleeves display his personal emblem, a white hart (punning on *riche-hart*). NATIONAL GALLERY, LONDON, GREAT BRITAIN / ART RESOURCE, NY.

The Crucifixion, Lapworth Missal, 1398

This late medieval manuscript illumination typically portrays the humanity of Christ: frail, eyes closed, head inclining on his shoulder. At the sides stand the Virgin mother, who swoons in the arms of Mary Magdalene, and St. John the evangelist. The skull signifies Golgotha (place of skulls), the site of the Crucifixion. According to medieval legend, the tree of knowledge had stood on the same site and Adam was buried there: thus the skull is that of Adam, whose original sin is being redeemed by the blood that the angels are collecting. The sun and moon symbolize the New and Old Testaments: as the sun illuminates the moon, the light of the New Testament reveals the hidden truths of the Old. Symbols of the four evangelists appear in the corners of the intricately decorated frame. CORPUS CHRISTI COLLEGE, UNIVERSITY OF OXFORD, MS 394.

Portrait of Chaucer, ca. 1411

In his poem *The Regiment of Princes*, Hoccleve, a younger disciple of Chaucer, memorializes "My maistir Chaucer, flour of eloquence, / Mirour of fructuous entendement, / O universel fadir in science!" One manuscript preserves a small portrait of Chaucer that Hoccleve placed in the margin so "That they that han of him lost thought and mynde / By this peynture may ageyn him fynde." Chaucer holds a rosary in his left hand; attached to his gown, a penknife (formerly used for making and mending quill pens) or pen case functions as a symbol of authorship. THE BRITISH LIBRARY, MS HARLEY 4866, FOLIO 88.

Manuscript illumination of pilgrims leaving Canterbury, ca. 1420

Chaucer's pilgrims never get to Canterbury, but they do in the prologue to John Lydgate's *The Siege of Thebes*. In the prologue, Lydgate, a monk of Bury St. Edmund's and an enthusiastic follower of Chaucer, tells how on his own pilgrimage to Canterbury he encounters Chaucer's pilgrims. The Host invites the monk to join the company on their return journey and calls on him to tell the first tale. Lydgate is the middle figure in a monk's cowl, costumed more soberly than Chaucer's Monk (pp. 247–48). The cathedral and walls of Canterbury appear in the background. THE BRITISH LIBRARY, MS ROYAL 18 D II, FOLIO 148.

Three hunting scenes, *Le Mireur du Monde,* French manuscript, ca. 1475

The medieval nobility regarded the hunt as both a sport and an art—a test of the skill and endurance of men, dogs, and quarry. These scenes of hunters stalking the deer, breaking up the carcass, and pursuing the boar correspond to the *Gawain* poet's elaborate descriptions of the first two hunts (pp. 209ff., 213ff., 219ff.). The stylized rhetoric describing the hunts both parallels and contrasts with the stylized exchanges between Gawain and the lady in the interspersed bedroom scenes where she is the hunter and he the quarry. BODLEIAN LIBRARY, UNIVERSITY OF OXFORD, MS Douce 338, FOLIO 60, 56, 78.

The Sixteenth Century
(1485–1603)

St. George and the Dragon (London version), Paolo Uccello, ca. 1455–60

A depiction by the Florentine artist Uccello of the legend that was to inspire Edmund Spenser in Book 1 of *The Faerie Queene*. Already held on a leash by the elegant lady—as if the struggle's outcome were not in doubt—the dragon submits to the knight's lance (thrust through the nose in a gesture that better recalls the domestication of cattle than the thwarting of an enemy). The desolate cave is strangely conjoined with the formal garden and the lady's elegant court dress: the story is imagined as located at once in the wilderness and at the very center of civilization. NATIONAL GALLERY, LONDON, GREAT BRITAIN / ART RESOURCE, NY.

Thomas More, Hans Holbein, 1527

Painted on the eve of More's great conflict with Henry VIII over the validity of the king's marriage to Catherine of Aragon, Holbein's portrait emphasizes both the chancellor's importance and his strength of character. More wears the heavy gold chain and rich dress of high office, which he had satirized a decade earlier in *Utopia*. In all probability, if early biographies of More can be believed, he also wears a hair shirt under the velvet and fur, a hidden, painful reminder of the vulnerable flesh that he secretly mortified. COPYRIGHT THE FRICK COLLECTION, NEW YORK.

Edward VI and the Pope: An Allegory of the Reformation, English school, ca. 1568–71

The dying Henry VIII hands over the mandate for church reform to his young son and heir, Prince Edward. This is a polemical attempt to depict the religious revolution that had a deep impact on English society and literature. The open book, proclaiming the Protestant emphasis on the Word of God in vernacular translation, crushes the pope and the taglines of Catholic corruption that surround him. The Council of Regency (appointed to guide the king, who was only nine when he ascended the throne) is in attendance; to the left, two monks flee the pope's downfall. In the upper right, a painting (or view from the window?) heralds the collapse of the Old Church and the breaking of its "idols." Several places in the painting are intended for inscriptions, but for unknown reasons these were never completed. NATIONAL PORTRAIT GALLERY, LONDON, UK / BRIDGEMAN ART LIBRARY.

The Wife and Daughter of a Chief,
John White, 1585

Accompanying Thomas Hariot's *Brief and True Report of the New-found Land of Virginia,* John White's watercolors chronicle Algonkian life as seen by the English voyagers. Here, a girl "of the age of 8 or 10 yeares" carries a European doll, dressed in full Elizabethan costume, that she has clearly been given as a gift by the strange visitors. The presentation of small gifts was a regular English practice, frequently alternating with murderous violence. White's drawing manages to convey both the exoticism and the dignity that Hariot and others perceived in the American natives. THE BRITISH MUSEUM.

Portrait of a Melancholy Young Man, Isaac Oliver, ca. 1590–95

Equally fashionable in attitude and dress, Oliver's young man displays the fascination of the English elite with the "melancholy humour." In addition to the sad expression, the black clothes and crossed arms are conventional markers of melancholy. Men in love, like Sidney's Astrophil (p. 1084) and Duke Orsino in *Twelfth Night* (p. 1188), found it particularly glamorous to parade their pensive dispositions. The romance of this "disease" figures in the couple just walking into the labyrinth-garden on the right. THE ROYAL COLLECTION © 2003, HER MAJESTY QUEEN ELIZABETH II.

Captain Thomas Lee, Marcus Gheeraerts the Younger, 1594

Restless, ambitious Thomas Lee was executed in 1601 for participating in the rebellion against the queen led by the Earl of Essex, but in 1594 he was in the midst of his bid for the position of chief negotiator between Ireland and the English Crown. His appearance refers both to his military service in Ireland and to his status at home: Lee sports the bare legs and open shirt of a "kerne," or Irish footsoldier, along with the rich brocade and armor of a wealthy English nobleman. Lee, whose hand had been injured in a skirmish, wishes to be compared with the Roman Gaius Mucius Scaevola, who demonstrated to the enemy Etruscans his resolution and indifference to pain by thrusting his right hand into a fire. Scaevola so impressed the Etruscans that their leader, Porsena, sued for peace. Painted in the tree to Lee's right is a quotation from Livy attributed to Scaevola: "Both to act and to suffer with fortitude is a Roman's part" (trans. Karen Hearn, ed. *Dynasties*). TATE GALLERY, LONDON / ART RESOURCE, NY.

C 12

The Life and Death of Sir Henry Unton, anonymous, ca. 1597

A masque of musicians and dancers performs for a dinner party of Unton's friends. Theatrical life in this period, which often included music and dancing, was not restricted to the playhouse; it extended into other social settings, such as this one. Theater here is depicted as incidental entertainment: some guests turn their backs on the pageant; the actors are considerably smaller than their patrons, an index of relative social importance. By COURTESY OF THE NATIONAL PORTRAIT GALLERY, LONDON.

The "Chandos" Portrait of William Shakespeare, anonymous, date unknown

The formal portrait of the playwright that appears in the First Folio edition of his works depicts him stiffly posed in a brocade jacket and a heavily starched collar. Here, in a portrait named after its owner, the Duke of Chandos, Shakespeare is presented less formally and more as his friends and colleagues may have known him. The artist is unknown, but some speculate that it may have been Shakespeare's fellow actor Richard Burbage. By COURTESY OF THE NATIONAL PORTRAIT GALLERY, LONDON.

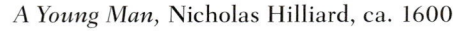

A Young Man, Nicholas Hilliard, ca. 1600

This tiny painting from a playing card approximately two inches square represents the "other side" of Elizabethan love poetry: passion replaces languor. The image of the lover tormented by the "fire" of his mistress's eyes or the hellish inner torment of desire was common. Though Sidney's Astrophil lives "in blackest winter night," he feels "the flames of hottest summer day" (p. 1099), while even disillusioned lovers in Shakespeare's sonnets do not know how "To shun the heaven that leads men to this hell" (p. 1183). The locket held by the young man presumably contains another miniature: a portrait of the beloved. VICTORIA & ALBERT MUSEUM, LONDON / ART RESOURCE, NY.

Elizabeth I in Procession, attributed to Robert Peake, ca. 1600

Carried on a litter like an image of the Virgin in the religious processions of previous centuries, the gorgeously arrayed Queen Elizabeth is shown here as a time-defying icon of purity and power. When the painting was executed, the queen was sixty-seven years old. Until the end of her life she continued her custom of going on "Progresses" through the realm: surrounded by her courtiers and ladies in waiting, she would venture forth to show herself to her people, many of whom nearly bankrupted themselves to entertain her in style. THE STAPLETON COLLECTION / BRIDGEMAN ART LIBRARY.

Henry Wriothesley, Third Earl of Southampton, John de Critz, 1603

Henry Wriothesley, the third Earl of Southampton, was nearly executed for his part in the rebellion against Queen Elizabeth led by his friend the Earl of Essex in 1601. Though he was eventually pardoned, Southampton was imprisoned for two years in the Tower of London, where he is here depicted along with his favorite cat. Tradition has it that the cat found its way to him in prison and reached him by coming down the chimney. An early patron of Shakespeare, the wealthy earl may be the "Mr. W. H." (his initials reversed) to whom the first edition of the sonnets is dedicated (p. 1170). On the eve of the Essex rebellion, Southampton seems to have instigated a performance of *Richard II* by Shakespeare's company to put the people of London in mind of deposition. The painting was clearly commissioned after his release, the date of which is painted on the tablet, along with the proud inscription "In Vinculis / Invictus" (Though in chains, unconquered). Private Collection / Bridgeman Art Library.

The Early Seventeenth Century
(1603–1660)

The Expulsion from Paradise, Masaccio, ca. 1427–28

This striking fresco shows an agonized Adam and Eve being driven from Eden by a sword-wielding angel. Adam is so overcome he buries his face in his hands; Eve's face is a mask of despair. They do not touch: each seems imprisoned in his or her own pain. Milton's representation of the expulsion at the end of Book 12 of *Paradise Lost* is very different, and the comparison is instructive (see pp. 2173ff.). SCALA / ART RESOURCE, NY.

The Three Graces (detail), *The Primavera*, Sandro Botticelli, ca. 1481

The Graces are a prominent allusive feature of seventeenth-century poetry and masques. At times they carry the allegorical significance suggested in Botticelli's portrayal of them as extensions of Venus, goddess of love and beauty, and as manifestations of the beauty, joy, and freshness of spring. Milton's "L'Allegro" (p. 1909) is couched as a literary hymn honoring Euphrosyne, the Grace who signifies youthful mirth; her sisters are Aglaia, splendor, and Thalia, abundance or pleasure. Their linked hands and postures are said to symbolize the giving and receiving of joy, bounty, and pleasure. ERICH LESSING / ART RESOURCE, NY.

Sacred and Profane Love, Titian, ca. 1515

This image might almost serve as an emblem for the two kinds of love celebrated and often contrasted in seventeenth-century verse. In Titian's Neoplatonic program, the nude figure bearing the torch is the celestial Venus, the principle of universal and eternal beauty and love; the clothed figure is the earthly Venus, who creates the perishable images of beauty in humans, flowers and trees, gold and gems, and works of art. Cupid is placed between them but somewhat closer to the terrestrial Venus. SCALA / ART RESOURCE, NY.

God Creating the Animals, Tintoretto, 1550–52

A remarkable rendering of the scene, with God the Father depicted as an immense figure, exuding power and energy, actively calling forth many varieties of animals. The conception invites comparison with Milton's rendering of the Genesis creation story in *Paradise Lost*, Book 7 (p. 2063). CAMARAPHOTO / ART RESOURCE, NY.

John Donne, anonymous, ca. 1595

This portrait presents Donne in the guise of a melancholy lover fond of self-display; the signs are his broad-brimmed black hat, soulful eyes, sensual lips, delicate hands, and united but expensive lace collar. Parts of Donne's *Songs and Sonnets* (pp. 1373ff.) date from this period. Melancholy, supposedly caused by an excess of black bile and often associated with the scholarly and artistic temperament, was identified in Robert Burton's massive and very popular *Anatomy of Melancholy* as a well-nigh universal attribute of the period. It is the temperament of many literary characters, among them Hamlet, Duke Orsino (in *Twelfth Night*, p. 1188), Jacques in *As You Like It*, and Milton's Il Penseroso (p. 1913). PRIVATE COLLECTION / BRIDGEMAN ART LIBRARY.

Lady Sidney and Six of Her Children, Marcus Gheeraerts the Younger, ca. 1596

This portrait of Barbara (Gamage) Sidney, wife of Sir Robert Sidney of Penshurst, provides an insight into domestic relations in the period, as well as an illuminating comment on Ben Jonson's poem "To Penshurst" (p. 1546). Robert Sidney (brother of Sir Philip Sidney) is absent, serving as governor of the English stronghold in Flushing. Lady Sidney is portrayed as a fruitful, fostering mother. Her hands rest on her two sons—both still in skirts, though the heir wears a sword; the four daughters are arranged in two pairs, the elder of each pair imitating her mother's nurturing gesture. The eldest daughter will become Lady Mary Wroth, author of *Urania* and the sonnet sequence *Pamphilia to Amphilanthus* (pp. 1560ff.). REPRODUCED BY KIND PERMISSION OF VISCOUNT DE L'ISLE, FROM HIS PRIVATE COLLECTION AT PENSHURST PLACE.

Lucy, Countess of Bedford, as a Masquer, attributed to John de Critz, ca. 1606

Lucy (Harrington) Russell, Countess of Bedford, prominent courtier, favorite of Queen Anne, patron of Donne and Jonson, and frequent planner of and participant in court masques, is shown in masquing costume for the wedding masque *Hymenaei*, by Ben Jonson and Inigo Jones. Jonson describes the masquing ladies as "attired richly and alike in the most celestial colors" associated with the rainbow, with elaborate headdresses and shoes, "all full of splendor, sovereignty, and riches." Their masque dances were "fully of subtlety and device." Woburn Abbey, Bedfordshire, UK / Bridgeman Art Library.

The Garden of Eden with the Fall of Man, Jan Brueghel the Elder and Peter Paul Rubens, ca. 1615

Possibly foreshadowing Milton's portrayal of Eden in *Paradise Lost*, the painting presents an idyllic scene with cavorting animals in a lush landscape and a graceful human pair—perhaps just enjoying the garden's fruit, but at least intimating the moment of the Fall as a seductive Eve hands Adam an apple and a snake looks on. A favorite painter of Charles I, Rubens designed and painted for the king the splendid ceiling of Whitehall, portraying King James in apotheosis, as a supporter of wisdom, justice, concord, and peace. Scala / Art Resource, NY.

Charles I on Horseback, Sir Anthony Van Dyck, 1637–38

One of Charles I's court painters, knighted and pensioned by the king, Van Dyck produced several portraits of the royal family and their circle at court. This magnificent equestrian portrait of the king in armor presents him as hero and warrior, in a pose that looks back to portraits and statues of Roman emperors on horseback. It was painted to be hung at the end of the Long Gallery in St. James Palace. NATIONAL GALLERY, LONDON, UK / BRIDGEMAN ART LIBRARY, NY.

The Penitent Magdalen, Georges de la Tour, ca. 1638–43

This remarkable image of a young woman in meditative pose, her face lit by candlelight and her hand touching a skull, can serve as an emblem for the extensive meditative literature of the period—the poetry and prose of Donne, Herbert, Vaughan, and Traherne, among others—on such topics as sickness, human mortality, the transience of life and beauty, and the inevitability of death. Réunion des Musées Nationaux / Art Resource, NY.

The Restoration and the Eighteenth Century (1660–1785)

Landscape with Apollo and the Muses, Claude Lorrain, 1652

Claude's poetic landscapes inspired many British landscape gardens. In this painting, a river god sprawls by the Castalian spring under Mount Parnassus; the white swans are sacred to Apollo. On the terrace to the left, Apollo plays his lyre, surrounded by the nine Muses, while four poets approach through the woods. At the upper left, below a temple, the fountain of Hippocrene pours forth its inspiring waters. The dreamlike distance of the figures in this mysterious, luminous scene is intended to draw the viewer in. Similarly, in landscape gardens visitors were invited to stroll amid temples, inscriptions, swans, and statues, gradually comprehending the master plan. NATIONAL GALLERY OF SCOTLAND, EDINBURGH, SCOTLAND / BRIDGEMAN ART LIBRARY.

Great Fire of London, Dutch school, 1666

The fire of London, described by Dryden in *Annus Mirabilis* and by Pepys in his diary, destroyed most of the central city. In the foreground of this panorama, huddled refugees carry their goods away from the city. Under a pall of smoke across the Thames, St. Paul's Cathedral blazes in the center, with London Bridge on the far left and the Tower on the far right. The fire raged for four days, after which a new city eventually rose from the ashes. MUSEUM OF LONDON, UK / BRIDGEMAN ART LIBRARY.

Embarkment for Cythera,
Jean Antoine Watteau, 1717

Cythera is one of the names of Venus, and in this painting elegant pilgrims visit an island of love to pay homage to Venus (whose statue is on the far right). Paired off, these lovers pass through a romantic, erotic dream-scape, related to the visionary landscape of Pope's *Eloisa to Abelard* (lines 155 ff., p. 2709). A ship of love waits on the left to carry the couples away. Are they going or coming to Cythera? In the grip of love, is the prevailing mood one of joy and anticipation, or of melancholy and surfeit? Critics differ; this painting does not reveal all its secrets. RÉUNION DES MUSÉES NATIONAUX / ART RESOURCE, NY.

Bristol Docks and Qua[y] anonymous, early eighteenth century

Bristol, in southwest England, profited enormously from the expansion of the slave trade. From this port, merchants sent trinkets[,] guns, and rum to West Africa in exchange for slaves, who were transported to North Americ[a] and the West Indies in exchange for money an[d] sugar. This painting shows a bustling metrop[-] olis whose trade makes possible the busy shops [on] the right and the great houses in the background. BRISTOL CITY MUSEUM AND ART GALLERY, UK / BRIDGEMAN ART LIBRAR[Y]

Gulliver Taking Leave of the Houyhnhnms, Sawrey Gilpin, 1769

In part 4 of *Gulliver's Travels* (pp. 2587 ff.), Swift cleverly makes use of the eighteenth-century British love of horses. Gulliver's infatuation with the dignity and nobility of the Houyhnhnms reflects the feelings of many hunters mounted for the chase or of gentlefolk promenading in the park; some preferred horses to human beings. Commercially, "horse painters" found eager and wealthy buyers, while Sawrey Gilpin tried to elevate horse painting by placing his horses against rich landscapes and in historical settings. PRIVATE COLLECTION / BRIDGEMAN ART LIBRARY.

The Beggar's Opera, act 3, scene 11, William Hogarth, 1729

The highwayman Macheath, in leg irons, stands at the center, flanked by the women between whom he cannot choose. To the left, Lucy kneels before the jailer Lockit; to the right, Polly kneels before her father, Peachum. In the rear, a group of prisoners waits for its cue. But the setting is not so much a prison as the theater; spectators are seated on each side of the stage. Hogarth connects the audience with the actors just as *The Beggar's Opera* does, suggesting corruption "through all the employments of life." Behind Peachum, John Gay confers with his producer, John Rich. Below them, seated at the far right, the duke of Bolton (note his Star of the Garter) exchanges a rapt gaze with Polly; a satyr points down at him. On opening night, the duke fell in love with the actor who played Polly, Lavinia Fenton. He returned every night, until she became his mistress—and, two decades later, his wife. Tate Gallery, London / Art Resource, NY.

Garrick between Tragedy and Comedy, Joshua Reynolds, 1762

Sir Joshua Reynolds specialized in portraits that characterized his subjects by alluding to classical literature and art. Here, the great actor David Garrick is torn between Comedy, on the left, and Tragedy, on the right. The picture parodies a well-known image, *Hercules between Virtue and Pleasure*, and alludes to Guido Reni (Tragedy) and Correggio (Comedy). Exalted Tragedy urges Garrick to follow her, but darling Comedy drags him away. SOMERSET MAUGHAM THEATRE COLLECTION, LONDON, UK / BRIDGEMAN ART LIBRARY.

A Philosopher Giving That Lecture on the Orrery, in Which a Lamp Is Put in Place of the Sun, Joseph Wright, 1766

Joseph Wright came from the English Midlands, where an intense interest in science helped spark the industrial revolution. The orrery, a mechanism that represents the movements of the planets around the sun, was one of many devices that taught the public to appreciate the wonders and pleasures of science. In this picture, the philosopher at the center bears a striking resemblance to portraits of Sir Isaac Newton, who had cast light on the solar system. Wright specialized in "candlelight pictures." Strong effects of light and shade play over the faces around the lamp, as if to reflect the literal meaning of enlightenment. GIRAUDON / ART RESOURCE, NY.

The Death of General Wolfe, Benjamin West, 1771

History painting—pictures that represent a famous legend or historical event—was the most prestigious genre of eighteenth-century art. West's painting of Wolfe, who fell on the day that he captured Quebec, revolutionized the genre by dressing the figures in contemporary clothes, not classical togas. Twelve years after his death, Wolfe had become an icon; the composition draws on images of mourners around the dead Christ. The poetic shading is also appropriate to Wolfe. The night before he died, he is supposed to have said of Gray's "Elegy" (p. 3051) that he "would rather have been the author of that piece than beat the French tomorrow"; and in his copy of the poem, he marked one passage: "The paths of glory lead but to the grave." PRIVATE COLLECTION / PHILLIPS, FINE ART AUCTIONEERS, NY / BRIDGEMAN ART LIBRARY.

The Parting of Abelard from Heloise, Angelika Kauffmann, ca. 1778

Angelika Kauffmann, born in Switzerland in 1741, was a child prodigy; at eleven she made a name in Italy for her portraits. From 1766 to 1781 she lived in England, where she was admired both as a singer and as a painter. During the eighteenth century the affair of Abelard and Heloise, which Pope depicted as a struggle between God and Eros, softened into a sentimental love story. Rousseau's novel *The New Heloise* (1761) helped transform the heroine into a saint of love. In an Age of Sensibility, Kauffmann portrays a youthful and feminized Abelard, not a wounded middle-aged scholar, and pathos, not repentance, marks this tender parting. COPYRIGHT © 2003 STATE HERMITAGE MUSEUM, ST. PETERSBURG, RUSSIA.

Within the illustration, a page of text reads:

Illustration for Gray's "Ode on the Death of a Favourite Cat," William Blake, 1798

In 1797, as a birthday gift for his wife, Nancy, the sculptor John Flaxman commissioned Blake to illustrate Gray's poems. These designs, in pen and watercolor, view the art of Gray through Blake's own vision. The charm of Gray's ode depends on picturing Selima both as a cat who tumbles for goldfish and as a "nymph" or "maid" who falls for gold. Blake mixes the two together in a cat and turns the goldfish (or "genii of the stream") into fleeing, finny human forms. Meanwhile, a lurking Fate cuts the thread of Selima's life, reminding us, in this interpretation of Gray, that perverted desires can be deadly. © YALE CENTER FOR BRITISH ART, PAUL MELLON COLLECTION, USA / BRIDGEMAN ART LIBRARY.

SCENE 2

[*Enter* DUCHESS *and* CARIOLA.]

DUCHESS   What hideous noise was that?

CARIOLA   'Tis the wild consort°   *band*
Of madmen, lady, which your tyrant brother
Hath placed about your lodging. This tyranny,
I think, was never practiced till this hour.

5   DUCHESS   Indeed, I thank him. Nothing but noise and folly
Can keep me in my right wits, whereas reason
And silence make me stark mad. Sit down;
Discourse to me some dismal tragedy.

CARIOLA   Oh, 'twill increase your melancholy.

DUCHESS   Thou art deceived:
10   To hear of greater grief would lessen mine.
This is a prison?

CARIOLA   Yes, but you shall live
To shake this durance° off.   *imprisonment*

DUCHESS   Thou art a fool:
The robin redbreast and the nightingale
Never live long in cages.

CARIOLA   Pray, dry your eyes.
What think you of, madam?

15   DUCHESS   Of nothing:
When I muse thus, I sleep.

CARIOLA   Like a madman, with your eyes open?

DUCHESS   Dost thou think we shall know one another in th' other world?

CARIOLA   Yes, out of question.

DUCHESS   Oh that it were possible we might
20   But hold some two days' conference with the dead!
From them I should learn somewhat, I am sure,
I never shall know here. I'll tell thee a miracle;
I am not mad yet, to my cause of sorrow:
Th' heaven o'er my head seems made of molten brass,
25   The earth of flaming sulphur, yet I am not mad.
I am acquainted with sad misery
As the tanned galley slave is with his oar;
Necessity makes me suffer constantly,
And custom makes it easy. Who do I look like now?

30   CARIOLA   Like to your picture in the gallery,
A deal of life in show, but none in practice;
Or rather like some reverend monument
Whose ruins are even pitied.

DUCHESS   Very proper.
And Fortune seems only to have her eyesight
35   To behold my tragedy.
How now! What noise is that?

[*Enter* SERVANT.]

SERVANT   I am come to tell you
Your brother hath intended you some sport.

A great physician, when the pope was sick
Of a deep melancholy, presented him
40 With several sorts of madmen, which wild object
Being full of change and sport, forced him to laugh,
And so the imposthume° broke. The selfsame cure   abscess
The duke intends on you.
DUCHESS   Let them come in.
SERVANT   There's a mad lawyer; and a secular priest;[1]
45 A doctor that hath forfeited his wits
By jealousy; an astrologian
That in his works said such a day o' th' month
Should be the day of doom, and, failing of 't,
Ran mad; an English tailor crazed i' th' brain
50 With the study of new fashions; a gentleman-usher°   doorkeeper
Quite beside himself with care to keep in mind
The number of his lady's salutations
Or "How do you's" she employed him in each morning;
A farmer, too, an excellent knave in grain,
55 Mad 'cause he was hindered transportation:[2]
And let one broker that's mad loose to these,
You'd think the devil were among them.
DUCHESS   Sit, Cariola. Let them loose when you please,
For I am chained to endure all your tyranny.
         [Enter MADMEN.]
         [Here by a MADMAN this song is sung to a dismal kind of music.]

60   Oh, let us howl some heavy note,
                 Some deadly dogged howl,
             Sounding as from the threatening throat
                 Of beasts and fatal fowl!
             As ravens, screech owls, bulls, and bears,
65   We'll bell° and bawl our parts,   cry
             Till irksome noise have cloyed your ears
                 And corrosived your hearts.
             At last, whenas our choir wants breath,
                 Our bodies being blest,
70   We'll sing, like swans, to welcome death,
                 And die in love and rest.

FIRST MADMAN   Doomsday not come yet? I'll draw it nearer by a perspective,[3]
   or make a glass that shall set all the world on fire upon an instant. I cannot sleep; my pillow is stuffed with a litter of porcupines.
75 SECOND MADMAN   Hell is a mere glasshouse, where the devils are continually blowing up women's souls on hollow irons, and the fire never goes out.
THIRD MADMAN   I will lie with every woman in my parish the tenth night;
   I will tithe them over like haycocks.[4]

4.2
1. One serving a parish, not a member of an order.
2. Forbidden to export.

3. Telescope.
4. As a priest takes his tenth ("tithe") of his
parishioners' crops. "Haycocks": haystacks.

FOURTH MADMAN Shall my pothecary outgo me because I am a cuckold? I
80 have found out his roguery; he makes alum of his wife's urine, and sells it
to puritans that have sore throats with overstraining.[5]
FIRST MADMAN I have skill in heraldry.
SECOND MADMAN Hast?
FIRST MADMAN You do give for your crest a woodcock's[6] head with the
85 brains picked out on 't; you are a very ancient gentleman.
THIRD MADMAN Greek is turned Turk: we are only to be saved by the Helvetian translation.[7]
FIRST MADMAN Come on, sir, I will lay the law to you.
SECOND MADMAN Oh, rather lay a corrosive: the law will eat to the bone.
90 THIRD MADMAN He that drinks but to satisfy nature is damned.
FOURTH MADMAN If I had my glass[8] here, I would show a sight should
make all the women here call me mad doctor.
FIRST MADMAN What's he? A rope maker?
SECOND MADMAN No, no, no, a snuffling knave that, while he shows the
95 tombs, will have his hand in a wench's placket.
THIRD MADMAN Woe to the caroche[9] that brought home my wife from the
masque at three o'clock in the morning! It had a large featherbed in it.
FOURTH MADMAN I have pared the devil's nails forty times, roasted them
in raven's eggs, and cured agues with them.
100 THIRD MADMAN Get me three hundred milchbats, to make possets[1] to procure sleep.
FOURTH MADMAN All the college may throw their caps[2] at me: I have made
a soap boiler costive;[3] it was my masterpiece.
[Here the dance, consisting of eight MADMEN, with music answerable
thereunto; after which BOSOLA, like an old man, enters.]
DUCHESS Is he mad too?
SERVANT   Pray, question him. I'll leave you.
[Exeunt SERVANT and MADMEN.]
BOSOLA I am come to make thy tomb.
105 DUCHESS   Ha! My tomb?
Thou speak'st as if I lay upon my deathbed,
Gasping for breath. Dost thou perceive me sick?
BOSOLA Yes, and the more dangerously, since thy sickness is insensible.[4]
DUCHESS Thou art not mad, sure. Dost know me?
110 BOSOLA Yes.
DUCHESS Who am I?
BOSOLA Thou art a box of worm-seed, at best but a salvatory of green
mummy. What's this flesh? A little crudded[5] milk, fantastical puff paste.
Our bodies are weaker than those paper prisons boys use to keep flies in,
115 more contemptible, since ours is to preserve earthworms. Didst thou ever
see a lark in a cage? Such is the soul in the body: this world is like her

5. In long prayers and sermons.
6. A proverbially stupid bird.
7. The Geneva Bible, a jibe at English Puritans who used that translation.
8. Looking glass.
9. Carriage. "Placket": slit in a skirt.
1. Sedative drafts, here made of bat's milk.
2. Despair of emulating.

3. Constipated.
4. Imperceptible.
5. Curdled. "Worm-seed" is a matter whose ultimate end is the generation of worms. "A salvatory of green mummy": the substance of mummified bodies was considered medicinal. The living body is a box ("salvatory") of such medicine, only not yet ready for use.

little turf of grass, and the heaven o'er our heads, like her looking glass, only gives us a miserable knowledge of the small compass of our prison.

DUCHESS   Am not I thy duchess?

120   BOSOLA   Thou art some great woman, sure, for riot[6] begins to sit on thy forehead, clad in gray hairs, twenty years sooner than on a merry milkmaid's. Thou sleep'st worse than if a mouse should be forced to take up her lodging in a cat's ear: a little infant that breeds its teeth,[7] should it lie with thee, would cry out, as if thou wert the more unquiet bedfellow.

125   DUCHESS   I am Duchess of Malfi still.

BOSOLA   That makes thy sleep so broken:
Glories, like glowworms, afar off shine bright,
But, looked to near, have neither heat nor light.

DUCHESS   Thou art very plain.

130   BOSOLA   My trade is to flatter the dead, not the living; I am a tombmaker.

DUCHESS   And thou com'st to make my tomb?

BOSOLA   Yes.

DUCHESS   Let me be a little merry. Of what stuff wilt thou make it?

BOSOLA   Nay, resolve° me first, of what fashion?   inform

135   DUCHESS   Why, do we grow fantastical in our deathbed? Do we affect fashion in the grave?

BOSOLA   Most ambitiously. Princes' images on their tombs do not lie, as they were wont, seeming to pray up to heaven, but with their hands under their cheeks, as if they died of the toothache. They are not carved
140   with their eyes fixed upon the stars, but as their minds were wholly bent upon the world, the selfsame way they seem to turn their faces.

DUCHESS   Let me know fully therefore the effect
Of this thy dismal preparation,
This talk fit for a charnel.[8]

BOSOLA   Now I shall.

[*Enter* EXECUTIONERS, *with a coffin, cords, and a bell.*]

145   Here is a present from your princely brothers;
And may it arrive welcome, for it brings
Last benefit, last sorrow.

DUCHESS   Let me see it:
I have so much obedience in my blood,
I wish it in their veins to do them good.

150   BOSOLA   This is your last presence chamber.[9]

CARIOLA   O my sweet lady!

DUCHESS   Peace, it affrights not me.

BOSOLA   I am the common bellman,
That usually° is sent to condemned persons   by custom
The night before they suffer.

DUCHESS   Even now thou said'st
Thou wast a tomb-maker.

155   BOSOLA   'Twas to bring you
By degrees to mortification.[1] Listen. [*rings the bell*]

---

6. Debauchery.
7. A teething infant.
8. A storage place for bones reserved from old

graves in the digging of new ones.
9. A noble person's reception room.
1. Repentance, also death and decomposition.

Hark, now everything is still
The screech owl and the whistler[2] shrill
Call upon our dame aloud,
160 And bid her quickly don her shroud!
Much you had of land and rent:
Your length in clay's now competent.°   *sufficient*
A long war disturbed your mind:
Here your perfect peace is signed.
165 Of what is 't fools make such vain keeping?
Sin their conception, their birth weeping,
Their life a general mist of error,
Their death a hideous storm of terror.
Strew your hair with powders sweet,
170 Don clean linen, bathe your feet,
And (the foul fiend more to check)
A crucifix let bless your neck:
'Tis now full tide 'tween night and day;
End your groan, and come away.

175 CARIOLA   Hence, villains, tyrants, murderers! Alas!
What will you do with my lady? Call for help.
DUCHESS   To whom? To our next neighbors? They are mad-folks.
BOSOLA   Remove that noise.
DUCHESS   Farewell, Cariola.
In my last will I have not much to give:
180 A many hungry guests have fed upon me;
Thine will be a poor reversion.°   *inheritance*
CARIOLA   I will die with her.
DUCHESS   I pray thee, look thou giv'st my little boy
Some syrup for his cold, and let the girl
Say her prayers ere she sleep.   [CARIOLA *is forced out by the* EXECUTIONERS.]
             Now what you please.
What death?
185 BOSOLA   Strangling: here are your executioners.
DUCHESS   I forgive them:
The apoplexy, catarrh, or cough o' th' lungs
Would do as much as they do.
BOSOLA   Doth not death fright you?
DUCHESS   Who would be afraid on 't,
190 Knowing to meet such excellent company
In th' other world?
BOSOLA   Yet, methinks,
The manner of your death should much afflict you:
This cord should terrify you.
DUCHESS   Not a whit.
What would it pleasure me to have my throat cut
195 With diamonds? Or to be smothered
With cassia?° Or to be shot to death with pearls?   *cinnamon*

2. A bird premonitory of death.

I know death hath ten thousand several doors
For men to take their exits, and 'tis found
They go on such strange geometrical hinges,
200 You may open them both ways.—Any way, for heaven sake,
So I were out of your whispering. Tell my brothers
That I perceive death, now I am well awake,
Best gift is they can give or I can take.
I would fain° put off my last woman's fault,   gladly
I'd not be tedious to you.
205 EXECUTIONER   We are ready.
DUCHESS   Dispose my breath how please you, but my body
Bestow upon my women, will you?
EXECUTIONER   Yes.
DUCHESS   Pull, and pull strongly, for your able strength
Must pull down heaven upon me—
210 Yet stay; heaven gates are not so high arched
As princes' palaces; they that enter there
Must go upon their knees. [*kneels*] Come, violent death.
Serve for mandragora³ to make me sleep!
Go tell my brothers, when I am laid out,
215 They then may feed in quiet.   [*They strangle her.*]
BOSOLA   Where's the waiting woman?
Fetch her. Some other strangle the children.
     [*Exeunt* EXECUTIONERS, *some of whom return with* CARIOLA.]
Look you, there sleeps your mistress.
CARIOLA   Oh, you are damned
Perpetually for this! My turn is next.
Is 't not so ordered?
220 BOSOLA   Yes, and I am glad
You are so well prepared for 't.
CARIOLA   You are deceived, sir,
I am not prepared for 't, I will not die;
I will first come to my answer,° and know   judicial hearing
How I have offended.
BOSOLA   Come, dispatch her.
225 You kept her counsel; now you shall keep ours.
CARIOLA   I will not die, I must not; I am contracted
To a young gentleman.
EXECUTIONER   Here's your wedding ring.   [*showing the noose*]
CARIOLA   Let me but speak with the duke; I'll discover°   reveal
Treason to his person.
BOSOLA   Delays! Throttle her.
EXECUTIONER   She bites and scratches.
230 CARIOLA   If you kill me now,
I am damned; I have not been at confession
This two years.
BOSOLA [*to* EXECUTIONERS]   When!
CARIOLA   I am quick with child.

---

3. The word is used loosely for a stupefying drug.

BOSOLA   Why, then,
  Your credit's saved.[4]   *[They strangle* CARIOLA.]
                 Bear her into th' next room;
  Let this lie still.   *[Exeunt the* EXECUTIONERS *with the body of* CARIOLA.]
      [Enter FERDINAND.]

FERDINAND   Is she dead?

BOSOLA   She is what

235   You'd have her. But here begin your pity.   *[Shows the children strangled.]*
  Alas, how have these offended?

FERDINAND   The death
  Of young wolves is never to be pitied.

BOSOLA   Fix
  Your eye here.

FERDINAND   Constantly.

BOSOLA   Do you not weep?
  Other sins only speak; murder shrieks out:

240   The element of water moistens the earth,
  But blood flies upwards and bedews the heavens.

FERDINAND   Cover her face; mine eyes dazzle: she died young.

BOSOLA   I think not so; her infelicity°   *unhappiness*
  Seemed to have years too many.

FERDINAND   She and I were twins;

245   And should I die this instant, I had lived
  Her time to a minute.

BOSOLA   It seems she was born first:
  You have bloodily approved° the ancient truth,   *given proof of*
  That kindred commonly do worse agree
  Than remote strangers.

FERDINAND   Let me see her face again.

250   Why didst not thou pity her? What an excellent
  Honest man mightst thou have been,
  If thou hadst borne her to some sanctuary!
  Or, bold in a good cause, opposed thyself,
  With thy advancèd sword above thy head,

255   Between her innocence and my revenge!
  I bade thee, when I was distracted of my wits,
  Go kill my dearest friend, and thou hast done 't.
  For let me but examine well the cause:
  What was the meanness of her match to me?

260   Only I must confess I had a hope,
  Had she continued widow, to have gained
  An infinite mass of treasure by her death:
  And that was the main cause, her marriage,
  That drew a stream of gall quite through my heart.

265   For thee, as we observe in tragedies
  That a good actor many times is cursed
  For playing a villain's part, I hate thee for 't,
  And, for my sake, say thou hast done much ill well.

---

4. Your reputation will now be safe.

BOSOLA Let me quicken your memory, for I perceive
270 You are falling into ingratitude: I challenge
The reward due to my service.
FERDINAND I'll tell thee
What I'll give thee.
BOSOLA Do.
FERDINAND I'll give thee a pardon
For this murder.
BOSOLA Ha!
FERDINAND Yes, and 'tis
The largest bounty I can study to do thee.
275 By what authority didst thou execute
This bloody sentence?
BOSOLA By yours.
FERDINAND Mine! Was I her judge?
Did any ceremonial form of law
Doom her to not-being? Did a complete° jury   *qualified*
Deliver her conviction up i' th' court?
280 Where shalt thou find this judgment registered,
Unless in hell? See, like a bloody fool,
Thou'st forfeited thy life, and thou shalt die for 't.
BOSOLA The office of justice is perverted quite
When one thief hangs another. Who shall dare
To reveal this?
285 FERDINAND Oh, I'll tell thee;
The wolf shall find her grave, and scrape it up,
Not to devour the corpse, but to discover
The horrid murder.
BOSOLA You, not I, shall quake for 't.
FERDINAND Leave me.
BOSOLA I will first receive my pension.
FERDINAND You are a villain.
290 BOSOLA When your ingratitude
Is judge, I am so.
FERDINAND Oh, horror!
That not the fear of Him which binds the devils
Can prescribe man obedience!
Never look upon me more.
BOSOLA Why, fare thee well.
295 Your brother and your self are worthy men:
You have a pair of hearts are rotten graves,
Rotten, and rotting others; and your vengeance,
Like two chained bullets, still° goes arm in arm.   *continually*
You may be brothers, for treason, like the plague,
300 Doth take much in a blood.[5] I stand like one
That long hath ta'en a sweet and golden dream.
I am angry with myself, now that I wake.

---

5. Treason and plague run in certain families.

FERDINAND Get thee into some unknown part o' th' world,
   That I may never see thee.
BOSOLA   Let me know
305   Wherefore I should be thus neglected. Sir,
   I served your tyranny, and rather strove
   To satisfy yourself than all the world,
   And though I loathed the evil, yet I loved
   You that did counsel it; and rather sought
310   To appear a true servant than an honest man.
FERDINAND I'll go hunt the badger by owl-light:
   'Tis a deed of darkness.   [*Exit.*]
BOSOLA He's much distracted. Off, my painted honor!
   While with vain hopes our faculties we tire,
315   We seem to sweat in ice and freeze in fire.
   What would I do, were this to do again?
   I would not change my peace of conscience
   For all the wealth of Europe.—She stirs; here's life.
   Return, fair soul, from darkness, and lead mine
320   Out of this sensible° hell.—She's warm, she breathes.   *living*
   Upon thy pale lips I will melt my heart,
   To store them with fresh color.—Who's there!
   Some cordial° drink!—Alas! I dare not call: *restorative*
   So pity would destroy pity.—Her eye opes,
325   And heaven in it seems to ope, that late was shut,
   To take me up to mercy.
DUCHESS Antonio!
BOSOLA   Yes, madam, he is living;
   The dead bodies you saw were but feigned statues:
   He's reconciled to your brothers: the pope hath wrought
   The atonement.°   *reconciliation*
330   DUCHESS   Mercy!   [*She dies.*]
BOSOLA Oh, she's gone again! There the cords of life broke.
   Oh, sacred innocence, that sweetly sleeps
   On turtles'[6] feathers, whilst a guilty conscience
   Is a black register wherein is writ
335   All our good deeds and bad, a perspective°   *telescope*
   That shows us hell! That we cannot be suffered°   *allowed*
   To do good when we have a mind to it!
   This is manly sorrow:
   These tears, I am very certain, never grew
340   In my mother's milk. My estate is sunk
   Below the degree of fear. Where were
   These penitent fountains while she was living?
   Oh, they were frozen up! Here is a sight
   As direful to my soul as is the sword
345   Unto a wretch hath slain his father. Come,
   I'll bear thee hence,

6. Turtledoves, emblems of a loving couple.

And execute thy last will; that's deliver
Thy body to the reverend dispose°   disposition
Of some good women: that the cruel tyrant
350   Shall not deny me. Then I'll post to Milan,
Where somewhat I will speedily enact
Worth my dejection.   [*Exit with the body.*]

Act 5

SCENE 1. *A public place in Milan.*

[*Enter* ANTONIO *and* DELIO.]

ANTONIO   What think you of my hope of reconcilement
To the Aragonian brethren?
DELIO   I misdoubt it;
For though they have sent their letters of safe conduct
For your repair° to Milan, they appear   resort
5   But nets to entrap you. The Marquis of Pescara,
Under whom you hold certain land in cheat,[1]
Much 'gainst his noble nature hath been moved
To seize those lands, and some of his dependents
Are at this instant making it their suit
10   To be invested in your revenues.[2]
I cannot think they mean well to your life
That do deprive you of your means of life,
Your living.
ANTONIO   You are still an heretic°   skeptic
To any safety I can shape myself.
15   DELIO   Here comes the marquis. I will make myself
Petitioner for some part of your land,
To know whither it is flying.
ANTONIO   I pray do.   [*Withdraws.*]
[*Enter* PESCARA.]
DELIO   Sir, I have a suit to you.
PESCARA   To me?
DELIO   An easy one.
20   There is the citadel of Saint Bennet,
With some demesnes,[3] of late in the possession
Of Antonio Bologna; please you bestow them on me.
PESCARA   You are my friend, but this is such a suit,
Nor fit for me to give, nor you to take.
DELIO   No, sir?
25   PESCARA   I will give you ample reason for 't
Soon in private.—Here's the cardinal's mistress.
[*Enter* JULIA.]
JULIA   My lord, I am grown your poor petitioner,
And should be an ill beggar, had I not

1. Escheat, i.e., subject to forfeiture under certain conditions.

2. I.e., to be given your rents.
3. Associated estates. "Saint Bennet": St. Benedict.

A great man's letter here, the cardinal's,
To court you in my favor.   [*Gives a letter.*]
30 PESCARA   He entreats for you
   The citadel of Saint Bennet, that belonged
   To the banished Bologna.
   JULIA   Yes.
   PESCARA   I could not
   Have thought of a friend I could rather pleasure with it;
   'Tis yours.
   JULIA   Sir, I thank you; and he shall know
35 How doubly I am engaged both in your gift,
   And speediness of giving, which makes your grant
   The greater.   [*Exit.*]
   ANTONIO [*aside*]   How they fortify themselves
   With my ruin!
   DELIO   Sir, I am little bound to you.
   PESCARA   Why?
   DELIO   Because you denied this suit to me, and gave 't
   To such a creature.
40 PESCARA   Do you know what it was?
   It was Antonio's land, not forfeited
   By course of law, but ravished from his throat
   By the cardinal's entreaty. It were not fit
   I should bestow so main° a piece of wrong   *egregious*
45 Upon my friend; 'tis a gratification
   Only due to a strumpet, for it is injustice.
   Shall I sprinkle the pure blood of innocents
   To make those followers I call my friends
   Look ruddier[4] upon me? I am glad
50 This land, ta'en from the owner by such wrong,
   Returns again unto so foul an use
   As salary for his lust. Learn, good Delio,
   To ask noble things of me, and you shall find
   I'll be a noble giver.
   DELIO   You instruct me well.
55 ANTONIO [*aside*]   Why, here's a man now would fright impudence
   From sauciest beggars.
   PESCARA   Prince Ferdinand's come to Milan,
   Sick, as they give out, of an apoplexy,°   *stroke*
   But some say 'tis a frenzy.° I am going   *insanity*
   To visit him.   [*Exit.*]
   ANTONIO   'Tis a noble old fellow.
60 DELIO   What course do you mean to take, Antonio?
   ANTONIO   This night I mean to venture all my fortune,
   Which is no more than a poor lingering life,
   To the cardinal's worst of malice. I have got
   Private access to his chamber, and intend
65 To visit him about the mid of night,

4. More agreeably, literally with a healthier (ruddy) complexion.

As once his brother did our noble duchess.
It may be that the sudden apprehension
Of danger—for I'll go in mine own shape—
When he shall see it fraught with love and duty,
70   May draw the poison out of him, and work
A friendly reconcilement. If it fail,
Yet it shall rid me of this infamous calling,
For better fall once than be ever falling.
DELIO   I'll second you in all danger, and, howe'er,
75   My life keeps rank with yours.
ANTONIO   You are still my loved and best friend.   [*Exeunt.*]

SCENE 2. *The scene continues.*

[*Enter* PESCARA *and* DOCTOR.]
PESCARA   Now, doctor, may I visit your patient?
DOCTOR   If 't please your lordship: but he's instantly°   *very shortly*
To take the air here in the gallery
By my direction.
PESCARA   Pray thee, what's his disease?
5   DOCTOR   A very pestilent disease, my lord,
They call lycanthropia.
PESCARA   What's that?
I need a dictionary to 't.
DOCTOR   I'll tell you.
In those that are possessed with 't there o'erflows
Such melancholy humor, they imagine
10   Themselves to be transformèd into wolves;
Steal forth to churchyards in the dead of night,
And dig dead bodies up: as two nights since
One met the duke 'bout midnight in a lane
Behind Saint Mark's Church, with the leg of a man
15   Upon his shoulder; and he howled fearfully;
Said he was a wolf, only the difference
Was, a wolf's skin was hairy on the outside,
His on the inside; bade them take their swords,
Rip up his flesh, and try. Straight° I was sent for,   *immediately*
20   And, having ministered to him, found his grace
Very well recovered.
PESCARA   I'm glad on 't.
DOCTOR   Yet not without some fear
Of a relapse. If he grow to his fit again,
I'll go a nearer way to work with him
25   Than ever Paracelsus¹ dreamed of: if
They'll give me leave, I'll buffet his madness
Out of him. Stand aside; he comes.
[*Enter* FERDINAND, MALATESTE, CARDINAL, *and* BOSOLA *apart.*]
FERDINAND   Leave me.

5.2
1. The great Swiss alchemist, famous for his cures by sympathetic magic.

MALATESTE   Why doth your lordship love this solitariness?

FERDINAND   Eagles commonly fly alone: they are crows, daws, and star-
lings that flock together. Look, what's that follows me?

MALATESTE   Nothing, my lord.

FERDINAND   Yes.

MALATESTE   'Tis your shadow.

FERDINAND   Stay it; let it not haunt me.

MALATESTE   Impossible, if you move, and the sun shine.

FERDINAND   I will throttle it.   [*Throws himself on the ground.*]

MALATESTE   O, my lord, you are angry with nothing.

FERDINAND   You are a fool: how is 't possible I should catch my shadow,
unless I fall upon 't? When I go to hell, I mean to carry a bribe; for, look
you, good gifts evermore make way for the worst persons.

PESCARA   Rise, good my lord.

FERDINAND   I am studying the art of patience.

PESCARA   'Tis a noble virtue.

FERDINAND   To drive six snails before me from this town to Moscow; neither use goad nor whip to them, but let them take their own time—the
patient'st man i' th' world match me for an experiment—and I'll crawl after
like a sheep-biter.[2]

CARDINAL   Force him up.   [*They raise him.*]

FERDINAND   Use me well, you were best. What I have done, I have done:
I'll confess nothing.

DOCTOR   Now let me come to him. Are you mad, my lord? Are you out of
your princely wits?

FERDINAND   What's he?

PESCARA   Your doctor.

FERDINAND   Let me have his beard sawed off, and his eyebrows filed more
civil.

DOCTOR   I must do mad tricks with him, for that's the only way on 't.[3] I have
brought your grace a salamander's skin to keep you from sunburning.

FERDINAND   I have cruel sore eyes.

DOCTOR   The white of a cockatrix's[4] egg is present remedy.

FERDINAND   Let it be a new-laid one, you were best. Hide me from him:
physicians are like kings—they brook no contradiction.

DOCTOR   Now he begins to fear me: now let me alone with him.

CARDINAL   How now? Put off your gown?

DOCTOR   Let me have some forty urinals filled with rosewater: he and I'll
go pelt one another with them. Now he begins to fear me. Can you fetch
a frisk, sir?[5] Let him go, let him go, upon my peril: I find by his eye he
stands in awe of me; I'll make him as tame as a dormouse.

FERDINAND   Can you fetch your frisks, sir? I will stamp him into a cullis,[6]
flay off his skin, to cover one of the anatomies[7] this rogue hath set i' th'
cold yonder in Barber-Surgeons' Hall. Hence, hence! You are all of you

---

2. A sheepdog.
3. I.e., to cure him.
4. A fabulous, and deadly poisonous, serpent, supposed to be hatched of a cock's egg.
5. Cut a caper, dance a jig.

6. Broth.
7. Anatomical skeletons hung up in the surgeon's college, which Ferdinand proposes to cover with the doctor's flayed skin.

like beasts for sacrifice: there's nothing left of you but tongue and belly,
flattery and lechery. [Exit.]

PESCARA Doctor, he did not fear you thoroughly.

DOCTOR   True;
I was somewhat too forward.

75 BOSOLA [aside]   Mercy upon me,
What a fatal judgment hath fall'n upon this Ferdinand!

PESCARA Knows your grace what accident hath brought
Unto the prince this strange distraction?

CARDINAL [aside] I must feign somewhat.—Thus they say it grew:
80   You have heard it rumored, for these many years
None of our family dies but there is seen
The shape of an old woman, which is given
By tradition to us to have been murdered
By her nephews for her riches. Such a figure
85   One night, as the prince sat up late at 's book,
Appeared to him; when, crying out for help,
The gentlemen of 's chamber found his grace
All on a cold sweat, altered much in face
And language; since which apparition,
90   He hath grown worse and worse, and I much fear
He cannot live.

BOSOLA   Sir, I would speak with you.

PESCARA We'll leave your grace,
Wishing to the sick prince, our noble lord,
All health of mind and body.

CARDINAL   You are most welcome.
            [Exeunt PESCARA, MALATESTE, and DOCTOR.]
95   Are you come? So. [Aside] This fellow must not know
By any means I had intelligence°   was accessory
In our duchess' death; for, though I counseled it,
The full of all th' engagement seemed to grow
From Ferdinand.—Now, sir, how fares our sister?
100 I do not think but sorrow makes her look
Like to an oft-dyed garment: she shall now
Taste comfort from me. Why do you look so wildly?
Oh, the fortune of your master here the prince
Dejects you, but be you of happy comfort:
105 If you'll do one thing for me I'll entreat,
Though he had a cold tombstone o'er his bones,
I'll make you what you would be.

BOSOLA   Anything;
Give it me in a breath, and let me fly to 't:
They that think long, small expedition win,
110 For musing much o' th' end cannot begin.
            [Enter JULIA.]

JULIA Sir, will you come in to supper?

CARDINAL   I am busy;
Leave me.

JULIA [aside] What an excellent shape hath that fellow!   [Exit.]

CARDINAL   'Tis thus. Antonio lurks here in Milan:
 Inquire him out, and kill him. While he lives,
115 Our sister cannot marry, and I have thought
 Of an excellent match for her. Do this, and style me
 Thy advancement.[8]
BOSOLA   But by what means shall I find him out?
CARDINAL   There is a gentleman called Delio
120 Here in the camp, that hath been long approved
 His loyal friend. Set eye upon that fellow;
 Follow him to Mass; maybe Antonio,
 Although he do account religion
 But a school-name,° for fashion of the world   *an idle phrase*
 May accompany him; or else go inquire out
125 Delio's confessor, and see if you can bribe
 Him to reveal it. There are a thousand ways
 A man might find to trace him; as to know
 What fellows haunt the Jews for taking up
 Great sums of money, for sure he's in want;
130 Or else to go to th' picture-makers, and learn
 Who bought her picture lately. Some of these
 Haply may take.
BOSOLA   Well, I'll not freeze i' th' business:°   *delay*
 I would see that wretched thing, Antonio,
 Above all sights i' th' world.
CARDINAL   Do, and be happy.   *[Exit.]*
135 BOSOLA   This fellow doth breed basilisks in 's eyes,
 He's nothing else but murder; yet he seems
 Not to have notice of the duchess' death.
 'Tis his cunning: I must follow his example;
 There cannot be a surer way to trace
 Than that of an old fox.
   [Reenter JULIA, *with a pistol.]*
140 JULIA   So, sir, you are well met.
BOSOLA   How now?
JULIA   Nay, the doors are fast enough.
 Now, sir, I will make you confess your treachery.
BOSOLA   Treachery?
JULIA   Yes, confess to me
 Which of my women 'twas, you hired to put
 Love-powder into my drink?
145 BOSOLA   Love powder?
JULIA   Yes, when I was at Malfi.
 Why should I fall in love with such a face else?°   *otherwise*
 I have already suffered for thee so much pain,
 The only remedy to do me good
 Is to kill my longing.
150 BOSOLA   Sure, your pistol holds
 Nothing but perfumes or kissing-comfits.[9]

---

8. Call me your means of promotion.
9. Candies to sweeten the breath.

Excellent lady! You have a pretty way on 't
To discover° your longing. Come, come, I'll disarm you,   *reveal*
And arm you thus:[1] yet this is wondrous strange.

155 JULIA   Compare thy form and my eyes together, you'll find
My love no such great miracle. Now you'll say
I am wanton: this nice° modesty in ladies   *fastidious*
Is but a troublesome familiar[2] that haunts them.

BOSOLA   Know you me, I am a blunt soldier.

JULIA   The better:

160 Sure, there wants° fire where there are no lively sparks   *lacks*
Of roughness.

BOSOLA   And I want compliment.[3]

JULIA   Why, ignorance
In courtship cannot make you do amiss,
If you have a heart to do well.

BOSOLA   You are very fair.

JULIA   Nay, if you lay beauty to my charge,
I must plead unguilty.

165 BOSOLA   Your bright eyes
Carry a quiver of darts in them, sharper
Than sunbeams.

JULIA   You will mar me with commendation,
Put yourself to the charge of courting me,
Whereas now I woo you.

170 BOSOLA *[aside]*   I have it, I will work upon this creature.—
Let us grow most amorously familiar.
If the great cardinal now should see me thus,
Would he not count me a villain?

JULIA   No, he might count me a wanton,

175 Not lay a scruple of offense on you;
For if I see and steal a diamond,
The fault is not i' th' stone, but in me the thief
That purloins it. I am sudden with you.
We that are great women of pleasure, use to cut off

180 These uncertain wishes and unquiet longings,
And in an instant join the sweet delight
And the pretty excuse together. Had you been i' th' street,
Under my chamber window, even there
I should have courted you.

BOSOLA   Oh, you are an excellent lady!

185 JULIA   Bid me do somewhat for you presently°   *right away*
To express I love you.

BOSOLA   I will, and if you love me,
Fail not to effect it.
The cardinal is grown wondrous melancholy;

---

1. Disarm (by taking away her pistol); arm (by embracing her).
2. Attendant spirit or demon.
3. I don't have the gift of flattery.

Demand the cause, let him not put you off
190 With feigned excuse; discover the main ground on 't.
JULIA   Why would you know this?
BOSOLA   I have depended on him,
    And I hear he is fallen in some disgrace
    With the emperor: if he be, like the mice
    That forsake falling houses, I would shift
195 To other dependence.
JULIA   You shall not need follow the wars;
    I'll be your maintenance.
BOSOLA   And I your loyal servant;
    But I cannot leave my calling.
JULIA   Not leave
    An ungrateful general for the love of a sweet lady?
200 You are like some cannot sleep in featherbeds,
    But must have blocks for their pillows.
BOSOLA   Will you do this?
JULIA   Cunningly.
BOSOLA   Tomorrow I'll expect th' intelligence.
JULIA   Tomorrow? Get you into my cabinet,°   inner chamber
    You shall have it with you. Do not delay me,
205 No more than I do you. I am like one
    That is condemned: I have my pardon promised,
    But I would see it sealed. Go, get you in;
    You shall see me wind my tongue about his heart
    Like a skein of silk.   [Exit BOSOLA.]
        [Reenter CARDINAL.]
CARDINAL   Where are you?
        [Enter SERVANTS.]
SERVANTS   Here.
210 CARDINAL   Let none, upon your lives,
    Have conference with the Prince Ferdinand,
    Unless I know it. [Aside] In this distraction
    He may reveal the murder.   [Exeunt SERVANTS.]
    Yond's my lingering consumption:
215 I am weary of her, and by any means
    Would be quit of.
JULIA   How now, my lord?
    What ails you?
CARDINAL   Nothing.
JULIA   Oh, you are much altered:
    Come, I must be your secretary,° and remove   confidante
    This lead from off your bosom.[4] What's the matter?
220 CARDINAL   I may not tell you.
JULIA   Are you so far in love with sorrow
    You cannot part with part of it? Or think you
    I cannot love your grace when you are sad

4. Secretaries opened letters addressed to their masters by removing the heavy lead seals.

As well as merry? Or do you suspect
225 I, that have been a secret to your heart
These many winters, cannot be the same
Unto your tongue?
CARDINAL   Satisfy thy longing—
The only way to make thee keep my counsel
Is not to tell thee.
230 JULIA   Tell your echo this,
Or flatterers, that like echoes still report
What they hear though most imperfect, and not me;
For if that you be true unto yourself,
I'll know.
CARDINAL   Will you rack° me?   *torture*
JULIA   No, judgment shall
Draw it from you: it is an equal fault,
235 To tell one's secrets unto all or none.
CARDINAL   The first argues folly.
JULIA   But the last, tyranny.
CARDINAL   Very well. Why, imagine I have committed
Some secret deed which I desire the world
May never hear of.
JULIA   Therefore may not I know it?
240 You have concealed for me as great a sin
As adultery. Sir, never was occasion
For perfect trial of my constancy
Till now: sir, I beseech you—
CARDINAL   You'll repent it.
JULIA   Never.
245 CARDINAL   It hurries thee to ruin: I'll not tell thee.
Be well advised, and think what danger 'tis
To receive a prince's secrets: they that do,
Had need have their breasts hooped with adamant°   *the hardest metal*
To contain them. I pray thee, yet be satisfied;
250 Examine thine own frailty; 'tis more easy
To tie knots than unloose them: 'tis a secret
That, like a lingering poison, may chance lie
Spread in thy veins, and kill thee seven year hence.
JULIA   Now you dally with me.
CARDINAL   No more; thou shalt know it.
255 By my appointment the great Duchess of Malfi
And two of her young children, four nights since,
Were strangled.
JULIA   O Heaven! Sir, what have you done?
CARDINAL   How now? How settles this? Think you your bosom
Will be a grave dark and obscure enough
For such a secret?
260 JULIA   You have undone yourself, sir.
CARDINAL   Why?
JULIA   It lies not in me to conceal it.
CARDINAL   No?

Come, I will swear you to 't upon this book.
JULIA   Most religiously.
CARDINAL   Kiss it.   [*She kisses the book.*]
                              Now you shall
265   Never utter it; thy curiosity
      Hath undone thee: thou'rt poisoned with that book.
      Because I knew thou couldst not keep my counsel,
      I have bound thee to 't by death.
              [*Reenter* BOSOLA.]
BOSOLA   For pity sake,
      Hold!
CARDINAL   Ha! Bosola?
JULIA   I forgive you
      This equal piece of justice you have done;
270   For I betrayed your counsel to that fellow:
      He overheard it; that was the cause I said
      It lay not in me to conceal it.
BOSOLA   O foolish woman,
      Couldst not thou have poisoned him?
JULIA   'Tis weakness,
      Too much to think what should have been done. I go
      I know not whither.   [*Dies.*]
275   CARDINAL   Wherefore com'st thou hither?
BOSOLA   That I might find a great man like yourself,
      Not out of his wits as the Lord Ferdinand,
      To remember my service.
CARDINAL   I'll have thee hewed in pieces.
BOSOLA   Make not yourself such a promise of that life
      Which is not yours to dispose of.
280   CARDINAL   Who placed thee here?
BOSOLA   Her lust, as she intended.
CARDINAL   Very well.
      Now you know me for your fellow murderer.
BOSOLA   And wherefore should you lay fair marble colors
      Upon your rotten purposes to me?[5]
285   Unless you imitate some that do plot great treasons,
      And when they have done, go hide themselves i' th' graves
      Of those were actors in 't?
CARDINAL   No more; there is
      A fortune attends thee.
BOSOLA   Shall I go sue to Fortune any longer?
      'Tis the fool's pilgrimage.
290   CARDINAL   I have honors in store for thee.
BOSOLA   There are a many ways that conduct to seeming
      Honor, and some of them very dirty ones.
CARDINAL   Throw to the devil
      Thy melancholy; the fire burns well,
      What need we keep a stirring of 't, and make

---

5. Plaster was often painted to look like marble.

295 A greater smother? Thou wilt kill Antonio?

BOSOLA   Yes.

CARDINAL   Take up that body.

BOSOLA   I think I shall
Shortly grow the common bier for churchyards!

CARDINAL   I will allow thee some dozen of attendants
To aid thee in the murder.

300 BOSOLA   Oh, by no means. Physicians that apply horse leeches to any rank
swelling use to cut off their tails, that the blood may run through them
the faster. Let me have no train[6] when I go to shed blood, lest it make me
have a greater when I ride to the gallows.[7]

CARDINAL   Come to me after midnight, to help to remove that body to her
305 own lodging. I'll give out she died of the plague; 'twill breed the less
inquiry after her death.

BOSOLA   Where's Castruccio her husband?

CARDINAL   He's rode to Naples to take possession of Antonio's citadel.

BOSOLA   Believe me, you have done a very happy turn.

310 CARDINAL   Fail not to come. There is the master key of our lodgings, and
by that you may conceive what trust I plant in you.

BOSOLA   You shall find me ready.   [*Exit* CARDINAL.]
Oh poor Antonio, though nothing be so needful
To thy estate as pity, yet I find
315 Nothing so dangerous. I must look to my footing;
In such slippery ice-pavements men had need
To be frost-nailed well;[8] they may break their necks else;
The precedent's here afore me. How this man
Bears up in blood! Seems fearless! Why, 'tis well:
320 Security some men call the suburbs of hell,
Only a dead° wall between. Well, good Antonio,   *bare*
I'll seek thee out, and all my care shall be
To put thee into safety from the reach
Of these most cruel biters that have got
325 Some of thy blood already. It may be,
I'll join with thee in a most just revenge:
The weakest arm is strong enough that strikes
With the sword of justice. Still methinks the duchess
Haunts me. There, there, 'tis nothing but my melancholy.
330 O Penitence, let me truly taste thy cup,
That throws men down only to raise them up!   [*Exit.*]

SCENE 3. *A fortification at Milan.*

[*Enter* ANTONIO *and* DELIO. *Echo from the* DUCHESS' *grave.*]

DELIO   Yond's the cardinal's window. This fortification
Grew from the ruins of an ancient abbey;
And to yond side o' th' river lies a wall,
Piece of a cloister, which in my opinion

---

6. Followers.
7. Criminals, carted through the streets to be

hanged at Tyburn, were followed by crowds.
8. To wear hobnailed boots.

5 Gives the best echo that you ever heard,
So hollow and so dismal, and withal°   *in addition*
So plain in the distinction of our words,
That many have supposed it is a spirit
That answers.

ANTONIO   I do love these ancient ruins.
10 We never tread upon them but we set
Our foot upon some reverend history:
And, questionless, here in this open court,
Which now lies naked to the injuries
Of stormy weather, some men lie interred
15 Loved the church so well, and gave so largely to 't,
They thought it should have canopied their bones
Till doomsday; but all things have their end:
Churches and cities, which have diseases like to men,
Must have like death that we have.

ECHO   "Like death that we have."
DELIO   Now the echo hath caught you.
20 ANTONIO   It groaned, methought, and gave
A very deadly accent.

ECHO   "Deadly accent."
DELIO   I told you 'twas a pretty one: you may make it
A huntsman, or a falconer, a musician,
Or a thing of sorrow.

ECHO   "A thing of sorrow."
ANTONIO   Aye, sure, that suits it best.
25 ECHO   "That suits it best."
ANTONIO   'Tis very like my wife's voice.

ECHO   "Aye, wife's voice."
DELIO   Come, let's walk further from 't. I would not have you
Go to th' cardinal's tonight: do not.

ECHO   "Do not."
DELIO   Wisdom doth not more moderate wasting sorrow
30 Than time: take time for 't; be mindful of thy safety.

ECHO   "Be mindful of thy safety."
ANTONIO   Necessity compels me:
Make° scrutiny throughout the passes   *if you make*
Of your own life, you'll find it impossible
To fly your fate.

ECHO   "Oh, fly your fate."
35 DELIO   Hark! The dead stones seem to have pity on you,
And give you good counsel.

ANTONIO   Echo, I will not talk with thee,
For thou art a dead thing.

ECHO   "Thou art a dead thing."
ANTONIO   My duchess is asleep now,
40 And her little ones, I hope sweetly: O heaven,
Shall I never see her more?

ECHO   "Never see her more."
ANTONIO   I marked° not one repetition of the echo   *attended to*

But that, and on the sudden a clear light
Presented me a face folded in sorrow.

DELIO   Your fancy merely.

45   ANTONIO   Come, I'll be out of this ague,°   fever
For to live thus is not indeed to live;
It is a mockery and abuse of life.
I will not henceforth save myself by halves;
Lose all, or nothing.

DELIO   Your own virtue save you!

50   I'll fetch your eldest son, and second you°   back you up
It may be that the sight of his own blood
Spread in so sweet a figure° may beget   face
The more compassion.

ANTONIO   However, fare you well.
Though in our miseries Fortune have a part,

55   Yet in our noble sufferings she hath none:
Contempt of pain, that we may call our own.   [*Exeunt.*]

SCENE 4. *A room in the* CARDINAL'S *palace.*

[*Enter* CARDINAL, PESCARA, MALATESTE, RODERIGO, *and* GRISOLAN.]

CARDINAL   You shall not watch tonight by the sick prince;
His grace is very well recovered.

MALATESTE   Good my lord, suffer° us.   allow

CARDINAL   Oh, by no means;
The noise and change of object in his eye

5   Doth more distract him. I pray, all to bed;
And though you hear him in his violent fit,
Do not rise, I entreat you.

PESCARA   So, sir; we shall not.

CARDINAL   Nay, I must have you promise upon your honors,
For I was enjoined to 't by himself; and he seemed
To urge it sensibly.°   with strong feeling

10   PESCARA   Let our honors bind
This trifle.

CARDINAL   Nor any of your followers.

MALATESTE   Neither.

CARDINAL   It may be, to make trial of your promise,
When he's asleep, myself will rise and feign

15   Some of his mad tricks, and cry out for help,
And feign myself in danger.

MALATESTE   If your throat were cutting,
I'd not come at you, now I have protested against it.

CARDINAL   Why, I thank you.   [*Withdraws.*]

GRISOLAN   'Twas a foul storm tonight.

RODERIGO   The Lord Ferdinand's chamber shook like an
osier.°   a willow wand

20   MALATESTE   'Twas nothing but pure kindness in the devil,
To rock his own child.   [*Exeunt all except the* CARDINAL.]

CARDINAL   The reason why I would not suffer° these   allow

About my brother is because at midnight
I may with better privacy convey
25 Julia's body to her own lodging. Oh, my conscience!
I would pray now, but the devil takes away my heart
For having any confidence in prayer.
About this hour I appointed Bosola
To fetch the body: when he hath served my turn,
30 He dies.   *[Exit.]*
        [Enter BOSOLA.*]*
BOSOLA   Ha! 'Twas the cardinal's voice; I heard him name
Bosola and my death. Listen! I hear
One's footing.
        [Enter FERDINAND.*]*
FERDINAND   Strangling is a very quiet death.
35 BOSOLA *[aside]*   Nay, then, I see I must stand upon my guard.
FERDINAND   What say to that? Whisper softly; do you agree to 't? So; it must
be done i' th' dark: the cardinal would not for a thousand pounds the doc-
tor should see it.   *[Exit.]*
BOSOLA   My death is plotted; here's the consequence of murder.
40 We value not desert nor Christian breath,
When we know black deeds must be cured with death.
        [Enter ANTONIO *and* SERVANT.*]*
SERVANT   Here stay, sir, and be confident, I pray:
I'll fetch you a dark lantern.   *[Exit.]*
ANTONIO   Could I take him at his prayers,
There were hope of pardon.
45 BOSOLA   Fall right, my sword!   *[Stabs him.]*
I'll not give thee so much leisure as to pray.
ANTONIO   Oh, I am gone! Thou hast ended a long suit[1]
In a minute.
BOSOLA   What art thou?
ANTONIO   A most wretched thing,
That only have thy benefit in death,
To appear myself.
        [Reenter SERVANT *with a lantern.]*
50 SERVANT   Where are you, sir?
ANTONIO   Very near my home. Bosola?
SERVANT   Oh, misfortune!
BOSOLA   Smother thy pity; thou art dead else.° Antonio?   *otherwise*
The man I would have saved 'bove mine own life!
We are merely the stars' tennis balls, struck and bandied
55 Which way please them.[2] O good Antonio,
I'll whisper one thing in thy dying ear
Shall make thy heart break quickly! Thy fair duchess
And two sweet children—
ANTONIO   Their very names
Kindle a little life in me.

5.4
1. Antonio thinks it is the cardinal, to whom he came to address a plea ("suit"), who has stabbed him.

2. The power of the stars over people's lives was a Renaissance commonplace.

BOSOLA   Are murdered.

60   ANTONIO   Some men have wished to die
       At the hearing of sad tidings; I am glad
       That I shall do 't in sadness: I would not now
       Wish my wounds balmed nor healed, for I have no use
       To put my life to. In all our quest of greatness,
65   Like wanton boys, whose pastime is their care,
       We follow after bubbles blown in th' air.
       Pleasure of life, what is't? Only the good hours
       Of an ague; merely a preparative to rest,
       To endure vexation. I do not ask
70   The process° of my death; only commend me   *reason, circumstances*
       To Delio.

BOSOLA   Break, heart!

ANTONIO   And let my son fly the courts of princes.   [*Dies.*]

BOSOLA   Thou seem'st to have loved Antonio?

SERVANT   I brought him hither
       To have reconciled him to the cardinal.

75   BOSOLA   I do not ask thee that.
       Take him up, if thou tender thine own life,
       And bear him where the lady Julia
       Was wont to lodge. Oh, my fate moves swift;
       I have this cardinal in the forge already;
80   Now I'll bring him to th' hammer. Oh direful
         misprision!°   *misunderstanding*
       I will not imitate things glorious,
       No more than base; I'll be mine own example.
       On, on, and look thou represent,° for silence,   *imitate*
       The thing thou bear'st.[3]   [*Exeunt.*]

SCENE 5. *The scene continues.*

[*Enter* CARDINAL, *with a book.*]

CARDINAL   I am puzzled in a question about hell:
       He says, in hell there's one material fire,
       And yet it shall not burn all men alike.
       Lay him by. How tedious is a guilty conscience!
5   When I look into the fish ponds in my garden,
       Methinks I see a thing armed with a rake,
       That seems to strike at me.

[*Enter* BOSOLA, *and* SERVANT *bearing* ANTONIO's *body.*]
                          Now, art thou come?
       Thou look'st ghastly:
       There sits in thy face some great determination
       Mixed with some fear.

10   BOSOLA   Thus it lightens° into action: *ignites*
       I am come to kill thee.

CARDINAL   Ha! Help! Our guard!

BOSOLA   Thou art deceived; they are out of thy howling.

---

3. The corpse.

CARDINAL   Hold; and I will faithfully divide
  Revenues with thee.
BOSOLA   Thy prayers and proffers
  Are both unseasonable.
15   CARDINAL   Raise the watch!
  We are betrayed!
BOSOLA   I have confined your flight:°   *cut off your escape*
  I'll suffer your retreat to Julia's chamber,
  But no further.
CARDINAL   Help! We are betrayed!
      [*Enter, above,* PESCARA, MALATESTE, RODERIGO, *and* GRISOLAN.]
MALATESTE   Listen.
CARDINAL   My dukedom for rescue!
RODERIGO   Fie upon his counterfeiting!
MALATESTE   Why, 'tis not the cardinal.
20   RODERIGO   Yes, yes, 'tis he,
  But I'll see him hanged ere I'll go down to him.
CARDINAL   Here's a plot upon me. I am assaulted! I am lost,
  Unless some rescue.
GRISOLAN   He doth this pretty well,
  But it will not serve to laugh me out of my honor.
CARDINAL   The sword's at my throat!
25   RODERIGO   You would not bawl so loud then.
MALATESTE   Come, come, let's go to bed. He told us thus much aforehand.
PESCARA   He wished you should not come at him; but, believe 't,
  The accent of the voice sounds not in jest:
  I'll down to him, howsoever, and with engines.°   *battering rams*
  Force ope the doors   [*Exit above.*]
30   RODERIGO   Let's follow him aloof,°   *at a distance*
  And note how the cardinal will laugh at him.
      [*Exeunt, above,* MALATESTE, RODERIGO, *and* GRISOLAN.]
BOSOLA   There's for you first,   [*He kills the* SERVANT.]
  'Cause you shall not unbarricade the door
  To let in rescue.
CARDINAL   What cause hast thou to pursue my life?
35   BOSOLA   Look there.
CARDINAL   Antonio?
BOSOLA   Slain by my hand unwittingly.
  Pray, and be sudden: when thou killed'st thy sister,
  Thou took'st from Justice her most equal balance,
  And left her naught but her sword.
CARDINAL   Oh, mercy!
40   BOSOLA   Now it seems thy greatness was only outward;
  For thou fall'st faster of thyself than calamity
  Can drive thee. I'll not waste longer time: there!   [*Stabs him.*]
CARDINAL   Thou hast hurt me.
BOSOLA   Again!   [*Stabs him again.*]
CARDINAL   Shall I die like a leveret,[1]

5.5
1. A baby hare.

Without any resistance? Help, help, help!
45 I am slain!
    [Enter FERDINAND.*]*
FERDINAND   Th' alarum? Give me a fresh horse;
   Rally the vaunt-guard, or the day is lost.
   Yield, yield! I give you the honor of arms,
   Shake my sword over you; will you yield?[2]
CARDINAL   Help me; I am your brother!
50 FERDINAND   The devil!
   My brother fight upon the adverse party?
    [He wounds the CARDINAL, *and, in the scuffle, gives* BOSOLA *his death*
    wound.]
   There flies your ransom.
CARDINAL   O justice!
   I suffer now for what hath former° been: *earlier*
   Sorrow is held the eldest child of sin.
55 FERDINAND   Now you're brave fellows. Caesar's fortune was harder than
   Pompey's; Caesar died in the arms of prosperity, Pompey at the feet of
   disgrace. You both died in the field. The pain's nothing: pain many times
   is taken away with the apprehension of greater, as the toothache with the
   sight of a barber that comes to pull it out: there's philosophy for you.
60 BOSOLA   Now my revenge is perfect. Sink, thou main cause
                          [He kills FERDINAND.*]*
   Of my undoing! The last part of my life
   Hath done me best service.
FERDINAND   Give me some wet hay; I am broken-winded.[3] I do account this
   world but a dog kennel: I will vault credit and affect high pleasures[4]
65 beyond death.
BOSOLA   He seems to come to himself, now he's so near the bottom.
FERDINAND   My sister, O my sister! There's the cause on 't.
   Whether we fall by ambition, blood, or lust,
   Like diamonds we are cut with our own dust.   *[Dies.]*
70 CARDINAL   Thou hast thy payment, too.
BOSOLA   Yes, I hold my weary soul in my teeth.
   'Tis ready to part from me. I do glory
   That thou, which stood'st like a huge pyramid
   Begun upon a large and ample base,
75 Shalt end in a little point, a kind of nothing.
    [Enter, below, PESCARA, MALATESTE, RODERIGO, *and* GRISOLAN.*]*
PESCARA   How now, my lord?
MALATESTE   O sad disaster!
RODERIGO   How comes this?
BOSOLA   Revenge for the Duchess of Malfi murdered
   By th' Aragonian brethren; for Antonio
   Slain by this hand; for lustful Julia
80 Poisoned by this man; and lastly for myself,

---

2. Ferdinand thinks he's on the field of battle and offering the "honor of arms" (liberal surrender terms) to his foes. "Vaunt-guard": vanguard.

3. Worn-out horses are said to be broken-winded.
4. Go beyond expectation and enjoy great pleasures.

That was an actor in the main of all,
Much 'gainst mine own good nature, yet i' th' end
Neglected.

PESCARA   How now, my lord?

CARDINAL   Look to my brother:
He gave us these large wounds as we were struggling
85 Here i' the rushes.[5] And now, I pray,
Let me be laid by and never thought of.   [*Dies.*]

PESCARA   How fatally, it seems, he did withstand
His own rescue!

MALATESTE   Thou wretched thing of blood,
How came Antonio by his death?

90 BOSOLA   In a mist: I know not how;
Such a mistake as I have often seen
In a play. Oh, I am gone!
We are only like dead walls or vaulted graves,
That, ruined, yield no echo. Fare you well.
95 It may be pain, but no harm to me to die
In so good a quarrel. Oh, this gloomy world,
In what a shadow or deep pit of darkness
Doth womanish and fearful mankind live!
Let worthy minds ne'er stagger in distrust
100 To suffer death or shame for what is just:
Mine is another voyage.   [*Dies.*]

PESCARA   The noble Delio, as I came to the palace,
Told me of Antonio's being here, and showed me
A pretty gentleman, his son and heir.
          [*Enter* DELIO *with* ANTONIO's SON.]

MALATESTE   O, sir, you come too late.

105 DELIO   I heard so, and
Was armed° for it ere I came. Let us make noble use   *prepared*
Of this great ruin, and join all our force
To establish this young hopeful° gentleman   *promising*
In 's mother's right. These wretched eminent things
110 Leave no more fame behind 'em, than should one
Fall in a frost, and leave his print in snow;
As soon as the sun shines, it ever melts
Both form and matter. I have ever thought
Nature doth nothing so great for great men
115 As when she's pleased to make them lords of truth:
Integrity of life is fame's best friend,
Which nobly, beyond death, shall crown the end.   [*Exeunt.*]

performed 1613   *published* 1623

---

5. Leafy plants, strewn over Elizabethan floors in lieu of carpets.

Gender Relations: Conflict and Counsel

What are women good for? By the English Renaissance, men had been debating this question for centuries. Seventeenth-century writing on the question of women's proper social place was an important topic in two quite different prose genres. On the one hand, rhetorically flashy polemics argued, often in a spirit of witty rhetorical gamesmanship, either that females were worthless or that they were superior to men. On the other hand, sober treatises of domestic management advised readers—generally presumptively male readers—how to choose a spouse and order a household. Of the selections here, Joseph Swetnam and Esther Speght exemplify the first kind of writing, and William Gouge the second.

Joseph Swetnam (ca. 1570?–1621) published his *Arraignment of Lewd, Idle, Froward, and Unconstant Women* in 1615, under the pseudonym Tom Tel-troth. Swetnam's rambling but lively attack on women cobbles together proverbs, rowdy jokes, and anecdotes, as well as often inexact or misattributed paraphrases of what various authorities had to say about women, evidently derived from anthologies and commonplace books. The latter were printed versions of the personal notebooks into which many readers were accustomed to copy, under various headings depending on interest and use, quotations and citations from their reading. *The Arraignment* touched off a pamphlet war between the years 1615 and 1620, including four reissues of Swetnam's book and at least eight rejoinders or related works. Two of the answers bear women's allegorical names, Esther Sowernam (a satiric play on Swe[e]tnam) and Constantia Munda ("steadfast world"); they may or may not have actually been written by women. Other works include a stage play, *Swetnam the Women-Hater Arraigned by Women* (1620), and two satires on cross-dressing (the satires are included in the supplemental ebook).

The first response to Swetnam, in 1617, and the only one of these tracts published under the author's own name, was *A Muzzle for Melastomus* (Black Mouth), by the nineteen-year-old Rachel Speght (ca 1597–?). Speght was the first Englishwoman to claim the role of polemicist and critic of gender ideology. Her tract defending women was published by, and perhaps solicited by, Swetnam's bookseller, Thomas Archer. While *A Muzzle* employs the railing attacks and witty ripostes expected in such a controversy, in most of the treatise Speght undertakes a serious argument. Her strategy resembles Aemelia Lanyer's in *Salve Deus Rex Judaeorum* (pp. 1431–36), reinterpreting controversial biblical texts to yield a more equitable concept of gender and challenging the stereotypes of female inferiority. Speght's father, a Calvinist clergyman and author himself, evidently provided her with some classical education—very rare for seventeenth-century women of any class. In her writings Rachel Speght displays a knowledge of Latin, some training in logic and rhetoric, and some familiarity with a range of learned authorities. In 1621 she published a long meditative poem, *Mortality's Memorandum*, which was occasioned by her mother's death. She prefaced it with an address to the reader reaffirming her authorship of *A Muzzle for Melastomus* and with a three-hundred-line autobiographical poem, "A Dream," available in the supplemental ebook, which vigorously defends the importance of education for women.

William Gouge (1575–1653) was a clergyman educated at King's College Cambridge, a prominent minister at St. Ann Blackfriars Church in London, and the father of thirteen children. His Puritan leanings occasionally led to friction with the authorities early in his career, but in the 1640s he was selected by Parliament to chair the committee that developed the Westminster Confession, a set of principles designed to reform the English church along Calvinist lines. The Protestant Reformation had altered attitudes toward marriage and family life; while the Catholic Church had honored celibacy and enjoined it for clergy, Protestants centered godly life on a harmonious marriage and the upbringing of devout children according to principles laid out in the Bible. This conviction spawned advice literature on the right ordering of the household, much of it written by ministers. *Of Domestical Duties*, perhaps the most thorough and popular of these manuals, was first published in 1622; new editions appeared in 1626 and 1634. Gouge not only devotes chapters to the proper roles of husband and wife but also discusses the obligations of children, and the relations between masters and servants. (All but the humblest seventeenth-century households employed domestic

Marriage. The Liturgy of Solemnizing Marriage from *The Book of Common Prayer* (1559), emphasized the purposes of marriage (with procreation primary), the indissolubility of marriage, and the biblical texts undergirding that definition of marriage. It also held up the ideal of mutual love and help, which is represented in this emblem from George Wither's *A Collection of Emblems* (1635). The Latin motto reads in English, "Hand Washes Hand."

help.) Gouge exemplifies moderate Puritan opinion, emphasizing the importance of love between married partners, and decrying the double sexual standard that tolerated adultery in the husband while condemning it in the wife. Yet Gouge is no feminist; he advocated a clear hierarchy in marriage, the husband firmly in charge and the wife embracing her submission willingly as her religious duty. The relation between a husband and wife, he argues, is analogous to the relationship between Christ and the church of which he is the head. It is interesting to compare Gouge's views to those of John Milton, another Puritan writer, in *Paradise Lost*.

JOSEPH SWETNAM

From The Arraignment of Lewd, Idle, Froward[1] and Unconstant Women: Or the Vanity of Them, Choose You Whether

Neither to the best, nor yet to the worst;
but to the common sort of women.

Musing with myself being idle, and having little ease to pass the time withal, and I being in a great choler[2] against some women, I mean more than one, and so in the rough of my fury, taking [I took] my pen in hand to beguile the time withal. Indeed, I might have employed myself to better use, than in such an idle business.

* * *

To the Reader. Read it, if you please, and like as you list: neither to the wisest clerk,[3] nor yet to the starkest fool, but unto the ordinary sort of giddy-headed young men, I send this greeting.

If thou mean to see the bearbaiting[4] of women, then trudge to this bear garden apace, and get in betimes,[5] and view every room where thou mayest best sit, for thy own pleasure, profit, and heart's ease, and bear with my rudeness if I chance to offend thee. But before I do open this trunk full of torments against women, I think it were not amiss . . . to drive all the women out of my hearing, for doubt lest this little spark kindle into such a flame, and raise so many stinging hornets humming about my ears, that all the wit I have will not quench the one, nor quiet the other. For I fear me I have set down more than they will like of, and yet a great deal less than they deserve: and for better proof, I refer myself to the judgment of men which have more experience than myself. For I esteem little of the malice of women, for men will be persuaded by reason, but women must be answered with silence, for I know women will bark more at me than Cerberus the two-headed dog did at Hercules, when he came into Hell to fetch out the fair Proserpina.[6]

* * *

---

1. Unruly, stubbornly willful.
2. Anger. Choler was one of the four humors, this one supposedly the source of anger and irascibility.
3. Scholar; originally, a clergyman (cleric).
4. Popular sport in medieval and early modern England in which a bear, chained to a post by his neck or one leg, was attacked by several dogs. The Paris Garden in Southwark was the largest

and most popular bear garden in London.
5. In good time.
6. Swetnam has confused several classical myths. Cerberus, the monster guarding the entrance to Hades, was said to have three (not two) heads, and Mercury (Hermes), not Hercules, was sent by Jove to release Proserpina. But the twelfth labor of Hercules was to bring Cerberus from Hades to the upper world.

Chapter I. This first chapter shows to what use women were made.
It also shows that most of them degenerate from the use they were framed
unto, by leading a proud, lazy, and idle life, to the great hindrance
of their poor husbands.

Moses describes a woman thus: at the first beginning (says he) a woman was made to be a helper unto man,[7] and so they are indeed: for she helps to spend and consume that which man painfully gets. He also says that they were made of the rib of a man,[8] and that their froward nature shows; for a rib is a crooked thing, good for nothing else, and women are crooked by nature, for small occasion will cause them to be angry.

Again, in a manner, she was no sooner made, but straightway her mind was set upon mischief, for by her aspiring mind and wanton will she quickly procured man's fall, and therefore ever since they are and have been a woe unto man, and follow the line of their first leader.[9]

For I pray you let us consider the times past, with the time present. First, that of David and Solomon, if they had occasion so many hundred years ago to exclaim so bitterly against women, for the one of them said, that it was better to be a doorkeeper, and better dwell in a den among lions, than to be in the house with a froward and wicked woman. And the other said, that the climbing up of a sandy hill to an aged man was nothing so wearisome as to be troubled with a froward woman.[1] . . . . If a woman hold an opinion, no man can draw her from it; tell her of her fault, she will not believe that she is in any fault; give her good counsel, but she will not take it. If you do but look after another woman, then she will be jealous, the more thou lovest her, the more she will disdain thee, and if thou threaten her, then she will be angry, flatter her, and then she will be proud, and if thou forbear her, it makes her bold, and if thou chasten her, then she will turn into a serpent. At a word, a woman will never forget an injury, nor give thanks for a good turn. What wise man then will exchange gold for dross, pleasure for pain, a quiet life, for wrangling brawls, from the which married men are never free.

And what of all this? Why nothing, but to tell thee that a woman is better lost than found, better forsaken than taken. Saint Paul says, that they which marry, do well, but he also says, that they which marry not, do better,[2] and he no doubt was well advised what he spoke. Then, if thou be wise, keep thy head out of the halter and take heed before thou have cause to curse thy hard pennyworth,[3] or wish the priest speechless which knit the knot.

---

7. Genesis 2.18: "And the Lord God said, It is not good that the man should be alone; I will make him an help meet for him."
8. Genesis 2.21–22.
9. I.e., Eve.
1. Swetnam evidently relies on his imperfect memory or on careless notes. The comparisons he paraphrases are not from Solomon or David but from the biblical Apocrypha, attributed in the Book of Ecclesiasticus to Jesus Son of Sir-

ach: "I had rather dwell with a lion and a dragon, than to keep house with a wicked woman. . . . As the climbing up a sandy way is to the feet of the aged, so is a wife full of words to a quiet man."
2. 1 Corinthians 7.38: "So then he that giveth her [his virgin] in marriage doeth well; but he that giveth her not in marriage doeth better." Swetnam takes the quote out of context.
3. Something, in this case a wife, that is worth only a penny.

The philosophers which lived in the old time, their opinions were so hard of marriage that they never delighted therein, for one of them being asked why he married not? he answered, that it was too soon. And afterwards when he was old, he was asked the same question, and he said then that it was too late.

* * *

If thou marriest a woman of evil report, her discredits will be a spot in thy brow; thou canst not go in the street with her without mocks, nor among thy neighbors without frumps.[4] And commonly the fairest women are soonest enticed to yield unto vanity. He that has a fair wife and a whetstone, everyone will be whetting thereon.[5] And a castle is hard to keep when it is assaulted by many, and fair women are commonly caught at. He that marries a fair woman, everyone will wish his death to enjoy her. And if thou be never so rich, and yet but a clown[6] in condition, then will thy fair wife have her credit to please her fancy, for a diamond has not his grace but in gold, no more has a fair woman her full commendations but in the ornament of her bravery,[7] by which means there are divers women whose beauty has brought their husbands into great poverty and discredit by their pride and whoredom. A fair woman commonly will go like a peacock, and her husband must go like a woodcock.[8]

1615

4. Derisive jeers.
5. A whetstone is an abrasive stone for sharpening knives or other edged tools. The bawdy joke suggests that "everyone" will make use of both the stone and the fair wife.
6. A countryman, one who is uncouth or ill-bred.
7. Her rich and showy clothing and jewelry.
8. A common European migratory bird with mottled brown plumage; easily taken in a snare, it was associated with gullibility.

RACHEL SPEGHT

From A Muzzle for Melastomus[1]

Not unto the veriest idiot that ever set pen to paper, but to the cynical[2] baiter of women, or metamorphosed Misogunes,[3] Joseph Swetnam.

From standing water, which soon putrifies, can no good fish be expected, for it produces no other creatures but those that are venomous or noisome, as snakes, and such like. Semblably,[4] no better stream can we look should issue from your idle corrupt brain than that whereto the rough of your fury (to use your own words) has moved you to open the sluice. In which excrement of your roving cognitions you have used such irregularities touching

1. Black mouth.
2. A play on the Latin *cynicus*, "canine," "dog-like."
3. Hater of women (Greek, cf. Misogynist).

Speght identifies Swetnam as the author of the *Arraignment*, which he had signed Thomas Telltroth.
4. Likewise.

concordance,[5] and observed so disordered a method, as I doubt not to tell you, that a very accidence scholar would have quite put you down[6] in both. You appear herein not unlike that painter who, seriously endeavoring to portray Cupid's bow, forgot the string.[7] For you, being greedy to botch up your mingle mangle invective against women, have not therein observed, in many places, so much as a grammar sense.[8] But the emptiest barrel makes the loudest sound, and so we will account of you.

Many propositions have you framed, which, as you think, make much against women, but if one would make a logical assumption, the conclusion would be flat against your own sex. Your dealing wants so much discretion that I doubt whether to bestow so good a name as the dunce upon you: but minority[9] bids me keep within my bounds. And therefore I only say unto you that your corrupt heart and railing tongue have made you a fit scribe for the Devil.

In that you have termed your virulent foam *The Bearbaiting of Women*, you have plainly displayed your own disposition to be cynical, in that there appears no other dog or bull to bait them, but yourself. Good had it been for you to have put on that muzzle which Saint James would have all Christians to wear: "Speak not evil one of another,"[1] and then you had not seemed so like the serpent Porphirus, as now you do; which, though full of deadly poison, yet being toothless, hurts none so much as himself.[2] For you having gone beyond the limits not of humanity alone but of Christianity, have done greater harm unto your own soul than unto women, as may plainly appear. First, in dishonoring of God by palpable blasphemy, wresting and perverting every place of Scripture that you have alleged, which by the testimony of Saint Peter, is to the destruction of them that do so.[3] Secondly, it appears by your disparaging of, and opprobrious speeches against, that excellent work of God's hands, which in his great love he perfected for the comfort of man. Thirdly, and lastly, by this your hodgepodge of heathenish sentences, similes, and examples, you have set forth yourself in your right colors unto the view of the world, and I doubt not but the judicious will account of you according to your demerit. As for the vulgar sort, which have no more learning than you have showed in your book, it is likely they will applaud you for your pains.

* * *

Of Woman's excellency, with the causes of her creation, and of the sympathy which ought to be in man and wife each toward other.

* * *

True it is, as is already confessed, that women first sinned, yet find we no mention of spiritual nakedness till man had sinned. Then it is said, "Their

---

5. Agreement of the parts of a sentence, according to the rules of grammar.
6. Revealed your errors and thereby disgraced you. "Accidence scholar": a schoolboy learning his Latin grammar.
7. This may refer not to an actual image, but rather to the omission of what is crucially important.
8. See his first sentence for an example.

9. Her own youth (she is just nineteen years old).
1. James 4.11. This and later biblical texts, marked (M) in these notes, are identified in the margins of Speght's original text as evidence of scholarly accuracy.
2. This toothless but venomous serpent is discussed in the naturalist Topsell's volume *Serpents*, though not the quality of hurting only himself.
3. 2 Peter 3.16 (M).

eyes were opened,"[4] the eyes of their mind and conscience, and then perceived they themselves naked, that is, not only bereft of their integrity which they originally had, but felt the rebellion and disobedience of their members in the disordered motions of their now corrupt nature, which made them for shame to cover their nakedness. Then, and not before, it is said that they saw it, as if sin were imperfect, and unable to bring a deprivation of a blessing received, or death on all mankind, till man, in whom lay the active power of generation, had transgressed. The offense therefore of Adam and Eve is by Saint Augustine thus distinguished, "the man sinned against God and himself, the woman against God, herself, and her husband."[5] Yet in her giving of the fruit to eat she had no malicious intent toward him, but did therein show a desire to make her husband partaker of that happiness which she thought by their eating they should both have enjoyed. This her giving Adam of that sauce wherewith Satan had served her, whose sourness before he had eaten she did not perceive, was that which made her sin to exceed his. Wherefore, that she might not of him who ought to honor her be abhorred, the first promise that was made in Paradise God made to woman, that by her seed should the serpent's head be broken.[6] Whereupon Adam calls her *Hevah*, life,[7] that as the woman had been an occasion of sin, so should woman bring forth the Savior from sin, which was in the fullness of time accomplished . . . so that by Eve's blessed seed (as Saint Paul affirms) it is brought to pass, "that male and female are all one in Christ Jesus."[8]

* * *

The efficient cause of woman's creation was Jehovah the Eternal, the truth of which is manifest in Moses his narration of the six days works, where he says, "God created them male and female."[9] And David, exhorting all the earth to sing unto the Lord, meaning, by a metonymy,[1] earth, all creatures that live on the earth of which nation or sex soever, gives this reason, "For the Lord hath made us."[2] That work, then, cannot choose but be good, yea very good, which is wrought by so excellent a workman as the Lord, for he being a glorious creator, must needs effect a worthy creature. . . .

Secondly, the material cause, or matter whereof woman was made, was of a refined mold, if I may so speak. For man was created of the dust of the earth, but woman was made of a part of man, after that he was a living soul. Yet was she not produced from Adam's foot, to be his too low inferior, nor from his head to be his superior, but from his side, near his heart, to be his equal. That where he is lord she may be lady: and therefore said God concerning man and woman jointly, "Let them rule over the fish of the sea,

4. Genesis 3.7 (M).
5. This formula became a commonplace, perhaps derived (very loosely) from some phrases in St. Augustine's sermon "De Adam et Eva et Sancta Maria."
6. Genesis 3.15 (M).
7. Genesis 3.20 (M).
8. Galatians 3.28 (M).
9. Genesis 1.27 (M). Speght here begins her analysis of woman's creation according to Aristotle's four causes of the making of any object: the efficient cause is the agent who made it; the material cause is the matter of which it is made; the formal cause is the plan or design by which it is formed; the final cause is the purpose for which it is made.
1. A figure of speech in which a part or attribute of a thing is used for the whole.
2. Psalms 100.3 (M).

and over the fowls of the heaven, and over every beast that moves upon the earth."[3] By which words he makes their authority equal, and all creatures to be in subjection unto them both. . . .

Thirdly, the formal cause, fashion, and proportion of a woman was excellent. For she was neither like the beasts of the earth, fowls of the air, fishes of the sea, or any other inferior creature, but man was the only object which she did resemble. For as God gave man a lofty countenance, that he might look up toward heaven, so did he likewise give unto woman. And as the temperature[4] of man's body is excellent, so is woman's. . . . And (that more is) in the image of God were they both created; yea and to be brief, all the parts of their bodies, both external and internal, were correspondent and meet each for other.

Fourthly and lastly, the final cause or end, for which woman was made, was to glorify God, and to be a collateral companion for man to glorify God, in using her body and all the parts, powers, and faculties thereof, as instruments for his honor.

* * *

To the Reader[5]

Although (courteous reader) I am young in years and more defective in knowledge, that little smattering in learning which I have obtained being only the fruit of such vacant hours as I could spare from affairs befitting my sex, yet am I not altogether ignorant of that analogy which ought to be used in a literate responsory.[6] But the bearbaiting of women, unto which I have framed my apologetical[7] answer, being altogether without method, irregular, without grammatical concordance, and a promiscuous mingle mangle, it would admit no such order to be observed in the answering thereof, as a regular responsory requires. * * *

1617

3. Genesis 1.26 (M).
4. Mixture or composition of elements.
5. This preface introduces a brief satiric treatise appended to *A Muzzle*, titled "Certain *Quaeres* to

the baiter of women, with confutation of some parts of his diabolical discipline."
6. Answer or reply.
7. Offering a defense or vindication.

WILLIAM GOUGE

From Of Domestical Duties

Of a wife's subjection in general.

The first point to be handled in the treatise of wives' particular duties is the general matter of all under which all other particulars are comprised, for it hath as large an extent as that honor which is required in the first commandment being applied to wives. When first the Lord declared unto the woman[1] her duty, he set it down under this phrase: "Thy desire shall be subject to thine husband" (Genesis 3:16).

Objection. That was a punishment inflicted on her for her transgression?

Answer. And a law too, for trial of her obedience, which if it be not observed, her nature will be more depraved, and her fault more increased. Besides, we cannot but think that the woman was made before the Fall, that the man might rule over her. Upon this ground the Prophets and Apostles have oft urged the same. Sarah is commended for this, that she was subject to her husband (1 Peter 3:6).[2] Hereby the Holy Ghost would teach wives, that subjection ought to be as salt to season every duty which they perform to their husband. Their very opinion, affection, speech, action, and all that concerneth the husband, must savor of subjection. Contrary is the disposition of many wives, whom ambition hath tainted and corrupted within and without: they cannot endure to hear of subjection: they imagine that they are made slaves thereby. But I hope partly by that which hath been before delivered[3] concerning those common duties which man and wife do mutually owe each to other, and partly by the particulars which under this general are comprised, but most especially by the duties which the husband in particular oweth to his wife, it will evidently appear, that this subjection is no servitude. But were it more than it is, seeing God requireth subjection of a wife to her husband, the wife is bound to yield it. And good reason it is that she who first drew man into sin, should be now subject to him, lest by the like womanish weakness she fall again.

Of an husband's superiority over a wife, to be acknowledged by the wife.

The subjection which is required of a wife to her husband implieth two things.

1. That she acknowledge her husband to be her superior.
2. That she respect him as her superior.

That acknowledgement of the husband's superiority is twofold,

1. General of any husband.
2. Particular of her own husband.

The general is the ground of the particular:[4] for till a wife be informed that an husband, by virtue of his place, is his wife's superior, she will not be persuaded that her own husband is above her, or hath any authority over her.

First therefore concerning the general, I will lay down some evident and undeniable proofs, to show that an husband is his wife's superior, and hath authority over her. The proofs are these following.

1. God of whom, the powers that be ordained, are (Romans 13:1), hath power to place his image in whom he will, and to whom God giveth superiority and authority, the same ought to be acknowledged to be due unto them. But God said of the man to the woman, he shall rule over thee (Genesis 3:16).

---

1. Eve, after the Fall in the Garden of Eden.
2. Sarah was the wife of the patriarch Abraham.
3. Earlier in Gouge's treatise.
4. Once the general premise (the superiority of all husbands) is established, the particular instance (the superiority of a woman's own husband) will follow logically from it.

2. Nature hath placed an eminency in the male over the female: so as where they are linked together in one yoke, it is given by nature that he should govern, she obey. This did the heathen by light of nature observe.

3. The titles and names, whereby an husband is set forth, do imply a superiority and authority in him, as "lord" (1 Peter 3:6), "master" (Esther), "guide" (Proverbs 2:17), "head" (1 Corinthians 2:3), "image and glory of God" (1 Corinthians 11:7).

4. The persons whom the husband by virtue of his place, and whom the wife by virtue of her place, represent, most evidently prove as much: for an husband representeth Christ, and a wife, the Church (Ephesians 5:23).

5. The circumstances noted by the Holy Ghost at the woman's creation imply no less, as that she was created after man, for man's good, and out of man's side (Genesis 2:18, etc.).

6. The very attire which nature and custom of all times and places have taught women to put on, comfirmeth the same: as long hair, veils, and other coverings over the head: this and the former argument doth the Apostle[5] himself use to this very purpose, (1 Corinthians 11:7, etc.).

The point then being so clear, wives ought in conscience to acknowledge as much: namely that an husband hath superiority and authority over a wife. The acknowledgement hereof is a main and principal duty, and a ground of all other duties. Till a wife be fully instructed therein and truly persuaded thereof, no duty can be performed by her as it ought: for subjection hath relation to superiority and authority. The very notation of the word implieth as much. How then can subjection be yielded, if husbands be not acknowledged superiors? It may be forced, as one king conquered in battle by another, may be compelled to yield homage to the conqueror, but yet because he still thinketh with himself, that he is no whit inferior, he will hardly be brought willingly to yield a subject's duty to him, but rather expect a time when he may free himself and take revenge of the conqueror.

Of a fond conceit[6] that husband and wife are equal.

Contrary to the forenamed subjection is the opinion of many wives, who think themselves every way as good as their husbands, and no way inferior to them.

The reason whereof seemeth to be that small inequality which is betwixt the husband and the wife: for of all degrees wherein there is any difference betwixt person and person, there is the least disparity betwixt man and wife. Though the man be as the head, yet is the woman as the heart, which is the most excellent part of the body next the head, far more excellent than any other member under the head, and almost equal to the head in many respects, and as necessary as the head. As an evidence, that a wife is to man as the heart to the head, she was at her first creation (Genesis 2:21) taken out of the side of man where his heart lieth; and though the woman was at first of the man (1 Corinthians 11:12) created out of his side, yet is the man also by the woman. Ever since the first creation man hath been born and brought forth out of the woman's womb: so as neither the man is without the woman, nor the woman without the man: yea, as the wife hath not power of his own

---

5. The Apostle Paul.   6. Foolish idea.

body, but he wife (1 Corinthians 7:4).[7] They are also heirs together of the grace of life (1 Peter 3:7). Besides, wives are mothers of the same children, whereof their husbands are fathers [for God said to both, multiply and increase (Genesis 1:28)] and mistresses of the same servants whereof they are masters [for Sarah is called mistress (Genesis 16:4)] and in many other respects there is common equity betwixt husbands and wives; whence many wives gather that in all things there ought to be a mutual equality.

But from some particulars to infer a general is a very weak argument.

1. Doth it follow, that because in many things there is a common equity betwixt judges of office, justices of peace, and constables of towns, that therefore there is in all things an equality betwixt them?

2. In many things there is not a common equity: for the husband may command his wife, but not she him.

3. Even in those things wherein there is a common equity, there is not an equality: for the husband hath ever even in all things a superiority: as if there be any difference even in the forenamed instances, the husband must have the stronger: as in giving the name of Rachel's youngest child, where the wife would have one name, the husband another, that name which the husband gave, stood (Genesis 35:18).

Though there seem to be never so little disparity, yet God having so expressly appointed subjection, it ought to be acknowledged: and though husband and wife may mutually serve one another through love: yet the Apostle suffereth not a woman to rule over a man. . . .

Of a wife's acknowledgment of her own husband's superiority.

The truth and life of that general acknowledgment of husbands' honor, consisteth in the particular application thereof unto their own proper husbands.

The next duty therefore is, that wives acknowledge their own husbands, even those to whom by God's providence they are joined in marriage, to be worthy of an husband's honor, and to be their superior: thus much the Apostle intendeth by that particle of restraint (Ephesians 5:22,24) which he useth very often: so likewise doth St. Peter, exhorting wives to be in subjection to their own husbands (1 Peter 3:1,5): and hereunto restraining the commendation of the ancient good wives, that they were in subjection to their own husbands.

Objection. What if a man of mean place be married to a woman of eminent place, or a servant to be married to his mistress, or an aged woman to a youth, must such a wife acknowledge such an husband her superior?

Answer. Yea, verily: for in giving herself to be his wife, and taking him to be her husband, she advanceth him above herself, and subjecteth herself unto him. It meaneth nothing what either of them were before marriage: by virtue of that matrimonial bond the husband is made the head of his wife, though the husband were before marriage a very beggar, and of mean parentage, and the wife very wealthy and of a noble stock; or though he were her prentice, or bondslave; which also holdeth in the case betwixt an aged woman and a youth: for the Scripture hath made no exception in any of those cases.

7. The text seems corrupt at this point: Corinthians 1.7.4 reads in full: "The wife hath not power of her own body, but the husband: and likewise also the husband hath not power of his own body, but the wife."

2. *Objection.* But what if a man of lewd and beastly conditions, as a drunkard, a glutton, a profane swaggerer, an impious swearer, and blasphemer, be married to a wife, sober, religious matron, must she account him her superior, and worthy of an husband's honor?

Answer. Surely she must. For the evil quality and disposition of his heart and life, doth not deprive a man of that civil honor which God hath given unto him. Though an husband in regard of evil qualities may carry the image of the devil, yet in regard of his place and office he beareth the image of God: so do magistrates in the commonwealth, ministers in the church, parents and masters in the same family. Note for our present purpose, the exhortation of St. Peter to Christian wives which had infidel husbands, Be in subjection to them: let your conversation be in fear (1 Peter 3:1,2). If infidels carry not the devil's image, and are not, so long as they are infidels, vessels of Satan, who are? Yet wives must be subject to them, and fear them.

Of wives denying honor to their own husbands.

Contrary thereunto is a very perverse disposition in some wives, who think they could better subject themselves to any husband, than their own. Though in general they acknowledge that an husband is his wife's superior, yet when the application cometh to themselves they fail, and cannot be brought to yield, that they are their husbands' inferiors. This is a vice worse than the former. For to acknowledge no husband to be superior over his wife, but to think man and wife in all things equal, may proceed from ignorance of mind, and error of judgment. But for a wife who knoweth and acknowledgeth the general, that an husband is above his wife, to imagine that she herself is not inferior to her husband, ariseth from monstrous self-conceit, and intolerable arrogancy, as if she herself were above her own sex, and more than a woman.

Contrary also is the practice of such women . . . as purposely marry a man so far lower than themselves, for this very end, that they may rule over their own husbands: and of others who being aged, for that end marry youths, if not very boys. A mind and practice very unseemly, and clean thwarting God's ordinance. But let them think of ruling what they list, the trust is, that they make themselves subjects both by God's law and man's: of which subjection such wives do oft feel the heaviest burden. Solomon noteth this to be one of the things for which the earth is disquieted, when a servant reigneth. Now when can a servant more domineer, than when he hath married his mistress? As for aged women who married youths, I may say, as in another case it was said, woe to thee, O wife whose husband is a child. Unmeet it is that an aged man should be married to a young maid, but much more unmeet for an aged woman to be married to a youth. . . .

Of a wife's obedience in general.

Hitherto of a wife's reverence, it followeth to speak of her obedience: The first law that ever was given to woman since her fall, laid upon her this duty of obedience to her husband, in these words, "Thy desire shall be to thine husband, and he shall rule over thee" (Genesis 3:16). How can an husband rule over a wife, if she obey not him? The principal part of that *submission* which in this text (Ephesians 5:22), and in many other places is required of a wife, consisteth in obedience: and therefore it is expressly commended unto wives in the example of Sarah who obeyed Abraham (1 Peter 3:6). Thus by obedience doth the Church manifest her subjection to Christ.

The place wherein God hath set an husband; namely, to be an head (Ephesians 5:23); the authority which he hath given unto him, to be a Lord (1 Peter 3:6), do all require obedience of a wife. Is not obedience to be yielded to an head, lord, and master? Take away all authority from an husband, if ye exempt a wife from obedience.

Contrary is the stoutness of such wives as must have their own will, and do what they list, or else all shall be out of quiet. *Their* will must be done, *they* must rule and over-rule all, *they* must command not only children and servants, but husbands also, if at least the husband will be at peace. Look into families, observe the estate and condition of many of them, and then tell me if these things be not so. If an husband be a man of courage, and seek to stand upon his right, and maintain his authority by requiring obedience of his wife, strange it is to behold what an hurly burly she will make in the house: but if he be a milksop, and basely yield unto his wife, and suffer her to rule, then, it may be, there shall be some outward quiet. The ground hereof is an ambitious and proud humor in women, who must needs rule, or else they think themselves slaves. But let them think as they list: assuredly herein they thwart God's ordinance, pervert the order of nature, deface the image of Christ, overthrow the ground of all duty, hinder the good of the family, become an ill pattern to children and servants, lay themselves open to Satan, and incur many other mischiefs which cannot but follow upon the violating of this main duty of obedience, which if it be not performed, how can other duties be expected?

1622

Inquiry and Experience

The problem of knowledge—what we know, how we know, what areas most demand attention, what methods are useful in studying those areas—came to be of pressing concern to many seventeenth-century thinkers and writers. Throughout Europe, experimental scientists were producing treatises describing their discoveries—Galileo on astronomy, William Harvey on the circulation of the blood, William Gilbert on magnetism—challenging the received wisdom of the past. The emphasis in many of these works is on the writer's direct personal experience, imagined as more immediate and convincing than any secondhand account.

But what experiences were worth recording? For Francis Bacon, individual peculiarities, as well as some traits of the mind and senses shared by all human beings, skew scientific objectivity and interfere with the search for truth. According to Bacon, the investigator must become conscious of these mental impediments, or "idols," and purge his mind of them insofar as he can. In *The New Atlantis*, Bacon proposes collaborative research institutes, which by pooling and orchestrating scientific inquiry, multiply the profitability of any individual's explorations while simultaneously reducing the destructive effect of his quirks. In his essays, Bacon adopted the voice of accumulated public wisdom, writing from the perspective of a man of affairs eager to make his way in the murky world of Jacobean court culture. Bacon was not, however, himself a distinguished experimental scientist. William Harvey, a physician who discovers the circulation of the blood, is less concerned than Bacon with a theory of knowledge and more with the detailed, matter-of-fact descriptions of his actual experiments: he effectively practices what Bacon preaches.

While writers like Bacon and Harvey championed "objective," dispassionate scientific experimentation, other writers, such as Robert Burton and Sir Thomas Browne, find human idiosyncrasy a fascinating subject of inquiry in itself. Indeed, a new ideal of objectivity possibly allows human foibles to be delineated in sharper, because contrasting, relief. Burton writes about melancholy, a psychological condition he regards as simultaneously pathological and universal; Browne, examining himself, revels in his own lack of systematic rigor.

In these and other writings of the period we see English prose developing remarkable stylistic range: sometimes epigrammatic, sometimes homely and vulgar, sometimes witty and boldly imagistic, sometimes learnedly allusive, sometimes ornately Latinate. While sixteenth-century prose typically employs long sentences with complex patterns of subordination and parallelism, early seventeenth-century prose favors broken rhythms, irregular phrasing, and more loosely organized sentences. Both the self-conscious embrace of whimsy and the tone of objective reportage—the latter visible not only in scientific writing but also in early journalism (see pp. 1834–41)—are key precursors to the rise of the novel.

SIR FRANCIS BACON

As a literary figure Sir Francis Bacon (1561–1626) played a central role in the development of the English essay and also inaugurated the genre of the scientific utopia in his *New Atlantis* (1627). But he was even more important to the intellectual and cultural history of the earlier seventeenth century for his treatises on reforming and promoting learning through experiment and induction. His life span closely overlapped that of Donne and Jonson, but unlike them he came from a noble family close to the centers of government and power. During Elizabeth's reign he studied law and entered Parliament. But it was under James I that his political fortunes took off: he was knighted in 1603, became attorney general in 1613, lord chancellor (the highest judicial post) and Baron Verulam in 1618, and Viscount St. Albans in 1621. That same year, however, he was convicted on twenty-three counts of corruption and accepting bribes, and was fined, imprisoned, and forced from office. Bacon admitted the truth of the charges (though they were in part politically motivated), merely observing that everyone took bribes and that bribery never influenced his judgment. He later commented: "I was the justest judge that was in England these fifty years, but it was the justest censure in Parliament that was these 200 years."

As an essayist Bacon stands at almost the opposite pole from his great French predecessor Michel de Montaigne (1533–1592), who proposed to learn about humankind by an intensive analysis of his own sensations, emotions, attitudes, and ideas. Bacon's essays are instead on topics "Civil and Moral." Montaigne's are tentative in structure; witty, expansive, and reflective in style; intimate, candid, and affable in tone; and he speaks constantly in the first person. By contrast, Bacon adopts an aphoristic structure and a curt, often disjunctive style, as well as a tone of cool objectivity and weighty sententiousness; he seldom uses "I," but instead presents himself as a mouthpiece for society's accumulated practical wisdom. The ten short pieces of the first edition of his essays (1597) are little more than collections of maxims placed in sequence; the thirty-eight of the second edition (1612) are longer and looser; the fifty-eight of the final edition (1625) are still longer, are smoother in texture, use more figurative language, and are more unified. In that last edition, more than half of the essays deal with public life, and many of the others—even on such topics as truth, marriage, and love—are written from the vantage point of a man of affairs rather than that of a profound moralist. They evoke an atmosphere of expediency and self-interest but also voice precepts of moral wisdom and public virtue, offering a penetrating insight into the thinking of the Jacobean ruling class.

Early in his life Bacon declared, "I have taken all knowledge to be my province." Whereas Donne, in the *First Anniversary*, saw human history as a process of inevitable degeneration and decay, Bacon saw it as progressive and believed that his new "scientific" method would lead humankind to a better future. He attempted a survey of the entire field of learning in *The Advancement of Learning* (1605), analyzing the principal obstacles to that advancement (rhetoric prompting the study of words rather than things, medieval scholasticism that ignores nature and promotes a barren rationalism, and pseudosciences such as astrology and alchemy); then he set forth what remains to be investigated. His *Novum Organum* (1620), written in Latin, urged induction—combining empirical investigation with carefully limited and tested generalizations—as the right method of investigating nature: the title challenged Aristotle's *Organon*, still the basis of university education, with its heavy reliance on deduction. *Novum Organum* includes a trenchant analysis of four kinds of "Idols"—

psychological dispositions and intellectual habits that hold humankind back in its quest for truth. But despite his emphasis on experiment, Bacon generally ignored major scientific discoveries by Galileo, Harvey, Gilbert and others; his true role was as a herald of the modern age. Despite his critique of rhetoric, he used the rich resources of figurative language—and of Utopian fiction in *The New Atlantis*—to urge a new faith in experiment and science. He segregated theology and science as "two truths," freeing science to go its own way unhampered by the old dogmas and unrestrained by the morality they supported. He is a primary creator of the myth of science as a pathway to Utopia; late in the century the Royal Society honored him as a prophet.

FROM ESSAYS[1]

Of Truth

"What is truth?" said jesting Pilate; and would not stay for an answer.[2] Certainly there be that delight in giddiness,[3] and count it a bondage to fix a belief; affecting free will in thinking, as well as in acting. And though the sects of philosophers of that kind be gone, yet there remain certain discoursing wits,[4] which are of the same veins, though there be not so much blood in them as was in those of the ancients. But it is not only the difficulty and labor which men take in finding out of truth; nor again, that when it is found, it imposeth upon[5] men's thoughts, that doth bring lies in favor; but a natural though corrupt love of the lie itself. One of the later school of the Grecians examineth the matter, and is at a stand[6] to think what should be in it, that men should love lies, where neither they make for pleasure, as with poets, nor for advantage, as with the merchant, but for the lie's sake. But I cannot tell: this same truth is a naked and open daylight, that doth not show the masques and mummeries and triumphs of the world half so stately and daintily as candlelights. Truth may perhaps come to the price of a pearl, that showeth best by day, but it will not rise to the price of a diamond or carbuncle,[7] that showeth best in varied lights. A mixture of a lie doth ever add pleasure. Doth any man doubt that if there were taken out of men's minds vain opinions, flattering hopes, false valuations, imaginations as one would, and the like, but it would leave the minds of a number of men poor shrunken things, full of melancholy and indisposition, and unpleasing to themselves? One of the fathers, in great severity, called poesy *vinum daemonum*,[8] because it filleth the imagination, and yet it is but with the shadow of a lie. But it is not the lie that passeth through the mind, but the lie that sinketh in, and settleth in it, that doth the hurt, such as we spake of before. But howsoever these things are thus in men's depraved judgments and affections, yet

---

1. Bacon's essays appeared in three editions, 1597 (10 essays), 1612 (38 essays), and 1625 (58 essays); we illustrate the very considerable stylistic differences between the earliest and latest collections by presenting two versions of "Of Studies." Otherwise, all selections are from the 1625 collection, in which "Of Truth" stands first.
2. See John 18.38 for Pilate's idle query to Jesus.
3. Foolish changeability. "That": those who.

4. Discursive minds. "Philosophers of that kind": the Greek Skeptics, who taught the uncertainty of all things.
5. Restricts, controls.
6. I.e., is baffled.
7. Ruby.
8. "The wine of devils"; St. Augustine is probably being cited.

truth, which only doth judge itself, teacheth that the inquiry of truth, which is the lovemaking or wooing of it, the knowledge of truth, which is the presence of it, and the belief of truth, which is the enjoying of it, is the sovereign good of human nature. The first creature[9] of God, in the works of the days, was the light of the sense; the last was the light of reason; and his sabbath work ever since is the illumination of his Spirit. First he breathed light upon the face of the matter, or chaos; then he breathed light into the face of man; and still he breatheth and inspireth light into the face of his chosen. The poet that beautified the sect that was otherwise inferior to the rest[1] saith yet excellently well: "It is a pleasure to stand upon the shore, and to see ships tossed upon the sea; a pleasure to stand in the window of a castle, and to see a battle, and the adventures thereof below; but no pleasure is comparable to the standing upon the vantage ground of truth" (a hill not to be commanded,[2] and where the air is always clear and serene), "and to see the errors, and wanderings, and mists, and tempests, in the vale below": so always that this prospect[3] be with pity, and not with swelling or pride. Certainly, it is heaven upon earth to have a man's mind move in charity, rest in providence, and turn upon the poles of truth.

To pass from theological and philosophical truth to the truth of civil business, it will be acknowledged even by those that practice it not, that clear and round[4] dealing is the honor of man's nature, and that mixture of falsehood is like alloy in coin of gold and silver, which may make the metal work the better, but it embaseth[5] it. For these winding and crooked courses are the goings of the serpent; which goeth basely upon the belly, and not upon the feet. There is no vice that doth so cover a man with shame as to be found false and perfidious. And therefore Montaigne saith prettily, when he inquired the reason why the word of the lie should be such a disgrace, and such an odious charge, saith he, "If it be well weighed, to say that a man lieth is as much to say as that he is brave towards God and a coward towards men."[6] For a lie faces God, and shrinks from man. Surely the wickedness of falsehood and breach of faith cannot possibly be so highly expressed, as in that it shall be the last peal to call the judgments of God upon the generations of men, it being foretold that when Christ cometh, he shall not "find faith upon the earth."[7]

1625

Of Marriage and Single Life

He that hath wife and children hath given hostages to fortune; for they are impediments to great enterprises, either of virtue or mischief. Certainly the best works, and of greatest merit for the public, have proceeded from the unmarried or childless men, which both in affection and means have mar-

---

9. Creation.
1. Lucretius's *On the Nature of Things* expressed the Epicurean creed, which Bacon thought inferior because it emphasized pleasure.
2. Topped by anything higher.

3. I.e., provided always that this observation.
4. Upright.
5. Debases.
6. *Essays* 2.18.
7. Luke 18.8.

ried and endowed the public. Yet it were great reason that those that have children should have greatest care of future times, unto which they know they must transmit their dearest pledges. Some there are who, though they lead a single life, yet their thoughts do end with themselves, and account future times impertinences.[1] Nay, there are some other that account wife and children but as bills of charges. Nay more, there are some foolish rich covetous men that take a pride in having no children, because they may be thought so much the richer. For perhaps they have heard some talk, "Such an one is a great rich man," and another except to it, "Yea, but he hath a great charge of children"; as if it were an abatement to his riches. But the most ordinary cause of a single life is liberty, especially in certain self-pleasing and humorous[2] minds, which are so sensible of every restraint, as they will go near to think their girdles and garters to be bonds and shackles. Unmarried men are best friends, best masters, best servants, but not always best subjects, for they are light to run away, and almost all fugitives are of that condition. A single life doth well with churchmen, for charity will hardly water the ground where it must first fill a pool. It is indifferent for judges and magistrates, for if they be facile[3] and corrupt, you shall have a servant five times worse than a wife. For soldiers, I find the generals commonly in their hortatives[4] put men in mind of their wives and children; and I think the despising of marriage amongst the Turks maketh the vulgar soldier more base. Certainly wife and children are a kind of discipline of humanity; and single men, though they be many times more charitable, because their means are less exhaust,[5] yet, on the other side, they are more cruel and hardhearted (good to make severe inquisitors), because their tenderness is not so oft called upon. Grave natures, led by custom, and therefore constant, are commonly loving husbands, as was said of Ulysses, *Vetulam suam praetulit immortalitati.*[6] Chaste women are often proud and froward,[7] as presuming upon the merit of their chastity. It is one of the best bonds, both of chastity and obedience, in the wife if she think her husband wise, which she will never do if she find him jealous. Wives are young men's mistresses, companions for middle age, and old men's nurses; so as a man may have a quarrel[8] to marry when he will. But yet he was reputed one of the wise men that made answer to the question when a man should marry: "A young man not yet, an elder man not at all."[9] It is often seen that bad husbands have very good wives; whether it be that it raiseth the price of their husbands' kindness when it comes, or that the wives take a pride in their patience. But this never fails, if the bad husbands were of their own choosing, against their friends' consent; for then they will be sure to make good their own folly.

1612, 1625

1. Irrelevant concerns.
2. Unbalanced, whimsical.
3. Pliable.
4. Exhortations.
5. Exhausted.
6. "He preferred his old wife to immortality." Ulysses might have had immortality with the nymph Calypso but preferred to go back to Penelope.
7. Ill-tempered.
8. Pretext.
9. Thales (6th century B.C.E.), one of the Seven Sages of Greece.

Of Great Place

Men in great place are thrice servants: servants of the sovereign or state, servants of fame, and servants of business. So as they have no freedom, neither in their persons, nor in their actions, nor in their times. It is a strange desire, to seek power and to lose liberty, or to seek power over others and to lose power over a man's self. The rising unto place is laborious, and by pains men come to greater pains; and it is sometimes base, and by indignities men come to dignities. The standing is slippery, and the regress is either a downfall or at least an eclipse, which is a melancholy thing: *Cum non sis qui fueris, non esse cur velis vivere.*[1] Nay, retire men cannot when they would, neither will they when it were reason; but are impatient of privateness, even in age and sickness, which require the shadow;[2] like old townsmen, that will be still sitting at their street door, though thereby they offer age to scorn. Certainly great persons had need to borrow other men's opinions to think themselves happy; for if they judge by their own feeling, they cannot find it; but if they think with themselves what other men think of them, and that other men would fain be as they are, then they are happy, as it were by report; when perhaps they find the contrary within. For they are the first that find their own griefs, though they be the last that find their own faults. Certainly men in great fortunes are strangers to themselves, and while they are in the puzzle of business they have no time to tend their health, either of body or mind. *Illi mors gravis incubat, qui notus nimis omnibus, ignotus moritur sibi.*[3] In place there is license to do good and evil, whereof the latter is a curse; for in evil the best condition is not to will, the second not to can.[4] But power to do good is the true and lawful end of aspiring; for good thoughts (though God accept them) yet towards men are little better than good dreams, except they be put in act; and that cannot be without power and place, as the vantage and commanding ground. Merit and good works is the end of man's motion, and conscience[5] of the same is the accomplishment of man's rest; for if a man can be partaker of God's theater,[6] he shall likewise be partaker of God's rest. *Et conversus Deus, ut aspiceret opera quae fecerunt manus suae, vidit quod omnia essent bona nimis;*[7] and then the Sabbath.

In the discharge of thy place set before thee the best examples, for imitation is a globe[8] of precepts. And after a time set before thee thine own example; and examine thyself strictly, whether thou didst not best at first. Neglect not also the examples of those that have carried themselves ill in the same place; not to set off thyself by taxing[9] their memory, but to direct thyself what to avoid. Reform, therefore, without bravery, or scandal[1] of former times and persons; but yet set it down to thyself, as well to create good precedents as to follow them. Reduce things to the first institution,[2] and observe wherein and how they have degenerate; but yet ask counsel of both times; of

---

1. "When you aren't what you were, there's no reason to live" (Cicero, *Familiar Letters* 7.3).
2. "The shadow" of retirement, out of the glare of public life.
3. "Death lies heavily on him who, while too well known to everyone else, dies unknown to himself" (Seneca, *Thyestes*).
4. Be able.

5. Consciousness.
6. Actions in the world.
7. "And God saw every thing that he had made, and, behold, it was very good" (Genesis 1.31).
8. World.
9. Blaming.
1. Defaming. "Bravery": ostentation.
2. To their original form.

the ancient time what is best, and of the latter time what is fittest. Seek to make thy course regular, that men may know beforehand what they may expect; but be not too positive and peremptory, and express thyself well when thou digressest from thy rule. Preserve the right of thy place, but stir not questions of jurisdiction; and rather assume thy right in silence and *de facto*,[3] than voice it with claims and challenges. Preserve likewise the rights of inferior places, and think it more honor to direct in chief than to be busy in all. Embrace and invite helps and advices touching the execution of thy place, and do not drive away such as bring thee information as meddlers, but accept of them in good part. The vices of authority are chiefly four: delays, corruption, roughness, and facility.[4] For delays, give easy access, keep times appointed, go through with that which is in hand, and interlace not business[5] but of necessity. For corruption, do not only bind thine own hands or thy servants' hands from taking, but bind the hands of suitors also from offering. For integrity used doth the one; but integrity professed, and with a manifest detestation of bribery, doth the other. And avoid not only the fault, but the suspicion. Whosoever is found variable and changeth manifestly, without manifest cause, giveth suspicion of corruption. Therefore, always when thou changest thine opinion or course, profess it plainly and declare it, together with the reasons that move thee to change; and do not think to steal it.[6] A servant or a favorite, if he be inward,[7] and no other apparent cause of esteem, is commonly thought but a byway to close[8] corruption. For roughness, it is a needless cause of discontent; severity breedeth fear, but roughness breedeth hate. Even reproofs from authority ought to be grave, and not taunting. As for facility, it is worse than bribery; for bribes come but now and then, but if importunity or idle respects[9] lead a man, he shall never be without. As Solomon saith, "To respect persons is not good, for such a man will transgress for a piece of bread."[1]

It is most true that was anciently spoken, "A place showeth the man"; and it showeth some to the better and some to the worse. *Omnium consensu capax imperii, nisi imperasset*,[2] saith Tacitus of Galba; but of Vespasian he saith, *Solus imperantium Vespasianus mutatus in melius*:[3] though the one was meant of sufficiency, the other of manners and affection. It is an assured sign of a worthy and generous spirit, whom honor amends.[4] For honor is, or should be, the place of virtue; and as in nature things move violently to their place and calmly in their place, so virtue in ambition is violent, in authority settled and calm. All rising to great place is by a winding stair; and if there be factions, it is good to side a man's self[5] whilst he is in the rising, and to balance himself when he is placed. Use the memory of thy predecessor fairly and tenderly; for if thou dost not, it is a debt will sure be paid when thou art gone. If thou have colleagues, respect them, and rather call them when they look not for it, than exclude them when they have reason to look to be called. Be not too sensible[6]

---

3. Without debate, as a matter of course.
4. Docility, too great obligingness.
5. I.e., do not carry on different businesses at the same time.
6. Change your mind without its being noticed.
7. In his master's confidence.
8. Secret.
9. Irrelevant considerations.
1. Cf. Proverbs 28.21.

2. "Everyone would have thought him a good ruler, if he had not ruled."
3. "Of all the emperors, only Vespasian changed for the better."
4. I.e., whom promotion improves. "Sufficiency": abilities. "Affection": disposition.
5. For a man to take sides.
6. Sensitive.

or too remembering of thy place in conversation and private answers to suitors; but let it rather be said, "When he sits in place he is another man."

1612, 1625

Of Superstition[1]

It were better to have no opinion of God at all than such an opinion as is unworthy of him. For the one is unbelief, the other is contumely:[2] and certainly superstition is the reproach of the deity. Plutarch saith well to that purpose: "Surely" (saith he) "I had rather a great deal men should say there was no such man at all as Plutarch, than that they should say that there was one Plutarch that would eat his children as soon as they were born"—as the poets speak of Saturn.[3] And as the contumely is greater towards God, so the danger is greater towards men. Atheism leaves a man to sense, to philosophy, to natural piety, to laws, to reputation, all which may be guides to an outward moral virtue, though religion were not. But superstition dismounts all these, and erecteth an absolute monarchy in the minds of men. Therefore atheism did never perturb states, for it makes men wary of themselves as looking no further;[4] and we see the times inclined to atheism (as the time of Augustus Caesar) were civil times. But superstition hath been the confusion of many states, and bringeth in a new *primum mobile*, that ravisheth all the spheres of government.[5] The master of superstition is the people, and in all superstition wise men follow fools, and arguments are fitted to practice in a reversed order. It was gravely said by some of the prelates in the council of Trent, where the doctrine of the schoolmen bare great sway, *that the schoolmen were like astronomers, which did feign eccentrics and epicycles and such engines of orbs to save the phenomena, though they knew there were no such things*;[6] and in like manner that the schoolmen had framed a number of subtle and intricate axioms and theorems to save the practice of the church.

The causes of superstition are: pleasing and sensual rites and ceremonies; excess of outward and pharisaical holiness;[7] overgreat reverence of traditions, which cannot but load the church; the stratagems of prelates for their own ambition and lucre; the favoring too much of good intentions, which openeth the gate to conceits[8] and novelties; the taking an aim at divine matters by human, which cannot but breed mixture of imaginations; and lastly barbarous times, especially joined with calamities and disasters. Supersti-

---

1. Irrational religious practices founded on fear or ignorance.
2. Contempt.
3. Saturn (Cronos), god of time (among other things), was reputed to have eaten all his children, as time does. Many of the sentiments in Bacon's essay come from Plutarch's essay "On Superstition."
4. I.e., not looking beyond their own personal lifetimes. The rule of Augustus Caesar (following) was marked by general peace and civil quiet (i.e., civilized). In this period of Roman history, many members of the elite no longer believed in the pagan gods, though they participated in the forms of state religion.
5. The prime mover (*primium mobile*) was supposed to control the motions of the other heavenly spheres; superstition is a second (and contrary) mover.
6. "Save the phenomena" means "explain appearances," as did the elaborate theories of pre-Copernican astronomers (epicycles, trepidation, and such concepts). So with the Scholastic philosophers ("schoolmen").
7. The Pharisees were the strict party among the Jews of Christ's time; they taught precise observance of the letter of Mosaic law.
8. Fancies.

tion without a veil is a deformed thing, for as it addeth deformity to an ape to be so like a man, so the similitude of superstition to religion makes it the more deformed. And as wholesome meat corrupteth to little worms, so good forms and orders corrupt into a number of petty observances. There is a superstition in avoiding superstition, when men think to do best if they go furthest from the superstition formerly received; therefore care would be had that (as it fareth in ill purgings) the good be not taken away with the bad, which commonly is done when the people is the reformer.[9]

1612, 1625

Of Plantations[1]

Plantations are amongst ancient, primitive, and heroical works. When the world was young it begat more children; but now it is old it begets fewer: for I may justly account new plantations to be the children of former kingdoms. I like a plantation in a pure soil; that is, where people are not displanted to the end to plant in others. For else it is rather an extirpation than a plantation. Planting of countries is like planting of woods; for you must make account to leese[2] almost twenty years profit, and expect your recompense in the end. For the principal thing that hath been the destruction of most plantations hath been the base and hasty drawing of profit in the first years. It is true, speedy profit is not to be neglected, as far as may stand[3] with the good of the plantation, but no further. It is a shameful and unblessed thing to take the scum of people, and wicked condemned men, to be the people with whom you plant; and not only so, but it spoileth the plantation, for they will ever live like rogues, and not fall to work, but be lazy, and do mischief, and spend victuals, and be quickly weary, and then certify over[4] to their country, to the discredit of the plantation. The people wherewith you plant ought to be gardeners, plowmen, laborers, smiths, carpenters, joiners,[5] fishermen, fowlers, with some few apothecaries, surgeons, cooks, and bakers.

In a country of plantation, first look about what kind of victual the country yields of itself to hand, as chestnuts, walnuts, pineapples, olives, dates, plums, cherries, wild honey, and the like, and make use of them. Then consider what victual or esculent[6] things there are which grow speedily and within the year, as parsnips, carrots, turnips, onions, radish, artichokes of

---

9. The final sentence is directed against Puritan reformers, who loathed ceremonies, traditions, liturgy, and images, which they considered "superstitions."

1. The planting of colonies had been a standard topic of political theory since Plato, with attention focused on such matters as the choice of site, the best mix of population, and the treatment of indigenous peoples. Sir Thomas More considered the matter in his *Utopia*, and it took on increased practical importance in the narratives of English explorers such as Sir Walter Ralegh, and especially in the early 17th century, with the establishment of the first permanent English settlements in the New World. Bacon's

essay largely avoids the most acute moral issues English colonization was posing: English participation in the brutal African slave trade, and the stocking of "plantations" in Ireland with Scottish Presbyterian settlers (to supplement genocidal policies that were starving the indigenous Roman Catholics). These policies sowed the seeds of slavery in America and civil war in Ireland.

2. Lose.
3. Be consistent.
4. Report.
5. Workers in fine carpentry.
6. Edible.

Jerusalem,[7] maize, and the like. For wheat, barley, and oats, they ask[8] too much labor; but with peas and beans you may begin, both because they ask less labor and because they serve for meat[9] as well as for bread. And of rice likewise cometh a great increase, and it is a kind of meat. Above all, there ought to be brought store of biscuit, oatmeal, flour, meal, and the like in the beginning, till bread may be had. For beasts or birds, take chiefly such as are least subject to diseases, and multiply fastest, as swine, goats, cocks, hens, turkeys, geese, house doves, and the like. The victual in plantations ought to be expended almost as in a besieged town; that is, with certain[1] allowance. And let the main part of the ground employed to gardens or corn be to[2] a common stock, and to be laid in and stored up and then delivered out in proportion; besides some spots of ground that any particular person will manure[3] for his own private. Consider likewise what commodities the soil where the plantation is doth naturally yield, that they may some way help to defray the charge of the plantation (so it be not, as was said, to the untimely prejudice of the main business), as it hath fared with tobacco in Virginia. Wood commonly aboundeth but too much, and therefore timber is fit to be one. If there be iron ore and streams whereupon to set the mills, iron is a brave commodity, where wood aboundeth.[4] Making of bay-salt, if the climate be proper for it, would be put in experience.[5] Growing silk likewise, if any be, is a likely commodity. Pitch and tar, where store of firs and pines are, will not fail; so drugs and sweet woods, where they are, cannot but yield great profit. Soap ashes likewise, and other things that may be thought of. But moil[6] not too much underground, for the hope of mines is very uncertain, and useth to make the planters lazy in other things.

For government, let it be in the hands of one, assisted with some counsel; and let them have commission to exercise martial laws, with some limitation. And above all, let men make that profit of being in the wilderness, as they have God always, and his service, before their eyes. Let not the government of the plantation depend upon too many counselors and undertakers[7] in the country that planteth, but upon a temperate number; and let those be rather noblemen and gentlemen than merchants, for they look ever to the present gain. Let there be freedoms from custom[8] till the plantation be of strength; and not only freedom from custom, but freedom to carry their commodities where they may make their best of them, except there be some special cause of caution. Cram not in people by sending too fast, company after company, but rather harken how they waste,[9] and send supplies proportionably, but so as the number may live well in the plantation, and not by surcharge[1] be in penury.

It hath been a great endangering to the health of some plantations, that they have built along the sea and rivers, in marish[2] and unwholesome grounds.

---

7. Jerusalem artichokes, a species of sunflower having an edible root. "Jerusalem" is a mistranslation of the Italian word for sunflower, *girasole*.
8. Require. "For": as for.
9. I.e., as a main dish.
1. Fixed.
2. For. "Corn": grain.
3. Cultivate.
4. Waterpower and wood fires were required for getting iron out of ore. "Brave": excellent.
5. I.e., should be tried. "Bay-salt" is a coarse salt

obtained by evaporating seawater. "Growing silk" (next sentence): vegetable silk.
6. Labor. "Soap ashes": ashes used for making soap.
7. Investors holding shares in the enterprise.
8. Customs duties.
9. I.e., observe at what rate the population declines.
1. I.e., by being overpopulated.
2. Marshy.

Therefore, though you begin there, to avoid carriage and other like discommodities,[3] yet build still rather upwards from the streams than along. It concerneth likewise the health of the plantation that they have good store of salt with them, that they may use it in their victuals when it shall be necessary. If you plant where savages are, do not only entertain them with trifles and jingles, but use them justly and graciously, with sufficient guard nevertheless; and do not win their favor by helping them to invade their enemies, but for their defense it is not amiss. And send oft of them over to the country that plants, that they may see a better condition than their own, and commend it when they return. When the plantation grows to strength, then it is time to plant with women as well as with men, that the plantation may spread into generations and not be ever pieced from without. It is the sinfullest thing in the world to forsake or destitute a plantation once in forwardness; for besides the dishonor it is the guiltiness of blood of many commiserable[4] persons.

1625

Of Negotiating

It is generally better to deal by speech than by letter, and by the mediation of a third than by a man's self. Letters are good when a man would draw an answer by letter back again, or when it may serve for a man's justification afterwards to produce his own letter, or where it may be danger to be interrupted or heard by pieces. To deal in person is good when a man's face breedeth regard, as commonly with inferiors, or in tender[1] cases, where a man's eye upon the countenance of him with whom he speaketh may give him a direction how far to go; and generally, where a man will reserve to himself liberty either to disavow or to expound. In choice of instruments, it is better to choose men of a plainer sort, that are like to do that that is committed to them, and to report back again faithfully the success,[2] than those that are cunning to contrive out of other men's business somewhat to grace themselves, and will help the matter in report for satisfaction sake. Use also such persons as affect[3] the business wherein they are employed, for that quickeneth much; and such as are fit for the matter, as bold men for expostulation, fairspoken men for persuasion, crafty men for inquiry and observation, froward and absurd men for business that doth not well bear out itself.[4] Use also such as have been lucky, and prevailed before in things wherein you have employed them; for that breeds confidence, and they will strive to maintain their prescription.[5] It is better to sound a person with whom one deals afar off, than to fall upon the point at first, except you mean to surprise him by some short question. It is better dealing with men in appetite,[6] than with those that are where they would be. If a man deal with another upon conditions, the start or

---

3. Disadvantages, inconveniences.
4. Worthy of compassion. "Destitute": abandon.
1. Delicate.
2. Result.
3. Like.

4. I.e., when your business is less than honest, use an ill-tempered or foolish person.
5. Keep up their reputation.
6. Who are hungry, i.e., ambitious men.

first performance is all, which a man cannot reasonably demand,[7] except either the nature of the thing be such which must go before, or else a man can persuade the other party that he shall still need him in some other thing, or else that he be counted the honester man. All practice is to discover or to work.[8] Men discover themselves in trust, in passion, at unawares, and of necessity, when they would have somewhat done and cannot find an apt pretext. If you would work any man, you must either know his nature and fashions, and so lead him; or his ends, and so persuade him; or his weakness and disadvantages, and so awe him; or those that have interest in him, and so govern him. In dealing with cunning persons, we must ever consider their ends, to interpret their speeches; and it is good to say little to them, and that which they least look for. In all negotiations of difficulty, a man may not look to sow and reap at once, but must prepare business, and so ripen it by degrees.

1597, 1625

Of Masques and Triumphs

These things are but toys to come amongst such serious observations; but yet, since princes will have such things, it is better they should be graced with elegancy, than daubed with cost. Dancing to song is a thing of great state and pleasure. I understand it that the song be in choir, placed aloft, and accompanied with some broken music,[1] and the ditty fitted to the device. Acting in song, especially in dialogues, hath an extreme good grace; I say acting, not dancing (for that is a mean and vulgar thing);[2] and the voices of the dialogue would be strong and manly (a bass and tenor, no treble), and the ditty high and tragical, not nice or dainty. Several choirs, placed one over against another, and taking the voices by catches anthem-wise, give great pleasure. Turning dances into figure[3] is a childish curiosity; and, generally, let it be noted, that those things which I here set down are such as to naturally take the sense, and not respect petty wonderments. It is true, the alterations of scenes, so it be quietly and without noise, are things of great beauty and pleasure for they feed and relieve the eye before it be full of the same object. Let the scenes abound with light, specially colored and varied; and let the masquers, or any other that are to come down from the scene,[4] have some motions upon the scene itself before their coming down; for it draws the eye strangely, and makes it with great pleasure to desire to see that it cannot perfectly discern. Let the songs be loud and cheerful, and not chirpings or pulings; let the music, likewise, be sharp and loud, and well placed. The colors that show best by candlelight[5] are

---

7. You cannot reasonably make special conditions favorable to you, except in the circumstances noted.
8. All sharp bargaining aims to find out what men are up to or to make use of them. "Discover" (next sentence): reveal.
1. Part-music, for different voices and different kinds of instruments.
2. Bacon's emphasis on dialogue and song (as opposed to dance) is in keeping with the increased emphasis on dialogue in later Jacobean and Caroline masques; dance, however, remains at the center of both early and late masques.
3. Patterns with allegorical or numerological significance.
4. To unmask at the end and come onto the floor, so as to take part in the general dancing (the revels) with members of the court.
5. The Banqueting Hall at Whitehall, the site of many court masques, was lit only by candlelight; viewers complained that some masques were hard to see.

white, carnation, and a kind of seawater green; and oes or spangs,[6] as they are of no great cost, so they are of most glory. As for rich embroidery, it is lost and not discerned. Let the suits of the masquers be graceful, and such as become the person when the vizors are off; not after examples of known attires, Turks, soldiers, mariners, and the like. Let antimasques[7] not be long; they have been commonly of fools, satyrs, baboons, wild men, antics, beasts, sprites, witches, Ethiopes, pigmies, turquets,[8] nymphs, rustics, Cupids, statues moving, and the like. As for angels, it is not comical enough to put them in antimasques; and anything that is hideous, as devils, giants, is, on the other side, as unfit; but, chiefly, let the music of them be recreative, and with some strange changes. Some sweet odors suddenly coming forth, without any drops falling, are, in such a company as there is steam and heat, things of great pleasure and refreshment. Double masques, one of men, another of ladies, addeth state and variety; but all is nothing, except the room be kept clear and neat.

For jousts, and tourneys, and barriers,[9] the glories of them are chiefly in the chariots, wherein the challengers make their entry; especially if they be drawn with strange beasts, as lions, bears, camels, and the like; or in the devices of their entrance, or in the bravery of their liveries, or in the goodly furniture of their horses and armor. But enough of these toys.

1625

Of Studies

[1597 version][1]

Studies serve for pastimes, for ornaments, and for abilities. Their chief use for pastime is in privateness[2] and retiring; for ornament, is in discourse; and for ability, is in judgment. For expert men[3] can execute, but learned men are fittest to judge or censure. To spend too much time in them is sloth; to use them too much for ornament is affectation; to make judgment wholly by their rules is the humor[4] of a scholar. They perfect nature, and are perfected by experience. Crafty men contemn them, simple men admire them, wise men use them, for they teach not their own use; but that[5] is a wisdom without them, and above them, won by observation. Read not to contradict nor to believe, but to weigh and consider. Some books are to be tasted, others to be swallowed, and some few to be chewed and digested; that is, some books are to be read only in parts; others to be read but cursorily; and some few to be read wholly, and with diligence and attention.

---

6. Spangles shaped like the letter "O."
7. The antic dances (presented by professionals) that preceded the main masque dances and represented the vices, follies, or disorders that are to be dispelled with the arrival of the main masques (royal and noble personages).
8. Turkish dwarfs.
9. One form of masque was the "joust," "tourney" (tournament), or "barriers," which chiefly involved knights, who represented allegorical qualities, tilting lances against each other.
1. This version of the essay illustrates Bacon's early epigrammatic, aphoristic style, featuring balance, parallelism, disjunction between sentences, and a curtness that is occasionally cryptic. The 1625 version keeps some aphoristic elements unchanged but provides more connectives and transitions, resulting in a smoother, more flowing style.
2. Private life.
3. Men of experience.
4. Disposition, implying folly.
5. I.e., the knowledge of how to use them. "Without" (following): outside.

Reading maketh a full man, conference[6] a ready man, and writing an exact man. And therefore, if a man write little, he had need have a great memory; if he confer little, he had need have a present wit;[7] and if he read little, he had need have much cunning, to seem to know that[8] he doth not. Histories make men wise; poets, witty;[9] the mathematics, subtle; natural philosophy,[1] deep; moral,[2] grave; logic and rhetoric, able to contend.

Of Studies

[1625 version]

Studies serve for delight, for ornament, and for ability. Their chief use for delight is in privateness[1] and retiring; for ornament, is in discourse; and for ability, is in the judgment and disposition of business. For expert men[2] can execute, and perhaps judge of particulars, one by one; but the general counsels, and the plots and marshaling of affairs, come best from those that are learned. To spend too much time in studies is sloth; to use them too much for ornament is affectation; to make judgment wholly by their rules is the humor[3] of a scholar. They perfect nature, and are perfected by experience; for natural abilities are like natural plants, that need pruning by study; and studies themselves do give forth directions too much at large, except they be bounded in by experience. Crafty men contemn studies, simple men admire them, and wise men use them, for they teach not their own use; but that[4] is a wisdom without them, and above them, won by observation. Read not to contradict and confute, nor to believe and take for granted, nor to find talk and discourse, but to weigh and consider. Some books are to be tasted, others to be swallowed, and some few to be chewed and digested; that is, some books are to be read only in parts; others to be read, but not curiously;[5] and some few to be read wholly, and with diligence and attention. Some books also may be read by deputy and extracts made of them by others, but that would be only in the less important arguments and the meaner sort of books; else distilled books are like common distilled waters,[6] flashy things. Reading maketh a full man, conference[7] a ready man, and writing an exact man. And therefore, if a man write little, he had need have a great memory; if he confer little, he had need have a present wit;[8] and if he read little, he had need have much cunning, to seem to know that[9] he doth not. Histories make men wise; poets, witty;[1] the mathematics, subtle; natural philosophy,[2] deep; moral, grave; logic and rhetoric, able to contend. *Abeunt studia in mores.*[3] Nay, there is no stond or impediment in the wit but may be wrought out by fit studies, like as diseases of the body may have appropriate exer-

---

6. Conversation.
7. Lively intelligence.
8. That which.
9. Clever.
1. Science.
2. Moral philosophy.
1. Private life.
2. Men of experience.
3. Folly.
4. I.e., the knowledge of how to use them. "Without" (following): outside.

5. Attentively.
6. Used as home remedies, without real value.
7. Conversation.
8. Lively intelligence.
9. That which.
1. Clever.
2. Science. "Moral" (following): i.e., moral philosophy.
3. "Studies culminate in manners" (Ovid, *Heroides*). "Stond" (following): stoppage.

cises. Bowling is good for the stone and reins,[4] shooting for the lungs and breast, gentle walking for the stomach, riding for the head, and the like. So if a man's wit be wandering, let him study the mathematics; for in demonstrations, if his wit be called away never so little, he must begin again. If his wit be not apt to distinguish or find differences, let him study the schoolmen, for they are *cumini sectores*.[5] If he be not apt to beat over matters[6] and to call up one thing to prove and illustrate another, let him study the lawyer's cases. So every defect of the mind may have a special receipt.[7]

From The Advancement of Learning

[THE ABUSES OF LANGUAGE][1]

Martin Luther, conducted (no doubt) by an higher providence, but in discourse of reason finding what a province he had undertaken against the bishop of Rome[2] and the degenerate traditions of the church, and finding his own solitude being no ways aided by the opinions of his own time, was enforced to awake all antiquity and to call former times to his succor to make a party against the present time, so that the ancient authors both in divinity and in humanity which had long time slept in libraries began generally to be read and revolved.[3] This by consequence did draw on a necessity of a more exquisite travail in the languages original wherein those authors did write,[4] for the better understanding of those authors and the better advantage of pressing and applying their words. And thereof grew again a delight in their manner of style and phrase, and an admiration of that kind of writing, which was much furthered and precipitated by the enmity and opposition that the propounders of those (primitive but seeming new) opinions had against the schoolmen, who were generally of the contrary part, and whose writings were altogether in a differing style and form, taking liberty to coin and frame new terms of art to express their own sense and to avoid circuit of speech, without regard to the pureness, pleasantness, and (as I may call it) lawfulness of the phrase or word.[5] And again, because the greatest labor then was with the people (of whom the Pharisees were wont to say, *Execrabilis ista turba, quae non novit legem*,[6]) for the winning and persuading of them there grew of necessity in chief price and request[7] eloquence and variety of discourse, as the fittest and forciblest access into the capacity of the

---

4. Gallstone and kidneys.
5. "Dividers of cuminseed," i.e., hairsplitters. "Schoolmen": Scholastic philosophers.
6. Discuss a subject thoroughly.
7. Cure, prescription.
1. Among the "three distempers of learning" that Bacon proposes to cure in this work, the most important involves "vain imaginations, vain altercations, and vain affectations"; to help explain these he offers a concise history of changes in the language of learned discourse since the Reformation.
2. The pope. "Province": task.
3. Considered. Luther (1483–1546) indeed looked back to the original languages of the Bible and to ancient authors in "divinity" (chiefly

Augustine), but he was not involved in the efforts of the humanists (including Erasmus and Sir Thomas More) to revive the classical languages and authors.
4. Classical Greek and Latin, and biblical Hebrew. "Exquisite travail": careful work.
5. The Scholastic philosophers ("schoolmen") used the living Latin of the Middle Ages, wrenching the language yet further from classical norms in applying it to subtle philosophical matters; the humanists denounced the Scholastics' Latin as barbarous and sought instead to imitate classical models, especially Cicero.
6. "This people who knoweth not the law are cursed" (John 7.49).
7. Worth and demand.

vulgar sort. So that these four causes concurring (the admiration of ancient authors, the hate of the schoolmen, the exact study of languages, and the efficacy of preaching) did bring in an affectionate study of eloquence and copy[8] of speech, which then began to flourish. This grew speedily to an excess, for men began to hunt more after words than matter, and more after the choiceness of the phrase, and the round and clean composition of the sentence, and the sweet falling of the clauses, and the varying and illustration of their works with tropes and figures[9] than after the weight of matter, worth of subject, soundness of argument, life of invention, or depth of judgment. Then grew the flowing and watery vein of Osorius, the Portugal bishop, to be in price. Then did Sturmius spend such infinite and curious pains upon Cicero the orator and Hermogenes the rhetorician, besides his own books of periods and imitation and the like.[1] Then did Carr of Cambridge and Ascham with their lectures and writings almost deify Cicero and Demosthenes, and allure all young men that were studious unto that delicate and polished kind of learning.[2] Then did Erasmus take occasion to make the scoffing echo, *Decem annos consumpsi in legendo Cicerone*, and the echo answered in Greek, *one, Asine*.[3] Then grew the learning of the schoolmen to be utterly despised as barbarous. In sum, the whole inclination and bent of those times was rather towards copy than weight.

Here therefore is the first distemper of learning, when men study words and not matter, whereof though I have represented an example of late times, yet it hath been and will be *secundum maius et minus*[4] in all time. And how is it possible but this should have an operation to discredit learning, even with vulgar capacities, when they see learned men's works like the first letter of a patent or limned[5] book, which though it hath large flourishes, yet it is but a letter? It seems to me that Pygmalion's frenzy[6] is a good emblem or portraiture of this vanity, for words are but the images of matter, and except they have life of reason and invention, to fall in love with them is all one as to fall in love with a picture.

But yet notwithstanding, it is a thing not hastily to be condemned to clothe and adorn the obscurity even of philosophy itself with sensible and plausible elocution. For hereof we have great examples in Xenophon, Cicero, Seneca, Plutarch, and of Plato also in some degree; and hereof likewise there is great use, for surely to the severe inquisition of truth and the deep progress into philosophy it is some hindrance, because it is too early satisfactory to the mind of man, and quencheth the desire of further search before we come to a just period; but then if a man be to have any use of such knowledge in civil occasions of conference, counsel, persuasion, discourse, or the like, then shall he find it prepared to his hands in those authors which write

8. Copiousness. "Affectionate": affected.
9. Figurative language.
1. Jeronimo Osorio (1506–1580) wrote a history of Portuguese conquests in a flowing style that caused him to be known as "the Portuguese Cicero." His contemporary, Johann Sturm, edited texts of Cicero and the Greek rhetorician Hermogenes; his "book of periods" was a rhetorical handbook.
2. Nicholas Carr was professor of Greek at Cambridge; Roger Ascham was tutor to Queen Elizabeth and author of *The Schoolmaster*. Both admired the rhetorical polish of the Roman orator Cicero and the Greek orator Demosthenes.
3. "I spent ten years in reading Cicero." Echo answers, "Ass!" The joke is in the *Colloquies* of Erasmus.
4. More or less, depending on circumstances.
5. Illuminated, i.e., illustrated, as with elaborate initial capitals. Royal grants ("patents") were also engrossed with fancy initial letters.
6. Pygmalion's "frenzy" (delirium) was to fall in love with a statue he had carved of a beautiful woman.

in that manner. But the excess of this is so justly contemptible that as Hercules, when he saw the image of Adonis, Venus' minion, in a temple, said in disdain, *Nil sacri es*;[7] so there is none of Hercules' followers in learning, that is, the more severe and laborious sort of inquirers into truth,[8] but will despise those delicacies and affectations as indeed capable of no divineness.

1605

From Novum Organum[1]

19

There are and can be only two ways of searching into and discovering truth. The one flies from the senses and particulars to the most general axioms, and from these principles, the truth of which it takes for settled and immovable, proceeds to judgment and to the discovery of middle axioms.[2] And this way is now in fashion. The other derives from the senses and particulars, rising by a gradual and unbroken ascent, so that it arrives at the most general axioms last of all.[3] This is the true way, but as yet untried.

* * *

22

Both ways set out from the senses and particulars, and rest in the highest generalities, but the difference between them is infinite. For the one just glances at experiment and particulars in passing, the other dwells duly and orderly among them. The one, again, begins at once by establishing certain abstract and useless generalities, the other rises by gradual steps to that which is prior and better known in the order of nature.

* * *

38

The idols and false notions which are now in possession of the human understanding and have taken deep root therein, not only so beset men's minds that truth can hardly find entrance, but even after entrance is obtained, they will again in the very instauration[4] of the sciences meet and

---

7. "You're nothing holy." Adonis was the lover ("minion") of Venus, deified after his death while boar hunting.

8. Hercules early in life was offered a choice between a life of ignoble ease and sensory delights and one of strenuous virtue. He chose the latter, and so do his followers in learning.

1. *Novum Organum*, or "The New Instrument of Learning," was written not in English but in Latin, for an international scholarly audience. Nonetheless it requires our attention here, as it is the keystone of Bacon's vast project to reform the structure of human learning from the

ground up. His reform called for careful observation of all aspects of nature and controlled experiment, but the first part of the book analyzes the stumbling blocks in the way—among them, famously, the various "idols," or delusive images of truth that lead people away from the exact knowledge of science.

2. The deductive method, associated with Aristotle and the Scholastic philosophers.

3. The inductive method that Bacon here champions.

4. Renovation, renewal.

trouble us, unless men being forewarned of the danger fortify themselves as far as may be against their assaults.

❊   ❊   ❊

41

The Idols of the Tribe have their foundation in human nature itself, and in the tribe or race of men. For it is a false assertion that the sense of man is the measure of things. On the contrary, all perceptions as well of the sense as of the mind are according to the measure of the individual and not according to the measure of the universe. And the human understanding is like a false mirror, which, receiving rays irregularly, distorts and discolors the nature of things by mingling its own nature with it.

42

The Idols of the Cave are the idols of the individual man. For everyone (besides the errors common to human nature in general) has a cave or den of his own, which refracts and discolors the light of nature, owing either to his own proper and peculiar nature, or to his education and conversation with others, or to the reading of books, and the authority of those whom he esteems and admires; or to the difference of impressions, accordingly as they take place in a mind preoccupied and predisposed or in a mind indifferent and settled, or the like. So that the spirit of man (according as it is meted out to different individuals) is in fact a thing variable and full of perturbation, and governed as it were by chance. Whence it was well observed by Heraclitus[5] that men look for sciences in their own lesser worlds, and not in the greater or common world.

43

There are also idols formed by the intercourse and association of men with each other, which I call Idols of the Marketplace, on account of the commerce and consort of men there. For it is by discourse that men associate, and words are imposed according to the apprehension of the vulgar. And therefore the fit and unfit choice of words wonderfully obstructs the understanding. Nor do the definitions or explanations wherewith in some things learned men are wont to guard and defend themselves, by any means set the matter right. But words plainly force and overrule the understanding, and throw all into confusion, and lead men away into numberless empty controversies and idle fancies.

44

Lastly, there are idols which have immigrated into men's minds from the various dogmas of philosophies, and also from wrong laws of demonstration.

5. Greek philosopher (ca. 513 B.C.E.) who considered knowledge to be based on perception by the senses and thought that everything was in flux.

These I call Idols of the Theater, because in my judgment all the received systems are but so many stage plays, representing worlds of their own creation after an unreal and scenic fashion. Nor is it only of the systems now in vogue or only of the ancient sects and philosophies that I speak; for many more plays of the same kind may yet be composed and in like artificial manner set forth, seeing that errors the most widely different have nevertheless causes for the most part alike. Neither again do I mean this only of entire systems, but also of the many principles and axioms in science, which by tradition, credulity, and negligence have come to be received.

* * *

59

But the Idols of the Marketplace are the most troublesome of all: idols which have crept into the understanding through the alliances of words and names. For men believe that their reason governs words; but it is also true that words react on the understanding; and this it is that has rendered philosophy and the sciences sophistical and inactive. Now words, being commonly framed and applied according to the capacity of the vulgar, follow those lines of division which are most obvious to the vulgar understanding. And whenever an understanding of greater acuteness or a more diligent observation would alter those lines to suit the true divisions of nature, words stand in the way and resist the change. Whence it comes to pass that the high and formal discussions of learned men end oftentimes in disputes about words and names; with which (according to the use[6] and wisdom of the mathematicians) it would be more prudent to begin, and so by means of definitions reduce them to order. Yet even definitions cannot cure this evil in dealing with natural and material things; since the definitions themselves consist of words, and those words beget others;[7] so that it is necessary to recur to individual instances, and those in due series and order; as I shall say presently when I come to the method and scheme for the formation of notions and axioms.

60

The idols imposed by words on the understanding are of two kinds. They are either names of things which do not exist (for as there are things left unnamed through lack of observation, so likewise are there names which result from fantastic suppositions and to which nothing in reality corresponds), or they are names of things which exist, but yet confused and ill-defined, and hastily and irregularly derived from realities. Of the former kind are Fortune, the Prime Mover, Planetary Orbits, Element of Fire, and like fictions which owe their origin to false and idle theories.[8] And this class

6. Custom.
7. Bacon's mistrust of words helped to prompt the Royal Society (founded in 1645) to cultivate a plain, stripped prose style for purposes of scientific communication.
8. The "Prime Mover" was a transparent sphere on the outside of the universe, supposed to move all the other spheres; the "Element of Fire" was an area of pure, invisible fire, supposed to exist above the atmosphere. By "Planetary Orbits" Bacon may be referring to the old notion of crystalline spheres in which the planets were supposed to be set. Obviously, these concepts could be based on no observation.

of idols is more easily expelled, because to get rid of them it is only necessary that all theories should be steadily rejected and dismissed as obsolete.[9]

But the other class, which springs out of a faulty and unskillful abstraction, is intricate and deeply rooted. Let us take for example such a word as *humid*; and see how far the several things which the word is used to signify agree with each other; and we shall find the word *humid* to be nothing else than a mark loosely and confusedly applied to denote a variety of actions which will not bear to be reduced to any constant meaning. For it both signifies that which easily spreads itself round any other body; and that which in itself is indeterminate and cannot solidize; and that which readily yields in every direction; and that which easily divides and scatters itself; and that which easily unites and collects itself; and that which readily flows and is put in motion; and that which readily clings to another body and wets it; and that which is easily reduced to a liquid, or being solid easily melts. Accordingly when you come to apply the word—if you take it in one sense, flame is humid; if in another, air is not humid; if in another, fine dust is humid; if in another, glass is humid. So that it is easy to see that the notion is taken by abstraction only from water and common and ordinary liquids, without any due verification.

There are however in words certain degrees of distortion and error. One of the least faulty kinds is that of names of substances, especially of lowest species and well-deduced (for the notion of *chalk* and of *mud* is good, of *earth* bad); a more faulty kind is that of actions, as *to generate, to corrupt, to alter*; the most faulty is of qualities (except such as are the immediate objects of the sense), as *heavy, light, rare, dense*, and the like. Yet in all these cases some notions are of necessity a little better than others, in proportion to the greater variety of subjects that fall within the range of the human sense.

* * *

62

Idols of the Theater, or of systems, are many, and there can be and perhaps will be yet many more. For were it not that now for many ages men's minds have been busied with religion and theology; and were it not that civil governments, especially monarchies, have been averse to such novelties, even in matters speculative, so that men labor therein to the peril and harming of their fortunes, not only unrewarded, but exposed also to contempt and envy; doubtless there would have arisen many other philosophical sects like to those which in great variety flourished once among the Greeks. For as on the phenomena of the heavens many hypotheses may be constructed, so likewise (and more also) many various dogmas may be set up and established on the phenomena of philosophy. And in the plays of this philosophical theater you may observe the same thing which is found in the theater of the poets, that stories invented for the stage are more compact and elegant, and more as one would wish them to be, than true stories out of history.

---

9. Bacon does not mean "theories" in the inclusive modern sense, but "abstractions loosely invoked to explain particular facts."

In general, however, there is taken for the material of philosophy either a great deal out of a few things, or a very little out of many things; so that on both sides philosophy is based on too narrow a foundation of experiment and natural history, and decides on the authority of too few cases. For the rational school of philosophers snatches from experience a variety of common instances, neither duly ascertained nor diligently examined and weighed, and leaves all the rest to meditation and agitation of wit.[1]

There is also another class of philosophers, who having bestowed much diligent and careful labor on a few experiments, have thence made bold to educe and construct systems; wresting all other facts in a strange fashion to conformity therewith.

And there is yet a third class, consisting of those who out of faith and veneration mix their philosophy with theology and traditions; among whom the vanity of some has gone so far aside as to seek the origin of sciences among spirits and genii. So that this parent stock of errors—this false philosophy—is of three kinds: the sophistical, the empirical, and the superstitious.

* * *

68

So much concerning the several classes of idols, and their equipage: all of which must be renounced and put away with a fixed and solemn determination, and the understanding thoroughly freed and cleansed; the entrance into the kingdom of man, founded on the sciences, being not much other than the entrance into the kingdom of heaven, whereinto none may enter except as a little child.

1620

From The New Atlantis[1]

[SOLOMON'S HOUSE]

We came at our day and hour, and I was chosen by my fellows for the private access.[2] We found him in a fair chamber, richly hanged, and carpeted under foot, without any degrees to the state.[3] He was set upon a low throne richly adorned, and a rich cloth of state over his head, of blue satin embroidered.

1. Bacon's enthusiasm for experiment at times led him to denigrate the value of reason, but what he chiefly opposes here is the excessive concern with logic he finds in the Scholastic philosophers.

1. Thomas More's *Utopia* (1516) set a fashion for accounts of imaginary communities with more or less ideal forms of government. Bacon's imaginary community has at its center an account of a research establishment, Solomon's House, that could exist in any society; indeed a version of it was established in England in 1662 as the Royal Society. Bacon's title alludes to the legendary island and ideal commonwealth in the Atlantic

Ocean described by Plato in *Critias;* in the 17th century it was sometimes located in the New World. Bacon places his island, Bensalem, in the Pacific, roughly where the Solomon Islands had been discovered in 1568. After an imaginary journey the nameless narrator and his shipmates discover an island cut off from Hebrew and Greek civilization (though given a special revelation of Christianity) and thereby freed to focus on the development of science.

2. Audience with one of the scientific "Fathers" of Solomon's House.

3. Without stairs leading up to the dais.

He was alone, save that he had two pages of honor, on either hand one, finely attired in white. His undergarments were the like that we saw him wear in the chariot;[4] but instead of his gown, he had on him a mantle with a cape of the same fine black, fastened about him. When we came in, as we were taught, we bowed low at our first entrance, and when we were come near his chair, he stood up, holding forth his hand ungloved and in posture of blessing; and we every one of us stooped down, and kissed the hem of his tippet.[5] That done, the rest departed, and I remained. Then he warned the pages forth of the room, and caused me to sit down beside him, and spake to me thus in the Spanish tongue:

"God bless thee, my son; I will give thee the greatest jewel I have. For I will impart unto thee, for the love of God and men, a relation of the true state of Solomon's House. Son, to make you know the true state of Solomon's House, I will keep this order. First, I will set forth unto you the end of our foundation. Secondly, the preparations and instruments we have for our works. Thirdly, the several employments and functions whereto our fellows are assigned. And fourthly, the ordinances and rites which we observe.

"The end of our foundation is the knowledge of causes, and secret motions of things; and the enlarging of the bounds of human empire, to the effecting of all things possible.

"The preparations and instruments are these. We have large and deep caves of several depths: the deepest are sunk six hundred fathom; and some of them are digged and made under great hills and mountains; so that if you reckon together the depth of the hill and the depth of the cave, they are, some of them, above three miles deep. For we find that the depth of a hill, and the depth of a cave from the flat, is the same thing; both remote alike from the sun and heaven's beams, and from the open air. These caves we call the Lower Region, and we use them for all coagulations, indurations,[6] refrigerations, and conservations of bodies. We use them likewise for the imitation of natural mines, and the producing also of new artificial metals, by compositions and materials which we use, and lay there for many years. We use them also sometimes (which may seem strange) for curing of some diseases, and for prolongation of life in some hermits that choose to live there, well accommodated of[7] all things necessary, and indeed live very long; by whom also we learn many things.

"We have burials in several earths, where we put divers cements,[8] as the Chinese do their porcelain. But we have them in greater variety, and some of them more fine. We have also great variety of composts and soils, for the making of the earth fruitful.

"We have high towers, the highest about half a mile in height, and some of them likewise set upon high mountains, so that the vantage of the hill, with the tower, is in the highest of them three miles at least. And these places we call the Upper Region, accounting the air between the high places and the low as a Middle Region. We use these towers, according to their several heights and situations, for insolation,[9] refrigeration, conservation, and for the view of divers meteors—as winds, rain, snow, hail; and some of the fiery meteors[1] also. And upon them, in some places, are dwellings of hermits, whom we visit sometimes, and instruct what to observe.

"We have great lakes, both salt and fresh, whereof we have use for the fish and fowl. We use them also for burials of some natural bodies, for we find a difference in things buried in earth, or in air below the earth, and things buried in water. We have also pools, of which some do strain fresh water out of salt, and others by art do turn fresh water into salt. We have also some rocks in the midst of the sea, and some bays upon the shore, for some works wherein is required the air and vapor of the sea. We have likewise violent streams and cataracts, which serve us for many motions; and likewise engines for multiplying and enforcing[2] of winds to set also on going divers motions.

"We have also a number of artificial wells and fountains, made in imitation of the natural sources and baths, as tincted upon[3] vitriol, sulphur, steel, brass, lead, niter, and other minerals; and again, we have little wells for infusions of many things, where the waters take the virtue[4] quicker and better than in vessels or basins. And amongst them we have a water which we call Water of Paradise, being by that we do to it, made very sovereign[5] for health and prolongation of life.

"We have also great and spacious houses, where we imitate and demonstrate meteors—as snow, hail, rain, some artificial rains of bodies and not of water, thunders, lightnings; also generations of bodies in air—as frogs, flies, and divers others.

"We have also certain chambers, which we call Chambers of Health, where we qualify[6] the air as we think good and proper for the cure of divers diseases and preservation of health.

"We have also fair and large baths, of several mixtures, for the cure of diseases and the restoring of man's body from arefaction;[7] and others for the confirming of it in strength of sinews, vital parts, and the very juice and substance of the body.

"We have also large and various orchards and gardens, wherein we do not so much respect beauty as variety of ground and soil, proper for divers trees and herbs, and some very spacious, where trees and berries are set, whereof we make divers kinds of drinks, besides the vineyards. In these we practice likewise all conclusions[8] of grafting and inoculating, as well of wild trees as fruit trees, which produceth many effects. And we make (by art) in the same orchards and gardens trees and flowers to come earlier or later than their seasons, and to come up and bear more speedily than by their natural course they do. We make them also by art greater much than their nature; and their fruit greater and sweeter, and of differing taste, smell, color, and figure, from their nature. And many of them we so order as they become of medicinal use.

"We have also means to make divers plants rise by mixtures of earths without seeds, and likewise to make divers new plants, differing from the vulgar,[9] and to make one tree or plant turn into another.

1. Anything that fell from the sky was, in Renaissance terminology, a meteor.
2. Reinforcing, strengthening.
3. Tinctured with.
4. Property (of the substances put into water).

5. Efficacious.
6. Modify.
7. Drying up.
8. Experiments.
9. Ordinary.

"We have also parks and enclosures of all sorts of beasts and birds; which we use not only for view or rareness, but likewise for dissections and trials,[1] that thereby we may take light what may be wrought upon the body of man. Wherein we find many strange effects: as continuing life in them, though divers parts, which you account vital, be perished and taken forth; resuscitating of some that seem dead in appearance; and the like. We try also all poisons and other medicines upon them, as well of chirurgery[2] as physic. By art likewise, we make them greater or taller than their kind is, and contrariwise dwarf them and stay their growth; we make them more fruitful and bearing than their kind is, and contrariwise barren and not generative. Also, we make them differ in color, shape, activity, many ways. We find means to make commixtures and copulations of different kinds, which have produced many new kinds,[3] and them not barren, as the general opinion is. We make a number of kinds of serpents, worms, fishes, flies, of putrefaction, whereof some are advanced (in effect) to be perfect creatures, like beasts or birds, and have sexes, and do propagate. Neither do we this by chance, but we know beforehand of what matter and commixture what kind of those creatures will arise.

"We have also particular pools where we make trials upon fishes, as we have said before of beasts and birds.

"We have also places for breed and generation of those kinds of worms and flies which are of special use; such as are with you your silkworms and bees."[4]

* * *

"For the several employments and offices of our fellows, we have twelve that sail into foreign countries under the names of other nations (for our own we conceal), who bring us the books and abstracts and patterns of experiments of all other parts. These we call Merchants of Light.

"We have three that collect the experiments which are in all books. These we call Depredators.

"We have three that collect the experiments of all mechanical arts, and also of liberal sciences, and also of practices which are not brought into arts. These we call Mystery-men.

"We have three that try new experiments, such as themselves think good. These we call Pioneers or Miners.

"We have three that draw the experiments of the former four into titles and tables, to give the better light for the drawing of observations and axioms out of them. These we call Compilers.

"We have three that bend themselves, looking into the experiments of their fellows, and cast about how to draw out of them things of use and practice for man's life and knowledge, as well for works as for plain demonstration of causes, means of natural divinations, and the easy and clear discovery of the virtues and parts of bodies. These we call Dowry-men or Benefactors.

1. Experiments.
2. Surgery.
3. Species. It was commonly supposed that all hybrids were sterile (see following).
4. The narrator continues to describe the various bakeries, vineyards, breweries, and kitchens operated by Solomon's House. He enumerates the medicines discovered there, as well as various experiments with heat. The researchers study light, sound, perfumes, mechanics, mathematics, and all ways of deceiving the senses.

"Then after divers meetings and consults of our whole number, to consider of the former labors and collections, we have three that take care out of them to direct new experiments, of a higher light, more penetrating into nature than the former. These we call Lamps.

"We have three others that do execute the experiments so directed, and report them. These we call Inoculators.

"Lastly, we have three that raise the former discoveries by experiments into greater observations, axioms, and aphorisms. These we call Interpreters of Nature.

"We have also, as you must think, novices and apprentices, that the succession of the former employed men do not fail; besides a great number of servants and attendants, men and women. And this we do also: we have consultations, which of the inventions and experiences which we have discovered shall be published, and which not; and take all an oath of secrecy for the concealing of those which we think fit to keep secret; though some of those we do reveal sometimes to the State, and some not.[5]

"For our ordinances and rites, we have two very long and fair galleries: in one of these we place patterns and samples of all manner of the more rare and excellent inventions; in the other we place the statues of all principal inventors. There we have the statue of your Columbus, that discovered the West Indies; also the inventor of ships; your monk that was the inventor of ordnance and of gunpowder;[6] the inventor of music; the inventor of letters; the inventor of printing; the inventor of observations of astronomy; the inventor of works in metal; the inventor of glass; the inventor of silk of the worm; the inventor of wine; the inventor of corn and bread; the inventor of sugars; and all these by more certain tradition than you have. Then we have divers inventors of our own, of excellent works, which since you have not seen, it were too long to make descriptions of them; and besides, in the right understanding of those descriptions you might easily err. For upon every invention of value we erect a statue to the inventor, and give him a liberal and honorable reward. These statues are some of brass, some of marble and touchstone,[7] some of cedar and other special woods gilt and adorned; some of iron, some of silver, some of gold.

"We have certain hymns and services, which we say daily, of laud and thanks to God for his marvelous works; and forms of prayer, imploring his aid and blessing for the illumination of our labors, and the turning of them into good and holy uses.

"Lastly, we have circuits or visits of divers principal cities of the kingdom; where, as it cometh to pass, we do publish such new profitable inventions as we think good. And we do also declare natural divinations of diseases, plagues, swarms of hurtful creatures, scarcity, tempests, earthquakes, great inundations, comets, temperature of the year, and divers other things; and we give counsel thereupon, what the people shall do for the prevention and remedy of them."

And when he had said this he stood up; and I, as I had been taught, kneeled down; and he laid his right hand upon my head, and said, "God bless

---

5. Bacon allows his scientists considerable autonomy in relation to the state.
6. Tradition credited Roger Bacon, a 13th- century monk, with the discovery of gunpowder.
7. A hard basaltic-type rock.

thee, my son, and God bless this relation which I have made. I give thee leave to publish it, for the good of other nations; for we here are in God's bosom, a land unknown." And so he left me; having assigned a value of about two thousand ducats for a bounty to me and my fellows. For they give great largesses, where they come, upon all occasions.

The rest was not perfected.

1627

WILLIAM HARVEY

William Harvey (1578–1657) received medical training at Cambridge University and then at the University of Padua, a leading center of anatomical research. Returning to England, he established a successful practice, serving as personal physician to King James and Charles as well as to many less exalted clients. After many years of investigation, in 1628 Harvey published a treatise arguing, against the authority of ancient writers, that blood circulated in the body, pumped by the heart. Because Harvey wished to engage a scientific readership not only in England but internationally, he published his treatise in Latin; the selection reproduced here comes from the first English translation, in 1653.

Direct observation of the circulation of the blood and of the heart in motion is challenging because, of course, in live bodies the process is concealed, and in dead ones it no longer occurs. Harvey's vivisection of animals—a skill he would have learned in Padua—allowed him to observe the movement of heart and arteries in the time between the opening of an animal's body and its death. Without a microscope, Harvey could not directly observe the capillaries, but he experimented with tourniquets on his own and others' bodies, which allowed him correctly to hypothesize that tiny vessels must transfer blood from the arteries, which carried the blood away from the heart, to the veins, which returned blood to the heart.

The excerpt demonstrates Harvey's lucid, methodical presentation of his observations and hypotheses. His experiments on beating hearts led him to a conclusion directly opposite of the accepted view: while previous writers had believed that the pulse was the effect of the heart dilating, Harvey argues instead that the heart is actively at work, and producing a pulse, when it compresses itself and forces blood into the arteries.

While Harvey's friend and patient Francis Bacon influentially elaborated the theory of science, Harvey actually performed the kind of innovative experiment Bacon was recommending. Harvey's objective, scientific prose constituted a stylistic model different from the rhetorically embellished, self-consciously artful prose of such sixteenth-century writers as Philip Sidney, and different as well from the style of Robert Burton or Sir Thomas Browne, which draws attention to the individual personality of the writer. Harvey's writings, striving for objectivity and the recording of detailed empirical fact, strongly influenced the founders of the Royal Society in the later seventeenth century.

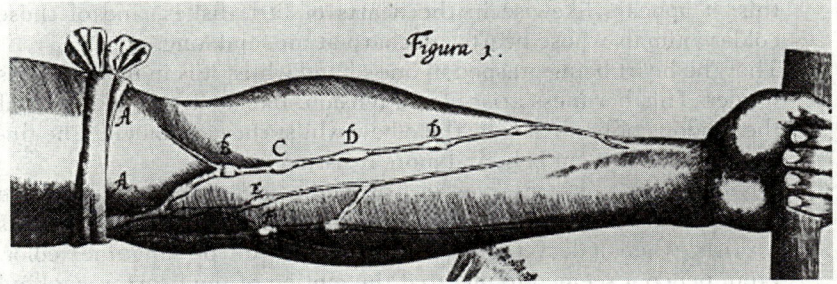

The Flow of Blood. This illustration from William Harvey's *On the Circulation of the Blood* (1628) depicts one of his experiments. Venal valves had already been discovered, but here Harvey shows that venal blood flows only toward the heart. He ligatured an arm to make obvious the veins and their valves, then pressed blood away from the heart and showed that the vein would remain empty because blocked by the valve.

The Anatomical Exercises of Dr. William Harvey Professor of Physic, and Physician to the King's Majesty, Concerning the Motion of the Heart and Blood. 1653

From *Chapter 2. What manner of motion the heart has in the dissection of living creatures.*

First then in the hearts of all creatures, being dissected whilst they are yet alive, opening the crest, and cutting up the capsule which immediately environeth the heart, you may observe that the heart moves sometimes, sometimes rests: and that there is a time when it moves, and when it moves not.

This is more evident in the hearts of colder creatures, as the toads, serpents, frogs, house-snails, shrimps, crevises,[1] and all manner of little fishes. For it shews itself more manifestly in the hearts of hotter bodies, as of dogs, swine, if you observe attentively till the heart begin to die, and move faintly, and life is as it were departing from it. Then you may clearly and plainly see that the motions of it are more slow and seldom, and the restings of it of a longer continuance: and you may observe and distinguish more easily, what manner of motion it is, and which ways it is made; in the resting of it, as likewise in death, the heart is yielding, flagging weak, and lies as it were drooping.

At the motion, and whilst it is moving, three things are chiefly to be observed.

1. That the heart is erected, and that it raises itself upwards into a point, insomuch that it beats the breast at that time, so as the pulsation is felt outwardly.
2. That there is a contraction of it every way, especially of the sides of it, so that it appears lesser, longer, and contracted. The heart of an eel, taken out, and laid upon a trencher,[2] or upon one's hand, doth evidence

---

1. Crayfish.   2. Plate.

this; it appears likewise in the hearts of little fishes, and of those colder animals whose hearts are sharp at top, and long.

3. That the heart being grasped in one's hand whilst it is in motion, feels harder. This hardness arises from tension, like as if one take hold of the tendons of one's arm by the elbow whilst they are moving the fingers, shall feel them bent and more resisting.

4. 'Tis moreover to be observed in fish, and colder animals which have blood, as serpents, frogs, at that time when the heart moves it becomes whitish, when it leaveth motion it appears full of sanguine[3] color. From hence it seemed to me, that the motion of the heart was a kind of tension in every part of it, according to the drawing and contraction of the fibers every way; because it appeared that in all its motions, it was erected, received vigor, grew lesser, and harder, and that the motion of it was like that of the muscles, where the contraction is made according to the drawing of the nervous parts, and fibers, for the muscles whilst they are in motion and in action, are invigorated and stretched, of soft become hard, they are uplifted and thickened; so likewise the heart.

From which observations with good reason we may gather that the heart at that time whilst it is in motion, suffers constriction, and is thickened in its outside, and so straitened in its ventricles, thrusting forth the blood contained within it: which from the fourth observation is evident because that in the tension it becomes white, having thrust out the blood contained within it, and presently after it in relaxation and rest, a purple and crimson color returns to the heart. But of this no man needs to make any further scruple, since upon the inflicting of a wound into the cavity of the ventricle, upon every motion and pulsation of the heart, in the very tension, you shall see the blood within contained to leap out.

So then these things happen at one and the same time: the tension of the heart, the erection of the point, and the beating (which is felt outwardly) by reason of its hitting against the breast, the incrassation[4] of the sides of it, and the forcible protrusion of the blood by constriction of the ventricles.

Hence the contrary of the commonly received opinion appears, which is, that the heart at that time when it beats against the breast, and the pulsation is outwardly felt, it is believed that the ventricles of the heart are dilated, and replete with blood, though you shall understand that it is otherwise, and that when the heart is contracted it is emptied. For that motion which is commonly thought the diastole[5] of the heart, is really the systole,[6] and so the proper motion of the heart is not a diastole but a systole, for the heart receives no vigor in the diastole, but in the systole, for then it is extended, moveth, and receiveth vigor.

---

3. Blood-red.
4. Compression.

5. Expansion.
6. Contraction.

ROBERT BURTON

Robert Burton's *Anatomy of Melancholy* assumes, unlike Bacon, that knowledge of psychology, not science, is humankind's greatest need. His enormous, baggy, delightful treatise analyzes in encyclopedic detail that ubiquitous Jacobean malady, melancholy, supposedly caused, according to contemporary humor theory, by an excess of black bile. It was responsible, according to Burton and others, for the wild passions and despair of lovers, the agonies and ecstasies of religious devotees, the frenzies of madmen, and the studious abstraction of scholars such as Shakespeare's Hamlet or Milton's Il Penseroso. But for Burton melancholy is more than a particular temperament or disease: it encompasses all the folly and madness intrinsic to the fallen human condition and so afflicts the whole world—necessarily including Burton himself.

Burton (1577–1640) was a scholar and cleric who lived in Christ Church College, Oxford, all his life: he never married, never traveled, never sought success in the world, but lived, as he says of himself in his preface, "a silent, sedentary, solitary, private life," researching his great book in the Bodleian Library and reading omnivorously in other topics. First published in 1621, the *Anatomy* went through five editions during the author's life, each one much augmented over the last. In his preface Burton creates a persona for himself, Democritus Junior, who proposes to complete the supposedly lost book on melancholy and madness by the Greek "laughing philosopher" Democritus. As Democritus Junior he promises not only to laugh but also to scoff, satirize, and lament.

The title term "anatomy" invites expectations of a clear, logical, ordered treatment of a medical subject after the manner of Vesalius, expectations also evoked by Donne in his *Anatomy of the World*. Burton's subtitle promises an analysis of "all the kinds, causes, symptoms, prognostics, and several cures" of melancholy, and a division into three parts—the Causes and Effects, the Cures, and the two principal kinds, Love Melancholy and Religious Melancholy—as well as various "sections, members, and subsections." But instead of such clarity and rigidity of structure, the categories collapse into each other. Since melancholy is universal, Burton finds warrant to be all-inclusive and digressive, to take us in picaresque disorder from one subject to the next, moving readily from the inner landscape to the world outside. The work contains a utopia, a treatise on climatology, and discourses on geography and meteorology, as well as case studies of various sufferers from melancholy: a man who thought he was glass; a man who thought he was butter; maids, nuns, and widows who suffer sexual deprivation; etc. Also, Burton cites every authority who wrote about any aspect of melancholy, from classical times to his present, but in no special order and without privileging even citations from Scripture. Such randomness and their own contradictions undercut the authorities, collapsing them all into the idiosyncratic style of Burton/Democritus Junior. Burton's prose style of long, loose sentences, with their pell-mell momentum as of thoughts rushing beyond the author's control, suggests a disorderly world not at all amenable to Baconian logic and science. Burton concludes by offering the pragmatic advice "Be not idle" as the only remedy against melancholy. His book, were we to read it all, would keep us from idleness for a good long time.

From The Anatomy[1] of Melancholy

From *Love Melancholy*

PART 3, SECTION 2, MEMBER 1, SUBSECTION 2: HOW LOVE TYRANNIZETH
OVER MEN. LOVE, OR HEROICAL MELANCHOLY, HIS DEFINITION, PART
AFFECTED.

You have heard how this tyrant Love rageth with brute beasts and spirits; now let us consider what passions it causeth amongst men. *Improbe amor quid non mortalia pectora cogis*,[2] How it tickles the hearts of mortal men, *horresco referens*,[3] I am almost afraid to relate, amazed, and ashamed, it hath wrought such stupend and prodigious effects, such foul offences. Love indeed (I may not deny) first united provinces, built cities, and by a perpetual generation makes and preserves mankind, propagates the Church; but if it rage, it is no more love, but burning lust, a disease, frenzy, madness, hell. *Est orcus ille, vis est immedicabilis, est rabies insana*; 'tis no virtuous habit this, but a vehement perturbation of the mind, a monster of nature, wit, and art, as Alexis in Athenaeus[4] sets it out, *viriliter audax, muliebriter timidium, furore praeceps, labore infractum, mel felleum, blanda percussio*, etc. It subverts kingdoms, overthrows cities, towns, families, mars, corrupts, and makes a massacre of men; thunder and lightning, wars, fires, plagues, have not done that mischief to mankind, as this burning lust, this brutish passion. Let Sodom and Gomorrah, Troy (which Dares Phrygius and Dictys Cretensis will make good)[5] and I know not how many cities bear record,—*et fuit ante Helenam*,[6] etc., all succeeding ages will subscribe: Joanna of Naples in Italy, Fredegunde and Brunhalt in France,[7] all histories are full of these basilisks.[8] Besides those daily monomachies,[9] murders, effusion of blood, rapes, riot, and immoderate expense, to satisfy their lusts, beggary, shame, loss, torture, punishment, disgrace, loathsome diseases that proceed from thence, worse than calentures[1] and pestilent fevers, those often gouts, pox,

---

1. A logical dissection of a topic into its several parts, on an analogy with a medical anatomy. (See also Donne, *An Anatomy of the World*, pp. 1399–1410.) Burton's full title plays wittily with the term while pointing to the massive scope of his work: *The Anatomy of Melancholy. What it is, with all the kinds, causes, symptoms, prognostics, & several cures of it. In three Partitions, with their several sections, members, & subsections. Philosophically, medicinally, historically opened & cut up.*
2. Depraved love, to what do you not force mortal breasts?
3. Burton immediately translates the Latin into English ("I am almost afraid to relate") as is his habit throughout *The Anatomy of Melancholy*. The notes here will provide translations only when Burton does not.
4. Alexis is one of the interlocutors in Athenaeus's series of dialogues, *Deipnosophistae* (*The Banquet of the Learned*) written in the 3rd century C.E., which features dinner conversations on topics that include food, poetry, philology, and sexual mores; the English classicist Isaac Casaubon revived interest in the work by publishing his edition in 1612.
5. In Genesis 18–19, God annihilates the towns Sodom and Gomorrah with a rain of fire and brimstone to punish their sexual wickedness; the Greeks destroyed Troy after the Trojan prince Paris eloped with the beautiful Helen, wife of the Greek king Menelaus. Dares Phrygius and Dictys Cretensis were the supposed authors of eyewitness accounts of the Trojan War; the texts, actually dating from late antiquity, were available in Latin and thus became the basis for the medieval knowledge of the Troy legend, in an era when Greek was not widely known in Western Europe.
6. And these were before Helen.
7. Joanna of Naples, 1327–1381, conspired to assassinate her first husband; most of the plotters were ferociously executed, but Joanna was eventually acquitted and married three more times. Fredegund (died 59 C.E.) was a servant of the Frankish king Chilperic, who killed his wife and made Fredegund his consort. Brunhalt or Brunhilda (543–613 C.E.), the sister of Chilperic's wife and married to Chilperic's brother, encouraged her husband to go to war to avenge this murder; years of bloody conflict ensued.
8. Legendary serpent with poisonous breath and lethal gaze.
9. Single combats; duels.
1. Feverish delirium.

arthritis, palsies, cramps, sciatica, convulsions, aches, combustions, etc., which torment the body, that feral[2] melancholy which crucifies the soul in this life, and everlastingly torments in the world to come.

Notwithstanding they know these and many such miseries, threats, tortures, will surely come upon them, rewards, exhortations, *e contra;*[3] yet either out of their own weakness, a depraved nature, or love's tyranny, which so furiously rageth, they suffer themselves to be led like an ox to the slaughter: (*Facilis descensus Averni*) they go down headlong to their own perdition, they will commit folly with beasts, men "leaving the natural use of women," as Paul saith, "burned in lust one towards another, and man with man wrought filthiness."[4]

* * *[5]

I come at last to that heroical love which is proper to men and women, is a frequent cause of melancholy, and deserves much rather to be called burning lust, than by such an honorable title. There is an honest love, I confess, which is natural, *laqueus occultus captivans corda hominum, ut a mulieribus non possint separari,* "a secret snare to captivate the hearts of men," as Christopher Fonseca proves,[6] a strong allurement, of a most attractive, occult, adamantine property, and powerful virtue, and no man living can avoid it. *Et qui vim non sensit amoris, aut lapis est, aut bellua.* He is not a man but a block, a very stone, *aut Numen, aut Nebuchadnezzar,*[7] he hath a gourd for his head, a pepon[8] for his heart, that hath not felt the power of it, and a rare creature to be found, one in an age, *qui nunquam visae flagravit amore puellae;*[9] for *semel insanivimus omnes,* dote we either young or old, as he said,[1] and none are excepted but Minerva and the Muses: so Cupid in Lucian[2] complains to his mother Venus, that amongst all the rest his arrows could not pierce them. But this nuptial love is a common passion, an honest, for men to love in the way of marriage; *ut materia appetit formam, sic mulier virum.*[3] You know marriage is honorable, a blessed calling, appointed by God himself in Paradise; it breeds true peace, tranquility, content, and happiness, *qua nulla est aut fuit unquam sanctior conjunctio,* as Daphnaeus in Plutarch[4] could well prove, *et quae generi humano immortalitatem parat,* when they live without jarring, scolding, lovingly as they should do.

> *Felices ter et amplius*
> *Quos irrupta tenet copula, nec ullis*
> *Divulsus querimoniis*
> *Suprema citius solvit amor die.*[5]

---

2. Deadly.
3. On the other hand.
4. In Romans 1.22–27, St. Paul writes that because of the pagans' idolatrous beliefs God "gave them up unto vile affections: for even their women did change the natural use into that which is against nature: And likewise also the men, leaving the natural use of the woman, burned in their lust one toward another."
5. In the omitted section, Burton provides, in Latin, a list of perverse loves as described by Ovid and other classical writers.
6. Quoting from the Spanish writer Christopher Fonseca's *Amphitheater of Love.*
7. "Either a god, or Nebuchadenezzar," i.e., an

extraordinary thing, quoting from the church father Tertullian's *Against Marcion,* book 4.
8. Pumpkin.
9. In whom the sight of a girl has never sparked love.
1. Chaucer.
2. Lucian, *Dialogue of the Gods* 19.
3. As matter seeks form, so a man seeks a woman.
4. Daphnaeus in Plutarch's *Dialogue on Love* argues for the sanctity of marital love, against Protogenes, who argues that true love is homosexual.
5. Quoting Horace, *Odes* 1.13; the translation follows immediately.

> Thrice happy they, and more than that,
> Whom bond of love so firmly ties,
> That without brawls till death them part,
> 'Tis undissolv'd and never dies.

As Seneca lived with his Paulina, Abraham and Sarah, Orpheus and Eurydice, Arria and Poetus, Artemisia and Mausolus,[6] Rubenius Celer, that would needs have it engraven on his tomb, he had led his life with Ennea, his dear wife, forty-three years eight months, and never fell out. There is no pleasure in this world comparable to it, 'tis *summum mortalitatis bonum, hominum divumque voluptas, Alma Venus; latet enim in muliere aliquid majus potentiusque, omnibus aliis humanis voluptatibus*, as one holds, there's something in a woman beyond all human delight; a magnetic virtue, a charming quality, an occult and powerful motive. The husband rules her as head, but she again commands his heart, he is her servant, she is only joy and content: no happiness is like unto it, no love so great as this of man and wife, no such comfort as *placens uxor*, a sweet wife: *omnis amor magnus, sed aperto in conjuge major*.[7] When they love at last as fresh as they did at first, *charaque charo consenescit conjugi*,[8] as Homer brings Paris kissing Helen, after they had been married ten years, protesting withal that he loved her as dear as he did the first hour that he was betrothed.[9] And in their old age, when they make much of one another, saying, as he did to his wife in the poet,

> *Uxor vivamus quod viximus, et moriamur,*
> *Servantes nomen sumpsimus in thalamo;*
> *Nec ferat ulla dies ut commutemur in aevo,*
> *Quin tibi sim juvenis, tuque puella mihi.*[1]

> Dear wife, let's live in love, and die together,
> As hitherto we have in all good will:
> Let no day change or alter our affections.
> But let's be young to one another still.

Such should conjugal love be, still the same, and as they are one flesh, so should they be of one mind, as in an aristocratical government, one consent, Geyron-like,[2] *coalescere in unum*, have one heart in two bodies, will and nill the same. A good wife, according to Plutarch,[3] should be as a looking-glass to represent her husband's face and passion: if he be pleasant, she should be merry: if he laugh, she should smile: if he look sad, she should participate of his sorrow, and bear a part with him, and so should they continue in mutual love one towards another.

> *Et me ab amore tuo deducet nulla senectus,*
> *Sive ego Tythonus, sive ego Nestor ero.*[4]

> No age shall part my love from thee, sweet wife,
> Though I live Nestor or Tithonus' life.

6. Famously compatible couples from classical history, mythology, and the Bible.
7. Love is always great, but greatest in marriage.
8. Remaining dear to one another as they grow old together.
9. In *The Iliad*, book 3.
1. The opening lines of the Latin poet Ausoni-us's "Epigram 20."
2. In classical mythology, a monster with one head and three bodies.
3. In his *Advice to the Bride and Groom*.
4. From the Latin love poet Propertius, *Elegies*, book 2: 25.

And she again to him, as the bride saluted the bridegroom of old in Rome, *Ubi tu Caius, ego semper Caia,* be thou still Caius, I'll be Caia.[5]

'Tis a happy state this[6] indeed, when the fountain is blessed (saith Solomon, Proverbs v.18), "and he rejoiceth with the wife of his youth, and she is to him as the loving hind and pleasant roe,[7] and he delights in her continually." But this love of ours is immoderate, inordinate, and not to be comprehended in any bounds. It will not contain itself within the union of marriage or apply to one object, but is a wandering, extravagant, a domineering, a boundless, an irrefragable,[8] a destructive passion; sometimes this burning lust rageth after marriage, and then it is properly called jealousy; sometimes before, and then it is called heroical melancholy; it extends sometimes to corrivals, etc., begets rapes, incests, murders: *Marcus Antoninus compressit Faustinam sororem, Caracalla Juliam novercam, Nero matrem, Caligula sorores, Cinyras Myrrham filiam,*[9] etc. But it is confined within no terms of blood, years, sex, or whatsoever else. Some furiously rage before they come to discretion or age. Quartilla in Petronius[1] never remembered she was a maid; and the Wife of Bath in Chaucer cracks,

> Since I was twelve years old, believe,
> Husbands at kirk-door had I five.[2]

Aretine's Lucretia sold her maidenhead a thousand times before she was twenty-four years old, *plus millies vendideram virginitatem, etc., neque te celabo, non deerant qui ut integram ambirent.*[3] Rahab, that harlot, began to be a professed quean at ten years of age, and was but fifteen when she hid the spies, as Hugh Broughton proves, to whom Serrarius the Jesuit, *quaest. 6 in cap. 2 Josue,* subscribes. Generally women begin *pubescere* as they call it, or *catulire* as Julius Pollux cites, *lib. 2, cap. 3 Onomast.* out of Aristophanes, at fourteen years old, then they do offer themselves, and some plainly rage. Leo Afer[4] saith that in Africa a man shall scarce find a maid at fourteen years of age, they are so forward, and many amongst us after they come into the teens do not live without husbands, but linger.[5] What pranks in this kind the middle age have played is not to be recorded, *si mihi sint centum linguae, sint oraque centum,*[6] no tongue can sufficiently declare, every story is full of men and women's insatiable lust, Neros, Heliogabali, Bonosi,[7] etc. *Coelius Aufilenum, et Quintius Aufilenam depereunt,*[8] etc. They

5. The ancient Roman marriage vow included these words: "where you (the man, Caius) are, so I (the woman, Caia) will be likewise."
6. I.e., the state of matrimony.
7. The hind is a female and the roebuck ("roe") a male deer.
8. Not to be questioned.
9. "Marc Antony slept with his sister Faustina, Caracalla with his stepmother Julia, Nero with his mother, Caligula with his sisters, Cinyras with his daughter Myrrha."
1. A character in the *Satyricon* of Petronius Arbiter (1st century C.E.).
2. Burton cites from memory, and inaccurately.
3. "Moreover, there were those who could restore it." The tale of Lucretia comes from a set of dialogues published by Pietro Aretino in 1534; they parody the dialogues of Plato and are set in a brothel. The "quean" (whore) Rahab (following)

appears in Joshua 2. Hugh Broughton (below) was a biblical scholar of Burton's day.
4. Leo Afer, or Africanus, was a 16th-century Spanish Moor who wrote one of the first accounts of Africa. *Pubescere*: mature sexually. *Catulire*: desire a male. Julius Pollux compiled a dictionary (*Onomasticon*) that Burton cites frequently.
5. I.e., they waste away if they are not married.
6. "If I had a hundred tongues, a hundred mouths."
7. Nero and Heliogabalus were sexually depraved Roman emperors, their vices described in lurid detail by Roman historians and moralists. Bonosus, a 3rd-century C.E. Roman usurper, was merely a drunk, but his close associate Proculus boasted of having deflowered one hundred virgins in a single night.
8. "Coelius had an itch for Aufilenus, Quintius for Aufilena." From Catullus, the Roman erotic poet.

neigh after other men's wives (as Jeremy, *cap.* v.8 complaineth) like fed horses, or range like town bulls, *raptores virginum et viduarum,*[9] as many of our great ones do. Solomon's wisdom was extinguished in this fire of lust, Samson's strength enervated, piety in Lot's daughters quite forgot, gravity of priesthood in Eli's sons, reverend old age in the elders that would violate Susanna, filial duty in Absalom to his stepmother, brotherly love in Amnon towards his sister.[1] Human, divine laws, precepts, exhortations, fear of God and men, fair, foul means, fame, fortunes, shame, disgrace, honor cannot oppose, stave off, or withstand the fury of it, *omnia vincit amor,*[2] etc. No cord nor cable can so forcibly draw, or hold so fast, as love can do with a twined thread. The scorching beams under the equinoctial or extremity of cold within the circle Arctic, where the very seas are frozen, cold or torrid zone cannot avoid or expel this heat, fury, and rage of mortal men.

> *Quo fugis? ah, demens! nulla est fuga, tu licet usque*
> *Ad Tanaim fugias, usque sequetur amor.*[3]

Of women's unnatural, unsatiable lust, what country, what village doth not complain? Mother and daughter sometimes dote on the same man; father and son, master and servant on one woman.

> *Sed amor, sed ineffrenata libido,*
> *Quid castum in terris intentatumque reliquit?*[4]

What breach of vows and oaths, fury, dotage, madness might I reckon up! Yet this is more tolerable in youth, and such as are still in their hot blood; but for an old fool to dote, to see an old lecher, what more odious, what can be more absurd? And yet what so common? Who so furious? *Amare ea aetate si occeperint, multo insaniunt acrius.*[5] Some dote then more than ever they did in their youth. How many decrepit, hoary, harsh, writhen, bursten-bellied, crooked, toothless, bald, blear-eyed, impotent, rotten old men shall you see flickering still in every place? One gets him a young wife, another a courtesan, and when he can scarce lift his leg over a sill and hath one foot already in Charon's boat,[6] when he hath the trembling in his joints, the gout in his feet, a perpetual rheum in his head, a continuate cough, "his sight fails him, thick of hearing, his breath stinks,"[7] all his moisture is dried up and gone, may not spit from him, a very child again, that cannot dress himself or cut his own meat, yet he will be dreaming of and honing after wenches; what can be more unseemly? Worse it is in women than in men; when she is *aetate declivis, diu vidua, mater olim, parum decore matrimonium sequi videtur,* an old widow, a mother so long since (in Pliny's opinion),[8] she doth very unseemly

---

9. "Ravishers of maids and widows." Jeremiah 5.8.
1. For these biblical stories see 1 Kings 11.3, Judges 16, Genesis 19.30–35, 1 Samuel 2.22, Daniel 13 (Apocrypha), 2 Samuel 16.22, 13.1–19.
2. "Love conquers all."
3. "Whither away? ah, madman! there is no escape. Flee to the remotest districts of the river Don, love will still follow." From Propertius, the Latin elegist.
4. "But love, unbridled passion, leaves nothing on earth untempted, nothing chaste." From Eurip-

ides, the Greek tragedian.
5. "When they start loving at that age, the madness takes them worse." From Plautus, the Roman comic dramatist.
6. Charon ferries the souls of the dead across the river Styx.
7. Quoted from Cyprian, 3rd-century bishop of Carthage.
8. Pliny, *Natural History* 8. The Latin is translated by Burton.

seek to marry; yet whilst she is so old, a crone, a beldam, she can neither see nor hear, go nor stand, a mere carcass, a witch, and scarce feel, she caterwauls and must have a stallion, a champion, she must and will marry again, and betroth herself to some young man that hates to look on her but for her goods, abhors the sight of her, to the prejudice of her good name, her own undoing, grief of friends, and ruin of her children.

But to enlarge or illustrate this power and effects of love is to set a candle in the sun. It rageth with all sorts and conditions of men, yet is most evident among such as are young and lusty, in the flower of their years, nobly descended, high fed, such as live idly and at ease; and for that cause (which our divines call burning lust) this *ferinus insanus amor*, this mad and beastly passion, as I have said, is named by our physicians heroical love, and a more honorable title put upon it, *amor nobilis* as Savonarola[9] styles it, because noble men and women make a common practice of it and are so ordinarily affected with it. Avicenna,[1] *lib. 3, fen.* 1, *tract.* 4, *cap.* 23, calleth this passion *Ilishi* and defines it to be "a disease or melancholy vexation or anguish of mind, in which a man continually meditates of the beauty, gesture, manners of his mistress, and troubles himself about it"; "desiring" (as Savonarola adds) "with all intentions and eagerness of mind to compass or enjoy her; as commonly hunters trouble themselves about their sports, the covetous about their gold and goods, so is he tormented still about his mistress." Arnoldus Villanovanus[2] in his book of heroical love defines it "a continual cogitation of that which he desires, with a confidence or hope of compassing it"; which definition his commentator cavils at. For continual cogitation is not the *genus* but a symptom of love; we continually think of that which we hate and abhor, as well as that which we love; and many things we covet and desire without all hope of attaining. Carolus à Lorme in his *Questions* makes a doubt *an amor sit morbus*, whether this heroical love be a disease: Julius Pollux, *Onomast.* lib. 6, *cap.* 44, determines it. They that are in love are likewise sick; *lascivus, salax, lasciviens, et qui in venerem furit, vere est aegrotus.*[3] Arnoldus will have it improperly so called, and a malady rather of the body than mind. Tully,[4] in his *Tusculans*, defines it a furious disease of the mind; Plato, madness itself; Ficinus, his commentator, *cap.* 12, a species of madness, "for many have run mad for women" (I Esdras iv.26); but Rhasis,[5] "a melancholy passion"; and most physicians make it a species or kind of melancholy (as will appear by the symptoms), and treat of it apart; whom I mean to imitate, and to discuss it in all his kinds, to examine his several causes, to show his symptoms, indications, prognostics, effects, that so it may be with more facility cured.

The part affected in the meantime, as Arnoldus supposeth, "is the former part of the head for want of moisture," which his commentator rejects. Langius, *Med. epist. lib.* 1, *cap.* 24, will have this passion sited in the liver, and to keep residence in the heart, "to proceed first from the eyes so carried

---

9. Not the Florentine reformer, but his grandfather Michele, a Paduan physician.

1. An encyclopedic Arabian physician of the 11th century.

2. Arnold of Villanova was a Spanish doctor, astrologer, and alchemist of the 13th and early 14th centuries.

3. "One who is lustful, lecherous, lascivious, and mad with desire is really sick."

4. I.e., Cicero.

5. Rhasis, or Rhazes, was an Arab physician of the 10th century.

by our spirits, and kindled with imagination in the liver and heart"; *cogit amare iecur,*[6] as the saying is. *Medium ferit per hepar,* as Cupid in Anacreon. For some such cause belike, Homer feigns Titius' liver (who was enamored of Latona) to be still gnawed by two vultures day and night in hell, "for that young men's bowels thus enamored are so continually tormented by love."[7] Gordonius, *cap. 2, part.* 2, "will have the testicles an immediate subject or cause, the liver an antecedent." Fracastorius agrees in this with Gordonius,[8] *inde primitus imaginatio venerea, erectio, etc.; titillatissimam partem vocat, ita ut nisi extruso semine gestiens voluptas non cessat, nec assidua veneris recordatio, addit Guastavinius, Comment.,* 4 *sect., prob.* 27 *Arist.*[9] But properly it is a passion of the brain, as all other melancholy, by reason of corrupt imagination, and so doth Jason Pratensis, cap. 19, *De morb. cerebri* (who writes copiously of this erotical love), place and reckon it amongst the affections of the brain. Melanchthon, *De anima,* confutes those that make the liver a part affected, and Guianerius, *tract.* 15, *cap.* 13 *et* 17, though many put all the affections in the heart, refers it to the brain. Ficinus, *cap. 7, In Convivium Platonis,* "will have the blood to be the part affected." Jo. Freitagius, *cap.* 14, *Noct. med.,* supposeth all four affected, heart, liver, brain, blood; but the major part concur upon the brain, 'tis *imaginatio laesa,*[1] and both imagination and reason are misaffected; because of his corrupt judgment and continual meditation of that which he desires, he may truly be said to be melancholy. If it be violent, or his disease inveterate, as I have determined in the precedent partitions, both imagination and reason are misaffected, first one, then the other.

1621, 1651

6. "The liver compels one to love"; and in the next phrase, "Love strikes through the liver." Anacreon was a Greek lyric poet.
7. *Odyssey* 11.
8. Gordonius, Guastavinius, Jason Pratensis, Guianerius, Freitagius, et al. (see following) are Renaissance physicians from the ragbag of Burton's encyclopedic reading. Two who stand out are Girolamo Fracastoro and Marsilio Ficino— the former a physician still remembered for his

work on communicable diseases, the latter known mostly for his learned commentaries on the dialogues of Plato.
9. "Whence at first come erotic imaginings, erection, etc.; it so rouses the most excitable part, adds Guastavinius, that until emission takes place, the longing pleasure does not cease, nor the constant recollection of lovemaking."
1. A wounded imagination.

SIR THOMAS BROWNE

Sir Thomas Browne (1605–1682) presents his best-known work, *Religio Medici* (A Doctor's Religion), as "the true Anatomy of myself." This work is not, as we might expect from the title, a spiritual autobiography relating, like many in the period, an angst-filled story of conversion or an account of providential experiences. Nor does Browne report the facts of his life: that he was born into the family of a cloth merchant, attended Winchester School and Pembroke College, Oxford, studied at the best medical schools (Montpelier, Padua, Leiden), practiced medicine in Yorkshire and Norwich, married in 1641, and fathered twelve children. Instead, this work is an exercise in delighted self-analysis, outlining Browne's own sometimes eccentric views on a wide variety of topics pertaining to religious doctrine and practice. For this purpose Browne constructs an engaging persona: the genial, speculative doctor who finds nothing human foreign to him and so is the very personification of charity and inclusiveness: he can readily participate in the customs of others in food, drink, or religion (even in certain Roman Catholic practices) but yet value his own.

In this two-part treatise divided into short numbered paragraphs, Browne voices his fondness for Anglo-Catholic ritual but also his belief in Calvinist predestination; he denounces religious persecution but thinks many religious martyrs not particularly admirable; he believes in witches but is skeptical of latter-day miracles. His love of mystery and wonder (in sharp contrast to Bacon) leads him to revel in metaphor and take positive joy in accepting things contrary to reason: "I love to lose myself in a mystery, to pursue my reason to an O *altitudo!*" According to his preface, he wrote the work around 1636 for himself only and circulated it in manuscript to a few friends but then was forced by a pirated edition (1642) to print a correct version (1643). Yet his decision to publish just as the king and Parliament took to the battlefield in the civil war was hardly fortuitous, and the treatise has political resonance. Describing himself as one who sympathizes with and has himself held several erroneous or heretical views, Browne disparages dogmatism and holds up to gentle irony those who claim exclusive possession of the path to salvation. At the same time, he deplores schism and is ready to conform his mind to the teachings and practices of the Church of England. His self-analysis comments on the wider world of church and state, posing his example of tolerant inclusiveness against reforming Puritans eager to rid the church of its errors.

Browne was a favorite prose stylist of many later writers, among them Samuel Taylor Coleridge, Charles Lamb, Thomas De Quincey, and Herman Melville: polysyllabic and Latinate, his prose mixes wit and sumptuous rhetoric, often rising to a resonant poetry.

From Religio Medici[1]

From *Part 1*

1. For my religion, though there be several circumstances that might persuade the world I have none at all—as the general scandal of my profession,[2] the natural course of my studies, the indifferency[3] of my behavior and discourse in matters of religion, neither violently defending one, nor with that common ardor and contention opposing another—yet in despite hereof I dare without usurpation assume the honorable style of a Christian. Not that I merely owe this title to the font,[4] my education, or clime wherein I was born, as being bred up either to confirm those principles my parents instilled into my unwary understanding, or by a general consent proceed in the religion of my country; but having in my riper years and confirmed judgment seen and examined all, I find myself obliged by the principles of grace

1. The Religion of a Doctor. Browne avoids any conflict between science and religion by a forthright "fideism"—entirely separating reason from faith and thereby exempting faith from any critique by reason, or any support from it. This was also the stance of some contemporary Roman Catholic skeptics, notably Montaigne and Pierre Charron.
2. Doctors were popularly reputed to be irreligious or atheistic.
3. Impartiality.
4. The baptismal font.

and the law of mine own reason to embrace no other name but this. Neither doth herein my zeal so far make me forget the general charity I owe unto humanity, as rather to hate than pity Turks, infidels, and (what is worse) Jews;[5] rather contenting myself to enjoy that happy style than maligning those who refuse so glorious a title.

2. But because the name of a Christian is become too general to express our faith—there being a geography of religions as well as lands, and every clime distinguished not only by their laws and limits, but circumscribed by their doctrines and rules of faith—to be particular, I am of that reformed new-cast religion wherein I mislike nothing but the name;[6] of the same belief our Savior taught, the apostles disseminated, the Fathers authorized, and the martyrs confirmed; but by the sinister ends of princes, the ambition and avarice of prelates, and the fatal corruption of times, so decayed, impaired, and fallen from its native beauty that it required the careful and charitable hands of these times to restore it to its primitive integrity. Now the accidental occasion whereon, the slender means whereby, the low and abject condition of the person by whom so good a work was set on foot,[7] which in our adversaries beget contempt and scorn, fills me with wonder, and is the very same objection the insolent pagans first cast at Christ and his disciples.

3. Yet have I not so shaken hands with those desperate resolutions—who had rather venture at large their decayed bottom[8] than bring her in to be new trimmed in the dock, who had rather promiscuously retain all than abridge any, and obstinately be what they are than what they have been—as to stand in diameter[9] and sword's point with them. We have reformed from them, not against them; for, omitting those improperations and terms of scurrility betwixt us, which only difference[1] our affections and not our cause, there is between us one common name and appellation, one faith and necessary body of principles common to us both; and therefore I am not scrupulous to converse and live with them, to enter their churches in defect of ours, and either pray with them or for them. I could never perceive any rational consequence from those many texts which prohibit the children of Israel to pollute themselves with the temples of the heathens; we being all Christians, and not divided by such detested impieties as might profane our prayers or the place wherein we make them; or that a resolved conscience may not adore her Maker anywhere, especially in places devoted to his service; where, if their devotions offend him, mine may please him, if theirs profane it, mine may hallow it. Holy water and crucifix, dangerous to the common people, deceive not my judgment nor abuse my devotion at all. I am, I confess, naturally inclined to that which misguided zeal terms superstition.[2] My common conversation I do acknowledge austere, my behavior full of rigor, sometimes not without morosity; yet at my devotion I love to use the civility of my knee, my hat, and hand, with all those outward and

---

5. Browne thought them worse because they had been given a better chance than the others to know and accept Christianity.
6. Protestantism, for its connotations of contentiousness.
7. Luther, who was a miner's son, began the Reformation.

8. The leaky ship of the Roman Catholic Church. "Shaken hands with": parted from.
9. In complete opposition.
1. Differentiate. "Improperations": reproaches.
2. He defines himself here and in the next few lines against Puritan iconoclasts who would uproot all such "superstitions."

sensible motions which may express or promote my invisible devotion. I should violate my own arm rather than a church, nor willingly deface the memory of saint or martyr. At the sight of a cross or crucifix I can dispense with my hat, but scarce with the thought and memory of my Savior. I cannot laugh at, but rather pity, the fruitless journeys of pilgrims, or contemn the miserable condition of friars; for though misplaced in circumstance, there is somewhat in it of devotion. I could never hear the Ave-Maria bell without an elevation,[3] or think it a sufficient warrant, because they erred in one circumstance, for me to err in all—that is, in silence and dumb contempt. Whilst, therefore, they directed their devotions to her, I offered mine to God, and rectified the errors of their prayers by rightly ordering mine own. At a solemn procession I have wept abundantly while my consorts,[4] blind with opposition and prejudice, have fallen into an excess of scorn and laughter. There are questionless, both in Greek, Roman, and African churches, solemnities and ceremonies whereof the wiser zeals do make a Christian use; and stand condemned by us, not as evil in themselves, but as allurements and baits of superstition to those vulgar heads that look asquint on the face of truth, and those unstable judgments that cannot consist[5] in the narrow point and center of virtue without a reel or stagger to the circumference.

4. As there were many reformers, so likewise many reformations; every country proceeding in a particular way and method, according as their national interest together with their constitution and clime inclined them: some angrily and with extremity, others calmly and with mediocrity,[6] not rending but easily dividing the community, and leaving an honest possibility of a reconciliation; which, though peaceable spirits do desire, and may conceive that revolution of time and the mercies of God may effect, yet that judgment that shall consider the present antipathies between the two extremes, their contrarieties in condition, affection, and opinion, may with the same hopes expect an union in the poles of heaven.

5. But—to difference myself nearer, and draw into a lesser circle—there is no church whose every part so squares unto my conscience, whose articles, constitutions, and customs seem so consonant unto reason, and as it were framed to my particular devotion, as this whereof I hold my belief: the Church of England, to whose faith I am a sworn subject, and therefore in a double obligation subscribe unto her articles and endeavor to observe her constitutions. Whatsoever is beyond, as points indifferent, I observe according to the rules of my private reason or the humor and fashion of my devotion; neither believing this because Luther affirmed it nor disapproving that because Calvin hath disavouched it. I condemn not all things in the council of Trent nor approve all in the synod of Dort.[7] In brief, where the Scripture is silent, the church is my text; where that speaks, 'tis but my comment; where there is a joint silence of both, I borrow not the rules of my religion from Rome or Geneva,[8] but the dictates of my own reason. It is an unjust

3. Exaltation of mind. "Ave-Maria bell": Angelus, rung daily at 6:00 and 12:00, morning and night.
4. Companions.
5. Stand firm. "Asquint": cross-eyed.
6. Moderation. "Extremity": violence.
7. The Council of Trent (1545–63), in Italy,

defined Catholic dogma after the Reformation; the Council of Dort (1618–19), in Holland, defined Calvinist doctrine.
8. Rome was the center of Catholicism; Geneva was a Calvinist city-state.

scandal of our adversaries and a gross error in ourselves to compute the nativity of our religion from Henry the Eighth, who, though he rejected the Pope, refused not the faith of Rome, and effected no more than what his own predecessors desired and essayed in ages past, and was conceived the state of Venice would have attempted in our days.[9] It is as uncharitable a point in us to fall upon those popular scurrilities and opprobrious scoffs of the bishop of Rome, to whom as a temporal prince we owe the duty of good language. I confess there is cause of passion between us. By his sentence I stand excommunicated: "heretic" is the best language he affords me; yet can no ear witness I ever returned to him the name of "antichrist," "man of sin," or "whore of Babylon."[1] It is the method of charity to suffer without reaction. Those usual satires and invectives of the pulpit may perchance produce a good effect on the vulgar, whose ears are opener to rhetoric than logic; yet do they in no wise confirm the faith of wiser believers, who know that a good cause needs not to be patroned by a passion, but can sustain itself upon a temperate dispute.

6. I could never divide myself from any man upon the difference of an opinion, or be angry with his judgment for not agreeing with me in that from which perhaps within a few days I should dissent myself. I have no genius to disputes in religion, and have often thought it wisdom to decline them, especially upon a disadvantage, or when the cause of truth might suffer in the weakness of my patronage. Where we desire to be informed, 'tis good to contest with men above ourselves; but to confirm and establish our opinions, 'tis best to argue with judgments below our own, that the frequent spoils and victories over their reasons may settle in ourselves an esteem and confirmed opinion of our own. Every man is not a proper champion for truth, nor fit to take up the gauntlet in the cause of verity. Many, from the ignorance of these maxims and an inconsiderate zeal unto truth, have too rashly charged the troops of error, and remain as trophies unto the enemies of truth. A man may be in as just possession of truth as of a city, and yet be forced to surrender. 'Tis therefore far better to enjoy her with peace than to hazard her on a battle. If therefore there rise any doubts in my way, I do forget them or at least defer them till my better settled judgment and more manly reason be able to resolve them; for I perceive every man's own reason is his best Oedipus,[2] and will upon a reasonable truce find a way to loose those bonds wherewith the subtleties of error have enchained our more flexible and tender judgments. In philosophy, where truth seems double-faced, there is no man more paradoxical than myself, but in divinity I love to keep the road; and, though not in an implicit, yet an humble faith, follow the great wheel of the church, by which I move, not reserving any proper poles or motion from the epicycle of my own brain.[3] By this means I leave no gap for heresies, schisms, or errors, of which at present I hope I shall not injure truth to say I have no taint or tincture. I must confess my greener studies have been polluted with two or three—not any begotten in the latter centuries, but old and obsolete, such as could never have been revived but by such extravagant

9. Though he repudiated the pope, Henry VIII was for long an ambiguous Protestant. Venice was excommunicated in 1606 for challenging papal authority.
1. Stock terms of anti-Catholic abuse.
2. Solver of riddles, as Oedipus solved that of the Sphinx.
3. In Ptolemaic astronomy, an "epicycle" is a small circle centered on the largest circle of a planet's orbit, hypothesized to account for inexplicable variations in the planet's motion.

and irregular heads as mine. For indeed heresies perish not with their authors, but like the river Arethusa, though they lose their currents in one place, they rise up again in another.[4] One general council is not able to extirpate one singular heresy. It may be canceled for the present, but revolution of time and the like aspects from heaven will restore it, when it will flourish till it be condemned again; for as though there were a metempsychosis, and the soul of one man passed into another, opinions do find after certain revolutions men and minds like those that first begat them. To see ourselves again we need not look for Plato's year.[5] Every man is not only himself; there have been many Diogenes and as many Timons,[6] though but few of that name. Men are lived over again; the world is now as it was in ages past. There was none then but there hath been someone since that parallels him, and is as it were his revived self.

* * *

9. As for those wingy mysteries in divinity and airy subtleties in religion, which have unhinged the brains of better heads, they never stretched the *pia mater*[7] of mine. Methinks there be not impossibilities enough in religion for an active faith. The deepest mysteries ours contains have not only been illustrated but maintained by syllogism and the rule of reason. I love to lose myself in a mystery, to pursue my reason to an *O altitudo!*[8] 'Tis my solitary recreation to pose my apprehension with those involved enigmas and riddles of the Trinity, with Incarnation and Resurrection. I can answer all the objections of Satan and my rebellious reason with that odd resolution I learned of Tertullian, *Certum est quia impossibile est.*[9] I desire to exercise my faith in the difficultest points, for to credit ordinary and visible objects is not faith but persuasion. Some believe the better for seeing Christ his sepulcher, and when they have seen the Red Sea doubt not of the miracle. Now, contrarily, I bless myself and am thankful that I lived not in the days of miracles, that I never saw Christ nor his disciples. I would not have been one of those Israelites that passed the Red Sea, nor one of Christ's patients on whom he wrought his wonders: then had my faith been thrust upon me, nor should I enjoy that greater blessing pronounced to all that believe and saw not. 'Tis an easy and necessary belief to credit what our eye and sense hath examined. I believe he was dead, buried, and rose again; and desire to see him in his glory rather than to contemplate him in his cenotaph or sepulcher. Nor is this much to believe. As we have reason, we owe this faith unto history; they only had the advantage of a bold and noble faith who lived before his coming, who upon obscure prophecies and mystical types[1] could raise a belief and expect apparent impossibilities.

* * *

4. In myth, when the nymph Arethusa, in Greece, was pursued by the river god Alpheus, she dived into the sea and came up again in Sicily as a fountain.
5. Browne's note on this reads: "A revolution of certain thousand years, when all things should return unto their former estate."
6. Diogenes was a Cynic philosopher, Timon a noted misanthrope, both Greek.
7. A membrane covering the brain, often used to refer to the brain itself.
8. From Romans 11.33: "O the depth [Latin Vulgate, *altitudo*] of the riches both of the wisdom and knowledge of God! How unsearchable are his judgments, and his ways past finding out!" The Latin term can also mean "heights."
9. Tertullian commenting on the Resurrection: "It is certain because it is impossible."
1. Foreshadowings of Christ in the Old Testament.

15. * * * I could never content my contemplation with those general pieces of wonder, the flux and reflux of the sea, the increase of Nile, the conversion of the needle to the north; and have studied to match and parallel those in the more obvious and neglected pieces of nature, which without further travel I can do in the cosmography of myself. We carry with us the wonders we seek without us: there is all Africa and her prodigies[2] in us. We are that bold and adventurous piece of nature which he that studies wisely learns in a compendium what others labor at in a divided piece and endless volume.

16. Thus are there two books from whence I collect my divinity: besides that written one of God, another of his servant nature, that universal and public manuscript that lies expansed unto the eyes of all. Those that never saw him in the one have discovered him in the other. This was the scripture and theology of the heathens: the natural motion of the sun made them more admire him than its supernatural station[3] did the children of Israel; the ordinary effects of nature wrought more admiration in them than in the other all his miracles. Surely the heathens knew better how to join and read these mystical letters than we Christians, who cast a more careless eye on these common hieroglyphics, and disdain to suck divinity from the flowers of nature. Nor do I so forget God as to adore the name of nature; which I define not, with the schools, the principle of motion and rest, but that straight and regular line, that settled and constant course the wisdom of God hath ordained the actions of his creatures according to their several kinds. To make a revolution every day is the nature of the sun, because that necessary course which God hath ordained it, from which it cannot swerve but by a faculty[4] from that voice which first did give it motion. Now this course of nature God seldom alters or perverts, but like an excellent artist hath so contrived his work that with the selfsame instrument, without a new creation, he may effect his obscurest designs. Thus he sweetened the water with a wood;[5] preserved the creatures in the Ark, which the blast of his mouth might have as easily created: for God is like a skillful geometrician, who when more easily and with one stroke of his compass he might describe or divide a right line, had yet rather do this in a circle or longer way according to the constituted and forelaid principles of his art. Yet this rule of his he doth sometimes pervert, to acquaint the world with his prerogative, lest the arrogancy of our reason should question his power and conclude he could not. And thus I call the effects of nature the works of God, whose hand and instrument she only is; and therefore to ascribe his actions unto her is to devolve the honor of the principal agent upon the instrument: which if with reason we may do, then let our hammers rise up and boast they have built our houses, and our pens receive the honor of our writings. I hold there is a general beauty in the works of God, and therefore no deformity in any kind or species of creature whatsoever. I cannot tell by what logic we call a toad, a bear, or an elephant ugly; they being created in those outward shapes and figures which best express the actions of their inward forms, and having passed that general visitation of God, who saw

2. Marvels.
3. Standing still, as at the battle of Gibeon (Joshua 10.13).

4. Authority.
5. Exodus 15.25 tells how the Lord sweetened the bitter waters of Marah with a special tree.

that all that he had made was good[6]—that is, conformable to his will, which abhors deformity and is the rule of order and beauty. There is therefore no deformity but in monstrosity; wherein notwithstanding there is a kind of beauty, nature so ingeniously contriving the irregular parts as they become sometimes more remarkable than the principal fabric. To speak yet more narrowly, there was never anything ugly or misshapen but the chaos; wherein notwithstanding (to speak strictly) there was no deformity because no form, nor was it yet impregnate by the voice of God. Now, nature is not at variance with art nor art with nature, they both being the servants of his providence: art is the perfection of nature. Were the world now as it was the sixth day, there were yet a chaos: nature hath made one world and art another. In brief, all things are artificial, for nature is the art of God.

* * *

34. These[7] are certainly the magisterial and masterpieces of the Creator; the flower or (as we may say) the best part of nothing; actually existing what we are but in hopes and probability. We are only that amphibious piece between a corporal and spiritual essence; that middle form that links those two together, and makes good the method of God and nature, that jumps not from extremes but unites the incompatible distances by some middle and participating natures. That we are the breath and similitude of God it is indisputable and upon record of holy Scripture; but to call ourselves a microcosm or little world I thought it only a pleasant trope of rhetoric[8] till my nearer judgment and second thoughts told me there was a real truth therein. For first we are a rude mass and in the rank of creatures which only are and have a dull kind of being not yet privileged with life or preferred to sense or reason. Next we live the life of plants, the life of animals, the life of men, and at last the life of spirits; running on, in one mysterious nature, those five kinds of existences which comprehend the creatures not only of the world but of the universe. Thus is man that great and true amphibium whose nature is disposed to live not only like other creatures in divers elements but in divided and distinguished worlds. For though there be but one world to sense, there are two to reason; the one visible, the other invisible, whereof Moses seems to have left no description, and of the other[9] so obscurely that some parts thereof are yet in controversy: and truly for the first chapters of Genesis I must confess a great deal of obscurity. Though divines have, to the power of human reason, endeavored to make all go in a literal meaning, yet those allegorical interpretations are also probable, and perhaps the mystical method of Moses bred up in the hieroglyphical schools of the Egyptians.[1]

* * *

59. Again, I am confident and fully persuaded, yet dare not take my oath of my salvation. I am as it were sure, and do believe without all doubt, that there is such a city as Constantinople; yet for me to take my oath thereon were a kind of perjury, because I hold no infallible warrant from my own sense to

6. Genesis 1.31.
7. The angels.
8. Figure of speech.
9. The visible world. Moses was supposed to have been the author of Genesis.

1. Some Neoplatonists thought that Moses, reared among the Egyptians, understood their hieroglyphic symbolism and imitated it in his own writing.

confirm me in the certainty thereof. And truly, though many pretend an absolute certainty of their salvation, yet when an humble soul shall contemplate her own unworthiness she shall meet with many doubts and suddenly find how little we stand in need of the precept of St. Paul, *Work out your salvation with fear and trembling*.[2] That which is the cause of my election I hold to be the cause of my salvation, which was the mercy and beneplacit[3] of God before I was or the foundation of the world. *Before Abraham was, I am*, is the saying of Christ;[4] yet is it true in some sense if I say it of myself, for I was not only before myself but Adam, that is, in the idea of God and the decree of that synod held from all eternity. And in this sense, I say, the world was before the creation and at an end before it had a beginning; and thus was I dead before I was alive. Though my grave be England, my dying place was Paradise, and Eve miscarried of me before she conceived of Cain.

* * *

From *Part 2*

1. Now for that other virtue of charity,[5] without which faith is mere notion, and of no existence, I have ever endeavored to nourish the merciful disposition and humane inclination I borrowed from my parents, and regulate it to the written and prescribed laws of charity; and if I hold the true anatomy of myself,[6] I am delineated and naturally framed to such a piece of virtue. For I am of a constitution so general that it comforts and sympathizeth with all things; I have no antipathy, or rather idiosyncrasy, in diet, humor, air, anything. I wonder not at the French for their dishes of frogs, snails, and toadstools, nor at the Jews for locusts and grasshoppers; but being amongst them, make them my common viands, and I find they agree with my stomach as well as theirs. I could digest a salad gathered in a churchyard as well as in a garden. I cannot start at the presence of a serpent, scorpion, lizard, or salamander, at the sight of a toad or viper I find in me no desire to take up a stone to destroy them. I feel not in myself those common antipathies that I can discover in others: those national repugnances do not touch me, nor do I behold with prejudice the French, Italian, Spaniard, or Dutch; but where I find their actions in balance with my countrymen's, I honor, love and embrace them in the same degree. I was born in the eighth climate,[7] but seem for to be framed and constellated unto all. I am no plant that will not prosper out of a garden. All places, all airs make unto me one country; I am in England everywhere and under any meridian. I have been shipwrecked,[8] yet am not enemy with the sea or winds; I can study, play, or sleep in a tempest. In brief, I am averse from nothing; my conscience would give me the lie if I should say I absolutely detest or hate any essence but the devil, or so at least abhor anything but that we might come to composition.[9] If there be any among those common objects of hatred I do contemn and laugh at, it is that great enemy of reason, virtue,

2. Philippians 2.12. "Election" (following): chosen by God for salvation.
3. Good pleasure.
4. John 8.58.
5. Like many theological manuals, Browne's first book concerns faith, the second charity.
6. If I have properly analyzed myself. See Donne, *An Anatomy of the World* (pp. 1399–1410), and Burton, *The Anatomy of Melancholy* (pp. 1690–96), for the way this term is used. "Delineated" (following): designed.
7. In the eighth of the twenty-four regions between the equator and the poles.
8. Browne was shipwrecked returning to England from Ireland in 1630.
9. Reach an agreement.

and religion, the multitude—that numerous piece of monstrosity which, taken asunder, seem men and the reasonable creatures of God, but confused together make but one great beast, and a monstrosity more prodigious than Hydra.[1] It is no breach of charity to call these fools; it is the style all holy writers have afforded them, set down by Solomon in canonical Scripture[2] and a point of our faith to believe so. Neither in the name of multitude do I only include the base and minor sort of people; there is a rabble even amongst the gentry, a sort of plebeian heads whose fancy moves with the same wheel as these; men in the same level with mechanics, though their fortunes do somewhat gild their infirmities, and their purses compound for their follies.[3] But as in casting account, three or four men together come short in account of one man placed by himself below them, so neither are a troop of these ignorant dorados[4] of that true esteem and value as many a forlorn person whose condition doth place him below their feet. Let us speak like politicians, there is a nobility without heraldry, a natural dignity whereby one man is ranked with another, another filed before him, according to the quality of his desert, and preeminence of his good parts. Though the corruption of these times and the bias of present practice wheel another way, thus it was in the first and primitive commonwealths, and is yet in the integrity and cradle of well-ordered polities, till corruption getteth ground, ruder desires laboring after that which wiser considerations contemn, everyone having a liberty to amass and heap up riches, and they a license or faculty to do or purchase anything.

1642 (pirated)
1643 (authorized)

---

1. In Greek mythology, a nine-headed serpent that grew two heads for every one that was cut off.
2. E.g., Proverbs 1.7: "fools despise wisdom and instruction."
3. With the growing rebelliousness of the Puri-

tan merchants and even some of the aristocracy as his point of reference, Browne redefines the rabble in terms of attitude and moral worth, not class.
4. Wealthy persons.

GEORGE HERBERT
1593–1633

George Herbert's style in his volume of religious poetry, *The Temple*, is deceptively simple and graceful, especially compared to the learned, witty style of his friend John Donne. But it is also marked by self-irony, a remarkable intellectual and emotional range, and an artistry evident in the poems' tight construction, exact diction, perfect control of tone, and enormously varied stanzaic forms and rhythmic patterns. These poems reflect Herbert's struggle to define his relationship to God through biblical metaphors invested with the tensions of relationships familiar in his own society: king and subject, lord and courtier, master and servant, father and child, bridegroom and bride, friends of unequal status. None of Herbert's secular English poems survives, so his reputation rests on this single volume, published posthumously. *The Temple* contains a long prefatory poem, "The Church-Porch," and a long concluding poem, "Church Militant," which together enclose a collection of 177 short lyrics entitled *The Church*, among which are sonnets, songs, hymns, laments, meditative poems, dialogue poems, acrostic poems, emblematic poems, and more. Herbert's own description of the collection is apt: "a picture of the many spiritual conflicts that have passed between God and my soul." Izaak Walton reports that Herbert gave the manuscript to his friend Nicholas Farrar, head of a quasi-monastic community at Little Gidding, with instructions to publish it if he thought it would "turn to the advantage of any dejected poor soul" and otherwise to burn it. Fortunately, Farrar chose to publish, and *The Temple* became the major influence on the religious lyric poets of the Caroline age: Henry Vaughan, Richard Crashaw, Thomas Traherne, and even Edward Taylor, the American colonial poet.

The fifth son of an eminent Welsh family, Herbert (and his nine siblings) had an upbringing carefully monitored by his mother, Magdalen Herbert, patron and friend of Donne and several other scholars and poets. Herbert was educated at Westminster School and at Trinity College, Cambridge, where he subsequently held a fellowship and wrote Latin poetry: elegies on the death of Prince Henry (1612), witty epigrams, poems on Christ's Passion and death, and poems defending the rites of the English church. In 1620 he was appointed "public orator," the official spokesman and correspondent for the university. This was a step toward a career at court or in public service, as was his election as the member of Parliament from Montgomery in 1624. But that route was closed off by the death of influential patrons and the change of monarchs. Like Donne, Herbert hesitated for some years before being ordained, but in 1630 he took up pastoral duties in the small country parish at Bemerton in Wiltshire. Whereas Donne preached to monarchs and statesmen, Herbert ministered to a few cottagers, and none of his sermons survive. His small book on the duties of his new life, *A Priest to the Temple; or, The Country Parson*, testifies to the earnestness and joy, but also to the aristocratic uneasiness, with which he embraced that role. In chronic bad health, he lived only three more years—performing pastoral duties assiduously, writing and revising his poems, playing music, and listening to the organ and choir at nearby Salisbury Cathedral.

George Herbert locates himself in the church through many poems that treat church liturgy, architecture, and art—e.g., "Church Monuments" and "The Windows"—but his primary emphasis is always on the soul's inner architecture. Unlike Donne, Herbert does not voice fears about his salvation or about his desperate sins; his anxieties center rather on his relationship with Christ, most often represented as that of friend with friend. Many poems register the speaker's distress over the vacillations and regressions in this relationship, over his lack of "fruition" in God's service, and over the instability of his own nature. In several dialogic poems the speaker's difficulties are alleviated by the voice of a divine friend heard within or recalled through a Scripture text (as

George Herbert. This engraving by Robert White was made from a portrait, now lost, painted during Herbert's lifetime and showing the poet in clerical garb. It was published in Isaak Walton's *Life of George Herbert* (1674).

in "The Collar"). In poem after poem he has to come to terms with the fact that his relationship with Christ is always radically unequal, that Christ must both initiate it and enable his own response. Herbert struggles constantly with the paradox that, as the works of a Christian poet, his poems ought to give fit praise to God but cannot possibly do so—an issue explored in "The Altar," the two "Jordan" poems, "Easter," "The Forerunners," and many more.

His recourse is to develop a biblical poetics that renounces conventional poetic styles—"fiction and false hair"—to depend instead on God's "art" wrought in his own soul and displayed in the language and symbolism of the Bible. He makes scant use of Donnean learned imagery, but his scriptural allusions carry profound significances. A biblical metaphor provides the unifying motif for the volume: the New Testament temple in the human heart (1 Corinthians 3.16). Another recurring biblical metaphor represents the Christian as plant or tree or flower in God's garden, needing pruning, rain, and nurture. Herbert was profoundly influenced by the genre of the emblem, which typically associated mysterious but meaningful pictures and mottoes with explanatory text. Shaped poems like "The Altar" or "Easter Wings" present image and picture at once; others, like "The Windows," resemble emblem commentary. Other poems allude to typological symbolism, which reads persons and events in the Old Testament as types or foreshadowings of Christ, the fulfillment or antitype. Often, as in "The Bunch of Grapes," Herbert locates both type and antitype in the speaker's soul.

From The Temple[1]

The Altar[2]

A broken ALTAR, Lord, thy servant rears,
Made of a heart, and cemented with tears:
Whose parts are as thy hand did frame;
No workman's tool hath touched the same.[3]
5   A HEART alone
Is such a stone,
As nothing but
Thy power doth cut.
Wherefore each part
10   Of my hard heart
Meets in this frame,
To praise thy Name:
That, if I chance to hold my peace,
These stones to praise thee may not cease.[4]
15 Oh let thy blessed SACRIFICE be mine,
And sanctify this ALTAR to be thine.

1. The title of Herbert's volume sets his poems in relation to David's psalms for the Temple at Jerusalem; his are "psalms" for the New Testament temple in the heart. All of the following poems come from this volume, published in 1633.

2. A variety of emblem poem. Emblems customarily have three parts: a picture, a motto, and a poem. This kind collapses picture and poem into one, presenting the emblem image by its very shape. Shaped poems have been used by authors

from Hellenistic times to Dylan Thomas.

3. A reference to Exodus 20.25, in which the Lord enjoins Moses to build an altar of uncut stones, not touched by any tool, and also to Psalm 51.17: "a broken and a contrite heart, O God, thou wilt not despise."

4. A reference to Luke 19.40: "I tell you that, if these should hold their peace, the stones would immediately cry out." Herbert's poems obtain much of their resonance from their biblical echoes.

Redemption[1]

Having been tenant long to a rich lord,
  Not thriving, I resolvèd to be bold,
And make a suit unto him, to afford
  A new small-rented lease, and cancel th' old.[2]

5 In heaven at his manor I him sought:
  They told me there that he was lately gone
About some land which he had dearly bought
  Long since on earth, to take possession.

I straight° returned, and knowing his great birth,   *at once*
10 Sought him accordingly in great resorts—
In cities, theaters, gardens, parks, and courts:
  At length I heard a ragged noise and mirth

Of thieves and murderers; there I him espied,
  Who straight, "Your suit is granted," said, and died.

Easter[1]

Rise, heart, thy lord is risen. Sing his praise
    Without delays,
Who takes thee by the hand, that thou likewise
    With him may'st rise;
5 That, as his death calcinèd° thee to dust,   *burned to powder*
His life may make thee gold, and, much more, just.

Awake, my lute, and struggle for thy part
    With all thy art.
The cross taught all wood to resound his name
10   Who bore the same.
His stretchèd sinews taught all strings what key
Is best to celebrate this most high day.

Consort, both heart and lute, and twist[2] a song
    Pleasant and long;
15 Or, since all music is but three parts vied[3]
    And multiplied,
Oh let thy blessèd spirit bear a part,
And make up our defects with his sweet art.

---

1. Literally, "buying back." In this beautifully concise sonnet Herbert figures God as a landlord, himself as a discontented tenant.
2. I.e., to ask him for a new lease, with a smaller rent; the figure points to the New Testament supplanting the Old.

1. The first three stanzas work out the poetics of writing hymns; then comes the hymn itself.
2. Weave. "Consort": harmonize.
3. Increased by repetition. Harmony is based on the triad, the chord.

The Song

I got me flowers to straw° thy way,[4]   *strew*
20 I got me boughs off many a tree;
But thou wast up by break of day
And brought'st thy sweets along with thee.

The sun arising in the east,
Though he give light and th' east perfume,
25 If they should offer to contest
With thy arising, they presume.

Can there be any day but this,
Though many suns to shine endeavor?
We count three hundred, but we miss:°   *misunderstand*
30 There is but one, and that one ever.

Easter Wings[1]

Lord, who createdst man in wealth and store,°   *abundance*
Though foolishly he lost the same,
Decaying more and more
Till he became
5   Most poor:
With thee
O let me rise
As larks, harmoniously,
And sing this day thy victories:
10 Then shall the fall further the flight in me.[2]

My tender age in sorrow did begin:
And still with sicknesses and shame
Thou didst so punish sin,
That I became
15   Most thin.
With thee
Let me combine,
And feel this day thy victory;
For, if I imp[3] my wing on thine,
20 Affliction shall advance the flight in me.

4. Evokes the scene of Christ's entry into Jerusalem (Matthew 21.8).
1. Another emblem poem whose shape presents
the emblem picture; the lines, increasing and
decreasing, imitate flight, and also the spiritual
experience of falling and rising. Early editions
printed the poem with the lines running verti-
cally, making the wing shape more apparent.
2. Refers to the "Fortunate Fall," which brought
humankind so great a redeemer.
3. In falconry, to insert feathers in a bird's wing.

Affliction (1)[1]

When first thou didst entice to thee my heart,
        I thought the service brave:°   *splendid*
So many joys I writ down for my part,
        Besides what I might have
5 Out of my stock of natural delights,
Augmented with thy gracious benefits.

I lookèd on thy furniture so fine,
        And made it fine to me;
Thy glorious household stuff did me entwine,
10   And 'tice° me unto thee.   *entice*
Such stars I counted mine: both heaven and earth
Paid me my wages in a world of mirth.

What pleasures could I want,° whose king I served,   *lack*
        Where joys my fellows were?
15 Thus argued into hopes, my thoughts reserved
        No place for grief or fear;
Therefore my sudden soul caught at the place,
And made her youth and fierceness seek thy face.

At first thou gav'st me milk and sweetnesses;
20   I had my wish and way:
My days were strawed° with flowers and happiness;   *strewn*
        There was no month but May.
But with my years sorrow did twist and grow,
And made a party unawares° for woe.   *unwittingly*

25 My flesh began unto° my soul in pain,   *started complaining to*
        Sicknesses cleave° my bones;   *penetrate*
Consuming agues° dwell in every vein,   *fevers with convulsions*
        And tune my breath to groans.
Sorrow was all my soul; I scarce believed,
30 Till grief did tell me roundly, that I lived.

When I got health, thou took'st away my life,
        And more; for my friends die:
My mirth and edge was lost: a blunted knife
        Was of more use than I.
35 Thus thin and lean without a fence or friend,
I was blown through with every storm and wind.

Whereas my birth and spirit rather took
        The way that takes the town,
Thou didst betray me to a lingering book,
40   And wrap me in a gown.°   *priest's garb*

---

1. Herbert sometimes used the same title for several poems, thereby associating them; editors distinguish them by adding numbers.

I was entangled in the world of strife,
Before I had the power to change my life.

Yet, for I threatened oft the siege to raise,
        Not simpering all mine age,
45 Thou often didst with academic praise
        Melt and dissolve my rage.
I took thy sweetened pill, till I came where
I could not go away, nor persevere.

Yet lest perchance I should too happy be
50   In my unhappiness,
Turning my purge° to food, thou throwest me   *laxative*
        Into more sicknesses.
Thus doth thy power cross-bias me,° not making   *turn me from my aim*
Thine own gift good, yet me from my ways taking.

55 Now I am here, what thou wilt do with me
        None of my books will show:
I read, and sigh, and wish I were a tree,
        For sure then I should grow
To fruit or shade; at least, some bird would trust
60 Her household to me, and I should be just.

Yet, though thou troublest me, I must be meek;
        In weakness must be stout.
Well, I will change the service, and go seek
        Some other master out.
65 Ah, my dear God! though I am clean forgot,
Let me not love thee, if I love thee not.

Prayer (1)[1]

Prayer, the church's banquet; angels' age,
    God's breath in man returning to his birth;
The soul in paraphrase,[2] heart in pilgrimage;
    The Christian plummet,[3] sounding heaven and earth;

5 Engine against th' Almighty, sinner's tower,
    Reversèd thunder, Christ-side-piercing spear,
The six-days' world transposing[4] in an hour;
    A kind of tune which all things hear and fear:

Softness and peace and joy and love and bliss;
10   Exalted manna,[5] gladness of the best;

1. This extraordinary sonnet is a series of epithets without a main verb, defining prayer by metaphor.
2. Clarifying by expansion.
3. A weight used to measure ("sound") the depth of water.
4. A musical term indicating sounds produced at another pitch from the original.
5. The food God supplied to the Israelites in the wilderness.

Heaven in ordinary,[6] man well dressed,
The milky way, the bird of paradise,

Church bells beyond the stars heard, the soul's blood,
The land of spices; something understood.

Jordan (1)[1]

Who says that fictions only and false hair
Become a verse? Is there in truth no beauty?
Is all good structure in a winding stair?
May no lines pass, except they do their duty°   *pay reverence*
5 Not to a true, but painted chair?[2]

Is it no verse, except enchanted groves
And sudden arbors shadow coarse-spun lines?[3]
Must purling° streams refresh a lover's loves?   *rippling*
Must all be veiled,[4] while he that reads, divines,
10 Catching the sense at two removes?

Shepherds[5] are honest people: let them sing;
Riddle who list,° for me, and pull for prime:[6]   *wishes*
I envy no man's nightingale or spring;
Nor let them punish me with loss of rhyme,
15 Who plainly say, *My God, My King.*[7]

Church Monuments[1]

While that my soul repairs to her devotion,
Here I entomb my flesh, that it betimes°   *while time remains*
May take acquaintance of this heap of dust
To which the blast of death's incessant motion,
5 Fed with the exhalation of our crimes,
Drives all at last. Therefore I gladly trust

My body to this school, that it may learn
To spell his elements and find his birth
Written in dusty heraldry and lines°   *engraving, genealogy*

---

6. I.e., everyday heaven.
1. The river Jordan, which the Israelites crossed to enter the Promised Land, was also taken as a symbol for baptism.
2. It was the custom for men to bow before a throne, whether it was occupied or not (see Donne, "Satire 3," lines 47–48, p. 1396), but to require bowing before a throne in a painting would be ridiculous.
3. "Sudden," i.e., that appear unexpectedly (an

artificial effect much sought after in landscape gardening). "Shadow": shade.
4. As in allegory.
5. Conventional pastoral poets.
6. To draw a lucky card in the game of primero. "For me": as far as I am concerned.
7. Echoes Psalm 145.1: "my God, O king."
1. The earlier, manuscript version of the poem does not divide it into stanzas.

10 Which dissolution sure doth best discern,
Comparing dust with dust and earth with earth.[2]
These laugh at jet and marble,[3] put for signs

To sever the good fellowship of dust
And spoil the meeting. What shall point out them[4]
15 When they shall bow and kneel and fall down flat
To kiss those heaps which now they have in trust?
Dear flesh, while I do pray, learn here thy stem
And true descent, that, when thou shalt grow fat

And wanton in thy cravings, thou mayest know
20 That flesh is but the glass° which holds the dust   *hourglass*
That measures all our time, which also shall
Be crumbled into dust. Mark here below
How tame these ashes are, how free from lust,
That thou mayest fit thyself against thy fall.

The Windows[1]

Lord, how can man preach thy eternal word?
He is a brittle, crazy° glass,   *flawed, distorting*
Yet in thy temple thou dost him afford
This glorious and transcendent place,
5   To be a window through thy grace.

But when thou dost anneal in glass[2] thy story,
Making thy life to shine within
The holy preachers, then the light and glory
More reverend grows, and more doth win,
10   Which else shows wat'rish, bleak, and thin.

Doctrine and life, colors and light, in one
When they combine and mingle, bring
A strong regard and awe; but speech alone
Doth vanish like a flaring thing,
15   And in the ear, not conscience, ring.

Denial

When my devotions could not pierce
        Thy silent ears,

---

2. Alludes to Genesis 3.19: "for dust thou art, and unto dust shalt thou return."
3. Jet (black basalt) and marble are used for tomb monuments. "These": i.e., dust and earth.
4. The inhabitants of the tombs.
1. From his little parish at Bemerton, Herbert used to walk twice a week across Salisbury Plain to the great cathedral, where he delighted not only in the music but in the stained-glass windows. This poem explores how the preacher himself may become such a window.
2. To burn colors into glass.

Then was my heart broken, as was my verse;
    My breast was full of fears
5   And disorder;[1]

My bent thoughts, like a brittle bow,
    Did fly asunder:
Each took his way; some would to pleasures go,
    Some to the wars and thunder
10   Of alarms.

As good go anywhere, they say,
    As to benumb
Both knees and heart in crying night and day,
    Come, come, my God, O come!
15   But no hearing.

O that thou shouldst give dust a tongue
    To cry to thee,
And then not hear it crying! All day long
    My heart was in my knee,
20   But no hearing.

Therefore my soul lay out of sight,
    Untuned, unstrung;
My feeble spirit, unable to look right,
    Like a nipped° blossom, hung   *frostbitten*
25   Discontented.

O cheer and tune my heartless breast;
    Defer no time,
That so thy favors granting my request,
    They and my mind may chime,°   *ring together, agree*
30   And mend my rhyme.

Virtue

Sweet day, so cool, so calm, so bright,
The bridal of the earth and sky:
The dew shall weep thy fall tonight,
    For thou must die.

5   Sweet rose, whose hue, angry and brave,[1]
Bids the rash gazer wipe his eye:
Thy root is ever in its grave,
    And thou must die.

---

1. Unrhymed, as are the concluding lines of each stanza except the last.

1. Splendid. "Angry": having the hue of anger, red.

Sweet spring, full of sweet days and roses,
10   A box where sweets° compacted lie;   *perfumes*
       My music shows ye have your closes,[2]
             And all must die.

       Only a sweet and virtuous soul,
       Like seasoned timber, never gives;
15   But though the whole world turn to coal,[3]
             Then chiefly lives.

Man

       My God, I heard this day
That none doth build a stately habitation,
       But he that means to dwell therein.
       What house more stately hath there been,
5   Or can be, than is man? to[1] whose creation
       All things are in decay.

       For man is every thing
And more; he is a tree, yet bears more[2] fruit;
       A beast, yet is or should be more;
10   Reason and speech we only bring.[3]
       Parrots may thank us, if they are not mute:
             They go upon the score.[4]

       Man is all symmetry,
Full of proportions, one limb to another,
15   And all to all the world besides;[5]
       Each part may call the farthest, brother;
For head with foot hath private amity,
             And both with moons and tides.

       Nothing hath got so far
20   But man hath caught and kept it as his prey.
       His eyes dismount° the highest star: *bring down to earth*
       He is in little all the sphere.°   *the universe*
Herbs gladly cure our flesh; because that they
             Find their acquaintance there.

25   For us the winds do blow,
The earth doth rest, heav'n move, and fountains flow;
       Nothing we see but means our good,

2. Concluding cadences in music. This poem
has often been set to music.
3. Will be reduced to a cinder at the Last Judgment.
1. Compared to.
2. A textual variant is "no."
3. Man has a vegetable, an animal, and a spiri-

tual nature; he is the only creature that speaks
and reasons.
4. Parrots are indebted to us for speech.
5. The notion of man as microcosm, whose parts
all correspond to features of the great world.
Cf. Donne, *Holy Sonnet* 5, p. 1411, and Browne,
Religio Medici, p. 1702.

As our delight, or as our treasure.
　The whole is either our cupboard of food,
30　　　Or cabinet of pleasure.

　The stars have us to bed;
Night draws the curtain which the sun withdraws,
　　Music and light attend our head.
　All things unto our flesh are kind°　　　　　　　　　*akin*
35　In their descent and being; to our mind
　　　In their ascent and cause.

　Each thing is full of duty.
Waters united are our navigation,
　　Distinguished,° our habitation;　　　　　　　　*separated*
40　　Below, our drink; above, our meat;[6]
Both are our cleanliness. Hath one such beauty?
　　　Then how are all things neat!

　More servants wait on man
Than he'll take notice of; in every path,
45　　He treads down that[7] which doth befriend him,
　　When sickness makes him pale and wan.
O mighty love! Man is one world, and hath
　　　Another to attend him.

　Since then, my God, thou hast
50　So brave° a palace built, O, dwell in it,　　　　*splendid*
　　That it may dwell with thee at last!
　Till then, afford us so much wit,
That, as the world serves us, we may serve thee,
　　　And both thy servants be.

Jordan (2)[1]

When first my lines of heavenly joys made mention,
　Such was their luster, they did so excel,
That I sought out quaint words and trim invention;
　My thoughts began to burnish,° sprout, and swell,　*burgeon*
5　Curling with metaphors a plain intention,
　Decking the sense, as if it were to sell.°　　　　*for sale*

Thousands of notions in my brain did run,
　Offering their service, if I were not sped:°　　*supplied, satisfied*
I often blotted what I had begun;
10　This was not quick° enough, and that was dead.　　*lively*

---

6. Oceans are valuable for navigation; the earth was created by dividing waters from waters (Genesis 1.6–7); on earth water is drink; from above it provides rain to grow our food ("meat").

7. The herb that will cure him when he's sick.
1. Cf. "Jordan (1)" (p. 1712), and Sidney, *Astrophil and Stella* 1 (p. 1084).

Nothing could seem too rich to clothe the sun,
Much less those joys which trample on his head.[2]

As flames do work and wind when they ascend,
So did I weave myself into the sense;
15   But while I bustled, I might hear a friend
Whisper, "How wide[3] is all this long pretense!
There is in love a sweetness ready penned:
Copy out only that, and save expense."

Time

Meeting with Time, "Slack thing," said I,[1]
"Thy scythe is dull; whet it for shame."
"No marvel, sir," he did reply,
"If it at length deserve some blame;
5   But where one man would have me grind it,
Twenty for one too sharp do find it."

"Perhaps some such of old did pass,
Who above all things loved this life;
To whom thy scythe a hatchet was,
10   Which now is but a pruning knife.[2]
Christ's coming hath made man thy debtor,
Since by thy cutting he grows better.

"And in his blessing thou art blessed,
For where thou only wert before
15   An executioner at best,
Thou art a gardener now, and more,
An usher to convey our souls
Beyond the utmost stars and poles.

"And this is that makes life so long,
20   While it detains us from our God.
Ev'n pleasures here increase the wrong,
And length of days lengthens the rod.°   *used for blows*
Who wants° the place where God doth dwell   *lacks*
Partakes already half of hell.

25   "Of what strange length must that needs be,
Which ev'n eternity excludes!"—
Thus far Time heard me patiently,
Then chafing said, "This man deludes:
What do I here before his door?
30   He doth not crave less time, but more."

2. The "joys which trample on" the sun's head
are heavenly joys (line 1).
3. Irrelevant, wide of the mark.
1. Herbert's speaker reports his dialogue with
Time.
2. A hatchet kills, a pruning knife improves growing things.

The Bunch of Grapes[1]

Joy, I did lock thee up;° but some bad man   *hold you fast*
    Hath let thee out again,
And now methinks I am where I began
    Sev'n years ago: one vogue° and vein,   *tendency*
5   One air of thoughts usurps my brain.
I did towards Canaan draw, but now I am
Brought back to the Red Sea, the sea of shame.[2]

For as the Jews of old by God's command
    Traveled, and saw no town,
10 So now each Christian hath his journeys spanned;
    Their story pens and sets us down.[3]
    A single deed is small renown.
God's works are wide, and let in future times;
His ancient justice overflows our crimes.

15 Then have we too our guardian fires and clouds;
    Our Scripture-dew° drops fast;   *manna*
We have our sands and serpents, tents and shrouds;°   *temporary shelters*
    Alas! our murmurings come not last.
    But where's the cluster? where's the taste
20 Of mine inheritance? Lord, if I must borrow,
Let me as well take up their joy as sorrow.

But can he want° the grape who hath the wine?   *lack*
    I have their fruit and more.
Blessèd be God, who prospered Noah's vine[4]
25   And made it bring forth grapes good store.
    But much more him I must adore
Who of the Law's sour juice[5] sweet wine did make,
Even God himself being pressèd for my sake.

The Pilgrimage

I traveled on, seeing the hill where lay
    My expectation.
    A long it was and weary way.
The gloomy cave of desperation

1. When the children of Israel almost lost hope in the wilderness, God inspired Moses to send forth scouts, who returned to report that Canaan was a land of milk and honey. They brought back a bunch of grapes so big they had to carry it between them on a pole (Numbers 13.23).
2. The Red Sea's color suggests blushing for shame. Because the Israelites complained about their long ordeal in the wilderness after leaving Egypt, God drove them back toward the Red Sea.
3. The wandering of the Israelites in the wilderness toward the land of Canaan was taken to be a type (prefiguration) of the Christian's trials on the path of salvation. "Spanned": measured out.
4. Noah's vine (Genesis 9) was taken as a type of the earth replenished by God after the Flood.
5. The severe rules of the Old Testament as contrasted with the sweeter and more liberal covenant of the New Testament, which Christ's crucifixion established.

5   I left on th' one, and on the other side
          The rock of pride.[1]

And so I came to fancy's meadow, strowed°   *strewn*
         With many a flower;
        Fain° would I here have made abode,   *gladly*
10   But I was quickened by my hour.[2]
So to care's copse° I came, and there got through   *thicket of trees*
         With much ado.

That led me to the wild of passion, which
        Some call the wold°—   *treeless plain, moor*
15   A wasted place but sometimes rich.
        Here I was robbed of all my gold
Save one good angel,[3] which a friend had tied
         Close to my side.

At length I got unto the gladsome hill
20   Where lay my hope,
     Where lay my heart; and, climbing still,
      When I had gained the brow and top,
A lake of brackish waters on the ground
         Was all I found.

25   With that abashed, and struck with many a sting
          Of swarming fears,
       I fell, and cried, "Alas, my king!
      Can both the way and end be tears?"
Yet taking heart I rose, and then perceived
30   I was deceived:

My hill was further; so I flung away,
         Yet heard a cry,
      Just as I went: *None goes that way*
     And lives: "If that be all," said I,
35   "After so foul a journey, death is fair,
         And but a chair."[4]

The Holdfast[1]

I threatened to observe the strict decree
   Of my dear God with all my power and might.
   But I was told by one, it could not be;
   Yet I might trust in God to be my light.

1. The rock and cave allude to Scylla and Charybdis, perils faced by Odysseus and often allegorized. The spiritual pilgrimage through allegorical perils was a frequent literary motif: cf. Bunyan's *Pilgrim's Progress* and Vaughan's "Regeneration" (pp. 1728–30).
2. Short span of life.
3. A golden coin as well as (punningly) a guardian angel.

4. "Chair" implies rest and relaxation but also a conveyance (a sedan chair).
1. Alludes to Psalm 73.27 in the Book of Common Prayer: "It is good for me to hold me fast by God." The poem dramatizes the entire reliance on grace—and the abnegation of any human capacity to cooperate with it or claim any merit—that was a cornerstone of Calvinist theology.

5   Then will I trust, said I, in him alone.
     Nay, ev'n to trust in him, was also his;
     We must confess, that nothing is our own.
   Then I confess that he my succor is.

   But to have naught is ours, not to confess
10   That we have naught. I stood amazed at this,
     Much troubled, till I heard a friend express,
   That all things were more ours by being his.
   What Adam had, and forfeited for all,
   Christ keepeth now, who cannot fail or fall.

The Collar[1]

I struck the board[2] and cried, "No more;
       I will abroad!
What? Shall I ever sigh and pine?
My lines and life are free, free as the road,
5   Loose as the wind, as large as store.
       Shall I be still in suit?[3]
Have I no harvest but a thorn
To let me blood, and not restore
What I have lost with cordial° fruit?   *restorative to the heart*
10   Sure there was wine
   Before my sighs did dry it; there was corn°   *grain*
     Before my tears did drown it.
   Is the year only lost to me?
     Have I no bays[4] to crown it,
15 No flowers, no garlands gay? All blasted?
       All wasted?
   Not so, my heart; but there is fruit,
     And thou hast hands.
     Recover all thy sigh-blown age
20 On double pleasures: leave thy cold dispute
Of what is fit and not. Forsake thy cage,
     Thy rope of sands,
Which petty thoughts have made, and made to thee
   Good cable,[5] to enforce and draw,
25   And be thy law,
While thou didst wink and wouldst not see.
     Away! Take heed;
     I will abroad.

1. The emblematic title suggests a clerical collar that has become a slave's collar; also, punningly, the speaker's choler (anger) and, perhaps, the caller that he at last hears.
2. Table, with an allusion to the Communion table.
3. Always in attendance, waiting on someone for a favor.
4. The poet's laurel wreath, a symbol of recognized accomplishment.
5. Christian restrictions on behavior, which the "petty thoughts" of the docile believer have made into strong bonds.

Call in thy death's-head[6] there; tie up thy fears.
30   He that forbears
        To suit and serve his need,
        Deserves his load."
But as I raved and grew more fierce and wild
        At every word,
35   Methoughts I heard one calling, *Child!*[7]
        And I replied, *My Lord.*

The Pulley[1]

        When God at first made man,
Having a glass of blessings standing by,
"Let us," said he, "pour on him all we can:
Let the world's riches, which dispersèd lie,
5   Contract into a span."

        So strength first made a way;
Then beauty flowed, then wisdom, honor, pleasure.
When almost all was out, God made a stay,
Perceiving that, alone of all his treasure,
10   Rest° in the bottom lay.   *repose*

        "For if I should," said He,
"Bestow this jewel also on my creature,
He would adore my gifts instead of me,
And rest in Nature, not the God of Nature;
15   So both should losers be.

        "Yet let him keep the rest,[2]
But keep them with repining restlessness:
Let him be rich and weary, that at least,
If goodness lead him not, yet weariness
20   May toss him to my breast."

The Flower

        How fresh, O Lord, how sweet and clean
Are thy returns! even as the flowers in spring,
        To which, besides their own demesne,°   *domain, demeanor*
The late-past frosts tributes of pleasure bring.

---

6. Skull, emblem of human mortality, and often used as an object for meditation.
7. The call "Child!" reminds the speaker of Paul's words (Romans 8.14–17) that Christians are not in "bondage again to fear" but are children of God, "and if children, then heirs."

1. The poem inverts the legend of Pandora's box, which released all manner of evils when opened but left Hope trapped inside.
2. "Rest" has two senses here: "remainder" and "repose."

5   Grief melts away
Like snow in May,
As if there were no such cold thing.

Who would have thought my shriveled heart
Could have recovered greenness? It was gone
10   Quite underground; as flowers depart
To see their mother-root, when they have blown,°   *bloomed*
Where they together
All the hard weather,
Dead to the world, keep house unknown.

15   These are thy wonders, Lord of power,
Killing and quickening, bringing down to hell
And up to heaven in an hour,
Making a chiming of a passing-bell.[1]
We say amiss
20   This or that is:
Thy word is all, if we could spell.°   *read*

O that I once past changing were,
Fast in thy Paradise, where no flower can wither!
Many a spring I shoot up fair,
25 Offering° at heaven, growing and groaning thither;   *aiming*
Nor doth my flower
Want a spring shower,°   *tears of contrition*
My sins and I joining together.

But while I grow in a straight line,
30 Still upwards bent,° as if heaven were mine own,   *directed*
Thy anger comes, and I decline:
What frost to that? What pole is not the zone
Where all things burn,
When thou dost turn,
35   And the least frown of thine is shown?[2]

And now in age I bud again,
After so many deaths I live and write;
I once more smell the dew and rain,
And relish versing. O my only light,
40   It cannot be
That I am he
On whom thy tempests fell all night.

These are thy wonders, Lord of love,
To make us see we are but flowers that glide;°   *slip silently away*
45   Which when we once can find and prove,°   *experience*

---

1. The "passing-bell," intended to mark the death of a parishioner, is tolled in a monotone; a "chiming" bell offers pleasant variety.

2. I.e., compared with God's wrath, what polar chill would not seem like the heat of the equator?

Thou hast a garden for us where to bide;
       Who would be more,
       Swelling through store,
Forfeit their Paradise by their pride.

The Forerunners

The harbingers are come: see, see their mark;
White is their color,[1] and behold my head.
But must they have my brain? Must they dispark°   turn out
Those sparkling notions which therein were bred?
5   Must dullness turn me to a clod?
Yet have they left me "Thou art still my God."[2]

Good men ye be to leave me my best room,
Even all my heart and what is lodgèd there:
I pass not,° I, what of the rest become,   care not
10   So "Thou art still my God" be out of fear.
       He will be pleasèd with that ditty;
And if I please Him, I write fine and witty.

Farewell, sweet phrases, lovely metaphors:
But will ye leave me thus? When ye before
15   Of stews° and brothels only knew the doors,   whorehouses
Then did I wash you with my tears, and more,
       Brought you to church well-dressed and clad:
My God must have my best, even all I had.

Lovely enchanting language, sugarcane,
20   Honey of roses, whither wilt thou fly?
Hath some fond lover 'ticed° thee to thy bane?°   enticed / poison
And wilt thou leave the church and love a sty?
       Fie! thou wilt soil thy 'broidered coat,
And hurt thyself and him that sings the note.

25   Let foolish lovers, if they will love dung,
With canvas, not with arras,° clothe their shame: fine cloth
Let Folly speak in her own native tongue.
True Beauty dwells on high; ours is a flame
       But borrowed thence to light us thither:
30   Beauty and beauteous words should go together.

Yet, if you go, I pass not;° take your way.   I don't care
For "Thou art still my God" is all that ye
Perhaps with more embellishment can say.

---

1. Harbingers rode ahead of a royal traveling party to requisition lodgings, marking the doors with chalk.

2. Echoes Psalm 31.14: "But I trusted in thee, O Lord: I said, Thou art my God."

Go, birds of spring; let winter have his fee;°   *due*
35   Let a bleak paleness chalk the door,
So all within be livelier than before.

Discipline

Throw away thy rod,
Throw away thy wrath:
      O my God,
Take the gentle path.

5   For my heart's desire
Unto thine is bent:
      I aspire
To a full consent.

Not a word or look
10   I affect° to own,   *wish, pretend*
      But by book,[1]
And thy book alone.

Though I fail, I weep:
Though I halt° in pace,   *limp*
15   Yet I creep
To the throne of grace.

Then let wrath remove;
Love will do the deed:
      For with love
20   Stony hearts will bleed.

Love is swift of foot;
Love's a man of war,[2]
      And can shoot,
And can hit from far.

25   Who can 'scape his bow?
That which wrought on thee,
      Brought thee low,
Needs must work on me.

Throw away thy rod;
30   Though man frailties hath,
      Thou art God:
Throw away thy wrath.

---

1. I.e., like an actor who follows his playbook.
2. The jubilant song sung by Moses in Exodus 15 calls the Lord "a man of war," but Herbert also alludes to Cupid, another divine bowman.

Death

Death, thou wast once an uncouth, hideous thing,
   Nothing but bones,
  The sad effect of sadder groans:
Thy mouth was open, but thou couldst not sing.

5 For we considered thee as at some six
    Or ten years hence,
  After the loss of life and sense,
Flesh being turned to dust and bones to sticks.

We looked on this side of thee, shooting short,
10   Where we did find
   The shells of fledge-souls left behind—
Dry dust, which sheds no tears, but may extort.[1]

But since our Savior's death did put some blood
    Into thy face,
15   Thou art grown fair and full of grace,
Much in request, much sought for as a good.

For we do now behold thee gay and glad
    As at doomsday,
   When souls shall wear their new array,
20 And all thy bones with beauty shall be clad.

Therefore we can go die as sleep, and trust
    Half that we have
   Unto an honest faithful grave,
Making our pillows either down or dust.

Love (3)

Love bade me welcome: yet my soul drew back,
  Guilty of dust and sin.
But quick-eyed Love, observing me grow slack°   *hesitant*
  From my first entrance in,
5 Drew nearer to me, sweetly questioning
  If I lacked anything.[1]

"A guest," I answered, "worthy to be here":
  Love said, "You shall be he."
"I, the unkind, ungrateful? Ah, my dear,

1. Souls that have left the body and gone to heaven are like fledgling chicks that have left the shell behind; that corpse ("dry dust") sheds no tears but may draw ("extort") tears from the survivors.

1. The first question of tavern waiters to an entering customer would be "What d'ye lack?" (i.e., want).

10   I cannot look on thee."
Love took my hand, and smiling did reply,
        "Who made the eyes but I?"

    "Truth, Lord; but I have marred them; let my shame
        Go where it doth deserve."
15 "And know you not," says Love, "who bore the blame?"
        "My dear, then I will serve."
    "You must sit down," says Love, "and taste my meat."
        So I did sit and eat.[2]

2. In addition to the sacrament of Communion, the reference is especially to the banquet in heaven, when the Lord "shall gird himself, and make them to sit down to meat, and will come forth and serve them" (Luke 12.37).

HENRY VAUGHAN
1621–1695

Born to a family with deep roots in Wales, Henry Vaughan was educated at Oxford and the Inns of Court but returned to his native county of Breconshire at the outbreak of the civil war and spent the rest of his life there. He served as secretary to the Welsh circuit courts until 1645; briefly fought for King Charles at Chester, just over the border with England; and in his later years took up the practice of medicine without much formal study. In a volume of verse published in 1651, *Olor Iscanus* (The Swan of Usk), he drew attention to his heritage by terming himself "the Silurist": the Silures were an ancient tribe from southeast Wales. Some features of Vaughan's poetry derive from the rich Welsh-language poetic tradition: the frequency of assonance, consonance, and alliteration; the multiplication of comparisons and similes (*dyfalu*); and the sensitivity to nature, especially the countryside around the Usk River.

Some of Vaughan's poetry is secular—*Poems with the Tenth Satire of Juvenal, Englished* (1646), *Olor Iscanus* (1651), and a late-published collection of earlier verse, *Thalia Rediviva* (1678). Vaughan's modern reputation, though, rests almost entirely on his religious poetry. In 1650 Vaughan published his major collection of religious verse, *Silex Scintillans* (The Flashing Flint); it was republished in 1655 with a second book added. A conversion experience may have prompted Vaughan's turn to religious themes: the title of the book is explicated by the emblem of a flint-like heart struck by a bolt of lightning from the hand of God.

In the preface to *Silex Scintillans* Vaughan places himself among the many "pious converts" gained by George Herbert's holy life and verse. While his secular poetry recalls Ben Jonson's, the religious poetry overtly models itself on Herbert's. Some twenty-six poems appropriate their titles from *The Temple*, several owe their metrical form to Herbert, and many begin by quoting one of Herbert's lines (compare Vaughan's "Unprofitableness" with Herbert's "The Flower"). Yet no one with an ear for poetry will mistake Vaughan's long, loose poetic lines for Herbert's artful precision. Vaughan's religious sensibility too differs markedly from Herbert's. Unable to locate himself in a national Church of England, now dismantled by war, he wanders unaccompanied through a landscape at once biblical, emblematic, and contemporary, mourning lost innocence. One unifying motif of the poems in *Silex Scintillans* is pilgrimage, though the arrival at the destination is typically deferred. Vaughan seems unable to experience Christ as a friend or supporter in present trials, as Herbert so often does; instead, he longs for a full relationship with the divine yet to come, at the Last Day. Despite his restless solitude, however, Vaughan finds vestiges of the divine everywhere. "I saw eternity the other night," he begins his most famous poem, "The World," situating the "ring of pure and endless light" in a specific, quotidian moment of illumination. Eternity hovers tantalizingly over the human world of strife, pain, and exploitation, apparently entirely detached from that world but in fact accessible to God's elect, who soar from earthly shadows into the light. Vaughan's twin brother, Thomas, introduced him to Hermetic philosophy, an esoteric brand of Neoplatonism that found occult correspondences between the visible world of matter and the invisible world of spirits. The influence of this philosophical system, so congenial to Vaughan's sensibility, is most apparent in the poem "Cock Crowing."

From Poems

A Song to Amoret[1]

If I were dead, and in my place,
    Some fresher youth designed,
To warm thee with new fires, and grace
    Those arms I left behind;

5   Were he as faithful as the sun,
    That's wedded to the sphere;[2]
His blood as chaste, and temperate run,
    As April's mildest tear;

Or were he rich, and with his heaps,
10   And spacious share of Earth,
Could make divine affection cheap,
    And court° his golden birth: *pay court to*

For all these arts I'ld not believe,
    (No though he should be thine)
15   The mighty amorist° could give   *lover*
    So rich a heart as mine.

Fortune and beauty thou mightst find,
    And greater men than I:
But my true resolvèd mind,
20   They never shall come nigh.

---

1. This poem comes from Vaughan's first collection, all on worldly themes and many on love. Amoret has sometimes been identified with Vaughan's first wife, but on no secure ground. Amoret (formed from *amor*, love) is a traditional name for a poet's beloved from classical literature; note Spenser's use of the name in *Faerie Queene* 3, and the variation on it in his sonnet sequence *Amoretti*.
2. In the Ptolemaic scheme, each of the planets (including the sun, which was regarded as a planet) occupied one of the spheres revolving around the earth.

For I not for an hour did love,
    Or for a day desire,
But with my soul had from above,
    This endless holy fire.

                    1646

FROM SILEX SCINTILLANS

Regeneration[1]

    A ward, and still in bonds,[2] one day
        I stole abroad;
It was high spring, and all the way
        Primrosed[3] and hung with shade;
5   Yet was it frost within,
        And surly winds
Blasted my infant buds, and sin
        Like clouds eclipsed my mind.

    Stormed thus, I straight perceived my spring
10   Mere stage and show,
My walk a monstrous, mountained thing,
        Roughcast with rocks and snow;
        And as a pilgrim's eye,
        Far from relief,
15 Measures the melancholy sky,
        Then drops and rains for grief,

    So sighed I upwards still; at last
        'Twixt steps and falls
I reached the pinnacle, where placed
20   I found a pair of scales;
I took them up and laid
        In th' one, late pains;
The other smoke and pleasures weighed,
        But proved the heavier grains.[4]

25 With that, some cried, "Away!" Straight° I   *immediately*
        Obeyed, and led
Full east, a fair, fresh field could spy;
        Some called it Jacob's bed,[5]

1. The poem allegorizes in rather precise Calvinist terms the experience of God's grace calling the elect and distinguishing between the regenerate and the unregenerate.
2. He begins as one in the Pauline "spirit of bondage" to fear because of sin and as one still in his minority ("wardship") under the Old Testament law. This contrasts with the "spirit of adoption" whereby we are children of God: "And if children then heirs; heirs of God and joint-heirs with Christ" (Romans 8.14–17).

3. Alluding to the adage that the "primrose path" leads to perdition.
4. He climbs Mount Sinai (tries to live by the Old Testament law) but finds his sins and follies far outweigh that effort.
5. Jacob slept in an open field, where he had a vision of a ladder leading to heaven (Genesis 28.11–19); that place, Bethel, was taken as a type or figure for the church. Vaughan's poem "Jacobs Pillow, and Pillar" works out this allegory.

A virgin soil which no
30   Rude feet ere trod,
Where, since he stepped there, only go
    Prophets and friends of God.

Here I reposed; but scarce well set,
    A grove descried°   *perceived*
35 Of stately height, whose branches met
    And mixed on every side;
    I entered, and once in,
      Amazed to see 't,
Found all was changed, and a new spring[6]
40   Did all my senses greet.

The unthrift sun shot vital gold,
    A thousand pieces,
And heaven its azure did unfold,
    Checkered with snowy fleeces;
45   The air was all in spice,
      And every bush
A garland wore; thus fed my eyes,
    But all the ear lay hush.°   *quiet*

Only a little fountain[7] lent
50   Some use for ears,
And on the dumb shades language spent
    The music of her tears;
    I drew her near, and found
      The cistern full
55 Of divers stones, some bright and round,
    Others ill-shaped and dull.[8]

The first, pray mark, as quick as light
    Danced through the flood;
But the last, more heavy than the night,
60   Nailed to the center stood.
    I wondered much, but tired
      At last with thought,
My restless eye that still desired
    As strange an object brought:

65 It was a bank of flowers, where I descried,
      Though 'twas midday,
Some fast asleep, others broad-eyed
    And taking in the ray;
    Here musing long, I heard

---

6. Imagery in the following lines—spring, perfumes, flowers—alludes to the Song of Solomon in which the bride is traditionally allegorized as the church or the beloved soul.

7. In the Song of Solomon 4.15 the "fountain of waters, a well of living waters" was traditionally allegorized as Christ.

8. Alludes to 1 Peter 2.5, which refers to the faithful as "lively stones." The different sorts of stones and flowers here suggest the elect and the reprobate.

70   A rushing wind
Which still increased, but whence it stirred
      Nowhere I could not find.

I turned me round, and to each shade
      Dispatched an eye
75 To see if any leaf had made
      Least motion or reply;
     But while I listening sought
        My mind to ease
By knowing where 'twas, or where not,
80   It whispered, "Where I please."[9]

"Lord," then said I, "on me one breath,
And let me die before my death!"

"Arise O North, and come thou South wind,
and blow upon my garden, that the spices
85 thereof may flow out."[1]

                                        1650

The Retreat

Happy those early days! when I
Shined in my angel infancy.
Before I understood this place
Appointed for my second race,[1]
5 Or taught my soul to fancy aught°   *anything*
But a white, celestial thought;
When yet I had not walked above
A mile or two from my first love,
And looking back, at that short space,
10 Could see a glimpse of His bright face;
When on some gilded cloud or flower
My gazing soul would dwell an hour,
And in those weaker glories spy
Some shadows of eternity;
15 Before I taught my tongue to wound
My conscience with a sinful sound,
Or had the black art to dispense
A several° sin to every sense,   *different*
But felt through all this fleshly dress
20 Bright shoots of everlastingness.

9. John 3.8: "The wind bloweth where it listeth, and thou hearest the sound thereof, but canst not tell whence it cometh, and whither it goeth, so is every one that is born of the Spirit."
1. Vaughan identifies this verse as Canticles (Song of Solomon) 5.17; it is properly 4.16.

1. The poem alludes throughout to the Platonic doctrine of preexistence, in conjunction with Christ's words (Mark 10.15): "Whosoever shall not receive the kingdom of God as a little child, he shall not enter therein." Comparisons are often made to Wordsworth's Immortality ode.

O, how I long to travel back,
And tread again that ancient track!
That I might once more reach that plain
Where first I left my glorious train,
25   From whence th' enlightened spirit sees
That shady city of palm trees.[2]
But, ah! my soul with too much stay°   *delay*
Is drunk, and staggers in the way.
Some men a forward motion love;
30   But I by backward steps would move,
And when this dust falls to the urn,
In that state I came, return.

1650

Silence, and Stealth of Days!

Silence, and stealth of days! 'tis now
    Since thou art gone[1]
Twelve hundred hours, and not a brow[2]
    But clouds hang on.
5   As he that in some cave's thick damp,
      Locked from the light,
Fixeth a solitary lamp
    To brave the night,
And walking from his sun, when past
10   That glimmering ray,
Cuts through the heavy mists in haste
    Back to his day,[3]
So o'er fled minutes I retreat
    Unto that hour
15   Which showed thee last, but did defeat
    Thy light and power;
I search and rack my soul to see
    Those beams again,
But nothing but the snuff[4] to me
20   Appeareth plain,
That dark and dead sleeps in its known
    And common urn;
But those[5] fled to their maker's throne,
    There shine and burn.
25   O could I track them! but souls must
    Track one the other,
And now the spirit, not the dust,

2. The New Jerusalem, the Heavenly City (for its identification with Jericho, the "city of Palm Trees," Deuteronomy 34.3).
1. As indicated in lines 27–28, the poem is on the loss of Vaughan's brother—not his twin brother, Thomas, the Hermetic philosopher, who did not die until 1666, but his younger brother, William,

who died in July 1648.
2. Mountain ridge, or forehead.
3. The miner fixes his lamp halfway down the dark shaft, ventures a little beyond it, but then beats a hasty retreat.
4. The burned wick of the lamp or candle.
5. The reference is back to "beams."

Must be thy brother.
Yet I have one pearl,[6] by whose light
30   All things I see,
And in the heart of earth and night,
Find heaven and thee.

1648   1650

Corruption

Sure it was so. Man in those early days
    Was not all stone and earth;
He shined a little, and by those weak rays
    Had some glimpse of his birth.
5   He saw heaven o'er his head, and knew from whence
    He came, condemnèd, hither;
And, as first love draws strongest, so from hence
    His mind sure progressed thither.
Things here were strange unto him: sweat and till,
10   All was a thorn or weed:[1]
Nor did those last, but (like himself) died still
    As soon as they did seed.
They seemed to quarrel with him, for that act
    That felled him foiled them all:
15 He drew the curse upon the world, and cracked
    The whole frame with his fall.[2]
This made him long for home, as loath to stay
    With murmurers and foes;
He sighed for Eden, and would often say,
20   "Ah! what bright days were those!"
Nor was heaven cold unto him; for each day
    The valley or the mountain
Afforded visits, and still Paradise lay
    In some green shade or fountain.
25 Angels lay lieger[3] here; each bush and cell,
    Each oak and highway knew them;
Walk but the fields, or sit down at some well,
    And he was sure to view them.
Almighty Love! where art thou now? Mad man
30   Sits down and freezeth on;
He raves, and swears to stir nor fire, nor fan,
    But bids the thread° be spun.   *thread of Fate*
I see, thy curtains are close-drawn; thy bow[4]
    Looks dim, too, in the cloud;

6. Probably the Bible. The reference is to Matthew 13.45–46, to the merchant who sold all he had to buy a pearl of great price, there likened to the Kingdom of Heaven.
1. God's curse on Adam for eating the forbidden fruit included a curse on the earth: "Thorns also and thistles shall it bring forth to thee"
(Genesis 3.18).
2. Cf. Donne, *An Anatomy of the World*, lines 199–200 (p. 1404).
3. As resident ambassadors (from heaven).
4. The rainbow, God's covenant with Noah after the Flood (Genesis 9.13).

35   Sin triumphs still, and man is sunk below
      The center, and his shroud.
  All's in deep sleep and night: thick darkness lies
      And hatcheth o'er thy people—
  But hark! what trumpet's that? what angel cries,
40   "Arise! thrust in thy sickle"?[5]

                        1650

Unprofitableness

How rich, O Lord! how fresh thy visits are![1]
'Twas but just now my bleak leaves hopeless hung,
    Sullied with dust and mud;
Each snarling blast shot through me, and did share°   *shear off*
5   Their youth and beauty; cold showers nipped and wrung
     Their spiciness and blood.
But since thou didst in one sweet glance survey
Their sad decays, I flourish, and once more
     Breathe all perfumes and spice;
10 I smell a dew like myrrh, and all the day
Wear in my bosom a full sun; such store
     Hath one beam from thy eyes.
But, ah, my God! what fruit hast thou of this?
What one poor leaf did ever I let[2] fall
15   To wait upon thy wreath?
Thus thou all day a thankless weed dost dress,
And when th' hast done, a stench or fog is all
     The odor I bequeath.

                        1650

The World

I saw eternity the other night,
Like a great ring of pure and endless light,
    All calm as it was bright;
And round beneath it, Time, in hours, days, years,
5   Driven by the spheres,[1]
Like a vast shadow moved, in which the world
    And all her train were hurled.
The doting lover in his quaintest° strain   *most ingenious*
    Did there complain;

---

5. Alludes to Revelation 14.15: "And another angel came out of the temple, crying with a loud voice to him that sat on the cloud, 'Thrust in thy sickle, and reap, for the harvest of the earth is now.'"

1. Cf. Herbert's "The Flower" (pp. 1721–23).
2. The original printed text reads "yet," emended here.
1. The concentric spheres of Ptolemaic astronomy.

10   Near him, his lute, his fancy, and his flights,°   *caprices*
        Wit's sour delights,
     With gloves and knots,° the silly snares of pleasure,   *love knots*
        Yet his dear treasure,
     All scattered lay, while he his eyes did pour
15   Upon a flower.

     The darksome statesman hung with weights and woe
     Like a thick midnight fog moved there so slow
        He did nor stay nor go;
     Condemning thoughts, like sad eclipses, scowl
20   Upon his soul,
     And clouds of crying witnesses[2] without
        Pursued him with one shout.
     Yet digged the mole,[3] and, lest his ways be found,
        Worked underground,
25   Where he did clutch his prey. But one did see
        That policy:°   *strategy*
     Churches and altars fed him; perjuries
        Were gnats and flies;
     It rained about him blood and tears; but he
30   Drank them as free.[4]

     The fearful miser on a heap of rust
     Sat pining all his life there, did scarce trust
        His own hands with the dust;
     Yet would not place° one piece above, but lives   *invest*
35   In fear of thieves.
     Thousands there were as frantic as himself,
        And hugged each one his pelf:
     The downright epicure placed heaven in sense,°   *the senses*
        And scorned pretense;
40   While others, slipped into a wide excess,
        Said little less;
     The weaker sort slight, trivial wares enslave,
        Who think them brave°   *fine, showy*
     And poor, despisèd Truth sat counting by°   *recording*
45   Their victory.

     Yet some, who all this while did weep and sing,
     And sing and weep, soared up into the ring;
        But most would use no wing.
     "O fools!" said I, "thus to prefer dark night
50   Before true light!
     To live in grots and caves, and hate the day
        Because it shows the way,
     The way which from this dead and dark abode
        Leads up to God,

---

2. In Hebrews 12, the "clouds of witnesses" testified to God's truth in past times. Here, these
champions of faith accuse one whose actions

deny God.
3. I.e., the "darksome statesman" (line 16).
4. I.e., as freely as they rained.

55 A way where you might tread the sun and be
    More bright than he!"
But as I did their madness so discuss,
    One whispered thus:
"This ring the bridegroom did for none provide,
60   But for his bride."[5]

John Chap. 2. ver. 16, 17

    All that is in the world, the lust of the flesh, the
lust of the eyes, and the pride of life, is not of the
Father, but is of the world.
    And the world passeth away, and the lusts thereof,
but he that doth the will of God abideth forever.

1650

They Are All Gone into the World of Light!

They are all gone into the world of light!
    And I alone sit ling'ring here;
Their very memory is fair and bright,
    And my sad thoughts doth clear.

5 It glows and glitters in my cloudy breast
    Like stars upon some gloomy grove,
Or those faint beams in which this hill is dressed
    After the sun's remove.

I see them walking in an air of glory,
10   Whose light doth trample on my days;
My days, which are at best but dull and hoary,°   *gray with age*
    Mere glimmering and decays.

O holy hope, and high humility,
    High as the heavens above!
15 These are your walks, and you have showed them me
    To kindle my cold love.

Dear, beauteous death! the jewel of the just,
    Shining nowhere but in the dark;
What mysteries do lie beyond thy dust,
20   Could man outlook that mark!°   *boundary*

He that hath found some fledged bird's nest may know
    At first sight if the bird be flown;

---

5. Alludes to Revelation 19.7–9, the marriage of the Lamb and his Bride, allegorized as Christ and the church or Christ and the regenerate soul: "Blessed are they which are called unto the marriage supper of the Lamb."

But what fair well° or grove he sings in now,   spring
    That is to him unknown.

25 And yet, as angels in some brighter dreams
    Call to the soul when man doth sleep,
So some strange thoughts transcend our wonted° themes,   accustomed
    And into glory peep.

If a star were confined into a tomb,
30   Her captive flames must needs burn there;
But when the hand that locked her up gives room,
    She'll shine through all the sphere.

O Father of eternal life, and all
    Created glories under thee!
35 Resume thy spirit from this world of thrall°   slavery
    Into true liberty!

Either disperse these mists, which blot and fill
    My pèrspective[1] still as they pass,
Or else remove me hence unto that hill
40   Where I shall need no glass.

                                  1655

Cock-Crowing[1]

Father of lights! what sunny seed,[2]
What glance of day hast thou confined
Into this bird? To all the breed
This busy ray thou hast assigned;
5   Their magnetism works all night,
      And dreams of Paradise and light.

Their eyes watch for the morning hue,
Their little grain expelling night
So shines and sings, as if it knew
10 The path unto the house of light.
      It seems their candle, howe'r done,
      Was tinned° and lighted at the sun.   kindled

1. Literally, telescope, but more freely, distant vision.
1. The poem calls upon the Hermetic notion of sympathetic attraction between earthly and heavenly bodies, e.g., the cock whose crowing announces the sun's rising because it bears within itself a "seed" of the sun. Vaughan finds here an analogy for the attraction the soul has for its Maker.
2. The opening lines recall a passage from Hen-ry's brother, the Hermetic philosopher Thomas Vaughan: "For she [the Anima or Soul] is guided in her operations by a spiritual metaphysical grain, a seed or glance of light . . . descending from the Father of lights." That term for God is from James 1.17. "Seed," "glance," "ray," and "grain" in line 8 are almost synonymous Hermetic terms for the bit of the sun implanted in the cock. "Magnetism" (line 5) refers to the attraction between the cock's "seed" and its source, the sun.

If such a tincture,[3] such a touch,
So firm a longing can impower,
15 Shall thy own image[4] think it much
To watch for thy appearing hour?
　　If a mere blast so fill the sail,
　　Shall not the breath of God[5] prevail?

O thou immortal light and heat!
20 Whose hand so shines through all this frame,°　　*universe*
That by the beauty of the seat,
We plainly see, who made the same.
　　Seeing thy seed abides in me,
　　Dwell thou in it, and I in thee.

25 To sleep without thee, is to die;
Yea, 'tis a death partakes of hell:
For where thou dost not close the eye
It never opens, I can tell.
　　In such a dark, Egyptian border,
30 　The shades of death dwell and disorder.[6]

If joys, and hopes, and earnest throes,
And hearts, whose pulse beats still for light
Are given to birds; who, but thee, knows
A love-sick soul's exalted flight?
35 　Can souls be tracked by any eye
　　But his, who gave them wings to fly?

Only this veil[7] which thou hast broke,
And must be broken yet in me,
This veil, I say, is all the cloak
40 And cloud which shadows thee from me.
　　This veil thy full-eyed love denies,
　　And only gleams and fractions spies.

O take it off! Make no delay,
But brush me with thy light, that I
45 May shine unto a perfect day,
And warm me at thy glorious eye!
　　O take it off! or till it flee,
　　Though with no lily,[8] stay with me!

1655

3. Alchemical term for a spiritual principle whose quality may be infused into material things.
4. Alludes to Genesis 1.27: "So God created man in his own image."
5. Alludes to Genesis 2.7: "And the Lord God formed man of the dust of the ground, and breathed into his nostrils the breath of life; and man became a living soul."
6. Alludes to Exodus 10.21, Moses bringing down the plague of "darkness over the land of Egypt, even darkness which may be felt."
7. Echoes Hebrews 10.20: "By a new and living way, which he [Christ] hath consecrated for us, through the veil, that is to say, his flesh."
8. Echoes Song of Solomon 2.16: "My beloved is mine, and I am his: he feedeth among the lilies."

The Night

John 3.2[1]

Through that pure virgin-shrine,
That sacred veil drawn o'er thy glorious noon,
That men might look and live as glowworms shine
    And face the moon,
5   Wise Nicodemus saw such light
    As made him know his God by night.

    Most blest believer he!
Who in that land of darkness and blind eyes
Thy long-expected healing wings[2] could see,
10   When thou didst rise,
    And what can never more be done,
    Did at midnight speak with the Sun!

    O who will tell me where
He found thee at that dead and silent hour?
15 What hallowed solitary ground did bear
      So rare a flower,
    Within whose sacred leaves did lie
    The fullness of the Deity?

    No mercy seat of gold,
20 No dead and dusty cherub nor carved stone,[3]
But his own living works did my Lord hold
      And lodge alone;
    Where trees and herbs did watch and peep
    And wonder while the Jews did sleep.

25   Dear night! this world's defeat,[4]
The stop to busy fools; care's check and curb;
The day of spirits; my soul's calm retreat
      Which none disturb!
    Christ's progress and his prayer time;
30   The hours to which high heaven doth chime;

    God's silent, searching flight,
When my Lord's head is filled with dew, and all
His locks are wet with the clear drops of night;
      His still, soft call;[5]

---

1. John 3.1–2 describes how a Pharisee named Nicodemus came to Jesus by night and said, "Rabbi, we know that thou art a teacher come from God."
2. Echoes Malachi 4.2: "The Sun of righteousness [shall] arise with healing in his wings."
3. God commanded the Israelites to cover the Ark of the Covenant with "a mercy seat of pure gold . . . and . . . two cherubims of gold, of beaten work . . . in the two ends of the mercy seat" (Exo-

dus 25.17–18).
4. The style of this stanza and the next imitates Herbert's "Prayer (1)" (pp. 1711–12).
5. Echoes Song of Solomon 5.2: "I sleep, but my heart waketh: it is the voice of my beloved that knocketh, saying, Open to me, my sister, my love, my dove, my undefiled: for my head is filled with dew, and my locks with the drops of the night." For the allegory see "The World," note 5.

35 His knocking time; the soul's dumb watch,
   When spirits their fair kindred catch.

    Were all my loud, evil days
  Calm and unhaunted as is thy dark tent,
  Whose peace but by some angel's wing or voice
40   Is seldom rent,
  Then I in heaven all the long year
  Would keep, and never wander here.

    But living where the sun
  Doth all things wake, and where all mix and tire
45 Themselves and others, I consent and run
    To every mire,
  And by this world's ill-guiding light
  Err more than I can do by night.

    There is in God (some say)
50 A deep but dazzling darkness,[6] as men here
  Say it is late and dusky, because they
    See not all clear.
  Oh for that night, where I in him
  Might live invisible and dim!

                  1655

The Waterfall[1]

With what deep murmurs through time's silent stealth
Doth thy transparent, cool, and watery wealth
    Here flowing fall,
    And chide, and call,
5 As if his liquid, loose retinue stayed
  Ling'ring, and were of this steep place afraid,
    The common pass
    Where, clear as glass,
    All must descend,
10   Not to an end,
  But quickened by this steep and rocky grave,
  Rise to a longer course more bright and brave.°   *resplendent*

  Dear stream! dear bank! where often I
  Have sat and pleased my pensive eye—
15 Why, since each drop of thy quick° store   *living*

6. Dionysius the Areopagite (ca. 5th century) deals with concepts of divine darkness, which the 14th-century philosopher Nicholas of Cusa later developed, referring to the "Darkness where truly dwells . . . the one who is beyond all" and "the superessential Darkness which is hidden by all the light that is in existing things."

1. The water, with its startling descent in a waterfall but ultimate circularity to its source, is for Vaughan an emblem of death and restoration of the soul to its source.

Runs thither whence it flowed before,
Should poor souls fear a shade or night,
Who came, sure, from a sea of light?
Or since those drops are all sent back
20 So sure to thee that none doth lack,
Why should frail flesh doubt any more
That what God takes he'll not restore?
O useful element and clear!
My sacred wash and cleanser here,
25 My first consigner° unto those   *in baptism*
Fountains of life where the Lamb goes![2]
What sublime truths and wholesome themes
Lodge in thy mystical deep streams!
Such as dull man can never find
30 Unless that Spirit lead his mind
Which first upon thy face did move
And hatched all with his quickening love.[3]
As this loud brook's incessant fall
In streaming rings restagnates° all   *makes still again*
35 Which reach by course the bank, and then
Are no more seen, just so pass men.
Oh my invisible estate,
My glorious liberty,[4] still late!
Thou art the channel my soul seeks,
40 Not this with cataracts and creeks.

1655

2. Echoes Revelation 7.17: "For the Lamb . . . shall lead them unto living fountains of waters."
3. Alludes to Genesis 1.2: "And the Spirit of God moved upon the face of the waters." The Latin Vulgate version, *incubabant*, is closer to Vaughan's "hatched" than to "moved."
4. Alludes to Romans 8.21, promising deliverance "from the bondage of corruption into the glorious liberty of the children of God."

RICHARD CRASHAW
ca. 1613–1649

Steps to the Temple (1646, 1648), the name of Richard Crashaw's collection of sacred poetry, clearly acknowledges George Herbert's primacy among devotional poets. Yet Crashaw is hardly Herbert's slavish disciple. A Roman Catholic convert, Crashaw was profoundly influenced by the Counter-Reformation, which reacted against Protestant austerity by linking heightened spirituality to vivid bodily experiences. He is the only major English poet in the tradition of the Continental baroque, a movement in literature and visual art that developed out of the Counter-Reformation. Baroque style is exuberant, sensuous, and elaborately ornamented, and it deliberately strains decorum, challenging formal restraints and generic limitations. Crashaw's favorite subjects are typical of baroque art: the infant Jesus surrounded by angels and cherubs; the crucified Savior, streaming blood; the sorrowful Virgin; the tearfully penitent Mary Magdalen; saintly martyrs wracked with ecstasy and pain. Although some have pronounced his images grotesque, Crashaw is alone among English poets in rendering the experience of rapture and religious ecstasy.

The son of a Puritan divine noted for hatred of popery, Crashaw was educated at Pembroke College, Cambridge, where he became an adherent of Laudian Anglicanism. In 1636 he was elected a fellow of Peterhouse, another Cambridge college. By 1639 he had become a priest of the Church of England, curate of Little St. Mary's, and a college lecturer. A contemporary wrote that his sermons "ravished more like poems," but apparently none survive. Crashaw called Peterhouse his "little contentful kingdom": his friends included the poet Abraham Cowley and George Herbert's literary executor Nicholas Ferrar, the founder of the Anglican monastic community Little Gidding. In 1643 the Puritans occupied Cambridge, violently disrupting Crashaw's life there. He fled to Paris and to the English court in exile, becoming a Roman Catholic in 1645. He was saved from destitution by obtaining various minor posts through the queen's influence, the last one at Loreto—thought to be Jesus' house at Nazareth, miraculously transported to Italy.

Crashaw's Latin epigrams, published as *Epigrammatum Sacrorum Liber* (1634), were much influenced by Jesuit epigram style and are among the best by an Englishman. In their Latin and later English versions, they are characterized by puns, paradoxes, and sometimes bizarre metaphors, as in the epigram on Luke 11. In 1646 Crashaw published, with the first version of *Steps to the Temple*, a book of secular poems, *The Delights of the Muses*, some of them in the restrained style of Ben Jonson. But the masterpiece of this book is "Music's Duel," a much-elaborated version of a poem by the Jesuit Famianus Strada about a contest between a nightingale and a lutenist, between melody and harmony. Crashaw imitates music by means of liquid vowels, gliding syntax, onomatopoeia, and the complex blending of sounds. Beyond that, he renders the ecstasy of the listening experience by collapsing one sense into another (synesthesia), creating an effect of continual metamorphosis.

Crashaw constantly revised his religious poems, usually making them longer. His posthumous volume, *Carmen Deo Nostro* (1652), includes emblems he may have executed himself, among them the padlocked heart prefixed to a poem urging the Countess of Denbigh to convert to Catholicism. Especially notable are the final versions of several hymns, ranging from the witty praise of St. Theresa in "The Flaming Heart" to the meltingly sweet "In the Holy Nativity."

FROM THE DELIGHTS OF THE MUSES

Music's Duel[1]

Now westward Sol° had spent the richest beams	*the sun*
Of noon's high glory, when hard by° the streams	*close to*
Of Tiber, on the scene of a green plat,	
Under protection of an oak, there sat	
5 A sweet lute's-master: in whose gentle airs	

1. Based on a much shorter Latin poem by the Jesuit Famianus Strada (1617), which also relates a contest between a nightingale and a lutenist, as a version of the contest between nature and art. Crashaw's poem also represents the contest of two kinds of music, melody (monody) and harmony (polyphony). The poem is especially remarkable for synesthesia, the blending of sensory images into one another, and sometimes the representation of one sense in the imagery of another.

He lost the day's heat, and his own hot cares.
    Close in the covert of the leaves there stood
A nightingale, come from the neighboring wood:
(The sweet inhabitant of each glad tree,
10 Their Muse, their Siren,[2] harmless Siren she)
There stood she listening, and did entertain
The music's soft report: and mold the same
In her own murmurs, that whatever mood
His curious° fingers lent, her voice made good: *skillful*
15 The man perceived his rival, and her art,
Disposed to give the light-foot lady sport
Awakes his lute, and 'gainst the fight to come
Informs it, in a sweet praeludium°   *prelude, introduction*
Of closer strains, and ere the war begin,
20 He lightly skirmishes on every string
Charged with a flying touch: and straightway she
Carves out her dainty voice as readily,
Into a thousand sweet distinguished tones,
And reckons up in soft divisions,°   *rapid melodic passages*
25 Quick volumes of wild notes; to let him know
By that shrill taste, she could do something too.
    His nimble hands instinct then taught each string
A cap'ring cheerfulness; and made them sing
To their own dance; now negligently rash
30 He throws his arm, and with a long drawn dash
Blends all together; then distinctly trips
From this to that; then quick returning skips
And snatches this again, and pauses there.
She measures every measure, everywhere
35 Meets art with art; sometimes as if in doubt
Not perfect yet, and fearing to be out°   *at a loss*
Trails her plain ditty[3] in one long-spun note
Through the sleek passage of her open throat:
A clear unwrinkled song, then doth she point it
40 With tender accents, and severely joint it
By short diminutives, that being reared
In controverting warbles evenly shared,
With her sweet self she wrangles; he amazed
That from so small a channel should be raised
45 The torrent of a voice, whose melody
Could melt into such sweet variety,
Strains higher yet; that tickled with rare art
The tattling° strings (each breathing in his part)   *prattling*
Most kindly do fall out;° the grumbling bass   *naturally quarrel*
50 In surly groans disdains the treble's grace.
The high-perched treble chirps at this, and chides,
Until his finger (moderator) hides
And closes the sweet quarrel, rousing all
Hoarse, shrill, at once; as when the trumpets call

2. The irresistible singing of sirens lures men to   3. Simple melody, without divisions.
their death.

55　Hot Mars to th'harvest of death's field, and woo
　　Men's hearts into their hands; this lesson too
　　She gives him back; her supple breast thrills out
　　Sharp airs, and staggers in a warbling doubt
　　Of dallying sweetness, hovers o'er her skill,
60　And folds in waved notes with a trembling bill,
　　The pliant series of her slippery song.
　　Then starts she suddenly into a throng
　　Of short thick sobs, whose thundering volleys float,
　　And roll themselves over her lubric° throat　　　　　　　　　smooth
65　In panting murmurs, stilled° out of her breast,　　　　　　distilled
　　That ever-bubbling spring; the sugared nest
　　Of her delicious soul, that there does lie
　　Bathing in streams of liquid melody;
　　Music's best seed-plot, whence in ripened airs
70　A golden-headed harvest fairly rears
　　His honey-dropping tops, plowed by her breath
　　Which there reciprocally laboreth
　　In that sweet soil. It seems a holy choir
　　Founded to th'name of great Apollo's[4] lyre.
75　Whose silver roof rings with the sprightly notes
　　Of sweet-lipped angel-imps, that swill their throats
　　In cream of morning Helicon,[5] and then
　　Prefer° soft anthems to the ears of men,　　　　　　　　　offer
　　To woo them from their beds, still murmuring
80　That men can sleep while they their matins sing:
　　(Most divine service) whose so early lay°　　　　　　　　　song
　　Prevents° the eyelids of the blushing day.　　　　comes before
　　There might you hear her kindle her soft voice,
　　In the close murmur of a sparkling noise,
85　And lay the groundwork of her hopeful song,
　　Still keeping in the forward stream, so long
　　Till a sweet whirlwind (striving to get out)
　　Heaves her soft bosom, wanders round about,
　　And makes a pretty earthquake in her breast,
90　Till the fledged notes at length forsake their nest;
　　Fluttering in wanton shoals, and to the sky
　　Winged with their own wild echoes prattling fly.
　　She opes the floodgate, and lets loose a tide
　　Of streaming sweetness, which in state doth ride
95　On the waved back of every swelling strain,
　　Rising and falling in a pompous train.
　　And while she thus discharges a shrill peal
　　Of flashing airs, she qualifies° their zeal　　　　　　　　moderates
　　With the cool epode° of a graver note,　　　　　　　　　　lyric
100　Thus high, thus low, as if her silver throat
　　Would reach the brazen voice of war's hoarse bird;°　　the raven
　　Her little soul is ravished: and so poured
　　Into loose ecstasies, that she is placed

4. God of music and poetry, father of the Muses.
5. Mountain in Greece, home of the Muses; sometimes, the fountains there.

Above herself, music's enthusiast.[6]
105　　Shame now and anger mixed a double stain
In the musician's face; yet once again,
Mistress, I come; now reach a strain, my lute,
Above her mock, or be forever mute.
Or tune a song of victory to me,
110　Or to thyself sing thine own obsequy;°　　　　　　*funeral song*
So said, his hands sprightly as fire he flings,
And with a quavering coyness tastes the strings.
The sweet-lipped sisters° musically frighted,　　　*the Muses*
Singing their fears are fearfully delighted.
115　Trembling as when Apollo's golden hairs
Are fanned and frizzled, in the wanton airs
Of his own breath; which married to his lyre
Doth tune the spheres, and make heaven's self look higher.
From this to that, from that to this he flies,
120　Feels music's pulse in all her arteries,
Caught in a net which there Apollo spreads,
His fingers struggle with the vocal threads,
Following those little rills,[7] he sinks into
A Sea of Helicon;[8] his hand does go
125　Those parts of sweetness, which with nectar drop,
Softer than that which pants in Hebe's[9] cup.
The humorous° strings expound his learned touch　　　*capricious*
By various glosses; now they seem to grutch°　　　　　*grumble*
And murmur in a buzzing din, then jingle
130　In shrill tongued accents: striving to be single.
Every smooth turn, every delicious stroke
Gives life to some new grace; thus doth h'invoke
Sweetness by all her names; thus, bravely° thus　　　*splendidly*
(Fraught with a fury so harmonious)
135　The lute's light genius now does proudly rise,
Heaved on the surges of swollen rhapsodies.
Whose flourish, meteor-like, doth curl the air
With flash of high-borne fancies; here and there
Dancing in lofty measures, and anon
140　Creeps on the soft touch of a tender tone:
Whose trembling murmurs melting in wild airs
Runs to and fro, complaining his sweet cares
Because those precious mysteries that dwell,
In music's ravished soul he dare not tell,
145　But whisper to the world: thus do they vary
Each string his note, as if they meant to carry
Their master's blest soul (snatched out at his ears
By a strong ecstasy) through all the spheres
Of music's heaven; and seat it there on high
150　In th' empyreum° of pure harmony.　　　　　　　*highest heaven*
At length (after so long, so loud a strife

6. Literally, one inspired by a god.
7. Small streams; also, passages of liquid notes.
8. Resort of Apollo and the Muses.

9. Greek goddess of youth and cupbearer to the gods.

Of all the strings, still breathing the best life
Of blest variety attending on
His finger's fairest revolution
155 In many a sweet rise, many as sweet a fall)
A full-mouthed diapason[1] swallows all.
    This done, he lists what she would say to this,
And she although her breath's late exercise
Had dealt too roughly with her tender throat,
160 Yet summons all her sweet powers for a note
Alas! in vain! for while, sweet soul, she tries
To measure all those wild diversities
Of chatt'ring strings, by the small size of one
Poor simple voice, raised in a natural tone,
165 She fails, and failing grieves, and grieving dies.
She dies; and leaves her life the victor's prize,
Falling upon his lute; o fit to have
(That lived so sweetly) dead, so sweet a grave!

1646

From Steps to the Temple

To the Infant Martyrs[1]

Go, smiling souls, your new-built cages° break: *their bodies*
In heaven you'll learn to sing, ere here to speak.[2]
Nor let the milky fonts that bathe your thirst
                Be your delay;
5 The place that calls you hence is, at the worst,
                Milk all the way.[3]

1646

I Am the Door[1]

And now th' art set wide ope, the spear's sad art,
Lo! hath unlocked thee at the very heart;
        He to himself (I fear the worst)
            And his own hope
5 Hath shut these doors of heaven, that durst
                Thus set them ope.

1646

---

1. A grand burst of harmony.
1. This epigram and the three following were originally written in Latin in a volume of "Sacred Epigrams" and then rendered in English versions. Epigrams are brief, pithy, witty poems with, as was often said, "a sting in the tail." This poem addresses the Holy Innocents, the infants murdered by Herod in an effort to destroy the new-born Jesus, who was honored as King of the Jews by the Magi (Matthew 2.16–18).
2. Infant comes from the Latin *infans*, meaning "unable to speak."
3. The Milky Way will replace their mothers' milk.
1. "I am the door; by me if any man enter in, he shall be saved" (1 John 10.9).

On the Wounds of Our Crucified Lord

O these wakeful wounds of thine!
   Are they mouths? or are they eyes?
Be they mouths, or be they eyne,[1]
   Each bleeding part some one supplies.[2]

5 Lo! a mouth, whose full-bloomed lips
   At too dear a rate are roses.
Lo! a bloodshot eye! that weeps
   And many a cruel tear discloses.

O thou that on this foot hast laid
10   Many a kiss and many a tear,
Now thou shalt have all repaid,
   Whatsoe'er thy charges were.

This foot hath got a mouth and lips
   To pay the sweet sum of thy kisses;
15 To pay thy tears, an eye that weeps
   Instead of tears such gems as this is.

The difference only this appears
   (Nor can the change offend),
The debt is paid in ruby-tears
20   Which thou in pearls didst lend.

1646

Luke 11.[27][1]
Blessed be the paps which Thou hast sucked

Suppose he had been tabled at thy teats,
   Thy hunger feels not what he eats:
He'll have his teat e're long (a bloody one)[2]
   The Mother then must suck the Son.

1646

---

1. Eyes, an old plural form.
2. I.e., each wound of Christ is either an eye or a mouth.
1. The verse identifies the addressee: "And it came to pass, as he [Jesus] spake these things, a certain woman of the company lifted up her voice, and said unto him, 'Blessed is the womb that bare thee, and the paps which thou hast sucked.'"
2. The wound in Christ's side, making his breast (the fountain of all graces) bloody.

FROM CARMEN DEO NOSTRO

In the Holy Nativity of Our Lord God: A Hymn Sung as by the Shepherds[1]

CHORUS   Come we shepherds whose blest sight
Hath met love's noon in nature's night;
   Come lift we up our loftier song,
And wake the sun that lies too long.

5   To all our world of well-stol'n joy
   He° slept, and dreamt of no such thing,   *the sun*
While we found out heaven's fairer eye,
   And kissed the cradle of our King.
Tell him he rises now too late
10   To show us aught worth looking at.

Tell him we now can show him more
   Than he e'er showed to mortal sight;
Than he himself e'er saw before,
   Which to be seen needs not his light.
15 Tell him, Tityrus, where th' hast been;
Tell him, Thyrsis,[2] what th' hast seen.

TITYRUS   Gloomy night embraced the place
   Where the noble infant lay.
The babe looked up and showed his face:
20   In spite of darkness, it was day.
It was thy day, sweet!° and did rise,   *sweet one*
Not from the east, but from thine eyes.
   CHORUS It was thy day, sweet, *etc.*

THYRSIS Winter chid aloud, and sent
25   The angry north to wage his wars;
The north forgot his fierce intent,
   And left perfumes instead of scars.
By those sweet eyes' persuasive powers,
Where he meant frost, he scattered flowers.
30   CHORUS By those sweet eyes', *etc.*

BOTH   We saw thee in thy balmy° nest,   *eastern, perfumed*
   Young dawn of our eternal day!
We saw thine eyes break from their east
   And chase the trembling shades away.
35 We saw thee; and we blessed the sight.
We saw thee by thine own sweet light.

---

1. See Luke 2.8–20. The poem's form, the inter-weaving of chorus and alternating soloists, is structurally comparable to an oratorio, an Italian musical form that Crashaw may well have known from his sojourns on the Continent. Its form invites comparison with Dryden's "Alexander's Feast"; and its subject with Milton's "On the Morning of Christ's Nativity" (pp. 1901–09). The last version of this poem (1652), printed here, differs considerably from the first version (1646).
2. Tityrus and Thyrsis are typical names for shepherds in classical pastoral poetry; Crashaw here identifies such pastoral figures with the biblical shepherds from the hillsides around Bethlehem.

TITYRUS   Poor world (said I), what wilt thou do
            To entertain this starry stranger?
      Is this the best thou canst bestow,
40   A cold, and not too cleanly, manger?
      Contend, ye powers of heaven and earth,
      To fit a bed for this huge birth.
          CHORUS   Contend, ye powers, *etc.*

THYRSIS   Proud world (said I), cease your contèst,
45   And let the Mighty Babe alone.
      The phoenix builds the phoenix' nest;[3]
          Love's architecture is his own.
      The Babe whose birth embraves° this morn   *makes splendid*
      Made his own bed ere he was born.
50   CHORUS   The Babe whose, *etc.*

TITYRUS   I saw the curl'd drops, soft and slow,
          Come hovering o'er the place's head,
      Offering their whitest sheets of snow
          To furnish the fair Infant's bed:
55   Forbear (said I), be not too bold;
      Your fleece is white, but 'tis too cold.
          CHORUS   Forbear (said I), *etc.*

THYRSIS   I saw the obsequious seraphims[4]
          Their rosy fleece of fire bestow,
60   For well they now can spare their wings
          Since heaven itself lies here below.
      Well done (said I), but are you sure
      Your down so warm will pass for pure?
          CHORUS   Well done (said I), *etc.*

65 TITYRUS   No, no; your King's not yet to seek
          Where to repose his royal head;
      See, see; how soon his new-bloomed cheek
          Twixt mother's breasts is gone to bed.
      Sweet choice (said we), no way but so
70   Not to lie cold, yet sleep in snow.
          CHORUS   Sweet choice (said we), *etc.*

BOTH   We saw thee in thy balmy nest,
          Bright dawn of our eternal day!
      We saw thine eyes break from their east
75   And chase the trembling shades away.
      We saw thee; and we blessed the sight.
      We saw thee, by thine own sweet light.
          CHORUS   We saw thee, *etc.*

---

3. The phoenix is the legendary bird of ancient Egypt, often taken as a symbol for Christ. Only one phoenix existed at any one time; after it had lived five hundred years, it was consumed in flame and a new phoenix rose from the ashes. Christ as Son of God took part in the making of the world long before his incarnation.

4. The highest order of angels, associated with fire because of their ardent love of God.

FULL CHORUS

Welcome, all wonders in one sight!
    Eternity shut in a span.
Summer in winter. Day in night.
    Heaven in earth, and God in man.
Great little one! whose all-embracing birth
Lifts earth to heaven, stoops heaven to earth.

Welcome! though not to gold nor silk,
    To more than Caesar's birthright is;
Two sister seas of virgin milk,
    With many a rarely tempered kiss
That breathes at once both maid° and mother,   *virgin*
Warms in the one, cools in the other.

Welcome! though not to those gay flies[5]
    Gilded i' th' beams of earthly kings—
Slippery souls in smiling eyes;
    But to poor shepherds, homespun things,
Whose wealth's their flock, whose wit to be
Well read in their simplicity.

Yet when young April's husband showers
    Shall bless the fruitful Maia's bed,[6]
We'll bring the firstborn of her flowers
    To kiss thy feet and crown thy head.
To thee, dread Lamb! whose love must keep
The shepherds more than they the sheep.

To Thee, meek Majesty! soft King
    Of simple graces and sweet loves,
Each of us his lamb will bring,
    Each his pair of silver doves,
Till burnt at last in fire of Thy fair eyes,
Ourselves become our own best sacrifice.

1646, 1652

5. Courtiers, stigmatized in three compressed lines as ephemeral, worldly, and hypocritical.
6. The showers of April make fruitful the bed of

May (from Maia, identified with an ancient Italian goddess of the spring).

NON VI.[1]

'Tis not the work of force but skill
To find the way into man's will.
'Tis love alone can hearts unlock.
Who knows the WORD, *he needs not knock.*

TO THE
Noblest & best of Ladies, the Countess of Denbigh.
Persuading her to Resolution in Religion, & to render herself without further delay into the Communion of the Catholic Church.[2]

What heaven-entreated heart is this,
Stands trembling at the gate of bliss,
Holds fast the door, yet dares not venture
Fairly to open it, and enter?
5 Whose definition is a doubt
'Twixt life and death, 'twixt in and out.
Say, lingering fair! why comes the birth
Of your brave soul so slowly forth?
Plead your pretenses (O you strong
10 In weakness!) why you choose so long
In labor of your self to lie,
Not daring quite to live nor die.
Ah, linger not, loved soul! A slow
And late consent was° a long no;   *would be*
15 Who grants at last, long time tried
And did his best to have denied.
What magic bolts, what mystic bars,
Maintain the will in these strange wars!
What fatal° yet fantastic bands   *fateful*
20 Keep the free heart from its own hands!

1. Not by force. Emblems were popular throughout Europe in the late Renaissance. Their elements were generally three: an image, an adage, and a poem explaining the relation of the other two. The image was often an enigma, with the poem often moralizing its various elements. Crashaw's poem to the Countess of Denbigh takes its departure from an enigmatic image but, like the best of the emblem poems, goes far beyond it. The heart here has a hinge on the right, to show that it can be opened, but is sealed on the left with a scroll or phylactery inscribed with letters standing for the Word, which alone enables one to open the heart. Crashaw is said to have engraved this image himself.
2. Susan, Countess of Denbigh, had been widowed in 1643, when her husband was killed fighting for the king. She went to Paris into exile with Queen Henrietta Maria in 1644 and, along with some other ladies attached to the court of that Roman Catholic queen, was herself attracted to that religion. Crashaw himself was a new convert; here he engages in a poetic version of the pressure often exerted by both Catholic priests and Anglican clergy on influential court ladies. As usual, he calls upon the imagery of erotic persuasion to urge her conversion.

So when the year takes cold, we see
Poor waters their own prisoners be;
Fettered and locked up fast they lie
In a sad self-captivity.
25   Th' astonished nymphs their flood's strange fate deplore,
To see themselves their own severer shore.
    Thou that alone canst thaw this cold,
And fetch the heart from its stronghold,
Almighty Love! end this long war,
30   And of a meteor make a star.[3]
O fix this fair indefinite;
And 'mongst thy shafts of sovereign° light   *supreme, effectual*
Choose out that sure decisive dart
Which has the key of this close heart,
35   Knows all the corners of 't, and can control
The self-shut cabinet of an unsearched soul.
O let it be at last love's hour!
Raise this tall trophy of thy power;
Come once the conquering way, not to confute,
40   But kill this rebel-word, *irresolute,*
That so, in spite of all this peevish strength
Of weakness, she may write, *resolved at length.*
    Unfold at length, unfold, fair flower,
And use the season of love's shower.
45   Meet his well-meaning wounds, wise heart,
And haste to drink the wholesome dart,
That healing shaft which heaven till now
Hath in love's quiver hid for you.
O dart of love! arrow of light!
50   O happy you, if it hit right;
It must not fall in vain, it must
Not mark the dry, regardless dust.
Fair one, it is your fate, and brings
Eternal worlds upon its wings.
55   Meet it with wide-spread arms, and see
Its seat your soul's just center be.
Disband dull fears; give faith the day.
To save your life, kill your delay.
It is love's siege, and sure to be
60   Your triumph, though his victory.
'Tis cowardice that keeps this field,
And want of courage not to yield.
Yield, then, O yield, that love may win
The fort at last, and let life in.
65   Yield quickly, lest perhaps you prove
Death's prey before the prize of love.
This fort of your fair self, if 't be not won,
He is repulsed indeed; but you are undone.

1652

3. Meteors were sublunary and therefore irregular and transient; stars, located above the moon, were
regular, fixed, and permanent.

The Flaming Heart

St. Teresa of Avila, a sixteenth-century Spanish mystic and founder of an ascetic order of barefoot Carmelite nuns, was one of the great figures of the Catholic Reformation. Her autobiography, popular throughout Europe and translated into English in 1642 as *The Flaming Heart*, describes not only her practical problems in establishing her order but also a series of ecstatic trances and visitations that represent union with the divine in sensual, indeed erotic, imagery. The Italian sculptor and architect Gianlorenzo Bernini portrayed a mystical experience described in the autobiography in a stunning baroque statue still in the church of Santa Maria della Vittoria, in Rome. It shows the saint in an attitude of ecstatic, swooning abandonment while a juvenile seraph stands over her, about to plunge a golden arrow into her heart. Crashaw may or may not have seen this statue while Bernini was at work on it (it was installed after Crashaw's death), but his poem addresses a painter who produced a picture of this episode conceived much as Bernini presented it.

THE
FLAMING HEART
UPON THE BOOK AND
Picture of the seraphical saint
TERESA,
(AS SHE IS USUALLY EX-
pressed with a SERAPHIM
beside her.)[1]

Well-meaning readers! you that come as friends,
And catch the precious name this piece pretends,°   *puts forward*
Make not too much haste to admire
That fair-cheeked fallacy of fire.
5 That is a seraphim, they say,
And this the great Teresia.
Readers, be ruled by me, and make
Here a well-placed and wise mistake:
You must transpose the picture quite
10 And spell° it wrong to read° it right;   *read / understand*
Read *him* for *her* and *her* for *him*,
And call the saint the seraphim.
   Painter, what didst thou understand,
To put her dart into his hand!
15 See, even the years and size of him
Shows this the mother seraphim.
This is the mistress-flame; and duteous he,
Her happy fireworks here comes down to see.
O most poor-spirited of men!
20 Had thy cold pencil kissed her pen[2]
Thou couldst not so unkindly err
To show us this faint shade for her.
Why, man, this speaks pure mortal frame,
And mocks with female frost love's manly flame.
25 One would suspect thou meant'st to paint
Some weak, inferior, woman saint.
But had thy pale-faced purple took
Fire from the burning cheeks of that bright book,
Thou wouldst on her have heaped up all
30 That could be found seraphical:

---

1. "Seraphim" is in fact the plural form of "seraph." This highest order of angels was thought to burn continuously in the fire of divine love.

2. I.e., if you'd only been properly inspired by her book.

Whate'er this youth of fire wears fair,
Rosy fingers, radiant hair,
Glowing cheek and glistering wings,
All those fair and flagrant° things,   *burning*
35   But before all, that fiery dart
Had filled the hand of this great heart.
     Do then as equal right requires,
Since his the blushes be, and hers the fires,
Resume and rectify thy rude design,
40   Undress thy seraphim into mine.
Redeem this injury of thy art,
Give him the veil, give her the dart.
     Give him the veil, that he may cover
The red cheeks° of a rivaled lover,   *blushes*
45   Ashamed that our world now can show
Nests of new seraphims here below.[3]
     Give her the dart, for it is she
(Fair youth) shoots both thy shaft and thee.
Say, all ye wise and well-pierced hearts
50   That live and die amidst her darts,°   *i.e., her writings*
What is 't your tasteful spirits do prove°   *experience*
In that rare life of her and love?
Say and bear witness. Sends she not
A seraphim at every shot?
55   What magazines of immortal arms there shine!
Heaven's great artillery in each love-spun line.
Give then the dart to her who gives the flame,
Give him the veil who kindly takes the shame.
     But if it be the frequent fate
60   Of worst faults to be fortunate;
If all's prescription,[4] and proud wrong
Hearkens not to an humble song,
For all the gallantry of him,
Give me the suffering seraphim.[5]
65   His be the bravery° of all those bright things,   *splendor*
The glowing cheeks, the glistering wings,
The rosy hand, the radiant dart;
Leave her alone the Flaming Heart.
     Leave her that, and thou shalt leave her
70   Not one loose shaft, but love's whole quiver.
For in love's field was never found
A nobler weapon than a wound.
Love's passives are his activ'st part,
The wounded is the wounding heart.
75   O heart! the equal poise of love's both parts,
Big alike with wounds and darts,

3. Teresa burns on earth in love, as seraphim do in heaven.
4. I.e., settled beforehand, by the decision of the artist.
5. If Teresa can't be transformed into the angel, Crashaw prefers her as the "suffering" lover.

Live in these conquering leaves,[6] live all the same;
And walk through all tongues one triumphant flame.
Live here, great heart; and love and die and kill,
80 And bleed and wound; and yield and conquer still.
Let this immortal life, where'er it comes,
Walk in a crowd of loves and martyrdoms.
Let mystic deaths wait on 't, and wise souls be
The love-slain witnesses of this life of thee.
85 O sweet incendiary! show here thy art,
Upon this carcass of a hard, cold heart;°   *Crashaw's heart*
Let all thy scattered shafts of light, that play
Among the leaves of thy large books of day,[7]
Combined against this breast, at once break in
90 And take away from me myself and sin!
This gracious robbery shall thy bounty be,
And my best fortunes such fair spoils of me.[8]
O thou undaunted daughter of desires!
By all thy dower of lights and fires;
95 By all the eagle in thee, all the dove;[9]
By all thy lives and deaths of love;
By thy large drafts of intellectual day,
And by thy thirsts of love more large than they;
By all thy brim-filled bowls of fierce desire,
100 By thy last morning's draft of liquid fire;
By the full kingdom of that final kiss
That seized thy parting soul, and sealed thee His;
By all the heavens thou hast in Him,
Fair sister of the seraphim,
105 By all of Him we have in thee,
Leave nothing of myself in me!
Let me so read thy life that I
Unto all life of mine may die!

1652

6. I.e., the leaves of St. Teresa's book.
7. Books filled with intellectual and spiritual light.
8. I.e., my best fortune will be to be despoiled in this way.
9. The eagle suggests wisdom and power, for its lofty flight and ability to look into the sun's eye; the dove suggests mercy and gentleness. Cf. Donne's "The Canonization," line 22 (pp. 1377–78).

ROBERT HERRICK
1591–1674

Robert Herrick was the most devoted of the Sons of Ben, though his epigrams and lyrics (like Jonson's) also show the direct influence of classical poets: Horace, Anacreon, Catullus, Tibullus, Ovid, and Martial. Born in London the son of a goldsmith and apprenticed for some years in that craft, Herrick took B.A. and M.A. degrees at Cambridge and consorted in the early 1620s with Jonson and his "tribe," who met regularly at the Apollo Room. After his ordination in 1623, he apparently served as chaplain to various noblemen and in that role joined Buckingham's failed military expedition to rescue French Protestants at Rhé in 1627. In 1630 he was installed as the vicar of Dean Prior in Devonshire. Expelled as a royalist in 1647, he apparently lived in London until the Restoration, when he was reinstated at Dean Prior and remained there until his death.

Herrick's single volume of poems, *Hesperides* (1648), with its appended book of religious poems, *Noble Numbers*, contains over four hundred short poems. Many are love poems on the carpe diem theme—seize the day, time is fleeting, make love now; a famous example is the elegant song "To the Virgins, to Make Much of Time." But Herrick's range is much wider than is sometimes recognized. He moves from the pastoral to the cynical, from an almost rococo elegance to coarse, even vulgar, epigrams, and from the didactic to the dramatic. Also, he derives mythic energy and power from certain recurring motifs. One is metamorphosis, "times transshifting," the transience of all natural things. Another is celebration—festivals and feasts—evoking the social, ritualistic, and even anthropological signficances and energies contained in rural harvest festivals ("The Hock Cart") or the May Day rituals described in what is perhaps his finest poem, "Corinna's Going A-Maying." Yet another is the classical but also perennial ideal of the "good life," defined in his terms as "cleanly wantonness." For Herrick this involves love devoid of high passion (the several mistresses he addresses seem interchangeable and not very real); the pleasures of food, drink, and song; delight in the beauty of surfaces (as in "Upon Julia's Clothes"); and, finally, the creation of poetry as bulwark against the ravages of time.

Published just months before the execution of Charles I, these poems seem merely playful and charming, almost oblivious to the catastrophes of the war. But they are not. Poems celebrating rural feasts and festivals, ceremonial social occasions, and the rituals of good fellowship reinforce the conservative values of social stability, tradition, and order threatened by the Puritans. Several poems that draw upon the Celtic mythology of fairy folk make their feasts, temples, worship, and ceremonies stand in for the forbidden ceremonies of the Laudian church and a life governed by ritual. Still other poems, like "The Hock Cart" and "Corinna's Going A-Maying," celebrate the kind of rural festivals that were at the center of the culture wars between royalists and Puritans. Both James I and Charles I urged such activities in their *Book of Sports* as a means of reinforcing traditional institutions in the countryside and deflecting discontent, while Puritans vigorously opposed them as occasions for drunkenness and licentiousness.

FROM HESPERIDES[1]

The Argument[2] of His Book

I sing of brooks, of blossoms, birds, and bowers,
Of April, May, of June, and July flowers.
I sing of Maypoles, hock carts, wassails, wakes,[3]
Of bridegrooms, brides, and of their bridal cakes.
5 I write of youth, of love, and have access
By these to sing of cleanly wantonness.
I sing of dews, of rains, and, piece by piece,
Of balm, of oil, of spice, and ambergris.[4]
I sing of times trans-shifting,° and I write   *changing*
10 How roses first came red and lilies white.
I write of groves, of twilights, and I sing
The court of Mab and of the fairy king.[5]
I write of hell; I sing (and ever shall)
Of heaven, and hope to have it after all.

Upon the Loss of His Mistresses[1]

I have lost, and lately, these
Many dainty mistresses:
Stately Julia, prime of all;
Sappho next, a principal;
5 Smooth Anthea, for a skin
White and heaven-like crystalline;
Sweet Electra, and the choice
Myrrha, for the lute and voice;
Next Corinna for her wit
10 And the graceful use of it,
With Perilla; all are gone,
Only Herrick's left alone,
For to number sorrows by
Their departures hence, and die.

1. In myth, the Hesperides, or Western Maidens, guarded an orchard and garden, also called Hesperides, in which grew a tree bearing golden apples. Herrick's title suggests that his poems are golden apples from his residence in western Devonshire; the following poems are all from that volume published in 1648.
2. Subject matter, theme.
3. Festive, not funerary, occasions, to celebrate the dedication of a new church. "Hock carts" carried home the last load of the harvest, so they were adorned and celebrated. "Wassails" were Twelfth Night celebrations.
4. A secretion of the sperm whale that is used in making perfume—hence it suggests something rare and delectable.
5. Mab was queen of the fairies and wife of their king, Oberon.
1. The ladies are imaginary, and their names are traditional in classical love poetry and pastoral poetry.

The Vine

I dreamed this mortal part of mine
Was metamorphosed to a vine,
Which, crawling one and every way,
Enthralled my dainty Lucia.[1]
5 Methought, her long small legs and thighs
I with my tendrils did surprise;
Her belly, buttocks, and her waist
By my soft nervelets were embraced.
About her head I writhing hung,
10 And with rich clusters (hid among
The leaves) her temples I behung,
So that my Lucia seemed to me
Young Bacchus ravished by his tree.°   the grapevine
My curls about her neck did crawl,
15 And arms and hands they did enthrall,
So that she could not freely stir
(All parts there made one prisoner).
But when I crept with leaves to hide
Those parts which maids keep unespied,
20 Such fleeting pleasures there I took
That with the fancy I awoke,
And found (ah me!) this flesh of mine
More like a stock° than like a vine.   hard stalk

Dreams

Here we are all, by day; by night, we're hurled
By dreams, each one into a several° world.   separate

Delight in Disorder[1]

A sweet disorder in the dress
Kindles in clothes a wantonness.
A lawn° about the shoulders thrown   fine linen scarf
Into a fine distraction;
5 An erring° lace, which here and there   wandering
Enthralls the crimson stomacher;[2]
A cuff neglectful, and thereby
Ribbons to flow confusedly;
A winning wave, deserving note,

1. For the sake of both rhyme and meter, the name of this lady is given three syllables here; in line 12 it has only two.
1. One of several poems in this period in which women's dress is a means by which to explore the relation of nature and art.
2. An ornamental covering of the chest, worn under the laces of the bodice.

10 In the tempestuous petticoat;
A careless shoestring, in whose tie
I see a wild civility:
Do more bewitch me than when art
Is too precise[3] in every part.

His Farewell to Sack[1]

Farewell, thou thing, time-past so known, so dear
To me as blood to life and spirit; near,
Nay, thou more near than kindred, friend, man, wife,
Male to the female, soul to body, life
5 To quick action, or the warm soft side
Of the resigning° yet resisting bride.   yielding
The kiss of virgins; first fruits of the bed;
Soft speech, smooth touch, the lips, the maidenhead;
These and a thousand sweets could never be
10 So near or dear as thou wast once to me.
O thou, the drink of gods and angels! Wine
That scatterest spirit and lust;° whose purest shine   pleasure
More radiant than the summer's sunbeams shows,
Each way illustrious, brave;° and like to those   splendid
15 Comets we see by night, whose shagg'd[2] portents
Foretell the coming of some dire events,
Or° some full flame which with a pride aspires,   or like to
Throwing about his wild and active fires.
'Tis thou, above nectar, O divinest soul!
20 (Eternal in thyself) that canst control
That which subverts whole nature: grief and care,
Vexation of the mind, and damned despair.
'Tis thou alone who with thy mystic fan[3]
Work'st more than wisdom, art, or nature can
25 To rouse the sacred madness,[4] and awake
The frost-bound blood and spirits, and to make
Them frantic with thy raptures, flashing through
The soul like lightning, and as active too.
'Tis not Apollo can, or those thrice three
30 Castalian sisters sing,[5] if wanting° thee.   lacking
Horace, Anacreon both had lost their fame
Had'st thou not filled them with thy fire and flame.[6]
Phoebean splendor! and thou Thespian spring![7]

3. "Precise" and "precision" were terms used satirically about Puritans. Herrick, in praising feminine disarray, is at one level praising the "sprezzatura," or careless grace, of Cavalier art.
1. Sherry wine, imported from Spain.
2. Hairy, referring to a comet's tail.
3. Instrument for winnowing grain; associated with Bacchus, god of wine.
4. Poetic inspiration or frenzy, often likened to intoxication.

5. Apollo, god of poetry, and the Nine Muses; the Castalian spring on Mount Parnassus was sacred to them.
6. Both Horace and Anacreon wrote about the pleasures of wine.
7. In addition to being an epithet of Apollo, *Phoebus* in Greek means bright, pure. The inhabitants of Thespiae, in Boeotia, worshipped the Muses and held an annual festival in their honor at the spring of Hippocrene, nearby.

Of which sweet swans must drink before they sing
35 Their true-paced numbers and their holy lays°   *songs*
Which makes them worthy cedar and the bays.[8]
But why? why longer do I gaze upon
Thee with the eye of admiration?
Since I must leave thee, and enforced must say
40 To all thy witching beauties, Go, away.
But if thy whimpering looks do ask me why,
Then know that nature bids thee go, not I.
'Tis her erroneous self has made a brain
Uncapable of such a sovereign
45 As is thy powerful self. Prithee not smile,
Or smile more inly, lest thy looks beguile
My vows denounced° in zeal, which thus much show thee, *proclaimed*
That I have sworn but by thy looks to know thee.
Let others drink thee freely, and desire
50 Thee and their lips espoused, while I admire
And love thee but not taste thee. Let my muse
Fail of thy former helps, and only use
Her inadulterate strength. What's done by me
Hereafter shall smell of the lamp, not thee.[9]

Corinna's Going A-Maying

Get up! Get up for shame! The blooming morn
Upon her wings presents the god unshorn.[1]
    See how Aurora throws her fair
    Fresh-quilted colors through the air:[2]
5   Get up, sweet slug-a-bed, and see
    The dew bespangling herb and tree.
Each flower has wept and bowed toward the east
Above an hour since, yet you not dressed;
    Nay, not so much as out of bed?
10   When all the birds have matins° said,   *morning prayer*
    And sung their thankful hymns, 'tis sin,
    Nay, profanation° to keep in,   *impiety*
Whenas a thousand virgins on this day
Spring, sooner than the lark, to fetch in May.[3]

15 Rise, and put on your foliage, and be seen
To come forth, like the springtime, fresh and green,
    And sweet as Flora.[4] Take no care
    For jewels for your gown or hair;

8. Cedar oil was used to preserve papyrus; the poet's crown is woven of bay (i.e., laurel) leaves.
9. To "smell of the lamp" is a proverbial expression for a laborious and uninspired literary production.
1. Apollo, the sun god; sunbeams are seen as his flowing locks.

2. Aurora is goddess of the dawn.
3. On May Day morning, it was the custom to gather whitethorn blossoms and trim the house with them.
4. Flora, Italian goddess of flowers, had her festival in the spring.

Fear not; the leaves will strew
20 Gems in abundance upon you;
Besides, the childhood of the day has kept,
Against° you come, some orient pearls[5] unwept;   *until*
    Come and receive them while the light
    Hangs on the dew-locks of the night,
25 And Titan° on the eastern hill   *the sun*
    Retires himself, or else stands still
Till you come forth. Wash, dress, be brief in praying:
Few beads[6] are best when once we go a-Maying.

Come, my Corinna, come; and, coming, mark
30 How each field turns° a street, each street a park   *turns into*
    Made green and trimmed with trees; see how
    Devotion gives each house a bough
    Or branch: each porch, each door ere this,
    An ark, a tabernacle is,[7]
35 Made up of whitethorn neatly interwove,
As if here were those cooler shades of love.
    Can such delights be in the street
    And open fields, and we not see 't?
    Come, we'll abroad; and let's obey
40 The proclamation[8] made for May,
And sin no more, as we have done, by staying;
But, my Corinna, come, let's go a-Maying.

There's not a budding boy or girl this day
But is got up and gone to bring in May;
45 A deal of youth, ere this, is come
    Back, and with whitethorn laden, home.
    Some have dispatched their cakes and cream
    Before that we have left to dream;
And some have wept, and wooed, and plighted troth,[9]
50 And chose their priest, ere we can cast off sloth.
    Many a green gown[1] has been given,
    Many a kiss, both odd and even;[2]
    Many a glance, too, has been sent
    From out the eye, love's firmament;°   *sky*
55 Many a jest told of the keys betraying
This night, and locks picked; yet we're not a-Maying.

Come, let us go while we are in our prime,
And take the harmless folly of the time.
    We shall grow old apace, and die
60 Before we know our liberty.

5. Pearls from the Orient were especially lustrous, like drops of dew.
6. Rosary beads of the "old" Catholic religion, but more generally, a casual term for prayers.
7. The doorways, ornamented with whitethorn, are like the Hebrew Ark of the Covenant or the sanctuary that housed it (Leviticus 23.40–42: "Ye shall take you on the first day the boughs of goodly trees . . .").
8. Probably a reference to Charles I's "Declaration to his subjects concerning lawful sports."
9. Engaged themselves to marry.
1. Got by rolling in the grass.
2. Kisses are odd and even in kissing games.

Our life is short, and our days run
As fast away as does the sun;
And, as a vapor or a drop of rain,
Once lost, can ne'er be found again,
65   So when or you or I are made
A fable, song, or fleeting shade,
All love, all liking, all delight
Lies drowned with us in endless night.[3]
Then while time serves, and we are but decaying,
70   Come, my Corinna, come, let's go a-Maying.

To the Virgins, to Make Much of Time

Gather ye rosebuds while ye may,
    Old time is still° a-flying;[1]   *always*
And this same flower that smiles today,
    Tomorrow will be dying.

5   The glorious lamp of heaven, the sun,
    The higher he's a-getting,
The sooner will his race be run,
    And nearer he's to setting.

That age is best which is the first,
10   When youth and blood are warmer;
But being spent, the worse, and worst
    Times still succeed the former.

Then be not coy, but use your time,
    And while ye may, go marry;
15   For having lost but once your prime,
    You may forever tarry.

The Hock Cart,[1] or Harvest Home

to the Right Honorable Mildmay, Earl of Westmoreland

Come, sons of summer, by whose toil
We are the lords of wine and oil;[2]
By whose tough labors and rough hands
We rip up first, then reap our lands.

---

3. Some echoes of the apocryphal book Wisdom of Solomon 2.1–8: "For the ungodly said . . . the breath of our nostrils is as smoke, and a little spark . . . and our life shall pass away as the trace of a cloud. . . . Come on therefore . . . Let us crown ourselves with rose buds before they be withered." This carpe diem sentiment is a frequent theme in classical love poetry.
1. Translates the Latin *tempus fugit*.

1. The last cart carrying home the harvest; hence the occasion for a rural festival, traditional throughout Europe. Mildmay Fane, Earl of Westmoreland (1628–1660), was one of Herrick's patrons.
2. Wine and oil are the yields of Mediterranean farming, connecting the English harvest festival to classical pastoral.

5 Crowned with the ears of corn,° now come   *grain*
And, to the pipe, sing harvest home.
Come forth, my lord, and see the cart
Dressed up with all the country art.
See here a maukin,° there a sheet,   *scarecrow*
10 As spotless pure as it is sweet,
The horses, mares, and frisking fillies
Clad all in linen, white as lilies,
The harvest swains° and wenches bound   *young men*
For joy to see the hock-cart crowned.
15   About the cart, hear how the rout
Of rural younglings raise the shout,
Pressing before, some coming after,
Those with a shout and these with laughter.
Some bless the cart, some kiss the sheaves,
20 Some prank° them up with oaken leaves;   *adorn*
Some cross the fill-horse,[3] some with great
Devotion stroke the home-borne wheat;
While other rustics, less attent
To prayers than to merriment,
25 Run after with their breeches rent.
   Well, on, brave boys, to your lord's hearth,
Glittering with fire; where, for your mirth,
Ye shall see first the large and chief
Foundation of your feast, fat beef;
30 With upper stories, mutton, veal,
And bacon,° which makes full the meal,   *pork*
With several dishes standing by,
As here a custard, there a pie,
And here all-tempting frumenty.°   *pudding*
35 And for to make the merry cheer,
If smirking° wine be wanting° here,   *sparkling / lacking*
There's that which drowns all care, stout beer:
Which freely drink to your lord's health,
Then to the plow (the common-wealth),
40 Next to your flails, your fans,[4] your vats,
Then to the maids with wheaten hats,
To the rough sickle and crook'd scythe,
Drink, frolic boys, till all be blithe.
   Feed, and grow fat; and, as ye eat,
45 Be mindful that the lab'ring neat,°   *cattle*
As you, may have their fill of meat.[5]
And know, besides, ye must revoke°   *call back*
The patient ox unto his yoke,
And all go back unto the plow
50 And harrow, though they're hanged up now.
And you must know, your lord's word's true,

3. The fill-horse is harnessed between the shafts of the cart. Crossing the horse and kissing the sheaves suggest the persistence of pre-Reformation rituals in the countryside.
4. "Flails" are threshing instruments; "fans" are used to winnow grain from chaff. The plow is the common source of everybody's wealth. In line with the anti-Puritan sentiments of the whole poem, the word "commonwealth," in this communal and earthy sense, invites a contrast with Puritan republican theories.
5. Food (grain or hay).

Feed him ye must whose food fills you,
And that this pleasure is like rain,
Not sent ye for to drown your pain
55 But for to make it spring again.[6]

How Roses Came Red[1]

Roses at first were white,
    Till they could not agree,
Whether my Sappho's breast,
    Or they more white should be.

5   But being vanquished quite,
    A blush their cheeks bespread;
Since which (believe the rest)
    The roses first came red.

Upon the Nipples of Julia's Breast

Have ye beheld (with much delight)
A red rose peeping through a white?
Or else a cherry (double graced)
Within a lily center-placed?
5   Or ever marked° the pretty beam   observed
A strawberry shows half drowned in cream?
Or seen rich rubies blushing through
A pure smooth pearl, and orient° too?   iridescent
So like to this, nay all the rest,
10 Is each neat niplet of her breast.

Upon Jack and Jill. Epigram[2]

When Jill complains to Jack for want of meat,
Jack kisses Jill, and bids her freely eat.
Jill says, Of what? Says Jack, On that sweet kiss,
Which full of nectar and ambrosia is,
5   The food of poets. So I thought, says Jill;
That makes them look so lank, so ghost-like still.
Let poets feed on air or what they will;
Let me feed full till that I fart, says Jill.

---

6. Spring is heralded by rain, but the lines also point to the continual renewal of the agricultural worker's pain and labor.
1. This poem and several others in the collection present minitransformations in witty allusion to Ovid's epiclike *Metamorphoses*.
2. Cf. Jonson, "On Giles and Joan," pp. 1541–42.

To Marigolds[3]

Give way, an° ye be ravished by the sun,   *if*
And hang the head whenas the act is done.
Spread as he spreads; wax less as he does wane,
And as he shuts, close up to maids° again.   *virgins*

His Prayer to Ben Jonson

When I a verse shall make,
Know I have prayed thee,
For old religion's sake,[4]
Saint Ben to aid me.

5   Make the way smooth for me
When I, thy Herrick,
Honoring thee, on my knee,
Offer my lyric.

Candles I'll give to thee
10   And a new altar;
And thou Saint Ben shalt be
Writ in my psalter.

The Bad Season Makes the Poet Sad[5]

Dull to myself and almost dead to these
My many fresh and fragrant mistresses,
Lost to all music now, since every thing
Puts on the semblance here of sorrowing.
5   Sick is the land to the heart, and doth endure
More dangerous faintings by her desperate cure.
But if that golden age would come again,
And Charles here rule as he before did reign,
If smooth and unperplexed the seasons were,
10   As when the sweet Maria livèd here,
I should delight to have my curls half drowned
In Tyrian dews,[6] and head with roses crowned,
And once more yet (ere I am laid out dead)
Knock at a star with my exalted head.[7]

3. The English pot marigold closes its flowers at dusk.
4. Herrick plays on the fact that Jonson was for a while a Catholic (of the "old religion"), as well as a saint in the mock religion of poetry.
5. The bad season is evidently political, not meteorological. Line 10 refers to Charles's queen, Henrietta Maria, so the poem must have been written after 1644, when she was forced to retire to France.
6. Perfume from Tyre was one of many Middle Eastern luxuries proverbial in Roman times.
7. The last line translates literally the last line of Horace's first ode, to his patron, Maecenas. Herrick hopes once more to have enlightened readers and an enlightened patron, so that he can feel something of Horace's exaltation.

The Night-Piece, to Julia

Her eyes the glowworm lend thee,
The shooting stars attend thee;
   And the elves also,
   Whose little eyes glow
5 Like the sparks of fire, befriend thee.

No Will-o'th'-Wisp mislight thee,[8]
Nor snake or slowworm° bite thee;   *adder*
   But on, on thy way,
   Not making a stay,
10 Since ghost there's none to affright thee.

Let not the dark thee cumber;
What though the moon does slumber?
   The stars of the night
   Will lend thee their light
15 Like tapers clear without number.

Then, Julia, let me woo thee,
Thus, thus to come unto me:
   And when I shall meet
   Thy silv'ry feet,
20 My soul I'll pour into thee.

Upon His Verses

What offspring other men have got,
The how, where, when I question not.
These are the children I have left;
Adopted some, none got by theft.
5 But all are touched (like lawful plate)[9]
And no verse illegitimate.

His Return to London

From the dull confines of the drooping west,[1]
To see the day spring from the pregnant east,
Ravished in spirit, I come, nay more, I fly
To thee, blest place of my nativity!
5 Thus, thus with hallowed foot I touch the ground

8. Will-o'-the-wisp traditionally draws travelers astray with false lights.
9. A special variety of quartz, known as basanite, was used to test gold and silver objects; the color of the smear left on the touchstone revealed its purity.
1. Devonshire, where his parish, Dean Prior, was located.

With thousand blessings by thy fortune crowned.
O fruitful Genius![2] that bestowest here
An everlasting plenty, year by year.
O place! O people! Manners! framed to please
10 All nations, customs, kindreds, languages!
I am a free-born Roman;[3] suffer then
That I amongst you live a citizen.
London my home is, though by hard fate sent
Into a long and irksome banishment;
15 Yet since called back, henceforward let me be,
O native country, repossessed by thee!
For, rather than I'll to the west return,
I'll beg of thee first here to have mine urn.
Weak I am grown, and must in short time fall;
20 Give thou my sacred relics burial.

1647?

Upon Julia's Clothes

Whenas in silks my Julia goes,°   *walks*
Then, then, methinks, how sweetly flows
That liquefaction of her clothes.

Next, when I cast mine eyes and see
5   That brave° vibration each way free,   *splendid*
Oh, how that glittering taketh me!

Upon Prue, His Maid[4]

In this little urn is laid
Prudence Baldwin, once my maid,
From whose happy spark here let
Spring the purple violet.

To His Book's End[5]

To his book's end this last line he'd have placed:
Jocund° his muse was, but his life was chaste.   *merry, sprightly*

---

2. In classical Rome, the genius of a place was
its guardian deity.
3. An ancient Roman born in the city was said to
be "free of it," i.e., entitled to its special rights

and privileges, including residence there.
4. This is an odd epitaph, since Prudence Baldwin died four years after Herrick.
5. The last poem of *Hesperides*.

From Noble Numbers

To His Conscience[6]

Can I not sin, but thou wilt be
My private protonotary?[7]
Can I not woo thee to pass by
A short and sweet iniquity?
5   I'll cast a mist and cloud upon
My delicate transgression
So utter dark as that no eye
Shall see the hugged° impiety.   cherished
Gifts blind the wise,[8] and bribes do please
10 And wind° all other witnesses: pervert
And wilt not thou with gold be tied
To lay thy pen and ink aside?
That in the mirk° and tongueless night   black, murky
Wanton I may, and thou not write?
15 It will not be; and therefore now
For times to come I'll make this vow,
From aberrations to live free,
So I'll not fear the Judge, or thee.

Another Grace for a Child

Here a little child I stand,
Heaving up my either hand;
Cold as paddocks° though they be,   frogs
Here I lift them up to thee,
5   For a benison° to fall   blessing
On our meat and on us all. *Amen.*

6. This and the following poem are from *Noble
Numbers*, the collection of Herrick's religious
poems that was bound together with *Hesperides*.

7. Chief recording clerk of a court.
8. Echoes Deuteronomy 16.19: "a gift doth blind
the eyes of the wise."

THOMAS CAREW
1595–1640

Thomas Carew (pronounced *Carey*) is perhaps the Cavalier poet with the greatest range and complexity. He gained his B.A. at Merton College, Oxford, studied law (his father's profession), held several minor positions in the diplomatic and
court bureaucracy, fought for his king in the ill-fated expedition against the Scots

(the First Bishops' War, 1639), and died of syphilis. A brilliant, dissolute young man, he was a great favorite with Charles I and Henrietta Maria.

His *Poems* (1640), published posthumously, are witty and often outrageous, but their emphasis on natural sensuality and the need for union between king and subjects encodes a serious critique of the Neoplatonic artifice of the Caroline court. Carew's spectacular court masque, *Coelum Britannicum*, performed at the Banqueting Hall at Whitehall on February 18, 1633, was based on a philosophical dialogue by Giordano Bruno. It combines a dramatization of serious social and political problems in the antimasque with wildly hyperbolic praise of the monarchs in the main masque. As a love poet Carew sometimes plays off Donnean situations and poems; elsewhere, as in "Ask me no more where Jove bestows," he imitates Jonson's most purely lyric vein. But his characteristic note is one of frank sexuality and emotional realism. "The Rapture," probably the most erotic poem of the era, describes the sexual act under the sustained metaphor of a voyage. He also wrote country-house poems that, unlike Jonson's "To Penshurst," describe Saxham and Wrest as places of refuge from the mounting dangers outside their gates. Carew's poems of literary criticism provide astute commentary on contemporary authors. "To Ben Jonson" evaluates Jonson with Jonsonian precision and judiciousness in weighing out praise and blame. His famous "Elegy" on Donne praises Donne's innovation, avoidance of classical tags, "giant fancy," and especially his tough masculinity of style, a feature Carew imitates in this poem's energetic runover couplets, quick changes of rhythms and images, and vigorous "strong lines."

An Elegy upon the Death of the Dean of Paul's, Dr. John Donne[1]

>   Can we not force from widowed poetry,
> Now thou art dead, great Donne, one elegy
> To crown thy hearse? Why yet dare we not trust,
> Though with unkneaded dough-baked[2] prose, thy dust,
> 5 Such as the unscissored[3] churchman from the flower
> Of fading rhetoric, short-lived as his hour,
> Dry as the sand that measures it,[4] should lay
> Upon thy ashes on the funeral day?
> Have we no voice, no tune? Didst thou dispense°   *lay out, use up*
> 10 Through all our language both the words and sense?
> 'Tis a sad truth. The pulpit may her plain
> And sober Christian precepts still retain;
> Doctrines it may, and wholesome uses,° frame,   *customs*
> Grave homilies and lectures; but the flame
> 15 Of thy brave soul, that shot such heat and light
> As burnt our earth and made our darkness bright,
> Committed holy rapes upon our will,
> Did through the eye the melting heart distill,
> And the deep knowledge of dark truths so teach

1. First appearing with a number of other elegies in the 1633 edition of Donne's poems, then reprinted in 1640 with some changes, Carew's tribute is notable among 17th-century poems on poetry for its technical precision.

2. I.e., tedious and flat.
3. With uncut hair.
4. The hourglass was used by preachers to keep track of time.

20 As sense might judge what fancy could not reach,[5]
Must be desired° forever. So the fire   *missed*
That fills with spirit and heat the Delphic choir,[6]
Which, kindled first by thy Promethean[7] breath,
Glowed here a while, lies quenched now in thy death.
25 The Muses' garden, with pedantic weeds
O'erspread, was purged by thee; the lazy seeds
Of servile imitation thrown away,
And fresh invention planted; thou didst pay
The debts of our penurious bankrupt age—
30 Licentious thefts, that make poetic rage
A mimic fury, when our souls must be
Possessed or with Anacreon's ecstasy,
Or Pindar's,[8] not their own. The subtle cheat
Of sly exchanges, and the juggling feat
35 Of two-edged words,[9] or whatsoever wrong
By ours was done the Greek or Latin tongue,
Thou hast redeemed, and opened us a mine
Of rich and pregnant fancy, drawn a line
Of masculine expression, which had good
40 Old Orpheus[1] seen, or all the ancient brood
Our superstitious fools admire, and hold
Their lead more precious than thy burnished gold,
Thou hadst been their exchequer,° and no more   *treasury*
They in each other's dust had raked for ore.
45 Thou shalt yield no precedence but of time
And the blind fate of language, whose tuned chime°   *rhyme*
More charms the outward sense; yet thou mayest claim
From so great disadvantage greater fame,
Since to the awe of thy imperious wit
50 Our stubborn language bends, made only fit
With her tough thick-ribbed hoops to gird about
Thy giant fancy, which had proved too stout
For their soft melting phrases. As in time
They had the start, so did they cull the prime
55 Buds of invention many a hundred year,
And left the rifled fields, besides the fear
To touch their harvest; yet from those bare lands
Of what is purely thine, thy only hands
(And that thy smallest work) have gleanèd more
60 Than all those times and tongues could reap before.
   But thou art gone, and thy strict laws will be
Too hard for libertines in poetry.
They will repeal° the goodly exiled train   *recall from banishment*
Of gods and goddesses, which in thy just reign

---

5. I.e., so that things too abstract to be imagined
might be made plain to sense.
6. The choir of poets, inspired by Apollo, whose
oracle was at Delphi.
7. Prometheus stole fire from heaven to aid
humankind.
8. Anacreon (6th and 5th centuries B.C.E.) and
Pindar (first half of the 5th century B.C.E.) were
famous Greek lyric poets.
9. "Sly exchanges": Carew seems to refer to the
habit of using English words in their Latin
senses. "Two-edged words" might be puns, but
these were a favorite device of Donne's.
1. Ancient Greek poet and prophet, often used
as the type of all poets.

65　Were banished nobler poems; now with these
　　The silenced tales o' th' *Metamorphoses*[2]
　　Shall stuff their lines and swell the windy page,
　　Till verse, refined by thee in this last age,
　　Turn ballad-rhyme, or those old idols be
70　Adored again with new apostasy.
　　　　O pardon me, that break with untuned verse
　　The reverend silence that attends thy hearse,
　　Whose awful° solemn murmurs were to thee,　　　　　　　*awesome*
　　More than these faint lines, a loud elegy,
75　That did proclaim in a dumb eloquence
　　The death of all of the arts, whose influence,
　　Grown feeble, in these panting numbers° lies　　　　　　*verses*
　　Gasping short-winded accents, and so dies:
　　So doth the swiftly turning wheel not stand
80　In th' instant we withdraw the moving hand,
　　But some small time maintain a faint weak course
　　By virtue of the first impulsive force;
　　And so whilst I cast on thy funeral pile
　　Thy crown of bays,° oh, let it crack awhile　　　　　　*poet's crown*
85　And spit disdain, till the devouring flashes
　　Suck all the moisture up; then turn to ashes.
　　　　I will not draw the envy to engross
　　All thy perfections, or weep all our loss;
　　Those are too numerous for an elegy,
90　And this too great to be expressed by me.
　　Though every pen should take a distinct part,
　　Yet art thou theme enough to tire° all art.[3]　　　　　*exhaust*
　　Let others carve the rest; it shall suffice
　　I on thy tomb this epitaph incise:

95　　*Here lies a king, that ruled as he thought fit*
　　　The universal monarchy of wit;
　　　Here lie two flamens,[4] *and both those the best:*
　　　Apollo's first, at last the true God's priest.

　　　　　　　　　　　　　　　　　　　　　1633, 1640

To Ben Jonson

Upon occasion of his Ode of Defiance annexed to his play of The New Inn[1]

'Tis true, dear Ben, thy just chastising hand
Hath fixed upon the sotted age a brand
To their swoll'n pride and empty scribbling due.

---

2. Ovid's tales in the *Metamorphoses* were a favorite stockpile of poetic properties for Renaissance poets, but Donne did not use them.
3. This line and the preceding one were omitted in the 1640 edition.
4. Priests of ancient Rome: Donne was first a priest of Apollo, the pagan god of poetry, and later a Christian priest.
1. Jonson's late play *The New Inn* was hissed from the stage in 1629 and published in 1631 with an angry "Ode to Himself" (pp. 1558–59) prefixed. Carew's remonstration must have been written shortly thereafter.

It can nor judge nor write; and yet 'tis true
5   Thy comic Muse from the exalted line
Touched by thy *Alchemist*[2] doth since decline
From that her zenith, and foretells a red
And blushing evening when she goes to bed—
Yet such as shall outshine the glimmering light
10 With which all stars shall gild the following night.
Nor think it much (since all thy eaglets may
Endure the sunny trial)[3] if we say,
This hath the stronger wing, or that doth shine
Tricked up in fairer plumes, since all are thine.
15 Who hath his flock of cackling geese compared
With thy tuned choir of swans? Or who hath dared
To call thy births deformed? But if thou bind
By city-custom, or by gavelkind,[4]
In equal shares thy love to all thy race,
20 We may distinguish of their sex and place:
Though one hand shape them and though one brain strike
Souls into all, they are not all alike.
Why should the follies then of this dull age
Draw from thy pen such an immodest rage
25 As seems to blast thy else-immortal bays,°   *the poet's crown*
When thine own tongue proclaims thy itch of praise?
Such thirst will argue drought. No, let be hurled
Upon thy works by the detracting world
What malice can suggest; let the rout° say   *rabble*
30 The running sands that, ere thou make a play,
Count the slow minutes might a Goodwin frame[5]
To swallow when th' hast done thy shipwrecked name.
Let them the dear° expense of oil upbraid,°   *extravagant / scold*
Sucked by thy watchful lamp that hath betrayed
35 To theft the blood of martyred authors, spilt
Into thy ink, while thou growest pale with guilt.[6]
Repine° not at the taper's thrifty waste,   *fret*
That sleeks thy terser poems; nor is haste
Praise, but excuse; and if thou overcome
40 A knotty writer, bring the booty home;
Nor think it theft if the rich spoils so torn
From conquered authors be as trophies worn.
Let others glut on the extorted praise
Of vulgar breath: trust thou to after days.
45 Thy labored works shall live when Time devours
Th' abortive offspring of their hasty hours.
Thou art not of their rank, the quarrel lies

---

2. Jonson's play (1610) about three confidence
tricksters.
3. To make sure the young birds in his nest are
genuine eaglets, the eagle is reputed to fly with
them up toward the sun; true eagles will not be
blinded by the rays.
4. "City-custom" (i.e., London City custom) and
"gavelkind" (a system of land tenure once common in Kent) were two legal ways of dividing an
estate equally among all the heirs—as opposed

to the normal English rule of primogeniture
(everything to the eldest son).
5. Goodwin Sands were shoals in the Strait of
Dover, shifty and treacherous, on which many
ships were lost. Jonson's slowness in composition
was proverbial.
6. The other great charge against Jonson was
that he copied or translated too liberally from
other authors.

Within thine own verge[7]—then let this suffice,
The wiser world doth greater thee confess
50   Than all men else, than thy self only less.

ca. 1631   1640

A Song[1]

Ask me no more where Jove bestows,
When June is past, the fading rose;
For in your beauties orient° deep,   *lustrous*
These flowers, as in their causes, sleep.[2]

5   Ask me no more whither do stray
The golden atoms of the day;
For in pure love heaven did prepare
Those powders to enrich your hair.

Ask me no more whither doth haste
10   The nightingale when May is past;
For in your sweet dividing[3] throat
She winters, and keeps warm her note.

Ask me no more where those stars light,
That downwards fall in dead of night;
15   For in your eyes they sit, and there
Fixèd become, as in their sphere.

Ask me no more if east or west
The phoenix builds her spicy nest;[4]
For unto you at last she flies,
20   And in your fragrant bosom dies.

                                                    1640

To Saxham[1]

Though frost and snow locked from mine eyes
That beauty which without door lies,
Thy gardens, orchards, walks, that so

---

7. I.e., within your own territory, against yourself. Duels cannot properly take place between two men of different rank, and as Jonson is out of everyone else's class, he can fight only himself.
1. Widely popular and several times set to music, this poem exists in different forms. Like Donne's "Go and catch a falling star" (pp. 1374–75), it is built around a series of impossibilities.
2. Aristotelian philosophy suggested that objects often lay latent in their causes. The lady is a summation of last summer and cause of the next one.
3. Warbling (from "division," or rapid melodic passage).
4. The phoenix, a legendary bird, builds her nest from spicy shrubs. She dies every five hundred years and a new bird springs from her ashes.
1. Little Saxham, near Bury Saint Edmunds, in Suffolk, was the country residence of Sir John Crofts, a friend of Carew's. Compare Jonson's "To Penshurst" (pp. 1546–48).

I might not all thy pleasures know,
5   Yet, Saxham, thou within thy gate
Art of thyself so delicate,
So full of native sweets, that bless
Thy roof with inward happiness,
As neither from nor to thy store
10   Winter takes aught, or spring adds more.
The cold and frozen air had starved°   *killed*
Much poor, if not by thee preserved,
Whose prayers have made thy table blest
With plenty, far above the rest.
15   The season hardly did afford
Coarse cates° unto thy neighbors' board,   *food*
Yet thou hadst dainties, as the sky
Had been thy only volary;°   *aviary*
Or else the birds, fearing the snow
20   Might to another Deluge[2] grow,
The pheasant, partridge, and the lark
Flew to thy house, as to the Ark.
The willing ox of himself came
Home to the slaughter, with the lamb,
25   And every beast did thither bring
Himself, to be an offering.
The scaly herd more pleasure took
Bathed in thy dish, than in the brook;
Water, earth, air did all conspire
30   To pay their tributes to thy fire;
Whose cherishing flames themselves divide
Through every room, where they deride
The night and cold abroad; whilst they,
Like suns within, keep endless day.
35   Those cheerful beams send forth their light
To all that wander in the night,
And seem to beckon from aloof
The weary pilgrim to thy roof,
Where, if refreshed, he will away,
40   He's fairly welcome; or if stay,
Far more; which he shall hearty find
Both from the master and the hind.°   *servant*
The stranger's welcome each man there
Stamped on his cheerful brow doth wear,
45   Nor doth this welcome or his cheer
Grow less 'cause he stays longer here;
There's none observes, much less repines,
How often this man sups or dines.
Thou hast no porter at the door
50   T'examine or keep back the poor,
Nor locks nor bolts: thy gates have been
Made only to let strangers in;
Untaught to shut, they do not fear

2. Noah's Flood (Genesis 7).

To stand wide open all the year,
55 Careless who enters, for they know
Thou never didst deserve a foe;
And as for thieves, thy bounty's such,
They cannot steal, thou giv'st so much.

A Rapture

I will enjoy thee now, my Celia, come
And fly with me to love's Elysium.[1]
The giant, Honor, that keeps cowards out,
Is but a masquer,° and the servile rout°   actor / rabble
5 Of baser subjects only bend in vain
To the vast idol, whilst the nobler train°   procession
Of valiant lovers daily sail between
The huge Colossus' legs,[2] and pass unseen
Unto the blissful shore. Be bold and wise,
10 And we shall enter; the grim Swiss[3] denies
Only tame fools a passage, that not know
He is but form and only frights in show
The duller eyes that look from far; draw near,
And thou shalt scorn what we were wont° to fear.   used
15 We shall see how the stalking pageant[4] goes
With borrowed legs, a heavy load to those
That made and bear him—not as we once thought
The seed of gods, but a weak model wrought
By greedy men, that seek to enclose the common,
20 And within private arms empale free woman.[5]
    Come then, and mounted on the wings of love,
We'll cut the flitting air and soar above
The monster's head, and in the noblest seats
Of those blessed shades, quench and renew our heats.
25 There shall the queens of love and innocence,
Beauty and nature banish all offense
From our close ivy twines, there I'll behold
Thy barèd snow and thy unbraided gold.
There my enfranchised hand on every side
30 Shall o'er thy naked polished ivory slide.
No curtain there, though of transparent lawn,°   fine linen
Shall be before thy virgin treasure drawn,
But the rich mine to the inquiring eye
Exposed, shall ready still° for mintage lie,   always

1. In classical mythology, the abode of the blessed spirits.
2. Tradition had it that the ancient Colossus of Rhodes bestrode the entrance to that harbor, so that ships entering or leaving passed between its legs.
3. The pope's Swiss Guard were renowned for their height.
4. Figure in a pageant, make-believe giant.
5. To "empale" is to surround with a fence, but the word has phallic overtones as well. The "enclosing" for landowners' private use of pastureland traditionally open to the whole community ("the commons") was a political issue in 17th-century England.

35　And we will coin young Cupids.[6] There a bed
　　Of roses and fresh myrtles shall be spread
　　Under the cooler shade of cypress groves;
　　Our pillows, of the down of Venus' doves,[7]
　　Whereon our panting limbs we'll gently lay
40　In the faint respites of our active play,
　　That so our slumbers may in dreams have leisure
　　To tell the nimble fancy our past pleasure,
　　And so our souls that cannot be embraced
　　Shall the embraces of our bodies taste.
45　Meanwhile the bubbling stream shall court the shore,
　　Th' enamored chirping wood-choir shall adore
　　In varied tunes the deity of love;
　　The gentle blasts of western winds shall move
　　The trembling leaves, and through their close boughs breathe
50　Still° music, while we rest ourselves beneath　　　　　　　　　*soft*
　　Their dancing shade; till a soft murmur, sent
　　From souls entranced in amorous languishment
　　Rouse us, and shoot into our veins fresh fire
　　Till we in their sweet ecstasy expire.
55　　　Then, as the empty bee, that lately bore
　　Into the common treasure all her store,
　　Flies 'bout the painted field with nimble wing,
　　Deflowering the fresh virgins of the spring,
　　So will I rifle all the sweets that dwell
60　In my delicious paradise, and swell
　　My bag with honey, drawn forth by the power
　　Of fervent kisses from each spicy flower.
　　I'll seize the rosebuds in their perfumed bed,
　　The violet knots, like curious mazes spread
65　O'er all the garden, taste the ripened cherry,
　　The warm, firm apple, tipped with coral berry.
　　Then will I visit with a wandering kiss
　　The vale of lilies and the bower of bliss,
　　And where the beauteous region both divide
70　Into two milky ways, my lips shall slide
　　Down those smooth alleys, wearing as I go
　　A track° for lovers on the printed snow.　　　　　　　　　*path*
　　Thence climbing o'er the swelling Apennine,
　　Retire into thy grove of eglantine,°　　　　　　　　　　*sweetbriar*
75　Where I will all those ravished sweets distill
　　Through love's alembic,[8] and with chemic skill
　　From the mixed mass one sovereign balm[9] derive,
　　Then bring that great elixir to thy hive.
　　　　Now in more subtle wreaths I will entwine
80　My sinewy thighs, my legs and arms with thine;
　　Thou like a sea of milk shalt lie displayed,

---

6. Behind this metaphor of mine, mint, and coin lies the ancient belief that in the creation of children woman contributes matter, and man, form (*materia and forma*).
7. Venus rides in a chariot drawn by a yoke of doves.

8. I.e., retort—a vessel used for distilling.
9. According to alchemical doctrine, skilled distillation could extract from common metals not only the philosopher's stone but an ointment ("sovereign balm"), good to prevent as well as to cure all diseases whatever.

Whilst I the smooth, calm ocèan invade
With such a tempest as when Jove of old
Fell down on Danaë in a storm of gold.[1]
85   Yet my tall pine shall in the Cyprian[2] strait
Ride safe at anchor and unlade her freight;
My rudder with thy bold hand like a tried
And skillful pilot thou shalt steer, and guide
My bark° into love's channel, where it shall   vessel
90   Dance as the bounding waves do rise or fall.
Then shall thy circling arms embrace and clip°   clasp
My naked body, and thy balmy lip
Bathe me in juice of kisses, whose perfume
Like a religious incense shall consume
95   And send up holy vapors to those powers
That bless our loves and crown our sportful hours,
That with such halcyon[3] calmness fix our souls
In steadfast peace, as no affright controls.°   overpowers
There no rude sounds shake us with sudden starts,
100 No jealous ears, when we unrip our hearts,
Suck our discourse in, no observing spies
This blush, that glance traduce;° no envious eyes   slander
Watch our close meetings, nor are we betrayed
To rivals by the bribèd chambermaid.
105 No wedlock bonds unwreathe our twisted loves,
We seek no midnight arbor, no dark groves
To hide our kisses; there the hated name
Of husband, wife, lust, modest, chaste, or shame
Are vain and empty words, whose very sound
110 Was never heard in the Elysian ground.
All things are lawful there that may delight
Nature or unrestrainèd appetite.
Like and enjoy, to will and act is one;
We only sin when love's rites are not done.
115   The Roman Lucrece there reads the divine
Lectures of love's great master, Aretine,
And knows as well as Laïs how to move
Her pliant body in the act of love.[4]
To quench the burning ravisher, she hurls
120 Her limbs into a thousand winding curls,
And studies artful postures, such as be
Carved on the bark of every neighboring tree
By learnèd hands, that so adorned the rind
Of those fair plants, which, as they lay entwined
125 Have fanned their glowing fires. The Grecian dame
That in her endless web toiled for a name
As fruitless as her work doth there display

1. Zeus (or Jove) wooed Danaë in a shower of
gold, begetting Perseus.
2. Cyprus was reputed the birthplace of the goddess of love, Venus, sometimes called simply "the
Cyprian." "Pine": mast, and by metonymy, ship.
3. While the halcyon (a legendary sea bird)
nests on the waves, the ocean remains calm.

4. In Elysium, Lucrece (chastest of Roman
matrons, who committed suicide to atone for the
disgrace of her rape by Tarquin) reads Aretino
(bawdiest of Italian pornographers) to provoke
her attacker to new efforts. Laïs was a famous
prostitute of Corinth.

Herself before the youth of Ithaca,
And th' amorous sport of gamesome nights prefer
130 Before dull dreams of the lost traveler.[5]
Daphne hath broke her bark, and that swift foot
Which th' angry gods had fastened with a root
To the fixed earth, doth now unfettered run
To meet th' embraces of the youthful sun.[6]
135 She hangs upon him like his Delphic lyre,[7]
Her kisses blow the old and breathe new fire;
Full of her god, she sings inspired lays,
Sweet odes of love, such as deserve the bays
Which she herself was.[8] Next her, Laura lies
140 In Petrarch's learnèd arms, drying those eyes
That did in such sweet smooth-paced numbers° flow,   verses
As made the world enamored of his woe.[9]
These and ten thousand beauties more, that died
Slave to the tyrant, now enlarged,[1] deride
145 His canceled laws, and for their time misspent
Pay into love's exchequer° double rent.   treasury
    Come then, my Celia, we'll no more forbear
To taste our joys, struck with a panic fear,
But will depose from his imperious sway
150 This proud usurper and walk free as they,
With necks unyoked; nor is it just that he
Should fetter your soft sex with chastity,
Which Nature made unapt for abstinence;
When yet this false impostor can dispense
155 With human justice and with sacred right,
And maugre° both their laws, command me fight   in spite of
With rivals or with emulous loves, that dare
Equal with thine their mistress' eyes or hair.
If thou complain of wrong, and call my sword
160 To carve out thy revenge, upon that word
He° bids me fight and kill, or else he brands   i.e., Honor
With marks of infamy my coward hands.
And yet religion bids from bloodshed fly,
And damns me for that act. Then tell me why
165 This goblin Honor which the world adores
Should make men atheists and not women whores.

1640

5. Penelope was the faithful wife of Odysseus ("the lost traveler"); during the twenty years he was away (at Troy and on the way back), she fended off her importunate suitors by weaving an endless web—she unwove by night what she wove by day—which she said she had to finish before she could marry again. But in Elysium, she welcomes "the youth of Ithaca" (the suitors) and enjoys "gamesome nights" with them.
6. Closely pursued by Apollo, god of poetry and the sun, Daphne cried out to her father, the river god Peneus, who turned her into a laurel bush or bay tree so that she could get away from Apollo.

7. The shrine of Apollo was at Delphi; he carries a lyre as an emblem of poetic harmony.
8. The songs she sings deserve the laurel crown of poetry—the laurel she had become.
9. Petrarch (1304–1374) wrote his celebrated sonnet sequence to Laura, mourning his unsatisfied desire in the first part, and Laura's death in the second.
1. The inhabitants of Elysium are liberated ("enlarged") from the prison of "the tyrant" Honor, in which woman must be chaste and men must fight duels.

RICHARD LOVELACE
1618–1657

The quintessential Cavalier, Richard Lovelace was described by a contemporary as "the most amiable and beautiful person that ever eye beheld." Born into a wealthy Kentish family, he was educated at Oxford and fought for Charles I in Scotland (in both expeditions, 1639 and 1640). He shared with his king a serious interest in art, especially the paintings of Rubens, Van Dyck, and Lely. He was imprisoned for a few months in 1642 for supporting the "Kentish Petition" that urged restoration of the king to his ancient rights; in "To Althea, from Prison," he finds freedom from external bondage in the Cavalier ideals of women, wine, and royalism. During 1643–46 he fought in Holland and France and in the king's armies in England and was wounded abroad. In a general roundup of known royalists in 1648 he was imprisoned for ten months, and while there prepared his poems for publication under the title *Lucasta* (1649). Besides witty and charming love songs, the volume includes the plaintive ballad about the conflict between love and honor, "To Lucasta, Going to the Wars," and also "The Grasshopper," a poem that presents the Cavalier ideal at its most attractive. Like that emblematic summer creature, the once-carefree Cavalier suffers in the Puritan "winter," but Lovelace finds in the fellowship of Cavalier friends a nobler version of the good life. After 1649 he endured years of penury, largely dependent on the largesse of his friend and fellow royalist, Charles Cotton. His remaining poems appeared in 1659 as *Lucasta: Postume Poems*.

From Lucasta

To Lucasta, Going to the Wars

Tell me not, sweet, I am unkind,
 That from the nunnery
Of thy chaste breast and quiet mind
 To war and arms I fly.

5 True, a new mistress now I chase,
 The first foe in the field;
And with a stronger faith embrace
 A sword, a horse, a shield.

Yet this inconstancy is such
10 As you too shall adore;
I could not love thee, dear, so much,
 Loved I not honor more.

1649

The Grasshopper[1]

To My Noble Friend, Mr. Charles Cotton

O thou that swing'st upon the waving hair
  Of some well-fillèd oaten beard,°   *head of grain*
Drunk every night with a delicious tear
  Dropped thee from heav'n, where now th' art reared,

5 The joys of earth and air are thine entire,
  That with thy feet and wings dost hop and fly;
And when thy poppy° works thou dost retire   *opiate*
  To thy carved acorn bed to lie.

Up with the day, the sun thou welcom'st then,
10 Sport'st in the gilt-plats° of his beams,   *golden fields*
And all these merry days mak'st merry men,
  Thyself, and melancholy streams.[2]

But ah, the sickle! golden ears are cropped,
  Ceres and Bacchus[3] bid goodnight;
15 Sharp frosty fingers all your flow'rs have topped,
  And what scythes spared, winds shave off quite.

Poor verdant fool! and now green ice! thy joys,
  Large and as lasting as thy perch of grass,
Bid us lay in 'gainst winter rain, and poise°   *counterbalance*
20 Their floods with an o'erflowing glass.

Thou best of men and friends! we will create
  A genuine summer in each other's breast;
And spite of this cold time and frozen fate
  Thaw us a warm seat to our rest.

25 Our sacred hearths shall burn eternally
  As vestal flames;[4] the North Wind, he
Shall strike his frost-stretched wings, dissolve, and fly
  This Etna in epitome.[5]

Dropping December shall come weeping in,
30 Bewail th' usurping of his reign;
But when in showers of old Greek we begin,
  Shall cry, he hath his crown again![6]

1. In *Aesop's Fables* the grasshopper lives in improvident, carefree idleness, in contrast with the industrious ant who lays up stores for the winter. The circumstances of the poem are those of the Interregnum, when a winter of Puritanism seemed, to royalists, to be settling over England and obliterating their mode of life. The grasshopper may also allude to the recently executed king, Charles I.
2. The three objects of "mak'st merry" are "men," "thyself," and "melancholy streams."
3. Goddess of grain and god of wine.
4. The Vestal Virgins, in Rome, were responsible for tending an eternal flame in the Temple of Vesta.
5. Boreas, the north wind, folding up ("striking") his wings, flees from the heat of the volcano within Mount Etna, a figure for the fires of friendship.
6. Greek wine was especially favored in the classical world. "Crown" here has multiple associations: the crown worn by "King Christmas" at the festivi-

Night as clear Hesper° shall our tapers whip   *the evening star*
 From the light casements where we play,
35 And the dark hag[7] from her black mantle strip,
 And stick there everlasting day.

Thus richer than untempted kings are we,
 That asking nothing, nothing need:
Though lord of all that seas embrace, yet he
40 That wants° himself is poor indeed.   *lacks*

1649

To Althea, from Prison

When Love with unconfinèd wings
 Hovers within my gates,
And my divine Althea brings
 To whisper at the grates;
5 When I lie tangled in her hair
 And fettered to her eye,
The gods[1] that wanton° in the air   *play*
 Know no such liberty.

When flowing cups run swiftly round,
10 With no allaying Thames,[2]
Our careless heads with roses bound,
 Our hearts with loyal flames;
When thirsty grief in wine we steep,
 When healths and drafts go free,
15 Fishes that tipple in the deep
 Know no such liberty.

When, like committed linnets,° I   *caged finches*
 With shriller throat shall sing
The sweetness, mercy, majesty,
20 And glories of my king;
When I shall voice aloud how good
 He is, how great should be,
Enlargèd winds, that curl the flood,
 Know no such liberty.

25 Stone walls do not a prison make,
 Nor iron bars a cage;
Minds innocent and quiet take
 That for an hermitage.
If I have freedom in my love,
30 And in my soul am free,

---

ties banned by Puritans; and the crown Cavaliers
hoped would soon be restored to Charles II.
7. Hecate, a daughter of Night.

1. Some versions read "birds" instead of "gods."
2. No mixture of water (as from the river Thames)
in the wine.

Angels alone, that soar above,
Enjoy such liberty.

1649

Love Made in the First Age.[1] To Chloris

In the nativity of time,
Chloris, it was not thought a crime
   In direct Hebrew for to woo.[2]
Now we make love as all on fire,
5 Ring retrograde[3] our loud desire,
   And court in English backward too.

Thrice happy was that golden age,
When compliment was construed rage,[4]
   And fine words in the center hid;
10 When cursèd *No* stained no maid's bliss,
And all discourse was summed in *Yes,*
   And naught forbade, but to forbid.

Love then unstinted, love did sip,
And cherries plucked fresh from the lip,
15 On cheeks and roses free he fed;
Lasses like autumn plums did drop,
And lads indifferently° did crop   *without preference*
   A flower and a maidenhead.

Then unconfinèd each did tipple
20 Wine from the bunch, milk from the nipple;
   Paps tractable as udders were;
Then equally the wholesome jellies
Were squeezed from olive trees and bellies,
   Nor suits of trespass did they fear.

25 A fragrant bank of strawberries,
Diapered° with violet's eyes,   *decorated, dappled*
   Was table, tablecloth, and fare;
No palace to the clouds did swell,
Each humble princess then did dwell
30 In the piazza[5] of her hair.

Both broken faith and th' cause of it,
All-damning gold, was damned to th' pit;

---

1. The Golden Age, described in Ovid's *Metamorphoses.*
2. Hebrew, supposed to be the original human language, is read from right to left; we have reversed this.
3. Backwards, in reverse. The term also has musical connotations, perhaps referring here to a pattern of bell ringing.
4. Passion. Compliments in the Golden Age were understood as ardent propositions.
5. Arcade, hence an artful structure.

Their troth, sealed with a clasp and kiss,
Lasted until that extreme day
35 In which they smiled their souls away,
And, in each other, breathed new bliss.

Because no fault, there was no tear;
No groan did grate the granting ear,
No false foul breath their del'cate smell:
40 No serpent kiss poisoned the taste,
Each touch was naturally chaste,
And their mere sense a miracle.

Naked as their own innocence,
And unembroidered from offense[6]
45 They went, above poor riches, gay;
On softer than the cygnet's° down,   *young swan*
In beds they tumbled of their own;
For each within the other lay.

Thus did they live; thus did they love,
50 Repeating only joys above;
And angels were, but with clothes on,
Which they would put off cheerfully,
To bathe them in the galaxy,°   *the Milky Way*
Then gird them with the heavenly zone.[7]

55 Now, Chloris, miserably crave°   *beg*
The offered bliss you would not have,
Which evermore I must deny,
Whilst ravished with these noble dreams
And crownèd with mine own soft beams,
60 Enjoying of my self I lie.

1659

---

6. I.e., not ornamented to hide an offense.   7. The zodiac of stars.

KATHERINE PHILIPS
1632–1664

The best-known woman poet of her own and the next generation, Katherine Philips was honored as "the Matchless Orinda," the classical name she chose for herself in her poetic addresses to a coterie of chiefly female friends, especially Mary Aubrey (M. A.) and Anne Owen (Lucasia). Sometimes reminiscent of Donne's love lyrics and sometimes of the ancient Greek Sappho's erotic lyrics to women, these poems develop an exalted ideal of female friendship as a Platonic union of souls. Born to a well-to-do Presbyterian family and educated at Mrs. Salmon's Presbyterian School, Philips was taken to Wales when her mother remarried. In 1648, at age seventeen, she was married to James Philips, a prominent member of Parliament. They lived together twelve years, chiefly in the small Welsh town of Cardigan, and had two children: Hector, whose death a few days after birth prompted one of her most moving poems, and Katherine, who lived to adulthood. A royalist despite her Puritan family connections, Philips forged connections with other displaced royalists. Her poems circulated in manuscript and elicited high praise from Vaughan in *Olor Iscanus*. They include elegies, epitaphs, poems at parting, and friendship poems to women and men, but also poetry on political themes: a denunciation of the regicide, "Upon the Double Murder of King Charles," and panegyrics on the restored Stuarts. After the Restoration, James Philips barely escaped execution as a regicide, had his estates confiscated, and lost his seat in Parliament, but Katherine became a favorite at court, promoted by her friend Sir Charles Cotterell ("Poliarchus"), who was master of ceremonies. In Ireland attempting (unsuccessfully) to redeem an investment, she translated Corneille's *Pompey* and her friend the Earl of Orrery produced and printed it in Dublin in 1663. The first edition of her poems, apparently pirated, appeared in 1664, the same year she died of smallpox. Her friend Cotterell brought out an authorized edition in 1667.

A Married State[1]

A married state affords but little ease
The best of husbands are so hard to please.
This in wives' careful° faces you may spell°   *full of cares / read*
Though they dissemble their misfortunes well.
5 A virgin state is crowned with much content;[2]
It's always happy as it's innocent.
No blustering husbands to create your fears;
No pangs of childbirth to extort your tears;
No children's cries for to offend your ears;
10 Few worldly crosses to distract your prayers:
Thus are you freed from all the cares that do
Attend on matrimony and a husband too.
Therefore Madam, be advised by me
Turn, turn apostate to love's levity,
15 Suppress wild nature if she dare rebel.
There's no such thing as leading apes in hell.[3]

ca. 1646   Ms; 1988

1. In a manuscript (Orielton MSS Box 24 at the National Library of Wales) this poem appears with another by Philips, addressed to Anne Barlow (whom she probably met in 1646); this one is probably also for Barlow. Both are signed by her maiden name, C. Fowler, so were evidently written before her marriage in 1648.
2. Praise of the single life is a common topic in women's poetry.
3. Proverbially, the fate of spinsters.

Upon the Double Murder of King Charles

In Answer to a Libelous Rhyme made by V. P.[1]

I think not on the state, nor am concerned
Which way soever that great helm[2] is turned,
But as that son whose father's danger nigh
Did force his native dumbness, and untie
5 His fettered organs: so here is a cause
That will excuse the breach of nature's laws.[3]
Silence were now a sin: nay passion now
Wise men themselves for merit would allow.[4]
What noble eye could see (and careless pass)
10 The dying lion kicked by every ass?
Hath Charles so broke God's laws, he must not have
A quiet crown, nor yet a quiet grave?
Tombs have been sanctuaries; thieves lie here
Secure from all their penalty and fear.
15 Great Charles his double misery was this,
Unfaithful friends, ignoble enemies;
Had any heathen been this prince's foe,
He would have wept to see him injured so.
His title was his crime, they'd reason good
20 To quarrel at the right they had withstood.
He broke God's laws, and therefore he must die,
And what shall then become of thee and I?
Slander must follow treason; but yet stay,
Take not our reason with our king away.
25 Though you have seized upon all our defense,
Yet do not sequester° our common sense.   confiscate
But I admire° not at this new supply: wonder
No bounds will hold those who at scepters fly.
Christ will be King, but I ne'er understood,
30 His subjects built his kingdom up with blood
(Except their own) or that he would dispense
With his commands, though for his own defense.
Oh! to what height of horror are they come
Who dare pull down a crown, tear up a tomb![5]

1649?   1664

1. The itinerant Welsh preacher Vavasour Powell was a Fifth Monarchist and an ardent republican who justified the regicide on the ground that Christ's second coming was imminent, when he would rule with his saints, putting down all earthly kings. His poem and Philips's answer were likely written shortly after Charles I's execution (January 30, 1649). Powell's poem has been published by Elizabeth H. Hageman in *English Manuscript Studies.*

2. Steering wheel for the "ships" of state.
3. Breaking the supposed law of nature that excludes women from speaking about public affairs.
4. Wise men, especially Stoic philosophers, normally counsel the firm control or elimination of passions.
5. Their slanders tear up Charles's tomb after his death.

Friendship's Mystery, To My Dearest *Lucasia*[1]

1

Come, my Lucasia, since we see
    That miracles men's faith do move,
By wonder and by prodigy
    To the dull angry world let's prove
5   There's a religion in our love.

2

For though we were designed t' agree,
    That fate no liberty destroys,
But our election is as free
    As angels, who with greedy choice
10   Are yet determined to their joys.[2]

3

Our hearts are doubled by the loss,
    Here mixture is addition grown;
We both diffuse,° and both engross:°   *spread out / collect*
    And we whose minds are so much one,
15   Never, yet ever are alone.

4

We court our own captivity
    Than thrones more great and innocent:
'Twere banishment to be set free,
    Since we wear fetters whose intent
20   Not bondage is, but ornament.

5

Divided joys are tedious found,
    And griefs united easier grow:
We are selves but by rebound,
    And all our titles shuffled so,
25   Both princes, and both subjects too.[3]

6

Our hearts are mutual victims laid,
    While they (such power in friendship lies)

---

1. This poem was first printed, with a musical setting by the royalist musician and composer Henry Lawes, as "Mutual Affection betweene *Orinda* and *Lucasia*" in Lawes's *The Second Book of Ayres* (1655); our text is from *Poems by the Most Deservedly Admired Mrs. Katherine Philips, the Matchless Orinda* (1667). Lucasia is Philips's name for her friend Anne Owen.
2. Angels, though created with free will, were thought to have become fixed in goodness when they turned toward God in the first moments after their creation.
3. Compare Donne, "The Sun Rising", line 21: "She is all states, and all princes, I" (p. 1376).

Are altars, priests, and off'rings made:
    And each heart which thus kindly° dies,   *benevolently, naturally*
30 Grows deathless by the sacrifice.

1655, 1664

To Mrs. M. A.[1] at Parting

I have examined and do find,
    Of all that favor me
There's none I grieve to leave behind
    But only only thee.
5 To part with thee I needs must die,
Could parting separate thee and I.

But neither chance nor compliment
    Did element our love:
'Twas sacred sympathy was lent
10   Us from the choir above.
(That friendship fortune did create,
Still fears a wound from time or fate.)

Our changed and mingled souls are grown
    To such acquaintance now,
15 That if each would resume their own,
    Alas! we know not how.
We have each other so engrossed°   *absorbed*
That each is in the union lost.[2]

And thus we can no absence know,
20   Nor shall we be confined;
Our active souls will daily go
    To learn each other's mind.
Nay, should we never meet to sense,°   *physically*
Our souls would hold intelligence.°   *would still commune*

25 Inspirèd with a flame divine,
    I scorn to court a stay;[3]
For from that noble soul of thine
    I ne'er can be away.
But I shall weep when thou dost grieve;
30 Nor can I die whilst thou dost live.

By my own temper I shall guess
    At thy felicity,

---

1. M. A. was Mary Aubrey, the first and, until she married, the dearest member of Philips's "Society of Friendship." Orinda's valedictory poem to her—which Keats admired enough to copy it out in full in an early letter—recalls some of Donne's lyrics, especially "A Valediction: For-

bidding Mourning" (pp. 1385–86).
2. These lines play upon the Neoplatonic idea of friendship and spiritual love—two souls become one.
3. Postponement (of their parting).

And only like my happiness
    Because it pleaseth thee.
35 Our hearts at any time will tell
    If thou or I be sick or well.

All honor, sure, I must pretend,°   *aspire to*
    All that is good or great:
She that would be Rosania's[4] friend
40   Must be at least complete.
If I have any bravery,°   *splendor*
    'Tis cause I have so much of thee.

Thy leiger° soul in me shall lie,   *ambassadorial*
    And all thy thoughts reveal;
45 Then back again with mine shall fly,
    And thence to me shall steal.
Thus still to one another tend:
    Such is the sacred name of friend.

Thus our twin souls in one shall grow,
50   And teach the world new love,
Redeem the age and sex, and show
    A flame fate dares not move:
And courting death to be our friend,
Our lives, together too, shall end.

55 A dew shall dwell upon our tomb
    Of such a quality
That fighting armies, thither come,
    Shall reconcilèd be.
We'll ask no epitaph, but say:
60 ORINDA and ROSANIA.

                                1664

On the Death of My First and Dearest Child, Hector Philips[1]

Twice forty months in wedlock[2] I did stay,
    Then had my vows crowned with a lovely boy.
And yet in forty days[3] he dropped away;
    O swift vicissitude of human joy!

5   I did but see him, and he disappeared,
    I did but touch the rosebud, and it fell;

---

4. The poetic name Philips gave to Mary Aubrey.
1. In Philips's manuscript the subtitle reads, "born the 23d of April, and died the 2d of May 1655. Set by Mr. Lawes." The musical setting has been published by Joan Applegate in *English*
Manuscript Studies.
2. Philips was married in August 1648.
3. The subtitle indicates that he lived barely ten days; the change here is clearly for the parallelism.

A sorrow unforeseen and scarcely feared,
 So ill can mortals their afflictions spell.°   *discern*

And now, sweet babe, what can my trembling heart
10   Suggest to right my doleful fate or thee?
Tears are my muse, and sorrow all my art,
 So piercing groans must be thy elegy.

Thus whilst no eye is witness of my moan,
 I grieve thy loss (ah, boy too dear to live!),
15 And let the unconcernèd world alone,
 Who neither will, nor can, refreshment give.

An off'ring too for thy sad tomb I have,
 Too just a tribute to thy early hearse.
Receive these gasping numbers to thy grave,
20   The last of thy unhappy mother's verse.[4]

1655   1667

4. This was not in fact Philips's last poem, but the sentiment is both true to human feeling and common in elegy. She had one other child, a year later—a daughter, Katherine, who survived her.

ANDREW MARVELL
1621–1678

Andrew Marvell's finest poems are second to none in this or any other period. He wrote less than Donne, Jonson, and Herbert did, but his range was in some ways greater, as he claimed both the private worlds of love and religion and the public worlds of political and satiric poetry and prose. His overriding concern with art, his elegant, well-crafted, limpid style, and the cool balance and reserve of some poems align him with Jonson. Yet his paradoxes and complexities of tone, his use of dramatic monologue, and his witty, dialectical arguments associate him with Donne. Above all, he is a supremely original poet, so complex and elusive that it is often hard to know what he really thought about the subjects he treated. Many of his poems were published posthumously in 1681, some thirty years after they were written, by a woman who claimed to be his widow but was probably his housekeeper. So their date and order of composition is often in doubt, as is his authorship of some anonymous works.

The son of a Church of England clergyman, Marvell grew up in Yorkshire, attended Trinity College, Cambridge (perhaps deriving the persistent strain of Neoplatonism in his poetry from the academics known as the Cambridge Platonists), ran off to London, and converted to Roman Catholicism until his father put an end to both ventures. He returned to Cambridge, took his degree in 1639, and stayed on as a scholar until his father's death in 1641. During the years of the civil wars (1642–48), he traveled in France, Italy, Holland, and Spain; much later he said of the Puritan "Good

Old Cause" that it was "too good to have been fought for." While his earliest poems associate him with royalists, those after 1649 celebrate the Commonwealth and Oliver Cromwell; although he is sometimes ambivalent, Marvell recognizes divine providence in the political changes. From 1650 to 1652 he lived at Nunappleton as tutor to the twelve-year-old daughter of Thomas Fairfax, who had given over his command of the parliamentary army to Cromwell because he was unwilling to invade Scotland. In these years of retirement and ease, Marvell probably wrote most of his love lyrics and pastorals as well as *Upon Appleton House*. Subsequently he was tutor to Cromwell's ward, William Dutton, and traveled with him on the Continent; in 1657 he joined the blind Milton, at Milton's request, in the post of Latin secretary to Cromwell's Council of State. Marvell accepted the Restoration but maintained his own independent vision and his abiding belief in religious toleration, a mixed state, and constitutional government. He helped his friend Milton avoid execution for his revolutionary polemics and helped negotiate Milton's release from a brief imprisonment. Elected a member of Parliament in 1659 from his hometown, Hull, in Yorkshire, he held that post until 1678, focusing his attention on the needs of his district; on two occasions he went on diplomatic missions—to Holland and Russia. His (necessarily anonymous) antiroyalist polemics of these years include several verse satires on Charles II and his ministers, as well as his best-known prose work, *The Rehearsal Transprosed* (1672–73), which defends Puritan dissenters and denounces censorship with verve and wit. He also wrote a brilliant poem of criticism and interpretation on Milton's *Paradise Lost* that was prefixed to the second edition (1674).

Many of Marvell's poems explore the human condition in terms of fundamental dichotomies that resist resolution. In religious or philosophical poems like "The Coronet" or "The Dialogue Between the Soul and Body," the conflict is between nature and grace, or body and soul, or poetic creation and sacrifice. In love poems such as "The Definition of Love" or "To His Coy Mistress," it is often between flesh and spirit, or physical sex and platonic love, or idealizing courtship and the ravages of time. In pastorals like the Mower poems and "The Garden," the opposition is between nature and art, or the fallen and the Edenic state, or violent passion and contentment. Marvell's most subtle and complex political poem, "An Horatian Ode upon Cromwell's Return from Ireland," sets stable traditional order and ancient right against providential revolutionary change, and the goods and costs of retirement and peace against those of action and war. *Upon Appleton House* also opposes the attractions of various kinds of retirement to the duties of action and reformation.

Marvell experimented with style and genre to striking effect. Many of his dramatic monologues are voiced by named, naive personas—the Mower, the Nymph—who stand at some remove from the author. "To His Coy Mistress," perhaps the best known of the century's carpe diem poems, is voiced by a witty and urbane speaker in balanced and artful couplets. But its rapid shifts from the world of fantasy to the charnal house of reality raise questions as to whether this is a clever seduction poem or a probing of existential angst, and whether Marvell intends to endorse or critique this speaker's view of passion and sex. In *Upon Appleton House* Marvell transforms the static, mythic features of Jonson's country-house poem "To Penshurst" to create a poem that incorporates history and the conflicts of contemporary society. It assimilates to the course of providential history the topographical features of the Fairfax estate, the Fairfax family myth of origin, the experiences of the poet-tutor on his progress around the estate, and the activities and projected future of the daughter of the house. In the poem's rich symbolism, biblical events—Eden, the first temptation, the Fall, the wilderness experience of the Israelites—find echoes in the experiences of the Fairfax family, the speaker, the history of the English Reformation, and the wanton destruction of the recent civil wars.

FROM POEMS[1]

The Coronet[2]

When for the thorns with which I long, too long,
    With many a piercing wound,
     My Savior's head have crowned,
I seek with garlands to redress that wrong,
5   Through every garden, every mead,
I gather flowers (my fruits are only flowers),
    Dismantling all the fragrant towers°   *high headdress*
That once adorned my shepherdess's head:
And now, when I have summed up all my store,
10   Thinking (so I myself deceive)
     So rich a chaplet° thence to weave   *wreath*
As never yet the King of Glory wore,
    Alas! I find the serpent old,[3]
     That, twining° in his speckled breast,   *entwining*
15   About the flowers disguised does fold
     With wreaths of fame and interest.[4]
Ah, foolish man, that wouldst debase with them,
    And mortal glory, heaven's diadem!
But thou who only couldst the serpent tame,
20   Either his slippery knots at once untie,
     And disentangle all his winding snare,
Or shatter too with him my curious frame,°   *elaborate construction*
And let these wither, so that he may die,
    Though set with skill and chosen out with care;
25   That they, while thou on both their spoils dost tread,[5]
May crown thy feet, that could not crown thy head.

1650–52   1681

Bermudas[1]

    Where the remote Bermudas ride
    In th' ocean's bosom unespied,
    From a small boat that rowed along,
    The listening winds received this song:

5   "What should we do but sing His praise
    That led us through the wat'ry maze

---

1. Marvell's lyrics were published posthumously in 1681.
2. A floral wreath, also a garland of poems of praise.
3. Alludes to the serpent that tempted Eve (Genesis 3), traditionally understood to be an instrument for Satan.
4. Self-glorification, self-advancement.
5. See the curse on the serpent (Genesis 3.15),

that the seed of Eve will bruise his head.
1. Otherwise known as the Summer Isles, the Bermudas were described in travel books like John Smith's *The General History of Virginia, New England, and the Summer Isles* (1624) as an Edenic paradise. The poem was probably written after 1653, when Marvell took up residence in the house of John Oxenbridge, who had twice visited the Bermudas.

Unto an isle so long unknown,
And yet far kinder than our own?
Where He the huge sea monsters wracks,[2]
10 That lift the deep upon their backs;
He lands us on a grassy stage,
Safe from the storms, and prelate's rage.[3]
He gave us this eternal spring
Which here enamels everything,
15 And sends the fowls to us in care,
On daily visits through the air;
He hangs in shades the orange bright,
Like golden lamps in a green night,
And does in the pomegranates close
20 Jewels more rich than Ormus[4] shows;
He makes the figs our mouths to meet,
And throws the melons at our feet;
But apples° plants of such a price,   *pineapples*
No tree could ever bear them twice;
25 With cedars, chosen by his hand
From Lebanon, he stores the land;
And makes the hollow seas that roar
Proclaim the ambergris[5] on shore;
He cast (of which we rather° boast)   *more properly*
30 The gospel's pearl upon our coast,
And in these rocks for us did frame
A temple, where to sound his name.
O let our voice his praise exalt
Till it arrive at heaven's vault,
35 Which, thence (perhaps) rebounding, may
Echo beyond the Mexique Bay."°   *Gulf of Mexico*

Thus sung they in the English boat
An holy and a cheerful note;
And all the way, to guide their chime,
40 With falling oars they kept the time.

ca. 1650–52   1681

A Dialogue Between the Soul and Body[1]

SOUL   O, who shall from this dungeon raise
A soul enslaved so many ways?[2]
With bolts of bones, that fettered stands

---

2. Probably an allusion to the event described in Edmund Waller's mock epic, a battle between the Bermudans and two stranded whales.
3. The Puritan settlers in Bermuda have escaped both the dangers of the sea voyage and religious persecution at home.
4. Hormuz, a pearl- and jewel-trading center in the Persian Gulf.

5. A substance found in sperm whales that was used in the manufacture of expensive perfume.
1. The poem derives from the medieval *debat* (debate) on this theme but alters the usual ending, which gives a clear victory to the soul.
2. The soul echoes Romans 7.24: "O wretched man that I am! who shall deliver me from the body of this death?"

In feet, and manacled in hands.
5   Here blinded with an eye, and there
Deaf with the drumming of an ear;
A soul hung up, as 'twere, in chains
Of nerves, and arteries, and veins;
Tortured, besides each other part,
10   In a vain head and double heart.

BODY   O, who shall me deliver whole
From bonds of this tyrannic soul?
Which, stretched upright, impales me so
That mine own precipice[3] I go;
15   And warms and moves this needless° frame   *without needs*
(A fever could but do the same),
And, wanting where° its spite to try,   *lacking an object*
Has made me live to let me die.
A body that could never rest
20   Since this ill spirit it possessed.

SOUL   What magic could me thus confine
Within another's grief to pine?
Where, whatsoever it complain,°   *suffer, complain of*
I feel, that cannot feel,[4] the pain;
25   And all my care itself employs,
That to preserve which me destroys;
Constrained not only to endure
Diseases, but, what's worse, the cure;
And, ready oft the port to gain,
30   Am shipwrecked into health again.

BODY   But physic° yet could never reach   *medicine*
The maladies thou me dost teach:
Whom first the cramp of hope does tear,
And then the palsy shakes of fear;
35   The pestilence of love does heat,
Or hatred's hidden ulcer eat;
Joy's cheerful madness does perplex,
Or sorrow's other madness vex;
Which knowledge forces me to know,
40   And memory will not forego.
What but a soul could have the wit
To build me up for sin so fit?
So architects do square and hew
Green trees that in the forest grew.

ca. 1650–52   1681

---

3. Having a soul allows humans to walk erect and so face the danger of falling.

4. The soul can sympathize ("feel") though it has no power of physical sensation.

The Nymph Complaining for the Death of Her Fawn[1]

The wanton troopers[2] riding by
Have shot my fawn, and it will die.
Ungentle men! They cannot thrive
To kill thee. Thou ne'er didst alive
5   Them any harm; alas, nor could
Thy death yet do them any good.
I'm sure I never wished them ill,
Nor do I for all this, nor will:
But if my simple prayers may yet
10   Prevail with heaven to forget
Thy murder, I will join my tears
Rather than fail. But, O my fears!
It cannot die so. Heaven's king
Keeps register of everything,
15   And nothing may we use in vain.
Even beasts must be with justice slain,
Else men are made their deodands.[3]
Though they should wash their guilty hands
In this warm lifeblood, which doth part
20   From thine, and wound me to the heart,
Yet could they not be clean; their stain
Is dyed in such a purple grain.
There is not such another in
The world to offer for their sin.
25   Unconstant Sylvio, when yet
I had not found him counterfeit,°   *false, deceitful*
One morning (I remember well),
Tied in this silver chain and bell,
Gave it to me; nay, and I know
30   What he said then, I'm sure I do.
Said he, Look how your huntsman here
Hath taught a fawn to hunt his dear.
But Sylvio soon had me beguiled;
This waxèd tame, while he grew wild,
35   And quite regardless of my smart,
Left me his fawn, but took his heart.[4]
     Thenceforth I set myself to play
My solitary time away
With this; and very well content
40   Could so mine idle life have spent.

---

1. The lament for the death of a pet is an ancient topic dating back to Catullus and Ovid; the closest analogue may be Virgil's story of Sylvia's deer killed wantonly by the Trojans (*Aeneid* 7.475ff). John Skelton has a mock-heroic poem on "Philip Sparrow." There are also echoes of the Song of Songs, which have prompted critical debate as to whether Marvell uses them with serious allegorical import or the nymph uses them quite inappropriately.

2. Soldiers of the invading Scots army were called "troopers" (ca. 1640), as were, sometimes, soldiers of Cromwell's New Model Army.
3. In English law, animals or objects forfeited to the Crown (literally, to God) because they were the immediate cause of a human being's death. The nymph applies the term to persons who cause the death of animals.
4. A pun: heart/hart (a deer); line 32 also puns on dear/deer.

For it was full of sport, and light
Of foot and heart, and did invite
Me to its game. It seemed to bless
Itself in me; how could I less
45 Than love it? O I cannot be
Unkind t' a beast that loveth me.
    Had it lived long, I do not know
Whether it too might have done so
As Sylvio did; his gifts might be
50 Perhaps as false or more than he.
But I am sure, for aught that I
Could in so short a time espy,
Thy love was far more better than
The love of false and cruel men.
55   With sweetest milk and sugar first
I it at mine own fingers nursed.
And as it grew, so every day
It waxed more sweet and white than they.
It had so sweet a breath! and oft
60 I blushed to see its foot more soft
And white—shall I say than my hand?—
Nay, any lady's of the land.
    It is a wondrous thing how fleet
'Twas on those little silver feet,
65 With what a pretty skipping grace
It oft would challenge me the race;
And when it had left me far away,
'Twould stay, and run again, and stay.
For it was nimbler much than hinds,[5]
70 And trod, as on the four winds.
    I have a garden of my own
But so with roses overgrown
And lilies that you would it guess
To be a little wilderness.
75 And all the springtime of the year
It only lovèd to be there.
Among the beds of lilies, I
Have sought it oft where it should lie,
Yet could not, till itself would rise,
80 Find it, although before mine eyes.
For in the flaxen lilies' shade
It like a bank of lilies laid.
Upon the roses it would feed,
Until its lips ev'n seemed to bleed;
85 And then to me 'twould boldly trip
And print those roses on my lip.
But all its chief delight was still
On roses thus itself to fill,
And its pure virgin limbs to fold
90 In whitest sheets of lilies cold.

5. I.e., full-grown deer.

Had it lived long, it would have been
Lilies without, roses within.
   O help! O help! I see it faint,
And die as calmly as a saint.
95 See how it weeps.[6] The tears do come
Sad, slowly dropping like a gum.
So weeps the wounded balsam, so
The holy frankincense doth flow.[7]
The brotherless Heliades
100 Melt in such amber tears as these.[8]
   I in a golden vial will
Keep these two crystal tears, and fill
It till it do o'erflow with mine,
Then place it in Diana's shrine.[9]
105   Now my sweet fawn is vanished to
Whither the swans and turtles° go,   *turtledoves*
In fair Elysium[1] to endure
With milk-white lambs and ermines pure.
O do not run too fast, for I
110 Will but bespeak° thy grave, and die.   *give orders for*
   First my unhappy statue shall
Be cut in marble, and withal,
Let it be weeping too; but there
Th' engraver sure his art may spare,
115 For I so truly thee bemoan
That I shall weep, though I be stone:[2]
Until my tears, still dropping, wear
My breast, themselves engraving there.
There at my feet shalt thou be laid,
120 Of purest alabaster made;
For I would have thine image be
White as I can, though not as thee.

ca. 1650–52   1681

To His Coy Mistress

   Had we but world enough, and time,
This coyness, lady, were no crime.
We would sit down, and think which way
To walk, and pass our long love's day.
5 Thou by the Indian Ganges' side
Shouldst rubies find; I by the tide

---

6. Deer were supposed to weep as they died.
7. Both balsam and frankincense are fragrant resins obtained a drop at a time from trees with holes bored in them.
8. The three daughters of the sun (Helios), grieving the death of their rash brother Phaëthon, were transformed to black poplar trees dropping "tears" of amber.
9. Diana was the goddess of chastity and woodland creatures; nymphs were her attendants.
1. The Elysian fields, a pagan version of heaven.
2. Niobe, lamenting the death of her many children, in whom she took inordinate pride, was turned to stone.

Of Humber would complain.[1] I would
Love you ten years before the Flood,
And you should, if you please, refuse
10 Till the conversion of the Jews.[2]
My vegetable love should grow
Vaster than empires, and more slow;
An hundred years should go to praise
Thine eyes, and on thy forehead gaze;
15 Two hundred to adore each breast,
But thirty thousand to the rest:
An age at least to every part,
And the last age should show your heart.
For, lady, you deserve this state,°   dignity
20 Nor would I love at lower rate.
   But at my back I always hear
Time's wingèd chariot hurrying near;
And yonder all before us lie
Deserts of vast eternity.
25 Thy beauty shall no more be found,
Nor, in thy marble vault, shall sound
My echoing song; then worms shall try
That long-preserved virginity,
And your quaint[3] honor turn to dust,
30 And into ashes all my lust:
The grave's a fine and private place,
But none, I think, do there embrace.
   Now therefore, while the youthful hue
Sits on thy skin like morning dew,[4]
35 And while thy willing soul transpires
At every pore with instant fires,[5]
Now let us sport us while we may,
And now, like amorous birds of prey,
Rather at once our time devour
40 Than languish in his slow-chapped[6] power.
Let us roll all our strength and all
Our sweetness up into one ball,
And tear our pleasures with rough strife
Thorough° the iron gates of life:[7]   through
45 Thus, though we cannot make our sun
Stand still, yet we will make him run.[8]

ca. 1650–52   1681

1. The exotic river Ganges in India is on one side of the world, the Humber River flows past Marvell's city, Hull, on the opposite side. Complaints are poems of plaintive, unavailing love.
2. Popular belief had it that the Jews were to be converted just before the Last Judgment. The exaggerated offers in this stanza play off against conventional hyperbolic declarations of love in Petrarchan poetry.
3. "Quaint" puns on "out of date" and *queynte*, a term for the female genitals.

4. The text reads "glew," which could be correct, but "dew" is a common emendation.
5. Urgent, sudden enthusiasm. "Transpires": breathes forth.
6. Slowly devouring jaws.
7. One manuscript reads "grates," a somewhat different figure for the sexual act proposed.
8. The sun stood still for Joshua (Joshua 10.12) in his war against Gibeon; see the very different resolution in Donne's "The Sun Rising" (p. 1376).

The Definition of Love

My Love is of a birth as rare
As 'tis, for object, strange and high;
It was begotten by Despair
Upon Impossibility.

5 Magnanimous Despair alone
Could show me so divine a thing,
Where feeble Hope could ne'er have flown
But vainly flapped its tinsel wing.

And yet I quickly might arrive
10 Where my extended soul is fixed;[1]
But Fate does iron wedges drive,
And always crowds itself betwixt.

For Fate with jealous eye does see
Two perfect loves, nor lets them close;°   *unite*
15 Their union would her ruin be,
And her tyrannic power depose.[2]

And therefore her decrees of steel
Us as the distant poles have placed
(Though Love's whole world on us doth wheel),[3]
20 Not by themselves to be embraced,

Unless the giddy heaven fall,
And earth some new convulsion tear,
And, us to join, the world should all
Be cramped into a planisphere.[4]

25 As lines, so loves oblique may well
Themselves in every angle greet;[5]
But ours, so truly parallel,
Though infinite, can never meet.

Therefore the Love which us doth bind,
30 But Fate so enviously debars,
Is the conjunction of the mind,
And opposition of the stars.[6]

ca. 1650–52   1681

1. The soul has extended itself from the speaker's body and fixed itself to his lover.
2. Two perfections, united, would not be subject to change and thereby to Fate.
3. Rotates as on its axis.
4. A two-dimensional map of the world; Marvell images a round globe collapsed into a flat pancake shape, top to bottom, which would bring the two poles together.
5. Oblique lines can touch in angles, as might "oblique" lovers that (in one meaning of the term) "deviate from right conduct or thought."
6. "Conjunction" is the coming together of two heavenly bodies in the same sign of the zodiac; "opposition" places them at diametrical opposites.

The Picture of Little T. C. in a Prospect of Flowers[1]

See with what simplicity
This nymph begins her golden days!
In the green grass she loves to lie,
And there with her fair aspect tames
5   The wilder flowers and gives them names,
But only with the roses plays,
    And them does tell
What color best becomes them and what smell.

Who can foretell for what high cause
10   This darling of the gods was born?
Yet this is she whose chaster laws
The wanton Love shall one day fear,
And under her command severe
See his bow broke and ensigns° torn.   *flags, pennants*
15   Happy who can
Appease this virtuous enemy of man!

O then let me in time compound°   *come to terms*
And parley with those conquering eyes
Ere they have tried their force to wound,
20   Ere with their glancing wheels they drive
In triumph over hearts that strive
And them that yield but more despise:
    Let me be laid
Where I may see thy glories from some shade.

25   Meantime, whilst every verdant thing
Itself does at thy beauty charm,
Reform the errors of the spring;
Make that the tulips may have share
Of sweetness, seeing they are fair;
30   And roses of their thorns disarm:
    But most procure
That violets may a longer age endure.

But O, young beauty of the woods,
Whom Nature courts with fruit and flowers,
35   Gather the flowers but spare the buds,
Lest Flora,[2] angry at thy crime
To kill her infants in their prime,
Do quickly make th' example yours;
    And ere we see,
40   Nip in the blossom all our hopes and thee.

ca. 1650–52   1681

---

1. The little girl, T. C., has not been identified with any certainty. "Prospect": landscape.   2. Roman goddess of flowers.

The Mower Against Gardens[1]

Luxurious° man, to bring his vice in use,[2]   *voluptuous*
 Did after him the world seduce,
And from the fields the flowers and plants allure,
 Where Nature was most plain and pure.
5 He first enclosed within the garden's square
 A dead and standing pool of air,
And a more luscious earth for them did knead,
 Which stupefied them while it fed.
The pink grew then as double as his mind;[3]
10 The nutriment did change the kind.
With strange perfumes he did the roses taint;
 And flowers themselves were taught to paint.
The tulip white did for complexion seek,
 And learned to interline its cheek;
15 Its onion root they then so high did hold,
 That one was for a meadow sold;[4]
Another world was searched through oceans new,
 To find the marvel of Peru;[5]
And yet these rarities might be allowed
20 To man, that sovereign thing and proud,
Had he not dealt between the bark and tree,[6]
 Forbidden mixtures there to see.
No plant now knew the stock from which it came;
 He grafts upon the wild the tame,
25 That the uncertain and adult'rate fruit
 Might put the palate in dispute.
His green seraglio[7] has its eunuchs too,
 Lest any tyrant him outdo;
And in the cherry he does Nature vex,
30 To procreate without a sex.[8]
'Tis all enforced, the fountain and the grot,°   *grotto*
 While the sweet fields do lie forgot,
Where willing Nature does to all dispense
 A wild and fragrant innocence;
35 And fauns and fairies do the meadows till
 More by their presence than their skill.
Their statues polished by some ancient hand
 May to adorn the gardens stand;

---

1. The four "Mower" poems are linked by their treatment of a distinctly unusual pastoral figure, a mower rather than a shepherd or goatherd, who provides a singular perspective on those familiar pastoral topics, nature versus art and nature's sympathy for man (the pathetic fallacy). As mower wielding a scythe, he evokes other figures (Time, Death).
2. Into common practice.
3. The double pink, or carnation, is a product of sophisticated ("double") minds.

4. A highly lucrative trade in Dutch tulip bulbs flourished during the 17th century.
5. *Mirabilis jalapa*, the four-o'clock, was an exotic, multicolored flower found originally in tropical America.
6. An adage for interfering between husband and wife, in reference, apparently, to grafting.
7. Enclosure, a harem in a sultan's palace.
8. Cherries were commonly propagated by grafting.

But, howsoe'er the figures do excel,
40   The gods themselves with us do dwell.

ca. 1650–52   1681

Damon the Mower

Hark how the mower Damon sung,
With love of Juliana stung![1]
While everything did seem to paint
The scene more fit for his complaint.[2]
5   Like her fair eyes the day was fair,
But scorching like his amorous care;
Sharp, like his scythe, his sorrow was,
And withered, like his hopes, the grass.

"Oh what unusual heats are here,
10   Which thus our sunburned meadows sear!
The grasshopper its pipe gives o'er,
And hamstringed° frogs can dance no more: disabled
But in the brook the green frog wades,
And grasshoppers seek out the shades.
15   Only the snake, that kept within,
Now glitters in its second skin.

"This heat the sun could never raise,
Nor Dog Star so inflame the days;[3]
It from an higher beauty grow'th,
20   Which burns the fields and mower both;
Which mads the dog, and makes the sun
Hotter than his own Phaëton.[4]
Not Jùly causeth these extremes,
But Juliana's scorching beams.

25   "Tell me where I may pass the fires
Of the hot day or hot desires,
To what cool cave shall I descend,
Or to what gelid° fountain bend?   icy
Alas! I look for ease in vain,
30   When remedies themselves complain:[5]
No moisture but my tears do rest,
No cold but in her icy breast.

1. Damon is a familiar classical name in pastoral; Juliana gets her name from July (lines 23–24).
2. The plaintive love song of an unrequited lover.
3. The Dog Star (Sirius in the constellation Canis Major) rises with the sun in late summer, producing the heats of "dog days."
4. Phaëthon, son of Helios, the sun god of Greek mythology; he tried to drive his father's chariot but let the horses run away and scorched the world.
5. I.e., fountain and cave themselves complain of unusual heat.

"How long wilt thou, fair shepherdess,
Esteem me and my presents less?
35   To thee the harmless snake I bring,
Disarmèd of its teeth and sting:
To thee chameleons, changing hue,
And oak leaves tipped with honeydew;
Yet thou, ungrateful, hast not sought
40   Nor what they are, nor who them brought.

"I am the mower Damon, known
Through all the meadows I have mown.
On me the morn her dew distills
Before her darling daffodils,
45   And if at noon my toil me heat,
The sun himself licks off my sweat;
While, going home, the evening sweet
In cowslip-water bathes my feet.

"What though the piping shepherd stock
50   The plains with an unnumbered flock?
This scythe of mine discovers° wide   *uncovers*
More ground than all his sheep do hide.
With this the golden fleece I shear
Of all these closes every year,[6]
55   And though in wool more poor than they,
Yet I am richer far in hay.

"Nor am I so deformed to sight
If in my scythe I lookèd right;
In which I see my picture done
60   As in a crescent moon the sun.
The deathless fairies take me oft
To lead them in their dances soft,
And when I tune myself to sing,
About me they contract their ring.[7]

65   "How happy might I still have mowed,
Had not Love here his thistles sowed!
But now I all the day complain,
Joining my labor to my pain;
And with my scythe cut down the grass,
70   Yet still my grief is where it was;
But when the iron blunter grows,
Sighing, I whet my scythe and woes."

While thus he threw his elbow round,
Depopulating all the ground,
75   And with his whistling scythe does cut
Each stroke between the earth and root,

---

6. Hay is the "wool" of the fields ("closes").
7. I.e., the "fairy ring," a discolored circle of grass popularly supposed to result from fairies dancing there.

The edgèd steel, by careless chance,
Did into his own ankle glance,
And there among the grass fell down[8]
80　By his own scythe the mower mown.

"Alas!" said he, "these hurts are slight
To those that die by Love's despite.
With shepherd's purse and clown's° all-heal[9]　　　　　*rustic's*
The blood I stanch and wound I seal.
85　Only for him no cure is found
Whom Juliana's eyes do wound.
'Tis Death alone that this must do;
For, Death, thou art a mower too."

ca. 1650–52　　　　　　　　　　　　　　　　　　　　　　　　1681

The Mower to the Glowworms

Ye living lamps, by whose dear light
The nightingale does sit so late,
And studying all the summer night
Her matchless songs does meditate,

5　Ye country comets, that portend
No war nor prince's funeral,
Shining unto no higher end
Than to presage the grass's fall;

Ye glowworms, whose officious° flame　　　　　　　*helpful*
10　To wand'ring mowers shows the way,
That in the night have lost their aim,
And after foolish fires° do stray;　　　　　　*will-o'-the-wisps*

Your courteous fires in vain you waste,
Since Juliana here is come,
15　For she my mind hath so displaced
That I shall never find my home.

ca. 1650–52　　　　　　　　　　　　　　　　　　　　　　　　1681

The Mower's Song

My mind was once the true survey
Of all these meadows fresh and gay,
And in the greenness of the grass

8. Evokes the biblical phrase "All flesh is grass"
(Isaiah 40.6).

9. Folk names for popular remedies to heal
wounds, found in fields and hedges.

Did see its hopes[1] as in a glass;°   *mirror*
5   When Juliana came, and she,
What I do to the grass, does to my thoughts and me.[2]

But these, while I with sorrow pine,
Grew more luxuriant still and fine,
That not one blade of grass you spied
10 But had a flower on either side;
When Juliana came, and she,
What I do to the grass, does to my thoughts and me.

Unthankful meadows, could you so
A fellowship so true forego,
15 And in your gaudy May-games[3] meet,
While I lay trodden under feet?
When Juliana came, and she,
What I do to the grass, does to my thoughts and me.

But what you in compassion ought
20 Shall now by my revenge be wrought,
And flowers, and grass, and I, and all,
Will in one common ruin fall;
For Juliana comes, and she,
What I do to the grass, does to my thoughts and me.

25 And thus ye meadows, which have been
Companions of my thoughts more green,
Shall now the heraldry become
With which I shall adorn my tomb;
For Juliana comes, and she,
30 What I do to the grass, does to my thoughts and me.

ca. 1650–52   1681

The Garden

How vainly men themselves amaze°   *bewilder*
To win the palm, the oak, or bays,[1]
And their uncessant labors see
Crowned from some single herb or tree,
5   Whose short and narrow-vergèd° shade   *edged*
Does prudently their toils upbraid;°   *reprove*
While all flowers and all trees do close°   *unite, agree*
To weave the garlands of repose!

1. Green is the color of hope.
2. The alexandrine (twelve-syllable line) used here is the only example of a refrain in Marvell.
3. Festivals and merrymaking marked the first of May, May Day.
1. Honors, respectively, for military, civic, and poetic achievement.

Fair Quiet, have I found thee here,
10   And Innocence, thy sister dear?
Mistaken long, I sought you then
In busy companies of men.
Your sacred plants, if here below,°   *on earth*
Only among the plants will grow;
15   Society is all but rude,
To° this delicious solitude.   *compared to*

No white nor red[2] was ever seen
So amorous as this lovely green.
Fond lovers, cruel as their flame,
20   Cut in these trees their mistress' name:
Little, alas, they know or heed
How far these beauties hers exceed!
Fair trees, wheresoe'er your barks I wound,
No name shall but your own be found.[3]

25   When we have run our passion's heat,
Love hither makes his best retreat.
The gods, that mortal beauty chase,
Still° in a tree did end their race: *always*
Apollo hunted Daphne so,
30   Only that she might laurel grow;
And Pan did after Syrinx speed,
Not as a nymph, but for a reed.[4]

What wondrous life is this I lead!
Ripe apples drop about my head;
35   The luscious clusters of the vine
Upon my mouth do crush their wine;
The nectarine and curious° peach   *exquisite*
Into my hands themselves do reach;
Stumbling on melons[5] as I pass,
40   Ensnared with flowers, I fall on grass.

Meanwhile the mind, from pleasure less,
Withdraws into its happiness;
The mind, that ocean where each kind
Does straight° its own resemblance find;[6]   *immediately*
45   Yet it creates, transcending these,
Far other worlds and other seas,

2. Colors traditionally associated with female beauty.
3. Marvell proposes to carve in the bark of trees not "Sylvia" or "Laura," but "Beech" and "Oak."
4. Apollo, the god of poetry, chased Daphne until she turned into a laurel (the emblematic reward of poets); Pan pursued Syrinx until she became a reed, out of which he made panpipes. The gods'

motives were, of course, sexual, not horticultural.
5. "Melons," with etymological roots in the Greek word for "apple," may recall the apple over which all humankind stumbled.
6. As the ocean supposedly contained a counterpart of every creature on land, so the ocean of the mind holds the innate ideas of all things (in Neoplatonic philosophy).

Annihilating all that's made
To a green thought in a green shade.

Here at the fountain's sliding foot,
50 Or at some fruit tree's mossy root,
Casting the body's vest° aside,   garment
My soul into the boughs does glide:
There like a bird it sits and sings,
Then whets° and combs its silver wings,   preens
55 And, till prepared for longer flight,
Waves in its plumes the various light.[7]

Such was that happy garden-state,
While man there walked without a mate:
After a place so pure and sweet,
60 What other help could yet be meet![8]
But 'twas beyond a mortal's share
To wander solitary there:
Two paradises 'twere in one
To live in paradise alone.

65 How well the skillful gardener drew
Of flowers and herbs this dial new,[9]
Where from above the milder sun
Does through a fragrant zodiac run;
And as it works, th' industrious bee
70 Computes its time[1] as well as we!
How could such sweet and wholesome hours
Be reckoned but with herbs and flowers?

ca. 1650–52   1681

An Horatian Ode

Upon Cromwell's Return from Ireland[1]

The forward° youth that would appear   eager, ambitious
Must now forsake his Muses dear,
    Nor in the shadows sing
    His numbers languishing:

7. The multicolored light of this world, contrasted with the white radiance of eternity.
8. Genesis 2.18 recounts the Lord's decision to make a "help meet" for Adam, Eve.
9. The garden itself is laid out as a sundial.
1. With a pun on "thyme."
1. Oliver Cromwell, the general primarily responsible for Parliament's victory in the civil war, returned from conquering Ireland in May 1650, about eighteen months after the execution of Charles I. The two events were persistently connected: Cromwell's success in Ireland was taken as a sign of God's favor to the new republican regime and to Cromwell as his chosen instrument. Pindaric odes (like Jonson's Cary-Morison ode, pp. 1551–55) are heroic and ecstatic; Horatian odes are poems of cool and balanced judgment, as this one is in its representations of Cromwell, Charles I, and the issues of power and providence.

The Execution of Charles I. A German print illustrates the beheading of Charles I before an enormous crowd, on a scaffold erected in front of the Banqueting House. At the top of the picture small portraits of General Fairfax and Cromwell, leaders of the Parliamentary forces, flank a portrait of King Charles, to whom an angel in the clouds is extending a heavenly crown. In the lower right corner, a woman faints.

5 'Tis time to leave the books in dust
And oil th' unusèd armor's rust,
Removing from the wall
The corselet° of the hall.[2]   *upper body armor*

So restless Cromwell could not cease
10 In the inglorious arts of peace,
But through adventurous war
Urgèd his active star;[3]

And, like the three-forked lightning, first
Breaking the clouds where it was nursed,
15 Did through his own side
His fiery way divide:[4]

2. Here as elsewhere there are allusions to Lucan's *Pharsalia*, a poem of civil war whose sympathies are with Pompey, Cato, and the Roman Republic against Caesar and the empire. The poem's allusions to Caesar are most often to Charles I, but sometimes to Cromwell.
3. Normally the stars are thought to control men's fates, but Cromwell presses his own star forward.
4. The "three-forked lightning" identifies him with Zeus, suggesting the elemental force by which he surpassed all those in his own party ("side") of radical Independents; the imagery of giving birth to himself also suggests going Caesar (born by cesarean section) one better.

For 'tis all one to courage high,
The emulous, or enemy;
    And with such, to enclose
20   Is more than to oppose.

Then burning through the air he went,
And palaces and temples rent;
    And Caesar's head at last
    Did through his laurels blast.[5]

25   'Tis madness to resist or blame
The force of angry heaven's flame;
    And if we would speak true,
    Much to the man is due,

Who from his private gardens, where
30   He lived reservèd and austere
    (As if his highest plot
    To plant the bergamot),[6]

Could by industrious valor climb
To ruin the great work of time,
35   And cast the kingdom old
    Into another mold;

Though Justice against Fate complain,
And plead the ancient rights in vain:
    But those do hold or break,
40   As men are strong or weak.

Nature that hateth emptiness,
Allows of penetration less,[7]
    And therefore must make room
    Where greater spirits come.

45   What field of all the civil wars
Where his were not the deepest scars?
    And Hampton shows what part
    He had of wiser art;[8]

Where, twining subtle fears with hope,
50   He wove a net of such a scope
    That Charles himself might chase
    To Caresbrooke's narrow case,

5. Royal crowns were made of laurel because they were supposed to protect from lightning.
6. A pear-shaped orange (from the Turkish, "prince's pear").
7. Nature abhors a vacuum, but even more, the penetration of one body's space by another body.
8. Charles was confined at Hampton Court after his defeat, as Parliament attempted to negotiate terms for his restoration. Cromwell was rumored to have connived at his escape to Carisbrooke Castle, on the Isle of Wight, in order to convince Parliament that he could not be trusted and must be executed. Cromwell has shown himself master of the two "arts" of rule defined by Machiavelli, namely, force and craft.

That thence the royal actor[9] borne,
The tragic scaffold might adorn;
55   While round the armèd bands
    Did clap their bloody hands.

He nothing common did or mean
Upon that memorable scene,
    But with his keener eye
60   The ax's edge[1] did try;

Nor called the gods with vulgar spite
To vindicate his helpless right;
    But bowed his comely head
    Down, as upon a bed.

65 This was that memorable hour,
Which first assured the forcèd power;
    So when they did design
    The Capitol's first line,

A bleeding head where they begun
70 Did fright the architects to run;
    And yet in that the state
    Foresaw its happy fate.[2]

And now the Irish are ashamed
To see themselves in one year tamed;
75   So much one man can do,
    That does both act and know.

They can affirm his praises best,
And have, though overcome, confessed
    How good he is, how just,
80   And fit for highest trust.[3]

Nor yet grown stiffer with command,
But still in the republic's hand—
    How fit he is to sway,
    That can so well obey.[4]

---

9. The theater metaphors used for Charles are even more powerful because the "tragic scaffold" was erected outside Whitehall, where so many royal masques were produced. See a depiction of the king's execution on p. 1807.

1. A play on the Latin *acies*, which means the edge of a sword or ax, a keen glance, and the vanguard of a battle. Cf. the newsbook account of the king's execution, p. 1838.

2. Livy and Pliny record that the workmen digging the foundations for a temple of Jupiter at Rome uncovered a bloody head which they were persuaded to take as an omen that Rome would be head (*caput*) of a great empire; the temple and the hill took the name Capitoline from that event.

3. Cromwell conducted a particularly brutal campaign in Ireland, and the Irish had no such testimonials for him; the lines are deeply equivocal.

4. The maxim about obedience fitting one to rule is a commonplace. The implications of "yet" and "still," along with the next stanza, suggest a Caesar figure who has not—but might—cross the Rubicon and defy the Republic, as Julius Caesar did.

85　He to the Commons' feet presents
　　A kingdom for his first year's rents;
　　　　And, what he may, forbears
　　　　His fame to make it theirs;[5]

　　And has his sword and spoils ungirt,
90　To lay them at the public's skirt:
　　　　So, when the falcon high
　　　　Falls heavy from the sky,

　　She, having killed, no more does search,
　　But on the next green bough to perch;
95　　　Where, when he first does lure,
　　　　The falconer has her sure.

　　What may not then our isle presume,
　　While victory his crest does plume!
　　　　What may not others fear,
100　　If thus he crown each year!

　　A Caesar he ere long to Gaul,
　　To Italy an Hannibal,
　　　　And to all states not free,
　　　　Shall climactèric be.[6]

105　The Pict no shelter now shall find
　　Within his parti-colored mind,
　　　　But from this valor sad,°　　　　　　　　*severe, solemn*
　　　　Shrink underneath the plaid;[7]

　　Happy if in the tufted brake
110　The English hunter him mistake,
　　　　Nor lay his hounds in near
　　　　The Caledonian° deer.　　　　　　　　　*Scottish*

　　But thou, the war's and Fortune's son,
　　March indefatigably on;
115　　　And for the last effect,
　　　　Still keep thy sword erect;

　　Besides the force it has to fright
　　The spirits of the shady night,[8]

---

5. Thus far, Cromwell gives the Republic credit for his victories.
6. It was thought that Cromwell's military acumen might subdue France and Italy (which threatened to attack the new republic to restore Charles II), just as did Caesar and Hannibal of old. "Climacteric": a period of crucial, epochal change— here, the expectation that the example of a successful English republic would topple absolute monarchs abroad.

7. Early Scots were called Picts (from the Latin *pictus*, painted), because the warriors painted themselves many colors; contemporary Scots are "parti-colored" (divided into many factions) like a scotch plaid. Cromwell was about to go to subdue Scotland, which had declared for Charles II.
8. A sword carried with the blade upright evokes the classical tradition that underworld spirits (here, the slain king and his followers) are frightened off by raised weapons.

The same arts that did gain
120   A power must it maintain.[9]

1650   1681

Upon Appleton House[1]

To My Lord Fairfax

1

Within this sober frame expect
Work of no foreign architect,
That unto caves the quarries drew,
And forests did to pastures hew;
5 Who of his great design in pain
Did for a model vault his brain,[2]
Whose columns should so high be raised
To arch the brows that on them gazed.

2

Why should of all things man unruled
10 Such unproportioned dwellings build?
The beasts are by their dens expressed,
And birds contrive an equal nest;[3]
The low-roofed tortoises do dwell
In cases fit of tortoiseshell:
15 No creature loves an empty space;
Their bodies measure out their place.

3

But he, superfluously spread,
Demands more room alive than dead;
And in his hollow palace goes
20 Where winds as he themselves may lose.
What need of all this marble crust

9. The maxim alludes to Machiavelli's advice that a kingdom won by force must for some time be maintained by force.

1. From 1651 to 1653, Marvell served as tutor to Mary Fairfax, daughter of Ann Vere and Thomas Fairfax, commander in chief of the parliamentary army throughout the civil wars. Fairfax opposed the regicide and in 1650 resigned his command rather than lead a preemptive strike against Scotland (which had declared for Charles II). Cromwell took over as Fairfax retired to his country estates in Yorkshire, especially Nunappleton, a comparatively simple brick structure on the site of a former Cistercian priory dissolved by Henry VIII along with all monasteries in 1542. The poem makes the house and its history figure the progress of the Reformation and the recent civil wars, played off against the Fall, the conflicts of the Israelites in the wilderness, and other biblical moments. The poem is structured as a journey around the estate, intersected by a long passage of family history. It was apparently written in the summer of 1651, when Mary Fairfax was twelve.

2. Did design in his brain the absurdly high vaulted ceilings of grand, magnificent houses built for showy display. This poem invites comparison and contrast with other country-house poems and the houses, estates, and society they describe: Jonson's "To Penshurst" (pp. 1546–48), Lanyer's "Description of Cookham" (pp. 1436–40), and Carew's "To Saxham" (pp. 1773–75).

3. I.e., a nest proportioned to their size.

T' impark the wanton mote of dust,
That thinks by breadth the world t' unite
Though the first builders[4] failed in height?

4

25　But all things are composèd here
Like nature, orderly and near:
In which we the dimensions find
Of what more sober age and mind,
When larger sizèd men did stoop
30　To enter at a narrow loop;
As practicing, in doors so strait,
To strain themselves through heaven's gate.

5

And surely when the after age
Shall hither come in pilgrimage,
35　These sacred places to adore,
By Vere and Fairfax trod before,
Men will dispute how their extent
Within such dwarfish confines went;
And some will smile at this as well
40　As Romulus his bee-like cell.[5]

6

Humility alone designs
Those short but admirable lines,
By which, ungirt and unconstrained,
Things greater are in less contained.
45　Let other vainly strive t'immure
The circle in the quadrature![6]
These holy mathematics can
In ev'ry figure equal man.[7]

7

Yet thus the laden house does sweat,
50　And scarce endures the master great:
But where he comes the swelling hall
Stirs, and the square grows spherical;[8]
More by his magnitude distressed,
Than he is by its straitness pressed;
55　And too officiously° it slights　　　　　　　　　　*overeagerly*
That in itself which him delights.

---

4. The proud builders of the Tower of Babel, who thought to make it reach to heaven (Genesis 11).
5. The thatched hut of the legendary founder of Rome.
6. To square the circle.
7. The circle symbolized perfection, the square variously virtue, justice, and prudence.
8. The square hall rises up into a domed cupola.

8

So honor better lowness bears,
Than that unwonted° greatness wears.   *unaccustomed*
Height with a certain grace does bend,
60 But low things clownishly° ascend.   *in rustic fashion*
And yet what needs there here excuse,
Where ev'ry thing does answer use?
Where neatness nothing can condemn,
Nor pride invent° what to contemn?   *find out*

9

65 A stately frontispiece of poor[9]
Adorns without the open door;
Nor less the rooms within commends
Daily new furniture of friends.
The house was built upon the place
70 Only as for a mark of grace;
And for an inn to entertain
Its lord a while, but not remain.[1]

10

Him Bishops-Hill, or Denton may,
Or Bilbrough, better hold than they;
75 But Nature here hath been so free
As if she said, Leave this to me.
Art would more neatly° have defaced   *elegantly*
What she had laid so sweetly waste;
In fragrant gardens, shady woods,
80 Deep meadows, and transparent floods.

11

While with slow eyes we these survey,
And on each pleasant footstep stay,
We opportunely may relate
The progress of this house's fate.
85 A nunnery first gave it birth
For virgin buildings oft brought forth.
And all that neighbor-ruin shows
The quarries whence this dwelling rose.

12

Near to this gloomy cloister's gates
90 There dwelt the blooming virgin Thwaites[2]

---

9. Poor people awaiting Fairfax's alms.
1. The house is described as an inn, with an allusion to Hebrews 11.13–16 and the faithful who proclaim themselves "strangers and pilgrims on the earth" as they "desire a better country, that is, an heavenly."

2. In 1518 the heiress Isabel Thwaites was to marry Thomas Fairfax's ancestor, William, but was confined by her guardian, the prioress of Nunappleton; William obtained an order for her release and then seized her by force and married her.

Fair beyond measure, and an heir
Which might deformity make fair.
And oft she spent the summer suns
Discoursing with the subtle nuns.
95 Whence in these words one to her weaved
(As 'twere by chance) thoughts long conceived.

13

"Within this holy leisure we
Live innocently as you see.
These walls restrain the world without,
100 But hedge° our liberty about.   defend
These bars inclose that wider den
Of those wild creatures, callèd men;
The cloister outward shuts its gates,
And, from us, locks on them the grates.

14

105 "Here we, in shining armor white,°   nun's habit
Like virgin amazons do fight:
And our chaste lamps we hourly trim,
Lest the great bridegroom find them dim.[3]
Our orient° breaths perfumed are   fresh
110 With incense of incessant pray'r.
And holy water of our tears
Most strangely our complexion clears:

15

"Not tears of grief; but such as those
With which calm pleasure overflows;
115 Or pity, when we look on you
That live without this happy vow.
How should we grieve that must be seen
Each one a spouse, and each a queen;
And can in heaven hence behold
120 Our brighter robes and crowns of gold?

16

"When we have prayed all our beads,
Some one the holy legend° reads;   a saint's life
While all the rest with needles paint
The face and graces of the saint.
125 But what the linen can't receive
They in their lives do interweave.
This work the saints best represents;
That serves for altar's ornaments.

---

3. Matthew 25.1–13 contrasts the wise virgins who kept their lamps lit for the bridegroom (Christ) and the foolish ones who did not and so were excluded from the marriage feast (heaven).

17

"But much it to our work would add
130 If here your hand, your face we had.
    By it we would our Lady touch;[4]
    Yet thus she you resembles much.
    Some of your features, as we sewed,
    Through every shrine should be bestowed:
135 And in one beauty we would take
    Enough a thousand saints to make.

18

"And (for I dare not quench the fire
    That me does for your good inspire)
    'Twere sacrilege a man t' admit
140 To holy things, for heaven fit.
    I see the angels in a crown
    On you the lilies show'ring down;
    And round about you glory breaks,
    That something more than human speaks.

19

145 "All beauty, when at such a height,
    Is so already consecrate.
    Fairfax I know; and long ere this
    Have marked the youth, and what he is.
    But can he such a rival seem
150 For whom you heav'n should disesteem?
    Ah, no! and 'twould more honor prove
    He your devoto° were, than love.   *devotee*

20

"Here live beloved, and obeyed,
    Each one your sister, each your maid.
155 And, if our rule seem strictly penned,
    The rule itself to you shall bend.
    Our abbess too, now far in age,
    Doth your succession near presage.
    How soft the yoke on us would lie,
160 Might such fair hands as yours it tie!

21

"Your voice, the sweetest of the choir,
    Shall draw heav'n nearer, raise us higher:
    And your example, if our head,
    Will soon us to perfection lead.
165 Those virtues to us all so dear,

---

4. We could come close to representing the Virgin Mary in our designs with you as model.

Will straight° grow sanctity when here: *immediately*
And that, once sprung, increase so fast
Till miracles it work at last.

22

"Nor is our order yet so nice,°   *precise*
170 Delight to banish as a vice.
Here pleasure piety doth meet,
One perfecting the other sweet.
So through the mortal fruit we boil
The sugar's uncorrupting oil;
175 And that which perished while we pull,
Is thus preserved clear and full.

23

"For such indeed are all our arts;
Still handling nature's finest parts.
Flow'rs dress the altars; for the clothes,
180 The sea-born amber[5] we compose;
Balms for the grieved° we draw; and pastes   *injured*
We mold, as baits for curious tastes.
What need is here of man? unless
These as sweet sins we should confess.

24

185 "Each night among us to your side
Appoint a fresh and virgin bride;
Whom if our Lord at midnight find,
Yet neither should be left behind.
Where you may lie as chaste in bed,
190 As pearls together billeted,
All night embracing arm in arm,
Like crystal pure with cotton warm.

25

"But what is this to all the store
Of joys you see, and may make more!
195 Try but a while, if you be wise:
The trial neither costs, nor ties."
Now Fairfax seek her promised faith:° *promise to wed*
Religion that dispensed hath;
Which she henceforward does begin:[6]
200 The nun's smooth tongue has sucked her in.

---

5. Ambergris from the sperm whale supplies the rich perfume for our altar cloths.

6. She now begins her "religious" life in the convent.

26

Oft, though he knew it was in vain,
Yet would he valiantly complain:
"Is this that sanctity so great,
An art by which you finelier cheat?
205   Hypocrite witches, hence avaunt,
Who though in prison yet enchant!
Death only can such thieves make fast,
As rob though in the dungeon cast.

27

"Were there but, when this house was made,
210   One stone that a just hand had laid,
It must have fall'n upon her head
Who first thee from thy faith misled.
And yet, how well soever meant,
With them 'twould soon grow fraudulent:
215   For like themselves they alter all,
And vice infects the very wall.

28

"But sure those buildings last not long,
Founded by folly, kept by wrong.
I know what fruit their gardens yield,
220   When they it think by night concealed.
Fly from their vices. 'Tis thy state,°   *estate*
Not thee, that they would consecrate.
Fly from their ruin. How I fear
Though guiltless lest thou perish there!"

29

225   What should he do? He would respect
Religion, but not right neglect;
For first religion taught him right,
And dazzled not but cleared his sight.
Sometimes resolved his sword he draws,
230   But reverenceth then the laws:
For justice still that courage led;
First from a judge, then soldier bred.[7]

30

Small honor would be in the storm.°   *storming the priory*
The court him grants the lawful form;
235   Which licensed either peace or force,
To hinder the unjust divorce.

---

7. His father was judge of the Common Pleas; his maternal grandfather was a heroic soldier.

Yet still the nuns his right debarred,
Standing upon their holy guard.
Ill-counseled women, do you know
240   Whom you resist, or what you do?

31

Is not this he whose offspring fierce
Shall fight through all the universe;
And with successive valor try
France, Poland, either Germany;
245   Till one, as long since prophesied,
His horse through conquered Britain ride?
Yet, against fate, his spouse they kept,
And the great race would intercept.[8]

32

Some to the breach against their foes
250   Their wooden saints in vain oppose.
Another bolder stands at push
With their old holy-water brush.
While the disjointed° abbess threads   *distracted*
The jingling chain-shot[9] of her beads.
255   But their loud'st cannon were their lungs;
And sharpest weapons were their tongues.

33

But, waving these aside like flies,
Young Fairfax through the wall does rise.
Then th' unfrequented vault appeared,
260   And superstitions vainly feared.
The relics false were set to view;
Only the jewels there were true—
But truly bright and holy Thwaites
That weeping at the altar waits.

34

265   But the glad youth away her bears
And to the nuns bequeaths her tears:
Who guiltily their prize bemoan,
Like gypsies that a child had stol'n.
Thenceforth (as when th' enchantment ends
270   The castle vanishes or rends)
The wasting cloister with the rest
Was in one instant dispossesed.[1]

---

8. Thomas Fairfax, son of William and Isabel Thwaites, fought in Italy and Germany; his descendants were also honored soldiers; the present Fairfax fulfilled the prophecy by his victories in the Civil War.

9. Cannonballs linked in a chain and fired together.

1. An allusion to Henry VIII's dissolution of the monasteries.

35

    At the demolishing, this seat
    To Fairfax fell as by escheat.[2]
275 And what both nuns and founders willed
    'Tis likely better thus fulfilled:
    For if the virgin proved not theirs,
    The cloister yet remained hers;
    Though many a nun there made her vow,
280 'Twas no religious house till now.

36

    From that blest bed the hero came,
    Whom France and Poland yet does fame;
    Who, when retired here to peace,
    His warlike studies could not cease;
285 But laid these gardens out in sport
    In the just figure of a fort;
    And with five bastions it did fence,
    As aiming one for ev'ry sense.[3]

37

    When in the east the morning ray
290 Hangs out the colors of the day,
    The bee through these known alleys hums,
    Beating the dian° with its drums.   *reveille*
    Then flow'rs their drowsy eyelids raise,
    Their silken ensigns each displays,
295 And dries its pan[4] yet dank with dew,
    And fills its flask° with odors new.   *powder flask*

38

    These, as their governor goes by,
    In fragrant volleys they let fly;
    And to salute their governess
300 Again as great a charge they press:
    None for the virgin nymph;[5] for she
    Seems with the flow'rs a flow'r to be.
    And think so still! though not compare[6]
    With breath so sweet, or cheek so fair.

39

305 Well shot ye firemen!° Oh how sweet,   *shooters*
    And round your equal fires do meet;

---

2. Legally, in the absence of an heir, the property reverted to him as lord of the manor; Henry gave monastery lands to his nobles.
3. The garden's five (seeming) bulwarks or fortifications aim at the five senses.
4. In a musket, the hollow part of the lock that receives the priming.
5. Mary Fairfax (Maria)—Marvell's pupil at Nunappleton.
6. The imperatives are addressed to the flowers.

Whose shrill report no ear can tell,
But echoes to the eye and smell.
See how the flow'rs, as at parade,
310 Under their colors stand displayed:
Each regiment in order grows,
That of the tulip, pink, and rose.

40

But when the vigilant patrol
Of stars walks round about the pole,
315 Their leaves, that to the stalks are curled,
Seem to their staves the ensigns furled.
Then in some flow'r's beloved hut
Each bee as sentinel is shut;
And sleeps so too: but, if once stirred,
320 She runs you through, nor asks the word.°   password

41

Oh thou,° that dear and happy isle   England
The garden of the world ere while,
Thou paradise of four⁷ seas,
Which heaven planted us to please,
325 But, to exclude the world, did guard
With wat'ry if not flaming sword;⁸
What luckless apple did we taste,
To make us mortal, and thee waste?

42

Unhappy! shall we never more
330 That sweet militia restore,
When gardens only had their tow'rs,
And all the garrisons were flow'rs;
When roses only arms might bear,
And men did rosy garlands wear?
335 Tulips, in several colors barred,
Were then the Switzers⁹ of our guard.

43

The gardener had the soldier's place,
And his more gentle forts did trace.
The nursery of all things green
340 Was then the only magazine.
The winter quarters were the stoves°   hothouses
Where he the tender plants removes.
But war all this doth overgrow;
We ordnance plant, and powder sow.

---

7. Pronounced with two syllables.
8. After the Fall, the garden in Eden was guarded
by angels with flaming swords.

9. The papal Swiss guards wore multicolored uniforms.

44

345 And yet there walks one on the sod
Who, had it pleased him and God,
Might once have made our gardens spring
Fresh as his own and flourishing.
But he preferred to the Cinque Ports[1]
350 These five imaginary forts;
And, in those half-dry trenches, spanned°   *restrained*
Pow'r which the ocean might command.

45

For he did, with his utmost skill,
Ambition weed, but conscience till.
355 Conscience, that heaven-nursèd plant,
Which most our earthly gardens want.°   *lack, need*
A prickling leaf it bears, and such
As that which shrinks at every touch;
But flow'rs eternal, and divine,
360 That in the crowns of saints do shine.

46

The sight does from these bastions ply
Th' invisible artillery;
And at proud Cawood Castle[2] seems
To point the batt'ry of its beams,
365 As if it quarreled in° the seat   *found fault with*
Th' ambition of its prelate great;
But o'er the meads below it plays,
Or innocently seems to gaze.

47

And now to the abyss I pass
370 Of that unfathomable grass,
Where men like grasshoppers appear,
But grasshoppers are giants[3] there:
They, in their squeaking laugh, contemn
Us as we walk more low than them:
375 And, from the precipices tall
Of the green spires, to us do call.

48

To see men through this meadow dive,
We wonder how they rise alive;

---

1. The five ports on the southeast coast of England, of which Fairfax was warden for a time; the "imaginary forts" (next line) are the "five bastions" of line 287.
2. Seat of the archbishop of York, two miles from Appleton House.
3. Cf. Numbers 13.33: "And there we saw the giants . . . and we were in our own sight as grasshoppers, and so we were in their sight."

As, underwater, none does know
380 Whether he fall through it or go;°   *move forward*
But as the mariners that sound
And show upon their lead the ground,[4]
They bring up flow'rs so to be seen,
And prove they've at the bottom been.

49

385 No scene° that turns with engines strange   *stage set*
Does oft'ner than these meadows change:
For when the sun the grass hath vexed,
The tawny mowers enter next;
Who seem like Israelites to be
390 Walking on foot through a green sea.
To them the grassy deeps divide
And crowd a lane to either side.[5]

50

With whistling scythe and elbow strong,
These massacre the grass along:
395 While one, unknowing, carves the rail,[6]
Whose yet unfeathered quills her fail.
The edge all bloody from its breast
He draws, and does his stroke detest;
Fearing the flesh untimely mowed
400 To him a fate as black forebode.

51

But bloody Thestylis[7] that waits
To bring the mowing camp their cates,°   *food*
Greedy as kites° has trussed it up,   *birds of prey*
And forthwith means on it to sup;
405 When on another quick she lights,
And cries, he[8] called us Israelites;
But now, to make his saying true,
Rails rain for quails, for manna dew.[9]

52

Unhappy birds! what does it boot°   *avail*
410 To build below the grasses' root,
When lowness is unsafe as height,

4. Plumb the depths and show the nature of the ground below.
5. The mowers produce a lane in the grassy meadow, like that formed when the Red Sea parted to allow the Israelites passage.
6. The corncrake (land rail), a field bird.
7. The cook for the harvest workers, comically given the name of a classical shepherdess.
8. The author, at line 389. The Puritans con-
stantly compared themselves and their revolution to the Israelites battling enemies and wandering in the wilderness en route to Canaan, the Promised Land.
9. Exodus 13–15 describes the quails and manna (left after the dew evaporated) with which the Israelites were miraculously fed after crossing the Red Sea.

And chance o'ertakes what scapeth spite?
And now your orphan parents' call
Sounds your untimely funeral.
415 Death-trumpets creak in such a note,
And 'tis the sourdine[1] in their throat.

53

Or° sooner hatch or higher build: *either*
The mower now commands the field;
In whose new traverse° seemeth wrought   *track*
420 A camp of battle newly fought:
Where, as the meads with hay, the plain
Lies quilted o'er with bodies slain;
The women that with forks it fling,
Do represent the pillaging.

54

425 And now the careless victors play,
Dancing the triumphs of the hay;[2]
Where every mower's wholesome heat
Smells like an Alexander's sweat,[3]
Their females fragrant as the mead
430 Which they in fairy circles tread:
When at their dance's end they kiss,
Their new-made hay not sweeter is.

55

When after this 'tis piled in cocks,°   *haystacks*
Like a calm sea it shows the rocks:
435 We wond'ring in the river near
How boats among them safely steer.
Or, like the desert Memphis[4] sand,
Short pyramids of hay do stand.
And such the Roman camps do rise[5]
440 In hills for soldiers' obsequies.

56

This scene° again withdrawing brings   *stage set*
A new and empty face of things;
A leveled space, as smooth and plain,
As cloths for Lely[6] stretched to stain.
445 The world when first created sure
Was such a table rase[7] and pure;

1. A small pipe put into the mouth of a trumpet to produce a low sound.
2. A country dance (with a pun).
3. Plutarch wrote that Alexander the Great's sweat smelled sweet.
4. An ancient Egyptian city near the pyramids.
5. Hillocks that served as burial mounds; they were actually British in origin, not Roman.
6. Canvases for the Dutch portrait painter Sir Peter Lely, who came to England in 1643.
7. *Tabula rasa* (Latin): a clean or blank slate.

Or rather such is the toril
Ere the bulls enter at Madril.[8]

57

For to this naked equal flat,
450 Which Levellers[9] take pattern at,
The villagers in common° chase   *common pasture*
Their cattle, which it closer rase;°   *crops*
And what below the scythe increased°   *grew*
Is pinched yet nearer by the beast.
455 Such, in the painted world, appeared,
Davenant with th' universal herd.[1]

58

They seem within the polished grass
A landscape drawn in looking glass;
And shrunk in the huge pasture show
460 As spots, so shaped, on faces do.[2]
Such fleas, ere they approach the eye,
In multiplying° glasses lie.   *magnifying*
They feed so wide, so slowly move,
As constellations do above.

59

465 Then, to conclude these pleasant acts,
Denton sets ope' its cataracts;[3]
And makes the meadow truly be
(What it but seemed before) a sea.
For, jealous of its lord's long stay,
470 It tries t' invite him thus away.
The river in itself is drowned
And isles th' astonished cattle round.

60

Let others tell the paradox,
How eels now bellow in the ox;[4]
475 How horses at their tails do kick,
Turned as they hang to leeches quick;[5]
How boats can over bridges sail,
And fishes do the stables scale;

---

8. Madrid. "Toril": bull ring.
9. A radical faction, the Diggers or True Levellers, who sought social and economic equality. A group of Diggers began to put their tenets into practice by taking over and cultivating the land on St. George Hill, part of Fairfax's domain. See Gerrard Winstanley (pp. 1849–55).
1. William Davenant, in his heroic poem *Gondibert* (2.6), describes a painting of creation, where on the sixth day "an universal herd" of animals appeared.

2. A landscape (or painted landscape) reflected in a mirror would be reduced in size.
3. Small waterfalls or dams. Denton, also a Fairfax estate (see line 73), was located on the Wharfe River, thirty miles from Nunappleton.
4. Because the ox swallowed them.
5. In popular superstition horse hairs in water became live leeches or eels.

How salmons trespassing are found,
480 And pikes are taken in the pound.°   *cattle pen*

61

But I, retiring from the flood,
Take sanctuary in the wood;
And, while it lasts, myself embark
In this yet green, yet growing ark;
485 Where the first carpenter[6] might best
Fit timber for his keel have pressed;°   *obtained*
And where all creatures might have shares,
Although in armies, not in pairs.

62

The double wood of ancient stocks
490 Linked in so thick an union locks,
It like two pedigrees[7] appears,
On one hand Fairfax, th' other Vere's:
Of whom though many fell in war,
Yet more to heaven shooting are:
495 And, as they nature's cradle decked,
Will in green age her hearse expect.

63

When first the eye this forest sees
It seems indeed as wood not trees;
As if their neighborhood° so old   *nearness*
500 To one great trunk them all did mold.
There the huge bulk takes place, as meant
To thrust up a fifth element;[8]
And stretches still so closely wedged
As if the night within were hedged.

64

505 Dark all without it knits; within
It opens passable and thin;
And in as loose an order grows
As the Corinthian porticoes.[9]
The arching boughs unite between
510 The columns of the temple green;
And underneath the winged choirs
Echo about their tuned fires.

---

6. Noah, who built an ark to escape a flood that would cover the earth (Genesis 6).
7. Genealogical trees, of the Fairfax and Vere families.

8. The so-called quintessence, beyond and superior to fire, air, water, and earth.
9. The most elaborate order of Greek columns.

65

The nightingale does here make choice
To sing the trials of her voice.
515 Low shrubs she sits in, and adorns
With music high the squatted thorns.
But highest oaks stoop down to hear,
And list'ning elders prick the ear.
The thorn, lest it should hurt her, draws
520 Within the skin its shrunken claws.

66

But I have for my music found
A sadder, yet more pleasing sound:
The stock doves,° whose fair necks are graced   *turtledoves*
With nuptial rings, their ensigns chaste;
525 Yet always, for some cause unknown,
Sad pair, unto the elms they moan.
O why should such a couple mourn,
That in so equal flames do burn!

67

Then as I careless on the bed
530 Of gelid strawberries do tread,
And through the hazels thick espy
The hatching throstle's shining eye,
The heron from the ash's top
The eldest of its young lets drop,
535 As if it stork-like[1] did pretend
That tribute to its lord to send.

68

But most the hewel's° wonders are,   *green woodpecker's*
Who here has the holtfelster's° care.   *woodcutter's*
He walks still upright from the root,
540 Meas'ring the timber with his foot;
And all the way, to keep it clean,
Doth from the bark the wood-moths glean.
He, with his beak, examines well
Which fit to stand and which to fell.

69

545 The good he numbers up, and hacks;
As if he marked them with the ax.
But where he, tinkling with his beak,

---

1. The stork upon leaving a nest was believed to leave behind one of its young as a tribute to the householder.

Does find the hollow oak[2] to speak,
That for his building he designs,
550 And through the tainted side he mines.
Who could have thought the tallest oak
Should fall by such a feeble stroke!

70

Nor would it, had the tree not fed
A traitor-worm, within it bred.
555 (As first our flesh corrupt within
Tempts impotent and bashful sin)
And yet that worm triumphs not long,
But serves to feed the hewel's young;
While the oak seems to fall content,
560 Viewing the treason's punishment.

71

Thus I, easy philosopher,
Among the birds and trees confer;
And little now to make me, wants°   lacks
Or° of the fowls, or of the plants.   either
565 Give me but wings as they, and I
Straight floating on the air shall fly:
Or turn me but, and you shall see
I was but an inverted tree.[3]

72

Already I begin to call
570 In their most learned original:
And where I language want, my signs
The bird upon the bough divines;
And more attentive there doth sit
Than if she were with lime[4] twigs knit.
575 No leaf does tremble in the wind
Which I returning cannot find.

73

Out of these scattered Sibyl's leaves
Strange prophecies my fancy weaves:[5]
And in one history consumes,
580 Like Mexique paintings, all the plumes.°   feathers
What Rome, Greece, Palestine, ere said
I in this light Mosaic[6] read.

---

2. The "royal" oak was traditionally an emblem of monarchy.
3. Originally classical, this is a widely used metaphor in the Renaissance.
4. Birdlime, a sticky substance smeared on twigs to trap birds.

5. The Cumaean Sibyl, in Virgil, committed her prophecies to leaves that Aeneas feared might be scattered (*Aeneid* 6.77).
6. The pattern formed by the trembling leaves; also the books of Moses, who was thought to have written the first five books of the Bible.

Thrice happy he who, not mistook,
Hath read in nature's mystic book.[7]

74

585 And see how chance's better wit
Could with a mask[8] my studies hit!
The oak-leaves me embroider all,
Between which caterpillars crawl;
And ivy, with familiar trails,
590 Me licks, and clasps, and curls, and hales.
Under this antic cope[9] I move
Like some great prelate of the grove.

75

Then, languishing with ease, I toss
On pallets swol'n of velvet moss;
595 While the wind, cooling through the boughs,
Flatters with air my panting brows.
Thanks for my rest, ye mossy banks,
And unto you, cool zephyrs,° thanks,   *gentle west winds*
Who, as my hair, my thoughts too shed,°   *part*
600 And winnow from the chaff my head.

76

How safe, methinks, and strong, behind
These trees have I encamped my mind;
Where beauty, aiming at the heart,
Bends in some tree its useless° dart;   *harmless*
605 And where the world no certain shot
Can make, or me it toucheth not.
But I on it securely play,
And gall its horsemen all the day.

77

Bind me ye woodbines in your twines,
610 Curl me about ye gadding vines,
And O so close your circles lace,
That I may never leave this place:
But, lest your fetters prove too weak,
Ere I your silken bondage break,
615 Do you, O brambles, chain me too,
And courteous briars, nail me through.[1]

---

7. The book of the creatures, or the book of
God's works.
8. Masque costume or disguise appropriate to
the speaker's studies.

9. Comic ecclesiastical vestment.
1. The imagery evokes imprisonment and crucifixion.

78

Here in the morning tie my chain,
Where the two woods have made a lane;
While, like a guard on either side,
620   The trees before their lord divide;
This, like a long and equal thread,
Betwixt two labyrinths does lead.
But, where the floods did lately drown,
There at the evening stake me down.

79

625   For now the waves are fall'n and dried,
And now the meadows fresher dyed;
Whose grass, with moister color dashed,
Seems as green silks but newly washed.
No serpent new nor crocodile
630   Remains behind our little Nile;[2]
Unless itself you will mistake,
Among these meads° the only snake.   *meadows*

80

See in what wanton harmless folds
It ev'rywhere the meadow holds;
635   And its yet muddy back doth lick,
Till as a crystal mirror slick;°   *smooth*
Where all things gaze themselves, and doubt
If they be in it or without.
And for his shade° which therein shines,   *shadow*
640   Narcissus-like, the sun too pines.[3]

81

Oh what a pleasure 'tis to hedge
My temples here with heavy sedge;
Abandoning my lazy side,
Stretched as a bank unto the tide;
645   Or to suspend my sliding foot
On th' osier's undermined root,
And in its branches tough to hang,
While at my lines the fishes twang!

82

But now away my hooks, my quills,°   *floats*
650   And angles, idle utensils.
The young Maria walks tonight:

2. Our river; serpents and crocodiles were
thought to be bred by spontaneous generation
from the mud of the Nile.

3. Narcissus lay beside water, staring at his
reflection, pining for himself.

Hide trifling youth thy pleasures slight.
'Twere shame that such judicious eyes
Should with such toys a man surprise;
655 She that already is the law
Of all her sex, her age's awe.

83

See how loose nature, in respect
To her, itself doth recollect;
And everything so whisht° and fine,   *hushed*
660 Starts forthwith to its bonne mine.°   *good appearance*
The sun himself, of Her aware,
Seems to descend with greater care;
And lest she see him go to bed,
In blushing clouds conceals his head.

84

665 So when the shadows laid asleep
From underneath these banks do creep,
And on the river as it flows
With ebon shuts° begin to close;   *black shutters*
The modest halcyon[4] comes in sight,
670 Flying betwixt the day and night;
And such an horror calm and dumb,
Admiring nature does benumb.

85

The viscous° air, wheresoe'r she fly,   *thick*
Follows and sucks her azure dye;
675 The jellying stream compacts° below,   *solidifies*
If it might fix her shadow so;
The stupid° fishes hang, as plain   *stupefied*
As flies in crystal overta'en;
And men the silent scene assist,°   *attend*
680 Charmed with the sapphire-wingèd mist.[5]

86

Maria such, and so° doth hush   *in like fashion*
The world, and through the ev'ning rush.
No newborn comet such a train
Draws through the sky, nor star new-slain.[6]
685 For straight those giddy rockets[7] fail,
Which from the putrid earth exhale,
But by her flames, in heaven tried,
Nature is wholly vitrified.°   *turned to glass*

---

4. The kingfisher, who by nesting on the waves
was believed to bring absolute calm to the sea.
5. The bird in its flight.

6. Meteor, or shooting star.
7. Vapors exhaled from the earth.

87

'Tis she that to these gardens gave
690 That wondrous beauty which they have;
She straightness on the woods bestows;
To her the meadow sweetness owes;
Nothing could make the river be
So crystal-pure but only she;
695 She yet more pure, sweet, straight, and fair,
Than gardens, woods, meads, rivers are.

88

Therefore what first she on them spent,
They gratefully again present:
The meadow, carpets where to tread;
700 The garden, flow'rs to crown her head;
And for a glass, the limpid brook,
Where she may all her beauties look;
But, since she would not have them seen,
The wood about her draws a screen.

89

705 For she, to higher beauties raised,
Disdains to be for lesser praised.
She counts her beauty to converse
In all the languages as hers;
Nor yet in those herself employs
710 But for the wisdom, not the noise;
Nor yet that wisdom would affect,
But as 'tis heaven's dialect.

90

Blest nymph! that couldst so soon prevent
Those trains° by youth against thee meant: *artillery*
715 Tears (wat'ry shot that pierce the mind)
And sighs (love's cannon charged with wind)
True praise (that breaks through all defense)
And feigned complying innocence;
But knowing where this ambush lay,
720 She scaped the safe, but roughest way.

91

This 'tis to have been from the first
In a domestic heaven nursed,
Under the discipline severe
Of Fairfax, and the starry Vere;
725 Where not one object can come nigh
But pure, and spotless as the eye;

And goodness doth itself entail
On females, if there want a male.[8]

92

Go now fond° sex that on your face   *foolish*
730   Do all your useless study place,
Nor once at vice your brows dare knit
Lest the smooth forehead wrinkled sit;
Yet your own face shall at you grin,
Thorough° the black-bag° of your skin;   *through / mask*
735   When knowledge only could have filled
And virtue all those furrows tilled.

93

Hence she with graces more divine
Supplies beyond her sex the line;
And, like a sprig of mistletoe,
740   On the Fairfacian oak doth grow;
Whence, for some universal good,
The priest shall cut the sacred bud;[9]
While her glad parents most rejoice,
And make their destiny their choice.

94

745   Meantime ye fields, springs, bushes, flow'rs,
Where yet she leads her studious hours
(Till fate her worthily translates,
And find a Fairfax for our Thwaites),
Employ the means you have by her,
750   And in your kind yourselves prefer;[1]
That, as all virgins she precedes,
So you all woods, streams, gardens, meads.

95

For you Thessalian Tempe's[2] seat
Shall now be scorned as obsolete;
755   Aranjuez, as less, disdained;
The Bel-Retiro[3] as constrained;
But name not the Idalian grove,[4]
For 'twas the seat of wanton Love;
Much less the dead's Elysian Fields,[5]
760   Yet nor to them your beauty yields.

---

8. Maria was the only child and heir of the Fair-
faxes.
9. Maria is, of course, intended for marriage.
1. Make yourselves the best you can.
2. The Vale of Tempe, in Greece, was a kind of
paradise.

3. Spanish palaces.
4. A favorite haunt of Aphrodite (Venus), goddess of love, on Cyprus.
5. The pleasant habitation of the good in the
classical underworld.

96

'Tis not, what once it was, the world,
But a rude heap together hurled;
All negligently overthrown,
Gulfs, deserts, precipices, stone.
765   Your lesser world[6] contains the same,
But in more decent order tame;
You heaven's center, nature's lap,
And paradise's only map.

97

But now the salmon-fishers moist
770   Their leathern boats begin to hoist;
And, like antipodes in shoes,
Have shod their heads in their canoes.[7]
How tortoise-like, but not so slow,
These rational amphibii[8] go!
775   Let's in; for the dark hemisphere
Does now like one of them appear.

1651   1681

---

6. Appleton House.
7. The men who dwell at the "antipodes," on the other side of the world are sometimes said to wear their shoes on their heads; these English fishermen transport their leather boats on their heads.
8. As men, the fishermen are "rational"; and they live in two elements, land and water.

Crisis of Authority

Most of the poets and prose writers who published in the "civil war decades," 1640 to 1660, registered in some way their responses to the conflicts swirling about them. The war and the issues over which it was fought shadow the poetry of Vaughan, Herrick, Lovelace, Suckling, and Marvell and the prose of Thomas Browne and Izaak Walton. Yet often such writers addressed the conflict only obliquely. When Marvell or Herrick celebrates peaceful gardens or fruitful countryside, when Vaughan envisions eternity as a "great ring of pure and endless light" suspended above all mortal turmoil, when Walton rhapsodizes about fishing, they create refuges of the imagination that might partially compensate for the trauma of war. Other writers confronted the issues of the age more straightforwardly. The readings included in this section sample some of this more explicitly political writing and exemplify some of the genres encouraged by the new conditions in which literary materials could be written and circulated.

With the restoration of Charles II in 1660, many of the radical voices of the 1640s and 1650s were muted. Yet the war decades left a lasting imprint upon English literature. They established a tradition of overtly political, often ambitiously literary writing without which it is hard to imagine the works of such authors as Dryden, Swift, and Pope. They established prose as a dominant literary medium, especially for the description and analysis of everyday life. They initiated a tradition of apparently ordinary people bearing witness in writing to extraordinary events: a vital precedent for the rise of the novel.

This section presents examples of several kinds of writing that flourished during the Civil War and its immediate aftermath: the journalistic reporting of current events; political theory; and careful descriptions of contemporary history, personal experience, and individual character. These excerpts demonstrate a variety of ways in which writers might respond to the disturbing and exciting developments around them: by reporting the details of dramatic, unprecedented occurences; by analyzing the political and social problems posed by the conflict; by ruminating upon the character of great men; by seizing new opportunities for autobiographical reflection. For other responses to the crisis of the war and other perspectives on the interregnum, go to the supplemental ebook, where you'll find the Leveler John Lilburne's call for a new government founded on popular sovereignty; the Fifth Monarchist Anna Trapnel's report of her visions, her travels, and her critique of Cromwell's government; and the Ranter Abiezer Coppe's radical denunciation of all human laws on the ground that he possesses the Spirit of God.

REPORTING THE NEWS

The following accounts of the king's trial and execution are excerpted from newsbooks, one of the most important new literary forms of the war years. In England the reportage of current events originated in the 1620s, when anxiety over the nation's entanglement in what would become the Thirty Years War on the Continent generated a demand for international news. In addition, in the 1620s and 1630s a few enterprising individuals provided "corantos," handwritten reports of court goings-on, to wealthy individuals in the provinces; these were technically considered private letters, although they sometimes circulated to several hundred paid subscribers. Yet even these modest ventures were always on legally shaky ground. The printing of domestic news, or commentary thereon, was strictly prohibited by Charles I, as it had been by his forebears.

In the early 1640s, censorship collapsed just when many people urgently wanted information about the momentous events transpiring in England, Scotland, and Ireland. The result was the explosive development of printed news. While in 1640 there were no newsbooks, by 1645 there were 755. Their format varied, but typically they were eight-page cheaply printed pamphlets, issued weekly. Most writers and compilers remained anonymous, though in some cases the identity of the authors was an open secret. Unlike the earlier corantos, the inexpensive newsbooks of the 1640s gave a broad spectrum of readers access to information about current events. Often, simultaneously, they propagandized on behalf of various parties to the developing conflict. The newsbooks thus encouraged an unprecedentedly wide and deep sense of civic involvement, and arguably also had the effect of hardening factional differences.

The newsbooks provided eyewitness, or what purported to be eyewitness, accounts of the king's trial and execution very shortly after they occurred. Both events were highly charged, with important and complex stakes on both sides. In the autumn of 1648, many in Parliament who had initially wanted to restrict the king's powers hesitated to remove him from the throne; they favored a negotiated end to hostilities. Yet the powerful leaders of the New Model Army, including Oliver Cromwell, were convinced that Charles was a threat to a reorganized commonwealth. Even if the king dealt with his opponents in good faith, which they doubted, he would be a constant rallying point for opposition to their policies. Conceivably, the war would never be over.

When Charles seemed to be planning to escape from his relatively light confinement on the Isle of Wight, the army council ordered him seized and brought to London, which the army occupied. Yet what were they to do with their captive? Simply to assassinate him would deprive his killers of any semblance of legitimacy. A formal trial, therefore, seemed necessary; but it was not easy to achieve. First, Parliament had to be purged of more than half its members, who disapproved of putting the king on trial. Once reconstituted so as to exclude opposition, Parliament then had to pass a law redefining treason as a crime against the state, not a crime against the king, of which the king himself could not logically have been guilty.

As in the case of most treason trials in the sixteenth and seventeenth centuries, a guilty verdict was a foregone conclusion. Yet the trial's value as propaganda was unpredictable. The judges and executioners pointedly assumed the regalia and symbolism of state power, and conducted both the trial and the execution with great punctiliousness, in order to bolster the impression of due process in the eyes of onlookers and newsbook readers. Charles's calmly defiant behavior, meanwhile, was not meant to secure his acquittal, which everyone knew would have been unforthcoming anyhow. Rather, he hoped to garner sympathy for his plight, to demonstrate publicly his unwavering adherence to his own principles, and to provoke prosecutors and judges into behaving like rabid zealots. Likewise, his conduct on the scaffold impressed even those who deplored his political position. While his judges and executioners strove to describe him as an overweening tyrant, Charles struggled to appear the heir to a Christian tradition of suffering innocence, a "martyr of the people." In 1660, as soon as the monarchy was restored, Charles I was canonized by the Church of England.

From The Moderate, No. 28

16–23 January 1649

[THE TRIAL OF KING CHARLES I, THE FIRST DAY]

At the high court of justice sitting in the Great Hall of Westminster, Sergeant Bradshaw President,[1] about 70 Members present. Oyez[2] made thrice, silence commanded. The president had the sword and mace carried before him, attended with Colonel Fox, and twenty other officers and gentlemen with partisans.[3] The act of the Commons in Parliament for trial of the king, read. After the court was called, and each member rising up as he was called. The king came into the court, his hat on, and the Commissioners with theirs on also; no congratulation or motion of hats at all.[4] The Sergeant ushered him in with the mace, Colonel Hacker[5] and about thirty officers and gentlemen more came as his guard; the president then spake in these words, viz.

"Charles Stuart, King of England, the Commons of England assembled in Parliament being sensible of the great calamities that have been brought upon this nation, of the innocent blood that hath been shed in this nation, which is referred[6] to you, as the author of it; and according to that duty which they owe to God, to the nation, and themselves, and according to that fundamental power and trust that is reposed in them by the people, have constituted this high court of justice before which you are now brought; and you are to hear the charge upon which the court will proceed."

Mr. Cook Solicitor General.[7] "My lord, in behalf of the Commons of England, and of all the people thereof, I do accuse Charles Stuart, here present, of high treason and high misdemeanors, and I do in the name of the Commons of England desire that the charge may be read unto him."

King. "Hold a little"—tapping the solicitor general twice on the shoulder with his cane, which drawing towards him again, the head thereon fell off, he stooping for it, put it presently[8] into his pocket. This is conceived will be very ominous.

Lord President. "Sir, the court commands the charge to be read; if you have any thing to say after, you may be heard."

The charge was read.

The king smiled often during the time, especially at those words therein, viz that Charles Stuart was a tyrant, traitor, murderer, and public enemy of the commonwealth.

---

1. John Bradshaw (1609–1659), chief justice of Cheshire and Wales, accepted the office of president after others declined. He lost this office after 1653, when he opposed Cromwell's consolidation of personal power. Bradshaw was posthumously convicted of treason at the Restoration in 1660; his body was exhumed and hanged in chains.
2. Hear ye (French).
3. John Fox (1610–1650) was commander of the Lord President's bodyguard, the members of which carried spears with a lobed base "partisan." The "sword and mace" symbolizes state power.

4. For either the king or the judges to doff their hats would be to acknowledge the others' superiority. "Congratulation": salutation.
5. Francis Hacker (1618–1660) commanded the soldiers who guarded the king, signed the king's death warrant, and supervised the guard on the scaffold. He was executed after the Restoration.
6. Attributed.
7. John Cook (1608–1660), a radical republican lawyer, served as chief prosecutor. He was executed after the Restoration.
8. Immediately.

Lord President. "Sir, you have now heard your charge read, containing such matter as appears in it: you find that in the close of it, it is prayed to the court in the behalf of all the Commons of England, that you answer to your charge. The court expects your answer."

King. "I would know by what power I am called hither. I was not long ago in the Isle of Wight; how I came hither is a larger story then I think is fit at this time for me to speak of: But there I entered into a treaty with the two Houses of Parliament, with as much public faith as is possibly to be had of any people in the world. I treated there with a number of honorable lords and gentlemen, and treated honestly and uprightly. I cannot say but they did deal very nobly with me. We were upon conclusion of a treaty. Now I would know by what authority—I mean lawful; there are many unlawful authorities in the world, thieves and robbers by the highways—but I would know by what authority I was brought from thence, and carried from place to place; and when I know by what lawful authority, I shall answer.

"Remember, I am your king, your lawful king; and what sin you bring upon your heads, and the judgments of God upon this land, think well upon it; I say think well upon it before you go further, from one sin to a greater.[9] Therefore let me know by what lawful authority I am seated here, and I shall not be unwilling to answer. In the meantime, I shall not betray my trust. I have a trust committed to me by God, by old and lawful descent. I will not betray it, to answer to a new and unlawful authority. Therefore resolve me that, and you shall hear more of me."

Lord President. "If you had been pleased to have observed what was hinted to you by the court at our first coming hither, you would have known by what authority; which authority requires you in the name of the people of England, of which you are elected king, to answer them."

King. "No sir, I deny that."

Lord President. "If you acknowledge not the authority of the court, they must proceed."

King. "I do tell you so, England was never an elective kingdom, but an hereditary kingdom, for near a thousand years; therefore let me know by what authority I am called hither. I do stand more for the liberty of my people than any here that come to be my pretended judges; and therefore let me know by what lawful authority I am seated here, and I will answer it; otherwise I will not answer it."

Lord President told him he did interrogate the court, which beseemed not one in his condition, and it was known how he had managed his trust.

* * *

King. "I desire that you would give me, and all the world, satisfaction in this. For let me tell you, it is not a slight thing you are about. I am sworn to keep the peace by the duty I owe to God and my country; and I will do it to the last breath of my body: And therefore you shall do well to satisfy first God and then the country by what authority you do it; if by a reserved[1] authority, you cannot answer it. There is a God in heaven that will call you, and all that give you power, to an account. Satisfy me in that, and I will

---

9. From rebellion to regicide.   1. Unexplained.

answer; otherwise, I betray my trust and the liberties of the people. And therefore think of that, and then I shall be willing. For I do vow, that it is as great a sin to withstand lawful authority, as it is to submit to a tyrannical or any otherways unlawful authority, And therefore satisfy me that, and you shall receive my answer."

Lord President. "The court expects a final answer. They are to adjourn till Monday. If you satisfy not yourself, though we tell you our authority, we are satisfied with our authority, and it is upon God's authority and the kingdom's; and that peace you speak of will be kept in the doing of justice; and that is our present work."

The court adjourned till Monday ten of clock to the Painted Chamber, and thence hither.

As the king went away, facing the court, the king said, "I fear not that," looking upon and meaning the sword.

Going down from the court, the people cried, "Justice, justice, justice!"

Jan. 21. The commissioners kept a fast this day in Whitehall. There preached before them Mr. Sprig, whose text was, "He that sheds blood, by man shall his blood be shed." Mr. Foxley's was "Judge not, lest you be judged." And Mr. Peters' was. "I will bind their kings in chains, and their nobles in fetters of iron."[2] The last sermon made amends for the two former.

1649

From A Perfect Diurnal of Some Passages in Parliament, No. 288

Tuesday, January 30

[THE EXECUTION OF CHARLES I]

This day the king was beheaded over against the Banqueting House by Whitehall.[1] The manner of execution and what passed before his death take thus.[2] He was brought from Saint James[3] about ten in the morning, walking on foot through the park with a regiment of foot for his guard, with colors flying, drums beating, his private guard of partisans,[4] with some of his gentlemen before, and some behind bareheaded, Dr. Juxon late Bishop of London[5] next behind him, and Colonel Tomlinson[6] (who had the charge of him) to the gallery in Whitehall, and so into the Cabinet Chamber where he used to lie, where he continued at his devotion, refusing to dine (having

2. The biblical texts are Genesis 9.6, Matthew 7.1, and Psalms 149.8. Hugh Peters (1598–1660), Independent preacher to Cromwell's New Model Army, passionately supported the king's execution. He was himself executed after the Restoration.
1. Whitehall Palace was the English monarch's principal residence from 1530 to 1698, when most of it was destroyed by fire. The Banqueting House, designed by Inigo Jones with ceilings painted by Peter Paul Rubens, was built for King James I in 1619–22 and was used to stage court masques. "Over against": just outside.
2. Accept the following account.

3. St. James Palace, near Whitehall.
4. Guards armed with partisans, spears with lobed points or halberds.
5. William Juxon (1582–1663), Charles I's personal chaplain, was bishop of London until 1649, when he was deprived of office. In the late 1630s he had also served as one of the king's financial advisers. After the Restoration he became archbishop of Canterbury.
6. Matthew Tomlinson commanded the guards assigned to Charles. He was tried after the Restoration but was spared because he had been courteous to the king.

before taken the sacrament) only about 12 at noon he drank a glass of claret wine, and eat a piece of bread. From thence he was accompanied by Dr. Juxon, Colonel Tomlinson, Colonel Hacker,[7] and the guards before mentioned through the Banqueting House adjoining to which the scaffold was erected between Whitehall Gate and the gate leading into the gallery from Saint James. The scaffold was hung round with black, and the floor covered with black, and the ax and block laid in the middle of the scaffold. There were divers companies of foot and horse on every side the scaffold, and the multitudes of people that came to be spectators very great. The king making a pass upon[8] the scaffold, looked very earnestly on the block, and asked Colonel Hacker if there were no higher; and then spake thus, directing his speech to the gentlemen upon the scaffold.

King. "I shall be very little heard of anybody here; I shall therefore speak a word unto you here. Indeed I could hold my peace[9] very well, if I did not think that holding my peace would make some men think that I did submit to the guilt as well as to the punishment. But I think it is my duty to God first, and to my country, for to clear myself both as an honest man, and a good king, and a good Christian. I shall begin first with my innocency. In troth I think it not very needful for me to insist long upon this, for all the world knows that I never did begin a war with the two Houses of Parliament, and I call God to witness, to whom I must shortly make an account, that I never did intend for to encroach upon their privileges; they began upon me. It is the militia they began upon;[1] they confessed that the militia was mine but they thought it fit to have it from me; and to be short, if anybody will look to the dates of commissions, theirs and mine, and likewise to the declarations,[2] will see clearly that they began these unhappy troubles, not I. So that as the guilt of these enormous crimes that are laid against me, I hope in God that God will clear me of it. I will not; I am in charity;[3] God forbid that I should lay it upon the two Houses of Parliament, there is no necessity of either.[4] I hope they are free of this guilt; for I do believe that ill instruments[5] between them and me has been the chief cause of all this bloodshed. So that by way of speaking, as I find myself clear of this, I hope and pray God that they may too. Yet for all this, God forbid that I should be so ill a Christian, as not to say that God's judgments are just upon me. Many times he does pay justice by an unjust sentence; that is ordinary. I only say this, that an unjust sentence (meaning Strafford)[6] that I suffered for to take effect, is punished now by an unjust sentence upon me. That is, so far I have said, to show you that I am an innocent man.

7. On Colonel Hacker, see p. 1836, note 5.
8. Traversing.
9. Remain silent. It was customary for condemned prisoners to address onlookers before their public executions. "You here": the small group standing on the scaffold, as distinguished from the large crowd watching the execution.
1. In 1642 Parliament's Militia Ordinance transferred local militias from the king's control to Parliament's. Despite its failure to secure Charles's assent to the measure, Parliament declared it legally binding.

2. "Commissions" and "declarations": warrants for enlisting troops and proclamations of war.
3. Practicing the charity that befits a Christian, I refuse to lay the blame for the war on my enemies.
4. Of blaming either side for the war.
5. Corrupt go-betweens.
6. In an attempt to appease his opponents in Parliament, Charles reluctantly consented to the execution of his adviser Thomas Wentworth, Earl of Strafford, for treason in 1641, despite lack of evidence that Strafford had committed any crime.

"Now for to show you that I am a good Christian, I hope there is" (pointing to Dr. Juxon) "a good man that will bear me witness that I have forgiven all the world, and those in particular that have been the chief causers of my death. Who they are, God knows; I do not desire to know. I pray God forgive them. But this is not all; my charity must go farther. I wish that they may repent, for indeed they have committed a great sin in that particular. I pray God with Saint Stephen that this be not laid to their charge;[7] nay, not only so, but that they may take the right way to the peace of the kingdom, for charity commands me not only to forgive particular men, but to endeavor to the last gasp the peace of the kingdom. Sirs, I do wish with all my soul, and I do hope there is some here will carry it further, that they may endeavor the peace of the kingdom.

"Now, sirs, I must show you both how you are out of the way, and will put you in a way.[8] First, you are out of the way, for certainly all the way[9] you ever have had yet as I could find by anything, is in the way of conquest. Certainly this is an ill way, for conquest, sir, in my opinion is never just, except there be a good just cause, either for matter of wrong or just title, and then if you go beyond it,[1] the first quarrel that you have to it, that makes it unjust at the end that was just at first. But if it be only matter of conquest, then it is a great robbery; as a pirate said to Alexander that he was a great robber, he was but a petty robber. And so, sir, I do think the way that you are in, is much out of the way. Now, sir, for to put you in the way, believe it you never do right, nor God will never prosper you,[2] until you give Him his due, the king his due (that is, my successors) and the people their due. I am as much for them[3] as any of you. You must give God his due by regulating rightly his Church, according to Scripture, which is now out of order. For to set you in a way particularly[4] now I cannot, but only this, a national synod freely called, freely debating among themselves, must settle this; when that every opinion is freely and clearly heard. For the king, indeed I will not—(Then turning to a gentleman that touched the ax, said, hurt not the ax that may hurt me.)—For the king, the laws of the land will clearly instruct you for that; therefore, because it concerns my own particular I only give you a touch of it.[5] For the people, and truly I desire their liberty and freedom, as much as anybody whomsoever; but I must tell you, that their liberty and their freedom consists in having of government, those laws by which their life and their goods may be most their own. It is not for having share in government, sir, that is nothing pertaining to them.[6] A subject and a sovereign are clean[7] different things; and therefore, until they do that, I mean, that you do put the people in that liberty as I say, certainly they will never enjoy themselves.[8] Sirs, it was for this[9] that now I am come here. If I would have given way to an arbitrary way, for to have all laws changed according to the power of the sword, I needed not to have come here; and

---

7. St. Stephen, the first Christian martyr, prayed that God not hold his persecutors responsible for their actions; recounted in Acts 7. "Particular" (previous line): regard.
8. Both show you how you are wrong and put you on a correct course.
9. All the rationale.
1. Beyond what is necessary to correct the wrong.

2. Allow you to flourish.
3. On the people's side.
4. In detail.
5. Because it concerns my own situation, I mention it only briefly.
6. Of their concern or responsibility.
7. Completely.
8. Be happy.
9. Because I upheld the liberty of the people.

therefore I tell you, and I pray God it be not laid to your charge, that I am the martyr of the people. In troth sirs, I shall not hold you much longer; for I will only say this to you, that in truth I could have desired some little time longer because that I would have put this that I have said in a little more order and a little better digested[1] than I have done; and therefore I hope you will excuse me. I have delivered[2] my conscience. I pray God that you do take those courses that are best for the good of the kingdom and your own salvations."

Dr. Juxon. "Will Your Majesty—though it may be very well known Your Majesty's affections to religion—yet it may be expected that you should say somewhat[3] for the world's satisfaction."

King. "I thank you very heartily, my lord, for that I had almost forgotten it. In troth, sirs, my conscience in religion I think is very well known to the world, and therefore I declare before you all that I die a Christian according to the profession of the Church of England as I found it left me by my father; and this honest man, I think, will witness it." Then turning to the officers said, "sirs, excuse me for this same.[4] I have a good cause, and I have a gracious God; I will say no more."

Then turning to Colonel Hacker, he said, "Take care that they do not put me to pain; and, sir, this, an it please you."[5] But then a gentleman coming near the ax, the king said, "Take heed of the ax, pray take heed of the ax." Then the king speaking to the executioner said, "I shall say but very short prayers, and then thrust out my hands."

Then the king called to Dr. Juxon for his nightcap, and having put it on he said to the executioner, "Does my hair trouble you?" Who desired him to put it all under his cap, which the king did accordingly, by the help of the executioner and the bishop. Then the king turning to Dr. Juxon said, "I have a good cause, and a gracious God on my side.

Dr. Juxon, "There is but one stage more. This stage is turbulent and troublesome; it is a short one: But you may consider it will soon carry you a very great way; it will carry you from earth to heaven, and there you shall find a great deal of cordial joy and comfort."

King. "I go from a corruptible to an incorruptible crown, where no disturbance can be."

Dr. Juxon. "You are exchanged from a temporal to an eternal crown, a good exchange."

Then the king took off his cloak and his George,[6] giving his George to Dr. Juxon, saying "Remember" (it is thought for the prince) and some other small ceremonies past. After which the king stooping down laid his neck upon the block, and after a very little pause stretching forth his hands, the executioner at one blow severed his head from his body. Then his body was put in a coffin covered with black velvet, and removed to his lodging chamber in Whitehall.

---

1. More methodically arranged.
2. Spoken
3. Something.
4. This religious profession. Charles did not accept the radical Protestantism espoused by many of his opponents.
5. As was customary, Charles tips Hacker, the person supervising the execution, in hopes of ensuring a quick death. "An": if.
6. A jeweled pendant representing St. George killing a dragon, worn by Knights of the Garter. The prince (following) is the king's eldest son, later King Charles II, who had escaped to exile in France.

POLITICAL WRITING

Not surprisingly, the tumult of civil war stimulated a good deal of thinking about the nature and ends of government. The four excerpts that follow give some idea of the arguments proposed by English political writers between 1630 and 1655.

Robert Filmer and Thomas Hobbes both favor an absolutist government that would concentrate power in the sovereign and deprive the people of any way to get rid of him. However, the two writers work from quite different premises. In *Patriarcha, or The Natural Power of Kings Defended Against the Unnatural Liberty of the People*, Filmer outlines a historical theory based on the authority of biblical patriarchs—Abraham, Isaac, and Jacob, for instance—over their families. God ratified kingly authority, Filmer argues, when he commanded the honoring of parents. Although many royalists retained a larger role for popular consent than Filmer did, Filmer's account of the king's fatherly care of his people, and the people's childlike incompetence to manage political affairs, was close to the Stuart kings' own view.

Unlike Filmer, Thomas Hobbes, a gifted mathematician, believed in working from clearly defined first principles to conclusions, grounding his political vision not on biblical history but upon a comprehensive philosophy of nature and of knowledge. He believed that human beings seek self-preservation as a primary goal, and power as a means to secure that goal; his politics spring directly from these premises. Since the best way to assure self-preservation, he argued, is to assent permanently to the creation of a strong authority, the founding political covenant cannot be revoked and rebellion against the sovereign is absurd. Hobbes's materialism and secularism—his virtual exclusion of God from politics—scandalized both the Puritans who opposed him, and many royalists as well.

The claims of royalists came under vigorous attack from the poet John Milton, who during the war years became one of the most effective polemicists for the parliamentary radicals. Milton wrote *The Tenure of Kings and Magistrates* in 1648, the days leading up to Charles's trial and execution, when many of those who had originally supported limiting the king's power shrank from actually beheading him. Milton decries this hesitation, seeing it as the effect of a misdirected awe for the privileges of monarchs. All political authorities, Milton argues, hold their power in trust from the people, and the people can revoke that trust whenever they choose.

Like Filmer, Milton bases his argument upon biblical history, but he cites very different passages. Filmer emphasizes the importance of fatherly authority in Genesis, which narrates the lives of Adam, Noah, Abraham, Isaac, Jacob, and Joseph. Milton acknowledges that the fall of Adam and Eve corrupted human nature so that individuals were henceforth unable to govern themselves properly without external discipline. Yet, he insists, since those charged with implementing that discipline are themselves sinners, they must be kept in check by laws and by strict limitations upon their authority. In Milton's account, problems with the exercise of authority became evident only gradually. Unlike Filmer, who assumes that the social arrangements described in Genesis are a pattern for modern political communities, Milton chooses his examples from later eras in Jewish history: for instance, the Book of Samuel, in which God disapproves of the Israelites' desire for a king.

For Filmer, Hobbes, and Milton, the central issue of the conflict between the king and Parliament is, who has ultimate authority, the king or the people? Gerrard Winstanley construes the problem differently, in primarily economic rather than political terms. Winstanley was a well-educated London linen draper who worked as a laborer in the countryside after suffering financial reverses during the war years. In his political writing, he concerns himself less with the way power is allocated than with the equitable distribution of wealth. The ownership of land is especially important to him, since it was the critical asset in a largely agrarian society. Members of the House of Commons, though they considered themselves the representatives of "the people," were actually fairly substantial property owners; indeed, those without land or income were not entitled to vote. In consequence, more than half the male population (and, of course, the entire female population) was denied the franchise. In *A New Year's Gift Sent to the Parliament and Army* (1650), Winstanley accuses Parliament of having merely transferred oppressive power from the king to itself, leaving most of England's population as impoverished and downtrodden as before.

Winstanley suggests a practical means to remedy his society's inequities: "the commons," undeveloped lands used for grazing, should be made available to poor people to farm communally. Since the commons, though traditionally used by all the residents on an estate, were legally the manorial landlord's private property, Winstanley's ideas were highly unpopular among landowners. Moreover, his proposal was not merely a theoretical recommendation. The year before he wrote *A New Year's Gift*, Winstanley and some of his followers, called Diggers, had settled on St. George's Hill in Surrey. They planted twelve acres of grain and built a number of makeshift houses before they were violently evicted.

Like Filmer and Milton, Winstanley turns to the Bible to justify his politics. Yet like them, he chooses passages that suit his argument. He reads contemporary history through the heady allegories of the Book of Revelation, as a confrontation between the powers of darkness and the powers of light. Jesus's concern for the poor and scorn for the rich loom large to him, and his social vision owes much to biblical accounts of early Christian communities, which held property in common and minimized class differences.

ROBERT FILMER

The eldest of eighteen children, Robert Filmer (1588–1653) attended Trinity College, Cambridge, and inherited his father's estate in Kent in 1629. When war broke out he was too old to participate as a soldier, but he was briefly imprisoned by Parliament as a known supporter of the king, and his property was seized and plundered. After his release, he published a number of treatises arguing for absolute monarchy, among them *The Anarchy of a Limited and Mixed Monarchy* (1648); *The Freeholder's Grand Inquest* (1648), which argued that Parliament could only meet at the will of the king; and a translation of excerpts from the works of the French absolutist Jean Bodin. However, Filmer's most important treatise, *Patriarcha*, was not among these publications. Scholars disagree about when it was written, but Filmer probably composed it in the early 1630s in the wake of Charles's conflicts with Parliament early in his reign. The treatise remained in manuscript until 1680. Printed during a heated debate between Tories (royalists) and Whigs (Parliamentarians) over the right of King Charles II's brother James to inherit the throne, *Patriarcha* was comprehensively savaged by John Locke in his *First Treatise of Government* (1690).

While Filmer's motive in writing *Patriarcha* was undoubtedly close-to-home disputes between the English king and his subjects, his explicit polemical target is not Charles's parliamentary opponents. Rather, Filmer argues against Continental political theorists such as the Jesuit Robert Cardinal Bellarmine, who had written a devastating critique of James I's treatises on monarchy earlier in the century. Bellarmine's aim had been to secure freedom of conscience and worship for Roman

Catholic subjects of a Protestant monarch, by arguing that the power of monarchs was constrained by their people. Charles's Puritan opponents would find many aspects of Bellarmine's line of reasoning irresistible. Since in the English-speaking tradition republican concepts eventually came to be strongly associated with Puritan dissent, it is worth remembering that for much of the sixteenth and early seventeenth centuries, it had been Protestants who advocated consolidating secular and spiritual power in the figure of a powerful king, and Catholics who had resisted that consolidation.

From Patriarcha, or The Natural Power of Kings Defended Against the Unnatural Liberty of the People

From Chapter 1: That the First Kings Were Fathers of Families

Since the time that school divinity[1] began to flourish there hath been a common opinion maintained, as well by divines as by divers other learned men, which affirms: "Mankind is naturally endowed and born with freedom from all subjection, and at liberty to choose what form of government it please, and that the power which any one man hath over others was at first bestowed according to the discretion of the multitude." This tenet was first hatched in the schools, and hath been fostered by all succeeding Papists for good divinity. The divines, also, of the reformed churches have entertained it, and the common people everywhere tenderly embrace it as being most plausible[2] to flesh and blood, for that it prodigally distributes a portion of liberty to the meanest of the multitude, who magnify liberty as if the height of human felicity were only to be found in it, never remembering that the desire of liberty was the first cause of the fall of Adam.

But howsoever this vulgar[3] opinion hath of late obtained a great reputation, yet it is not to be found in the ancient fathers and doctors of the primitive church. It contradicts the doctrine and history of the holy scriptures, the constant practice of all ancient monarchies, and the very principles of the law of nature. It is hard to say whether it be more erroneous in divinity or dangerous in policy.[4]

* * *

That the patriarchs[5] . . . were endowed with kingly power, their deeds to testify; for as Adam was lord of his children, so his children under him had a command and power over their own children, but still with subordination to the first parent, who is lord-paramount over his children's children to all generations, as being the grandfather of his people.

I see not then how the children of Adam, or of any man else, can be free from subjection to their parents. And this subjection of children being the fountain of all regal authority, by the ordination of God himself, it follows that civil power not only in general is by divine institution, but even the assignment of it specifically to the eldest parents, which quite takes away

---

1. Systematic theology, as undertaken by medieval philosophers in the universities ("schools").
2. Agreeable.
3. Commonly held.

4. The conduct of public affairs.
5. Forefathers of the Jews, including Adam, Noah, Abraham, Isaac, Jacob, and Jacob's twelve sons.

that new and common distinction which refers only power universal and absolute to God, but power respective[6] in regard of the special form of government to the choice of the people.

This lordship which Adam by command had over the whole world, and by right descending from him the patriarchs did enjoy, was as large and ample as the absolutest dominion of any monarch which hath been since the Creation. For dominion of life and death we find that Judah, the father, pronounced sentence of death against Thamar, his daughter-in-law, for playing the harlot. "Bring her forth," saith he, "that she may be burnt."[7] Touching war, we see that Abraham commanded an army of three hundred and eighteen soldiers of his own family. And Esau met his brother Jacob with four hundred men at arms. For matter of peace, Abraham made a league with Abimelech, and ratified the articles with an oath. These acts of judging in capital crimes, of making war, and concluding peace, are the chiefest marks of sovereignty that are found in any monarch.

*　*　*

It may seem absurd to maintain that kings now are the fathers of their people, since experience shows the contrary. It is true, all kings be not the natural parents of their subjects, yet they all either are, or are to be reputed, the next heirs to those first progenitors who were at first the natural parents of the whole people, and in their right succeed to the exercise of supreme jurisdiction; and such heirs are not only lords of their own children, but also of their brethren, and all others that were subject to their fathers. And therefore we find that God told Cain of his brother Abel, "His desires shall he subject unto thee, and thou shalt rule over him." Accordingly, when Jacob bought his brother's birthright, Isaac blessed him thus: "Be lord over thy brethren, and let the sons of thy mother bow before thee."[8]

As long as the first fathers of families lived, the name of patriarchs did aptly belong unto them; but after a few descents, when the true fatherhood itself was extinct, and only the right of the father descends to the true heir, then the title of prince or king was more significant to express the power of him who succeeds only to the right of that fatherhood which his ancestors did naturally enjoy. By this means it comes to pass that many a child, by succeeding a king, hath the right of a father over many a gray-headed multitude, and hath the title of *pater patriae*.[9]

To confirm this natural right of regal power, we find in the Decalogue[1] that the law which enjoins obedience to kings is delivered in the terms of "Honor thy father," as if all power were originally in the father. If obedience to parents be immediately due by a natural law, and subjection to princes but by the mediation of a human ordinance, what reason is there that the laws of nature should give place to the laws of men, as we see the power of the father over his child gives place and is subordinate to the power of the magistrate?

If we compare the natural rights of a father with those of a king, we find them all one, without any difference at all but only in the latitude or extent

6. Partial, limited.
7. Genesis 38.24. The examples following also come from Genesis, 14.14, 32.6, and 21.22–27.
8. The first reference is to Genesis 4.7, which Filmer reads tendentiously as establishing the elder brother Cain's authority over the younger Abel, and the second is to Genesis 27.29.
9. Father of his country.
1. Ten Commandments.

of them: as the father over one family, so the king, as father over many families, extends his care to preserve, feed, clothe, instruct, and defend the whole commonwealth. His war, his peace, his courts of justice, and all his acts of sovereignty, tend only to preserve and distribute to every subordinate and inferior father, and to their children, their rights and privileges, so that all the duties of a king are summed up in an universal fatherly care of his people.

1620s–40s   1680

JOHN MILTON[1]

From The Tenure[2] of Kings and Magistrates

If men within themselves would be governed by reason, and not generally give up their understanding to a double tyranny, of custom from without, and blind affections[3] within, they would discern better what it is to favor and uphold the tyrant of a nation. But being slaves within doors,[4] no wonder that they strive so much to have the public state conformably governed to the inward vicious rule by which they govern themselves. For indeed none can love freedom heartily but good men; the rest love not freedom but license; which never hath more scope or more indulgence than under tyrants. Hence it is that tyrants are not oft offended nor stand much in doubt of bad men, as being all naturally servile; but in whom[5] virtue and true worth most is eminent, them they fear in earnest as by right their masters; against them lies all their hatred and suspicion. Consequently neither do bad men hate tyrants, but have been always readiest with the falsified names of loyalty, and obedience, to color over their base compliances.[6] And although sometimes for shame, and when it comes to their own grievances, of purse especially, they would seem good patriots and side with the better cause, yet when others for the deliverance of their country, endued with fortitude and heroic virtue to fear nothing by the curse written against those "that do the work of the lord negligently,"[7] would go on to remove not only the calamities and thralldoms of a people but the roots and causes whence they spring, straight these men and sure helpers at need, as if they hated only the miseries but not the mischiefs,[8] after they have juggled and paltered[9] with the world, bandied and borne arms against their king, divested him, disanointed him, nay cursed him all over in their pulpits and their pamphlets, to the engaging of sincere and real men beyond what is possible or honest to retreat from, not only turn revolters from those prin-

---

1. See headnote to Milton, pp. 1897–1901.
2. Terms of holding office.
3. Impulses, passions.
4. I.e., within their own selves.
5. Those in whom.
6. Make their slavishness look good.

7. Milton apparently refers to Jeremiah 48.10: "Cursed be he that doeth the work of the Lord deceitfully, and cursed be he that keepeth back his sword from blood."
8. The suffering but not its causes.
9. Played fast and loose.

ciples which only could at first move them, but lay the stain of disloyalty and worse on those proceedings which are the necessary consequences of their own former actions; nor disliked by themselves, were they managed to the entire advantages of their own faction; not considering the while that he toward whom they boasted their new fidelity counted them accessory;[1] and by those statutes and laws which they so impotently brandish against others would have doomed them to a traitor's death for what they have done already. 'Tis true, that most men are apt enough to civil wars and commotions as a novelty, and for a flash hot and active; but through sloth or inconstancy, and weakness of spirit either fainting ere their own pretences,[2] though never so just, be half attained, or through an inbred falsehood and wickedness, betray ofttimes to destruction with themselves men of noblest temper[3] joined with them for causes whereof they in their rash undertakings[4] were not capable.

* * *

No man who knows aught, can be so stupid to deny that all men naturally were born free, being the image and resemblance of God Himself, and were by privilege above all the creatures born to command and not to obey, and that they lived so. Till from the root of Adam's transgression,[5] falling among themselves to do wrong and violence, and foreseeing that such courses must needs tend to the destruction of them all, they agreed by common league to bind each other from mutual injury, and jointly to defend themselves against any that gave disturbance or opposition to such agreement. Hence came cities, towns, and commonwealths. And because no faith in all was found sufficiently binding,[6] they saw it needful to ordain some authority that might restrain by force and punishment what was violated against peace and common right. This authority and power of self-defense and preservation being originally and naturally in every one of them, and unitedly in them all, for ease, for order, and lest each man should be his own partial[7] judge, they communicated and derived[8] either to one, whom for the eminence of his wisdom and integrity they chose above the rest, or to more than one whom they thought of equal deserving: the first was called a king, the other magistrates. Not to be their lords and masters (though afterward those names in some places were given voluntarily to such as had been authors[9] of inestimable good to the people) but to be their deputies and commissioners, to execute, by virtue of their entrusted power, that justice which else every man by the bond of nature and of convenant must have executed for himself and for one another. And to him that shall consider well why among free persons, one man by civil right[1] should bear authority and jurisdiction over another, no other end or reason can be imaginable. These[2] for a while governed well, and with much equity decided all things at their own arbitrament:[3] till the temptation of such a power left absolute in their hands,

1. Guilty of being accessories to a crime.
2. Purposes.
3. Character.
4. Attempts, enterprises.
5. Adam's fall introduced sin and violence into human life.
6. Because merely trusting people to behave themselves did not suffice to control them.
7. Biased.
8. Delegated.
9. Doers.
1. Law.
2. Kings and magistrates.
3. Judgment.

perverted them at length to injustice and partiality. Then did they who now by trial[4] had found the danger and inconveniences of committing arbitrary power to any, invent laws either framed or consented to by all, that should confine and limit the authority of whom they chose to govern them: that so man,[5] of whose failing they had proof, might no more rule over them, but law and reason abstracted as much as might be from personal errors and frailties. While[6] as the magistrate was set above the people, so the law was set above the magistrate. When this would not serve, but that the law was either not executed or misapplied, they were constrained from that time, the only remedy left them, to put conditions[7] and take oaths from all kings and magistrates at their first installment to do impartial justice by law: who upon those terms and no other received allegiance from the people, that is to say, bond or covenant to obey them in execution of those laws which they the people had themselves made or assented to. And this ofttimes with express warning, that if the king or magistrate proved unfaithful to his trust, the people would be disengaged.[8] They added also counselors and parliaments, nor to be only at his beck,[9] but with him or without him, at set times, or at all times when any danger threatened to have care of the public safety.

* * *

It being thus manifest that the power of kings and magistrates is nothing else but what is only derivative, transferred and committed to them in trust from the people, to the common good of them all, in whom the power yet remains fundamentally, and cannot be taken from them without a violation of their natural birthright; and seeing that from hence Aristotle[1] and the best of political writers have defined a king, him who governs to the good and profit of his people and not for his own ends, it follows from necessary causes that the titles of sovereign lord, natural lord, and the like, are either arrogancies or flatteries, not admitted[2] by emperors and kings of best note, and disliked by the church both of Jews, Isaiah 26.13, and ancient Christians, as appears by Tertullian and others.[3] Although generally the people of Asia, and with them the Jews also, especially since the time they chose a king against the advice and counsel of God,[4] are noted by wise authors much inclinable to slavery.

Secondly, that to say, as is usual, the king hath as good right to his crown and dignity as any man to his inheritance, is to make the subject no better than the king's slave, his chattel or his possession that may be bought and sold. And doubtless if hereditary title were sufficiently inquired, the best foundation of it would be found either but in courtesy or convenience. But suppose it to be of right hereditary, what can be more just and legal, if a

---

4. Experience. "They": the people who had delegated power to the kings and magistrates.
5. An individual man.
6. Thus.
7. Specify restrictions on.
8. Freed from having to obey.
9. The king's command. Charles had claimed that Parliament could not assemble unless called into session by the king.
1. In *Nicomachean Ethics* 8.11.1.

2. Permitted.
3. Isaiah 26.13: "O Lord our God, other lords beside thee have had dominion over us; but by thee only will we make mention of thy name." The Church Father Tertullian wrote against earthly monarchs in *On the Crown*.
4. The Israelites, traditionally governed by judges, demanded a king despite God's warning against monarchy, as conveyed by the prophet Samuel (1 Samuel 8).

subject for certain crimes be to forfeit by law from himself, and posterity,[5] all his inheritance to the king, than that a king for crimes proportional should forfeit all his title and inheritance to the people: unless the people must be thought created all for him, he not for them, and they all in one body inferior to him single, which were a kind of treason against the dignity of mankind to affirm.

Thirdly it follows that to say kings are accountable to none but God is the overturning of all law and government. For if they may refuse to give account, then all covenants made with them at coronation, all oaths are in vain and mere mockeries, all laws which they swear to keep made to no purpose; for if the king fear not God—as how many of them do not?—we hold then our lives and estates by the tenure of his mere grace and mercy, as from a God, not a mortal magistrate, a position that none but court parasites or men besotted would maintain.

* * *

It follows lastly, that since the king or magistrate holds his authority of the people, both originally and naturally for their good in the first place, and not his own, then may the people as oft as they shall judge it for the best, either choose him or reject him, retain him or depose him though no tyrant, merely by the liberty and right of freeborn men to be governed as seems to them best.

1649

5. Convicted felons forfeited their property to the king.

GERRARD WINSTANLEY

The demand for democratic elections by a political faction called the Levelers raised the fear in Cromwell and his conservative associates that, with unpropertied voters outnumbering the propertied by five to one, they might divide or even abolish private property. That was in fact the program of a small group calling themselves True Levelers or, later, Diggers, who were a group of Christian communists. Their leader was Gerrard Winstanley (1609–1676?), a failed businessman and subsequently a hired laborer, who began to publish tracts in 1648, became notorious in 1649 with the attempted enactment of the Diggers' program, and lapsed back into obscurity after his last published work in 1652.

In the spring of 1649 the Diggers began to put their ideals into practice, digging up the wasteland of St. George's Hill in Surrey and preparing it for crops. Though this land was not enclosed, all over England landowners claimed property rights in such common land, and the Diggers' gesture of cultivation here and in a few other Digger communities made a threatening counterclaim on behalf of the poor and propertyless. Their aim was at one level practical: at least one-third of England, they claimed, was barren waste, and if properly cultivated could vastly increase the food supply, to the great benefit of the poor. At another level their aim was ideological, a fundamental challenge to the concept of private ownership of land, as the tract excerpted here argues—at least in regard to the common land. The army and the civil authorities were not very hard on the Diggers, but the local landholders were, beating them up, expelling them, and destroying their several settlements. But their often-eloquent tracts survived to inspire later communes.

From A New Year's Gift[1] Sent to the Parliament and Army

Gentlemen of the Parliament and army: you and the common people have assisted each other to cast out the head of oppression which was kingly power seated in one man's hand, and that work is now done; and till that work was done you called upon the people to assist you to deliver this distressed, bleeding, dying nation out of bondage; and the people came and failed you not, counting neither purse nor blood too dear to part with to effect this work.

The Parliament after this have made an act to cast out kingly power, and to make England a free commonwealth. These acts the people are much rejoiced with, as being words forerunning their freedom, and they wait for their accomplishment that their joy may be full; for as words without action are a cheat and kills the comfort of a righteous spirit, so words performed in action does comfort and nourish the life thereof.

Now, sirs, wheresoever we spy out kingly power, no man I hope shall be troubled to declare it, nor afraid to cast it out, having both act of Parliament, the soldiers' oath, and the common people's consent on his side; for kingly power is like a great spread tree, if you lop the head or top bough, and let the other branches and root stand, it will grow again and recover fresher strength.

If any ask me what kingly power is, I answer, there is a twofold kingly power. The one is the kingly power of righteousness, and this is the power of almighty God, ruling the whole creation in peace and keeping it together. And this is the power of universal love, leading people into all truth, teaching everyone to do as he would be done unto: now once more striving with flesh and blood, shaking down everything that cannot stand, and bringing everyone into the unity of himself, the one spirit of love and righteousness, and so will work a thorough restoration. But this kingly power is above all and will tread all covetousness, pride, envy, and self-love, and all other enemies whatsoever, under his feet, and take the kingdom and government of the creation out of the hand of self-seeking and self-honoring flesh,[2] and rule the alone king of righteousness in the earth; and this indeed is Christ himself, who will cast out the curse.[3] But this is not that kingly power intended by that act of Parliament to be cast out, but pretended to be set up, though this kingly power be much fought against both by Parliament, army, clergy, and people; but when they are made to see him, then they shall mourn because they have persecuted him.[4]

---

1. In 17th-century England, gifts were customarily exchanged on New Year's Day, not at Christmas.
2. "Flesh" is imagined as everything mortal and fallible, that which rebels against divine righteousness.
3. The curse upon mankind that was the punishment of Adam's fall.
4. I.e., Parliament and the army do not expressly intend to cast out God's kingly power, but rather they act as if they are conforming to God's teachings, and yet often they resist God until they are brought to recognize him.

But the other kingly power is the power of unrighteousness, which indeed is the devil. And O, that there were such a heart in Parliament and army as to perform your own act.[5] Then people would never complain of you for breach of covenant, for your covetousness, pride, and too much self-seeking that is in you. And you on the other side would never have cause to complain of the people's murmurings against you. Truly this jarring that is between you and the people is the kingly power; yea that very kingly power which you have made an act to cast out. Therefore see it be fulfilled on your part; for the kingly power of righteousness expects it, or else he will cast you out for hypocrites and unsavory salt;[6] for he looks upon all your actions, and truly there is abundance of rust about your actings, which makes them that they do not shine bright.

This kingly power is covetousness in his branches,[7] or the power of self-love ruling in one or in many men over others and enslaving those who in the creation are their equals; nay, who are in the strictness of equity rather their masters. And this kingly power is usually set in the chair of government under the name of prerogative[8] when he rules in one over other: and under the name of state privilege of Parliament when he rules in many over others: and this kingly power is always raised up and established by the sword, and therefore he is called the murderer, or the great red dragon which fights against Michael,[9] for he enslaves the weakness of the people under him, denying an equal freedom in the earth to everyone, which the law of righteousness gave every man in his creation. This I say is kingly power under darkness; and as he rules in men, so he makes men jar one against another, and is the cause of all wars and complainings. He is known by his outward actions, and his action at this very day fills all places; for this power of darkness rules, and would rule, and is that only enemy that fights against creation and national freedom. And this kingly power is he which you have made an act of Parliament to cast out. And now, you rulers of England, play the men and be valiant for the truth, which is Christ: for assure yourselves God will not be mocked, nor the devil will not be mocked. For first you say and profess you own[1] the scriptures of prophets and apostles, and God looks that you should perform that word in action. Secondly you have declared against the devil, and if you do not now go through with your work but slack your hand by hypocritical self-love, and so suffer this dark kingly power to rise higher and rule, you shall find he will maul both you and yours to purpose.[2]

* * *

In the time of the kings, who came in as conquerors and ruled by the power of the sword, not only the common land but the enclosures[3] also were

---

5. Enforce the act already passed by Parliament.
6. Matthew 5.13: "Ye are the salt of the earth: but if the salt have lost his savour, wherewith shall it be salted? it is thenceforth good for nothing, but to be cast out, and to be trodden under foot of men."
7. I.e., covetousness is one manifestation of unrighteous kingly power.
8. The monarch's special powers.
9. Revelation 12.3–9: "And there appeared another wonder in heaven; and behold a great red dragon, having seven heads and ten horns, and seven crowns upon his heads. . . . And there was war in heaven: Michael and his angels fought against the dragon; and the dragon fought and his angels, / and prevailed not; neither was their place found any more in heaven. / And the great dragon was cast out, that old serpent, called the Devil, and Satan, which deceiveth the whole world."
1. Acknowledge.
2. Thoroughly.
3. Privately held land.

captivated under the will of those kings, till now of late that our later kings granted more freedom to the gentry than they had presently after the Conquest:[4] yet under bondage still. For what are prisons, whips, and gallows in the times of peace but the laws and power of the sword, forcing and compelling obedience, and so enslaving as if the sword raged in the open field? England was in such a slavery under the kingly power that both gentry and commonalty[5] groaned under bondage; and to ease themselves, they endeavored to call a parliament, that by their counsels and decrees they might find some freedom.

But Charles the then king perceiving that the freedom they strove for would derogate from his prerogative tyranny,[6] thereupon he goes into the north to raise a war against the Parliament; and took William the Conqueror's sword into his hand again, thereby to keep under the former conquered English, and to uphold his kingly power of self-will and prerogative, which was the power got by former conquests; that is, to rule over the lives and estates of all men at his will, and so to make us pure slaves and vassals.

Well, this Parliament, that did consist of the chief lords, lords of manors, and gentry, and they seeing that the king, by raising an army, did thereby declare his intent to enslave all sorts to him by the sword; and being in distress and in a low ebb, they call upon the common people to bring in their plate, monies, taxes, free-quarter, excise,[7] and to adventure their lives with them, and they would endeavor to recover England from that Norman yoke and make us a free people. And the common people assent hereunto, and call this the Parliament's cause, and own it and adventure person and purse to preserve it; and by the joint assistance of Parliament and people the king was beaten in the field, his head taken off, and his kingly power voted down. And we the commons thereby virtually have recovered ourselves from the Norman conquest; we want nothing but possession of the spoil,[8] which is a free use of the land for our livelihood.

And from hence we the common people, or younger brothers,[9] plead our property in the common land as truly our own by virtue of this victory over the king, as our elder brothers can plead property in their enclosures; and that for three reasons in England's law.

First, by a lawful purchase or contract between the Parliament and us; for they were our landlords and lords of manors, that held the freedom of the commons from us[1] while the king was in his power; for they held title thereunto from him,[2] he being the head and they branches of the kingly power that enslaved the people by that ancient conqueror's sword, that was the ruling power. For they said, "Come and help us against the king that enslaves us, that we may be delivered from his tyranny, and we will make you a free people."

---

4. The conquest of England by the Norman William the Conqueror in 1066. Winstanley argued that the oppression of the poor and the landless was a consequence of nearly six centuries of occupation of England by a foreign power.
5. Common people.
6. Absolute rule.
7. A tax on domestically manufactured goods, first imposed by Parliament in 1643 to finance the war against the king. "Plate": silver plate. "Free-

quarter": free room and board for soldiers, or its monetary equivalent imposed as a tax.
8. Reward of victory.
9. Estates commonly passed to the eldest brother, leaving the younger brothers landless.
1. Kept the right to use the common lands from us, the common people.
2. Under the feudal system, the great lords held their lands on grant from the king, in return for their allegiance.

Now they cannot make us free unless they deliver us from the bondage[3] which they themselves held us under; and that is, they held the freedom of the earth from us: for we in part with them have delivered ourselves from the king. Now we claim freedom from that bondage you have and yet do hold us under, by the bargain and contract between Parliament and us, who, I say, did consist of lords of manors and landlords, whereof Mr. Drake,[4] who hath arrested me for digging upon the common, was one at that time. Therefore by the law of bargain and sale we claim of them our freedom, to live comfortably with them in this land of our nativity; and this we cannot do so long as we lie under poverty, and must not be suffered to plant the commons and wasteland for our livelihood. For take away the land from any people, and those people are in a way of continual dearth and misery; and better not to have had a body, than not to have food and raiment for it. But, I say, they have sold us our freedom in the common, and have been largely paid for it; for by means of our bloods and money they sit in peace: for if the king had prevailed, they had lost all, and been in slavery to the meanest cavalier, if the king would.[5] Therefore we the commons say, give us our bargain: if you deny us our bargain, you deny God, Christ, and scriptures; and all your profession[6] then is and hath been hypocrisy.

Secondly, the commons and crown land is our property by equal conquest over the kingly power: for the Parliament did never stir up the people by promises and covenant to assist them to cast out the king and to establish them in the king's place and prerogative power. No, but all their declarations were for the safety and peace of the whole nation.

Therefore the common people being part of the nation, and especially they that bore the greatest heat of the day in casting out the oppressor; and the nation cannot be in peace so long as the poor oppressed are in wants and the land is entangled and held from them by bondage.

But the victory being obtained over the king, the spoil, which is properly the land, ought in equity to be divided now between the two parties, that is Parliament and common people. The Parliament, consisting of lords of manors and gentry, ought to have their enclosure lands free to them without molestation. . . . And the common people, consisting of soldiers and such as paid taxes and free-quarter, ought to have the freedom of all waste and common land and crown land equally among them. The soldiery ought not in equity to have all, nor the other people that paid them to have all; but the spoil ought to be divided between them that stayed at home and them that went to war; for the victory is for the whole nation.

And as the Parliament declared they did all for the nation, and not for themselves only; so we plead with the army, they did not fight for themselves, but for the freedom of the nation: and I say, we have bought our freedom of them likewise by taxes and free-quarter. Therefore we claim an equal freedom with them in this conquest over the king.

---

3. Technically bondage refers to the services and goods legally required by feudal landowners of their tenants.
4. Sir Francis Drake, a member of Parliament who owned St. George's Hill, on which Winstanley and his followers had established a com-mune. At first sympathetic to the Diggers, Drake eventually took legal action to have them evicted.
5. To the lowest soldier of the king, if the king so commanded.
6. Statement of principles.

Thirdly, we claim an equal portion in the victory over the king by virtue of the two acts of Parliament: the one to make England a free commonwealth, the other to take away kingly power. Now the kingly power, you have heard, is a power that rules by the sword in covetousness and self, giving the earth to some and denying it to others: and this kingly power was not in the hand of the king alone, but lords, and lords of manors, and corrupt judges and lawyers especially held it up likewise. For he was the head and they, with the tithing priests,[7] are the branches of that tyrannical kingly power; and all the several limbs and members must be cast out before kingly power can be pulled up root and branch. Mistake me not, I do not say, cast out the persons of men. No, I do not desire their fingers to ache;[8] but I say, cast out their power whereby they hold the people in bondage, as the king held them in bondage. And I say, it is our own freedom we claim, both by bargain and by equality in the conquest; as well as by the law of righteous creation which gives the earth to all equally.

And the power of lords of manors lies in this: they deny the common people the use and free benefit of the earth, unless they give them leave and pay them for it, either in rent, in fines, in homages or heriots.[9] Surely the earth was never made by God that the younger brother should not live in the earth unless he would work for and pay his elder brother rent for the earth. No, this slavery came in by conquest, and it is part of the kingly power; and England cannot be a free commonwealth till this bondage be taken away. You have taken away the king; you have taken away the House of Lords. Now step two steps further, and take away the power of lords of manors and of tithing priests, and the intolerable oppressions of judges by whom laws are corrupted; and your work will be honorable.

Fourthly, if this freedom be denied the common people, to enjoy the common land; then Parliament, army, and judges will deny equity and reason, whereupon the laws of a well-governed commonwealth ought to be built. And if this equity be denied, then there can be no law but club law[1] among the people: and if the sword must reign, then every party will be striving to bear the sword; and then farewell peace; nay, farewell religion and gospel, unless it be made use of to entrap one another, as we plainly see some priests and others make it a cloak for their knavery. If I adventure my life and fruit of my labor equal with you, and obtain what we strive for; it is both equity and reason that I should equally divide the spoil with you, and not you to have all and I none. And if you deny us this, you take away our property from us, our monies and blood, and give us nothing for it.

Therefore, I say, the common land is my own land, equal with my fellow-commoners, and our true property, by the law of creation. It is everyone's, but not one single one's. . . . True religion and undefiled is this, to make restitution of the earth, which hath been taken and held from the common people by the power of conquests formerly, and so set the oppressed free. Do not

---

7. Priests of the Church of England were legally entitled to a tenth, or "tithe," of every parishioner's goods; those people who wished to separate from the established church fiercely resented the involuntary nature of the tithe.

8. Wish the least physical harm to them.
9. Fees or goods paid by tenants to landlords in addition to rent.
1. That is, might makes right.

all strive to enjoy the land? The gentry strive for land, the clergy strive for land, the common people strive for land; and buying and selling is an art whereby people endeavor to cheat one another of the land. Now if any can prove from the law of righteousness that the land was made peculiar to him and his successively,[2] shutting others out, he shall enjoy it freely for my part. But I affirm it was made for all; and true religion is to let everyone enjoy it. Therefore, you rulers of England, make restitution of the lands which the kingly power holds from us: set the oppressed free, and come in and honor Christ, who is the restoring power, and you shall find rest.

1650

2. By inheritance.

THOMAS HOBBES

The English civil war and its aftermath raised fundamental questions about the nature and legitimacy of state power. In 1651 Thomas Hobbes (1588–1679) attempted to answer those questions in his ambitious masterwork of political philosophy, *Leviathan*. He grounded his political vision upon a comprehensive philosophy of nature and knowledge. Hobbes held that everything in the universe is composed only of matter; spirit does not exist. All knowledge is gained through sensory impressions, which are nothing but matter in motion. What we call the self is, for Hobbes, simply a tissue of sensory impressions—clear and immediate in the presence of the objects that evoke them, vague and less vivid in their absence. As a result, an iron determinism of cause and effect governs everything in the universe, including human action.

Because, Hobbes argues, all humans are roughly equal mentally and physically, they possess equal hopes of attaining goods, as well as equal fears of danger from others. In the state of nature, before the foundation of some sovereign power to keep them in awe, everyone is continually at war with everyone else, and life, in Hobbes's memorable phrase, is "solitary, poor, nasty, brutish, and short." To escape this ghastly strife, humans covenant with one another to establish a sovereign government over all of them. That sovereign power—which need not be a king but is always indivisible—incorporates the wills and individuality of them all, so that the people no longer have rights or liberties apart from the sovereign's will. The sovereign's dominion over his subjects extends to the right to pronounce on all matters of religion.

While other versions of covenant theory, for instance Milton's *Tenure of Kings and Magistrates*, insisted that the power transferred by the people to the sovereign could be limited or revoked, in Hobbes's system, the founding political covenant must be a permanent one, since no tyranny can be so evil as the state of war that the sovereign power prevents. Yet if the sovereign power should be overthrown, the individual ruler has no further claim, and the people, for their safety, must accept the new sovereign unconditionally. Hobbes was generally associated with the royalist cause, as a tutor to the Cavendish family and as an exile in Paris from 1640 to 1651, where he tutored the future Charles II. Yet his argument made no distinction between a legitimate monarch and a successful usurper, like Oliver Cromwell. Moreover, Hobbes's philosophical materialism led many to suspect him of atheism;

after the Restoration, the publication of many of his books, including a history of the civil war entitled *Behemoth*, was prohibited for a number of years. Undeterred, Hobbes continued to write on a variety of psychological, political, and mathematical topics, completing a translation of Homer's *Iliad* and *Odyssey* at the age of eighty-six.

Hobbes's political theory did not fit easily into the established patterns of English thought partly because his perspective was essentially cosmopolitan. Educated at Oxford as a classicist, Hobbes traveled widely in Europe between 1610 and 1660 as a companion and tutor of noblemen, often remaining abroad for years at a time. During these lengthy sojourns he became acquainted with many of the leading intellectuals and scientists on the Continent, including Galileo, Descartes, and the prominent French mathematician Pierre Gassendi, who argued that the universe was governed entirely by mechanical principles. The most important political philosophers for Hobbes were also Continental figures: the Italian Niccolò Machiavelli, who saw human beings as naturally competitive and power hungry, and Jean Bodin, a French theorist of indivisible, absolute monarchy. One English writer who did influence Hobbes profoundly was Francis Bacon, whose amanuensis Hobbes had been in Bacon's last years. Ironically, Hobbes was not invited to join the Royal Society, established after the Restoration on Baconian principles, because his religious views were suspect and because he had quarreled with several of the society's founders. Yet Hobbes is truly Bacon's heir, sharing Bacon's utter lack of sentimentality and a memorably astringent prose style.

From Leviathan[1]

From *The Introduction*

[THE ARTIFICIAL MAN]

Nature (the art whereby God hath made and governs the world) is by the art of man, as in many other things, so in this also imitated, that it can make an artificial[2] animal. For seeing life is but a motion of limbs, the beginning whereof is in some principal part within, why may we not say that all automata (engines that move themselves by springs and wheels as doth a watch) have an artificial life?[3] For what is the heart but a spring; and the nerves but so many strings; and the joints but so many wheels, giving motion to the whole body such as was intended by the artificer? Art goes yet further, imitating that rational and most excellent work of nature, man. For by art is created that great Leviathan called a Commonwealth or State (in Latin, *Civitas*), which is but an artificial man, though of greater stature and strength than the natural, for whose protection and defense it was intended; and in which the sovereignty is an artificial soul, as giving life and motion to the whole body; the magistrates and other officers of judicature and execution, artificial joints; reward and punishment (by which, fastened to the seat of the sovereignty, every joint and member is moved to perform his duty) are the nerves, that do the same in the body natural; the wealth and riches

---

1. The title refers to the primordial sea creature Leviathan, described in Job 41 as the prime evidence of and analogue to God's power, beyond all human measure and comprehension. Hobbes takes him as figure for the sovereign power in the state. Leviathan was also sometimes taken as a figure for Satan, on the basis of Job 41.34: "he is a king over all the children of pride."
2. Made by art.
3. Hobbes's definition of life as motion collapses the distinction between the life of humans and the life of machines or institutions.

of all the particular members are the strength; *salus populi* (the people's safety) its business; counselors, by whom all things needful for it to know are suggested unto it, are the memory; equity and laws an artificial reason and will; concord, health; sedition, sickness; and civil war, death. Lastly, the pacts and covenants by which the parts of this body politic were at first made, set together, and united, resemble that *Fiat* or the "let us make man," pronounced by God in the creation.[4]

* * *

From *Part 1. Of Man*

CHAPTER 1. OF SENSE

Concerning the thoughts of man, I will consider them first singly and afterwards in train or dependence upon one another. Singly, they are every one a representation or appearance of some quality or other accident of a body without us, which is commonly called an object. Which object worketh on the eyes, ears, and other parts of man's body, and by diversity of working produceth diversity of appearances.

The original of them all is that which we call sense. (For there is no conception in a man's mind which hath not at first, totally or by parts, been begotten upon the organs of sense.)[5] The rest are derived from that original.

To know the natural cause of sense is not very necessary to the business now in hand, and I have elsewhere written of the same at large. Nevertheless, to fill each part of my present method, I will briefly deliver the same in this place.

The cause of sense is the external body or object which presseth the organ proper to each sense, either immediately as in the taste and touch, or mediately, as in seeing, hearing, and smelling; which pressure, by the mediation of nerves and other strings and membranes of the body continued inwards to the brain and heart, causeth there a resistance or counterpressure or endeavor of the heart to deliver itself;[6] which endeavor, because outward, seemeth to be some matter without. And this seeming or fancy is that which men call sense; and consisteth, as to the eye, in a light or color figured; to the ear, in a sound; to the nostril in an odor; to the tongue and palate in a savor; and to the rest of the body in heat, cold, hardness, softness, and such other qualities as we discern by feeling. All which qualities called "sensible"[7] are, in the object that causeth them, but so many several motions of the matter by which it presseth our organs diversely. Neither, in us that are pressed, are they anything else but diverse motions; for motion produceth nothing but motion. But their appearance to us is fancy, the same waking, that dreaming. And as pressing, rubbing, or striking the eye makes us fancy a light; and pressing the ear produceth a din; so do the bodies also we see or hear produce the same by their strong though unobserved actions. For if those colors and sounds were in the bodies or objects that cause them, they

4. Genesis 1.26.
5. This view of the mind as a blank sheet written on by physical experience will influence the philosophy of John Locke and David Hume.

6. Hobbes's physiology of sense is, in keeping with his premises, strictly mechanical.
7. I.e., accessible through the senses.

Leviathan. Abraham Bosse's frontispiece for *Leviathan* was based on a sketch by Hobbes. The "Leviathan" or commonwealth is shown as a gigantic human figure holding a scepter and a sword; the figure is made up of many tiny individual humans who have joined together in the social contract. Hobbes's royalist sympathies are betrayed in the figure's face, which is that of King Charles. The small pictures in the lower part of the engraving display the various attributes of civil power on the left, and ecclesiastical power on the right.

could not be severed from them, as by glasses[8] and in echoes by reflection we see they are; where we know the thing we see is in one place, the appearance in another. And though at some certain distance the real and very object seem invested with the fancy it begets in us, yet still the object is one thing, the image or fancy is another. So that sense in all cases is nothing

8. Mirrors.

else but original fancy, caused (as I have said) by the pressure, that is by the motion, of external things upon our eyes, ears, and other organs thereunto ordained.

But the philosophy schools[9] through all the universities of Christendom, grounded upon certain texts of Aristotle, teach another doctrine, and say for the cause of vision, that the thing seen sendeth forth on every side a visible species—in English, a visible show, apparition, or aspect, or a being seen— the receiving whereof into the eye is seeing. And for the cause of hearing, that the thing heard sendeth forth an audible species, that is an audible aspect or audible being seen, which entering at the ear maketh hearing. Nay for the cause of understanding also they say the thing understood sendeth forth intelligible species, that is an intelligible being seen, which coming into the understanding makes us understand. I say not this as disapproving the use of universities, but because I am to speak hereafter of their office in a commonwealth, I must let you see on all occasions by the way what things would be amended in them; amongst which the frequency of insignificant speech[1] is one.

* * *

CHAPTER 13. OF THE NATURAL CONDITION OF MANKIND AS CONCERNING THEIR FELICITY AND MISERY

Nature hath made men so equal in the faculties of body and mind as that, though there be found one man sometimes manifestly stronger in body or of quicker mind than another, yet when all is reckoned together, the difference between man and man is not so considerable as that one man can thereupon claim to himself any benefit, to which another may not pretend as well as he. For as to the strength of body, the weakest has strength enough to kill the strongest, either by secret machination, or by confederacy[2] with others that are in the same danger with himself.

And as to the faculties of the mind—setting aside the arts grounded upon words, and especially that skill of proceeding upon general and infallible rules, called science; which very few have, and but in few things; as being not a native faculty, born with us; nor attained, as prudence, while we look after somewhat else—I find yet a greater equality amongst men than that of strength. For prudence is but experience, which equal time equally bestows on all men, in those things they equally apply themselves unto. That which may perhaps make such equality incredible is but a vain conceit of one's own wisdom, which almost all men think they have in a greater degree than the vulgar—that is, than all men but themselves and a few others, whom by fame, or for concurring with themselves, they approve. For such is the nature of men, that howsoever they may acknowledge many others to be more witty, or more eloquent, or more learned, yet they will hardly believe there be many so wise as themselves; for they see their own wit at hand, and other men's at a distance. But this proveth rather that men are in that point equal, than unequal. For there is not ordinarily a greater

9. Led by the Scholastic philosophers (schoolmen).
1. Unmeaningful speech. Cf. Bacon's critique of the idols of the marketplace and the theater in *Novum Organum* 43–44 and 59–62.
2. Alliance.

sign of the equal distribution of anything than that every man is contented with his share.

From this equality of ability ariseth equality of hope in the attaining of our ends. And therefore if any two men desire the same thing, which nevertheless they cannot both enjoy, they become enemies; and in the way to their end (which is principally their own conservation, and sometimes their delectation[3] only) endeavor to destroy or subdue one another. And from hence it comes to pass, that where an invader hath no more to fear than another man's single power, if one plant, sow, build, or possess a convenient seat, others may probably be expected to come prepared with forces united, to dispossess and deprive him, not only of the fruit of his labor, but also of his life or liberty. And the invader again is in the like danger of another.

And from this diffidence[4] of one another, there is no way for any man to secure himself so reasonable as anticipation; that is, by force or wiles to master the persons of all men he can, so long, till he see no other power great enough to endanger him; and this is no more than his own conservation requireth, and is generally allowed. Also because there be some, that taking pleasure in contemplating their own power in the acts of conquest, which they pursue farther than their security requires; if others that otherwise would be glad to be at ease within modest bounds, should not by invasion increase their power, they would not be able long time, by standing only on their defense, to subsist. And by consequence, such augmentation of dominion over men being necessary to a man's conservation, it ought to be allowed him.

Again, men have no pleasure, but on the contrary a great deal of grief, in keeping company, where there is no power able to overawe them all. For every man looketh that his companion should value him at the same rate he sets upon himself; and upon all signs of contempt, or undervaluing, naturally endeavors, as far as he dares (which amongst them that have no common power to keep them in quiet, is far enough to make them destroy each other), to extort a greater value from his contemners[5] by damage, and from others by the example.

So that in the nature of man, we find three principal causes of quarrel. First, competition; secondly, diffidence; thirdly, glory.

The first maketh men invade for gain; the second, for safety; and the third, for reputation. The first use violence to make themselves masters of other men's persons, wives, children, and cattle; the second, to defend them; the third, for trifles, as a word, a smile, a different opinion, and any other sign of undervalue, either direct in their persons, or by reflection in their kindred, their friends, their nation, their profession, or their name.

Hereby it is manifest that during the time men live without a common power to keep them all in awe, they are in that condition which is called war; and such a war as is of every man against every man. For war consisteth not in battle only, or the act of fighting, but in a tract of time wherein the will to contend by battle is sufficiently known; and therefore the notion of time is to be considered in the nature of war, as it is in the nature of weather. For as the nature of foul weather lieth not in a shower or two of rain, but in an

3. Pleasure.
4. Lack of faith, mistrust.
5. Scorners.

inclination thereto of many days together; so the nature of war consisteth not in actual fighting, but in the known disposition thereto, during all the time there is no assurance to the contrary. All other time is peace.

Whatsoever therefore is consequent to a time of war, where every man is enemy to every man, the same is consequent to the time wherein men live without other security than what their own strength and their own invention shall furnish them withal. In such condition there is no place for industry, because the fruit thereof is uncertain, and consequently no culture of the earth; no navigation, nor use of the commodities that may be imported by sea; no commodious building; no instruments of moving, and removing, such things as require much force; no knowledge of the face of the earth; no account of time; no arts; no letters; no society; and, which is worst of all, continual fear, and danger of violent death; and the life of man, solitary, poor, nasty, brutish, and short.

It may seem strange to some man that has not well weighed these things, that nature should thus dissociate and render men apt to invade and destroy one another; and he may therefore, not trusting to this inference, made from the passions, desire perhaps to have the same confirmed by experience. Let him therefore consider with himself, when taking a journey, he arms himself and seeks to go well accompanied; when going to sleep, he locks his doors; when even in his house he locks his chests; and this when he knows there be laws, and public officers, armed, to revenge all injuries shall be done him; what opinion he has of his fellow subjects, when he rides armed; of his fellow citizens, when he locks his doors; and of his children and servants, when he locks his chests. Does he not there as much accuse mankind by his actions, as I do by my words? But neither of us accuse man's nature in it. The desires and other passions of man are in themselves no sin. No more are the actions that proceed from those passions, till they know a law that forbids them, which, till laws be made, they cannot know; nor can any law be made, till they have agreed upon the person that shall make it.

It may peradventure be thought there was never such a time nor condition of war as this; and I believe it was never generally so, over all the world; but there are many places where they live so now. For the savage people in many places of America, except the government of small families, the concord whereof dependeth on natural lust, have no government at all and live at this day in that brutish manner as I said before. Howsoever, it may be perceived what manner of life there would be, where there were no common power to fear, by the manner of life which men that have formerly lived under a peaceful government use to degenerate into in a civil war.[6]

But though there had never been any time wherein particular men were in a condition of war one against another, yet in all times, kings and persons of sovereign authority, because of their independency, are in continual jealousies, and in the state and posture of gladiators; having their weapons pointing, and their eyes fixed on one another; that is, their forts, garrisons, and guns upon the frontiers of their kingdoms, and continual spies upon their neighbors, which is a posture of war. But because they uphold thereby

---

6. Hobbes is thinking of the recent civil wars in England, and perhaps also of the Greek civil wars described by Thucydides (whom he translated).

the industry of their subjects, there does not follow from it that misery which accompanies the liberty of particular men.

To this war of every man against every man, this also is consequent: that nothing can be unjust. The notions of right and wrong, justice and injustice, have there no place. Where there is no common power, there is no law; where no law, no injustice. Force and fraud are in war the two cardinal virtues. Justice and injustice are none of the faculties neither of the body nor mind. If they were, they might be in a man that were alone in the world, as well as his senses and passions. They are qualities that relate to men in society, not in solitude. It is consequent also to the same condition that there be no propriety,[7] no dominion, no *mine* and *thine* distinct; but only that to be every man's, that he can get; and for so long as he can keep it. And thus much for the ill condition which man by mere nature is actually placed in; though with a possibility to come out of it, consisting partly in the passions, partly in his reason.

The passions that incline men to peace are fear of death, desire of such things as are necessary to commodious living, and a hope by their industry to obtain them. And reason suggesteth convenient articles of peace, upon which men may be drawn to agreement. These articles are they which otherwise are called the Laws of Nature, whereof I shall speak more particularly in the two following chapters.

FROM CHAPTER 14. OF THE FIRST AND SECOND NATURAL LAWS

The Right of Nature, which writers commonly call *ius naturale*, is the liberty each man hath to use his own power as he will himself for the preservation of his own nature, that is to say, of his own life; and consequently of doing anything which in his own judgment and reason he shall conceive to be the aptest means thereunto.

By Liberty is understood, according to the proper signification of the word, the absence of external impediments, which impediments may oft take away part of a man's power to do what he would, but cannot hinder him from using the power left him according as his judgment and reason shall dictate to him.

A Law of Nature (*lex naturalis*) is a precept or general rule found out by reason, by which a man is forbidden to do that which is destructive of his life or taketh away the means of preserving the same; and to omit that by which he thinketh it may be best preserved. For though they that speak of this subject use to confound[8] *Ius* and *Lex*, *Right* and *Law*, yet they ought to be distinguished, because Right consisteth in liberty to do or to forbear, whereas Law determineth and bindeth to one of them: so that Law and Right differ as much as obligation and liberty, which in one and the same matter are inconsistent.

And because the condition of man (as hath been declared in the precedent chapter) is a condition of war of every one against every one, in which case every one is governed by his own reason, and there is nothing he can make use of that may not be a help unto him in preserving his life against his enemies: it followeth that in such a condition every man has a right to

---

7. Property.   8. Confuse.

every thing, even to one another's body. And therefore as long as this natural right of every man to every thing endureth, there can be no security to any man (how strong or wise soever he be) of living out the time which nature ordinarily alloweth men to live. And consequently it is a precept or general rule of reason, *That every man ought to endeavor peace, as far as he has hope of obtaining it; and when he cannot obtain it, that he may seek and use all helps and advantages of war.* The first branch of which rule containeth the first and fundamental law of nature, which is *to seek peace and follow it.* The second, the sum of the right of nature, which is, *by all means we can to defend ourselves.*

From this fundamental law of nature, by which men are commanded to endeavor peace, is derived this second law: *That a man be willing, when others are so too, as far-forth as[9] for peace and defense of himself he shall think it necessary, to lay down this right to all things, and be contented with so much liberty against other men as he would allow other men against himself.* For as long as any man holdeth this right of doing anything he liketh, so long are all men in the condition of war. But if other men will not lay down their right, as well as he, then there is no reason for anyone to divest himself of his. For that were to expose himself to prey (which no man is bound to) rather than to dispose himself to peace. This is that law of the Gospel: *Whatsoever you require that others should do to you, that do ye to them.*[1]

* * *

FROM CHAPTER 15. OF OTHER LAWS OF NATURE

From that law of nature by which we are obliged to transfer to another such rights as, being retained, hinder the peace of mankind, there followeth a third, which is this: *That men perform their covenants made:*[2] without which, covenants are in vain, and but empty words; and, the right of all men to all things remaining, we are still in the condition of war.

And in this law of nature consisteth the fountain and original of Justice. For where no covenant hath preceded, there hath no right been transferred, and every man has right to every thing; and consequently no action can be unjust. But when a covenant is made, then to break it is unjust; and the definition of injustice is no other than *the not performance of covenant.* And whatsoever is not unjust is just. * * *

For the question is not of promises mutual where there is no security of performance on either side, as when there is no civil power erected over the parties promising; for such promises are no covenants. But either where one of the parties has performed already, or where there is a power to make him perform: there is the question whether it be against reason, that is against the benefit of the other, to perform or not. And I say it is not against reason.[3] For the manifestation whereof, we are to consider: first, that when a man doth a thing which (notwithstanding anything can be foreseen and

9. Insofar as.
1. The Golden Rule: Matthew 7.12, Luke 6.31.
2. Though the terms are general, Hobbes refers in this chapter especially to the covenants men make with each other when they transfer power to the sovereign. Milton makes very different use of covenant theory to justify the rebellion and regicide in *The Tenure of Kings and Magistrates.*
3. I.e., to perform the promise.

reckoned on) tendeth to his own destruction, howsoever[4] some accident, which he could not expect, arriving may turn it to his benefit; yet such events do not make it reasonably or wisely done. Secondly, that in a condition of war, wherein every man to every man, for want of a common power to keep them all in awe, is an enemy, there is no man can hope by his own strength or wit to defend himself from destruction without the help of confederates; where everyone expects the same defense by the confederation that anyone else does. And therefore he which declares he thinks it reason to deceive those that help him can in reason expect no other means of safety than what can be had from his own single power. He therefore that breaketh his covenant, and consequently declareth that he thinks he may with reason do so, cannot be received into any society that unite themselves for peace and defense, but by the error of them that receive him; nor when he is received be retained in it without seeing the danger of their error; which errors a man cannot reasonably reckon upon as the means of his security. And therefore if he be left or cast out of society, he perisheth; and if he live in society, it is by the errors of other men, which he could not foresee nor reckon upon; and consequently against the reason of his preservation; and so as all men that contribute not to his destruction forbear him only out of ignorance of what is good for themselves.

As for the instance of gaining the secure and perpetual felicity of heaven by any way, it is frivolous: there being but one way imaginable, and that is not breaking, but keeping of covenant.

And for the other instance of attaining sovereignty by rebellion, it is manifest that though the event follow, yet because it cannot reasonably be expected, but rather the contrary; and because by gaining it so others are taught to gain the same in like manner, the attempt thereof is against reason. Justice therefore, that is to say, keeping of covenant, is a rule of reason, by which we are forbidden to do anything destructive to our life, and consequently a law of nature.

* * *

From *Part 2: Of Commonwealth*

CHAPTER 17. OF THE CAUSES, GENERATION, AND DEFINITION OF A COMMONWEALTH

The final cause, end, or design of men, who naturally love liberty and dominion over others, in the introduction of that restraint upon themselves in which we see them live in commonwealths, is the foresight of their own preservation and of a more contented life thereby—that is to say, of getting themselves out from their miserable condition of war which is necessarily consequent, as has been shown (Chapter 13), to the natural passions of men when there is no visible power to keep them in awe and tie them by fear of punishment to the performance of their convenants and observation of those laws of nature set down in the fourteenth and fifteenth chapters.

4. Even though.

For the laws of nature—as justice, equity, modesty, mercy, and, in sum, doing to others as we would be done to—of themselves, without the terror of some power to cause them to be observed, are contrary to our natural passions, that carry us to partiality,[5] pride, revenge, and the like. And covenants without the sword are but words, and of no strength to secure a man at all. Therefore, notwithstanding the laws of nature (which everyone has then kept when he had the will to keep them, when he can do it safely), if there be no power erected, or not great enough for our security, every man will—and may lawfully—rely on his own strength and art for caution[6] against all other men. And in all places where men have lived by small families, to rob and spoil one another has been a trade, and so far from being reputed against the law of nature that the greater spoils they gained, the greater was their honor; and men observed no other laws therein but the laws of honor—that is to abstain from cruelty, leaving to men their lives and instruments of husbandry. And as small families did then, so now do cities and kingdoms, which are but greater families, for their own security enlarge their dominions upon all pretenses of danger and fear of invasion or assistance that may be given to invaders, and endeavor as much as they can to subdue or weaken their neighbors by open force and secret arts, for want of other caution, justly; and are remembered for it in after ages with honor.

Nor is it the joining together of a small number of men that gives them this security, because in small numbers small additions on the one side or the other make the advantage of strength so great as is sufficient to carry the victory, and therefore gives encouragement to an invasion. The multitude sufficient to confide in for our security is not determined by any certain number but by comparison with the enemy we fear, and is then sufficient when the odds of the enemy is not of so visible and conspicuous moment to determine the event[7] of war as to move him to attempt.

And be there never so great a multitude, yet if their actions be directed according to their particular judgments and particular appetites, they can expect thereby no defense nor protection, neither against a common enemy nor against the injuries of one another. For being distracted in opinion[8] concerning the best use and application of their strength, they do not help but hinder one another, and reduce their strength by mutual opposition to nothing; whereby they are easily not only subdued by a very few that agree together, but also, when there is no common enemy, they make war upon each other for their particular interest. For if we could suppose a great multitude of men to consent in the observation of justice and other laws of nature without a common power to keep them all in awe, we might as well suppose all mankind to do the same, then there neither would be, nor need to be, any civil government or commonwealth at all, because there would be peace without subjection.

Nor is it enough for the security which men desire should last all the time of their life that they be governed and directed by one judgment for a limited time, as in one battle or one war. For though they obtain a victory by their unanimous endeavor against a foreign enemy, yet afterwards, when either

---

5. Favoritism, to oneself or another.
6. Precaution, defense.

7. Outcome.
8. I.e., by opinions.

they have no common enemy or he that by one part is held for an enemy is by another part held for a friend, they must needs, by the difference of their interests, dissolve and fall again into a war among themselves.

It is true that certain living creatures, as bees and ants, live sociably one with another—which are therefore by Aristotle numbered among political creatures—and have no other direction than their particular judgments and appetites, nor speech whereby one of them can signify to another what he thinks expedient for the common benefit; and therefore some man may perhaps desire to know why mankind cannot do the same. To which I answer:

First, that men are continually in competition for honor and dignity, which these creatures are not; and consequently among men there arises on that ground envy and hatred and finally war, but among these not so.

Secondly, that among these creatures the common good differs not from the private; and being by nature inclined to their private, they procure thereby the common benefit. But man, whose joy consists in comparing himself with other men, can relish nothing but what is eminent.

Thirdly, that these creatures—having not, as man, the use of reason—do not see nor think they see any fault in the administration of their common business; whereas among men there are very many that think themselves wiser and abler to govern the public better than the rest, and these strive to reform and innovate, one this way, another that way, and thereby bring it into distraction and civil war.

Fourthly, that these creatures, though they have some use of voice in making known to one another their desires and other affections, yet they want that art of words by which some men can represent to others that which is good in the likeness of evil, and evil in the likeness of good, and augment or diminish this apparent greatness of good and evil, discontenting men and troubling their peace at their pleasure.

Fifthly, irrational creatures cannot distinguish between injury and damage, and therefore, as long as they be at ease, they are not offended with their fellows; whereas man is then most troublesome when he is most at ease, for then it is that he loves to show his wisdom and control the actions of them that govern the commonwealth.

Lastly, the agreement of these creatures is natural, that of men is by covenant only, which is artificial, and therefore it is no wonder if there be somewhat else required besides covenant to make their agreement constant and lasting, which is a common power to keep them in awe and to direct their actions to the common benefit.

The only way to erect such a common power as may be able to defend them from the invasion of foreigners and the injuries of one another, and thereby to secure them in such sort as that by their own industry and by the fruits of the earth they may nourish themselves and live contentedly, is to confer all their power and strength upon one man, or upon one assembly of men that may reduce all their wills, by plurality of voices, into one will, which is as much as to say, to appoint one man or assembly of men to bear their person, and everyone to own and acknowledge himself to be the author of whatsoever he that so bears their person shall act or cause to be acted in those things which concern the common peace and safety, and therein to submit their wills everyone to his will, and their judgments to his judgment. This is more than consent or concord; it is a real unity of them all in one and the same person, made by covenant of every man with every man, in such manner as if every man should say to every man, "I authorize and give up my right of governing myself to this man, or to this assembly of men, on the condition that you give up your right to him and authorize all his actions in like manner." This done, the multitude so united in one person is called a commonwealth, in Latin *civitas*. This is the generation of that great Leviathan (or rather, to speak more reverently, of that mortal god) to whom we owe, under the immortal God, our peace and defense. For by this authority, given him by every particular man in the commonwealth, he has the use of so much power and strength conferred on him that, by terror thereof, he is enabled to form the wills of them all to peace at home and mutual aid against their enemies abroad. And in him consists the essence of the commonwealth, which, to define it, is one person, of whose acts a great multitude, by mutual covenants one with another, have made themselves everyone the author, to the end he may use the strength and means of them all as he shall think expedient for their peace and common defense. And he that carries this person is called sovereign and said to have sovereign power; and everyone besides, his subject.

1651

Writing the Self

The seventeenth century saw an explosion of interest in the intimate texture of day-to-day experience, in the sometimes surprising twists and turns of individual lives, in the relationship between character and destiny. Of course, such concerns were not entirely new: Chaucer's *Canterbury Tales* had dwelt lovingly upon the quirky diversity of its pilgrims. Some seventeenth-century writers looked back as well to classical or foreign precedents: the *Lives* of the late-classical biographer Plutarch, with their marvelously revelatory anecdotes and shrewd assessments of human moral complexity, the essays of the French Michel de Montaigne, who described his own opinions and experiences in frank detail. Both Plutarch and Montaigne profoundly influenced William Shakespeare, whose unparalleled gift for delineating character has led one recent critic to credit him with having "invented the human." Other writers, particularly religious ones, owed much to the medieval tradition of hagiography, or the narrating of the lives of saints and martyrs as models for the faithful to admire and imitate. Isaak Walton, in biographies of John Donne, George Herbert, and other worthies that draw upon his personal experience with them as well as upon his research, was one practitioner in a Protestant hagiographic tradition (p. 1424). Other Protestants directed their gaze inward, convinced of the importance of spiritual self-scrutiny ummediated by ritual or clergyman. Many Puritans kept spiritual accountings in writing—part diaries, part prayers—that effectively substituted for the Catholic practice of oral confession to a priest.

During the civil war and its aftermath, interest in "writing the self" only intensified. For the autobiographically inclined, the physical and ideological turmoil of midcentury could intensify a sense of the individual's isolation and uniqueness, forcing (or permitting) him to experience a range of events for which his upbringing could not have prepared him. Those who reflected upon the history of the period, as Lucy Hutchinson and Edward Hyde did, were often enthralled by the clash of strong personalities as well as the struggle between political principles, social trends, or cultural movements. Both Hutchinson and Hyde, from their different ends of the political spectrum, saw Cromwell and Charles I as locked in a fateful rivalry, each leader a complex mixture of personal strengths and failings.

The prominence of women writers in this section is no accident. Even though women were excluded from formal political participation, the war contributed to the development of their political interests and consciousness, and sometimes allowed them to play important informal or improvised roles in momentous events. The resourceful, adventurous Anne Halkett obviously relished her daring contribution to the rescue of the Duke of York. Some women writers explicitly eschewed a feminist agenda: Lucy Hutchinson's trenchant historical analysis coexists with thoroughly traditional beliefs about the proper submission of wife to husband and about the danger of women with political ambition, notably Charles I's queen. She excuses her own writing, to others and perhaps also to herself, by casting her work as a tribute to her beloved husband. In other cases, a challenge to political authority is inextricable from an assault on male privilege. Dorothy Waugh, a Quaker, refused like others of her faith to defer to political or religious authorities and insisted on the spiritual equality between women and men. Waugh suffered as much on account of her sex as on account of her religion, for she describes how the mayor of Carlisle is outraged not only by her unauthorized preaching but by the fact that the preacher is female. She is punished by being forced to wear a "scold's bridle," a traditional humiliation meted out to outspoken, argumentative women who refused to obey their husbands.

LUCY HUTCHINSON

Lucy Hutchinson, née Apsley (1620–1681), whose life centered in the North Country city of Nottingham, was a staunch republican, memoirist, poet, translator of Lucretius, and biographer and historian of the revolutionary period. In a fragmentary autobiography, she relates that she could read English perfectly by the age of four, and that "having a great memory, I was carried to sermons, and while I was very young could remember and repeat them . . . exactly." Her parents allowed her to receive at home as good an education as her brothers got at school (for an account of that education see the supplemental ebook). She reports that her future husband learned of her existence by noticing some of her Latin books. She was married at eighteen to John Hutchinson, a man of unyielding conviction and courage: he fought in the Puritan armies, served as governor of Nottingham Castle, sat in the Long Parliament, voted for the execution of Charles I, supported the republican commonwealth (1649–53), but withdrew support from Cromwell when he overrode and dismissed parliaments. Hutchinson was arrested after the Restoration and died in prison in 1664. After his death his devoted wife of twenty-six years wrote her *Memoirs of the Life of Colonel John Hutchinson*, purportedly to preserve his memory for her children. But within that eyewitness account of the remarkable period they had lived through, she enfolded a broad history of and commentary upon the Puritan movement and the revolution (for her account of the cultural crisis over sports, masques, and recreation, see the supplemental ebook). Almost certainly she hoped for a broader audience of nonconformists and republicans who might someday revive the "Good Old Cause," though because of its politics this work was not published until 1806. Also unpublished in her lifetime were several recently uncovered elegiac and satiric poems, as well as most of a long but unfinished epic poem, *Order and Disorder*, which treats biblical history from the Creation to the story of Jacob in twenty cantos, the first five of which were published in 1679. Much of the poem is indebted to *Paradise Lost*.

From Memoirs of the Life of Colonel John Hutchinson

[CHARLES I AND HENRIETTA MARIA]

The face of the court was much changed in the change of the king; for King Charles was temperate, chaste, and serious, so that the fools and bawds, mimics and catamites[1] of the former court grew out of fashion; and the nobility and courtiers, who did not quite abandon their debaucheries, yet so reverenced the king as to retire into corners to practice them. Men of learning and ingenuity in all arts were in esteem, and received encouragement from the king, who was a most excellent judge and great lover of paintings, carvings, gravings,[2] and many other ingenuities, less offensive than the bawdry and profane abusive[3] wit which was the only exercise of the other court. But, as in the primitive times,[4] it is observed that the best emperors were some of them stirred up by Satan to be the bitterest persecutors of the church, so this king was a worse encroacher upon the civil and spiritual liberties of his people by far than his father. He married a papist,[5] a French lady of a haughty spirit, and a great wit and beauty, to whom he became a most uxorious husband. By this means the court was replenished with papists, and many who hoped to advance themselves by the change, turned to that religion. All the papists in the kingdom were favored, and, by the king's example, matched into the best families. The puritans were more than ever discountenanced[6] and persecuted, insomuch that many of them chose to abandon their native country and leave their dearest relations, to retire into any foreign soil or plantation[7] where they might amidst all outward inconveniences enjoy the free exercise of God's worship. Such as could not flee were tormented in the bishops' court,[8] fined, whipped, pilloried, imprisoned, and suffered to enjoy no rest, so that death was better than life to them; and notwithstanding their patient sufferance of all these things, yet was not the king satisfied till the whole land was reduced to perfect slavery. The example of the French king[9] was propounded to him, and he thought himself no monarch so long as his will was confined to the bounds of any law; but knowing that the people of England were not pliable to an arbitrary rule, he plotted to subdue them to his yoke by a foreign

1. Clowns and homosexuals.
2. Engravings.
3. Satiric.
4. Early Christian period.
5. Roman Catholic.
6. Thwarted, out of favor.
7. Colony, such as the Massachusetts Bay Colony, founded in 1630. "Inconveniences" (following): misfortunes.
8. Courts administered by the Church of England tried and punished those who refused to attend church services, frequented alternative religious gatherings, or disputed church doctrines or policies.
9. The French king reigned without a parliament.

force;[1] and till he could effect it made no conscience of granting anything to the people, which he resolved should not oblige him longer than it served his turn; for he was a prince that had nothing of faith or truth, justice or generosity in him. He was the most obstinate person in his self-will that ever was, and so bent upon being an absolute, uncontrollable sovereign that he was resolved either to be such a king or none. His firm adherence to prelacy[2] was not for conscience of one religion more than another, for it was his principle that an honest man might be saved in any profession; but he had a mistaken principle that kingly government in the state could not stand without episcopal government in the church; and therefore, as the bishops flattered him with preaching up his prerogative,[3] and inveighing against the puritans as factious and disloyal, so he protected them in their pomp and pride and insolent practices against all the godly and sober people of the land.

* * *

But above all these the king had another instigator of his own violent purpose, more powerful than all the rest; and that was the queen, who, grown out of her childhood, began to turn her mind from those vain extravagancies she lived in at first to that which did less become her, and was more fatal to the kingdom; which is never in any place happy where the hands which were made only for distaffs affect[4] the management of scepters. If any one object the fresh example of Queen Elizabeth, let them remember that the felicity of her reign was the effect of her submission to her masculine and wise counselors; but wherever male princes are so effeminate as to suffer women of foreign birth and different religions to intermeddle with the affairs of state, it is always found to produce sad desolations; and it hath been observed that a French queen never brought any happiness to England. Some kind of fatality[5] too the English imagined to be in her name of Marie, which, it is said, the king rather chose to have her called by than her other, Henrietta, because the land should find a blessing in that name which had been more unfortunate;[6] but it was not in his power, though a great prince, to control destiny. This lady being by her priests affected with the meritoriousness of advancing her own religion, whose principle it is to subvert all other, applied that way her great wit and parts,[7] and the power her haughty spirit kept over her husband, who was enslaved in his affection only to her, though she had no more passion for him than what served to promote her design. Those brought her into a very good correspondence with the archbishop[8] and his prelatical crew, both joining in the cruel design of rooting the godly out of the land. . . . But how much soever their designs were framed in the dark, God revealed

1. Puritans suspected that Charles planned to invite Catholic forces to invade his realm in order to consolidate his own power.
2. Rule of the church by bishops.
3. Kingly powers.
4. Aspire to. "Distaff": spinning staff, emblem of female household management.
5. Fatefulness.
6. "Bloody Mary" Tudor, queen of England from 1553 to 1558, reintroduced Roman Catholicism

to England and burned many Protestants for heresy; the Scottish Mary, Queen of Scots, also Catholic, was executed in 1587 for plotting to assassinate Elizabeth I.
7. Abilities.
8. William Laud, archbishop of Canterbury, favored a highly ritualized form of worship that Puritans considered tantamount to Roman Catholicism. He was executed by the Parliamentarians in 1645.

them to his servants, and most miraculously ordered providences for their preservation.

1806

EDWARD HYDE, EARL OF CLARENDON

E dward Hyde (1609–1674) was educated at Oxford and during the 1630s practiced law. From about 1641 onward, he was among the chief supporters and advisers of Charles I; he went into exile with the boy who was to become Charles II and was privy to the various plots and plans of the royalists to restore him to power. After the Restoration he became lord chancellor and prime minister to Charles II, and he was instrumental in enacting the so-called Clarendon Code, a series of harsh laws against all nonconformists to the reestablished Church of England. He was impeached in 1667, owing partly to England's ill success in the Dutch War, and spent the last seven years of his life in France.

Clarendon wrote part of his great *History of the Rebellion* amid the events it describes. For the Muse of History such a short view can be a mixed blessing. But Clarendon's learning—legal, classical, and historical—and the formality of his method save him from many of the failings of partisanship. He wrote with dignity and for posterity. His *History*, which first appeared in print thirty years after his death, was remarkable not only for the largeness of its canvas but also for the force and coherence of the conservative social philosophy informing it. As a historian and rhetorician Clarendon invites comparison with his classical models, Thucydides and Tacitus. As an evaluator of character he invites comparison with Plutarch, whose judiciousness he shares.

From The History of the Rebellion

[THE CHARACTER OF OLIVER CROMWELL][1]

About the middle of August he was seized on by a common tertian ague,[2] from which he believed a little ease and divertissement at Hampton Court[3] would have freed him; but the fits grew stronger and his spirits much abated, so that he returned again to Whitehall,[4] when his physicians began to think him in danger, though the preachers who prayed always about him and told God Almighty what great things he had done for Him, and how much more need He had still of his service, declared as from God that he should recover, and he himself did not think he should die, till even the time that his spirits failed him, and then declared to them that he did appoint his

---

1. After the manner of ancient historians, Clarendon describes the last days, sickness, and death of Cromwell, then summarizes his character. The Protector, who had been depressed for some time by the death of a favorite daughter, first grew ill in the summer of 1658.
2. An acute fever, with paroxysms recurring every third day.
3. Hampton Court, built by Cardinal Wolsey and ceded by him to Henry VIII, is a splendid old palace up the Thames from London. "Divertissement": diversion.
4. Whitehall, in London, was the traditional residence of the head of state.

son to succeed him, his eldest son Richard. And so expired upon the third day of September (a day he thought always very propitious to him, and on which he had triumphed for several victories),[5] 1658, a day very memorable for the greatest storm of wind that had been ever known for some hours before and after his death, which overthrew trees, houses, and made great wrecks at sea, and was so universal that there were terrible effects of it both in France and Flanders, where all people trembled at it, besides the wrecks all along the coast, many boats having been cast away in the very rivers; and within few days after, that circumstance of his death that accompanied that storm was known.

He was one of those men *quos vituperare ne inimici quidem possunt, nisi ut simul laudent,*[6] for he could never have done half that mischief without great parts of courage and industry and judgment, and he must have had a wonderful understanding in the natures and humors of men, and as great a dexterity in the applying them, who from a private and obscure birth (though of a good family), without interest of estate, alliance, or friendships, could raise himself to such a height, and compound and knead such opposite and contradictory tempers, humors, and interests into a consistence that contributed to his designs and to their own destruction, whilst himself grew insensibly powerful enough to cut off those by whom he had climbed, in the instant that they projected to demolish their own building.[7] What Velleius Paterculus said of Cinna may very justly be said of him, *Ausum eum quae nemo auderet bonus, perfecisse quae a nullo nisi fortissimo perfici possunt.*[8] Without doubt no man with more wickedness ever attempted anything, or brought to pass what he desired more wickedly, more in the face and contempt of religion and moral honesty; yet wickedness as great as his could never have accomplished those trophies without the assistance of a great spirit, an admirable circumspection and sagacity, and a most magnanimous resolution. When he appeared first in the Parliament he seemed to have a person in no degree gracious, no ornament of discourse, none of those talents which use to reconcile the affections of the standers-by; yet as he grew into place and authority, his parts[9] seemed to be renewed, as if he had concealed faculties till he had occasion to use them, and when he was to act the part of a great man, he did it without any indecency[1] through the want of custom.

After he was confirmed and invested Protector by the Humble Petition and Advice,[2] he consulted with very few upon any action of importance, nor communicated any enterprise he resolved upon with more than those who were to have principal parts in the execution of it, nor to them sooner than was absolutely necessary. What he once resolved, in which he was not rash, he would not be dissuaded from, nor endure any contradiction of his power

5. Dunbar and Worcester were important battles that Cromwell had won on September 3.
6. "Whom not even his enemies could curse without praising him." The source of the phrase is unknown.
7. Clarendon's judgment can be compared with that of Marvell in "An Horatian Ode" (pp. 1806–11). "Insensibly": imperceptibly.
8. "He dared undertake what no good man would have tried and triumphed where only the strongest of men could have succeeded." Velleius

Paterculus (died 30 C.E.) wrote a concise *History of Rome;* the quotation is from 2.24.
9. Personal qualities.
1. Indecorum.
2. In December 1653, Cromwell was invested as Protector under a written constitution called the Instrument of Government. In 1657 another constitution, the Humble Petition and Advice, invested him with quasi-monarchical powers and restored the House of Lords.

and authority, but extorted obedience from them who were not willing to yield it.

When he had laid some very extraordinary tax upon the city, one Cony, an eminent fanatic,[3] and one who had heretofore served him very notably, positively refused to pay his part and loudly dissuaded others from submitting to it, as an imposition notoriously against the law and the property of the subject, which all honest men were bound to defend. Cromwell sent for him and cajoled him with the memory of the old kindness and friendship that had been between them, and that of all men he did not expect this opposition from him in a matter that was so necessary for the good of the commonwealth. But it was always his fortune to meet with the most rude and obstinate behavior from those who had formerly been absolutely governed by him, and they commonly put him in mind of some expressions and sayings of his own in cases of the like nature. So this man remembered[4] him how great an enemy he had expressed himself to such grievances, and declared that all who submitted to them and paid illegal taxes were more to blame, and greater enemies to their country, than they who imposed them; and that the tyranny of princes could never be grievous but by the tameness and stupidity of the people.

When Cromwell saw that he could not convert him, he told him that he had a will as stubborn as his, and he would try which of them two should be master, and thereupon with some terms of reproach and contempt he committed the man to prison—whose courage was nothing abated by it, but as soon as the term came, he brought his *habeas corpus*[5] in the King's Bench, which they then called the Upper Bench. Maynard, who was of counsel with the prisoner, demanded his liberty with great confidence, both upon the illegality of the commitment and the illegality of the imposition,[6] as being laid without any lawful authority. The judges could not maintain or defend either, but enough declared what their sentence would be, and therefore the Protector's attorney required a further day to answer what had been urged. Before that day, Maynard was committed to the Tower for presuming to question or make doubt of his authority, and the judges were sent for and severely reprehended for suffering that license; and when they with all humility mentioned the law, and Magna Carta, Cromwell told them their Magna Carta should not control his actions, which he knew were for the safety of the commonwealth. He asked them who made them judges; whether they had any authority to sit there but what he gave them, and that if his authority were at an end, they knew well enough what would become of themselves. And therefore advised them to be more tender of that which could only preserve them, and so dismissed them with caution that they should not suffer the lawyers to prate what it would not become them to hear.

Thus he subdued a spirit that had been often troublesome to the most sovereign power, and made Westminster Hall[7] as obedient and subservient to his commands as any of the rest of his quarters. In all other matters which did not concern the life of his jurisdiction, he seemed to have great

---

3. In Clarendon's vocabulary, a radical Puritan. "The city": the City of London.
4. Reminded.
5. Writ to release a prisoner.
6. I.e., the original tax.

7. The center of the law courts and legal profession. Clarendon never tells us what happened to poor George Cony; the lawyer and judges made their submission and got off, but the fate of the plaintiff remains obscure.

reverence for the law, and rarely interposed between party and party; and as he proceeded with this kind of indignation and haughtiness with those who were refractory and dared to contend with his greatness, so towards those who complied with his good pleasure and courted his protection he used a wonderful civility, generosity, and bounty.

To reduce three nations which perfectly hated him to an entire obedience to all his dictates, to awe and govern those nations by an army that was indevoted to him and wished his ruin, was an instance of a very prodigious address;[8] but his greatness at home was but a shadow of the glory he had abroad. It was hard to discover which feared him most, France, Spain, or the Low Countries, where his friendship was current at the value he put upon it; and as they did all sacrifice their honor and their interest to his pleasure, so there is nothing he could have demanded that either of them would have denied him.

* * *

He was not a man of blood, and totally declined Machiavel's method, which prescribes upon any alteration of a government, as a thing absolutely necessary, to cut off all the heads of those, and extirpate their families, who are friends to the old;[9] and it was confidently reported in the Council of Officers, it was more than once proposed that there might be a general massacre of all the royal party as the only expedient to secure the government, but Cromwell would never consent to it, it may be out of too much contempt of his enemies. In a word, as he had all the wickednesses against which damnation is denounced and for which hellfire is prepared, so he had some virtues which have caused the memory of some men in all ages to be celebrated, and he will be looked upon by posterity as a brave, bad man.

1702–4

8. Skill. "Indevoted": Clarendon's word, carefully coined to express the far from unanimous feelings of the army.
9. See *The Prince*, chapters 3 and 7.

LADY ANNE HALKETT

Lady Anne Halkett, née Anne Murray (1622–1699), was born into a family of the royal household; her father was a tutor to Prince Charles, later Charles I. Her allegiance to the royalist cause was an attachment by comparison with which her several love affairs were mere incidents. Halkett was a tough and active partisan who, more directly than most women of her day, engaged in the intrigues of the civil wars. With one of her particular admirers, Colonel Bamfield, she assisted the young Duke of York (future King James II of England) in making his escape from parliamentary custody. Her account of this adventure appeared in her memoirs, published many years later. We pick up the story in April 1648 with the question of Colonel Bamfield's intentions.

From The Memoirs

[SPRING THE DUKE]

This gentleman came to see me sometimes in the company of ladies who had been my mother's neighbors in St. Martin's Lane, and sometimes alone, but whenever he came his discourse was serious, handsome, and tending to impress the advantages of piety, loyalty, and virtue; and these subjects were so agreeable to my own inclination that I could not but give them a good reception, especially from one that seemed to be so much an owner of them himself. After I had been used to freedom of discourse with him, I told him I approved much of his advice to others, but I thought his own practice contradicted much of his profession, for one of his acquaintance had told me he had not seen his wife in a twelvemonth, and it was impossible in my opinion for a good man to be an ill husband; and therefore he must defend himself from one before I could believe the other of him. He said it was not necessary to give everyone that might condemn him the reason of his being so long from her, yet to satisfy me he would tell me the truth, which was that, he being engaged in the king's service,[1] he was obliged to be at London where it was not convenient for her to be with him, his stay in any place being uncertain; besides, she lived amongst her friends who, though they were kind to her, yet were not so to him, for most of that country had declared for the Parliament and were enemies to all that had or did serve the king, and therefore his wife, he was sure, would not condemn him for what he did by her own consent. This seeming reasonable, I did insist no more upon that subject.

At this time he had frequent letters from the king, who employed him in several affairs, but that of the greatest concern which he was employed in was to contrive the Duke of York's escape out of St. James[2] (where His Highness and the Duke of Gloucester and the Princess Elizabeth lived under the care of the Earl of Northumberland and his lady). The difficulties of it was represented by Colonel Bamfield; but His Majesty still pressed it, and I remember this expression was in one of the letters: "I believe it will be difficult, and if he miscarry in the attempt, it will be the greatest affliction that can arrive to me; but I look upon James's escape as Charles's preservation,[3] and nothing can content me more; therefore be careful what you do."

This letter, amongst others, he showed me, and where the king approved of his choice of me to entrust with it, for to get the duke's clothes made and to dress him in his disguise. So now all Colonel Bamfield's business and care was how to manage this business of so important concern, which could not be performed without several persons' concurrence in it, for he being generally known as one whose stay at London was in order to serve the king, few of those who were entrusted by the Parliament in public concerns durst own converse or hardly civility to him, lest they should have been suspect

---

1. The service of Charles I, then a close prisoner of the parliamentary army under Cromwell. In less than a year he would be executed.
2. St. James's Palace, the royal residence. The two named below were other children of Charles I.

3. Charles I must have feared the capture or assassination of the heir apparent, Prince Charles, then in France with his mother, Queen Henrietta Maria. If the younger son, James, were alive and at liberty, there would be no point in such an attempt to cut off the succession.

by their party, which made it difficult for him to get access to the duke. But, to be short, having communicated the design to a gentleman attending His Highness who was full of honor and fidelity, by his means he had private access to the duke, to whom he presented the king's letter and order to His Highness for consenting to act what Colonel Bamfield should contrive for his escape, which was so cheerfully entertained and so readily obeyed, that being once designed there was nothing more to do than to prepare all things for the execution. I had desired him to take a ribbon with him and bring me the bigness of the duke's waist and his length, to have clothes made fit for him. In the meantime, Colonel Bamfield was to provide money for all necessary expense, which was furnished by an honest citizen. When I gave the measure to my tailor to inquire how much mohair would serve to make a petticoat and waistcoat to a young gentlewoman of that bigness and stature, he considered it a long time, and said he had made many gowns and suits, but he had never made any to such a person in his life. I thought he was in the right; but his meaning was he had never seen any woman of so low a stature have so big a waist. However, he made it as exactly fit as if he had taken the measure himself. It was a mixed mohair of a light hair color and black, and the under-petticoat was scarlet.

All things being now ready, upon the 20th of April 1648 in the evening was the time resolved for the duke's escape. And in order to that, it was designed for a week before every night as soon as the duke had supped he and those servants that attended His Highness (till the Earl of Northumberland and the rest of the house had supped) went to a play called *hide and seek*,[4] and sometimes he would hide himself so well that in half an hour's time they could not find him. His Highness had so used them to this that when he went really away they thought he was but at the usual sport. A little before the duke went to supper that night, he called for the gardener, who only had a treble key besides that which the duke had, and bid him give him that key till his own was mended, which he did. And after His Highness had supped, he immediately called to go to the play, and went down the privy stairs into the garden, and opened the gate that goes into the park, treble locking all the doors behind him. And at the garden gate Colonel Bamfield waited for His Highness, and putting on a cloak and periwig, hurried him away to the park gate, where a coach waited that carried them to the waterside, and, taking the boat that was appointed for that service, they rowed to the stairs next the bridge, where I and Miriam[5] waited in a private house hard by that Colonel Bamfield had prepared for dressing His Highness, where all things were in a readiness. But I had many fears, for Colonel Bamfield had desired me, if they came not there precisely by ten o'clock, to shift for myself, for then I might conclude they were discovered, and so my stay there could do no good but prejudice myself. Yet this did not make me leave the house though ten o'clock did strike, and he that was entrusted often went to the landing place and saw no boat coming was much discouraged, and asked me what I would do. I told him I came there with a resolution to serve His Highness, and I was fully determined not to leave that place till I was out of hopes of doing what

---

4. As a boy of fourteen, James could play such a game without arousing suspicion and could be disguised without too much difficulty in wom-en's clothes.

5. Anne Murray's personal maidservant.

I came there for, and would take my hazard. He left me to go again to the waterside, and while I was fortifying myself against what might arrive to me, I heard a great noise of many as I thought coming upstairs, which I expected to be soldiers to take me, but it was a pleasing disappointment, for the first that came in was the duke, who with much joy I took in my arms and gave God thanks for his safe arrival. His Highness called "Quickly, quickly, dress me!"; and, putting off his clothes, I dressed him in the women's habit that was prepared, which fitted His Highness very well, and was very pretty in it.

After he had eaten something I made ready while I was idle, lest His Highness should be hungry, and having sent for a Wood Street cake (which I knew he loved) to take in the barge, with as much haste as could be His Highness went cross the bridge to the stairs where the barge lay, Colonel Bamfield leading him; and immediately the boatmen plied the oar so well that they were soon out of sight, having both wind and tide with them. But I afterwards heard the wind changed, and was so contrary that Colonel Bamfield told me he was terribly afraid they should have been blown back again. And the duke said, "Do anything with me rather than let me go back again," which put Colonel Bamfield to seek help where it was only to be had, and, after he had most fervently supplicated assistance from God, presently the wind blew fair, and they came safely to their intended landing place. But I heard there was some difficulty before they got to the ship at Gravesend, which had like to have discovered them had not Colonel Washington's lady[6] assisted them.

After the duke's barge was out of sight of the bridge, I and Miriam went where I appointed the coach to stay for me, and made drive as fast as the coachman could to my brother's house, where I stayed. I met none in the way that gave me any apprehension that the design was discovered, nor was it noised abroad till the next day, for (as I related before) the duke having used to play at hide and seek, and to conceal himself a long time, when they missed him at the same play, thought he would have discovered himself as formerly when they had given over seeking him. But a much longer time being passed than usually was spent in that divertissement, some began to apprehend that His Highness was gone in earnest past their finding, which made the Earl of Northumberland (to whose care he was committed), after strict search made in the house of St. James and all thereabouts to no purpose, to send and acquaint the Speaker of the House of Commons that the duke was gone, but how or by what means he knew not, but desired that there might be orders sent to the Cinque Ports[7] for stopping all ships going out till the passengers were examined and search made in all suspected places where His Highness might be concealed.

Though this was gone about with all the vigilancy imaginable, yet it pleased God to disappoint them of their intention by so infatuating those several persons who were employed for writing orders that none of them were able to write one right, but ten or twelve of them were cast by before one was according to their mind. This account I had from Mr. N. who was mace-bearer to the Speaker all that time and a witness of it. This disorder of the clerks

6. Most likely, the wife of Colonel Henry Washington, a royalist soldier (and distant relative of George Washington).
7. A group of channel ports, originally five in number (*cinque* is French for "five"); most English shipping to or from the Continent passed through them.

contributed much to the duke's safety, for he was at sea before any of the orders came to the ports, and so was free from what was designed if they had taken His Highness. Though several were suspected for being accessory to the escape, yet they could not charge any with it but the person who went away, and he being out of their reach, they took no notice as either to examine or imprison others.[8]

1778

8. Despite this romantic beginning to their friendship, Colonel Bamfield and Murray never did get together, because Bamfield's estranged wife was still living. In 1656 Murray married Sir James Halkett.

DOROTHY WAUGH

Around 1647, a group of disciples began forming around the charismatic itinerant preacher George Fox. Like many religious radicals of the period, Fox taught the importance of relying upon the Inner Light—one's own conscience as guided by the Holy Spirit—in preference to human law or holy writ. Fox believed that the days of prophecy and revelation had not ended in biblical times but were ongoing, so that the teachings of Scripture were open to revision. Moreover, sacred illumination was available to all sincere believers regardless of sex, education, or social rank. Fox's followers were derisively called "Quakers" because, in the grip of a visitation by the Holy Spirit, they would suffer paroxysms similar to epileptic convulsions.

Because Quakers believed all human beings to be spiritually equal, they refused to perform the acts of deference that permeated social life in seventeenth-century England—bowing before and doffing the hat to superiors or addressing them with the honorific "you" rather than the familiar "thou." They felt called upon to testify to their beliefs wherever, and whenever, the Inner Light prompted, answering back to ministers in the pulpit, inveighing against what they considered social injustices, and sermonizing without a license in public places. Often, their outspokenness enraged secular and ecclesiastical authorities.

Dorothy Waugh (ca. 1636–?) worked as a maidservant in Preston Patrick, in northwest England, a hotbed of Quaker activity. She probably became one of Fox's followers in the early 1650s, when she was still a teenager. Like Fox and a number of other missionary spirits, sometimes called "the Valiant Sixty," she traveled through England on foot, spreading the Quaker message to all who would listen. In 1656, aged about twenty, she was one of the Friends who arrived in Boston, Massachusetts, aboard the *Speedwell:* the party was imprisoned for ten days by the staunch Puritan governor John Endicott, and then forced to return to England. Undaunted, Waugh embarked for the colonies again, with another small group of missionary Quakers, the following year, this time landing in New Amsterdam (modern New York). They were no more welcome here than they had been in Boston. After a brief imprisonment they were shipped in shackles to the colony of Rhode Island, where complete religious toleration was the rule. In the late 1650s, probably between voyages to the New World, Waugh married William Lotherington of Yorkshire, but nothing is known about her later life or the circumstances of her death. Other Quakers traveled even further than Waugh on missionary expeditions; one woman made it as far as the Ottoman Empire and gave a sermon before the Grand Turk; when she failed to convert him, she walked back home to England.

Waugh's account of her treatment in Carlisle was published in *The Lamb's Defence Against Lies*, a collection in which various Quakers testified to their maltreatment by secular and religious authorities. Although the Friends were pacifists who refused to retaliate physically or verbally against their persecutors, they were fully aware of the propaganda value of unmerited suffering—indeed, their enemies believed that they deliberately courted abuse as a publicity stunt. More probably, their bad reception only reinforced their conviction that they constituted a tiny remnant of holiness, bravely resisting the overwhelming powers of worldliness and evil. The Quakers' published accounts of their victimization, typically reported in understated, factual, but gruesome detail, owed much to the sixteenth-century writer John Foxe's influential tales of Protestant martyrdom under the Catholic queen "Bloody Mary" Tudor. In the years between 1650 and 1700, numerous male and female Friends published memoirs of their arduous lives, producing some of the first printed autobiographical writing in English by women and by people of humble status.

A Relation Concerning Dorothy Waugh's Cruel Usage by the Mayor of Carlisle

Upon a seventh day about the time called Michaelmas in the year of the world's account 1655[1] I was moved of the Lord to go into the market of Carlisle, to speak against all deceit and ungodly practices, and the mayor's officer came and violently haled me off the cross[2] and put me in prison, not having anything to lay to my charge. And presently the mayor came up where I was, and asked me from whence I came; and I said, "Out of Egypt,[3] where thou lodgest." But after these words, he was so violent and full of passion he scarce asked me any more questions, but called to one of his followers to bring the bridle[4] as he called it to put upon me, and was to be on three hours. And that which they called so was like a steel cap and my hat being violently plucked off which was pinned to my head whereby they tore my clothes to put on their bridle as they called it, which was a stone weight of iron by the relation of their own generation,[5] and three bars of iron to come over my face, and a piece of it was put in my mouth, which was so unreasonable big a thing for that place as cannot be well related, which was locked to my head. And so I stood their time with my hands bound behind me, with the stone weight of iron upon my head and the bit in my mouth to keep me from speaking. And the mayor said he would make me an example to all that should ever come in that name.[6] And the people to see me so violently abused were broken into tears, but he cried out on them and said, "For foolish pity, one may spoil a whole city." And the man that kept the prison door demanded two pence of everyone that came to see me while

---

1. Quakers saw themselves as separated from "the world" and its conventional means of marking dates, particularly objecting to terms left over from medieval Catholicism, like "Michaelmas," or the Mass of the Archangel Michael, celebrated on September 29. "Seventh day": Sabbath.
2. A large stone cross marked the main intersection of most English towns; public speakers could mount the steps in order to be heard better.

3. In the Bible, the place where God's chosen people were enslaved and where most of the population worshipped false gods.
4. An instrument of torture and humiliation, typically used to punish women who "scolded" their husbands or neighbors in public.
5. By their own report. A stone is fourteen pounds.
6. As professed Friends, or Quakers.

their bridle remained upon me. Afterwards it was taken off and they kept me in prison for a little season, and after a while the mayor came again and caused it to be put on again, and sent me out of the city with it on, and gave me very vile and unsavory words, which were not fit to proceed out of any man's mouth, and charged the officer to whip me out of the town, from constable to constable to send me till I came to my own home, whenas[7] they had not anything to lay to my charge.

1656

7. Inasmuch as.

THOMAS TRAHERNE
1637–1674

Thomas Traherne's most remarkable works—his stanzaic poems, free verse *Thanksgivings*, and the brilliant prose meditative sequence *Centuries of Meditations*—were lost for over two centuries. With them was lost a unique religious and aesthetic sensibility that conceives of heavenly felicity as a state that can be enjoyed in this world by recovering the perspective of lost childhood innocence. In 1673 Traherne published a polemic against Roman Catholics (*Roman Forgeries*), and some works of moral philosophy, meditation, and devotion received posthumous publication over the next several years. But his poems and the *Centuries* were discovered in manuscript only in 1896–97, and at first his poems were attributed to Henry Vaughan. Little is known of Traherne's life. The son of a Herefordshire shoemaker, he received a degree from Brasenose College, Oxford; took orders and became rector of Credenhill in Herefordshire in 1661; became chaplain about 1660 to Sir Orlando Bridgeman, Lord Keeper of the Great Seal; and spent his last years in and near London. The *Centuries* consists of four books of one hundred items each and a fifth unfinished. They contain prose meditations (which are often ecstatic prose poems) and some interpolated poems; the work was addressed to Traherne's good friend Mrs. Susanna Hopton, to help her attain "felicity." The poems render moments of spiritual experience: the speaker's enjoyment of a wondrous heavenly felicity in childhood, his painful loss of it in maturity, and his successful efforts to recover that heavenly perspective.

From Centuries of Meditation

From The Third Century

3

The corn was orient and immortal wheat, which never should be reaped, nor was ever sown. I thought it had stood from everlasting to everlasting. The dust and stones of the street were as precious as gold: the gates were at first the end of the world. The green trees when I saw them first through one of the gates transported and ravished me; their sweetness and unusual beauty made my heart to leap, and almost mad with ecstasy, they were such strange and wonderful things. The men! O what venerable and reverend creatures did the aged seem! Immortal cherubims! And young men glittering and sparkling angels, and maids strange seraphic pieces of life and beauty! Boys and girls tumbling in the street, and playing, were moving jewels. I knew not that they were born or should die; but all things abided eternally as they were in their proper places. Eternity was manifest in the light of the day, and something infinite behind everything appeared, which talked with my expectation and moved my desire. The city seemed to stand in Eden, or to be built in Heaven. The streets were mine, the temple was mine, the people were mine, their clothes and gold and silver were mine, as much as their sparkling eyes, fair skins, and ruddy faces. The skies were mine, and so were the sun and moon and stars, and all the world was mine; and I the only spectator and enjoyer of it. I knew no churlish proprieties,[1] nor bounds, nor divisions: but all proprieties and divisions were mine: all treasures and the possessors of them. So that with much ado I was corrupted, and made to learn the dirty devices of this world, which now I unlearn, and become, as it were, a little child again that I may enter into the Kingdom of God.

1908

Wonder

How like an angel came I down!
  How bright are all things here!
When first among his works I did appear,
  O how their glory me did crown!
5 The world resembled his eternity,
    In which my soul did walk,
And everything that I did see
    Did with me talk.

The skies in their magnificence,
10   The lively, lovely air;
O how divine, how soft, how sweet, how fair!
The stars did entertain my sense,[1]
And all the works of God so bright and pure,
    So rich and great did seem,
15 As if they ever must endure,
    In my esteem.

A native health and innocence
    Within my bones did grow,
And while my God did all his glories show,
20   I felt a vigor in my sense

---

1. Private property rights.   1. Sight.

That was all Spirit. I within did flow
    With seas of life like wine;
  I nothing in the world did know
    But 'twas divine.

25   Harsh ragged objects were concealed,
      Oppression's tears and cries,
  Sins, griefs, complaints, dissensions, weeping eyes,
    Were hid; and only things revealed
  Which heavenly spirits and the angels prize.
30   The state of innocence
    And bliss, not trades and poverties,
      Did fill my sense.

The streets were paved with golden stones,
    The boys and girls were mine,
35 O how did all their lovely faces shine!
    The sons of men were holy ones.
Joy, beauty, welfare did appear to me
    And everything which here I found
  While like an angel I did see,
40   Adorned the ground.

Rich diamond and pearl and gold
    In every place was seen;
Rare splendors, yellow, blue, red, white, and green,
    Mine eyes did everywhere behold.
45 Great wonders clothed with glory did appear,
    Amazement was my bliss.
That and my wealth was everywhere:
    No joy to this!°   *compared to this*

Cursed and devised proprieties,[2]
50   With envy, avarice,
And fraud, those fiends that spoil even paradise,
    Fled from the splendor of mine eyes.
And so did hedges, ditches, limits, bounds:
    I dreamed not aught of those,
55 But wandered over all men's grounds,
      And found repose.

Proprieties themselves were mine,
    And hedges ornaments;
Walls, boxes, coffers, and their rich contents
60   Did not divide my joys, but shine.
Clothes, ribbons, jewels, laces, I esteemed
    My joys by others worn;
For me they all to wear them seemed
    When I was born.

1903

2. Private property rights.

On Leaping over the Moon

I saw new worlds beneath the water lie,
  New people, and another sky
    And sun, which seen by day
    Might things more clear display.
5   Just such another[1]
     Of late my brother[2]
Did in his travel see, and saw by night,
  A much more strange and wondrous sight;
Nor could the world exhibit such another
10   So great a sight, but in a brother.

Adventure strange! no such in story we
  New or old, true or feignèd see.
    On earth he seemed to move,
    Yet heaven went above;[3]
15   Up in the skies
     His body flies,
In open, visible, yet magic sort:
  As he along the way did sport,
Like Icarus[4] over the flood he soars
20   Without the help of wings or oars.

As he went tripping o'er the king's highway,
  A little pearly river lay
    O'er which, without a wing
    Or oar, he dared to swim,
25   Swim through the air
     On body fair;
He would not use nor trust Icarian wings[5]
  Lest they should prove deceitful things;
For had he fallen, it had been wondrous high,
30   Not from, but from above, the sky.

He might have dropped through that thin element
  Into a fathomless descent
    Unto the nether sky
    That did beneath him lie
35   And there might tell
     What wonders dwell
On earth above. Yet bold he briskly runs,
  And soon the danger overcomes,
Who, as he leapt, with joy related soon
40   How happy he o'erleaped the moon.

---

1. Another world.
2. Traherne's brother Philip.
3. I.e., yet went above the heavens.
4. Icarus soared on waxen wings.
5. Icarus's wings melted in the sun, and he fell into the sea.

What wondrous things upon the earth are done
   Beneath and yet above the sun!
      Deeds all appear again
      In higher spheres; remain
45   In clouds as yet:
      But there they get
Another light, and in another way
   Themselves to us above display.
The skies themselves this earthly globe surround;
50   We're even here within them found.

On heavenly ground within the skies we walk,
   And in this middle center talk:
      Did we but wisely move
      On earth in heaven above,
55   We then should be
      Exalted high
Above the sky: from whence whoever falls,
   Through a long dismal precipice,°   *headlong fall*
Sinks to the deep abyss where Satan crawls,
60   Where horrid death and dèspair lies.

As much as others thought themselves to lie
   Beneath the moon, so much more high
      Himself he thought to fly
      Above the starry sky,
65   As that he spied
      Below the tide.
Thus did he yield me in the shady night
   A wondrous and instructive light,
Which taught me that under our feet there is,
70   As o'er our heads, a place of bliss.

1910

MARGARET CAVENDISH
1623–1673

Margaret (Lucas) Cavendish, Duchess of Newcastle, wrote and published numerous works during the Interregnum and Restoration era, in a great variety of genres: poetry (*Poems and Fancies*, 1653); essays (*Philosophical Fancies*, 1653; *The World's Olio*, 1655), short fiction (*Nature's Pictures*, 1656), autobiography (*A True Relation of My Birth, Breeding, and Life*, 1656), Utopian romance (*The Blazing World*, 1666), scientific essays chiefly critical of the new science, letters, a biography of her husband (*The Life of . . . William Cavendish*, 1667), and some eighteen plays, of which one, *The Forced Marriage*, was produced in 1670. Most were published in lavish editions at the Newcastles' own expense. At the time they elicited more derision than praise: for a woman, especially an aristocratic woman, to publish works dealing so intimately with her desires, opinions, personal circumstances, and aspirations to fame and authorship seemed to many disgraceful. Samuel Pepys concluded, after reading her life of her husband the duke, that she was "a mad, conceited, ridiculous woman, and he an ass to suffer [her] to write what she writes to him and of him." Her fantastic dress and sometimes idiosyncratic behavior abetted that characterization: she took pride in "singularity" and even paid a visit to the all-male Royal Society. But the philosopher Thomas Hobbes thought well of her, and her rediscoverers in recent decades have praised her works and her self-construction as a female author.

Cavendish's autobiography analyzes her responses to the circumstances of her life. Born into a wealthy royalist family that encouraged her disposition to read and write, she became maid of honor to Queen Henrietta Maria, whom she followed into exile in Paris. There she married, in 1645, the widowed William Cavendish, thirty years her senior, who was one of Charles I's generals and later Duke of Newcastle. Exiled for fifteen years on the Continent, where (his estates having been sequestered) they ran up exorbitant debts, they were restored to status and fortune after the Restoration. The duke, who was himself a poet, playwright, and philosopher, supported and promoted Margaret's literary endeavors, for which she was profoundly grateful. In polemical prefaces to her several works, she develops a fragmentary poetics, trenchantly defends her right to publish and to participate in contemporary intellectual exchange, defends women's rational powers, and decries their educational disadvantages and exclusion from the public domain.

From Poems and Fancies

The Poetess's Hasty Resolution

Reading my verses, I liked them so well,
Self-love did make my judgment to rebel.
Thinking them so good, I thought more to write;
Considering not how others would them like.
5   I writ so fast, I thought, if I lived long,
A pyramid of fame[1] to build thereon.
Reason observing which way I was bent,
Did stay my hand, and asked me what I meant;
Will you, said she, thus waste your time in vain,
10   On that which in the world small praise shall gain?
For shame, leave off, said she, the printer spare,
He'll lose by your ill poetry, I fear.
Besides the world hath already such a weight
Of useless books, as it is overfraught.[2]
15   Then pity take, do the world a good turn,
And all you write cast in the fire, and burn.
Angry I was, and Reason struck away,
When I did hear, what she to me did say.

---

1. A poetic monument.
2. Like a ship with too heavy a cargo, in danger of sinking.

Then all in haste I to the press it sent,
20 Fearing persuasion might my book prevent.
But now 'tis done, with grief repent do I,
Hang down my head with shame, blush, sigh, and cry.
Take pity, and my drooping spirits raise,
Wipe off my tears with handkerchiefs of praise.

1653

The Hunting of the Hare

Betwixt two ridges of plowed land lay Wat,[1]
Pressing his body close to earth lay squat.
His nose upon his two forefeet close lies,
Glazing obliquely with his great gray eyes.
5 His head he always sets against the wind,
If turn his tail, his hairs blow up behind:
Which he too cold will grow, but he is wise,
And keeps his coat still° down, so warm he lies.   constantly
Then resting all the day, till, sun doth set,
10 Then riseth up, his relief for to get.
Walking about until the sun doth rise,
Then back returns, down in his form° he lies.   nest
At last, poor Wat was found, as he there lay,
By huntsmen, with their dogs which came that way.
15 Seeing, gets up, and fast begins to run,
Hoping some ways the cruel dogs to shun.
But they by nature have so quick a scent,
That by their nose they trace what way he went.
And with their deep, wide mouths set forth a cry,
20 Which answered was by echoes in the sky.
Then Wat was struck with terror, and with fear,
Thinks every shadow still the dogs they were.
And running out some distance from the noise,
To hide himself, his thoughts he new employs.
25 Under a clod of earth in sand pit wide,
Poor Wat sat close, hoping himself to hide.
There long he had not sat, but straight° his ears   immediately
The winding° horns and crying dogs he hears: blowing
Staring with fear, up leaps, then doth he run,
30 And with such speed, the ground scarce treads upon.
Into a great thick wood he straightway gets.
Where underneath a broken bough he sits.
At every leaf that with the wind did shake,
Did bring such terror, made his heart to ache.
35 That place he left, to champaign° plains he went,   open
Winding about, for to deceive their scent.
And while they snuffling were, to find his track,

1. Conventional name for a hare.

Poor Wat, being weary, his swift pace did slack.
On his two hinder legs for ease did sit,
His forefeet rubbed his face from dust, and sweat.
Licking his feet, he wiped his ears so clean,
That none could tell that Wat had hunted been.
But casting round about his fair great eyes,
The hounds in full career he near him spies:
To Wat it was so terrible a sight,
Fear gave him wings, and made his body light.
Though weary was before, by running long,
Yet now his breath he never felt more strong.
Like those that dying are, think health returns,
When 'tis but a faint blast, which life out burns.
For spirits seek to guard the heart about,
Striving with death, but death doth quench them out.
Thus they so fast came on, with such loud cries,
That he no hopes hath left, nor help espies.
With that the winds did pity poor Wat's case,
And with their breath the scent blew from the place.
Then every nose is busily employed,
And every nostril is set open wide,
And every head doth seek a several° way, *different*
To find what grass, or track, the scent on lay.
Thus quick industry° that is not slack, *clever work*
Is like to witchery,° brings lost things back. *witchcraft*
For though the wind had tied the scent up close,
A busy dog thrust in his snuffling nose
And drew it out, with it did foremost run,
Then horns blew loud, for th'rest to follow on.
The great slow hounds, their throats did set a bass,
The fleet swift hounds, as tenors next in place,
The little beagles they a treble sing,
And through the air their voices round did ring.
Which made a consort, as they ran along;
If they but words could speak, might sing a song.
The horns kept time, the hunters shout for joy,
And valiant seem, poor Wat for to destroy:
Spurring their horses to a full career,
Swim rivers deep, leap ditches without fear;
Endanger life and limbs so fast will ride,
Only to see how patiently Wat died.
At last,[2] the dogs so near his heels did get,
That they their sharp teeth in his breech did set;
Then tumbling down, did fall with weeping eyes,
Gives up his ghost, and thus poor Wat he dies.
Men whooping loud, such acclamations make,
As if the Devil they did prisoner take.
When they do but a shiftless° creature kill; *helpless*
To hunt, there needs no valiant soldier's skill.
But man doth think that exercise and toil,

2. From the 1664 edition; 1653 has "For why."

To keep their health, is best, which makes most spoil.
Thinking that food and nourishment so good,
90   And appetite, that feeds on flesh and blood.
When they do lions, wolves, bears, tigers see,
To kill poor sheep, straight say, they cruel be,
But for themselves all creatures think too few
For luxury, wish God would make them new.
95   As if that God made creatures for man's meat,
To give them life and sense, for man to eat;
Or else for sport, or recreation's sake,
Destroy those lives that God saw good to make:
Making their stomachs, graves, which full they fill
100   With murdered bodies that in sport they kill.
Yet man doth think himself so gentle, mild,
When he of creatures is most cruel wild.
And is so proud, thinks only he shall live,
That God a godlike nature did him give.
105   And that all creatures for his sake alone
Was made for him, to tyrannize upon.

1653, 1664

From A True Relation of My Birth, Breeding, and Life[1]

As for my breeding, it was according to my birth and the nature of my sex, for my birth was not lost in my breeding; for as my sisters had been bred, so was I in plenty, or rather with superfluity. . . . 'Tis true my mother might have increased her daughters' portions by a thrifty sparing, yet she chose to bestow it on our breeding, honest pleasures, and harmless delight, out of an opinion that if she bred us with needy necessity it might chance to create in us shark-ing[2] qualities, mean thoughts, and base actions, which she knew my father as well as herself did abhor. Likewise we were bred tenderly, for my mother naturally did strive to please and delight her children, not to cross or torment them, terrifying them with threats or lashing them with slavish whips. But instead of threats, reason was used to persuade us, and instead of lashes, the deformities of vices was discovered,[3] and the graces and virtues were presented unto us.

*   *   *

After the Queen went from Oxford, and so out of England, I was parted from them.[4] For when the Queen was in Oxford I had a great desire to be one of her maids of honor. . . . And though I might have learned more wit,

1. Cavendish's autobiography is a concise account, factual and at times self-reflective, of her early life. It comprises the final section of *Nature's Pictures* (1656), a collection of her fiction written during the Newcastles' exile in Antwerp during the Cromwell regime. "Breeding": upbringing.
2. Greedy.
3. Shown.

4. Her mother and family; her father had died when she was two years old. In 1643 Charles I moved his family and court to Oxford, where Margaret became maid of honor to Queen Henrietta Maria; in 1644 the queen fled with some supporters, Margaret among them, to her native Paris, to urge support for the royalist cause.

and advanced my understanding by living in a court, yet being dull, fearful, and bashful, I neither heeded what was said or practiced, but just what belonged to my loyal duty and my own honest reputation. And indeed I was so afraid to dishonor my friends and family by my indiscreet actions that I rather chose to be accounted a fool than to be thought rude or wanton. In truth my bashfulness and fears made me repent my going from home to see the world abroad. . . .

So I continued almost two years, until such time as I was married from thence. For my Lord the Marquis of Newcastle did approve of those bashful fears which many condemned, and would choose such a wife as he might bring to his own humors,[5] and not such an one as was wedded to self-conceit, or one that had been tempered to the humors of another, for which he wooed me for his wife. And though I did dread marriage, and shunned men's companies as much as I could, yet I could not nor had not the power to refuse him, by reason my affections were fixed on him, and he was the only person I ever was in love with. Neither was I ashamed to own it, but gloried therein, for it was not amorous love. I never was infected therewith—it is a disease, or a passion, or both, I know by relation, not by experience. Neither could title, wealth, power, or person entice me to love. But my love was honest and honorable, being placed upon merit; which affection joyed at the fame of his worth, pleased with delight in his wit, proud of the respects he used to me, and triumphing in the affections he professed for me. . . . And though my lord hath lost his estate, and banished out of his country for his loyalty to his king and country, yet neither despised poverty nor pinching necessity could make him break the bonds of friendship, or weaken his loyal duty to his king or country.

* * *

When I am writing any sad feigned stories or serious humors or melancholy passions, I am forced many times to express them with the tongue before I can write them with the pen, by reason those thoughts that are sad, serious, and melancholy are apt to contract and to draw back too much, which oppression doth as it were overpower or smother the conception in the brain. But when some of those thoughts are sent out in words, they give the rest more liberty to place themselves in a more methodical order, marching more regularly with my pen on the ground of white paper. But my letters seem rather as a ragged rout, than a well-armed body, for the brain being quicker in creating than the hand in writing, or the memory in retaining, many fancies are lost by reason they ofttimes outrun the pen. Where I, to keep speed in the race, write so fast as I stay not so long as to write my letters plain, insomuch as some have taken my handwriting for some strange character.[6] . . . My only trouble is lest my brain should grow barren, or that the root of my fancies should become insipid, withering into a dull stupidity, for want of maturing subjects to write on.

* * *

---

5. Disposition. William Cavendish (1593–1676), a general in the king's army, fled to the Continent in 1644. Margaret was his second wife, whom he married in 1645 in Paris.
6. Alphabet.

Since I have writ in general thus far of my life, I think it fit, I should speak something of my humor, particular practice, and disposition. As for my humor, I was from my childhood given to contemplation, being more taken or delighted with thoughts than in conversation with a society, in so much as I would walk two or three hours, and never rest, in a musing, considering, contemplating manner, reasoning with myself of everything my senses did present. . . . Likewise I had a natural stupidity towards the learning of any other language than my native tongue, for I could sooner and with more facility understand the sense than remember the words, and for want of such memory makes me so unlearned in foreign languages as I am: as for my practice,[7] I was never very active, by reason I was given so much to contemplation. . . . As for my study of books it was little, yet I chose rather to read, than to employ my time in any other work, or practice, and when I read what I understood not, I would ask my brother, the lord Lucas, he being learned, the sense of meaning thereof; but my serious study could not be much, by reason I took great delight in attiring, fine dressing, and fashions, especially such fashions as I did invent myself, not taking that pleasure in such fashions as was invented by others: also I did dislike any should follow my fashions, for I always took delight in a singularity, even in the accoutrements of habits, but whatsoever I was addicted to, either in fashion of clothes, contemplations of thoughts, actions of life, they were lawful, honorable, and modest, of which I can avouch to the world with a great confidence, because it is a pure truth.

* * *

I am a great emulator; for though I wish none worse than they are, yet it is lawful for me to wish myself the best, and to do my honest endeavor thereunto; for I think it no crime to wish myself the exactest[8] of Nature's works, my thread of life the longest, my chain of destiny the strongest, my mind the peaceablest, my life the pleasantest, my death the easiest, and the greatest saint in heaven. Also to do my endeavor, so far as honor and honesty doth allow of, to be the highest on fortune's wheel, and to hold the wheel from turning if I can; and if it be commendable to wish another's good, it were a sin not to wish my own; for as envy is a vice, so emulation is a virtue, but emulation is in the way to ambition, or indeed it is a noble ambition. But I fear my ambition inclines to vainglory, for I am very ambitious; yet 'tis neither for beauty, wit, titles, wealth, or power, but as they are steps to raise me to fame's tower, which is to live by remembrance on after-ages. . . . But I hope my readers will not think me vain for writing my life, since there have been many that have done the like, as Caesar, Ovid,[9] and many more, both men and women, and I know no reason I may not do it as well as they: but I verily believe some censuring readers will scornfully say, Why hath this lady writ her own life? since none cares to know whose daughter she was, or whose wife she is, or how she was bred, or what fortunes she had, or how she lived, or what humor or disposition she was of? I answer that it is true, that

---

7. Refers, probably, to practicing a musical instrument, music being an accomplishment cultivated by highborn young ladies.
8. Most perfect.

9. Julius Caesar wrote an account of his military campaigns (*Commentaries*); the Roman poet Ovid wrote poems ostensibly about his own life and loves.

'tis to no purpose to the readers, but it is to the authoress, because I write it for my own sake, not theirs; neither did I intend this piece for to delight, but to divulge; not to please the fancy but to tell the truth, lest after-ages should mistake, in not knowing I was daughter to one Master Lucas[1] of St. Johns, near Colchester, in Essex, second wife to the Lord Marquis of Newcastle; for my lord having had two wives, I might easily have been mistaken, especially if I should die and my lord marry again.

1656

The Blazing World   Part romance, part utopia, and part science fiction, *The Blazing World* is also an idealized version of Cavendish's own fantasies in that it portrays the effortless rise of a woman to absolute power. It begins in the vein of romance: a young woman is abducted and miraculously saved as a tempest carries the abductors' boat to the North Pole and on to another universe, the Blazing World, whose emperor promptly marries her and turns over the entire government of the realm to her. It takes on a utopian character, as the new empress learns from the fantastically diverse inhabitants about their numerous scientific experiments and about the royalist politics and religious uniformity of the place. The empress then brings Margaret Cavendish to be her scribe and returns with Margaret (in the state of disembodied spirits and Platonic friends) to visit and learn about Margaret's world; she also puts down a rebellion at home and subjects other nations to her beneficent rule. Cavendish's preface makes a bold claim for authorial self-sufficiency, equating her creation of and rule over her textual world with the conquering and ruling of empires by Caesar and Alexander. She emphasizes the satisfactions of authorship, but in doing so she also underscores the social and political restrictions on women that have confined her sphere of action to an imagined world.

The Description of a New World, Called The Blazing World[1]

To the Reader

* * *This is the reason, why I added this piece of fancy to my philosophical observations, and joined them as two worlds at the ends of their poles; both for my own sake, to divert my studious thoughts, which I employed in the contemplation thereof, and to delight the reader with variety, which is always pleasing. But lest my fancy should stray too much, I chose such a fiction as would be agreeable to the subject treated of in the former parts; it is a description of a new world, not such as Lucian's or the French-man's world in the moon;[2] but a world of my own creating, which I call the Blazing World: the first part whereof is romancical, the second philosophical, and the third is merely fancy, or (as I may call it) fantastical, which if it add

---

1. Thomas Lucas (ca. 1573–1625), a gentleman of large fortune and estates. Margaret describes him as "not a peer of the realm, yet there were few peers who had much greater estates, or lived more noble therewith."
1. *The Blazing World* was published in 1666 and 1668, together with Newcastle's *Observations upon Experimental Philosophy*, a critique of the new science emphasizing the limitations of experiment founded on human perception and such instruments as the microscope and the telescope.
2. Cyrano de Bergerac (1619–1655), author of *Histoire comique des états et empires de la lune* (1656). The Greek satirist Lucian of Samosata (125–200? C.E.) wrote dialogues about an imaginary voyage, translated in 1634.

any satisfaction to you, I shall account myself a happy creatoress; if not, I must be content to live a melancholy life in my own world; I cannot call it a poor world, if poverty be only want of gold, silver, and jewels; for there is more gold in it than all the chemists ever did, and (as I verily believe) will ever be able to make. As for the rocks of diamonds, I wish with all my soul they might be shared amongst my noble female friends, and upon that condition, I would willingly quit my part; and of the gold I should only desire so much as might suffice to repair my noble lord and husband's losses:[3] for I am not covetous, but as ambitious as ever any of my sex was, is, or can be; which makes, that though I cannot be Henry the Fifth, or Charles the Second, yet I endeavor to be Margaret the First; and although I have neither power, time nor occasion to conquer the world as Alexander and Caesar did; yet rather than not to be mistress of one, since fortune and the fates would give me none, I have made a world of my own: for which nobody, I hope, will blame me, since it is in everyone's power to do the like.

---

* * *No sooner was the lady brought before the emperor, but he conceived her to be some goddess, and offered to worship her; which she refused, telling him, (for by that time she had pretty well learned their language) that although she came out of another world, yet was she but a mortal; at which the emperor rejoicing, made her his wife, and gave her an absolute power to rule and govern all that world as she pleased. But her subjects, who could hardly be persuaded to believe her mortal, tendered her all the veneration and worship due to a deity. . . .

Their priests and governors were princes of the imperial blood, and made eunuchs for that purpose; and as for the ordinary sort of men in that part of the world where the emperor resided, they were of several complexions; not white, black, tawny, olive or ash-colored; but some appeared of an azure, some of a deep purple, some of a grass-green, some of a scarlet, some of an orange color, etc. Which colors and complexions, whether they were made by the bare reflection of light, without the assistance of small particles, or by the help of well-ranged and ordered atoms; or by a continual agitation of little globules; or by some pressing and reacting motion, I am not able to determine. The rest of the inhabitants of that world, were men of several different sorts, shapes, figures, dispositions, and humors, as I have already made mention heretofore; some were bear-men, some worm-men, some fish- or mear-men,[4] otherwise called sirens; some bird-men, some fly-men, some ant-men, some geese-men, some spider-men, some lice-men, some fox-men, some ape-men, some jackdaw-men, some magpie-men, some parrot-men, some satyrs, some giants, and many more, which I cannot all remember; and of these several sorts of men, each followed such a profession as was most proper for the nature of their species, which the empress encouraged them in, especially those that had applied themselves to the study of several arts and sciences; for they were as ingenious and witty in the invention of profit-

---

3. Cavendish's husband, William, was formally banished from England and his estates confiscated in 1649; they were all restored after the Restoration. During his banishment Margaret estimated that he suffered financial losses of around £940,000.
4. Mermen, the male counterparts of mermaids.

able and useful arts, as we are in our world, nay, more; and to that end she erected schools, and founded several societies. The bear-men were to be her experimental philosophers, the bird-men her astronomers, the fly-, worm-, and fish-men her natural philosophers, the ape-men her chemists, the satyrs her Galenic physicians, the fox-men her politicians, the spider- and lice-men her mathematicians, the jackdaw-, magpie-, and parrot-men her orators and logicians, the giants her architects, etc. But before all things, she having got a sovereign power from the emperor over all the world, desired to be informed both of the manner of their religion and government, and to that end she called the priests and statesmen, to give her an account of either. Of the statesmen she inquired, first, why they had so few laws? To which they answered, that many laws made many divisions, which most commonly did breed factions, and at last break out into open wars. Next, she asked, why they preferred the monarchical form of government before any other? They answered, that as it was natural for one body to have but one head, so it was also natural for a politic body to have but one governor; and that a commonwealth, which had many governors, was like a monster with many heads: besides, said they, a monarchy is a divine form of government, and agrees most with our religion; for as there is but one God, whom we all unanimously worship and adore with one faith, so we are resolved to have but one emperor, to whom we all submit with one obedience.

Then the empress seeing that the several sorts of her subjects had each their churches apart, asked the priests whether they were of several religions? They answered Her Majesty, that there was no more but one religion in all that world, nor no diversity of opinions in that same religion; for though there were several sorts of men, yet had they all but one opinion concerning the worship and adoration of God. The empress asked them, whether they were Jews, Turks, or Christians? We do not know, said they, what religions those are; but we do all unanimously acknowledge, worship, and adore the only, omnipotent, and eternal God, with all reverence, submission, and duty. Again, the empress inquired, whether they had several forms of worship? They answered, no: for our devotion and worship consists only in prayers, which we frame according to our several necessities, in petitions, humiliations, thanksgiving, etc. Truly, replied the empress, I thought you had been either Jews, or Turks, because I never perceived any women in your congregations; but what is the reason, you bar them from your religious assemblies? It is not fit, said they, that men and women should be promiscuously together in time of religious worship; for their company hinders devotion, and makes many, instead of praying to God, direct their devotion to their mistresses. But, asked the empress, have they no congregation of their own, to perform the duties of divine worship, as well as men? No, answered they: but they stay at home, and say their prayers by themselves in their closets.[5] Then the empress desired to know the reason why the priests and governors of their world were made eunuchs? They answered, to keep them from marriage: for women and children most commonly make disturbance both in church and state. But, said she, women and children have no employment in church or state. 'Tis true, answered they; but although they are not admitted to public

5. Private chambers.

employments, yet are they so prevalent[6] with their husbands and parents, that many times by their importunate persuasions, they cause as much, nay, more mischief secretly, than if they had the management of public affairs.

* * *

[THE EMPRESS BRINGS THE DUCHESS OF NEWCASTLE TO THE BLAZING WORLD]

After some time, when the spirits had refreshed themselves in their own vehicles, they sent one of their nimblest spirits, to ask the empress, whether she would have a scribe.* * * Then the spirit asked her, whether she would have the soul of a living or a dead man? Why, said the empress, can the soul quit a living body, and wander or travel abroad? Yes, answered he, for according to Plato's doctrine, there is a conversation of souls, and the souls of lovers live in the bodies of their beloved. Then I will have, answered she, the soul of some ancient famous writer, either of Aristotle, Pythagoras, Plato, Epicurus,[7] or the like. The spirit said, that those famous men were very learned, subtle, and ingenious writers, but they were so wedded to their own opinions, that they would never have the patience to be scribes. Then, said she, I'll have the soul of one of the most famous modern writers, as either of Galileo, Gassendus, Descartes, Helmont, Hobbes, H. More,[8] etc. The spirit answered, that they were fine ingenious writers, but yet so self-conceited, that they would scorn to be scribes to a woman. But, said he, there's a lady, the Duchess of Newcastle, which although she is not one of the most learned, eloquent, witty, and ingenious, yet is she a plain and rational writer, for the principle of her writings, is sense and reason, and she will without question, be ready to do you all the service she can. This lady then, said the empress, will I choose for my scribe, neither will the emperor have reason to be jealous, she being one of my own sex. In truth, said the spirit, husbands have reason to be jealous of platonic lovers, for they are very dangerous, as being not only very intimate and close, but subtle and insinuating. You say well, replied the empress; wherefore I pray send me the Duchess of Newcastle's soul; which the spirit did; and after she came to wait on the empress, at her first arrival the empress embraced and saluted her with a spiritual kiss.

* * *

[THE DUCHESS WANTS A WORLD TO RULE]

Well, said the duchess, setting aside this dispute, my ambition is, that I would fain be as you are, that is, an empress of a world, and I shall never be at quiet until I be one. I love you so well, replied the empress, that I wish

---

6. I.e., they prevail so much.
7. Classical philosophers and founders, respectively, of schools of philosophy: the Peripatetics, the Pythagoreans, the Academics, the Epicureans.
8. Galileo Galilei (1564–1642), Italian astronomer and defender of the Copernican system; Pierre Gassendi (1592–1655), proponent of a mechanistic theory of matter; René Descartes (1596–1650),

French mathematician and philosopher who had a major influence on the new science; Jan Baptista van Helmont (1579–1644), Flemish chemist; Thomas Hobbes, English mechanistic philosopher and political scientist, author of *Leviathan*; Henry More (1614–1687), one of the antimaterialist Cambridge Platonists.

with all my soul, you had the fruition of your ambitious desire, and I shall not fail to give you my best advice how to accomplish it; the best informers are the immaterial spirits, and they'll soon tell you, whether it be possible to obtain your wish. But, said the duchess, I have little acquaintance with them, for I never knew any before the time you sent for me. They know you, replied the empress; for they told me of you, and were the means and instrument of your coming hither: wherefore I'll confer with them, and inquire whether there be not another world, whereof you may be empress as well as I am of this. No sooner had the empress said this, but some immaterial spirits came to visit her, of whom she inquired, whether there were but three worlds in all, to wit, the Blazing World where she was in, the world which she came from, and the world where the duchess lived? The spirits answered, that there were more numerous worlds than the stars which appeared in these three mentioned worlds. Then the empress asked, whether it was not possible, that her dearest friend the Duchess of Newcastle, might be empress of one of them.[9] Although there be numerous, nay, infinite worlds, answered the spirits, yet none is without government. But is none of these worlds so weak, said she, that it may be surprised or conquered? The spirits answered, that Lucian's world of lights, had been for some time in a snuff,[1] but of late years one Helmont had got it, who since he was emperor of it, had so strengthened the immortal parts thereof with mortal outworks, as it was for the present impregnable. Said the empress, if there be such an infinite number of worlds, I am sure, not only my friend, the duchess, but any other might obtain one. Yes, answered the spirits, if those worlds were uninhabited; but they are as populous as this, your majesty governs. Why, said the empress, it is not impossible to conquer a world. No, answered the spirits, but, for the most part, conquerors seldom enjoy their conquest, for they being more feared than loved, most commonly come to an untimely end. If you will but direct me, said the duchess to the spirits, which world is easiest to be conquered, her Majesty will assist me with means, and I will trust to fate and fortune; for I had rather die in the adventure of noble achievements, than live in obscure and sluggish security; since by the one, I may live in a glorious fame, and by the other I am buried in oblivion. The spirits answered, that the lives of fame were like other lives; for some lasted long, and some died soon. 'Tis true, said the duchess; but yet the shortest-lived fame lasts longer than the longest life of man. But, replied the spirits, if occasion does not serve you, you must content yourself to live without such achievements that may gain you a fame: but we wonder, proceeded the spirits, that you desire to be empress of a terrestrial world, whenas you can create yourself a celestial world if you please. What, said the empress, can any mortal be a creator? Yes, answered the spirits; for every human creature can create an immaterial world fully inhabited by immaterial creatures, and populous of immaterial subjects, such as we are, and all this within the compass of the head or skull; nay, not only so, but he may create a world of what fashion and government he will, and give the creatures thereof such motions, figures, forms, colors, perceptions, etc. as he pleases, and make whirlpools, lights, pressures,

9. Speculation about multiple inhabited worlds was an occasional topic in texts on the new astronomy. Milton's Raphael introduces the idea to Adam (*Paradise Lost* 8.140–58).

1. On the point of extinction.

and reactions, etc. as he thinks best; nay, he may make a world full of veins, muscles, and nerves, and all these to move by one jolt or stroke: also he may alter that world as often as he pleases, or change it from a natural world, to an artificial; he may make a world of ideas, a world of atoms, a world of lights, or whatsoever his fancy leads him to. And since it is in your power to create such a world, what need you to venture life, reputation and tranquility, to conquer a gross material world? . . . You have converted me, said the duchess to the spirits, from my ambitious desire; wherefore I'll take your advice, reject and despise all the worlds without me, and create a world of my own.

* * *

The Epilogue to the Reader

By this poetical description, you may perceive, that my ambition is not only to be empress, but authoress of a whole world; and that the worlds I have made, both the Blazing and the other Philosophical World, mentioned in the first part of this description, are framed and composed of the most pure, that is, the rational parts of matter, which are the parts of my mind; which creation was more easily and suddenly effected, than the conquests of the two famous monarchs of the world, Alexander and Caesar:[2] neither have I made such disturbances, and caused so many dissolutions of particulars, otherwise named deaths, as they did; for I have destroyed but some few men in a little boat, which died through the extremity of cold, and that by the hand of justice, which was necessitated to punish their crime of stealing away a young and beauteous lady.[3] And in the formation of those worlds, I take more delight and glory, than ever Alexander or Caesar did in conquering this terrestrial world; and though I have made my Blazing World, a peaceable world, allowing it but one religion, one language, and one government; yet could I make another world, as full of factions, divisions, and wars, as this is of peace and tranquility; and the rational figures of my mind might express as much courage to fight, as Hector and Achilles had; and be as wise as Nestor, as eloquent as Ulysses, and as beautiful as Helen.[4] But I esteeming peace before war, wit before policy,[5] honesty before beauty; instead of the figures of Alexander, Caesar, Hector, Achilles, Nestor, Ulysses, Helen, etc. chose rather the figure of honest Margaret Newcastle, which now I would not change for all this terrestrial world; and if any should like the world I have made, and be willing to be my subjects, they may imagine themselves such, and they are such, I mean, in their minds, fancies, or imaginations; but if they cannot endure to be subjects, they may create worlds of their own, and govern themselves as they please: but yet let them have a care, not to prove unjust usurpers, and to rob me of mine; for concerning the Philosophical World, I am empress of it myself; and

---

2. Alexander the Great and Julius Caesar were both famed as conquerors of much of the world known to them.
3. A reference to the romancelike incident with which *The Blazing World* begins, the abduction of a young woman by a party of adventurers whose boat is blown in a tempest to the North Pole, where they perish (except for the woman, who enters into the Blazing World).

4. Hector the Trojan and Achilles the Greek are the principal heroes of Homer's *Iliad*; Nestor, wise adviser to the Greeks; Ulysses, hero of Homer's *Odyssey*, Helen, the one whose beauty caused the Trojan War, as it prompted the Trojan Paris to steal her away from her Greek husband, Menelaus.
5. Intelligence before cunning.

as for the Blazing World, it having an empress already, who rules it with great wisdom and conduct, which empress is my dear platonic friend; I shall never prove so unjust, treacherous, and unworthy to her, as to disturb her government, much less to depose her from her imperial throne, for the sake of any other; but rather choose to create another world for another friend.

1666, 1668

JOHN MILTON
1608–1674

As a young man, John Milton proclaimed himself the future author of a great English epic. He promised a poem devoted to the glory of the nation, centering on the deeds of King Arthur or some other ancient hero. When Milton finally published his epic thirty years later, readers found instead a poem about the Fall of Satan and humankind, set in Heaven, Hell, and the Garden of Eden, in which traditional heroism is denigrated and England not once mentioned. What lay between the youthful promise and the eventual fulfillment was a career marked by private tragedy and public controversy.

In his poems and prose tracts Milton often alludes to crises in his own life: his choice of a vocation, the early death of friends, painful disappointment in marriage, and the catastrophe of blindness. At the same time, no other major English poet has been so deeply involved in the great questions and political crises of his times. His works reflect upon and help develop some basic Western concepts that were taking modern form in his lifetime: companionate marriage, the new science, freedom of the press, religious liberty and toleration, republicanism, and more. It is scarcely possible to treat Milton's career separately from the history of England in his lifetime, not only because he was an active participant in affairs of church and state, but also because when he signed himself, as he often did, "John Milton, Englishman," he was presenting himself as England's prophetic bard. He considered himself the spokesman for the nation as a whole even when he found himself in a minority of one.

No English poet before Milton fashioned himself quite so self-consciously as an author. The young Milton deliberately set out to follow the steps of the ideal poetic

Milton.

career—beginning with pastoral (the mode of several of his early poems) and ending with epic. His models for this progression were Virgil and Spenser: he called the latter "a better teacher than Scotus or Aquinas." In his systematic approach to his vocation he stood at the opposite end of the spectrum from such Cavalier contemporaries as Richard Lovelace, who turned to verse with an air of studied carelessness. Milton resembles Spenser especially in his constant use of myth and archetype and also in his readiness to juxtapose biblical and classical stories. He is everywhere concerned with the conventions of genre, yet he infused every genre he used with new energy, transforming it for later practitioners. The Western literary and intellectual heritage impinged on his writing as immediately and directly as the circumstances of his own life, but he continually reconceived the ideas, literary forms, and values of this heritage to make them relevant to himself and to his age.

Milton's family was bourgeois, cultured, and staunchly Protestant. His father was a scrivener—a combination solicitor, investment adviser, and moneylender—as well as an amateur composer with some reputation in musical circles. Milton had a younger brother, Christopher, who practiced law, and an elder sister, Anne. At age seventeen he wrote a funeral elegy for the death of Anne's infant daughter and later educated her two sons, Edward and John (Edward wrote his biography). Milton had private tutors at home and also attended one of the finest schools in the land, St. Paul's. At school he began a close friendship with Charles Diodati, with whom he exchanged Latin poems and letters over several years, and for whose death in 1638 he wrote a moving Latin elegy. Milton's excellent early education gave him special facility in languages (Latin, Greek, Hebrew and its dialects, Italian, and French; later he learned Spanish and Dutch).

In 1625 Milton entered Christ's College, Cambridge. He was briefly suspended during his freshman year over some dispute with his tutor, but he graduated in 1629 and was made Master of Arts three years later. As his surviving student orations indicate, he was profoundly disappointed in his university education, reviling the scholastic logic and Latin rhetorical exercises that still formed its core as "futile and barren controversies and wordy disputes" that "stupefy and benumb the mind." He went to university with the serious intention of taking orders in the Church of England—the obvious vocation for a young man of his scholarly and religious bent—but became increasingly disenchanted with the lack of reformation in the church under Archbishop William Laud, and in the hindsight of 1642 he proclaimed himself "church-outed by the prelates." No doubt his change of direction was also linked to the fastidious contempt he expressed for the ignorant and clownish clergymen-in-the-making who were his fellow students at Cambridge: "They thought themselves gallant men, and I thought them fools." Those students retaliated by dubbing Milton "the Lady of Christ's College."

Above all, Milton came to believe more and more strongly that he was destined to serve his language, his country, and his God as a poet. He began by writing occasional poetry in Latin, the usual language for collegiate poets and for poets who sought a European audience. Milton wrote some of the century's best Latin poems, but as early as 1628 he announced to a university audience his determination to glorify England and the English language in poetry. In his first major English poem (at age twenty-one), the hymn "On the Morning of Christ's Nativity," Milton already portrayed himself as a prophetic bard. This poem is very different from Richard Crashaw's Nativity hymn, with its Spenserian echoes, its allusion to Roman Catholic and Laudian "idolatry" in the long passage on the expulsion of the pagan gods, and its stunning moves from the Creation to Doomsday, from the manger at Bethlehem to the cosmos, and from the shepherd's chatter to the music of the spheres. Two or three years later, probably, Milton wrote the companion poems "L'Allegro" and "Il Penseroso," achieving a stylistic tour de force by creating from the same meter (octosyllabic couplets) entirely different sound qualities, rhythmic effects, and moods. These poems celebrate, respectively, Mirth and Melancholy, defining them by their ancestry, lifestyles, associates, landscapes, activities, music, and literature. In 1634, at the invitation of his musician friend Henry Lawes, he wrote the masque called *Comus*, in which the villain is portrayed as a refined, seductive, and dissolute Cavalier. *Comus* challenges the absolutist politics of previous court masques by locating true virtue and good pleasure in the households of the country aristocracy rather than at court.

After university, as part of his preparation for a poetic career, Milton undertook a six-year program of self-directed reading in ancient and modern theology, philosophy, history, science, politics, and literature. He was profoundly grateful to his father for sparing him the grubby business of making money and for financing these years of private study, followed by a fifteen-month "grand tour" of France, Italy, and Switzerland. In 1638 Milton contributed the pastoral elegy "Lycidas" to a Cambridge volume lamenting the untimely death of a college contemporary. This greatest of English funeral elegies explores Milton's deep anxieties about poetry as a vocation, confronts the terrors of mortality in language of astonishing resonance and power, and incorporates a furious apocalyptic diatribe on the corrupt Church of England clergy. Nonetheless, while he was in Italy he exchanged verses and learned compliments with various Catholic intellectuals and men of letters, some of whom became his friends. Milton could always maintain friendships and family relationships across ideological divides. In 1645 his English and Latin poems were published together in a two-part volume, *Poems of Mr. John Milton*.

Upon his return to England, Milton opened a school and was soon involved in Presbyterian efforts to depose the bishops and reform church liturgy, writing five "antiprelatical tracts" denouncing and satirizing bishops. These were the first in a series of political interventions Milton produced over the next twenty years, characterized by remarkable courage and independence of thought. He wrote successively on church government, divorce, education, freedom of the press, regicide, and republicanism. From the outbreak of the Civil War in 1642 until his death, Milton allied himself with the Puritan cause, but his religious opinions developed throughout his life, from relative orthodoxy in his youth to ever more heretical positions in his later years. And while his family belonged to the class that benefited most directly from Europe's first bourgeois revolution, his brother, Christopher, fought on the royalist side. The Milton brothers, like most of their contemporaries, did not see these wars as a confrontation of class interests, but as a conflict between radically differing theories of government and, above all, religion.

Some of Milton's treatises were prompted by personal concerns. He interrupted his polemical tract, *The Reason of Church Government Urged Against Prelaty* (1642), to devote several pages to a discussion of his poetic vocation and the great works he hoped to produce in the future. His tracts about divorce, which can hardly have seemed the most pressing of issues in the strife-torn years 1643–45, were motivated by his own disastrous marriage. Aged thirty-three, inexperienced with women, and idealistic about marriage as in essence a union of minds and spirits, he married a young woman of seventeen, Mary Powell, who returned to her royalist family just a few months after the wedding. In response, Milton wrote several tracts vigorously advocating divorce on the grounds of incompatibility and with the right to remarry—a position almost unheard of at the time and one that required a boldly antiliteral reading of the Gospels. The fact that these tracts could not be licensed and were roundly denounced in Parliament, from pulpits, and in print prompted him to write *Areopagitica* (1644), an impassioned defense of a free press and the free commerce in ideas against a Parliament determined to restore effective censorship. He saw these personal issues—reformed poetry, domestic liberty achieved through needful divorce, and a free press—as vital to the creation of a reformed English culture.

In 1649, just after Charles I was executed, Milton published *The Tenure of Kings and Magistrates* (go to pages 1846–49 and see the supplemental ebook for extracts from the *Tenure*), which defends the revolution and the regicide and was of considerable importance in developing a "contract theory" of government based on the inalienable sovereignty of the people—a version of contract very different from that of Thomas Hobbes. Milton was appointed Latin Secretary to the Commonwealth government (1649–53) and to Oliver Cromwell's Protectorate (1654–58), which meant that he wrote the official letters—mostly in Latin—to foreign governments and heads of state. He also wrote polemical defenses of the new government: *Eikonoklastes* (1649), to counter the powerful emotional effect of *Eikon Basilike*, supposedly written by the king just before his death (an excerpt is included in the supplemental ebook), and two Latin *Defenses* upholding the regicide and the new republic to European audiences.

During these years Milton suffered a series of agonizing tragedies. Mary Powell returned to him in 1645 but died in childbirth in 1652, leaving four children; the only son, John, died a few months later. That same year Milton became totally blind; he thought his boyhood habit of reading until midnight had weakened his eyesight and that writing his first *Defense* to answer the famous French scholar Claudius Salmasius had destroyed it. Milton married again in 1656, apparently happily, but his new wife, Katherine Woodcock, was dead two years later, along with their infant daughter. Katherine is probably the subject of his sonnet "Methought I Saw My Late Espoused Saint," a moving dream vision poignant with the sense of loss—both of sight and of love. Milton had little time for poetry in these years, but his few sonnets revolutionized the genre, overlaying the Petrarchan metrical structure with an urgent rhetorical voice and using the small sonnet form, hitherto confined mainly to matters of love, for new and grand subjects: praises of Cromwell and other statesmen mixed with admonition and political advice; a prophetic denunciation calling down God's vengeance for Protestants massacred in Piedmont; and an emotion-filled account of his continuing struggle to come to terms with his blindness as part of God's providence.

Cromwell's death in 1658 led to mounting chaos and a growing belief that a restored Stuart monarchy was inevitable. Milton held out against that tide. His several tracts of 1659–60 developed radical arguments for broad toleration, church disestablishment, and republican government. And just as he was among the first to attack the power of the bishops, so he was virtually the last defender of the "Good Old Cause" of the Revolution; the second edition of his *Ready and Easy Way to Establish a Free Commonwealth* appeared in late April 1660, scarcely two weeks before the monarchy was restored. For several months after that event, Milton was in hiding, his life in danger. Friends, especially the poet Andrew Marvell, managed to secure his pardon and later his release from a brief imprisonment. He lived out his last years in reduced circumstances, plagued by ever more serious attacks of gout but grateful for the domestic comforts provided by his third wife, Elizabeth Minshull, whom he married in 1663 and who survived him.

In such conditions, dismayed by the defeat of his political and religious cause, totally blind and often ill, threatened by the horrific plague of 1665 and the great fire of 1666, and entirely dependent on amanuenses and friends to transcribe his dictation, he completed his great epic poem. *Paradise Lost* (1667/74) radically reconceives the epic genre and epic heroism, choosing as protagonists a domestic couple rather than martial heroes and degrading the military glory celebrated in epic tradition in favor of "the better fortitude / Of patience and heroic martyrdom." It offers a sweeping imaginative vision of Hell, Chaos, and Heaven; prelapsarian life in Eden; the power of the devil's political rhetoric; the psychology of Satan, Adam, and Eve; and the high drama of the Fall and its aftermath.

In his final years, Milton published works on grammar and logic chiefly written during his days as a schoolmaster, a history of Britain (1670) from the earliest times to the Norman Conquest, and a treatise urging toleration for Puritan dissenters (1673). He also continued work on his *Christian Doctrine*, a Latin treatise that reveals how far he had moved from the orthodoxies of his day. The work denies the Trinity (making the Son and the Holy Spirit much inferior to God the Father), insists upon free will against Calvinist predestination, and privileges the inspiration of the Spirit even above the Scriptures and the Ten Commandments. Such radical and heterodox positions could not be made public in his lifetime, certainly not in the repressive conditions of the Restoration, and Milton's *Christian Doctrine* was subsequently lost to view for over 150 years.

In 1671 Milton published two poems that resonated with the harsh repression and the moral and political challenges all Puritan dissenters faced after the Restoration. *Paradise Regained*, a brief epic in four books, treats Jesus' Temptation in the Wilderness as an intellectual struggle through which the hero comes to understand both himself and his mission and through which he defeats Satan by renouncing the whole panoply of faulty versions of the good life and of God's kingdom. *Samson Agonistes*, a classical tragedy, is the more harrowing for the resemblances between its tragic hero and its author. The deeply flawed, pain-wracked, blind, and defeated Samson struggles, in dialogues with his visitors, to gain self-knowledge, discovering at last a desperate way to triumph over his captors and offer his people a chance to regain their freedom. (The tragedy in its entirety is available in the supplemental ebook.) In these last poems Milton sought to educate his readers in moral and political wisdom and virtue. Only through such inner transformation, Milton now firmly believed, would men and women come to value—and so perhaps reclaim—the intellectual, religious, and political freedom he so vigorously promoted in his prose and poetry.

FROM POEMS

On the Morning of Christ's Nativity[1]

1

This is the month, and this the happy morn
Wherein the son of Heaven's eternal King,
Of wedded maid and virgin mother born,
Our great redemption from above did bring;
5 For so the holy sages once did sing,
    That he our deadly forfeit[2] should release,
And with his Father work us a perpetual peace.

2

That glorious form, that light unsufferable,°   *unable to be endured*
And that far-beaming blaze of majesty
10 Wherewith he wont° at Heaven's high council-table   *was accustomed*

---

1. This ode was written on Christmas 1629, a few weeks after Milton's twenty-first birthday. He placed it first in the 1645 edition of his poems, claiming in it his vocation as inspired poet. The poem often looks back to Spenser: the first four stanzas are an adaptation of the Spenserian stanza; there are several Spenserian archaisms (y- prefixes) and some Spenser-like onamatopoeia

(lines 156, 172). Comparison with Crashaw's Nativity poem (pp. 1747–49) will highlight some important differences between Roman Catholic and Puritan aesthetics in this period.
2. The sentence of death consequent on the Fall. "Holy sages": for example, the prophet Isaiah (chaps. 9 and 40) and Job (chap. 19) were thought to have foretold Christ as Messiah.

To sit the midst of Trinal Unity,[3]
He laid aside; and here with us to be,
  Forsook the courts of everlasting day,
And chose with us a darksome house of mortal clay.

3

15 Say, heavenly Muse, shall not thy sacred vein
Afford a present to the infant God?
Hast thou no verse, no hymn, or solemn strain,
To welcome him to this his new abode,
Now while the heaven by the sun's team untrod[4]
20   Hath took no print of the approaching light,
And all the spangled host° keep watch in squadrons bright?   *angels*

4

See how from far upon the eastern road
The star-led wizards[5] haste with odors sweet:
O run, prevent° them with thy humble ode,   *anticipate*
25 And lay it lowly at his blessèd feet;
Have thou the honor first thy Lord to greet,
  And join thy voice unto the angel choir,
From out His secret altar touched with hallowed fire.[6]

The Hymn

1

It was the winter wild
30 While the Heaven-born child
  All meanly wrapped in the rude manger lies;
Nature in awe to him
Had doffed her gaudy trim[7]
  With her great Master so to sympathize;
35 It was no season then for her
To wanton with the sun, her lusty paramour.

2

Only with speeches fair
She woos the gentle air
  To hide her guilty front° with innocent snow,   *brow*
40 And on her naked shame,
Pollute with sinful blame,
  The saintly veil of maiden white to throw,[8]

---

3. The Trinity: Father, Son (incarnate in Christ), and Holy Ghost.
4. In classical myth, the sun (Phoebus Apollo) drove across heaven in a chariot drawn by horses.
5. The Magi who followed the star of Bethlehem to find and adore the infant Christ.

6. Isaiah's lips were touched by a burning coal from the altar, purifying him and confirming him as a prophet (Isaiah 6.7).
7. Put off her garments of leaves and flowers.
8. Nature fell also with the Fall, so she is a harlot (line 36), not a pure maiden, despite her white garment of snow.

Confounded that her Maker's eyes
Should look so near upon her foul deformities.

3

45 But he her fears to cease
Sent down the meek-eyed Peace;
    She, crowned with olive green, came softly sliding
Down through the turning sphere,[9]
His ready harbinger,°   *forerunner*
50   With turtle[1] wing the amorous clouds dividing,
And waving wide her myrtle wand,
She strikes a universal peace through sea and land.

4

No war or battle's sound
Was heard the world around;[2]
55   The idle spear and shield were high up-hung;
The hookèd chariot[3] stood
Unstained with hostile blood,
    The trumpet spake not to the armèd throng,
And kings sat still with awful° eye,   *filled with awe*
60 As if they surely knew their sovereign Lord was by.

5

But peaceful was the night
Wherein the Prince of Light
    His reign of peace upon the earth began:
The winds, with wonder whist,°   *hushed*
65 Smoothly the waters kissed,
    Whispering new joys to the mild oceàn,
Who now hath quite forgot to rave,
While birds of calm[4] sit brooding on the charmèd wave.

6

The stars with deep amaze
70 Stand fixed in steadfast gaze,
    Bending one way their precious influence,
And will not take their flight
For all the morning light,
    Or Lucifer[5] that often warned them thence;
75 But in their glimmering orbs did glow
Until their Lord himself bespake,° and bid them go.   *spoke out*

---

9. The Ptolemaic spheres, revolving around the earth.
1. Like a turtledove, which, like the myrtle (next line), is an emblem of Venus (Love), as the olive crown is of peace.
2. Around the time of Christ's birth, the "Peace of Augustus" held, during which no major wars disturbed the Roman Empire; that peace was sometimes attributed to Christ.
3. War chariots were built with scythelike hooks on the axles, to wound and kill.
4. Kingfishers (halcyons) were thought to calm the seas during the time they nested on its waves.
5. Not Satan but the morning star, Venus.

7

And though the shady gloom
Had given day her room,
   The sun himself withheld his wonted speed,
80 And hid his head for shame
As° his inferior flame   *as if*
   The new-enlightened world no more should need;
He saw a greater Sun[6] appear
Than his bright throne or burning axletree° could bear.   *chariot axle*

8

85 The shepherds on the lawn
Or ere the point of° dawn   *just before*
   Sat simply chatting in a rustic row;
Full little thought they than°   *then*
That the mighty Pan[7]
90   Was kindly[8] come to live with them below;
Perhaps their loves or else their sheep
Was all that did their silly° thoughts so busy keep.   *simple, humble*

9

When such music sweet
Their hearts and ears did greet
95   As never was by mortal finger struck,
Divinely warbled voice
Answering the stringèd noise,
   As all their souls in blissful rapture took;
The air, such pleasure loath to lose,
100 With thousand echoes still prolongs each heavenly close.°   *cadence*

10

Nature that heard such sound
Beneath the hollow round
   Of Cynthia's seat,[9] the airy region thrilling,°   *piercing, delighting*
Now was almost won
105 To think her part was done,
   And that her reign had here its last fulfilling;
She knew such harmony alone
Could hold all heaven and earth in happier uniòn.

11

At last surrounds their sight
110 A globe of circular light

---

6. The familiar Son/sun pun.
7. Pan, patron of shepherds, is a merry, goat-footed god, but he was often conceived in more exalted terms and identified with Christ, because his name in Greek means "all."
8. By nature; also, benevolently.

9. Cynthia is the moon. Nature rules below the moon (the region of the four elements and subject to decay). The unchanging, perfect region above the moon is normally the only place one could hear either angels' hymnody or the music of the spheres.

That with long beams the shamefaced night arrayed;°   *adorned with rays*
The helmèd cherubim
And sworded seraphim[1]
Are seen in glittering ranks with wings displayed,
115   Harping in loud and solemn choir
With unexpressive° notes to Heaven's newborn heir.   *inexpressible*

12

Such music (as 'tis said)
Before was never made,
     But when of old the sons of morning sung,[2]
120   While the Creator great
His constellations set,
     And the well-balanced world on hinges° hung,   *the two poles*
And cast the dark foundations deep,
And bid the welt'ring waves their oozy channel keep.

13

125   Ring out, ye crystal spheres,
Once bless our human ears
     (If ye have power to touch our senses so),
And let your silver chime
Move in melodious time,
130   And let the bass of Heaven's deep organ blow;
And with your ninefold harmony[3]
Make up full consort to th' angelic symphony.

14

For if such holy song
Enwrap our fancy long,
135   Time will run back and fetch the age of gold;[4]
And speckled vanity
Will sicken soon and die,
     And leprous sin will melt from earthly mold,
And Hell itself will pass away,
140   And leave her dolorous mansions to the peering day.

15

Yea, Truth and Justice then
Will down return to men,
     Th' enameled arras° of the rainbow wearing,   *brightly colored fabric*

---

1. Seraphim and cherubim are the highest of the traditional nine orders of angels; they are often portrayed in martial attire.
2. Job 38.4–7: "Where wast thou when I laid the foundations of the earth? . . . / When the morning stars sang together and all the sons of God shouted for joy?"
3. In Pythagorean theory, each of the nine moving spheres sounds a distinctive note (the tenth, the primum mobile, does not move). It was supposed that, after the Fall, this harmonious music of the spheres could not be heard on earth. Earth would be the "bass" of the cosmic organ, sounding under that planetary harmony.
4. The first age, of human innocence, classical mythology's equivalent to the Garden of Eden.

And Mercy set between,[5]
145 Throned in celestial sheen,
    With radiant feet the tissued[6] clouds down steering;
And Heaven, as at some festival,
Will open wide the gates of her high palace hall.

16

But wisest Fate says no,
150 This must not yet be so;
    The Babe lies yet in smiling infancy[7]
That on the bitter cross
Must redeem our loss,
    So both himself and us to glorify;
155 Yet first to those ychained[8] in sleep
The wakeful trump of doom must thunder through the deep,

17

With such a horrid clang
As on Mount Sinai rang
    While the red fire and smoldering clouds outbrake;
160 The agèd earth, aghast
With terror of that blast,
    Shall from the surface to the center shake,
When at the world's last sessiòn,
The dreadful Judge in middle air shall spread His throne.[9]

18

165 And then at last our bliss
Full and perfect is,
    But now begins; for from this happy day
Th' old dragon under ground,[1]
In straiter limits bound,
170   Not half so far casts his usurpèd sway,
And wroth to see his kingdom fail,
Swinges° the scaly horror of his folded tail.   *lashes*

19

The oracles are dumb;[2]
No voice or hideous hum
175   Runs through the archèd roof in words deceiving.

---

5. This allegorical scene, suggesting a masque descent, alludes to Psalm 85.10, part of the liturgy for Christmas: "Mercy and truth are met together; righteousness and peace have kissed each other." Peace, in the poem, has already descended (lines 45–52). The lines also evoke the flight of Astraea, the classical goddess of justice, at the end of the Golden Age, and her return with its restoration, celebrated by Virgil in his fourth eclogue, applied by him to the birth of Pollio but by Christians to Christ.
6. Cloth woven with silver and gold.

7. The Latin word, *infans*, means, literally, "non-speaking."
8. One of Spenser's archaic *y*- prefixes.
9. Moses received the Ten Commandments amid thunder and lightning atop Mount Sinai (Exodus 19); the Last Judgment will take place amid similar uproar. "Session": court proceeding.
1. The devil (Revelation 20.2).
2. An ancient tradition held that pagan oracles ceased with the coming of Christ; another identified the pagan gods with the fallen angels.

Apollo from his shrine
Can no more divine,
   With hollow shriek the steep of Delphos leaving.[3]
No nightly trance or breathèd spell
180 Inspires the pale-eyed priest from the prophetic cell.

20

The lonely mountains o'er
And the resounding shore
   A voice of weeping heard and loud lament;
From haunted spring and dale
185 Edged with the poplar pale,
   The parting genius[4] is with sighing sent;
With flower-in-woven tresses torn
The nymphs in twilight shade of tangled thickets mourn.

21

In consecrated earth
190 And on the holy hearth,
   The lars and lemures[5] moan with midnight plaint;
In urns and altars round
A drear and dying sound
   Affrights the flamens[6] at their service quaint;
195 And the chill marble seems to sweat,
While each peculiar power forgoes his wonted seat.

22

Peor and Baalim[7]
Forsake their temples dim,
   With that twice-battered god of Palestine,[8]
200 And moonèd Ashtaroth,[9]
Heaven's queen and mother both,
   Now sits not girt with tapers' holy shine;
The Libyc Hammon[1] shrinks° his horn;   *draws in*
In vain the Tyrian maids their wounded Thammuz mourn.[2]

23

205 And sullen Moloch,[3] fled,
Hath left in shadows dread
   His burning idol all of blackest hue;

3. Apollo's main shrine was at Delphi, on the slopes of Mount Parnassus.
4. A local deity guarding a particular place.
5. Spirits of the dead. "Lars": household gods.
6. Roman priests.
7. Other manifestations of Baal, a Canaanite sun god.
8. Dagon, the Philistine god whose image at Ashdod was twice thrown down when the Ark of the Covenant was placed beside it (1 Samuel 5.2–4).
9. Ashtaroth, also known as Astarte, was a Phoe-nician fertility goddess identified with the moon.
1. Hammon, also Ammon, an Egyptian and Lib-yan god, depicted as a ram.
2. Thammuz, lover of Ashtaroth, was killed by a boar and lamented by the Phoenician women; he was taken into the Greek pantheon as Adonis.
3. Moloch was a Phoenician fire god, a brazen idol with a human body and a calf's, head; the statue ("his burning idol," line 207) was heated flaming hot and children were thrown into its embrace, with cymbals drowning out their cries (2 Kings 22.10).

In vain with cymbals' ring
They call the grisly king
210 In dismal dance about the furnace blue;
The brutish gods of Nile as fast,[4]
Isis and Orus and the dog Anubis haste.

24

Nor is Osiris seen
In Memphian grove or green,
215 Trampling the unshowered° grass with lowings loud, *rainless*
Nor can he be at rest
Within his sacred chest;
Naught but profoundest Hell can be his shroud.
In vain with timbrelled anthems dark
220 The sable-stolèd sorcerers bear his worshipped ark.[5]

25

He feels from Judah's land
The dreaded Infant's hand,
The rays of Bethlehem blind his dusky eyne;° *eyes*
Nor all the gods beside
225 Longer dare abide,
Not Typhon huge, ending in snaky twine;
Our Babe, to show his godhead true,
Can in his swaddling bands control the damnèd crew.[6]

26

So when the sun in bed,
230 Curtained with cloudy red,
Pillows his chin upon an orient° wave, *eastern, bright*
The flocking shadows pale
Troop to th' infernal jail;
Each fettered ghost slips to his several° grave; *separate*
235 And the yellow-skirted fays
Fly after the night-steeds, leaving their moon-loved maze.[7]

27

But see! the Virgin blessed
Hath laid her Babe to rest.
Time is our tedious song should here have ending.
240 Heaven's youngest-teemèd° star *latest born*
Hath fixed her polished car,° *gleaming chariot*

---

4. Egyptian gods had some features of animals: Isis (next line) was represented with cow's horns, Orus, or Horus, with a hawk's head; Osiris (lines 213–15) sometimes had the shape of a bull.
5. Osiris's image was carried from temple to temple in a wooden chest, and his priests accompanied it with tambourines ("timbrels").

6. Typhon was a hundred-headed monster who was a serpent below the waist, a figure for the devil. The infant Christ controlling him calls up (as a foreshadowing) the story of the infant Hercules strangling two giant serpents in his cradle.
7. Fairy rings. "Night-steeds": horses drawing Night's chariot.

Her sleeping Lord with handmaid lamp attending:
And all about the courtly stable
Bright-harnessed° angels sit in order serviceàble.   *bright-armored*

1629   1645

On Shakespeare[1]

What needs my Shakespeare for his honored bones
The labor of an age in pilèd stones,
Or that his hallowed relics should be hid
Under a star-ypointing[2] pyramid?
5   Dear son of memory,[3] great heir of fame,
What° need'st thou such weak witness of thy name?   *why*
Thou in our wonder and astonishment
Hast built thyself a livelong° monument.   *enduring*
For whilst to th' shame of slow-endeavoring art
10   Thy easy numbers° flow, and that each heart   *verses*
Hath from the leaves of thy unvalued° book   *invaluable*
Those Delphic[4] lines with deep impression took,
Then thou, our fancy of itself bereaving,
Dost make us marble with too much conceiving;[5]
15   And so sepùlchered in such pomp dost lie,
That kings for such a tomb would wish to die.

1630   1632

L'Allegro[1]

Hence loathèd Melancholy,[2]
Of Cerberus[3] and blackest midnight born,
In Stygian[4] cave forlorn
    'Mongst horrid shapes, and shrieks, and sights unholy,
5   Find out some uncouth° cell,   *desolate*

1. This tribute, Milton's first published poem, appeared in the Second Folio of Shakespeare's plays (1632).
2. A Spenserian archaism.
3. As "son of memory" Shakespeare is a brother of the Muses, who are the daughters of Mnemosyne (Memory).
4. Apollo, god of poetry, had his oracle at Delphi.
5. Shakespeare's mesmerized readers are themselves his ("marble") monument.
1. The companion poems "L'Allegro" and "Il Penseroso" are both written in tetrameter couplets, except for the first ten lines, but Milton's virtuosity produces entirely different tempos and sound qualities in the two poems. The Italian titles name, respectively, the cheerful, mirthful man and the melancholy, contemplative man.

The poems are carefully balanced and their different values celebrated, though "Il Penseroso's" greater length and final coda may intimate that life's superiority. Mirth, the presiding deity of "L'Allegro," is described in terms that evoke Botticelli's presentation of the Grace Euphrosyne (youthful mirth) and her sisters in his *Primavera*.
2. The black melancholy recognized and here exorcized by Mirth's man is a disease leading to madness. "Il Penseroso" celebrates "white" melancholy as the temperament of the scholarly, contemplative man, represented in Dürer's famous engraving *Melancholy*. Burton's *Anatomy of Melancholy* treats the entire range of possibilities.
3. The three-headed hellhound of classical mythology.
4. Near the river Styx, in the underworld.

Where brooding Darkness spreads his jealous wings,
And the night raven sings;
There under ebon shades and low-browed rocks,
As ragged as thy locks,
10   In dark Cimmerian[5] desert ever dwell.
But come thou goddess fair and free,
In heaven yclept Euphrosyne,[6]
And by men, heart-easing Mirth,
Whom lovely Venus at a birth
15   With two sister Graces more
To ivy-crownèd Bacchus bore;
Or whether (as some sager sing)
The frolic wind that breathes the spring,
Zephyr with Aurora playing,
20   As he met her once a-Maying,
There on beds of violets blue,
And fresh-blown° roses washed in dew,   *newly opened*
Filled her with thee a daughter fair,
So buxom,° blithe, and debonair.   *lively*
25   Haste thee nymph, and bring with thee
Jest and youthful Jollity,
Quips° and Cranks,° and wanton Wiles,   *witty sayings / jokes*
Nods, and Becks,° and wreathèd Smiles,   *beckonings*
Such as hang on Hebe's[7] cheek,
30   And love to live in dimple sleek;
Sport that wrinkled Care derides,
And Laughter holding both his sides.
Come, and trip it° as ye go   *dance*
On the light fantastic toe,
35   And in thy right hand lead with thee
The mountain nymph, sweet Liberty;
And if I give thee honor due,
Mirth, admit me of thy crew
To live with her and live with thee,
40   In unreprovèd° pleasures free;   *irreproachable*
To hear the lark begin his flight,
And, singing, startle the dull night,
From his watch tower in the skies,
Till the dappled dawn doth rise;
45   Then to come in spite of° sorrow,   *in defiance of*
And at my window bid good morrow,
Through the sweetbriar or the vine,
Or the twisted eglantine.
While the cock with lively din
50   Scatters the rear of darkness thin,

---

5. Homer's Cimmereans (*Odyssey* 11.13–19) live on the outer edge of the world, in perpetual darkness.
6. The three Graces—Euphrosyne (four syllables) figuring Youthful Mirth; Aglaia, Brilliance; and Thalia, Bloom—were commonly taken to be offspring of Venus (Love and Beauty) and Bacchus (god of wine). Milton proceeds, however, to devise another, more innocent parentage for Euphrosyne (ascribing it to "some sager," lines 17–24): Zephyr, the West Wind, and Aurora, goddess of the Dawn.
7. Goddess of youth and cupbearer to the gods.

And to the stack or the barn door,
Stoutly struts his dames before;
Oft listening how the hounds and horn
Cheerly rouse the slumbering morn,
55 From the side of some hoar° hill,   *ancient*
Through the high wood echoing shrill.
Sometime walking not unseen
By hedgerow elms, on hillocks green,
Right against the eastern gate,
60 Where the great sun begins his state,[8]
Robed in flames and amber light,
The clouds in thousand liveries dight;°   *dressed*
While the plowman near at hand
Whistles o'er the furrowed land,
65 And the milkmaid singeth blithe,
And the mower whets his scythe,
And every shepherd tells his tale
Under the hawthorn in the dale.
Straight° mine eye hath caught new pleasures   *immediately*
70 Whilst the landscape round it measures,
Russet lawns and fallows° gray,   *plowed land*
Where the nibbling flocks do stray,
Mountains on whose barren breast
The laboring clouds do often rest;
75 Meadows trim with daisies pied,°   *multicolored*
Shallow brooks, and rivers wide.
Towers and battlements it sees
Bosomed high in tufted trees,
Where perhaps some beauty lies,
80 The cynosure[9] of neighboring eyes.
Hard by, a cottage chimney smokes
From betwixt two agèd oaks,
Where Corydon and Thyrsis met
Are at their savory dinner set
85 Of herbs and other country messes,
Which the neat-handed° Phyllis dresses;   *dexterous*
And then in haste her bower she leaves,
With Thestylis[1] to bind the sheaves;
Or if the earlier season lead
90 To the tanned° haycock in the mead.   *sun-dried*
Sometimes with secure° delight   *careless*
The upland hamlets will invite,
When the merry bells ring round
And the jocund rebecks[2] sound
95 To many a youth and many a maid,
Dancing in the checkered shade;
And young and old come forth to play

8. Stately procession, as by a monarch.
9. Literally, the bright polestar, or North Star, by which mariners steer; here, a splendid object, much gazed at.
1. Milton uses traditional names from classical pastoral—Corydon, Thyrsis, Phyllis, Thestylis—for his rustic English shepherds.
2. A small three-stringed fiddle. "Jocund": merry, sprightly.

On a sunshine holiday,
Till the livelong daylight fail;
100 Then to the spicy nut-brown ale,
With stories told of many a feat,
How fairy Mab the junkets[3] eat;
She was pinched and pulled, she said,
And he, by friar's lantern led,
105 Tells how the drudging goblin[4] sweat
To earn his cream bowl duly set,
When in one night, ere glimpse of morn,
His shadowy flail hath threshed the corn
That ten day laborers could not end;
110 Then lies him down the lubber fiend,[5]
And stretched out all the chimney's° length,   *fireplace's*
Basks at the fire his hairy strength;
And crop-full° out of doors he flings   *satiated*
Ere the first cock his matin rings.
115 Thus done the tales, to bed they creep,
By whispering winds soon lulled asleep.
Towered cities please us then,
And the busy hum of men,
Where throngs of knights and barons bold
120 In weeds of peace high triumphs[6] hold,
With store of ladies, whose bright eyes
Rain influence,[7] and judge the prize
Of wit or arms, while both contend
To win her grace, whom all commend.
125 There let Hymen[8] oft appear
In saffron robe, with taper clear,
And pomp and feast and revelry,
With masque and antique° pageantry;   *ancient, also antic*
Such sights as youthful poets dream
130 On summer eves by haunted stream.
Then to the well-trod stage anon,
If Jonson's learned sock be on,
Or sweetest Shakespeare, fancy's child,
Warble his native woodnotes wild.[9]
135 And ever against eating cares;[1]
Lap me in soft Lydian airs,[2]
Married to immortal verse
Such as the meeting soul may pierce

---

3. Sweetmeats, especially with cream. Queen Mab is the fairy queen, consort of Oberon. "She" and "he" in the next two lines are country folk telling of their experiences with fairies.
4. Robin Goodfellow, alias Puck, Pook, or Hobgoblin. "Friar's lantern": will-o'-the-wisp.
5. Puck, here identified with the folktale goblin, Lob-lie-by-the-fire. Robin traditionally did all manner of drudging work for people, to be rewarded with a bowl of cream.
6. Pageants. "Weeds of peace": courtly raiment.
7. The ladies' eyes are stars and so have astrological influence over the men.
8. Roman god of marriage. An orange-yellow ("saffron") robe and a torch are his attributes.
9. It was conventional to contrast Jonson as a "learned" poet and Shakespeare as a "natural" one, but L'Allegro's views and choices of literature also suits with his nature. "Sock": the comedian's low-heeled slipper, contrasted with the tragedian's buskin, a high-heeled boot.
1. "Eating cares" (Horace, *Odes* 2.11.18) is one of many classical echoes in the poem.
2. Plato considered "Lydian airs" to be enervating, soft, and sensual; he preferred the solemn Doric mode. Some others thought Lydian airs relaxing and delightful.

In notes with many a winding bout°   *circuit*
140 Of linkèd sweetness long drawn out,
With wanton heed and giddy cunning,
The melting voice through mazes running,
Untwisting all the chains that tie
The hidden soul of harmony;
145 That Orpheus' self may heave his head
From golden slumber on a bed
Of heapèd Elysian flowers, and hear
Such strains as would have won the ear
Of Pluto, to have quite set free
150 His half-regained Eurydice.³
These delights if thou canst give,
Mirth, with thee I mean to live.⁴

ca. 1631   1645

Il Penseroso¹

Hence vain deluding joys,²
  The brood of Folly without father bred,
How little you bestead,°   *avail*
  Or fill the fixèd mind with all your toys°   *trifles*
5 Dwell in some idle brain,
  And fancies fond° with gaudy shapes possess,   *foolish*
As thick and numberless
  As the gay motes that people the sunbeams,
Or likest hovering dreams,
10 The fickle pensioners of Morpheus'³ train.
But hail thou Goddess sage and holy,
Hail, divinest Melancholy,
Whose saintly visage is too bright
To hit° the sense of human sight,   *suit*
15 And therefore to our weaker view
O'erlaid with black, staid wisdom's hue;⁴
Black, but such as in esteem,
Prince Memnon's sister⁵ might beseem,
Or that starred Ethiope queen⁶ that strove

3. Orpheus's music so moved Pluto that he agreed to release Orpheus's dead wife Eurydice (four syllables, accent on the second) from the underworld (Elysium), but he violated the condition set—that he not look back at her—and so lost her again. Milton often uses Orpheus as a figure for the poet.
4. The final lines echo Marlowe's "The Passionate Shepherd to His Love" (p. 1126): "If these delights thy mind may move, / Then live with me and be my love."
1. Il Penseroso whose name is Italian for "the thoughtful one," celebrates a melancholy that does not produce madness but the scholarly temperament, ruled by Saturn. See note 2 on p. 1909 to "L'Allegro."

2. In "Il Penseroso," Mirth is not the innocent joys of "L'Allegro," but "vain deluding joys."
3. Morpheus is the god of sleep. "Pensioners": followers.
4. The melancholy humor, caused by black bile, was thought to make the face dark or saturnine—from the ancient god Saturn, allegorized in Neoplatonic philosophy as "the collective angelic mind."
5. Memnon, in *Odyssey* 11, was a handsome Ethiopian prince; his sister Himera's beauty was mentioned by later commentators. Cf. Song of Solomon 1.5, "I am black but comely."
6. Cassiopeia was turned into a constellation ("starred") for bragging that she was more beautiful than the sea nymphs.

20 To set her beauty's praise above
The sea nymphs, and their powers offended.
Yet thou art higher far descended;
Thee bright-haired Vesta long of yore
To solitary Saturn bore;[7]
25 His daughter she (in Saturn's reign
Such mixture was not held a stain).
Oft in glimmering bowers and glades
He met her, and in secret shades
Of woody Ida's inmost grove,
30 While yet there was no fear of Jove.
Come pensive nun, devout and pure,
Sober, steadfast, and demure,
All in a robe of darkest grain,°   color
Flowing with majestic train,
35 And sable stole[8] of cypress lawn
Over thy decent° shoulders drawn.   comely, modestly covered
Come, but keep thy wonted° state,°   usual / dignity
With even step and musing gait,
And looks commercing with the skies,
40 Thy rapt soul sitting in thine eyes:
There held in holy passion still,
Forget thyself to marble,[9] till
With a sad° leaden downward cast°   grave, dignified / glance
Thou fix them on the earth as fast.
45 And join with thee calm Peace and Quiet,
Spare Fast, that oft with gods doth diet,
And hears the Muses in a ring
Aye° round about Jove's altar sing.   continually
And add to these retired Leisure,
50 That in trim gardens takes his pleasure;
But first, and chiefest, with thee bring
Him that yon soars on golden wing,
Guiding the fiery-wheelèd throne,
The cherub Contemplatìon;[1]
55 And the mute Silence hist° along,   summon
'Less Philomel[2] will deign a song,
In her sweetest, saddest plight,°   mood
Smoothing the rugged brow of night,
While Cynthia[3] checks her dragon yoke
60 Gently o'er th' accustomed oak;
Sweet bird that shunn'st the noise of folly,

7. Vesta, daughter of Saturn, was goddess of the household and a virgin, as were her priestesses. Milton invented the story of her sexual congress with Saturn on Mount Ida, resulting in Melancholy's birth. Saturn ruled the gods and the world during the Golden Age, which ended when he was murdered by his son Jove.
8. A delicate black cloth.
9. Still as a statue.
1. The special function of cherubim is contemplation of God; Milton alludes also (line 53) to their identification with the wheels of the mystical chariot/throne of God described by Ezekiel (Ezekiel 10).
2. The nightingale (the bird into which Philomela was transformed after her rape by her brother-in-law Tereus) traditionally sings a mournful song. "'Less": unless.
3. Goddess of the moon, also associated with Hecate, goddess of the underworld, who drives a pair of sleepless dragons.

Most musical, most melancholy!
Thee chantress oft the woods among
I woo to hear thy evensong;[4]
65   And missing thee, I walk unseen
On the dry smooth-shaven green,
To behold the wandering moon,
Riding near her highest noon,
Like one that had been led astray
70   Through the heaven's wide pathless way;
And oft as if her head she bowed,
Stooping through a fleecy cloud.
Oft on a plat° of rising ground,   *plot, open field*
I hear the far-off curfew sound
75   Over some wide-watered shore,
Swinging slow with sullen° roar;   *deep, mournful*
Or if the air will not permit,
Some still removèd place will fit,
Where glowing embers through the room
80   Teach light to counterfeit a gloom,
Far from all resort of mirth,
Save the cricket on the hearth,
Or the bellman's[5] drowsy charm,
To bless the doors from nightly harm;
85   Or let my lamp at midnight hour
Be seen in some high lonely tower,
Where I may oft outwatch the Bear,[6]
With thrice-great Hermes, or unsphere
The spirit of Plato[7] to unfold
90   What words or what vast regions hold
The immortal mind that hath forsook
Her mansion in this fleshly nook;
And of those demons[8] that are found
In fire, air, flood, or underground,
95   Whose power hath a true consent°   *agreement*
With planet, or with element.
Sometime let gorgeous Tragedy
In sceptered pall[9] come sweeping by,
Presenting Thebes, or Pelops' line,
100 Or the tale of Troy divine,[1]
Or what (though rare) of later age
Ennobled hath the buskined[2] stage.

4. The evening liturgy traditionally sung by cloistered monks and nuns ("chantress" evokes such a singer); "L'Allegro's" cock, by contrast, calls hearers to the morning liturgy, "matins" (line 114).
5. Night watchman who rang a bell to mark the hours.
6. The Great Bear constellation never sets in northern skies.
7. Various esoteric books (actually written in the 3rd and 4th centuries) were attributed to an ancient Egyptian, Hermes Trismegistus ("thrice great"). Neoplatonists made him the father of all knowledge; later he became a patron of magicians and alchemists. To "unsphere" Plato is to bring him magically back to earth from whatever sphere he now inhabits—in practical terms, by reading his books.
8. Demons (daemons), halfway between gods and men, preside over the four elements.
9. Royal robe, worn by tragic actors.
1. Tragedies about Thebes include Sophocles' *Oedipus* cycle, those about the line of Pelops, Aeschylus's *Oresteia*, and those about Troy, Euripedes' *Trojan Women*.
2. The buskin (high boot) of tragedy, contrasted with the "sock" of comedy ("L'Allegro," line 132).

But, O sad virgin, that thy power
Might raise Musaeus[3] from his bower,
105   Or bid the soul of Orpheus[4] sing
Such notes as, warbled to the string,
Drew iron tears down Pluto's cheek,
And made Hell grant what love did seek.
Or call up him[5] that left half told
110   The story of Cambuscan bold,
Of Camball and of Algarsife,
And who had Canacee to wife,
That owned the virtuous° ring and glass,   *having magical*
And of the wondrous horse of brass,   *powers*
115   On which the Tartar king did ride;
And if aught° else great bards beside   *anything*
In sage and solemn tunes have sung,
Of tourneys and of trophies hung,
Of forests and enchantments drear,
120   Where more is meant than meets the ear.[6]
Thus, Night, oft see me in thy pale career,
Till civil-suited Morn appear,
Not tricked and frounced as she was wont
With the Attic boy to hunt,[7]
125   But kerchiefed in a comely cloud,
While rocking winds are piping loud,
Or ushered with a shower still,°   *gentle*
When the gust hath blown his fill,
Ending on the rustling leaves,
130   With minute drops from off the eaves.
And when the sun begins to fling
His flaring beams, me, Goddess, bring
To archèd walks of twilight groves,
And shadows brown that Sylvan[8] loves
135   Of pine or monumental oak,
Where the rude ax with heavèd stroke
Was never heard the nymphs to daunt,
Or fright them from their hallowed haunt.
There in close covert° by some brook,   *hidden place*
140   Where no profaner eye may look,
Hide me from day's garish eye,
While the bee with honeyed thigh,
That at her flowery work doth sing,
And the waters murmuring
145   With such consort° as they keep,   *musical harmony*
Entice the dewy-feathered sleep;
And let some strange mysterious dream
Wave at his wings in airy stream

3. Mythical poet-priest of the pre-Homeric age, supposedly a son or pupil of Orpheus.
4. For the story of Orpheus, see "L'Allegro," line 145, and note 3 (on line 150).
5. Chaucer, whose Squire's Tale is unfinished.
6. A capsule definition of allegory.

7. The now soberly dressed Aurora, goddess of the dawn, once fell in love with Cephalus ("the Attic boy") and hunted with him. "Tricked and frounced": adorned and with frizzled hair.
8. Roman god of woodlands.

Of lively portraiture displayed
150 Softly on my eyelids laid.
And as I wake, sweet music breathe
Above, about, or underneath,
Sent by some spirit to mortals good,
Or th' unseen genius° of the wood.   *guardian deity*
155 But let my due feet never fail
To walk the studious cloister's pale,°   *enclosure*
And love the high embowèd roof,
With antic pillars massy proof,⁹
And storied windows richly dight,¹
160 Casting a dim religious light.
There let the pealing organ blow
To the full-voiced choir below,
In service high and anthems clear,
As may with sweetness, through mine ear,
165 Dissolve me into ecstasies,
And bring all heaven before mine eyes.
And may at last my weary age
Find out the peaceful hermitage,
The hairy gown and mossy cell,
170 Where I may sit and rightly spell°   *study*
Of every star that heaven doth shew,
And every herb that sips the dew,
Till old experience do attain
To something like prophetic strain.
175 These pleasures, Melancholy, give,²
And I with thee will choose to live.

ca. 1631   1645

Lycidas   Milton wrote this pastoral elegy for a volume of Latin, Greek, and English poems, *Justa Eduourdo King Naufrago* (1638), commemorating the death by shipwreck of his college classmate Edward King, three years younger than himself. King was not a close friend, but Milton's deepest emotions, anxieties, and fears are engaged here because, as poet and minister, King could serve Milton as a kind of alter ego. Still engaged in preparing himself, at the age of twenty-nine, for his projected poetic career, Milton was forced to recognize the uncertainty of all human endeavors. King's death posed the problem of mortality in its most agonizing form: the death of the young, the unfulfilled, the good seems to deny all meaning to life, to demonstrate the uselessness of exceptional talent, lofty ambition, and noble ideals of service to God.

While the poem expresses Milton's anxieties, it also serves as an announcement of his grand ambitions. Like Edmund Spenser, Milton saw mastery of the pastoral mode as the first step in a great poetic career. In "Lycidas" that mastery is complete. In the tradition that Milton received from classical and Renaissance predecessors,

---

9. Massive and strong. "Antic": covered with quaint or grotesque carvings, also antique.
1. Dressed. "Storied windows": stained-glass windows depicting biblical stories.

2. Compare "L'Allegro," lines 151–52 (p. 1913), and the final lines of Marlowe's "Passionate Shepherd" (p. 1126).

including Theocritus, Virgil, Petrarch, and Spenser, the pastoral landscape was invested with profound significances that had little indeed to do with the hard life of agricultural labor. In lines 25–36, Milton evokes the conventional pastoral topic of carefree shepherds who engage in singing contests, watch contentedly over their grazing sheep, fall in love, and write poetry, offering an image of human life in harmony with nature and the seasonal processes of fruition and mellowing before the winter of death. That classical image of the shepherd as poet is mingled with the Christian understanding of the shepherd as pastor (Christ is the Good Shepherd), and sometimes as the prophet called to his mission from the fields, like David or Isaiah. Milton calls on all these associations, along with other motifs specific to pastoral funeral elegy: the recollection of past friendship, a questioning of destiny for cutting short this life, a procession of mourners (often mythological figures), and a "flower passage" in which nature pays tribute to the dead shepherd.

"Lycidas" uses but continually tests and challenges the assumptions and conventions of pastoral elegy, making for profound tensions and clashes of tone. The pastoral "oaten flute" is interrupted by divine pronouncements and bitter invective; nature seems rife with examples of meaningless waste and early death; the "blind Fury" often cuts off the poet's "thin-spun life" before he can win fame; good pastors die young while corrupt "Blind mouths" remain; and Nature cannot even pay her tribute of flowers to Lycidas's funeral bier since he welters in the deep, his bones hurled to the "bottom of the monstrous world." In response to these fierce challenges come pronouncements by Apollo and St. Peter, and images of protection and resurrection in nature and myth, culminating in a new vision of pastoral: in heaven Lycidas enjoys a perfected pastoral existence, and in the coda the consoled shepherd arises and carries his song to "pastures new." Milton's questioning leads to a final reassertion of confidence in his calling as national poet. Moreover, in the headnote added in the 1645 volume of his *Poems*, he lays claim to prophetic authority, for the Church of England clergy he denounced as corrupt in 1638 had mostly been expelled from their livings by Puritan reformers in 1645.

Lycidas

In this monody[1] the author bewails a learned friend, unfortunately drowned in his passage from Chester on the Irish seas, 1637. And by occasion foretells the ruin of our corrupted clergy, then in their height.

	Yet once more, O ye laurels, and once more	
	Ye myrtles brown, with ivy never sere,[2]	
	I come to pluck your berries harsh and crude,°	*unripe*
	And with forced fingers rude,°	*unskilled*
5	Shatter your leaves before the mellowing year.	
	Bitter constraint, and sad occasion dear,°	*heartfelt, also dire*
	Compels me to disturb your season due;	
	For Lycidas is dead, dead ere his prime,[3]	
	Young Lycidas, and hath not left his peer.	

1. A dirge sung by a single voice, though this one incorporates several other voices. Milton added this headnote in the edition of 1645; it identifies Milton as a prophet in the passage denouncing the clergy in this 1638 poem (lines 112–31) and invites the reader to remember Milton's 1641–42 polemics against the English bishops and church government (now dismantled).

2. "Laurels," associated with Apollo and poetry; "myrtle," associated with Venus and love; "ivy," associated with Bacchus and frenzy (also learning). All three are evergreens ("never sere") linked to poetic inspiration.

3. King was twenty-five.

10 Who would not sing for Lycidas? He knew
Himself to sing, and build the lofty rhyme.[4]
He must not float upon his watery bier
Unwept, and welter° to the parching wind,   *be tossed about*
Without the meed° of some melodious tear.°   *reward / elegy*
15   Begin then, sisters of the sacred well[5]
That from beneath the seat of Jove doth spring,
Begin, and somewhat loudly sweep the string.
Hence with denial vain, and coy excuse;
So may some gentle muse[6]
20 With lucky words favor my destined urn,
And as he passes turn,
And bid fair peace be to my sable shroud.
For we were nursed upon the selfsame hill,
Fed the same flock, by fountain, shade, and rill.
25   Together both, ere the high lawns° appeared   *upland pastures*
Under the opening eyelids of the morn,
We drove afield, and both together heard
What time the grayfly winds her sultry horn,[7]
Battening° our flocks with the fresh dews of night,   *feeding fat*
30 Oft till the star that rose at evening bright[8]
Toward heaven's descent had sloped his westering wheel.
Meanwhile the rural ditties were not mute,
Tempered to th' oaten flute,[9]
Rough satyrs danced, and fauns with cloven heel
35 From the glad sound would not be absent long,
And old Damoetas[1] loved to hear our song.
    But O the heavy change, now thou art gone,
Now thou art gone, and never must return!
Thee, shepherd, thee the woods and desert caves,
40 With wild thyme and the gadding° vine o'ergrown,   *wandering*
And all their echoes mourn.
The willows and the hazel copses° green   *thickets of trees*
Shall now no more be seen,
Fanning their joyous leaves to thy soft lays.
45 As killing as the canker° to the rose,   *cankerworm*
Or taint-worm[2] to the weanling herds that graze,
Or frost to flowers that their gay wardrobe wear
When first the white-thorn blows;[3]
Such, Lycidas, thy loss to shepherd's ear.
50   Where were ye, nymphs,[4] when the remorseless deep
Closed o'er the head of your loved Lycidas?
For neither were ye playing on the steep

---

4. King had written several poems of compliment in the patronage mode, chiefly on members of the royal family.
5. The nine (sister) Muses called (probably) from the fountain Aganippe, near Mount Helicon.
6. Here, some kindly poet.
7. I.e., heard the grayfly when she buzzes.
8. Hesperus, the evening star.
9. Panpipes, played traditionally by shepherds in pastoral.

1. A type name from pastoral poetry, possibly referring to some particular tutor at Cambridge. "Satyrs": goat-legged woodland creatures, Pan's boisterous attendants.
2. Internal parasite fatal to newly weaned lambs.
3. Hawthorn blooms.
4. Nature deities.

Where your old bards, the famous Druids,[5] lie,
Nor on the shaggy top of Mona high,
55 Nor yet where Deva spreads her wizard stream:[6]
Ay me! I fondly dream—
Had ye been there—for what could that have done?
What could the Muse[7] herself that Orpheus bore,
The Muse herself, for her enchanting[8] son
60 Whom universal Nature did lament,
When by the rout that made the hideous roar
His gory visage down the stream was sent,
Down the swift Hebrus to the Lesbian shore?[9]
    Alas! What boots° it with incessant care   *profits*
65 To tend the homely slighted shepherd's trade,
And strictly meditate the thankless muse?[1]
Were it not better done as others use,
To sport with Amaryllis in the shade,
Or with the tangles of Neaera's hair?[2]
70 Fame is the spur that the clear spirit doth raise
(That last infirmity of noble mind)
To scorn delights, and live laborious days;
But the fair guerdon° when we hope to find,   *reward*
And think to burst out into sudden blaze,
75 Comes the blind Fury[3] with th' abhorrèd shears,
And slits the thin-spun life. "But not the praise,"
Phoebus replied, and touched my trembling ears;[4]
"Fame is no plant that grows on mortal soil,
Nor in the glistering foil[5]
80 Set off to th' world, nor in broad rumor lies,
But lives and spreads aloft by those pure eyes,
And perfect witness of all-judging Jove;
As he pronounces lastly on each deed,
Of so much fame in heaven expect thy meed."°   *reward*
85   O fountain Arethuse, and thou honored flood,
Smooth-sliding Mincius, crowned with vocal reeds,
That strain I heard was of a higher mood.[6]
    But now my oat° proceeds,   *pastoral flute*

5. Priestly poet-kings of Celtic Britain, who worshipped the forces of nature. They are buried on the mountain ("steep") Kerig-y-Druidion in Wales.
6. Mona is the island of Anglesey. Deva, the river Dee in Cheshire, was magic ("wizard") because its shifting stream foretold prosperity or dearth for the land. All these places are in the West Country, near where King drowned.
7. Calliope, Muse of epic poetry, was the mother of Orpheus.
8. Implies both song and magic; the root word survives in "incantation."
9. Orpheus's song was drowned out by the screams of a mob ("rout") of Thracian women, the Bacchantes, who then were able to tear him to pieces and throw his gory head into the river Hebrus, which carried it—still singing—to the island of Lesbos, bringing that island the gift of poetry.

1. I.e., study to write poetry (a Virgilian phrase).
2. "Amaryllis" and "Neaera" (*Nee-eye-ra*), conventional names for pretty shepherdesses wooed in song by pastoral shepherds.
3. Atropos, one of the three Fates, whose scissors cuts the thread of human life after her sisters spin and measure it. Milton makes her a savage, and blind, Fury.
4. Phoebus Apollo, god of poetic inspiration. In *Eclogue* 6.3–4 he plucked Virgil's ears, warning him against impatient ambition.
5. Flashy, glittering metal foil, set under a gem to enhance its brilliance.
6. Arethusa was a fountain in Sicily associated with Greek pastoral poetry (Theocritus), Mincius a river in Lombardy associated with Latin pastoral (Virgil); Milton invokes them as a return to the pastoral after the "higher mood" of Apollo's speech.

And listens to the herald of the sea[7]
90 That came in Neptune's plea.
He asked the waves, and asked the felon° winds,   *savage*
"What hard mishap hath doomed this gentle swain?"°   *shepherd*
And questioned every gust of rugged° wings   *stormy*
That blows from off each bekèd promontory;
95 They knew not of his story,
And sage Hippotades[8] their answer brings,
That not a blast was from his dungeon strayed;
The air was calm, and on the level brine,
Sleek Panope[9] with all her sisters played.
100 It was that fatal and perfidious bark,
Built in th' eclipse,[1] and rigged with curses dark,
That sunk so low that sacred head of thine.
    Next Camus,[2] reverend sire, went footing slow,
His mantle hairy, and his bonnet sedge,°   *formed of reeds*
105 Inwrought with figures dim, and on the edge
Like to that sanguine flower inscribed with woe.[3]
"Ah! who hath reft," quoth he, "my dearest pledge?"
Last came and last did go
The pilot of the Galilean lake;[4]
110 Two massy keys he bore of metals twain
(The golden opes, the iron shuts amain).°   *forever*
He shook his mitered locks, and stern bespake:
"How well could I have spared for° thee, young swain,   *in place of*
Enow° of such as for their bellies' sake   *enough (plural)*
115 Creep and intrude and climb into the fold![5]
Of other care they little reckoning make,
Than how to scramble at the shearers' feast,[6]
And shove away the worthy bidden guest.
Blind mouths![7] that scarce themselves know how to hold
120 A sheep-hook, or have learned aught else the least
That to the faithful herdsman's art belongs!
What recks it them? What need they? They are sped;[8]
And when they list,° their lean° and flashy songs   *choose / meager*
Grate on their scrannel° pipes of wretched straw.   *harsh, thin*

7. Triton, who comes gathering evidence about the accident for Neptune's court.
8. Aeolus, god of winds.
9. The chief Nereid, or sea nymph.
1. Eclipses were taken as evil omens.
2. God of the river Cam, representing Cambridge University.
3. Like the *AI AI* cry of grief supposedly found on the hyacinth, a "sanguine flower" sprung from the blood of the youth Hyacinthus, beloved of Apollo and accidentally killed by him.
4. St. Peter, originally a fisherman on the sea of Galilee, was Christ's chief apostle; his keys open and shut the gates of heaven. He wears a bishop's miter (line 112): Milton in his "antiprelatical tracts" allows for a special role for apostles but denies any distinction in office between bishops and ministers in the later church.

5. Cf. John 10.1: "He that entereth not by the door into the sheepfold, but climbeth up some other way, the same is a thief and a robber."
6. Festive suppers for the sheepshearers (hence, the material rewards of their ministry). "Worthy bidden guest" (next line): cf. Matthew 22.8, the parable of the marriage feast, "they which were bidden were not worthy."
7. Collapsing blindness with greed, this audacious metaphor accuses churchmen of shirking oversight (*episcopus*, bishop, means "supervision") and of glutting themselves, although pastors ought to feed their flocks. "Sheep-hook" (next line): the bishop's staff is in the form of a shepherd's crook.
8. Provided for. "What recks it them?": what do they care?

125 The hungry sheep look up, and are not fed,
But swol'n with wind, and the rank mist they draw,°   *inhale*
Rot inwardly,[9] and foul contagion spread,
Besides what the grim wolf with privy paw[1]
Daily devours apace, and nothing said.
130 But that two-handed engine at the door[2]
Stands ready to smite once, and smite no more."
   Return, Alpheus,[3] the dread voice is past,
That shrunk thy streams; return, Sicilian muse,
And call the vales, and bid them hither cast
135 Their bells and flowerets of a thousand hues.[4]
Ye valleys low where the mild whispers use,°   *frequent*
Of shades and wanton winds, and gushing brooks,
On whose fresh lap the swart star[5] sparely looks,
Throw hither all your quaint enameled eyes,[6]
140 That on the green turf suck the honeyed showers,
And purple all the ground with vernal flowers.
Bring the rathe° primrose that forsaken dies,   *early*
The tufted crow-toe, and pale jessamine,[7]
The white pink, and the pansy freaked° with jet,   *flecked*
145 The glowing violet,
The musk rose, and the well-attired woodbine,
With cowslips wan° that hang the pensive head,   *pale*
And every flower that sad embroidery wears:
Bid amaranthus[8] all his beauty shed,
150 And daffadillies fill their cups with tears,
To strew the laureate hearse° where Lycid lies.   *laurel-decked bier*
For so to interpose a little ease,
Let our frail thoughts dally with false surmise.[9]
Ay me! whilst thee the shores and sounding seas
155 Wash far away, where'er thy bones are hurled,
Whether beyond the stormy Hebrides,[1]
Where thou perhaps under the whelming° tide *roaring, overwhelming*
Visit'st the bottom of the monstrous world;
Or whether thou, to our moist vows denied,
160 Sleep'st by the fable of Bellerus old,[2]
Where the great vision of the guarded mount

---

9. Sheep rot is used as an allegory of church corruption by both Petrarch and Dante.
1. I.e., Roman Catholicism, whole agents operated in secret ("privy"). Conversions in the court of the Roman Catholic queen Henrietta Maria were notorious.
2. A celebrated crux, variously explained as the two houses of Parliament, St. Peter's keys, the two-edged sword of the Book of Revelation, a sword wielded by two hands, and by other guesses; what is clear is the denunciation of impending, apocalyptic vengeance. In Matthew 24.33 the Last Judgment is said to be "even at the doors."
3. A river in Arcadia, fabled to pass unmixed through the sea before mixing its waters with the "fountain Arethuse" in Sicily, again reviving the pastoral mode after the fierce denunciation of Peter (see lines 85–87).

4. A catalogue of flowers was a common pastoral topic. "Bells": bell-shaped flowers.
5. The Dog Star, Sirius, associated with the heats of late summer.
6. Flowers curiously patterned and adorned with many colors.
7. White jasmine. "Tufted crow-toe": hyacinth or buttercup, growing in clusters. "Woodbine" (line 146): honeysuckle.
8. In Greek, "unfading," a legendary flower of immortality, one that never fades.
9. False, because Lycidas's body is not here to receive floral and poetic tributes.
1. Islands off the coast of Scotland, the northern terminus of the Irish Sea.
2. A fabulous giant invented by Milton as the origin of the Latin name for Land's End in Cornwall, *Bellerium*. "Monstrous world" (line 158): filled with monsters, also, immense.

Looks toward Namancos and Bayona's hold;[3]
Look homeward angel now, and melt with ruth:°   *pity*
And, O ye dolphins,[4] waft the hapless youth.
165   Weep no more, woeful shepherds, weep no more,
For Lycidas your sorrow is not dead,
Sunk though he be beneath the wat'ry floor;
So sinks the daystar° in the ocean bed,   *the sun*
And yet anon repairs his drooping head,
170   And tricks° his beams, and with new-spangled ore   *adorns, trims*
Flames in the forehead of the morning sky:
So Lycidas sunk low, but mounted high,
Through the dear might of him that walked the waves,[5]
Where, other groves and other streams along,[6]
175   With nectar pure his oozy° locks he laves,   *moist*
And hears the unexpressive nuptial song,[7]
In the blest kingdoms meek of joy and love.
There entertain him all the saints above,
In solemn troops and sweet societies
180   That sing, and singing in their glory move,
And wipe the tears forever from his eyes.
Now, Lycidas, the shepherds weep no more;
Henceforth thou art the Genius[8] of the shore,
In thy large recompense, and shalt be good
185   To all that wander in that perilous flood.
       Thus sang the uncouth swain[9] to th' oaks and rills,
While the still morn went out with sandals gray;
He touched the tender stops of various quills,[1]
With eager thought warbling his Doric[2] lay:
190   And now the sun had stretched out all the hills,
And now was dropped into the western bay;
At last he rose, and twitched his mantle blue:[3]
Tomorrow to fresh woods, and pastures new.

November 1637   1638

---

3. "The guarded mount" is St. Michael's Mount in Cornwall, where the archangel was said to have appeared to fishermen in 495, and from which he is envisioned as looking over the Atlantic toward a region and fortress ("Bayona's hold") in northern Spain, thereby guarding Protestant England against the continuing Roman Catholic threat.
4. Dolphins brought the Greek poet Arion safely ashore, for love of his verse, and also performed other sea rescues.
5. Christ, who rescued Peter when he tried and failed to walk on the Sea of Galilee (Matthew 14.25–31).

6. See Revelation 22.1–2, on the "pure river of water of life," and the "tree of life, which bare twelve manner of fruits."
7. Inexpressible hymn of joy sung at "the marriage supper of the Lamb" (Revelation 19).
8. Local guardian spirit.
9. Another voice now seems to take over from the previously heard voice of the "uncouth swain" (unknown, unskilled shepherd).
1. The oaten stalks of panpipes.
2. Rustic, the dialect of Theocritus and other famous Greek pastoral poets.
3. The color of hope. "Twitched": pulled up around his shoulders.

From The Reason of Church Government Urged Against Prelaty[1]

[PLANS AND PROJECTS]

* * * Concerning therefore this wayward subject against prelaty,[2] the touching whereof is so distasteful and disquietous[3] to a number of men, as by what hath been said I may deserve of charitable readers to be credited that neither envy nor gall hath entered me upon this controversy, but the enforcement of conscience only and a preventive fear lest the omitting of this duty should be against me when I would store up to myself the good provision of peaceful hours; so lest it should be still imputed to me, as I have found it hath been, that some self-pleasing humor of vainglory hath incited me to contest with men of high estimation, now while green years are upon my head;[4] from this needless surmisal I shall hope to dissuade the intelligent and equal auditor, if I can but say successfully that which in this exigent[5] behooves me; although I would be heard only, if it might be, by the elegant and learned reader, to whom principally for a while I shall beg leave I may address myself. To him it will be no new thing though I tell him that if I hunted after praise by the ostentation of wit and learning, I should not write thus out of mine own season when I have neither yet completed to my mind the full circle of my private studies,[6] although I complain not of any insufficiency to the matter in hand; or, were I ready to my wishes, it were a folly to commit anything elaborately composed to the careless and interrupted listening of these tumultuous times. Next, if I were wise only to mine own ends, I would certainly take such a subject as of itself might catch applause, whereas this hath all the disadvantages on the contrary, and such a subject as the publishing whereof might be delayed at pleasure, and time enough to pencil it over with all the curious touches of art, even to the perfection of a faultless picture; whenas in this argument the not deferring is of great moment to the good speeding,[7] that if solidity have leisure to do her office, art cannot have much. Lastly, I should not choose this manner of writing, wherein knowing myself inferior to myself, led by the genial power of nature[8] to another task, I have the use, as I may account it, but of my left hand. And though I shall be foolish in saying more to this purpose, yet, since it will be such a folly as wisest men going about to commit have only confessed and so

---

1. This was the fourth of five tracts Milton published attacking the bishops, liturgy, and church government of the Church of England, in support of Presbyterian reform, though these tracts also show signs of the more radical positions he will soon adopt. This 1642 treatise is the first one to carry his name, so the autobiographical passage is in part to introduce himself to the reader and explain why, though a layman and a young man, he feels himself called, and well prepared, to write on theology and ecclesiastical order. Beyond that rhetorical purpose, this is also the fullest account Milton ever set forth of his poetics: his sense of the poet's calling, of the nature and multiple uses of poetry, and of the several genres he already has employed or hopes to attempt. It also registers his inner conflict between duty (to serve God and his church with

his learning) and desire (to write poetry).
2. Government by prelates (bishops). "Wayward": untoward, unpromising.
3. Distressing.
4. Milton's opponents, Bishops Joseph Hall, James Ussher, and Lancelot Andrewes, were famous, and he was still almost unknown, at age thirty-four.
5. Urgent occasion. "Equal": impartial.
6. After taking his B.A. and M.A. degrees from Cambridge, Milton spent nearly six more years in private study at home; he was still continuing that program of reading.
7. Prompt publication is essential in polemic, so substance rather than art must be the priority. "Office": duty.
8. Intellectual gifts or natural disposition.

committed, I may trust with more reason, because with more folly, to have courteous pardon. For although a poet, soaring in the high region of his fancies with his garland and singing robes about him, might without apology speak more of himself than I mean to do, yet for me sitting here below in the cool element of prose, a mortal thing among many readers of no empyreal conceit,[9] to venture and divulge unusual things of myself, I shall petition to the gentler sort, it may not be envy[1] to me.

I must say, therefore, that after I had from my first years by the ceaseless diligence and care of my father (whom God recompense) been exercised to the tongues and some sciences, as my age would suffer,[2] by sundry masters and teachers both at home and at the schools, it was found that whether aught was imposed me by them that had the overlooking, or betaken to of mine own choice in English or other tongue, prosing or versing (but chiefly this latter), the style, by certain vital signs it had, was likely to live. But much latelier in the private academies of Italy,[3] whither I was favored to resort—perceiving that some trifles which I had in memory, composed at under twenty or thereabout (for the manner is that everyone must give some proof of his wit[4] and reading there) met with acceptance above what was looked for, and other things which I had shifted in scarcity of books and conveniences to patch up amongst them, were received with written encomiums,[5] which the Italian is not forward to bestow on men of this side the Alps—I began thus far to assent both to them and divers of my friends here at home, and not less to an inward prompting which now grew daily upon me, that by labor and intent study (which I take to be my portion in this life) joined with the strong propensity of nature, I might perhaps leave something so written to aftertimes, as they should not willingly let it die. These thoughts at once possessed me, and these other: that if I were certain to write as men buy leases, for three lives and downward,[6] there ought no regard be sooner had than to God's glory by the honor and instruction of my country. For which cause, and not only for that I knew it would be hard to arrive at the second rank among the Latins, I applied myself to that resolution which Ariosto followed against the persuasions of Bembo,[7] to fix all the industry and art I could unite to the adorning of my native tongue; not to make verbal curiosities the end—that were a toilsome vanity—but to be an interpreter and relater of the best and sagest things among mine own citizens throughout this island in the mother dialect. That what the greatest and choicest wits of Athens, Rome, or modern Italy, and those Hebrews of old did for their country, I, in my proportion, with this over and above of being a Christian,[8] might do for mine; not caring to be once named abroad, though perhaps I could attain to that, but content with these British islands as my world; whose fortune hath hitherto been that if the Athenians, as

---

9. Without sublime and elevated conceits.

1. Cause for odium or disrespect.

2. Admit. "Tongues": foreign languages. In *Ad Patrem* Milton says that as a boy he learned Latin, Greek, French, Italian, and Hebrew.

3. When on the grand tour of the Continent (1638–39) Milton enjoyed attending academies in Rome and especially Florence, which were centers for literary, scientific, and social exchange.

4. Ingenuity, creative powers; Milton read some of his Latin poems to the academies.

5. Praises. Milton published five of these encomiums, four in Latin, one in Italian, as prefatory material to the Latin part of his 1645 *Poems*.

6. Leases were often drawn for a tenancy to run through the longest-lived of three named persons.

7. Rejecting Cardinal Bembo's advice, Ariosto said he would rather be first among the Italian poets than second among those writing Latin.

8. The advantage would be in having "true" subjects to write about.

some say, made their small deeds great and renowned by their eloquent writers, England hath had her noble achievements made small by the unskillful handling of monks and mechanics.

Time serves not now, and perhaps I might seem too profuse to give any certain account of what the mind at home in the spacious circuits of her musing hath liberty to propose to herself, though of highest hope and hardest attempting: whether that epic form whereof the two poems of Homer and those other two of Virgil and Tasso are a diffuse, and the book of Job a brief, model;[9] or whether the rules of Aristotle herein are strictly to be kept, or nature to be followed,[1] which in them that know art and use judgment is no transgression but an enriching of art; and lastly, what king or knight before the conquest[2] might be chosen in whom to lay the pattern of a Christian hero. And as Tasso gave to a prince of Italy his choice whether he would command him to write of Godfrey's expedition against the infidels, or Belisarius against the Goths, or Charlemagne against the Lombards;[3] if to the instinct of nature and the emboldening of art aught may be trusted, and that there be nothing adverse in our climate[4] or the fate of this age, it haply would be no rashness from an equal diligence and inclination to present the like offer in our own ancient stories; or whether those dramatic constitutions[5] wherein Sophocles and Euripides reign shall be found more doctrinal and exemplary to a nation. The Scripture also affords us a divine pastoral drama in the Song of Solomon, consisting of two persons and a double chorus, as Origen rightly judges. And the Apocalypse of St. John is the majestic image of a high and stately tragedy, shutting up and intermingling her solemn scenes and acts with a sevenfold chorus of hallelujahs and harping symphonies; and this my opinion the grave authority of Paraeus, commenting that book, is sufficient to confirm.[6] Or if occasion shall lead to imitate those magnific odes and hymns wherein Pindarus and Callimachus[7] are in most things worthy, some others in their frame judicious, in their matter most an end[8] faulty. But those frequent songs throughout the law and prophets beyond all these, not in their divine argument alone, but in the very critical art of composition, may be easily made appear over all the kinds of lyric poesy to be incomparable.[9] These abilities, wheresoever they be found, are the inspired gift of God rarely bestowed, but yet to some

---

9. The great models for the "diffuse" or long, epic were Homer's *Iliad* and *Odyssey*, Virgil's *Aeneid*, and Torquato Tasso's *Gerusalemme liberata*; there was also a long tradition of reading the Book of Job as a "brief" epic, a moral conflict between Job and Satan. Milton's brief epic, *Paradise Regained* (1671), makes some use of that model. For all the genres he discusses, Milton cites both classical and biblical models.

1. One contemporary debate concerned whether the Aristotelian rule of beginning in medias res was to be followed, or Ariosto's "natural" method of beginning at the beginning of the story.

2. At first Milton considered as potential epic subjects King Arthur, who fought against invading Saxons, and King Alfred, who warred with invading Danes; he excluded those after the Norman Conquest.

3. Tasso offered this choice to his patron, Alfonso II d'Este, Duke of Ferrara.

4. Milton often speculated that the cold climate

of England might not be conducive to poetry, as the warmer climate of Italy and Greece had been.

5. Plays.

6. Sophocles and Euripides are supreme examples of Greek tragedy; the Scripture models for drama are the Song of Solomon as a "divine pastoral drama" (Milton cites Origen, an Alexandrine Father of the 3rd century), and the Book of Revelation as a "high and stately tragedy" (he cites David Paraeus, a German theologian of the 16th and 17th centuries).

7. Pindar, a 5th century B.C.E. Greek poet, wrote numerous odes especially on winners of the Olympic games; Callimachus, a 3rd century B.C.E. Alexandrine Greek, wrote elegant elegiac verse on the origin of various myths and rituals.

8. Almost entirely.

9. He thinks especially of the Psalms, often compared to classical lyric.

(though most abuse) in every nation; and are of power beside the office of a pulpit to inbreed and cherish in a great people the seeds of virtue and public civility, to allay the perturbations of the mind and set the affections in right tune, to celebrate in glorious and lofty hymns the throne and equipage of God's almightiness, and what he works and what he suffers to be wrought with high providence in his church, to sing the victorious agonies of martyrs and saints, the deeds and triumphs of just and pious nations doing valiantly through faith against the enemies of Christ, to deplore the general relapses of kingdoms and states from justice and God's true worship. Lastly, whatsoever in religion is holy and sublime, in virtue amiable or grave, whatsoever hath passion or admiration in all the changes of that which is called fortune from without or the wily subtleties and refluxes of man's thoughts from within, all these things with a solid and treatable smoothness to paint out and describe.[1] Teaching over the whole book of sanctity and virtue through all the instances of example, with such delight to those especially of soft and delicious temper,[2] who will not so much as look upon truth herself unless they see her elegantly dressed, that whereas the paths of honesty and good life appear now rugged and difficult, though they be indeed easy and pleasant, they would then appear to all men both easy and pleasant, though they were rugged and difficult indeed. And what a benefit this would be to our youth and gentry may be soon guessed by what we know of the corruption and bane which they suck in daily from the writings and interludes of libidinous and ignorant poetasters,[3] who, having scarce ever heard of that which is the main consistence of a true poem, the choice of such persons as they ought to introduce, and what is moral and decent to each one, do for the most part lap up[4] vicious principles in sweet pills to be swallowed down, and make the taste of virtuous documents harsh and sour.

But because the spirit of man cannot demean[5] itself lively in this body without some recreating intermission of labor and serious things, it were happy for the commonwealth if our magistrates, as in those famous governments of old, would take into their care, not only the deciding of our contentious law cases and brawls, but the managing of our public sports and festival pastimes, that they might be, not such as were authorized a while since,[6] the provocations of drunkenness and lust, but such as may inure and harden our bodies by martial exercises to all warlike skill and performance, and may civilize, adorn, and make discreet our minds by the learned and affable meeting of frequent academies, and the procurement of wise and artful recitations sweetened with eloquent and graceful enticements to the love and practice of justice, temperance, and fortitude, instructing and bettering the nation at all opportunities, that the call of wisdom and virtue may be heard everywhere, as Solomon saith: "She crieth without, she uttereth her voice in the streets, in the top of high places, in the chief concourse, and

---

1. See the wide range of kinds and subjects and functions suggested for the serious national poet.
2. Temperament. Milton here paraphrases Horace's formula echoed by Sidney and Jonson, that poetry both teaches and delights, and that it encourages virtuous endeavor.
3. Some of the pseudo-poets of the Cavalier court who wrote on lascivious topics.
4. Roll up.
5. Comport.
6. Charles I's republication (1633) of James I's *Book of Sports*, encouraging sports, dancing, and rural festivals on Sundays—anathema to Puritans.

in the openings of the gates."[7] Whether this may not be, not only in pulpits, but after another persuasive method,[8] at set and solemn panegyries, in theaters, porches,[9] or what other place or way may win most upon the people to receive at once both recreation and instruction, let them in authority consult.

The thing which I had to say, and those intentions which have lived within me ever since I could conceive myself anything worth to my country, I return to crave excuse that urgent reason hath plucked from me by an abortive and foredated discovery.[1] And the accomplishment of them lies not but in a power above man's to promise; but that none hath by more studious ways endeavored, and with more unwearied spirit that none shall, that I dare almost aver of myself as far as life and free leisure will extend; and that the land had once enfranchised herself from this impertinent[2] yoke of prelaty, under whose inquisitorious and tyrannical duncery no free and splendid wit can flourish. Neither do I think it shame to covenant with any knowing reader that for some few years yet I may go on trust with him toward the payment of what I am now indebted, as being a work not to be raised from the heat of youth or the vapors of wine, like that which flows at waste from the pen of some vulgar amorist or the trencher fury of a rhyming parasite, nor to be obtained by the invocation of Dame Memory and her siren daughters,[3] but by devout prayer to that Eternal Spirit who can enrich with all utterance and knowledge, and sends out his seraphim with the hallowed fire of his altar to touch and purify the lips of whom he pleases.[4] To this must be added industrious and select reading, steady observation, insight into all seemly and generous arts and affairs; till which in some measure be compassed, at mine own peril and cost I refuse not to sustain this expectation.* * * But were it the meanest under-service, if God by his secretary conscience enjoin it, it were sad for me if I should draw back; for me especially, now when all men offer their aid to help ease and lighten the difficult labors of the church, to whose service by the intentions of my parents and friends I was destined of a child, and in mine own resolutions: till coming to some maturity of years and perceiving what tyranny had invaded the church, that he who would take orders must subscribe slave and take an oath withal,[5] which, unless he took with a conscience that would retch, he must either straight perjure or split his faith; I thought it better to prefer a blameless silence before the sacred office of speaking, bought and begun with servitude and forswearing. Howsoever, thus church-outed by the prelates,

---

7. The phrases are from Proverbs 1.20–21 and 8.2–3. Milton would not ban recreation or festival pastimes but reform them: his models are the lofty encomiastic poems and recitations Plato would admit into his *Republic*, the literary and social exchanges of the Italian academies, and martial exercises (to prepare the citizenry for war, now imminent).
8. I.e., poetry.
9. Porticos. "Panegyries": solemn public meetings.
1. I.e., I have been forced to write for my country's sake and to reveal my poetic plans before I was ready to do either.
2. Unsuitable, absurd.
3. True poetry comes, not from youth, wine, a

full plate, or even Memory (and her daughters the Muses): tradition alone does not make a poet.
4. The coal from the altar that purifies the prophet's lips (Isaiah 6.6–7): the passage makes poetry first and foremost the product of inspiration, but Milton also insists on his need to attain well-nigh universal knowledge and experience.
5. Milton was not willing to subscribe the oath affirming that the Book of Common Prayer and the present government of the church by bishops were according to the word of God; still less was he willing to subscribe the notorious "etcetera" oath required in 1640, that the minister would never seek to alter the government of the church "by archbishops, bishops, deacons, and archdeacons, etc."

hence may appear the right I have to meddle in these matters, as before the necessity and constraint appeared.

1642

Areopagitica   This passionate, trenchant defense of intellectual liberty has had a powerful influence on the evolving liberal conception of freedom of speech, press, and thought. Milton's specific target is the Press Ordinance of June 14, 1643, Parliament's attempt to crack down on the flood of pamphlets (including Milton's own controversial treatises on divorce) that poured forth both from legal and from underground presses as the Civil War raged. Like Tudor and Stuart censorship laws, Parliament's ordinance demanded that works be registered with the stationers and licensed by the censors before publication, and that both author and publisher be identified, on pain of fines and imprisonment for both. Milton vigorously protests the prepublication licensing of books, arguing that such measures have only been used by, and are only fit for, degenerate cultures. In the regenerate English nation, now "rousing herself like a strong man after sleep," men and women must be allowed to develop in virtue by participating in the clash and conflict of ideas. Truth will always overcome falsehood in reasoned debate. Thus, in opposition to the Presbyterians then in power, Milton defends widespread religious toleration, though with restrictions on Roman Catholicism, which, like most of his Protestant contemporaries, he viewed as a political threat and a tyranny binding individual conscience to the pope.

The title associates the tract with the speech of the Greek orator Isocrates to the Areopagus, the Council of the Wise in Athens. Learned readers would have recognized the irony of this. While Isocrates instructed the council to reform Athens by careful supervision of the private lives of citizens, Milton argues that only liberty and removal of censorship can advance reformation. This association explains the oratorical tone of the tract, which was, in fact, subtitled "A Speech." In this most literary of his tracts, Milton's style is elevated, eloquent, dense with poetic figures, and ranges in tone from satire and ridicule to urgent pleading and florid praise. His arguments and principles are often couched in striking images and phrases. One example is his passionate testimony to the potency and inestimable value of books: "As good almost kill a man as kill a good book . . ." Most memorable is his ringing credo that echoes down the centuries to protest every new tyranny: "Give me the liberty to know, to utter, and to argue freely according to conscience, above all liberties."

From Areopagitica

I deny not, but that it is of greatest concernment in the church and commonwealth, to have a vigilant eye how books demean[1] themselves as well as men; and thereafter to confine, imprison, and do sharpest justice on them as malefactors:[2] For books are not absolutely dead things, but do contain a potency of life in them to be as active as that soul was whose progeny they are; nay they do preserve as in a vial the purest efficacy and extraction of that living intellect that bred them. I know they are as lively, and as vigorously

---

1. Behave.
2. Milton allows that books may be called to account after publication, if they are proved to contain libels or other manifest crimes (he leaves this quite vague).

productive, as those fabulous dragon's teeth; and being sown up and down, may chance to spring up armed men.[3] And yet on the other hand unless wariness be used, as good almost kill a man as kill a good book; who kills a man kills a reasonable creature, God's image; but he who destroys a good book, kills reason itself, kills the image of God, as it were in the eye. Many a man lives a burden to the earth; but a good book is the precious lifeblood of a master spirit, embalmed and treasured up on purpose to a life beyond life. 'Tis true, no age can restore a life, whereof perhaps there is no great loss; and revolutions of ages do not oft recover the loss of a rejected truth, for the want of which whole nations fare the worse. We should be wary therefore what persecution we raise against the living labors of public men, how we spill that seasoned life of man preserved and stored up in books; since we see a kind of massacre, whereof the execution ends not in the slaying of an elemental life, but strikes at that ethereal and fifth essence,[4] the breath of reason itself, slays an immortality rather than a life. But lest I should be condemned of introducing licence, while I oppose licensing, I refuse not the pains to be so much historical, as will serve to show what hath been done by ancient and famous commonwealths, against this disorder, till the very time that this project of licensing crept out of the Inquisition,[5] was catched up by our prelates, and hath caught some of our presbyters.[6] * * *

* * * *Good and evil we know in the field of this world grow up together almost inseparably; and the knowledge of good is so involved and interwoven with the knowledge of evil, and in so many cunning resemblances hardly to be discerned, that those confused seeds which were imposed on Psyche as an incessant labor to cull out and sort asunder were not more intermixed.[7] It was from out the rind of one apple tasted, that the knowledge of good and evil, as two twins cleaving together, leaped forth into the world. And perhaps this is that doom which Adam fell into of knowing good and evil, that is to say of knowing good by evil.

As therefore the state of man now is, what wisdom can there be to choose, what continence to forbear, without the knowledge of evil? He that can apprehend and consider vice with all her baits and seeming pleasures, and yet abstain, and yet distinguish, and yet prefer that which is truly better, he is the true wayfaring[8] Christian. I cannot praise a fugitive and cloistered virtue, unexercised and unbreathed,[9] that never sallies out and sees her adversary, but slinks out of the race where that immortal garland is to be run for, not without dust and heat. Assuredly we bring not innocence into the world, we bring impurity much rather; that which purifies us is

3. After Cadmus killed a dragon on his way to founding Thebes, on a god's advice he sowed the dragon's teeth, which sprang up as an army, the belligerent forefathers of Sparta.
4. Quintessence, a pure, mystical substance above the four elements (fire, air, water, earth).
5. The Roman Catholic institution for suppressing heresy, especially strong in Spain.
6. The Presbyterians, powerful in the Parliament, were striving to establish theirs as the national church and suppress others. Milton, who began by supporting them in *The Reason of Church Government* and his other antiprelatical tracts (1641–42), now rejects them, in large part because they seek to supplant one repressive

church with another.
7. Angry at her son Cupid's love for Psyche, Venus set the girl many trials, among them to sort out a vast mound of mixed seeds, but the ants took pity on her and did the work.
8. The printed text reads "wayfaring," calling up the image of the Christian pilgrim; several presentation copies correct it (by hand) to "warfaring," calling up the image of the Christian warrior. Both suit the passage.
9. Not forced by exertion to breathe hard. "Immortal garland" (next line): the prize for the winner of a race, as figure for the "crown of life" promised to those who endure temptation (James 1.12).

trial, and trial is by what is contrary. That virtue therefore which is but a youngling in the contemplation of evil, and knows not the utmost that vice promises to her followers, and rejects it, is but a blank virtue, not a pure; her whiteness is but an excremental[1] whiteness; which was the reason why our sage and serious poet Spenser (whom I dare be known to think a better teacher than Scotus or Aquinas), describing true temperance under the person of Guyon, brings him in with his Palmer through the Cave of Mammon and the Bower of Earthly Bliss,[2] that he might see and know, and yet abstain.

Since therefore the knowledge and survey of vice is in this world so necessary to the constituting of human virtue, and the scanning of error to the confirmation of truth, how can we more safely, and with less danger, scout into the regions of sin and falsity than by reading all manner of tractates and hearing all manner of reason? And this is the benefit which may be had of books promiscuously read.

But of the harm that may result hence, three kinds are usually reckoned. First is feared the infection that may spread; but then all human learning and controversy in religious points must remove out of the world, yea, the Bible itself; for that ofttimes relates blasphemy not nicely,[3] it describes the carnal sense of wicked men not unelegantly, it brings in holiest men passionately murmuring against providence through all the arguments of Epicurus;[4] in other great disputes it answers dubiously and darkly to the common reader.[5]

*   *   *

To sequester out of the world into Atlantic and Utopian politics,[6] which never can be drawn into use, will not mend our condition, but to ordain wisely as in this world of evil, in the midst whereof God hath placed us unavoidably. . . . Impunity and remissness, for certain, are the bane of a commonwealth; but here the great art lies, to discern in what the law is to bid restraint and punishment, and in what things persuasion only is to work. If every action which is good or evil in man at ripe years were to be under pittance[7] and prescription and compulsion, what were virtue but a name, what praise could be then due to well-doing, what gramercy[8] to be sober, just, or continent?

Many there be that complain of divine providence for suffering Adam to transgress; foolish tongues! When God gave him reason, he gave him freedom to choose, for reason is but choosing; he had been else a mere artificial Adam, such an Adam as he is in the motions.[9] We ourselves esteem not of that obedience, or love, or gift, which is of force: God therefore left him

---

1. Exterior only.
2. John Duns Scotus and Thomas Aquinas, major Scholastic theologians. Guyon (following), the hero of Book 2 of the *Faerie Queene*, passes through the Cave of Mammon (symbolic of all worldly goods and honors) without his Palmer-guide, but that figure does accompany him through the Bower of Bliss.
3. Daintily.
4. Greek philosopher (342–270 B.C.E.) who taught that happiness is the greatest good, and that virtue should be practiced because it brings happiness; some of his followers equated happiness with sensual enjoyment. Milton may be thinking of the biblical book of Ecclesiastes.
5. Milton goes on to argue that a fool can find material for folly in the best books, and a wise person material for wisdom in the worst. Also, one cannot remove evil by censoring books without also censoring ballads, fiddlers, clothing, conversation, and all social life.
6. Milton alludes to More's *Utopia* and Bacon's *New Atlantis*.
7. Rationing.
8. Reward, thanks.
9. Puppet shows.

free, set before him a provoking object, ever almost in his eyes; herein consisted his merit, herein the right of his reward, the praise of his abstinence.[1] Wherefore did he create passions within us, pleasures round about us, but that these rightly tempered are the very ingredients of virtue? They are not skillful considerers of human things, who imagine to remove sin by removing the matter of sin; for, besides that it is a huge heap increasing under the very act of diminishing, though some part of it may for a time be withdrawn from some persons, it cannot from all, in such a universal thing as books are; and when this is done, yet the sin remains entire. Though ye take from a covetous man all his treasure, he has yet one jewel left: ye cannot bereave him of his covetousness. Banish all objects of lust, shut up all youth into the severest discipline that can be exercised in any hermitage, ye cannot make them chaste that came not thither so: such great care and wisdom is required to the right managing of this point.

Suppose we could expel sin by this means; look how much we thus expel of sin, so much we expel of virtue: for the matter of them both is the same; remove that, and ye remove them both alike. This justifies the high providence of God, who, though he commands us temperance, justice, continence, yet pours out before us, even to a profuseness, all desirable things, and gives us minds that can wander beyond all limit and satiety. Why should we then affect a rigor contrary to the manner of God and of nature, by abridging or scanting those means, which books freely permitted are, both to the trial of virtue and the exercise of truth? It would be better done to learn that the law must needs be frivolous which goes to restrain things uncertainly and yet equally working to good and to evil. And were I the chooser, a dram of well-doing should be preferred before many times as much the forcible hindrance of evil-doing. For God sure esteems the growth and completing of one virtuous person more than the restraint of ten vicious.

* * *

What advantage is it to be a man over it is to be a boy at school, if we have only scaped the ferula to come under the fescue of an *imprimatur*;[2] if serious and elaborate writings, as if they were no more than the theme of a grammarlad under his pedagogue, must not be uttered without the cursory eyes of a temporizing and extemporizing licenser?[3] He who is not trusted with his own actions, his drift not being known to be evil, and standing to the hazard of law and penalty, has no great argument to think himself reputed, in the commonwealth wherein he was born, for other than a fool or a foreigner.

When a man writes to the world, he summons up all his reason and deliberation to assist him; he searches, meditates, is industrious, and likely consults and confers with his judicious friends, after all which done he takes himself to be informed in what he writes, as well as any that writ before him. If in this the most consummate act of his fidelity and ripeness, no years, no industry, no former proof of his abilities can bring him to that state

---

1. Compare Milton's representation of Adam and Eve in Eden in *Paradise Lost*.
2. "Ferula": a schoolmaster's rod; "fescue": a pointer, "imprimatur": "it may be printed" (Latin), appears on the title page of books approved by the Roman Catholic censors. Milton's keen sense of the affront to scholars and scholarship, and to himself, is evident in this passage.
3. He temporizes in following the times, and acts by whim (extemporizes).

of maturity as not to be still mistrusted and suspected (unless he carry all his considerate diligence, all his midnight watchings, and expense of Palladian[4] oil, to the hasty view of an unleisured licenser, perhaps much his younger, perhaps far his inferior in judgment, perhaps one who never knew the labor of book-writing), and if he be not repulsed, or slighted, must appear in print like a puny[5] with his guardian, and his censor's hand on the back of his title to be his bail and surety that he is no idiot, or seducer; it cannot be but a dishonor and derogation to the author, to the book, to the privilege and dignity of learning.* * *

And how can a man teach with authority, which is the life of teaching, how can he be a doctor[6] in his book as he ought to be, or else had better be silent, whenas all he teaches, all he delivers, is but under the tuition, under the correction of his patriarchal[7] licenser to blot or alter what precisely accords not with the hide-bound humor which he calls his judgment? When every acute reader upon the first sight of a pedantic license, will be ready with these like words to ding the book a quoit's[8] distance from him: "I hate a pupil teacher, I endure not an instructor that comes to me under the wardship of an overseeing fist. I know nothing of the licenser, but that I have his own hand here for his arrogance; who shall warrant me his judgment?"

"The state, sir," replies the stationer,[9] but has a quick return: "The state shall be my governors, but not my critics; they may be mistaken in the choice of a licenser, as easily as this licenser may be mistaken in an author."

*　　*　　*

Well knows he who uses to consider, that our faith and knowledge thrives by exercise, as well as our limbs and complexion.[1] Truth is compared in Scripture to a streaming fountain;[2] if her waters flow not in a perpetual progression, they sicken into a muddy pool of conformity and tradition. A man may be a heretic in the truth; and if he believe things only because his pastor says so, or the Assembly[3] so determines, without knowing other reason, though his belief be true, yet the very truth he holds becomes his heresy.

*　　*　　*

Truth indeed came once into the world with her Divine Master, and was a perfect shape most glorious to look on: but when he ascended, and his apostles after him were laid asleep, then straight arose a wicked race of deceivers, who, as that story goes of the Egyptian Typhon with his conspirators, how they dealt with the good Osiris,[4] took the virgin Truth, hewed her lovely form into a thousand pieces, and scattered them to the four winds. From that time ever since, the sad friends of Truth, such as durst appear, imitating the careful search that Isis made for the mangled body of Osiris,

---

4. Pertaining to Pallas Athena, goddess of wisdom.
5. A minor, hence, young, unseasoned.
6. Teacher.
7. Taking on the role of a father; also, standing in for ecclesiastical patriarchs or prelates (like Archbishop Laud).
8. A flat disc of stone or metal, thrown as an exercise of strength or skill.
9. Printer, who was responsible for submitting

books before publication to the "licenser" (censor).
1. Constitution, the proper mingling of qualities in the body.
2. In Psalm 85.11.
3. The Westminster Assembly, convened by Parliament in 1643 to reorganize the English church along Presbyterian lines.
4. Plutarch tells, in "Isis and Osiris," of Typhon's scattering the fragments of his brother Osiris and of Isis's efforts to recover them.

went up and down gathering up limb by limb, still as they could find them. We have not yet found them all, Lords and Commons, nor ever shall do, till her Master's second coming; he shall bring together every joint and member, and shall mold them into an immortal feature of loveliness and perfection. Suffer not these licensing prohibitions to stand at every place of opportunity, forbidding and disturbing them that continue seeking, that continue to do our obsequies[5] to the torn body of our martyred saint.

We boast our light; but if we look not wisely on the sun itself, it smites us into darkness. Who can discern those planets that are oft combust,[6] and those stars of brightest magnitude that rise and set with the sun, until the opposite motion of their orbs bring them to such a place in the firmament where they may be seen evening or morning? The light which we have gained was given us, not to be ever staring on, but by it to discover onward things more remote from our knowledge. It is not the unfrocking of a priest, the unmitering of a bishop, and the removing him from off the Presbyterian shoulders, that will make us a happy nation. No, if other things as great in the church, and in the rule of life both economical and political, be not looked into and reformed, we have looked so long upon the blaze that Zwinglius and Calvin[7] hath beaconed up to us, that we are stark blind.

There be who perpetually complain of schisms and sects, and make it such a calamity that any man dissents from their maxims. 'Tis their own pride and ignorance which causes the disturbing, who neither will hear with meekness, nor can convince; yet all must be suppressed which is not found in their syntagma.[8] They are the troublers, they are the dividers of unity, who neglect and permit not others to unite those disseevered pieces which are yet wanting to the body of Truth. To be still searching what we know not by what we know, still closing up truth to truth as we find it (for all her body is homogeneal and proportional), this is the golden rule in theology as well as in arithmetic, and makes up the best harmony in a church; not the forced and outward union of cold and neutral and inwardly divided minds.

Lords and Commons of England, consider what nation it is whereof ye are, and whereof ye are the governors: a nation not slow and dull, but of a quick, ingenious, and piercing spirit, acute to invent, subtle and sinewy to discourse, not beneath the reach of any point the highest that human capacity can soar to. Therefore the studies of learning in her deepest sciences have been so ancient and so eminent among us, that writers of good antiquity and ablest judgment have been persuaded that even the school of Pythagoras and the Persian wisdom took beginning from the old philosophy of this island.[9] And that wise and civil Roman, Julius Agricola,[1] who governed once here for Caesar, preferred the natural wits of Britain before the labored studies of the French. Nor is it for nothing that the grave and

---

5. Funeral or commemorative rites.

6. Burned up; in astrology, so close to the sun as not to be visible.

7. Zwingli and Calvin, famous Protestant reformers, were mainstays of the Presbyterian cause. "Economical": domestic.

8. Compilations of beliefs, creeds.

9. Some speculation existed as to whether the Pythagorean notion of the transmigration of souls might trace back to the Druids, but the notion was mostly denied.

1. The "civil" (cultured, civilized) Agricola's opinion of the British intellect is found in Tacitus's *Life of Agricola*. Transylvania (following; now Romania) was an independent Protestant country whose citizens sometimes came to England to study. "Hercynian wilderness": Roman name for a forested and mountainous region of Germany.

frugal Transylvanian[2] sends out yearly from as far as the mountainous borders of Russia, and beyond the Hercynian wilderness, not their youth, but their staid men, to learn our language and our theologic arts.

Yet that which is above all this, the favor and the love of heaven we have great argument to think in a peculiar manner propitious and propending[3] towards us. Why else was this nation chosen before any other, that out of her, as out of Zion,[4] should be proclaimed and sounded forth the first tidings and trumpet of Reformation to all Europe? And had it not been the obstinate perverseness of our prelates against the divine and admirable spirit of Wycliffe to suppress him as a schismatic and innovator, perhaps neither the Bohemian Huss and Jerome,[5] no, nor the name of Luther or of Calvin, had been ever known: the glory of reforming all our neighbors had been completely ours. But now, as our obdurate clergy have with violence demeaned the matter, we are become hitherto the latest and the backwardest scholars of whom[6] God offered to have made us the teachers.

Now once again by all concurrence of signs, and by the general instinct of holy and devout men, as they daily and solemnly express their thoughts, God is decreeing to begin some new and great period in his church, even to the reforming of Reformation itself; what does he then but reveal himself to his servants, and as his manner is, first to his Englishmen? I say, as his manner is, first to us, though we mark not the method of his counsels, and are unworthy. Behold now this vast city: a city of refuge,[7] the mansion house of liberty, encompassed and surrounded with his protection; the shop of war hath not there more anvils and hammers waking, to fashion out the plates[8] and instruments of armed justice in defense of beleaguered truth, than there be pens and heads there, sitting by their studious lamps, musing, searching, revolving new notions and ideas wherewith to present, as with their homage and their fealty, the approaching Reformation: others as fast reading, trying all things, assenting to the force of reason and convincement.

What could a man require more from a nation so pliant and so prone to seek after knowledge? What wants there to such a towardly and pregnant[9] soil, but wise and faithful laborers, to make a knowing people, a nation of prophets,[1] of sages, and of worthies? We reckon more than five months yet to harvest; there need not be five weeks; had we but eyes to lift up, the fields are white already.[2] Where there is much desire to learn, there of necessity will be much arguing, much writing, many opinions; for opinion in good men is but knowledge in the making. Under these fantastic terrors of sect and schism we wrong the earnest and zealous thirst after knowledge and understanding which God hath stirred up in this city.

---

2. The Protestant princes of Transylvania encouraged their theologians and humanist scholars to study at English universities.
3. Inclining, favorable. "Argument": reason.
4. Mount Zion, in Jerusalem, the site of the Temple.
5. John Wycliffe was a 14th-century English reformer and translator of the Bible, whose books were forbidden by Pope Alexander V in 1409. John Huss spread Wycliffe's doctrines on the Continent; he was burned at the stake in 1415, as was (the next year) his follower Jerome of Prague.
6. Of those whom. "Demeaned": conducted, degraded.
7. Numbers 35 instructs the Jews to establish "cities of refuge" where those accused of crimes will be protected from "revengers of blood."
8. Plate mail, for armor.
9. Favorable and fertile.
1. In Numbers 11.29 Moses reproaches Joshua, who complained of the presence of other prophets: "Enviest thou for my sake? Would God that all the Lord's people were prophets."
2. Milton is paraphrasing Christ's words to his disciples (John 4.35): "Lift up your eyes, and look on the fields: for they are white already to harvest."

What some lament of, we rather should rejoice at, should rather praise this pious forwardness among men, to reassume the ill-deputed care of their religion into their own hands again. A little generous prudence, a little forbearance of one another, and some grain of charity might win all these diligences to join, and unite into one general and brotherly search after truth; could we but forgo this prelatical tradition of crowding free consciences and Christian liberties into canons and precepts of men. I doubt not, if some great and worthy stranger should come among us, wise to discern the mold and temper of a people, and how to govern it, observing the high hopes and aims, the diligent alacrity of our extended thoughts and reasonings in the pursuance of truth and freedom, but that he would cry out as Pyrrhus did, admiring the Roman docility and courage: "If such were my Epirots, I would not despair the greatest design that could be attempted, to make a church or kingdom happy."[3] Yet these are the men cried out against for schismatics and sectaries;[4] as if, while the temple of the Lord was building, some cutting, some squaring the marble, others hewing the cedars, there should be a sort of irrational men, who could not consider there must be many schisms and many dissections[5] made in the quarry and in the timber, ere the house of God can be built. And when every stone is laid artfully together, it cannot be united into a continuity, it can but be contiguous in this world; neither can every piece of the building be of one form; nay rather the perfection consists in this, that out of many moderate varieties and brotherly dissimilitudes that are not vastly disproportional, arises the goodly and the graceful symmetry that commends the whole pile and structure. Let us therefore be more considerate builders, more wise in spiritual architecture, when great reformation is expected. For now the time seems come, wherein Moses the great prophet may sit in heaven rejoicing to see that memorable and glorious wish of his fulfilled, when not only our seventy elders, but all the Lord's people, are become prophets.[6]

* * *

Methinks I see in my mind a noble and puissant nation rousing herself like a strong man after sleep, and shaking her invincible locks:[7] methinks I see her as an eagle mewing her mighty youth, and kindling her undazzled eyes at the full midday beam;[8] purging and unsealing her long-abused sight at the fountain itself of heavenly radiance; while the whole noise of timorous and flocking birds, with those also that love the twilight, flutter about, amazed at what she means, and in their envious gabble would prognosticate[9] a year of sects and schisms.

What should ye do then, should ye suppress all this flowery crop of knowledge and new light sprung up and yet springing daily in this city? Should ye

3. Though King Pyrrhus of Epirus beat the Roman armies at Heraclea in 280 B.C.E., he was much impressed by their discipline.
4. "Schismatics": those who cut up or divide the church; "sectaries": members of Protestant communions outside the national church.
5. Milton is playing on the literal meaning of "schism," cutting up or dividing.
6. Again alluding to Numbers 11.29, Milton equates the English assembly of clergy to set doctrine and church order (the Westminster Assembly) with the Jewish Sanhedrin of seventy elders.
7. The allusion is to Samson, whose uncut hair made him invincible, when he frustrated the first three attempts of Delilah and the Philistines to subdue him in sleep (Judges 16.6–14).
8. Eagles were thought to be able to look directly at the sun. "Mewing": molting, when the eagle sheds it feathers and thereby renews its coat.
9. Predict.

set an oligarchy of twenty engrossers[1] over it, to bring a famine upon our minds again, when we shall know nothing but what is measured to us by their bushel? Believe it, Lords and Commons, they who counsel ye to such a suppressing do as good as bid ye suppress yourselves; and I will soon show how.[2]

* * *

And now the time in special is by privilege to write and speak what may help to the further discussing of matters in agitation. The temple of Janus with his two controversial faces might now not unsignificantly be set open.[3] And though all the winds of doctrine were let loose to play upon the earth, so Truth be in the field, we do injuriously by licensing and prohibiting to misdoubt her strength. Let her and Falsehood grapple; who ever knew Truth put to the worse in a free and open encounter? Her[4] confuting is the best and surest suppressing. He who hears what praying there is for light and clearer knowledge to be sent down among us would think of other matters to be constituted beyond the discipline of Geneva framed and fabriced already to our hands.[5]

Yet when the new light which we beg for shines in upon us, there be who envy and oppose if it come not first in at their casements. What a collusion is this, whenas we are exhorted by the wise man to use diligence, to seek for wisdom as for hidden treasures early and late,[6] that another order shall enjoin us to know nothing but by statute. When a man hath been laboring the hardest labor in the deep mines of knowledge, hath furnished out his findings in all their equipage, drawn forth his reasons as it were a battle[7] ranged, scattered and defeated all objections in his way, calls out his adversary into the plain, offers him the advantage of wind and sun if he please, only that he may try the matter by dint of argument; for his opponents then to skulk, to lay ambushments, to keep a narrow bridge of licensing where the challenger should pass, though it be valor enough in soldiership, is but weakness and cowardice in the wars of Truth.

For who knows not that Truth is strong, next to the Almighty? She needs no policies nor stratagems nor licensings to make her victorious—those are the shifts and the defenses that error uses against her power. Give her but room, and do not bind her when she sleeps, for then she speaks not true, as the old Proteus[8] did, who spake oracles only when he was caught and bound, but then rather she turns herself into all shapes except her own, and perhaps tunes her voice according to the time, as Micaiah did before Ahab,[9] until she be adjured into her own likeness.

---

1. Engrossers, much hated in the English countryside, bought up great quantities of grain and held it for times of famine, selling it at high prices; Milton equates them with the twenty authorized printers, the stationers.
2. Milton goes on to argue that Parliament, by its own liberalizing reforms to date, has created the vigorous and inquiring minds it now seeks to suppress.
3. Janus, as god of beginnings and endings, had two faces looking in opposite directions; a door dedicated to him in Rome was kept open in time of war, closed in time of peace.
4. I.e., Falsehood's.

5. Milton was already disenchanted with Genevan "Discipline" (Presbyterian church government) and within a year or so would be writing "New *presbyter* is but old *priest*, writ large." "Fabriced": fabricated.
6. Solomon's advice in Proverbs 8.11.
7. Line of battle. Wind and sun (below) were significant advantages in a fight with swords.
8. The sea god who could change shape at will, to avoid capture (*Odyssey* 4).
9. Micaiah, a prophet of God, tried for a time to disguise an unpleasant prophecy from King Ahab but then spoke truth when adjured to do so (1 Kings 22.10–28).

Yet it is not impossible that she may have more shapes than one. What else is all that rank of things indifferent, wherein Truth may be on this side or on the other without being unlike herself? What but a vain shadow else is the abolition of those ordinances, that handwriting nailed to the cross?[1] What great purchase is this Christian liberty which Paul so often boasts of? His doctrine is that he who eats or eats not, regards a day or regards it not, may do either to the Lord.[2] How many other things might be tolerated in peace and left to conscience, had we but charity, and were it not the chief stronghold of our hypocrisy to be ever judging one another? I fear yet this iron yoke of outward conformity hath left a slavish print upon our necks; the ghost of a linen decency[3] yet haunts us. We stumble and are impatient at the least dividing of one visible congregation from another, though it be not in fundamentals; and through our forwardness to suppress and our backwardness to recover any enthralled piece of truth out of the grip of custom, we care not[4] to keep truth separated from truth, which is the fiercest rent and disunion of all. We do not see that while we still affect by all means a rigid and external formality, we may as soon fall again into a gross conforming stupidity, a stark and dead congealment of "wood and hay and stubble,"[5] forced and frozen together, which is more to the sudden degenerating of a church than many subdichotomies of petty schisms.

Not that I can think well of every light separation, or that all in a church is to be expected "gold and silver and precious stones." It is not possible for man to sever the wheat from the tares, the good fish from the other fry; that must be the angels' ministry at the end of mortal things.[6] Yet if all cannot be of one mind—as who looks they should be?—this doubtless is more wholesome, more prudent, and more Christian, that many be tolerated rather than all compelled. I mean not tolerated popery and open superstition, which, as it extirpates all religions and civil supremacies, so itself should be extirpate, provided first that all charitable and compassionate means be used to win and regain the weak and the misled; that also which is impious or evil absolutely, either against faith or manners,[7] no law can possibly permit that intends not to unlaw itself; but those neighboring differences or rather indifferences are what I speak of, whether in some point of doctrine or of discipline, which though they may be many yet need not interrupt "the unity of spirit," if we could but find among us the "bond of peace."[8]

In the meanwhile, if anyone would write and bring his helpful hand to the slow-moving reformation which we labor under, if truth have spoken to him before others, or but seemed at least to speak, who hath so bejesuited[9] us that we should trouble that man with asking license to do so worthy a deed? And not consider this, that if it come to prohibiting, there is not aught more likely to be prohibited than truth itself; whose first appearance to our

---

1. The locution, from Colossians 2.14, implies that the Crucifixion canceled all the rules and penalties of the Mosaic law. Paul's doctrine of Christian liberty (below) is expressed in Galatians 5 and elsewhere.
2. In the Lord's service.
3. White bands around the necks of clergymen are made emblems of formal piety.
4. Scruple not.

5. The contrast between "wood and hay and stubble" and "gold and silver and precious stones" (next paragraph) is from 1 Corinthians 3.12.
6. In Matthew 13.24–30, 36–43, Christ in a parable tells his disciples to let the wheat and tares (weeds) grow up together till harvest time.
7. Morals.
8. The quoted phrases are from Ephesians 4.3.
9. Imposed on us Jesuit ideas (of censorship).

eyes bleared and dimmed with prejudice and custom is more unsightly and unplausible than many errors, even as the person is of many a great man slight and contemptible to see to. And what do they tell us vainly of new opinions, when this very opinion of theirs, that none must be heard but whom they like, is the worst and newest opinion of all others, and is the chief cause why sects and schisms do so much abound, and true knowledge is kept at distance from us; besides yet a greater danger which is in it. For when God shakes a kingdom[1] with strong and healthful commotions to a general reforming, it is not untrue that many sectaries and false teachers are then busiest in seducing; but yet more true it is that God then raises to his own work men of rare abilities and more than common industry, not only to look back and revise what hath been taught heretofore, but to gain further and go on some new enlightened steps in the discovery of truth.

1644

Sonnets   Milton wrote twenty-four sonnets between 1630 and 1658. Five in Italian constitute a mini-Petrarchan sequence on a perhaps imaginary Italian lady. The rest, in English, are individual poems on a wide variety of topics and occasions, though not on the usual sonnet topics (love, as in the sequences of Sidney, Spenser, and Shakespeare, or religious devotion, as in that of Donne). Milton writes sometimes about personal crises (his blindness, the death of his wife), sometimes about political issues or personages (Cromwell, the persecuting Parliament), sometimes about friends and friendship (Cyriack Skinner, Lady Margaret Ley), sometimes about historical events (a threatened royalist attack on London, the massacre of Protestants in Piedmont). His tone ranges from Jonsonian urbanity to prophetic denunciation. The form of the sonnets is Petrarchan (see "Poetic Forms and Literary Terminology," in the appendices to this volume), but in the later sonnets especially (e.g., the Blindness and Piedmont sonnets) the sense runs on from line to line, overriding the expected end-stopped lines and the octave/sestet shift. There is some precedent for this in the Italian sonneteer Giovanni della Casa, but not for the powerful tension Milton creates as meaning and emotion strive within and against the formal metrics of the Petrarchan sonnet. Milton's new ways with the sonnet had a profound and acknowledged influence on the Romantic poets, especially Wordsworth and Shelley.

SONNETS

How Soon Hath Time

> How soon hath Time, the subtle thief of youth,
>   Stol'n on his wing my three and twentieth year!
>   My hasting days fly on with full career,
>   But my late spring no bud or blossom shew'th.
> 5 Perhaps my semblance might deceive[1] the truth,

---

1. Milton alludes to Haggai 2.7: "I will shake all nations, and the desire of all nations shall come, and I will fill this house with glory, saith the Lord of hosts."

1. Misrepresent. "Semblance": appearance.

That I to manhood am arrived so near,
And inward ripeness doth much less appear,
That some more timely-happy spirits endu'th.°   *endows*
Yet be it less or more, or soon or slow,
10   It shall be still in strictest measure even[2]
To that same lot, however mean or high,
Toward which Time leads me, and the will of Heaven;
All is, if I have grace to use it so,
As ever in my great Taskmaster's eye.[3]

1632?   1645

On the New Forcers of Conscience under the Long Parliament[1]

Because you have thrown off your prelate lord,[2]
And with stiff vows renounced his liturgy,
To seize the widowed whore Plurality[3]
From them whose sin ye envied, not abhorred,
5   Dare ye for this adjure° the civil sword[4]   *invoke*
To force our consciences that Christ set free,
And ride us with a classic hierarchy[5]
Taught ye by mere A. S. and Rutherford?[6]
Men whose life, learning, faith, and pure intent
10   Would have been held in high esteem with Paul
Must now be named and printed heretics
By shallow Edwards and Scotch what-d'ye-call:[7]
But we do hope to find out all your tricks,
Your plots and packing° worse than those of Trent,[8]   *fraudulent*
15   That so the Parliament[9]   *dealings*

2. Equal, adequate. "It": Milton's inner growth. "Even / To that same lot": conformed to my appointed destiny.
3. The final lines allow for various readings. "Taskmaster" identifies God with the parable (Matthew 20.1–16) in which a vineyard keeper takes on workers throughout the day, paying the same wages to those hired at the first and at the eleventh hour.
1. The sonnet targets the Presbyterians, whom Milton in *The Reason of Church Government* (pp. 1924–29) and other antiprelatical tracts of 1641–42 had supported against the bishops. Now that they have overthrown the bishops and dominate the Long Parliament, they seek to become the national church, repressing all others. This *sonetto cauduto*, or "tailed sonnet" (an Italian form) has the usual fourteen lines followed by two "tails" of three lines each.
2. Bishops and the ecclesiastical church structure.
3. The practice of holding several benefices at once; she is a "widowed whore" because her earlier lovers, the Anglican clergy, can no longer possess her.

4. State authority.
5. The Presbyterian church order comprised of synods and classes as governing boards and disciplinary courts.
6. Adam Stuart and Samuel Rutherford, Scottish Presbyterian pamphleteers who urged the establishment of an English national Presbyterian church on the Scottish model.
7. Thomas Edwards analyzed hundreds of so-called heresies in a book picturesquely titled *Gangraena* (1645, 1646). It even identifies Milton as the founder of a sect of Divorcers, promoting "divorce at pleasure." "Scotch what-d'ye-call" may refer to another Scots cleric, Robert Baillie, or may simply be a sneer at the unpronounceability of Scottish names.
8. The Council of Trent, held by the Roman Church to deal with the Protestant Reformation, was notorious as a scene of political jockeying.
9. In the previous few months Independents and more secular-minded republicans had gained some strength in the Parliament, so Milton could hope they might weigh in against Presbyterian repression.

> May with their wholesome and preventive shears
> Clip your phylacteries,[1] though balk your ears,[2]
>> And succor our just fears
> When they shall read this clearly in your charge:
> 20 New *presbyter* is but old *priest* writ large.[3]

ca. 1646   1673

To the Lord General Cromwell, May 1652[1]

> Cromwell, our chief of men, who through a cloud
> Not of war only, but detractions[2] rude,
> Guided by faith and matchless fortitude
> To peace and truth[3] thy glorious way hast ploughed,
> 5 And on the neck of crownèd Fortune proud
> Hast reared God's trophies,[4] and his work pursued,
> While Darwen stream with blood of Scots imbrued[5]
> And Dunbar field resounds thy praises loud,
> And Worcester's laureate wreath;[6] yet much remains
> 10 To conquer still; peace hath her victories
> No less renowned than war; new foes arise,
> Threatening to bind our souls with secular chains:[7]
> Help us to save free conscience from the paw
> Of hireling wolves[8] whose gospel is their maw.°   *belly*

1652   1694

---

1. Little scrolls containing texts from the Penta-teuch, worn on the forehead and arm by obser-vant Jews; Milton takes them as a symbol of self-righteous ostentation.

2. "Balk": spare. Mutilation by cutting off the ears was a punishment formerly suffered by sev-eral Presbyterian leaders, as Milton hereby reminds them. Milton changed the rather cruel manuscript version of this line—"Crop ye as close as marginal P——'s ears"—alluding to the ultraprolific pamphleteer William Prynne, who stuffed his margins with citations, and who had his ears cropped twice.

3. "Priest" is, etymologically, a contracted form of "Presbyter."

1. The sonnet appeals to Cromwell, a longtime supporter of religious toleration but also of some kind of loosely defined national church, to oppose recent proposals by Independents to set up a national church with a paid clergy and some limits to toleration. This is the only Milton son-net to end with an epigrammatic couplet. It could not be published in the 1673 *Poems* of Milton because the subject would have offended the restored Stuart monarchy.

2. Cromwell was a target of slander and vitu-peration from royalists and from extreme radi-cals.

3. The words "Truth and Peace" were on a coin issued by Parliament to honor Cromwell's victo-ries over the Scots at Preston (1648), Dunbar (1650), and Worcester (1651).

4. Alluding to the ancient Greek custom of erecting trophies of victory on the battlefield.

5. Stained with blood. The river Darwen runs through Preston, site of a major victory by Crom-well over the Scots.

6. Cromwell described his victory at Worcester as his "crowning mercy."

7. Alluding to the new proposals that Parlia-ment, the secular power, repress heresies and blasphemy.

8. Milton fiercely opposed a paid clergy, believ-ing they should support themselves or be sup-ported by their congregations.

When I Consider How My Light Is Spent[1]

When I consider how my light is spent,°   *extinguished*
Ere half my days,[2] in this dark world and wide,
And that one talent which is death to hide[3]
Lodged with me useless, though my soul more bent
5   To serve therewith my Maker, and present
     My true account, lest he returning chide;
     "Doth God exact day-labor, light denied?"[4]
I fondly° ask; but Patience to prevent°   *foolishly / forestall*
That murmur, soon replies, "God doth not need
10   Either man's work or his own gifts; who best
     Bear his mild yoke, they serve him best. His state°   *splendor*
Is kingly.[5] Thousands at his bidding speed
And post o'er land and ocean without rest:
They also serve who only stand and wait."

1652?   1673

On the Late Massacre in Piedmont[1]

Avenge,[2] O Lord, thy slaughtered saints, whose bones
Lie scattered on the Alpine mountains cold;
Even them who kept thy truth so pure of old
When all our fathers worshiped stocks and stones,[3]
5   Forget not: in thy book[4] record their groans
Who were thy sheep and in their ancient fold
Slain by the bloody Piemontese that rolled

---

1. Apparently written soon after Milton lost his sight entirely in 1652.
2. Milton was forty-three in 1652; he is obviously not thinking of the biblical lifespan of seventy, but perhaps of that of his father, who died at eighty-four.
3. In the parable of the talents (Matthew 25.14–30), a crucial text for Puritans, the servants who put their master's money ("talents") to earn interest for him were praised, while the servant who buried the single talent he was given was deprived of it and cast into outer darkness. Milton puns on "literary talent." "Useless" (line 4) carries a pun on "usury," the return expected by the Master.
4. Milton alludes here to the parable of the vineyard keeper (see "How Soon Hath Time," note 3), and also to John 9.4, spoken by Jesus before curing a blind man: "I must work the works of him that sent me, while it is day: the night cometh, when no man can work."
5. The changed metaphor for God—from master who needs to profit from his workers to king—allows the inference that those who "stand and wait" may be placed nearest the throne.
1. The Waldensians (or Vaudois) were a proto-Protestant sect dating to the 12th century who lived in the valleys of northern Italy (the Pied-

mont) and southern France; Protestants considered them a remnant retaining apostolic purity, free of Catholic superstitions and graven images ("stocks and stones," line 4). The treaty that had allowed them freedom of worship was bypassed in 1655 when the armies of the Catholic duke of Savoy conducted a massacre, razing villages, committing unspeakable atrocities, and hurling women and children from the mountaintops. Protestant Europe was outraged, and in his capacity as Cromwell's Latin secretary Milton translated and wrote several letters about the episode. The sonnet incorporates details from such letters and the contemporary newsbooks. Here Milton transforms the sonnet into a prophetic denunciation.
2. Cf. Revelation 6.9–10: "the souls of them that were slain for the word of God . . . cried with a loud voice, saying, 'How long, O Lord, holy and true, dost thou not judge and avenge our blood . . . ?'"
3. Pagan gods of wood and stone, but with allusion to Roman Catholic "idols."
4. Cf. Revelation 20.12: "the dead were judged out of those things which were written in the books, according to their works." "Sheep" (next line) echoes Romans 8.36: "we are accounted as sheep for the slaughter."

Mother with infant down the rocks. Their moans
The vales redoubled to the hills, and they
10 To heaven. Their martyred blood and ashes sow
O'er all th' Italian fields, where still doth sway
The triple tyrant:[5] that from these may grow
A hundredfold, who having learnt thy way
Early may fly the Babylonian woe.[6]

1655   1673

Methought I Saw My Late Espousèd Saint[1]

Methought I saw my late espousèd saint
Brought to me like Alcestis[2] from the grave,
Whom Jove's great son to her glad husband gave,
Rescued from death by force though pale and faint.
5 Mine, as whom[3] washed from spot of childbed taint,
Purification in the old law did save,[4]
And such, as yet once more I trust to have
Full sight of her in heaven without restraint,
Came vested all in white, pure as her mind.
10 Her face was veiled, yet to my fancied sight[5]
Love, sweetness, goodness, in her person shined
So clear, as in no face with more delight.
But O, as to embrace me she inclined,
I waked, she fled, and day brought back my night.

1658   1673

Paradise Lost   The setting of Milton's great epic encompasses Heaven, Hell, primordial Chaos, and the planet earth. It features battles among immortal spirits, voyages through space, and lakes of fire. Yet its protagonists are a married couple living in a garden, and its climax consists in the eating of a piece of fruit. *Paradise Lost* is ultimately about the human condition, the Fall that caused "all our woe," and the promise and means of restoration. It is also about knowing and choosing, about free will. In the opening passages of Books 1, 3, 7, and 9, Milton highlights

5. The pope, wearing his tiara with three crowns. The passage alludes to Tertullian's maxim that "the blood of the martyrs is the seed of the church"; also to the parable of the sower (Matthew 13.3), some of whose seed brought forth fruit "an hundredfold" (see next line); and also to Cadmus, who sowed dragon's teeth that sprang forth armed men.

6. Protestants often identified the Roman Church with the whore of Babylon (Revelation 17–18).

1. There is some debate as to whether this poem refers to Milton's first wife, Mary Powell, who died in May 1652, three days after giving birth to her third daughter, or his second wife, Katherine Woodcock, who died in February 1658, after giving birth (in October 1657) to a daughter. The

text can support either, but the latter seems more likely. The sonnet is couched as a dream vision.

2. In Euripides' *Alcestis*, Alcestis, wife of Admetus, is rescued from the underworld by Hercules ("Jove's great son," next line) and restored, veiled, to Admetus; he is overjoyed when he lifts the veil, but she must remain silent until she is ritually cleansed.

3. As one whom.

4. The Mosaic Law (Leviticus 12.2–8) prescribed periods for the purification of women after childbirth (eighty days for a daughter).

5. She is veiled like Alcestis, and Milton's sight of her is only "fancied"; he never saw the face of his second wife, Katherine, because of his blindness.

the choices and difficulties he faced in creating his poem. His central characters—Satan, Beelzebub, Abdiel, Adam, and Eve—are confronted with hard choices under the pressure of powerful desires and sometimes devious temptations. Milton's readers, too, are continually challenged to choose and to reconsider their most basic assumptions about freedom, heroism, work, pleasure, language, nature, and love. The great themes of *Paradise Lost* are intimately linked to the political questions at stake in the English Revolution and the Restoration, but the connection is by no means simple or straightforward. This is a poem in which Satan leads a revolution against an absolute monarch and in which questions of tyranny, servitude, and liberty are debated in a parliament in Hell. Milton's readers are hereby challenged to rethink these topics and, like Abdiel debating with Satan in Books 5 and 6, to make crucial distinctions between God as monarch and earthly kings.

In Milton's time, the conventions of epic poetry followed a familiar recipe. The action was to begin *in medias res* (in the middle of things), following the poet's statement of his theme and invocation of his Muse. The reader could expect grand battles and love affairs, supernatural intervention, a descent into the underworld, catalogues of warriors, and epic similes. Milton had absorbed the epic tradition in its entirety, and his poem abounds with echoes of Homer and Virgil, the fifteenth-century Italians Tasso and Ariosto, and the English Spenser. But in *Paradise Lost* he at once heightens epic conventions and values and utterly transforms them. This is the epic to end all epics. Milton gives us the first and greatest of all wars (between God and Satan) and the first and greatest of love affairs (between Adam and Eve). His theme is the destiny of the entire human race, caught up in the temptation and Fall of our first "grand parents."

Milton challenges his readers in *Paradise Lost*, at once fulfilling and defying all of our expectations. Nothing in the epic tradition or in biblical interpretation can prepare us for the Satan who hurtles into view in Book 1, with his awesome energy and defiance, incredible fortitude, and, above all, magnificent rhetoric. For some readers, including Blake and Shelley, Satan is the true hero of the poem. But Milton is engaged in a radical reevaluation of epic values, and Satan's version of heroism must be contrasted with those of the loyal Abdiel and the Son of God. Moreover, the poem's truly epic action takes place not on the battlefield but in the moral and domestic arena. Milton's Adam and Eve are not conventional epic heroes, but neither are they the conventional Adam and Eve. Their state of innocence is not childlike, tranquil, and free of sexual desire. Instead, the first couple enjoy sex, experience tension and passion, make mistakes of judgment, and grow in knowledge. Their task is to prune what is unruly in their own natures as they prune the vegetation in their garden, for both have the capacity to grow wild. Their relationship exhibits gender hierarchy, but Milton's early readers may have been surprised by the fullness and complexity of Eve's character and the centrality of her role, not only in the Fall but in the promised restoration.

We expect in epics a grand style, and Milton's style engulfs us from the outset with its energy and power, as those rushing, enjambed, blank-verse lines propel us along with only a few pauses for line endings or grammar (there is only one full stop in the first twenty-six lines). The elevated diction and complex syntax, the sonorities and patternings make a magnificent music. But that music is an entire orchestra of tones, including the high political rhetoric of Satan in Books 1 and 2, the evocative sensuousness of the descriptions of Eden, the delicacy of Eve's love lyric to Adam in Book 4, the relatively plain speech of God in Book 3, and the speech rhythms of Adam and Eve's marital quarrel in Book 9. This majestic achievement depends on the poet's rejection of heroic couplets, the norm for epic and tragedy in the Restoration, vigorously defended by Dryden but denounced by Milton in his note on "The Verse." The choice of verse form was, like so many other things in Milton's life, in part a question of politics. Milton's terms associate the "troublesome and modern bondage of rhyming" with Restoration monarchy and the repression of dissidents and present his use of unrhymed blank verse as a recovery of "ancient liberty."

The first edition (1667) presented *Paradise Lost* in ten books; the second (1674) recast it into twelve books, after the Virgilian model, splitting the original Books 7 and 10. We present the twelve-book epic in its entirety, to allow readers to experience the impact of the whole.

PARADISE LOST

SECOND EDITION (1674)

The Verse

The measure is English heroic verse without rhyme, as that of Homer in Greek and of Virgil in Latin; rhyme being no necessary adjunct or true ornament of poem or good verse, in longer works especially, but the invention of a barbarous age, to set off wretched matter[1] and lame meter; graced indeed since by the use of some famous modern poets,[2] carried away by custom, but much to their own vexation, hindrance, and constraint to express many things otherwise, and for the most part worse than else they would have expressed them. Not without cause therefore some both Italian[3] and Spanish poets of prime note have rejected rhyme both in longer and shorter works, as have also long since our best English tragedies, as a thing of itself, to all judicious ears, trivial and of no true musical delight; which consists only in apt numbers,[4] fit quantity of syllables, and the sense variously drawn out from one verse into another, not in the jingling sound of like endings, a fault avoided by the learned ancients both in poetry and all good oratory. This neglect then of rhyme so little is to be taken for a defect, though it may seem so perhaps to vulgar readers, that it rather is to be esteemed an example set, the first in English, of ancient liberty recovered to heroic poem from the troublesome and modern bondage of rhyming.

Book 1

The Argument[1]

This first book proposes, first in brief, the whole subject, man's disobedience, and the loss thereupon of Paradise wherein he was placed: then touches the prime cause of his fall, the Serpent, or rather Satan in the Serpent; who revolting from God, and drawing to his side many legions of angels, was by the command of God driven out of Heaven with all his crew

---

1. Perhaps the bawdy content of the Latin songs composed by goliardic poets of the Middle Ages; they learned rhyme from medieval hymns.
2. Notably, Dryden. See his *Essay of Dramatic Poesy*.
3. Trissino and Tasso.
4. Appropriate rhythm.

1. *Paradise Lost* appeared originally without any sort of prose aid to the reader, but the printer asked Milton for some "Arguments," or summary explanations of the action in the various books, and these were prefixed to later issues of the poem. We reprint the "Argument" for the first book.

into the great deep. Which action passed over, the poem hastes into the midst of things,[2] presenting Satan with his angels now fallen into Hell, described here, not in the center[3] (for Heaven and Earth may be supposed as yet not made, certainly not yet accursed) but in a place of utter darkness, fitliest called Chaos: here Satan with his angels lying on the burning lake, thunderstruck and astonished, after a certain space recovers, as from confusion, calls up him who next in order and dignity lay by him; they confer of their miserable fall. Satan awakens all his legions, who lay till then in the same manner confounded; they rise, their numbers, array of battle, their chief leaders named, according to the idols known afterwards in Canaan and the countries adjoining. To these Satan directs his speech, comforts them with hope yet of regaining Heaven, but tells them lastly of a new world and new kind of creature to be created, according to an ancient prophecy or report in Heaven; for that angels were long before this visible creation, was the opinion of many ancient Fathers.[4] To find out the truth of this prophecy, and what to determine[5] thereon he refers to a full council. What his associates thence attempt. Pandemonium the palace of Satan rises, suddenly built out of the deep: the infernal peers there sit in council.

Of man's first disobedience, and the fruit[1]
Of that forbidden tree, whose mortal° taste   *deadly*
Brought death into the world, and all our woe,
With loss of Eden, till one greater Man[2]
5   Restore us, and regain the blissful seat,
Sing Heav'nly Muse,[3] that on the secret top
Of Oreb, or of Sinai, didst inspire
That shepherd, who first taught the chosen seed,
In the beginning how the heav'ns and earth
10 Rose out of Chaos: or if Sion hill[4]
Delight thee more, and Siloa's brook that flowed
Fast by the oracle of God; I thence
Invoke thy aid to my advent'rous song,
That with no middle flight intends to soar
15 Above th' Aonian mount,[5] while it pursues
Things unattempted yet in prose or rhyme.[6]
And chiefly thou O Spirit,[7] that dost prefer
Before all temples th' upright heart and pure,
Instruct me, for thou know'st; thou from the first
20 Wast present, and with mighty wings outspread

---

2. According to Horace, the epic poet should begin, "in medias res."
3. I.e., of the earth.
4. Church Fathers, the Christian writers of the first centuries.
5. I.e., what action to take.
1. Eve's apple, and all the consequences of eating it. This first proem (lines 1–26) combines the epic statement of theme and invocation.
2. Christ, the second Adam.
3. In Greek mythology, Urania, Muse of astronomy; here, however, by the references to Oreb (Horeb) and Sinai (following), identified with the Muse who inspired Moses ("that shepherd")

to write Genesis and the other four books of the Pentateuch for the instruction of the Jews ("the chosen seed").
4. Mount Zion: the site of Solomon's Temple. "Siloa's brook" (next line): a spring near the Temple where Christ cured a blind man.
5. Helicon, home of the classical Muses. Milton will attempt to surpass Homer and Virgil.
6. Paradoxically, Milton vaunts his originality in a translated line from Ariosto's *Orlando Furioso* 1.2. The allusion also challenges the romantic epic in Ariosto's tradition.
7. Here identified with God's creating power.

Dove-like sat'st brooding[8] on the vast abyss
And mad'st it pregnant: what in me is dark
Illumine, what is low raise and support;
That to the height of this great argument°   *subject, theme*
25 I may assert Eternal Providence,
And justify° the ways of God to men.   *show the justice of*
    Say first, for Heav'n hides nothing from thy view
Nor the deep tract of Hell, say first what cause[9]
Moved our grand parents in that happy state,
30 Favored of Heav'n so highly, to fall off
From their Creator, and transgress his will
For° one restraint, lords of the world besides?°   *because of / otherwise*
Who first seduced them to that foul revolt?
Th' infernal Serpent; he it was, whose guile
35 Stirred up with envy and revenge, deceived
The mother of mankind, what time° his pride   *when*
Had cast him out from Heav'n, with all his host
Of rebel angels, by whose aid aspiring
To set himself in glory above his peers,°   *equals*
40 He trusted to have equaled the Most High,
If he opposed; and with ambitious aim
Against the throne and monarchy of God
Raised impious war in Heav'n and battle proud
With vain attempt. Him the Almighty Power
45 Hurled headlong flaming from th' ethereal sky
With hideous ruin and combustion down
To bottomless perdition, there to dwell
In adamantine[1] chains and penal fire,
Who durst defy th' Omnipotent to arms.
50 Nine times the space[2] that measures day and night
To mortal men, he with his horrid crew
Lay vanquished, rolling in the fiery gulf
Confounded though immortal: but his doom
Reserved him to more wrath; for now the thought
55 Both of lost happiness and lasting pain
Torments him; round he throws his baleful° eyes   *malignant*
That witnessed huge affliction and dismay
Mixed with obdúrate pride and steadfast hate:
At once as far as angels' ken° he views   *range of sight*
60 The dismal situation waste and wild,
A dungeon horrible, on all sides round
As one great furnace flamed, yet from those flames
No light, but rather darkness visible
Served only to discover sights of woe,
65 Regions of sorrow, doleful shades, where peace

---

8. A composite of phrases and ideas from Genesis 1.2 ("And the earth was without form, and void, and darkness was upon the face of the deep. And the Spirit of God moved upon the face of the waters"). Only a small number of Milton's many allusions to the Bible (in many versions) can be indicated in the notes. Milton's brooding dove image comes from the Latin (Tremellius) Bible version, *incubabat*, "incubated."
9. An opening question like this is an epic convention.
1. A mythical substance of great hardness.
2. Extent of time.

And rest can never dwell, hope never comes
That comes to all;[3] but torture without end
Still urges,° and a fiery deluge, fed   *always provokes*
With ever-burning sulphur unconsumed:
70 Such place Eternal Justice had prepared
For those rebellious, here their prison ordained
In utter darkness, and their portion set
As far removed from God and light of Heav'n
As from the center thrice to th' utmost pole.[4]
75 O how unlike the place from whence they fell!
There the companions of his fall, o'erwhelmed
With floods and whirlwinds of tempestuous fire,
He soon discerns, and welt'ring° by his side   *rolling in the waves*
One next himself in power, and next in crime,
80 Long after known in Palestine, and named
Beëlzebub.[5] To whom th' Arch-Enemy,
And thence in Heav'n called Satan,[6] with bold words
Breaking the horrid silence thus began.
    "If thou beest he; but O how fall'n![7] how changed
85 From him, who in the happy realms of light
Clothed with transcendent brightness didst outshine
Myriads though bright: if he whom mutual league,
United thoughts and counsels, equal hope
And hazard in the glorious enterprise,
90 Joined with me once, now misery hath joined
In equal ruin: into what pit thou seest
From what height fall'n, so much the stronger proved
He with his thunder:° and till then who knew   *thunderbolt*
The force of those dire arms? Yet not for those,
95 Nor what the potent victor in his rage
Can else inflict, do I repent or change,
Though changed in outward luster, that fixed mind
And high disdain, from sense of injured merit,
That with the mightiest raised me to contend,
100 And to the fierce contention brought along
Innumerable force of spirits armed
That durst dislike his reign, and me preferring,
His utmost power with adverse power opposed
In dubious° battle on the plains of Heav'n,   *of uncertain outcome*
105 And shook his throne. What though the field be lost?
All is not lost; the unconquerable will,
And study° of revenge, immortal hate,   *intense consideration*

---

3. The phrase alludes to Dante ("All hope abandon, ye who enter here").
4. Milton makes use of various images of the cosmos in *Paradise Lost:* (1) the earth is the center of the (Ptolemaic) cosmos of ten concentric spheres; (2) the earth and the whole cosmos are an appendage hanging from Heaven by a golden chain; (3) the cosmos seems Copernican from the angels' perspective (see Book 8). Here, the fall from Heaven to Hell is described as thrice as far as the distance from the center (earth) to the outermost sphere.

5. A Phoenician deity, or Baal (the name means "Lord of Flies"). He is called the prince of devils in Matthew 12.24. As with the other fallen angels, his angelic name has been obliterated, and he is now called by the name he will bear as a pagan deity. That literary strategy evokes all the evil associations attaching to those names in human history.
6. In Hebrew the name means "adversary."
7. Alludes to Isaiah 14.12: "How art thou fallen from heaven, O Lucifer, Son of the morning."

And courage never to submit or yield:
And what is else not to be overcome?[8]
110 That glory never shall his wrath or might
Extort from me. To bow and sue for grace
With suppliant knee, and deify his power
Who from the terror of this arm so late
Doubted° his empire, that were low indeed,   *feared for*
115 That were an ignominy and shame beneath
This downfall; since by fate the strength of gods[9]
And this empyreal substance cannot fail,°   *cease to exist*
Since through experience of this great event
In arms not worse, in foresight much advanced,
120 We may with more successful hope resolve
To wage by force or guile eternal war
Irreconcilable, to our grand foe,
Who now triúmphs, and in th' excess of joy
Sole reigning holds the tyranny of Heav'n."
125   So spake th' apostate angel, though in pain,
Vaunting aloud, but racked with deep despair:
And him thus answered soon his bold compeer.°   *comrade*
   "O Prince, O Chief of many thronéd Powers,
That led th' embattled Seraphim[1] to war
130 Under thy conduct, and in dreadful deeds
Fearless, endangered Heav'ns perpetual King;
And put to proof his high supremacy,
Whether upheld by strength, or chance, or fate;
Too well I see and rue the dire event,°   *outcome*
135 That with sad overthrow and foul defeat
Hath lost us Heav'n, and all this mighty host
In horrible destruction laid thus low,
As far as gods and heav'nly essences
Can perish: for the mind and spirit remains
140 Invincible, and vigor soon returns,
Though all our glory extinct, and happy state
Here swallowed up in endless misery.
But what if he our conqueror (whom I now
Of force° believe almighty, since no less   *necessarily*
145 Than such could have o'erpow'red such force as ours)
Have left us this our spirit and strength entire
Strongly to suffer and support our pains,
That we may so suffice° his vengeful ire,   *satisfy*
Or do him mightier service as his thralls
150 By right of war, whate'er his business be
Here in the heart of Hell to work in fire,
Or do his errands in the gloomy deep;
What can it then avail though yet we feel

---

8. I.e., what else does it mean not to be overcome?
9. A term commonly used in the poem for angels.
But to Satan and his followers it means more, as
Satan claims the position of a god, subject to fate
but nothing else. Their substance is "empyreal"
(next line), of the empyrean.

1. According to tradition, there were nine orders
of angels, arranged hierarchically—seraphim,
cherubim, thrones, dominions, virtues, powers,
principalities, archangels, and angels. The poem
makes use of some of these titles but does not
keep this hierarchy.

Strength undiminished, or eternal being
155 To undergo eternal punishment?"
Whereto with speedy words th' Arch-Fiend replied.
"Fall'n Cherub, to be weak is miserable
Doing or suffering: but of this be sure,
To do aught° good never will be our task,   *anything*
160 But ever to do ill our sole delight,
As being the contrary to his high will
Whom we resist. If then his providence
Out of our evil seek to bring forth good,
Our labor must be to pervert that end,
165 And out of good still to find means of evil;
Which ofttimes may succeed, so as perhaps
Shall grieve him, if I fail° not, and disturb   *err*
His inmost counsels from their destined aim.
But see the angry victor hath recalled
170 His ministers of vengeance and pursuit
Back to the gates of Heav'n: the sulphurous hail
Shot after us in storm, o'erblown hath laid°   *calmed*
The fiery surge, that from the precipice
Of Heav'n received us falling, and the thunder,
175 Winged with red lightning and impetuous rage,
Perhaps hath spent his shafts, and ceases now
To bellow through the vast and boundless deep.
Let us not slip° th' occasion, whether scorn,   *let slip*
Or satiate fury yield it from our foe.
180 Seest thou yon dreary plain, forlorn and wild,
The seat of desolation, void of light,
Save what the glimmering of these livid° flames   *bluish*
Casts pale and dreadful? Thither let us tend
From off the tossing of these fiery waves,
185 There rest, if any rest can harbor there,
And reassembling our afflicted powers,°   *armies*
Consult how we may henceforth most offend°   *harm, vex*
Our enemy, our own loss how repair,
How overcome this dire calamity,
190 What reinforcement we may gain from hope,
If not what resolution from despair."[2]
Thus Satan talking to his nearest mate
With head uplift above the wave, and eyes
That sparkling blazed, his other parts besides
195 Prone on the flood, extended long and large
Lay floating many a rood,[3] in bulk as huge
As whom° the fables name of monstrous size,   *as those whom*
Titanian, or Earth-born, that warred on Jove,
Briareos or Typhon,[4] whom the den

---

2. Five of the last nine lines of Satan's speech rhyme.
3. An old unit of measure, between six and eight yards.
4. Both the Titans, led by Briareos (said to have had a hundred hands), and the earth-born

Giants, represented by Typhon (who lived in Cilicea near Tarsus and was said to have had a hundred heads), fought with Jove. They were punished by being thrown into the underworld. Christian mythographers found in these stories an analogy to Satan's revolt and punishment.

200   By ancient Tarsus held, or that sea-beast
       Leviathan,[5] which God of all his works
       Created hugest that swim th' ocean stream:
       Him haply° slumb'ring on the Norway foam   *perhaps*
       The pilot of some small night-foundered° skiff,   *overcome by night*
205   Deeming some island, oft, as seamen tell,[6]
       With fixèd anchor in his scaly rind
       Moors by his side under the lee,° while night   *out of the wind*
       Invests° the sea, and wishèd morn delays: *covers*
       So stretched out huge in length the Arch-Fiend lay
210   Chained on the burning lake, nor ever thence
       Had ris'n or heaved his head, but that the will
       And high permission of all-ruling Heaven
       Left him at large to his own dark designs,
       That with reiterated crimes he might
215   Heap on himself damnation, while he sought
       Evil to others, and enraged might see
       How all his malice served but to bring forth
       Infinite goodness, grace, and mercy shown
       On man by him seduced, but on himself
220   Treble confusion, wrath, and vengeance poured.
       Forthwith upright he rears from off the pool
       His mighty stature; on each hand the flames
       Driv'n backward slope their pointing spires,° and rolled   *points of flames*
       In billows, leave i' th' midst a horrid° vale.   *dreadful, bristling*
225   Then with expanded wings he steers his flight
       Aloft, incumbent on° the dusky air   *resting on*
       That felt unusual weight, till on dry land
       He lights,° if it were land that ever burned   *alights*
       With solid, as the lake with liquid fire,
230   And such appeared in hue; as when the force
       Of subterranean wind transports a hill
       Torn from Pelorus, or the shattered side
       Of thund'ring Etna,[7] whose combustible
       And fueled entrails thence conceiving fire,
235   Sublimed° with mineral fury, aid the winds,   *vaporized*
       And leave a singèd bottom all involved°   *enveloped*
       With stench and smoke: such resting found the sole
       Of unblest feet. Him followed his next mate,
       Both glorying to have scaped the Stygian° flood   *Styxlike, hellish*
240   As gods, and by their own recovered strength,
       Not by the sufferance° of supernal power.   *permission*
       "Is this the region, this the soil, the clime,"
       Said then the lost Archangel, "this the seat°   *estate*
       That we must change for Heav'n, this mournful gloom
245   For that celestial light? Be it so, since he
       Who now is sov'reign can dispose and bid

5. The whale, often identified with the great sea monster and enemy of the Lord in Isaiah 17.1 and the crocodile-like dragon of Job 41. Both were also identified with Satan.
6. The story of the deceived sailor and the illusory island was a commonplace, but the reference to Norway suggests a 16th-century version by Olaus Magnus, a Swedish historian.
7. Pelorus and Etna are volcanic mountains in Sicily.

What shall be right: farthest from him is best
Whom reason hath equaled, force hath made supreme
Above his equals. Farewell happy fields
250 Where joy forever dwells: Hail horrors, hail
Infernal world, and thou profoundest Hell
Receive thy new possessor: one who brings
A mind not to be changed by place or time.
The mind is its own place, and in itself
255 Can make a Heav'n of Hell, a Hell of Heav'n.[8]
What matter where, if I be still the same,
And what I should be, all but less than° he   *barely less than*
Whom thunder hath made greater? Here at least
We shall be free; th' Almighty hath not built
260 Here for his envy,[9] will not drive us hence:
Here we may reign secure, and in my choice
To reign is worth ambition though in Hell:
Better to reign in Hell, than serve in Heav'n.[1]
But wherefore let we then our faithful friends,
265 Th' associates and copartners of our loss
Lie thus astonished° on th' oblivious pool,[2]   *stunned*
And call them not to share with us their part
In this unhappy mansion, or once more
With rallied arms to try what may be yet
270 Regained in Heav'n, or what more lost in Hell?"
      So Satan spake, and him Beëlzebub
Thus answered. "Leader of those armies bright,
Which but th' Omnipotent none could have foiled,
If once they hear that voice, their liveliest pledge
275 Of hope in fears and dangers, heard so oft
In worst extremes, and on the perilous edge°   *front lines*
Of battle when it raged, in all assaults
Their surest signal, they will soon resume
New courage and revive, though now they lie
280 Groveling and prostrate on yon lake of fire,
As we erewhile, astounded and amazed,
No wonder, fall'n such a pernicious highth."
      He scarce had ceased when the superior Fiend
Was moving toward the shore; his ponderous shield
285 Ethereal temper,[3] massy, large and round,
Behind him cast; the broad circumference
Hung on his shoulders like the moon, whose orb
Through optic glass the Tuscan artist views[4]
At evening from the top of Fesole,
290 Or in Valdarno, to descry new lands,
Rivers or mountains in her spotty globe.

8. Compare Satan's soliloquy, 4.32–113.
9. I.e., because he desires this place.
1. An ironic echo of *Odyssey* 11.489–91, where
the shade of Achilles tells Odysseus that it is better to be a farmhand on earth than king among
the dead.
2. The epithet "oblivious" is transferred from
the fallen angels to the pool into which they have

fallen.
3. I.e., tempered in celestial fire.
4. Galileo, who looked through a telescope
("optic glass") from the hill town of Fiesole, outside Florence, in the valley of the Arno River
("Valdarno," val d'Arno, line 290). In 1610 he
published a book describing the mountains on
the moon.

His spear, to equal which the tallest pine
Hewn on Norwegian hills, to be the mast
Of some great ammiral,° were but a wand   admiral's ship
295 He walked with to support uneasy steps
Over the burning marl,° not like those steps   soil
On heaven's azure; and the torrid clime
Smote on him sore besides, vaulted with fire;
Nathless° he so endured, till on the beach   nevertheless
300 Of that inflamed° sea, he stood and called   flaming
His legions, angel forms, who lay entranced
Thick as autumnal leaves that strow the brooks
In Vallombrosa,⁵ where th' Etrurian shades
High overarched embow'r;° or scattered sedge°   form bowers / seaweed
305 Afloat, when with fierce winds Orion armed
Hath vexed the Red Sea coast,⁶ whose waves o'erthrew
Busiris⁷ and his Memphian chivalry,
While with perfidious hatred they pursued
The sojourners of Goshen, who beheld
310 From the safe shore their floating carcasses
And broken chariot wheels; so thick bestrown
Abject and lost lay these, covering the flood,
Under amazement of their hideous change.
He called so loud, that all the hollow deep
315 Of Hell resounded. "Princes, Potentates,
Warriors, the flow'r of Heav'n, once yours, now lost,
If such astonishment as this can seize
Eternal Spirits: or have ye chos'n this place
After the toil of battle to repose
320 Your wearied virtue,° for the ease you find   strength, valor
To slumber here, as in the vales of Heav'n?
Or in this abject posture have ye sworn
To adore the conqueror? who now beholds
Cherub and Seraph rolling in the flood
325 With scattered arms and ensigns,° till anon   battle flags
His swift pursuers from Heav'n gates discern
Th' advantage, and descending tread us down
Thus drooping, or with linkèd thunderbolts
Transfix us to the bottom of this gulf.
330 Awake, arise, or be forever fall'n."
     They heard, and were abashed, and up they sprung
Upon the wing, as when men wont° to watch   accustomed
On duty, sleeping found by whom they dread,
Rouse and bestir themselves ere well awake.
335 Nor did they not perceive the evil plight
In which they were, or the fierce pains not feel;⁸

---

5. The name means "shady valley" and refers to a region high in the Apennines, about twenty miles from Florence, in Tuscany ("Etruria"). Similes comparing the numberless dead to falling leaves are frequent in epic (e.g., *Aeneid* 6.309–10).
6. Orion is a constellation whose rising near sunset in late summer and autumn was associated with storms in the Red Sea.

7. Mythical Egyptian pharaoh, whom Milton associates with the pharaoh of Exodus 14, who pursued the Israelites ("sojourners of Goshen," line 309) into the Red Sea, which God parted for them. His "chivalry" (following) are horsemen from Memphis.
8. The double negatives make a positive: they did perceive both plight and pain.

Yet to their general's voice they soon obeyed
Innumerable. As when the potent rod
Of Amram's son[9] in Egypt's evil day
340 Waved round the coast, up called a pitchy cloud
Of locusts, warping° on the eastern wind,   *swarming*
That o'er the realm of impious Pharaoh hung
Like night, and darkened all the land of Nile:
So numberless were those bad angels seen
345 Hovering on wing under the cope° of Hell   *roof*
'Twixt upper, nether, and surrounding fires;
Till, as a signal giv'n, th' uplifted spear
Of their great Sultan[1] waving to direct
Their course, in even balance down they light
350 On the firm brimstone, and fill all the plain;
A multitude, like which the populous north
Poured never from her frozen loins, to pass
Rhene or the Danaw, when her barbarous sons
Came like a deluge on the south, and spread
355 Beneath Gibraltar to the Libyan sands.[2]
Forthwith from every squadron and each band
The heads and leaders thither haste where stood
Their great commander; godlike shapes and forms
Excelling human, princely dignities,
360 And powers that erst° in Heaven sat on thrones;   *formerly*
Though of their names in heav'nly records now
Be no memorial, blotted out and razed°   *erased*
By their rebellion, from the Books of Life.
Nor had they yet among the sons of Eve
365 Got them new names, till wand'ring o'er the earth,
Through God's high sufferance for the trial of man,
By falsities and lies the greatest part
Of mankind they corrupted to forsake
God their Creator, and th' invisible
370 Glory of him that made them, to transform
Oft to the image of a brute, adorned
With gay religions° full of pomp and gold,   *showy rites*
And devils to adore for deities:
Then were they known to men by various names,
375 And various idols through the heathen world.
    Say, Muse, their names then known, who first, who last,[3]
Roused from the slumber on that fiery couch,
At their great emperor's call, as next in worth
Came singly° where he stood on the bare strand,   *one at a time*
380 While the promiscuous° crowd stood yet aloof.   *mixed*
    The chief were those who from the pit of Hell
Roaming to seek their prey on earth, durst fix

---

9. Moses, who drew down a plague of locusts on Egypt (Exodus 10.12–15).
1. A first use of this description of Satan as an Oriental despot.
2. The barbarian invasions of Rome began with crossings of the Rhine ("Rhene") and Danube ("Danaw") rivers and spread across Spain, via Gibraltar, to North Africa.
3. The catalogue of gods here is an epic convention; Homer catalogues ships; Virgil, warriors.

Their seats long after next the seat of God,[4]
Their altars by his altar, gods adored
385 Among the nations round, and durst abide
Jehovah thund'ring out of Zion, throned
Between the Cherubim;[5] yea, often placed
Within his sanctuary itself their shrines,
Abomination; and with cursèd things
390 His holy rites, and solemn feasts profaned,
And with their darkness durst affront his light.
First Moloch,[6] horrid king besmeared with blood
Of human sacrifice, and parents' tears,
Though for the noise of drums and timbrels° loud   *tambourines*
395 Their children's cries unheard, that passed through fire
To his grim idol. Him the Ammonite[7]
Worshipped in Rabba and her wat'ry plain,
In Argob and in Basan, to the stream
Of utmost Arnon. Nor content with such
400 Audacious neighborhood, the wisest heart
Of Solomon he led by fraud to build
His temple right against the temple of God
On that opprobrious hill, and made his grove
The pleasant valley of Hinnom, Tophet thence
405 And black Gehenna called, the type of Hell.[8]
Next Chemos,[9] th' obscene dread of Moab's sons,
From Aroer to Nebo, and the wild
Of southmost Abarim; in Hesebon
And Horanaim, Seon's realm, beyond
410 The flow'ry dale of Sibma clad with vines,
And Elealè to th' Asphaltic Pool.[1]
Peor[2] his other name, when he enticed
Israel in Sittim on their march from Nile
To do him wanton rites, which cost them woe.
415 Yet thence his lustful orgies he enlarged
Even to that hill of scandal,[3] by the grove
Of Moloch homicide, lust hard by° hate;   *close by*
Till good Josiah drove them thence to Hell.
With these came they, who from the bord'ring flood
420 Of old Euphrates to the brook that parts

4. The first group of devils come from the Middle East, close neighbors of Jehovah "throned" in his sanctuary in Jerusalem.
5. Golden cherubim adorned opposite ends of the gold cover on the Ark of the Covenant.
6. Moloch was a sun god, sometimes represented as a roaring bull or with a calf's head, within whose brazen image living children were supposedly burned as sacrifices.
7. The Ammonites lived east of the Jordan River. "Rabba" (next line) is modern Amman, in Jordan; "Argob," "Basan," "utmost Arnon" (lines 398–99) are lands east of the Dead Sea.
8. The rites of Moloch on "that opprobrious hill" (the Mount of Olives), just opposite the Jewish temple, and in the valley of Hinnom so polluted those places that they were turned into the refuse dump of Jerusalem. Under the name "Tophet" and "Gehenna," Hinnom became a type of Hell.
9. Chemos, or Chemosh, associated with Moloch in 1 Kings 11.7, was the god of the Moabites, whose lands (many drawn from Isaiah 15–16) are mentioned in the following lines.
1. The Dead Sea.
2. The story of Peor seducing the Israelites in Sittim is told in Numbers 25.
3. The Mount of Olives, where Solomon built temples for Chemos and Moloch (1 Kings 11.7); epithets were commonly attached to the names of gods, as in the next line, Moloch "homicide." Josiah (following line) destroyed pagan idols in Jerusalem and other cities (2 Chronicles 34).

Egypt from Syrian ground,[4] had general names
Of Baalim and Ashtaroth, those male,
These feminine.[5] For Spirits when they please
Can either sex assume, or both; so soft
425   And uncompounded is their essence pure,
Not tied or manacled with joint or limb,
Nor founded on the brittle strength of bones,
Like cumbrous flesh; but in what shape they choose
Dilated or condensed, bright or obscure,
430   Can execute their airy purposes,
And works of love or enmity fulfill.
For those the race of Israel oft forsook
Their Living Strength, and unfrequented left
His righteous altar, bowing lowly down
435   To bestial gods; for which their heads as low
Bowed down in battle, sunk before the spear
Of despicable foes. With these in troop
Came Astoreth, whom the Phoenicians called
Astartè, queen of Heav'n, with crescent horns;
440   To whose bright image nightly by the moon
Sidonian virgins[6] paid their vows and songs,
In Sion also not unsung, where stood
Her temple on th' offensive mountain,[7] built
By that uxorious king, whose heart though large,
445   Beguiled by fair idolatresses, fell
To idols foul. Thammuz[8] came next behind,
Whose annual wound in Lebanon allured
The Syrian damsels to lament his fate
In amorous ditties all a summer's day,
450   While smooth Adonis[9] from his native work
Ran purple to the sea, supposed with blood
Of Thammuz yearly wounded: the love-tale
Infected Sion's daughters with like heat,
Whose wanton passions in the sacred porch
455   Ezekiel[1] saw, when by the vision led
His eye surveyed the dark idolatries
Of alienated Judah. Next came one
Who mourned in earnest, when the captive ark
Maimed his brute image, head and hands lopped off
460   In his own temple, on the grunsel edge,[2]
Where he fell flat, and shamed his worshippers:

4. Palestine lies between the Euphrates and "the brook Besor" (1 Samuel 30.10).
5. Plural forms, masculine and feminine, respectively, denoting aspects of the sun god Baal and the moon goddess Astarte (called "Astoreth" in line 438, below).
6. Sidon and Tyre were the chief cities of Phoenicia.
7. The Mount of Olives again. "That uxorious king" (next line) is Solomon, who "loved many strange women" (2 Kings 11.1–8).
8. A Syrian god, supposedly killed by a boar in Lebanon; his Greek form was Adonis, beloved of

Aphrodite and god of the solar year. Annual festivals mourned his death and celebrated his revival as signifying the death and rebirth of vegetation.
9. Here, the Lebanese river named for the deity because every spring it turned bloodred from sedimentary mud.
1. The prophet complained that Jewish women were worshipping Thammuz (Ezekiel 8.14).
2. When the Philistines stole the ark of God, they placed it in the temple of their sea god, Dagon, but in the morning the mutilated statue of Dagon was found on the threshhold ("grunsel edge") (1 Samuel 5.1–5).

Dagon his name, sea monster, upward man
And downward fish: yet had his temple high
Reared in Azotus, dreaded through the coast
465   Of Palestine, in Gath and Ascalon
And Accaron and Gaza's[3] frontier bounds.
Him followed Rimmon,[4] whose delightful seat
Was fair Damascus, on the fertile banks
Of Abbana and Pharphar, lucid streams.
470   He also against the house of God was bold:
A leper once he lost and gained a king,
Ahaz his sottish conqueror, whom he drew
God's altar to disparage and displace
For one of Syrian mode,[5] whereon to burn
475   His odious off'rings, and adore the gods
Whom he had vanquished. After these appeared
A crew who under names of old renown,
Osiris, Isis, Orus[6] and their train
With monstrous shapes and sorceries abused
480   Fanatic Egypt and her priests, to seek
Their wand'ring gods disguised in brutish forms
Rather than human. Nor did Israel scape
Th' infection when their borrowed gold composed
The calf in Oreb:[7] and the rebel king
485   Doubled that sin in Bethel and in Dan,
Lik'ning his Maker to the grazèd ox,[8]
Jehovah, who in one night when he passed
From Egypt marching, equaled° with one stroke   **leveled**
Both her firstborn and all her bleating gods.[9]
490   Belial came last,[1] than whom a spirit more lewd
Fell not from Heaven, or more gross to love
Vice for itself: to him no temple stood
Or altar smoked; yet who more oft than he
In temples and at altars, when the priest
495   Turns atheist, as did Eli's sons,[2] who filled
With lust and violence the house of God.
In courts and palaces he also reigns
And in luxurious cities, where the noise
Of riot ascends above their loftiest tow'rs,
500   And injury and outrage: and when night

3. The five chief cities of the Philistines, sites of Dagon's worship.
4. A Phoenician god whose temple was in Damascus.
5. A Syrian general, Naaman, was cured of leprosy and converted from worship of Rimmon by the waters of the Jordan (2 Kings 5), while King Ahaz, an Israelite monarch who conquered Damascus, was converted there to Rimmon's worship.
6. The second group of devils includes the Egyptian gods driven from Heaven by the revolt of the giants (Ovid, *Metamorphoses* 5) and forced to wander in "monstrous" (next line) animal disguises.
7. In the wilderness of Egypt, while Moses was receiving the Law, Aaron made a golden calf, thought to be an idol of the Egyptian god Apis and made of ornaments brought out of Egypt (Exodus 32).
8. Jeroboam, "the rebel king" who led the ten tribes of Israel in revolt against Solomon's son, Rehoboam; he doubled Aaron's sin by making two golden calves (1 Kings 12.25–30).
9. Jehovah smote the firstborn of all Egyptian families as well as their gods (Exodus 12.12).
1. Belial was never worshipped as a god; his name means "wickedness," but its use in phrases like "sons of Belial" encouraged personification.
2. Priests who were termed "sons of Belial" because they seized for themselves offerings made to God and lay with women who assembled at the door of the tarbernacle (1 Samuel 2.12–22).

Darkens the streets, then wander forth the sons
Of Belial, flown° with insolence and wine.[3]   *flushed*
Witness the streets of Sodom, and that night
In Gibeah, when the hospitable door
505 Exposed a matron to avoid worse rape.[4]
    These were the prime in order and in might;
The rest were long to tell, though far renowned,
Th' Ionian gods, of Javan's issue held
Gods, yet confessed later than Heav'n and Earth
510 Their boasted parents;[5] Titan Heav'n's firstborn
With his enormous brood, and birthright seized
By younger Saturn, he from mightier Jove,
His own and Rhea's son, like measure found;
So Jove usurping reigned:[6] these first in Crete
515 And Ida known, thence on the snowy top
Of cold Olympus ruled the middle air
Their highest heav'n; or on the Delphian cliff,
Or in Dodona, and through all the bounds
Of Doric land;[7] or who with Saturn old
520 Fled over Adria to th' Hesperian fields,
And o'er the Celtic roamed the utmost isles.[8]
    All these and more came flocking; but with looks
Downcast and damp,° yet such wherein appeared   *depressed, dazed*
Obscure some glimpse of joy, to have found their chief
525 Not in despair, to have found themselves not lost
In loss itself; which on his count'nance cast
Like doubtful hue:[9] but he his wonted° pride   *accustomed*
Soon recollecting, with high words, that bore
Semblance of worth, not substance, gently raised
530 Their fainting courage, and dispelled their fears.
Then straight° commands that at the warlike sound   *immediately*
Of trumpets loud and clarions be upreared
His mighty standard; that proud honor claimed
Azazel[1] as his right, a Cherub tall:
535 Who forthwith from the glittering staff unfurled
Th' imperial ensign, which full high advanced
Shone like a meteor streaming to the wind
With gems and golden luster rich emblazed,
Seraphic arms and trophies:[2] all the while

3. This passage, with its present-tense verbs, invites application to current examples—at court and in Restoration London.
4. Lot begged the Sodomites to rape his daughters rather than his (male) angel guests (Genesis 19); in Gibeah a Levite avoided "worse" (homosexual) rape by surrendering his concubine to riotous "sons of Belial" (Judges 19.21–30).
5. The Ionian Greeks ("Javan's issue," i.e., of the line of Javan, grandson of Noah) regarded the Titans as gods; their supposed parents were Heaven (Uranus) and Earth (Gaia).
6. The Titan Cronos, or Saturn, deposed his father, married his sister Rhea, and ruled until he was deposed by his son, Zeus (Jove), who had been reared in secret on Mount Ida in Crete.

7. Zeus and the other Olympian gods had their seat on Mount Olympus, in "middle air"; they were worshipped in Delphi, Dodona, and throughout Greece ("Doric lands").
8. Saturn, after his downfall, fled over "Adria" (the Adriatic Sea) to the "Hesperian fields" (Italy), crossed the "Celtic" fields of France, and thence to Britain, the "utmost isles."
9. Satan's face reflected the same mixed emotions.
1. Traditionally, one of the four standard-bearers in Satan's army. "Clarions" (line 532): small, shrill trumpets.
2. Their flags bear the heraldic arms of the various orders of angels and memorials of their battles.

540	Sonorous metal° blowing martial sounds:	*trumpets*
	At which the universal host upsent	
	A shout that tore Hell's concave,° and beyond	*vault*
	Frighted the reign of Chaos and old Night.[3]	
	All in a moment through the gloom were seen	
545	Ten thousand banners rise into the air	
	With orient° colors waving: with them rose	*lustrous*
	A forest huge of spears: and thronging helms	
	Appeared, and serried° shields in thick array	*pushed close together*
	Of depth immeasurable: anon they move	
550	In perfect phalanx to the Dorian[4] mood	
	Of flutes and soft recorders; such as raised	
	To highth of noblest temper heroes old	
	Arming to battle, and instead of rage	
	Deliberate valor breathed, firm and unmoved	
555	With dread of death to flight or foul retreat,	
	Nor wanting power to mitigate and swage°	*assuage*
	With solemn touches, troubled thoughts, and chase	
	Anguish and doubt and fear and sorrow and pain	
	From mortal or immortal minds. Thus they	
560	Breathing united force with fixèd thought	
	Moved on in silence to soft pipes that charmed	
	Their painful steps o'er the burnt soil; and now	
	Advanced in view they stand, a horrid° front	*bristling with spears*
	Of dreadful length and dazzling arms, in guise	
565	Of warriors old with ordered spear and shield,	
	Awaiting what command their mighty chief	
	Had to impose. He through the armèd files	
	Darts his experienced eye, and soon traverse°	*across*
	The whole battalion views, their order due,	
570	Their visages and stature as of gods,	
	Their number last he sums. And now his heart	
	Distends with pride, and hard'ning in his strength	
	Glories: for never since created man[5]	
	Met such embodied force, as named° with these	*composed*
575	Could merit more than that small infantry	
	Warred on by cranes:[6] though all the giant brood	
	Of Phlegra with th' heroic race were joined	
	That fought at Thebes and Ilium,[7] on each side	
	Mixed with auxiliar° gods; and what resounds	*allied*
580	In fable or romance of Uther's son	
	Begirt with British and Armoric knights;	
	And all who since, baptized or infidel	
	Jousted in Aspramont or Montalban,	
	Damasco, or Morocco, or Trebisond,	

3. In *Paradise Lost* 2.894–909, 959–70 Chaos and Night rule the region of unformed matter between Heaven and earth.
4. Severe, martial music used by the Spartans marching to battle. "Phalanx": battle formation.
5. I.e., since the creation of man.
6. Pygmies (little people, with a pun, in "infantry" on "infants") had periodic fights with the cranes, in Pliny's account. Compared with Satan's forces, all other armies are puny.
7. In Greek mythology, the Giants fought the gods at Phlegra in Macedonia; in Roman myth, it was at Phlegra in Italy. Satan's forces surpass them, even if joined with the Seven who fought against Thebes and the whole Greek host that besieged Troy ("Ilium").

585 Or whom Biserta sent from Afric shore
When Charlemagne with all his peerage fell
By Fontarabia.[8] Thus far these beyond
Compare of mortal prowess, yet observed°   *obeyed*
Their dread commander: he above the rest
590 In shape and gesture proudly eminent
Stood like a tow'r; his form had yet not lost
All her[9] original brightness, nor appeared
Less than Archangel ruined, and th' excess
Of glory obscured: as when the sun new-ris'n
595 Looks through the horizontal° misty air   *on the horizon*
Shorn of his beams, or from behind the moon
In dim eclipse disastrous° twilight sheds   *ill-starred*
On half the nations, and with fear of change
Perplexes monarchs. Darkened so, yet shone
600 Above them all th' Archangel: but his face
Deep scars of thunder had intrenched,° and care   *furrowed*
Sat on his faded cheek, but under brows
Of dauntless courage, and considerate° pride   *conscious, deliberate*
Waiting revenge: cruel his eye, but cast
605 Signs of remorse and passion° to behold   *compassion, pain*
The fellows of his crime, the followers rather
(Far other once beheld in bliss) condemned
Forever now to have their lot in pain,
Millions of Spirits for his fault amerced°   *deprived*
610 Of Heav'n, and from eternal splendors flung
For his revolt, yet faithful how they stood,
Their glory withered: as when Heaven's fire
Hath scathed° the forest oaks, or mountain pines,   *damaged*
With singèd top their stately growth though bare
615 Stands on the blasted heath. He now prepared
To speak; whereat their doubled ranks they bend
From wing to wing, and half enclose him round
With all his peers: attention held them mute.
Thrice he essayed,° and thrice, in spite of scorn,   *attempted*
620 Tears such as angels weep burst forth: at last
Words interwove with sighs found out their way.
   "O myriads of immortal Spirits, O Powers
Matchless, but with th' Almighty, and that strife
Was not inglorious, though th' event° was dire,   *outcome*
625 As this place testifies, and this dire change
Hateful to utter: but what power of mind
Foreseeing or presaging, from the depth
Of knowledge past or present, could have feared,
How such united force of gods, how such
630 As stood like these, could ever know repulse?
For who can yet believe, though after loss,

---

8. Satan's forces also surpass the "British and Armoric" (from Brittany) knights who fought with King Arthur ("Uther's son") and all the romance knights who fought at the famous named sites in the following lines. Roncesvalles, near Fontara-bia, was the place where Charlemagne's "peer-age," including his best knight, Roland, were defeated in battle (though not Charlemagne himself).
9. *Forma* in Latin is feminine.

That all these puissant° legions, whose exile   *potent, powerful*
Hath emptied Heav'n, shall fail to reascend
Self-raised, and repossess their native seat?
635   For me, be witness all the host of Heav'n,
If counsels different,° or danger shunned   *contradictory*
By me, have lost our hopes. But he who reigns
Monarch in Heav'n, till then as one secure
Sat on his throne, upheld by old repute,
640   Consent or custom, and his regal state
Put forth at full, but still° his strength concealed,   *always*
Which tempted our attempt, and wrought our fall.
Henceforth his might we know, and know our own
So as not either to provoke, or dread
645   New war, provoked; our better part remains
To work in close design, by fraud or guile
What force effected not: that he no less
At length from us may find, who overcomes
By force, hath overcome but half his foe.
650   Space may produce new worlds; whereof so rife°   *common*
There went a fame° in Heav'n that he ere long   *rumor*
Intended to create, and therein plant
A generation, whom his choice regard
Should favor equal to the sons of Heaven:
655   Thither, if but to pry, shall be perhaps
Our first eruption,° thither or elsewhere: *breaking out*
For this infernal pit shall never hold
Celestial Spirits in bondage, not th' abyss
Long under darkness cover. But these thoughts
660   Full counsel must mature: peace is despaired,
For who can think submission? War then, war
Open or understood° must be resolved."   *covert*
    He spake: and to confirm his words, out flew
Millions of flaming swords, drawn from the thighs
665   Of mighty Cherubim; the sudden blaze
Far round illumined Hell: highly they raged
Against the Highest, and fierce with graspèd arms
Clashed on their sounding shields the din of war,[1]
Hurling defiance toward the vault of Heav'n.
670   There stood a hill not far whose grisly top
Belched fire and rolling smoke; the rest entire
Shone with a glossy scurf,° undoubted sign   *crust*
That in his womb was hid metallic ore,
The work of sulphur.[2] Thither winged with speed
675   A numerous brígade hastened. As when bands
Of pioneers° with spade and pickax armed   *military engineers*
Forerun the royal camp, to trench a field,
Or cast a rampart. Mammon[3] led them on,

---

1. Like Roman legionnaires, the fallen angels applaud by beating swords on shields.
2. Sulfur and mercury were considered the basic substances of all metals.
3. "Mammon," an abstract word for riches, came to be personified and associated with the god of wealth, Plutus, and so with Pluto, god of the underworld. Cf. Matthew 6.24: "Ye cannot serve God and mammon."

Mammon, the least erected Spirit that fell
680　From Heav'n, for ev'n in Heav'n his looks and thoughts
Were always downward bent, admiring more
The riches of Heav'n's pavement, trodden gold,
Than aught divine or holy else enjoyed
In vision beatific: by him first
685　Men also, and by his suggestion taught,
Ransacked the center, and with impious hands
Rifled the bowels of their mother earth
For treasures better hid. Soon had his crew
Opened into the hill a spacious wound
690　And digged out ribs of gold. Let none admire°　　　*wonder*
That riches grow in Hell; that soil may best
Deserve the precious bane.° And here let those　　　*poison*
Who boast in mortal things, and wond'ring tell
Of Babel, and the works of Memphian kings,[4]
695　Learn how their greatest monuments of fame,
And strength and art are easily outdone
By Spirits reprobate, and in an hour
What in an age they with incessant toil
And hands innumerable scarce perform.
700　Nigh on the plain in many cells prepared,
That underneath had veins of liquid fire
Sluiced from the lake, a second multitude
With wondrous art founded° the massy ore,　　　*melted*
Severing° each kind, and scummed the bullion dross:°　*separating / boiling dregs*
705　A third as soon had formed within the ground
A various mold, and from the boiling cells
By strange conveyance filled each hollow nook,
As in an organ from one blast of wind
To many a row of pipes the soundboard breathes.
710　Anon out of the earth a fabric huge
Rose like an exhalation, with the sound
Of dulcet symphonies and voices sweet,
Built like a temple,[5] where pilasters° round　　　*columns set in a wall*
Were set, and Doric pillars[6] overlaid
715　With golden architrave; nor did there want
Cornice or frieze, with bossy° sculptures grav'n;　　*embossed*
The roof was fretted° gold. Not Babylon,　　　*richly ornamented*
Nor great Alcairo such magnificence
Equaled in all their glories, to enshrine
720　Belus or Serapis[7] their gods, or seat
Their kings, when Egypt with Assyria strove
In wealth and luxury. Th' ascending pile
Stood fixed° her stately height, and straight° the doors　*complete / at once*

---

4. The Tower of Babel and the pyramids of Egypt.
5. After melting the gold with fire from the lake and pouring it into molds, the devils cause their building to rise as by magic, to the sounds of marvelous music.
6. Doric pillars are severe and plain. The devils' palace combines classical architectural features with elaborate ornamentation, suggesting, perhaps, St. Peter's in Rome.
7. At Babylon, in Assyria, there were temples to "Belus" or Baal; at Alcairo (modern Cairo, ancient Memphis), in Egypt, they were to Osiris ("Serapis").

Opening their brazen folds discover° wide   *reveal*
725 Within, her ample spaces, o'er the smooth
And level pavement: from the archèd roof
Pendent by subtle magic many a row
Of starry lamps and blazing cressets[8] fed
With naphtha and asphaltus yielded light
730 As from a sky. The hasty multitude
Admiring entered, and the work some praise
And some the architect: his hand was known
In Heav'n by many a towered structure high,
Where sceptered angels held their residence,
735 And sat as princes, whom the Súpreme King
Exalted to such power, and gave to rule,
Each in his hierarchy, the orders bright.
Nor was his name unheard or unadored
In ancient Greece and in Ausonian land
740 Men called him Mulciber[9] and how he fell
From Heav'n, they fabled, thrown by angry Jove
Sheer o'er the crystal battlements: from morn
To noon he fell, from noon to dewy eve,
A summer's day; and with the setting sun
745 Dropped from the zenith like a falling star,
On Lemnos th' Aégean isle: thus they relate,
Erring; for he with this rebellious rout
Fell long before; nor aught availed him now
To have built in Heav'n high tow'rs; nor did he scape
750 By all his engines, but was headlong sent
With his industrious crew to build in Hell.
  Meanwhile the wingèd heralds by command
Of sov'reign power, with awful ceremony
And trumpet's sound throughout the host proclaim
755 A solemn council forthwith to be held
At Pandemonium,[1] the high capitol
Of Satan and his peers:° their summons called   *nobles*
From every band and squarèd regiment
By place° or choice° the worthiest; they anon   *rank / election*
760 With hundreds and with thousands trooping came
Attended: all access was thronged, the gates
And porches wide, but chief the spacious hall
(Though like a covered field, where champions bold
Wont ride in armed, and at the soldan's° chair   *sultan's*
765 Defied the best of paynim° chivalry   *pagan*
To mortal combat or career with lance)
Thick swarmed, both on the ground and in the air,
Brushed with the hiss of rustling wings. As bees
In springtime, when the sun with Taurus rides,[2]
770 Pour forth their populous youth about the hive

8. Basketlike lamps, hung from the ceiling.
9. Hephaestus, or Vulcan, was sometimes known in "Ausonian land" (Italy) as "Mulciber." The story of Jove's tossing him out of Heaven (see following lines) is told in Book 1 of the *Iliad*.

1. "Pandemonium" (a Miltonic coinage) means literally "all demons," an inversion of "pantheon," "all gods."
2. The sun is in the zodiacal sign of Taurus from about April 19 to May 20.

In clusters; they among fresh dews and flowers
Fly to and fro, or on the smoothèd plank,
The suburb of their straw-built citadel,
New rubbed with balm, expatiate and confer[3]
775 Their state affairs. So thick the aery crowd
Swarmed and were straitened; till the signal giv'n,
Behold a wonder! They but now who seemed
In bigness to surpass Earth's giant sons
Now less than smallest dwarfs, in narrow room
780 Throng numberless, like that Pygmean race
Beyond the Indian mount,[4] or fairy elves,
Whose midnight revels, by a forest side
Or fountain some belated peasant sees,
Or dreams he sees, while overhead the moon
785 Sits arbitress,° and nearer to the earth   witness
Wheels her pale course: they on their mirth and dance
Intent, with jocund° music charm his ear;[5]   merry
At once with joy and fear his heart rebounds.
Thus incorporeal Spirits to smallest forms
790 Reduced their shapes immense, and were at large,
Though without number still amidst the hall
Of that infernal court. But far within
And in their own dimensions like themselves
The great Seraphic Lords and Cherubim
795 In close recess and secret conclave sat,
A thousand demigods on golden seats,
Frequent and full.[6] After short silence then
And summons read, the great consult[7] began.

Book 2

High on a throne of royal state, which far
Outshone the wealth of Ormus and of Ind,[1]
Or where the gorgeous East with richest hand
Show'rs on her kings barbaric pearl and gold,
5 Satan exalted sat, by merit raised
To that bad eminence; and from despair
Thus high uplifted beyond hope, aspires
Beyond thus high, insatiate to pursue
Vain war with Heav'n, and by success° untaught   the outcome
10 His proud imaginations° thus displayed.   schemes
   "Powers and Dominions,[2] deities of Heaven,
For since no deep within her gulf can hold

---

3. Spread out and discuss. Bee similes were
common in epic from Homer on; also, the bees'
(royalist) society was often cited in political
argument. The simile prepares for the sudden
contraction of the devils, who can shrink or
dilate at will.
4. The pygmies were supposed to live beyond

the Himalayas.
5. The belated peasant's.
6. Crowded together, and in full complement.
7. Consultation, often secret and seditious.
1. India. "Ormus": an island in the Persian Gulf,
modern Hormuz, famous for pearls.
2. Angelic orders.

Immortal vigor, though oppressed and fall'n,
I give not Heav'n for lost. From this descent
15 Celestial Virtues rising, will appear
More glorious and more dread than from no fall,
And trust themselves to fear no second fate.
Me though just right, and the fixed laws of Heav'n
Did first create your leader, next, free choice,
20 With what besides, in counsel or in fight,
Hath been achieved of merit, yet this loss
Thus far at least recovered, hath much more
Established in a safe unenvied throne
Yielded with full consent. The happier state
25 In Heav'n, which follows dignity, might draw
Envy from each inferior; but who here
Will envy whom the highest place exposes
Foremost to stand against the Thunderer's aim
Your bulwark, and condemns to greatest share
30 Of endless pain? Where there is then no good
For which to strive, no strife can grow up there
From faction; for none sure will claim in Hell
Precédence, none, whose portion is so small
Of present pain, that with ambitious mind
35 Will covet more. With this advantage then
To union, and firm faith, and firm accord,
More than can be in Heav'n, we now return
To claim our just inheritance of old,
Surer to prosper than prosperity
40 Could have assured us;³ and by what best way,
Whether of open war or covert guile,⁴
We now debate; who can advise, may speak."
    He ceased, and next him Moloch, sceptered king
Stood up, the strongest and the fiercest Spirit
45 That fought in Heav'n; now fiercer by despair:
His trust was with th' Eternal to be deemed
Equal in strength, and rather than be less
Cared not to be at all; with that care lost
Went all his fear: of God, or Hell, or worse
50 He recked° not, and these words thereafter spake.   cared
    "My sentence° is for open war: of wiles,   judgment
More unexpért,° I boast not: them let those   less experienced
Contrive who need, or when they need, not now.
For while they sit contriving, shall the rest,
55 Millions that stand in arms, and longing wait
The signal to ascend, sit lingering here
Heav'n's fugitives, and for their dwelling place
Accept this dark opprobrious den of shame,
The prison of his tyranny who reigns
60 By our delay? No, let us rather choose

---

3. Note the play on "surer," "prosper," "prosperity," "assured," a favorite device of Milton's.
4. A typical epic convention (in Homer, Virgil,
Tasso, and elsewhere) involved councils debating
war or peace, with spokesmen on each side. Satan
offers only the option of war, open or covert.

Armed with Hell flames and fury all at once
O'er Heav'n's high tow'rs to force resistless way,
Turning our tortures into horrid° arms   *bristling, horrifying*
Against the Torturer; when to meet the noise
65 Of his almighty engine° he shall hear   *the thunderbolt*
Infernal thunder, and for lightning see
Black fire and horror shot with equal rage
Among his angels; and his throne itself
Mixed with Tartarean[5] sulfur, and strange fire,
70 His own invented torments. But perhaps
The way seems difficult and steep to scale
With upright wing against a higher foe.
Let such bethink them, if the sleepy drench°   *large draught*
Of that forgetful° lake benumb not still,   *causing oblivion*
75 That in our proper° motion we ascend   *natural to us*
Up to our native seat: descent and fall
To us is adverse. Who but felt of late
When the fierce foe hung on our broken rear
Insulting,[6] and pursued us through the deep,
80 With what compulsion and laborious flight
We sunk thus low? Th' ascent is easy then;
Th' event° is feared; should we again provoke   *outcome*
Our stronger, some worse way his wrath may find
To our destruction: if there be in Hell
85 Fear to be worse destroyed: what can be worse
Than to dwell here, driven out from bliss, condemned
In this abhorrèd deep to utter woe;
Where pain of unextinguishable fire
Must exercise° us without hope of end   *vex, afflict*
90 The vassals[7] of his anger, when the scourge
Inexorably, and the torturing hour
Calls us to penance? More destroyed than thus
We should be quite abolished and expire.
What fear we then? What° doubt we to incense   *why*
95 His utmost ire? which to the height enraged,
Will either quite consume us, and reduce
To nothing this essential,° happier far   *essence*
Than miserable to have eternal being:
Or if our substance be indeed divine,
100 And cannot cease to be, we are at worst
On this side nothing;[8] and by proof we feel
Our power sufficient to disturb his Heav'n,
And with perpetual inroads to alarm,
Though inaccessible, his fatal[9] throne:
105 Which if not victory is yet revenge."
    He ended frowning, and his look, denounced°   *portended*
Desperate revenge, and battle dangerous
To less than gods. On th' other side up rose

---

5. Tartarus is a classical name for hell.
6. With the Latin sense of stamping on; also, triumphantly scorning.
7. Servants, but perhaps also vessels. See Romans

9.22: "vessels of wrath fitted to destruction."
8. I.e., we cannot be worse off than we are now, and still live.
9. Established by Fate; also, deadly.

Belial, in act more graceful and humane;°   *civil, polite*
110 A fairer person lost not Heav'n; he seemed
For dignity composed and high exploit:
But all was false and hollow; though his tongue
Dropped manna, and could make the worse appear
The better reason,[1] to perplex and dash°   *confuse*
115 Maturest counsels: for his thoughts were low;
To vice industrious, but to nobler deeds
Timorous and slothful: yet he pleased the ear,
And with persuasive accent thus began.
   "I should be much for open war, O Peers,
120 As not behind in hate; if what was urged
Main reason to persuade immediate war,
Did not dissuade me most, and seem to cast
Ominous conjecture on the whole success:
When he who most excels in fact° of arms,   *feat*
125 In what he counsels and in what excels
Mistrustful, grounds his courage on despair
And utter dissolution, as the scope
Of all his aim, after some dire revenge.
First, what revenge? The tow'rs of Heav'n are filled
130 With armèd watch, that render all access
Impregnable; oft on the bordering deep
Encamp their legions, or with óbscure wing
Scout far and wide into the realm of Night,
Scorning surprise. Or could we break our way
135 By force, and at our heels all Hell should rise
With blackest insurrection, to confound
Heav'n's purest light, yet our great enemy
All incorruptible would on his throne
Sit unpolluted, and th' ethereal mold[2]
140 Incapable of stain would soon expel
Her mischief, and purge off the baser fire
Victorious. Thus repulsed, our final hope
Is flat despair: we must exasperate
Th' almighty victor to spend all his rage,
145 And that must end us, that must be our cure,
To be no more; sad cure; for who would lose,
Though full of pain, this intellectual being,
Those thoughts that wander through eternity,
To perish rather, swallowed up and lost
150 In the wide womb of uncreated night,
Devoid of sense and motion? And who knows,
Let this be good, whether our angry foe
Can give it, or will ever? How he can
Is doubtful; that he never will is sure.
155 Will he, so wise, let loose at once his ire,

1. The Sophists, mercenary teachers of rhetoric in ancient Greece, were denounced by Plato for making "the worse appear / The better reason." "His tongue / Dropped manna": his honeyed words seemed like the manna supplied to the Israelites in the desert.
2. Heavenly substance, derived from "ether," the fifth and purest element, thought to be incorruptible.

Belike° through impotence, or unaware,   *perhaps*
To give his enemies their wish, and end
Them in his anger, whom his anger saves
To punish endless? 'Wherefore cease we then?'
160   Say they who counsel war, 'We are decreed,
Reserved and destined to eternal woe;
Whatever doing, what can we suffer more,
What can we suffer worse?' Is this then worst,
Thus sitting, thus consulting, thus in arms?
165   What when we fled amain,° pursued and strook°   *headlong / struck*
With Heav'n's afflicting thunder, and besought
The deep to shelter us? This Hell then seemed
A refuge from those wounds. Or when we lay
Chained on the burning lake? That sure was worse.
170   What if the breath that kindled those grim fires
Awaked should blow them into sevenfold rage
And plunge us in the flames? Or from above
Should intermitted° vengeance arm again   *suspended*
His red right hand to plague us? What if all
175   Her° stores were opened, and this firmament°   *Hell's / sky*
Of Hell should spout her cataracts° of fire,   *cascades*
Impendent[3] horrors, threat'ning hideous fall
One day upon our heads; while we perhaps
Designing or exhorting glorious war,
180   Caught in a fiery tempest shall be hurled
Each on his rock transfixed, the sport and prey
Of racking whirlwinds, or forever sunk
Under yon boiling ocean, wrapped in chains;
There to converse with everlasting groans,
185   Unrespited, unpitied, unreprieved,
Ages of hopeless end; this would be worse.
War therefore, open or concealed, alike
My voice dissuades; for what can force or guile[4]
With him, or who deceive his mind, whose eye
190   Views all things at one view? He from Heav'n's high
All these our motions° vain, sees and derides;   *proposals*
Not more almighty to resist our might
Than wise to frustrate all our plots and wiles.
Shall we then live thus vile, the race of Heav'n
195   Thus trampled, thus expelled to suffer here
Chains and these torments? Better these than worse
By my advice; since fate inevitable
Subdues us, and omnipotent decree,
The victor's will. To suffer, as to do,
200   Our strength is equal, nor the law unjust
That so ordains: this was at first resolved,
If we were wise, against so great a foe
Contending, and so doubtful what might fall.
I laugh, when those who at the spear are bold

3. In the Latin sense, hanging down, threatening.

4. The verb "accomplish" or "achieve" is understood.

205 And vent'rous, if that fail them, shrink and fear
What yet they know must follow, to endure
Exile, or ignominy, or bonds, or pain,
The sentence of their conqueror: This is now
Our doom; which if we can sustain and bear,
210 Our Súpreme Foe in time may much remit
His anger, and perhaps thus far removed
Not mind us not offending, satisfied
With what is punished; whence these raging fires
Will slacken, if his breath stir not their flames.
215 Our purer essence then will overcome
Their noxious vapor, or inured° not feel,   *accustomed*
Or changed at length, and to the place conformed
In temper and in nature, will receive
Familiar the fierce heat, and void of pain;
220 This horror will grow mild, this darkness light,
Besides what hope the never-ending flight
Of future days may bring, what chance, what change
Worth waiting, since our present lot appears
For happy though but ill, for ill not worst,[5]
225 If we procure not to ourselves more woe."
      Thus Belial, with words clothed in reason's garb,
Counseled ignoble ease and peaceful sloth,
Not peace: and after him thus Mammon spake.
      "Either to disenthrone the King of Heav'n
230 We war, if war be best, or to regain
Our own right lost: him to unthrone we then
May hope when everlasting Fate shall yield
To fickle Chance, and Chaos judge the strife:
The former vain to hope argues° as vain   *proves*
235 The latter: for what place can be for us
Within Heav'n's bound, unless Heav'n's Lord supreme
We overpower? Suppose he should relent
And publish grace to all, on promise made
Of new subjection; with what eyes could we
240 Stand in his presence humble, and receive
Strict laws imposed, to celebrate his throne
With warbled hymns, and to his Godhead sing
Forced hallelujahs; while he lordly sits
Our envied Sov'reign, and his altar breathes
245 Ambrosial° odors and ambrosial flowers,   *fragrant, immortal*
Our servile offerings. This must be our task
In Heav'n, this our delight; how wearisome
Eternity so spent in worship paid
To whom we hate. Let us not then pursue
250 By force impossible, by leave obtained
Unácceptable, though in Heav'n, our state
Of splendid vassalage,° but rather seek   *servitude*
Our own good from ourselves, and from our own
Live to ourselves, though in this vast recess,

---

5. I.e., from the point of view of happiness, the devils are in an ill state, but it could be worse.

255 Free, and to none accountable, preferring
Hard liberty before the easy yoke
Of servile pomp. Our greatness will appear
Then most conspicuous, when great things of small,
Useful of hurtful, prosperous of adverse
260 We can create, and in what place soe'er
Thrive under evil, and work ease out of pain
Through labor and endurance. This deep world
Of darkness do we dread? How oft amidst
Thick clouds and dark doth Heav'n's all-ruling Sire
265 Choose to reside, his glory unobscured,
And with the majesty of darkness round
Covers his throne; from whence deep thunders roar
Must'ring their rage, and Heav'n resembles Hell?
As he our darkness, cannot we his light
270 Imitate when we please? This desert soil
Wants° not her hidden luster, gems and gold; *lacks*
Nor want we skill or art, from whence to raise
Magnificence; and what can Heav'n show more?
Our torments also may in length of time
275 Become our elements, these piercing fires
As soft as now severe, our temper° changed *constitution*
Into their temper; which must needs remove
The sensible of pain.[6] All things invite
To peaceful counsels, and the settled state
280 Of order, how in safety best we may
Compose° our present evils, with regard *come to terms with*
Of what we are and where, dismissing quite
All thoughts of war: ye have what I advise."
   He scarce had finished, when such murmur filled
285 Th' assembly, as when hollow rocks retain
The sound of blust'ring winds, which all night long
Had roused the sea, now with hoarse cadence lull
Seafaring men o'erwatched,° whose bark by chance *worn out from watching*
Or pinnace° anchors in a craggy bay *boat*
290 After the tempest: such applause was heard
As Mammon ended, and his sentence pleased,
Advising peace: for such another field° *battlefield*
They dreaded worse than Hell: so much the fear
Of thunder and the sword of Michaël[7]
295 Wrought still within them; and no less desire
To found this nether empire, which might rise
By policy,° and long process of time, *statecraft*
In emulation opposite to Heav'n.
Which then Beëlzebub perceived, than whom,
300 Satan except, none higher sat, with grave
Aspect he rose, and in his rising seemed
A pillar of state; deep on his front° engraven *brow*
Deliberation sat and public care;
And princely counsel in his face yet shone,

6. Pain felt by the senses.

7. The warrior angel, chief of the angelic armies.

305 Majestic though in ruin: sage he stood
With Atlantean[8] shoulders fit to bear
The weight of mightiest monarchies; his look
Drew audience and attention still as night
Or summer's noontide air, while thus he spake.
310   "Thrones and imperial Powers, offspring of Heav'n
Ethereal Virtues; or these titles[9] now
Must we renounce, and changing style° be called   *title*
Princes of Hell? for so the popular vote
Inclines, here to continue, and build up here
315 A growing empire. Doubtless! while we dream,
And know not that the King of Heav'n hath doomed
This place our dungeon, not our safe retreat
Beyond his potent arm, to live exempt
From Heav'n's high jurisdiction, in new league
320 Banded against his throne, but to remain
In strictest bondage, though thus far removed,
Under th' inevitable curb, reserved
His captive multitude: for he, be sure,
In height or depth, still first and last will reign
325 Sole King, and of his kingdom lose no part
By our revolt, but over Hell extend
His empire, and with iron scepter rule
Us here, as with his golden those in Heav'n.
What° sit we then projecting peace and war?   *why*
330 War hath determined us,[1] and foiled with loss
Irreparable; terms of peace yet none
Vouchsafed° or sought; for what peace will be giv'n   *granted*
To us enslaved, but custody severe,
And stripes, and arbitrary punishment
335 Inflicted? And what peace can we return,
But, to our power,[2] hostility and hate,
Untamed reluctance,° and revenge though slow,   *resistance*
Yet ever plotting how the conqueror least
May reap his conquest, and may least rejoice
340 In doing what we most in suffering feel?
Nor will occasion want,° nor shall we need   *be lacking*
With dangerous expedition to invade
Heav'n, whose high walls fear no assault or siege,
Or ambush from the deep. What if we find
345 Some easier enterprise? There is a place
(If ancient and prophetic fame° in Heav'n   *rumor*
Err not) another world, the happy seat
Of some new race called Man, about this time
To be created like to us, though less
350 In power and excellence, but favored more
Of him who rules above; so was his will
Pronounced among the gods, and by an oath,

8. Worthy of Atlas, the Titan who as a punishment for rebellion was condemned to hold up the heavens on his shoulders.
9. The official titles of angelic orders.

1. I.e., war has decided the question for us, but also limited us.
2. I.e., to the best of our power.

That shook Heav'n's whole circumference, confirmed.
Thither let us bend all our thoughts, to learn
355 What creatures there inhabit, of what mold,
Or substance, how endued,° and what their power,   *endowed*
And where their weakness, how attempted° best,   *attacked, tempted*
By force or subtlety. Though Heav'n be shut,
And Heav'n's high arbitrator sit secure
360 In his own strength, this place may lie exposed,
The utmost border of his kingdom, left
To their defense who hold it:³ here perhaps
Some advantageous act may be achieved
By sudden onset, either with hellfire
365 To waste° his whole creation, or possess   *lay waste*
All as our own, and drive as we were driven,
The puny habitants, or if not drive,
Seduce them to our party, that their God
May prove their foe, and with repenting hand
370 Abolish his own works.⁴ This would surpass
Common revenge, and interrupt his joy
In our confusion, and our joy upraise
In his disturbance; when his darling sons
Hurled headlong to partake with us, shall curse
375 Their frail original,° and faded bliss,   *originator, parent*
Faded so soon. Advise° if this be worth   *consider*
Attempting, or to sit in darkness here
Hatching vain empires." Thus Beëlzebub
Pleaded his devilish counsel, first devised
380 By Satan, and in part proposed: for whence,
But from the author of all ill could spring
So deep a malice, to confound° the race   *ruin*
Of mankind in one root,⁵ and earth with Hell
To mingle and involve, done all to spite
385 The great Creator? But their spite still serves
His glory to augment. The bold design
Pleased highly those infernal States,° and joy   *nobles*
Sparkled in all their eyes; with full assent
They vote: whereat his speech he thus renews.
390   "Well have ye judged, well ended long debate,
Synod of gods, and like to what ye are,
Great things resolved, which from the lowest deep
Will once more lift us up, in spite of fate,
Nearer our ancient seat; perhaps in view
395 Of those bright confines, whence with neighboring arms
And opportune excursion we may chance
Reenter Heav'n; or else in some mild zone
Dwell not unvisited of Heav'n's fair light
Secure, and at the bright'ning orient° beam   *lustrous*
400 Purge off this gloom; the soft delicious air,

3. To be defended by the occupants.
4. Cf. Genesis 6.7: "And the Lord said, 'I will destroy man [and all other creatures]; for it repen-

teth me that I have made them.'"
5. Adam, the first man, is the "root" of the human race.

To heal the scar of these corrosive fires
Shall breathe her balm. But first whom shall we send
In search of this new world, whom shall we find
Sufficient? Who shall tempt° with wand'ring feet   *attempt, venture*
405 The dark unbottomed infinite abyss
And through the palpable obscure[6] find out
His uncouth° way, or spread his aery flight   *unknown*
Upborne with indefatigable wings
Over the vast abrupt,[7] ere he arrive
410 The happy isle? What strength, what art can then
Suffice, or what evasion bear him safe
Through the strict senteries° and stations thick   *sentries*
Of angels watching round? Here he had need
All circumspection, and we now no less
415 Choice° in our suffrage; for on whom we send,   *discrimination*
The weight of all and our last hope relies."
     This said, he sat; and expectation held
His look suspense,[8] awaiting who appeared
To second, or oppose, or undertake
420 The perilous attempt: but all sat mute,
Pondering the danger with deep thoughts; and each
In other's count'nance read his own dismay
Astonished. None among the choice and prime
Of those Heav'n-warring champions could be found
425 So hardy as to proffer or accept
Alone the dreadful voyage; till at last
Satan, whom now transcendent glory raised
Above his fellows, with monarchal pride
Conscious of highest worth, unmoved thus spake.
430 "O progeny of Heav'n, empyreal Thrones,
With reason hath deep silence and demur°   *hesitation*
Seized us, though undismayed: long is the way
And hard, that out of Hell leads up to light;
Our prison strong, this huge convex of fire,
435 Outrageous to devour, immures us round
Ninefold,[9] and gates of burning adamant
Barred over us prohibit all egress.
These passed, if any pass, the void profound
Of unessential Night receives him next
440 Wide gaping, and with utter loss of being
Threatens him, plunged in that abortive gulf.[1]
If thence he scape into whatever world,
Or unknown region, what remains him less°   *awaits him except*
Than unknown dangers and as hard escape?
445 But I should ill become this throne, O Peers,
And this imperial sov'reignty, adorned

6. Darkness so thick it can be felt (cf. Exodus 10.21).
7. Chaos, a striking example of sound imitating sense.
8. I.e., he sat waiting in suspense.
9. Hell's fiery walls and gates have nine thick-

nesses (see lines 645ff.). "Adamant" (following): a fabulously hard metal.
1. Chaos is a womb in which all potential forms fragment (see lines 895ff.) "Unessential" (line 439): i.e., having no real essence.

With splendor, armed with power, if aught proposed
And judged of public moment,° in the shape   *importance*
Of difficulty or danger could deter
450 Me from attempting. Wherefore do I assume
These royalties, and not refuse to reign,
Refusing° to accept as great a share   *if I refuse*
Of hazard as of honor, due alike
To him who reigns, and so much to him due
455 Of hazard more, as he above the rest
High honored sits? Go therefore mighty Powers,
Terror of Heav'n, though fall'n; intend° at home,   *consider*
While here shall be our home, what best may ease
The present misery, and render Hell
460 More tolerable; if there be cure or charm
To respite or deceive, or slack the pain
Of this ill mansion: intermit no watch
Against a wakeful foe, while I abroad
Through all the coasts° of dark destruction seek   *districts*
465 Deliverance for us all: this enterprise
None shall partake with me." Thus saying rose
The monarch, and prevented° all reply,   *forestalled*
Prudent, lest from his resolution raised°   *roused*
Others among the chief might offer now
470 (Certain to be refused) what erst° they feared;   *formerly*
And so refused might in opinion stand
His rivals, winning cheap the high repute
Which he through hazard huge must earn. But they
Dreaded not more th' adventure than his voice
475 Forbidding; and at once with him they rose;
Their rising all at once was as the sound
Of thunder heard remote. Towards him they bend
With awful° reverence prone; and as a god   *full of awe*
Extol him equal to the Highest in Heav'n:
480 Nor failed they to express how much they praised,
That for the general safety he despised
His own: for neither do the Spirits damned
Lose all their virtue; lest bad men should boast
Their specious° deeds on earth, which glory excites, *pretending to worth*
485 Or close° ambition varnished o'er with zeal.   *secret*
  Thus they their doubtful consultations dark
Ended rejoicing in their matchless chief:
As when from mountaintops the dusky clouds
Ascending, while the north wind sleeps, o'erspread
490 Heav'n's cheerful face, the louring element°   *threatening sky*
Scowls o'er the darkened landscape snow, or show'r;
If chance the radiant sun with farewell sweet
Extend his evening beam, the fields revive,
The birds their notes renew, and bleating herds
495 Attest their joy, that hill and valley rings.
O shame to men! Devil with devil damned
Firm concord holds, men only disagree
Of creatures rational, though under hope

Of heavenly grace: and God proclaiming peace,
500 Yet live in hatred, enmity, and strife
Among themselves, and levy cruel wars,
Wasting the earth, each other to destroy:
As if (which might induce us to accord)
Man had not hellish foes enow° besides,   enough
505 That day and night for his destruction wait.
    The Stygian° council thus dissolved; and forth   Styx-like, hellish
In order came the grand infernal peers:
Midst came their mighty paramount,° and seemed   supreme ruler
Alone th' antagonist of Heav'n, nor less
510 Than Hell's dread emperor with pomp supreme,
And godlike imitated state; him round
A globe° of fiery Seraphim enclosed   band, circle
With bright emblazonry and horrent[2] arms.
Then of their session ended they bid cry
515 With trumpet's regal sound the great result:
Toward the four winds four speedy Cherubim
Put to their mouths the sounding alchemy[3]
By herald's voice explained; the hollow abyss
Heard far and wide, and all the host of Hell
520 With deaf'ning shout, returned them loud acclaim.
Thence more at ease their minds and somewhat raised
By false presumptuous hope, the rangèd° powers   arrayed in ranks
Disband, and wand'ring, each his several way
Pursues, as inclination or sad choice
525 Leads him perplexed, where he may likeliest find
Truce to his restless thoughts, and entertain
The irksome hours, till his great chief return.
Part on the plain, or in the air sublime°   aloft
Upon the wing, or in swift race contend,
530 As at th' Olympian games or Pythian fields;[4]
Part curb their fiery steeds, or shun the goal[5]
With rapid wheels, or fronted° brígades form.   confronting
As when to warn proud cities war appears
Waged in the troubled sky, and armies rush
535 To battle in the clouds,[6] before each van°   vanguard
Prick° forth the aery knights, and couch their spears   spur
Till thickest legions close; with feats of arms
From either end of Heav'n the welkin° burns.   sky
Others with vast Typhoean[7] rage more fell°   fierce
540 Rend up both rocks and hills, and ride the air
In whirlwind; Hell scarce holds the wild uproar.
As when Alcides from Oechalia crowned
With conquest, felt th' envenomed robe, and tore
Through pain up by the roots Thessalian pines,

---

2. Bristling. "Emblazonry": decorated shields.
3. Trumpets (made of the goldlike alloy brass).
4. The Olympic games were held at Olympia, the Pythian games at Delphi. Games celebrating a (usually dead) hero are an epic convention.
5. To drive a chariot as close as possible around a column without hitting it.
6. The appearance of warfare in the skies, reported before several notable battles, portends trouble on earth.
7. Like that of Typhon, the hundred-headed Titan (see 1.199).

545 And Lichas from the top of Oeta threw
     Into th' Euboic sea.[8] Others more mild,
     Retreated in a silent valley, sing
     With notes angelical to many a harp
     Their own heroic deeds and hapless fall
550 By doom of battle; and complain that fate
     Free virtue should enthrall to force or chance.
     Their song was partial,° but the harmony   *prejudiced*
     (What could it less when Spirits immortal sing?)
     Suspended° Hell, and took with ravishment   *held in suspense*
555 The thronging audience. In discourse more sweet
     (For eloquence the soul, song charms the sense)
     Others apart sat on a hill retired,
     In thoughts more elevate, and reasoned high
     Of providence, foreknowledge, will, and fate,
560 Fixed fate, free will, foreknowledge absolute,
     And found no end, in wand'ring mazes lost.
     Of good and evil much they argued then,
     Of happiness and final misery,
     Passion and apathy,[9] and glory and shame,
565 Vain wisdom all, and false philosophy:
     Yet with a pleasing sorcery could charm
     Pain for a while or anguish, and excite
     Fallacious hope, or arm th' obdurèd° breast   *hardened*
     With stubborn patience as with triple steel.
570 Another part in squadrons and gross° bands,   *solid, dense*
     On bold adventure to discover wide
     That dismal world, if any clime perhaps
     Might yield them easier habitation, bend
     Four ways their flying march, along the banks
575 Of four infernal rivers that disgorge
     Into the burning lake their baleful streams:[1]
     Abhorrèd Styx the flood of deadly hate,
     Sad Acheron of sorrow, black and deep;
     Cocytus, named of lamentation loud
580 Heard on the rueful stream; fierce Phlegethon
     Whose waves of torrent fire inflame with rage.
     Far off from these a slow and silent stream,
     Lethe the river of oblivion rolls
     Her wat'ry labyrinth, whereof who drinks,
585 Forthwith his former state and being forgets,
     Forgets both joy and grief, pleasure and pain.
     Beyond this flood a frozen continent
     Lies dark and wild, beat with perpetual storms
     Of whirlwind and dire hail, which on firm land
590 Thaws not, but gathers heap,[2] and ruin seems

---

8. Wearing a poisoned robe given him in a deception, Hercules ("Alcides") in his dying agonies
threw his beloved companion Lichas, along with a
good part of Mount Oeta, into the Euboean Sea,
near Thermopylae.
9. The Stoic goal of freedom from passion.
1. These four rivers are traditional in hellish

geography. Milton distinguishes them by the original meanings of their Greek names: Styx means
"hateful," Acheron "woeful," etc. Lethe is "far
off" and quite different from the others, oblivion
being a desired state in Hell.
2. In a heap, resembling the ruin of an old building ("ancient pile," next line).

Of ancient pile; all else deep snow and ice,
A gulf profound as that Serbonian bog[3]
Betwixt Damiata and Mount Casius old,
Where armies whole have sunk: the parching air
595 Burns frore,° and cold performs th' effect of fire.   *frozen*
Thither by harpy-footed[4] Furies haled,°   *driven*
At certain revolutions° all the damned   *recurring times*
Are brought: and feel by turns the bitter change
Of fierce extremes, extremes by change more fierce,
600 From beds of raging fire to starve° in ice   *make numb*
Their soft ethereal warmth, and there to pine
Immovable, infixed, and frozen round,
Periods of time; thence hurried back to fire.
They ferry over this Lethean sound
605 Both to and fro, their sorrow to augment,
And wish and struggle, as they pass, to reach
The tempting stream, with one small drop to lose
In sweet forgetfulness all pain and woe,
All in one moment, and so near the brink;
610 But fate withstands, and to oppose th' attempt
Medusa[5] with Gorgonian terror guards
The ford, and of itself the water flies
All taste of living wight,° as once it fled   *creature*
The lip of Tantalus.[6] Thus roving on
615 In cónfused march forlorn, th' advent'rous bands
With shudd'ring horror pale, and eyes aghast
Viewed first their lamentable lot, and found
No rest: through many a dark and dreary vale
They passed, and many a region dolorous,
620 O'er many a frozen, many a fiery alp,°   *volcano*
Rocks, caves, lakes, fens, bogs, dens, and shades of death,
A universe of death, which God by curse
Created evil, for evil only good,
Where all life dies, death lives, and nature breeds,
625 Perverse, all monstrous, all prodigious things,
Abominable, inutterable, and worse
Than fables yet have feigned, or fear conceived,
Gorgons and Hydras, and Chimeras[7] dire.
     Meanwhile the Adversary[8] of God and man,
630 Satan, with thoughts inflamed of highest design,
Puts on swift wings,° and towards the gates of Hell   *flies swiftly*
Explores his solitary flight; sometimes
He scours the right-hand coast, sometimes the left,
Now shaves with level wing the deep, then soars

---

3. Lake Serbonis, once famous for its quicksands, lies near the city of Damietta ("Damiata," next line), just east of the Nile.
4. Taloned. In Greek mythology the Harpies (monsters with women's faces) carried off individuals to the Furies, who avenged crimes.
5. One of the three Gorgons, women with snaky hair, scaly bodies, and boar's tusks, the sight of whose faces changed men to stone.

6. Tantalus, afflicted with a raging thirst, stood in the middle of a lake, the water of which always receded when he tried to drink (hence, "tantalize").
7. The Hydra was a serpent whose multiple heads grew back when severed; the Chimera was a fire-breathing creature, part lion, part dragon, part goat.
8. *Satan* in Hebrew means "adversary."

635　Up to the fiery concave° tow'ring high.   *vault*
 As when far off at sea a fleet descried
 Hangs on the clouds, by equinoctial° winds   *from the equator*
 Close sailing from Bengala,° or the isles   *Bengal*
 Of Ternate and Tidore,⁹ whence merchants bring
640　Their spicy drugs: they on the trading flood
 Through the wide Ethiopian to the Cape
 Ply stemming nightly toward the pole:¹ so seemed
 Far off the flying Fiend. At last appear
 Hell bounds high reaching to the horrid roof,
645　And thrice threefold the gates; three folds were brass,
 Three iron, three of adamantine rock,
 Impenetrable, impaled with circling fire,
 Yet unconsumed. Before the gates there sat
 On either side a formidable shape;²
650　The one seemed woman to the waist, and fair,
 But ended foul in many a scaly fold
 Voluminous and vast, a serpent armed
 With mortal sting: about her middle round
 A cry° of hellhounds never ceasing barked   *pack*
655　With wide Cerberean³ mouths full loud, and rung
 A hideous peal: yet, when they list,° would creep,   *wish*
 If aught disturbed their noise, into her womb,
 And kennel there, yet there still barked and howled,
 Within unseen. Far less abhorred than these
660　Vexed Scylla⁴ bathing in the sea that parts
 Calabria from the hoarse Trinacrian shore:
 Nor uglier follow the night-hag,⁵ when called
 In secret, riding through the air she comes
 Lured with the smell of infant blood, to dance
665　With Lapland witches, while the laboring° moon   *troubled*
 Eclipses at their charms.° The other shape,   *magic*
 If shape it might be called that shape had none
 Distinguishable in member, joint, or limb,
 Or substance might be called that shadow seemed,
670　For each seemed either; black it stood as night,
 Fierce as ten Furies, terrible as hell,
 And shook a dreadful dart; what seemed his head
 The likeness of a kingly crown had on.
 Satan was now at hand, and from his seat
675　The monster moving onward came as fast
 With horrid strides. Hell trembled as he strode.

---

9. Two of the Moluccas, or Spice Islands, modern Indonesia.
1. The South Pole. "Ethiopian": the Indian Ocean. "The Cape" is the Cape of Good Hope.
2. The allegorical figures of Sin and Death are founded on James 1.15: "Then when lust hath conceived, it bringeth forth sin: and sin, when it is finished, bringeth forth death." But the incestuous relations of Sin and Death are Milton's own invention. Physically, Sin is modeled on Virgil's or Ovid's Scylla, with some touches adopted from Spenser's Error. Death is a traditional figure,

vague and vast.
3. Like Cerberus, the multiheaded hound of Hell.
4. Circe, out of jealousy, threw poison into the water where Scylla bathed, in the straits between Calabria and Sicily ("Trinacria," next line); the poison caused Scylla to develop a ring of barking, snapping dogs around her waist.
5. Hecate (three syllables), goddess of sorcery. She attends orgies of witches in Lapland (line 665, famous for witchcraft), drawn by the blood of babies sacrificed for the occasion.

PARADISE LOST, BOOK 2 | 1979

Th' undaunted Fiend what this might be admired,°   *wondered*
Admired, not feared; God and his Son except,
Created thing naught valued he nor shunned;
680 And with disdainful look thus first began.
    "Whence and what art thou, execrable shape,
That dar'st, though grim and terrible, advance
Thy miscreated front° athwart my way   *misshapen face*
To yonder gates? Through them I mean to pass,
685 That be assured, without leave asked of thee:
Retire, or taste° thy folly, and learn by proof,   *experience*
Hell-born, not to contend with Spirits of Heav'n."
    To whom the goblin full of wrath replied:
"Art thou that traitor angel, art thou he,
690 Who first broke peace in Heav'n and faith, till then
Unbroken, and in proud rebellious arms
Drew after him the third part of Heav'n's sons
Conjured° against the Highest, for which both thou   *sworn together*
And they outcast from God, are here condemned
695 To waste eternal days in woe and pain?
And reckon'st thou thyself with Spirits of Heav'n,
Hell-doomed, and breath'st defiance here and scorn,
Where I reign king, and to enrage thee more,
Thy king and lord? Back to thy punishment,
700 False fugitive, and to thy speed add wings,
Lest with a whip of scorpions I pursue
Thy ling'ring, or with one stroke of this dart
Strange horror seize thee, and pangs unfelt before."
    So spake the grisly terror, and in shape,
705 So speaking and so threat'ning, grew tenfold
More dreadful and deform: on th' other side
Incensed with indignation Satan stood
Unterrified, and like a comet burned
That fires the length of Ophiuchus[6] huge
710 In th' arctic sky, and from his horrid° hair   *bristling*
Shakes pestilence and war. Each at the head
Leveled his deadly aim; their fatal hands
No second stroke intend, and such a frown
Each cast at th' other, as when, two black clouds
715 With Heav'n's artillery fraught,[7] come rattling on
Over the Caspian,[8] then stand front to front
Hov'ring a space, till winds the signal blow
To join their dark encounter in mid-air:
So frowned the mighty combatants, that Hell
720 Grew darker at their frown, so matched they stood;
For never but once more was either like
To meet so great a foe.[9] And now great deeds
Had been achieved, whereof all Hell had rung,
Had not the snaky sorceress that sat

---

6. A vast northern constellation, "the Serpent Bearer."
7. Loaded with thunderbolts.

8. The Caspian is a particularly stormy area.
9. I.e., the Son of God.

725 Fast by Hell gate, and kept the fatal key,
Ris'n, and with hideous outcry rushed between.
    "O father, what intends thy hand," she cried,
"Against thy only son?[1] What fury O son,
Possesses thee to bend that mortal dart
730 Against thy father's head? And know'st for whom;
For him who sits above and laughs the while
At thee ordained his drudge, to execute
Whate'er his wrath, which he calls justice, bids,
His wrath which one day will destroy ye both."
735   She spake, and at her words the hellish pest
Forbore, then these to her Satan returned.
    "So strange thy outcry, and thy words so strange
Thou interposest, that my sudden hand
Prevented° spares to tell thee yet by deeds   *forestalled*
740 What it intends; till first I know of thee,
What thing thou art, thus double-formed, and why
In this infernal vale first met thou call'st
Me father, and that phantasm call'st my son?
I know thee not, nor ever saw till now
745 Sight more detestable than him and thee."
    T' whom thus the portress of Hell gate replied:
"Hast thou forgot me then, and do I seem
Now in thine eye so foul, once deemed so fair
In Heav'n, when at th' assembly, and in sight
750 Of all the Seraphim with thee combined
In bold conspiracy against Heav'n's King,
All on a sudden miserable pain
Surprised thee, dim thine eyes, and dizzy swum
In darkness, while thy head flames thick and fast
755 Threw forth, till on the left side op'ning wide,
Likest to thee in shape and count'nance bright,
Then shining heav'nly fair, a goddess armed
Out of thy head I sprung:[2] amazement seized
All th' host of Heav'n; back they recoiled afraid
760 At first, and called me Sin, and for a sign
Portentous held me; but familiar grown,
I pleased, and with attractive graces won
The most averse, thee chiefly, who full oft
Thyself in me thy perfect image viewing
765 Becam'st enamored, and such joy thou took'st
With me in secret, that my womb conceived
A growing burden. Meanwhile war arose,
And fields were fought in Heav'n; wherein remained
(For what could else) to our almighty foe
770 Clear victory, to our part loss and rout
Through all the empyrean: down they fell
Driv'n headlong from the pitch° of Heaven, down   *summit*

---

1. Sin, Death, and Satan, in their various inter-
relations, parody obscenely the relations between
God and the Son, Adam and Eve.

2. As Athena sprang full grown from the head of
Zeus.

Into this deep, and in the general fall
I also; at which time this powerful key
775 Into my hand was giv'n, with charge to keep
These gates forever shut, which none can pass
Without my op'ning. Pensive here I sat
Alone, but long I sat not, till my womb
Pregnant by thee, and now excessive grown
780 Prodigious motion felt and rueful throes.
At last this odious offspring whom thou seest
Thine own begotten, breaking violent way
Tore through my entrails, that with fear and pain
Distorted, all my nether shape thus grew
785 Transformed: but he my inbred enemy
Forth issued, brandishing his fatal dart
Made to destroy: I fled, and cried out 'Death';
Hell trembled at the hideous name, and sighed
From all her caves, and back resounded 'Death.'
790 I fled, but he pursued (though more, it seems,
Inflamed with lust than rage) and swifter far,
Me overtook his mother all dismayed,
And in embraces forcible and foul
Engend'ring with me, of that rape begot
795 These yelling monsters that with ceaseless cry
Surround me, as thou saw'st, hourly conceived
And hourly born, with sorrow infinite
To me, for when they list,° into the womb   wish
That bred them they return, and howl and gnaw
800 My bowels, their repast; then bursting forth
Afresh with conscious terrors vex me round,
That rest or intermission none I find.
Before mine eyes in opposition sits
Grim Death my son and foe, who sets them on,
805 And me his parent would full soon devour
For want of other prey, but that he knows
His end with mine involved; and knows that I
Should prove a bitter morsel, and his bane,°   poison
Whenever that shall be; so fate pronounced.
810 But thou O father, I forewarn thee, shun
His deadly arrow; neither vainly hope
To be invulnerable in those bright arms,
Though tempered heav'nly, for that mortal dint,°   blow
Save he who reigns above, none can resist."
815   She finished, and the subtle Fiend his lore°   lesson
Soon learned, now milder, and thus answered smooth.
"Dear daughter, since thou claim'st me for thy sire,
And my fair son here show'st me, the dear pledge
Of dalliance had with thee in Heav'n, and joys
820 Then sweet, now sad to mention, through dire change
Befall'n us unforeseen, unthought of, know
I come no enemy, but to set free
From out this dark and dismal house of pain,
Both him and thee, and all the heav'nly host

825 Of Spirits that in our just pretenses° armed   *claims*
Fell with us from on high: from them I go
This uncouth errand[3] sole, and one for all
Myself expose, with lonely steps to tread
Th' unfounded° deep, and through the void immense   *bottomless*
830 To search with wand'ring quest a place foretold
Should be, and, by concurring signs, ere now
Created vast and round, a place of bliss
In the purlieus° of Heav'n, and therein placed   *outskirts*
A race of upstart creatures, to supply
835 Perhaps our vacant room, though more removed,
Lest Heav'n surcharged° with potent multitude   *overcrowded*
Might hap to move new broils:° be this or aught   *controversies*
Than this more secret now designed, I haste
To know, and this once known, shall soon return,
840 And bring ye to the place where thou and Death
Shall dwell at ease, and up and down unseen
Wing silently the buxom° air, embalmed°   *yielding / made fragrant*
With odors; there ye shall be fed and filled
Immeasurably, all things shall be your prey."
845 He ceased, for both seemed highly pleased, and Death
Grinned horrible a ghastly smile, to hear
His famine° should be filled, and blessed his maw°   *ravenous hunger / belly*
Destined to that good hour: no less rejoiced
His mother bad, and thus bespake her sire.
850   "The key of this infernal pit by due,
And by command of Heav'n's all-powerful King
I keep, by him forbidden to unlock
These adamantine gates; against all force
Death ready stands to interpose his dart,
855 Fearless to be o'ermatched by living might.
But what owe I to his commands above
Who hates me, and hath hither thrust me down
Into this gloom of Tartarus profound,
To sit in hateful office here confined,
860 Inhabitant of Heav'n, and heav'nly-born,
Here in perpetual agony and pain,
With terrors and with clamors compassed round
Of mine own brood, that on my bowels feed?
Thou art my father, thou my author, thou
865 My being gav'st me; whom should I obey
But thee, whom follow? Thou wilt bring me soon
To that new world of light and bliss, among
The gods who live at ease, where I shall reign
At thy right hand voluptuous,[4] as beseems
870 Thy daughter and thy darling, without end."
    Thus saying, from her side the fatal key,
Sad instrument of all our woe, she took;
And towards the gate rolling her bestial train,[5]

---

3. Unknown journey—a parody of Christ's errand on earth (3.236–65).
4. As the Son sits at God's right hand, Sin will at Satan's, a blasphemous parody of the Apostles' Creed and of *Paradise Lost* 3.250–80.
5. I.e. propelling her yelping offspring.

Forthwith the huge portcullis high up drew,
875 Which but herself not all the Stygian powers°   *armies of Hell*
Could once have moved; then in the keyhole turns
Th' intrícate wards, and every bolt and bar
Of massy iron or solid rock with ease
Unfastens: on a sudden open fly
880 With impetuous recoil and jarring sound
Th' infernal doors, and on their hinges grate
Harsh thunder, that the lowest bottom shook
Of Erebus.° She opened, but to shut   *Hell*
Excelled° her power; the gates wide open stood,   *exceeded*
885 That with extended wings a bannered host
Under spread ensigns° marching might pass through   *flags, standards*
With horse and chariots ranked in loose array;
So wide they stood, and like a furnace mouth
Cast forth redounding° smoke and ruddy flame.   *billowing*
890 Before their eyes in sudden view appear
The secrets of the hoary° deep, a dark   *ancient*
Illimitable° ocean without bound,   *without limit*
Without dimension, where length, breadth, and height,
And time and place are lost; where eldest Night
895 And Chaos, ancestors of Nature, hold
Eternal anarchy, amidst the noise
Of endless wars, and by confusion stand.
For Hot, Cold, Moist, and Dry, four champions fierce
Strive here for mastery, and to battle bring
900 Their embryon atoms;[6] they around the flag
Of each his faction, in their several clans,
Light-armed or heavy, sharp, smooth, swift or slow,
Swarm populous, unnumbered as the sands
Of Barca or Cyrene's torrid soil,[7]
905 Levied to side with warring winds, and poise[8]
Their lighter wings. To whom these most adhere,
He rules a moment; Chaos[9] umpire sits,
And by decision more embroils the fray
By which he reigns: next him high arbiter
910 Chance governs all. Into this wild abyss,
The womb of Nature and perhaps her grave,
Of neither sea, nor shore, nor air, nor fire,
But all these in their pregnant causes° mixed   *seeds*
Confus'dly, and which thus must ever fight,
915 Unless th' Almighty Maker them ordain
His dark materials to create more worlds,
Into this wild abyss the wary Fiend
Stood on the brink of Hell and looked a while,
Pondering his voyage; for no narrow frith°   *channel, firth*

---

6. These subatomic qualities combine together in
nature to form the four elements, fire, earth,
water, and air, but they struggle endlessly in
Chaos, where the atoms of these elements remain
undeveloped (in "embryo").
7. Cities built on the shifting sands of North
Africa.
8. Give weight to. "Levied": both enlisted and
raised up.
9. Chaos is both the place where confusion
reigns and personified confusion itself.

920 He had to cross. Nor was his ear less pealed°　　　　*dinned*
　　With noises loud and ruinous (to compare
　　Great things with small) than when Bellona[1] storms,
　　With all her battering engines bent to raze
　　Some capital city; or less than if this frame°　　　　*structure*
925 Of Heav'n were falling, and these elements
　　In mutiny had from her axle torn
　　The steadfast earth. At last his sail-broad vans°　　　　*wings*
　　He spreads for flight, and in the surging smoke
　　Uplifted spurns the ground, thence many a league
930 As in a cloudy chair ascending rides
　　Audacious, but that seat soon failing, meets
　　A vast vacuity: all unawares
　　Flutt'ring his pennons[2] vain plumb down he drops
　　Ten thousand fathom deep, and to this hour
935 Down had been falling, had not by ill chance
　　The strong rebuff° of some tumultuous cloud　　　　*counterblast*
　　Instinct° with fire and niter° hurried him　　　　*filled / saltpeter*
　　As many miles aloft: that fury stayed,
　　Quenched in a boggy Syrtis,[3] neither sea,
940 Nor good dry land: nigh foundered° on he fares,　　　　*drowned*
　　Treading the crude consistence, half on foot,
　　Half flying; behoves° him now both oar and sail.　　　　*befits*
　　As when a griffin through the wilderness
　　With wingèd course o'er hill or moory° dale,　　　　*marshy*
945 Pursues the Arimaspian, who by stealth
　　Had from his wakeful custody purloined
　　The guarded gold:[4] so eagerly the Fiend
　　O'er bog or steep, through strait, rough, dense, or rare,
　　With head, hands, wings, or feet pursues his way,
950 And swims or sinks, or wades, or creeps, or flies:
　　At length a universal hubbub wild
　　Of stunning sounds and voices all confused
　　Borne through the hollow dark assaults his ear
　　With loudest vehemence: thither he plies,
955 Undaunted to meet there whatever Power
　　Or Spirit of the nethermost abyss
　　Might in that noise reside, of whom to ask
　　Which way the nearest coast of darkness lies
　　Bordering on light; when straight behold the throne
960 Of Chaos, and his dark pavilion spread
　　Wide on the wasteful deep; with him enthroned
　　Sat sable-vested Night, eldest of things,
　　The consort of his reign; and by them stood
　　Orcus and Ades,[5] and the dreaded name
965 Of Demogorgon,[6] Rumor next and Chance,

---

1. Goddess of war.
2. Useless wings ("pinions").
3. Quicksand in North African gulfs, famous for their shifting sandbars.
4. Griffins, mythical creatures, half-eagle, half-lion, hoarded gold that was stolen from them by the one-eyed Arimaspians.
5. Latin and Greek names of Pluto, god of Hell.
6. A mysterious deity associated with Fate; Milton elsewhere identifies him with Chaos.

And Tumult and Confusion all embroiled,
And Discord with a thousand various mouths.
   T' whom Satan turning boldly, thus. "Ye Powers
And Spirits of this nethermost abyss,
970 Chaos and ancient Night, I come no spy,
With purpose to explore or to disturb
The secrets of your realm, but by constraint
Wand'ring this darksome desert, as my way
Lies through your spacious empire up to light,
975 Alone, and without guide, half lost, I seek
What readiest path leads where your gloomy bounds
Confine with° Heav'n; or if some other place   *border on*
From your dominion won, th' Ethereal King
Possesses lately, thither to arrive
980 I travel this profound;° direct my course;   *deep pit*
Directed, no mean recompense it brings
To your behoof,° if I that region lost,   *on your behalf*
All usurpation thence expelled, reduce
To her original darkness and your sway
985 (Which is my present journey)[7] and once more
Erect the standard there of ancient Night;
Yours be th' advantage all, mine the revenge."
   Thus Satan; and him thus the anarch[8] old
With falt'ring speech and visage incomposed°   *disordered*
990 Answered. "I know thee, stranger, who thou art,
That mighty leading angel, who of late
Made head against Heav'n's King, though overthrown.
I saw and heard, for such a numerous host
Fled not in silence through the frighted deep
995 With ruin upon ruin, rout on rout,
Confusion worse confounded; and Heav'n gates
Poured out by millions her victorious bands
Pursuing. I upon my frontiers here
Keep residence; if all I can will serve,
1000 That little which is left so to defend,
Encroached on still° through our intestine broils°   *constantly / civil wars*
Weak'ning the scepter of old Night: first Hell
Your dungeon stretching far and wide beneath;
Now lately heaven and earth,[9] another world
1005 Hung o'er my realm, linked in a golden chain
To that side Heav'n from whence your legions fell:
If that way be your walk, you have not far;
So much the nearer danger; go and speed;
Havoc and spoil and ruin are my gain."
1010   He ceased; and Satan stayed not to reply,
But glad that now his sea should find a shore,
With fresh alacrity and force renewed

---

7. The purpose of my present journey.
8. Chaos is not monarch of his realm but, appropriately, "anarch," nonruler.

9. The cosmos, with its own "heaven" (not the empyrean, the Heaven of God and the angels).

Springs upward like a pyramid of fire
Into the wild expanse, and through the shock
1015 Of fighting elements, on all sides round
Environed wins his way; harder beset
And more endangered, than when Argo passed
Through Bosporus betwixt the justling rocks:[1]
Or when Ulysses on the larboard shunned
1020 Charybdis, and by th' other whirlpool steered.[2]
So he with difficulty and labor hard
Moved on, with difficulty and labor he;
But he once passed, soon after when man fell,
Strange alteration! Sin and Death amain°   at full speed
1025 Following his track, such was the will of Heav'n,
Paved after him a broad and beaten way
Over the dark abyss, whose boiling gulf
Tamely endured a bridge of wondrous length
From Hell continued reaching th' utmost orb[3]
1030 Of this frail world; by which the Spirits perverse
With easy intercourse pass to and fro
To tempt or punish mortals, except whom
God and good angels guard by special grace.
But now at last the sacred influence
1035 Of light appears, and from the walls of Heav'n
Shoots far into the bosom of dim Night
A glimmering dawn; here Nature first begins
Her farthest verge,° and Chaos to retire   threshold
As from her outmost works a broken foe
1040 With tumult less and with less hostile din,
That° Satan with less toil, and now with ease   so that
Wafts on the calmer wave by dubious light
And like a weather-beaten vessel holds°   makes for
Gladly the port, though shrouds and tackle torn;
1045 Or in the emptier waste, resembling air
Weighs° his spread wings, at leisure to behold   balances
Far off th' empyreal Heav'n, extended wide
In circuit, undetermined square or round,
With opal tow'rs and battlements adorned
1050 Of living sapphire, once his native seat;
And fast by hanging in a golden chain
This pendent world,° in bigness as a star   universe
Of smallest magnitude close by the moon.
Thither full fraught with mischievous revenge,
1055 Accursed, and in a cursèd hour, he hies.

1. Jason and his fifty Argonauts, sailing through the Bosporus to the Black Sea in pursuit of the Golden Fleece, had to pass through the Symplegades, or clashing rocks.
2. Homer's Ulysses, sailing where Italy almost touches Sicily, had to pass between Charybdis, a whirlpool, and Scylla, a monster who devoured six of his men (not another whirlpool, as used here).
3. The bridge ends on the outermost sphere of the ten concentric spheres making up the universe.

Book 3

Hail holy Light, offspring of Heav'n firstborn,
Or of th' Eternal coeternal beam
May I express thee unblamed?[1] Since God is light,
And never but in unapproachèd light
5   Dwelt from eternity, dwelt then in thee,
Bright effluence of bright essence increate.°   *uncreated, eternal*
Or hear'st thou rather[2] pure ethereal stream,
Whose fountain who shall tell? Before the sun,
Before the heavens thou wert, and at the voice
10   Of God, as with a mantle, didst invest°   *cover*
The rising world of waters dark and deep,
Won from the void and formless infinite.
Thee I revisit now with bolder wing,
Escaped the Stygian pool, though long detained
15   In that obscure sojourn, while in my flight
Through utter and through middle darkness[3] borne
With other notes than to th' Orphéan lyre[4]
I sung of Chaos and eternal Night,
Taught by the Heav'nly Muse[5] to venture down
20   The dark descent, and up to reascend,
Though hard and rare: thee I revisit safe,
And feel thy sov'reign vital lamp; but thou
Revisit'st not these eyes, that roll in vain
To find thy piercing ray, and find no dawn;
25   So thick a drop serene hath quenched their orbs,
Or dim suffusion[6] veiled. Yet not the more
Cease I to wander where the Muses haunt
Clear spring, or shady grove, or sunny hill,
Smit with the love of sacred song; but chief
30   Thee Sion[7] and the flow'ry brooks beneath
That wash thy hallowed feet, and warbling flow,
Nightly I visit: nor sometimes forget°   *always remember*
Those other two equaled with me in fate,[8]
So were I equaled with them in renown,
35   Blind Thamyris and blind Maeonides,
And Tiresias and Phineus prophets old,[9]
Then feed on thoughts, that voluntary move
Harmonious numbers;° as the wakeful bird°   *verses / nightingale*
Sings darkling,° and in shadiest covert hid   *in the dark*

1. This second proem or invocation (3.1–55) is a hymn to Light, addressed either as the first creature of God or as coeternal with God, with allusion to 1 John 1.5, "God is Light, and in him is no darkness at all."
2. I.e., would you rather be called (a Latinism).
3. Hell is "utter" (i.e., outer) darkness; Chaos is middle darkness.
4. One of the so-called Orphic hymns is "To Night," and Orpheus himself visited the underworld. But Milton's song, Christian and epic, is of a different kind.
5. Urania (though not named until 7.1).
6. Cataract—*suffusio nigra*. "Drop serene": *gutta serena*, the medical term for Milton's kind of blindness.
7. The mountain of scriptural inspiration, with its brooks Siloa and Kidron.
8. I.e., blind like me.
9. Thamyris was a blind Thracian poet who lived before Homer; "Maeonides" is an epithet of Homer; Tiresias was the blind prophet of Thebes; Phineus was a blind king and seer (*Aeneid* 3).

40   Tunes her nocturnal note. Thus with the year
      Seasons return, but not to me returns
      Day, or the sweet approach of ev'n or morn,
      Or sight of vernal bloom, or summer's rose,
      Or flocks, or herds, or human face divine;
45   But cloud instead, and ever-during° dark   *everlasting*
      Surrounds me, from the cheerful ways of men
      Cut off, and for the book of knowledge° fair   *Book of Nature*
      Presented with a universal blank
      Of nature's works to me expunged and razed,°   *erased*
50   And wisdom at one entrance quite shut out.
      So much the rather thou celestial Light
      Shine inward, and the mind through all her powers
      Irradiate, there plant eyes, all mist from thence
      Purge and disperse, that I may see and tell
55   Of things invisible to mortal sight.
        Now had the Almighty Father from above,
      From the pure empyrean° where he sits   *Heaven*
      High throned above all height, bent down his eye,
      His own works and their works at once to view:
60   Above him all the sanctities° of Heaven   *angels*
      Stood thick as stars, and from his sight received
      Beatitude past utterance; on his right
      The radiant image of his glory sat,
      His only Son; on earth he first beheld
65   Our two first parents, yet the only two
      Of mankind, in the happy garden placed,
      Reaping immortal fruits of joy and love,
      Uninterrupted joy, unrivaled love
      In blissful solitude; he then surveyed
70   Hell and the gulf between, and Satan there
      Coasting the wall of Heav'n on this side Night
      In the dun° air sublime,° and ready now   *dusky / aloft*
      To stoop° with wearied wings, and willing feet   *swoop down*
      On the bare outside of this world,° that seemed   *universe*
75   Firm land embosomed without firmament,°   *atmosphere*
      Uncertain which, in ocean or in air.
      Him God beholding from his prospect high,
      Wherein past, present, future he beholds,
      Thus to his only Son foreseeing spake.
80   "Only begotten Son, seest thou what rage
      Transports our Adversary, whom no bounds
      Prescribed, no bars of Hell, nor all the chains
      Heaped on him there, nor yet the main° abyss   *vast*
      Wide interrupt[1] can hold; so bent he seems
85   On desperate revenge, that shall redound°   *flow back*
      Upon his own rebellious head. And now
      Through all restraint broke loose he wings his way
      Not far off Heav'n, in the precincts of light,
      Directly towards the new-created world,

---

1. Forming a wide breach between Heaven and Hell.

90　And man there placed, with purpose to essay°　　　　　　　　*try*
　　If him by force he can destroy, or worse,
　　By some false guile pervert; and shall pervert;
　　For man will hearken to his glozing° lies,　　　　　　　　*flattering*
　　And easily transgress the sole command,
95　Sole pledge of his obedience: so will fall
　　He and his faithless progeny: whose fault?
　　Whose but his own? Ingrate, he had of me
　　All he could have; I made him just and right,
　　Sufficient to have stood, though free to fall.
100　Such I created all th' ethereal Powers
　　And Spirits, both them who stood and them who failed;
　　Freely they stood who stood, and fell who fell.
　　Not free, what proof could they have giv'n sincere
　　Of true allegiance, constant faith or love,
105　Where only what they needs must do, appeared,
　　Not what they would? What praise could they receive?
　　What pleasure I from such obedience paid,
　　When will and reason (reason also is choice)
　　Useless and vain, of freedom both despoiled,
110　Made passive both, had served necessity,
　　Not me. They therefore as to right belonged,
　　So were created, nor can justly accuse
　　Their Maker, or their making, or their fate,
　　As if predestination overruled
115　Their will, disposed by absolute decree
　　Or high foreknowledge; they themselves decreed
　　Their own revolt, not I: if I foreknew,
　　Foreknowledge had no influence on their fault,
　　Which had no less proved certain unforeknown.[2]
120　So without least impulse or shadow of fate,
　　Or aught by me immutably foreseen,
　　They trespass, authors to themselves in all
　　Both what they judge and what they choose; for so
　　I formed them free, and free they must remain,
125　Till they enthrall themselves: I else must change
　　Their nature, and revoke the high decree
　　Unchangeable, eternal, which ordained
　　Their freedom, they themselves ordained their fall.
　　The first sort[3] by their own suggestion fell,
130　Self-tempted, self-depraved: man falls deceived
　　By the other first: man therefore shall find grace,
　　The other none: in mercy and justice both,
　　Through Heav'n and earth, so shall my glory excel,
　　But mercy first and last shall brightest shine."
135　　　Thus while God spake, ambrosial° fragrance filled　　*fragrant, immortal*
　　All Heav'n, and in the blessèd Spirits elect°　　　　　　　*unfallen*
　　Sense of new joy ineffable° diffused:　　　　　　　　*inexpressible*
　　Beyond compare the Son of God was seen
　　Most glorious, in him all his Father shone

2. I.e., if I had not foreknown it.　　　　　3. Satan and his crew.

140 Substantially expressed, and in his face
Divine compassion visibly appeared,
Love without end, and without measure grace,
Which uttering thus he to his Father spake.
    "O Father, gracious was that word which closed
145 Thy sov'reign sentence, that man should find grace;
For which both Heav'n and earth shall high extol
Thy praises, with th' innumerable sound
Of hymns and sacred songs, wherewith thy throne
Encompassed shall resound thee ever blessed.
150 For should man finally be lost, should man
Thy creature late so loved, thy youngest son
Fall circumvented thus by fraud, though joined
With his own folly? That be from thee far,
That far be from thee, Father, who art judge
155 Of all things made, and judgest only right.[4]
Or shall the Adversary thus obtain
His end, and frustrate thine, shall he fulfill
His malice, and thy goodness bring to naught,
Or proud return though to his heavier doom,
160 Yet with revenge accomplished, and to Hell
Draw after him the whole race of mankind,
By him corrupted? Or wilt thou thyself
Abolish thy creation, and unmake,
For him, what for thy glory thou hast made?
165 So should thy goodness and thy greatness both
Be questioned and blasphemed° without defense."   profaned
    To whom the great Creator thus replied.
"O Son, in whom my soul hath chief delight,
Son of my bosom, Son who art alone
170 My Word, my wisdom, and effectual might,[5]
All hast thou spoken as my thoughts are, all
As my eternal purpose hath decreed:
Man shall not quite be lost, but saved who will,
Yet not of will in him, but grace in me
175 Freely vouchsafed;° once more I will renew   bestowed
His lapsèd powers, though forfeit and enthralled
By sin to foul exorbitant desires;
Upheld by me, yet once more he shall stand
On even ground against his mortal foe,
180 By me upheld, that he may know how frail
His fall'n condition is, and to me owe
All his deliv'rance, and to none but me.
Some I have chosen of peculiar grace
Elect above the rest;[6] so is my will:

---

4. The Son echoes (or rather foreshadows) Abraham pleading with the Lord to spare Sodom: "That be far from thee to do after this manner, to slay the righteous with the wicked . . . that be far from thee: Shall not the Judge of all the earth do right?" (Genesis 18.25).

5. God's speech is rhythmic and sometimes rhymed.

6. In this speech, Milton's God rejects the Calvinist doctrine that he had from the beginning predestined the damnation or salvation of each individual soul; he claims rather that grace sufficient for salvation is offered to all, enabling everyone, if they choose to do so, to believe and persevere. He does, however, assert his right to give special grace to some.

185 The rest shall hear me call, and oft be warned°   *warned about*
     Their sinful state, and to appease betimes
     Th' incensèd Deity, while offered grace
     Invites; for I will clear their senses dark,
     What may suffice, and soften stony hearts
190 To pray, repent, and bring obedience due.
     To prayer, repentance, and obedience due,
     Though but endeavored with sincere intent,
     Mine ear shall not be slow, mine eye not shut.
     And I will place within them as a guide
195 My umpire conscience, whom if they will hear,
     Light after light well used they shall attain,[7]
     And to the end persisting, safe arrive.
     This my long sufferance and my day of grace
     They who neglect and scorn, shall never taste;
200 But hard be hardened, blind be blinded more,
     That they may stumble on, and deeper fall;
     And none but such from mercy I exclude.
     But yet all is not done; man disobeying,
     Disloyal breaks his fealty, and sins
205 Against the high supremacy of Heav'n,
     Affecting° Godhead, and so losing all,   *aspiring to*
     To expiate his treason hath naught left,
     But to destruction sacred and devote,°   *consecrated*
     He with his whole posterity must die,
210 Die he or justice must; unless for him
     Some other able, and as willing, pay
     The rigid satisfaction, death for death.
     Say heav'nly Powers, where shall we find such love,
     Which of ye will be mortal to redeem
215 Man's mortal crime,[8] and just th' unjust to save,
     Dwells in all Heaven charity so dear?"
       He asked, but all the heav'nly choir stood mute,[9]
     And silence was in Heav'n; on man's behalf
     Patron or intercessor none appeared,
220 Much less that durst upon his own head draw
     The deadly forfeiture, and ransom set.
     And now without redemption all mankind
     Must have been lost, adjudged to death and Hell
     By doom severe, had not the Son of God,
225 In whom the fullness dwells of love divine,
     His dearest mediation° thus renewed.   *intercession*
       "Father, thy word is passed, man shall find grace;
     And shall grace not find means, that finds her way,
     The speediest of thy wingèd messengers,
230 To visit all thy creatures, and to all
     Comes unprevented,° unimplored, unsought,   *unanticipated*
     Happy for man, so coming; he her aid

---

7. By using the light of conscience well they will gain more light.
8. "Mortal" means "human" in line 214, but "deadly" in line 215.
9. Compare the devils in the Great Consult, 2.420–26.

Can never seek, once dead in sins and lost;
Atonement for himself or offering meet,°   *fitting*
235 Indebted and undone, hath none to bring:
Behold me then, me for him, life for life
I offer, on me let thine anger fall;
Account me man; I for his sake will leave
Thy bosom, and this glory next to thee
240 Freely put off, and for him lastly die
Well pleased, on me let Death wreak all his rage;
Under his gloomy power I shall not long
Lie vanquished; thou hast giv'n me to possess
Life in myself forever, by thee I live,
245 Though now to Death I yield, and am his due
All that of me can die, yet that debt paid,
Thou wilt not leave me in the loathsome grave
His prey, nor suffer my unspotted soul
Forever with corruption there to dwell;
250 But I shall rise victorious, and subdue
My vanquisher, spoiled of his vaunted spoil;
Death his death's wound shall then receive, and stoop
Inglorious, of his mortal sting disarmed.
I through the ample air in triumph high
255 Shall lead Hell captive maugre° Hell, and show   *in spite of*
The powers of darkness bound. Thou at the sight
Pleased, out of Heaven shalt look down and smile,
While by thee raised I ruin[1] all my foes,
Death last, and with his carcass glut the grave:
260 Then with the multitude of my redeemed
Shall enter Heaven long absent, and return,
Father, to see thy face, wherein no cloud
Of anger shall remain, but peace assured,
And reconcilement; wrath shall be no more
265 Thenceforth, but in thy presence joy entire."
　　His words here ended, but his meek aspéct
Silent yet spake, and breathed immortal love
To mortal men, above which only shone
Filial obedience: as a sacrifice
270 Glad to be offered, he attends the will
Of his great Father. Admiration° seized   *wonder*
All Heav'n, what this might mean, and whither tend
Wond'ring; but soon th' Almighty thus replied:
　　"O thou in Heav'n and earth the only peace
275 Found out for mankind under wrath, O thou
My sole complacence!° well thou know'st how dear   *pleasure, delight*
To me are all my works, nor man the least
Though last created, that for him I spare
Thee from my bosom and right hand, to save,
280 By losing thee a while, the whole race lost.
Thou therefore whom[2] thou only canst redeem,

1. In the Latin sense, throw down.
2. The antecedent of "whom" is, loosely construed, the "their nature" that follows it.

Their nature also to thy nature join;
And be thyself man among men on earth,
Made flesh, when time shall be, of virgin seed,
285 By wondrous birth: be thou in Adam's room
The head of all mankind, though Adam's son.[3]
As in him perish all men, so in thee
As from a second root shall be restored,
As many as are restored, without thee none.
290 His crime makes guilty all his sons; thy merit
Imputed shall absolve them who renounce
Their own both righteous and unrighteous deeds,
And live in thee transplanted, and from thee
Receive new life.[4] So man, as is most just,
295 Shall satisfy for man, be judged and die,
And dying rise, and rising with him raise
His brethren, ransomed with his own dear life.
So heav'nly love shall outdo hellish hate,
Giving to death, and dying to redeem,
300 So dearly to redeem what hellish hate
So easily destroyed, and still destroys
In those who, when they may, accept not grace.
Nor shalt thou by descending to assume
Man's nature, lessen or degrade thine own.
305 Because thou hast, though throned in highest bliss
Equal to God, and equally enjoying
Godlike fruition,° quitted all to save   pleasurable possession
A world from utter loss, and hast been found
By merit more than birthright Son of God,[5]
310 Found worthiest to be so by being good,
Far more than great or high; because in thee
Love hath abounded more than glory abounds.
Therefore thy humiliation shall exalt
With thee thy manhood also to this throne;
315 Here shalt thou sit incarnate, here shalt reign
Both God and man, Son both of God and man,
Anointed[6] universal King; all power
I give thee, reign forever, and assume
Thy merits; under thee as Head Supreme
320 Thrones, Princedoms, Powers, Dominions[7] I reduce:
All knees to thee shall bow, of them that bide
In Heaven, or earth, or under earth in Hell;
When thou attended gloriously from Heav'n
Shalt in the sky appear, and from thee send
325 The summoning Archangels to proclaim
Thy dread tribunal: forthwith from all winds°   directions

The living, and forthwith the cited° dead   *summoned*
Of all past ages to the general doom°   *judgment*
Shall hasten, such a peal shall rouse their sleep.
330   Then all thy saints assembled, thou shalt judge
Bad men and angels, they arraigned° shall sink   *accursed*
Beneath thy sentence; Hell, her numbers full,
Thenceforth shall be forever shut. Meanwhile
The world shall burn, and from her ashes spring
335   New heav'n° and earth, wherein the just shall dwell,[8]   *sky, cosmos*
And after all their tribulations long
See golden days, fruitful of golden deeds,
With joy and love triumphing, and fair truth.
Then thou thy regal scepter shalt lay by,
340   For regal scepter then no more shall need,°   *be needed*
God shall be all in all. But all ye gods,°   *angels*
Adore him, who to compass all this dies,
Adore the Son, and honor him as me."
    No sooner had th' Almighty ceased, but all
345   The multitude of angels with a shout
Loud as from numbers without number, sweet
As from blest voices, uttering joy, Heav'n rung[9]
With jubilee, and loud hosannas filled
Th' eternal regions: lowly reverent
350   Towards either throne[1] they bow, and to the ground
With solemn adoration down they cast
Their crowns inwove with amarant[2] and gold,
Immortal amarant, a flow'r which once
In Paradise, fast by the Tree of Life
355   Began to bloom, but soon for man's offense
To Heav'n removed where first it grew, there grows,
And flow'rs aloft shading the Fount of Life,
And where the river of bliss through midst of Heav'n
Rolls o'er Elysian[3] flow'rs her amber stream;
360   With these that never fade the Spirits elect
Bind their resplendent locks inwreathed with beams,
Now in loose garlands thick thrown off, the bright
Pavement that like a sea of jasper shone
Impurpled with celestial roses smiled.
365   Then crowned again their golden harps they took,
Harps ever tuned, that glittering by their side
Like quivers hung, and with preamble sweet
Of charming symphony they introduce
Their sacred song, and waken raptures high;
370   No voice exempt,° no voice but well could join   *excluded*
Melodious part, such concord is in Heav'n.

8. Milton's description of the Last Judgment draws on several biblical texts, including Matthew 24.30–31 and 25.31–32; the account of the burning and re-creation of the heavens and earth is from 2 Peter 3.12–13.
9. "Multitude" (line 345) is the subject of the sentence, "rung" the verb, and "Heav'n" the object.
1. Thrones of God and the Son.
2. In Greek, "unfading," a legendary immortal flower.
3. Milton draws freely, for his Christian Heaven, on descriptions of the classical paradisal place, the Elysian Fields.

Thee Father first they sung omnipotent,
Immutable, immortal, infinite,
Eternal King; thee Author of all being,
375 Fountain of light, thyself invisible
Amidst the glorious brightness where thou sitt'st
Throned inaccessible, but° when thou shad'st   *except*
The full blaze of thy beams, and through a cloud
Drawn round about thee like a radiant shrine,[4]
380 Dark with excessive bright thy skirts appear,
Yet dazzle Heav'n, that brightest Seraphim
Approach not, but with both wings veil their eyes.
Thee next they sang of all creation first,[5]
Begotten Son, Divine Similitude,
385 In whose conspicuous count'nance, without cloud
Made visible, th' Almighty Father shines,
Whom else no creature can behold;[6] on thee
Impressed th' effulgence of his glory abides,
Transfused on thee his ample spirit rests.
390 He Heav'n of heavens and all the Powers therein
By thee created, and by thee threw down
Th' aspiring Dominations.[7] Thou that day
Thy Father's dreadful thunder didst not spare,
Nor stop thy flaming chariot wheels, that shook
395 Heav'n's everlasting frame, while o'er the necks
Thou drov'st of warring angels disarrayed.
Back from pursuit thy Powers° with loud acclaim   *angels*
Thee only extolled, Son of thy Father's might,
To execute fierce vengeance on his foes,
400 Not so on man; him through their malice fall'n,
Father of mercy and grace, thou didst not doom
So strictly, but much more to pity incline:
No sooner did thy dear and only Son
Perceive thee purposed not to doom° frail man   *judge*
405 So strictly, but much more to pity inclined,
He to appease thy wrath, and end the strife
Of mercy and justice in thy face discerned,
Regardless of the bliss wherein he sat
Second to thee, offered himself to die
410 For man's offense. O unexampled love,
Love nowhere to be found less than divine!
Hail Son of God, Savior of men, thy name
Shall be the copious matter of my[8] song
Henceforth, and never shall my harp thy praise
415 Forget, nor from thy Father's praise disjoin.
Thus they in Heav'n, above the starry sphere,
Their happy hours in joy and hymning spent.
Meanwhile upon the firm opacous° globe   *opaque*

4. The turn from theological debate to images that evoke a more mystical aspect of God.
5. The Son is not eternal, as in Trinitarian doctrine, but rather, God's first creation.
6. If it were not for the Son who is God's image,
no creature could see God.
7. The rebel angels.
8. Either Milton here quotes the angels singing as a single chorus, or he associates himself with their song, or both.

Of this round world, whose first convex divides
420 The luminous inferior orbs, enclosed
From Chaos and th' inroad of Darkness old,
Satan alighted walks:[9] a globe far off
It seemed, now seems a boundless continent
Dark, waste, and wild, under the frown of Night
425 Starless exposed, and ever-threatening storms
Of Chaos blust'ring round, inclement sky;
Save on that side which from the wall of Heav'n
Though distant far some small reflection gains
Of glimmering air less vexed with tempest loud:
430 Here walked the Fiend at large in spacious field.
As when a vulture on Imaus bred,
Whose snowy ridge the roving Tartar bounds,[1]
Dislodging from a region scarce of prey
To gorge the flesh of lambs or yeanling° kids   *newborn*
435 On hills where flocks are fed, flies toward the springs
Of Ganges or Hydaspes, Indian streams;[2]
But in his way lights on the barren plains
Of Sericana, where Chineses drive
With sails and wind their cany wagons light:
440 So on this windy sea of land, the Fiend
Walked up and down alone bent on his prey,
Alone, for other creature in this place
Living or lifeless to be found was none,
None yet, but store hereafter from the earth
445 Up hither like aërial vapors flew
Of all things transitory and vain, when sin
With vanity had filled the works of men:
Both all things vain, and all who in vain things
Built their fond° hopes of glory or lasting fame,   *foolish*
450 Or happiness in this or th' other life;
All who have their reward on earth, the fruits
Of painful superstition and blind zeal,
Naught seeking but the praise of men, here find
Fit retribution, empty as their deeds;
455 All th' unaccomplished° works of nature's hand,   *imperfect*
Abortive, monstrous, or unkindly° mixed,   *unnaturally*
Dissolved on earth, fleet° hither, and in vain,   *float*
Till final dissolution, wander here,
Not in the neighboring moon, as some[3] have dreamed;
460 Those argent° fields more likely habitants,   *silver*
Translated saints,[4] or middle Spirits hold
Betwixt th' angelical and human kind:

---

9. Satan is on the outermost of the ten concentric spheres that make up the cosmos.
1. Imaus, a ridge of mountains beyond the modern Himalayas, runs north through Asia from modern Afghanistan to the Arctic Circle.
2. Both the Ganges and the Hydaspes (a tributary of the Indus) rise from the mountains of northern India. Sericana (line 438) is a region in northwest China.

3. Milton's Paradise of Fools (named in line 496) was inspired by Ariosto's Limbo of Vanity in *Orlando Furioso* (Book 34, lines 73ff.); Milton's region is reserved for deluded victims of misplaced devotion, chiefly Roman Catholics.
4. Holy men like Enoch and Elijah, transported to Heaven while yet alive. (Genesis 5.24; 2 Kings 2.11–12).

Hither of ill-joined sons and daughters born
First from the ancient world those giants came
465   With many a vain exploit, though then renowned:[5]
The builders next of Babel on the plain
Of Sennaär,[6] and still with vain design
New Babels, had they wherewithal, would build:
Others came single; he who to be deemed
470   A god, leaped fondly° into Etna flames,   *foolishly*
Empedocles, and he who to enjoy
Plato's Elysium, leaped into the sea,
Cleombrotus, and many more too long,[7]
Embryos and idiots, eremites° and friars   *hermits*
475   White, black, and gray, with all their trumpery.[8]
Here pilgrims roam, that strayed so far to seek
In Golgotha[9] him dead, who lives in Heav'n;
And they who to be sure of paradise
Dying put on the weeds° of Dominic,   *garments*
480   Or in Franciscan think to pass disguised;[1]
They pass the planets seven, and pass the fixed,
And that crystalline sphere whose balance weighs
The trepidation talked, and that first moved;[2]
And now Saint Peter at Heav'n's wicket seems
485   To wait them with his keys, and now at foot
Of Heav'n's ascent they lift their feet, when lo
A violent crosswind from either coast
Blows them transverse ten thousand leagues awry
Into the devious° air. Then might ye see   *erratic*
490   Cowls, hoods, and habits[3] with their wearers tossed
And fluttered into rags; then relics, beads,
Indulgences, dispenses, pardons, bulls,
The sport of winds: all these upwhirled aloft
Fly o'er the backside° of the world far off   *rump*
495   Into a limbo large and broad, since called
The Paradise of Fools, to few unknown
Long after, now unpeopled, and untrod;
All this dark globe the Fiend found as he passed,
And long he wandered, till at last a gleam
500   Of dawning light turned thitherward in haste
His traveled° steps; far distant he descries   *travel-weary*
Ascending by degrees° magnificent   *steps*
Up to the wall of Heaven a structure high,

---

5. Giants, born of unnatural marriages between the "sons of God" and the daughters of men (Genesis 6.4), are creatures unkindly mixed.
6. Shinar, the plain of Babel (Genesis 11.2–9); the Tower of Babel is an emblem of human pride and folly.
7. I.e., it would take too long to name them. Both Empedocles and Cleombrotus foolishly carried piety to the point of suicide.
8. Religious paraphernalia. The white friars are Carmelites; the black, Dominicans; and the gray, Franciscans.
9. Place where Christ was crucified.
1. Some try to trick God into granting them sal-

vation by wearing on their deathbeds the garb of various religious orders.
2. Milton follows their souls through the spheres of the moon and sun, the five then-known planets, the fixed stars, and the sphere responsible for the "trepidation" (a periodic corrective shudder of the cosmos), up to the primum mobile, or prime mover. The next step seems to be the empyreal Heaven.
3. The dress of religious orders, together with (next lines) saints' relics, rosary beads, various kinds of pardon for sins, and papal decrees ("bulls").

At top whereof, but far more rich appeared
505 The work as of a kingly palace gate
With frontispiece° of diamond and gold   *pediment*
Embellished; thick with sparkling orient° gems   *lustrous*
The portal shone, inimitable on earth,
By model, or by shading pencil drawn.
510 The stairs were such as whereon Jacob saw
Angels ascending and descending, bands
Of guardians bright, when he from Esau fled
To Padan-Aram in the field of Luz,
Dreaming by night under the open sky,
515 And waking cried, "This is the gate of Heav'n."⁴
Each stair mysteriously was meant, nor stood
There always, but drawn up to Heav'n sometimes
Viewless,° and underneath a bright sea flowed   *invisible*
Of jasper, or of liquid pearl, whereon
520 Who after came from earth, sailing arrived,
Wafted by angels, or flew o'er the lake
Rapt in a chariot drawn by fiery steeds.⁵
The stairs were then let down, whether to dare
The Fiend by easy ascent, or aggravate
525 His sad exclusion from the doors of bliss.
Direct against which opened from beneath,
Just o'er the blissful seat of Paradise,
A passage down to th' earth, a passage wide,⁶
Wider by far than that of aftertimes
530 Over Mount Zion, and, though that were large,
Over the Promised Land to God so dear,
By which, to visit oft those happy tribes,
On high behests his angels to and fro
Passed frequent, and his eye with choice° regard   *discriminating*
535 From Paneas the fount of Jordan's flood
To Beërsaba, where the Holy Land
Borders on Egypt and the Arabian shore;⁷
So wide the op'ning seemed, where bounds were set
To darkness, such as bound the ocean wave.
540 Satan from hence now on the lower stair
That scaled by steps of gold to Heaven gate
Looks down with wonder at the sudden view
Of all this world at once. As when a scout
Through dark and desert ways with peril gone
545 All night; at last by break of cheerful dawn
Obtains° the brow of some high-climbing hill,   *gains*
Which to his eye discovers unaware
The goodly prospect of some foreign land
First seen, or some renowned metropolis
550 With glistering spires and pinnacles adorned,

---

4. The story of Jacob's vision is summarized from Genesis 28.1–19; the stairs of the ladder (next line) allegorically ("mysteriously") represent stages of spiritual growth.
5. Elijah was wafted to heaven in a chariot.

6. A passage through the crystalline spheres, otherwise impenetrable.
7. From Paneas (or Dan) in northern Palestine to Beersaba, or Beersheba, near the Egyptian border—the entire land of Israel.

Which now the rising sun gilds with his beams.
Such wonder seized, though after Heaven seen,
The Spirit malign, but much more envy seized
At sight of all this world beheld so fair.
555 Round he surveys, and well might, where he stood
So high above the circling canopy
Of night's extended shade; from eastern point
Of Libra to the fleecy star that bears
Andromeda far off Atlantic seas[8]
560 Beyond th' horizon; then from pole to pole
He views in breadth, and without longer pause
Down right into the world's first region throws
His flight precipitant, and winds with ease
Through the pure marble° air his oblique way   *sparkling*
565 Amongst innumerable stars, that shone
Stars distant, but nigh hand seemed other worlds,
Or other worlds they seemed, or happy isles,
Like those Hesperian gardens famed of old,
Fortunate fields, and groves and flow'ry vales,[9]
570 Thrice happy isles, but who dwelt happy there
He stayed not to inquire: above them all
The golden sun in splendor likest Heaven
Allured his eye: thither his course he bends
Through the calm firmament;° but up or down   *sky*
575 By center, or eccentric, hard to tell,
Or longitude,[1] where the great luminary
Aloof the vulgar constellations thick,
That from his lordly eye keep distance due,
Dispenses light from far; they as they move
580 Their starry dance in numbers that compute
Days, months, and years, towards his all-cheering lamp
Turn swift their various motions, or are turned
By his magnetic beam, that gently warms
The universe, and to each inward part
585 With gentle penetration, though unseen,
Shoots invisible virtue° even to the deep: *influence, strength*
So wondrously was set his station bright.
      There lands the Fiend, a spot like which perhaps
Astronomer in the sun's lucent orb
590 Through his glazed optic tube yet never saw.[2]
The place he found beyond expression bright,
Compared with aught on earth, metal or stone;
Not all parts like, but all alike informed
With radiant light, as glowing iron with fire;
595 If metal, part seemed gold, part silver clear;
If stone, carbuncle most or chrysolite,[3]
Ruby or topaz, to the twelve that shone

8. In the zodiac, Libra is diametrically opposite
Aries, or the Ram ("the fleecy star"), which seems
to carry the constellation Andromeda on its back.
9. The gardens of the Hesperides and the "fortunate isles" of Greek mythology, classical versions
of paradise, lay far out in the Atlantic.

1. The passage leaves open whether the sun or
the earth is at the center of the cosmos.
2. Galileo first observed sunspots through his
telescope in 1609.
3. Any green stone. "Carbuncle": any red stone.

In Aaron's breastplate,[4] and a stone besides
Imagined rather oft than elsewhere seen,[5]
600 That stone, or like to that which here below
Philosophers in vain so long have sought,[6]
In vain, though by their powerful art they bind
Volátile Hermes, and call up unbound
In various shapes old Proteus from the sea,
605 Drained through a limbec to his native form.[7]
What wonder then if fields and regions here
Breathe forth elixir pure,[8] and rivers run
Potable° gold, when with one virtuous° touch   *drinkable / powerful*
Th' arch-chemic° sun so far from us remote   *chief alchemist*
610 Produces with terrestrial humor° mixed   *earth's moisture*
Here in the dark so many precious things
Of color glorious and effect so rare?
Here matter new to gaze the Devil met
Undazzled, far and wide his eye commands,
615 For sight no obstacle found here, nor shade,
But all sunshine, as when his beams at noon
Culminate from th' equator, as they now
Shot upward still direct, whence no way round
Shadow from body opaque can fall,[9] and the air,
620 Nowhere so clear, sharpened his visual ray
To objects distant far,[1] whereby he soon
Saw within ken° a glorious angel stand,   *range of vision*
The same whom John saw also in the sun:[2]
His back was turned, but not his brightness hid;
625 Of beaming sunny rays, a golden tiar°   *tiara, crown*
Circled his head, nor less his locks behind
Illustrous° on his shoulders fledge° with wings   *lustrous / feathered*
Lay waving round; on some great charge employed
He seemed, or fixed in cogitation deep.
630 Glad was the Spirit impure; as now in hope
To find who might direct his wand'ring flight
To Paradise the happy seat of man,
His journey's end and our beginning woe.
But first he casts° to change his proper shape,   *contrives*
635 Which else might work him danger or delay:
And now a stripling Cherub he appears,
Not of the prime,[3] yet such as in his face
Youth smiled celestial, and to every limb
Suitable grace diffused, so well he feigned;

---

4. In Exodus 28.15–20, Aaron's "breastplate" is described as decorated with twelve different gems, of which Milton lists the first four.
5. I.e., elsewhere imagined more often than seen.
6. Alchemists had identified the "philosophers" store with the *urim* on Aaron's breastplate (Exodus 28.30); that stone reputedly could heal all diseases, restore paradise, and transmute base metals to gold.
7. "Hermes": the winged god and the element mercury, which evaporated readily ("volatile"). "Proteus": the shape-shifting sea god, a symbol of matter. Alchemists would "bind" (solidify)

mercury and dissolve or refine matter to its "native form" in a vessel (alembic, "limbec").
8. The liquid form of the philosopher's stone. "Here": in the sun.
9. Before the Fall (and the consequent tipping of the earth's axis) the sun at noon, on the equator, never cast a shadow. "Culminate": reach their zenith.
1. The eye was thought to emit a beam into the object perceived.
2. "I saw an angel standing in the sun" (Revelation 19.17).
3. Not yet in the prime of life.

640 Under a coronet his flowing hair
In curls on either cheek played, wings he wore
Of many a colored plume sprinkled with gold,
His habit fit for speed succinct,° and held   *close-fitting*
Before his decent° steps a silver wand.   *comely*
645 He drew not nigh unheard; the angel bright,
Ere he drew nigh, his radiant visage turned,
Admonished by his ear, and straight° was known   *immediately*
Th' Archangel Uriel, one of the sev'n
Who in God's presence, nearest to his throne[4]
650 Stand ready at command, and are his eyes
That run through all the heav'ns, or down to th' earth
Bear his swift errands over moist and dry,
O'er sea and land: him Satan thus accosts:
"Uriel, for thou of those sev'n Spirits that stand
655 In sight of God's high throne, gloriously bright,
The first art wont° his great authentic° will   *used / authoritative*
Interpreter through highest Heav'n to bring,
Where all his sons thy embassy attend;
And here art likeliest by supreme decree
660 Like honor to obtain, and as his eye
To visit oft this new creation round;
Unspeakable desire to see, and know
All these his wondrous works, but chiefly man,
His chief delight and favor,° him for whom   *favorite*
665 All these his works so wondrous he ordained,
Hath brought me from the choirs of Cherubim
Alone thus wand'ring. Brightest Seraph tell
In which of all these shining orbs hath man
His fixèd seat, or fixèd seat hath none,
670 But all these shining orbs his choice to dwell;
That I may find him, and with secret gaze,
Or open admiration him behold
On whom the great Creator hath bestowed
Worlds, and on whom hath all these graces poured;
675 That both in him and all things, as is meet,°   *fitting*
The Universal Maker we may praise;
Who justly hath driv'n out his rebel foes
To deepest Hell, and to repair that loss
Created this new happy race of men
680 To serve him better: wise are all his ways."
So spake the false dissembler unperceived;
For neither man nor angel can discern
Hypocrisy, the only evil that walks
Invisible, except to God alone,
685 By his permissive will, through Heav'n and earth:
And oft though wisdom wake, suspicion sleeps
At wisdom's gate, and to simplicity
Resigns her charge, while goodness thinks no ill

---

4. Uriel—in Hebrew, "light" (or "fire") of God—is the angel named first (in 2 Esdras 4.1–5, *apocrypha*)
among the seven angels who stood before God's throne.

Where no ill seems: which now for once beguiled
690 Uriel, though regent of the sun, and held
The sharpest-sighted Spirit of all in Heav'n;
Who to the fraudulent impostor foul
In his uprightness answer thus returned:
    "Fair angel, thy desire which tends° to know   *inclines*
695 The works of God, thereby to glorify
The great Work-Master, leads to no excess
That reaches blame, but rather merits praise
The more it seems excess, that led thee hither
From thy empyreal mansion thus alone,
700 To witness with thine eyes what some perhaps
Contented with report hear only in Heav'n:
For wonderful indeed are all his works,
Pleasant to know, and worthiest to be all
Had in remembrance always with delight;
705 But what created mind can comprehend
Their number, or the wisdom infinite
That brought them forth, but hid their causes deep.
I saw when at his word the formless mass,
This world's material mold,° came to a heap: *substance*
710 Confusion heard his voice, and wild uproar
Stood ruled, stood vast infinitude confined;
Till at his second bidding darkness fled,
Light shone, and order from disorder sprung:
Swift to their several quarters hasted then
715 The cumbrous elements, earth, flood, air, fire,
And this ethereal quintessence[5] of Heav'n
Flew upward, spirited with various forms,
That rolled orbicular,[6] and turned to stars
Numberless, as thou seest, and how they move;
720 Each had his place appointed, each his course,
The rest in circuit walls this universe.
Look downward on that globe whose hither side
With light from hence, though but reflected, shines;
That place is earth the seat of man, that light
725 His day, which else as th' other hemisphere
Night would invade, but there the neighboring moon
(So call that opposite fair star) her aid
Timely interposes, and her monthly round
Still ending, still renewing through mid-Heav'n,
730 With borrowed light her countenance triform[7]
Hence[8] fills and empties to enlighten th' earth,
And in her pale dominion checks the night.
That spot to which I point is Paradise,
Adam's abode, those lofty shades his bow'r.
735 Thy way thou canst not miss, me mine requires."

5. The fifth element, of which the incorruptible
heavenly bodies were made.
6. The spherical shape of the stars and their
orbits. "Spirited with various forms": presided
over or inhabited by various angelic spirits or
intelligences (Plato, *Timaeus* 41E).
7. The moon was said to have a triple nature:
Luna in Heaven, Diana on earth, and Hecate in
Hell.
8. From here (the sun).

Thus said, he turned, and Satan bowing low,
As to superior Spirits is wont in Heav'n,
Where honor due and reverence none neglects,
Took leave, and toward the coast of earth beneath,
740 Down from th' ecliptic,° sped with hoped success,   *the sun's orbit*
Throws his steep flight in many an airy wheel,
Nor stayed, till on Niphates' top[9] he lights.

Book 4

O for that warning voice, which he who saw
Th' Apocalypse, heard cry in Heaven aloud,
Then when the Dragon, put to second rout,
Came furious down to be revenged on men,
5 "Woe to the inhabitants on earth!"[1] that now,
While time was, our first parents had been warned
The coming of their secret foe, and scaped
Haply° so scaped his mortal° snare; for now   *perhaps / deadly*
Satan, now first inflamed with rage, came down,
10 The tempter ere° th' accuser of mankind,   *before being*
To wreak° on innocent frail man his loss   *avenge*
Of that first battle, and his flight to Hell:
Yet not rejoicing in his speed, though bold,
Far off and fearless, nor with cause to boast,
15 Begins his dire attempt, which nigh the birth
Now rolling, boils in his tumultuous breast,
And like a devilish engine back recoils
Upon himself; horror and doubt distract
His troubled thoughts, and from the bottom stir
20 The Hell within him, for within him Hell
He brings, and round about him, nor from Hell
One step no more than from himself can fly
By change of place: now conscience wakes despair
That slumbered, wakes the bitter memory
25 Of what he was, what is, and what must be
Worse; of worse deeds worse sufferings must ensue.
Sometimes towards Eden which now in his view
Lay pleasant, his grieved look he fixes sad,
Sometimes towards Heav'n and the full-blazing sun,
30 Which now sat high in his meridian tow'r:[2]
Then much revolving,° thus in sighs began.   *pondering*
 "O thou that with surpassing glory crowned,[3]
Look'st from thy sole dominion like the god
Of this new world: at whose sight all the stars
35 Hide their diminished heads; to thee I call,
But with no friendly voice, and add thy name

---

9. A mountain in Assyria.
1. John of Patmos, in Revelation 12.3–12, hears such a cry during a second war in Heaven, between the Dragon and the angels.
2. At midday, the height of noon.

3. Milton's nephew, Edward Phillips, said that this soliloquy was written "several years before the poem was begun," and was intended to begin a drama on the topic, *Adam Unparadised*.

O sun, to tell thee how I hate thy beams
That bring to my remembrance from what state
I fell, how glorious once above thy sphere;
40 Till pride and worse ambition threw me down
Warring in Heav'n against Heav'n's matchless King:
Ah wherefore! he deserved no such return
From me, whom he created what I was
In that bright eminence, and with his good
45 Upbraided[4] none, nor was his service hard.
What could be less than to afford him praise,
The easiest recompense, and pay him thanks,
How due! yet all his good proved ill in me,
And wrought but malice; lifted up so high
50 I 'sdained° subjection, and thought one step higher   *disdained*
Would set me highest, and in a moment quit°   *pay*
The debt immense of endless gratitude,
So burthensome still° paying, still to owe;   *always*
Forgetful what from him I still received,
55 And understood not that a grateful mind
By owing owes not, but still pays, at once
Indebted and discharged; what burden then?
O had his powerful destiny ordained
Me some inferior angel, I had stood
60 Then happy; no unbounded hope had raised
Ambition. Yet why not? some other Power°   *angel*
As great might have aspired, and me though mean
Drawn to his part; but other Powers as great
Fell not, but stand unshaken, from within
65 Or from without, to all temptations armed.
Hadst thou[5] the same free will and power to stand?
Thou hadst: whom hast thou then or what to accuse,
But Heav'n's free love dealt equally to all?
Be then his love accursed, since love or hate,
70 To me alike, it deals eternal woe.
Nay cursed be thou; since against his thy will
Chose freely what it now so justly rues.
Me miserable![6] which way shall I fly
Infinite wrath, and infinite despair?
75 Which way I fly is Hell; myself am Hell;[7]
And in the lowest deep a lower deep
Still threat'ning to devour me opens wide,
To which the Hell I suffer seems a Heav'n.
O then at last relent! is there no place
80 Left for repentance, none for pardon left?
None left but by submission; and that word
Disdain forbids me, and my dread of shame
Among the Spirits beneath, whom I seduced
With other promises and other vaunts

4. Reproached (James 1.5).
5. Compare Satan's address to himself here with Adam's soliloquy in parallel circumstances (10.758ff.).

6. A Latinism, *me miserum!*
7. Compare Satan's earlier claim that "the mind is its own place" (1.254).

85   Than to submit, boasting I could subdue
     Th' Omnipotent. Ay me, they little know
     How dearly I abide° that boast so vain,   *pay the penalty far*
     Under what torments inwardly I groan:
     While they adore me on the throne of Hell,
90   With diadem and scepter high advanced
     The lower still I fall, only supreme
     In misery; such joy ambition finds.
     But say I could repent and could obtain
     By act of grace[8] my former state; how soon
95   Would heighth recall high thoughts, how soon unsay
     What feigned submission swore: ease would recant
     Vows made in pain, as violent° and void.   *forced*
     For never can true reconcilement grow
     Where wounds of deadly hate have pierced so deep:
100   Which would but lead me to a worse relapse,
     And heavier fall: so should I purchase dear
     Short intermission bought with double smart.
     This knows my punisher; therefore as far
     From granting he, as I from begging peace:
105   All hope excluded thus, behold instead
     Of us outcast, exiled, his new delight,
     Mankind created, and for him this world.
     So farewell hope, and with hope farewell fear,
     Farewell remorse: all good to me is lost;
110   Evil be thou my good; by thee at least
     Divided empire with Heav'n's King I hold
     By thee, and more than half perhaps will reign;
     As man ere long, and this new world shall know."
        Thus while he spake, each passion dimmed his face
115   Thrice changed with pale,° ire, envy, and despair,   *pallor*
     Which marred his borrowed visage, and betrayed
     Him counterfeit, if any eye beheld.
     For heav'nly minds from such distempers foul
     Are ever clear. Whereof he soon aware,
120   Each perturbation smoothed with outward calm,
     Artificer of fraud; and was the first
     That practiced falsehood under saintly show,
     Deep malice to conceal, couched° with revenge: *hidden*
     Yet not enough had practiced to deceive
125   Uriel once warned; whose eye pursued him down
     The way he went, and on th' Assyrian mount°   *Niphates*
     Saw him disfigured, more than could befall
     Spirit of happy sort: his gestures fierce
     He marked and mad demeanor, then alone,
130   As he supposed, all unobserved, unseen.
        So on he fares, and to the border comes
     Of Eden, where delicious Paradise,[9]
     Now nearer, crowns with her enclosure green,

---

8. The technical term for a formal pardon.
9. Paradise is a delightful ("delicious") garden on top of a steep hill situated in the east of the land of Eden.

As with a rural mound the champaign head°   *open summit*
135 Of a steep wilderness, whose hairy sides
With thicket overgrown, grotesque[1] and wild,
Access denied; and overhead up grew
Insuperable heighth of loftiest shade,
Cedar, and pine, and fir, and branching palm,
140 A sylvan scene, and as the ranks ascend
Shade above shade, a woody theater[2]
Of stateliest view. Yet higher than their tops
The verdurous wall of Paradise up sprung:
Which to our general sire gave prospect large
145 Into his nether empire neighboring round.
And higher than that wall a circling row
Of goodliest trees loaden with fairest fruit,
Blossoms and fruits at once of golden hue
Appeared, with gay enameled° colors mixed: *bright*
150 On which the sun more glad impressed his beams
Than in fair evening cloud, or humid bow,°   *rainbow*
When God hath show'red the earth; so lovely seemed
That landscape: and of pure now purer air[3]
Meets his approach, and to the heart inspires°   *infuses*
155 Vernal delight and joy, able to drive°   *drive out*
All sadness but despair: now gentle gales
Fanning their odoriferous° wings dispense   *fragrance-bearing*
Native perfumes, and whisper whence they stole
Those balmy spoils. As when to them who sail
160 Beyond the Cape of Hope,° and now are past   *Cape of Good Hope*
Mozambic, off at sea northeast winds blow
Sabean odors from the spicy shore
Of Araby the Blest,[4] with such delay
Well pleased they slack their course, and many a league
165 Cheered with the grateful° smell old Ocean smiles.   *pleasing*
So entertained those odorous sweets the Fiend
Who came their bane,° though with them better pleased   *poison*
Than Asmodeus with the fishy fume,
That drove him, though enamored, from the spouse
170 Of Tobit's son, and with a vengeance sent
From Media post to Egypt, there fast bound.[5]
  Now to th'ascent of that steep savage° hill   *wooded, wild*
Satan had journeyed on, pensive and slow;
But further way found none, so thick entwined,
175 As one continued brake,° the undergrowth   *thicket*
Of shrubs and tangling bushes had perplexed
All path of man or beast that passed that way:
One gate there only was, and that looked east

---

1. Characterized by interwoven, tangled vines and branches.
2. As if in a Greek amphitheater, the trees are set row on row.
3. The air becomes still purer.
4. *Arabia Felix* (modern Yemen). "Sabean": the biblical Sheba.
5. The Apocryphal book of Tobit tells of Tobias,

Tobit's son, who married Sara and avoided the fate of her previous seven husbands (killed on their wedding night by the demon Asmodeus) by following the instructions of the angel Raphael and making a fishy smell to drive him off; Asmodeus then fled to Egypt, where Raphael bound him.

On th' other side: which when th' arch-felon saw
180 Due entrance he disdained, and in contempt,
At one slight bound high overleaped all bound
Of hill or highest wall, and sheer within
Lights on his feet. As when a prowling wolf,
Whom hunger drives to seek new haunt for prey,
185 Watching where shepherds pen their flocks at eve
In hurdled cotes° amid the field secure,   *pens of woven reeds*
Leaps o'er the fence with ease into the fold:
Or as a thief bent to unhoard the cash
Of some rich burgher, whose substantial doors,
190 Cross-barred and bolted fast, fear no assault,
In at the window climbs, or o'er the tiles;
So clomb° this first grand thief into God's fold: *climbed*
So since into his church lewd hirelings[6] climb.
Thence up he flew, and on the Tree of Life,
195 The middle tree and highest there that grew,
Sat like a cormorant;[7] yet not true life
Thereby regained, but sat devising death
To them who lived; nor on the virtue° thought   *power*
Of that life-giving plant, but only used
200 For prospect,° what well used had been the pledge   *as a lookout*
Of immortality. So little knows
Any, but God alone, to value right
The good before him, but perverts best things
To worst abuse, or to their meanest use.
205   Beneath him with new wonder now he views
To all delight of human sense exposed
In narrow room nature's whole wealth, yea more,
A heav'n on earth: for blissful Paradise
Of God the garden was, by him in the east
210 Of Eden planted; Eden stretched her line
From Auran eastward to the royal tow'rs
Of great Seleucia, built by Grecian kings,
Or where the sons of Eden long before
Dwelt in Telassar:[8] in this pleasant soil
215 His far more pleasant garden God ordained;
Out of the fertile ground he caused to grow
All trees of noblest kind for sight, smell, taste;
And all amid them stood the Tree of Life,
High eminent, blooming ambrosial° fruit   *divinely fragrant*
220 Of vegetable gold; and next to life
Our death the Tree of Knowledge grew fast by,
Knowledge of good bought dear by knowing ill.
Southward through Eden went a river large,[9]
Nor changed his course, but through the shaggy hill
225 Passed underneath engulfed, for God had thrown

6. Base men interested only in money; Milton would have clergymen not paid by required tithes or by the state, to ensure their purity of motive.
7. A sea bird, noted for gluttony.
8. Auran is the province of Hauran on the eastern border of Israel. Selucia, a powerful city on the Tigris, near modern Baghdad, was founded by one of Alexander's generals ("built by Grecian kings"). Telassar is another Near Eastern kingdom.
9. The Tigris (identified at 9.71) flowed under the hill.

That mountain as his garden mold° high raised   *rich earth*
Upon the rapid current, which through veins
Of porous earth with kindly° thirst up drawn,   *natural*
Rose a fresh fountain, and with many a rill
230   Watered the garden; thence united fell
Down the steep glade, and met the nether flood,
Which from his darksome passage now appears,
And now divided into four main streams,
Runs diverse, wand'ring many a famous realm
235   And country whereof here needs no account,
But rather to tell how, if art could tell,
How from that sapphire fount the crispèd° brooks,   *wavy, rippling*
Rolling on orient pearl and sands of gold,
With mazy error¹ under pendent shades
240   Ran nectar, visiting each plant, and fed
Flow'rs worthy of Paradise which not nice° art   *fastidious*
In beds and curious knots, but nature boon°   *bounteous*
Poured forth profuse on hill and dale and plain,
Both where the morning sun first warmly smote
245   The open field, and where the unpierced shade
Embrowned° the noontide bow'rs. Thus was this place, *darkened*
A happy rural seat of various view,²
Groves whose rich trees wept odorous gums and balm,
Others whose fruit burnished with golden rind
250   Hung amiable,° Hesperian fables true,³   *lovely*
If true, here only, and of delicious taste:
Betwixt them lawns, or level downs,° and flocks   *uplands*
Grazing the tender herb, were interposed,
Or palmy hillock, or the flow'ry lap
255   Of some irriguous° valley spread her store,   *well-watered*
Flow'rs of all hue, and without thorn the rose:
Another side, umbrageous° grots and caves   *shady*
Of cool recess, o'er which the mantling° vine   *enveloping*
Lays forth her purple grape, and gently creeps
260   Luxuriant; meanwhile murmuring waters fall
Down the slope hills, dispersed, or in a lake,
That to the fringèd bank with myrtle crowned,
Her crystal mirror holds, unite their streams.
The birds their choir apply; airs,⁴ vernal airs,
265   Breathing the smell of field and grove, attune
The trembling leaves, while universal Pan⁵
Knit° with the Graces and the Hours in dance   *clasping hands*
Led on th' eternal spring. Not that fair field
Of Enna, where Proserpine gathering flow'rs
270   Herself a fairer flow'r by gloomy Dis
Was gathered, which cost Ceres all that pain
To seek her through the world; nor that sweet grove

---

1. From Latin *errare*, wandering.
2. Like a country estate, with a variety of prospects.
3. These were real golden apples, by contrast to those feigned golden apples of the Hesperides, fabled paradisal islands in the Western Ocean.
4. Both breezes and melodies. "Their choir apply": practice their songs.
5. The god of all nature—*pan* in Greek means "all."

Of Daphne by Orontes, and th' inspired
Castalian spring, might with this Paradise
275 Of Eden strive;[6] nor that Nyseian isle
Girt with the river Triton, where old Cham,
Whom Gentiles Ammon call and Libyan Jove,
Hid Amalthea and her florid° son   *wine-flushed*
Young Bacchus from his stepdame Rhea's eye;[7]
280 Nor where Abassin kings their issue guard,
Mount Amara,[8] though this by some supposed
True Paradise under the Ethiop line°   *equator*
By Nilus'° head, enclosed with shining rock,   *Nile's*
A whole day's journey high, but wide remote
285 From this Assyrian garden,° where the Fiend *Eden*
Saw undelighted all delight, all kind
Of living creatures new to sight and strange:
    Two of far nobler shape erect and tall,
Godlike erect, with native honor clad
290 In naked majesty seemed lords of all,
And worthy seemed, for in their looks divine
The image of their glorious Maker shone,
Truth, wisdom, sanctitude severe and pure,
Severe but in true filial freedom placed;
295 Whence true authority in men;[9] though both
Not equal, as their sex not equal seemed;
For contemplation he and valor formed,
For softness she and sweet attractive grace,
He for God only, she for God in him:[1]
300 His fair large front° and eye sublime declared *forehead*
Absolute rule; and hyacinthine[2] locks
Round from his parted forelock manly hung
Clust'ring, but not beneath his shoulders broad:
She as a veil down to the slender waist
305 Her unadorned golden tresses wore
Disheveled, but in wanton° ringlets waved   *unrestrained*
As the vine curls her tendrils,[3] which implied
Subjection, but required° with gentle sway,° *requested / persuasion*
And by her yielded, by him best received,
310 Yielded with coy° submission, modest pride, *shyly reserved*
And sweet reluctant amorous delay.
Nor those mysterious parts were then concealed,
Then was not guilty shame, dishonest° shame *unchaste*

6. Milton compares Paradise with famous beauty spots of antiquity. Enna in Sicily was a lovely meadow from which Proserpine was kidnapped by "gloomy Dis" (i.e., Pluto); her mother Ceres sought her throughout the world. The grove of Daphne, near Antioch and the Orontes River in the Near East, had a spring called "Castalia" after the Muses' fountain near Parnassus.

7. The isle of Nysa in the river Triton in Tunisia was where Ammon (an Egyptian god, identified with Cham, or Ham, the son of Noah) hid Bacchus, his child by Amalthea (who later became the god of wine), away from the eyes of his wife Rhea.

8. Atop Mount Amara, the "Abassin" (Abyssinian) king had a splendid palace in a paradisal garden.

9. This phrase underscores Milton's idea that true freedom involves obedience to natural superiors (i.e., God).

1. The phrase has as its context 1 Corinthians 11.3: "The head of every man is Christ; and the head of the woman is the man."

2. A classical metaphor for hair curled in the form of hyacinth petals, and perhaps also implying dark or flowing.

3. Eve's hair is curly, abundant, not subjected to rigid control, like the vegetation in Paradise.

Of nature's works, honor dishonorable,
315 Sin-bred, how have ye troubled all mankind
With shows instead, mere shows of seeming pure,
And banished from man's life his happiest life,
Simplicity and spotless innocence.
So passed they naked on, nor shunned the sight
320 Of God or angel, for they thought no ill:
So hand in hand they passed, the loveliest pair
That ever since in love's embraces met,
Adam the goodliest man of men since born
His sons, the fairest of her daughters Eve.
325 Under a tuft of shade that on a green
Stood whispering soft, by a fresh fountain side
They sat them down, and after no more toil
Of their sweet gard'ning labor than sufficed
To recommend cool Zephyr,[4] and made ease
330 More easy, wholesome thirst and appetite
More grateful, to their supper fruits they fell,
Nectarine° fruits which the compliant boughs   *sweet as nectar*
Yielded them, sidelong as they sat recline
On the soft downy bank damasked with flow'rs:
335 The savory pulp they chew, and in the rind
Still as they thirsted scoop the brimming stream;
Nor gentle purpose,° nor endearing smiles   *conversation*
Wanted,° nor youthful dalliance as beseems   *lacked*
Fair couple, linked in happy nuptial league,
340 Alone as they. About them frisking played
All beasts of th' earth, since wild, and of all chase°   *game animals*
In wood or wilderness, forest or den;
Sporting the lion ramped,° and in his paw   *stood on hind legs*
Dandled the kid; bears, tigers, ounces,° pards°   *lynxes / leopards*
345 Gamboled before them; th' unwieldy elephant
To make them mirth used all his might, and wreathed
His lithe proboscis;° close the serpent sly   *trunk*
Insinuating,° wove with Gordian twine   *writhing, twisting*
His braided train,[5] and of his fatal guile
350 Gave proof unheeded; others on the grass
Couched, and now filled with pasture gazing sat,
Or bedward ruminating:° for the sun   *chewing the cud*
Declined was hasting now with prone° career   *sinking*
To th' Ocean Isles,° and in th' ascending scale   *the Azores*
355 Of Heav'n the stars that usher evening rose:
When Satan still in gaze, as first he stood,
Scarce thus at length failed speech recovered sad.
    "O Hell! what do mine eyes with grief behold,
Into our room of bliss thus high advanced
360 Creatures of other mold, earth-born perhaps,
Not Spirits, yet to heav'nly Spirits bright
Little inferior; whom my thoughts pursue

---

4. I.e., to make a cool breeze welcome.
5. Checkered body. "Gordian twine": cords as
convoluted as the Gordian knot that Alexander
the Great had to cut with his sword.

With wonder, and could love, so lively shines
In them divine resemblance, and such grace
365 The hand that formed them on their shape hath poured.
Ah gentle pair, ye little think how nigh
Your change approaches, when all these delights
Will vanish and deliver ye to woe,
More woe, the more your taste is now of joy;
370 Happy, but for so happy° ill secured   *such happiness*
Long to continue, and this high seat your heav'n
Ill fenced for Heav'n to keep out such a foe
As now is entered; yet no purposed foe
To you whom I could pity thus forlorn
375 Though I unpitied: league with you I seek,
And mutual amity so strait,° so close,   *intimate*
That I with you must dwell, or you with me
Henceforth; my dwelling haply° may not please   *perhaps*
Like this fair Paradise, your sense, yet such
380 Accept your Maker's work; he gave it me,
Which I as freely give; Hell shall unfold,
To entertain you two, her widest gates,
And send forth all her kings; there will be room,
Not like these narrow limits, to receive
385 Your numerous offspring; if no better place,
Thank him who puts me loath to this revenge
On you who wrong me not for° him who wronged.   *in place of*
And should I at your harmless innocence
Melt, as I do, yet public reason just,
390 Honor and empire with revenge enlarged
By conquering this new world, compels me now
To do what else though damned I should abhor."[6]
    So spake the Fiend, and with necessity,
The tyrant's plea, excused his devilish deeds.
395 Then from his lofty stand on that high tree
Down he alights among the sportful herd
Of those four-footed kinds, himself now one,
Now other, as their shape served best his end
Nearer to view his prey, and unespied
400 To mark what of their state he more might learn
By word or action marked: about them round
A lion now he stalks with fiery glare,
Then as a tiger, who by chance hath spied
In some purlieu° two gentle fawns at play,   *outskirts of a forest*
405 Straight° couches close, then rising changes oft   *at once*
His couchant watch, as one who chose his ground
Whence rushing he might surest seize them both
Gripped in each paw: when Adam first of men
To first of women Eve thus moving speech
410 Turned him all ear to hear new utterance flow:
    "Sole partner and sole° part of all these joys,   *chief*
Dearer thyself than all; needs must the Power

---

6. Satan's excuse—reason of state, public interest, empire, etc.—is called "the tyrant's plea" in line 394.

That made us, and for us this ample world
Be infinitely good, and of his good
415 As liberal and free as infinite,
That raised us from the dust and placed us here
In all this happiness, who at his hand
Have nothing merited, nor can perform
Aught whereof he hath need, he who requires
420 From us no other service than to keep
This one, this easy charge, of all the trees
In Paradise that bear delicious fruit
So various, not to taste that only Tree
Of Knowledge, planted by the Tree of Life,
425 So near grows death to life, whate'er death is,
Some dreadful thing no doubt; for well thou know'st
God hath pronounced it death to taste that Tree,
The only sign of our obedience left
Among so many signs of power and rule
430 Conferred upon us, and dominion giv'n
Over all other creatures that possess
Earth, air, and sea. Then let us not think hard
One easy prohibition, who enjoy
Free leave so large to all things else, and choice
435 Unlimited of manifold delights:
But let us ever praise him, and extol
His bounty, following our delightful task
To prune these growing plants, and tend these flow'rs,
Which were it toilsome, yet with thee were sweet."
440   To whom thus Eve replied. "O thou for whom
And from whom I was formed flesh of thy flesh,
And without whom am to no end, my guide
And head, what thou hast said is just and right.
For we to him indeed all praises owe,
445 And daily thanks, I chiefly who enjoy
So far the happier lot, enjoying thee
Preeminent by so much odds,° while thou   *advantage*
Like consort to thyself canst nowhere find.
That day I oft remember, when from sleep
450 I first awaked, and found myself reposed°   *resting*
Under a shade on flowers, much wond'ring where
And what I was, whence thither brought, and how.
Not distant far from thence a murmuring sound
Of waters issued from a cave and spread
455 Into a liquid plain, then stood unmoved
Pure as th' expanse of Heav'n; I thither went
With unexperienced thought, and laid me down
On the green bank, to look into the clear
Smooth lake, that to me seemed another sky.
460 As I bent down to look, just opposite,
A shape within the wat'ry gleam appeared
Bending to look on me, I started back,
It started back, but pleased I soon returned,
Pleased it returned as soon with answering looks

465 Of sympathy and love; there I had fixed
Mine eyes till now, and pined with vain° desire,[7]   *futile*
Had not a voice thus warned me, 'What thou seest,
What there thou seest fair creature is thyself,
With thee it came and goes: but follow me,
470 And I will bring thee where no shadow stays°   *hinders*
Thy coming, and thy soft embraces, he
Whose image thou art, him thou shall enjoy
Inseparably thine, to him shalt bear
Multitudes like thyself, and thence be called
475 Mother of human race': what could I do,
But follow straight° invisibly thus led?   *at once*
Till I espied thee, fair indeed and tall,
Under a platan,° yet methought less fair,   *plane tree*
Less winning soft, less amiably mild,
480 Than that smooth wat'ry image; back I turned,
Thou following cried'st aloud, 'Return fair Eve,
Whom fli'st thou? Whom thou fli'st, of him thou art,
His flesh, his bone; to give thee being I lent
Out of my side to thee, nearest my heart
485 Substantial life, to have thee by my side
Henceforth an individual° solace dear;   *inseparable, distinct*
Part of my soul I seek thee, and thee claim
My other half': with that thy gentle hand
Seized mine, I yielded, and from that time see
490 How beauty is excelled by manly grace
And wisdom, which alone is truly fair."
     So spake our general mother, and with eyes
Of conjugal attraction unreproved,
And meek surrender, half embracing leaned
495 On our first father, half her swelling breast
Naked met his under the flowing gold
Of her loose tresses hid: he in delight
Both of her beauty and submissive charms
Smiled with superior love, as Jupiter
500 On Juno smiles, when he impregns° the clouds   *impregnates*
That shed May flowers; and pressed her matron lip
With kisses pure: aside the Devil turned
For envy, yet with jealous leer malign
Eyed them askance, and to himself thus plained.°   *complained*
505   "Sight hateful, sight tormenting! thus these two
Imparadised in one another's arms
The happier Eden, shall enjoy their fill
Of bliss on bliss, while I to Hell am thrust,
Where neither joy nor love, but fierce desire,
510 Among our other torments not the least,
Still° unfulfilled with pain of longing pines;   *always*
Yet let me not forget what I have gained
From their own mouths; all is not theirs it seems:

---

7. Eve's experience reprises (but with significant differences) the story of Narcissus, who fell in love with his own reflection and was transformed into a flower.

One fatal tree there stands of Knowledge called,
515 Forbidden them to taste: knowledge forbidden?
Suspicious, reasonless. Why should their Lord
Envy° them that? Can it be sin to know,   *begrudge*
Can it be death? And do they only stand
By ignorance, is that their happy state,
520 The proof of their obedience and their faith?
O fair foundation laid whereon to build
Their ruin! Hence I will excite their minds
With more desire to know, and to reject
Envious commands, invented with design
525 To keep them low whom knowledge might exalt
Equal with gods; aspiring to be such,
They taste and die: what likelier can ensue?
But first with narrow search I must walk round
This garden, and no corner leave unspied;
530 A chance, but chance[8] may lead where I may meet
Some wand'ring Spirit of Heav'n, by fountain side,
Or in thick shade retired, from him to draw
What further would be learnt. Live while ye may,
Yet happy pair; enjoy, till I return,
535 Short pleasures, for long woes are to succeed."
     So saying, his proud step he scornful turned,
But with sly circumspection, and began
Through wood, through waste, o'er hill, o'er dale his roam.°   *act of wandering*
Meanwhile in utmost longitude, where heav'n°   *the sky*
540 With earth and ocean meets, the setting sun
Slowly descended, and with right aspéct
Against the eastern gate of Paradise
Leveled his evening rays.[9] It was a rock
Of alabaster,[1] piled up to the clouds,
545 Conspicuous far, winding with one ascent
Accessible from earth, one entrance high;
The rest was craggy cliff, that overhung
Still as it rose, impossible to climb.
Betwixt these rocky pillars Gabriel[2] sat
550 Chief of th' angelic guards, awaiting night;
About him exercised heroic games
Th' unarmèd youth of Heav'n, but nigh at hand
Celestial armory, shields, helms, and spears
Hung high with diamond flaming, and with gold.
555 Thither came Uriel, gliding through the even
On a sunbeam, swift as a shooting star
In autumn thwarts° the night, when vapors fired   *passes across*
Impress the air, and shows the mariner
From what point of his compass to beware
560 Impetuous winds:[3] he thus began in haste.

---

8. An opportunity, even if only by luck.
9. Setting in the west, the sun struck the eastern gate from the inside, at a ninety-degree angle.
1. White, translucent marble veined with colors.
2. In Hebrew, "strength of God." A tradition (cf. 1

Enoch 20.7) gave Gabriel charge of Paradise.
3. Shooting stars were thought to indicate by the direction of their fall the source of oncoming storms. "Vapors fired": heat lightning.

"Gabriel, to thee thy course by lot hath giv'n
Charge and strict watch that to this happy place
No evil thing approach or enter in;
This day at height of noon came to my sphere
565 A Spirit, zealous, as he seemed, to know
More of th' Almighty's works, and chiefly man
God's latest image: I described° his way   *descried, observed*
Bent all on speed, and marked his airy gait;°   *path*
But in the mount that lies from Eden north,
570 Where he first lighted, soon discerned his looks
Alien from Heav'n, with passions foul obscured:
Mine eye pursued him still, but under shade°   *trees*
Lost sight of him; one of the banished crew
I fear, hath ventured from the deep, to raise
575 New troubles; him thy care must be to find."
     To whom the winged warrior thus returned:
"Uriel, no wonder if thy perfect sight,
Amid the sun's bright circle where thou sitt'st,
See far and wide. In at this gate none pass
580 The vigilance here placed, but such as come
Well known from Heav'n; and since meridian hour°   *noon*
No creature thence: if Spirit of other sort,
So minded, have o'erleaped these earthy bounds
On purpose, hard thou know'st it to exclude
585 Spiritual substance with corporeal bar.
But if within the circuit of these walks,
In whatsoever shape he lurk, of whom
Thou tell'st, by morrow dawning I shall know."
     So promised he, and Uriel to his charge
590 Returned on that bright beam, whose point now raised
Bore him slope downward to the sun now fall'n
Beneath th' Azorès; whether the prime orb,
Incredible how swift, had thither rolled
Diurnal,° or this less volúble° earth   *daily / swift-turning*
595 By shorter flight to th' east,[4] had left him there
Arraying with reflected purple and gold
The clouds that on his western throne attend.
Now came still evening on, and twilight gray
Had in her sober livery all things clad;
600 Silence accompanied, for beast and bird,
They to their grassy couch, these to their nests
Were slunk, all but the wakeful nightingale;
She all night long her amorous descant° sung;   *melody*
Silence was pleased: now glowed the firmament
605 With living sapphires: Hesperus[5] that led
The starry host, rode brightest, till the moon
Rising in clouded majesty, at length
Apparent° queen unveiled her peerless light,   *clearly seen*

---

4. Here and elsewhere Milton leaves open the question of whether the sun moves around the earth, or vice versa.

5. Called Venus when it appears in the evening sky.

And o'er the dark her silver mantle threw.

610   When Adam thus to Eve: "Fair consort, th' hour
Of night, and all things now retired to rest
Mind us of like repose, since God hath set
Labor and rest, as day and night to men
Successive, and the timely dew of sleep

615 Now falling with soft slumbrous weight inclines
Our eyelids; other creatures all day long
Rove idle unemployed, and less need rest;
Man hath his daily work of body or mind
Appointed, which declares his dignity,

620 And the regard of Heav'n on all his ways;
While other animals unactive range,
And of their doings God takes no account.
Tomorrow ere fresh morning streak the east
With first approach of light, we must be ris'n,

625 And at our pleasant labor, to reform
Yon flow'ry arbors, yonder alleys green,
Our walk at noon, with branches overgrown,
That mock our scant manuring,° and require   *cultivating*
More hands than ours to lop their wanton° growth: *luxuriant*

630 Those blossoms also, and those dropping gums,
That lie bestrown unsightly and unsmooth,
Ask riddance,° if we mean to tread with ease;   *need to be cleared*
Meanwhile, as nature wills, night bids us rest."
    To whom thus Eve with perfect beauty adorned.

635 "My author and disposer, what thou bidd'st
Unargued I obey; so God ordains,
God is thy law, thou mine: to know no more
Is woman's happiest knowledge and her praise.
With thee conversing I forget all time.

640 All seasons° and their change, all please alike.   *times of day*
Sweet[6] is the breath of morn, her rising sweet,
With charm[7] of earliest birds; pleasant the sun
When first on this delightful land he spreads
His orient° beams, on herb, tree, fruit, and flow'r,   *lustrious, eastern*

645 Glist'ring with dew; fragrant the fertile earth
After soft showers; and sweet the coming on
Of grateful evening mild, then silent night
With this her solemn bird° and this fair moon,   *the nightingale*
And these the gems of heav'n, her starry train:

650 But neither breath of morn when she ascends
With charm of earliest birds, nor rising sun
On this delightful land, nor herb, fruit, flow'r,
Glist'ring with dew, nor fragrance after showers,
Nor grateful evening mild, nor silent night

655 With this her solemn bird, nor walk by moon,
Or glittering starlight without thee is sweet.

---

6. With this embedded lyric, beginning here, Eve displays her literary talents in an elegant love song, sonnetlike and replete with striking rhetorical figures of circularity and repetition.
7. Blended singing of many birds.

But wherefore all night long shine these, for whom
This glorious sight, when sleep hath shut all eyes?"
    To whom our general ancestor replied.
660 "Daughter of God and man, accomplished[8] Eve,
Those have their course to finish, round the earth,
By morrow evening, and from land to land
In order, though to nations yet unborn,
Minist'ring light prepared, they set and rise;
665 Lest total darkness should by night regain
Her old possession, and extinguish life
In nature and all things, which these soft° fires   *agreeable*
Not only enlighten, but with kindly° heat   *natural, benevolent*
Of various influence foment° and warm,   *foster*
670 Temper or nourish, or in part shed down
Their stellar virtue on all kinds that grow
On earth, made hereby apter to receive
Perfection from the sun's more potent ray.[9]
These then, though unbeheld in deep of night,
675 Shine not in vain, nor think, though men were none,
That heav'n would want° spectators, God want praise;   *lack*
Millions of spiritual creatures walk the earth
Unseen, both when we wake, and when we sleep:
All these with ceaseless praise his works behold
680 Both day and night: how often from the steep
Of echoing hill or thicket have we heard
Celestial voices to the midnight air,
Sole, or responsive each to other's note
Singing their great Creator: oft in bands
685 While they keep watch, or nightly rounding walk,
With heav'nly touch of instrumental sounds
In full harmonic number joined, their songs
Divide[1] the night, and lift our thoughts to Heaven."
    Thus talking hand in hand alone they passed
690 On to their blissful bower; it was a place
Chos'n by the sov'reign Planter, when he framed°   *fashioned*
All things to man's delightful use; the roof
Of thickest covert was inwoven shade
Laurel and myrtle, and what higher grew
695 Of firm and fragrant leaf; on either side
Acanthus, and each odorous bushy shrub
Fenced up the verdant wall; each beauteous flow'r,
Iris all hues, roses, and jessamine°   *jasmine*
Reared high their flourished° heads between, and wrought   *flowering*
700 Mosaic; underfoot the violet,
Crocus, and hyacinth with rich inlay
Broidered the ground, more colored than with stone
Of costliest emblem:° other creature here   *inlaid work*
Beast, bird, insect, or worm durst enter none,

8. Having many talents and achievements; perfect, complete.
9. The stars were thought to have their own occult influence, and also to moderate that of the sun.
1. Mark the watches of the night; also, perform musical "divisions," elaborate melodic passages.

705 Such was their awe of man. In shadier bower
More sacred and sequestered,° though but feigned,   *secluded*
Pan or Silvanus never slept, nor nymph,
Nor Faunus[2] haunted. Here in close recess
With flowers, garlands, and sweet-smelling herbs
710 Espousèd Eve decked first her nuptial bed,
And heav'nly choirs the hymenean° sung,   *wedding song*
What day the genial[3] angel to our sire
Brought her in naked beauty more adorned,
More lovely than Pandora, whom the gods
715 Endowed with all their gifts, and O too like
In sad event,° when to the unwiser son   *outcome*
Of Japhet brought by Hermes, she ensnared
Mankind with her fair looks, to be avenged
On him who had stole Jove's authentic fire.[4]
720   Thus at their shady lodge arrived, both stood,
Both turned, and under open sky adored
The God that made both sky, air, earth, and heav'n
Which they beheld, the moon's resplendent globe
And starry pole:° "Thou also mad'st the night,   *sky*
725 Maker Omnipotent, and thou the day,
Which we in our appointed work employed
Have finished happy in our mutual help
And mutual love, the crown of all our bliss
Ordained by thee, and this delicious place
730 For us too large, where thy abundance wants
Partakers, and uncropped falls to the ground.
But thou hast promised from us two a race
To fill the earth, who shall with us extol
Thy goodness infinite, both when we wake,
735 And when we seek, as now, thy gift of sleep."
    This said unanimous, and other rites
Observing none, but adoration pure
Which God likes best,[5] into their inmost bow'r
Handed° they went; and eased° the putting off   *hand in hand / spared*
740 These troublesome disguises which we wear,
Straight side by side were laid, nor turned I ween°   *surmise*
Adam from his fair spouse, nor Eve the rites
Mysterious[6] of connubial love refused:
Whatever hypocrites austerely talk
745 Of purity and place and innocence,
Defaming as impure what God declares
Pure, and commands to some, leaves free to all.

---

2. Forest and field divinities of classical mythology.

3. Presiding over marriage and generation.

4. Pandora (the name means "all gifts") was an artificial woman, molded of clay, bestowed by the gods on Epimetheus, brother of Prometheus (who angered Jove by stealing fire from heaven). She brought a box that foolish Epimetheus opened, releasing all the ills of the human race, leaving only hope inside. The brothers were sons of Iapetos, whom Milton identifies with Japhet,

Noah's third son. The Eve-Pandora parallel was often noted.

5. Like many Puritans, Milton objected to set forms of prayer, so Adam and Eve pray spontaneously (therefore sincerely), but also, paradoxically, together. Their prayer develops variations on Psalm 104.20–24.

6. Ephesians 5.32 calls the union of man and woman a "mystery" paralleling that of Christ and the church.

Our Maker bids increase,[7] who bids abstain
But our destroyer, foe to God and man?
750 Hail wedded Love, mysterious law, true source
Of human offspring, sole propriety°   *private property*
In Paradise of all things common else.
By thee adulterous lust was driv'n from men
Among the bestial herds to range, by thee
755 Founded in reason, loyal, just, and pure,
Relations dear, and all the charities°   *loves*
Of father, son, and brother first were known.
Far be it, that I should write thee sin or blame,
Or think thee unbefitting holiest place,
760 Perpetual fountain of domestic sweets,
Whose bed is undefiled and chaste pronounced,
Present, or past, as saints and patriarchs used.[8]
Here Love his golden shafts employs,[9] here lights
His constant lamp, and waves his purple wings,
765 Reigns here and revels; not in the bought smile
Of harlots, loveless, joyless, unendeared,
Casual fruition, nor in court amours,
Mixed dance, or wanton masque, or midnight ball,
Or serenade, which the starved° lover sings   *deprived*
770 To his proud fair, best quitted with disdain.
These lulled by nightingales embracing slept,
And on their naked limbs the flow'ry roof
Show'red roses, which the morn repaired.° Sleep on,   *replaced*
Blest pair; and O yet happiest if ye seek
775 No happier state, and know to know no more.[1]
     Now had night measured with her shadowy cone
Halfway up hill this vast sublunar vault,[2]
And from their ivory port the Cherubim
Forth issuing at th' accustomed hour stood armed
780 To their night watches in warlike parade,
When Gabriel to his next in power thus spake:
     "Uzziel,[3] half these draw off, and coast° the south   *skirt*
With strictest watch; these other wheel[4] the north,
Our circuit meets full west." As flame they part
785 Half wheeling to the shield, half to the spear.
From these, two strong and subtle Spirits he called
That near him stood, and gave them thus in charge:
     "Ithuriel and Zephon,[5] with winged speed
Search through this garden, leave unsearched no nook,
790 But chiefly where those two fair creatures lodge,
Now laid perhaps asleep secure of° harm.   *from*

7. Genesis 1.28: "Be fruitful and multiply, and replenish the earth."
8. Throughout history ("present or past"), Old and New Testament worthies have "used" matrimony as a noble estate.
9. The "golden shafts" (arrows) of Cupid produce true love, his lead-tipped arrows, hate.
1. Know enough to be content with what you know.

2. The conical shadow cast by the earth has moved halfway up to its zenith, so it is 9 P.M., the end of the first three-hour watch.
3. Hebrew, "my strength is God."
4. "Wheel": turn to (military term); "shield" (line 785) is left, "spear" is right.
5. Hebrew, "a looking out." "Ithuriel": Hebrew, "discovery of God."

This evening from the sun's decline arrived
Who° tells of some infernal Spirit seen   *one who*
Hitherward bent; who could have thought? escaped
795   The bars of Hell, on errand bad no doubt:
Such where ye find, seize fast, and hither bring."
      So saying, on he led his radiant files,
Dazzling the moon; these to the bower direct
In search of whom they sought: him there they found
800   Squat like a toad, close at the ear of Eve;
Assaying° by his devilish art to reach   *attempting*
The organs of her fancy,[6] and with them forge
Illusions as he list,° phantasms and dreams;   *pleased*
Or if, inspiring° venom, he might taint   *breathing*
805   Th' animal spirits that from pure blood arise
Like gentle breaths from rivers pure, thence raise
At least distempered,° discontented thoughts,   *disordered*
Vain hopes, vain aims, inordinate desires
Blown up with high conceits° engend'ring pride.   *notions*
810   Him thus intent Ithuriel with his spear
Touched lightly; for no falsehood can endure
Touch of celestial temper,[7] but returns
Of force to its own likeness: up he starts
Discovered and surprised. As when a spark
815   Lights on a heap of nitrous powder,[8] laid
Fit for the tun some magazine to store
Against a rumored war, the smutty° grain   *black*
With sudden blaze diffused, inflames the air:
So started up in his own shape the Fiend.
820   Back stepped those two fair angels half amazed
So sudden to behold the grisly king;
Yet thus, unmoved with fear, accost him soon:
      "Which of those rebel Spirits adjudged to Hell
Com'st thou, escaped thy prison; and transformed,
825   Why sat'st thou like an enemy in wait
Here watching at the head of these that sleep?"
      "Know ye not then," said Satan, filled with scorn,
"Know ye not me? Ye knew me once no mate
For you, there sitting where ye durst not soar;
830   Not to know me argues° yourselves unknown,   *proves*
The lowest of your throng; or if ye know,
Why ask ye, and superfluous begin
Your message, like to end as much in vain?"
      To whom thus Zephon, answering scorn with scorn:
835   "Think not, revolted Spirit, thy shape the same,
Or undiminished brightness, to be known
As when thou stood'st in Heav'n upright and pure;
That glory then, when thou no more wast good,
Departed from thee, and thou resembl'st now

---

6. The faculty of forming mental images.
7. Anything, like the spear, made ("tempered")
in Heaven.
8. Alights or kindles ("lights") gunpowder

("nitrous powder"), ready (next lines) to be stored
in some barrel ("tun") laid up in some storehouse
("magazine"), in preparation for ("against")
rumors of war.

840 Thy sin and place of doom obscure° and foul.   *dark*
But come, for thou, be sure, shalt give account
To him who sent us, whose charge is to keep
This place inviolable, and these from harm."
    So spake the Cherub, and his grave rebuke

845 Severe in youthful beauty, added grace
Invincible: abashed the Devil stood,
And felt how awful° goodness is, and saw   *awe-inspiring*
Virtue in her shape how lovely, saw, and pined°   *mourned*
His loss; but chiefly to find here observed

850 His luster visibly impaired; yet seemed
Undaunted. "If I must contend," said he,
"Best with the best, the sender not the sent,
Or all at once; more glory will be won,
Or less be lost." "Thy fear," said Zephon bold,

855 "Will save us trial what the least can do
Single° against thee wicked, and thence weak."   *in single combat*
    The Fiend replied not, overcome with rage;
But like a proud steed reined, went haughty on,
Champing his iron curb: to strive or fly

860 He held it vain; awe from above had quelled
His heart, not else dismayed. Now drew they nigh
The western point, where those half-rounding guards
Just met, and closing stood in squadron joined
Awaiting next command. To whom their chief

865 Gabriel from the front thus called aloud:
    "O friends, I hear the tread of nimble feet
Hasting this way, and now by glimpse discern
Ithuriel and Zephon through the shade,°   *trees*
And with them comes a third of regal port,°   *bearing*

870 But faded splendor wan;° who by his gait   *faint, dark*
And fierce demeanor seems the Prince of Hell,
Not likely to part hence without contést;
Stand firm, for in his look defiance lours."°   *frowns*
    He scarce had ended, when those two approached

875 And brief related whom they brought, where found,
How busied, in what form and posture couched.
    To whom with stern regard thus Gabriel spake:
"Why hast thou, Satan, broke the bounds prescribed
To thy transgressions, and disturbed the charge°   *responsibility*

880 Of others, who approve not to transgress
By thy example, but have power and right
To question thy bold entrance on this place;
Employed it seems to violate sleep, and those
Whose dwelling God hath planted here in bliss?"

885   To whom thus Satan, with contemptuous brow:
"Gabriel, thou hadst in Heav'n th' esteem° of wise,   *reputation of being*
And such I held thee; but this question asked
Puts me in doubt. Lives there who loves his pain?
Who would not, finding way, break loose from Hell,

890 Though thither doomed? Thou wouldst thyself, no doubt,
And boldly venture to whatever place

Farthest from pain, where thou mightst hope to change°   *exchange*
Torment with ease, and soonest recompense
Dole° with delight, which in this place I sought;   *pain, grief*
895   To thee no reason, who know'st only good,
But evil hast not tried: and wilt object⁹
His will who bound us? Let him surer bar
His iron gates, if he intends our stay
In that dark durance:° thus much what was asked.¹   *confinement*
900   The rest is true, they found me where they say;
But that implies not violence or harm."
    Thus he in scorn. The warlike angel moved,
Disdainfully half smiling thus replied:
"O loss of one in Heav'n to judge of wise,
905   Since Satan fell, whom folly overthrew,²
And now returns him from his prison scaped,
Gravely in doubt whether to hold them wise
Or not, who ask what boldness brought him hither
Unlicensed from his bounds in Hell prescribed;
910   So wise he judges it to fly from pain
However,° and to scape his punishment.   *howsoever*
So judge thou still, presumptuous, till the wrath,
Which thou incurr'st by flying, meet thy flight
Sevenfold, and scourge that wisdom back to Hell,
915   Which taught thee yet no better, that no pain
Can equal anger infinite provoked.
But wherefore thou alone? Wherefore with thee
Came not all Hell broke loose? Is pain to them
Less pain, less to be fled, or thou than they
920   Less hardy to endure? Courageous chief,
The first in flight from pain, hadst thou alleged
To thy deserted host this cause of flight,
Thou surely hadst not come sole fugitive."
    To which the Fiend thus answered frowning stern:
925   "Not that I less endure, or shrink from pain,
Insulting angel, well thou know'st I stood°   *withstood*
Thy fiercest, when in battle to thy aid
The blasting volleyed thunder made all speed
And seconded thy else not dreaded spear.
930   But still thy words at random, as before,
Argue thy inexperience what behoves
From° hard assays° and ill successes past   *after / attempts*
A faithful leader, not to hazard all
Through ways of danger by himself untried.
935   I therefore, I alone first undertook
To wing the desolate abyss, and spy
This new-created world, whereof in Hell
Fame° is not silent, here in hope to find   *rumor*
Better abode, and my afflicted powers°   *downcast armies*

9. Put forward as an objection.
1. I.e., thus much (answers) what was asked.
2. Irony: "O what a loss to Heaven to lose such a
judge of wisdom as Satan, whose folly led to his fall."

940 To settle here on earth, or in midair;[3]
Though for possession put° to try once more   *forced*
What thou and thy gay° legions dare against;   *showy*
Whose easier business were to serve their Lord
High up in Heav'n, with songs to hymn his throne,
945 And practiced distances to cringe, not fight."[4]
    To whom the warrior angel soon replied:
"To say and straight unsay, pretending first
Wise to fly pain, professing next the spy,
Argues no leader, but a liar traced,°   *found out*
950 Satan, and couldst thou faithful add? O name,
O sacred name of faithfulness profaned!
Faithful to whom? To thy rebellious crew?
Army of fiends, fit body to fit head;
Was this your discipline and faith engaged,
955 Your military obedience, to dissolve
Allegiance to th' acknowledged Power Supreme?
And thou sly hypocrite, who now wouldst seem
Patron of liberty, who more than thou
Once fawned, and cringed, and servilely adored
960 Heav'n's awful Monarch?[5] Wherefore but in hope
To dispossess him, and thyself to reign?
But mark what I areed° thee now, avaunt;°   *advise / be gone*
Fly thither whence thou fledd'st: if from this hour
Within these hallowed limits thou appear,
965 Back to th' infernal pit I drag thee chained,
And seal thee so, as henceforth not to scorn
The facile° gates of Hell too slightly barred."   *easily moved*
    So threatened he, but Satan to no threats
Gave heed, but waxing° more in rage replied: *growing*
970   "Then when I am thy captive talk of chains,
Proud limitary[6] Cherub, but ere then
Far heavier load thyself expect to feel
From my prevailing arm, though Heaven's King
Ride on thy wings, and thou with thy compeers,
975 Used to the yoke, draw'st his triumphant wheels
In progress through the road of heav'n star-paved."
    While thus he spake, th' angelic squadron bright
Turned fiery red, sharp'ning in moonèd horns[7]
Their phalanx, and began to hem him round
980 With ported[8] spears, as thick as when a field
Of Ceres[9] ripe for harvest waving bends
Her bearded grove of ears, which way the wind
Sways them; the careful plowman doubting stands
Lest on the threshing floor his hopeful sheaves

---

3. Satan will become "prince of the power of the air" (Ephesians 2.2).

4. Satan contemptuously parallels the angels' courtly deference ("distances") before God's throne and keeping a safe distance from battle. "Cringe": bow or kneel in fear or servility.

5. See 5.617 for Satan's "servile" adoration on the day of the Son's exaltation, when he "seemed well pleased" but was not.

6. Frontier guard, also, one of limited authority.

7. A crescent-shaped military formation.

8. Held slantwise in front.

9. Roman goddess of grain; here, the grain itself. A Homeric simile compares an excited army to windswept corn (*Iliad* 2.147–50).

985   Prove chaff. On th' other side Satan alarmed°   *called to arms*
      Collecting all his might dilated stood,
      Like Tenerife or Atlas[1] unremoved:°   *unremovable*
      His stature reached the sky, and on his crest
      Sat Horror plumed; nor wanted in his grasp
990   What seemed both spear and shield: now dreadful deeds
      Might have ensued, nor only Paradise
      In this commotion, but the starry cope°   *vault*
      Of Heav'n perhaps, or all the elements
      At least had gone to wrack, disturbed and torn
995   With violence of this conflict, had not soon
      Th' Eternal to prevent such horrid fray
      Hung forth in Heav'n his golden scales, yet seen
      Betwixt Astraea and the Scorpion sign,[2]
      Wherein all things created first he weighed,
1000   The pendulous round earth with balanced air
      In counterpoise, now ponders all events,
      Battles and realms: in these he put two weights
      The sequel each of parting and of fight;[3]
      The latter quick up flew, and kicked the beam;
1005   Which Gabriel spying, thus bespake the Fiend:
        "Satan, I know thy strength, and thou know'st mine,
      Neither our own but giv'n; what folly then
      To boast what arms can do, since thine no more
      Than Heav'n permits, nor mine, though doubled now
1010   To trample thee as mire: for proof look up,
      And read thy lot in yon celestial sign
      Where thou art weighed, and shown how light, how weak,[4]
      If thou resist." The Fiend looked up and knew
      His mounted scale aloft: nor more; but fled
1015   Murmuring, and with him fled the shades of night.

Book 5

      Now Morn her rosy steps in th' eastern clime
      Advancing, sowed the earth with orient pearl,°   *sparkling dew*
      When Adam waked, so customed, for his sleep
      Was aery light, from pure digestion bred,
5   And temperate vapors bland,° which th' only sound   *gentle, balmy*
      Of leaves and fuming rills, Aurora's fan,[1]
      Lightly dispersed, and the shrill matin° song   *morning*
      Of birds on every bough; so much the more
      His wonder was to find unwakened Eve

---

1. A mountain in Morocco. "Tenerife": a mountain in the Canary Islands.
2. The zodiac sign Libra, represented by a pair of scales, is between Virgo (identified with Astraea, goddess of Justice, who fled the earth at the end of the Golden Age) and Scorpio.
3. In several classical epic similes the fates of opposing heroes are weighed in scales by the gods, but here God "ponders" (weighs the consequences of) all events, including parting or fighting. Battle, desired by Satan, proves lighter ("kicked the beam," line 1004).
4. Cf. Daniel 5.27: "Thou art weighed in the balances, and art found wanting."
1. Rustling leaves and streams ("rills") stirred by Aurora, goddess of the dawn.

10 With tresses discomposed, and glowing cheek,
As through unquiet rest: he on his side
Leaning half-raised, with looks of cordial° love   *heartfelt*
Hung over her enamored, and beheld
Beauty, which whether waking or asleep,
15 Shot forth peculiar° graces; then with voice   *its own*
Mild, as when Zephyrus on Flora² breathes,
Her hand soft touching, whispered thus: "Awake
My fairest, my espoused, my latest found,
Heav'n's last best gift, my ever new delight,
20 Awake, the morning shines, and the fresh field
Calls us, we lose the prime, to mark how spring
Our tended plants, how blows° the citron grove,   *blooms*
What drops the myrrh, and what the balmy reed,°   *balsam*
How nature paints her colors, how the bee
25 Sits on the bloom extracting liquid sweet."³
　　　Such whispering waked her, but with startled eye
On Adam, whom embracing, thus she spake:
　　　"O sole in whom my thoughts find all repose,
My glory, my perfection, glad I see
30 Thy face, and morn returned, for I this night,
Such night till this I never passed, have dreamed,
If dreamed, not as I oft am wont,° of thee,   *accustomed*
Works of day past, or morrow's next design,
But of offense and trouble, which my mind
35 Knew never till this irksome night. Methought
Close at mine ear one called me forth to walk
With gentle voice, I thought it thine; it said,
'Why sleep'st thou Eve? Now is the pleasant time,
The cool, the silent, save where silence yields
40 To the night-warbling bird, that now awake
Tunes sweetest his love-labored song; now reigns
Full-orbed the moon, and with more pleasing light
Shadowy sets off the face of things, in vain,
If none regard; heav'n wakes with all his eyes,°   *stars*
45 Whom to behold but thee, nature's desire,
In whose sight all things joy, with ravishment
Attracted by thy beauty still° to gaze.'   *continually*
I rose as at thy call, but found thee not;
To find thee I directed then my walk;
50 And on, me thought, alone I passed through ways
That brought me on a sudden to the tree
Of interdicted knowledge: fair it seemed,
Much fairer to my fancy than by day:
And as I wond'ring looked, beside it stood
55 One shaped and winged like one of those from Heav'n
By us oft seen; his dewy locks distilled

2. Zephyrus is god of the gentle west wind, Flora goddess of flowers.
3. Adam sings a morning love song (*aubade*) to Eve, which works variations on Song of Solomon 2.10–12: "Rise up, my love, my fair one, and come away. . . . The flowers appear on the earth; the time of the singing of birds is come." Compare Satan's serenade (5.38–47), a parody of Adam's *aubade* and the Song of Solomon. "Prime" (line 21): first hour of the day.

Ambrosia;° on that tree he also gazed;   *heavenly fragrance*
And 'O fair plant,' said he, 'with fruit surcharged,°   *overburdened*
Deigns none to ease thy load and taste thy sweet,
60 Nor god,° nor man? Is knowledge so despised?   *angel*
Or envy, or what reserve forbids to taste?[4]
Forbid who will, none shall from me withhold
Longer thy offered good, why else set here?'
This said he paused not, but with vent'rous arm
65 He plucked, he tasted; me damp horror chilled
At such bold words vouched with° a deed so bold: *backed by*
But he thus overjoyed, 'O fruit divine,
Sweet of thyself, but much more sweet thus cropped,
Forbidden here, it seems, as only fit
70 For gods, yet able to make gods of men:
And why not gods of men, since good, the more
Communicated, more abundant grows,
The author not impaired,° but honored more?   *injured, diminished*
Here, happy creature, fair angelic Eve,
75 Partake thou also; happy though thou art,
Happier thou may'st be, worthier canst not be:
Taste this, and be henceforth among the gods
Thyself a goddess, not to earth confined,
But sometimes in the air, as we, sometimes
80 Ascend to Heav'n, by merit thine, and see
What life the gods live there, and such live thou.'
So saying, he drew nigh, and to me held,
Even to my mouth of that same fruit held part
Which he had plucked; the pleasant savory smell
85 So quickened appetite, that I, methought,
Could not but taste. Forthwith up to the clouds
With him I flew, and underneath beheld
The earth outstretched immense, a prospect wide
And various: wond'ring at my flight and change
90 To this high exaltation: suddenly
My guide was gone, and I, methought, sunk down,
And fell asleep; but O how glad I waked
To find this but a dream!" Thus Eve her night
Related, and thus Adam answered sad.°   *gravely, soberly*
95   "Best image of myself and dearer half,
The trouble of thy thoughts this night in sleep
Affects me equally; nor can I like
This uncouth° dream, of evil sprung I fear;   *strange, unpleasant*
Yet evil whence? In thee can harbor none,
100 Created pure. But know that in the soul
Are many lesser faculties[5] that serve
Reason as chief; among these fancy next
Her office holds; of all external things,
Which the five watchful senses represent,

---

4. I.e., does envy or some other barrier ("reserve") forbid your being tasted?
5. Adam's explanation of the dream (lines 100–116) summarizes the orthodox faculty psychol- ogy and dream theory of Milton's time—one among many kinds of knowledge with which unfallen man was endowed.

105 She forms imaginations,° aery shapes,   *images*
Which reason joining or disjoining, frames
All what we affirm or what deny, and call
Our knowledge or opinion; then retires
Into her private cell when nature rests.
110 Oft in her absence mimic fancy wakes
To imitate her; but misjoining shapes,
Wild work produces oft, and most in dreams,
Ill matching words and deeds long past or late.
Some such resemblances methinks I find
115 Of our last evening's talk in this thy dream,[6]
But with addition strange; yet be not sad.
Evil into the mind of god[7] or man
May come and go, so unapproved,[8] and leave
No spot or blame behind: which gives me hope
120 That what in sleep thou didst abhor to dream,
Waking thou never wilt consent to do.
Be not disheartened then, nor cloud those looks
That wont to be° more cheerful and serene   *usually are*
Than when fair morning first smiles on the world,
125 And let us to our fresh employments rise
Among the groves, the fountains, and the flow'rs
That open now their choicest bosomed smells
Reserved from night, and kept for thee in store."
    So cheered he his fair spouse, and she was cheered,
130 But silently a gentle tear let fall
From either eye, and wiped them with her hair;
Two other precious drops that ready stood,
Each in their crystal sluice, he ere they fell
Kissed as the gracious signs of sweet remorse
135 And pious awe, that feared to have offended.
    So all was cleared, and to the field they haste.
But first from under shady arborous° roof,   *consisting of trees*
Soon as they forth were come to open sight
Of day-spring,° and the sun, who scarce up risen   *daybreak*
140 With wheels yet hov'ring o'er the ocean brim,
Shot parallel to the earth his dewy ray,
Discovering in wide landscape all the east
Of Paradise and Eden's happy plains,
Lowly they bowed adoring, and began
145 Their orisons,° each morning duly paid   *prayers*
In various style, for neither various style
Nor holy rapture° wanted they to praise   *ecstasy*
Their Maker, in fit strains pronounced or sung
Unmeditated,[9] such prompt eloquence
150 Flowed from their lips, in prose or numerous° verse,   *rhythmic*
More tuneable° than needed lute or harp   *melodious*

---

6. Adam recalls his own words in 4.411–39.
7. Probably "angel" as elsewhere, but perhaps God, whose omniscience must encompass knowledge of evil as well as good.
8. If not willed (approved of) or not acted on

(put to the proof).
9. In a variety of styles or forms of speech and song, which harmonize together but are at the same time impromptu, spontaneous, and ecstatic.

To add more sweetness, and they thus began:
  "These are thy glorious works, Parent of good,[1]
Almighty, thine this universal frame,

155 Thus wondrous fair; thyself how wondrous then!
Unspeakable, who sitt'st above these heavens,
To us invisible or dimly seen
In these thy lowest works, yet these declare
Thy goodness beyond thought, and power divine:

160 Speak ye who best can tell, ye sons of light,
Angels, for ye behold him, and with songs
And choral symphonies,° day without night,   *music in parts*
Circle his throne rejoicing, ye in Heav'n,
On earth join all ye creatures to extol

165 Him first, him last, him midst, and without end.
Fairest of stars,[2] last in the train° of night,   *procession*
If better thou belong not to the dawn,
Sure pledge of day, that crown'st the smiling morn
With thy bright circlet, praise him in thy sphere

170 While day arises, that sweet hour of prime.
Thou sun, of this great world both eye and soul,
Acknowledge him thy greater, sound his praise
In thy eternal course, both when thou climb'st,
And when high noon hast gained, and when thou fall'st.

175 Moon, that now meet'st the orient sun, now fli'st
With the fixed stars, fixed in their orb that flies,
And ye five other wand'ring fires that move
In mystic dance not without song,[3] resound
His praise, who out of darkness called up light.

180 Air, and ye elements the eldest birth
Of nature's womb, that in quaternion[4] run
Perpetual circle, multiform, and mix
And nourish all things, let your ceaseless change
Vary to our great Maker still° new praise.   *continually*

185 Ye mists and exhalations that now rise
From hill or steaming lake, dusky or gray,
Till the sun paint your fleecy skirts with gold,
In honor to the world's great Author rise,
Whether to deck with clouds the uncolored sky,

190 Or wet the thirsty earth with falling showers,
Rising or falling still advance his praise.
His praise ye winds, that from four quarters blow,
Breathe soft or loud; and wave your tops, ye pines,
With every plant, in sign of worship wave.

195 Fountains and ye, that warble, as ye flow,
Melodious murmurs, warbling tune his praise.
Join voices all ye living souls: ye birds,

---

1. Their morning hymn works variations on Psalms 148, 104, and 19, as well as the canticle "Benedicite."
2. Venus, the morning star and (as Hesperus) the evening star.
3. The planets, unlike the fixed stars, change their relative positions; their motion produces the music of the spheres, audible to unfallen humans.
4. The fourfold changing relationship of the four elements.

That singing up to heaven gate ascend,
Bear on your wings and in your notes his praise.
200 Ye that in waters glide, and ye that walk
The earth, and stately tread, or lowly creep;
Witness if I be silent, morn or even,
To hill, or valley, fountain, or fresh shade
Made vocal by my song, and taught his praise.
205 Hail universal Lord, be bounteous still°   *always*
To give us only good; and if the night
Have gathered aught of evil or concealed,
Disperse it, as now light dispels the dark."
 So prayed they innocent, and to their thoughts
210 Firm peace recovered soon and wonted calm.
On to their morning's rural work they haste
Among sweet dews and flow'rs; where any row
Of fruit trees over-woody° reached too far   *too bushy*
Their pampered boughs, and needed hands to check
215 Fruitless embraces: or they led the vine
To wed her elm;[5] she spoused about him twines
Her marriageable arms, and with her brings
Her dow'r th' adopted clusters, to adorn
His barren leaves. Them thus employed beheld
220 With pity Heav'n's high King, and to him called
Raphael, the sociable Spirit, that deigned
To travel with Tobias, and secured
His marriage with the seven-times-wedded maid.[6]
 "Raphael," said he, "thou hear'st what stir on earth
225 Satan from Hell scaped through the darksome gulf
Hath raised in Paradise, and how disturbed
This night the human pair, how he designs
In them at once to ruin all mankind.
Go therefore, half this day as friend with friend
230 Converse with Adam, in what bow'r or shade
Thou find'st him from the heat of noon retired,
To respite his day labor with repast,
Or with repose; and such discourse bring on,
As may advise him of his happy state,
235 Happiness in his power left free to will,
Left to his own free will, his will though free,
Yet mutable; whence warn him to beware
He swerve not too secure:° tell him withal   *overconfident*
His danger, and from whom, what enemy
240 Late fall'n himself from Heav'n, is plotting now
The fall of others from like state of bliss;
By violence, no, for that shall be withstood,
But by deceit and lies; this let him know,
Lest wilfully transgressing he pretend°   *plead*
245 Surprisal, unadmonished, unforewarned."

5. A familiar emblem of matrimony, the elm symbolizing masculine strength, and the vine, feminine fruitfulness, softness, and sweetness; note, however, the matriarchal implications of "adopted clusters" (line 218).

6. Raphael (in Hebrew, "health of God") was the adviser of Tobias in winning his wife (see 4.168–71 and note).

So spake th' Eternal Father, and fulfilled
All justice: nor delayed the wingèd saint°   *angel*
After his charge received; but from among
Thousand celestial ardors,[7] where he stood
250 Veiled with his gorgeous wings, up springing light
Flew through the midst of Heav'n; th' angelic choirs
On each hand parting, to his speed gave way
Through all th' empyreal road; till at the gate
Of Heav'n arrived, the gate self-opened wide
255 On golden hinges turning, as by work°   *mechanism*
Divine the sov'reign Architect had framed.
From hence, no cloud, or, to obstruct his sight,
Star interposed, however small he sees,
Not unconform to other shining globes,
260 Earth and the gard'n of God, with cedars crowned
Above all hills. As when by night the glass°   *telescope*
Of Galileo, less assured, observes
Imagined lands and regions in the moon:
Or pilot from amidst the Cyclades
265 Delos or Samos first appearing kens°   *discerns*
A cloudy spot.[8] Down thither prone° in flight   *bent forward*
He speeds, and through the vast ethereal sky
Sails between worlds and worlds, with steady wing
Now on the polar wings, then with quick fan
270 Winnows the buxom air; till within soar
Of tow'ring eagles,[9] to all the fowls he seems
A phoenix, gazed by all, as that sole bird
When to enshrine his relics in the sun's
Bright temple, to Egyptian Thebes he flies.[1]
275 At once on th' eastern cliff of Paradise
He lights, and to his proper shape returns
A Seraph winged; six wings he wore, to shade
His lineaments° divine; the pair that clad   *parts of the body*
Each shoulder broad, came mantling° o'er his breast   *draping*
280 With regal ornament; the middle pair
Girt like a starry zone° his waist, and round   *belt*
Skirted his loins and thighs with downy gold
And colors dipped in Heav'n; the third his feet
Shadowed from either heel with feathered mail[2]
285 Sky-tinctured grain.° Like Maia's son[3] he stood,   *dye*
And shook his plumes, that heav'nly fragrance filled
The circuit wide. Straight° knew him all the bands   *at once*
Of angels under watch; and to his state,°   *rank*
And to his message° high in honor rise;   *mission*

7. Bright spirits burning in love; the Hebrew *seraph* means "to bum."
8. The Cyclades are a circular group of islands in the south Aegean Sea; the two islands seen as "spots" from within the archipelago are Delos (the traditional center but famous for having floated adrift) and Samos (outside the group).
9. Raphael sails with steady wing, turns at the pole, beats ("fans") with his wings the yielding ("buxom") air, and then comes within range of the eagle's soaring flight.
1. The phoenix was a mythical, unique ("sole") bird that lived five hundred years, was consumed by fire, and was reborn from the ashes, which it then carried to the temple of the sun at Heliopolis in Egypt.
2. Plumage suggesting scale armor.
3. Mercury, messenger of the gods.

290 For on some message high they guessed him bound.
Their glittering tents he passed, and now is come
Into the blissful field; through groves of myrrh,
And flow'ring odors, cassia, nard, and balm;[4]
A wilderness of sweets; for nature here

295 Wantoned° as in her prime, and played° at will   *reveled / acted out*
Her virgin fancies, pouring forth more sweet,
Wild above rule or art; enormous° bliss.   *immense, beyond rule*
Him through the spicy forest onward come
Adam discerned, as in the door he sat[5]

300 Of his cool bow'r, while now the mounted sun
Shot down direct his fervid rays, to warm
Earth's inmost womb, more warmth than Adam needs;
And Eve within, due° at her hour prepared   *fittingly*
For dinner savory fruits, of taste to please

305 True appetite and not disrelish thirst,
Of nectarous drafts between, from milky stream,
Berry or grape: to whom thus Adam called:
    "Haste hither Eve, and worth thy sight behold
Eastward among those trees, what glorious shape

310 Comes this way moving; seems another morn
Ris'n on mid-noon; some great behest from Heav'n
To us perhaps he brings, and will vouchsafe
This day to be our guest. But go with speed,
And what thy stores contain, bring forth and pour

315 Abundance, fit to honor and receive
Our heav'nly stranger; well we may afford
Our givers their own gifts, and large bestow
From large bestowed, where nature multiplies
Her fertile growth, and by disburd'ning grows

320 More fruitful, which instructs us not to spare."
    To whom thus Eve. "Adam, earth's hallowed mold,[6]
Of God inspired, small store will serve, where store,[7]
All seasons, ripe for use hangs on the stalk;
Save what by frugal storing firmness gains

325 To nourish, and superfluous moist consumes:
But I will haste and from each bough and brake
Each plant and juiciest gourd will pluck such choice
To entertain our angel guest, as he
Beholding shall confess that here on earth

330 God hath dispensed his bounties as in Heav'n."
    So saying, with dispatchful looks in haste
She turns, on hospitable thoughts intent
What choice to choose for delicacy best,
What order, so contrived as not to mix

335 Tastes, not well joined, inelegant, but bring
Taste after taste upheld° with kindliest° change,   *maintained / most natural*

---

4. "Odors": aromatic substances; "cassia": cinnamon; "nard": spikenard; "balm": balsam—all were used to make perfumed ointments.
5. Raphael's visit to Adam is modeled on Abraham's entertainment of three angels (Genesis 18.1–16).
6. Revered shape of earth's substance. The name "Adam" signifies red earth.
7. A great quantity. "Small store": few stored foods.

Bestirs her then, and from each tender stalk
Whatever earth all-bearing mother yields
In India east or west, or middle shore
340 In Pontus or the Punic coast,[8] or where
Alcinous reigned, fruit of all kinds, in coat,
Rough, or smooth-rined, or bearded husk, or shell
She gathers, tribute large, and on the board
Heaps with unsparing hand; for drink the grape
345 She crushes, inoffensive must, and meaths[9]
From many a berry, and from sweet kernels pressed
She tempers° dulcet creams, nor these to hold   *blends*
Wants° her fit vessels pure, then strews the ground   *lacks*
With rose and odors from the shrub unfumed.[1]
350 Meanwhile our primitive° great sire, to meet   *original*
His godlike guest, walks forth, without more train°   *attendants*
Accompanied than with his own complete
Perfections, in himself was all his state,°   *dignity, authority*
More solemn° than the tedious pomp that waits   *awe-inspiring*
355 On princes, when their rich retínue long
Of horses led, and grooms besmeared with gold
Dazzles the crowd, and sets them all agape.
Nearer his presence Adam though not awed,
Yet with submiss approach and reverence meek,
360 As to a superior nature, bowing low,
    Thus said: "Native of Heav'n, for other place:
None can than Heav'n such glorious shape contain;
Since by descending from the thrones above,
Those happy places thou hast deigned° a while   *condescended*
365 To want,° and honor these, vouchsafe with us   *be parted from*
Two only, who yet by sov'reign gift possess
This spacious ground, in yonder shady bow'r
To rest, and what the garden choicest bears
To sit and taste, till this meridian° heat   *noontime*
370 Be over, and the sun more cool decline."
    Whom thus the angelic Virtue[2] answered mild:
"Adam, I therefore came, nor art thou such
Created, or such place hast here to dwell,
As may not oft invite, though Spirits of Heav'n
375 To visit thee; lead on then where thy bow'r
O'ershades; for these mid-hours, till evening rise
I have at will." So to the sylvan lodge
They came, that like Pomona's[3] arbor smiled
With flow'rets decked° and fragrant smells; but Eve   *covered*
380 Undecked, save with herself more lovely fair
Than wood nymph, or the fairest goddess feigned

---

8. The "middle shore" includes Pontus, the south coast of the Black Sea, famous for nuts and fruits, and the "Punic" (Carthaginian) coast of North Africa on the Mediterranean, famous for figs; the gardens of Alcinous (next line) are described in the *Odyssey* 7.113–21 as perpetually fruitful.
9. Meads, drinks sweetened with honey. "Must":
unfermented fruit juice.
1. Naturally scented, not burned for incense.
2. Milton uses these angelic titles freely, in the Protestant manner, not as designations of the nine traditional orders (Raphael was called "Seraph" at line 277).
3. The Roman goddess of fruit trees.

Of three that in Mount Ida naked strove,[4]
Stood to entertain her guest from Heav'n; no veil
She needed, virtue-proof,° no thought infirm   *armored in virtue*
385 Altered her cheek. On whom the Angel "Hail"
Bestowed, the holy salutation used
Long after to blest Mary, second Eve.[5]
  "Hail mother of mankind, whose fruitful womb
Shall fill the world more numerous with thy sons
390 Than with these various fruits the trees of God
Have heaped this table." Raised of grassy turf
Their table was, and mossy seats had round,
And on her ample square from side to side
All autumn piled, though spring and autumn here
395 Danced hand in hand. A while discourse they hold;
No fear lest dinner cool; when thus began
Our author:° "Heav'nly stranger, please to taste   *forefather*
These bounties which our Nourisher, from whom
All perfect good unmeasured out, descends,
400 To us for food and for delight hath caused
The earth to yield; unsavory food perhaps
To spiritual natures; only this I know,
That one Celestial Father gives to all."
  To whom the angel: "Therefore what he gives
405 (Whose praise be ever sung) to man in part
Spiritual, may of° purest Spirits be found   *by*
No ingrateful food: and food alike those pure
Intelligential substances require[6]
As doth your rational; and both contain
410 Within them every lower faculty
Of sense, whereby they hear, see, smell, touch, taste,
Tasting concoct, digest, assimilate,[7]
And corporeal to incorporeal turn.
For know, whatever was created, needs
415 To be sustained and fed; of elements
The grosser feeds the purer, earth the sea,
Earth and the sea feed air, the air those fires
Ethereal, and as lowest first the moon;
Whence in her visage round those spots, unpurged
420 Vapors not yet into her substance turned.[8]
Nor doth the moon no nourishment exhale
From her moist continent to higher orbs.[9]
The sun that light imparts to all, receives

---

4. On Mount Ida, Venus, Juno, and Minerva "strove" naked for the title of the most beautiful; Paris awarded the prize (the apple of discord) to Venus, which led to the rape of Helen and the Trojan War.
5. Cf. the angel's words to Mary announcing that she would bear a son, Jesus (Luke 1.28): "Hail, thou that art highly favored, the Lord is with thee: blessed art thou among women."
6. Milton's angels ("intelligential substances") require real food, even as "rational" men do (see below, lines 430–38). As a monist (believer that

all creation is of one matter), Milton denied the more common (dualistic) idea that angels are pure spirit, holding instead that they are of a very highly refined material substance.
7. Three stages in digestion.
8. Here Raphael describes lunar spots as still-undigested vapors (in keeping with his exposition of the universal need of nourishment); in 1.287–91 he referred to moon spots in Galileo's terms, as landscape features.
9. A double negative: the moon does exhale such nourishment to other planets.

From all his alimental° recompense   *nourishing*
425 In humid exhalations, and at even
Sups with the ocean:[1] though in Heav'n the trees
Of life ambrosial° fruitage bear, and vines   *divinely fragrant*
Yield nectar,[2] though from off the boughs each morn
We brush mellifluous° dews, and find the ground   *honey-flowing*
430 Covered with pearly grain; yet God hath here
Varied his bounty so with new delights,
As may compare with Heaven; and to taste
Think not I shall be nice."° So down they sat,   *fastidious, finicky*
And to their viands fell, nor seemingly°   *in show*
435 The angel, nor in mist, the common gloss°   *explanation*
Of theologians, but with keen dispatch
Of real hunger, and concoctive° heat   *digestive*
To transubstantiate;[3] what redounds, transpires
Through Spirits with ease; nor wonder, if by fire
440 Of sooty coal the empiric° alchemist   *experimental*
Can turn, or holds it possible to turn
Metals of drossiest ore to perfect gold
As from the mine. Meanwhile at table Eve
Ministered naked, and their flowing cups
445 With pleasant liquors crowned.° O innocence   *filled to the brim*
Deserving Paradise! if ever, then,
Then had the Sons of God excuse t' have been
Enamored at that sight,[4] but in those hearts
Love unlibidinous° reigned, nor jealousy   *without lust*
450 Was understood, the injured lover's hell.
     Thus when with meats and drinks they had sufficed,
Not burdened nature, sudden mind arose
In Adam, not to let th' occasion pass
Given him by this great conference to know
455 Of things above his world, and of their being
Who dwell in Heav'n, whose excellence he saw
Transcend his own so far, whose radiant forms
Divine effulgence,° whose high power so far   *shining forth*
Exceeded human, and his wary speech
460 Thus to th' empyreal minister he framed:
"Inhabitant with God, now know I well
Thy favor, in this honor done to man,
Under whose lowly roof thou hast vouchsafed
To enter and these earthly fruits to taste,
465 Food not of angels, yet accepted so,
As that more willingly thou couldst not seem

---

1. Milton explains evaporation as the sun dining off moisture exhaled from the oceans.
2. Ambrosia is the food and nectar the drink of the classical gods; Milton adds "pearly grain" (line 430), like the manna showered on the Israelites in the desert (Exodus 16.14–15).
3. In common theological use, transubstantiation is the Roman Catholic doctrine that the bread and wine of the Eucharist become the body and blood of Christ. Milton vigorously denied that doctrine, but he describes the angels' transforming of earthly food into their more highly refined spiritual substance as a true transubstantiation. The excess ("what redounds") is exhaled ("transpires") through angelic pores.
4. Genesis 6.2 tells of the marriage of "the daughters of men" with "the sons of God," usually identified as sons of Seth, but a patristic tradition (alluded to here) identifies them as angels.

At Heav'n's high feasts t' have fed: yet what compare?"
　　To whom the wingèd hierarch° replied:　　　　　　　　　*authority*
"O Adam, one Almighty is, from whom
470 All things proceed, and up to him return,
If not depraved from good, created all
Such to perfection, one first matter all,[5]
Endued with various forms, various degrees
Of substance, and in things that live, of life;
475 But more refined, more spiritous, and pure,
As nearer to him placed or nearer tending
Each in their several active spheres assigned,
Till body up to spirit work, in bounds
Proportioned to each kind.[6] So from the root
480 Springs lighter the green stalk, from thence the leaves
More airy, last the bright consummate flow'r
Spirits odorous breathes:[7] flow'rs and their fruit
Man's nourishment, by gradual scale sublimed°　　　　　　*purified*
To vital spirits aspire, to animal,
485 To intellectual, give both life and sense,
Fancy° and understanding, whence the soul　　　　　　　*imagination*
Reason receives, and reason is her being,
Discursive, or intuitive;[8] discourse
Is oftest yours, the latter most is ours,
490 Differing but in degree, of kind the same.
Wonder not then, what God for you saw good
If I refuse not, but convert, as you,
To proper° substance; time may come when men　　　　　　*our own*
With angels may participate, and find
495 No inconvenient diet, nor too light fare:
And from these corporal nutriments perhaps
Your bodies may at last turn all to spirit,
Improved by tract° of time, and winged ascend　　　　　　*passage*
Ethereal as we, or may at choice
500 Here or in heav'nly paradises dwell;
If ye be found obedient, and retain
Unalterably firm his love entire
Whose progeny you are. Meanwhile enjoy
Your fill what happiness this happy state
505 Can comprehend, incapable° of more."　　　　　　　*unable to contain*

---

5. Milton held that the universe was created out of Chaos, not out of nothing: the primal matter of Chaos had its origin in God, who subsequently created all things from that matter (see 7.168–73, 210–42). This materialist "monism" denies sharp distinctions between angels and men, spirit and matter: all beings are of one substance, of varying degrees of refinement and life.
6. Milton's version of the chain of being qualifies natural hierarchy by allowing for movement up or down; beings may become increasingly spiritual ("more spiritous") or increasingly gross (as the rebel angels do), depending on their moral choices—"nearer tending."
7. The plant figure—root, stalk, leaves, flowers, and fruit—provides an illustration of the dyna-

mism of being in the universe and further explains why Raphael can eat the fruit. Such food is then transformed (next lines) into various orders of "spirits"—"vital," "animal," and "intellectual" (fluids in the blood that sustain life, sensation, motion, and finally intellect and its functions, "fancy," "understanding," and "reason"), indicating that the soul is also material.
8. Traditionally, on the dualist assumption that angels are pure spirit and humans a combination of matter and spirit, angelic intuition (immediate apprehension of truth) was absolutely distinguished from human "discourse" of reason (arguing from premises to conclusions). Milton, denying that assumption, makes the distinction only relative, a matter of "degree" (line 490).

To whom the patriarch of mankind replied:
"O favorable Spirit, propitious guest,
Well hast thou taught the way that might direct
Our knowledge, and the scale of nature set
510 From center to circumference, whereon
In contemplation of created things
By steps we may ascend to God. But say,
What meant that caution joined, 'If ye be found
Obedient'? Can we want° obedience then   lack
515 To him, or possibly his love desert
Who formed us from the dust, and placed us here
Full to the utmost measure of what bliss
Human desires can seek or apprehend?"
    To whom the angel: "Son of Heav'n and earth,
520 Attend: that thou art happy, owe° to God;   attribute
That thou continu'st such, owe to thyself,
That is, to thy obedience; therein stand.
This was that caution giv'n thee; be advised.
God made thee perfect, not immutable;°   unchangeable
525 And good he made thee, but to persevere
He left it in thy power, ordained thy will
By nature free, not overruled by fate
Inextricable, or strict necessity,
Our voluntary service he requires,
530 Not our necessitated, such with him
Finds no acceptance, nor can find, for how
Can hearts, not free, be tried whether they serve
Willing or no, who will but what they must
By destiny, and can no other choose?
535 Myself and all th' angelic host that stand
In sight of God enthroned, our happy state
Hold, as you yours, while our obedience holds;
On other surety° none; freely we serve,   guarantee
Because we freely love, as in our will
540 To love or not; in this we stand or fall:
And some are fall'n, to disobedience fall'n,
And so from Heav'n to deepest Hell; O fall
From what high state of bliss into what woe!"
    To whom our great progenitor: "Thy words
545 Attentive, and with more delighted ear,
Divine instructor, I have heard, than when
Cherubic songs° by night from neighboring hills   songs of Cherubim
Aerial music send: nor knew I not[9]
To be both will and deed created free;
550 Yet that we never shall forget to love
Our Maker, and obey him whose command
Single, is yet° so just, my constant thoughts   also
Assured me, and still assure: though what thou tell'st
Hath passed in Heav'n, some doubt within me move,
555 But more desire to hear, if thou consent,

9. A double negative; i.e., "I did know."

The full relation, which must needs be strange,
Worthy of sacred silence to be heard;
And we have yet large° day, for scarce the sun   *ample*
Hath finished half his journey, and scarce begins
His other half in the great zone of Heav'n."
　　Thus Adam made request, and Raphael
After short pause assenting, thus began:
　　"High matter[1] thou enjoin'st me, O prime of men,
Sad task and hard, for how shall I relate
To human sense th' invisible exploits
Of warring Spirits; how without remorse
The ruin of so many glorious once
And perfect while they stood; how last unfold
The secrets of another world, perhaps
Not lawful to reveal? Yet for thy good
This is dispensed, and what surmounts the reach
Of human sense, I shall delineate so,
By lik'ning spiritual to corporal forms,
As may express them best, though what if earth
Be but the shadow of Heav'n, and things therein
Each to other like, more than on earth is thought?
　　"As yet this world was not, and Chaos wild
Reigned where these heav'ns now roll, where earth now rests
Upon her center poised, when on a day
(For time, though in eternity, applied
To motion, measures all things durable
By present, past, and future)[2] on such day
As Heav'n's great year[3] brings forth, th' empyreal host
Of angels by imperial summons called,
Innumerable before th' Almighty's throne
Forthwith from all the ends of Heav'n appeared
Under their hierarchs° in orders bright.   *leaders*
Ten thousand thousand ensigns high advanced,
Standards, and gonfalons° twixt van and rear   *banners*
Stream in the air, and for distinction serve
Of hierarchies, of orders, and degrees;
Or in their glittering tissues° bear emblazed   *cloth*
Holy memorials, acts of zeal and love
Recorded eminent. Thus when in orbs
Of circuit° inexpressible they stood,   *circumference*
Orb within orb, the Father Infinite,
By whom in bliss embosomed sat the Son,
Amidst as from a flaming mount, whose top
Brightness had made invisible, thus spake:
　　"'Hear all ye angels, progeny of Light,

---

1. Raphael's account of the war in Heaven is an epic device, a narrative of past action; it is also a mini-epic itself, with traditional battles, challenges, and single combats. As an "epic" poet treating sacred matter, Raphael confronts a narrative challenge similar to Milton's own.
2. Countering a long philosophical tradition,

Milton asserts the existence of time in Heaven, before the creation of the universe.
3. Plato and others defined the "great year" as the cycle completed when all the heavenly bodies simultaneously return to the positions they held at the cycle's beginning.

Thrones, Dominations, Princedoms, Virtues, Powers,
Hear my decree, which unrevoked shall stand.
This day I have begot whom I declare
My only Son, and on this holy hill
605 Him have anointed,[4] whom ye now behold
At my right hand; your head I him appoint;
And by myself have sworn to him shall bow
All knees in Heav'n, and shall confess him Lord:
Under his great vicegerent[5] reign abide
610 United as one individual° soul   indivisible
Forever happy: him who° disobeys   whoever
Me disobeys, breaks union, and that day
Cast out from God and blessèd vision, falls
Into utter° darkness, deep engulfed, his place   outer, total
615 Ordained without redemption, without end.'
      "So spake th' Omnipotent, and with his words
All seemed well pleased, all seemed, but were not all.
That day, as other solemn° days, they spent   ceremonial
In song and dance about the sacred hill,
620 Mystical dance, which yonder starry sphere
Of planets and of fixed° in all her wheels   fixed stars
Resembles nearest, mazes intricate,
Eccentric,° intervolved,° yet regular   off center / intertwined
Then most, when most irregular they seem:
625 And in their motions harmony divine
So smooths her charming tones,[6] that God's own ear
Listens delighted. Evening now approached
(For we have also our evening and our morn,
We ours for change delectable, not need)
630 Forthwith from dance to sweet repast they turn
Desirous; all in circles as they stood,
Tables are set, and on a sudden piled
With angels' food, and rubied nectar flows
In pearl, in diamond, and massy gold,
635 Fruit of delicious vines, the growth of Heav'n.
On flow'rs reposed, and with fresh flow'rets crowned,
They eat, they drink, and in communion sweet
Quaff immortality and joy, secure
Of surfeit where full measure only bounds
640 Excess, before th' all-bounteous King, who show'red
With copious hand, rejoicing in their joy.
Now when ambrosial° night with clouds exhaled   fragrant
From that high mount of God, whence light and shade
Spring both, the face of brightest Heav'n had changed
645 To grateful° twilight (for night comes not there   pleasing
In darker veil) and roseate° dews disposed   rose-scented

---

4. Cf. Psalm 2.7: "I will declare the decree: . . .
Thou art my Son; this day have I begotten thee."
The episode refers to the exaltation of the Son as
King, not his actual begetting, since he is else-
where described as "of all creation first" (3.383)
and as God's agent in creating the angels and

everything else.
5. Vice-regent, one appointed by the supreme
ruler (here, God) to wield his authority.
6. The movements of the angels in their dance
produce harmony, like those of the planets in the
Pythagorean theory of the music of the spheres.

All but the unsleeping eyes of God to rest,
Wide over all the plain, and wider far
Than all this globous earth in plain outspread,
650 (Such are the courts of God) th' angelic throng
Dispersed in bands and files their camp extend
By living streams among the trees of life,
Pavilions numberless, and sudden reared,
Celestial tabernacles, where they slept
655 Fanned with cool winds, save those who in their course
Melodious hymns about the sov'reign throne
Alternate all night long: but not so waked
Satan, so call him now, his former name
Is heard no more in Heav'n; he of the first,
660 If not the first Archangel, great in power,
In favor and preeminence, yet fraught
With envy against the Son of God, that day
Honored by his great Father, and proclaimed
Messiah[7] King anointed, could not bear
665 Through pride that sight, and thought himself impaired.
Deep malice thence conceiving and disdain,
Soon as midnight brought on the dusky hour
Friendliest to sleep and silence, he resolved
With all his legions to dislodge,° and leave   *leave camp*
670 Unworshipped, unobeyed the throne supreme
Contemptuous, and his next subordinate[8]
Awak'ning, thus to him in secret spake:
   "'Sleep'st thou companion dear, what sleep can close
Thy eyelids? and remember'st what decree
675 Of yesterday, so late hath passed the lips
Of Heav'n's Almighty. Thou to me thy thoughts
Wast wont,° I mine to thee was wont to impart;   *in the habit of*
Both waking we were one; how then can now
Thy sleep dissent? New laws thou seest imposed;
680 New laws from him who reigns, new minds° may raise   *purposes*
In us who serve, new counsels, to debate
What doubtful may ensue, more in this place
To utter is not safe. Assemble thou
Of all those myriads which we lead the chief;
685 Tell them that by command, ere yet dim night
Her shadowy cloud withdraws, I am to haste,
And all who under me their banners wave,
Homeward with flying march where we possess
The quarters of the north, there to prepare
690 Fit entertainment to receive our King
The great Messiah, and his new commands,
Who speedily through all the hierarchies
Intends to pass triumphant, and give laws.'
   "So spake the false Archangel, and infused
695 Bad influence into th' unwary breast

---

7. Hebrew, "anointed."
8. His original name in Heaven is lost (1.356–63), but he will come to be known as Beelzebub.

Of his associate; he together calls,
Or several one by one, the regent powers,
Under him regent, tells, as he was taught,
That the Most High commanding, now ere night,
700 Now ere dim night had disencumbered Heav'n,
The great hierarchal standard was to move;
Tells the suggested° cause, and casts between   *insinuated*
Ambitious words and jealousies, to sound°   *make trials of*
Or taint integrity; but all obeyed
705 The wonted signal, and superior voice
Of their great potentate° for great indeed   *ruler*
His name, and high was his degree in Heav'n;
His count'nance as the morning star that guides
The starry flock, allured them, and with lies
710 Drew after him the third part of Heav'n's host:
Meanwhile, th' Eternal Eye, whose sight discerns
Abstrusest° thoughts, from forth his holy mount   *most secret*
And from within the golden lamps that burn
Nightly before him, saw without their light
715 Rebellion rising, saw in whom, how spread
Among the sons of morn, what multitudes
Were banded to oppose his high decree;
And smiling to his only Son thus said:
    "'Son, thou in whom my glory I behold
720 In full resplendence, heir of all my might,
Nearly it now concerns us to be sure
Of our omnipotence, and with what arms
We mean to hold what anciently we claim
Of deity or empire, such a foe
725 Is rising, who intends to erect his throne
Equal to ours, throughout the spacious north;
Nor so content, hath in his thought to try
In battle, what our power is, or our right.
Let us advise, and to this hazard draw
730 With speed what force is left, and all employ
In our defense, lest unawares we lose
This our high place, our sanctuary, our hill.'
    "To whom the Son with calm aspect and clear
Lightning divine, ineffable, serene,
735 Made answer: 'Mighty Father, thou thy foes
Justly hast in derision, and secure
Laugh'st at their vain designs and tumults vain,⁹
Matter to me of glory, whom their hate
Illustrates,° when they see all regal power   *makes illustrious*
740 Giv'n me to quell their pride, and in event°   *in the outcome*
Know whether I be dextrous to subdue
Thy rebels, or be found the worst in Heav'n.'
    "So spake the Son, but Satan with his powers°   *armies*
Far was advanced on wingèd speed, an host

---

9. Cf. Psalm 2.4: "He that sitteth in the heavens shall laugh: the Lord shall have them in derision."

745   Innumerable as the stars of night,
       Or stars of morning, dewdrops, which the sun
       Impearls on every leaf and every flower.
       Regions they passed, the mighty regencies°   *dominions*
       Of Seraphim and Potentates and Thrones
750   In their triple degrees, regions to° which   *compared to*
       All thy dominion, Adam, is no more
       Than what this garden is to all the earth,
       And all the sea, from one entire globose°   *globe*
       Stretched into longitude° which having passed   *spread out flat*
755   At length into the limits° of the north   *regions*
       They came, and Satan to his royal seat
       High on a hill, far blazing, as a mount
       Raised on a mount, with pyramids and tow'rs
       From diamond quarries hewn, and rocks of gold,
760   The palace of great Lucifer (so call
       That structure in the dialect of men
       Interpreted) which not long after, he
       Affecting° all equality with God,   *arrogating*
       In imitation of that mount whereon
765   Messiah was declared in sight of Heav'n,
       The Mountain of the Congregation called;
       For thither he assembled all his train,
       Pretending so commanded to consult
       About the great reception of their King,
770   Thither to come, and with calumnious art
       Of counterfeited truth thus held their ears:
       "'Thrones, Dominations, Princedoms, Virtues, Powers,
       If these magnific titles yet remain
       Not merely titular, since by decree
775   Another now hath to himself engrossed°   *monopolized*
       All power, and us eclipsed under the name
       Of King anointed, for whom all this haste
       Of midnight march, and hurried meeting here,
       This only to consult how we may best
780   With what may be devised of honors new
       Receive him coming to receive from us
       Knee-tribute yet unpaid, prostration vile,
       Too much to one, but double how endured,
       To one and to his image now proclaimed?
785   But what if better counsels might erect
       Our minds and teach us to cast off this yoke?
       Will ye submit your necks, and choose to bend
       The supple knee? Ye will not, if I trust
       To know ye right, or if ye know yourselves
790   Natives and sons of Heav'n possessed before
       By none, and if not equal all, yet free,
       Equally free; for orders and degrees
       Jar not with liberty, but well consist.
       Who can in reason then or right assume
795   Monarchy over such as live by right

His equals,[1] if in power and splendor less,
In freedom equal? or can introduce
Law and edíct on us, who without law
Err not, much less for this to be our Lord,
800 And look for adoration to th' abuse
Of those imperial titles which assert
Our being ordained to govern, not to serve?'
    "Thus far his bold discourse without control°   *hindrance*
Had audience, when among the Seraphim
805 Abdiel,[2] than whom none with more zeal adored
The Deity, and divine commands obeyed,
Stood up, and in a flame of zeal severe
The current of his fury thus opposed:
    "'O argument blasphémous, false and proud!
810 Words which no ear ever to hear in Heav'n
Expected, least of all from thee, ingrate,
In place thyself so high above thy peers.
Canst thou with impious obloquy condemn
The just decree of God, pronounced and sworn,
815 That to his only Son by right endued
With regal scepter, every soul in Heav'n
Shall bend the knee, and in that honor due
Confess him rightful King? Unjust thou says't,
Flatly unjust, to bind with laws the free,
820 And equal over equals to let reign,
One over all with unsucceeded° power.   *without successor*
Shalt thou give law to God, shalt thou dispute
With him the points of liberty, who made
Thee what thou art, and formed the pow'rs of Heav'n
825 Such as he pleased, and circumscribed their being?
Yet by experience taught we know how good,
And of our good, and of our dignity
How provident he is, how far from thought
To make us less, bent rather to exalt
830 Our happy state under one head more near
United. But to grant it thee unjust,
That equal over equals monarch reign:
Thyself though great and glorious dost thou count,
Or all angelic nature joined in one,
835 Equal to him begotten Son, by whom
As by his Word the mighty Father made
All things, ev'n thee, and all the Spirits of Heav'n
By him created in their bright° degrees,   *illustrious*
Crowned them with glory, and to their glory named
840 Thrones, Dominations, Princedoms, Virtues, Powers,
Essential Powers, nor by his reign obscured,
But more illustrious made, since he the head

---

1. Satan here paraphrases the republican theory against earthly monarchy like that urged by Milton in his *Tenure of Kings and Magistrates* (1649); see pp. 1846–49. Abdiel, however, insists

(lines 809–41) that the argument from equality cannot pertain to God and the angels.
2. Hebrew, "servant of God."

One of our number thus reduced becomes,[3]
His laws our laws, all honor to him done
845   Returns our own. Cease then this impious rage,
And tempt not these; but hasten to appease
Th' incensèd Father and th' incensèd Son,
While pardon may be found in time besought.'
      "So spake the fervent angel, but his zeal
850   None seconded, as out of season judged,
Or singular and rash, whereat rejoiced
Th' Apostate,° and more haughty thus replied.   religious renegade
'That we were formed then say'st thou? and the work
Of secondary hands, by task transferred
855   From Father to his Son? Strange point and new!
Doctrine which we would know whence learnt: who saw
When this creation was? Remember'st thou
Thy making, while the Maker gave thee being?
We know no time when we were not as now;
860   Know none before us, self-begot, self-raised,
By our own quick'ning power, when fatal course°   the course of fate
Had circled his full orb, the birth mature
Of this our native Heav'n, ethereal sons.[4]
Our puissance° is our own, our own right hand   power
865   Shall teach us highest deeds, by proof to try
Who is our equal: then thou shalt behold
Whether by supplication we intend
Address, and to begirt th' Almighty throne
Beseeching or besieging. This report,
870   These tidings carry to th' anointed King;
And fly, ere evil intercept thy flight.'
      "He said, and as the sound of waters deep
Hoarse murmur echoed to his words applause
Through the infinite host, nor less for that
875   The flaming Seraph fearless, though alone
Encompassed round with foes, thus answered bold:
      "'O alienate from God, O Spirit accurst,
Forsaken of all good; I see thy fall
Determined, and thy hapless crew involved
880   In this perfidious fraud, contagion spread
Both of thy crime and punishment: henceforth
No more be troubled how to quit the yoke
Of God's Messiah; those indulgent laws
Will not be now vouchsafed, other decrees
885   Against thee are gone forth without recall;
That golden scepter which thou didst reject
Is now an iron rod to bruise and break
Thy disobedience. Well thou didst advise,
Yet not for thy advice or threats I fly
890   These wicked tents devoted,° lest the wrath   doomed

3. Abdiel suggests that the Son's appointment as the angels' king is something like an "incarnation" for them.
4. Satan's (illogical) argument is that since the angels cannot remember their creation, they created themselves. Cf. Adam's comment on his recollection of origins (8.250–51, 270–79).

Impendent,° raging into sudden flame   *impending*
Distinguish not: for soon expect to feel
His thunder on thy head, devouring fire.
Then who created thee lamenting learn,
895 When who can uncreate thee thou shalt know.'
    "So spake the Seraph Abdiel faithful found,
Among the faithless, faithful only he;
Among innumerable false, unmoved,
Unshaken, unseduced, unterrified
900 His loyalty he kept, his love, his zeal;
Nor number, nor example with him wrought
To swerve from truth, or change his constant mind
Though single. From amidst them forth he passed,
Long way through hostile scorn, which he sustained
905 Superior, nor of violence feared aught;°   *anything*
And with retorted scorn his back he turned
On those proud tow'rs to swift destruction doomed."

Book 6

All night the dreadless angel[1] unpursued
Through Heav'n's wide champaign° held his way, till Morn,   *plain*
Waked by the circling Hours,[2] with rosy hand
Unbarred the gates of light. There is a cave
5 Within the mount of God, fast° by his throne,   *close*
Where light and darkness in perpetual round
Lodge and dislodge by turns, which makes through Heav'n
Grateful vicissitude,° like day and night;   *delightful change*
Light issues forth, and at the other door
10 Obsequious° darkness enters, till her hour   *compliant*
To veil the Heav'n, though darkness there might well
Seem twilight here; and now went forth the Morn
Such as in highest Heav'n, arrayed in gold
Empyreal;° from before her vanished night,   *heavenly*
15 Shot through with orient beams: when all the plain
Covered with thick embattled° squadrons bright,   *in battle array*
Chariots and flaming arms, and fiery steeds
Reflecting blaze on blaze, first met his view:
War he perceived, war in procinct,° and found   *preparation*
20 Already known what he for news had thought
To have reported: gladly then he mixed
Among those friendly Powers who him received
With joy and acclamations loud, that one
That of so many myriads fall'n, yet one
25 Returned not lost: on to the sacred hill
They led him high applauded, and present
Before the seat supreme; from whence a voice:

---

1. I.e., Abdiel.
2. Daughters of Jove, who control the seasons
and guard the gates of Heaven. "Morn": Aurora, goddess of dawn.

From midst a golden cloud thus mild was heard.
"'Servant of God,[3] well done, well hast thou fought
30   The better fight, who single hast maintained
Against revolted multitudes the cause
Of truth, in word mightier than they in arms;
And for the testimony of truth hast borne
Universal reproach, far worse to bear
35   Than violence: for this was all thy care
To stand approved in sight of God, though worlds
Judged thee perverse: the easier conquest now
Remains thee, aided by this host of friends,
Back on thy foes more glorious to return
40   Than scorned thou didst depart, and to subdue
By force, who reason for their law refuse,
Right reason° for their law, and for their King   *upright, true reason*
Messiah, who by right of merit reigns.
Go Michael of celestial armies prince,
45   And thou in military prowess next
Gabriel, lead forth to battle these my sons°   *angels*
Invincible, lead forth my armèd saints
By thousands and by millions ranged for fight;
Equal in number to that godless crew
50   Rebellious,[4] them with fire and hostile arms
Fearless assault, and to the brow of Heav'n
Pursuing drive them out from God and bliss,
Into their place of punishment, the gulf
Of Tartarus,° which ready opens wide   *Hell*
55   His fiery chaos to receive their fall.'
    "So spake the Sovereign Voice, and clouds began
To darken all the hill, and smoke to roll
In dusky wreaths reluctant° flames, the sign   *writhing*
Of wrath awaked: nor with less dread the loud
60   Ethereal trumpet from on high gan° blow: *began to*
At which command the powers militant,
That stood for Heav'n, in mighty quadrate[5] joined
Of union irresistible, moved on
In silence their bright legions, to the sound
65   Of instrumental harmony that breathed
Heroic ardor to advent'rous deeds
Under their godlike leaders, in the cause
Of God and his Messiah. On they move
Indissolubly firm; nor obvious° hill,   *standing in the way*
70   Nor strait'ning vale,[6] nor wood, nor stream divides
Their perfect ranks; for high above the ground
Their march was, and the passive air upbore
Their nimble tread; as when the total kind
Of birds in orderly array on wing
75   Came summoned over Eden to receive

---

3. The literal meaning (Hebrew) of the name Abdiel.
4. God sends out only an equal force to match the one-third of the angelic host that rebelled, not the two-thirds that remained loyal.
5. A square military formation.
6. A narrow valley would force other armies to march in a file.

Their names of thee; so over many a tract
Of Heav'n they marched, and many a province wide
Tenfold the length of this terrene:° at last   *earth, terrain*
Far in th' horizon to the north appeared
80 From skirt to skirt a fiery region, stretched
In battailous° aspéct, and nearer view   *warlike*
Bristled with upright beams° innumerable   *shafts*
Of rigid spears, and helmets thronged, and shields
Various, with boastful argument° portrayed,   *heraldic devices*
85 The banded powers of Satan hasting on
With furious expedition;° for they weened°   *speed / thought*
That selfsame day by fight, or by surprise
To win the mount of God, and on his throne
To set the envier of his state, the proud
90 Aspirer, but their thoughts proved fond° and vain   *foolish*
In the mid-way: though strange to us it seemed
At first, that angel should with angel war,
And in fierce hosting[7] meet, who wont° to meet   *were accustomed*
So oft in festivals of joy and love
95 Unanimous, as sons of one great Sire
Hymning th' Eternal Father: but the shout
Of battle now began, and rushing sound
Of onset ended soon each milder thought.
High in the midst exalted as a god
100 Th' Apostate in his sun-bright chariot sat
Idol of majesty divine, enclosed
With flaming Cherubim, and golden shields;
Then lighted from his gorgeous throne, for now
'Twixt host° and host but narrow space was left,   *army*
105 A dreadful interval, and front to front°   *face to face*
Presented stood in terrible array
Of hideous length: before the cloudy van,°   *frowning vanguard*
On the rough edge of battle° ere it joined,   *front line*
Satan with vast and haughty strides advanced,
110 Came tow'ring, armed in adamant and gold;
Abdiel that sight endured not, where he stood
Among the mightiest, bent on highest deeds,
And thus his own undaunted heart explores:
    "'O Heav'n! that such resemblance of the Highest
115 Should yet remain, where faith and realty°   *sincerity*
Remain not; wherefore should not strength and might
There fail where virtue fails, or weakest prove
Where boldest; though to sight° unconquerable?   *seemingly*
His puissance,° trusting in th' Almighty's aid,   *power*
120 I mean to try, whose reason I have tried°   *proved by trial*
Unsound and false; nor is it aught but just,
That he who in debate of truth hath won,
Should win in arms, in both disputes alike
Victor; though brutish that contést and foul,
125 When reason hath to deal with force, yet so

7. Hostile encounter.

Most reason is that reason overcome.'
    "So pondering, and from his armèd peers
Forth stepping opposite, halfway he met
His daring foe, at this prevention° more   *obstruction*
130 Incensed, and thus securely° him defied: *confidently*
    "'Proud, art thou met? Thy hope was to have reached
The height of thy aspiring unopposed,
The throne of God unguarded, and his side
Abandoned at the terror of thy power
135 Or potent tongue; fool, not to think how vain
Against the Omnipotent to rise in arms;
Who out of smallest things could without end
Have raised incessant armies to defeat
Thy folly; or with solitary hand
140 Reaching beyond all limit at one blow
Unaided could have finished thee, and whelmed
Thy legions under darkness; but thou seest
All are not of thy train; there be° who faith   *there are those*
Prefer, and piety° to God, though then   *devotion*
145 To thee not visible, when I alone
Seemed in thy world erroneous to dissent
From all: my sect[8] thou seest, now learn too late
How few sometimes may know, when thousand err.'
    "Whom the grand Foe with scornful eye askance
150 Thus answered. 'Ill for thee, but in wished hour
Of my revenge, first sought for thou return'st
From flight, seditious angel, to receive
Thy merited reward, the first assay
Of this right hand provoked, since first that tongue
155 Inspired with contradiction durst oppose
A third part of the gods, in synod met
Their deities to assert, who while they feel
Vigor divine within them, can allow
Omnipotence to none. But well thou com'st
160 Before thy fellows, ambitious to win
From me some plume, that thy success[9] may show
Destruction to the rest: this pause between
(Unanswered lest thou boast)[1] to let thee know;
At first I thought that liberty and Heav'n
165 To heav'nly souls had been all one;° but now   *one and the same*
I see that most through sloth had rather serve,
Minist'ring Spirits, trained up in feast and song;
Such hast thou armed, the minstrelsy[2] of Heav'n,
Servility° with freedom to contend,   *bondage, obsequiousness*

---

8. The term carries political resonance, since the national English church, Anglican or (during the revolution) Presbyterian, sought to suppress and persecute the sects who separated from it (Baptists, Quakers, Socinians, and others), often denouncing them as heretics. Satan claims that a "synod" (line 156, term for a Presbyterian assembly) has proclaimed the truth of the rebel angels' case; Abdiel insists that truth may rather reside (as here) with a single "dissenter" or a sect of a few.

9. The outcome of your action. "Plume": token of victory.

1. I.e., lest thou boast that I did not answer your argument.

2. Satan's contemptuous pun links together the loyal angels' service ("Minist'ring," line 167) with their song, likened to the street songs of minstrels.

170　As both their deeds compared this day shall prove.'
　　　　"To whom in brief thus Abdiel stern replied:
　　　'Apostate, still thou err'st, nor end wilt find
　　　Of erring, from the path of truth remote:
　　　Unjustly thou deprav'st° it with the name　　　　　　　　　　*vilify*
175　Of servitude to serve whom God ordains,
　　　Or nature; God and nature bid the same,
　　　When he who rules is worthiest, and excels
　　　Them whom he governs. This is servitude,
　　　To serve th' unwise, or him who hath rebelled
180　Against his worthier, as thine now serve thee,
　　　Thyself not free, but to thyself enthralled;[3]
　　　Yet lewdly° dar'st our minist'ring upbraid.　　　　　*ignorantly, basely*
　　　Reign thou in Hell thy kingdom, let me serve
　　　In Heav'n God ever blest, and his divine
185　Behests obey, worthiest to be obeyed;
　　　Yet chains in Hell, not realms expect: meanwhile
　　　From me returned, as erst° thou saidst, from flight,　　　　*formerly*
　　　This greeting on thy impious crest receive.'
　　　　"So saying, a noble stroke he lifted high,
190　Which hung not, but so swift with tempest fell
　　　On the proud crest of Satan, that no sight,
　　　Nor motion of swift thought, less could his shield
　　　Such ruin intercept: ten paces huge
　　　He back recoiled; the tenth on bended knee
195　His massy spear upstayed; as if on earth
　　　Winds under ground or waters forcing way
　　　Sidelong, had pushed a mountain from his seat
　　　Half sunk with all his pines. Amazement seized
　　　The rebel Thrones,[4] but greater rage to see
200　Thus foiled their mightiest: ours joy filled, and shout,
　　　Presage of victory and fierce desire
　　　Of battle: whereat Michaël bid sound
　　　Th' Archangel trumpet; through the vast of Heav'n
　　　It sounded, and the faithful armies rung
205　Hosanna to the Highest: nor stood at gaze
　　　The adverse legions, nor less hideous joined
　　　The horrid shock: now storming fury rose,
　　　And clamor such as heard in Heav'n till now
　　　Was never, arms on armor clashing brayed[5]
210　Horrible discord, and the madding° wheels　　　　*whirling madly*
　　　Of brazen chariots raged; dire was the noise
　　　Of conflict; overhead the dismal° hiss　　　　　　　　*dreadful*
　　　Of fiery darts in flaming volleys flew,
　　　And flying vaulted either host with fire.
215　So under fiery cope° together rushed　　　　　　　　　　*sky*

---

3. Abdiel cites the "natural law" principle that rule rightly belongs to the best or worthiest, and that tyrants are enslaved to their own passions.
4. Here as elsewhere Milton uses the name of one angelic order to stand for all. But the choice of "Thrones" here carries political resonance, linking monarchs with rebels against God's kingdom.
5. Made a harsh, jarring sound.

Both battles main,[6] with ruinous assault
And inextinguishable rage; all Heav'n
Resounded, and had earth been then, all earth
Had to her center shook. What wonder? when
220 Millions of fierce encount'ring angels fought
On either side, the least of whom could wield
These elements,[7] and arm him with the force
Of all their regions: how much more of power
Army against army numberless to raise
225 Dreadful combustion° warring, and disturb,   *tumult*
Though not destroy, their happy native seat;
Had not th' Eternal King Omnipotent
From his stronghold of Heav'n high overruled
And limited their might; though numbered such
230 As each divided legion might have seemed
A numerous host, in strength each armèd hand
A legion; led in fight, yet leader seemed
Each warrior single as in chief,[8] expert
When to advance, or stand, or turn the sway°   *force*
235 Of battle, open when, and when to close
The ridges° of grim war; no thought of flight,   *ranks*
None of retreat, no unbecoming deed
That argued fear; each on himself relied,
As° only in his arm the moment[9] lay   *as if*
240 Of victory; deeds of eternal fame
Were done, but infinite: for wide was spread
That war and various; sometimes on firm ground
A standing fight, then soaring on main° wing   *strong, powerful*
Tormented° all the air; all air seemed then   *agitated*
245 Conflicting fire: long time in even scale
The battle hung; till Satan, who that day
Prodigious power had shown, and met in arms
No equal, ranging through the dire attack
Of fighting Seraphim confused, at length
250 Saw where the sword of Michael smote, and felled
Squadrons at once; with huge two-handed sway
Brandished aloft the horrid edge came down
Wide-wasting; such destruction to withstand
He hasted, and opposed the rocky orb
255 Of tenfold adamant, his ample shield[1]
A vast circumference: at his approach
The great Archangel from his warlike toil
Surceased, and glad as hoping here to end
Intestine war° in Heav'n, the Arch-Foe subdued   *civil war*
260 Or captive dragged in chains, with hostile frown
And visage all inflamed first thus began:

6. The principal body of an army, as opposed to
the van, rear, and wing.
7. The four elements—fire, air, water, earth—
that constitute the several "regions" (next line) of
planet earth.
8. I.e., the angelic legions had leaders, yet each

single warrior seemed like such a leader.
9. Weight that will tip the scales.
1. Satan's shield is a rocklike ("rocky") circle,
made of impenetrable "adamant" (probably diamond), ten layers thick.

"'Author of evil, unknown till thy revolt,
Unnamed in Heav'n, now plenteous, as thou seest
These acts of hateful strife, hateful to all,
265 Though heaviest by just measure on thyself
And thy adherents: how hast thou disturbed
Heav'n's blessèd peace, and into nature brought
Misery, uncreated till the crime
Of thy rebellion! how hast thou instilled
270 Thy malice into thousands, once upright
And faithful, now proved false! But think not here
To trouble holy rest; Heav'n casts thee out
From all her confines. Heav'n the seat of bliss
Brooks° not the works of violence and war.   *endures*
275 Hence then, and evil go with thee along
Thy offspring, to the place of evil, Hell,
Thou and thy wicked crew; there mingle° broils,   *concoct*
Ere this avenging sword begin thy doom,
Or some more sudden vengeance winged from God
280 Precipitate thee with augmented pain.'
    "So spake the Prince of Angels; to whom thus
The Adversary: 'Nor think thou with wind
Of airy threats to awe whom yet with deeds
Thou canst not. Hast thou turned the least of these
285 To flight, or if to fall, but that they rise
Unvanquished, easier to transact with me
That thou shouldst hope, imperious, and with threats
To chase me hence?[2] Err not that so shall end
The strife which thou call'st evil, but we style
290 The strife of glory: which we mean to win,
Or turn this Heav'n itself into the Hell
Thou fablest, here however to dwell free,
If not to reign: meanwhile thy utmost force,
And join him named Almighty to thy aid,
295 I fly not, but have sought thee far and nigh.'
    "They ended parle,° and both addressed° for fight   *parley / prepared*
Unspeakable; for who, though with the tongue
Of angels, can relate, or to what things
Liken on earth conspicuous, that may lift
300 Human imagination to such height
Of godlike power: for likest gods they seemed,
Stood they or moved, in stature, motion, arms
Fit to decide the empire of great Heav'n.
Now waved their fiery swords, and in the air
305 Made horrid circles; two broad suns their shields
Blazed opposite, while Expectation stood[3]
In horror; from each hand with speed retired
Where erst° was thickest fight, th' angelic throng,   *ever*
And left large field, unsafe within the wind

---

2. I.e., Have you made even the least of my followers flee, or seen them fall and fail to rise, that
you would hope "imperiously" to deal ("transact") otherwise with me, driving me off by mere
threats? "Err not" (following): don't falsely suppose.
3. Personifying the angels' apprehension.

310 Of such commotion, such as to set forth
Great things by small, if nature's concord broke,
Among the constellations war were sprung,
Two planets rushing from aspéct malign
Of fiercest opposition in midsky,
315 Should combat, and their jarring spheres confound.[4]
Together both with next to almighty arm,
Uplifted imminent one stroke they aimed
That might determine,° and not need repeat,°   *end / repetition*
As not of power,[5] at once; nor odds° appeared   *inequality*
320 In might or swift prevention;° but the sword   *anticipation*
Of Michael from the armory of God
Was giv'n him tempered so, that neither keen
Nor solid might resist that edge: it met
The sword of Satan with steep force to smite
325 Descending, and in half cut sheer, nor stayed,
But with swift wheel reverse, deep ent'ring shared°   *cut off*
All his right side; then Satan first knew pain,
And writhed him to and fro convolved;° so sore   *contorted*
The griding° sword with discontinuous° wound *keenly cutting / gaping*
330 Passed through him, but th' ethereal substance closed
Not long divisible, and from the gash
A stream of nectarous humor issuing flowed
Sanguine,° such as celestial Spirits may bleed,   *blood-red*
And all his armor stained erewhile so bright.
335 Forthwith on all sides to his aid was run
By angels many and strong, who interposed
Defense, while others bore him on their shields
Back to his chariot, where it stood retired
From off the files of war; there they him laid
340 Gnashing for anguish and despite and shame
To find himself not matchless, and his pride
Humbled by such rebuke, so far beneath
His confidence to equal God in power.
Yet soon he healed; for Spirits that live throughout
345 Vital in every part, not as frail man
In entrails, heart or head, liver or reins,°   *kidneys*
Cannot but by annihilating die;
Nor in their liquid texture mortal wound
Receive, no more than can the fluid air:
350 All heart they live, all head, all eye, all ear,
All intellect, all sense, and as they please,
They limb themselves,[6] and color, shape, or size
Assume, as likes° them best, condense or rare.   *pleases*
  "Meanwhile in other parts like deeds deserved
355 Memorial, where the might of Gabriel fought,

---

4. An epic simile comparing the clash of these armies ("great things") with war among the planets, in which two planets clashing together from diametrically opposed positions ("aspect malign"), would cast the planetary system and its music ("jarring spheres") into confusion ("confound").
5. I.e., because they would not have power to repeat the blow.
6. I.e., provide themselves with limbs. "Condense or rare" (line 353): dense or airy.

And with fierce ensigns pierced the deep array
Of Moloch furious king,[7] who him defied,
And at his chariot wheels to drag him bound
Threatened, nor from the Holy One of Heav'n
360 Refrained his tongue blasphémous; but anon
Down clov'n to the waist, with shattered arms
And uncouth° pain fled bellowing. On each wing   *unfamiliar*
Uriel and Raphael his vaunting foe,
Though huge, and in a rock of diamond armed,
365 Vanquished Adramelech, and Asmadai,[8]
Two potent Thrones, that to be less than gods
Disdained, but meaner thoughts learned in their flight,
Mangled with ghastly wounds through plate and mail.
Nor stood unmindful Abdiel to annoy°   *injure*
370 The atheist° crew, but with redoubled blow   *impious*
Ariel and Arioch, and the violence
Of Ramiel[9] scorched and blasted overthrew.
I might relate of thousands, and their names
Eternize here on earth; but those elect
375 Angels contented with their fame in Heav'n
Seek not the praise of men: the other sort
In might though wondrous and in acts of war,
Nor of renown less eager, yet by doom
Canceled from Heav'n and sacred memory,
380 Nameless in dark oblivion let them dwell.
For strength from truth divided and from just,
Illaudable,° naught merits but dispraise   *unworthy of praise*
And ignominy, yet to glory aspires
Vainglorious, and through infamy seeks fame:
385 Therefore eternal silence be their doom.
    "And now their mightiest quelled, the battle swerved,[1]
With many an inroad gored; deformèd rout
Entered, and foul disorder; all the ground
With shivered armor strown, and on a heap
390 Chariot and charioteer lay overturned
And fiery foaming steeds; what° stood, recoiled   *those who*
O'erwearied, through the faint Satanic host
Defensive scarce,[2] or with pale fear surprised,°   *seized unexpectedly*
Then first with fear surprised and sense of pain
395 Fled ignominious, to such evil brought
By sin of disobedience, till that hour
Not liable to fear or flight or pain.
Far otherwise th' inviolable saints
In cubic phalanx° firm advanced entire,   *formation*
400 Invulnerable, impenetrably armed:
Such high advantages their innocence
Gave them above their foes, not to have sinned,

---

7. With his companies ("ensigns") he pierced Moloch's troops in their dense formation ("deep array").
8. Asmodeus, a Persian god (cf. 4.167–71). "Adramelech": "king of fire," a god worshipped at Samaria with human sacrifice.
9. "Ariel": "lion of God." "Arioch": "lionlike." "Ramiel": "thunder of God."
1. I.e., the army gave way.
2. Scarcely defending themselves.

Not to have disobeyed; in fight they stood
Unwearied, unobnoxious° to be pained   *not liable*
405   By wound, though from their place by violence moved.
       "Now night her course began, and over Heav'n
Inducing darkness, grateful truce imposed,
And silence on the odious din of war:
Under her cloudy covert both retired,
410   Victor and vanquished: on the foughten field
Michaël and his angels prevalent°   *victorious*
Encamping, placed in guard their watches round,
Cherubic waving fires: on th' other part
Satan with his rebellious disappeared,
415   Far in the dark dislodged,° and void of rest,   *shifted quarters*
His potentates to council called by night;
And in the midst thus undismayed began:
       "'O now in danger tried, now known in arms
Not to be overpowered, companions dear,
420   Found worthy not of liberty alone,
Too mean pretense,° but what we more affect,³   *low aim*
Honor, dominion, glory, and renown,
Who have sustained one day in doubtful° fight,   *indecisive*
(And if one day, why not eternal days?)
425   What Heaven's Lord had powerfullest to send
Against us from about his throne, and judged
Sufficient to subdue us to his will,
But proves not so: then fallible, it seems,
Of future° we may deem him, though till now   *in the future*
430   Omniscient thought. True is, less firmly armed,
Some disadvantage we endured and pain,
Till now not known, but known as soon contemned,⁴
Since now we find this our empyreal form
Incapable of mortal injury
435   Imperishable, and though pierced with wound,
Soon closing, and by native vigor healed.
Of evil then so small as easy think
The remedy; perhaps more valid° arms,   *powerful*
Weapons more violent, when next we meet,
440   May serve to better us, and worse° our foes,   *injure*
Or equal what between us made the odds,
In nature none: if other hidden cause
Left them superior, while we can preserve
Unhurt our minds, and understanding sound,
445   Due search and consultation will disclose.'
       "He sat; and in th' assembly next upstood
Nisroch,⁵ of Principalities the prime;
As one he stood escaped from cruel fight,
Sore toiled, his riven arms to havoc hewn,°   *cut to pieces*
450   And cloudy in aspéct thus answering spake:
'Deliverer from new lords, leader to free

---

3. Aspire to.   5. An Assyrian god; the Hebrew name was said
4. No sooner known than despised.   to mean flight or luxurious temptation.

Enjoyment of our right as gods; yet hard
For gods, and too unequal work we find
Against unequal arms to fight in pain,
455   Against unpained, impassive;[6] from which evil
Ruin must needs ensue; for what avails
Valor or strength, though matchless, quelled with pain
Which all subdues, and makes remiss° the hands   *slack, weak*
Of mightiest. Sense of pleasure we may well
460   Spare out of life perhaps, and not repine,
But live content, which is the calmest life:
But pain is perfect misery, the worst
Of evils, and excessive, overturns
All patience. He who therefore can invent
465   With what more forcible we may offend°   *attack*
Our yet unwounded enemies, or arm
Ourselves with like defense, to me° deserves   *in my opinion*
No less than for deliverance what we owe.'[7]
    "Whereto with look composed Satan replied.
470   'Not uninvented that, which thou aright
Believ'st so main° to our success, I bring;   *essential*
Which of us who beholds the bright surfáce
Of this ethereous mold° whereon we stand,   *ethereal matter*
This continent of spacious Heav'n, adorned
475   With plant, fruit, flow'r ambrosial, gems and gold,
Whose eye so superfically surveys
These things, as not to mind° from whence they grow   *consider*
Deep underground, materials dark and crude,
Of spiritous and fiery spume,° till touched   *frothy matter*
480   With Heav'n's ray, and tempered they shoot forth
So beauteous, op'ning to the ambient° light.   *enveloping*
These in their dark nativity the deep
Shall yield us, pregnant with infernal° flame,   *from underground*
Which into hollow engines° long and round   *cannon*
485   Thick-rammed, at th' other bore[8] with touch of fire
Dilated and infuriate° shall send forth   *raging*
From far with thund'ring noise among our foes
Such implements of mischief as shall dash
To pieces, and o'erwhelm whatever stands
490   Adverse, that they shall fear we have disarmed
The Thunderer of his only° dreaded bolt.   *unique*
Nor long shall be our labor, yet ere dawn,
Effect shall end our wish. Meanwhile revive;
Abandon fear; to strength and counsel joined
495   Think nothing hard, much less to be despaired.'
    He ended, and his words their drooping cheer°   *spirits*
Enlightened, and their languished hope revived.
Th' invention all admired,° and each, how he   *marveled at*
To be th' inventor missed, so easy it seemed

---

6. Not liable to suffering.
7. I.e., we would owe such a one our deliverance.
8. The touchhole into which fine powder was

poured to serve as fuse for the charge. "Thick":
compactly.

500 Once found, which yet unfound most would have thought
Impossible: yet haply° of thy race   *possibly*
In future days, if malice should abound,
Someone intent on mischief, or inspired
With dev'lish machination might devise
505 Like instrument to plague the sons of men
For sin, on war and mutual slaughter bent.
Forthwith from council to the work they flew,
None arguing stood, innumerable hands
Were ready, in a moment up they turned
510 Wide the celestial soil, and saw beneath
Th' originals° of nature in their crude   *original elements*
Conception; sulphurous and nitrous foam[9]
They found, they mingled, and with subtle art,
Concocted° and adjusted° they reduced   *heated / dried*
515 To blackest grain, and into store conveyed:
Part hidden veins digged up (nor hath this earth
Entrails unlike) of mineral and stone,
Whereof to found° their engines and their balls   *cast*
Of missive° ruin; part incentive° reed   *missile / kindling*
520 Provide, pernicious° with one touch to fire.   *quick, destructive*
So all ere day-spring,° under conscious[1] night   *dawn*
Secret they finished, and in order set,
With silent circumspection unespied.
Now when fair morn orient in Heav'n appeared
525 Up rose the victor angels, and to arms
The matin° trumpet sung: in arms they stood   *morning*
Of golden panoply, refulgent° host,   *shining*
Soon banded; others from the dawning hills
Looked round, and scouts each coast light-armèd scour,
530 Each quarter, to descry the distant foe,
Where lodged, or whither fled, or if for fight,
In motion or in alt:° him soon they met   *halt*
Under spread ensigns moving nigh, in slow
But firm battalion; back with speediest sail
535 Zophiel,[2] of Cherubim the swiftest wing,
Came flying, and in mid-air aloud thus cried:
   "'Arm, warriors, arm for fight, the foe at hand,
Whom fled we thought, will save us long pursuit
This day, fear not his flight; so thick a cloud
540 He comes, and settled in his face I see
Sad° resolution and secure:° let each   *sober / confident*
His adamantine° coat gird well, and each   *of hardest metal*
Fit well his helm, gripe fast his orbèd shield,
Borne ev'n° or high, for this day will pour down,   *straight out*
545 If I conjecture° aught, no drizzling shower,   *interpret signs*
But rattling storm of arrows barbed with fire.'
So warned he them aware themselves, and soon
In order, quit of all impediment;°   *hindrance*

9. Saltpeter ("nitrous foam") and sulphur are the ingredients of gunpowder.

1. Aware, as an accessory to a crime.
2. Hebrew, "spy of God."

Instant without disturb° they took alarm,   *disorder*
550 And onward move embattled;° when behold   *in battle order*
Not distant far the heavy pace the foe
Approaching gross° and huge; in hollow cube   *compact*
Training° his devilish enginry, impaled°   *hauling / fenced in*
On every side with shadowing squadrons deep,
555 To hide the fraud. At interview° both stood   *at mutual view*
A while, but suddenly at head appeared
Satan: and thus was heard commanding loud:
 "'Vanguard, to right and left the front unfold;
That all may see who hate us, how we seek
560 Peace and composure,° and with open breast   *agreement*
Stand ready to receive them, if they like
Our overture,³ and turn not back perverse;
But that I doubt, however witness Heaven,
Heav'n witness thou anon, while we discharge
565 Freely our part: ye who appointed stand
Do as you have in charge, and briefly touch
What we propound, and loud that all may hear.'
 "So scoffing in ambiguous words, he scarce
Had ended; when to right and left the front
570 Divided, and to either flank retired.
Which to our eyes discovered new and strange,
A triple-mounted° row of pillars laid   *in three rows*
On wheels (for like to pillars most they seemed
Or hollowed bodies made of oak or fir
575 With branches lopped, in wood or mountain felled)
Brass, iron, stony mold,° had not their mouths   *matter*
With hideous orifice gaped on us wide,
Portending hollow truce; at each behind
A Seraph stood, and in his hand a reed
580 Stood waving tipped with fire; while we suspense,° *in suspense*
Collected stood within our thoughts amused,°   *puzzled*
Not long, for sudden all at once their reeds
Put forth, and to a narrow vent applied
With nicest° touch. Immediate in a flame,   *most exact*
585 But soon obscured with smoke, all Heav'n appeared,
From those deep-throated engines belched,⁴ whose roar
Emboweled° with outrageous noise the air,   *disemboweled*
And all her entrails tore, disgorging foul
Their devilish glut, chained⁵ thunderbolts and hail
590 Of iron globes, which on the victor host
Leveled, with such impetuous fury smote,
That whom they hit, none on their feet might stand,
Though standing else as rocks, but down they fell
By thousands, Angel on Archangel rolled,

---

3. A pun on "offer to negotiate" and "opening" (aperture), the hole or muzzle of the cannon. The passage is full of puns: e.g., "perverse" (line 562, peevish, turned the wrong way), "discharge" (line 564), "charge," "touch," "propound," "loud" (lines 566–67), "hollow" (line 578).
4. See the sustained debased imagery relating to bodily functions, e.g., "belched," "emboweled," "entrails."
5. Chainshot, which was linked cannonballs.

595 The sooner for their arms; unarmed they might
Have easily as Spirits evaded swift
By quick contraction or remove; but now
Foul dissipation° followed and forced rout;   dispersal
Nor served it to relax their serried files.[6]
600 What should they do? If on they rushed, repulse
Repeated, and indecent° overthrow   shameful
Doubled, would render them yet more despised,
And to their foes a laughter; for in view
Stood ranked of Seraphim another row
605 In posture to displode° their second dire°   explode / volley
Of thunder: back defeated to return
They worse abhorred. Satan beheld their plight,
And to his mates thus in derision called:
    "'O friends, why come not on these victors proud?
610 Erewhile they fierce were coming, and when we,
To entertain them fair with open front°   candid face
And breast,° (what could we more?) propounded[7] terms   heart
Of composition, straight they changed their minds,
Flew off, and into strange vagaries° fell,   eccentric motions
615 As they would dance, yet for a dance they seemed
Somewhat extravagant and wild, perhaps
For joy of offering peace: but I suppose
If our proposals once again were heard
We should compel them to a quick result.'
620   "To whom thus Belial in like gamesome mood:
'Leader, the terms we sent were terms of weight,
Of hard contents, and full of force urged home,
Such as we might perceive amused them[8] all,
And stumbled many: who receives them right,
625 Had need from head to foot well understand;
Not understood, this gift they have besides,
They show us when our foes walk not upright."
    "So they among themselves in pleasant° vein   jesting
Stood scoffing, heightened in their thoughts beyond
630 All doubt of victory, Eternal Might
To match with their inventions they presumed
So easy, and of his thunder made a scorn,
And all his host derided, while they° stood   the good angels
A while in trouble; but they stood not long,
635 Rage prompted them at length, and found them arms
Against such hellish mischief fit to oppose.
Forthwith (behold the excellence, the power,
Which God hath in his mighty angels placed)
Their arms away they threw, and to the hills
640 (For earth hath this variety from Heav'n
Of pleasure situate in hill and dale)

---

6. I.e., nor did it do any good ("served it") to
loosen up ("relax") their rows pressed close
together ("serried files").
7. More puns, on "propounded," "terms of composition," "flew off."

8. A pun on "held their attention" and "bewildered them." Belial also puns on (among other
terms) "stumbled" ("nonplussed" and "tripped
up") and "understand" ("comprehend" and "prop
up").

Light as the lightning glimpse they ran, they flew,
From their foundations loos'ning to and fro
They plucked the seated hills with all their load,[9]
645   Rocks, waters, woods, and by the shaggy tops
Uplifting bore them in their hands: amaze,°   *astonishment, panic*
Be sure, and terror seized the rebel host,
When coming towards them so dread they saw
The bottom of the mountains upward turned,
650   Till on those cursèd engines' triple-row
They saw them whelmed, and all their confidence
Under the weight of mountains buried deep,
Themselves invaded° next, and on their heads   *attacked*
Main° promontories flung, which in the air   *great, solid*
655   Came shadowing, and oppressed° whole legions armed.   *pressed down*
Their armor helped their harm, crushed in and bruised
Into their substance pent,° which wrought them pain   *closely confined*
Implacable, and many a dolorous groan,
Long struggling undernearth, ere they could wind
660   Out of such prison, though Spirits of purest light,
Purest at first, now gross by sinning grown.
The rest in imitation to like arms
Betook them, and the neighboring hills uptore;
So hills amid the air encountered hills
665   Hurled to and fro with jaculation° dire,   *hurling*
That underground they fought in dismal shade;
Infernal noise; war seemed a civil° game   *humane, refined*
To° this uproar; horrid confusion heaped   *compared to*
Upon confusion rose: and now all Heav'n
670   Had gone to wrack, with ruin overspread,
Had not th' Almighty Father where he sits
Shrined in his sanctuary of Heav'n secure,
Consulting° on the sum of things, foreseen   *considering*
This tumult, and permitted all, advised:°   *deliberately*
675   That his great purpose he might so fulfill,
To honor his anointed Son avenged
Upon his enemies, and to declare
All power on him transferred: whence to his Son
Th' assessor[1] of his throne he thus began:
680   "'Effulgence° of my glory, Son beloved,   *radiance*
Son in whose face invisible is beheld
Visibly,[2] what by Deity I am,
And in whose hand what by decree I do,
Second Omnipotence,[3] two days are passed,
685   Two days, as we compute the days of Heav'n,
Since Michael and his powers went forth to tame

9. The hurling of hills as missiles is taken from the war between the Olympian gods and the Giants, in Hesiod's *Theogony*.
1. One who sits beside, an associate.
2. Cf. Colossians 1.15: "Who is the image of the invisible God."
3. Two omnipotences are a logical impossibility;

the phrase underscores Milton's view that the Son receives all power from the Father. Cf. John 5.19, "The Son can do nothing of himself, but what he seeth the Father do," which Milton cites in *Christian Doctrine* 1.5 to argue that the Son derives all power from the Father.

These disobedient; sore hath been their fight,
As likeliest was, when two such foes met armed;
For to themselves I left them, and thou know'st,
690 Equal in their creation they were formed,
Save what sin hath impaired, which yet hath wrought
Insensibly,° for I suspend their doom;   *imperceptively*
Whence in perpetual fight they needs must last
Endless, and no solution will be found:
695 War wearied hath performed what war can do,
And to disordered rage let loose the reins,
With mountains as with weapons armed, which makes
Wild work in Heav'n, and dangerous to the main.°   *whole continent*
Two days are therefore passed, the third is thine;
700 For thee I have ordained it, and thus far
Have suffered,° that the glory may be thine   *permitted*
Of ending this great war, since none but thou
Can end it. Into thee such virtue and grace
Immense I have transfused, that all may know
705 In Heav'n and Hell thy power above compare,
And this perverse commotion governed thus,
To manifest thee worthiest to be heir
Of all things, to be heir and to be King
By sacred unction,° thy deservèd right.   *anointing*
710 Go then thou mightiest in thy Father's might,
Ascend my chariot, guide the rapid wheels
That shake Heav'n's basis, bring forth all my war,°   *instruments of war*
My bow and thunder, my almighty arms
Gird on, and sword upon thy puissant thigh;
715 Pursue these sons of darkness, drive them out
From all Heav'n's bounds into the utter° deep: *outer*
There let them learn, as likes them, to despise
God and Messiah his anointed[4] King.'
      "He said, and on his Son with rays direct
720 Shone full, he all his Father full expressed
Ineffably° into his face received,   *inexpressibly*
And thus the Filial Godhead answering spake:
      "'O Father, O Supreme of heav'nly Thrones,
First, highest, holiest, best, thou always seek'st
725 To glorify thy Son, I always thee,
As is most just; this I my glory account,
My exaltation, and my whole delight,
That thou in me well pleased, declar'st thy will
Fulfilled, which to fulfill is all my bliss.
730 Scepter and power, thy giving, I assume,
And gladlier shall resign, when in the end
Thou shalt be all in all, and I in thee
Forever, and in me all whom thou lov'st:
But whom thou hat'st, I hate, and can put on
735 Thy terrors, as I put thy mildness on,
Image of thee in all things; and shall soon,

---

4. The literal meaning of "messiah."

Armed with thy might, rid Heav'n of these rebelled,
To their prepared ill mansion driven down
To chains of darkness, and th' undying worm,
740 That from thy just obedience could revolt,
Whom to obey is happiness entire.
Then shall thy saints unmixed, and from th' impure
Far separate, circling thy holy mount
Unfeignèd hallelujahs to thee sing,
745 Hymns of high praise, and I among them chief.'
So said, he o'er his scepter bowing, rose
From the right hand of Glory where he sat,
And the third sacred morn began to shine
Dawning through Heav'n: forth rushed with whirlwind sound
750 The chariot of Paternal Deity,
Flashing thick flames, wheel within wheel undrawn,
Itself instinct with° spirit, but convoyed   animated by
By four Cherubic shapes, four faces each⁵
Had wondrous, as with stars their bodies all
755 And wings were set with eyes, with eyes the wheels
Of beryl, and careering fires between;⁶
Over their heads a crystal firmament,
Whereon a sapphire throne, inlaid with pure
Amber, and colors of the show'ry arch.°   rainbow
760 He in celestial panoply all armed
Of radiant urim,⁷ work divinely wrought,
Ascended, at his right hand Victory
Sat eagle-winged, beside him hung his bow
And quiver with three-bolted thunder stored,⁸
765 And from about him fierce effusion° rolled   copious emission
Of smoke and bickering° flame, and sparkles dire;   flickering
Attended with ten thousand thousand saints,
He onward came, far off his coming shone,
And twenty thousand⁹ (I their number heard)
770 Chariots of God, half on each hand were seen:
He on the wings of Cherub rode sublime°   lifted up
On the crystálline sky, in sapphire throned,
Illustrious° far and wide, but by his own   shining
First seen: them unexpected joy surprised,
775 When the great ensign of Messiah blazed
Aloft by angels borne, his sign in Heav'n:
Under whose conduct Michael soon reduced°   led back
His army, circumfused° on either wing,   spread around
Under their Head embodied all in one.
780 Before him Power Divine his way prepared;
At his command the uprooted hills retired

---

5. The Son's living chariot, with its four-faced
Cherubim—the faces being man, lion, ox, and
eagle—is taken from Ezekiel 1 (especially 1.10)
and 10.
6. Cf. Ezekiel 10.12: "And their whole body, and
their backs, and their hands, and their wings,
and the wheels, were full of eyes round about,
even the wheels that they four had."

7. Gems worn by Aaron in his "breastplate of
judgment" (Exodus 28.30).
8. Jove's bird was the eagle; his weapon was the
thunderbolt.
9. Cf. Psalm 68.17: "The chariots of God are
twenty thousand, even thousands of angels: the
Lord is among them."

Each to his place, they heard his voice and went
Obsequious,° Heav'n his wonted face renewed,   *dutiful*
And with fresh flow'rets hill and valley smiled.
785 This saw his hapless foes but stood obdured,°   *hardened*
And to rebellious fight rallied their powers
Insensate, hope conceiving from despair.
In heav'nly Spirits could such perverseness dwell?
But to convince the proud what signs avail,
790 Or wonders move th' obdúrate to relent?
They hardened more by what might most reclaim,
Grieving° to see his glory, at the sight   *aggrieved*
Took envy, and aspiring to his height,
Stood re-embattled[1] fierce, by force or fraud
795 Weening° to prosper, and at length prevail   *thinking*
Against God and Messiah, or to fall
In universal ruin last, and now
To final battle drew; disdaining flight,
Or faint retreat; when the great Son of God
800 To all his host on either hand thus spake:
   "'Stand still in bright array ye saints, here stand
Ye angels armed, this day from battle rest;[2]
Faithful hath been your warfare, and of God
Accepted, fearless in his righteous cause,
805 And as ye have received, so have ye done
Invincibly; but of this cursed crew
The punishment to other hand belongs,
Vengeance is his,[3] or whose he sole appoints;
Number to this day's work is not ordained
810 Nor multitude, stand only and behold
God's indignation on these godless poured
By me, not you but me they have despised,
Yet envied; against me is all their rage,
Because the Father, t' whom in Heav'n supreme
815 Kingdom and power and glory appertains,
Hath honored me according to his will.
Therefore to me their doom he hath assigned;
That they may have their wish, to try with me
In battle which the stronger proves, they all,
820 Or I alone against them, since by strength
They measure all, of other excellence
Not emulous,° nor care who them excels;   *desirous of rivaling*
Nor other strife with them do I vouchsafe.'°   *grant*
   "So spake the Son, and into terror changed
825 His count'nance too severe to be beheld
And full of wrath bent on his enemies.
At once the Four[4] spread out their starry wings
With dreadful shade contiguous, and the orbs

---

1. Drawn up again in battle formation.
2. Echoes Moses' words when God destroyed the Egyptians in the Red Sea (Exodus 14.13): "Fear ye not, stand still, and see the salvation of the Lord, which he will shew to you to day."
3. Cf. Romans 12.19: "Vengeance is mine; I will repay, saith the Lord."
4. The four "Cherubic shapes" of line 753.

Of his fierce chariot rolled, as with the sound
830 Of torrent floods, or of a numerous host.
He on his impious foes right onward drove,
Gloomy as night; under his burning wheels
The steadfast empyrean shook throughout,
All but the throne itself of God. Full soon
835 Among them he arrived; in his right hand
Grasping ten thousand thunders, which he sent
Before him, such as in their souls infixed
Plagues; they astonished° all resistance lost,   *struck with fear*
All courage; down their idle weapons dropped;
840 O'er shields and helms, and helmèd heads he rode
Of Thrones and mighty Seraphim prostráte,
That wished the mountains now might be again
Thrown on them as a shelter from his ire.
Nor less on either side tempestuous fell
845 His arrows, from the fourfold-visaged Four,
Distinct° with eyes, and from the living wheels,   *adorned*
Distinct alike with multitude of eyes;
One spirit in them ruled, and every eye
Glared lightning, and shot forth pernicious° fire   *deadly*
850 Among th' accursed, that withered all their strength,
And of their wonted° vigor left them drained,   *accustomed*
Exhausted, spiritless, afflicted, fall'n.
Yet half his strength he put not forth, but checked
His thunder in mid-volley, for he meant
855 Not to destroy, but root them out of Heav'n:
The overthrown he raised, and as a herd
Of goats or timorous flock together thronged
Drove them before him thunderstruck, pursued
With terrors and with furies to the bounds
860 And crystal wall of Heav'n, which op'ning wide,
Rolled inward, and a spacious gap disclosed
Into the wasteful° deep; the monstrous sight   *desolate*
Strook them with horror backward, but far worse
Urged them behind; headlong themselves they threw
865 Down from the verge of Heav'n, eternal wrath
Burnt after them to the bottomless pit.
   "Hell heard th' unsufferable noise, Hell saw
Heav'n ruining° from Heav'n, and would have fled   *falling headlong*
Affrighted; but strict fate had cast too deep
870 Her dark foundations, and too fast had bound.
Nine days they fell; confounded Chaos roared,
And felt tenfold confusion in their fall
Through his wild anarchy, so huge a rout°   *defeated army*
Encumbered° him with ruin: Hell at last   *burdened*
875 Yawning received them whole, and on them closed,
Hell their fit habitation fraught with fire
Unquenchable, the house of woe and pain.
Disburdened Heav'n rejoiced, and soon repaired
Her mural° breach, returning whence it rolled.   *in the wall*
880 Sole victor from th' expulsion of his foes

Messiah his triumphal chariot turned:
To meet him all his saints, who silent stood
Eyewitnesses of his almighty acts,
With jubilee° advanced; and as they went,   *joyful shouts*
885 Shaded with branching palm, each order bright
Sung triumph, and him sung victorious King,
Son, Heir, and Lord, to him dominion giv'n,
Worthiest to reign: he celebrated rode
Triumphant through mid-Heav'n, into the courts
890 And temple of his mighty Father throned
On high: who into glory him received,
Where now he sits at the right hand of bliss.
   "Thus measuring things in Heav'n by things on earth
At thy request, and that thou may'st beware
895 By what is past, to thee I have revealed
What might have else to human race been hid;
The discord which befell, and war in Heav'n
Among th' angelic powers,° and the deep fall   *armies*
Of those too high aspiring, who rebelled
900 With Satan, he who envies now thy state,
Who now is plotting how he may seduce
Thee also from obedience, that with him
Bereaved of happiness thou may'st partake
His punishment, eternal misery;
905 Which would be all his solace and revenge,
As a despite° done against the Most High,   *malicious act*
Thee once to gain companion of his woe.
But listen not to his temptations, warn
Thy weaker;[5] let it profit thee to have heard
910 By terrible example the reward
Of disobedience; firm they might have stood,
Yet fell; remember, and fear to transgress."

Book 7

Descend from Heav'n Urania,[1] by that name
If rightly thou art called, whose voice divine
Following, above th' Olympian hill I soar,
Above the flight of Pegasean wing.[2]
5 The meaning, not the name I call: for thou
Nor of the muses nine, nor on the top
Of old Olympus dwell'st, but heav'nly born
Before the hills appeared, or fountain flowed,

---

5. Eve, who is, however, present for this story.
1. Urania, the Greek Muse of astronomy, had been made into the Muse of Christian poetry by du Bartas and other religious poets. Milton, however, constructs another derivation for her (line 5ff.). Milton begins Book 7 with a third

proem (lines 1–39).
2. Pegasus, the flying horse of inspired poetry, suggests (in connection with Bellerophon, line 18) Milton's sense of perilous audacity in writing this poem.

Thou with eternal Wisdom[3] didst converse,°   *associate*
10 Wisdom thy sister, and with her didst play
In presence of th' Almighty Father, pleased
With thy celestial song. Up led by thee
Into the Heav'n of Heav'ns I have presumed,
An earthly guest, and drawn empyreal air,
15 Thy temp'ring;° with like safety guided down   *made suitable by thee*
Return me to my native element:
Lest from this flying steed unreined (as once
Bellerophon,[4] though from a lower clime)°   *region*
Dismounted, on th' Aleian field I fall
20 Erroneous° there to wander and forlorn.   *straying*
Half yet remains unsung, but narrower bound
Within the visible diurnal sphere;[5]
Standing on earth, not rapt° above the pole,   *transported, enraptured*
More safe I sing with mortal voice, unchanged
25 To hoarse or mute, though fall'n on evil days,
On evil days though fall'n, and evil tongues;
In darkness, and with dangers compassed round,[6]
And solitude; yet not alone, while thou
Visit'st my slumbers nightly, or when morn
30 Purples the east: still govern thou my song,
Urania, and fit audience find, though few.
But drive far off the barbarous dissonance
Of Bacchus and his revelers, the race
Of that wild rout that tore the Thracian bard
35 In Rhodope, where woods and rocks had ears
To rapture, till the savage clamor drowned
Both harp and voice;[7] nor could the Muse defend
Her son.[8] So fail not thou, who thee implores:
For thou art heav'nly, she an empty dream.
40 Say goddess, what ensued when Raphael,
The affable Archangel, had forewarned
Adam by dire example to beware
Apostasy, by what befell in Heaven
To those apostates, lest the like befall
45 In Paradise to Adam or his race,
Charged not to touch the interdicted tree,
If they transgress, and slight that sole command,

3. In Proverbs 8.24–31 Wisdom tells of her activities before the Creation: "Then I was by him [God], as one brought up with him: and I was daily his delight, rejoicing always before him." Milton describes "eternal Wisdom" as a daughter of God (personification of his wisdom) and devises a myth in which the Muse of divine poetry ("celestial song," line 12) is Wisdom's "sister"—also, thereby, originating from God.
4. Bellerophon incurred the gods' anger when he tried to fly to heaven upon Pegasus; Zeus sent an insect to sting the horse, and Bellerophon fell down to the "Aleian field" (plain of error), where he wandered alone and blind until his death.
5. The universe, which appears to rotate daily.
6. After the Restoration of Charles II (May 1660) and until the passage of the Act of Obliv-

ion (August 1660), Milton was in danger of death and dismemberment (like Orpheus, lines 34–35); several of his republican colleagues were hanged, disemboweled, and quartered for their part in the revolution and regicide.
7. The music of the "Thracian bard" Orpheus, type of the poet, charmed even "woods and rocks," but his song was drowned out by the Bacchantes, a "wild rout" of screaming women who murdered and dismembered him and threw his body parts into the Hebrus River, which rises in the "Rhodope" mountains. Milton fears that a similar "barbarous dissonance" unleashed by the Restoration will drown out his voice and threaten his life.
8. Orpheus's mother is Calliope, Muse of epic poetry.

So easily obeyed amid the choice
Of all tastes else° to please their appetite,   *besides*
50 Though wand'ring. He with his consorted° Eve   *wedded*
The story heard attentive, and was filled
With admiration,° and deep muse to hear   *amazement*
Of things so high and strange, things to their thought
So unimaginable as hate in Heav'n,
55 And war so near the peace of God in bliss
With such confusion: but the evil soon
Driv'n back redounded° as a flood on those   *flowed back*
From whom it sprung, impossible to mix
With blessedness. Whence Adam soon repealed°   *abandoned*
60 The doubts that in his heart arose: and now
Led on, yet sinless, with desire to know
What nearer might concern him, how this world
Of Heav'n and earth conspicuous° first began,   *visible*
When, and whereof created, for what cause,
65 What within Eden or without was done
Before his memory, as one whose drouth°   *thirst*
Yet scarce allayed still eyes the current° stream,   *flowing*
Whose liquid murmur heard new thirst excites,
Proceeded thus to ask his heav'nly guest:
70   "Great things, and full of wonder in our ears,
Far differing from this world, thou hast revealed
Divine interpreter, by favor sent
Down from the empyrean to forewarn
Us timely of what might else° have been our loss,   *otherwise*
75 Unknown, which human knowledge could not reach:
For which to the Infinitely Good we owe
Immortal thanks, and his admonishment
Receive with solemn purpose to observe
Immutably his sov'reign will, the end°   *purpose*
80 Of what we are. But since thou hast vouchsafed
Gently for our instruction to impart
Things above earthly thought, which yet concerned
Our knowing, as to Highest Wisdom seemed,
Deign to descend now lower, and relate
85 What may no less perhaps avail us known,
How first began this Heav'n which we behold
Distant so high, with moving fires adorned
Innumerable, and this which yields or fills
All space, the ambient° air wide interfused   *yielding*
90 Embracing round this florid° earth, what cause   *flowery*
Moved the Creator in his holy rest
Through all eternity so late to build
In Chaos,[9] and the work begun, how soon
Absolved,° if unforbid thou may'st unfold   *finished*
95 What we, not to explore the secrets ask

9. Adam's question about God's actions before   cially when, as here, it implies mutability in God.
the Creation was often cited as an example of   But in Milton's Eden, error that is not deliberate
presumptuous and dangerous speculation, espe-   is not sinful.

Of his eternal empire, but the more
To magnify° his works, the more we know.   *glorify*
And the great light of day yet wants to run
Much of his race though steep, suspense° in Heav'n   *attentive, suspended*
100 Held by thy voice, thy potent voice he hears,
And longer will delay to hear thee tell
His generation,° and the rising birth   *creation*
Of nature from the unapparent[1] deep:
Or if the star of evening and the moon
105 Haste to thy audience, night with her will bring
Silence, and sleep list'ning to thee will watch,°   *stay awake*
Or we can bid his absence, till thy song
End, and dismiss thee ere the morning shine."
        Thus Adam his illustrious guest besought:
110   And thus the godlike angel answered mild:
"This also thy request with caution asked
Obtain: though to recount almighty works
What words or tongue of Seraph can suffice,
Or heart of man suffice to comprehend?
115 Yet what thou canst attain, which best may serve
To glorify the Maker, and infer°   *make, render*
Thee also happier, shall not be withheld
Thy hearing, such commission from above
I have received, to answer thy desire
120 Of knowledge within bounds; beyond abstain
To ask, nor let thine own inventions° hope   *speculations*
Things not revealed, which th' invisible King,
Only omniscient, hath suppressed in night,
To none communicable in earth or Heaven:
125 Enough is left besides to search and know.
But knowledge is as food, and needs no less
Her temperance over appetite, to know
In measure what the mind may well contain,
Oppresses else with surfeit, and soon turns
130 Wisdom to folly, as nourishment to wind.
        "Know then, that after Lucifer from Heav'n
(So call him, brighter once amidst the host
Of angels, than that star the stars among)[2]
Fell with his flaming legions through the deep
135 Into his place, and the great Son returned
Victorious with his saints, th' Omnipotent
Eternal Father from his throne beheld
Their multitude, and to his Son thus spake:
        "'At least our envious foe hath failed, who thought
140 All like himself rebellious, by whose aid
This inaccessible high strength, the seat
Of Deity supreme, us dispossessed,[3]
He trusted to have seized, and into fraud°   *deception, error*

1. Invisible, because dark and without form.   among the stars.
2. I.e., Lucifer (Satan) was once brighter among   3. I.e., once he had dispossessed us.
the angels than the star bearing his name is

Drew many, whom their place knows here no more;
145 Yet far the greater part have kept, I see,
Their station, Heav'n yet populous retains
Number sufficient to possess her realms
Though wide, and this high temple to frequent
With ministeries due and solemn rites:
150 But lest his heart exalt him in the harm
Already done, to have dispeopled Heav'n,
My damage fondly° deemed, I can repair   *foolishly*
That detriment, if such it be to lose
Self-lost, and in a moment will create
155 Another world, out of one man a race
Of men innumerable, there to dwell,
Not here, till by degrees of merit raised
They open to themselves at length the way
Up hither, under long obedience tried,
160 And earth be changed to Heav'n and Heav'n to earth,
One kingdom, joy and union without end.
Meanwhile inhabit lax,° ye Powers of Heav'n;   *spread out*
And thou my Word, begotten Son, by thee
This I perform, speak thou, and be it done:[4]
165 My overshadowing Spirit and might with thee
I send along, ride forth, and bid the deep
Within appointed bounds be heav'n and earth,
Boundless the deep, because I am who fill
Infinitude, nor vacuous the space.
170 Though I uncircumscribed myself retire,
And put not forth my goodness, which is free
To act or not,[5] necessity and chance
Approach not me, and what I will is fate.'
    "So spake th' Almighty and to what he spake
175 His Word, the Filial Godhead, gave effect.
Immediate are the acts of God, more swift
Than time or motion, but to human ears
Cannot without process of speech be told,
So told as earthly notion° can receive.[6]   *human understanding*
180 Great triumph and rejoicing was in Heav'n
When such was heard declared the Almighty's will;
'Glory' they sung to the Most High, 'good will
To future men, and in their dwellings peace:
Glory to him whose just avenging ire
185 Had driven out th' ungodly from his sight
And th' habitations of the just; to him
Glory and praise, whose wisdom had ordained
Good out of evil to create, instead

---

4. God identifies himself as Creator, the Son as his agent to speak his creating Word.
5. Milton's God creates out of Chaos, not out of nothing; the matter of Chaos emanated from God, and Chaos is therefore "infinite" because God fills it even while he withholds his "goodness" (creating power) from it. Neither necessity

nor chance affect in any way God's freely willed creative act.
6. Raphael explains the principle of accommodation, whereby God's acts are said to be translated into terms humans can understand: here, a six-day creation. This principle allows for an escape from biblical literalism.

Of Spirits malign a better race to bring
190 Into their vacant room, and thence diffuse
His good to worlds and ages infinite.'
So sang the hierarchies: meanwhile the Son
On his great expedition now appeared,
Girt with omnipotence, with radiance crowned
195 Of majesty divine, sapience° and love   *wisdom*
Immense, and all his Father in him shone.
About his chariot numberless were poured
Cherub and Seraph, Potentates and Thrones,
And Virtues, winged Spirits, and chariots winged,
200 From the armory of God, where stand of old
Myriads between two brazen mountains lodged
Against° a solemn day, harnessed at hand,   *in preparation for*
Celestial equipage; and now came forth
Spontaneous, for within them spirit lived,
205 Attendant on their Lord: Heav'n opened wide
Her ever-during° gates, harmonious sound   *lasting*
On golden hinges moving, to let forth
The King of Glory[7] in his powerful Word
And Spirit coming to create new worlds.
210 On heav'nly ground they stood, and from the shore
They viewed the vast immeasurable abyss
Outrageous° as a sea, dark, wasteful, wild,   *enormous, violent*
Up from the bottom turned by furious winds
And surging waves, as mountains to assault
215 Heav'n's height, and with the center mix the pole.
    "'Silence, ye troubled waves, and thou deep, peace,'
Said then th' Omnific° Word, 'your discord end':   *all-creating*
    "Nor stayed, but on the wings of Cherubim
Uplifted, in paternal glory rode
220 Far into Chaos, and the world unborn;
For Chaos heard his voice: him all his train
Followed in bright procession to behold
Creation, and the wonders of his might.
Then stayed the fervid° wheels, and in his hand   *burning*
225 He took the golden compasses, prepared
In God's eternal store, to circumscribe
This universe, and all created things:
One foot he centered, and the other turned
Round through the vast profundity obscure,
230 And said, 'Thus far extend, thus far thy bounds,
This be thy just° circumference O world.'   *exact*
Thus God the heav'n° created, thus the earth,   *the sky*
Matter unformed and void: darkness profound
Covered th' abyss: but on the wat'ry calm
235 His brooding wings the Spirit of God outspread,
And vital virtue° infused, and vital warmth   *power*
Throughout the fluid mass, but downward purged

---

7. Cf. Psalm 24.9: "Lift up your heads, O ye gates; even lift them up, ye everlasting doors; and the King of glory shall come in."

The black tartareous cold infernal dregs[8]
Adverse to life: then founded, then conglobed
240 Like things to like, the rest to several place
Disparted, and between spun out the air,
And earth self-balanced on her center hung.
　　"'Let there be light,' said God,[9] and forthwith light
Ethereal, first of things, quintessence[1] pure
245 Sprung from the deep, and from her native east
To journey through the airy gloom began,
Sphered in a radiant cloud, for yet the sun
Was not; she in a cloudy tabernacle
Sojourned the while. God saw the light was good;
250 And light from darkness by the hemisphere
Divided: light the day, and darkness night
He named. Thus was the first day ev'n and morn:[2]
Nor passed uncelebrated, nor unsung
By the celestial choirs, when orient light
255 Exhaling° first from darkness they beheld;　　　　　*rising as vapor*
Birthday of heav'n° and earth; with joy and shout　　　*the sky*
The hollow universal orb they filled,
And touched their golden harps, and hymning praised
God and his works, Creator him they sung,
260 Both when first evening was, and when first morn.
　　"Again, God said, 'Let there be firmament
Amid the waters, and let it divide
The waters from the waters': and God made
The firmament, expanse of liquid,° pure,　　　　　　*clear, bright*
265 Transparent, elemental air diffused
In circuit to the uttermost convex°　　　　　　　　*vault*
Of this great round:° partition firm and sure,　　　*universe*
The waters underneath from those above
Dividing: for as earth, so he the world
270 Built on circumfluous° waters calm, in wide　　　　*flowing around*
Crystálline ocean, and the loud misrule
Of Chaos far removed, lest fierce extremes
Contiguous might distemper the whole frame:[3]
And heav'n° he named the firmament: so ev'n　　　　*the sky*
275 And morning chorus sung the second day.
　　"The earth was formed, but in the womb as yet
Of waters, embryon[4] immature involved°　　　　　*enfolded*
Appeared not: over all the face of earth
Main° ocean flowed, not idle, but with warm　　　　*of great expanse*
280 Prolific humor° soft'ning all her globe,　　　　　*generative moisture*

---

8. Crusty, gritty stuff left over from the elements
infused with life that make up the universe; it is
associated with Hell ("infernal," "tartarous") and
presumably used in its composition.
9. God's creating words, here and later, are
quoted from Genesis 1–2, but Milton freely elaborates the creatures' responses to those words.
1. Ether was thought to be a fifth element or
"quintessence," the substance of the celestial

bodies above the moon.
2. One twenty-four-hour period measured in the
Hebrew manner from sundown to sundown.
3. Disturb the order and mixture of the elements and the created "frame" of the universe.
4. The earth is at first the "embryo" enveloped in
a "womb of waters" and is then herself the "great
mother" (line 281), made ready ("fermented") to
conceive and bear every other being.

Fermented the great mother to conceive,
Satiate with genial° moisture, when God said,   *generative*
'Be gathered now ye waters under heav'n
Into one place, and let dry land appear.'
285 Immediately the mountains huge appear
Emergent, and their broad bare backs upheave
Into the clouds, their tops ascend the sky:
So high as heaved the tumid° hills, so low   *swollen*
Down sunk a hollow bottom broad and deep,
290 Capacious bed of waters: thither they
Hasted with glad precipitance,° uprolled   *headlong fall*
As drops on dust conglobing from the dry;
Part rise in crystal wall, or ridge direct°   *surge forward*
For haste; such flight the great command impressed
295 On the swift floods: as armies at the call
Of trumpet (for of armies thou hast heard)
Troop to their standard, so the wat'ry throng,
Wave rolling after wave, where way they found,
If steep, with torrent rapture,° if through plain,   *force*
300 Soft-ebbing; nor withstood them rock or hill,
But they, or° underground, or circuit wide   *whether*
With serpent error° wand'ring, found their way,   *winding course*
And on the washy ooze deep channels wore;
Easy, ere God had bid the ground be dry,
305 All but within those banks, where rivers now
Stream, and perpetual draw their humid train.°   *following*
The dry land, earth, and the great receptacle
Of congregated waters he called seas:
And saw that it was good, and said, 'Let th' earth
310 Put forth the verdant grass, herb yielding seed,
And fruit tree yielding fruit after her kind;
Whose seed is in herself upon the earth.'
He scarce had said, when the bare earth, till then
Desert and bare, unsightly, unadorned,
315 Brought forth the tender grass, whose verdure clad
Her universal face with pleasant green,
Then herbs of every leaf, that sudden flow'red
Op'ning their various colors, and made gay
Her bosom smelling sweet: and these scarce blown,°   *blossomed*
320 Forth flourished thick the clust'ring vine, forth crept
The swelling gourd, up stood the corny° reed   *hard as horn*
Embattled in her field: add the humble° shrub,   *low-growing*
And bush with frizzled hair implicit:° last   *tangled*
Rose as in dance the stately trees, and spread
325 Their branches hung with copious fruit; or gemmed°   *put forth buds*
Their blossoms: with high woods the hills were crowned,
With tufts the valleys and each fountain side,
With borders long the rivers. That earth now
Seemed like to Heav'n, a seat where gods might dwell,
330 Or wander with delight, and love to haunt
Her sacred shades: though God had yet not rained
Upon the earth, and man to till the ground

None was, but from the earth a dewy mist
Went up and watered all the ground, and each
335 Plant of the field, which ere it was in the earth
God made, and every herb, before it grew
On the green stem; God saw that it was good:
So ev'n and morn recorded the third day.
    "Again th' Almighty spake: 'Let there be lights
340 High in th' expanse of heaven° to divide   *the sky*
The day from night; and let them be for signs,
For seasons, and for days, and circling years,
And let them be for lights as I ordain
Their office° in the firmament of heav'n   *function*
345 To give light on the earth'; and it was so.
And God made two great lights, great for their use
To man, the greater to have rule by day,
The less by night altern:° and made the stars,   *in turns*
And set them in the firmament of heav'n
350 To illuminate the earth, and rule the day
In their vicissitude,° and rule the night,   *regular alternation*
And light from darkness to divide. God saw,
Surveying his great work, that it was good:
For of celestial bodies first the sun
355 A mighty sphere he framed, unlightsome first,
Though of ethereal mold:° then formed the moon   *fashioned from ether*
Globose, and every magnitude of stars,
And sowed with stars the heav'n thick as a field:
Of light by far the greater part he took,
360 Transplanted from her cloudy shrine,[5] and placed
In the sun's orb, made porous to receive
And drink the liquid light, firm to retain
Her gathered beams, great palace now of light.
Hither as to their fountain other stars
365 Repairing,° in their golden urns draw light,   *resorting*
And hence the morning planet gilds her horns;[6]
By tincture° or reflection they augment   *absorption*
Their small peculiar,° though from human sight   *own small light*
So far remote, with dimunition seen.
370 First in his east the glorious lamp was seen,
Regent of day, and all th' horizon round
Invested with bright rays, jocund° to run   *merry*
His longitude° through heav'n's high road: the gray   *distance*
Dawn, and the Pleiades[7] before him danced
375 Shedding sweet influence: less bright the moon,
But opposite in leveled west was set
His mirror, with full face borrowing her light
From him, for other light she needed none
In that aspect,° and still that distance keeps   *when full*
380 Till night, then in the east her turn she shines,

5. The "cloudy tabernacle" of line 248.
6. Venus, which Galileo's telescope found to be
crescent-shaped in her first quarter.

7. A cluster of seven stars in the constellation
Taurus. They appear at dawn ahead of the sun.
See Job 38.31.

Revolved on heav'n's great axle, and her reign
With thousand lesser lights dividual° holds,   *divided*
With thousand thousand stars, that then appeared
Spangling the hemisphere: then first adorned
385 With their bright luminaries that set and rose,
Glad° evening and glad morn crowned the fourth day.   *bright, gay*
    And God said, 'Let the waters generate
Reptile° with spawn abundant, living soul: *creeping animals*
And let fowl fly above the earth, with wings
390 Displayed° on the op'n firmament of heav'n.'   *spread out*
And God created the great whales, and each
Soul living, each that crept, which plenteously
The waters generated by their kinds,
And every bird of wing after his kind;
395 And saw that it was good, and blessed them, saying,
'Be fruitful, multiply, and in the seas
And lakes and running streams the waters fill;
And let the fowl be multiplied on the earth.'
Forthwith the sounds and seas, each creek and bay
400 With fry° innumerable swarm, and shoals   *young fish*
Of fish that with their fins and shining scales
Glide under the green wave, in sculls that oft
Bank the mid-sea:[8] part single or with mate
Graze the seaweed their pasture, and through groves
405 Of coral stray, or sporting with quick glance
Show to the sun their waved° coats dropped° with gold,   *striped / flecked*
Or in their pearly shells at ease, attend°   *watch for*
Moist nutriment, or under rocks their food
In jointed armor watch: on smooth the seal,
410 And bended[9] dolphins play: part huge of bulk
Wallowing unwieldy, enormous in their gait
Tempest° the ocean: there leviathan[1]   *stir up*
Hugest of living creatures, on the deep
Stretched like a promontory sleeps or swims,
415 And seems a moving land, and at his gills
Draws in, and at his trunk spouts out a sea.
Meanwhile the tepid caves, and fens and shores
Their brood as numerous hatch, from th' egg that soon
Bursting with kindly° rupture forth disclosed   *natural*
420 Their callow° young, but feathered soon and fledge   *without feathers*
They summed their pens,[2] and soaring th' air sublime
With clang° despised the ground, under a cloud   *harsh cry*
In prospect;[3] there the eagle and the stork
On cliffs and cedar tops their eyries build:
425 Part loosely° wing the region,° part more wise   *separately / sky*
In common, ranged in figure wedge their way,[4]
Intelligent° of seasons, and set forth   *understanding*

8. The fishes' darting motions resemble boats
oared now on one side, now on the other
("sculls"), as they turn they seem to form banks
within the sea.
9. Curved in leaping. "Smooth": a stretch of

calm water.
1. The great whale (see 1.200–208).
2. Brought their feathers to full growth.
3. The ground seems covered by a cloud of birds.
4. Fly in a wedge formation.

Their aery caravan high over seas
Flying, and over lands with mutual wing
430 Easing their flight;[5] so steers the prudent crane
Her annual voyage, borne on winds; the air
Floats,° as they pass, fanned with unnumbered plumes: *undulates*
From branch to branch the smaller birds with song
Solaced the woods, and spread their painted wings
435 Till ev'n, nor then the solemn nightingale
Ceased warbling, but all night tuned her soft lays:°   *songs*
Others on silver lakes and rivers bathed
Their downy breast; the swan, with archèd neck
Between her white wings mantling proudly, rows
440 Her state with oary feet:[6] yet oft they quit
The dank,° and rising on stiff pennons, tow'r°   *pool / soar into*
The mid-aerial sky: others on ground
Walked firm; the crested cock whose clarion sounds
The silent hours, and th' other° whose gay train   *the peacock*
445 Adorns him, colored with the florid hue
Of rainbows and starry eyes. The waters thus
With fish replenished,° and the air with fowl,   *fully supplied*
Evening and morn solemnized the fifth day.
    "The sixth, and of creation last arose
450 With evening harps and matin,° when God said,   *morning*
'Let th' earth bring forth soul living in her kind,
Cattle and creeping things, and beast of the earth,
Each in their kind.' The earth obeyed, and straight
Op'ning her fertile womb teemed° at a birth   *brought forth*
455 Innumerous living creatures, perfect forms,
Limbed and full grown: out of the ground up rose
As from his lair the wild beast where he wons°   *dwells*
In forest wild, in thicket, brake, or den;
Among the trees in pairs they rose, they walked:
460 The cattle in the fields and meadows green:
Those rare and solitary, these[7] in flocks
Pasturing at once,° and in broad herds upsprung.   *immediately*
The grassy clods° now calved, now half appeared   *mounds of earth*
The tawny lion, pawing to get free
465 His hinder parts, then springs as broke from bonds,
And rampant shakes his brinded° mane; the ounce,°   *streaked / lynx*
The libbard,° and the tiger, as the mole   *leopard*
Rising, the crumbled earth above them threw
In hillocks; the swift stag from underground
470 Bore up his branching head: scarce from his mold
Behemoth[8] biggest born of earth upheaved
His vastness: fleeced the flocks and bleating rose,
As plants: ambiguous between sea and land

5. Birds were thought to support each other
with their wings when they flew in formation.
6. The swan's outstretched ("mantling") wings
form a mantle, and it seems like a monarch on a
royal barge rowed by its own "oary" feet.
7. "These" are the domestic cattle who come

forth in "flocks" and "herds" in pastures; "those"
are the wild beasts who come forth "in pairs"
(line 459), and spread out ("rare") at wide intervals.
8. A huge biblical beast (Job 40.15), often identified with the elephant.

The river-horse[9] and scaly crocodile.
475 At once came forth whatever creeps the ground,
Insect or worm;[1] those waved their limber fans
For wings, and smallest lineaments exact
In all the liveries decked of summer's pride
With spots of gold and purple, azure and green:
480 These as a line their long dimension drew,
Streaking the ground with sinuous trace; not all
Minims° of nature; some of serpent kind   *smallest animals*
Wondrous in length and corpulence involved°   *coiled*
Their snaky folds, and added wings. First crept
485 The parsimonious emmet,° provident   *thrifty ant*
Of future, in small room large heart° enclosed,   *great wisdom*
Pattern of just equality perhaps
Hereafter, joined in her popular tribes
Of commonalty:[2] swarming next appeared
490 The female bee that feeds her husband drone
Deliciously, and builds her waxen cells
With honey stored: the rest are numberless,
And thou their natures know'st, and gav'st them names,[3]
Needless to thee repeated; nor unknown
495 The serpent subtlest beast of all the field,
Of huge extent sometimes, with brazen eyes
And hairy mane[4] terrific,° though to thee   *terrifying*
Not noxious, but obedient at thy call.
Now heav'n in all her glory shone, and rolled
500 Her motions, as the great First Mover's hand
First wheeled their course; earth in her rich attire
Consummate° lovely smiled; air, water, earth,   *complete, perfect*
By fowl, fish, beast, was flown, was swum, was walked
Frequent;° and of the sixth day yet remained;   *in throngs*
505 There wanted yet the master work, the end°   *purpose*
Of all yet done; a creature who not prone
And brute as other creatures, but endued
With sanctity of reason, might erect
His stature,[5] and upright with front° serene   *brow, face*
510 Govern the rest, self-knowing, and from thence
Magnanimous to correspond[6] with Heav'n,
But grateful to acknowledge whence his good
Descends, thither with heart and voice and eyes
Directed in devotion, to adore
515 And worship God supreme, who made him chief
Of all his works: therefore th' Omnipotent
Eternal Father (for where is not he

---

9. Translates the Greek name "hippopotamus."
1. Any creeping creature, including serpents.
2. The ant will become the symbol of a frugal and self-governing republic ("pattern of just equality") with the "popular" (populous, plebian) tribes of common people ("commonalty") joined in rule (lines 486–89); Milton made it such a symbol in his prose tract *The Ready and Easy Way*. Bees here (lines 489–93) suggest delightful ease but are not yet (as in 1.768–75) a symbol of monarchy and associated with Hell.
3. See 8.342–54, and Genesis 2.19–20.
4. Sea serpents were so described in *Aeneid* 2.203–7.
5. Both "stand erect" and "elevate his condition": his erect stance was understood to signify that he was created for Heaven.
6. Both "be in harmony" and "communicate."

Present) thus to his Son audibly spake:
    "'Let us make now man in our image, man
520 In our similitude, and let them rule
Over the fish and fowl of sea and air,
Beast of the field, and over all the earth,
And every creeping thing that creeps the ground.'
This said, he formed thee, Adam, thee O man
525 Dust of the ground, and in thy nostrils breathed
The breath of life; in his own image he
Created thee, in the image of God
Express,° and thou becam'st a living soul.   *exact, manifest*
Male he created thee, but thy consort
530 Female for race; then blessed mankind, and said,
'Be fruitful, multiply, and fill the earth,
Subdue it, and throughout dominion hold
Over fish of the sea, and fowl of the air,
And every living thing that moves on the earth.'
535 Wherever thus created, for no place
Is yet distinct by name, thence,° as thou know'st   *from there*
He brought thee into this delicious° grove,   *delightful*
This garden, planted with the trees of God,
Delectable both to behold and taste;
540 And freely all their pleasant fruit for food
Gave thee, all sorts are here that all th' earth yields,
Variety without end; but of the tree
Which tasted works knowledge of good and evil,
Thou may'st not; in the day thou eat'st, thou di'st;
545 Death is the penalty imposed, beware,
And govern well thy appetite, lest Sin
Surprise thee, and her black attendant Death.
Here finished he, and all that he had made
Viewed, and behold all was entirely good;
550 So ev'n and morn accomplished the sixth day:
Yet not till the Creator from his work
Desisting, though unwearied, up returned
Up to the Heav'n of Heav'ns his high abode,
Thence to behold his new-created world
555 Th' addition of his empire, how it showed
In prospect from his throne, how good, how fair,
Answering his great Idea.[7] Up he rode
Followed with acclamation and the sound
Symphonious of ten thousand harps that tuned°   *performed*
560 Angelic harmonies: the earth, the air
Resounded (thou remember'st, for thou heard'st),
The heav'ns and all the constellations rung,
The planets in their stations list'ning stood,
While the bright pomp° ascended jubilant.   *triumphal procession*
565   "'Open, ye everlasting gates,' they sung,
'Open, ye Heav'ns, your living doors; let in
The great Creator from his work returned

---

7. Eternal archetype or pattern, as in Plato: concept in the mind of God.

Magnificent,[8] his six days' work, a world;
Open, and henceforth oft; for God will deign
570 To visit oft the dwellings of just men
Delighted, and with frequent intercourse
Thither will send his wingèd messengers
On errands of supernal° grace.' So sung   *heavenly*
The glorious train ascending: he through Heav'n,
575 That opened wide her blazing° portals, led   *radiant*
To God's eternal house direct the way,
A broad and ample road, whose dust is gold
And pavement stars, as stars to thee appear,
Seen in the galaxy, that Milky Way
580 Which nightly as a circling zone° thou seest   *belt*
Powdered with stars. And now on earth the seventh
Evening arose in Eden, for the sun
Was set, and twilight from the east came on,
Forerunning night; when at the holy mount
585 Of Heav'n's high-seated top, th' imperial throne
Of Godhead, fixed forever firm and sure,
The Filial Power arrived, and sat him down
With his great Father, for he[9] also went
Invisible, yet stayed (such privilege
590 Hath Omnipresence) and the work ordained,°   *ordered, enacted*
Author and end of all things, and from work
Now resting, blessed and hallowed the sev'nth day,
As resting on that day from all his work,
But not in silence holy kept; the harp
595 Had work and rested not, the solemn pipe,
And dulcimer, all organs° of sweet stop,   *wind instruments*
All sounds on fret[1] by string or golden wire
Tempered° soft tunings, intermixed with voice   *brought into harmony*
Choral° or unison: of incense clouds   *in parts*
600 Fuming from golden censers hid the mount.
    "Creation and the six days' acts they sung:
'Great are thy works, Jehovah, infinite
Thy power; what thought can measure thee or tongue
Relate thee; greater now in thy return
605 Than from the giant[2] angels; thee that day
Thy thunders magnified; but to create
Is greater than created to destroy.
Who can impair thee, Mighty King, or bound
Thy empire? Easily the proud attempt
610 Of Spirits apostate and their counsels vain
Thou hast repelled, while impiously they thought
Thee to diminish, and from thee withdraw
The number of thy worshippers. Who seeks
To lessen thee, against his purpose serves

---

8. Cf. Psalm 24.7: "Lift up your heads, O ye gates; and be ye lift up, ye everlasting doors; and the King of glory shall come in."
9. The Father.
1. Bar on the fingerboard of a stringed instru-

ment. "Dulcimer": the Hebrew bagpipe (Daniel 3.5).
2. The allusion implies that the myth of the Giants' revolt against Jove is a classical type or version of the angels' rebellion.

615 To manifest the more thy might: his evil
Thou usest, and from thence creat'st more good.
Witness this new-made world, another heav'n
From Heaven gate not far, founded in view
On the clear hyaline,[3] the glassy sea;
620 Of amplitude almost immense,° with stars   *immeasurable*
Numerous, and every star perhaps a world
Of destined habitation; but thou know'st
Their seasons: among these the seat of men,
Earth with her nether ocean circumfused,°   *surrounded, bathed*
625 Their pleasant dwellingplace. Thrice happy men,
And sons of men, whom God hath thus advanced,
Created in his image, there to dwell
And worship him, and in reward to rule
Over his works, on earth, in sea, or air,
630 And multiply a race of worshippers
Holy and just: thrice happy if they know
Their happiness, and persevere upright.'
    "So sung they, and the empyrean rung,
With hallelujahs:[4] thus was Sabbath kept.
635 And thy request think now fulfilled, that asked
How first this world and face of things began,
And what before thy memory was done
From the beginning, that posterity
Informed by thee might know; if else thou seek'st
640 Aught, not surpassing human measure, say."

Book 8

The angel ended, and in Adam's ear
So charming° left his voice, that he a while   *spell-binding*
Thought him still speaking, still stood fixed to hear;
Then as new-waked thus gratefully replied:[1]
5 "What thanks sufficient, or what recompense
Equal have I to render thee, divine
Historian, who thus largely hast allayed
The thirst I had of knowledge, and vouchsafed
This friendly condescension to relate
10 Things else by me unsearchable, now heard
With wonder, but delight, and, as is due,
With glory attributed to the high
Creator; something yet of doubt remains,
Which only thy solution° can resolve.   *explanation*
15 When I behold this goodly frame,° this world   *the universe*
Of heav'n and earth consisting, and compute

---

3. From the Greek word for glass (Revelation 4.6), the waters above the firmament as contrasted with the "nether ocean" (line 624), the earth's seas.
4. Hebrew, "praise the Lord."

1. When Milton divided Book 7 of the ten-book version of 1667 into the present Books 7 and 8, he replaced a line reading "To whom thus Adam gratefully replied" with these introductory lines.

Their magnitudes, this earth a spot, a grain,
An atom, with the firmament compared
And all her numbered° stars, that seem to roll   numerous
20 Spaces incomprehensible (for such
Their distance argues and their swift return
Diurnal)° merely to officiate° light   daily / supply
Round this opacous° earth, this punctual° spot,   dark / pointlike
One day and night; in all their vast survey
25 Useless besides; reasoning I oft admire,°   wonder
How Nature wise and frugal could commit
Such disproportions, with superfluous hand
So many nobler bodies to create,
Greater so manifold,° to this one use,   so much greater
30 For aught appears,° and on their orbs impose   as it seems
Such restless revolution day by day
Repeated, while the sedentary° earth,   motionless
That better might with far less compass° move,   circular course
Served by more noble than herself, attains
35 Her end without least motion, and receives,
As tribute such a sumless° journey brought   incalculable
Of incorporeal° speed, her warmth and light;   like that of spirits
Speed, to describe whose swiftness number fails."
    So spake our sire, and by his count'nance seemed
40 Ent'ring on studious thoughts abstruse, which Eve
Perceiving where she sat retired in sight,
With lowliness majestic from her seat,
And grace that won who saw to wish her stay,
Rose, and went forth among her fruits and flow'rs,
45 To visit° how they prospered, bud and bloom,   see
Her nursery;² they at her coming sprung
And touched by her fair tendance gladlier grew.
Yet went she not as not with such discourse
Delighted, or not capable her ear
50 Of what was high: such pleasure she reserved,
Adam relating, she sole auditress;
Her husband the relater she preferred
Before the angel, and of him to ask
Chose rather;³ he, she knew, would intermix
55 Grateful° digressions, and solve high dispute   gratifying
With conjugal caresses, from his lip
Not words alone pleased her. O when meet now
Such pairs, in love and mutual honor joined?
With goddess-like demeanor forth she went;
60 Not unattended, for on her as queen
A pomp° of winning Graces⁴ waited still,   procession
And from about her shot darts of desire
Into all eyes to wish her still in sight.

2. Her garden, where she "nurses" her flowers and plants.
3. The emphasis on choice suggests that Eve is not bound in Eden by the Pauline directive (1 Corinthians 14.34–35) that women refrain from speaking in church and instead learn at home from their husbands, but she voluntarily and for her own pleasure observes this hierarchical decorum.
4. The Graces attended on Venus.

And Raphael now to Adam's doubt proposed
65 Benevolent and facile° thus replied.   *easy, affable*
     "To ask or search I blame thee not, for heav'n
Is as the book of God before thee set,
Wherein to read his wondrous works, and learn
His seasons, hours, or days, or months, or years:
70 This to attain, whether heav'n move or earth,
Imports not, if thou reckon right; the rest[5]
From man or angel the great Architect
Did wisely to conceal, and not divulge
His secrets to be scanned° by them who ought   *judged critically*
75 Rather admire;° or if they list to try   *marvel*
Conjecture, he his fabric° of the heav'ns   *design*
Hath left to their disputes, perhaps to move
His laughter at their quaint opinions wide°   *wide of the mark*
Hereafter, when they come to model heav'n
80 And calculate the stars, how they will wield
The mighty frame, how build, unbuild, contrive
To save appearances,[6] how gird the sphere
With centric and eccentric scribbled o'er,
Cycle and epicycle,[7] orb in orb:
85 Already by thy reasoning this I guess,
Who art to lead thy offspring, and supposest
That bodies bright and greater should not serve
The less not bright, nor heav'n such journeys run,
Earth sitting still, when she alone receives
90 The benefit: consider first, that great
Or bright infers° not excellence: the earth   *implies*
Though, in comparison of heav'n, so small,
Nor glistering, may of solid good contain
More plenty than the sun that barren shines,
95 Whose virtue on itself works no effect,
But in the fruitful earth; there first received
His beams, unactive° else, their vigor find.   *ineffective*
Yet not to earth are those bright luminaries
Officious,° but to thee earth's habitant.   *attentive, dutiful*
100 And for the heav'n's wide circuit, let it speak
The Maker's high magnificence, who built
So spacious, and his line stretched out so far;
That man may know he dwells not in his own;
An edifice too large for him to fill,
105 Lodged in a small partition, and the rest
Ordained for uses to his Lord best known.
The swiftness of those circles° áttribute,   *orbits*
Though numberless,° to his omnipotence,   *innumerable*
That to corporeal substances could add

---

5. Presumably, God's ways with other worlds and other creatures inhabiting them (if any).
6. To find ways of explaining discrepancies between their hypotheses and observed facts.
7. In the Ptolemaic system, observed irregularities in the motion of heavenly bodies were first explained by hypothesizing eccentric orbits, then by adding epicycles, which were smaller orbits whose centers ride on the circumference of the main eccentric circles and carry the planets. The Copernican system also had some recourse to epicycles.

110 Speed almost spiritual;° me thou think'st not slow, *that of angels*
  Who since the morning hour set out from Heav'n
  Where God resides, and ere midday arrived
  In Eden, distance inexpressible
  By numbers that have name. But this I urge,
115 Admitting motion in the heav'ns, to show
  Invalid that which thee to doubt it moved;
  Not that I so affirm, though so it seem
  To thee who hast thy dwelling here on earth.[8]
  God to remove his ways from human sense,
120 Placed heav'n from earth so far, that earthly sight,
  If it presume, might err in things too high,
  And no advantage gain. What if the sun
  Be center to the world, and other stars
  By his attractive virtue° and their own *magnetism*
125 Incited, dance about him various rounds?° *circles*
  Their wand'ring course now high, now low, then hid,
  Progressive, retrograde,° or standing still, *backward*
  In six thou seest,[9] and what if sev'nth to these
  The planet earth, so steadfast though she seem,
130 Insensibly three different motions move?[1]
  Which else to several spheres thou must ascribe,
  Moved contrary with thwart obliquities,[2]
  Or save the sun his labor, and that swift
  Nocturnal and diurnal rhomb[3] supposed,
135 Invisible else above all stars, the wheel
  Of day and night; which needs not thy belief,
  If earth industrious of herself fetch day
  Traveling east, and with her part averse
  From the sun's beam meet night, her other part
140 Still luminous by his ray. What if that light
  Sent from her through the wide transpicuous° air, *transparent*
  To the terrestrial moon be as a star
  Enlight'ning her by day, as she by night
  This earth? Reciprocal, if land be there,
145 Fields and inhabitants: her spots thou seest
  As clouds, and clouds may rain, and rain produce
  Fruits in her softened soil, for some to eat
  Allotted there; and other suns perhaps
  With their attendant moons thou wilt descry
150 Communicating male° and female° light, *original / reflected*
  Which two great sexes animate° the world, *endow with life*

8. Raphael declines to "reveal" astronomical truth to Adam, leaving that matter open to human scientific speculation. He suggests here that Adam's Ptolemaic assumptions result from his earthbound perspective, and he implies that angels see the universe in different terms. In the following lines (122–58) he sets forth advanced scientific notions Adam had not imagined: not only Copernican astronomy but multiple universes and other inhabited planets.
9. Mercury, Venus, Mars, Jupiter, Saturn, and the moon. In the Ptolemaic system the "seventh"

is the sun; in the Copernican, earth.
1. Copernicus described the three motions as daily, annual, and "motion in declination" whereby the earth's axis swerved so as always to point in the same direction.
2. Oblique paths that cross each other.
3. Wheel, that is, the primum mobile, which (if we accept the Ptolemaic system and "save the sun his labor") revolves around the universe every twenty-four hours, carrying the planets and their spheres with it.

Stored in each orb perhaps with some that live.
For such vast room in nature unpossessed
By living soul, desert and desolate,
155 Only to shine, yet scarce to cóntribute
Each orb a glimpse of light, conveyed so far
Down to this habitable,° which returns   *inhabited place*
Light back to them, is obvious to dispute.°   *open to dispute*
But whether thus these things, or whether not,
160 Whether the sun predominant in heav'n
Rise on the earth, or earth rise on the sun,
He from the east his flaming road begin,
Or she from west her silent course advance
With inoffensive° pace that spinning sleeps   *unobstructed, harmless*
165 On her soft axle, while she paces ev'n,
And bears thee soft with the smooth air along,
Solicit° not thy thoughts with matters hid,   *disturb*
Leave them to God above, him serve and fear;
Of other creatures, as him pleases best,
170 Wherever placed, let him dispose: joy thou
In what he gives to thee, this Paradise
And thy fair Eve; heav'n is for thee too high
To know what passes there; be lowly wise:
Think only what concerns thee and thy being;
175 Dream not of other worlds, what creatures there
Live, in what state, condition, or degree,
Contented that thus far hath been revealed
Not of earth only but of highest Heav'n."
    To whom thus Adam cleared of doubt, replied:
180 "How fully hast thou satisfied me, pure
Intelligence° of Heav'n, angel serene,   *spirit*
And freed from intricacies, taught to live
The easiest way, nor with perplexing thoughts
To interrupt the sweet of life, from which
185 God hath bid dwell far off all anxious cares,
And not molest us, unless we ourselves
Seek them with wand'ring thoughts, and notions vain.
But apt the mind or fancy is to rove
Unchecked, and of her roving is no end;
190 Till warned, or by experience taught, she learn,
That not to know at large of things remote
From use, obscure and subtle, but to know
That which before us lies in daily life,
Is the prime wisdom; what is more, is fume,°   *vapor*
195 Or emptiness, or fond impertinence,°   *foolish irrelevance*
And renders us in things that most concern
Unpracticed, unprepared, and still to seek.°   *always searching*
Therefore from this high pitch let us descend
A lower flight, and speak of things at hand
200 Useful, whence haply° mention may arise   *perhaps*
Of something not unseasonable to ask
By sufferance,° and thy wonted° favor deigned.   *permission / usual*
Thee I have heard relating what was done

Ere my remembrance: now hear me relate
205 My story, which perhaps thou hast not heard;
And day is yet not spent; till then thou seest
How subtly to detain thee I devise,
Inviting thee to hear while I relate,
Fond,° were it not in hope of thy reply: *foolish*
210 For while I sit with thee, I seem in Heav'n,
And sweeter thy discourse is to my ear
Than fruits of palm tree pleasantest to thirst
And hunger both, from labor, at the hour
Of sweet repast; they satiate, and soon fill,
215 Though pleasant, but thy words with grace divine
Imbued, bring to their sweetness no satiety."
    To whom thus Raphael answered heav'nly meek:
"Nor are thy lips ungraceful, sire of men,
Nor tongue ineloquent; for God on thee
220 Abundantly his gifts hath also poured
Inward and outward both, his image fair:
Speaking or mute all comeliness and grace
Attends thee, and each word, each motion forms.
Nor less think we in Heav'n of thee on earth
225 Than of our fellow-servant, and inquire
Gladly into the ways of God with man:
For God we see hath honored thee, and set
On man his equal love: say therefore on;
For I that day was absent, as befell,
230 Bound on a voyage uncouth° and obscure,   *strange*
Far on excursion toward the gates of Hell;
Squared in full legion (such command we had)
To see that none thence issued forth a spy,
Or enemy, while God was in his work,
235 Lest he incensed at such eruption bold,
Destruction with creation might have mixed.
Not that they durst without his leave attempt,
But us he sends upon his high behests
For state,° as sov'reign King, and to inure°   *ceremony / strengthen*
240 Our prompt obedience. Fast we found, fast shut
The dismal gates, and barricadoed strong;
But long ere our approaching heard within
Noise, other than the sound of dance or song,
Torment, and loud lament, and furious rage.
245 Glad we returned up to the coasts of light
Ere Sabbath evening: so we had in charge.
But thy relation now; for I attend,
Pleased with thy words no less than thou with mine."
    So spake the godlike Power, and thus our sire:
250 "For man to tell how human life began
Is hard; for who himself beginning knew?[4]
Desire with thee still longer to converse

---

4. Compare Satan's inability to remember his origins (5.856–63), from which he infers self-creation, whereas Adam infers a Maker (line 278).

Induced me. As new-waked from soundest sleep
Soft on the flow'ry herb I found me laid
255 In balmy sweat, which with his beams the sun
Soon dried, and on the reeking° moisture fed.   *steaming*
Straight toward heav'n my wond'ring eyes I turned,
And gazed a while the ample sky, till raised
By quick instinctive motion up I sprung
260 As thitherward endeavoring, and upright
Stood on my feet; about me round I saw
Hill, dale, and shady woods, and sunny plains,
And liquid lapse° of murmuring streams; by these, *flow*
Creatures that lived, and moved, and walked, or flew,
265 Birds on the branches warbling; all things smiled,
With fragrance and with joy my heart o'erflowed.
Myself I then perused, and limb by limb
Surveyed, and sometimes went,° and sometimes ran *walked*
With supple joints, as lively vigor led:
270 But who I was, or where, or from what cause,
Knew not; to speak I tried, and forthwith spake,
My tongue obeyed and readily could name
Whate'er I saw.[5] 'Thou sun,' said I, 'fair light,
And thou enlightened earth, so fresh and gay,
275 Ye hills and dales, ye rivers, woods, and plains,
And ye that live and move, fair creatures, tell,
Tell, if ye saw, how came I thus, how here?
Not of myself; by some great Maker then,
In goodness and in power preeminent;
280 Tell me, how may I know him, how adore,
From whom I have that thus I move and live,
And feel that I am happier than I know.'
While thus I called, and strayed I knew not whither,
From where I first drew air, and first beheld
285 This happy light, when answer none returned,
On a green shady bank profuse of flow'rs
Pensive I sat me down; there gentle sleep
First found me, and with soft oppression seized
My drowsèd sense, untroubled, though I thought
290 I then was passing to my former state
Insensible, and forthwith to dissolve:
When suddenly stood at my head a dream,
Whose inward apparition gently moved
My fancy to believe I yet had being,
295 And lived: one came, methought, of shape divine,
And said, 'Thy mansion° wants° thee, Adam, rise, *habitation / lacks*
First man, of men innumerable ordained
First father, called by thee I come thy guide
To the garden of bliss, thy seat° prepared.'   *residence*
300 So saying, by the hand he took me raised,
And over fields and waters, as in air
Smooth sliding without step, last led me up

---

5. Adam's ability to name the creatures was said to signify his intuitive understanding of their natures.

A woody mountain whose high top was plain,
A circuit wide, enclosed, with goodliest trees
305 Planted, with walks, and bowers, that what I saw
Of earth before scarce pleasant seemed. Each tree
Load'n with fairest fruit, that hung to the eye
Tempting, stirred in me sudden appetite
To pluck and eat; whereat I waked, and found
310 Before mine eyes all real, as the dream
Had lively° shadowed: here had new begun   *vividly*
My wand'ring, had not he who was my guide
Up hither, from among the trees appeared,
Presence Divine. Rejoicing, but with awe
315 In adoration at his feet I fell
Submiss:° he reared me, and 'Whom thou sought'st I am,'   *submissive*
Said mildly, 'Author of all this thou seest
Above, or round about thee or beneath.
This Paradise I give thee, count it thine
320 To till and keep,° and of the fruit to eat: *care for*
Of every tree that in the garden grows
Eat freely with glad heart; fear here no dearth:
But of the tree whose operation° brings   *action*
Knowledge of good and ill, which I have set
325 The pledge of thy obedience and thy faith,
Amid the garden by the Tree of Life,
Remember what I warn thee, shun to taste,
And shun the bitter consequence: for know,
The day thou eat'st thereof, my sole command
330 Transgressed, inevitably thou shalt die;
From that day mortal, and this happy state
Shalt lose, expelled from hence into a world
Of woe and sorrow.'⁶ Sternly he pronounced
The rigid interdiction,° which resounds   *prohibition*
335 Yet dreadful in mine ear, though in my choice
Not to incur; but soon his clear aspéct°   *untroubled expression*
Returned and gracious purpose° thus renewed: *speech*
'Not only these fair bounds, but all the earth
To thee and to thy race I give; as lords
340 Possess it, and all things that therein live,
Or live in sea, or air, beast, fish, and fowl.
In sign whereof each bird and beast behold
After their kinds; I bring them to receive
From thee their names, and pay thee fealty
345 With low subjection; understand the same
Of fish within their wat'ry residence,
Not hither summoned, since they cannot change
Their element to draw the thinner air.'
As thus he spake, each bird and beast behold
350 Approaching two and two, these° cow'ring low   *the beasts*
With blandishment,° each bird stooped on his wing.   *flattering gesture*
I named them, as they passed, and understood

---

6. Compare God's commands to Adam (Genesis 1.28–30, 2.16–17) with Milton's elaboration here.

Their nature, with such knowledge God endued
My sudden apprehension:[7] but in these
355 I found not what methought I wanted still;
And to the heav'nly Vision thus presumed:
  "'O by what name, for thou above all these,
Above mankind, or aught than mankind higher,
Surpassest far my naming,[8] how may I
360 Adore thee, Author of this universe,
And all this good to man, for whose well-being
So amply, and with hands so liberal
Thou hast provided all things: but with me
I see not who partakes. In solitude
365 What happiness, who can enjoy alone,
Or all enjoying, what contentment find?'
Thus I presumptuous; and the Vision bright,
As with a smile more brightened, thus replied:
  "'What call'st thou solitude? Is not the earth
370 With various living creatures, and the air
Replenished,° and all these at thy command   *fully stocked*
To come and play before thee? Know'st thou not
Their language and their ways? They also know,°   *have understanding*
And reason not contemptibly; with these
375 Find pastime, and bear rule; thy realm is large.'
So spake the Universal Lord, and seemed
So ordering. I with leave of speech implored,
And humble deprecation thus replied:
  "'Let not my words offend thee, Heav'nly Power,
380 My Maker, be propitious while I speak.
Hast thou not made me here thy substitute,
And these inferior far beneath me set?
Among unequals what society
Can sort,° what harmony or true delight?   *agree*
385 Which must be mutual, in proportion due
Giv'n and received; but in disparity
The one intense, the other still remiss
Cannot well suit with either,[9] but soon prove
Tedious alike. Of fellowship I speak
390 Such as I seek, fit to participate°   *partake of*
All rational delight, wherein the brute
Cannot be human consort; they rejoice
Each with their kind, lion with lioness;
So fitly them in pairs thou hast combined;
395 Much less can bird with beast, or fish with fowl
So well converse, nor with the ox the ape;
Worse then can man with beast, and least of all.'
  "Whereto th' Almighty answered, not displeased:

---

7. Adam had already begun naming the sun and
features of the earth (lines 272–74), but here he
names (and thereby shows he understands) all
living creatures.
8. Adam reasons, as the Scholastics did, from
the creatures to the fact of a Creator, but he can-

not name (and so indicates that he cannot
understand) God, except as God reveals himself.
9. As with poorly matched musical instruments,
Adam's string is too taut ("intense") and the animals' is too slack ("remiss") to be in harmony
("suit").

'A nice° and subtle happiness I see   *fastidious*
400 Thou to thyself proposest, in the choice
Of thy associates, Adam, and wilt taste
No pleasure, though in pleasure, solitary.
What think'st thou then of me, and this my state?
Seem I to thee sufficiently possessed
405 Of happiness, or not? who am alone
From all eternity, for none I know
Second to me or like, equal much less.
How have I then with whom to hold converse
Save with the creatures which I made, and those
410 To me inferior, infinite descents
Beneath what other creatures are to thee?'
    "He ceased, I lowly answered: 'To attain
The height and depth of thy eternal ways
All human thoughts come short, Supreme of things;
415 Thou in thyself art perfect, and in thee
Is no deficience found; not so is man,
But in degree, the cause of his desire
By conversation with his like to help,
Or solace his defects.[1] No need that thou
420 Shouldst propagate, already infinite;
And through all numbers absolute, though One;
But man by number is to manifest
His single imperfection, and beget
Like of his like, his image multiplied,
425 In unity defective,[2] which requires
Collateral° love, and dearest amity.   *mutual*
Thou in thy secrecy° although alone,   *seclusion*
Best with thyself accompanied, seek'st not
Social communication, yet so pleased,
430 Canst raise thy creature to what height thou wilt
Of union or communion, deified;
I by conversing cannot these erect
From prone, nor in their ways complacence° find.'   *satisfaction*
Thus I emboldened spake, and freedom used
435 Permissive,° and acceptance found, which gained   *permitted*
This answer from the gracious Voice Divine:
    "'Thus far to try thee, Adam, I was pleased,
And find thee knowing not of beasts alone,
Which thou hast rightly named, but of thyself,
440 Expressing well the spirit within thee free,
My image, not imparted to the brute,
Whose fellowship therefore unmeet° for thee   *unsuitable*
Good reason was thou freely shouldst dislike,
And be so minded still. I, ere thou spak'st,
445 Knew it not good for man to be alone,

1. God is absolutely perfect, man only relatively
so ("in degree"), and thereby needs companionship with a fit mate to assuage ("solace") the
"defects" arising from solitude.
2. God, "though One," (line 421), contains all
numbers, but man has to remedy the "imperfection" of being single (line 423) by procreating
and thereby multiplying his single and thereby
"defective" image (line 425).

And no such company as then thou saw'st
Intended thee, for trial only brought,
To see how thou couldst judge of fit and meet:
What next I bring shall please thee, be assured,
450 Thy likeness, thy fit help, thy other self,
Thy wish, exactly to thy heart's desire.'[3]
   "He ended, or I heard no more, for now
My earthly by his heav'nly overpowered,
Which it had long stood under,° strained to the height   *been exposed to*
455 In that celestial colloquy sublime,
As with an object that excels° the sense,   *exceeds*
Dazzled and spent, sunk down, and sought repair
Of sleep, which instantly fell on me, called
By nature as in aid, and closed mine eyes.
460 Mine eyes he closed, but open left the cell
Of fancy° my internal sight, by which   *imagination*
Abstract° as in a trance methought I saw,   *withdrawn*
Though sleeping, where I lay, and saw the shape
Still glorious before whom awake I stood;
465 Who stooping opened my left side, and took
From thence a rib, with cordial° spirits warm,   *from the heart*
And lifeblood streaming fresh; wide was the wound,
But suddenly with flesh filled up and healed:
The rib he formed and fashioned with his hands;
470 Under his forming hands a creature grew,[4]
Manlike, but different sex, so lovely fair
That what seemed fair in all the world seemed now
Mean, or in her summed up, in her contained
And in her looks, which from that time infused
475 Sweetness into my heart, unfelt before,
And into all things from her air° inspired   *mien, look*
The spirit of love and amorous delight.
She disappeared, and left me dark, I waked
To find her, or forever to deplore
480 Her loss, and other pleasures all abjure:
When out of hope, behold her, not far off,
Such as I saw her in my dream, adorned
With what all earth or heaven could bestow
To make her amiable:° on she came,   *lovely*
485 Led by her heav'nly Maker, though unseen,[5]
And guided by his voice, nor uninformed
Of nuptial sanctity and marriage rites:
Grace was in all her steps, Heav'n in her eye,
In every gesture dignity and love.
490 I overjoyed could not forbear aloud:
   "'This turn hath made amends; thou hast fulfilled
Thy words, Creator bounteous and benign,
Giver of all things fair, but fairest this

---

3. Compare the account in Genesis 2.18 with
Milton's elaboration.
4. Go to the online StudySpace to see the *Creation of Eve* by the Italian painter Paolo Veronese

(1528–1588).
5. Compare Eve's version of these events
(4.440–91).

Of all thy gifts, nor enviest.° I now see   *given reluctantly*
495 Bone of my bone, flesh of my flesh, my self
Before me; woman is her name, of man
Extracted; for this cause he shall forgo
Father and mother, and to his wife adhere;
And they shall be one flesh, one heart, one soul.'°
500   "She heard me thus, and though divinely brought,
Yet innocence and virgin modesty,
Her virtue and the conscience° of her worth   *consciousness*
That would be wooed, and not unsought be won,
Not obvious,° not obtrusive,° but retired,   *bold / forward*
505 The more desirable, or to say all,
Nature herself, though pure of sinful thought,
Wrought in her so that, seeing me, she turned;
I followed her, she what was honor knew,
And with obsequious° majesty approved   *compliant*
510 My pleaded reason. To the nuptial bow'r
I led her blushing like the morn: all heav'n,
And happy constellations on that hour
Shed their selectest influence; the earth
Gave sign of gratulation,° and each hill;   *rejoicing, congratulation*
515 Joyous the birds; fresh gales and gentle airs[7]
Whispered it to the woods, and from their wings
Flung rose, flung odors from the spicy shrub,
Disporting,° till the amorous bird of night°   *frolicking / nightingale*
Sung spousal, and bid haste the evening star°   *Venus*
520 On his hill top, to light the bridal lamp.
    Thus I have told thee all my state, and brought
My story to the sum of earthly bliss
Which I enjoy, and must confess to find
In all things else delight indeed, but such
525 As used or not, works in the mind no change,
Nor vehement desire, these delicacies
I mean of taste, sight, smell, herbs, fruits, and flow'rs,
Walks, and the melody of birds; but here
Far otherwise, transported° I behold,   *enraptured*
530 Transported touch; here passion first I felt,
Commotion° strange, in all enjoyments else   *mental agitation*
Superior and unmoved, here only weak
Against the charm of beauty's powerful glance.
Or° nature failed in me, and left some part   *either*
535 Not proof enough such object to sustain,°   *withstand*
Or from my side subducting,° took perhaps   *subtracting*
More than enough; at least on her bestowed
Too much of ornament, in outward show
Elaborate, of inward less exact.
540 For well I understand in the prime end
Of nature her th' inferior, in the mind
And inward faculties, which most excel,
In outward also her resembling less

6. Compare the account in Genesis 2.23–24.
7. Both breezes and melodies. "Gales": winds.

His image who made both, and less expressing
545 The character of that dominion giv'n
O'er other creatures; yet when I approach
Her loveliness, so absolute° she seems   *perfect, independent*
And in herself complete, so well to know
Her own, that what she wills to do or say,
550 Seems wisest, virtuousest, discreetest, best;
All higher knowledge in her presence falls
Degraded, wisdom in discourse with her
Loses discount'nanced,° and like folly shows;   *disconcerted, abashed*
Authority and reason on her wait,
555 As one intended first, not after made
Occasionally;° and to consúmmate all,   *incidentally*
Greatness of mind and nobleness their seat
Build in her loveliest, and create an awe
About her, as a guard angelic placed."
560 To whom the angel with contracted brow:
  "Accuse not nature, she hath done her part;
Do thou but thine, and be not diffident°   *mistrustful*
Of wisdom, she deserts thee not, if thou
Dismiss not her, when most thou need'st her nigh,
565 By áttributing overmuch to things
Less excellent, as thou thyself perceiv'st.
For what admir'st thou, what transports thee so,
An outside? Fair no doubt, and worthy well
Thy cherishing, thy honoring, and thy love,
570 Not thy subjection: weigh with her thyself;
Then value: ofttimes nothing profits more
Than self-esteem, grounded on just and right
Well managed; of that skill the more thou know'st,
The more she will acknowledge thee her head,[8]
575 And to realities yield all her shows:
Made so adorn for thy delight the more,
So awful,° that with honor thou may'st love   *awe-inspiring*
Thy mate, who sees when thou art seen least wise.
But if the sense of touch whereby mankind
580 Is propagated seem such dear delight
Beyond all other, think the same vouchsafed
To cattle and each beast; which would not be
To them made common and divulged,° if aught   *imparted generally*
Therein enjoyed were worthy to subdue
585 The soul of man, or passion in him move.
What higher in her society thou find'st
Attractive, human, rational, love still;
In loving thou dost well, in passion not,
Wherein true love consists not; love refines
590 The thoughts, and heart enlarges, hath his seat
In reason, and is judicious, is the scale[9]

---

8. See 1 Corinthians 11.3: "the head of every man is Christ; and the head of the woman is the man; and the head of Christ is God."
9. The ladder of love, a Neoplatonic concept for the movement from sensual love to higher forms, and ultimately to love of God (see Castiglione's *Courtier*, p. 706).

By which to heav'nly love thou may'st ascend,
Not sunk in carnal pleasure, for which cause
Among the beasts no mate for thee was found."
595   To whom thus half abashed Adam replied.
"Neither her outside formed so fair, nor aught
In procreation common to all kinds
(Though higher of the genial[1] bed by far,
And with mysterious reverence I deem)
600   So much delights me, as those graceful acts,
Those thousand decencies° that daily flow   *fitting acts*
From all her words and actions, mixed with love
And sweet compliance, which declare unfeigned
Union of mind, or in us both one soul;
605   Harmony to behold in wedded pair
More grateful than harmonious sound to the ear.
Yet these subject not; I to thee disclose
What inward thence I feel, not therefore foiled,°   *overcome*
Who meet with various objects, from the sense
610   Variously representing;[2] yet still free
Approve the best, and follow what I approve.
To love thou blam'st me not, for love thou say'st
Leads up to Heav'n, is both the way and guide;
Bear with me then, if lawful what I ask;
615   Love not the heav'nly Spirits, and how their love
Express they, by looks only, or do they mix
Irradiance, virtual or immediate° touch?"   *actual*
        To whom the angel with a smile that glowed
Celestial rosy red, love's proper hue,[3]
620   Answered. "Let it suffice thee that thou know'st
Us happy, and without love no happiness.
Whatever pure thou in the body enjoy'st
(And pure thou wert created) we enjoy
In eminence,° and obstacle find none   *higher degree*
625   Of membrane, joint, or limb, exclusive bars:
Easier than air with air, if Spirits embrace,
Total they mix, union of pure with pure
Desiring; nor restrained conveyance need
As flesh to mix with flesh, or soul with soul.
630   But I can now no more; the parting sun
Beyond the earth's green cape and verdant isles
Hesperian sets,[4] my signal to depart.
Be strong, live happy, and love, but first of all
Him whom to love is to obey, and keep
635   His great command; take heed lest passion sway

1. Both "nuptial" and "generative." Adam takes respectful issue with the apparent denigration of human sex in Raphael's account of the Neoplatonic ladder, which prompts his question about angelic sex (lines 615–17).
2. I.e., various objects, variously represented to me by my senses.
3. This is not likely to be an embarrassed blush:

red is the color traditionally associated with Seraphim, who burn with ardor. Raphael's smile also glows with friendship for Adam and appreciation of his perceptive inference about angelic love.
4. Cape Verde, near Dakar, and the islands off that coast are the westernmost ("Hesperian") points of Africa.

Thy judgment to do aught, which else free will
Would not admit;° thine and of all thy sons   *permit*
The weal or woe in thee is placed; beware.
I in thy persevering shall rejoice,
640 And all the blest: stand fast; to stand or fall
Free in thine own arbitrament° it lies.   *determination*
Perfect within, no outward aid require;°   *depend on*
And all temptation to transgress repel."
     So saying, he arose; whom Adam thus
645 Followed with benediction. "Since to part,
Go heavenly guest, ethereal messenger,
Sent from whose sov'reign goodness I adore.
Gentle to me and affable hath been
Thy condescension, and shall be honored ever
650 With grateful memory: thou to mankind
Be good and friendly still,° and oft return."   *always*
     So parted they, the angel up to Heav'n
From the thick shade, and Adam to his bow'r.

Book 9

No more of talk where God or angel guest
With man, as with his friend, familiar used
To sit indulgent, and with him partake
Rural repast, permitting him the while
5   Venial° discourse unblamed: I now must change   *permissible*
Those notes to tragic; foul distrust, and breach
Disloyal on the part of man, revolt,
And disobedience: on the part of Heav'n
Now alienated, distance and distaste,°   *aversion*
10   Anger and just rebuke, and judgment giv'n,
That brought into this world a world of woe,
Sin and her shadow Death, and misery
Death's harbinger:° sad task, yet argument°   *forerunner / subject*
Not less but more heroic than the wrath
15   Of stern Achilles on his foe pursued
Thrice fugitive about Troy wall; or rage
Of Turnus for Lavinia disespoused,
Or Neptune's ire or Juno's, that so long
Perplexed the Greek and Cytherea's son;[1]
20   If answerable° style I can obtain   *fitting*
Of my celestial patroness, who deigns

---

1. In this fourth proem (lines 1–47), after sig-
naling his change from pastoral to tragic mode
(lines 1–6), Milton emphasizes tragic elements
in several classical epics: Achilles pursuing Hector three times around the wall of Troy before
killing him (*Iliad* 22); Turnus fighting Aeneas

over the loss of his betrothed Lavinia, and then
killed by Aeneas; Odysseus ("the Greek") and
Aeneas ("Cytherea's son," i.e., Venus's son) tormented ("perplexed") by Neptune (Poseidon)
and Juno, respectively.

Her nightly visitation unimplored,[2]
And dictates to me slumb'ring, or inspires
Easy my unpremeditated verse:
25 Since first this subject for heroic song
Pleased me long choosing, and beginning late;
Not sedulous° by nature to indite   *eager*
Wars, hitherto the only argument°   *subject*
Heroic deemed, chief mastery to dissect
30 With long and tedious havoc fabled knights
In battles feigned; the better fortitude
Of patience and heroic martyrdom
Unsung; or to describe races and games,
Or tilting furniture, emblazoned shields,
35 Impresses quaint, caparisons and steeds;
Bases[3] and tinsel trappings, gorgeous knights
At joust and tournament; then marshaled feast
Served up in hall with sewers,° and seneschals;°   *waiters / stewards*
The skill of artifice° or office mean,   *mechanic art*
40 Not that which justly gives heroic name
To person or to poem. Me of these
Nor skilled nor studious, higher argument
Remains,[4] sufficient of itself to raise
That name, unless an age too late, or cold
45 Climate, or years damp my intended wing
Depressed, and much they may, if all be mine,
Not hers who brings it nightly to my ear.
    The sun was sunk, and after him the star
Of Hesperus,[5] whose office is to bring
50 Twilight upon the earth, short arbiter
'Twixt day and night, and now from end to end
Night's hemisphere had veiled the horizon round:
When Satan who late° fled[6] before the threats   *recently*
Of Gabriel out of Eden, now improved°   *increased*
55 In meditated fraud and malice, bent
On man's destruction, maugre what might hap
Of heavier on himself,[7] fearless returned.
By night he fled, and at midnight returned
From compassing the earth, cautious of day,
60 Since Uriel regent of the sun descried
His entrance, and forewarned the Cherubim
That kept their watch; thence full of anguish driv'n,
The space of seven continued nights he rode

---

2. Milton does not here invoke the Muse but testifies to her customary nightly visits. Milton's nephew reports that he often awoke in the morning with lines of poetry fully formed in his head, ready to dictate them to a scribe.
3. Cloth coverings for horses; "tilting furniture": equipment for jousting; "impresses quaint": cunningly designed heraldic devices on shields; "caparisons": ornamental trappings or armor for horses. After rejecting the classical epic subjects, Milton here rejects the familiar topics of romance.

4. For a heroic poem. He proceeds to recap worries he has voiced before: that the times might not be receptive to such poems ("age too late"), that the "cold Climate" of England or his own advanced age might "damp" (benumb, dampen) his "intended wing / Depressed" (poetic flights held down, kept from soaring).
5. Venus, the evening star.
6. At the end of Book 4.
7. I.e., despite ("maugre") what might result in heavier punishments for himself.

With darkness, thrice the equinoctial line°   *equator*
65 He circled, four times crossed the car of Night
From pole to pole, traversing each colure;[8]
On the eighth returned, and on the coast averse°   *turned away*
From entrance on Cherubic watch, by stealth
Found unsuspected way. There was a place,
70 Now not, though sin, not time, first wrought the change,
Where Tigris at the foot of Paradise
Into a gulf shot underground, till part
Rose up a fountain by the Tree of Life;
In with the river sunk, and with it rose
75 Satan involved° in rising mist, then sought   *enveloped*
Where to lie hid. Sea he had searched and land
From Eden over Pontus,[9] and the pool
Maeotis, up beyond the river Ob;
Downward as far Antarctic; and in length
80 West from Orontes to the ocean barred
At Darien, thence to the land where flows
Ganges and Indus: thus the orb he roamed
With narrow° search; and with inspection deep   *strict*
Considered every creature, which of all
85 Most opportune might serve his wiles, and found
The serpent subtlest beast of all the field.[1]
Him after long debate, irresolute°   *undecided*
Of° thoughts revolved, his final sentence° chose *among / decision*
Fit vessel, fittest imp° of fraud, in whom   *offshoot*
90 To enter, and his dark suggestions hide
From sharpest sight: for in the wily snake,
Whatever sleights° none would suspicious mark, *artifices*
As from his wit and native subtlety
Proceeding, which in other beasts observed
95 Doubt° might beget of diabolic pow'r   *suspicion*
Active within beyond the sense of brute.
Thus he resolved, but first from inward grief
His bursting passion into plaints thus poured:
   "O earth, how like to Heav'n, if not preferred
100 More justly, seat worthier of gods, as built
With second thoughts, reforming what was old!
For what God after better worse would build?
Terrestrial heav'n, danced round by other heav'ns
That shine, yet bear their bright officious° lamps, *dutiful*
105 Light above light, for thee alone, as seems,[2]
In thee concent'ring all their precious beams

---

8. The colures are two great circles that intersect at right angles at the poles. By circling the globe from east to west at the equator and then over the north and south poles, Satan can remain in darkness, keeping the earth between himself and the sun. "Car of Night" (line 65): the earth's shadow, imagined as the chariot of the goddess Night.
9. The Black Sea. Satan's journey (lines 77–82) takes him from there to the Sea of Azov in Russia ("Maeotis"), beyond the river "Ob" in Siberia,

which flows into the Arctic Ocean, then south to Antarctica; thence west from "Orontes" (a river in Syria) across the Atlantic to "Darien" (the Isthmus of Panama), then across the Pacific and Asia to India where the "Ganges" and "Indus" rivers flow.
1. The serpent is so described in Genesis 3.1.
2. Like Adam (8.15ff.) and Eve (4.657–58) but not Raphael (8.114–78), Satan assumes a Ptolemaic universe centered on the earth and humankind.

Of sacred influence: as God in Heav'n
Is center, yet extends to all, so thou
Centring receiv'st from all those orbs; in thee,
110   Not in themselves, all their known virtue appears
Productive in herb, plant, and nobler birth
Of creatures animate with gradual life
Of growth, sense, reason,[3] all summed up in man.
With what delight could I have walked thee round,
115   If I could joy in aught, sweet interchange
Of hill and valley, rivers, woods and plains,
Now land, now sea, and shores with forest crowned,
Rocks, dens, and caves; but I in none of these
Find place or refuge; and the more I see
120   Pleasures about me, so much more I feel
Torment within me, as from the hateful siege°   *conflict*
Of contraries; all good to me becomes
Bane,° and in Heav'n much worse would be my state.   *poison*
But neither here seek I, no nor in Heav'n
125   To dwell, unless by mastering Heav'n's Supreme;
Nor hope to be myself less miserable
By what I seek, but others to make such
As I, though thereby worse to me redound:
For only in destroying I find ease
130   To my relentless thoughts; and him[4] destroyed,
Or won to what may work his utter loss,
For whom all this was made, all this will soon
Follow, as to him linked in weal or woe:
In woe then; that destruction wide may range:
135   To me shall be the glory sole among
The infernal Powers, in one day to have marred
What he Almighty styled,° six nights and days   *called*
Continued making, and who knows how long
Before had been contriving, though perhaps
140   Not longer than since I in one night freed
From servitude inglorious well-nigh half
Th' angelic name, and thinner left the throng
Of his adorers. He to be avenged,
And to repair his numbers thus impaired,
145   Whether such virtue° spent of old now failed   *power*
More angels to create, if they at least
Are his created, or to spite us more,
Determined to advance into our room
A creature formed of earth, and him endow,
150   Exalted from so base original,°   *origin*
With Heav'nly spoils, our spoils: what he decreed
He effected; man he made, and for him built
Magnificent this world, and earth his seat,
Him lord pronounced, and, O indignity!
155   Subjected to his service angel wings,

3. Graduated in steps ("gradual," 112) from vegetable to animal to rational forms (souls); cf. 5.469–90.
4. Adam. "This" (line 132): the universe.

And flaming ministers to watch and tend
Their earthy charge: of these the vigilance
I dread, and to elude, thus wrapped in mist
Of midnight vapor glide obscure, and pry
160 In every bush and brake, where hap° may find   *luck*
The serpent sleeping, in whose mazy folds
To hide me, and the dark intent I bring.
O foul descent! that I who erst contended
With gods to sit the highest, am now constrained
165 Into a beast, and mixed with bestial slime,
This essence to incarnate and imbrute,[5]
That to the height of deity aspired;
But what will not ambition and revenge
Descend to? Who aspires must down as low
170 As high he soared, obnoxious° first or last   *exposed*
To basest things. Revenge, at first though sweet,
Bitter ere long back on itself recoils;
Let it; I reck° not, so it light well aimed,   *care*
Since higher I fall short, on him who next
175 Provokes my envy, this new favorite
Of Heav'n, this man of clay, son of despite,
Whom us the more to spite his Maker raised
From dust: spite then with spite is best repaid."
    So saying, through each thicket dank or dry,
180 Like a black mist low creeping, he held on
His midnight search, where soonest he might find
The serpent: him fast sleeping soon he found
In labyrinth of many a round self-rolled,
His head the midst, well stored with subtle wiles:
185 Not yet in horrid shade or dismal den,
Nor nocent° yet, but on the grassy herb   *harmful, guilty*
Fearless unfeared he slept: in at his mouth
The Devil entered, and his brutal° sense,   *animal*
In heart or head, possessing soon inspired
190 With act intelligential: but his sleep
Disturbed not, waiting close° th' approach of morn.   *hidden*
Now whenas sacred light began to dawn
In Eden on the humid flow'rs, that breathed
Their morning incense, when all things that breathe,
195 From th' earth's great altar send up silent praise
To the Creator, and his nostrils fill
With grateful° smell, forth came the human pair   *pleasing*
And joined their vocal worship to the choir
Of creatures wanting° voice; that done, partake   *lacking*
200 The season, prime° for sweetest scents and airs: *best*
Then cómmune how that day they best may ply
Their growing work; for much their work outgrew
The hands' dispatch of two gard'ning so wide.
And Eve first to her husband thus began:

5. Satan "imbruting" himself in a snake parodies, grotesquely, the Son's incarnation in human form, as Christ.

205   "Adam, well may we labor still° to dress   *continually*
   This garden, still to tend plant, herb, and flow'r,
   Our pleasant task enjoined, but till more hands
   Aid us, the work under our labor grows,
   Luxurious° by restraint; what we by day   *luxuriant*
210   Lop overgrown, or prune, or prop, or bind,
   One night or two with wanton° growth derides,   *unrestrained*
   Tending to wild. Thou therefore now advise
   Or hear what to my mind first thoughts present,
   Let us divide our labors, thou where choice
215   Leads thee, or where most needs, whether to wind
   The woodbine round this arbor, or direct
   The clasping ivy where to climb, while I
   In yonder spring° of roses intermixed   *growth*
   With myrtle, find what to redress° till noon: *set upright*
220   For while so near each other thus all day
   Our task we choose, what wonder if so near
   Looks intervene and smiles, or object new
   Casual discourse draw on, which intermits°   *interrupts*
   Our day's work brought to little, though begun
225   Early, and th' hour of supper comes unearned."
      To whom mild answer Adam thus returned:
   "Sole Eve, associate sole,[6] to me beyond
   Compare above all living creatures dear,
   Well hast thou motioned,° well thy thoughts employed   *proposed*
230   How we might best fulfill the work which here
   God hath assigned us, nor of me shalt pass
   Unpraised: for nothing lovelier can be found
   In woman, than to study household good,
   And good works in her husband to promote.[7]
235   Yet not so strictly hath our Lord imposed
   Labor, as to debar us when we need
   Refreshment, whether food, or talk between,
   Food of the mind, or this sweet intercourse
   Of looks and smiles, for smiles from reason flow,
240   To brute denied, and are of love the food,
   Love not the lowest end of human life.
   For not to irksome toil, but to delight
   He made us, and delight to reason joined.
   These paths and bowers doubt not but our joint hands
245   Will keep from wilderness with ease, as wide
   As we need walk, till younger hands ere long
   Assist us: but if much convérse perhaps
   Thee satiate, to short absence I could yield.
   For solitude sometimes is best society,
250   And short retirement urges sweet return.
   But other doubt possesses me, lest harm
   Befall thee severed from me; for thou know'st
   What hath been warned us, what malicious foe

---

6. Adam puns on "sole" as "unrivaled" and "only" (cf. 4.411).
7. Adam's compliments resemble the praises of a good wife in Proverbs 31.

Envying our happiness, and of his own
255   Despairing, seeks to work us woe and shame
By sly assault; and somewhere nigh at hand
Watches, no doubt, with greedy hope to find
His wish and best advantage, us asunder,
Hopeless to circumvent us joined, where each
260   To other speedy aid might lend at need;
Whether his first design be to withdraw
Our fealty° from God, or to disturb   *allegiance*
Conjugal love, than which perhaps no bliss
Enjoyed by us excites his envy more;
265   Or° this, or worse, leave not the faithful side   *whether*
That gave thee being, still shades thee and protects.
The wife, where danger or dishonor lurks,
Safest and seemliest by her husband stays,
Who guards her, or with her the worst endures."
270   To whom the virgin[8] majesty of Eve,
As one who loves, and some unkindness meets,
With sweet austere composure thus replied.
     "Offspring of Heav'n and earth, and all earth's lord,
That such an enemy we have, who seeks
275   Our ruin, both by thee informed I learn,
And from the parting angel overheard
As in a shady nook I stood behind,
Just then returned at shut of evening flow'rs.[9]
But that thou shouldst my firmness therefore doubt
280   To God or thee, because we have a foe
May tempt it, I expected not to hear.
His violence thou fear'st not, being such,
As we, not capable of death or pain,
Can either not receive, or can repel.
285   His fraud is then thy fear, which plain infers
Thy equal fear that my firm faith and love
Can by his fraud be shaken or seduced;
Thoughts, which how found they harbor in thy breast,
Adam, misthought of° her to thee so dear?"   *misapplied to*
290   To whom with healing words Adam replied.
     "Daughter of God and man, immortal Eve,
For such thou art, from sin and blame entire:°   *untouched*
Not diffident° of thee do I dissuade   *distrustful*
Thy absence from my sight, but to avoid
295   Th' attempt itself, intended by our foe.
For he who tempts, though in vain, at least asperses°   *bespatters*
The tempted with dishonor foul, supposed
Not incorruptible of faith, not proof
Against temptation: thou thyself with scorn
300   And anger wouldst resent the offered wrong,

8. The term here means unspotted or peerless; Milton has insisted at the end of Books 4 and 8 that Adam and Eve have sex.
9. Somewhat confusing, since Eve heard the full story of the war in Heaven and Raphael's earlier warnings; Raphael's parting words (8.630–43) overheard by Eve do not specifically mention Satan but warn Adam to resist his passion for Eve. He does, however, reiterate the charge to obey the "great command" and repel temptation.

Though ineffectual found; misdeem not then,
If such affront I labor to avert
From thee alone, which on us both at once
The enemy, though bold, will hardly dare,
305 Or daring, first on me th' assault shall light.
Nor thou his malice and false guile contemn;° *despise*
Subtle he needs must be, who could seduce
Angels, nor think superfluous others' aid.
I from the influence of thy looks receive
310 Access° in every virtue, in thy sight *increase*
More wise, more watchful, stronger, if need were
Of outward strength; while shame, thou looking on,
Shame to be overcome or overreached° *outwitted*
Would utmost vigor raise, and raised unite.
315 Why shouldst not thou like sense within thee feel
When I am present, and thy trial choose
With me, best witness of thy virtue tried."
　　So spake domestic Adam in his care
And matrimonial love; but Eve, who thought
320 Less° attribúted to her faith sincere, *too little*
Thus her reply with accent sweet renewed.
　　"If this be our condition, thus to dwell
In narrow circuit straitened° by a foe, *confined*
Subtle or violent, we not endued
325 Single with like defense, wherever met,
How are we happy, still° in fear of harm? *always*
But harm precedes not sin: only our foe
Tempting affronts us with his foul esteem
Of our integrity: his foul esteem
330 Sticks no dishonor on our front,° but turns *forehead*
Foul on himself; then wherefore shunned or feared
By us? who rather double honor gain
From his surmise proved false, find peace within,
Favor from Heav'n, our witness from th' event.° *outcome*
335 And what is faith, love, virtue unassayed
Alone, without exterior help sustained?[1]
Let us not then suspect our happy state
Left so imperfect by the Maker wise,
As not secure to single° or combined. *one alone*
340 Frail is our happiness, if this be so,
And Eden were no Eden thus exposed."
　　To whom thus Adam fervently replied.
"O woman, best are all things as the will
Of God ordained them, his creating hand
345 Nothing imperfect or deficient left
Of all that he created, much less man,
Or aught that might his happy state secure,
Secure from outward force; within himself
The danger lies, yet lies within his power:

---

1. Compare and contrast *Areopagitica*, pp. 1929–39.

350 Against his will he can receive no harm.
But God left free the will, for what obeys
Reason, is free, and reason he made right,[2]
But bid her well beware, and still erect,°   *ever-alert*
Lest by some fair appearing good surprised
355 She dictate false, and misinform the will
To do what God expressly hath forbid.
Not then mistrust, but tender love enjoins,
That I should mind° thee oft, and mind thou me. *remind, pay heed to*
Firm we subsist,° yet possible to swerve,   *stand, exist*
360 Since reason not impossibly may meet
Some specious° object by the foe suborned, *deceptively attractive*
And fall into deception unaware,
Not keeping strictest watch, as she was warned.
Seek not temptation then, which to avoid
365 Were better, and most likely if from me
Thou sever not: trial will come unsought.
Wouldst thou approve° thy constancy, approve   *prove*
First thy obedience; th' other who can know,
Not seeing thee attempted, who attest?
370 But if thou think, trial unsought may find
Us both securer° than thus warned thou seem'st, *overconfident*
Go; for thy stay, not free, absents thee more;
Go in thy native innocence, rely
On what thou hast of virtue, summon all,
375 For God towards thee hath done his part, do thine."
  So spake the patriarch of mankind, but Eve
Persisted, yet submiss, though last, replied:
  "With thy permission then, and thus forewarned
Chiefly by what thy own last reasoning words
380 Touched only, that our trial, when least sought,
May find us both perhaps far less prepared,
The willinger I go, nor much expect
A foe so proud will first the weaker seek;
So bent, the more shall shame him his repulse."
385 Thus saying, from her husband's hand her hand
Soft she withdrew, and like a wood nymph light[3]
Oread or Dryad, or of Delia's train,
Betook her to the groves, but Delia's self
In gait surpassed and goddess-like deport,°   *bearing*
390 Though not as she with bow and quiver armed,
But with such gardening tools as art yet rude,
Guiltless of fire[4] had formed, or angels brought.
To Pales, or Pomona, thus adorned,
Likest she seemed Pomona when she fled

2. Right reason, a classical concept accommodated to Christian thought, is the God-given
power to apprehend truth and moral law.
3. Light-footed, with overtones of "fickle" or
"frivolous." "Oread" (next line): a mountain
nymph. "Dryad": a wood nymph. "Delia": Diana,

born on the isle of Delos, hunted with a "train"
of nymphs.
4. Having no experience of fire, not needed in
Paradise. Milton may be alluding to the guilt of
Prometheus, who stole fire from heaven.

395 Vertumnus, or to Ceres in her prime,
　　 Yet virgin of Proserpina from Jove.[5]
　　 Her long with ardent look his eye pursued
　　 Delighted, but desiring more her stay.
　　 Oft he to her his charge of quick return
400 Repeated, she to him as oft engaged
　　 To be returned by noon amid the bow'r,
　　 And all things in best order to invite
　　 Noontide repast, or afternoon's repose.
　　 O much deceived, much failing,° hapless° Eve,   *erring / unlucky*
405 Of thy presumed return! event° perverse!   *outcome*
　　 Thou never from that hour in Paradise
　　 Found'st either sweet repast, or sound repose;
　　 Such ambush hid among sweet flow'rs and shades
　　 Waited with hellish rancor imminent
410 To intercept thy way, or send thee back
　　 Despoiled of innocence, of faith, of bliss.
　　 For now, and since first break of dawn the Fiend,
　　 Mere serpent in appearance, forth was come,
　　 And on his quest, where likeliest he might find
415 The only two of mankind, but in them
　　 The whole included race, his purposed prey.
　　 In bow'r and field he sought, where any tuft
　　 Of grove or garden plot more pleasant lay,
　　 Their tendance or plantation for delight,[6]
420 By fountain or by shady rivulet
　　 He sought them both, but wished his hap° might find   *luck*
　　 Eve separate; he wished, but not with hope
　　 Of what so seldom chanced, when to his wish,
　　 Beyond his hope, Eve separate he spies,
425 Veiled in a cloud of fragrance, where she stood,
　　 Half spied, so thick the roses bushing round
　　 About her glowed, oft stooping to support
　　 Each flow'r of slender stalk, whose head though gay
　　 Carnation, purple, azure, or specked with gold,
430 Hung drooping unsustained, them she upstays
　　 Gently with myrtle band, mindless° the while,   *heedless*
　　 Herself, though fairest unsupported flow'r
　　 From her best prop so far, and storm so nigh.[7]
　　 Nearer he drew, and many a walk traversed
435 Of stateliest covert, cedar, pine, or palm,
　　 Then voluble° and bold, now hid, now seen   *undulating*
　　 Among thick-woven arborets° and flow'rs   *small trees*
　　 Embordered on each bank, the hand° of Eve: *handiwork*
　　 Spot more delicious than those gardens feigned

5. These goddesses, like Eve, are associated with agriculture (lines 393–96)—Pales, with flocks and pastures; Pomona, with fruit trees; Ceres, with harvests—and the latter two foreshadow Eve's situation. Pomona was chased by the wood god "Vertumnus" in many guises before surrendering to him; Ceres was impreg-nated by Jove with Proserpina—later carried off to Hades by Pluto.
6. I.e., which they had cultivated or planted for their pleasure.
7. The conceit of the flower-gatherer who is herself gathered evokes the story of Proserpina, to whom it was applied in 4.269–71.

440	Or° of revived Adonis, or renowned	*either*
	Alcinous, host of old Laertes' son,	
	Or that, not mystic, where the sapient king	
	Held dalliance with his fair Egyptian spouse.[8]	
	Much he the place admired, the person more.	
445	As one who long in populous city pent,	
	Where houses thick and sewers annoy° the air,	*make noisome, befoul*
	Forth issuing on a summer's morn to breathe	
	Among the pleasant villages and farms	
	Adjoined, from each thing met conceives delight,	
450	The smell of grain, or tedded grass, or kine,[9]	
	Or dairy, each rural sight, each rural sound;	
	If chance with nymph-like step fair virgin pass,	
	What pleasing seemed, for° her now pleases more,	*because of*
	She most, and in her look sums all delight.	
455	Such pleasure took the Serpent to behold	
	This flow'ry plat,° the sweet recess° of Eve	*plot / retreat*
	Thus early, thus alone; her heav'nly form	
	Angelic, but more soft, and feminine,	
	Her graceful innocence, her every air°	*manner*
460	Of gesture or least action overawed	
	His malice, and with rapine sweet[1] bereaved	
	His fierceness of the fierce intent it brought:	
	That space the Evil One abstracted° stood	*withdrawn*
	From his own evil, and for the time remained	
465	Stupidly good,° of enmity disarmed,	*good because stupefied*
	Of guile, of hate, of envy, of revenge;	
	But the hot hell that always in him burns,	
	Though in mid-Heav'n, soon ended his delight,	
	And tortures him now more, the more he sees	
470	Of pleasure not for him ordained: then soon	
	Fierce hate he recollects,° and all his thoughts	
	Of mischief gratulating,° thus excites:	*greeting*
	"Thoughts, whither have ye led me, with what sweet	
	Compulsion thus transported to forget	
475	What hither brought us, hate, not love, nor hope	
	Of Paradise for Hell, hope here to taste	
	Of pleasure, but all pleasure to destroy,	
	Save what is in destroying, other joy	
	To me is lost. Then let me not let pass	
480	Occasion which now smiles, behold alone	
	The woman, opportune° to all attempts,	*open*
	Her husband, for I view far round, not nigh,	
	Whose higher intellectual more I shun,	
	And strength, of courage haughty,° and of limb	*exalted*
485	Heroic built, though of terrestrial° mold,	*earthly*

8. The gardens of Adonis were beauty spots named for the lovely youth loved by Venus, killed by a boar, and subsequently revived; Odysseus ("Laertes' son") was entertained by Alcinous in his beautiful gardens; Solomon ("the sapient king") entertained his "fair Egyptian spouse," the Queen of Sheba, in a real garden (not "mystic," or "feigned," as the others were).
9. Cattle. "Tedded": spread out to dry, like hay.
1. From Latin *rapere*, to seize, the root of both "rape" and "rapture," underscoring the paradox of the ravisher (temporarily) ravished.

Foe not informidable, exempt from wound,
I not; so much hath Hell debased, and pain
Enfeebled me, to what I was in Heav'n.
She fair, divinely fair, fit love for gods,
490 Not terrible,° though terror be in love   *terrifying*
And beauty, not° approached by stronger hate,   *unless*
Hate stronger, under show of love well feigned,
The way which to her ruin now I tend."
  So spake the Enemy of mankind, enclosed
495 In serpent, inmate bad, and toward Eve
Addressed his way, not with indented° wave,   *zigzag*
Prone on the ground, as since, but on his rear,
Circular base of rising folds, that tow'red
Fold above fold a surging maze, his head
500 Crested aloft, and carbuncle° his eyes;   *deep red*
With burnished neck of verdant° gold, erect   *green*
Amidst his circling spires,° that on the grass   *coils*
Floated redundant:° pleasing was his shape,   *in swelling waves*
And lovely, never since of serpent kind
505 Lovelier, not those that in Illyria changed
Hermione and Cadmus, or the god
In Epidaurus;[2] nor to which transformed
Ammonian Jove, or Capitoline was seen,
He with Olympias, this with her who bore
510 Scipio, the height of Rome.[3] With tract° oblique *course*
At first, as one who sought accéss, but feared
To interrupt, sidelong he works his way.
As when a ship by skillful steersman wrought
Nigh river's mouth or foreland, where the wind
515 Veers oft, as oft so steers, and shifts her sail;
So varied he, and of his tortuous train°   *twisting length*
Curled many a wanton° wreath in sight of Eve, *luxuriant, sportive*
To lure her eye; she busied heard the sound
Of rustling leaves, but minded not, as used
520 To such disport before her through the field,
From every beast, more duteous at her call,
Than at Circean call the herd disguised.[4]
He bolder now, uncalled before her stood;
But as in gaze admiring: oft he bowed
525 His turret crest, and sleek enameled° neck,   *multicolored*
Fawning, and licked the ground whereon she trod.
His gentle dumb expression turned at length
The eye of Eve to mark his play; he glad
Of her attention gained, with serpent tongue
530 Organic, or impulse of vocal air,[5]

---

2. The legendary founder of Thebes, Cadmus, and his wife Harmonia (Milton's "Hermione") were changed to serpents when they went to Illyria in old age; Aesculapius, god of healing, sometimes came forth as a serpent from his temple in Epidaurus.
3. Jupiter Ammon ("Ammonian Jove") made love to Olympias in the form of a snake and sired Alexander the Great; the Jupiter worshipped in Rome ("Capitoline"), also in serpent form, sired Scipio Africanus, the savior and great leader ("height") of Rome.
4. Circe, in the *Odyssey*, transformed men to beasts and was attended by an obedient herd.
5. Satan either used the actual tongue of the serpent or impressed the air with his own voice.

His fraudulent temptation thus began.
   "Wonder not, sovereign mistress, if perhaps
Thou canst, who art sole wonder, much less arm
Thy looks, the heav'n of mildness, with disdain,
535 Displeased that I approach thee thus, and gaze
Insatiate, I thus single, nor have feared
Thy awful° brow, more awful thus retired.   *awe-inspiring*
Fairest resemblance of thy Maker fair,
Thee all things living gaze on, all things thine
540 By gift, and thy celestial beauty adore
With ravishment beheld, there best beheld
Where universally admired; but here
In this enclosure wild, these beasts among,
Beholders rude, and shallow to discern
545 Half what in thee is fair, one man except,
Who sees thee? (and what is one?) who shouldst be seen
A goddess among gods, adored and served
By angels numberless, thy daily train."[6]
   So glozed° the Tempter, and his proem° tuned;   *flattered / prelude*
550 Into the heart of Eve his words made way,
Though at the voice much marveling; at length
Not unamazed she thus in answer spake.
"What may this mean? Language of man pronounced
By tongue of brute, and human sense expressed?
555 The first at least of these I thought denied
To beasts, whom God on their creation day
Created mute to all articulate sound;
The latter I demur,° for in their looks   *hesitate about*
Much reason, and in their actions oft appears.
560 Thee, Serpent, subtlest beast of all the field
I knew, but not with human voice endued;°   *endowed*
Redouble then this miracle, and say,
How cam'st thou speakable° of mute, and how   *able to speak*
To me so friendly grown above the rest
565 Of brutal kind, that daily are in sight?
Say, for such wonder claims attention due."
   To whom the guileful Tempter thus replied:
"Empress of this fair world, resplendent Eve,
Easy to me it is to tell thee all
570 What thou command'st, and right thou shouldst be obeyed:
I was at first as other beasts that graze
The trodden herb, of abject thoughts and low,
As was my food, nor aught but food discerned
Or sex, and apprehended nothing high:
575 Till on a day roving the field, I chanced
A goodly tree far distant to behold
Loaden with fruit of fairest colors mixed,
Ruddy and gold: I nearer drew to gaze;
When from the boughs a savory odor blown,
580 Grateful to appetite, more pleased my sense

6. Satan's entire speech is couched in the extravagant praises of the Petrarchan love convention.

Than smell of sweetest fennel, or the teats
Of ewe or goat dropping with milk at ev'n,[7]
Unsucked of lamb or kid, that tend their play.
To satisfy the sharp desire I had
585 Of tasting those fair apples, I resolved
Not to defer;° hunger and thirst at once,   *delay*
Powerful persuaders, quickened at the scent
Of that alluring fruit, urged me so keen.
About the mossy trunk I wound me soon,
590 For high from ground the branches would require
Thy utmost reach or Adam's: round the tree
All other beasts that saw, with like desire
Longing and envying stood, but could not reach.
Amid the tree now got, where plenty hung
595 Tempting so nigh, to pluck and eat my fill
I spared° not, for such pleasure till that hour   *refrained*
At feed or fountain never had I found.
Sated at length, ere long I might perceive
Strange alteration in me, to degree
600 Of reason in my inward powers, and speech
Wanted° not long, though to this shape retained.[8]   *lacked*
Thenceforth to speculations high or deep
I turned my thoughts, and with capacious mind
Considered all things visible in Heav'n,
605 Or earth, or middle,° all things fair and good;   *regions between*
But all that fair and good in thy divine
Semblance, and in thy beauty's heav'nly ray
United I beheld; no fair° to thine   *beauty*
Equivalent or second, which compelled
610 Me thus, though importune° perhaps, to come   *inopportunely*
And gaze, and worship thee of right declared
Sov'reign of creatures, universal dame."[9]
     So talked the spirited[1] sly snake; and Eve
Yet more amazed unwary thus replied:
615   "Serpent, thy overpraising leaves in doubt
The virtue° of that fruit, in thee first proved: *power*
But say, where grows the tree, from hence how far?
For many are the trees of God that grow
In Paradise, and various, yet unknown
620 To us, in such abundance lies our choice,
As leaves a greater store of fruit untouched,
Still hanging incorruptible, till men
Grow up to their provision,[2] and more hands
Help to disburden nature of her birth."
625   To whom the wily adder, blithe and glad:

7. According to Pliny, serpents ate fennel to aid in shedding their skins and to sharpen their eyesight; folklore had it that they drank the milk of sheep and goats.
8. There is no precedent in Genesis or the interpretative tradition for Satan's powerfully persuasive argument by analogy based on the snake's supposed experience of attaining to reason and speech by eating the forbidden fruit.
9. Satan continues his Petrarchan language of courtship.
1. Both inspired by and possessed by an evil spirit, Satan.
2. I.e., until the numbers of the human race are such as to consume the food God has provided.

"Empress, the way is ready, and not long,
Beyond a row of myrtles, on a flat,
Fast by° a fountain, one small thicket past   *close by*
Of blowing myrrh and balm;³ if thou accept
630 My conduct,° I can bring thee thither soon."   *guidance*
    "Lead then," said Eve. He leading swiftly rolled
In tangles, and made intricate seem straight,
To mischief swift. Hope elevates, and joy
Brightens his crest, as when a wand'ring fire,°   *will-o'-the-wisp*
635 Compact° of unctuous° vapor, which the night   *composed / oily*
Condenses, and the cold environs round,
Kindled through agitation to a flame,
Which oft, they say, some evil spirit attends,
Hovering and blazing with delusive light,
640 Misleads th' amazed° night-wanderer from his way   *bewildered*
To bogs and mires, and oft through pond or pool,
There swallowed up and lost, from succor far.
So glistered the dire snake, and into fraud
Led Eve our credulous mother, to the tree
645 Of prohibition, root of all our woe;
Which when she saw, thus to her guide she spake:
    "Serpent, we might have spared our coming hither,
Fruitless to me, though fruit be here to excess,
The credit of whose virtue° rest with thee,   *power*
650 Wondrous indeed, if cause of such effects.
But of this tree we may not taste nor touch;
God so commanded, and left that command
Sole daughter of his voice;⁴ the rest, we live
Law to ourselves, our reason is our law."
655   To whom the Tempter guilefully replied:
"Indeed? hath God then said that of the fruit
Of all these garden trees ye shall not eat,
Yet lords declared of all in earth or air?"
    To whom thus Eve yet sinless: "Of the fruit
660 Of each tree in the garden we may eat,
But of the fruit of this fair tree amidst
The garden, God hath said, 'Ye shall not eat
Thereof, nor shall ye touch it, lest ye die.'"⁵
    She scarce had said, though brief, when now more bold
665 The Tempter, but with show of zeal and love
To man, and indignation at his wrong,
New part puts on, and as to passion moved,
Fluctuates disturbed, yet comely, and in act
Raised,⁶ as of some great matter to begin.
670 As when of old some orator renowned

3. Blooming trees that exude the aromatic gums
myrrh and balm (balsam).
4. God's only direct commandment (in Hebrew,
Bath Kol, "daughter of a voice" from heaven).
Otherwise (see following), they follow the moral
law of nature, known to them perfectly by their
unfallen reason, "our reason is our law."

5. Eve's formulation indicates her "sufficient"
understanding of the prohibition and the conditions of life in Eden. See 3.98–101.
6. Drawn up to full dignity. Satan as the snake
takes on the role of a Greek or Roman orator
defending liberty (lines 670–72), a Demosthenes
or a Cicero.

In Athens or free Rome, where eloquence
Flourished, since mute, to some great cause addressed,
Stood in himself collected, while each part,
Motion, each act won audience ere the tongue,°   *before speaking*
675 Sometimes in height began, as no delay
Of preface brooking[7] through his zeal of right.
So standing, moving, or to high upgrown
The Tempter all impassioned thus began:
   "O sacred, wise, and wisdom-giving plant,
680 Mother of science,° now I feel thy power   *knowledge*
Within me clear, not only to discern
Things in their causes, but to trace the ways
Of highest agents, deemed however wise.
Queen of this universe, do not believe
685 Those rigid threats of death; ye shall not die:
How should ye? By the fruit? It gives you life
To knowledge.[8] By the Threat'ner? Look on me,
Me who have touched and tasted, yet both live,
And life more perfect have attained than fate
690 Meant me, by vent'ring higher than my lot.
Shall that be shut to man, which to the beast
Is open? Or will God incense his ire
For such a petty trespass, and not praise
Rather your dauntless virtue,° whom the pain   *courage*
695 Of death denounced,° whatever thing death be,   *threatened*
Deterred not from achieving what might lead
To happier life, knowledge of good and evil;
Of good, how just?[9] Of evil, if what is evil
Be real, why not known, since easier shunned?
700 God therefore cannot hurt ye, and be just;
Not just, not God; not feared then,[1] nor obeyed:
Your fear itself of death removes the fear.
Why then was this forbid? Why but to awe,
Why but to keep ye low and ignorant,
705 His worshippers; he knows that in the day
Ye eat thereof, your eyes that seem so clear,
Yet are but dim, shall perfectly be then
Opened and cleared, and ye shall be as gods,[2]
Knowing both good and evil as they know.
710 That ye should be as gods, since I as man,
Internal man, is but proportion meet,
I of brute human, ye of human gods.[3]
So ye shall die perhaps, by putting off
Human, to put on gods, death to be wished,
715 Though threatened, which no worse than this can bring.

---

7. Bursting into the middle of his speech without a preface, and "upgrown" to the impassioned high style ("high") at once (lines 675–78).
8. I.e., life as well as knowledge, and a better life enhanced by knowledge, which Satan in the snake presents as a magical property of the tree.
9. I.e., how can it be just to forbid the knowledge of good?

1. Satan's sophism invites atheism: if God forbids knowledge of good and evil he is not just, therefore not God, therefore his threat of death need not be feared.
2. Hereafter, Satan speaks of "gods," not God.
3. Satan invites the aspiration to divinity, based on analogy to the supposed experience of the snake.

And what are gods that man may not become
As they, participating° godlike food?   *partaking of*
The gods are first, and that advantage use
On our belief, that all from them proceeds;
720   I question it, for this fair earth I see,
Warmed by the sun, producing every kind,
Them nothing: if they all° things, who enclosed   *produce all*
Knowledge of good and evil in this tree,
That whoso eats thereof, forthwith attains
725   Wisdom without their leave? And wherein lies
Th' offense, that man should thus attain to know?
What can your knowledge hurt him, or this tree
Impart against his will if all be his?
Or is it envy, and can envy dwell
730   In heav'nly breasts? These, these and many more
Causes import° your need of this fair fruit.   *prove*
Goddess humane,[4] reach then, and freely taste."
     He ended, and his words replete with guile
Into her heart too easy entrance won:
735   Fixed on the fruit she gazed, which to behold
Might tempt alone, and in her ears the sound
Yet rung of his persuasive words, impregned°   *impregnated*
With reason, to her seeming, and with truth;
Meanwhile the hour of noon drew on, and waked
740   An eager appetite, raised by the smell
So savory of that fruit, which with desire,
Inclinable now grown to touch or taste,
Solicited her longing eye; yet first
Pausing a while, thus to herself she mused:
745   "Great are thy virtues,° doubtless, best of fruits,   *powers*
Though kept from man, and worthy to be admired,
Whose taste, too long forborne, at first assay°   *try*
Gave elocution to the mute, and taught
The tongue not made for speech to speak thy praise:
750   Thy praise he also who forbids thy use,
Conceals not from us, naming thee the Tree
Of Knowledge, knowledge both of good and evil;
Forbids us then to taste, but his forbidding
Commends thee more, while it infers° the good   *implies*
755   By thee communicated, and our want:°   *lack*
For good unknown, sure is not had, or had
And yet unknown, is as not had at all.
In plain° then, what forbids he but to know,   *in plain words*
Forbids us good, forbids us to be wise?
760   Such prohibitions bind not. But if death
Bind us with after-bands,° what profits then   *later bonds*
Our inward freedom? In the day we eat
Of this fair fruit, our doom is, we shall die.
How dies the serpent? He hath eat'n and lives,
765   And knows, and speaks, and reasons, and discerns,

---

4. Both "human" and "gracious" or "kindly."

Irrational till then. For us alone
Was death invented? Or to us denied
This intellectual food, for beasts reserved?
For beasts it seems: yet that one beast which first
770 Hath tasted, envies° not, but brings with joy   *begrudges*
The good befall'n him, author unsuspect,[5]
Friendly to man, far from deceit or guile.
What fear I then, rather what know to fear
Under this ignorance of good and evil,
775 Of God or death, of law or penalty?
Here grows the cure of all, this fruit divine,
Fair to the eye, inviting to the taste,
Of virtue° to make wise: what hinders then   *power*
To reach, and feed at once both body and mind?"
780   So saying, her rash hand in evil hour
Forth reaching to the fruit, she plucked, she eat.[6]
Earth felt the wound, and nature from her seat
Sighing through all her works gave signs of woe,
That all was lost. Back to the thicket slunk
785 The guilty serpent, and well might, for Eve
Intent now wholly on her taste, naught else
Regarded, such delight till then, as seemed,
In fruit she never tasted, whether true
Or fancied so, through expectation high
790 Of knowledge, nor was godhead from her thought.
Greedily she engorged without restraint,
And knew not eating death:[7] satiate at length,
And heightened as with wine, jocund° and boon,°   *merry / jolly*
Thus to herself she pleasingly began:
795   "O sov'reign, virtuous, precious of all trees
In Paradise, of operation blest
To sapience, hitherto obscured, infamed,[8]
And thy fair fruit let hang, as to no end
Created; but henceforth my early care,
800 Not without song, each morning, and due praise
Shall tend thee, and the fertile burden ease
Of thy full branches offered free to all;
Till dieted by thee I grow mature
In knowledge, as the gods who all things know;
805 Though others envy what they cannot give;
For had the gift been theirs,[9] it had not here
Thus grown. Experience, next to thee I owe,
Best guide; not following thee, I had remained
In ignorance, thou open'st wisdom's way,
810 And giv'st accéss, though secret° she retire.   *hidden*
And I perhaps am secret;° Heav'n is high,   *unseen*
High and remote to see from thence distinct

---

5. An authority or informant beyond suspicion.
6. Ate: an accepted past tense, pronounced *et*.
7. I.e., she is eating death and doesn't know it, or experience it yet, but also, punning, death is eating her too.

8. Slandered. "Sapience": both knowledge and tasting (Latin *sapere*).
9. Like Satan, Eve now conflates gods and God, ascribing envy but also lack of power to "them."

Each thing on earth; and other care perhaps
May have diverted from continual watch
815 Our great Forbidder, safe with all his spies
About him. But to Adam in what sort°   *guise*
Shall I appear? Shall I to him make known
As yet my change, and give him to partake
Full happiness with me, or rather not,
820 But keep the odds° of knowledge in my power   *advantage*
Without copartner? so to add what wants°   *lacks*
In female sex, the more to draw his love,
And render me more equal, and perhaps,
A thing not undesirable, sometime
825 Superior; for inferior who is free?[1]
This may be well: but what if God have seen,
And death ensue? Then I shall be no more,
And Adam wedded to another Eve,
Shall live with her enjoying, I extinct;
830 A death to think. Confirmed then I resolve,
Adam shall share with me in bliss or woe:
So dear I love him, that with him all deaths
I could endure, without him live no life."
        So saying, from the tree her step she turned,
835 But first low reverence done, as to the power
That dwelt within,[2] whose presence had infused
Into the plant sciential° sap, derived   *knowledge-producing*
From nectar, drink of gods. Adam the while
Waiting desirous her return, had wove
840 Of choicest flow'rs a garland to adorn
Her tresses, and her rural labors crown,
As reapers oft are wont° their harvest queen.   *accustomed*
Great joy he promised to his thoughts, and new
Solace in her return, so long delayed;
845 Yet oft his heart, divine of° something ill,   *foreboding*
Misgave him; he the falt'ring measure° felt;   *heartbeat*
And forth to meet her went, the way she took
That morn when first they parted; by the Tree
Of Knowledge he must pass; there he her met,
850 Scarce from the tree returning; in her hand
A bough of fairest fruit that downy smiled,
New gathered, and ambrosial° smell diffused.   *fragrant*
To him she hasted, in her face excuse
Came prologue,[3] and apology to prompt,
855 Which with bland° words at will she thus addressed.   *mild, coaxing*
        "Hast thou not wondered, Adam, at my stay?
Thee I have missed, and thought it long, deprived
Thy presence, agony of love till now
Not felt, nor shall be twice, for never more
860 Mean I to try, what rash untried I sought,

1. Cf. Satan, 1.248–63, 5.790–97.
2. Eve ends with idolatry, worship of the tree.
3. I.e., excuse came like the prologue in a play,
and apology (justification, self-defense) served
as prompter.

The pain of absence from thy sight. But strange
Hath been the cause, and wonderful to hear:
This tree is not as we are told, a tree
Of danger tasted,° nor to evil unknown   *if tasted*
865 Op'ning the way, but of divine effect
To open eyes, and make them gods who taste;
And hath been tasted such: the serpent wise,
Or° not restrained as we, or not obeying,   *either*
Hath eaten of the fruit, and is become,
870 Not dead, as we are threatened, but thenceforth
Endued with human voice and human sense,
Reasoning to admiration,° and with me   *wonderfully well*
Persuasively° hath so prevailed, that I   *by persuasion*
Have also tasted, and have also found
875 Th' effects to correspond, opener mine eyes,
Dim erst,° dilated spirits, ampler heart,   *before*
And growing up to godhead; which for thee
Chiefly I sought, without thee can despise.
For bliss, as thou hast part, to me is bliss,
880 Tedious, unshared with thee, and odious soon.
Thou therefore also taste, that equal lot
May join us, equal joy, as equal love;
Lest thou not tasting, different degree°   *rank*
Disjoin us, and I then too late renounce
885 Deity for thee, when fate will not permit."[4]
    Thus Eve with count'nance blithe her story told;
But in her cheek distemper[5] flushing glowed.
On th' other side, Adam, soon as he heard
The fatal trespass done by Eve, amazed,°   *stunned*
890 Astonied° stood and blank, while horror chill   *petrified*
Ran through his veins, and all his joints relaxed;
From his slack hand the garland wreathed for Eve
Down dropped, and all the faded roses shed:
Speechless he stood and pale, till thus at length
895 First to himself he inward silence broke:
    "O fairest of creation, last and best
Of all God's works, creature in whom excelled
Whatever can to sight or thought be formed,
Holy, divine, good, amiable, or sweet!
900 How art thou lost, how on a sudden lost,
Defaced, deflow'red, and now to death devote?°   *doomed*
Rather how hast thou yielded to transgress
The strict forbiddance, how to violate
The sacred° fruit forbidd'n! Some cursèd fraud   *consecrated*
905 Of enemy hath beguiled thee, yet unknown,
And me with thee hath ruined, for with thee
Certain my resolution is to die;
How can I live without thee, how forgo
Thy sweet converse and love so dearly joined,

---

4. Compare Eve in soliloquy, lines 817–33.
5. I.e., disorder arising from disturbance of the balance of humors in the body, intoxication.

910 To live again in these wild woods forlorn?
Should God create another Eve, and I
Another rib afford, yet loss of thee
Would never from my heart; no no, I feel
The link of nature draw me: flesh of flesh,
915 Bone of my bone thou art,[6] and from thy state
Mine never shall be parted, bliss or woe."
　　So having said, as one from sad dismay
Recomforted, and after thoughts disturbed
Submitting to what seemed remédiless,
920 Thus in calm mood his words to Eve he turned:
　　"Bold deed thou hast presumed, advent'rous Eve,
And peril great provoked, who thus hast dared
Had it been only coveting to eye
That sacred fruit, sacred° to abstinence,　　　　　　　　　　*set apart*
925 Much more to taste it under ban to touch.
But past who can recall, or done undo?
Not God omnipotent, nor fate; yet so
Perhaps thou shalt not die, perhaps the fact°　　　　　　　　　*deed*
Is not so heinous now, foretasted fruit,
930 Profaned first by the serpent, by him first
Made common and unhallowed ere our taste;
Nor yet on him found deadly, he yet lives,
Lives, as thou saidst, and gains to live as man
Higher degree of life, inducement strong
935 To us, as likely tasting to attain
Proportional ascent, which cannot be
But to be gods, or angels demigods.
Nor can I think that God, Creator wise,
Though threat'ning, will in earnest so destroy
940 Us his prime creatures, dignified so high,
Set over all his works, which in our fall,
For us created, needs with us must fail,
Dependent made; so God shall uncreate,
Be frustrate, do, undo, and labor lose,
945 Not well conceived of God, who though his power
Creation could repeat, yet would be loath
Us to abolish, lest the Adversary°　　　　　　　　　　　　　*Satan*
Triumph and say; 'Fickle their state whom God
Most favors, who can please him long? Me first
950 He ruined, now mankind; whom will he next?'
Matter of scorn, not to be given the Foe.
However I with thee have fixed my lot,
Certain° to undergo like doom; if death　　　　　　　　　　　*resolved*
Consort° with thee, death is to me as life;　　　　　　　　　　*associate*
955 So forcible within my heart I feel
The bond of nature draw me to my own,
My own in thee, for what thou art is mine;
Our state cannot be severed, we are one,
One flesh; to lose thee were to lose myself."

6. Adam echoes Genesis 2.23–24.

960   So Adam, and thus Eve to him replied:
"O glorious trial of exceeding[7] love,
Illustrious evidence, example high!
Engaging me to emulate, but short
Of thy perfection, how shall I attain,
965 Adam, from whose dear side I boast me sprung,
And gladly of our union hear thee speak,
One heart, one soul in both; whereof good proof
This day affords, declaring thee resolved,
Rather than death or aught° than death more dread   *anything other*
970 Shall separate us, linked in love so dear,
To undergo with me one guilt, one crime,
If any be, of tasting this fair fruit,
Whose virtue,° for of good still good proceeds,   *power*
Direct, or by occasion° hath presented   *indirectly*
975 This happy trial of thy love, which else
So eminently never had been known.
Were it° I thought death menaced would ensue°   *if / result from*
This my attempt, I would sustain alone
The worst, and not persuade thee, rather die
980 Deserted, than oblige° thee with a fact°   *bind / deed*
Pernicious to thy peace, chiefly assured
Remarkably so late of thy so true,
So faithful love unequaled;[8] but I feel
Far otherwise th' event,° not death, but life   *result*
985 Augmented, opened eyes, new hopes, new joys,
Taste so divine, that what of sweet before
Hath touched my sense, flat seems to this, and harsh.
On my experience, Adam, freely taste,
And fear of death deliver to the winds."
990   So saying, she embraced him, and for joy
Tenderly wept, much won that he his love
Had so ennobled, as of choice to incur
Divine displeasure for her sake, or death.
In recompense (for such compliance bad
995 Such recompense best merits) from the bough
She gave him of that fair enticing fruit
With liberal hand: he scrupled not to eat
Against his better knowledge, not deceived,[9]
But fondly° overcome with female charm.   *foolishly*
1000 Earth trembled from her entrails, as again
In pangs, and nature gave a second groan;
Sky loured, and muttering thunder, some sad drops
Wept at completing of the mortal sin
Original;[1] while Adam took no thought,
1005 Eating his fill, nor Eve to iterate°   *repeat*

---

7. The word, which Eve intends as praise, carries the implication of "excessive."
8. I.e., since I have so recently been assured of your unparalleled love.
9. Cf. 1 Timothy 2.14: "And Adam was not deceived, but the woman being deceived was in the transgression."
1. The theological doctrine that all Adam's descendants are stained by Adam's sin and are thereby subject to physical death and (unless saved by grace) to damnation.

Her former trespass feared, the more to soothe
Him with her loved society, that now
As with new wine intoxicated both
They swim in mirth, and fancy that they feel
1010 Divinity within them breeding wings
Wherewith to scorn the earth: but that false fruit
Far other operation first displayed,
Carnal desire inflaming, he on Eve
Began to cast lascivious eyes, she him
1015 As wantonly repaid; in lust they burn:
Till Adam thus 'gan Eve to dalliance move:
    "Eve, now I see thou art exact of taste,
And elegant, of sapience[2] no small part,
Since to each meaning savor we apply,
1020 And palate call judicious; I the praise
Yield thee, so well this day thou hast purveyed.°   *provided*
Much pleasure we have lost, while we abstained
From this delightful fruit, nor known till now
True relish, tasting; if such pleasure be
1025 In things to us forbidden, it might be wished,
For this one tree had been forbidden ten.
But come, so well refreshed, now let us play,
As meet° is, after such delicious fare;   *appropriate*
For never did thy beauty since the day
1030 I saw thee first and wedded thee, adorned
With all perfections, so inflame my sense
With ardor to enjoy thee, fairer now
Than ever, bounty of this virtuous tree."
    So said he, and forbore not glance or toy°   *caress*
1035 Of amorous intent, well understood
Of° Eve, whose eye darted contagious fire.   *by*
Her hand he seized, and to a shady bank,
Thick overhead with verdant roof embow'red
He led her nothing loath; flow'rs were the couch,
1040 Pansies, and violets, and asphodel,
And hyacinth, earth's freshest softest lap.
There they their fill of love and love's disport
Took largely, of their mutual guilt the seal,
The solace of their sin, till dewy sleep
1045 Oppressed them, wearied with their amorous play.
Soon as the force of that fallacious fruit,
That with exhilarating vapor bland°   *pleasing*
About their spirits had played, and inmost powers
Made err, was now exhaled, and grosser sleep
1050 Bred of unkindly fumes,° with conscious dreams   *unnatural vapors*
Encumbered,° now had left them, up they rose   *oppressed*
As from unrest, and each the other viewing,
Soon found their eyes how opened, and their minds
How darkened; innocence, that as a veil

---

2. Adam commends Eve for her fine ("exact") and discriminating ("elegant") taste, as a part of "sapience," which means both "taste" and "wisdom."

1055	Had shadowed them from knowing ill, was gone,
	Just confidence, and native righteousness,
	And honor from about them, naked left
	To guilty shame: he° covered, but his robe
	Uncovered more. So rose the Danite strong
1060	Hercúlean Samson from the harlot-lap
	Of Philistéan Dálilah, and waked
	Shorn of his strength,[3] they destitute and bare
	Of all their virtue: silent, and in face
	Confounded long they sat, as strucken mute,
1065	Till Adam, though not less than Eve abashed,
	At length gave utterance to these words constrained:°
	"O Eve, in evil[4] hour thou didst give ear
	To that false worm, of whomsoever taught
	To counterfeit man's voice, true in our fall,
1070	False in our promised rising; since our eyes
	Opened we find indeed, and find we know
	Both good and evil, good lost and evil got,[5]
	Bad fruit of knowledge, if this be to know,
	Which leaves us naked thus, of honor void,
1075	Of innocence, of faith, of purity,
	Our wonted° ornaments now soiled and stained,
	And in our faces evident the signs
	Of foul concupiscence;[6] whence evil store;
	Even shame, the last of evils; of the first
1080	Be sure then. How shall I behold the face
	Henceforth of God or angel, erst with joy
	And rapture so oft beheld? Those heav'nly shapes
	Will dazzle now this earthly, with their blaze
	Insufferably bright. O might I here
1085	In solitude live savage, in some glade
	Obscured, where highest woods impenetrable
	To star or sunlight, spread their umbrage° broad,
	And brown as evening: cover me ye pines,
	Ye cedars, with innumerable boughs
1090	Hide me, where I may never see them more.
	But let us now, as in bad plight, devise
	What best may for the present serve to hide
	The parts of each from other, that seem most
	To shame obnoxious,° and unseemliest seen,
1095	Some tree whose broad smooth leaves together sewed,
	And girded on our loins, may cover round
	Those middle parts, that this newcomer, shame,
	There sit not, and reproach us as unclean."

Marginal glosses:
- *shame* (line 1058)
- *forced* (line 1066)
- *accustomed* (line 1076)
- *shadow, foliage* (line 1087)
- *exposed* (line 1094)

3. Samson, of the tribe of Dan, told the "harlot" Philistine Delilah that the secret of his strength (like that of Hercules) lay in his hair; she sheared it off while he slept, and when he awoke he was easily captured and blinded by his enemies.
4. Adam's bitter pun—Eve, evil—repudiates the actual etymology of Eve, "life," which Adam will later reaffirm (11.159–61).
5. Milton, like most commentators, derives the

tree's name from the event (4.222, 11.84–89).
6. The theological term for the unruly human passions and desires seen as one effect of the Fall, a sign of abundance ("store") of evils. If "shame" (see following lines) is the "last" evil, the "first" is probably the guiltiness that produces it, according to Milton's *Christian Doctrine* (1.12).

So counseled he, and both together went
1100 Into the thickest wood, there soon they chose
The fig tree,[7] not that kind for fruit renowned,
But such as at this day to Indians known
In Malabar or Deccan spreads her arms
Branching so broad and long, that in the ground
1105 The bended twigs take root, and daughters grow
About the mother tree, a pillared shade
High overarched, and echoing walks between;
There oft the Indian herdsman shunning heat
Shelters in cool, and tends his pasturing herds
1110 At loopholes cut through thickest shade: those leaves
They gathered, broad as Amazonian targe,°   shields
And with what skill they had, together sewed,
To gird their waist, vain covering if to hide
Their guilt and dreaded shame. O how unlike
1115 To that first naked glory. Such of late
Columbus found th' American so girt
With feathered cincture,° naked else and wild,   belt
Among the trees on isles and woody shores.
Thus fenced, and as they thought, their shame in part
1120 Covered, but not at rest or ease of mind,
They sat them down to weep, nor only tears
Rained at their eyes, but high winds worse within
Began to rise, high passions, anger, hate,
Mistrust, suspicion, discord, and shook sore
1125 Their inward state of mind, calm region once
And full of peace, now tossed and turbulent:
For understanding ruled not, and the will
Heard not her lore, both in subjection now
To sensual appetite, who from beneath
1130 Usurping over sov'reign reason claimed
Superior sway: from thus distempered breast,[8]
Adam, estranged° in look and altered style,   unlike himself
Speech intermitted° thus to Eve renewed: interrupted
        "Would thou hadst hearkened to my words, and stayed
1135 With me, as I besought thee, when that strange
Desire of wand'ring this unhappy morn,
I know not whence possessed thee; we had then
Remained still happy, not as now, despoiled
Of all our good, shamed, naked, miserable.
1140 Let none henceforth seek needless cause to approve°   prove
The faith they owe; when earnestly they seek
Such proof, conclude, they then begin to fail."
        To whom soon moved with touch of blame thus Eve:
"What words have passed thy lips, Adam severe,
1145 Imput'st thou that to my default, or will
Of wand'ring, as thou call'st it, which who knows

---

7. The banyan, or Indian fig, has small leaves, but the account Milton draws on from Gerard's *Herbal* (1597) contains the details of lines 1104–11; Malabar and Deccan (line 1103) are in south-ern India.

8. The immediate psychological effects of the Fall are evident in the subjection of reason to the lower faculties of sensual appetite.

But might as ill have happened thou being by,
Or to thyself perhaps: hadst thou been there,
Or here th' attempt, thou couldst not have discerned
1150 Fraud in the serpent, speaking as he spake;
No ground of enmity between us known,
Why he should mean me ill, or seek to harm.
Was I to have never parted from thy side?
As good have grown there still a lifeless rib.
1155 Being as I am, why didst not thou the head
Command me absolutely not to go,
Going into such danger as thou saidst?
Too facile° then thou didst not much gainsay,°   *easy, mild / oppose*
Nay didst permit, approve, and fair dismiss.
1160 Hadst thou been firm and fixed in thy dissent,
Neither had I transgressed, nor thou with me."
    To whom then first incensed Adam replied.
"Is this the love, is this the recompense
Of mine to thee, ingrateful Eve, expressed°   *demonstrated*
1165 Immutable when thou wert lost, not I,
Who might have lived and joyed immortal bliss,
Yet willingly chose rather death with thee:
And am I now upbraided, as the cause
Of thy transgressing? not enough severe,
1170 It seems, in thy restraint: what could I more?
I warned thee, I admonished thee, foretold
The danger, and the lurking enemy
That lay in wait; beyond this had been force,
And force upon free will hath here no place.
1175 But confidence then bore thee on, secure°   *self-assured*
Either to meet no danger, or to find
Matter of glorious trial; and perhaps
I also erred in overmuch admiring
What seemed in thee so perfect, that I thought
1180 No evil durst attempt thee, but I rue
That error now, which is become my crime,
And thou th' accuser. Thus it shall befall
Him who to worth in women overtrusting
Lets her will rule; restraint she will not brook,°   *accept*
1185 And left to herself, if evil thence ensue,
She first his weak indulgence will accuse."
    Thus they in mutual accusation spent
The fruitless hours, but neither self-condemning,
And of their vain contést appeared no end.

Book 10

Meanwhile the heinous and despiteful act
Of Satan done in Paradise, and how
He in the serpent had perverted Eve,
Her husband she, to taste the fatal fruit,

5   Was known in Heav'n; for what can scape the eye
    Of God all-seeing, or deceive his heart
    Omniscient, who in all things wise and just,
    Hindered not Satan to attempt the mind
    Of man, with strength entire, and free will armed,
10   Complete° to have discovered and repulsed   *fully equipped*
    Whatever wiles of foe or seeming friend.
    For still they knew, and ought to have still° remembered   *always*
    The high injunction not to taste that fruit,
    Whoever tempted; which they not obeying,
15   Incurred, what could they less, the penalty,
    And manifold in sin, deserved to fall.
    Up into Heav'n from Paradise in haste
    Th' angelic guards ascended, mute and sad
    For man, for of his state by this° they knew,   *this time*
20   Much wond'ring how the subtle Fiend had stol'n
    Entrance unseen. Soon as th' unwelcome news
    From earth arrived at Heaven gate, displeased
    All were who heard, dim sadness did not spare
    That time celestial visages, yet mixed
25   With pity, violated not their bliss.
    About the new-arrived, in multitudes
    Th' ethereal people ran, to hear and know
    How all befell: they towards the throne supreme
    Accountable made haste to make appear
30   With righteous plea, their utmost vigilance,
    And easily approved;[1] when the Most High
    Eternal Father from his secret cloud,
    Amidst in thunder uttered thus his voice:
       "Assembled Angels, and ye Powers returned
35   From unsuccessful charge, be not dismayed,
    Nor troubled at these tidings from the earth,
    Which your sincerest care could not prevent,
    Foretold so lately what would come to pass,
    When first this tempter crossed the gulf from Hell.
40   I told ye then he should prevail and speed°   *succeed*
    On his bad errand, man should be seduced
    And flattered out of all, believing lies
    Against his Maker; no decree of mine
    Concurring to necessitate his fall,
45   Or touch with lightest moment[2] of impulse
    His free will, to her own inclining left
    In even scale. But fall'n he is, and now
    What rests,° but that the mortal sentence pass   *remains*
    On his transgression, death denounced° that day,   *decreed*
50   Which he presumes already vain and void,
    Because not yet inflicted, as he feared,
    By some immediate stroke; but soon shall find

---

1. The angels, "accountable" for guarding Eden, rush to God's throne to explain that they had exercised "utmost vigilance"; their plea is readily accepted ("easily approved").
2. The smallest weight that would tip the scales.

Forbearance no acquittance ere day end.[3]
Justice shall not return as bounty scorned.
55 But whom send I to judge them? Whom but thee
Vicegerent Son, to thee I have transferred
All judgment, whether in Heav'n, or earth, or Hell.[4]
Easy it may be seen that I intend
Mercy colleague with justice, sending thee
60 Man's friend, his mediator, his designed
Both ransom and redeemer voluntary,
And destined man himself to judge man fall'n."
    So spake the Father, and unfolding bright
Toward the right hand his glory, on the Son
65 Blazed forth unclouded deity; he full
Resplendent all his Father manifest
Expressed, and thus divinely answered mild:
    "Father Eternal, thine is to decree,
Mine both in Heav'n and earth to do thy will
70 Supreme, that thou in me thy Son beloved
May'st ever rest well pleased. I go to judge
On earth these thy transgressors; but thou know'st,
Whoever judged, the worst on me must light,
When time shall be, for so I undertook
75 Before thee; and not repenting, this obtain
Of right, that I may mitigate their doom
On me derived,° yet I shall temper so   diverted
Justice with mercy, as may illustrate most°   best show
Them fully satisfied, and thee appease.
80 Attendance none shall need, nor train,° where none   attendants
Are to behold the judgment, but the judged,
Those two; the third best absent is condemned,
Convict° by flight, and rebel to all law: proved guilty
Conviction to the serpent none belongs."
85   Thus saying, from his radiant seat he rose
Of high collateral° glory: him Thrones and Powers,   placed side by side
Princedoms, and Dominations ministrant
Accompanied to Heaven gate, from whence
Eden and all the coast° in prospect lay.   region
90 Down he descended straight; the speed of gods
Time counts not,[5] though with swiftest minutes winged.
Now was the sun in western cadence° low   falling
From noon, and gentle airs due at their hour
To fan the earth now waked, and usher in
95 The evening cool, when he from wrath more cool
Came the mild Judge and Intercessor both
To sentence man: the voice of God they heard
Now walking in the garden, by soft winds
Brought to their ears, while day declined; they heard,

---

3. A proverb: "Abstinence from enforcing a debt
is not release from it." Next line: My justice must
not be scorned as my generosity has been.
4. Cf. John 5.22: "For the Father judgeth no
man, but hath committed all judgment unto the

Son."
5. The Son's descent is immediate; Raphael had
taken much of the morning to travel from
Heaven to earth (8.110–14).

100 And from his presence hid themselves among
The thickest trees, both man and wife, till God
Approaching, thus to Adam called aloud.
    "Where art thou Adam, wont° with joy to meet   *used before*
My coming seen far off? I miss thee here,
105 Not pleased, thus entertained with solitude,
Where obvious duty erewhile appeared unsought:
Or come I less conspicuous, or what change
Absents thee, or what chance detains? Come forth."
He came, and with him Eve, more loath, though first
110 To offend, discount'nanced both, and discomposed;
Love was not in their looks, either to God
Or to each other, but apparent° guilt,   *easily seen*
And shame, and perturbation, and despair,
Anger, and obstinacy, and hate, and guile.
115 Whence Adam falt'ring long, thus answered brief:
    "I heard thee in the garden, and of thy voice
Afraid, being naked, hid myself." To whom
The gracious Judge without revile° replied: *abuse*
    "My voice thou oft hast heard, and hast not feared,
120 But still° rejoiced, how is it now become   *always*
So dreadful to thee? That thou art naked, who
Hath told thee? Hast thou eaten of the tree
Whereof I gave thee charge thou shouldst not eat?"
    To whom thus Adam sore beset replied.
125 "O Heav'n! in evil strait this day I stand
Before my Judge, either to undergo
Myself the total crime, or to accuse
My other self, the partner of my life;
Whose failing, while her faith to me remains,
130 I should conceal, and not expose to blame
By my complaint; but strict necessity
Subdues me, and calamitous constraint,
Lest on my head both sin and punishment,
However insupportable, be all
135 Devolved;° though should I hold my peace, yet thou   *fallen on*
Wouldst easily detect what I conceal.
This woman whom thou mad'st to be my help,
And gav'st me as thy perfect gift, so good,
So fit, so acceptáble, so divine,
140 That from her hand I could suspect no ill,
And what she did, whatever in itself,
Her doing seemed to justify the deed;
She gave me of the tree, and I did eat."[6]
    To whom the Sov'reign Presence thus replied.
145 "Was she thy God, that her thou didst obey
Before his voice, or was she made thy guide,
Superior, or but equal, that to her
Thou didst resign thy manhood, and the place

6. Compare Adam's speech in Genesis 3.12, and the elements Milton adds of complaint, veiled accusation of God, and self-exculpation; also compare Eve's answer in Genesis 3.13 and in lines 159–62 below.

Wherein God set thee above her made of thee,
150 And for thee,[7] whose perfection far excelled
Hers in all real dignity: adorned
She was indeed, and lovely to attract
Thy love, not thy subjection, and her gifts
Were such as under government well seemed,
155 Unseemly to bear rule, which was thy part
And person,[8] hadst thou known thyself aright."
    So having said, he thus to Eve in few°   *few words*
"Say woman, what is this which thou hast done?"
    To whom sad Eve with shame nigh overwhelmed,
160 Confessing soon, yet not before her Judge
Bold or loquacious, thus abashed replied:
"The serpent me beguiled and I did eat."
    Which when the Lord God heard, without delay
To judgment he proceeded on th' accused
165 Serpent though brute, unable to transfer
The guilt on him who made him instrument
Of mischief, and polluted from the end°   *purpose*
Of his creation; justly then accursed,
As vitiated in nature:[9] more to know
170 Concerned not man (since he no further knew)
Nor altered his offense; yet God at last
To Satan first in sin his doom applied,
Though in mysterious terms, judged as then best:
And on the serpent thus his curse let fall.
175   "Because thou hast done this, thou art accursed
Above all cattle, each beast of the field;
Upon thy belly groveling thou shalt go,
And dust shalt eat all the days of thy life.
Between thee and the woman I will put
180 Enmity, and between thine and her Seed;
Her Seed shall bruise thy head, thou bruise his heel."[1]
    So spake this oracle, then verified
When Jesus son of Mary second Eve,
Saw Satan fall like lightning down from Heav'n,[2]
185 Prince of the air; then rising from his grave
Spoiled Principalities and Powers, triumphed
In open show, and with ascension bright
Captivity led captive through the air,
The realm itself of Satan long usurped,
190 Whom he shall tread at last under our feet;
Ev'n he who now foretold his fatal bruise,

---

7. Cf. 1 Corinthians 11.8–9: "For the man is not of the woman; but the woman of the man. / Neither was the man created for the woman; but the woman for the man."
8. Role and character (persona), as in a drama.
9. The serpent was "unable to transfer" (line 165) his own guilt in being "polluted" from his proper end and nature onto Satan, who made him "instrument," so he was "justly . . . accursed," but the terms of that judgment have a "mysterious" (line 173) or hidden meaning that applies to Satan.

1. This is the so-called protoevangelion or judgment of the Serpent (Satan) that contains at the same time the promise of the Redeemer ("her Seed"); Adam and Eve are led to understand it by degrees.
2. Cf. Christ's comment to his disciples (Luke 10.18: "I beheld Satan as lightning fall from heaven"), and also Colossians 2.15 and Ephesians 4.8, to the following lines, 185–88.

And to the woman thus his sentence turned.
   "Thy sorrow I will greatly multiply
By thy conception; children thou shalt bring
195 In sorrow forth, and to thy husband's will
Thine shall submit, he over thee shall rule."
   On Adam last thus judgment he pronounced.
"Because thou hast hearkened to the voice of thy wife,
And eaten of the tree concerning which
200 I charged thee, saying: Thou shalt not eat thereof,
Cursed is the ground for thy sake, thou in sorrow
Shalt eat thereof all the days of thy life;
Thorns also and thistles it shall bring thee forth
Unbid, and thou shalt eat th' herb of the field,
205 In the sweat of thy face shalt thou eat bread,
Till thou return unto the ground, for thou
Out of the ground wast taken: know thy birth,
For dust thou art, and shalt to dust return."
   So judged he man, both judge and savior sent,
210 And th' instant stroke of death denounced° that day   *announced*
Removed far off; then pitying how they stood
Before him naked to the air, that now
Must suffer change, disdained not to begin
Thenceforth the form of servant to assume,
215 As when he washed his servants' feet,[3] so now
As father of his family he clad
Their nakedness with skins of beasts, or° slain,   *either*
Or as the snake with youthful coat repaid;
And thought not much° to clothe his enemies: *too much*
220 Nor he their outward only with the skins
Of beasts, but inward nakedness, much more
Opprobrious, with his robe of righteousness,
Arraying covered from his Father's sight.
To him with swift ascent he up returned,
225 Into his blissful bosom reassumed
In glory as of old, to him appeased
All, though all-knowing, what had passed with man
Recounted, mixing intercession sweet.
   Meanwhile ere thus was sinned and judged on earth,
230 Within the gates of Hell sat Sin and Death,
In counterview within the gates, that now
Stood open wide, belching outrageous° flame   *unrestrained*
Far into Chaos, since the Fiend passed through,
Sin opening, who thus now to Death began:
235   "O son, why sit we here each other viewing
Idly, while Satan our great author° thrives   *father*
In other worlds, and happier seat provides
For us his offspring dear? It cannot be,
But that success attends him; if mishap,
240 Ere this he had returned, with fury driv'n

3. Cf. Philippians 2.7: "[Christ] took upon him the form of a servant"; John 13.5: "he poureth water into a basin, and began to wash the disciples' feet."

By his avengers, since no place like° this   *as well as*
Can fit his punishment, or their revenge.
Methinks I feel new strength within me rise,
Wings growing, and dominion giv'n me large
245   Beyond this deep; whatever draws me on,
Or sympathy, or some connatural force
Powerful at greatest distance to unite
With secret amity things of like kind
By secretest conveyance.[4] Thou my shade
250   Inseparable must with me along:
For Death from Sin no power can separate.
But lest the difficulty of passing back
Stay his return perhaps over this gulf
Impassable, impervious,° let us try   *impenetrable*
255   Advent'rous work, yet to thy power and mine
Not unagreeable, to found° a path   *establish*
Over this main from Hell to that new world
Where Satan now prevails, a monument
Of merit high to all th' infernal host,
260   Easing their passage hence, for intercourse,°   *passing back and forth*
Or transmigration,° as their lot shall lead.   *emigration*
Nor can I miss the way, so strongly drawn
By this new-felt attraction and instínct."
      Whom thus the meager° shadow answered soon: *emaciated*
265   "Go whither fate and inclination strong
Leads thee, I shall not lag behind, nor err
The way, thou leading, such a scent I draw
Of carnage, prey innumerable, and taste
The savor of death from all things there that live:
270   Nor shall I to the work thou enterprisest
Be wanting, but afford thee equal aid."
      So saying, with delight he snuffed the smell
Of mortal change on earth. As when a flock
Of ravenous fowl, though many a league remote,
275   Against° the day of battle, to a field,   *anticipating*
Where armies lie encamped, come flying, lured
With scent of living carcasses designed°   *marked out*
For death, the following day, in bloody fight.
So scented the grim feature,° and upturned   *form, shape*
280   His nostril wide into the murky air,
Sagacious° of his quarry from so far.   *keenly smelling, wise*
Then both from out Hell gates into the waste
Wide anarchy of Chaos damp and dark
Flew diverse,° and with power (their power was great)   *in different directions*
285   Hovering upon the water, what they met
Solid or slimy, as in raging sea
Tossed up and down, together crowded drive
From each side shoaling° towards the mouth of Hell.   *assembling*
As when two polar winds blowing adverse

---

4. Sin feels an attraction ("sympathy") drawing two things together, or an innate ("connatural") force, linking her to Satan.

290 Upon the Cronian Sea,[5] together drive
Mountains of ice, that stop th' imagined way
Beyond Petsora eastward, to the rich
Cathaian coast. The aggregated soil
Death with his mace petrific,[6] cold and dry,
295 As with a trident smote, and fixed as firm
As Delos floating once; the rest his look
Bound with Gorgonian rigor not to move,[7]
And with asphaltic slime;° broad as the gate,   *pitch*
Deep to the roots of Hell the gathered beach
300 They fastened, and the mole° immense wrought on   *pier*
Over the foaming deep high-arched, a bridge
Of length prodigious joining to the wall°   *outer shell*
Immovable of this now fenceless world
Forfeit to Death; from hence a passage broad,
305 Smooth, easy, inoffensive° down to Hell.   *free from obstacle*
So, if great things to small may be compared,
Xerxes,[8] the liberty of Greece to yoke,
From Susa his Memnonian palace high
Came to the sea, and over Hellespont
310 Bridging his way, Europe with Asia joined,
And scourged with many a stroke th' indignant waves.
Now had they brought the work by wondrous art
Pontifical,[9] a ridge of pendent rock
Over the vexed° abyss, following the track   *stormy*
315 Of Satan, to the selfsame place where he
First lighted from his wing, and landed safe
From out of Chaos to the outside bare
Of this round world: with pins of adamant
And chains they made all fast, too fast they made
320 And durable; and now in little space
The confines° met of empyrean Heav'n   *boundaries*
And of this world, and on the left hand Hell
With long reach interposed; three sev'ral ways
In sight, to each of these three places led.[1]
325 And now their way to earth they had descried,°   *perceived*
To Paradise first tending, when behold
Satan in likeness of an angel bright
Betwixt the Centaur and the Scorpion[2] steering
His zenith, while the sun in Aries rose:
330 Disguised he came, but those his children dear

5. The Arctic Ocean; the "imagined way" (lines 291–93) is the Northeast Passage to North China ("Cathay") from Pechora ("Petsora"), a river in Siberia, which Henry Hudson could only imagine (in 1608) because it was blocked with ice.
6. Turning things to stone.
7. Anything the Gorgon Medusa looked upon turned to stone. Death's materials are the "cold and dry" elements; his mace is associated with Neptune's "trident," which was said to have "fixed" the floating Greek island of Delos.
8. The Persian king Xerxes ordered the sea whipped when it destroyed the bridge of ships he built over the Hellespont (linking Europe and Asia) so as to invade Greece. "Susa" (next line): Xerxes' winter residence, founded by the mythical prince Memnon.
9. Bridge-building, with a pun on "papal" (the pope had the title "pontifex maximus").
1. The golden staircase or chain linking the universe to Heaven, the new bridge linking it to Hell, and the passage through the spheres down to earth.
2. Satan steered between Sagittarius ("the Centaur") and Scorpio, thereby passing through Anguis, the constellation of the Serpent.

Their parent soon discerned, though in disguise.
He, after Eve seduced, unminded° slunk   *unnoticed*
Into the wood fast by, and changing shape
To observe the sequel, saw his guileful act
335   By Eve, though all unweeting,° seconded   *unaware*
Upon her husband, saw their shame that sought
Vain covertures;° but when he saw descend   *garments*
The Son of God to judge them, terrified
He fled, not hoping to escape, but shun
340   The present, fearing guilty what his wrath
Might suddenly inflict; that past, returned
By night, and list'ning where the hapless pair
Sat in their sad discourse, and various plaint,
Thence gathered his own doom, which understood
345   Not instant, but of future time.[3] With joy
And tidings fraught, to Hell he now returned,
And at the brink of Chaos, near the foot
Of this new wondrous pontifice,° unhoped   *bridge*
Met who to meet him came, his offspring dear.
350   Great joy was at their meeting, and at sight
Of that stupendous bridge his joy increased.
Long he admiring stood, till Sin, his fair
Enchanting daughter, thus the silence broken:
     "O parent, these are thy magnific deeds,
355   Thy trophies,[4] which thou view'st as not thine own,
Thou art their author and prime architect:
For I no sooner in my heart divined,
My heart, which by a secret harmony
Still moves with thine, joined in connection sweet,
360   That thou on earth hadst prospered, which thy looks
Now also evidence, but straight° I felt   *at once*
Though distant from thee worlds between, yet felt
That I must after thee with this thy son;
Such fatal consequence[5] unites us three:
365   Hell could no longer hold us in her bounds,
Nor this unvoyageable gulf obscure
Detain from following thy illustrious track.
Thou hast achieved our liberty, confined
Within Hell gates till now, thou us empow'red
370   To fortify thus far, and overlay
With this portentous° bridge the dark abyss.   *marvelous, ominous*
Thine now is all this world, thy virtue° hath won   *power, courage*
What thy hands builded not, thy wisdom gained
With odds° what war hath lost, and fully avenged   *advantage*
375   Our foil in Heav'n; here thou shalt monarch reign,
There didst not; there let him still victor sway,
As battle hath adjudged, from this new world

---

3. This evidently refers to the plaints and discourse of Adam and Eve (lines 720–1104 below), which therefore precede Satan's return to Hell (lines 345–609).
4. Objects or persons captured in battle were displayed in the Triumphs accorded Roman generals and emperors who had won a great military victory; the term casts Satan's conquests in Eden in such terms.
5. Connection of cause and effect.

Retiring, by his own doom alienated,
And henceforth monarchy with thee divide
380 Of all things parted by th' empyreal bounds,
His quadrature, from thy orbicular world,[6]
Or try° thee now more dangerous to his throne."   *discover by experience*
    Whom thus the Prince of Darkness answered glad:
"Fair daughter, and thou son and grandchild both,
385 High proof ye now have giv'n to be the race
Of Satan (for I glory in the name,
Antagonist[7] of Heav'n's Almighty King)
Amply have merited of me, of all
Th' infernal empire, that so near Heav'n's door
390 Triumphal with triumphal act[8] have met,
Mine with this glorious work, and made one realm
Hell and this world, one realm, one continent
Of easy thoroughfare. Therefore while I
Descend through darkness, on your road with ease
395 To my associate powers, them to acquaint
With these successes, and with them rejoice,
You two this way, among those numerous orbs
All yours, right down to Paradise descend;
There dwell and reign in bliss, thence on the earth
400 Dominion exercise and in the air,
Chiefly on man, sole lord of all declared,
Him first make sure your thrall,° and lastly kill.   *slave*
My substitutes I send ye, and create
Plenipotent° on earth, of matchless might   *with full power*
405 Issuing from me: on your joint vigor now
My hold of this new kingdom all depends,
Through Sin to Death exposed by my exploit.
If your joint power prevail, th' affairs of Hell
No detriment need fear, go and be strong."
410   So saying he dismissed them, they with speed
Their course through thickest constellations held
Spreading their bane;° the blasted° stars looked wan,   *poison / ruined*
And planets, planet-strook,[9] real eclipse
Then suffered. Th' other way Satan went down
415 The causey° to Hell gate; on either side   *causeway*
Disparted Chaos over-built exclaimed,
And with rebounding surge the bars assailed,
That scorned his indignation.[1] Through the gate,
Wide open and unguarded, Satan passed,
420 And all about found desolate; for those[2]
Appointed to sit there, had left their charge,

---

6. Revelation 21.16 describes the City of God as "foursquare, and the length is as large as the breadth"; Satan's new conquest, earth, is an orb. Sin may imply its superiority (being a sphere).
7. The name "Satan" means "adversary" or "antagonist."
8. The repeated word emphasizes that Satan is enacting a Triumph, passing over a triumphal bridge rather than through triumphal arches;

the scene would likely evoke the "Roman" Triumph and triumphal arches celebrating the Restoration of Charles II.
9. Suffering not merely a temporary eclipse but a real loss of light, as from the malign influence of an adverse planet.
1. Chaos is the instinctive enemy of all order, so hostile to the bridge built over it.
2. Sin and Death.

Flown to the upper world; the rest were all
Far to the inland retired, about the walls
Of Pandemonium, city and proud seat
425 Of Lucifer, so by allusion° called,   *metaphor*
Of that bright star to Satan paragoned.[3]
There kept their watch the legions, while the grand[4]
In council sat, solicitous° what chance   *anxious*
Might intercept their emperor sent, so he
430 Departing gave command, and they observed.
As when the Tartar from his Russian foe
By Astracan over the snowy plains
Retires, or Bactrian Sophi from the horns
Of Turkish crescent, leaves all waste beyond
435 The realm of Aladule, in his retreat
To Tauris or Casbeen:[5] so these the late
Heav'n-banished host, left desert utmost Hell
Many a dark league, reduced° in careful watch   *drawn together*
Round their metropolis, and now expecting
440 Each hour their great adventurer from the search
Of foreign worlds: he through the midst unmarked,°   *unnoticed*
In show plebeian angel militant
Of lowest order, passed; and from the door
Of that Plutonian[6] hall, invisible
445 Ascended his high throne, which under state°   *canopy*
Of richest texture spread, at th' upper end
Was placed in regal luster. Down a while
He sat, and round about him saw unseen:
At last as from a cloud his fulgent head
450 And shape star-bright appeared, or brighter, clad
With what permissive° glory since his fall   *permitted*
Was left him, or false glitter: all amazed
At that so sudden blaze the Stygian[7] throng
Bent their aspéct, and whom they wished beheld,
455 Their mighty chief returned: loud was th' acclaim:
Forth rushed in haste the great consulting peers,
Raised from their dark divan,[8] and with like joy
Congratulant approached him, who with hand
Silence, and with these words attention won:
460   "Thrones, Dominations, Princedoms, Virtues, Powers,
For in possession such, not only of right,
I call ye[9] and declare ye now, returned
Successful beyond hope, to lead ye forth

3. Satan before his fall was Lucifer, the Light-
bringer, and the morning star is named Lucifer
because it is compared ("paragoned") to him.
4. The "grand infernal peers" who govern (cf.
2.507).
5. The simile, begun in line 431, compares the
fallen angels, withdrawn from other regions of
Hell to guard their metropolis, to Tartars retiring before attacking Russians and Persians
retreating before the attacking Turks. "Astracan": a region west of the Caspian Sea inhabited
by Russia and defended against Turks and Tar-

tars; "Aladule": the region of Armenia, from
which the last Persian ruler, called Anadule, a
"Bactrian Sophi" (Persian shah), was forced to
retreat from the Turks, to Tabriz ("Tauris") and
Kazvin ("Casbeen").
6. Pertaining to Pluto, ruler of the classical
underworld.
7. Of the river Styx in Hades, the river of hate.
8. The Turkish Council of State.
9. I.e., you now have these titles not only by
right but by possession (from the conquest on
earth).

Triumphant out of this infernal pit
465 Abominable, accurst, the house of woe,
And dungeon of our tyrant: now possess,
As lords, a spacious world, to our native Heaven
Little inferior, by my adventure hard
With peril great achieved. Long were to tell
470 What I have done, what suffered, with what pain
Voyaged th' unreal,° vast, unbounded deep   *unformed*
Of horrible confusion, over which
By Sin and Death a broad way now is paved
To expedite your glorious march; but I
475 Toiled out my uncouth° passage, forced to ride   *strange*
Th' untractable abyss, plunged in the womb
Of unoriginal[1] Night and Chaos wild,
That jealous of their secrets fiercely opposed
My journey strange, with clamorous uproar
480 Protesting Fate[2] supreme; thence how I found
The new-created world, which fame in Heav'n
Long had foretold, a fabric wonderful
Of absolute perfection, therein man
Placed in a paradise, by our exile
485 Made happy: him by fraud I have seduced
From his Creator, and the more to increase
Your wonder, with an apple. He thereat
Offended, worth your laughter, hath giv'n up
Both his beloved man and all his world,
490 To Sin and Death a prey, and so to us,
Without our hazard, labor, or alarm,
To range in, and to dwell, and over man
To rule, as over all he should have ruled.
True is, me also he hath judged, or rather
495 Me not, but the brute serpent in whose shape
Man I deceived; that which to me belongs,
Is enmity, which he will put between
Me and mankind; I am to bruise his heel;
His seed, when is not set, shall bruise my head:
500 A world who would not purchase with a bruise,
Or much more grievous pain? Ye have th' account
Of my performance: what remains, ye gods,
But up and enter now into full bliss."[3]
     So having said, a while he stood, expecting
505 Their universal shout and high applause
To fill his ear, when contrary he hears
On all sides, from innumerable tongues
A dismal universal hiss, the sound
Of public scorn; he wondered, but not long
510 Had leisure, wond'ring at himself now more;
His visage drawn he felt to sharp and spare,

1. Having no origin, uncreated.
2. Protesting both to and against Fate.
3. Ironically, the final word of Satan's proud, triumphal speech rhymes with and so prepares for the "hiss" (line 508) that will soon greet him, as his would-be triumph is turned by God to abject humiliation.

His arms clung to his ribs, his legs entwining
Each other, till supplanted° down he fell   *tripped up*
A monstrous serpent on his belly prone,
515 Reluctant,° but in vain, a greater power   *struggling*
Now ruled him, punished in the shape he sinned,
According to his doom: he would have spoke,
But hiss for hiss returned with forkèd tongue
To forkèd tongue, for now were all transformed
520 Alike, to serpents[4] all as accessories
To his bold riot:° dreadful was the din   *revolt*
Of hissing through the hall, thick swarming now
With complicated° monsters, head and tail,   *tangled*
Scorpion and asp, and amphisbaena dire,
525 Cerastes horned, hydrus, and ellops drear,
And dipsas[5] (not so thick swarmed once the soil
Bedropped with blood of Gorgon, or the isle
Ophiusa)[6] but still greatest he the midst,
Now dragon grown, larger than whom the sun
530 Engendered in the Pythian vale on slime,
Huge Python,[7] and his power no less he seemed
Above the rest still to retain; they all
Him followed issuing forth to th' open field,
Where all yet left of that revolted rout
535 Heav'n-fall'n, in station stood or just array,[8]
Sublime° with expectation when to see   *raised up*
In triumph issuing forth their glorious chief;
They saw, but other sight instead, a crowd
Of ugly serpents; horror on them fell,
540 And horrid sympathy; for what they saw,
They felt themselves now changing; down their arms,
Down fell both spear and shield, down they as fast,
And the dire hiss renewed, and the dire form
Catched by contagion, like in punishment,
545 As in their crime. Thus was th' applause they meant,
Turned to exploding hiss, triumph to shame
Cast on themselves from their own mouths. There stood
A grove hard by, sprung up with this their change,
His will who reigns above, to aggravate
550 Their penance,° laden with fair fruit, like that   *punishment*
Which grew in Paradise, the bait of Eve
Used by the Tempter: on that prospect strange
Their earnest eyes they fixed, imagining
For one forbidden tree a multitude
555 Now ris'n, to work them further woe or shame;

---

4. The scene recalls Dante's vivid description of
the thieves metamorphosed to snakes in *Inferno*
24–25.
5. The "scorpion" has a venomous sting at the
tip of the tail; "asp" is a small Egyptian viper;
"amphisbaena" supposedly had a head at each
end; "Cerastes" is an asp with horny projections
over each eye; "hydrus" and "ellops" were mythical water snakes; "dipsas" was a mythical snake
whose bite caused raging thirst.
6. Drops of blood from the Gorgon Medusa's
severed head turned into snakes; "Ophiusa" in
Greek means "isle of snakes."
7. A gigantic serpent engendered from the slime
left by Deucalion's flood; Apollo slew him and
appropriated the "Pythian" vale and shrine at
Delphi.
8. I.e., at their posts or on parade.

Yet parched with scalding thirst and hunger fierce,
Though to delude them sent, could not abstain,
But on they rolled in heaps, and up the trees
Climbing, sat thicker than the snaky locks
560 That curled Megaera:[9] greedily they plucked
The fruitage fair to sight, like that which grew
Near that bituminous lake where Sodom flamed;[1]
This more delusive, not the touch, but taste
Deceived; they fondly° thinking to allay   *foolishly*
565 Their appetite with gust,° instead of fruit   *relish*
Chewed bitter ashes, which th' offended taste
With spattering noise rejected: oft they assayed,°   *attempted*
Hunger and thirst constraining, drugged as oft,
With hatefulest disrelish writhed their jaws
570 With soot and cinders filled; so oft they fell
Into the same illusion, not as man
Whom they triumphed once lapsed.[2] Thus were they plagued
And worn with famine, long and ceaseless hiss,
Till their lost shape, permitted, they resumed,[3]
575 Yearly enjoined, some say, to undergo
This annual humbling certain numbered days,
To dash their pride, and joy for man seduced.
However some tradition they dispersed
Among the heathen of their purchase° got,   *plunder*
580 And fabled how the serpent, whom they called
Ophion with Eurynome, the wide-
Encroaching Eve perhaps, had first the rule
Of high Olympus, thence by Saturn driv'n
And Ops, ere yet Dictaean Jove was born.[4]
585 Meanwhile in Paradise the hellish pair
Too soon arrived, Sin there in power before,
Once actual, now in body, and to dwell
Habitual habitant;[5] behind her Death
Close following pace for pace, not mounted yet
590 On his pale horse:[6] to whom Sin thus began:
  "Second of Satan sprung, all-conquering Death,
What think'st thou of our empire now, though earned
With travail° difficult, not better far   *labor*
Than still at Hell's dark threshold to have sat watch,
595 Unnamed, undreaded, and thyself half-starved?"
  Whom thus the Sin-born monster answered soon:

9. One of three Furies with snaky hair.
1. Sodom apples reputedly grew on the spot where the accursed city once stood, now the Dead Sea ("that bituminous lake"); the apples look good but dissolve into ashes when eaten.
2. Unlike man who fell once, they try to eat the dissolving apples over and over again.
3. God permitted them to regain their "lost shape" as fallen angels; but they are undergoing a slower, natural metamorphosis into grosser substance by their continuing commitment to and choice of evil.
4. The Titan Ophion (whose name means

"snake") and his wife Eurynome ("the wide-reacher") ruled Olympus until driven away by "Saturn" and his wife Ops, who were in turn overthrown by Jove, who lived on the mountain Dicte. Milton suggests that these may represent versions of the story transmitted by the fallen angels to the pagans (lines 578–79).
5. Sin was present in Eden in the actual sins committed by Adam and Eve; now she will dwell there in her own body and in all other bodies.
6. Cf. Revelation 6.8: "behold a pale horse: and his name that sat on him was Death, and Hell followed with him."

"To me, who with eternal famine pine,
Alike is Hell, or Paradise, or Heaven,
There best, where most with ravin° I may meet;   prey
600 Which here, though plenteous, all too little seems
To stuff this maw, this vast unhidebound corpse."[7]
    To whom th' incestuous mother thus replied:
"Thou therefore on these herbs, and fruits, and flow'rs
Feed first, on each beast next, and fish, and fowl,
605 No homely morsels, and whatever thing
Thy scythe of Time mows down, devour unspared,
Till I in man residing through the race,
His thoughts, his looks, words, actions all infect,
And season him thy last and sweetest prey."
610   This said, they both betook them several ways,
Both to destroy, or unimmortal make
All kinds, and for destruction to mature
Sooner or later; which th' Almighty seeing,
From his transcendent seat the saints among,
615 To those bright orders uttered thus his voice:
    "See with what heat these dogs of Hell advance
To waste and havoc° yonder world, which I   plunder
So fair and good created, and had still
Kept in that state, had not the folly of man
620 Let in these wasteful furies, who impute
Folly to me, so doth the Prince of Hell
And his adherents, that with so much ease
I suffer them to enter and possess
A place so heav'nly, and conniving seem
625 To gratify my scornful enemies,
That laugh, as if transported with some fit
Of passion, I to them had quitted all,°   handed everything over
At random yielded up to their misrule;
And know not that I called and drew them thither
630 My hellhounds, to lick up the draff° and filth   dregs
Which man's polluting sin with taint hath shed
On what was pure, till crammed and gorged, nigh burst
With sucked and glutted offal, at one sling
Of thy victorious arm, well-pleasing Son,
635 Both Sin, and Death, and yawning grave at last
Through Chaos hurled, obstruct the mouth of Hell
Forever, and seal up his ravenous jaws.
Then Heav'n and earth renewed shall be made pure
To sanctity that shall receive no stain:
640 Till then the curse pronounced on both precedes."°   takes precedence
    He ended, and the heav'nly audience loud
Sung hallelujah, as the sound of seas,
Through multitude that sung: "Just are thy ways,
Righteous are thy decrees on all thy works;
645 Who can extenuate° thee? Next, to the Son,   disparage
Destined restorer of mankind, by whom

7. Its hide does not cling close to its bones: Death's hunger is such that it can never fill its skin.

New heav'n and earth shall to the ages rise,
Or down from Heav'n descend." Such was their song,
While the Creator calling forth by name
650 His mighty angels gave them several charge,   *suited*
As sorted° best with present things. The sun
Had first his precept so to move, so shine,
As might affect the earth with cold and heat
Scarce tolerable, and from the north to call
655 Decrepit winter, from the south to bring
Solstitial summer's heat. To the blank° moon   *white, pale*
Her office they prescribed, to th' other five
Their planetary motions and aspécts[8]
In sextile, square, and trine, and opposite,
660 Of noxious efficacy, and when to join
In synod° unbenign, and taught the fixed°   *conjunction / fixed stars*
Their influence malignant when to show'r,
Which of them rising with the sun, or falling,
Should prove tempestuous:° to the winds they set   *productive of storms*
665 Their corners, when with bluster to confound
Sea, air, and shore, the thunder when to roll
With terror through the dark aerial hall.
Some say[9] he bid his angels turn askance
The poles of earth twice ten degrees and more
670 From the sun's axle; they with labor pushed
Oblique the centric globe:° some say the sun   *the earth*
Was bid turn reins from th' equinoctial road°   *the equator*
Like distant breadth to Taurus[1] with the sev'n
Atlantic Sisters, and the Spartan Twins
675 Up to the Tropic Crab; thence down amain°   *at full speed*
By Leo and the Virgin and the Scales,
As deep as Capricorn, to bring in change
Of seasons to each clime; else° had the spring   *otherwise*
Perpetual smiled on earth with vernant° flow'rs,   *spring*
680 Equal in days and nights, except to those
Beyond the polar circles; to them day
Had unbenighted° shone, while the low sun   *without any night*
To recompense his distance, in their sight
Had rounded still° th' horizon, and not known   *always*
685 Or° east or west, which had forbid the snow   *either*
From cold Estotiland, and south as far
Beneath Magellan.[2] At that tasted fruit
The sun, as from Thyestean banquet, turned
His course intended;[3] else how had the world

8. Astrological positions. The next line names positions of 60, 90, 120, and 180 degrees, respectively.
9. The poem offers both a Ptolemaic and a Copernican explanation of the shifts made in the cosmic order so as to change the prelapsarian eternal spring. The Copernican explanation (offered first) proposes that the earth's axis is now tilted (lines 668–71); the Ptolemaic explanation is that the plane of the sun's orbit is tilted (lines 671–78).

1. Lines 673–78 trace the sun's apparent (Ptolemaic) journey from Aries through Taurus and the rest of the zodiac over the course of the year.
2. The region of the Straits of Magellan, at the tip of South America. "Estotiland" (line 686): northern Labrador.
3. As a revenge, Atreus killed one of the sons of his brother Thyestes and served him in a banquet to that brother; the sun changed course to avoid the sight.

690　Inhabited, though sinless, more than now,
　　Avoided pinching cold and scorching heat?
　　These changes in the heav'ns, though slow, produced
　　Like change on sea and land, sideral blast,[4]
　　Vapor, and mist, and exhalation hot,
695　Corrupt and pestilent: now from the north
　　Of Norumbega, and the Samoed shore
　　Bursting their brazen dungeon, armed with ice
　　And snow and hail and stormy gust and flaw,°　　　　squall
　　Boreas and Caecias and Argestes loud
700　And Thrascias rend the woods and seas upturn;
　　With adverse blast upturns them from the south
　　Notus and Afer black with thund'rous clouds
　　From Serraliona,[5] thwart of these as fierce
　　Forth rush the Levant and the ponent° winds　　　　opposing
705　Eurus and Zephyr with their lateral noise,
　　Sirocco and Libecchio.[6] Thus began
　　Outrage from lifeless things; but Discord first
　　Daughter of Sin, among th' irrational,
　　Death introduced through fierce antipathy:[7]
710　Beast now with beast gan war, and fowl with fowl,
　　And fish with fish; to graze the herb° all leaving,　　grass
　　Devour'd each other; nor stood much in awe
　　Of man, but fled him, or with count'nance grim
　　Glared on him passing: these were from without
715　The growing miseries, which Adam saw
　　Already in part, though hid in gloomiest shade,
　　To sorrow abandoned, but worse felt within,
　　And in a troubled sea of passion tossed,
　　Thus to disburden sought with sad complaint:
720　　"O miserable of happy![8] Is this the end
　　Of this new glorious world, and me so late
　　The glory of that glory, who now become
　　Accurst of blessèd, hide me from the face
　　Of God, whom to behold was then my height
725　Of happiness: yet well, if here would end
　　The misery, I deserved it, and would bear
　　My own deservings; but this will not serve;
　　All that I eat or drink, or shall beget,
　　Is propagated[9] curse. O voice once heard
730　Delightfully, 'Increase and multiply,'
　　Now death to hear! For what can I increase

4. Malevolent stellar influences. "Norumbega" (line 696): northern New England and maritime Canada; "Samoed" Shore: northeastern Siberia.
5. Winds (701–6) from the south ("Notus," "Afer") come from Sierra Leone ("Serraliona") on the west coast of Africa; "Boreas," "Caecias," "Argestes," and "Thrascias" are all winds that blow from the north, northeast, and northwest, bursting from the cave ("brazen dungeon") in which Aeolus imprisoned the winds (lines 695–700).
6. Crossing the north and south winds ("thwart,"

line 703) are the "Levant" (from the east) and "Eurus" (east southeast), from the west "Zephyr," the west wind; "Sirocco" and "Libecchio" come from the southeast and southwest, respectively.
7. Discord (personified as daughter of Sin) introduced Death among the animals ("th' irrational") by stirring up "antipathy" among them.
8. Adam's complaint begins with the classical formula for a tragic fall, or peripeteia, the change from happiness to misery.
9. Handed down from one generation to the next.

Or multiply, but curses on my head?
Who of all ages to succeed, but feeling
The evil on him brought by me, will curse
735 My head: 'Ill fare our ancestor impure,
For this we may thank Adam'; but his thanks
Shall be the execration; so besides
Mine own that bide upon me, all from me
Shall with a fierce reflux on me redound,
740 On me as on their natural center light
Heavy, though in their place.[1] O fleeting joys
Of Paradise, dear bought with lasting woes!
Did I request thee, Maker, from my clay
To mold me man, did I solicit thee
745 From darkness to promote me, or here place
In this delicious garden? As my will
Concurred not to my being, it were but right
And equal° to reduce me to my dust,   just
Desirous to resign, and render back
750 All I received, unable to perform
Thy terms too hard, by which I was to hold
The good I sought not. To the loss of that,
Sufficient penalty, why hast thou added
The sense of endless woes? Inexplicable
755 Thy justice seems; yet to say truth, too late
I thus contest; then should have been refused
Those terms whatever, when they were proposed:
Thou[2] didst accept them; wilt thou enjoy the good,
Then cavil° the conditions? And though God   object frivolously to
760 Made thee without thy leave, what if thy son
Prove disobedient, and reproved, retort,
'Wherefore didst thou beget me? I sought it not':
Wouldst thou admit for his contempt of thee
That proud excuse? Yet him not thy election,°   choice
765 But natural necessity begot.
God made thee of choice his own, and of his own
To serve him, thy reward was of his grace,
Thy punishment then justly is at his will.
Be it so, for I submit, his doom is fair,
770 That dust I am, and shall to dust return:
O welcome hour whenever! Why delays
His hand to execute what his decree
Fixed on this day? Why do I overlive,
Why am I mocked with death, and lengthened out
775 To deathless pain? How gladly would I meet
Mortality my sentence, and be earth
Insensible, how glad would lay me down
As in my mother's lap! There I should rest
And sleep secure; his dreadful voice no more

---

1. I.e., Adam's "own" curse will remain ("bide") with him, and the curse ("execration") of "all" who descend from him will "redound" on him as to their "natural center"; objects so placed ("in their place") were thought to be weightless ("light"), but these curses will be "heavy."
2. Adam turns from addressing God to address himself.

780 Would thunder in my ears, no fear of worse
To me and to my offspring would torment me
With cruel expectation. Yet one doubt
Pursues me still, lest all I° cannot die,   *all of me*
Lest that pure breath of life, the spirit of man
785 Which God inspired, cannot together perish
With this corporeal clod; then in the grave,
Or in some other dismal place, who knows
But I shall die a living death? O thought
Horrid, if true! Yet why? It was but breath
790 Of life that sinned; what dies but what had life
And sin? The body properly hath neither.
All of me then shall die:[3] let this appease
The doubt, since human reach no further knows.
For though the Lord of all be infinite,
795 Is his wrath also? Be it, man is not so,
But mortal doomed. How can he exercise
Wrath without end on man whom death must end?
Can he make deathless death? That were to make
Strange contradiction, which to God himself
800 Impossible is held, as argument
Of weakness, not of power. Will he draw out,
For anger's sake, finite to infinite
In punished man, to satisfy his rigor
Satisfied never; that were to extend
805 His sentence beyond dust and nature's law,
By which all causes else according still
To the reception of their matter act,
Not to th' extent of their own sphere.[4] But say
That death be not one stroke, as I supposed,
810 Bereaving° sense, but endless misery   *taking away*
From this day onward, which I feel begun
Both in me, and without° me, and so last   *outside of*
To perpetuity; ay me, that fear
Comes thund'ring back with dreadful revolution°   *return*
815 On my defenseless head; both Death and I
Am found eternal, and incorporate° both,   *made one body*
Nor I on my part single, in me all
Posterity stands cursed: fair patrimony
That I must leave ye, sons; O were I able
820 To waste it all myself, and leave ye none!
So disinherited how would ye bless
Me now your curse! Ah, why should all mankind
For one man's fault thus guiltless be condemned,
If guiltless? But from me what can proceed,
825 But all corrupt, both mind and will depraved,
Not to do° only, but to will the same   *act*

3. After debating the matter, Adam concludes that the soul dies with the body; Milton in his *Christian Doctrine* worked out this "mortalist" doctrine, with its corollary, that both soul and body rise at the Last Judgment.

4. Adam convinces himself that "finite" matter (line 802) cannot suffer "infinite" punishment by an axiom of traditional philosophy, that by "nature's law" (line 805) the actions of agents are limited by the nature of the object they act upon.

With me? How can they then acquitted stand
In sight of God? Him after all disputes
Forced I absolve: all my evasions vain
830 And reasonings, though through mazes, lead me still
But to my own conviction: first and last
On me, me only, as the source and spring
Of all corruption, all the blame lights due;
So might the wrath.⁵ Fond° wish! Couldst thou support   *foolish*
835 That burden heavier than the earth to bear,
Than all the world much heavier, though divided
With that bad woman? Thus what thou desir'st,
And what thou fear'st, alike destroys all hope
Of refuge, and concludes thee miserable
840 Beyond all past example and future,
To Satan only like both crime and doom.
O conscience, into what abyss of fears
And horrors hast thou driv'n me; out of which
I find no way, from deep to deeper plunged!"
845   Thus Adam to himself lamented loud
Through the still night, not now, as ere man fell,
Wholesome and cool, and mild, but with black air
Accompanied, with damps° and dreadful gloom,   *noxious vapors*
Which to his evil conscience represented
850 All things with double terror: on the ground
Outstretched he lay, on the cold ground, and oft
Cursed his creation, Death as oft accused
Of tardy execution, since denounced°   *pronounced*
The day of his offense: "Why comes not Death,"
855 Said he, "with one thrice-ácceptáble stroke
To end me? Shall Truth fail to keep her word,
Justice divine not hasten to be just?
But Death comes not at call, Justice divine
Mends not her slowest pace for prayers or cries.
860 O woods, O fountains, hillocks, dales, and bow'rs,
With other echo late I taught your shades
To answer, and resound far other song."⁶
Whom thus afflicted when sad Eve beheld,
Desolate where she sat, approaching nigh,
865 Soft words to his fierce passion she assayed;°   *attempted*
But her with stern regard he thus repelled:
    "Out of my sight, thou serpent,⁷ that name best
Befits thee with him leagued, thyself as false
And hateful; nothing wants,° but that thy shape,   *is lacking*
870 Like his, and color serpentine may show
Thy inward fraud, to warn all creatures from thee
Henceforth; lest that too heav'nly form, pretended⁸
To hellish falsehood, snare them. But° for thee   *except*
I had persisted happy, had not thy pride

5. Cf. the Son's offer to accept all humankind's guilt (3.236–41), and Eve's similar offer (10.933–36).
6. Cf. their morning hymn (5.153–208).
7. Adam's bitter, misogynistic outcry begins with reference to the patristic notion that the name Eve, aspirated, means "serpent."
8. Held in front, as a cover or mask.

875 And wand'ring vanity, when least was safe,
Rejected my forewarning, and disdained
Not to be trusted, longing to be seen
Though by the Devil himself, him overweening°   *overconfident*
To overreach, but with the serpent meeting
880 Fooled and beguiled, by him thou, I by thee,
To trust thee from my side, imagined wise,
Constant, mature, proof against all assaults,
And understood not all was but a show
Rather than solid virtue, all but a rib
885 Crooked by nature, bent, as now appears,
More to the part siníster° from me drawn,   *the left side*
Well if thrown out, as supernumerary
To my just number found.⁹ O why did God,
Creator wise, that peopled highest heav'n
890 With Spirits masculine,¹ create at last
This novelty on earth, this fair defect
Of nature,² and not fill the world at once
With men as angels without feminine,
Or find some other way to generate
895 Mankind? This mischief had not then befall'n,
And more that shall befall, innumerable
Disturbances on earth through female snares,
And strait conjunction³ with this sex: for either
He never shall find out fit mate, but such
900 As some misfortune brings him, or mistake,
Or whom he wishes most shall seldom gain
Through her perverseness, but shall see her gained
By a far worse, or if she love, withheld
By parents, or his happiest choice too late
905 Shall meet, already linked and wedlock-bound
To a fell° adversary, his hate or shame: *bitter*
Which infinite calamity shall cause
To human life, and household peace confound."
        He added not, and from her turned, but Eve
910 Not so repulsed, with tears that ceased not flowing,
And tresses all disordered, at his feet
Fell humble, and embracing them, besought
His peace, and thus proceeded in her plaint:
        "Forsake me not thus, Adam, witness Heav'n
915 What love sincere, and reverence in my heart
I bear thee, and unweeting° have offended,   *unintentionally*
Unhappily deceived; thy suppliant
I beg, and clasp thy knees;⁴ bereave me not,
Whereon I live, thy gentle looks, thy aid,

---

9. It was supposed that Adam had thirteen ribs on the left side, so he could spare one for the creation of Eve and still retain the proper ("just") number, twelve.
1. The Miltonic bard indicated that angels can assume at will "either sex . . . or both" (1.424).
2. Aristotle had claimed that the female is a defective male.
3. Close, hard-pressing, binding union: Adam then projects the problems of future marriages.
4. Eve assumes the posture of the classical suppliant, clasping the knees of the one she begs from.

920 Thy counsel in this uttermost distress,
My only strength and stay: forlorn of thee,
Whither shall I betake me, where subsist?
While yet we live, scarce one short hour perhaps,
Between us two let there be peace, both joining,
925 As joined in injuries, one enmity
Against a foe by doom express° assigned us, *explicit judgment*
That cruel serpent: on me exercise not
Thy hatred for this misery befall'n,
On me already lost, me than thyself
930 More miserable; both have sinned, but thou
Against God only, I against God and thee,
And to the place of judgment will return,
There with my cries importune Heaven, that all
The sentence from thy head removed may light
935 On me, sole cause to thee of all this woe,
Me me only just object of his ire."[5]
  She ended weeping, and her lowly plight,° *posture*
Immovable till peace obtained from fault
Acknowledged and deplored, in Adam wrought
940 Commiseration; soon his heart relented
Towards her, his life so late and sole delight,
Now at his feet submissive in distress,
Creature so fair his reconcilement seeking,
His counsel whom she had displeased, his aid;
945 As one disarmed, his anger all he lost,
And thus with peaceful words upraised her soon:
  "Unwary, and too desirous, as before,
So now of what thou know'st not, who desir'st
The punishment all on thyself; alas!
950 Bear thine own first, ill able to sustain
His full wrath whose thou feel'st as yet least part,
And my displeasure bear'st so ill.[6] If prayers
Could alter high decrees, I to that place
Would speed before thee, and be louder heard,
955 That on my head all might be visited,
Thy frailty and infirmer sex forgiv'n,
To me committed and by me exposed.
But rise, let us no more contend, nor blame
Each other, blamed enough elsewhere, but strive
960 In offices of love, how we may light'n
Each other's burden in our share of woe;
Since this day's death denounced, if aught I see,
Will prove no sudden, but a slow-paced evil,
A long day's dying to augment our pain,
965 And to our seed (O hapless seed!) derived."° *passed on*
  To whom thus Eve, recovering heart, replied:
"Adam, by sad experiment I know

5. Eve also echoes the Son's offer (3.236–41).
Cf. Adam's cry (10.832–34).
6. I.e., you could hardly bear God's "full wrath"
since you are so distraught when you feel only
the smallest part of it, and you can "ill" bear my
displeasure.

How little weight my words with thee can find,
Found so erroneous, thence by just event°   *consequence*
970 Found so unfortunate; nevertheless,
Restored by thee, vile as I am, to place
Of new acceptance, hopeful to regain
Thy love, the sole contentment of my heart
Living or dying, from thee I will not hide
975 What thoughts in my unquiet breast are ris'n,
Tending to some relief of our extremes,
Or end, though sharp and sad, yet tolerable,
As in our evils, and of easier choice.
If care of our descent perplex us most,[7]
980 Which must be born to certain woe, devoured
By Death at last, and miserable it is
To be to others cause of misery,
Our own begotten, and of our loins to bring
Into this cursèd world a woeful race,
985 That after wretched life must be at last
Food for so foul a monster, in thy power
It lies, yet ere conception to prevent
The race unblest, to being yet unbegot.
Childess thou art, childless remain; so Death
990 Shall be deceived° his glut, and with us two   *cheated of*
Be forced to satisfy his rav'nous maw.
But if thou judge it hard and difficult,
Conversing, looking, loving, to abstain
From love's due rites, nuptial embraces sweet,
995 And with desire to languish without hope,
Before the present object[8] languishing
With like desire, which would be misery
And torment less than none of what we dread,
Then both ourselves and seed at once to free
1000 From what we fear for both, let us make short,°   *lose no time*
Let us seek Death, or he not found, supply
With our own hands his office on ourselves;
Why stand we longer shivering under fears,
That show no end but death, and have the power,
1005 Of many ways to die the shortest choosing,
Destruction with destruction to destroy."
    She ended here, or vehement despair
Broke off the rest; so much of death her thoughts
Had entertained, as dyed her cheeks with pale.
1010 But Adam with such counsel nothing swayed,
To better hopes his more attentive mind
Laboring had raised, and thus to Eve replied.
    "Eve thy contempt of life and pleasure seems
To argue in thee something more sublime
1015 And excellent than what thy mind contemns;°   *despises*

---

7. I.e., if concern for our descendants most torment ("perplex") us.

8. I.e., Eve herself, who then projects her own
frustrated desire if they were to forgo sex.

But self-destruction therefore sought, refutes
That excellence thought in thee, and implies,
Not thy contempt, but anguish and regret
For loss of life and pleasure overloved.
1020 Or if thou covet death, as utmost end
Of misery, so thinking to evade
The penalty pronounced, doubt not but God
Hath wiselier armed his vengeful ire than so
To be forestalled; much more I fear lest death
1025 So snatched will not exempt us from the pain
We are by doom to pay: rather such acts
Of contumácy° will provoke the Highest   *contempt*
To make death in us live. Then let us seek
Some safer resolution, which methinks
1030 I have in view, calling to mind with heed
Part of our sentence, that thy seed shall bruise
The serpent's head; piteous amends, unless
Be meant, whom I conjecture, our grand foe
Satan, who in the serpent hath contrived
1035 Against us this deceit: to crush his head
Would be revenge indeed; which will be lost
By death brought on ourselves, or childless days
Resolved, as thou proposest; so our foe
Shall scape his punishment ordained, and we
1040 Instead shall double ours upon our heads.
No more be mentioned then of violence
Against ourselves, and willful barrenness,
That cuts us off from hope, and savors only
Rancor and pride, impatience and despite,
1045 Reluctance° against God and his just yoke   *resistance*
Laid on our necks. Remember with what mild
And gracious temper he both heard and judged
Without wrath or reviling; we expected
Immediate dissolution, which we thought
1050 Was meant by death that day, when lo, to thee
Pains only in childbearing were foretold,
And bringing forth, soon recompensed with joy,
Fruit of thy womb:[9] on me the curse aslope
Glanced on the ground,[1] with labor I must earn
1055 My bread; what harm? Idleness had been worse;
My labor will sustain me; and lest cold
Or heat should injure us, his timely care
Hath unbesought provided, and his hands
Clothed us unworthy, pitying while he judged;
1060 How much more, if we pray him, will his ear
Be open, and his heart to pity incline,

9. Adam's prophetic echo of Elizabeth's address to Mary, mother of Jesus (Luke 1.41–42), "blessed is the fruit of thy womb," lays the ground for their fuller understanding of the promise about the "seed" of the woman.
1. I.e., the curse, like a spear that almost missed its target, glanced aside and hit the ground.

And teach us further by what means to shun
Th' inclement seasons, rain, ice, hail, and snow,
Which now the sky with various face begins

1065 To show us in this mountain, while the winds
Blow moist and keen, shattering° the graceful locks   *scattering*
Of these fair spreading trees; which bids us seek
Some better shroud,° some better warmth to cherish   *shelter*
Our limbs benumbed, ere this diurnal star°   *the sun*

1070 Leave cold the night, how we his gathered beams
Reflected, may with matter sere° foment,   *dry*
Or by collision of two bodies grind
The air attrite to fire,[2] as late the clouds
Justling or pushed with winds rude in their shock

1075 Tine° the slant lightning, whose thwart° flame driv'n down   *ignite / slanting*
Kindles the gummy bark of fir or pine,
And sends a comfortable heat from far,
Which might supply° the sun: such fire to use,   *take the place of*
And what may else be remedy or cure

1080 To evils which our own misdeeds have wrought,
He will instruct us praying, and of grace
Beseeching him, so as we need not fear
To pass commodiously this life, sustained
By him with many comforts, till we end

1085 In dust, our final rest and native home.
What better can we do, than to the place
Repairing where he judged us, prostrate fall
Before him reverent, and there confess
Humbly our faults, and pardon beg, with tears

1090 Watering the ground, and with our sighs the air
Frequenting,° sent from hearts contrite, in sign   *filling*
Of sorrow unfeigned, and humiliation meek.
Undoubtedly he will relent and turn
From his displeasure; in whose look serene,

1095 When angry most he seemed and most severe,
What else but favor, grace, and mercy shone?"
    So spake our father penitent, nor Eve
Felt less remorse: they forthwith to the place
Repairing where he judged them prostrate fell

1100 Before him reverent, and both confessed
Humbly their faults, and pardon begged, with tears
Watering the ground, and with their sighs the air
Frequenting, sent from hearts contrite, in sign
Of sorrow unfeigned, and humiliation meek.[3]

2. Adam projects the invention of fire: they
might, by striking two bodies together, rub
("attrite") the air into fire by friction; or else (lines
1070–71) focus reflected sunbeams (through
some equivalent of glass) on dry ("sere") matter.

3. The final six lines repeat, almost word for
word, lines 1086–92, as the poet describes
Adam's proposed gesture of repentance carried
out in every detail.

Book 11

Thus they in lowliest plight repentant stood[1]
Praying, for from the mercy-seat above
Prevenient grace[2] descending had removed
The stony from their hearts, and made new flesh
5   Regenerate grow instead, that sighs now breathed
Unutterable, which the spirit of prayer
Inspired, and winged for Heav'n with speedier flight
Than loudest oratory: yet their port
Not of mean suitors, nor important less
10   Seemed their petition, than when th' ancient pair
In fables old, less ancient yet than these,
Deucalion and chaste Pyrrha to restore
The race of mankind drowned, before the shrine
Of Themis stood devout.[3] To Heav'n their prayers
15   Flew up, nor missed the way, by envious winds
Blown vagabond or frustrate:[4] in they passed
Dimensionless through heav'nly doors; then clad
With incense, where the golden altar fumed,
By their great Intercessor, came in sight
20   Before the Father's throne: them the glad° Son   *pleased*
Presenting, thus to intercede began:
    "See Father, what firstfruits on earth are sprung
From thy implanted grace in man, these sighs
And prayers, which in this golden censer, mixed
25   With incense, I thy priest before thee bring,
Fruits of more pleasing savor from thy seed
Sown with contrition in his heart, than those
Which his own hand manuring° all the trees   *cultivating*
Of Paradise could have produced, ere fall'n
30   From innocence. Now therefore bend thine ear
To supplication, hear his sighs though mute;
Unskillful with what words to pray, let me
Interpret for him, me his advocate
And propitiation, all his works on me
35   Good or not good ingraft,[5] my merit those
Shall perfect, and for these my death shall pay.
Accept me, and in me from these receive
The smell of peace toward mankind, let him live
Before thee reconciled, at least his days

---

1. "Stood" may mean "remained," or that, after prostrating themselves (10.1099) they prayed standing upright; their demeanor ("port") was "Not of mean suitors" (11.8–9), and they had stood to pray before (4.720).
2. Grace given before the human will can turn from sin, enabling it to do so.
3. In Greek myth, when Deucalion and his wife Pyrrha (like Noah's family) alone survived a universal flood, they sought direction from Themis, goddess of justice; she told them to throw stones behind them, which became men and women.
4. I.e., their prayers were not scattered ("blown vagabond") by spiteful ("envious") winds, or prevented ("frustrate") from reaching their goal. "Dimensionless": without physical extension.
5. The theological term for Christ's standing in the place of humankind, taking onto himself all their deeds, perfecting the good by his merit, and, by his death, "paying" (see next line) the debt due God's justice for their evil deeds.

40 Numbered, though sad, till death, his doom (which I
    To mitigate thus plead, not to reverse)
    To better life shall yield him, where with me
    All my redeemed may dwell in joy and bliss,
    Made one with me as I with thee am one."
45   To whom the Father, without cloud, serene:
    "All thy request for man, accepted Son,
    Obtain, all thy request was my decree:
    But longer in that Paradise to dwell,
    The law I gave to nature him forbids:
50 Those pure immortal elements that know
    No gross, no unharmonious mixture foul,
    Eject him tainted now, and purge him off
    As a distemper, gross to air as gross,
    And mortal food,[6] as may dispose him best
55 For dissolution° wrought by sin, that first   *death*
    Distempered all things, and of incorrupt
    Corrupted. I at first with two fair gifts
    Created him endowed, with happiness
    And immortality: that fondly° lost,   *foolishly*
60 This other served but to eternize woe;
    Till I provided death; so death becomes
    His final remedy, and after life
    Tried in sharp tribulation, and refined
    By faith and faithful works, to second life,
65 Waked in the renovation[7] of the just,
    Resigns him up with Heav'n and earth renewed.
    But let us call to synod° all the blest   *assembly*
    Through Heav'n's wide bounds; from them I will not hide
    My judgments, how with mankind I proceed,
70 As how with peccant° angels late they saw;   *sinning*
    And in their state, though firm, stood more confirmed."
        He ended, and the Son gave signal high
    To the bright minister that watched, he blew
    His trumpet, heard in Oreb[8] since perhaps
75 When God descended, and perhaps once more
    To sound at general doom. Th' angelic blast
    Filled all the regions: from their blissful bow'rs
    Of amarantine° shade, fountain or spring,   *unfading*
    By the waters of life, where'er they sat
80 In fellowships of joy, the sons of light
    Hasted, resorting to the summons high,
    And took their seats; till from his throne supreme
    Th' Almighty thus pronounced his sov'reign will:
        "O sons, like one of us man is become
85 To know both good and evil, since his taste

---

6. The pure elements of the Garden of Eden will
themselves "purge" Adam and Eve as an impurity
or disorder ("distemper"), ejecting them to a
place where the air and food are more gross, like
themselves.
7. The resurrection and renewal of body and
soul on the Last Day.
8. Where God delivered the Ten Commandments to the sound of a trumpet (Exodus 19.19);
it will sound again at the Last Judgment ("general doom," line 76).

Of that defended° fruit; but let him boast   *forbidden*
His knowledge of good lost, and evil got,
Happier, had it sufficed him to have known
Good by itself, and evil not at all.
90 He sorrows now, repents, and prays contrite,
My motions° in him; longer than they move,   *promptings*
His heart I know, how variable and vain
Self-left.⁹ Lest therefore his now bolder hand
Reach also of the Tree of Life, and eat,
95 And live forever, dream at least to live
Forever,¹ to remove him I decree,
And send him from the garden forth to till
The ground whence he was taken, fitter soil.
    "Michael, this my behest have thou in charge,
100 Take to thee from among the Cherubim
Thy choice of flaming warriors, lest the Fiend
Or° in behalf of man, or to invade   *either*
Vacant possession some new trouble raise:
Haste thee, and from the Paradise of God
105 Without remorse° drive out the sinful pair,   *pity*
From hallowed ground th' unholy, and denounce
To them and to their progeny from thence
Perpetual banishment. Yet lest they faint°   *lose courage*
At the sad sentence rigorously urged,
110 For I behold them softened and with tears
Bewailing their excess,° all terror hide.   *violation of law*
If patiently thy bidding they obey,
Dismiss them not disconsolate; reveal
To Adam what shall come in future days,
115 As I shall thee enlighten,² intermix
My cov'nant in the woman's seed renewed;
So send them forth, though sorrowing, yet in peace:
And on the east side of the garden place,
Where entrance up from Eden easiest climbs,
120 Cherubic watch, and of a sword the flame
Wide-waving, all approach far off to fright,
And guard all passage to the Tree of Life:³
Lest Paradise a receptácle prove
To spirits foul, and all my trees their prey,
125 With whose stol'n fruit man once more to delude."
    He ceased; and th' archangelic power prepared
For swift descent, with him the cohort bright

---

9. Left to itself, without my continual promptings ("motions," line 91), I know his heart to be
"variable and vain."
1. Milton adds the phrase "dream at least to live
forever" to suggest that parts of God's speech
(especially lines 84–85 and 93–95, closely
quoted from Genesis 3.22) are ironic.
2. God, it seems, has to "enlighten" Michael
with knowledge of humankind's future at the
same time Michael presents that future to Adam

(cf. 12.128); Michael is told to "intermix" in his
account God's "cov'nant in the woman's seed"
(lines 115–16), the "mysterious" promise of the
redeemer hinted when the Son pronounced judgment on the serpent (10.179–81).
3. Cf. Genesis 3.24: "he placed at the east of the
garden of Eden Cherubims, and a flaming sword
which turned every way, to keep the way of the
tree of life."

Of watchful Cherubim; four faces each[4]
Had, like a double Janus, all their shape
130 Spangled with eyes more numerous than those
Of Argus, and more wakeful than to drowse,
Charmed with Arcadian pipe, the pastoral reed
Of Hermes, or his opiate rod. Meanwhile
To resalute the world with sacred light
135 Leucóthea[5] waked, and with fresh dews embalmed
The earth, when Adam and first matron Eve
Had ended now their orisons, and found
Strength added from above, new hope to spring
Out of despair, joy, but with fear yet linked;
140 Which thus to Eve his welcome words renewed:
    "Eve, easily may faith admit, that all
The good which we enjoy, from Heav'n descends;
But that from us aught should ascend to Heav'n
So prevalent° as to concern the mind   *influential*
145 Of God high-blest, or to incline his will,
Hard to belief may seem; yet this will prayer,
Or one short sigh of human breath, upborne
Ev'n to the seat of God. For since I sought
By prayer th' offended Deity to appease,
150 Kneeled and before him humbled all my heart,
Methought I saw him placable and mild,
Bending his ear; persuasion in me grew
That I was heard with favor; peace returned
Home to my breast, and to my memory
155 His promise, that thy seed shall bruise our foe;
Which then not minded in dismay, yet now
Assures me that the bitterness of death
Is past, and we shall live. Whence hail to thee,
Eve rightly called, mother of all mankind,
160 Mother of all things living, since by thee
Man is to live, and all things live for man."[6]
    To whom thus Eve with sad demeanor meek:
"Ill-worthy I such title should belong
To me transgressor, who for thee ordained
165 A help, became thy snare; to me reproach
Rather belongs, distrust and all dispraise:
But infinite in pardon was my Judge,
That I who first brought death on all, am graced
The source of life; next favorable thou,
170 Who highly thus to entitle me vouchsaf'st,
Far other name deserving. But the field
To labor calls us now with sweat imposed,

---

4. Ezekiel 1.6 Janus (line 129), the Roman god of doorways, had two faces; in one version he had four, corresponding to the four seasons and the four quarters of the earth. Argus (line 131), a giant with one hundred eyes, was set by Juno to watch Jove's mistress Io, but Hermes (Mercury) put all of his eyes to sleep with his music ("pipe")

and his sleep-producing caduceus ("opiate rod").
5. Roman goddess of the dawn.
6. The name Eve is cognate with the Hebrew word meaning "life." In Genesis 3.20 Adam names his wife Eve only after the Fall; Milton's Adam has named her before (4.481) and now affirms that that name is right.

Though after sleepless night; for see the morn,
All unconcerned with our unrest, begins
175   Her rosy progress smiling; let us forth,
I never from thy side henceforth to stray,
Where'er our day's work lies, though now enjoined
Laborious, till day droop; while here we dwell,
What can be toilsome in these pleasant walks?
180   Here let us live, though in fall'n state, content."
    So spake, so wished much-humbled Eve, but fate
Subscribed not; nature first gave signs,° impressed   *omens*
On bird, beast, air, air suddenly eclipsed°   *darkened*
After short blush of morn; nigh in her sight
185   The bird of Jove, stooped from his airy tow'r,[7]
Two birds of gayest plume before him drove:
Down from a hill the beast that reigns in woods,[8]
First hunter then, pursued a gentle brace,°   *pair*
Goodliest of all the forest, hart and hind;
190   Direct to th' eastern gate was bent their flight.
Adam observed, and with his eye the chase
Pursuing, not unmoved to Eve thus spake:
    "O Eve, some further change awaits us nigh,
Which Heaven by these mute signs in nature shows
195   Forerunners of his purpose, or to warn
Us haply too secure° of our discharge   *overconfident*
From penalty, because from death released
Some days; how long, and what till then our life,
Who knows, or more than this, that we are dust,
200   And thither must return and be no more.
Why else this double object in our sight
Of flight pursued in th' air and o'er the ground
One way the selfsame hour? Why in the east
Darkness ere day's mid-course, and morning light
205   More orient° in yon western cloud that draws   *bright*
O'er the blue firmament a radiant white,
And slow descends, with something heav'nly fraught."°   *laden*
    He erred not, for by this° the heav'nly bands   *by this time*
Down from a sky of jasper lighted° now   *alighted, shone*
210   In Paradise, and on a hill made alt,°   *halt*
A glorious apparition, had not doubt
And carnal fear that day dimmed Adam's eye.
Not that more glorious, when the angels met
Jacob in Mahanaim,[9] where he saw
215   The field pavilioned with his guardians bright;
Nor that which on the flaming mount appeared
In Dothan, covered with a camp of fire,
Against the Syrian king, who to surprise
One man, assassin-like had levied war,

---

7. The eagle swooped ("stooped") from his soaring flight ("tow'r").
8. The lion.

9. Jacob gave that name, meaning "armies" or "camps" ("field pavilioned," line 215), to a place where he saw an army of angels (Genesis 32.2).

220 War unproclaimed.[1] The princely hierarch[2]
In their bright stand, there left his powers to seize
Possession of the garden; he alone,
To find where Adam sheltered, took his way,
Not unperceived of Adam, who to Eve,
225 While the great visitant approached, thus spake:
    "Eve, now expect great tidings, which perhaps
Of us will soon determine,° or impose   *make an end*
New laws to be observed; for I descry
From yonder blazing cloud that veils the hill
230 One of the heav'nly host, and by his gait
None of the meanest, some great potentate
Or of the Thrones above, such majesty
Invests him coming; yet not terrible,
That I should fear, nor sociably mild,
235 As Raphael, that I should much confide,
But solemn and sublime, whom not to offend,
With reverence I must meet, and thou retire."
He ended; and th' Archangel soon drew nigh,
Not in his shape celestial, but as man
240 Clad to meet man; over his lucid arms
A military vest of purple flowed
Livelier than Meliboean, or the grain
Of Sarra,[3] worn by kings and heroes old
In time of truce; Iris[4] had dipped the woof;
245 His starry helm unbuckled showed him prime
In manhood where youth ended; by his side
As in a glistering zodiac° hung the sword,   *belt*
Satan's dire dread, and in his hand the spear.
Adam bowed low, he kingly from his state°   *stately bearing*
250 Inclined not, but his coming thus declared:
    "Adam, Heav'n's high behest no preface needs:
Sufficient that thy prayers are heard, and Death,
Then due by sentence when thou didst transgress,
Defeated° of his seizure° many days   *cheated / possession*
255 Giv'n thee of grace, wherein thou may'st repent,
And one bad act with many deeds well done
May'st cover: well may then thy Lord appeased
Redeem thee quite from Death's rapacious claim;
But longer in this Paradise to dwell
260 Permits not; to remove thee I am come,
And send thee from the garden forth to till
The ground whence thou wast taken, fitter soil."
    He added not, for Adam at the news
Heart-strook with chilling gripe° of sorrow stood,   *spasm*
265 That all his senses bound; Eve, who unseen
Yet all had heard, with audible lament

---

1. He had levied war against "Dothan" (line 217) in order to capture Elisha the prophet ("One man," line 219), but the Lord saved him by sending "horses and chariots of fire" (2 Kings 6.8ff.).
2. Michael, who left his angelic forces ("pow-

ers") in their formation ("stand") to take possession of the garden (lines 221–22).
3. Both Meliboea and Tyre ("Sarra") in Thessaly were famous for purple dye.
4. Goddess of the rainbow.

Discovered° soon the place of her retire: *revealed*
   "O unexpected stroke, worse than of Death!
Must I thus leave thee Paradise? thus leave
270 Thee native soil,[5] these happy walks and shades,
Fit haunt of gods? where I had hope to spend,
Quiet though sad, the respite° of that day   *delay*
That must be mortal to us both. O flow'rs,
That never will in other climate grow,
275 My early visitation, and my last
At ev'n which I bred up with tender hand
From the first op'ning bud, and gave ye names,[6]
Who now shall rear ye to the sun, or rank
Your tribes,° and water from th' ambrosial° fount? *species / fragrant*
280 Thee lastly nuptial bower, by me adorned
With what to sight or smell was sweet; from thee
How shall I part, and whither wander down
Into a lower world, to° this obscure   *compared to*
And wild, how shall we breathe in other air
285 Less pure, accustomed to immortal fruits?"
   Whom thus the angel interrupted mild:
"Lament not Eve, but patiently resign
What justly thou hast lost; nor set thy heart,
Thus overfond, on that which is not thine;
290 Thy going is not lonely, with thee goes
Thy husband, him to follow thou art bound;
Where he abides, think there thy native soil."
   Adam by this from the cold sudden damp°   *dejection*
Recovering, and his scattered spirits returned,
295 To Michael thus his humble words addressed:
   "Celestial, whether among the Thrones, or named
Of them the highest, for such of shape may seem
Prince above princes, gently hast thou told
Thy message, which might else in telling wound,
300 And in performing end us; what besides
Of sorrow and dejection and despair
Our frailty can sustain, thy tidings bring,
Departure from this happy place, our sweet
Recess, and only consolation left
305 Familiar to our eyes, all places else
Inhospitable appear and desolate,
Nor knowing us nor known: and if by prayer
Incessant I could hope to change the will
Of him who all things can,° I would not cease *knows, can do*
310 To weary him with my assiduous cries:
But prayer against his absolute decree
No more avails than breath against the wind,
Blown stifling back on him that breathes it forth:
Therefore to his great bidding I submit.

---

5. Unlike Adam, Eve was created in the Paradise of Eden.
6. Departing from Genesis 2.19–20, in which Adam alone gives names, Milton has Eve name the flowers, an action that signifies (like Adam's naming of the beasts, 8.352–54) intuitive knowledge of their nature.

315 This most afflicts me, that departing hence,
As from his face I shall be hid, deprived
His blessed count'nance; here I could frequent,
With worship, place by place where he vouchsafed
Presence Divine, and to my sons relate:
320 'On this mount he appeared, under this tree
Stood visible, among these pines his voice
I heard, here with him at this fountain talked:'
So many grateful altars I would rear
Of grassy turf, and pile up every stone
325 Of luster from the brook, in memory,
Or monument to ages, and thereon
Offer sweet-smelling gums and fruits and flow'rs:
In yonder nether world where shall I seek
His bright appearances, or footstep trace?
330 For though I fled him angry, yet recalled
To life prolonged and promised race,[7] I now
Gladly behold though but his utmost skirts
Of glory, and far off his steps adore."
  To whom thus Michael with regard benign:
335 "Adam, thou know'st Heav'n his, and all the earth,
Not this rock only; his omnipresence fills
Land, sea, and air, and every kind that lives,
Fomented° by his virtual° power and warmed: *nurtured / potent*
All th' earth he gave thee to possess and rule,
340 No despicable gift; surmise not then
His presence to these narrow bounds confined
Of Paradise or Eden: this had been
Perhaps thy capital seat, from whence had spread
All generations, and had hither come
345 From all the ends of th' earth, to celebrate
And reverence thee their great progenitor.
But this preeminence thou hast lost, brought down
To dwell on even ground now with thy sons:
Yet doubt not but in valley and in plain
350 God is as here, and will be found alike
Present, and of his presence many a sign
Still following thee, still compassing thee round
With goodness and paternal love, his face
Express, and of his steps the track divine.
355 Which that thou may'st believe, and be confirmed,
Ere thou from hence depart, know I am sent
To show thee what shall come in future days
To thee and to thy offspring,[8] good with bad
Expect to hear, supernal° grace contending   *heavenly*
360 With sinfulness of men; thereby to learn
True patience, and to temper joy with fear
And pious sorrow, equally inured°   *tempered*

---

7. His descendants, from whom will spring the "promised Seed." See 10.180–81 and note 1, and 12.623.
8. Prophetic visions are a common feature in epic, e.g., Aeneas's vision of his descendants culminating in the Roman Empire (Virgil, *Aeneid* 6.754–854).

By moderation either state to bare,
Prosperous or adverse: so shalt thou lead
365 Safest thy life, and best prepared endure
Thy mortal passage when it comes. Ascend
This hill; let Eve (for I have drenched her eyes)[9]
Here sleep below while thou to foresight wak'st,
As once thou slept'st while she to life was formed."
370   To whom thus Adam gratefully replied:
"Ascend, I follow thee, safe guide, the path
Thou lead'st me, and to the hand of Heav'n submit,
However chast'ning, to the evil turn
My obvious° breast, arming to overcome   *exposed*
375 By suffering, and earn rest from labor won,
If so I may attain." So both ascend
In the visions of God: it was a hill
Of Paradise the highest, from whose top
The hemisphere of earth in clearest ken°   *view*
380 Stretched out to amplest reach of prospect lay.
Not higher that hill nor wider looking round,
Whereon for different cause the Tempter set
Our second Adam in the wilderness,
To show him all earth's kingdoms and their glory.[1]
385 His eye might there command wherever stood
City of old or modern fame, the seat
Of mightiest empire, from the destined walls
Of Cambalu, seat of Cathaian Can,
And Samarkand by Oxus, Temir's throne,
390 To Paquin of Sinaean kings, and thence
To Agra and Lahore of Great Mogul
Down to the golden Chersonese,[2] or where
The Persian in Ecbatan sat, or since
In Hispahan, or where the Russian czar
395 In Moscow, or the sultan in Bizance,
Turkéstan-born;[3] nor could his eye not ken°   *view*
Th' empire of Negus to his utmost port
Ercoco and the less maritime kings
Mombaza, and Quiloa, and Melind,
400 And Sofala thought Ophir, to the realm
Of Congo, and Angola farthest south;[4]

---

9. Put a soporific liquid ("drench") in her eyes.
1. When Satan tempted Christ (the subject of Milton's "brief epic" *Paradise Regained*), he took him up to "an exceeding high mountain" and showed him "all the kingdoms of the world, and the glory of them" (Matthew 4.8). The passage that follows details the places "he" (Christ and / or Adam) might see (lines 386–411).
2. His first views are of "destined" (yet to come) great kingdoms in Asia: "Cambalu," capital of "Cathay," the region of North China ruled by such khans as Genghis and Kublai; "Samarkand," ruled by Tamburlaine ("Temir"), near the "Oxus" river near modern Uzbekistan; Beijing ("Paquin," Peking), ruled by Chinese ("Sinaean") kings; "Agra" and "Lahore," capitals in northern India ruled by the "Great Mogul"; "golden Cher-

sonese," an area sometimes identified with the Malay Peninsula.
3. Next, Persian and Turkish kingdoms. From Persia (Iran): Ecbatana ("Ecbatan"), a summer residence of Persian kings, and the 16th-century Persian capital Isfahan ("Hispahan"); and Byzantium ("Bizance," Constantinople, Istanbul), capital of the Ottoman Empire after falling to the Turks in 1453.
4. From Africa: Abyssinia (empire of King "Negus"); Arkiko ("Ercoco") in Ethiopia, a Red Sea port; Mombasa ("Mombaza") and Malindi ("Melind") in Kenya; Kilwa ("Quiloa") in Tanzania; "Sofala," sometimes identified with the biblical "Ophir" from which Solomon took gold for his Temple (1 Kings 9.28); and "Congo" and "Angola" on the west coast.

Or thence from Niger flood to Atlas mount
The kingdoms of Almansor, Fez and Sus,
Marocco and Algiers, and Tremisen;[5]
405 On Europe thence, and where Rome was to sway
The world: in spirit perhaps he also saw
Rich Mexico the seat of Motezume,
And Cuzsco in Peru, the richer seat
Of Atabalipa, and yet unspoiled
410 Guiana, whose great city Geryon's sons
Call El Dorado:[6] but to nobler sights
Michael from Adam's eyes the film removed
Which that false fruit that promised clearer sight
Had bred; then purged with euphrasy and rue[7]
415 The visual nerve, for he had much to see;
And from the well of life three drops instilled.
So deep the power of these ingredients pierced,
Ev'n to the inmost seat of mental sight,
That Adam now enforced to close his eyes,
420 Sunk down and all his spirits became entranced:
But him the gentle angel by the hand
Soon raised, and his attention thus recalled:
  "Adam, now ope thine eyes, and first behold
Th' effects which thy original crime hath wrought
425 In some to spring from thee, who never touched
Th' excepted° tree, nor with the snake conspired,   forbidden
Nor sinned thy sin, yet from that sin derive
Corruption to bring forth more violent deeds."
  His eyes he opened, and beheld a field,
430 Part arable and tilth,° whereon were sheaves   cultivated
New-reaped, the other part sheep-walks and folds;
I' th' midst an altar as the landmark° stood   boundary marker
Rustic, of grassy sord;° thither anon   turf
A sweaty reaper from his tillage brought
435 Firstfruits, the green ear, and the yellow sheaf,
Unculled,° as came to hand; a shepherd next   picked at random
More meek came with the firstlings of his flock
Choicest and best; then sacrificing, laid
The inwards and their fat, with incense strewed,
440 On the cleft wood, and all due rites performed.
His off'ring soon propitious fire from Heav'n
Consumed with nimble glance, and grateful steam;

5. In North Africa: the kingdoms of "Almansor" (the name shared by various Muslim rulers, here referring probably to Abu-Amir al Ma-Ma'afiri, caliph of Cordova) reached from the "Niger" River in northern Morocco to the "Atlas" Mountains in Algeria, taking in Morocco (and its capital, "Fez"), Tunis ("Sus"), and part of Algeria called Tiemecen ("Tremisen").
6. Because they lay on the other side of the spherical earth, Christ and/or Adam could only see places in the New World "in spirit" (line 406): Mexico, the seat of Montezuma ("Mote-

zume"), the last Aztec emperor; "Cuzsco in Peru," seat of Atahualpa ("Atabalipa"), the last Incan emperor (murdered by Pizarro); and "Guiana" (a region including Surinam, Guyana, and parts of Venezuela and Brazil). Unlike Mexico and Peru it was "yet unspoiled" by the Spaniards (sons of the evil monster "Geryon," in Spenser an allegory of the great power and oppression of Spain), though they identified its chief city, Manoa, with the fabled city of gold, "El Dorado."
7. Both herbs were thought to sharpen eyesight.

The other's not, for his was not sincere;[8]
Whereat he inly raged, and as they talked,
445 Smote him into the midriff with a stone
That beat out life; he fell, and deadly pale
Groaned out his soul with gushing blood effused.
Much at that sight was Adam in his heart
Dismayed, and thus in haste to th' angel cried:
450 "O teacher, some great mischief hath befall'n
To that meek man, who well had sacrificed;
Is piety thus and pure devotion paid?"
  T' whom Michael thus, he also moved, replied:
"These two are brethren, Adam, and to come
455 Out of thy loins;[9] th' unjust the just hath slain,
For envy that his brother's offering found
From Heav'n acceptance; but the bloody fact°   *crime*
Will be avenged, and th' other's faith approved
Lose no reward, though here thou see him die,
460 Rolling in dust and gore." To which our sire:
  "Alas, both for the deed and for the cause!
But have I now seen death? Is this the way
I must return to native dust? O sight
Of terror, foul and ugly to behold,
465 Horrid to think, how horrible to feel!"
  To whom thus Michaël: "Death thou hast seen
In his first shape on man; but many shapes
Of Death, and many are the ways that lead
To his grim cave, all dismal; yet to sense
470 More terrible at th' entrance than within.
Some, as thou saw'st, by violent stroke shall die,
By fire, flood, famine; by intemperance more
In meats and drinks, which on the earth shall bring
Diseases dire, of which a monstrous crew
475 Before thee shall appear; that thou may'st know
What misery th' inabstinence of Eve
Shall bring on men." Immediately a place[1]
Before his eyes appeared, sad,° noisome, dark,   *lamentable*
A lazar-house it seemed, wherein were laid
480 Numbers of all diseased, all maladies
Of ghastly spasm, or racking torture, qualms
Of heartsick agony, all feverous kinds,
Convulsions, epilepsies, fierce catarrhs,
Intestine stone and ulcer, colic pangs,
485 Demoniac frenzy, moping melancholy
And moonstruck madness,° pining atrophy,   *lunacy*
Marasmus, and wide-wasting pestilence,[2]
Dropsies, and asthmas, and joint-racking rheums.

---

8. Milton's version of the Cain and Abel story (Genesis 4.1–16) provides a clear reason for God's rejection of Cain's sacrifice.
9. Adam has to be told that these are his own sons, not simply descendants.
1. This is the only nonbiblical sight shown to Adam, a "lazar-house" (line 479)—a hospital for leprosy and infectious diseases, especially syphilis.
2. The plague. "Marasmus": a wasting disease of the body.

Dire was the tossing, deep the groans, Despair
490 Tended the sick busiest from couch to couch;
And over them triumphant Death his dart
Shook, but delayed to strike, though oft invoked
With vows, as their chief good, and final hope.
Sight so deform what heart of rock could long
495 Dry-eyed behold? Adam could not, but wept,
Though not of woman born; compassion quelled
His best of man,° and gave him up to tears   *manliness, courage*
A space, till firmer thoughts restrained excess,
And scarce recovering words his plaint renewed:
500   "O miserable mankind, to what fall
Degraded, to what wretched state reserved!
Better end here unborn. Why is life giv'n
To be thus wrested from us? Rather why
Obtruded on us thus? who if we knew
505 What we receive, would either not accept
Life offered, or soon beg to lay it down,
Glad to be so dismissed in peace. Can thus
Th' image of God in man created once
So goodly and erect, though faulty since,
510 To such unsightly sufferings be debased
Under inhuman pains? Why should not man,
Retaining still divine similitude
In part, from such deformities be free,
And for his Maker's image sake exempt?"
515   "Their Maker's image," answered Michael, "then
Forsook them, when themselves they vilified°   *debased*
To serve ungoverned appetite, and took°   *took away*
His image whom they served, a brutish vice,
Inductive° mainly to° the sin of Eve.   *produced / from*
520 Therefore so abject is their punishment,
Disfiguring not God's likeness, but their own,
Or if his likeness, by themselves defaced
While they pervert pure nature's healthful rules
To loathsome sickness, worthily,° since they   *deservedly*
525 God's image did not reverence in themselves."
    "I yield it just," said Adam, "and submit.
But is there yet no other way, besides
These painful passages, how we may come
To death, and mix with our connatural dust?"
530   "There is," said Michael, "if thou well observe
The rule of not too much, by temperance taught
In what thou eat'st and drink'st, seeking from thence
Due nourishment, not gluttonous delight,
Till many years over thy head return:
535 So may'st thou live, till like ripe fruit thou drop
Into thy mother's[3] lap, or be with ease
Gathered, not harshly plucked, for death mature:
This is old age; but then thou must outlive

---

3. "Mother" earth.

Thy youth, thy strength, thy beauty, which will change
540 To withered weak and gray; thy senses then
Obtuse, all taste of pleasure must forgo,
To what thou hast, and for the air of youth
Hopeful and cheerful, in thy blood will reign
A melancholy damp° of cold and dry   *depression of spirits*
545 To weigh thy spirits down, and last consume
The balm° of life." To whom our ancestor: *preservative essence*
    "Henceforth I fly not death, nor would prolong
Life much, bent rather how I may be quit
Fairest and easiest of this cumbrous charge,
550 Which I must keep till my appointed day
Of rend'ring up, and patiently attend°   *await*
My dissolution." Michaël replied:
    "Nor love thy life, nor hate; but what thou liv'st
Live well, how long or short permit to Heav'n:
555 And now prepare thee for another sight."
    He looked and saw a spacious plain,[4] whereon
Were tents of various hue; by some were herds
Of cattle grazing: others, whence the sound
Of instruments that made melodious chime
560 Was heard, of harp and organ; and who moved
Their stops and chords was seen: his volant touch
Instinct through all proportions low and high
Fled and pursued transverse the resonant fugue.[5]
In other part stood one[6] who at the forge
565 Laboring, two massy clods of iron and brass
Had melted (whether found where casual° fire   *accidental*
Had wasted woods on mountain or in vale,
Down to the veins of earth, thence gliding hot
To some cave's mouth, or whether washed by stream
570 From underground) the liquid ore he drained
Into fit molds prepared; from which he formed
First his own tools; then, what might else be wrought
Fusile° or grav'n in metal. After these,   *cast*
But on the hither side a different sort[7]
575 From the high neighboring hills, which was their seat,
Down to the plain descended: by their guise
Just men they seemed, and all their study bent
To worship God aright, and know his works
Not hid,[8] nor those things last which might preserve
580 Freedom and peace to men: they on the plain
Long had not walked, when from the tents behold
A bevy of fair women, richly gay

---

4. Adam's third vision is based on Genesis 4.19–22; "tents" (next line) identifies these as the descendants of Cain, described as "such as dwell in tents."
5. Genesis 4.21 describes Cain's descendant Jubal as "father of all such as handle the harp and organ." "Volant": nimble; "instinct": instinctive; "proportions": ratios of pitches; "fugue": musical form in which one statement of the theme seems to chase another.
6. Tubal-cain, "instructor of every artificer in brass and iron" (Genesis 4.22).
7. The descendants of Seth, Adam's third son (Genesis 5.3); "hither side": away from the "east" (Genesis 4.16), where Cain's sons lived.
8. They studied God's visible works, not the "matters hid" that Raphael had warned Adam against.

In gems and wanton dress; to the harp they sung
Soft amorous ditties, and in dance came on:
585 The men though grave, eyed them, and let their eyes
Rove without rein, till in the amorous net
Fast caught, they liked, and each his liking chose;
And now of love they treat till th' evening star[9]
Love's harbinger appeared; then all in heat
590 They light the nuptial torch, and bid invoke
Hymen,[1] then first to marriage rites invoked;
With feast and music all the tents resound.
Such happy interview and fair event°   outcome
Of love and youth not lost, songs, garlands, flow'rs,
595 And charming symphonies attached° the heart   seized
Of Adam, soon° inclined to admit delight,   easily
The bent of nature; which he thus expressed:
    "True opener of mine eyes, prime angel blest,
Much better seems this vision, and more hope
600 Of peaceful days portends, than those two past;
Those were of hate and death, or pain much worse,
Here nature seems fulfilled in all her ends."
    To whom thus Michael: "Judge not what is best
By pleasure, though to nature seeming meet,°   appropriate
605 Created, as thou art, to nobler end
Holy and pure, conformity divine.
Those tents thou saw'st so pleasant, were the tents
Of wickedness, wherein shall dwell his race
Who slew his brother; studious they appear
610 Of arts that polish life, inventors rare,
Unmindful of their Maker, though his spirit
Taught them, but they his gifts acknowledged none.
Yet they a beauteous offspring shall beget;
For that fair female troop thou saw'st, that seemed
615 Of goddesses, so blithe, so smooth, so gay,
Yet empty of all good wherein consists
Woman's domestic honor and chief praise;
Bred only and completed° to the taste   accomplished
Of lustful appetence,° to sing, to dance,   desire
620 To dress, and troll° the tongue, and roll the eye.   move
To these that sober race of men, whose lives
Religious titled them the sons of God,[2]
Shall yield up all their virtue, all their fame
Ignobly, to the trains° and to the smiles   wiles, snares
625 Of these fair atheists, and now swim in joy,
(Erelong to swim at large) and laugh; for which
The world erelong a world of tears must weep."
    To whom thus Adam of short joy bereft:
"O pity and shame, that they who to live well
630 Entered so fair, should turn aside to tread

9. Venus.
1. God of marriage.
2. Like many exegetes, Milton identifies the

"sons of God" as the descendants of Seth, and
the "daughters of men" whom they wed (Genesis
6.2) as the descendants of Cain.

Paths indirect, or in the mid-way faint!
But still I see the tenor of man's woe
Holds on the same, from woman to begin."
"From man's effeminate slackness it begins,"
635 Said th' angel, "who should better hold his place
By wisdom, and superior gifts received.
But now prepare thee for another scene."
   He looked and saw wide territory spread
Before him, towns, and rural works between,
640 Cities of men with lofty gates and tow'rs,
Concourse° in arms, fierce faces threat'ning war,   *encounters*
Giants[3] of mighty bone, and bold emprise;°   *chivalric adventure*
Part wield their arms, part curb the foaming steed,
Single or in array of battle ranged°   *drawn up in ranks*
645 Both horse and foot, nor idly must'ring stood;
One way a band select from forage drives
A herd of beeves, fair oxen and fair kine
From a fat meadow ground; or fleecy flock,
Ewes and their bleating lambs over the plain,
650 Their booty; scarce with life the shepherds fly,
But call in aid, which makes a bloody fray;
With cruel tournament the squadrons join;
Where cattle pastured late, now scattered lies
With carcasses and arms th' ensanguined° field   *blood-stained*
655 Deserted: others to a city strong
Lay siege, encamped; by battery, scale, and mine,[4]
Assaulting; others from the wall defend
With dart and jav'lin, stones and sulphurous fire;
On each hand slaughter and gigantic deeds.
660 In other part the sceptered heralds call
To council in the city gates: anon
Gray-headed men and grave, with warriors mixed,
Assemble, and harangues are heard, but soon
In factious opposition, till at last
665 Of middle age one[5] rising, eminent
In wise deport, spake much of right and wrong,
Of justice, of religion, truth and peace,
And judgment from above: him old and young
Exploded,° and had seized with violent hands,   *mocked*
670 Had not a cloud descending snatched him thence
Unseen amid the throng: so violence
Proceeded, and oppression, and sword-law
Through all the plain, and refuge none was found.
Adam was all in tears, and to his guide
675 Lamenting turned full sad; "O what are these,
Death's ministers, not men, who thus deal death

---

3. Adam's fourth vision, based on Genesis 6.4, is
of the "Giant" offspring of the previous marriages (identified at lines 683–84); Milton makes
them exemplify false heroism and false glory
sought through military might and conquest
(lines 689–99).

4. I.e., by battering, scaling, and tunneling
under the walls.
5. Enoch, who "walked with God: and he was
not; for God took him" (Genesis 5.24); Milton
elaborates on the story.

Inhumanly to men, and multiply
Ten-thousandfold the sin of him who slew
His brother; for of whom such massacre
680 Make they but of their brethren, men of men?
But who was that just man, whom had not Heav'n
Rescued, had in his righteousness been lost?"
    To whom thus Michael: "These are the product
Of those ill-mated marriages thou saw'st:
685 Where good with bad were matched, who of themselves
Abhor to join; and by imprudence mixed,
Produce prodigious births of body or mind.
Such were these giants, men of high renown;
For in those days might only shall be admired,
690 And valor and heroic virtue called;
To overcome in battle, and subdue
Nations, and bring home spoils with infinite
Manslaughter, shall be held the highest pitch
Of human glory, and for glory done
695 Of triumph, to be styled great conquerors,
Patrons of mankind, gods, and sons of gods,
Destroyers rightlier called and plagues of men.
Thus fame shall be achieved, renown on earth,
And what most merits fame in silence hid.
700 But he the sev'nth from thee,[6] whom thou beheld'st
The only righteous in a world perverse,
And therefore hated, therefore so beset
With foes for daring single to be just,
And utter odious truth, that God would come
705 To judge them with his saints: him the Most High
Rapt in a balmy cloud with winged steeds
Did, as thou saw'st, receive, to walk with God
High in salvation and the climes of bliss,
Exempt from death; to show thee what reward
710 Awaits the good, the rest what punishment;
Which now direct thine eyes and soon behold."
    He looked, and saw the face of things quite changed;
The brazen throat of war had ceased to roar,
All now was turned to jollity and game,
715 To luxury° and riot,° feast and dance,   *lust / debauchery*
Marrying or prostituting, as befell,
Rape or adultery, where passing fair°   *surpassing beauty*
Allured them; thence from cups to civil broils.
At length a reverend sire[7] among them came,
720 And of their doings great dislike declared,
And testified against their ways; he oft
Frequented their assemblies, whereso met,
Triumphs or festivals, and to them preached

6. Here Enoch is more precisely identified by generation, but neither he nor the other biblical personages in these pageants are named. Apparently, Michael and Adam together see the pageants, and Michael (by God's illumination) can interpret them rightly, but neither of the two knows the names these persons will later bear.
7. Noah. Milton's account is based on Genesis 6–9.

Conversion and repentance, as to souls
725　In prison under judgments imminent:
But all in vain: which when he saw, he ceased
Contending, and removed his tents far off;
Then from the mountain hewing timber tall,
Began to build a vessel of huge bulk,
730　Measured by cubit, length, and breadth, and height,
Smeared round with pitch, and in the side a door
Contrived, and of provisions laid in large
For man and beast: when lo a wonder strange!
Of every beast, and bird, and insect small
735　Came sevens and pairs, and entered in, as taught
Their order: last the sire and his three sons
With their four wives; and God made fast the door.
Meanwhile the south wind rose, and with black wings
Wide hovering, all the clouds together drove
740　From under heav'n; the hills to their supply°　　　　　assistance
Vapor, and exhalation dusk° and moist,　　　　　　　　dark mist
Sent up amain;° and now the thickened sky　　　with main force
Like a dark ceiling stood; down rushed the rain
Impetuous, and continued till the earth
745　No more was seen; the floating vessel swum
Uplifted; and secure with beakèd prow
Rode tilting o'er the waves, all dwellings else
Flood overwhelmed, and them with all their pomp
Deep underwater rolled; sea covered sea,
750　Sea without shore;[8] and in their palaces
Where luxury late reigned, sea monsters whelped
And stabled; of mankind, so numerous late,
All left, in one small bottom° swum embarked.　　　　　boat
How didst thou grieve then, Adam, to behold
755　The end of all thy offspring, end so sad,
Depopulation; thee another flood,
Of tears and sorrow a flood thee also drowned,
And sunk thee as thy sons; till gently reared
By th' angel, on thy feet thou stood'st at last,
760　Though comfortless, as when a father mourns
His children, all in view destroyed at once;
And scarce to th' angel utter'dst thus thy plaint:
　　"O visions ill foreseen! Better had I
Lived ignorant of future, so had borne
765　My part of evil only, each day's lot
Enough to bear; those now, that were dispensed
The burd'n of many ages, on me light
At once, by my foreknowledge[9] gaining birth
Abortive, to torment me ere their being,
770　With thought that they must be. Let no man seek

8. The "sea without shore" and some other features of this description are taken from Ovid's account of Deucalion's Flood (*Metamorphoses* 1.292–300, Sandys, translation).
9. The term suggests that Adam is experiencing

something akin to God's foreknowledge, which the poem insists is not predestination. Adam knows what is to happen but can neither cause it nor prevent it.

Henceforth to be foretold what shall befall
Him or his children, evil he may be sure,
Which neither his foreknowing can prevent,
And he the future evil shall no less
775   In apprehension than in substance feel
Grievous to bear: but that care now is past,
Man is not whom to warn:[1] those few escaped
Famine and anguish will at last consume
Wand'ring that wat'ry desert: I had hope
780   When violence was ceased, and war on earth,
All would have then gone well, peace would have crowned
With length of happy days the race of man;
But I was far deceived; for now I see
Peace to corrupt no less than war to waste.
785   How comes it thus? Unfold, celestial guide,
And whether here the race of man will end."
    To whom thus Michael: "Those whom last thou saw'st
In triumph and luxurious wealth, are they
First seen in acts of prowess eminent
790   And great exploits, but of true virtue void;
Who having spilt much blood, and done much waste
Subduing nations, and achieved thereby
Fame in the world, high titles, and rich prey,
Shall change their course to pleasure, ease, and sloth,
795   Surfeit, and lust, till wantonness and pride
Raise out of friendship hostile deeds in peace.
The conquered also, and enslaved by war
Shall with their freedom lost all virtue lose
And fear of God, from whom their piety feigned
800   In sharp contést of battle found no aid
Against invaders; therefore cooled in zeal
Thenceforth shall practice how to live secure,
Worldly or dissolute, on what their lords
Shall leave them to enjoy, for th' earth shall bear
805   More than enough, that temperance may be tried:
So all shall turn degenerate, all depraved,
Justice and temperance, truth and faith forgot;[2]
One man except, the only son of light
In a dark age, against example good,
810   Against allurement, custom, and a world
Offended;° fearless of reproach and scorn,   *hostile*
Or violence, he of their wicked ways
Shall them admonish, and before them set
The paths of righteousness, how much more safe,
815   And full of peace, denouncing° wrath to come   *proclaiming*
On their impenitence; and shall return
Of them derided, but of God observed
The one just man alive; by his command

---

1. I.e., there is no man to warn, all will die.
2. This passage (lines 797–807) may also allude to the backsliding Puritans who betrayed the Commonwealth in 1660 and have now taken on the vices of the restored royalists.

Shall build a wondrous ark, as thou beheld'st,
820 To save himself and household from amidst
A world devote° to universal wrack.   *doomed*
No sooner he with them of man and beast
Select for life shall in the ark be lodged,
And sheltered round, but all the cataracts°   *floodgates*
825 Of heav'n set open on the earth shall pour
Rain day and night, all fountains of the deep
Broke up, shall heave the ocean to usurp
Beyond all bounds, till inundation rise
Above the highest hills: then shall this mount
830 Of Paradise by might of waves be moved
Out of his place, pushed by the hornèd flood,[3]
With all his verdure spoiled, and trees adrift
Down the great river to the op'ning gulf,[4]
And there take root an island salt and bare,
835 The haunt of seals and ores,° and sea mews'° clang. *sea monsters / seagulls*
To teach thee that God áttributes to place
No sanctity, if none be thither brought
By men who there frequent, or therein dwell.
And now what further shall ensue, behold."
840   He looked, and saw the ark hull° on the flood,   *drift*
Which now abated, for the clouds were fled,
Driv'n by a keen north wind, that blowing dry
Wrinkled the face of deluge, as decayed;
And the clear sun on his wide wat'ry glass
845 Gazed hot, and of the fresh wave largely drew,
As after thirst, which made their flowing shrink
From standing lake to tripping° ebb, that stole   *running*
With soft foot towards the deep, who now had stopped
His sluices, as the heav'n his windows shut.
850 The ark no more now floats, but seems on ground
Fast on the top of some high mountain fixed.[5]
And now the tops of hills as rocks appear;
With clamor thence the rapid currents drive
Towards the retreating sea their furious tide.
855 Forthwith from out the ark a raven flies,
And after him, the surer messenger,
A dove sent forth once and again to spy
Green tree or ground whereon his foot may light;
The second time returning, in his bill
860 An olive leaf he brings, pacific sign:
Anon dry ground appears, and from his ark
The ancient sire descends with all his train;
Then with uplifted hands, and eyes devout,
Grateful to Heav'n, over his head beholds
865 A dewy cloud, and in the cloud a bow
Conspicuous with three listed colors gay,[6]

---

3. Classical river gods were often depicted as horned.
4. I.e., down the Euphrates to the Persian Gulf.
5. Mount Ararat (Genesis 8.4).
6. The primary colors, red, yellow, and blue.

Betok'ning peace from God, and covenant new.
Whereat the heart of Adam erst so sad
Greatly rejoiced, and thus his joy broke forth:
870   "O thou who future things canst represent
As present, heav'nly instructor, I revive
At this last sight, assured that man shall live
With all the creatures, and their seed preserve.
Far less I now lament for one whole world
875   Of wicked sons destroyed, than I rejoice
For one man found so perfect and so just,
That God vouchsafes to raise another world
From him, and all his anger to forget.[7]
But say, what mean those colored streaks in heav'n,
880   Distended° as the brow of God appeased,   *spread out*
Or serve they as a flow'ry verge to bind
The fluid skirts of that same wat'ry cloud,
Lest it again dissolve and show'r the earth?"
          To whom th' Archangel: "Dextrously thou aim'st;
885   So willingly doth God remit his ire,
Though late repenting him of man depraved,
Grieved at his heart, when looking down he saw
The whole earth filled with violence, and all flesh
Corrupting each their way; yet those removed,
890   Such grace shall one just man find in his sight,
That he relents, not to blot out mankind,
And makes a cov'nant[8] never to destroy
The earth again by flood, nor let the sea
Surpass his bounds, nor rain to drown the world
895   With man therein or beast; but when he brings
Over the earth a cloud, will therein set
His triple-colored bow, whereon to look
And call to mind his cov'nant: day and night,
Seed-time and harvest, heat and hoary frost
900   Shall hold their course, till fire purge all things new,
Both heav'n and earth, wherein the just shall dwell."[9]

Book 12

As one who in his journey bates° at noon,   *stops for refreshment*
Though bent on speed, so here the Archangel paused
Betwixt the world destroyed and world restored,
If Adam aught perhaps might interpose;

---

7. The language invites recognition of Noah as a type (foreshadowing) of Christ, the one "perfect" and "just" who will cause God to forget his anger.
8. The language of covenant makes this promise—that God will not again destroy the earth by flood—a type of the "covenant of grace"

through which God will save humankind.
9. The restoration of the orderly processes of nature after the Flood is identified as a type (foreshadowing) of the final renewal of all things after the final conflagration at the Last Judgment.

5   Then with transition sweet new speech resumes:[1]
      "Thus thou hast seen one world begin and end;
    And man as from a second stock proceed.
    Much thou hast yet to see, but I perceive
    Thy mortal sight to fail; objects divine
10   Must needs impair and weary human sense:
    Henceforth what is to come I will relate,[2]
    Thou therefore give due audience, and attend.
    This second source of men, while yet but few,
    And while the dread of judgment past remains
15   Fresh in their minds, fearing the Deity,
    With some regard to what is just and right
    Shall lead their lives, and multiply apace,
    Laboring the soil, and reaping plenteous crop,
    Corn, wine, and oil; and from the herd or flock,
20   Oft sacrificing bullock, lamb, or kid,
    With large wine-offerings poured, and sacred feast,
    Shall spend their days in joy unblamed, and dwell
    Long time in peace by families and tribes
    Under paternal rule; till one[3] shall rise
25   Of proud ambitious heart, who not content
    With fair equality, fraternal state,
    Will arrogate dominion undeserved
    Over his brethren, and quite dispossess
    Concord and law of nature from the earth;
30   Hunting (and men not beasts shall be his game)
    With war and hostile snare such as refuse
    Subjection to his empire tyrannous:
    A mighty hunter thence he shall be styled°   *called*
    Before the Lord, as in despite of Heav'n,
35   Or from Heav'n claiming second sov'reignty;[4]
    And from rebellion shall derive his name,
    Though of rebellion others he accuse.
    He with a crew, whom like ambition joins
    With him or under him to tyrannize,
40   Marching from Eden towards the west, shall find
    The plain, wherein a black bituminous gurge°   *whirlpool*
    Boils out from underground, the mouth of Hell;
    Of brick, and of that stuff they cast° to build   *set about*
    A city and tow'r,[5] whose top may reach to Heav'n;
45   And get themselves a name, lest far dispersed
    In foreign lands their memory be lost,
    Regardless whether good or evil fame.

---

1. The first five lines were added when Book 10 of the 1667 edition was divided to make Books 11 and 12 of the 1674 edition.
2. Adam no longer sees visions or pageants, as before, but simply listens to Michael's narration.
3. Nimrod (Genesis 10.8–10) is described as the first king, in terms that equate kingship itself with tyranny (lines 25–29).
4. Milton offers two explanations of the biblical phrase "Before the Lord": either he openly defied God ("despite") or he claimed divine right ("second sov'reignty") like the Stuart kings. Drawing on the (false) etymology linking the name Nimrod with the Hebrew word meaning "to rebel," Milton implies that the paradox developed in the next two lines (that he accuses others of rebellion but is himself a rebel against God) extends to other kings, especially Charles I, who accused his opponents in the civil war of rebellion.
5. Babylon is the city, Babel the tower.

But God who oft descends to visit men
Unseen, and through their habitations walks
50   To mark their doings, them beholding soon,
Comes down to see their city, ere the tower
Obstruct Heav'n tow'rs, and in derision sets
Upon their tongues a various° spirit to raze   *divisive*
Quite out their native language, and instead
55   To sow a jangling noise of words unknown:
Forthwith a hideous gabble[6] rises loud
Among the builders; each to other calls
Not understood, till hoarse, and all in rage,
As mocked they storm; great laughter was in Heav'n
60   And looking down, to see the hubbub strange
And hear the din; thus was the building left
Ridiculous, and the work Confusion[7] named."
      Whereto thus Adam fatherly displeased:
"O execrable son so to aspire
65   Above his brethren, to himself assuming
Authority usurped, from God not giv'n:
He gave us only over beast, fish, fowl
Dominion absolute; that right we hold
By his donation; but man over men
70   He made not lord; such title to himself
Reserving, human left from human free.[8]
But this usurper his encroachment proud
Stays not on man; to God his tower intends
Siege and defiance: wretched man! What food
75   Will he convey up thither to sustain
Himself and his rash army, where thin air
Above the clouds will pine° his entrails gross,   *waste away*
And famish him of breath, if not of bread?"
      To whom thus Michael: "Justly thou abhorr'st
80   That son, who on the quiet state of men
Such trouble brought, affecting° to subdue   *aspiring*
Rational liberty; yet know withal,
Since thy original lapse, true liberty
Is lost, which always with right reason dwells
85   Twinned, and from her hath no dividual° being:[9]   *separate*
Reason in man obscured, or not obeyed,
Immediately inordinate desires
And upstart passions catch the government
From reason, and to servitude reduce
90   Man till then free. Therefore since he permits

6. Genesis 11.1–9 recounts the building of the Tower of Babel reaching to Heaven; God punished this presumption by confounding the builders' original language into multiple languages.
7. "Confusion" was taken to be the meaning of "Babel."
8. Adam states the assumption Milton often invokes to support republicanism.
9. As Milton (following classical theorists) often

did, and as Abdiel did earlier (6.178–81), Michael links political to psychological servitude, and political liberty to inner freedom, i.e., the exercise of "right reason" and the control of passion. Loss of liberty is often (though not always) God's just punishment for national decline (lines 81–100). The long passage alludes to the "baseness" of the English in restoring monarchy in 1660.

Within himself unworthy powers to reign
Over free reason, God in judgment just
Subjects him from without to violent lords;
Who oft as undeservedly enthrall
His outward freedom: tyranny must be,
Though to the tyrant thereby no excuse.
Yet sometimes nations will decline so low
From virtue, which is reason, that no wrong,
But justice, and some fatal curse annexed
Deprives them of their outward liberty,
Their inward lost: witness th' irreverent son[1]
Of him who built the ark, who for the shame
Done to his father, heard this heavy curse,
'Servant of servants,' on his vicious race.[2]
Thus will this latter, as the former world,
Still tend from bad to worse, till God at last
Wearied with their iniquities, withdraw
His presence from among them, and avert
His holy eyes; resolving from thenceforth
To leave them to their own polluted ways;
And one peculiar° nation to select *special*
From all the rest, of whom to be invoked,
A nation from one faithful man[3] to spring:
Him on this side Euphrates yet residing,
Bred up in idol-worship; O that men
(Canst thou believe?) should be so stupid grown,
While yet the patriarch[4] lived, who scaped the Flood,
As to forsake the living God, and fall
To worship their own work in wood and stone
For gods! Yet him God the Most High vouchsafes
To call by vision from his father's house,
His kindred and false gods, into a land
Which he will show him, and from him will raise
A mighty nation, and upon him show'r
His benediction so, that in his seed
All nations shall be blest; he straight° obeys, *immediately*
Not knowing to what land, yet firm believes:
I see him, but thou canst not,[5] with what faith
He leaves his gods, his friends, and native soil
Ur[6] of Chaldaea, passing now the ford
To Haran, after him a cumbrous train
Of herds and flocks, and numerous servitude;° *servants and slaves*
Not wand'ring poor, but trusting all his wealth

1. Ham, son of Noah, who looked on the nakedness of his father and brought down the curse that his descendants would be "servant of servants" to their brethren (Genesis 9.22–25).
2. Tribe. "Race" did not then bear its modern sense, so Milton is probably thinking of the Canaanites (descendants of Ham's son Canaan), rather than black Africans; blacks were, however, classed among Ham's descendants, and this biblical text was often used to justify slavery.
3. Abraham, whose name means "father of many nations"; the passage is based on Genesis 11.27 to 25.10.
4. Noah, who lived for 350 years after the Flood.
5. Michael evidently continues to see the stories he recounts as visionary scenes or pageants; Adam must accept the story of Abraham "by faith," analogous to the faith Abraham himself displays.
6. Ur was on one bank of the Euphrates, Haran (line 131) on the other, to the northwest.

With God, who called him, in a land unknown.
135 Canaan he now attains, I see his tents
Pitched about Sechem, and the neighboring plain
Of Moreh; there by promise he receives
Gift to his progeny of all that land;
From Hamath northward to the desert south
140 (Things by their names I call, though yet unnamed)
From Hermon east to the great western sea,[7]
Mount Hermon, yonder sea, each place behold
In prospect, as I point them; on the shore
Mount Carmel; here the double-founted stream
145 Jordan, true limit eastward; but his sons
Shall dwell to Senir, that long ridge of hills.[8]
This ponder, that all nations of the earth
Shall in his seed be blessed; by that Seed
Is meant thy great Deliverer,[9] who shall bruise
150 The Serpent's head; whereof to thee anon
Plainlier shall be revealed. This patriarch blest,
Whom 'faithful Abraham'[1] due time shall call,
A son, and of his son a grandchild leaves,
Like him in faith, in wisdom, and renown;
155 The grandchild with twelve sons increased, departs
From Canaan, to a land hereafter called
Egypt, divided by the river Nile;
See where it flows,[2] disgorging at seven mouths
Into the sea: to sojourn in that land
160 He comes invited by a younger son[3]
In time of dearth,° a son whose worthy deeds   *famine*
Raise him to be the second in that realm
Of Pharaoh: there he dies, and leaves his race
Growing into a nation, and now grown
165 Suspected to° a sequent° king, who seeks   *by / successive*
To stop their overgrowth, as inmate° guests   *foreign*
Too numerous; whence of guests he makes them slaves
Inhospitably, and kills their infant males:
Till by two brethren (those two brethren call
170 Moses and Aaron) sent from God to claim
His people from enthrallment, they return
With glory and spoil back to their promised land.[4]
But first the lawless tyrant, who denies°   *refuses*

---

7. The Promised Land was bounded on the north by Hamath, a city on the Orontes River in west Syria; on the south by the wilderness "desert" of Zin; on the east by Mount Hermon; and on the west by the Mediterranean, the "great western sea."
8. "Mount Carmel": a mountain range near Haifa, on the Mediterranean coast of Israel; "Jordan": the river thought incorrectly to have two sources ("double-founted"), the Jor and the Dan; "Senir": a peak of Mount Hermon.
9. Michael interprets the promise to Abraham (Genesis 17.5, "a father of many nations have I made thee") typologically, as to be fulfilled in Christ, the "Woman's Seed." See 10.180–81 and

note 1, and 12.322–28, 12.600–601, 12.623.
1. Echoes Galatians 3.9: "So then they which be of faith are blessed with faithful Abraham." His son (line 153) is Isaac, and his grandson, Jacob.
2. Adam can see geographical features from his mountaintop, though not the scenes Michael sees and describes.
3. Joseph, the next youngest of Jacob's twelve sons, invited the Israelites to Egypt to escape famine, but they were subsequently made slaves (Genesis 21–50).
4. The story of Moses and Aaron leading the Israelites from captivity to the Promised Land is told in Exodus and Deuteronomy.

To know their God, or message to regard,
175 Must be compelled by signs and judgments dire;[5]
To blood unshed the rivers must be turned,
Frogs, lice, and flies must all his palace fill
With loathed intrusion, and fill all the land;
His cattle must of rot and murrain° die,   *cattle plague*
180 Botches and blains must all his flesh emboss,[6]
And all his people; thunder mixed with hail,
Hail mixed with fire must rend th' Egyptian sky
And wheel on th' earth, devouring where it rolls;
What it devours not, herb, or fruit, or grain,
185 A darksome cloud of locusts swarming down
Must eat, and on the ground leave nothing green:
Darkness must overshadow all his bounds,
Palpable darkness, and blot out three days;
Last with one midnight stroke all the firstborn
190 Of Egypt must lie dead. Thus with ten wounds°   *plagues*
The river-dragon[7] tamed at length submits
To let his sojourners depart, and oft
Humbles his stubborn heart, but still as ice
More hardened after thaw, till in his rage
195 Pursuing whom he late dismissed, the sea
Swallows him with his host, but them lets pass
As on dry land between two crystal walls,
Awed by the rod of Moses so to stand
Divided, till his rescued gain their shore:[8]
200 Such wondrous power God to his saint will lend,
Though present in his angel, who shall go
Before them in a cloud, and pillar of fire,
By day a cloud, by night a pillar of fire,
To guide them in their journey,[9] and remove
205 Behind them, while th' obdúrate king pursues:
All night he will pursue, but his approach
Darkness defends° between till morning watch;   *prevents*
Then through the fiery pillar and the cloud
God looking forth will trouble all his host
210 And craze° their chariot wheels: when by command   *shatter*
Moses once more his potent rod extends
Over the sea; the sea his rod obeys;
On their embattled ranks the waves return,
And overwhelm their war:° the race elect   *armies*
215 Safe towards Canaan from the shore advance
Through the wild desert, not the readiest way,
Lest ent'ring on the Canaanite alarmed°   *prepared to fight*
War terrify them inexpert, and fear

---

5. The ten plagues, recounted in lines 176–90.
6. "Botches": boils; "blains": blisters; "emboss": cover as with studs.
7. The Egyptian pharaoh is termed "the great dragon that lieth in the midst of his rivers" (Ezekiel 29.3).
8. The Red Sea was parted by the rod of Moses; the Israelites passed through, but Pharaoh's pur-

suing forces drowned as the water rushed back (Exodus 13.17–22 and 14.5–31).
9. Milton repeats here a view developed in his *Christian Doctrine*, that God was "present in his angel," not in his own person, in the cloud and pillar of fire that led the Israelites on their journey (Exodus 13.21–22).

Return them back to Egypt, choosing rather
220   Inglorious life with servitude; for life
To noble and ignoble is more sweet
Untrained in arms, where rashness leads not on.[1]
This also shall they gain by their delay
In the wide wilderness, there they shall found
225   Their government, and their great senate[2] choose
Through the twelve tribes, to rule by laws ordained:
God from the mount of Sinai, whose gray top
Shall tremble, he descending, will himself
In thunder, lightning, and loud trumpet's sound
230   Ordain them laws; part such as appertain
To civil justice, part religious rites
Of sacrifice,[3] informing them, by types
And shadows, of that destined Seed to bruise
The Serpent, by what means he shall achieve
235   Mankind's deliverance.[4] But the voice of God
To mortal ear is dreadful; they beseech
That Moses might report to them his will,
And terror cease; he grants what they besought
Instructed that to God is no access
240   Without mediator, whose high office now
Moses in figure[5] bears, to introduce
One greater, of whose day he shall foretell,
And all the prophets in their age the times
Of great Messiah shall sing. Thus laws and rites
245   Established, such delight hath God in men
Obedient to his will, that he vouchsafes
Among them to set up his tabernacle,
The Holy One with mortal men to dwell:
By his prescript a sanctuary is framed
250   Of cedar, overlaid with gold, therein
An ark, and in the ark his testimony,
The records of his cov'nant, over these
A mercy-seat of gold between the wings
Of two bright Cherubim, before him burn
255   Seven lamps as in a zodiac° representing   *like the planets*
The heav'nly fires; over the tent a cloud
Shall rest by day, a fiery gleam by night,
Save when they journey, and at length they come,
Conducted by his angel to the land
260   Promised to Abraham and his seed: the rest
Were long to tell, how many battles fought,
How many kings destroyed, and kingdoms won,
Or how the sun shall in mid-heav'n stand still

---

1. I.e., unless prompted by "rashness," those "untrained in arms" will choose servitude rather than battle.
2. The "Seventy Elders" of the Sanhedrin, whom Milton cites as a model for republican government in his *Ready and Easy Way*.
3. God delivered ceremonial, civil, and moral/religious laws (the Ten Commandments) to Moses on Mount Sinai, with thunder and lightning (lines 227–32; Exodus 19–31).
4. The principle of typology, whereby persons and events in the Old Testament are seen to prefigure Christ or matters pertaining to his life or the Christian church.
5. Moses is a type of Christ in his role as mediator between the people and God.

A day entire, and night's due course adjourn,
265 Man's voice commanding, 'Sun in Gibeon stand,
And thou moon in the vale of Aialon,
Till Israel overcome';[6] so call the third
From Abraham, son of Isaac, and from him
His whole descent,[7] who thus shall Canaan win."
270   Here Adam interposed: "O sent from Heav'n,
Enlight'ner of my darkness, gracious things
Thou hast revealed, those chiefly which concern
Just Abraham and his seed: now first I find
Mine eyes true op'ning, and my heart much eased,
275 Erewhile perplexed with thoughts what would become
Of me and all mankind; but now I see
His day, in whom all nations shall be blest,[8]
Favor unmerited by me, who sought
Forbidden knowledge by forbidden means.
280 This yet I apprehend not, why to those
Among whom God will deign to dwell on earth
So many and so various laws are giv'n;
So many laws argue so many sins
Among them; how can God with such reside?"
285   To whom thus Michael: "Doubt not but that sin
Will reign among them, as of thee begot;
And therefore was law given them to evince°   *make evident*
Their natural pravity,° by stirring up   *original sin*
Sin against law to fight; that when they see
290 Law can discover sin, but not remove,
Save by those shadowy expiations weak,
The blood of bulls and goats, they may conclude
Some blood more precious must be paid for man,
Just for unjust, that in such righteousness
295 To them by faith imputed, they may find
Justification towards God, and peace
Of conscience,[9] which the law by ceremonies
Cannot appease, nor man the moral part
Perform, and not performing cannot live.[1]
300 So law appears imperfect, and but giv'n
With purpose to resign° them in full time   *yield*
Up to a better cov'nant, disciplined
From shadowy types to truth, from flesh to spirit,
From imposition of strict laws, to free
305 Acceptance of large grace, from servile fear

6. The story of Joshua, at whose bidding the sun stood still in Gibeon, and the moon in Ajalon (both a few miles north of Jerusalem), until Israel won its battle against the Amorites (Joshua 10.12–23).
7. Isaac's son Jacob was named Israel, and his descendants after him (Genesis 33.28).
8. Adam supposes that the promise made to him is fulfilled in the covenant with Abraham; he has yet to understand that in this Abraham is a type of Christ.
9. The ceremonial sacrifices of "bulls and goats"

under the Law are types, "shadowy expiations," pointing to Christ's efficacious sacrifice that alone can win "Justification" for humankind, by Christ's merits being "imputed" (attributed vicariously) to them through faith (lines 290–96).
1. The theological doctrine that the Law is intended to lead humans to the "better cov'nant" (line 302) of grace, by demonstrating that fallen men cannot fulfill the commandments of the Law or appease God through ceremonial sacrifices (lines 297–302).

To filial, works of law to works of faith.[2]
And therefore shall not Moses, though of God
Highly beloved, being but the minister
Of law, his people into Canaan lead;
310 But Joshua whom the Gentiles Jesus call,[3]
His name and office bearing, who shall quell
The adversary Serpent, and bring back
Through the world's wilderness long-wandered man
Safe to eternal paradise of rest.
315 Meanwhile they in their earthly Canaan placed
Long time shall dwell and prosper, but when sins
National interrupt their public peace,
Provoking God to raise them enemies:
From whom as oft he saves them penitent°   *when penitent*
320 By judges first, then under kings; of whom
The second, both for piety renowned
And puissant° deeds, a promise shall receive   *mighty*
Irrevocable, that his regal throne
Forever shall endure;[4] the like shall sing
325 All prophecy, that of the royal stock
Of David (so I name this king) shall rise
A son, the Woman's Seed to thee foretold,[5]
Foretold to Abraham, as in whom shall trust
All nations, and to kings foretold, of kings
330 The last, for of his reign shall be no end.
But first a long succession must ensue,
And his next son for wealth and wisdom famed,
The clouded ark of God till then in tents
Wand'ring, shall in a glorious temple enshrine.[6]
335 Such follow him, as shall be registered
Part good, part bad, of bad the longer scroll,
Whose foul idolatries and other faults
Heaped° to the popular sum, will so incense   *added*
God, as to leave them, and expose their land,
340 Their city, his temple, and his holy ark
With all his sacred things, a scorn and prey
To that proud city, whose high walls thou saw'st
Left in confusion, Babylon thence called.
There in captivity he lets them dwell
345 The space of seventy years,[7] then brings them back,
Rememb'ring mercy, and his cov'nant sworn
To David, stablished as the days of Heav'n.
Returned from Babylon by leave of kings[8]

---

2. A more complete explanation of the principle of typology.
3. "Jesus" is the Greek equivalent of the Hebrew "Joshua," who, rather than Moses, led the children of Israel into the Promised Land of Canaan, being in this a type of Christ.
4. The history summarized in lines 315–30 is recounted in Judges, Samuel, and Kings.
5. The Messiah was prophesied to come of David's line, and Jesus was referred to as the

"Son of David."
6. Solomon, son of David, built a "glorious temple" to house the Ark of the Covenant.
7. The seventy-year Babylonian Captivity of the Jews and destruction of the Temple (6th century B.C.E.).
8. The Persian kings Cyrus the Great, Darius, and Artaxerxes allowed the Jews to return from Babylon and rebuild the Temple.

	Their lords, whom God disposed,° the house of God	*made well-disposed*
350	They first re-edify, and for a while	
	In mean estate live moderate, till grown	
	In wealth and multitude, factious they grow;	
	But first among the priests dissension springs,	
	Men who attend the altar, and should most	
355	Endeavor peace: their strife pollution brings	
	Upon the Temple itself: at last they seize	
	The scepter, and regard not David's sons,°	*descendants*
	Then lose it to a stranger,[9] that the true	
	Anointed King Messiah might be born	
360	Barred of his right; yet at his birth a star	
	Unseen before in heav'n proclaims him come,	
	And guides the eastern sages,° who inquire	*the Magi*
	His place, to offer incense, myrrh, and gold;	
	His place of birth a solemn° angel tells	*awe-inspiring*
365	To simple shepherds, keeping watch by night;	
	They gladly thither haste, and by a choir	
	Of squadroned angels hear his carol sung.	
	A virgin is his mother, but his sire	
	The Power of the Most High; he shall ascend	
370	The throne hereditary, and bound his reign	
	With earth's wide bounds, his glory with the heav'ns."	

He ceased, discerning Adam with such joy
Surcharged,° as had like grief been dewed in tears,   *overwhelmed*
Without the vent of words, which these he breathed:

	"O prophet of glad tidings, finisher	
375	Of utmost hope! now clear I understand	
	What oft my steadiest thoughts have searched in vain,	
	Why our great expectation should be called	
	The Seed of Woman: Virgin Mother, hail,	
380	High in the love of Heav'n, yet from my loins	
	Thou shalt proceed, and from thy womb the Son	
	Of God Most High; so God with man unites.	
	Needs must the Serpent now his capital° bruise	*on the head, fatal*
	Expect with mortal pain: say where and when	
385	Their fight, what stroke shall bruise the victor's heel."	

To whom thus Michael: "Dream not of their fight,
As of a duel, or the local wounds
Of head or heel: not therefore joins the Son
Manhood to Godhead, with more strength to foil

390	Thy enemy; nor so is overcome	
	Satan, whose fall from Heav'n, a deadlier bruise,	
	Disabled not to give thee thy death's wound:	
	Which he who comes thy Savior, shall recure,°	*heal*
	Not by destroying Satan, but his works	
395	In thee and in thy seed: nor can this be,	

---

9. Antiochus, father of Herod the Great (who ruled at the time of Christ's birth), was made governor of Jerusalem in 61 B.C.E. by the Romans, and procurator of Judaea in 47 B.C.E. Prior to this (lines 353–57), strife among the priests allowed the Seleucid king Antiochus IV to sack Jerusalem and pollute the Temple; then one of the Maccabees seized the throne, disregarding the claims of David's dynasty.

But by fulfilling that which thou didst want,°   *lack*
Obedience to the law of God, imposed
On penalty of death, and suffering death,
The penalty to thy transgression due,
400 And due to theirs which out of thine will grow:
So only can high justice rest apaid.°   *satisfied*
The law of God exact he shall fulfill
Both by obedience and by love, though love
Alone fulfill the law; thy punishment
405 He shall endure by coming in the flesh
To a reproachful life and cursèd death,
Proclaiming life to all who shall believe
In his redemption, and that his obedience
Imputed becomes theirs by faith, his merits
410 To save them, not their own, though legal works.[1]
For this he shall live hated, be blasphemed,
Seized on by force, judged, and to death condemned
A shameful and accursed, nailed to the cross
By his own nation, slain for bringing life;
415 But to the cross he nails thy enemies,
The law that is against thee, and the sins
Of all mankind, with him there crucified,
Never to hurt them more who rightly trust
In this his satisfaction; so he dies,
420 But soon revives, Death over him no power
Shall long usurp; ere the third dawning light
Return, the stars of morn shall see him rise
Out of his grave, fresh as the dawning light,
Thy ransom paid, which man from Death redeems,
425 His death for man, as many as offered life
Neglect not,[2] and the benefit embrace
By faith not void of works: this Godlike act
Annuls thy doom, the death thou shouldst have died,
In sin forever lost from life; this act
430 Shall bruise the head of Satan, crush his strength
Defeating Sin and Death, his two main arms,
And fix far deeper in his head their stings
Than temporal death shall bruise the victor's heel,
Or theirs whom he redeems, a death like sleep,
435 A gentle wafting to immortal life.
Nor after resurrection shall he stay
Longer on earth than certain times to appear
To his disciples, men who in his life
Still followed him; to them shall leave in charge
440 To teach all nations what of him they learned
And his salvation, them who shall believe
Baptizing in the profluent° stream, the sign   *flowing*
Of washing them from guilt of sin to life

---

1. Michael restates the theological doctrine that humans can be saved only by Christ's merits attributed to them vicariously ("imputed"), not by their own good works performed according to God's law ("legal").

2. I.e., for as many as accept ("neglect not") his offer of life.

Pure, and in mind prepared, if so befall,
445 For death, like that which the Redeemer died.
All nations they shall teach; for from that day
Not only to the sons of Abraham's loins
Salvation shall be preached, but to the sons
Of Abraham's faith wherever through the world;
450 So in his seed all nations shall be blest.[3]
Then to the Heav'n of Heav'ns he shall ascend
With victory, triumphing through the air
Over his foes and thine; there shall surprise
The Serpent, prince of air, and drag in chains
455 Through all his realm, and there confounded leave;
Then enter into glory, and resume
His seat at God's right hand, exalted high
Above all names in Heav'n; and thence shall come,
When this world's dissolution shall be ripe
460 With glory and power to judge both quick° and dead,   living
To judge th' unfaithful dead, but to reward
His faithful, and receive them into bliss,
Whether in Heav'n or earth, for then the earth
Shall all be paradise, far happier place
465 Than this of Eden, and far happier days."
     So spake th' Archangel Michaël, then paused,
As at the world's great period;° and our sire   consummation
Replete with joy and wonder thus replied:
     "O goodness infinite, goodness immense!
470 That all this good of evil shall produce,
And evil turn to good; more wonderful
Than that which by creation first brought forth
Light out of darkness! Full of doubt I stand,
Whether I should repent me now of sin
475 By me done and occasioned, or rejoice
Much more, that much more good thereof shall spring,
To God more glory, more good will to men
From God, and over wrath grace shall abound.[4]
But say, if our Deliverer up to Heav'n
480 Must reascend, what will betide the few
His faithful, left among th' unfaithful herd,
The enemies of truth; who then shall guide
His people, who defend? Will they not deal
Worse with his followers than with him they dealt?"
485   "Be sure they will," said th' angel; "but from Heav'n
He to his own a Comforter will send,[5]
The promise of the Father, who shall dwell
His Spirit within them, and the law of faith

---

3. Michael spells out the application to Christ of the promise offered typologically to Abraham's seed.
4. These lines do not formulate the medieval idea of the *felix culpa*—that the Fall was fortunate in bringing humans greater happiness than they would otherwise have enjoyed—only that

the Fall has provided God an occasion to bring still greater good out of evil. The poem makes clear that Adam and Eve would have grown in perfection and advanced to Heaven had they not sinned.
5. The Holy Spirit, who for Milton is much subordinate to both Father and Son.

Working through love, upon their hearts shall write,
490 To guide them in all truth, and also arm
With spiritual armor, able to resist
Satan's assaults, and quench his fiery darts,[6]
What° man can do against them, not afraid,   *as much as*
Though to the death, against such cruelties
495 With inward consolations recompensed,
And oft supported so as shall amaze
Their proudest persecutors: for the Spirit
Poured first on his apostles, whom he sends
To evangelize the nations, then on all
500 Baptized, shall them with wondrous gifts endue°   *endow*
To speak all tongues, and do all miracles,
As did their Lord before them. Thus they win
Great numbers of each nation to receive
With joy the tidings brought from Heav'n: at length
505 Their ministry performed, and race well run,
Their doctrine and their story written left,[7]
They die; but in their room, as they forewarn,
Wolves shall succeed for teachers, grievous wolves,
Who all the sacred mysteries of Heav'n
510 To their own vile advantages shall turn
Of lucre° and ambition, and the truth   *wealth*
With superstitions and traditions taint,[8]
Left only in those written records pure,
Though not but by the Spirit understood.
515 Then shall they seek to avail themselves of names,°   *honors*
Places° and titles, and with these to join   *offices*
Secular power, though feigning still to act
By spiritual, to themselves appropriating
The Spirit of God, promised alike and giv'n
520 To all believers; and from that pretense,
Spiritual laws by carnal° power shall force   *fleshly, worldly*
On every conscience;[9] laws which none shall find
Left them enrolled, or what the Spirit within
Shall on the heart engrave.[1] What will they then
525 But force the Spirit of Grace itself, and bind
His consort Liberty; what, but unbuild
His living temples,[2] built by faith to stand,

---

6. Cf. Ephesians 6.11–16: "Put on the whole armor of God, that ye may be able to stand against the wiles of the devil. . . . Above all, taking the shield of faith, wherewith ye shall be able to quench all the fiery darts of the wicked." The subsequent history (lines 493–507) is that of the early Christian church in apostolic times.
7. I.e., in the Gospels and Epistles.
8. The history summarized in lines 508–40 is of the corruption of the Christian church by superstitions, traditions, and persecutions of conscience in patristic times under the popes and the Christian emperors, but also extending to the Last Day. The terms point especially to what Milton saw as the revival of "popish" superstitions in the English church of the Restoration

and to the fierce persecution of dissenters.
9. These lines affirm the Protestant principle of every Christian's right to interpret Scripture according to the "inner light" of the Spirit, and denounce (as Milton consistently did in his tracts) the use of civil ("carnal") power to enforce orthodoxy.
1. I.e., there is nothing in Scripture or in the Spirit's inner teaching that sanctions persecution for conscience.
2. Cf. 1 Corinthians 3.16: "Know ye not that ye are the temple of God?" "His consort Liberty": Milton typically insists that Christ's gospel and the Spirit of God teach liberty, religious and civil, alluding as here to 2 Corinthians 3.17: "where the Spirit of the Lord is, there is liberty."

Their own faith not another's: for on earth
Who against faith and conscience can be heard
530 Infallible?[3] Yet many will presume:
Whence heavy persecution shall arise
On all who in the worship persevere
Of Spirit and Truth; the rest, far greater part,
Will deem in outward rites and specious forms
535 Religion satisfied; Truth shall retire
Bestuck with sland'rous darts, and works of faith
Rarely be found: so shall the world go on,
To good malignant, to bad men benign,
Under her own weight groaning, till the day
540 Appear of respiration° to the just,   *respite*
And vengeance to the wicked, at return
Of him so lately promised to thy aid,
The Woman's Seed,[4] obscurely then foretold,
Now ampler known thy Savior and thy Lord,
545 Last in the clouds from Heav'n to be revealed
In glory of the Father, to dissolve
Satan with his perverted world, then raise
From the conflagrant mass,° purged and refined,   *the burning world*
New heav'ns, new earth, ages of endless date
550 Founded in righteousness and peace of love,
To bring forth fruits joy and eternal bliss."
      He ended; and thus Adam last replied:
"How soon hath thy prediction, seer blest,
Measured this transient world, the race of time,
555 Till time stand fixed: beyond is all abyss,
Eternity, whose end no eye can reach.
Greatly instructed I shall hence depart,
Greatly in peace of thought, and have my fill
Of knowledge, what° this vessel can contain;   *as much as*
560 Beyond which was my folly to aspire.
Henceforth I learn, that to obey is best,
And love with fear the only God, to walk
As in his presence, ever to observe
His providence, and on him sole depend,
565 Merciful over all his works, with good
Still overcoming evil, and by small
Accomplishing great things, by things deemed weak
Subverting worldly strong, and worldly wise
By simply meek; that suffering for truth's sake
570 Is fortitude to highest victory,
And to the faithful death the gate of life;
Taught this by his example whom I now
Acknowledge my Redeemer ever blest."
      To whom thus also th' angel last replied:
575 "This having learnt, thou hast attained the sum

---

3. An attack on papal claims to infallibility, asserted though not yet proclaimed as doctrine.
4. Michael's story ends with the full explication of the promised "Woman's Seed" as Christ, and with the renewal of all things after the Last Judgment (lines 545–51).

Of wisdom; hope no higher, though all the stars
Thou knew'st by name,[5] and all th' ethereal powers,
All secrets of the deep, all nature's works,
Or works of God in heav'n, air, earth, or sea,
580 And all the riches of this world enjoy'dst,
And all the rule, one empire; only add
Deeds to thy knowledge answerable,° add faith,   *corresponding*
Add virtue, patience, temperance, add love,
By name to come called charity, the soul
585 Of all the rest: then wilt thou not be loath
To leave this Paradise, but shalt possess
A paradise within thee, happier far.
Let us descend now therefore from this top
Of speculation;° for the hour precise   *hill of speculation*
590 Exacts° our parting hence; and see the guards,   *requires*
By me encamped on yonder hill, expect
Their motion,° at whose front a flaming sword,   *await their orders*
In signal of remove, waves fiercely round;
We may no longer stay: go, waken Eve;
595 Her also I with gentle dreams have calmed
Portending good, and all her spirits composed
To meek submission: thou at season fit
Let her with thee partake what thou hast heard,
Chiefly what may concern her faith to know,
600 The great deliverance by her seed to come
(For by the Woman's Seed) on all mankind.
That ye may live, which will be many days,
Both in one faith unanimous though sad,
With cause for evils past, yet much more cheered
605 With meditation on the happy end."
     He ended, and they both descend the hill;
Descended, Adam to the bow'r where Eve
Lay sleeping ran before, but found her waked;
And thus with words not sad she him received:
610 "Whence thou return'st, and whither went'st, I know;
For God is also in sleep, and dreams advise,[6]
Which he hath sent propitious, some great good
Presaging, since with sorrow and heart's distress
Wearied I fell asleep: but now lead on;
615 In me is no delay; with thee to go,
Is to stay here; without thee here to stay,
Is to go hence unwilling; thou to me
Art all things under heav'n, all places thou,[7]
Who for my willful crime art banished hence.
620 This further consolation yet secure

---

5. Michael glances back at Raphael's warning in Book 8 that Adam should concern himself first with matters pertaining to his own life and world, rather than speculating overmuch about the cosmos.

6. The lines suggest that Eve's dream has provided her a parallel (if lesser) prophecy to Adam's visions and instruction. Cf. Numbers 12.6: "If there be a prophet among you, I the Lord will make myself known unto him in a vision, and will speak unto him in a dream."

7. Eve's lines—the final speech in the poem— recall her prelapsarian love song to Adam (4.641ff.) and Ruth's promise to accompany her mother-in-law, Naomi (Ruth 1.16).

I carry hence; though all by me is lost,
Such favor I unworthy am vouchsafed,
By me the promised Seed shall all restore."
   So spake our mother Eve, and Adam heard
625 Well pleased, but answered not; for now too nigh
Th' Archangel stood, and from the other hill
To their fixed station, all in bright array
The Cherubim descended; on the ground
Gliding metéorous,° as evening mist   *like a meteor*
630 Ris'n from a river o'er the marish° glides,   *marsh*
And gathers ground fast at the laborer's heel
Homeward returning. High in front advanced,
The brandished sword of God before them blazed
Fierce as a comet; which with torrid heat,
635 And vapor° as the Libyan air adust,°   *smoke / parched*
Began to parch that temperate clime; whereat
In either hand the hast'ning angel caught
Our ling'ring parents, and to th' eastern gate
Led them direct, and down the cliff as fast
640 To the subjected° plain; then disappeared.   *low-lying*
They looking back, all th' eastern side beheld
Of Paradise, so late their happy seat,°   *estate*
Waved over by that flaming brand,° the gate   *sword*
With dreadful faces thronged and fiery arms:
645 Some natural tears they dropped, but wiped them soon;
The world was all before them, where to choose
Their place of rest, and Providence their guide:
They hand in hand with wand'ring steps and slow,
Through Eden took their solitary way.

1674

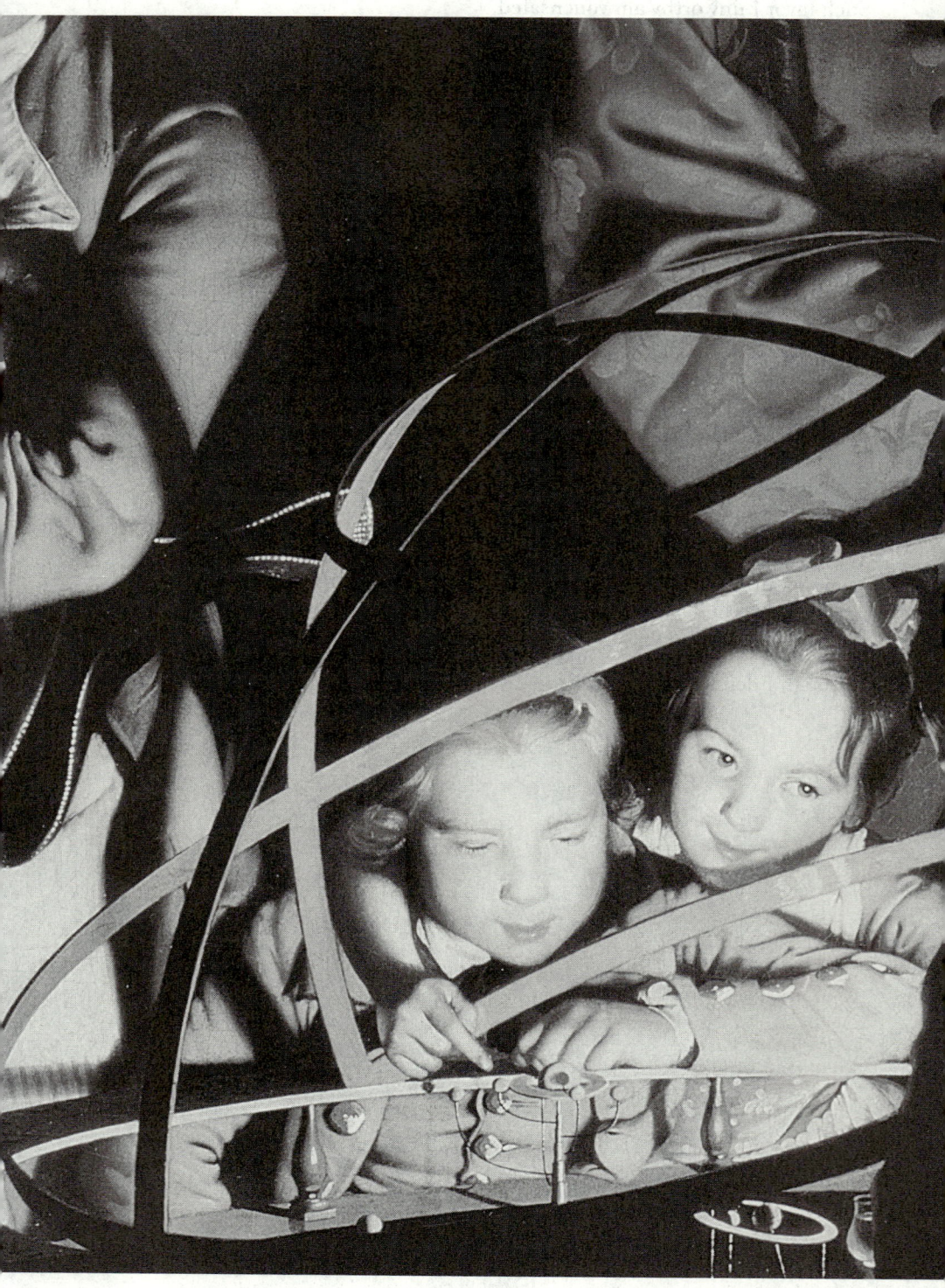

The Restoration and the Eighteenth Century 1660–1785

1660:	Charles II restored to the English throne
1688–89:	The Glorious Revolution: deposition of James II and accession of William of Orange
1700:	Death of John Dryden
1707:	Act of Union unites Scotland and England, creating the nation of "Great Britain"
1714:	Rule by House of Hanover begins with accession of George I
1744–45:	Deaths of Alexander Pope and Jonathan Swift
1784:	Death of Samuel Johnson

The Restoration and the eighteenth century brought vast changes to the island of Great Britain, which became a single nation after 1707, when the Act of Union joined Scotland to England and Wales. After the prolonged civil and religious strife of the seventeenth century, Britain attained political stability and unprecedented commercial vigor. The countryside kept its seemingly timeless agricultural rhythms, even as the nation's great families consolidated their control over the land and those who worked it. Change came most dramatically to cities, which absorbed much of a national population that nearly doubled in the period, to ten million. Britons came together in civil society—the public but nongovernmental institutions and practices that became newly powerful in the period. The theaters (reopened at the Restoration),

A Philosopher Giving That Lecture on the Orrery, in Which a Lamp Is Put in Place of the Sun (detail), 1766, Joseph Wright. For more information about this painting, see the color insert in this volume.

coffeehouses, concert halls, pleasure gardens, lending libraries, picture exhibitions, and shopping districts gave life in London and elsewhere a feeling of bustle and friction. Reflecting and stimulating this activity, an expanding assortment of printed works vied to interest literate women and men, whose numbers grew to include most of the middle classes and many among the poor. Civil society also linked people to an increasingly global economy, as they shopped for diverse goods from around the world. The rich and even the moderately well off could profit or go broke from investments in joint-stock companies, which controlled much of Britain's international trade, including its lucrative traffic in slaves. At home, new systems of canals and turnpikes stimulated domestic trade, industry, and travel, bringing distant parts of the country closer together. The cohesion of the nation also depended on ideas of social order—some old and clear, many subtle and new. An ethos of politeness came to prevail, a standard of social behavior to which more and more could aspire yet that served to distinguish the privileged sharply from the rude and vulgar. This and other ideas, of order and hierarchy, of liberty and rights, of sentiment and sympathy, helped determine the ways in which an expanding diversity of people could seek to participate in Britain's thriving cultural life.

RELIGION AND POLITICS

The Restoration of 1660—the return of Charles Stuart and, with him, the monarchy to England—brought hope to a divided nation, exhausted by years of civil war and political turmoil. Almost all of Charles's subjects welcomed him home. After the abdication of Richard Cromwell in 1659 the country had seemed at the brink of chaos, and Britons were eager to believe that their king would bring order and law and a spirit of mildness back into the national life. But no political settlement could be stable until the religious issues had been resolved. The restoration of the monarchy meant that the established church would also be restored, and though Charles was willing to pardon or ignore many former enemies (such as Milton), the bishops and Anglican clergy were less tolerant of dissent. When Parliament reimposed the Book of Common Prayer in 1662 and then in 1664 barred Nonconformists from religious meetings outside the established church, thousands of clergymen resigned their livings, and the jails were filled with preachers like John Bunyan who refused to be silenced. In 1673 the Test Act required all holders of civil and military offices to take the sacrament in an Anglican church and to deny belief in transubstantiation. Thus Protestant Dissenters and Roman Catholics were largely excluded from public life; for instance, Alexander Pope, a Catholic, could not attend a university, own land, or vote. The scorn of Anglicans for Nonconformist zeal or "enthusiasm" (a belief in private revelation) bursts out in Samuel Butler's popular *Hudibras* (1663), a caricature of Presbyterians and Independents. And English Catholics were widely regarded as potential traitors and (wrongly) thought to have set the Great Fire that destroyed much of London in 1666.

Yet the triumph of the established church did not resolve the constitutional issues that had divided Charles I and Parliament. Charles II had promised to govern through Parliament but slyly tried to consolidate royal power. Steering away from crises, he hid his Catholic sympathies and avoided a test of strength with Parliament—except on one occasion. In 1678 the report of the Popish Plot, in which Catholics would rise and murder their Protestant foes, terrified London; and though the charge turned out to be a fraud, the House of Commons exploited the fear by trying to force Charles to exclude his Catholic brother, James, duke of York, from succession to the throne. The turmoil of this period is captured brilliantly by Dryden's *Absalom and Achitophel* (1681). Finally, Charles defeated the Exclusion Bill by dissolving Parliament. But the crisis resulted in a basic division of the country between two new political parties: the Tories, who supported the king, and the Whigs, the king's opponents.

Neither party could live with James II. After he came to the throne in 1685, he claimed the right to make his own laws, suspended the Test Act, and began to fill the army and government with fellow Catholics. The birth of James's son in 1688 brought matters to a head, confronting the nation with the prospect of a Catholic dynasty. Secret negotiations paved the way for the Dutchman William of Orange, a champion of Protestantism and the husband of James's Protestant daughter Mary. William landed with a small army in southwestern England and marched toward London. As he advanced the king's allies melted away, and James fled to a permanent exile in France. But the house of Stuart would be heard from again. For more than half a century some loyal Jacobites (from the Latin *Jacobus,* "James"), especially in Scotland, supported James, his son ("the Old Pretender"), and his grandson ("the Young Pretender" or "Bonnie Prince Charlie") as the legitimate rulers of Britain. Moreover, a good many writers, from Aphra Behn and Dryden (and arguably Pope and Johnson) to Robert Burns, privately sympathized with Jacobitism. But after the failure of one last rising in 1745, the cause would dwindle gradually into a wistful sentiment. In retrospect, the coming of William and Mary in 1688—the Glorious, or Bloodless, Revolution— came to be seen as the beginning of a stabilized, unified Great Britain.

A number of innovations made this stability possible. In 1689 a Bill of Rights revoked James's actions; it limited the powers of the Crown, reaffirmed the supremacy of Parliament, and guaranteed some individual rights. The same year the Toleration Act relaxed the strain of religious conflict by granting a limited freedom of worship to Dissenters (although not to Catholics or Jews) so long as they swore allegiance to the Crown. This proved to be a workable compromise. The passage of the Act of Settlement in 1701 seemed finally to resolve the difficult problem of succession that had bedeviled the monarchy. Sophia, the electress of Hanover, and her descendants were put in line for the throne. As the granddaughter of James I, she was the closest Protestant relative of Princess Anne, James II's younger daughter (whose sole surviving child died in that year). The principles established in these years endured unaltered in essentials until the Reform Bill of 1832.

But the political rancor that often animates contests for power did not vanish, and during Anne's reign (1702–14), new tensions embittered the nation. In the War of the Spanish Succession (1702–13), England and its allies defeated France and Spain. As these commercial rivals were weakened and war profits flowed in, the Whig lords and London merchants supporting the war grew rich. The spoils included new colonies and the *asiento,* a contract to supply slaves to the Spanish Empire. The hero of the war, Captain-General John Churchill, duke of Marlborough, won the famous victory of Blenheim; was showered with honors and wealth; and, with his duchess, dominated the queen until 1710. But the Whigs and Marlborough pushed their luck too hard. When the Whigs tried to reward the Dissenters for their loyalty by removing the Test, Anne fought back to defend the established church. She dismissed her Whig ministers and the Marlboroughs and called in Robert Harley and the brilliant young Henry St. John to form a Tory ministry. These ministers employed prominent writers like Defoe and Swift and commissioned Matthew Prior to negotiate the Peace of Utrecht (1713). But to Swift's despair—he later burlesqued events at court in *Gulliver's Travels*—a bitter rivalry broke out between Harley (now earl of Oxford) and St. John (now Viscount Bolingbroke). Though Bolingbroke succeeded in ousting Oxford, the death of Anne in 1714 reversed his fortunes. The Whigs returned to power, and George I (Sophia's son) became the first Hanoverian king (he would reign until 1727). Harley was imprisoned in the Tower of London until 1717; and Bolingbroke, charged with being a Jacobite traitor, fled to France. Government was now securely in the hands of the Whigs.

The political principles of the Whig and Tory parties, which bring so much fire to eighteenth-century public debate, evolved through the period to address changing circumstances. Now we tend to think of Tories as conservative and Whigs as liberal. (Members of today's Conservative Party in the United Kingdom are sometimes called Tories.) During the Exclusion Crisis of the 1680s the Whigs asserted the liberties of the English subject against the royal prerogatives of Charles II, whom Tories such as Dryden supported. After both parties survived the 1688 Glorious Revolution, the Tories guarded the preeminence of the established church (sometimes styling themselves the Church Party), while Whigs tended to support toleration of Dissenters. Economically, too, Tories defined themselves as traditionalists, affirming landownership as the proper basis of wealth, power, and privilege (though most thought trade honorable), whereas the Whigs came to be seen as supporting a new "moneyed interest" (as Swift called it): managers of the Bank of England (founded 1694), contrivers of the system of public credit, and investors in the stock market. But conservatism and liberalism did not exist as ideological labels in the period, and the vicissitudes of party dispute offer many surprises. When Bolingbroke returned to England in 1724 after being pardoned, he led a Tory opposition that decried the "ministerial tyranny" of the Whig government. This opposition patriotically hailed liberty in a manner recalling the Whig rhetoric of earlier decades, appealed to both landed gentry and urban merchants, and anticipated the antigovernment radicalism of the end of the eighteenth century. Conversely, the Whigs sought to secure a centralized fiscal and military state machine and a web of financial interdependence controlled by the wealthiest aristocrats.

The great architect of this Whig policy was Robert Walpole, who came to power as a result of the "South Sea bubble" (1720), a stock market crash. His ability to restore confidence and keep the country running smoothly, as well as to juggle money, would mark his long ascendancy. Coming to be known as Britain's first "prime" minister, he consolidated his power during the reign of George II (1727–60). More involved in British affairs than his essentially German father, George II came to appreciate the efficient administration of the patronage system under Walpole, who installed dependents in government offices and controlled the House of Commons by financially rewarding its members. Many great writers found these methods offensive and embraced Bolingbroke's new Tory rhetoric extolling the Englishman's fierce independence from the corrupting power of centralized government and concentrations of wealth. Gay's *Beggar's Opera* (1728) and Fielding's *Jonathan Wild* (1743) draw parallels between great criminals and great politicians, and Pope's *Dunciad* uses Walpole as an emblem of the venal commercialization of the whole social fabric. This distaste, however, did not prevent Pope himself from marketing his poems as cleverly as he wrote them.

Walpole fell in 1742 because he was unwilling to go to war against the French and Spanish, a war he thought would cost too much but that many perceived would enhance Britain's wealth still further. The next major English statesman, William Pitt the Elder, appealed to a spirit of patriotism and called for the expansion of British power and commerce overseas. The defeat of the French in the Seven Years' War (1756–63), especially in North America, was largely his doing. The long reign of George III (1760–1820) was dominated by two great concerns: the emergence of Britain as a colonial power and the cry for a new social order based on liberty and radical reform. In 1763 the Peace of Paris consolidated British rule over Canada and India, and not even the later loss of the American colonies could stem the rise of the empire. Great Britain was no longer an isolated island but a nation with interests and responsibilities around the world.

At home, however, there was discontent. The wealth brought to England by industrialism and foreign trade had not spread to the great mass of the poor. For much of the century, few had questioned the idea that those at the top of the social hierarchy rightfully held power. Rich families' alliances and rivalries, national and local, dominated politics; while male property owners could vote in Parliamentary elections, they and others of the middle classes and the poor had mostly followed the powerful people who could best help them thrive or at least survive. But toward the end of the century it seemed to many that the bonds of custom that once held people together had finally broken, and now money alone was respected. Protestants turned against Catholics; in 1780 the Gordon Riots put London temporarily under mob rule. The king was popular with his subjects and tried to take government into his own hands, rising above partisanship, but his efforts often backfired—as when the American colonists took him for a tyrant. From 1788 to the end of his life, moreover, an inherited disease (porphyria) periodically unhinged his mind, as in a memorable scene described by Frances Burney. Meanwhile, reformers such as John Wilkes, Richard Price, and Catherine Macaulay called for a new political republic. Fear of their radicalism would contribute to the British reaction against the French Revolution. In the last decades of the century British authors would be torn between two opposing attitudes: loyalty to the old traditions of subordination, mutual obligations, and local self-sufficiency, and yearning for a new dispensation founded on principles of liberty, the rule of reason, and human rights.

THE CONTEXT OF IDEAS

Much of the most powerful writing after 1660 exposed divisions in the nation's thinking inherited from the tumult of earlier decades. As the possibility of a Christian Commonwealth receded, the great republican John Milton published *Paradise Lost* (final version, 1674), and John Bunyan's immensely popular masterwork *Pilgrim's Progress* (1679) expressed the conscience of a Nonconformist. Conversely, an aristocratic culture, led by Charles II himself, aggressively celebrated pleasure and the right of the elite to behave as they wished. Members of the court scandalized respectable London citizens and considered their wives and daughters fair game. The court's hero, the earl of Rochester, became a celebrity for enacting the creed of a libertine and rake. The delights of the court also took more refined forms. French and Italian musicians, as well as painters from the Low Countries, migrated to England; and playhouses—closed by the Puritans since 1642—sprang back to life. In 1660 Charles authorized two new companies of actors, the King's Players and the Duke's; their repertory included witty, bawdy comedies written and acted by women as well as men. But as stark as the contrasts were during the Restoration between libertine and religious intellectuals, royalists and republicans, High Churchmen and Nonconformists, the court and the rest of the country, a spirit of compromise was brewing.

Perhaps the most widely shared intellectual impulse of the age was a distrust of dogmatism. Nearly everybody blamed it for the civil strife through which the nation had recently passed. Opinions varied widely about which dogmatism was most dangerous—Puritan enthusiasm, papal infallibility, the divine right of kings, medieval scholastic or modern Cartesian philosophy—but these were denounced in remarkably similar terms. As far apart intellectually and temperamentally as Rochester and Milton were, both portray overconfidence in human reasoning as the supreme disaster. It is the theme of Butler's *Hudibras* and much of the work of Dryden. Many philosophers, scientists, and divines began to embrace a mitigated skepticism, which argued that human beings could readily achieve a sufficient degree of necessary knowledge (sometimes called "moral certainty") but also contended that the pursuit of absolute certainty was vain, mad, and socially calamitous. If, as the commentator Martin Clifford put it in *A Treatise of Humane Reason* (1675), "in this vast latitude of probabilities," a person thinks "there is none can lead one to salvation, but the path wherein he treads himself, we may see the evident and necessary consequence of eternal troubles and confusions." Such writers insist that a distrust of human capacities is fully compatible with religious faith: for them the inability of reason and sensory evidence to settle important questions reveals our need to accept Christian mysteries as our intellectual foundation. Dryden's poem *Religio Laici* (1682) explains: "So pale grows reason in religion's sight; / So dies, and so dissolves in supernatural light."

Far from inhibiting fresh thinking, however, the distrust of old dogmas inspired new theories, projects, and explorations. In *Leviathan* (1651), Thomas Hobbes jettisoned the notion of a divine basis for kingly authority, proposing instead a naturalistic argument for royal absolutism begun from the claim that mere "matter in motion" composes the universe: if not checked by an absolute sovereign, mankind's "perpetual and restless desire

Frontispiece to Thomas Sprat's *History of the Royal Society*;
Wenceslaus Hollar, engraving, London, 1667. A bust of King
Charles II, called the "author and patron of the Royal Society"
(Latin), is being crowned by Fame. To the left is the Royal Society's
president, Lord Bruckner; to the right, Francis Bacon, pointing to
mathematical and military technology. On the left side are shelves
full of books, and in the background, more scientific instruments,
including Robert Boyle's air pump (center left).

of power after power" could lead to civic collapse. Other materialist philosophies derived from ancient Epicurean thought, which was Christianized by
the French philosopher Pierre Gassendi (1592–1655). The Epicurean doctrine that the universe consists only of minuscule atoms and void unnerved
some thinkers—Swift roundly mocks it in *A Tale of a Tub*—but it also energized efforts to examine the world with deliberate, acute attention. This
new scientific impulse advanced Francis Bacon's program of methodical
experimentation and inductive reasoning formulated earlier in the century.

Charles II gave official approval to the scientific revolution by charter-
ing the Royal Society of London for the Improving of Natural Knowledge in
1662. But observations of nature advanced both formally and informally in an
eclectic range of areas: the specialized, professional "scientist" we know today
did not yet exist. And new features of the world were disclosed to everyone
who had the chance to look. Two wonderful inventions, the microscope and

telescope, had begun to reveal that nature is more extravagant—teeming with tiny creatures and boundless galaxies—than anyone had ever imagined. One book that stayed popular for more than a century, Fontenelle's *Conversations on the Plurality of Worlds* (1686; translated from French by Behn and later by Burney), suggested that an infinite number of alternate worlds and living creatures might exist, not only in outer space but under our feet, invisibly small. Travels to unfamiliar regions of the globe also enlarged understandings of what nature could do: Behn's classifying and collecting of South American flora and fauna in *Oroonoko* show how the appetite for wondrous facts kept pace with the economic motives of world exploration and colonization. Encounters with hitherto little known societies in the Far East, Africa, and the Americas enlarged Europeans' understanding of human norms as well. In *Gulliver's Travels*, Swift shows the comical, painful ways in which the discovery of new cultures forces one average Briton to reexamine his own.

Scientific discovery and exploration also affected religious attitudes. Alongside "natural history" (the collection and description of facts of nature) and "natural philosophy" (the study of the causes of what happens in nature), thinkers of the period placed "natural religion" (the study of nature as a book written by God). Newly discovered natural laws, such as Newton's laws of optics and celestial mechanics, seemed evidence of a universal order in creation, which implied God's hand in the design of the universe, as a watch implies a watchmaker. Expanded knowledge of peoples around the world who had never heard of Christianity led theologians to formulate supposedly universal religious tenets available to all rational beings. Some intellectuals embraced Deism, the doctrine that religion need not depend on mystery or biblical truths and could rely on reason alone, which recognized the goodness and wisdom of natural law and its creator. Natural religion could not, however, discern an active God who punished vice and rewarded virtue in this life; evidently the First Cause had withdrawn from the universe He set in motion. Many orthodox Christians shuddered at the vision of a vast, impersonal machine of nature. Instead they rested their faith on the revelation of Scripture, the scheme of salvation in which Christ died to redeem our sins. Other Christians, such as Pope in *An Essay on Man* and Thomson in *The Seasons,* espoused arguments for natural religion that they felt did not conflict with or diminish orthodox belief.

Some people began to argue that the achievements of modern inquiry had eclipsed those of the ancients (and the fathers of the church), who had not known about the solar system, the New World, microscopic organisms, or the circulation of the blood. The school curriculum still began with years of Latin and Greek, inculcating a long-established humanistic tradition cherished by many authors, including Swift and Pope. A battle of the books erupted in the late seventeenth century between champions of ancient and of modern learning. Swift crusaded fiercely in this battle: *Gulliver's Travels* denounces the pointlessness and arrogance he saw in experiments of the Royal Society, while "A Modest Proposal" depicts a peculiar new cruelty and indifference to moral purpose made possible by statistics and economics (two fields pioneered by Royal Society member Sir William Petty). But as sharp as such disagreements were, accommodation was also possible. Even as works such as Newton's *Principia* (1687) and *Opticks* (1704) revolutionized previously held views of the world, Newton himself maintained a seemly diffidence, comparing himself to "a boy playing on the sea-shore" "whilst the great ocean of truth lay all undiscovered before me." He and other modest modern inquirers such as Locke won the admiration of Pope and many ardent defenders of the past.

The widespread devotion to the direct observation of experience established empiricism as the dominant intellectual attitude of the age, which would become Britain's great legacy to world philosophy. Locke and his heirs George Berkeley and David Hume pursue the experiential approach in widely divergent directions. But even when they reach conclusions shocking to common sense, they tend to reassert the security of our prior knowledge. Berkeley insists we know the world only through our senses and thus cannot prove that any material thing exists, but he uses that argument to demonstrate the necessity of faith, because reality amounts to no more than a perception in the mind of God. Hume's famous argument about causation—that "causes and effects are discoverable, not by reason but by experience"—grounds our sense of the world not on rational reflection but on spontaneous, unreflective beliefs and feelings. Perhaps Locke best expresses the temper of his times in the *Essay Concerning Human Understanding* (1690):

> If by this inquiry into the nature of the understanding, I can discover the powers thereof; how far they reach; to what things they are in any degree proportionate; and where they fail us, I suppose it may be of use, to prevail with the busy mind of man to be more cautious in meddling with things exceeding its comprehension; to stop when it is at the utmost extent of its tether; and to sit down in a quiet ignorance of those things which, upon examination, are found to be beyond the reach of our capacities. . . . Our business here is not to know all things, but those which concern our conduct.

Such a position is Swift's, when he inveighs against metaphysics, abstract logical deductions, and theoretical science. It is similar to Pope's warning against human presumption in *An Essay on Man*. It prompts Johnson to talk of "the business of living" and to restrain the flights of unbridled imagination. And it helps account for the Anglican clergy's dislike of emotion and "enthusiasm" in religion and for their emphasis on good works, rather than faith, as the way to salvation. Locke's attitudes pervaded eighteenth-century British thought on politics, education, and morals as well as philosophy; Johnson's great *Dictionary* (1755) uses more than fifteen hundred illustrations from his writings.

Yet one momentous new idea at the turn of the eighteenth century was set against Lockean thinking. The groundbreaking intellectual Mary Astell, in *A Serious Proposal to the Ladies* (1694) and *Some Reflections upon Marriage* (1700, 1706), initiated a powerful strain of modern feminism, arguing for the establishment of women's educational institutions and decrying the tyranny that husbands legally exercised over their wives. She nonetheless mocked the calls for political rights and liberty by Locke and other Whig theorists, rights that pointedly did not extend to women. Instead, she and other early feminists, including Sarah Fyge Egerton and Mary, Lady Chudleigh, embraced the Tory principle of obedience to royal and church authority. Women's advocates had to fight "tyrant Custom" (in Egerton's words), rooted in ancient traditions of domestic power and enshrined in the Bible and mythic human prehistory. This struggle seemed distinct from public political denunciations of the tyranny of some relatively recent Charles or James. Astell feared that the doctrines of male revolutionaries could produce civil chaos and so jeopardize the best that women could hope for in her day: the freedom to become fully educated, practice their religion, and marry (or not) according to their own enlightened judgment.

Other thinkers, male and female, began to advocate improving women's education as part of a wider commitment to enhancing and extending sociability. Richard Steele's periodical *The Toiler* satirized Astell as "Madonella" because she seemed to recommend women to a nun-like, "recluse life." In *The Spectator* (1711–12; 1714), conversely, Steele and Joseph Addison encouraged women to learn to participate in an increasingly sociable, intellectually sophisticated, urbane world, where all sorts of people could mingle, as in the streets, parks, and pleasure grounds of a thriving city like London. Such peri-

Robert Dighton, *Mr. Deputy Dumpling and Family Enjoying a Summer Afternoon*, 1781. A family of the middling sort, the father self-important, the mother beaming, visit Bagnigge Wells, one of many resorts in London catering to specific classes.

odicals sought to teach as large a readership as possible to think and behave politely. On a more aristocratic plane, the *Characteristics of Men, Manners, Opinions, and Times* (1711) by the third earl of Shaftesbury similarly asserted the naturally social meaning of human character and meditated on the affections, the witty intercourse, and the standards of politeness that bind people together. Such ideas led to the popularity around mid-century of a new word, *sentimental,* which locates the bases of social conduct in instinctual feeling rather than divinely sanctioned moral codes. Religion itself, according to Laurence Sterne, might be a "Great Sensorium," a sort of central nervous system that connects the feelings of all living creatures in one great benevolent soul. And people began to feel exquisite pleasure in the exercise of charity. The cult of sensibility fostered a philanthropy that led to social reforms seldom envisioned in earlier times—to the improvement of jails, the relief of imprisoned debtors, the establishment of foundling hospitals and of homes for penitent prostitutes, and ultimately the abolition of the slave trade. And it also loosed a ready flow of sympathetic responses to the joys and sorrows of fellow human beings.

As they cultivated fine feelings, Britons also pursued their fascination with the material world. Scientific discoveries increasingly found practical applications in industry, the arts, and even entertainment. By the late 1740s, as knowledge of electricity advanced, public experiments offered fashionable British crowds the opportunity to electrocute themselves. Amateurs everywhere amused themselves with air pumps and chemical explosions. Birmingham became famous as a center where science and manufacturing were combining to change the world: in the early 1760s Matthew Boulton (1728–1809) established the most impressive factory of the age just outside town, producing vast quantities of pins, buckles, and buttons; in subsequent decades, his applications and manufacture of the new steam engine invented by Scotsman James Watt (1736–1819) helped build an industry to drive all others. Practical chemistry also led to industrial improvements: domestic porcelain production became established in the 1750s; and from the 1760s Josiah Wedgwood (1730–1795) developed glazing, manufacturing, and marketing techniques that enabled British ceramics to compete with China for fashionable taste. (In 1765 he named his creamware "Queen's ware" to remind customers of its place on Queen Charlotte's table.) Wedgwood and others answered an ever-increasing demand in Britain for beautiful objects. Artist William Hogarth satirized this appetite of the upper and middle classes for the accumulation of finery: a chaotic collection of china figurines crowds the mantel in Plate 2 of *Marriage A-la-Mode* (1743–45). Yet the images that made Hogarth famous would soon decorate English ceramic teapots and plates and be turned into porcelain figurines themselves.

New forms of religious devotion sprang up amid Britain's spectacular material success. The evangelical revival known as Methodism began in the 1730s, led by three Oxford graduates: John Wesley (1703–1791), his brother Charles (1707–1788), and George Whitefield (1714–1770). The Methodists took their gospel to the common people, warning that all were sinners and damned, unless they accepted "amazing grace," salvation through faith. Often denied the privilege of preaching in village churches, evangelicals preached to thousands in barns or the open fields. The emotionalism of such revival meetings repelled the somnolent Anglican Church and the upper

classes, who feared that the fury and zeal of the Puritan sects were returning. Methodism was sometimes related to madness; convinced that he was
damned forever, the poet William Cowper broke down and became a recluse.
But the religious awakening persisted and affected many clergymen and laymen within the Establishment, who reanimated the church and promoted
unworldliness and piety. Nor did the insistence of Methodists on faith over
works as the way to salvation prevent them or their Anglican allies from
fighting for social reforms. The campaign to abolish slavery and the slave
trade was driven largely by a passion to save souls.

Sentimentalism, evangelicalism, and the pursuits of wealth and luxury
in different ways all placed a new importance on individuals—the gratification of their tastes and ambitions or their yearning for personal encounters
with each other or a personal God. Diary keeping, elaborate letter writing, and the novel also testified to the growing importance of the private,
individual life. Few histories of kings or nations could rival Richardson's
novel *Clarissa* in length, popularity, or documentary detail: it was subtitled
"the History of a Young Lady." The older hierarchical system had tended
to subordinate individuals to their social rank or station. In the eighteenth
century that fixed system began to break down, and people's sense of themselves began to change. By the end of the century many issues of politics
and the law revolve around rights, not traditions. The modern individual
had been invented; no product of the age is more enduring.

CONDITIONS OF LITERARY PRODUCTION

Publishing boomed as never before in eighteenth-century Britain, as the
number of titles appearing annually and the periodicals published in London and the provincial towns dramatically increased. This expansion in part
resulted from a loosening of legal restraints on printing. Through much of
the previous three centuries, the government had licensed the texts deemed
suitable for publication and refused to license those it wanted suppressed (a
practice called "prior restraint"). After the Restoration, the new Printing
Act (1662) tightened licensing controls, though unlike his Stuart predecessors Charles II now shared this power with Parliament. But in 1695, during
the reign of William III, the last in a series of printing acts was not renewed.
Debate in Parliament on the matter was more practical than idealistic: it
was argued that licensing fettered the printing trades and was ineffective
at preventing obnoxious publications anyway, which could be better constrained after publication by enforcing laws against seditious libel, obscenity,
and treason. As the two-party system consolidated, both Whigs and Tories
seemed to realize that prepublication censorship could bite them when their
own side happened to be out of power. Various governments attempted to
revive licensing during political crises throughout the eighteenth century,
but it was gone for good.

This did not end the legal liabilities, and the prosecutions, of authors.
Daniel Defoe, for instance, was convicted of seditious libel and faced the
pillory and jail for his satirical pamphlet "The Shortest Way with the Dissenters" (1702), which imitated High Church zeal so extravagantly that it
provoked both the Tories and the Dissenters he had set about to defend. And

licensing of the stage returned: irritated especially by Henry Fielding's anti-government play *The Historical Register for the Year 1736*, Robert Walpole pushed the Stage Licensing Act through Parliament in 1737, which authorized the Lord Chamberlain to license all plays and reduced the number of London theaters to two (Drury Lane and Covent Garden), closing Fielding's New Theatre in the Haymarket and driving him to a new career as a novelist. But despite such constraints, Hume could begin his essay "Of the Liberty of the Press" (1741) by citing "the extreme liberty we enjoy in this country of communicating whatever we please to the public" as an internationally recognized commonplace. This freedom allowed eighteenth-century Britain to build an exemplary version of what historians have called "the public sphere": a cultural arena, free of direct government control, consisting of not just published comment on matters of national interest but also the public venues—coffeehouses, clubs, taverns—where readers circulated, discussed, and conceived responses to it. The first regular daily London newspaper, the *Daily Courant*, appeared in 1702; in 1731, the first magazine, the *Gentleman's Magazine*. The latter was followed both by imitations and by successful literary journals like the *Monthly Review* (1749) and the *Critical Review* (1756). Each audience attracted some periodical tailored to it, as with the *Female Tatler* (1709) and Eliza Haywood's *Female Spectator* (1744–46).

After 1695, the legal status of printed matter became ambiguous, and in 1710 Parliament enacted the Statute of Anne—"An Act for the Encouragement of Learning by Vesting the Copies of Printed Books in the Authors or Purchasers of Such Copies"—the first copyright law in British history not tied to government approval of works' contents. Typically, these copyrights were held by booksellers, who operated much as publishers do today (in the eighteenth century, *publisher* referred to one who distributed books). A bookseller paid an author for a work's copyright and, after registering the work with the Stationers' Company for a fee, had exclusive right for fourteen years to publish it; if alive when this term expired, he owned it another fourteen years. Payments to authors for copyright varied. Pope got £15 for the 1714 version of *The Rape of the Lock*, while Samuel Johnson's *Rasselas* earned him £100. The Statute of Anne spurred the book trade by enhancing booksellers' control over works and hence their chance to profit by them. But the government soon introduced a new constraint. In 1712, the first Stamp Act put a tax on all newspapers, advertisements, paper, and pamphlets (effectively any work under a hundred pages or so): all printed matter had to carry the stamp indicating the taxes had been paid. Happily for Anne and her ministry, the act both raised government revenue and drove a number of the more irresponsible, ephemeral newspapers out of business, though the *Spectator* simply doubled its price and thrived. Stamp Acts were in effect throughout the century, and duties tended to increase when the government needed to raise money and rein in the press, as during the Seven Years' War in 1757.

But such constraints were not heavy enough to hold back the publishing market, which began to sustain the first true professional class of authors in British literary history. The lower echelon of the profession was called "Grub Street," which was, as Johnson's *Dictionary* explains, "originally the name of a street in Moorfields in London, much inhabited by writers of small histories, dictionaries, and temporary poems." The market increasingly motivated the literary elite too, and Johnson himself came to remark that "no man but a blockhead ever wrote, except for money." As a young writer, he sold articles to the *Gentleman's Magazine*, and many other men and women struggled to survive doing piecework for periodicals. The enhanced opportunity to sell their works on the open market meant that fewer authors needed to look to aristocratic patrons for support. But a new practice, publication by subscription, blended elements of patronage and literary capitalism and created the century's most spectacular authorial fortunes. Wealthy readers could subscribe to a work in progress, usually by agreeing to pay the author half in advance and half upon receipt of the book. Subscribers were rewarded with an edition more sumptuous than the common run and the appearance of their names in a list in the book's front pages. Major works by famous authors, such as Dryden's translation of Virgil (1697) and the 1718 edition of Prior's poems, generated the most subscription sales; the grandest success was Pope's translation of Homer's *Iliad* (1715–20), which gained him about £5000; his *Odyssey* (1725–26) raised nearly that much. But smaller projects deemed to need special encouragement also sold by subscription, including nearly all books of poetry by women, such as Mary Leapor's poems (1751).

Not all entered the literary market with equal advantages; and social class played a role, though hardly a simple one, in preparing authors for success. The better educated were better placed to be taken seriously: many eminent male writers, including Dryden, Locke, Addison, Swift, Hume, Johnson, Burke—the list could go on and on—had at least some university education, either at Oxford or Cambridge or at Scottish or Irish universities, where attendance by members of the laboring classes was virtually nil. Also, universities were officially closed to non-Anglicans. Some important writers attended the Dissenting academies that sprang up to fulfill Nonconformists' educational aspirations: Defoe went to an excellent one at Newington Green. A few celebrated authors such as Rochester and Henry Fielding had aristocratic backgrounds, but many came from the "middle class," though those in this category show how heterogeneous it was. Pope, a Catholic, obtained his education privately, and his father was a linen wholesaler, but he eventually became intimate with earls and viscounts, whereas Richardson, who had a family background in trade and (as he said) "only common school-learning," was a successful printer before he became a novelist. Both were middle class in a sense and made their own fortunes in eighteenth-century print culture, yet they inhabited vastly different social worlds.

Despite the general exclusion of the poor from education and other means of social advancement, some self-educated writers of the laboring classes fought their way into print. A few became celebrities, aided by the increasing popularity of the idea, famously expressed by Gray in his "Elegy Written in a Country Churchyard," that there must be unknown geniuses among the poor. Stephen Duck, an agricultural worker from Wiltshire, published his popular *Poems on Several Subjects* in 1730, which included "The Thresher's Labor" (he became known as the Thresher Poet). Queen Caroline herself retained him to be keeper of her library in Richmond. Several authors of the "common sort" followed in Duck's wake, including Mary Collier, whose poem "The Woman's Labor: An Epistle to Mr. Duck" (1739) defended country women against charges of idleness. Apart from such visible successes, eighteenth-century print culture afforded work for many from lower socioeconomic levels, if not as authors, then as hawkers of newspapers on city streets and singers of political ballads (who were often illiterate and female), bookbinders, papermakers, and printing-press workers. The vigor of the literary market demanded the labor of all classes.

As all women were barred from universities and faced innumerable other disadvantages and varieties of repression, the story of virtually every woman author in the period is one of self-education, courage, and extraordinary initiative. Yet women did publish widely for the first time in the period, and the examples that can be assembled are as diverse as they are impressive. During the Restoration and early eighteenth century, a few aristocratic women poets were hailed as marvelous exceptions and given fanciful names: the poems of Katherine Philips (1631–1664), "the matchless Orinda," were published posthumously in 1667; and others, including Anne Finch, Anne Killigrew, and later, Lady Mary Wortley Montagu, printed poems or circulated them in manuscript among fashionable circles. A more broadly public sort of female authorship was more ambivalently received. Though Aphra Behn built a successful career in the theater and in print, her sexually frank works were sometimes denounced as unbecoming a woman. Many women writers of popular

Richard Samuel, *Portraits in the Characters of the Muses in the Temple of Apollo* (*The Nine Living Muses of Great Britain*), 1778. A mythological depiction of some "bluestockings," women who made outstanding contributions to British literature and culture after the mid-18th century. *Standing, left to right:* Elizabeth Carter, Anna Barbauld, Elizabeth Sheridan, Hannah More, and Charlotte Lennox; *seated, left to right:* Angelica Kauffmann, Catherine Macaulay, Elizabeth Montagu, and Elizabeth Griffith.

literature after her in the early eighteenth century assumed "scandalous" public roles. Delarivier Manley published transparent fictionalizations of the doings of the Whig nobility, including *The New Atalantis* (1709), while Eliza Haywood produced stories about seduction and sex (though her late works, including *The History of Miss Betsy Thoughtless*, 1751, courted a rising taste for morality). Male defenders of high culture found it easy to denounce these women and their works as affronts simultaneously to sexual decency and to good literary taste: Pope's *Dunciad* (1728) awards Haywood as the prize in a pissing contest between scurrilous male booksellers.

Many women writers after midcentury were determined to be more moral than their predecessors. Around 1750, intellectual women established clubs of their own under the leadership of Elizabeth Vesey and Elizabeth Montagu, cousin to Lady Mary. Proclaiming a high religious and intellectual standard, these women came to be called "bluestockings" (after the inelegant worsted hose of an early member). Eminent men joined the bluestockings for literary conversation, including Samuel Johnson, Samuel Richardson, Horace Walpole (novelist, celebrated letter writer, and son of the prime minister), and David Garrick, preeminent actor of his day. The literary accomplishments of bluestockings ranged widely: in 1758 Elizabeth Carter published her translation of the Greek philosopher Epictetus, while Hannah More won fame as a poet, abolitionist, and educational theorist. Some of the most considerable literary achievements of women after mid-century came in the novel, a form increasingly directed at women readers, often exploring the moral difficulties of young women approaching marriage. The satirical novel *The Female Quixote* (1752) by Charlotte Lennox describes one such heroine deluded by the extravagant romances she reads, while Frances Burney's *Evelina* (1778) unfolds the sexual and other dangers besetting its naïve but good-hearted heroine.

Readers' abilities and inclinations to consume literature helped determine the volume and variety of published works. While historians disagree about how exactly the literacy rate changed in Britain through the early modern period, there is widespread consensus that by 1800 between 60 and 70 percent of adult men could read, in contrast to 25 percent in 1600. Since historians use the ability to sign one's name as an indicator of literacy, the evidence is even sketchier for women, who were less often parties to legal contracts: perhaps a third of women could read by the mid-eighteenth century. Reading was commoner among the relatively well off than among the very poor, and among the latter, more prevalent in urban centers than the countryside. Most decisively, cultural commentators throughout the century portrayed literacy as a good in itself: everyone in a Protestant country such as Britain, most thought, would benefit from direct access to the Bible and devotional works, and increasingly employers found literacy among servants and other laborers useful, especially those working in cities. Moral commentators did their best to steer inexperienced readers away from the frivolous and idle realm of popular imaginative literature, though literacy could not but give its new possessors freedom to explore their own tastes and inclinations.

Cost placed another limit on readership: few of the laboring classes would have disposable income to buy a cheap edition of Milton (around two shillings at mid-century) or even a copy of the *Gentleman's Magazine* (six pence), let alone the spare time or sense of entitlement to peruse such things. Nonetheless, reading material was widely shared (Addison optimistically calculated "twenty readers to every paper" of the *Spectator*), and occasionally servants were given access to the libraries of their employers or the rich family of the neighborhood. In the 1740s, circulating libraries began to emerge in cities and towns throughout Britain. Though the yearly fee they usually charged put them beyond the reach of the poor, these libraries gave the middle classes access to a wider array of books than they could afford to assemble on their own. Records of such libraries indicate that travels, histories, letters, and novels were most popular, though patrons borrowed many specialized, technical works as well. One fascinating index of change in the character of the reading public was the very look of words on the page. In the past, printers had rather capriciously capitalized many nouns—words as common as *Wood* or *Happiness*—and frequently italicized various words for emphasis. But around the middle of the eighteenth century, new conventions arose: initial capitals were reserved for proper names, and the use of italics was reduced. Such changes indicate that the reading public was becoming sophisticated enough not to require such overt pointing to the meanings of what they read. The modern, eighteenth-century reader had come to expect that all English writing, no matter how old or new, on any topic, in any genre, would be printed in the same consistent, uncluttered style. No innovation of the eighteenth-century culture of reading more immediately demonstrates its linkage to our own.

LITERARY PRINCIPLES

The literature appearing between 1660 and 1785 divides conveniently into three shorter periods of about forty years each. The first, extending to the death of Dryden in 1700, is characterized by an effort to bring a new refinement to English literature according to sound critical principles of what is fitting and right; the second, ending with the deaths of Pope in 1744 and Swift in 1745, extends that effort to a wider circle of readers, with special satirical attention to what is unfitting and wrong; the third, concluding with the death of Johnson in 1784 and the publication of Cowper's *The Task* in 1785, confronts the old principles with revolutionary ideas that would come to the fore in the Romantic movement of the late eighteenth and early nineteenth centuries.

A sudden change of taste seemed to occur around 1660. The change had been long prepared, however, by a trend in European culture, especially in seventeenth-century France: the desire for an elegant simplicity. Reacting against the difficulty and occasional extravagance of late Renaissance literature, writers and critics called for a new restraint, clarity, regularity, and good sense. Donne's "metaphysics" and Milton's bold storming of heaven, for instance, seemed overdone to some Restoration readers. Hence Dryden and Andrew Marvell both were tempted to revise *Paradise Lost*, smoothing away its sublime but arduous idiosyncrasies. As daring and imaginative as Dryden's verse is, he tempers even its highly dramatic moments with an ease and sense of control definitive of the taste of his times.

This movement produced in France an impressive body of classical literature that distinguished the age of Louis XIV. In England it produced a literature often termed "Augustan," after the writers who flourished during the reign of Augustus Caesar, the first Roman emperor. Rome's Augustan Age reestablished stability after the civil war that followed the assassination of Julius Caesar. Its chief poets, Virgil, Horace, and Ovid, addressed their polished works to a sophisticated aristocracy among whom they looked for patrons. Dryden's generation took advantage of the analogy between post–civil war England and Augustan Rome. Later generations would be suspicious of that analogy; after 1700 most writers stressed that Augustus had been a tyrant who thought himself greater than the law. But in 1660 there was hope that Charles would be a better Augustus, bringing England the civilized virtues of an Augustan age without its vices.

Charles and his followers brought back from exile an admiration of French literature as well as French fashions, and the theoretical "correctness" of such writers as Pierre Corneille, René Rapin, and Nicolas Boileau came into vogue. England also had a native tradition of classicism, derived from Ben Jonson and his followers, whose couplets embodied a refinement Dryden eagerly inherited and helped codify. The effort to formulate rules of good writing appealed to many critics of the age. Even Shakespeare had sometimes been careless; and although writers could not expect to surpass his genius, they might hope to avoid his faults. But "neoclassical" English literature aimed to be not only classical but *new*. Rochester and Dryden drew on literary traditions of variety, humor, and freewheeling fancy represented by Chaucer, Spenser, Shakespeare, Jonson, and Milton to infuse fresh life into Greek or Latin or French classical models.

Above all, the new simplicity of style aimed to give pleasure to readers—to express passions that everyone could recognize in language that everyone could understand. According to Dryden, Donne's amorous verse misguidedly "perplexes the minds of the fair sex with nice speculations of philosophy, when he should engage their hearts, and entertain them with the softnesses of love." Dryden's poems would not make that mistake; like subsequent English critics, he values poetry according to its power to move an audience. Thus Timotheus, in Dryden's "Alexander's Feast," is not only a musician but an archetypal poet who can make Alexander tearful or loving or angry at will. Readers, in turn, were supposed to cooperate with authors through the exercise of their own imaginations, creating pictures in the mind. When Timotheus describes vengeful ghosts holding torches, Alexander hallucinates in response and seizes a torch "with zeal to destroy." Much eighteenth-century poetry demands to be visualized. A phrase from Horace's *Art of Poetry, ut pictura poesis* (as in painting, so in poetry), was interpreted to mean that poetry ought to be a visual as well as verbal art. Pope's "Eloisa to Abelard," for instance, begins by picturing two rival female personifications: "heavenly-pensive contemplation" and "ever-musing melancholy" (in the older typographical style, the nouns would be capitalized). Readers were expected to *see* these figures: Contemplation, in the habit of a nun, whose eyes roll upward toward heaven; and the black goddess Melancholy, in wings and drapery, who broods upon the darkness. These two competing visions fight for Eloisa's soul throughout the poem, which we see entirely through her perspective. Eighteenth-century readers knew how to translate words into pictures, and modern readers can share their pleasure by learning to see poetic images in the mind's eye.

What poets most tried to see and represent was *Nature*—a word of many meanings. The Augustans focused especially on one: Nature as the universal and permanent elements in human experience. External nature, the landscape, attracted attention throughout the eighteenth century as a source of pleasure and an object of inquiry. But as Finch muses on the landscape, in "A Nocturnal Reverie," it is her own soul she discovers. Pope's injunction to the critic, "First follow Nature," has primarily *human* nature in view. Nature consists of the enduring, general truths that have been, are, and will be true for everyone in all times, everywhere. Hence the business of the poet, according to Johnson's *Rasselas,* is "to examine, not the individual, but the species; to remark general properties and large appearances . . . to exhibit in his portraits of nature such prominent and striking features as recall the original to every mind." Yet if human nature was held to be uniform, human beings were known to be infinitely varied. Pope praises Shakespeare's characters as "Nature herself," but continues that "every single character in Shakespeare is as much an individual as those in life itself; it is . . . impossible to find any two alike." The general need not exclude the particular. In *The Vanity of Human Wishes*, Johnson describes the sorrows of an old woman: "Now kindred Merit fills the sable Bier, / Now lacerated Friendship claims a tear." Here "kindred Merit" refers particularly to a worthy relative who has died, and "lacerated Friendship" refers to a friend who has been wasted by violence or disease. Yet Merit and Friendship are also personifications, and the lines imply that the woman may be mourning the passing of goodness like her own or a broken friendship; values and sympathies can die as well as people. This play on words is not a pun. Rather, it indicates a state of mind in which life assumes the form of a perpetual allegory and some abiding truth shines through each circumstance as it passes. The particular is already the general, in good eighteenth-century verse.

To study Nature was also to study the ancients. Nature and Homer, according to Pope, were the same; and both Pope and his readers applied Horace's satires on Rome to their own world, because Horace had expressed the perennial forms of life. Moreover, modern writers could learn from the ancients how to practice their craft. If a poem is an object to be made, the *poet* (a word derived from the Greek for "maker") must make the object to proper specifications. Thus poets were taught to plan their works in one of the classical "kinds" or genres—epic, tragedy, comedy, pastoral, satire, or ode—to choose a language appropriate to that genre, and to select the right style and tone and rhetorical figures. The rules of art, as Pope had said, "are Nature methodized." At the same time, however, writers needed *wit*: quickness of mind, inventiveness, a knack for conceiving images and metaphors and for perceiving resemblances between things apparently unlike. Shakespeare had surpassed the ancients themselves in wit, and no one could deny that Pope was witty. Hence a major project of the age was to combine good method with wit, or judgment with fancy. Nature intended them to be one, and the role of judgment was not to suppress passion, energy, and originality but to make them more effective through discipline: "The winged courser, like a generous horse, / Shows most true mettle when you check his course."

The test of a poet's true mettle is language. When Wordsworth, in the preface to *Lyrical Ballads* (1800), declared that he wrote "in a selection of the language really used by men," he went on to attack eighteenth-century poets for their use of an artificial and stock "poetic diction." Many poets did employ a special language. It is characterized by personification, representing a thing or abstraction in human form, as when an "Ace of Hearts steps forth" or "Melancholy frowns"; by periphrasis (a roundabout way of avoiding homely words: "finny tribes" for *fish*, or "household feathery people" for *chickens*); by stock phrases such as "shining sword," "verdant mead," "bounding main," and "checkered shade"; by words used in their original Latin sense, such as "genial," "gelid," and "horrid"; and by English sentences forced into Latin syntax ("Here rests his head upon the lap of Earth / A youth to Fortune and to Fame unknown," where *youth* is the subject of the verb *rests*). This language originated in the attempt of Renaissance poets to rival the elegant diction of Virgil and other Roman writers, and Milton depended on it to help him obtain "answerable style" for the lofty theme of *Paradise Lost*. When used mechanically it could become a mannerism. But Thomas Gray contrives subtle, expressive effects from artificial diction and syntax, as in the ironic inflation of "Ode on the Death of a Favorite Cat" or a famous stanza from "Elegy Written in a Country Churchyard":

> The boast of heraldry, the pomp of power,
> And all that beauty, all that wealth e'er gave,
> Awaits alike the inevitable hour.
> The paths of glory lead but to the grave.

It is easy to misread the first sentence. What is the subject of *awaits*? The answer must be *hour* (the only available singular noun), which lurks at the end of the sentence, ready to spring a trap not only on the reader but on all those aristocratic, powerful, beautiful, wealthy people who forget that their hour will come. Moreover, the intricacy of that sentence sets off the simplicity of the next, which says the same thing with deadly directness. The artful mix in the "Elegy" of a special poetic language—a language that nobody speaks—with sentiments that everybody feels helps account for the poem's enduring popularity.

Versification also tests a poet's skill. The heroic couplet was brought to such perfection by Pope, Johnson thought, that "to attempt any further improvement of versification will be dangerous." Pope's couplets, in rhymed iambic pentameter, typically present a complete statement, closed by a punctuation mark. Within the binary system of these two lines, a world of distinctions can be compressed. The second line of the couplet might closely parallel the first in structure and meaning, for instance, or the two lines might antithetically play against each other. Similarly, because a slight pause called a "caesura" often divides the typical pentameter line ("Know then thyself, presume not God to scan"), one part of the line can be made parallel with or antithetical to the other or even to one part of the following line. An often quoted and parodied passage of Sir John Denham's "Cooper's Hill" (1642) illustrates these effects. The poem addresses the Thames and builds up a witty comparison between the flow of a river and the flow of verse (italics are added to highlight the terms compared):

"Here rests his head . . ." Through a crumbling Gothic arch appears a youth reading the epitaph on a tombstone that concludes Thomas Gray's "Elegy Written in a Country Churchyard." Illustration, *Designs by Mr. R. Bentley for Six Poems by Mr. T. Gray* (1753).

	O could I flow like thee, | and make thy stream
Parallelism:	*My great example,* | *as it is my theme!*
Double balance:	Though *deep,* yet *clear,* | though *gentle,* yet not *dull,*
Double balance:	*Strong* without *rage,* | without *o'erflowing, full.*

Once Dryden and Pope had bound such passages more tightly together with alliteration and assonance, the typical metrical-rhetorical wit of the new age had been perfected. For most of the eighteenth century its only metrical rival was blank verse: iambic pentameter that does not rhyme and is not closed in couplets. Milton's blank verse in *Paradise Lost* provided one model, and the dramatic blank verse of Shakespeare and Dryden provided another. This more expansive form appealed to poets who cared less for wit than for stories and thoughts with plenty of room to develop. Blank verse was favored as the best medium for descriptive and meditative poems, from Thomson's *Seasons* (1726–30) to Cowper's *The Task* (1785), and the tradition continued in Wordsworth's "Tintern Abbey" and *Prelude.*

Yet not all poets chose to compete with Pope's wit or Milton's heroic striving. Ordinary people also wrote and read verse, and many of them neither knew nor regarded the classics. Only a minority of men, and very few women, had the chance to study Latin and Greek, but that did not keep a good many from playing with verse as a pastime or writing about their own lives. Hence the eighteenth century is the first age to reflect the modern tension between "high" and "low" art. While the heroic couplet was being perfected, doggerel also thrived, and Milton's blank verse was sometimes reduced to describing a drunk or an oyster. Burlesque and broad humor characterize the common run of eighteenth-century verse. As the audience for poetry became more diversified, so did the subject matter. No readership was too small to address; Isaac Watts, and later Anna Laetitia Barbauld and William Blake, wrote songs for children. The rise of unconventional forms and topics of verse subverted an older poetic ideal: the Olympian art that only a handful of the elect could possibly master. The eighteenth century brought poetry down to earth. In the future, art that claimed to be high would have to find ways to distinguish itself from the low.

RESTORATION LITERATURE, 1660–1700

Dryden brought England a *modern* literature between 1660 and 1700. He combined a cosmopolitan outlook on the latest European trends with some of the richness and variety he admired in Chaucer and Shakespeare. In most of the important contemporary forms—occasional verse, comedy, tragedy, heroic play, ode, satire, translation, and critical essay—both his example and his precepts influenced others. As a critic, he spread the word that English literature, particularly his own, could vie with the best of the past. As a translator, he made such classics as Ovid and Virgil available to a wide public; for the first time, a large number of women and men without a formal education could feel included in the literary world.

Restoration prose clearly indicated the desire to reach a new audience. The styles of Donne's sermons, Milton's pamphlets, or Browne's treatises now seemed too elaborate and rhetorical for simple communication. By contrast, Pepys and Behn head straight to the point, informally and unselfconsciously. The Royal Society asked its members to employ a plain, utilitarian prose style that spelled out scientific truths; rhetorical flourishes and striking metaphors might be acceptable in poetry, which engaged the emotions, but they had no place in rational discourse. In polite literature, exemplified by Cowley, Dryden, and Sir William Temple, the ideal of good prose came to be a style with the ease and poise of well-bred urbane conversation. This is a social prose for a sociable age. Later, it became the mainstay of essayists like Addison and Steele, of eighteenth-century novelists, and of the host of brilliant eighteenth-century letter writers, including Montagu, Horace Walpole, Gray, Cowper, and Burney, who still give readers the sense of being their intimate friends.

Yet despite its broad appeal to the public, Restoration literature kept its ties to an aristocratic heroic ideal. The "fierce wars and faithful loves" of epic poems were expected to offer patterns of virtue for noble emulation. These ideals lived on in popular French prose romances and in Behn's *Oroonoko*. But the ideal was most fully expressed in heroic plays like those written by Dryden, which push to extremes the conflict between love and honor in the hearts of impossibly valiant heroes and impossibly high-minded and attractive heroines. Dryden's best serious drama, however, was his blank verse tragedy *All for Love* (produced 1677), based on the story of Antony and Cleopatra. Instead of Shakespeare's worldwide panorama, his rapid shifts of scene and complex characters, this version follows the unities of time, place, and action, compressing the plot to the tragic last hours of the lovers. Two other tragic playwrights were celebrated in the Restoration and for a long time to come: Nathaniel Lee (ca. 1649–1692), known for violent plots and wild ranting, and the passionately sensitive Thomas Otway (1652–1685).

But comedy was the real distinction of Restoration drama. The best plays of Sir George Etherege (*The Man of Mode*, 1676), William Wycherley (*The Country Wife*, 1675), Aphra Behn (*The Rover*, 1677), William Congreve (*Love for Love*, 1695; *The Way of the World*, 1700), and later George Farquhar (*The Beaux' Stratagem*, 1707) can still hold the stage today. These "comedies of manners" pick social behavior apart, exposing the nasty struggles for power among the upper classes, who use wit and manners as weapons. Human nature in these plays often conforms to the worst fears of Hobbes; sensual, false-hearted, selfish characters prey on each other. The male hero lives for pleasure and for the money and women that he can conquer. The object of his game of sexual intrigue is a beautiful, witty, pleasure-loving, and emancipated lady, every bit his equal in the strategies of love. What makes the favored couple stand out is the true wit and well-bred grace with which they step through the minefield of the plot. But during the 1690s "Societies for the Reformation of Manners" began to attack the blasphemy and obscenity they detected in such plays, and they sometimes brought offenders to trial. When Dryden died in 1700, a more respectable society was coming into being.

EIGHTEENTH-CENTURY LITERATURE, 1700–1745

Early in the eighteenth century a new and brilliant group of writers emerged: Swift, with *A Tale of a Tub* (1704–10); Addison, with *The Campaign* (1705), a poetic celebration of the battle of Blenheim; Prior, with *Poems on Several Occasions* (1707); Steele, with the *Tatler* (1709); and the youthful Pope, in the same year, with his *Pastorals*. These writers consolidate and popularize the social graces of the previous age. Determined to preserve good sense and civilized values, they turn their wit against fanaticism and innovation. Hence this is a great age of satire. Deeply conservative but also playful, their finest works often cast a strange light on modern times by viewing them through the screen of classical myths and classical forms. Thus Pope exposes the frivolity of fashionable London, in *The Rape of the Lock*, through the incongruity of verse that casts the idle rich as epic heroes. Similarly, Swift uses epic similes to mock the moderns in *The Battle of the Books*, and John Gay's *Trivia, or the Art of Walking the Streets of London* (1716) uses mock georgics to order his tour of the city. Such incongruities are not entirely negative. They also provide a fresh perspective on things that had once seemed too low for poetry to notice—for instance, in *The Rape of the Lock*, a girl putting on her makeup. In this way a parallel with classical literature can show not only how far the modern world has fallen but also how fascinating and magical it is when seen with "quick, poetic eyes."

The Augustans' effort to popularize and enforce high literary and social values was set against the new mass and multiplicity of writings that responded more spontaneously to the expanding commercial possibilities of print. The array of popular prose genres—news, thinly disguised political allegories, biographies of notorious criminals, travelogues, gossip, romantic tales—often blended facts and patently fictional elements, cemented by a rich lode of exaggeration, misrepresentations, and outright lies. Out of this matrix the modern novel would come to be born. The great master of such works was Daniel Defoe, producing first-person accounts such as *Robinson Crusoe* (1719), the famous castaway, and *Moll Flanders* (1722), mistress of lowlife crime. Claims that such works present (as the "editor" of *Crusoe* says) "a just history of fact," believed or not, sharpened the public's avidity for them. Defoe shows his readers a world plausibly like the one they know, where ordinary people negotiate familiar, entangled problems of financial, emotional, and spiritual existence. Jane Barker, Mary Davys, and many others brought women's work and daily lives as well as love affairs to fiction. Such stories were not only amusing but also served as models of conduct; they influenced the stories that real people told about themselves.

The theater also began to change its themes and effects to appeal to a wider audience. The clergyman Jeremy Collier had vehemently taken Dryden, Wycherley, and Congreve to task in *A Short View of the Immorality and Profaneness of the English Stage* (1698), which spoke for the moral outrage of the pious middle classes. The wits retreated. The comedy of manners was replaced by a new kind, later called "sentimental" not only because goodness triumphs over vice but also because it deals in high moral sentiments rather than witty dialogue and because the embarrassments of its heroines and heroes move the audience not to laughter but to tears. Virtue refuses to bow to aristocratic codes. In one crucial scene of Steele's influential play *The Conscious Lovers* (1722) the hero would rather accept dishonor than fight a duel with a friend. Piety and middle-class values typify tragedies such as George Lillo's *London Merchant* (1731). One luxury invented in eighteenth-century Europe was the delicious pleasure of weeping, and comedies as well as tragedies brought that pleasure to playgoers through many decades. Some plays resisted the tide. Gay's cynical *Beggar's Opera* (1728) was a tremendous success, and later in the century the comedies of Goldsmith and Sheridan proved that sentiment is not necessarily an enemy to wit and laughter. Yet larger and larger audiences responded more to spectacles and special effects than to sophisticated writing. Although the *stage* prospered during the eighteenth century, and the star system produced idolized actors and actresses (such as David Garrick and Sarah Siddons), the authors of *drama* tended to fade to the background.

Despite the sociable impulses of much the period's writing, readers also craved less crowded, more meditative works. Since the seventeenth century, no poems had been more popular than those about the pleasures of retirement, which invited the reader to dream about a safe retreat in the country or to meditate, like Finch, on scenery and the soul. But after 1726, when Thomson published *Winter*, the first of his cycle on the seasons, the poetry of natural description came into its own. A taste for gentle, picturesque beauty found expression not only in verse but in the elaborate, cultivated art of landscape gardening, and finally in the cherished English art of landscape painting in watercolor or oils (often illustrating Thomson's *Seasons*). Many readers also learned to enjoy a thrilling pleasure or fear in the presence of the sublime in nature: rushing waters, wild prospects, and mountains shrouded in mist. Whether enthusiasts went to the landscape in search of God or merely of heightened sensations, they came back feeling that they had been touched by something beyond the life they knew, by something that could hardly be expressed. Tourists as well as poets roamed the countryside, frequently quoting verse as they gazed at some evocative scene. A partiality for the sublime passed from Thomson to Collins to inspire the poetry of the Romantic age to come.

THE EMERGENCE OF NEW LITERARY THEMES AND MODES, 1740–85

When Matthew Arnold called the eighteenth century an "age of prose," he meant to belittle its poetry, but he also stated a significant fact: great prose does dominate the age. Until the 1740s, poetry tended to set the standards of literature. But the growth of new kinds of prose took the initiative away from verse. Novelists became better known than poets. Intellectual prose also flourished, with the achievements of Johnson in the essay and literary criticism, of Boswell in biography, of Hume in philosophy, of Burke in politics, of Edward Gibbon in history, of Sir Joshua Reynolds in aesthetics, of Gilbert White in natural history, and of Adam Smith in economics. Each of these authors is a master stylist, whose effort to express himself clearly and fully demands an art as carefully wrought as poetry. Other writers of prose were more informal. The memoirs of such women as Laetitia Pilkington, Charlotte Charke, Hester Thrale Piozzi, and Frances Burney bring each reader into their private lives and also remind us that the new print culture created celebrities, who wrote not only about themselves but about other celebrities they knew. The interest of readers in Samuel Johnson helped sell his own books as well as a host of books that quoted his sayings. But the prose of the age also had to do justice to difficult and complicated ideas. An unprecedented effort to formulate the first principles of philosophy, history, psychology, and art required a new style of persuasion.

Johnson helped codify that language, not only with his writings but with the first great English *Dictionary* (1755). This work established him as a national man of letters; eventually the period would be known as "the Age of Johnson." But his dominance was based on an ideal of service to others. The *Dictionary* illustrates its definitions with more than 114,000 quotations from the best English writers, thus building a bridge from past to present usage; and Johnson's essays, poems, and criticism also reflect his desire to preserve the lessons of the past. Yet he looks to the future as well, trying both to reach and to mold a nation of readers. If Johnson speaks for his age, one reason is his faith in common sense and the common reader. "By the common sense of readers uncorrupted with literary prejudices," he wrote in the last of his *Lives of the Poets* (1781), "must be finally decided all claim to poetical honors." A similar respect for the good judgment of ordinary people, and for standards of taste and behavior that anyone can share, marks many writers of the age. Both Burke, the great conservative statesman and author, and Thomas Paine, his radical adversary, proclaim themselves apostles of common sense.

No prose form better united availability to the common reader and seriousness of artistic purpose than the novel in the hands of two of its early masters, Samuel Richardson and Henry Fielding. Like many writers of fiction earlier in the century, Richardson initially did not set out to entertain the public with an avowedly invented tale: he conceived *Pamela, or Virtue Rewarded* (1740) while compiling a little book of model letters. The letters grew into a story about a captivating young servant who resists her master's base designs on her virtue until he gives up and marries her. The combination of a high moral tone with sexual titillation and a minute analysis of the heroine's emotions and state of mind proved irresistible to readers, in Britain and in Europe at large. Richardson topped *Pamela's* success with *Clarissa* (1747–48), another epistolary novel, which explored the conflict between the libertine Lovelace, an attractive and diabolical aristocrat, and the angelic Clarissa, a middle-class paragon who struggles to stay pure. The sympathy that readers felt for Clarissa was magnified by a host of sentimental novels, including Frances Sheridan's *Memoirs of Miss Sidney Bidulph* (1761), Rousseau's *Julie, or The New Heloise* (1761), and Henry Mackenzie's *The Man of Feeling* (1771).

Henry Fielding made his entrance into the novel by turning *Pamela* farcically upside-down, as the hero of *Joseph Andrews* (1742), Pamela's brother, defends his chastity from the lewd advances of Lady Booby. Fielding's true model, however, is Cervantes's great *Don Quixote* (1605–15), from which he took an ironic, antiromantic style; a plot of wandering around the countryside; and an idealistic central character (Parson Adams) who keeps mistaking appearances for reality. The ambition of writing what Fielding called "a comic epic-poem in prose" went still further in *The History of Tom Jones, a Foundling* (1749). Crowded with incidents and comments on the state of England, the novel contrasts a good-natured, generous, wayward hero (who needs to learn prudence) with cold-hearted people who use moral codes and the law for their own selfish interests. This emphasis on instinctive virtue and vice, instead of Richardson's devotion to good principles, put off respectable readers like Johnson and Burney. But Coleridge thought that *Tom Jones* (along with *Oedipus Rex* and Jonson's *Alchemist*) was one of "the three most perfect plots ever planned."

An age of great prose can burden its poets. To Gray, Collins, Mark Akenside, and the brothers Joseph and Thomas Warton, it seemed that the spirit of poetry might be dying, driven out by the spirit of prose, by uninspiring truth, by the end of superstitions that had once peopled the land with poetic fairies and demons. In an age barren of magic, they ask, where has poetry gone? That question haunts many poems, suffusing them with melancholy. Poets who muse in silence are never far from thoughts of death, and a morbid fascination with suicide and the grave preoccupies many at midcentury. Such an attitude has little in common with that of poets like Dryden and Pope, social beings who live in a crowded world and seldom confess their private feelings in public. Pope's *Essay on Man* had taken a sunny view of providence; Edward Young's *The Complaint: or Night Thoughts on Life, Death, and Immortality* (1742–46), an immensely long poem in blank verse, is darkened by Christian fear of the life to come.

Often the melancholy poet withdraws into himself and yearns to be living in some other time and place. In his "Ode to Fancy" (1746), Joseph Warton associated "fancy" with visions in the wilderness and spontaneous passions; the true poet was no longer defined as a craftsman or maker but as a seer or nature's priest. "The public has seen all that art can do," William Shenstone wrote in 1761, welcoming James Macpherson's *Ossian*, "and they want the more striking efforts of wild, original, enthusiastic genius." Macpherson filled the bill. His primitive, sentimental epics, supposedly translated from an ancient Gaelic warrior-bard, won the hearts of readers around the world; Napoleon and Thomas Jefferson, for instance, both thought that Ossian was greater than Homer. Poets began to cultivate archaic language and antique forms. Inspired by Thomas Percy's edition of *Reliques of Ancient English Poetry* (1765), Thomas Chatterton passed off his own ballads as medieval; he died at seventeen, soon after his forgeries were exposed, but the Romantics later idolized his precocious genius.

The most remarkable consequence of the medieval revival, however, was the invention of the Gothic novel. Horace Walpole set *The Castle of Otranto* (1765), a dreamlike tale of terror, in a simulacrum of Strawberry Hill, his own tiny, pseudo-medieval castle, which helped revive a taste for Gothic architecture. Walpole created a mode of fiction that retains its popularity to the present day. In a typical Gothic romance, amid the glooms and secret passages of some remote castle, the laws of nightmare replace the laws of probability. Forbidden themes—incest, murder, necrophilia, atheism, and the torments of sexual desire—are allowed free play. Most such romances, like William Beckford's *Vathek* (1786) and Matthew Lewis's *The Monk* (1796), revel in sensationalism and the grotesque. The Gothic vogue suggested that classical canons of taste—simplicity and harmonious balance—might count for less than the pleasures of fancy—intricate puzzles and a willful excess. But Gothicism also resulted in works, like Ann Radcliffe's, that temper romance with reality as well as in serious novels of social purpose, like William Godwin's *Caleb Williams* (1794) and Mary Wollstonecraft's *Maria, or The Wrongs of Woman* (1798); and Mary Shelley, the daughter of Wollstonecraft and

Bertie Greatheed, *Diego and Jaquez Frightened by the Giant Foot*, 1791. A scene from Horace Walpole's Gothic novel *The Castle of Otranto* (1764), showing servants terrified by the supernatural appearance of an oversize stone foot in the castle.

Godwin, eventually composed a romantic nightmare, *Frankenstein* (1818), that continues to haunt our dreams.

The century abounded in other remarkable experiments in fiction, anticipating many of the forms that novelists still use today. Tobias Smollett's picaresque *Roderick Random* (1748) and *Humphry Clinker* (1771) delight in coarse practical jokes, the freaks and strong odors of life. But the most *novel* novelist of the age was Laurence Sterne, a humorous, sentimental clergyman who loves to play tricks on his readers. *The Life and Opinions of Tristram Shandy* (1760–67) abandons clock time for psychological time, whimsically follows chance associations, interrupts its own stories, violates the conventions of print by putting chapters 18 and 19 after chapter 25, sneaks in double entendres, and seems ready to go on forever. And yet these games get us inside the characters' minds, as if the world were as capricious as our thoughts. Sterne's self-conscious art implies that people's private obsessions shape their lives—or help create reality itself. As unique as Sterne's fictional world is, his interest in private life matched the concerns of the novel toward the end of the century: depictions of characters' intimate feelings dominated the tradition of domestic fiction that included Burney, Radcliffe, and, later, Maria Edgeworth, culminating in the masterworks of Jane Austen. A more "masculine" orientation emerged at the beginning of the next century, as Walter Scott's works, with their broad historical scope and outdoor scenes of men at work and war, appealed to a large readership. Yet the copious, acute, often ironic attention to details of private life by Richardson, Sterne, and Austen continued to influence the novel profoundly through its subsequent history.

CONTINUITY AND REVOLUTION

The history of eighteenth-century literature was first composed by the Romantics, who wrote it to serve their own interests. Prizing originality, they naturally preferred to stress how different they were from writers of the previous age. Later historians have tended to follow their lead, competing to prove that everything changed in 1776, or 1789, or 1798. This revolutionary view of history accounts for what happened to the word *revolution*. The older meaning referred to a movement around a point, a recurrence or cycle, as in the revolutions of the planets; the newer meaning signified a violent break with the past, an overthrow of the existing order, as in the Big Bang or the French Revolution. Romantic rhetoric made heavy use of such dramatic upheavals. Yet every history devoted to truth must take account of both sorts of revolution, of continuities as well as changes. The ideals that many Romantics made their own—the passion for liberty and equality, the founding of justice on individual rights, the distrust of institutions, the love of nature, the reverence for imagination, and even the embrace of change— grew from seeds that had been planted long before. Nor did Augustan literature abruptly vanish on that day in 1798 when Wordsworth and Coleridge anonymously published a small and unsuccessful volume of poems called *Lyrical Ballads*. Even when they rebel against the work of Pope and Johnson and Gray, Romantic writers incorporate much of their language and values.

What Restoration and eighteenth-century literature passed on to the future, in fact, was chiefly a set of unresolved problems. The age of Enlightenment was also, in England, an age that insisted on holding fast to older beliefs and customs; the age of population explosion was also an age of individualism; the age that developed the slave trade was also the age that gave rise to the abolitionist movement; the age that codified rigid standards of conduct for women was also an age when many women took the chance to read and write and think for themselves; the age of reason was also the age when sensibility flourished; the last classical age was also the first modern age. These contradictions are far from abstract; writers were forced to choose their own directions. When young James Boswell looked for a mentor whose biography he might write, he considered not only Samuel Johnson but also David Hume, whose skeptical views of morality, truth, and religion were everything Johnson abhorred. The two writers seem to inhabit different worlds, yet Boswell traveled freely between them. That was exciting and also instructive. "Without Contraries is no progression," according to one citizen of Johnson's London, William Blake, who also thought that "Opposition is true Friendship." Good conversation was a lively eighteenth-century art, and sharp disagreements did not keep people from talking. The conversations the period started have not ended yet.

The Restoration and
The Eighteenth Century

TEXTS	CONTEXTS
1660 Samuel Pepys begins his diary	1660 Charles II restored to the throne. Reopening of the theaters
1662 Samuel Butler, *Hudibras,* part 1	1662 Act of Uniformity requires all clergy to obey the Church of England. Chartering of the Royal Society
	1664–66 Great Plague of London
	1666 Fire destroys the City of London
1667 John Milton, *Paradise Lost*	
1668 John Dryden, *Essay of Dramatic Poesy*	1668 Dryden becomes poet laureate
	1673 Test Act requires all officeholders to swear allegiance to Anglicanism
1678 John Bunyan, *Pilgrim's Progress,* part 1	1678 The "Popish Plot" inflames anti-Catholic feeling
1681 Dryden, *Absalom and Achitophel*	1681 Charles II dissolves Parliament
	1685 Death of Charles II. James II, his Catholic brother, takes the throne
1687 Sir Isaac Newton, *Principia Mathematica*	
1688 Aphra Behn, *Oroonoko*	1688–89 The Glorious Revolution. James II exiled and succeeded by his Protestant daughter, Mary, and her husband, William of Orange
1690 John Locke, *An Essay Concerning Human Understanding*	
1700 William Congreve, *The Way of the World.* Mary Astell, *Some Reflections upon Marriage*	
	1702 War of the Spanish Succession begins. Death of William III. Succession of Anne (Protestant daughter of James II)
1704 Jonathan Swift, *A Tale of a Tub.* Newton, *Opticks*	
	1707 Act of Union with Scotland
	1710 Tories take power
1711 Alexander Pope, *An Essay on Criticism.* Joseph Addison and Sir Richard Steele, *Spectator* (1711–12, 1714)	
	1713 Treaty of Utrecht ends War of the Spanish Succession
	1714 Death of Queen Anne. George I (great-grandson of James I) becomes the first Hanoverian king. Tory government replaced by Whigs
1716 Lady Mary Wortley Montagu writes her letters from Turkey (1716–18)	
1717 Pope, *The Rape of the Lock* (final version)	

TEXTS	CONTEXTS
1719 Daniel Defoe, *Robinson Crusoe*	
	1720 South Sea Bubble collapses
	1721 Robert Walpole comes to power
1726 Swift, *Gulliver's Travels*	
	1727 George I dies. George II succeeds
1728 John Gay, *The Beggar's Opera*	
1733 Pope, *An Essay on Man*	
	1737 Licensing Act censors the stage
1740 Samuel Richardson, *Pamela*	
1742 Henry Fielding, *Joseph Andrews*	**1742** Walpole resigns
1743 Pope, *The Dunciad* (final version). William Hogarth, *Marriage A-la-Mode*	
1746 William Collins's *Odes*	**1746** Charles Edward Stuart's defeat at Culloden ends the last Jacobite rebellion
1747 Richardson, *Clarissa*	
1749 Fielding, *Tom Jones*	
1751 Thomas Gray, "Elegy Written in a Country Churchyard"	**1751** Robert Clive seizes Arcot, the prelude to English control of India
1755 Samuel Johnson, *Dictionary*	
	1756 Beginning of Seven Years' War
1759 Johnson, *Rasselas*. Voltaire, *Candide*	**1759** James Wolfe's capture of Quebec ensures British control of Canada
1760 Laurence Sterne, *Tristram Shandy* (1760–67)	**1760** George III succeeds to the throne
1765 Johnson's edition of Shakespeare	
	1768 Captain James Cook voyages to Australia and New Zealand
1770 Oliver Goldsmith, "The Deserted Village"	
	1775 American Revolution (1775–83). James Watt produces steam engines
1776 Adam Smith, *The Wealth of Nations*	
1778 Frances Burney, *Evelina*	
1779 Johnson, *Lives of the Poets* (1779–81)	
	1780 Gordon Riots in London
1783 George Crabbe, *The Village*	**1783** William Pitt becomes prime minister
1785 William Cowper, *The Task*	

JOHN DRYDEN
1631–1700

Although John Dryden's parents seem to have sided with Parliament against the king, there is no evidence that the poet grew up in a strict Puritan family. His father, a country gentleman of moderate fortune, gave his son a gentleman's education at Westminster School, under the renowned Dr. Richard Busby, who used the rod as a pedagogical aid in imparting a sound knowledge of the learned languages and literatures to his charges (among others John Locke and Matthew Prior). From Westminster, Dryden went to Trinity College, Cambridge, where he took his A.B. in 1654. His first important poem, "Heroic Stanzas" (1659), was written to commemorate the death of Cromwell. The next year, however, in "Astraea Redux," Dryden joined his countrymen in celebrating the return of Charles II to his throne. During the rest of his life Dryden was to remain entirely loyal to Charles and to his successor, James II.

Dryden is the commanding literary figure of the last four decades of the seventeenth century. Every important aspect of the life of his times—political, religious, philosophical, artistic—finds expression somewhere in his writings. Dryden is the least personal of poets. He is not at all the solitary, subjective poet listening to the murmur of his own voice and preoccupied with his own feelings but rather a citizen of the world commenting publicly on matters of public concern.

From the beginning to the end of his literary career, Dryden's nondramatic poems are most typically occasional poems, which commemorate particular events of a public character—a coronation, a military victory, a death, or a political crisis. Such poems are social and often ceremonial, written not for the self but for the nation. Dryden's principal achievements in this form are the two poems on the king's return and his coronation; *Annus Mirabilis* (1667), which celebrates the English naval victory over the Dutch and the fortitude of the people of London and the king during the Great Fire, both events of that "wonderful year," 1666; the political poems; the lines on the death of Oldham (1684); and odes such as "Alexander's Feast."

Between 1664 and 1681, however, Dryden was mainly a playwright. The newly chartered theaters needed a modern repertory, and he set out to supply the need. Dryden wrote his plays, as he frankly confessed, to please his audiences, which were not heterogeneous like Shakespeare's but were largely drawn from the court and from people of fashion. In the style of the time, he produced rhymed heroic plays, in which incredibly noble heroes and heroines face incredibly difficult choices between love and honor; comedies, in which male and female rakes engage in intrigue and bright repartee; and later, libretti for the newly introduced dramatic form, the opera. His one great tragedy, *All for Love* (1677), in blank verse, adapts Shakespeare's *Antony and Cleopatra* to the unities of time, place, and action. As his *Essay of Dramatic Poesy* (1668) shows, Dryden had studied the works of the great playwrights of Greece and Rome, of the English Renaissance, and of contemporary France, seeking sound theoretical principles on which to construct the new drama that the age demanded. Indeed, his fine critical intelligence always supported his creative powers, and, because he took literature seriously and enjoyed discussing it, he became, almost casually, what Samuel Johnson called him: "the father of English criticism." His abilities as both poet and dramatist brought him to the attention of the king, who in 1668 made him poet laureate. Two years later the post of historiographer royal was added to the laureateship at a combined stipend of £200, enough money to live comfortably on.

Between 1678 and 1681, when he was nearing fifty, Dryden discovered his great gift for writing formal verse satire. A quarrel with the playwright Thomas Shadwell prompted the mock-heroic episode "Mac Flecknoe," probably written in 1678 or 1679 but not published until 1682. Out of the stresses occasioned by the Popish Plot (1678) and its political aftermath came his major political satires, *Absalom and Achitophel* (1681), and "The Medal" (1682), his final attack on the villain of *Absalom and Achitophel,* the earl of Shaftesbury. Twenty years' experience as poet and playwright had prepared him technically for the triumph of *Absalom and Achitophel.* He had mastered the heroic couplet, having fashioned it into an instrument suitable in his hands for every sort of discourse from the thrust and parry of quick logical argument, to lyric feeling, rapid narrative, or forensic declamation. Thanks to this long discipline, he was able in one stride to rival the masters of verse satire: Horace, Juvenal, Persius, in ancient Rome, and Boileau, his French contemporary.

The consideration of religious and political questions that the events of 1678–81 forced on Dryden brought a new seriousness to his mind and works. In 1682 he published *Religio Laici,* a poem in which he examined the grounds of his religious faith and defended the middle way of the Anglican Church against the rationalism of Deism on the one hand and the authoritarianism of Rome on the other. But he had moved closer to Rome than he perhaps realized when he wrote the poem. Charles II died in 1685 and was succeeded by his Catholic brother, James II. Within a year Dryden and his two sons converted to Catholicism. Though his enemies accused him of opportunism, he proved his sincerity by his steadfast loyalty to the Roman Church after James abdicated and the Protestant William and Mary came in; as a result he was to lose his offices and their much-needed stipends. From his new position as a Roman Catholic, Dryden wrote in 1687 *The Hind and the Panther,* in which a milk-white Hind (the Roman Church) and a spotted Panther (the Anglican Church) eloquently debate theology. The Hind has the better of the argument, but Dryden already knew that James's policies were failing, and with them the Catholic cause in England.

Dryden was now nearing sixty, with a family to support on a much-diminished income. To earn a living, he resumed writing plays and turned to translations. In 1693 appeared his versions of Juvenal and Persius, with a long dedicatory epistle on satire; and in 1697, his greatest achievement in this mode, the works of Virgil. At the very end, two months before his death, came the *Fables Ancient and Modern,* prefaced by one of the finest of his critical essays and made up of translations from Ovid, Boccaccio, and Chaucer.

Dryden's foremost achievement was to bring the pleasures of literature to the ever-increasing reading public of Britain. As a critic and translator, he made many classics available to men and women who lacked a classical education. His canons of taste and theoretical principles would set the standard for the next generation. As a writer of prose, he helped establish a popular new style, shaped to the cadences of good conversation. Johnson praised its apparent artlessness: "every word seems to drop by chance, though it falls into its proper place. Nothing is cold or languid; the whole is airy, animated, and vigorous . . . though all is easy, nothing is feeble; though all seems careless, there is nothing harsh." Although Dryden's plays went out of fashion, his poems did not. His satire inspired the most brilliant verse satirist of the next century, Alexander Pope, and the energy and variety of his metrics launched the long-standing vogue of heroic couplets. Augustan style is at its best in his poems: lively, dignified, precise, and always musical—a flexible instrument of public speech. "By him we were taught *sapere et fari,* to think naturally and express forcibly," Johnson concluded. "What was said of Rome, adorned by Augustus, may be applied by an easy metaphor to English poetry embellished by Dryden, *lateritiam invenit, marmoream reliquit,* he found it brick, and he left it marble."

From Annus Mirabilis[1]

* * *

[LONDON REBORN]

845   Yet London, empress of the northern clime,
        By an high fate thou greatly didst expire;
    Great as the world's, which at the death of time
        Must fall, and rise a nobler frame by fire.[2]

    As when some dire usurper Heaven provides,
850   To scourge his country with a lawless sway:[3]
    His birth, perhaps, some petty village hides,
        And sets his cradle out of fortune's way:

    Till fully ripe his swelling fate breaks out,
        And hurries him to mighty mischiefs on:
855   His Prince, surprised at first, no ill could doubt,°   *fear*
        And wants the power to meet it when 'tis known:

    Such was the rise of this prodigious fire,
        Which in mean buildings first obscurely bred,
    From thence did soon to open streets aspire,
860   And straight to palaces and temples spread.

* * *

    Me-thinks already, from this chymic° flame,   *alchemic, transmuting*
1170   I see a city of more precious mold:
    Rich as the town which gives the Indies name,°   *Mexico*
        With silver paved, and all divine with gold.

    Already, laboring with a mighty fate,
        She shakes the rubbish from her mounting brow,
1175   And seems to have renewed her charter's date,
        Which Heaven will to the death of time allow.

    More great than human, now, and more August,[4]
        New deified she from her fires does rise:

---

1. 1666 was a "year of wonders" (*annus mirabilis*): war, plague, and the Great Fire of London. According to the enemies of Charles II, God was visiting His wrath on the English people to signify that the reign of an unholy king would soon come to an end. Dryden's long "historical poem" *Annus Mirabilis*, written the same year, interprets the wonders differently: as trials sent by God to punish rebellious spirits and to bind the king and his people together. "Never had prince or people more mutual reason to love each other," Dryden wrote, "if suffering for each other can endear affection." Charles had endured rejection and exile, England had been torn by civil wars. Dryden views these sufferings as a covenant, a pledge of better times to come. Out of Charles's troubles, he predicts in heroic stanzas modeled on Virgil, the king shall arise like a new Augustus, the ruler of a great empire, and out of fire, London shall arise like the phoenix, ready to take its place as trade center for the world, in the glory of a new Augustan age.

2. Dryden's footnote cites Ovid, *Metamorphoses* I, which foretells that the world will be purged by fire. The fire of London, which utterly consumed the central city, burned for four days, September 2–6. By September 10, Christopher Wren had already submitted a plan, much of it later adopted, for rebuilding the city on a grander scale. For a dramatic contemporary depiction of the event, see *The Great Fire of London, 1666*, in the color insert in this volume.

3. Probably a reference to Oliver Cromwell.

4. Augusta, the old name of London [Dryden's note].

Her widening streets on new foundations trust,
1180   And, opening, into larger parts she flies.

Before, she like some shepherdess did show,
    Who sat to bathe her by a river's side:
Not answering to her fame, but rude and low,
    Nor taught the beauteous arts of modern pride.

1185 Now, like a Maiden Queen, she will behold,
    From her high turrets, hourly suitors come:
The East with incense, and the West with gold,
    Will stand, like suppliants, to receive her doom.°   *judgment, decree*

The silver Thames, her own domestic flood,
1190   Shall bear her vessels like a sweeping train;
And often wind (as of his mistress proud)
    With longing eyes to meet her face again.

The wealthy Tagus, and the wealthier Rhine,
    The glory of their towns no more shall boast;
1195 And Seine, that would with Belgian rivers join,[5]
    Shall find her luster stained, and traffic lost.

The venturous merchant, who designed° more far,   *intended to go*
    And touches on our hospitable shore,
Charmed with the splendor of this northern star,
1200   Shall here unlade him, and depart no more.

Our powerful navy shall no longer meet,
    The wealth of France or Holland to invade;
The beauty of this Town, without a fleet,
    From all the world shall vindicate° her trade.   *defend, protect*

1205 And while this famed emporium we prepare,
    The British ocean shall such triumphs boast,
That those who now disdain our trade to share,
    Shall rob like pirates on our wealthy coast.

Already we have conquered half the war,
1210   And the less dangerous part is left behind:
Our trouble now is but to make them dare,
    And not so great to vanquish as to find.

Thus to the eastern wealth through storms we go,
    But now, the Cape once doubled,° fear no more;   *sailed around*
1215 A constant trade-wind will securely blow,
    And gently lay us on the spicy shore.

1666   1667

---

5. France and Holland (which then included Belgium) had made an alliance for trade, as well as war, against England. The river Tagus flows into the Atlantic at Lisbon.

Song from *Marriage à la Mode*

1

Why should a foolish marriage vow,
    Which long ago was made,
Oblige us to each other now,
    When passion is decayed?
5   We loved, and we loved, as long as we could,
    Till our love was loved out in us both;
But our marriage is dead when the pleasure is fled:
    'Twas pleasure first made it an oath.

2

If I have pleasures for a friend,
10   And farther love in store,
What wrong has he whose joys did end,
    And who could give no more?
'Tis a madness that he should be jealous of me,
    Or that I should bar him of another:
15   For all we can gain is to give ourselves pain,
    When neither can hinder the other.

ca. 1672   1673

Absalom and Achitophel   In 1678 a dangerous crisis, both religious and political, threatened to undo the Restoration settlement and to precipitate England once again into civil war. The Popish Plot and its aftermath not only whipped up extreme anti-Catholic passions, but led between 1679 and 1681 to a bitter political struggle between Charles II (whose adherents came to be called Tories) and the earl of Shaftesbury (whose followers were termed Whigs). The issues were nothing less than the prerogatives of the crown and the possible exclusion of the king's Catholic brother, James, duke of York, from his position as heir-presumptive to the throne. Charles's cool courage and brilliant, if unscrupulous, political genius saved the throne for his brother and gave at least temporary peace to his people.

Charles was a Catholic at heart—he received the last rites of that church on his deathbed—and was eager to do what he could do discreetly for the relief of his Catholic subjects, who suffered severe civil and religious disabilities imposed by their numerically superior Protestant compatriots. James openly professed the Catholic religion, an awkward fact politically, for he was next in line of succession because Charles had no legitimate children. The household of the duke, as well as that of Charles's neglected queen, Catherine of Braganza, inevitably became the center of Catholic life and intrigue at court and consequently of Protestant prejudice and suspicion.

No one understood, however, that the situation was explosive until 1678, when Titus Oates (a renegade Catholic convert of infamous character) offered sworn testimony of the existence of a Jesuit plot to assassinate the king, burn London, massacre Protestants, and reestablish the Roman Church.

The country might have kept its head and come to realize (what no historian has doubted) that Oates and his confederates were perjured rascals, as Charles himself quickly perceived. But panic was created by the discovery of the body of a prominent London justice of the peace, Sir Edmund Berry Godfrey, who a few days before had received for safekeeping a copy of Oates's testimony. The murder, immediately ascribed to the Catholics, has never been solved. Fear and indignation reached a hysterical pitch when the seizure of the papers of the duke of York's secretary revealed that he had been in correspondence with the confessor of Louis XIV regarding the reestablishment of the Roman Church in England. Before the terror subsided many innocent men were executed on the increasingly bold and always false evidence of Oates and his accomplices.

The earl of Shaftesbury, the duke of Buckingham, and others quickly took advantage of the situation. With the support of the Commons and the City of London, they moved to exclude the duke of York from the succession. Between 1679 and 1681 Charles and Shaftesbury were engaged in a mighty struggle. The Whigs found a candidate of their own in the king's favorite illegitimate son, the handsome and engaging duke of Monmouth, whom they advanced as a proper successor to his father. They urged Charles to legitimize him, and when he refused, they whispered that there was proof that the king had secretly married Monmouth's mother. The young man allowed himself to be used against his father. He was sent on a triumphant progress, through western England, where he was enthusiastically received. Twice an Exclusion Bill nearly passed both houses. But by early 1681 Charles had secured his own position by secretly accepting from Louis XIV a three-year subsidy that made him independent of Parliament, which had tried to force his hand by refusing to vote him funds. He summoned Parliament to meet at Oxford in the spring of 1681, and a few moments after the Commons had passed the Exclusion Bill, in a bold stroke he abruptly dissolved Parliament, which never met again during his reign. Already, as Charles was aware, a reaction had set in against the violence of the Whigs. In midsummer, when he felt it safe to move against his enemies, Shaftesbury was sent to the Tower of London, charged with high treason. In November, the grand jury, packed with Whigs, threw out the indictment, and the earl was free, but his power was broken, and he lived only two more years.

Shortly before the grand jury acted, Dryden published anonymously the first part of *Absalom and Achitophel,* apparently hoping to influence their verdict. The issues in question were grave; the chief actors, the most important men in the realm. Dryden, therefore, could not use burlesque and caricature as had Butler, or the mock heroic as he himself had done in "Mac Flecknoe." Only a heroic style and manner were appropriate to his weighty material, and the poem is most original in its blending of the heroic and the satiric. Dryden's task called for all his tact and literary skill; he had to mention, but to gloss over, the king's faults: his indolence and love of pleasure; his neglect of his wife, and his devotion to his mistresses—conduct that had left him with many children, but no heir except his Catholic brother. He had to deal gently with Monmouth, whom Charles still loved. And he had to present, or appear to present, the king's case objectively.

The remarkable parallels between the rebellion of Absalom against his father, King David (2 Samuel 13–18), had already been remarked in sermons, satires, and pamphlets. Dryden took the hint and gave contemporary events a due distance and additional dignity by approaching them indirectly through their biblical analogues. The poem is famous for its brilliant portraits of the king's enemies and friends, but equally admirable are the temptation scene (which, like other passages, is indebted to *Paradise Lost*) and the remarkably astute analysis of the Popish Plot itself.

A second part of *Absalom and Achitophel* appeared in 1682. Most of it is the work of Nahum Tate, but lines 310–509, which include the devastating portraits of Doeg and Og (two Whig poets, Elkanah Settle and Thomas Shadwell), are certainly by Dryden.

Absalom and Achitophel: A Poem

In pious times, ere priestcraft[1] did begin,
Before polygamy was made a sin;
When man on many multiplied his kind,
Ere one to one was cursedly confined;
5   When nature prompted and no law denied
Promiscuous use of concubine and bride;
Then Israel's monarch after Heaven's own heart,[2]
His vigorous warmth did variously impart
To wives and slaves; and, wide as his command,
10   Scattered his Maker's image through the land.
Michal,[3] of royal blood, the crown did wear,
A soil ungrateful to the tiller's care:
Not so the rest; for several mothers bore
To godlike David several sons before.
15   But since like slaves his bed they did ascend,
No true succession could their seed attend.
Of all this numerous progeny was none
So beautiful, so brave, as Absalom:[4]
Whether, inspired by some diviner lust,
20   His father got him with a greater gust,°   *relish, pleasure*
Or that his conscious destiny made way,
By manly beauty, to imperial sway.
Early in foreign fields he won renown,
With kings and states allied to Israel's crown:[5]
25   In peace the thoughts of war he could remove,
And seemed as he were only born for love.
Whate'er he did, was done with so much ease,
In him alone 'twas natural to please;
His motions all accompanied with grace;
30   And paradise was opened in his face.
With secret joy indulgent David viewed
His youthful image in his son renewed:
To all his wishes nothing he denied;
And made the charming Annabel[6] his bride.
35   What faults he had (for who from faults is free?)
His father could not, or he would not see.
Some warm excesses which the law forbore,
Were cònstrued youth that purged by boiling o'er:
And Amnon's murther,[7] by a specious name,
40   Was called a just revenge for injured fame.
Thus praised and loved the noble youth remained,

---

1. "Religious frauds; management of wicked priests to gain power" (Johnson's *Dictionary*).
2. David ("a man after [God's] own heart," according to 1 Samuel 13.14) represents Charles II.
3. One of David's wives, who represents the childless queen, Catherine of Braganza.
4. James Scott, duke of Monmouth (1649–1685).
5. Monmouth had won repute as a soldier fighting for France against Holland and for Holland against France.
6. Anne Scott, duchess of Buccleuch (pronounced *Bue-cloo*), a beauty and a great heiress.
7. Absalom killed his half-brother Amnon, who had raped Absalom's sister Tamar (2 Samuel 13.28–29). The parallel with Monmouth is vague. He is known to have committed acts of violence in his youth, but certainly not fratricide.

	While David, undisturbed, in Sion° reigned.	*London*
	But life can never be sincerely° blest;	*wholly*
	Heaven punishes the bad, and proves° the best.	*tests*
45	The Jews,° a headstrong, moody, murmuring race,	*English*
	As ever tried the extent and stretch of grace;	
	God's pampered people, whom, debauched with ease,	
	No king could govern, nor no God could please	
	(Gods they had tried of every shape and size	
50	That god-smiths could produce, or priests devise);[8]	
	These Adam-wits, too fortunately free,	
	Began to dream they wanted liberty;[9]	
	And when no rule, no precedent was found,	
	Of men by laws less circumscribed and bound,	
55	They led their wild desires to woods and caves,	
	And thought that all but savages were slaves.	
	They who, when Saul was dead, without a blow,	
	Made foolish Ishbosheth[1] the crown forgo;	
	Who banished David did from Hebron[2] bring,	
60	And with a general shout proclaimed him king:	
	Those very Jews, who, at their very best,	
	Their humor° more than loyalty expressed,	*caprice*
	Now wondered why so long they had obeyed	
	An idol monarch, which their hands had made;	
65	Thought they might ruin him they could create,	
	Or melt him to that golden calf,[3] a state.°	*republic*
	But these were random bolts;° no formed design	*shots*
	Nor interest made the factious crowd to join:	
	The sober part of Israel, free from stain,	
70	Well knew the value of a peaceful reign;	
	And, looking backward with a wise affright,	
	Saw seams of wounds, dishonest° to the sight:	*disgraceful*
	In contemplation of whose ugly scars	
	They cursed the memory of civil wars.	
75	The moderate sort of men, thus qualified,°	*assuaged*
	Inclined the balance to the better side;	
	And David's mildness managed it so well,	
	The bad found no occasion to rebel.	
	But when to sin our biased[4] nature leans,	
80	The careful Devil is still at hand with means;	
	And providently pimps for ill desires:	
	The Good Old Cause[5] revived, a plot requires.	
	Plots, true or false, are necessary things,	
	To raise up commonwealths and ruin kings.	
85	The inhabitants of old Jerusalem	

---

8. Dryden recalls the political and religious controversies that, since the Reformation, had divided England and finally caused civil wars.
9. Adam rebelled because he felt that he lacked ("wanted") liberty, because he was forbidden to eat the fruit of one tree.
1. Saul's son. He stands for Richard Cromwell, who succeeded his father as lord protector. "Saul": Oliver Cromwell.
2. Where David reigned over Judah after the death of Saul and before he became king of Israel (2 Samuel 1–5). Charles had been crowned in Scotland in 1651.
3. The image worshiped by the children of Israel during the period that Moses spent on Mount Sinai, receiving the law from God.
4. Inclined (cf. "Mac Flecknoe," line 189 and n. 5, p. 2242).
5. The Commonwealth. Dryden stigmatizes the Whigs by associating them with subversion.

Were Jebusites;[6] the town so called from them;
And theirs the native right.
But when the chosen people° grew more strong,   *Protestants*
The rightful cause at length became the wrong;
90 And every loss the men of Jebus bore,
They still were thought God's enemies the more.
Thus worn and weakened, well or ill content,
Submit they must to David's government:
Impoverished and deprived of all command,
95 Their taxes doubled as they lost their land;
And, what was harder yet to flesh and blood,
Their gods disgraced, and burnt like common wood.[7]
This set the heathen priesthood° in a flame;   *Roman Catholic clergy*
For priests of all religions are the same:
100 Of whatsoe'er descent their godhead be,
Stock, stone, or other homely pedigree,
In his defense his servants are as bold,
As if he had been born of beaten gold.
The Jewish rabbins,° though their enemies,   *Anglican clergy*
105 In this conclude them honest men and wise:
For 'twas their duty, all the learned think,
To espouse his cause, by whom they eat and drink.
From hence began that Plot, the nation's curse,
Bad in itself, but represented worse;
110 Raised in extremes, and in extremes decried;
With oaths affirmed, with dying vows denied;
Not weighed or winnowed by the multitude;
But swallowed in the mass, unchewed and crude.
Some truth there was, but dashed° and brewed with lies,   *adulterated*
115 To please the fools, and puzzle all the wise.
Succeeding times did equal folly call,
Believing nothing, or believing all.
The Egyptian rites the Jebusites embraced,
Where gods were recommended by their taste.[8]
120 Such savory deities must needs be good,
As served at once for worship and for food.
By force they could not introduce these gods,
For ten to one in former days was odds;
So fraud was used (the sacrificer's trade):
125 Fools are more hard to conquer than persuade.
Their busy teachers mingled with the Jews,
And raked for converts even the court and stews:°   *brothels*
Which Hebrew priests the more unkindly took,
Because the fleece accompanies the flock.[9]
130 Some thought they God's anointed° meant to slay   *the king*
By guns, invented since full many a day:

6. Roman Catholics. The original name of Jerusalem (here, London) was Jebus.
7. Such oppressive laws against Roman Catholics date from the time of Elizabeth I.
8. Here Dryden sneers at the doctrine of transubstantiation. "Egyptian": French, therefore

Catholic.
9. Dryden charges that the Anglican clergy ("Hebrew priests") resented proselytizing by Catholics chiefly because they stood to lose their tithes ("fleece").

Our author swears it not; but who can know
How far the Devil and Jebusites may go?
This Plot, which failed for want of common sense,
135   Had yet a deep and dangerous consequence:
For, as when raging fevers boil the blood,
The standing lake soon floats into a flood,
And every hostile humor,[1] which before
Slept quiet in its channels, bubbles o'er;
140   So several factions from this first ferment
Work up to foam, and threat the government.
Some by their friends, more by themselves thought wise,
Opposed the power to which they could not rise.
Some had in courts been great, and thrown from thence,
145   Like fiends were hardened in impenitence;
Some, by their monarch's fatal mercy, grown
From pardoned rebels kinsmen to the throne,
Were raised in power and public office high;
Strong bands, if bands ungrateful men could tie.
150   Of these the false Achitophel[2] was first;
A name to all succeeding ages cursed:
For close designs, and crooked counsels fit;
Sagacious, bold, and turbulent of wit;°   *unruly imagination*
Restless, unfixed in principles and place;
155   In power unpleased, impatient of disgrace:
A fiery soul, which, working out its way, ⎫
Fretted the pygmy body to decay,   ⎬
And o'er-informed the tenement of clay.[3] ⎭
A daring pilot in extremity;
160   Pleased with the danger, when the waves went high,
He sought the storms; but, for a calm unfit,
Would steer too nigh the sands, to boast his wit.
Great wits° are sure to madness near allied,[4]   *men of genius*
And thin partitions do their bounds divide;
165   Else why should he, with wealth and honor blest,
Refuse his age the needful hours of rest?
Punish a body which he could not please;
Bankrupt of life, yet prodigal of ease?
And all to leave what with his toil he won,
170   To that unfeathered two-legged thing,[5] a son;
Got, while his soul did huddled° notions try;   *confused, hurried*
And born a shapeless lump, like anarchy.
In friendship false, implacable in hate,
Resolved to ruin or to rule the state.

1. Bodily fluid. Such fluids were thought to determine health and temperament.
2. Anthony Ashley Cooper, first earl of Shaftesbury (1621–1683). He had served in the parliamentary army and been a member of Cromwell's council of state. He later helped bring back Charles and, in 1670, was made a member of the notorious Cabal Ministry, which formed an alliance with Louis XIV in which England betrayed her ally, Holland, and joined France in war against that country. In 1672 he became lord chancellor, but with the dissolution of the cabal in 1673, he was removed from office. Lines 146–49 apply perfectly to him.
3. The soul is thought of as the animating principle, the force that puts the body in motion. Shaftesbury's body seemed too small to house his fiery, energetic soul.
4. That genius and madness are akin is a very old idea.
5. Cf. Plato's definition of a human: "a featherless biped."

175 To compass this the triple bond[6] he broke,
   The pillars of the public safety shook,
   And fitted Israel for a foreign yoke;
   Then seized with fear, yet still affecting fame,
   Usurped a patriot's all-atoning name.
180 So easy still it proves in factious times,
   With public zeal to cancel private crimes.
   How safe is treason, and how sacred ill,
   Where none can sin against the people's will!
   Where crowds can wink, and no offense be known,
185 Since in another's guilt they find their own!
   Yet fame deserved, no enemy can grudge;
   The statesman we abhor, but praise the judge.
   In Israel's courts ne'er sat an Abbethdin[7]
   With more discerning eyes, or hands more clean;
190 Unbribed, unsought, the wretched to redress;
   Swift of dispatch, and easy of access.
   Oh, had he been content to serve the crown,
   With virtues only proper to the gown°   *judge's robe*
   Or had the rankness of the soil been freed
195 From cockle,° that oppressed the noble seed;   *weeds*
   David for him his tuneful harp had strung,
   And Heaven had wanted one immortal song.[8]
   But wild Ambition loves to slide, not stand,
   And Fortune's ice prefers to Virtue's land.
200 Achitophel, grown weary to possess
   A lawful fame, and lazy happiness,
   Disdained the golden fruit to gather free,
   And lent the crowd his arm to shake the tree.
   Now, manifest of° crimes contrived long since,   *detected in*
205 He stood at bold defiance with his prince;
   Held up the buckler of the people's cause
   Against the crown, and skulked behind the laws.
   The wished occasion of the Plot he takes;
   Some circumstances finds, but more he makes.
210 By buzzing emissaries fills the ears
   Of listening crowds with jealousies° and fears   *suspicions*
   Of arbitrary counsels brought to light,
   And proves the king himself a Jebusite.
   Weak arguments! which yet he knew full well
215 Were strong with people easy to rebel.
   For, governed by the moon, the giddy Jews
   Tread the same track when she the prime renews;
   And once in twenty years, their scribes record,[9]

---

6. The triple alliance of England, Sweden, and Holland against France, 1668. Shaftesbury helped bring about the war against Holland in 1672.
7. The chief of the seventy elders who composed the Jewish supreme court. The allusion is to Shaftesbury's serving as lord chancellor from 1672 to 1673. Dryden's praise of Shaftesbury's integrity in this office, by suggesting a balanced judgment, makes his condemnation of the statesman more effective than it might otherwise have been.

8. I.e., David would have had occasion to write one fewer song of praise to heaven. The reference may be to 2 Samuel 22 or to Psalm 4.
9. The moon "renews her prime" when its several phases recur on the same day of the solar calendar (i.e., complete a cycle) as happens approximately every twenty years. The crisis between Charles I and Parliament began to grow acute about 1640; Charles II returned in 1660; it is now 1680 and a full cycle has been completed.

By natural instinct they change their lord.
220 Achitophel still wants a chief, and none
Was found so fit as warlike Absalom:
Not that he wished his greatness to create
(For politicians neither love nor hate),
But, for he knew his title not allowed,
225 Would keep him still depending on the crowd,
That° kingly power, thus ebbing out, might be   *so that*
Drawn to the dregs of a democracy.[1]
Him he attempts with studied arts to please,
And sheds his venom in such words as these:
230   "Auspicious prince, at whose nativity
Some royal planet[2] ruled the southern sky;
Thy longing country's darling and desire;
Their cloudy pillar and their guardian fire:
Their second Moses, whose extended wand
235 Divides the seas, and shows the promised land;[3]
Whose dawning day in every distant age
Has exercised the sacred prophet's rage:
The people's prayer, the glad diviners' theme,
The young men's vision, and the old men's dream![4]
240 Thee, savior, thee, the nation's vows[5] confess,
And, never satisfied with seeing, bless:
Swift unbespoken° pomps thy steps proclaim,   *spontaneous*
And stammering babes are taught to lisp thy name.
How long wilt thou the general joy detain,
245 Starve and defraud the people of thy reign?
Content ingloriously to pass thy days
Like one of Virtue's fools that feeds on praise;
Till thy fresh glories, which now shine so bright,
Grow stale and tarnish with our daily sight.
250 Believe me, royal youth, thy fruit must be
Or gathered ripe, or rot upon the tree.
Heaven has to all allotted, soon or late,
Some lucky revolution of their fate;
Whose motions if we watch and guide with skill
255 (For human good depends on human will),
Our Fortune rolls as from a smooth descent,
And from the first impression takes the bent;
But, if unseized, she glides away like wind,
And leaves repenting Folly far behind.
260 Now, now she meets you with a glorious prize,
And spreads her locks before her as she flies.[6]
Had thus old David, from whose loins you spring,

1. I.e., mob rule. To Dryden, *democracy* meant popular government.
2. A planet whose influence destines him to kingship.
3. After their exodus from Egypt under the leadership of Moses, whose "extended wand" separated the waters of the Red Sea so that they crossed over on dry land, the Israelites were led in their forty-year wandering in the wilderness by a pillar of cloud by day and a pillar of fire by night (Exodus 13–14).
4. Cf. Joel 2.28.
5. Solemn promises of fidelity.
6. Achitophel gives to Fortune the traditional attributes of the allegorical personification of Opportunity: bald except for a forelock, she can be seized only as she approaches.

2220 | JOHN DRYDEN

Not dared, when Fortune called him, to be king,
At Gath[7] an exile he might still remain,
265 And heaven's anointing[8] oil had been in vain.
Let his successful youth your hopes engage;
But shun the example of declining age;
Behold him setting in his western skies,
The shadows lengthening as the vapors rise.
270 He is not now, as when on Jordan's sand[9]
The joyful people thronged to see him land,
Covering the beach, and blackening all the strand;
But, like the Prince of Angels, from his height
Comes tumbling downward with diminished light;[1]
275 Betrayed by one poor plot to public scorn
(Our only blessing since his cursed return),
Those heaps of people which one sheaf did bind,
Blown off and scattered by a puff of wind.
What strength can he to your designs oppose,
280 Naked of friends, and round beset with foes?
If Pharaoh's[2] doubtful succor he should use,
A foreign aid would more incense the Jews:
Proud Egypt would dissembled friendship bring;
Foment the war, but not support the king:
285 Nor would the royal party e'er unite
With Pharaoh's arms to assist the Jebusite;
Or if they should, their interest soon would break,
And with such odious aid make David weak.
All sorts of men by my successful arts,
290 Abhorring kings, estrange their altered hearts
From David's rule: and 'tis the general cry,
'Religion, commonwealth, and liberty.'[3]
If you, as champion of the public good,
Add to their arms a chief of royal blood,
295 What may not Israel hope, and what applause
Might such a general gain by such a cause?
Not barren praise alone, that gaudy flower
Fair only to the sight, but solid power;
And nobler is a limited command,
300 Given by the love of all your native land,
Than a successive title,[4] long and dark,
Drawn from the moldy rolls of Noah's ark."
      What cannot praise effect in mighty minds,
When flattery soothes, and when ambition blinds!
305 Desire of power, on earth a vicious weed,
Yet, sprung from high, is of celestial seed:
In God 'tis glory; and when men aspire,

---

7. Brussels, where Charles spent his last years in exile. David took refuge from Saul in Gath (1 Samuel 27.4).
8. After God rejected Saul, he sent Samuel to anoint the boy David, as a token that he should finally come to the throne (1 Samuel 16.1–13).
9. The seashore at Dover, where Charles landed (May 25, 1660).

1. Cf. the fall of Satan in *Paradise Lost* 1.50–124, which dims the brightness of the archangel. The choice of the undignified word *tumbling* is deliberate.
2. Pharaoh is Louis XIV of France.
3. Cf. line 82 and n. 5.
4. A title to the crown based on succession.

'Tis but a spark too much of heavenly fire.
The ambitious youth, too covetous of fame,
310   Too full of angels' metal[5] in his frame,
Unwarily was led from virtue's ways,
Made drunk with honor, and debauched with praise.
Half loath, and half consenting to the ill
(For loyal blood within him struggled still),
315   He thus replied: "And what pretense have I
To take up arms for public liberty?
My father governs with unquestioned right;
The faith's defender, and mankind's delight,
Good, gracious, just, observant of the laws:
320   And heaven by wonders has espoused his cause.
Whom has he wronged in all his peaceful reign?
Who sues for justice to his throne in vain?
What millions has he pardoned of his foes,
Whom just revenge did to his wrath expose?
325   Mild, easy, humble, studious of our good,
Inclined to mercy, and averse from blood;
If mildness ill with stubborn Israel suit,
His crime is God's beloved attribute.
What could he gain, his people to betray,
330   Or change his right for arbitrary sway?
Let haughty Pharaoh curse, with such a reign
His fruitful Nile, and yoke a servile train.
If David's rule Jerusalem displease,
The Dog Star[6] heats their brains to this disease.
335   Why then should I, encouraging the bad,
Turn rebel and run popularly mad?
Were he a tyrant, who, by lawless might
Oppressed the Jews, and raised the Jebusite,
Well might I mourn; but nature's holy bands
340   Would curb my spirits and restrain my hands:
The people might assert° their liberty,   *claim*
But what was right in them were crime in me.
His favor leaves me nothing to require;
Prevents my wishes, and outruns desire.
345   What more can I expect while David lives?
All but his kingly diadem he gives:
And that"—But there he paused; then sighing, said—
"Is justly destined for a worthier head.
For when my father from his toils shall rest
350   And late augment the number of the blest,
His lawful issue shall the throne ascend,
Or the collateral line,[7] where that shall end.
His brother, though oppressed with vulgar spite,[8]

---

5. An alternative spelling of *mettle* (i.e., spirit).
But a pun on *metal* is intended, as is obvious from
the pun *angel* (a purely intellectual being and a
coin). Ambition caused the revolt of the angels in
heaven.
6. Sirius, which in midsummer rises and sets
with the sun and is thus associated with the

maddening heat of the "dog days."
7. In the event of Charles's dying without legitimate issue, the throne would constitutionally
pass to his brother, James, or his descendants,
the "collateral line."
8. Anger of the common people.

Yet dauntless, and secure of native right,
355 Of every royal virtue stands possessed;
Still dear to all the bravest and the best.
His courage foes, his friends his truth proclaim;
His loyalty the king, the world his fame.
His mercy even the offending crowd will find,
360 For sure he comes of a forgiving kind.[9]
Why should I then repine at heaven's decree,
Which gives me no pretense to royalty?
Yet O that fate, propitiously inclined,
Had raised my birth, or had debased my mind;
365 To my large soul not all her treasure lent,
And then betrayed it to a mean descent!
I find, I find my mounting spirits bold,
And David's part disdains my mother's mold.
Why am I scanted by a niggard birth?[1]
370 My soul disclaims the kindred of her earth;
And, made for empire, whispers me within,
'Desire of greatness is a godlike sin.'"
        Him staggering so when hell's dire agent found,
While fainting Virtue scarce maintained her ground,
375 He pours fresh forces in, and thus replies:
        "The eternal god, supremely good and wise,
Imparts not these prodigious gifts in vain:
What wonders are reserved to bless your reign!
Against your will, your arguments have shown,
380 Such virtue's only given to guide a throne.
Not that your father's mildness I contemn,
But manly force becomes the diadem.
'Tis true he grants the people all they crave;
And more, perhaps, than subjects ought to have:
385 For lavish grants suppose a monarch tame,
And more his goodness than his wit° proclaim.   intelligence
But when should people strive their bonds to break,
If not when kings are negligent or weak?
Let him give on till he can give no more,
390 The thrifty Sanhedrin[2] shall keep him poor;
And every shekel which he can receive,
Shall cost a limb of his prerogative.[3]
To ply him with new plots shall be my care;
Or plunge him deep in some expensive war;
395 Which when his treasure can no more supply,
He must, with the remains of kingship, buy.
His faithful friends our jealousies and fears
Call Jebusites, and Pharaoh's pensioners;
Whom when our fury from his aid has torn,
400 He shall be naked left to public scorn.

9. Race, in the sense of family.
1. I.e., why does my mean birth impose such
limits on me?
2. The highest judicial counsel of the Jews,
here, Parliament.

3. The Whigs hoped to limit the special privileges of the Crown (the royal "prerogative") by
refusing to vote money to Charles. He circumvented them by living on French subsidies and
refusing to summon Parliament.

The next successor, whom I fear and hate,
My arts have made obnoxious to the state;
Turned all his virtues to his overthrow,
And gained our elders[4] to pronounce a foe.

405 His right, for sums of necessary gold,
Shall first be pawned, and afterward be sold;
Till time shall ever-wanting David draw,
To pass your doubtful title into law:
If not, the people have a right supreme

410 To make their kings; for kings are made for them.
All empire is no more than power in trust,
Which, when resumed,° can be no longer just.   *taken back*
Succession, for the general good designed,
In its own wrong a nation cannot bind;

415 If altering that the people can relieve,
Better one suffer than a nation grieve.
The Jews well know their power: ere Saul they chose,[5]
God was their king, and God they durst depose.
Urge now your piety,[6] your filial name,

420 A father's right and fear of future fame;
The public good, that universal call,
To which even heaven submitted, answers all.
Nor let his love enchant your generous mind;
'Tis Nature's trick to propagate her kind.

425 Our fond begetters, who would never die,
Love but themselves in their posterity.
Or let his kindness by the effects be tried,
Or let him lay his vain pretense aside.
God said he loved your father; could he bring

430 A better proof than to anoint him king?
It surely showed he loved the shepherd well,
Who gave so fair a flock as Israel.
Would David have you thought his darling son?
What means he then, to alienate[7] the crown?

435 The name of godly he may blush to bear:
'Tis after God's own heart[8] to cheat his heir.
He to his brother gives supreme command;
To you a legacy of barren land,[9]
Perhaps the old harp, on which he thrums his lays,

440 Or some dull Hebrew ballad in your praise.
Then the next heir, a prince severe and wise,
Already looks on you with jealous eyes;
Sees through the thin disguises of your arts,
And marks your progress in the people's hearts.

445 Though now his mighty soul its grief contains,

---

4. The chief magistrates and rulers of the Jews. Shaftesbury had won over ("gained") country gentlemen and nobles to his hostile view of James.
5. Before Saul, the first king of Israel, came to the throne, the Jews were governed by judges. Similarly Oliver Cromwell as lord protector took over the reins of government, after he had dissolved the Rump Parliament in 1653.

6. Dutifulness to a parent.
7. In law, to convey the title to property to another person.
8. An irony (cf. line 7 and n. 2).
9. James was given the title of generalissimo in 1678. In 1679 Monmouth was banished and withdrew to Holland.

He meditates revenge who least complains;
And, like a lion, slumbering in the way,
Or sleep dissembling, while he waits his prey,
His fearless foes within his distance draws,
450   Constrains his roaring, and contracts his paws;
Till at the last, his time for fury found,
He shoots with sudden vengeance from the ground;
The prostrate vulgar° passes o'er and spares,   *common people*
But with a lordly rage his hunters tears.
455   Your case no tame expedients will afford:
Resolve on death, or conquest by the sword,
Which for no less a stake than life you draw;
And self-defense is nature's eldest law.
Leave the warm people no considering time;
460   For then rebellion may be thought a crime.
Prevail yourself of what occasion gives,
But try your title while your father lives;
And that your arms may have a fair pretense,°   *pretext*
Proclaim you take them in the king's defense;
465   Whose sacred life each minute would expose
To plots, from seeming friends, and secret foes.
And who can sound the depth of David's soul?
Perhaps his fear his kindness may control.
He fears his brother, though he loves his son,
470   For plighted vows too late to be undone.
If so, by force he wishes to be gained,
Like women's lechery, to seem constrained.°   *forced*
Doubt not; but when he most affects the frown,
Commit a pleasing rape upon the crown.
475   Secure his person to secure your cause:
They who possess the prince, possess the laws."
    He said, and this advice above the rest
With Absalom's mild nature suited best:
Unblamed of life (ambition set aside),
480   Not stained with cruelty, nor puffed with pride,
How happy had he been, if destiny
Had higher placed his birth, or not so high!
His kingly virtues might have claimed a throne,
And blest all other countries but his own.
485   But charming greatness since so few refuse,
'Tis juster to lament him than accuse.
Strong were his hopes a rival to remove,
With blandishments to gain the public love;
To head the faction while their zeal was hot,
490   And popularly prosecute the Plot.
To further this, Achitophel unites
The malcontents of all the Israelites;
Whose differing parties he could wisely join,
For several ends, to serve the same design:
495   The best (and of the princes some were such),
Who thought the power of monarchy too much;
Mistaken men, and patriots in their hearts;

Not wicked, but seduced by impious arts.
By these the springs of property were bent,
500 And wound so high, they cracked the government.
The next for interest sought to embroil the state,
To sell their duty at a dearer rate;
And make their Jewish markets of the throne,
Pretending public good, to serve their own.
505 Others thought kings an useless heavy load,
Who cost too much, and did too little good.
These were for laying honest David by,
On principles of pure good husbandry.°   economy
With them joined all the haranguers of the throng,
510 That thought to get preferment by the tongue.
Who follow next, a double danger bring,
Not only hating David, but the king:
The Solymaean rout,[1] well-versed of old
In godly faction, and in treason bold;
515 Cowering and quaking at a conqueror's sword,
But lofty to a lawful prince restored;
Saw with disdain an ethnic[2] plot begun,
And scorned by Jebusites to be outdone.
Hot Levites[3] headed these; who, pulled before
520 From the ark, which in the Judges' days they bore,
Resumed their cant, and with a zealous cry
Pursued their old beloved theocracy:
Where Sanhedrin and priest enslaved the nation,
And justified their spoils by inspiration:
525 For who so fit for reign as Aaron's race,[4]
If once dominion they could found in grace?
These led the pack; though not of surest scent,
Yet deepest-mouthed[5] against the government.
A numerous host of dreaming saints[6] succeed,
530 Of the true old enthusiastic breed:
'Gainst form and order they their power employ,
Nothing to build, and all things to destroy.
But far more numerous was the herd of such,
Who think too little, and who talk too much.
535 These out of mere instinct, they knew not why,
Adored their fathers' God and property;
And, by the same blind benefit of fate,
The Devil and the Jebusite did hate:
Born to be saved, even in their own despite,

1. I.e., London rabble. Solyma was a name for Jerusalem.
2. Gentile; here, Roman Catholic.
3. I.e., Presbyterian clergymen. The tribe of Levi, assigned to duties in the tabernacle, carried the Ark of the Covenant during the forty-year sojourn in the wilderness (Numbers 4). Under the Commonwealth ("in the Judges' days") Presbyterianism became the state religion, and its clergy, therefore, "bore the ark." The Act of Uniformity (1662) forced the Presbyterian clergy out of their livings: in short, before the Popish Plot, they had been

"pulled from the ark." They are represented here as joining the Whigs in the hope of restoring the commonwealth, "their old beloved theocracy."
4. Priests had to be descendants of Aaron (Exodus 28.1, Numbers 18.7).
5. Loudest. The phrase is applied to hunting dogs. "Pack" and "scent" sustain the image.
6. Term used by certain Dissenters for those elected to salvation. The extreme fanaticism of the "saints" and their claims to inspiration are characterized as a form of religious madness ("enthusiastic," line 530).

540 Because they could not help believing right.
Such were the tools; but a whole Hydra more
Remains, of sprouting heads too long to score.°   count
Some of their chiefs were princes of the land:
In the first rank of these did Zimri[7] stand;
545 A man so various, that he seemed to be
Not one, but all mankind's epitome:
Stiff in opinions, always in the wrong;
Was everything by starts, and nothing long;
But, in the course of one revolving moon,
550 Was chymist,° fiddler, statesman, and buffoon: chemist
Then all for women, painting, rhyming, drinking,
Besides ten thousand freaks that died in thinking.
Blest madman, who could every hour employ,
With something new to wish, or to enjoy!
555 Railing° and praising were his usual themes;   reviling, abusing
And both (to show his judgment) in extremes:
So over-violent, or over-civil,
That every man, with him, was God or Devil.
In squandering wealth was his peculiar art:
560 Nothing went unrewarded but desert.
Beggared by fools, whom still° he found° too late,   constantly / found out
He had his jest, and they had his estate.
He laughed himself from court; then sought relief
By forming parties, but could ne'er be chief;
565 For, spite of him, the weight of business fell
On Absalom and wise Achitophel:
Thus, wicked but in will, of means bereft,
He left not faction, but of that was left.
   Titles and names 'twere tedious to rehearse
570 Of lords, below the dignity of verse.
Wits, warriors, Commonwealth's men, were the best;
Kind husbands, and mere nobles, all the rest.
And therefore, in the name of dullness, be
The well-hung Balaam and cold Caleb, free;
575 And canting Nadab let oblivion damn,
Who made new porridge for the paschal lamb.[8]
Let friendship's holy band some names assure;
Some their own worth, and some let scorn secure.
Nor shall the rascal rabble here have place,
580 Whom kings no titles gave, and God no grace:

7. George Villiers, second duke of Buckingham (1628–1687), wealthy, brilliant, dissolute, and unstable. He had been an influential member of the cabal, but after 1673 had joined Shaftesbury in opposition to the court party. This is the least political of the satirical portraits in the poem. Buckingham had been the chief author of *The Rehearsal* (1671), the play that satirized heroic tragedy and ridiculed Dryden in the character of Mr. Bayes. Politics gave Dryden an opportunity to retaliate. He comments on this portrait in his "A Discourse Concerning the Original and Progress of Satire." Dryden had two biblical Zimris in mind: the Zimri destroyed for his lustfulness and

blasphemy (Numbers 25) and the conspirator and regicide of 1 Kings 16.8–20 and 2 Kings 9.31.
8. The lamb slain during Passover; here, Christ. The identities of Balaam, Caleb, and Nadab have not been certainly established, although various Whig nobles have been suggested. For Balaam see Numbers 22–24; for Caleb, Numbers 13–14; and for Nadab, Leviticus 10.1–2. "Well-hung": fluent of speech or sexually potent or both. "Cold": contrasts with the second meaning of *well-hung*. "Canting": points to a Nonconformist, as does "new porridge," for Dissenters referred to the Book of Common Prayer contemptuously as "porridge," a hodgepodge, unsubstantial stuff.

Not bull-faced Jonas,[9] who could statutes draw
To mean rebellion, and make treason law.
But he, though bad, is followed by a worse,
The wretch who heaven's anointed dared to curse:
585 Shimei,[1] whose youth did early promise bring
Of zeal to God and hatred to his king,
Did wisely from expensive sins refrain,
And never broke the Sabbath, but for gain;
Nor ever was he known an oath to vent,
590 Or curse, unless against the government.
Thus heaping wealth, by the most ready way
Among the Jews, which was to cheat and pray,
The city, to reward his pious hate
Against his master, chose him magistrate.
595 His hand a vare° of justice did uphold;   staff
His neck was loaded with a chain of gold.
During his office, treason was no crime;
The sons of Belial[2] had a glorious time;
For Shimei, though not prodigal of pelf,
600 Yet loved his wicked neighbor as himself.
When two or three were gathered to declaim ⎤
Against the monarch of Jerusalem,   ⎬
Shimei was always in the midst of them;   ⎦
And if they cursed the king when he was by,
605 Would rather curse than break good company.
If any durst his factious friends accuse,
He packed a jury of dissenting Jews;
Whose fellow-feeling in the godly cause
Would free the suffering saint from human laws.
610 For laws are only made to punish those
Who serve the king, and to protect his foes.
If any leisure time he had from power
(Because 'tis sin to misemploy an hour),
His business was, by writing, to persuade
615 That kings were useless, and a clog to trade;
And, that his noble style he might refine,
No Rechabite[3] more shunned the fumes of wine.
Chaste were his cellars, and his shrieval board[4]
The grossness of a city feast abhorred:
620 His cooks, with long disuse, their trade forgot;
Cool was his kitchen, though his brains were hot,
Such frugal virtue malice may accuse,
But sure 'twas necessary to the Jews:

9. Sir William Jones, attorney general, had been largely responsible for the passage of the first Exclusion Bill by the House of Commons. He prosecuted the accused in the Popish Plot.
1. Shimei cursed and stoned David when he fled into the wilderness during Absalom's revolt (2 Samuel 16.5–14). His name is used here for one of the two sheriffs of London: Slingsby Bethel, a Whig, former republican, and virulent enemy of Charles. He packed juries with Whigs and so secured the acquittal of enemies of the court, among them Shaftesbury himself.
2. Sons of wickedness (cf. Milton, *Paradise Lost* 1.490–505). Dryden probably intended a pun on Balliol, the Oxford college in which leading Whigs stayed during the brief and fateful meeting of Parliament at Oxford in 1681.
3. An austere Jewish sect that drank no wine (Jeremiah 35.2–19).
4. Sheriff's dinner table.

For towns once burnt[5] such magistrates require
625   As dare not tempt God's providence by fire.
      With spiritual food he fed his servants well,
      But free from flesh that made the Jews rebel;
      And Moses' laws he held in more account,
      For forty days of fasting in the mount.[6]
630   To speak the rest, who better are forgot,
      Would tire a well-breathed witness of the Plot.
      Yet, Corah,[7] thou shalt from oblivion pass:
      Erect thyself, thou monumental brass,
      High as the serpent of thy metal made,[8]
635   While nations stand secure beneath thy shade.
      What though his birth were base, yet comets rise
      From earthy vapors, ere they shine in skies.
      Prodigious actions may as well be done
      By weaver's issue,[9] as by prince's son.
640   This arch-attestor for the public good
      By that one deed ennobles all his blood.
      Who ever asked the witnesses' high race
      Whose oath with martyrdom did Stephen[1] grace?
      Ours was a Levite, and as times went then,
645   His tribe were God Almighty's gentlemen.
      Sunk were his eyes, his voice was harsh and loud,
      Sure signs he neither choleric° was nor proud: *prone to anger*
      His long chin proved his wit; his saintlike grace
      A church vermilion, and a Moses' face.[2]
650   His memory, miraculously great,
      Could plots, exceeding man's belief, repeat;
      Which therefore cannot be accounted lies,
      For human wit could never such devise.
      Some future truths are mingled in his book;
655   But where the witness failed, the prophet spoke:
      Some things like visionary flights appear;
      The spirit caught him up, the Lord knows where,
      And gave him his rabbinical degree,
      Unknown to foreign university.[3]
660   His judgment yet his memory did excel;
      Which pieced his wondrous evidence so well,
      And suited to the temper of the times,
      Then groaning under Jebusitic crimes.
      Let Israel's foes suspect his heavenly call,
665   And rashly judge his writ apocryphal;[4]

---

5. London burned in 1666.
6. Mount Sinai, where, during a fast of forty days, Moses received the law (Exodus 34.28).
7. Or Korah, a rebellious Levite, swallowed up by the earth because of his crimes (Numbers 16). Corah is Titus Oates, the self-appointed, perjured, and "well-breathed" (long-winded) witness of the plot.
8. Moses erected a brazen serpent to heal the Jews bitten by fiery serpents (Numbers 21.4–9). *Brass* also means impudence or shamelessness.
9. Oates's father, a clergyman, belonged to an obscure family of ribbon weavers.
1. The first Christian martyr, accused by false witnesses (Acts 6–7).
2. Moses' face shone when he came down from Mount Sinai with the tables of the law (Exodus 34.29–30). Oates's face suggests high living, not spiritual illumination.
3. Oates falsely claimed to be a doctor of divinity in the University of Salamanca.
4. Not inspired and hence excluded from Holy Writ.

Our laws for such affronts have forfeits made:
He takes his life, who takes away his trade.
Were I myself in witness Corah's place,
The wretch who did me such a dire disgrace
670 Should whet my memory, though once forgot,
To make him an appendix of my plot.
His zeal to heaven made him his prince despise,
And load his person with indignities;
But zeal peculiar privilege affords,
675 Indulging latitude to deeds and words;
And Corah might for Agag's[5] murder call,
In terms as coarse as Samuel used to Saul.
What others in his evidence did join
(The best that could be had for love or coin),
680 In Corah's own predicament will fall;
For *witness* is a common name to all.
    Surrounded thus with friends of every sort,
Deluded Absalom forsakes the court:
Impatient of high hopes, urged with renown,
685 And fired with near possession of a crown.
The admiring crowd are dazzled with surprise,
And on his goodly person feed their eyes:
His joy concealed, he sets himself to show,
On each side bowing popularly[6] low;
690 His looks, his gestures, and his words he frames,
And with familiar ease repeats their names.
Thus formed by nature, furnished out with arts,
He glides unfelt into their secret hearts.
Then, with a kind compassionating look,
695 And sighs, bespeaking pity ere he spoke,
Few words he said; but easy those and fit,
More slow than Hybla-drops,[7] and far more sweet.
    "I mourn, my countrymen, your lost estate;
Though far unable to prevent your fate:
700 Behold a banished man, for your dear cause
Exposed a prey to arbitrary laws!
Yet oh! that I alone could be undone,
Cut off from empire, and no more a son!
Now all your liberties a spoil are made; ⎤
705 Egypt° and Tyrus° intercept your trade, ⎬   *France / Holland*
And Jebusites your sacred rites invade. ⎦
My father, whom with reverence yet I name,
Charmed into ease, is careless of his fame;
And, bribed with petty sums of foreign gold,
710 Is grown in Bathsheba's[8] embraces old;
Exalts his enemies, his friends destroys;

---

5. Agag is probably one of the five Catholic peers executed for the Popish Plot in 1680, most likely Lord Stafford, against whom Oates fabricated testimony. He is almost certainly not, as is usually suggested, Sir Edmund Berry Godfrey (see head-note, pp. 2212–13). "Agag's murder" and Samuel's coarse terms to Saul are in 1 Samuel 15.

6. "So as to please the crowd" (Johnson's *Dictionary*).
7. The famous honey of Hybla in Sicily.
8. Bathsheba is the woman with whom David committed adultery (2 Samuel 11). Here, Charles II's French mistress, Louise de Keroualle, duchess of Portsmouth.

And all his power against himself employs.
He gives, and let him give, my right away;
But why should he his own, and yours betray?
715 He only, he can make the nation bleed,
And he alone from my revenge is freed.
Take then my tears (with that he wiped his eyes),
'Tis all the aid my present power supplies:
No court-informer can these arms accuse;
720 These arms may sons against their fathers use:
And 'tis my wish, the next successor's reign
May make no other Israelite complain."

Youth, beauty, graceful action seldom fail;
But common interest always will prevail;
725 And pity never ceases to be shown
To him who makes the people's wrongs his own.
The crowd (that still believe their kings oppress)
With lifted hands their young Messiah bless:
Who now begins his progress to ordain
730 With chariots, horsemen, and a numerous train;
From east to west his glories he displays,[9]
And, like the sun, the promised land surveys.
Fame runs before him as the morning star,
And shouts of joy salute him from afar:
735 Each house receives him as a guardian god,
And consecrates the place of his abode:
But hospitable treats did most commend
Wise Issachar,[1] his wealthy western friend.
This moving court, that caught the people's eyes,
740 And seemed but pomp, did other ends disguise:
Achitophel had formed it, with intent
To sound the depths, and fathom, where it went,
The people's hearts; distinguish friends from foes,
And try their strength, before they came to blows.
745 Yet all was colored with a smooth pretense
Of specious love, and duty to their prince.
Religion, and redress of grievances,
Two names that always cheat and always please,
Are often urged; and good King David's life
750 Endangered by a brother and a wife.[2]
Thus, in a pageant show, a plot is made,
And peace itself is war in masquerade.
O foolish Israel! never warned by ill,
Still the same bait, and circumvented still!
755 Did ever men forsake their present ease,
In midst of health imagine a disease;
Take pains contingent mischiefs to foresee,
Make heirs for monarchs, and for God decree?

---

9. In 1680 Monmouth made a progress through the west of England, seeking popular support for his cause.
1. Thomas Thynne of Longleat. He entertained Monmouth on his journey in the west. *Wise* is, of

course, ironic.
2. Titus Oates had sworn that both James, duke of York, and the queen were involved in a similar plot to poison Charles II.

What shall we think! Can people give away
760 Both for themselves and sons, their native sway?
Then they are left defenseless to the sword
Of each unbounded, arbitrary lord:
And laws are vain, by which we right enjoy,
If kings unquestioned can those laws destroy.
765 Yet if the crowd be judge of fit and just,
And kings are only officers in trust,
Then this resuming covenant was declared
When kings were made, or is forever barred.
If those who gave the scepter could not tie
770 By their own deed their own posterity,
How then could Adam bind his future race?
How could his forfeit on mankind take place?
Or how could heavenly justice damn us all,
Who ne'er consented to our father's fall?
775 Then kings are slaves to those whom they command,
And tenants to their people's pleasure stand.
Add, that the power for property allowed
Is mischievously seated in the crowd;
For who can be secure of private right,
780 If sovereign sway may be dissolved by might?
Nor is the people's judgment always true:
The most may err as grossly as the few;
And faultless kings run down, by common cry,
For vice, oppression, and for tyranny.
785 What standard is there in a fickle rout,
Which, flowing to the mark,° runs faster out?   *highwater mark*
Nor only crowds, but Sanhedrins may be
Infected with this public lunacy,[3]
And share the madness of rebellious times,
790 To murder monarchs for imagined crimes.[4]
If they may give and take whene'er they please,
Not kings alone (the Godhead's images),
But government itself at length must fall
To nature's state, where all have right to all.
795 Yet, grant our lords the people kings can make,
What prudent men a settled throne would shake?
For whatsoe'er their sufferings were before,
That change they covet makes them suffer more.
All other errors but disturb a state,
800 But innovation is the blow of fate.
If ancient fabrics nod, and threat to fall,
To patch the flaws, and buttress up the wall,
Thus far 'tis duty; but here fix the mark;
For all beyond it is to touch our ark.[5]
805 To change foundations, cast the frame anew,
Is work for rebels, who base ends pursue,

3. The fickle crowd flows and ebbs like the tide, which is pulled back and forth by the moon (hence "lunacy," after the Latin *luna*, or "moon").
4. An allusion to the execution of Charles I.

5. Uzzah was struck dead because he sacrilegiously touched the Ark of the Covenant (2 Samuel 6.6–7).

At once divine and human laws control,
And mend the parts by ruin of the whole.
The tampering world is subject to this curse,
810 To physic their disease into a worse.
    Now what relief can righteous David bring?
How fatal 'tis to be too good a king!
Friends he has few, so high the madness grows:
Who dare be such, must be the people's foes:
815 Yet some there were, even in the worst of days;
Some let me name, and naming is to praise.
    In this short file Barzillai[6] first appears;
Barzillai, crowned with honor and with years:
Long since, the rising rebels he withstood
820 In regions waste, beyond the Jordan's flood:
Unfortunately brave to buoy the State;
But sinking underneath his master's fate:
In exile with his godlike prince he mourned;
For him he suffered, and with him returned.
825 The court he practiced, not the courtier's art:
Large was his wealth, but larger was his heart:
Which well the noblest objects knew to choose,
The fighting warrior, and recording Muse.
His bed could once a fruitful issue boast;
830 Now more than half a father's name is lost.
His eldest hope,[7] with every grace adorned,
By me (so Heaven will have it) always mourned,
And always honored, snatched in manhood's prime
By unequal fates, and Providence's crime:
835 Yet not before the goal of honor won, ⎫
All parts fulfilled of subject and of son; ⎬
Swift was the race, but short the time to run. ⎭
O narrow circle, but of power divine,
Scanted in space, but perfect in thy line!
840 By sea, by land, thy matchless worth was known,
Arms thy delight, and war was all thy own:
Thy force, infused, the fainting Tyrians° propped;   *the Dutch*
And haughty Pharaoh found his fortune stopped.
Oh ancient honor! Oh unconquered hand,
845 Whom foes unpunished never could withstand!
But Israel was unworthy of thy name:
Short is the date of all immoderate fame.
It looks as Heaven our ruin had designed,
And durst not trust thy fortune and thy mind.
850 Now, free from earth, thy disencumbered soul
Mounts up, and leaves behind the clouds and starry pole:
From thence thy kindred legions mayst thou bring,

6. James Butler, duke of Ormond (1610–1688). He was famous for his loyalty to the Stuart cause. He fought for Charles I in Ireland, and when that cause was hopeless, he joined Charles II in his exile abroad. He spent a large fortune on behalf of the king and continued to serve him loyally after the Restoration. Six of his ten children were dead (see line 830). Cf. 2 Samuel 19.31–39.
7. Ormond's son, Thomas, earl of Ossory (1634–1680), a famous soldier and, like his father, devoted to Charles II.

To aid the guardian angel of thy king.
Here stop my Muse, here cease thy painful flight;
855 No pinions can pursue immortal height:
Tell good Barzillai thou canst sing no more,
And tell thy soul she should have fled before:
Or fled she with his life, and left this verse
To hang on her departed patron's hearse?
860 Now take thy steepy flight from heaven, and see
If thou canst find on earth another *he*:
Another *he* would be too hard to find;
See then whom thou canst see not far behind.
Zadoc the priest, whom, shunning power and place,
865 His lowly mind advanced to David's grace:
With him the Sagan[8] of Jerusalem,
Of hospitable soul, and noble stem;
Him of the western dome, whose weighty sense
Flows in fit words and heavenly eloquence.
870 The prophets' sons,[9] by such example led,
To learning and to loyalty were bred:
For colleges on bounteous kinds depend,
And never rebel was to arts a friend.
To these succeed the pillars of the laws,
875 Who best could plead, and best can judge a cause.
Next them a train of loyal peers ascend;
Sharp-judging Adriel,[1] the Muses' friend,
Himself a Muse—in Sanhedrin's debate
True to his prince, but not a slave of state:
880 Whom David's love with honors did adorn,
That from his disobedient son were torn.
Jotham[2] of piercing wit, and pregnant thought,
Indued by nature, and by learning taught
To move assemblies, who but only tried
885 The worse a while, then chose the better side;
Nor chose alone, but turned the balance too;
So much the weight of one brave man can do.
Hushar,[3] the friend of David in distress,
In public storms, of manly steadfastness:
890 By foreign treaties he informed his youth,
And joined experience to his native truth.
His frugal care supplied the wanting throne,
Frugal for that, but bounteous of his own:
'Tis easy conduct when exchequers flow,
895 But hard the task to manage well the low;
For sovereign power is too depressed or high,
When kings are forced to sell, or crowds to buy.
Indulge one labor more, my weary Muse,
For Amiel:[4] who can Amiel's praise refuse?

---

8. Henry Compton, bishop of London. "Zadoc":
William Sancroft, archbishop of Canterbury.
9. The boys of Westminster School, which
Dryden had attended. "Him of the western dome":
John Dolben, dean of Westminster.

1. John Sheffield, earl of Mulgrave.
2. George Savile, marquis of Halifax.
3. Laurence Hyde, earl of Rochester.
4. Edward Seymour, speaker of the House of
Commons.

900 Of ancient race by birth, but nobler yet
In his own worth, and without title great:
The Sanhedrin long time as chief he ruled,
Their reason guided, and their passion cooled:
So dexterous was he in the crown's defense,
905 So formed to speak a loyal nation's sense,
That, as their band was Israel's tribes in small,
So fit was he to represent them all.
Now rasher charioteers the seat ascend,
Whose loose careers his steady skill commend°: *set off to advantage*
910 They like the unequal ruler of the day,
Misguide the seasons, and mistake the way;
While he withdrawn at their mad labor smiles,
And safe enjoys the sabbath of his toils.
  These were the chief, a small but faithful band ⎤
915 Of worthies, in the breach who dared to stand, ⎬
And tempt the united fury of the land. ⎦
With grief they viewed such powerful engines bent,
To batter down the lawful government:
A numerous faction, with pretended frights,
920 In Sanhedrins to plume° the regal rights; *pluck, plunder*
The true successor from the court removed:[5]
The Plot, by hireling witnesses, improved.
These ills they saw, and, as their duty bound,
They showed the king the danger of the wound:
925 That no concessions from the throne would please,
But lenitives° fomented the disease; *pain relievers*
That Absalom, ambitious of the crown,
Was made the lure to draw the people down;
That false Achitophel's pernicious hate
930 Had turned the Plot to ruin Church and State:
The council violent, the rabble worse;
That Shimei taught Jerusalem to curse.
  With all these loads of injuries oppressed,
And long revolving, in his careful breast,
935 The event of things, at last, his patience tired,
Thus from his royal throne, by Heaven inspired,
The godlike David spoke: with awful fear
His train their Maker in their master hear.
  "Thus long have I, by native mercy swayed,
940 My wrongs dissembled, my revenge delayed:
So willing to forgive the offending age,
So much the father did the king assuage.
But now so far my clemency they slight,
The offenders question my forgiving right.
945 That one was made for many, they contend;
But 'tis to rule; for that's a monarch's end.
They call my tenderness of blood, my fear;
Though manly tempers can the longest bear.
Yet, since they will divert my native course,

5. The duke of York had been banished from England.

950   'Tis time to show I am not good by force.
       Those heaped affronts that haughty subjects bring,
       Are burdens for a camel, not a king:
       Kings are the public pillars of the State,
       Born to sustain and prop the nation's weight:
955   If my young Samson will pretend a call
       To shake the column, let him share the fall:[6]
       But, oh, that yet he would repent and live!
       How easy 'tis for parents to forgive!
       With how few tears a pardon might be won
960   From nature, pleading for a darling son!
       Poor pitied youth, by my paternal care
       Raised up to all the height his frame could bear:
       Had God ordained his fate for empire born,
       He would have given his soul another turn:
965   Gulled° with a patriot's name, whose modern sense   *deceived*
       Is one that would by law supplant his prince:
       The people's brave,° the politician's tool;   *bully*
       Never was patriot yet, but was a fool.
       Whence comes it that religion and the laws
970   Should more be Absalom's than David's cause?
       His old instructor,[7] ere he lost his place,
       Was never thought indued with so much grace.
       Good heavens, how faction can a patriot paint!
       My rebel ever proves my people's saint:
975   Would *they* impose an heir upon the throne?
       Let Sanhedrins be taught to give their own.
       A king's at least a part of government,
       And mine as requisite as their consent;
       Without my leave a future king to choose,
980   Infers a right the present to depose:
       True, they petition me to approve their choice;
       But Esau's hands suit ill with Jacob's voice.[8]
       My pious subjects for my safety pray,
       Which to secure, they take my power away.
985   From plots and treasons Heaven preserve my years,
       But save me most from my petitioners.
       Unsatiate as the barren womb or grave;
       God cannot grant so much as they can crave.
       What then is left but with a jealous eye
990   To guard the small remains of royalty?
       The law shall still direct my peaceful sway,
       And the same law teach rebels to obey:
       Votes shall no more established power control—
       Such votes as make a part exceed the whole:
995   No groundless clamors shall my friends remove,
       Nor crowds have power to punish ere they prove:
       For gods and godlike kings, their care express,
       Still to defend their servants in distress.

6. Judges 16.   8. Genesis 27.22.
7. The earl of Shaftesbury.

O that my power to saving were confined:
1000 Why am I forced, like Heaven, against my mind,
To make examples of another kind?
Must I at length the sword of justice draw?
O curst effects of necessary law!
How ill my fear they by my mercy scan°!   judge
1005 Beware the fury of a patient man.
Law they require, let Law then show her face;
They could not be content to look on Grace,
Her hinder parts, but with a daring eye
To tempt the terror of her front and die.[9]
1010 By their own arts, 'tis righteously decreed,
Those dire artificers of death shall bleed.
Against themselves their witnesses will swear,
Till viper-like their mother Plot they tear:
And suck for nutriment that bloody gore,
1015 Which was their principle of life before.
Their Belial with their Belzebub[1] will fight;
Thus on my foes, my foes shall do me right:
Nor doubt the event; for factious crowds engage,
In their first onset, all their brutal rage.
1020 Then let 'em take an unresisted course,
Retire and traverse,° and delude their force: thwart
But when they stand all breathless, urge the fight,
And rise upon 'em with redoubled might:
For lawful power is still superior found,
1025 When long driven back, at length it stands the ground."
    He said. The Almighty, nodding, gave consent;
And peals of thunder shook the firmament.
Henceforth a series of new time began,
The mighty years in long procession ran:
1030 Once more the godlike David was restored,
And willing nations knew their lawful lord.

1681

Mac Flecknoe

The target of this superb satire, which is cast in the form of a mock-heroic episode, is Thomas Shadwell (1640–1692), the playwright, with whom Dryden had been on good terms for a number of years, certainly as late as March 1678. Shadwell considered himself the successor of Ben Jonson and the champion of the type of comedy that Jonson had written, the "comedy of humors," in which each character is presented under the domination of a single psychological trait or eccentricity, his humor. His plays are not without merit, but they are often clumsy and prolix and certainly much inferior to Jonson's. For many years he had conducted a public argument with Dryden on the merits of Jonson's comedies, which he thought Dryden undervalued. Exactly what moved Dryden to attack him is a matter of conjecture: he may simply have grown progressively bored and irritated by Shadwell and his tedious argument. The poem seems to have been written in late 1678 or 1679

---

9. Moses was not allowed to see the countenance of Jehovah (Exodus 33.20–23).

1. A god of the Philistines. "Belial": the incarnation of all evil.

and to have circulated only in manuscript until it was printed in 1682 in a pirated edition by an obscure publisher. By that time, the two playwrights were alienated by politics as well as by literary quarrels. Shadwell was a violent Whig and the reputed author of a sharp attack on Dryden as the Tory author of *Absalom and Achitophel* and "The Medal." It was probably for this reason that the printer added the subtitle referring to Shadwell's Whiggism in the phrase "true-blue-Protestant poet." Political passions were running high, and sales would be helped if the poem seemed to refer to the events of the day.

Whereas Butler had debased and degraded his victims by using burlesque, caricature, and the grotesque, Dryden exposed Shadwell to ridicule by using the devices of mock epic, which treats the low, mean, or absurd in the grand language, lofty style, and solemn tone of epic poetry. The obvious disparity between subject and style makes the satiric point. In 1678, a prolific, untalented writer, Richard Flecknoe, died. Dryden conceived the idea of presenting Shadwell (the self-proclaimed heir of Ben Jonson, the laureate) as the son and successor of Flecknoe (an irony also because Flecknoe was a Catholic priest)—hence *Mac* (son of) *Flecknoe*—from whom he inherits the throne of dullness. Flecknoe in the triple role of king, priest, and poet hails his successor, pronounces a panegyric on his perfect fitness for the throne, anoints and crowns him, foretells his glorious reign, and as he sinks (leaden dullness cannot soar), leaves his mantle to fall symbolically on Shadwell's shoulders. The poem abounds in literary allusions—to Roman legend and history and to the *Aeneid*, to Cowley's fragmentary epic *The Davideis*, to *Paradise Lost*, and to Shadwell's own plays. Biblical allusions add an unexpected dimension of incongruous dignity to the low scene. The coronation takes place in the City, to the plaudits of the citizens, who are fit to admire only what is dull. In 217 lines, Dryden created an image of Shadwell that has fixed his reputation to this day.

Mac Flecknoe

Or a Satire upon the True-Blue-Protestant Poet, T. S.

> All human things are subject to decay,
> And when fate summons, monarchs must obey.
> This Flecknoe found, who, like Augustus,[1] young
> Was called to empire, and had governed long;
> 5   In prose and verse, was owned, without dispute,
> Through all the realms of Nonsense, absolute.
> This aged prince, now flourishing in peace,
> And blest with issue of a large increase,
> Worn out with business, did at length debate
> 10   To settle the succession of the state;
> And, pondering which of all his sons was fit
> To reign, and wage immortal war with wit,
> Cried: " 'Tis resolved; for nature pleads that he
> Should only rule, who most resembles me.
> 15   Sh——[2] alone my perfect image bears,
> Mature in dullness from his tender years:
> Sh——alone, of all my sons, is he

---

1. In 31 B.C.E. Octavian became the first Roman emperor, at the age of thirty-two. He assumed the title Augustus in 27 B.C.E.
2. Thomas Shadwell. The initial and second letter of the name followed by a dash give the appearance, but only the appearance, of protecting Dryden's victim by concealing his name. A common device in the satire of the period.

Who stands confirmed in full stupidity.
The rest to some faint meaning make pretense,
20   But Sh—— never deviates into sense.
Some beams of wit on other souls may fall,
Strike through, and make a lucid interval;
But Sh——'s genuine night admits no ray,
His rising fogs prevail upon the day.
25   Besides, his goodly fabric³ fills the eye,
And seems designed for thoughtless majesty:
Thoughtless as monarch oaks that shade the plain,
And, spread in solemn state, supinely reign.
Heywood and Shirley were but types of thee,⁴
30   Thou last great prophet of tautology.⁵
Even I, a dunce of more renown than they,
Was sent before but to prepare thy way;
And, coarsely clad in Norwich drugget,° came   *coarse woolen cloth*
To teach the nations in thy greater name.⁶
35   My warbling lute, the lute I whilom° strung,   *formerly*
When to King John of Portugal⁷ I sung,
Was but the prelude to that glorious day,
When thou on silver Thames didst cut thy way,
With well-timed oars before the royal barge,
40   Swelled with the pride of thy celestial charge;
And big with hymn, commander of a host,
The like was ne'er in Epsom blankets tossed.⁸
Methinks I see the new Arion⁹ sail,
The lute still trembling underneath thy nail.
45   At thy well-sharpened thumb from shore to shore
The treble squeaks for fear, the basses roar;
Echoes from Pissing Alley Sh—— call,
And Sh—— they resound from Aston Hall.
About thy boat the little fishes throng,
50   As at the morning toast° that floats along.   *sewage*
Sometimes, as prince of thy harmonious band,
Thou wield'st thy papers in thy threshing hand,
St. André's¹ feet ne'er kept more equal time,
Not ev'n the feet of thy own *Psyche's* rhyme;
55   Though they in number as in sense excel:
So just, so like tautology, they fell,
That, pale with envy, Singleton² forswore

---

3. His body. Shadwell was a corpulent man.
4. Thomas Heywood (ca. 1570–1641) and James Shirley (1596–1666), playwrights popular before the closing of the theaters in 1642 but now out of fashion. They are introduced here as "types" (i.e., prefigurings) of Shadwell, in the sense that Solomon was regarded as an Old Testament prefiguring of Christ, the "last [final] great prophet."
5. Unnecessary repetition of meaning in different words.
6. The parallel between Flecknoe, as forerunner of Shadwell, and John the Baptist, as forerunner of Jesus, is made plain in lines 32–34 by the use of details and even words taken from Matthew 3.3–4 and John 1.23.

7. Flecknoe boasted of the patronage of the Portuguese king.
8. A reference to Shadwell's comedy *Epsom Wells* and to the farcical scene in his *Virtuoso*, in which Sir Samuel Hearty is tossed in a blanket.
9. A legendary Greek poet. Returning home by sea, he was robbed and thrown overboard by the sailors, but was saved by a dolphin that had been charmed by his music.
1. A French dancer who designed the choreography of Shadwell's opera *Psyche* (1675). Dryden's sneer at the mechanical metrics of the songs in *Psyche* is justified.
2. John Singleton (d. 1686), a musician at the Theatre Royal.

The lute and sword, which he in triumph bore, ⎱
And vowed he ne'er would act Villerius[3] more." ⎰
60 Here stopped the good old sire, and wept for joy
In silent raptures of the hopeful boy.
All arguments, but most his plays, persuade,
That for anointed dullness[4] he was made.
   Close to the walls which fair Augusta° bind   *London*
65 (The fair Augusta much to fears inclined),[5]
An ancient fabric,° raised to inform the sight,   *building*
There stood of yore, and Barbican it hight:°   *was called*
A watchtower once; but now, so fate ordains,
Of all the pile an empty name remains.
70 From its old ruins brothel houses rise,
Scenes of lewd loves, and of polluted joys,
Where their vast courts the mother-strumpets keep,
And, undisturbed by watch, in silence sleep.
Near these a Nursery[6] erects its head,
75 Where queens are formed, and future heroes bred;
Where unfledged actors learn to laugh and cry, ⎱
Where infant punks° their tender voices try, ⎬ *prostitutes*
And little Maximins[7] the gods defy.   ⎰
Great Fletcher never treads in buskins here,
80 Nor greater Jonson dares in socks[8] appear;
But gentle Simkin[9] just reception finds
Amidst this monument of vanished minds:
Pure clinches° the suburbian Muse affords,   *puns*
And Panton[1] waging harmless war with words.
85 Here Flecknoe, as a place to fame well known,
Ambitiously design'd his Sh——'s throne;
For ancient Dekker[2] prophesied long since, ⎱
That in this pile would reign a mighty prince, ⎬
Born for a scourge of wit, and flail of sense; ⎰
90 To whom true dullness should some *Psyches* owe,
But worlds of *Misers* from his pen should flow;
Humorists and *Hypocrites*[3] it should produce,
Whole Raymond families, and tribes of Bruce.
   Now Empress Fame had published the renown
95 Of Sh——'s coronation through the town.
Roused by report of Fame, the nations meet,
From near Bunhill, and distant Watling Street.[4]

---

3. A character in Sir William Davenant's *Siege of Rhodes* (1656), the first English opera.
4. The anticipated phrase is "anointed *majesty*." English kings are anointed with oil at their coronations.
5. This line alludes to the fears excited by the Popish Plot (cf. *Absalom and Achitophel*, p. 2212).
6. The name of a training school for young actors.
7. Maximin is the cruel emperor, in Dryden's *Tyrannic Love* (1669), notorious for his bombast.
8. "Buskins" and "socks" were the symbols of tragedy and comedy, respectively. John Fletcher (1579–1625), the playwright and collaborator with Francis Beaumont (ca. 1584–1616).
9. A popular character in low farces.

1. Said to have been a celebrated punster.
2. Thomas Dekker (ca. 1572–1632), the playwright, whom Jonson had satirized in *The Poetaster*.
3. Three of Shadwell's plays; *The Hypocrite*, a failure, was not published. "Raymond" and "Bruce" (line 93) are characters in *The Humorists* and *The Virtuoso*, respectively.
4. Because Bunhill is about a quarter mile and Watling Street little more than a half mile from the site of the Nursery, where the coronation is held, Shadwell's fame is narrowly circumscribed. Moreover, his subjects live in the heart of the City, regarded by men of wit and fashion as the abode of bad taste and middle-class vulgarity.

No Persian carpets spread the imperial way,
But scattered limbs of mangled poets lay;
100 From dusty shops neglected authors come,
Martyrs of pies, and relics of the bum.[5]
Much Heywood, Shirley, Ogilby[6] there lay,
But loads of Sh—— almost choked the way.
Bilked stationers for yeomen stood prepared,
105 And Herringman was captain of the guard.[7]
The hoary prince in majesty appeared,
High on a throne of his own labors reared.
At his right hand our young Ascanius sate,
Rome's other hope, and pillar of the state.
110 His brows thick fogs, instead of glories, grace,
And lambent dullness played around his face.[8]
As Hannibal did to the altars come,
Sworn by his sire a mortal foe to Rome,[9]
So Sh—— swore, nor should his vow be vain,
115 That he till death true dullness would maintain;
And, in his father's right, and realm's defense,
Ne'er to have peace with wit, nor truce with sense.
The king himself the sacred unction[1] made,
As king by office, and as priest by trade.
120 In his siníster° hand, instead of ball,   left
He placed a mighty mug of potent ale;
Love's Kingdom to his right he did convey,
At once his scepter, and his rule of sway;
Whose righteous lore the prince had practiced young,
125 And from whose loins recorded *Psyche* sprung.
His temples, last, with poppies were o'erspread,
That nodding seemed to consecrate his head.[2]
Just at that point of time, if fame not lie,
On his left hand twelve reverend owls did fly.[3]
130 So Romulus, 'tis sung, by Tiber's brook,
Presage of sway from twice six vultures took.
The admiring throng loud acclamations make,
And omens of his future empire take.
The sire then shook the honors[4] of his head,
135 And from his brows damps of oblivion shed

5. Unsold books were used to line pie plates and as toilet paper.
6. John Ogilby, a translator of Homer and Virgil, ridiculed by both Dryden and Pope as a bad poet.
7. "Bilked stationers": cheated publishers, acting as "yeomen" of the guard, led by Henry Herringman, who until 1679 was the publisher of both Shadwell and Dryden.
8. Ascanius, or Iulus, was the son of Aeneas. Virgil referred to him as *"spes altera Romae"* ("Rome's other hope," *Aeneid* 12.168). As Troy fell, he was marked as favored by the gods when a flickering ("lambent") flame played round his head (*Aeneid* 2.680–84).
9. Hannibal, who almost conquered Rome in 216 B.C.E., during the second Punic War, took this oath at the age of nine (Livy 21.1).
1. The sacramental oil, used in the coronation.
2. During the coronation a British monarch holds two symbols of the throne: a globe ("ball") representing the world in the left hand and a scepter in the right. Shadwell's symbols of monarchy are a mug of ale; Flecknoe's dreary play *Love's Kingdom;* and a crown of poppies, which suggest heaviness, dullness, and drowsiness. The poppies also refer obliquely to Shadwell's addiction to opium.
3. Birds of night. Appropriate substitutes for the twelve vultures whose flight confirmed to Romulus the destined site of Rome, of which he was founder and king.
4. Ornaments, hence locks.

Full on the filial dullness: long he stood, ⎫
Repelling from his breast the raging god; ⎬
At length burst out in this prophetic mood: ⎭
    "Heavens bless my son, from Ireland let him reign

140 To far Barbadoes on the western main;[5]
Of his dominion may no end be known,
And greater than his father's be his throne;
Beyond *Love's Kingdom* let him stretch his pen!"
He paused, and all the people cried, "Amen."

145 Then thus continued he: "My son, advance
Still in new impudence, new ignorance.
Success let others teach, learn thou from me
Pangs without birth, and fruitless industry.
Let *Virtuosos* in five years be writ;

150 Yet not one thought accuse thy toil of wit.
Let gentle George[6] in triumph tread the stage,
Make Dorimant betray, and Loveit rage;
Let Cully, Cockwood, Fopling, charm the pit,
And in their folly show the writer's wit.

155 Yet still thy fools shall stand in thy defense,
And justify their author's want of sense.
Let 'em be all by thy own model made
Of dullness, and desire no foreign aid;
That they to future ages may be known,

160 Not copies drawn, but issue of thy own.
Nay, let thy men of wit too be the same,
All full of thee, and differing but in name.
But let no alien S—dl—y[7] interpose,
To lard with wit[8] thy hungry *Epsom* prose.

165 And when false flowers of rhetoric thou wouldst cull,
Trust nature, do not labor to be dull;
But write thy best, and top; and, in each line,
Sir Formal's[9] oratory will be thine:
Sir Formal, though unsought, attends thy quill,

170 And does thy northern dedications[1] fill.
Nor let false friends seduce thy mind to fame,
By arrogating Jonson's hostile name.
Let father Flecknoe fire thy mind with praise,
And uncle Ogilby thy envy raise.

175 Thou art my blood, where Jonson has no part:
What share have we in nature, or in art?
Where did his wit on learning fix a brand,
And rail at arts he did not understand?
Where made he love in Prince Nicander's vein,[2]

---

5. Shadwell's empire is vast but empty.
6. Sir George Etherege (ca. 1635–1691), a writer of brilliant comedies. In the next couplet Dryden names characters from his plays.
7. Sir Charles Sedley (1638–1701), wit, rake, poet, and playwright. Dryden hints that he contributed more than the prologue to Shadwell's *Epsom Wells*.

8. This phrase recalls a sentence in Burton's *Anatomy of Melancholy*: "They lard their lean books with the fat of others' works."
9. Sir Formal Trifle, the ridiculous and vapid orator in *The Virtuoso*.
1. Shadwell frequently dedicated his works to the duke of Newcastle and members of his family.
2. In *Psyche*.

180 Or swept the dust in *Psyche's* humble strain?
Where sold he bargains, 'whip-stitch,³ kiss my arse,'
Promised a play and dwindled to a farce?⁴
When did his Muse from Fletcher scenes purloin,
As thou whole Eth'rege dost transfuse to thine?
185 But so transfused, as oil on water's flow,
His always floats above, thine sinks below.
This is thy province, this thy wondrous way,
New humors to invent for each new play:
This is that boasted bias⁵ of thy mind,
190 By which one way, to dullness, 'tis inclined;
Which makes thy writings lean on one side still,
And, in all changes, that way bends thy will.
Nor let thy mountain-belly make pretense
Of likeness; thine's a tympany⁶ of sense.
195 A tun° of man in thy large bulk is writ,   *large cask*
But sure thou'rt but a kilderkin° of wit.   *small cask*
Like mine, thy gentle numbers feebly creep;
Thy tragic Muse gives smiles, thy comic sleep.
With whate'er gall thou sett'st thyself to write,
200 Thy inoffensive satires never bite.
In thy felonious heart though venom lies,
It does but touch thy Irish pen,⁷ and dies.
Thy genius calls thee not to purchase fame
In keen iambics,° but mild anagram.   *sharp satire*
205 Leave writing plays, and choose for thy command
Some peaceful province in acrostic land.
There thou may'st wings display and altars raise,⁸
And torture one poor word ten thousand ways.
Or, if thou wouldst thy different talent suit,
210 Set thy own songs, and sing them to thy lute."
    He said: but his last words were scarcely heard ⎤
For Bruce and Longville had a trap prepared,   ⎬
And down they sent the yet declaiming bard.⁹ ⎦
Sinking he left his drugget robe behind,
215 Borne upwards by a subterranean wind.
The mantle fell to the young prophet's part,¹
With double portion of his father's art.

ca. 1679   1682

3. A nonsense word frequently used by Sir Samuel Hearty in *The Virtuoso*. "Sell bargains": to answer an innocent question with a coarse or indecent phrase, as in this line.
4. Low comedy that depends largely on situation rather than wit, consistently condemned by Dryden and other serious playwrights.
5. In bowling, the spin given to the bowl that causes it to swerve. Dryden closely parodies a passage in Shadwell's epilogue to *The Humorists*.
6. A swelling in some part of the body caused by wind.
7. Dryden accuses Flecknoe and his "son" of being Irish. Ireland suggested only poverty, superstition, and barbarity to 17th-century Londoners.
8. "Wings" and "altars" refer to poems in the shape of these objects as in George Herbert's "Easter Wings" (p. 1709) and "The Altar" (p. 1707). "Anagram": the transposition of letters in a word so as to make a new one. "Acrostic": a poem in which the first letter of each line, read downward, makes up the name of the person or thing that is the subject of the poem. Dryden is citing instances of triviality and overingenuity in literature.
9. In *The Virtuoso*, Bruce and Longville play this trick on Sir Formal Trifle while he makes a speech.
1. When the prophet Elijah was carried to heaven in a chariot of fire borne on a whirlwind, his mantle fell on his successor, the younger prophet Elisha (2 Kings 2.8–14). Flecknoe, prophet of dullness, naturally cannot ascend, but must sink.

To the Memory of Mr. Oldham[1]

Farewell, too little, and too lately known,
Whom I began to think and call my own:
For sure our souls were near allied, and thine
Cast in the same poetic mold with mine.
5   One common note on either lyre did strike,
And knaves and fools[2] we both abhorred alike.
To the same goal did both our studies drive;
The last set out the soonest did arrive.
Thus Nisus fell upon the slippery place,
10   While his young friend[3] performed and won the race.
O early ripe! to thy abundant store
What could advancing age have added more?
It might (what nature never gives the young)
Have taught the numbers° of thy native tongue.   °metrics, verse
15   But satire needs not those, and wit will shine
Through the harsh cadence of a rugged line.[4]
A noble error, and but seldom made,
When poets are by too much force betrayed.
Thy generous fruits, though gathered ere their prime,
20   Still showed a quickness;[5] and maturing time
But mellows what we write to the dull sweets of rhyme.
Once more, hail and farewell;[6] farewell, thou young,
But ah too short, Marcellus[7] of our tongue;
Thy brows with ivy, and with laurels bound;[8]
25   But fate and gloomy night encompass thee around.

1684

A Song for St. Cecilia's Day[1]

1

From harmony, from heavenly harmony
This universal frame began:

1. John Oldham (1653–1683), the young poet whose *Satires upon the Jesuits* (1681), which Dryden admired, were written in 1679, before Dryden's major satires appeared (see line 8). This elegy was published in Oldham's *Remains in Verse and Prose* (1684).
2. Objects of satire.
3. Nisus, on the point of winning a footrace, slipped in a pool of blood. His "young friend" was Euryalus (Virgil's *Aeneid* 5.315–39).
4. Dryden repeats the Renaissance idea that the satirist should avoid smoothness and affect rough meters ("harsh cadence").
5. Sharpness of flavor.
6. Dryden echoes the famous words that conclude Catullus's elegy to his brother: *"Atque in perpetuum, frater, ave atque vale"* (And forever, brother, hail and farewell!).

7. The nephew of Augustus, adopted by him as his successor. After winning military fame as a youth, he died at the age of twenty. Virgil celebrated him in the *Aeneid* 6.854–86. The last line of Dryden's poem is a reminiscence of *Aeneid* 6.866.
8. The poet's wreath (cf. Milton's *Lycidas*, lines 1–2, p. 1918).
1. St. Cecilia, a Roman lady, was an early Christian martyr. She has long been regarded as the patroness of music and the supposed inventor of the organ. Celebrations of her festival day (November 22) in England were usually devoted to music and the praise of music, and from about 1683 to 1703 the Musical Society in London annually commemorated it with a religious service and a public concert. This concert always included an ode written and set to music for the occasion, of which the two by Dryden ("A Song for St. Cecilia's

When Nature underneath a heap
  Of jarring atoms lay,
5   And could not heave her head,
The tuneful voice was heard from high:
  "Arise, ye more than dead."
Then cold, and hot, and moist, and dry,[2]
In order to their stations leap,
10   And Music's power obey.
From harmony, from heavenly harmony
  This universal frame began:
  From harmony to harmony
Through all the compass of the notes it ran,
15 The diapason[3] closing full in man.

2

What passion cannot Music raise and quell![4]
  When Jubal struck the corded shell,[5]
His listening brethren stood around,
And, wondering, on their faces fell
20   To worship that celestial sound.
Less than a god they thought there could not dwell
  Within the hollow of that shell
  That spoke so sweetly and so well.
What passion cannot Music raise and quell!

3

25 The trumpet's loud clangor
  Excites us to arms,
With shrill notes of anger,
  And mortal alarms.
The double double double beat
30   Of the thundering drum
Cries: "Hark! the foes come;
Charge, charge, 'tis too late to retreat."

Day," 1687, and "Alexander's Feast," 1697) are the most distinguished. G. B. Draghi, an Italian brought to England by Charles II, set this ode to music; but Handel's fine score, composed in 1739, has completely obscured the original setting. This is an irregular ode in the manner of Cowley. In stanzas 3–6, Dryden boldly attempted to suggest in the sounds of his words the characteristic tones of the instruments mentioned.

2. "Nature": created nature, ordered by the Divine Wisdom out of chaos, which Dryden, adopting the physics of the Greek philosopher Epicurus, describes as composed of the warring and discordant ("jarring") atoms of the four elements: earth, fire, water, and air ("cold," "hot," "moist," and "dry").

3. The entire compass of tones in the scale.

Dryden is thinking of the Chain of Being, the ordered creation from inanimate nature up to humans, God's latest and final work. The just gradations of notes in a scale are analogous to the equally just gradations in the ascending scale of created beings. Both are the result of harmony.

4. The power of music to describe, evoke, or subdue emotion ("passion") is a frequent theme in 17th-century literature. In stanzas 2–6, the poet considers music as awakening religious awe, warlike courage, sorrow for unrequited love, jealousy and fury, and the impulse to worship God.

5. According to Genesis 4.21, Jubal was the inventor of the lyre and the pipe. Dryden imagines Jubal's lyre to have been made of a tortoiseshell ("corded shell").

4

The soft complaining flute
In dying notes discovers
35   The woes of hopeless lovers,
Whose dirge is whispered by the warbling lute.

5

Sharp violins[6] proclaim
Their jealous pangs, and desperation,
Fury, frantic indignation,
40   Depth of pains, and height of passion,
For the fair, disdainful dame.

6

But O! what art can teach,
What human voice can reach,
The sacred organ's praise?
45   Notes inspiring holy love,
Notes that wing their heavenly ways
To mend the choirs above.

7

Orpheus[7] could lead the savage race;
And trees unrooted left their place,
50   Sequacious of° the lyre;   *following*
But bright Cecilia raised the wonder higher:
When to her organ vocal breath was given,
An angel heard, and straight appeared,[8]
Mistaking earth for heaven.

GRAND CHORUS

55   *As from the power of sacred lays*
        The spheres began to move,
And sung the great Creator's praise[9]
        To all the blest above;
So, when the last and dreadful hour
60   *This crumbling pageant[1] shall devour,*
The trumpet shall be heard on high,⎫
The dead shall live, the living die,⎬
And Music shall untune the sky.[2]⎭

1687

6. A reference to the bright tone of the modern violin, introduced into England at the Restoration. The tone of the old-fashioned viol is much duller.
7. Legendary poet, son of one of the Muses, who played so wonderfully on the lyre that wild beasts ("the savage race") grew tame and followed him, as did even rocks and trees.
8. According to the legend, it was Cecilia's piety, not her music, that brought an angel to visit her.
9. As it was harmony that ordered the universe,

so it was angelic song ("sacred lays") that put the celestial bodies ("spheres") in motion. The harmonious chord that results from the traditional "music of the spheres" is a hymn of "praise" sung by created nature to its "Creator."
1. The universe, the stage on which the drama of human salvation has been acted out.
2. The "last trump" of 1 Corinthians 15.52, which will announce the Resurrection and the Last Judgment.

Epigram on Milton[1]

Three poets,[2] in three distant ages born,
Greece, Italy, and England did adorn.
The first in loftiness of thought surpassed,
The next in majesty, in both the last:
5 The force of Nature could no farther go;
To make a third, she joined the former two.

1688

Alexander's Feast[1]

Or the Power of Music; An Ode in Honor of St. Cecilia's Day

I

'Twas at the royal feast, for Persia won
      By Philip's[2] warlike son:
    Aloft in awful state
    The godlike hero sate
5   On his imperial throne;
His valiant peers were placed around;
Their brows with roses and with myrtles[3] bound:
  (So should desert in arms be crowned).
The lovely Thaïs, by his side,
10 Sate like a blooming Eastern bride
In flower of youth and beauty's pride.
    Happy, happy, happy pair!
    None but the brave,
    None but the brave,
15   None but the brave deserves the fair.

CHORUS

Happy, happy, happy pair!
None but the brave,
None but the brave,
None but the brave deserves the fair.

---

1. Engraved beneath the portrait of Milton in Jacob Tonson's edition of *Paradise Lost* (1688).
2. I.e., Homer, Virgil, and Milton.
1. After his defeat of the Persian emperor Darius III and the fall of the Persian capital Persepolis (331 B.C.E.), Alexander the Great held a feast for his officers. Thaïs his Athenian mistress, persuaded him to set fire to the palace in revenge for the burning of Athens by the Persians under Xerxes in 480 B.C.E. According to Plutarch, Alexander was moved by love and wine, not by music,

but Dryden, perhaps altering an old tradition that Alexander's musician Timotheus once by his flute-playing caused the hero to start up and arm himself, attributes the burning of Persepolis to the power of music. The original music was by Jeremiah Clarke, but Handel's score of 1736 is better known.
2. King Philip II of Macedonia, father of Alexander the Great.
3. Emblems of love. The Greeks and Romans wore wreaths of flowers at banquets.

2

20 Timotheus, placed on high
    Amid the tuneful choir,
    With flying fingers touched the lyre:
The trembling notes ascend the sky,
    And heavenly joys inspire.
25 The song began from Jove,
Who left his blissful seats above
(Such is the power of mighty love).
A dragon's fiery form belied the god:[4]
Sublime on radiant spires[5] he rode,
30   When he to fair Olympia pressed;
    And while he sought her snowy breast:
Then, round her slender waist he curled,
And stamped an image of himself, a sovereign of the world.
The listening crowd admire° the lofty sound: *wonder at*
35 "A present deity," they shout around;
"A present deity," the vaulted roofs rebound.
    With ravished ears
    The monarch hears,
    Assumes the god,
40   Affects to nod,
And seems to shake the spheres.[6]

CHORUS

With ravished ears
The monarch hears,
Assumes the god,
45 *Affects to nod,*
    And seems to shake the spheres.

3

The praise of Bacchus° then the sweet musician sung,   *god of wine*
    Of Bacchus ever fair and ever young:
    The jolly god in triumph comes;
50   Sound the trumpets; beat the drums;
    Flushed with a purple grace
    He shows his honest face:
Now give the hautboys° breath; he comes, he comes!   *oboes*
    Bacchus, ever fair and young
55   Drinking joys did first ordain;
    Bacchus' blessings are a treasure,
    Drinking is a soldier's pleasure;
    Rich the treasure,

---

4. An oracle had declared that Alexander was the son of Zeus ("Jove") by Philip's wife Olympias (not, as Dryden calls her in line 30, "Olympia"), thus conferring on him that semidivinity often claimed by heroes. Zeus habitually conducted his amours with mortals in the guise of an animal, in this case a dragon.

5. High on shining coils ("radiant spires"). "Spires" for the coils of a serpent is derived from the Latin word *spira*, which Virgil use in this sense, *Aeneid* 2.217 (cf. *Paradise Lost* 9.502).
6. According to Virgil (*Aeneid* 10.115) the nod of Jove causes earthquakes.

Sweet the pleasure,
60   Sweet is pleasure after pain.

CHORUS

Bacchus' blessings are a treasure,
Drinking is the soldier's pleasure;
Rich the treasure,
Sweet the pleasure,
65   *Sweet is pleasure after pain.*

4

Soothed with the sound, the king grew vain;
Fought all his battles o'er again,
And thrice he routed all his foes, and thrice he slew the slain.
The master saw the madness rise,
70   His glowing cheeks, his ardent eyes;
And, while he° heaven and earth defied,   *Alexander*
Changed his° hand, and checked his° pride.   *Timotheus's / Alexander's*
He chose a mournful Muse,
Soft pity to infuse:
75   He sung Darius great and good,
By too severe a fate
Fallen, fallen, fallen, fallen,
Fallen from his high estate,
And weltering in his blood;
80   Deserted at his utmost need
By those his former bounty fed;
On the bare earth exposed he lies,
With not a friend to close his eyes.[7]
With downcast looks the joyless victor sate,
85   Revolving° in his altered soul   *pondering*
The various turns of chance below;
And, now and then, a sigh he stole,
And tears began to flow.

CHORUS

Revolving in his altered soul
90   *The various turns of chance below;*
And, now and then, a sigh he stole,
And tears began to flow.

5

The mighty master smiled to see
That love was in the next degree;
95   'Twas but[8] a kindred sound to move,
For pity melts the mind to love.
Softly sweet, in Lydian[9] measures,

---

7. After his final defeat by Alexander, Darius was assassinated by his own followers.
8. I.e., it was necessary only.

9. In Greek music the Lydian mode expressed the plaintive and the sad.

Soon he soothed his soul to pleasures.
"War," he sung, "is toil and trouble;
100 Honor, but an empty bubble.
　　Never ending, still beginning,
Fighting still, and still destroying:
　　If the world be worth thy winning,
Think, O think it worth enjoying.
105　　Lovely Thaïs sits beside thee,
Take the good the gods provide thee."
The many° rend the skies with loud applause;　　　*crowd, retinue*
So Love was crowned, but Music won the cause.
　　The prince, unable to conceal his pain,
110　　　　Gazed on the fair
　　　　Who caused his care,
And sighed and looked, sighed and looked,
Sighed and looked, and sighed again:
At length, with love and wine at once oppressed,
115 The vanquished victor sunk upon her breast.

CHORUS

The prince, unable to conceal his pain,
　　Gazed on the fair
　　Who caused his care,
And sighed and looked, sighed and looked,
120 *Sighed and looked, and sighed again:*
　　At length, with love and wine at once oppressed,
　　The vanquished victor sunk upon her breast.

6

Now strike the golden lyre again:
A louder yet, and yet a louder strain.
125 Break his bands of sleep asunder,
And rouse him, like a rattling peal of thunder.
　　Hark, hark, the horrid° sound　　　　　　　*rough*
　　　　Has raised up his head:
　　　　As waked from the dead,
130　　　And amazed, he stares around,
"Revenge, revenge!" Timotheus cries,
　　　"See the Furies[1] arise!
　　See the snakes that they rear,
　　How they hiss in their hair,
135　And the sparkles that flash from their eyes!
　　　Behold a ghastly band,
　　　Each a torch in his hand!
Those are Grecian ghosts, that in battle were slain,
　　　And unburied remain[2]
140　　　Inglorious on the plain:
　　　Give the vengeance due

---

1. The Erinyes of the Greeks, avengers of crimes against the natural and the social orders. They are described as women with snakes in their hair and wrapped around their waists and arms.
2. According to Greek beliefs, the shades of the dead could not rest until their bodies were buried.

To the valiant crew.
Behold how they toss their torches on high,
How they point to the Persian abodes,
145 And glittering temples of their hostile gods!"
The princes applaud, with a furious joy;
And the king seized a flambeau° with zeal to destroy;   *torch*
Thaïs led the way,
To light him to his prey,
150 And, like another Helen, fired another Troy.[3]

CHORUS

And the king seized a flambeau with zeal to destroy;
Thaïs led the way,
To light him to his prey,
And, like another Helen, fired another Troy.

7

155 Thus long ago,
Ere heaving bellows learned to blow,
While organs yet were mute;
Timotheus, to his breathing flute,
And sounding lyre,
160 Could swell the soul to rage, or kindle soft desire.
At last, divine Cecilia came,
Inventress of the vocal frame;°   *organ*
The sweet enthusiast,[4] from her sacred store,
Enlarged the former narrow bounds,
165 And added length to solemn sounds,
With nature's mother wit, and arts unknown before.
Let old Timotheus yield the prize,
Or both divide the crown:
He raised a mortal to the skies;
170 She drew an angel down.

GRAND CHORUS

At last, divine Cecilia came,
Inventress of the vocal frame;
The sweet enthusiast, from her sacred store,
Enlarged the former narrow bounds,
175 *And added length to solemn sounds,*
With nature's mother wit, and arts unknown before.
Let old Timotheus yield the prize,
Or both divide the crown:
He raised a mortal to the skies;
180 *She drew an angel down.*

1697

3. Helen's elopement to Troy with Paris brought on the Trojan War and the ultimate destruction of the city by the Greeks.
4. Usually at this time a disparaging word, frequently, though not always, applied to a religious zealot or fanatic. Here it is used approvingly and in its literal sense, "possessed by a god," an allusion to Cecilia's angelic companion referred to in line 170 (but see "Song for St. Cecilia's Day," line 53 and n. 8, p. 2245).

CRITICISM

Dryden's impulse to write criticism came from his practical urge to explain and justify his own writings; his attraction to clear, ordered theoretical principles; and his growing sense of himself as a leader of English literary taste and judgment. The Elizabethans, largely impelled by the example of Italian humanists, had produced an interesting but unsystematic body of critical writings. Dryden could look back to such pioneer works as George Puttenham's *Art of English Poesy* (1589), Sir Philip Sidney's *Defense of Poesy* (1595), Samuel Daniel's *Defense of Rhyme* (ca. 1603), and Ben Jonson's *Timber, or Discoveries* (1641). These and later writings Dryden knew, as he knew the ancients and the important contemporary French critics, notably Pierre Corneille, René Rapin, and Nicolas Boileau. Taken as a whole, his critical prefaces and dedications, which appeared between 1664 and 1700, are the work of a man of independent mind who has made his own synthesis of critical canons from wide reading, a great deal of thinking, and the constant practice of the art of writing. As a critic he is no one's disciple, and he has the saving grace of being always willing to change his mind.

All but a very few of Dryden's critical works (most notably *An Essay of Dramatic Poesy*) grew out of the works to which they served as prefaces: comedies, heroic plays, tragedies, translations, and poems of various sorts. Each work posed problems that Dryden was eager to discuss with his readers, and the topics that he treated proved to be important in the development of the new literature of which he was the principal apologist. He dealt with the processes of literary creation, the poet's relation to tradition, the forms of modern drama, the craft of poetry, and above all the genius of earlier poets: Shakespeare, Jonson, Chaucer, Juvenal, Horace, Homer, and Virgil. For nearly forty years this voice was heard in the land; and when it was finally silenced, a set of critical standards had come into existence and a new age had been given its direction.

From An Essay of Dramatic Poesy[1]

[TWO SORTS OF BAD POETRY]

* * * "I have a mortal apprehension of two poets,[2] whom this victory, with the help of both her wings, will never be able to escape." "'Tis easy to guess

---

1. With the reopening of the theaters in 1660, older plays were revived, but despite their power and charm, they seemed old-fashioned. Although new playwrights, ambitious to create a modern English drama, soon appeared, they were uncertain of their direction. What, if anything, useful could they learn from the dramatic practice of the ancients? Should they ignore the English dramatists of the late 16th and early 17th centuries? Should they make their example the vigorous contemporary drama of France? Dryden addresses himself to these and other problems in this essay, his first extended piece of criticism. Its purpose, he tells us, was "chiefly to vindicate the honor of our English writers from the censure of those who unjustly prefer the French before them." Its method is skeptical: Dryden presents several points of view, but imposes none. The form is a dialogue among friends, like the *Tusculan Disputations* or the *Brutus* of Cicero. Crites praises the drama of the ancients; Eugenius protests against their authority and argues for the idea of progress in the arts; Lisideius urges the

excellence of French plays; and Neander, speaking in the climactic position, defends the native tradition and the greatness of Shakespeare, Fletcher, and Jonson. The dialogue takes place on June 3, 1665, in a boat on the Thames. The four friends are rowed downstream to listen to the cannonading of the English and Dutch fleets, engaged in battle off the Suffolk coast. As the gunfire recedes they are assured of victory and order their boatman to return to London, and naturally enough they fall to discussing the number of bad poems that the victory will evoke.

2. Crites here is probably referring to Robert Wilde and possibly to Richard Flecknoe, whom Dryden later ridiculed in "Mac Flecknoe." Their actual identity is unimportant, for they merely represent two extremes in poetry, both deplorable: the fantastic and extravagant manner of decadent metaphysical wit and its opposite, the flat and the dull. The new poetry was to seek a mean between these extremes (cf. Pope, *An Essay on Criticism* 2.239–42 and 289–300, pp. 2674 and 2675–76).

whom you intend," said Lisideius; "and without naming them, I ask you if one of them does not perpetually pay us with clenches[3] upon words, and a certain clownish kind of raillery?[4] if now and then he does not offer at a catachresis or Clevelandism, wresting and torturing a word into another meaning: in fine, if he be not one of those whom the French would call *un mauvais buffon;*[5] one who is so much a well-willer to the satire, that he spares no man; and though he cannot strike a blow to hurt any, yet ought to be punished for the malice of the action, as our witches are justly hanged, because they think themselves so, and suffer deservedly for believing they did mischief, because they meant it." "You have described him," said Crites, "so exactly that I am afraid to come after you with my other extremity of poetry. He is one of those who, having had some advantage of education and converse, knows better than the other what a poet should be, but puts it into practice more unluckily than any man; his style and matter are everywhere alike: he is the most calm, peaceable writer you ever read: he never disquiets your passions with the least concernment, but still leaves you in as even a temper as he found you; he is a very Leveller[6] in poetry: he creeps along with ten little words in every line, and helps out his numbers with *for to,* and *unto,* and all the pretty expletives[7] he can find, till he drags them to the end of another line; while the sense is left tired halfway behind it: he doubly starves all his verses, first for want of thought, and then of expression; his poetry neither has wit in it, nor seems to have it; like him in Martial:

Pauper videri Cinna vult, et est pauper.[8]

"He affects plainness, to cover his want of imagination: when he writes the serious way, the highest flight of his fancy is some miserable antithesis, or seeming contradiction; and in the comic he is still reaching at some thin conceit, the ghost of a jest, and that too flies before him, never to be caught; these swallows which we see before us on the Thames are the just resemblance of his wit: you may observe how near the water they stoop, how many proffers they make to dip, and yet how seldom they touch it; and when they do, it is but the surface: they skim over it but to catch a gnat, and then mount into the air and leave it."

[THE WIT OF THE ANCIENTS: THE UNIVERSAL][9]

* * * "A thing well said will be wit in all languages; and though it may lose something in the translation, yet to him who reads it in the original, 'tis still the same: he has an idea of its excellency, though it cannot pass from his mind into any other expression or words than those in which he finds it. When Phaedria, in the *Eunuch,*[1] had a command from his mistress to be

---

3. Puns.
4. Boorish banter.
5. A malicious jester (French). "Catachresis": the use of a word in a sense remote from its normal meaning. A legitimate figure of speech used by all poets, it had been abused by John Cleveland (1613–1658), who was at first admired for his ingenuity, but whose reputation declined rapidly after the Restoration. A Clevelandism: "The marigold, whose courtier's face / *Echoes* the sun."
6. The Levellers were radical egalitarians and

republicans, a powerful political force in the Puritan army about 1648. They were suppressed by Cromwell. "Passions": emotions. "Still": always.
7. Words used merely to fill out a line of verse (cf. Pope, *An Essay on Criticism* 2.346–47, p. 2676).
8. Cinna wishes to seem poor, and he is poor (Latin; *Epigrams* 8.19).
9. Eugenius is in the midst of remarks about the limitations of the ancients.
1. A comedy by the Roman poet Terence (ca. 185–159 B.C.E.).

absent two days, and, encouraging himself to go through with it, said, 'Tandem ego non ilia caream, si sit opus, vel totum triduum?'[2]—Parmeno, to mock the softness of his master, lifting up his hands and eyes, cries out, as it were in admiration, 'Hui! universum triduum!'[3] the elegancy of which universum, though it cannot be rendered in our language, yet leaves an impression on our souls: but this happens seldom in him; in Plautus[4] oftener, who is infinitely too bold in his metaphors and coining words, out of which many times his wit is nothing; which questionless was one reason why Horace falls upon him so severely in those verses:

> Sed proavi nostri Plautinos et numeros et
> Laudavere sales, nimium patienter utrumque,
> Ne dicam stolide.[5]

For Horace himself was cautious to obtrude a new word on his readers, and makes custom and common use the best measure of receiving it into our writings:

> Multa renascentur quae nunc cecidere, cadentque
> Quae nunc sunt in honore vocabula, si volet usus,
> Quem penes arbitrium est, et jus, et norma loquendi.[6]

"The not observing this rule is that which the world has blamed in our satirist, Cleveland: to express a thing hard and unnaturally is his new way of elocution. 'Tis true no poet but may sometimes use a catachresis: Virgil does it—

> Mistaque ridenti colocasia fundet acantho—[7]

in his eclogue of Pollio; and in his seventh Aeneid:

> mirantur et undae,
> Miratur nemus insuetum fulgentia longe
> Scuta virum fluvio pictasque innare carinas.[8]

And Ovid once so modestly that he asks leave to do it:

> quem, si verbo audacia detur,
> Haud metuam summi dixisse Palatia caeli.[9]

calling the court of Jupiter by the name of Augustus his palace; though in another place he is more bold, where he says, 'et longas visent Capitolia pompas.'[1] But to do this always, and never be able to write a line without it,

---

2. Shall I not then do without her, if need be, for three whole days? (Latin).
3. The wit of Parmeno's exclamation, "Oh, three entire days," depends on universum, which suggests that a lover may regard three days as an eternity. "Admiration": wonder.
4. Titus Maccus Plautus, (ca. 254–184 B.C.E.), Roman comic poet.
5. But our ancestors too tolerantly (I do not say foolishly) praised both the verse and the wit of Plautus (Latin; Art of Poetry, lines 270–72). Dryden misquotes slightly.
6. Many words that have perished will be born again, and those shall perish that are now esteemed, if usage wills it, in whose power are the judgment, the law, and the pattern of speech

(Latin; Art of Poetry, lines 70–72).
7. [The earth] shall give forth the Egyptian bean, mingled with the smiling acanthus (Latin; Eclogues 4.20). "Smiling acanthus" is a catachresis.
8. Actually Aeneid 8.91–93. Dryden's paraphrase makes the point clearly: "The woods and waters wonder at the gleam / Of shields and painted ships that stem the stream" (Latin; Aeneid. 8.125–26). "Wonder" is a catachresis.
9. [This is the place] which, if boldness of expression be permitted, I shall not hesitate to call the Palace of high heaven (Latin; Metamorphoses 1.175–76).
1. And the Capitol shall see the long processions (Latin; Metamorphoses 1.561).

though it may be admired by some few pedants, will not pass upon those who know that wit is best conveyed to us in the most easy language; and is most to be admired when a great thought comes dressed in words so commonly received that it is understood by the meanest apprehensions, as the best meat is the most easily digested: but we cannot read a verse of Cleveland's without making a face at it, as if every word were a pill to swallow: he gives us many times a hard nut to break our teeth, without a kernel for our pains. So that there is this difference betwixt his satires and Doctor Donne's; that the one gives us deep thoughts in common language, though rough cadence; the other gives us common thoughts in abstruse words: 'tis true in some places his wit is independent of his words, as in that of the *Rebel Scot:*

> Had Cain been Scot, God would have changed his doom;
> Not forced him wander, but confined him home.[2]

"*Si sic omnia dixisset!*[3] This is wit in all languages: it is like mercury, never to be lost or killed: and so that other—

> For beauty, like white powder, makes no noise,
> And yet the silent hypocrite destroys.[4]

You see that the last line is highly metaphorical, but it is so soft and gentle that it does not shock us as we read it."

[SHAKESPEARE AND BEN JONSON COMPARED][5]

"To begin, then, with Shakespeare. He was the man who of all modern, and perhaps ancient poets, had the largest and most comprehensive soul. All the images of Nature were still present to him, and he drew them, not laboriously, but luckily; when he describes anything, you more than see it, you feel it too. Those who accuse him to have wanted learning, give him the greater commendation: he was naturally learned; he needed not the spectacles of books to read Nature; he looked inwards, and found her there. I cannot say he is everywhere alike; were he so, I should do him injury to compare him with the greatest of mankind. He is many times flat, insipid; his comic wit degenerating into clenches, his serious swelling into bombast. But he is always great when some great occasion is presented to him; no man can say he ever had a fit subject for his wit and did not then raise himself as high above the rest of poets,

Quantum lenta solent inter viburna cupressi[6]

The consideration of this made Mr. Hales[7] of Eton say that there was no subject of which any poet ever writ, but he would produce it much better treated of in Shakespeare; and however others are now generally preferred before him, yet the age wherein he lived, which had contemporaries with

---

2. Lines 63–64.
3. Had he said everything thus! (Latin; Juvenal's *Satires* 10.123–24).
4. From *Rupertismus*, lines 39–40. Mercury is said to be "killed" if its fluidity is destroyed.
5. Neander's contrast of Shakespeare and Jonson introduces an extended commentary on the

latter's play *Epicoene; or the Silent Woman.*
6. As do cypresses among the bending shrubs (Latin; Virgil's *Eclogues* 1.25).
7. The learned John Hales (1584–1656), provost of Eton. He is reputed to have said this to Jonson himself.

him Fletcher and Jonson, never equaled them to him in their esteem: and in the last king's court, when Ben's reputation was at highest, Sir John Suckling,[8] and with him the greater part of the courtiers, set our Shakespeare far above him. . . .

"As for Jonson, to whose character I am now arrived, if we look upon him while he was himself (for his last plays were but his dotages), I think him the most learned and judicious writer which any theater ever had. He was a most severe judge of himself, as well as others. One cannot say he wanted wit, but rather that he was frugal of it. In his works you find little to retrench[9] or alter. Wit, and language, and humor also in some measure, we had before him; but something of art[1] was wanting to the drama till he came. He managed his strength to more advantage than any who preceded him. You seldom find him making love in any of his scenes or endeavoring to move the passions; his genius was too sullen and saturnine[2] to do it gracefully, especially when he knew he came after those who had performed both to such an height. Humor was his proper sphere: and in that he delighted most to represent mechanic people.[3] He was deeply conversant in the ancients, both Greek and Latin, and he borrowed boldly from them: there is scarce a poet or historian among the Roman authors of those times whom he has not translated in *Sejanus* and *Catiline*.[4] But he has done his robberies so openly, that one may see he fears not to be taxed by any law. He invades authors like a monarch; and what would be theft in other poets is only victory in him. With the spoils of these writers he so represents old Rome to us, in its rites, ceremonies, and customs, that if one of their poets had written either of his tragedies, we had seen less of it than in him. If there was any fault in his language, 'twas that he weaved it too closely and laboriously, in his serious plays:[5] perhaps, too, he did a little too much Romanize our tongue, leaving the words which he translated almost as much Latin as he found them: wherein, though he learnedly followed the idiom of their language, he did not enough comply with the idiom of ours. If I would compare him with Shakespeare, I must acknowledge him the more correct poet, but Shakespeare the greater wit.[6] Shakespeare was the Homer, or father of our dramatic poets; Jonson was the Virgil, the pattern of elaborate writing; I admire him, but I love Shakespeare. To conclude of him; as he has given us the most correct plays, so in the precepts which he has laid down in his *Discoveries,* we have as many and profitable rules for perfecting the stage, as any wherewith the French can furnish us."

1668

---

8. Courtier, poet, playwright, much admired in Dryden's time for his wit and the easy naturalness of his style. "King's court": that of Charles I.
9. Delete.
1. Craftsmanship.
2. Heavy.
3. I.e., artisans. In Jonson's comedies the characters are seen under the domination of some psychological trait, ruling passion, or affectation—i.e.,

some "humor"—that makes them unique and ridiculous.
4. Jonson's two Roman plays, dated 1605 and 1611, respectively.
5. This is the reading of the first edition. Curiously enough, in the second edition Dryden altered the phrase to "in his comedies especially."
6. Genius.

From The Author's Apology for Heroic Poetry and Heroic License[1]

["BOLDNESS" OF FIGURES AND TROPES DEFENDED: THE APPEAL TO "NATURE"]

* * * They, who would combat general authority with particular opinion, must first establish themselves a reputation of understanding better than other men. Are all the flights of heroic poetry to be concluded bombast, unnatural, and mere madness, because they are not affected with their excellencies? It is just as reasonable as to conclude there is no day, because a blind man cannot distinguish of light and colors. Ought they not rather, in modesty, to doubt of their own judgments, when they think this or that expression in Homer, Virgil, Tasso, or Milton's *Paradise* to be too far strained, than positively to conclude that 'tis all fustian and mere nonsense? 'Tis true there are limits to be set betwixt the boldness and rashness of a poet; but he must understand those limits who pretends to judge as well as he who undertakes to write: and he who has no liking to the whole ought, in reason, to be excluded from censuring of the parts. He must be a lawyer before he mounts the tribunal; and the judicature of one court, too, does not qualify a man to preside in another. He may be an excellent pleader in the Chancery, who is not fit to rule the Common Pleas.[2] But I will presume for once to tell them that the boldest strokes of poetry, when they are managed artfully, are those which most delight the reader.

Virgil and Horace, the severest writers of the severest age, have made frequent use of the hardest metaphors and of the strongest hyperboles; and in this case the best authority is the best argument, for generally to have pleased, and through all ages, must bear the force of universal tradition. And if you would appeal from thence to right reason, you will gain no more by it in effect than, first, to set up your reason against those authors, and, secondly, against all those who have admired them. You must prove why that ought not to have pleased which has pleased the most learned and the most judicious; and, to be thought knowing, you must first put the fool upon all mankind. If you can enter more deeply than they have done into the causes and resorts[3] of that which moves pleasure in a reader, the field is open, you may be heard: but those springs of human nature are not so easily discovered by every superficial judge: it requires philosophy, as well as poetry, to sound the depth of all the passions, what they are in themselves, and how they are to be provoked; and in this science the best poets have excelled. * * * From hence have sprung the tropes and figures,[4] for which they wanted a name who first practiced them and succeeded in them. Thus I grant you

---

1. This essay was prefixed to Dryden's *State of Innocence,* the libretto for an opera (never produced), based on *Paradise Lost.* Dryden had been ridiculed for the extravagant and bold imagery and rhetorical figures that are typical of the style of his rhymed heroic plays. This preface is a defense not only of his own predilection for what Samuel Johnson described as "wild and daring sallies of sentiment, in the irregular and eccentric violence of wit" but also of the theory that heroic and idealized materials should be treated in lofty

and boldly metaphorical style; hence his definition of wit as propriety.
2. Court in which civil actions could be brought by one subject against another. "Chancery": a high court presided over by the lord chancellor.
3. Mechanical springs that set something in motion.
4. I.e., such figures of speech as metaphors and similes. "Tropes": the uses of words in a figurative sense.

that the knowledge of Nature was the original rule, and that all poets ought to study her, as well as Aristotle and Horace, her interpreters.[5] But then this also undeniably follows, that those things which delight all ages must have been an imitation of Nature—which is all I contend. Therefore is rhetoric made an art; therefore the names of so many tropes and figures were invented, because it was observed they had such and such effect upon the audience. Therefore catachreses and hyperboles[6] have found their place amongst them; not that they were to be avoided, but to be used judiciously and placed in poetry as heightenings and shadows are in painting, to make the figure bolder, and cause it to stand off to sight. * * *

[WIT AS "PROPRIETY"]

* * * [Wit] is a propriety of thoughts and words; or, in other terms, thought and words elegantly adapted to the subject. If our critics will join issue on this definition, that we may *convenire in aliquo tertio;*[7] if they will take it as a granted principle, it will be easy to put an end to this dispute. No man will disagree from another's judgment concerning the dignity of style in heroic poetry; but all reasonable men will conclude it necessary that sublime subjects ought to be adorned with the sublimest, and, consequently, often with the most figurative expressions. * * *

1677

From A Discourse Concerning the Original and Progress of Satire[1]

[THE ART OF SATIRE]

* * * How easy is it to call rogue and villain, and that wittily! But how hard to make a man appear a fool, a blockhead, or a knave without using any of those opprobrious terms! To spare the grossness of the names, and to do the thing yet more severely, is to draw a full face, and to make the nose and cheeks stand out, and yet not to employ any depth of shadowing.[2] This is the mystery of that noble trade, which yet no master can teach to his apprentice; he may give the rules, but the scholar is never the nearer in his practice. Neither is it true that this fineness of raillery[3] is offensive. A witty man is tickled while he is hurt in this manner, and a fool feels it not. The occasion

5. In the words of the French critic René Rapin, the rules (largely derived from Aristotle's *Poetics* and Horace's *Art of Poetry*) were made to "reduce Nature to method" (cf. Pope, *An Essay on Criticism* 1.88–89, p. 2671).
6. Deliberate overstatement or exaggeration. "Catachresis": the use of a word in a sense remote from its normal meaning.
7. To find some means of agreement, in a third term, between the two opposites [Latin].
1. This passage is an excerpt from the long and rambling preface that served as the dedication of a translation of the satires of the Roman satirists Juvenal and Persius to Charles Sackville, sixth earl of Dorset. The translations were made by

Dryden and other writers, among them William Congreve. Dryden traces the origin and development of verse satire in Rome and in a very fine passage contrasts Horace and Juvenal as satiric poets. It is plain that he prefers the "tragic" satire of Juvenal to the urbane and laughing satire of Horace. But in the passage printed here, he praises his own satiric character of Zimri (the duke of Buckingham) in *Absalom and Achitophel* for the very reason that it is modeled on Horatian "raillery," not Juvenalian invective.
2. Early English miniaturists prided themselves on the art of giving roundness to the full face without painting in shadows.
3. Satirical mirth, good-natured satire.

of an offense may possibly be given, but he cannot take it. If it be granted that in effect this way does more mischief; that a man is secretly wounded, and though he be not sensible himself, yet the malicious world will find it out for him; yet there is still a vast difference betwixt the slovenly butchering of a man, and the fineness of a stroke that separates the head from the body, and leaves it standing in its place. A man may be capable, as Jack Ketch's[4] wife said of his servant, of a plain piece of work, a bare hanging; but to make a malefactor die sweetly was only belonging to her husband. I wish I could apply it to myself, if the reader would be kind enough to think it belongs to me. The character of Zimri in my *Absalom*[5] is, in my opinion, worth the whole poem: it is not bloody, but it is ridiculous enough; and he, for whom it was intended, was too witty to resent it as an injury. If I had railed,[6] I might have suffered for it justly; but I managed my own work more happily, perhaps more dexterously. I avoided the mention of great crimes, and applied myself to the representing of blindsides, and little extravagancies; to which, the wittier a man is, he is generally the more obnoxious.[7] It succeeded as I wished; the jest went round, and he was laughed at in his turn who began the frolic. * * *

1693

From The Preface to *Fables Ancient and Modern*[1]

[IN PRAISE OF CHAUCER]

In the first place, as he is the father of English poetry, I hold him in the same degree of veneration as the Grecians held Homer, or the Romans Virgil. He is a perpetual fountain of good sense; learned in all sciences;[2] and, therefore, speaks properly on all subjects. As he knew what to say, so he knows also when to leave off; a continence which is practiced by few writers, and scarcely by any of the ancients, excepting Virgil and Horace. * * *

Chaucer followed Nature everywhere, but was never so bold to go beyond her; and there is a great difference of being *poeta* and *nimis poeta*,[3] if we may believe Catullus, as much as betwixt a modest behavior and affectation. The verse of Chaucer, I confess, is not harmonious to us; but 'tis like the eloquence of one whom Tacitus commends, it was *auribus istius temporis accommodata:*[4] they who lived with him, and some time after him, thought it musical; and it continues so, even in our judgment, if compared with the

---

4. A notorious public executioner of Dryden's time (d. 1686). His name later became a generic term for all members of his profession.
5. *Absalom and Achitophel*, lines 544–68 (p. 2226).
6. Reviled, abused. Observe that the verb differed in meaning from its noun, defined above.
7. Liable.
1. Dryden's final work, published in the year of his death, was a collection of translations from Homer, Ovid, Boccaccio, and Chaucer, and one or two other pieces. The Preface is Dryden's ripest and finest critical essay. He is not concerned here with critical theory or with a formalistic approach

to literature but is simply a man, grown old in the reading and writing of poetry, who is eager to talk informally with his readers about some of his favorite authors. His praise of Chaucer (unusually sympathetic and perceptive for 1700) is animated by that love of great literature that is manifest in everything that Dryden wrote.
2. Branches of learning.
3. A poet (*"poeta"*) and too much of a poet (*"nimis poeta"*). The phrase is not from Catullus but from Martial (*Epigrams* 3.44).
4. Suitable to the ears of that time (Latin). Tacitus (ca. 55–ca. 117 C.E.), Roman historian and writer on oratory.

numbers of Lydgate and Gower,[5] his contemporaries; there is the rude sweetness of a Scotch tune in it, which is natural and pleasing, though not perfect. 'Tis true I cannot go so far as he who published the last edition of him;[6] for he would make us believe the fault is in our ears, and that there were really ten syllables in a verse where we find but nine; but this opinion is not worth confuting; 'tis so gross and obvious an error that common sense (which is a rule in everything but matters of faith and revelation) must convince the reader that equality of numbers in every verse which we call heroic[7] was either not known, or not always practiced in Chaucer's age. It were an easy matter to produce some thousands of his verses which are lame for want of half a foot, and sometimes a whole one, and which no pronunciation can make otherwise. We can only say that he lived in the infancy of our poetry, and that nothing is brought to perfection at the first. * * *

He must have been a man of a most wonderful comprehensive nature, because, as it has been truly observed of him, he has taken into the compass of his *Canterbury Tales* the various manners and humors (as we now call them) of the whole English nation in his age. Not a single character has escaped him. All his pilgrims are severally distinguished from each other; and not only in their inclinations but in their very physiognomies and persons. Baptista Porta[8] could not have described their natures better than by the marks which the poet gives them. The matter and manner of their tales, and of their telling, are so suited to their different educations, humors, and callings that each of them would be improper in any other mouth. Even the grave and serious characters are distinguished by their several sorts of gravity: their discourses are such as belong to their age, their calling, and their breeding; such as are becoming of them, and of them only. Some of his persons are vicious, and some virtuous; some are unlearned, or (as Chaucer calls them) lewd, and some are learned. Even the ribaldry of the low characters is different: the Reeve, the Miller, and the Cook are several[9] men, and distinguished from each other as much as the mincing Lady Prioress and the broad-speaking, gap-toothed Wife of Bath. But enough of this; there is such a variety of game springing up before me that I am distracted in my choice, and know not which to follow. 'Tis sufficient to say, according to the proverb, that here is God's plenty. * * *

1700

5. John Gower (d. 1408), poet and friend of Chaucer. "Numbers": versification. John Lydgate (ca. 1370–ca. 1449) wrote poetry that shows the influence of Chaucer.
6. Thomas Speght's Chaucer, which Dryden used, was first published in 1598; the second edition, published in 1602, was reprinted in 1687.
7. The pentameter line. In Dryden's time few readers knew how to pronounce Middle English, especially the syllabic *e*. Moreover, Chaucer's works were known only in corrupt printed texts. As a consequence Chaucer's verse seemed rough and irregular.
8. Giambattista della Porta (ca. 1535–1615), author of a Latin treatise on physiognomy.
9. Different.

SAMUEL PEPYS
1633–1703

S amuel Pepys (pronounced "Peeps") was the son of a London tailor. With the help of a scholarship he took a degree at Cambridge; with the help of a cousin he found a place in the Navy Office. Eventually, through hard work and an eye for detail, he rose to secretary of the Admiralty. His defense of the Navy Office and himself before Parliament in 1668 won him a reputation as a good administrator, and his career continued to prosper until it was broken, first by false accusations of treason in 1679 and finally by the fall of James II in 1688. But Pepys was more than a bureaucrat. A Londoner to his core, he was interested in all the activities of the city: the theater, music, the social whirl, business, religion, literary life, and the scientific experiments of the Royal Society (which he served as president from 1684 to 1686). He also found plenty of chances to indulge his two obsessions: chasing after women and making money.

Pepys kept his diary from 1660 to 1669 (when his eyesight began to fail). Writing in shorthand and sometimes in code, he was utterly frank in recording the events of his day, both public and private, the major affairs of state or his quarrels with his wife. Altogether he wrote about 1.3 million words. When the diary was first deciphered and published in the nineteenth century, it made him newly famous. As a document of social history it is unsurpassed for its rich detail, honesty, and immediacy. But more than that, it gives us a sense of somebody else's world: what it was like to live in the Restoration, and what it was like to see through the eyes of Pepys.

From The Diary

[THE GREAT FIRE]

September 2, 1666

Lords day. Some of our maids sitting up late last night to get things ready against our feast today, Jane called us up, about 3 in the morning, to tell us of a great fire they saw in the City.[1] So I rose, and slipped on my nightgown and went to her window, and thought it to be on the back side of Mark Lane[2] at the furthest; but being unused to such fires as followed, I thought it far enough off, and so went to bed again and to sleep. About 7 rose again to dress myself, and there looked out at the window and saw the fire not so much as it was, and further off. So to my closet[3] to set things to rights after yesterday's cleaning. By and by Jane comes and tells me that she hears that above 300 houses have been burned down tonight by the fire we saw, and that it was now burning down all Fish Street by London Bridge. So I made myself ready presently,[4] and walked to the Tower and there got up upon one of the high places,

---

1. The fire of London, which was to destroy four-fifths of the central city, had begun an hour earlier. For another description see Dryden's *Annus Mirabilis* (p. 2210).

2. Near Pepys's own house in Seething Lane.
3. A small private room or study.
4. Immediately.

Sir J. Robinson's little son going up with me; and there I did see the houses at that end of the bridge all on fire, and an infinite great fire on this and the other side the end of the bridge—which, among other people, did trouble me for poor little Michell and our Sarah[5] on the Bridge. So down, with my heart full of trouble, to the Lieutenant of the Tower, who tells me that it begun this morning in the King's baker's house in Pudding Lane, and that it hath burned down St. Magnus' Church and most part of Fish Street already. So I down to the waterside and there got a boat and through bridge, and there saw a lamentable fire. Poor Michell's house, as far as the Old Swan,[6] already burned that way and the fire running further, that in a very little time it got as far as the Steelyard while I was there. Everybody endeavoring to remove their goods, and flinging into the river or bringing them into lighters[7] that lay off. Poor people staying in their houses as long as till the very fire touched them, and then running into boats or clambering from one pair of stair by the waterside to another. And among other things, the poor pigeons I perceive were loath to leave their houses, but hovered about the windows and balconies till they were some of them burned, their wings, and fell down.

Having stayed, and in an hour's time seen the fire rage every way, and nobody to my sight endeavoring to quench it, but to remove their goods and leave all to the fire; and having seen it get as far as the Steelyard, and the wind mighty high and driving it into the city, and everything, after so long a drought, proving combustible, even the very stones of churches, and among other things, the poor steeple by which pretty Mrs. [8] lives, and whereof my old school-fellow Elborough is parson, taken fire in the very top and there burned till it fell down—I to Whitehall[9] with a gentleman with me who desired to go off from the Tower to see the fire in my boat—to Whitehall, and there up to the King's closet in the chapel, where people came about me and I did give them an account dismayed them all; and word was carried in to the King, so I was called for and did tell the King and Duke of York what I saw, and that unless his Majesty did command houses to be pulled down, nothing could stop the fire. They seemed much troubled, and the King commanded me to go to my Lord Mayor from him and command him to spare no houses but to pull down before the fire every way. The Duke of York bid me tell him that if he would have any more soldiers, he shall; and so did my Lord Arlington afterward, as a great secret. Here meeting with Captain Cocke, I in his coach, which he lent me, and Creed with me, to Paul's;[1] and there walked along Watling Street as well as I could, every creature coming away loaden with goods to save—and here and there sick people carried away in beds. Extraordinary good goods carried in carts and on backs. At last met my Lord Mayor in Canning Street, like a man spent, with a hankercher[2] about his neck. To the King's message, he cried like a fainting woman, "Lord, what can I do? I am spent. People will not obey me. I have been pulling down houses. But the fire overtakes us faster than we can do it." That he needed no more soldiers; and that for himself, he must go and refresh himself, having been up

5. William Michell and his wife, Betty, one of Pepys's old flames, lived near London Bridge. Sarah had been a maid of the Pepyses'.
6. A tavern in Thames Street, near the source of the fire.
7. Barges.

8. Mrs. Horsely, a beauty admired and pursued by Pepys.
9. Palace in central London.
1. St. Paul's Cathedral, later ravaged by the fire.
2. Handkerchief.

all night. So he left me, and I him, and walked home—seeing people all almost distracted and no manner of means used to quench the fire. The houses too, so very thick thereabouts, and full of matter for burning, as pitch and tar, in Thames Street—and warehouses of oil and wines and brandy and other things. Here I saw Mr. Isaak Houblon, that handsome man—prettily dressed and dirty at his door at Dowgate, receiving some of his brothers' things whose houses were on fire; and as he says, have been removed twice already, and he doubts[3] (as it soon proved) that they must be in a little time removed from his house also—which was a sad consideration. And to see the churches all filling with goods, by people who themselves should have been quietly there at this time.

By this time it was about 12 o'clock, and so home and there find my guests, which was Mr. Wood and his wife, Barbary Shelden, and also Mr. Moone— she mighty fine, and her husband, for aught I see, a likely[4] man. But Mr. Moone's design and mine, which was to look over my closet and please him with the sight thereof, which he hath long desired, was wholly disappointed, for we were in great trouble and disturbance at this fire, not knowing what to think of it. However, we had an extraordinary good dinner, and as merry as at this time we could be.

While at dinner, Mrs. Batelier came to enquire after Mr. Woolfe and Stanes (who it seems are related to them), whose houses in Fish Street are all burned, and they in a sad condition. She would not stay in the fright.

As soon as dined, I and Moone away and walked through the City, the streets full of nothing but people and horses and carts loaden with goods, ready to run over one another, and removing goods from one burned house to another—they now removing out of Canning Street (which received goods in the morning) into Lumbard Street and further; and among others, I now saw my little goldsmith Stokes receiving some friend's goods, whose house itself was burned the day after. We parted at Paul's, he home and I to Paul's Wharf, where I had appointed a boat to attend me; and took in Mr. Carcasse and his brother, whom I met in the street, and carried them below and above bridge, to and again, to see the fire, which was now got further, both below and above, and no likelihood of stopping it. Met with the King and Duke of York in their barge, and with them to Queenhithe and there called Sir Rd. Browne[5] to them. Their order was only to pull down houses apace, and so below bridge at the waterside; but little was or could be done, the fire coming upon them so fast. Good hopes there was of stopping it at the Three Cranes above, and at Buttolph's Wharf below bridge, if care be used; but the wind carries it into the City, so as we know not by the water-side what it doth there. River full of lighters and boats taking in goods, and good goods swimming in the water; and only, I observed that hardly one lighter or boat in three that had the goods of a house in, but there was a pair of virginals[6] in it. Having seen as much as I could now, I away to Whitehall by appointment, and there walked to St. James's Park, and there met my wife and Creed and Wood and his wife and walked to my boat, and there upon the water again, and to the fire up and down, it still increasing and the wind

3. Fears.
4. Promising.
5. Sir Richard Browne was a former lord mayor.

"Queenhithe": harbor in Thames Street.
6. Table-size harpsichord, popular at the time.

great. So near the fire as we could for smoke; and all over the Thames, with one's face in the wind you were almost burned with a shower of firedrops— this is very true—so as houses were burned by these drops and flakes of fire, three or four, nay five or six houses, one from another. When we could endure no more upon the water, we to a little alehouse on the Bankside over against the Three Cranes, and there stayed till it was dark almost and saw the fire grow; and as it grew darker, appeared more and more, and in corners and upon steeples and between churches and houses, as far as we could see up the hill of the City, in a most horrid malicious bloody flame, not like the fine flame of an ordinary fire. Barbary[7] and her husband away before us. We stayed till, it being darkish, we saw the fire as only one entire arch of fire from this to the other side the bridge, and in a bow up the hill, for an arch of above a mile long. It made me weep to see it. The churches, houses, and all on fire and flaming at once, and a horrid noise the flames made, and the cracking of houses at their ruin. So home with a sad heart, and there find everybody discoursing and lamenting the fire; and poor Tom Hater came with some few of his goods saved out of his house, which is burned upon Fish Street hill. I invited him to lie at my house, and did receive his goods: but was deceived in his lying there,[8] the noise coming every moment of the growth of the fire, so as we were forced to begin to pack up our own goods and prepare for their removal. And did by moonshine (it being brave,[9] dry, and moonshine and warm weather) carry much of my goods into the garden, and Mr. Hater and I did remove my money and iron chests into my cellar—as thinking that the safest place. And got my bags of gold into my office ready to carry away, and my chief papers of accounts also there, and my tallies[1] into a box by themselves. So great was our fear, as Sir W. Batten had carts come out of the country to fetch away his goods this night. We did put Mr. Hater, poor man, to bed a little; but he got but very little rest, so much noise being in my house, taking down of goods.

September 5, 1666

I lay down in the office again upon W. Hewer's[2] quilt, being mighty weary and sore in my feet with going till I was hardly able to stand. About 2 in the morning my wife calls me up and tells of new cries of "Fire!"—it being come to Barking Church, which is the bottom of our lane. I up; and finding it so, resolved presently to take her away; and did, and took my gold (which was about £2350), W. Hewer, and Jane down by Poundy's boat to Woolwich.[3] But Lord, what a sad sight it was by moonlight to see the whole City almost on fire—that you might see it plain at Woolwich, as if you were by it. There when I came, I find the gates shut, but no guard kept at all; which troubled me, because of discourses now begun that there is plot in it and that the French had done it.[4] I got the gates open, and to Mr. Shelden's,[5] where I

---

7. The actress Elizabeth Knepp, another of Pepys's mistresses. He calls her "Barbary" because she had enchanted him by singing *Barbary Allen*.
8. I.e., mistaken in asking him to stay.
9. Fine.
1. Receipts notched on sticks.
2. William Hewer, Pepys's chief clerk. Pepys had packed or sent away all his own goods.

3. Suburb on the east side of London.
4. There were rumors that the French had set the fire and were invading the city. "Gates": at the dockyard.
5. William Shelden, a Woolwich official at whose home Mrs. Pepys had stayed the year before, during the plague.

locked up my gold and charged my wife and W. Hewer never to leave the room without one of them in it night nor day. So back again, by the way seeing my goods well in the lighters at Deptford and watched well by people. Home, and whereas I expected to have seen our house on fire, it being now about 7 o'clock, it was not. But to the fire, and there find greater hopes than I expected; for my confidence of finding our office on fire was such, that I durst not ask anybody how it was with us, till I came and saw it not burned. But going to the fire, I find, by the blowing up of houses and the great help given by the workmen out of the King's yards, sent up by Sir W. Penn, there is a good stop given to it, as well at Mark Lane end as ours—it having only burned the dial[6] of Barking Church, and part of the porch, and was there quenched. I up to the top of Barking steeple, and there saw the saddest sight of desolation that I ever saw. Everywhere great fires. Oil cellars and brimstone and other things burning. I became afeared to stay there long; and therefore down again as fast as I could, the fire being spread as far as I could see it, and to Sir W. Penn's and there eat a piece of cold meat, having eaten nothing since Sunday but the remains of Sunday's dinner.

Here I met with Mr. Young and Whistler; and having removed all my things, and received good hopes that the fire at our end is stopped, they and I walked into the town and find Fanchurch Street, Gracious Street, and Lumbard Street all in dust. The Exchange a sad sight, nothing standing there of all the statues or pillars but Sir Tho. Gresham's picture in the corner.[7] Walked into Moore-fields (our feet ready to burn, walking through the town among the hot coals) and find that full of people, and poor wretches carrying their goods there, and everybody keeping his goods together by themselves (and a great blessing it is to them that it is fair weather for them to keep abroad[8] night and day); drank there, and paid twopence for a plain penny loaf.

Thence homeward, having passed through Cheapside and Newgate Market, all burned—and seen Anthony Joyce's house in fire. And took up (which I keep by me) a piece of glass of Mercer's Chapel in the street, where much more was, so melted and buckled with the heat of the fire, like parchment. I also did see a poor cat taken out of a hole in the chimney joining to the wall of the Exchange, with the hair all burned off the body and yet alive. So home at night, and find there good hopes of saving our office—but great endeavors of watching all night and having men ready; and so we lodged them in the office and had drink and bread and cheese for them. And I lay down and slept a good night about midnight—though when I rose, I hear that there had been a great alarm of French and Dutch being risen—which proved nothing. But it is a strange thing to see how long this time did look since Sunday, having been always full of variety of actions, and little sleep, that it looked like a week or more. And I had forgot almost the day of the week.[9]

---

6. Clock. "Yards": i.e., dockyards.
7. Sir Thomas Gresham had founded the Royal Exchange, a center for shopping and trading, in 1568. It was rebuilt in 1669.

8. Out of doors.
9. A day later the fire was under control. Pepys's own house was spared.

[THE DEB WILLET AFFAIR]

October 25, 1668

Lords day. Up, and discoursing with my wife about our house and many new things we are doing of; and so to church I, and there find Jack Fen come, and his wife, a pretty black[1] woman; I never saw her before, nor took notice of her now. So home and to dinner; and after dinner, all the afternoon got my wife and boy[2] to read to me. And at night W. Batelier comes and sups with us; and after supper, to have my head combed by Deb,[3] which occasioned the greatest sorrow to me that ever I knew in this world; for my wife, coming up suddenly, did find me embracing the girl con my hand sub su coats; and indeed, I was with my main in her cunny.[4] I was at a wonderful loss upon it, and the girl also; and I endeavored to put it off, but my wife was struck mute and grew angry, and as her voice came to her, grew quite out of order; and I do say little, but to bed; and my wife said little also, but could not sleep all night; but about 2 in the morning waked me and cried, and fell to tell me as a great secret that she was a Roman Catholic and had received the Holy Sacrament;[5] which troubled me but I took no notice of it, but she went on from one thing to another, till at last it appeared plainly her trouble was at what she saw; but yet I did not know how much she saw and therefore said nothing to her. But after her much crying and reproaching me with inconstancy and preferring a sorry girl before her, I did give her no provocations but did promise all fair usage to her, and love, and foreswore any hurt that I did with her—till at last she seemed to be at ease again; and so toward morning, a little sleep; [*Oct. 26*] and so I, with some little repose and rest, rose, and up and by water to Whitehall, but with my mind mightily troubled for the poor girl, whom I fear I have undone by this, my wife telling me that she would turn her out of door. However, I was obliged to attend the Duke of York, thinking to have had a meeting of Tanger[6] today, but had not; but he did take me and Mr. Wren into his closet, and there did press me to prepare what I had to say upon the answers of my fellow-officers to his great letter; which I promised to do against[7] his coming to town again the next week; and so to other discourse, finding plainly that he is in trouble and apprehensions of the reformers, and would be found to do what he can towards reforming himself. And so thence to my Lord Sandwich; where after long stay, he being in talk with others privately, I to him; and there he taking physic and keeping his chamber, I had an hour's talk with him about the ill posture of things at this time, while the King gives countenance to Sir Ch. Sidly and Lord Buckhurst,[8] telling him their late story of running up and down the streets a little while since all night, and their being beaten and clapped up all night by the constable, who is since chid and imprisoned for his pains.

---

1. Dark-haired.
2. Servant. Pepys had no children.
3. Deborah Willett, Mrs. Pepys's maid.
4. With his hand under her skirts and in her vulva.
5. When unhappy with her husband, Elizabeth Pepys sometimes threatened to convert to the Church of Rome. She never did.
6. Committee supervising the British naval base at Tangier, later evacuated under Pepys's supervision.
7. Before. Pepys had drafted a letter for the duke of York (later James II), high admiral of the navy, defending him from charges of mismanagement.
8. Sir Charles Sedley and Lord Buckhurst were riotous rakes and well-known writers; they are often identified with Lisideius and Eugenius in Dryden's *Essay of Dramatic Poesy*.

He tells me that he thinks his matters do stand well with the King—and hopes to have dispatch to his mind;[9] but I doubt it, and do see that he doth fear it too. He told me my Lady Carteret's trouble about my writing of that letter of the Duke of York's lately to the office; which I did not own, but declared to be of no injury to G. Carteret[1] and that I would write a letter to him to satisfy him therein. But this I am in pain how to do without doing myself wrong, and the end I had, of preparing a justification to myself hereafter, when the faults of the Navy come to be found out. However, I will do it in the best manner I can.

Thence by coach home and to dinner, finding my wife mightily discontented and the girl sad, and no words from my wife to her. So after dinner, they out[2] with me about two or three things; and so home again, I all the evening busy and my wife full of trouble in her looks; and anon to bed—where about midnight, she wakes me and there falls foul on me again, affirming that she saw me hug and kiss the girl; the latter I denied, and truly; the other I confessed and no more. And upon her pressing me, did offer to give her under my hand that I would never see Mrs. Pierce more, nor Knepp, but did promise her particular demonstrations of my true love to her, owning some indiscretion in what I did, but that there was no harm in it. She at last on these promises was quiet, and very kind we were, and so to sleep; [Oct. 27] and in the morning up, but with my mind troubled for the poor girl, with whom I could not get opportunity to speak; but to the office, my mind mighty full of sorrow for her, where all the morning, and to dinner with my people and to the office all the afternoon; and so at night home and there busy to get some things ready against tomorrow's meeting of Tanger; and that being done and my clerks gone, my wife did towards bedtime begin to be in a mighty rage from some new matter that she had got in her head, and did most part of the night in bed rant at me in most high terms, of threats of publishing[3] my shame; and when I offered to rise, would have rose too, and caused a candle to be lit, to burn by her all night in the chimney while she ranted; while I, that knew myself to have given some grounds for it, did make it my business to appease her all I could possibly, and by good words and fair promises did make her very quiet; and so rested all night and rose with perfect good peace, being heartily afflicted for this folly of mine that did occasion it; but was forced to be silent about the girl, which I have no mind to part with, but much less that the poor girl should be undone by my folly. [Oct. 28] So up, with mighty kindness from my wife and a thorough peace; and being up, did by a note advise the girl what I had done and owned, which note I was in pain for till she told me that she had burned it. This evening, Mr. Spong came and sat late with me, and first told me of the instrument called Parrallogram,[4] which I must have one of, showing me his practice thereon by a map of England.

---

9. A message to his liking.
1. Sir George Carteret, former treasurer of the navy (which Pepys had plans to reform), was later censured for having kept poor accounts.
2. Went out.
3. Making public.
4. The pantograph, a mechanism for copying maps or plans.

November 14, 1668

Up, and had a mighty mind to have seen or given a note to Deb or to have given her a little money; to which purpose I wrapped up 40s in a paper, thinking to give her; but my wife rose presently, and would not let me be out of her sight; and went down before me into the kitchen, and came up and told me that she was in the kitchen, and therefore would have me go round the other way; which she repeating, and I vexed at it, answered her a little angrily; upon which she instantly flew out into a rage, calling me dog and rogue, and that I had a rotten heart; all which, knowing that I deserved it, I bore with; and word being brought presently up that she was gone away by coach with her things, my wife was friends; and so all quiet, and I to the office with my heart sad, and find that I cannot forget the girl, and vexed I know not where to look for her—and more troubled to see how my wife is by this means likely for ever to have her hand over me, that I shall for ever be a slave to her; that is to say, only in matters of pleasure, but in other things she will make her business, I know, to please me and to keep me right to her— which I will labor to be indeed, for she deserves it of me, though it will be I fear a little time before I shall be able to wear Deb out of my mind. At the office all the morning, and merry at noon at dinner; and after dinner to the office, where all the afternoon and doing much business late; my mind being free of all troubles, I thank God, but[5] only for my thoughts of this girl, which hang after her. And so at night home to supper, and there did sleep with great content with my wife. I must here remember that I have lain with my moher[6] as a husband more times since this falling-out then in I believe twelve months before—and with more pleasure to her then I think in all the time of our marriage before.

November 18, 1668

Lay long in bed, talking with my wife, she being unwilling to have me go abroad, being and declaring herself jealous of my going out, for fear of my going to Deb; which I do deny—for which God forgive me, for I was no sooner out about noon but I did go by coach directly to Somerset House and there inquired among the porters there for Dr. Allbun;[7] and the first I spoke with told me he knew him, and that he was newly gone into Lincoln's Inn fields, but whither he could not tell me, but that one of his fellows, not then in the way, did carry a chest of drawers thither with him, and that when he comes he would ask him. This put me in some hopes; and I to Whitehall and thence to Mr. Povy's, but he at dinner; and therefore I away and walked up and down the Strand between the two turnstiles,[8] hoping to see her out of a window; and then employed a porter, one Osbeston, to find out this doctor's lodgings thereabouts; who by appointment comes to me to Hercules' Pillars, where I dined alone, but tells me that he cannot find out any such but will inquire further. Thence back to Whitehall to the treasury a while, and thence to the Strand; and towards night did meet with the porter that car- ried the chest of drawers with this doctor, but he would not tell me where he

5. Except.
6. Woman or wife (*mujer* in Spanish).
7. Pepys's wife had told him that Deb was stay-

ing with a man named Allbon.
8. To keep traffic, except for pedestrians, out of the street.

lived, being his good master he told me; but if I would have a message to him, he would deliver it. At last, I told him my business was not with him, but a little gentlewoman, one Mrs. Willet, that is with him; and sent him to see how she did, from her friend in London, and no other token. He goes while I walk in Somerset House walk there in the court; at last he comes back and tells me she is well, and that I may see her if I will—but no more. So I could not be commanded by my reason, but I must go this very night; and so by coach, it being now dark, I to her, close by my tailor's; and there she came into the coach to me, and yo did besar her and tocar her thing, but ella was against it and labored with much earnestness, such as I believed to be real; and yet at last yo did make her tener mi cosa in her mano, while mi mano was sobra her pectus, and so did hazer[9] with grand delight. I did nevertheless give her the best counsel I could, to have a care of her honor and to fear God and suffer no man para haver to do con her—as yo have done—which she promised. Yo did give her 20s and directions para laisser sealed in paper at any time the name of the place of her being, at Herringman's my bookseller in the Change[1]—by which I might go para her. And so bid her good-night, with much content to my mind and resolution to look after her no more till I heard from her. And so home, and there told my wife a fair tale, God knows, how I spent the whole day; with which the poor wretch was satisfied, or at least seemed so; and so to supper and to bed, she having been mighty busy all day in getting of her house in order against tomorrow, to hang up our new hangings and furnishing our best chamber.

November 19, 1668

Up, and at the office all the morning, with my heart full of joy to think in what a safe condition all my matters now stand between my wife and Deb and me; and at noon, running upstairs to see the upholsters, who are at work upon hanging my best room and setting up my new bed, I find my wife sitting sad in the dining-room; which inquiring into the reason of, she begun to call me all the false, rotten-hearted rogues in the world, letting me understand that I was with Deb yesterday; which, thinking impossible for her ever to understand, I did a while deny; but at last did, for the ease of my mind and hers, and for ever to discharge my heart of this wicked business, I did confess all; and above-stairs in our bed-chamber there, I did endure the sorrow of her threats and vows and curses all the afternoon. And which was worst, she swore by all that was good that she would slit the nose of this girl, and be gone herself this very night from me; and did there demand 3 or 400*l* of me to buy my peace, that she might be gone without making any noise, or else protested that she would make all the world know of it. So, with most perfect confusion of face and heart, and sorrow and shame, in the greatest agony in the world, I did pass this afternoon, fearing that it will never have an end; but at last I did call for W. Hewer, who I was forced to make privy now to all; and the poor fellow did cry like a child and obtained what I could not, that she would be pacified, upon condition that I would give it under my hand never to see or speak with Deb while I live, as I did before of Pierce

---

9. Carry on. "Besar": kiss. "Tocar": touch. "Ella": she. "Tener mi cosa in her mano": take my thing in her hand. "Mi mano was sobra her pectus": my hand was on her breast.
1. I.e., the Royal Exchange, a center for shopping, business, and trade. "Para laisser": to leave.

and Knepp; and which I did also, God knows, promise for Deb too, but I have the confidence to deny it, to the perjuring of myself. So before it was late, there was, beyond my hopes as well as desert, a tolerable peace; and so to supper, and pretty kind words, and to bed, and there yo did hazer con ella to her content; and so with some rest spent the night in bed, being most absolutely resolved, if ever I can master this bout, never to give her occasion while I live of more trouble of this or any other kind, there being no curse in the world so great as this of the difference between myself and her; and therefore I do by the grace of God promise never to offend her more, and did this night begin to pray to God upon my knees alone in my chamber; which God knows I cannot yet do heartily, but I hope God will give me the grace more and more every day to fear Him, and to be true to my poor wife. This night the upholsters did finish the hanging of my best chamber, but my sorrow and trouble is so great about this business, that put me out of all joy in looking upon it or minding how it was.[2]

2. Despite his promises, Pepys continued to hanker for Deb, and they had a few brief encounters. Mrs. Pepys accused him of talking to Deb in his dreams, and she once threatened him with red-hot tongs. But so far as is known the affair was never consummated.

JOHN BUNYAN
1628–1688

John Bunyan is one of the most remarkable figures in seventeenth-century literature. The son of a poor Bedfordshire tinker (a maker and mender of metal pots), he received only meager schooling and then learned his father's craft. Nothing in the circumstances of his early life could have suggested that he would become a writer known the world over.

Grace Abounding to the Chief of Sinners (1666), his spiritual autobiography, records his transformation from a self-doubting sinner into an eloquent and fearless Baptist preacher. Preachers, both male and female, often even less educated than Bunyan, were common phenomena among the sects during the Commonwealth. They wished no ordination but the "call," and they could dispense with learning because they abounded in inspiration, inner light, and the gifts conferred by the Holy Spirit. In November 1660, the Anglican Church began to persecute and silence the dissenting sects. Jails filled with unlicensed Nonconformist preachers, and Bunyan was one of the prisoners. Refusing to keep silent, he chose imprisonment and so for twelve years remained in Bedford jail, preaching to his fellow prisoners and writing religious books. Upon his release, he was called to the pastorate of a Nonconformist group in Bedford. It was during a second imprisonment, in 1675, when the Test Act was once again rigorously enforced against Nonconformists, that he wrote his greatest work, *The Pilgrim's Progress from This World to That Which Is to Come* (1678), revised and augmented in the third edition (1679). Bunyan was a prolific writer: part 2 of *The Pilgrim's Progress*, dealing with the journey of Christian's wife and children, appeared in 1684; *The Life and Death of Mr. Badman*, in 1680; *The Holy War*, in 1682. And these major works form only a small part of all his writings.

The Pilgrim's Progress is the most popular allegory in English. Its basic metaphor—life is a journey—is simple and familiar; the objects that the pilgrim Christian meets are homely and commonplace: a quagmire, the highway, the bypaths and shortcuts through pleasant meadows, the inn, the steep hill, the town fair on market day, and the river that must be forded. As in the equally homely parables of Jesus, however, these simple things are charged with spiritual significance. Moreover, this is a tale of adventure. If the road that Christian travels is the King's Highway, it is also a perilous path along which we encounter giants, wild beasts, hobgoblins, and the terrible Apollyon, "the angel of the bottomless pit," whom Christian must fight. Bunyan keeps the tale firmly based on human experience, and his style, modeled on the prose of the English Bible, together with his concrete language and carefully observed details, enables even the simplest reader to share the experiences of the characters. What could be better than the following sentence? "Some cry out against sin even as the mother cries out against her child in her lap, when she calleth it slut and naughty girl, and then falls to hugging and kissing it." *The Pilgrim's Progress* is no longer a household book, but it survives in the phrases it gave to our language: "the slough of despond," "the house beautiful," "Mr. Worldly-Wiseman," and "Vanity Fair." And it lives again for anyone who reads beyond the first page.

From The Pilgrim's Progress

From This World to That Which Is to Come:
Delivered under the Similitude of a Dream

[CHRISTIAN SETS OUT FOR THE CELESTIAL CITY]

As I walked through the wilderness of this world, I lighted on a certain place where was a den, and I laid me down in that place to sleep; and, as I slept, I dreamed a dream. I dreamed, and behold I saw a man clothed with rags, standing in a certain place, with his face from his own house, a book in his hand, and a great burden upon his back (Isaiah lxiv.6; Luke xiv.33; Psalms xxxviii.4; Habakkuk ii.2; Acts xvi.31). I looked and saw him open the book and read therein; and, as he read, he wept, and trembled; and not being able longer to contain, he brake out with a lamentable cry, saying, "What shall I do?" (Acts ii.37).

In this plight, therefore, he went home and refrained himself as long as he could, that his wife and children should not perceive his distress; but he could not be silent long, because that his trouble increased. Wherefore at length he brake his mind to his wife and children; and thus he began to talk to them. O my dear wife, said he, and you the children of my bowels, I your dear friend am in myself undone by reason of a burden that lieth hard upon me; moreover, I am for certain informed that this our city will be burned with fire from heaven, in which fearful overthrow both myself, with thee, my wife, and you, my sweet babes, shall miserably come to ruin, except (the which yet I see not) some way of escape can be found, whereby we may be delivered. At this his relations were sore amazed; not for that they believed that what he had said to them was true, but because they thought that some frenzy distemper[1] had got into his head; therefore, it drawing towards night, and they

---

1. A malady causing madness. The use of *frenzy* as an adjective was not uncommon in the 17th century.

hoping that sleep might settle his brains, with all haste they got him to bed; but the night was as troublesome to him as the day; wherefore, instead of sleeping, he spent it in sighs and tears. So when the morning was come, they would know how he did. He told them, Worse and worse; he also set to talking to them again, but they began to be hardened. They also thought to drive away his distemper by harsh and surly carriages[2] to him: sometimes they would deride, sometimes they would chide, and sometimes they would quite neglect him. Wherefore he began to retire himself to his chamber, to pray for and pity them, and also to condole his own misery; he would also walk solitarily in the fields, sometimes reading, and sometimes praying; and thus for some days he spent his time.

Now I saw, upon a time, when he was walking in the fields, that he was (as he was wont) reading in this book, and greatly distressed in his mind; and as he read, he burst out, as he had done before, crying, "What shall I do to be saved?"

I saw also that he looked this way and that way, as if he would run; yet he stood still, because (as I perceived) he could not tell which way to go. I looked then, and saw a man named Evangelist[3] coming to him, who asked, Wherefore dost thou cry? (Job xxxiii.23). He answered, Sir, I perceive by the book in my hand that I am condemned to die, and after that to come to judgment (Hebrews ix.27), and I find that I am not willing to do the first (Job xvi.21), nor able to do the second (Ezekiel xxii.14). . . .

Then said Evangelist, Why not willing to die, since this life is attended with so many evils? The man answered, Because I fear that this burden that is upon my back will sink me lower than the grave, and I shall fall into Tophet[4] (Isaiah xxx.33). And, sir, if I be not fit to go to prison, I am not fit to go to judgment, and from thence to execution; and the thoughts of these things make me cry.[5]

Then said Evangelist, If this be thy condition, why standest thou still? He answered, Because I know not whither to go. Then he gave him a parchment roll, and there was written within, "Fly from the wrath to come" (Matthew iii.7).

The man therefore read it, and looking upon Evangelist very carefully,[6] said, Whither must I fly? Then said Evangelist, pointing with his finger over a very wide field, Do you see yonder wicketgate?[7] (Matthew vii. 13, 14.) The man said, No. Then said the other, Do you see yonder shining light? (Psalms cxix.105; II Peter i.19.) He said, I think I do. Then said Evangelist, Keep that light in your eye, and go up directly thereto; so shalt thou see the gate; at which when thou knockest it shall be told thee what thou shalt do.

So I saw in my dream that the man began to run. Now, he had not run far from his own door, but his wife and children perceiving it, began to cry after him to return; but the man put his fingers in his ears, and ran on, crying, Life! life! eternal life! (Luke xiv.26.) So he looked not behind him, but fled towards the middle of the plain (Genesis xix.17).

---

2. Behavior.
3. A preacher of the Gospel; literally, a bearer of good news.
4. The place near Jerusalem where bodies and filth were burned; hence, by association, a name for hell.
5. Cry out.
6. Sorrowfully.
7. A small gate in or beside a larger gate.

The neighbors also came out to see him run (Jeremiah xx.10); and as he ran some mocked, others threatened, and some cried after him to return; and, among those that did so, there were two that resolved to fetch him back by force. The name of the one was Obstinate, and the name of the other Pliable. Now by this time the man was got a good distance from them; but, however, they were resolved to pursue him, which they did, and in a little time they overtook him. Then said the man, Neighbors, wherefore are ye come? They said, To persuade you to go back with us. But he said, That can by no means be; you dwell, said he, in the City of Destruction (the place also where I was born) I see it to be so; and, dying there, sooner or later, you will sink lower than the grave, into a place that burns with fire and brimstone; be content, good neighbors, and go along with me.

OBST. What! said Obstinate, and leave our friends and our comforts behind us?

CHR. Yes, said Christian (for that was his name), because that ALL which you shall forsake is not worthy to be compared with a little of that which I am seeking to enjoy (II Corinthians v.17); and, if you will go along with me, and hold it, you shall fare as I myself; for there, where I go, is enough and to spare (Luke xv.17). Come away, and prove my words.

OBST. What are the things you seek, since you leave all the world to find them?

CHR. I seek an inheritance incorruptible, undefiled, and that fadeth not away (I Peter i.4), and it is laid up in heaven, and safe there (Hebrews xi.16), to be bestowed, at the time appointed, on them that diligently seek it. Read it so, if you will, in my book.

OBST. Tush! said Obstinate, away with your book; will you go back with us or no?

CHR. No, not I, said the other, because I have laid my hand to the plow (Luke ix.62).

OBST. Come, then, neighbor Pliable, let us turn again, and go home without him; there is a company of these crazed-headed coxcombs, that, when they take a fancy[8] by the end, are wiser in their own eyes than seven men that can render a reason (Proverbs xxvi.16).

PLI. Then said Pliable, Don't revile; if what the good Christian says is true, the things he looks after are better than ours; my heart inclines to go with my neighbor.

OBST. What! more fools still? Be ruled by me, go back; who knows whither such a brain-sick fellow will lead you? Go back, go back, and be wise.

CHR. Nay, but do thou come with thy neighbor, Pliable; there are such things to be had which I spoke of, and many more glories besides. If you believe not me, read here in this book; and for the truth of what is expressed therein, behold, all is confirmed by the blood of Him that made it (Hebrews ix.17–22; xiii.20).

PLI. Well, neighbor Obstinate, said Pliable, I begin to come to a point,[9] I intend to go along with this good man, and to cast in my lot with him: but, my good companion, do you know the way to this desired place?

8. Delusion. "Coxcombs": fools.   9. Decision.

CHR. I am directed by a man, whose name is Evangelist, to speed me to a little gate that is before us, where we shall receive instructions about the way.

PLI. Come, then, good neighbor, let us be going. Then they went both together. * * *

[THE SLOUGH OF DESPOND]

Now I saw in my dream, that just as they had ended this talk they drew near to a very miry slough,[1] that was in the midst of the plain; and they, being heedless, did both fall suddenly into the bog. The name of the slough was Despond. Here, therefore, they wallowed for a time, being grievously bedaubed with dirt; and Christian, because of the burden that was on his back, began to sink in the mire.

PLI. Then said Pliable, Ah, neighbor Christian, where are you now?

CHR. Truly, said Christian, I do not know.

PLI. At that Pliable began to be offended, and angrily said to his fellow, Is this the happiness you have told me all this while of? If we have such ill speed at our first setting out, what may we expect 'twixt this and our journey's end? May I get out again with my life, you shall possess the brave[2] country alone for me. And, with that, he gave a desperate struggle or two, and got out of the mire on that side of the slough which was next[3] to his own house: so away he went, and Christian saw him no more.

Wherefore Christian was left to tumble in the Slough of Despond alone: but still he endeavored to struggle to that side of the slough that was further from his own house, and next to the wicket-gate; the which he did, but could not get out, because of the burden that was upon his back: but I beheld in my dream, that a man came to him, whose name was Help, and asked him what he did there?

CHR. Sir, said Christian, I was bid go this way by a man called Evangelist, who directed me also to yonder gate, that I might escape the wrath to come; and as I was going thither I fell in here.

HELP. But why did not you look for the steps?

CHR. Fear followed me so hard that I fled the next way, and fell in.

HELP. Then said he, Give me thy hand; so he gave him his hand, and he drew him out, and set him upon sound ground, and bid him go on his way.

Then I stepped to him that plucked him out, and said, Sir, wherefore, since over this place is the way from the City of Destruction to yonder gate, is it that this plat[4] is not mended, that poor travelers might go thither with more security? And he said unto me, This miry slough is such a place as cannot be mended; it is the descent whither the scum and filth that attends conviction for sin doth continually run, and therefore it was called the Slough of Despond; for still, as the sinner is awakened about his lost condition, there ariseth in his soul many fears, and doubts, and discouraging apprehensions, which all of them get together, and settle in his place. And this is the reason of the badness of this ground. * * *

---

1. Swamp (pronounced to rhyme with *now*).
2. Fine.
3. Nearest.
4. A plot of ground.

[VANITY FAIR][5]

Then I saw in my dream, that when they were got out of the wilderness, they presently saw a town before them, and the name of that town is Vanity; and at the town there is a fair kept, called Vanity Fair; it is kept all the year long; it beareth the name of Vanity Fair because the town where it is kept is lighter than vanity; and also because all that is there sold, or that cometh thither, is vanity. As is the saying of the wise, "All that cometh is vanity" (Ecclesiastes i.2, 14; ii.11, 17; xi.8; Isaiah xl.17).

This fair is no new-erected business, but a thing of ancient standing; I will show you the original of it.

Almost five thousand years agone, there were pilgrims walking to the Celestial City, as these two honest persons are; and Beelzebub, Apollyon, and Legion,[6] with their companions, perceiving by the path that the pilgrims made, that their way to the city lay through this town of Vanity, they contrived here to set up a fair; a fair wherein should be sold all sorts of vanity, and that it should last all the year long. Therefore at this fair are all such merchandise sold, as houses, lands, trades, places, honors, preferments,[7] titles, countries, kingdoms, lusts, pleasures, and delights of all sorts, as whores, bawds, wives, husbands, children, masters, servants, lives, blood, bodies, souls, silver, gold, pearls, precious stones, and what not.

And, moreover, at this fair there is at all times to be seen jugglings, cheats, games, plays, fools, apes, knaves, and rogues, and that of every kind.

Here are to be seen, too, and that for nothing, thefts, murders, adulteries, false swearers, and that of a blood-red color.

And as in other fairs of less moment, there are the several rows and streets, under their proper names, where such and such wares are vended; so here likewise you have the proper places, rows, streets (viz., countries and kingdoms), where the wares of this fair are soonest to be found. Here is the Britain Row, the French Row, the Italian Row, the Spanish Row, the German Row, where several sorts of vanities are to be sold. But, as in other fairs, some one commodity is as the chief of all the fair, so the ware of Rome and her merchandise[8] is greatly promoted in this fair; only our English nation, with some others, have taken a dislike thereat.

Now, as I said, the way to the Celestial City lies just through this town where this lusty[9] fair is kept; and he that will go to the City, and yet not go through this town, must needs "go out of the world" (I Corinthians v.10). The Prince of princes himself, when here, went through this town to his

---

5. In this, perhaps the best-known episode in the book, Bunyan characteristically turns one of the most familiar institutions in contemporary England—annual fairs—into an allegory of universal spiritual significance. Christian and his companion Faithful pass through the town of Vanity at the season of the local fair. *Vanity* means "emptiness" or "worthlessness," and hence the fair is an allegory of worldliness and the corruption of the religious life through the attractions of the world. From earliest times numerous fairs were held for stated periods throughout Britain; to them the most important merchants from all over Europe brought their wares. The serious business of buying and selling was accompanied by all sorts of diversions—eating, drinking, and other fleshly pleasures, as well as spectacles of strange animals, acrobats, and other wonders.

6. The "unclean spirit" sent by Jesus into the Gadarene swine (Mark 5.9). Beelzebub, prince of the devils (Matthew 12.24). Apollyon, the destroyer, "the Angel of the bottomless pit" (Revelation 9.11).

7. Appointments and promotions to political or ecclesiastical positions.

8. The practices and the temporal power of the Roman Catholic Church.

9. Cheerful, lustful.

own country, and that upon a fair-day too,[1] yea, and as I think, it was Beelzebub, the chief lord of this fair, that invited him to buy of his vanities; yea, would have made him lord of the fair, would he but have done him reverence as he went through the town. (Matthew iv.8; Luke iv.5–7.) Yea, because he was such a person of honor, Beelzebub had him from street to street, and showed him all the kingdoms of the world in a little time, that he might, if possible, allure the Blessed One to cheapen[2] and buy some of his vanities; but he had no mind to the merchandise, and therefore left the town, without laying out so much as one farthing upon these vanities. This fair, therefore, is an ancient thing, of long standing, and a very great fair.

Now these pilgrims, as I said, must needs go through this fair. Well, so they did; but, behold, even as they entered into the fair, all the people in the fair were moved, and the town itself as it were in a hubbub about them; and that for several reasons: for

First, The pilgrims were clothed with such kind of raiment as was diverse from the raiment of any that traded in that fair. The people, therefore, of the fair, made a great gazing upon them: some said they were fools, some they were bedlams, and some they are outlandish[3] men. (I Corinthians ii.7, 8.)

Secondly, And as they wondered at their apparel, so they did likewise at their speech; for few could understand what they said; they naturally spoke the language of Canaan, but they that kept the fair were the men of this world; so that, from one end of the fair to the other, they seemed barbarians[4] each to the other.

Thirdly, But that which did not a little amuse the merchandisers was that these pilgrims set very light by all their wares; they cared not so much as to look upon them; and if they called upon them to buy, they would put their fingers in their ears, and cry, "Turn away mine eyes from beholding vanity," and look upwards, signifying that their trade and traffic was in heaven. (Psalms cxix.37; Philippians iii.19, 20.)

One chanced mockingly, beholding the carriages of the men, to say unto them, What will ye buy? But they, looking gravely upon him, said, "We buy the truth" (Proverbs xxiii.23). At that there was an occasion taken to despise the men the more; some mocking, some taunting, some speaking reproachfully, and some calling upon others to smite them. At last things came to an hubbub and great stir in the fair, insomuch that all order was confounded. Now was word presently brought to the great one of the fair, who quickly came down, and deputed some of his most trusty friends to take these men into examination, about whom the fair was almost overturned. So the men were brought to examination; and they that sat upon them[5] asked them whence they came, whither they went, and what they did there, in such an unusual garb? The men told them that they were pilgrims and strangers in the world, and that they were going to their own country, which was the Heavenly Jerusalem (Hebrews xi.13–16); and that they had given no occasion to the men of the town, nor yet to the merchandisers, thus to abuse them,

---

1. The temptation of Jesus in the wilderness (Matthew 4.1–11).
2. Ask the price of.
3. Foreign. "Bedlams": lunatics from Bethlehem Hospital, the insane asylum in London.
4. The Greeks and Romans so designated all those who spoke a foreign tongue. "Canaan": the Promised Land, ultimately conquered by the Children of Israel (Joshua 4) and settled by them; hence the pilgrims speak the language of the Bible and of the true religion. Dissenters were notorious for their habitual use of biblical language.
5. Interrogated and tried them.

and to let[6] them in their journey, except it was for that, when one asked them what they would buy, they said they would buy the truth. But they that were appointed to examine them did not believe them to be any other than bedlams and mad, or else such as came to put all things into a confusion in the fair. Therefore they took them and beat them, and besmeared them with dirt, and then put them into the cage, that they might be made a spectacle to all the men of the fair. * * *

[THE RIVER OF DEATH AND THE CELESTIAL CITY]

So I saw that when they[7] awoke, they addressed themselves to go up to the City; but, as I said, the reflection of the sun upon the City (for the City was pure gold, Revelation xxi.18) was so extremely glorious, that they could not, as yet, with open face behold it, but through an instrument made for that purpose. (II Corinthians iii.18.) So I saw that as I went on, there met them two men, in raiment that shone like gold; also their faces shone as the light.

These men asked the pilgrims whence they came; and they told them. They also asked them where they had lodged, what difficulties and dangers, what comforts and pleasures they had met in the way; and they told them. Then said the men that met them, You have but two difficulties more to meet with, and then you are in the City.

Christian then and his companion asked the men to go along with them; so they told them they would. But, said they, you must obtain it by your own faith. So I saw in my dream that they went on together till they came in sight of the gate.

Now I further saw that betwixt them and the gate was a river, but there was no bridge to go over; the river was very deep. At the sight, therefore, of this river, the pilgrims were much stunned;[8] but the men that went with them said, You must go through, or you cannot come at the gate.

The pilgrims then began to inquire if there was no other way to the gate; to which they answered, Yes; but there hath not any, save two, to wit, Enoch and Elijah,[9] been permitted to tread that path, since the foundation of the world, nor shall, until the last trumpet shall sound. (I Corinthians xv.51, 52.) The pilgrims then, especially Christian, began to despond in his mind, and looked this way and that, but no way could be found by them by which they might escape the river. Then they asked the men if the waters were all of a depth. They said no; yet they could not help them in that case; for, said they, you shall find it deeper or shallower, as you believe in the King of the place.

They then addressed themselves to the water; and entering, Christian began to sink, and crying out to his good friend Hopeful, he said, I sink in deep waters; the billows go over my head, all his waves go over me! Selah.[1]

Then said the other, Be of good cheer, my brother, I feel the bottom, and it is good. Then said Christian, Ah, my friend, the sorrows of death have compassed me about; I shall not see the land that flows with milk and honey. And with that a great darkness and horror fell upon Christian, so that he

6. Hinder.
7. Christian and his companion, Hopeful. Ignorance, who appears tragically in the final paragraph, had tried to accompany the two pilgrims but had dropped behind because of his hobbling gait.

8. Amazed.
9. Both were "translated" alive to heaven (Genesis 5.24, Hebrews 11.5, 2 Kings 2.11–12).
1. A word of uncertain meaning that occurs frequently at the end of a verse in the Psalms. Bunyan may have supposed it to signify the end.

could not see before him. Also here he in great measure lost his senses, so that he could neither remember nor orderly talk of any of those sweet refreshments that he had met with in the way of his pilgrimage. But all the words that he spake still tended to discover[2] that he had horror of mind, and heart-fears that he should die in that river, and never obtain entrance in at the gate. Here also, as they that stood by perceived, he was much in the troublesome thoughts of the sins that he had committed, both since and before he began to be a pilgrim. 'Twas also observed that he was troubled with apparitions of hobgoblins and evil spirits; for ever and anon he would intimate so much by words. Hopeful, therefore, here had much ado to keep his brother's head above water; yea, sometimes he would be quite gone down, and then, ere a while, he would rise up again half dead. Hopeful also would endeavor to comfort him, saying, Brother, I see the gate and men standing by to receive us; but Christian would answer, 'Tis you, 'tis you they wait for; you have been Hopeful ever since I knew you. And so have you, said he to Christian. Ah, brother, said he, surely if I was right he would now arise to help me; but for my sins he hath brought me into the snare, and hath left me. Then said Hopeful, My brother, you have quite forgot the text, where it is said of the wicked, "There are no bands in their death, but their strength is firm. They are not in trouble as other men, neither are they plagued like other men" (Psalms lxxiii.4, 5). These troubles and distresses that you go through in these waters are no sign that God hath forsaken you, but are sent to try you, whether you will call to mind that which heretofore you have received of his goodness, and live upon him in your distresses.

Then I saw in my dream that Christian was as in a muse[3] a while, to whom also Hopeful added this word, Be of good cheer. Jesus Christ maketh thee whole. And with that Christian brake out with a loud voice, Oh, I see him again! and he tells me, "When thou passest through the waters, I will be with thee; and through the rivers, they shall not overflow thee" (Isaiah xliii.2). Then they both took courage, and the Enemy was after that as still as a stone, until they were gone over. Christian therefore presently found ground to stand upon, and so it followed that the rest of the river was but shallow. Thus they got over. Now, upon the bank of the river on the other side, they saw the two Shining Men again, who there waited for them. Wherefore, being come out of the river, they saluted[4] them saying, We are ministering spirits, sent forth to minister for those that shall be heirs of salvation. Thus they went along towards the gate. * * *

Now when they were come up to the gate, there was written over it in letters of gold, "Blessed are they that do his commandments, that they may have right to the tree of life, and may enter in through the gates into the city" (Revelation xxii.14).

Then I saw in my dream, that the Shining Men bid them call at the gate; the which, when they did, some from above looked over the gate, to wit, Enoch, Moses, and Elijah, etc., to whom it was said, These pilgrims are come from the City of Destruction, for the love that they bear to the King of this place; and then the pilgrims gave in unto them each man his certificate, which they had received in the beginning; those, therefore, were carried in

2. Reveal.
3. A deep meditation.
4. Greeted.

to the King, who, when he had read them, said, Where are the men? To whom it was answered, They are standing without the gate. The King then commanded to open the gate, "That the righteous nation," said he, "which keepeth the truth, may enter in" (Isaiah xxvi.2).

Now I saw in my dream that these two men went in at the gate; and lo, as they entered, they were transfigured, and they had raiment put on that shone like gold. There was also that met them with harps and crowns, and gave them to them: the harps to praise withal, and the crowns in token of honor. Then I heard in my dream that all the bells in the city rang again for joy, and that it was said unto them, "ENTER YE INTO THE JOY OF OUR LORD" (Matthew xxv.21). I also heard the men themselves, that they sang with a loud voice, saying, "BLESSING AND HONOR, GLORY AND POWER, BE TO HIM THAT SITTETH UPON THE THRONE, AND TO THE LAMB FOREVER AND EVER" (Revelation v.13).

Now just as the gates were opened to let in the men, I looked in after them, and, behold, the City shone like the sun; the streets also were paved with gold, and in them walked many men, with crowns on their heads, palms in their hands, and golden harps to sing praises withal.

There were also of them that had wings, and they answered one another without intermission, saying, "Holy, holy, holy is the Lord" (Revelation iv.8). And after that they shut up the gates, which when I had seen I wished myself among them.

Now while I was gazing upon all these things, I turned my head to look back, and saw Ignorance come up to the riverside; but he soon got over, and that without half that difficulty which the other two men met with. For it happened that there was then in that place one Vain-hope, a ferryman, that with his boat helped him over; so he, as the other, I saw, did ascend the hill to come up to the gate, only he came alone; neither did any man meet him with the least encouragement. When he was come up to the gate, he looked up to the writing that was above, and then began to knock, supposing that entrance should have been quickly administered to him; but he was asked by the men that looked over the top of the gate, Whence came you? and what would you have? He answered, I have eat and drank in the presence of the King, and he has taught in our streets. Then they asked him for his certificate, that they might go in and show it to the King; so he fumbled in his bosom for one, and found none. Then said they, Have you none? But the man answered never a word. So they told the King, but he would not come down to see him, but commanded the two Shining Ones that conducted Christian and Hopeful to the City, to go out and take Ignorance, and bind him hand and foot, and have him away. Then they took him up, and carried him through the air, to the door that I saw in the side of the hill, and put him in there. Then I saw that there was a way to hell, even from the gates of heaven, as well as from the City of Destruction. So I awoke, and behold it was a dream.

1678

JOHN LOCKE
1632–1704

John Locke's *Essay Concerning Human Understanding* (1690) is "a history-book," according to Laurence Sterne, "of what passes in a man's own mind." Like Montaigne's essays, it aims to explore the human mind in general by closely watching one particular mind. When Locke analyzed his ideas, the ways they were acquired and put together, he found they were clear when they were based on direct experience and adequate when they were clear. Usually, it appeared, problems occurred when basic ideas were blurred or confused or did not refer to anything determinate. Thus a critical analysis of the ideas in an individual mind could lead straight to a rule about adequate ideas in general and the sort of subject where adequate ideas were possible. On the basis of such a limitation, individuals might reach rational agreement with one another and so set up an area of natural law, within which a common rule of understanding was available.

Locke's new "way of ideas" strikes a humble, antidogmatic note, but readers quickly perceived its far-reaching implications. By basing knowledge on the ideas immediately "before the mind," Locke comports with and helps codify the movement of his times away from the authority of traditions of medieval, scholastic philosophy. His approach also alarmed some divines who argued that the foundation of human life—the mysteries of faith—could never be reduced to clear, distinct ideas. Locke indirectly accepts the Christian scriptures in the *Essay* in the midst of his famous critique of "enthusiasm," the belief in private revelation, but his main impulse is to restrain rather than to encourage religious speculations. (His fullest theological work, *The Reasonableness of Christianity*, 1695, argues that scriptural revelation is necessary for right-thinking people but not incompatible with ordinary reasonable beliefs gathered from personal experience and history.) The *Essay* also contains an unsettling discussion of personal identity (in the chapter "Of Identity and Diversity" added to the second edition in 1694). Locke argues that a person's sense of selfhood derives not from the "identity of soul" but rather from "consciousness of present and past actions": I am myself now because I remember my past, not because a unique substance ("me") underlies everything I experience. This account drew critical responses from numerous distinguished thinkers throughout the eighteenth century, notably Bishop Joseph Butler (1692–1752).

Locke spent his life in thought. His background and connections were all with the Puritan movement, but he was disillusioned early with the enthusiastic moods and persecutions to which he found the Puritans prone. Having a small but steady private income, he became a student, chiefly at Oxford, learning enough medicine to act as a physician, holding an occasional appointive office, but never allowing any of these activities to limit his controlling passion: the urge to think. After 1667, he was personal physician and tutor in the household of a violent, crafty politician, the first earl of Shaftesbury (Dryden's "Achitophel"). But Locke himself was always a grave, dispassionate man. On one occasion, Shaftesbury's political enemies at Oxford had Locke watched for several years on end, during which he was not heard to say one word either critical of the government or favorable to it. When times are turbulent, so much discretion is suspicious in itself, and Locke found it convenient to go abroad for several years during the 1680s. He lived quietly in Holland and pursued his thoughts. The Glorious Revolution of 1688–89 and the accession of William III brought him back to England and made possible the publication of the *Essay*, on which he had been working for many years. Its publication foreshadowed the coming age, not only in the positive ideas that the book advanced but in the quiet way it set aside as insoluble a range of problems about absolute authority and absolute assurance that had torn society apart earlier in the seventeenth century:

From An Essay Concerning Human Understanding

From *The Epistle to the Reader*

Reader,

I here put into thy hands what has been the diversion of some of my idle and heavy hours; if it has the good luck to prove so of any of thine, and thou hast but half so much pleasure in reading as I had in writing it, thou wilt as little think thy money, as I do my pains, ill-bestowed. Mistake not this for a commendation of my work; nor conclude, because I was pleased with the doing of it, that therefore I am fondly taken with it now it is done. He that hawks at larks and sparrows, has no less sport, though a much less considerable quarry, than he that flies at nobler game: and he is little acquainted with the subject of this treatise, the Understanding, who does not know, that as it is the most elevated faculty of the soul, so it is employed with a greater and more constant delight than any of the other. Its searches after truth are a sort of hawking and hunting, wherein the very pursuit makes a great part of the pleasure. Every step the mind takes in its progress towards knowledge makes some discovery, which is not only new, but the best, too, for the time at least.

For the understanding, like the eye, judging of objects only by its own sight, cannot but be pleased with what it discovers, having less regret for what has escaped it, because it is unknown. Thus he who has raised himself above the alms-basket, and, not content to live lazily on scraps of begged opinions, sets his own thoughts on work to find and follow truth, will (whatever he lights on) not miss the hunter's satisfaction; every moment of his pursuit will reward his pains with some delight, and he will have reason to think his time not ill-spent, even when he cannot much boast of any great acquisition.

This, reader, is the entertainment of those who let loose their own thoughts, and follow them in writing; which thou oughtest not to envy them, since they afford thee an opportunity of the like diversion, if thou wilt make use of thy own thoughts in reading. It is to them, if they are thy own, that I refer myself; but if they are taken upon trust from others, it is no great matter what they are, they not following truth, but some meaner consideration; and it is not worthwhile to be concerned what he says or thinks, who says or thinks only as he is directed by another. If thou judgest for thyself, I know thou wilt judge candidly; and then I shall not be harmed or offended, whatever be thy censure. For, though it be certain that there is nothing in this treatise of the truth whereof I am not fully persuaded, yet I consider myself as liable to mistakes as I can think thee; and know that this book must stand or fall with thee, not by any opinion I have of it, but thy own. If thou findest little in it new or instructive to thee, thou art not to blame me for it. It was not meant for those that had already mastered this subject, and made a thorough acquaintance with their own understandings, but for my own information, and the satisfaction of a few friends, who acknowledged themselves not to have sufficiently considered it. Were it fit to trouble thee with the history of this Essay, I should tell thee, that five or six friends, meeting at my chamber, and discoursing on a subject very remote from this, found themselves quickly at a stand by the difficulties that rose on every side. After we had awhile puzzled ourselves, without coming any nearer a resolution of those doubts which perplexed us, it came into my thoughts, that we took a wrong course; and that, before we set ourselves upon inquiries of that nature, it was necessary to examine our own abilities, and see what objects our understandings were or were not fitted to deal with. This I proposed to the company, who all readily assented; and thereupon it was agreed, that this should be our first inquiry. Some hasty and undigested thoughts, on a subject I had never before considered, which I set down against[1] our next meeting, gave the first entrance into this discourse, which, having been thus begun by chance, was continued by entreaty; written by incoherent parcels; and, after long intervals of neglect, resumed again, as my humor or occasions permitted; and at last, in a retirement, where an attendance on my health gave me leisure, it was brought into that order thou now seest it.

This discontinued way of writing may have occasioned, besides others, two contrary faults; viz., that too little and too much may be said in it. If thou findest anything wanting, I shall be glad that what I have writ gives thee any desire that I should have gone farther: if it seems too much to thee, thou must blame the subject; for when I first put pen to paper, I thought all I should have to say on this matter would have been contained in one sheet of paper; but the farther I went, the larger prospect I had: new discoveries led me still on, and so it grew insensibly to the bulk it now appears in. I will not deny but possibly it might be reduced to a narrower compass than it is; and that some parts of it might be contracted; the way it has been writ in, by catches,[2] and many long intervals of interruption, being apt to cause some repetitions. But, to confess the truth, I am now too lazy or too busy to make it shorter.

* * * I pretend not to publish this Essay for the information of men of large thoughts and quick apprehensions; to such masters of knowledge, I profess myself a scholar, and therefore warn them beforehand not to expect anything here but what, being spun out of my own coarse thoughts, is fitted to men of my own size, to whom, perhaps, it will not be unacceptable that I have taken some pains to make plain and familiar to their thoughts some truths, which established prejudice or the abstractness of the ideas themselves might render difficult. * * *

* * * The commonwealth of learning is not at this time without master-builders, whose mighty designs in advancing, the sciences will leave lasting monuments to the admiration of posterity: but everyone must not hope to be a Boyle or a Sydenham; and in an age that produces such masters as the great Huygenius, and the incomparable Mr. Newton,[3] with some other of that strain, it is ambition enough to be employed as an under-laborer in

1. Before.
2. Fragments.
3. Sir Isaac Newton. Robert Boyle, the great Anglo-Irish chemist and physicist. Thomas Sydenham, a physician and authority on the treatment of fevers. Christiaan Huygens, Dutch mathematician and astronomer.

clearing the ground a little, and removing some of the rubbish that lies in the way to knowledge; which certainly had been very much more advanced in the world, if the endeavors of ingenious and industrious men had not been much cumbered with the learned but frivolous use of uncouth, affected, or unintelligible terms introduced into the sciences, and there made an art of to that degree that philosophy, which is nothing but the true knowledge of things, was thought unfit or uncapable to be brought into well-bred company and polite conversation.[4] Vague and insignificant forms of speech, and abuse of language, have so long passed for mysteries of science; and hard or misapplied words, with little or no meaning, have, by prescription, such a right to be mistaken for deep learning and height of speculation; that it will not be easy to persuade either those who speak or those who hear them, that they are but the covers of ignorance, and hindrance of true knowledge. * * *

The booksellers, preparing for the fourth edition of my Essay, gave me notice of it, that I might, if I had leisure, make any additions or alterations I should think fit. Whereupon I thought it convenient to advertise the reader, that besides several corrections I had made here and there, there was one alteration which it was necessary to mention, because it ran through the whole book, and is of consequence to be rightly understood. What I thereupon said, was this:—

"Clear and distinct ideas" are terms which, though familiar and frequent in men's mouths, I have reason to think everyone who uses does not perfectly understand. And possibly it is but here and there one who gives himself the trouble to consider them so far as to know what he himself or others precisely mean by them. I have therefore, in most places, chose to put "determinate" or "determined,"[5] instead of "clear" and "distinct," as more likely to direct men's thoughts to my meaning in this matter. By those denominations, I mean some object in the mind, and consequently determined, i.e., such as it is there seen and perceived to be. This, I think, may fitly be called a "determinate" or "determined" idea, when such as it is at any time objectively in the mind, and so determined there, it is annexed, and without variation determined, to a name or articulate sound which is to be steadily the sign of that very same object of the mind, or determinate idea.

To explain this a little more particularly: By "determinate," when applied to a simple idea, I mean that simple appearance which the mind has in its view, or perceives in itself, when that idea is said to be in it. By "determined," when applied to a complex idea, I mean such an one as consists of a determinate number of certain simple or less complex ideas, joined in such a proportion and situation as the mind has before its view, and sees in itself, when that idea is present in it, or should be present in it, when a man gives a name to it. I say "should be"; because it is not everyone, nor perhaps anyone, who is so careful of his language as to use no word till he views in his mind the precise determined idea which he resolves to make it the sign of. The want

4. Locke was tutor to Anthony Ashley Cooper, third earl of Shaftesbury, whose philosophical writings make of genteel social conversation and civilized good humor something like guides to ultimate truth.

5. Definite, limited, fixed in value.

of this is the cause of no small obscurity and confusion in men's thoughts and discourses.

I know there are not words enough in any language to answer all the variety of ideas that enter into men's discourses and reasonings. But this hinders not but that when anyone uses any term, he may have in his mind a determined idea which he makes it the sign of, and to which he should keep it steadily annexed during that present discourse. Where he does not or cannot do this, he in vain pretends to clear or distinct ideas: it is plain his are not so; and therefore there can be expected nothing but obscurity and confusion, where such terms are made use of which have not such a precise determination.

Upon this ground I have thought "determined ideas" a way of speaking less liable to mistake than "clear and distinct"; and where men have got such determined ideas of all that they reason, inquire, or argue about, they will find a great part of their doubts and disputes at an end; the greatest part of the questions and controversies that perplex mankind depending on the doubtful and uncertain use of words, or (which is the same) indetermined ideas, which they are made to stand for. I have made choice of these terms to signify, 1. Some immediate object of the mind, which it perceives and has before it, distinct from the sound it uses as a sign of it. 2. That this idea, thus determined, i.e., which the mind has in itself, and knows and sees there, be determined without any change to that name, and that name determined to that precise idea. If men had such determined ideas in their inquiries and discourses, they would both discern how far their own inquiries and discourses went, and avoid the greatest part of the disputes and wranglings they have with others.

* * *

1690, 1700

SIR ISAAC NEWTON
1642–1727

Isaac Newton was the posthumous son of a Lincolnshire farmer. As a boy, he invented machines; as an undergraduate, he made major discoveries in optics and mathematics; and in 1667—at twenty-five—he was elected a fellow of Trinity College, Cambridge. Two years later his teacher, Isaac Barrow, resigned the Lucasian Chair of Mathematics in his favor. By then, in secret, Newton had already begun to rethink the universe. His mind worked incessantly, at the highest level of insight, both theoretical and experimental. He designed the first reflecting telescope and explained why the sky looks blue; contemporaneously with Leibniz, he invented calculus; he revolutionized the study of mechanics and physics with three basic laws of motion; and as everyone knows, he discovered the universal law of gravity. Although Newton's *Principia* (*Mathematical Principles of Natural Philosophy*, 1687) made possible the modern understanding of the cosmos, his *Opticks* (1704) had a still greater impact on his contemporaries, not only for its discoveries about light and color but also for its formulation of a proper scientific method.

Newton reported most of his scientific findings in Latin, the language of international scholarship; but when he chose, he could express himself in crisp and vigorous English. His early experiments on light and color were described in a letter to Henry Oldenburg, secretary of the Royal Society, and quickly published in the society's journal. By analyzing the spectrum, Newton had discovered something amazing, the "oddest if not the most considerable detection, which hath hitherto been made in the operations of nature": light is not homogeneous, as everyone thought, but a compound of heterogeneous rays, and white is not the absence of color but a composite of all sorts of colors. Newton assumes that a clear account of his experiments and reasoning will compel assent; when, at the end of his summary, he drops a very heavy word, he clinches the point like a carpenter nailing a box shut. But other scientists resisted the theory. In years to come, Newton would be more wary; eventually he would leave the university to become master of the mint in London and to devote himself to religious studies. Yet all the while his fame would continue to grow. "There could be only one Newton," Napoleon was told a century later: "there was only one world to discover."

From A Letter of Mr. Isaac Newton, Professor of the Mathematics in the University of Cambridge, Containing His New Theory about Light and Colors

Sent by the Author to the Publisher from Cambridge, Febr. 6, 1672, in order to Be Communicated to the Royal Society

Sir,

To perform my late promise to you, I shall without further ceremony acquaint you that in the beginning of the year 1666 (at which time I applied myself to the grinding of optic glasses of other figures than spherical) I procured me a triangular glass prism to try therewith the celebrated phenomena of colors. And in order thereto having darkened my chamber and made a small hole in my window-shuts to let in a convenient quantity of the sun's light, I placed my prism at his entrance that it might be thereby refracted[1] to the opposite wall. It was at first a very pleasing divertissement to view the vivid and intense colors produced thereby; but after a while, applying myself to consider them more circumspectly, I became surprised to see them in an *oblong* form, which according to the received laws of refraction I expected should have been *circular*.

They were terminated at the sides with straight lines, but at the ends the decay of light was so gradual that it was difficult to determine justly what was their figure; yet they seemed *semicircular*.

Comparing the length of this colored spectrum with its breadth, I found it about five times greater, a disproportion so extravagant that it excited me to a more than ordinary curiosity of examining from whence it might proceed. I could scarce think that the various thickness of the glass or the termina-

---

1. I.e., that the light's direction might be diverted from a straight path.

tion with shadow or darkness could have any influence on light to produce such an effect; yet I thought it not amiss first to examine those circumstances, and so tried what would happen by transmitting light through parts of the glass of divers thicknesses, or through holes in the window of divers bignesses, or by setting the prism without, so that the light might pass through it and be refracted before it was terminated by the hole. But I found none of those circumstances material. The fashion of the colors was in all these cases the same.

Then I suspected whether by any unevenness in the glass or other contingent irregularity these colors might be thus dilated. And to try this, I took another prism like the former and so placed it that the light, passing through them both, might be refracted contrary ways, and so by the latter returned into that course from which the former had diverted it. For by this means I thought the regular effects of the first prism would be destroyed by the second prism, but the irregular ones more augmented by the multiplicity of refractions. The event was that the light, which by the first prism was diffused into an oblong form, was by the second reduced into an orbicular one with as much regularity as when it did not at all pass through them. So that, whatever was the cause of that length, 'twas not any contingent irregularity.[2]

* * *

The gradual removal of these suspicions at length led me to the *experimentum crucis*,[3] which was this: I took two boards, and placed one of them close behind the prism at the window, so that the light might pass through a small hole made in it for the purpose and fall on the other board, which I placed at about 12 foot distance, having first made a small hole in it also, for some of that incident[4] light to pass through. Then I placed another prism behind this second board so that the light, trajected through both the boards, might pass through that also, and be again refracted before it arrived at the wall. This done, I took the first prism in my hand, and turned it to and fro slowly about its axis, so much as to make the several parts of the image, cast on the second board, successively pass through the hole in it, that I might observe to what places on the wall the second prism would refract them. And I saw by the variation of those places that the light, tending to that end of the image towards which the refraction of the first prism was made, did in the second prism suffer a refraction considerably greater than the light tending to the other end. And so the true cause of the length of that image was detected to be no other than that light consists of rays *differently refrangible*, which, without any respect to a difference in their incidence, were, according to their degrees of refrangibility, transmitted towards divers parts of the wall.[5]

* * *

2. Newton goes on to describe several experiments and calculations by which he disposed of alternative theories—that rays coming from different parts of the sun caused the diffusion of light into an oblong, or that the rays of light traveled in curved paths after leaving the prism.
3. Crucial experiment (Latin); turning point.
4. From the Latin *incidere*, to fall into or onto. Newton uses it of light striking an obstacle.

5. This insight enables Newton to design a greatly improved telescope, which uses reflections to correct the distortions caused by the scattering of refracted rays. He adds in passing that his experiments were interrupted for two years by the plague; but at last he returns to some further and even more important characteristics of light. "Refrangible": susceptible to being refracted.

I shall now proceed to acquaint you with another more notable diffor-mity[6] in its rays, wherein the *origin of colors* is infolded. A naturalist[7] would scarce expect to see the science of those become mathematical, and yet I dare affirm that there is as much certainty in it as in any other part of optics. For what I shall tell concerning them is not an hypothesis but most rigid consequence, not conjectured by barely inferring 'tis thus because not otherwise or because it satisfied all phenomena (the philosophers' universal topic) but evinced by the mediation of experiments concluding directly and without any suspicion of doubt. * * *

The doctrine you will find comprehended and illustrated in the following propositions.

1. As the rays of light differ in degrees of refrangibility, so they also dif-fer in their disposition to exhibit this or that particular color. Colors are not *qualifications of light*, derived from refractions or reflections of natural bodies (as 'tis generally believed), but *original and connate properties* which in divers rays are divers. Some rays are disposed to exhibit a red color and no other; some a yellow and no other, some a green and no other, and so of the rest. Nor are there only rays proper and particular to the more eminent colors, but even to all their intermediate gradations.

2. To the same degree of refrangibility ever belongs the same color, and to the same color ever belongs the same degree of refrangibility. The least refrangible rays are all disposed to exhibit a red color, and contrarily those rays which are disposed to exhibit a red color are all the least refrangible. So the most refrangible rays are all disposed to exhibit a deep violet color, and contrarily those which are apt to exhibit such a violet color are all the most refrangible. And so to all the intermediate colors in a continued series belong intermediate degrees of refrangibility. And this analogy 'twixt colors and refrangibility is very precise and strict; the rays always either exactly agreeing in both or proportionally disagreeing in both.

3. The species of color and degree of refrangibility proper to any partic-ular sort of rays is not mutable by refraction, nor by reflection from natural bodies, nor by any other cause that I could yet observe. When any one sort of rays hath been well parted from those of other kinds, it hath afterwards obstinately retained its color, notwithstanding my utmost endeavors to change it. I have refracted it with prisms and reflected it with bodies which in daylight were of other colors; I have intercepted it with the colored film of air interceding two compressed plates of glass; transmitted it through colored mediums and through mediums irradiated with other sorts of rays, and diversely terminated it; and yet could never produce any new color out of it. It would by contracting or dilating become more brisk or faint and by the loss of many rays in some cases very obscure and dark; but I could never see it changed *in specie*.[8]

4. Yet seeming transmutations of colors may be made, where there is any mixture of divers sorts of rays. For in such mixtures, the component colors appear not, but by their mutual allaying each other constitute a middling color. And therefore, if by refraction or any other of the aforesaid causes the difform rays latent in such a mixture be separated, there shall emerge colors

---

6. Diversity of forms.
7. A student of physics or "natural philosophy."

8. In kind.

different from the color of the composition. Which colors are not new generated, but only made apparent by being parted; for if they be again entirely mixed and blended together, they will again compose that color which they did before separation. And for the same reason, transmutations made by the convening of divers colors are not real; for when the difform rays are again severed, they will exhibit the very same colors which they did before they entered the composition—as you see blue and yellow powders when finely mixed appear to the naked eye green, and yet the colors of the component corpuscles are not thereby transmuted, but only blended. For, when viewed with a good microscope, they still appear blue and yellow interspersedly.

5. There are therefore two sorts of colors: the one original and simple, the other compounded of these. The original or primary colors are red, yellow, green, blue, and a violet-purple, together with orange, indigo, and an indefinite variety of intermediate graduations.

6. The same colors *in specie* with these primary ones may be also produced by composition. For a mixture of yellow and blue makes green; of red and yellow makes orange; of orange and yellowish green makes yellow. And in general, if any two colors be mixed which, in the series of those generated by the prism, are not too far distant one from another, they by their mutual alloy compound that color which in the said series appeareth in the mid-way between them. But those which are situated at too great a distance, do not so. Orange and indigo produce not the intermediate green, nor scarlet and green the intermediate yellow.

7. But the most surprising and wonderful composition was that of *whiteness*. There is no one sort of rays which alone can exhibit this. 'Tis ever compounded, and to its composition are requisite all the aforesaid primary colors, mixed in a due proportion. I have often with admiration beheld that all the colors of the prism, being made to converge, and thereby to be again mixed as they were in the light before it was incident upon the prism, reproduced light entirely and perfectly white, and not at all sensibly differing from a direct light of the sun, unless when the glasses I used were not sufficiently clear; for then they would a little incline it to *their* color.

8. Hence therefore it comes to pass that *whiteness* is the usual color of light, for light is a confused aggregate of rays endued with all sorts of colors, as they are promiscuously darted from the various parts of luminous bodies. And of such a confused aggregate, as I said, is generated whiteness, if there be a due proportion of the ingredients; but if any one predominate, the light must incline to that color, as it happens in the blue flame of brimstone, the yellow flame of a candle, and the various colors of the fixed stars.

9. These things considered, the manner how colors are produced by the prism is evident. For of the rays constituting the incident light, since those which differ in color proportionally differ in refrangibility, they by their unequal refractions must be severed and dispersed into an oblong form in an orderly succession from the least refracted scarlet to the most refracted violet. And for the same reason it is that objects, when looked upon through a prism, appear colored. For the difform rays, by their unequal refractions, are made to diverge towards several parts of the retina, and there express the images of things colored, as in the former case they did the sun's image upon a wall. And by this inequality of refractions they become not only colored, but also very confused and indistinct.

10. Why the colors of the rainbow appear in falling drops of rain is also from hence evident. For those drops which refract the rays disposed to appear purple in greatest quantity to the spectator's eye, refract the rays of other sorts so much less as to make them pass beside it;[9] and such are the drops on the inside of the primary bow and on the outside of the secondary or exterior one. So those drops which refract in greatest plenty the rays apt to appear red toward the spectator's eye, refract those of other sorts so much more as to make them pass beside it; and such are the drops on the exterior part of the primary and interior part of the secondary bow.

* * *

13. I might add more instances of this nature, but I shall conclude with this general one, that the colors of all natural bodies have no other origin than this, that they are variously qualified to reflect one sort of light in greater plenty than another. And this I have experimented in a dark room by illuminating those bodies with uncompounded light of divers colors. For by that means any body may be made to appear of any color. They have there no appropriate color, but ever appear of the color of the light cast upon them, but yet with this difference, that they are most brisk and vivid in the light of their own daylight color. *Minium* appeareth there of any color indifferently with which 'tis illustrated, but yet most luminous in red, and so *Bise*[1] appeareth indifferently of any color with which 'tis illustrated, but yet most luminous in blue. And therefore *minium* reflecteth rays of any color, but most copiously those endued with red; and consequently when illustrated with daylight, that is, with all sorts of rays promiscuously blended, those qualified with red shall abound most in the reflected light, and by their prevalence cause it to appear of that color. And for the same reason *bise,* reflecting blue most copiously, shall appear blue by the excess of those rays in its reflected light; and the like of other bodies. And that this is the entire and adequate cause of their colors is manifest, because they have no power to change or alter the colors of any sort of rays incident apart, but put on all colors indifferently with which they are enlightened.

These things being so, it can no longer be disputed whether there be colors in the dark, nor whether they be the qualities of the objects we see, no, nor perhaps whether light be a body. For since colors are the qualities of light, having its rays for their entire and immediate subject,[2] how can we think those rays qualities also, unless one quality may be the subject of and sustain another—which in effect is to call it substance. We should not know bodies for substances were it not for their sensible qualities, and the principal of those being now found due to something else, we have as good reason to believe that to be a substance also.[3]

Besides, who ever thought any quality to be a heterogeneous aggregate, such as light is discovered to be? But to determine more absolutely what light is, after what manner refracted, and by what modes or actions it pro-

9. I.e., disappear alongside it.

1. Azurite blue. "Minium": red lead. "Illustrated": illuminated.

2. That of which a thing consists.

3. I.e., the only way we know bodies are substances is that our senses perceive their qualities.

The chief of these qualities, color, is now known to be a quality of light, not body; our conclusion can perfectly well be that light is a form of substance, as well as body, and that we know it to be so through its quality, color.

duceth in our minds the phantasms of colors, is not so easy. And I shall not mingle conjectures with certainties.

* * *

1672

SAMUEL BUTLER
1612–1680

Samuel Butler passed his middle years during the fury of the civil wars and under the Commonwealth, sardonically observing the behavior and lovingly memorizing the faults of the Puritan rulers. He despised them and found relief for his feelings by satirizing them, though, naturally enough, he could not publish while they were in power. He served as clerk to several Puritan justices of the peace in the west of England, one of whom, according to tradition, was the original of Sir Hudibras (the s is pronounced). *Hudibras,* part 1, was published late in 1662 (the edition bears the date 1663) and pleased the triumphant Royalists. King Charles II admired and often quoted the poem and rewarded its author with a gift of £300; it was, after all, a relief to laugh at what he had earlier hated and feared. The first part, attacking Presbyterians and Independents, proved more vigorous and effective than parts 2 and 3, which followed in 1664 and 1678, respectively. After his initial success,

William Hogarth, *Hudibras, the Manner How He Sallied Forth*; engraving, 1726. Hudibras riding out to go a-coloneling, with his squire Ralph. From *Hudibras,* by Samuel Butler (1793).

Butler was neglected by the people he had pleased. He died in poverty, and not until 1721 was a monument to his memory erected in Westminster Abbey.

Hudibras is a travesty, or burlesque: it takes a serious subject and debases it by using a low style or distorts it by grotesque exaggeration. Butler carried this mode even into his verse, for he reduced the iambic tetrameter line (used subtly and seriously by such seventeenth-century poets as John Donne, John Milton, and Andrew Marvell) to something approaching doggerel, and his boldly comic rhymes add to the effect of broad comedy that he sought to create. Burlesque was a popular form of satire during the seventeenth century, especially after the French poet Paul Scarron published his *Virgile Travesti* (1648), which retells the *Aeneid* in slang. Butler's use of burlesque expresses his contempt for the Puritans and their commonwealth; the history of England from 1642 to 1660 is made to appear mere sound and fury.

Butler took his hero's name from Spenser's *Faerie Queene* 2.2, where Sir Huddibras appears briefly as a rash adventurer and lover. The questing knight of chivalric romance is degraded into the meddling, hypocritical busybody Hudibras, who goes out, like an officer in Cromwell's army, "a-coloneling" against the popular sport of bear baiting. The knight and his squire, Ralph, suggest Don Quixote and Sancho Panza, but the temper of Butler's mind is as remote from Cervantes's warm humanity as it is from Spenser's ardent idealism. Butler had no illusions; he was skeptical in philosophy and conservative in politics, distrusting theoretical reasoning and the new science, disdainful of claims of inspiration and illumination, contemptuous of Catholicism and dubious of bishops, Anglican no less than Roman. It is difficult to think of anything that he approved unless it was peace, common sense, and the wisdom that emerges from the experience of humankind through the ages.

From Hudibras

From *Part 1, Canto 1*

THE ARGUMENT

Sir Hudibras, his passing worth,
The manner how he sallied forth,
His arms and equipage are shown,
His horse's virtues and his own:
The adventure of the Bear and Fiddle
Is sung, but breaks off in the middle.

> When civil fury[1] first grew high,
> And men fell out, they knew not why;
> When hard words, jealousies, and fears
> Set folks together by the ears
> 5 And made them fight, like mad or drunk,
> For Dame Religion as for punk,°   prostitute
> Whose honesty they all durst swear for,
> Though not a man of them knew wherefore;
> When gospel-trumpeter, surrounded
> 10 With long-eared rout,[2] to battle sounded,

1. The civil wars between Royalists and Parliamentarians (1642–49).
2. A mob of Puritans or Roundheads, so called because they wore their hair short instead of in flowing curls and thus exposed their ears, which to many satirists suggested the long ears of the ass. "Gospel-trumpeter": a Presbyterian minister vehemently preaching rebellion.

And pulpit, drum ecclesiastic,[3]
Was beat with fist instead of a stick;
Then did Sir Knight abandon dwelling,
And out he rode a-coloneling.[4]
15   A wight° he was whose very sight would   *creature*
Entitle him Mirror of Knighthood;
That never bent his stubborn knee
To anything but chivalry,
Nor put up blow but that which laid
20   Right worshipful on shoulder blade;[5]
Chief of domestic knights and errant,
Either for chartel or for warrant;
Great on the bench, great in the saddle,[6]
That could as well bind o'er as swaddle.[7]
25   Mighty he was at both of these,
And styled of war as well as peace.
(So some rats of amphibious nature
Are either for the land or water.)
But here our authors make a doubt
30   Whether he were more wise or stout.
Some hold the one and some the other;
But howsoe'er they make a pother,
The difference was so small his brain
Outweighed his rage but half a grain;
35   Which made some take him for a tool
That knaves do work with, called a fool,
And offer to lay wagers that,
As Montaigne, playing with his cat,
Complains she thought him but an ass,[8]
40   Much more she would Sir Hudibras
(For that's the name our valiant knight
To all his challenges did write).
But they're mistaken very much,
'Tis plain enough he was no such.
45   We grant, although he had much wit,
He was very shy of using it;
As being loath to wear it out,
And therefore bore it not about,
Unless on holidays, or so,
50   As men their best apparel do.
Beside, 'tis known he could speak Greek
As naturally as pigs squeak;

3. The Presbyterian clergy were said to have preached the country into the civil wars. Hence, in pounding their pulpits with their fists, they are said to beat their ecclesiastical drums.
4. Here pronounced *có-lo-nel-ing*.
5. When a man is knighted he kneels and is tapped on the shoulder by his overlord's sword.
6. "Chartel": a written challenge to combat, such as a knight-errant sends. But Hudibras, as justice of the peace ("domestic knight"), could also issue a "warrant" (a writ authorizing an arrest, a seizure, or a search). Hence he is satirically called

"great on the [justice's] bench" as well as in the saddle. "Errant" was spelled and pronounced *arrant*.
7. Both justice of the peace and soldier, he is equally able to "bind over" a malefactor to be tried at the next sessions or, in his role of colonel, to beat ("swaddle") him.
8. In his "Apology for Raymond Sebond," Michel de Montaigne (1533–1592), French skeptic and essayist, wondered whether he played with his cat or his cat played with him.

That Latin was no more difficile
Than to a blackbird 'tis to whistle.
55 Being rich in both, he never scanted
His bounty unto such as wanted,
But much of either would afford
To many that had not one word.
For Hebrew roots, although they're found
60 To flourish most in barren ground,[9]
He had such plenty as sufficed
To make some think him circumcised;
And truly so perhaps he was,
'Tis many a pious Christian's case.
65   He was in logic a great critic,
Profoundly skilled in analytic.
He could distinguish and divide
A hair 'twixt south and southwest side;
On either which he would dispute,
70 Confute, change hands, and still confute.
He'd undertake to prove, by force
Of argument, a man's no horse;
He'd prove a buzzard is no fowl,
And that a lord may be an owl,
75 A calf an alderman, a goose a justice,
And rooks committee-men and trustees.[1]
He'd run in debt by disputation,
And pay with ratiocination.
All this by syllogism true,
80 In mood and figure,[2] he would do.
    For rhetoric, he could not ope
His mouth but out there flew a trope°   figure of speech
And when he happened to break off
In the middle of his speech, or cough,[3]
85 He had hard words ready to show why,
And tell what rules he did it by.
Else, when with greatest art he spoke,
You'd think he talked like other folk;
For all a rhetorician's rules
90 Teach nothing but to name his tools.
His ordinary rate of speech
In loftiness of sound was rich,
A Babylonish dialect,[4]
Which learned pedants much affect.
95 It was a parti-colored dress
Of patched and piebald languages;
'Twas English cut on Greek and Latin,

9. Hebrew, the language of Adam, was thought of as the primitive language, the one that people in a state of nature would naturally speak.
1. Committees were set up in the counties by Parliament and given authority to imprison Royalists and to sequestrate their estates. "Rooks": a kind of blackbird; here, cheats (slang).
2. The "figure" of a syllogism is "the proper dispo-

sition of the middle term with the parts of the question." "Mood": the form of an argument.
3. Some pulpit orators regarded hemming and coughing as ornaments of speech.
4. Pedants affected the use of foreign words. "Babylonish" alludes to the confusion of languages with which God afflicts the builders of the Tower of Babel (Genesis 11.4–9).

Like fustian heretofore on satin.[5]
It had an odd promiscuous tone,
100 As if he had talked three parts in one;
Which made some think, when he did gabble,
They had heard three laborers of Babel,
Or Cerberus himself pronounce
A leash of languages at once.[6]
105 This he as volubly would vent
As if his stock would ne'er be spent;
And truly, to support that charge,
He had supplies as vast and large.
For he could coin or counterfeit
110 New words with little or no wit;[7]
Words so debased and hard no stone
Was hard enough to touch them on.[8]
And when with hasty noise he spoke 'em,
The ignorant for current took 'em;
115 That had the orator, who once
Did fill his mouth with pebble-stones
When he harangued,[9] but known his phrase,
He would have used no other ways.
    In mathematics he was greater
120 Than Tycho Brahe, or Erra Pater:[1]
For he, by geometric scale,
Could take the size of pots of ale;
Resolve by sines and tangents straight,
If bread or butter wanted weight;
125 And wisely tell what hour o' the day
The clock does strike, by algebra.
    Beside, he was a shrewd philosopher,
And had read every text and gloss over;
Whate'er the crabbed'st author hath,
130 He understood by implicit faith;
Whatever skeptic could inquire for,
For every *why* he had a *wherefore*;
Knew more than forty of them do,
As far as words and terms could go.
135 All which he understood by rote
And, as occasion served, would quote,
No matter whether right or wrong;
They might be either said or sung.
His notions fitted things so well
140 That which was which he could not tell,
But oftentimes mistook the one

---

5. Clothes made of coarse cloth ("fustian") were slashed to display the richer satin lining. "Fustian" also means pompous, banal speech.
6. The sporting term "leash" denotes a group of three dogs, hawks, deer, etc., hence, three in general. Cerberus was the three-headed dog that guarded the entrance to Hades.
7. The Presbyterians and other sects invented a special religious vocabulary, much ridiculed by Anglicans: *out-goings, workings-out, gospel-walking-times,* etc.
8. Touchstones were used to test gold and silver for purity.
9. Demosthenes cured a stutter by speaking with pebbles in his mouth.
1. Butler's contemptuous name for the popular astrologer William Lilly (1602–1681). Brahe (1546–1601), a Danish astronomer.

For the other, as great clerks° have done.[2] scholars
He could reduce all things to acts,
And knew their natures by abstracts;
145 Where entity and quiddity,
The ghosts of defunct bodies,[3] fly;
Where truth in person does appear,
Like words congealed in northern air.[4]
He knew what's what, and that's as high
150 As metaphysic wit can fly.
      In school-divinity° as able scholastic theology
As he that hight Irrefragable;
Profound in all the nominal
And real ways beyond them all;[5]
155 And with as delicate a hand
Could twist as tough a rope of sand;
And weave fine cobwebs, fit for skull
That's empty when the moon is full;[6]
Such as take lodgings in a head
160 That's to be let unfurnishèd
He could raise scruples dark and nice,[7]
And after solve 'em in a trice;
As if divinity had catched
The itch on purpose to be scratched,
165 Or, like a mountebank,[8] did wound
And stab herself with doubts profound,
Only to show with how small pain
The sores of faith are cured again;
Although by woeful proof we find
170 They always leave a scar behind.
He knew the seat of paradise,[9]
Could tell in what degree it lies;
And, as he was disposed, could prove it
Below the moon, or else above it;
175 What Adam dreamt of when his bride
Came from her closet in his side;
Whether the devil tempted her
By a High Dutch interpreter;
If either of them had a navel;
180 Who first made music malleable;[1]

2. Elsewhere Butler wrote, "Notions are but pictures of things in the imagination of man, and if they agree with their originals in nature, they are true, and if not, false."
3. In the hairsplitting logic of medieval Scholastic philosophy, a distinction was drawn between the "entity," or *being,* and the "quiddity," or *essence,* of bodies. Butler calls entity and quiddity "ghosts" because they were held to be independent realities and so to survive the bodies in which they lodge.
4. The notion, as old as the Greek wit Lucian, that in arctic regions words freeze as they are uttered and become audible only when they thaw.
5. These lines refer to the debate, continuous throughout the Middle Ages, about whether the objects of our concepts exist in nature or are mere intellectual abstractions. The "nominalists" denied their objective reality, the "realists" affirmed it. Alexander of Hales (d. 1245) was called "Irrefragable," i.e., unanswerable, because his system seemed incontrovertible.
6. The frenzies of the insane were supposed to wax and wane with the moon (hence "lunatic").
7. Obscure ("dark") and subtle ("nice") intellectual perplexities ("scruples").
8. A seller of quack medicines.
9. The problem of the precise location of the Garden of Eden and the similar problems listed in the ensuing dozen lines had all been the subject of controversy among theologians.
1. Capable of being fashioned into form. Pythagoras is said to have organized sounds into the musical scale.

Whether the serpent at the fall
Had cloven feet or none at all:
All this without a gloss or comment
He could unriddle in a moment,
185 In proper terms, such as men smatter
When they throw out and miss the matter.
    For his religion, it was fit
To match his learning and his wit:
'Twas Presbyterian true blue,[2]
190 For he was of that stubborn crew
Of errant saints[3] whom all men grant
To be the true church militant,
Such as do build their faith upon
The holy text of pike and gun;
195 Decide all controversies by
Infallible artillery,
And prove their doctrine orthodox
By apostolic blows and knocks;
Call fire, and sword, and desolation
200 A godly, thorough reformation,
Which always must be carried on
And still be doing, never done;
As if religion were intended
For nothing else but to be mended.
205 A sect whose chief devotion lies
In odd, perverse antipathies;[4]
In falling out with that or this,
And finding somewhat still amiss;
More peevish, cross, and splènetic
210 Than dog distract or monkey sick;
That with more care keep holiday
The wrong, than others the right way;
Compound for° sins they are inclined to   excuse
By damning those they have no mind to;
215 Still so perverse and opposite
As if they worshiped God for spite.
The selfsame thing they will abhor
One way and long another for.
Free-will they one way disavow,[5]
220 Another, nothing else allow:
All piety consists therein
In them, in other men all sin.
Rather than fail, they will defy
That which they love most tenderly;

---

2. Supporters of Scotland's (Presbyterian) National Covenant adopted blue as their color, in contrast to the Royalist red. Blue is the color of constancy; hence, "true blue," staunch, unwavering.

3. A pun: *arrant*, meaning "unmitigated," and *errant*, meaning "wandering," were both pronounced *arrant*. The Puritans frequently called themselves "saints."

4. The hostility of the sects to everything Anglican or Roman Catholic laid them open to the charge of opposing innocent practices out of mere perverse antipathy. Some extreme Presbyterians fasted at Christmas, instead of following the old custom of feasting and rejoicing (cf. lines 211–12).

5. By the doctrine of predestination.

225 Quarrel with minced pies and disparage
Their best and dearest friend, plum-porridge;
Fat pig and goose itself oppose,
And blaspheme custard through the nose.[6]

1663

6. A reference to the nasal whine of the pious sectarians.

JOHN WILMOT, SECOND EARL OF ROCHESTER
1647–1680

John Wilmot, second earl of Rochester, was the precocious son of one of Charles II's most loyal followers in exile. He won the king's favor at the Restoration and, in 1664, after education at Oxford and on the Continent, took a place at court, at the age of seventeen. There he soon distinguished himself as "the man who has the most wit and the least honor in England." For one escapade, the abduction of Elizabeth Malet, an heiress, he was imprisoned in the Tower of London. But he regained his position by courageous service in the naval war against the Dutch, and in 1667 he married Malet. The rest of his career was no less stormy. His satiric wit, directed not only at ordinary mortals but at Dryden and Charles II himself, embroiled him in constant quarrels and exiles; his practical jokes, his affairs, and his dissipation were legendary. He circulated his works, always intellectually daring and often obscene, to a limited court readership in manuscripts executed by professional scribes—a common way of handling writing deemed too ideologically or morally scandalous for print. An early printed collection of his poems did appear in 1680, though the title page read "Antwerp," probably to hide its London origin. The air of scandal and disguise surrounding his writing only intensified his notoriety as the exemplar of the dissolute, libertine ways of court culture. He told his biographer, Gilbert Burnet, that "for five years together he was continually drunk." Just before his death, however, he was converted to Christian repentance, and for posterity, Rochester became a favorite moral topic: the libertine who had seen the error, of his ways.

Wit, in the Restoration, meant not only a clever turn of phrase but mental capacity and intellectual power. Rochester was famous for both kinds of wit. His fierce intelligence, impatient of sham and convention, helped design a way of life based on style, cleverness, and self-interest—a way of life observable in Restoration plays (Dorimant, in Etherege's *The Man of Mode,* strongly resembles Rochester). Stylistically, Rochester infuses forms such as the heroic couplet with a volatility that contrasts with the pointed and balanced manner of its other masters. From the very first line of "A Satire against Reason and Mankind"—"Were I (who to my cost already am"—he plunges the reader into a couplet mode energized by speculation, self-interruption, and enjambment; and he frequently employs extravagant effects (such as the alliterations "love's lesser lightning" and "balmy brinks of bliss" in "The Imperfect Enjoyment") to flaunt his delight in dramatizing situations, sensations, and himself. "The Disabled Debauchee," composed in "heroic stanzas" like those of Dryden's *Annus Mirabilis,* subverts the very notion of heroism by turning conventions upside down. Philosophically, Rochester is daring and destabilizing. In "A Satire," he rejects high-flown, theoretical reason and consigns its "misguided follower" to an abyss of doubt. The poem's speaker himself happily embraces the "right reason" of instinct, celebrating the life of a "natural man." The poem thus accords with Hobbes's doctrine that all laws, even our notions of good and evil, are artificial social checks on natural human desires. Yet it remains unclear, in Rochester's world of intellectual risk and conflict, whether he thinks humanity's paradoxical predicament can ever finally be escaped. Often called a skeptic himself, he seems to hint that the doubt raised by reason's collapse may surge to engulf him too.

The Disabled Debauchee

As some brave admiral, in former war
    Deprived of force, but pressed with courage still,
Two rival fleets appearing from afar,
    Crawls to the top of an adjacent hill;

5 From whence, with thoughts full of concern, he views
    The wise and daring conduct of the fight,
And each bold action to his mind renews
    His present glory and his past delight;

From his fierce eyes flashes of fire he throws,
10   As from black clouds when lightning breaks away;
Transported, thinks himself amidst his foes,
    And absent, yet enjoys the bloody day;

So, when my days of impotence approach,
    And I'm by pox° and wine's unlucky chance   *syphilis*
15 Forced from the pleasing billows of debauch
    On the dull shore of lazy temperance,

My pains at least some respite shall afford
    While I behold the battles you maintain
When fleets of glasses sail about the board,°   *table*
20   From whose broadsides[1] volleys of wit shall rain.

Nor shall the sight of honorable scars,
    Which my too forward valor did procure,
Frighten new-listed° soldiers from the wars: *newly enlisted*
    Past joys have more than paid what I endure.

25 Should any youth (worth being drunk) prove nice,°   *coy, fastidious*
    And from his fair inviter meanly shrink,
'Twill please the ghost of my departed vice
    If, at my counsel, he repent and drink.

---

1. The sides of the table; artillery on a ship; sheets on which satirical verses were printed.

Or should some cold-complexioned sot forbid,
30 With his dull morals, our bold night-alarms,
I'll fire his blood by telling what I did
When I was strong and able to bear arms.

I'll tell of whores attacked, their lords at home;
Bawds' quarters beaten up, and fortress won;
35 Windows demolished, watches° overcome;   watchmen
And handsome ills by my contrivance done.

Nor shall our love-fits, Chloris, be forgot,
When each the well-looked linkboy² strove t' enjoy,
And the best kiss was the deciding lot
40 Whether the boy used³ you, or I the boy.

With tales like these I will such thoughts inspire
As to important mischief shall incline:
I'll make him long some ancient church to fire,
And fear no lewdness he's called to by wine.

45 Thus, statesmanlike, I'll saucily impose,
And safe from action, valiantly advise;
Sheltered in impotence, urge you to blows,
And being good for nothing else, be wise.

1680

The Imperfect Enjoyment¹

Naked she lay, clasped in my longing arms,
I filled with love, and she all over charms;
Both equally inspired with eager fire,
Melting through kindness, flaming in desire.
5 With arms, legs, lips close clinging to embrace,
She clips° me to her breast, and sucks me to her face.   hugs
Her nimble tongue, Love's lesser lightning, played
Within my mouth, and to my thoughts conveyed
Swift orders that I should prepare to throw
10 The all-dissolving thunderbolt below.
My fluttering soul, sprung² with the pointed kiss,
Hangs hovering o'er her balmy brinks of bliss.
But whilst her busy hand would guide that part
Which should convey my soul up to her heart,
15 In liquid raptures I dissolve all o'er,
Melt into sperm, and spend at every pore.

2. Good-looking boy employed to light the way
with a link or torch.
3. The meaning of "used," which appears in the
first printed version and many manuscript versions, includes but extends beyond that of
"fucked," another prevalent alternative and one
preferred by most modern editors.

1. The genre of poems about the downfall of male
"pride"—not only a swelled head but an
erection—derives from Ovid's *Amores* 3.7. For a
woman's treatment of this situation, see Aphra
Behn's "The Disappointment" (p. 2310).
2. Startled from cover, like a game bird.

A touch from any part of her had done 't:
Her hand, her foot, her very look's a cunt.
   Smiling, she chides in a kind murmuring noise,
20 And from her body wipes the clammy joys,
When, with a thousand kisses wandering o'er
My panting bosom, "Is there then no more?"
She cries. "All this to love and rapture's due;
Must we not pay a debt to pleasure too?"
25   But I, the most forlorn, lost man alive,
To show my wished obedience vainly strive:
I sigh, alas! and kiss, but cannot swive.°   *screw*
Eager desires confound my first intent, ⎤
Succeeding shame does more success prevent, ⎬
30 And rage at last confirms me impotent. ⎦
Ev'n her fair hand, which might bid heat return
To frozen age, and make cold hermits burn,
Applied to my dead cinder, warms no more
Than fire to ashes could past flames restore.
35 Trembling, confused, despairing, limber, dry,
A wishing, weak, unmoving lump I lie.
This dart of love, whose piercing point, oft tried,
With virgin blood ten thousand maids have dyed;
Which nature still directed with such art
40 That it through every cunt reached every heart—
Stiffly resolved, 'twould carelessly invade ⎤
Woman or man, nor aught° its fury stayed: ⎬   *anything*
Where'er it pierced, a cunt it found or made— ⎦
Now languid lies in this unhappy hour,
45 Shrunk up and sapless like a withered flower.
   Thou treacherous, base deserter of my flame,
False to my passion, fatal to my fame,
Through what mistaken magic dost thou prove
So true to lewdness, so untrue to love?
50 What oyster-cinder-beggar-common whore
Didst thou e'er fail in all thy life before?
When vice, disease, and scandal lead the way,
With what officious haste dost thou obey!
Like a rude, roaring hector° in the streets   *bully*
55 Who scuffles, cuffs, and justles all he meets,
But if his King or country claim his aid,
The rakehell villain shrinks and hides his head;
Ev'n so thy brutal valor is displayed,
Breaks every stew,[3] does each small whore invade,
60 But when great Love the onset does command,
Base recreant to thy prince, thou dar'st not stand.
Worst part of me, and henceforth hated most,
Through all the town a common fucking post,
On whom each whore relieves her tingling cunt
65 As hogs on gates do rub themselves and grunt,
Mayst thou to ravenous chancres be a prey,

3. Breaks into every brothel.

Or in consuming weepings waste away;
May strangury and stone[4] thy days attend;
May'st thou ne'er piss, who didst refuse to spend
70   When all my joys did on false thee depend.
    And may ten thousand abler pricks agree
    To do the wronged Corinna right for thee.

                                            1680

Upon Nothing

Nothing, thou elder brother even to shade,
Thou hadst a being ere the world was made
And (well fixed) art alone of ending not afraid.

Ere time and place were, time and place were not,
5   When primitive Nothing Something straight begot,
Then all proceeded from the great united *What*.

Something, the general attribute of all,
Severed from thee, its sole original,
Into thy boundless self must undistinguished fall.

10   Yet Something did thy mighty power command
And from thy fruitful emptiness's hand
Snatched men, beasts, birds, fire, water, air, and land.

Matter, the wick'dst offspring of thy race,
By form assisted, flew from thy embrace,
15   And rebel light obscured thy reverend dusky face.

With form and matter, time and place did join,
Body thy foe, with these did leagues combine[1]
To spoil thy peaceful realm and ruin all thy line.

But turncoat time assists the foe in vain
20   And bribed by thee destroys their short-lived reign
And to thy hungry womb drives back thy slaves again.

Though mysteries are barred from laic eyes[2]
And the divine alone with warrant pries
Into thy bosom where thy truth in private lies,

25   Yet this of thee the wise may truly say:
Thou from the virtuous, nothing tak'st away,[3]
And to be part of thee, the wicked wisely pray.

---

4. "Strangury" and "stone" cause slow and painful urination. "Chancres" and "weepings" are signs of venereal disease.
1. Form, matter, time, and place combined in alliances against Nothing.

2. I.e., the eyes of the laity, who are uninitiated in Nothing's mysteries.
3. You, Nothing, do not take anything away from the virtuous.

Great negative, how vainly would the wise
Enquire, define, distinguish, teach, devise,
30 Didst thou not stand to point° their blind philosophies. *expose*

Is or Is Not, the two great ends of fate,
And true or false, the subject of debate
That perfect or destroy the vast designs of state,

When they have racked the politician's breast,
35 Within thy bosom most securely rest
And when reduced to thee are least unsafe and best.

But Nothing, why does Something still permit
That sacred monarchs should at council sit
With persons highly thought, at best, for nothing fit;

40 Whilst weighty Something modestly abstains
From princes' coffers[4] and from statesmen's brains
And Nothing there like stately Something reigns?

Nothing, who dwellst with fools in grave disguise,
For whom they reverend shapes and forms devise,
45 Lawn-sleeves and furs and gowns,[5] when they like thee look wise;

French truth, Dutch prowess, British policy,
Hibernian° learning, Scotch civility, *Irish*
Spaniards' dispatch, Danes' wit[6] are mainly seen in thee;

The great man's gratitude to his best friend,
50 Kings' promises, whores' vows, towards thee they bend,
Flow swiftly into thee and in thee ever end.

1679

A Satire against Reason and Mankind

"He had a strange vivacity of thought, and vigor of expression," said Bishop Gilbert Burnet of his friend and contemporary, Rochester: "his wit had a subtility and sublimity both, that were scarce imitable." Rochester displays these characteristics nowhere more vividly than in his most famous poem, "A Satire against Reason and Mankind." Many of the thoughts in the poem were familiar by Rochester's time. The idea that animals are better equipped to lead successful lives than human beings, for instance, had been a commonplace among moralists for centuries: Michel de Montaigne (1533–1592) makes much of it in his best-known, most comprehensively skeptical essay, "An Apology for Raymond Sebond." Other elements of the skeptical tradition, particularly a comic appreciation of the weakness of reason, receive ample play in the "Satire." The poem in general loosely follows *Satire VIII* by the highly influential French neoclassical poet and critic, Nicolas Boileau (1636–1711). But everywhere Rochester's energetic intellectual distinctiveness bursts through. Perhaps most unnervingly, he both

4. Charles II's coffers were notably empty, and he was forced to declare bankruptcy in 1672.
5. "Furs and gowns" were worn by judges. "Lawn": a fine linen or cotton fabric, worn by bishops.
6. All proverbial deficiencies of the various nationalities mentioned, many of them exposed during the Anglo-Dutch war (1672–74).

claims to restrict his thinking to immediate, instinctual reason and gestures toward the "limits of the boundless universe" and "mysterious truths, which no man can conceive." Framed as it is by paradoxes and mysteries, his commonsensical instinct has seemed less stable to many readers than Rochester himself would have us believe. Still, these and other extravagant conflicts surely suit Rochester's fundamental aim: to throw as dramatic a light as he can on himself and his thinking.

A Satire against Reason and Mankind

Were I (who to my cost already am
One of those strange prodigious creatures, man)
A spirit free to choose, for my own share,
What case of flesh and blood I pleased to wear, }
5 I'd be a dog, a monkey, or a bear;
Or anything but that vain animal
Who is so proud of being rational.
The senses are too gross, and he'll contrive
A sixth[1] to contradict the other five:
10 And before certain instinct will prefer
Reason, which fifty times for one does err.
Reason, an ignis fatuus[2] of the mind,
Which leaving light of nature, sense, behind,
Pathless and dangerous wandering ways it takes,
15 Through Error's fenny bogs and thorny brakes:°   *thickets*
Whilst the misguided follower climbs with pain
Mountains of whimsies heaped in his own brain;
Stumbling from thought to thought, falls headlong down
Into doubt's boundless sea, where like° to drown,   *likely*
20 Books bear him up awhile, and make him try
To swim with bladders[3] of philosophy;
In hopes still to o'ertake th'escaping light, ⎤
The vapor dances in his dazzled sight, }
Till spent, it leaves him to eternal night. ⎦
25 Then old age and experience, hand in hand,
Lead him to death, and make him understand,
After a search so painful and so long,
That all his life he has been in the wrong.
Huddled in dirt the reasoning engine° lies,   *brain*
30 Who was so proud, so witty and so wise.
Pride drew him in (as cheats their bubbles° catch)   *dupes*
And made him venture to be made a wretch.
His wisdom did his happiness destroy,
Aiming to know that world he should enjoy;
35 And wit was his vain frivolous pretence
Of pleasing others at his own expense:
For wits are treated just like common whores,
First they're enjoyed and then kicked out of doors.

1. Here, reason.
2. Foolish fire (Latin). Sometimes called the will-o'-the-wisp, a light appearing in marshy lands that

proverbially misleads travelers.
3. Inflated animal bladders used for buoyancy in the water.

Jacob Huysmans, *Lord Rochester with a Monkey and a Book*, 1665–70. Rochester bestowing a laurel wreath, symbol of poetic excellence, on a monkey, who holds a page torn from a book.

The pleasure past, a threatening doubt remains,
40   That frights th'enjoyer with succeeding pains:[4]
Women and men of wit are dangerous tools,
And ever fatal to admiring fools.
Pleasure allures, and when the fops escape,
'Tis not that they're beloved, but fortunate;
45   And therefore what they fear, at heart they hate.[5]
     But now methinks some formal band and beard[6]
Takes me to task. Come on, Sir, I'm prepared:
"Then by your favor any thing that's writ
Against this gibing,° jingling knack called wit,   *jeering*
50   Likes° me abundantly, but you take care   *pleases*
Upon this point not to be too severe.
Perhaps my Muse were fitter for this part,
For I profess I can be very smart
On wit, which I abhor with all my heart.

4. The doubt that wits leave behind resembles venereal disease left by "common whores."
5. Though allured by wits, fops also fear and hate them.
6. Clergyman, wearing a clerical collar.

55   I long to lash it in some sharp essay,   ⎫
      But your grand indiscretion bids me stay, ⎬
      And turns my tide of ink another way.   ⎭
      What rage ferments in your degenerate mind,
      To make you rail at reason and mankind?

60   Blest glorious man! to whom alone kind heaven
      An everlasting soul has freely given;
      Whom his creator took such care to make,
      That from himself he did the image take,
      And this fair frame° in shining reason dressed,   *physical body*

65   To dignify his nature above beast.
      Reason, by whose aspiring influence
      We take a flight beyond material sense;
      Dive into mysteries, then soaring pierce
      The flaming limits of the universe;

70   Search heaven and hell, find out what's acted there,
      And give the world true grounds of hope and fear."[7]
          Hold, mighty man, I cry, all this we know,
      From the pathetic pen of Ingelo,
      From Patrick's *Pilgrim,* Sibbs'[8] soliloquies;

75   And 'tis this very reason I despise;
      This supernatural gift, that makes a mite
      Think he's the image of the infinite,
      Comparing his short life, void of all rest,
      To the eternal and the ever blest;

80   This busy puzzling stirrer-up of doubt,
      That frames deep mysteries, then finds them out;
      Filling with frantic crowds of thinking fools
      Those reverend Bedlams,° colleges and schools;   *madhouses*
      Borne on whose wings each heavy sot can pierce

85   The limits of the boundless universe;
      So charming ointments make an old witch fly,
      And bear a crippled carcass through the sky.
      'Tis this exalted power whose business lies
      In nonsense and impossibilities.

90   This made a whimsical philosopher
      Before the spacious world his tub prefer.[9]
      And we have modern cloistered coxcombs, who
      Retire to think, 'cause they have naught to do:
      But thoughts are given for action's government,

95   Where action ceases, thought's impertinent.
      Our sphere of action is life's happiness,
      And he who thinks beyond, thinks like an ass.
      Thus, whilst against false reasoning I inveigh,
      I own° right reason, which I would obey: *avow*

100   That reason which distinguishes by sense,

---

7. Teach the world about salvation and damnation.

8. Richard Sibbes, Puritan preacher who published volumes of sermons, though none called "soliloquies." Nathaniel Ingelo (d. 1683), author of the long religious allegory *Bentivolio and Ura-*

nia (1660). Simon Patrick (1626–1707), author of the devotional work *The Parable of the Pilgrim* (1665).

9. Diogenes the Cynic (5th century B.C.E.), who lived in a tub to exemplify the virtues of asceticism.

And gives us rules of good and ill from thence;
That bounds desires with a reforming will,
To keep them more in vigor, not to kill.
Your reason hinders, mine helps to enjoy,
105 Renewing appetites yours would destroy.
My reason is my friend, yours is a cheat,
Hunger calls out, my reason bids me eat;
Perversely, yours your appetites does mock:
They ask for food, that answers, "what's a clock?"
110 This plain distinction, Sir, your doubt secures,°   *resolves*
'Tis not true reason I despise, but yours.
    Thus I think reason righted, but for man,
I'll ne'er recant, defend him if you can.
For all his pride and his philosophy, ⎫
115 'Tis evident beasts are, in their degree, ⎬
As wise at least, and better far than he. ⎭
Those creatures are the wisest who attain
By surest means, the ends at which they aim.
If therefore Jowler[1] finds and kills his hares
120 Better than Meres[2] supplies committee chairs,
Though one's a statesman, th'other but a hound,
Jowler in justice would be wiser found.
You see how far man's wisdom here extends;
Look next if human nature makes amends;
125 Whose principles most generous are and just,
And to whose morals you would sooner trust.
Be judge yourself, I'll bring it to the test,
Which is the basest creature, man or beast.
Birds feed on birds, beasts on each other prey,
130 But savage man alone does man betray;
Pressed by necessity they kill for food,
Man undoes man to do himself no good.
With teeth and claws by nature armed, they hunt
Nature's allowance to supply their want.
135 But man with smiles, embraces, friendship, praise,
Inhumanly his fellow's life betrays;
With voluntary° pains works his distress,   *deliberate*
Not through necessity, but wantonness.
For hunger or for love they fight and tear,
140 Whilst wretched man is still° in arms for fear;   *always*
For fear he arms, and is of arms afraid,
By fear to fear successively betrayed.
Base fear! The source whence his best passion came,
His boasted honor, and his dear bought fame;
145 That lust of power to which he's such a slave,
And for the which alone he dares be brave,
To which his various projects are designed,
Which makes him generous, affable, and kind;
For which he takes such pains to be thought wise

1. A common name for hunting dogs.
2. Sir Thomas Meres (1635–1715), a busy parliamentarian of the day.

150 And screws his actions in a forced disguise;
     Leading a tedious life in misery
     Under laborious mean hypocrisy.
     Look to the bottom of his vast design,
     Wherein man's wisdom, power, and glory join;
155 The good he acts, the ill he does endure,
     'Tis all from fear to make himself secure.
     Merely for safety after fame we thirst,
     For all men would be cowards if they durst.
     And honesty's against all common sense;
160 Men must be knaves, 'tis in their own defense.
     Mankind's dishonest, if you think it fair
     Amongst known cheats to play upon the square,°   *honestly*
     You'll be undone—
     Nor can weak truth your reputation save;
165 The knaves will all agree to call you knave.
     Wronged shall he live, insulted o'er, oppressed,
     Who dares be less a villain than the rest.
          Thus Sir, you see what human nature craves:
     Most men are cowards, all men should be knaves.
170 The difference lies, as far as I can see,
     Not in the thing itself, but the degree,
     And all the subject matter of debate
     Is only who's a knave of the first rate.

          Addition[3]

     All this with indignation have I hurled
175 At the pretending° part of the proud world,   *affected*
     Who swollen with selfish vanity, devise
     False freedoms, holy cheats, and formal lies, ⎫
     Over their fellow slaves to tyrannize.   ⎭
          But if in court so just a man there be
180 (In court a just man yet unknown to me),
     Who does his needful flattery direct,
     Not to oppress and ruin, but protect
     (Since flattery, which way so ever laid,
     Is still a tax on that unhappy trade);[4]
185 If so upright a statesman you can find,
     Whose passions bend to his unbiased mind;
     Who does his arts and policies apply
     To raise his country, not his family,
     Nor while his pride owned avarice withstands,
190 Receives close bribes from friends' corrupted hands[5]—
          Is there a churchman who on God relies,
     Whose life his faith and doctrine justifies?
     Not one blown up with vain prelatic[6] pride,
     Who for reproof of sins does man deride;

3. The second part was also circulated as a separate poem.
4. Even good men must pay the tax of flattery if they "trade" at the royal court at Whitehall.
5. Nor while he proudly rejects open greed, still arranges that his friends collect secret bribes for him.
6. Of prelates, high church officials.

195 Whose envious heart makes preaching a pretense,
With his obstreperous saucy eloquence,
To chide at kings, and rail at men of sense;
Who from his pulpit vents more peevish lies,
More bitter railings, scandals, calumnies,
200 Than at a gossiping are thrown about
When the good wives get drunk and then fall out;
None of that sensual tribe, whose talents lie
In avarice, pride, sloth and gluttony,
Who hunt good livings,[7] but abhor good lives,
205 Whose lust exalted to that height arrives,
They act adultery with their own wives;[8]
And ere a score of years completed be,
Can from the lofty pulpit proudly see
Half a large parish their own progeny.
210 Nor doating° bishop who would be adored   senile
For domineering at the council board,[9]
A greater fop in business at fourscore,
Fonder of serious toys,° affected more   trifles
Than the gay glittering fool at twenty proves,
215 With all his noise, his tawdry clothes and loves;
    But a meek humble man of honest sense,
Who, preaching peace, does practice continence;
Whose pious life's a proof he does believe
Mysterious truths, which no man can conceive;
220 If upon earth there dwell such God-like men,
I'll here recant my paradox[1] to them;
Adore those shrines of virtue, homage pay,
And with the rabble world, their laws obey.
    If such there be, yet grant me this at least,
225 Man differs more from man, than man from beast.

1679

7. Ecclesiastical appointments.
8. Married women of their parishes. Rochester also suggests that these clergymen act out their adulterous lusts with their own spouses.
9. In the Privy Council, a meeting of advisers to the monarch.
1. That beasts are superior to humans.

APHRA BEHN
1640?–1689

A woman wit has often graced the stage," Dryden wrote in 1681. Soon after actresses first appeared in English public theaters, there was an even more striking debut by a woman writer who boldly signed her plays and talked back to her critics. In a dozen years, Aphra Behn turned out at least that many plays, discovering fresh dramatic possibilities in casts that included women with warm bodies and clever heads. She also drew attention as a warm and witty poet of love. When writing for the stage became less profitable, she turned to the emerging field of prose fiction, composing a pioneering epistolary novel, *Love Letters between a Nobleman and His Sister,* and diverse short tales—not to mention a raft of translations from the French, pindarics to her beloved Stuart rulers, compilations, prologues, complimentary verses, all the piecework and puffery that were the stock in trade of the Restoration town wit. She worked in haste and with flair for nearly two decades and more than held her own as a professional writer. In the end, no author of her time—except Dryden himself—proved more versatile, more alive to new currents of thought, or more inventive in recasting fashionable forms.

Much of Behn's life remains a mystery. Although her books have been accompanied—and often all but buried—by volumes of rumor, hard facts are elusive. She was almost certainly from East Kent; she may well have been named Johnson. But she herself seems to have left no record of her date and place of birth, her family name and upbringing, or the identity of the shadowy Mr. Behn whom she reportedly married. Her many references to nuns and convents, as well as praise for prominent Catholic lords (*Oroonoko* is dedicated to one), have prompted speculation that she may have been raised as a Catholic and educated in a convent abroad. Without doubt, she drew on a range of worldly experience that would be closed to women in the more genteel ages to come. The circumstantial detail of *Oroonoko* supports her claim that she was in the new sugar colony of Surinam early in 1664. Perhaps she exaggerated her social position to enhance her tale, but many particulars—from dialect words and the location of plantations to methods of selling and torturing slaves—can be authenticated. During the trade war that broke out in 1665—which left her "vast and charming world" a Dutch prize—Behn traveled to the Low Countries on a spying mission for King Charles II. The king could be lax about payment, however, and Behn had to petition desperately to escape debtor's prison. In 1670 she brought out her first plays, "forced to write for bread," she confessed, "and not ashamed to own it."

In London, Behn flourished in the cosmopolitan world of the playhouse and the court. Dryden and other wits encouraged her; she mixed with actresses and managers and playwrights and exchanged verses with a lively literary set that she called her "cabal." Surviving letters record a passionate, troubled attachment to a lawyer named John Hoyle, a bisexual with libertine views. She kept up with the most advanced thinking and joined public debates with pointed satire against the Whigs. But the festivity of the Restoration world was fading out in bitter party acrimony. In 1682 Behn was placed under arrest for "abusive reflections" on the king's illegitimate son, the Whig duke of Monmouth (Dryden's Absalom). Her Royalist opinions and the immodesty of her public role made her a target; gleeful lampoons declared that she was aging and ill and once again poor. She responded by bringing out her works at a still faster rate, composing *Oroonoko*, her dedication claims, "in a few hours . . . for I never rested my pen a moment for thought." In some last works she recorded her hope that her writings would live: "I value fame as much as if I had been born a hero." When she died she was buried in Westminster Abbey.

"All women together ought to let flowers fall upon the grave of Aphra Behn," Virginia Woolf wrote, "for it was she who earned them the right to speak their minds." Behn herself spoke her mind. She scorned hypocrisy and calculation in her society and commented freely on religion, science, and philosophy. Moreover, she spoke as a woman. Denied the classical education of most male authors, she dismissed "musty rules" and lessons and relished the immediate human appeal of popular forms. Her first play, *The Forced Marriage,* exposes the bondage of matches arranged for money and status, and many later works invoke the powerful natural force of love, whose energy breaks through conventions. In a range of genres, from simple pastoral songs to complex plots of intrigue, she candidly explores the sexual feelings of women, their schooling in disguise, their need to "love upon the honest square" (for this her work was later denounced as coarse and impure). *Oroonoko* represents another departure for Behn and prose fiction. It achieves something new both in its narrative form and in extending some of her favorite themes to an original subject: the destiny of a black male hero on a world historical stage.

Oroonoko cannot be classified as fact or fiction, realism or romance. In the still unshaped field of prose narrative—where a "history" could mean any story, true or false—Behn combined the attractions of three older forms. First, she presents the work as a memoir, a personal account of what she has heard and seen. According to a friend, Behn had told this tale over and over; perhaps that explains the conversational ease with which she turns back and forth, interpreting faraway scenes for her readers at home. Second, *Oroonoko* is a travel narrative in three parts. It turns west to a new world often extolled as a paradise, then east to Africa and the amorous intrigues of a corrupt old-world court (popular reading fare), then finally west again with its hero across the infamous "Middle Passage"—over which millions of slaves would be transported during the next century—to the conflicts of a raw colonial world. Exotic scenes fascinate Behn, but she wants even more to talk to people and learn about their ways of life. As in imaginary voyages, from Sir Thomas More's *Utopia* to *Gulliver's Travels* and *Rasselas,* encounters with foreign cultures sharply challenge Europeans to reexamine themselves. Behn's primitive Indians and noble Africans live by a code of virtue, by principles of fidelity and honor, that "civilized" Christians often ignore or betray. Oroonoko embodies this code. Above all, the book is his biography. Courageous, high-minded, and great hearted, he rivals the heroes of classical epics and Plutarch's *Lives* and is equally worthy of fame. Nor does he lack gentler virtues. Like the heroes of seventeenth-century heroic dramas and romances, he shines in the company of women and proves his nobility by his passionate and constant love for Imoinda, his ideal counterpart. Yet finally a contradiction dooms Oroonoko: he is at once prince and chattel, a "royal slave."

Behn handles her forms dynamically, drawing out their inner discords and tensions. In the biography, Oroonoko's deepest values are turned against him. His trust in friendship and scrupulous truth to his word expose him to the treachery of Europeans who calculate human worth on a yardstick of profit. A hero cannot survive in such a world. His self-respect demands action, even when he can find no clear path through the tangle of assurances and lies. Moreover, the colony too seems tangled in contradictions. Behn's travel narrative reveals a broken paradise where, in the absence of secure authority, the settlers descend into a series of unstable alliances, improvised power relations, and escalating suspicions. Here every term—friend and foe, tenderness and brutality, savagery and civilization—can suddenly turn into its opposite. And the author also seems caught between worlds. The cultivated Englishwoman who narrates and acts in this memoir thinks highly of her hero's code of honor and shares his contempt for the riffraff who plague him. Yet her own role is ambiguous: she lacks the power to save Oroonoko and might even be viewed as implicated in his downfall. Only as a writer can she take control, preserving the hero in her work.

The story of Oroonoko did not end with Behn. Compassion for the royal slave and outrage at his fate were enlisted in the long battle against the slave trade. Reprinted, translated, serialized, dramatized, and much imitated, *Oroonoko* helped teach a mass audience to feel for all victims of the brutal commerce in human beings. A hundred years later, the popular writer Hannah More testified to the widening influence of the story: "No individual griefs my bosom melt, / For millions feel what Oroonoko felt." Women especially identified with the experience of personal injustice and everyday indignity—the pain of being treated as something less than fully human. Perhaps it is appropriate that the writer who made the suffering of the royal slave famous had known the pride and lowliness of being "a female pen."

The Disappointment[1]

One day the amorous Lysander,
By an impatient passion swayed,
Surprised fair Cloris, that loved maid,
Who could defend herself no longer.
5   All things did with his love conspire;
The gilded planet of the day,°   *the sun*
In his gay chariot drawn by fire,
Was now descending to the sea,
And left no light to guide the world
10   But what from Cloris' brighter eyes was hurled.

In a lone thicket made for love,
Silent as yielding maid's consent,
She with a charming languishment,
Permits his force, yet gently strove;
15   Her hands his bosom softly meet,
But not to put him back designed,
Rather to draw 'em on inclined:
Whilst he lay trembling at her feet,
Resistance 'tis in vain to show:
20   She wants° the power to say—*Ah! what d'ye do?*   *lacks*

Her bright eyes sweet and yet severe,
Where love and shame confusedly strive,
Fresh vigor to Lysander give;
And breathing faintly in his ear,
25   She cried—*Cease, cease—your vain desire,*
Or I'll call out—what would you do?
My dearer honor even to you
I cannot, must not give—Retire,
Or take this life, whose chiefest part
30   *I gave you with the conquest of my heart.*

But he as much unused to fear,
As he was capable of love,
The blessed minutes to improve
Kisses her mouth, her neck, her hair;
35   Each touch her new desire alarms;
His burning, trembling hand he pressed
Upon her swelling snowy breast,
While she lay panting in his arms.
All her unguarded beauties lie
40   The spoils and trophies of the enemy.

---

1. This variation on the "imperfect enjoyment" genre compares with Rochester's (p. 2298); it first appeared in a collection of his poems. But Behn gives the theme of impotence her own twist. Freely translating a French poem, Cantenac's "The Lost Chance Recovered," she cuts the conclusion, in which the French lover regained his potency, and she highlights the woman's feelings as well as the man's.

And now without respect or fear
He seeks the object of his vows
(His love no modesty allows)
By swift degrees advancing—where
45   His daring hand that altar seized,
Where gods of love do sacrifice:
That awful throne, that paradise
Where rage is calmed, and anger pleased;
That fountain where delight still flows,
50   And gives the universal world repose.

Her balmy lips encountering his,
Their bodies, as their souls, are joined;
Where both in transports unconfined
Extend themselves upon the moss.
55   Cloris half dead and breathless lay;
Her soft eyes cast a humid light
Such as divides the day and night;
Or falling stars, whose fires decay:
And now no signs of life she shows,
60   But what in short-breathed sighs returns and goes.

He saw how at her length she lay;
He saw her rising bosom bare;
Her loose thin robes, through which appear
A shape designed for love and play;
65   Abandoned by her pride and shame
She does her softest joys dispense,
Offering her virgin innocence
A victim to love's sacred flame;
While the o'er-ravished shepherd lies
70   Unable to perform the sacrifice.

Ready to taste a thousand joys,
The too transported hapless swain
Found the vast pleasure turned to pain;
Pleasure which too much love destroys:
75   The willing garments by he laid,[2]
And heaven all opened to his view.
Mad to possess, himself he threw
On the defenseless lovely maid.
But oh what envying god conspires
80   To snatch his power, yet leave him the desire!

Nature's support (without whose aid
She can no human being give)
Itself now wants the art[3] to live;
Faintness its slackened nerves invade:
85   In vain th'enraged youth essayed
To call its fleeting vigor back;

2. He took off her compliant clothes.   3. Lacks the capacity.

No motion 'twill from motion take;
Excess of love his love betrayed:
In vain he toils, in vain commands:
90   The insensible[4] fell weeping in his hand.

In this so amorous cruel strife,
Where love and fate were too severe,
The poor Lysander in despair
Renounced his reason with his life:
95   Now all the brisk and active fire
That should the nobler part inflame
Served to increase his rage and shame,
And left no spark for new desire:
Not all her naked charms could move
100   Or calm that rage that had debauched his love.

Cloris returning from the trance
Which love and soft desire had bred,
Her timorous hand she gently laid
(Or guided by design or chance)
105   Upon that fabulous Priapus,[5]
That potent god, as poets feign:
But never did young shepherdess,
Gathering the fern upon the plain,
More nimbly draw her fingers back,
110   Finding beneath the verdant leaves a snake,

Than Cloris her fair hand withdrew,
Finding that god of her desires
Disarmed of all his awful fires,
And cold as flowers bathed in the morning dew.
115   Who can the nymph's confusion guess?
The blood forsook the hinder place,
And strewed with blushes all her face,
Which both disdain and shame expressed:
And from Lysander's arms she fled,
120   Leaving him fainting on the gloomy bed.

Like lightning through the grove she hies,
Or Daphne from the Delphic god;[6]
No print upon the grassy road
She leaves, to instruct pursuing eyes.
125   The wind that wantoned in her hair
And with her ruffled garments played,
Discovered in the flying maid
All that the gods e'er made, if fair.
So Venus, when her love[7] was slain,
130   With fear and haste flew o'er the fatal plain.

---

4. Devoid of feeling and too small to be noticed.
5. Phallus. The ancient god Priapus is always pictured with an outstanding erection.

6. Apollo, from whom the Greek nymph Daphne fled until she turned into a laurel tree.
7. Adonis, who was killed by a boar.

> The nymph's resentments none but I
> Can well imagine or condole:
> But none can guess Lysander's soul,
> But those who swayed his destiny.
> 135   His silent griefs swell up to storms,
> And not one god his fury spares;
> He cursed his birth, his fate, his stars;
> But more the shepherdess's charms,
> Whose soft bewitching influence
> 140   Had damned him to the hell of impotence.[8]

1680

Oroonoko; or, The Royal Slave[1]

I do not pretend, in giving you the history of this royal slave, to entertain my reader with the adventures of a feigned hero, whose life and fortunes fancy may manage at the poet's pleasure; nor in relating the truth, design to adorn it with any accidents but such as arrived in earnest to him. And it shall come simply into the world, recommended by its own proper merits and natural intrigues, there being enough of reality to support it, and to render it diverting, without the addition of invention.

I was myself an eyewitness to a great part of what you will find here set down, and what I could not be witness of, I received from the mouth of the chief actor in this history, the hero himself, who gave us the whole transactions of his youth; and though I shall omit for brevity's sake a thousand little accidents of his life, which, however pleasant to us, where history was scarce and adventures very rare, yet might prove tedious and heavy to my reader, in a world where he finds diversions for every minute, new and strange. But we who were perfectly charmed with the character of this great man were curious to gather every circumstance of his life.

The scene of the last part of his adventures lies in a colony in America called Surinam,[2] in the West Indies.

But before I give you the story of this gallant slave, 'tis fit I tell you the manner of bringing them to these new colonies, for those they make use of there are not natives of the place; for those we live with in perfect amity, without daring to command 'em, but on the contrary caress 'em with all the brotherly and friendly affection in the world, trading with 'em for their fish, venison, buffaloes, skins, and little rarities; as marmosets, a sort of monkey as big as a rat or weasel but of a marvelous and delicate shape, and has face and hands like a human creature, and *cousheries*,[3] a little beast in the form and fashion of a lion, as big as a kitten, but so exactly made in all parts like

---

8. Blaming the woman for an imperfect enjoyment is typical of the genre.

1. The text, prepared by Joanna Lipking, is based on the 1688 edition, the sole edition published during Behn's lifetime. The critical edition of G. C. Duchovnay (diss., Indiana, 1971), which collates the four 17th-century editions, has been consulted.

2. A British sugar colony on the South American coast east of Venezuela; later Dutch Guiana, now the Republic of Suriname.

3. A name appearing in local descriptions, but the animal is not clearly identified; probably the lion-headed marmoset or perhaps the *cujara* (Portuguese), a rodent known as the rice rat. "Buffaloes": wild oxen of various species.

that noble beast, that it is it in miniature. Then for little parakeetoes, great parrots, macaws, and a thousand other birds and beasts of wonderful and surprising forms, shapes, and colors. For skins of prodigious snakes, of which there are some threescore yards in length, as is the skin of one that may be seen at his Majesty's antiquaries'; where are also some rare flies[4] of amazing forms and colors, presented to 'em by myself, some as big as my fist, some less, and all of various excellencies, such as art cannot imitate. Then we trade for feathers, which they order into all shapes, make themselves little short habits of 'em, and glorious wreaths for their heads, necks, arms and legs, whose tinctures are unconceivable. I had a set of these presented to me, and I gave 'em to the King's theater, and it was the dress of the Indian Queen,[5] infinitely admired by persons of quality, and were unimitable. Besides these, a thousand little knacks and rarities in nature, and some of art, as their baskets, weapons, aprons, et cetera. We dealt with 'em with beads of all colors, knives, axes, pins and needles, which they used only as tools to drill holes with in their ears, noses, and lips, where they hang a great many little things, as long beads, bits of tin, brass, or silver beat thin, and any shining trinket. The beads they weave into aprons about a quarter of an ell long, and of the same breadth,[6] working them very prettily in flowers of several colors of beads; which apron they wear just before 'em, as Adam and Eve did the fig leaves, the men wearing a long stripe of linen which they deal with us for. They thread these beads also on long cotton threads and make girdles to tie their aprons to, which come twenty times or more about the waist, and then cross, like a shoulder belt, both ways, and round their necks, arms, and legs. This adornment, with their long black hair, and the face painted in little specks or flowers here and there, makes 'em a wonderful figure to behold.

Some of the beauties which indeed are finely shaped, as almost all are, and who have pretty features, are very charming and novel; for they have all that is called beauty, except the color, which is a reddish yellow; or after a new oiling, which they often use to themselves, they are of the color of a new brick, but smooth, soft, and sleek. They are extreme[7] modest and bashful, very shy and nice of being touched. And though they are all thus naked, if one lives forever among 'em there is not to be seen an indecent action or glance; and being continually used to see one another so unadorned, so like our first parents before the Fall, it seems as if they had no wishes; there being nothing to heighten curiosity, but all you can see you see at once, and every moment see, and where there is no novelty there can be no curiosity. Not but I have seen a handsome young Indian dying for love of a very beautiful young Indian maid; but all his courtship was to fold his arms, pursue her with his eyes, and sighs were all his language; while she, as if no such lover were present, or rather, as if she desired none such, carefully guarded her eyes from beholding him, and never approached him but she looked down with all the blushing modesty I have seen in the most severe and cautious of our world. And these people represented to me an absolute idea of the first state of innocence, before man knew how to sin. And 'tis most evident and

---

4. Butterflies. "Antiquaries": probably the natural history museum of the Royal Society.
5. The title character in the 1664 heroic play by Sir Robert Howard and John Dryden, which was noted for its lavish production. There are contemporary records of "speckled plumes" and feather headdresses.
6. About a foot square.
7. Extremely.

plain that simple Nature is the most harmless, inoffensive, and virtuous mistress. 'Tis she alone, if she were permitted, that better instructs the world than all the inventions of man. Religion would here but destroy that tranquillity they possess by ignorance, and laws would but teach 'em to know offense, of which now they have no notion. They once made mourning and fasting for the death of the English governor, who had given his hand to come on such a day to 'em and neither came nor sent, believing when once a man's word was passed, nothing but death could or should prevent his keeping it. And when they saw he was not dead, they asked him what name they had for a man who promised a thing he did not do. The governor told them, such a man was a liar, which was a word of infamy to a gentleman. Then one of 'em replied, "Governor, you are a liar, and guilty of that infamy." They have a native justice which knows no fraud, and they understand no vice or cunning, but when they are taught by the white men. They have plurality of wives, which, when they grow old, they serve those that succeed 'em, who are young, but with a servitude easy and respected; and unless they take slaves in war, they have no other attendants.

Those on that continent where I was had no king, but the oldest war captain was obeyed with great resignation. A war captain is a man who has led them on to battle with conduct[8] and success, of whom I shall have occasion to speak more hereafter, and of some other of their customs and manners, as they fall in my way.

With these people, as I said, we live in perfect tranquillity and good understanding, as it behooves us to do, they knowing all the places where to seek the best food of the country and the means of getting it, and for very small and unvaluable trifles, supply us with what 'tis impossible for us to get; for they do not only in the wood and over the savannas, in hunting, supply the parts of hounds, by swiftly scouring through those almost impassable places, and by the mere activity of their feet run down the nimblest deer and other eatable beasts; but in the water one would think they were gods of the rivers, or fellow citizens of the deep, so rare an art they have in swimming, diving, and almost living in water, by which they command the less swift inhabitants of the floods. And then for shooting, what they cannot take, or reach with their hands, they do with arrows, and have so admirable an aim that they will split almost a hair; and at any distance that an arrow can reach, they will shoot down oranges and other fruit, and only touch the stalk with the dart's point, that they may not hurt the fruit. So that they being, on all occasions, very useful to us, we find it absolutely necessary to caress 'em as friends, and not to treat 'em as slaves; nor dare we do other, their numbers so far surpassing ours in that continent.

Those then whom we make use of to work in our plantations of sugar are Negroes, black slaves altogether, which are transported thither in this manner. Those who want slaves make a bargain with a master or captain of a ship and contract to pay him so much apiece, a matter of twenty pound a head for as many as he agrees for, and to pay for 'em when they shall be delivered on such a plantation. So that when there arrives a ship laden with slaves, they who have so contracted go aboard and receive their number by lot; and perhaps in one lot that may be for ten, there may happen to be three

8. Capacity to lead.

or four men, the rest women and children. Or be there more or less of either sex, you are obliged to be contented with your lot.

Coramantien,[9] a country of blacks so called, was one of those places in which they found the most advantageous trading for these slaves, and thither most of our great traders in that merchandise trafficked; for that nation is very warlike and brave, and having a continual campaign, being always in hostility with one neighboring prince or other, they had the fortune to take a great many captives; for all they took in battle were sold as slaves, at least those common men who could not ransom themselves. Of these slaves so taken, the general only has all the profit; and of these generals, our captains and masters of ships buy all their freights.

The King of Coramantien was himself a man of a hundred and odd years old, and had no son, though he had many beautiful black wives; for most certainly there are beauties that can charm of that color. In his younger years he had had many gallant men to his sons, thirteen of which died in battle, conquering when they fell; and he had only left him for his successor one grandchild, son to one of these dead victors, who, as soon as he could bear a bow in his hand and a quiver at his back, was sent into the field, to be trained up by one of the oldest generals to war; where, from his natural inclination to arms and the occasions given him, with the good conduct of the old general, he became, at the age of seventeen, one of the most expert captains and bravest soldiers that ever saw the field of Mars. So that he was adored as the wonder of all that world, and the darling of the soldiers. Besides, he was adorned with a native beauty so transcending all those of his gloomy race that he struck an awe and reverence even in those that knew not his quality; as he did in me, who beheld him with surprise and wonder, when afterwards he arrived in our world.

He had scarce arrived at his seventeenth year, when fighting by his side, the general was killed with an arrow in his eye, which the Prince Oroonoko (for so was this gallant Moor[1] called) very narrowly avoided; nor had he, if the general, who saw the arrow shot, and perceiving it aimed at the Prince, had not bowed his head between, on purpose to receive it in his own body rather than it should touch that of the Prince, and so saved him.

'Twas then, afflicted as Oroonoko was, that he was proclaimed general in the old man's place; and then it was, at the finishing of that war, which had continued for two years, that the Prince came to court, where he had hardly been a month together from the time of his fifth year to that of seventeen; and 'twas amazing to imagine where it was he learned so much humanity; or to give his accomplishments a juster name, where 'twas he got that real greatness of soul, those refined notions of true honor, that absolute generosity, and that softness that was capable of the highest passions of love and gallantry, whose objects were almost continually fighting men, or those mangled or dead; who heard no sounds but those of war and groans. Some part of it we may attribute to the care of a Frenchman of wit and learning, who, finding it turn to very good account to be a sort of royal tutor to this

---

9. Not a country but a British-held fort and slave market on the Gold Coast of Africa, in modern-day Ghana. As the slave trade expanded, the slaves and workers shipped out from the region (who came to be called Cormantines) impressed many European observers by their beauty and bearing, their fierceness in war, and their extreme dignity under captivity or torture.
1. Loosely used for any dark-skinned person.

young black, and perceiving him very ready, apt, and quick of apprehension, took a great pleasure to teach him morals, language, and science, and was for it extremely beloved and valued by him. Another reason was, he loved, when he came from war, to see all the English gentlemen that traded thither, and did not only learn their language but that of the Spaniards also, with whom he traded afterwards for slaves.

I have often seen and conversed with this great man, and been a witness to many of his mighty actions, and do assure my reader the most illustrious courts could not have produced a braver man, both for greatness of courage and mind, a judgment more solid, a wit more quick, and a conversation more sweet and diverting. He knew almost as much as if he had read much. He had heard of and admired the Romans; he had heard of the late civil wars in England, and the deplorable death of our great monarch,[2] and would discourse of it with all the sense and abhorrence of the injustice imaginable. He had an extreme good and graceful mien, and all the civility of a well-bred great man. He had nothing of barbarity in his nature, but in all points addressed himself as if his education had been in some European court.

This great and just character of Oroonoko gave me an extreme curiosity to see him, especially when I knew he spoke French and English, and that I could talk with him. But though I had heard so much of him, I was as greatly surprised when I saw him as if I had heard nothing of him, so beyond all report I found him. He came into the room and addressed himself to me, and some other women, with the best grace in the world. He was pretty tall, but of a shape the most exact that can be fancied. The most famous statuary[3] could not form the figure of a man more admirably turned from head to foot. His face was not of that brown, rusty black which most of that nation are, but a perfect ebony or polished jet. His eyes were the most awful that could be seen, and very piercing, the white of 'em being like snow, as were his teeth. His nose was rising and Roman, instead of African and flat; his mouth the finest shaped that could be seen, far from those great turned lips which are so natural to the rest of the Negroes. The whole proportion and air of his face was so noble and exactly formed that, bating[4] his color, there could be nothing in nature more beautiful, agreeable, and handsome. There was no one grace wanting that bears the standard of true beauty. His hair came down to his shoulders by the aids of art; which was by pulling it out with a quill and keeping it combed, of which he took particular care. Nor did the perfections of his mind come short of those of his person, for his discourse was admirable upon almost any subject; and whoever had heard him speak would have been convinced of their errors, that all fine wit is confined to the white men, especially to those of Christendom, and would have confessed that Oroonoko was as capable even of reigning well, and of governing as wisely, had as great a soul, as politic[5] maxims, and was as sensible of

2. Charles I, beheaded in 1649 during the civil wars between Royalists and Parliamentarians. In 1688 this remark and others would have signaled Behn's ardent support of James II, the last of the Stuart kings, who would be forced into exile within the year.
3. Sculptor.
4. Except for. The singling out of Africans with

European looks or moral values is by no means unique to Behn; for example, Edward Long's 1774 *History of Jamaica* reports of the Cormantines that "their features are very different from the rest of the African Negroes, being smaller, and more of the European turn."
5. Shrewd, sagacious.

power, as any prince civilized in the most refined schools of humanity and learning, or the most illustrious courts.

This prince, such as I have described him, whose soul and body were so admirably adorned, was (while yet he was in the court of his grandfather), as I said, as capable of love as 'twas possible for a brave and gallant man to be; and in saying that, I have named the highest degree of love, for sure, great souls are most capable of that passion.

I have already said, the old general was killed by the shot of an arrow, by the side of this prince, in battle, and that Oroonoko was made general. This old dead hero had one only daughter left of his race, a beauty that, to describe her truly, one need say only she was female to the noble male, the beautiful black Venus to our young Mars, as charming in her person as he, and of deli-cate virtues. I have seen an hundred white men sighing after her, and making a thousand vows at her feet, all vain and unsuccessful. And she was, indeed, too great for any but a prince of her own nation to adore.

Oroonoko coming from the wars (which were now ended), after he had made his court to his grandfather, he thought in honor he ought to make a visit to Imoinda, the daughter of his foster-father, the dead general; and to make some excuses to her, because his preservation was the occasion of her father's death; and to present her with those slaves that had been taken in this last battle, as the trophies of her father's victories. When he came, attended by all the young soldiers of any merit, he was infinitely surprised at the beauty of this fair queen of night, whose face and person was so exceed-ing all he had ever beheld; that lovely modesty with which she received him; that softness in her look, and sighs, upon the melancholy occasion of this honor that was done by so great a man as Oroonoko, and a prince of whom she had heard such admirable things: the awfulness[6] wherewith she received him, and the sweetness of her words and behavior while he stayed, gained a perfect conquest over his fierce heart, and made him feel the victor could be subdued. So that having made his first compliments, and presented her a hundred and fifty slaves in fetters, he told her with his eyes that he was not insensible of her charms; while Imoinda, who wished for nothing more than so glorious a conquest, was pleased to believe she understood that silent language of newborn love, and from that moment put on all her additions to beauty.

The Prince returned to court with quite another humor than before; and though he did not speak much of the fair Imoinda, he had the pleasure to hear all his followers speak of nothing but the charms of that maid, inso-much that, even in the presence of the old king, they were extolling her and heightening, if possible, the beauties they had found in her. So that nothing else was talked of, no other sound was heard in every corner where there were whisperers, but "Imoinda! Imoinda!"

'Twill be imagined Oroonoko stayed not long before he made his second visit, nor, considering his quality, not much longer before he told her he adored her. I have often heard him say that he admired by what strange inspiration he came to talk things so soft and so passionate, who never knew love, nor was used to the conversation[7] of women; but (to use his own words)

---

6. Reverence.

7. Company. "Admired": marveled.

he said, most happily some new and till then unknown power instructed his heart and tongue in the language of love, and at the same time, in favor of him, inspired Imoinda with a sense of his passion. She was touched with what he said, and returned it all in such answers as went to his very heart, with a pleasure unknown before. Nor did he use those obligations[8] ill that love had done him, but turned all his happy moments to the best advantage; and as he knew no vice, his flame aimed at nothing but honor, if such a distinction may be made in love; and especially in that country, where men take to themselves as many as they can maintain, and where the only crime and sin with woman is to turn her off, to abandon her to want, shame, and misery. Such ill morals are only practiced in Christian countries, where they prefer the bare name of religion, and, without virtue or morality, think that's sufficient. But Oroonoko was none of those professors, but as he had right notions of honor, so he made her such propositions as were not only and barely such; but contrary to the custom of his country, he made her vows she should be the only woman he would possess while he lived; that no age or wrinkles should incline him to change, for her soul would be always fine and always young, and he should have an eternal idea in his mind of the charms she now bore, and should look into his heart for that idea when he could find it no longer in her face.

After a thousand assurances of his lasting flame, and her eternal empire over him, she condescended to receive him for her husband, or rather, received him as the greatest honor the gods could do her.

There is a certain ceremony in these cases to be observed, which I forgot ᴑ ask him how performed; but 'twas concluded on both sides that, in obedi-ce to him, the grandfather was to be first made acquainted with the design, ʰey pay a most absolute resignation to the monarch, especially when he ᵁrent also.

he other side, the old king, who had many wives and many concu-ᴵnted not court flatterers to insinuate in his heart a thousand ten-ʰts for this young beauty, and who represented her to his fancy as ᵃrming he had ever possessed in all the long race of his numer-this character his old heart, like an extinguished brand, most felt new sparks of love and began to kindle; and now grown ᴵildhood, longed with impatience to behold this gay thing, ʰe could but innocently play. But how he should be con-wonder, before he used his power to call her to court ʳ came, unless for the King's private use), he was next ʰe was so doing, he had intelligence brought him that ᴵnly mistress to the Prince Oroonoko. This gave him gave him also an opportunity, one day when the ᴵt on a man of quality, as his slave and attendant, ᵉsent to Imoinda as from the Prince; he should ᴵnaid, and have an opportunity to hear what ᴵnce for his present, and from thence gather ᵒf her inclination. This was put in execu-ᵇurned. He found her all he had heard, and would not delay his happiness, but found he should have some obstacle to overcome her heart; for she expressed her sense of the present the Prince had sent her in terms so sweet, so soft and pretty, with an air of love and joy that could not be dissembled, insomuch that 'twas past doubt whether she loved Oroonoko entirely. This gave the old king some affliction, but he salved it with this, that the obedience the people pay their king was not at all inferior to what they paid their gods; and what love would not oblige Imoinda to do, duty would compel her to.

He was therefore no sooner got to his apartment but he sent the royal veil to Imoinda, that is, the ceremony of invitation: he sends the lady he has a mind to honor with his bed a veil, with which she is covered, and secured for the King's use; and 'tis death to disobey, besides held a most impious disobedience.

'Tis not to be imagined the surprise and grief that seized this lovely maid at this news and sight. However, as delays in these cases are dangerous and pleading worse than treason, trembling, and almost fainting, she was obliged to suffer herself to be covered and led away.

They brought her thus to court; and the King, who had caused a very rich bath to be prepared, was led into it, where he sat under a canopy, in state, to receive this longed-for virgin; whom he having commanded should be brought to him, they (after disrobing her) led her to the bath, and making fast the doors, left her to descend. The King, without more courtship, bade her throw off her mantle and come to his arms. But Imoinda, all in tears, threw herself on the marble, on the brink of the bath, and besought him to hear her. She told him, as she was a maid, how proud of the divine glory she should have been, of having it in her power to oblige her king; but as by the laws he could not, and from his royal goodness would not, take from any man his wedded wife, so she believed she should be the occasion of making him commit a great sin, if she did not reveal her state and condition, and tell him she was another's, and could not be so happy to be his.

The King, enraged at this delay, hastily demanded the name of the bold man that had married a woman of her degree without his consent. Imoinda seeing his eyes fierce and his hands tremble (whether with age or anger, know not, but she fancied the last), almost repented she had said so much, now she feared the storm would fall on the Prince. She therefore said a th sand things to appease the raging of his flame, and to prepare him to who it was with calmness; but before she spoke, he imagined who she me but would not seem to do so, but commanded her to lay aside her mantl suffer herself to receive his caresses; or by his gods, he swore that happ whom she was going to name should die, though it were even Oroonok self. "Therefore," said he, "deny this marriage, and swear thyself a "That," replied Imoinda, "by all our powers I do, for I am not yet know husband." "'Tis enough," said the King; "'tis enough to satisfy both science and my heart." And rising from his seat, he went and le the bath, it being in vain for her to resist.

In this time the Prince, who was returned from hunting, went Imoinda, but found her gone; and not only so, but heard she h the royal veil. This raised him to a storm, and in his madness th ado to save him from laying violent hands on himself. Force fi and then reason. They urged all to him that might oppose his r ing weighed so greatly with him as the King's old age, uncapable of injuring him with Imoinda. He would give way to that hope, because it pleased him most, and flattered best his heart. Yet this served not altogether to make him cease his different passions, which sometimes raged within him, and sometimes softened into showers. 'Twas not enough to appease him, to tell him his grandfather was old and could not that way injure him, while he retained that awful duty which the young men are used there to pay to their grave relations. He could not be convinced he had no cause to sigh and mourn for the loss of a mistress he could not with all his strength and courage retrieve. And he would often cry, "O my friends! Were she in walled cities or confined from me in fortifications of the greatest strength, did enchantments or monsters detain her from me, I would venture through any hazard to free her. But here, in the arms of a feeble old man, my youth, my violent love, my trade in arms, and all my vast desire of glory avail me nothing. Imoinda is as irrecoverably lost to me as if she were snatched by the cold arms of Death. Oh! she is never to be retrieved. If I would wait tedious years, till fate should bow the old king to his grave, even that would not leave me Imoinda free; but still that custom that makes it so vile a crime for a son to marry his father's wives or mistresses would hinder my happiness, unless I would either ignobly set an ill precedent to my successors, or abandon my country and fly with her to some unknown world, who never heard our story."

But it was objected to him that his case was not the same; for Imoinda being his lawful wife, by solemn contract, 'twas he was the injured man and might if he so pleased take Imoinda back, the breach of the law being on his grandfather's side; and that if he could circumvent him and redeem her from the Otan, which is the palace of the King's women, a sort of seraglio, it was both just and lawful for him so to do.

This reasoning had some force upon him, and he should have been entirely comforted, but for the thought that she was possessed by his grandfather. However, he loved so well that he was resolved to believe what most favored his hope, and to endeavor to learn from Imoinda's own mouth what only she could satisfy him in, whether she was robbed of that blessing which was only due to his faith and love. But as it was very hard to get a sight of the women (for no men ever entered into the Otan but when the King went to entertain himself with some one of his wives or mistresses, and 'twas death at any other time for any other to go in), so he knew not how to contrive to get a sight of her.

While Oroonoko felt all the agonies of love, and suffered under a torment the most painful in the world, the old king was not exempted from his share of affliction. He was troubled for having been forced by an irresistible passion to rob his son[9] of a treasure he knew could not but be extremely dear to him, since she was the most beautiful that ever had been seen, and had besides all the sweetness and innocence of youth and modesty, with a charm of wit surpassing all. He found that, however she was forced to expose her lovely person to his withered arms, she could only sigh and weep there, and think of Oroonoko; and oftentimes could not forbear speaking of him, though her life were, by custom, forfeited by owning her passion. But she spoke not of a lover only, but of a prince dear to him to whom she spoke, and

9. I.e., grandson.

of the praises of a man who, till now, filled the old man's soul with joy at every recital of his bravery, or even his name. And 'twas this dotage on our young hero that gave Imoinda a thousand privileges to speak of him without offending, and this condescension in the old king that made her take the satisfaction of speaking of him so very often.

Besides, he many times inquired how the Prince bore himself; and those of whom he asked, being entirely slaves to the merits and virtues of the Prince, still answered what they thought conduced best to his service; which was to make the old king fancy that the Prince had no more interest in Imoinda, and had resigned her willingly to the pleasure of the King; that he diverted himself with his mathematicians, his fortifications, his officers, and his hunting.

This pleased the old lover, who failed not to report these things again to Imoinda, that she might, by the example of her young lover, withdraw her heart, and rest better contented in his arms. But however she was forced to receive this unwelcome news, in all appearance with unconcern and content, her heart was bursting within, and she was only happy when she could get alone, to vent her griefs and moans with sighs and tears.

What reports of the Prince's conduct were made to the King, he thought good to justify as far as possibly he could by his actions, and when he appeared in the presence of the King, he showed a face not at all betraying his heart. So that in a little time, the old man being entirely convinced that he was no longer a lover of Imoinda, he carried him with him in his train to the Otan, often to banquet with his mistress. But as soon as he entered, one day, into the apartment of Imoinda with the King, at the first glance from her eyes, notwithstanding all his determined resolution, he was ready to sink in the place where he stood, and had certainly done so but for the support of Aboan, a young man who was next to him; which, with his change of countenance, had betrayed him, had the King chanced to look that way. And I have observed, 'tis a very great error, in those who laugh when one says a Negro can change color, for I have seen 'em as frequently blush, and look pale, and that as visibly as ever I saw in the most beautiful white. And 'tis certain that both these changes were evident, this day, in both these lovers. And Imoinda, who saw with some joy the change in the Prince's face, and found it in her own, strove to divert the King from beholding either by a forced caress, with which she met him, which was a new wound in the heart of the poor dying Prince. But as soon as the King was busied in looking on some fine thing of Imoinda's making, she had time to tell the Prince with her angry but love-darting eyes that she resented his coldness, and bemoaned her own miserable captivity. Nor were his eyes silent, but answered hers again, as much as eyes could do, instructed by the most tender and most passionate heart that ever loved. And they spoke so well and so effectually, as Imoinda no longer doubted but she was the only delight and the darling of that soul she found pleading in 'em its right of love, which none was more willing to resign than she. And 'twas this powerful language alone that in an instant conveyed all the thoughts of their souls to each other, that[1] they both found there wanted but opportunity to make them both entirely happy. But when he saw another door opened by Onahal, a former old wife of the King's

---

1. So that.

who now had charge of Imoinda, and saw the prospect of a bed of state made ready with sweets and flowers for the dalliance of the King, who immediately led the trembling victim from his sight into that prepared repose, what rage, what wild frenzies seized his heart! which forcing to keep within bounds, and to suffer without noise, it became the more insupportable, and rent his soul with ten thousand pains. He was forced to retire to vent his groans, where he fell down on a carpet and lay struggling a long time, and only breathing now and then, "—O Imoinda!"

When Onahal had finished her necessary affair within, shutting the door, she came forth to wait till the King called; and hearing someone sighing in the other room, she passed on, and found the Prince in that deplorable condition, which she thought needed her aid. She gave him cordials, but all in vain, till finding the nature of his disease by his sighs and naming Imoinda. She told him, he had not so much cause as he imagined to afflict himself, for if he knew the King so well as she did, he would not lose a moment in jealousy, and that she was confident that Imoinda bore, at this minute, part in his affliction. Aboan was of the same opinion, and both together persuaded him to reassume his courage; and all sitting down on the carpet, the Prince said so many obliging things to Onahal that he half persuaded her to be of his party. And she promised him she would thus far comply with his just desires, that she would let Imoinda know how faithful he was, what he suffered, and what he said.

This discourse lasted till the King called, which gave Oroonoko a certain satisfaction, and with the hope Onahal had made him conceive, he assumed a look as gay as 'twas possible a man in his circumstances could do; and presently after, he was called in with the rest who waited without. The King commanded music to be brought, and several of his young wives and mistresses came all together by his command to dance before him; where Imoinda performed her part with an air and grace so passing all the rest as her beauty was above 'em, and received the present ordained as a prize. The Prince was every moment more charmed with the new beauties and graces he beheld in this fair one. And while he gazed, and she danced, Onahal was retired to a window with Aboan.

This Onahal, as I said, was one of the cast mistresses of the old king; and 'twas these (now past their beauty) that were made guardians or governants[2] to the new and the young ones, and whose business it was to teach them all those wanton arts of love with which they prevailed and charmed heretofore in their turn; and who now treated the triumphing happy ones with all the severity, as to liberty and freedom, that was possible, in revenge of those honors they rob them of; envying them those satisfactions, those gallantries and presents, that were once made to themselves, while youth and beauty lasted, and which they now saw pass regardless by, and paid only to the bloomings. And certainly nothing is more afflicting to a decayed beauty than to behold in itself declining charms that were once adored, and to find those caresses paid to new beauties to which once she laid a claim; to hear 'em whisper as she passes by, "That once was a delicate woman." These abandoned ladies therefore endeavor to revenge all the despites[3] and decays

---

2. Female teachers or chaperones. "Cast": i.e., cast-off.
3. Insults.

of time on these flourishing happy ones. And 'twas this severity that gave Oroonoko a thousand fears he should never prevail with Onahal to see Imoinda. But, as I said, she was now retired to a window with Aboan.

This young man was not only one of the best quality,[4] but a man extremely well made and beautiful; and coming often to attend the King to the Otan, he had subdued the heart of the antiquated Onahal, which had not forgot how pleasant it was to be in love. And though she had some decays in her face, she had none in her sense and wit; she was there agreeable still, even to Aboan's youth, so that he took pleasure in entertaining her with discourses of love. He knew also that to make his court to these she-favorites was the way to be great, these being the persons that do all affairs and business at court. He had also observed that she had given him glances more tender and inviting than she had done to others of his quality. And now, when he saw that her favor could so absolutely oblige the Prince, he failed not to sigh in her ear and to look with eyes all soft upon her, and give her hope that she had made some impressions on his heart. He found her pleased at this, and making a thousand advances to him; but the ceremony ending and the King departing broke up the company for that day, and his conversation.

Aboan failed not that night to tell the Prince of his success, and how advantageous the service of Onahal might be to his amour with Imoinda. The Prince was overjoyed with this good news and besought him, if it were possible, to caress her so as to engage her entirely, which he could not fail to do, if he complied with her desires. "For then," said the Prince, "her life lying at your mercy, she must grant you the request you make in my behalf." Aboan understood him, and assured him he would make love so effectually that he would defy the most expert mistress of the art to find out whether he dissembled it or had it really. And 'twas with impatience they waited the next opportunity of going to the Otan.

The wars came on, the time of taking the field approached, and 'twas impossible for the Prince to delay his going at the head of his army to encounter the enemy. So that every day seemed a tedious year till he saw his Imoinda, for he believed he could not live if he were forced away without being so happy. 'Twas with impatience, therefore, that he expected the next visit the King would make, and according to his wish, it was not long.

The parley of the eyes of these two lovers had not passed so secretly but an old jealous lover could spy it; or rather, he wanted not flatterers who told him they observed it. So that the Prince was hastened to the camp, and this was the last visit he found he should make to the Otan; he therefore urged Aboan to make the best of this last effort, and to explain himself so to Onahal that she, deferring her enjoyment of her young lover no longer, might make way for the Prince to speak to Imoinda.

The whole affair being agreed on between the Prince and Aboan, they attended the King, as the custom was, to the Otan, where, while the whole company was taken up in beholding the dancing and antic postures the women-royal made to divert the King, Onahal singled out Aboan, whom she found most pliable to her wish. When she had him where she believed she could not be heard, she sighed to him, and softly cried, "Ah, Aboan! When will you be sensible of my passion? I confess it with my mouth, because I

4. Rank.

would not give my eyes the lie; and you have but too much already perceived they have confessed my flame. Nor would I have you believe that because I am the abandoned mistress of a king, I esteem myself altogether divested of charms. No, Aboan; I have still a rest[5] of beauty enough engaging, and have learned to please too well not to be desirable. I can have lovers still, but will have none but Aboan." "Madam," replied the half-feigning youth, "you have already, by my eyes, found you can still conquer, and I believe 'tis in pity of me you condescend to this kind confession. But, Madam, words are used to be so small a part of our country courtship, that 'tis rare one can get so happy an opportunity as to tell one's heart, and those few minutes we have are forced to be snatched for more certain proofs of love than speaking and sighing; and such I languish for."

He spoke this with such a tone that she hoped it true, and could not forbear believing it; and being wholly transported with joy, for having subdued the finest of all the King's subjects to her desires, she took from her ears two large pearls and commanded him to wear 'em in his. He would have refused 'em, crying, "Madam, these are not the proofs of your love that I expect; 'tis opportunity, 'tis a lone hour only, that can make me happy." But forcing the pearls into his hand, she whispered softly to him, "Oh! Do not fear a woman's invention, when love sets her a-thinking." And pressing his hand, she cried, "This night you shall be happy. Come to the gate of the orange groves behind the Otan, and I will be ready, about midnight, to receive you." 'Twas thus agreed, and she left him, that no notice might be taken of their speaking together.

The ladies were still dancing, and the King, laid on a carpet, with a great deal of pleasure was beholding them, especially Imoinda, who that day appeared more lovely than ever, being enlivened with the good tidings Onahal had brought her of the constant passion the Prince had for her. The Prince was laid on another carpet at the other end of the room, with his eyes fixed on the object of his soul; and as she turned or moved, so did they, and she alone gave his eyes and soul their motions. Nor did Imoinda employ her eyes to any other use than in beholding with infinite pleasure the joy she produced in those of the Prince. But while she was more regarding him than the steps she took, she chanced to fall, and so near him as that, leaping with extreme force from the carpet, he caught her in his arms as she fell; and 'twas visible to the whole presence[6] the joy wherewith he received her. He clasped her close to his bosom, and quite forgot that reverence that was due to the mistress of a king, and that punishment that is the reward of a boldness of this nature; and had not the presence of mind of Imoinda (fonder of his safety than her own) befriended him, in making her spring from his arms and fall into her dance again, he had at that instant met his death; for the old king, jealous to the last degree, rose up in rage, broke all the diversion, and led Imoinda to her apartment, and sent out word to the Prince to go immediately to the camp, and that if he were found another night in court he should suffer the death ordained for disobedient offenders.

You may imagine how welcome this news was to Oroonoko, whose unseasonable transport and caress of Imoinda was blamed by all men that loved

---

5. Remnant.   6. Company.

him; and now he perceived his fault, yet cried that for such another moment, he would be content to die.

All the Otan was in disorder about this accident; and Onahal was particularly concerned, because on the Prince's stay depended her happiness, for she could no longer expect that of Aboan. So that ere they departed, they contrived it so that the Prince and he should come both that night to the grove of the Otan, which was all of oranges and citrons, and that there they should wait her orders.

They parted thus, with grief enough, till night, leaving the King in possession of the lovely maid. But nothing could appease the jealousy of the old lover. He would not be imposed on, but would have it that Imoinda made a false step on purpose to fall into Oroonoko's bosom, and that all things looked like a design on both sides; and 'twas in vain she protested her innocence. He was old and obstinate, and left her more than half assured that his fear was true.

The King going to his apartment sent to know where the Prince was, and if he intended to obey his command. The messenger returned and told him, he found the Prince pensive and altogether unpreparing for the campaign, that he lay negligently on the ground, and answered very little. This confirmed the jealousy of the King, and he commanded that they should very narrowly and privately watch his motions, and that he should not stir from his apartment but one spy or other should be employed to watch him. So that the hour approaching wherein he was to go to the citron grove, and taking only Aboan along with him, he leaves his apartment, and was watched to the very gate of the Otan, where he was seen to enter, and where they left him, to carry back the tidings to the King.

Oroonoko and Aboan were no sooner entered but Onahal led the Prince to the apartment of Imoinda, who, not knowing anything of her happiness, was laid in bed. But Onahal only left him in her chamber, to make the best of his opportunity, and took her dear Aboan to her own, where he showed the heighth of complaisance for his prince, when, to give him an opportunity, he suffered himself to be caressed in bed by Onahal.

The Prince softly wakened Imoinda, who was not a little surprised with joy to find him there; and yet she trembled with a thousand fears. I believe he omitted saying nothing to this young maid that might persuade her to suffer him to seize his own, and take the rights of love; and I believe she was not long resisting those arms where she so longed to be; and having opportunity, night and silence, youth, love and desire, he soon prevailed, and ravished in a moment what his old grandfather had been endeavoring for so many months.

'Tis not to be imagined the satisfaction of these two young lovers; nor the vows she made him that she remained a spotless maid till that night, and that what she did with his grandfather had robbed him of no part of her virgin honor, the gods in mercy and justice having reserved that for her plighted lord, to whom of right it belonged. And 'tis impossible to express the transports he suffered, while he listened to a discourse so charming from her loved lips, and clasped that body in his arms for whom he had so long languished; and nothing now afflicted him but his sudden departure from her; for he told her the necessity and his commands, but should depart satisfied in this, that since the old king had hitherto not been able to deprive him of those enjoyments which only belonged to him, he believed for the future he would be less able to injure him; so that abating the scandal of the veil, which was no otherwise so than that she was wife to another, he believed her safe, even in the arms of the King, and innocent; yet would he have ventured at the conquest of the world, and have given it all, to have had her avoided that honor of receiving the royal veil. 'Twas thus, between a thousand caresses, that both bemoaned the hard fate of youth and beauty, so liable to that cruel promotion. 'Twas a glory that could well have been spared here, though desired and aimed at by all the young females of that kingdom.

But while they were thus fondly employed, forgetting how time ran on, and that the dawn must conduct him far away from his only happiness, they heard a great noise in the Otan, and unusual voices of men; at which the Prince, starting from the arms of the frighted Imoinda, ran to a little battle-ax he used to wear by his side, and having not so much leisure as to put on his habit, he opposed himself against some who were already opening the door; which they did with so much violence that Oroonoko was not able to defend it, but was forced to cry out with a commanding voice, "Whoever ye are that have the boldness to attempt to approach this apartment thus rudely, know that I, the Prince Oroonoko, will revenge it with the certain death of him that first enters. Therefore stand back, and know, this place is sacred to love and me this night; tomorrow 'tis the King's."

This he spoke with a voice so resolved and assured that they soon retired from the door, but cried, "'Tis by the King's command we are come; and being satisfied by thy voice, O Prince, as much as if we had entered, we can report to the King the truth of all his fears, and leave thee to provide for thy own safety, as thou art advised by thy friends."

At these words they departed, and left the Prince to take a short and sad leave of his Imoinda, who, trusting in the strength of her charms, believed she should appease the fury of a jealous king by saying she was surprised, and that it was by force of arms he got into her apartment. All her concern now was for his life, and therefore she hastened him to the camp, and with much ado prevailed on him to go. Nor was it she alone that prevailed; Aboan and Onahal both pleaded, and both assured him of a lie that should be well enough contrived to secure Imoinda. So that at last, with a heart sad as death, dying eyes, and sighing soul, Oroonoko departed and took his way to the camp.

It was not long after the King in person came to the Otan, where, beholding Imoinda with rage in his eyes, he upbraided her wickedness and perfidy, and threatening her royal lover, she fell on her face at his feet, bedewing the floor with her tears and imploring his pardon for a fault which she had not with her will committed, as Onahal, who was also prostrate with her, could testify; that unknown to her, he had broke into her apartment, and ravished her. She spoke this much against her conscience, but to save her own life 'twas absolutely necessary she should feign this falsity. She knew it could not injure the Prince, he being fled to an army that would stand by him against any injuries that should assault him. However, this last thought of Imoinda's being ravished changed the measures of his revenge; and whereas before he designed to be himself her executioner, he now resolved she should not die. But as it is the greatest crime in nature amongst 'em to touch a woman after having been possessed by a son, a father, or a brother, so now he looked on Imoinda as a polluted thing, wholly unfit for his embrace; nor would he resign her to his grandson, because she had received the royal veil. He therefore removes her from the Otan, with Onahal; whom he put into safe hands, with order they should be both sold off as slaves to another country, either Christian or heathen; 'twas no matter where.

This cruel sentence, worse than death, they implored might be reversed; but their prayers were vain, and it was put in execution accordingly, and that with so much secrecy that none, either without or within the Otan, knew anything of their absence or their destiny.

The old king, nevertheless, executed this with a great deal of reluctancy; but he believed he had made a very great conquest over himself, when he had once resolved, and had performed what he resolved. He believed now that his love had been unjust, and that he could not expect the gods, or Captain of the Clouds (as they call the unknown power), should suffer a better consequence from so ill a cause. He now begins to hold Oroonoko excused, and to say he had reason for what he did. And now everybody could assure the King how passionately Imoinda was beloved by the Prince; even those confessed it now, who said the contrary before his flame was abated. So that the King being old, and not able to defend himself in war, and having no sons of all his race remaining alive but only this, to maintain him on his throne; and looking on this as a man disobliged, first by the rape of his mistress, or rather wife; and now by depriving of him wholly of her, he feared, might make him desperate and do some cruel thing, either to himself or his old grandfather, the offender: he began to repent him extremely of the contempt he had, in his rage, put on Imoinda. Besides, he considered he ought in honor to have killed her for this offense, if it had been one. He ought to have had so much value and consideration for a maid of her quality as to have nobly put her to death, and not to have sold her like a common slave, the greatest revenge and the most disgraceful of any; and to which they a thousand times prefer death, and implore it, as Imoinda did, but could not obtain that honor. Seeing therefore it was certain that Oroonoko would highly resent this affront, he thought good to make some excuse for his rashness to him; and to that end he sent a messenger to the camp, with orders to treat with him about the matter, to gain his pardon, and to endeavor to mitigate his grief; but that by no means he should tell him she was sold, but secretly put to death, for he knew he should never obtain his pardon for the other.

When the messenger came, he found the Prince upon the point of engaging with the enemy; but as soon as he heard of the arrival of the messenger, he commanded him to his tent, where he embraced him and received him with joy; which was soon abated by the downcast looks of the messenger, who was instantly demanded the cause by Oroonoko, who, impatient of delay, asked a thousand questions in a breath, and all concerning Imoinda. But there needed little return, for he could almost answer himself of all he demanded, from his sighs and eyes. At last, the messenger casting himself at the Prince's feet, and kissing them with all the submission of a man that had something to implore which he dreaded to utter, he besought him to hear with calmness what he had to deliver to him, and to call up all his noble and heroic courage to encounter with his words, and defend himself against the ungrateful[7] things he must relate. Oroonoko replied, with a deep sigh and a

7. Offensive.

languishing voice, "I am armed against their worst efforts—; for I know they will tell me, Imoinda is no more—and after that, you may spare the rest." Then, commanding him to rise, he laid himself on a carpet, under a rich pavilion, and remained a good while silent, and was hardly heard to sigh. When he was come a little to himself, the messenger asked him leave to deliver that part of his embassy which the Prince had not yet divined. And the Prince cried, "I permit thee—." Then he told him the affliction the old king was in, for the rashness he had committed in his cruelty to Imoinda; and how he deigned to ask pardon for his offense, and to implore the Prince would not suffer that loss to touch his heart too sensibly, which now all the gods could not restore him, but might recompense him in glory, which he begged he would pursue; and that Death, that common revenger of all injuries, would soon even the account between him and a feeble old man.

Oroonoko bade him return his duty to his lord and master, and to assure him, there was no account of revenge to be adjusted between them; if there were, 'twas he was the aggressor, and that Death would be just and, maugre[8] his age, would see him righted; and he was contented to leave his share of glory to youths more fortunate and worthy of that favor from the gods. That henceforth he would never lift a weapon or draw a bow, but abandon the small remains of his life to sighs and tears, and the continual thoughts of what his lord and grandfather had thought good to send out of the world, with all that youth, that innocence, and beauty.

After having spoken this, whatever his greatest officers and men of the best rank could do, they could not raise him from the carpet, or persuade him to action and resolutions of life; but commanding all to retire, he shut himself into his pavilion all that day, while the enemy was ready to engage; and wondering at the delay, the whole body of the chief of the army then addressed themselves to him, and to whom they had much ado to get admittance. They fell on their faces at the foot of his carpet, where they lay and besought him with earnest prayers and tears to lead 'em forth to battle, and not let the enemy take advantages of them; and implored him to have regard to his glory, and to the world, that depended on his courage and conduct. But he made no other reply to all their supplications but this, that he had now no more business for glory; and for the world, it was a trifle not worth his care. "Go," continued he, sighing, "and divide it amongst you; and reap with joy what you so vainly prize, and leave me to my more welcome destiny."

They then demanded what they should do, and whom he would constitute in his room, that the confusion of ambitious youth and power might not ruin their order and make them a prey to the enemy. He replied, he would not give himself the trouble—; but wished 'em to choose the bravest man amongst 'em, let his quality or birth be what it would. "For, O my friends!" said he, "it is not titles make men brave or good, or birth that bestows courage and generosity, or makes the owner happy. Believe this, when you behold Oroonoko, the most wretched and abandoned by fortune of all the creation of the gods." So turning himself about, he would make no more reply to all they could urge or implore.

The army, beholding their officers return unsuccessful, with sad faces and ominous looks that presaged no good luck, suffered a thousand fears

---

8. In spite of. Oroonoko is saying that he will die before the king does.

to take possession of their hearts, and the enemy to come even upon 'em, before they would provide for their safety by any defense; and though they were assured by some, who had a mind to animate 'em, that they should be immediately headed by the Prince, and that in the meantime Aboan had orders to command as general, yet they were so dismayed for want of that great example of bravery that they could make but a very feeble resistance; and at last downright fled before the enemy, who pursued 'em to the very tents, killing 'em. Nor could all Aboan's courage, which that day gained him immortal glory, shame 'em into a manly defense of themselves. The guards that were left behind about the Prince's tent, seeing the soldiers flee before the enemy and scatter themselves all over the plain, in great disorder, made such outcries as roused the Prince from his amorous slumber, in which he had remained buried for two days without permitting any sustenance to approach him. But in spite of all his resolutions, he had not the constancy of grief to that degree, as to make him insensible of the danger of his army; and in that instant he leaped from his couch and cried, "—Come, if we must die, let us meet Death the noblest way; and 'twill be more like Oroonoko to encounter him at an army's head, opposing the torrent of a conquering foe, than lazily on a couch to wait his lingering pleasure, and die every moment by a thousand wrecking[9] thoughts; or be tamely taken by an enemy, and led a whining, lovesick slave to adorn the triumphs of Jamoan, that young victor, who already is entered beyond the limits I had prescribed him."

While he was speaking, he suffered his people to dress him for the field, and sallying out of his pavilion, with more life and vigor in his countenance than ever he showed, he appeared like some divine power descended to save his country from destruction; and his people had purposely put on him all things that might make him shine with most splendor, to strike a reverend awe into the beholders. He flew into the thickest of those that were pursuing his men, and being animated with despair, he fought as if he came on purpose to die, and did such things as will not be believed that human strength could perform, and such as soon inspired all the rest with new courage and new order. And now it was that they began to fight indeed, and so as if they would not be outdone even by their adored hero; who, turning the tide of the victory, changing absolutely the fate of the day, gained an entire conquest; and Oroonoko having the good fortune to single out Jamoan, he took him prisoner with his own hand, having wounded him almost to death.

This Jamoan afterwards became very dear to him, being a man very gallant and of excellent graces and fine parts; so that he never put him amongst the rank of captives, as they used to do, without distinction, for the common sale or market; but kept him in his own court, where he retained nothing of the prisoner but the name, and returned no more into his own country, so great an affection he took for Oroonoko; and by a thousand tales and adventures of love and gallantry flattered[1] his disease of melancholy and languishment, which I have often heard him say had certainly killed him, but for the conversation of this prince and Aboan, and the French governor he had from his childhood, of whom I have spoken before, and who was a man of admirable wit, great ingenuity and learning, all which he had infused into his young pupil. This Frenchman was banished out of his own country for

9. Racking.   1. Soothed.

some heretical notions he held, and though he was a man of very little religion, he had admirable morals and a brave soul.

After the total defeat of Jamoan's army, which all fled, or were left dead
upon the place, they spent some time in the camp, Oroonoko choosing rather
to remain a while there in his tents than enter into a palace or live in a court
where he had so lately suffered so great a loss. The officers, therefore, who
saw and knew his cause of discontent, invented all sorts of diversions and
sports to entertain their prince; so that what with those amusements abroad
and others at home, that is, within their tents, with the persuasions, arguments, and care of his friends and servants that he more peculiarly prized, he
wore off in time a great part of that chagrin and torture of despair which the
first efforts of Imoinda's death had given him. Insomuch as having received a
thousand kind embassies from the King, and invitations to return to court,
he obeyed, though with no little reluctancy; and when he did so, there was
a visible change in him, and for a long time he was much more melancholy
than before. But time lessens all extremes, and reduces 'em to mediums and
unconcern; but no motives or beauties, though all endeavored it, could
engage him in any sort of amour, though he had all the invitations to it, both
from his own youth and others' ambitions and designs.

Oroonoko was no sooner returned from this last conquest, and received
at court with all the joy and magnificence that could be expressed to a young
victor, who was not only returned triumphant but beloved like a deity, when
there arrived in the port an English ship.

This person[2] had often before been in these countries and was very well
known to Oroonoko, with whom he had trafficked for slaves, and had used
to do the same with his predecessors.

This commander was a man of a finer sort of address and conversation,
better bred and more engaging than most of that sort of men are, so that he
seemed rather never to have been bred out of a court than almost all his life
at sea. This captain therefore was always better received at court than most
of the traders to those countries were; and especially by Oroonoko, who was
more civilized, according to the European mode, than any other had been,
and took more delight in the white nations, and above all men of parts and
wit. To this captain he sold abundance of his slaves, and for the favor and
esteem he had for him, made him many presents, and obliged him to stay at
court as long as possibly he could. Which the captain seemed to take as a
very great honor done him, entertaining the Prince every day with globes
and maps, and mathematical discourses and instruments; eating, drinking,
hunting, and living with him with so much familiarity that it was not to be
doubted but he had gained very greatly upon the heart of this gallant young
man. And the captain, in return of all these mighty favors, besought the
Prince to honor his vessel with his presence, some day or other, to dinner,
before he should set sail; which he condescended to accept, and appointed
his day. The captain, on his part, failed not to have all things in a readiness,
in the most magnificent order he could possibly. And the day being come, the
captain in his boat, richly adorned with carpets and velvet cushions, rowed
to the shore to receive the Prince, with another longboat where was placed
all his music and trumpets, with which Oroonoko was extremely delighted;

2. The ship's captain.

who met him on the shore attended by his French governor, Jamoan, Aboan, and about a hundred of the noblest of the youths of the court. And after they had first carried the Prince on board, the boats fetched the rest off; where they found a very splendid treat, with all sorts of fine wines, and were as well entertained as 'twas possible in such a place to be.

The Prince, having drunk hard of punch and several sorts of wine, as did all the rest (for great care was taken they should want nothing of that part of the entertainment), was very merry, and in great admiration of the ship, for he had never been in one before; so that he was curious of beholding every place where he decently might descend. The rest, no less curious, who were not quite overcome with drinking, rambled at their pleasure fore and aft, as their fancies guided 'em. So that the captain, who had well laid his design before, gave the word, and seized on all his guests; they clapping great irons suddenly on the Prince, when he was leaped down in the hold to view that part of the vessel, and locking him fast down, secured him. The same treachery was used to all the rest; and all in one instant, in several places of the ship, were lashed fast in irons, and betrayed to slavery. That great design over, they set all hands to work to hoise[3] sail; and with as treacherous and fair a wind, they made from the shore with this innocent and glorious prize, who thought of nothing less than such an entertainment.

Some have commended this act as brave in the captain; but I will spare my sense of it, and leave it to my reader to judge as he pleases.

It may be easily guessed in what manner the Prince resented this indignity, who may be best resembled to a lion taken in a toil; so he raged, so he struggled for liberty, but all in vain; and they had so wisely managed his fetters that he could not use a hand in his defense, to quit himself of a life that would by no means endure slavery, nor could he move from the place where he was tied to any solid part of the ship, against which he might have beat his head, and have finished his disgrace that way. So that being deprived of all other means, he resolved to perish for want of food. And pleased at last with that thought, and toiled and tired by rage and indignation, he laid himself down, and sullenly resolved upon dying, and refused all things that were brought him.

This did not a little vex the captain, and the more so because he found almost all of 'em of the same humor; so that the loss of so many brave slaves, so tall and goodly to behold, would have been very considerable. He therefore ordered one to go from him (for he would not be seen himself) to Oroonoko, and to assure him he was afflicted for having rashly done so unhospitable a deed, and which could not be now remedied, since they were far from shore; but since he resented it in so high a nature, he assured him he would revoke his resolution, and set both him and his friends ashore on the next land they should touch at; and of this the messenger gave him his oath, provided he would resolve to live. And Oroonoko, whose honor was such as he never had violated a word in his life himself, much less a solemn asseveration, believed in an instant what this man said, but replied, he expected for a confirmation of this to have his shameful fetters dismissed. This demand was carried to the captain, who returned him answer that the offense had been so great which he had put upon the Prince that he durst not trust him with liberty

3. Hoist.

while he remained in the ship, for fear lest by a valor natural to him, and a revenge that would animate that valor, he might commit some outrage fatal to himself and the King his master, to whom his vessel did belong. To this Oroonoko replied, he would engage his honor to behave himself in all friendly order and manner, and obey the command of the captain, as he was lord of the King's vessel and general of those men under his command.

This was delivered to the still doubting captain, who could not resolve to trust a heathen, he said, upon his parole,[4] a man that had no sense or notion of the God that he worshipped. Oroonoko then replied, he was very sorry to hear that the captain pretended to the knowledge and worship of any gods who had taught him no better principles than not to credit as he would be credited; but they told him the difference of their faith occasioned that distrust. For the captain had protested to him upon the word of a Christian, and sworn in the name of a great god, which if he should violate, he would expect eternal torment in the world to come. "Is that all the obligation he has to be just to his oath?" replied Oroonoko. "Let him know I swear by my honor; which to violate, would not only render me contemptible and despised by all brave and honest men, and so give myself perpetual pain, but it would be eternally offending and diseasing all mankind, harming, betraying, circumventing and outraging all men; but punishments hereafter are suffered by one's self, and the world takes no cognizances whether this god have revenged 'em or not, 'tis done so secretly and deferred so long. While the man of no honor suffers every moment the scorn and contempt of the honester world, and dies every day ignominiously in his fame, which is more valuable than life. I speak not this to move belief, but to show you how you mistake, when you imagine that he who will violate his honor will keep his word with his gods." So turning from him with a disdainful smile, he refused to answer him, when he urged him to know what answer he should carry back to his captain; so that he departed without saying any more.

The captain pondering and consulting what to do, it was concluded that nothing but Oroonoko's liberty would encourage any of the rest to eat, except the Frenchman, whom the captain could not pretend to keep prisoner, but only told him he was secured because he might act something in favor of the Prince, but that he should be freed as soon as they came to land. So that they concluded it wholly necessary to free the Prince from his irons, that he might show himself to the rest; that they might have an eye upon him, and that they could not fear a single man.

This being resolved, to make the obligation the greater, the captain himself went to Oroonoko; where after many compliments, and assurances of what he had already promised, he receiving from the Prince his parole and his hand for his good behavior, dismissed his irons and brought him to his own cabin; where after having treated and reposed him a while, for he had neither eat[5] nor slept in four days before, he besought him to visit those obstinate people in chains, who refused all manner of sustenance, and entreated him to oblige 'em to eat, and assure 'em of their liberty the first opportunity.

Oroonoko, who was too generous not to give credit to his words, showed himself to his people, who were transported with excess of joy at the sight of their darling prince, falling at his feet and kissing and embracing 'em,

---

4. Word of honor.   5. The past form of *eat*.

believing, as some divine oracle, all he assured 'em. But he besought 'em to bear their chains with that bravery that became those whom he had seen act so nobly in arms; and that they could not give him greater proofs of their love and friendship, since 'twas all the security the captain (his friend) could have, against the revenge, he said, they might possibly justly take for the injuries sustained by him. And they all with one accord assured him, they could not suffer enough, when it was for his repose and safety.

After this they no longer refused to eat, but took what was brought 'em, and were pleased with their captivity, since by it they hoped to redeem the Prince, who, all the rest of the voyage, was treated with all the respect due to his birth, though nothing could divert his melancholy; and he would often sigh for Imoinda, and think this a punishment due to his misfortune, in having left that noble maid behind him that fatal night, in the Otan, when he fled to the camp.

Possessed with a thousand thoughts of past joys with this fair young person, and a thousand griefs for her eternal loss, he endured a tedious voyage, and at last arrived at the mouth of the river of Surinam, a colony belonging to the King of England, and where they were to deliver some part of their slaves. There the merchants and gentlemen of the country going on board to demand those lots of slaves they had already agreed on, and, amongst those, the overseers of those plantations where I then chanced to be, the captain, who had given the word, ordered his men to bring up those noble slaves in fetters whom I have spoken of; and having put 'em some in one and some in other lots, with women and children (which they call pickaninnies), they sold 'em off as slaves to several merchants and gentlemen; not putting any two in one lot, because they would separate 'em far from each other, not daring to trust 'em together, lest rage and courage should put 'em upon contriving some great action, to the ruin of the colony.

Oroonoko was first seized on, and sold to our overseer, who had the first lot, with seventeen more of all sorts and sizes, but not one of quality with him. When he saw this, he found what they meant, for, as I said, he understood English pretty well; and being wholly unarmed and defenseless, so as it was in vain to make any resistance, he only beheld the captain with a look all fierce and disdainful, upbraiding him with eyes that forced blushes on his guilty cheeks; he only cried, in passing over the side of the ship, "Farewell, sir. 'Tis worth my suffering, to gain so true a knowledge both of you and of your gods by whom you swear." And desiring those that held him to forbear their pains, and telling 'em he would make no resistance, he cried, "Come, my fellow slaves; let us descend, and see if we can meet with more honor and honesty in the next world we shall touch upon." So he nimbly leaped into the boat, and showing no more concern, suffered himself to be rowed up the river with his seventeen companions.

The gentleman that bought him was a young Cornish gentleman whose name was Trefry, a man of great wit and fine learning, and was carried into those parts by the Lord——, Governor,[6] to manage all his affairs. He reflecting on the last words of Oroonoko to the captain, and beholding the richness of his vest,[7] no sooner came into the boat but he fixed his eyes on him; and

---

6. Lord Willoughby of Parham, coproprietor of Surinam by royal grant. John Treffry was his plantation overseer.
7. An outer garment or robe.

finding something so extraordinary in his face, his shape and mien, a greatness of look and haughtiness in his air, and finding he spoke English, had a great mind to be inquiring into his quality and fortune; which, though Oroonoko endeavored to hide, by only confessing he was above the rank of common slaves, Trefry soon found he was yet something greater than he confessed, and from that moment began to conceive so vast an esteem for him that he ever after loved him as his dearest brother, and showed him all the civilities due to so great a man.

Trefry was a very good mathematician and a linguist, could speak French and Spanish; and in the three days they remained in the boat (for so long were they going from the ship to the plantation) he entertained Oroonoko so agreeably with his art and discourse, that he was no less pleased with Trefry than he was with the Prince; and he thought himself at least fortunate in this, that since he was a slave, as long as he would suffer himself to remain so, he had a man of so excellent wit and parts for a master. So that before they had finished their voyage up the river, he made no scruple of declaring to Trefry all his fortunes, and most part of what I have here related, and put himself wholly into the hands of his new friend, whom he found resenting all the injuries were done him, and was charmed with all the greatness of his actions; which were recited with that modesty and delicate sense as wholly vanquished him, and subdued him to his interest. And he promised him on his word and honor, he would find the means to reconduct him to his own country again, assuring him, he had a perfect abhorrence of so dishonorable an action, and that he would sooner have died than have been the author of such a perfidy. He found the Prince was very much concerned to know what became of his friends, and how they took their slavery; and Trefry promised to take care about the inquiring after their condition, and that he should have an account of 'em.

Though, as Oroonoko afterwards said, he had little reason to credit the words of a *backearary*,[8] yet he knew not why, but he saw a kind of sincerity and awful truth in the face of Trefry; he saw an honesty in his eyes, and he found him wise and witty enough to understand honor; for it was one of his maxims, a man of wit could not be a knave or villain.

In their passage up the river they put in at several houses for refreshment, and ever when they landed, numbers of people would flock to behold this man; not but their eyes were daily entertained with the sight of slaves, but the fame of Oroonoko was gone before him, and all people were in admiration of his beauty. Besides, he had a rich habit on, in which he was taken, so different from the rest, and which the captain could not strip him of, because he was forced to surprise his person in the minute he sold him. When he found his habit made him liable, as he thought, to be gazed at the more, he begged Trefry to give him something more befitting a slave, which he did, and took off his robes. Nevertheless, he shone through all; and his osenbrigs (a sort of brown holland[9] suit he had on) could not conceal the graces of his looks and mien, and he had no less admirers than when he had his dazzling habit on. The royal youth appeared in spite of the slave, and people could not help

---

8. White person or master; a variant of *backra*, from an Ibo word transported with the slaves to Surinam and the Caribbean.

9. Coarse cotton or linen, sometimes called osnaburg, after a German cloth-manufacturing town.

treating him after a different manner, without designing it. As soon as they approached him, they venerated and esteemed him; his eyes insensibly commanded respect, and his behavior insinuated it into every soul. So that there was nothing talked of but this young and gallant slave, even by those who yet knew not that he was a prince.

I ought to tell you that the Christians never buy any slaves but they give 'em some name of their own, their native ones being likely very barbarous and hard to pronounce; so that Mr. Trefry gave Oroonoko that of Caesar, which name will live in that country as long as that (scarce more) glorious one of the great Roman; for 'tis most evident, he wanted[1] no part of the personal courage of that Caesar, and acted things as memorable, had they been done in some part of the world replenished with people and historians that might have given him his due. But his misfortune was to fall in an obscure world, that afforded only a female pen to celebrate his fame; though I doubt not but it had lived from others' endeavors, if the Dutch, who immediately after his time took that country,[2] had not killed, banished, and dispersed all those that were capable of giving the world this great man's life, much better than I have done. And Mr. Trefry, who designed it, died before he began it, and bemoaned himself for not having undertook it in time.

For the future, therefore, I must call Oroonoko Caesar, since by that name only he was known in our western world, and by that name he was received on shore at Parham House, where he was destined a slave. But if the King himself (God bless him) had come ashore, there could not have been greater expectations by all the whole plantation, and those neighboring ones, than was on ours at that time; and he was received more like a governor than a slave. Notwithstanding, as the custom was, they assigned him his portion of land, his house, and his business, up in the plantation. But as it was more for form than any design to put him to his task, he endured no more of the slave but the name, and remained some days in the house, receiving all visits that were made him, without stirring towards that part of the plantation where the Negroes were.

At last he would needs go view his land, his house, and the business assigned him. But he no sooner came to the houses of the slaves, which are like a little town by itself, the Negroes all having left work, but they all came forth to behold him, and found he was that prince who had, at several times, sold most of 'em to these parts; and from a veneration they pay to great men, especially if they know 'em, and from the surprise and awe they had at the sight of him, they all cast themselves at his feet, crying out in their language, "Live, O King! Long live, O King!" and kissing his feet, paid him even divine homage.

Several English gentlemen were with him; and what Mr. Trefry had told 'em was here confirmed, of which he himself before had no other witness than Caesar himself. But he was infinitely glad to find his grandeur confirmed by the adoration of all the slaves.

Caesar, troubled with their over-joy and over-ceremony, besought 'em to rise and to receive him as their fellow slave, assuring them he was no better. At which they set up with one accord a most terrible and hideous mourning

---

1. Lacked.
2. In 1667 the Dutch attacked and conquered

Surinam, and England ceded it by treaty in exchange for New York.

and condoling, which he and the English had much ado to appease; but at last they prevailed with 'em, and they prepared all their barbarous music, and everyone killed and dressed something of his own stock (for every family has their land apart, on which, at their leisure times, they breed all eatable things), and clubbing it together,[3] made a most magnificent supper, inviting their *Grandee Captain,* their prince, to honor it with his presence; which he did, and several English with him; where they all waited on him, some playing, others dancing before him all the time, according to the manners of their several nations, and with unwearied industry endeavoring to please and delight him.

While they sat at meat Mr. Trefry told Caesar that most of these young slaves were undone in love with a fine she-slave, whom they had had about six months on their land. The Prince, who never heard the name of love without a sigh, nor any mention of it without the curiosity of examining further into that tale, which of all discourses was most agreeable to him, asked how they came to be so unhappy as to be all undone for one fair slave. Trefry, who was naturally amorous and loved to talk of love as well as anybody, proceeded to tell him, they had the most charming black that ever was beheld on their plantation, about fifteen or sixteen years old, as he guessed; that for his part, he had done nothing but sigh for her ever since she came, and that all the white beauties he had seen never charmed him so absolutely as this fine creature had done; and that no man, of any nation, ever beheld her that did not fall in love with her; and that she had all the slaves perpetually at her feet, and the whole country resounded with the fame of Clemene, "for so," said he, "we have christened her. But she denies us all with such a noble disdain, that 'tis a miracle to see that she, who can give such eternal desires, should herself be all ice and all unconcern. She is adorned with the most graceful modesty that ever beautified youth; the softest sigher—that, if she were capable of love, one would swear she languished for some absent happy man; and so retired, as if she feared a rape even from the god of day,[4] or that the breezes would steal kisses from her delicate mouth. Her task of work some sighing lover every day makes it his petition to perform for her, which she accepts blushing and with reluctancy, for fear he will ask her a look for a recompense, which he dares not presume to hope, so great an awe she strikes into the hearts of her admirers." "I do not wonder," replied the Prince, "that Clemene should refuse slaves, being as you say so beautiful, but wonder how she escapes those who can entertain her as you can do; or why, being your slave, you do not oblige her to yield." "I confess," said Trefry, "when I have, against her will, entertained her with love so long as to be transported with my passion, even above decency, I have been ready to make use of those advantages of strength and force nature has given me. But oh! she disarms me with that modesty and weeping, so tender and so moving that I retire, and thank my stars she overcame me." The company laughed at his civility to a slave, and Caesar only applauded the nobleness of his passion and nature, since that slave might be noble or, what was better, have true notions of honor and virtue in her. Thus passed they this night, after having received from the slaves all imaginable respect and obedience.

---

3. Contributing jointly.   4. The sun.

The next day Trefry asked Caesar to walk, when the heat was allayed, and designedly carried him by the cottage of the fair slave, and told him she whom he spoke of last night lived there retired. "But," says he, "I would not wish you to approach, for I am sure you will be in love as soon as you behold her." Caesar assured him he was proof against all the charms of that sex, and that if he imagined his heart could be so perfidious to love again, after Imoinda, he believed he should tear it from his bosom. They had no sooner spoke, but a little shock dog[5] that Clemene had presented her, which she took great delight in, ran out; and she, not knowing anybody was there, ran to get it in again, and bolted out on those who were just speaking of her. When seeing them, she would have run in again, but Trefry caught her by the hand and cried, "Clemene, however you fly a lover, you ought to pay some respect to this stranger" (pointing to Caesar). But she, as if she had resolved never to raise her eyes to the face of a man again, bent 'em the more to the earth when he spoke, and gave the Prince the leisure to look the more at her. There needed no long gazing or consideration to examine who this fair creature was; he soon saw Imoinda all over her; in a minute he saw her face, her shape, her air, her modesty, and all that called forth his soul with joy at his eyes, and left his body destitute of almost life; it stood without motion, and for a minute knew not that it had a being; and I believe he had never come to himself, so oppressed he was with over-joy, if he had not met with this allay, that he perceived Imoinda fall dead in the hands of Trefry. This awakened him, and he ran to her aid and caught her in his arms, where by degrees she came to herself; and 'tis needless to tell with what transports, what ecstasies of joy, they both a while beheld each other, without speaking; then snatched each other to their arms; then gaze again, as if they still doubted whether they possessed the blessing they grasped; but when they recovered their speech, 'tis not to be imagined what tender things they expressed to each other, wondering what strange fate had brought 'em again together. They soon informed each other of their fortunes, and equally bewailed their fate; but at the same time they mutually protested that even fetters and slavery were soft and easy, and would be supported with joy and pleasure, while they could be so happy to possess each other and to be able to make good their vows. Caesar swore he disdained the empire of the world while he could behold his Imoinda; and she despised grandeur and pomp, those vanities of her sex, when she could gaze on Oroonoko. He adored the very cottage where she resided, and said that little inch of the world would give him more happiness than all the universe could do; and she vowed it was a palace, while adorned with the presence of Oroonoko.

Trefry was infinitely pleased with this novel,[6] and found this Clemene was the fair mistress of whom Caesar had before spoke; and was not a little satisfied that heaven was so kind to the Prince as to sweeten his misfortunes by so lucky an accident; and leaving the lovers to themselves, was impatient to come down to Parham House (which was on the same plantation) to give me an account of what had happened. I was as impatient to make these lovers a visit, having already made a friendship with Caesar, and from his own mouth learned what I have related; which was confirmed by his French-

5. A long-haired dog or poodle, especially associated with women of fashion.
6. I.e., novel event or piece of news.

man, who was set on shore to seek his fortunes, and of whom they could not make a slave, because a Christian, and he came daily to Parham Hill to see and pay his respects to his pupil prince. So that concerning and interesting myself in all that related to Caesar, whom I had assured of liberty as soon as the Governor arrived, I hasted presently to the place where the lovers were, and was infinitely glad to find this beautiful young slave (who had already gained all our esteems, for her modesty and her extraordinary prettiness) to be the same I had heard Caesar speak so much of. One may imagine then we paid her a treble respect; and though, from her being carved in fine flowers and birds all over her body, we took her to be of quality before, yet when we knew Clemene was Imoinda, we could not enough admire her.

I had forgot to tell you that those who are nobly born of that country are so delicately cut and rased[7] all over the forepart of the trunk of their bodies, that it looks as if it were japanned, the works being raised like high point round the edges of the flowers. Some are only carved with a little flower or bird at the sides of the temples, as was Caesar; and those who are so carved over the body resemble our ancient Picts,[8] that are figured in the chronicles, but these carvings are more delicate.

From that happy day Caesar took Clemene for his wife, to the general joy of all people; and there was as much magnificence as the country would afford at the celebration of this wedding: and in a very short time after she conceived with child, which made Caesar even adore her, knowing he was the last of his great race. This new accident made him more impatient of liberty, and he was every day treating with Trefry for his and Clemene's liberty, and offered either gold or a vast quantity of slaves, which should be paid before they let him go, provided he could have any security that he should go when his ransom was paid. They fed him from day to day with promises, and delayed him till the Lord Governor should come; so that he began to suspect them of falsehood, and that they would delay him till the time of his wife's delivery and make a slave of that too, for all the breed is theirs to whom the parents belong. This thought made him very uneasy, and his sullenness gave them some jealousies[9] of him; so that I was obliged, by some persons who feared a mutiny (which is very fatal sometimes in those colonies, that abound so with slaves that they exceed the whites in vast numbers), to discourse with Caesar, and to give him all the satisfaction I possibly could; they knew he and Clemene were scarce an hour in a day from my lodgings, that they eat with me, and that I obliged 'em in all things I was capable of. I entertained him with the lives of the Romans, and great men, which charmed him to my company, and her with teaching her all the pretty works[1] that I was mistress of, and telling her stories of nuns, and endeavoring to bring her to the knowledge of the true God. But of all discourses Caesar liked that the worst, and would never be reconciled to our notions of the Trinity, of which he ever made a jest; it was a riddle, he said, would turn his brain to conceive, and one could not make him understand what faith was. However, these conversations failed not altogether so well to divert him that he liked the company of us women much above the men, for he could

---

7. Incised. The carving is likened to figured lacquerwork in the Japanese style and to elaborate "high point" lace.
8. A North British people appearing in histories of England and Scotland.
9. Suspicions.
1. Decorative needlework or other handiwork.

not drink, and he is but an ill companion in that country that cannot. So that obliging him to love us very well, we had all the liberty of speech with him, especially myself, whom he called his Great Mistress; and indeed my word would go a great way with him. For these reasons, I had opportunity to take notice to him that he was not well pleased of late as he used to be; was more retired and thoughtful; and told him I took it ill he should suspect we would break our words with him, and not permit both him and Clemene to return to his own kingdom, which was not so long a way but when he was once on his voyage he would quickly arrive there. He made me some answers that showed a doubt in him, which made me ask him what advantage it would be to doubt. It would but give us a fear of him, and possibly compel us to treat him so as I should be very loath to behold; that is, it might occasion his confinement. Perhaps this was not so luckily spoke of me, for I perceived he resented that word, which I strove to soften again in vain. However, he assured me that whatsoever resolutions he should take, he would act nothing upon the white people; and as for myself and those upon that plantation where he was, he would sooner forfeit his eternal liberty, and life itself, than lift his hand against his greatest enemy on that place. He besought me to suffer no fears upon his account, for he could do nothing that honor should not dictate; but he accused himself for having suffered slavery so long; yet he charged that weakness on Love alone, who was capable of making him neglect even glory itself, and for which now he reproaches himself every moment of the day. Much more to this effect he spoke, with an air impatient enough to make me know he would not be long in bondage; and though he suffered only the name of a slave, and had nothing of the toil and labor of one, yet that was sufficient to render him uneasy; and he had been too long idle, who used to be always in action and in arms. He had a spirit all rough and fierce, and that could not be tamed to lazy rest; and though all endeavors were used to exercise himself in such actions and sports as this world afforded, as running, wrestling, pitching the bar, hunting and fishing, chasing and killing tigers of a monstrous size, which this continent affords in abundance, and wonderful snakes, such as Alexander is reported to have encountered at the river of Amazons,[2] and which Caesar took great delight to overcome, yet these were not actions great enough for his large soul, which was still panting after more renowned action.

Before I parted that day with him, I got, with much ado, a promise from him to rest yet a little longer with patience, and wait the coming of the Lord Governor, who was every day expected on our shore; he assured me he would, and this promise he desired me to know was given perfectly in complaisance to me, in whom he had an entire confidence.

After this, I neither thought it convenient to trust him much out of our view, nor did the country, who feared him; but with one accord it was advised to treat him fairly, and oblige him to remain within such a compass, and that he should be permitted as seldom as could be to go up to the plantations of the Negroes or, if he did, to be accompanied by some that should be rather in appearance attendants than spies. This care was for some time taken, and

---

2. Alexander the Great is supposed to have encountered both snakes and Amazons in a campaign against India. "Pitching the bar": game in which players compete in throwing a heavy bar or rod. "Tigers": wild cats, including the South American jaguar and cougar.

Caesar looked upon it as a mark of extraordinary respect, and was glad his discontent had obliged 'em to be more observant to him. He received new assurance from the overseer, which was confirmed to him by the opinion of all the gentlemen of the country, who made their court to him. During this time that we had his company more frequently than hitherto we had had, it may not be unpleasant to relate to you the diversions we entertained him with, or rather he us.

My stay was to be short in that country, because my father died at sea, and never arrived to possess the honor was designed him (which was lieutenant general of six and thirty islands, besides the continent[3] of Surinam) nor the advantages he hoped to reap by them; so that though we were obliged to continue on our voyage, we did not intend to stay upon the place. Though, in a word, I must say thus much of it, that certainly had his late Majesty, of sacred memory, but seen and known what a vast and charming world he had been master of in that continent, he would never have parted so easily with it to the Dutch. 'Tis a continent whose vast extent was never yet known, and may contain more noble earth than all the universe besides, for, they say, it reaches from east to west, one way as far as China and another to Peru. It affords all things both for beauty and use; 'tis there eternal spring, always the very months of April, May, and June; the shades are perpetual, the trees bearing at once all degrees of leaves and fruit, from blooming buds to ripe autumn: groves of oranges, lemons, citrons, figs, nutmegs, and noble aromatics, continually bearing their fragrancies. The trees appearing all like nosegays adorned with flowers of different kinds; some are all white, some purple, some scarlet, some blue, some yellow; bearing, at the same time, ripe fruit and blooming young, or producing every day new. The very wood of all these trees has an intrinsic value above common timber, for they are, when cut, of different colors, glorious to behold, and bear a price considerable, to inlay withal. Besides this they yield rich balm and gums, so that we make our candles of such an aromatic substance as does not only give a sufficient light, but, as they burn, they cast their perfumes all about. Cedar is the common firing, and all the houses are built with it. The very meat we eat, when set on the table, if it be native, I mean of the country, perfumes the whole room; especially a little beast called an armadilly, a thing which I can liken to nothing so well as a rhinoceros; 'tis all in white armor, so jointed that it moves as well in it as if it had nothing on; this beast is about the bigness of a pig of six weeks old. But it were endless to give an account of all the diverse wonderful and strange things that country affords, and which we took a very great delight to go in search of, though those adventures are oftentimes fatal and at least dangerous. But while we had Caesar in our company on these designs we feared no harm, nor suffered any.

As soon as I came into the country, the best house in it was presented me, called St. John's Hill. It stood on a vast rock of white marble, at the foot of which the river ran a vast depth down, and not to be descended on that side; the little waves still dashing and washing the foot of this rock made the softest murmurs and purlings in the world; and the opposite bank was adorned with such vast quantities of different flowers eternally blowing,[4] and

3. "Land not disjoined by the sea from other lands" (Johnson's *Dictionary*).
4. Blooming.

every day and hour new, fenced behind 'em with lofty trees of a thousand rare forms and colors, that the prospect was the most ravishing that fancy can create. On the edge of this white rock, towards the river, was a walk or grove of orange and lemon trees, about half the length of the Mall[5] here, whose flowery and fruit-bearing branches met at the top and hindered the sun, whose rays are very fierce there, from entering a beam into the grove; and the cool air that came from the river made it not only fit to entertain people in, at all the hottest hours of the day, but refreshed the sweet blossoms and made it always sweet and charming; and sure the whole globe of the world cannot show so delightful a place as this grove was. Not all the gardens of boasted Italy can produce a shade to outvie this, which nature had joined with art to render so exceeding fine; and 'tis a marvel to see how such vast trees, as big as English oaks, could take footing on so solid a rock and in so little earth as covered that rock; but all things by nature there are rare, delightful, and wonderful. But to our sports.

Sometimes we would go surprising,[6] and in search of young tigers in their dens, watching when the old ones went forth to forage for prey; and oftentimes we have been in great danger and have fled apace for our lives when surprised by the dams. But once, above all other times, we went on this design, and Caesar was with us, who had no sooner stolen a young tiger from her nest but, going off, we encountered the dam, bearing a buttock of a cow which he[7] had torn off with his mighty paw, and going with it towards his den. We had only four women, Caesar, and an English gentleman, brother to Harry Martin, the great Oliverian;[8] we found there was no escaping this enraged and ravenous beast. However, we women fled as fast as we could from it; but our heels had not saved our lives if Caesar had not laid down his cub, when he found the tiger quit her prey to make the more speed towards him, and taking Mr. Martin's sword, desired him to stand aside, or follow the ladies. He obeyed him, and Caesar met this monstrous beast of might, size, and vast limbs, who came with open jaws upon him; and fixing his awful stern eyes full upon those of the beast, and putting himself into a very steady and good aiming posture of defense, ran his sword quite through his breast down to his very heart, home to the hilt of the sword. The dying beast stretched forth her paw, and going to grasp his thigh, surprised with death in that very moment, did him no other harm than fixing her long nails in his flesh very deep, feebly wounded him, but could not grasp the flesh to tear off any. When he had done this, he hallooed to us to return, which, after some assurance of his victory, we did, and found him lugging out the sword from the bosom of the tiger, who was laid in her blood on the ground; he took up the cub, and with an unconcern that had nothing of the joy or gladness of a victory, he came and laid the whelp at my feet. We all extremely wondered at his daring, and at the bigness of the beast, which was about the heighth of a heifer but of mighty, great, and strong limbs.

Another time, being in the woods, he killed a tiger which had long infested that part, and borne away abundance of sheep and oxen, and other things

---

5. Fashionable walk in St. James's Park in London.
6. A military term for making sudden raids.
7. The jarring mixture of pronouns in the two accounts of the tigers (wild cats) may suggest a reluctance to use a feminine pronoun in moments of extreme violence. The first account was left uncorrected in all four 17th-century editions.
8. Supporter of Oliver Cromwell.

that were for the support of those to whom they belonged; abundance of people assailed this beast, some affirming they had shot her with several bullets quite through the body at several times, and some swearing they shot her through the very heart, and they believed she was a devil rather than a mortal thing. Caesar had often said he had a mind to encounter this monster, and spoke with several gentlemen who had attempted her, one crying, "I shot her with so many poisoned arrows," another with his gun in this part of her, and another in that; so that he, remarking all these places where she was shot, fancied still he should overcome her by giving her another sort of a wound than any had yet done; and one day said (at the table), "What trophies and garlands, ladies, will you make me, if I bring you home the heart of this ravenous beast that eats up all your lambs and pigs?" We all promised he should be rewarded at all our hands. So taking a bow, which he choosed out of a great many, he went up in the wood, with two gentlemen, where he imagined this devourer to be; they had not passed very far in it but they heard her voice, growling and grumbling, as if she were pleased with something she was doing. When they came in view, they found her muzzling in the belly of a new ravished sheep, which she had torn open; and seeing herself approached, she took fast hold of her prey with her forepaws and set a very fierce raging look on Caesar, without offering to approach him, for fear at the same time of losing what she had in possession. So that Caesar remained a good while, only taking aim, and getting an opportunity to shoot her where he designed; 'twas some time before he could accomplish it, and to wound her and not kill her would but have enraged her more, and endangered him. He had a quiver of arrows at his side, so that if one failed he could be supplied; at last, retiring a little, he gave her opportunity to eat, for he found she was ravenous, and fell to as soon as she saw him retire, being more eager of her prey than of doing new mischiefs. When he going softly to one side of her, and hiding his person behind certain herbage that grew high and thick, he took so good aim that, as he intended, he shot her just into the eye, and the arrow was sent with so good a will and so sure a hand that it stuck in her brain, and made her caper and become mad for a moment or two; but being seconded by another arrow, he fell dead upon the prey. Caesar cut him open with a knife, to see where those wounds were that had been reported to him, and why he did not die of 'em. But I shall now relate a thing that possibly will find no credit among men, because 'tis a notion commonly received with us, that nothing can receive a wound in the heart and live; but when the heart of this courageous animal was taken out, there were seven bullets of lead in it, and the wounds seamed up with great scars, and she lived with the bullets a great while, for it was long since they were shot. This heart the conqueror brought up to us, and 'twas a very great curiosity, which all the country came to see, and which gave Caesar occasion of many fine discourses, of accidents in war and strange escapes.

At other times he would go a-fishing; and discoursing on that diversion, he found we had in that country a very strange fish, called a numb eel[9] (an eel of which I have eaten), that while it is alive, it has a quality so cold, that those who are angling, though with a line of never so great a length with a rod at the end of it, it shall, in the same minute the bait is touched by this eel, seize

9. Electric eel.

him or her that holds the rod with benumbedness, that shall deprive 'em of sense for a while; and some have fallen into the water, and others dropped as dead on the banks of the rivers where they stood, as soon as this fish touches the bait. Caesar used to laugh at this, and believed it impossible a man could lose his force at the touch of a fish, and could not understand that philoso-phy,[1] that a cold quality should be of that nature. However, he had a great curiosity to try whether it would have the same effect on him it had on others, and often tried, but in vain. At last the sought for fish came to the bait, as he stood angling on the bank; and instead of throwing away the rod or giving it a sudden twitch out of the water, whereby he might have caught both the eel and have dismissed the rod, before it could have too much power over him, for experiment sake he grasped it but the harder, and faint-ing fell into the river; and being still possessed of the rod, the tide carried him, senseless as he was, a great way, till an Indian boat took him up, and perceived when they touched him a numbness seize them, and by that knew the rod was in his hand; which with a paddle (that is, a short oar) they struck away, and snatched it into the boat, eel and all. If Caesar were almost dead with the effect of this fish, he was more so with that of the water, where he had remained the space of going a league, and they found they had much ado to bring him back to life. But at last they did, and brought him home, where he was in a few hours well recovered and refreshed, and not a little ashamed to find he should be overcome by an eel, and that all the people who heard his defiance would laugh at him. But we cheered him up; and he being convinced, we had the eel at supper, which was a quarter of an ell about and most deli-cate meat, and was of the more value, since it cost so dear as almost the life of so gallant a man.

About this time we were in many mortal fears about some disputes the English had with the Indians, so that we could scarce trust ourselves, with-out great numbers, to go to any Indian towns or place where they abode, for fear they should fall upon us, as they did immediately after my coming away; and that it was in the possession of the Dutch, who used 'em not so civilly as the English, so that they cut in pieces all they could take, getting into houses and hanging up the mother and all her children about her, and cut a foot-man I left behind me all in joints, and nailed him to trees.

This feud began while I was there, so that I lost half the satisfaction I proposed, in not seeing and visiting the Indian towns. But one day, bemoan-ing of our misfortunes upon this account, Caesar told us we need not fear, for if we had a mind to go, he would undertake to be our guard. Some would, but most would not venture; about eighteen of us resolved and took barge, and after eight days arrived near an Indian town. But approaching it, the hearts of some of our company failed, and they would not venture on shore; so we polled who would and who would not. For my part, I said if Caesar would, I would go; he resolved; so did my brother and my woman, a maid of good courage. Now none of us speaking the language of the people, and imagining we should have a half diversion in gazing only and not knowing what they said, we took a fisherman that lived at the mouth of the river, who had been a long inhabitant there, and obliged him to go with us. But because he was known to the Indians, as trading among 'em, and being by long living

---

1. "Hypothesis or system upon which natural effects are explained" (Johnson's *Dictionary*).

there become a perfect Indian in color, we, who resolved to surprise 'em by making 'em see something they never had seen (that is, white people), resolved only myself, my brother and woman should go; so Caesar, the fisherman, and the rest, hiding behind some thick reeds and flowers that grew on the banks, let us pass on towards the town, which was on the bank of the river all along. A little distant from the houses, or huts, we saw some dancing, others busied in fetching and carrying of water from the river. They had no sooner spied us but they set up a loud cry, that frighted us at first; we thought it had been for those that should kill us, but it seems it was of wonder and amazement. They were all naked, and we were dressed so as is most commode for the hot countries, very glittering and rich, so that we appeared extremely fine; my own hair was cut short, and I had a taffety cap with black feathers on my head; my brother was in a stuff[2] suit, with silver loops and buttons and abundance of green ribbon. This was all infinitely surprising to them, and because we saw them stand still till we approached 'em, we took heart and advanced, came up to 'em, and offered 'em our hands; which they took, and looked on us round about, calling still for more company; who came swarming out, all wondering and crying out *"Tepeeme,"* taking their hair up in their hands and spreading it wide to those they called out to, as if they would say (as indeed it signified) "Numberless wonders," or not to be recounted, no more than to number the hair of their heads. By degrees they grew more bold, and from gazing upon us round, they touched us, laying their hands upon all the features of our faces, feeling our breasts and arms, taking up one petticoat, then wondering to see another; admiring our shoes and stockings, but more our garters, which we gave 'em, and they tied about their legs, being laced with silver lace at the ends, for they much esteem any shining things. In fine, we suffered 'em to survey us as they pleased, and we thought they would never have done admiring us. When Caesar and the rest saw we were received with such wonder, they came up to us; and finding the Indian trader whom they knew (for 'tis by these fishermen, called Indian traders, we hold a commerce with 'em, for they love not to go far from home, and we never go to them), when they saw him therefore they set up a new joy, and cried, in their language, "Oh! here's our *tiguamy*, and we shall now know whether those things can speak." So advancing to him, some of 'em gave him their hands and cried, *"Amora tiguamy,"* which is as much as, "How do you?" or "Welcome, friend," and all with one din began to gabble to him, and asked if we had sense and wit; if we could talk of affairs of life and war, as they could do; if we could hunt, swim, and do a thousand things they use. He answered 'em, we could. Then they invited us into their houses, and dressed venison and buffalo for us; and going out, gathered a leaf of a tree called a *sarumbo* leaf, of six yards long, and spread it on the ground for a tablecloth; and cutting another in pieces instead of plates, setting us on little bow Indian stools, which they cut out of one entire piece of wood and paint in a sort of japan work. They serve everyone their mess[3] on these pieces of leaves, and it was very good, but too high seasoned with pepper. When we had eat, my brother and I took out our flutes and played to 'em, which gave 'em new wonder; and I soon perceived, by an admiration that is natural to these people, and by the extreme ignorance and simplicity of 'em, it were not

---

2. Woven fabric, worsted. "Commode": suitable.   3. Meal.

difficult to establish any unknown or extravagant religion among them, and to impose any notions or fictions upon 'em. For seeing a kinsman of mine set some paper afire with a burning glass, a trick they had never before seen, they were like to have adored him for a god, and begged he would give them the characters or figures of his name, that they might oppose it against winds and storms; which he did, and they held it up in those seasons, and fancied it had a charm to conquer them, and kept it like a holy relic. They are very superstitious, and called him the great *Peeie*, that is, prophet. They showed us their Indian *Peeie*, a youth of about sixteen years old, as handsome as nature could make a man. They consecrate a beautiful youth from his infancy, and all arts are used to complete him in the finest manner, both in beauty and shape. He is bred to all the little arts and cunning they are capable of, to all the legerdemain tricks and sleight of hand, whereby he imposes upon the rabble, and is both a doctor in physic[4] and divinity; and by these tricks makes the sick believe he sometimes eases their pains, by drawing from the afflicted part little serpents, or odd flies, or worms, or any strange thing; and though they have besides undoubted good remedies for almost all their diseases, they cure the patient more by fancy than by medicines, and make themselves feared, loved, and reverenced. This young *Peeie* had a very young wife, who seeing my brother kiss her, came running and kissed me; after this they kissed one another, and made it a very great jest, it being so novel; and new admiration and laughing went round the multitude, that they never will forget that ceremony, never before used or known. Caesar had a mind to see and talk with their war captains, and we were conducted to one of their houses, where we beheld several of the great captains, who had been at council. But so frightful a vision it was to see 'em no fancy can create; no such dreams can represent so dreadful a spectacle. For my part I took 'em for hobgoblins or fiends rather than men; but however their shapes appeared, their souls were very humane and noble; but some wanted their noses, some their lips, some both noses and lips, some their ears, and others cut through each cheek with long slashes, through which their teeth appeared; they had other several formidable wounds and scars, or rather dismemberings. They had *comitias* or little aprons before 'em, and girdles of cotton, with their knives naked, stuck in it; a bow at their backs and a quiver of arrows on their thighs; and most had feathers on their heads of diverse colors. They cried *"Amora tiguamy"* to us at our entrance, and were pleased we said as much to 'em; they seated us, and gave us drink of the best sort, and wondered, as much as the others had done before, to see us. Caesar was marveling as much at their faces, wondering how they should all be so wounded in war; he was impatient to know how they all came by those frightful marks of rage or malice, rather than wounds got in noble battle. They told us, by our interpreter, that when any war was waging, two men chosen out by some old captain whose fighting was past, and who could only teach the theory of war, these two men were to stand in competition for the generalship, or great war captain; and being brought before the old judges, now past labor, they are asked what they dare do to show they are worthy to lead an army. When he who is first asked, making no reply, cuts off his nose, and throws it contemptibly[5] on the ground; and the other does something to

4. Medicine.

5. With contempt.

himself that he thinks surpasses him, and perhaps deprives himself of lips and an eye; so they slash on till one gives out, and many have died in this debate. And 'tis by a passive valor they show and prove their activity, a sort of courage too brutal to be applauded by our black hero; nevertheless he expressed his esteem of 'em.

In this voyage Caesar begot so good an understanding between the Indians and the English that there were no more fears or heart-burnings during our stay, but we had a perfect, open, and free trade with 'em. Many things remarkable and worthy reciting we met with in this short voyage, because Caesar made it his business to search out and provide for our entertainment, especially to please his dearly adored Imoinda, who was a sharer in all our adventures; we being resolved to make her chains as easy as we could, and to compliment the Prince in that manner that most obliged him.

As we were coming up again, we met with some Indians of strange aspects; that is, of a larger size and other sort of features than those of our country. Our Indian slaves that rowed us asked 'em some questions, but they could not understand us; but showed us a long cotton string with several knots on it, and told us, they had been coming from the mountains so many moons as there were knots. They were habited in skins of a strange beast, and brought along with 'em bags of gold dust, which, as well as they could give us to understand, came streaming in little small channels down the high mountains when the rains fell; and offered to be the convoy to any body or persons that would go to the mountains. We carried these men up to Parham, where they were kept till the Lord Governor came. And because all the country was mad to be going on this golden adventure, the Governor by his letters commanded (for they sent some of the gold to him) that a guard should be set at the mouth of the river of Amazons[6] (a river so called, almost as broad as the river of Thames) and prohibited all people from going up that river, it conducting to those mountains of gold. But we going off for England before the project was further prosecuted, and the Governor being drowned in a hurricane, either the design died, or the Dutch have the advantage of it. And 'tis to be bemoaned what his Majesty lost by losing that part of America.

Though this digression is a little from my story, however since it contains some proofs of the curiosity and daring of this great man, I was content to omit nothing of his character.

It was thus for some time we diverted him; but now Imoinda began to show she was with child, and did nothing but sigh and weep for the captivity of her lord, herself, and the infant yet unborn, and believed if it were so hard to gain the liberty of two, 'twould be more difficult to get that for three. Her griefs were so many darts in the great heart of Caesar; and taking his opportunity one Sunday when all the whites were overtaken in drink, as there were abundance of several trades and slaves for four years[7] that inhabited among the Negro houses, and Sunday was their day of debauch (otherwise they were a sort of spies upon Caesar), he went pretending out of goodness to 'em to feast amongst 'em; and sent all his music, and ordered a great treat for the whole gang, about three hundred Negroes; and about a hundred and fifty were able to bear arms, such as they had, which were

---

6. The mouth of the Amazon, in Brazil, is far distant from Surinam.

7. Whites who, for crimes or debt, were indentured for a fixed period. "Trades": tradesman.

sufficient to do execution[8] with spirits accordingly. For the English had none but rusty swords that no strength could draw from a scabbard, except the people of particular quality, who took care to oil 'em and keep 'em in good order. The guns also, unless here and there one, or those newly carried from England, would do no good or harm; for 'tis the nature of that country to rust and eat up iron, or any metals but gold and silver. And they are very unexpert at the bow, which the Negroes and Indians are perfect masters of.

Caesar, having singled out these men from the women and children, made an harangue to 'em of the miseries and ignominies of slavery, counting up all their toils and sufferings, under such loads, burdens, and drudgeries as were fitter for beasts than men, senseless brutes than human souls. He told 'em, it was not for days, months, or years, but for eternity; there was no end to be of their misfortunes. They suffered not like men, who might find a glory and fortitude in oppression, but like dogs that loved the whip and bell,[9] and fawned the more they were beaten. That they had lost the divine quality of men and were become insensible asses, fit only to bear; nay, worse: an ass, or dog, or horse, having done his duty, could lie down in retreat and rise to work again, and while he did his duty endured no stripes; but men, villainous, senseless men such as they, toiled on all the tedious week till Black Friday;[1] and then, whether they worked or not, whether they were faulty or meriting, they promiscuously, the innocent with the guilty, suffered the infamous whip, the sordid stripes, from their fellow slaves, till their blood trickled from all parts of their body, blood whose every drop ought to be revenged with a life of some of those tyrants that impose it. "And why," said he, "my dear friends and fellow sufferers, should we be slaves to an unknown people? Have they vanquished us nobly in fight? Have they won us in honorable battle? And are we by the chance of war become their slaves? This would not anger a noble heart, this would not animate a soldier's soul; no, but we are bought and sold like apes or monkeys, to be the sport of women, fools, and cowards, and the support of rogues, runagades,[2] that have abandoned their own countries for rapine, murders, thefts, and villainies. Do you not hear every day how they upbraid each other with infamy of life, below the wildest savages; and shall we render obedience to such a degenerate race, who have no one human virtue left to distinguish 'em from the vilest creatures? Will you, I say, suffer the lash from such hands?" They all replied, with one accord, "No, no, no; Caesar has spoke like a great captain, like a great king."

After this he would have proceeded, but was interrupted by a tall Negro of some more quality than the rest; his name was Tuscan; who bowing at the feet of Caesar, cried, "My lord, we have listened with joy and attention to what you have said, and, were we only men, would follow so great a leader through the world. But oh! consider, we are husbands and parents too, and have things more dear to us than life, our wives and children, unfit for travel in these unpassable woods, mountains, and bogs; we have not only difficult lands to overcome, but rivers to wade, and monsters to encounter, ravenous

---

8. Harm, slaughter.
9. Proverbial for something that distracts from comfort or pleasure, from the protective charm on chariots of triumphing generals in ancient Rome.

1. Here a day of customary beating; more widely, a Friday bringing some notable disaster, from students' slang for examination day.
2. Renegades or fugitives.

beasts of prey—." To this, Caesar replied that honor was the first principle in nature that was to be obeyed; but as no man would pretend to that, without all the acts of virtue, compassion, charity, love, justice, and reason, he found it not inconsistent with that to take an equal care of their wives and children as they would of themselves; and that he did not design, when he led them to freedom and glorious liberty, that they should leave that better part of themselves to perish by the hand of the tyrant's whip. But if there were a woman among them so degenerate from love and virtue to choose slavery before the pursuit of her husband, and with the hazard of her life to share with him in his fortunes, that such a one ought to be abandoned, and left as a prey to the common enemy.

To which they all agreed—and bowed. After this, he spoke of the impassable woods and rivers, and convinced 'em, the more danger, the more glory. He told them that he had heard of one Hannibal, a great captain, had cut his way through mountains of solid rocks;[3] and should a few shrubs oppose them, which they could fire before 'em? No, 'twas a trifling excuse to men resolved to die or overcome. As for bogs, they are with a little labor filled and hardened; and the rivers could be no obstacle, since they swam by nature, at least by custom, from their first hour of their birth. That when the children were weary they must carry them by turns, and the woods and their own industry would afford them food. To this they all assented with joy.

Tuscan then demanded what he would do. He said, they would travel towards the sea, plant a new colony, and defend it by their valor; and when they could find a ship, either driven by stress of weather or guided by Providence that way, they would seize it and make it a prize, till it had transported them to their own countries; at least, they should be made free in his kingdom, and be esteemed as his fellow sufferers, and men that had the courage and the bravery to attempt, at least, for liberty; and if they died in the attempt it would be more brave than to live in perpetual slavery.

They bowed and kissed his feet at this resolution, and with one accord vowed to follow him to death. And that night was appointed to begin their march; they made it known to their wives, and directed them to tie their hamaca[4] about their shoulder and under their arm like a scarf, and to lead their children that could go, and carry those that could not. The wives, who pay an entire obedience to their husbands, obeyed, and stayed for 'em where they were appointed. The men stayed but to furnish themselves with what defensive arms they could get; and all met at the rendezvous, where Caesar made a new encouraging speech to 'em, and led 'em out.

But as they could not march far that night, on Monday early, when the overseers went to call 'em all together to go to work, they were extremely surprised to find not one upon the place, but all fled with what baggage they had. You may imagine this news was not only suddenly spread all over the plantation, but soon reached the neighboring ones; and we had by noon about six hundred men they call the militia of the county, that came to assist us in the pursuit of the fugitives. But never did one see so comical an army march forth to war. The men of any fashion would not concern themselves, though it were almost the common cause; for such revoltings are very ill

3. The Carthaginian general and his troops literally hacked their way down the Alps into Italy to attack Rome.
4. Hammock.

examples, and have very fatal consequences oftentimes in many colonies. But they had a respect for Caesar, and all hands were against the Parhamites, as they called those of Parham plantation, because they did not, in the first place, love the Lord Governor, and secondly they would have it that Caesar was ill used, and baffled with;[5] and 'tis not impossible but some of the best in the country was of his counsel in this flight, and depriving us of all the slaves; so that they of the better sort would not meddle in the matter. The deputy governor,[6] of whom I have had no great occasion to speak, and who was the most fawning fair-tongued fellow in the world and one that pretended the most friendship to Caesar, was now the only violent man against him; and though he had nothing, and so need fear nothing, yet talked and looked bigger than any man. He was a fellow whose character is not fit to be mentioned with the worst of the slaves. This fellow would lead his army forth to meet Caesar, or rather to pursue him; most of their arms were of those sort of cruel whips they call cat with nine tails; some had rusty useless guns for show, others old basket hilts[7] whose blades had never seen the light in this age, and others had long staffs and clubs. Mr. Trefry went along, rather to be a mediator than a conqueror in such a battle; for he foresaw and knew, if by fighting they put the Negroes into despair, they were a sort of sullen fellows that would drown or kill themselves before they would yield; and he advised that fair means was best. But Byam was one that abounded in his own wit and would take his own measures.

It was not hard to find these fugitives; for as they fled they were forced to fire and cut the woods before 'em, so that night or day they pursued 'em by the light they made and by the path they had cleared. But as soon as Caesar found he was pursued, he put himself in a posture of defense, placing all the women and children in the rear, and himself with Tuscan by his side, or next to him, all promising to die or conquer. Encouraged thus, they never stood to parley, but fell on pell-mell upon the English, and killed some and wounded a good many, they having recourse to their whips as the best of their weapons. And as they observed no order, they perplexed the enemy so sorely with lashing 'em in the eyes; and the women and children seeing their husbands so treated, being of fearful cowardly dispositions, and hearing the English cry out, "Yield and live, yield and be pardoned," they all run in amongst their husbands and fathers, and hung about 'em, crying out, "Yield, yield; and leave Caesar to their revenge"; that by degrees the slaves abandoned Caesar, and left him only Tuscan and his heroic Imoinda; who, grown big as she was, did nevertheless press near her lord, having a bow and a quiver full of poisoned arrows, which she managed with such dexterity that she wounded several, and shot the governor[8] into the shoulder; of which wound he had like to have died, but that an Indian woman, his mistress, sucked the wound and cleansed it from the venom. But however, he stirred not from the place till he had parleyed with Caesar, who he found was resolved to die fighting, and would not be taken; no more would Tuscan, or Imoinda. But he, more thirsting after revenge of another sort than that of depriving him of life, now made use of all his art of talking and dissembling,

5. Cheated.
6. William Byam. There are recorded complaints against him for high-handedness and from him about insubordination by settlers and slaves.
7. Swords with protective hilt guards.
8. I.e., Byam, the deputy governor.

and besought Caesar to yield himself upon terms which he himself should propose, and should be sacredly assented to and kept by him. He told him, it was not that he any longer feared him, or could believe the force of two men, and a young heroine, could overcome all them, with all the slaves now on their side also; but it was the vast esteem he had for his person, the desire he had to serve so gallant a man, and to hinder himself from the reproach hereafter of having been the occasion of the death of a prince whose valor and magnanimity deserved the empire of the world. He protested to him, he looked upon this action as gallant and brave, however tending to the prejudice of his lord and master, who would by it have lost so considerable a number of slaves; that this flight of his should be looked on as a heat of youth, and rashness of a too forward courage, and an unconsidered impatience of liberty, and no more; and that he labored in vain to accomplish that which they would effectually perform as soon as any ship arrived that would touch on his coast. "So that if you will be pleased," continued he, "to surrender yourself, all imaginable respect shall be paid you; and yourself, your wife, and child, if it be here born, shall depart free out of our land."

But Caesar would hear of no composition;[9] though Byam urged, if he pursued and went on in his design, he would inevitably perish, either by great snakes, wild beasts, or hunger; and he ought to have regard to his wife, whose condition required ease, and not the fatigues of tedious travel, where she could not be secured from being devoured. But Caesar told him, there was no faith in the white men or the gods they adored, who instructed 'em in principles so false that honest men could not live amongst 'em; though no people professed so much, none performed so little; that he knew what he had to do when he dealt with men of honor, but with them a man ought to be eternally on his guard, and never to eat and drink with Christians without his weapon of defense in his hand; and for his own security, never to credit one word they spoke. As for the rashness and inconsiderateness of his action, he would confess the governor is in the right; and that he was ashamed of what he had done, in endeavoring to make those free who were by nature slaves, poor wretched rogues, fit to be used as Christians' tools; dogs, treacherous and cowardly, fit for such masters; and they wanted only but to be whipped into the knowledge of the Christian gods to be the vilest of all creeping things, to learn to worship such deities as had not power to make 'em just, brave, or honest. In fine, after a thousand things of this nature, not fit here to be recited, he told Byam he had rather die than live upon the same earth with such dogs. But Trefry and Byam pleaded and protested together so much that Trefry, believing the governor to mean what he said, and speaking very cordially himself, generously put himself into Caesar's hands, and took him aside and persuaded him, even with tears, to live, by surrendering himself, and to name his conditions. Caesar was overcome by his wit and reasons, and in consideration of Imoinda; and demanding what he desired, and that it should be ratified by their hands in writing, because he had perceived that was the common way of contract between man and man, amongst the whites. All this was performed, and Tuscan's pardon was put in, and they surrender to the governor, who walked peaceably down into the plantation with 'em, after giving order to bury their dead. Caesar was very much toiled with the

9. Settlement.

bustle of the day, for he had fought like a fury; and what mischief was done he and Tuscan performed alone, and gave their enemies a fatal proof that they durst do anything and feared no mortal force.

But they were no sooner arrived at the place where all the slaves receive their punishments of whipping, but they laid hands on Caesar and Tuscan, faint with heat and toil; and surprising them, bound them to two several stakes, and whipped them in a most deplorable and inhuman manner, rending the very flesh from their bones; especially Caesar, who was not perceived to make any moan or to alter his face, only to roll his eyes on the faithless governor, and those he believed guilty, with fierceness and indignation; and to complete his rage, he saw every one of those slaves, who but a few days before adored him as something more than mortal, now had a whip to give him some lashes, while he strove not to break his fetters; though if he had, it were impossible. But he pronounced a woe and revenge from his eyes, that darted fire that 'twas at once both awful and terrible to behold.

When they thought they were sufficiently revenged on him, they untied him, almost fainting with loss of blood from a thousand wounds all over his body, from which they had rent his clothes, and led him bleeding and naked as he was, and loaded him all over with irons; and then rubbed his wounds, to complete their cruelty, with Indian pepper, which had like to have made him raving mad; and in this condition made him so fast to the ground that he could not stir, if his pains and wounds would have given him leave. They spared Imoinda, and did not let her see this barbarity committed towards her lord, but carried her down to Parham and shut her up; which was not in kindness to her, but for fear she should die with the sight, or miscarry, and then they should lose a young slave and perhaps the mother.

You must know, that when the news was brought on Monday morning that Caesar had betaken himself to the woods and carried with him all the Negroes, we were possessed with extreme fear, which no persuasions could dissipate, that he would secure himself till night, and then that he would come down and cut all our throats. This apprehension made all the females of us fly down the river, to be secured; and while we were away they acted this cruelty. For I suppose I had authority and interest enough there, had I suspected any such thing, to have prevented it; but we had not gone many leagues but the news overtook us that Caesar was taken and whipped like a common slave. We met on the river with Colonel Martin, a man of great gallantry, wit, and goodness, and whom I have celebrated in a character of my new comedy[1] by his own name, in memory of so brave a man. He was wise and eloquent and, from the fineness of his parts, bore a great sway over the hearts of all the colony. He was a friend to Caesar, and resented this false dealing with him very much. We carried him back to Parham, thinking to have made an accommodation; when we came, the first news we heard was that the governor was dead of a wound Imoinda had given him; but it was not so well. But it seems he would have the pleasure of beholding the revenge he took on Caesar, and before the cruel ceremony was finished, he dropped down; and then they perceived the wound he had on his shoulder was by a venomed arrow, which, as I said, his Indian mistress healed by sucking the wound.

---

1. *The Younger Brother; or, The Amorous Jilt,* not produced until 1696 despite this piece of promotion.

We were no sooner arrived but we went up to the plantation to see Caesar, whom we found in a very miserable and unexpressible condition; and I have a thousand times admired how he lived, in so much tormenting pain. We said all things to him that trouble, pity, and good nature could suggest, protesting our innocency of the fact and our abhorrence of such cruelties; making a thousand professions of services to him and begging as many pardons for the offenders, till we said so much that he believed we had no hand in his ill treatment; but told us he could never pardon Byam; as for Trefry, he confessed he saw his grief and sorrow for his suffering, which he could not hinder, but was like to have been beaten down by the very slaves for speaking in his defense. But for Byam, who was their leader, their head—and should, by his justice and honor, have been an example to 'em—for him, he wished to live, to take a dire revenge of him, and said, "It had been well for him if he had sacrificed me, instead of giving me the contemptible[2] whip." He refused to talk much, but begging us to give him our hands, he took 'em, and protested never to lift up his to do us any harm. He had a great respect for Colonel Martin, and always took his counsel like that of a parent, and assured him he would obey him in anything but his revenge on Byam. "Therefore," said he, "for his own safety, let him speedily dispatch me; for if I could dispatch myself I would not, till that justice were done to my injured person,[3] and the contempt of a soldier. No, I would not kill myself, even after a whipping, but will be content to live with that infamy, and be pointed at by every grinning slave, till I have completed my revenge; and then you shall see that Oroonoko scorns to live with the indignity that was put on Caesar." All we could do could get no more words from him; and we took care to have him put immediately into a healing bath to rid him of his pepper, and ordered a chirurgeon[4] to anoint him with healing balm, which he suffered; and in some time he began to be able to walk and eat. We failed not to visit him every day, and to that end had him brought to an apartment at Parham.

The governor was no sooner recovered, and had heard of the menaces of Caesar, but he called his council; who (not to disgrace them, or burlesque the government there) consisted of such notorious villains as Newgate[5] never transported; and possibly originally were such who understood neither the laws of God or man, and had no sort of principles to make 'em worthy the name of men; but at the very council table would contradict and fight with one another, and swear so bloodily that 'twas terrible to hear and see 'em. (Some of 'em were afterwards hanged when the Dutch took possession of the place, others sent off in chains.) But calling these special rulers of the nation together, and requiring their counsel in this weighty affair, they all concluded that (Damn 'em) it might be their own cases; and that Caesar ought to be made an example to all the Negroes, to fright 'em from daring to threaten their betters, their lords and masters; and at this rate no man was safe from his own slaves; and concluded, *nemine contradicente*,[6] that Caesar should be hanged.

Trefry then thought it time to use his authority, and told Byam his command did not extend to his lord's plantation, and that Parham was as much

---

2. Showing contempt.
3. Body or character.
4. Surgeon.

5. The major London prison, from which criminals were transported to the colonies.
6. No one disagreeing (Latin).

exempt from the law as Whitehall,[7] and that they ought no more to touch the servants of the Lord——(who there represented the King's person) than they could those about the King himself; and that Parham was a sanctuary; and though his lord were absent in person, his power was still in being there, which he had entrusted with him as far as the dominions of his particular plantations reached, and all that belonged to it; the rest of the country, as Byam was lieutenant to his lord, he might exercise his tyranny upon. Trefry had others as powerful, or more, that interested themselves in Caesar's life, and absolutely said he should be defended. So turning the governor and his wise council out of doors (for they sat at Parham House), they set a guard upon our landing place, and would admit none but those we called friends to us and Caesar.

The governor having remained wounded at Parham till his recovery was completed, Caesar did not know but he was still there; and indeed, for the most part his time was spent there, for he was one that loved to live at other people's expense; and if he were a day absent, he was ten present there, and used to play and walk and hunt and fish with Caesar. So that Caesar did not at all doubt, if he once recovered strength, but he should find an opportunity of being revenged on him. Though after such a revenge, he could not hope to live, for if he escaped the fury of the English mobile,[8] who perhaps would have been glad of the occasion to have killed him, he was resolved not to survive his whipping; yet he had, some tender hours, a repenting softness, which he called his fits of coward, wherein he struggled with Love for the victory of his heart, which took part with his charming Imoinda there; but for the most part his time was passed in melancholy thought and black designs. He considered, if he should do this deed and die, either in the attempt or after it, he left his lovely Imoinda a prey, or at best a slave, to the enraged multitude; his great heart could not endure that thought. "Perhaps," said he, "she may be first ravished by every brute, exposed first to their nasty lusts and then a shameful death." No; he could not live a moment under that apprehension, too insupportable to be borne. These were his thoughts and his silent arguments with his heart, as he told us afterwards; so that now resolving not only to kill Byam but all those he thought had enraged him, pleasing his great heart with the fancied slaughter he should make over the whole face of the plantation, he first resolved on a deed, that (however horrid it at first appeared to us all), when we had heard his reasons, we thought it brave and just. Being able to walk and, as he believed, fit for the execution of his great design, he begged Trefry to trust him into the air, believing a walk would do him good, which was granted him; and taking Imoinda with him, as he used to do in his more happy and calmer days, he led her up into a wood, where, after (with a thousand sighs, and long gazing silently on her face, while tears gushed, in spite of him, from his eyes) he told her his design first of killing her, and then his enemies, and next himself, and the impossibility of escaping, and therefore he told her the necessity of dying, he found the heroic wife faster pleading for death than he was to propose it, when she found his fixed resolution, and on her knees besought him not to leave her a prey to his enemies. He (grieved to death) yet pleased at her

7. The king's palace in London. Trefry stands as Lord Willoughby's deputy on his private land, Byam in the colony at large.
8. Common people or mob.

noble resolution, took her up, and embracing her with all the passion and languishment of a dying lover, drew his knife to kill this treasure of his soul, this pleasure of his eyes; while tears trickled down his cheeks, hers were smiling with joy she should die by so noble a hand, and be sent in her own country (for that's their notion of the next world) by him she so tenderly loved and so truly adored in this; for wives have a respect for their husbands equal to what any other people pay a deity, and when a man finds any occasion to quit his wife, if he love her, she dies by his hand; if not, he sells her, or suffers some other to kill her. It being thus, you may believe the deed was soon resolved on; and 'tis not to be doubted but the parting, the eternal leave-taking of two such lovers, so greatly born, so sensible,[9] so beautiful, so young, and so fond, must be very moving, as the relation of it was to me afterwards.

C. Grignion, after J. Barralet, *Mr. Savigny in the Character of Oroonoko*; engraving, 1785. Through the 18th century, the story of *Oroonoko* was known mostly in a 1696 play adapted from Behn's work by Thomas Southerne. His version makes Imoinda white, as this scene from a 1775 production shows. The actor plays Oroonoko in blackface, here on the verge of killing Imoinda. In *Oroonoko. A tragedy. Written by Thomas Southern, Marked with the variations in the manager's book, at the Theatre-Royal in Drury-Lane* (1785).

All that love could say in such cases being ended, and all the intermitting irreso-lutions being adjusted, the lovely, young, and adored victim lays herself down before the sacrificer; while he, with a hand resolved and a heart break-ing within, gave the fatal stroke; first cutting her throat, and then severing her yet smiling face from that delicate body, pregnant as it was with fruits of tenderest love. As soon as he had done, he laid the body decently on leaves and flowers, of which he made a bed, and concealed it under the same cover-lid of nature; only her face he left yet bare to look on. But when he found she was dead and past all retrieve, never more to bless him with her eyes and soft language, his grief swelled up to rage; he tore, he raved, he roared, like some monster of the wood, calling on the loved name of Imoinda. A thousand times he turned the fatal knife that did the deed toward his own heart, with a resolution to go immediately after her; but dire revenge, which now was a

9. Sensitive.

thousand times more fierce in his soul than before, prevents him; and he would cry out, "No; since I have sacrificed Imoinda to my revenge, shall I lose that glory which I have purchased so dear as at the price of the fairest, dearest, softest creature that ever nature made? No, no!" Then, at her name, grief would get the ascendant of rage, and he would lie down by her side and water her face with showers of tears, which never were wont to fall from those eyes. And however bent he was on his intended slaughter, he had not power to stir from the sight of this dear object, now more beloved and more adored than ever.

He remained in this deploring condition for two days, and never rose from the ground where he had made his sad sacrifice. At last, rousing from her side, and accusing himself with living too long now Imoinda was dead, and that the deaths of those barbarous enemies were deferred too long, he resolved now to finish the great work; but offering to rise, he found his strength so decayed that he reeled to and fro, like boughs assailed by contrary winds; so that he was forced to lie down again, and try to summon all his courage to his aid. He found his brains turned round, and his eyes were dizzy, and objects appeared not the same to him they were wont to do; his breath was short, and all his limbs surprised with a faintness he had never felt before. He had not eat in two days, which was one occasion of this feebleness, but excess of grief was the greatest; yet still he hoped he should recover vigor to act his design, and lay expecting it yet six days longer, still mourning over the dead idol of his heart, and striving every day to rise, but could not.

In all this time you may believe we were in no little affliction for Caesar and his wife; some were of opinion he was escaped never to return; others thought some accident had happened to him. But however, we failed not to send out an hundred people several ways to search for him; a party of about forty went that way he took, among whom was Tuscan, who was perfectly reconciled to Byam. They had not gone very far into the wood but they smelt an unusual smell, as of a dead body; for stinks must be very noisome that can be distinguished among such a quantity of natural sweets as every inch of that land produces. So that they concluded they should find him dead, or somebody that was so. They passed on towards it, as loathsome as it was, and made such a rustling among the leaves that lie thick on the ground, by continual falling, that Caesar heard he was approached; and though he had during the space of these eight days endeavored to rise, but found he wanted strength, yet looking up and seeing his pursuers, he rose and reeled to a neighboring tree, against which he fixed his back; and being within a dozen yards of those that advanced and saw him, he called out to them and bid them approach no nearer, if they would be safe. So that they stood still, and hardly believing their eyes, that would persuade them that it was Caesar that spoke to 'em, so much was he altered, they asked him what he had done with his wife, for they smelt a stink that almost struck them dead. He, pointing to the dead body, sighing, cried, "Behold her there." They put off the flowers that covered her with their sticks, and found she was killed, and cried out, "Oh, monster! that hast murdered thy wife." Then asking him why he did so cruel a deed, he replied, he had no leisure to answer impertinent questions. "You may go back," continued he, "and tell the faithless governor he may thank fortune that I am breathing my last, and that my arm is too feeble to obey my heart in what it had designed him." But his tongue faltering, and trembling, he could scarce end what he was saying. The English, taking advantage by his weakness, cried, "Let us take him alive by all means." He heard 'em; and as if he had revived from a fainting, or a dream, he cried out, "No, gentlemen, you are deceived; you will find no more Caesars to be whipped, no more find a faith in me. Feeble as you think me, I have strength yet left to secure me from a second indignity." They swore all anew, and he only shook his head and beheld them with scorn. Then they cried out, "Who will venture on this single man? Will nobody?" They stood all silent while Caesar replied, "Fatal will be the attempt to the first adventurer, let him assure himself," and at that word, held up his knife in a menacing posture. "Look ye, ye faithless crew," said he, "'tis not life I seek, nor am I afraid of dying," and at that word cut a piece of flesh from his own throat, and threw it at 'em; "yet still I would live if I could, till I had perfected my revenge. But oh! it cannot be; I feel life gliding from my eyes and heart, and if I make not haste, I shall yet fall a victim to the shameful whip." At that, he ripped up his own belly, and took his bowels and pulled 'em out, with what strength he could; while some, on their knees imploring, besought him to hold his hand. But when they saw him tottering, they cried out, "Will none venture on him?" A bold English cried, "Yes, if he were the devil" (taking courage when he saw him almost dead); and swearing a horrid oath for his farewell to the world, he rushed on him; Caesar, with his armed hand, met him so fairly as stuck him to the heart, and he fell dead at his feet. Tuscan, seeing that, cried out, "I love thee, O Caesar, and therefore will not let thee die, if possible." And running to him, took him in his arms; but at the same time warding a blow that Caesar made at his bosom, he received it quite through his arm; and Caesar having not the strength to pluck the knife forth, though he attempted it, Tuscan neither pulled it out himself nor suffered it to be pulled out, but came down with it sticking in his arm; and the reason he gave for it was, because the air should not get into the wound. They put their hands across, and carried Caesar between six of 'em, fainted as he was, and they thought dead, or just dying; and they brought him to Parham, and laid him on a couch, and had the chirurgeon immediately to him, who dressed his wounds and sewed up his belly, and used means to bring him to life, which they effected. We ran all to see him, and if before we thought him so beautiful a sight, he was now so altered that his face was like a death's head blacked over, nothing but teeth and eyeholes. For some days we suffered nobody to speak to him, but caused cordials to be poured down his throat, which sustained his life; and in six or seven days he recovered his senses. For you must know that wounds are almost to a miracle cured in the Indies, unless wounds in the legs, which rarely ever cure.

When he was well enough to speak, we talked to him, and asked him some questions about his wife, and the reasons why he killed her; and he then told us what I have related of that resolution, and of his parting; and he besought us we would let him die, and was extremely afflicted to think it was possible he might live; he assured us if we did not dispatch him, he would prove very fatal to a great many. We said all we could to make him live, and gave him new assurances; but he begged we would not think so poorly of him, or of his love to Imoinda, to imagine we could flatter him to life again; but the chirurgeon assured him he could not live, and therefore he need not fear. We were all (but Caesar) afflicted at this news; and the sight was gashly;[1] his discourse was sad, and the earthly smell about him so strong that I was persuaded to leave the place for some time (being myself but sickly, and very apt to fall into fits of dangerous illness upon any extraordinary melancholy). The servants and Trefry and the chirurgeons promised all to take what possible care they could of the life of Caesar, and I, taking boat, went with other company to Colonel Martin's, about three days' journey down the river; but I was no sooner gone, but the governor taking Trefry about some pretended earnest business a day's journey up the river, having communicated his design to one Banister, a wild Irishman and one of the council, a fellow of absolute barbarity, and fit to execute any villainy, but was rich: he came up to Parham, and forcibly took Caesar, and had him carried to the same post where he was whipped; and causing him to be tied to it, and a great fire made before him, he told him he should die like a dog, as he was. Caesar replied, this was the first piece of bravery that ever Banister did, and he never spoke sense till he pronounced that word; and if he would keep it, he would declare, in the other world, that he was the only man of all the whites that ever he heard speak truth. And turning to the men that bound him, he said, "My friends, am I to die, or to be whipped?" And they cried, "Whipped! No, you shall not escape so well." And then he replied, smiling, "A blessing on thee," and assured them they need not tie him, for he would stand fixed like a rock, and endure death so as should encourage them to die. "But if you whip me," said he, "be sure you tie me fast."

He had learned to take tobacco; and when he was assured he should die, he desired they would give him a pipe in his mouth, ready lighted, which they did; and the executioner came, and first cut off his members,[2] and threw them into the fire; after that, with an ill-favored knife, they cut his ears, and his nose, and burned them; he still smoked on, as if nothing had touched him. Then they hacked off one of his arms, and still he bore up, and held his pipe; but at the cutting off the other arm, his head sunk, and his pipe dropped, and he gave up the ghost, without a groan or a reproach. My mother and sister were by him all the while, but not suffered to save him, so rude and wild were the rabble, and so inhuman were the justices, who stood by to see the execution, who after paid dearly enough for their insolence. They cut Caesar in quarters, and sent them to several of the chief plantations. One quarter was sent to Colonel Martin, who refused it, and swore he had rather see the quarters of Banister and the governor himself than those of Caesar on his plantations, and that he could govern his Negroes without terrifying and grieving them with frightful spectacles of a mangled king.

Thus died this great man, worthy of a better fate, and a more sublime wit than mine to write his praise; yet, I hope, the reputation of my pen is considerable enough to make his glorious name to survive to all ages, with that of the brave, the beautiful, and the constant Imoinda.

1688

---

1. Ghastly.   2. Genitals.

WILLIAM CONGREVE
1670–1729

Both of William Congreve's parents came from well-to-do and prominent county families. His father, a younger son, obtained a commission as lieutenant in the army and moved to Ireland in 1674. There the future playwright was educated at Kilkenny School and Trinity College, Dublin; at both places he was a younger contemporary of Swift. In 1691 he took rooms in the Middle Temple and began to study law, but soon found he preferred the wit of the coffeehouses and the theater. Within a year he had so distinguished himself at Will's Coffeehouse that he had become intimate with the great Dryden himself, and his brief career as a dramatist began shortly thereafter.

The success of *The Old Bachelor* (produced in 1693) immediately established him as the most promising young dramatist in London. It had the then phenomenally long run of fourteen days, and Dryden declared it the best first play he had ever read. *The Double Dealer* (produced in 1693) was a near failure, though it evoked one of Dryden's most graceful and gracious poems, in which he praised Congreve as the superior of Jonson and Fletcher and the equal of Shakespeare. *Love for Love* (produced in 1695) was an unqualified success and remains Congreve's most frequently revived play. In 1697 he brought out a well-received tragedy, *The Mourning Bride*. Congreve's most elegant comedy of manners, *The Way of the World*, received a brilliant production in 1700, but it did not have a long run. During the rest of his life he wrote no more plays. Instead he held a minor government post, which, although a Whig, he was allowed to keep during the Tory ministry of Oxford and Bolingbroke; after the accession of George I he was given a more lucrative government sinecure. Despite the political animosities of the first two decades of the century, he managed to remain on friendly terms with Swift and Pope, and Pope dedicated to him his translation of the *Iliad*. Congreve's final years were perplexed by poor health but were made bearable by the love of Henrietta, second duchess of Marlborough, whose last child, a daughter, was in all probability the playwright's.

The Way of the World is one of the wittiest plays ever written, a play to read slowly and savor. Like an expert jeweler, Congreve polished the Restoration comedy of manners to its ultimate sparkle and gloss. The dialogue is epigrammatic and brilliant, the plot is an intricate puzzle, and the characters shine with surprisingly complex facets. Yet the play is not all dazzling surface; it also has depths. Most Restoration comedies begin with the struggle for power, sex, and money and end with a marriage. In an age that viewed property, not romance, as the basis of marriage, the hero shows his prowess by catching an heiress. *The Way of the World* reflects that standard plot; it is a battle more over a legacy than over a woman, a battle in which sexual attraction is used as a weapon. Yet Congreve, writing after such conventions had been thoroughly explored, reveals the weakness of those who treat love as a war or a game: "each deceiver to his cost may find/That marriage frauds too oft are paid in kind." If "the way of the world" is cynical self-interest, it is also the worldly prudence that sees through the ruses of power and turns them to better ends. In this world generosity and affection win the day and true love conquers—with the help of some clever plotting.

At the center of the action are four fully realized characters—Mirabell and Millamant, the hero and heroine, and Fainall and Mrs. Marwood, the two villains—whose stratagems and relations move the play. Around them are characters who serve in one way or another as foils: Witwoud, the would-be wit, with whom we contrast the true wit of Mirabell and Millamant; Petulant, a "humor" character, who affects bluff candor and cynical realism, but succeeds only in being offensive; and Sir Wilfull Witwoud, the booby squire from the country, who serves with Petulant to throw into relief the high good breeding and fineness of nature of the hero and heroine. Finally there is one of Congreve's finest creations, Lady Wishfort ("wish for it"), who though aging and ugly still longs for love, gallantry, and courtship and who is led by her appetites into the trap that Mirabell lays for her.

Because of the complexity of the plot, a summary of the situation at the rise of the curtain may prove helpful. Mirabell (a reformed rake) is sincerely in love with and wishes to marry Millamant, who, though a coquette and a highly sophisticated wit, is a virtuous woman. Mirabell some time before has married off his former mistress, the daughter of Lady Wishfort, to his friend Fainall. Fainall has grown tired of his wife and has been squandering her money on his mistress, Mrs. Marwood. In order to gain access to Millamant, Mirabell has pretended to pay court to the elderly and amorous Lady Wishfort, who is the guardian of Millamant and as such controls half her fortune. But his game has been spoiled by Mrs. Marwood, who nourishes a secret love for Mirabell and, to separate him from Millamant, has made Lady Wishfort aware of Mirabell's duplicity. Lady Wishfort now loathes Mirabell for making a fool of her—an awkward situation, because if Millamant should marry without her guardian's consent she would lose half her fortune, and Mirabell cannot afford to marry any but a rich wife. It is at this point that the action begins. Mirabell perfects a plot to get such power over Lady Wishfort as to force her to agree to the marriage, while Millamant continues to doubt whether she wishes to marry at all.

The Way of the World

Dramatis Personae[1]

Men

FAINALL, *in love with* MRS. MARWOOD
MIRABELL, *in love with* MRS. MILLAMANT
WITWOUD ⎫
PETULANT ⎭ *followers of* MRS. MILLAMANT
SIR WILFULL WITWOUD, *half brother to* WITWOUD, *and nephew to*
  LADY WISHFORT
WAITWELL, *servant to* MIRABELL

Women

LADY WISHFORT, *enemy to* MIRABELL, *for having falsely pretended love to her*
MRS. MILLAMANT, *a fine lady, niece to* LADY WISHFORT, *and loves* MIRABELL
MRS. MARWOOD, *friend to* MR. FAINALL, *and likes* MIRABELL
MRS. FAINALL, *daughter to* LADY WISHFORT, *and wife to* FAINALL, *formerly friend*
  to MIRABELL
FOIBLE, *woman to* LADY WISHFORT
MINCING, *woman to* MRS. MILLAMANT

---

1. The names of the principal characters reveal their dominant traits: e.g., Fainall would *fain* have *all,* with perhaps also the suggestion that he is the complete hypocrite, who *feigns*; Witwoud is the *would-be wit*; Wishfort suggests *wish for it*; Millamant is the lady with a thousand lovers (French *mille amants*); Marwood *would* willingly *mar* (injure) the lovers; Mincing has an air of affected gentility (i.e., she *minces*), which clashes with her vulgar English. "Mrs." is "Mistress," a title then used by young unmarried ladies as well as by the married Mrs. Fainall.

BETTY, *waitress at the chocolate house*
PEG, *under-servant to* LADY WISHFORT
DANCERS, FOOTMEN, *and* ATTENDANTS

SCENE—*London.*

Prologue

SPOKEN BY MR. BETTERTON[2]

Of those few fools, who with ill stars are cursed,
Sure scribbling fools, called poets, fare the worst:
For they're a sort of fools which Fortune makes,
And after she has made 'em fools, forsakes.
5 With nature's oafs 'tis quite a different case,
For Fortune favors all her idiot race.
In her own nest the cuckoo eggs we find,
O'er which she broods to hatch the changeling kind.[3]
No portion for her own she has to spare,
10 So much she dotes on her adopted care.
    Poets are bubbles,° by the town drawn in,   *dupes*
Suffered at first some trifling stakes to win:
But what unequal hazards do they run!
Each time they write they venture all they've won:
15 The squire that's buttered still,° is sure to be undone. *constantly flattered*
This author, heretofore, has found your favor,
But pleads no merit from his past behavior;
To build on that might prove a vain presumption,
Should grants to poets made, admit resumption:[4]
20 And in Parnassus[5] he must lose his seat,
If that be found a forfeited estate.[6]
    He owns,° with toil he wrought the following scenes,   *admits*
But if they're naught ne'er spare him for his pains:
Damn him the more; have no commiseration
25 For dullness on mature deliberation.
He swears he'll not resent one hissed-off scene
Nor, like those peevish wits, his play maintain,°   *defend*
Who, to assert their sense, your taste arraign.
Some plot we think he has, and some new thought;
30 Some humor too, no farce; but that's a fault.
Satire, he thinks, you ought not to expect,
For so reformed a town,[7] who dares correct?
To please, this time, has been his sole pretense,
He'll not instruct, lest it should give offense.

---

2. Thomas Betterton (ca. 1635–1710), the greatest actor of the period, played Fainall in the original production of this play.
3. Simpletons; children supposed to have been secretly exchanged in infancy for others. The cuckoo lays its eggs in the nests of other birds.
4. The Crown could both grant and take back ("resume") estates.
5. Greek mountain sacred to the Muses.
6. *Seat* rhymed with *estate*; in the next couplet,

scenes and *pains* rhymed. A few lines later *scene* is similarly pronounced to rhyme with *maintain,* and *fault* (the *l* being silent) is rhymed with *thought.*
7. A sarcasm, directed against the general movement to reform manners and morals and, more particularly, against Jeremy Collier's attack on actors and playwrights in his *Short View of the Profaneness and Immorality of the English Stage* (1698).

35 Should he by chance a knave or fool expose,
    That hurts none here; sure here are none of those.
    In short, our play shall (with your leave to show it)
    Give you one instance of a passive poet
    Who to your judgments yields all resignation;
40 So save or damn after your own discretion.

Act 1—*A chocolate house.*

MIRABELL *and* FAINALL *rising from cards,* BETTY *waiting.*

MIRABELL   You are a fortunate man, Mr. Fainall.

FAINALL   Have we done?

MIRABELL   What you please. I'll play on to entertain you.

FAINALL   No, I'll give you your revenge another time, when you are not so indifferent; you are thinking of something else now, and play too negligently. The coldness of a losing gamester lessens the pleasure of the winner. I'd no more play with a man that slighted his ill fortune than I'd make love to a woman who undervalued the loss of her reputation.

MIRABELL   You have a taste extremely delicate, and are for refining on your pleasures.

FAINALL   Prithee, why so reserved? Something has put you out of humor.

MIRABELL   Not at all. I happen to be grave today, and you are gay; that's all.

FAINALL   Confess, Millamant and you quarreled last night after I left you; my fair cousin has some humors that would tempt the patience of a stoic. What, some coxcomb came in, and was well received by her, while you were by?

MIRABELL   Witwoud and Petulant; and what was worse, her aunt, your wife's mother, my evil genius; or to sum up all in her own name, my old Lady Wishfort came in.

FAINALL   O, there it is then—she has a lasting passion for you, and with reason. What, then my wife was there?

MIRABELL   Yes, and Mrs. Marwood and three or four more, whom I never saw before. Seeing me, they all put on their grave faces, whispered one another; then complained aloud of the vapors,[8] and after fell into a profound silence.

FAINALL   They had a mind to be rid of you.

MIRABELL   For which good reason I resolved not to stir. At last the good old lady broke through her painful taciturnity, with an invective against long visits. I would not have understood her, but Millamant joining in the argument, I rose and with a constrained smile told her I thought nothing was so easy as to know when a visit began to be troublesome. She reddened and I withdrew, without expecting[9] her reply.

FAINALL   You were to blame to resent what she spoke only in compliance with her aunt.

MIRABELL   She is more mistress of herself than to be under the necessity of such a resignation.

FAINALL   What? though half her fortune depends upon her marrying with my lady's approbation?

---

8. Melancholy.   9. Awaiting.

MIRABELL   I was then in such a humor that I should have been better pleased if she had been less discreet.

FAINALL   Now I remember, I wonder not they were weary of you: last night was one of their cabal[1] nights; they have 'em three times a week, and meet by turns, at one another's apartments, where they come together like the coroner's inquest, to sit upon the murdered reputations of the week. You and I are excluded; and it was once proposed that all the male sex should be excepted; but somebody moved that to avoid scandal there might be one man of the community; upon which Witwoud and Petulant were enrolled members.

MIRABELL   And who may have been the foundress of this sect? My Lady Wishfort, I warrant, who publishes her detestation of mankind, and full of the vigor of fifty-five, declares for a friend and ratafia;[2] and let posterity shift for itself, she'll breed no more.

FAINALL   The discovery of your sham addresses to her, to conceal your love to her niece, has provoked this separation. Had you dissembled better, things might have continued in the state of nature.[3]

MIRABELL   I did as much as man could, with any reasonable conscience: I proceeded to the very last act of flattery with her, and was guilty of a song in her commendation. Nay, I got a friend to put her into a lampoon and compliment her with the imputation of an affair with a young fellow, which I carried so far that I told her the malicious town took notice that she was grown fat of a sudden; and when she lay in of a dropsy, persuaded her she was reported to be in labor. The devil's in't, if an old woman is to be flattered further, unless a man should endeavor downright personally to debauch her; and that my virtue forbade me. But for the discovery of this amour, I am indebted to your friend, or your wife's friend, Mrs. Marwood.

FAINALL   What should provoke her to be your enemy, unless she has made you advances, which you have slighted? Women do not easily forgive omissions of that nature.

MIRABELL   She was always civil to me, till of late. I confess I am not one of those coxcombs who are apt to interpret a woman's good manners to her prejudice, and think that she who does not refuse 'em everything, can refuse 'em nothing.

FAINALL   You are a gallant man, Mirabell; and though you may have cruelty enough not to satisfy a lady's longing, you have too much generosity not to be tender of her honor. Yet you speak with an indifference which seems to be affected, and confesses you are conscious of a negligence.

MIRABELL   You pursue the argument with a distrust that seems to be unaffected, and confesses you are conscious of a concern for which the lady is more indebted to you than is your wife.

FAINALL   Fie, fie, friend, if you grow censorious I must leave you.—I'll look upon the gamesters in the next room.

MIRABELL   Who are they?

---

1. Secret organization designed for intrigue.
2. A liqueur flavored with fruit kernels (pronounced *rat-a-fé-a*).

3. Lady Wishfort's natural inclination for you would have continued.

FAINALL Petulant and Witwoud. [*To* BETTY.] Bring me some chocolate. [*Exit* FAINALL.]

MIRABELL Betty, what says your clock?

BETTY Turned of the last canonical hour,[4] sir. [*Exit* BETTY.]

MIRABELL How pertinently the jade answers me! Ha? almost one a clock! [*Looking on his watch.*]—O, y'are come—
      [*Enter a* FOOTMAN.]

MIRABELL Well, is the grand affair over? You have been something tedious.[5]

FOOTMAN Sir, there's such coupling at Pancras[6] that they stand behind one another, as 'twere in a country dance. Ours was the last couple to lead up; and no hopes appearing of dispatch, besides, the parson growing hoarse, we were afraid his lungs would have failed before it came to our turn; so we drove around to Duke's Place, and there they were riveted in a trice.

MIRABELL So, so, you are sure they are married?

FOOTMAN Married and bedded, sir. I am witness.

MIRABELL Have you the certificate?

FOOTMAN Here it is, sir.

MIRABELL Has the tailor brought Waitwell's clothes home, and the new liveries?

FOOTMAN Yes, sir.

MIRABELL That's well. Do you go home again, d'ye hear, and adjourn the consummation till farther order. Bid Waitwell shake his ears, and Dame Partlet rustle up her feathers, and meet me at one a clock by Rosamond's Pond, that I may see her before she returns to her lady: and as you tender your ears,[7] be secret. [*Exit* FOOTMAN.]
      [*Re-enter* FAINALL, BETTY.]

FAINALL Joy of your success, Mirabell; you look pleased.

MIRABELL Aye, I have been engaged in a matter of some sort of mirth, which is not yet ripe for discovery. I am glad this is not a cabal night. I wonder, Fainall, that you who are married, and of consequence should be discreet, will suffer your wife to be of such a party.

FAINALL Faith, I am not jealous. Besides, most who are engaged are women and relations; and for the men, they are of a kind too contemptible to give scandal.

MIRABELL I am of another opinion. The greater the coxcomb, always the more the scandal: for a woman who is not a fool can have but one reason for associating with a man who is one.

FAINALL Are you jealous as often as you see Witwoud entertained by Millamant?

MIRABELL Of her understanding I am, if not of her person.

FAINALL You do her wrong; for to give her her due, she has wit.

MIRABELL She has beauty enough to make any man think so; and complaisance enough not to contradict him who shall tell her so.

---

4. The hours in which marriage can legally be performed in the Anglican Church, then eight to twelve noon.
5. Taken a long time.
6. The Church of St. Pancras, like that of St. James in Duke's Place (referred to later in the same speech), was notorious for a thriving trade in unlicensed marriages.
7. If you don't want your ears cropped. Rosamond's Pond is in St. James's Park. "Dame Partlet": Pertelote, the hen-wife of the cock Chauntecleer in Chaucer's *The Nun's Priest's Tale.*

FAINALL   For a passionate lover, methinks you are a man somewhat too discerning in the failings of your mistress.

MIRABELL   And for a discerning man, somewhat too passionate a lover; for I like her with all her faults, nay, like her for her faults. Her follies are so natural, or so artful, that they become her, and those affectations which in another woman would be odious, serve but to make her more agreeable. I'll tell thee, Fainall, she once used me with that insolence that in revenge I took her to pieces; sifted her, and separated her failings; I studied 'em, and got 'em by rote. The catalogue was so large that I was not without hopes, one day or other, to hate her heartily: to which end I so used myself to think of 'em that at length, contrary to my design and expectation, they gave me every hour less and less disturbance, till in a few days it became habitual to me to remember 'em without being displeased. They are now grown as familiar to me as my own frailties, and in all probability in a little time longer I shall like 'em as well.

FAINALL   Marry her, marry her; be half as well acquainted with her charms as you are with her defects, and my life on't, you are your own man again.

MIRABELL   Say you so?

FAINALL   Aye, aye, I have experience; I have a wife, and so forth.

[*Enter a* MESSENGER.]

MESSENGER   Is one Squire Witwoud here?

BETTY   Yes. What's your business?

MESSENGER   I have a letter for him, from his brother Sir Wilfull, which I am charged to deliver into his own hands.

BETTY   He's in the next room, friend—that way. [*Exit* MESSENGER.]

MIRABELL   What, is the chief of that noble family in town, Sir Wilfull Witwoud?

FAINALL   He is expected today. Do you know him?

MIRABELL   I have seen him. He promises to be an extraordinary person; I think you have the honor to be related to him.

FAINALL   Yes; he is half brother to this Witwoud by a former wife, who was sister to my Lady Wishfort, my wife's mother. If you marry Millamant, you must call cousins too.

MIRABELL   I had rather be his relation than his acquaintance.

FAINALL   He comes to town in order to equip himself for travel.

MIRABELL   For travel! Why the man that I mean is above forty.[8]

FAINALL   No matter for that; 'tis for the honor of England that all Europe should know that we have blockheads of all ages.

MIRABELL   I wonder there is not an Act of Parliament to save the credit of the nation, and prohibit the exportation of fools.

FAINALL   By no means, 'tis better as 'tis; 'tis better to trade with a little loss than to be quite eaten up with being overstocked.

MIRABELL   Pray, are the follies of this knight-errant, and those of the squire his brother, anything related?

8. The grand tour of the Continent was rapidly becoming a part of the education of gentlemen, but it was usually made in company with a tutor after a young man had graduated from a university, not after a man had passed the age of forty.

FAINALL   Not at all. Witwoud grows by the knight, like a medlar grafted on a crab.[9] One will melt in your mouth, and t'other set your teeth on edge; one is all pulp, and the other all core.

MIRABELL   So one will be rotten before he be ripe, and the other will be rotten without ever being ripe at all.

FAINALL   Sir Wilfull is an odd mixture of bashfulness and obstinacy. But when he's drunk, he's as loving as the monster in the *Tempest*;[1] and much after the same manner. To give t'other his due, he has something of good nature, and does not always want wit.

MIRABELL   Not always; but as often as his memory fails him, and his commonplace of comparisons.[2] He is a fool with a good memory, and some few scraps of other folks' wit. He is one whose conversation can never be approved, yet it is now and then to be endured. He has indeed one good quality, he is not exceptious,[3] for he so passionately affects the reputation of understanding raillery that he will construe an affront into a jest; and call downright rudeness and ill language, satire and fire.

FAINALL   If you have a mind to finish his picture, you have an opportunity to do it at full length. Behold the original.

[*Enter* WITWOUD.]

WITWOUD   Afford me your compassion, my dears; pity me, Fainall, Mirabell, pity me.

MIRABELL   I do from my soul.

FAINALL   Why, what's the matter?

WITWOUD   No letters for me, Betty?

BETTY   Did not a messenger bring you one but now, sir?

WITWOUD   Aye, but no other?

BETTY   No, sir.

WITWOUD   That's hard, that's very hard. A messenger, a mule, a beast of burden, he has brought me a letter from the fool my brother, as heavy as a panegyric in a funeral sermon, or a copy of commendatory verses from one poet to another. And what's worse, 'tis as sure a forerunner of the author as an epistle dedicatory.

MIRABELL   A fool, and your brother, Witwoud!

WITWOUD   Aye, aye, my half brother. My half brother he is, no nearer upon honor.

MIRABELL   Then 'tis possible he may be but half a fool.

WITWOUD   Good, good, Mirabell, *le drôle!*[4] Good, good. Hang him, don't let's talk of him. Fainall, how does your lady? Gad. I say anything in the world to get this fellow out of my head. I beg pardon that I should ask a man of pleasure and the town a question at once so foreign and domestic. But I talk like an old maid at a marriage, I don't know what I say: but she's the best woman in the world.

---

9. Crabapple. "Medlar": a fruit eaten when it is overripe.
1. Trinculo, in the adaptation of Shakespeare's *Tempest* by Sir William Davenant and Dryden (1667), having made Caliban drunk, says, "The poor monster is loving in his drink" (2.2).
2. One recognized sign of wit was the ability to quickly discover resemblances between objects apparently unlike. Witwoud specializes in this kind of wit, but Mirabell suggests that they are all obvious and collected from others, like observations copied in a notebook, or "commonplace" book.
3. Quarrelsome.
4. The witty fellow (French).

FAINALL 'Tis well you don't know what you say, or else your commendation would go near to make me either vain or jealous.

WITWOUD No man in town lives well with a wife but Fainall. Your judgment, Mirabell?

MIRABELL You had better step and ask his wife, if you would be credibly informed.

WITWOUD Mirabell.

MIRABELL Aye.

WITWOUD My dear, I ask ten thousand pardons—gad, I have forgot what I was going to say to you.

MIRABELL I thank you heartily, heartily.

WITWOUD No, but prithee excuse me—my memory is such a memory.

MIRABELL Have a care of such apologies, Witwoud—for I never knew a fool but he affected to complain, either of the spleen[5] or his memory.

FAINALL What have you done with Petulant?

WITWOUD He's reckoning his money—my money it was.—I have no luck today.

FAINALL You may allow him to win of you at play—for you are sure to be too hard for him at repartee. Since you monopolize the wit that is between you, the fortune must be his of course.

MIRABELL I don't find that Petulant confesses the superiority of wit to be your talent, Witwoud.

WITWOUD Come, come, you are malicious now, and would breed debates.— Petulant's my friend, and a very honest fellow, and a very pretty fellow, and has a smattering—faith and troth a pretty deal of an odd sort of a small wit: nay, I'll do him justice. I'm his friend, I won't wrong him.— And if he had any judgment in the world—he would not be altogether contemptible. Come, come, don't detract from the merits of my friend.

FAINALL You don't take your friend to be over-nicely bred.

WITWOUD No, no, hang him, the rogue has no manners at all, that I must own—no more breeding than a bum-bailey,[6] that I grant you.— 'Tis pity; the fellow has fire and life.

MIRABELL What, courage?

WITWOUD Hum, faith I don't know as to that—I can't say as to that.— Yes, faith, in a controversy he'll contradict anybody.

MIRABELL Though 'twere a man whom he feared, or a woman whom he loved.

WITWOUD Well, well, he does not always think before he speaks—we have all our failings; you are too hard upon him, you are, faith. Let me excuse him—I can defend most of his faults, except one or two. One he has, that's the truth on't, if he were my brother, I could not acquit him.—That indeed I could wish were otherwise.

MIRABELL Aye marry, what's that, Witwoud?

WITWOUD O, pardon me—expose the infirmities of my friend?—No, my dear, excuse me there.

FAINALL What, I warrant he's unsincere, or 'tis some such trifle.

5. Depression.   6. Bumbailiff, the lowest arresting officer.

WITWOUD   No, no, what if he be? 'Tis no matter for that, his wit will excuse that. A wit should no more be sincere than a woman constant; one argues a decay of parts[7] as t'other of beauty.

MIRABELL   Maybe you think him too positive?

WITWOUD   No, no, his being positive is an incentive to argument, and keeps up conversation.

FAINALL   Too illiterate.

WITWOUD   That! that's his happiness.—His want of learning gives him the more opportunities to show his natural parts.

MIRABELL   He wants words.

WITWOUD   Aye; but I like him for that now; for his want of words gives me the pleasure very often to explain his meaning.

FAINALL   He's impudent.

WITWOUD   No, that's not it.

MIRABELL   Vain.

WITWOUD   No.

MIRABELL   What, he speaks unseasonable truths sometimes, because he has not wit enough to invent an evasion.

WITWOUD   Truths! Ha, ha, ha! No, no, since you will have it—I mean, he never speaks truth at all—that's all. He will lie like a chambermaid, or a woman of quality's porter. Now that is a fault.

[*Enter* COACHMAN.]

COACHMAN   Is Master Petulant here, mistress?

BETTY   Yes.

COACHMAN   Three gentlewomen in a coach would speak with him.

FAINALL   O brave Petulant, three!

BETTY   I'll tell him.

COACHMAN   You must bring two dishes of chocolate and a glass of cinnamon water.

[*Exeunt* BETTY, COACHMAN.]

WITWOUD   That should be for two fasting strumpets, and a bawd troubled with wind. Now you may know what the three are.

MIRABELL   You are free with your friend's acquaintance.

WITWOUD   Aye, aye, friendship without freedom is as dull as love without enjoyment, or wine without toasting; but to tell you a secret, these are trulls[8] whom he allows coach-hire, and something more by the week, to call on him once a day at public places.

MIRABELL   How!

WITWOUD   You shall see he won't go to 'em because there's no more company here to take notice of him.—Why this is nothing to what he used to do, before he found out this way. I have known him call for himself.—

FAINALL   Call for himself? What dost thou mean?

WITWOUD   Mean? Why he would slip you out of this chocolate house, just when you had been talking to him.—As soon as your back was turned—whip he was gone—then trip to his lodging, clap on a hood and scarf, and a mask, slap into a hackney coach, and drive hither to the door again in a trice; where he would send in for himself, that I mean, call for him-

---

7. Talents.　　　　　8. Prostitutes.

self, wait for himself, nay and what's more, not finding himself, sometimes leave a letter for himself.

MIRABELL   I confess this is something extraordinary.—I believe he waits
for himself now, he is so long a-coming. O, I ask his pardon.

[*Enter* PETULANT, BETTY.]

BETTY   Sir, the coach stays.

PETULANT   Well, well; I come.—'Sbud,[9] a man had as good be a professed
midwife, as a professed whoremaster, at this rate; to be knocked up and
raised at all hours, and in all places. Pox on 'em, I won't come.—D'ye
hear, tell 'em I won't come.—Let 'em snivel and cry their hearts out.

FAINALL   You are very cruel, Petulant.

PETULANT   All's one, let it pass—I have a humor to be cruel.

MIRABELL   I hope they are not persons of condition[1] that you use at this
rate.

PETULANT   Condition, condition's a dried fig, if I am not in humor.—By
this hand, if they were your—a—a—your what-dee-call-'ems themselves, they must wait or rub off,[2] if I want appetite.

MIRABELL   What-de-call-ems! What are they, Witwoud?

WITWOUD   Empresses, my dear.—By your what-dee-call-'ems he means
sultana queens.

PETULANT   Aye, Roxolanas.[3]

MIRABELL   Cry you mercy.

FAINALL   Witwoud says they are—

PETULANT   What does he say th' are?

WITWOUD   I? Fine ladies I say.

PETULANT   Pass on, Witwoud.—Harkee, by this light his relations—two
coheiresses his cousins, and an old aunt, who loves caterwauling better
than a conventicle.[4]

WITWOUD   Ha, ha, ha; I had a mind to see how the rogue would come
off.—Ha, ha, ha; gad, I can't be angry with him, if he had said they were
my mother and my sisters.

MIRABELL   No!

WITWOUD   No; the rogue's wit and readiness of invention charm me, dear
Petulant.

BETTY   They are gone, sir, in great anger.

PETULANT   Enough, let 'em trundle.[5] Anger helps complexion, saves paint.[6]

FAINALL   This continence is all dissembled; this is in order to have something to brag of the next time he makes court to Millamant, and swear
he had abandoned the whole sex for her sake.

MIRABELL   Have you not left off your impudent pretensions there yet? I
shall cut your throat, sometime or other, Petulant, about that business.

PETULANT   Aye, aye, let that pass.—There are other throats to be cut.—

MIRABELL   Meaning mine, sir?

---

9. God's body.
1. High social standing.
2. Go away.
3. "Empresses," "sultana queens," and "Roxolanas" were terms for prostitutes. Roxolana is the

wife of the Sultan in Davenant's *Siege of Rhodes*
(1656).
4. Nonconformist religious meeting.
5. Move along.
6. Makeup.

PETULANT   Not I—I mean nobody—I know nothing. But there are uncles
and nephews in the world—and they may be rivals—What then? All's
one for that—

MIRABELL   How! Harkee, Petulant, come hither—explain, or I shall call
your interpreter.

PETULANT   Explain? I know nothing.—Why, you have an uncle, have you
not, lately come to town, and lodges by my Lady Wishfort's?

MIRABELL   True.

PETULANT   Why, that's enough.—You and he are not friends; and if he
should marry and have a child, you may be disinherited, ha?

MIRABELL   Where hast thou stumbled upon all this truth?

PETULANT   All's one for that; why, then, say I know something.

MIRABELL   Come, thou art an honest fellow, Petulant, and shalt make love
to my mistress, thou sha't, faith. What hast thou heard of my uncle?

PETULANT   I, nothing, I. If throats are to be cut, let swords clash; snug's
the word, I shrug and am silent.

MIRABELL   O raillery, raillery. Come, I know thou art in the women's
secrets.—What, you're a cabalist. I know you stayed at Millamant's last
night, after I went. Was there any mention made of my uncle or me? Tell
me; if thou hadst but good nature equal to thy wit, Petulant, Tony Witwoud, who is now thy competitor in fame, would show as dim by thee as
a dead whiting's eye by a pearl of Orient. He would no more be seen by
thee than Mercury is by the sun: come, I'm sure thou wo't tell me.

PETULANT   If I do, will you grant me common sense then, for the future?

MIRABELL   Faith, I'll do what I can for thee, and I'll pray that Heaven
may grant it thee in the meantime.

PETULANT   Well, harkee.

[MIRABELL *and* PETULANT *talk privately.*]

FAINALL   Petulant and you both will find Mirabell as warm a rival as a
lover.

WITWOUD   Pshaw, pshaw, that she laughs at Petulant is plain. And for my
part—but that it is almost a fashion to admire her, I should—harkee—
to tell you a secret, but let it go no further—between friends, I shall
never break my heart for her.

FAINALL   How!

WITWOUD   She's handsome; but she's a sort of an uncertain woman.

FAINALL   I thought you had died for her.

WITWOUD   Umh—no—

FAINALL   She has wit.

WITWOUD   'Tis what she will hardly allow anybody else.—Now, demme,[7]
I should hate that, if she were as handsome as Cleopatra. Mirabell is
not so sure of her as he thinks for.

FAINALL   Why do you think so?

WITWOUD   We stayed pretty late there last night, and heard something of
an uncle to Mirabell, who is lately come to town—and is between him
and the best part of his estate. Mirabell and he are at some distance, as
my Lady Wishfort has been told; and you know she hates Mirabell, worse

---

7. Damn me.

than a Quaker hates a parrot,[8] or than a fishmonger hates a hard frost. Whether this uncle has seen Mrs. Millamant or not, I cannot say; but there were items of such a treaty being in embryo; and if it should come to life, poor Mirabell would be in some sort unfortunately fobbed[9] i' faith.

FAINALL 'Tis impossible Millamant should harken to it.

WITWOUD Faith, my dear, I can't tell; she's a woman and a kind of a humorist.[1]

[MIRABELL, PETULANT *privately*.]

MIRABELL And this is the sum of what you could collect last night.

PETULANT The quintessence. Maybe Witwoud knows more, he stayed longer.—Besides they never mind him; they say anything before him.

MIRABELL I thought you had been the greatest favorite.

PETULANT Aye, *tête à tête*;[2] but not in public, because I make remarks.

MIRABELL You do?

PETULANT Aye, aye, pox, I'm malicious, man. Now he's soft, you know, they are not in awe of him.—The fellow's well bred, he's what you call a—what-d'ye-call-'em. A fine gentleman, but he's silly withal.

MIRABELL I thank you, I know as much as my curiosity requires. Fainall, are you for the Mall?[3]

FAINALL Aye, I'll take a turn before dinner.

WITWOUD Aye, we'll all walk in the park, the ladies talked of being there.

MIRABELL I thought you were obliged to watch for your brother Sir Wilfull's arrival.

WITWOUD No, no, he's come to his aunt's, my Lady Wishfort. Pox on him, I shall be troubled with him too. What shall I do with the fool?

PETULANT Beg him for his estate, that I may beg you afterwards, and so have but one trouble with you both.

WITWOUD O rare Petulant; thou art as quick as fire in a frosty morning; thou shalt to the Mall with us; and we'll be very severe.

PETULANT Enough, I'm in a humor to be severe.

MIRABELL Are you? Pray then walk by yourselves.—Let not us be accessory to your putting the ladies out of countenance with your senseless ribaldry, which you roar out aloud as often as they pass by you; and when you have made a handsome woman blush, then you think you have been severe.

PETULANT What, what? Then let 'em either show their innocence by not understanding what they hear, or else show their discretion by not hearing what they would not be thought to understand.

MIRABELL But hast not thou then sense enough to know that thou ought'st to be most ashamed thyself, when thou hast put another out of countenance?

PETULANT Not I, by this hand.—I always take blushing either for a sign of guilt, or ill breeding.

---

8. In his *Apology for the True Christian Divinity* (1678), the Quaker Robert Barclay says that professing belief in Christ without spiritual revelation is like "the prattling of a parrot."
9. Tricked.

1. A capricious person.
2. Face to face (French); i.e., in private.
3. A walk in St. James's Park, one of the fashionable public places of London.

MIRABELL   I confess you ought to think so. You are in the right, that you may plead the error of your judgment in defense of your practice.

> Where modesty's ill manners, 'tis but fit
> That impudence and malice pass for wit.

Act 2—St. James's Park.

[*Enter* MRS. FAINALL *and* MRS. MARWOOD.]

MRS. FAINALL   Aye, aye, dear Marwood, if we will be happy, we must find the means in ourselves, and among ourselves. Men are ever in extremes; either doting or averse. While they are lovers, if they have fire and sense, their jealousies are insupportable: and when they cease to love (we ought to think at least) they loathe. They look upon us with horror and distaste; they meet us like the ghosts of what we were, and as from such, fly from us.

MRS. MARWOOD   True, 'tis an unhappy circumstance of life that love should ever die before us; and that the man so often should outlive the lover. But say what you will, 'tis better to be left than never to have been loved. To pass over youth in dull indifference, to refuse the sweets of life because they once must leave us, is as preposterous as to wish to have been born old, because we one day must be old. For my part, my youth may wear and waste, but it shall never rust in my possession.

MRS. FAINALL   Then it seems you dissemble an aversion to mankind only in compliance to my mother's humor.

MRS. MARWOOD   Certainly. To be free,[4] I have no taste of those insipid dry discourses with which our sex of force must entertain themselves apart from men. We may affect endearments to each other, profess eternal friendships, and seem to dote like lovers; but 'tis not in our natures long to persevere. Love will resume his empire in our breasts, and every heart, or soon or late, receive and readmit him as its lawful tyrant.

MRS. FAINALL   Bless me, how have I been deceived! Why, you profess[5] a libertine.

MRS. MARWOOD   You see my friendship by my freedom. Come, be as sincere, acknowledge that your sentiments agree with mine.

MRS. FAINALL   Never.

MRS. MARWOOD   You hate mankind?

MRS. FAINALL   Heartily, inveterately.

MRS. MARWOOD   Your husband?

MRS. FAINALL   Most transcendently; aye, though I say it, meritoriously.

MRS. MARWOOD   Give me your hand upon it.

MRS. FAINALL   There.

MRS. MARWOOD   I join with you. What I have said has been to try you.

MRS. FAINALL   Is it possible? Dost thou hate those vipers men?

MRS. MARWOOD   I have done hating 'em, and am now come to despise 'em; the next thing I have to do is eternally to forget 'em.

MRS. FAINALL   There spoke the spirit of an Amazon, a Penthesilea.[6]

---

4. To speak freely.
5. Talk like.

6. Queen of the Amazons (a legendary nation of women warriors).

MRS. MARWOOD   And yet I am thinking sometimes to carry my aversion further.

MRS. FAINALL   How?

MRS. MARWOOD   Faith, by marrying. If I could but find one that loved me very well, and would be thoroughly sensible of ill usage, I think I should do myself the violence of undergoing the ceremony.

MRS. FAINALL   You would not make him a cuckold?

MRS. MARWOOD   No; but I'd make him believe I did, and that's as bad.

MRS. FAINALL   Why had not you as good do it?

MRS. MARWOOD   O, if he should ever discover it, he would then know the worst, and be out of his pain; but I would have him ever to continue upon the rack of fear and jealousy.

MRS. FAINALL   Ingenious mischief! Would thou wert married to Mirabell.

MRS. MARWOOD   Would I were.

MRS. FAINALL   You change color.

MRS. MARWOOD   Because I hate him.

MRS. FAINALL   So do I; but I can hear him named. But what reason have you to hate him in particular?

MRS. MARWOOD   I never loved him; he is and always was insufferably proud.

MRS. FAINALL   By the reason you give for your aversion, one would think it dissembled; for you have laid a fault to his charge of which his enemies must acquit him.

MRS. MARWOOD   O then it seems you are one of his favorable enemies. Methinks you look a little pale, and now you flush again.

MRS. FAINALL   Do I? I think I am a little sick o' the sudden.

MRS. MARWOOD   What ails you?

MRS. FAINALL   My husband. Don't you see him? He turned short upon me unawares, and has almost overcome me.

[*Enter* FAINALL *and* MIRABELL.]

MRS. MARWOOD   Ha, ha, ha; he comes opportunely for you.

MRS. FAINALL   For you, for he has brought Mirabell with him.

FAINALL   My dear.

MRS. FAINALL   My soul.

FAINALL   You don't look well today, child.

MRS. FAINALL   D'ye think so?

MIRABELL   He is the only man that does, madam.

MRS. FAINALL   The only man that would tell me so at least; and the only man from whom I could hear it without mortification.

FAINALL   O my dear, I am satisfied of your tenderness; I know you cannot resent anything from me, especially what is an effect of my concern.

MRS. FAINALL   Mr. Mirabell, my mother interrupted you in a pleasant relation last night. I would fain hear it out.

MIRABELL   The persons concerned in that affair have yet a tolerable reputation.—I am afraid Mr. Fainall will be censorious.

MRS. FAINALL   He has a humor more prevailing than his curiosity, and will willingly dispense with the hearing of one scandalous story to avoid giving an occasion to make another by being seen to walk with his wife. This way, Mr. Mirabell, and I dare promise you will oblige us both.

[*Exeunt* MIRABELL *and* MRS. FAINALL.]

FAINALL   Excellent creature! Well, sure if I should live to be rid of my wife, I should be a miserable man.

MRS. MARWOOD   Aye!

FAINALL   For having only that one hope, the accomplishment of it of consequence must put an end to all my hopes; and what a wretch is he who must survive his hopes! Nothing remains when that day comes but to sit down and weep like Alexander, when he wanted other worlds to conquer.

MRS. MARWOOD   Will you not follow 'em?

FAINALL   Faith, I think not.

MRS. MARWOOD   Pray let us; I have a reason.

FAINALL   You are not jealous?

MRS. MARWOOD   Of whom?

FAINALL   Of Mirabell.

MRS. MARWOOD   If I am, is it inconsistent with my love to you that I am tender of your honor?

FAINALL   You would intimate then, as if there were a fellow-feeling between my wife and him.

MRS. MARWOOD   I think she does not hate him to that degree she would be thought.

FAINALL   But he, I fear, is too insensible.[7]

MRS. MARWOOD   It may be you are deceived.

FAINALL   It may be so. I do now begin to apprehend it.

MRS. MARWOOD   What?

FAINALL   That I have been deceived, Madam, and you are false.

MRS. MARWOOD   That I am false! What mean you?

FAINALL   To let you know I see through all your little arts.—Come, you both love him; and both have equally dissembled your aversion. Your mutual jealousies of one another have made you clash till you have both struck fire. I have seen the warm confession reddening on your cheeks, and sparkling from your eyes.

MRS. MARWOOD   You do me wrong.

FAINALL   I do not.—'Twas for my ease to oversee[8] and willfully neglect the gross advances made him by my wife; that by permitting her to be engaged I might continue unsuspected in my pleasures; and take you oftener to my arms in full security. But could you think, because the nodding husband would not wake, that e'er the watchful lover slept?

MRS. MARWOOD   And wherewithal can you reproach me?

FAINALL   With infidelity, with loving another, with love of Mirabell.

MRS. MARWOOD   'Tis false. I challenge you to show an instance that can confirm your groundless accusation. I hate him.

FAINALL   And wherefore do you hate him? He is insensible, and your resentment follows his neglect. An instance! The injuries you have done him are a proof: your interposing in his love. What cause had you to make discoveries of his pretended passion? To undeceive the credulous aunt, and be the officious obstacle of his match with Millamant?

7. Indifferent.   8. Overlook.

MRS. MARWOOD   My obligations to my lady[9] urged me. I had professed a friendship to her, and could not see her easy nature so abused by that dissembler.

FAINALL   What, was it conscience then? Professed a friendship! O the pious friendships of the female sex!

MRS. MARWOOD   More tender, more sincere, and more enduring than all the vain and empty vows of men, whether professing love to us, or mutual faith to one another.

FAINALL   Ha, ha, ha; you are my wife's friend too.

MRS. MARWOOD   Shame and ingratitude! Do you reproach me? You, you upbraid me! Have I been false to her, through strict fidelity to you, and sacrificed my friendship to keep my love inviolate? And have you the baseness to charge me with the guilt, unmindful of the merit! To you it should be meritorious that I have been vicious: and do you reflect that guilt upon me, which should lie buried in your bosom?

FAINALL   You misinterpret my reproof. I meant but to remind you of the slight account you once could make of strictest ties, when set in competition with your love to me.

MRS. MARWOOD   'Tis false, you urged it with deliberate malice.—'Twas spoke in scorn, and I never will forgive it.

FAINALL   Your guilt, not your resentment, begets your rage. If yet you loved, you could forgive a jealousy, but you are stung to find you are discovered.

MRS. MARWOOD   It shall be all discovered. You too shall be discovered; be sure you shall. I can but be exposed.—If I do it myself, I shall prevent[1] your baseness.

FAINALL   Why, what will you do?

MRS. MARWOOD   Disclose it to your wife; own what has passed between us.

FAINALL   Frenzy!

MRS. MARWOOD   By all my wrongs I'll do't—I'll publish to the world the injuries you have done me, both in my fame and fortune: with both I trusted you, you bankrupt in honor, as indigent of wealth.

FAINALL   Your fame[2] I have preserved. Your fortune has been bestowed as the prodigality of your love would have it, in pleasures which we both have shared. Yet, had not you been false, I had e'er this repaid it.—'Tis true—had you permitted Mirabell with Millamant to have stolen their marriage, my lady had been incensed beyond all means of reconcilement: Millamant had forfeited the moiety[3] of her fortune, which then would have descended to my wife—and wherefore did I marry, but to make lawful prize of a rich widow's wealth, and squander it on love and you?

MRS. MARWOOD   Deceit and frivolous pretense.

FAINALL   Death, am I not married? What's pretense? Am I not imprisoned, fettered? Have I not a wife? Nay, a wife that was a widow, a young widow, a handsome widow; and would be again a widow, but that I have a heart of proof,[4] and something of a constitution to bustle through the ways of wedlock and this world. Will you yet be reconciled to truth and me?

---

9. Lady Wishfort.
1. Anticipate.
2. Good name.

3. Half.
4. I.e., a proved or tempered heart.

MRS. MARWOOD   Impossible. Truth and you are inconsistent—I hate you, and shall forever.

FAINALL   For loving you?

MRS. MARWOOD   I loathe the name of love after such usage; and next to the guilt with which you would asperse me, I scorn you most. Farewell.

FAINALL   Nay, we must not part thus.

MRS. MARWOOD   Let me go.

FAINALL   Come, I'm sorry.

MRS. MARWOOD   I care not.—Let me go.—Break my hands, do—I'd leave 'em to get loose.

FAINALL   I would not hurt you for the world. Have I no other hold to keep you here?

MRS. MARWOOD   Well, I have deserved it all.

FAINALL   You know I love you.

MRS. MARWOOD   Poor dissembling!—O that—Well, it is not yet—

FAINALL   What? What is it not? What is it not yet? It is not yet too late—

MRS. MARWOOD   No, it is not yet too late—I have that comfort.

FAINALL   It is, to love another.

MRS. MARWOOD   But not to loathe, detest, abhor mankind, myself, and the whole treacherous world.

FAINALL   Nay, this is extravagance.—Come, I ask your pardon.—No tears.—I was to blame. I could not love you and be easy in my doubts.—Pray forbear.—I believe you; I'm convinced I've done you wrong; and any way, every way will make amends.—I'll hate my wife yet more, damn her, I'll part with her, rob her of all she's worth, and we'll retire somewhere, anywhere, to another world. I'll marry thee.—Be pacified.—'Sdeath, they come, hide your face, your tears.—You have a mask,[5] wear it a moment. This way, this way, be persuaded. [*Exeunt* FAINALL *and* MRS. MARWOOD.]
   [*Enter* MIRABELL *and* MRS. FAINALL.]

MRS. FAINALL   They are here yet.

MIRABELL   They are turning into the other walk.

MRS. FAINALL   While I only hated my husband, I could bear to see him, but since I have despised him, he's too offensive.

MIRABELL   O, you should hate with prudence.

MRS. FAINALL   Yes, for I have loved with indiscretion.

MIRABELL   You should have just so much disgust for your husband as may be sufficient to make you relish your lover.

MRS. FAINALL   You have been the cause that I have loved without bounds, and would you set limits to that aversion, of which you have been the occasion? Why did you make me marry this man?

MIRABELL   Why do we daily commit disagreeable and dangerous actions? To save that idol, reputation. If the familiarities of our loves had produced that consequence, of which you were apprehensive, where could you have fixed a father's name with credit, but on a husband? I knew Fainall to be a man lavish of his morals, an interested and professing friend, a false and a designing lover; yet one whose wit and outward fair

5. Often worn in public places by fashionable women of the time to preserve their complexions; they were also useful to disguise a woman and so to protect her reputation when she was carrying on an illicit affair.

behavior have gained a reputation with the town, enough to make that woman stand excused who has suffered herself to be won by his addresses. A better man ought not to have been sacrificed to the occasion; a worse had not answered to the purpose. When you are weary of him, you know your remedy.

MRS. FAINALL   I ought to stand in some degree of credit with you, Mirabell.

MIRABELL   In justice to you, I have made you privy to my whole design, and put it in your power to ruin or advance my fortune.

MRS. FAINALL   Whom have you instructed to represent your pretended uncle?

MIRABELL   Waitwell, my servant.

MRS. FAINALL   He is an humble servant to Foibles,[6] my mother's woman, and may win her to your interest.

MIRABELL   Care is taken for that.—She is won and worn by this time. They were married this morning.

MRS. FAINALL   Who?

MIRABELL   Waitwell and Foible. I would not tempt my servant to betray me by trusting him too far. If your mother, in hopes to ruin me, should consent to marry my pretended uncle, he might, like Mosca in *The Fox*, stand upon terms;[7] so I made him sure beforehand.

MRS. FAINALL   So, if my poor mother is caught in a contract, you will discover the imposture betimes; and release her by producing a certificate of her gallant's former marriage.

MIRABELL   Yes, upon condition that she consent to my marriage with her niece, and surrender the moiety of her fortune in her possession.

MRS. FAINALL   She talked last night of endeavoring at a match between Millamant and your uncle.

MIRABELL   That was by Foible's direction, and my instruction, that she might seem to carry it more privately.

MRS. FAINALL   Well, I have an opinion of your success, for I believe my lady will do anything to get an husband; and when she has this, which you have provided for her, I suppose she will submit to anything to get rid of him.

MIRABELL   Yes, I think the good lady would marry anything that resembled a man, though 'twere no more than what a butler could pinch out of a napkin.

MRS. FAINALL   Female frailty! We must all come to it, if we live to be old, and feel the craving of a false appetite when the true is decayed.

MIRABELL   An old woman's appetite is depraved like that of a girl—'tis the greensickness[8] of a second childhood; and like the faint offer of a latter spring, serves but to usher in the fall and withers in an affected bloom.

MRS. FAINALL   Here's your mistress.

[*Enter* MRS. MILLAMANT, WITWOUD, *and* MINCING.]

---

6. I.e., he is Foible's lover.
7. To insist on conditions; here, to blackmail. "Mosca": the scheming parasite in Ben Jonson's *Volpone*, who in the end tries to blackmail

Volpone.
8. The anemia that sometimes affects girls at puberty.

MIRABELL   Here she comes, i'faith, full sail, with her fan spread and streamers out, and a shoal of fools for tenders.—Ha, no, I cry her mercy.

MRS. FAINALL   I see but one poor empty sculler, and he tows her woman after him.

MIRABELL   You seem to be unattended, madam.—You used to have the *beau monde* throng after you; and a flock of gay fine perukes[9] hovering round you.

WITWOUD   Like moths about a candle—I had like to have lost my comparison for want of breath.

MILLAMANT   O, I have denied myself airs today. I have walked as fast through the crowd—

WITWOUD   As a favorite just disgraced; and with as few followers.

MILLAMANT   Dear Mr. Witwoud, truce with your similitudes: For I am as sick of 'em—

WITWOUD   As a physician of a good air—I cannot help it, madam, though 'tis against myself.

MILLAMANT   Yet again! Mincing, stand between me and his wit.

WITWOUD   Do, Mrs. Mincing, like a screen before a great fire. I confess I do blaze today, I am too bright.

MRS. FAINALL   But dear Millamant, why were you so long?

MILLAMANT   Long! Lord, have I not made violent haste? I have asked every living thing I met for you; I have inquired after you, as after a new fashion.

WITWOUD   Madam, truce with your similitudes.—No, you met her husband, and did not ask him for her.

MIRABELL   By your leave, Witwoud, that were like inquiring after an old fashion, to ask a husband for his wife.

WITWOUD   Hum, a hit, a hit, a palpable hit,[1] I confess it.

MRS. FAINALL   You were dressed before I came abroad.

MILLAMANT   Aye, that's true.—O, but then I had—Mincing, what had I? Why was I so long?

MINCING   O mem, your la'ship stayed to peruse a packet of letters.

MILLAMANT   O, aye, letters—I had letters—I am persecuted with letters—I hate letters.—Nobody knows how to write letters; and yet one has 'em, one does not know why.—They serve one to pin up one's hair.

WITWOUD   Is that the way? Pray, madam, do you pin up your hair with all your letters? I find I must keep copies.

MILLAMANT   Only with those in verse, Mr. Witwoud. I never pin up my hair with prose. I think I tried once, Mincing.

MINCING   O mem, I shall never forget it.

MILLAMANT   Aye, poor Mincing tiffed[2] and tiffed all the morning.

MINCING   Till I had the cramp in my fingers, I'll vow, mem. And all to no purpose. But when your la'ship pins it up with poetry, it sits so pleasant the next day as anything, and is so pure and so crips.[3]

WITWOUD   Indeed, so crips?

MINCING   You're such a critic, Mr. Witwoud.

9. Periwigs, worn by fashionable men (cf. Pope's *Rape of the Lock* 1.101). "*Beau monde*": fashionable world (French).
1. An allusion to the dueling scene in *Hamlet*
5.2.
2. Dressed the hair.
3. A dialectal form of "crisp," curly.

MILLAMANT Mirabell, did not you take exceptions last night? O, aye, and went away.—Now I think on't I'm angry.—No, now I think on't I'm pleased—for I believe I gave you some pain.

MIRABELL Does that please you?

MILLAMANT Infinitely; I love to give pain.

MIRABELL You would affect a cruelty which is not in your nature; your true vanity is in the power of pleasing.

MILLAMANT O, I ask your pardon for that—one's cruelty is one's power, and when one parts with one's cruelty, one parts with one's power; and when one has parted with that, I fancy one's old and ugly.

MIRABELL Aye, aye, suffer your cruelty to ruin the object of your power, to destroy your lover.—And then how vain, how lost a thing you'll be! Nay, 'tis true: you are no longer handsome when you've lost your lover; your beauty dies upon the instant: for beauty is the lover's gift; 'tis he bestows your charms—your glass is all a cheat. The ugly and the old, whom the looking glass mortifies, yet after commendation can be flattered by it, and discover beauties in it: for that reflects our praises, rather than your face.

MILLAMANT O, the vanity of these men! Fainall, d'ye hear him? If they did not commend us, we were not handsome! Now you must know they could not commend one, if one was not handsome. Beauty the lover's gift?—Lord, what is a lover, that it can give? Why, one makes lovers as fast as one pleases, and they live as long as one pleases, and they die as soon as one pleases: and then if one pleases one makes more.

WITWOUD Very pretty. Why, you make no more of making of lovers, madam, than of making so many card-matches.[4]

MILLAMANT One no more owes one's beauty to a lover than one's wit to an echo.—They can but reflect what we look and say; vain empty things if we are silent or unseen, and want a being.

MIRABELL Yet, to those two vain empty things, you owe two of the greatest pleasures of your life.

MILLAMANT How so?

MIRABELL To your lover you owe the pleasure of hearing yourselves praised; and to an echo the pleasure of hearing yourselves talk.

WITWOUD But I know a lady that loves talking so incessantly she won't give an echo fair play; she has that everlasting rotation of tongue, that an echo must wait till she dies before it can catch her last words.

MILLAMANT O, fiction; Fainall, let us leave these men.

MIRABELL [Aside to MRS. FAINALL.] Draw off Witwoud.

MRS. FAINALL Immediately; I have a word or two for Mr. Witwoud.

[Exeunt WITWOUD and MRS. FAINALL.]

MIRABELL I would beg a little private audience too.—You had the tyranny to deny me last night, though you knew I came to impart a secret to you that concerned my love.

MILLAMANT You saw I was engaged.

MIRABELL Unkind. You had the leisure to entertain a herd of fools, things who visit you from their excessive idleness, bestowing on your easiness that time, which is the encumbrance of their lives. How can

---

4. Matches made by dipping pieces of card in melted sulfur.

you find delight in such society? It is impossible they should admire you, they are not capable: or if they were, it should be to you as a mortification; for sure to please a fool is some degree of folly.

MILLAMANT   I please myself—besides, sometimes to converse with fools is for my health.

MIRABELL   Your health! Is there a worse disease than the conversation of fools?

MILLAMANT   Yes, the vapors; fools are physic for it, next to asafetida.[5]

MIRABELL   You are not in a course[6] of fools?

MILLAMANT   Mirabell, if you persist in this offensive freedom, you'll displease me. I think I must resolve after all not to have you.—We shan't agree.

MIRABELL   Not in our physic, it may be.

MILLAMANT   And yet our distemper in all likelihood will be the same, for we shall be sick of one another. I shan't endure to be reprimanded nor instructed; 'tis so dull to act always by advice, and so tedious to be told of one's faults.—I can't bear it. Well, I won't have you, Mirabell—I'm resolved—I think—you may go—ha, ha, ha. What would you give that you could help loving me?

MIRABELL   I would give something that you did not know I could not help it.

MILLAMANT   Come, don't look grave then. Well, what do you say to me?

MIRABELL   I say that a man may as soon make a friend by his wit, or a fortune by his honesty, as win a woman with plain-dealing and sincerity.

MILLAMANT   Sententious Mirabell! prithee don't look with that violent and inflexible wise face, like Solomon at the dividing of the child in an old tapestry hanging.[7]

MIRABELL   You are merry, madam, but I would persuade you for a moment to be serious.

MILLAMANT   What, with that face? No, if you keep your countenance, 'tis impossible I should hold mine. Well, after all, there is something very moving in a lovesick face. Ha, ha, ha.—Well I won't laugh, don't be peevish—heigho! Now I'll be melancholy, as melancholy as a watchlight.[8] Well, Mirabell, if ever you will win me, woo me now. Nay, if you are so tedious, fare you well; I see they are walking away.

MIRABELL   Can you not find in the variety of your disposition one moment—

MILLAMANT   To hear you tell me Foible's married and your plot like to speed.—No.

MIRABELL   But how you came to know it—

MILLAMANT   Without the help of the devil, you can't imagine; unless she should tell me herself. Which of the two it may have been, I will leave you to consider; and when you have done thinking of that, think of me.

[*Exeunt* MILLAMANT *and* MINCING.]

MIRABELL   I have something more.—Gone!—Think of you! To think of a whirlwind, though 'twere in a whirlwind, were a case of more steady contemplation, a very tranquility of mind and mansion. A fellow that

5. An evil-smelling resin used for medicinal purposes.
6. Plan of medical treatment.

7. The Judgment of Solomon (1 Kings 3.16–27) was a favorite subject in painting and tapestry.
8. Nightlight.

lives in a windmill has not a more whimsical dwelling than the heart of a man that is lodged in a woman. There is no point of the compass to which they cannot turn, and by which they are not turned; and by one as well as another, for motion, not method, is their occupation. To know this, and yet continue to be in love, is to be made wise from the dictates of reason, and yet persevere to play the fool by the force of instinct. O, here come my pair of turtles[9]—what, billing so sweetly! Is not Valentine's Day over with you yet?

[*Enter* WAITWELL *and* FOIBLE.]

MIRABELL Sirrah[1] Waitwell, why sure you think you were married for your own recreation and not for my conveniency.

WAITWELL Your pardon, sir. With submission, we have indeed been solacing in lawful delights, but still with an eye to business, sir. I have instructed her as well as I could. If she can take your directions as readily as my instructions, sir, your affairs are in a prosperous way.

MIRABELL Give you joy, Mrs. Foible.

FOIBLE O-las, sir, I'm so ashamed—I'm afraid my lady has been in a thousand inquietudes for me. But I protest, sir, I made as much haste as I could.

WAITWELL That she did indeed, sir. It was my fault that she did not make more.

MIRABELL That I believe.

FOIBLE But I told my lady as you instructed me, sir. That I had a prospect of seeing Sir Rowland your uncle, and that I would put her ladyship's picture in my pocket to show him; which I'll be sure to say has made him so enamored of her beauty that he burns with impatience to lie at her ladyship's feet and worship the original.

MIRABELL Excellent, Foible! Matrimony has made you eloquent in love.

WAITWELL I think she has profited, sir. I think so.

FOIBLE You have seen Madam Millamant, sir?

MIRABELL Yes.

FOIBLE I told her, sir, because I did not know that you might find an opportunity; she had so much company last night.

MIRABELL Your diligence will merit more—in the meantime—

[*Gives money.*]

FOIBLE O dear sir, your humble servant.

WAITWELL Spouse.

MIRABELL Stand off, sir, not a penny. Go on and prosper, Foible. The lease shall be made good and the farm stocked if we succeed.[2]

FOIBLE I don't question your generosity, sir. And you need not doubt of success. If you have no more commands, sir, I'll be gone; I'm sure my lady is at her toilet,[3] and can't dress till I come. O dear, I'm sure that [*Looking out.*] was Mrs. Marwood that went by in a mask; if she has seen me with you I'm sure she'll tell my lady. I'll make haste home and prevent her. Your servant, sir. B'w'y,[4] Waitwell. [*Exit* FOIBLE.]

---

9. I.e., turtledoves, remarkable for their affectionate billing and cooing. Birds were popularly supposed to choose their mates on St. Valentine's Day.
1. Form of address to an inferior.
2. Mirabell has promised to lease a farm for the couple for helping him.
3. Vanity, makeup table.
4. A shortened form of "God be with you" (our word *good-bye*). "Prevent her": arrive before she does.

WAITWELL Sir Rowland, if you please. The jade's so pert upon her prefer-ment she forgets herself.

MIRABELL Come, sir, will you endeavor to forget yourself—and trans-form into Sir Rowland.

WAITWELL Why, sir, it will be impossible I should remember myself—married, knighted, and attended[5] all in one day! 'Tis enough to make any man forget himself. The difficulty will be how to recover my acquain-tance and familiarity with my former self; and fall from my transforma-tion to a reformation into Waitwell. Nay, I shan't be quite the same Waitwell neither—for now I remember me, I'm married and can't be my own man again.

> Aye, there's my grief; that's the sad change of life;
> To lose my title, and yet keep my wife.

Act 3—*A room in* LADY WISHFORT's *house.*

LADY WISHFORT *at her toilet,* PEG *waiting.*

LADY WISHFORT Merciful, no news of Foible yet?

PEG No, madam.

LADY WISHFORT I have no more patience. If I have not fretted myself till I am pale again, there's no veracity in me. Fetch me the red—the red, do you hear, sweetheart? An errant ash color, as I'm a person. Look you how this wench stirs! Why dost thou not fetch me a little red? Didst thou not hear me, mopus?[6]

PEG The red ratafia does your ladyship mean, or the cherry brandy?

LADY WISHFORT Ratafia, fool. No, fool. Not the ratafia, fool. Grant me patience! I mean the Spanish paper,[7] idiot—complexion, darling. Paint, paint, paint, dost thou understand that, changeling, dangling thy hands like bobbins before thee? Why dost thou not stir, puppet? Thou wooden thing upon wires.

PEG Lord, madam, your ladyship is so impatient.—I cannot come at the paint, madam. Mrs. Foible has locked it up and carried the key with her.

LADY WISHFORT A pox take you both!—Fetch me the cherry brandy then. [*Exit* PEG.] I'm as pale and as faint, I look like Mrs. Qualmsick, the curate's wife, that's always breeding. Wench, come, come, wench, what art thou doing? Sipping? Tasting? Save thee, dost thou not know the bottle?

[*Re-enter* PEG *with a bottle and china cup.*]

PEG Madam, I was looking for a cup.

LADY WISHFORT A cup, save thee, and what a cup hast thou brought! Dost thou take me for a fairy, to drink out of an acorn? Why didst thou not bring thy thimble? Hast thou ne'er a brass thimble clinking in thy pocket with a bit of nutmeg? I warrant thee. Come, fill, fill.—So—again. See who that is.—[*A knock is heard.*]—Set down the bottle first. Here, here, under the table.—What, wouldst thou go with the bottle in thy hand like a tapster?[8] As I'm a person, this wench has lived in an inn upon

---

5. By servants.
6. Dull, stupid person.

7. Rouge.
8. Bartender.

the road before she came to me, like Maritornes the Asturian[9] in *Don Quixote*. No Foible yet?

PEG   No, madam, Mrs. Marwood.

LADY WISHFORT   O Marwood, let her come in. Come in, good Marwood.
   [*Enter* MRS. MARWOOD.]

MRS. MARWOOD   I'm surprised to find your ladyship in *deshabillé*[1] at this time of day.

LADY WISHFORT   Foible's a lost thing; has been abroad since morning, and never heard of since.

MRS. MARWOOD   I saw her but now, as I came masked through the park, in conference with Mirabell.

LADY WISHFORT   With Mirabell! you call my blood into my face, with mentioning that traitor. She durst not have the confidence. I sent her to negotiate an affair, in which if I'm detected I'm undone. If that wheedling villain has wrought upon Foible to detect me, I'm ruined. O my dear friend, I'm a wretch of wretches if I'm detected.

MRS. MARWOOD   O madam, you cannot suspect Mrs. Foible's integrity.

LADY WISHFORT   O, he carries poison in his tongue that would corrupt integrity itself. If she has given him an opportunity, she has as good as put her integrity into his hands. Ah dear Marwood, what's integrity to an opportunity? Hark! I hear her—dear friend, retire into my closet,[2] that I may examine her with more freedom. You'll pardon me, dear friend, I can make bold with you. There are books over the chimney—Quarles and Prynne, and the *Short View of the Stage*,[3] with Bunyan's works to entertain you. [*Exit* MRS. MARWOOD; *to* PEG.] Go, you thing, and send her in. [*Exit* PEG.]
   [*Enter* FOIBLE.]

LADY WISHFORT   O Foible, where hast thou been? What hast thou been doing?

FOIBLE   Madam, I have seen the party.

LADY WISHFORT   But what hast thou done?

FOIBLE   Nay, 'tis your ladyship has done, and are to do; I have only promised. But a man so enamored—so transported! Well, if worshiping of pictures be a sin—poor Sir Rowland, I say.

LADY WISHFORT   The miniature has been counted like[4]—but hast thou not betrayed me, Foible? Hast thou not detected me to that faithless Mirabell?—What hadst thou to do with him in the park? Answer me, has he got nothing out of thee?

FOIBLE [*Aside.*]   So, the devil has been beforehand with me. What shall I say?—Alas, madam, could I help it if I met that confident thing? Was I in fault? If you had heard how he used me, and all upon your ladyship's account, I'm sure you would not suspect my fidelity. Nay, if that had

9. The servant at the inn where Don Quixote and Sancho Panza are taken care of.
1. In her negligee (French).
2. Private room.
3. By Collier; see n. 7, p. 2411. Francis Quarles (1592–1644), a religious poet, by 1700 regarded with contempt, but formerly greatly admired, especially among the Puritans. William Prynne (1600–1669), Puritan pamphleteer, author of *Histriomastix* (1632), a violent attack on the stage. Congreve, who had been the object of much of Collier's vituperation, slyly identifies his enemy with Puritans and Nonconformists, whom Collier, an ardent High Churchman, despised.
4. Considered a good likeness.

been the worst I could have borne; but he had a fling at your ladyship too; and then I could not hold; but i' faith I gave him his own.

LADY WISHFORT   Me? What did the filthy fellow say?

FOIBLE   O madam; 'tis a shame to say what he said—with his taunts and his fleers, tossing up his nose. Humh (says he) what, you are a-hatching some plot (says he) you are so early abroad, or catering (says he), ferreting for some disbanded[5] officer, I warrant—half pay is but thin subsistence (says he).—Well, what pension does your lady propose? Let me see (says he) what, she must come down pretty deep now, she's superannuated (says he) and—

LADY WISHFORT   Ods my life, I'll have him—I'll have him murdered. I'll have him poisoned. Where does he eat? I'll marry a drawer[6] to have him poisoned in his wine. I'll send for Robin from Locket's[7]—immediately.

FOIBLE   Poison him? Poisoning's too good for him. Starve him, madam, starve him; marry Sir Rowland, and get him disinherited. O, you would bless yourself, to hear what he said.

LADY WISHFORT   A villain!—superannuated!

FOIBLE   Humh (says he) I hear you are laying designs against me too (says he) and Mrs. Millamant is to marry my uncle; (he does not suspect a word of your ladyship) but (says he) I'll fit you for that, I warrant you (says he) I'll hamper you for that (says he) you and your old frippery[8] too (says he). I'll handle you—

LADY WISHFORT   Audacious villain! handle me, would he durst—frippery? old frippery! Was there ever such a foul-mouthed fellow? I'll be married tomorrow, I'll be contracted tonight.

FOIBLE   The sooner the better, madam.

LADY WISHFORT   Will Sir Rowland be here, say'st thou? When, Foible?

FOIBLE   Incontinently, madam. No new sheriff's wife expects the return of her husband after knighthood, with that impatience in which Sir Rowland burns for the dear hour of kissing your ladyship's hand after dinner.

LADY WISHFORT   Frippery! Superannuated frippery! I'll frippery the villain, I'll reduce him to frippery and rags. A tatterdemalion—I hope to see him hung with tatters, like a Long Lane penthouse,[9] or a gibbet-thief. A slander-mouthed railer—I warrant the spendthrift prodigal's in debt as much as the million lottery, or the whole court upon a birthday. I'll spoil his credit with his tailor. Yes, he shall have my niece with her fortune, he shall.

FOIBLE   He! I hope to see him lodge in Ludgate first, and angle into Black-friars for brass farthings with an old mitten.[1]

LADY WISHFORT   Aye, dear Foible; thank thee for that, dear Foible. He has put me out of all patience. I shall never recompose my features to receive

---

5. When a regiment was "disbanded," its officers went on half pay, often for life. "Fleers": jeers. "Catering": procuring (i.e., pimping for Lady Wishfort).

6. One who draws wine from casks and serves it.

7. A fashionable tavern near Charing Cross.

8. Old, cast-off clothes; an insulting metaphor to apply to Lady Wishfort.

9. A shed, supported by the wall toward which it is inclined. "Tatterdemalion": ragamuffin. Long Lane was a street where old clothes were sold.

1. Prisoners begged by letting down a mitten on a string; passers-by dropped coins into it. Ludgate was a debtor's prison, adjoining the district of Blackfriars in London.

Sir Rowland with any economy of face. This wretch has fretted me that I am absolutely decayed. Look, Foible.

FOIBLE Your ladyship has frowned a little too rashly, indeed, madam. There are some cracks discernible in the white varnish.

LADY WISHFORT Let me see the glass.—Cracks, say'st thou? Why I am arrantly flayed—I look like an old peeled wall. Thou must repair me, Foible, before Sir Rowland comes, or I shall never keep up to my picture.

FOIBLE I warrant you, madam; a little art once made your picture like you and now a little of the same art must make you like your picture. Your picture must sit for you, madam.

LADY WISHFORT But art thou sure Sir Rowland will not fail to come? Or will a' not fail[2] when he does come? Will he be importunate, Foible, and push? For if he should not be importunate—I shall never break decorums.—I shall die with confusion, if I am forced to advance.—Oh, no, I can never advance.—I shall swoon if he should expect advances. No, I hope Sir Rowland is better bred than to put a lady to the necessity of breaking her forms. I won't be too coy neither—I won't give him despair—but a little disdain is not amiss; a little scorn is alluring.

FOIBLE A little scorn becomes your ladyship.

LADY WISHFORT Yes, but tenderness becomes me best.—A sort of dyingness—You see that picture has a sort of a—Ha, Foible? A swimmingness in the eyes—Yes, I'll look so—my niece affects it; but she wants features.[3] Is Sir Rowland handsome? Let my toilet be removed—I'll dress above. I'll receive Sir Rowland here. Is he handsome? Don't answer me. I won't know: I'll be surprised. I'll be taken by surprise.

FOIBLE By storm, madam. Sir Rowland's a brisk man.

LADY WISHFORT Is he! O, then he'll importune, if he's a brisk man, I shall save decorums if Sir Rowland importunes. I have a mortal terror at the apprehension of offending against decorums. O, I'm glad he's a brisk man. Let my things be removed, good Foible. [*Exit* LADY WISHFORT.]
[*Enter* MRS. FAINALL.][4]

MRS. FAINALL O Foible, I have been in a fright, lest I should come too late. That devil Marwood saw you in the park with Mirabell, and I'm afraid will discover it to my lady.

FOIBLE Discover what, madam?

MRS. FAINALL Nay, nay, put not on that strange face. I am privy to the whole design and know Waitwell, to whom thou wert this morning married, is to personate[5] Mirabell's uncle, and as such, winning my lady, to involve her in those difficulties from which Mirabell only must release her, by his making his conditions to have my cousin and her fortune left to her own disposal.

FOIBLE O dear madam, I beg your pardon. It was not my confidence in your ladyship that was deficient, but I thought the former good correspondence between your ladyship and Mr. Mirabell might have hindered his communicating this secret.

MRS. FAINALL Dear Foible, forget that.

---

2. I.e., will *he* not fail?
3. Lacks the looks for it.
4. The subsequent conversation is sometimes

staged to show Mrs. Marwood overhearing it.
5. I.e., impersonate.

FOIBLE   O dear madam, Mr. Mirabell is such a sweet winning gentleman—but your ladyship is the pattern of generosity. Sweet lady, to be so good! Mr. Mirabell cannot choose but to be grateful. I find your ladyship has his heart still. Now, madam, I can safely tell your ladyship our success. Mrs. Marwood had told my lady; but I warrant I managed myself. I turned it all for the better. I told my lady that Mr. Mirabell railed at her. I laid horrid things to his charge, I'll vow; and my lady is so incensed that she'll be contracted to Sir Rowland tonight, she says—I warrant I worked her up, that he may have her for asking for, as they say of a Welsh maidenhead.

MRS. FAINALL   O rare Foible!

FOIBLE   Madam, I beg your ladyship to acquaint Mr. Mirabell of his success. I would be seen as little as possible to speak to him—besides, I believe Madam Marwood watches me. She has a month's mind,[6] but I know Mr. Mirabell can't abide her. [*Calls.*] John, remove my lady's toilet. Madam, your servant. My lady is so impatient, I fear she'll come for me if I stay.

MRS. FAINALL   I'll go with you up the back stairs, lest I should meet her.
    [*Exeunt* MRS. FAINALL, FOIBLE.]
    [*Enter* MRS. MARWOOD.]

MRS. MARWOOD   Indeed, Mrs. Engine,[7] is it thus with you? Are you become a go-between of this importance? Yes, I shall watch you. Why, this wench is the *passe-partout,* a very master key to everybody's strongbox. My friend Fainall,[8] have you carried it so swimmingly? I thought there was something in it; but it seems it's over with you. Your loathing is not from a want of appetite, then, but from a surfeit. Else you could never be so cool to fall from a principal to be an assistant; to procure for him! A pattern of generosity, that I confess. Well, Mr. Fainall, you have met with your match. O, man, man! Woman, woman! The devil's an ass: If I were a painter, I would draw him like an idiot, a driveler with a bib and bells. Man should have his head and horns, and woman the rest of him. Poor simple fiend! Madam Marwood has a month's mind, but he can't abide her.—'Twere better for him you had not been his confessor in that affair without you could have kept his counsel closer. I shall not prove another pattern of generosity.—He has not obliged me to that with those excesses of himself; and now I'll have none of him. Here comes the good lady, panting ripe, with a heart full of hope and a head full of care, like any chemist upon the day of projection.[9]
    [*Enter* LADY WISHFORT.]

LADY WISHFORT   O dear Marwood, what shall I say for this rude forgetfulness—but my dear friend is all goodness.

MRS. MARWOOD   No apologies, dear madam. I have been very well entertained.

LADY WISHFORT   As I'm a person I am in a very chaos to think I should so forget myself—but I have such an olio[1] of affairs really I know not what

---

6. An inclination (toward Mirabell).
7. A person who serves as an instrument or tool of others in an intrigue.
8. Mrs. Fainall.

9. An alchemical term denoting the final step in the transmutation of baser metals into gold.
1. Hodgepodge.

to do—[*Calls.*] Foible—I expect my nephew Sir Wilfull every moment too.—Why, Foible!—He means to travel for improvement.

MRS. MARWOOD   Methinks Sir Wilfull should rather think of marrying than traveling at his years. I hear he is turned of forty.

LADY WISHFORT   O, he's in less danger of being spoiled by his travels.—I am against my nephew's marrying too young. It will be time enough when he comes back and has acquired discretion to choose for himself.

MRS. MARWOOD   Methinks Mrs. Millamant and he would make a very fit match. He may travel afterwards. 'Tis a thing very usual with young gentlemen.

LADY WISHFORT   I promise you I have thought on't—and since 'tis your judgment, I'll think on't again. I assure you I will; I value your judgment extremely. On my word I'll propose it.

[*Enter* FOIBLE.]

LADY WISHFORT   Come, come Foible—I had forgot my nephew will be here before dinner.—I must make haste.

FOIBLE   Mr. Witwoud and Mr. Petulant are come to dine with your ladyship.

LADY WISHFORT   O dear, I can't appear till I am dressed. Dear Marwood, shall I be free with you again and beg you to entertain 'em? I'll make all imaginable haste. Dear friend, excuse me.

[*Exeunt* LADY WISHFORT *and* FOIBLE.]
[*Enter* MRS. MILLAMANT *and* MINCING.]

MILLAMANT   Sure never anything was so unbred as that odious man.— Marwood, your servant.

MRS. MARWOOD   You have a color. What's the matter?

MILLAMANT   That horrid fellow Petulant has provoked me into a flame—I have broke my fan.—Mincing, lend me yours; is not all the powder out of my hair?

MRS. MARWOOD   No. What has he done?

MILLAMANT   Nay, he has done nothing; he has only talked.—Nay, he has said nothing neither; but he has contradicted everything that has been said. For my part, I thought Witwoud and he would have quarreled.

MINCING   I vow, mem, I thought once they would have fit.[2]

MILLAMANT   Well, 'tis a lamentable thing, I swear, that one has not the liberty of choosing one's acquaintance as one does one's clothes.

MRS. MARWOOD   If we had that liberty, we should be as weary of one set of acquaintance, though never so good, as we are of one suit, though never so fine. A fool and a doily stuff[3] would now and then find days of grace, and be worn for variety.

MILLAMANT   I could consent to wear 'em, if they would wear alike; but fools never wear out—they are such drap-de-Berry[4] things! Without one could give 'em to one's chambermaid after a day or two.

MRS. MARWOOD   'Twere better so indeed. Or what think you of the play house?[5] A fine gay glossy fool should be given there, like a new masking habit after the masquerade is over, and we have done with the disguise.

---

2. Fought. Millamant turns Mincing's word to refer to clothing in her next remark.
3. A woolen cloth.
4. Coarse woolen cloth, made in the Berry dis-

trict of France.
5. Fine gentlemen and ladies sometimes donated their old clothes to the playhouses.

For a fool's visit is always a disguise, and never admitted by a woman of wit, but to blind her affair with a lover of sense. If you would but appear barefaced now and own Mirabell, you might as easily put off Petulant and Witwoud as your hood and scarf. And indeed 'tis time, for the town has found it: the secret is grown too big for the pretense: 'tis like Mrs. Primly's great belly; she may lace it down before, but it burnishes[6] on her hips. Indeed, Millamant, you can no more conceal it than my Lady Strammel can her face, that goodly face, which in defiance of her Rhenish-wine tea will not be comprehended in a mask.[7]

MILLAMANT   I'll take my death, Marwood, you are more censorious than a decayed beauty, or a discarded toast.[8] Mincing, tell the men they may come up. My aunt is not dressing here; their folly is less provoking than your malice. [*Exit* MINCING.] "The town has found it." What has it found? That Mirabell loves me is no more a secret than it is a secret that you discovered it to my aunt, or than the reason why you discovered it is a secret.

MRS. MARWOOD   You are nettled.

MILLAMANT   You're mistaken. Ridiculous!

MRS. MARWOOD   Indeed, my dear, you'll tear another fan if you don't mitigate those violent airs.

MILLAMANT   O silly! Ha, ha, ha. I could laugh immoderately. Poor Mirabell! His constancy to me has quite destroyed his complaisance for all the world beside. I swear, I never enjoined it him, to be so coy.—If I had the vanity to think he would obey me, I would command him to show more gallantry.—'Tis hardly well bred to be so particular on one hand and so insensible on the other. But I despair to prevail, and so let him follow his own way. Ha, ha, ha. Pardon me, dear creature, I must laugh, ha, ha, ha; though I grant you 'tis a little barbarous, ha, ha, ha.

MRS. MARWOOD   What pity 'tis, so much fine raillery, and delivered with so significant gesture, should be so unhappily directed to miscarry.

MILLAMANT   Ha? Dear creature, I ask your pardon—I swear I did not mind you.

MRS. MARWOOD   Mr. Mirabell and you both may think it a thing impossible, when I shall tell him by telling you—

MILLAMANT   O dear, what? For it is the same thing, if I hear it—Ha, ha, ha.

MRS. MARWOOD   That I detest him, hate him, madam.

MILLAMANT   O madam, why so do I—and yet the creature loves me, ha, ha, ha. How can one forbear laughing to think of it?—I am a sibyl[9] if I am not amazed to think what he can see in me. I'll take my death, I think you are handsomer—and within a year or two as young. If you could but stay for me, I should overtake you.—But that cannot be.—Well, that thought makes me melancholy.—Now I'll be sad.

MRS. MARWOOD   Your merry note may be changed sooner than you think.

---

6. Spreads out.
7. Lady Strammel (the name means "a lean, ill-favored person") tries to lose weight by drinking Rhenish wine, but still her face is too large to be contained ("comprehended") in a mask.
8. A lady to whom toasts are no longer drunk.
9. A prophetess.

MILLAMANT   D'ye say so? Then I'm resolved I'll have a song to keep up my
   spirits.
   [*Enter* MINCING.]
MINCING   The gentlemen stay but to comb,[1] madam, and will wait on you.
MILLAMANT   Desire Mrs. ——[2] that is in the next room to sing the song I
   would have learnt yesterday. You shall hear it, madam—not that there's
   any great matter in it—But 'tis agreeable to my humor.

[SONG. SET BY MR. JOHN ECCLES]

I

Love's but the frailty of the mind,
   When 'tis not with ambition joined;
A sickly flame, which if not fed expires;
And feeding, wastes in self-consuming fires.

2

'Tis not to wound a wanton boy
   Or amorous youth, that gives the joy;
But 'tis the glory to have pierced a swain,
For whom inferior beauties sighed in vain.

3

Then I alone the conquest prize,
   When I insult a rival's eyes:
If there's delight in love, 'tis when I see
That heart which others bleed for, bleed for me.

   [*Enter* PETULANT, WITWOUD.]
MILLAMANT   Is your animosity composed, gentlemen?
WITWOUD   Raillery, raillery, madam, we have no animosity. We hit off a
   little wit now and then, but no animosity. The falling out of wits is like
   the falling out of lovers—we agree in the main, like treble and bass. Ha,
   Petulant!
PETULANT   Aye, in the main. But when I have a humor to contradict—
WITWOUD   Aye, when he has a humor to contradict, then I contradict too.
   What, I know my cue. Then we contradict one another like two bat-
   tledores,[3] for contradictions beget one another like Jews.
PETULANT   If he says black's black—if I have a humor to say 'tis blue—let
   that pass.—All's one for that. If I have a humor to prove it, it must be
   granted.
WITWOUD   Not positively must—but it may—it may.
PETULANT   Yes, it positively must, upon proof positive.
WITWOUD   Aye, upon proof positive it must; but upon proof presumptive
   it only may. That's a logical distinction now, madam.

---

1. I.e., to comb their periwigs.
2. The name of the singer was to be inserted.
The music was by John Eccles (d. 1735), a popular composer for the theater.

3. Rackets used to strike the shuttlecock, or
bird, in the old game from which badminton is
descended.

MRS. MARWOOD   I perceive your debates are of importance and very learnedly handled.

PETULANT   Importance is one thing, and learning's another; but a debate's a debate, that I assert.

WITWOUD   Petulant's an enemy to learning; he relies altogether on his parts.[4]

PETULANT   No, I'm no enemy to learning; it hurts not me.

MRS. MARWOOD   That's a sign indeed it's no enemy to you.

PETULANT   No, no, it's no enemy to anybody but them that have it.

MILLAMANT   Well, an illiterate man's my aversion. I wonder at the impudence of any illiterate man, to offer to make love.

WITWOUD   That I confess I wonder at too.

MILLAMANT   Ah! to marry an ignorant! that can hardly read or write.

PETULANT   Why should a man be any further from being married though he can't read than he is from being hanged. The ordinary's[5] paid for setting the Psalm, and the parish priest for reading the ceremony. And for the rest which is to follow in both cases, a man may do it without book.—So all's one for that.

MILLAMANT   D'ye hear the creature? Lord, here's company, I'll be gone.
          [*Exeunt* MILLAMANT *and* MINCING.]

WITWOUD   In the name of Bartlemew and his Fair, what have we here?[6]

MRS. MARWOOD   'Tis your brother, I fancy. Don't you know him?

WITWOUD   Not I.—Yes, I think it is he—I've almost forgot him; I have not seen him since the Revolution.[7]
          [*Enter* SIR WILFUL WITWOUD *in riding clothes, and a* FOOTMAN *to* LADY WISHFORT.]

FOOTMAN   Sir, my lady's dressing. Here's company; if you please to walk in, in the meantime.

SIR WILFULL   Dressing! What, it's but morning here, I warrant, with you in London; we should count it towards afternoon in our parts, down in Shropshire. Why, then belike my aunt han't dined yet—ha, friend?

FOOTMAN   Your aunt, Sir?

SIR WILFULL   My aunt, sir, yes, my aunt, sir, and your lady, sir; your lady is my aunt, sir.—Why, what do'st thou not know me, friend? Why, then send somebody hither that does. How long hast thou lived with thy lady, fellow, ha?

FOOTMAN   A week, sir; longer than anybody in the house, except my lady's woman.

SIR WILFULL   Why, then belike thou dost not know thy lady, if thou see'st her, ha, friend?

FOOTMAN   Why truly, sir, I cannot safely swear to her face in a morning, before she is dressed. 'Tis like I may give a shrewd guess at her by this time.

SIR WILFULL   Well, prithee try what thou canst do; if thou canst not guess, inquire her out, do'st hear, fellow? And tell her her nephew, Sir Wilfull Witwoud, is in the house.

4. Native abilities.
5. The clergyman appointed to prepare condemned prisoners for death.
6. A feature of St. Bartholomew's Fair, held during August in Smithfield, London, was the exhibition of monsters and freaks of nature.
7. The Glorious Revolution of 1688, which forced the abdication of James II.

FOOTMAN   I shall, sir.

SIR WILFULL   Hold ye, hear me, friend; a word with you in your ear. Prithee who are these gallants?

FOOTMAN   Really, sir, I can't tell; there come so many here, 'tis hard to know 'em all. [*Exit* FOOTMAN.]

SIR WILFULL   Oons,[8] this fellow knows less than a starling; I don't think a'knows his own name.

MRS. MARWOOD   Mr. Witwoud, your brother is not behind hand in forgetfulness—I fancy he has forgot you too.

WITWOUD   I hope so.—The devil take him that remembers first, I say.

SIR WILFULL   Save you, gentlemen and lady.

MRS. MARWOOD   For shame, Mr. Witwoud; why don't you speak to him?— And you, sir.

WITWOUD   Petulant, speak.

PETULANT   And you, sir.

SIR WILFULL   [*Salutes*[9] MARWOOD.]   No offense, I hope.

MRS. MARWOOD   No sure, sir.

WITWOUD   This is a vile dog, I see that already. No offense! Ha, ha, ha, to him; to him, Petulant, smoke him.[1]

PETULANT   [*Surveying him round.*]   It seems as if you had come a journey, sir. Hem, hem.

SIR WILFULL   Very likely, sir, that it may seem so.

PETULANT   No offense, I hope, sir.

WITWOUD   Smoke the boots, the boots, Petulant, the boots. Ha, ha, ha.

SIR WILFULL   Maybe not, sir; thereafter as 'tis meant, sir.

PETULANT   Sir, I presume upon the information of your boots.

SIR WILFULL   Why, 'tis like you may, sir: If you are not satisfied with the information of my boots, sir, if you will step to the stable, you may inquire further of my horse, sir.

PETULANT   Your horse, sir! Your horse is an ass, sir!

SIR WILFULL   Do you speak by way of offense, sir?

MRS. MARWOOD   The gentleman's merry, that's all, sir.—[*Aside.*] 'Slife,[2] we shall have a quarrel betwixt an horse and an ass, before they find one another out. [*Aloud.*] You must not take anything amiss from your friends, sir. You are among your friends, here, though it may be you don't know it.—If I am not mistaken, you are Sir Wilfull Witwoud.

SIR WILFULL   Right, lady; I am Sir Wilfull Witwoud, so I write myself; no offense to anybody, I hope; and nephew to the Lady Wishfort of this mansion.

MRS. MARWOOD   Don't you know this gentleman, sir?

SIR WILFULL   Hum! What, sure, 'tis not—yea by'r Lady, but 'tis—'sheart, I know not whether 'tis or no.—Yea but 'tis, by the Wrekin.[3] Brother Antony! What, Tony, i'faith! What, do'st thou not know me? By'r Lady, nor I thee, thou art so becravated and so beperriwigged—'sheart, why do'st not speak? Art thou o'erjoyed?

WITWOUD   Odso, brother, is it you? Your servant, brother.

8. An uncouth oath: God's wounds.
9. Kisses.
1. Make fun of him.

2. God's life.
3. A solitary mountain peak in Shropshire, near the Welsh border. "'Sheart": God's heart.

SIR WILFULL Your servant! Why, yours, sir. Your servant again—'sheart, and your friend and servant to that—and a—[*Puff.*]—and a flapdragon for your service, sir: and a hare's foot, and a hare's scut[4] for your service, sir; an you be so cold and so courtly!

WITWOUD No offense, I hope, brother.

SIR WILFULL 'Sheart, sir, but there is, and much offense. A pox, is this your Inns o'Court[5] breeding, not to know your friends and your relations, your elders and your betters?

WITWOUD Why, Brother Wilfull of Salop, you may be as short as a Shrewsbury cake,[6] if you please. But I tell you 'tis not modish to know relations in town. You think you're in the country, where great lubberly brothers slabber and kiss one another when they meet, like a call of sergeants.[7]— 'Tis not the fashion here; 'tis not indeed, dear brother.

SIR WILFULL The fashion's a fool; and you're a fop, dear brother. 'Sheart, I've suspected this—by'r Lady, I conjectured you were a fop, since you began to change the style of your letters and write in a scrap of paper gilt round the edges, no bigger than a subpoena. I might expect this when you left off "Honored Brother" and "hoping you are in good health," and so forth—to begin with a "Rat me, knight, I'm so sick of a last night's debauch"—'od's heart, and then tell a familiar tale of a cock and bull, and a whore and a bottle, and so conclude—You could write news before you were out of your time, when you lived with honest Pumple-Nose, the attorney of Furnival's Inn[8]—You could entreat to be remembered then to your friends round the Wrekin. We could have gazettes then, and Dawks's *Letter,* and the Weekly Bill,[9] till of late days.

PETULANT 'Slife, Witwoud, were you ever an attorney's clerk? Of the family of the Furnivals. Ha, ha, ha!

WITWOUD Aye, aye, but that was but for a while. Not long, not long; pshaw, I was not in my own power then. An orphan, and this fellow was my guardian; aye, aye, I was glad to consent to that man to come to London. He had the disposal of me then. If I had not agreed to that, I might have been bound 'prentice to a felt-maker in Shrewsbury; this fellow would have bound me to a maker of felts.

SIR WILFULL 'Sheart, and better than to be bound to a maker of fops; where, I suppose, you have served your time; and now you may set up for yourself.

MRS. MARWOOD You intend to travel, sir, as I'm informed.

SIR WILFULL Belike I may, madam. I may chance to sail upon the salt seas, if my mind hold.

PETULANT And the wind serve.

---

4. Rabbit's tail. "Flapdragon": something worthless.
5. The buildings—Gray's Inn, Lincoln's Inn, the Inner Temple, the Middle Temple—housing the four legal societies that have the sole right to admit persons to the practice of law.
6. Shortcake, in the modern meaning of the term. Witwoud puns, using "short" also in the sense of "abrupt." "Salop": ancient name of Shropshire.
7. Witwoud refers to the mutual greetings and

felicitations of a group of barristers ("sergeants") newly admitted to the bar. "Lubberly": loutish.
8. One of the inns of Chancery, attached to Lincoln's Inn. Attorneys were looked down on socially; hence Petulant's ill-natured mirth in his next speech. "Before you were out of your time": before you had served out your apprenticeship.
9. The official list of the deaths occurring in London. "Gazettes": newspapers. "Dawks's [*News*] *Letter*": a popular source of news in the country.

SIR WILFULL   Serve or not serve, I shan't ask license of you, sir; nor the weather-cock[1] your companion. I direct my discourse to the lady, sir. 'Tis like my aunt may have told you, madam—Yes, I have settled my concerns, I may say now, and am minded to see foreign parts. If an' how that the peace[2] holds, whereby, that is, taxes abate.

MRS. MARWOOD   I thought you had designed for France at all adventures.[3]

SIR WILFULL   I can't tell that; 'tis like I may and 'tis like I may not. I am somewhat dainty in making a resolution, because when I make it I keep it, I don't stand shill I, shall I,[4] then; if I say't, I'll do't. But I have thoughts to tarry a small matter in town, to learn somewhat of your lingo first, before I cross the seas. I'd gladly have a spice of your French as they say, whereby to hold discourse in foreign countries.

MRS. MARWOOD   Here's an academy in town for that use.

SIR WILFULL   There is? 'Tis like there may.

MRS. MARWOOD   No doubt you will return very much improved.

WITWOUD   Yes, refined like a Dutch skipper from a whale-fishing.

[Enter LADY WISHFORT and FAINALL.]

LADY WISHFORT   Nephew, you are welcome.

SIR WILFULL   Aunt, your servant.

FAINALL   Sir Wilfull, your most faithful servant.

SIR WILFULL   Cousin Fainall, give me your hand.

LADY WISHFORT   Cousin Witwoud, your servant; Mr. Petulant, your servant.—Nephew, you are welcome again. Will you drink anything after your journey, nephew, before you eat? Dinner's almost ready.

SIR WILFULL   I'm very well, I thank you, aunt. However, I thank you for your courteous offer. 'Sheart, I was afraid you would have been in the fashion too, and have remembered to have forgot your relations. Here's your cousin Tony, belike, I mayn't call him brother for fear of offense.

LADY WISHFORT   O, he's a rallier, nephew—my cousin's a wit; and your great wits always rally their best friends to choose.[5] When you have been abroad, nephew, you'll understand raillery better.

[FAINALL and MRS. MARWOOD talk apart.]

SIR WILFULL   Why then let him hold his tongue in the meantime, and rail when that day comes.

[Enter MINCING.]

MINCING   Mem, I come to acquaint your la'ship that dinner is impatient.

SIR WILFULL   Impatient? Why then belike it won't stay till I pull off my boots. Sweetheart, can you help me to a pair of slippers?—My man's with his horses, I warrant.

LADY WISHFORT   Fie, fie, nephew, you would not pull off your boots here. Go down into the hall.—Dinner shall stay for you. My nephew's a little unbred; you'll pardon him, madam.—Gentlemen, will you walk? Marwood?

MRS. MARWOOD   I'll follow you, madam—before Sir Wilfull is ready.

[Exeunt all but MRS. MARWOOD, FAINALL.]

---

1. Weathervane.
2. The peace established by the Treaty of Ryswick in 1697, which concluded the war against France waged under the leadership of William III by England, the Empire, Spain, and Holland. It endured until the spring of 1702, when the War of the Spanish Succession began.
3. No matter what happens.
4. Shilly-shally. "Dainty": scrupulous, cautious.
5. By choice.

FAINALL   Why then Foible's a bawd, an errant, rank, match-making bawd. And I it seems am a husband, a rank husband; and my wife a very errant, rank wife—all in the way of the world. 'Sdeath, to be a cuckold by anticipation, a cuckold in embryo? Sure I was born with budding antlers like a young satyr, or a citizen's child.[6] 'Sdeath, to be outwitted, to be outjilted—outmatrimonied. If I had kept my speed like a stag, 'twere somewhat, but to crawl after, with my horns like a snail, and be outstripped by my wife—'tis scurvy wedlock.

MRS. MARWOOD   Then shake it off. You have often wished for an opportunity to part, and now you have it. But first prevent their plot.—The half of Millamant's fortune is too considerable to be parted with to a foe, to Mirabell.

FAINALL   Damn him, that had been mine—had you not made that fond[7] discovery.—That had been forfeited, had they been married. My wife had added luster to my horns. By that increase of fortune, I could have worn 'em tipped with gold, though my forehead had been furnished like a Deputy-Lieutenant's hall.[8]

MRS. MARWOOD   They may prove a cap of maintenance[9] to you still, if you can away with your wife. And she's no worse than when you had her—I dare swear she had given up her game, before she was married.

FAINALL   Hum! That may be—She might throw up her cards; but I'll be hanged if she did not put Pam[1] in her pocket.

MRS. MARWOOD   You married her to keep you, and if you can contrive to have her keep you better than you expected, why should you not keep her longer than you intended?

FAINALL   The means, the means.

MRS. MARWOOD   Discover to my lady your wife's conduct; threaten to part with her.—My lady loves her and will come to any composition to save her reputation. Take the opportunity of breaking it, just upon the discovery of this imposture. My lady will be enraged beyond bounds and sacrifice niece and fortune and all at that conjuncture. And let me alone to keep her warm; if she should flag in her part, I will not fail to prompt her.

FAINALL   Faith, this has an appearance.[2]

MRS. MARWOOD   I'm sorry I hinted to my lady to endeavor a match between Millamant and Sir Wilfull. That may be an obstacle.

FAINALL   O, for that matter leave me to manage him; I'll disable him for that; he will drink like a Dane; after dinner, I'll set his hand in.

MRS. MARWOOD   Well, how do you stand affected towards your lady?

FAINALL   Why, faith, I'm thinking of it. Let me see—I am married already; so that's over. My wife has played the jade with[3] me—well, that's over too. I never loved her, or if I had, why that would have been over too by this time. Jealous of her I cannot be, for I am certain; so there's an end of

---

6. "Satyr": a sylvan deity, usually represented with a goat's legs and horns. A cuckold is said to wear horns. Because the wives of "citizens" (merchants living in the old city of London, not the fashionable suburbs) were regarded by the rakes as their natural and easy prey, a "citizen's child" was born to be cuckolded.
7. Foolish. Fainall blames her for revealing to Lady Wishfort that Mirabell was not interested

in her.
8. I.e., the great hall in the house of the deputy lieutenant of a shire. Fainall imagines it ornamented with numerous antlers taken from deer slain in the hunt.
9. In heraldry, a cap with two points like horns.
1. Jack of clubs, high card in the game of loo.
2. It's a promising scheme.
3. Cheated on.

jealousy. Weary of her I am and shall be—no, there's no end of that; no, no, that were too much to hope. Thus far concerning my repose. Now for my reputation. As to my own, I married not for it; so that's out of the question. And as to my part in my wife's—why, she had parted with hers before; so bringing none to me, she can take none from me; 'tis against all rule of play that I should lose to one who has not wherewithal to stake.

MRS. MARWOOD Besides you forget, marriage is honorable.

FAINALL Hum! Faith, and that's well thought on; marriage is honorable, as you say; and if so, wherefore should cuckoldom be a discredit, being derived from so honorable a root?

MRS. MARWOOD Nay, I know not; if the root be honorable, why not the branches?[4]

FAINALL So, so, why this point's clear.[5] Well, how do we proceed?

MRS. MARWOOD I will contrive a letter which shall be delivered to my lady at the time when that rascal who is to act Sir Rowland is with her. It shall come as from an unknown hand—for the less I appear to know of the truth, the better I can play the incendiary. Besides, I would not have Foible provoked if I could help it, because you know she knows some passages—nay, I expect all will come out. But let the mine be sprung first, and then I care not if I am discovered.

FAINALL If the worst come to the worst, I'll turn my wife to grass[6]—I have already a deed of settlement of the best part of her estate, which I wheedled out of her; and that you shall partake at least.

MRS. MARWOOD I hope you are convinced that I hate Mirabell now: you'll be no more jealous?

FAINALL Jealous, no—by this kiss.—Let husbands be jealous, but let the lover still believe. Or if he doubt, let it be only to endear his pleasure and prepare the joy that follows, when he proves his mistress true. But let husbands' doubts convert to endless jealousy; or if they have belief, let it corrupt to superstition and blind credulity. I am single, and will herd no more with 'em. True, I wear the badge, but I'll disown the order. And since I take my leave of 'em, I care not if I leave 'em a common motto to their common crest.

> All husbands must, or pain, or shame, endure;
> The wise too jealous are, fools too secure.

[*Exeunt* FAINALL *and* MRS. MARWOOD.]

Act 4—Scene continues.

[*Enter* LADY WISHFORT *and* FOIBLE.]

LADY WISHFORT Is Sir Rowland coming, say'st thou, Foible? and are things in order?

FOIBLE Yes, madam. I have put wax lights in the sconces, and placed the footmen in a row in the hall, in their best liveries, with the coachman and postilion to fill up the equipage.

---

4. I.e., of the cuckold's horns.
5. Cleared up.

6. Turn out to pasture. A "grass widow" is divorced or separated from her husband.

LADY WISHFORT Have you pulvilled[7] the coachman and postilion, that they may not stink of the stable, when Sir Rowland comes by?

FOIBLE Yes, madam.

LADY WISHFORT And are the dancers and the music ready, that he may be entertained in all points with correspondence to his passion?

FOIBLE All is ready, madam.

LADY WISHFORT And—well—and how do I look, Foible?

FOIBLE Most killing well, madam.

LADY WISHFORT Well, and how shall I receive him? In what figure shall I give his heart the first impression? There is a great deal in the first impression. Shall I sit?—No, I won't sit—I'll walk.—Aye, I'll walk from the door upon his entrance; and then turn full upon him.—No, that will be too sudden. I'll lie—aye, I'll lie down—I'll receive him in my little dressing-room, there's a couch.—Yes, yes, I'll give the first impression on a couch.—I won't lie neither, but loll and lean upon one elbow; with one foot a little dangling off, jogging in a thoughtful way—yes—and then as soon as he appears, start, aye, start and be surprised, and rise to meet him in a pretty disorder—yes. O, nothing is more alluring than a levee[8] from a couch in some confusion. It shows the foot to advantage and furnishes with blushes and recomposing airs beyond comparison. Hark! There's a coach.

FOIBLE 'Tis he, madam.

LADY WISHFORT O dear, has my nephew made his addresses to Millamant? I ordered him.

FOIBLE Sir Wilfull is set in to drinking, madam, in the parlor.

LADY WISHFORT 'Ods my life, I'll send him to her. Call her down, Foible; bring her hither. I'll send him as I go.—When they are together, then come to me, Foible, that I may not be too long alone with Sir Rowland.
[Exit LADY WISHFORT.]

[Enter MRS. MILLAMANT and MRS. FAINALL.]

FOIBLE Madam, I stayed here to tell your ladyship that Mr. Mirabell has waited this half hour for an opportunity to talk with you. Though my lady's orders were to leave you and Sir Wilfull together. Shall I tell Mr. Mirabell that you are at leisure?

MILLAMANT No—What would the dear man have? I am thoughtful and would amuse myself.—Bid him come another time.

> There never yet was woman made,
> Nor shall, but to be cursed.[9]

[Repeating and walking about.]

That's hard!

MRS. FAINALL You are very fond of Sir John Suckling today, Millamant, and the poets.

MILLAMANT He? Aye, and filthy verses—so I am.

FOIBLE Sir Wilfull is coming, madam. Shall I send Mr. Mirabell away?

7. Sprinkled with perfumed powder.
8. A rising.
9. The opening lines of a poem by Sir John Suckling. Impelled by her love to accept Mirabell, but reluctant to give herself, Millamant broods over poems that speak of the brief happiness of lovers and the falseness of men.

MILLAMANT   Aye, if you please, Foible, send him away—or send him hither, just as you will, dear Foible. I think I'll see him—Shall I? Aye, let the wretch come.

> Thyrsis, a youth of the inspirèd train.[1]

> [*Repeating.*]

Dear Fainall, entertain Sir Wilfull.—Thou hast philosophy to undergo a fool, thou art married and hast patience.—I would confer with my own thoughts.

MRS. FAINALL   I am obliged to you that you would make me your proxy in this affair, but I have business of my own.

[*Enter* SIR WILFULL.]

MRS. FAINALL   O Sir Wilfull; you are come at the critical instant. There's your mistress up to the ears in love and contemplation. Pursue your point, now or never.

SIR WILFULL   Yes; my aunt will have it so.—I would gladly have been encouraged with a bottle or two, because I'm somewhat wary at first, before I am acquainted; [*This while* MILLAMANT *walks about repeating to herself.*]—but I hope, after a time, I shall break my mind[2]—that is upon further acquaintance.—So for the present, cousin, I'll take my leave.—If so be you'll be so kind to make my excuse, I'll return to my company.—

MRS. FAINALL   O fie, Sir Wilfull! What, you must not be daunted.

SIR WILFULL   Daunted, no, that's not it; it is not so much for that—for if so be that I set on't, I'll do't. But only for the present, 'tis sufficient till further acquaintance, that's all.—Your servant.

MRS. FAINALL   Nay, I'll swear you shall never lose so favorable an opportunity if I can help it. I'll leave you together and lock the door. [*Exit* MRS. FAINFALL.]

SIR WILFULL   Nay, nay, cousin—I have forgot my gloves.—What d'ye do? 'Sheart, a'has locked the door indeed, I think.—Nay, cousin Fainall, open the door.—Pshaw, what a vixen trick is this? Nay, now a'has seen me too.—Cousin, I made bold to pass through, as it were.—I think this door's enchanted.—

MILLAMANT   [*Repeating.*]

> I prithee spare me, gentle boy,
> Press me no more for that slight toy.[3]

SIR WILFULL   Anan?[4] Cousin, your servant.
MILLAMANT.   —"That foolish trifle of a heart"—Sir Wilfull!
SIR WILFULL   Yes—your servant. No offense I hope, cousin.
MILLAMANT   [*Repeating.*]

> I swear it will not do its part,
> Though thou dost thine, employ'st thy power and art.

Natural, easy Suckling!

---

1. The first line of Edmund Waller's "The Story of Phoebus and Daphne Applied." In the flight of the virgin nymph from the embraces of the amorous god, Millamant finds an emblem of her relations with Mirabell.
2. Speak more openly.
3. The first lines of a song by Suckling, which she continues in her next lines.
4. How's that?

SIR WILFULL Anan? Suckling? No such suckling neither, cousin, nor stripling: I thank heaven I'm no minor.

MILLAMANT Ah rustic, ruder than Gothic.[5]

SIR WILFULL Well, well, I shall understand your lingo one of these days, cousin. In the meanwhile I must answer in plain English.

MILLAMANT Have you any business with me, Sir Wilfull?

SIR WILFULL Not at present, cousin.—Yes, I made bold to see, to come and know if that how you were disposed to fetch a walk this evening, if so be that I might not be troublesome, I would have sought a walk with you.

MILLAMANT A walk? What then?

SIR WILFULL Nay nothing—only for the walk's sake, that's all—

MILLAMANT I nauseate walking; 'tis a country diversion. I loathe the country and everything that relates to it.

SIR WILFULL Indeed! Hah! Look ye, look ye, you do? Nay, 'tis like you may.—Here are choice of pastimes here in town, as plays and the like; that must be confessed indeed.—

MILLAMANT Ah, l'étourdi.[6] I hate the town too.

SIR WILFULL Dear heart, that's much—Hah! that you should hate 'em both! Hah! 'tis like you may; there are some can't relish the town, and others can't away with the country—'tis like you may be one of those, cousin.

MILLAMANT Ha, ha, ha. Yes, 'tis like I may. You have nothing further to say to me?

SIR WILFULL Not at present, cousin. 'Tis like when I have an opportunity to be more private, I may break my mind in some measure.—I conjecture you partly guess—however, that's as time shall try; but spare to speak and spare to speed, as they say.

MILLAMANT If it is of no great importance, Sir Wilfull, you will oblige me to leave me. I have just now a little business.

SIR WILFULL Enough, enough, cousin. Yes, yes, all a case—when you're disposed, when you're disposed. Now's as well as another time; and another time as well as now. All's one for that.—Yes, yes, if your concerns call you, there's no haste; it will keep cold as they say.—Cousin, your servant. I think this door's locked.

MILLAMANT You may go this way, sir.

SIR WILFULL Your servant—then with your leave I'll return to my company.

[*Exit* SIR WILFULL]

MILLAMANT Aye, aye. Ha, ha, ha.

Like Phoebus sung the no less amorous Boy.[7]

[*Enter* MIRABELL.]

MIRABELL

Like Daphne she, as lovely and as coy.

---

5. To the new age with its classical taste, medieval art, especially architecture, seemed crude ("rude").
6. Oh, the silly fellow (French); also the title of a comedy by Molière.
7. This, and the line that Mirabell caps it with, are also from Waller's "The Story of Phoebus and Daphne Applied."

Do you lock yourself up from me, to make my search more curious?[8] Or is this pretty artifice contrived to signify that here the chase must end, and my pursuit be crowned, for you can fly no further?

MILLAMANT Vanity! No—I'll fly and be followed to the last moment. Though I am upon the very verge of matrimony, I expect you should solicit me as much as if I were wavering at the grate of a monastery,[9] with one foot over the threshold. I'll be solicited to the very last, nay and afterwards.

MIRABELL What, after the last?

MILLAMANT O, I should think I was poor and had nothing to bestow, if I were reduced to an inglorious ease; and freed from the agreeable fatigues of solicitation.

MIRABELL But do not you know that when favors are conferred upon instant and tedious solicitation, that they diminish in their value and that both the giver loses the grace, and the receiver lessens his pleasure?

MILLAMANT It may be in things of common application, but never sure in love. O, I hate a lover that can dare to think he draws a moment's air, independent on the bounty of his mistress. There is not so impudent a thing in nature as the saucy look of an assured man, confident of success. The pedantic arrogance of a very husband has not so pragmatical[1] an air. Ah! I'll never marry, unless I am first made sure of my will and pleasure.

MIRABELL Would you have 'em both before marriage? Or will you be contented with the first now, and stay for the other till after grace?

MILLAMANT Ah, don't be impertinent.—My dear liberty, shall I leave thee? My faithful solitude, my darling contemplation, must I bid you then adieu? Ay-h adieu—My morning thoughts, agreeable wakings, indolent slumbers, all ye *douceurs,* ye *sommeils du matin,*[2] adieu.—I can't do't, 'tis more than impossible.—Positively, Mirabell, I'll lie abed in a morning as long as I please.

MIRABELL Then I'll get up in a morning as early as I please.

MILLAMANT Ah, idle creature, get up when you will.—and d'ye hear? I won't be called names after I'm married; positively I won't be called names.

MIRABELL Names!

MILLAMANT Aye, as wife, spouse, my dear, joy, jewel, love, sweetheart, and the rest of that nauseous cant, in which men and their wives are so fulsomely familiar—I shall never bear that.—Good Mirabell, don't let us be familiar or fond, nor kiss before folks, like my Lady Fadler[3] and Sir Francis; nor go to Hyde Park together the first Sunday in a new chariot, to provoke eyes and whispers; and then never be seen there together again, as if we were proud of one another the first week, and ashamed of one another ever after. Let us never visit together, nor go to a play together, but let us be very strange[4] and well bred; let us be as strange as if we had been married a great while; and as well bred as if we were not married at all.

---

8. Intricate, laborious.
9. The grated door of a convent.
1. Self-assured, conceited.

2. Soft (pleasures) and morning naps (French).
3. I.e., Fondler.
4. Reserved.

MIRABELL   Have you any more conditions to offer? Hitherto your demands are pretty reasonable.

MILLAMANT   Trifles—as liberty to pay and receive visits to and from whom I please; to write and receive letters, without interrogatories or wry faces on your part; to wear what I please; and choose conversation with regard only to my own taste; to have no obligation upon me to converse with wits that I don't like, because they are your acquaintance; or to be intimate with fools, because they may be your relations. Come to dinner when I please, dine in my dressing room when I'm out of humor, without giving a reason. To have my closet inviolate; to be sole empress of my tea table, which you must never presume to approach without first asking leave. And lastly, wherever I am, you shall always knock at the door before you come in. These articles subscribed, if I continue to endure you a little longer, I may by degrees dwindle into a wife.

MIRABELL   Your bill of fare is something advanced in this latter account. Well, have I liberty to offer conditions—that when you are dwindled into a wife, I may not be beyond measure enlarged into a husband?

MILLAMANT   You have free leave, propose your utmost, speak and spare not.

MIRABELL   I thank you. *Imprimis*[5] then, I covenant that your acquaintance be general; that you admit no sworn confidante or intimate of your own sex; no she-friend to screen her affairs under your countenance and tempt you to make trial of a mutual secrecy. No decoy duck to wheedle you a fop—scrambling to the play in a mask—then bring you home in a pretended fright, when you think you shall be found out—and rail at me for missing the play, and disappointing the frolic which you had to pick me up and prove my constancy.

MILLAMANT   Detestable *imprimis!* I go to the play in a mask!

MIRABELL   *Item,* I article,[6] that you continue to like your own face as long as I shall; and while it passes current with me, that you endeavor not to new coin it. To which end, together with all vizards for the day, I prohibit all masks for the night, made of oiled-skins and I know not what—hog's bones, hare's gall, pig water, and the marrow of a roasted cat.[7] In short, I forbid all commerce with the gentlewoman in what-d'ye-call-it court. *Item,* I shut my doors against all bawds with baskets, and pennyworths of muslin, china, fans, atlases,[8] etc. *Item,* when you shall be breeding—

MILLAMANT   Ah! Name it not.

MIRABELL   Which may be presumed, with a blessing on our endeavors—

MILLAMANT   Odious endeavors!

MIRABELL   I denounce against all strait lacing, squeezing for a shape, till you mold my boy's head like a sugar loaf; and instead of a man-child, make me father to a crooked billet.[9] Lastly, to the dominion of the tea table I submit.—But with proviso that you exceed not in your province; but restrain yourself to native and simple tea-table drinks, as tea, chocolate, and coffee. As likewise to genuine and authorized tea-table talk—such as mending of fashions, spoiling reputations, railing at absent

---

5. In the first place (Latin), as in legal documents.
6. I stipulate. *"Item":* used to introduce each item in a list.
7. Cosmetics were made of materials as repulsive

as those that Mirabell names. "Vizards": masks.
8. Rich silk fabrics.
9. I.e., a crooked piece of firewood.

friends, and so forth—but that on no account you encroach upon the men's prerogative, and presume to drink healths, or toast fellows; for prevention of which, I banish all foreign forces, all auxiliaries to the tea table, as orange brandy, all aniseed, cinnamon, citron and Barbados waters, together with ratafia and the most noble spirit of clary.[1]—But for cowslip-wine, poppy water, and all dormitives,[2] those I allow. These provisos admitted, in other things I may prove a tractable and complying husband.

MILLAMANT   O, horrid provisos! filthy strong waters! I toast fellows, odious men! I hate your odious provisos.

MIRABELL   Then we're agreed. Shall I kiss your hand upon the contract? And here comes one to be a witness to the sealing of the deed.

[Enter MRS. FAINALL.]

MILLAMANT   Fainall, what shall I do? Shall I have him? I think I must have him.

MRS. FAINALL   Aye, aye, take him, take him. What should you do?

MILLAMANT   Well then—I'll take my death I'm in a horrid fright— Fainall, I shall never say it—well—I think—I'll endure you.

MRS. FAINALL   Fy, fy, have him, have him, and tell him so in plain terms: for I am sure you have a mind to him.

MILLAMANT   Are you? I think I have—and the horrid man looks as if he thought so too.—Well, you ridiculous thing you, I'll have you.—I won't be kissed, nor I won't be thanked.—Here kiss my hand though.—So, hold your tongue now, don't say a word.

MRS. FAINALL   Mirabell, there's a necessity for your obedience—you have neither time to talk nor stay. My mother is coming; and in my conscience if she should see you, would fall into fits, and maybe not recover, time enough to return to Sir Rowland; who, as Foible tells me, is in a fair way to succeed. Therefore spare your ecstasies for another occasion, and slip down the back stairs, where Foible waits to consult you.

MILLAMANT   Aye, go, go. In the meantime I suppose you have said something to please me.

MIRABELL   I am all obedience.

[Exit MIRABELL.]

MRS. FAINALL   Yonder Sir Wilfull's drunk, and so noisy that my mother has been forced to leave Sir Rowland to appease him; but he answers her only with singing and drinking.—What they may have done by this time I know not, but Petulant and he were upon quarreling as I came by.

MILLAMANT   Well, if Mirabell should not make a good husband, I am a lost thing; for I find I love him violently.

MRS. FAINALL   So it seems, for you mind not what's said to you.—If you doubt him, you had best take up with Sir Wilfull.

MILLAMANT   How can you name that superannuated lubber? foh!

[Enter WITWOUD from drinking.]

MRS. FAINALL   So, is the fray made up, that you have left 'em?

WITWOUD   Left 'em? I could stay no longer—I have laughed like ten christenings—I am tipsy with laughing.—If I had stayed any longer, I

---

1. A sweet liqueur made of wine, honey, and spices. "Aniseed, cinnamon, citron and Barbados waters": alcoholic drinks.
2. Sedatives.

should have burst—I must have been let out and pieced in the sides like an unsized camlet.[3]—Yes, yes, the fray is composed; my lady came in like a *nolle prosequi*[4] and stopped the proceedings.

MILLAMANT   What was the dispute?

WITWOUD   That's the jest; there was no dispute. They could neither of 'em speak for rage; and so fell a-sputtering at one another like two roasting apples.

[*Enter* PETULANT *drunk.*]

WITWOUD   Now, Petulant? All's over, all's well? Gad, my head begins to whim it about.—Why dost thou not speak? Thou art both as drunk and as mute as a fish.

PETULANT   Look you, Mrs. Millamant—if you can love me, dear nymph— say it—and that's the conclusion—pass on, or pass off—that's all.

WITWOUD   Thou hast uttered volumes, folios, in less than decimo sexto, my dear Lacedemonian.[5] Sirrah Petulant, thou art an epitomizer of words.

PETULANT   Witwoud—You are an annihilator of sense.

WITWOUD   Thou art a retailer of phrases, and dost deal in remnants of remnants, like a maker of pincushions. Thou art in truth (metaphorically speaking) a speaker of shorthand.

PETULANT   Thou art (without a figure) just one-half of an ass, and Baldwin yonder, thy half brother, is the rest.—A Gemini[6] of asses split, would make just four of you.

WITWOUD   Thou dost bite, my dear mustard-seed; kiss me for that.

PETULANT   Stand off—I'll kiss no more males.—I have kissed your twin yonder in a humor of reconciliation, till he—[*Hiccup.*]—rises upon my stomach like a radish.

MILLAMANT   Eh! filthy creature.—What was the quarrel?

PETULANT   There was no quarrel—there might have been a quarrel.

WITWOUD   If there had been words enow between 'em to have expressed provocation, they had gone together by the ears like a pair of castanets.

PETULANT   You were the quarrel.

MILLAMANT   Me!

PETULANT   If I have a humor to quarrel, I can make less matters conclude premises.[7]—If you are not handsome, what then, if I have a humor to prove it?—If I shall have my reward, say so; if not, fight for your face the next time yourself.—I'll go sleep.

WITWOUD   Do, wrap thyself up like a woodlouse, and dream revenge— and hear me, if thou canst learn to write by tomorrow morning, pen me a challenge.—I'll carry it for thee.

PETULANT   Carry your mistress's monkey a spider—go flea dogs, and read romances—I'll go to bed to my maid.[8]

MRS. FAINALL   He's horridly drunk—how came you all in this pickle?

---

3. A fabric made by mixing wool and silk; "unsized" because not stiffened with some glutinous substance.
4. A Latin phrase indicating the withdrawal of a lawsuit.
5. Spartans; people of few words. "Folios": books of the largest size. "Decimo sexto": a book of the smallest size.
6. The two Roman deities, the twins Castor and Pollux, for whom one of the signs of the zodiac is

named. "Baldwin": the name of the ass in the beast epic *Reynard the Fox* (ca. 1175–1250).
7. I can argue successfully about matters less significant than you.
8. Monkeys were supposed to eat spiders. Petulant scornfully contrasts what he imagines to be Witwoud's technique with his lady with his own more vigorous and direct program for the rest of the evening.

WITWOUD   A plot, a plot, to get rid of the knight—your husband's advice; but he sneaked off.

[*Enter* SIR WILFULL *drunk, and* LADY WISHFORT.]

LADY WISHFORT   Out upon't, out upon't! At years of discretion, and comport yourself at this rantipole[9] rate!

SIR WILFULL   No offense, aunt.

LADY WISHFORT   Offense? As I'm a person, I'm ashamed of you.—Fogh! how you stink of wine! D'ye think my niece will ever endure such a borachio![1] you're an absolute borachio.

SIR WILFULL   Borachio!

LADY WISHFORT   At a time when you should commence an amour, and put your best foot foremost—

SIR WILFULL   'Sheart, an you grutch[2] me your liquor, make a bill.—Give me more drink, and take my purse.

[*Sings.*]   Prithee fill me the glass
                'Till it laugh in my face,
        With ale that is potent and mellow;
              He that whines for a lass
              Is an ignorant ass,
        For a bumper[3] has not its fellow.

But if you would have me marry my cousin—say the word and I'll do't—Wilfull will do't, that's the word—Wilfull will do't, that's my crest—my motto I have forgot.[4]

LADY WISHFORT   My nephew's a little overtaken, cousin—but 'tis with drinking your health—O' my word you are obliged to him—

SIR WILFULL   *In vino veritas*,[5] aunt.—If I drunk your health today, cousin—I am a borachio. But if you have a mind to be married, say the word, and send for the piper; Wilfull will do't. If not, dust[6] it away, and let's have t'other round.—Tony, 'ods heart, where's Tony?—Tony's an honest fellow, but he spits after a bumper, and that's a fault—

[*Sings.*]   We'll drink and we'll never ha' done, boys,
        Put the glass then around with the sun, boys,
              Let Apollo's example invite us;
              For he's drunk every night,
              And that makes him so bright,
        That he's able next morning to light us.

The sun's a good pimple,[7] an honest soaker, he has a cellar at your Antipodes. If I travel, aunt, I touch at your Antipodes.—Your Antipodes are a good rascally sort of topsy-turvy fellows.—If I had a bumper, I'd stand upon my head and drink a health to 'em.—A match or no match, cousin, with the hard name?—aunt, Wilfull will do't. If she has her maidenhead, let her look to't; if she has not, let her keep her own counsel in the meantime, and cry out at the nine months' end.

9. Rakish.
1. Drunkard (Spanish).
2. Grudge.
3. A wineglass filled to the brim. The word comes from the custom of touching (bumping) glasses when drinking toasts.

4. A coat of arms had a crest—a helmet surmounting the shield—and a motto. In his drunkenness, Sir Wilfull confuses the two.
5. In wine [there is] truth (Latin).
6. Throw.
7. Fellow.

MILLAMANT   Your pardon, madam, I can stay no longer—Sir Wilfull grows
very powerful. Egh! how he smells! I shall be overcome if I stay. Come,
cousin.

[*Exeunt* MRS. MILLAMANT *and* MRS. FAINALL.]

LADY WISHFORT   Smells! he would poison a tallow-chandler[8] and his family. Beastly creature, I know not what to do with him. Travel, quoth a';
aye, travel, travel, get thee gone, get thee but far enough, to the Saracens,
or the Tartars, or the Turks—for thou art not fit to live in a Christian
commonwealth, thou beastly pagan.

SIR WILFULL   Turks, no; no Turks, aunt. Your Turks are infidels, and believe
not in the grape. Your Mahometan, your Mussulman is a dry stinkard.—
No offense, aunt. My map says that your Turk is not so honest a man as
your Christian.—I cannot find by the map that your Mufti[9] is orthodox—
whereby it is a plain case, that orthodox is a hard word, aunt, and—[*Hiccup.*]—Greek for claret.

[*Sings.*]   To drink is a Christian diversion.
          Unknown to the Turk or the Persian:
               Let Mahometan fools
               Live by heathenish rules,
          And be damned over tea cups and coffee.
          But let British lads sing,
               Crown a health to the king,
          And a fig for your sultan and sophy.[1]

Ah, Tony!   [*Enter* FOIBLE, *and whispers to* LADY WISHFORT.]

LADY WISHFORT   Sir Rowland impatient? Good lack! what shall I do with
this beastly tumbrel?[2]—Go lie down and sleep, you sot—or as I'm a person, I'll have you bastinadoed[3] with broomsticks. Call up the wenches
with broomsticks. [*Exit* FOIBLE.]

SIR WILFULL   Ahay? Wenches, where are the wenches?

LADY WISHFORT   Dear cousin Witwoud, get him away, and you will bind
me to you inviolably. I have an affair of moment that invades me with
some precipitation—you will oblige me to all futurity.

WITWOUD   Come, knight.—Pox on him, I don't know what to say to him.—
Will you go to a cockmatch?

SIR WILFULL   With a wench, Tony? Is she a shakebag,[4] sirrah? Let me bite
your cheek for that.

WITWOUD   Horrible! He has a breath like a bagpipe.—Aye, aye, come,
will you march, my Salopian?[5]

SIR WILFULL   Lead on, little Tony—I'll follow thee, my Anthony, my Tantony. Sirrah, thou shalt be my Tantony, and I'll be thy pig.[6]

—And a fig for your sultan and sophy.

---

8. Candle maker.
9. The Grand Mufti, head of the state religion of
Turkey. Muslims do not drink alcohol.
1. The shah of Persia.
2. Dung cart.
3. Punished by beating the soles of the feet.

4. Gamecock.
5. Inhabitant of Shropshire.
6. St. Anthony (hence "Tantony"), the patron
of swineherds, was represented accompanied by
a pig.

LADY WISHFORT   This will never do. It will never make a match—at least before he has been abroad.

[*Exeunt* SIR WILFULL, *singing, and* WITWOUD.]

[*Enter* WAITWELL, *disguised as* SIR ROWLAND.]

LADY WISHFORT   Dear Sir Rowland, I am confounded with confusion at the retrospection of my own rudeness—I have more pardons to ask than the Pope distributes in the Year of Jubilee. But I hope where there is likely to be so near an alliance—we may unbend the severity of decorum—and dispense with a little ceremony.

WAITWELL   My impatience, madam, is the effect of my transport—and till I have the possession of your adorable person, I am tantalized on the rack; and do but hang, madam, on the tenter[7] of expectation.

LADY WISHFORT   You have excess of gallantry, Sir Rowland; and press things to a conclusion, with a most prevailing vehemence.—But a day or two for decency of marriage.—

WAITWELL   For decency of funeral, madam. The delay will break my heart—or if that should fail, I shall be poisoned. My nephew will get an inkling of my designs, and poison me—and I would willingly starve him before I die—I would gladly go out of the world with that satisfaction.—That would be some comfort to me, if I could but live so long as to be revenged on that unnatural viper.

LADY WISHFORT   Is he so unnatural, say you? Truly I would contribute much both to the saving of your life and the accomplishment of your revenge—Not that I respect[8] myself; though he has been a perfidious wretch to me.

WAITWELL   Perfidious to you!

LADY WISHFORT   O Sir Rowland, the hours that he has died away at my feet, the tears that he has shed, the oaths that he has sworn, the palpitations that he has felt, the trances and the tremblings, the ardors and the ecstasies, the kneelings, and the risings, the heart-heavings and the hand-gripings, the pangs and the pathetic regards of his protesting eyes! Oh, no memory can register.

WAITWELL   What, my rival! Is the rebel my rival? a'dies.

LADY WISHFORT   No, don't kill him at once, Sir Rowland, starve him gradually inch by inch.

WAITWELL   I'll do't. In three weeks he shall be barefoot; in a month out at knees with begging an alms—he shall starve upward and upward, till he has nothing living but his head, and then go out in a stink like a candle's end upon a saveall.[9]

LADY WISHFORT   Well, Sir Rowland, you have the way.—You are no novice in the labyrinth of love—you have the clue—but as I am a person, Sir Rowland, you must not attribute my yielding to any sinister appetite, or indigestion of widowhood; nor impute my complacency to any lethargy of continence.—I hope you do not think me prone to any iteration of nuptials.—

---

7. A frame for stretching cloth on hooks so that it may dry without losing its original shape (cf. the phrase "to be on tenterhooks").

8. Consider.

9. A small pan inserted into a candlestick to catch the drippings of the candle.

WAITWELL Far be it from me—

LADY WISHFORT If you do, I protest I must recede—or think that I have made a prostitution of decorums, but in the vehemence of compassion, and to save the life of a person of so much importance—

WAITWELL I esteem it so—

LADY WISHFORT Or else you wrong my condescension—

WAITWELL I do no, I do not—

LADY WISHFORT Indeed you do.

WAITWELL I do not, fair shrine of virtue.

LADY WISHFORT If you think the least scruple of carnality was an ingredient—

WAITWELL Dear madam, no. You are all camphire[1] and frankincense, all chastity and odor.

LADY WISHFORT Or that—

[Enter FOIBLE.]

FOIBLE Madam, the dancers are ready, and there's one with a letter, who must deliver it into your own hands.

LADY WISHFORT Sir Rowland, will you give me leave? Think favorably, judge candidly, and conclude you have found a person who would suffer racks in honor's cause, dear Sir Rowland, and will wait on you incessantly.[2]

[Exit LADY WISHFORT.]

WAITWELL Fie, fie!—What a slavery have I undergone; spouse, hast thou any cordial? I want spirits.

FOIBLE What a washy rogue art thou, to pant thus for a quarter of an hour's lying and swearing to a fine lady?

WAITWELL O, she is the antidote to desire. Spouse, thou wilt fare the worse for't—I shall have no appetite for iteration of nuptials—this eight and forty hours—by this hand I'd rather be a chairman in the dog days[3]—than act Sir Rowland till this time tomorrow.

[Re-enter LADY WISHFORT, with a letter.]

LADY WISHFORT Call in the dancers.—Sir Rowland, we'll sit, if you please, and see the entertainment.

[Dance.]

Now with your permission, Sir Rowland, I will peruse my letter.—I would open it in your presence, because I would not make you uneasy. If it should make you uneasy, I would burn it—speak if it does—but you may see, the superscription is like a woman's hand.

FOIBLE [To him.] By heaven! Mrs. Marwood's, I know it—my heart aches—get it from her.—

WAITWELL A woman's hand? No, madam, that's no woman's hand, I see that already. That's somebody whose throat must be cut.

LADY WISHFORT Nay, Sir Rowland, since you give me a proof of your passion by your jealousy, I promise you I'll make a return, by a frank communication—you shall see it—we'll open it together—look you here.—[Reads.]—Madam, though unknown to you (Look you there, 'tis from nobody that I know.)—I have that honor for your character, that I

---

1. Camphor was considered an effective antidote to sexual desire.
2. Immediately.
3. I.e., one who carries a sedan chair during the hottest part of the summer. July and August are called the "dog days" because during these months the Dog Star, Sirius, rises and sets with the sun.

think myself obliged to let you know you are abused. He who pretends to be Sir Rowland is a cheat and a rascal—O Heavens! what's this?

FOIBLE Unfortunate, all's ruined.

WAITWELL How, how, let me see, let me see—[*Reads.*]—*A rascal and disguised, and suborned for that imposture*—O villainy! O villainy!—*by the contrivance of*—

LADY WISHFORT I shall faint, I shall die, oh!

FOIBLE [*To him.*] Say, 'tis your nephew's hand.—Quickly, his plot, swear, swear it.—

WAITWELL Here's a villain! Madam, don't you perceive it, don't you see it?

LADY WISHFORT Too well, too well. I have seen too much.

WAITWELL I told you at first I knew the hand—A woman's hand? The rascal writes a sort of a large hand, your Roman hand—I saw there was a throat to be cut presently. If he were my son, as he is my nephew, I'd pistol him—

FOIBLE O treachery! But are you sure, Sir Rowland, it is his writing?

WAITWELL Sure? Am I here? Do I live? Do I love this pearl of India? I have twenty letters in my pocket from him in the same character.

LADY WISHFORT How!

FOIBLE O, what luck it is, Sir Rowland, that you were present at this juncture! This was the business that brought Mr. Mirabell disguised to Madam Millamant this afternoon. I thought something was contriving, when he stole by me and would have hid his face.

LADY WISHFORT How, how!—I heard the villain was in the house indeed; and now I remember, my niece went away abruptly, when Sir Wilfull was to have made his addresses.

FOIBLE Then, then, madam, Mr. Mirabell waited for her in her chamber; but I would not tell your ladyship to discompose you when you were to receive Sir Rowland.

WAITWELL Enough, his date is short.[4]

FOIBLE No, good Sir Rowland, don't incur the law.

WAITWELL Law! I care not for law. I can but die, and 'tis in a good cause—my lady shall be satisfied of my truth and innocence, though it cost me my life.

LADY WISHFORT No, dear Sir Rowland, don't fight. If you should be killed I must never show my face—or be hanged—O, consider my reputation, Sir Rowland—no, you shan't fight—I'll go and examine my niece; I'll make her confess. I conjure you, Sir Rowland, by all your love not to fight.

WAITWELL I am charmed, madam, I obey. But some proof you must let me give you—I'll go for a black box, which contains the writings of my whole estate, and deliver that into your hands.

LADY WISHFORT Aye, dear Sir Rowland, that will be some comfort. Bring the black box.

WAITWELL And may I presume to bring a contract to be signed this night? May I hope so far?

LADY WISHFORT Bring what you will; but come alive, pray come alive. O, this is a happy discovery.

---

4. He won't live long.

WAITWELL   Dead or alive I'll come—and married we will be in spite of treachery; aye, and get an heir that shall defeat the last remaining glimpse of hope in my abandoned nephew. Come, my buxom widow:

> E'er long you shall substantial proof receive
> That I'm an arrant[5] knight———

FOIBLE   Or arrant knave.

Act 5—Scene continues.

[*Enter* LADY WISHFORT *and* FOIBLE.]

LADY WISHFORT   Out of my house, out of my house, thou viper, thou serpent, that I have fostered; thou bosom traitress, that I raised from nothing.—Begone, begone, begone, go, go—that I took from washing of old gauze and weaving of dead hair,[6] with a bleak blue nose over a chafing dish of starved embers, and dining behind a traverse rag,[7] in a shop no bigger than a bird cage—go, go, starve again, do, do.

FOIBLE   Dear madam, I'll beg pardon on my knees.

LADY WISHFORT   Away, out, out, go set up for yourself again.—Do, drive a trade, do, with your three-pennyworth of small ware, flaunting upon a packthread, under a brandy-seller's bulk or against a dead wall[8] by a ballad-monger. Go, hang out an old frisoneer-gorget, with a yard of yellow colberteen[9] again; do; an old gnawed mask, two rows of pins and a child's fiddle; a glass necklace with the beads broken, and a quilted nightcap with one ear. Go, go, drive a trade—these were your commodities, you treacherous trull, this was the merchandise you dealt in when I took you into my house, placed you next myself, and made you governante[1] of my whole family. You have forgot this, have you, now you have feathered your nest?

FOIBLE   No, no, dear madam. Do but hear me, have but a moment's patience—I'll confess all. Mr. Mirabell seduced me; I am not the first that he has wheedled with his dissembling tongue. Your ladyship's own wisdom has been deluded by him, then how should I, a poor ignorant, defend myself? O madam, if you knew but what he promised me, and how he assured me your ladyship should come to no damage—or else the wealth of the Indies should not have bribed me to conspire against so good, so sweet, so kind a lady as you have been to me.

LADY WISHFORT   No damage? What, to betray me, to marry me to a cast[2] servingman; to make me a receptacle, an hospital for a decayed pimp? No damage? O, thou frontless[3] impudence, more than a big-bellied actress.

FOIBLE   Pray do but hear me, madam. He could not marry your ladyship, madam.—No, indeed, his marriage was to have been void in law; for he was married to me first, to secure your ladyship. He could not have bed-

---

5. The two words *errant* ("wandering," as in "knight-errant") and *arrant* ("thorough-going," "notorious") were originally the same and were still pronounced alike. This makes possible Foible's pun.
6. Foible had been a wigmaker.
7. A worn cloth, used to curtain off part of a room.

8. A continuous, unbroken wall. "Bulk": stall.
9. A French imitation of Italian lace. "Frisoneer-gorget": a woolen garment that covers the neck and breast.
1. Housekeeper.
2. Cast off, discharged.
3. Shameless.

ded your ladyship; for if he had consummated with your ladyship, he must have run the risk of the law, and been put upon his clergy.[4]—Yes, indeed, I inquired of the law in that case before I would meddle or make.[5]

LADY WISHFORT   What, then I have been your property, have I? I have been convenient to you, it seems.—While you were catering for Mirabell, I have been broker for you? What, have you made a passive bawd of me?—This exceeds all precedent; I am brought to fine uses, to become a botcher of second-hand marriages between Abigails and Andrews![6] I'll couple you. Yes, I'll baste you together, you and your philander.[7] I'll Duke's-Place[8] you, as I'm a person. Your turtle is in custody already: you shall coo in the same cage, if there be constable or warrant in the parish. [*Exit* LADY WISHFORT.]

FOIBLE   O, that ever I was born, O, that I was ever married.—A bride, aye, I shall be a Bridewell-bride.[9] Oh!
[*Enter* MRS. FAINALL.]

MRS. FAINALL   Poor Foible, what's the matter?

FOIBLE   O madam, my lady's gone for a constable. I shall be had to a justice, and put to Bridewell to beat hemp; poor Waitwell's gone to prison already.

MRS. FAINALL   Have a good heart, Foible. Mirabell's gone to give security for him. This is all Marwood's and my husband's doing.

FOIBLE   Yes, yes, I know it, madam; she was in my lady's closet, and overheard all that you said to me before dinner. She sent the letter to my lady; and that missing effect,[1] Mr. Fainall laid this plot to arrest Waitwell, when he pretended to go for the papers; and in the meantime Mrs. Marwood declared all to my lady.

MRS. FAINALL   Was there no mention made of me in the letter?—My mother does not suspect my being in the confederacy? I fancy Marwood has not told her, though she has told my husband.

FOIBLE   Yes, madam; but my lady did not see that part. We stifled the letter before she read so far. Has that mischievous devil told Mr. Fainall of your ladyship then?

MRS. FAINALL   Aye, all's out, my affair with Mirabell, everything discovered. This is the last day of our living together, that's my comfort.

FOIBLE   Indeed, madam, and so 'tis a comfort if you knew all.—He has been even with your ladyship; which I could have told you long enough since, but I love to keep peace and quietness by my good will. I had rather bring friends together than set 'em at distance. But Mrs. Marwood and he are nearer related than ever their parents thought for!

MRS. FAINALL   Say'st thou so, Foible? Canst thou prove this?

FOIBLE   I can take my oath of it, madam. So can Mrs. Mincing; we have had many a fair word from Madam Marwood, to conceal something that

---

4. I.e., pleaded "benefit of clergy," originally the privilege of the clergy to be tried for felony before ecclesiastical, not secular, courts; by Congreve's time it had become the privilege to plead exemption from a penal sentence granted a person who could read and was a first offender.
5. A dialectal phrase; the two words mean approximately the same thing.
6. Generic names for maidservants and serving-

men. "Botcher": a mender of old clothes. Lady Wishfort means something like "a patcher-up of marriages."
7. Lover. "Baste": sew together loosely.
8. Notorious for its thriving trade in unlicensed marriages.
9. House of correction for women, in London.
1. Not working.

passed in our chamber one evening when you were at Hyde Park—and we were thought to have gone a-walking; but we went up unawares—though we were sworn to secrecy too; Madam Marwood took a book and swore us upon it, but it was but a book of poems.—So long as it was not a Bible-oath, we may break it with a safe conscience.

MRS. FAINALL This discovery is the most opportune thing I could wish. Now, Mincing?

[*Enter* MINCING.]

MINCING My lady would speak with Mrs. Foible, mem. Mr. Mirabell is with her; he has set your spouse at liberty, Mrs. Foible, and would have you hide yourself in my lady's closet, till my old lady's anger is abated. O, my old lady is in a perilous passion, at something Mr. Fainall has said; he swears, and my old lady cries. There's a fearful hurricane, I vow. He says, mem, how that he'll have my lady's fortune made over to him, or he'll be divorced.

MRS. FAINALL Does your lady or Mirabell know that?

MINCING Yes, mem, they have sent me to see if Sir Wilfull be sober, and to bring him to them. My lady is resolved to have him, I think, rather than lose such a vast sum as six thousand pound. O, come, Mrs. Foible, I hear my old lady.

MRS. FAINALL Foible, you must tell Mincing that she must prepare to vouch when I call her.

FOIBLE Yes, yes, madam.

MINCING O yes, mem, I'll vouch anything for your ladyship's service, be what it will. [*Exit* MINCING, FOIBLE.]

[*Enter* LADY WISHFORT *and* MRS. MARWOOD.]

LADY WISHFORT O my dear friend, how can I enumerate the benefit that I have received from your goodness? To you I owe the timely discovery of the false vows of Mirabell; to you I owe the detection of the imposter Sir Rowland. And now you are become an intercessor with my son-in-law, to save the honor of my house, and compound for the frailties of my daughter. Well, friend, you are enough to reconcile me to the bad world, or else I would retire to deserts and solitudes, and feed harmless sheep by groves and purling streams. Dear Marwood, let us leave the world and retire by ourselves and be shepherdesses.

MRS. MARWOOD Let us first dispatch the affair in hand, madam. We shall have leisure to think of retirement afterwards. Here is one who is concerned in the treaty.

LADY WISHFORT O daughter, daughter, is it possible thou should'st be my child, bone of my bone, and flesh of my flesh, and as I may say, another me, and yet transgress the most minute particle of severe virtue? Is it possible you should lean aside to iniquity, who have been cast in the direct mold of virtue? I have not only been a mold but a pattern for you, and a model for you, after you were brought into the world.

MRS. FAINALL I don't understand your ladyship.

LADY WISHFORT Not understand? Why, have you not been naught?[2] Have you not been sophisticated?[3] Not understand? Here I am ruined to com-

---

2. Wicked.   3. Corrupted.

pound[4] for your caprices and your cuckoldoms. I must pawn my plate and my jewels, and ruin my niece, and all little enough—

MRS. FAINALL I am wronged and abused, and so are you. 'Tis a false accusation, as false as hell, as false as your friend there, aye, or your friend's friend, my false husband.

MRS. MARWOOD My friend, Mrs. Fainall? Your husband my friend, what do you mean?

MRS. FAINALL I know what I mean, madam, and so do you; and so shall the world at a time convenient.

MRS. MARWOOD I am sorry to see you so passionate, madam. More temper[5] would look more like innocence. But I have done. I am sorry my zeal to serve your ladyship and family should admit of misconstruction, or make me liable to affront. You will pardon me, madam, if I meddle no more with an affair in which I am not personally concerned.

LADY WISHFORT O dear friend, I am so ashamed that you should meet with such returns.—You ought to ask pardon on your knees, ungrateful creature; she deserves more from you than all your life can accomplish—O, don't leave me destitute in this perplexity—no, stick to me, my good genius.

MRS. FAINALL I tell you, madam, you're abused—Stick to you? aye, like a leech, to suck your best blood—She'll drop off when she's full. Madam, you shan't pawn a bodkin, nor part with a brass counter,[6] in composition for me. I defy 'em all. Let 'em prove their aspersions; I know my own innocence, and dare stand a trial. [*Exit* MRS. FAINALL.]

LADY WISHFORT Why, if she should be innocent, if she should be wronged after all, ha? I don't know what to think—and I promise you, her education has been unexceptionable—I may say it; for I chiefly made it my own care to initiate her very infancy in the rudiments of virtue, and to impress upon her tender years a young odium and aversion to the very sight of men.—Aye, friend, she would have shrieked if she had but seen a man, till she was in her teens. As I'm a person, 'tis true—she was never suffered to play with a male child, though but in coats. Nay, her very babies[7] were of the feminine gender—O, she never looked a man in the face but her own father, or the chaplain, and him we made a shift to put upon her for a woman, by the help of his long garments, and his sleek face; till she was going in her fifteen.

MRS. MARWOOD 'Twas much she should be deceived so long.

LADY WISHFORT I warrant you, or she would never have borne to have been catechized by him; and have heard his long lectures against singing and dancing, and such debaucheries; and going to filthy plays; and profane music-meetings, where the lewd trebles squeek nothing but bawdry, and the basses roar blasphemy. O, she would have swooned at the sight or name of an obscene play-book—and can I think after all this, that my daughter can be naught? What, a whore? And thought it excommunication to set her foot within the door of a playhouse? O dear friend, I can't believe it, no, no; as she says, let him prove it, let him prove it.

4. I.e., come to terms by making a monetary settlement.
5. Moderation.
6. An imitation coin, used in games of chance.

"Bodkin": ornamental hairpin. "In composition for me": to settle my debts.
7. Dolls. "In coats": in the dress common to young children of both genders.

MRS. MARWOOD   Prove it, madam? What, and have your name prostituted in a public court; yours and your daughter's reputation worried at the bar by a pack of bawling lawyers? To be ushered in with an O *Yes* of scandal; and have your case opened by an old fumbler lecher in a quoif[8] like a man midwife, to bring your daughter's infamy to light; to be a theme for legal punsters, and quibblers by the statute; and become a jest, against a rule of court, where there is no precedent for a jest in any record, not even in Doomsday Book;[9] to discompose the gravity of the bench, and provoke naughty interrogatories in more naughty law-Latin; while the good judge, tickled with the proceeding, simpers under a gray beard, and fidges off and on his cushion as if he had swallowed cantharides, or sate upon cowhage.[1]

LADY WISHFORT   O, 'tis very hard!

MRS. MARWOOD   And then to have my young revelers of the Temple take notes, like 'prentices at a conventicle; and after talk it over again in commons,[2] or before drawers in an eating house.

LADY WISHFORT   Worse and worse.

MRS. MARWOOD   Nay, this is nothing; if it would end here 'twere well. But it must after this be consigned by the shorthand writers to the public press; and from thence be transferred to the hands, nay into the throats and lungs of hawkers, with voices more licentious than the loud flounderman's or the woman that cries gray peas;[3] and this you must hear till you are stunned; nay, you must hear nothing else for some days.

LADY WISHFORT   O, 'tis insupportable. No, no, dear friend, make it up, make it up; aye, aye, I'll compound. I'll give up all, myself and my all, my niece and her all—anything, everything for composition.

MRS. MARWOOD   Nay, madam, I advise nothing; I only lay before you, as a friend, the inconveniencies which perhaps you have overseen.[4] Here comes Mr. Fainall. If he will be satisfied to huddle up all in silence, I shall be glad. You must think I would rather congratulate than condole with you.

    [*Enter* FAINALL.]

LADY WISHFORT   Aye, aye, I do not doubt it, dear Marwood. No, no, I do not doubt it.

FAINALL   Well, madam; I have suffered myself to be overcome by the importunity of this lady, your friend, and am content you shall enjoy your own proper estate during life; on condition you oblige yourself never to marry, under such penalty as I think convenient.

LADY WISHFORT   Never to marry?

FAINALL   No more Sir Rowlands—the next imposture may not be so timely detected.

MRS. MARWOOD   That condition, I dare answer, my lady will consent to, without difficulty; she has already but too much experienced the

---

8. The cap of a sergeant-at-law. "O *Yes*": The formula for opening court, a variant of Old French *Oyez*, "Hear ye."
9. Or Domesday Book, the survey of England made in 1085–86 by William the Conqueror.
1. A plant that causes intolerable itching. "Fidges": fidgets. "Cantharides": Spanish fly, an

irritant.
2. In the dining hall. "Revelers": here, law students. The Temple is one of the Inns of Court. "Conventicle": clandestine meeting of Protestant Dissenters.
3. Street vendors known for their stridency.
4. Overlooked.

perfidiousness of men. Besides, madam, when we retire to our pastoral solitude we shall bid adieu to all other thoughts.

LADY WISHFORT Aye, that's true; but in case of necessity; as of health, or some such emergency—

FAINALL O, if you are prescribed marriage, you shall be considered; I will only reserve to myself the power to choose for you. If your physic be wholesome, it matters not who is your apothecary. Next, my wife shall settle on me the remainder of her fortune, not made over already; and for her maintenance depend entirely on my discretion.

LADY WISHFORT This is most inhumanly savage; exceeding the barbarity of a Muscovite husband.

FAINALL I learned it from His Czarish Majesty's retinue,[5] in a winter evening's conference over brandy and pepper, amongst other secrets of matrimony and policy, as they are at present practiced in the northern hemisphere. But this must be agreed unto, and that positively. Lastly, I will be endowed, in right of my wife, with that six thousand pound, which is the moiety of Mrs. Millamant's fortune in your possession; and which she has forfeited (as will appear by the last will and testament of your deceased husband, Sir Jonathan Wishfort) by her disobedience in contracting herself against your consent or knowledge; and by refusing the offered match with Sir Wilfull Witwoud, which you, like a careful aunt, had provided for her.

LADY WISHFORT My nephew was *non compos*,[6] and could not make his addresses.

FAINALL I come to make demands—I'll hear no objections.

LADY WISHFORT You will grant me time to consider?

FAINALL Yes, while the instrument[7] is drawing, to which you must set your hand till more sufficient deeds can be perfected: which I will take care shall be done with all possible speed. In the meanwhile I will go for the said instrument, and till my return you may balance this matter in your own discretion. [*Exit* FAINALL.]

LADY WISHFORT This insolence is beyond all precedent, all parallel; must I be subject to this merciless villain?

MRS. MARWOOD 'Tis severe indeed, madam, that you should smart for your daughter's wantonness.

LADY WISHFORT 'Twas against my consent that she married this barbarian, but she would have him, though her year was not out.[8]—Ah! her first husband, my son Languish, would not have carried it thus. Well, that was my choice, this is hers; she is matched now with a witness[9]—I shall be mad, dear friend. Is there no comfort for me? Must I live to be confiscated at this rebel-rate?—Here comes two more of my Egyptian plagues,[1] too.

[*Enter* MRS. MILLAMANT *and* SIR WILFULL.]

SIR WILFULL Aunt, your servant.

LADY WISHFORT Out, caterpillar, call not me aunt; I know thee not.

5. Peter the Great of Russia visited London in 1698.
6. I.e., *non compos mentis* (of unsound mind, Latin).
7. Legal contract.
8. The conventional period of mourning for a widow was one year.
9. With a vengeance.
1. The plagues visited by God on Pharaoh until he agreed to release the Israelites from bondage (Exodus 7–12).

SIR WILFULL I confess I have been a little in disguise,[2] as they say—'Sheart! and I'm sorry for't. What would you have? I hope I committed no offense, aunt—and if I did, I am willing to make satisfaction; and what can a man say fairer? If I have broke anything, I'll pay for't, an' it cost a pound. And so let that content for what's past, and make no more words. For what's to come, to pleasure you I'm willing to marry my cousin. So, pray, let's all be friends. She and I are agreed upon the matter before a witness.

LADY WISHFORT How's this, dear niece? Have I any comfort? Can this be true?

MILLAMANT I am content to be a sacrifice to your repose, madam; and to convince you that I had no hand in the plot, as you were misinformed, I have laid my commands on Mirabell to come in person, and be a witness that I give my hand to this flower of knighthood; and for the contract that passed between Mirabell and me, I have obliged him to make a resignation of it in your ladyship's presence.—He is without, and waits your leave for admittance.

LADY WISHFORT Well, I'll swear I am something revived at this testimony of your obedience; but I cannot admit that traitor—I fear I cannot fortify myself to support his appearance. He is as terrible to me as a Gorgon;[3] if I see him, I fear I shall turn to stone, petrify incessantly.

MILLAMANT If you disoblige him, he may resent your refusal, and insist upon the contract still. Then 'tis the last time he will be offensive to you.

LADY WISHFORT Are you sure it will be the last time?—If I were sure of that—Shall I never see him again?

MILLAMANT Sir Wilfull, you and he are to travel together, are you not?

SIR WILFULL 'Sheart, the gentleman's a civil gentleman, aunt, let him come in; why, we are sworn brothers and fellow travelers. We are to be Pylades and Orestes,[4] he and I. He is to be my interpreter in foreign parts. He has been overseas once already; and with proviso that I marry my cousin, will cross 'em once again, only to bear my company.—'Sheart, I'll call him in—an I set on't once, he shall come in; and see who'll hinder him. [*Exit* SIR WILFULL.]

MRS. MARWOOD This is precious fooling, if it would pass; but I'll know the bottom of it.

LADY WISHFORT O dear Marwood, you are not going?

MARWOOD Not far, madam; I'll return immediately. [*Exit* MRS. MARWOOD.]
[*Re-enter* SIR WILFULL *and* MIRABELL.]

SIR WILFULL [*Aside.*] Look up, man, I'll stand by you. 'Sbud an she do frown, she can't kill you—besides—harkee, she dare not frown desperately, because her face is none of her own. 'Sheart, an she should her forehead would wrinkle like the coat of a cream cheese; but mum for that, fellow traveler.

MIRABELL If a deep sense of the many injuries I have offered to so good a lady, with a sincere remorse, and a hearty contrition, can but obtain the least glance of compassion, I am too happy—Ah madam, there was

---

2. Drunk.
3. In Greek mythology, a hideous monster with snakes in her hair. Her glance turned people to stone.

4. Pylades was the constant friend who journeyed with Orestes, the son and avenger of the murdered king Agamemnon.

a time—but let it be forgotten—I confess I have deservedly forfeited the high place I once held of sighing at your feet. Nay kill me not by turning from me in disdain—I come not to plead for favor—nay not for pardon. I am a suppliant only for pity—I am going where I never shall behold you more—

SIR WILFULL [*Aside*.] How, fellow traveler!—You shall go by yourself then.

MIRABELL Let me be pitied first, and afterwards forgotten—I ask no more.

SIR WILFULL By'r Lady a very reasonable request, and will cost you nothing, aunt.—Come, come, forgive and forget, aunt. Why you must, an you are a Christian.

MIRABELL Consider, madam, in reality you could not receive much prejudice; it was an innocent device, though I confess it had a face of guiltiness.—It was at most an artifice which love contrived—and errors which love produces have ever been accounted venial. At least think it is punishment enough that I have lost what in my heart I hold most dear, that to your cruel indignation, I have offered up this beauty, and with her my peace and quiet; nay, all my hopes of future comfort.

SIR WILFULL An he does not move me, would I may never be o' the quorum[5]—An it were not as good a deed as to drink, to give her to him again—I would I might never take shipping.—Aunt, if you don't forgive quickly I shall melt, I can tell you that. My contract went no farther than a little mouth glue,[6] and that's hardly dry.—One doleful sigh more from my fellow traveler and 'tis dissolved.

LADY WISHFORT Well, nephew, upon your account—Ah, he has a false insinuating tongue.—Well, sir, I will stifle my just resentment at my nephew's request. I will endeavor what I can to forget—but on proviso that you resign the contract with my niece immediately.

MIRABELL It is in writing and with papers of concern, but I have sent my servant for it and will deliver it to you, with all acknowledgements for your transcendent goodness.

LADY WISHFORT [*Aside*.] O, he has witchcraft in his eyes and tongue; when I did not see him I could have bribed a villain to his assassination; but his appearance rakes the embers which have so long lain smothered in my breast.—

[*Enter* FAINALL *and* MRS. MARWOOD.]

FAINALL Your date of deliberation, madam, is expired. Here is the instrument; are you prepared to sign?

LADY WISHFORT If I were prepared, I am not empowered. My niece exerts a lawful claim, having matched herself by my direction to Sir Wilfull.

FAINALL That sham is too gross to pass on me—though 'tis imposed on you, madam.

MILLAMANT Sir, I have given my consent.

MIRABELL And, sir, I have resigned my pretensions.

---

5. Justices of the peace, who were required to be present at the sessions of a court.
6. Literally, glue to be used by moistening with the tongue; but here, "glue made of mere words" and therefore not binding.

SIR WILFULL   And, sir, I assert my right; and will maintain it in defiance of you, sir, and of your instrument. 'Sheart, an you talk of an instrument, sir, I have an old fox by my thigh shall hack your instrument of ram vellum[7] to shreds, sir. It shall not be sufficient for a *mittimus*[8] or a tailor's measure; therefore withdraw your instrument, sir, or by'r Lady I shall draw mine.

LADY WISHFORT   Hold, nephew, hold.

MILLAMANT   Good Sir Wilfull, respite your valor.

FAINALL   Indeed? Are you provided of your guard, with your single beefeater[9] there? But I'm prepared for you; and insist upon my first proposal. You shall submit your own estate to my management and absolutely make over my wife's to my sole use, as pursuant to the purport and tenor of this other covenant. I suppose, madam, your consent is not requisite in this case; nor, Mr. Mirabell, your resignation; nor, Sir Wilfull, your right— You may draw your fox if you please, sir, and make a bear garden[1] flourish somewhere else: for here it will not avail. This, my Lady Wishfort, must be subscribed, or your darling daughter's turned adrift, like a leaky hulk to sink or swim, as she and the current of this lewd town can agree.

LADY WISHFORT   Is there no means, no remedy, to stop my ruin? Ungrateful wretch! Dost thou not owe thy being, thy subsistence to my daughter's fortune?

FAINALL   I'll answer you when I have the rest of it in my possession.

MIRABELL   But that you would not accept of a remedy from my hands—I own I have not deserved you should owe any obligation to me; or else perhaps I could advise—

LADY WISHFORT   O, what? what? to save me and my child from ruin, from want, I'll forgive all that's past; nay, I'll consent to anything to come, to be delivered from this tyranny.

MIRABELL   Aye, madam, but that is too late; my reward is intercepted. You have disposed of her who only could have made me a compensation for all my services; but be it as it may, I am resolved I'll serve you. You shall not be wronged in this savage manner.

LADY WISHFORT   How! Dear Mr. Mirabell, can you be so generous at last! But it is not possible. Harkee, I'll break my nephew's match, you shall have my niece yet, and all her fortune, if you can but save me from this imminent danger.

MIRABELL   Will you? I take you at your word. I ask no more. I must have leave for two criminals to appear.

LADY WISHFORT   Aye, aye, anybody, anybody.

MIRABELL   Foible is one, and a penitent.

　　　[*Enter* MRS. FAINALL, FOIBLE, *and* MINCING.]

MRS. MARWOOD   O, my shame! These corrupt things are brought hither to expose me. [MIRABELL *and* LADY WISHFORT *go to* MRS. FAINALL *and* FOIBLE.]

---

7. The legal instrument to be signed is written on vellum. "Fox": a kind of sword.
8. A warrant, committing a felon to jail.

9. Yeoman of the guard.
1. The place for bear baiting, frequented by a vulgar and unruly crowd. "Draw": track by scent.

FAINALL   If it must all come out, why let 'em know it, 'tis but *the way of the world*. That shall not urge me to relinquish or abate one tittle of my terms; no, I will insist the more.

FOIBLE   Yes, indeed, madam, I'll take my Bible-oath of it.

MINCING   And so will I, mem.

LADY WISHFORT   O Marwood, Marwood, art thou false? My friend deceive me? Hast thou been a wicked accomplice with that profligate man?

MRS. MARWOOD   Have you so much ingratitude and injustice, to give credit against your friend to the aspersions of two such mercenary trulls?

MINCING   Mercenary, mem? I scorn your words. 'Tis true we found you and Mr. Fainall in the blue garret; by the same token, you swore us to secrecy upon Messalina's[2] poems. Mercenary? No, if we would have been mercenary, we should have held our tongues; you would have bribed us sufficiently.

FAINALL   Go, you are an insignificant thing. Well, what are you the better for this! Is this Mr. Mirabell's expedient? I'll be put off no longer. You, thing that was a wife, shall smart for this. I will not leave thee wherewithal to hide thy shame: your body shall be naked as your reputation.

MRS. FAINALL   I despise you and defy your malice.—You have aspersed me wrongfully.—I have proved your falsehood.—Go, you and your treacherous—I will not name it, but starve together—perish.

FAINALL   Not while you are worth a groat, indeed, my dear. Madam, I'll be fooled no longer.

LADY WISHFORT   Ah, Mr. Mirabell, this is small comfort, the detection of this affair.

MIRABELL   O, in good time—Your leave for the other offender and penitent to appear, madam.

[*Enter* WAITWELL *with a box of writings.*]

LADY WISHFORT   O Sir Rowland—Well, rascal.

WAITWELL   What your ladyship pleases—I have brought the black box at last, madam.

MIRABELL   Give it me. Madam, you remember your promise.

LADY WISHFORT   Aye, dear sir.

MIRABELL   Where are the gentlemen?

WAITWELL   At hand, sir, rubbing their eyes, just risen from sleep.

FAINALL   'Sdeath, what's this to me? I'll not wait your private concerns.

[*Enter* PETULANT *and* WITWOUD.]

PETULANT   How now? What's the matter? Whose hand's out?[3]

WITWOUD   Heyday! What, are you all got together, like players at the end of the last act?

MIRABELL   You may remember, gentlemen, I once requested your hands as witnesses to a certain parchment.

WITWOUD   Aye, I do, my hand I remember—Petulant set his mark.

MIRABELL   You wrong him, his name is fairly written, as shall appear. You do not remember, gentlemen, anything of what that parchment contained—[*Undoing the box.*]

---

2. Mincing means *Miscellany*, a collection of poems by various writers, such as Dryden's popular *Miscellanies*. Messalina was the viciously debauched wife of the Roman emperor Claudius.
3. I.e., Whose game's over?

WITWOUD   No.

PETULANT   Not I. I writ, I read nothing.

MIRABELL   Very well, now you shall know. Madam, your promise.

LADY WISHFORT   Aye, aye, sir, upon my honor.

MIRABELL   Mr. Fainall, it is now time that you should know that your lady, while she was at her own disposal, and before you had by your insinuations wheedled her out of a pretended settlement of the greatest part of her fortune—

FAINALL   Sir! Pretended!

MIRABELL   Yes, sir. I say that this lady while a widow, having, it seems, received some cautions respecting your inconstancy and tyranny of temper, which from her own partial opinion and fondness of you she could never have suspected—she did, I say, by the wholesome advice of friends and of sages learned in the laws of this land, deliver this same as her act and deed to me in trust, and to the uses within mentioned. You may read if you please—[*Holding out the parchment.*]—though perhaps what is written on the back may serve your occasions.

FAINALL   Very likely, sir. What's here? Damnation!—[*Reads.*] A *deed of conveyance of the whole estate real of Arabella Languish, widow, in trust to Edward Mirabell.* Confusion!

MIRABELL   Even so, sir, 'tis the way of the world, sir; of the widows of the world. I suppose this deed may bear an elder date than what you have obtained from your lady.

FAINALL   Perfidious fiend! Then thus I'll be revenged.

[*Offers to run at* MRS. FAINALL.]

SIR WILFULL   Hold, sir, now you may make your bear garden flourish somewhere else, sir.

FAINALL   Mirabell, you shall hear of this, sir, be sure you shall. Let me pass, oaf. [*Exit* FAINALL.]

MRS. FAINALL   Madam, you seem to stifle your resentment: you had better give it vent.

MRS. MARWOOD   Yes, it shall have vent—and to your confusion, or I'll perish in the attempt. [*Exit* MRS. MARWOOD.]

LADY WISHFORT   O daughter, daughter, 'tis plain thou hast inherited thy mother's prudence.

MRS. FAINALL   Thank Mr. Mirabell, a cautious friend, to whose advice all is owing.

LADY WISHFORT   Well, Mr. Mirabell, you have kept your promise and I must perform mine. First I pardon for your sake Sir Rowland there and Foible.—The next thing is to break the matter to my nephew—and how to do that—

MIRABELL   For that, madam, give yourself no trouble—let me have your consent.—Sir Wilfull is my friend; he has had compassion upon lovers, and generously engaged a volunteer in this action, for our service; and now designs to prosecute his travels.

SIR WILFULL   'Sheart, aunt, I have no mind to marry. My cousin's a fine lady, and the gentleman loves her, and she loves him, and they deserve one another. My resolution is to see foreign parts—I have set on't—and when I'm set on't, I must do't. And if these two gentlemen would travel too, I think they may be spared.

PETULANT   For my part, I say little—I think things are best off or on.

WITWOUD   Igad, I understand nothing of the matter—I'm in a maze yet; like a dog in a dancing school.

LADY WISHFORT   Well, sir, take her, and with her all the joy I can give you.

MILLAMANT   Why does not the man take me? Would you have me give myself to you over again?

MIRABELL   Aye, and over and over again—[*Kisses her hand.*]—I would have you as often as possibly I can. Well, Heaven grant I love you not too well, that's all my fear.

SIR WILFULL   'Sheart, you'll have time enough to toy after you're married; or if you will toy now, let us have a dance in the meantime; that we who are not lovers may have some other employment, besides looking on.

MIRABELL   With all my heart, dear Sir Wilfull. What shall we do for music?

FOIBLE   O, sir, some that were provided for Sir Rowland's entertainment are yet within call.

[A DANCE.]

LADY WISHFORT   As I am a person I can hold out no longer.—I have wasted my spirits so today already, that I am ready to sink under the fatigue; and I cannot but have some fears upon me yet, that my son Fainall will pursue some desperate course.

MIRABELL   Madam, disquiet not yourself on that account; to my knowledge his circumstances are such, he must of force comply. For my part, I will contribute all that in me lies to a reunion: in the meantime, madam—[*To* MRS. FAINALL.]—let me before these witnesses restore to you this deed of trust; it may be a means, well managed, to make you live easily together.

> From hence let those be warned, who mean to wed;
> Lest mutual falsehood stain the bridal bed:
> For each deceiver to his cost may find,
> That marriage frauds too oft are paid in kind.

[*Exeunt omnes.*]

Epilogue

SPOKEN BY MRS. BRACEGIRDLE[4]

After our Epilogue this crowd dismisses,
I'm thinking how this play'll be pulled to pieces.
But pray consider, e'er you doom its fall,
How hard a thing 'twould be to please you all.
5   There are some critics so with spleen diseased,
They scarcely come inclining to be pleased;
And sure he must have more than mortal skill,
Who pleases anyone against his will.
Then, all bad poets we are sure are foes,
10   And how their number's swelled the town well knows:

---

4. Anne Bracegirdle (ca. 1663–1748), the most brilliant actress of her generation. She created the role of Millamant. Congreve loved her, and it was rumored that they were secretly married.

In shoals, I've marked 'em judging in the pit; ⎤
Though they're on no pretence for judgment fit, ⎬
But that they have been damned for want of wit. ⎦
Since when, they by their own offenses taught

15 Set up for spies on plays, and finding fault.
Others there are whose malice we'd prevent; ⎤
Such, who watch plays, with scurrilous intent ⎬
To mark out who by characters are meant. ⎦
And though no perfect likeness they can trace,

20 Yet each pretends to know the copied face.
These, with false glosses feed their own ill-nature,
And turn to libel, what was meant a *satire*.[5]
May such malicious fops this fortune find,
To think themselves alone the fools designed:

25 If any are so arrogantly vain, ⎤
To think they singly can support a scene, ⎬
And furnish fool enough to entertain. ⎦
For well the learn'd and the judicious know, ⎤
That satire scorns to stoop so meanly low, ⎬

30 As any one abstracted° fop to show. ⎦   separated
For, as when painters form a matchless face,
They from each fair one catch some different grace,
And shining features in one portrait blend,
To which no single beauty must pretend:

35 So poets oft do in one piece expose
Whole *belles assemblées* of coquettes and beaux.

1700

5. Pronounce *nā-ter* and *sā-ter*.

MARY ASTELL
1666–1731

Daughter of a Newcastle merchant, Mary Astell was encouraged and educated by her uncle, a clergyman. She never forgot what he taught her: a confidence in her own reason and a religious faith entirely compatible with reason. In her twenties she moved to Chelsea, on the outskirts of London, where she spent the rest of her life. There she championed the causes of women and the Church of England, and her vigorous way of arguing (not only in print but in person) won her many admirers, both male and female. Her political and religious polemics also put her at odds with many important writers, including John Locke and Daniel Defoe (for her response to Lockean arguments for political liberty, see p. 3019). One of her best-known works, *A Serious Proposal to the Ladies* (1694), was, like the rest of her writings, published anonymously ("by a Lover of her Sex"). It advocates the founding of a monastic school or retreat for women, where a rigorous, wide-ranging education could be combined with moral and religious discipline. Though the idea was never carried out, it had a broad influence on later plans for educating women as well as on literature. At the end of Johnson's *Rasselas,* both Pekuah's dream of leading a religious order and Nekayah's desire to found a college of learned women owe something to Astell.

To question the customs and laws of marriage is to question society itself, its distribution of money and power and love. During the eighteenth century many of the terms of marriage were renegotiated. The older view of the wife as a chattel, bound by contract to a husband whom others had chosen for her and whom she was sworn to obey, was hotly debated and challenged. The witty arguments of Congreve's *The Way of the World* (1700) reflect this growing debate between the sexes. Another work published in the same year, *Some Reflections upon Marriage,* takes a more independent position. Marriage, according to Astell, is all too often a trap. She insists that a woman should be guided by reason, not only in choosing a mate but in choosing whether or not to marry at all (Astell herself never married). So long as the institution of marriage perpetuates inequality rather than a true partnership of minds, women had better beware of flattery and look to themselves or to God, not to men, for the hope of a better life. The debate on marriage continued throughout the century in works such as Defoe's *Roxana,* Hogarth's *Marriage A-la-Mode,* the novels of Samuel Richardson, *Rasselas,* and eventually the writings of Mary Wollstonecraft and William Godwin. It still continues today. In her sharp, lively style and the pertinent questions she raised, Astell has come to be seen as ahead of her time.

From Some Reflections upon Marriage[1]

If marriage be such a blessed state, how comes it, may you say, that there are so few happy marriages? Now in answer to this, it is not to be wondered that so few succeed; we should rather be surprised to find so many do, considering how imprudently men engage, the motives they act by, and the very strange conduct they observe throughout.

For pray, what do men propose to themselves in marriage? What qualifications do they look after in a spouse? What will she bring? is the first enquiry: How many acres? Or how much ready coin? Not that this is altogether an unnecessary question, for marriage without a competency,[2] that is, not only a bare subsistence, but even a handsome and plentiful provision, according to the quality[3] and circumstances of the parties, is no very comfortable condition. They who marry for love, as they call it, find time enough to repent their rash folly, and are not long in being convinced, that whatever fine speeches might be made in the heat of passion, there could be no *real kindness* between those who can agree to make each other miserable. But as an estate is to be considered, so it should not be the *main,* much less the *only* consideration; for happiness does not depend on wealth.

* * *

But suppose a man does not marry for money, though for one that does not, perhaps there are thousands that do; suppose he marries for love, an heroic action, which makes a mighty noise in the world, partly because of its

---

1. The text is from the first edition.
2. Sufficient income.
3. Social position.

rarity, and partly in regard of its extravagancy, and what does his marrying for love amount to? There's no great odds between his marrying for the love of money, or for the love of beauty; the man does not act according to reason in either case, but is governed by irregular appetites. But he loves her wit perhaps, and this, you'll say, is more spiritual, more refined: not at all, if you examine it to the bottom. For what is that which nowadays passes under the name of wit? A bitter and ill-natured raillery, a pert repartee, or a confident talking at all; and in such a multitude of words, it's odds if something or other does not pass that is surprising, though every thing that surprises does not please; some things are wondered at for their ugliness, as well as others for their beauty. True wit, durst one venture to describe it, is quite another thing; it consists in such a sprightliness of imagination, such a reach and turn of thought, so properly expressed, as strikes and pleases a judicious taste.[4]

* * *

Thus, whether it be wit or beauty that a man's in love with, there's no great hopes of a lasting happiness; beauty, with all the helps of art, is of no very lasting date; the more it is helped, the sooner it decays; and he, who only or chiefly chose for beauty, will in a little time find the same reason for another choice. Nor is that sort of wit which he prefers, of a more sure tenure; or allowing it to last, it will not always please. For that which has not a real excellency and value in itself entertains no longer than that giddy humor which recommended it to us holds; and when we can like on no just, or on very little ground, 'tis certain a dislike will arise, as lightly and as unaccountably. And it is not improbable that such a husband may in a little time, by ill usage, provoke such a wife to exercise her wit, that is, her spleen[5] on him, and then it is not hard to guess how very agreeable it will be to him.

* * *

But do the women never choose amiss? Are the men only in fault? That is not pretended; for he who will be just must be forced to acknowledge that neither sex is always in the right. A woman, indeed, can't properly be said to choose; all that is allowed her, is to refuse or accept what is offered. And when we have made such reasonable allowances as are due to the sex, perhaps they may not appear so much in fault as one would at first imagine, and a generous spirit will find more occasion to pity than to reprove. But sure I transgress—it must not be supposed that the ladies can do amiss! He is but an ill-bred fellow who pretends that they need amendment! They are, no doubt on't, always in the right, and most of all when they take pity on distressed lovers; whatever they *say* carries an authority that no reason can resist, and all that they *do* must needs be exemplary! This is the modish language, nor is there a man of honor amongst the whole tribe that would not venture his life, nay and his salvation too, in their defense, if any but himself attempts to injure them. But I must ask pardon if I can't come up to these heights, nor flatter them with the having no faults, which is only a malicious way of continuing and increasing their mistakes.

4. Cf. Pope's *An Essay on Criticism* 2.297–304 (p. 2675).
5. Bad temper.

* * *

But, alas! what poor woman is ever taught that she should have a higher design than to get her a husband? Heaven will fall in of course; and if she make but an obedient and dutiful wife, she cannot miss of it. A husband indeed is thought by both sexes so very valuable, that scarce a man who can keep himself clean and make a bow, but thinks he is good enough to pretend[6] to any woman; no matter for the difference of birth or fortune, a husband is such a wonder-working name as to make an equality, or something more, whenever it is pronounced.

* * *

To wind up this matter: if a woman were duly principled and taught to know the world, especially the true sentiments that men have of her, and the traps they lay for her under so many gilded compliments, and such a seemingly great respect, that disgrace would be prevented which is brought upon too many families; women would marry more discreetly, and demean[7] themselves better in a married state than some people say they do.

* * *

But some sage persons may perhaps object, that were women allowed to improve themselves, and not, amongst other discouragements, driven back by the wise jests and scoffs that are put upon a woman of sense or learning, a philosophical lady, as she is called by way of ridicule, they would be too wise, and too good for the men. I grant it, for vicious and foolish men. Nor is it to be wondered that he is afraid he should not be able to govern them were their understandings improved, who is resolved not to take too much pains with his own. But these, 'tis to be hoped, are no very considerable number, the foolish at least; and therefore this is so far from being an argument against their improvement, that it is a strong one for it, if we do but suppose the men to be as capable of improvement as the women; but much more if, according to tradition, we believe they have greater capacities. This, if anything, would stir them up to be what they ought, not permit them to waste their time and abuse their faculties in the service of their irregular appetites and unreasonable desires, and so let poor contemptible women, who have been their slaves, excel them in all that is truly excellent. This would make them blush at employing an immortal mind no better than in making provision for the flesh to fulfill the lusts thereof, since women, by a wiser conduct, have brought themselves to such a reach of thought, to such exactness of judgment, such clearness and strength of reasoning, such purity and elevation of mind, such command of their passions, such regularity of will and affection, and, in a word, to such a pitch of perfection as the human soul is capable of attaining even in this life by the grace of God; such true wisdom, such real greatness, as though it does not qualify them to make a noise in this world, to found or overturn empires, yet it qualifies them for what is infinitely better, a Kingdom that cannot be moved, an incorruptible crown of glory.

---

6. Aspire or lay claim.　　　　　7. Behave.

* * *

Again, it may be said, if a wife's case be as it is here represented, it is not good for a woman to marry, and so there's an end of human race. But this is no fair consequence, for all that can justly be inferred from hence is that a woman has no mighty obligations to the man who makes love to her; she has no reason to be fond of being a wife, or to reckon it a piece of preferment when she is taken to be a man's upper-servant;[8] it is no advantage to her in this world; if rightly managed it may prove one as to the next. For she who marries purely to do good, to educate souls for heaven, who can be so truly mortified as to lay aside her own will and desires, to pay such an entire submission for life, to one whom she cannot be sure will always deserve it, does certainly perform a more heroic action than all the famous masculine heroes can boast of; she suffers a continual martyrdom to bring glory to God, and benefit to mankind; which consideration indeed may carry her through all difficulties, I know not what else can, and engage her to love him who proves perhaps so much worse than a brute, as to make this condition yet more grievous than it needed to be. She has need of a strong reason, of a truly Christian and well-tempered spirit, of all the assistance the best education can give her, and ought to have some good assurance of her own firmness and virtue, who ventures on such a trial; and for this reason 'tis less to be wondered at that women marry off in haste, for perhaps if they took time to consider and reflect upon it, they seldom would.

1700

8. High-ranking servant. "Preferment": advancement in rank.

DANIEL DEFOE
ca. 1660–1731

By birth, education, and occupations Daniel Defoe was a stranger to the sphere of refined tastes and classical learning that dominated polite literature during his lifetime. Middle class in his birth, Presbyterian in his religion, he belonged among the hardy Nonconformist tradesfolk who, after the Restoration, slowly increased their wealth and toward the end of the seventeenth century began to achieve political importance.

He began adult life as a small merchant and for a while prospered, but he was not overscrupulous in his dealings, and in 1692 he found himself bankrupt, with debts amounting to £17,000. This was the first of his many financial crises, crises that drove him to make his way, like his own heroes and heroines, by whatever means presented themselves. And however double his dealings, he seems always to have found the way to reconcile them with his genuine Nonconformist piety. His restless mind was fertile in "projects," both for himself and for the country, and his itch for politics made the role of passive observer impossible for him.

An ardent Whig, he first gained notoriety by political verses and pamphlets, and for one of them, "The Shortest Way with the Dissenters" (1702), in which he ironically defended Anglican oppression, he stood in the pillory three times and was sentenced to jail. He was released through the influence of Robert Harley (later earl of Oxford), who recognized in Defoe, as he was to do in Swift, a useful ally. For the next eleven years Defoe served his benefactor secretly as a political spy and confidential agent, traveling throughout England and Scotland, reporting and perhaps influencing opinion. As founder and editor of the *Review,* he endeavored to gain support for Harley's policies, even when, in 1710, Harley became head of a Tory ministry. It is characteristic of Defoe that, after the fall of the Tories in 1714, he went over to the triumphant Whigs and served them as loyally as he had their enemy.

When he was nearly sixty, Defoe's energy and inventiveness enabled him to break new ground, indeed to begin a new career. *Robinson Crusoe,* which appeared in 1719, is the first of a series of tales of adventure for which Defoe is now admired, but which brought him little esteem from the polite world, however much they gratified the less cultivated readers in the City or the servants' hall. In *Robinson Crusoe* and other tales that followed, Defoe was able to use all his greatest gifts: the ability to re-create a milieu vividly, through the cumulative effect of carefully observed, often petty details; a special skill in writing easygoing prose, the language of actual speech, which seems to reveal the consciousness of the first-person narrator; a wide knowledge of the society in which he lived, both the trading classes and the rogues who preyed on them; and an absorption in the spectacle of lonely human beings, whether Crusoe on his island or Moll Flanders in England and Virginia, somehow bending a stubborn and indifferent environment to their own ends of survival or profits. There is something of himself in all his protagonists: enormous vitality, humanity, and a scheming and sometimes sneaky ingenuity. In these fictitious autobiographies of adventurers or rogues—*Captain Singleton* (1720), *Moll Flanders* (1722), *Colonel Jack* (1722), and *Roxana* (1724)—Defoe spoke for and to the members of his own class. Like them, he was engrossed by property and success, and his way of writing made all he touched seem true.

From Roxana[1]

[THE CONS OF MARRIAGE]

One morning, in the middle of our unlawful freedoms—that is to say, when we were in bed together—he sighed, and told me he desired my leave to ask me one question, and that I would give him an answer to it with the same ingenuous freedom and honesty that I had used to[2] treat him with. I told him I would. Why, then, his question was, why I would not marry him, seeing I allowed him all the freedom of a husband. "Or," says he, "my dear, since you have been so kind as to take me to your bed, why will you not make

1. *Roxana; or, The Fortunate Mistress,* is the story, told by herself, of a beautiful and ambitious courtesan. A bad marriage and early poverty drive her to a career of prostitution, at which she succeeds brilliantly until eventually her past catches up with her. The story is set in the Restoration, and even the title reflects the decadence associated with the period: admirers give "Roxana" her name after she has displayed herself provocatively in Turkish costume at a ball (*Roxalana,* a sultana in Sir William Davenant's *The Siege of Rhodes,* 1656, had come to mean "whore"). In this excerpt the narrator, who has been saved from ruin and allowed herself to be seduced by an honest Dutch merchant, expresses her liberated views of marriage.
2. Been accustomed to.

me your own, and take me for good and all, that we may enjoy ourselves without any reproach to one another?"

I told him, that as I confessed it was the only thing I could not comply with him in, so it was the only thing in all my actions that I could not give him a reason for; that it was true I had let him come to bed to me, which was supposed to be the greatest favor a woman could grant; but it was evident, and he might see it, that as I was sensible of the obligation I was under to him for saving me from the worst circumstance it was possible for me to be brought to, I could deny him nothing; and if I had had any greater favor to yield him, I should have done it, *that of matrimony only excepted,* and he could not but see that I loved him to an extraordinary degree, in every part of my behavior to him; but that as to marrying, which was giving up my liberty, it was what once he knew I had done, and he had seen how it had hurried me up and down in the world, and what it had exposed me to;[3] that I had an aversion to it, and desired he would not insist upon it. He might easily see I had no aversion to him; and that, if I was with child by him, he should see a testimony of my kindness to the father, for that I would settle all I had in the world upon the child.

He was mute a good while. At last says he, "Come, my dear, you are the first woman in the world that ever lay with a man and then refused to marry him, and therefore there must be some other reason for your refusal; and I have therefore one other request, and that is, if I guess at the true reason, and remove the objection, will you then yield to me?" I told him, if he removed the objection I must needs comply, for I should certainly do everything that I had no objection against.

"Why then, my dear, it must be that either you are already engaged or married to some other man, or you are not willing to dispose of your money to me, and expect to advance yourself higher with your fortune. Now, if it be the first of these, my mouth will be stopped, and I have no more to say; but if it be the last, I am prepared effectually to remove the objection, and answer all you can say on that subject."

I took him up short at the first of these, telling him he must have base thoughts of me indeed, to think that I could yield to him in such a manner as I had done, and continue it with so much freedom as he found I did, if I had a husband, or were engaged to any other man; and that he might depend upon it that was not my case, nor any part of my case.

"Why then," said he, "as to the other, I have an offer to make to you that shall take off all the objections, viz., that I will not touch one pistole[4] of your estate more than shall be with your own voluntary consent, neither now or at any other time, but you shall settle it as you please for your life, and upon who you please after your death." That I should see he was able to maintain me without it; and that it was not for that that he followed me from Paris.

I was indeed surprised at that part of his offer, and he might easily perceive it; it was not only what I did not expect, but it was what I knew not what answer to make to. He had, indeed, removed my principal objection, nay, all

---

3. The Dutch merchant thinks that Roxana is the widow of a jeweler, whose death had left her alone and friendless; actually she was the jeweler's mistress and has since been the lover of a French prince.

4. A Spanish coin.

my objections, and it was not possible for me to give any answer; for, if upon so generous an offer I should agree with him, I then did as good as confess that it was upon the account of my money that I refused him; and that though I could give up my virtue, and expose myself, yet I would not give up my money, which, though it was true, yet was really too gross for me to acknowledge, and I could not pretend to marry him upon that principle neither. Then as to having him, and make over all my estate out of his hands, so as not to give him the management of what I had, I thought it would be not only a little Gothic[5] and inhumane, but would be always a foundation of unkindness between us, and render us suspected one to another; so that, upon the whole, I was obliged to give a new turn to it, and talk upon a kind of an elevated strain, which really was not in my thoughts, at first, at all; for I own, as above, the divesting myself of my estate and putting my money out of my hand was the sum of the matter that made me refuse to marry; but, I say, I gave it a new turn upon this occasion, as follows.

I told him I had, perhaps, different notions of matrimony from what the received custom had given us of it; that I thought a woman was a free agent as well as a man, and was born free, and could she manage herself suitably, might enjoy that liberty to as much purpose as the men do; that the laws of matrimony were indeed otherwise, and mankind at this time acted quite upon other principles, and those such that a woman gave herself entirely away from herself, in marriage, and capitulated only to be, at best, but an upper servant, and from the time she took the man she was no better or worse than the servant among the Israelites, who had his ears bored—that is, nailed to the doorpost—who by that act gave himself up to be a servant during life.[6] That the very nature of the marriage contract was, in short, nothing but giving up liberty, estate, authority, and everything to the man, and the woman was indeed a mere woman ever after—that is to say, a slave.

He replied, that though in some respects it was as I had said, yet I ought to consider that, as an equivalent to this, the man had all the care of things devolved upon him; that the weight of business lay upon his shoulders, and as he had the trust, so he had the toil of life upon him; his was the labor, his the anxiety of living; that the woman had nothing to do but to eat the fat and drink the sweet; to sit still and look around her, be waited on and made much of, be served and loved and made easy, especially if the husband acted as became him; and that, in general, the labor of the man was appointed to make the woman live quiet and unconcerned in the world; that they had the name of subjection without the thing; and if in inferior families they had the drudgery of the house and care of the provisions upon them, yet they had indeed much the easier part; for in general, the women had only the care of managing—that is, spending what their husbands get—and that a woman had the name of subjection, indeed, but that they very generally commanded not the men only, but all they had; managed all for themselves; and where the man did his duty, the woman's life was all ease and tranquility, and that she had nothing to do but to be easy, and to make all that were about her both easy and merry.

5. Barbaric.

6. Cf. Exodus 21.5–6. "Upper": high-ranking.

I returned, that while a woman was single, she was a masculine in her politic capacity;[7] that she had then the full command of what she had, and the full direction of what she did; that she was a man in her separated capacity, to all intents and purposes that a man could be so to himself; that she was controlled by none, because accountable to none, and was in subjection to none. So I sung these two lines of Mr ————'s:[8]

> Oh! 'tis pleasant to be free,
> The sweetest Miss is Liberty.

I added, that whoever the woman was that had an estate, and would give it up to be the slave of *a great man,* that woman was a fool, and must be fit for nothing but a beggar; that it was my opinion a woman was as fit to govern and enjoy her own estate without a man as a man was without a woman; and that, if she had a mind to gratify herself as to sexes, she might entertain a man as a man does a mistress; that while she was thus single she was her own, and if she gave away that power she merited to be as miserable as it was possible that any creature could be.

All he could say could not answer the force of this, as to argument; only this, that the other way was the ordinary method that the world was guided by; that he had reason to expect I should be content with that which all the world was contented with; that he was of the opinion that a sincere affection between a man and his wife answered all the objections that I had made about the being a slave, a servant, and the like; and where there was a mutual love, there could be no bondage, but that there was but one interest, one aim, one design, and all conspired to make both very happy.

"Aye," said I, "that is the thing I complain of. The pretense of affection takes from a woman everything that can be called *herself*; she is to have no interest, no aim, no view, but all is the interest, aim, and view of the husband; she is to be the passive creature you spoke of," said I. "She is to lead a life of perfect indolence, and living by faith (not in God, but) in her husband, she sinks or swims, as he is either fool or wise man, unhappy or prosperous; and in the middle of what she thinks is her happiness and prosperity, she is engulfed in misery and beggary, which she had not the least notice, knowledge, or suspicion of. How often have I seen a woman living in all the splendor that a plentiful fortune ought to allow her, with her coaches and equipages, her family and rich furniture, her attendants and friends, her visitors and good company, all about her today; tomorrow surprised with a disaster, turned out of all by a commission of bankrupt, stripped to the clothes on her back; her jointure, suppose she had it, is sacrificed to the creditors so long as her husband lived, and she turned into the street, and left to live on the charity of her friends, *if she has any,* or follow the monarch, her husband, into the Mint,[9] and live there on the wreck of his fortunes, till he is forced to run away from her even there; and then she sees her children starve, herself miserable, breaks her heart, and cries herself to death! This," says I, "is the state of many a lady that has had ten thousand pound to her portion."

---

7. A male in her function of making prudent decisions.
8. Charles Cotton (1630–1687), from his poem "The Joys of Marriage" (1689). Ironically, Cotton's poem denounces women as incompatible with men's happiness.
9. Debtors took refuge in the area near the Mint, where they could not be arrested. "A commission": a writ. "Jointure": property settled on a wife.

He did not know how feelingly I spoke this, and what extremities I had gone through of this kind; how near I was to the very last article above, viz., crying myself to death; and how I really starved for almost two years together.[1]

But he shook his head, and said, where had I lived? and what dreadful families had I lived among, that had frighted me into such terrible apprehensions of things? that these things indeed might happen where men run into hazardous things in trade, and without prudence or due consideration, launched their fortunes in a degree beyond their strength, grasping at adventures beyond their stocks, and the like; but that, as he was stated[2] in the world, if I would embark with him, he had a fortune equal with mine; that together we should have no occasion of engaging in business any more; but that in any part of the world where I had a mind to live, whether England, France, Holland, or where I would, we might settle, and live as happily as the world could make any one live; that if I desired the management of our estate, when put together, if I would not trust him with mine, he would trust me with his; that we would be upon one bottom,[3] and I should steer. "Ay," says I, "you'll allow me to steer—that is, hold the helm—but you'll con[4] the ship, as they call it; that is, as at sea, a boy serves to stand at the helm, but he that gives him the orders is pilot."

He laughed at my simile. "No," says he; "you shall be pilot then; you shall con the ship." "Ay," says I, "as long as you please, but you can take the helm out of my hand when you please, and bid me go spin.[5] It is not you," says I, "that I suspect, but the laws of matrimony puts the power into your hands, bids you do it, commands you to command, and binds me, forsooth, to obey. You, that are now upon even terms with me, and I with you," says I, "are the next hour set up upon the throne, and the humble wife placed at your footstool; all the rest, all that you call oneness of interest, mutual affection, and the like, is courtesy and kindness then, and a woman is indeed infinitely obliged where she meets with it; but can't help herself where it fails."

Well, he did not give it over yet, but came to the serious part, and there he thought he should be too many for me. He first hinted, that marriage was decreed by Heaven; that it was the fixed state of life, which God had appointed for man's felicity, and for establishing a legal posterity; that there could be no legal claim of estates by inheritance but by children born in wedlock; that all the rest was sunk under scandal and illegitimacy; and very well he talked upon that subject indeed.

But it would not do; I took him short there. "Look you, sir," said I, "you have an advantage of me there indeed, in my particular case; but it would not be generous to make use of it. I readily grant that it were better for me to have married you than to admit you to the liberty I have given you; but as I could not reconcile my judgment to marriage, for the reasons above, and had kindness enough for you, and obligation too much on me to resist you, I suffered your rudeness and gave up my virtue. But I have two things before me to heal up that breach of honor without that desperate one of marriage, and those are, repentance for what is past, and putting an end to it for time to come."

1. Roxana's first husband, a profligate brewer, had run off, leaving her destitute.
2. Established, a person of standing.
3. One ship (literally, lowest part of a hull).
4. Direct the steering of.
5. I.e., spin yarn (women's work).

He seemed to be concerned to think that I should take him in that manner. He assured me that I misunderstood him; that he had more manners as well as more kindness for me, and more justice, than to reproach me with what he had been the aggressor in, and had surprised me into; that what he spoke referred to my words above, that the woman, if she thought fit, might entertain a man, as a man did a mistress; and that I seemed to mention that way of living as justifiable, and setting it as a lawful thing, and in the place of matrimony.

Well, we strained some compliments upon those points, not worth repeating; and I added, I supposed when he got to bed to me he thought himself sure of me; and indeed, in the ordinary course of things, after he had lain with me he ought to think so; but that, upon the same foot of argument which I had discoursed with him upon, it was just the contrary; and when a woman had been weak enough to yield up the last point before wedlock, it would be adding one weakness to another to take the man afterwards, to pin down the shame of it upon herself all the days of her life, and bind herself to live all her time with the only man that could upbraid her with it; that in yielding at first, she must be a fool, but to take the man is to be sure to be called fool; that to resist a man is to act with courage and vigor, and to cast off the reproach, which, in the course of things, drops out of knowledge and dies. The man goes one way and the woman another, as fate and the circumstances of living direct; and if they keep one another's counsel, the folly is heard no more of. "But to take the man," says I, "is the most preposterous thing in nature, and (saving your presence) is to befoul one's self, and live always in the smell of it. No, no," added I; "after a man has lain with me as a mistress, he ought never to lie with me as a wife; that's not only preserving the crime in memory, but it is recording it in the family. If the woman marries the man afterwards, she bears the reproach of it to the last hour; if her husband is not a man of a hundred thousand, he some time or other upbraids her with it. If he has children, they fail not one way or other to hear of it. If the children are virtuous, they do their mother the justice to hate her for it; if they are wicked, they give her the mortification of doing the like, and giving her for the example. On the other hand, if the man and the woman part, there is an end of the crime and an end of the clamor. Time wears out the memory of it; or a woman may remove[6] but a few streets, and she soon outlives it, and hears no more of it."

He was confounded at this discourse, and told me he could not say but I was right in the main. That as to that part relating to managing estates, it was arguing *à la cavalier*;[7] it was in some sense right, if the woman were able to carry it on so, but that in general the sex were not capable of it; their heads were not turned for it, and they had better choose a person capable and honest, that knew how to do them justice as women, as well as to love them; and that then the trouble was all taken off of their hands.

I told him it was a dear way of purchasing their ease; for very often when the trouble was taken off of their hands, so was their money too; and that I thought it was far safer for the sex not to be afraid of the trouble, but to be really afraid of their money; that if nobody was trusted, nobody would be deceived; and the staff in their own hands was the best security in the world.

---

6. Move away.

7. Cavalierly, rashly (French).

He replied, that I had started a new thing in the world; that however I might support it by subtle reasoning, yet it was a way of arguing that was contrary to the general practice, and that he confessed he was much disappointed in it; that had he known I would have made such a use of it, he would never have attempted what he did, which he had no wicked design in, resolving to make me reparation, and that he was very sorry he had been so unhappy;[8] that he was very sure he should never upbraid me with it hereafter, and had so good an opinion of me as to believe I did not suspect him; but seeing I was positive in refusing him, notwithstanding what had passed, he had nothing to do but secure me from reproach by going back again to Paris, that so, according to my own way of arguing, it might die out of memory, and I might never meet with it again to my disadvantage.

* * *

Thus blinded by my own vanity, I threw away the only opportunity I then had to have effectually settled my fortunes, and secured them for this world; and I am a memorial to all that shall read my story, a standing monument of the madness and distraction which pride and infatuations from hell run us into; how ill our passions guide us; and how dangerously we act, when we follow the dictates of an ambitious mind.

1724

8. Troublesome.

ANNE FINCH, COUNTESS OF WINCHILSEA
1661–1720

Born into an ancient country family, Anne Kingsmill became a maid of honor at the court of Charles II. There she met Colonel Heneage Finch; in 1684 they married. During the short reign of James II they prospered at court, but at the king's fall in 1688 they were forced to retire, eventually settling on a beautiful family estate at Eastwell, in Kent, near the south coast of England. Here Colonel Finch became, in 1712, earl of Winchilsea, and here Anne Finch wrote most of her poems, influenced, she said, by "the solitude and security of the country," and by "objects naturally inspiring soft and poetical imaginations." Her *Miscellany Poems on Several Occasions, Written by a Lady* were published in 1713. One poem, "The Spleen," a description of the mysterious melancholic illness from which she and many other fashionable people suffered, achieved some fame; Pope seems to refer to it when he invokes the goddess Spleen in *The Rape of the Lock*. But Finch's larger reputation began only a century later, when Wordsworth praised her for keeping her eye on external nature and for a style "often admirable, chaste, tender, and vigorous."

Three things conspired to keep Finch's poems in the shade: she was an aristocrat, her nature was retiring, and she was a woman. Any one of these might have made her shrink from exposing herself to the jeers that still, at the turn of the century, greeted any effort by a "scribbling lady." Many of her best poems, for instance "The Petition for an Absolute Retreat," celebrate the joys of solitude. Nevertheless, remarkably, she chose to publish. The reason for Finch's push to publish may be found in her contempt for the notion that women are fit for nothing but trivial pursuits. In "The Introduction" (to her poems) she insists that women are "education's, more than nature's fools," and she often comments on the damaging exclusion of half the human race from public life. But Finch is her own best example of what a woman can be: keen-eyed and self-sufficient and a poet.

The Introduction[1]

Did I my lines intend for public view,
How many censures would their faults pursue!
Some would, because such words they do affect,
Cry they're insipid, empty, uncorrect.
5   And many have attained, dull and untaught,
The name of wit, only by finding fault.[2]
True judges might condemn their want of wit;
And all might say, they're by a woman writ.
Alas! a woman that attempts the pen,
10   Such an intruder on the rights of men,
Such a presumptuous creature is esteemed,
The fault can by no virtue be redeemed.
They tell us we mistake our sex and way;
Good breeding, fashion, dancing, dressing, play
15   Are the accomplishments we should desire;
To write, or read, or think, or to enquire,
Would cloud our beauty, and exhaust our time,
And interrupt the conquests of our prime;
Whilst the dull manage of a servile house
20   Is held by some our utmost art and use.
     Sure 'twas not ever thus, nor are we told
Fables,[3] of women that excelled of old;
To whom, by the diffusive hand of heaven,
Some share of wit and poetry was given.
25   On that glad day on which the Ark[4] returned,
The holy pledge for which the land had mourned,
The joyful tribes attend it on the way,
The Levites do the sacred charge convey,
Whilst various instruments before it play;
30   Here holy virgins in the concert join,[5]
The louder notes to soften and refine,
And with alternate verse[6] complete the hymn divine.
     Lo! the young poet,° after God's own heart,   David

By Him inspired and taught the Muses' art,
35   Returned from conquest a bright chorus meets,
That sing his slain ten thousand in the streets.[7]
In such loud numbers[8] they his acts declare,
Proclaim the wonders of his early war,
That Saul upon the vast applause does frown,
40   And feels its mighty thunder shake the crown.
What can the threatened judgment now prolong?[9]
Half of the kingdom is already gone;
The fairest half, whose influence guides the rest,
Have David's empire o'er their hearts confessed.
45   A woman here leads fainting Israel on,
She fights, she wins, she triumphs with a song,[1]
Devout, majestic, for the subject fit,
And far above her arms, exalts her wit,
Then to the peaceful, shady palm withdraws,
50   And rules the rescued nation with her laws.
     How are we fallen! fallen by mistaken rules,
And education's, more than nature's fools;
Debarred from all improvements of the mind,
And to be dull, expected and designed:°   *intended*
55   And if some one would soar above the rest,
With warmer fancy and ambition pressed,
So strong the opposing faction still appears,
The hopes to thrive can ne'er outweigh the fears.
Be cautioned, then, my Muse, and still retired;
60   Nor be despised, aiming to be admired;
Conscious of wants, still with contracted wing,
To some few friends and to thy sorrows sing.
For groves of laurel thou wert never meant;
Be dark enough thy shades, and be thou there content.

1689?   1903

A Nocturnal Reverie

In such a night,[1] when every louder wind
Is to its distant cavern safe confined;
And only gentle Zephyr fans his wings,
And lonely Philomel,° still waking, sings;   *nightingale*
5   Or from some tree, famed for the owl's delight,
She, hollowing clear, directs the wanderer right:
In such a night, when passing clouds give place,
Or thinly veil the heavens' mysterious face;

7. 1 Samuel 18.6–7.
8. Measures of music and verse.
9. What can now stave off the threatened judgment? Saul's doom ("judgment") had been prophesied: God would replace him with a better king.
1. The prophet and judge Deborah sang to praise the Lord for the victory she herself had brought about (Judges 4–5).
1. This phrase, repeated twice below, echoes the same repeated phrase in the night piece that opens act 5 of *The Merchant of Venice.*

When in some river, overhung with green,
10 The waving moon and trembling leaves are seen;
When freshened grass now bears itself upright,
And makes cool banks to pleasing rest invite,
Whence springs the woodbind, and the bramble-rose,
And where the sleepy cowslip sheltered grows;
15 Whilst now a paler hue the foxglove takes,
Yet checkers still with red the dusky brakes:°   thickets
When scattered glow-worms, but in twilight fine,
Show trivial beauties watch their hour to shine;
Whilst Salisbury[2] stands the test of every light,
20 In perfect charms, and perfect virtue bright:
When odors, which declined repelling day,
Through temperate air uninterrupted stray;
When darkened groves their softest shadows wear,
And falling waters we distinctly hear;
25 When through the gloom more venerable shows
Some ancient fabric,° awful in repose,   edifice
While sunburnt hills their swarthy looks conceal,
And swelling haycocks thicken up the vale:
When the loosed horse now, as his pasture leads,
30 Comes slowly grazing through the adjoining meads,
Whose stealing pace, and lengthened shade we fear,
Till torn-up forage in his teeth we hear:
When nibbling sheep at large pursue their food,
And unmolested kine rechew the cud;
35 When curlews cry beneath the village walls,
And to her straggling brood the partridge calls;
Their shortlived jubilee the creatures keep,
Which but endures, whilst tyrant man does sleep;
When a sedate content the spirit feels,
40 And no fierce light disturbs, whilst it reveals;
But silent musings urge the mind to seek
Something, too high for syllables to speak;
Till the free soul to a composedness charmed,
Finding the elements of rage disarmed,
45 O'er all below a solemn quiet grown,
Joys in the inferior world,[3] and thinks it like her own:
In such a night let me abroad remain,
Till morning breaks, and all's confused again;
Our cares, our toils, our clamors are renewed,
50 Or pleasures, seldom reached, again pursued.

1713

---

2. Probably Lady Salisbury, the daughter of a friend. The sense is that this lady differs from others more trivial, who like glowworms look fine only one hour a day.

3. The world of nature (compared to the world of the soul).

Low People and High People

As more and more people learned to read and write in seventeenth- and eighteenth-century Britain, the world of literature changed. Sharp divisions between persons of rank and commoners had always defined the social and cultural life of the nation, and poets who learned their trade in the universities or at the court appealed to an elite group of like-minded readers and patrons. Even at Shakespeare's Globe, where all sorts came to see the plays, high people mostly sat in galleries above the stage, while, for a penny, low people stood below in the yard. But in the mid-seventeenth century the world turned briefly upside down: Oliver Cromwell, a farmer and country gentleman of modest means, became a soldier, took the reins of power, joined in condemning the king to death, and proclaimed a republic. His way had been prepared by a torrent of writing—rebellious books, papers, broadsheets, and pamphlets, often illicitly printed. One group, called Levellers, declared that in the eyes of God working-class people were the same as the wealthy and privileged and were entitled to equal rights. And though that movement and the republic did not last long, print culture continued to grow. By the end of the eighteenth century the reading public had tripled; it included all sorts of middle- and lower-class men and women who had seldom attracted attention before. New kinds of writing developed to satisfy them: newspapers, periodical essays and journals, how-to books, gazetteers, novels. And many poets catered to what Samuel Johnson called "the common reader" rather than to an elite. Moreover, an unprecedented number of writers began to publish (or hoped to publish) their work. English literature no longer belonged solely to those of means.

All genres of writing reflected these changes in content as well as in style. In earlier periods drama had usually focused on persons of standing, the monarchs, aristocrats, and military commanders whose fates affected the entire social order. Shakespeare's wonderful lower-class characters breathe comic life into his plays, but they are not protagonists; only the noble heroes and heroines speak in blank verse. In the eighteenth century the stage found room for stories of apprentices and criminals and middle-class lovers, who talked in prose like ordinary people. "Greatness" itself became suspect; the joke of *The Beggar's Opera* is that robbers act just like the ruling classes, and vice versa. Prose fiction went through still more radical alterations. French romances had pictured the loves and adventures of courtly heroes and glittering ladies. But John Bunyan's enormously popular *Pilgrim's Progress*, written in prison in 1675, follows a "plain man's" journey to salvation, and its homely, biblical language turns away from the speech and values of people of fashion. Later Daniel Defoe impersonated the voices of hard-working men and fallen women in stories that seemed to be reported instead of invented. And eventually, in the 1740s, the vogue of novels brought masses of readers close to characters not far removed from their own lives. Class conflicts thread through those novels: the wealthy and the poor interact and sometimes grapple with one another. The rigid hierarchies of the old class system seemed to be breaking down; a servant might marry her master, a footman might preach to his betters. And even the names of Fanny Andrews and Tom Jones suggested typical Englishwomen and -men, who might have lived in anyone's neighborhood.

Meanwhile, the language of poetry slowly came down to earth. Renaissance poets were supposed to be learned; they studied Latin and Greek and mastered ingenious forms, such as the sonnet, passed along from Italy and France. Moreover, they took much of their style and diction from classical texts. As late as 1715, Pope called

Frederik Hendrik van Hove, *An Emblem of the Athenian Society*; engraving, 1692. The **Athenian Society**, founded by John Dunton to promote his periodical *The Athenian Mercury* (1690–97), solicited questions from the public on any topic. *The Mercury* published answers from "a society of experts," here shown on top, with different social strata ranged beneath: one man, accosted by a woman with a knife and club, shouts, "Help help noble athenians." From Charles Gildon, *The History of the Athenian Society* (1692).

Homer "the father of poetic diction, the first who taught that language of the gods to men." Poems striving for an exalted tone not only adopted a special vocabulary and appropriate figures of speech but also incorporated the classical gods; it was poetic to point to "Phoebus" rather than to "the sun." Milton heightened his style with Latinate syntax and pagan myths, though he was careful to denounce the false gods he named. But nobody really talked that way, and Samuel Butler, Jonathan Swift, and other satirists mocked poets who prattled about ancient idols. Hence much of eighteenth-century poetry is driven by a revolutionary project: to write about ordinary people in a language that ordinary people could understand. It was a difficult task. Readers accustomed to the traditional forms and artifices of verse could hardly recognize that such unassuming pictures of life— plain styles that dealt with everyday affairs—deserved the name of poetry. Matthew Prior's "Epitaph" on Jack and Joan, and Johnson's tribute to the humble Robert Levet, challenge the prejudices of such readers. When Oliver Goldsmith idealized *The Deserted Village* of bygone days, George Crabbe deflated his dreams and his language. But Gray's "Elegy Written in a Country Churchyard" was the poem that meant most to eighteenth-century readers. The sensitive, educated speaker turns away from the well-born people entombed in the church and sympathizes with the common folk buried in the graveyard. Here was evidence that a great poem might reject the trappings of greatness. Even so, the refined and labored style of the poem seems very distant from the words of the people it mourns. It was left to William Wordsworth, half a century later, to complete the eighteenth-century project by cherishing country folk in a language that he imagined to be like their own.

Yet low people did not need high people to put words into their mouths. As literacy spread, the tools of verse were taken up by would-be writers at the bottom of the social ladder: a thresher, a kitchen maid, a shoemaker, a footman, a milkmaid, a plowboy. Often these poets wrote directly about the hardships they faced, a daily grind that earlier poetry had rarely touched. Whatever they lacked in education, they had something to say: their lives too could inspire poetic feelings and thoughts. And though the privileged sometimes smiled at these efforts, many were also moved. Rich patrons frequently took an interest in working-class poets and tried to better their lot—usually without success, because such poets, cut off from their roots, felt lost in high society. But the most lasting effect of the verse that ordinary people published was a new attitude toward poetry itself. Evidently it could flourish anywhere and cover any subject; the test was whether it was interesting, not whether it was learned.

Still more important, some poets were born, not made; they seemed to be the children of nature. By the end of the eighteenth century, when Thomas Chatterton and Robert Burns were lionized as geniuses, "low people" could no longer be ignored. In the future, British literature would have to find a place for them.

HENRY FIELDING

Henry Fielding's career as an inventor and a master of the English novel in the eighteenth century was one of many he undertook in response to his frustrated social expectations. Fielding (1707–1754) was the eldest of several children in a family with wealthy and aristocratic, even noble, connections, but his prodigal father, a military officer (eventually a general), squandered the fortune that his son would need in order to live the gentleman's life he thought he deserved. The literary projects the young man began after graduating from Eton were always intended to make money. Perhaps with the help of his cousin Lady Mary Wortley Montagu, his first play was staged when Fielding was twenty, and in time the writer developed into the most important London dramatist of the 1730s. His farces so powerfully satirized Robert Walpole's government that they ushered in a new era of stage censorship: the Licensing Act of 1737 aimed to rein Fielding in and closed the Haymarket Theater, where his plays were produced. He then studied for the legal profession and also tried his hand at prose fiction. In 1741 he published *Shamela*, a parody of Samuel Richardson's wildly successful novel *Pamela, or Virtue Rewarded* (1740), which narrates a housemaid's trouble with and eventual marriage to her sexually harassing master. Fielding's version poked fun at the manipulations and cunning that made this crossing of class lines possible, as well as at *Pamela*'s epistolary form. In 1742, *The History of the Adventures of Joseph Andrews* appeared. Not only does this work continue Fielding's parody of Richardson (Joseph, Pamela's brother, is a footman harassed by his lustful employer, Lady Booby); it also fully develops a new kind of comic fiction, which the preface defines as "a comic Epic-Poem in Prose." Fielding would perfect this mode in his masterpiece, *Tom Jones* (1749), and take a more Richardsonian direction in his sentimental novel *Amelia* (1751). He found an idealized model for the heroines of those novels in his first wife, Charlotte, who had brought him a sizable dowry and died in 1744. In 1747 he excited scandal by marrying her maid, Mary Daniel, then six months pregnant. Late in the 1740s he found yet another way to make a historic contribution to English society: as chief magistrate of London, with his half brother, he founded the Bow Street Runners, often called London's first police force. Though Fielding was born into the high life, his experiences gave him insight into all social ranks, from street criminals to the nobility (extremes, in his eyes, often resembling each other). His literary output reflects his range of vision.

The selection here from *Joseph Andrews* exemplifies the subtle skepticism with which Fielding views distinctions of rank. When Parson Adams, a hero of the novel, brings the servant girl Fanny Goodwill to one of the many inns in the story, they encounter Joseph Andrews, Fanny's betrothed, and Mrs. Slipslop, the household manager of Lady Booby, who pretends not to recognize Fanny even though they had worked together for years. Fielding goes on to articulate ideas that run through all his treatments of social hierarchy: individuals occupy different ranks due to arbitrary circumstances; a given status or occupation can tell us little about the virtue or vice of the person associated with it; and people make fools of themselves when they take social distinctions too seriously. The social structure described in the chapter is a parody of the "great chain of being," an ancient philosophical view of the hierarchical nature of the universe, explained in Pope's *Essay on Man* and Joseph Addison's *Spectator* #519. Fielding's attitude is borne out in the plots of *Joseph Andrews* and *Tom Jones*, which at last reveal that major characters have origins and parentage vastly different from what had been supposed; the hectic comedy of these resolutions parodies the conventions of romance and makes the point that moral character is ultimately more important than the identities society gives us. But though Fielding finds the social hierarchy largely absurd and uninformative about true character, he nowhere suggests it is so unjust that it ought to be radically transformed. His skepticism, like that of many gentlemen of mid-century, extended also to those whose political schemes and visions of a more equal society would upset the social order as it stood.

From The History of the Adventures of Joseph Andrews: "A Dissertation Concerning High People and Low People . . ."

It will doubtless seem extremely odd to many readers, that Mrs. Slipslop, who had lived several years in the same house with Fanny, should in a short separation utterly forget her. And indeed the truth is, that she remembered her very well. As we would not willingly therefore, that any thing should appear unnatural in this our history, we will endeavor to explain the reasons of her conduct; nor do we doubt being able to satisfy the most curious reader, that Mrs. Slipslop did not in the least deviate from the common road in this behavior; and indeed, had she done otherwise, she must have descended below herself, and would have very justly been liable to censure.

Be it known then, that the human species are divided into two sorts of people, to wit, *High* People and *Low* People. As by High People, I would not be understood to mean persons literally born higher in their dimensions than the rest of the species, nor metaphorically those of exalted characters or abilities; so by Low People I cannot be construed to intend the reverse. High People signify no other than people of fashion, and Low People those of no fashion. Now this word *fashion* hath by long use lost its original meaning, from which at present it gives us a very different idea: for I am deceived, if by persons of fashion, we do not generally include a conception of birth and accomplishments superior to the herd of mankind; whereas in reality, nothing more was originally meant by a person of fashion, than a person who dressed himself in the fashion of the times; and the word really and truly signifies no more at this day. Now the world being thus divided into people of fashion, and people of no fashion, a fierce contention arose between them, nor would those of one party, to avoid suspicion, be seen publicly to speak to those of the other; though they often held a very good correspondence in private. In this contention, it is difficult to say which party succeeded; for whilst the people of fashion seized several places to their own use, such as courts,[1] assemblies, operas, balls, etc., the people of no fashion, besides one royal place called His Majesty's Bear Garden,[2] have been in constant posses-

---

1. Social world attending a sovereign.
2. Place of entertainment where spectators watched trained dogs attack a chained bear. In Fielding's time the principal bear garden was at Hockley-in-the-Hole, near Clerkenwell Green in central London (see note to *Beggar's Opera*, 1.6, p. 2795).

sion of all hops,[3] fairs, revels, etc. Two places have been agreed to be divided between them, namely the church and the playhouse; where they segregate themselves from each other in a remarkable manner: for as the people of fashion exalt themselves at church over the heads of the people of no fashion; so in the playhouse they abase themselves in the same degree under their feet.[4] This distinction I have never met with anyone able to account for; it is sufficient, that so far from looking on each other as brethren in the Christian language, they seem scarce to regard each other as of the same species. This the terms *strange persons, people one does not know, the creature, wretches, beasts, brutes*, and many other appellations evidently demonstrate; which Mrs. Slipslop having often heard her mistress use, thought she also had a right to use in her turn: and perhaps she was not mistaken; for these two parties, especially those bordering nearly on each other, to wit the lowest of the High, and the highest of the Low, often change their parties according to place and time; for those who are people of fashion in one place, are often people of no fashion in another: and with regard to time, it may not be unpleasant to survey the picture of dependence like a kind of ladder; as for instance, early in the morning arises the postilion, or some other boy which great families no more than great ships are without, and falls to brushing the clothes, and cleaning the shoes of John the footman, who being dressed himself, applies his hands to the same labors for Mr. Second-hand the Squire's Gentleman; the Gentleman in the like manner, a little later in the day, attends the Squire; the Squire is no sooner equipped, than he attends the levee[5] of my Lord; which is no sooner over, than my Lord himself is seen at the levee of the Favorite,[6] who after his hour of homage is at an end, appears himself to pay homage to the levee of his Sovereign. Nor is there perhaps, in the whole ladder of dependence, any one step at a greater distance from the other, than the first from the second: so that to a philosopher the question might only seem whether you would choose to be a great man at six in the morning, or at twelve. And yet there are scarce two of these, who do not think the least familiarity with the persons below them a condescension,[7] and if they were to go one step farther, a degradation.

And now, reader, I hope thou wilt pardon this long digression, which seemed to me necessary to vindicate the character of Mrs. Slipslop, from what Low People who have never seen High People might think an absurdity; but we who know them, must have daily found High Persons know us in one place and not in another, today, and not tomorrow; all which, it is difficult to account for, otherwise than I have here endeavored; and perhaps, if the gods, according to the opinion of some, made men only to laugh at them, there is no part of our behavior which answers to the end of our creation better than this.

But to return to our history. Adams, who knew no more of this than the cat who sat on the table, imagining Mrs. Slipslop's memory had been much worse than it really was, followed her into the next room, crying out, "Madam Slipslop, here is one of your old acquaintance: do but see what a fine woman

---

3. Informal dance parties.
4. In eighteenth-century playhouses the cheap seats were in the upper galleries, the expensive ones in the pit and the lower boxes.
5. Morning reception of visitors.

6. Person high in the sovereign's esteem and confidence.
7. A temporary giving up of the privileges of superiority in kindness to an inferior.

she is grown since she left Lady Booby's service." "I think I *reflect*[8] something of her," answered she with great dignity, "but I can't remember all the inferior servants in our family."

1742

8. Mrs. Slipslop often misuses words and here means "recollect."

MATTHEW PRIOR

Matthew Prior (1664–1721) is a rare example in his time of a person from humble beginnings who, with luck, talent, and diligence, rose to a prominent place in the political and literary life of his nation. His father, a carpenter, was prosperous enough to send him to Westminster School, though at his father's death the boy had to withdraw. The earl of Dorset discovered him at age twelve in his brother's tavern reading Horace in Latin, and the great man was impressed enough to finance the rest of Prior's schooling. A scholarship enabled him to attend Cambridge University, where he made connections that led him later in life to be a tutor and secretary to aristocrats, a member of Parliament, and finally an important diplomat, negotiating the Treaty of Utrecht (1713) for the earl of Oxford's Tory ministry, which ended the War of the Spanish Succession. When the Tories fell in 1713, Prior's diplomatic and political career over, he undertook to publish by subscription his *Poems on Several Occasions* (1718), which earned him the vast sum of four thousand guineas and enabled him to spend the rest of his life in comfort.

Prior's best poems are graceful Horatian lyrics, whose ease and directness are intended to hide the great skill and sophistication that went into their composition. His poem "An Epitaph" undercuts a fantasy that goes back at least as far as Horace, very popular among seventeenth- and eighteenth-century readers, best expressed by John Pomfret's poem "The Choice" (1700): the ideal human life is to be found on a small country estate, with sufficient income to enjoy the modest pleasures of companionship, healthy food and fortifying wine, and a life free of labor—modest by comparison not to the actual lives of most people in the countryside but to the splendor chased by the age's ambitious men. "An Epitaph" quietly questions the guarantee of virtue that a country life without ambition seemed to promise.

An Epitaph

> Interred beneath this marble stone
> Lie sauntering Jack and idle Joan.
> While rolling threescore years and one
> Did round this globe their courses run;
> 5 If human things went ill or well;
> If changing empires rose or fell;
> The morning passed, the evening came,
> And found this couple still the same.
> They walked and ate, good folks: what then?
> 10 Why then they walked and ate again.

They soundly slept the night away;
They did just nothing all the day;
And having buried children four,
Would not take pains to try for more.
15   Nor sister either had, nor brother:
They seemed just tallied for each other.
    Their moral° and economy[1]   *morality*
Most perfectly they made agree:
Each virtue kept its proper bound,
20   Nor trespassed on the other's ground.
Nor fame, nor censure they regarded:
They neither punished, nor rewarded.
He cared not what the footmen did;
Her maids she neither praised, nor chid:
25   So every servant took his course;
And bad at first, they all grew worse.
Slothful disorder filled his stable,
And sluttish plenty decked her table.
Their beer was strong; their wine was port;
30   Their meal was large; their grace was short.
They gave the poor the remnant-meat
Just when it grew not fit to eat.
    They paid the church and parish rate,°   *tax*
And took, but read not the receipt;
35   For which they claimed their Sunday's due
Of slumbering in an upper pew.
    No man's defects sought they to know,
So never made themselves a foe.
No man's good deeds did they commend,
40   So never raised themselves a friend.
Nor cherished they relations poor:
That might decrease their present store;
Nor barn nor house did they repair:
That might oblige their future heir.
45   They neither added, nor confounded;°   *wasted*
They neither wanted, nor abounded.
Each Christmas they accompts° did clear;   *accounts*
And wound their bottom[2] round the year.
Nor tear nor smile did they employ
50   At news of public grief or joy.
When bells were rung and bonfires made,
If asked, they ne'er denied their aid;
Their jug was to the ringers carried,
Whoever either died, or married.
55   Their billet° at the fire was found,   *firewood*
Whoever was deposed, or crowned.
    Nor good, nor bad, nor fools, nor wise;
They would not learn, nor could advise;
Without love, hatred, joy, or fear,

1. Household management.
2. Wound up their skein of thread; i.e., they set the year nicely to rights.

60   They led—a kind of—as it were;
        Nor wished, nor cared, nor laughed, nor cried;
        And so they lived; and so they died.

1718

WORKING-CLASS GENIUSES

Decades before Thomas Gray's famous speculation appeared in "Elegy Written in a Country Churchyard" (see pp. 3051–54) that "some mute inglorious Milton" (line 59) may be hidden among the nation's working people, the notion of the natural, untutored genius had emerged in Britain's literary landscape. Stephen Duck (1705–1756), the first and most celebrated such poet of the century, attended a charity school until the age of fourteen; and as he worked subsequently as an agricultural laborer by day, by night he read Milton, Dryden, *The Spectator*, Matthew Prior, and other literature. By 1729, Duck had begun writing the poems that would make him first a Wiltshire celebrity, then a national one. In 1730 he came to the attention of Queen Caroline, who gave him an annuity and a house, and eventually various official posts; after Caroline's death Duck studied successfully to become a clergyman. But his transformed life cut him off from his roots, and he finally killed himself by drowning in a river behind a tavern. A pirated edition of three of his poems had appeared in 1730 and went through ten editions in that year alone. The work included "The Thresher's Labor," a poem of nearly 300 lines, advertising Duck's wages for that job on the title page ("four shillings and six pence per week") and gaining him the nickname the Thresher Poet. It is from this edition that the excerpt here is taken. Because Duck was unhappy with the pirated texts, he put out an authorized *Poems on Several Occasions* (1736). The language of the earlier version is fresher, though still exhibiting his high literary ambitions: he alludes to classical mythology and (skeptically) to pastoral conventions, and he structures "The Thresher's Labor" to follow the seasons of the year as experienced by farmworkers. The second selection from Duck, "On Mites, to a Lady," from his 1736 collection, wryly comments on human pretensions (of which his new place in high society gave him a good view) by employing the magnifying perspective afforded by modern science.

Mary Collier (1699?–1762), another poet and laborer, was provoked by passages in "The Thresher's Labor" that depicted working women as lazy, "prattling females." At her own expense, she printed "The Woman's Labor: An Epistle to Mr. Duck" in 1739, an explicit, second-person retort to "great Duck," whom she calls an "Immortal Bard!" Lacking any schooling, as her autobiographical note to a 1761 edition of her poems says, she was "set to such labor as the country afforded. My recreation was reading, I bought and borrowed many books." "The Woman's Labor," a poem of about 250 lines, portrays the range of women's work that Collier knew firsthand: washing clothes, polishing the brass and silver of gentry employers, brewing beer, and the field labor, household chores, and child rearing that the excerpt describes. Though she never attained the fame that Duck did, she vividly describes the hardships faced by working women. After Duck and Collier, writings of several other country laborers would find their way into print, including those of Mary Leapor (see pp. 2783–87) and Ann Yearsley, the "Milkmaid Poet," who published her work in 1785. Sponsored and condescended to by wealthy patrons, often seen as mere curiosities in the period's literary culture, these authors speak in vigorous, singular voices, for the first time in literature, of experiences shared by multitudes of working people and inaugurate a tradition of working-class writing that would transform the literary, social, and political consciousness of the nation.

STEPHEN DUCK

From The Thresher's Labor

❆   ❆   ❆

Soon as the harvest hath laid bare the plains,
And barns well filled reward the farmer's pains;
15 What corn° each sheaf will yield, intent to hear,   *grain*
And guess from thence the profits of the year;
Or else impending ruin to prevent,
By paying, timely, threatening landlord's rent,
He calls his threshers[1] forth: around we stand,
20 With deep attention waiting his command.
To each our tasks he readily divides,
And pointing, to our different stations guides.
As he directs, to different barns we go;
Here two for wheat, and there for barley two,
25 But first, to show what he expects to find,
These words, or words like these, disclose his mind:
"So dry the corn was carried from the field,
So easily will thresh, so well 'twill yield.
Sure large day's work I well may hope for now;
30 Come, strip, and try, let's see what you can do."
Divested of our clothes, with flail in hand,
At a just distance, front to front we stand;
And first the threshall's° gently swung, to prove   *flail*
Whether with just exactness it will move.
35 That once secure, more quick we whirl them round,
From the strong planks our crab-tree staves rebound, ⎤
And echoing barns return the rattling sound.   ⎦
Now in the air our knotty weapons fly,
And now with equal force descend from high:
40 Down one, one up, so well they keep the time,
The Cyclops' hammers could not truer chime;
Nor with more heavy strokes could Aetna groan,
When Vulcan forged the arms for Thetis' son.[2]
In briny streams our sweat descends apace,
45 Drops from our locks, or trickles down our face.
No intermission in our works we know;
The noisy threshall must for ever go.
Their master absent, others safely play;
The sleeping threshall doth itself betray.

---

1. Those who separate grains from their husks with a flail, a wooden staff with a short, heavy stick attached by a chain at the end.
2. Thetis's son is Achilles, hero of Homer's *Iliad*; Vulcan, Roman god identified with the Greek god Hephaestus, who made Achilles' shield in the volcano "Aetna," Sicily. The Cyclops were Hephaestus' workers. These lines echo a passage from the fourth of Virgil's *Georgics* (29 B.C.E.), which depict rural labor, as translated by Dryden.

50 Nor yet the tedious labor to beguile,
    And make the passing minutes sweetly smile,
    Can we, like shepherds, tell a merry tale;[3]
    The voice is lost, drowned by the noisy flail.
    But we may think—Alas! what pleasing thing
55 Here to the mind can the dull fancy bring?
    The eye beholds no pleasant object here;
    No cheerful sound diverts the listening ear.
    The shepherd well may tune his voice to sing,
    Inspired by all the beauties of the spring,
60 No fountains murmur here, no lambkins play,
    No linnets warble, and no fields look gay.
    'Tis all a dull and melancholy scene,
    Fit only to provoke the muses' spleen.

*　*　*

1730, 1736

On Mites, to a Lady

'Tis but by way of Simile.
Prior[1]

Dear Madam, did you never gaze,
Through optic°-glass, on rotten cheese?   *magnifying*
There, Madam, did you ne'er perceive
A crowd of dwarfish creatures live?
5 The little things, elate with pride,
Strut to and fro, from side to side:
In tiny pomp, and pertly vain,
Lords of their pleasing orb, they reign;
And, filled with hardened curds and cream,
10 Think the whole dairy made for them.
So men, conceited lords of all,
Walk proudly o'er this pendent ball,°   *earth*
Fond of their little spot below,
Nor greater beings care to know;
15 But think, those worlds, which deck the skies,
Were only formed to please their eyes.

1736

---

3. Duck refers to themes, conventional in pastoral poetry, about the literary leisure of shepherds'
lives.

1. From Matthew Prior's "A Simile," which compares poets to squirrels in a cage.

MARY COLLIER

From The Woman's Labor

* * *

When harvest comes, into the field we go,
And help to reap the wheat as well as you;
Or else we go the ears of corn to glean°;   *gather*
90   No labor scorning, be it e'er so mean;
But in the work we freely bear a part,
And what we can, perform with all our heart.
To get a living we so willing are,
Our tender babes into the field we bear,
95   And wrap them in our clothes to keep them warm,
While round about we gather up the corn;
And often unto them our course do bend,
To keep them safe, that nothing them offend:
Our children that are able, bear a share
100   In gleaning corn, such is our frugal care.
When night comes on, unto our home we go,
Our corn we carry, and our infant too;
Weary, alas! but 'tis not worth our while
Once to complain, or *rest at ev'ry stile;*[1]
105   We must make haste, for when we home are come,
Alas! we find our work but just begun;
So many things for our attendance call,
Had we ten hands, we could employ them all.
Our children put to bed, with greatest care
110   We all things for your coming home prepare:
You sup, and go to bed without delay,
And rest yourselves till the ensuing day;
While we, alas! but little sleep can have,
Because our froward° children cry and rave;   *unruly*
115   Yet, without fail, soon as day-light doth spring,
We in the field again our work begin,
And there, with all our strength, our toil renew,
Till Titan's golden rays[2] have dried the dew;
Then home we go unto our children dear,
120   Dress, feed, and bring them to the field with care.
Were this your case, you justly might complain
That day nor night you are secure from pain;
Those mighty troubles which perplex your mind
(*Thistles* before, and *Females* come behind)[3]

---

1. What Duck says the exhausted men must do on the way home after a day's work ("Thresher's Labor," line 151). Stile: steps over or through a fence, allowing people but not livestock to cross.
2. The sun. Homer calls the sun Titan after the Titan god Hyperion, though other Greek literature identifies the sun with Hyperion's son, Helios.
3. At "Thresher's Labor," lines 241–43, Duck complains about thistles and women in the fields.

125   Would vanish soon, and quickly disappear,
        Were you, like us, encumbered thus with care,

* * *

1739

MARY BARBER

The Irish poet Mary Barber (ca. 1685–1755) was, according to her friend and countryman Jonathan Swift, "the best poetess of both kingdoms" (Ireland and Britain), who had "a true poetical genius" that was surprisingly well cultivated, he thought, for a woman married to a Dublin woolen salesman. Though known as modest and retiring, she was at times involved in controversy, as when she was arrested in England for holding manuscript copies of Swift's poems attacking the government of Robert Walpole. Her *Poems on Several Occasions* (1734), which sold over nine hundred copies by subscription, with Swift's support, contains numerous poems to her sons; verse about social life in Bath, Tunbridge Wells, and other fashionable places; and humorous verse such as the selection here, written in Swiftian tetrameter couplets.

Barber is well represented, alongside Aphra Behn, Anne Finch, Mary Wortley Montagu, Mary Leapor, and others, in two important anthologies of women's poetry in the eighteenth century: *Poems by Eminent Ladies*, 2 vols. (1755), and an expanded version, *Poems by the Most Eminent Ladies of Great Britain and Ireland*, 2 vols. (1785).

An Unanswerable Apology for the Rich

    "All-bounteous heaven," Castalio cries,
    With bended knees, and lifted eyes,
    "When shall I have the power to bless,
    And raise up merit in distress?"

5   How do our hearts deceive us here!
    He gets ten thousand pounds a year.
    With this the pious youth is able
    To build, and plant, and keep a table.
    But then, the poor he must not treat;
10   Who asks the wretch that wants to eat?
    Alas! to ease their woes he wishes,
    But cannot live without ten dishes.
    Though six would serve as well, 'tis true;
    But one must live as others do.
15   He now feels wants, unknown before,
    Wants still increasing with his store.°   *supply*
    The good Castalio must provide
    Brocade, and jewels, for his bride.

Her toilet° shines with plate° embossed,   *dressing table / wrought silver*
20   What sums her lace and linen cost!
The clothes that must his person° grace   *body*
Shine with embroidery and lace.
The costly pride of Persian looms,
And Guido's[1] paintings, grace his rooms.
25   His wealth Castalio will not waste,
But must have every thing in taste.
He's an economist° confessed,   *thrifty*
But what he buys must be the best.
For common use, a set of plate;
30   Old china, when he dines in state;
A coach and six, to take the air;
Besides a chariot and a chair.°   *sedan chair*
All these important calls supplied,
Calls of necessity, not pride,
35   His income's regularly spent;
He scarcely saves to pay his rent.
No man alive would do more good,
Or give more freely, if he could.
He grieves, whene'er the wretched sue;°   *ask for aid*
40   But what can poor Castalio do?

Would heaven but send ten thousand more,
He'd give—just as he did before.

1734

1. Guido Reni, Italian painter (1575–1642).

MARY JONES

I can't say they, any of 'em, answered to my expectations," Mary Jones (1707–1778) joked of her humble ancestors—except her grandmother, "counted the best housewife in the village." Daughter of a cooper (a maker or repairer of casks or tubs) in Oxford, Jones found a way to learn French and Italian, and then worked as a governess in aristocratic households. Her connections in high social circles helped her bring a volume of poems and witty letters, *Miscellanies in Prose and Verse* (1750), into print, with a subscribers' list of around fourteen hundred names. As the project was conceived, she again adopted a droll tone: despairing of fame, she says, "I must even stick by my first mover, riches: and as to the other, if it comes, why let it." Fame did come to Jones. *The Monthly Review* declared that "her compositions in verse are superior to those of any other female writer since the days of *Catherine Philips*" (for Philips's poems, see pp. 1783–89).

Jones's work, like Mary Barber's, was represented extensively in the major anthologies of women's poetry in the century. Though she was keenly aware of the social disparity between her and her wealthy friends, her literary reputation brought its own kind of distinction. She was befriended by Thomas Warton, a poet and Oxford professor, who helped her make another important literary friend, Samuel Johnson. As one biographical notice declared, "Oxford is deservedly called the seat of the muses while this ingenious lady resides there."

Soliloquy, on an Empty Purse

Alas! my purse! how lean and low!
My silken purse! what art thou now!
Once I beheld—but stocks will fall—
When both thy ends had wherewithal.
5   When I within thy slender fence
My fortune placed, and confidence,
A poet's fortune!—not immense:
Yet mixed with keys and coins among,
Chinked to the melody of song.

10 Canst thou forget when, high in air,
I saw thee fluttering at a fair?
And took thee, destined to be sold
My lawful purse, to have and hold?
Yet used so oft to disembogue,°   *empty*
15 No prudence could thy fate prorogue.°   *delay*
Like wax thy silver melted down,
Touch but the brass, and lo! 'twas gone:
And gold would never with thee stay,
For gold had wings, and flew away.

20 Alas, my purse! yet still be proud,
For see the Virtues round thee crowd!
See, in the room° of paltry wealth,   *place*
Calm Temperance rise, the nurse of Health;
And Self-denial, slim and spare,
25 And Fortitude, with look severe;
And Abstinence, to leanness prone,
And Patience, worn to skin and bone:
Prudence and Foresight on thee wait,
And Poverty lies here in state!
30 Hopeless her spirits to recruit,°   *reinvigorate*
For every Virtue is a mute.

Well then, my purse, thy sabbaths keep;
Now thou art empty, I shall sleep.
No silver sounds shall thee molest,
35 Nor golden dreams disturb my breast.
Safe shall I walk the streets along,
Amidst temptations thick and strong;
Catched by the eye, no more shall stop
At Wildey's toys, or Pinchbeck's shop;

40 Nor, cheap'ning° Payne's ungodly books,[1] *bargaining for*
  Be drawn aside by pastry cooks:
  But fearless now we both may go
  Where Ludgate's mercers[2] bow so low;
  Beholding all with equal eye,
45 Nor moved at "Madam, what d'ye buy?"

  Away, far hence each worldly care!
  Nor dun,° nor pick-purse shalt thou fear,   *creditor*
  Nor flatterer base annoy my ear.
  Snug shalt thou travel through the mob,
50 For who a poet's purse will rob?
  And softly sweet, in garret high.
  Will I thy virtues magnify;
  Outsoaring flatterers' stinking breath,
  And gently rhyming rats to death.

1750

1. Thomas Payne, successful bookseller and publisher. George Wildey ran the Great Toy, Spectacle, Chinaware & Print Shop in St. Paul's churchyard; "toys" refers not just to playthings but to a variety of inexpensive articles. The Pinchbecks were a famous family of makers of clocks and musical toys.
2. Tradesmen in an area just west of the City of London.

LAURENCE STERNE

In his stylistic playfulness and love of unconstrained exploration, Laurence Sterne (1713–1768) stands apart among the great eighteenth-century novelists, but none more than he influenced experiments in the art of fiction in the centuries to come. Born in Ireland to English parents, Sterne obtained bachelor's and master's degrees from Cambridge University and settled into a quiet career as a country parson near York, in the north of England. Though he wrote a little about provincial politics, he remained virtually unknown until 1759. After trying unsuccessfully that year to interest a London bookseller in the first two volumes of his masterpiece, *The Life and Opinions of Tristram Shandy, Gentleman,* he published them at his own expense in York; soon he was famous in London literary circles and, soon after that, throughout Europe. Over the next seven years he brought out seven more volumes of *Tristram,* the work comprising nine volumes in all. As the narrator Tristram comically struggles to account for his own life from the moment of his conception, the book depicts intimate transactions of the fictional Shandy family circle, mostly of Tristram's father and uncle and their male associates, and satirizes arcane, learned theorizing. While immensely popular, *Tristram* began increasingly to be condemned for its bawdy humor when its author's vocation as a clergyman became known. Sterne perhaps thought of his second and last novel, *A Sentimental Journey through France and Italy,* as a morally delicate alternative to *Tristram Shandy* that would placate his critics. Plagued by ill health (he had bouts of tuberculosis since his college days, and they worsened through his final years) and in an unhappy marriage, Sterne began a sentimental attachment in 1767 to a young married woman named Elizabeth Draper: a journal addressed to her, written in the fulsome language of fine feeling, was discovered in an attic in the nineteenth century and published as the *Journal to Eliza* in 1904. Sterne died of tuberculosis the year that *A Sentimental Journey* appeared. The list of his admirers in succeeding generations could scarcely be more impressive: Goethe and Dickens, Gogol and Tolstoy all paid tribute to him; modernists such as Proust and Joyce, postmodernists including Italo Calvino, Salman Rushdie, and Carlos Fuentes found his experimentation inspiring; the philosopher Friedrich Nietzsche called him "the most liberated spirit of all time."

In two short volumes, *A Sentimental Journey* presents a series of episodes about travel in France (two planned volumes on Italy would never be written), narrated by the protagonist Parson Yorick, Sterne's alter ego, named after the jester in *Hamlet*, whose skull occasions Hamlet's reflections in the graveyard scene. Yorick had also appeared in *Tristram Shandy*. The interlude of Yorick and the unnamed grisset in a Paris shop is here presented complete—she never reappears in the story—and well exemplifies the complexity of Sterne's renderings of sentimental exchanges. The literature of sensibility had a great vogue in the second half of the eighteenth century, often emphasizing the high-mindedness and purity of male protagonists such as Harley, in Henry Mackenzie's popular novel *The Man of Feeling* (1771). In Sterne's hands, fine feelings of benevolence, most politely expressed, have a way of getting mixed up in a range of ambiguous motives. The scene layers many kinds of commerce—economic, sociable, erotic—that unfold in the class distance between the learned parson and the shopgirl. The pauses in their thoughts and in their dialogue, represented by Sterne's characteristically copious use of dashes, seem to invite the reader to fill them with various interpretative suspicions. The social meaning of shopping, especially complex as carried on between male buyers and female sellers, had been an important topic in eighteenth-century writing from at least as early as Addison and Steele's *Spectator* (1711–14), and the culture of consumerism fascinated readers and writers alike (as Mary Jones's poem "Soliloquy, on an Empty Purse" attests). However well moralized Yorick's encounter with the grisset is here, Sterne allows us to ponder the ironies of kindness and sensitive contact that attend transactions between people of different social stations and genders.

From A Sentimental Journey through France and Italy

[THE BEAUTIFUL GRISSET]
THE PULSE.
PARIS.

Hail ye small sweet courtesies of life, for smooth do ye make the road of it! like grace and beauty which beget inclinations to love at first sight; 'tis ye who open this door and let the stranger in.

—Pray, Madame, said I, have the goodness to tell me which way I must turn to go to the Opera Comique.[1]—Most willingly, Monsieur, said she, laying aside her work—

I had given a cast with my eye into half a dozen shops as I came along in search of a face not likely to be disordered by such an interruption; till at last, this hitting my fancy, I had walked in.

She was working a pair of ruffles as she sat in a low chair on the far side of the shop facing the door—

1. Paris theater presenting opera and other musical entertainment.

Très volontiers; most willingly, said she, laying her work down upon a chair next her, and rising up from the low chair she was sitting in, with so cheerful a movement and so cheerful a look, that had I been laying out fifty louis d'ors[2] with her, I should have said—"This woman is grateful."

You must turn, Monsieur, said she, going with me to the door of the shop, and pointing the way down the street I was to take—you must turn first to your left hand—*mais prenez garde*[3]—there are two turns; and be so good as to take the second—then go down a little way and you'll see a church, and when you are past it, give yourself the trouble to turn directly to the right, and that will lead you to the foot of the *pont neuf*,[4] which you must cross—and there, any one will do himself the pleasure to show you—

She repeated her instructions three times over to me with the same good-natured patience the third time as the first; —and if *tones* and *manners* have a meaning, which certainly they have, unless to hearts which shut them out—she seemed really interested, that I should not lose myself.

I will not suppose it was the woman's beauty, notwithstanding she was the handsomest grisset,[5] I think, I ever saw, which had much to do with the sense I had of her courtesy; only I remember, when I told her how much I was obliged to her, that I looked very full into her eyes,—and that I repeated my thanks as often as she had done her instructions.

I had not got ten paces from the door, before I found I had forgot every tittle of what she had said—so looking back, and seeing her still standing in the door of the shop as if to look whether I went right or not—I returned back, to ask her whether the first turn was to my right or left—for that I had absolutely forgot.—Is it possible! said she, half laughing.—'Tis very possible, replied I, when a man is thinking more of a woman, than of her good advice.

As this was the real truth—she took it, as every woman takes a matter of right, with a slight courtesy.[6]

Attendez![7] said she, laying her hand upon my arm to detain me, whilst she called a lad out of the back-shop to get ready a parcel of gloves. I am just going to send him, said she, with a packet into that quarter, and if you will have the complaisance to step in, it will be ready in a moment, and he shall attend you to the place.—So I walked in with her to the far side of the shop, and taking up the ruffle in my hand which she laid upon the chair, as if I had a mind to sit, she sat down herself in her low chair, and I instantly sat myself down besides her.

—He will be ready, Monsieur, said she, in a moment—And in that moment, replied I, most willingly would I say something very civil to you for all these courtesies. Any one may do a casual act of good nature, but a continuation of them shows it is a part of the temperature; and certainly, added I, if it is the same blood which comes from the heart, which descends to the extremes (touching her wrist) I am sure you must have one of the best pulses of any woman in the world—Feel it, said she, holding out her arm. So laying down my hat, I took hold of her fingers in one hand, and applied the two fore-fingers of my other to the artery—

---

2. A *louis d'or* is a French gold coin that in 1717 had its value fixed in England at 17 shillings.
3. But be careful (French).
4. New Bridge (French), the oldest standing bridge in Paris.
5. French shopgirl or seamstress.
6. Curtsy.
7. Wait a moment! (French).

—Would to heaven! my dear Eugenius,[8] thou hadst passed by, and beheld me sitting in my black coat, and in my lack-a-day-sical[9] manner, counting the throbs of it, one by one, with as much true devotion as if I had been watching the critical ebb or flow of her fever—How wouldst thou have laughed and moralized upon my new profession?—and thou shouldst have laughed and moralized on—Trust me, my dear Eugenius, I should have said, "there are worse occupations in this world *than feeling a woman's pulse*."—But a Grisset's! thou wouldst have said—and in an open shop! Yorick—

So much the better: for when my views are direct,[1] Eugenius, I care not if all the world saw me feel it.

THE HUSBAND.
PARIS.

I had counted twenty pulsations, and was going on fast towards the fortieth, when her husband coming unexpected from a back parlor into the shop, put me a little out in my reckoning.—'Twas nobody but her husband, she said—so I began a fresh score—Monsieur is so good, quoth she, as he passed by us, as to give himself the trouble of feeling my pulse—The husband took off his hat, and making me a bow, said, I did him too much honor—and having said that, he put on his hat and walked out.

Good God! said I to myself, as he went out—and can this man be the husband of this woman?

Let it not torment the few who know what must have been the grounds of this exclamation, if I explain it to those who do not.

In London a shopkeeper and a shopkeeper's wife seem to be one bone and one flesh:[2] in the several endowments of mind and body, sometimes the one, sometimes the other has it, so as in general to be upon a par, and to tally with each other as nearly as man and wife need to do.

In Paris, there are scarce two orders of beings more different: for the legislative and executive powers of the shop not resting in the husband, he seldom comes there—in some dark and dismal room behind, he sits commerceless in his thrum night-cap,[3] the same rough son of Nature that Nature left him.

The genius of a people where nothing but the monarchy is *salique*,[4] having ceded this department, with sundry others, totally to the women—by a continual higgling[5] with customers of all ranks and sizes from morning to night, like so many rough pebbles shook long together in a bag, by amicable collisions, they have worn down their asperities and sharp angles, and not only become round and smooth, but will receive, some of them, a polish like a brilliant—Monsieur *le Mari*[6] is little better than the stone under your foot—

—Surely—surely man! it is not good for thee to sit alone[7]—thou wast made for social intercourse and gentle greetings, and this improvement of our natures from it, I appeal to, as my evidence.

8. The name Sterne uses in his fiction for his friend John Hall-Stevenson.
9. *OED* gives this use as the first instance of the word *lackadaisical*. Black coat: Yorick wears the coat of an English clergyman.
1. Straightforward, true, upright.
2. See Genesis 2.23–24.

3. Cap made of waste thread and yarn.
4. Law that excludes women from accession to the throne, as in France (unlike Britain).
5. Haggling.
6. The husband (French). Brilliant: finely cut diamond.
7. See Genesis 2.18.

—And how does it beat, Monsieur? said she. —With all the benignity, said I, looking quietly in her eyes, that I expected—She was going to say something civil in return—but the lad came into the shop with the gloves— A *propos*, said I; I want a couple of pair myself.

THE GLOVES.
PARIS.

The beautiful Grisset rose up when I said this, and going behind the counter, reached down a parcel and untied it: I advanced to the side over-against her: they were all too large. The beautiful Grisset measured them one by one across my hand—It would not alter the dimensions—she begged I would try a single pair, which seemed to be the least—She held it open—my hand slipped into it at once—It will not do, said I, shaking my head a little—No, said she, doing the same thing.

There are certain combined looks of simple subtlety—where whim, and sense, and seriousness, and nonsense, are so blended, that all the languages of Babel set loose together could not express them—they are communicated and caught so instantaneously, that you can scarce say which party is the infecter. I leave it to your men of words to swell pages about it—it is enough in the present to say again, the gloves would not do; so folding our hands within our arms, we both lolled upon the counter—it was narrow, and there was just room for the parcel to lay between us.

The beautiful Grisset looked sometimes at the gloves, then side-ways to the window, then at the gloves—and then at me. I was not disposed to break silence—I followed her example: so I looked at the gloves, then to the window, then at the gloves, and then at her—and so on alternately.

I found I lost considerably in every attack—she had a quick black eye, and shot through two such long and silken eye-lashes with such penetration, that she looked into my very heart and reins[8]—It may seem strange, but I could actually feel she did—

—It is no matter, said I, taking up a couple of the pairs next me, and putting them into my pocket.

I was sensible the beautiful Grisset had not asked above a single livre[9] above the price—I wished she had asked a livre more, and was puzzling my brains how to bring the matter about—Do you think, my dear Sir, said she, mistaking my embarrassment, that I could ask a sous[1] too much of a stranger—and of a stranger whose politeness, more than his want of gloves, has done me the honor to lay himself at my mercy? *M'en croyez capable?*[2]— Faith! not I, said I; and if you were, you are welcome—So counting the money into her hand, and with a lower bow than one generally makes to a shopkeeper's wife, I went out, and her lad with his parcel followed me.

1768

---

8. A biblical term (literally, kidneys) referring to the bodily seat of affections and feelings.
9. French unit of money valued at about one franc.
1. A sou was the twentieth part of a livre.
2. Do you think I'm capable of it? (French).

THOMAS CHATTERTON

Thomas Chatterton was born in Bristol on November 20, 1752, three months after the death of his father, a schoolteacher. Raised in poverty by his mother, who worked as a seamstress, he went to a charity school and at fourteen was bound apprentice to an attorney. But by then he had already begun to write poems, and his imagination was kindled by parchments his father had salvaged from a chest in a medieval church, St. Mary Redcliffe. Soon Chatterton fabricated documents of his own, and invented a fifteenth-century poet-priest, Thomas Rowley, under whose name he created a fully realized world of local color and verse. Some of these forgeries appealed to credulous antiquarians and found their way into print. But Chatterton felt frustrated in Bristol. In April 1770 he moved to London, hoping for fame and fortune as a writer. Whether he would have succeeded can never be known, because on August 24, in a London garret, at age seventeen, he died from an overdose of arsenic.

Yet Chatterton's legend was only beginning. After his death a scholarly edition of the Rowley poems ignited a controversy in which the authenticity of the works was savagely attacked and defended. Even skeptics who saw through the forgeries, however, were amazed that an unknown adolescent could have produced them. "This is the most extraordinary young man that has encountered my knowledge," Johnson told Boswell: "It is wonderful how the whelp has written such things." Eventually the story of Chatterton's neglected genius and tragic early death grew into a Romantic obsession. When Wordsworth broods on the fate of poets, in "Resolution and Independence," one example comes first to mind: "I thought of Chatterton, the marvelous Boy, / The sleepless Soul that perished in its pride." Blake admired Chatterton as much as he did any other poet; Coleridge's first published poem mourns him; Keats dedicated *Endymion* to him; and later, Dante Gabriel Rossetti compared him to Shakespeare. Yet in modern times Chatterton's reputation remains unsettled. Some critics view him as the first great Romantic poet, and others ignore him. Even his suicide is disputed: the dose of arsenic might

Artist unknown, ***Thomas Chatterton***, 1797. This contemporary portrait, whose authenticity has not been determined, appeared in *The Monthly Visitor* (1797), which declared that "the person of Chatterton, like his genius, was premature; he had a manliness and dignity beyond his years, and there was something about him uncommonly prepossessing. His most remarkable feature was his eyes, which, though grey, were uncommonly piercing; when he was warmed in argument, they sparkled with fire, and one eye, it is said, was still more remarkable than the other."

have been a medicine for venereal disease. But the questions raised by his brief career are still alive. Can a brilliant hoax be equal to true creative invention? Are poets and other storytellers essentially masters of impersonation, whose art depends on mimicking many voices and styles? And is the final test of genius to be found in performance or in potential, in the work that genius produces or in the inspiration that it reveals?

"An Excelente Balade of Charitie" is one of Chatterton's last poems. Its story, modeled on the parable of the Good Samaritan, contrasts the selfishness of a high and mighty abbot with the altruism of a humble friar. But it also has a sharp personal edge. In Chatterton's imaginary world, the make-believe Rowley was supported by a generous patron, William Canynge, a wealthy merchant who actually lived in fifteenth-century Bristol, served as mayor, and rebuilt St. Mary Redcliffe. Yet that was a dream of the past: no such patrons lived in eighteenth-century Bristol, and no one now supported poets in need. The storm that rages in the poem sets the stage for an angry climax. Not all low people were willing to suffer in silence; a revolution was coming.

An Excelente Balade of Charitie:[1]
As wroten bie the gode Prieste Thomas Rowley,[2] 1464

In Virgyne the sweltrie sun gan sheene,[3]	
And hotte upon the mees° did caste his raie;	*meads* (C)
The apple rodded° from its palie greene,	*reddened, ripened* (C)
And the mole° peare did bende the leafy spraie;	*soft* (C)
5 The peede chelandri° sunge the livelong daie;	*pied goldfinch* (C)
'Twas nowe the pride, the manhode of the yeare,	
And eke the grounde was dighte in its mose defte aumere.[4]	
The sun was glemeing in the midde of daie,	
Deadde still the aire, and eke the welken° blue,	*the sky, the atmosphere* (C)
10 When from the sea arist° in drear arraie	*arose*
A hepe of cloudes of sable sullen hue,	
The which full fast unto the woodlande drewe,	
Hiltring attenes the sunnis fetive face,[5]	
And the blacke tempeste swolne and gatherd up apace.	
15 Beneathe an holme,° faste by a pathwaie side,	*holly*
Which dide unto Seyncte Godwine's covent[6] lede,	

---

1. Like all the works attributed to Rowley, this "Balade" (the verse form is rime royal) is written in a language Chatterton invented to fit his idea of 15th-century English. Mining Nathan Bailey's etymological dictionary, he mixed together traces of Chaucer, William Camden, Spenser, and the ballads collected by Thomas Percy in *Reliques of Ancient English Poetry* (1765), and peppered words with extra consonants and final *es*. At first this artificial dialect looks hard to understand, but reading it aloud will often clarify the meaning. Chatterton himself provided glosses, which are marked in the text here with a "C."

2. "Thomas Rowley, the author, was born at Norton Mal-reward in Somersetshire, educated at the Convent of St. Kenna at Keynesham, and died at Westbury in Gloucestershire" (C).
3. In Virgo the sultry (or sweltering) sun began to shine.
4. And also the ground was clothed in a most handsome robe.
5. *Hiltring:* "hiding, shrouding"; *attenes:* "at once"; *fetive:* "beauteous" (C).
6. "It would have been *charitable*, if the author had not pointed at personal characters in this Ballad of Charity. The Abbot of St. Godwin's at

A hapless pilgrim moneynge° did abide,   *moaning*
  Pore in his viewe, ungentle° in his weede,   *beggarly* (C)
  Longe bretful° of the miseries of neede,   *filled with* (C)
20   Where from the hail-stone coulde the almer° flie?   *beggar* (C)
He had no housen theere, ne anie covent nie.

  Look in his glommed[7] face, his sprighte there scanne;
  Howe woe-be-gone, how withered, forwynd,° deade!   *dry, sapless* (C)
  Haste to thie church-glebe-house,° asshrewed°   *the grave / accursed,*
    manne!   *unfortunate* (C)
25   Haste to thie kiste,° thie onlie dortoure° bedde.   *coffin* (C) / *a sleeping room* (C)
  Cale,° as the claie whiche will gre on thie hedde,   *cold*
  Is Charitie and Love aminge highe elves;°   *nobles*
Knightis and Barons live for pleasure and themselves.

  The gatherd storme is rype; the bigge drops falle;
30   The forswat° meadowes smethe,° and drenche°   *sun-burnt* (C) /
    the raine;   *smoke* (C) / *drink* (C)
  The comyng ghastness do the cattle pall,[8]
  And the full flockes are drivynge ore the plaine;
  Dashde from the cloudes the waters flott° againe;   *fly* (C)
  The welkin opes; the yellow levynne° flies;   *lightning* (C)
35   And the hot fierie smothe° in the wide lowings°   *steam, vapours* (C) /
    dies.   *flames* (C)

  Liste! now the thunder's rattling clymmynge° sound   *noisy* (C)
  Cheves° slowlie on, and then embollen° clangs,   *moves* (C) / *swelled,*
  Shakes the hie spyre, and losst, dispended, drown'd,   *strengthened* (C)
  Still on the gallard° eare of terroure hanges;   *frighted* (C)
40   The windes are up; the lofty elmen swanges;
  Again the levynne and the thunder poures,
And the full cloudes are braste° attenes in stonen° showers.   *burst* (C) / *stony*

  Spurreynge his palfrie oere the watrie plaine,
  The Abbote of Seyncte Godwynes convente came;
45   His chapournette[9] was drented with the reine,
  And his pencte° gyrdle met with mickle shame;   *painted* (C)
  He aynewarde tolde his bederoll[1] at the same;
  The storme encreasen, and he drew aside,
With the mist° almes craver neere to the holme to bide.   *poor, needy* (C)

50   His cope° was all of Lyncolne clothe so fyne,   *a cloke* (C)
  With a gold button fasten'd neere his chynne;

---

the time of the writing of this was Ralph de Bellomont, a great stickler for the Lancastrian family. Rowley was a Yorkist" (C).

7. "Cloudy, dejected. A person of some note in the literary world is of opinion, that *glum* and *glom* are modern cant words; and from this circumstance doubts the authenticity of Rowley's Manuscripts. Glum-mong in the Saxon signifies twilight, a dark or dubious light; and the mod-ern word *gloomy* is derived from the Saxon *glum*" (C).

8. "*Pall,* a contraction from *appall,* to fright" (C).

9. "A small round hat, not unlike the shapournette in heraldry, formerly worn by Ecclesiastics and Lawyers" (C).

1. "He told his beads backwards; a figurative expression to signify cursing" (C).

His autremete[2] was edged with golden twynne,
And his shoone pyke° a loverds° mighte have binne;   *shoelaces / a lord* (C)
Full well it shewn he thoughten coste no sinne:
55   The trammels of the palfrye pleasde his sighte,
For the horse-millanare[3] his head with roses dighte.

An almes, sir prieste! the droppynge pilgrim saide,
O! let me waite within your covente dore,
Till the sunne sheneth hie above our heade,
60   And the loude tempeste of the aire is oer;
Helpless and ould am I alas! and poor;
No house, ne friend, ne moneie in my pouche;
All yatte I call my owne is this my silver crouche.°   *cross*

Varlet, replyd the Abbatte, cease your dinne;
65   This is no season almes and prayers to give;
Mie porter never lets a faitour° in;   *a beggar, or vagabond* (C)
None touch mie rynge who not in honour live.
And now the sonne with the blacke cloudes did stryve,
And shettynge° on the grounde his glairie raie,   *shedding*
70   The Abbatte spurrde his steede, and eftsoones° roadde awaie.   *forthwith*

Once moe the skie was blacke, the thounder rolde;
Faste reyneynge oer the plaine a prieste was seen;
Ne dighte full proude, ne buttoned up in golde;
His cope and jape[4] were graie, and eke were clene;
75   A Limitoure[5] he was of order seene;
And from the pathwaie side then turned hee,
Where the pore almer laie binethe the holmen tree.

An almes, sir priest! the droppynge pilgrim sayde,
For sweete Seyncte Marie and your order sake.
80   The Limitoure then loosen'd his pouche threade,
And did thereoute a groate of silver take;
The mister pilgrim dyd for halline° shake.   *joy* (C)
Here take this silver, it maie eathe° thie care;   *ease* (C)
We are Goddes stewards all, nete° of oure owne we bare.   *nought* (C)

85   But ah! unhailie° pilgrim, lerne of me,   *unhappy* (C)
Scathe° anie give a rentrolle[6] to their Lorde.   *scarcely*
Here take my semecope,° thou arte bare I see;   *a short under-cloke* (C)
Tis thyne; the Seynctes will give me mie rewarde.
He left the pilgrim, and his waie aborde.°   *advanced on*
90   Virgynne and hallie Seyncte, who sitte yn gloure,°   *Glory* (C)
Or give the mittee° will, or give the gode man power.   *mighty, rich* (C)

1777

2. "A loose white robe, worn by Priests" (C).
3. Hat-maker. "I believe that this trade is still in being, though but seldom employed" (C).
4. "A short surplice, worn by Friars of an inferior class, and secular priests" (C).
5. A friar granted begging rights within a limited area.
6. An account of "rents" or income, owed to God by his stewards.

William Hogarth, *Heads of Six of Hogarth's Servants*, ca. 1750–55. The painting assembles six portrait studies and originally hung in Hogarth's studio, displaying his talent for capturing character. It conveys the servants' individualized personalities, not defined merely by the jobs they do for their master.

SAMUEL JOHNSON

After Johnson's wife died in 1752, he took in an odd assortment of needy houseguests. Levet, an unlicensed physician who tended to the very poor, lived with Johnson for many years and died in 1782. According to Boswell, "He was of a strange grotesque appearance, stiff and formal in his manner, and seldom said a word while any company was present." This poem is one of the few in which a great writer plays tribute to someone so lowly and unregarded.

On the Death of Dr. Robert Levet

Condemned to Hope's delusive mine,
    As on we toil from day to day,
By sudden blasts, or slow decline,
    Our social comforts drop away.

5   Well tried through many a varying year,
    See Levet to the grave descend;

Officious,[1] innocent, sincere,
   Of every friendless name the friend.

Yet still he fills Affection's eye,
10   Obscurely wise, and coarsely kind;
Nor, lettered Arrogance, deny
   Thy praise to merit unrefined.

When fainting Nature called for aid,
   And hovering Death prepared the blow,
15   His vigorous remedy displayed
   The power of art without the show.

In Misery's darkest caverns known,
   His useful care was ever nigh,
Where hopeless Anguish poured his groan,
20   And lonely Want retired to die.

No summons mocked by chill delay,
   No petty gain disdained by pride,
The modest wants of every day
   The toil of every day supplied.

25   His virtues walked their narrow round,
   Nor made a pause, nor left a void;
And sure the Eternal Master found
   The single talent well employed.[2]

The busy day, the peaceful night,
30   Unfelt, uncounted, glided by;
His frame was firm, his powers were bright,
   Though now his eightieth year was nigh.

Then with no throbbing fiery pain,
   No cold gradations of decay,
35   Death broke at once the vital chain,
   And freed his soul the nearest way.

1783

---

1. "Kind, doing good offices" (Johnson's *Dictionary*).
2. In the parable of the talents (Matthew 25.14–30), Jesus suggests that salvation will be granted to those who make good use of their abilities, however small.

GEORGE CRABBE

George Crabbe (1754–1832) survived through the Romantic period, but his first successful poem is very much a part of eighteenth-century literature. Born to poverty in a small, decayed Suffolk seaport, Aldeburgh, he was apprenticed to a surgeon but could not manage to earn a living by practicing in his native village. In 1780 Crabbe went to London where, finding neither a patron nor a position, and reduced to desperate straits, he sent an appeal to Edmund Burke, who recognized his merit and gave him timely help. Through Burke's influence, *The Library* was published; Samuel Johnson agreed to correct *The Village* (1783); and Crabbe was ordained a minister in the Anglican Church. His appointment as chaplain to the Duke of Rutland enabled him to marry the woman to whom he had long been engaged.

After 1785 Crabbe published nothing until 1807, when *The Parish Register* appeared. It was followed by *The Borough* (1810), *Tales* (1812), and *Tales of the Hall* (1819). In these poems, which won the admiration of William Wordsworth, Sir Walter Scott, and Lord Byron, Crabbe developed his powers of narrative and characterization. *The Village* was widely read, although its unrelieved realism and gloom set it sharply apart from conventional poems on rural life. Indeed, it is an angry, scornful reply to the sentimental cult of rural simplicity, innocence, and happiness. It mocks the naïveté of pastoral conventions and systematically answers Oliver Goldsmith's idealization of villagers, and their life, in *The Deserted Village*. Crabbe had experienced the degrading effect of hopeless poverty; he had observed rural vice; and he knew the gulf that sometimes separated the landed gentry from their laboring tenants. Out of recollections of Aldeburgh and the neighboring seacoast, he fashioned for his poem a setting whose withered nature seems the only proper background for the rugged people who inhabit it. The accuracy of the details created a poetry of the ugly and the barren that has always appealed to readers who prefer plain truth to pretty illusions.

From The Village

From *Book 1*

> The village life, and every care that reigns
> O'er youthful peasants and declining swains;
> What labor yields, and what, that labor past,
> Age, in its hour of languor, finds at last;
> 5   What forms the real picture of the poor,
> Demand a song—the Muse can give no more.
>   Fled are those times when, in harmonious strains,
> The rustic poet praised his native plains.
> No shepherds now, in smooth altérnate° verse,   *metrically regular*
> 10   Their country's beauty or their nymphs' rehearse;
> Yet still for these we frame the tender strain,
> Still in our lays fond Corydons[1] complain,

---

1. "Corydon" is a stock name for a shepherd in pastorals, used by both Theocritus and Virgil.

And shepherds' boys their amorous pains reveal,
The only pains, alas! they never feel.
15   On Mincio's banks, in Caesar's bounteous reign,
If Tityrus found the Golden Age again,
Must sleepy bards the flattering dream prolong,
Mechanic echoes of the Mantuan song?[2]
From Truth and Nature shall we widely stray,
20   Where Virgil, not where Fancy, leads the way?
        Yes, thus the Muses sing of happy swains,
Because the Muses never knew their pains.
They boast their peasants' pipes; but peasants now
Resign their pipes and plod behind the plow;
25   And few, amid the rural tribe, have time
To number syllables, and play with rhyme;
Save honest Duck,[3] what son of verse could share
The poet's rapture, and the peasant's care?
Or the great labors of the field degrade,
30   With the new peril of a poorer trade?
        From this chief cause these idle praises spring,
That themes so easy few forbear to sing;
For no deep thought the trifling subjects ask:
To sing of shepherds is an easy task.
35   The happy youth assumes the common strain,
A nymph his mistress, and himself a swain;
With no sad scenes he clouds his tuneful prayer,
But all, to look like her, is painted fair.
        I grant indeed that fields and flocks have charms
40   For him that grazes or for him that farms;
But when amid such pleasing scenes I trace
The poor laborious natives of the place,
And see the midday sun, with fervid ray,
On their bare heads and dewy temples play;
45   While some, with feebler heads and fainter hearts,
Deplore their fortune, yet sustain their parts:
Then shall I dare these real ills to hide
In tinsel trappings of poetic pride?
        No; cast by Fortune on a frowning coast,
50   Which neither groves nor happy valleys boast;
Where other cares than those the Muse relates,
And other shepherds dwell with other mates;
By such examples taught, I paint the cot,°   cottage
As Truth will paint it, and as bards will not:
55   Nor you, ye poor, of lettered scorn complain,
To you the smoothest song is smooth in vain;
O'ercome by labor, and bowed down by time,
Feel you the barren flattery of a rhyme?
Can poets soothe you, when you pine for bread,
60   By winding myrtles round your ruined shed?

---

2. Virgil was born near Mantua, in Italy, not far
from the river Mincius. Tityrus is one of the
speakers in Virgil's *Eclogues* 1.
3. Stephen Duck (1705–1756), the "Thresher

Poet," was a self-educated agricultural laborer
whose verses attracted attention and finally won
him the patronage of Queen Caroline (see pp.
2443–44).

Can their light tales your weighty griefs o'erpower,
Or glad with airy mirth the toilsome hour?
   Lo! where the heath, with withering brake grown o'er,
Lends the light turf that warms the neighboring poor;
65 From thence a length of burning sand appears,
Where the thin harvest waves its withered ears;
Rank weeds, that every art and care defy,
Reign o'er the land, and rob the blighted rye:
There thistles stretch their prickly arms afar,
70 And to the ragged infant threaten war;
There poppies, nodding, mock the hope of toil;
There the blue bugloss paints the sterile soil;
Hardy and high, above the slender sheaf,
The slimy mallow waves her silky leaf;
75 O'er the young shoot the charlock throws a shade,
And clasping tares cling round the sickly blade;
With mingled tints the rocky coasts abound,
And a sad splendor vainly shines around.
So looks the nymph whom wretched arts adorn,
80 Betrayed by man, then left for man to scorn;
Whose cheek in vain assumes the mimic rose,
While her sad eyes the troubled breast disclose;
Whose outward splendor is but folly's dress,
Exposing most, when most it gilds distress.
85   Here joyless roam a wild amphibious race,
With sullen woe displayed in every face;
Who far from civil arts and social fly,
And scowl at strangers with suspicious eye.
   Here too the lawless merchant of the main
90 Draws from his plow the intoxicated swain;
Want only claimed the labor of the day,
But vice now steals his nightly rest away.
   Where are the swains, who, daily labor done,
With rural games played down the setting sun;
95 Who struck with matchless force the bounding ball,
Or made the ponderous quoit obliquely fall;
While some huge Ajax, terrible and strong,
Engaged some artful stripling of the throng,
And fell beneath him, foiled, while far around
100 Hoarse triumph rose, and rocks returned the sound?
Where now are these?—Beneath yon cliff they stand,
To show the freighted pinnace where to land;[4]
To load the ready steed with guilty haste;
To fly in terror o'er the pathless waste;
105 Or, when detected in their straggling course,
To foil their foes by cunning or by force;
Or yielding part (which equal knaves demand)
To gain a lawless passport[5] through the land.
   Here, wandering long amid these frowning fields,

4. Smuggling was common on the East Anglian coast.
5. License to import or travel.

110 I sought the simple life that Nature yields;
Rapine and Wrong and Fear usurped her place,
And a bold, artful, surly, savage race;
Who, only skilled to take the finny tribe,
The yearly dinner, or septennial bribe,[6]
115 Wait on the shore, and, as the waves run high,
On the tossed vessel bend their eager eye,
Which to their coast directs its venturous way;
Theirs, or the ocean's, miserable prey.
   As on their neighboring beach yon swallows stand,
120 And wait for favoring winds to leave the land,
While still for flight the ready wing is spread:
So waited I the favoring hour, and fled;
Fled from these shores where guilt and famine reign,
And cried, "Ah! hapless they who still remain;
125 Who still remain to hear the ocean roar,
Whose greedy waves devour the lessening shore;
Till some fierce tide, with more imperious sway,
Sweeps the low hut and all it holds away;
When the sad tenant weeps from door to door,
130 And begs a poor protection from the poor!"
   But these are scenes where Nature's niggard hand
Gave a spare portion to the famished land;
Hers is the fault, if here mankind complain
Of fruitless toil and labor spent in vain.
135 But yet in other scenes, more fair in view,
Where Plenty smiles—alas! she smiles for few—
And those who taste not, yet behold her store,
Are as the slaves that dig the golden ore,
The wealth around them makes them doubly poor. }
140 Or will you deem them amply paid in health,
Labor's fair child, that languishes with wealth?
Go, then! and see them rising with the sun,
Through a long course of daily toil to run;
See them beneath the dog star's raging heat,
145 When the knees tremble and the temples beat;
Behold them, leaning on their scythes, look o'er
The labor past, and toils to come explore;
See them alternate suns and showers engage,
And hoard up aches and anguish for their age;
150 Through fens and marshy moors their steps pursue,
When their warm pores imbibe the evening dew;
Then own that labor may as fatal be
To these thy slaves, as thine excess to thee.
   Amid this tribe too oft a manly pride
155 Strives in strong toil the fainting heart to hide;
There may you see the youth of slender frame
Contend, with weakness, weariness, and shame;
Yet, urged along, and proudly loath to yield,

6. Paid to electors by candidates for election to Parliament. Because Parliaments is elected at least every seven years, the bribes are "septennial."

He strives to join his fellows of the field;
160 Till long-contending nature droops at last,
Declining health rejects his poor repast,
His cheerless spouse the coming danger sees,
And mutual murmurs urge the slow disease.
    Yet grant them health, 'tis not for us to tell,
165 Though the head droops not, that the heart is well;
Or will you praise that homely, healthy fare,
Plenteous and plain, that happy peasants share?
Oh! trifle not with wants you cannot feel,
Nor mock the misery of a stinted meal,
170 Homely, not wholesome; plain, not plenteous; such
As you who praise would never deign to touch.
    Ye gentle souls, who dream of rural ease,
Whom the smooth stream and smoother sonnet please;
Go! if the peaceful cot your praises share,
175 Go, look within, and ask if peace be there:
If peace be his—that drooping weary sire,
Or theirs, that offspring round their feeble fire;
Or hers, that matron pale, whose trembling hand
Turns on the wretched hearth the expiring brand!

* * *

1780–83   1783

JONATHAN SWIFT
1667–1745

Jonathan Swift—a posthumous child—was born of English parents in Dublin. Through the generosity of an uncle he was educated at Kilkenny School and Trinity College, Dublin, but before he could fix on a career, the troubles that followed upon James II's abdication and subsequent invasion of Ireland drove Swift along with other Anglo-Irish to England. Between 1689 and 1699 he was more or less continuously a member of the household of his kinsman Sir William Temple, an urbane, civilized man, a retired diplomat, and a friend of King William. During these years Swift read widely, rather reluctantly decided on the church as a career and so took orders, and discovered his astonishing gifts as a satirist. About 1696–97 he wrote his powerful satires on corruptions in religion and learning, *A Tale of a Tub* and *The Battle of the Books,* which were published in 1704 and reached their final form only in the fifth edition of 1710. These were the years in which he slowly came to maturity. When, at the age of thirty-two, he returned to Ireland as chaplain to the lord justice, the earl of Berkeley, he had a clear sense of his genius.

For the rest of his life, Swift devoted his talents to politics and religion—not clearly separated at the time—and most of his works in prose were written to further a specific cause. As a clergyman, a spirited controversialist, and a devoted supporter of the Anglican Church, he was hostile to all who seemed to threaten it: Deists, freethinkers, Roman Catholics, Nonconformists, or merely Whig politicians. In 1710 he abandoned the Whigs, because he opposed their indifference to the welfare of the Anglican Church in Ireland and their desire to repeal the Test Act, which required all holders of offices of state to take the Sacrament according to the Anglican rites, thus excluding Roman Catholics and Dissenters. Welcomed by the Tories, he became the most brilliant political journalist of the day, serving the government of Oxford and Bolingbroke as editor of the party organ, the *Examiner,* and as author of its most powerful articles as well as writing longer pamphlets in support of important policies, such as that favoring the Peace of Utrecht (1713). He was greatly valued by the two ministers, who admitted him to social intimacy, although never to their counsels. The reward of his services was not the English bishopric that he had a right to expect, but the deanship of St. Patrick's Cathedral in Dublin, which came to him in 1713, a year before the death of Queen Anne and the fall of the Tories put an end to all his hopes of preferment in England.

In Ireland, where he lived unwillingly, he became not only an efficient ecclesiastical administrator but also, in 1724, the leader of Irish resistance to English oppression. Under the pseudonym "M. B. Drapier," he published the famous series of public letters that aroused the country to refuse to accept £100,000 in new copper coins (minted in England by William Wood, who had obtained his patent through court corruption), which, it was feared, would further debase the coinage of the already poverty-stricken kingdom. Although his authorship of the letters was known to all Dublin, no one could be found to earn the £300 offered by the government for information as to the identity of the drapier. Swift is still venerated in Ireland as a national hero. He earned the right to refer to himself in the epitaph that he wrote for his tomb as a vigorous defender of liberty.

His last years were less happy. Swift had suffered most of his adult life from what we now recognize as Ménière's disease, which affects the inner ear, causing dizziness, nausea, and deafness. After 1739, when he was seventy-two years old, his infirmities cut him off from his duties as dean, and from then on his social life dwindled. In 1742 guardians were appointed to administer his affairs, and his last three years were spent in gloom and lethargy. But this dark ending should not put his earlier life, so full of energy and humor, into a shadow. The writer of the satires was a man in full control of great intellectual powers.

He also had a gift for friendship. Swift was admired and loved by many of the distinguished men of his time. His friendships with Joseph Addison, Alexander Pope, John Arbuthnot, John Gay, Matthew Prior, Lord Oxford, and Lord Bolingbroke, not to mention those in his less brilliant but amiable Irish circle, bear witness to his moral integrity and social charm. Nor was he, despite some of his writings, indifferent to women. Esther Johnson (Swift's "Stella") was the daughter of Temple's steward, and when Swift first knew her, she was little more than a child. He educated her, formed her character, and came to love her as he was to love no other person. After Temple's death she moved to Dublin, where she and Swift met constantly, but never alone. While working with the Tories in London, he wrote letters to her, later published as *The Journal to Stella* (1766), and they exchanged poems as well. Whether they were secretly married or never married—and in either case why—has been often debated. A marriage of any sort seems most unlikely; and however perplexing their relationship was to others, it seems to have satisfied them. Not even the violent passion that Swift awakened, no doubt unwittingly, in the much younger woman Hester Vanhomrigh (pronounced *Van-úm-mery*)—with her pleadings and reproaches and early death—could unsettle his devotion to Stella. An enigmatic account of his relations with "Vanessa," as he called Vanhomrigh, is given in his poem "Cadenus and Vanessa."

For all his involvement in public affairs, Swift seems to stand apart from his contemporaries—a striking figure among the statesmen of the time, a writer who towered above others by reason of his imagination, mordant wit, and emotional intensity. He has been called a misanthrope, a hater of humanity, and *Gulliver's Travels* has been considered an expression of savage misanthropy. It is true that Swift proclaimed himself a misanthrope in a letter to Pope, declaring that, though he loved individuals, he hated "that animal called man" in general and offering a new definition of the species not as *animal rationale* ("a rational animal") but as merely *animal rationis capax* ("an animal *capable* of reason"). This, he declared, is the "great foundation" on which his "misanthropy" was erected. Swift was stating not his hatred of his fellow creatures but his antagonism to the current optimistic view that human nature is essentially good. To the "philanthropic" flattery that sentimentalism and Deistic rationalism were paying to human nature, Swift opposed a more ancient view: that human nature is deeply and permanently flawed and that we can do nothing with or for the human race until we recognize its moral and intellectual limitations. In his epitaph he spoke of the "fierce indignation" that had torn his heart, an indignation that found superb expression in his greatest satires. It was provoked by the constant spectacle of creatures capable of reason, and therefore of reasonable conduct, steadfastly refusing to live up to their capabilities.

Swift is a master of prose. He defined a good style as "proper words in proper places," a more complex and difficult saying than at first appears. Clear, simple, concrete diction; uncomplicated syntax; and economy and conciseness of language mark all his writings. His is a style that shuns ornaments and singularity of all kinds, a style that grows more tense and controlled the more fierce the indignation that it is called on to express. The virtues of his prose are those of his poetry, which shocks us with its hard look at the facts of life and the body. It is unpoetic poetry, devoid of, indeed as often as not mocking at, inspiration, romantic love, cosmetic beauty, easily assumed literary attitudes, and conventional poetic language. Like the prose, it is predominantly satiric in purpose, but not without its moments of comedy and lightheartedness, though most often written less to divert than to agitate the reader.

A Description of a City Shower

Careful observers may foretell the hour
(By sure prognostics) when to dread a shower:
While rain depends,[1] the pensive cat gives o'er
Her frolics, and pursues her tail no more.
5 Returning home at night, you'll find the sink°   *sewer*
Strike your offended sense with double stink.
If you be wise, then go not far to dine;
You'll spend in coach hire more than save in wine.
A coming shower your shooting corns presage,
10 Old achés throb, your hollow tooth will rage.
Sauntering in coffeehouse is Dulman seen;
He damns the climate and complains of spleen.[2]
    Meanwhile the South, rising with dabbled wings,
A sable cloud athwart the welkin flings,
15 That swilled more liquor than it could contain,

1. Impends, is imminent. An example of elevated diction used frequently throughout the poem.
2. The English tendency to melancholy ("the spleen") was often attributed to the rainy climate. "Dulman": a type name (from "dull man"), like Congreve's "Petulant" or "Witwoud."

And, like a drunkard, gives it up again.
Brisk Susan whips her linen from the rope,
While the first drizzling shower is borne aslope:
Such is that sprinkling which some careless quean°   *wench, slut*
20 Flirts on you from her mop, but not so clean:
You fly, invoke the gods; then turning, stop
To rail; she singing, still whirls on her mop.
Not yet the dust had shunned the unequal strife,
But, aided by the wind, fought still for life,
25 And wafted with its foe by violent gust,
'Twas doubtful which was rain and which was dust.
Ah! where must needy poet seek for aid,
When dust and rain at once his coat invade?
Sole coat, where dust cemented by the rain
30 Erects the nap,[3] and leaves a mingled stain.
  Now in contiguous drops the flood comes down,
Threatening with deluge this devoted town.
To shops in crowds the daggled° females fly,   *mud-spattered*
Pretend to cheapen° goods, but nothing buy.   *bargain for*
35 The Templar spruce, while every spout's abroach,[4]
Stays till 'tis fair, yet seems to call a coach.
The tucked-up sempstress walks with hasty strides,
While streams run down her oiled umbrella's sides.
Here various kinds, by various fortunes led,
40 Commence acquaintance underneath a shed.
Triumphant Tories and desponding Whigs
Forget their feuds,[5] and join to save their wigs.
Boxed in a chair° the beau impatient sits,   *sedan chair*
While spouts run clattering o'er the roof by fits,
45 And ever and anon with frightful din
The leather sounds;[6] he trembles from within.
So when Troy chairmen bore the wooden steed,
Pregnant with Greeks impatient to be freed
(Those bully Greeks, who, as the moderns do,
50 Instead of paying chairmen, run them through),[7]
Laocoön struck the outside with his spear,
And each imprisoned hero quaked for fear.[8]
  Now from all parts the swelling kennels[9] flow,
And bear their trophies with them as they go:
55 Filth of all hues and odors seem to tell
What street they sailed from, by their sight and smell.
They, as each torrent drives with rapid force,
From Smithfield or St. Pulchre's shape their course,
And in huge confluence joined at Snow Hill ridge,
60 Fall from the conduit prone to Holborn Bridge.[1]

---

3. Stiffens the coat's surface.
4. Pouring out water. "The Templar": a young man engaged in studying law.
5. The Whig ministry had just fallen and the Tories, led by Harley and St. John, were forming the government with which Swift was to be closely associated until the death of the queen in 1714.

6. The roof of the sedan chair was made of leather.
7. I.e., with their swords.
8. *Aeneid* 2.40–53.
9. The open gutters in the middle of the street.
1. An accurate description of the drainage system of this part of London—the eastern edge of Holborn and West Smithfield, which lie outside the

Sweepings from butchers' stalls, dung, guts, and blood,
Drowned puppies, stinking sprats,[2] all drenched in mud,   } small
Dead cats, and turnip tops, come tumbling down the flood.[3] } herrings

1710

Verses on the Death of Dr. Swift

Occasioned by Reading a Maxim in Rochefoucauld[1]

*Dans l'adversité de nos meilleurs amis nous trouvons toujours quelque
chose, qui ne nous déplaît pas.*[2]

As Rochefoucauld his maxims drew
From nature, I believe 'em true:
They argue no corrupted mind
In him; the fault is in mankind.
5   This maxim more than all the rest
Is thought too base for human breast:
"In all distresses of our friends
We first consult our private ends,
While Nature, kindly bent to ease us,
10   Points out some circumstance to please us."
      If this perhaps your patience move,°   should agitate
Let reason and experience prove.
      We all behold with envious eyes
Our equal raised above our size.
15   Who would not at a crowded show
Stand high himself, keep others low?
I love my friend as well as you,
But why should he obstruct my view?
Then let me have the higher post;
20   I ask but for an inch at most.
      If in a battle you should find
One, whom you love of all mankind,
Had some heroic action done,
A champion killed, or trophy won;
25   Rather than thus be overtopped,
Would you not wish his laurels cropped?
      Dear honest Ned is in the gout,
Lies racked with pain, and you without:

---

old walls west and east of Newgate. The great
cattle and sheep markets were in Smithfield. The
church of St. Sepulchre ("St. Pulchre's") stood
opposite Newgate Prison. Holborn Conduit was
at the foot of Snow Hill. It drained into Fleet
Ditch, an evil-smelling open sewer, at Holborn
Bridge.
2. Small herrings.
3. In Faulkner's edition of Swift's *Works* (Dublin,
1735) a note almost certainly suggested by Swift
points to the concluding triplet, with its resonant
final alexandrine, as a burlesque of a mannerism
of Dryden and other Restoration poets and claims

that Swift's ridicule banished the triplet from
contemporary poetry.
1. François de la Rochefoucauld (1613–1680),
writer of witty, cynical maxims. Writing to Pope
(November 26, 1725), Swift, opposing the optimistic philosophy that Pope and Bolingbroke (see
n. 4) were at that time developing, professed to
have founded his whole character on these
maxims.
2. In the misfortune of our best friends we
always find something that does not displease us
(French).

How patiently you hear him groan!
30 How glad the case is not your own!
   What poet would not grieve to see
His brethren write as well as he?
But rather than they should excel,
He'd wish his rivals all in hell.
35   Her end when Emulation misses,
She turns to envy, stings, and hisses:
The strongest friendship yields to pride,
Unless the odds be on our side.
   Vain humankind! fantastic race!
40 Thy various follies who can trace?
Self-love, ambition, envy, pride,
Their empire in our hearts divide.
Give others riches, power, and station;
'Tis all on me an usurpation;
45 I have no title to aspire,
Yet, when you sink, I seem the higher.
In Pope I cannot read a line,
But with a sigh I wish it mine:
When he can in one couplet fix
50 More sense than I can do in six,
It gives me such a jealous fit,
I cry, "Pox take him and his wit!"
   I grieve to be outdone by Gay
In my own humorous biting way.
55 Arbuthnot[3] is no more my friend,
Who dares to irony pretend,
Which I was born to introduce,
Refined it first, and showed its use.
St. John, as well as Pulteney,[4] knows
60 That I had some repute for prose;
And, till they drove me out of date,
Could maul a minister of state.
If they have mortified my pride,
And made me throw my pen aside;
65 If with such talents Heaven hath blessed 'em,
Have I not reason to detest 'em?
   To all my foes, dear Fortune, send
Thy gifts, but never to my friend:
I tamely can endure the first,
70 But this with envy makes me burst.
   Thus much may serve by way of proem;
Proceed we therefore to our poem.
   The time is not remote, when I

---

3. A physician and wit, friend of Swift and Pope (see Pope's *Epistle to Dr. Arbuthnot*, p. 2721). Gay is the author of *The Beggar's Opera* and an intimate friend of Swift and Pope. His *Trivia, or the Art of Walking the Streets of London* (1716) owes something to Swift's "City Shower."
4. Henry St. John, Lord Bolingbroke (see headnote to *An Essay on Man*, p. 2713), though debarred from the House of Lords and from public office, had become the center of a group of Tories and discontented young Whigs (of whom William Pulteney was one) who united in opposing Sir Robert Walpole, the chief minister. They published a political periodical, the *Craftsman*, thus rivaling Swift in his role of political pamphleteer and enemy of Sir Robert.

Must by the course of nature die;
75 When, I foresee, my special friends
Will try to find their private ends:
Though it is hardly understood
Which way my death can do them good;
Yet thus, methinks, I hear 'em speak:
80 "See how the Dean begins to break!
Poor gentleman! he droops apace!
You plainly find it in his face.
That old vertigo[5] in his head
Will never leave him till he's dead.
85 Besides, his memory decays;
He recollects not what he says;
He cannot call his friends to mind;
Forgets the place where last he dined;
Plies you with stories o'er and o'er;
90 He told them fifty times before.
How does he fancy we can sit
To hear his out-of-fashion'd wit?
But he takes up with younger folks,
Who for his wine will bear his jokes.
95 Faith, he must make his stories shorter,
Or change his comrades once a quarter;
In half the time, he talks them round;
There must another set be found.
    "For poetry, he's past his prime;
100 He takes an hour to find a rhyme;
His fire is out, his wit decayed,
His fancy sunk, his Muse a jade.[6]
I'd have him throw away his pen—
But there's no talking to some men."
105   And then their tenderness appears
By adding largely to my years:
"He's older than he would be reckoned,
And well remembers Charles the Second.
He hardly drinks a pint of wine;
110 And that, I doubt, is no good sign.
His stomach, too, begins to fail;
Last year we thought him strong and hale;
But now he's quite another thing;
I wish he may hold out till spring."
115 Then hug themselves, and reason thus:
"It is not yet so bad with us."
    In such a case they talk in tropes,°   *figures of speech*
And by their fears express their hopes.
Some great misfortune to portend
120 No enemy can match a friend.
    With all the kindness they profess,

5. Johnson in his *Dictionary* authorizes Swift's pronunciation: *ver-tì-go*.
6. A worn-out horse, in contrast to Pegasus, the winged horse of Greek mythology, emblem of poetic inspiration.

The merit of a lucky guess
(When daily how-d'ye's come of course,
And servants answer, "Worse and worse!")
125 Would please 'em better, than to tell
That God be praised! the Dean is well.
Then he who prophesied the best,
Approves his foresight to the rest:
"You know I always feared the worst,
130 And often told you so at first."
He'd rather choose that I should die,
Than his prediction prove a lie.
Not one foretells I shall recover,
But all agree to give me over.
135   Yet, should some neighbor feel a pain
Just in the parts where I complain,
How many a message would he send?
What hearty prayers that I should mend?
Inquire what regimen I kept;
140 What gave me ease, and how I slept,
And more lament, when I was dead,
Than all the snivelers round my bed.
    My good companions, never fear;
For though you may mistake a year,
145 Though your prognostics run too fast,
They must be verified at last.
    Behold the fatal day arrive!
"How is the Dean?"—"He's just alive."
Now the departing prayer is read.
150 "He hardly breathes"—"The Dean is dead."
Before the passing bell begun,
The news through half the town has run.
"Oh! may we all for death prepare!
What has he left? and who's his heir?"
155 "I know no more than what the news is;
'Tis all bequeathed to public uses."
"To public use! a perfect whim!
What had the public done for him?
Mere envy, avarice, and pride:
160 He gave it all—but first he died.
And had the Dean in all the nation
No worthy friend, no poor relation?
So ready to do strangers good,
Forgetting his own flesh and blood?"
165 Now Grub Street[7] wits are all employed;
With elegies the town is cloyed;
Some paragraph in every paper
To curse the Dean, or bless the Drapier.[8]
    The doctors, tender of their fame,

---

7. Originally a street in London largely inhabited by hack writers; later, a generic term applied to all such writers.
8. It was in the character of M. B., a Dublin dra- pier, that Swift aroused the Irish people to resistance against the importation of Wood's halfpence (see headnote, p. 2465)

170 Wisely on me lay all the blame.
"We must confess his case was nice;[9]
But he would never take advice.
Had he been ruled, for aught appears,
He might have lived these twenty years:
175 For, when we opened him, we found,
That all his vital parts were sound."
    From Dublin soon to London spread,
'Tis told at court, "The Dean is dead."
Kind Lady Suffolk, in the spleen,[1]
180 Runs laughing up to tell the Queen.
The Queen, so gracious, mild and good,
Cries, "Is he gone? 'tis time he should.
He's dead, you say; why, let him rot:
I'm glad the medals were forgot.[2]
185 I promised him, I own; but when?
I only was the Princess then;
But now, as consort of the King,
You know, 'tis quite a different thing."
    Now Chartres, at Sir Robert's levee,[3]
190 Tells with a sneer the tidings heavy:
"Why, is he dead without his shoes?"
Cries Bob, "I'm sorry for the news:
Oh, were the wretch but living still,
And in his place my good friend Will![4]
195 Or had a miter on his head,
Provided Bolingbroke were dead!"
    Now Curll[5] his shop from rubbish drains:
Three genuine tomes of Swift's remains.
And then, to make them pass the glibber,
200 Revised by Tibbalds, Moore, and Cibber.[6]
He'll treat me as he does my betters,
Publish my will, my life, my letters;
Revive the libels born to die,
Which Pope must bear, as well as I.
205   Here shift the scene, to represent
How those I love, my death lament.
Poor Pope will grieve a month, and Gay
A week, and Arbuthnot a day.
    St. John himself will scarce forbear
210 To bite his pen, and drop a tear.

9. Delicate; hence demanding careful diagnosis and treatment.
1. In low spirits. The phrase is ironic, as "laughing" makes clear. Lady Suffolk was George II's mistress, with whom Swift became friendly during his visit to Pope in 1726.
2. Queen Caroline had promised Swift some medals when she was princess of Wales during the same year.
3. Morning reception. Colonel Francis Chartres was a debauchee, often satirized by Pope. Sir Robert Walpole is meant here.
4. William Pulteney (see n. 4, p. 2469).

5. Edmund Curll, shrewd and disreputable bookseller, published pirated works, scandalous biographies, and works falsely ascribed to notable writers of the time.
6. Colley Cibber (1671–1757), comic actor, playwright, and supremely untalented poet laureate. He succeeded Theobald as king of the Dunces in Pope's *The Dunciad* of 1743. Lewis Theobald (1688–1744), Shakespeare scholar and editor, already enthroned as king of the Dunces in *The Dunciad* of 1728. Like Pope, Swift spells the name phonetically. James Moore Smythe, poetaster and playwright, an enemy of Pope.

The rest will give a shrug, and cry,
"I'm sorry—but we all must die."
 Indifference clad in wisdom's guise
All fortitude of mind supplies:
215 For how can stony bowels melt
In those who never pity felt?
When *we* are lashed, *they* kiss the rod,
Resigning to the will of God.
 The fools, my juniors by a year,
220 Are tortured with suspense and fear;
Who wisely thought my age a screen,
When death approached, to stand between:
The screen removed, their hearts are trembling;
They mourn for me without dissembling.
225 My female friends, whose tender hearts
Have better learned to act their parts,
Receive the news in doleful dumps:
"The Dean is dead (and what is trumps?)
Then, Lord have mercy on his soul!
230 (Ladies, I'll venture for the vole.)[7]
Six deans, they say, must bear the pall.
(I wish I knew what king to call.)
Madam, your husband will attend
The funeral of so good a friend?"
235 "No, madam, 'tis a shocking sight;
And he's engaged tomorrow night:
My Lady Club would take it ill,
If he should fail her at quadrille.
He loved the Dean—(I lead a heart)
240 But dearest friends, they say, must part.
His time was come; he ran his race;
We hope he's in a better place."
 Why do we grieve that friends should die?
No loss more easy to supply.
245 One year is past; a different scene;
No further mention of the Dean,
Who now, alas! no more is missed,
Than if he never did exist.
Where's now this favorite of Apollo?[8]
250 Departed—and his works must follow,
Must undergo the common fate;
His kind of wit is out of date.
 Some country squire to Lintot[9] goes,
Inquires for *Swift* in verse and prose.
255 Says Lintot, "I have heard the name;
He died a year ago."—"The same."
He searches all his shop in vain.
"Sir, you may find them in Duck Lane:[1]

7. The equivalent in the card game quadrille of bidding a grand slam in bridge.
8. Poet who is inspired by the god of poetry (Apollo).
9. Bernard Lintot, a bookseller and the publisher of Pope's Homer and some of his early poems.
1. London street where secondhand books and publishers' remainders were sold.

I sent them, with a load of books,
260 Last Monday to the pastry-cook's.[2]
To fancy they could live a year!
I find you're but a stranger here.
The Dean was famous in his time,
And had a kind of knack at rhyme.
265 His way of writing now is past:
The town has got a better taste.
I keep no antiquated stuff;
But spick and span I have enough.
Pray do but give me leave to show 'em:
270 Here's Colley Cibber's birthday poem.[3]
This ode you never yet have seen
By Stephen Duck[4] upon the Queen.
Then here's a letter finely penned
Against the *Craftsman*[5] and his friend;
275 It clearly shows that all reflection
On ministers is disaffection.
Next, here's Sir Robert's vindication,[6]
And Mr. Henley's last oration.[7]
The hawkers have not got 'em yet:
280 Your honor please to buy a set?
　　"Here's Woolston's[8] tracts, the twelfth edition;
'Tis read by every politician:
The country members, when in town,
To all their boroughs send them down;
285 You never met a thing so smart;
The courtiers have them all by heart;
Those maids of honor (who can read)
Are taught to use them for their creed.
The reverend author's good intention
290 Has been rewarded with a pension.
He does an honor to his gown,
By bravely running priestcraft down;
He shows, as sure as God's in Gloucester,[9]
That Jesus was a grand impostor;
295 That all his miracles were cheats,
Performed as jugglers do their feats:
The Church had never such a writer;
A shame he hath not got a miter!"
　　Suppose me dead; and then suppose
300 A club assembled at the Rose;[1]
Where, from discourse of this and that,

---

2. To be used as waste paper for lining baking dishes and wrapping parcels.

3. The laureate Cibber was obliged to celebrate each of the king's birthdays with a poem.

4. "The Thresher Poet," an agricultural laborer whose verse brought him to the notice and patronage of Queen Caroline.

5. See n. 4, p. 2469

6. Walpole hires a string of party scribblers who do nothing else but write in his defense [Swift's note].

7. "Orator" John Henley, an Independent preacher who dazzled unlearned audiences with his oratory and who wrote treatises on elocution.

8. Thomas Woolston (1670–1733), a Cambridge scholar (hence wearing a "gown" in line 291) whose *Discourses on the Miracles of Our Saviour* had recently earned him notoriety.

9. Proverbially, Gloucestershire was full of monks.

1. A fashionable tavern in Covent Garden.

I grow the subject of their chat:
And while they toss my name about,
With favor some, and some without,
305 One, quite indifferent in the cause,
My character impartial draws:
    "The Dean, if we believe report,
Was never ill received at court.
As for his works in verse and prose,
310 I own myself no judge of those;
Nor can I tell what critics thought 'em:
But this I know, all people bought 'em,
As with a moral view designed
To cure the vices of mankind.
315   "His vein, ironically grave,
Exposed the fool and lashed the knave;
To steal a hint was never known,
But what he writ was all his own.
    "He never thought an honor done him,
320 Because a duke was proud to own him;
Would rather slip aside and choose
To talk with wits in dirty shoes;
Despised the fools with stars and garters,[2]
So often seen caressing Chartres.
325 He never courted men in station,
Nor persons held in admiration;
Of no man's greatness was afraid,
Because he sought for no man's aid.
Though trusted long in great affairs,
330 He gave himself no haughty airs;
Without regarding private ends,
Spent all his credit for his friends;
And only chose the wise and good;
No flatterers, no allies in blood;
335 But succored virtue in distress,
And seldom failed of good success;
As numbers in their hearts must own,
Who, but for him, had been unknown.
    "With princes kept a due decorum,
340 But never stood in awe before 'em.
He followed David's lesson just;
In princes never put thy trust:[3]
And would you make him truly sour,
Provoke him with a slave in power.
345 The Irish senate if you named,
With what impatience he declaimed!
Fair Liberty was all his cry,
For her he stood prepared to die;
For her he boldly stood alone;
350 For her he oft exposed his own.
Two kingdoms, just as faction led,

2. Emblems of knighthood.   3. Psalm 146.3.

Had set a price upon his head,
But not a traitor could be found,
To sell him for six hundred pound.[4]
355 "Had he but spared his tongue and pen,
He might have rose like other men;
But power was never in his thought,
And wealth he valued not a groat:
Ingratitude he often found,
360 And pitied those who meant the wound;
But kept the tenor of his mind,
To merit well of human kind:
Nor made a sacrifice of those
Who still were true, to please his foes.
365 He labored many a fruitless hour,
To reconcile his friends in power;
Saw mischief by a faction brewing,
While they pursued each other's ruin.
But, finding vain was all his care,
370 He left the court in mere despair.[5]
 "And, oh! how short are human schemes!
Here ended all our golden dreams.
What St. John's skill in state affairs,
What Ormonde's[6] valor, Oxford's cares,
375 To save their sinking country lent,
Was all destroyed by one event.[7]
Too soon that precious life was ended,
On which alone our weal depended.
When up a dangerous faction starts,[8]
380 With wrath and vengeance in their hearts;
By solemn League and Covenant bound,
To ruin, slaughter, and confound;
To turn religion to a fable,
And make the government a Babel;
385 Pervert the laws, disgrace the gown,
Corrupt the senate, rob the crown;
To sacrifice old England's glory,
And make her infamous in story:
When such a tempest shook the land,
390 How could unguarded Virtue stand?
With horror, grief, despair, the Dean
Beheld the dire destructive scene:

4. In 1714 the government offered £300 for the discovery of the author of Swift's "Public Spirit of the Whigs," and in 1724 the Irish government offered a similar amount for the discovery of the author of the fourth of Swift's *Drapier's Letters.*
5. The antagonism between the two chief ministers (his dear friends), Robert Harley, earl of Oxford, and Bolingbroke, paralyzed the Tory ministry in the crucial last months of Queen Anne's life and drove Swift to retirement in Ireland, whence he returned in 1714 to make a final effort to heal the breach and save the government,
which failed.
6. James Butler, duke of Ormond, who succeeded to the command of the English armies on the Continent when, in 1711, the duke of Marlborough was stripped of his offices by Anne. He went into exile in 1714 and was active in Jacobite intrigue.
7. The death of Queen Anne.
8. Swift feared the policies of the "dangerous faction" (the Whig party) because its toleration of Dissenters threatened the Church of England.

His friends in exile, or the Tower,[9]
Himself within the frown of power,
395 Pursued by base envenomed pens,
Far to the land of slaves and fens;°   *Ireland*
A servile race in folly nursed,
Who truckle most, when treated worst.
"By innocence and resolution,
400 He bore continual persecution;
While numbers to preferment rose,
Whose merits were to be his foes;
When even his own familiar friends,
Intent upon their private ends,
405 Like renegadoes now he feels,
Against him lifting up their heels.
"The Dean did, by his pen, defeat
An infamous destructive cheat;[1]
Taught fools their interest how to know,
410 And gave them arms to ward the blow.
Envy has owned it was his doing,
To save that hapless land from ruin;
While they who at the steerage[2] stood,
And reaped the profit, sought his blood.
415 "To save them from their evil fate,
In him was held a crime of state.
A wicked monster on the bench,[3]
Whose fury blood could never quench;
As vile and profligate a villain,
420 As modern Scroggs, or old Tresilian;[4]
Who long all justice had discarded,
Nor feared he God, nor man regarded;
Vowed on the Dean his rage to vent,
And make him of his zeal repent:
425 But Heaven his innocence defends,
The grateful people stand his friends;
Not strains of law, nor judge's frown,
Nor topics° brought to please the crown,   *arguments*
Nor witness hired, nor jury picked,
430 Prevail to bring him in convict.
"In exile, with a steady heart,
He spent his life's declining part;
Where folly, pride, and faction sway,

9. Bolingbroke was in exile. Oxford was sent to the Tower of London by the Whigs.
1. The scheme to introduce Wood's copper halfpence into Ireland in 1723–24.
2. Literally the steering of a ship. Here the direction and management of public affairs in Ireland.
3. William Whitshed, lord chief justice of the King's Bench of Ireland. In 1720, when the jury refused to find Swift's anonymous pamphlet "Proposal for the Universal Use of Irish Manufacture" wicked and seditious, Whitshed sent them back nine times, hoping to force them to another ver-dict. In 1724 he presided over the trial of Harding, the printer of the fourth of Swift's *Drapier's Letters*, but again was unable, despite bullying, to force a verdict of guilty.
4. In 1381, Sir Robert Tresilian punished with great severity men who had participated in the Peasants' Revolt; he was impeached and in 1387 was hanged. Sir William Scroggs, lord chief justice of England at the time of the Popish Plot, 1678 (see Dryden's *Absalom and Achitophel*, p. 2212), was impeached for his misdemeanors in office in 1680.

Remote from St. John, Pope, and Gay.
435   "His friendships there, to few confined,
Were always of the middling kind;
No fools of rank, a mongrel breed,
Who fain would pass for lords indeed:
Where titles give no right or power,
440 And peerage is a withered flower;
He would have held it a disgrace,
If such a wretch had known his face.
On rural squires, that kingdom's bane,
He vented oft his wrath in vain;
445 Biennial squires[5] to market brought:
Who sell their souls and votes for naught;
The nation stripped, go joyful back,
To rob the church, their tenants rack,
Go snacks° with rogues and rapparees;°   *shares / highwaymen*
450 And keep the peace to pick up fees;
In every job to have a share,
A jail or barrack to repair;
And turn the tax for public roads
Commodious to their own abodes.
455   "Perhaps I may allow the Dean
Had too much satire in his vein;
And seemed determined not to starve it,
Because no age could more deserve it.
Yet malice never was his aim;
460 He lashed the vice, but spared the name;
No individual could resent,
Where thousands equally were meant;
His satire points at no defect,
But what all mortals may correct;
465 For he abhorred that senseless tribe
Who call it humor when they gibe:
He spared a hump, or crooked nose,
Whose owners set not up for beaux.
True genuine dullness moved his pity,
470 Unless it offered to be witty.
Those who their ignorance confessed,
He ne'er offended with a jest;
But laughed to hear an idiot quote
A verse from Horace learned by rote.
475   "He knew an hundred pleasant stories,
With all the turns of Whigs and Tories:
Was cheerful to his dying day;
And friends would let him have his way.
    "He gave the little wealth he had
480 To build a house for fools and mad;[6]
And showed by one satiric touch,
No nation wanted it so much.

5. Members of the Irish Parliament.
6. Swift left funds to endow a hospital for the insane.

That kingdom he hath left his debtor,
I wish it soon may have a better."

1731   1739

From A Tale of a Tub

A Digression Concerning the Original, the Use, and Improvement of Madness in a Commonwealth[1]

Nor shall it any ways detract from the just reputation of this famous sect,[2] that its rise and institution are owing to such an author as I have described Jack to be, a person whose intellectuals were overturned, and his brain shaken out of its natural position; which we commonly suppose to be a distemper, and call by the name of madness or frenzy. For, if we take a survey of the greatest actions that have been performed in the world, under the influence of single men, which are the establishment of new empires by conquest, the advance and progress of new schemes in philosophy, and the contriving, as well as the propagating, of new religions, we shall find the authors of them all to have been persons whose natural reason had admitted great revolutions from their diet, their education, the prevalency of some certain temper, together with the particular influence of air and climate. Besides, there is something individual in human minds, that easily kindles at the accidental approach and collision of certain circumstances, which, though of paltry and mean appearance, do often flame out into the greatest emergencies of life. For great turns are not always given by strong hands, but by lucky adaption, and at proper seasons; and it is of no import where the fire was kindled, if the vapor has once got up into the brain. For the upper region of man is furnished like the middle region of the air; the materials are formed from causes of the widest difference, yet produce at last the same substance and effect. Mists arise from the earth, steams from dunghills, exhalations from the sea, and smoke from fire; yet all clouds are the same in composition as well as consequences, and the fumes issuing from a jakes[3] will furnish as comely and useful a vapor as incense from an altar. Thus far, I suppose, will easily be granted me; and then it will follow, that as the face of nature never produces rain but when it is overcast and disturbed, so human understanding, seated in the brain, must be troubled and overspread by vapors, ascending from the lower faculties to water the invention and render it fruitful. Now, although these vapors (as it hath been

---

1. *A Tale of a Tub*, Swift's first major work, recounts the adventures of three brothers: Peter (Roman Catholicism), Martin (Luther, here regarded as inspiring the Church of England), and Jack (Calvin, the spirit of Protestant dissent). But the most memorable character of the book is its narrator, who interrupts the story with numerous digressions (including even "A Digression in Praise of Digressions") and whose pride in learning and lack of common sense represent the zealous modern insanity that Swift takes as his target for satire. "A Digression Concerning Madness," this narrator's masterpiece, is based on Swift's

ironical doctrine of "the mechanical operation of the spirit": the notion that all spiritual and mental states derive from physical causes—in this case, the ascent of "vapors" to the brain. Beneath his whimsy, however, the author raises a fearful question: what right has any human being to trust that he or she is sane?
2. The Aeolists, who "maintain the original cause of all things to be wind," are equated by Swift with religious dissenters who believe themselves to be inspired by the Holy Spirit.
3. Latrine.

2480 | JONATHAN SWIFT

already said) are of as various original as those of the skies, yet the crop they produce differs both in kind and degree, merely according to the soil. I will produce two instances to prove and explain what I am now advancing.

A certain great prince[4] raised a mighty army, filled his coffers with infinite treasures, provided an invincible fleet, and all this without giving the least part of his design to his greatest ministers or his nearest favorites. Immediately the whole world was alarmed; the neighboring crowns in trembling expectation towards what point the storm would burst; the small politicians everywhere forming profound conjectures. Some believed he had laid a scheme for universal monarchy; others, after much insight, determined the matter to be a project for pulling down the Pope, and setting up the reformed religion, which had once been his own. Some again, of a deeper sagacity, sent him into Asia to subdue the Turk, and recover Palestine. In the midst of all these projects and preparations, a certain state-surgeon,[5] gathering the nature of the disease by these symptoms, attempted the cure, at one blow performed the operation, broke the bag, and out flew the vapor; nor did anything want to render it a complete remedy, only that the prince unfortunately happened to die in the performance. Now, is the reader exceeding curious to learn whence this vapor took its rise, which had so long set the nations at a gaze? What secret wheel, what hidden spring, could put into motion so wonderful an engine? It was afterwards discovered that the movement of this whole machine had been directed by an absent female, whose eyes had raised a protuberancy, and before emission, she was removed into an enemy's country. What should an unhappy prince do in such ticklish circumstances as these? He tried in vain the poet's never-failing receipt of *corpora quaeque*;[6] for,

> *Idque petit corpus mens unde est saucia amore:*
> *Unde feritur, eo tendit, gestitque coire.*—LUCRETIUS[7]

Having to no purpose used all peaceable endeavors, the collected part of the semen, raised and inflamed, became adust,[8] converted to choler, turned head upon the spinal duct, and ascended to the brain. The very same principle that influences a bully to break the windows of a whore who has jilted him, naturally stirs up a great prince to raise mighty armies, and dream of nothing but sieges, battles, and victories.

> ——*Teterrima belli*
> *Causa*——[9]

The other instance is what I have read somewhere in a very ancient author, of a mighty king,[1] who, for the space of above thirty years, amused himself to take and lose towns, beat armies, and be beaten, drive princes out of their dominions; fright children from their bread and butter; burn, lay

---

4. "This was Harry the Great of France" [Swift's note]. Henry IV (1553–1610), infatuated with the princesse de Condé, whose husband had removed her to the Spanish Netherlands, prepared an expedition to bring her back.
5. Ravillac, who stabbed Henry the Great in his coach [Swift's note].
6. Any available bodies (Latin). "Receipt": recipe.
7. The body strives for that which sickens the

mind with love. . . . Stretches out toward that which smites it, and yearns to couple (Latin; *De Rerum Natura* 4.1048ff.).
8. Burned up.
9. "The most abominable cause of war" (Latin) in olden days, according to Horace, *Satires* 1.3.107–08, was a whore.
1. This is meant of the present French king [Louis XIV] [Swift's note].

waste, plunder, dragoon, massacre subject and stranger, friend and foe, male and female. 'Tis recorded, that the philosophers of each country were in grave dispute upon causes natural, moral, and political, to find out where they should assign an original solution of this phenomenon. At last the vapor or spirit, which animated the hero's brain, being in perpetual circulation, seized upon that region of the human body, so renowned for furnishing the *zibeta occidentalis*,[2] and gathering there into a tumor, left the rest of the world for that time in peace. Of such mighty consequence it is where those exhalations fix, and of so little from whence they proceed. The same spirits which, in their superior progress, would conquer a kingdom, descending upon the anus, conclude in a fistula.[3]

Let us next examine the great introducers of new schemes in philosophy, and search till we can find from what faculty of the soul the disposition arises in mortal man, of taking it into his head to advance new systems with such an eager zeal, in things agreed on all hands impossible to be known; from what seeds this disposition springs, and to what quality of human nature these grand innovators have been indebted for their number of disciples. Because it is plain, that several of the chief among them, both ancient and modern, were usually mistaken by their adversaries, and indeed by all except their own followers, to have been persons crazed, or out of their wits; having generally proceeded, in the common course of their words and actions, by a method very different from the vulgar dictates of unrefined reason; agreeing for the most part in their several models, with their present undoubted successors in the academy of modern Bedlam[4] (whose merits and principles I shall farther examine in due place). Of this kind were *Epicurus, Diogenes, Apollonius, Lucretius, Paracelsus, Descartes*,[5] and others, who, if they were now in the world, tied fast, and separate from their followers, would, in this our undistinguishing age, incur manifest danger of phlebotomy,[6] and whips, and chains, and dark chambers, and straw. For what man, in the natural state or course of thinking, did ever conceive it in his power to reduce the notions of all mankind exactly to the same length, and breadth, and height of his own? Yet this is the first humble and civil design of all innovators in the empire of reason. Epicurus modestly hoped, that one time or other a certain fortuitous concourse of all men's opinions, after perpetual justlings, the sharp with the smooth, the light and the heavy, the round and the square, would by certain *clinamina*[7] unite in the notions of atoms and void, as these did in the originals of all things. Cartesius reckoned to see, before he died, the sentiments of all philosophers, like so many lesser stars in his romantic system, wrapped and drawn within his own vortex.[8] Now, I would gladly be informed, how it is possible to account for such imaginations as these in particular men without recourse to my phenomenon of

2. Paracelsus, who was so famous for chemistry, tried an experiment upon human excrement, to make a perfume of it, which when he had brought to perfection, he called *zibeta occidentalis,* or western-civet, the back parts of man . . . being the west [Swift's note].
3. Ulcer shaped like a pipe.
4. Bethlehem hospital, London's lunatic asylum.
5. Each of these famous speculative thinkers was known as a materialist, hence suspected by Swift

of encouraging atheism.
6. Medical bloodletting.
7. Swerves. The Greek philosopher Epicurus held that the universe was formed by atoms swerving together. Swift implies that a similar miracle would be required for people to join in agreement with Epicurus.
8. The physics of René Descartes (1596–1650) is based on a theory of vortices. Swift considered the theory pure romance.

vapors, ascending from the lower faculties to overshadow the brain, and there distilling into conceptions for which the narrowness of our mother-tongue has not yet assigned any other name beside that of madness or frenzy. Let us therefore now conjecture how it comes to pass, that none of these great prescribers do ever fail providing themselves and their notions with a number of implicit disciples. And, I think, the reason is easy to be assigned: for there is a peculiar string in the harmony of human understanding, which in several individuals is exactly of the same tuning. This, if you can dexterously screw up to its right key, and then strike gently upon it, whenever you have the good fortune to light among those of the same pitch, they will, by a secret necessary sympathy, strike exactly at the same time. And in this one circumstance lies all the skill or luck of the matter; for if you chance to jar the string among those who are either above or below your own height, instead of subscribing to your doctrine, they will tie you fast, call you mad, and feed you with bread and water. It is therefore a point of the nicest conduct to distinguish and adapt this noble talent, with respect to the differences of persons and of times. Cicero understood this very well, when writing to a friend in England, with a caution, among other matters, to beware of being cheated by our hackney-coachmen (who, it seems, in those days were as arrant rascals as they are now), has these remarkable words: *Est quod gaudeas te in ista loca venisse, ubi aliquid sapere viderere.*[9] For, to speak a bold truth, it is a fatal miscarriage so ill to order affairs, as to pass for a fool in one company, when in another you might be treated as a philosopher. Which I desire some certain gentlemen of my acquaintance to lay up in their hearts, as a very seasonable *innuendo*.

This, indeed, was the fatal mistake of that worthy gentleman, my most ingenious friend, Mr. W—tt—n,[1] a person, in appearance, ordained for great designs, as well as performances; whether you will consider his notions or his looks. Surely no man ever advanced into the public with fitter qualifications of body and mind, for the propagation of a new religion. Oh, had those happy talents, misapplied to vain philosophy, been turned into their proper channels of dreams and visions, where distortion of mind and countenance are of such sovereign use, the base detracting world would not then have dared to report that something is amiss, that his brain has undergone an unlucky shake; which even his brother modernists themselves, like ungrates, do whisper so loud, that it reaches up to the very garret I am now writing in.

Lastly, whosoever pleases to look into the fountains of enthusiasm,[2] from whence, in all ages, have eternally proceeded such fattening streams, will find the springhead to have been as troubled and muddy as the current. Of such great emolument is a tincture of this vapor, which the world calls madness, that without its help, the world would not only be deprived of those two great blessings, conquests and systems, but even all mankind would unhappily be reduced to the same belief in things invisible. Now, the former *postulatum* being held, that it is of no import from what originals this vapor

---

9. It is ground for rejoicing that you have come to such places, where anyone can seem wise (Latin; Cicero's *Familiar Epistles* 7.10).
1. William Wotton (who had championed modern authors against Swift's patron, Sir William Temple, a spokesman for the ancients) is ridiculed

in Swift's *The Battle of the Books,* published in the same volume as *A Tale of a Tub* (1704).
2. For much of the 18th century the word *enthusiasm* (literally, "possessed by a god") signified a deluded belief in personal revelation.

proceeds, but either in what angles it strikes and spreads over the understanding, or upon what species of brain it ascends; it will be a very delicate point to cut the feather, and divide the several reasons to a nice and curious reader, how this numerical difference in the brain can produce effects of so vast a difference from the same vapor, as to be the sole point of individuation between Alexander the Great, Jack of Leyden[3] and Monsieur Descartes. The present argument is the most abstracted that ever I engaged in; it strains my faculties to their highest stretch; and I desire the reader to attend with utmost perpensity;[4] for I now proceed to unravel this knotty point.

There is in mankind a certain[5] • • • • • • •
• • • • • • • • •
Hic multa • • • • • •
desiderantur. • • • • • •
• • • • • • And this I take to be a clear solution of the matter.

Having therefore so narrowly passed through this intricate difficulty, the reader will, I am sure, agree with me in the conclusion, that if the moderns mean by madness, only a disturbance or transposition of the brain, by force of certain vapors issuing up from the lower faculties, then has this madness been the parent of all those mighty revolutions that have happened in empire, in philosophy, and in religion. For the brain, in its natural position and state of serenity, disposeth its owner to pass his life in the common forms, without any thought of subduing multitudes to his own power, his reasons, or his visions; and the more he shapes his understanding by the pattern of human learning, the less he is inclined to form parties after his particular notions, because that instructs him in his private infirmities, as well as in the stubborn ignorance of the people. But when a man's fancy gets astride on his reason, when imagination is at cuffs[6] with the senses, and common understanding, as well as common sense, is kicked out of doors, the first proselyte he makes is himself; and when that is once compassed, the difficulty is not so great in bringing over others; a strong delusion always operating from without as vigorously as from within. For cant[7] and vision are to the ear and the eye, the same that tickling is to the touch. Those entertainments and pleasures we most value in life, are such as dupe and play the wag with the senses. For, if we take an examination of what is generally understood by happiness, as it has respect either to the understanding or the senses, we shall find all its properties and adjuncts will herd under this short definition, that it is a perpetual possession of being well deceived. And first, with relation to the mind or understanding, 'tis manifest what mighty advantages fiction has over truth; and the reason is just at our elbow, because imagination can build nobler scenes, and produce more wonderful revolutions, than fortune or nature will be at expense to furnish. Nor is

---

3. John of Leyden, a tailor and prophet, briefly established a revolutionary Anabaptist community, the "New Jerusalem," in the city of Münster early in the 16th century.
4. Consideration.
5. "Here is another defect in the manuscript, but I think the author did wisely, and that the matter which thus strained his faculties, was not worth a solution; and it were well if all metaphysical cobweb problems were no otherwise answered" [Swift's note]. The Latin phrase (Much is missing here) indicates a gap in the text Swift pretends to be "editing."
6. In conflict.
7. "Sudden exclamations, whining, unusual tones, and in fine all praying and preaching like the unlearned of the Presbyterians" (*Spectator* 147).

mankind so much to blame in his choice thus determining him, if we consider that the debate merely lies between things past and things conceived; and so the question is only this: whether things that have place in the imagination, may not as properly be said to exist, as those that are seated in the memory; which may be justly held in the affirmative, and very much to the advantage of the former, since this is acknowledged to be the womb of things, and the other allowed to be no more than the grave. Again, if we take this definition of happiness, and examine it with reference to the senses, it will be acknowledged wonderfully adapt. How fading and insipid do all objects accost us, that are not conveyed in the vehicle of delusion! How shrunk is everything, as it appears in the glass of nature! So that if it were not for the assistance of artificial mediums, false lights, refracted angles, varnish, and tinsel, there would be a mighty level in the felicity and enjoyments of mortal men. If this were seriously considered by the world, as I have a certain reason to suspect it hardly will, men would no longer reckon among their high points of wisdom, the art of exposing weak sides, and publishing infirmities; an employment, in my opinion, neither better nor worse than that of unmasking, which, I think, has never been allowed[8] fair usage, either in the world, or the playhouse.

In the proportion that credulity is a more peaceful possession of the mind than curosity, so far preferable is that wisdom, which converses about the surface, to that pretended philosophy which enters into the depth of things, and then comes gravely back with informations and discoveries, that in the inside they are good for nothing. The two senses, to which all objects first address themselves, are the sight and the touch; these never examine farther than the color, the shape, the size, and whatever other qualities dwell, or are drawn by art upon the outward of bodies; and then comes reason officiously with tools for cutting, and opening, and mangling, and piercing, offering to demonstrate, that they are not of the same consistence quite through. Now I take all this to be the last degree of perverting nature; one of whose eternal laws it is, to put her best furniture forward. And therefore, in order to save the charges of all such expensive anatomy for the time to come, I do here think fit to inform the reader, that in such conclusions as these, reason is certainly in the right, and that in most corporeal beings, which have fallen under my cognizance, the outside has been infinitely preferable to the in; whereof I have been farther convinced from some late experiments. Last week I saw a woman flayed, and you will hardly believe how much it altered her person for the worse. Yesterday I ordered the carcass of a beau to be stripped in my presence; when we were all amazed to find so many unsuspected faults under one suit of clothes. Then I laid open his brain, his heart, and his spleen; but I plainly perceived at every operation, that the farther we proceeded, we found the defects increase upon us in number and bulk; from all which, I justly formed this conclusion to myself: that whatever philosopher or projector[9] can find out an art to solder and patch up the flaws and imperfections of nature, will deserve much better of mankind, and teach us a more useful science, than that so much in present esteem, of widening and exposing them (like him who held anatomy to be the ultimate end of physic).[1]

---

8. Admitted to be.
9. Someone given to speculative experiments.

1. Medical practice.

And he, whose fortunes and dispositions have placed him in a convenient station to enjoy the fruits of this noble art; he that can with Epicurus content his ideas with the films and images that fly off upon his senses from the superficies[2] of things; such a man, truly wise, creams off nature, leaving the sour and the dregs for philosophy and reason to lap up. This is the sublime and refined point of felicity, called the possession of being well deceived; the serene peaceful state of being a fool among knaves.

But to return to madness. It is certain, that according to the system I have above deduced, every species thereof proceeds from a redundancy of vapors; therefore, as some kinds of frenzy give double strength to the sinews, so there are of other species, which add vigor, and life, and spirit to the brain. Now, it usually happens, that these active spirits, getting possession of the brain, resemble those that haunt other waste and empty dwellings, which for want of business, either vanish, and carry away a piece of the house, or else stay at home and fling it all out of the windows. By which are mystically displayed the two principal branches of madness, and which some philosophers, not considering so well as I, have mistaken to be different in their causes, over-hastily assigning the first to deficiency, and the other to redundance.

I think it therefore manifest, from what I have here advanced, that the main point of skill and address is to furnish employment for this redundancy of vapor, and prudently to adjust the season of it; by which means it may certainly become of cardinal and catholic emolument, in a commonwealth. Thus one man, choosing a proper juncture, leaps into a gulf, from thence proceeds a hero, and is called the saver of his country; another achieves the same enterprise, but unluckily timing it, has left the brand of madness fixed as a reproach upon his memory; upon so nice a distinction, are we taught to repeat the name of Curtius with reverence and love, that of Empedocles[3] with hatred and contempt. Thus also it is usually conceived, that the elder Brutus only personated the fool and madman for the good of the public; but this was nothing else than a redundancy of the same vapor long misapplied, called by the Latins, *ingenium par negotiis;*[4] or (to translate it as nearly as I can) a sort of frenzy, never in its right element, till you take it up in business of the state.

Upon all which, and many other reasons of equal weight, though not equally curious, I do here gladly embrace an opportunity I have long sought for, of recommending it as a very noble undertaking to Sir Edward Seymour, Sir Christopher Musgrave, Sir John Bowls, John How, Esq.,[5] and other patriots concerned, that they would move for leave to bring in a bill for appointing commissioners to inspect into Bedlam, and the parts adjacent; who shall be empowered to send for persons, papers, and records, to examine into the merits and qualifications of every student and professor, to observe with utmost exactness their several dispositions and behavior, by which means, duly distinguishing and adapting their talents, they might produce

2. Surfaces. Epicurus considered the senses, directly affected by objects, more trustworthy than reason.
3. Committed suicide by leaping into the crater of Mount Etna. The Roman hero Marcus Curtius appeased the gods by hurling himself into an omi-nous crack in the earth of the Forum.
4. A talent for business (Latin). Lucius Junius Brutus, like Hamlet, pretended madness to deceive his murderous uncle, Tarquin the Proud.
5. Members of Parliament.

admirable instruments for the several offices in a state, . . . ,[6] civil, and military, proceeding in such methods as I shall here humbly propose. And I hope the gentle reader will give some allowance to my great solicitudes in this important affair, upon account of the high esteem I have borne that honorable society, whereof I had some time the happiness to be an unworthy member.

Is any student tearing his straw in piece-meal, swearing and blaspheming, biting his grate, foaming at the mouth, and emptying his piss-pot in the spectators' faces? Let the right worshipful the commissioners of inspection give him a regiment of dragoons, and send him into Flanders among the rest. Is another eternally talking, sputtering, gaping, bawling in a sound without period or article? What wonderful talents are here mislaid! Let him be furnished immediately with a green bag and papers, and threepence in his pocket,[7] and away with him to Westminster Hall. You will find a third gravely taking the dimensions of his kennel, a person of foresight and insight, though kept quite in the dark; forwhy, like Moses, *ecce cornuta erat ejus facies*.[8] He walks duly in one pace, entreats your penny with due gravity and ceremony, talks much of hard times, and taxes, and the whore of Babylon, bars up the wooden window of his cell constantly at eight o'clock, dreams of fire, and shoplifters, and court-customers, and privileged places. Now, what a figure would all these acquirements amount to, if the owner were sent into the city[9] among his brethren! Behold a fourth, in much and deep conversation with himself, biting his thumbs at proper junctures, his countenance checkered with business and design, sometimes walking very fast, with his eyes nailed to a paper that he holds in his hands; a great saver of time, somewhat thick of hearing, very short of sight, but more of memory; a man ever in haste, a great hatcher and breeder of business, and excellent at the famous art of whispering nothing; a huge idolator of monosyllables and procrastination, so ready to give his word to everybody, that he never keeps it; one that has forgot the common meaning of words, but an admirable retainer of the sound; extremely subject to the looseness,[1] for his occasions are perpetually calling him away. If you approach his grate in his familiar intervals, "Sir," says he, "give me a penny, and I'll sing you a song; but give me the penny first." (Hence comes the common saying, and commoner practice, of parting with money for a song.) What a complete system of court skill is here described in every branch of it, and all utterly lost with wrong application! Accost the hole of another kennel, first stopping your nose, you will behold a surly, gloomy, nasty, slovenly mortal, raking in his own dung, and dabbling in his urine. The best part of his diet is the reversion of his own ordure, which expiring into steams, whirls perpetually about, and at last re-infunds.[2] His complexion is of a dirty yellow, with a thin scattered beard, exactly agreeable to that of his diet upon its first declination, like other insects, who having their birth and education in an excre-

---

6. Swift omits the third office, ecclesiastical. "Instruments": useful persons.
7. "A lawyer's coach-hire" [Swift's note] from the Inns of Court to Westminster. Most lawyers carried green bags.
8. "Cornutus is either horned or shining, and by this term, Moses is described in the vulgar Latin of the Bible" [Swift's note]. Swift puns on

the Latin phrase (behold his face was shining) by suggesting someone kept in the dark through being "horned," i.e., a cuckold. "Forwhy": because.
9. The commercial center of London.
1. Diarrhea.
2. Pours in again.

ment, from thence borrow their color and their smell. The student of this apartment is very sparing of his words, but somewhat over-liberal of his breath; he holds his hand out ready to receive your penny, and immediately upon receipt withdraws to his former occupations. Now, is it not amazing to think, the society of Warwick-lane[3] should have no more concern for the recovery of so useful a member, who, if one may judge from these appearances, would become the greatest ornament to that illustrious body? Another student struts up fiercely to your teeth, puffing with his lips, half squeezing out his eyes, and very graciously holds you out his hand to kiss. The keeper desires you not to be afraid of this professor, for he will do you no hurt; to him alone is allowed the liberty of the antechamber, and the orator of the place gives you to understand, that this solemn person is a tailor run mad with pride. This considerable student is adorned with many other qualities, upon which at present I shall not farther enlarge.————*Hark in your ear*[4]————I am strangely mistaken, if all his address, his motions, and his airs, would not then be very natural, and in their proper element.

I shall not descend so minutely, as to insist upon the vast number of beaux, fiddlers, poets, and politicians, that the world might recover by such a reformation; but what is more material, besides the clear gain redounding to the commonwealth, by so large an acquisition of persons to employ, whose talents and acquirements, if I may be so bold as to affirm it, are now buried, or at least misapplied; it would be a mighty advantage accruing to the public from this inquiry, that all these would very much excel, and arrive at great perfection in their several kinds; which, I think, is manifest from what I have already shown, and shall enforce by this one plain instance: that even I myself, the author of these momentous truths, am a person, whose imaginations are hard-mouthed,[5] and exceedingly disposed to run away with his reason, which I have observed from long experience to be a very light rider, and easily shook off; upon which account, my friends will never trust me alone, without a solemn promise to vent my speculations in this, or the like manner, for the universal benefit of human kind; which perhaps the gentle, courteous, and candid reader, brimful of that modern charity and tenderness usually annexed to his office, will be very hardly persuaded to believe.

1704

Gulliver's Travels

Gulliver's Travels is Swift's most enduring satire. Although full of allusions to recent and current events, it still rings true today, for its objects are human failings and the defective political, economic, and social institutions that they call into being. Swift adopts an ancient satirical device: the imaginary voyage. Lemuel Gulliver, the narrator, is a ship's surgeon, a moderately well educated man, kindly, resourceful, cheerful, inquiring, patriotic, truthful, and rather unimaginative—in short, a reasonably decent example of humanity, with whom a reader can readily identify. He undertakes four voyages, all of which end disastrously among "several remote nations of the world." In the first, Gulliver is shipwrecked in the empire of

---

3. Royal College of Physicians.
4. I cannot conjecture what the author means here, or how this chasm could be filled, though it

is capable of more than one interpretation [Swift's note].
5. (Of a horse) apt to reject control by the bit.

Lilliput, where he finds himself a giant among a diminutive people, charmed by their miniature city and amused by their toylike prettiness. But in the end they prove to be treacherous, malicious, ambitious, vengeful, and cruel. As we read we grow disenchanted with the inhabitants of this fanciful kingdom, and then gradually we begin to recognize our likeness to them, especially in the disproportion between our natural pettiness and our boundless and destructive passions. In the second voyage, Gulliver is abandoned by his shipmates in Brobdingnag, a land of giants, creatures ten times as large as Europeans. Though he fears that such monsters must be brutes, the reverse proves to be the case. Brobdingnag is something of a utopia, governed by a humane and enlightened prince who is the embodiment of moral and political wisdom. In the long interview in which Gulliver pridefully enlarges on the glories of England and its political institutions, the king reduces him to resentful silence by asking questions that reveal the difference between what England is and what it ought to be. In Brobdingnag, Gulliver finds himself a Lilliputian, his pride humbled by his helpless state and his human vanity diminished by the realization that his body must have seemed as disgusting to the Lilliputians as do the bodies of the Brobdingnagians to him.

In the third voyage, to Laputa, Swift is chiefly concerned with attacking extremes of theoretical and speculative reasoning, whether in science, politics, or economics. Much of this voyage is an allegory of political life under the administration of the Whig minister, Sir Robert Walpole. The final voyage sets Gulliver between a race of horses, Houyhnhnms (prounced *Hwín-ims*), who live entirely by reason except for a few well-controlled and muted social affections, and their slaves, the Yahoos, whose bodies are obscene caricatures of the human body and who have no glimmer of reason but are mere creatures of appetite and passion.

When *Gulliver's Travels* first appeared, everyone read it—children for the story and politicians for the satire of current affairs—and ever since it has retained a hold on readers of every kind. Almost unique in world literature, it is simple enough for children, complex enough to carry adults beyond their depth. Swift's art works on many levels. First of all, there is the sheer playfulness of the narrative. Through Gulliver's eyes, we gaze on marvel after marvel: a tiny girl who threads an invisible needle with invisible silk or a white mare who threads a needle between pastern and hoof. The travels, like a fairy story, transport us to imaginary worlds that function with a perfect, fantastic logic different from our own; Swift exercises our sense of vision. But beyond that, he exercises our perceptions of meaning. In *Gulliver's Travels,* things are seldom what they seem; irony, probing or corrosive, underlies almost every word. In the last chapter, Gulliver insists that the example of the Houyhnhnms has made him incapable of telling a lie—but the oath he swears is quoted from Sinon, whose lies to the Trojans persuaded them to accept the Trojan *horse*. Swift trains us to read alertly, to look beneath the surface. Yet on its deepest level, the book does not offer final meanings, but a question: What is a human being? Voyaging through imaginary worlds, we try to find ourselves. Are we prideful insects or lords of creation? brutes or reasonable beings? In the last voyage, Swift pushes such questions, and Gulliver himself, almost beyond endurance; hating his own humanity, Gulliver forgets who he is. For the reader, however, the outcome cannot be so clear. Swift does not set out to satisfy our minds but to vex and unsettle them. And he leaves us at the moment when the mixed face of humanity—the pettiness of the Lilliputians, the savagery of the Yahoos, the innocence of Gulliver himself—begins to look strangely familiar, like our own faces in a mirror.

Swift's full title for this work was *Travels into Several Remote Nations of the World. In Four Parts. By Lemuel Gulliver, First a Surgeon, and then a Captain of several Ships.* In the first edition (1726), either the bookseller or Swift's friends Charles Ford, Pope, and others, who were concerned in getting the book anonymously into print, altered and omitted so much of the original manuscript (because of its dangerous political implications) that Swift was seriously annoyed. When, in 1735, the Dublin bookseller George Faulkner brought out an edition of Swift's works, the dean seems to have taken pains, surreptitiously, to see that a more authentic version of the work was published. This text is the basis of modern editions.

From Gulliver's Travels

A Letter from Captain Gulliver to His Cousin Sympson[1]

I hope you will be ready to own publicly, whenever you shall be called to it, that by your great and frequent urgency you prevailed on me to publish a very loose and uncorrect account of my travels; with direction to hire some young gentlemen of either University to put them in order, and correct the style, as my Cousin Dampier[2] did by my advice, in his book called *A Voyage round the World*. But I do not remember I gave you power to consent that anything should be omitted, and much less that anything should be inserted: therefore, as to the latter, I do here renounce everything of that kind; particularly a paragraph about her Majesty the late Queen Anne, of most pious and glorious memory; although I did reverence and esteem her more than any of human species. But you, or your interpolator, ought to have considered that as it was not my inclination, so was it not decent to praise any animal of our composition before my master Houyhnhnm; and besides, the fact was altogether false; for to my knowledge, being in England during some part of her Majesty's reign, she did govern by a chief Minister; nay, even by two successively; the first whereof was the Lord of Godolphin, and the second the Lord of Oxford; so that you have made me *say the thing that was not*. Likewise, in the account of the Academy of Projectors, and several passages of my discourse to my master Houyhnhnm, you have either omitted some material circumstances, or minced or changed them in such a manner, that I do hardly know mine own work. When I formerly hinted to you something of this in a letter, you were pleased to answer that you were afraid of giving offense; that people in power were very watchful over the press; and apt not only to interpret, but to punish everything which looked like an *innuendo* (as I think you called it). But pray, how could that which I spoke so many years ago, and at above five thousand leagues distance, in another reign, be applied to any of the Yahoos, who now are said to govern the herd; especially, at a time when I little thought on or feared the unhappiness of living under them. Have not I the most reason to complain, when I see these very Yahoos carried by Houyhnhnms in a vehicle, as if these were brutes, and those the rational creatures? And, indeed, to avoid so monstrous and detestable a sight was one principal motive of my retirement hither.[3]

Thus much I thought proper to tell you in relation to yourself, and to the trust I reposed in you.

---

1. In this letter, first published in 1735, Swift complains, among other matters, of the alterations in his original text made by the publisher, Benjamin Motte, in the interest of what he considered political discretion.

2. William Dampier (1652–1715), the explorer, whose account of his circumnavigation of the globe Swift had read.
3. To Nottinghamshire.

I do in the next place complain of my own great want of judgment, in being prevailed upon by the intreaties and false reasonings of you and some others, very much against mine own opinion, to suffer my travels to be published. Pray bring to your mind how often I desired you to consider, when you insisted on the motive of public good, that the Yahoos were a species of animals utterly incapable of amendment by precepts or examples; and so it hath proved; for instead of seeing a full stop put to all abuses and corruptions, at least in this little island, as I had reason to expect, behold, after above six months warning, I cannot learn that my book hath produced one single effect according to mine intentions; I desired you would let me know by a letter, when party and faction were extinguished; judges learned and upright; pleaders honest and modest, with some tincture of common sense; and Smithfield blazing with pyramids of law books; the young nobility's education entirely changed; the physicians banished; the female Yahoos abounding in virtue, honor, truth, and good sense; courts and levees of great ministers thoroughly weeded and swept; wit, merit, and learning rewarded; all disgracers of the press in prose and verse, condemned to eat nothing but their own cotton,[4] and quench their thirst with their own ink. These, and a thousand other reformations, I firmly counted upon by your encouragement; as indeed they were plainly deducible from the precepts delivered in my book. And, it must be owned that seven months were a sufficient time to correct every vice and folly to which Yahoos are subject; if their natures had been capable of the least disposition to virtue or wisdom; yet so far have you been from answering mine expectation in any of your letters, that on the contrary, you are loading our carrier every week with libels, and keys, and reflections, and memoirs, and second parts; wherein I see myself accused of reflecting upon great statesfolk; of degrading human nature (for so they have still the confidence to style it) and of abusing the female sex. I find likewise, that the writers of those bundles are not agreed among themselves; for some of them will not allow me to be author of mine own travels; and others make me author of books to which I am wholly a stranger.

I find likewise that your printer hath been so careless as to confound the times, and mistake the dates of my several voyages and returns; neither assigning the true year, or the true month, or day of the month; and I hear the original manuscript is all destroyed, since the publication of my book. Neither have I any copy left; however, I have sent you some corrections, which you may insert, if ever there should be a second edition; and yet I cannot stand to them, but shall leave that matter to my judicious and candid readers, to adjust it as they please.

I hear some of our sea Yahoos find fault with my sea language, as not proper in many parts, nor now in use. I cannot help it. In my first voyages, while I was young, I was instructed by the oldest mariners, and learned to speak as they did. But I have since found that the sea Yahoos are apt, like the land ones, to become new fangled in their words; which the latter change every year; insomuch, as I remember upon each return to mine own country, their old dialect was so altered, that I could hardly understand the new. And I observe, when any Yahoo comes from London out of curiosity to visit me at

---

4. Presumably their paper. "Pleaders": lawyers. Smithfield was a part of London containing many bookshops. "Levees": morning receptions.

mine own house, we neither of us are able to deliver our conceptions in a manner intelligible to the other.[5]

If the censure of Yahoos could any way affect me, I should have great reason to complain that some of them are so bold as to think my book of travels a mere fiction out of mine own brain; and have gone so far as to drop hints that the Houyhnhnms, and Yahoos have no more existence than the inhabitants of Utopia.

Indeed I must confess that as to the people of Lilliput, Brobdingrag (for so the word should have been spelled, and not erroneously Brobdingnag) and Laputa, I have never yet heard of any Yahoo so presumptuous as to dispute their being, or the facts I have related concerning them; because the truth immediately strikes every reader with conviction. And, is there less probability in my account of the Houyhnhnms or Yahoos, when it is manifest as to the latter, there are so many thousands even in this city, who only differ from their brother brutes in Houyhnhnmland, because they use a sort of a jabber, and do not go naked. I wrote for their amendment, and not their approbation. The united praise of the whole race would be of less consequence to me, than the neighing of those two degenerate Houyhnhnms I keep in my stable; because, from these, degenerate as they are, I still improve in some virtues, without any mixture of vice.

Do these miserable animals presume to think that I am so far degenerated as to defend my veracity; Yahoo as I am, it is well known through all Houyhnhnmland, that by the instructions and example of my illustrious master, I was able in the compass of two years (although I confess with the utmost difficulty) to remove that infernal habit of lying, shuffling, deceiving, and equivocating, so deeply rooted in the very souls of all my species; especially the Europeans.

I have other complaints to make upon this vexatious occasion; but I forbear troubling myself or you any further. I must freely confess that since my last return, some corruptions of my Yahoo nature have revived in me by conversing with a few of your species, and particularly those of mine own family, by an unavoidable necessity; else I should never have attempted so absurd a project as that of reforming the Yahoo race in this kingdom; but I have now done with all such visionary schemes for ever.

1727?   1735

The Publisher to the Reader

The author of these travels, Mr. Lemuel Gulliver, is my ancient and intimate friend; there is likewise some relation between us by the mother's side. About three years ago Mr. Gulliver, growing weary of the concourse of curious people coming to him at his house in Redriff,[6] made a small purchase of land, with a convenient house, near Newark, in Nottinghamshire, his native country; where he now lives retired, yet in good esteem among his neighbors.

5. Swift was the inveterate enemy of slang.
6. Rotherhithe, a district in southern London, below Tower Bridge, then frequented by sailors.

Although Mr. Gulliver were born in Nottinghamshire, where his father dwelt, yet I have heard him say his family came from Oxfordshire; to confirm which, I have observed in the churchyard at Banbury, in that county, several tombs and monuments of the Gullivers.

Before he quitted Redriff, he left the custody of the following papers in my hands, with the liberty to dispose of them as I should think fit. I have carefully perused them three times; the style is very plain and simple; and the only fault I find is that the author, after the manner of travelers, is a little too circumstantial. There is an air of truth apparent through the whole; and indeed the author was so distinguished for his veracity, that it became a sort of proverb among his neighbors at Redriff, when anyone affirmed a thing, to say, it was as true as if Mr. Gulliver had spoke it.

By the advice of several worthy persons, to whom, with the author's permission, I communicated these papers, I now venture to send them into the world; hoping they may be, at least for some time, a better entertainment to our young noblemen, than the common scribbles of politics and party.

This volume would have been at least twice as large, if I had not made bold to strike out innumerable passages relating to the winds and tides, as well as to the variations and bearings in the several voyages; together with the minute descriptions of the management of the ship in storms, in the style of sailors; likewise the account of the longitudes and latitudes, wherein I have reason to apprehend that Mr. Gulliver may be a little dissatisfied; but I was resolved to fit the work as much as possible to the general capacity of readers. However, if my own ignorance in sea affairs shall have led me to commit some mistakes, I alone am answerable for them; and if any traveler hath a curiosity to see the whole work at large, as it came from the hand of the author, I will be ready to gratify him.

As for any further particulars relating to the author, the reader will receive satisfaction from the first pages of the book.

RICHARD SYMPSON

Part 1. A Voyage to Lilliput

CHAPTER 1. *The author gives some account of himself and family; his first inducements to travel. He is shipwrecked, and swims for his life; gets safe on shore in the country of Lilliput; is made a prisoner, and carried up the country.*

My father had a small estate in Nottinghamshire; I was the third of five sons. He sent me to Emanuel College in Cambridge, at fourteen years old, where I resided three years, and applied myself close to my studies: but the charge of maintaining me (although I had a very scanty allowance) being too great for a narrow fortune, I was bound apprentice to Mr. James Bates, an eminent surgeon in London, with whom I continued four years; and my father now and then sending me small sums of money, I laid them out in learning navigation, and other parts of the mathematics, useful to those who intend to travel, as I always believed it would be some time or other my fortune to do. When I left Mr. Bates, I went down to my father; where, by the assistance of him and my uncle John, and some other relations, I got forty pounds, and a promise of thirty pounds a year to maintain me at Leyden:[7] there I studied physic two years and seven months, knowing it would be useful in long voyages.

Soon after my return from Leyden, I was recommended by my good master Mr. Bates, to be surgeon to the *Swallow*, Captain Abraham Pannell commander; with whom I continued three years and a half, making a voyage or two into the Levant[8] and some other parts. When I came back, I resolved to settle in London, to which Mr. Bates, my master, encouraged me; and by him I was recommended to several patients. I took part of a small house in the Old Jury; and being advised to alter my condition, I married Mrs.[9] Mary Burton, second daughter to Mr. Edmond Burton, hosier, in Newgate Street, with whom I received four hundred pounds for a portion.

But, my good master Bates dying in two years after, and I having few friends, my business began to fail; for my conscience would not suffer me to imitate the bad practice of too many among my brethren. Having therefore consulted with my wife, and some of my acquaintance, I determined to go again to sea. I was surgeon successively in two ships, and made several voyages, for six years, to the East and West Indies; by which I got some addition to my fortune. My hours of leisure I spent in reading the best authors, ancient and modern, being always provided with a good number of books; and when I was ashore, in observing the manners and dispositions of the people, as well as learning their language; wherein I had a great facility by the strength of my memory.

The last of these voyages not proving very fortunate, I grew weary of the sea, and intended to stay at home with my wife and family. I removed from the Old Jury to Fetter Lane, and from thence to Wapping, hoping to get business among the sailors; but it would not turn to account. After three years' expectation that things would mend, I accepted an advantageous offer from Captain William Prichard, master of the *Antelope*, who was making a voyage to the South Sea. We set sail from Bristol, May 4th, 1699, and our voyage at first was very prosperous.

It would not be proper, for some reasons, to trouble the reader with the particulars of our adventures in those seas: let it suffice to inform him, that in our passage from thence to the East Indies we were driven by a violent storm to the northwest of Van Diemen's Land.[1] By an observation, we found ourselves in the latitude of 30 degrees 2 minutes south. Twelve of our crew were dead by immoderate labor, and ill food, the rest were in a very weak condition. On the fifth of November, which was the beginning of summer in those parts, the weather being very hazy, the seamen spied a rock, within half a cable's length[2] of the ship; but the wind was so strong, that we were driven directly upon it, and immediately split. Six of the crew, of whom I was one, having let down the boat into the sea, made a shift to get clear of the ship, and the rock. We rowed by my computation about three leagues, till we were able to work no longer, being already spent with labor while we were in

7. The University of Leyden, in Holland, was a center for the study of medicine ("physic").
8. The eastern Mediterranean.
9. The title (pronounced *mistress*) designated any woman, married or unmarried. "Old Jury": a
street (once "Old Jewry") in the City of London.
1. Tasmania.
2. A cable is about six hundred feet (one hundred fathoms).

the ship. We therefore trusted ourselves to the mercy of the waves; and in about half an hour the boat was overset by a sudden flurry from the north. What became of my companions in the boat, as well as of those who escaped on the rock, or were left in the vessel, I cannot tell; but conclude they were all lost. For my own part, I swam as fortune directed me, and was pushed forward by wind and tide. I often let my legs drop, and could feel no bottom; but when I was almost gone, and able to struggle no longer, I found myself within my depth; and by this time the storm was much abated. The declivity was so small, that I walked near a mile before I got to the shore, which I conjectured was about eight o'clock in the evening. I then advanced forward near half a mile, but could not discover any sign of houses or inhabitants; at least I was in so weak a condition, that I did not observe them. I was extremely tired, and with that, and the heat of the weather, and about half a pint of brandy that I drank as I left the ship, I found myself much inclined to sleep. I lay down on the grass, which was very short and soft, where I slept sounder than ever I remember to have done in my life, and as I reckoned, above nine hours; for when I awaked, it was just daylight. I attempted to rise, but was not able to stir: for as I happened to lie on my back, I found my arms and legs were strongly fastened on each side to the ground; and my hair, which was long and thick, tied down in the same manner. I likewise felt several slender ligatures across my body, from my armpits to my thighs. I could only look upwards; the sun began to grow hot, and the light offended my eyes. I heard a confused noise about me, but in the posture I lay, could see nothing except the sky. In a little time I felt something alive moving on my left leg, which advancing gently forward over my breast, came almost up to my chin; when bending my eyes downwards as much as I could, I perceived it to be a human creature not six inches high,[3] with a bow and arrow in his hands, and a quiver at his back. In the meantime, I felt at least forty more of the same kind (as I conjectured) following the first. I was in the utmost astonishment, and roared so loud, that they all ran back in a fright; and some of them, as I was afterwards told, were hurt with the falls they got by leaping from my sides upon the ground. However, they soon returned; and one of them, who ventured so far as to get a full sight of my face, lifting up his hands and eyes by way of admiration,[4] cried out in a shrill, but distinct voice, *Hekinah Degul:* the others repeated the same words several times, but I then knew not what they meant. I lay all this while, as the reader may believe, in great uneasiness; at length, struggling to get loose, I had the fortune to break the strings, and wrench out the pegs that fastened my left arm to the ground; for, by lifting it up to my face, I discovered the methods they had taken to bind me; and, at the same time, with a violent pull, which gave me excessive pain, I a little loosened the strings that tied down my hair on the left side; so that I was just able to turn my head about two inches. But the creatures ran off a second time, before I could seize them; whereupon there was a great shout in a very shrill accent; and after it ceased, I heard one of them cry aloud, *Tolgo phonac;* when in an instant I felt above an hundred arrows discharged on my left hand, which pricked me like so many needles; and besides they shot another flight into the air, as we do bombs in

3. Lilliput is scaled, fairly consistently, at one-twelfth of Gulliver's world.
4. Wonderment.

Europe, whereof many, I suppose, fell on my body (though I felt them not) and some on my face, which I immediately covered with my left hand. When this shower of arrows was over, I fell a groaning with grief and pain; and then striving again to get loose, they discharged another volley larger than the first, and some of them attempted with spears to stick me in the sides; but, by good luck, I had on me a buff jerkin,[5] which they could not pierce. I thought it the most prudent method to lie still; and my design was to continue so till night, when, my left hand being already loose, I could easily free myself: and as for the inhabitants, I had reason to believe I might be a match for the greatest armies they could bring against me, if they were all of the same size with him that I saw. But fortune disposed otherwise of me. When the people observed I was quiet, they discharged no more arrows: but by the noise increasing, I knew their numbers were greater; and about four yards from me, over-against my right ear, I heard a knocking for above an hour, like people at work; when turning my head that way, as well as the pegs and strings would permit me, I saw a stage erected about a foot and a half from the ground, capable of holding four of the inhabitants, with two or three ladders to mount it: from whence one of them, who seemed to be a person of quality, made me a long speech, whereof I understood not one syllable. But I should have mentioned, that before the principal person began his oration, he cried out three times, *Langro Dehul san:* (these words and the former were afterwards repeated and explained to me). Whereupon immediately about fifty of the inhabitants came, and cut the strings that fastened the left side of my head, which gave me the liberty of turning it to the right, and of observing the person and gesture of him who was to speak. He appeared to be of a middle age, and taller than any of the other three who attended him; whereof one was a page who held up his train, and seemed to be somewhat longer than my middle finger; the other two stood one on each side to support him. He acted every part of an orator, and I could observe many periods[6] of threatenings, and others of promises, pity and kindness. I answered in a few words, but in the most submissive manner, lifting up my left hand and both my eyes to the sun, as calling him for a witness; and being almost famished with hunger, having not eaten a morsel for some hours before I left the ship, I found the demands of nature so strong upon me, that I could not forbear showing my impatience (perhaps against the strict rules of decency) by putting my finger frequently on my mouth, to signify that I wanted food. The *Hurgo* (for so they call a great lord, as I afterwards learned) understood me very well. He descended from the stage, and commanded that several ladders should be applied to my sides, on which above an hundred of the inhabitants mounted, and walked towards my mouth, laden with baskets full of meat, which had been provided and sent thither by the King's orders upon the first intelligence he received of me. I observed there was the flesh of several animals, but could not distinguish them by the taste. There were shoulders, legs, and loins shaped like those of mutton, and very well dressed, but smaller than the wings of a lark. I eat them by two or three at a mouthful, and took three loaves at a time, about the bigness of musket bullets. They supplied me as fast as they could,

---

5. Leather jacket.
6. In rhetoric, complete, well-constructed sentences.

showing a thousand marks of wonder and astonishment at my bulk and appetite. I then made another sign that I wanted drink. They found by my eating that a small quantity would not suffice me; and being a most ingenious people, they slung up with great dexterity one of their largest hogsheads; then rolled it towards my hand, and beat out the top; I drank it off at a draught, which I might well do, for it hardly held half a pint, and tasted like a small wine of Burgundy, but much more delicious. They brought me a second hogshead, which I drank in the same manner, and made signs for more, but they had none to give me. When I had performed these wonders, they shouted for joy, and danced upon my breast, repeating several times as they did at first, *Hekinah Degul.* They made me a sign that I should throw down the two hogsheads, but first warned the people below to stand out of the way, crying aloud, *Borach Mivola,* and when they saw the vessels in the air, there was an universal shout of *Hekinah Degul.* I confess I was often tempted, while they were passing backwards and forwards on my body, to seize forty or fifty of the first that came in my reach, and dash them against the ground. But the remembrance of what I had felt, which probably might not be the worst they could do; and the promise of honor I made them, for so I interpreted my submissive behavior, soon drove out those imaginations. Besides, I now considered myself as bound by the laws of hospitality to a people who had treated me with so much expense and magnificence. However, in my thoughts I could not sufficiently wonder at the intrepidity of these diminutive mortals, who durst venture to mount and walk on my body, while one of my hands was at liberty, without trembling at the very sight of so prodigious a creature as I must appear to them. After some time, when they observed that I made no more demands for meat, there appeared before me a person of high rank from his Imperial Majesty. His Excellency, having mounted on the small of my right leg, advanced forwards up to my face, with about a dozen of his retinue. And producing his credentials under the Signet Royal, which he applied[7] close to my eyes, spoke about ten minutes, without any signs of anger, but with a kind of determinate resolution; often pointing forwards, which, as I afterwards found, was towards the capital city, about half a mile distant, whither it was agreed by his Majesty in council that I must be conveyed. I answered in a few words, but to no purpose, and made a sign with my hand that was loose, putting it to the other (but over his Excellency's head, for fear of hurting him or his train) and then to my own head and body, to signify that I desired my liberty. It appeared that he understood me well enough; for he shook his head by way of disapprobation, and held his hand in a posture to show that I must be carried as a prisoner. However, he made other signs to let me understand that I should have meat and drink enough, and very good treatment. Whereupon I once more thought of attempting to break my bonds; but again, when I felt the smart of their arrows upon my face and hands, which were all in blisters, and many of the darts still sticking in them; and observing likewise that the number of my enemies increased; I gave tokens to let them know that they might do with me what they pleased. Upon this the *Hurgo* and his train withdrew, with much civility and cheerful countenances. Soon after I heard a general shout, with frequent repetitions of the words, *Peplom Selan,* and I felt great

---

7. Brought.

numbers of the people on my left side relaxing the cords to such a degree, that I was able to turn upon my right, and to ease myself with making water; which I very plentifully did, to the great astonishment of the people, who conjecturing by my motions what I was going to do, immediately opened to the right and left on that side, to avoid the torrent which fell with such noise and violence from me. But before this, they had daubed my face and both my hands with a sort of ointment very pleasant to the smell, which in a few minutes removed all the smart of their arrows. These circumstances, added to the refreshment I had received by their victuals and drink, which were very nourishing, disposed me to sleep. I slept about eight hours, as I was afterwards assured; and it was no wonder; for the physicians, by the Emperor's order, had mingled a sleeping potion in the hogsheads of wine.

It seems that upon the first moment I was discovered sleeping on the ground after my landing, the Emperor had early notice of it by an express; and determined in council that I should be tied in the manner I have related (which was done in the night while I slept), that plenty of meat and drink should be sent me, and a machine prepared to carry me to the capital city.

This resolution perhaps may appear very bold and dangerous, and I am confident would not be imitated by any prince in Europe on the like occasion; however, in my opinion it was extremely prudent as well as generous. For supposing these people had endeavored to kill me with their spears and arrows while I was asleep; I should certainly have awaked with the first sense of smart, which might so far have roused my rage and strength, as to enable me to break the strings wherewith I was tied; after which, as they were not able to make resistance, so they could expect no mercy.

These people are most excellent mathematicians, and arrived to a great perfection in mechanics by the countenance and encouragement of the Emperor, who is a renowned patron of learning. This prince hath several machines fixed on wheels, for the carriage of trees and other great weights. He often builds his largest men of war, whereof some are nine foot long, in the woods where the timber grows, and has them carried on these engines[8] three or four hundred yards to the sea. Five hundred carpenters and engineers were immediately set at work to prepare the greatest engine they had. It was a frame of wood raised three inches from the ground, about seven foot long and four wide, moving upon twenty-two wheels. The shout I heard was upon the arrival of this engine, which it seems set out in four hours after my landing. It was brought parallel to me as I lay. But the principal difficulty was to raise and place me in this vehicle. Eighty poles, each of one foot high, were erected for this purpose, and very strong cords of the bigness of packthread were fastened by hooks to many bandages, which the workmen had girt round my neck, my hands, my body, and my legs. Nine hundred of the strongest men were employed to draw up these cords by many pulleys fastened on the poles; and thus, in less than three hours, I was raised and slung into the engine, and there tied fast. All this I was told, for while the whole operation was performing, I lay in a profound sleep, by the force of that soporiferous[9] medicine infused into my liquor. Fifteen hundred of the Emperor's largest horses, each about four inches and a half high, were employed to draw me towards the metropolis, which, as I said, was half a mile distant.

---

8. Contrivances.

9. Inducing unnatural sleep.

About four hours after we began our journey, I awaked by a very ridiculous accident; for, the carriage being stopped a while to adjust something that was out of order, two or three of the young natives had the curiosity to see how I looked when I was asleep; they climbed up into the engine, and advancing very softly to my face, one of them, an officer in the guards, put the sharp end of his half-pike a good way up into my left nostril, which tickled my nose like a straw, and made me sneeze violently: whereupon they stole off unperceived, and it was three weeks before I knew the cause of my awaking so suddenly. We made a long march the remaining part of the day, and rested at night with five hundred guards on each side of me half with torches, and half with bows and arrows, ready to shoot me if I should offer to stir. The next morning at sunrise we continued our march, and arrived within two hundred yards of the city gates about noon. The Emperor and all his court came out to meet us, but his great officers would by no means suffer his Majesty to endanger his person by mounting on my body.

At the place where the carriage stopped, there stood an ancient temple, esteemed to be the largest in the whole kingdom, which having been polluted some years before by an unnatural murder,[1] was, according to the zeal of those people, looked on as profane, and therefore had been applied to common use, and all the ornaments and furniture carried away. In this edifice it was determined I should lodge. The great gate fronting to the north was about four foot high, and almost two foot wide, through which I could easily creep. On each side of the gate was a small window not above six inches from the ground: into that on the left side, the King's smiths conveyed fourscore and eleven chains, like those that hang to a lady's watch in Europe, and almost as large, which were locked to my left leg with six and thirty padlocks. Over against this temple, on the other side of the great highway, at twenty foot distance, there was a turret at least five foot high. Here the Emperor ascended with many principal lords of his court, to have an opportunity of viewing me, as I was told, for I could not see them. It was reckoned that above an hundred thousand inhabitants came out of the town upon the same errand; and in spite of my guards, I believe there could not be fewer than ten thousand, at several times, who mounted upon my body by the help of ladders. But a proclamation was soon issued to forbid it upon pain of death. When the workmen found it was impossible for me to break loose, they cut all the strings that bound me; whereupon I rose up with as melancholy a disposition as ever I had in my life. But the noise and astonishment of the people at seeing me rise and walk are not to be expressed. The chains that held my left leg were about two yards long, and gave me not only the liberty of walking backwards and forwards in a semicircle; but, being fixed within four inches of the gate, allowed me to creep in, and lie at my full length in the temple.

CHAPTER 2. *The Emperor of Lilliput, attended by several of the nobility, comes to see the author in his confinement. The Emperor's person and habit described. Learned men appointed to teach the author their language. He gains favor by his mild disposition. His pockets are searched, and his sword and pistols taken from him.*

1. Presumably a reference to the execution of Charles I, who was sentenced in Westminster Hall.

When I found myself on my feet, I looked about me, and must confess I never beheld a more entertaining prospect. The country round appeared like a continued garden, and the inclosed fields, which were generally forty foot square, resembled so many beds of flowers. These fields were intermingled with woods of half a stang,[2] and the tallest trees, as I could judge, appeared to be seven foot high. I viewed the town on my left hand, which looked like the painted scene of a city in a theater.

I had been for some hours extremely pressed by the necessities of nature; which was no wonder, it being almost two days since I had last disburthened myself. I was under great difficulties between urgency and shame. The best expedient I could think on, was to creep into my house, which I accordingly did; and shutting the gate after me, I went as far as the length of my chain would suffer; and discharged my body of that uneasy load. But this was the only time I was ever guilty of so uncleanly an action; for which I cannot but hope the candid reader will give some allowance, after he hath maturely and impartially considered my case, and the distress I was in. From this time my constant practice was, as soon as I rose, to perform that business in open air, at the full extent of my chain, and due care was taken every morning before company came, that the offensive matter should be carried off in wheelbarrows by two servants appointed for that purpose. I would not have dwelt so long upon a circumstance, that perhaps at first sight may appear not very momentous, if I had not thought it necessary to justify my character in point of cleanliness to the world; which I am told some of my maligners have been pleased, upon this and other occasions, to call in question.

When this adventure was at an end, I came back out of my house, having occasion for fresh air. The Emperor was already descended from the tower, and advancing on horseback towards me, which had like to have cost him dear; for the beast, although very well trained, yet wholly unused to such a sight, which appeared as if a mountain moved before him, reared up on his hinder feet: but that prince, who is an excellent horseman, kept his seat, until his attendants ran in, and held the bridle, while his Majesty had time to dismount. When he alighted, he surveyed me round with great admiration, but kept beyond the length of my chains. He ordered his cooks and butlers, who were already prepared, to give me victuals and drink, which they pushed forward in a sort of vehicles upon wheels until I could reach them. I took these vehicles, and soon emptied them all; twenty of them were filled with meat, and ten with liquor; each of the former afforded me two or three good mouthfuls, and I emptied the liquor of ten vessels, which was contained in earthen vials, into one vehicle, drinking it off at a draught; and so I did with the rest. The Empress, and young princes of the blood, of both sexes, attended by many ladies, sat at some distance in their chairs; but upon the accident that happened to the Emperor's horse, they alighted, and came near his person; which I am now going to describe. He is taller, by almost the breadth of my nail, than any of his court, which alone is enough to strike an awe into the beholders. His features are strong and masculine, with an Austrian lip, and arched nose, his complexion olive, his countenance[3] erect,

---

2. A quarter of an acre.
3. Bearing, appearance. Swift may be satirically

idealizing George I, whom most of the British thought gross.

his body and limbs well proportioned, all his motions graceful, and his deportment majestic. He was then past his prime, being twenty-eight years and three quarters old, of which he had reigned about seven, in great felicity, and generally victorious. For the better convenience of beholding him, I lay on my side, so that my face was parallel to his, and he stood but three yards off: however, I have had him since many times in my hand, and therefore cannot be deceived in the description. His dress was very plain and simple, the fashion of it between the Asiatic and the European; but he had on his head a light helmet of gold, adorned with jewels, and a plume on the crest. He held his sword drawn in his hand, to defend himself, if I should happen to break loose; it was almost three inches long, the hilt and scabbard were gold enriched with diamonds. His voice was shrill, but very clear and articulate, and I could distinctly hear it when I stood up. The ladies and courtiers were all most magnificently clad, so that the spot they stood upon seemed to resemble a petticoat spread on the ground, embroidered with figures of gold and silver. His Imperial Majesty spoke often to me, and I returned answers, but neither of us could understand a syllable. There were several of his priests and lawyers present (as I conjectured by their habits) who were commanded to address themselves to me, and I spoke to them in as many languages as I had the least smattering of, which were High and Low Dutch, Latin, French, Spanish, Italian, and Lingua Franca;[4] but all to no purpose. After about two hours the court retired, and I was left with a strong guard, to prevent the impertinence, and probably the malice of the rabble, who were very impatient to crowd about me as near as they durst; and some of them had the impudence to shoot their arrows at me as I sat on the ground by the door of my house, whereof one very narrowly missed my left eye. But the colonel ordered six of the ringleaders to be seized, and thought no punishment so proper as to deliver them bound into my hands, which some of his soldiers accordingly did, pushing them forwards with the butt-ends of their pikes into my reach; I took them all in my right hand, put five of them into my coat-pocket; and as to the sixth, I made a countenance as if I would eat him alive. The poor man squalled terribly, and the colonel and his officer were in much pain, especially when they saw me take out my penknife: but I soon put them out of fear; for, looking mildly, and immediately cutting the strings he was bound with, I set him gently on the ground, and away he ran. I treated the rest in the same manner, taking them one by one out of my pocket, and I observed both the soldiers and people were highly obliged at this mark of my clemency, which was represented very much to my advantage at court.

Towards night I got with some difficulty into my house, where I lay on the ground, and continued to do so about a fortnight; during which time the Emperor gave orders to have a bed prepared for me. Six hundred beds of the common measure were brought in carriages, and worked up in my house; an hundred and fifty of their beds sewn together made up the breadth and length, and these were four double, which however kept me but very indifferently from the hardness of the floor, that was of smooth stone. By the

---

4. A jargon, based on Italian, used by traders in the Mediterranean. "High and Low Dutch": German and Dutch, respectively.

same computation they provided me with sheets, blankets, and coverlets, tolerable enough for one who had been so long enured to hardships as I.

As the news of my arrival spread through the kingdom, it brought prodigious numbers of rich, idle, and curious people to see me; so that the villages were almost emptied, and great neglect of tillage and household affairs must have ensued, if his Imperial Majesty had not provided by several proclamations and orders of state against this inconveniency. He directed that those who had already beheld me should return home, and not presume to come within fifty yards of my house without license from court; whereby the secretaries of state got considerable fees.

In the mean time, the Emperor held frequent councils to debate what course should be taken with me; and I was afterwards assured by a particular friend, a person of great quality, who was as much in the secret as any, that the court was under many difficulties concerning me. They apprehended[5] my breaking loose, that my diet would be very expensive, and might cause a famine. Sometimes they determined to starve me, or at least to shoot me in the face and hands with poisoned arrows, which would soon dispatch me: but again they considered, that the stench of so large a carcass might produce a plague in the metropolis, and probably spread through the whole kingdom. In the midst of these consultations, several officers of the army went to the door of the great council chamber; and two of them being admitted, gave an account of my behavior to the six criminals above-mentioned; which made so favorable an impression in the breast of his Majesty, and the whole board, in my behalf, that an imperial commission was issued out, obliging all the villages nine hundred yards round the city to deliver in every morning six beeves, forty sheep, and other victuals for my sustenance; together with a proportionable quantity of bread and wine, and other liquors: for the due payment of which his Majesty gave assignments[6] upon his treasury. For this prince lives chiefly upon his own demesnes; seldom except upon great occasions raising any subsidies upon his subjects, who are bound to attend him in his wars at their own expense. An establishment was also made of six hundred persons to be my domestics, who had board-wages allowed for their maintenance, and tents built for them very conveniently on each side of my door. It was likewise ordered, that three hundred tailors should make me a suit of clothes after the fashion of the country: that six of his Majesty's greatest scholars should be employed to instruct me in their language: and, lastly, that the Emperor's horses, and those of the nobility, and troops of guards, should be exercised in my sight, to accustom themselves to me. All these orders were duly put in execution; and in about three weeks I made a great progress in learning their language; during which time the Emperor frequently honored me with his visits, and was pleased to assist my masters in teaching me. We began already to converse together in some sort; and the first words I learned, were to express my desire that he would please to give me my liberty; which I every day repeated on my knees.[7] His answer, as I could apprehend, was, that this must be a work of time, not to be thought on without the advice of his council; and that first I must *Lumos*

5. Anticipated with fear.
6. Formal mandates of revenue.
7. Gulliver's plea for liberty and the threat of star-vation or rebellion he represents to his captors suggest the situation of Ireland with respect to England.

kelmin pesso desmar lon emposo; that is, swear a peace with him and his kingdom. However, that I should be used with all kindness; and he advised me to acquire by my patience and discreet behavior, the good opinion of himself and his subjects. He desired I would not take it ill, if he gave orders to certain proper officers to search me; for probably I might carry about me several weapons, which must needs be dangerous things, if they answered the bulk of so prodigious a person.[8] I said, his Majesty should be satisfied, for I was ready to strip myself, and turn up my pockets before him. This I delivered part in words, and part in signs. He replied, that by the laws of the kingdom, I must be searched by two of his officers; that he knew this could not be done without my consent and assistance; that he had so good an opinion of my generosity and justice, as to trust their persons in my hands; that whatever they took from me should be returned when I left the country, or paid for at the rate which I would set upon them. I took up the two officers in my hands, put them first into my coat-pockets, and then into every other pocket about me, except my two fobs, and another secret pocket which I had no mind should be searched, wherein I had some little necessaries of no consequence to any but myself. In one of my fobs there was a silver watch, and in the other a small quantity of gold in a purse. These gentlemen, having pen, ink, and paper about them, made an exact inventory of everything they saw; and when they had done, desired I would set them down, that they might deliver it to the Emperor. This inventory I afterwards translated into English, and is word for word as follows.

Imprimis,[9] In the right coat-pocket of the Great Man-Mountain (for so I interpret the words *Quinbus Flestrin*) after the strictest search, we found only one great piece of coarse cloth, large enough to be a foot-cloth for your Majesty's chief room of state. In the left pocket, we saw a huge silver chest, with a cover of the same metal, which we the searchers were not able to lift. We desired it should be opened; and one of us, stepping into it, found himself up to the mid leg in a sort of dust, some part whereof flying up to our faces, set us both a sneezing for several times together. In his right waistcoat-pocket, we found a prodigious bundle of white thin substances, folded one over another, about the bigness of three men, tied with a strong cable, and marked with black figures; which we humbly conceive to be writings; every letter almost half as large as the palm of our hands. In the left there was a sort of engine, from the back of which were extended twenty long poles, resembling the palisados[1] before your Majesty's court; wherewith we conjecture the Man-Mountain combs his head; for we did not always trouble him with questions, because we found it a great difficulty to make him understand us. In the large pocket on the right side of his middle cover (so I translate the word *ranfu-lo,* by which they meant my breeches) we saw a hollow pillar of iron, about the length of a man, fastened to a strong piece of timber, larger than the pillar; and upon one side of the pillar were huge pieces of iron sticking out, cut into strange figures; which we know not

---

8. When the Whigs came into power in 1715, the leading Tories, who included Swift's friends Oxford and Bolingbroke (Robert Harley and Henry St. John) as well as Swift himself, were investigated by a committee of secrecy.
9. In the first place (Latin).
1. Fences of stakes.

what to make of. In the left pocket, another engine of the same kind. In the smaller pocket on the right side, were several round flat pieces of white and red metal, of different bulk; some of the white, which seemed to be silver, were so large and heavy, that my comrade and I could hardly lift them. In the left pocket were two black pillars irregularly shaped: we could not, without difficulty, reach the top of them as we stood at the bottom of his pocket. One of them was covered, and seemed all of a piece; but at the upper end of the other, there appeared a white round substance, about twice the bigness of our heads. Within each of these was inclosed a prodigious plate of steel; which, by our orders, we obliged him to show us, because we apprehended they might be dangerous engines. He took them out of their cases, and told us, that in his own country his practice was to shave his beard with one of these, and to cut his meat with the other. There were two pockets which we could not enter: these he called his fobs; they were two large slits cut into the top of his middle cover, but squeezed close by the pressure of his belly. Out of the right fob hung a great silver chain, with a wonderful kind of engine at the bottom. We directed him to draw out whatever was at the end of the chain, which appeared to be a globe, half silver, and half of some transparent metal: for on the transparent side we saw certain strange figures circularly drawn, and thought we could touch them, until we found our fingers stopped with that lucid substance. He put this engine to our ears, which made an incessant noise like that of a water-mill. And we conjecture it is either some unknown animal, or the god that he worships: but we are more inclined to the latter opinion, because he assured us (if we understood him right, for he expressed himself very imperfectly), that he seldom did any thing without consulting it. He called it his oracle, and said it pointed out the time for every action of his life. From the left fob he took out a net almost large enough for a fisher-man, but contrived to open and shut like a purse, and served him for the same use: we found therein several massy pieces of yellow metal, which if they be of real gold, must be of immense value.

Having thus, in obedience to your Majesty's commands, diligently searched all his pockets, we observed a girdle[2] about his waist made of the hide of some prodigious animal; from which, on the left side, hung a sword of the length of five men; and on the right, a bag or pouch divided into cells; each cell capable of holding three of your Majesty's subjects. In one of these cells were several globes or balls of a most ponderous metal, about the bigness of our heads, and required a strong hand to lift them: the other cell contained a heap of certain black grains, but of no great bulk or weight, for we could hold above fifty of them in the palms of our hands.

This is an exact inventory of what we found about the body of the Man-Mountain; who used us with great civility, and due respect to your Majesty's commission. Signed and sealed on the fourth day of the eighty-ninth moon of your Majesty's auspicious reign.

CLEFREN FRELOCK, MARSI FRELOCK.

2. Belt.

When this inventory was read over to the Emperor, he directed me to deliver up the several particulars. He first called for my scimitar, which I took out, scabbard and all. In the meantime he ordered three thousand of his choicest troops (who then attended him) to surround me at a distance, with their bows and arrows just ready to discharge: but I did not observe it; for my eyes were wholly fixed upon his Majesty. He then desired me to draw my scimitar, which, although it had got some rust by the sea water, was in most parts exceeding bright. I did so, and immediately all the troops gave a shout between terror and surprise; for the sun shone clear, and the reflection dazzled their eyes, as I waved the scimitar to and fro in my hand. His Majesty, who is a most magnanimous[3] prince, was less daunted than I could expect; he ordered me to return it into the scabbard, and cast it on the ground as gently as I could, about six foot from the end of my chain. The next thing he demanded was one of the hollow iron pillars, by which he meant my pocket-pistols. I drew it out, and at his desire, as well as I could, expressed to him the use of it, and charging it only with powder, which by the closeness of my pouch happened to escape wetting in the sea (an inconvenience that all prudent mariners take special care to provide against), I first cautioned the Emperor not to be afraid; and then I let it off in the air. The astonishment here was much greater than at the sight of my scimitar. Hundreds fell down as if they had been struck dead; and even the Emperor, although he stood his ground, could not recover himself in some time. I delivered up both my pistols in the same manner as I had done my scimitar, and then my pouch of powder and bullets; begging him that the former might be kept from fire; for it would kindle with the smallest spark, and blow up his imperial palace into the air. I likewise delivered up my watch, which the Emperor was very curious to see; and commanded two of his tallest yeomen of the guards to bear it on a pole upon their shoulders, as draymen in England do a barrel of ale. He was amazed at the continual noise it made, and the motion of the minute-hand, which he could easily discern; for their sight is much more acute than ours: he asked the opinions of his learned men about him, which were various and remote, as the reader may well imagine without my repeating; although indeed I could not very perfectly understand them. I then gave up my silver and copper money, my purse with nine large pieces of gold, and some smaller ones; my knife and razor, my comb and silver snuffbox, my handkerchief and journal book. My scimitar, pistols, and pouch, were conveyed in carriages to his Majesty's stores; but the rest of my goods were returned me.

I had, as I before observed, one private pocket which escaped their search, wherein there was a pair of spectacles (which I sometimes use for the weakness of my eyes), a pocket perspective,[4] and several other little conveniences; which, being of no consequence to the Emperor, I did not think myself bound in honor to discover, and I apprehended they might be lost or spoiled if I ventured them out of my possession.

---

3. Courageous, great-spirited. Magnanimity, the relation (direct or inverse) between the size of the body and the soul, is a central concern of the first two parts of the *Travels*.
4. Telescope.

CHAPTER 3. *The author diverts the Emperor and his nobility of both sexes in a very uncommon manner. The diversions of the court of Lilliput described. The author hath his liberty granted him upon certain conditions.*

My gentleness and good behavior had gained so far on the Emperor and his court, and indeed upon the army and people in general, that I began to conceive hopes of getting my liberty in a short time. I took all possible methods to cultivate this favorable disposition. The natives came by degrees to be less apprehensive of any danger from me. I would sometimes lie down, and let five or six of them dance on my hand. And at last the boys and girls would venture to come and play at hide-and-seek in my hair. I had now made a good progress in understanding and speaking their language. The Emperor had a mind one day to entertain me with several of the country shows; wherein they exceed all nations I have known, both for dexterity and magnificence. I was diverted with none so much as that of the rope-dancers, performed upon a slender white thread, extended about two foot, and twelve inches from the ground. Upon which I shall desire liberty, with the reader's patience, to enlarge a little.

This diversion is only practiced by those persons who are candidates for great employments, and high favor, at court. They are trained in this art from their youth, and are not always of noble birth, or liberal education. When a great office is vacant either by death or disgrace (which often happens) five or six of those candidates petition the Emperor to entertain his Majesty and the court with a dance on the rope; and whoever jumps the highest without falling, succeeds in the office. Very often the chief ministers themselves are commanded to show their skill, and to convince the Emperor that they have not lost their faculty. Flimnap,[5] the Treasurer, is allowed to cut a caper on the strait rope, at least an inch higher than any other lord in the whole empire. I have seen him do the summerset several times together upon a trencher[6] fixed on the rope, which is no thicker than a common packthread in England. My friend Reldresal, Principal Secretary for Private Affairs, is, in my opinion, if I am not partial, the second after the Treasurer; the rest of the great officers are much upon a par.

These diversions are often attended with fatal accidents, whereof great numbers are on record. I myself have seen two or three candidates break a limb. But the danger is much greater when the ministers themselves are commanded to show their dexterity; for, by contending to excel themselves and their fellows, they strain so far, that there is hardly one of them who hath not received a fall; and some of them two or three. I was assured, that a year or two before my arrival, Flimnap would have infallibly broke his neck, if one of the King's cushions,[7] that accidentally lay on the ground, had not weakened the force of his fall.

There is likewise another diversion, which is only shown before the Emperor and Empress, and first minister, upon particular occasions. The Emperor lays on a table three fine silken threads of six inches long. One is blue, the other red, and the third green.[8] These threads are proposed as

---

5. Sir Robert Walpole, the Whig head of the government, was notorious in Swift's circle for his political acrobatics.
6. Plate. "Summerset": somersault.

7. A mistress of George I was supposed to have helped restore Walpole to office in 1721.
8. The Orders of the Garter, the Bath, and the Thistle, conferred for services to the king.

prizes for those persons whom the Emperor hath a mind to distinguish by a peculiar mark of his favor. The ceremony is performed in his Majesty's great chamber of state; where the candidates are to undergo a trial of dexterity very different from the former, and such as I have not observed the least resemblance of in any other country of the old or the new world. The Emperor holds a stick in his hands, both ends parallel to the horizon, while the candidates, advancing one by one, sometimes leap over the stick, sometimes creep under it backwards and forwards several times, according as the stick is advanced or depressed. Sometimes the Emperor holds one end of the stick, and his first minister the other; sometimes the minister has it entirely to himself. Whoever performs his part with most agility, and holds out the longest in *leaping* and *creeping*, is rewarded with the blue-colored silk; the red is given to the next, and the green to the third, which they all wear girt twice round about the middle; and you see few great persons about this court who are not adorned with one of these girdles.

The horses of the army, and those of the royal stables, having been daily led before me, were no longer shy, but would come up to my very feet, without starting. The riders would leap them over my hand as I held it on the ground; and one of the Emperor's huntsmen, upon a large courser, took[9] my foot, shoe and all; which was indeed a prodigious leap. I had the good fortune to divert the Emperor one day after a very extraordinary manner. I desired he would order several sticks of two foot high, and the thickness of an ordinary cane, to be brought me; whereupon his Majesty commanded the master of his woods to give directions accordingly; and the next morning six woodmen arrived with as many carriages, drawn by eight horses to each. I took nine of these sticks, and fixing them firmly in the ground in a quadrangular figure, two foot and a half square, I took four other sticks, and tied them parallel at each corner, about two foot from the ground; then I fastened my handkerchief to the nine sticks that stood erect, and extended it on all sides till it was as tight as the top of a drum; and the four parallel sticks, rising about five inches higher than the handkerchief, served as ledges on each side. When I had finished my work, I desired the Emperor to let a troop of his best horse, twenty-four in number, come and exercise upon this plain. His Majesty approved of the proposal, and I took them up one by one in my hands, ready mounted and armed, with the proper officers to exercise them. As soon as they got into order, they divided into two parties, performed mock skirmishes, discharged blunt arrows, drew their swords, fled and pursued, attacked and retired; and in short discovered the best military discipline I ever beheld. The parallel sticks secured them and their horses from falling over the stage; and the Emperor was so much delighted, that he ordered this entertainment to be repeated several days; and once was pleased to be lifted up, and give the word of command; and, with great difficulty, persuaded even the Empress herself to let me hold her in her close chair[1] within two yards of the stage, from whence she was able to take a full view of the whole performance. It was my good fortune that no ill accident happened in these entertainments, only once a fiery horse that belonged to one of the captains pawing with his hoof struck a hole in my handkerchief, and his foot slipping, he overthrew his rider and himself; but I immediately

9. Jumped over.   1. An enclosed or sedan chair.

relieved them both; for covering the hole with one hand, I set down the troop with the other, in the same manner as I took them up. The horse that fell was strained in the left shoulder, but the rider got no hurt, and I repaired my handkerchief as well as I could; however, I would not trust to the strength of it any more in such dangerous enterprises.

About two or three days before I was set at liberty, as I was entertaining the court with these kinds of feats, there arrived an express to inform his Majesty that some of his subjects, riding near the place where I was first taken up, had seen a great black substance lying on the ground, very oddly shaped, extending its edges round as wide as his Majesty's bedchamber, and rising up in the middle as high as a man; that it was no living creature, as they at first apprehended, for it lay on the grass without motion, and some of them had walked round it several times; that by mounting upon each other's shoulders, they had got to the top, which was flat and even; and stamping upon it they found it was hollow within; that they humbly conceived it might be something belonging to the Man-Mountain, and if his Majesty pleased, they would undertake to bring it with only five horses. I presently[2] knew what they meant; and was glad at heart to receive this intelligence. It seems upon my first reaching the shore after our shipwreck, I was in such confusion, that before I came to the place where I went to sleep, my hat, which I had fastened with a string to my head while I was rowing, and had stuck on all the time I was swimmings, fell off after I came to land; the string, as I conjecture, breaking by some accident which I never observed, but thought my hat had been lost at sea. I intreated his Imperial Majesty to give orders it might be brought to me as soon as possible, describing to him the use and the nature of it: and the next day the wagoners arrived with it, but not in a very good condition; they had bored two holes in the brim, within an inch and half of the edge, and fastened two hooks in the holes; these hooks were tied by a long cord to the harness, and thus my hat was dragged along for above half an English mile: but the ground in that country being extremely smooth and level, it received less damage than I expected.

Two days after this adventure, the Emperor, having ordered that part of his army which quarters in and about his metropolis to be in a readiness, took a fancy of diverting himself in a very singular manner. He desired I would stand like a colossus, with my legs as far asunder as I conveniently could. He then commanded his general (who was an old experienced leader, and a great patron of mine) to draw up the troops in close order, and march them under me; the foot[3] by twenty-four in a breast, and the horse by sixteen, with drums beating, colors flying, and pikes advanced. This body consisted of three thousand foot, and a thousand horse. His Majesty gave orders, upon pain of death, that every soldier in his march should observe the strictest decency with regard to my person; which, however, could not prevent some of the younger officers from turning up their eyes as they passed under me. And, to confess the truth, my breeches were at that time in so ill a condition, that they afforded some opportunities for laughter and admiration.

I had sent so many memorials and petitions for my liberty, that his Majesty at length mentioned the matter first in the cabinet, and then in a full

2. Immediately.   3. Foot soldiers or infantry.

council; where it was opposed by none, except Skyresh Bolgolam,[4] who was pleased, without any provocation, to be my mortal enemy. But it was carried against him by the whole board, and confirmed by the Emperor. That minister was *Galbet*, or Admiral of the Realm; very much in his master's confidence, and a person well versed in affairs, but of a morose and sour complexion.[5] However, he was at length persuaded to comply; but prevailed that the articles and conditions upon which I should be set free, and to which I must swear, should be drawn up by himself. These articles were brought to me by Skyresh Bolgolam in person, attended by two undersecretaries, and several persons of distinction. After they were read, I was demanded to swear to the performance of them; first in the manner of my own country, and afterwards in the method prescribed by their laws; which was to hold my right foot in my left hand, to place the middle finger of my right hand on the crown of my head, and my thumb on the tip of my right ear. But because the reader may perhaps be curious to have some idea of the style and manner of expression peculiar to that people, as well as to know the articles upon which I recovered my liberty, I have made a translation of the whole instrument,[6] word for word, as near as I was able; which I here offer to the public.

> GOLBASTO MOMAREN EVLAME GURDILO SHEFIN MULLY ULLY GUE, most mighty Emperor of Lilliput, delight and terror of the universe, whose dominions extend five thousand blustrugs (about twelve miles in circumference) to the extremities of the globe; Monarch of all Monarchs; taller than the sons of men; whose feet press down to the center, and whose head strikes against the sun; at whose nod the princes of the earth shake their knees; pleasant as the spring, comfortable as the summer, fruitful as autumn, dreadful as winter. His most sublime Majesty proposeth to the Man-Mountain, lately arrived at our celestial dominions, the following articles, which by a solemn oath he shall be obliged to perform.
>
> First, The Man-Mountain shall not depart from our dominions, without our license under our great seal.
>
> Secondly, He shall not presume to come into our metropolis, without our express order; at which time the inhabitants shall have two hours warning, to keep within their doors.
>
> Thirdly, The said Man-Mountain shall confine his walks to our principal high roads; and not offer to walk or lie down in a meadow, or field of corn.
>
> Fourthly, As he walks the said roads, he shall take the utmost care not to trample upon the bodies of any of our loving subjects, their horses, or carriages, nor take any of our said subjects into his hands, without their own consent.
>
> Fifthly, If an express require extraordinary dispatch, the Man-Mountain shall be obliged to carry in his pocket the messenger and horse, a six days' journey once in every moon, and return the said messenger back (if so required) safe to our Imperial Presence.

---

4. The earl of Nottingham, an enemy of Swift.   6. A formal legal document.
5. Disposition.

Sixthly, He shall be our ally against our enemies in the island of Blefuscu, and do his utmost to destroy their fleet, which is now preparing to invade us.

Seventhly, That the said Man-Mountain shall, at his times of leisure, be aiding and assisting to our workmen, in helping to raise certain great stones, towards covering the wall of the principal park, and other our royal buildings.

Eighthly, That the said Man-Mountain shall, in two moons' time, deliver in an exact survey of the circumference of our dominions by a computation of his own paces round the coast.

Lastly, That upon his solemn oath to observe all the above articles, the said Man-Mountain shall have a daily allowance of meat and drink sufficient for the support of 1,728 of our subjects; with free access to our Royal Person, and other marks of our favor. Given at our palace at Belfaborac the twelfth day of the ninety-first moon of our reign.

I swore and subscribed to these articles with great cheerfulness and content, although some of them were not so honorable as I could have wished; which proceeded wholly from the malice of Skyresh Bolgolam the High Admiral: whereupon my chains were immediately unlocked, and I was at full liberty: the Emperor himself in person did me the honor to be by at the whole ceremony. I made my acknowledgements by prostrating myself at his Majesty's feet: but he commanded me to rise; and after many gracious expressions, which, to avoid the censure of vanity, I shall not repeat, he added, that he hoped I should prove a useful servant, and well deserve all the favors he had already conferred upon me, or might do for the future.

The reader may please to observe, that in the last article for the recovery of my liberty, the Emperor stipulates to allow me a quantity of meat and drink, sufficient for the support of 1,728 Lilliputians. Some time after, asking a friend at court how they came to fix on that determinate number, he told me, that his Majesty's mathematicians, having taken the height of my body by the help of a quadrant, and finding it to exceed theirs in the proportion of twelve to one, they concluded from the similarity of their bodies, that mine must contain at least 1,728 of theirs, and consequently would require as much food as was necessary to support that number of Lilliputians. By which, the reader may conceive an idea of the ingenuity of that people, as well as the prudent and exact economy of so great a prince.

CHAPTER 4. *Mildendo, the metropolis of Lilliput, described, together with the Emperor's palace. A conversation between the author and a principal secretary, concerning the affairs of that empire; the author's offers to serve the Emperor in his wars.*

The first request I made after I had obtained my liberty, was, that I might have license to see Mildendo, the metropolis; which the Emperor easily granted me, but with a special charge to do no hurt, either to the inhabitants, or their houses. The people had notice by proclamation of my design to visit the town. The wall which encompassed it is two foot and an half high, and at least eleven inches broad, so that a coach and horses may be driven very safely round it; and it is flanked with strong towers at ten foot distance.

I stepped over the great western gate, and passed very gently, and sideling[7] through the two principal streets, only in my short waistcoat, for fear of damaging the roofs and eaves of the houses with the skirts of my coat. I walked with the utmost circumspection, to avoid treading on any stragglers, who might remain in the streets, although the orders were very strict, that all people should keep in their houses, at their own peril. The garret windows and tops of houses were so crowded with spectators, that I thought in all my travels I had not seen a more populous place. The city is an exact square, each side of the wall being five hundred foot long. The two great streets, which run cross and divide it into four quarters, are five foot wide. The lanes and alleys, which I could not enter, but only viewed them as I passed, are from twelve to eighteen inches. The town is capable of holding five hundred thousand souls. The houses are from three to five stories. The shops and markets well provided.

The Emperor's palace is in the center of the city, where the two great streets meet. It is enclosed by a wall of two foot high, and twenty foot distant from the buildings. I had his Majesty's permission to step over this wall; and the space being so wide between that and the palace, I could easily view it on every side. The outward court is a square of forty foot, and includes two other courts: in the inmost are the royal apartments, which I was very desirous to see, but found it extremely difficult; for the great gates, from one square into another, were but eighteen inches high, and seven inches wide. Now the buildings of the outer court were at least five foot high; and it was impossible for me to stride over them, without infinite damage to the pile, although the walls were strongly built of hewn stone, and four inches thick. At the same time the Emperor had a great desire that I should see the magnificence of his palace; but this I was not able to do till three days after, which I spent in cutting down with my knife some of the largest trees in the royal park, about an hundred yards distance from the city. Of these trees I made two stools, each about three foot high, and strong enough to bear my weight. The people having received notice a second time, I went again through the city to the palace, with my two stools in my hands. When I came to the side of the outer court, I stood upon one stool, and took the other in my hand: this I lifted over the roof, and gently set it down on the space between the first and second court, which was eight foot wide. I then stepped over the buildings very conveniently from one stool to the other, and drew up the first after me with a hooked stick. By this contrivance I got into the inmost court; and lying down upon my side, I applied my face to the windows of the middle stories, which were left open on purpose, and discovered the most splendid apartments that can be imagined. There I saw the Empress, and the young princes in their several lodgings, with their chief attendants about them. Her Imperial Majesty was pleased to smile very graciously upon me and gave me out of the window her hand to kiss.

But I shall not anticipate the reader with farther descriptions of this kind, because I reserve them for a greater work, which is now almost ready for the press; containing a general description of this empire, from its first erection, through a long series of princes, with a particular account of their wars and politics, laws, learning, and religion; their plants and animals,

7. Sideways.

their peculiar manners and customs, with other matters very curious and useful; my chief design at present being only to relate such events and transactions as happened to the public, or to myself, during a residence of about nine months in that empire.

One morning, about a fortnight after I had obtained my liberty, Reldresal, Principal Secretary (as they style him) of Private Affairs, came to my house, attended only by one servant. He ordered his coach to wait at a distance, and desired I would give him an hour's audience; which I readily consented to, on account of his quality, and personal merits, as well as of the many good offices he had done me during my solicitations at court. I offered to lie down, that he might the more conveniently reach my ear; but he chose rather to let me hold him in my hand during our conversation. He began with compliments on my liberty, said he might pretend to some merit in it; but, however, added, that if it had not been for the present situation of things at court, perhaps I might not have obtained it so soon. For, said he, as flourishing a condition as we appear to be in to foreigners, we labor under two mighty evils; a violent faction at home, and the danger of an invasion by a most potent enemy from abroad. As to the first, you are to understand, that for above seventy moons past, there have been two struggling parties in the empire, under the names of *Tramecksan*, and *Slamecksan*,[8] from the high and low heels on their shoes, by which they distinguish themselves.

It is alleged indeed, that the high heels are most agreeable to our ancient constitution: but however this be, his Majesty hath determined to make use of only low heels in the administration of the government and all offices in the gift of the crown; as you cannot but observe; and particularly, that his Majesty's imperial heels are lower at least by a *drurr* than any of his court; (*drurr* is a measure about the fourteenth part of an inch). The animosities between these two parties run so high, that they will neither eat nor drink, nor talk with each other. We compute the *Tramecksan*, or High-Heels, to exceed us in number; but the power is wholly on our side. We apprehend his Imperial Highness, the heir to the crown, to have some tendency towards the High-Heels; at least we can plainly discover one of his heels higher than the other, which gives him a hobble in his gait.[9] Now, in the midst of these intestine disquiets, we are threatened with an invasion from the island of Blefuscu,[1] which is the other great empire of the universe, almost as large and powerful as this of his Majesty. For as to what we have heard you affirm, that there are other kingdoms and states in the world, inhabited by human creatures as large as yourself, our philosophers are in much doubt; and would rather conjecture that you dropped from the moon, or one of the stars; because it is certain, that an hundred mortals of your bulk would, in a short time, destroy all the fruits and cattle of his Majesty's dominions. Besides, our histories of six thousand moons make no mention of any other regions, than the two great empires of Lilliput and Blefuscu. Which two mighty powers have, as I was going to tell you, been engaged in a most obstinate war for six and thirty moons past. It began upon the following occasion. It is allowed on all hands, that the primitive way of breaking eggs before we

---

8. Tory (High Church) and Whig (Low Church), respectively.
9. The prince of Wales (later George II) had

friends in both parties.
1. France.

eat them, was upon the larger end: but his present Majesty's grandfather, while he was a boy, going to eat an egg, and breaking it according to the ancient practice, happened to cut one of his fingers. Whereupon the Emperor his father published an edict, commanding all his subjects, upon great penalties, to break the smaller end of their eggs. The people so highly resented this law, that our histories tell us there have been six rebellions raised on that account; wherein one emperor lost his life, and another his crown.[2] These civil commotions were constantly fomented by the monarchs of Blefuscu; and when they were quelled, the exiles always fled for refuge to that empire. It is computed, that eleven thousand persons have, at several times, suffered death, rather than submit to break their eggs at the smaller end. Many hundred large volumes have been published upon this controversy: but the books of the Big-Endians have been long forbidden, and the whole party rendered incapable by law of holding employments.[3] During the course of these troubles, the emperors of Blefuscu did frequently expostulate by their ambassadors, accusing us of making a schism in religion, by offending against a fundamental doctrine of our great prophet Lustrog, in the fifty-fourth chapter of the *Brundecral* (which is their Alcoran[4]). This, however, is thought to be a mere strain upon the text: for the words are these; *That all true believers shall break their eggs at the convenient end:* and which is the convenient end, seems, in my humble opinion, to be left to every man's conscience, or at least in the power of the chief magistrate[5] to determine. Now the Big-Endian exiles have found so much credit in the Emperor of Blefuscu's court, and so much private assistance and encouragement from their party here at home, that a bloody war hath been carried on between the two empires for six and thirty moons with various success;[6] during which time we have lost forty capital ships, and a much greater number of smaller vessels, together with thirty thousand of our best seamen and soldiers; and the damage received by the enemy is reckoned to be somewhat greater than ours. However, they have now equipped a numerous fleet, and are just preparing to make a descent upon us; and his Imperial Majesty, placing great confidence in your valor and strength, hath commanded me to lay this account of his affairs before you.

I desired the Secretary to present my humble duty to the Emperor, and to let him know, that I thought it would not become me, who was a foreigner, to interfere with parties; but I was ready, with the hazard of my life, to defend his person and state against all invaders.

CHAPTER 5. *The author by an extraordinary stratagem prevents an invasion. A high title of honor is conferred upon him. Ambassadors arrive from the Emperor of Blefuscu, and sue for peace. The Empress's apartment on fire by an accident; the author instrumental in saving the rest of the palace.*

---

2. Swift's satirical allegory of the strife between Catholics (Big-Endians) and Protestants (Little-Endians) touches on Henry VIII (who "broke" with the Pope), Charles I (who lost his life), and James II (who lost his crown).
3. The Test Act (1673) prevented Catholics and Nonconformists from holding office unless they accepted the Anglican Sacrament.
4. Koran.
5. Ruler, sovereign. Swift himself accepted the right of the king to determine religious observances.
6. Reminiscent of the War of the Spanish Succession (1702–13).

The empire of Blefuscu is an island situated to the north north-east side of Lilliput, from whence it is parted only by a channel of eight hundred yards wide. I had not yet seen it, and upon this notice of an intended invasion, I avoided appearing on that side of the coast, for fear of being discovered by some of the enemy's ships, who had received no intelligence of me; all intercourse between the two empires having been strictly forbidden during the war, upon pain of death; and an embargo laid by our Emperor upon all vessels whatsoever. I communicated to his Majesty a project I had formed of seizing the enemy's whole fleet; which, as our scouts assured us, lay at anchor in the harbor ready to sail with the first fair wind. I consulted the most experienced seamen upon the depth of the channel, which they had often plumbed; who told me, that in the middle at high water it was seventy *glumgluffs* deep, which is about six foot of European measure; and the rest of it fifty *glumgluffs* at most. I walked to the northeast coast over against Blefuscu; where, lying down behind a hillock, I took out my small pocket perspective glass, and viewed the enemy's fleet at anchor, consisting of about fifty men of war, and a great number of transports: I then came back to my house, and gave order (for which I had a warrant) for a great quantity of the strongest cable and bars of iron. The cable was about as thick as packthread and the bars of the length and size of a knitting-needle. I trebled the cable to make it stronger, and for the same reason I twisted three of the iron bars together, bending the extremities into a hook. Having thus fixed fifty hooks to as many cables, I went back to the northeast coast, and putting off my coat, shoes, and stockings, walked into the sea in my leathern jerkin, about half an hour before high water. I waded with what haste I could, and swam in the middle about thirty yards until I felt the ground; I arrived at the fleet in less than half an hour. The enemy was so frighted when they saw me, that they leaped out of their ships, and swam to shore, where there could not be fewer than thirty thousand souls. I then took my tackling, and fastening a hook to the hole at the prow of each, I tied all the cords together at the end. While I was thus employed, the enemy discharged several thousand arrows, many of which stuck in my hands and face; and besides the excessive smart, gave me much disturbance in my work. My greatest apprehension was for my eyes, which I should have infallibly lost, if I had not suddenly thought of an expedient. I kept, among other little necessaries, a pair of spectacles in a private pocket, which, as I observed before, had escaped the Emperor's searchers. These I took out, and fastened as strongly as I could upon my nose; and thus armed went on boldly with my work in spite of the enemy's arrows; many of which struck against the glasses of my spectacles, but without any other effect, further than a little to discompose them. I had now fastened all the hooks, and taking the knot in my hand, began to pull; but not a ship would stir, for they were all too fast by their anchors, so that the boldest part of my enterprise remained. I therefore let go the cord, and leaving the hooks fixed to the ships, I resolutely cut with my knife the cables that fastened the anchors, receiving about two hundred shots in my face and hands; then I took up the knotted end of the cables to which my hooks were tied; and with great ease drew fifty of the enemy's largest men-of-war after me.

The Blefuscudians, who had not the least imagination of what I intended, were at first confounded with astonishment. They had seen me cut the cables, and thought my design was only to let the ships run adrift, or fall foul on each other: but when they perceived the whole fleet moving in order, and saw me pulling at the end, they set up such a scream of grief and despair, that it is almost impossible to describe or conceive. When I had got out of danger, I stopped a while to pick out the arrows that stuck in my hands and face, and rubbed on some of the same ointment that was given me at my first arrival, as I have formerly mentioned. I then took off my spectacles, and waiting about an hour until the tide was a little fallen, I waded through the middle with my cargo, and arrived safe at the royal port of Lilliput.

The Emperor and his whole court stood on the shore, expecting the issue of this great adventure. They saw the ships move forward in a large half-moon, but could not discern me, who was up to my breast in water. When I advanced to the middle of the channel, they were yet more in pain, because I was under water to my neck. The Emperor concluded me to be drowned, and that the enemy's fleet was approaching in a hostile manner: but he was soon eased of his fears, for the channel growing shallower every step I made, I came in a short time within hearing; and holding up the end of the cable by which the fleet was fastened, I cried in a loud voice, Long live the most puissant Emperor of Lilliput! This great prince received me at my landing with all possible encomiums, and created me a *Nardac* upon the spot, which is the highest title of honor among them.

His Majesty desired I would take some other opportunity of bringing all the rest of his enemy's ships into his ports. And so unmeasurable is the ambition of princes, that he seemed to think of nothing less than reducing the whole empire of Blefuscu into a province, and governing it by a viceroy; of destroying the Big-Endian exiles, and compelling that people to break the smaller end of their eggs, by which he would remain sole monarch of the whole world. But I endeavored to divert him from this design, by many arguments drawn from the topics of policy as well as justice: and I plainly protested, that I would never be an instrument of bringing a free and brave people into slavery. And when the matter was debated in council, the wisest part of the ministry were of my opinion.

This open bold declaration of mine was so opposite to the schemes and politics of his Imperial Majesty, that he could never forgive me; he mentioned it in a very artful manner at council, where I was told that some of the wisest appeared, at least by their silence, to be of my opinion; but others, who were my secret enemies, could not forbear some expressions, which by a side-wind[7] reflected on me. And from this time began an intrigue between his Majesty and a junta of ministers maliciously bent against me, which broke out in less than two months, and had like to have ended in my utter destruction. Of so little weight are the greatest services to princes, when put into the balance with a refusal to gratify their passions.[8]

About three weeks after this exploit, there arrived a solemn embassy from Blefuscu, with humble offers of a peace; which was soon concluded upon conditions very advantageous to our Emperor; wherewith I shall not trouble the reader. There were six ambassadors, with a train of about five hundred persons; and their entry was very magnificent, suitable to the grandeur of

7. Indirectly.
8. After a series of British naval victories, the Treaty of Utrecht (1713) had ended the war with France, but the Tory ministers who engineered the peace were subsequently accused of having sold out to the enemy.

their master, and the importance of their business. When their treaty was finished, wherein I did them several good offices by the credit I now had, or at least appeared to have at court, their Excellencies, who were privately told how much I had been their friend, made me a visit in form. They began with many compliments upon my valor and generosity; invited me to that kingdom in the Emperor their master's name; and desired me to show them some proofs of my prodigious strength, of which they had heard so many wonders; wherein I readily obliged them, but shall not interrupt the reader with the particulars.

When I had for some time entertained their Excellencies to their infinite satisfaction and surprise, I desired they would do me the honor to present my most humble respects to the Emperor their master, the renown of whose virtues had so justly filled the whole world with admiration, and whose royal person I resolved to attend before I returned to my own country. Accordingly, the next time I had the honor to see our Emperor, I desired his general license to wait on the Blefuscudian monarch, which he was pleased to grant me, as I could plainly perceive, in a very cold manner; but could not guess the reason, till I had a whisper from a certain person, that Flimnap and Bolgolam had represented my intercourse with those ambassadors as a mark of disaffection, from which I am sure my heart was wholly free. And this was the first time I began to conceive some imperfect idea of courts and ministers.

It is to be observed, that these ambassadors spoke to me by an interpreter; the languages of both empires differing as much from each other as any two in Europe, and each nation priding itself upon the antiquity, beauty, and energy of their own tongues, with an avowed contempt for that of their neighbor; yet our Emperor, standing upon the advantage he had got by the seizure of their fleet, obliged them to deliver their credentials, and make their speech, in the Lilliputian tongue. And it must be confessed, that from the great intercourse of trade and commerce between both realms, from the continual reception of exiles, which is mutual among them, and from the custom in each empire to send their young nobility and richer gentry to the other, in order to polish themselves, by seeing the world, and understanding men and manners, there are few persons of distinction, or merchants, or seamen, who dwell in the maritime parts, but what can hold conversation in both tongues; as I found some weeks after, when I went to pay my respects to the Emperor of Blefuscu, which in the midst of great misfortunes, through the malice of my enemies, proved a very happy adventure to me, as I shall relate in its proper place.

The reader may remember, that when I signed those articles upon which I recovered my liberty, there were some which I disliked upon account of their being too servile, neither could any thing but an extreme necessity have forced me to submit. But being now a *Nardac*, of the highest rank in that empire, such offices[9] were looked upon as below my dignity, and the Emperor (to do him justice) never once mentioned them to me. However, it was not long before I had an opportunity of doing his Majesty, at least as I then thought, a most signal service. I was alarmed at midnight with the cries of many hundred people at my door; by which being suddenly awaked, I was in some kind of terror. I heard the word *burglum* repeated incessantly;

9. Duties.

several of the Emperor's court, making their way through the crowd, intreated me to come immediately to the palace, where her Imperial Majesty's apartment was on fire, by the carelessness of a maid of honor, who fell asleep while she was reading a romance. I got up in an instant; and orders being given to clear the way before me, and it being likewise a moonshine night, I made a shift to get to the palace without trampling on any of the people. I found they had already applied ladders to the walls of the apartment, and were well provided with buckets, but the water was at some distance. These buckets were about the size of a large thimble, and the poor people supplied me with them as fast as they could; but the flame was so violent, that they did little good. I might easily have stifled it with my coat, which I unfortunately left behind me for haste, and came away only in my leathern jerkin. The case seemed wholly desperate and deplorable; and this magnificent palace would have infallibly been burnt down to the ground, if, by a presence of mind, unusual to me, I had not suddenly thought of an expedient. I had the evening before drank plentifully of a most delicious wine, called *glimigrim* (the Blefuscudians call it *flunec*, but ours is esteemed the better sort), which is very diuretic. By the luckiest chance in the world, I had not discharged myself of any part of it. The heat I had contracted by coming very near the flames, and by my laboring to quench them, made the wine begin to operate by urine; which I voided in such a quantity, and applied so well to the proper places, that in three minutes the fire was wholly extinguished; and the rest of that noble pile, which had cost so many ages in erecting, preserved from destruction.

It was now daylight, and I returned to my house, without waiting to congratulate with the Emperor; because, although I had done a very eminent piece of service, yet I could not tell how his Majesty might resent the manner by which I had performed it: for, by the fundamental laws of the realm, it is capital[1] in any person, of what quality soever, to make water within the precincts of the palace. But I was a little comforted by a message from his Majesty, that he would give orders to the Grand Justiciary for passing my pardon in form; which, however, I could not obtain. And I was privately assured, that the Empress, conceiving the greatest abhorrence of what I had done,[2] removed to the most distant side of the court, firmly resolved that those buildings should never be repaired for her use; and, in the presence of her chief confidents, could not forbear vowing revenge.

CHAPTER 6. *Of the inhabitants of Lilliput; their learning, laws, and customs, the manner of educating their children. The author's way of living in that country. His vindication of a great lady.*

Although I intend to leave the description of this empire to a particular treatise, yet in the mean time I am content to gratify the curious reader with some general ideas. As the common size of the natives is somewhat under six inches, so there is an exact proportion in all other animals, as well as plants and trees: for instance, the tallest horses and oxen are between four and five inches in height, the sheep an inch and a half, more or less; their geese

---

1. Punishable by death.
2. Queen Anne, whom Swift called "a royal

prude," strongly objected to the coarseness of *A Tale of a Tub.*

about the bigness of a sparrow; and so the several gradations downwards, till you come to the smallest, which, to my sight, were almost invisible; but nature hath adapted the eyes of the Lilliputians to all objects proper for their view: they see with great exactness, but at no great distance. And to show the sharpness of their sight towards objects that are near, I have been much pleased with observing a cook pulling[3] a lark, which was not so large as a common fly; and a young girl threading an invisible needle with invisible silk. Their tallest trees are about seven foot high; I mean some of those in the great royal park, the tops whereof I could but just reach with my fist clinched. The other vegetables[4] are in the same proportion; but this I leave to the reader's imagination.

I shall say but little at present of their learning, which for many ages hath flourished in all its branches among them: but their manner of writing is very peculiar; being neither from the left to the right, like the Europeans; nor from the right to the left, like the Arabians; nor from up to down, like the Chinese; nor from down to up, like the Cascagians;[5] but aslant from one corner of the paper to the other, like ladies in England.

They bury their dead with their heads directly downwards; because they hold an opinion that in eleven thousand moons they are all to rise again; in which period, the earth (which they conceive to be flat) will turn upside down, and by this means they shall, at their resurrection, be found ready standing on their feet. The learned among them confess the absurdity of this doctrine; but the practice still continues, in compliance to the vulgar.[6]

There are some laws and customs in this empire very peculiar; and if they were not so directly contrary to those of my own dear country, I should be tempted to say a little in their justification. It is only to be wished, that they were as well executed. The first I shall mention relateth to informers. All crimes against the state are punished here with the utmost severity; but if the person accused make his innocence plainly to appear upon his trial, the accuser is immediately put to an ignominious death; and out of his goods or lands, the innocent person is quadruply recompensed for the loss of his time, for the danger he underwent, for the hardship of his imprisonment, and for all the charges he hath been at in making his defense. Or, if that fund be deficient, it is largely[7] supplied by the crown. The Emperor doth also confer on him some public mark of his favor; and proclamation is made of his innocence through the whole city.

They look upon fraud as a greater crime than theft, and therefore seldom fail to punish it with death; for they allege, that care and vigilance, with a very common understanding, may preserve a man's goods from thieves; but honesty hath no fence against superior cunning: and since it is necessary that there should be a perpetual intercourse of buying and selling, and dealing upon credit, where fraud is permitted or connived at, or hath no law to punish it, the honest dealer is always undone, and the knave gets the advantage. I remember when I was once interceding with the King for a criminal who had wronged his master of a great sum of money, which he had received by order, and ran away with; and happening to tell his Majesty, by way of

---

3. Plucking.
4. Plants.
5. Swift's invention.

6. The (beliefs of the) common people.
7. Fully.

extenuation, that it was only a breach of trust, the Emperor thought it monstrous in me to offer, as a defense, the greatest aggravation of the crime: and truly, I had little to say in return, farther than the common answer, that different nations had different customs; for, I confess, I was heartily ashamed.

Although we usually call reward and punishment the two hinges upon which all government turns, yet I could never observe this maxim to be put in practice by any nation, except that of Lilliput. Whoever can there bring sufficient proof that he hath strictly observed the laws of his country for seventy-three moons, hath a claim to certain privileges, according to his quality[8] and condition of life, with a proportionable sum of money out of a fund appropriated for that use: he likewise acquires the title of *Snilpall*, or *Legal*, which is added to his name, but doth not descend to his posterity. And these people thought it a prodigious defect of policy among us, when I told them that our laws were enforced only by penalties, without any mention of reward. It is upon this account that the image of Justice, in their courts of judicature, is formed with six eyes, two before, as many behind, and on each side one, to signify circumspection; with a bag of gold open in her right hand, and a sword sheathed in her left, to show she is more disposed to reward than to punish.

In choosing persons for all employments, they have more regard to good morals than to great abilities; for, since government is necessary to mankind, they believe that the common size of human understandings is fitted to some station or other; and that Providence never intended to make the management of public affairs a mystery, to be comprehended only by a few persons of sublime genius, of which there seldom are three born in an age: but they suppose truth, justice, temperance, and the like, to be in every man's power; the practice of which virtues, assisted by experience and a good intention, would qualify any man for the service of his country, except where a course of study is required. But they thought the want of moral virtues was so far from being supplied by superior endowments of the mind, that employments could never be put into such dangerous hands as those of persons so qualified; and at least, that the mistakes committed by ignorance in a virtuous disposition would never be of such fatal consequence to the public weal, as the practices of a man whose inclinations led him to be corrupt, and had great abilities to manage, to multiply, and defend his corruptions.

In like manner, the disbelief of a divine Providence renders a man uncapable of holding any public station; for since kings avow themselves to be the deputies of Providence, the Lilliputians think nothing can be more absurd than for a prince to employ such men as disown the authority under which he acteth.

In relating these and the following laws, I would only be understood to mean the original institutions, and not the most scandalous corruptions into which these people are fallen by the degenerate nature of man. For as to that infamous practice of acquiring great employments by dancing on the ropes, or badges of favor and distinction by leaping over sticks, and creeping under them, the reader is to observe, that they were first introduced by the grandfather of the Emperor now reigning; and grew to the present height by the gradual increase of party and faction.

8. Social position.

Ingratitude is among them a capital crime, as we read it to have been in some other countries; for they reason thus, that whoever makes ill returns to his benefactor, must needs be a common enemy to the rest of mankind, from whom he hath received no obligation; and therefore such a man is not fit to live.

Their notions relating to the duties of parents and children differ extremely from ours. For, since the conjunction of male and female is founded upon the great law of nature, in order to propagate and continue the species, the Lilliputians will needs have it, that men and women are joined together like other animals, by the motives of concupiscence; and that their tenderness towards their young proceedeth from the like natural principle: for which reason they will never allow, that a child is under any obligation to his father for begetting him, or to his mother for bringing him into the world; which, considering the miseries of human life, was neither a benefit in itself, nor intended so by his parents, whose thoughts in their love-encounters were otherwise employed. Upon these, and the like reasonings, their opinion is, that parents are the last of all others to be trusted with the education of their own children: and therefore they have in every town public nurseries, where all parents, except cottagers[9] and laborers, are obliged to send their infants of both sexes to be reared and educated when they come to the age of twenty moons; at which time they are supposed to have some rudiments of docility. These schools are of several kinds, suited to different qualities, and to both sexes. They have certain professors[1] well skilled in preparing children for such a condition of life as befits the rank of their parents, and their own capacities as well as inclinations. I shall first say something of the male nurseries, and then of the female.

The nurseries for males of noble or eminent birth are provided with grave and learned professors, and their several deputies. The clothes and food of the children are plain and simple. They are bred up in the principles of honor, justice, courage, modesty, clemency, religion, and love of their country; they are always employed in some business, except in the times of eating and sleeping, which are very short, and two hours for diversions, consisting of bodily exercises. They are dressed by men until four years of age, and then are obliged to dress themselves, although their quality be ever so great; and the women attendants, who are aged proportionably to ours at fifty, perform only the most menial offices. They are never suffered to converse with servants, but go together in small or greater numbers to take their diversions, and always in the presence of a professor, or one of his deputies; whereby they avoid those early bad impressions of folly and vice to which our children are subject. Their parents are suffered to see them only twice a year; the visit is not to last above an hour; they are allowed to kiss the child at meeting and parting; but a professor, who always standeth by on those occasions, will not suffer them to whisper, or use any fondling expressions, or bring any presents of toys, sweetmeats, and the like.

The pension from each family for the education and entertainment[2] of a child, upon failure of due payment, is levied by the Emperor's officers.

---

9. Agricultural workers, peasants.
1. Professional teachers.

2. Sustenance.

The nurseries for children of ordinary gentlemen, merchants, traders, and handicrafts, are managed proportionably after the same manner; only those designed for trades are put out apprentices at seven years old; whereas those of persons of quality continue in their exercises until fifteen, which answers to one and twenty with us: but the confinement is gradually lessened for the last three years.

In the female nurseries, the young girls of quality are educated much like the males, only they are dressed by orderly servants of their own sex, but always in the presence of a professor or deputy, until they come to dress themselves, which is at five years old. And if it be found that these nurses ever presume to entertain the girls with frightful or foolish stories, or the common follies practiced by chambermaids among us, they are publicly whipped thrice about the city, imprisoned for a year, and banished for life to the most desolate parts of the country. Thus the young ladies there are as much ashamed of being cowards and fools as the men; and despise all personal ornaments beyond decency and cleanliness: neither did I perceive any difference in their education, made by their difference of sex, only that the exercises of the females were not altogether so robust; and that some rules were given them relating to domestic life, and a smaller compass of learning was enjoined them: for their maxim is, that among people of quality, a wife should be always a reasonable and agreeable companion, because she cannot always be young. When the girls are twelve years old, which among them is the marriageable age, their parents or guardians take them home, with great expressions of gratitude to the professors, and seldom without tears of the young lady and her companions.

In the nurseries of females of the meaner sort, the children are instructed in all kinds of works proper for their sex, and their several degrees:[3] those intended for apprentices are dismissed at seven years old, the rest are kept to eleven.

The meaner families who have children at these nurseries are obliged, besides their annual pension, which is as low as possible, to return to the steward of the nursery a small monthly share of their gettings, to be a portion for the child; and therefore all parents are limited in their expenses by the law. For the Lilliputians think nothing can be more unjust, than that people, in subservience to their own appetites, should bring children into the world, and leave the burthen of supporting them on the public. As to persons of quality, they give security to appropriate a certain sum for each child, suitable to their condition; and these funds are always managed with good husbandry, and the most exact justice.

The cottagers and laborers keep their children at home, their business being only to till and cultivate the earth; and therefore their education is of little consequence to the public; but the old and diseased among them are supported by hospitals: for begging is a trade unknown in this empire.

And here it may perhaps divert the curious reader, to give some account of my domestic,[4] and my manner of living in this country, during a residence of nine months and thirteen days. Having a head mechanically turned, and being likewise forced by necessity, I had made for myself a table and chair

---

3. Various social ranks.

4. Household.

convenient enough, out of the largest trees in the royal park. Two hundred sempstresses were employed to make me shirts, and linen for my bed and table, all of the strongest and coarsest kind they could get; which, however, they were forced to quilt together in several folds; for the thickest was some degrees finer than lawn. Their linen is usually three inches wide, and three foot make a piece. The sempstresses took my measure as I lay on the ground, one standing at my neck, and another at my mid-leg, with a strong cord extended, that each held by the end, while the third measured the length of the cord with a rule of an inch long. Then they measured my right thumb, and desired no more; for by a mathematical computation, that twice round the thumb is one round the wrist, and so on to the neck and the waist; and by the help of my old shirt, which I displayed on the ground before them for a pattern, they fitted me exactly. Three hundred tailors were employed in the same manner to make me clothes; but they had another contrivance for taking my measure. I kneeled down, and they raised a ladder from the ground to my neck; upon this ladder one of them mounted, and let fall a plumb-line from my collar to the floor, which just answered the length of my coat; but my waist and arms I measured myself. When my clothes were finished, which was done in my house (for the largest of theirs would not have been able to hold them), they looked like the patchwork made by the ladies in England, only that mine were all of a color.

I had three hundred cooks to dress my victuals, in little convenient huts built about my house, where they and their families lived, and prepared me two dishes apiece. I took up twenty waiters in my hand, and placed them on the table; an hundred more attended below on the ground, some with dishes of meat, and some with barrels of wine, and other liquors, slung on their shoulders; all which the waiters above drew up as I wanted, in a very ingenious manner, by certain cords, as we draw the bucket up a well in Europe. A dish of their meat was a good mouthful, and a barrel of their liquor a reasonable draught. Their mutton yields to ours, but their beef is excellent. I have had a sirloin so large, that I have been forced to make three bites of it; but this is rare. My servants were astonished to see me eat it bones and all, as in our country we do the leg of a lark. Their geese and turkeys I usually eat at a mouthful, and I must confess they far exceed ours. Of their smaller fowl I could take up twenty or thirty at the end of my knife.

One day his Imperial Majesty, being informed of my way of living, desired that himself and his royal consort, with the young princes of the blood of both sexes, might have the happiness (as he was pleased to call it) of dining with me. They came accordingly, and I placed them upon chairs of state on my table, just over against me, with their guards about them. Flimnap the Lord High Treasurer attended there likewise, with his white staff; and I observed he often looked on me with a sour countenance, which I would not seem to regard, but eat more than usual, in honor to my dear country, as well as to fill the court with admiration. I have some private reasons to believe, that this visit from his Majesty gave Flimnap an opportunity of doing me ill offices to his master. That minister had always been my secret enemy, although he outwardly caressed me more than was usual to the moroseness of his nature. He represented to the Emperor the low condition of his treasury; that he was forced to take up money at great discount; that exchequer bills[5] would not circulate under nine per cent below par; that I had cost his Majesty above a million and a half of *sprugs* (their greatest gold coin, about the bigness of a spangle); and upon the whole, that it would be advisable in the Emperor to take the first fair occasion of dismissing me.

I am here obliged to vindicate the reputation of an excellent lady, who was an innocent sufferer upon my account. The Treasurer took a fancy to be jealous of his wife, from the malice of some evil tongues, who informed him that her Grace had taken a violent affection for my person; and the court-scandal ran for some time that she once came privately to my lodging. This I solemnly declare to be a most infamous falsehood, without any grounds, farther than that her Grace was pleased to treat me with all innocent marks of freedom and friendship. I own she came often to my house, but always publicly, nor ever without three more in the coach, who were usually her sister and young daughter, and some particular acquaintance; but this was common to many other ladies of the court. And I still appeal to my servants round, whether they at any time saw a coach at my door without knowing what persons were in it. On those occasions, when a servant had given me notice, my custom was to go immediately to the door; and, after paying my respects, to take up the coach and two horses very carefully in my hands (for if there were six horses, the postillion always unharnessed four) and place them on a table, where I had fixed a moveable rim quite round, of five inches high, to prevent accidents. And I have often had four coaches and horses at once on my table full of company, while I sat in my chair leaning my face towards them; and when I was engaged with one set, the coachmen would gently drive the others round my table. I have passed many an afternoon very agreeably in these conversations. But I defy the Treasurer, or his two informers (I will name them, and let them make their best of it) Clustril and Drunlo, to prove that any person ever came to me *incognito*, except the Secretary Reldresal, who was sent by express command of his Imperial Majesty, as I have before related. I should not have dwelt so long upon this particular, if it had not been a point wherein the reputation of a great lady is so nearly concerned, to say nothing of my own; although I had the honor to be a *Nardac*, which the Treasurer himself is not; for all the world knows he is only a *Clumglum*, a title inferior by one degree, as that of a marquis is to a duke in England; yet I allow he preceded me in right of his post. These false informations, which I afterwards came to the knowledge of, by an accident not proper to mention, made the Treasurer show his lady for some time an ill countenance, and me a worse; for although he was at last undeceived and reconciled to her, yet I lost all credit with him; and found my interest decline very fast with the Emperor himself, who was indeed too much governed by that favorite.

CHAPTER 7. *The author, being informed of a design to accuse him of high treason, makes his escape to Blefuscu. His reception there.*

Before I proceed to give an account of my leaving this kingdom, it may be proper to inform the reader of a private intrigue which had been for two months forming against me.

---

5. Government bills of credit. Walpole was noted as a canny financier.

I had been hitherto all my life a stranger to courts, for which I was unqualified by the meanness of my condition. I had indeed heard and read enough of the dispositions of great princes and ministers; but never expected to have found such terrible effects of them in so remote a country, governed, as I thought, by very different maxims from those in Europe.

When I was just preparing to pay my attendance on the Emperor of Blefuscu, a considerable person at court (to whom I had been very serviceable at a time when he lay under the highest displeasure of his Imperial Majesty) came to my house very privately at night in a close chair, and without sending his name, desired admittance. The chairmen were dismissed; I put the chair, with his Lordship in it, into my coat-pocket; and giving orders to a trusty servant to say I was indisposed and gone to sleep, I fastened the door of my house, placed the chair on the table, according to my usual custom, and sat down by it. After the common salutations were over, observing his Lordship's countenance full of concern, and enquiring into the reason, he desired I would hear him with patience, in a matter that highly concerned my honor and my life. His speech was to the following effect, for I took notes of it as soon as he left me.

You are to know, said he, that several committees of council have been lately called in the most private manner on your account: and it is but two days since his Majesty came to a full resolution.

You are very sensible that Skyresh Bolgolam (*Galbet*, or High Admiral) hath been your mortal enemy almost ever since your arrival. His original reasons I know not; but his hatred is much increased since your great success against Blefuscu, by which his glory, as Admiral, is obscured. This lord, in conjunction with Flimnap the High Treasurer, whose enmity against you is notorious on account of his lady, Limtoc the General, Lalcon the Chamberlain, and Balmuff the Grand Justiciary, have prepared articles of impeachment against you, for treason, and other capital crimes.[6]

This preface made me so impatient, being conscious of my own merits and innocence, that I was going to interrupt; when he entreated me to be silent, and thus proceeded.

Out of gratitude for the favors you have done me, I procured information of the whole proceedings, and a copy of the articles, wherein I venture my head for your service.

Articles of Impeachment against Quinbus Flestrin (*the* Man-Mountain).

ARTICLE I

Whereas, by a statute made in the reign of his Imperial Majesty Calin Deffar Plune, it is enacted, that whoever shall make water within the precincts of the royal palace shall be liable to the pains and penalties of high treason: notwithstanding, the said Quinbus Flestrin, in open breach of the said law, under color of extinguishing the fire kindled in the apartment of his Majesty's most dear imperial consort, did maliciously, traitorously, and devilishly, by discharge of his urine, put out

---

6. After the Whigs had investigated Oxford and Bolingbroke, both were impeached for high treason, on charges of being sympathetic to the Jacobites and the French.

the said fire kindled in the said apartment, lying and being within the precincts of the said royal palace; against the statute in that case provided, etc., against the duty, etc.

ARTICLE 2

That the said Quinbus Flestrin, having brought the imperial fleet of Blefuscu into the royal port, and being afterwards commanded by his Imperial Majesty to seize all the other ships of the said empire of Blefuscu, and reduce that empire to a province, to be governed by a viceroy from hence; and to destroy and put to death not only all the Big-Endian exiles, but likewise all the people of that empire who would not immediately forsake the Big-Endian heresy: he, the said Flestrin, like a false traitor against his most auspicious, serene, Imperial Majesty, did petition to be excused from the said service, upon pretense of unwillingness to force the consciences, or destroy the liberties and lives of an innocent people.

ARTICLE 3

That, whereas certain ambassadors arrived from the court of Blefuscu to sue for peace in his Majesty's court: he the said Flestrin did, like a false traitor, aid, abet, comfort, and divert the said ambassadors; although he knew them to be servants to a prince who was lately an open enemy to his Imperial Majesty, and in open war against his said Majesty.

ARTICLE 4

That the said Quinbus Flestrin, contrary to the duty of a faithful subject, is now preparing to make a voyage to the court and empire of Blefuscu, for which he hath received only verbal license from his Imperial Majesty; and under color of the said license, doth falsely and traitorously intend to take the said voyage, and thereby to aid, comfort, and abet the Emperor of Blefuscu, so late an enemy, and in open war with his Imperial Majesty aforesaid.

There are some other articles, but these are the most important, of which I have read you an abstract.

In the several debates upon this impeachment, it must be confessed that his Majesty gave many marks of his great *lenity*; often urging the services you had done him, and endeavoring to extenuate your crimes. The Treasurer and Admiral insisted that you should be put to the most painful and ignominious death, by setting fire on your house at night; and the General was to attend with twenty thousand men armed with poisoned arrows, to shoot you on the face and hands. Some of your servants were to have private orders to strew a poisonous juice on your shirts and sheets, which would soon make you tear your own flesh, and die in the utmost torture. The General came into the same opinion; so that for a long time there was a majority against you. But his Majesty resolving, if possible, to spare your life, at last brought off[7] the Chamberlain.

---

7. Won over.

Upon this incident, Reldresal, Principal Secretary for Private Affairs, who always approved[8] himself your true friend, was commanded by the Emperor to deliver his opinion, which he accordingly did; and therein justified the good thoughts you have of him. He allowed your crimes to be great; but that still there was room for mercy, the most commendable virtue in a prince, and for which his Majesty was so justly celebrated. He said, the friendship between you and him was so well known to the world, that perhaps the most honorable board might think him partial: however, in obedience to the command he had received, he would freely offer his sentiments. That if his Majesty, in consideration of your services, and pursuant to his own merciful disposition, would please to spare your life, and only give order to put out both your eyes, he humbly conceived, that by this expedient justice might in some measure be satisfied, and all the world would applaud the *lenity* of the Emperor, as well as the fair and generous proceedings of those who have the honor to be his counselors. That the loss of your eyes would be no impediment to your bodily strength, by which you might still be useful to his Majesty. That blindness is an addition to courage, by concealing dangers from us; that the fear you had for your eyes was the greatest difficulty in bringing over the enemy's fleet; and it would be sufficient for you to see by the eyes of the ministers, since the greatest princes do no more.

This proposal was received with the utmost disapprobation by the whole board. Bolgolam, the Admiral, could not preserve his temper; but rising up in fury, said, he wondered how the Secretary durst presume to give his opinion for preserving the life of a traitor: that the services you had performed were, by all true reasons of state, the great aggravation of your crimes; that you, who were able to extinguish the fire by discharge of urine in her Majesty's apartment (which he mentioned with horror), might, at another time, raise an inundation by the same means, to drown the whole palace; and the same strength which enabled you to bring over the enemy's fleet might serve, upon the first discontent, to carry it back: that he had good reasons to think you were a Big-Endian in your heart; and as treason begins in the heart before it appears in overt acts, so he accused you as a traitor on that account, and therefore insisted you should be put to death.

The Treasurer was of the same opinion; he showed to what straits his Majesty's revenue was reduced by the charge of maintaining you, which would soon grow insupportable: that the Secretary's expedient of putting out your eyes was so far from being a remedy against this evil, that it would probably increase it; as it is manifest from the common practice of blinding some kind of fowl, after which they fed the faster, and grew sooner fat: that his sacred Majesty, and the council, who are your judges, were in their own consciences fully convinced of your guilt; which was a sufficient argument to condemn you to death, without the formal proofs required by the strict letter of the law.

But his Imperial Majesty, fully determined against capital punishment, was graciously pleased to say, that since the council thought the loss of your eyes too easy a censure, some other may be inflicted hereafter. And your friend the Secretary humbly desiring to be heard again, in answer to what the Treasurer had objected concerning the great charge his Majesty was at

8. Proved.

in maintaining you, said, that his Excellency, who had the sole disposal of the Emperor's revenue, might easily provide against this evil, by gradually lessening your establishment; by which, for want of sufficient food, you would grow weak and faint, and lose your appetite, and consequently decay and consume in a few months; neither would the stench of your carcass be then so dangerous, when it should become more than half diminished; and immediately upon your death, five or six thousand of his Majesty's subjects might, in two or three days, cut your flesh from your bones, take it away by cart-loads, and bury it in distant parts to prevent infection; leaving the skeleton as a monument of admiration to posterity.

Thus by the great friendship of the Secretary, the whole affair was compromised. It was strictly enjoined, that the project of starving you by degrees should be kept a secret; but the sentence of putting out your eyes was entered on the books; none dissenting except Bolgolam the Admiral, who being a creature of the Empress, was perpetually instigated by her Majesty to insist upon your death; she having borne perpetual malice against you, on account of that infamous and illegal method you took to extinguish the fire in her apartment.

In three days your friend the Secretary will be directed to come to your house, and read before you the articles of impeachment; and then to signify the great lenity and favor of his Majesty and council; whereby you are only condemned to the loss of your eyes, which his Majesty doth not question you will gratefully and humbly submit to; and twenty of his Majesty's surgeons will attend, in order to see the operation well performed, by discharging very sharp-pointed arrows into the balls of your eyes, as you lie on the ground.

I leave to your prudence what measures you will take; and to avoid suspicion, I must immediately return in as private a manner as I came.

His Lordship did so, and I remained alone, under many doubts and perplexities of mind.

It was a custom introduced by this prince and his ministry (very different, as I have been assured, from the practices of former times), that after the court had decreed any cruel execution, either to gratify the monarch's resentment, or the malice of a favorite, the Emperor always made a speech to his whole council, expressing his great lenity and tenderness, as qualities known and confessed by all the world. This speech was immediately published through the kingdom; nor did any thing terrify the people so much as those encomiums on his Majesty's mercy; because it was observed, that the more these praises were enlarged and insisted on, the more inhuman was the punishment, and the sufferer more innocent. Yet as to myself, I must confess, having never been designed for a courtier, either by my birth or education, I was so ill a judge of things, that I could not discover the lenity and favor of this sentence, but conceived it (perhaps erroneously) rather to be rigorous than gentle. I sometimes thought of standing my trial; for although I could not deny the facts alleged in the several articles, yet I hoped they would admit of some extenuations. But having in my life perused many state trials, which I ever observed to terminate as the judges thought fit to direct, I durst not rely on so dangerous a decision, in so critical a juncture, and against such powerful enemies. Once I was strongly bent upon resistance: for while I had liberty, the whole strength of that empire could hardly subdue me, and I might easily with stones pelt the metropolis to pieces; but

I soon rejected that project with horror, by remembering the oath I had made to the Emperor, the favors I received from him, and the high title of *Nardac* he conferred upon me. Neither had I so soon learned the gratitude of courtiers, to persuade myself that his Majesty's present severities acquitted me of all past obligations.

At last I fixed upon a resolution, for which it is probable I may incur some censure, and not unjustly; for I confess I owe the preserving my eyes, and consequently my liberty, to my own great rashness and want of experience: because if I had then known the nature of princes and ministers, which I have since observed in many other courts, and their methods of treating criminals less obnoxious than myself, I should with great alacrity and readiness have submitted to so *easy* a punishment. But hurried on by the precipitancy of youth, and having his Imperial Majesty's license to pay my attendance upon the Emperor of Blefuscu, I took this opportunity, before the three days were elapsed, to send a letter to my friend the Secretary, signifying my resolution of setting out that morning for Blefuscu,[9] pursuant to the leave I had got; and without waiting for an answer, I went to that side of the island where our fleet lay. I seized a large man of war, tied a cable to the prow, and lifting up the anchors, I stripped myself, put my clothes (together with my coverlet, which I carried under my arm) into the vessel; and drawing it after me, between wading and swimming, arrived at the royal port of Blefuscu, where the people had long expected me. They lent me two guides to direct me to the capital city, which is of the same name; I held them in my hands until I came within two hundred yards of the gate; and desired them to signify my arrival to one of the secretaries, and let him know, I there waited his Majesty's commands. I had an answer in about an hour, that his Majesty, attended by the royal family, and great officers of the court, was coming out to receive me. I advanced a hundred yards; the Emperor, and his train, alighted from their horses, the Empress and ladies from their coaches; and I did not perceive they were in any fright or concern. I lay on the ground to kiss his Majesty's and the Empress's hand. I told his Majesty that I was come according to my promise, and with the license of the Emperor my master, to have the honor of seeing so mighty a monarch, and to offer him any service in my power, consistent with my duty to my own prince; not mentioning a word of my disgrace, because I had hitherto no regular information of it, and might suppose myself wholly ignorant of any such design; neither could I reasonably conceive that the Emperor would discover the secret while I was out of his power: wherein, however, it soon appeared I was deceived.

I shall not trouble the reader with the particular account of my reception at this court, which was suitable to the generosity of so great a prince; nor of the difficulties I was in for want of a house and bed, being forced to lie on the ground, wrapped up in my coverlet.

CHAPTER 8. *The author, by a lucky accident, finds means to leave Blefuscu; and, after some difficulties, returns safe to his native country.*

Three days after my arrival, walking out of curiosity to the northeast coast of the island, I observed, about half a league off, in the sea, somewhat that

9. Before his trial for treason could be held, Bolingbroke had escaped to France.

looked like a boat overturned. I pulled off my shoes and stockings, and wading two or three hundred yards, I found the object to approach nearer by force of the tide; and then plainly saw it to be a real boat, which I supposed might, by some tempest, have been driven from a ship. Whereupon I returned immediately towards the city, and desired his Imperial Majesty to lend me twenty of the tallest vessels he had left after the loss of his fleet, and three thousand seamen under the command of his Vice Admiral. This fleet sailed round, while I went back the shortest way to the coast where I first discovered the boat; I found the tide had driven it still nearer; the seamen were all provided with cordage, which I had beforehand twisted to a sufficient strength. When the ships came up, I stripped myself, and waded till I came within an hundred yards of the boat; after which I was forced to swim till I got up to it. The seamen threw me the end of the cord, which I fastened to a hole in the forepart of the boat, and the other end to a man of war: but I found all my labor to little purpose; for being out of my depth, I was not able to work. In this necessity, I was forced to swim behind, and push the boat forwards as often as I could, with one of my hands; and the tide favoring me, I advanced so far, that I could just hold up my chin and feel the ground. I rested two or three minutes, and then gave the boat another shove, and so on till the sea was no higher than my armpits. And now the most laborious part being over, I took out my other cables which were stowed in one of the ships, and fastening them first to the boat, and then to nine of the vessels which attended me, the wind being favorable, the seamen towed, and I shoved till we arrived within forty yards of the shore; and waiting till the tide was out, I got dry to the boat, and by the assistance of two thousand men, with ropes and engines, I made a shift to turn it on its bottom, and found it was but little damaged.

I shall not trouble the reader with the difficulties I was under by the help of certain paddles, which cost me ten days making, to get my boat to the royal port of Blefuscu; where a mighty concourse of people appeared upon my arrival, full of wonder at the sight of so prodigious a vessel. I told the Emperor that my good fortune had thrown this boat in my way, to carry me to some place from whence I might return into my native country; and begged his Majesty's orders for getting materials to fit it up, together with license to depart; which, after some kind expostulations, he was pleased to grant.

I did very much wonder, in all this time, not to have heard of any express relating to me from our Emperor to the court of Blefuscu. But I was afterwards given privately to understand, that his Imperial Majesty, never imagining I had the least notice of his designs, believed I was only gone to Blefuscu in performance of my promise, according to the license he had given me, which was well known at our court; and would return in a few days when that ceremony was ended. But he was at last in pain at my long absence; and, after consulting with the Treasurer, and the rest of that cabal, a person of quality was dispatched with the copy of the articles against me. This envoy had instructions to represent to the monarch of Blefuscu the great lenity of his master, who was content to punish me no further than with the loss of my eyes; that I had fled from justice, and if I did not return in two hours, I should be deprived of my title of *Nardac*, and declared a traitor. The envoy further added, that in order to maintain the peace and amity between both empires, his master expected, that his brother of Blefuscu would give orders to have me sent back to Lilliput, bound hand and foot, to be punished as a traitor.

The Emperor of Blefuscu, having taken three days to consult, returned an answer consisting of many civilities and excuses. He said, that as for sending me bound, his brother knew it was impossible; that although I had deprived him of his fleet, yet he owed great obligations to me for many good offices I had done him in making the peace. That however, both their Majesties would soon be made easy; for I had found a prodigious vessel on the shore, able to carry me on the sea, which he had given order to fit up with my own assistance and direction; and he hoped in a few weeks both empires would be freed from so insupportable an incumbrance.

With this answer the envoy returned to Lilliput, and the monarch of Blefuscu related to me all that had passed, offering me at the same time (but under the strictest confidence) his gracious protection, if I would continue in his service; wherein although I believed him sincere, yet I resolved never more to put any confidence in princes or ministers, where I could possibly avoid it; and therefore, with all due acknowledgements for his favorable intentions, I humbly begged to be excused. I told him, that since fortune, whether good or evil, had thrown a vessel in my way, I was resolved to venture myself in the ocean, rather than be an occasion of difference between two such mighty monarchs. Neither did I find the Emperor at all displeased; and I discovered by a certain accident, that he was very glad of my resolution, and so were most of his ministers.

These considerations moved me to hasten my departure somewhat sooner than I intended; to which the court, impatient to have me gone, very readily contributed. Five hundred workmen were employed to make two sails to my boat, according to my directions, by quilting thirteen fold of their strongest linen together. I was at the pains of making ropes and cables, by twisting ten, twenty or thirty of the thickest and strongest of theirs. A great stone that I happened to find, after a long search by the seashore, served me for an anchor. I had the tallow of three hundred cows for greasing my boat, and other uses. I was at incredible pains in cutting down some of the largest timber trees for oars and masts, wherein I was, however, much assisted by his Majesty's ship-carpenters, who helped me in smoothing them, after I had done the rough work.

In about a month, when all was prepared, I sent to receive his Majesty's commands, and to take my leave. The Emperor and royal family came out of the palace; I lay down on my face to kiss his hand, which he very graciously gave me: so did the Empress, and young princes of the blood. His Majesty presented me with fifty purses of two hundred *sprugs* apiece, together with his picture at full length, which I put immediately into one of my gloves, to keep it from being hurt. The ceremonies at my departure were too many to trouble the reader with at this time.

I stored the boat with the carcasses of an hundred oxen, and three hundred sheep, with bread and drink proportionable, and as much meat ready dressed as four hundred cooks could provide. I took with me six cows and two bulls alive, with as many ewes and rams, intending to carry them into my own country, and propagate the breed. And to feed them on board, I had a good bundle of hay, and a bag of corn.[1] I would gladly have taken a dozen of the natives; but this was a thing the Emperor would by no means permit; and besides a diligent search into my pockets, his Majesty engaged my honor not to carry away any of his subjects, although with their own consent and desire.

Having thus prepared all things as well as I was able, I set sail on the twenty-fourth day of September, 1701, at six in the morning; and when I had gone about four leagues to the northward, the wind being at southeast, at six in the evening, I descried a small island about half a league to the northwest. I advanced forward, and cast anchor on the lee-side of the island, which seemed to be uninhabited. I then took some refreshment, and went to my rest. I slept well, and as I conjecture at least six hours; for I found the day broke in two hours after I awaked. It was a clear night; I eat my breakfast before the sun was up; and heaving anchor, the wind being favorable, I steered the same course that I had done the day before, wherein I was directed by my pocket compass. My intention was to reach, if possible, one of those islands which I had reason to believe lay to the northeast of Van Diemen's Land. I discovered nothing all that day; but upon the next, about three in the afternoon, when I had by my computation made twenty-four leagues from Blefuscu, I descried a sail steering to the southeast; my course was due east. I hailed her, but could get no answer; yet I found I gained upon her, for the wind slackened. I made all the sail I could, and in half an hour she spied me, then hung out her ancient,[2] and discharged a gun. It is not easy to express the joy I was in upon the unexpected hope of once more seeing my beloved country, and the dear pledges[3] I had left in it. The ship slackened her sails, and I came up with her between five and six in the evening, September 26; but my heart leapt within me to see her English colors. I put my cows and sheep into my coat-pockets and got on board with all my little cargo of provisions. The vessel was an English merchantman, returning from Japan by the North and South Seas;[4] the captain, Mr. John Biddel of Deptford, a very civil man, and an excellent sailor. We were now in the latitude of 30 degrees south; there were about fifty men in the ship; and here I met an old comrade of mine, one Peter Williams, who gave me a good character to the captain. This gentleman treated me with kindness, and desired I would let him know what place I came from last, and whither I was bound; which I did in few words; but he thought I was raving, and that the dangers I underwent had disturbed my head; whereupon I took my black cattle and sheep out of my pocket, which, after great astonishment, clearly convinced him of my veracity. I then showed him the gold given me by the Emperor of Blefuscu, together with his Majesty's picture at full length, and some other rarities of that country. I gave him two purses of two hundred *sprugs* each, and promised, when we arrived in England, to make him a present of a cow and a sheep big with young.

I shall not trouble the reader with a particular account of this voyage; which was very prosperous for the most part. We arrived in the Downs[5] on the 13th of April, 1702. I had only one misfortune, that the rats on board car-

---

1. Generic term for any cereal or grain crop (here, wheat).
2. Flag.
3. Hostages (i.e., his family).

4. North and South Pacific.
5. A rendezvous for ships off the southeast coast of England.

ried away one of my sheep; I found her bones in a hole, picked clean from the flesh. The rest of my cattle I got safe on shore, and set them a grazing in a bowling-green at Greenwich, where the fineness of the grass made them feed very heartily, though I had always feared the contrary; neither could I possibly have preserved them in so long a voyage, if the captain had not allowed me some of his best biscuit, which rubbed to powder, and mingled with water, was their constant food. The short time I continued in England, I made a considerable profit by showing my cattle to many persons of quality, and others: and before I began my second voyage, I sold them for six hundred pounds. Since my last return, I find the breed is considerably increased, especially the sheep; which I hope will prove much to the advantage of the woolen manufacture, by the fineness of the fleeces.

I stayed but two months with my wife and family; for my insatiable desire of seeing foreign countries would suffer me to continue no longer. I left fifteen hundred pounds with my wife, and fixed her in a good house at Redriff. My remaining stock I carried with me, part in money, and part in goods, in hopes to improve my fortunes. My eldest uncle, John, had left me an estate in land, near Epping, of about thirty pounds a year; and I had a long lease of the Black Bull in Fetter Lane, which yielded me as much more: so that I was not in any danger of leaving my family upon the parish.[6] My son Johnny, named so after his uncle, was at the grammar school, and a towardly[7] child. My daughter Betty (who is now well married, and has children) was then at her needlework. I took leave of my wife, and boy and girl, with tears on both sides; and went on board the *Adventure*, a merchant-ship of three hundred tons, bound for Surat, Captain John Nicholas of Liverpool, Commander. But my account of this voyage must be referred to the second part of my *Travels*.

Part 2. A Voyage to Brobdingnag

CHAPTER 1. *A great storm described. The longboat sent to fetch water; the Author goes with it to discover the country. He is left on shore, is seized by one of the natives, and carried to a farmer's house. His reception there, with several accidents that happened there. A description of the inhabitants.*

Having been condemned by nature and fortune to an active and restless life, in ten months after my return I again left my native country, and took shipping in the Downs on the 20th day of June, 1702, in the *Adventure*, Captain John Nicholas, a Cornish man, Commander, bound for Surat.[8] We had a very prosperous gale till we arrived at the Cape of Good Hope, where we landed for fresh water, but discovering a leak we unshipped our goods and wintered there; for the Captain falling sick of an ague, we could not leave the Cape till the end of March. We then set sail, and had a good voyage till we passed the Straits of Madagascar; but having got northward of that island, and to about five degrees south latitude, the winds, which in those seas are

6. On welfare (living on charity given by the parish).
7. Promising.
8. In India. The geography of the voyage (described next) is simple: The *Adventure*, after sailing up the east coast of Africa to about five degrees south of the equator (the "Line"), is blown past India into the Malay Archipelago, north of the islands of Buru and Ceram. The storm then drives the ship northward and eastward, away from the coast of Siberia ("Great Tartary") into the northeast Pacific, at that time unexplored. Brobdingnag lies somewhere in the vicinity of Alaska.

observed to blow a constant equal gale between the north and west from the beginning of December to the beginning of May, on the 19th of April began to blow with much greater violence and more westerly than usual, continuing so far twenty days together, during which time we were driven a little to the east of the Molucca Islands and about three degrees northward of the Line, as our Captain found by an observation he took the 2nd of May, at which time the wind ceased, and it was a perfect calm, whereat I was not a little rejoiced. But he, being a man well experienced in the navigation of those seas, bid us all prepare against a storm, which accordingly happened the day following: for a southern wind, called the southern monsoon, began to set in.

Finding it was likely to overblow,[9] we took in our spritsail, and stood by to hand the foresail; but making foul weather, we looked the guns were all fast, and handed the mizzen. The ship lay very broad off, so we thought it better spooning before the sea, than trying or hulling. We reefed the foresail and set him, we hauled aft the foresheet; the helm was hard aweather. The ship wore bravely. We belayed the fore-downhaul; but the sail was split, and we hauled down the yard and got the sail into the ship, and unbound all the things clear of it. It was a very fierce storm; the sea broke strange and dangerous. We hauled off upon the lanyard of the whipstaff, and helped the man at helm. We would not get down our topmast, but let all stand, because she scudded before the sea very well, and we knew that the topmast being aloft, the ship was the wholesomer, and made better way through the sea, seeing we had searoom. When the storm was over, we set foresail and mainsail, and brought the ship to. Then we set the mizzen, main topsail and the fore topsail. Our course was east-northeast, the wind was at southwest. We got the starboard tacks aboard, we cast off our weather braces and lifts; we set in the lee braces, and hauled forward by the weather bowlings, and hauled them tight, and belayed them, and hauled over the mizzen tack to windward, and kept her full and by as near as she would lie.

During this storm, which was followed by a strong wind west-southwest, we were carried by my computation about five hundred leagues to the east, so that the oldest sailor on board could not tell in what part of the world we were. Our provisions held out well, our ship was staunch, and our crew all in good health; but we lay in the utmost distress for water. We thought it best to hold on the same course rather than turn more northerly, which might have brought us to the northwest parts of Great Tartary, and into the frozen sea.

On the 16th day of June, 1703, a boy on the topmast discovered land. On the 17th we came in full view of a great island or continent (for we knew not whether) on the south side whereof was a small neck of land jutting out into the sea, and a creek[1] too shallow to hold a ship of above one hundred tons. We cast anchor within a league of this creek, and our Captain sent a dozen of his men well armed in the longboat, with vessels for water if any could be found. I desired his leave to go with them that I might see the country and make what discoveries I could. When we came to land we saw no river or spring, nor any sign of inhabitants. Our men therefore wandered on the shore to find out some fresh water near the sea, and I walked alone about a mile on

---

9. This paragraph is taken almost literally from Samuel Sturmy's *Mariner's Magazine* (1669). Swift is ridiculing the use of technical terms by

writers of popular voyages.
1. A small bay or cove, affording anchorage.

the other side, where I observed the country all barren and rocky. I now began to be weary, and seeing nothing to entertain my curiosity, I returned gently down towards the creek; and the sea being full in my view, I saw our men already got into the boat, and rowing for life to the ship. I was going to hollow after them, although it had been to little purpose, when I observed a huge creature walking after them in the sea as fast as he could; he waded not much deeper than his knees and took prodigious strides, but our men had the start of him half a league, and the sea thereabouts being full of sharp-pointed rocks, the monster was not able to overtake the boat. This I was afterwards told, for I durst not stay to see the issue of that adventure, but ran as fast as I could the way I first went, and then climbed up a steep hill, which gave me some prospect of the country. I found it fully cultivated; but that which first surprised me was the length of the grass, which, in those grounds that seemed to be kept for hay, was about twenty foot high.[2]

I fell into a highroad, for so I took it to be, although it served to the inhabitants only as a footpath through a field of barley. Here I walked on for some time, but could see little on either side, it being now near harvest, and the corn[3] rising at least forty foot. I was an hour walking to the end of this field, which was fenced in with a hedge of at least one hundred and twenty foot high, and the trees so lofty that I could make no computation of their altitude. There was a stile to pass from this field into the next: it had four steps, and a stone to cross over when you came to the utmost. It was impossible for me to climb this stile, because every step was six foot high, and the upper stone above twenty. I was endeavoring to find some gap in the hedge when I discovered one of the inhabitants in the next field advancing towards the stile, of the same size with him whom I saw in the sea pursuing our boat. He appeared as tall as an ordinary spire-steeple, and took about ten yards at every stride, as near as I could guess. I was struck with the utmost fear and astonishment, and ran to hide myself in the corn, from whence I saw him at the top of the stile, looking back into the next field on the right hand; and heard him call in a voice many degrees louder than a speaking trumpet; but the noise was so high in the air that at first I certainly thought it was thunder. Whereupon seven monsters like himself came towards him with reaping hooks in their hands, each hook about the largeness of six scythes. These people were not so well clad as the first, whose servants or laborers they seemed to be. For, upon some words he spoke, they went to reap the corn in the field where I lay. I kept from them at as great a distance as I could, but was forced to move with extreme difficulty, for the stalks of the corn were sometimes not above a foot distant, so that I could hardly squeeze my body betwixt them. However, I made a shift to go forward till I came to a part of the field where the corn had been laid by the rain and wind; here it was impossible for me to advance a step, for the stalks were so interwoven that I could not creep through, and the beards of the fallen ears so strong and pointed that they pierced through my clothes into my flesh. At the same time I heard the reapers not above an hundred yards behind me. Being quite dispirited with toil, and wholly overcome by grief and despair, I lay down

2. Swift's intention, not always carried out accurately, is that everything in Brobdingnag should be, in relation to our familiar world, on a scale of ten to one.
3. Here, barley.

between two ridges and heartily wished I might there end my days. I bemoaned my desolate widow and fatherless children; I lamented my own folly and willfulness in attempting a second voyage against the advice of all my friends and relations. In this terrible agitation of mind, I could not forbear thinking of Lilliput, whose inhabitants looked upon me as the greatest prodigy that ever appeared in the world; where I was able to draw an imperial fleet in my hand, and perform those other actions which will be recorded forever in the chronicles of that empire, while posterity shall hardly believe them, although attested by millions. I reflected what a mortification it must prove to me to appear as inconsiderable in this nation as one single Lilliputian would be among us. But this I conceived was to be the least of my misfortunes; for as human creatures are observed to be more savage and cruel in proportion to their bulk, what could I expect but to be a morsel in the mouth of the first among these enormous barbarians who should happen to seize me? Undoubtedly philosophers are in the right when they tell us that nothing is great or little otherwise than by comparison. It might have pleased fortune to let the Lilliputians find some nation where the people were as diminutive with respect to them as they were to me. And who knows but that even this prodigious race of mortals might be equally overmatched in some distant part of the world, whereof we have yet no discovery?

Scared and confounded as I was, I could not forbear going on with these reflections; when one of the reapers approaching within ten yards of the ridge where I lay, made me apprehend that with the next step I should be squashed to death under his foot, or cut in two with his reaping hook. And therefore when he was again about to move, I screamed as loud as fear could make me. Whereupon the huge creature trod short, and looking round about under him for some time, at last espied me as I lay on the ground. He considered a while with the caution of one who endeavors to lay hold on a small dangerous animal in such a manner that it shall not be able either to scratch or to bite him, as I myself have sometimes done with a weasel in England. At length he ventured to take me up behind by the middle between his forefinger and thumb, and brought me within three yards of his eyes, that he might behold my shape more perfectly. I guessed his meaning, and my good fortune gave me so much presence of mind that I resolved not to struggle in the least as he held me in the air about sixty foot from the ground, although he grievously pinched my sides, for fear I should slip through his fingers. All I ventured was to raise mine eyes towards the sun, and place my hands together in a supplicating posture, and to speak some words in an humble melancholy tone, suitable to the condition I then was in. For I apprehended every moment that he would dash me against the ground, as we usually do any little hateful animal which we have a mind to destroy. But my good star would have it that he appeared pleased with my voice and gestures, and began to look upon me as a curiosity, much wondering to hear me pronounce articulate words, although he could not understand them. In the meantime I was not able to forbear groaning and shedding tears and turning my head towards my sides, letting him know, as well as I could, how cruelly I was hurt by the pressure of his thumb and finger. He seemed to apprehend my meaning; for, lifting up the lappet[4] of his coat, he put me gently into it, and immediately ran along

4. Flap or fold.

with me to his master, who was a substantial farmer, and the same person I had first seen in the field.

The farmer having (as I supposed by their talk) received such an account of me as his servant could give him, took a piece of a small straw about the size of a walking staff, and therewith lifted up the lappets of my coat, which it seems he thought to be some kind of covering that nature had given me. He blew my hairs aside to take a better view of my face. He called his hinds[5] about him, and asked them (as I afterwards learned) whether they had ever seen in the fields any little creature that resembled me. He then placed me softly on the ground upon all four; but I got immediately up, and walked slowly backwards and forwards, to let those people see I had no intent to run away. They all sat down in a circle about me, the better to observe my motions. I pulled off my hat, and made a low bow towards the farmer; I fell on my knees, and lifted up my hands and eyes, and spoke several words as loud as I could; I took a purse of gold out of my pocket, and humbly presented it to him. He received it on the palm of his hand, then applied it close to his eye to see what it was, and afterwards turned it several times with the point of a pin (which he took out of his sleeve), but could make nothing of it. Whereupon I made a sign that he should place his hand on the ground; I then took the purse, and opening it, poured all the gold into his palm. There were six Spanish pieces of four pistoles each, beside twenty or thirty smaller coins. I saw him wet the tip of his little finger upon his tongue, and take up one of my largest pieces, and then another; but he seemed to be wholly ignorant what they were. He made me a sign to put them again into my purse, and the purse again into my pocket, which after offering to him several times, I thought it best to do.

The farmer by this time was convinced I must be a rational creature. He spoke often to me, but the sound of his voice pierced my ears like that of a water mill, yet his words were articulate enough. I answered as loud as I could in several languages, and he often laid his ear within two yards of me, but all in vain, for we were wholly unintelligible to each other. He then sent his servants to their work, and taking his handkerchief out of his pocket, he doubled and spread it on his hand, which he placed flat on the ground with the palm upwards, making me a sign to step into it, as I could easily do, for it was not above a foot in thickness. I thought it my part to obey, and for fear of falling, laid myself at full length upon the handkerchief, with the remainder of which he lapped me up to the head for further security, and in this manner carried me home to his house. There he called his wife, and showed me to her; but she screamed and ran back as women in England do at the sight of a toad or a spider. However, when she had a while seen my behavior, and how well I observed the signs her husband made, she was soon reconciled, and by degrees grew extremely tender of me.

It was about twelve at noon, and a servant brought in dinner. It was only one substantial dish of meat (fit for the plain condition of an husbandman) in a dish of about four-and-twenty foot diameter. The company were the farmer and his wife, three children, and an old grandmother. When they were sat down, the farmer placed me at some distance from him on the table, which was thirty foot high from the floor. I was in a terrible fright, and kept as far

5. Farm servants.

as I could from the edge, for fear of falling. The wife minced a bit of meat, then crumbled some bread on a trencher, and placed it before me. I made her a low bow, took out my knife and fork, and fell to eat; which gave them exceeding delight. The mistress sent her maid for a small dram cup, which held about two gallons, and filled it with drink; I took up the vessel with much difficulty in both hands, and in a most respectful manner drank to her ladyship's health, expressing the words as loud as I could in English; which made the company laugh so heartily that I was almost deafened with the noise. This liquor tasted like a small cider,[6] and was not unpleasant. Then the master made me a sign to come to his trencher side; but as I walked on the table, being in great surprise all the time, as the indulgent reader will easily conceive and excuse, I happened to stumble against a crust, and fell flat on my face, but received no hurt. I got up immediately, and observing the good people to be in much concern, I took my hat (which I held under my arm out of good manners) and waving it over my head, made three huzzas to show I had got no mischief by my fall. But advancing forwards toward my master (as I shall henceforth call him), his youngest son who sat next him, an arch boy of about ten years old, took me up by the legs, and held me so high in the air that I trembled every limb; but his father snatched me from him, and at the same time gave him such a box on the left ear as would have felled an European troop of horse to the earth, ordering him to be taken from the table. But being afraid the boy might owe me a spite, and well remembering how mischievous all children among us naturally are to sparrows, rabbits, young kittens, and puppy dogs, I fell on my knees, and pointing to the boy, made my master to understand, as well as I could, that I desired his son might be pardoned. The father complied, and the lad took his seat again; whereupon I went to him and kissed his hand, which my master took, and made him stroke me gently with it.

In the midst of dinner, my mistress's favorite cat leaped into her lap. I heard a noise behind me like that of a dozen stocking weavers at work; and turning my head, I found it proceeded from the purring of this animal, who seemed to be three times larger than an ox, as I computed by the view of her head and one of her paws, while her mistress was feeding and stroking her. The fierceness of this creature's countenance altogether discomposed me, although I stood at the farther end of the table, about fifty foot off, and although my mistress held her fast for fear she might give a spring and seize me in her talons. But it happened there was no danger, for the cat took not the least notice of me when my master placed me within three yards of her. And as I have been always told, and found true by experience in my travels, that flying or discovering[7] fear before a fierce animal is a certain way to make it pursue or attack you, so I resolved in this dangerous juncture to show no manner of concern. I walked with intrepidity five or six times before the very head of the cat, and came within half a yard of her; whereupon she drew herself back, as if she were more afraid of me. I had less apprehension concerning the dogs, whereof three or four came into the room, as it is usual in farmers' houses; one of which was a mastiff, equal in bulk to four elephants, and a greyhound, somewhat taller than the mastiff, but not so large.

6. I.e., weak cider.   7. Revealing.

When dinner was almost done, the nurse came in with a child of a year old in her arms, who immediately spied me, and began a squall that you might have heard from London Bridge to Chelsea, after the usual oratory of infants, to get me for a plaything. The mother out of pure indulgence took me up, and put me towards the child, who presently seized me by the middle, and got my head in his mouth, where I roared so loud that the urchin was frighted and let me drop; and I should infallibly have broke my neck if the mother had not held her apron under me. The nurse to quiet her babe made use of a rattle, which was a kind of hollow vessel filled with great stones, and fastened by a cable to the child's waist: but all in vain, so that she was forced to apply the last remedy by giving it suck. I must confess no object ever disgusted me so much as the sight of her monstrous breast, which I cannot tell what to compare with so as to give the curious reader an idea of its bulk, shape, and color. It stood prominent six foot, and could not be less than sixteen in circumference. The nipple was about half the bigness of my head, and the hue both of that and the dug so varified with spots, pimples, and freckles that nothing could appear more nauseous: for I had a near sight of her, she sitting down the more conveniently to give suck, and I standing on the table. This made me reflect upon the fair skins of our English ladies, who appear so beautiful to us, only because they are of our own size, and their defects not to be seen but through a magnifying glass, where we find by experiment that the smoothest and whitest skins look rough and coarse and ill colored.

I remember when I was at Lilliput, the complexion of those diminutive people appeared to me the fairest in the world; and talking upon this subject with a person of learning there, who was an intimate friend of mine, he said that my face appeared much fairer and smoother when he looked on me from the ground than it did upon a nearer view when I took him up in my hand and brought him close, which he confessed was at first a very shocking sight. He said he could discover great holes in my skin; that the stumps of my beard were ten times stronger than the bristles of a boar, and my complexion made up of several colors altogether disagreeable: although I must beg leave to say for myself that I am as fair as most of my sex and country and very little sunburnt by all my travels. On the other side, discoursing of the ladies in that Emperor's court, he used to tell me one had freckles, another too wide a mouth, a third too large a nose; nothing of which I was able to distinguish. I confess this reflection was obvious enough; which however I could not forbear, lest the reader might think those vast creatures were actually deformed: for I must do them justice to say they are a comely race of people; and particularly the features of my master's countenance, although he were but a farmer, when I beheld him from the height of sixty foot, appeared very well proportioned.

When dinner was done, my master went out to his laborers; and as I could discover by his voice and gesture, gave his wife a strict charge to take care of me. I was very much tired and disposed to sleep, which my mistress perceiving, she put me on her own bed, and covered me with a clean white handkerchief, but larger and coarser than the mainsail of a man-of-war.

I slept about two hours, and dreamed I was at home with my wife and children, which aggravated my sorrows when I awaked and found myself alone in a vast room, between two and three hundred foot wide, and above two hundred high, lying in a bed twenty yards wide. My mistress was gone about her household affairs, and had locked me in. The bed was eight yards from the floor. Some natural necessities required me to get down; I durst not presume to call, and if I had, it would have been in vain with such a voice as mine at so great a distance from the room where I lay to the kitchen where the family kept. While I was under these circumstances, two rats crept up the curtains, and ran smelling backwards and forwards on the bed. One of them came up almost to my face; whereupon I rose in a fright, and drew out my hanger[8] to defend myself. These horrible animals had the boldness to attack me on both sides, and one of them held his forefeet at my collar; but I had the good fortune to rip up his belly before he could do me any mischief. He fell down at my feet; and the other seeing the fate of his comrade, made his escape, but not without one good wound on the back, which I gave him as he fled, and made the blood run trickling from him. After this exploit I walked gently to and fro on the bed, to recover my breath and loss of spirits. These creatures were of the size of a large mastiff, but infinitely more nimble and fierce; so that if I had taken off my belt before I went to sleep, I must have infallibly been torn to pieces and devoured. I measured the tail of the dead rat, and found it to be two yards long, wanting an inch; but it went against my stomach to drag the carcass off the bed, where it lay still bleeding; I observed it had yet some life, but with a strong slash cross the neck, I thoroughly dispatched it.

Soon after, my mistress came into the room, who seeing me all bloody, ran and took me up in her hand. I pointed to the dead rat, smiling and making other signs to show I was not hurt, whereat she was extremely rejoiced, calling the maid to take up the dead rat with a pair of tongs, and throw it out of the window. Then she set me on a table, where I showed her my hanger all bloody, and wiping it on the lappet of my coat, returned it to the scabbard. I was pressed to do more than one thing, which another could not do for me, and therefore endeavored to make my mistress understand that I desired to be set down on the floor; which after she had done, my bashfulness would not suffer me to express myself farther than by pointing to the door, and bowing several times. The good woman with much difficulty at last perceived what I would be at, and taking me up again in her hand, walked into the garden, where she set me down. I went on one side about two hundred yards; and beckoning to her not to look or to follow me, I hid myself between two leaves of sorrel, and there discharged the necessities of nature.

I hope the gentle reader will excuse me for dwelling on these and the like particulars, which however insignificant they may appear to groveling vulgar minds, yet will certainly help a philosopher[9] to enlarge his thoughts and imagination, and apply them to the benefit of public as well as private life, which was my sole design in presenting this and other accounts of my travels to the world; wherein I have been chiefly studious of truth, without affecting any ornaments of learning or of style. But the whole scene of this voyage made so strong an impression on my mind, and is so deeply fixed in my memory, that in committing it to paper I did not omit one material circumstance; however, upon a strict review, I blotted out several passages of less

8. A short, broad sword.
9. Scientist, in contrast to the "vulgar" (commonplace, uncultivated).

moment which were in my first copy, for fear of being censured as tedious and trifling, whereof travelers are often, perhaps not without justice, accused.

CHAPTER 2. *A description of the farmer's daughter. The Author carried to a market town, and then to the metropolis. The particulars of his journey.*

My mistress had a daughter of nine years old, a child of towardly parts for her age, very dexterous at her needle, and skillful in dressing her baby.[1] Her mother and she contrived to fit up the baby's cradle for me against night: the cradle was put into a small drawer of a cabinet, and the drawer placed upon a hanging shelf for fear of the rats. This was my bed all the time I stayed with those people, although made more convenient by degrees as I began to learn their language, and make my wants known. This young girl was so handy, that after I had once or twice pulled off my clothes before her, she was able to dress and undress me, although I never gave her that trouble when she would let me do either myself. She made me seven shirts, and some other linen of as fine cloth as could be got, which indeed was coarser than sackcloth, and these she constantly washed for me with her own hands. She was likewise my schoolmistress to teach me the language: when I pointed to anything, she told me the name of it in her own tongue, so that in a few days I was able to call for whatever I had a mind to. She was very good-natured, and not above forty foot high, being little for her age. She gave me the name of *Grildrig*, which the family took up, and afterwards the whole kingdom. The word imports what the Latins call *nanunculus*, the Italian *homunceletino*, and the English *mannikin*.[2] To her I chiefly owe my preservation in that country: we never parted while I was there; I called her my *Glumdalclitch*, or little nurse: and I should be guilty of great ingratitude if I omitted this honorable mention of her care and affection towards me, which I heartily wish it lay in my power to requite as she deserves, instead of being the innocent but unhappy instrument of her disgrace, as I have too much reason to fear.

It now began to be known and talked of in the neighborhood that my master had found a strange animal in the field, about the bigness of a *splacknuck*, but exactly shaped in every part like a human creature, which it likewise imitated in all its actions: seemed to speak in a little language of its own, had already learned several words of theirs, went erect upon two legs, was tame and gentle, would come when it was called, do whatever it was bid, had the finest limbs in the world, and a complexion fairer than a nobleman's daughter of three years old. Another farmer who lived hard by, and was a particular friend of my master, came on a visit on purpose to inquire into the truth of this story. I was immediately produced, and placed upon a table, where I walked as I was commanded, drew my hanger, put it up again, made my reverence to my master's guest, asked him in his own language how he did, and told him he was welcome, just as my little nurse had instructed me. This man, who was old and dimsighted, put on his spectacles to behold me better, at which I could not forbear laughing very heartily, for his eyes

---

1. Doll. "Towardly parts": promising abilities.
2. Little man, dwarf. The Latin and Italian words are Swift's own coinages, as, of course, are

the various words from the Brobdingnagian language.

appeared like the full moon shining into a chamber at two windows. Our people, who discovered the cause of my mirth, bore me company in laughing, at which the old fellow was fool enough to be angry and out of countenance. He had the character of a great miser, and to my misfortune he well deserved it by the cursed advice he gave my master to show me as a sight upon a market day in the next town, which was half an hour's riding, about two and twenty miles from our house. I guessed there was some mischief contriving when I observed my master and his friend whispering long together, sometimes pointing at me; and my fears made me fancy that I overheard and understood some of their words. But the next morning Glumdalclitch, my little nurse, told me the whole matter, which she had cunningly picked out from her mother. The poor girl laid me on her bosom, and fell a weeping with shame and grief. She apprehended some mischief would happen to me from rude vulgar folks, who might squeeze me to death, or break one of my limbs by taking me in their hands. She had also observed how modest I was in my nature, how nicely I regarded my honor, and what an indignity I should conceive it to be exposed for money as a public spectacle to the meanest of the people. She said her papa and mamma had promised that Grildrig should be hers; but now she found they meant to serve her as they did last year, when they pretended to give her a lamb, and yet, as soon as it was fat, sold it to a butcher. For my own part, I may truly affirm that I was less concerned than my nurse. I had a strong hope, which never left me, that I should one day recover my liberty; and as to the ignominy of being carried about for a monster, I considered myself to be a perfect stranger in the country, and that such a misfortune could never be charged upon me as a reproach, if ever I should return to England; since the King of Great Britain himself, in my condition, must have undergone the same distress.

My master, pursuant to the advice of his friend, carried me in a box the next market day to the neighboring town, and took along with him his little daughter, my nurse, upon a pillion[3] behind him. The box was close on every side, with a little door for me to go in and out, and a few gimlet holes to let in air. The girl had been so careful to put the quilt of her baby's bed into it, for me to lie down on. However, I was terribly shaken and discomposed in this journey, although it were but of half an hour. For the horse went about forty foot at every step, and trotted so high that the agitation was equal to the rising and falling of a ship in a great storm, but much more frequent. Our journey was somewhat further than from London to St. Albans.[4] My master alighted at an inn which he used to frequent; and after consulting a while with the innkeeper, and making some necessary preparations, he hired the *Grultrud*, or crier, to give notice through the town of a strange creature to be seen at the Sign of the Green Eagle, not so big as a *splacknuck* (an animal in that country very finely shaped, about six foot long), and in every part of the body resembling an human creature; could speak several words and perform an hundred diverting tricks.

I was placed upon a table in the largest room of the inn, which might be near three hundred foot square. My little nurse stood on a low stool close to the table, to take care of me, and direct what I should do. My master, to

---

3. A pad attached to the hinder part of a saddle, on which a second person, usually a woman, could ride.
4. About twenty miles.

avoid a crowd, would suffer only thirty people at a time to see me. I walked about on the table as the girl commanded; she asked me questions as far as she knew my understanding of the language reached, and I answered them as loud as I could. I turned about several times to the company, paid my humble respects, said they were welcome, and used some other speeches I had been taught. I took up a thimble filled with liquor, which Glumdalclitch had given me for a cup, and drank their health. I drew out my hanger, and flourished with it after the manner of fencers in England. My nurse gave me part of a straw, which I exercised as pike, having learned the art in my youth. I was that day shown to twelve sets of company, and as often forced to go over again with the same fopperies, till I was half dead with weariness and vexation. For those who had seen me made such wonderful reports that the people were ready to break down the doors to come in. My master for his own interest would not suffer anyone to touch me except my nurse; and, to prevent danger, benches were set round the table at such a distance as put me out of everybody's reach. However, an unlucky schoolboy aimed a hazelnut directly at my head, which very narrowly missed me; otherwise, it came with so much violence that it would have infallibly knocked out my brains, for it was almost as large as a small pumpion:[5] but I had the satisfaction to see the young rogue well beaten, and turned out of the room.

My master gave public notice that he would show me again the next market day, and in the meantime he prepared a more convenient vehicle for me, which he had reason enough to do; for I was so tired with my first journey, and with entertaining company for eight hours together, that I could hardly stand upon my legs or speak a word. It was at least three days before I recovered my strength; and that I might have no rest at home, all the neighboring gentlemen from an hundred miles round, hearing of my fame, came to see me at my master's own house. There could not be fewer than thirty persons with their wives and children (for the country is very populous); and my master demanded the rate of a full room whenever he showed me at home, although it were only to a single family. So that for some time I had but little ease every day of the week (except Wednesday, which is their Sabbath) although I were not carried to the town.

My master finding how profitable I was like to be, resolved to carry me to the most considerable cities of the kingdom. Having therefore provided himself with all things necessary for a long journey, and settled his affairs at home, he took leave of his wife; and upon the 17th of August, 1703, about two months after my arrival, we set out for the metropolis, situated near the middle of that empire, and about three thousand miles distance from our house. My master made his daughter Glumdalclitch ride behind him. She carried me on her lap in a box tied about her waist. The girl had lined it on all sides with the softest cloth she could get, well quilted underneath, furnished it with her baby's bed, provided me with linen and other necessaries, and made everything as convenient as she could. We had no other company but a boy of the house, who rode after us with the luggage.

My master's design was to show me in all the towns by the way, and to step out of the road for fifty or an hundred miles to any village or person of quality's house where he might expect custom. We made easy journeys of not

5. Pumpkin.

above seven or eight score miles a day: for Glumdalclitch, on purpose to spare me, complained she was tired with the trotting of the horse. She often took me out of my box at my own desire, to give me air and show me the country, but always held me fast by leading strings.[6] We passed over five or six rivers many degrees broader and deeper than the Nile or the Ganges; and there was hardly a rivulet so small as the Thames at London Bridge. We were ten weeks in our journey, and I was shown in eighteen large towns, besides many large villages and private families.

On the 26th day of October, we arrived at the metropolis, called in their language *Lorbrulgrud*, or Pride of the Universe. My master took a lodging in the principal street of the city, not far from the royal palace, and put out bills in the usual form, containing an exact description of my person and parts. He hired a large room between three and four hundred foot wide. He provided a table sixty foot in diameter, upon which I was to act my part, and palisadoed it round three foot from the edge, and as many high, to prevent my falling over. I was shown ten times a day to the wonder and satisfaction of all people. I could now speak the language tolerably well, and perfectly understood every word that was spoken to me. Besides, I had learned their alphabet, and could make a shift to explain a sentence here and there; for Glumdalclitch had been my instructor while we were at home, and at leisure hours during our journey. She carried a little book in her pocket, not much larger than a Sanson's *Atlas*;[7] it was a common treatise for the use of young girls, giving a short account of their religion: out of this she taught me my letters, and interpreted the words.

CHAPTER 3. *The Author sent for to Court. The Queen buys him of his master, the farmer, and presents him to the King. He disputes with his Majesty's great scholars. An apartment at Court provided for the Author. He is in high favor with the Queen. He stands up for the honor of his own country. His quarrels with the Queen's dwarf.*

The frequent labors I underwent every day made in a few weeks a very considerable change in my health: the more my master got by me, the more unsatiable he grew. I had quite lost my stomach, and was almost reduced to a skeleton. The farmer observed it, and concluding I soon must die, resolved to make as good a hand of me as he could. While he was thus reasoning and resolving with himself, a *Slardral*, or Gentleman Usher, came from Court, commanding my master to carry me immediately thither for the diversion of the Queen and her ladies. Some of the latter had already been to see me and reported strange things of my beauty, behavior, and good sense. Her Majesty and those who attended her were beyond measure delighted with my demeanor. I fell on my knees and begged the honor of kissing her Imperial foot; but this gracious princess held out her little finger towards me (after I was set on a table), which I embraced in both my arms, and put the tip of it, with the utmost respect, to my lip. She made me some general questions about my country and my travels, which I answered as distinctly and in as few words as I could. She asked whether I would be content to live at Court. I bowed down to the board of the table, and humbly answered that I was my

---

6. Used to guide children learning to walk. 7. I.e., over two feet long and about two feet wide.

master's slave, but if I were at my own disposal, I should be proud to devote my life to her Majesty's service. She then asked my master whether he were willing to sell me at a good price. He, who apprehended I could not live a month, was ready enough to part with me, and demanded a thousand pieces of gold, which were ordered him on the spot, each piece being about the bigness of eight hundred moidores;[8] but, allowing for the proportion of all things between that country and Europe, and the high price of gold among them, was hardly so great a sum as a thousand guineas would be in England. I then said to the Queen, since I was now her Majesty's most humble creature and vassal, I must beg the favor that Glumdalclitch, who had always tended me with so much care and kindness, and understood to do it so well, might be admitted into her service, and continue to be my nurse and instructor. Her Majesty agreed to my petition, and easily got the farmer's consent, who was glad enough to have his daughter preferred at Court; and the poor girl herself was not able to hide her joy. My late master withdrew, bidding me farewell, and saying he had left me in a good service; to which I replied not a word, only making him a slight bow.

The Queen observed my coldness, and when the farmer was gone out of the apartment, asked me the reason. I made bold to tell her Majesty that I owed no other obligation to my late master than his not dashing out the brains of a poor harmless creature found by chance in his field; which obligation was amply recompensed by the gain he had made in showing me through half the kingdom, and the price he had now sold me for. That the life I had since led was laborious enough to kill an animal of ten times my strength. That my health was much impaired by the continual drudgery of entertaining the rabble every hour of the day; and that if my master had not thought my life in danger, her Majesty perhaps would not have got so cheap a bargain. But as I was out of all fear of being ill treated under the protection of so great and good an Empress, the Ornament of Nature, the Darling of the World, the Delight of her Subjects, the Phoenix of the Creation; so I hoped my late master's apprehensions would appear to be groundless, for I already found my spirits to revive by the influence of her most august presence.

This was the sum of my speech, delivered with great improprieties and hesitation; the latter part was altogether framed in the style peculiar to that people, whereof I learned some phrases from Glumdalclitch, while she was carrying me to Court.

The Queen, giving great allowance for my defectiveness in speaking, was however surprised at so much wit and good sense in so diminutive an animal. She took me in her own hand, and carried me to the King, who was then retired to his cabinet.[9] His Majesty, a prince of much gravity, and austere countenance, not well observing my shape at first view, asked the Queen after a cold manner how long it was since she grew fond of a *splacknuck*; for such it seems he took me to be, as I lay upon my breast in her Majesty's right hand. But this princess, who hath an infinite deal of wit and humor, set me gently on my feet upon the scrutore,[1] and commanded me to give his Majesty an account of myself, which I did in a very few words; and Glumdalclitch,

8. Portuguese coins.
9. Private apartment.

1. Writing desk.

who attended at the cabinet door, and could not endure I should be out of her sight, being admitted, confirmed all that had passed from my arrival at her father's house.

The King, although he be as learned a person as any in his dominions, had been educated in the study of philosophy and particularly mathematics; yet when he observed my shape exactly, and saw me walk erect, before I began to speak, conceived I might be a piece of clockwork (which is in that country arrived to a very great perfection) contrived by some ingenious artist. But when he heard my voice, and found what I delivered to be regular and rational, he could not conceal his astonishment. He was by no means satisfied with the relation I gave him of the manner I came into his kingdom, but thought it a story concerted between Glumdalclitch and her father, who had taught me a set of words to make me sell at a higher price. Upon this imagination he put several other questions to me, and still received rational answers, no otherwise defective than by a foreign accent, and an imperfect knowledge in the language, with some rustic phrases which I had learned at the farmer's house, and did not suit the polite style of a court.

His Majesty sent for three great scholars who were then in their weekly waiting (according to the custom in that country). These gentlemen, after they had a while examined my shape with much nicety, were of different opinions concerning me. They all agreed that I could not be produced according to the regular laws of nature, because I was not framed with a capacity of preserving my life, either by swiftness, or climbing of trees, or digging holes in the earth. They observed by my teeth, which they viewed with great exactness, that I was a carnivorous animal; yet most quadrupeds being an overmatch for me, and field mice, with some others, too nimble, they could not imagine how I should be able to support myself, unless I fed upon snails and other insects; which they offered, by many learned arguments, to evince that I could not possibly do. One of them seemed to think that I might be an embryo, or abortive birth. But this opinion was rejected by the other two, who observed my limbs to be perfect and finished, and that I had lived several years, as it was manifested from my beard, the stumps whereof they plainly discovered through a magnifying glass. They would not allow me to be a dwarf, because my littleness was beyond all degrees of comparison; for the Queen's favorite dwarf, the smallest ever known in that kingdom, was nearly thirty foot high. After much debate, they concluded unanimously that I was only *relplum scalcath*, which is interpreted literally, *lusus naturae*; a determination exactly agreeable to the modern philosophy of Europe, whose professors, disdaining the old evasion of *occult causes*, whereby the followers of Aristotle endeavor in vain to disguise their ignorance, have invented this wonderful solution of all difficulties, to the unspeakable advancement of human knowledge.[2]

After this decisive conclusion, I entreated to be heard a word or two. I applied myself to the King, and assured his Majesty that I came from a country which abounded with several millions of both sexes, and of my own

2. Swift had contempt for both the medieval Schoolmen, who discussed "occult causes," the unknown causes of observable effects, and modern scientists, who, he believed, often concealed their ignorance by using equally meaningless terms. "*Lusus naturae*": one of nature's sports, or roughly, freaks.

stature, where the animals, trees, and houses were all in proportion, and where by consequence I might be as able to defend myself, and to find sustenance, as any of his Majesty's subjects could do here; which I took for a full answer to those gentlemen's arguments. To this they only replied with a smile of contempt, saying that the farmer had instructed me very well in my lesson. The King, who had a much better understanding, dismissing his learned men, sent for the farmer, who by good fortune was not yet gone out of town; having therefore first examined him privately, and then confronted him with me and the young girl, his Majesty began to think that what we told him might possibly be true. He desired the Queen to order that a particular care should be taken of me, and was of opinion that Glumdalclitch should still continue in her office of tending me, because he observed we had a great affection for each other. A convenient apartment was provided for her at Court; she had a sort of governess appointed to take care of her education, a maid to dress her, and two other servants for menial offices; but the care of me was wholly appropriated to herself. The Queen commanded her own cabinetmaker to contrive a box that might serve me for a bedchamber, after the model that Glumdalclitch and I should agree upon. This man was a most ingenious artist, and according to my directions, in three weeks finished for me a wooden chamber of sixteen foot square and twelve high, with sash windows, a door, and two closets, like a London bedchamber. The board that made the ceiling was to be lifted up and down by two hinges, to put in a bed ready furnished by her Majesty's upholsterer, which Glumdalclitch took out every day to air, made it with her own hands, and letting it down at night, locked up the roof over me. A nice[3] workman, who was famous for little curiosities, undertook to make me two chairs, with backs and frames, of a substance not unlike ivory, and two tables, with a cabinet to put my things in. The room was quilted on all sides, as well as the floor and the ceiling, to prevent any accident from the carelessness of those who carried me, and to break the force of a jolt when I went in a coach. I desired a lock for my door to prevent rats and mice from coming in: the smith, after several attempts, made the smallest that ever was seen among them, for I have known a larger at the gate of a gentleman's house in England. I made a shift[4] to keep the key in a pocket of my own, fearing Glumdalclitch might lose it. The Queen likewise ordered the thinnest silks that could be gotten, to make me clothes, not much thicker than an English blanket, very cumbersome till I was accustomed to them. They were after the fashion of the kingdom, partly resembling the Persian, and partly the Chinese, and are a very grave, decent habit.

The Queen became so fond of my company that she could not dine without me. I had a table placed upon the same at which her Majesty ate, just at her left elbow, and a chair to sit on. Glumdalclitch stood upon a stool on the floor, near my table, to assist and take care of me. I had an entire set of silver dishes and plates, and other necessaries, which, in proportion to those of the Queen, were not much bigger than what I have seen of the same kind in a London toyshop,[5] for the furniture of a baby-house: these my little nurse

3. Exact.
4. Contrived.

5. A shop for selling knickknacks.

kept in her pocket in a silver box and gave me at meals as I wanted them, always cleaning them herself. No person dined with the Queen but the two Princesses Royal, the elder sixteen years old, and the younger at that time thirteen and a month. Her Majesty used to put a bit of meat upon one of my dishes, out of which I carved for myself; and her diversion was to see me eat in miniature. For the Queen (who had indeed but a weak stomach) took up at one mouthful as much as a dozen English farmers could eat at a meal, which to me was for some time a very nauseous sight. She would craunch the wing of a lark, bones and all, between her teeth, although it were nine times as large as that of a full-grown turkey; and put a bit of bread into her mouth as big as two twelve-penny loaves. She drank out of a golden cup, above a hogshead at a draught. Her knives were twice as long as a scythe set straight upon the handle. The spoons, forks, and other instruments were all in the same proportion. I remember when Glumdalclitch carried me out of curiosity to see some of the tables at Court, where ten or a dozen of these enormous knives and forks were lifted up together, I thought I had never till then beheld so terrible a sight.

It is the custom that every Wednesday (which, as I have before observed, was their Sabbath) the King and Queen, with the royal issue of both sexes, dine together in the apartment of his Majesty, to whom I was now become a favorite; and at these times my little chair and table were placed at his left hand, before one of the salt-cellars. This prince took a pleasure in conversing with me, inquiring into the manners, religion, laws, government, and learning of Europe; wherein I gave him the best account I was able. His apprehension was so clear, and his judgment so exact, that he made very wise reflections and observations upon all I said. But I confess that after I had been a little too copious in talking of my own beloved country, of our trade and wars by sea and land, of our schisms in religion and parties in the state, the prejudices of his education prevailed so far that he could not forbear taking me up in his right hand, and stroking me gently with the other, after an hearty fit of laughing, asked me whether I were a Whig or a Tory. Then turning to his first minister, who waited behind him with a white staff, near as tall as the mainmast of the *Royal Sovereign*,[6] he observed how contemptible a thing was human grandeur, which could be mimicked by such diminutive insects as I: "and yet," said he, "I dare engage, these creatures have their titles and distinctions of honor; they contrive little nests and burrows, that they call houses and cities; they make a figure in dress and equipage; they love, they fight, they dispute, they cheat, they betray." And thus he continued on, while my color came and went several times with indignation to hear our noble country, the mistress of arts and arms, the scourge of France, the arbitress of Europe, the seat of virtue, piety, honor, and truth, the pride and envy of the world, so contemptuously treated.

But as I was not in a condition to resent injuries, so, upon mature thoughts, I began to doubt whether I were injured or no. For, after having been accustomed several months to the sight and converse of this people, and observed every object upon which I cast my eyes to be of proportionable magnitude, the horror I had first conceived from their bulk and aspect was so far worn

---

6. One of the largest ships in the Royal Navy. At the English court the lord treasurer bore a "white staff" as the symbol of his office.

off that if I had then beheld a company of English lords and ladies in their finery and birthday clothes,[7] acting their several parts in the most courtly manner of strutting and bowing and prating, to say the truth, I should have been strongly tempted to laugh as much at them as this King and his grandees did at me. Neither indeed could I forbear smiling at myself when the Queen used to place me upon her hand towards a looking glass, by which both our persons appeared before me in full view together; and there could be nothing more ridiculous than the comparison; so that I really began to imagine myself dwindled many degrees below my usual size.

Nothing angered and mortified me so much as the Queen's dwarf, who being of the lowest stature that was ever in that country (for I verily think he was not full thirty foot high) became so insolent at seeing a creature so much beneath him that he would always affect to swagger and look big as he passed by me in the Queen's antechamber, while I was standing on some table talking with the lords or ladies of the court; and he seldom failed of a smart word or two upon my littleness, against which I could only revenge myself by calling him brother, challenging him to wrestle, and such repartees as are usual in the mouths of Court pages. One day at dinner this malicious little cub was so nettled with something I had said to him that, raising himself upon the frame of Her Majesty's chair, he took me up by the middle, as I was sitting down, not thinking any harm, and let me drop into a large silver bowl of cream, and then ran away as fast as he could. I fell over head and ears, and if I had not been a good swimmer, it might have gone very hard with me; for Glumdalclitch in that instant happened to be at the other end of the room, and the Queen was in such a fright that she wanted presence of mind to assist me. But my little nurse ran to my relief, and took me out, after I had swallowed above a quart of cream. I was put to bed; however, I received no other damage than the loss of a suit of clothes, which was utterly spoiled. The dwarf was soundly whipped, and as further punishment, forced to drink up the bowl of cream into which he had thrown me; neither was he ever restored to favor: for soon after the Queen bestowed him to a lady of high quality, so that I saw him no more, to my very great satisfaction; for I could not tell to what extremity such a malicious urchin might have carried his resentment.

He had before served me a scurvy trick, which set the Queen a laughing, although at the same time she were heartily vexed, and would have immediately cashiered him, if I had not been so generous as to intercede. Her Majesty had taken a marrow bone upon her plate, and after knocking out the marrow, placed the bone again in the dish, erect as it stood before; the dwarf watching his opportunity, while Glumdalclitch was gone to the sideboard, mounted upon the stool she stood on to take care of me at meals, took me up in both hands, and squeezing my legs together, wedged them into the marrow bone above my waist, where I stuck for some time, and made a very ridiculous figure. I believe it was near a minute before anyone knew what was become of me, for I thought it below me to cry out. But, as princes seldom get their meat hot, my legs were not scalded, only my stockings and breeches in a sad condition. The dwarf at my entreaty had no other punishment than a sound whipping.

<hr>

7. Courtiers dressed with special splendor on the monarch's birthday.

I was frequently rallied by the Queen upon account of my fearfulness, and she used to ask me whether the people of my country were as great cowards as myself. The occasion was this. The kingdom is much pestered with flies in summer, and these odious insects, each of them as big as a Dunstable lark, hardly gave me any rest while I sat at dinner, with their continual humming and buzzing about my ears. They would sometimes alight upon my victuals, and leave their loathsome excrement or spawn behind, which to me was very visible, although not to the natives of that country, whose large optics were not so acute as mine in viewing smaller objects. Sometimes they would fix upon my nose or forehead, where they stung me to the quick, smelling very offensively; and I could easily trace that viscous matter, which our naturalists tell us enables those creatures to walk with their feet upwards upon a ceiling. I had much ado to defend myself against these detestable animals, and could not forbear starting when they came on my face. It was the common practice of the dwarf to catch a number of these insects in his hand, as schoolboys do among us, and let them out suddenly under my nose, on purpose to frighten me, and divert the Queen. My remedy was to cut them in pieces with my knife as they flew in the air, wherein my dexterity was much admired.

I remember one morning when Glumdalclitch had set me in my box upon a window, as she usually did in fair days to give me air (for I durst not venture to let the box be hung on a nail out of the window, as we do with cages in England), after I had lifted up one of my sashes, and sat down at my table to eat a piece of sweet cake for my breakfast, above twenty wasps, allured by the smell, came flying into the room, humming louder than the drones of as many bagpipes. Some of them seized my cake, and carried it piecemeal away; others flew about my head and face, confounding me with the noise, and putting me in the utmost terror of their stings. However, I had the courage to rise and draw my hanger, and attack them in the air. I dispatched four of them, but the rest got away, and I presently shut my window. These insects were as large as partridges; I took out their stings, found them an inch and a half long, and as sharp as needles. I carefully preserved them all, and having since shown them with some other curiosities in several parts of Europe, upon my return to England I gave three of them to Gresham College,[8] and kept the fourth for myself.

CHAPTER 4. *The country described. A proposal for correcting modern maps. The King's palace, and some account of the metropolis. The Author's way of traveling. The chief temple described.*

I now intend to give the reader a short description of this country, as far as I had traveled in it, which was not above two thousand miles round Lorbrulgrud the metropolis. For the Queen, whom I always attended, never went further when she accompanied the King in his progresses, and there stayed till his Majesty returned from viewing his frontiers. The whole extent of this prince's dominions reacheth about six thousand miles in length, and from three to five in breadth. From whence I cannot but conclude that our

---

8. The Royal Society, in its earliest years, met in Gresham College.

geographers of Europe are in a great error by supposing nothing but sea between Japan and California: for it was ever my opinion that there must be a balance of earth to counterpoise the great continent of Tartary; and therefore they ought to correct their maps and charts by joining this vast tract of land to the northwest parts of America, wherein I shall be ready to lend them my assistance.

The kingdom is a peninsula, terminated to the northeast by a ridge of mountains thirty miles high, which are altogether impassable by reason of the volcanoes upon the tops. Neither do the most learned know what sort of mortals inhabit beyond those mountains, or whether they be inhabited at all. On the three other sides it is bounded by the ocean. There is not one seaport in the whole kingdom; and those parts of the coasts into which the rivers issue are so full of pointed rocks, and the sea generally so rough, that there is no venturing with the smallest of their boats; so that these people are wholly excluded from any commerce with the rest of the world. But the large rivers are full of vessels, and abound with excellent fish, for they seldom get any from the sea, because the sea fish are of the same size with those in Europe, and consequently not worth catching; whereby it is manifest that nature, in the production of plants and animals of so extraordinary a bulk, is wholly confined to this continent, of which I leave the reasons to be determined by philosophers. However, now and then they take a whale that happens to be dashed against the rocks, which the common people feed on heartily. These whales I have known so large that a man could hardly carry one upon his shoulders; and sometimes for curiosity they are brought in hampers to Lorbrulgrud: I saw one of them in a dish at the King's table, which passed for a rarity, but I did not observe he was fond of it; for I think indeed the bigness disgusted him, although I have seen one somewhat larger in Greenland.

The country is well inhabited, for it contains fifty-one cities, near an hundred walled towns, and a great number of villages. To satisfy my curious reader, it may be sufficient to describe Lorbrulgrud. This city stands upon almost two equal parts on each side the river that passes through. It contains above eight thousand houses, and about six hundred thousand inhabitants. It is in length three *glonglungs* (which make about fifty-four English miles) and two and a half in breadth, as I measured it myself in the royal map made by the King's order, which was laid on the ground on purpose for me, and extended an hundred feet; I paced the diameter and circumference several times barefoot, and computing by the scale, measured it pretty exactly.

The King's palace is no regular edifice, but an heap of buildings about seven miles round: the chief rooms are generally two hundred and forty foot high, and broad and long in proportion. A coach was allowed to Glumdalclitch and me, wherein her governess frequently took her out to see the town, go among the shops; and I was always of the party, carried in my box, although the girl at my own desire would often take me out, and hold me in her hand, that I might more conveniently view the houses and the people as we passed along the streets. I reckoned our coach to be about a square of Westminster Hall,[9] but not altogether so high; however, I cannot be very

---

9. The ancient hall, now incorporated into the Houses of Parliament, where the law courts then sat. Swift presumably means the square of its breadth (just under sixty-eight feet).

exact. One day the governess ordered our coachman to stop at several shops, where the beggars, watching their opportunity, crowded to the sides of the coach, and gave me the most horrible spectacles that ever an English eye beheld. There was a woman with a cancer in her breast, swelled to a monstrous size, full of holes, in two or three of which I could have easily crept, and covered my whole body. There was a fellow with a wen in his neck, larger than five woolpacks, and another with a couple of wooden legs, each about twenty foot high. But the most hateful sight of all was the lice crawling on their clothes. I could see distinctly the limbs of these vermin with my naked eye, much better than those of an European louse through a microscope, and their snouts with which they rooted like swine. They were the first I had ever beheld; and I should have been curious enough to dissect one of them if I had proper instruments (which I unluckily left behind me in the ship), although indeed the sight was so nauseous that it perfectly turned my stomach.

Besides the large box in which I was usually carried, the Queen ordered a smaller one to be made for me, of about twelve foot square and ten high, for the convenience of traveling, because the other was somewhat too large for Glumdalclitch's lap, and cumbersome in the coach; it was made by the same artist, whom I directed in the whole contrivance. This traveling closet was an exact square with a window in the middle of three of the squares, and each window was latticed with iron wire on the outside, to prevent accidents in long journeys. On the fourth side, which had no windows, two strong staples were fixed, through which the person that carried me, when I had a mind to be on horseback, put in a leathern belt, and buckled it about his waist. This was always the office of some grave trusty servant in whom I could confide, whether I attended the King and Queen in their progresses, or were disposed to see the gardens, or pay a visit to some great lady or minister of state in the court, when Glumdalclitch happened to be out of order: for I soon began to be known and esteemed among the greatest officers, I suppose more upon account of their Majesties' favor than any merit of my own. In journeys, when I was weary of the coach, a servant on horseback would buckle my box, and place it on a cushion before him; and there I had a full prospect of the country on three sides from my three windows. I had in this closet a field bed[1] and a hammock hung from the ceiling, two chairs and a table, neatly screwed to the floor to prevent being tossed about by the agitation of the horse or the coach. And having been long used to sea voyages, those motions, although sometimes very violent, did not much discompose me.

When I had a mind to see the town, it was always in my traveling closet, which Glumdalclitch held in her lap in a kind of open sedan, after the fashion of the country, borne by four men, and attended by two others in the Queen's livery. The people, who had often heard of me, were very curious to crowd about the sedan; and the girl was complaisant enough to make the bearers stop, and to take me in her hand that I might be more conveniently seen.

I was very desirous to see the chief temple, and particularly the tower belonging to it, which is reckoned the highest in the kingdom. Accordingly one day my nurse carried me thither, but I may truly say I came back disap-

---

1. Folding bed, cot.

pointed; for the height is not above three thousand foot, reckoning from the ground to the highest pinnacle top; which, allowing for the difference between the size of those people and us in Europe, is no great matter for admiration, nor at all equal in proportion (if I rightly remember) to Salisbury steeple.[2] But, not to detract from a nation to which during my life I shall acknowledge myself extremely obliged, it must be allowed that whatever this famous tower wants in height is amply made up in beauty and strength. For the walls are near an hundred foot thick, built of hewn stone, whereof each is about forty foot square, and adorned on all sides with statues of gods and emperors cut in marble larger than the life, placed in their several niches. I measured a little finger which had fallen down from one of these statues, and lay unperceived among some rubbish, and found it exactly four foot and an inch in length. Glumdalclitch wrapped it up in a handkerchief, and carried it home in her pocket to keep among other trinkets, of which the girl was very fond, as children at her age usually are.

The King's kitchen is indeed a noble building, vaulted at top, and about six hundred foot high. The great oven is not so wide by ten paces as the cupola at St. Paul's:[3] for I measured the latter on purpose after my return. But if I should describe the kitchen grate, the prodigious pots and kettles, the joints of meat turning on the spits, with many other particulars, perhaps I should be hardly believed; at least a severe critic would be apt to think I enlarged a little, as travelers are often suspected to do. To avoid which censure, I fear I have run too much into the other extreme, and that if this treatise should happen to be translated into the language of Brobdingnag (which is the general name of that kingdom) and transmitted thither, the King and his people would have reason to complain that I had done them an injury by a false and diminutive representation.

His Majesty seldom keeps above six hundred horses in his stables: they are generally from fifty-four to sixty foot high. But when he goes abroad on solemn days, he is attended for state by a militia guard of five hundred horse, which indeed I thought was the most splendid sight that could be ever beheld, till I saw part of his army in battalia,[4] whereof I shall find another occasion to speak.

CHAPTER 5. *Several adventures that happened to the Author. The execution of a criminal. The Author shows his skill in navigation.*

I should have lived happy enough in that country if my littleness had not exposed me to several ridiculous and troublesome accidents, some of which I shall venture to relate. Glumdalclitch often carried me into the gardens of the court in my smaller box, and would sometimes take me out of it and hold me in her hand, or set me down to walk. I remember, before the dwarf left the Queen, he followed us one day into those gardens; and my nurse having set me down, he and I being close together near some dwarf apple trees, I must needs show my wit by a silly allusion between him and the trees, which happens to hold in their language as it doth in ours. Whereupon, the

---

2. One of the most beautiful Gothic steeples in England is that of Salisbury Cathedral, 404 feet high.

3. The cupola of St. Paul's Cathedral in London is 108 feet in diameter.
4. Battle array.

malicious rogue watching his opportunity, when I was walking under one of them, shook it directly over my head, by which a dozen apples, each of them near as large as a Bristol barrel, came tumbling about my ears; one of them hit me on the back as I chanced to stoop, and knocked me down flat on my face, but I received no other hurt; and the dwarf was pardoned at my desire, because I had given the provocation.

Another day Glumdalclitch left me on a smooth grassplot to divert myself while she walked at some distance with her governess. In the meantime there suddenly fell such a violent shower of hail that I was immediately by the force of it struck to the ground: and when I was down, the hailstones gave me such cruel bangs all over the body as if I had been pelted with tennis balls;[5] however I made a shift to creep on all four, and shelter myself by lying on my face on the lee side of a border of lemon thyme, but so bruised from head to foot that I could not go abroad in ten days. Neither is this at all to be wondered at, because nature in that country observing the same proportion through all her operations, a hailstone is near eighteen hundred times as large as one in Europe; which I can assert upon experience, having been so curious to weigh and measure them.

But a more dangerous accident happened to me in the same garden when my little nurse, believing she had put me in a secure place, which I often entreated her to do that I might enjoy my own thoughts, and having left my box at home to avoid the trouble of carrying it, went to another part of the garden with her governess and some ladies of her acquaintance. While she was absent and out of hearing, a small white spaniel belonging to one of the chief gardeners, having got by accident into the garden, happened to range near the place where I lay. The dog following the scent, came directly up, and taking me in his mouth, ran straight to his master, wagging his tail, and set me gently on the ground. By good fortune he had been so well taught that I was carried between his teeth without the least hurt, or even tearing my clothes. But the poor gardener, who knew me well, and had a great kindness for me, was in a terrible fright. He gently took me up in both his hands, and asked me how I did; but I was so amazed and out of breath that I could not speak a word. In a few minutes I came to myself, and he carried me safe to my little nurse, who by this time had returned to the place where she left me, and was in cruel agonies when I did not appear nor answer when she called; she severely reprimanded the gardener on account of his dog. But the thing was hushed up and never known at court; for the girl was afraid of the Queen's anger; and truly, as to myself, I thought it would not be for my reputation that such a story should go about.

This accident absolutely determined Glumdalclitch never to trust me abroad for the future out of her sight. I had been long afraid of this resolution, and therefore concealed from her some little unlucky adventures that happened in those times when I was left by myself. Once a kite hovering over the garden made a stoop[6] at me, and if I had not resolutely drawn my hanger, and run under a thick espalier, he would have certainly carried me away in his talons. Another time walking to the top of a fresh molehill, I fell to my neck in the hole through which that animal had cast up the earth, and

---

5. Eighteenth-century tennis balls, unlike the modern, were very hard.

6. Swoop. "Kite": a bird of prey.

coined some lie, not worth remembering, to excuse myself for spoiling my clothes. I likewise broke my right shin against the shell of a snail, which I happened to stumble over, as I was walking alone, and thinking on poor England.

I cannot tell whether I were more pleased or mortified to observe in those solitary walks that the smaller birds did not appear to be at all afraid of me; but would hop about within a yard distance, looking for worms and other food with as much indifference and security as if no creature at all were near them. I remember a thrush had the confidence to snatch out of my hand with his bill a piece of cake that Glumdalclitch had just given me for my breakfast. When I attempted to catch any of these birds, they would boldly turn against me, endeavoring to pick my fingers, which I durst not venture within their reach; and then they would hop back unconcerned to hunt for worms or snails, as they did before. But one day I took a thick cudgel, and threw it with all my strength so luckily at a linnet that I knocked him down, and seizing him by the neck with both my hands, ran with him in triumph to my nurse. However, the bird, who had only been stunned, recovering himself, gave me so many boxes with his wings on both sides of my head and body, though I held him at arm's length, and was out of the reach of his claws, that I was twenty times thinking to let him go. But I was soon relieved by one of our servants, who wrung off the bird's neck, and I had him next day for dinner, by the Queen's command. This linnet, as near as I can remember, seemed to be somewhat larger than an English swan.

The Maids of Honor often invited Glumdalclitch to their apartments, and desired she would bring me along with her, on purpose to have the pleasure of seeing and touching me. They would often strip me naked from top to toe and lay me at full length in their bosoms; wherewith I was much disgusted, because, to say the truth, a very offensive smell came from their skins, which I do not mention or intend to the disadvantage of those excellent ladies, for whom I have all manner of respect; but I conceive that my sense was more acute in proportion to my littleness, and that those illustrious persons were no more disagreeable to their lovers, or to each other, than people of the same quality are with us in England. And, after all, I found their natural smell was much more supportable than when they used perfumes, under which I immediately swooned away. I cannot forget that an intimate friend of mine in Lilliput took the freedom in a warm day, when I had used a good deal of exercise, to complain of a strong smell about me, although I am as little faulty that way as most of my sex: but I suppose his faculty of smelling was as nice with regard to me as mine was to that of this people. Upon this point, I cannot forbear doing justice to the Queen, my mistress, and Glumdalclitch, my nurse, whose persons were as sweet as those of any lady in England.

That which gave me most uneasiness among these Maids of Honor, when my nurse carried me to visit them, was to see them use me without any manner of ceremony, like a creature who had no sort of consequence. For they would strip themselves to the skin and put on their smocks in my presence, while I was placed on their toilet[7] directly before their naked bodies; which, I am sure, to me was very far from being a tempting sight, or from

7. Toilet table.

giving me any other emotions than those of horror and disgust. Their skins appeared so coarse and uneven, so variously colored, when I saw them near, with a mole here and there as broad as a trencher, and hairs hanging from it thicker than packthreads, to say nothing further concerning the rest of their persons. Neither did they at all scruple, while I was by, to discharge what they had drunk, to the quantity of at least two hogsheads, in a vessel that held above three tuns. The handsomest among these Maids of Honor, a pleasant frolicsome girl of sixteen, would sometimes set me astride upon one of her nipples, with many other tricks, wherein the reader will excuse me for not being over particular. But I was so much displeased that I entreated Glumdalclitch to contrive some excuse for not seeing that young lady any more.

One day a young gentleman, who was nephew to my nurse's governess, came and pressed them both to see an execution. It was of a man who had murdered one of that gentleman's intimate acquaintance. Glumdalclitch was prevailed on to be of the company, very much against her inclination, for she was naturally tender-hearted: and as for myself, although I abhorred such kind of spectacles, yet my curiosity tempted me to see something that I thought must be extraordinary. The malefactor was fixed in a chair upon a scaffold erected for the purpose, and his head cut off at a blow with a sword of about forty foot long. The veins and arteries spouted up such a prodigious quantity of blood, and so high in the air, that the great *jet d'eau* at Versailles was not equal for the time it lasted; and the head, when it fell on the scaffold floor, gave such a bounce,[8] as made me start, although I were at least half an English mile distant.

The Queen, who often used to hear me talk of my sea voyages, and took all occasions to divert me when I was melancholy, asked me whether I understood how to handle a sail or an oar, and whether a little exercise of rowing might not be convenient for my health. I answered that I understood both very well. For although my proper employment had been to be surgeon or doctor to the ship, yet often, upon a pinch, I was forced to work like a common mariner. But I could not see how this could be done in their country, where the smallest wherry was equal to a first-rate man-of-war among us, and such a boat as I could manage would never live in any of their rivers. Her Majesty said, if I would contrive a boat, her own joiner should make it, and she would provide a place for me to sail in. The fellow was an ingenious workman and, by my instructions, in ten days finished a pleasure boat with all its tackling, able conveniently to hold eight Europeans. When it was finished, the Queen was so delighted that she ran with it in her lap to the King, who ordered it to be put in a cistern full of water, with me in it, by way of trial; where I could not manage my two sculls, or little oars, for want of room. But the Queen had before contrived another project. She ordered the joiner to make a wooden trough of three hundred foot long, fifty broad, and eight deep; which being well pitched to prevent leaking, was placed on the floor along the wall in an outer room of the palace. It had a cock near the bottom to let out the water when it began to grow stale, and two servants could easily fill it in half an hour. Here I often used to row for my own diversion, as well as that of the Queen and her ladies, who thought themselves

---

8. A sudden noise. "*Jet d'eau* at Versailles": this fountain rose over forty feet in the air.

well entertained with my skill and agility. Sometimes I would put up my sail, and then my business was only to steer, while the ladies gave me a gale with their fans; and when they were weary, some of the pages would blow my sail forward with their breath, while I showed my art by steering starboard or larboard as I pleased. When I had done, Glumdalclitch always carried my boat into her closet, and hung it on a nail to dry.

In this exercise I once met an accident which had like to have cost me my life. For one of the pages having put my boat into the trough, the governess who attended Glumdalclitch very officiously lifted me up to place me in the boat; but I happened to slip through her fingers, and should have infallibly fallen down forty foot upon the floor, if by the luckiest chance in the world I had not been stopped by a corking-pin that stuck in the good gentlewoman's stomacher;[9] the head of the pin passed between my shirt and the waistband of my breeches, and thus I was held by the middle in the air until Glumdalclitch ran to my relief.

Another time, one of the servants, whose office it was to fill my trough every third day with fresh water, was so careless to let a huge frog (not perceiving it) slip out of his pail. The frog lay concealed till I was put into my boat, but then seeing a resting place, climbed up, and made it lean so much on one side that I was forced to balance it with all my weight on the other, to prevent overturning. When the frog was got in, it hopped at once half the length of the boat, and then over my head, backwards and forwards, daubing my face and clothes with its odious slime. The largeness of its features made it appear the most deformed animal that can be conceived. However, I desired Glumdalclitch to let me deal with it alone. I banged it a good while with one of my sculls, and at last forced it to leap out of the boat.

But the greatest danger I ever underwent in that kingdom was from a monkey, who belonged to one of the clerks of the kitchen. Glumdalclitch had locked me up in her closet, while she went somewhere upon business or a visit. The weather being very warm, the closet window was left open, as well as the windows in the door of my bigger box, in which I usually lived, because of its largeness and conveniency. As I sat quietly meditating at my table, I heard something bounce in at the closet window, and skip about from one side to the other, whereat, although I was much alarmed, yet I ventured to look out, but stirred not from my seat; and then I saw this frolicsome animal, frisking and leaping up and down, till at last he came to my box, which he seemed to view with great pleasure and curiosity, peeping in at the door and every window. I retreated to the farther corner of my room, or box, but the monkey looking in at every side, put me into such a fright that I wanted presence of mind to conceal myself under the bed, as I might easily have done. After some time spent in peeping, grinning, and chattering, he at last espied me, and reaching one of his paws in at the door, as a cat does when she plays with a mouse, although I often shifted place to avoid him, he at length seized the lappet of my coat (which, being made of that country cloth, was very thick and strong) and dragged me out. He took me up in his right forefoot, and held me as a nurse does a child she is going to suckle, just as I have seen the same sort of creature do with a kitten in Europe: and when I offered to

9. An ornamental covering for the front and upper part of the body. "Officiously": kindly, dutifully. "Corking-pin": a pin of the largest size.

struggle, he squeezed me so hard that I thought it more prudent to submit. I have good reason to believe that he took me for a young one of his own species, by his often stroking my face very gently with his other paw. In these diversions he was interrupted by a noise at the closet door, as if somebody were opening it, whereupon he suddenly leaped up to the window at which he had come in, and thence upon the leads and gutters, walking upon three legs, and holding me in the fourth, till he clambered up to a roof that was next to ours. I heard Glumdalclitch give a shriek at the moment he was carrying me out. The poor girl was almost distracted: that quarter of the palace was all in an uproar; the servants ran for ladders; the monkey was seen by hundreds in the court, sitting upon the ridge of a building, holding me like a baby in one of his forepaws and feeding me with the other, by cramming into my mouth some victuals he had squeezed out of the bag on one side of his chaps, and patting me when I would not eat; whereat many of the rabble below could not forebear laughing; neither do I think they justly ought to be blamed, for without question the sight was ridiculous enough to everybody but myself. Some of the people threw up stones, hoping to drive the monkey down; but this was strictly forbidden, or else very probably my brains had been dashed out.

The ladders were now applied, and mounted by several men; which the monkey observing, and finding himself almost encompassed, not being able to make speed enough with his three legs, let me drop on a ridge tile, and made his escape. Here I sat for some time three hundred yards from the ground, expecting every moment to be blown down by the wind, or to fall by my own giddiness, and come tumbling over and over from the ridge to the eaves. But an honest lad, one of my nurse's footmen, climbed up, and putting me into his breeches pocket, brought me down safe.

I was almost choked with the filthy stuff the monkey had crammed down my throat; but my dear little nurse picked it out of my mouth with a small needle, and then I fell a vomiting, which gave me great relief. Yet I was so weak and bruised in the sides with the squeezes given me by this odious animal that I was forced to keep my bed a fortnight. The King, Queen, and all the Court sent every day to inquire after my health, and her Majesty made me several visits during my sickness. The monkey was killed, and an order made that no such animal should be kept about the palace.

When I attended the King after my recovery, to return him thanks for his favors, he was pleased to rally me a good deal upon this adventure. He asked me what my thoughts and speculations were while I lay in the monkey's paw, how I liked the victuals he gave me, his manner of feeding, and whether the fresh air on the roof had sharpened my stomach. He desired to know what I would have done upon such an occasion in my own country. I told his Majesty that in Europe we had no monkeys, except such as were brought for curiosities from other places, and so small that I could deal with a dozen of them together, if they presumed to attack me. And as for that monstrous animal with whom I was so lately engaged (it was indeed as large as an elephant), if my fears had suffered me to think so far as to make use of my hanger (looking fiercely and clapping my hand upon the hilt as I spoke) when he poked his paw into my chamber, perhaps I should have given him such a wound as would have made him glad to withdraw it with more haste than he put it in. This I delivered in a firm tone, like a person who was jealous lest his courage should be called in question. However, my speech produced nothing else besides a loud laughter, which all the respect due to his Majesty from those about him could not make them contain. This made me reflect how vain an attempt it is for a man to endeavor doing himself honor among those who are out of all degree of equality or comparison with him. And yet I have seen the moral of my own behavior very frequent in England since my return, where a little contemptible varlet, without the least title to birth, person, wit, or common sense, shall presume to look with importance, and put himself upon a foot with the greatest persons of the kingdom.

I was every day furnishing the court with some ridiculous story; and Glumdalclitch, although she loved me to excess, yet was arch enough to inform the Queen whenever I committed any folly that she thought would be diverting to her Majesty. The girl, who had been out of order,[1] was carried by her governess to take the air about an hour's distance, or thirty miles from town. They alighted out of the coach near a small footpath in a field, and Glumdalclitch setting down my traveling box, I went out of it to walk. There was a cow dung in the patch, and I must needs try my activity by attempting to leap over it. I took a run, but unfortunately jumped short, and found myself just in the middle up to my knees. I waded through with some difficulty, and one of the footmen wiped me as clean as he could with his handkerchief; for I was filthily bemired, and my nurse confined me to my box till we returned home, where the Queen was soon informed of what had passed and the footmen spread it about the Court, so that all the mirth, for some days, was at my expense.

CHAPTER 6. *Several contrivances of the Author to please the King and Queen. He shows his skill in music. The King inquires into the state of Europe, which the Author relates to him. The King's observations thereon.*

I used to attend the King's levee once or twice a week, and had often seen him under the barber's hand, which indeed was at first very terrible to behold. For the razor was almost twice as long as an ordinary scythe. His Majesty, according to the custom of the country, was only shaved twice a week. I once prevailed on the barber to give me some of the suds or lather, out of which I picked forty or fifty of the strongest stumps of hair. I then took a piece of fine wood, and cut it like the back of a comb, making several holes in it at equal distance with as small a needle as I could get from Glumdalclitch. I fixed in the stumps so artificially,[2] scraping and sloping them with my knife towards the points, that I made a very tolerable comb; which was a seasonable supply, my own being so much broken in the teeth that it was almost useless; neither did I know any artist in that country so nice and exact as would undertake to make me another.

And this puts me in mind of an amusement wherein I spent many of my leisure hours. I desired the Queen's woman to save for me the combings of her Majesty's hair, whereof in time I got a good quantity; and consulting with my friend the cabinetmaker, who had received general orders to do little jobs for me, I directed him to make two chair frames, no larger than those I had in my box, and then to bore little holes with a fine awl round

---

1. Not feeling well.   2. Skillfully.

those parts where I designed the backs and seats; through these holes I wove the strongest hairs I could pick out, just after the manner of cane chairs in England. When they were finished, I made a present of them to her Majesty, who kept them in her cabinet, and used to show them for curiosities, as indeed they were the wonder of every one that beheld them. The Queen would have made me sit upon one of these chairs, but I absolutely refused to obey her, protesting I would rather die a thousand deaths than place a dishonorable part of my body on those precious hairs that once adorned her Majesty's head. Of these hairs (as I had always a mechanical genius) I likewise made a neat little purse above five foot long, with her Majesty's name deciphered in gold letters, which I gave to Glumdalclitch by the Queen's consent. To say the truth, it was more for show than use, being not of strength to bear the weight of the larger coins; and therefore she kept nothing in it but some little toys[3] that girls are fond of.

The King, who delighted in music, had frequent consorts[4] at court, to which I was sometimes carried, and set in my box on a table to hear them; but the noise was so great that I could hardly distinguish the tunes. I am confident that all the drums and trumpets of a royal army, beating and sounding together just at your ears, could not equal it. My practice was to have my box removed from the places where the performers sat, as far as I could, then to shut the doors and windows of it, and draw the window curtains, after which I found their music not disagreeable.

I had learned in my youth to play a little upon the spinet. Glumdalclitch kept one in her chamber, and a master attended twice a week to teach her: I call it a spinet, because it somewhat resembled that instrument, and was played upon in the same manner. A fancy came into my head that I would entertain the King and Queen with an English tune upon this instrument. But this appeared extremely difficult: for the spinet was near sixty foot long, each key being almost a foot wide; so that, with my arms extended, I could not reach to above five keys, and to press them down required a good smart stroke with my fist, which would be too great a labor and to no purpose. The method I contrived was this: I prepared two round sticks about the bigness of common cudgels; they were thicker at one end than the other, and I covered the thicker ends with a piece of a mouse's skin, that by rapping on them I might neither damage the tops of the keys, nor interrupt the sound. Before the spinet a bench was placed, about four foot below the keys, and I was put upon the bench. I ran sideling upon it that way and this, as fast as I could, banging the proper keys with my two sticks; and made a shift to play a jig, to the great satisfaction of both their Majesties: but it was the most violent exercise I ever underwent, and yet I could not strike above sixteen keys, nor, consequently, play the bass and treble together, as other artists do; which was a great disadvantage to my performance.

The King, who, as I before observed, was a prince of excellent understanding, would frequently order that I should be brought in my box and set upon the table in his closet. He would then command me to bring one of my chairs out of the box, and sit down within three yards distance upon the top of the cabinet, which brought me almost to a level with his face. In this manner I had several conversations with him. I one day took the freedom to tell his

---

3. Trifles. 4. Concerts.

Majesty that the contempt he discovered towards Europe, and the rest of the world, did not seem answerable to those excellent qualities of mind that he was master of. That reason did not extend itself with the bulk of the body: on the contrary, we observed in our country that the tallest persons were usually least provided with it. That among other animals, bees and ants had the reputation of more industry, art, and sagacity than many of the larger kinds; and that, as inconsiderable as he took me to be, I hoped I might live to do his Majesty some signal service. The King heard me with attention, and began to conceive a much better opinion of me than he had before. He desired I would give him as exact an account of the government of England as I possibly could; because, as fond as princes commonly are of their own customs (for so he conjectured of other monarchs, by my former discourses), he should be glad to hear of anything that might deserve imitation.

Imagine with thyself, courteous reader, how often I then wished for the tongue of Demosthenes or Cicero,[5] that might have enabled me to celebrate the praise of my own dear native country in a style equal to its merits and felicity.

I began my discourse by informing his Majesty that our dominions consisted of two islands, which composed three mighty kingdoms under one sovereign, beside our plantations in America. I dwelt long upon the fertility of our soil, and the temperature of our climate. I then spoke at large upon the constitution of an English Parliament, partly made up of an illustrious body called the House of Peers,[6] persons of the noblest blood, and of the most ancient and ample patrimonies. I described that extraordinary care always taken of their education in arts and arms, to qualify them for being counselors born to the king and kingdom; to have a share in the legislature, to be members of the highest Court of Judicature, from whence there could be no appeal; and to be champions always ready for the defense of their prince and country, by their valor, conduct, and fidelity. That these were the ornament and bulwark of the kingdom, worthy followers of their most renowned ancestors, whose honor had been the reward of their virtue, from which their posterity were never once known to degenerate. To these were joined several holy persons, as part of that assembly, under the title of Bishops, whose peculiar business it is to take care of religion, and of those who instruct the people therein. These were searched and sought out through the whole nation, by the prince and his wisest counselors, among such of the priesthood as were most deservedly distinguished by the sanctity of their lives and the depth of their erudition, who were indeed the spiritual fathers of the clergy and the people.

That the other part of the Parliament consisted of an assembly called the House of Commons, who were all principal gentlemen, freely picked and culled out by the people themselves, for their great abilities and love of their country, to represent the wisdom of the whole nation. And these two bodies make up the most august assembly in Europe, to whom, in conjunction with the prince, the whole legislature is committed.

I then descended to the Courts of Justice, over which the Judges, those venerable sages and interpreters of the law, presided, for determining the

5. Great orators of Athens and Rome, respectively.

6. The House of Lords. "Temperature": temperateness.

disputed rights and properties of men, as well as for the punishment of vice, and protection of innocence. I mentioned the prudent management of our treasury, the valor and achievements of our forces by sea and land. I computed the number of our people, by reckoning how many millions there might be of each religious sect, or political party among us. I did not omit even our sports and pastimes, or any other particular which I thought might redound to the honor of my country. And I finished all with a brief historical account of affairs and events in England for about an hundred years past.

This conversation was not ended under five audiences, each of several hours, and the King heard the whole with great attention, frequently taking notes of what I spoke, as well as memorandums of several questions he intended to ask me.

When I had put an end to these long discourses, his Majesty in a sixth audience consulting his notes, proposed many doubts, queries, and objections, upon every article. He asked what methods were used to cultivate the minds and bodies of our young nobility, and in what kind of business they commonly spent the first and teachable part of their lives. What course was taken to supply that assembly when any noble family became extinct. What qualifications were necessary in those who were to be created new lords. Whether the humor[7] of the prince, a sum of money to a Court lady or a prime minister, or a design of strengthening a party opposite to the public interest, ever happened to be motives in those advancements. What share of knowledge these lords had in the laws of their country, and how they came by it, so as to enable them to decide the properties of their fellow subjects in the last resort. Whether they were always so free from avarice, partialities, or want that a bribe or some other sinister view could have no place among them. Whether those holy lords I spoke of were constantly promoted to that rank upon account of their knowledge in religious matters, and the sanctity of their lives; had never been compliers with the times while they were common priests, or slavish prostitute chaplains to some nobleman, whose opinions they continued servilely to follow after they were admitted into that assembly.

He then desired to know what arts were practiced in electing those whom I called Commoners. Whether a stranger with a strong purse might not influence the vulgar voters to choose him before their own landlord or the most considerable gentleman in the neighborhood. How it came to pass that people were so violently bent upon getting into this assembly, which I allowed to be a great trouble and expense, often to the ruin of their families, without any salary or pension: because this appeared such an exalted strain of virtue and public spirit that his Majesty seemed to doubt it might possibly not be always sincere; and he desired to know whether such zealous gentlemen could have any views of refunding themselves for the charges and trouble they were at, by sacrificing the public good to the designs of a weak and vicious prince in conjunction with a corrupted ministry. He multiplied his questions, and sifted me thoroughly upon every part of this head, proposing numberless inquiries and objections, which I think it not prudent or convenient to repeat.

7. Whim.

Upon what I said in relation to our Courts of Justice, his Majesty desired to be satisfied in several points: and this I was the better able to do, having been formerly almost ruined by a long suit in chancery, which was decreed for me with costs. He asked what time was usually spent in determining between right and wrong, and what degree of expense. Whether advocates and orators had liberty to plead in causes manifestly known to be unjust, vexatious, or oppressive. Whether party in religion or politics were observed to be of any weight in the scale of justice. Whether those pleading orators were persons educated in the general knowledge of equity, or only in provincial, national, and other local customs. Whether they or their judges had any part in penning those laws which they assumed the liberty of interpreting and glossing upon at their pleasure. Whether they had ever at different times pleaded for and against the same cause, and cited precedents to prove contrary opinions. Whether they were a rich or a poor corporation. Whether they received any pecuniary reward for pleading or delivering their opinions. And particularly whether they were ever admitted as members in the lower senate.

He fell next upon the management of our treasury, and said he thought my memory had failed me, because I computed our taxes at about five or six millions a year, and when I came to mention the issues,[8] he found they sometimes amounted to more than double, for the notes he had taken were very particular in this point; because he hoped, as he told me, that the knowledge of our conduct might be useful to him, and he could not be deceived in his calculations. But if what I told him were true, he was still at a loss how a kingdom could run out of its estate like a private person. He asked me, who were our creditors? and where we should find money to pay them? He wondered to hear me talk of such chargeable and extensive wars; that certainly we must be a quarrelsome people, or live among very bad neighbors, and that our generals must needs be richer than our kings.[9] He asked what business we had out of our own islands, unless upon the score of trade or treaty or to defend the coasts with our fleet. Above all, he was amazed to hear me talk of a mercenary standing army[1] in the midst of peace, and among a free people. He said if we were governed by our own consent in the persons of our representatives, he could not imagine of whom we were afraid, or against whom we were to fight; and would hear my opinion whether a private man's house might not better be defended by himself, his children, and family, than by half a dozen rascals picked up at a venture[2] in the streets for small wages, who might get an hundred times more by cutting their throats.

He laughed at my odd kind of arithmetic (as he was pleased to call it) in reckoning the numbers of our people by a computation drawn from the several sects among us in religion and politics. He said he knew no reason why those who entertain opinions prejudicial to the public should be obliged to change, or should not be obliged to conceal them. And as it was tyranny in any government to require the first, so it was weakness not to enforce the

---

8. Expenditures.
9. An allusion to the enormous fortune gained by the duke of Marlborough, formerly captain-general of the army, whom Swift detested.
1. Since the declaration of the Bill of Rights (1689), a standing army without authorization by Parliament had been illegal. Swift and the Tories in general were vigilant in their opposition to such an army.
2. By chance.

second: for a man may be allowed to keep poisons in his closet, but not to vend them about for cordials.[3]

He observed that among the diversions of our nobility and gentry I had mentioned gaming. He desired to know at what age this entertainment was usually taken up, and when it was laid down; how much of their time it employed; whether it ever went so high as to affect their fortunes; whether mean, vicious people, by their dexterity in that art, might not arrive at great riches, and sometimes keep our very nobles in dependence, as well as habituate them to vile companions, wholly take them from the improvement of their minds, and force them, by the losses they received, to learn and practice that infamous dexterity upon others.

He was perfectly astonished with the historical account I gave him of our affairs during the last century, protesting it was only an heap of conspiracies, rebellions, murders, massacres, revolutions, banishments, the very worst effects that avarice, faction, hypocrisy, perfidiousness, cruelty, rage, madness, hatred, envy, lust, malice, or ambition could produce.

His Majesty in another audience was at the pains to recapitulate the sum of all I had spoken; compared the questions he made with the answers I had given; then taking me into his hands, and stroking me gently, delivered himself in these words, which I shall never forget, nor the manner he spoke them in. "My little friend Grildrig, you have made a most admirable panegyric upon your country. You have clearly proved that ignorance, idleness, and vice are the proper ingredients for qualifying a legislator. That laws are best explained, interpreted, and applied by those whose interests and abilities lie in perverting, confounding, and eluding them. I observe among you some lines of an institution which in its original might have been tolerable; but these half erased, and the rest wholly blurred and blotted by corruptions. It doth not appear from all you have said how any one virtue is required towards the procurement of any one station among you; much less that men are ennobled on account of their virtue, that priests are advanced for their piety or learning, soldiers for their conduct or valor, judges for their integrity, senators for the love of their country, or counselors for their wisdom. As for yourself," continued the King, "who have spent the greatest part of your life in traveling, I am well disposed to hope you may hitherto have escaped many vices of your country. But by what I have gathered from your own relation, and the answers I have with much pains wringed and extorted from you, I cannot but conclude the bulk of your natives to be the most pernicious race of little odious vermin that nature ever suffered to crawl upon the surface of the earth."

CHAPTER 7. *The Author's love of his country. He makes a proposal of much advantage to the King; which is rejected. The King's great ignorance in politics. The learning of that country very imperfect and confined. Their laws, and military affairs, and parties in the State.*

Nothing but an extreme love of truth could have hindered me from concealing this part of my story. It was in vain to discover my resentments, which were always turned into ridicule: and I was forced to rest with patience while

3. Medicines to stimulate the heart, or, equally commonly, liqueurs.

my noble and most beloved country was so injuriously treated. I am heartily sorry as any of my readers can possibly be that such an occasion was given, but this prince happened to be so curious and inquisitive upon every particular that it could not consist either with gratitude or good manners to refuse giving him what satisfaction I was able. Yet thus much I may be allowed to say in my own vindication: that I artfully eluded many of his questions, and gave to every point a more favorable turn by many degrees than the strictness of truth would allow. For I have always borne that laudable partiality to my own country, which Dionysius Halicarnassensis[4] with so much justice recommends to an historian. I would hide the frailties and deformities of my political mother, and place her virtues and beauties in the most advantageous light. This was my sincere endeavor in those many discourses I had with that mighty monarch, although it unfortunately failed of success.

But great allowances should be given to a King who lives wholly secluded from the rest of the world, and must therefore be altogether unacquainted with the manners and customs that most prevail in other nations: the want of which knowledge will ever produce many *prejudices,* and a certain *narrowness of thinking,* from which we and the politer countries of Europe are wholly exempted. And it would be hard indeed if so remote a prince's notions of virtue and vice were to be offered as a standard for all mankind.

To confirm what I have now said, and further to show the miserable effects of a *confined education,* I shall here insert a passage which will hardly obtain belief. In hopes to ingratiate myself farther into his Majesty's favor, I told him of an invention discovered between three and four hundred years ago, to make a certain powder, into an heap of which the smallest spark of fire falling would kindle the whole in a moment, although it were as big as a mountain, and make it all fly up in the air together, with a noise and agitation greater than thunder. That a proper quantity of this powder rammed into an hollow tube of brass or iron, according to its bigness, would drive a ball of iron or lead with such violence and speed as nothing was able to sustain its force. That the largest balls thus discharged would not only destroy whole ranks of an army at once, but batter the strongest walls to the ground; sink down ships with a thousand men in each, to the bottom of the sea; and, when linked together by a chain, would cut through masts and rigging; divide hundreds of bodies in the middle, and lay all waste before them. That we often put this powder into large hollow balls of iron, and discharged them by an engine into some city we were besieging; which would rip up the pavements, tear the houses to pieces, burst and throw splinters on every side, dashing out the brains of all who came near. That I knew the ingredients very well, which were cheap and common; I understood the manner of compounding them, and could direct his workmen how to make those tubes of a size proportionable to all other things in his Majesty's kingdom, and the largest need not be above two hundred foot long; twenty or thirty of which tubes, charged with the proper quantity of powder and balls, would batter down the walls of the strongest town in his dominions in a few hours; or destroy the whole metropolis, if ever it should pretend to dispute his absolute commands. This I humbly, offered to his Majesty as a small tribute of

---

4. A Greek rhetorician and historian, who flourished ca. 25 B.C.E. His history of Rome was written to reconcile the Greeks to their Roman masters.

acknowledgement in return of so many marks that I had received of his royal favor and protection.

The King was struck with horror at the description I had given of those terrible engines and the proposal I had made. He was amazed how so impotent and groveling an insect as I (these were his expressions) could entertain such inhuman ideas, and in so familiar a manner as to appear wholly unmoved at all the scenes of blood and desolation which I had painted as the common effects of those destructive machines; whereof he said some evil genius, enemy to mankind, must have been the first contriver. As for himself, he protested that although few things delighted him so much as new discoveries in art or in nature, yet he would rather lose half his kingdom than be privy to such a secret, which he commanded me, as I valued my life, never to mention any more.

A strange effect of *narrow principles* and *short views!* that a prince possessed of every quality which procures veneration, love, and esteem; of strong parts, great wisdom, and profound learning; endued with admirable talents for government, and almost adored by his subjects; should from a *nice, unnecessary scruple,* whereof in Europe we can have no conception, let slip an opportunity put into his hands that would have made him absolute master of the lives, the liberties, and the fortunes of his people. Neither do I say this with the least intention to detract from the many virtues of that excellent King, whose character I am sensible will on this account be very much lessened in the opinion of an English reader: but I take this defect among them to have risen from their ignorance; they not having hitherto reduced politics into a science, as the more acute wits of Europe have done. For I remember very well, in a discourse one day with the King, when I happened to say there were several thousand books among us written upon the art of government, it gave him (directly contrary to my intention) a very mean opinion of our understandings. He professed both to abominate and despise all *mystery, refinement,* and *intrigue,* either in a prince or a minister. He could not tell what I meant by *secrets of state,* where an enemy or some rival nation were not in the case. He confined the knowledge of governing within very *narrow bounds:* to common sense and reason, to justice and lenity, to the speedy determination of civil and criminal causes, with some other obvious topics which are not worth considering. And he gave it for his opinion that whoever could make two ears of corn or two blades of grass to grow upon a spot of ground where only one grew before would deserve better of mankind and do more essential service to his country than the whole race of politicians[5] put together.

The learning of this people is very defective, consisting only in morality, history, poetry, and mathematics; wherein they must be allowed to excel. But the last of these is wholly applied to what may be useful in life, to the improvement of agriculture and all mechanical arts; so that among us it would be little esteemed. And as to ideas, entities, abstractions, and transcendentals,[6] I could never drive the least conception into their heads.

No law of that country must exceed in words the number of letters in their alphabet, which consists only in two and twenty. But indeed few of them

5. Swift means something like our modern political scientists or theorists.

6. In Swift's time, *transcendental* was practically synonymous with *metaphysical.*

extend even to that length. They are expressed in the most plain and simple terms, wherein those people are not mercurial enough to discover above one interpretation. And to write a comment upon any law is a capital crime. As to the decision of civil causes, or proceedings against criminals, their precedents are so few that they have little reason to boast of any extraordinary skill in either.

They have had the art of printing as well as the Chinese, time out of mind. But their libraries are not very large; for that of the King's, which is reckoned the biggest, doth not amount to above a thousand volumes, placed in a gallery of twelve hundred foot long, from whence I had liberty to borrow what books I pleased. The Queen's joiner had contrived in one of the Glumdalclitch's rooms a kind of wooden machine five and twenty foot high, formed like a standing ladder; the steps were each fifty foot long. It was indeed a movable pair of stairs, the lowest end placed at ten foot distance from the wall of the chamber. The book I had a mind to read was put up leaning against the wall. I first mounted to the upper step of the ladder, and turning my face towards the book began at the top of the page, and so walking to the right and left about eight or ten paces according to the length of the lines, till I had gotten a little below the level of mine eyes, and then descending gradually till I came to the bottom: after which I mounted again, and began the other page in the same manner, and so turned over the leaf, which I could easily do with both my hands, for it was as thick and stiff as a pasteboard, and in the largest folios not above eighteen or twenty foot long.

Their style is clear, masculine, and smooth, but not florid; for they avoid nothing more than multiplying unnecessary words or using various expressions. I have perused many of their books, especially those in history and morality. Among the rest, I was much diverted with a little old treatise, which always lay in Glumdalclitch's bedchamber, and belonged to her governess, a grave elderly gentlewoman, who dealt in writings of morality and devotion. The book treats of the weakness of human kind, and is in little esteem, except among the women and the vulgar. However, I was curious to see what an author of that country could say upon such a subject. This writer went through all the usual topics of European moralists: showing how diminutive, contemptible, and helpless an animal was man in his own nature; how unable to defend himself from the inclemencies of the air, or the fury of wild beasts; how much he was excelled by one creature in strength, by another in speed, by a third in foresight, by a fourth in industry. He added that nature was degenerated in these latter declining ages of the world, and could now produce only small abortive births in comparison of those in ancient times. He said it was very reasonable to think, not only that the species of men were originally much larger, but also that there must have been giants in former ages; which, as it is asserted by history and tradition, so it hath been confirmed by huge bones and skulls casually dug up in several parts of the kingdom, far exceeding the common dwindled race of man in our days. He argued that the very laws of nature absolutely required we should have been made in the beginning of a size more large and robust, not so liable to destruction from every little accident of a tile falling from a house, or a stone cast from the hand of a boy, or of being drowned in a little brook. From this way of reasoning, the author drew several moral applications useful in the conduct of life, but needless here to repeat. For my own part, I could not avoid reflecting how universally this talent was spread, of drawing lectures in morality, or indeed rather matter of discontent and repining, from the quarrels we raise with nature. And I believe, upon a strict inquiry, those quarrels might be shown as ill grounded among us as they are among that people.

As to their military affairs, they boast that the King's army consists of an hundred and seventy-six thousand foot and thirty-two thousand horse: if that may be called an army which is made up of tradesmen in the several cities, and farmers in the country, whose commanders are only the nobility and gentry, without pay or reward. They are indeed perfect enough in their exercises, and under very good discipline, wherein I saw no great merit; for how should it be otherwise, where every farmer is under the command of his own landlord, and every citizen under that of the principal men in his own city, chosen after the manner of Venice by ballot?

I have often seen the militia of Lorbrulgrud drawn out to exercise in a great field near the city, of twenty miles square. They were in all not above twenty-five thousand foot, and six thousand horse; but it was impossible for me to compute their number, considering the space of ground they took up. A cavalier mounted on a large steed might be about an hundred foot high. I have seen this whole body of horse, upon a word of command, draw their swords at once, and brandish them in the air. Imagination can figure nothing so grand, so surprising, and so astonishing. It looked as if ten thousand flashes of lightning were darting at the same time from every quarter of the sky.

I was curious to know how this prince, to whose dominions there is no access from any other country, came to think of armies, or to teach his people the practice of military discipline. But I was soon informed, both by conversation and reading their histories. For in the course of many ages they have been troubled with the same disease to which the whole race of mankind is subject: the nobility often contending for power, the people for liberty, and the King for absolute dominion. All which, however happily tempered by the laws of the kingdom, have been sometimes violated by each of the three parties, and have more than once occasioned civil wars, the last whereof was happily put an end to by this prince's grandfather in a general composition;[7] and the militia, then settled with common consent, hath been ever since kept in the strictest duty.

CHAPTER 8. *The King and Queen make a progress to the frontiers. The Author attends them. The manner in which he leaves the country very particularly related. He returns to England.*

I had always a strong impulse that I should some time recover my liberty, though it were impossible to conjecture by what means, or to form any project with the least hope of succeeding. The ship in which I sailed was the first ever known to be driven within sight of that coast; and the King had given strict orders that if at any time another appeared, it should be taken ashore, and with all its crew and passengers brought in a tumbrel[8] to Lorbrulgrud.

7. A political settlement based on general agreement of all parties.
8. A farm wagon.

He was strongly bent to get me a woman of my own size, by whom I might propagate the breed: but I think I should rather have died than undergone the disgrace of leaving a posterity to be kept in cages like tame canary birds, and perhaps in time sold about the kingdom to persons of quality for curiosities. I was indeed treated with much kindness: I was the favorite of a great King and Queen, and the delight of the whole Court, but it was upon such a foot as ill became the dignity of human kind. I could never forget those domestic pledges I had left behind me. I wanted to be among people with whom I could converse upon even terms, and walk about the streets and fields without fear of being trod to death like a frog or a young puppy. But my deliverance came sooner than I expected, and in a manner not very common; the whole story and circumstances of which I shall faithfully relate.

I had now been two years in this country; and about the beginning of the third, Glumdalclitch and I attended the King and Queen in progress to the south coast of the kingdom. I was carried as usual in my traveling box, which, as I have already described, was a very convenient closet of twelve foot wide. I had ordered a hammock to be fixed by silken ropes from the four corners at the top, to break the jolts when a servant carried me before him on horseback, as I sometimes desired; and would often sleep in my hammock while we were upon the road. On the roof of my closet, set not directly over the middle of the hammock, I ordered the joiner to cut out a hole of a foot square to give me air in hot weather as I slept, which hole I shut at pleasure with a board that drew backwards and forwards through a groove.

When we came to our journey's end, the King thought proper to pass a few days at a palace he hath near Flanflasnic, a city within eighteen English miles of the seaside. Glumdalclitch and I were much fatigued; I had gotten a small cold, but the poor girl was so ill as to be confined to her chamber. I longed to see the ocean, which must be the only scene of my escape, if ever it should happen. I pretended to be worse than I really was, and desired leave to take the fresh air of the sea with a page whom I was very fond of, and who had sometimes been trusted with me. I shall never forget with what unwillingness Glumdalclitch consented, nor the strict charge she gave the page to be careful of me, bursting at the same time into a flood of tears, as if she had some foreboding of what was to happen. The boy took me out in my box about half an hour's walk from the palace, towards the rocks on the seashore. I ordered him to set me down, and lifting up one of my sashes, cast many a wistful melancholy look towards the sea. I found myself not very well, and told the page that I had a mind to take a nap in my hammock, which I hoped would do me good. I got in, and the boy shut the window close down, to keep out the cold. I soon fell asleep: and all I can conjecture is that while I slept, the page, thinking no danger could happen, went among the rocks to look for birds' eggs; having before observed him from my window searching about, and picking up one or two in the clefts. Be that as it will, I found myself suddenly awaked with a violent pull upon the ring which was fastened at the top of my box for the conveniency of carriage. I felt my box raised very high in the air, and then borne forward with prodigious speed. The first jolt had like to have shaken me out of my hammock, but afterwards the motion was easy enough. I called out several times as loud as I could raise my voice, but all to no purpose. I looked towards my windows, and could see nothing but the clouds and sky. I heard a noise just over my head like the clapping of wings, and then began to perceive the woeful condition I was in; that some eagle had got the ring of my box in his beak, with an intent to let it fall on a rock, like a tortoise in a shell, and then pick out my body and devour it. For the sagacity and smell of this bird enable him to discover his quarry at a great distance, although better concealed than I could be within a two-inch board.

In a little time I observed the noise and flutter of wings to increase very fast, and my box was tossed up and down like a signpost in a windy day. I heard several bangs or buffets, as I thought, given to the eagle (for such I am certain it must have been that held the ring of my box in his beak), and then all on a sudden felt myself falling perpendicularly down for above a minute, but with such incredible swiftness that I almost lost my breath. My fall was topped by a terrible squash, that sounded louder to mine ears than the cataract of Niagara; after which I was quite in the dark for another minute, and then my box began to rise so high that I could see light from the tops of my windows. I now perceived that I was fallen into the sea. My box, by the weight of my body, the goods that were in, and the broad plates of iron fixed for strength at the four corners of the top and bottom, floated above five foot deep in water. I did then and do now suppose that the eagle which flew away with my box was pursued by two or three others, and forced to let me drop while he was defending himself against the rest, who hoped to share in the prey. The plates of iron fastened at the bottom of the box (for those were the strongest) preserved the balance while it fell, and hindered it from being broken on the surface of the water. Every joint of it was well grooved, and the door did not move on hinges, but up and down like a sash; which kept my closet so tight that very little water came in. I got with much difficulty out of my hammock, having first ventured to draw back the slip-board on the roof already mentioned, contrived on purpose to let in air, for want of which I found myself almost stifled.

How often did I then wish myself with my dear Glumdalclitch, from whom one single hour had so far divided me! And I may say with truth that in the midst of my own misfortune, I could not forbear lamenting my poor nurse, the grief she would suffer for my loss, the displeasure of the Queen, and the ruin of her fortune. Perhaps many travelers have not been under greater difficulties and distress than I was at this juncture, expecting every moment to see my box dashed in pieces, or at least overset by the first violent blast or a rising wave. A breach in one single pane of glass would have been immediate death, nor could anything have preserved the windows but the strong lattice wires placed on the outside against accidents in traveling. I saw the water ooze in at several crannies, although the leaks were not considerable, and I endeavored to stop them as well as I could. I was not able to lift up the roof of my closet, which otherwise I certainly should have done, and sat on the top of it, where I might at least preserve myself from being shut up, as I may call it, in the hold. Or, if I escaped these dangers for a day or two, what could I expect but a miserable death of cold and hunger! I was four hours under these circumstances, expecting and indeed wishing every moment to be my last.

I have already told the reader that there were two strong staples fixed upon that side of my box which had no window and into which the servant, who used to carry me on horseback, would put a leathern belt, and buckle it about his waist. Being in this disconsolate state, I heard, or at least thought I heard, some kind of grating noise on that side of my box where the staples were fixed; and soon after I began to fancy that the box was pulled or towed along in the sea; for I now and then felt a sort of tugging, which made the waves rise near the tops of my windows, leaving me almost in the dark. This gave me some faint hopes of relief, although I was not able to imagine how it could be brought about. I ventured to unscrew one of my chairs, which were always fastened to the floor; and having made a hard shift to screw it down again directly under the slipping-board that I had lately opened, I mounted on the chair, and putting my mouth as near as I could to the hole, I called for help in a loud voice, and in all the languages I understood. I then fastened my handkerchief to a stick I usually carried, and thrusting it up the hole, waved it several times in the air, that if any boat or ship were near, the seamen might conjecture some unhappy mortal to be shut up in the box.

I found no effect from all I could do, but plainly perceived my closet to be moved along; and in the space of an hour or better, that side of the box where the staples were, and had no window, struck against something that was hard. I apprehended it to be a rock, and found myself tossed more than ever. I plainly heard a noise upon the cover of my closet, like that of a cable, and the grating of it as it passed through the ring. I then found myself hoisted up by degrees at least three foot higher than I was before. Where-upon I again thrust up my stick and handkerchief, calling for help till I was almost hoarse. In return to which, I heard a great shout repeated three times, giving me such transports of joy as are not to be conceived but by those who feel them. I now heard a trampling over my head, and somebody calling through the hole with a loud voice in the English tongue: "If there be anybody below, let them speak." I answered, I was an Englishman, drawn by ill fortune into the greatest calamity that ever any creature underwent, and begged, by all that was moving, to be delivered out of the dungeon I was in. The voice replied, I was safe, for my box was fastened to their ship; and the carpenter should immediately come and saw an hole in the cover, large enough to pull me out. I answered, that was needless and would take up too much time, for there was no more to be done but let one of the crew put his finger into the ring, and take the box out of the sea into the ship, and so into the captain's cabin. Some of them, upon hearing me talk so wildly, thought I was mad; others laughed; for indeed it never came into my head that I was now got among people of my own stature and strength. The carpenter came, and in a few minutes sawed a passage about four foot square; then let down a small ladder, upon which I mounted, and from thence was taken into the ship in a very weak condition.

The sailors were all in amazement, and asked me a thousand questions, which I had no inclination to answer. I was equally confounded at the sight of so many pygmies, for such I took them to be, after having so long accustomed my eyes to the monstrous objects I had left. But the Captain, Mr. Thomas Wilcocks, an honest, worthy Shropshire man, observing I was ready to faint, took me into his cabin, gave me a cordial to comfort me, and made me turn in upon his own bed, advising me to take a little rest, of which I had great need. Before I went to sleep I gave him to understand that I had some valuable furniture in my box, too good to be lost, a fine hammock, an handsome field bed, two chairs, a table, and a cabinet; that my closet was hung on all sides, or rather quilted with silk and cotton; that if he would let one of the crew bring my closet into his cabin, I would open it before him and show him my goods. The Captain, hearing me utter these absurdities, concluded I was raving; however (I suppose to pacify me), he promised to give order as I desired, and going upon deck, sent some of his men down into my closet, from whence (as I afterwards found) they drew up all my goods and stripped off the quilting; but the chairs, cabinet, and bedstead, being screwed to the floor, were much damaged by the ignorance of the seamen, who tore them up by force. Then they knocked off some of the boards for the use of the ship; and when they had got all they had a mind for, let the hulk drop into the sea, which, by reason of many breaches made in the bottom and sides, sunk to rights.[9] And indeed I was glad not to have been a spectator of the havoc they made, because I am confident it would have sensibly touched me, by bringing former passages into my mind, which I had rather forget.

I slept some hours, but perpetually disturbed with dreams of the place I had left, and the dangers I had escaped. However, upon waking, I found myself much recovered. It was now about eight o'clock at night, and the Captain ordered supper immediately, thinking I had already fasted too long. He entertained me with great kindness, observing me not to look wildly, or talk inconsistently; and when we were left alone, desired I would give him a relation of my travels, and by what accident I came to be set adrift in that monstrous wooden chest. He said that about twelve o'clock at noon, as he was looking through his glass, he spied it at a distance, and thought it was a sail, which he had a mind to make,[1] being not much out of his course, in hopes of buying some biscuit, his own beginning to fall short. That, upon coming nearer, and finding his error, he sent out his longboat to discover what I was; that his men came back in a fright, swearing they had seen a swimming house. That he laughed at their folly, and went himself in the boat, ordering his men to take a strong cable along with them. That the weather being calm, he rowed round me several times, observed my windows, and the wire lattices that defended them. That he discovered two staples upon one side, which was all of boards, without any passage for light. He then commanded his men to row up to that side, and fastening a cable to one of the staples, ordered his men to tow my chest (as he called it) towards the ship. When it was there, he gave directions to fasten another cable to the ring fixed in the cover, and to raise up my chest with pulleys, which all the sailors were not able to do above two or three foot. He said they saw my stick and handkerchief thrust out of the hole, and concluded that some unhappy man must be shut up in the cavity. I asked whether he or the crew had seen any prodigious birds in the air about the time he first discovered me. To which he answered that, discoursing this matter with the sailors while I was asleep, one of them said he had observed three eagles flying towards the north, but remarked nothing of their being larger than the usual size (which I suppose must be imputed to the great height they were at), and he could not guess the reason of my question. I then asked the Captain how far he reckoned we might be from land; he said, by the best computation he could make, we were at least an hundred leagues. I assured him that he must be mistaken by almost half; for I had not left the country from whence I came above two

---

9. At once, altogether.   1. Overtake.

hours before I dropped into the sea. Whereupon he began again to think that my brain was disturbed, of which he gave me a hint, and advised me to go to bed in a cabin he had provided. I assured him I was well refreshed with his good entertainment and company, and as much in my senses as ever I was in my life. He then grew serious and desired to ask me freely whether I were not troubled in mind by the consciousness of some enormous crime, for which I was punished at the command of some prince, by exposing me in that chest, as great criminals in other countries have been forced to sea in a leaky vessel without provisions; for although he should be sorry to have taken so ill[2] a man into his ship, yet he would engage his word to set me safe on shore in the first port where we arrived. He added that his suspicions were much increased by some very absurd speeches I had delivered at first to the sailors, and afterwards to himself, in relation to my closet or chest, as well as by my odd looks and behavior while I was at supper.

I begged his patience to hear me tell my story, which I faithfully did from the last time I left England to the moment he first discovered me. And as truth always forceth its way into rational minds, so this honest, worthy gentleman, who had some tincture of learning, and very good sense, was immediately convinced of my candor and veracity. But further to confirm all I had said, I entreated him to give order that my cabinet should be brought, of which I kept the key in my pocket (for he had already informed me how the seamen disposed of my closet). I opened it in his presence and showed him the small collection of rarities I made in the country from whence I had been so strangely delivered. There was the comb I had contrived out of the stumps of the King's beard, and another of the same materials, but fixed into a paring of her Majesty's thumbnail, which served for the back. There was a collection of needles and pins from a foot to half a yard long; four wasp-stings, like joiners' tacks; some combings of the Queen's hair; a gold ring which one day she made me a present of in a most obliging manner, taking it from her little finger, and throwing it over my head like a collar. I desired the Captain would please to accept this ring in return for his civilities, which he absolutely refused. I showed him a corn that I had cut off with my own hand from a Maid of Honor's toe; it was about the bigness of a Kentish pippin, and grown so hard that, when I returned to England, I got it hollowed into a cup and set in silver. Lastly, I desired him to see the breeches I had then on, which were made of a mouse's skin.

I could force nothing on him but a footman's tooth, which I observed him to examine with great curiosity, and found he had a fancy for it. He received it with abundance of thanks, more than such a trifle could deserve. It was drawn by an unskillful surgeon in a mistake from one of Glumdalclitch's men, who was afflicted with the toothache; but it was as sound as any in his head. I got it cleaned, and put it into my cabinet. It was about a foot long, and four inches in diameter.

The Captain was very well satisfied with this plain relation I had given him, and said he hoped when we returned to England I would oblige the world by putting it in paper and making it public. My answer was that I thought we were already overstocked with books of travels; that nothing could now pass which was not extraordinary; wherein I doubted some authors

2. Evil.

less consulted truth than their own vanity or interest, or the diversion of ignorant readers. That my story could contain little besides common events, without those ornamental descriptions of strange plants, trees, birds, and other animals, or the barbarous customs and idolatry of savage people, with which most writers abound. However, I thanked him for his good opinion, and promised to take the matter into my thoughts.

He said he wondered at one thing very much, which was to hear me speak so loud, asking me whether the King or Queen of that country were thick of hearing. I told him it was what I had been used to for above two years past, and that I admired[3] as much at the voices of him and his men, who seemed to me only to whisper, and yet I could hear them well enough. But, when I spoke in that country, it was like a man talking in the street to another looking out from the top of a steeple, unless when I was placed on a table, or held in any person's hand. I told him I had likewise observed another thing: that when I first got into the ship, and the sailors stood all about me, I thought they were the most little contemptible creatures I had ever beheld. For indeed while I was in that prince's country, I could never endure to look in a glass after my eyes had been accustomed to such prodigious objects, because the comparison gave me so despicable a conceit[4] of myself. The Captain said that while we were at supper he observed me to look at everything with a sort of wonder, and that I often seemed hardly able to contain my laughter; which he knew not well how to take, but imputed it to some disorder in my brain. I answered, it was very true; and I wondered how I could forbear, when I saw his dishes of the size of a silver threepence, a leg of pork hardly a mouthful, a cup not so big as a nutshell; and so I went on, describing the rest of his household stuff and provisions after the same manner. For, although the Queen had ordered a little equipage of all things necessary for me while I was in her service, yet my ideas were wholly taken up with what I saw on every side of me, and I winked at my own littleness, as people do at their own faults. The Captain understood my raillery very well, and merrily replied with the old English proverb, that he doubted[5] my eyes were bigger than my belly, for he did not observe my stomach so good, although I had fasted all day; and continuing in his mirth, protested he would have gladly given an hundred pounds to have seen my closet in the eagle's bill, and afterwards in its fall from so great an height into the sea; which would certainly have been a most astonishing object, worthy to have the description of it transmitted to future ages: and the comparison of Phaeton[6] was so obvious, that he could not forbear applying it, although I did not much admire the conceit.

The Captain having been at Tonquin,[7] was in his return to England driven northeastward to the latitude of 44 degrees, and of longitude 143. But meeting a trade wind two days after I came on board him, we sailed southward a long time, and coasting New Holland[8] kept our course west-southwest, and then south-southwest till we doubled the Cape of Good Hope. Our voyage was very prosperous, but I shall not trouble the reader with a journal of it. The Captain called in at one or two ports, and sent in his longboat for provi-

---

3. Wondered.
4. Notion.
5. Feared.
6. Son of Helios, the sun god, whose unsuccessful attempt to drive his father's chariot led to his

death, when he lost control and was hurled by Zeus from the sky, falling into the river Eridanus, where he drowned.
7. Tonkin, now in Vietnam.
8. Australia.

sions and fresh water; but I never went out of the ship till we came into the Downs, which was on the third day of June, 1706, about nine months after my escape. I offered to leave my goods in security for payment of my freight; but the Captain protested he would not receive one farthing. We took kind leave of each other, and I made him promise he would come to see me at my house in Redriff. I hired a horse and guide for five shillings, which I borrowed of the Captain.

As I was on the road, observing the littleness of the houses, the trees, the cattle, and the people, I began to think myself in Lilliput. I was afraid of trampling on every traveler I met, and often called aloud to have them stand out of the way, so that I had like to have gotten one or two broken heads for my impertinence.

When I came to my own house, for which I was forced to inquire, one of the servants opening the door, I bent down to go in (like a goose under a gate) for fear of striking my head. My wife ran out to embrace me, but I stooped lower than her knees, thinking she could otherwise never be able to reach my mouth. My daughter kneeled to ask my blessing, but I could not see her till she arose, having been so long used to stand with my head and eyes erect to above sixty foot; and then I went to take her up with one hand by the waist. I looked down upon the servants and one or two friends who were in the house, as if they had been pygmies and I a giant. I told my wife she had been too thrifty; for I found she had starved herself and her daughter to nothing. In short, I behaved myself so unaccountably that they were all of the Captain's opinion when he first saw me, and concluded I had lost my wits. This I mention as an instance of the great power of habit and prejudice.

In a little time I and my family and friends came to a right understanding; but my wife protested I should never go to sea any more, although my evil destiny so ordered that she had not power to hinder me; as the reader may know hereafter. In the meantime I here conclude the second part of my unfortunate voyages.

From *Part 3. A Voyage to Laputa, Balnibarbi, Glubbdubdrib, Luggnagg, and Japan*

* * *

[THE FLYING ISLAND OF LAPUTA][9]

CHAPTER 2. *The humors and dispositions of the Laputans described. An account of their learning. Of the King and his court. The author's reception there. The inhabitants subject to fears and disquietudes. An account of the women.*

At my alighting I was surrounded by a crowd of people, but those who stood nearest seemed to be of better quality. They beheld me with all the marks and circumstances of wonder; neither indeed was I much in their debt, having never till then seen a race of mortals so singular in their shapes, habits, and countenances. Their heads were all reclined to the right, or the

---

9. In the first chapter of part 3 Gulliver starts on his third voyage, but is captured by pirates and set adrift. Just as he is about to despair, a vast flying island appears in the sky, and the inhabitants draw him up with pulleys.

left; one of their eyes turned inward, and the other directly up to the zenith. Their outward garments were adorned with the figures of suns, moons, and stars, interwoven with those of fiddles, flutes, harps, trumpets, guitars, harpsichords, and many more instruments of music, unknown to us in Europe.[1] I observed here and there many in the habits of servants, with a blown bladder fastened like a flail to the end of a short stick, which they carried in their hands. In each bladder was a small quantity of dried pease or little pebbles (as I was afterwards informed). With these bladders they now and then flapped the mouths and ears of those who stood near them, of which practice I could not then conceive the meaning. It seems, the minds of these people are so taken up with intense speculations, that they neither can speak, or attend to the discourses of others, without being roused by some external taction[2] upon the organs of speech and hearing; for which reason those persons who are able to afford it always keep a flapper (the original is *climenole*) in their family, as one of their domestics; nor ever walk abroad or make visits without him. And the business of this officer is, when two or more persons are in company, gently to strike with his bladder the mouth of him who is to speak, and the right ear of him or them to whom the speaker addresseth himself. This flapper is likewise employed diligently to attend his master in his walks, and upon occasion to give him a soft flap on his eyes, because he is always so wrapped up in cogitation, that he is in manifest danger of falling down every precipice, and bouncing his head against every post; and in the streets, of jostling others, or being jostled himself into the kennel.[3]

It was necessary to give the reader this information, without which he would be at the same loss with me, to understand the proceedings of these people, as they conducted me up the stairs to the top of the island, and from thence to the royal palace. While we were ascending, they forgot several times what they were about, and left me to myself, till their memories were again roused by their flappers; for they appeared altogether unmoved by the sight of my foreign habit and countenance, and by the shouts of the vulgar, whose thoughts and minds were more disengaged.

At last we entered the palace, and proceeded into the chamber of presence; where I saw the King seated on his throne, attended on each side by persons of prime quality. Before the throne was a large table filled with globes and spheres, and mathematical instruments of all kinds. His Majesty took not the least notice of us, although our entrance was not without sufficient noise, by the concourse of all persons belonging to the court. But he was then deep in a problem, and we attended at least an hour before he could solve it. There stood by him on each side a young page, with flaps in their hands, and when they saw he was at leisure, one of them gently struck his mouth, and the other his right ear; at which he started like one awaked on the sudden, and looking towards me, and the company I was in, recollected the occasion of our coming, whereof he had been informed before. He spoke some words, whereupon immediately a young man with a flap came up to my side, and flapped me gently on the right ear; but I made signs as well as I could, that I had no occasion for such an instrument; which as I

1. The Laputans represent contemporary speculation, deplored by Swift, about abstract theories of science, mathematics, and music. Both the Royal Society and Sir Isaac Newton took an interest in the mathematical basis of music.
2. Touch.
3. Gutter.

afterwards found gave his Majesty and the whole court a very mean opinion of my understanding. The King, as far as I could conjecture, asked me several questions, and I addressed myself to him in all the languages I had. When it was found that I could neither understand nor be understood, I was conducted by his order to an apartment in his palace (this prince being distinguished above all his predecessors for his hospitality to strangers),[4] where two servants were appointed to attend me. My dinner was brought, and four persons of quality, whom I remembered to have seen very near the King's person, did me the honor to dine with me. We had two courses, of three dishes each. In the first course there was a shoulder of mutton, cut into an equilateral triangle; a piece of beef into a rhomboid; and a pudding into a cycloid. The second course was two ducks, trussed up into the form of fiddles; sausages and pudding resembling flutes and haut-boys,[5] and a breast of veal in the shape of a harp. The servants cut our bread into cones, cylinders, parallelograms, and several other mathematical figures.

While we were at dinner, I made bold to ask the names of several things in their language, and those noble persons, by the assistance of their flappers, delighted to give me answers, hoping to raise my admiration of their great abilities, if I could be brought to converse with them. I was soon able to call for bread and drink, or whatever else I wanted.

After dinner my company withdrew, and a person was sent to me by the King's order, attended by a flapper. He brought with him pen, ink, and paper, and three or four books; giving me to understand by signs, that he was sent to teach me the language. We sat together four hours, in which time I wrote down a great number of words in columns, with the translations over against them. I likewise made a shift to learn several short sentences. For my tutor would order one of my servants to fetch something, to turn about, to make a bow, to sit, or stand, or walk, and the like. Then I took down the sentence in writing. He showed me also in one of his books the figures of the sun, moon, and stars, the zodiac, the tropics and polar circles, together with the denominations of many figures of planes and solids. He gave me the names and descriptions of all the musical instruments, and the general terms of art in playing on each of them. After he had left me, I placed all my words with their interpretations in alphabetical order. And thus in a few days, by the help of a very faithful memory, I got some insight into their language.

The word, which I interpret the *Flying* or *Floating Island*, is in the original *Laputa*; whereof I could never learn the true etymology. *Lap* in the old obsolete language signifieth *high*, and *untuh* a *governor*; from which they say by corruption was derived *Laputa*, from *Lapuntuh*. But I do not approve of this derivation, which seems to be a little strained. I ventured to offer to the learned among them a conjecture of my own, that *Laputa* was *quasi Lap outed; Lap* signifying properly the dancing of the sunbeams in the sea, and *outed* a wing, which however I shall not obtrude, but submit to the judicious reader.[6]

Those to whom the King had entrusted me, observing how ill I was clad, ordered a tailor to come next morning, and take my measure for a suit of

4. George I, a patron of music and science, had filled his court with Hanoverians when he came to England in 1714.

5. Oboes.

6. Gulliver overlooks a likelier etymology: Spanish *la puta,* "the whore."

clothes. This operator did his office after a different manner from those of his trade in Europe. He first took my altitude by a quadrant, and then, with rule and compasses, described the dimensions and outlines of my whole body; all which he entered upon paper, and in six days brought my clothes very ill made, and quite out of shape, by happening to mistake a figure in the calculation. But my comfort was, that I observed such accidents very frequent, and little regarded.

During my confinement for want of clothes, and by an indisposition that held me some days longer, I much enlarged my dictionary; and when I went next to court, was able to understand many things the King spoke, and to return him some kind of answers. His Majesty had given orders that the island should move northeast and by east, to the vertical point over Lagado, the metropolis of the whole kingdom, below upon the firm earth. It was about ninety leagues distant, and our voyage lasted four days and a half. I was not in the least sensible of the progressive motion made in the air by the island. On the second morning, about eleven o'clock, the King himself in person, attended by his nobility, courtiers, and officers, having prepared all their musical instruments, played on them for three hours without intermission, so that I was quite stunned with the noise; neither could I possibly guess the meaning, till my tutor informed me. He said, that the people of their island had their ears adapted to hear the music of the spheres, which always played at certain periods; and the court was now prepared to bear their part in whatever instrument they most excelled.

In our journey towards Lagado, the capital city, his Majesty ordered that the island should stop over certain towns and villages, from whence he might receive the petitions of his subjects. And to this purpose, several pack-threads were let down with small weights at the bottom. On these pack-threads the people strung their petitions, which mounted up directly like the scraps of paper fastened by schoolboys at the end of the string that holds their kite.[7] Sometimes we received wine and victuals from below, which were drawn up by pulleys.

The knowledge I had in mathematics gave me great assistance in acquiring their phraseology, which depended much upon that science and music; and in the latter I was not unskilled. Their ideas are perpetually conversant in lines and figures. If they would, for example, praise the beauty of a woman, or any other animal, they describe it by rhombs, circles, parallelograms, ellipses, and other geometrical terms; or else by words of art drawn from music, needless here to repeat. I observed in the King's kitchen all sorts of mathematical and musical instruments, after the figures of which they cut up the joints that were served to his Majesty's table.

Their houses are very ill built, the walls bevil, without one right angle in any apartment; and this defect ariseth from the contempt they bear for practical geometry; which they despise as vulgar and mechanic, those instructions they give being too refined for the intellectuals of their workmen; which occasions perpetual mistakes. And although they are dextrous enough upon a piece of paper, in the management of the rule, the pencil, and the divider, yet in the common actions and behavior of life I have not seen a more clumsy,

---

7. Petitioners, that is, might as well go fly a kite. Throughout this section Swift satirizes the "distance" of George I (who spent much of his time in Hanover) from his British subjects.

awkward, and unhandy people, nor so slow and perplexed in their conceptions upon all other subjects, except those of mathematics and music. They are very bad reasoners, and vehemently given to opposition, unless when they happen to be of the right opinion, which is seldom their case. Imagination, fancy, and invention, they are wholly strangers to, nor have any words in their language by which those ideas can be expressed; the whole compass of their thoughts and mind being shut up within the two forementioned sciences.

Most of them, and especially those who deal in the astronomical part, have great faith in judicial astrology, although they are ashamed to own it publicly. But what I chiefly admired,[8] and thought altogether unaccountable, was the strong disposition I observed in them towards news and politics; perpetually enquiring into public affairs, giving their judgments in matters of state; and passionately disputing every inch of a party opinion. I have indeed observed the same disposition among most of the mathematicians I have known in Europe; although I could never discover the least analogy between the two sciences; unless those people suppose, that because the smallest circle hath as many degrees as the largest, therefore the regulation and management of the world require no more abilities than the handling and turning of a globe. But I rather take this quality to spring from a very common infirmity of human nature, inclining us to be more curious and conceited in matters where we have least concern, and for which we are least adapted either by study or nature.

These people are under continual disquietudes, never enjoying a minute's peace of mind; and their disturbances proceed from causes which very little affect the rest of mortals. Their apprehensions arise from several changes they dread in the celestial bodies. For instance; that the earth, by the continual approaches of the sun towards it, must in course of time be absorbed or swallowed up. That the face of the sun will by degrees be encrusted with its own effluvia,[9] and give no more light to the world. That the earth very narrowly escaped a brush from the tail of the last comet, which would have infallibly reduced it to ashes; and that the next, which they have calculated for one and thirty years hence, will probably destroy us.[1] For, if in its perihelion it should approach within a certain degree of the sun (as by their calculations they have reason to dread), it will conceive a degree of heat ten thousand times more intense than that of red-hot glowing iron; and in its absence from the sun, carry a blazing tail ten hundred thousand and fourteen miles long; through which if the earth should pass at the distance of one hundred thousand miles from the nucleus, or main body of the comet, it must in its passage be set on fire, and reduced to ashes. That the sun daily spending its rays without any nutriment to supply them, will at last be wholly consumed and annihilated; which must be attended with the destruction of this earth, and of all the planets that receive their light from it.

They are so perpetually alarmed with the apprehensions of these and the like impending dangers, that they can neither sleep quietly in their beds, nor have any relish for the common pleasures or amusements of life. When they meet an acquaintance in the morning, the first question is about the

8. Wondered at.
9. Sunspots.
1. Halley's comet, some astronomers had feared, might strike the earth on its next appearance

(1758). All the disasters that disquiet the Laputans had occurred to English scientists as possible implications of Newtonian theory.

sun's health, how he looked at his setting and rising, and what hopes they have to avoid the stroke of the approaching comet. This conversation they are apt to run into with the same temper that boys discover in delighting to hear terrible stories of sprites and hobgoblins, which they greedily listen to, and dare not go to bed for fear.

The women of the island have abundance of vivacity; they contemn their husbands, and are exceedingly fond of strangers, whereof there is always a considerable number from the continent below, attending at court, either upon affairs of the several towns and corporations, or their own particular occasions; but are much despised, because they want[2] the same endowments. Among these the ladies choose their gallants: but the vexation is, that they act with too much ease and security; for the husband is always so rapt in speculation, that the mistress and lover may proceed to the greatest familiarities before his face, if he be but provided with paper and implements, and without his flapper at his side.

The wives and daughters lament their confinement to the island, although I think it the most delicious spot of ground in the world; and although they live here in the greatest plenty and magnificence, and are allowed to do whatever they please, they long to see the world, and take the diversions of the metropolis, which they are not allowed to do without a particular license from the King; and this is not easy to be obtained, because the people of quality have found by frequent experience, how hard it is to persuade their women to return from below. I was told that a great court lady, who had several children, is married to the prime minister, the richest subject in the kingdom, a very graceful person, extremely fond of her, and lives in the finest palace of the island, went down to Lagado, on the pretense of health, there hid herself for several months, till the King sent a warrant to search for her, and she was found in an obscure eating-house all in rags, having pawned her clothes to maintain an old deformed footman, who beat her every day, and in whose company she was taken much against her will. And although her husband received her with all possible kindness, and without the least reproach, she soon after contrived to steal down again with all her jewels, to the same gallant, and hath not been heard of since.

This may perhaps pass with the reader rather for an European or English story, than for one of a country so remote. But he may please to consider, that the caprices of womankind are not limited by any climate or nation; and that they are much more uniform than can be easily imagined.

In about a month's time I had made a tolerable proficiency in their language, and was able to answer most of the King's questions, when I had the honor to attend him. His Majesty discovered not the least curiosity to enquire into the laws, government, history, religion, or manners of the countries where I had been; but confined his questions to the state of mathematics, and received the account I gave him with great contempt and indifference, though often roused by his flapper on each side.[3]

* * *

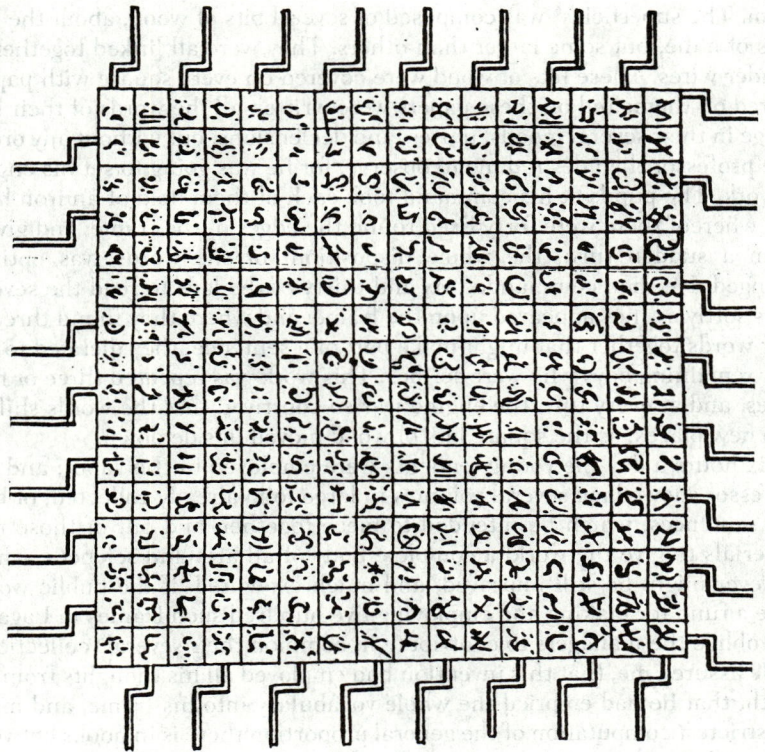

[THE ACADEMY OF LAGADO][4]
FROM CHAPTER 5.

The first professor I saw was in a very large room, with forty pupils about him. After salutation, observing me to look earnestly upon a frame, which took up the greatest part of both the length and breadth of the room, he said, perhaps I might wonder to see him employed in a project for improving speculative knowledge by practical and mechanical operations. But the world would soon be sensible[5] of its usefulness, and he flattered himself that a more noble, exalted thought never sprang in any other man's head. Everyone knew how laborious the usual method is of attaining to arts and sciences; whereas by his contrivance the most ignorant person at a reasonable charge, and with a little bodily labor, may write books in philosophy, poetry, politics, law, mathematics, and theology, without the least assistance from genius or study. He then led me to the frame, about the sides whereof all his pupils stood in ranks. It was twenty foot square, placed in the middle of the

---

4. The Grand Academy of Lagado satirizes the impractical scientists. In the Grand Academy of Lagado he meets many professors who are contriving such perverse "improvements" as making clothes from cobwebs or breeding naked sheep. Then he visits the part of the academy devoted to speculative learning.

Royal Society of London, an organization founded in 1662 to encourage the pursuit of scientific knowledge. Some of the projects described by Swift resemble the experiments or speculations of British scientists at the time.
5. Aware.

room. The superficies[6] was composed of several bits of wood, about the bigness of a die, but some larger than others. They were all linked together by slender wires. These bits of wood were covered on every square with papers pasted on them; and on these papers were written all the words of their language in their several moods, tenses, and declensions, but without any order. The professor then desired me to observe, for he was going to set his engine at work. The pupils at his command took each of them hold of an iron handle, whereof there were forty fixed round the edges of the frame; and giving them a sudden turn, the whole disposition[7] of the words was entirely changed. He then commanded six and thirty of the lads to read the several lines softly as they appeared upon the frame; and where they found three or four words together that might make part of a sentence, they dictated to the four remaining boys who were scribes. This work was repeated three or four times, and at every turn the engine was so contrived that the words shifted into new places, as the square bits of wood moved upside down.

Six hours a day the young students were employed in this labor; and the professor showed me several volumes in large folio already collected, of broken sentences, which he intended to piece together, and out of those rich materials to give the world a complete body of all arts and sciences; which however might be still improved, and much expedited, if the public would raise a fund for making and employing five hundred such frames in Lagado, and oblige the managers to contribute in common their several[8] collections.

He assured me, that this invention had employed all his thoughts from his youth, that he had emptied the whole vocabulary into his frame, and made the strictest computation of the general proportion there is in books between the numbers of particles, nouns, and verbs, and other parts of speech.

I made my humblest acknowledgments to this illustrious person for his great communicativeness, and promised if ever I had the good fortune to return to my native country, that I would do him justice, as the sole inventor of this wonderful machine; the form and contrivance of which I desired leave to delineate upon paper as in the figure here annexed. I told him, although it were the custom of our learned in Europe to steal inventions from each other, who had thereby at least this advantage, that it became a controversy which was the right owner, yet I would take such caution, that he should have the honor entire without a rival.

We next went to the school of languages, where three professors sat in consultation upon improving that of their own country.[9]

The first project was to shorten discourse by cutting polysyllables into one, and leaving out verbs and participles, because in reality all things imaginable are but nouns.

The other was a scheme for entirely abolishing all words whatsoever; and this was urged as a great advantage in point of health as well as brevity. For it is plain, that every word we speak is in some degree a diminution of our lungs by corrosion, and consequently contributes to the shortening of our lives. An expedient was therefore offered, that since words are only names for *things*, it would be more convenient for all men to carry about them such

6. Surface.
7. Arrangement.
8. Separate.
9. Many contemporary scientists had proposed a philosophical language that would eliminate the treacherous disparity between words and things and thus allow accurate scientific discourse.

things as were necessary to express the particular business they are to discourse on. And this invention would certainly have taken place, to the great ease as well as health of the subject, if the women in conjunction with the vulgar and illiterate had not threatened to raise a rebellion, unless they might be allowed the liberty to speak with their tongues, after the manner of their forefathers. Such constant irreconcilable enemies to science[1] are the common people. However, many of the most learned and wise adhere to the new scheme of expressing themselves by *things*, which hath only this inconvenience attending it, that if a man's business be very great, and of various kinds, he must be obliged in proportion to carry a greater bundle of *things* upon his back, unless he can afford one or two strong servants to attend him. I have often beheld two of those sages almost sinking under the weight of their packs, like pedlars among us, who when they met in the streets would lay down their loads, open their sacks, and hold conversation for an hour together, then put up their implements, help each other to resume their burdens, and take their leave.

But for short conversations a man may carry implements in his pockets and under his arms, enough to supply him, and in his house he cannot be at a loss; therefore the room where company meet who practice this art is full of all *things* ready at hand, requisite to furnish matter for this kind of artificial converse.[2]

Another great advantage proposed by this invention was that it would serve as an universal language to be understood in all civilized nations, whose goods and utensils are generally of the same kind, or nearly resembling, so that their uses might easily be comprehended. And thus, ambassadors would be qualified to treat with foreign princes or ministers of state to whose tongues they were utter strangers.

I was at the mathematical school, where the master taught his pupils after a method scarce imaginable to us in Europe. The proposition and demonstration were fairly written on a thin wafer, with ink composed of a cephalic tincture.[3] This the student was to swallow upon a fasting stomach, and for three days following eat nothing but bread and water. As the wafer digested, the tincture mounted to his brain, bearing the proposition along with it. But the success hath not hitherto been answerable, partly by some error in the *quantum* or composition, and partly by the perverseness of lads, to whom this bolus[4] is so nauseous that they generally steal aside, and discharge it upwards before it can operate; neither have they been yet persuaded to use so long an abstinence as the prescription requires.[5]

* * *

1. Knowledge.
2. The Royal Society had sponsored a collection intended to contain one specimen of every thing in the world.
3. A solution or dye directed toward the head.
4. A large pill. *"Quantum"*: amount.
5. In the omitted chapters Gulliver hears projects

for improving politics and offers some of his own. He sails to Glubbdubdrib, the Island of Sorcerers, where he talks with the spirits of the dead; he learns that history is a pack of lies and that humanity has degenerated since ancient times. He is then received by the king of Luggnagg.

[THE STRULDBRUGGS]

CHAPTER 10. *The Luggnaggians commended. A particular description of the struldbruggs, with many conversations between the author and some eminent persons upon that subject.*

The Luggnaggians are a polite[6] and generous people, and although they are not without some share of that pride which is peculiar to all eastern countries, yet they show themselves courteous to strangers, especially such who are countenanced by the court. I had many acquaintance among persons of the best fashion, and being always attended by my interpreter, the conversation we had was not disagreeable.

One day in much good company, I was asked by a person of quality, whether I had seen any of their *struldbruggs* or *immortals.* I said I had not; and desired he would explain to me what he meant by such an appellation, applied to a mortal creature. He told me, that sometimes, although very rarely, a child happened to be born in a family with a red circular spot in the forehead, directly over the left eyebrow, which was an infallible mark that it should never die. The spot, as he described it, was about the compass of a silver threepence, but in the course of time grew larger, and changed its color; for at twelve years old it became green, so continued till five and twenty, then turned to a deep blue; at five and forty it grew coal black, and as large as an English shilling; but never admitted any farther alteration. He said these births were so rare, that he did not believe there could be above eleven hundred *struldbruggs* of both sexes in the whole kingdom, of which he computed about fifty in the metropolis, and among the rest a young girl born about three years ago. That these productions were not peculiar to any family, but a mere effect of chance; and the children of the *struldbruggs* themselves were equally mortal with the rest of the people.

I freely own myself to have been struck with inexpressible delight upon hearing this account: and the person who gave it me happening to understand the Balnibarbian language, which I spoke very well, I could not forbear breaking out into expressions perhaps a little too extravagant. I cried out as in a rapture: Happy nation, where every child hath at least a chance for being immortal! Happy people who enjoy so many living examples of ancient virtue, and have masters ready to instruct them in the wisdom of all former ages! But happiest beyond all comparison are those excellent *struldbruggs*, who being born exempt from that universal calamity of human nature, have their minds free and disengaged, without the weight and depression of spirits caused by the continual apprehension of death. I discovered my admiration that I had not observed any of these illustrious persons at court; the black spot on the forehead being so remarkable a distinction, that I could not have easily overlooked it; and it was impossible that his Majesty, a most judicious prince, should not provide himself with a good number of such wise and able counselors. Yet perhaps the virtue of those reverend sages was too strict for the corrupt and libertine manners of a court. And we often find by experience that young men are too opinionative[7] and volatile to be guided by the sober dictates of their seniors. How-

---

6. Refined, cultivated.

7. Speculative, impractical.

ever, since the King was pleased to allow me access to his royal person, I was resolved upon the very first occasion to deliver my opinion to him on this matter freely, and at large by the help of my interpreter; and whether he would please to take my advice or no, yet in one thing I was determined, that his Majesty having frequently offered me an establishment in this country, I would with great thankfulness accept the favor, and pass my life here in the conversation of those superior beings the *struldbruggs,* if they would please to admit me.

The gentleman to whom I addressed my discourse, because (as I have already observed) he spoke the language of Balnibarbi, said to me with a sort of a smile, which usually ariseth from pity to the ignorant, that he was glad of any occasion to keep me among them, and desired my permission to explain to the company what I had spoke. He did so; and they talked together for some time in their own language, whereof I understood not a syllable, neither could I observe by their countenances what impression my discourse had made on them. After a short silence the same person told me, that his friends and mine (so he thought fit to express himself) were very much pleased with the judicious remarks I had made on the great happiness and advantages of immortal life; and they were desirous to know in a particular manner, what scheme of living I should have formed to myself, if it had fallen to my lot to have been born a *struldbrugg.*

I answered, it was easy to be eloquent on so copious and delightful a subject, especially to me who have been often apt to amuse myself with visions of what I should do if I were a king, a general, or a great lord; and upon this very case I had frequently run over the whole system how I should employ myself, and pass the time if I were sure to live forever.

That, if it had been my good fortune to come into the world a *struldbrugg,* as soon as I could discover my own happiness by understanding the difference between life and death, I would first resolve by all arts and methods whatsoever to procure myself riches: in the pursuit of which, by thrift and management, I might reasonably expect in about two hundred years to be the wealthiest man in the kingdom. In the second place, I would from my earliest youth apply myself to the study of arts and sciences, by which I should arrive in time to excel all others in learning. Lastly, I would carefully record every action and event of consequence that happened in the public, impartially draw the characters of the several successions of princes, and great ministers of state; with my own observations on every point. I would exactly set down the several changes in customs, languages, fashions of dress, diet and diversions. By all which acquirements, I should be a living treasury of knowledge and wisdom, and certainly become the oracle of the nation.

I would never marry after threescore, but live in an hospitable manner, yet still on the saving side. I would entertain myself in forming and directing the minds of hopeful young men, by convincing them from my own remembrance, experience and observation, fortified by numerous examples, of the usefulness of virtue in public and private life. But my choice and constant companions should be a set of my own immortal brotherhood, among whom I would elect a dozen from the most ancient down to my own contemporaries. Where any of these wanted fortunes, I would provide them with convenient lodges round my own estate, and have some of them always at my table, only mingling a few of the most valuable among you mortals, whom length of time would harden me to lose with little or no reluctance, and treat your posterity after the same manner; just as a man diverts himself with the annual succession of pinks and tulips in his garden, without regretting the loss of those which withered the preceding year.

These *struldbruggs* and I would mutually communicate our observations and memorials[8] through the course of time; remark the several gradations by which corruption steals into the world, and oppose it in every step, by giving perpetual warning and instruction to mankind; which, added to the strong influence of our own example, would probably prevent that continual degeneracy of human nature, so justly complained of in all ages.

Add to all this, the pleasure of seeing the various revolutions of states and empires; the changes in the lower and upper world;[9] ancient cities in ruins; and obscure villages become the seats of kings. Famous rivers lessening into shallow brooks; the ocean leaving one coast dry, and overwhelming another; the discovery of many countries yet unknown. Barbarity overrunning the politest nations, and the most barbarous becoming civilized. I should then see the discovery of the longitude, the perpetual motion, the universal medicine,[1] and many other great inventions brought to the utmost perfection.

What wonderful discoveries should we make in astronomy, by outliving and confirming our own predictions, by observing the progress and returns of comets, with the changes of motion in the sun, moon and stars.

I enlarged upon many other topics, which the natural desire of endless life and sublunary happiness could easily furnish me with. When I had ended, and the sum of my discourse had been interpreted as before to the rest of the company, there was a good deal of talk among them in the language of the country, not without some laughter at my expense. At last the same gentleman who had been my interpreter said, he was desired by the rest to set me right in a few mistakes, which I had fallen into through the common imbecility[2] of human nature, and upon that allowance was less answerable for them. That this breed of *struldbruggs* was peculiar to their country, for there were no such people either in Balnibarbi or Japan, where he had the honor to be ambassador from his Majesty, and found the natives in both those kingdoms very hard to believe that the fact was possible; and it appeared from my astonishment when he first mentioned the matter to me, that I received it as a thing wholly new, and scarcely to be credited. That in the two kingdoms above mentioned, where during his residence he had conversed very much, he observed long life to be the universal desire and wish of mankind. That whoever had one foot in the grave was sure to hold back the other as strongly as he could. That the oldest had still hopes of living one day longer, and looked on death as the greatest evil, from which nature always prompted him to retreat; only in this island of Luggnagg the appetite for living was not so eager, from the continual example of the *struldbruggs* before their eyes.

That the system of living contrived by me was unreasonable and unjust, because it supposed a perpetuity of youth, health, and vigor, which no man could be so foolish to hope, however extravagant he might be in his wishes.

8. Memories.
9. Earth and heaven; figuratively, common people and the ruling class. "Revolutions": cycles.
1. The *elixir vitae*, an alchemical formula to pre-serve life forever, was considered by Swift an impossible dream, like a method for calculating longitude at sea, or a perpetual motion machine.
2. Weakness.

That the question therefore was not whether a man would choose to be always in the prime of youth, attended with prosperity and health; but how he would pass a perpetual life under all the usual disadvantages which old age brings along with it. For although few men will avow their desires of being immortal upon such hard conditions, yet in the two kingdoms before mentioned of Balnibarbi and Japan, he observed that every man desired to put off death for some time longer, let it approach ever so late; and he rarely heard of any man who died willingly, except he were incited by the extremity of grief or torture. And he appealed to me whether in those countries I had traveled, as well as my own, I had not observed the same general disposition.

After this preface he gave me a particular account of the *struldbruggs* among them. He said they commonly acted like mortals, till about thirty years old, after which by degrees they grew melancholy and dejected, increasing in both till they came to fourscore. This he learned from their own confession; for otherwise there not being above two or three of that species born in an age, they were too few to form a general observation by. When they came to fourscore years, which is reckoned the extremity of living in this country, they had not only all the follies and infirmities of other old men, but many more which arose from the dreadful prospect of never dying. They were not only opinionative, peevish, covetous, morose, vain, talkative; but uncapable of friendship, and dead to all natural affection, which never descended below their grandchildren. Envy and impotent desires are their prevailing passions. But those objects against which their envy seems principally directed, are the vices of the younger sort, and the deaths of the old. By reflecting on the former, they find themselves cut off from all possibility of pleasure; and whenever they see a funeral, they lament and repine that others are gone to an harbor of rest, to which they themselves never can hope to arrive. They have no remembrance of anything but what they learned and observed in their youth and middle age, and even that is very imperfect. And for the truth or particulars of any fact, it is safer to depend on common traditions than upon their best recollections. The least miserable among them appear to be those who turn to dotage, and entirely lose their memories; these meet with more pity and assistance, because they want many bad qualities which abound in others.

If a *struldbrugg* happen to marry one of his own kind, the marriage is dissolved of course by the courtesy of the kingdom, as soon as the younger of the two comes to be fourscore. For the law thinks it a reasonable indulgence, that those who are condemned without any fault of their own to a perpetual continuance in the world, should not have their misery doubled by the load of a wife.

As soon as they have completed the term of eighty years, they are looked on as dead in law; their heirs immediately succeed to their estates, only a small pittance is reserved for their support; and the poor ones are maintained at the public charge. After that period they are held incapable of any employment of trust or profit; they cannot purchase land, or take leases, neither are they allowed to be witnesses in any cause, either civil or criminal, not even for the decision of meers[3] and bounds.

---

3. Boundaries.

At ninety they lose their teeth and hair; they have at that age no distinction of taste, but eat and drink whatever they can get, without relish or appetite. The diseases they were subject to still continue without increasing or diminishing. In talking they forget the common appellation of things, and the names of persons, even of those who are their nearest friends and relations. For the same reason they never can amuse themselves with reading, because their memory will not serve to carry them from the beginning of a sentence to the end, and by this defect they are deprived of the only entertainment whereof they might otherwise be capable.

The language of this country being always upon the flux, the *struldbruggs* of one age do not understand those of another; neither are they able after two hundred years to hold any conversation (farther than by a few general words) with their neighbors the mortals; and thus they lie under the disadvantage of living like foreigners in their own country.

This was the account given me of the *struldbruggs*, as near as I can remember. I afterwards saw five or six of different ages, the youngest not above two hundred years old, who were brought to me at several times by some of my friends; but although they were told that I was a great traveler, and had seen all the world, they had not the least curiosity to ask me a question; only desired I would give them *slumskudask*, or a token of remembrance; which is a modest way of begging, to avoid the law that strictly forbids it, because they are provided for by the public, although indeed with a very scanty allowance.

They are despised and hated by all sorts of people; when one of them is born, it is reckoned ominous, and their birth is recorded very particularly; so that you may know their age by consulting the registry, which however hath not been kept above a thousand years past, or at least hath been destroyed by time or public disturbances. But the usual way of computing how old they are, is by asking them what kings or great persons they can remember, and then consulting history; for infallibly the last prince in their mind did not begin his reign after they were fourscore years old.

They were the most mortifying sight I ever beheld; and the women more horrible than the men. Besides the usual deformities in extreme old age, they acquired an additional ghastliness in proportion to their number of years, which is not to be described; and among half a dozen I soon distinguished which was the oldest, although there were not above a century or two between them.

The reader will easily believe, that from what I had heard and seen, my keen appetite for perpetuity of life was much abated. I grew heartily ashamed of the pleasing visions I had formed; and thought no tyrant could invent a death into which I would not run with pleasure from such a life. The King heard of all that had passed between me and my friends upon this occasion, and rallied[4] me very pleasantly; wishing I would send a couple of *struldbruggs* to my own country, to arm our people against the fear of death; but this it seems is forbidden by the fundamental laws of the kingdom; or else I should have been well content with the trouble and expense of transporting them.

I could not but agree, that the laws of this kingdom relating to the *struldbruggs*, were founded upon the strongest reasons, and such as any other

4. Ridiculed.

country would be under the necessity of enacting in the like circumstances. Otherwise, as avarice is the necessary consequent of old age, those immortals would in time become proprietors of the whole nation, and engross[5] the civil power; which, for want of abilities to manage, must end in the ruin of the public.[6]

* * *

Part 4. A Voyage to the Country of the Houyhnhnms[7]

CHAPTER 1. *The Author sets out as Captain of a ship. His men conspire against him, confine him a long time to his cabin, set him on shore in an unknown land. He travels up into the country. The Yahoos, a strange sort of animal, described. The Author meets two Houyhnhnms.*

I continued at home with my wife and children about five months in a very happy condition, if I could have learned the lesson of knowing when I was well. I left my poor wife big with child, and accepted an advantageous offer made me to be Captain of the *Adventure,* a stout merchantman of 350 tons; for I understood navigation well, and being grown weary of a surgeon's employment at sea, which however I could exercise upon occasion, I took a skillful young man of that calling, one Robert Purefoy, into my ship. We set sail from Portsmouth upon the 7th day of September, 1710; on the 14th we met with Captain Pocock of Bristol, at Tenariff, who was going to the Bay of Campeachy[8] to cut logwood. On the 16th he was parted from us by a storm; I heard since my return that his ship foundered and none escaped, but one cabin boy. He was an honest man and a good sailor, but a little too positive in his own opinions, which was the cause of his destruction, as it hath been of several others. For if he had followed my advice, he might at this time have been safe at home with his family as well as myself.

I had several men died in my ship of calentures,[9] so that I was forced to get recruits out of Barbadoes and the Leeward Islands, where I touched by the direction of the merchants who employed me; which I had soon too much cause to repent, for I found afterwards that most of them had been buccaneers. I had fifty hands on board; and my orders were that I should trade with the Indians in the South Sea, and make what discoveries I could. These rogues whom I had picked up debauched my other men, and they all formed a conspiracy to seize the ship and secure me; which they did one morning, rushing into my cabin, and binding me hand and foot, threatening to throw me overboard, if I offered to stir. I told them I was their prisoner, and would submit. This they made me swear to do, and then unbound me, only fastening one of my legs with a chain near my bed, and placed a sentry at my door with his piece charged, who was commanded to shoot me dead if I attempted my liberty. They sent me down victuals and drink, and took the government of the ship to themselves. Their design was to turn pirates and

5. Absorb, monopolize.
6. In the omitted chapter, Gulliver sails to Japan, where a Dutch ship provides him passage back to Europe.
7. Pronounced *hwin-ims.* The word suggests the neigh characteristic of a horse.

8. Campeche, in the Gulf of Mexico. Teneriffe is one of the Canary Islands.
9. "A distemper peculiar to sailors, in hot climates; wherein they imagine the sea to be green fields, and will throw themselves into it, if not restrained" (Johnson's *Dictionary*).

plunder the Spaniards, which they could not do, till they got more men. But first they resolved to sell the goods in the ship, and then go to Madagascar for recruits, several among them having died since my confinement. They sailed many weeks, and traded with the Indians; but I knew not what course they took, being kept close prisoner in my cabin, and expecting nothing less than to be murdered, as they often threatened me.

Upon the 9th day of May, 1711, one James Welch came down to my cabin; and said he had orders from the Captain to set me ashore. I expostulated with him, but in vain; neither would he so much as tell me who their new Captain was. They forced me into the longboat, letting me put on my best suit of clothes, which were as good as new, and a small bundle of linen, but no arms except my hanger; and they were so civil as not to search my pockets, into which I conveyed what money I had, with some other little necessaries. They rowed about a league, and then set me down on a strand. I desired them to tell me what country it was; they all swore, they knew no more than myself, but said that the Captain (as they called him) was resolved, after they had sold the lading, to get rid of me in the first place where they discovered land. They pushed off immediately, advising me to make haste, for fear of being overtaken by the tide, and bade me farewell.

In this desolate condition I advanced forward, and soon got upon firm ground, where I sat down on a bank to rest myself, and consider what I had best to do. When I was a little refreshed, I went up into the country, resolving to deliver myself to the first savages I should meet, and purchase my life from them by some bracelets, glass rings, and other toys, which sailors usually provide themselves with in those voyages, and whereof I had some about me. The land was divided by long rows of trees, not regularly planted, but naturally growing; there was great plenty of grass, and several fields of oats. I walked very circumspectly for fear of being surprised, or suddenly shot with an arrow from behind, or on either side. I fell into a beaten road, where I saw many tracks of human feet, and some of cows, but most of horses. At last I beheld several animals in a field, and one or two of the same kind sitting in trees. Their shape was very singular, and deformed, which a little discomposed me, so that I lay down behind a thicket to observe them better. Some of them coming forward near the place where I lay, gave me an opportunity of distinctly marking their form. Their heads and breasts were covered with a thick hair, some frizzled and others lank; they had beards like goats, and a long ridge of hair down their backs, and the fore parts of their legs and feet; but the rest of their bodies were bare, so that I might see their skins, which were of a brown buff color. They had no tails, nor any hair at all on their buttocks, except about the anus; which, I presume Nature had placed there to defend them as they sat on the ground; for this posture they used, as well as lying down, and often stood on their hind feet. They climbed high trees, as nimbly as a squirrel, for they had strong extended claws before and behind, terminating in sharp points, and hooked. They would often spring, and bound, and leap with prodigious agility. The females were not so large as the males; they had long lank hair on their heads, and only a sort of down on the rest of their bodies, except about the anus, and pudenda. Their dugs hung between their forefeet, and often reached almost to the ground as they walked. The hair of both sexes was of several colors, brown, red, black, and yellow. Upon the whole, I never beheld in all my travels so disagreeable an animal, or one against which I naturally conceived so strong an antipathy. So that thinking I had seen enough, full of contempt and aversion, I got up and pursued the beaten road, hoping it might direct me to the cabin of some Indian. I had not gone far when I met one of these creatures full in my way, and coming up directly to me. The ugly monster, when he saw me, distorted several ways every feature of his visage, and stared as at an object he had never seen before; then approaching nearer, lifted up his forepaw, whether out of curiosity or mischief, I could not tell; but I drew my hanger, and gave him a good blow with the flat side of it; for I durst not strike him with the edge, fearing the inhabitants might be provoked against me, if they should come to know that I had killed or maimed any of their cattle. When the beast felt the smart, he drew back, and roared so loud, that a herd of at least forty came flocking about me from the near field, howling and making odious faces; but I ran to the body of a tree, and leaning my back against it, kept them off, by waving my hanger. Several of this cursed brood getting hold of the branches behind, leaped up into the tree, from whence they began to discharge their excrements on my head; however, I escaped pretty well, by sticking close to the stem of the tree, but was almost stifled with the filth, which fell about me on every side.

In the midst of this distress, I observed them all to run away on a sudden as fast as they could; at which I ventured to leave the tree, and pursue the road, wondering what it was that could put them into this fright. But looking on my left hand, I saw a horse walking softly in the field; which my persecutors having sooner discovered, was the cause of their flight. The horse started a little when he came near me, but soon recovering himself, looked full in my face with manifest tokens of wonder; he viewed my hands and feet, walking round me several times. I would have pursued my journey, but he placed himself directly in the way, yet looking with a very mild aspect, never offering the least violence. We stood gazing at each other for some time; at last I took the boldness, to reach my hand towards his neck, with a design to stroke it; using the common style and whistle of jockies when they are going to handle a strange horse. But this animal, seeming to receive my civilities with disdain, shook his head, and bent his brows, softly raising up his left forefoot to remove my hand. Then he neighed three or four times, but in so different a cadence, that I almost began to think he was speaking to himself in some language of his own.

While he and I were thus employed, another horse came up; who applying himself to the first in a very formal manner, they gently struck each other's right hoof before, neighing several times by turns, and varying the sound, which seemed to be almost articulate. They went some paces off, as if it were to confer together, walking side by side, backward and forward, like persons deliberating upon some affair of weight; but often turning their eyes towards me, as it were to watch that I might not escape. I was amazed to see such actions and behavior in brute beasts; and concluded with myself that if the inhabitants of this country were endued with a proportionable degree of reason, they must needs be the wisest people upon earth. This thought gave me so much comfort, that I resolved to go forward until I could discover some house or village, or meet with any of the natives, leaving the two horses to discourse together as they pleased. But the first, who was a dapple grey, observing me to steal off, neighed after me in so expressive a tone that

I fancied myself to understand what he meant; whereupon I turned back, and came near him, to expect his farther commands; but concealing my fear as much as I could; for I began to be in some pain, how this adventure might terminate; and the reader will easily believe I did not much like my present situation.

The two horses came up close to me, looking with great earnestness upon my face and hands. The grey steed rubbed my hat all round with his right fore hoof, and discomposed it so much that I was forced to adjust it better, by taking it off, and settling it again; whereat both he and his companion (who was a brown bay) appeared to be much surprised; the latter felt the lappet of my coat, and finding it to hang loose about me, they both looked with new signs of wonder. He stroked my right hand, seeming to admire the softness, and color; but he squeezed it so hard between his hoof and his pastern, that I was forced to roar; after which they both touched me with all possible tenderness. They were under great perplexity about my shoes and stockings, which they felt very often, neighing to each other, and using various gestures, not unlike those of a philosopher, when he would attempt to solve some new and difficult phenomenon.

Upon the whole, the behavior of these animals was so orderly and rational, so acute and judicious, that I at last concluded, they must needs be magicians, who had thus metamorphosed themselves upon some design; and seeing a stranger in the way, were resolved to divert themselves with him; or perhaps were really amazed at the sight of a man so very different in habit, feature, and complexion from those who might probably live in so remote a climate. Upon the strength of this reasoning, I ventured to address them in the following manner: "Gentlemen, if you be conjurers, as I have good cause to believe, you can understand any language; therefore I make bold to let your worships know that I am a poor distressed Englishman, driven by his misfortunes upon your coast; and I entreat one of you, to let me ride upon his back, as if he were a real horse, to some house or village, where I can be relieved. In return of which favor, I will make you a present of this knife and bracelet" (taking them out of my pocket). The two creatures stood silent while I spoke, seeming to listen with great attention; and when I had ended, they neighed frequently towards each other, as if they were engaged in serious conversation. I plainly observed, that their language expressed the passions very well, and the words might with little pains be resolved into an alphabet more easily than the Chinese.

I could frequently distinguish the word *Yahoo*,[1] which was repeated by each of them several times; and although it were impossible for me to conjecture what it meant, yet while the two horses were busy in conversation, I endeavored to practice this word upon my tongue; and as soon as they were silent, I boldly pronounced "Yahoo" in a loud voice, imitating, at the same time, as near as I could, the neighing of a horse; at which they were both visibly surprised, and the grey repeated the same word twice, as if he meant to teach me the right accent, wherein I spoke after him as well as I could, and found myself perceivably to improve every time, although very far from any degree of perfection. Then the bay tried me with a second word, much

---

1. Perhaps compounded from two expressions of disgust, *yah* and *ugh* (or *hoo*), common in the 18th century.

harder to be pronounced; but reducing it to the English orthography, may be spelt thus, *Houyhnhnm*. I did not succeed in this so well as the former, but after two or three farther trials, I had better fortune; and they both appeared amazed at my capacity.

After some farther discourse, which I then conjectured might relate to me, the two friends took their leaves, with the same compliment of striking each other's hoof; and the grey made me signs that I should walk before him; wherein I thought it prudent to comply, till I could find a better director. When I offered to slacken my pace, he would cry, "Hhuun, Hhuun"; I guessed his meaning, and gave him to understand, as well as I could that I was weary, and not able to walk faster; upon which, he would stand a while to let me rest.

CHAPTER 2. *The Author conducted by a Houyhnhnm to his house. The house described. The Author's reception. The food of the Houyhnhnms. The Author in distress for want of meat is at last relieved. His manner of feeding in that country.*

Having traveled about three miles, we came to a long kind of building, made of timber, stuck in the ground, and wattled across; the roof was low, and covered with straw. I now began to be a little comforted, and took out some toys, which travelers usually carry for presents to the savage Indians of America and other parts, in hopes the people of the house would be thereby encouraged to receive me kindly. The horse made me a sign to go in first; it was a large room with a smooth clay floor, and a rack and manger extending the whole length on one side. There were three nags, and two mares, not eating, but some of them sitting down upon their hams, which I very much wondered at; but wondered more to see the rest employed in domestic business. The last seemed but ordinary cattle; however this confirmed my first opinion, that a people who could so far civilize brute animals must needs excel in wisdom all the nations of the world. The grey came in just after, and thereby prevented any ill treatment, which the others might have given me. He neighed to them several times in a style of authority, and received answers.

Beyond this room there were three others, reaching the length of the house, to which you passed through three doors, opposite to each other, in the manner of a vista; we went through the second room towards the third; here the grey walked in first, beckoning me to attend.[2] I waited in the second room, and got ready my presents, for the master and mistress of the house; they were two knives, three bracelets of false pearl, a small looking glass and a bead necklace. The horse neighed three or four times, and I waited to hear some answers in a human voice, but I heard no other returns than in the same dialect, only one or two a little shriller than his. I began to think that this house must belong to some person of great note among them, because there appeared so much ceremony before I could gain admittance. But, that a man of quality should be served all by horses, was beyond my comprehension. I feared my brain was disturbed by my sufferings and misfortunes; I roused myself, and looked about me in the room where I was left

---

2. To wait. "Vista": a long, open corridor.

alone; this was furnished as the first, only after a more elegant manner. I rubbed my eyes often, but the same objects still occurred. I pinched my arms and sides, to awaken myself, hoping I might be in a dream. I then absolutely concluded that all these appearances could be nothing else but necromancy and magic. But I had no time to pursue these reflections; for the grey horse came to the door, and made me a sign to follow him into the third room; where I saw a very comely mare, together with a colt and foal, sitting on their haunches, upon mats of straw, not unartfully made, and perfectly neat and clean.

The mare soon after my entrance, rose from her mat, and coming up close, after having nicely observed my hands and face, gave me a most contemptuous look; then turning to the horse, I heard the word Yahoo often repeated betwixt them; the meaning of which word I could not then comprehend, although it were the first I had learned to pronounce; but I was soon better informed, to my everlasting mortification: for the horse beckoning to me with his head, and repeating the word, "Hhuun, Hhuun," as he did upon the road, which I understood was to attend him, led me out into a kind of court, where was another building at some distance from the house. Here we entered, and I saw three of those detestable creatures, which I first met after my landing, feeding upon roots, and the flesh of some animals, which I afterwards found to be that of asses and dogs, and now and then a cow dead by accident or disease. They were all tied by the neck with strong withes,[3] fastened to a beam; they held their food between the claws of their forefeet, and tore it with their teeth.

The master horse ordered a sorrel nag, one of his servants, to untie the largest of these animals, and take him into a yard. The beast and I were brought close together; and our countenances diligently compared, both by master and servant, who thereupon repeated several times the word "Yahoo." My horror and astonishment are not to be described, when I observed, in this abominable animal, a perfect human figure; the face of it indeed was flat and broad, the nose depressed, the lips large, and the mouth wide; but these differences are common to all savage nations, where the lineaments of the countenance are distorted by the natives suffering their infants to lie groveling on the earth, or by carrying them on their backs, nuzzling with their face against the mother's shoulders. The forefeet of the Yahoo differed from my hands in nothing else but the length of the nails, the coarseness and brownness of the palms, and the hairiness on the backs. There was the same resemblance between our feet, with the same differences, which I knew very well, although the horses did not, because of my shoes and stockings; the same in every part of our bodies, except as to hairiness and color, which I have already described.

The great difficulty that seemed to stick with the two horses was to see the rest of my body so very different from that of a Yahoo, for which I was obliged to my clothes, whereof they had no conception; the sorrel nag offered me a root, which he held (after their manner, as we shall describe in its proper place) between his hoof and pastern; I took it in my hand, and having smelled it, returned it to him again as civilly as I could. He brought out of the Yahoo's kennel a piece of ass's flesh, but it smelled so offensively

---

3. Slender, flexible branches.

that I turned from it with loathing; he then threw it to the Yahoo, by whom it was greedily devoured. He afterwards showed me a wisp of hay, and a fetlock full of oats; but I shook my head, to signify that neither of these were food for me. And indeed, I now apprehended that I must absolutely starve, if I did not get to some of my own species; for as to those filthy Yahoos, although there were few greater lovers of mankind, at that time, than myself, yet I confess I never saw any sensitive being so detestable on all accounts; and the more I came near them, the more hateful they grew, while I stayed in that country. This the master horse observed by my behavior, and therefore sent the Yahoo back to his kennel. He then put his forehoof to his mouth, at which I was much surprised, although he did it with ease, and with a motion that appeared perfectly natural; and made other signs to know what I would eat; but I could not return him such an answer as he was able to apprehend; and if he had understood me, I did not see how it was possible to contrive any way for finding myself nourishment. While we were thus engaged, I observed a cow passing by; whereupon I pointed to her, and expressed a desire to let me go and milk her. This had its effect; for he led me back into the house, and ordered a mare-servant to open a room, where a good store of milk lay in earthen and wooden vessels, after a very orderly and cleanly manner. She gave me a large bowl full, of which I drank very heartily, and found myself well refreshed.

About noon I saw coming towards the house a kind of vehicle, drawn like a sledge by four Yahoos. There was in it an old steed, who seemed to be of quality; he alighted with his hind feet forward, having by accident got a hurt in his left forefoot. He came to dine with our horse, who received him with great civility. They dined in the best room, and had oats boiled in milk for the second course, which the old horse eat warm, but the rest cold. Their mangers were placed circular in the middle of the room, and divided into several partitions, round which they sat on their haunches upon bosses[4] of straw. In the middle was a large rack with angles answering to every partition of the manger. So that each horse and mare eat their own hay, and their own mash of oats and milk, with much decency and regularity. The behavior of the young colt and foal appeared very modest; and that of the master and mistress extremely cheerful and complaisant to their guest. The grey ordered me to stand by him; and much discourse passed between him and his friend concerning me, as I found by the stranger's often looking on me, and the frequent repetition of the word Yahoo.

I happened to wear my gloves; which the master grey observing, seemed perplexed; discovering signs of wonder what I had done to my forefeet; he put his hoof three or four times to them, as if he would signify, that I should reduce them to their former shape, which I presently did, pulling off both my gloves, and putting them into my pocket. This occasioned farther talk, and I saw the company was pleased with my behavior, whereof I soon found the good effects. I was ordered to speak the few words I understood; and while they were at dinner, the master taught me the names for oats, milk, fire, water, and some others which I could readily pronounce after him, having from my youth a great facility in learning languages.

---

4. Seats of bundled grasses.

When dinner was done, the master horse took me aside, and by signs and words made me understand the concern he was in that I had nothing to eat. Oats in their tongue are called *hlunnh*. This word I pronounced two or three times; for although I had refused them at first, yet upon second thoughts, I considered that I could contrive to make a kind of bread, which might be sufficient with milk to keep me alive, till I could make my escape to some other country, and to creatures of my own species. The horse immediately ordered a white mare-servant of his family to bring me a good quantity of oats in a sort of wooden tray. These I heated before the fire as well as I could, and rubbed them till the husks came off, which I made a shift to winnow from the grain; I ground and beat them between two stones, then took water, and made them into a paste or cake, which I toasted at the fire, and eat warm with milk. It was at first a very insipid diet, although common enough in many parts of Europe, but grew tolerable by time; and having been often reduced to hard fare in my life, this was not the first experiment I had made how easily nature is satisfied. And I cannot but observe that I never had one hour's sickness, while I staid in this island. It is true, I sometimes made a shift to catch a rabbit, or bird, by springes[5] made of Yahoos' hairs; and I often gathered wholesome herbs, which I boiled, or eat as salads with my bread; and now and then, for a rarity, I made a little butter, and drank the whey. I was at first at a great loss for salt; but custom soon reconciled the want of it; and I am confident that the frequent use of salt among us is an effect of luxury, and was first introduced only as a provocative to drink; except where it is necessary for preserving of flesh in long voyages, or in places remote from great markets. For we observe no animal to be fond of it but man;[6] and as to myself, when I left this country, it was a great while before I could endure the taste of it in anything that I eat.

This is enough to say upon the subject of my diet, wherewith other travelers fill their books, as if the readers were personally concerned whether we fare well or ill. However, it was necessary to mention this matter, lest the world should think it impossible that I could find sustenance for three years in such a country, and among such inhabitants.

When it grew towards evening, the master horse ordered a place for me to lodge in; it was but six yards from the house, and separated from the stable of the Yahoos. Here I got some straw, and covering myself with my own clothes, slept very sound. But I was in a short time better accommodated, as the reader shall know hereafter, when I come to treat more particularly about my way of living.

CHAPTER 3. *The Author studious to learn the language, the Houyhnhnm his master assists in teaching him. The language described. Several Houyhnhnms of quality come out of curiosity to see the Author. He gives his master a short account of his voyage.*

My principal endeavor was to learn the language, which my master (for so I shall henceforth call him) and his children, and every servant of his house were desirous to teach me. For they looked upon it as a prodigy, that a brute

---

5. Snares.
6. Gulliver is, of course, in error; many animals require salt.

animal should discover such marks of a rational creature. I pointed to every-thing, and enquired the name of it, which I wrote down in my journal book when I was alone, and corrected my bad accent, by desiring those of the family to pronounce it often. In this employment, a sorrel nag, one of the under servants, was very ready to assist me.

In speaking, they pronounce through the nose and throat, and their lan-guage approaches nearest to the High Dutch or German, of any I know in Europe; but is much more graceful and significant. The Emperor Charles V made almost the same observation, when he said, that if he were to speak to his horse, it should be in High Dutch.[7]

The curiosity and impatience of my master were so great, that he spent many hours of his leisure to instruct me. He was convinced (as he after-wards told me) that I must be a Yahoo, but my teachableness, civility, and cleanliness astonished him; which were qualities altogether so opposite to those animals. He was most perplexed about my clothes, reasoning some-times with himself whether they were a part of my body; for I never pulled them off till the family were asleep, and got them on before they waked in the morning. My master was eager to learn from whence I came; how I acquired those appearances of reason, which I discovered in all my actions; and to know my story from my own mouth, which he hoped he should soon do by the great proficiency I made in learning and pronouncing their words and sentences. To help my memory, I formed all I learned into the English alphabet, and writ the words down with the translations. This last, after some time, I ventured to do in my master's presence. It cost me much trouble to explain to him what I was doing; for the inhabitants have not the least idea of books or literature.

In about ten weeks time I was able to understand most of his questions; and in three months could give him some tolerable answers. He was extremely curious to know from what part of the country I came, and how I was taught to imitate a rational creature; because the Yahoos (whom he saw I exactly resembled in my head, hands, and face, that were only visible) with some appearance of cunning, and the strongest disposition to mischief, were observed to be the most unteachable of all brutes. I answered that I came over the sea, from a far place, with many others of my own kind, in a great hollow vessel made of the bodies of trees; that my companions forced me to land on this coast, and then left me to shift for myself. It was with some dif-ficulty, and by the help of many signs, that I brought him to understand me. He replied that I must needs be mistaken, or that I *said the thing which was not.* (For they have no word in their language to express lying or falsehood.) He knew it was impossible that there could be a country beyond the sea, or that a parcel of brutes could move a wooden vessel whither they pleased upon water. He was sure no Houyhnhnm alive could make such a vessel, or would trust Yahoos to manage it.

The word Houyhnhnm, in their tongue, signifies a Horse; and in its ety-mology, the Perfection of Nature. I told my master that I was at a loss for expression, but would improve as fast as I could; and hoped in a short time I should be able to tell him wonders. He was pleased to direct his own mare,

---

7. The emperor is supposed to have said that he would speak to his God in Spanish, to his mistress in Italian, and to his horse in German.

his colt, and foal, and the servants of the family to take all opportunities of instructing me; and every day for two or three hours, he was at the same pains himself. Several horses and mares of quality in the neighborhood came often to our house, upon the report spread of a wonderful Yahoo, that could speak like a Houyhnhnm, and seemed in his words and actions to discover some glimmerings of reason. These delighted to converse with me; they put many questions, and received such answers as I was able to return. By all which advantages, I made so great a progress, that in five months from my arrival, I understood whatever was spoke, and could express myself tolerably well.

The Houyhnhnms who came to visit my master, out of a design of seeing and talking with me, could hardly believe me to be a right Yahoo, because my body had a different covering from others of my kind. They were astonished to observe me without the usual hair or skin, except on my head, face, and hands; but I discovered that secret to my master, upon an accident, which happened about a fortnight before.

I have already told the reader, that every night when the family were gone to bed, it was my custom to strip and cover myself with my clothes; it happened one morning early, that my master sent for me, by the sorrel nag, who was his valet; when he came, I was fast asleep, my clothes fallen off on one side, and my shirt above my waist. I awaked at the noise he made, and observed him to deliver his message in some disorder; after which he went to my master, and in a great fright gave him a very confused account of what he had seen. This I presently discovered; for going as soon as I was dressed, to pay my attendance upon his honor, he asked me the meaning of what his servant had reported; that I was not the same thing when I slept as I appeared to be at other times; that his valet assured him, some part of me was white, some yellow, at least not so white, and some brown.

I had hitherto concealed the secret of my dress, in order to distinguish myself as much as possible, from that cursed race of Yahoos; but now I found it in vain to do so any longer. Besides, I considered that my clothes and shoes would soon wear out, which already were in a declining condition, and must be supplied by some contrivance from the hides of Yahoos, or other brutes; whereby the whole secret would be known. I therefore told my master, that in the country from whence I came, those of my kind always covered their bodies with the hairs of certain animals prepared by art, as well for decency, as to avoid inclemencies of air both hot and cold; of which, as to my own person I would give him immediate conviction, if he pleased to command me; only desiring his excuse, if I did not expose those parts that Nature taught us to conceal. He said, my discourse was all very strange, but especially the last part; for he could not understand why Nature should teach us to conceal what Nature had given. That neither himself nor family were ashamed of any parts of their bodies; but however I might do as I pleased. Whereupon, I first unbuttoned my coat, and pulled it off. I did the same with my waistcoat; I drew off my shoes, stockings, and breeches. I let my shirt down to my waist, and drew up the bottom, fastening it like a girdle about my middle to hide my nakedness.

My master observed the whole performance with great signs of curiosity and admiration. He took up all my clothes in his pastern, one piece after another, and examined them diligently; he then stroked my body very gently, and looked round me several times; after which he said, it was plain I must be a perfect Yahoo; but that I differed very much from the rest of my species, in the whiteness and smoothness of my skin, my want of hair in several parts of my body, the shape and shortness of my claws behind and before, and my affectation of walking continually on my two hinder feet. He desired to see no more; and gave me leave to put on my clothes again, for I was shuddering with cold.

I expressed my uneasiness at his giving me so often the appellation of Yahoo, an odious animal, for which I had so utter an hatred and contempt. I begged he would forbear applying that word to me, and take the same order in his family, and among his friends whom he suffered to see me. I requested likewise, that the secret of my having a false covering to my body might be known to none but himself, at least as long as my present clothing should last; for as to what the sorrel nag his valet had observed, his honor might command him to conceal it.

All this my master very graciously consented to; and thus the secret was kept till my clothes began to wear out, which I was forced to supply by several contrivances, that shall hereafter be mentioned. In the meantime, he desired I would go on with my utmost diligence to learn their language, because he was more astonished at my capacity for speech and reason, than at the figure of my body, whether it were covered or no; adding that he waited with some impatience to hear the wonders which I promised to tell him.

From thenceforward he doubled the pains he had been at to instruct me; he brought me into all company, and made them treat me with civility, because, as he told them privately, this would put me into good humor, and make me more diverting.

Every day when I waited on him, beside the trouble he was at in teaching, he would ask me several questions concerning myself, which I answered as well as I could; and by those means he had already received some general ideas, although very imperfect. It would be tedious to relate the several steps, by which I advanced to a more regular conversation, but the first account I gave of myself in any order and length was to this purpose:

That, I came from a very far country, as I already had attempted to tell him, with about fifty more of my own species; that we traveled upon the seas, in a great hollow vessel made of wood, and larger than his honor's house. I described the ship to him in the best terms I could; and explained by the help of my handkerchief displayed, how it was driven forward by the wind. That, upon a quarrel among us, I was set on shore on this coast, where I walked forward without knowing whither, till he delivered me from the persecution of those execrable Yahoos. He asked me who made the ship, and how it was possible that the Houyhnhnms of my country would leave it to the management of brutes? My answer was that I durst proceed no farther in my relation, unless he would give me his word and honor that he would not be offended; and then I would tell him the wonders I had so often promised. He agreed; and I went on by assuring him, that the ship was made by crea-tures like myself, who in all the countries I had traveled, as well as in my own, were the only governing, rational animals; and that upon my arrival hither, I was as much astonished to see the Houyhnhnms act like rational beings, as he or his friends could be in finding some marks of reason in a creature he was pleased to call a Yahoo; to which I owned my resemblance in every part, but could not account for their degenerate and brutal nature. I said farther, that if good fortune ever restored me to my native country, to relate my travels hither, as I resolved to do, everybody would believe that I *said the thing which was not,* that I invented the story out of my own head; and with all possible respect to himself, his family, and friends, and under his promise of not being offended, our countrymen would hardly think it probable, that a Houyhnhnm should be the presiding creature of a nation, and a Yahoo the brute.

CHAPTER 4. *The Houyhnhnms' notion of truth and falsehood. The Author's discourse disapproved by his master. The Author gives a more particular account of himself, and the accidents of his voyage.*

My master heard me with great appearances of uneasiness in his countenance; because *doubting* or *not believing* are so little known in this country, that the inhabitants cannot tell how to behave themselves under such circumstances. And I remember in frequent discourses with my master concerning the nature of manhood, in other parts of the world, having occasion to talk of *lying* and *false representation,* it was with much difficulty that he comprehended what I meant; although he had otherwise a most acute judgment. For he argued thus: that the use of speech was to make us understand one another, and to receive information of facts; now if anyone *said the thing which was not,* these ends were defeated; because I cannot properly be said to understand him; and I am so far from receiving information, that he leaves me worse than in ignorance; for I am led to believe a thing *black* when it is *white,* and *short* when it is *long.* And these were all the notions he had concerning the faculty of *lying,* so perfectly well understood, and so universally practiced among human creatures.

To return from this digression; when I asserted that the Yahoos were the only governing animals in my country, which my master said was altogether past his conception, he desired to know, whether we had Houyhnhnms among us, and what was their employment. I told him we had great numbers; that in summer they grazed in the fields, and in winter were kept in houses, with hay and oats, where Yahoo servants were employed to rub their skins smooth, comb their manes, pick their feet, serve them with food, and make their beds. "I understand you well," said my master; "it is now very plain from all you have spoken, that whatever share of reason the Yahoos pretend to, the Houyhnhnms are your masters; I heartily wish our Yahoos would be so tractable." I begged his honor would please to excuse me from proceeding any farther, because I was very certain that the account he expected from me would be highly displeasing. But he insisted in commanding me to let him know the best and the worst; I told him he should be obeyed. I owned that the Houyhnhnms among us, whom we called Horses, were the most generous[8] and comely animal we had; that they excelled in strength and swiftness; and when they belonged to persons of quality, employed in traveling, racing, and drawing chariots, they were treated with much kindness and care, till they fell into diseases, or became foundered in the feet; but then they were sold, and used to all kind of drudgery till they died; after which their skins

8. Noble.

were stripped and sold for what they were worth, and their bodies left to be devoured by dogs and birds of prey. But the common race of horses had not so good fortune, being kept by farmers and carriers, and other mean people, who put them to greater labor, and feed them worse. I described as well as I could, our way of riding; the shape and use of a bridle, a saddle, a spur, and a whip; of harness and wheels. I added, that we fastened plates of a certain hard substance called iron at the bottom of their feet, to preserve their hoofs from being broken by the stony ways on which we often traveled.

My master, after some expressions of great indignation, wondered how we dared to venture upon a Houyhnhnm's back; for he was sure, that the weakest servant in his house would be able to shake off the strongest Yahoo; or by lying down, and rolling upon his back, squeeze the brute to death. I answered that our horses were trained up from three or four years old to the several uses we intended them for; that if any of them proved intolerably vicious, they were employed for carriages; that they were severely beaten while they were young for any mischievous tricks; that the males, designed for the common use of riding or draught, were generally castrated about two years after their birth, to take down their spirits, and make them more tame and gentle; that they were indeed sensible of rewards and punishments; but his honor would please to consider that they had not the least tincture of reason any more than the Yahoos in this country.

It put me to the pains of many circumlocutions to give my master a right idea of what I spoke; for their language doth not abound in variety of words, because their wants and passions are fewer than among us. But it is impossible to express his noble resentment at our savage treatment of the Houyhnhnm race; particularly after I had explained the manner and use of castrating horses among us, to hinder them from propagating their kind, and to render them more servile. He said, if it were possible there could be any country where Yahoos alone were endued with reason, they certainly must be the governing animal, because reason will in time always prevail against brutal strength. But, considering the frame of our bodies, and especially of mine, he thought no creature of equal bulk was so ill-contrived for employing that reason in the common offices of life; whereupon he desired to know whether those among whom I lived resembled me or the Yahoos of his country. I assured him that I was as well shaped as most of my age; but the younger and the females were much more soft and tender, and the skins of the latter generally as white as milk. He said I differed indeed from other Yahoos, being much more cleanly, and not altogether so deformed; but in point of real advantage, he thought I differed for the worse. That my nails were of no use either to my fore or hinder feet; as to my forefeet, he could not properly call them by that name, for he never observed me to walk upon them; that they were too soft to bear the ground; that I generally went with them uncovered, neither was the covering I sometimes wore on them of the same shape, or so strong as that on my feet behind. That I could not walk with any security; for if either of my hinder feet slipped, I must inevitably fall. He then began to find fault with other parts of my body; the flatness of my face, the prominence of my nose, my eyes placed directly in front, so that I could not look on either side without turning my head; that I was not able to feed myself without lifting one of my forefeet to my mouth; and therefore nature had placed those joints to answer that necessity. He knew not what could be the use of those several clefts and divisions in my feet behind; that these were too soft to bear the hardness and sharpness of stones without a covering made from the skin of some other brute; that my whole body wanted a fence against heat and cold, which I was forced to put on and off every day with tediousness and trouble. And lastly, that he observed every animal in his country naturally to abhor the Yahoos, whom the weaker avoided, and the stronger drove from them. So that supposing us to have the gift of reason, he could not see how it were possible to cure that natural antipathy which every creature discovered against us; nor consequently, how we could tame and render them serviceable. However, he would (as he said) debate the matter no farther, because he was more desirous to know my own story, the country where I was born, and the several actions and events of my life before I came hither.

I assured him how extremely desirous I was that he should be satisfied in every point; but I doubted much whether it would be possible for me to explain myself on several subjects whereof his honor could have no conception, because I saw nothing in his country to which I could resemble them. That however, I would do my best, and strive to express myself by similitudes, humbly desiring his assistance when I wanted proper words; which he was pleased to promise me.

I said, my birth was of honest parents, in an island called England, which was remote from this country, as many days journey as the strongest of his honor's servants could travel in the annual course of the sun. That I was bred a surgeon, whose trade it is to cure wounds and hurts in the body, got by accident or violence. That my country was governed by a female man, whom we called a queen. That I left it to get riches, whereby I might maintain myself and family when I should return. That in my last voyage, I was Commander of the ship and had about fifty Yahoos under me, many of which died at sea, and I was forced to supply them by others picked out from several nations. That our ship was twice in danger of being sunk; the first time by a great storm, and the second, by striking against a rock. Here my master interposed, by asking me, how I could persuade strangers out of different countries to venture with me, after the losses I had sustained, and the hazards I had run. I said, they were fellows of desperate fortunes, forced to fly from the places of their birth, on account of their poverty or their crimes. Some were undone by lawsuits; others spent all they had in drinking, whoring, and gaming; others fled for treason; many for murder, theft, poisoning, robbery, perjury, forgery, coining false money; for committing rapes or sodomy; for flying from their colors, or deserting to the enemy; and most of them had broken prison. None of these durst return to their native countries for fear of being hanged, or of starving in a jail; and therefore were under a necessity of seeking a livelihood in other places.

During this discourse, my master was pleased often to interrupt me. I had made use of many circumlocutions in describing to him the nature of the several crimes, for which most of our crew had been forced to fly their country. This labor took up several days conversation before he was able to comprehend me. He was wholly at a loss to know what could be the use or necessity of practicing those vices. To clear up which I endeavored to give him some ideas of the desire of power and riches; of the terrible effects of lust, intemperance, malice, and envy. All this I was forced to define and describe by putting of cases, and making suppositions. After which, like one whose imagination was struck with something never seen or heard of before, he would lift up his eyes with amazement and indignation. Power, government, war, law, punishment, and a thousand other things had no terms, wherein that language could express them; which made the difficulty almost insuperable to give my master any conception of what I meant; but being of an excellent understanding, much improved by contemplation and converse, he at last arrived at a competent knowledge of what human nature in our parts of the world is capable to perform; and desired I would give him some particular account of that land, which we call Europe, especially, of my own country.

CHAPTER 5. *The Author, at his master's commands, informs him of the state of England. The causes of war among the princes of Europe. The Author begins to explain the English Constitution.*

The reader may please to observe that the following extract of many conversations I had with my master contains a summary of the most material points, which were discoursed at several times for above two years; his honor often desiring fuller satisfaction as I farther improved in the Houyhnhnm tongue. I laid before him, as well as I could, the whole state of Europe; I discoursed of trade and manufactures, of arts and sciences; and the answers I gave to all the questions he made, as they arose upon several subjects, were a fund of conversation not to be exhausted. But I shall here only set down the substance of what passed between us concerning my own country, reducing it into order as well as I can, without any regard to time or other circumstances, while I strictly adhere to truth. My only concern is that I shall hardly be able to do justice to my master's arguments and expressions; which must needs suffer by my want of capacity, as well as by a translation into our barbarous English.

In obedience therefore to his honor's commands, I related to him the Revolution under the Prince of Orange; the long war with France entered into by the said Prince, and renewed by his successor the present queen; wherein the greatest powers of Christendom were engaged, and which still continued. I computed at his request, that about a million of Yahoos might have been killed in the whole progress of it; and perhaps a hundred or more cities taken, and five times as many ships burned or sunk.[9]

He asked me what were the usual causes or motives that made one country to go to war with another. I answered, they were innumerable; but I should only mention a few of the chief. Sometimes the ambition of princes, who never think they have land or people enough to govern; sometimes the corruption of ministers, who engage their master in a war in order to stifle or divert the clamor of the subjects against their evil administration. Difference in opinions hath cost many millions of lives; for instance, whether flesh be bread, or bread be flesh; whether the juice of a certain berry be blood or wine; whether whistling be a vice or a virtue; whether it be better to kiss a post, or throw it into the fire; what is the best color for a coat, whether black,

---

9. Gulliver relates recent English history: the Glorious Revolution (1688–89) and the War of Spanish Succession (1701–13). He greatly exaggerates the casualties in the war.

white, red, or grey; and whether it should be long or short, narrow or wide, dirty or clean;[1] with many more. Neither are any wars so furious and bloody, or of so long continuance, as those occasioned by difference in opinion, especially if it be in things indifferent.[2]

Sometimes the quarrel between two princes is to decide which of them shall dispossess a third of his dominions, where neither of them pretend to any right. Sometimes one prince quarreleth with another, for fear the other should quarrel with him. Sometimes a war is entered upon, because the enemy is too strong, and sometimes because he is too weak. Sometimes our neighbors want the things which we have, or have the things which we want; and we both fight, till they take ours or give us theirs. It is a very justifiable cause of war to invade a country after the people have been wasted by famine, destroyed by pestilence, or embroiled by factions amongst themselves. It is justifiable to enter into a war against our nearest ally, when one of his towns lies convenient for us, or a territory of land, that would render our dominions round and compact. If a prince send forces into a nation, where the people are poor and ignorant, he may lawfully put half of them to death, and make slaves of the rest, in order to civilize and reduce them from their barbarous way of living. It is a very kingly, honorable, and frequent practice, when one prince desires the assistance of another to secure him against an invasion, that the assistant, when he hath driven out the invader, should seize on the dominions himself, and kill, imprison, or banish the prince he came to relieve. Alliance by blood or marriage is a sufficient cause of war between princes; and the nearer the kindred is, the greater is their disposition to quarrel. Poor nations are hungry, and rich nations are proud; and pride and hunger will ever be at variance. For these reasons, the trade of a soldier is held the most honorable of all others: because a soldier is a Yahoo hired to kill in cold blood as many of his own species, who have never offended him, as possibly he can.

There is likewise a kind of beggarly princes in Europe, not able to make war by themselves, who hire out their troops to richer nations for so much a day to each man; of which they keep three fourths to themselves, and it is the best part of their maintenance; such are those in many northern parts of Europe.[3]

"What you have told me," said my master, "upon the subject of war, doth indeed discover most admirably the effects of that reason you pretend to. However, it is happy that the shame is greater than the danger; and that Nature hath left you utterly uncapable of doing much mischief; for your mouths lying flat with your faces, you can hardly bite each other to any purpose, unless by consent. Then, as to the claws upon your feet before and behind, they are so short and tender, that one of our Yahoos would drive a dozen of yours before him. And therefore in recounting the numbers of those who have been killed in battle, I cannot but think that you have *said the thing which is not.*"

I could not forbear shaking my head and smiling a little at his ignorance. And, being no stranger to the art of war, I gave him a description of cannons,

---

1. Gulliver refers to the religious controversies of the Reformation and Counter-Reformation: the doctrine of transubstantiation, the use of music in church services, the veneration of the crucifix, and the wearing of priestly vestments.
2. Of little consequence.
3. A satiric glance at George I, who, as elector of Hanover, had dealt in this trade.

culverins, muskets, carabines, pistols, bullets, powder, swords, bayonets, battles, sieges, retreats, attacks, undermines, countermines, bombardments, sea fights; ships sunk with a thousand men; twenty thousand killed on each side; dying groans, limbs flying in the air; smoke, noise, confusion, trampling to death under horses' feet; flight, pursuit, victory; fields strewed with carcasses left for food to dogs, and wolves, and birds of prey; plundering, stripping, ravishing, burning, and destroying. And, to set forth the valor of my own dear countrymen, I assured him that I had seen them blow up a hundred enemies at once in a siege, and as many in a ship; and beheld the dead bodies drop down in pieces from the clouds, to the great diversion of all the spectators.

I was going on to more particulars, when my master commanded me silence. He said, whoever understood the nature of Yahoos might easily believe it possible for so vile an animal, to be capable of every action I had named, if their strength and cunning equaled their malice. But, as my discourse had increased his abhorrence of the whole species, so he found it gave him a disturbance in his mind, to which he was wholly a stranger before. He thought his ears being used to such abominable words, might by degrees admit them with less detestation. That, although he hated the Yahoos of this country, yet he no more blamed them for their odious qualities, than he did a *gnnayh* (a bird of prey) for its cruelty, or a sharp stone for cutting his hoof. But, when a creature pretending to reason could be capable of such enormities, he dreaded lest the corruption of that faculty might be worse than brutality itself. He seemed therefore confident, that instead of reason, we were only possessed of some quality fitted to increase our natural vices; as the reflection from a troubled stream returns the image of an ill-shapen body, not only larger, but more distorted.

He added that he had heard too much upon the subject of war, both in this and some former discourses. There was another point which a little perplexed him at present. I had said that some of our crew left their country on account of being ruined by law: that I had already explained the meaning of the word; but he was at a loss how it should come to pass, that the law which was intended for every man's preservation, should be any man's ruin. Therefore he desired to be farther satisfied what I meant by law, and the dispensers thereof, according to the present practice in my own country; because he thought Nature and Reason were sufficient guides for a reasonable animal, as we pretended to be, in showing us what we ought to do, and what to avoid.

I assured his honor that law was a science wherein I had not much conversed, further than by employing advocates, in vain, upon some injustices that had been done me. However, I would give him all the satisfaction I was able.

I said there was a society of men among us, bred up from their youth in the art of proving by words multiplied for the purpose, that white is black, and black is white, according as they are paid. To this society all the rest of the people are slaves.

"For example. If my neighbor hath a mind to my cow, he hires a lawyer to prove that he ought to have my cow from me. I must then hire another to defend my right; it being against all rules of law that any man should be allowed to speak for himself. Now in this case, I who am the true owner lie under two great disadvantages. First, my lawyer being practiced almost from his cradle in defending falsehood is quite out of his element when he would be an advocate for justice, which as an office unnatural, he always attempts with great awkwardness, if not with ill-will. The second disadvantage is that my lawyer must proceed with great caution, or else he will be reprimanded by the judges, and abhorred by his brethren, as one who would lessen the practice of the law. And therefore I have but two methods to preserve my cow. The first is to gain over my adversary's lawyer with a double fee; who will then betray his client, by insinuating that he hath justice on his side. The second way is for my lawyer to make my cause appear as unjust as he can; by allowing the cow to belong to my adversary; and this if it be skillfully done, will certainly bespeak the favor of the bench.

"Now, your honor is to know that these judges are persons appointed to decide all controversies of property, as well as for the trial of criminals; and picked out from the most dextrous lawyers who are grown old or lazy; and having been biased all their lives against truth and equity, lie under such a fatal necessity of favoring fraud, perjury, and oppression, that I have known some of them to have refused a large bribe from the side where justice lay, rather than injure the faculty,[4] by doing anything unbecoming their nature or their office.

"It is a maxim among these lawyers, that whatever hath been done before may legally be done again; and therefore they take special care to record all the decisions formerly made against common justice and the general reason of mankind. These, under the name of *precedents*, they produce as authorities to justify the most iniquitous opinions; and the judges never fail of directing accordingly.

"In pleading, they studiously avoid entering into the merits of the cause; but are loud, violent, and tedious in dwelling upon all circumstances which are not to the purpose. For instance, in the case already mentioned, they never desire to know what claim or title my adversary hath to my cow; but whether the said cow were red or black; her horns long or short; whether the field I graze her in be round or square; whether she were milked at home or abroad; what diseases she is subject to, and the like. After which they consult precedents, adjourn the cause, from time to time, and in ten, twenty, or thirty years come to an issue.

"It is likewise to be observed, that this society hath a peculiar cant and jargon of their own, that no other mortal can understand, and wherein all their laws are written, which they take special care to multiply; whereby they have wholly confounded the very essence of truth and falsehood, of right and wrong; so that it will take thirty years to decide whether the field, left me by my ancestors for six generations, belong to me, or to a stranger three hundred miles off.

"In the trial of persons accused for crimes against the state, the method is much more short and commendable: the judge first sends to sound the disposition of those in power; after which he can easily hang or save the criminal, strictly preserving all the forms of law."

Here my master interposing said it was a pity that creatures endowed with such prodigious abilities of mind as these lawyers, by the description I gave of them, must certainly be, were not rather encouraged to be instructors of

4. Profession.

others in wisdom and knowledge. In answer to which, I assured his honor that in all points out of their own trade, they were usually the most ignorant and stupid generation among us, the most despicable in common conversation, avowed enemies to all knowledge and learning; and equally disposed to pervert the general reason of mankind, in every other subject of discourse as in that of their own profession.

CHAPTER 6. *A continuation of the state of England, under Queen Anne. The character of a first minister in the courts of Europe.*

My master was yet wholly at a loss to understand what motives could incite this race of lawyers to perplex, disquiet, and weary themselves by engaging in a confederacy of injustice, merely for the sake of injuring their fellow animals; neither could he comprehend what I meant in saying they did it for hire. Whereupon I was at much pains to describe to him the use of money, the materials it was made of, and the value of the metals; that when a Yahoo had got a great store of this precious substance, he was able to purchase whatever he had a mind to; the finest clothing, the noblest houses, great tracts of land, the most costly meats and drinks; and have his choice of the most beautiful females. Therefore since money alone was able to perform all these feats, our Yahoos thought they could never have enough of it to spend or to save, as they found themselves inclined from their natural bent either to profusion or avarice. That the rich man enjoyed the fruit of the poor man's labor, and the latter were a thousand to one in proportion to the former. That the bulk of our people was forced to live miserably, by laboring every day for small wages to make a few live plentifully. I enlarged myself much on these and many other particulars to the same purpose, but his honor was still to seek,[5] for he went upon a supposition that all animals had a title to their share in the productions of the earth; and especially those who presided over the rest. Therefore he desired I would let him know what these costly meats were, and how any of us happened to want them. Whereupon I enumerated as many sorts as came into my head, with the various methods of dressing them, which could not be done without sending vessels by sea to every part of the world, as well for liquors to drink, as for sauces, and innumerable other conveniencies. I assured him, that this whole globe of earth must be at least three times gone round, before one of our better female Yahoos could get her breakfast, or a cup to put it in. He said, "That must needs be a miserable country which cannot furnish food for its own inhabitants." But what he chiefly wondered at, was how such vast tracts of ground as I described, should be wholly without fresh water, and the people put to the necessity of sending over the sea for drink. I replied that England (the dear place of my nativity) was computed to produce three times the quantity of food, more than its inhabitants are able to consume, as well as liquors extracted from grain, or pressed out of the fruit of certain trees, which made excellent drink; and the same proportion in every other convenience of life. But, in order to feed the luxury and intemperance of the males, and the vanity of the females, we sent away the greatest part of our necessary things to other countries, from whence in return we brought the materials of diseases, folly, and vice,

---

5. Still did not understand.

to spend among ourselves. Hence it follows of necessity, that vast numbers of our people are compelled to seek their livelihood by begging, robbing, stealing, cheating, pimping, forswearing, flattering, suborning, forging, gaming, lying, fawning, hectoring, voting, scribbling, star gazing, poisoning, whoring, canting, libeling, freethinking, and the like occupations; every one of which terms, I was at much pains to make him understand.

That, wine was not imported among us from foreign countries, to supply the want of water or other drinks, but because it was a sort of liquid which made us merry, by putting us out of our senses; diverted all melancholy thoughts, begat wild extravagant imaginations in the brain, raised our hopes, and banished our fears; suspended every office of reason for a time, and deprived us of the use of our limbs, until we fell into a profound sleep; although it must be confessed, that we always awaked sick and dispirited; and that the use of this liquor filled us with diseases, which made our lives uncomfortable and short.

But beside all this, the bulk of our people supported themselves by furnishing the necessities or conveniencies of life to the rich, and to each other. For instance, when I am at home and dressed as I ought to be, I carry on my body the workmanship of an hundred tradesmen; the building and furniture of my house employ as many more; and five times the number to adorn my wife.

I was going on to tell him of another sort of people, who get their livelihood by attending the sick; having upon some occasions informed his honor that many of my crew had died of diseases. But here it was with the utmost difficulty that I brought him to apprehend what I meant. He could easily conceive that a Houyhnhnm grew weak and heavy a few days before his death; or by some accident might hurt a limb. But that nature, who worketh all things to perfection, should suffer any pains to breed in our bodies, he thought impossible; and desired to know the reason of so unaccountable an evil. I told him, we fed on a thousand things which operated contrary to each other; that we eat when we were not hungry, and drank without the provocation of thirst; that we sat whole nights drinking strong liquors without eating a bit, which disposed us to sloth, inflamed our bodies, and precipitated or prevented digestion. That, prostitute female Yahoos acquired a certain malady, which bred rottenness in the bones of those who fell into their embraces; that this and many other diseases were propagated from father to son; so that great numbers come into the world with complicated maladies upon them; that it would be endless to give him a catalogue of all diseases incident to human bodies; for they could not be fewer than five or six hundred, spread over every limb, and joint; in short, every part, external and intestine, having diseases appropriated to each. To remedy which, there was a sort of people bred up among us, in the profession or pretense of curing the sick. And because I had some skill in the faculty, I would in gratitude to his honor let him know the whole mystery and method by which they proceed.

Their fundamental is that all diseases arise from repletion; from whence they conclude, that a great evacuation of the body is necessary, either through the natural passage, or upwards at the mouth. Their next business is, from herbs, minerals, gums, oils, shells, salts, juices, seaweed, excrements, barks of trees, serpents, toads, frogs, spiders, dead men's flesh and bones, birds, beasts and fishes, to form a composition for smell and taste the most abominable, nauseous, and detestable, that they can possibly contrive, which the stomach immediately rejects with loathing, and this they call a vomit. Or else from the same storehouse, with some other poisonous additions, they command us to take in at the orifice above or below (just as the physician then happens to be disposed) a medicine equally annoying and disgustful to the bowels; which relaxing the belly, drives down all before it; and this they call a purge, or a clyster. For nature (as the physicians allege) having intended the superior anterior orifice only for the intromission of solids and liquids, and the inferior posterior for ejection, these artists ingeniously considering that in all diseases nature is forced out of her seat; therefore to replace her in it, the body must be treated in a manner directly contrary, by interchanging the use of each orifice; forcing solids and liquids in at the anus, and making evacuations at the mouth.

But, besides real diseases, we are subject to many that are only imaginary, for which the physicians have invented imaginary cures; these have their several names, and so have the drugs that are proper for them; and with these our female Yahoos are always infested.

One great excellency in this tribe is their skill at prognostics, wherein they seldom fail; their predictions in real diseases, when they rise to any degree of malignity, generally portending death, which is always in their power, when recovery is not, and therefore, upon any unexpected signs of amendment, after they have pronounced their sentence, rather than be accused as false prophets, they know how to approve[6] their sagacity to the world by a seasonable dose.

They are likewise of special use to husbands and wives, who are grown weary of their mates; to eldest sons, to great ministers of state, and often to princes.

I had formerly upon occasion discoursed with my master upon the nature of government in general, and particularly of our own excellent constitution, deservedly the wonder and envy of the whole world. But having here accidently mentioned a minister of state, he commanded me some time after to inform him what species of Yahoo I particularly meant by that appellation.

I told him that a first or chief minister of state, whom I intended to describe, was a creature wholly exempt from joy and grief, love and hatred, pity and anger; at least makes use of no other passions but a violent desire of wealth, power, and titles; that he applies his words to all uses, except to the indication of his mind; that he never tells a truth, but with an intent that you should take it for a lie; nor a lie, but with a design that you should take it for a truth; that those he speaks worst of behind their backs are in the surest way to preferment; and whenever he begins to praise you to others or to yourself, you are from that day forlorn. The worst mark you can receive is a promise, especially when it is confirmed with an oath; after which every wise man retires, and gives over all hopes.

There are three methods by which a man may rise to be chief minister: the first is by knowing how with prudence to dispose of a wife, a daughter, or a sister; the second, by betraying or undermining his predecessor; and the third is by a furious zeal in public assemblies against the corruptions of

6. Prove.

the court. But a wise prince would rather choose to employ those who practice the last of these methods; because such zealots prove always the most obsequious and subservient to the will and passions of their master. That, these ministers having all employments at their disposal, preserve themselves in power by bribing the majority of a senate or great council; and at last by an expedient called an Act of Indemnity[7] (whereof I described the nature to him) they secure themselves from after reckonings, and retire from the public, laden with the spoils of the nation.

The palace of a chief minister is a seminary to breed up others in his own trade; the pages, lackies, and porter, by imitating their master, become ministers of state in their several districts, and learn to excel in the three principal ingredients, of insolence, lying, and bribery. Accordingly, they have a subaltern court paid to them by persons of the best rank; and sometimes by the force of dexterity and impudence, arrive through several gradations to be successors to their lord.

He is usually governed by a decayed wench, or favorite footman, who are the tunnels through which all graces are conveyed, and may properly be called, in the last resort, the governors of the kingdom.

One day, my master, having heard me mention the nobility of my country, was pleased to make me a compliment which I could not pretend to deserve: that, he was sure, I must have been born of some noble family, because I far exceeded in shape, color, and cleanliness, all the Yahoos of his nation, although I seemed to fail in strength, and agility, which must be imputed to my different way of living from those other brutes; and besides, I was not only endowed with the faculty of speech, but likewise with some rudiments of reason, to a degree, that with all his acquaintance I passed for a prodigy.

He made me observe, that among the Houyhnhnms, the white, the sorrel, and the iron grey were not so exactly shaped as the bay, the dapple grey, and the black; nor born with equal talents of mind, or a capacity to improve them; and therefore continued always in the condition of servants, without ever aspiring to match out of their own race, which in that country would be reckoned monstrous and unnatural.

I made his honor my most humble acknowledgments for the good opinion he was pleased to conceive of me; but assured him at the same time, that my birth was of the lower sort, having been born of plain, honest parents, who were just able to give me a tolerable education; that, nobility among us was altogether a different thing from the idea he had of it; that, our young noblemen are bred from their childhood in idleness and luxury; that, as soon as years will permit, they consume their vigor, and contract odious diseases among lewd females; and when their fortunes are almost ruined, they marry some woman of mean birth, disagreeable person, and unsound constitution, merely for the sake of money, whom they hate and despise. That, the productions of such marriages are generally scrofulous, rickety or deformed children; by which means the family seldom continues above three generations, unless the wife take care to provide a healthy father among her neighbors, or domestics, in order to improve and continue the breed. That a weak diseased body, a meager countenance, and sallow complexion are the true

---

7. An act passed at each session of Parliament to protect ministers of state who in good faith might have acted illegally.

marks of noble blood; and a healthy robust appearance is so disgraceful in a man of quality, that the world concludes his real father to have been a groom or a coachman. The imperfections of his mind run parallel with those of his body; being a composition of spleen, dullness, ignorance, caprice, sensuality, and pride.

Without the consent of this illustrious body, no law can be enacted, repealed, or altered, and these nobles have likewise the decision of all our possessions without appeal.

CHAPTER 7. *The Author's great love of his native country. His master's observations upon the constitution and administration of England, as described by the Author, with parallel cases and comparisons. His master's observations upon human nature.*

The reader may be disposed to wonder how I could prevail on myself to give so free a representation of my own species, among a race of mortals who were already too apt to conceive the vilest opinion of humankind, from that entire congruity betwixt me and their Yahoos. But I must freely confess that the many virtues of those excellent quadrupeds placed in opposite view to human corruptions had so far opened my eyes, and enlarged my understanding, that I began to view the actions and passions of man in a very different light; and to think the honor of my own kind not worth managing;[8] which, besides, it was impossible for me to do before a person of so acute a judgment as my master, who daily convinced me of a thousand faults in myself, whereof I had not the least perception before, and which with us would never be numbered even among human infirmities. I had likewise learned from his example an utter detestation of all falsehood or disguise; and truth appeared so amiable to me, that I determined upon sacrificing everything to it.

Let me deal so candidly with the reader as to confess that there was yet a much stronger motive for the freedom I took in my representation of things. I had not been a year in this country, before I contracted such a love and veneration for the inhabitants, that I entered on a firm resolution never to return to humankind, but to pass the rest of my life among these admirable Houyhnhnms in the contemplation and practice of every virtue; where I could have no example or incitement to vice. But it was decreed by fortune, my perpetual enemy, that so great a felicity should not fall to my share. However, it is now some comfort to reflect that in what I said of my countrymen, I extenuated their faults as much as I durst before so strict an examiner; and upon every article, gave as favorable a turn as the matter would bear. For, indeed, who is there alive that will not be swayed by his bias and partiality to the place of his birth?

I have related the substance of several conversations I had with my master, during the greatest part of the time I had the honor to be in his service; but have indeed for brevity sake omitted much more than is here set down.

When I had answered all his questions, and his curiosity seemed to be fully satisfied; he sent for me one morning early, and commanding me to sit down at some distance (an honor which he had never before conferred upon me), he said he had been very seriously considering my whole story, as

8. Taking care of.

far as it related both to myself and my country; that, he looked upon us as a sort of animals to whose share, by what accident he could not conjecture, some small pittance of reason had fallen, whereof we made no other use than by its assistance to aggravate our natural corruptions, and to acquire new ones which nature had not given us. That we disarmed ourselves of the few abilities she had bestowed; had been very successful in multiplying our original wants, and seemed to spend our whole lives in vain endeavors to supply them by our own inventions. That, as to myself, it was manifest I had neither the strength or agility of a common Yahoo; that I walked infirmly on my hinder feet; had found out a contrivance to make my claws of no use or defense, and to remove the hair from my chin, which was intended as a shelter from the sun and the weather. Lastly, that I could neither run with speed, nor climb trees like my brethren (as he called them) the Yahoos in this country.

That our institutions of government and law were plainly owing to our gross defects in reason, and by consequence, in virtue; because reason alone is sufficient to govern a rational creature; which was therefore a character we had no pretense to challenge, even from the account I had given of my own people; although he manifestly perceived, that in order to favor them, I had concealed many particulars, and often *said the thing which was not*.

He was the more confirmed in this opinion, because he observed that I agreed in every feature of my body with other Yahoos, except where it was to my real disadvantage in point of strength, speed, and activity, the shortness of my claws, and some other particulars where Nature had no part; so, from the representation I had given him of our lives, our manners, and our actions, he found as near a resemblance in the disposition of our minds. He said the Yahoos were known to hate one another more than they did any different species of animals; and the reason usually assigned was the odiousness of their own shapes, which all could see in the rest, but not in themselves. He had therefore begun to think it not unwise in us to cover our bodies, and by that invention, conceal many of our deformities from each other, which would else be hardly supportable. But he now found he had been mistaken; and that the dissensions of those brutes in his country were owing to the same cause with ours, as I had described them. For, if (said he) you throw among five Yahoos as much food as would be sufficient for fifty, they will instead of eating peaceably, fall together by the ears, each single one impatient to have all to itself; and therefore a servant was usually employed to stand by while they were feeding abroad, and those kept at home were tied at a distance from each other. That, if a cow died of age or accident, before a Houyhnhnm could secure it for his own Yahoos, those in the neighborhood would come in herds to seize it, and then would ensue such a battle as I had described, with terrible wounds made by their claws on both sides, although they seldom were able to kill one another, for want of such convenient instruments of death as we had invented. At other times the like battles have been fought between the Yahoos of several neighborhoods without any visible cause; those of one district watching all opportunities to surprise the next before they are prepared. But if they find their project hath miscarried, they return home, and for want of enemies, engage in what I call a civil war among themselves.

That, in some fields of his country, there are certain shining stones of several colors, whereof the Yahoos are violently fond; and when part of these stones are fixed in the earth, as it sometimes happeneth, they will dig with their claws for whole days to get them out, and carry them away, and hide them by heaps in their kennels; but still looking round with great caution, for fear their comrades should find out their treasure. My master said he could never discover the reason of this unnatural appetite, or how these stones could be of any use to a Yahoo; but now he believed it might proceed from the same principle of avarice, which I had ascribed to mankind. That he had once, by way of experiment, privately removed a heap of these stones from the place where one of his Yahoos had buried it, whereupon, the sordid animal missing his treasure, by his loud lamenting brought the whole herd to the place, there miserably howled, then fell to biting and tearing the rest; began to pine away, would neither eat nor sleep, nor work, till he ordered a servant privately to convey the stones into the same hole, and hide them as before; which when his Yahoo had found, he presently recovered his spirits and good humor; but took care to remove them to a better hiding place; and hath ever since been a very serviceable brute.

My master farther assured me, which I also observed myself, that in the fields where these shining stones abound, the fiercest and most frequent battles are fought, occasioned by perpetual inroads of the neighboring Yahoos.

He said it was common when two Yahoos discovered such a stone in a field, and were contending which of them should be the proprietor, a third would take the advantage, and carry it away from them both; which my master would needs contend to have some resemblance with our suits at law; wherein I thought it for our credit not to undeceive him; since the decision he mentioned was much more equitable than many decrees among us; because the plaintiff and defendant there lost nothing beside the stone they contended for; whereas our courts of equity would never have dismissed the cause while either of them had anything left.

My master continuing his discourse said there was nothing that rendered the Yahoos more odious, than their undistinguished appetite to devour everything that came in their way, whether herbs, roots, berries, corrupted flesh of animals, or all mingled together; and it was peculiar in their temper, that they were fonder of what they could get by rapine or stealth at a greater distance, than much better food provided for them at home. If their prey held out, they would eat till they were ready to burst, after which nature had pointed out to them a certain root that gave them a general evacuation.

There was also another kind of root very juicy, but something rare and difficult to be found, which the Yahoos sought for with much eagerness, and would suck it with great delight; it produced the same effects that wine hath upon us. It would make them sometimes hug, and sometimes tear one another; they would howl and grin, and chatter, and reel, and tumble, and then fall asleep in the mud.

I did indeed observe that the Yahoos were the only animals in this country subject to any diseases; which however, were much fewer than horses have among us, and contracted not by any ill treatment they meet with, but by the nastiness and greediness of that sordid brute. Neither has their language any more than a general appellation for those maladies; which is borrowed from the name of the beast, and called *Hnea Yahoo,* or the Yahoo's Evil; and the cure prescribed is a mixture of their own dung and urine, forcibly put down the Yahoo's throat. This I have since often known to have been taken with success, and do here freely recommend it to my countrymen, for the public good, as an admirable specific[9] against all diseases produced by repletion.

As to learning, government, arts, manufactures, and the like, my master confessed he could find little or no resemblance between the Yahoos of that country and those in ours. For he only meant to observe what parity there was in our natures. He had heard indeed some curious Houyhnhnms observe that in most herds there was a sort of ruling Yahoo (as among us there is generally some leading or principal stag in a park) who was always more deformed in body, and mischievous in disposition, than any of the rest. That this leader had usually a favorite as like himself as he could get, whose employment was to lick his master's feet and posteriors, and drive the female Yahoos to his kennel; for which he was now and then rewarded with a piece of ass's flesh. This favorite is hated by the whole herd; and therefore to protect himself, keeps always near the person of his leader. He usually continues in office till a worse can be found; but the very moment he is discarded, his successor, at the head of all the Yahoos in that district, young and old, male and female, come in a body, and discharge their excrements upon him from head to foot. But how far this might be applicable to our courts and favorites, and ministers of state, my master said I could best determine.

I durst make no return to this malicious insinuation, which debased human understanding below the sagacity of a common hound, who hath judgment enough to distinguish and follow the cry of the ablest dog in the pack, without being ever mistaken.

My master told me there were some qualities remarkable in the Yahoos, which he had not observed me to mention, or at least very slightly, in the accounts I had given him of humankind. He said, those animals, like other brutes, had their females in common; but in this they differed, that the she-Yahoo would admit the male while she was pregnant; and that the hes would quarrel and fight with the females as fiercely as with each other. Both which practices were such degrees of infamous brutality, that no other sensitive creature ever arrived at.

Another thing he wondered at in the Yahoos was their strange disposition to nastiness and dirt; whereas there appears to be a natural love of cleanliness in all other animals. As to the two former accusations, I was glad to let them pass without any reply, because I had not a word to offer upon them in defense of my species, which otherwise I certainly had done from my own inclinations. But I could have easily vindicated humankind from the imputation of singularity upon the last article, if there had been any swine in that country (as unluckily for me there were not) which although it may be a sweeter quadruped than a Yahoo, cannot I humbly conceive in justice pretend to more cleanliness; and so his honor himself must have owned, if he had seen their filthy way of feeding, and their custom of wallowing and sleeping in the mud.

My master likewise mentioned another quality, which his servants had discovered in several Yahoos, and to him was wholly unaccountable. He said, a fancy would sometimes take a Yahoo, to retire into a corner, to lie down and howl, and groan, and spurn away all that came near him, although he were young and fat, and wanted neither food nor water; nor did the ser-

---

9. Remedy.

vants imagine what could possibly ail him. And the only remedy they found was to set him to hard work, after which he would infallibly come to himself. To this I was silent out of partiality to my own kind; yet here I could plainly discover the true seeds of spleen,[1] which only seizeth on the lazy, the luxurious, and the rich; who, if they were forced to undergo the same regimen, I would undertake for the cure.

His Honor had farther observed, that a female Yahoo would often stand behind a bank or a bush, to gaze on the young males passing by, and then appear, and hide, using many antic gestures and grimaces; at which time it was observed, that she had a most offensive smell; and when any of the males advanced, would slowly retire, looking back, and with a counterfeit show of fear, run off into some convenient place where she knew the male would follow her.

At other times, if a female stranger came among them, three or four of her own sex would get about her, and stare and chatter, and grin, and smell her all over; and then turn off with gestures that seemed to express contempt and disdain.

Perhaps my master might refine a little in these speculations, which he had drawn from what he observed himself, or had been told by others; however, I could not reflect without some amazement, and much sorrow, that the rudiments of lewdness, coquetry, censure, and scandal, should have place by instinct in womankind.

I expected every moment that my master would accuse the Yahoos of those unnatural appetites in both sexes, so common among us. But Nature it seems hath not been so expert a schoolmistress; and these politer pleasures are entirely the productions of art and reason, on our side of the globe.

CHAPTER 8. *The Author relateth several particulars of the Yahoos. The great virtues of the Houyhnhnms. The education and exercises of their youth. Their general assembly.*

As I ought to have understood human nature much better than I supposed it possible for my master to do, so it was easy to apply the character he gave of the Yahoos to myself and my countrymen; and I believed I could yet make farther discoveries from my own observation. I therefore often begged his honor to let me go among the herds of Yahoos in the neighborhood; to which he always very graciously consented, being perfectly convinced that the hatred I bore those brutes would never suffer me to be corrupted by them; and his honor ordered one of his servants, a strong sorrel nag, very honest and good-natured, to be my guard; without whose protection I durst not undertake such adventures. For I have already told the reader how much I was pestered by those odious animals upon my first arrival. I afterwards failed very narrowly three or four times of falling into their clutches, when I happened to stray at any distance without my hanger. And I have reason to believe, they had some imagination that I was of their own species, which I often assisted myself, by stripping up my sleeves, and shewing my naked arms and breast in their sight, when my protector was with me; at which times they would approach as near as they durst, and imitate my actions after the

1. Depression.

manner of monkeys, but ever with great signs of hatred; as a tame jackdaw with cap and stockings is always persecuted by the wild ones, when he happens to be got among them.

They are prodigiously nimble from their infancy; however, I once caught a young male of three years old, and endeavored by all marks of tenderness to make it quiet; but the little imp fell a squalling, scratching, and biting with such violence, that I was forced to let it go; and it was high time, for a whole troop of old ones came about us at the noise; but finding the cub was safe (for away it ran) and my sorrel nag being by, they durst not venture near us. I observed the young animal's flesh to smell very rank, and the stink was somewhat between a weasel and a fox, but much more disagreeable. I forgot another circumstance (and perhaps I might have the reader's pardon, if it were wholly omitted) that while I held the odious vermin in my hands, it voided its filthy excrements of a yellow liquid substance, all over my clothes; but by good fortune there was a small brook hard by, where I washed myself as clean as I could; although I durst not come into my master's presence until I were sufficiently aired.

By what I could discover, the Yahoos appear to be the most unteachable of all animals, their capacities never reaching higher than to draw or carry burdens. Yet I am of opinion, this defect ariseth chiefly from a perverse, restive disposition. For they are cunning, malicious, treacherous and revengeful. They are strong and hardy, but of a cowardly spirit, and by consequence insolent, abject, and cruel. It is observed that the red-haired of both sexes are more libidinous and mischievous than the rest, whom yet they much exceed in strength and activity.

The Houyhnhnms keep the Yahoos for present use in huts not far from the house; but the rest are sent abroad to certain fields, where they dig up roots, eat several kinds of herbs, and search about for carrion, or sometimes catch weasels and *luhimuhs* (a sort of wild rat) which they greedily devour. Nature hath taught them to dig deep holes with their nails on the side of a rising ground, wherein they lie by themselves; only the kennels of the females are larger, sufficient to hold two or three cubs.

They swim from their infancy like frogs, and are able to continue long under water, where they often take fish, which the females carry home to their young. And upon this occasion, I hope the reader will pardon my relating an odd adventure.

Being one day abroad with my protector the sorrel nag, and the weather exceeding hot, I entreated him to let me bathe in a river that was near. He consented, and I immediately stripped myself stark naked, and went down softly into the stream. It happened that a young female Yahoo standing behind a bank, saw the whole proceeding; and inflamed by desire, as the nag and I conjectured, came running with all speed, and leaped into the water within five yards of the place where I bathed. I was never in my life so terribly frighted; the nag was grazing at some distance, not suspecting any harm. She embraced me after a most fulsome manner; I roared as loud as I could, and the nag came galloping towards me, whereupon she quitted her grasp, with the utmost reluctancy, and leaped upon the opposite bank, where she stood gazing and howling all the time I was putting on my clothes.

This was matter of diversion to my master and his family, as well as of mortification to myself. For now I could no longer deny that I was a real

Yahoo, in every limb and feature, since the females had a natural propensity to me as one of their own species; neither was the hair of this brute of a red color (which might have been some excuse for an appetite a little irregular) but black as a sloe, and her countenance did not make an appearance altogether so hideous as the rest of the kind; for I think, she could not be above eleven years old.

Having already lived three years in this country, the reader I suppose will expect that I should, like other travelers, give him some account of the manners and customs of its inhabitants, which it was indeed my principal study to learn.

As these noble Houyhnhnms are endowed by Nature with a general disposition to all virtues, and have no conceptions or ideas of what is evil in a rational creature; so their grand maxim is to cultivate reason, and to be wholly governed by it. Neither is reason among them a point problematical as with us, where men can argue with plausibility on both sides of a question; but strikes you with immediate conviction; as it must needs do where it is not mingled, obscured, or discolored by passion and interest. I remember it was with extreme difficulty that I could bring my master to understand the meaning of the word "opinion," or how a point could be disputable; because reason taught us to affirm or deny only where we are certain; and beyond our knowledge we cannot do either. So that controversies, wranglings, disputes, and positiveness in false or dubious propositions are evils unknown among the Houyhnhnms. In the like manner when I used to explain to him our several systems of natural philosophy,[2] he would laugh that a creature pretending to reason should value itself upon the knowledge of other people's conjectures, and in things, where that knowledge, if it were certain, could be of no use. Wherein he agreed entirely with the sentiments of Socrates, as Plato delivers them, which I mention as the highest honor I can do that prince of philosophers. I have often since reflected what destruction such a doctrine would make in the libraries of Europe; and how many paths to fame would be then shut up in the learned world.

Friendship and benevolence are the two principal virtues among the Houyhnhnms; and these not confined to particular objects, but universal to the whole race. For a stranger from the remotest part is equally treated with the nearest neighbor, and wherever he goes, looks upon himself as at home. They preserve decency and civility in the highest degrees, but are altogether ignorant of ceremony. They have no fondness for their colts or foals; but the care they take in educating them proceedeth entirely from the dictates of reason. And I observed my master to show the same affection to his neighbor's issue that he had for his own. They will have it that Nature teaches them to love the whole species, and it is reason only that maketh a distinction of persons, where there is a superior degree of virtue.

When the matron Houyhnhnms have produced one of each sex, they no longer accompany with their consorts, except they lose one of their issue by some casualty, which very seldom happens; but in such a case they meet again; or when the like accident befalls a person whose wife is past bearing, some other couple bestows on him one of their own colts, and then go together a second time, until the mother be pregnant. This caution is

2. Science.

necessary to prevent the country from being overburdened with numbers. But the race of inferior Houyhnhnms bred up to be servants is not so strictly limited upon this article; these are allowed to produce three of each sex, to be domestics in the noble families.

In their marriages they are exactly careful to choose such colors as will not make any disagreeable mixture in the breed. Strength is chiefly valued in the male, and comeliness in the female; not upon the account of love, but to preserve the race from degenerating; for, where a female happens to excel in strength, a consort is chosen with regard to comeliness. Courtship, love, presents, jointures, settlements, have no place in their thoughts, or terms whereby to express them in their language. The young couple meet and are joined, merely because it is the determination of their parents and friends; it is what they see done every day; and they look upon it as one of the necessary actions in a reasonable being. But the violation of marriage, or any other unchastity, was never heard of; and the married pair pass their lives with the same friendship and mutual benevolence that they bear to all others of the same species who come in their way, without jealousy, fondness, quarreling, or discontent.

In educating the youth of both sexes, their method is admirable, and highly deserveth our imitation. These are not suffered to taste a grain of oats, except upon certain days, till eighteen years old; nor milk, but very rarely; and in summer they graze two hours in the morning, and as many in the evening, which their parents likewise observe; but the servants are not allowed above half that time; and a great part of the grass is brought home, which they eat at the most convenient hours when they can be best spared from work.

Temperance, industry, exercise, and cleanliness are the lessons equally enjoined to the young ones of both sexes; and my master thought it monstrous in us to give the females a different kind of education from the males, except in some articles of domestic management; whereby, as he truly observed, one half of our natives were good for nothing but bringing children into the world; and to trust the care of their children to such useless animals, he said was yet a greater instance of brutality.

But the Houyhnhnms train up their youth to strength, speed, and hardiness, by exercising them in running races up and down steep hills, or over hard stony grounds; and when they are all in a sweat, they are ordered to leap over head and ears into a pond or a river. Four times a year the youth of certain districts meet to show their proficiency in running, and leaping, and other feats of strength or agility; where the victor is rewarded with a song made in his or her praise. On this festival the servants drive a herd of Yahoos into the field, laden with hay, and oats, and milk for a repast to the Houyhnhnms; after which these brutes are immediately driven back again, for fear of being noisome to the assembly.

Every fourth year, at the vernal equinox, there is a representative council of the whole nation, which meets in a plain about twenty miles from our house, and continueth about five or six days. Here they inquire into the state and condition of the several districts; whether they abound or be deficient in hay or oats, or cows or Yahoos? And wherever there is any want (which is but seldom) it is immediately supplied by unanimous consent and contribution. Here likewise the regulation of children is settled: as for instance, if a Houyhnhnm hath two males, he changeth one of them with another who hath two females, and when a child hath been lost by any casualty, where the mother is past breeding, it is determined what family in the district shall breed another to supply the loss.

CHAPTER 9. *A grand debate at the general assembly of the Houyhnhnms, and how it was determined. The learning of the Houyhnhnms. Their buildings. Their manner of burials. The defectiveness of their language.*

One of these grand assemblies was held in my time, about three months before my departure, whither my master went as the representative of our district. In this council was resumed their old debate, and indeed, the only debate that ever happened in their country; whereof my master after his return gave me a very particular account.

The question to be debated was whether the Yahoos should be exterminated from the face of the earth. One of the members for the affirmative offered several arguments of great strength and weight, alleging that, as the Yahoos were the most filthy, noisome, and deformed animal which nature ever produced, so they were the most restive and indocible,[3] mischievous, and malicious; they would privately suck the teats of the Houyhnhnms' cows; kill and devour their cats, trample down their oats and grass, if they were not continually watched; and commit a thousand other extravagancies. He took notice of a general tradition, that Yahoos had not been always in their country, but that many ages ago, two of these brutes appeared together upon a mountain; whether produced by the heat of the sun upon corrupted mud and slime, or from the ooze and froth of the sea, was never known. That these Yahoos engendered, and their brood in a short time grew so numerous as to overrun and infest the whole nation. That the Houyhnhnms to get rid of this evil, made a general hunting, and at last enclosed the whole herd; and destroying the older, every Houyhnhnm kept two young ones in a kennel, and brought them to such a degree of tameness as an animal so savage by nature can be capable of acquiring, using them for draught and carriage. That there seemed to be much truth in this tradition, and that those creatures could not be *ylnhniamshy* (or aborigines of the land) because of the violent hatred the Houyhnhnms as well as all other animals bore them; which although their evil disposition sufficiently deserved, could never have arrived at so high a degree, if they had been aborigines, or else they would have long since been rooted out. That the inhabitants taking a fancy to use the service of the Yahoos, had very imprudently neglected to cultivate the breed of asses, which were a comely animal, easily kept, more tame and orderly, without any offensive smell, strong enough for labor, although they yield to the other in agility of body; and if their braying be no agreeable sound, it is far preferable to the horrible howlings of the Yahoos.

Several others declared their sentiments to the same purpose, when my master proposed an expedient to the assembly, whereof he had indeed borrowed the hint from me. He approved of the tradition, mentioned by the honorable member, who spoke before; and affirmed, that the two Yahoos said to be first seen among them, had been driven thither over the sea; that

3. Unteachable.

coming to land, and being forsaken by their companions, they retired to the mountains, and degenerating by degrees, became in process of time much more savage than those of their own species in the country from whence these two originals came. The reason of his assertion was that he had now in his possession a certain wonderful Yahoo (meaning myself) which most of them had heard of, and many of them had seen. He then related to them how he first found me; that my body was all covered with an artificial composure of the skins and hairs of other animals; that I spoke in a language of my own, and had thoroughly learned theirs; that I had related to him the accidents which brought me thither; that when he saw me without my covering, I was an exact Yahoo in every part, only of a whiter color, less hairy and with shorter claws. He added how I had endeavored to persuade him that in my own and other countries the Yahoos acted as the governing, rational animal, and held the Houyhnhnms in servitude; that he observed in me all the qualities of a Yahoo, only a little more civilized by some tincture of reason, which however was in a degree as far inferior to the Houyhnhnm race as the Yahoos of their country were to me; that among other things, I mentioned a custom we had of castrating Houyhnhnms when they were young, in order to render them tame; that the operation was easy and safe; that it was no shame to learn wisdom from brutes, as industry is taught by the ant, and building by the swallow (for so I translate the world *lyhannh,* although it be a much larger fowl). That this invention might be practiced upon the younger Yahoos here, which, besides rendering them tractable and fitter for use, would in an age put an end to the whole species without destroying life. That in the meantime the Houyhnhnms should be exhorted to cultivate the breed of asses, which, as they are in all respects more valuable brutes, so they have this advantage, to be fit for service at five years old, which the other are not till twelve.

This was all my master thought fit to tell me at that time, of what passed in the grand council. But he was pleased to conceal one particular, which related personally to myself, whereof I soon felt the unhappy effect, as the reader will know in its proper place, and from whence I date all the succeeding misfortunes of my life.

The Houyhnhnms have no letters, and consequently, their knowledge is all traditional. But there happening few events of any moment among a people so well united, naturally disposed to every virtue, wholly governed by reason, and cut off from all commerce with other nations, the historical part is easily preserved without burdening their memories. I have already observed that they are subject to no diseases, and therefore can have no need of physicians. However, they have excellent medicines composed of herbs, to cure accidental bruises and cuts in the pastern or frog[4] of the foot by sharp stones, as well as other maims and hurts in the several parts of the body.

They calculate the year by the revolution of the sun and the moon, but use no subdivisions into weeks. They are well enough acquainted with the motions of those two luminaries, and understand the nature of eclipses; and this is the utmost progress of their astronomy.

In poetry they must be allowed to excel all other mortals; wherein the justness of their similes, and the minuteness, as well as exactness of their

4. Sole.

descriptions, are indeed inimitable. Their verses abound very much in both of these, and usually contain either some exalted notions of friendship and benevolence, or the praises of those who were victors in races and other bodily exercises. Their buildings, although very rude and simple, are not inconvenient, but well contrived to defend them from all injuries of cold and heat. They have a kind of tree, which at forty years old loosens in the root, and falls with the first storm; it grows very straight, and being pointed like stakes with a sharp stone (for the Houyhnhnms know not the use of iron), they stick them erect in the ground about ten inches asunder, and then weave in oat straw, or sometimes wattles, betwixt them. The roof is made after the same manner, and so are the doors.

The Houyhnhnms use the hollow part between the pastern and the hoof of their forefeet as we do our hands, and this with greater dexterity than I could at first imagine. I have seen a white mare of our family thread a needle (which I lent her on purpose) with that joint. They milk their cows, reap their oats, and do all the work which requires hands in the same manner. They have a kind of hard flints, which by grinding against other stones they form into instruments that serve instead of wedges, axes, and hammers. With tools made of these flints, they likewise cut their hay, and reap their oats, which there groweth naturally in several fields. The Yahoos draw home the sheaves in carriages, and the servants tread them in certain covered huts, to get out the grain, which is kept in stores. They make a rude kind of earthen and wooden vessels, and bake the former in the sun.

If they can avoid casualties, they die only of old age, and are buried in the obscurest places that can be found, their friends and relations expressing neither joy nor grief at their departure; nor does the dying person discover the least regret that he is leaving the world, any more than if he were upon returning home from a visit to one of his neighbors; I remember my master having once made an appointment with a friend and his family to come to his house upon some affair of importance; on the day fixed, the mistress and her two children came very late; she made two excuses, first for her husband, who, as she said, happened that very morning to *lhnuwnh*. The word is strongly expressive in their language, but not easily rendered into English; it signifies, *to retire to his first Mother*. Her excuse for not coming sooner was that her husband dying late in the morning, she was a good while consulting her servants about a convenient place where his body should be laid; and I observed she behaved herself at our house, as cheerfully as the rest. She died about three months after.

They live generally to seventy or seventy-five years, very seldom to fourscore; some weeks before their death they feel a gradual decay, but without pain. During this time they are much visited by their friends, because they cannot go abroad with their usual ease and satisfaction. However, about ten days before their death, which they seldom fail in computing, they return the visits that have been made by those who are nearest in the neighborhood, being carried in a convenient sledge drawn by Yahoos; which vehicle they use, not only upon this occasion, but when they grow old, upon long journeys, or when they are lamed by any accident. And therefore when the dying Houyhnhnms return those visits, they take a solemn leave of their friends, as if they were going to some remote part of the country, where they designed to pass the rest of their lives.

I know not whether it may be worth observing, that the Houyhnhnms have no word in their language to express anything that is evil, except what they borrow from the deformities or ill qualities of the Yahoos. Thus they denote the folly of a servant, an omission of a child, a stone that cuts their feet, a continuance of foul or unseasonable weather, and the like, by adding to each the epithet of Yahoo. For instance, *hhnm Yahoo, whnaholm Yahoo, ynlhmndwihlma Yahoo,* and an ill-contrived house, *ynholmhnmrohlnw Yahoo.*

I could with great pleasure enlarge farther upon the manners and virtues of this excellent people; but intending in a short time to publish a volume by itself expressly upon that subject, I refer the reader thither. And in the meantime, proceed to relate my own sad catastrophe.

CHAPTER 10. *The Author's economy, and happy life among the Houyhnhnms. His great improvement in virtue, by conversing with them. Their conversations. The Author hath notice given him by his master that he must depart from the country. He falls into a swoon for grief, but submits. He contrives and finishes a canoe, by the help of a fellow servant, and puts to sea at a venture.*

I had settled my little economy to my own heart's content. My master had ordered a room to be made for me after their manner, about six yards from the house; the sides and floors of which I plastered with clay, and covered with rush mats of my own contriving; I had beaten hemp, which there grows wild, and made of it a sort of ticking; this I filled with the feathers of several birds I had taken with springes made of Yahoos' hairs, and were excellent food. I had worked two chairs with my knife, the sorrel nag helping me in the grosser and more laborious part. When my clothes were worn to rags, I made myself others with the skins of rabbits, and of a certain beautiful animal about the same size, called *nnuhnoh,* the skin of which is covered with a fine down. Of these I likewise made very tolerable stockings. I soled my shoes with wood which I cut from a tree, and fitted to the upper leather, and when this was worn out, I supplied it with the skins of Yahoos, dried in the sun. I often got honey out of hollow trees, which I mingled with water, or eat it with my bread. No man could more verify the truth of these two maxims, that *Nature is very easily satisfied;* and, that *Necessity is the mother of invention.* I enjoyed perfect health of body, and tranquility of mind; I did not feel the treachery or inconstancy of a friend, nor the inquiries of a secret or open enemy. I had no occasion of bribing, flattering, or pimping to procure the favor of any great man, or of his minion. I wanted no fence against fraud or oppression; here was neither physician to destroy my body, nor lawyer to ruin my fortune; no informer to watch my words and actions, or forge accusations against me for hire; here were no gibers, censurers, backbiters, pickpockets, highwaymen, housebreakers, attorneys, bawds, buffoons, gamesters, politicians, wits, splenetics, tedious talkers, controvertists, ravishers, murderers, robbers, virtuosos;[5] no leaders or followers of party and faction; no encouragers to vice, by seducement or examples; no dungeons, axes, gibbets, whipping posts, or pillories; no cheating shopkeepers or mechanics; no pride, vanity or affectation; no fops, bullies, drunkards, strolling whores, or poxes; no ranting, lewd, expensive wives; no stupid, proud pedants; no importunate, over-

5. Those who pursue special interests in the arts or sciences.

bearing, quarrelsome, noisy, roaring, empty, conceited, swearing companions; no scoundrels raised from the dust upon the merit of their vices; or nobility thrown into it on account of their virtues; no lords, fiddlers, judges, or dancing masters.

I had the favor of being admitted to several Houyhnhnms, who came to visit or dine with my master; where his honor graciously suffered me to wait in the room, and listen to their discourse. Both he and his company would often descend to ask me questions, and receive my answers. I had also sometimes the honor of attending my master in his visits to others. I never presumed to speak, except in answer to a question; and then I did it with inward regret, because it was a loss of so much time for improving myself; but I was infinitely delighted with the station of an humble auditor in such conversations, where nothing passed but what was useful, expressed in the fewest and most significant words; where (as I have already said) the greatest decency was observed, without the least degree of ceremony; where no person spoke without being pleased himself, and pleasing his companions; where there was no interruption, tediousness, heat, or difference of sentiments. They have a notion, that when people are met together, a short silence doth much improve conversation; this I found to be true; for during those little intermissions of talk, new ideas would arise in their minds, which very much enlivened the discourse. Their subjects are generally on friendship and benevolence; on order and economy; sometimes upon the visible operations of nature, or ancient traditions; upon the bounds and limits of virtue; upon the unerring rules of reason; or upon some determinations, to be taken at the next great assembly; and often upon the various excellencies of poetry. I may add, without vanity, that my presence often gave them sufficient matter for discourse, because it afforded my master an occasion of letting his friends into the history of me and my country, upon which they were all pleased to descant in a manner not very advantageous to human kind; and for that reason I shall not repeat what they said; only I maybe allowed to observe that his honor, to my great admiration, appeared to understand the nature of Yahoos much better than myself. He went through all our vices and follies, and discovered many which I had never mentioned to him; by only supposing what qualities a Yahoo of their country, with a small proportion of reason, might be capable of exerting; and concluded, with too much probability, how vile as well as miserable such a creature must be.

I freely confess, that all the little knowledge I have of any value was acquired by the lectures I received from my master, and from hearing the discourses of him and his friends; to which I should be prouder to listen, than to dictate to the greatest and wisest assembly in Europe. I admired the strength, comeliness, and speed of the inhabitants; and such a constellation of virtues in such amiable persons produced in me the highest veneration. At first, indeed, I did not feel that natural awe which the Yahoos and all other animals bear towards them; but it grew upon me by degrees, much sooner than I imagined, and was mingled with a respectful love and gratitude, that they would condescend to distinguish me from the rest of my species.

When I thought of my family, my friends, my countrymen, or human race in general, I considered them as they really were, Yahoos in shape and disposition, perhaps a little more civilized, and qualified with the gift of speech; but making no other use of reason than to improve and multiply those vices, whereof their brethren in this country had only the share that nature allotted them. When I happened to behold the reflection of my own form in a lake or fountain, I turned away my face in horror and detestation of myself, and could better endure the sight of a common Yahoo than of my own person. By conversing with the Houyhnhnms, and looking upon them with delight, I fell to imitate their gait and gesture, which is now grown into a habit; and my friends often tell me in a blunt way, that I trot like a horse; which, however, I take for a great compliment. Neither shall I disown, that in speaking I am apt to fall into the voice and manner of the Houyhnhnms, and hear myself ridiculed on that account without the least mortification.

In the midst of this happiness, when I looked upon myself to be fully settled for life, my master sent for me one morning a little earlier than his usual hour. I observed by his countenance that he was in some perplexity, and at a loss how to begin what he had to speak. After a short silence, he told me, he did not know how I would take what he was going to say; that, in the last general assembly, when the affair of the Yahoos was entered upon, the representatives had taken offense at his keeping a Yahoo (meaning myself) in his family more like a Houyhnhnm than a brute animal. That he was known frequently to converse with me, as if he could receive some advantage of pleasure in my company; that such a practice was not agreeable to reason or nature, or a thing ever heard of before among them. The assembly did therefore exhort him, either to employ me like the rest of my species, or command me to swim back to the place from whence I came. That the first of these expedients was utterly rejected by all the Houyhnhnms who had ever seen me at his house or their own; for, they alleged, that because I had some rudiments of reason, added to the natural pravity[6] of those animals, it was to be feared, I might be able to seduce them into the woody and mountainous parts of the country, and bring them in troops by night to destroy the Houyhnhnms' cattle, as being naturally of the ravenous kind, and averse from labor.

My master added that he was daily pressed by the Houyhnhnms of the neighborhood to have the assembly's exhortation executed, which he could not put off much longer. He doubted[7] it would be impossible for me to swim to another country; and therefore wished I would contrive some sort of vehicle resembling those I had described to him, that might carry me on the sea; in which work I should have the assistance of his own servants, as well as those of his neighbors. He concluded that for his own part he could have been content to keep me in his service as long as I lived; because he found I had cured myself of some bad habits and dispositions, by endeavoring, as far as my inferior nature was capable, to imitate the Houyhnhnms.

I should here observe to the reader, that a decree of the general assembly in this country is expressed by the word *hnhloayn*, which signifies an exhortation, as near as I can render it; for they have no conception how a rational creature can be compelled, but only advised, or exhorted; because no person can disobey reason without giving up his claim to be a rational creature.

I was struck with the utmost grief and despair at my master's discourse; and being unable to support the agonies I was under, I fell into a swoon at his feet; when I came to myself, he told me that he concluded I had been

---

6. Corruption.　　　　　　7. Feared.

dead (for these people are subject to no such imbecilities of nature). I answered, in a faint voice, that death would have been too great an happiness; that although I could not blame the assembly's exhortation, or the urgency of his friends; yet in my weak and corrupt judgment, I thought it might consist with reason to have been less rigorous. That I could not swim a league, and probably the nearest land to theirs might be distant above an hundred; that many materials, necessary for making a small vessel to carry me off, were wholly wanting in this country, which, however, I would attempt in obedience and gratitude to his honor, although I concluded the thing to be impossible, and therefore looked on myself as already devoted to destruction. That the certain prospect of an unnatural death was the least of my evils; for, supposing I should escape with life by some strange adventure, how could I think with temper[8] of passing my days among Yahoos, and relapsing into my old corruptions, for want of examples to lead and keep me within the paths of virtue. That I knew too well upon what solid reasons all the determinations of the wise Houyhnhnms were founded, not to be shaken by arguments of mine, a miserable Yahoo; and therefore after presenting him with my humble thanks for the offer of his servants' assistance in making a vessel, and desiring a reasonable time for so difficult a work, I told him I would endeavor to preserve a wretched being; and, if ever I returned to England, was not without hopes of being useful to my own species by celebrating the praises of the renowned Houyhnhnms, and proposing their virtues to the imitation of mankind.

My master in a few words made me a very gracious reply, allowed me the space of two months to finish my boat, and ordered the sorrel nag, my fellow servant (for so at this distance I may presume to call him), to follow my instructions, because I told my master that his help would be sufficient, and I knew he had a tenderness for me.

In his company my first business was to go to that part of the coast where my rebellious crew had ordered me to be set on shore. I got upon a height, and looking on every side into the sea, fancied I saw a small island towards the northeast; I took out my pocket glass, and could then clearly distinguish it about five leagues off, as I computed; but it appeared to the sorrel nag to be only a blue cloud; for, as he had no conception of any country besides his own, so he could not be as expert in distinguishing remote objects at sea, as we who so much converse in that element.

After I had discovered this island, I considered no farther; but resolved, it should, if possible, be the first place of my banishment, leaving the consequence to fortune.

I returned home, and consulting with the sorrel nag, we went into a copse at some distance, where I with my knife, and he with a sharp flint fastened very artificially,[9] after their manner, to a wooden handle, cut down several oak wattles about the thickness of a walking staff, and some larger pieces. But I shall not trouble the reader with a particular description of my own mechanics; let it suffice to say, that in six weeks time, with the help of the sorrel nag, who performed the parts that required most labor, I finished a sort of Indian canoe; but much larger, covering it with the skins of Yahoos, well stitched together, with hempen threads of my own making. My sail was

---

8. Equanimity. "Devoted": doomed.   9. Artfully.

likewise composed of the skins of the same animal; but I made use of the youngest I could get, the older being too tough and thick; and I likewise provided myself with four paddles. I laid in a stock of boiled flesh, of rabbits and fowls; and took with me two vessels, one filled with milk, and the other with water.

I tried my canoe in a large pond near my master's house, and then corrected in it what was amiss, stopping all the chinks with Yahoo's tallow, till I found it staunch, and able to bear me and my freight. And when it was as complete as I could possibly make it, I had it drawn on a carriage very gently by Yahoos, to the seaside, under the conduct of the sorrel nag and another servant.

When all was ready, and the day came for my departure, I took leave of my master and lady, and the whole family, my eyes flowing with tears and my heart quite sunk with grief.[1] But his honor, out of curiosity, and perhaps (if I may speak it without vanity) partly out of kindness, was determined to see me in my canoe; and got several of his neighboring friends to accompany him. I was forced to wait above an hour for the tide, and then observing the wind very fortunately bearing towards the island to which I intended to steer my course, I took a second leave of my master; but as I was going to prostrate myself to kiss his hoof, he did me the honor to raise it gently to my mouth. I am not ignorant how much I have been censured for mentioning this last particular. Detractors are pleased to think it improbable that so illustrious a person should descend to give so great a mark of distinction to a creature so inferior as I. Neither have I forgot how apt some travelers are to boast of extraordinary favors they have received. But, if these censurers were better acquainted with the noble and courteous disposition of the Houyhnhnms, they would soon change their opinion. I paid my respects to the rest of the Houyhnhnms in his honor's company; then getting into my canoe, I pushed off from shore.

CHAPTER 11. *The Author's dangerous voyage. He arrives at New Holland, hoping to settle there. Is wounded with an arrow by one of the natives. Is seized and carried by force into a Portuguese ship. The great civilities of the Captain. The Author arrives at England.*

I began this desperate voyage on February 15, 1714/5,[2] at 9 o'clock in the morning. The wind was very favorable; however, I made use at first only of my paddles; but considering I should soon be weary, and that the wind might probably chop about, I ventured to set up my little sail, and thus, with the help of the tide, I went at the rate of a league and a half an hour, as near as I could guess. My master and his friends continued on the shore, till I was almost out of sight; and I often heard the sorrel nag (who always loved me) crying out, *"Hnuy illa nyha maiah Yahoo"* ("Take care of thyself, gentle Yahoo").

My design was, if possible, to discover some small island uninhabited, yet sufficient by my labor to furnish me with necessaries of life, which I would have thought a greater happiness than to be first minister in the politest

---

1. For a depiction of this scene by Sawrey Gilpin, see the color insert in this volume.

2. I.e., 1715, by modern dating. The year began on March 25.

court of Europe, so horrible was the idea I conceived of returning to live in the society and under the government of Yahoos. For in such a solitude as I desired, I could at least enjoy my own thoughts, and reflect with delight on the virtues of those inimitable Houyhnhnms, without any opportunity of degenerating into the vices and corruptions of my own species.

The reader may remember what I related when my crew conspired against me, and confined me to my cabin, how I continued there several weeks, without knowing what course we took; and when I was put ashore in the longboat, how the sailors told me with oaths, whether true or false, that they knew not in what part of the world we were. However, I did then believe us to be about 10 degrees southward of the Cape of Good Hope, or about 45 degrees southern latitude, as I gathered from some general words I overheard among them, being I supposed to the southeast in their intended voyage to Madagascar. And although this were but little better than conjecture, yet I resolved to steer my course eastward, hoping to reach the southwest coast of New Holland, and perhaps some such island as I desired, lying westward of it. The wind was full west, and by six in the evening I computed I had gone eastward at least eighteen leagues; when I spied a very small island about half a league off, which I soon reached. It was nothing but a rock with one creek, naturally arched by the force of tempests. Here I put in my canoe, and climbing a part of the rock, I could plainly discover land to the east, extending from south to north. I lay all night in my canoe; and repeating my voyage early in the morning, I arrived in seven hours to the southeast point of New Holland. This confirmed me in the opinion I have long entertained, that the maps and charts place this country at least three degrees more to the east than it really is; which thought I communicated many years ago to my worthy friend Mr. Herman Moll,[3] and gave him my reasons for it, although he hath rather chosen to follow other authors.

I saw no inhabitants in the place where I landed; and being unarmed, I was afraid of venturing far into the country. I found some shellfish on the shore, and eat them raw, not daring to kindle a fire, for fear of being discovered by the natives. I continued three days feeding on oysters and limpets, to save my own provisions; and I fortunately found a brook of excellent water, which gave me great relief.

On the fourth day, venturing out early a little too far, I saw twenty or thirty natives upon a height, not above five hundred yards from me. They were stark naked, men, women, and children round a fire, as I could discover by the smoke. One of them spied me, and gave notice to the rest; five of them advanced towards me, leaving the women and children at the fire. I made what haste I could to the shore, and getting into my canoe, shoved off; the savages observing me retreat, ran after me; and before I could get far enough into the sea, discharged an arrow, which wounded me deeply on the inside of my left knee. (I shall carry the mark to my grave.) I apprehended the arrow might be poisoned; and paddling out of the reach of their darts (being a calm day) I made a shift to suck the wound, and dress it as well as I could.

I was at a loss what to do, for I durst not return to the same landing place, but stood to the north, and was forced to paddle; for the wind, although very gentle, was against me, blowing northwest. As I was looking about for a

3. A famous contemporary map maker.

secure landing place, I saw a sail to the north northeast, which appearing every minute more visible, I was in some doubt whether I should wait for them or no; but at last my detestation of the Yahoo race prevailed; and turning my canoe, I sailed and paddled together to the south, and got into the same creek from whence I set out in the morning, choosing rather to trust myself among these barbarians than live with European Yahoos. I drew up my canoe as close as I could to the shore, and hid myself behind a stone by the little brook, which, as I have already said, was excellent water.

The ship came within half a league of this creek, and sent out her longboat with vessels to take in fresh water (for the place it seems was very well known), but I did not observe it until the boat was almost on shore; and it was too late to seek another hiding place. The seamen at their landing observed my canoe, and rummaging it all over, easily conjectured that the owner could not be far off. Four of them well armed searched every cranny and lurking hole, till at last they found me flat on my face behind the stone. They gazed a while in admiration at my strange uncouth dress; my coat made of skins, my wooden-soled shoes, and my furred stockings; from whence, however, they concluded I was not a native of the place, who all go naked. One of the seamen in Portuguese bid me rise, and asked who I was. I understood that language very well, and getting upon my feet, said I was a poor Yahoo, banished from the Houyhnhnms, and desired they would please to let me depart. They admired to hear me answer them in their own tongue, and saw by my complexion I must be an European; but were at a loss to know what I meant by Yahoos and Houyhnhnms, and at the same time fell a laughing at my strange tone in speaking, which resembled the neighing of a horse. I trembled all the while betwixt fear and hatred; I again desired leave to depart, and was gently moving to my canoe; but they laid hold on me, desiring to know what country I was of? whence I came? with many other questions. I told them I was born in England, from whence I came about five years ago, and then their country and ours was at peace. I therefore hoped they would not treat me as an enemy, since I meant them no harm, but was a poor Yahoo, seeking some desolate place where to pass the remainder of his unfortunate life.

When they began to talk, I thought I never heard or saw any thing so unnatural; for it appeared to me as monstrous as if a dog or a cow should speak in England, or a Yahoo in Houyhnhnmland. The honest Portuguese were equally amazed at my strange dress, and the odd manner of delivering my words, which however they understood very well. They spoke to me with great humanity, and said they were sure their Captain would carry me *gratis* to Lisbon, from whence I might return to my own country; that two of the seamen would go back to the ship, to inform the Captain of what they had seen, and receive his orders; in the meantime, unless I would give my solemn oath not to fly, they would secure me by force. I thought it best to comply with their proposal. They were very curious to know my story, but I gave them very little satisfaction; and they all conjectured, that my misfortunes had impaired my reason. In two hours the boat, which went laden with vessels of water, returned with the Captain's commands to fetch me on board. I fell on my knees to preserve my liberty; but all was in vain, and the men having tied me with cords, heaved me into the boat, from whence I was taken into the ship, and from thence into the Captain's cabin.

His name was Pedro de Mendez; he was a very courteous and generous person; he entreated me to give some account of myself, and desired to know what I would eat or drink; said I should be used as well as himself, and spoke so many obliging things, that I wondered to find such civilities from a Yahoo. However, I remained silent and sullen; I was ready to faint at the very smell of him and his men. At last I desired something to eat out of my own canoe; but he ordered me a chicken and some excellent wine, and then directed that I should be put to bed in a very clean cabin. I would not undress myself, but lay on the bedclothes; and in half an hour stole out, when I thought the crew was at dinner; and getting to the side of the ship, was going to leap into the sea, and swim for my life, rather than continue among Yahoos. But one of the seamen prevented me, and having informed the Captain, I was chained to my cabin.

After dinner Don Pedro came to me, and desired to know my reason for so desperate an attempt; assured me he only meant to do me all the service he was able; and spoke so very movingly, that at last I descended to treat him like an animal which had some little portion of reason. I gave him a very short relation of my voyage; of the conspiracy against me by my own men; of the country where they set me on shore, and of my five years residence there. All which he looked upon as if it were a dream or a vision; whereat I took great offense; for I had quite forgot the faculty of lying, so peculiar to Yahoos in all countries where they preside, and consequently the disposition of suspecting truth in others of their own species. I asked him whether it were the custom of his country to *say the thing that was not?* I assured him I had almost forgot what he meant by falsehood; and if I had lived a thousand years in Houyhnhnmland, I should never have heard a lie from the meanest servant. That I was altogether indifferent whether he believed me or no; but however, in return for his favors, I would give so much allowance to the corruption of his nature, as to answer any objection he would please to make; and he might easily discover the truth.

The Captain, a wise man, after many endeavors to catch me tripping in some part of my story, at last began to have a better opinion of my veracity. But he added that since I professed so inviolable an attachment to truth, I must give him my word of honor to bear him company in this voyage without attempting anything against my life; or else he would continue me a prisoner till we arrived at Lisbon. I gave him the promise he required; but at the same time protested that I would suffer the greatest hardships rather than return to live among Yahoos.

Our voyage passed without any considerable accident. In gratitude to the Captain I sometimes sat with him at his earnest request, and strove to conceal my antipathy against humankind, although it often broke out; which he suffered to pass without observation. But the greatest part of the day, I confined myself to my cabin, to avoid seeing any of the crew. The Captain had often entreated me to strip myself of my savage dress, and offered to lend me the best suit of clothes he had. This I would not be prevailed on to accept, abhorring to cover myself with anything that had been on the back of a Yahoo. I only desired he would lend me two clean shirts, which having been washed since he wore them, I believed would not so much defile me. These I changed every second day, and washed them myself.

We arrived at Lisbon, Nov. 5, 1715. At our landing, the Captain forced me to cover myself with his cloak, to prevent the rabble from crowding about me. I was conveyed to his own house; and at my earnest request, he led me up to the highest room backwards.[4] I conjured him to conceal from all persons what I had told him of the Houyhnhnms; because the least hint of such a story would not only draw numbers of people to see me, but probably put me in danger of being imprisoned, or burned by the Inquisition. The Captain persuaded me to accept a suit of clothes newly made; but I would not suffer the tailor to take my measure; however, Don Pedro being almost of my size, they fitted me well enough. He accoutered me with other necessaries, all new, which I aired for twenty-four hours before I would use them.

The Captain had no wife, nor above three servants, none of which were suffered to attend at meals; and his whole deportment was so obliging, added to very good human understanding, that I really began to tolerate his company. He gained so far upon me, that I ventured to look out of the back window. By degrees I was brought into another room, from whence I peeped into the street, but drew my head back in a fright. In a week's time he seduced me down to the door. I found my terror gradually lessened, but my hatred and contempt seemed to increase. I was at last bold enough to walk the street in his company, but kept my nose well stopped with rue, or sometimes with tobacco.

In ten days, Don Pedro, to whom I had given some account of my domestic affairs, put it upon me as a point of honor and conscience that I ought to return to my native country, and live at home with my wife and children. He told me there was an English ship in the port just ready to sail, and he would furnish me with all things necessary. It would be tedious to repeat his arguments, and my contradictions. He said it was altogether impossible to find such a solitary island as I had desired to live in; but I might command in my own house, and pass my time in a manner as recluse as I pleased.

I complied at last, finding I could not do better. I left Lisbon the 24th day of November, in an English merchantman, but who was the Master I never inquired. Don Pedro accompanied me to the ship, and lent me twenty pounds. He took kind leave of me, and embraced me at parting; which I bore as well as I could. During this last voyage I had no commerce with the Master, or any of his men; but pretending I was sick kept close in my cabin. On the fifth of December, 1715, we cast anchor in the Downs about nine in the morning, and at three in the afternoon I got safe to my house at Redriff.

My wife and family received me with great surprise and joy, because they concluded me certainly dead; but I must freely confess, the sight of them filled me only with hatred, disgust, and contempt; and the more, by reflecting on the near alliance I had to them. For although since my unfortunate exile from the Houyhnhnm country, I had compelled myself to tolerate the sight of Yahoos, and to converse with Don Pedro de Mendez; yet my memory and imaginations were perpetually filled with the virtues and ideas of those exalted Houyhnhnms. And when I began to consider that by copulating with one of the Yahoo species, I had become a parent of more, it struck me with the utmost shame, confusion, and horror.

4. At the rear.

As soon as I entered the house, my wife took me in her arms, and kissed me; at which, having not been used to the touch of that odious animal for so many years, I fell in a swoon for almost an hour. At the time I am writing, it is five years since my last return to England. During the first year I could not endure my wife or children in my presence, the very smell of them was intolerable; much less could I suffer them to eat in the same room. To this hour they dare not presume to touch my bread, or drink out of the same cup; neither was I ever able to let one of them take me by the hand. The first money I laid out was to buy two young stone-horses,[5] which I keep in a good stable, and next to them the groom is my greatest favorite; for I feel my spirits revived by the smell he contracts in the stable. My horses understand me tolerably well; I converse with them at least four hours every day. They are strangers to bridle or saddle; they live in great amity with me, and friendship to each other.

CHAPTER 12. *The Author's veracity. His design in publishing this work. His censure of those travelers who swerve from the truth. The Author clears himself from any sinister ends in writing. His native country commended. The right of the crown to those countries described by the Author is justified. The difficulty of conquering them. The Author takes his last leave of the reader; proposeth his manner of living for the future; gives good advice, and concludeth.*

Thus gentle reader, I have given thee a faithful history of my travels for sixteen years, and above seven months; wherein I have not been so studious of ornament as of truth. I could perhaps like others have astonished thee with strange improbable tales; but I rather chose to relate plain matter of fact in the simplest manner and style; because my principal design was to inform, and not to amuse thee.

It is easy for us who travel into remote countries, which are seldom visited by Englishmen or other Europeans, to form descriptions of wonderful animals both at sea and land. Whereas a traveler's chief aim should be to make men wiser and better, and to improve their minds by the bad as well as good example of what they deliver concerning foreign places.

I could heartily wish a law were enacted, that every traveler, before he were permitted to publish his voyages, should be obliged to make oath before the Lord High Chancellor that all he intended to print was absolutely true to the best of his knowledge; for then the world would no longer be deceived as it usually is, while some writers, to make their works pass the better upon the public, impose the grossest falsities on the unwary reader. I have perused several books of travels with great delight in my younger days; but, having since gone over most parts of the globe, and been able to contradict many fabulous accounts from my own observation, it hath given me a great disgust against this part of reading, and some indignation to see the credulity of mankind so impudently abused. Therefore, since my acquaintance were pleased to think my poor endeavors might not be unacceptable to my country, I imposed on myself as a maxim, never to be swerved from, that I would *strictly adhere to truth*; neither indeed can I be ever under the least temptation to vary from it, while I retain in my mind the lectures and example of my

5. Stallions.

noble master, and the other illustrious Houyhnhnms, of whom I had so long the honor to be an humble hearer.

———*Nec si miserum Fortuna Sinonem*
Finxit, vanum etiam, mendacemque improba finget.[6]

I know very well how little reputation is to be got by writings which require neither genius nor learning, nor indeed any other talent, except a good memory, or an exact journal. I know likewise, that writers of travels, like dictionary-makers, are sunk into oblivion by the weight and bulk of those who come last, and therefore lie uppermost. And it is highly probable that such travelers who shall hereafter visit the countries described in this work of mine, may be detecting my errors (if there be any) and adding many new discoveries of their own, jostle me out of vogue, and stand in my place, making the world forget that ever I was an author. This indeed would be too great a mortification if I wrote for fame; but, as my sole intention was the Public Good, I cannot be altogether disappointed. For, who can read the virtues I have mentioned in the glorious Houyhnhnms, without being ashamed of his own vices, when he considers himself as the reasoning, governing animal of his country? I shall say nothing of those remote nations where Yahoos preside; amongst which the least corrupted are the Brobdingnagians, whose wise maxims in morality and government it would be our happiness to observe. But I forbear descanting further, and rather leave the judicious reader to his own remarks and applications.

I am not a little pleased that this work of mine can possibly meet with no censurers; for what objections can be made against a writer who relates only plain facts that happened in such distant countries, where we have not the least interest with respect either to trade or negotiations? I have carefully avoided every fault with which common writers of travels are often too justly charged. Besides, I meddle not the least with any party, but write without passion, prejudice, or ill-will against any man or number of men whatsoever. I write for the noblest end, to inform and instruct mankind, over whom I may, without breach of modesty, pretend to some superiority, from the advantages I received by conversing so long among the most accomplished Houyhnhnms. I write without any view towards profit or praise. I never suffer a word to pass that may look like a reflection,[7] or possibly give the least offense even to those who are most ready to take it. So that, I hope, I may with justice pronounce myself an Author perfectly blameless; against whom the tribes of answerers, considerers, observers, reflectors, detecters, remarkers will never be able to find matter for exercising their talents.

I confess it was whispered to me that I was bound in duty as a subject of England, to have given in a memorial[8] to a secretary of state, at my first coming over; because, whatever lands are discovered by a subject, belong to the Crown. But I doubt whether our conquests in the countries I treat of would be as easy as those of Ferdinando Cortez over the naked Americans. The Lilliputians, I think, are hardly worth the charge of a fleet and army to reduce them; and I question whether it might be prudent or safe to attempt the Brob-

---

6. Nor if Fortune had molded Sinon for misery, will she also in spite mold him as false and lying (Latin; Virgil's *Aeneid* 2.79–80).

7. Censure, criticism.

8. Statement of facts for government use.

dingnagians; or, whether an English army would be much at their ease with the Flying Island over their heads. The Houyhnhnms, indeed, appear not to be so well prepared for war, a science to which they are perfect strangers, and especially against missive weapons. However, supposing myself to be a minister of state, I could never give my advice for invading them. Their prudence, unanimity, unacquaintedness with fear, and their love of their country would amply supply all defects in the military art. Imagine twenty thousand of them breaking into the midst of an European army, confounding the ranks, overturning the carriages, battering the warriors' faces into mummy, by terrible yerks from their hinder hoofs: for they would well deserve the character given to Augustus, *Recalcitrat undique tutus.*[9] But instead of proposals for conquering that magnanimous nation, I rather wish they were in a capacity or disposition to send a sufficient number of their inhabitants for civilizing Europe; by teaching us the first principles of Honor, Justice, Truth, Temperance, Public Spirit, Fortitude, Chastity, Friendship, Benevolence, and Fidelity. The names of all which virtues are still retained among us in most languages, and are to be met with in modern as well as ancient authors, which I am able to assert from my own small reading.

But I had another reason which made me less forward to enlarge his majesty's dominions by my discoveries: to say the truth, I had conceived a few scruples with relation to the distributive justice of princes upon those occasions. For instance, a crew of pirates are driven by a storm they know not whither; at length a boy discovers land from the topmast; they go on shore to rob and plunder; they see an harmless people, are entertained with kindness, they give the country a new name, they take formal possession of it for the king, they set up a rotten plank or a stone for a memorial, they murder two or three dozen of the natives, bring away a couple more by force for a sample, return home, and get their pardon. Here commences a new dominion acquired with a title by Divine Right. Ships are sent with the first opportunity; the natives driven out or destroyed, their princes tortured to discover their gold; a free license given to all acts of inhumanity and lust; the earth reeking with the blood of its inhabitants: and this execrable crew of butchers employed in so pious an expedition is a *modern colony* sent to convert and civilize an idolatrous and barbarous people.

But this description, I confess, doth by no means affect the British nation, who may be an example to the whole world for their wisdom, care, and justice in planting colonies; their liberal endowments for the advancement of religion and learning; their choice of devout and able pastors to propagate Christianity; their caution in stocking their provinces with people of sober lives and conversations from this the Mother Kingdom; their strict regard to the distribution of justice, in supplying the civil administration through all their colonies with officers of the greatest abilities, utter strangers to corruption: and to crown all, by sending the most vigilant and virtuous governors, who have no other views than the happiness of the people over whom they preside, and the honor of the king their master.

But, as those countries which I have described do not appear to have any desire of being conquered, and enslaved, murdered, or driven out by colonies,

---

9. He kicks backward, at every point on his guard (Latin; Horace's *Satires* 2.1.20). "Mummy": pulp. "Yerks": kicks.

nor abound either in gold, silver, sugar, or tobacco, I did humbly conceive they were by no means proper objects of our zeal, our valor, or our interest. However, if those whom it may concern, think fit to be of another opinion, I am ready to depose, when I shall be lawfully called, that no European did ever visit these countries before me. I mean, if the inhabitants ought to be believed.

But, as to the formality of taking possession in my sovereign's name, it never came once into my thoughts; and if it had, yet as my affairs then stood, I should perhaps in point of prudence and self-preservation have put it off to a better opportunity.

Having thus answered the only objection that can be raised against me as a traveler, I here take a final leave of my courteous readers, and return to enjoy my own speculations in my little garden at Redriff; to apply those excellent lessons of virtue which I learned among the Houyhnhnms; to instruct the Yahoos of my own family as far as I shall find them docible animals; to behold my figure often in a glass, and thus if possible habituate myself by time to tolerate the sight of a human creature; to lament the brutality of Houyhnhnms in my own country, but always treat their persons with respect, for the sake of my noble master, his family, his friends, and the whole Houyhnhnm race, whom these of ours have the honor to resemble in all their lineaments, however their intellectuals came to degenerate.

I began last week to permit my wife to sit at dinner with me, at the farthest end of a long table; and to answer (but with the utmost brevity) the few questions I ask her. Yet the smell of a Yahoo continuing very offensive, I always keep my nose well stopped with rue, lavender, or tobacco leaves. And although it be hard for a man late in life to remove old habits, I am not altogether out of hopes in some time to suffer a neighbor Yahoo in my company, without the apprehensions I am yet under of his teeth or his claws.

My reconcilement to the Yahoo kind in general might not be so difficult, if they would be content with those vices and follies only which nature hath entitled them to. I am not in the least provoked at the sight of a lawyer, a pickpocket, a colonel, a fool, a lord, a gamester, a politician, a whoremonger, a physician, an evidence,[1] a suborner, an attorney, a traitor, or the like: this is all according to the due course of things. But when I behold a lump of deformity, and diseases both in body and mind, smitten with *pride,* it immediately breaks all the measures of my patience; neither shall I be ever able to comprehend how such an animal and such a vice could tally together. The wise and virtuous Houyhnhnms, who abound in all excellencies that can adorn a rational creature, have no name for this vice in their language, which hath no terms to express anything that is evil, except those whereby they describe the detestable qualities of their Yahoos, among which they were not able to distinguish this of pride, for want of thoroughly understanding human nature, as it showeth itself in other countries, where that animal presides. But I, who had more experience, could plainly observe some rudiments of it among the wild Yahoos.

But the Houyhnhnms, who live under the government of reason, are no more proud of the good qualities they possess, than I should be for not wanting a leg or an arm, which no man in his wits would boast of, although he must be miserable without them. I dwell the longer upon this subject from

1. Witness.

the desire I have to make the society of an English Yahoo by any means not insupportable; and therefore I here entreat those who have any tincture of this absurd vice, that they will not presume to appear in my sight.

1726, 1735

A Modest Proposal[1]

FOR PREVENTING THE CHILDREN OF POOR PEOPLE IN IRELAND FROM BEING A BURDEN TO THEIR PARENTS OR COUNTRY, AND FOR MAKING THEM BENEFICIAL TO THE PUBLIC

It is a melancholy object to those who walk through this great town[2] or travel in the country, when they see the streets, the roads, and cabin doors, crowded with beggars of the female sex, followed by three, four, or six children, all in rags and importuning every passenger for an alms. These mothers, instead of being able to work for their honest livelihood, are forced to employ all their time in strolling to beg sustenance for their helpless infants, who, as they grow up, either turn thieves for want of work, or leave their dear native country to fight for the Pretender in Spain, or sell themselves to the Barbadoes.[3]

I think it is agreed by all parties that this prodigious number of children in the arms, or on the backs, or at the heels of their mothers, and frequently of their fathers, is in the present deplorable state of the kingdom a very great additional grievance; and therefore whoever could find out a fair, cheap, and easy method of making these children sound, useful members of the commonwealth would deserve so well of the public as to have his statue set up for a preserver of the nation.

But my intention is very far from being confined to provide only for the children of professed beggars; it is of a much greater extent, and shall take in the whole number of infants at a certain age who are born of parents in effect as little able to support them as those who demand our charity in the streets.

As to my own part, having turned my thoughts for many years upon this important subject, and maturely weighed the several schemes of other projectors,[4] I have always found them grossly mistaken in their computation. It is true, a child just dropped from its dam may be supported by her milk for a

1. "A Modest Proposal" is an example of Swift's favorite satiric devices used with superb effect. Irony (from the deceptive adjective *modest* in the title to the very last sentence) pervades the piece. A rigorous logic deduces ghastly arguments from a premise so quietly assumed that readers assent before they are aware of what that assent implies. Parody, at which Swift is adept, allows him to glance sardonically at the by then familiar figure of the benevolent humanitarian (forerunner of the modern sociologist, social worker, and economic planner) concerned to correct a social evil by means of a theoretically conceived plan. The proposer, as naive as he is apparently logical and kindly, ignores and therefore emphasizes for the reader the enormity of his plan. The whole is an elaboration of a rather trite metaphor: "The English are devouring the Irish." But there is nothing trite about the pamphlet, which expresses in Swift's most controlled style his revulsion at the contemporary state of Ireland and his indignation at the rapacious English absentee landlords, who were bleeding the country white with the silent approbation of Parliament, ministers, and the crown.

2. Dublin.

3. James Francis Edward Stuart (1688–1766), the son of James II, was claimant ("Pretender") to the throne of England from which the Glorious Revolution had barred his succession. Catholic Ireland was loyal to him, and Irishmen joined him in his exile on the Continent. Because of the poverty in Ireland, many Irishmen emigrated to the West Indies and other British colonies in America; they paid their passage by binding themselves to work for a stated period for one of the planters.

4. Devisers of schemes.

solar year, with little other nourishment; at most not above the value of two shillings, which the mother may certainly get, or the value in scraps, by her lawful occupation of begging; and it is exactly at one year old that I propose to provide for them in such a manner as instead of being a charge upon their parents or the parish, or wanting food and raiment for the rest of their lives, they shall on the contrary contribute to the feeding, and partly to the clothing, of many thousands.

There is likewise another great advantage in my scheme, that it will prevent those voluntary abortions, and that horrid practice of women murdering their bastard children, alas, too frequent among us, sacrificing the poor innocent babes, I doubt, more to avoid the expense than the shame, which would move tears and pity in the most savage and inhuman breast.

The number of souls in this kingdom[5] being usually reckoned one million and a half, of these I calculate there may be about two hundred thousand couple whose wives are breeders; from which number I subtract thirty thousand couples who are able to maintain their own children, although I apprehend there cannot be so many under the present distresses of the kingdom; but this being granted, there will remain an hundred and seventy thousand breeders. I again subtract fifty thousand for those women who miscarry, or whose children die by accident or disease within the year. There only remain an hundred and twenty thousand children of poor parents annually born. The question therefore is, how this number shall be reared and provided for, which, as I have already said, under the present situation of affairs, is utterly impossible by all the methods hitherto proposed. For we can neither employ them in handicraft or agriculture; we neither build houses (I mean in the country) nor cultivate land. They can very seldom pick up a livelihood by stealing till they arrive at six years old, except where they are of towardly parts;[6] although I confess they learn the rudiments much earlier, during which time they can however be looked upon only as probationers, as I have been informed by a principal gentleman in the county of Cavan, who protested to me that he never knew above one or two instances under the ages of six, even in a part of the kingdom so renowned for the quickest proficiency in that art.

I am assured by our merchants that a boy or a girl before twelve years old is no salable commodity; and even when they come to this age they will not yield above three pounds, or three pounds and half a crown at most on the Exchange; which cannot turn to account either to the parents or the kingdom, the charge of nutriment and rags having been at least four times that value.

I shall now therefore humbly propose my own thoughts, which I hope will not be liable to the least objection.

I have been assured by a very knowing American of my acquaintance in London, that a young healthy child well nursed is at a year old a most delicious, nourishing, and wholesome food, whether stewed, roasted, baked, or boiled; and I make no doubt that it will equally serve in a fricassee or a ragout.[7]

I do therefore humbly offer it to public consideration that of the hundred and twenty thousand children, already computed, twenty thousand may be reserved for breed, whereof only one fourth part to be males, which is more than we allow to sheep, black cattle, or swine; and my reason is that these

5. Ireland.
6. Promising abilities.

7. A highly seasoned meat stew.

children are seldom the fruits of marriage, a circumstance not much regarded by our savages, therefore one male will be sufficient to serve four females. That the remaining hundred thousand may at a year old be offered in sale to the persons of quality and fortune through the kingdom, always advising the mother to let them suck plentifully in the last month, so as to render them plump and fat for a good table. A child will make two dishes at an entertainment for friends; and when the family dines alone, the fore or hind quarter will make a reasonable dish, and seasoned with a little pepper or salt will be very good boiled on the fourth day, especially in winter.

I have reckoned upon a medium that a child just born will weigh twelve pounds, and in a solar year if tolerably nursed increaseth to twenty-eight pounds.

I grant this food will be somewhat dear, and therefore very proper for landlords, who, as they have already devoured most of the parents, seem to have the best title to the children.

Infant's flesh will be in season throughout the year, but more plentiful in March, and a little before and after. For we are told by a grave author, an eminent French physician,[8] that fish being a prolific diet, there are more children born in Roman Catholic countries about nine months after Lent than at any other season; therefore, reckoning a year after Lent, the markets will be more glutted than usual, because the number of popish infants is at least three to one in this kingdom; and therefore it will have one other collateral advantage, by lessening the number of Papists among us.

I have already computed the charge of nursing a beggar's child (in which list I reckon all cottagers, laborers, and four fifths of the farmers) to be about two shillings per annum, rags included; and I believe no gentleman would repine to give ten shillings for the carcass of a good fat child, which, as I have said, will make four dishes of excellent nutritive meat, when he hath only some particular friend or his own family to dine with him. Thus the squire will learn to be a good landlord, and grow popular among the tenants; the mother will have eight shillings net profit, and be fit for the work till she produces another child.

Those who are more thrifty (as I must confess the times require) may flay the carcass; the skin of which artificially[9] dressed will make admirable gloves for ladies, and summer boots for fine gentlemen.

As to our city of Dublin, shambles[1] may be appointed for this purpose in the most convenient parts of it, and butchers we may be assured will not be wanting; although I rather recommend buying the children alive, and dressing them hot from the knife as we do roasting pigs.

A very worthy person, a true lover of his country, and whose virtues I highly esteem, was lately pleased in discoursing on this matter to offer a refinement upon my scheme. He said that many gentlemen of this kingdom, having of late destroyed their deer, he conceived that the want of venison might be well supplied by the bodies of young lads and maidens, not exceeding fourteen years of age nor under twelve, so great a number of both sexes in every county being now ready to starve for want of work and service; and these to be disposed of by their parents, if alive, or otherwise by their nearest

---

8. François Rabelais (ca. 1494–1553), a humorist and satirist, by no means grave.

9. Skillfully.
1. Slaughterhouses.

relations. But with due deference to so excellent a friend and so deserving a patriot, I cannot be altogether in his sentiments; for as to the males, my American acquaintance assured me from frequent experience that their flesh was generally tough and lean, like that of our schoolboys, by continual exercise, and their taste disagreeable; and to fatten them would not answer the charge. Then as to the females, it would, I think with humble submission, be a loss to the public, because they soon would become breeders themselves; and besides, it is not improbable that some scrupulous people might be apt to censure such a practice (although indeed very unjustly) as a little bordering upon cruelty; which I confess, hath always been with me the strongest objection against any project, how well soever intended.

But in order to justify my friend, he confessed that this expedient was put into his head by the famous Psalmanazar,[2] a native of the island Formosa, who came from thence to London above twenty years ago, and in conversation told my friend that in his country when any young person happened to be put to death, the executioner sold the carcass to persons of quality as a prime dainty; and that in his time the body of a plump girl of fifteen, who was crucified for an attempt to poison the emperor, was sold to his Imperial Majesty's prime minister of state, and other great mandarins of the court, in joints from the gibbet, at four hundred crowns. Neither indeed can I deny that if the same use were made of several plump young girls in this town, who without one single groat to their fortunes cannot stir abroad without a chair, and appear at the playhouse and assemblies in foreign fineries which they never will pay for, the kingdom would not be the worse.

Some persons of a desponding spirit are in great concern about that vast number of poor people who are aged, diseased, or maimed, and I have been desired to employ my thoughts what course may be taken to ease the nation of so grievous an encumbrance. But I am not in the least pain upon that matter, because it is very well known that they are every day dying and rotting by cold and famine, and filth and vermin, as fast as can be reasonably expected. And as to the younger laborers, they are now in almost as hopeful a condition. They cannot get work, and consequently pine away for want of nourishment to a degree that if at any time they are accidentally hired to common labor, they have not strength to perform it; and thus the country and themselves are happily delivered from the evils to come.

I have too long digressed, and therefore shall return to my subject. I think the advantages by the proposal which I have made are obvious and many, as well as of the highest importance.

For first, as I have already observed, it would greatly lessen the number of Papists, with whom we are yearly overrun, being the principal breeders of the nation as well as our most dangerous enemies; and who stay at home on purpose to deliver the kingdom to the Pretender, hoping to take their advantage by the absence of so many good Protestants, who have chosen rather to leave their country than stay at home and pay tithes against their conscience to an Episcopal curate.[3]

---

2. George Psalmanazar (ca. 1679–1763), a famous impostor. A Frenchman, he imposed himself on English bishops, noblemen, and scientists as a Formosan. He wrote an entirely fictitious account of Formosa, in which he described human sacrifices and cannibalism.

3. Ireland had many Protestant sectarians who did not support the "Episcopal" (Anglican) Church of Ireland.

Secondly, the poorer tenants will have something valuable of their own, which by law may be made liable to distress,[4] and help to pay their landlord's rent, their corn and cattle being already seized and money a thing unknown.

Thirdly, whereas the maintenance of an hundred thousand children, from two years old and upwards, cannot be computed at less than ten shillings a piece per annum, the nation's stock will be thereby increased fifty thousand pounds per annum, besides the profit of a new dish introduced to the tables of all gentlemen of fortune in the kingdom who have any refinement in taste. And the money will circulate among ourselves, the goods being entirely of our own growth and manufacture.

Fourthly, the constant breeders, besides the gain of eight shillings sterling per annum by the sale of their children, will be rid of the charge of maintaining them after the first year.

Fifthly, this food would likewise bring great custom to taverns, where the vintners will certainly be so prudent as to procure the best receipts[5] for dressing it to perfection, and consequently have their houses frequented by all the fine gentlemen, who justly value themselves upon their knowledge in good eating; and a skillful cook, who understands how to oblige his guests, will contrive to make it as expensive as they please.

Sixthly, this would be a great inducement to marriage, which all wise nations have either encouraged by rewards or enforced by laws and penalties. It would increase the care and tenderness of mothers toward their children, when they were sure of a settlement for life to the poor babes, provided in some sort by the public, to their annual profit instead of expense. We should see an honest emulation among the married women, which of them could bring the fattest child to the market. Men would become as fond of their wives during the time of their pregnancy as they are now of their mares in foal, their cows in calf, or sows when they are ready to farrow; nor offer to beat or kick them (as is too frequent a practice) for fear of a miscarriage.

Many other advantages might be enumerated. For instance, the addition of some thousand carcasses in our exportation of barreled beef, the propagation of swine's flesh, and improvement in the art of making good bacon, so much wanted among us by the great destruction of pigs, too frequent at our tables, which are no way comparable in taste or magnificence to a well-grown, fat, yearling child, which roasted whole will make a considerable figure at a lord mayor's feast or any other public entertainment. But this and many others I omit, being studious of brevity.

Supposing that one thousand families in this city would be constant customers for infants' flesh, besides others who might have it at merry meetings, particularly weddings and christenings, I compute that Dublin would take off annually about twenty thousand carcasses, and the rest of the kingdom (where probably they will be sold somewhat cheaper) the remaining eighty thousand.

I can think of no one objection that will probably be raised against this proposal, unless it should be urged that the number of people will be thereby much lessened in the kingdom. This I freely own, and it was indeed one principal design in offering it to the world. I desire the reader will observe,

4. Distraint, i.e., the seizing, through legal action, of property for the payment of debts and other obligations. "Corn": grain.
5. Recipes.

that I calculate my remedy for this one individual kingdom of Ireland and for no other that ever was, is, or I think ever can be upon earth. Therefore let no man talk to me of other expedients: of taxing our absentees at five shillings a pound: of using neither clothes nor household furniture except what is of our own growth and manufacture: of utterly rejecting the materials and instruments that promote foreign luxury: of curing the expensiveness of pride, vanity, idleness, and gaming in our women: of introducing a vein of parsimony, prudence, and temperance: of learning to love our country, in the want of which we differ even from Laplanders and the inhabitants of Topinamboo:[6] of quitting our animosities and factions, nor acting any longer like the Jews, who were murdering one another at the very moment their city was taken:[7] of being a little cautious not to sell our country and conscience for nothing: of teaching landlords to have at least one degree of mercy toward their tenants: lastly, of putting a spirit of honesty, industry, and skill into our shopkeepers; who, if a resolution could now be taken to buy only our native goods, would immediately unite to cheat and exact upon us in the price, the measure, and the goodness, nor could ever yet be brought to make one fair proposal of just dealing, though often and earnestly invited to it.[8]

Therefore I repeat, let no man talk to me of these and the like expedients, till he hath at least some glimpse of hope that there will ever be some hearty and sincere attempt to put them in practice.

But as to myself, having been wearied out for many years with offering vain, idle, visionary thoughts, and at length utterly despairing of success, I fortunately fell upon this proposal, which, as it is wholly new, so it hath something solid and real, of no expense and little trouble, full in our own power, and whereby we can incur no danger in disobliging England. For this kind of commodity will not bear exportation, the flesh being of too tender a consistence to admit a long continuance in salt, although perhaps I could name a country which would be glad to eat up our whole nation without it.[9]

After all, I am not so violently bent upon my own opinion as to reject any offer proposed by wise men, which shall be found equally innocent, cheap, easy, and effectual. But before something of that kind shall be advanced in contradiction to my scheme, and offering a better, I desire the author or authors will be pleased maturely to consider two points. First, as things now stand, how they will be able to find food and raiment for an hundred thousand useless mouths and backs. And secondly, there being a round million of creatures in human figure throughout this kingdom, whose sole subsistence put into a common stock would leave them in debt two millions of pounds sterling, adding those who are beggars by profession to the bulk of farmers, cottagers, and laborers, with their wives and children who are beggars in effect; I desire those politicians who dislike my overture, and may perhaps be so bold to attempt an answer, that they will first ask the parents of these mortals whether they would not at this day think it a great happiness to have been sold for food at a year old in the manner I prescribe, and thereby have avoided

6. I.e., even Laplanders love their frozen, infertile country and the savage tribes of Brazil love their jungle more than the Anglo-Irish love Ireland.
7. During the siege of Jerusalem by the Roman Titus (later emperor), who captured and destroyed the city in 70 C.E., bloody fights broke out between

fanatical factions among the defenders.
8. Swift himself had made all these proposals in various pamphlets. In editions printed during his lifetime the various proposals were italicized to indicate Swift's support for them.
9. England.

such a perpetual sense of misfortunes as they have since gone through by the oppression of landlords, the impossibility of paying rent without money or trade, the want of common sustenance, with neither house nor clothes to cover them from the inclemencies of the weather, and the most inevitable prospect of entailing the like or greater miseries upon their breed forever.

I profess, in the sincerity of my heart, that I have not the least personal interest in endeavoring to promote this necessary work, having no other motive than the public good of my country, by advancing our trade, providing for infants, relieving the poor, and giving some pleasure to the rich. I have no children by which I can propose to get a single penny; the youngest being nine years old, and my wife past childbearing.

1729

JOSEPH ADDISON *and* SIR RICHARD STEELE
1672–1719   1672–1729

The friendship of Joseph Addison and Richard Steele began when they were schoolboys together in London. Their careers ran parallel courses and brought them for a while into fruitful collaboration. Addison, although charming when among friends, was by nature reserved, calculating, and prudent. Steele was impulsive and rakish when young (but ardently devoted to his beautiful wife), often imprudent, and frequently in want of money. Addison never stumbled in his progress to financial security, a late marriage to a widowed countess, and a successful political career; walking less surely, Steele experienced many vicissitudes and faced serious financial problems during his last years.

Both men attended Oxford, where Addison took his degree, won a fellowship, and gained a reputation for Latin verse; the less scholarly Steele left the university before earning a degree to take a commission in the army. For a while he cut a dashing figure in London, even, to his horror, seriously wounding a man in a duel. Both men enjoyed the patronage of the great Whig magnates; and except during the last four years of Queen Anne's reign, when the Tories were in the ascendancy, they were generously treated. Steele edited and wrote the *London Gazette*, an official newspaper that normally appeared twice a week, listing government appointments and reporting domestic and foreign news—much like a modern paper. He served in Parliament, was knighted by George I, and later became manager of the Theatre Royal, Drury Lane. Addison held more important positions: he was secretary to the lord lieutenant of Ireland and later an undersecretary of state; finally, toward the end of his life, he became secretary of state. Both men wrote plays: Addison's *Cato*, a frigid and very "correct" tragedy, had great success in 1713, and Steele's later plays at Drury Lane (especially *The Conscious Lovers*, 1722) were instrumental in establishing the popularity of sentimental comedy throughout the eighteenth century.

Steele's debts and Addison's loss of office in 1710 drove them to journalistic enterprises, through which they developed one of the most characteristic types of eighteenth-century literature, the periodical essay. Steele's experience as gazetteer had involved him in journalism and, in need of money, in 1709 he launched the

Tatler under the pseudonym Isaac Bickerstaff. He sought to attract the largest possible audience: the title was a bid for female readers, and the mixture of news with personal reflections soon became popular in coffeehouses and at breakfast tables. The paper appeared three times a week from April 1709 to January 1711. Steele wrote by far the greater number of *Tatlers*, but Addison contributed helpfully, as did other friends. When the *Spectator* began its run two months after the last *Tatler*, the new periodical drew on and expanded the readership Steele had reached and influenced. The *Spectator* appeared daily except Sunday from March 1711 to December 1712 (and was briefly resumed by Addison in 1714). It was the joint undertaking of the two friends, although it was dominated by Addison. Both the *Spectator* and the *Tatler* had many imitators in their own day and throughout the rest of the century. There was a *Female Tatler* and a *Female Spectator*, as well as Samuel Johnson's *Rambler* and *Idler* and Oliver Goldsmith's brief *Bee*.

The periodical writing of Addison and Steele is remarkable for its comprehensive attention to diverse aspects of English life—good manners, daily happenings in London, going to church, shopping, investing in the stock market, the fascinations of trade and commerce, proper gender roles and relations, the personality types found in society, the town's offerings of high and low entertainment, tastes in literature and luxury goods, philosophical speculations—and the seamless way all were shown to be elements of a single vast, agreeable world. In this unifying spirit, both Steele and Addison set the divisive political battles of the day, so vigorously fought in other periodicals and newspapers, at a distance: they portray the ardor for political dispute more as a personal quirk than as a provocation to true civil unrest. Less formal and didactic than the essays of Francis Bacon, less personal than those of Charles Lamb and William Hazlitt in the next century, these essays promote morality among their readers by praising and enacting sociability and set standards of good taste and polite behavior with a light but firm and unwavering grace. They thereby sought to establish a new social-literary ethos transcending the narrowness of Puritan morality and the exorbitance of the fashionable court culture of the last century.

In the *Spectator*, Steele and especially Addison set out to break down the distinction between educating their readers and entertaining them with winning characters, vivid scenes, and even playfully visionary allegories. In the second number, Steele introduces us to the members of Mr. Spectator's Club: a man about town, a student of law and literature, a churchman, a soldier, a Tory country squire, and—interestingly enough—a London merchant. The development of these characters shows how the very manner in which the *Spectator* makes distinctions tends to smooth away conflict. As a Whig, Steele sympathized with the new moneyed class in London and evidently intended to pit the merchant Sir Andrew Freeport, the representative of the new order, against the Tory Sir Roger de Coverley, representative of the one passing away. Addison, however, preferred to present Sir Roger in episodes set in town and in country as an endearing, eccentric character, often absurd but always amiable and innocent. He is a prominent ancestor of a long line of similar characters in fiction in the following two centuries. Addison's scholarly interests broadened the material to include not only social criticism but the popularization of current philosophical and scientific notions. He wrote important critical papers distinguishing true and false wit; an extended series of Saturday essays evaluating *Paradise Lost*; and an influential series on "the pleasures of the imagination," which treated the visual effect of beautiful, "great," and uncommon objects in nature and art. Altogether, the *Spectator* fulfilled his ambition (outlined in "The Aims of the Spectator") to be considered an agreeable modern Socrates.

The best description of Addison's prose is Samuel Johnson's in his *Life of Addison*: "His prose is the model of the middle style; on grave subjects not formal, on light occasions not groveling; pure without scrupulosity, and exact without apparent elaboration; always equable, and always easy, without glowing words or pointed sentences."

And he concludes: "Whoever wishes to attain an English style, familiar but not coarse, and elegant but not ostentatious, must give his days and nights to the volumes of Addison"—a course of study that a good many aspiring writers during the century seem to have undertaken.

THE PERIODICAL ESSAY: MANNERS, SOCIETY, GENDER

STEELE: [The Spectator's Club]

The Spectator, *No. 2, Friday, March 2, 1711*

——*Ast alii sex*
Et plures uno conclamant ore.[1]
—JUVENAL, *Satire* 7.167–68

The first of our society is a gentleman of Worcestershire, of ancient descent, a baronet, his name Sir Roger de Coverley. His great-grandfather was inventor of that famous country-dance which is called after him. All who know the shire are very well acquainted with the parts and merits of Sir Roger. He is a gentleman that is very singular in his behavior, but his singularities proceed from his good sense, and are contradictions to the manners of the world only as he thinks the world is in the wrong. However, this humor creates him no enemies, for he does nothing with sourness or obstinacy; and his being unconfined to modes and forms[2] makes him but the readier and more capable to please and oblige all who know him. When he is in town, he lives in Soho Square. It is said he keeps himself a bachelor by reason he was crossed in love by a perverse, beautiful widow of the next county to him. Before this disappointment, Sir Roger was what you call a fine gentleman, had often supped with my Lord Rochester and Sir George Etherege, fought a duel upon his first coming to town, and kicked Bully Dawson[3] in a public coffeehouse for calling him "youngster." But being ill used by the above-mentioned widow, he was very serious for a year and a half; and though, his temper being naturally jovial, he at last got over it, he grew careless of himself, and never dressed afterwards. He continues to wear a coat and doublet of the same cut that were in fashion at the time of his repulse, which, in his merry humors, he tells us, has been in and out twelve times since he first wore it. 'Tis said Sir Roger grew humble in his desires after he had forgot this cruel beauty, insomuch that it is reported he has frequently offended in point of chastity with beggars and gypsies; but this is looked upon by his friends rather as matter of raillery than truth. He is now in his fifty-sixth year, cheerful, gay, and hearty; keeps a good house both in town and country; a great lover of mankind; but there is such a mirthful cast in his behavior that he is rather beloved than esteemed. His tenants grow rich, his servants look satisfied, all the young women profess love to him, and the young men are glad of his company; when he comes into a house he calls the servants by their names, and talks all the way upstairs to a visit. I must not omit that Sir Roger is a justice of the

1. Six more at least join their consenting voice (Latin).
2. Social conventions.
3. Notorious cardsharp of the period. John

Wilmot, second earl of Rochester (1647–1680), British poet, Etherege (ca. 1634–1691), playwright, rake, and close companion of the king and Rochester.

quorum, that he fills the chair at a quarter-session with great abilities; and, three months ago, gained universal applause by explaining a passage in the Game Act.[4]

The gentleman next in esteem and authority among us is another bachelor, who is a member of the Inner Temple; a man of great probity, wit, and understanding; but he has chosen his place of residence rather to obey the direction of an old humorsome[5] father, than in pursuit of his own inclinations. He was placed there to study the laws of the land, and is the most learned of any of the house in those of the stage. Aristotle and Longinus are much better understood by him than Littleton or Coke.[6] The father sends up, every post, questions relating to marriage articles, leases, and tenures, in the neighborhood; all which questions he agrees with an attorney to answer and take care of in the lump. He is studying the passions themselves, when he should be inquiring into the debates among men which arise from them. He knows the argument of each of the orations of Demosthenes and Tully,[7] but not one case in the reports of our own courts. No one ever took him for a fool, but none, except his intimate friends, know he has a great deal of wit. This turn makes him at once both disinterested and agreeable; as few of his thoughts are drawn from business, they are most of them fit for conversation. His taste of books is a little too just[8] for the age he lives in; he has read all, but approves of very few. His familiarity with the customs, manners, actions, and writings of the ancients makes him a very delicate observer of what occurs to him in the present world. He is an excellent critic, and the time of the play is his hour of business; exactly at five he passes through New Inn, crosses through Russell Court, and takes a turn at Will's till the play begins; he has his shoes rubbed and his periwig powdered at the barber's as you go into the Rose.[9] It is for the good of the audience when he is at a play, for the actors have an ambition to please him.

The person of next consideration is Sir Andrew Freeport, a merchant of great eminence in the city of London, a person of indefatigable industry, strong reason, and great experience. His notions of trade are noble and generous, and (as every rich man has usually some sly way of jesting which would make no great figure were he not a rich man) he calls the sea the British Common. He is acquainted with commerce in all its parts, and will tell you that it is a stupid and barbarous way to extend dominion by arms; for true power is to be got by arts and industry. He will often argue that if this part of our trade were well cultivated, we should gain from one nation; and if another, from another. I have heard him prove that diligence makes more lasting acquisitions than valor, and that sloth has ruined more nations than the sword. He abounds in several frugal maxims, among which the

4. In 1671 the act gave the gentry (Sir Roger's class) broad legal powers to prevent poaching and hence granted them a virtual monopoly on hunting. "Justice of the quorum": a country justice of the peace, presiding over quarterly sessions of the court.
5. Temperamental. "Inner Temple": one of the Inns of Court, where lawyers resided or had their offices and where students studied law.
6. In other words, he is more familiar with the laws of literature than those of England. The *Poetics* of Aristotle and the Greek treatise *On the Sublime* (reputedly by Longinus) were in high favor

among the critics of the time. Sir Thomas Littleton, 15th-century jurist, was author of a renowned treatise on *Tenures*. Sir Edward Coke (1552–1634) was the judge and writer whose *Reports* and *Institutes of the Laws of England* (known as *Coke upon Littleton*) have exerted a great influence on the interpretation of English law.
7. Marcus Tullius Cicero.
8. Exact.
9. A tavern near Drury Lane. "Will's": the coffeehouse in Covent Garden associated with literature and criticism since Dryden had begun to frequent it in the 1660s.

greatest favorite is, "A penny saved is a penny got." A general trader of good sense is pleasanter company than a general scholar; and Sir Andrew having a natural unaffected eloquence, the perspicuity of his discourse gives the same pleasure that wit would in another man. He has made his fortunes himself, and says that England may be richer than other kingdoms by as plain methods as he himself is richer than other men; though at the same time I can say this of him, that there is not a point in the compass but blows home a ship in which he is an owner.

Next to Sir Andrew in the clubroom sits Captain Sentry, a gentleman of great courage, good understanding, but invincible modesty. He is one of those that deserve very well, but are very awkward at putting their talents within the observation of such as should take notice of them. He was some years a captain, and behaved himself with great gallantry in several engagements and at several sieges; but having a small estate of his own, and being next heir to Sir Roger, he has quitted a way of life in which no man can rise suitably to his merit who is not something of a courtier as well as a soldier. I have heard him often lament that in a profession where merit is placed in so conspicuous a view, impudence should get the better of modesty. When he has talked to this purpose I never heard him make a sour expression, but frankly confess that he left the world because he was not fit for it. A strict honesty and an even, regular behavior are in themselves obstacles to him that must press through crowds who endeavor at the same end with himself—the favor of a commander. He will, however, in his way of talk, excuse generals for not disposing according to men's desert, or inquiring into it, "for," says he, "that great man who has a mind to help me, has as many to break through to come at me as I have to come at him"; therefore he will conclude that the man who would make a figure, especially in a military way, must get over all false modesty, and assist his patron against the importunity of other pretenders by a proper assurance in his own vindication. He says it is a civil cowardice to be backward in asserting[1] what you ought to expect, as it is a military fear to be slow in attacking when it is your duty. With this candor does the gentleman speak of himself and others. The same frankness runs through all his conversation. The military part of his life has furnished him with many adventures, in the relation of which he is very agreeable to the company; for he is never overbearing, though accustomed to command men in the utmost degree below him; nor ever too obsequious from an habit of obeying men highly above him.

But that our society may not appear a set of humorists[2] unacquainted with the gallantries and pleasures of the age, we have among us the gallant Will Honeycomb, a gentleman who, according to his years, should be in the decline of his life, but having ever been very careful of his person, and always had a very easy fortune, time has made but very little impression either by wrinkles on his forehead or traces in his brain. His person is well turned, of a good height. He is very ready at that sort of discourse with which men usually entertain women. He has all his life dressed very well, and remembers habits[3] as others do men. He can smile when one speaks to him, and laughs easily. He knows the history of every mode, and can inform you from which of the French king's wenches our wives and daughters had this manner of

1. Claiming.
2. Eccentrics.
3. Clothes.

curling their hair, that way of placing their hoods; whose frailty was covered by such a sort of petticoat, and whose vanity to show her foot made that part of the dress so short in such a year. In a word, all his conversation and knowledge has been in the female world. As other men of his age will take notice to you what such a minister said upon such and such an occasion, he will tell you when the Duke of Monmouth[4] danced at court such a woman was then smitten, another was taken with him at the head of his troop in the Park. In all these important relations, he has ever about the same time received a kind glance or a blow of a fan from some celebrated beauty, mother of the present Lord Such-a-one. If you speak of a young commoner that said a lively thing in the House, he starts up: "He has good blood in his veins; Tom Mirabell begot him, the rogue cheated me in that affair; that young fellow's mother used me more like a dog than any woman I ever made advances to." This way of talking of his very much enlivens the conversation among us of a more sedate turn; and I find there is not one of the company but myself, who rarely speak at all, but speaks of him as of that sort of man who is usually called a well-bred, fine gentleman. To conclude his character, where women are not concerned he is an honest, worthy man.

I cannot tell whether I am to account him whom I am next to speak of as one of our company, for he visits us but seldom; but when he does, it adds to every man else a new enjoyment of himself. He is a clergyman, a very philosophic man, of general learning, great sanctity of life, and the most exact good breeding. He has the misfortune to be of a very weak constitution, and consequently cannot accept of such cares and business as preferments in his function would oblige him to; he is therefore among divines what a chamber-counselor[5] is among lawyers. The probity of his mind and the integrity of his life create him followers, as being eloquent or loud advances others. He seldom introduces the subject he speaks upon; but we are so far gone in years that he observes, when he is among us, an earnestness to have him fall on some divine topic, which he always treats with much authority, as one who has no interest in this world, as one who is hastening to the object of all his wishes and conceives hope from his decays and infirmities. These are my ordinary companions.

ADDISON: [The Aims of the *Spectator*]

The Spectator, No. 10, Monday, March 12, 1711

Non aliter quam qui adverso vix flumine lembum
Remigiis subigit, si bracchia forte remisit,
Atque illum in præceps prono rapit alveus amni.[1]
—VIRGIL, *Georgics* 1.201–3

It is with much satisfaction that I hear this great city inquiring day by day after these my papers, and receiving my morning lectures with a becoming seriousness and attention. My publisher tells me that there are already three

---

4. The illegitimate son of Charles II, the ill-fated Absalom of Dryden's *Absalom and Achitophel.*
5. A lawyer who gives opinions in private, not in court.

1. Like him whose oars can hardly force his boat against the current, if by chance he relaxes his arms, the boat sweeps him headlong down the stream (Latin).

thousand of them distributed every day. So that if I allow twenty readers to every paper, which I look upon as a modest computation, I may reckon about three-score thousand disciples in London and Westminster, who I hope will take care to distinguish themselves from the thoughtless herd of their ignorant and unattentive brethren. Since I have raised to myself so great an audience, I shall spare no pains to make their instruction agreeable, and their diversion useful. For which reasons I shall endeavor to enliven morality with wit, and to temper wit with morality, that my readers may, if possible, both ways find their account in the speculation of the day. And to the end that their virtue and discretion may not be short, transient, intermitting starts of thought, I have resolved to refresh their memories from day to day, till I have recovered them out of that desperate state of vice and folly into which the age is fallen. The mind that lies fallow but a single day sprouts up in follies that are only to be killed by a constant and assiduous culture. It was said of Socrates that he brought philosophy down from heaven, to inhabit among men; and I shall be ambitious to have it said of me that I have brought philosophy out of closets[2] and libraries, schools and colleges, to dwell in clubs and assemblies, at tea tables and in coffeehouses.

I would therefore in a very particular manner recommend these my speculations to all well-regulated families that set apart an hour in every morning for tea and bread and butter; and would earnestly advise them for their good to order this paper to be punctually served up, and to be looked upon as a part of the tea equipage.

Sir Francis Bacon observes that a well-written book, compared with its rivals and antagonists, is like Moses's serpent, that immediately swallowed up and devoured those of the Egyptians.[3] I shall not be so vain as to think that where *The Spectator* appears the other public prints will vanish; but shall leave it to my reader's consideration whether is it not much better to be let into the knowledge of one's self, than to hear what passes in Muscovy or Poland; and to amuse ourselves with such writings as tend to the wearing out of ignorance, passion, and prejudice, than such as naturally conduce to inflame hatreds, and make enmities irreconcilable?

In the next place, I would recommend this paper to the daily perusal of those gentlemen whom I cannot but consider as my good brothers and allies, I mean the fraternity of spectators who live in the world without having anything to do in it; and either by the affluence of their fortunes or laziness of their dispositions have no other business with the rest of mankind but to look upon them. Under this class of men are comprehended all contemplative tradesmen, titular physicians, fellows of the Royal Society, Templars[4] that are not given to be contentious, and statesmen that are out of business; in short, everyone that considers the world as a theater, and desires to form a right judgment of those who are the actors on it.

There is another set of men that I must likewise lay a claim to, whom I have lately called the blanks of society, as being altogether unfurnished with ideas, till the business and conversation of the day has supplied them. I have often considered these poor souls with an eye of great commiseration, when

---

2. Private rooms, studies.
3. In *The Advancement of Learning* 2, "To the King." But it was the rod of Aaron, not of Moses, that turned into a devouring serpent (Exodus 7.10–12).

4. Lawyers or students of the law who live or have their offices ("chambers") in the Middle or Inner Temple, one of the Inns of Court.

I have heard them asking the first man they have met with, whether there was any news stirring? and by that means gathering together materials for thinking. These needy persons do not know what to talk of till about twelve o'clock in the morning; for by that time they are pretty good judges of the weather, know which way the wind sits, and whether the Dutch mail[5] be come in. As they lie at the mercy of the first man they meet, and are grave or impertinent all the day long, according to the notions which they have inbibed in the morning, I would earnestly entreat them not to stir out of their chambers till they have read this paper, and do promise them that I will daily instil into them such sound and wholesome sentiments as shall have a good effect on their conversation for the ensuing twelve hours.

But there are none to whom this paper will be more useful than to the female world. I have often thought there has not been sufficient pains taken in finding out proper employments and diversions for the fair ones. Their amusements seem contrived for them, rather as they are women, than as they are reasonable creatures; and are more adapted to the sex than to the species. The toilet[6] is their great scene of business, and the right adjusting of their hair the principal employment of their lives. The sorting of a suit of ribbons is reckoned a very good morning's work; and if they make an excursion to a mercer's or a toyshop,[7] so great a fatigue makes them unfit for anything else all the day after. Their more serious occupations are sewing and embroidery, and their greatest drudgery the preparation of jellies and sweetmeats. This, I say, is the state of ordinary women; though I know there are multitudes of those of a more elevated life and conversation, that move in an exalted sphere of knowledge and virtue, that join all the beauties of the mind to the ornaments of dress, and inspire a kind of awe and respect, as well as love, into their male beholders. I hope to increase the number of these by publishing this daily paper, which I shall always endeavor to make an innocent if not improving entertainment, and by that means at least divert the minds of my female readers from greater trifles. At the same time, as I would fain give some finishing touches to those which are already the most beautiful pieces in human nature, I shall endeavor to point all those imperfections that are the blemishes, as well as those virtues which are the embellishments, of the sex. In the meanwhile I hope these my gentle readers, who have so much time on their hands, will not grudge throwing away a quarter of an hour in a day on this paper, since they may do it without any hindrance to business.

I know several of my friends and well-wishers are in great pain for me, lest I should not be able to keep up the spirit of a paper which I oblige myself to furnish every day: but to make them easy in this particular, I will promise them faithfully to give it over as soon as I grow dull. This I know will be matter of great raillery to the small wits; who will frequently put me in mind of my promise, desire me to keep my word, assure me that it is high time to give over, with many other little pleasantries of the like nature, which men of a little smart genius cannot forbear throwing out against their best friends, when they have such a handle given them of being witty. But let them remember that I do hereby enter my caveat against this piece of raillery.

---

5. Bringing the latest war news.
6. Dressing table.
7. A shop where baubles and trifles are sold. "Suit of ribbons": A set of ribbons to be worn together. "Mercer": a seller of such notions as tape, ribbon, and fringe.

STEELE: [Inkle and Yarico]

The Spectator, No. 11, Tuesday, March 13, 1711

Dat veniam corvis, vexat censura columbas.[1]
—JUVENAL, *Satire* 2.63

Arietta is visited by all persons of both sexes who have any pretence to wit and gallantry. She is in that time of life which is neither affected with the follies of youth or infirmities of age; and her conversation is so mixed with gaiety and prudence that she is agreeable both to the young and the old. Her behavior is very frank without being in the least blamable; as she is out of the tract[2] of any amorous or ambitious pursuits of her own, her visitants entertain her with accounts of themselves very freely, whether they concern their passions or their interests. I made her a visit this afternoon, having been formerly introduced to the honor of her acquaintance by my friend Will Honeycomb, who has prevailed upon her to admit me sometimes into her assembly as a civil, inoffensive man. I found her accompanied with one person only, a commonplace talker who upon my entrance arose and after a very slight civility sat down again; then turning to Arietta pursued his discourse, which I found was upon the old topic of constancy in love. He went on with great facility in repeating what he talks every day of his life; and with the ornaments of insignificant laughs and gestures enforced his arguments by quotations out of plays and songs which allude to the perjuries of the fair and the general levity[3] of women. Methought he strove to shine more than ordinarily in his talkative way that he might insult my silence, and distinguish himself before a woman of Arietta's taste and understanding. She had often an inclination to interrupt him but could find no opportunity, till the larum ceased of itself; which it did not till he had repeated and murdered the celebrated story of the Ephesian Matron.[4]

Arietta seemed to regard this piece of raillery as an outrage done to her sex, as indeed I have always observed that women, whether out of a nicer regard to their honor or what other reason I cannot tell, are more sensibly touched with those general aspersions which are cast upon their sex than men are by what is said of theirs.

When she had a little recovered her self from the serious anger she was in, she replied in the following manner.

Sir, when I consider how perfectly new all you have said on this subject is, and that the story you have given us is not quite two thousand years old, I cannot but think it a piece of presumption to dispute with you. But your quotations put in me in mind of the fable of the Lion and the Man.[5] The man walking with that noble animal showed him, in the ostentation of human superiority, a sign of a man killing a lion. Upon which the lion said very justly, "We lions are none of us painters, else we could show a hundred men killed by lions, for one lion killed by a man." You men are writers and can represent us women as unbecoming as you please in your works, while

---

1. Censure acquits the raven, but pursues the dove (Latin).
2. Course, way of acting.
3. Frivolity.
4. A story from Petronius's *Satyricon*, satirizing a supposedly grieving widow who allows a soldier to seduce her and to steal her husband's body. Cf. Haywood's *Fantomina*, p. 2740. "Larum": clamor.
5. Attributed to Aesop, the name under which a body of beast fables from Greek antiquity and later are collected. Cf. Chaucer, *The Wife of Bath's Prologue*, line 698.

we are unable to return the injury. You have twice or thrice observed in your discourse that hypocrisy is the very foundation of our education; and that an ability to dissemble our affections is a professed part of our breeding. These and such other reflections are sprinkled up and down the writings of all ages by authors who leave behind them memorials of their resentment against the scorn of particular women in invectives against the whole sex. Such a writer, I doubt not, was the celebrated Petronius, who invented the pleasant aggravations of the frailty of the Ephesian Lady; but when we consider this question between the sexes, which has been either a point of dispute or raillery ever since there were men and women, let us take facts from plain people, and from such as have not either ambition or capacity to embellish their narrations with any beauties of imagination. I was the other day amusing myself with Ligon's account of Barbados; and in answer to your well-wrought tale, I will give you (as it dwells upon my memory) out of that honest traveler, in his fifty fifth page, the history of Inkle and Yarico.[6]

Mr. Thomas Inkle of London, aged twenty years, embarked in the Downs[7] on the good ship called the Achilles, bound for the West Indies, on the 16th of June 1647, in order to improve his fortune by trade and merchandise. Our adventurer was the third son of an eminent citizen,[8] who had taken particular care to instill into his mind an early love of gain by making him a perfect master of numbers, and consequently giving him a quick view of loss and advantage, and preventing the natural impulses of his passions by prepossession towards his interests. With a mind thus turned, young Inkle had a person[9] every way agreeable, a ruddy vigor in his countenance, strength in his limbs, with ringlets of fair hair loosely flowing on his shoulders. It happened in the course of the voyage that the Achilles, in some distress, put into a creek on the main[1] of America in search of provisions. The youth, who is the hero of my story, among others went ashore on this occasion. From their first landing they were observed by a party of Indians who hid themselves in the woods for that purpose. The English unadvisedly marched a great distance from the shore into the country, and were intercepted by the natives, who slew the greatest number of them. Our adventurer escaped among others by flying into a forest. Upon his coming into a remote and pathless part of the wood, he threw himself, tired and breathless, on a little hillock, when an Indian maid rushed from a thicket behind him. After the first surprise, they appeared mutually agreeable to each other. If the European was highly charmed with the limbs, features, and wild graces of the naked American, the American was no less taken with the dress, complexion, and shape of an European, covered from head to foot. The Indian grew immediately enamored of him, and consequently solicitous for his preservation. She therefore conveyed him to a cave, where she gave him a delicious repast of fruits, and led him to a stream to slake his thirst. In the midst of these good offices, she would sometimes play with his hair and delight in the opposition of its color to that of her fingers; then open his bosom, then laugh at him for covering it. She was, it seems, a person of distinction, for she every day came to him in a different dress of the most beautiful shells,

---

6. In *A True and Exact History of the Island of Barbados* (1657), Richard Ligon tells the first version of this story, which was retold throughout the eighteenth century. Steele invents the names of the lovers and many incidental details.
7. An anchorage off the southeast coast of England.
8. Inhabitant of a city (especially London), often identified as "a man of trade, not a gentleman" (Johnson's *Dictionary*).
9. Physical appearance.
1. Mainland.

bugles and bredes.[2] She likewise brought him a great many spoils which her other lovers had presented to her; so that his cave was richly adorned with all the spotted skins of beasts and most parti-colored feathers of fowls which that world afforded. To make his confinement more tolerable, she would carry him in the dusk of the evening or by the favor of moonlight to unfrequented groves and solitudes, and show him where to lie down in safety and sleep amidst the falls of waters and melody of nightingales. Her part was to watch and hold him awake in her arms for fear of her countrymen, and wake him on occasions to consult his safety. In this manner did the lovers pass away their time, till they had learned a language of their own in which the voyager communicated to his mistress how happy he should be to have her in his country, where she should be clothed in such silks as his waistcoat was made of and be carried in houses drawn by horses, without being exposed to wind or weather. All this he promised her the enjoyment of, without such fears and alarms as they were there tormented with. In this tender correspondence these lovers lived for several months, when Yarico, instructed by her lover, discovered a vessel on the coast, to which she made signals, and in the night, with the utmost joy and satisfaction, accompanied him to a ships' crew of his countrymen bound for Barbados. When a vessel from the main arrives in that island, it seems the planters come down to the shore, where there is an immediate market of the Indians and other slaves, as with us of horses and oxen.

To be short, Mr. Thomas Inkle, now coming into English territories, began seriously to reflect upon his loss of time and to weigh with himself how many days' interest of his money he had lost during his stay with Yarico. This thought made the young man very pensive and careful what account he should be able to give his friends[3] of his voyage. Upon which considerations, the prudent and frugal young man sold Yarico to a Barbadian merchant; notwithstanding that the poor girl, to incline him to commiserate her condition, told him that she was with child by him. But he only made use of that information to rise in his demands upon the purchaser.

I was so touched with this story (which I think should be always a counterpart to the Ephesian Matron) that I left the room with tears in my eyes; which a woman of Arietta's good sense did, I am sure, take for greater applause than any compliments I could make her.

ADDISON: [The Royal Exchange]

The Spectator, No. 69, Saturday, May 19, 1711

> Hic segetes, illic veniunt felicius uvae:
> Arborei foetus alibi, atque injussa virescunt
> Gramina. Nonne vides, croceos ut Tmolus odores,
> India mittit ebur, molles sua thura Saboei?
> At Chalybes nudi ferrum, virosaque Pontus
> Castorea, Eliadum palmas Epirus equarum?
> Continuo has leges aeternaque foedera certis
> Imposuit Natura locis . . .
>   —VIRGIL, Georgics 1.54–61[1]

---

2. Tube-shaped glass beads and braided or interwoven ornaments.
3. Family members and other connections.

1. Here grain, there grapes grow more successfully, and elsewhere young trees and grasses sprout up spontaneously. Don't you see how Tmolus sends

The bustle of the **Royal Exchange** in the 18th century. Etching 1788a by Francesco Bartolozzi.

There is no place in the town which I so much love to frequent as the Royal Exchange.[2] It gives me a secret satisfaction, and in some measure gratifies my vanity as I am an Englishman, to see so rich an assembly of countrymen and foreigners consulting together upon the private business of mankind, and making this metropolis a kind of emporium for the whole earth. I must confess I look upon High Change[3] to be a great council in which all considerable nations have their representatives. Factors[4] in the trading world are what ambassadors are in the politic world; they negotiate affairs, conclude treaties, and maintain a good correspondence between those wealthy societies of men that are divided from one another by seas and oceans or live on the different extremities of a continent. I have often been pleased to hear disputes adjusted between an inhabitant of Japan and an alderman of London, or to see a subject of the Great Mogul entering into a league with one of the Czar of Muscovy.[5] I am infinitely delighted in mixing with these several ministers of commerce as they are distinguished by their different walks[6] and different languages. Sometimes I am justled among a body of Armenians; sometimes I am lost in a crowd of Jews; and sometimes make one in a group of Dutchmen. I am a Dane, Swede, or Frenchman at different times; or rather fancy myself like the old philosopher,[7] who upon being asked what countryman he was, replied that he was a citizen of the world.

Though I very frequently visit this busy multitude of people, I am known to nobody there but my friend Sir Andrew, who often smiles upon me as he sees me bustling in the crowd, but at the same time connives[8] at my presence without taking any further notice of me. There is indeed a merchant of Egypt who just knows me by sight, having formerly remitted me some money to Grand Cairo; but as I am not versed in the modern Coptic,[9] our conferences go no further than a bow and a grimace.

This grand scene of business gives me an infinite variety of solid and substantial entertainments. As I am a great lover of mankind, my heart naturally overflows with pleasure at the sight of a prosperous and happy multitude, insomuch that at many public solemnities I cannot forbear expressing my joy with tears that have stolen down my cheeks. For this reason I am wonderfully delighted to see such a body of men thriving in their own private fortunes and at the same time promoting the public stock; or in other words, raising estates for their own families by bringing into their country whatever is wanting, and carrying out of it whatever is superfluous.

Nature seems to have taken a particular care to disseminate her blessings among the different regions of the world with an eye to this mutual intercourse and traffic among mankind, that the natives of the several parts of the globe might have a kind of dependence upon one another and be united together by their common interest. Almost every degree[1] produces something peculiar to it. The food often grows in one country and the sauce in another. The fruits of Portugal are corrected by the products of Barbados; the infusion of a China plant sweetened with the pith of an Indian cane. The Philippick Islands[2] give a flavor to our European bowls. The single dress of a woman of quality is often the product of an hundred climates. The muff and the fan come together from the different ends of the earth. The scarf is sent from the torrid zone and the tippet[3] from beneath the pole. The brocade petticoat rises out of the mines of Peru and the diamond necklace out of the bowels of Indostan.[4]

If we consider our own country in its natural prospect without any of the benefits and advantages of commerce, what a barren uncomfortable spot of earth falls to our share! Natural historians tell us that no fruit grows originally among us besides hips and haws, acorns and pig-nuts, with other delicacies of the like nature; that our climate of itself and without the assistances of art can make no further advances towards a plum than to a sloe and carries an apple to no greater a perfection than a crab;[5] that our melons, our peaches, our figs, our apricots, and cherries are strangers among us, imported in different ages and naturalized in our English gardens; and that they would all degenerate and fall away into the trash of our own country, if they were wholly neglected by the planter and left to the mercy of our sun and soil. Nor has traffic[6] more enriched our vegetable world than it has

---

7. Diogenes the Cynic (4th century B.C.E.).
8. Winks.
9. Language of the Copts, a sect of Egyptian Christians.
1. Here, a degree of latitude, hence a particular position on the earth's surface.
2. The Philippines.

3. A cape or other hanging part of a woman's dress.
4. India.
5. Crabapple. "Hips and haws": rosehips and the berries of the hawthorn tree. "Pig-nuts": or groundnuts, the tuber of *Bunium flexuosum*.
6. Trade.

improved the whole face of nature among us. Our ships are laden with the harvest of every climate; our tables are stored with spices, and oils, and wines; our rooms are filled with pyramids of China and adorned with the workmanship of Japan; our morning's draught comes to us from the remotest corners of the earth. We repair our bodies by the drugs of America and repose ourselves under Indian canopies. My friend Sir Andrew calls the vineyards of France our gardens; the Spice-Islands our hot-beds; the Persians our silk-weavers, and the Chinese our potters. Nature indeed furnishes us with the bare necessaries of life, but traffic gives us great variety of what is useful, and at the same time supplies us with every thing that is convenient and ornamental. Nor is it the least part of this our happiness that whilst we enjoy the remotest products of the north and south, we are free from those extremities of weather which give them birth; that our eyes are refreshed with the green fields of Britain at the same time that our palates are feasted with fruits that rise between the tropics.

For these reasons there are no more useful members in a commonwealth than merchants. They knit mankind together in a mutual intercourse of good offices, distribute the gifts of nature, find work for the poor, add wealth to the rich, and magnificence to the great. Our English merchant converts the tin of his own country into gold and exchanges his wool for rubies. The Mahometans are clothed in our British manufacture and the inhabitants of the frozen zone warmed with the fleeces of our sheep.

When I have been upon the 'Change, I have often fancied one of our old kings standing in person where he is represented in effigy, and looking down upon the wealthy concourse of people with which that place is every day filled. In this case, how would he be surprised to hear all the languages of Europe spoken in this little spot of his former dominions, and to see so many private men, who in his time would have been the vassals of some powerful baron, negotiating like princes for greater sums of money than were formerly to be met with in the Royal Treasury! Trade, without enlarging the British territories, has given us a kind of additional empire. It has multiplied the number of the rich, made our landed estates infinitely more valuable than they were formerly, and added to them an accession of other estates as valuable as the lands themselves.

THE PERIODICAL ESSAY: IDEAS

ADDISON: [Wit: True, False, Mixed]

The Spectator, No. 62, Friday, March 11, 1711

Scribendi recte sapere est et principium et fons.[1]
—HORACE, *Ars Poetica* 309

Mr. Locke has an admirable reflection upon the difference of wit and judgment, whereby he endeavors to show the reason why they are not always the talents of the same person. His words are as follow: "And hence, perhaps,

---

1. Discernment is the source and fount of writing well (Latin).

may be given some reason of that common observation, that men who have a great deal of wit and prompt memories, have not always the clearest judgment, or deepest reason. For wit lying most in the assemblage of ideas, and putting those together with quickness and variety, wherein can be found any resemblance or congruity, thereby to make up pleasant pictures and agreeable visions in the fancy; judgment, on the contrary, lies quite on the other side, in separating carefully one from another, ideas wherein can be found the least difference, thereby to avoid being misled by similitude, and by affinity to take one thing for another. This is a way of proceeding quite contrary to metaphor and allusion; wherein, for the most part, lies that entertainment and pleasantry of wit which strikes so lively on the fancy, and is therefore so acceptable to all people."[2]

This is, I think, the best and most philosophical account that I have ever met with of wit, which generally, though not always, consists in such a resemblance and congruity of ideas as this author mentions. I shall only add to it, by way of explanation, that every resemblance of ideas is not that which we call wit, unless it be such an one that gives delight and surprise to the reader. These two properties seem essential to wit, more particularly the last of them. In order therefore that the resemblance in the ideas be wit, it is necessary that the ideas should not lie too near one another in the nature of things; for where the likeness is obvious, it gives no surprise. To compare one man's singing to that of another, or to represent the whiteness of any object by that of milk and snow, or the variety of its colors by those of the rainbow, cannot be called wit, unless, besides this obvious resemblance, there be some further congruity discovered in the two ideas that is capable of giving the reader some surprise. Thus when a poet tells us, the bosom of his mistress is as white as snow, there is no wit in the comparison; but when he adds, with a sigh, that it is as cold too, it then grows into wit. Every reader's memory may supply him with innumerable instances of the same nature. For this reason, the similitudes in heroic poets, who endeavor rather to fill the mind with great conceptions, than to divert it with such as are new and surprising, have seldom anything in them that can be called wit. Mr. Locke's account of wit, with this short explanation, comprehends most of the species of wit, as metaphors, similitudes, allegories, enigmas, mottoes, parables, fables, dreams, visions, dramatic writings, burlesque, and all the methods of allusion:[3] as there are many other pieces of wit (how remote soever they may appear at first sight from the foregoing description) which upon examination will be found to agree with it.

As true wit generally consists in this resemblance and congruity of ideas, false wit chiefly consists in the resemblance and congruity sometimes of single letters, as in anagrams, chronograms, lipograms, and acrostics; sometimes of syllables, as in echoes and doggerel rhymes; sometimes of words, as in puns and quibbles; and sometimes of whole sentences or poems, cast into the figures of eggs, axes, or altars:[4] nay, some carry the notion of wit so far,

2. John Locke's *An Essay Concerning Human Understanding* 2.11.2.
3. Wordplay; more broadly, any covert or symbolic use of language.
4. E.g., George Herbert's "The Altar" (p. 1707), and "Easter Wings" (p. 1709). "Chronogram": phrase in which certain letters express a date; e.g., "LorD haVe MerCIe Vpon Vs"; the capital letters (in Roman numerals) add up to 1666, the *annus mirabilis* of fire, plague, and war. "Lipograms": compositions omitting all words that contain a certain letter or letters.

as to ascribe it even to external mimicry; and to look upon a man as an ingenious person, that can resemble the tone, posture, or face of another.

As true wit consists in the resemblance of ideas, and false wit in the resemblance of words, according to the foregoing instances; there is another kind of wit which consists partly in the resemblance of ideas, and partly in the resemblance of words; which for distinction's sake I shall call mixed wit. This kind of wit is that which abounds in Cowley, more than in any author that ever wrote. Mr. Waller has likewise a great deal of it. Mr. Dryden is very sparing in it. Milton had a genius much above it. Spenser is in the same class with Milton. The Italians, even in their epic poetry, are full of it. Monsieur Boileau,[5] who formed himself upon the ancient poets, has everywhere rejected it with scorn. If we look after mixed wit among the Greek writers, we shall find it nowhere but in the epigrammatists. There are indeed some strokes of it in the little poem ascribed to Musaeus,[6] which by that, as well as many other marks, betrays itself to be a modern composition. If we look into the Latin writers, we find none of this mixed wit in Virgil, Lucretius, or Catullus; very little in Horace, but a great deal of it in Ovid, and scarce anything else in Martial.

Out of the innumerable branches of mixed wit, I shall choose one instance which may be met with in all the writers of this class. The passion of love in its nature has been thought to resemble fire; for which reason the words fire and flame are made use of to signify love. The witty poets therefore have taken an advantage from the doubtful meaning of the word fire, to make an infinite number of witticisms. Cowley, observing the cold regard of his mistress's eyes,[7] and at the same time their power of producing love in him, considers them as burning-glasses made of ice; and finding himself able to live in the greatest extremities of love, concludes the torrid zone to be habitable. When his mistress has read his letter written in juice of lemon by holding it to the fire, he desires her to read it over a second time by love's flames. When she weeps, he wishes it were inward heat that distilled those drops from the limbec.[8] When she is absent he is beyond eighty, that is, thirty degrees nearer the pole than when she is with him. His ambitious love is a fire that naturally mounts upwards; his happy love is the beams of heaven, and his unhappy love flames of hell. When it does not let him sleep, it is a flame that sends up no smoke; when it is opposed by counsel and advice, it is a fire that rages the more by the wind's blowing upon it. Upon the dying of a tree in which he had cut his loves, he observes that his written flames had burned up and withered the tree. When he resolves to give over his passion, he tells us that one burnt like him for ever dreads the fire. His heart is an Aetna, that instead of Vulcan's shop[9] encloses Cupid's forge in it. His endeavoring to drown his love in wine is throwing oil upon the fire. He would insinuate to his mistress that the fire of love, like that of the sun (which produces so many living creatures), should not only warm but beget. Love in another place cooks pleasure at his fire. Sometimes the poet's heart is frozen in every breast, and sometimes

---

5. Nicolas Boileau (1636–1711), French neoclassicist who wrote a verse *Art of Poetry* (1674), which was translated by Dryden.
6. A poem called *Hero and Leander*, attributed to the ancient Greek poet Musaeus, was first published in 1635.

7. In *The Mistress, or Several Copies of Love-Verses* (1647).
8. Or alembic, an apparatus used in distilling.
9. Mount Etna was supposed to be the workshop of Vulcan, the Roman god of fire and metalworking.

scorched in every eye. Sometimes he is drowned in tears, and burnt in love, like a ship set on fire in the middle of the sea.

The reader may observe in every one of these instances that the poet mixes the qualities of fire with those of love; and in the same sentence speaking of it both as a passion, and as real fire, surprises the reader with those seeming resemblances or contradictions that make up all the wit in this kind of writing. Mixed wit therefore is a composition of pun and true wit, and is more or less perfect as the resemblance lies in the ideas or in the words. Its foundations are laid partly in falsehood and partly in truth: reason puts in her claim for one half of it, and extravagance for the other. The only province therefore for this kind of wit is epigram, or those little occasional poems that in their own nature are nothing else but a tissue of epigrams. I cannot conclude this head of mixed wit without owning that the admirable poet out of whom I have taken the examples of it had as much true wit as any author that ever writ; and indeed all other talents of an extraordinary genius.

It may be expected, since I am upon this subject, that I should take notice of Mr. Dryden's definition of wit; which, with all the deference that is due to the judgment of so great a man, is not so properly a definition of wit, as of good writing in general. Wit, as he defines it, is "a propriety of words and thoughts adapted to the subject."[1] If this be a true definition of wit, I am apt to think that Euclid[2] was the greatest wit that ever set pen to paper: it is certain there never was a greater propriety of words and thoughts adapted to the subject than what that author has made use of in his elements. I shall only appeal to my reader, if this definition agrees with any notion he has of wit: if it be a true one, I am sure Mr. Dryden was not only a better poet, but a greater wit than Mr. Cowley; and Virgil a much more facetious man than either Ovid or Martial.

Bouhours,[3] whom I look upon to be the most penetrating of all the French critics, has taken pains to show that it is impossible for any thought to be beautiful which is not just, and has not its foundation in the nature of things; that the basis of all wit is truth; and that no thought can be valuable, of which good sense is not the groundwork. Boileau has endeavored to inculcate the same notion in several parts of his writings, both in prose and verse. This is that natural way of writing, that beautiful simplicity, which we so much admire in the compositions of the ancients; and which nobody deviates from, but those who want strength of genius to make a thought shine in its own natural beauties. Poets who want this strength of genius to give that majestic simplicity to nature, which we so much admire in the works of the ancients, are forced to hunt after foreign ornaments, and not to let any piece of wit of what kind soever escape them. I look upon these writers as Goths in poetry, who, like those in architecture, not being able to come up to the beautiful simplicity of the old Greeks and Romans, have endeavored to supply its place with all the extravagances of an irregular fancy. Mr. Dryden makes a very handsome observation on Ovid's writing a letter from Dido to Aeneas, in the following words:[4] "Ovid" (says he, speaking of Virgil's fiction of Dido and Aeneas) "takes it up after him, even in the same age, and makes an ancient

1. Adapted from Dryden's "Apology for Heroic Poetry."
2. Hellenic mathematician (ca. 300 B.C.E.).
3. Dominique Bouhours (1628–1702), who wrote

Art of Criticism.
4. From Dryden's dedication to his translation of the *Aeneid* (1697).

heroine of Virgil's new-created Dido; dictates a letter for her just before her death to the ungrateful fugitive; and, very unluckily for himself, is for measuring a sword with a man so much superior in force to him, on the same subject. I think I may be judge of this, because I have translated both. The famous author of the Art of Love[5] has nothing of his own; he borrows all from a greater master in his own profession, and, which is worse, improves nothing which he finds: nature fails him, and being forced to his old shift, he has recourse to witticism. This passes indeed with his soft admirers, and gives him the preference to Virgil in their esteem."

Were not I supported by so great an authority as that of Mr. Dryden, I should not venture to observe that the taste of most of our English poets, as well as readers, is extremely Gothic. He quotes Monsieur Segrais for a threefold distinction of the readers of poetry: in the first of which he comprehends the rabble of readers, whom he does not treat as such with regard to their quality,[6] but to their numbers and the coarseness of their taste. His words are as follow: "Segrais has distinguished the readers of poetry, according to their capacity of judging, into three classes. [He might have said the same of writers too, if he had pleased.] In the lowest form he places those whom he calls *les petits esprits*,[7] such things as are our upper-gallery audience in a play-house; who like nothing but the husk and rind of wit, prefer a quibble, a conceit, an epigram, before solid sense and elegant expression: these are mob-readers. If Virgil and Martial stood for parliament-men, we know already who would carry it.[8] But though they make the greatest appearance in the field, and cry the loudest, the best on 't is they are but a sort of French Huguenots, or Dutch boors,[9] brought over in herds, but not naturalized; who have not lands of two pounds per annum in Parnassus, and therefore are not privileged to poll.[1] Their authors are of the same level, fit to represent them on a mountebank's stage, or to be masters of the ceremonies in a bear-garden:[2] yet these are they who have the most admirers. But it often happens, to their mortification, that as their readers improve their stock of sense (as they may by reading better books, and by conversation with men of judgment), they soon forsake them."

I must not dismiss this subject without observing, that as Mr. Locke in the passage above-mentioned has discovered the most fruitful source of wit, so there is another of a quite contrary nature to it, which does likewise branch itself out into several kinds. For not only the resemblance but the opposition of ideas does very often produce wit; as I could show in several little points, turns, and antitheses, that I may possibly enlarge upon in some future speculation.[3]

---

5. Ovid.
6. Social standing. Jean Regnauld de Segrais (1624–1701), who had translated Virgil into French, is quoted extensively by Dryden.
7. The small minded (French).
8. I.e., the witty Martial would easily defeat the weighty Virgil in an election.
9. Peasants. Huguenots and the Dutch were the largest class of immigrants in England. "On 't": that one can say.
1. Vote. Only freeholders worth £2 a year could go to the polls, and these readers of little taste hold no land in Parnassus (where the Muses live).
2. Place for bearbaiting and other violent exhibitions.
3. For such an "enlargement," see Samuel Johnson's remarks on wit in the life of Cowley (p. 2947).

ADDISON: [*Paradise Lost*: General Critical Remarks]

The Spectator, No. 267, Saturday, January 5, 1712

Cedite Romani scriptores, cedite Graii.[1]
—PROPERTIUS, *Elegies* 2.34.65

There is nothing in nature so irksome as general discourses, especially when they turn chiefly upon words. For this reason I shall waive the discussion of that point which was started some years since, Whether Milton's *Paradise Lost* may be called an heroic poem? Those who will not give it that title may call it (if they please) a *divine poem*. It will be sufficient to its perfection, if it has in it all the beauties of the highest kind of poetry; and as for those who allege it is not an heroic poem, they advance no more to the diminution of it, than if they should say Adam is not Aeneas, nor Eve Helen.

I shall therefore examine it by the rules of epic poetry,[2] and see whether it falls short of the *Iliad* or *Aeneid*, in the beauties which are essential to that kind of writing. The first thing to be considered in an epic poem is the fable,[3] which is perfect or imperfect, according as the action which it relates is more or less so. This action should have three qualifications in it. First, it should be but one action. Secondly, it should be an entire action; and thirdly, it should be a great action. To consider the action of the *Iliad, Aeneid,* and *Paradise Lost,* in these three several lights. Homer to preserve the unity of his action hastens into the midst of things, as Horace has observed:[4] had he gone up to Leda's egg, or begun much later, even at the rape of Helen, or the investing of Troy, it is manifest that the story of the poem would have been a series of several actions. He therefore opens his poem with the discord of his princes, and with great art interweaves in the several succeeding parts of it, an account of everything material which relates to them and had passed before that fatal dissension. After the same manner Aeneas makes his first appearance in the Tyrrhene seas, and within sight of Italy, because the action proposed to be celebrated was that of his settling himself in Latium.[5] But because it was necessary for the reader to know what had happened to him in the taking of Troy, and in the preceding parts of his voyage, Virgil makes his hero relate it by way of episode[6] in the second and third books of the *Aeneid*. The contents of both which books come before those of the first book in the thread of the story, though for preserving of this unity of action, they follow them in the disposition of the poem. Milton, in imitation of these two great poets, opens his *Paradise Lost* with an infernal council plotting the fall of man, which is the action he proposed to celebrate; and as for those great

---

1. Yield place, ye Roman and ye Grecian writers, yield (Latin).
2. The rules for the conduct of an epic poem—derived out of the poems of Homer and Virgil, the *Poetics* of Aristotle, and the *Art of Poetry* of Horace—had been given their most systematic and complete statement in Père René Le Bossu's *Traité du poème épique* (1675), which was immediately absorbed into English critical thought. Addison writes of *Paradise Lost* with Le Bossu well in sight, but he is no slavish disciple.
3. The plot of a drama or poem.
4. *Art of Poetry*, 147–49. Helen, whose abduction from her husband Menelaus by the Trojan prince

Paris brought on the Trojan War, was the daughter of Leda, who was visited by Zeus in the guise of a swan.
5. The kingdom of the Latini, where Aeneas was hospitably received when he landed at the mouth of the Tiber. He married Lavinia, the daughter of King Latinus, and later ruled the kingdom. "Tyrrhene seas": that part of the Mediterranean west of Italy, bounded by the islands of Sicily, Sardinia, and Corsica.
6. An incidental narration or digression in an epic that arises naturally from the subject but is separable from the main action.

actions which preceded in point of time, the battle of the angels, and the creation of the world (which would have entirely destroyed the unity of his principal action, had he related them in the same order that they happened), he cast them into the fifth, sixth, and seventh books, by way of episode to this noble poem.

Aristotle himself allows that Homer has nothing to boast of as to the unity of his fable, though at the same time that great critic and philosopher endeavors to palliate this imperfection in the Greek poet, by imputing it in some measure to the very nature of an epic poem. Some have been of opinion that the *Aeneid* labors also in this particular, and has episodes which maybe looked upon as excrescences rather than as parts of the action. On the contrary, the poem which we have now under our consideration hath no other episodes than such as naturally arise from the subject, and yet is filled with such a multitude of astonishing incidents that it gives us at the same time a pleasure of the greatest variety, and of the greatest simplicity.

I must observe also that as Virgil, in the poem which was designed to celebrate the original of the Roman Empire, has described the birth of its great rival, the Carthaginian commonwealth, Milton with the like art in his poem on the Fall of Man, has related the fall of those angels who are his professed enemies. Besides the many other beauties in such an episode, its running parallel with the great action of the poem hinders it from breaking the unity so much as another episode would have done that had not so great an affinity with the principal subject. In short, this is the same kind of beauty which the critics admire in the *Spanish Friar, or The Double Discovery*,[7] where the two different plots look like counterparts and copies of one another.

The second qualification required in the action of an epic poem is that it should be an *entire* action. An action is entire when it is complete in all its parts; or as Aristotle describes it, when it consists of a beginning, a middle, and an end. Nothing should go before it, be intermixed with it, or follow after it, that is not related to it. As on the contrary, no single step should be omitted in that just and regular process which it must be supposed to take from its original to its consummation. Thus, we see the anger of Achilles in its birth, its continuance, and effects; and Aeneas's settlement in Italy, carried on through all the oppositions in his way to it both by sea and land. The action in Milton excels (I think) both the former in this particular: we see it contrived in hell, executed upon earth, and punished by heaven. The parts of it are told in the most distinct manner, and grow out of one another in the most natural method.

The third qualification of an epic poem is its *greatness*. The anger of Achilles was of such consequence that it embroiled the kings of Greece, destroyed the heroes of Troy, and engaged all the gods in factions. Aeneas's settlement in Italy produced the Caesars, and gave birth to the Roman Empire. Milton's subject was still greater than either of the former; it does not determine the fate of single persons or nations, but of a whole species. The united powers of hell are joined together for the destruction of mankind, which they effected in part, and would have completed, had not Omnipotence itself interposed. The principal actors are man in his greatest perfection, and woman in her highest beauty. Their enemies are the fallen angels: the Messiah their friend,

---

7. A comedy by Dryden.

and the Almighty their protector. In short, everything that is great in the whole circle of being, whether within the verge of nature, or out of it, has a proper part assigned it in this noble poem.

In poetry, as in architecture, not only the whole, but the principal members, and every part of them, should be great. I will not presume to say, that the book of games in the *Aeneid*, or that in the *Iliad*, are not of this nature, nor to reprehend Virgil's simile of the top,[8] and many other of the same nature in the *Iliad*, as liable to any censure in this particular; but I think we may say, without derogating from those wonderful performances, that there is an unquestionable magnificence in every part of *Paradise Lost*, and indeed a much greater than could have been formed upon any pagan system.

But Aristotle, by the greatness of the action, does not only mean that it should be great in its nature, but also in its duration, or in other words, that it should have a due length in it, as well as what we properly call greatness. The just measure of the kind of magnitude he explains by the following similitude. An animal no bigger than a mite cannot appear perfect to the eye, because the sight takes it in at once, and has only a confused idea of the whole, and not a distinct idea of all its parts: if on the contrary you should suppose an animal of ten thousand furlongs in length, the eye would be so filled with a single part of it, that it would not give the mind an idea of the whole. What these animals are to the eye, a very short or a very long action would be to the memory. The first would be, as it were, lost and swallowed up by it, and the other difficult to be contained in it. Homer and Virgil have shown their principal art in this particular; the action of the *Iliad*, and that of the *Aeneid*, were in themselves exceeding short, but are so beautifully extended and diversified by the invention of episodes, and the machinery[9] of gods, with the like poetical ornaments, that they make up an agreeable story sufficient to employ the memory without overcharging it. Milton's action is enriched with such a variety of circumstances that I have taken as much pleasure in reading the contents of his books as in the best invented story I ever met with. It is possible that the traditions on which the *Iliad* and *Aeneid* were built had more circumstances in them than the history of the Fall of Man, as it is related in Scripture. Besides it was easier for Homer and Virgil to dash the truth with fiction, as they were in no danger of offending the religion of their country by it. But as for Milton, he had not only a very few circumstances upon which to raise his poem, but was also obliged to proceed with the greatest caution in everything that he added out of his own invention. And, indeed, notwithstanding all the restraints he was under, he has filled his story with so many surprising incidents, which bear so close an analogy with what is delivered in Holy Writ, that it is capable of pleasing the most delicate reader, without giving offense to the most scrupulous.

The modern critics have collected from several hints in the *Iliad* and *Aeneid* the space of time which is taken up by the action of each of these poems; but as a great part of Milton's story was transacted in regions that lie out of the reach of the sun and the sphere of day, it is impossible to gratify the reader with such a calculation, which indeed would be more

---

8. In book VII of the *Aeneid*, Virgil compares Amata, enraged at the engagement of her daughter to Aeneas, to a top whipped by young boys.
9. The technical term (from *deus ex machina*) in critical theory for the supernatural beings who oversee and intervene in the affairs of the characters in epic poems.

curious than instructive; none of the critics, either ancient or modern, having laid down rules to circumscribe the action of an epic poem with any determined number of years, days, or hours.

This Piece of Criticism on Milton's Paradise Lost *shall be carried on in the following Saturdays' papers.*[1]

ADDISON: [The Pleasures of the Imagination]

The Spectator, No. 411, Saturday, June 21, 1712

> *Avia Pieridum peragro loca, nullius ante*
> *Trita solo; juvat integros accedere fonts [fonteis];*
> *Atque haurire:. . .*
> —LUCRETIUS, *De Rerum Natura,* 1.926–8[1]

Our sight is the most perfect and most delightful of all our senses. It fills the mind with the largest variety of ideas, converses with its objects at the greatest distance, and continues the longest in action without being tired or satiated with its proper enjoyments. The sense of feeling can indeed give us a notion of extension, shape, and all other ideas that enter at the eye, except colors; but at the same time it is very much straitened and confined in its operations, to the number, bulk, and distance of its particular objects. Our sight seems designed to supply all these defects, and may be considered as a more delicate and diffusive kind of touch, that spreads itself over an infinite multitude of bodies, comprehends the largest figures, and brings into our reach some of the most remote parts of the universe.

It is this sense which furnishes the imagination with its ideas; so that by the pleasures of the imagination or fancy (which I shall use promiscuously[2]) I here mean such as arise from visible objects, either when we have them actually in our view or when we call up their ideas into our minds by paintings, statues, descriptions, or any the like occasion. We cannot indeed have a single image in the fancy that did not make its first entrance through the sight; but we have the power of retaining, altering, and compounding those images which we have once received into all the varieties of picture and vision that are most agreeable to the imagination; for by this faculty a man in a dungeon is capable of entertaining himself with scenes and landscapes more beautiful than any that can be found in the whole compass of nature.

There are few words in the English language which are employed in a more loose and uncircumscribed sense than those of the fancy and the imagination. I therefore thought it necessary to fix and determine the notion of these two words, as I intend to make use of them in the thread of my following speculations, that the reader may conceive rightly what is the subject which I proceed upon. I must therefore desire him to remember that by the pleasures of the imagination I mean only such pleasures as arise originally from sight, and that I divide these pleasures into two kinds: my design being first of all to discourse of those primary pleasures of the imagination which entirely proceed from such objects as are before our eyes; and in the next place to

---

1. The series on *Paradise Lost* contains eighteen essays.
1. I wander paths of the Pierides [muses] not traveled before and joy to be the first to drink at untasted springs (Latin).
2. Without discriminating between them.

speak of those secondary pleasures of the imagination which flow from the ideas of visible objects when the objects are not actually before the eye, but are called up into our memories, or formed into agreeable visions of things that are either absent or fictitious.

The pleasures of the imagination taken in their full extent are not so gross as those of sense nor so refined as those of the understanding. The last are indeed more preferable, because they are founded on some new knowledge or improvement in the mind of man; yet it must be confessed that those of the imagination are as great and as transporting as the other. A beautiful prospect delights the soul as much as a demonstration; and a description in Homer has charmed more readers than a chapter in Aristotle. Besides, the pleasures of the imagination have this advantage above those of the understanding, that they are more obvious and more easy to be acquired. It is but opening the eye, and the scene enters. The colors paint themselves on the fancy with very little attention of thought or application of mind in the beholder. We are struck, we know not how, with the symmetry of any thing we see, and immediately assent to the beauty of an object without enquiring into the particular causes and occasions of it.

A man of a polite imagination is let into a great many pleasures that the vulgar[3] are not capable of receiving. He can converse with a picture and find an agreeable companion in a statue. He meets with a secret refreshment in a description, and often feels a greater satisfaction in the prospect of fields and meadows than another does in the possession. It gives him indeed a kind of property in everything he sees, and makes the most rude, uncultivated parts of nature administer to his pleasure; so that he looks upon the world, as it were, in another light, and discovers in it a multitude of charms that conceal themselves from the generality of mankind.

There are indeed but very few who know how to be idle and innocent, or have a relish of any pleasures that are not criminal; every diversion they take is at the expense of some one virtue or another, and their very first step out of business is into vice or folly. A man should endeavor, therefore, to make the sphere of his innocent pleasures as wide as possible, that he may retire into them with safety, and find in them such a satisfaction as a wise man would not blush to take. Of this nature are those of the imagination, which do not require such a bent of thought as is necessary to our more serious employments, nor at the same time suffer the mind to sink into that negligence and remissness which are apt to accompany our more sensual delights, but, like a gentle exercise to the faculties, awaken them from sloth and idleness without putting them upon any labor or difficulty.

We might here add that the pleasures of the fancy are more conducive to health than those of the understanding, which are worked out by dint of thinking and attended with too violent a labor of the brain. Delightful scenes, whether in nature, painting, or poetry, have a kindly influence on the body as well as the mind, and not only serve to clear and brighten the imagination but are able to disperse grief and melancholy, and to set the animal spirits[4] in pleasing and agreeable motions. For this reason Sir Francis Bacon in his Essay upon Health[5] has not thought it improper to prescribe to his reader a poem or

---

3. The ordinary sort of person. "Polite": cultivated, refined.
4. Principle of animating bodily energy.

5. Bacon's Essay 30, "Of Regiment of Health," appeared in his *Essays* (1597).

a prospect, where he particularly dissuades him from knotty and subtle disquisitions, and advises him to pursue studies that fill the mind with splendid and illustrious objects, as histories, fables, and contemplations of nature.

I have in this paper, by way of introduction, settled the notion of those pleasures of the imagination which are the subject of my present undertaking, and endeavored by several considerations to recommend to my reader the pursuit of those pleasures. I shall in my next paper examine the several sources from whence these pleasures are derived.[6]

ADDISON: [On the Scale of Being]

The Spectator, No. 519, October 25, 1712

Inde hominum pecudumque genus, vitaeque volantum,
Et quae marmoreo fert monstra sub aequore pontus.[1]
—VIRGIL, *Aeneid* 6.728–29

Though there is a great deal of pleasure in contemplating the material world, by which I mean that system of bodies into which nature has so curiously wrought the mass of dead matter, with the several relations which those bodies bear to one another, there is still, methinks, something more wonderful and surprising in contemplations on the world of life, by which I mean all those animals with which every part of the universe is furnished. The material world is only the shell of the universe: the world of life are its inhabitants.

If we consider those parts of the material world which lie the nearest to us and are, therefore, subject to our observations and inquiries, it is amazing to consider the infinity of animals with which it is stocked. Every part of matter is peopled. Every green leaf swarms with inhabitants. There is scarce a single humor in the body of a man, or of any other animal, in which our glasses[2] do not discover myriads of living creatures. The surface of animals is also covered with other animals which are, in the same manner, the basis of other animals that live upon it; nay, we find in the most solid bodies, as in marble itself, innumerable cells and cavities that are crowded with such imperceptible inhabitants as are too little for the naked eye to discover. On the other hand, if we look into the more bulky parts of nature, we see the seas, lakes, and rivers teeming with numberless kinds of living creatures. We find every mountain and marsh, wilderness and wood, plentifully stocked with birds and beasts, and every part of matter affording proper necessaries and conveniences for the livelihood of multitudes which inhabit it.

The author of *The Plurality of Worlds*[3] draws a very good argument upon this consideration for the peopling of every planet, as indeed it seems very probable from the analogy of reason that, if no part of matter which we are

---

6. Addison wrote eleven papers on various aspects of the pleasures of the imagination (*Spectator* nos. 411–21), of which this is first.
1. Thence the race of men and beasts, the life of flying creatures, and the monsters that ocean bears beneath her smooth surface (Latin).
2. Microscopes. "Humor": fluid.

3. Bernard de Fontenelle (1657–1757). This popular book, a series of dialogues between a scientist and a countess concerning the possibility of other inhabited planets and the new astrophysics in general, was published in 1686 in France and was translated in 1688 by both John Glanvill and Aphra Behn.

acquainted with lies waste and useless, those great bodies, which are at such a distance from us, should not be desert and unpeopled, but rather that they should be furnished with beings adapted to their respective situations.

Existence is a blessing to those beings only which are endowed with perception and is, in a manner, thrown away upon dead matter any further than as it is subservient to beings which are conscious of their existence. Accordingly, we find from the bodies which lie under our observation that matter is only made as the basis and support of animals and that there is no more of the one than what is necessary for the existence of the other.

Infinite Goodness is of so communicative a nature that it seems to delight in the conferring of existence upon every degree of perceptive being. As this is a speculation which I have often pursued with great pleasure to myself, I shall enlarge farther upon it, by considering that part of the scale of beings which comes within our knowledge.

There are some living creatures which are raised but just above dead matter. To mention only that species of shellfish, which are formed in the fashion of a cone, that grow to the surface of several rocks and immediately die upon their being severed from the place where they grow. There are many other creatures but one remove from these, which have no other sense besides that of feeling and taste. Others have still an additional one of hearing; others of smell, and others of sight. It is wonderful to observe by what a gradual progress the world of life advances through a prodigious variety of species before a creature is formed that is complete in all its senses; and, even among these, there is such a different degree of perfection in the sense which one animal enjoys, beyond what appears in another, that, though the sense in different animals be distinguished by the same common denomination, it seems almost of a different nature. If after this we look into the several inward perfections of cunning and sagacity, or what we generally call instinct, we find them rising after the same manner, imperceptibly, one above another, and receiving additional improvements, according to the species in which they are implanted. This progress in nature is so very gradual that the most perfect of an inferior species comes very near to the most imperfect of that which is immediately above it.

The exuberant and overflowing goodness of the Supreme Being, whose mercy extends to all his works, is plainly seen, as I have before hinted, from his having made so very little matter, at least what falls within our knowledge, that does not swarm with life. Nor is his goodness less seen in the diversity than in the multitude of living creatures. Had he only made one species of animals, none of the rest would have enjoyed the happiness of existence; he has, therefore, *specified* in his creation every degree of life, every capacity of being. The whole chasm in nature, from a plant to a man, is filled up with diverse kinds of creatures, rising one over another by such a gentle and easy ascent that the little transitions and deviations from one species to another are almost insensible. This intermediate space is so well husbanded and managed that there is scarce a degree of perception which does not appear in some one part of the world of life. Is the goodness or wisdom of the Divine Being more manifested in this his proceeding?

There is a consequence, besides those I have already mentioned, which seems very naturally deducible from the foregoing considerations. If the scale of being rises by such a regular progress so high as man, we may by a parity of reason[4] suppose that it still proceeds gradually through those beings which are of a superior nature to him, since there is an infinitely greater space and room for different degrees of perfection between the Supreme Being and man than between man and the most despicable insect. This consequence of so great a variety of beings which are superior to us, from that variety which is inferior to us, is made by Mr. Locke[5] in a passage which I shall here set down after having premised that, notwithstanding there is such infinite room between man and his Maker for the creative power to exert itself in, it is impossible that it should ever be filled up, since there will be still an infinite gap or distance between the highest created being and the Power which produced him:

> That there should be more species of intelligent creatures above us than there are of sensible and material below, is probable to me from hence: That in all the visible corporeal world we see no chasms or no gaps. All quite down from us, the descent is by easy steps and a continued series of things that, in each remove, differ very little from the other. There are fishes that have wings and are not strangers to the airy region; and there are some birds that are inhabitants of the water, whose blood is cold as fishes and their flesh so like in taste that the scrupulous are allowed them on fish days.[6] There are animals so near of kin both to birds and beasts that they are in the middle between both: amphibious animals link the terrestrial and aquatic together; seals live at land and at sea, and porpoises have the warm blood and entrails of a hog, not to mention what is confidently reported of mermaids or seamen. There are some brutes that seem to have as much knowledge and reason as some that are called men; and the animal and vegetable kingdoms are so nearly joined that, if you will take the lowest of one and the highest of the other, there will scarce be perceived any great difference between them; and so on, till we come to the lowest and the most inorganical parts of matter, we shall find everywhere that the several species are linked together and differ but in almost insensible degrees. And when we consider the infinite power and wisdom of the Maker, we have reason to think that it is suitable to the magnificent harmony of the universe and the great design and infinite goodness of the Architect, that the species of creatures should also, by gentle degrees, ascend upward from us toward his infinite perfection, as we see they gradually descend from us downward; which, if it be probable, we have reason to be persuaded that there are far more species of creatures above us than there are beneath, we being in degrees of perfection much more remote from the infinite being of God than we are from the lowest state of being and that which approaches nearest to nothing. And yet of all those distinct species we have no clear distinct ideas.

In this system of being, there is no creature so wonderful in its nature, and which so much deserves our particular attention, as man, who fills up the middle space between the animal and intellectual nature, the visible and

---

4. A reasonable analogy or equivalence.
5. John Locke, in his *Essay Concerning Human Understanding*, 3.6.12.
6. Days of religious observance when fish instead of meat is eaten.

invisible world, and is that link in the chain of beings which has been often termed the *nexus utriusque mundi*.[7] So that he who, in one respect, is associated with angels and archangels, may look upon a Being of infinite perfection as his father, and the highest order of spirits as his brethren, may, in another respect, say to corruption, "Thou art my father," and to the worm, "Thou art my mother and my sister."[8]

7. The binding together of both worlds (Latin).   8. Job 17.14.

ALEXANDER POPE
1688–1744

Alexander Pope is the only important writer of his generation who was solely a man of letters. Because he could not, as a Roman Catholic, attend a university, vote, or hold public office, he was excluded from the sort of patronage that was bestowed by statesmen on many writers during the reign of Anne. This disadvantage he turned into a positive good, for the translation of Homer's *Iliad* and *Odyssey*, which he undertook for profit as well as for fame, gave him ample means to live the life of an independent suburban gentleman. After 1718 he lived hospitably in his villa by the Thames at Twickenham (then pronounced *Twit'nam*), entertaining his friends and converting his five acres of land into a diminutive landscape garden. Almost exactly a century earlier, William Shakespeare had earned enough to retire to a country estate at Stratford—but he had been an actor-manager as well as a playwright; Pope was the first English writer to build a lucrative, lifelong career by publishing his works.

Ill health plagued Pope almost from birth. Crippled early by tuberculosis of the bone, he never grew taller than four and a half feet. In later life he suffered from violent headaches and required constant attention from servants. But Pope did not allow his infirmities to hold him back; he was always a master at making the best of what he had. Around 1700 his father, a well-to-do, retired London merchant, moved to a small property at Binfield in Windsor Forest. There, in rural surroundings, young Pope completed his education by reading whatever he pleased, "like a boy gathering flowers in the woods and fields just as they fall in his way"; and there, encouraged by his father, he began to write verse. He was already an accomplished poet in his teens; no English poet has ever been more precocious.

Pope's first striking success as a poet was *An Essay on Criticism*. (1711), which brought him Joseph Addison's approval and an intemperate personal attack from the critic John Dennis, who was angered by a casual reference to himself in the poem. *The Rape of the Lock*, both in its original shorter version of 1712 and in its more elaborate version of 1714, proved the author a master not only of metrics and of language but also of witty, urbane satire. In *An Essay on Criticism*, Pope had excelled all his predecessors in writing a didactic poem after the example of Horace; in the *Rape*, he had written the most brilliant mock epic in the language. But there was another vein in Pope's youthful poetry, a tender concern with natural beauty and love. The *Pastorals* (1709), his first publication, and *Windsor Forest* (1713; much of it was written earlier) abound in visual imagery and descriptive passages of ideally ordered nature; they remind us that Pope was an amateur painter. The "Elegy to the Memory of an Unfortunate Lady" and *Eloisa to Abelard,* published in the collected poems of 1717, dwell on the pangs of unhappy lovers (Pope himself never married). And even the long task of translating Homer, the "dull duty" of editing Shakespeare, and, in middle age, his dedication to ethical and satirical poetry did not make less fine his keen sense of beauty in nature and art.

Pope's early poetry brought him to the attention of literary men, with whom he began to associate in the masculine world of coffeehouse and tavern, where he liked to play the rake. Between 1706 and 1711 he came to know, among many others, William Congreve; William Walsh, the critic and poet; and Richard Steele and Joseph Addison. As it happened, all were Whigs. Pope could readily ignore politics in the excitement of taking his place among the leading wits of the town. But after the fall of the Whigs in 1710 and the formation of the Tory government under Robert Harley (later the earl of Oxford) and Henry St. John (later Viscount Bolingbroke), party loyalties bred bitterness among the wits as among the politicians. By 1712, Pope had made the acquaintance of another group of writers, all Tories, who were soon his intimate friends: Jonathan Swift, by then the close associate of Harley and St. John and the principal propagandist for their policies; Dr. John Arbuthnot, physician to the queen, a learned scientist, a wit, and a man of humanity and integrity; John Gay, the poet, who in 1728 was to create *The Beggar's Opera,* the greatest theatrical success of the century; and the poet Thomas Parnell. Through them he became the friend and admirer of Oxford and later the intimate of Bolingbroke. In 1714 this group, at the instigation of Pope, formed a club for satirizing all sorts of false learning. The friends proposed to write jointly the biography of a learned fool whom they named Martinus Scriblerus (Martin the Scribbler), whose life and opinions would be a running commentary on educated nonsense. Some amusing episodes were later rewritten and published as the *Memoirs of Martinus Scriblerus* (1741). The real importance of the club, however, is that it fostered a satiric temper that would be expressed in such mature works of the friends as *Gulliver's Travels, The Beggar's Opera,* and *The Dunciad.*

"The life of a wit is a warfare on earth," said Pope, generalizing from his own experience. His very success as a poet (and his astonishing precocity brought him success very early) made enemies who were to plague him in pamphlets, verse satires, and squibs in the journals throughout his entire literary career. He was attacked for his writings, his religion, and his physical deformity. Although he smarted under the jibes of his detractors, he was a fighter who struck back, always giving better than he got. Pope's literary warfare began in 1713, when he announced his intention of translating the *Iliad* and sought subscribers to a deluxe edition of the work. Subscribers came in droves, but the Whig writers who surrounded Addison at Button's Coffee House did all they could to discredit the venture. The eventual success of the first published installment of his *Iliad* in 1715 did not obliterate Pope's resentment against Addison and his "little senate"; and he took his revenge in the damaging portrait of Addison (under the name of Atticus), which was later included in the *Epistle to Dr. Arbuthnot* (1735), lines 193–214. The not unjustified attacks on Pope's edition of Shakespeare (1725) by the learned Shakespeare scholar Lewis Theobald (Pope always spelled and pronounced the name "Tibbald" in his satires) led to Theobald's appearance as king of the dunces in *The Dunciad* (1728). In this impressive poem Pope stigmatized his literary enemies as agents of all that he disliked and feared in the tendencies of his time—the vulgarization of taste and the arts consequent on the rapid growth of the reading public and the development of journalism, magazines, and other popular and cheap publications, which spread scandal, sensationalism, and political partisanship—in short the new commercial spirit of the nation that was corrupting not only the arts but, as Pope saw it, the national life itself.

In the 1730s Pope moved on to philosophical, ethical, and political subjects in *An Essay on Man,* the *Epistles to Several Persons,* and the *Imitations of Horace.* The reigns of George I and George II appeared to him, as to Swift and other Tories, a period of rapid moral, political, and cultural deterioration. The agents of decay fed on the rise of moneyed (as opposed to landed) wealth, which accounted for the political corruption encouraged by Sir Robert Walpole and the court party and the corruption of all aspects of the national life by a vulgar class of *nouveaux riches*. Pope assumed the role of the champion of traditional values: of right reason, humanistic learning, sound art, good taste, and public virtue. It was fortunate that many of his enemies happened to illustrate various degrees of unreason, pedantry, bad art, vulgar taste, and at best, indifferent morals.

The satirist traditionally deals in generally prevalent evils and generally observable human types, not with particular individuals. So too with Pope; the bulk of his satire can be read and enjoyed without much biographical information. Usually he used fictional or type names, although he most often had an individual in mind—Sappho, Atossa, Atticus, Sporus—and when he named individuals (as he consistently did in *The Dunciad*), his purpose was to raise his victims to emblems of folly and vice. To judge and censure the age, Pope also created the *I* of the satires (not identical with Alexander Pope of Twickenham). This semifictional figure is the detached observer, somewhat removed from the City, town, and court, the centers of corruption; he is the friend of the virtuous, whose friendship for him testifies to his integrity; he is fond of peace, country life, the arts, morality, and truth; and he detests their opposites that flourish in the great world. In such an age, Pope implies, it is impossible for such a man—honest, truthful, blunt—not to write satire.

Pope was a master of style. From first to last, his verse is notable for its rhythmic variety, despite the apparently rigid metrical unit—the heroic couplet—in which he wrote; for the precision of meaning and the harmony (or expressive disharmony) of his language; and for the union of maximum conciseness with maximum complexity. Variety and harmony can be observed in even so short a passage as lines 71–76 of the pastoral "Summer" (1709), lines so lyrical that, in *Semele*, Handel set them to music. In the passage quoted below (as also in the quotation that follows), only those rhetorical stresses that distort the normal iambic flow of the verse have been marked; these distortions often stem from a slight emphasis given to "you," Summer, the addressee of the passage, on the off beat. Internal pauses within the line are indicated by single and double bars, alliteration and assonance by italics.

> Óh déign to visit our *f*orsaken *s*eats,
>
> The mossy *f*ountains || and the *gr*een re*tr*eats!
>
> Where'er yóu wálk || cóol *g*áles shall *f*an the glade,
>
> Trées whére yóu sít || shall crowd into a shade:
>
> Where'er yóu tŕead || the bl*u*shing *f*lowers shall rise,
>
> And all thíngs *f*lóurish where yóu túrn your eyes.

Pope has attained metrical variety by the free substitution of trochees and spondees for the normal iambs; he has achieved rhythmic variety by arranging phrases and clauses (units of syntax and logic) of different lengths within single lines and couplets, so that the passage moves with the sinuous fluency of thought and feeling; and he not only has chosen musical combinations of words but has also subtly modulated the harmony of the passage by unobtrusive patterns of alliteration and assonance.

Contrast with this pastoral passage lines 16–25 of the "Epilogue to the Satires, Dialogue 2" (1738), in which Pope is not making music but imitating actual conversation so realistically that the metrical pattern and the integrity of the couplet and individual line seem to be destroyed (although in fact they remain in place). In a dialogue with a friend who warns him that his satire is too personal, indeed mere libel, the poet-satirist replies:

Yé státesmen, | priests of one religion all!

Yé trádesmen vile || in army, court, or hall!

Yé réverend atheists. || F. Scandal! | name them, | Who?

 P. Why that's the thing you bid me not to do.

Whó stárved a sister, || who foreswore a debt,

Í néver named; || the town's inquiring yet.

The poisoning dame—| F. Yóu méan—| P. I don't—| F. Yóu dó.

 P. Sée, nów Í kéep the secret, || and nót yóu!

The bribing statesman—| F. Hóld, || tóo hígh you go.

 P. The bribed elector—|| F. There you stoop tóo lów.

In such a passage the language and rhythms of poetry merge with the language and rhythms of impassioned living speech.

 A fine example of Pope's ability to derive the maximum of meaning from the most economic use of language and image is the description of the manor house in which lives old Cotta, the miser (*Epistle to Lord Bathurst,* lines 187–96):

> Like some lone Chartreuse stands the good old Hall,
> Silence without, and fasts within the wall;
> No raftered roofs with dance and tabor sound,
> No noontide bell invites the country round;
> Tenants with sighs the smokeless towers survey,
> And turn the unwilling steeds another way;
> Benighted wanderers, the forest o'er,
> Curse the saved candle and unopening door;
> While the gaunt mastiff growling at the gate,
> Affrights the beggar whom he longs to eat.

The first couplet of this passage associates the "Hall," symbol of English rural hospitality, with the Grande Chartreuse, the monastery in the French Alps, which, although a place of "silence" and "fasts" for the monks, afforded food and shelter to all travelers. Then the dismal details of Cotta's miserly dwelling provide a stark contrast, and the meaning of the scene is concentrated in the grotesque image of the last couplet: the half-starved watchdog and the frightened beggar confronting each other in mutual hunger.

 But another sort of variety derives from Pope's respect for the idea that the different kinds of literature have their different and appropriate styles. Thus *An Essay on Criticism,* an informal discussion of literary theory, is written, like Horace's *Art of Poetry* (a similarly didactic poem), in a plain style, the easy language of well-bred talk. *The Rape of the Lock,* "a heroi-comical poem" (that is, a comic poem that treats trivial material in an epic style), employs the lofty heroic language that John Dryden had perfected in his translation of Virgil and introduces amusing parodies of passages in *Paradise Lost,* parodies later raised to truly Miltonic sublimity and complexity by the conclusion of *The Dunciad. Eloisa to Abelard* renders the brooding, passionate voice of its heroine in a declamatory language, given to sudden outbursts and shifts of tone, that recalls the stage. The grave epistles that make up *An Essay on Man,* a philosophical discussion of such majestic themes as the Creator and His creation, the universe, human nature, society, and happiness, are written in a stately forensic language and tone and constantly employ the traditional rhetorical figures. The *Imitations of Horace* and, above all, the *Epistle to Dr. Arbuthnot,* his finest poem "in the Horatian way," reveal Pope's final mastery of the plain style of Horace's epistles and satires and support his image of himself as the heir of the Roman poet.

In short, no other poet of the century can equal Pope in the range of his materials, the diversity of his poetic styles, and the wizardry of his technique.

An Essay on Criticism
There is no pleasanter introduction to the canons of taste in the English Augustan age than Pope's *An Essay on Criticism*. As Addison said in his review in *Spectator* 253, it assembles the "most known and most received observations on the subject of literature and criticism." Pope was attempting to do for his time what Horace, in his *Art of Poetry*, and what Nicolas Boileau (French poet, of the age of Louis XIV), in his *L'Art Poétique*, had done for theirs. Horace is Pope's model not only for principles of criticism but also for style, especially in the simple, conversational language and the tone of well-bred ease.

In framing his critical creed, Pope did not try for novelty: he wished merely to give to generally accepted doctrines pleasing and memorable expression and make them useful to modern poets. Here one meets the key words of neoclassical criticism: *wit, Nature, ancients, rules,* and *genius. Wit* in the poem is a word of many meanings—a clever remark or the person who makes it, a conceit, liveliness of mind, inventiveness, fancy, genius, a genius, and poetry itself, among others. *Nature* is an equally ambiguous word, meaning not "things out there" or "the outdoors" but most important that which is representative, universal, permanent in human experience as opposed to the idiosyncratic, the individual, the temporary. In line 21, *Nature* comes close to meaning "intuitive knowledge." In line 52, it means that half-personified power manifested in the cosmic order, which in its modes of working is a model for art. The reverence felt by most Augustans for the great writers of ancient Greece and Rome raised the question how far the authority of these *ancients* extended. Were their works to be received as models to be conscientiously imitated? Were the *rules* received from them or deducible from their works to be accepted as prescriptive laws or merely convenient guides? Was individual *genius* to be bound by what has been conventionally held to be *Nature,* by the authority of the *ancients,* and by the legalistic pedantry of *rules*? Or could it go its own way?

In part 1 of the *Essay,* Pope constructs a harmonious system in which he effects a compromise among all these conflicting forces—a compromise that is typical of his times. Part 2 analyzes the causes of faulty criticism. Part 3 characterizes the good critic and praises the great critics of the past.

An Essay on Criticism

Part 1

'Tis hard to say, if greater want of skill
Appear in writing or in judging ill;
But of the two less dangerous is the offense
To tire our patience than mislead our sense.
5 Some few in that, but numbers err in this,
Ten censure° wrong for one who writes amiss;   *judge*
A fool might once himself alone expose,
Now one in verse makes many more in prose.
   'Tis with our judgments as our watches, none
10 Go just alike, yet each believes his own.
In poets as true genius is but rare,
True taste as seldom is the critic's share;
Both must alike from Heaven derive their light,

These born to judge, as well as those to write.
15 Let such teach others who themselves excel,
And censure freely who have written well.
Authors are partial to their wit, 'tis true,
But are not critics to their judgment too?
Yet if we look more closely, we shall find
20 Most have the seeds of judgment in their mind:
Nature affords at least a glimmering light;
The lines, though touched but faintly, are drawn right.
But as the slightest sketch, if justly traced, ⎤
Is by ill coloring but the more disgraced, ⎬
25 So by false learning is good sense defaced: ⎦
Some are bewildered in the maze of schools,
And some made coxcombs[1] Nature meant but fools.
In search of wit these lose their common sense,
And then turn critics in their own defense:
30 Each burns alike, who can, or cannot write,
Or with a rival's or an eunuch's spite.
All fools have still an itching to deride,
And fain would be upon the laughing side.
If Maevius[2] scribble in Apollo's spite,
35 There are who judge still worse than he can write.
    Some have at first for wits, then poets passed,
Turned critics next, and proved plain fools at last.
Some neither can for wits nor critics pass,
As heavy mules are neither horse nor ass.
40 Those half-learn'd witlings, numerous in our isle,
As half-formed insects on the banks of Nile;[3]
Unfinished things, one knows not what to call,
Their generation's so equivocal:
To tell° them would a hundred tongues require,   reckon, count
45 Or one vain wit's, that might a hundred tire.
    But you who seek to give and merit fame,
And justly bear a critic's noble name,
Be sure yourself and your own reach to know,
How far your genius, taste, and learning go;
50 Launch not beyond your depth, but be discreet,
And mark that point where sense and dullness meet.
    Nature to all things fixed the limits fit,
And wisely curbed proud man's pretending° wit.   aspiring
As on the land while here the ocean gains,
55 In other parts it leaves wide sandy plains;
Thus in the soul while memory prevails,
The solid power of understanding fails;
Where beams of warm imagination play,
The memory's soft figures melt away.
60 One science° only will one genius fit,   branch of learning
So vast is art, so narrow human wit.
Not only bounded to peculiar arts,

---

1. Superficial pretenders to learning.
2. A silly poet alluded to contemptuously by Virgil in *Eclogue* 3 and by Horace in *Epode* 10.

3. The ancients believed that many forms of life were spontaneously generated in the fertile mud of the Nile.

But oft in those confined to single parts.
Like kings we lose the conquests gained before,
65 By vain ambition still to make them more;
Each might his several province well command,
Would all but stoop to what they understand.
    First follow Nature, and your judgment frame
By her just standard, which is still the same;
70 Unerring Nature, still divinely bright,
One clear, unchanged, and universal light,
Life, force, and beauty must to all impart,
At once the source, and end, and test of art.
Art from that fund each just supply provides,
75 Works without show, and without pomp presides.
In some fair body thus the informing soul
With spirits feeds, with vigor fills the whole,
Each motion guides, and every nerve sustains;
Itself unseen, but in the effects remains.
80 Some, to whom Heaven in wit has been profuse,
Want as much more to turn it to its use;
For wit and judgment often are at strife,
Though meant each other's aid, like man and wife.
'Tis more to guide than spur the Muse's steed,
85 Restrain his fury than provoke his speed;
The wingèd courser,[4] like a generous° horse,   spirited, highly bred
Shows most true mettle when you check his course.
    Those rules of old discovered, not devised,
Are Nature still, but Nature methodized;
90 Nature, like liberty, is but restrained
By the same laws which first herself ordained.
    Hear how learn'd Greece her useful rules indites,
When to repress and when indulge our flights:
High on Parnassus' top her sons she showed,
95 And pointed out those arduous paths they trod;
Held from afar, aloft, the immortal prize,
And urged the rest by equal steps to rise.
Just precepts thus from great examples given,
She drew from them what they derived from Heaven.
100 The generous critic fanned the poet's fire,
And taught the world with reason to admire.
Then criticism the Muse's handmaid proved,
To dress her charms, and make her more beloved:
But following wits from that intention strayed,
105 Who could not win the mistress, wooed the maid;
Against the poets their own arms they turned,
Sure to hate most the men from whom they learned.
So modern 'pothecaries, taught the art
By doctors's bills° to play the doctor's part,   prescriptions
110 Bold in the practice of mistaken rules,
Prescribe, apply, and call their masters fools.
Some on the leaves of ancient authors prey,

---

4. Pegasus, associated with the Muses and poetic inspiration.

Nor time nor moths e'er spoiled so much as they.
Some dryly plain, without invention's aid,
115 Write dull receipts[5] how poems may be made.
These leave the sense their learning to display,
And those explain the meaning quite away.
     You then whose judgment the right course would steer,
Know well each ancient's proper character;
120 His fable,[6] subject, scope° in every page;   aim, purpose
Religion, country, genius of his age:
Without all these at once before your eyes,
Cavil you may, but never criticize.
Be Homer's works your study and delight,
125 Read them by day, and meditate by night;
Thence form your judgment, thence your maxims bring,
And trace the Muses upward to their spring.
Still with itself compared, his text peruse;
And let your comment be the Mantuan Muse.
130   When first young Maro[7] in his boundless mind
A work to outlast immortal Rome designed,
Perhaps he seemed above the critic's law,
And but from Nature's fountains scorned to draw;
But when to examine every part he came,
135 Nature and Homer were, he found, the same.
Convinced, amazed, he checks the bold design, ⎤
And rules as strict his labored work confine ⎬
As if the Stagirite[8] o'erlooked each line.   ⎦
Learn hence for ancient rules a just esteem;
140 To copy Nature is to copy them.
     Some beauties yet no precepts can declare,
For there's a happiness as well as care.[9]
Music resembles poetry, in each   ⎤
Are nameless graces which no methods teach, ⎬
145 And which a master hand alone can reach. ⎦
If, where the rules not far enough extend
(Since rules were made but to promote their end)
Some lucky license answers to the full
The intent proposed, that license is a rule.
150 Thus Pegasus, a nearer way to take,
May boldly deviate from the common track.
Great wits sometimes may gloriously offend,
And rise to faults true critics dare not mend;
From vulgar bounds with brave disorder part,
155 And snatch a grace beyond the reach of art,
Which, without passing through the judgment, gains

---

5. Formulas for preparing a dish; recipes. Pope himself wrote an amusing burlesque, "Receipt to Make an Epic Poem," first published in the *Guardian* 78 (1713).
6. Plot or story of a play or poem.
7. Virgil, who was born in a village adjacent to Mantua in Italy, hence "Mantuan Muse." His epic, the *Aeneid,* was modeled on Homer's *Iliad* and *Odyssey* and was considered to be a refinement, of the Greek poems. Thus it could be thought of as a

commentary ("comment") on Homer's poems.
8. Aristotle, a native of Stagira, from whose *Poetics* later critics formulated strict rules for writing tragedy and the epic.
9. I.e., no rules ("precepts") can explain ("declare") some beautiful effects in a work of art that can be the result only of inspiration or good luck ("happiness"), not of painstaking labor ("care").

The heart, and all its end at once attains.
In prospects thus, some objects please our eyes,   }
Which out of Nature's common order rise,
160 The shapeless rock, or hanging precipice.
But though the ancients thus their rules invade°   *violate*
(As kings dispense with laws themselves have made)
Moderns, beware! or if you must offend
Against the precept, ne'er transgress its end;
165 Let it be seldom, and compelled by need;
And have at least their precedent to plead.
The critic else proceeds without remorse,
Seizes your fame, and puts his laws in force.
     I know there are, to whose presumptuous thoughts
170 Those freer beauties, even in them, seem faults.[1]
Some figures monstrous and misshaped appear,
Considered singly, or beheld too near,
Which, but proportioned to their light or place,
Due distance reconciles to form and grace.
175 A prudent chief not always must display
His powers in equal ranks and fair array,
But with the occasion and the place comply,
Conceal his force, nay seem sometimes to fly.
Those oft are stratagems which errors seem,
180 Nor is it Homer nods, but we that dream.
     Still green with bays each ancient altar stands
Above the reach of sacrilegious hands,
Secure from flames, from envy's fiercer rage,
Destructive war, and all-involving age.
185 See, from each clime the learn'd their incense bring!
Here in all tongues consenting° paeans ring!   *agreeing, concurring*
In praise so just let every voice be joined,[2]
And fill the general chorus of mankind.
Hail, bards triumphant! born in happier days,
190 Immortal heirs of universal praise!
Whose honors with increase of ages grow,
As streams roll down, enlarging as they flow;
Nations unborn your mighty names shall sound,
And worlds applaud that must not yet be found!
195 Oh, may some spark of your celestial fire,
The last, the meanest of your sons inspire
(That on weak wings, from far, pursues your flights,
Glows while he reads, but trembles as he writes)
To teach vain wits a science little known,
200 To admire superior sense, and doubt their own!

Part 2

     Of all the causes which conspire to blind
Man's erring judgment, and misguide the mind,
What the weak head with strongest bias rules,

---

1. Pronounced *fawts*.   2. Pronounced *jined*.

Is pride, the never-failing vice of fools.
205 Whatever Nature has in worth denied,
She gives in large recruits° of needful pride;　　　　*supplies*
For as in bodies, thus in souls, we find
What wants in blood and spirits, swelled with wind:
Pride, where wit fails, steps in to our defense,
210 And fills up all the mighty void of sense.
If once right reason drives that cloud away,
Truth breaks upon us with resistless day.
Trust not yourself: but your defects to know,
Make use of every friend—and every foe.
215　　A little learning is a dangerous thing;
Drink deep, or taste not the Pierian spring.³
There shallow draughts intoxicate the brain,
And drinking largely sobers us again.
Fired at first sight with what the Muse imparts,
220 In fearless youth we tempt° the heights of arts,　　　*attempt*
While from the bounded level of our mind
Short views we take, nor see the lengths behind;
But more advanced, behold with strange surprise
New distant scenes of endless science rise!
225 So pleased at first the towering Alps we try,
Mount o'er the vales, and seem to tread the sky,
The eternal snows appear already past,
And the first clouds and mountains seem the last;
But, those attained, we tremble to survey
230 The growing labors of the lengthened way,
The increasing prospect tires our wandering eyes,
Hills peep o'er hills, and Alps on Alps arise!
　　A perfect judge will read each work of wit
With the same spirit that its author writ:
235 Survey the whole, nor seek slight faults to find
Where Nature moves, and rapture warms the mind;
Nor lose, for that malignant dull delight,
The generous pleasure to be charmed with wit.
But in such lays as neither ebb nor flow,
240 Correctly cold, and regularly low,
That, shunning faults, one quiet tenor keep,
We cannot blame indeed—but we may sleep.
In wit, as nature, what affects our hearts
Is not the exactness of peculiar° parts;　　　　*particular*
245 'Tis not a lip, or eye, we beauty call,
But the joint force and full result of all.
Thus when we view some well-proportioned dome⁴
(The world's just wonder, and even thine, O Rome!),
No single parts unequally surprise,
250 All comes united to the admiring eyes:
No monstrous height, or breadth, or length appear;
The whole at once is bold and regular.

---

3. The spring in Pieria on Mount Olympus, sacred to the Muses.

4. The dome of St. Peter's, designed by Michelangelo.

Whoever thinks a faultless piece to see,
Thinks what ne'er was, nor is, nor e'er shall be.
255 In every work regard the writer's end,
Since none can compass more than they intend;
And if the means be just, the conduct true,
Applause, in spite of trivial faults, is due.
As men of breeding, sometimes men of wit,
260 To avoid great errors must the less commit,
Neglect the rules each verbal critic lays,
For not to know some trifles is a praise.
Most critics, fond of some subservient art,
Still make the whole depend upon a part:
265 They talk of principles, but notions prize,
And all to one loved folly sacrifice.
    Once on a time La Mancha's knight,[5] they say,
A certain bard encountering on the way,
Discoursed in terms as just, with looks as sage,
270 As e'er could Dennis,[6] of the Grecian stage;
Concluding all were desperate sots and fools
Who durst depart from Aristotle's rules.
Our author, happy in a judge so nice,
Produced his play, and begged the knight's advice;
275 Made him observe the subject and the plot,
The manners, passions, unities; what not?
All which exact to rule were brought about,
Were but a combat in the lists left out.
"What! leave the combat out?" exclaims the knight.
280 "Yes, or we must renounce the Stagirite."
"Not so, by Heaven!" he answers in a rage,
"Knights, squires, and steeds must enter on the stage."
"So vast a throng the stage can ne'er contain."
"Then build a new, or act it in a plain."
285   Thus critics of less judgment than caprice,
Curious,° not knowing, not exact, but nice,°   *laborious / fussy*
Form short ideas, and offend in arts
(As most in manners), by a love to parts.
    Some to conceit[7] alone their taste confine,
290 And glittering thoughts struck out at every line;
Pleased with a work where nothing's just or fit,
One glaring chaos and wild heap of wit.
Poets, like painters, thus unskilled to trace
The naked nature and the living grace,
295 With gold and jewels cover every part,
And hide with ornaments their want of art.
True wit is Nature to advantage dressed,
What oft was thought, but ne'er so well expressed;
Something whose truth convinced at sight we find,

---

5. Don Quixote. The story comes not from Cervantes's novel, but from a spurious sequel to it by Don Alonzo Fernandez de Avellaneda.
6. John Dennis (1657–1734), although one of the leading critics of the time, was frequently ridiculed by the wits for his irascibility and pomposity. Pope apparently did not know Dennis personally, but his jibe at him in part 3 of this poem made him a bitter enemy.
7. Pointed wit, ingenuity and extravagance, or affectation in the use of figures, especially similes and metaphors.

300   That gives us back the image of our mind.
      As shades more sweetly recommend the light,
      So modest plainness sets off sprightly wit;
      For works may have more wit than does them good,
      As bodies perish through excess of blood.
305   Others for language all their care express,
      And value books, as women men, for dress.
      Their praise is still—the style is excellent;
      The sense they humbly take upon content.°   mere acquiescence
      Words are like leaves; and where they most abound,
310   Much fruit of sense beneath is rarely found.
      False eloquence, like the prismatic glass,
      Its gaudy colors spreads on every place;[8]
      The face of Nature we no more survey,
      All glares alike, without distinction gay.
315   But true expression, like the unchanging sun,⎤
      Clears and improves whate'er it shines upon; ⎬
      It gilds all objects, but it alters none.   ⎦
      Expression is the dress of thought, and still
      Appears more decent as more suitable.
320   A vile conceit in pompous words expressed
      Is like a clown° in regal purple dressed: country bumpkin
      For different styles with different subjects sort,
      As several garbs with country, town, and court.
      Some by old words to fame have made pretense,
325   Ancients in phrase, mere moderns in their sense.
      Such labored nothings, in so strange a style,
      Amaze the unlearn'd, and make the learned smile;
      Unlucky as Fungoso[9] in the play,   ⎤
      These sparks with awkward vanity display   ⎬
330   What the fine gentleman wore yesterday;   ⎦
      And but so mimic ancient wits at best,
      As apes our grandsires in their doublets dressed.
      In words as fashions the same rule will hold,
      Alike fantastic if too new or old:
335   Be not the first by whom the new are tried,
      Nor yet the last to lay the old aside.
         But most by numbers° judge a poet's song,   versification
      And smooth or rough with them is right or wrong.
      In the bright Muse though thousand charms conspire,
340   Her voice is all these tuneful fools admire,
      Who haunt Parnassus but to please their ear,   ⎤
      Not mend their minds; as some to church repair,⎬
      Not for the doctrine, but the music there.   ⎦
      These equal syllables alone require,
345   Though oft the ear the open vowels tire,[1]
      While expletives[2] their feeble aid do join,

8. A very up-to-date scientific reference. Newton's *Opticks,* which dealt with the prism and the
spectrum, had been published in 1704, although
his theories had been known earlier.
9. A character in Ben Jonson's comedy *Every
Man out of His Humor* (1599).

1. In lines 345–57 Pope cleverly contrives to make
his own metrics or diction illustrate the faults
that he is exposing.
2. Words used merely to achieve the necessary
number of feet in a line of verse.

And ten low words oft creep in one dull line:
While they ring round the same unvaried chimes,
With sure returns of still expected rhymes;
350 Where'er you find "the cooling western breeze,"
In the next line, it "whispers through the trees";
If crystal streams "with pleasing murmurs creep,"
The reader's threatened (not in vain) with "sleep";
Then, at the last and only couplet fraught
355 With some unmeaning thing they call a thought,
A needless Alexandrine[3] ends the song
That, like a wounded snake, drags its slow length along.
Leave such to tune their own dull rhymes, and know
What's roundly smooth or languishingly slow;
360 And praise the easy vigor of a line
Where Denham's strength and Waller's sweetness join.[4]
True ease in writing comes from art, not chance,
As those move easiest who have learned to dance.
'Tis not enough no harshness gives offense,
365 The sound must seem an echo to the sense.
Soft is the strain when Zephyr gently blows,
And the smooth stream in smoother numbers flows;
But when loud surges lash the sounding shore,
The hoarse, rough verse should like the torrent roar.
370 When Ajax strives some rock's vast weight to throw,
The line too labors, and the words move slow;
Not so when swift Camilla[5] scours the plain,
Flies o'er the unbending corn, and skims along the main.
Hear how Timotheus'[6] varied lays surprise,
375 And bid alternate passions fall and rise!
While at each change the son of Libyan Jove°   *Alexander the Great*
Now burns with glory, and then melts with love;
Now his fierce eyes with sparkling fury glow,
Now sighs steal out, and tears begin to flow:
380 Persians and Greeks like turns of nature[7] found
And the world's victor stood subdued by sound!
The power of music all our hearts allow,
And what Timotheus was, is Dryden now.
　　Avoid extremes; and shun the fault of such
385 Who still are pleased too little or too much.
At every trifle scorn to take offense:
That always shows great pride, or little sense.
Those heads, as stomachs, are not sure the best,
Which nauseate all, and nothing can digest.
390 Yet let not each gay turn thy rapture move;
For fools admire,° but men of sense approve:[8]   *wonder*
As things seem large which we through mists descry,

---

3. A line of verse containing six iambic feet; it is illustrated in the next line.
4. Dryden, whom Pope echoes here, considered Sir John Denham (1615–1669) and Edmund Waller (1606–1687) to have been the principal shapers of the closed pentameter couplet. He had distinguished the "strength" of the one and the "sweetness" of the other.
5. Fleet-footed virgin warrior (*Aeneid* 7, 11).
6. The musician in Dryden's "Alexander's Feast." Pope retells the story of that poem in the following lines.
7. Alternations of feelings.
8. Judge favorably only after due deliberation.

Dullness is ever apt to magnify.
 Some foreign writers, some our own despise;
395 The ancients only, or the moderns prize.
Thus wit, like faith, by each man is applied
To one small sect, and all are damned beside.
Meanly they seek the blessing to confine,
And force that sun but on a part to shine,
400 Which not alone the southern wit sublimes,°   *raises up, purifies*
But ripens spirits in cold northern climes;
Which from the first has shone on ages past,
Enlights the present, and shall warm the last;
Though each may feel increases and decays,
405 And see now clearer and now darker days.
Regard not then if wit be old or new,
But blame the false and value still the true.
 Some ne'er advance a judgment of their own,
But catch the spreading notion of the town;
410 They reason and conclude by precedent,
And own° stale nonsense which they ne'er invent.   *lay claim to*
Some judge of authors' names, not works, and then
Nor praise nor blame the writings, but the men.
Of all this servile herd the worst is he
415 That in proud dullness joins with quality,[9]
A constant critic at the great man's board,
To fetch and carry nonsense for my lord.
What woeful stuff this madrigal would be
In some starved hackney sonneteer° or me!   *hireling poet*
420 But let a lord once own the happy lines,
How the wit brightens! how the style refines!
Before his sacred name flies every fault,
And each exalted stanza teems with thought!
 The vulgar thus through imitation err;
425 As oft the learn'd by being singular;
So much they scorn the crowd, that if the throng
By chance go right, they purposely go wrong.
So schismatics[1] the plain believers quit,
And are but damned for having too much wit.
430 Some praise at morning what they blame at night,
But always think the last opinion right.
A Muse by these is like a mistress used,
This hour she's idolized, the next abused;
While their weak heads like towns unfortified,
435 'Twixt sense and nonsense daily change their side.
Ask them the cause; they're wiser still, they say;
And still tomorrow's wiser than today.
We think our fathers fools, so wise we grow;
Our wiser sons, no doubt, will think us so.
440 Once school divines[2] this zealous isle o'erspread;

---

9. People of high rank.
1. Those who have divided the church on points of theology. Pope stressed the first syllable, the pronunciation approved by Johnson in his *Dic-*

tionary.
2. The medieval theologians, such as the followers of Duns Scotus and St. Thomas Aquinas, mentioned below.

Who knew most sentences[3] was deepest read.
Faith, Gospel, all seemed made to be disputed,
And none had sense enough to be confuted.
Scotists and Thomists now in peace remain
445 Amidst their kindred cobwebs in Duck Lane.[4]
If faith itself has different dresses worn,
What wonder modes in wit should take their turn?
Oft, leaving what is natural and fit,
The current folly proves the ready wit;
450 And authors think their reputation safe,
Which lives as long as fools are pleased to laugh.
    Some valuing those of their own side or mind,
Still make themselves the measure of mankind:
Fondly° we think we honor merit then,   *foolishly*
455 When we but praise ourselves in other men.
Parties in wit attend on those of state,
And public faction doubles private hate.
Pride, Malice, Folly against Dryden rose,
In various shapes of parsons, critics, beaux;
460 But sense survived, when merry jests were past;
For rising merit will buoy up at last.
Might he return and bless once more our eyes,
New Blackmores and new Milbourns[5] must arise.
Nay, should great Homer lift his awful head,
465 Zoilus[6] again would start up from the dead.
Envy will merit, as its shade, pursue,
But like a shadow, proves the substance true;
For envied wit, like Sol eclipsed, makes known
The opposing body's grossness, not its own.
470 When first that sun too powerful beams displays,
It draws up vapors which obscure its rays;
But even those clouds at last adorn its way,
Reflect new glories, and augment the day.
    Be thou the first true merit to befriend;
475 His praise is lost who stays till all commend.
Short is the date, alas! of modern rhymes,
And 'tis but just to let them live betimes.°   *for a brief time*
No longer now that golden age appears,
When patriarch wits survived a thousand years:
480 Now length of fame (our second life) is lost,
And bare threescore is all even that can boast;
Our sons their fathers' failing language see,
And such as Chaucer is, shall Dryden be.[7]
So when the faithful pencil has designed
485 Some bright idea of the master's mind,

---

3. Allusion to Peter Lombard's *Book of Sentences,*
a book esteemed by Scholastic philosophers.
4. Street where publishers' remainders and secondhand books were sold.
5. Luke Milbourn had attacked Dryden's translation of Virgil. Sir Richard Blackmore, physician and poet, had attacked Dryden for the
immorality of his plays.

6. A Greek critic of the 4th century B.C.E. who
wrote a book of carping criticism of Homer.
7. The radical changes that took place in the
English language between the death of Chaucer
in 1400 and the death of Dryden in 1700 suggested that in another three hundred years
Dryden would be unintelligible.

Where a new world leaps out at his command,
And ready Nature waits upon his hand;
When the ripe colors soften and unite,
And sweetly melt into just shade and light;
490 When mellowing years their full perfection give,
And each bold figure just begins to live,
The treacherous colors the fair art betray,
And all the bright creation fades away!
Unhappy° wit, like most mistaken things,   ill-fated
495 Atones not for that envy which it brings.
In youth alone its empty praise we boast,
But soon the short-lived vanity is lost;
Like some fair flower the early spring supplies,
That gaily blooms, but even in blooming dies.
500 What is this wit, which must our cares employ?
The owner's wife, that other men enjoy;
Then most our trouble still when most admired,
And still the more we give, the more required;
Whose fame with pains we guard, but lose with ease,
505 Sure some to vex, but never all to please;
'Tis what the vicious fear, the virtuous shun,
By fools 'tis hated, and by knaves undone!
If wit so much from ignorance undergo,
Ah, let not learning too commence its foe!
510 Of old those met rewards who could excel,
And such were praised who but endeavored well;
Though triumphs were to generals only due,
Crowns were reserved to grace the soldiers too.[8]
Now they who reach Parnassus' lofty crown
515 Employ their pains to spurn° some others down;   kick
And while self-love each jealous writer rules,
Contending wits become the sport of fools;
But still the worst with most regret commend,
For each ill author is as bad a friend.
520 To what base ends, and by what abject ways,
Are mortals urged through sacred° lust of praise![9]   accursed
Ah, ne'er so dire a thirst of glory boast,
Nor in the critic let the man be lost!
Good nature and good sense must ever join;
525 To err is human, to forgive divine.
But if in noble minds some dregs remain
Not yet purged off, of spleen° and sour disdain,   rancor
Discharge that rage on more provoking crimes,
Nor fear a dearth in these flagitious° times.   scandalously wicked
530 No pardon vile obscenity should find,
Though wit and art conspire to move your mind;
But dullness with obscenity must prove
As shameful sure as impotence in love.
In the fat age of pleasure, wealth, and ease

8. To celebrate Roman victories, valiant soldiers were decorated with a variety of crowns.

9. The phrase imitates Virgil's *auri sacra famis,* "accursed hunger for gold" (*Aeneid* 3.57).

535 Sprung the rank weed, and thrived with large increase:
 When love was all an easy monarch's[1] care,
 Seldom at council, never in a war;
 Jilts[2] ruled the state, and statesmen farces writ;
 Nay, wits had pensions, and young lords had wit;
540 The fair sat panting at a courtier's play,
 And not a mask[3] went unimproved away;
 The modest fan was lifted up no more,
 And virgins smiled at what they blushed before.
 The following license of a foreign reign
545 Did all the dregs of bold Socinus[4] drain;
 Then unbelieving priests reformed the nation,
 And taught more pleasant methods of salvation;
 Where Heaven's free subjects might their rights dispute,
 Lest God himself should seem too absolute;
550 Pulpits their sacred satire learned to spare,
 And Vice admired° to find a flatterer there!   *wondered*
 Encouraged thus, wit's Titans braved the skies,
 And the press groaned with licensed blasphemies.
 These monsters, critics! with your darts engage,
555 Here point your thunder, and exhaust your rage!
 Yet shun their fault, who, scandalously nice,°   *subtle*
 Will needs mistake an author into vice;
 All seems infected that the infected spy,
 As all looks yellow to the jaundiced eye.

Part 3

560 Learn then what morals critics ought to show,
 For 'tis but half a judge's task, to know.
 'Tis not enough, taste, judgment, learning, join;
 In all you speak, let truth and candor° shine: *kindness, impartiality*
 That not alone what to your sense is due
565 All may allow; but seek your friendship too.
  Be silent always when you doubt your sense;
 And speak, though sure, with seeming diffidence:
 Some positive, persisting fops we know,
 Who, if once wrong, will needs be always so;
570 But you, with pleasure own your errors past,
 And make each day a critic° on the last.   *critique*
  'Tis not enough, your counsel still be true;
 Blunt truths more mischief than nice falsehoods do;
 Men must be taught as if you taught them not,
575 And things unknown proposed as things forgot.
 Without good breeding, truth is disapproved;
 That only makes superior sense beloved.
  Be niggards of advice on no pretense;

1. Charles II. The concluding lines of part 2 discuss the corruption of wit and poetry under this monarch.
2. Mistresses of the king.
3. A woman wearing a mask.

4. The name of two Italian theologians of the 16th century who denied the divinity of Jesus. Pope charges that freethinkers attained the upper hand during the "foreign reign" of William III, a Dutchman.

For the worst avarice is that of sense.
580 With mean complacence[5] ne'er betray your trust,
Nor be so civil as to prove unjust.
Fear not the anger of the wise to raise;
Those best can bear reproof, who merit praise.
'Twere well might critics still this freedom take;
585 But Appius reddens at each word you speak,
And stares, tremendous! with a threatening eye,
Like some fierce tyrant in old tapestry.[6]
Fear most to tax an honorable fool,
Whose right it is, uncensured to be dull;
590 Such, without wit, are poets when they please,
As without learning they can take degrees.[7]
Leave dangerous truths to unsuccessful satyrs,°   satires
And flattery to fulsome dedicators,
Whom, when they praise, the world believes no more,
595 Than when they promise to give scribbling o'er.
'Tis best sometimes your censure to restrain,
And charitably let the dull be vain:
Your silence there is better than your spite,
For who can rail so long as they can write?
600 Still humming on, their drowsy course they keep,
And lashed so long, like tops, are lashed asleep.[8]
False steps but help them to renew the race,
As, after stumbling, jades° will mend their pace.   worn-out horses
What crowds of these, impenitently bold,
605 In sounds and jingling syllables grown old,
Still run on poets, in a raging vein,
Even to the dregs and squeezings of the brain,
Strain out the last dull droppings of their sense,
And rhyme with all the rage of impotence.
610   Such shameless bards we have, and yet 'tis true,
There are as mad, abandoned critics too.
The bookful blockhead, ignorantly read,
With loads of learned lumber° in his head,   rubbish
With his own tongue still edifies his ears,
615 And always listening to himself appears.
All books he reads, and all he reads assails,
From Dryden's *Fables* down to Durfey's *Tales*.[9]
With him, most authors steal their works, or buy;
Garth did not write his own *Dispensary*.[1]
620 Name a new play, and he's the poet's friend,
Nay showed his faults—but when would poets mend?
No place so sacred from such fops is barred,

---

5. Softness of manners; desire of pleasing.
6. "This picture was taken to himself by John Dennis, a furious old critic by profession, who, upon no other provocation, wrote against this Essay and its author, in a manner perfectly lunatic" [Pope's note, 1744]. Pope *did* intend to ridicule Dennis, whose *Appius and Virginia* had failed on the stage in 1709 and who was known for his stare and his use of the word *tremendous* (see line 270).
7. Honorary degrees were granted to unqualified

men of rank.
8. Tops "sleep" when they spin so rapidly that they seem not to move.
9. Thomas D'Urfey's *Tales* (1704) were notorious potboilers. Dryden's *Fables* (1700), a set of translations, were among his most admired works.
1. Samuel Garth (1661–1719), who had been accused of plagiarizing his mock-epic poem *The Dispensary* (1699), was admired and defended by Pope.

Nor is Paul's church more safe than Paul's churchyard:[2]
Nay, fly to altars; *there* they'll talk you dead:
625 For fools rush in where angels fear to tread.
Distrustful sense with modest caution speaks, ⎤
It still looks home, and short excursions makes; ⎬
But rattling nonsense in full volleys breaks, ⎦
And never shocked, and never turned aside,
630 Bursts out, resistless, with a thundering tide.
　　But where's the man, who counsel can bestow,
Still pleased to teach, and yet not proud to know?
Unbiased, or° by favor, or by spite: 　　　　　　　　*either*
Not dully prepossessed, nor blindly right;
635 Though learned, well-bred; and though well-bred, sincere;
Modestly bold, and humanly severe:
Who to a friend his faults can freely show,
And gladly praise the merit of a foe?
Blessed with a taste exact, yet unconfined;
640 A knowledge both of books and humankind;
Gen'rous converse;[3] a soul exempt from pride;
And love to praise, with reason on his side?
　　Such once were critics; such the happy few,
Athens and Rome in better ages knew.
645 The mighty Stagirite° first left the shore, 　　　　　*Aristotle*
Spread all his sails, and durst the deeps explore;
He steered securely, and discovered far,
Led by the light of the Maeonian star.[4]
Poets, a race long unconfined, and free,
650 Still fond and proud of savage liberty,
Received his laws; and stood convinced 'twas fit,
Who conquered nature, should preside o'er wit.
　　Horace still charms with graceful negligence,
And without method talks us into sense;
655 Will, like a friend, familiarly convey
The truest notions in the easiest° way. 　　　　　*least formal*
He, who supreme in judgment, as in wit,
Might boldly censure, as he boldly writ,
Yet judged with coolness, though he sung with fire;
660 His precepts teach but what his works inspire.
Our critics take a contrary extreme,
They judge with fury, but they write with fle'me.° 　　*phlegmatically*
Nor suffers Horace more in wrong translations
By wits, than critics[5] in as wrong quotations.
665 　　See Dionysius[6] Homer's thoughts refine,
And call new beauties forth from every line!
　　Fancy and art in gay Petronius[7] please,
The scholar's learning, with the courtier's ease.

---

2. Booksellers' district near St. Paul's Cathedral, whose aisles were used as a place to meet and do business.
3. Well-bred conversation.
4. Homer, who was supposed to have been born in Maeonia.

5. I.e., than by critics. Phrases from Horace's *Art of Poetry* were quoted incessantly by critics.
6. Dionysius of Halicarnassus (1st century B.C.E.) wrote an important treatise on the artistic arrangement of words.
7. Author of the *Satyricon* (1st century C.E.).

In grave Quintilian's[8] copious work, we find
670 The justest rules, and clearest method joined:
Thus useful arms in magazines° we place,   *storehouses, arsenals*
All ranged in order, and disposed with grace,
But less to please the eye, than arm the hand,
Still fit for use, and ready at command.
675   Thee, bold Longinus![9] all the nine° inspire,   *Muses*
And bless their critic with a poet's fire.
An ardent judge, who, zealous in his trust,
With warmth gives sentence, yet is always just;
Whose own example strengthens all his laws,
680 And is himself that great sublime he draws.
    Thus long succeeding critics justly reigned,
License repressed, and useful laws ordained.
Learning and Rome alike in empire grew;
And arts still followed where her eagles[1] flew;
685 From the same foes, at last, both felt their doom,
And the same age saw learning fall, and Rome.
With tyranny, then superstition joined,
As that the body, this enslaved the mind;
Much was believed, but little understood,
690 And to be dull was construed to be good;
A second deluge learning thus o'errun,
And the monks finished what the Goths begun.[2]
    At length Erasmus, that great, injured name
(The glory of the priesthood, and the shame!),[3]
695 Stemmed the wild torrent of a barb'rous age,
And drove those holy Vandals off the stage.
    But see! each Muse, in Leo's golden days,
Starts from her trance, and trims her withered bays![4]
Rome's ancient Genius, o'er its ruins spread,
700 Shakes off the dust, and rears his reverend head.
Then sculpture and her sister-arts revive;
Stones leaped to form, and rocks began to live;
With sweeter notes each rising temple rung;
A Raphael painted, and a Vida[5] sung.
705 Immortal Vida: on whose honored brow
The poet's bays and critic's ivy grow:
Cremona now shall ever boast thy name,
As next in place to Mantua, next in fame![6]
    But soon by impious arms from Latium[7] chased,

8. Author of the *Institutio Oratorio* (ca. 95 C.E.),
a famous treatise on rhetoric. Here as elsewhere,
Pope's terms of praise are drawn from the author
he is praising.
9. Supposed author of the influential treatise
On the Sublime (1st century C.E.), greatly in
vogue at the time of Pope.
1. Emblems on the standards of the Roman army.
2. Pope thought that the Scholastic theologians
of the Middle Ages were "holy Vandals" who had
"sacked" learning as the Goths and Vandals had
sacked Rome.
3. Erasmus (1466–1536), the great humanist
scholar, was the "glory of the priesthood" because

of his goodness and learning and its "shame"
because he was persecuted.
4. The wreath of poetry. Leo X, pope from 1513
to 1521, was notable for his encouragement of
artists.
5. "M. Hieronymus Vida, an excellent Latin
poet, who writ an Art of Poetry in verse. He flourished in the time of Leo the Tenth" [Pope's note].
Raphael (1483–1520) painted many of his greatest works under the patronage of Leo X.
6. Vida came from Cremona, near Mantua, the
birthplace of Virgil, his favorite poet.
7. Italy. German and Spanish troops sacked
Rome in 1527.

710 Their ancient bounds the banished Muses passed;
Thence arts o'er all the northern world advance,
But critic-learning flourished most in France:
The rules a nation, born to serve, obeys;
And Boileau still in right of Horace sways.[8]

715 But we, brave Britons, foreign laws despised,
And kept unconquered—and uncivilized;
Fierce for the liberties of wit, and bold,
We still defied the Romans, as of old.
Yet some there were, among the sounder few

720 Of those who less presumed, and better knew,
Who durst assert the juster ancient cause,
And here restored wit's fundamental laws.
Such was the Muse, whose rules and practice tell,
"Nature's chief masterpiece is writing well."[9]

725 Such was Roscommon,[1] not more learned than good,
With manners gen'rous as his noble blood;
To him the wit of Greece and Rome was known,
And every author's merit, but his own.
Such late was Walsh—the Muse's[2] judge and friend,

730 Who justly knew to blame or to commend;
To failings mild, but zealous for desert;
The clearest head, and the sincerest heart.
This humble praise, lamented shade! receive,
This praise at least a grateful Muse may give:

735 The Muse, whose early voice you taught to sing,
Prescribed her heights, and pruned her tender wing,
(Her guide now lost) no more attempts to rise,
But in low numbers° short excursions tries: *humble verses*
Content, if hence the unlearned their wants may view,

740 The learned reflect on what before they knew:
Careless of° censure, nor too fond of fame;   *unconcerned at*
Still pleased to praise, yet not afraid to blame;
Averse alike to flatter, or offend;
Not free from faults, nor yet too vain to mend.

1709   1711

The Rape of the Lock

The Rape of the Lock is based on an actual episode that provoked a quarrel between two prominent Catholic families. Pope's friend John Caryll, to whom the poem is addressed (line 3), suggested that Pope write it, in the hope that a little laughter might serve to soothe ruffled tempers. Lord Petre had cut off a lock of hair from the head of the lovely Arabella Fermor (often spelled "Farmer" and doubtless so pronounced), much to the indignation of the lady and her relatives. In its original version of two cantos and 334 lines, published in 1712, *The Rape of the Lock* was a great success. In 1713 a new version was undertaken

8. Boileau's *L'Art Poétique* (1674) regularized and modernized the lessons of Horace's *Art of Poetry*.
9. Quoted from an *Essay on Poetry* by John Sheffield, duke of Buckingham (1648–1721), who had befriended the young Pope.
1. Wentworth Dillon, earl of Roscommon, wrote

the important *Essay on Translated Verse* (1684).
2. Here, Pope himself. William Walsh (1663–1708), whom Dryden once called "the best critic of our nation," had advised Pope to work at becoming the first great "correct" poet in English.

against the advice of Addison, who considered the poem perfect as it was first written. Pope greatly expanded the earlier version, adding the delightful "machinery" (i.e., the supernatural agents in epic action) of the Sylphs, Belinda's toilet, the card game, and the visit to the Cave of Spleen in canto 4. In 1717, with the addition of Clarissa's speech on good humor, the poem assumed its final form.

With delicate fancy and playful wit, Pope elaborated the trivial episode that occasioned the poem into the semblance of an epic in miniature, the most nearly perfect heroicomical poem in English. The verse abounds in parodies and echoes of the *Iliad,* the *Aeneid,* and *Paradise Lost,* thus constantly forcing the reader to compare small things with great. The familiar devices of epic are observed, but the incidents or characters are beautifully proportioned to the scale of mock epic. The *Rape* tells of war, but it is the drawing-room war between the sexes; it has its heroes and heroines, but they are beaux and belles; it has its supernatural characters ("machinery"), but they are Sylphs (borrowed, as Pope tells us in his dedicatory letter, from Rosicrucian lore)—creatures of the air, the souls of dead coquettes, with tasks appropriate to their nature—or the Gnome Umbriel, once a prude on earth; it has its epic game, played on the "velvet plain" of the card table, its feasting heroes, who sip coffee and gossip, and its battle, fought with the clichés of compliment and conceits, with frowns and angry glances, with snuff and bodkin; it has the traditional epic journey to the underworld—here the Cave of Spleen, emblematic of the ill nature of female hypochondriacs. And Pope creates a world in which these actions take place, a world that is dense with beautiful objects: brocades, ivory and tortoiseshell, cosmetics and diamonds, lacquered furniture, silver teapot, delicate chinaware. It is a world that is constantly in motion and that sparkles and glitters with light, whether the light of the sun or of Belinda's eyes or that light into which the "fluid" bodies of the Sylphs seem to dissolve as they flutter in shrouds and around the mast of Belinda's ship. Pope laughs at this world, its ritualized triviality, its irrational, upper-class women and feminized men—and remembers that a grimmer, darker world surrounds it (3.19–24 and 5.145–48); but he also makes us aware of its beauty and charm.

The epigraph may be translated, "I was unwilling, Belinda, to ravish your locks; but I rejoice to have conceded this to your prayers" (Martial's *Epigrams* 12.84.1–2). Pope substituted his heroine for Martial's Polytimus. The epigraph is intended to suggest that the poem was published at Miss Fermor's request.

The Rape of the Lock

An Heroi-Comical Poem

Nolueram, Belinda, tuos violare capillos;
sed juvat hoc precibus me tribuisse tuis.
—MARTIAL

TO MRS. ARABELLA FERMOR

MADAM,

It will be in vain to deny that I have some regard for this piece, since I dedicate it to you. Yet you may bear me witness, it was intended only to divert a few young ladies, who have good sense and good humor enough to laugh not only at their sex's little unguarded follies, but at their own. But as it was communicated with the air of a secret, it soon found its way into the world. An imperfect copy having been offered to a bookseller, you had the good nature for my sake to consent to the publication of one more correct; this I was forced to, before I had executed half my design, for the machinery was entirely wanting to complete it.

The machinery, Madam, is a term invented by the critics, to signify that part which the deities, angels, or demons are made to act in a poem; for the ancient poets are in one respect like many modern ladies: let an action be never so trivial in itself, they always make it appear of the utmost importance. These machines I determined to raise on a very new and odd foundation, the Rosicrucian[1] doctrine of spirits.

I know how disagreeable it is to make use of hard words before a lady; but 'tis so much the concern of a poet to have his works understood, and particularly by your sex, that you must give me leave to explain two or three difficult terms.

The Rosicrucians are a people I must bring you acquainted with. The best account I know of them is in a French book called *Le Comte de Gabalis*,[2] which both in its title and size is so like a novel, that many of the fair sex have read it for one by mistake. According to these gentlemen, the four elements are inhabited by spirits, which they call Sylphs, Gnomes, Nymphs, and Salamanders. The Gnomes or Demons of earth delight in mischief; but the Sylphs, whose habitation is in the air, are the best-conditioned creatures imaginable. For they say, any mortals may enjoy the most intimate familiarities with these gentle spirits, upon a condition very easy to all true adepts, an inviolate preservation of chastity.

As to the following cantos, all the passages of them are as fabulous as the vision at the beginning, or the transformation at the end (except the loss of your hair, which I always mention with reverence). The human persons are as fictitious as the airy ones; and the character of Belinda, as it is now managed, resembles you in nothing but in beauty.

If this poem had as many graces as there are in your person, or in your mind, yet I could never hope it should pass through the world half so uncensured as you have done. But let its fortune be what it will, mine is happy enough, to have given me this occasion of assuring you that I am, with the truest esteem,

MADAM,
Your most obedient, humble servant,
A. POPE

Canto 1

> What dire offense from amorous causes springs,
> What mighty contests rise from trivial things,
> I sing—This verse to Caryll, Muse! is due:
> This, even Belinda may vouchsafe to view:
> 5 Slight is the subject, but not so the praise,
> If she inspire, and he approve my lays.
> Say what strange motive, Goddess! could compel
> A well-bred lord to assault a gentle belle?
> Oh, say what stranger cause, yet unexplored,
> 10 Could make a gentle belle reject a lord?

---

1. A system of arcane philosophy introduced into England from Germany in the 17th century.

2. By the Abbé de Montfaucon de Villars, published in 1670.

In tasks so bold can little men engage,
And in soft bosoms dwells such mighty rage?
    Sol through white curtains shot a timorous ray,
And oped those eyes that must eclipse the day.
15 Now lapdogs give themselves the rousing shake,
And sleepless lovers, just at twelve, awake:
Thrice rung the bell, the slipper knocked the ground,
And the pressed watch[3] returned a silver sound.
Belinda still her downy pillow pressed,
20 Her guardian Sylph prolonged the balmy rest.
'Twas he had summoned to her silent bed
The morning dream that hovered o'er her head.
A youth more glittering than a birthnight beau[4]
(That even in slumber caused her cheek to glow)
25 Seemed to her ear his winning lips to lay,
And thus in whispers said, or seemed to say:
    "Fairest of mortals, thou distinguished care
Of thousand bright inhabitants of air!
If e'er one vision touched thy infant thought,
30 Of all the nurse and all the priest have taught,
Of airy elves by moonlight shadows seen,
The silver token, and the circled green,[5]
Or virgins visited by angel powers,
With golden crowns and wreaths of heavenly flowers,
35 Hear and believe! thy own importance know,
Nor bound thy narrow views to things below.
Some secret truths, from learned pride concealed,
To maids alone and children are revealed:
What though no credit doubting wits may give?
40 The fair and innocent shall still believe.
Know, then, unnumbered spirits round thee fly,
The light militia of the lower sky:
These, though unseen, are ever on the wing,
Hang o'er the box, and hover round the Ring.[6]
45 Think what an equipage thou hast in air,
And view with scorn two pages and a chair.°   *sedan chair*
As now your own, our beings were of old,
And once enclosed in woman's beauteous mold;
Thence, by a soft transition, we repair
50 From earthly vehicles to these of air.
Think not, when woman's transient breath is fled,
That all her vanities at once are dead:
Succeeding vanities she still regards,
And though she plays no more, o'erlooks the cards.
55 Her joy in gilded chariots, when alive,
And love of ombre,[7] after death survive.

---

3. A watch that chimes the hour and the quarter hour when the stem is pressed down. "Knocked the ground": summons to a maid.
4. Courtiers wore especially fine clothes on the sovereign's birthday.
5. Rings of bright green grass, which are common in England even in winter, were held to be caused by the round dances of fairies. According to popular belief, fairies skim off the cream from jugs of milk left standing overnight and leave a coin ("silver token") in payment.
6. The "box" in the theater and the fashionable circular drive ("Ring") in Hyde Park.
7. The popular card game (see n. 1, p. 2694).

For when the Fair in all their pride expire,
To their first elements[8] their souls retire:
The sprites of fiery termagants in flame
60   Mount up, and take a Salamander's[9] name.
Soft yielding minds to water glide away,
And sip, with Nymphs, their elemental tea.[1]
The graver prude sinks downward to a Gnome,
In search of mischief still on earth to roam.
65   The light coquettes in Sylphs aloft repair,
And sport and flutter in the fields of air.
    "Know further yet; whoever fair and chaste
Rejects mankind, is by some Sylph embraced:
For spirits, freed from mortal laws, with ease
70   Assume what sexes and what shapes they please.[2]
What guards the purity of melting maids,
In courtly balls, and midnight masquerades,
Safe from the treacherous friend, the daring spark,
The glance by day, the whisper in the dark,
75   When kind occasion prompts their warm desires,
When music softens, and when dancing fires?
'Tis but their Sylph, the wise Celestials° know,   *heavenly beings*
Though Honor is the word with men below.
    "Some nymphs[3] there are, too conscious of their face,
80   For life predestined to the Gnomes' embrace.
These swell their prospects and exalt their pride,
When offers are disdained, and love denied:
Then gay ideas° crowd the vacant brain,   *showy images*
While peers, and dukes, and all their sweeping train,
85   And garters, stars, and coronets[4] appear,
And in soft sounds, 'your Grace'° salutes their ear.   *a duchess*
'Tis these that early taint the female soul,
Instruct the eyes of young coquettes to roll,
Teach infant cheeks a bidden blush to know,
90   And little hearts to flutter at a beau.
    "Oft, when the world imagine women stray,
The Sylphs through mystic mazes guide their way,
Through all the giddy circle they pursue,
And old impertinence° expel by new.   *trifle*
95   What tender maid but must a victim fall
To one man's treat, but for another's ball?
When Florio speaks, what virgin could withstand,
If gentle Damon did not squeeze her hand?
With varying vanities, from every part,
100   They shift the moving toyshop[5] of their heart;

---

8. The four elements out of which all things were believed to have been made were fire, water, earth, and air. One or another of these elements was supposed to be predominant in both the physical and the psychological makeup of each human being. In this context they are spoken of as "humors."
9. A lizardlike animal, in antiquity believed to live in fire. Each element was inhabited by a spirit, as the following lines explain. "Terma-

gants": shrewish or overbearing women.
1. Pronounced *tay*.
2. Cf. *Paradise Lost* 1.427–31; this is one of many allusions to that poem in the *Rape*.
3. Here and after, a fanciful name for a young woman, to be distinguished from the "Nymphs" (water spirits) in line 62.
4. Emblems of nobility.
5. A shop stocked with baubles and trifles.

Where wigs with wigs, with sword-knots sword-knots strive,
Beaux banish beaux, and coaches coaches drive.
This erring mortals levity may call;
Oh, blind to truth! the Sylphs contrive it all.
105   "Of these am I, who thy protection claim,
A watchful sprite, and Ariel is my name.
Late, as I ranged the crystal wilds of air,
In the clear mirror of thy ruling star
I saw, alas! some dread event impend,
110 Ere to the main this morning sun descend,
But Heaven reveals not what, or how, or where:
Warned by thy Sylph, O pious maid, beware!
This to disclose is all thy guardian can:
Beware of all, but most beware of Man!"
115   He said; when Shock,[6] who thought she slept too long,
Leaped up, and waked his mistress with his tongue.
'Twas then, Belinda, if report say true,
Thy eyes first opened on a billet-doux;
Wounds, charms, and ardors were no sooner read,
120 But all the vision vanished from thy head.
   And now, unveiled, the toilet stands displayed,
Each silver vase in mystic order laid.
First, robed in white, the nymph intent adores,
With head uncovered, the cosmetic powers.
125 A heavenly image in the glass appears;
To that she bends, to that her eyes she rears.
The inferior priestess, at her altar's side,
Trembling begins the sacred rites of Pride.
Unnumbered treasures ope at once, and here
130 The various offerings of the world appear;
From each she nicely culls with curious toil,
And decks the goddess with the glittering spoil.
This casket India's glowing gems unlocks,
And all Arabia breathes from yonder box.
135 The tortoise here and elephant unite,
Transformed to combs, the speckled and the white.
Here files of pins extend their shining rows,
Puffs, powders, patches, Bibles,[7] billet-doux.
Now awful° Beauty puts on all its arms;   *awe-inspiring*
140 The fair each moment rises in her charms,
Repairs her smiles, awakens every grace,
And calls forth all the wonders of her face;
Sees by degrees a purer blush arise,
And keener lightnings quicken in her eyes.
145 The busy Sylphs surround their darling care,
These set the head, and those divide the hair,
Some fold the sleeve, whilst others plait the gown;
And Betty's[8] praised for labors not her own.

---

6. A long-haired poodle, Belinda's lapdog.
7. It has been suggested that Pope intended here not "Bibles," but "bibelots" (trinkets), but this interpretation has not gained wide acceptance.
8. Belinda's maid, the "inferior priestess" mentioned in line 127.

Canto 2

Not with more glories, in the ethereal plain,
The sun first rises o'er the purpled main,
Than, issuing forth, the rival of his beams
Launched on the bosom of the silver Thames.
5   Fair nymphs and well-dressed youths around her shone,
But every eye was fixed on her alone.
On her white breast a sparkling cross she wore,
Which Jews might kiss, and infidels adore.
Her lively looks a sprightly mind disclose,
10   Quick as her eyes, and as unfixed as those:
Favors to none, to all she smiles extends;
Oft she rejects, but never once offends.
Bright as the sun, her eyes the gazers strike,
And, like the sun, they shine on all alike.
15   Yet graceful ease, and sweetness void of pride,
Might hide her faults, if belles had faults to hide:
If to her share some female errors fall,
Look on her face, and you'll forget 'em all.
     This nymph, to the destruction of mankind,
20   Nourished two locks which graceful hung behind
In equal curls, and well conspired to deck
With shining ringlets her smooth ivory neck.
Love in these labyrinths his slaves detains,
And mighty hearts are held in slender chains.
25   With hairy springes[9] we the birds betray,
Slight lines of hair surprise the finny prey,
Fair tresses man's imperial race ensnare,
And beauty draws us with a single hair.
     The adventurous Baron the bright locks admired,
30   He saw, he wished, and to the prize aspired.
Resolved to win, he meditates the way,
By force to ravish, or by fraud betray;
For when success a lover's toil attends,
Few ask if fraud or force attained his ends.
35   For this, ere Phoebus° rose, he had implored   *the sun*
Propitious Heaven, and every power adored,
But chiefly Love—to Love an altar built,
Of twelve vast French romances, neatly gilt.
There lay three garters, half a pair of gloves,
40   And all the trophies of his former loves.
With tender billet-doux he lights the pyre,
And breathes three amorous sighs to raise the fire.
Then prostrate falls, and begs with ardent eyes
Soon to obtain, and long possess the prize:
45   The powers gave ear, and granted half his prayer,
The rest the winds dispersed in empty air.
     But now secure the painted vessel glides,
The sunbeams trembling on the floating tides,

9. Snares (pronounced *sprin-jez*).

While melting music steals upon the sky,
50 And softened sounds along the waters die.
Smooth flow the waves, the zephyrs gently play,
Belinda smiled, and all the world was gay.
All but the Sylph—with careful thoughts oppressed,
The impending woe sat heavy on his breast.
55 He summons straight his denizens of air;
The lucid squadrons round the sails repair:
Soft o'er the shrouds aërial whispers breathe
That seemed but zephyrs to the train beneath.
Some to the sun their insect-wings unfold,
60 Waft on the breeze, or sink in clouds of gold.
Transparent forms too fine for mortal sight,
Their fluid bodies half dissolved in light,
Loose to the wind their airy garments flew,
Thin glittering textures of the filmy dew,
65 Dipped in the richest tincture of the skies,
Where light disports in ever-mingling dyes,
While every beam new transient colors flings,
Colors that change whene'er they wave their wings.
Amid the circle, on the gilded mast,
70 Superior by the head was Ariel placed;
His purple[1] pinions opening to the sun,
He raised his azure wand, and thus begun:
   "Ye Sylphs and Sylphids, to your chief give ear!
Fays, Fairies, Genïi, Elves, and Daemons, hear!
75 Ye know the spheres and various tasks assigned
By laws eternal to the aërial kind.
Some in the fields of purest ether play,
And bask and whiten in the blaze of day.
Some guide the course of wandering orbs on high,
80 Or roll the planets through the boundless sky.
Some less refined, beneath the moon's pale light
Pursue the stars that shoot athwart the night,
Or suck the mists in grosser air below,
Or dip their pinions in the painted bow,°   *rainbow*
85 Or brew fierce tempests on the wintry main,
Or o'er the glebe° distill the kindly rain.   *cultivated field*
Others on earth o'er human race preside,
Watch all their ways, and all their actions guide:
Of these the chief the care of nations own,
90 And guard with arms divine the British Throne.
   "Our humbler province is to tend the Fair,
Not a less pleasing, though less glorious care:
To save the powder from too rude a gale,
Nor let the imprisoned essences° exhale;   *perfumes*
95 To draw fresh colors from the vernal flowers;
To steal from rainbows e'er they drop in showers
A brighter wash;° to curl their waving hairs,   *cosmetic lotion*

1. In 18th-century poetic diction the word might mean bloodred, purple, or simply (as is likely here) brightly colored. The word derives from Virgil's *Eclogue* 9.40, *purpureum*. An example of the Latin-ate nature of some poetic diction of the period.

Assist their blushes, and inspire their airs,
Nay oft, in dreams invention we bestow,
100 To change a flounce, or add a furbelow.
    "This day black omens threat the brightest fair,
That e'er deserved a watchful spirit's care;
Some dire disaster, or by force or slight,
But what, or where, the Fates have wrapped in night:
105 Whether the nymph shall break Diana's[2] law,
Or some frail china jar receive a flaw,
Or stain her honor, or her new brocade,
Forget her prayers, or miss a masquerade,
Or lose her heart, or necklace, at a ball;
110 Or whether Heaven has doomed that Shock must fall.
Haste, then, ye spirits! to your charge repair:
The fluttering fan be Zephyretta's care;
The drops[3] to thee, Brillante, we consign;
And, Momentilla, let the watch be thine;
115 Do thou, Crispissa,[4] tend her favorite Lock;
Ariel himself shall be the guard of Shock.
    "To fifty chosen Sylphs, of special note,
We trust the important charge, the petticoat;
Oft have we known that sevenfold fence to fail,
120 Though stiff with hoops, and armed with ribs of whale.[5]
Form a strong line about the silver bound,
And guard the wide circumference around.
    "Whatever spirit, careless of his charge,
His post neglects, or leaves the fair at large,
125 Shall feel sharp vengeance soon o'ertake his sins,
Be stopped in vials, or transfixed with pins,
Or plunged in lakes of bitter washes lie,
Or wedged whole ages in a bodkin's[6] eye;
Gums and pomatums shall his flight restrain,
130 While clogged he beats his silken wings in vain,
Or alum styptics with contracting power
Shrink his thin essence like a riveled[7] flower:
Or, as Ixion[8] fixed, the wretch shall feel
The giddy motion of the whirling mill,
135 In fumes of burning chocolate shall glow,
And tremble at the sea that froths below!"
    He spoke; the spirits from the sails descend;
Some, orb in orb, around the nymph extend;
Some thread the mazy ringlets of her hair;
140 Some hang upon the pendants of her ear:
With beating hearts the dire event they wait,
Anxious, and trembling for the birth of Fate.

---

2. Diana was the goddess of chastity.
3. Diamond earrings. Observe the appropriateness of the names of the Sylphs to their assigned functions.
4. From Latin crispere, "to curl."
5. Corsets and the hoops of hoopskirts were made of whalebone.
6. A blunt needle with a large eye used for draw-

ing ribbon through eyelets in the edging of women's garments.
7. To "rivel" is to "contract into wrinkles and corrugations" (Johnson's Dictionary).
8. In the Greek myth, he was punished in the underworld by being bound on an everturning wheel.

Canto 3

    Close by those meads, forever crowned with flowers,
Where Thames with pride surveys his rising towers,
There stands a structure of majestic frame,
Which from the neighboring Hampton[9] takes its name.
5 Here Britain's statesmen oft the fall foredoom
Of foreign tyrants and of nymphs at home;
Here thou, great Anna! whom three realms obey,
Dost sometimes counsel take—and sometimes tea.
    Hither the heroes and the nymphs resort,
10 To taste awhile the pleasures of a court;
In various talk the instructive hours they passed,
Who gave the ball, or paid the visit last;
One speaks the glory of the British Queen,
And one describes a charming Indian screen;
15 A third interprets motions, looks, and eyes;
At every word a reputation dies.
Snuff, or the fan, supply each pause of chat,
With singing, laughing, ogling, and all that.
    Meanwhile, declining from the noon of day,
20 The sun obliquely shoots his burning ray;
The hungry judges soon the sentence sign,
And wretches hang that jurymen may dine;
The merchant from the Exchange returns in peace,
And the long labors of the toilet cease.
25 Belinda now, whom thirst of fame invites,
Burns to encounter two adventurous knights,
At ombre[1] singly to decide their doom,
And swells her breast with conquests yet to come.
Straight the three bands prepare in arms to join,
30 Each band the number of the sacred nine.
Soon as she spreads her hand, the aërial guard
Descend, and sit on each important card:
First Ariel perched upon a Matadore,
Then each according to the rank they bore;
35 For Sylphs, yet mindful of their ancient race,
Are, as when women, wondrous fond of place.
    Behold, four Kings in majesty revered,
With hoary whiskers and a forky beard;
And four fair Queens whose hands sustain a flower,
40 The expressive emblem of their softer power;
Four Knaves in garbs succinct,° a trusty band,   *girded up*
Caps on their heads, and halberts in their hand;

---

9. Hampton Court, the royal palace, about fifteen miles up the Thames from London.
1. The game of ombre that Belinda plays against the baron and another young man is too complicated for complete explication here. Pope has carefully arranged the cards so that Belinda wins. The baron's hand is strong enough to be a threat, but the third player's is of little account. The hand is played exactly according to the rules of ombre, and Pope's description of the cards is equally accurate. Each player holds nine cards (line 30). The "Matadores" (line 33), when spades are trump, are "Spadillio" (line 49), the ace of spades; "Manillio" (line 51), the two of spades; and "Basto" (line 53), the ace of clubs. Belinda holds all three of these. (For a more complete description of ombre, see *The Rape of the Lock and Other Poems*, ed. Geoffrey Tillotson, in the Twickenham Edition of Pope's poems, vol. 2, Appendix C.)

And parti-colored troops, a shining train,
Draw forth to combat on the velvet plain.
45   The skillful nymph reviews her force with care;
"Let Spades be trumps!" she said, and trumps they were.
     Now move to war her sable Matadores,
In show like leaders of the swarthy Moors.
Spadillio first, unconquerable lord!
50   Led off two captive trumps, and swept the board.
As many more Manillio forced to yield,
And marched a victor from the verdant field.
Him Basto followed, but his fate more hard
Gained but one trump and one plebeian card.
55   With his broad saber next, a chief in years,
The hoary Majesty of Spades appears,
Puts forth one manly leg, to sight revealed,
The rest his many-colored robe concealed.
The rebel Knave, who dares his prince engage,
60   Proves the just victim of his royal rage.
Even mighty Pam,[2] that kings and queens o'erthrew
And mowed down armies in the fights of loo,
Sad chance of war! now destitute of aid,
Falls undistinguished by the victor Spade.
65   Thus far both armies to Belinda yield;
Now to the Baron fate inclines the field.
His warlike amazon her host invades,
The imperial consort of the crown of Spades.
The Club's black tyrant first her victim died,
70   Spite of his haughty mien and barbarous pride.
What boots° the regal circle on his head,   *avails*
His giant limbs, in state unwieldy spread?
That long behind he trails his pompous robe,
And of all monarchs only grasps the globe?[3]
75   The Baron now his Diamonds pours apace;
The embroidered King who shows but half his face,
And his refulgent Queen, with powers combined,
Of broken troops an easy conquest find.
Clubs, Diamonds, Hearts, in wild disorder seen,
80   With throngs promiscuous strew the level green.
Thus when dispersed a routed army runs,
Of Asia's troops, and Afric's sable sons,
With like confusion different nations fly,
Of various habit, and of various dye,
85   The pierced battalions disunited fall
In heaps on heaps; one fate o'erwhelms them all.
     The Knave of Diamonds tries his wily arts,
And wins (oh, shameful chance!) the Queen of Hearts.
At this, the blood the virgin's cheek forsook,
90   A livid paleness spreads o'er all her look;
She sees, and trembles at the approaching ill,

2. The knave of clubs, the highest trump in the
game of loo.

3. In the English deck, only the king of clubs
holds an imperial orb.

Just in the jaws of ruin, and Codille.[4]
And now (as oft in some distempered state)
On one nice trick depends the general fate.
95   An Ace of Hearts steps forth: the King unseen
Lurked in her hand, and mourned his captive Queen.
He springs to vengeance with an eager pace,
And falls like thunder on the prostrate Ace.
The nymph exulting fills with shouts the sky,
100 The walls, the woods, and long canals reply.
      O thoughtless mortals! ever blind to fate,
Too soon dejected, and too soon elate:
Sudden these honors shall be snatched away,
And cursed forever this victorious day.
105   For lo! the board with cups and spoons is crowned,
The berries crackle, and the mill turns round;[5]
On shining altars of Japan[6] they raise
The silver lamp; the fiery spirits blaze:
From silver spouts the grateful liquors glide,
110 While China's earth receives the smoking tide.
At once they gratify their scent and taste,
And frequent cups prolong the rich repast.
Straight hover round the fair her airy band;
Some, as she sipped, the fuming liquor fanned,
115 Some o'er her lap their careful plumes displayed,
Trembling, and conscious of the rich brocade.
Coffee (which makes the politician wise,
And see through all things with his half-shut eyes)
Sent up in vapors to the Baron's brain
120 New stratagems, the radiant Lock to gain.
Ah, cease, rash youth! desist ere 'tis too late,
Fear the just Gods, and think of Scylla's[7] fate!
Changed to a bird, and sent to flit in air,
She dearly pays for Nisus' injured hair!
125   But when to mischief mortals bend their will,
How soon they find fit instruments of ill!
Just then, Clarissa drew with tempting grace
A two-edged weapon from her shining case:
So ladies in romance assist their knight,
130 Present the spear, and arm him for the fight.
He takes the gift with reverence, and extends
The little engine on his fingers' ends;
This just behind Belinda's neck he spread,
As o'er the fragrant steams she bends her head.
135 Swift to the Lock a thousand sprites repair,
A thousand wings, by turns, blow back the hair,
And thrice they twitched the diamond in her ear,

---

4. The term applied to losing a hand at cards.
5. I.e., coffee is roasted and ground.
6. I.e., small, lacquered tables. "Altars" suggests the ritualistic character of coffee drinking in Belinda's world.
7. Scylla, daughter of Nisus, was turned into a

sea bird because, for the sake of her love for Minos of Crete, who was besieging her father's city of Megara, she cut from her father's head the purple lock on which his safety depended. She is not the Scylla of "Scylla and Charybdis."

Thrice she looked back, and thrice the foe drew near.
Just in that instant, anxious Ariel sought
140 The close recesses of the virgin's thought;
As on the nosegay in her breast reclined,
He watched the ideas rising in her mind,
Sudden he viewed, in spite of all her art,
An earthly lover lurking at her heart.
145 Amazed, confused, he found his power expired,
Resigned to fate, and with a sigh retired.
    The Peer now spreads the glittering forfex° wide,   *scissors*
To enclose the Lock; now joins it, to divide.
Even then, before the fatal engine closed,
150 A wretched Sylph too fondly interposed;
Fate urged the shears, and cut the Sylph in twain
(But airy substance soon unites again):
The meeting points the sacred hair dissever
From the fair head, forever and forever!
155   Then flashed the living lightning from her eyes,
And screams of horror rend the affrighted skies.
Not louder shrieks to pitying heaven are cast,
When husbands, or when lapdogs breathe their last;
Or when rich china vessels fallen from high,
160 In glittering dust and painted fragments lie!
"Let wreaths of triumph now my temples twine,"
The victor cried, "the glorious prize is mine!
While fish in streams, or birds delight in air,
Or in a coach and six the British fair,
165 As long as *Atalantis*[8] shall be read,
Or the small pillow grace a lady's bed,
While visits shall be paid on solemn days,
When numerous wax-lights in bright order blaze,
While nymphs take treats,° or assignations give,   *free refreshments*
170 So long my honor, name, and praise shall live!
    "What time would spare, from steel receives its date,
And monuments, like men, submit to fate!
Steel could the labor of the Gods destroy,
And strike to dust the imperial towers of Troy;
175 Steel could the works of mortal pride confound,
And hew triumphal arches to the ground.
What wonder then, fair nymph! thy hairs should feel,
The conquering force of unresisted steel?"

Canto 4

    But anxious cares the pensive nymph oppressed,
And secret passions labored in her breast.
Not youthful kings in battle seized alive,
Not scornful virgins who their charms survive,
5 Not ardent lovers robbed of all their bliss,

---

8. Delarivier Manley's *New Atalantis* (1709) was notorious for its thinly concealed allusions to contemporary scandals.

Not ancient ladies when refused a kiss,
Not tyrants fierce that unrepenting die,
Not Cynthia when her manteau's° pinned awry,   *wrap*
E'er felt such rage, resentment, and despair,
10   As thou, sad virgin! for thy ravished hair.
     For, that sad moment, when the Sylphs withdrew
And Ariel weeping from Belinda flew,
Umbriel,⁹ a dusky, melancholy sprite
As ever sullied the fair face of light,
15   Down to the central earth, his proper scene,
Repaired to search the gloomy Cave of Spleen.°   *Ill Humor*
     Swift on his sooty pinions flits the Gnome,
And in a vapor reached the dismal dome.
No cheerful breeze this sullen region knows,
20   The dreaded east is all the wind that blows.
Here in a grotto, sheltered close from air,
And screened in shades from day's detested glare,
She sighs forever on her pensive bed,
Pain at her side, and Megrim° at her head.   *headache*
25   Two handmaids wait the throne: alike in place
But differing far in figure and in face.
Here stood Ill-Nature like an ancient maid,
Her wrinkled form in black and white arrayed;
With store of prayers for mornings, nights, and noons,
30   Her hand is filled; her bosom with lampoons.
     There Affectation, with a sickly mien,
Shows in her cheek the roses of eighteen,
Practiced to lisp, and hang the head aside,
Faints into airs, and languishes with pride,
35   On the rich quilt sinks with becoming woe,
Wrapped in a gown, for sickness and for show.
The fair ones° feel such maladies as these,   *women*
When each new nightdress gives a new disease.
     A constant vapor¹ o'er the palace flies,
40   Strange phantoms rising as the mists arise;
Dreadful as hermit's dreams in haunted shades,
Or bright as visions of expiring maids.
Now glaring fiends, and snakes on rolling spires,°   *coils*
Pale specters, gaping tombs, and purple fires;
45   Now lakes of liquid gold, Elysian scenes,
And crystal domes, and angels in machines.²
     Unnumbered throngs on every side are seen
Of bodies changed to various forms by Spleen.
Here living teapots stand, one arm held out,
50   One bent; the handle this, and that the spout:
A pipkin° there, like Homer's tripod,³ walks;   *earthen pot*
Here sighs a jar, and there a goose pie talks;

---

9. The name suggests shade and darkness.
1. Emblematic of "the vapors," a fashionable hypochondria, melancholy, or peevishness.
2. Mechanical devices used in the theaters for spectacular effects. The catalog of hallucinations draws on the sensational stage effects popular with contemporary audiences.
3. In the *Iliad* (18.373–77), Vulcan furnishes the gods with self-propelling "tripods" (three-legged stools).

Men prove with child, as powerful fancy works,
And maids, turned bottles, call aloud for corks.
55   Safe passed the Gnome through this fantastic band,
A branch of healing spleenwort[4] in his hand.
Then thus addressed the Power: "Hail, wayward Queen!
Who rule the sex to fifty from fifteen:
Parent of vapors and of female wit,
60 Who give the hysteric or poetic fit,
On various tempers act by various ways,
Make some take physic,° others scribble plays;   *medicine*
Who cause the proud their visits to delay,
And send the godly in a pet to pray.
65 A nymph there is that all your power disdains,
And thousands more in equal mirth maintains.
But oh! if e'er thy Gnome could spoil a grace,
Or raise a pimple on a beauteous face,
Like citron-waters[5] matrons' cheeks inflame,
70 Or change complexions at a losing game;
If e'er with airy horns[6] I planted heads,
Or rumpled petticoats, or tumbled beds,
Or caused suspicion when no soul was rude,
Or discomposed the headdress of a prude,
75 Or e'er to costive lapdog gave disease,
Which not the tears of brightest eyes could ease,
Hear me, and touch Belinda with chagrin:°   *ill humor*
That single act gives half the world the spleen."
     The Goddess with a discontented air
80 Seems to reject him though she grants his prayer.
A wondrous bag with both her hands she binds,
Like that where once Ulysses held the winds;[7]
There she collects the force of female lungs,
Sighs, sobs, and passions, and the war of tongues.
85 A vial next she fills with fainting fears,
Soft sorrows, melting griefs, and flowing tears.
The Gnome rejoicing bears her gifts away,
Spreads his black wings, and slowly mounts to day.
     Sunk in Thalestris'[8] arms the nymph he found,
90 Her eyes dejected and her hair unbound.
Full o'er their heads the swelling bag he rent,
And all the Furies issued at the vent.
Belinda burns with more than mortal ire,
And fierce Thalestris fans the rising fire.
95 "O wretched maid!" she spread her hands, and cried
(While Hampton's echoes, "Wretched maid!" replied),

---

4. An herb, efficacious against diseases of the spleen. Pope alludes to the golden bough that Aeneas and the Cumaean sibyl carry with them for protection into the underworld in *Aeneid* 6.
5. Brandy flavored with orange or lemon peel.
6. The symbol of the cuckold, the man whose wife has been unfaithful to him; here "airy," because they exist only in the jealous suspicions of the husband, the victim of the mischievous Umbriel.

7. Aeolus (later conceived of as god of the winds) gave Ulysses a bag containing all the winds adverse to his voyage home. When his ship was in sight of Ithaca, his companions opened the bag and the storms that ensued drove Ulysses far away (*Odyssey* 10.19ff.).
8. The name is borrowed from a queen of the Amazons, hence a fierce and warlike woman.

"Was it for this you took such constant care
The bodkin, comb, and essence to prepare?
For this your locks in paper durance bound,
100 For this with torturing irons wreathed around?
For this with fillets strained your tender head,
And bravely bore the double loads of lead?[9]
Gods! shall the ravisher display your hair,
While the fops envy, and the ladies stare!
105 Honor forbid! at whose unrivaled shrine
Ease, pleasure, virtue, all, our sex resign.
Methinks already I your tears survey,
Already hear the horrid things they say,
Already see you a degraded toast,
110 And all your honor in a whisper lost!
How shall I, then, your helpless fame defend?
'Twill then be infamy to seem your friend!
And shall this prize, the inestimable prize,
Exposed through crystal to the gazing eyes,
115 And heightened by the diamond's circling rays,
On that rapacious hand forever blaze?
Sooner shall grass in Hyde Park Circus grow,
And wits take lodgings in the sound of Bow;[1]
Sooner let earth, air, sea, to chaos fall,
120 Men, monkeys, lapdogs, parrots, perish all!"
　　She said; then raging to Sir Plume repairs,
And bids her beau demand the precious hairs
(Sir Plume of amber snuffbox justly vain,
And the nice conduct of a clouded° cane).   *marbled, veined*
125 With earnest eyes, and round unthinking face,
He first the snuffbox opened, then the case,
And thus broke out—"My Lord, why, what the devil!
Z—ds! damn the lock! 'fore Gad, you must be civil!
Plague on 't! 'tis past a jest—nay prithee, pox!
130 Give her the hair"—he spoke, and rapped his box.
　　"It grieves me much," replied the Peer again,
"Who speaks so well should ever speak in vain.
But by this Lock, this sacred Lock I swear
(Which never more shall join its parted hair;
135 Which never more its honors shall renew,
Clipped from the lovely head where late it grew),
That while my nostrils draw the vital air,
This hand, which won it, shall forever wear."
He spoke, and speaking, in proud triumph spread
140 The long-contended honors[2] of her head.
　　But Umbriel, hateful Gnome, forbears not so;
He breaks the vial whence the sorrows flow.
Then see! the nymph in beauteous grief appears,
Her eyes half languishing, half drowned in tears;

9. The frame on which the elaborate coiffures of the day were arranged.
1. A person born within sound of the bells of St. Mary-le-Bow in Cheapside is said to be a cock-ney. No fashionable wit would have so vulgar an address.
2. Ornaments, hence locks; a Latinism.

145 On her heaved bosom hung her drooping head,
Which with a sigh she raised, and thus she said:
"Forever cursed be this detested day,
Which snatched my best, my favorite curl away!
Happy! ah, ten times happy had I been,
150 If Hampton Court these eyes had never seen!
Yet am not I the first mistaken maid,
By love of courts to numerous ills betrayed.
Oh, had I rather unadmired remained
In some lone isle, or distant northern land;
155 Where the gilt chariot never marks the way,
Where none learn ombre, none e'er taste bohea![3]
There kept my charms concealed from mortal eye,
Like roses that in deserts bloom and die.
What moved my mind with youthful lords to roam?
160 Oh, had I stayed, and said my prayers at home!
'Twas this the morning omens seemed to tell;
Thrice from my trembling hand the patch box[4] fell;
The tottering china shook without a wind,
Nay, Poll sat mute, and Shock was most unkind!
165 A Sylph too warned me of the threats of fate,
In mystic visions, now believed too late!
See the poor remnants of these slighted hairs!
My hands shall rend what e'en thy rapine spares.
These in two sable ringlets taught to break,
170 Once gave new beauties to the snowy neck.
The sister lock now sits uncouth, alone,
And in its fellow's fate foresees its own;
Uncurled it hangs, the fatal shears demands,
And tempts once more thy sacrilegious hands.
175 Oh, hadst thou, cruel! been content to seize
Hairs less in sight, or any hairs but these!"

Canto 5

She said: the pitying audience melt in tears.
But Fate and Jove had stopped the Baron's ears.
In vain Thalestris with reproach assails,
For who can move when fair Belinda fails?
5 Not half so fixed the Trojan[5] could remain,
While Anna begged and Dido raged in vain.
Then grave Clarissa graceful waved her fan;
Silence ensued, and thus the nymph began:
"Say, why are beauties praised and honored most,
10 The wise man's passion, and the vain man's toast?
Why decked with all that land and sea afford,
Why angels called, and angel-like adored?
Why round our coaches crowd the white-gloved beaux,

3. A costly sort of tea.
4. To hold the ornamental patches of court plaster worn on the face by both sexes.
5. Aeneas, who forsook Dido at the bidding of the gods, despite her reproaches and the supplications of her sister Anna. Virgil compares him to a steadfast oak that withstands a storm (Aeneid 4.437–43).

Why bows the side box from its inmost rows?
15 How vain are all these glories, all our pains,
Unless good sense preserve what beauty gains;
That men may say when we the front box grace,
'Behold the first in virtue as in face!'
Oh! if to dance all night, and dress all day,
20 Charmed the smallpox, or chased old age away,
Who would not scorn what housewife's cares produce,
Or who would learn one earthly thing of use?
To patch, nay ogle, might become a saint,
Nor could it sure be such a sin to paint.
25 But since, alas! frail beauty must decay,
Curled or uncurled, since locks will turn to gray;
Since painted, or not painted, all shall fade,
And she who scorns a man must die a maid;
What then remains but well our power to use,
30 And keep good humor still whate'er we lose?
And trust me, dear, good humor can prevail
When airs, and flights, and screams, and scolding fail.
Beauties in vain their pretty eyes may roll;
Charms strike the sight, but merit wins the soul."⁶
35   So spoke the dame, but no applause ensued;
Belinda frowned, Thalestris called her prude.
"To arms, to arms!" the fierce virago cries,
And swift as lightning to the combat flies.
All side in parties, and begin the attack;
40 Fans clap, silks rustle, and tough whalebones crack;
Heroes' and heroines' shouts confusedly rise,
And bass and treble voices strike the skies.
No common weapons in their hands are found,
Like Gods they fight, nor dread a mortal wound.
45   So when bold Homer makes the Gods engage,
And heavenly breasts with human passions rage;
'Gainst Pallas, Mars; Latona, Hermes arms;
And all Olympus rings with loud alarms:
Jove's thunder roars, heaven trembles all around,
50 Blue Neptune storms, the bellowing deeps resound:
Earth shakes her nodding towers, the ground gives way,
And the pale ghosts start at the flash of day!
   Triumphant Umbriel on a sconce's⁷ height
Clapped his glad wings, and sat to view the fight:
55 Propped on the bodkin spears, the sprites survey
The growing combat, or assist the fray.
   While through the press enraged Thalestris flies,
And scatters death around from both her eyes,
A beau and witling perished in the throng,
60 One died in metaphor, and one in song.
"O cruel nymph! a living death I bear,"
Cried Dapperwit, and sunk beside his chair.

---

6. The speech is a close parody of Pope's own translation of the speech of Sarpedon to Glaucus, first published in 1709 and slightly revised in his version of the *Iliad* (12.371–96).
7. A sconce is a candlestick fastened on the wall.

A mournful glance Sir Fopling upwards cast,
"Those eyes are made so killing"—was his last.
65 Thus on Maeander's flowery margin lies
The expiring swan,[8] and as he sings he dies.
    When bold Sir Plume had drawn Clarissa down,
Chloe stepped in, and killed him with a frown;
She smiled to see the doughty hero slain,
70 But, at her smile, the beau revived again.
    Now Jove suspends his golden scales in air,
Weighs the men's wits against the lady's hair;
The doubtful beam long nods from side to side;
At length the wits mount up, the hairs subside.
75   See, fierce Belinda on the Baron flies,
With more than usual lightning in her eyes;
Nor feared the chief the unequal fight to try,
Who sought no more than on his foe to die.
    But this bold lord with manly strength endued,
80 She with one finger and a thumb subdued:
Just where the breath of life his nostrils drew,
A charge of snuff the wily virgin threw;
The Gnomes direct, to every atom just,
The pungent grains of titillating dust.
85 Sudden, with starting tears each eye o'erflows,
And the high dome re-echoes to his nose.
    "Now meet thy fate," incensed Belinda cried,
And drew a deadly bodkin[9] from her side.
(The same, his ancient personage to deck,
90 Her great-great-grandsire wore about his neck,
In three seal rings; which after, melted down,
Formed a vast buckle for his widow's gown:
Her infant grandame's whistle next it grew,
The bells she jingled, and the whistle blew;
95 Then in a bodkin graced her mother's hairs,
Which long she wore, and now Belinda wears.)
    "Boast not my fall," he cried, "insulting foe!
Thou by some other shalt be laid as low.
Nor think to die dejects my lofty mind:
100 All that I dread is leaving you behind!
Rather than so, ah, let me still survive,
And burn in Cupid's flames—but burn alive."
    "Restore the Lock!" she cries; and all around
"Restore the Lock!" the vaulted roofs rebound.
105 Not fierce Othello in so loud a strain
Roared for the handkerchief that caused his pain.[1]
But see how oft ambitious aims are crossed,
And chiefs contend till all the prize is lost!
The lock, obtained with guilt, and kept with pain,
110 In every place is sought, but sought in vain:
With such a prize no mortal must be blessed,

8. The Maeander, a river in Asia Minor, was famous in mythology for its swans.
9. Here, an ornamental hairpin shaped like a

dagger.
1. *Othello* 3.4.

So Heaven decrees! with Heaven who can contest?
   Some thought it mounted to the lunar sphere,
Since all things lost on earth are treasured there.
¹¹⁵ There heroes' wits are kept in ponderous vases,
And beaux' in snuffboxes and tweezer cases.
There broken vows and deathbed alms are found,
And lovers' hearts with ends of riband bound,
The courtier's promises, and sick man's prayers,
¹²⁰ The smiles of harlots, and the tears of heirs,
Cages for gnats, and chains to yoke a flea,
Dried butterflies, and tomes of casuistry.
   But trust the Muse—she saw it upward rise,
Though marked by none but quick, poetic eyes
¹²⁵ (So Rome's great founder to the heavens withdrew,[2]
To Proculus alone confessed in view);
A sudden star, it shot through liquid air,
And drew behind a radiant trail of hair.
Not Berenice's locks first rose so bright,[3]
¹³⁰ The heavens bespangling with disheveled light.
The Sylphs behold it kindling as it flies,
And pleased pursue its progress through the skies.
   This the beau monde shall from the Mall[4] survey,
And hail with music its propitious ray.
¹³⁵ This the blest lover shall for Venus take,
And send up vows from Rosamonda's Lake.[5]
This Partridge[6] soon shall view in cloudless skies,
When next he looks through Galileo's eyes;°   *telescope*
And hence the egregious wizard shall foredoom
¹⁴⁰ The fate of Louis, and the fall of Rome.
   Then cease, bright nymph! to mourn thy ravished hair,
Which adds new glory to the shining sphere!
Not all the tresses that fair head can boast
Shall draw such envy as the Lock you lost.
¹⁴⁵ For, after all the murders of your eye,
When, after millions slain, yourself shall die:
When those fair suns shall set, as set they must,
And all those tresses shall be laid in dust,
This Lock the Muse shall consecrate to fame,
¹⁵⁰ And 'midst the stars inscribe Belinda's name.

1712   1714, 1717

2. Romulus, the "founder" and first king of Rome, was snatched to heaven in a storm cloud while reviewing his army in the Campus Martius (Livy 1.16).
3. Berenice, the wife of Ptolemy III, dedicated a lock of her hair to the gods to ensure her husband's safe return from war. It was turned into a constellation.
4. A walk laid out by Charles II in St. James's Park (London), a resort for strollers of all sorts.
5. In St. James's Park; associated with unhappy lovers.
6. John Partridge, an astrologer whose annually published predictions (among them that Louis XIV and the Catholic Church would fall) had been amusingly satirized by Swift and other wits in 1708.

Eloisa to Abelard

Like Ovid's *Sappho to Phaon*, which Pope had translated in his teens, *Eloisa to Abelard* is a heroic epistle: strictly defined, a versified love letter, involving historical persons, which dramatizes the feelings of a woman who has been forsaken. Pope took his subject from one of the most famous affairs of history. Peter Abelard (1079–1142), a brilliant Scholastic theologian, seduced a young girl, his pupil Heloise; eventually she bore him a child, and they were secretly married. Enraged at the betrayal of trust, and what he regarded as the casting off of Heloise, her uncle Fulbert revenged himself by having Abelard castrated. The lovers separated; each of them entered a monastery and went on to a distinguished career in the church. Yet their greatest fame derives from the letters they are supposed to have exchanged late in their lives (some scholars have cast doubt on the authenticity of Heloise's letters). It is this correspondence, made newly popular by French and English translations of the original Latin, that inspired Pope's poem.

The heroic epistle challenges authors in two ways: they must exert historical imagination, projecting themselves into another time and place; and they must enter the mind and passions of a woman, acting her part, and showing everything from her point of view. Historically, Pope draws on his knowledge of Roman Catholic ritual to envelop Eloisa in a rich medieval atmosphere. The dark Gothic convent, situated in an imaginary landscape of grottos, mountains, and pine forests, embodies the eighteenth-century sense of the romantic: fantastic, legendary, and extravagant. Here Eloisa is cloistered, not only physically but mentally, by religious mysticism that surrounds her with a melancholy as palpable as the image of her lover. The greatest triumph of the poem, however, is psychological. In *Eloisa,* for the only time in his career, Pope tells a story wholly in another's voice. Confused and tormented, the heroine tosses between two kinds of love: an erotic passion for the earthly lover whose memory she cannot quell and the divine, chaste love that must content a nun. Abelard and God, within her fantasy, compete for her soul. Pope brings these internal struggles to the surface by externalizing them in bold dramatic rhetoric, formal and intense as an aria in an opera (the poem was long a favorite for reading aloud). Eloisa views herself theatrically, if only because, in the letter, she is trying to make Abelard visualize the pathos of her situation. There is literally no way out for her, and at the end of the poem, she can break the static circle of desire and loneliness only by picturing herself in the peace of death. Yet the high reputation of the work, well into the Romantic era, owes less to its theatrics than to its convincing image of a mind in pain. "If you search for passion," Lord Byron wrote more than a century later, "where is it to be found stronger than in the Epistle from Eloisa to Abelard?"

For a depiction of an incident in this famous love story, see Angelika Kauffmann's painting *The Parting of Abelard from Heloise* (ca. 1778), in the color insert in this volume.

Eloisa to Abelard

The Argument

Abelard and Eloisa flourished in the twelfth century; they were two of the most distinguished persons of their age in learning and beauty, but for nothing more famous than for their unfortunate passion. After a long course of calamities, they retired each to a several[1] convent, and consecrated the remainder of their days to religion. It was many years after this separation,

1. Separate.

that a letter of Abelard's to a friend which contained the history of his misfortune, fell into the hands of Eloisa. This awakening all her tenderness, occasioned those celebrated letters (out of which the following is partly extracted)[2] which give so lively a picture of the struggles of grace and nature, virtue and passion.

> In these deep solitudes and awful cells,
> Where heavenly-pensive contemplation dwells,
> And ever-musing melancholy reigns;
> What means this tumult in a vestal's[3] veins?
> 5 Why rove my thoughts beyond this last retreat?
> Why feels my heart its long-forgotten heat?
> Yet, yet I love!—From Abelard it[4] came,
> And Eloisa yet must kiss the name.
>   Dear fatal name! rest ever unrevealed,
> 10 Nor pass these lips in holy silence sealed.
> Hide it, my heart, within that close disguise,
> Where mixed with God's, his loved idea° lies.   *mental image*
> O write it not, my hand—the name appears
> Already written—wash it out, my tears!
> 15 In vain lost Eloisa weeps and prays,
> Her heart still dictates, and her hand obeys.
>   Relentless walls! whose darksome round contains
> Repentant sighs, and voluntary pains:
> Ye rugged rocks! which holy knees have worn;
> 20 Ye grots and caverns shagged with horrid° thorn!   *bristling*
> Shrines! where their vigils pale-eyed virgins keep,
> And pitying saints, whose statues learn to weep![5]
> Tho' cold like you, unmoved, and silent grown,
> I have not yet forgot myself to stone.
> 25 All is not Heaven's while Abelard has part,
> Still rebel nature holds out half my heart;
> Nor prayers nor fasts its stubborn pulse restrain,
> Nor tears, for ages taught to flow in vain.
>   Soon as thy letters trembling I unclose,
> 30 That well-known name awakens all my woes.
> Oh name for ever sad! for ever dear!
> Still breathed in sighs, still ushered with a tear.
> I tremble too, where'er my own I find,
> Some dire misfortune follows close behind.
> 35 Line after line my gushing eyes o'erflow,
> Led through a sad variety of woe:
> Now warm in love, now withering in my bloom,
> Lost in a convent's solitary gloom!
> There stern religion quenched the unwilling flame,
> 40 There died the best of passions, love and fame.
>   Yet write, oh write me all, that I may join

---

2. Pope's source was a highly romanticized English version of the letters by John Hughes, published in 1713.

3. Nun's. Here, as elsewhere, Eloisa substitutes a pagan form for a Christian; nor is she in fact a virgin (vestal).

4. The letter to which Eloisa is replying.

5. In damp places, stone "weeps" through condensation.

Griefs to thy griefs, and echo sighs to thine.
Nor foes nor fortune take this power away.
And is my Abelard less kind than they?
45   Tears still are mine, and those I need not spare,
Love but demands what else were shed in prayer;
No happier task these faded eyes pursue,
To read and weep is all they now can do.
      Then share thy pain, allow that sad relief;
50   Ah, more than share it! give me all thy grief.
Heaven first taught letters for some wretch's aid,
Some banished lover, or some captive maid;
They live, they speak, they breathe what love inspires,
Warm from the soul, and faithful to its fires,
55   The virgin's wish without her fears impart,
Excuse the blush, and pour out all the heart,
Speed the soft intercourse from soul to soul,
And waft a sigh from Indus to the Pole.[6]
      Thou knowest how guiltless first I met thy flame,
60   When love approached me under friendship's name;
My fancy formed thee of angelic kind,
Some emanation of the all-beauteous Mind.[7]
Those smiling eyes, attempering° every ray, *moderating, assuaging*
Shone sweetly lambent with celestial day:
65   Guiltless I gazed; heaven listened while you sung;
And truths divine came mended from that tongue.[8]
From lips like those what precept failed to move?
Too soon they taught me 'twas no sin to love.
Back through the paths of pleasing sense I ran,
70   Nor wished an angel whom I loved a man.
Dim and remote the joys of saints I see,
Nor envy them, that heaven I lose for thee.
      How oft, when pressed to marriage, have I said,
Curse on all laws but those which love has made!
75   Love, free as air, at sight of human ties,
Spreads his light wings, and in a moment flies.
Let wealth, let honor, wait the wedded dame,
August her deed, and sacred be her fame;
Before true passion all those views remove,° *depart*
80   Fame, wealth, and honor! what are you to love?
The jealous god, when we profane his fires,
Those restless passions in revenge inspires,
And bids them make mistaken mortals groan,
Who seek in love for aught but love alone.
85   Should at my feet the world's great master fall,
Himself, his throne, his world, I'd scorn 'em all:
Nor Caesar's empress would I deign to prove;° *try*
No, make me mistress to the man I love;
If there be yet another name more free,

---

6. From the Indus River, in South Asia, to the North Pole.
7. God, conceived (as is proper to a student of philosophy) in Platonic terms.
8. He was her preceptor in philosophy and divinity [Pope's note].

90　More fond than mistress, make me that to thee!
　　Oh happy state! when souls each other draw,
　　When love is liberty, and nature, law:
　　All then is full, possessing, and possessed,
　　No craving void left aching in the breast:
95　Even thought meets thought ere from the lips it part,
　　And each warm wish springs mutual from the heart.
　　This sure is bliss (if bliss on earth there be)
　　And once the lot of Abelard and me.
　　　　Alas how changed! what sudden horrors rise!
100　A naked lover bound and bleeding lies!
　　Where, where was Eloise? her voice, her hand,
　　Her poniard,° had opposed the dire command.　　　　　　*dagger*
　　Barbarian, stay! that bloody stroke restrain;
　　The crime was common,° common be the pain.°　　*shared / punishment*
105　I can no more; by shame, by rage suppressed,
　　Let tears, and burning blushes speak the rest.
　　　　Canst thou forget that sad, that solemn day,
　　When victims at yon altar's foot we lay?
　　Canst thou forget what tears that moment fell,
110　When, warm in youth, I bade the world farewell?
　　As with cold lips I kissed the sacred veil,
　　The shrines all trembled, and the lamps grew pale:
　　Heaven scarce believed the conquest it surveyed,
　　And saints with wonder heard the vows I made.
115　Yet then, to those dread altars as I drew,
　　Not on the Cross my eyes were fixed, but you;
　　Not grace, or zeal, love only was my call,
　　And if I lose thy love, I lose my all.
　　Come! with thy looks, thy words, relieve my woe;
120　Those still at least are left thee to bestow.
　　Still on that breast enamored let me lie,
　　Still drink delicious poison from thy eye,
　　Pant on thy lip, and to thy heart be pressed;
　　Give all thou canst—and let me dream the rest.
125　Ah no! instruct me other joys to prize,
　　With other beauties charm my partial[9] eyes,
　　Full in my view set all the bright abode,
　　And make my soul quit Abelard for God.
　　　　Ah think at least thy flock deserves thy care,
130　Plants of thy hand, and children of thy prayer.
　　From the false world in early youth they fled,
　　By thee to mountains, wilds, and deserts led.
　　You raised these hallowed walls;[1] the desert smiled,
　　And paradise was opened in the wild.
135　No weeping orphan saw his father's stores
　　Our shrines irradiate,[2] or emblaze the floors;
　　No silver saints, by dying misers given,

9. Fond; seeing only a part.
1. "He founded the monastery" [Pope's note]. Abelard erected the "Paraclete," a modest oratory near Troyes, in 1122; seven years later, when the nunnery of which Heloise was prioress was evicted from its property, he ceded the lands of the Paraclete to her.
2. Adorn with splendor.

Here bribed the rage of ill-requited heaven:
But such plain roofs as piety could raise,
140 And only vocal with the Maker's[3] praise.
In these lone walls (their day's eternal bound)
These moss-grown domes with spiry turrets crowned,
Where awful arches make a noon-day night,
And the dim windows shed a solemn light,
145 Thy eyes diffused a reconciling ray,
And gleams of glory brightened all the day.
But now no face divine contentment wears,
'Tis all blank sadness, or continual tears.
See how the force of others' prayers I try,
150 (O pious fraud of amorous charity!)
But why should I on others' prayers depend?
Come thou, my father, brother, husband, friend!
Ah let thy handmaid, sister, daughter move,
And all those tender names in one, thy love!
155 The darksome pines that o'er yon rocks reclined
Wave high, and murmur to the hollow wind,
The wandering streams that shine between the hills,
The grots that echo to the tinkling rills,
The dying gales that pant upon the trees,
160 The lakes that quiver to the curling breeze;
No more these scenes my meditation aid,
Or lull to rest the visionary[4] maid.
But o'er the twilight groves and dusky caves,
Long-sounding isles,[5] and intermingled graves,
165 Black Melancholy sits, and round her throws
A death-like silence, and a dread repose:
Her gloomy presence saddens all the scene,
Shades every flower, and darkens every green,
Deepens the murmur of the falling floods,
170 And breathes a browner horror on the woods.[6]
        Yet here for ever, ever must I stay;
Sad proof how well a lover can obey!
Death, only death, can break the lasting chain;
And here, even then, shall my cold dust remain,
175 Here all its frailties, all its flames resign,
And wait, till 'tis no sin to mix with thine.
        Ah wretch! believed the spouse of God in vain,
Confessed within the slave of love and man.
Assist me, heaven! but whence arose that prayer?
180 Sprung it from piety, or from despair?
Even here, where frozen chastity retires,
Love finds an altar for forbidden fires.
I ought to grieve, but cannot what I ought;
I mourn the lover, not lament the fault;

---

3. God's or Abelard's.
4. Given to visions.
5. Sounds reverberate over water as in the *aisles* of a church.
6. The image of the Goddess Melancholy sitting over the convent, and, as it were, expanding her dreadful wings over its whole circuit, and diffusing her gloom all around it, is truly sublime, and strongly conceived [Joseph Warton's note].

185 I view my crime, but kindle at the view,
Repent old pleasures, and solicit new;
Now turned to heaven, I weep my past offense,
Now think of thee, and curse my innocence.
Of all affliction taught a lover yet,
190 'Tis sure the hardest science° to forget!   knowledge
How shall I lose the sin, yet keep the sense,[7]
And love the offender, yet detest the offense?
How the dear object from the crime remove,
Or how distinguish penitence from love?
195 Unequal task! a passion to resign,
For hearts so touched, so pierced, so lost as mine.
Ere such a soul regains its peaceful state,
How often must it love, how often hate!
How often hope, despair, resent, regret,
200 Conceal, disdain—do all things but forget.
But let heaven seize it, all at once 'tis fired,
Not touched, but rapt; not wakened, but inspired![8]
Oh come! oh teach me nature to subdue,
Renounce my love, my life, my self—and you.
205 Fill my fond heart with God alone, for he
Alone can rival, can succeed to thee.
      How happy is the blameless vestal's lot!
The world forgetting, by the world forgot.
Eternal sun-shine of the spotless mind!
210 Each prayer accepted, and each wish resigned;
Labor and rest, that equal periods keep;
"Obedient slumbers that can wake and weep;"[9]
Desires composed, affections ever even;
Tears that delight, and sighs that waft to heaven.
215 Grace shines around her with serenest beams,
And whispering angels prompt her golden dreams.
For her the unfading rose of Eden blooms,
And wings of seraphs shed divine perfumes,
For her the Spouse prepares the bridal ring,
220 For her white virgins hymenaeals[1] sing,
To sounds of heavenly harps she dies away,
And melts in visions of eternal day.
      Far other dreams my erring soul employ,
Far other raptures, of unholy joy:
225 When at the close of each sad, sorrowing day,
Fancy restores what vengeance snatched away,
Then conscience sleeps, and leaving nature free,
All my loose soul unbounded springs to thee.
O curst, dear horrors of all-conscious night![2]
230 How glowing guilt exalts the keen delight!
Provoking daemons all restraint remove,

---

7. Both perception and sensation.
8. I.e., when touched, at once rapt; when wakened, at once inspired.
9. From *Description of a Religious House* (1648), by Richard Crashaw.

1. Wedding hymns. Every nun is the bride of Christ, her spouse.
2. The night knows everything, and Eloisa is conscious (guiltily aware) all through the night.

And stir within me every source of love.
I hear thee, view thee, gaze o'er all thy charms,
And round thy phantom glue my clasping arms.
235 I wake—no more I hear, no more I view,
The phantom flies me, as unkind as you.
I call aloud; it hears not what I say;
I stretch my empty arms; it glides away:
To dream once more I close my willing eyes;
240 Ye soft illusions, dear deceits, arise!
Alas, no more!—methinks we wandering go
Through dreary wastes, and weep each other's woe;
Where round some moldering tower pale ivy creeps,
And low-browed rocks hang nodding o'er the deeps.
245 Sudden you mount! you beckon from the skies;
Clouds interpose, waves roar, and winds arise.
I shriek, start up, the same sad prospect find,
And wake to all the griefs I left behind.
    For thee the fates, severely kind, ordain
250 A cool suspense° from pleasure and from pain;   *suspension*
Thy life a long dead calm of fixed repose;
No pulse that riots, and no blood that glows.
Still as the sea, ere winds were taught to blow,
Or moving spirit bade the waters flow;
255 Soft as the slumbers of a saint forgiven,
And mild as opening gleams of promised heaven.
    Come, Abelard! for what hast thou to dread?
The torch of Venus burns not for the dead.
Nature stands checked; religion disapproves;
260 Even thou art cold—yet Eloisa loves.
Ah hopeless, lasting flames! like those that burn
To light the dead, and warm the unfruitful urn.[3]
    What scenes appear where'er I turn my view?
The dear ideas, where I fly, pursue,
265 Rise in the grove, before the altar rise,
Stain all my soul, and wanton in my eyes!
I waste the matin lamp in sighs for thee,
Thy image steals between my God and me,
Thy voice I seem in every hymn to hear,
270 With every bead I drop too soft a tear.
When from the censer clouds of fragrance roll,
And swelling organs lift the rising soul,
One thought of thee puts all the pomp to flight,
Priests, tapers, temples, swim before my sight:
275 In seas of flame[4] my plunging soul is drowned,
While altars blaze, and angels tremble round.
    While prostrate here in humble grief I lie,
Kind, virtuous drops just gathering in my eye,
While praying, trembling, in the dust I roll,
280 And dawning grace is opening on my soul:
Come, if thou dar'st, all charming as thou art!

3. Perpetual fires were placed in Roman tombs.   4. Love or hell.

Oppose thyself to heaven; dispute° my heart;   *contend for*
Come, with one glance of those deluding eyes
Blot out each bright idea of the skies.
285 Take back that grace, those sorrows, and those tears,
Take back my fruitless penitence and prayers,
Snatch me, just mounting, from the blest abode,
Assist the fiends and tear me from my God!
   No, fly me, fly me! far as pole from pole;
290 Rise Alps between us! and whole oceans roll!
Ah come not, write not, think not once of me,
Nor share one pang of all I felt for thee.
Thy oaths I quit,° thy memory resign,   *absolve*
Forget, renounce me, hate whate'er was mine.
295 Fair eyes, and tempting looks (which yet I view!)
Long loved, adored ideas! all adieu!
O grace serene! oh virtue heavenly fair!
Divine oblivion of low-thoughted care!
Fresh blooming hope, gay daughter of the sky!
300 And faith, our early immortality!
Enter, each mild, each amicable guest;
Receive, and wrap me in eternal rest!
   See in her cell sad Eloisa spread,
Propped on some tomb, a neighbor of the dead!
305 In each low wind methinks a spirit calls,
And more than echoes talk along the walls.
Here, as I watched the dying lamps around,
From yonder shrine I heard a hollow sound.
"Come, sister, come! (it said, or seemed to say)
310 Thy place is here, sad sister, come away!
Once like thyself, I trembled, wept, and prayed,
Love's victim then, tho' now a sainted maid:
But all is calm in this eternal sleep;
Here grief forgets to groan, and love to weep,
315 Even superstition loses every fear:
For God, not man, absolves our frailties here."
   I come, I come! prepare your roseate bowers,
Celestial palms, and ever-blooming flowers.
Thither, where sinners may have rest, I go,
320 Where flames refined in breasts seraphic glow.
Thou, Abelard! the last sad office pay,
And smooth my passage to the realms of day;
See my lips tremble, and my eyeballs roll,
Suck my last breath, and catch my flying soul!
325 Ah no—in sacred vestments may'st thou stand,
The hallowed taper trembling in thy hand,
Present the Cross before my lifted eye,
Teach me at once, and learn of° me to die.   *from*
Ah then, thy once-loved Eloisa see!
330 It will be then no crime to gaze on me.
See from my cheek the transient roses fly!
See the last sparkle languish in my eye!
Till every motion, pulse, and breath be o'er;

And even my Abelard be loved no more.
335 O death all-eloquent! you only prove
What dust we doat on, when 'tis man we love.
    Then too, when fate shall thy fair frame destroy,
(That cause of all my guilt, and all my joy)
In trance ecstatic may thy pangs be drowned,
340 Bright clouds descend, and angels watch thee round,
From opening skies may streaming glories shine,
And saints embrace thee with a love like mine.
    May one kind grave unite each hapless name,[5]
And graft my love immortal on thy fame!
345 Then, ages hence, when all my woes are o'er,
When this rebellious heart shall beat no more;
If ever chance two wandering lovers brings
To Paraclete's white walls, and silver springs,
O'er the pale marble shall they join their heads,
350 And drink the falling tears each other sheds,
Then sadly say, with mutual pity moved,
"Oh may we never love as these have loved!"
From the full choir when loud Hosannas rise,
And swell the pomp of dreadful sacrifice,[6]
355 Amid that scene if some relenting eye
Glance on the stone where our cold relics lie,
Devotion's self shall steal a thought from heaven,
One human tear shall drop, and be forgiven.
And sure if fate some future bard shall join
360 In sad similitude of griefs to mine,
Condemned whole years in absence to deplore,[7]
And image° charms he must behold no more,   *imagine, depict*
Such if there be, who loves so long, so well,
Let him our sad, our tender story tell;
365 The well-sung woes will sooth my pensive ghost;
He best can paint 'em, who shall feel 'em most.

1717

An Essay on Man

Pope's philosophical poem *An Essay on Man* represents the beginnings of an ambitious but never completed plan for what he called his "ethic work," intended to be a large survey of human nature, society, and morals. He dedicated the *Essay* to Henry St. John (pronounced *Sín-jun*), Viscount Bolingbroke (1678–1751), the brilliant, erratic secretary of state in the Tory ministry of 1710–14. After the accession of George I, Bolingbroke fled to France, but he was allowed to return in 1723, settling near Pope at Dawley Farm. The two formed a close friendship and talked through the ideas expressed in the *Essay* and in Bolingbroke's own philosophical writings (some of which are addressed to Pope). But

---

5. Abelard and Eloisa were interred in the same grave, or in monuments adjoining, in the monastery of the Paraclete [Pope's note].
6. The celebration of the Eucharist (mass).
7. Lament. Pope, imagining himself imagined by Eloisa, hints that he too is separated from a loved one; perhaps Lady Mary Wortley Montagu, who was in Turkey. Pope and Montagu later quarreled, and she appears as Sappho in Epistle 2, *To a Lady*, in the *Epistle to Dr. Arbuthnot*, and in other places in his work.

Pope's poem has many sources in the thought of his times and the philosophical tradition at large, and he says himself in the poem's little preface that his intention is to formulate a widely acceptable system of obvious, familiar truths. Pope's "optimism"—his insistence that everything must be "RIGHT" in a universe created and superintended by God—skips over the tragic elements of experience that much great literary, philosophical, and religious expression confronts. But the strains and contradictions of the poem are themselves deeply revealing about the thinking of Pope and his age, as he both presents and withholds a comprehensive view of the universe and reasons out reason's drastic limitations.

Pope's purpose is to "vindicate the ways of God to man," a phrase that consciously echoes *Paradise Lost* 1.26. Like John Milton, Pope faces the problem of the existence of evil in a world presumed to be the creation of a good god. *Paradise Lost* is biblical in content, Christian in doctrine; *An Essay on Man* avoids all specifically Christian doctrines, not because Pope disbelieved them but because "man," the subject of the poem, includes millions who never heard of Christianity and Pope is concerned with the universal. Milton tells a Judeo-Christian story. Pope writes in abstract terms.

The *Essay* is divided into four epistles. In the first Pope asserts the essential order and goodness of the universe and the rightness of our place in it. The other epistles deal with how we may emulate in our nature and in society the cosmic harmony revealed in the first epistle. The second seeks to show how we may attain a psychological harmony that can become the basis of a virtuous life through the cooperation of self-love and the passions (both necessary to our complete humanity) with reason, the controller and director. The third is concerned with the individual in society, which, it teaches, was created through the cooperation of self-love (the egoistic drives that motivate us) and social love (our dependence on others, our inborn benevolence). The fourth is concerned with happiness, which lies within the reach of all for it is dependent on virtue, which becomes possible when—though only when—self-love is transmuted into love of others and love of God. Such, in brief summary, are Pope's main ideas, expressed in many phrases so memorable that they have detached themselves from the poem and become part of daily speech.

From An Essay on Man

TO HENRY ST. JOHN, LORD BOLINGBROKE

Epistle 1. Of the Nature and State of Man,
with Respect to the Universe

> Awake, my St. John! leave all meaner things
> To low ambition, and the pride of kings.
> Let us (since life can little more supply
> Than just to look about us and to die)
> 5 Expatiate free° o'er all this scene of man;   *range freely*
> A mighty maze! but not without a plan;
> A wild, where weeds and flowers promiscuous shoot,
> Or garden, tempting with forbidden fruit.
> Together let us beat this ample field,[1]
> 10 Try what the open, what the covert yield;
> The latent tracts, the giddy heights, explore

---

1. Pope and Bolingbroke will try to drive truth into the open, like hunters beating the bushes for game.

Of all who blindly creep, or sightless soar;
Eye Nature's walks, shoot folly as it flies,
And catch the manners living as they rise;
15   Laugh where we must, be candid° where we can;   *favorably disposed*
But vindicate the ways of God to man.

    1. Say first, of God above, or man below,
What can we reason, but from what we know?
Of man, what see we but his station here,
20   From which to reason, or to which refer?
Through worlds unnumbered though the God be known,
'Tis ours to trace him only in our own.
He, who through vast immensity can pierce,
See worlds on worlds compose one universe,
25   Observe how system into system runs,
What other planets circle other suns,
What varied being peoples every star,
May tell why Heaven has made us as we are.
But of this frame° the bearings, and the ties,   *the universe*
30   The strong connections, nice dependencies,
Gradations just, has thy pervading soul
Looked through? or can a part contain the whole?
    Is the great chain, that draws all to agree,
And drawn supports, upheld by God, or thee?[2]

35   2. Presumptuous man! the reason wouldst thou find,
Why formed so weak, so little, and so blind?
First, if thou canst, the harder reason guess,
Why formed no weaker, blinder, and no less!
Ask of thy mother earth, why oaks are made
40   Taller or stronger than the weeds they shade?
Or ask of yonder argent fields above,
Why Jove's satellites[3] are less than Jove?
    Of systems possible, if 'tis confessed
That Wisdom Infinite must form the best,
45   Where all must full or not coherent be,
And all that rises, rise in due degree;
Then, in the scale of reasoning life, 'tis plain,
There must be, somewhere, such a rank as man:
And all the question (wrangle e'er so long)
50   Is only this, if God has placed him wrong?
    Respecting man, whatever wrong we call,
May, must be right, as relative to all.
In human works, though labored on with pain,
A thousand movements scarce one purpose gain;
55   In God's, one single can its end produce;
Yet serves to second too some other use.
So man, who here seems principal alone,
Perhaps acts second to some sphere unknown,

---

2. For the chain of being, see Addison's *The*
Spectator 519 (p. 2662) and lines 207–58.

3. In his *Dictionary,* Johnson notes and condemns
Pope's giving this word four syllables, as in Latin.

Touches some wheel, or verges to some goal;
60   'Tis but a part we see, and not a whole.
        When the proud steed shall know why man restrains
      His fiery course, or drives him o'er the plains;
      When the dull ox, why now he breaks the clod,
      Is now a victim, and now Egypt's god:[4]
65   Then shall man's pride and dullness comprehend
      His actions', passions', being's use and end;
      Why doing, suffering, checked, impelled; and why
      This hour a slave, the next a deity.
        Then say not man's imperfect, Heaven in fault;
70   Say rather, man's as perfect as he ought;
      His knowledge measured to his state and place,
      His time a moment, and a point his space.
      If to be perfect in a certain sphere,[5]
      What matter, soon or late, or here or there?
75   The blest today is as completely so,
      As who began a thousand years ago.

        3. Heaven from all creatures hides the book of Fate,
      All but the page prescribed, their present state:
      From brutes what men, from men what spirits know:
80   Or who could suffer being here below?
      The lamb thy riot° dooms to bleed today,   feast
      Had he thy reason, would he skip and play?
      Pleased to the last, he crops the flowery food,
      And licks the hand just raised to shed his blood.
85   O blindness to the future! kindly given,
      That each may fill the circle marked by Heaven:
      Who sees with equal eye, as God of all,
      A hero perish, or a sparrow fall,
      Atoms or systems° into ruin hurled,   solar systems
90   And now a bubble burst, and now a world.
        Hope humbly then; with trembling pinions soar;
      Wait the great teacher Death, and God adore!
      What future bliss, he gives not thee to know,
      But gives that hope to be thy blessing now.
95   Hope springs eternal in the human breast:
      Man never is, but always to be blest:
      The soul, uneasy and confined from home,
      Rests and expatiates in a life to come.
        Lo! the poor Indian, whose untutored mind
100   Sees God in clouds, or hears him in the wind;
      His soul proud Science never taught to stray
      Far as the solar walk, or milky way;
      Yet simple Nature to his hope has given,
      Behind the cloud-topped hill, an humbler heaven;
105   Some safer world in depth of woods embraced,
      Some happier island in the watery waste,
      Where slaves once more their native land behold,

4. The Egyptians worshiped a bull called Apis.   5. I.e., in one's "state and place."

No fiends torment, no Christians thirst for gold!
To be, contents his natural desire,
110   He asks no angel's wing, no seraph's fire;
But thinks, admitted to that equal° sky,   *impartial*
His faithful dog shall bear him company.

4. Go, wiser thou! and, in thy scale of sense,
Weigh thy opinion against Providence;
115   Call imperfection what thou fancy'st such,
Say, here he gives too little, there too much;
Destroy all creatures for thy sport or gust,[6]
Yet cry, if man's unhappy, God's unjust;
If man alone engross not Heaven's high care,
120   Alone made perfect here, immortal there:
Snatch from his hand the balance and the rod,[7]
Rejudge his justice, be the God of God!
In pride, in reasoning pride, our error lies;
All quit their sphere, and rush into the skies.
125   Pride still is aiming at the blest abodes,
Men would be angels, angels would be gods.
Aspiring to be gods, if angels fell,
Aspiring to be angels, men rebel:
And who but wishes to invert the laws
130   Of order, sins against the Eternal Cause.

5. Ask for what end the heavenly bodies shine,
Earth for whose use? Pride answers, " 'Tis for mine:
For me kind Nature wakes her genial power,
Suckles each herb, and spreads out every flower;
135   Annual for me, the grape, the rose renew
The juice nectareous, and the balmy dew;
For me, the mine a thousand treasures brings;
For me, health gushes from a thousand springs;
Seas roll to waft me, suns to light me rise;
140   My footstool earth, my canopy the skies."
But errs not Nature from this gracious end,
From burning suns when livid deaths descend,
When earthquakes swallow, or when tempests sweep
Towns to one grave, whole nations to the deep?
145   "No," 'tis replied, "the first Almighty Cause
Acts not by partial, but by general laws;
The exceptions few; some change since all began,
And what created perfect?"—Why then man?
If the great end be human happiness,
150   Then Nature deviates; and can man do less?
As much that end a constant course requires
Of showers and sunshine, as of man's desires;
As much eternal springs and cloudless skies,
As men forever temperate, calm, and wise.
155   If plagues or earthquakes break not Heaven's design,

6. "Sense of tasting" (Johnson's *Dictionary*).   7. Symbols of judgment and punishment.

Why then a Borgia, or a Catiline?[8]
Who knows but he whose hand the lightning forms,
Who heaves old ocean, and who wings the storms,
Pours fierce ambition in a Caesar's mind,
160 Or turns young Ammon° loose to scourge mankind?   *Alexander the*
From pride, from pride, our very reasoning springs;   *Great*
Account for moral, as for natural things:
Why charge we Heaven in those, in these acquit?
In both, to reason right is to submit.
165   Better for us, perhaps, it might appear,
Were there all harmony, all virtue here;
That never air or ocean felt the wind;
That never passion discomposed the mind:
But ALL subsists by elemental strife;
170 And passions are the elements of life.
The general ORDER, since the whole began,
Is kept in Nature, and is kept in man.

6. What would this man? Now upward will he soar,
And little less than angel, would be more;
175 Now looking downwards, just as grieved appears
To want the strength of bulls, the fur of bears.
Made for his use all creatures if he call,
Say what their use, had he the powers of all?
Nature to these, without profusion, kind,
180 The proper organs, proper powers assigned;
Each seeming want compènsated of course,°   *as a matter of course*
Here with degrees of swiftness, there of force;
All in exact proportion to the state;
Nothing to add, and nothing to abate.
185 Each beast, each insect, happy in its own;
Is Heaven unkind to man, and man alone?
Shall he alone, whom rational we call,
Be pleased with nothing, if not blessed with all?
The bliss of man (could pride that blessing find)
190 Is not to act or think beyond mankind;
No powers of body or of soul to share,
But what his nature and his state can bear.
Why has not man a microscopic eye?
For this plain reason, man is not a fly.
195 Say what the use, were finer optics given,
To inspect a mite, not comprehend the heaven?
Or touch, if tremblingly alive all o'er,
To smart and agonize at every pore?
Or quick effluvia[9] darting through the brain,

---

8. The Italian Renaissance family the Borgias was notorious for its ruthless lust for power, cruelty, rapaciousness, treachery, and murder (especially by poisoning). Cesare Borgia (1476–1507), son of Pope Alexander VI, is here referred to. Lucius Sergius Catiline (ca. 108–62 B.C.E.), an ambitious, greedy, and cruel conspirator against the Roman state, was denounced in Cicero's famous orations before the senate and in the Forum.

9. According to the philosophy of Epicurus (adopted by Robert Boyle, the chemist, and other 17th-century scientists), the senses are stirred to perception by being bombarded through the pores by steady streams of "effluvia," incredibly thin

200   Die of a rose in aromatic pain?
       If nature thundered in his opening ears,
       And stunned him with the music of the spheres,
       How would he wish that Heaven had left him still
       The whispering zephyr, and the purling rill?
205   Who finds not Providence all good and wise,
       Alike in what it gives, and what denies?

       7. Far as creation's ample range extends,
       The scale of sensual,° mental powers ascends: *sensory*
       Mark how it mounts, to man's imperial race,
210   From the green myriads in the peopled grass:
       What modes of sight betwixt each wide extreme,
       The mole's dim curtain, and the lynx's beam:[1]
       Of smell, the headlong lioness between,
       And hound sagacious° on the tainted green: *quick of scent*
215   Of hearing, from the life that fills the flood,
       To that which warbles through the vernal wood:
       The spider's touch, how exquisitely fine!
       Feels at each thread, and lives along the line:
       In the nice° bee, what sense so subtly true   *exact, accurate*
220   From poisonous herbs extracts the healing dew:
       How instinct varies in the groveling swine,
       Compared, half-reasoning elephant, with thine!
       'Twixt that, and reason, what a nice barrier,[2]
       Forever separate, yet forever near!
225   Remembrance and reflection how allied;
       What thin partitions sense from thought divide:
       And middle natures, how they long to join,
       Yet never pass the insuperable line!
       Without this just gradation, could they be
230   Subjected, these to those, or all to thee?
       The powers of all subdued by thee alone,
       Is not thy reason all these powers in one?

       8. See, through this air, this ocean, and this earth,
       All matter quick, and bursting into birth.
235   Above, how high progressive life may go!
       Around, how wide! how deep extend below!
       Vast Chain of Being! which from God began,
       Natures ethereal, human, angel, man,
       Beast, bird, fish, insect, what no eye can see,
240   No glass can reach! from Infinite to thee,
       From thee to nothing.—On superior powers
       Were we to press, inferior might on ours:
       Or in the full creation leave a void,
       Where, one step broken, the great scale's destroyed:
245   From Nature's chain whatever link you strike,
       Tenth or ten thousandth, breaks the chain alike.

---

and tiny—but material—images of the objects
that surround us.
1. One of several early theories of vision held
that the eye casts a beam of light that makes
objects visible.
2. Pronounced *ba-réer.*

And, if each system in gradation roll
Alike essential to the amazing whole,
The least confusion but in one, not all
250 That system only, but the whole must fall.
Let earth unbalanced from her orbit fly,
Planets and suns run lawless through the sky,
Let ruling angels from their spheres be hurled,
Being on being wrecked, and world on world,
255 Heaven's whole foundations to their center nod,
And Nature tremble to the throne of God:
All this dread ORDER break—for whom? for thee?
Vile worm!—oh, madness, pride, impiety!

9. What if the foot, ordained the dust to tread,
260 Or hand, to toil, aspired to be the head?
What if the head, the eye, or ear repined
To serve mere engines to the ruling Mind?[3]
Just as absurd, for any part to claim
To be another, in this general frame.
265 Just as absurd, to mourn the tasks or pains,
The great directing MIND of ALL ordains.
All are but parts of one stupendous whole,
Whose body Nature is, and God the soul;
That, changed through all, and yet in all the same,
270 Great in the earth, as in the ethereal frame,
Warms in the sun, refreshes in the breeze,
Glows in the stars, and blossoms in the trees,
Lives through all life, extends through all extent,
Spreads undivided, operates unspent,
275 Breathes in our soul, informs our mortal part,
As full, as perfect, in a hair as heart;
As full, as perfect, in vile man that mourns,
As the rapt seraph that adores and burns;
To him no high, no low, no great, no small;
280 He fills, he bounds, connects, and equals all.

10. Cease then, nor ORDER imperfection name:
Our proper bliss depends on what we blame.
Know thy own point: this kind, this due degree
Of blindness, weakness, Heaven bestows on thee.
285 Submit—In this, or any other sphere,
Secure to be as blest as thou canst bear:
Safe in the hand of one disposing Power,
Or in the natal, or the mortal hour.
All Nature is but art, unknown to thee;
290 All chance, direction, which thou canst not see;
All discord, harmony not understood;
All partial evil, universal good:
And, spite of pride, in erring reason's spite,
One truth is clear: Whatever IS, is RIGHT.

3. Cf. 1 Corinthians 12.14–26.

From *Epistle 2. Of the Nature and State of Man with Respect to Himself, as an Individual*

    1. Know then thyself, presume not God to scan;°   *judge*
    The proper study of mankind is Man.
    Placed on this isthmus of a middle state,
    A being darkly wise, and rudely great:
5   With too much knowledge for the skeptic side,
    With too much weakness for the Stoic's pride,
    He hangs between; in doubt to act, or rest,
    In doubt to deem himself a god, or beast;
    In doubt his mind or body to prefer,
10 Born but to die, and reasoning but to err;
    Alike in ignorance, his reason such,
    Whether he thinks too little, or too much:
    Chaos of thought and passion, all confused;
    Still by himself abused, or disabused;
15 Created half to rise, and half to fall;
    Great lord of all things, yet a prey to all;
    Sole judge of truth, in endless error hurled:
    The glory, jest, and riddle of the world!

*   *   *

1733

Epistle to Dr. Arbuthnot

Dr. John Arbuthnot (1667–1735), to whom Pope addressed his best-known verse epistle, was distinguished both as a physician and as a man of wit. He had been one of the liveliest members of the Martinus Scriblerus Club, helping his friends create the character and shape the career of the learned pedant whose memoirs the club had undertaken to write.

Pope had long been meditating such a poem, which was to be both an attack on his detractors and a defense of his own character and career. In his usual way, he had jotted down hints, lines, couplets, and fragments over a period of two decades, but the poem might never have been completed had it not been for two events: Arbuthnot, from his deathbed, wrote to urge Pope to continue his abhorrence of vice and to express it in his writings and, during 1733, Pope was the victim of two bitter attacks by "persons of rank and fortune," as the Advertisement has it. The "Verses Addressed to the Imitator of Horace" was the work of Lady Mary Wortley Montagu, helped by her friend Lord Hervey (pronounced *Harvey*), a close friend and confidant of Queen Caroline. "An Epistle to a Doctor of Divinity from a Nobleman at Hampton Court" was the work of Lord Hervey alone. Montagu had provocation enough, especially in Pope's recent reference to her in "The First Satire of the Second Book of Horace," lines 83–84; but Hervey had little to complain of beyond occasional covert references to him as "Lord Fanny." At any rate, the two scurrilous attacks goaded Pope into action, and he completed the poem by the end of the summer of 1734.

The *Epistle* is the most brilliant and daring execution of the techniques that Pope used in many of the autobiographical poems of the 1730s. He presents himself in a theatrical array of postures: the comically exaggerating complainer, the admired man of genius, the true friend, the unpretentiously honest man, the satirist-hero of his country, the "manly" defender of virtue, the tender son mothering his own mother. Part of what cements this mixture is the verve with which he modulates from role to role, implying that none of them exhaustively defines him. Pope tries to force the reader to take sides, for him and what he claims to represent, or against him. Thus reading becomes an ethical exercise; readers must make up their own minds about his moral superiority, his exquisitely crafted portraits of his enemies, his social self-positioning, or his self-righteous politics. Pope solicits our judgment of his character and his professed ideals, and no other poet in English does so with so much artistic energy, resourcefulness, and success.

It is not clear that Pope intended the poem to be thought of as a dialogue, as it has usually been printed since Warburton's edition of 1751. The original edition, while suggesting interruptions in the flow of the monologue, kept entirely to the form of a letter. The introduction of the friend, who speaks from time to time, converts the original letter into a dramatic dialogue.

Epistle to Dr. Arbuthnot

Advertisement

TO THE FIRST PUBLICATION OF THIS *Epistle*

This paper is a sort of bill of complaint, begun many years since, and drawn up by snatches, as the several occasions offered. I had no thoughts of publishing it, till it pleased some persons of rank and fortune (the authors of *Verses to the Imitator of Horace*, and of an *Epistle to a Doctor of Divinity from a Nobleman at Hampton Court*) to attack, in a very extraordinary manner, not only my writings (of which, being public, the public is judge) but my person, morals, and family, whereof, to those who know me not, a truer information may be requisite. Being divided between the necessity to say something of myself, and my own laziness to undertake so awkward a task, I thought it the shortest way to put the last hand[1] to this epistle. If it have anything pleasing, it will be that by which I am most desirous to please, the truth and the sentiment; and if anything offensive, it will be only to those I am least sorry to offend, the vicious or the ungenerous.

Many will know their own pictures in it, there being not a circumstance but what is true; but I have, for the most part, spared their names, and they may escape being laughed at, if they please.

I would have some of them know, it was owing to the request of the learned and candid friend to whom it is inscribed, that I make not as free use of theirs as they have done of mine. However, I shall have this advantage, and honor, on my side, that whereas, by their proceeding, any abuse may be directed at any man, no injury can possibly be done by mine, since a nameless character can never be found out, but by its truth and likeness. P.

> P. Shut, shut the door, good John![2] (fatigued, I said),
> Tie up the knocker, say I'm sick, I'm dead.
> The Dog Star[3] rages! nay 'tis past a doubt
> All Bedlam,[4] or Parnassus, is let out:
> 5   Fire in each eye, and papers in each hand,

1. Finish.
2. John Serle, Pope's gardener.
3. Sirius, associated with the period of greatest heat (and hence of madness) because it sets with the sun in late summer. August, in ancient Rome, was the season for reciting poetry.
4. Bethlehem Hospital for the insane, in London.

They rave, recite, and madden round the land.
    What walls can guard me, or what shades can hide?
They pierce my thickets, through my grot[5] they glide,
By land, by water, they renew the charge,
10 They stop the chariot, and they board the barge.
No place is sacred, not the church is free;
Even Sunday shines no Sabbath day to me:
Then from the Mint[6] walks forth the man of rhyme,
Happy! to catch me just at dinner time.
15   Is there a parson, much bemused in beer,
A maudlin poetess, a rhyming peer,
A clerk foredoomed his father's soul to cross,
Who pens a stanza when he should engross?[7]
Is there who, locked from ink and paper,[8] scrawls
20 With desperate charcoal round his darkened walls?
All fly to Twit'nam,[9] and in humble strain
Apply to me to keep them mad or vain.
Arthur,[1] whose giddy son neglects the laws,
Imputes to me and my damned works the cause:
25 Poor Cornus[2] sees his frantic wife elope,
And curses wit, and poetry, and Pope.
    Friend to my life (which did not you prolong,
The world had wanted° many an idle song)   *missed*
What drop or nostrum° can this plague remove?   *medicine*
30 Or which must end me, a fool's wrath or love?
A dire dilemma! either way I'm sped,°   *killed*
If foes, they write, if friends, they read me dead.
Seized and tied down to judge, how wretched I!
Who can't be silent, and who will not lie.
35 To laugh were want of goodness and of grace,
And to be grave exceeds all power of face.
I sit with sad civility, I read
With honest anguish and an aching head,
And drop at last, but in unwilling ears,
40 This saving counsel, "Keep your piece nine years."[3]
    "Nine years!" cries he, who high in Drury Lane,[4]
Lulled by soft zephyrs through the broken pane,
Rhymes ere he wakes, and prints before term[5] ends,
Obliged by hunger and request of friends:
45 "The piece, you think, is incorrect? why, take it,
I'm all submission, what you'd have it, make it."
    Three things another's modest wishes bound,

---

5. The subterranean passage under the road that separated his house at Twickenham from his garden became, in Pope's hands, a romantic grotto ornamented with shells and mirrors.
6. A place in Southwark where debtors were free from arrest (they could not be arrested anywhere on Sundays).
7. Write out legal documents.
8. Is there some madman who, locked up without ink or paper . . . ?
9. I.e., Twickenham, Pope's villa on the bank of the Thames; a few miles above Hampton Court.
1. Arthur Moore, whose son, James Moore

Smythe, dabbled in literature. Moore Smythe had earned Pope's enmity by using in one of his plays some unpublished lines from Pope's "Epistle 2. To a Lady" in spite of Pope's objections.
2. Latin for "horn," the traditional emblem of the cuckold.
3. The advice of Horace in *Art of Poetry* (line 388).
4. I.e., living in a garret in Drury Lane, site of one of the theaters and the haunt of the profligate.
5. One of the four annual periods in which the law courts are in session and with which the publishing season coincided.

My friendship, and a prologue,[6] and ten pound.
    Pitholeon[7] sends to me: "You know his Grace,
50 I want a patron; ask him for a place."
Pitholeon libeled me—"but here's a letter
Informs you, sir, 'twas when he knew no better.
Dare you refuse him? Curll[8] invites to dine,
He'll write a *Journal,* or he'll turn divine."[9]
55 Bless me! a packet.—" 'Tis a stranger sues,°   *asks for help*
A virgin tragedy, an orphan Muse."
If I dislike it, "Furies, death, and rage!"
If I approve, "Commend it to the stage."
There (thank my stars) my whole commission ends,
60 The players and I are, luckily, no friends.
Fired that the house° reject him, " 'Sdeath, I'll print it,   *playhouse*
And shame the fools—Your interest, sir, with Lintot!"[1]
Lintot, dull rogue, will think your price too much.
"Not, sir, if you revise it, and retouch."
65 All my demurs but double his attacks;
At last he whispers, "Do; and we go snacks."°   *shares*
Glad of a quarrel, straight I clap the door,
"Sir, let me see your works and you no more."
    'Tis sung, when Midas' ears began to spring
70 (Midas, a sacred person and a king),
His very minister who spied them first,
(Some say his queen) was forced to speak, or burst.[2]
And is not mine, my friend, a sorer case,
When every coxcomb perks them in my face?
75   A. Good friend, forbear! you deal in dangerous things.
I'd never name queens, ministers, or kings;
Keep close to ears,° and those let asses prick;   *whisper*
'Tis nothing——P. Nothing? if they bite and kick?
Out with it, *Dunciad!* let the secret pass,
80 That secret to each fool, that he's an ass:
The truth once told (and wherefore should we lie?)
The queen of Midas slept, and so may I.
    You think this cruel? take it for a rule,
No creature smarts so little as a fool.
85 Let peals of laughter, Codrus![3] round thee break,
Thou unconcerned canst hear the mighty crack.
Pit, box, and gallery in convulsions hurled,
Thou stand'st unshook amidst a bursting world.
Who shames a scribbler? break one cobweb through,

6. Famous poets helped playwrights by contributing prologues to their plays.
7. "A foolish poet of Rhodes, who pretended much to Greek" [Pope's note]. He is Leonard Welsted, who translated Longinus and had attacked and slandered Pope (see line 375).
8. Edmund Curll, shrewd and disreputable bookseller, published pirated works, works falsely ascribed to reputable writers, scandalous biographies, and other ephemera. Pope had often attacked him and had assigned to him a low role in The Dunciad.
9. I.e., he will attack Pope in the *London Journal*

or write a treatise on theology, as Welsted in fact did.
1. Bernard Lintot, publisher of Pope's Homer and other early works.
2. Midas, king of ancient Lydia, had the bad taste to prefer the flute-playing of Pan to that of Apollo, whereupon the god endowed him with ass's ears. It was his barber (not his wife or his minister) who discovered the secret and whispered it into a hole in the earth. The reference to "queen" and "minister" makes it plain that Pope is alluding to George II, Queen Caroline, and Walpole.
3. Poet ridiculed by Virgil and Juvenal.

90 He spins the slight, self-pleasing thread anew:
    Destroy his fib or sophistry, in vain;
    The creature's at his dirty work again,
    Throned in the center of his thin designs,
    Proud of a vast extent of flimsy lines.
95 Whom have I hurt? has poet yet or peer
    Lost the arched eyebrow or Parnassian sneer?
    And has not Colley still his lord and whore?
    His butchers Henley?[4] his freemasons Moore?
    Does not one table Bavius still admit?
100 Still to one bishop Philips[5] seem a wit?
    Still Sappho[6]——A. Hold! for god's sake—you'll offend.
    No names—be calm—learn prudence of a friend.
    I too could write, and I am twice as tall;
    But foes like these!——P. One flatterer's worse than all.
105 Of all mad creatures, if the learn'd are right,
    It is the slaver kills, and not the bite.
    A fool quite angry is quite innocent:
    Alas! 'tis ten times worse when they repent.

        One dedicates in high heroic prose,
110 And ridicules beyond a hundred foes;
    One from all Grub Street[7] will my fame defend,
    And, more abusive, calls himself my friend.
    This prints my letters,[8] that expects a bribe,
    And others roar aloud, "Subscribe, subscribe!"[9]
115   There are, who to my person pay their court:
    I cough like Horace,[1] and, though lean, am short;
    Ammon's great son[2] one shoulder had too high,
    Such Ovid's nose,[3] and "Sir! you have an eye—"
    Go on, obliging creatures, make me see
120 All that disgraced my betters met in me.
    Say for my comfort, languishing in bed,
    "Just so immortal Maro° held his head":   *Virgil*
    And when I die, be sure you let me know
    Great Homer died three thousand years ago.

125   Why did I write? what sin to me unknown
    Dipped me in ink, my parents', or my own?
    As yet a child, nor yet a fool to fame,
    I lisped in numbers,° for the numbers came.   *verses*

---

4. John Henley, known as "Orator" Henley, an independent preacher of marked eccentricity, was popular among the common people, especially for his elocution. Colley Cibber, the poet laureate.
5. The "bishop" is Hugh Boulter, bishop of Armagh. He had employed as his secretary Ambrose Philips (1674–1749), whose insipid simplicity of manner in poetry earned him the nickname of "Namby-Pamby." Bavius, the bad poet alluded to in Virgil's *Eclogue* 3.
6. Lady Mary Wortley Montagu.
7. A term denoting the whole society of literary, political, and journalistic hack writers.

8. In 1726 Curll had surreptitiously acquired and published without permission some of Pope's letters to Henry Cromwell.
9. To ensure the financial success of a work, wealthy readers were often asked to "subscribe" to it before printing was undertaken. Pope's Homer was published in this manner.
1. Horace, who mentions a cough in a few poems, was plump and short.
2. Alexander the Great, whose head inclined to his left shoulder, resembling Pope's hunchback.
3. Ovid's family name, Naso, suggests the Latin word *nasus* ("nose"), hence the pun.

I left no calling for this idle trade,
130 No duty broke, no father disobeyed.
The Muse but served to ease some friend, not wife,
To help me through this long disease, my life,
To second, Arbuthnot! thy art and care,
And teach the being you preserved, to bear.°   *endure*
135 A. But why then publish? P. Granville the polite,
And knowing Walsh, would tell me I could write;
Well-natured Garth inflamed with early praise,
And Congreve loved, and Swift endured my lays;
The courtly Talbot, Somers, Sheffield, read;
140 Even mitered Rochester would nod the head,
And St. John's self (great Dryden's friends before)
With open arms received one poet more.[4]
Happy my studies, when by these approved!
Happier their author, when by these beloved!
145 From these the world will judge of men and books,
Not from the Burnets, Oldmixons, and Cookes.[5]
      Soft were my numbers; who could take offense
While pure description held the place of sense?
Like gentle Fanny's[6] was my flowery theme,
150 A painted mistress, or a purling stream.
Yet then did Gildon draw his venal quill;[7]
I wished the man a dinner, and sat still.
Yet then did Dennis[8] rave in furious fret;
I never answered, I was not in debt.
155 If want provoked, or madness made them print,
I waged no war with Bedlam or the Mint.
      Did some more sober critic come abroad?
If wrong, I smiled; if right, I kissed the rod.
Pains, reading, study are their just pretense,
160 And all they want is spirit, taste, and sense.
Commas and points they set exactly right,
And 'twere a sin to rob them of their mite.
Yet ne'er one sprig of laurel graced these ribalds,
From slashing Bentley down to piddling Tibbalds.[9]
165 Each wight who reads not, and but scans and spells,
Each word-catcher that lives on syllables,
Even such small critics some regard may claim,

4. The purpose of this list is to establish Pope as the successor of Dryden and thus to place him far above his Grub Street persecutors. George Granville, Lord Lansdowne, poet, and statesman; William Walsh, poet and critic; Sir Samuel Garth, physician and mock-epic poet; William Congreve, the playwright; Charles Talbot, duke of Shrewsbury, Lord Sommers; John Sheffield, duke of Buckinghamshire; and Francis Atterbury, bishop of Rochester, statesmen, had all been associated with Dryden in his later years and had all encouraged the young Pope.
5. Thomas Burnet, John Oldmixon, and Thomas Cooke: Pope identifies them in a note as "authors of secret and scandalous history."
6. John, Lord Hervey, whom Pope satirizes in the character of Sporus (lines 305–33).

7. Charles Gildon, minor critic and scribbler, who, Pope believed, early attacked him at the instigation of Addison; hence "venal quill."
8. John Dennis (see *An Essay on Criticism*, n. 6, p. 2675).
9. Lewis Theobald (1688–1744), whose minute learning in Elizabethan literature had enabled him to expose Pope's defects as an editor of Shakespeare in 1726. Pope made him king of the Dunces in *The Dunciad* of 1728. Richard Bentley (1662–1742), the eminent classical scholar, seemed to both Pope and Swift the perfect type of the pedant: he is called "slashing" because, in his edition of *Paradise Lost* (1732), he had set in square brackets all passages that he disliked on the grounds they had been slipped into the poem without the blind poet's knowledge.

Preserved in Milton's or in Shakespeare's name.
Pretty! in amber to observe the forms
170   Of hairs, or straws, or dirt, or grubs, or worms!
The things, we know, are neither rich nor rare,
But wonder how the devil they got there.
      Were others angry? I excused them too;
Well might they rage; I gave them but their due.
175   A man's true merit 'tis not hard to find;
But each man's secret standard in his mind,
That casting weight[1] pride adds to emptiness,
This, who can gratify? for who can guess?
The bard[2] whom pilfered pastorals renown,
180   Who turns a Persian tale for half a crown,
Just writes to make his barrenness appear,
And strains from hard-bound brains eight lines a year:
He, who still wanting, though he lives on theft,
Steals much, spends little, yet has nothing left;
185   And he who now to sense, now nonsense leaning,
Means not, but blunders round about a meaning:
And he whose fustian's so sublimely bad,
It is not poetry, but prose run mad:
All these, my modest satire bade translate,
190   And owned that nine such poets made a Tate.[3]
How did they fume, and stamp, and roar, and chafe!
And swear, not Addison himself was safe.
      Peace to all such! but were there one whose fires
True Genius kindles, and fair Fame inspires;
195   Blessed with each talent and each art to please,
And born to write, converse, and live with ease:
Should such a man, too fond to rule alone,
Bear, like the Turk, no brother near the throne;[4]
View him with scornful, yet with jealous eyes,
200   And hate for arts that caused himself to rise;
Damn with faint praise, assent with civil leer,
And without sneering, teach the rest to sneer;
Willing to wound, and yet afraid to strike,
Just hint a fault, and hesitate dislike;
205   Alike reserved to blame or to commend,
A timorous foe, and a suspicious friend;
Dreading even fools; by flatterers besieged,
And so obliging that he ne'er obliged;
Like Cato, give his little senate[5] laws,
210   And sit attentive to his own applause;

1. The weight that turns the scale; here, the "deciding factor."
2. Philips, Pope's rival in pastoral poetry in 1709, when their pastorals were published in Tonson's 6th *Miscellany*. Philips had also translated some Persian tales (see line 100 and n. 5, p. 2725).
3. Nahum Tate, poet laureate from 1692 to 1715. His popular rewriting of Shakespeare's *King Lear* provided a happy ending; he wrote most of part 2 of *Absalom and Achitophel*. The line refers to the old adage that it takes nine tailors to make one man.
4. Turkish monarchs proverbially killed off their nearest rivals.
5. Addison's tragedy *Cato* had been a sensational success in 1713. Pope had written the prologue, in which occurs the line, "While Cato gives his little senate laws." The satirical reference here is to Addison in the role of arbiter of taste among his friends and admirers, mostly Whigs, at Button's Coffee House. This group worked against the success of Pope's Homer.

While wits and Templars° every sentence raise,   *law students*
And wonder with a foolish face of praise—
Who but must laugh, if such a man there be?
Who would not weep, if Atticus[6] were he?
215   What though my name stood rubric° on the walls   *in red letters*
Or plastered posts, with claps,° in capitals?   *posters*
Or smoking forth, a hundred hawkers' load,
On wings of winds came flying all abroad?
I sought no homage from the race that write;
220   I kept, like Asian monarchs, from their sight:
Poems I heeded (now berhymed so long)
No more than thou, great George! a birthday song.
I ne'er with wits or witlings passed my days
To spread about the itch of verse and praise;
225   Nor like a puppy daggled through the town
To fetch and carry sing-song up and down;
Nor at rehearsals sweat, and mouthed, and cried,
With handkerchief and orange at my side;
But sick of fops, and poetry, and prate,
230   To Bufo left the whole Castalian[7] state.
     Proud as Apollo on his forkèd hill,[8]
Sat full-blown Bufo, puffed° by every quill;°   *flattered / pen*
Fed with soft dedication all day long,
Horace and he went hand in hand in song.
235   His library (where busts of poets dead
And a true Pindar stood without a head)
Received of wits an undistinguished race,
Who first his judgment asked, and then a place:
Much they extolled his pictures, much his seat,[9]
240   And flattered every day, and some days eat:
Till grown more frugal in his riper days,
He paid some bards with port, and some with praise;
To some a dry rehearsal was assigned,
And others (harder still) he paid in kind.
245   Dryden alone (what wonder?) came not nigh;
Dryden alone escaped this judging eye:
But still the great have kindness in reserve;
He helped to bury whom he helped to starve.
     May some choice patron bless each gray goose quill!
250   May every Bavius have his Bufo still!
So when a statesman wants a day's defense,
Or envy holds a whole week's war with sense,
Or simple pride for flattery makes demands,
May dunce by dunce be whistled off my hands!
255   Blessed be the great! for those they take away,
And those they left me—for they left me Gay;[1]

---

6. Pope's satiric pseudonym for Addison. Atticus (109–32 B.C.E.), a wealthy man of letters and a friend of Cicero, was known as wise and disinterested.
7. The Castalian spring on Mount Parnassus was sacred to Apollo and the Muses. "Bufo": a type of tasteless patron of the arts. (*Bufo* means "toad" in Latin.)
8. Mount Parnassus had two peaks, one sacred to Apollo, one to Bacchus.
9. Estate. Pronounced *sate* and rhymed in next line with "eat" (*ate*).
1. John Gay (1685–1732), author of *The Beggar's Opera*, dear friend of Swift and Pope. His failure

Left me to see neglected genius bloom,
Neglected die, and tell it on his tomb;
Of all thy blameless life the sole return
260 My verse, and Queensberry weeping o'er thy urn!
Oh, let me live my own, and die so too!
("To live and die is all I have to do")[2]
Maintain a poet's dignity and ease,
And see what friends, and read what books I please;
265 Above a patron, though I condescend
Sometimes to call a minister my friend.
I was not born for courts or great affairs;
I pay my debts, believe, and say my prayers,
Can sleep without a poem in my head,
270 Nor know if Dennis be alive or dead.
    Why am I asked what next shall see the light?
Heavens! was I born for nothing but to write?
Has life no joys for me? or (to be grave)
Have I no friend to serve, no soul to save?
275 "I found him close with Swift"—"Indeed? no doubt"
Cries prating Balbus,[3] "something will come out."
'Tis all in vain, deny it as I will.
"No, such a genius never can lie still,"
And then for mine obligingly mistakes
280 The first lampoon Sir Will or Bubo[4] makes.
Poor guiltless I! and can I choose but smile,
When every coxcomb knows me by my style?
    Cursed be the verse, how well soe'er it flow,
That tends to make one worthy man my foe,
285 Give virtue scandal, innocence a fear,
Or from the soft-eyed virgin steal a tear!
But he who hurts a harmless neighbor's peace,
Insults fallen worth, or beauty in distress,
Who loves a lie, lame slander helps about,
290 Who writes a libel, or who copies out:
That fop whose pride affects a patron's name,
Yet absent, wounds an author's honest fame;
Who can your merit selfishly approve,
And show the sense of it without the love;
295 Who has the vanity to call you friend,
Yet wants the honor, injured, to defend;
Who tells whate'er you think, whate'er you say,
And, if he lie not, must at least betray:
Who to the dean and silver bell can swear,
300 And sees at Cannons what was never there:[5]

---

to obtain patronage from the court intensified
Pope's hostility to the Whig administration and
the queen. Gay spent the last years of his life
under the protection of the duke and duchess of
Queensberry. Pope wrote his epitaph.
2. A quotation from John Denham's poem "Of
Prudence."
3. Latin for *stammering*.
4. Sir William Yonge, Whig politician and poet-

aster. George Bubb ("Bubo") Dodington, a Whig
patron of letters.
5. Pope's enemies had accused him of satirizing
Cannons, the ostentatious estate of the duke of
Chandos, in his description of Timon's villa in
the *Epistle to Burlington*. This Pope quite justly
denied. The bell of Timon's chapel was of silver,
and there preached a dean who "never mentions
Hell to ears polite."

Who reads but with a lust to misapply,
Make satire a lampoon, and fiction, lie:
A lash like mine no honest man shall dread,
But all such babbling blockheads in his stead.

305   Let Sporus[6] tremble——A. What? that thing of silk,
Sporus, that mere white curd of ass's milk?[7]
Satire or sense, alas! can Sporus feel?
Who breaks a butterfly upon a wheel?
    P. Yet let me flap this bug with gilded wings,

310 This painted child of dirt, that stinks and stings;
Whose buzz the witty and the fair annoys,
Yet wit ne'er tastes, and beauty ne'er enjoys;
So well-bred spaniels civilly delight
In mumbling of the game they dare not bite.

315 Eternal smiles his emptiness betray,
As shallow streams run dimpling all the way.
Whether in florid impotence he speaks,
And, as the prompter breathes, the puppet squeaks;
Or at the ear of Eve,[8] familiar toad,

320 Half froth, half venom, spits himself abroad,
In puns, or politics, or tales, or lies,
Or spite, or smut, or rhymes, or blasphemies.
His wit all seesaw between *that* and *this,*
Now high, now low, now master up, now miss,

325 And he himself one vile antithesis.
Amphibious thing! that acting either part,
The trifling head or the corrupted heart,
Fop at the toilet, flatterer at the board,
Now trips a lady, and now struts a lord.

330 Eve's tempter thus the rabbins[9] have expressed,
A cherub's face, a reptile all the rest;
Beauty that shocks you, parts that none will trust,
Wit that can creep, and pride that licks the dust.
    Not fortune's worshiper, nor fashion's fool,

335 Not lucre's madman, nor ambition's tool,
Not proud, nor servile, be one poet's praise,
That if he pleased, he pleased by manly ways:
That flattery, even to kings, he held a shame,
And thought a lie in verse or prose the same:

340 That not in fancy's maze he wandered long,
But stooped[1] to truth, and moralized his song:
That not for fame, but virtue's better end,
He stood the furious foe, the timid friend,
The damning critic, half approving wit,

345 The coxcomb hit, or fearing to be hit;

---

6. John, Lord Hervey, effeminate courtier and confidant of Queen Caroline (see headnote, p. 2721). The original Sporus was a boy, whom the emperor Nero publicly married (see Suetonius's life of Nero in *The Twelve Caesars*).
7. Drunk by invalids.

8. The queen; the allusion is to *Paradise Lost* (4.799–809).
9. Scholars of and authorities on Jewish law and doctrine.
1. The falcon is said to "stoop" to its prey when it swoops down and seizes it in flight.

Laughed at the loss of friends he never had,
The dull, the proud, the wicked, and the mad;
The distant threats of vengeance on his head,
The blow unfelt, the tear he never shed;
350 The tale revived, the lie so oft o'erthrown,
The imputed trash, and dullness not his own;
The morals blackened when the writings 'scape,
The libeled person, and the pictured shape;[2]
Abuse on all he loved, or loved him, spread,
355 A friend in exile, or a father dead;
The whisper, that to greatness still too near,
Perhaps yet vibrates on his Sovereign's ear—
Welcome for thee, fair virtue! all the past:
For thee, fair virtue! welcome even the last!
360   A. But why insult the poor, affront the great?
P. A knave's a knave to me in every state:
Alike my scorn, if he succeed or fail,
Sporus at court, or Japhet[3] in a jail,
A hireling scribbler, or a hireling peer,
365 Knight of the post[4] corrupt, or of the shire,
If on a pillory, or near a throne,
He gain his prince's ear, or lose his own.[5]
   Yet soft by nature, more a dupe than wit,
Sappho° can tell you how this man was bit:°   *Montagu / deceived*
370 This dreaded satirist Dennis will confess
Foe to his pride, but friend to his distress:[6]
So humble, he has knocked at Tibbald's door,
Has drunk with Cibber, nay, has rhymed for Moore.
Full ten years slandered, did he once reply?
375 Three thousand suns went down on Welsted's lie.[7]
To please a mistress one aspersed his life;
He lashed him not, but let her be his wife.
Let Budgell charge low Grub Street on his quill,
And write whate'er he pleased, except his will;[8]
380 Let the two Curlls of town and court,[9] abuse
His father, mother, body, soul, and muse.
Yet why? that father held it for a rule,
It was a sin to call our neighbor fool;
That harmless mother thought no wife a whore:
385 Hear this, and spare his family, James Moore!
Unspotted names, and memorable long,
If there be force in virtue, or in song.
   Of gentle blood (part shed in honor's cause,
While yet in Britain honor had applause)

2. Pope's deformity was frequently ridiculed and occasionally caricatured.
3. Japhet Crook, a notorious forger.
4. One who lives by selling false evidence.
5. Those punished in the pillory often also had their ears cropped.
6. Pope wrote the prologue to Cibber's *Provoked Husband* (1728) when that play was performed for Dennis's benefit, shortly before the old critic died.

7. "This man had the impudence to tell in print that Mr. P. had occasioned a Lady's death, and to name a person he had never heard of" [Pope's note].
8. Eustace Budgell attacked the *Grub Street Journal* for publishing what he took to be a squib by Pope charging him with having forged the will of Dr. Matthew Tindal.
9. I.e., the publisher and Lord Hervey.

390 Each parent sprung——A. What fortune, pray?——P. Their own,
     And better got than Bestia's[1] from the throne.
     Born to no pride, inheriting no strife,
     Nor marrying discord in a noble wife,
     Stranger to civil and religious rage,
395 The good man walked innoxious through his age.
     No courts he saw, no suits would ever try,
     Nor dared an oath,[2] nor hazarded a lie.
     Unlearn'd, he knew no schoolman's subtle art,
     No language but the language of the heart.
400 By nature honest, by experience wise,
     Healthy by temperance, and by exercise;
     His life, though long, to sickness passed unknown,
     His death was instant, and without a groan.
     Oh, grant me thus to live, and thus to die!
405 Who sprung from kings shall know less joy than I.
        O friend! may each domestic bliss be thine!
     Be no unpleasing melancholy mine:
     Me, let the tender office long engage,
     To rock the cradle of reposing age,
410 With lenient arts extend a mother's breath,
     Make languor smile, and smooth the bed of death,
     Explore the thought, explain the asking eye,
     And keep a while one parent from the sky![3]
     On cares like these if length of days attend,
415 May Heaven, to bless those days, preserve my friend,
     Preserve him social, cheerful, and serene,
     And just as rich as when he served a Queen![4]
        A. Whether that blessing be denied or given,
     Thus far was right—the rest belongs to Heaven.

1735

The Dunciad: Book the Fourth

The fourth book of *The Dunciad*, Pope's last major work, was originally intended as a continuation of *An Essay on Man*. To Jonathan Swift, the spiritual ancestor of the poem, Pope confided in 1736 that he was at work on a series of epistles on the uses of human reason and learning, to conclude with "a satire against the misapplication of all these, exemplified by pictures, characters, and examples." But the epistles never appeared; instead, the satire grew until it took their place. As Pope surveyed England in his last years, the complex literary and social order that had sustained him seemed to be crumbling. It was a time for desperate measures, for satire. And the means of retribution was at hand, in the structure of Pope's own *Dunciad*, the long work that had already impaled so many enemies.

---

1. Probably the duke of Marlborough, whose vast fortune was made through the favor of Queen Anne. The actual Bestia was a corrupt Roman consul.
2. As a Catholic, Pope's father refused to take the Oaths of Allegiance and Supremacy and the oath against the pope. He thus rendered himself vulnerable to the many repressive anti-Catholic laws then in force.
3. Pope was a tender and devoted son. His mother had died in 1733. The earliest version of these lines dates from 1731, when the poet was nursing her through a serious illness.
4. Pope alludes to the fact that Arbuthnot, a man of strict probity, left the queen's service no wealthier than when he entered it.

The first *Dunciad*, published in three books in 1728, is a mock-epic reply to Pope's critics and other petty authors. Its hero and victim, Lewis Theobald, had attacked Pope's edition of Shakespeare (1725); other victims had offended Pope either by personal abuse or simply by ineptitude. Inspired by Dryden's "Mac Flecknoe," *The Dunciad* celebrates the triumph of the hordes of Grub Street. Indeed, so many obscure hacks were mentioned that a *Dunciad Variorum* (1729) was soon required, in which mock-scholarly notes identify the victims, "since it is only in this monument that they must expect to survive." But a modern reader need not catch every reference to enjoy the dazzling wit of the poem, or the sheer sense of fun with which Pope remakes the London literary world into a tiny insane fairground of his own.

The New Dunciad (1742), however, plays a far more serious game: here Pope takes aim at the rot of the whole social fabric. The satire goes deep and works at many levels, which for convenience may be divided into four. (1) Politics: From 1721 to 1742 England had been ruled by the Whig supremacy of Robert Walpole, first minister. To Pope and his circle, the immensely powerful Walpole (no friend of poets) seemed crass and greedy, like his monarch George II. It is no accident, in the kingdom of *The Dunciad*, that Dulness personified sits on a throne. (2) Society: Just as the action of the *Aeneid* had been the removal of the empire of Troy to Latium, the action of *The Dunciad*, according to Pope, is "the removal of the empire of Dulness from the City of London to the polite world, Westminster"; that is, the abdication of civility in favor of commerce and financial interests. In modern England, authors write for money, and ministers govern for profit; conspicuous consumption (especially the consumption of paper by scribblers) has replaced the old values of the yeoman and the aristocrat. In 1743 Pope revised the original *Dunciad*, substituting the actor and poet laureate Colley Cibber for Theobald as the hero and incorporating *The New Dunciad* as the fourth book (the version printed here). Dulness, he implies, has achieved her final triumph; Cibber is laureate in England. (3) Education: The word *dunce* is derived from the Scholastic philosopher John Duns Scotus (ca. 1265–1308), whose name had come to stand for silly and useless subtlety, logical hairsplitting. Pope, as an heir of the Renaissance, believes that the central subject of education must always be its relevance for human behavior: "The proper study of mankind is Man," and moral philosophy, the relation of individuals to each other and to the world, should be the teacher's first and last concern. By contrast, Dunces waste their time on grammar (words alone) or the "science" of the collector (things alone); they never comprehend that word and thing, like spirit and matter, are essentially dead unless they join. (4) Religion: At its deepest level, the subject of *The Dunciad* is the undoing of God's creation. Many passages from the fourth book echo *Paradise Lost*, and one of Pope's starting places seems to be Satan's threat to return the world to its original darkness, chaos, and ancient night (*Paradise Lost* 2.968–87). *The Dunciad* ends in a great apocalypse, with a yawn that signals the death of *Logos*; as words have become meaningless, so has the whole creation, which the Lord called forth with words. Here Pope invokes, with sublime intensity, the old idea that God was the first poet, one whose poem was the world, and suggests that the sickness of the word has infected all nature. Such a cosmic collapse allows Pope to realize in full the aim of his satirical poetry: to depict the evil of his enemies in all its excessive might and magnitude. As matter without spirit and substance without essence prevail in the final *Dunciad* over Pope's own ideals, the poem perversely confirms his poetic power, and the destruction of art permits his ultimate artistic triumph.

From The Dunciad

From *Book the Fourth*

Yet, yet a moment, one dim ray of light
Indulge, dread Chaos, and eternal Night!
Of darkness visible[1] so much be lent,
As half to show, half veil the deep intent.
5 Ye Powers![2] whose mysteries restored I sing,
To whom Time bears me on his rapid wing,
Suspend a while your force inertly strong,
Then take at once the poet and the song.
      Now flamed the Dog-star's[3] unpropitious ray,
10 Smote every brain, and withered every bay,[4]
Sick was the sun, the owl forsook his bower,
The moon-struck prophet felt the madding hour:
Then rose the seed[5] of Chaos, and of Night,
To blot out Order, and extinguish Light,
15 Of dull and venal a new world to mold,
And bring Saturnian days of lead and gold.[6]
      She mounts the throne: her head a cloud concealed,
In broad effulgence all below revealed,
('Tis thus aspiring Dulness ever shines)
20 Soft on her lap her Laureate son[7] reclines.
      Beneath her foot-stool, Science groans in chains,
And Wit dreads exile, penalties and pains.
There foamed rebellious Logic, gagged and bound,
There, stripped, fair Rhetoric languished on the ground;
25 His blunted arms by Sophistry are borne,
And shameless Billingsgate[8] her robes adorn.
Morality, by her false guardians drawn,
Chicane in furs, and Casuistry in lawn,[9]
Gasps, as they straighten at each end the cord,
30 And dies, when Dulness gives her Page[1] the word.

*   *   *

[THE EDUCATOR]

135   Now crowds on crowds around the Goddess press,
Each eager to present the first address.[2]
Dunce scorning dunce beholds the next advance,

---

1. Cf. *Paradise Lost* 1.63.
2. Chaos and Night, invoked in place of the Muse, because "the restoration of their empire is the action of the poem" [Pope's note].
3. Sirius, associated with the heat of summer and the madness of poets (see *Epistle to Dr. Arbuthnot*, line 3, p. 2722).
4. The laurel, whose garlands are bestowed on poets.
5. The Goddess Dulness.
6. Saturn ruled during the golden age; the new age of "gold" will be reestablished by the dull and venal.

7. Colley Cibber, the poet laureate.
8. Fishmarket slang, which now covers the noble science of rhetoric.
9. Chicanery (legal trickery) wears the ermine robe of a judge. Casuistry wears the linen ("lawn") sleeves of a bishop.
1. Sir Francis Page, a notorious hanging judge; or court page, used to strangle criminals in Turkey; or page of writing on which a dull author "kills" moral sentiments.
2. The goddess, newly enthroned, is receiving petitions and congratulations.

But fop shows fop superior complaisance.
When lo! a specter[3] rose, whose index-hand
140   Held forth the virtue of the dreadful wand;
His beavered brow a birchen garland wears,[4]
Dropping with infant's blood, and mother's tears.
O'er every vein a shuddering horror runs;
Eton and Winton shake through all their sons.
145   All flesh is humbled, Westminster's bold race[5]
Shrink, and confess the Genius[6] of the place:
The pale boy-Senator yet tingling stands,
And holds his breeches close with both his hands.
    Then thus. "Since Man from beast by words is known,
150   Words are Man's province, words we teach alone.
When reason doubtful, like the Samian letter,[7]
Points him two ways, the narrower is the better.
Placed at the door of learning, youth to guide,
We never suffer it to stand too wide.
155   To ask, to guess, to know, as they commence,
As fancy opens the quick springs of sense,
We ply the memory, we load the brain,
Bind rebel wit, and double chain on chain,
Confine the thought, to exercise the breath;[8]
160   And keep them in the pale of words till death.
Whate'er the talents, or howe'er designed,
We hang one jingling padlock on the mind:
A poet the first day, he dips his quill;
And what the last? a very poet still.
165   Pity! the charm works only in our wall,
Lost, lost too soon in yonder House or Hall."[9]

*   *   *

[THE CARNATION AND THE BUTTERFLY]

Then thick as locusts blackening all the ground,
A tribe,[1] with weeds and shells fantastic crowned,
Each with some wondrous gift approached the Power,
400   A nest, a toad, a fungus, or a flower.
But far the foremost, two, with earnest zeal,
And aspect ardent to the throne appeal.
    The first thus opened: "Hear thy suppliant's call,
Great Queen, and common mother of us all!
405   Fair from its humble bed I reared this flower,

---

3. The ghost of Dr. Busby, stern headmaster of Westminster School.
4. He wears a hat (beaver) and a garland of birch twigs, used for flogging. "Wand": cane used for beating.
5. Alumni of Westminster School, with a play on the justices and members of Parliament who meet at Westminster Hall.
6. I.e., admit that Dr. Busby is the presiding deity (Genius).
7. The letter Y, which Pythagoras (a native of Samos) used as an emblem of the different roads of virtue and vice.
8. Students are taught only to recite the classic poets by heart.
9. The House of Commons and Westminster Hall, where law cases were heard. The eloquence learned by rote disappears on occasions for public speaking.
1. The Virtuosi, or amateur scientists and collectors.

Suckled, and cheer'd, with air, and sun, and shower,
Soft on the paper ruff its leaves I spread,
Bright with the gilded button tipped its head,
Then throned in glass, and named it CAROLINE:[2]
410 Each maid cried, charming! and each youth, divine!
Did Nature's pencil ever blend such rays,
Such varied light in one promiscuous blaze?
Now prostrate! dead! behold that Caroline:
No maid cries, charming! and no youth, divine!
415 And lo the wretch! whose vile, whose insect lust
Laid this gay daughter of the Spring in dust.
Oh punish him, or to th' Elysian shades
Dismiss my soul, where no carnation fades."
       He ceased, and wept. With innocence of mien,
420 The accused stood forth, and thus addressed the Queen.
       "Of all th' enameled race,° whose silvery wing   colored insects
Waves to the tepid zephyrs of the spring,
Or swims along the fluid atmosphere,
Once brightest shined this child of heat and air.
425 I saw, and started from its vernal bower
The rising game, and chased from flower to flower.
It fled, I followed; now in hope, now pain;
It stopped, I stopped; it moved, I moved again.
At last it fixed, 'twas on what plant it pleased,
430 And where it fixed, the beauteous bird° I seized: flying creature
Rose or carnation was below my care;
I meddle, Goddess! only in my sphere.
I tell the naked fact without disguise,
And, to excuse it, need but show the prize;
435 Whose spoils this paper offers to your eye,
Fair even in death! this peerless Butterfly."
       "My sons!" she answered, "both have done your parts;
Live happy both, and long promote our arts.
But hear a mother, when she recommends
440 To your fraternal care, our sleeping friends.
The common soul, of heaven's more frugal make,
Serves but to keep fools pert, and knaves awake:
A drowsy watchman, that just gives a knock,
And breaks our rest, to tell us what's a clock.[3]
445 Yet by some object every brain is stirred;
The dull may waken to a hummingbird;
The most recluse, discreetly opened, find
Congenial matter in the cockle-kind;[4]
The mind, in metaphysics at a loss,
450 May wander in a wilderness of moss;
The head that turns at super-lunar things,
Poised with a tail, may steer on Wilkins' wings.[5]

---

2. Queen Caroline, an enthusiastic gardener, is an appropriate choice to lend her name to the perfect carnation.
3. In the 18th century, watchmen kept guard in the streets and announced the hours.
4. Cockleshells, popular with collectors, as were hummingbirds and varieties of moss.
5. John Wilkins (1614–1672), one of the founders of the Royal Society, had speculated "that a man may be able to fly, by the application of wings to his own body."

"O! would the Sons of Men once think their eyes
And reason given them but to study *flies!*[6]
455 See Nature in some partial narrow shape,
And let the Author of the whole escape:
Learn but to trifle; or, who most observe,
To wonder at their Maker, not to serve."

* * *

[THE TRIUMPH OF DULNESS]

Then blessing all,[7] "Go children of my care!
580 To practice now from theory repair.
All my commands are easy, short, and full:
My sons! be proud, be selfish, and be dull.
Guard my prerogative, assert my throne:
This nod confirms each privilege your own.
585 The cap and switch be sacred to his Grace;[8]
With staff and pumps[9] the Marquis lead the race;
From stage to stage the licensed[1] Earl may run,
Paired with his fellow-charioteer the sun;
The learned baron butterflies design,
590 Or draw to silk Arachne's subtle line;°   *spiderweb*
The Judge to dance his brother Sergeant[2] call;
The Senator at cricket urge the ball;
The Bishop stow (pontific luxury!)
An hundred souls of turkeys in a pie;[3]
595 The sturdy squire to Gallic masters° stoop,   *French chefs*
And drown his lands and manors in a soup.
Others import yet nobler arts from France,
Teach kings to fiddle, and make senates dance.
Perhaps more high some daring son may soar,[4]
600 Proud to my list to add one monarch more;
And nobly conscious, Princes are but things
Born for First Ministers, as slaves for kings,
Tyrant supreme! shall three estates command,
And MAKE ONE MIGHTY DUNCIAD OF THE LAND!"
605 More she had spoke, but yawned—All Nature nods:
What mortal can resist the yawn of Gods?
Churches and chapels instantly it reached;
(St. James's first, for leaden Gilbert[5] preached)
Then catched the schools; the Hall scarce kept awake;
610 The Convocation gaped,[6] but could not speak:

6. Cf. *An Essay on Man* 1.189–96 (p. 2718).
7. Having conferred her titles, Dulness bids each eminent dunce to indulge in the triviality closest to his heart.
8. His Grace, a duke who loves horse racing, is to use the cap and switch of a jockey.
9. Footmen, who wore pumps (low-cut shoes for running), were matched in races.
1. The license required by the owner of a stage-coach; also privileged or licentious.
2. A lawyer or legislative officer. Formal ceremonies at the Inns of Court are said to have resembled a country dance.
3. According to Pope, a hundred turkeys had been "not unfrequently deposited in one Pye in the Bishopric of Durham."
4. A bold, direct attack on Walpole.
5. Dr. John Gilbert, dean of Exeter.
6. The Convocation, an assembly of clergy consulting on ecclesiastical affairs, had been adjourned since 1717.

Lost was the Nation's Sense,° nor could be found,   *Parliament*
While the long solemn unison went round:
Wide, and more wide, it spread o'er all the realm;
Even Palinurus[7] nodded at the helm:
615   The vapor mild o'er each committee crept;
Unfinished treaties in each office slept;
And chiefless armies dozed out the campaign;
And navies yawned for orders on the main.
        O Muse! relate (for you can tell alone,
620   Wits have short memories, and dunces none)
Relate, who first, who last resigned to rest;
Whose heads she partly, whose completely blessed;
What charms could faction, what ambition lull,
The venal quiet, and entrance the dull;
625   'Till drowned was sense, and shame, and right, and wrong—
O sing, and hush the nations with thy song!
. . . .
In vain, in vain,—the all-composing Hour
Resistless falls: The Muse obeys the Power.
She comes! she comes![8] the sable throne behold
630   Of Night primeval, and of Chaos old!
Before her, Fancy's gilded clouds decay,
And all its varying rainbows die away.
Wit shoots in vain its momentary fires,
The meteor drops, and in a flash expires.
635   As one by one, at dread Medea's strain,
The sickening stars fade off the ethereal plain;[9]
As Argus' eyes by Hermes' wand oppressed,
Closed one by one to everlasting rest;[1]
Thus at her felt approach, and secret might,
640   Art after Art goes out, and all is Night.
See skulking Truth to her old cavern fled,[2]
Mountains of casuistry heaped o'er her head!
Philosophy, that leaned on Heaven before,
Shrinks to her second cause,[3] and is no more.
645   Physic[4] of Metaphysic begs defense,
And Metaphysic calls for aid on Sense!
See Mystery[5] to Mathematics fly!
In vain! they gaze, turn giddy, rave, and die.
Religion blushing veils her sacred fires,
650   And unawares Morality expires.
Nor public flame, nor private, dares to shine;
Nor human spark is left, nor glimpse divine!

---

7. The pilot of Aeneas's ship; here Walpole.
8. Having triumphed in the contemporary world of affairs, Dulness (like her antitype Christ) has a Second Coming, a prophetic vision in which she extinguishes the light of the arts and sciences.
9. In Seneca's *Medea*, the stars obey the curse of Medea, a magician and avenger.
1. Argus, Hera's hundred-eyed watchman, was charmed to sleep and slain by Hermes.
2. Alluding to the saying of Democritus, that

Truth lay at the bottom of a deep well [Pope's note].
3. Science (philosophy) no longer accepts God as the first cause or final explanation of how all things came to be; instead, it accepts only the second or material cause and tries to account for all things by physical principles alone.
4. Natural science in general.
5. A religious truth known only through divine revelation.

Lo! thy dread Empire, CHAOS! is restored;
Light dies before thy uncreating word:[6]
655 Thy hand, great Anarch! lets the curtain fall;
And Universal Darkness buries All.

1743

6. Cf. God's first creating words in Genesis, "Let there be light."

ELIZA HAYWOOD
1693?–1756

Not much is known about the early life of Elizabeth Fowler or about the "unfortunate marriage," as she described it, that made her Eliza Haywood. She first came before the public as an actress in 1714 in Dublin, then moved to London. But "the stage not answering my expectation," as she later confessed, soon "made me turn my genius another way," to the life of a professional writer. Her first novel, the racy, best-selling *Love in Excess; or, the Fatal Inquiry* (1719), launched her long career as one of the most popular, prolific, and versatile authors of her time. She retailed gossip and also was gossiped about, becoming involved with the poet Richard Savage—a friend of Pope and later of Samuel Johnson—and with William Hatchett, a, playwright and actor who seems to have been her longtime companion. Pope mocked her scandal-mongering, and her two illegitimate children, in his own scandalmongering *Dunciad* (1728), and Fielding caricatured her as "Mrs. Novel." But nothing could keep her from writing. In addition to many kinds of fiction, she produced poems, translations, plays, political satires, essays, criticism, and books of advice and conduct—whatever might sell. In the 1730s she returned to the stage, as a playwright and actress, until the government cracked down on the theater in 1737. From 1744 to 1746 she had another great success with the *Female Spectator*, a wide-ranging periodical written for women. Later, *The History of Miss Betsy Thoughtless* (1751), the story of an indiscreet charmer who eventually reforms and finds her Mr. Trueworth, proved how well Haywood could adjust to the new style of edifying novels. And right up to the moment of her death she continued to work.

Fantomina first appeared among Haywood's *Secret Histories, Novels, and Poems* (1725), and the title page calls it "A Secret History of an Amour between Two Persons of Condition." The popular genre of "secret histories" promised a peep at what went on behind the scenes of fashionable society; and even though Haywood's story is obviously made up, it suggests that private lives, and especially love lives, are very different from what the public sees. Right at the start, the aristocratic heroine (whose name we never learn) is fascinated by the dalliance between "respectable" gentlemen and loose women of the town. She soon becomes a player herself. Cleverly switching roles, she gratifies her own desire by exploiting her lover's fickle passions. The story unsettles conventional views of social position, identity, morality, and gender. But most of all it shows that love is not only an irresistible impulse but also a risky, exciting game.

Fantomina; or, Love in a Maze

In love the victors from the vanquished fly.
They fly that wound, and they pursue that die.
                                            —Waller[1]

A young lady of distinguished birth, beauty, wit, and spirit, happened to be in a box one night at the playhouse; where, though there were a great number of celebrated toasts,[2] she perceived several gentlemen extremely pleased themselves with entertaining a woman who sat in a corner of the pit and, by her air and manner of receiving them, might easily be known to be one of those who come there for no other purpose, than to create acquaintance with as many as seem desirous of it. She could not help testifying her contempt of men who, regardless either of the play or circle, threw away their time in such a manner, to some ladies that sat by her. But they, either less surprised by being more accustomed to such sights than she who had been bred for the most part in the country, or not of a disposition to consider anything very deeply, took but little notice of it. She still thought of it, however; and the longer she reflected on it, the greater was her wonder that men, some of whom she knew were accounted to have wit, should have tastes so very depraved.—This excited a curiosity in her to know in what manner these creatures were addressed.—She was young, a stranger to the world, and consequently to the dangers of it; and having nobody in town, at that time, to whom she was obliged to be accountable for her actions, did in everything as her inclinations or humors rendered most agreeable to her: therefore thought it not in the least a fault to put in practice a little whim which came immediately into her head, to dress herself as near as she could in the fashion of those women who make sale of their favors, and set herself in the way of being accosted as such a one, having at that time no other aim than the gratification of an innocent curiosity.—She no sooner designed this frolic than she put it in execution; and muffling her hoods over her face, went the next night into the gallery-box, and practicing, as much as she had observed at that distance, the behavior of that woman, was not long before she found her disguise had answered the ends she wore it for.—A crowd of purchasers of all degrees and capacities were in a moment gathered about her, each endeavoring to outbid the other, in offering her a price for her embraces.—She listened to 'em all, and was not a little diverted in her mind at the disappointment she should give to so many, each of which thought himself secure of gaining her.—She was told by 'em all, that she was the most lovely woman in the world; and some cried, *Gad, she is mighty like my fine Lady Such-a-one*—naming her own name. She was naturally vain, and received no small pleasure in hearing herself praised, though in the person of another, and a supposed prostitute; but she dispatched as soon as she could all that had hitherto attacked her, when she saw the accomplished *Beauplaisir*[3] was making his way through the crowd as fast as he was able, to reach the bench she sat on. She had often seen him in the drawing-room, had talked with him; but then her quality[4] and reputed virtue kept him from using her with that freedom she now

1. Edmund Waller, "To A. H., of the different successes of their loves" (1645).
2. Women to whose charms men drink.
3. Fine pleasure (French).
4. Social standing.

expected he would do, and had discovered something in him which had made her often think she should not be displeased, if he would abate some part of his reserve.—Now was the time to have her wishes answered.—He looked in her face, and fancied, as many others had done, that she very much resembled that lady whom she really was; but the vast disparity there appeared between their characters prevented him from entertaining even the most distant thought that they could be the same.—He addressed her at first with the usual salutations of her pretended profession, as, *Are you engaged, Madam?—Will you permit me to wait on you home after the play?—By Heaven, you are a fine girl!—How long have you used this house?*—and such like questions; but perceiving she had a turn of wit, and a genteel manner in her raillery, beyond what is frequently to be found among those wretches, who are for the most part gentlewomen but by necessity, few of 'em having had an education suitable to what they affect to appear, he changed the form of his conversation, and showed her it was not because he understood no better, that he had made use of expressions so little polite.—In fine, they were infinitely charmed with each other. He was transported to find so much beauty and wit in a woman who he doubted not but on very easy terms he might enjoy; and she found a vast deal of pleasure in conversing with him in this free and unrestrained manner. They passed their time all the play with an equal satisfaction; but when it was over, she found herself involved in a difficulty which before never entered into her head, but which she knew not well how to get over.—The passion he professed for her was not of that humble nature which can be content with distant adorations.—He resolved not to part from her without the gratifications of those desires she had inspired; and presuming on the liberties which her supposed function allowed of, told her she must either go with him to some convenient house of his procuring, or permit him to wait on her to her own lodgings.—Never had she been in such a *dilemma.* Three or four times did she open her mouth to confess her real quality; but the influence of her ill stars prevented it, by putting an excuse into her head which did the business as well, and at the same time did not take from her the power of seeing and entertaining him a second time with the same freedom she had done this.—She told him, she was under obligations to a man who maintained her, and whom she durst not disappoint, having promised to meet him that night at a house hard by.—This story, so like what those ladies sometimes tell, was not at all suspected, by *Beauplaisir;* and assuring her he would be far from doing her a prejudice,[5] desired that in return for the pain he should suffer in being deprived of her company that night, that she would order her affairs so as not to render him unhappy the next. She gave a solemn promise to be in the same box on the morrow evening, and they took leave of each other; he to the tavern to drown the remembrance of his disappointment; she in a hackney-chair[6] hurried home to indulge contemplation on the frolic she had taken, designing nothing less on her first reflections than to keep the promise she had made him, and hugging herself with joy, that she had the good luck to come off undiscovered.

But these cogitations were but of a short continuance, they vanished with the hurry of her spirits, and were succeeded by others vastly different and

---

5. Harm.

6. A small hired coach, carried by two men.

ruinous.—All the charms of *Beauplaisir* came fresh into her mind; she languished, she almost died for another opportunity of conversing with him; and not all the admonitions of her discretion were effectual to oblige her to deny laying hold of that which offered itself the next night.—She depended on the strength of her virtue to bear her fate through trials more dangerous than she apprehended this to be, and never having been addressed by him as Lady—, was resolved to receive his devoirs as a town-mistress,[7] imagining a world of satisfaction to herself in engaging him in the character of such a one and in observing the surprise he would be in to find himself refused by a woman who he supposed granted her favors without exception.—Strange and unaccountable were the whimsies she was possessed of—wild and incoherent her desires—unfixed and undetermined her resolutions, but in that of seeing *Beauplaisir* in the manner she had lately done. As for her proceedings with him, or how a second time to escape him without discovering who she was, she could neither assure herself, nor whether or not in the last extremity she would do so.—Bent, however, on meeting him, whatever should be the consequence, she went out some hours before the time of going to the playhouse, and took lodgings in a house not very far from it, intending, that if he should insist on passing some part of the night with her, to carry him there, thinking she might with more security to her honor entertain him at a place where she was mistress than at any of his own choosing.

The appointed hour being arrived, she had the satisfaction to find his love in his assiduity. He was there before her; and nothing could be more tender than the manner in which he accosted her. But from the first moment she came in, to that of the play being done, he continued to assure her no consideration should prevail with him to part from her again, as she had done the night before; and she rejoiced to think she had taken that precaution of providing herself with a lodging, to which she thought she might invite him without running any risk, either of her virtue or reputation.—Having told him she would admit of his accompanying her home, he seemed perfectly satisfied; and leading her to the place, which was not above twenty houses distant, would have ordered a collation to be brought after them. But she would not permit it, telling him she was not one of those who suffered themselves to be treated at their own lodgings; and as soon she was come in, sent a servant belonging to the house to provide a very handsome supper and wine, and everything was served to table in a manner which showed the director neither wanted money, nor was ignorant how it should be laid out.

This proceeding, though it did not take from him the opinion that she was what she appeared to be, yet it gave him thoughts of her which he had not before.—He believed her a *mistress,* but believed her to be one of a superior rank, and began to imagine the possession of her would be much more expensive than at first he had expected. But not being of a humor to grudge anything for his pleasures, he gave himself no farther trouble than what were occasioned by fears of not having money enough to reach her price about him.

Supper being over, which was intermixed with a vast deal of amorous conversation, he began to explain himself more than he had done; and both by his words and behavior let her know he would not be denied that happiness the freedoms she allowed had made him hope.—It was in vain; she would

7. Prostitute. "Devoirs": dutiful compliments.

have retracted the encouragement she had given.—In vain she endeavored to delay, till the next meeting, the fulfilling of his wishes.—She had now gone too far to retreat.—*He* was bold;—he was resolute. *She* fearful—confused, altogether unprepared to resist in such encounters, and rendered more so by the extreme liking she had to him.—Shocked, however, at the apprehension of really losing her honor, she struggled all she could, and was just going to reveal the whole secret of her name and quality, when the thoughts of the liberty he had taken with her, and those he still continued to prosecute, prevented her, with representing the danger of being exposed, and the whole affair made a theme for public ridicule.—Thus much, indeed, she told him, that she was a virgin, and had assumed this manner of behavior only to engage him. But that he little regarded, or if he had, would have been far from obliging him to desist;—nay, in the present burning eagerness of desire, 'tis probable, that had he been acquainted both with who and what she really was, the knowledge of her birth would not have influenced him with respect sufficient to have curbed the wild exuberance of his luxurious wishes, or made him in that longing, that impatient moment, change the form of his addresses. In fine, she was undone; and he gained a victory, so highly rapturous, that had he known over whom, scarce could he have triumphed more. Her tears, however, and the distraction she appeared in, after the ruinous ecstasy was past, as it heightened his wonder, so it abated his satisfaction.—He could not imagine for what reason a woman, who, if she intended not to be a *mistress,* had counterfeited the part of one, and taken so much pains to engage him, should lament a consequence which she could not but expect, and till the last test, seemed inclinable to grant; and was both surprised and troubled at the mystery.—He omitted nothing that he thought might make her easy; and still retaining an opinion that the hope of interest[8] had been the chief motive which had led her to act in the manner she had done, and believing that she might know so little of him as to suppose, now she had nothing left to give, he might not make that recompense she expected for her favors: to put her out of that pain, he pulled out of his pocket a purse of gold, entreating her to accept of that as an earnest of what he intended to do for her; assuring her, with ten thousand protestations, that he would spare nothing which his whole estate could purchase, to procure her content and happiness. This treatment made her quite forget the part she had assumed, and throwing it from her with an air of disdain, Is this a reward (*said she*) for condescensions,[9] such as I have yielded to?—Can all the wealth you are possessed of make a reparation for my loss of honor?—Oh! no, I am undone beyond the power of heaven itself to help me!—She uttered many more such exclamations; which the amazed *Beauplaisir* heard without being able to reply to, till by degrees sinking from that rage of temper, her eyes resumed their softening glances, and guessing at the consternation he was in, No, my dear *Beauplaisir,* (*added she*) your love alone can compensate for the shame you have involved me in; be you sincere and constant, and I hereafter shall, perhaps, be satisfied with my fate, and forgive myself the folly that betrayed me to you.

Beauplaisir thought he could not have a better opportunity than these words gave him of inquiring who she was, and wherefore she had feigned

---

8. Profit.   9. Humiliations.

herself to be of a profession which he was now convinced she was not; and after he had made her a thousand vows of an affection as inviolable and ardent as she could wish to find in him, entreated she would inform him by what means his happiness had been brought about, and also to whom he was indebted for the bliss he had enjoyed.—Some remains of yet unextinguished modesty, and sense of shame, made her blush exceedingly at this demand; but recollecting herself in a little time, she told him so much of the truth, as to what related to the frolic she had taken of satisfying her curiosity in what manner *mistresses*, of the sort she appeared to be, were treated by those who addressed them; but forbore discovering her true name and quality, for the reasons she had done before, resolving, if he boasted of this affair, he should not have it in his power to touch her character. She therefore said she was the daughter of a country gentleman, who was come to town to buy clothes, and that she was called *Fantomina*. He had no reason to distrust the truth of this story, and was therefore satisfied with it; but did not doubt by the beginning of her conduct, but that in the end she would be in reality the thing she so artfully had counterfeited; and had good nature enough to pity the misfortunes he imagined would be her lot. But to tell her so, or offer his advice in that point, was not his business, at least as yet.

They parted not till towards morning; and she obliged him to a willing vow of visiting her the next day at three in the afternoon. It was too late for her to go home that night, therefore she contented herself with lying there. In the morning she sent for the woman of the house to come up to her; and easily perceiving, by her manner, that she was a woman who might be influenced by gifts, made her a present of a couple of broad pieces,[1] and desired her, that if the gentleman who had been there the night before should ask any questions concerning her, that he should be told, she was lately come out of the country, had lodged there about a fortnight, and that her name was *Fantomina*. I shall (*also added she*) lie but seldom here; nor, indeed, ever come but in those times when I expect to meet him. I would, therefore, have you order it so, that he may think I am but just gone out, if he should happen by any accident to call when I am not here; for I would not, for the world, have him imagine I do not constantly lodge here. The landlady assured her she would do everything as she desired, and gave her to understand she wanted not[2] the gift of secrecy.

Everything being ordered at this home for the security of her reputation, she repaired to the other, where she easily excused to an unsuspecting aunt, with whom she boarded, her having been abroad all night, saying, she went with a gentleman and his lady in a barge to a little country seat of theirs up the river, all of them designing to return the same evening; but that one of the bargemen happening to be taken ill on the sudden, and no other waterman to be got that night, they were obliged to tarry till morning. Thus did this lady's wit and vivacity assist her in all but where it was most needful.— She had discernment to foresee and avoid all those ills which might attend the loss of her *reputation*, but was wholly blind to those of the ruin of her *virtue*; and having managed her affairs so as to secure the *one*, grew perfectly easy with the remembrance she had forfeited the *other*.—The more she reflected on the merits of *Beauplaisir*, the more she excused herself for what

---

1. Gold coins.   2. Did not lack.

she had done; and the prospect of that continued bliss she expected to share with him took from her all remorse for having engaged in an affair which promised her so much satisfaction, and in which she found not the least danger of misfortune.—If he is really (*said she, to herself*) the faithful, the constant lover he has sworn to be, how charming will be our amour?—And if he should be false, grow satiated, like other men, I shall but, at the worst, have the private vexation of knowing I have lost him;—the intrigue being a secret, my disgrace will be so too.—I shall hear no whispers as I pass,—She is forsaken.—The odious word *forsaken* will never wound my ears; nor will my wrongs excite either the mirth or pity of the talking world.—It would not be even in the power of my undoer himself to triumph over me; and while he laughs at, and perhaps despises the fond, the yielding *Fantomina,* he will revere and esteem the virtuous, the reserved lady.—In this manner did she applaud her own conduct, and exult with the imagination that she had more prudence than all her sex beside. And it must be confessed, indeed, that she preserved an economy[3] in the management of this intrigue beyond what almost any woman but herself ever did: in the first place, by making no person in the world a confidant in it; and in the next, in concealing from *Beauplaisir* himself the knowledge who she was; for though she met him three or four days in a week at that lodging she had taken for that purpose, yet as much as he employed her time and thoughts, she was never missed from any assembly she had been accustomed to frequent.—The business of her love has engrossed her till six in the evening, and before seven she has been dressed in a different habit, and in another place.—Slippers, and a nightgown loosely flowing, has been the garb in which he has left the languishing *Fantomina;*—laced and adorned with all the blaze of jewels has he, in less than an hour after, beheld at the royal chapel, the palace gardens, drawing-room, opera, or play, the haughty awe-inspiring lady.—A thousand times has he stood amazed at the prodigious likeness between his little mistress and this court beauty; but was still as far from imagining they were the same as he was the first hour he had accosted her in the playhouse, though it is not impossible but that her resemblance to this celebrated lady might keep his inclination alive something longer than otherwise they would have been; and that it was to the thoughts of this (as he supposed) unenjoyed charmer she owed in great measure the vigor of his latter caresses.

But he varied not so much from his sex as to be able to prolong desire to any great length after possession. The rifled charms of *Fantomina* soon lost their poignancy,[4] and grew tasteless and insipid; and when the season of the year inviting the company to the *Bath,*[5] she offered to accompany him, he made an excuse to go without her. She easily perceived his coldness, and the reason why he pretended her going would be inconvenient, and endured as much from the discovery as any of her sex could do. She dissembled it, however, before him, and took her leave of him with the show of no other concern than his absence occasioned. But this she did to take from him all suspicion of her following him, as she intended, and had already laid a scheme for.— From her first finding out that he designed to leave her behind, she plainly saw it was for no other reason than that being tired of her conversation, he

---

3. Careful regulation.
4. Pungency.

5. A fashionable resort, one hundred miles west of London.

was willing to be at liberty to pursue new conquests; and wisely considering that complaints, tears, swoonings, and all the extravagancies which women make use of in such cases have little prevalence over a heart inclined to rove, and only serve to render those who practice them more contemptible, by robbing them of that beauty which alone can bring back the fugitive lover, she resolved to take another course; and remembering the height of transport she enjoyed when the agreeable *Beauplaisir* kneeled at her feet, imploring her first favors, she longed to prove the same again. Not but a woman of her beauty and accomplishments might have beheld a thousand in that condition *Beauplaisir* had been; but with her sex's modesty, she had not also thrown off another virtue equally valuable, though generally unfortunate, *constancy.* She loved *Beauplaisir;* it was only he whose solicitations could give her pleasure; and had she seen the whole species despairing, dying for her sake, it might, perhaps, have been a satisfaction to her pride, but none to her more tender inclination.—Her design was once more to engage him; to hear him sigh, to see him languish, to feel the strenuous pressures of his eager arms, to be compelled, to be sweetly forced to what she wished with equal ardor, was what she wanted, and what she had formed a stratagem to obtain, in which she promised herself success.

She no sooner heard he had left the town, than making a pretense to her aunt that she was going to visit a relation in the country, went towards *Bath,* attended but by two servants, who she found reasons to quarrel with on the road and discharged. Clothing herself in a habit she had brought with her, she forsook the coach and went into a wagon, in which equipage she arrived at *Bath.* The dress she was in was a round-eared cap, a short red petticoat, and a little jacket of gray stuff; all the rest of her accoutrements were answerable to[6] these, and joined with a broad country dialect, a rude unpolished air, which she, having been bred in these parts, knew very well how to imitate, with her hair and eye-brows blacked, made it impossible for her to be known, or taken for any other than what she seemed. Thus disguised did she offer herself to service in the house where *Beauplaisir* lodged, having made it her business to find out immediately where he was. Notwithstanding this metamorphosis she was still extremely pretty; and the mistress of the house happening at that time to want a maid, was very glad of the opportunity of taking her. She was presently[7] received into the family; and had a post in it (such as she would have chose, had she been left at her liberty), that of making the gentlemen's beds, getting them their breakfasts, and waiting on them in their chambers. Fortune in this exploit was extremely on her side; there were no others of the male sex in the house than an old gentleman who had lost the use of his limbs with the rheumatism, and had come thither for the benefit of the waters, and her beloved *Beauplaisir;* so that she was in no apprehensions of any amorous violence, but where she wished to find it. Nor were her designs disappointed. He was fired with the first sight of her; and though he did not presently take any farther notice of her than giving her two or three hearty kisses, yet she, who now understood that language but too well, easily saw they were the prelude to more substantial joys.—Coming the next morning to bring his chocolate, as he had ordered, he catched her by the pretty leg, which the shortness of her petticoat did not in the least oppose;

6. In harmony with. 7. Immediately.

then pulling her gently to him, asked her, how long she had been at service?—
How many sweethearts she had? If she had ever been in love? and many other
such questions, befitting one of the degree[8] she appeared to be. All which she
answered with such seeming innocence, as more enflamed the amorous
heart of him who talked to her. He compelled her to sit in his lap; and gazing
on her blushing beauties, which, if possible, received addition from her plain
and rural dress, he soon lost the power of containing himself.—His wild
desires burst out in all his words and actions: he called her little angel, cherubim, swore he must enjoy her, though death were to be the consequence,
devoured her lips, her breasts with greedy kisses, held to his burning bosom
her half-yielding, half-reluctant body, nor suffered her to get loose till he had
ravaged all, and glutted each rapacious sense with the sweet beauties of the
pretty *Celia*, for that was the name she bore in this second expedition.—
Generous as liberality itself to all who gave him joy this way, he gave her a
handsome sum of gold, which she durst not now refuse, for fear of creating
some mistrust, and losing the heart she so lately had regained; therefore taking it with an humble curtsy, and a well counterfeited show of surprise and
joy, cried, O law, Sir! what must I do for all this? He laughed at her simplicity,
and kissing her again, though less fervently than he had done before, bad her
not be out of the way when he came home at night. She promised she would
not, and very obediently kept her word.

His stay at *Bath* exceeded not a month; but in that time his supposed country lass had persecuted him so much with her fondness that in spite of the
eagerness with which he first enjoyed her, he was at last grown more weary of
her than he had been of *Fantomina*: which she perceiving, would not be
troublesome, but quitting her service remained privately in the town till she
heard he was on his return; and in that time provided herself of another disguise to carry on a third plot, which her inventing brain had furnished her
with, once more to renew his twice-decayed ardors. The dress she had
ordered to be made was such as widows wear in their first mourning, which,
together with the most afflicted and penitential countenance that ever was
seen, was no small alteration to her who used to seem all gaiety.—To add to
this, her hair, which she was accustomed to wear very loose, both when *Fantomina* and *Celia*, was now tied back so straight, and her pinners[9] coming so
very forward, that there was none of it to be seen. In fine, her habit and her
air were so much changed, that she was not more difficult to be known in the
rude country *girl*, than she was now in the sorrowful *widow*.

She knew that *Beauplaisir* came alone in his chariot to the *Bath*, and in
the time of her being servant in the house where he lodged, heard nothing
of anybody that was to accompany him to *London*, and hoped he would
return in the same manner he had gone. She therefore hired horses and a
man to attend her to an inn about ten miles on this side *Bath*, where having
discharged them, she waited till the chariot should come by; which when it
did, and she saw that he was alone in it, she called to him that drove it to
stop a moment, and going to the door saluted the master with these words:

The distressed and wretched, Sir (*said she*), never fail to excite compassion in a generous mind; and I hope I am not deceived in my opinion that

8. Social class.
9. Long flaps on the sides of a cap worn by women of rank.

yours is such.—You have the appearance of a gentleman, and cannot, when you hear my story, refuse that assistance which is in your power to give to an unhappy woman, who without it may be rendered the most miserable of all created beings.

It would not be very easy to represent the surprise so odd an address created in the mind of him to whom it was made.—She had not the appearance of one who wanted charity; and what other favor she required he could not conceive; but telling her she might command anything in his power, gave her encouragement to declare herself in this manner. You may judge (*resumed she*), by the melancholy garb I am in, that I have lately lost all that ought to be valuable to womankind; but it is impossible for you to guess the greatness of my misfortune, unless you had known my husband, who was master of every perfection to endear him to a wife's affections.— But, notwithstanding I look on myself as the most unhappy of my sex in out-living him, I must so far obey the dictates of my discretion as to take care of the little fortune he left behind him, which being in the hands of a brother of his in *London*, will be all carried off to *Holland*, where he is going to settle; if I reach not the town before he leaves it, I am undone for ever.—To which end I left *Bristol*, the place where we lived, hoping to get a place in the stage[1] at *Bath*, but they were all taken up before I came; and being, by a hurt I got in a fall, rendered incapable of traveling any long journey on horseback, I have no way to go to *London*, and must be inevitably ruined in the loss of all I have on earth, without[2] you have good nature enough to admit me to take part of your chariot.

Here the feigned widow ended her sorrowful tale, which had been several times interrupted by a parenthesis of sighs and groans; and *Beauplaisir*, with a complaisant and tender air, assured her of his readiness to serve her in things of much greater consequence than what she desired of him; and told her it would be an impossibility of denying a place in his chariot to a lady, who he could not behold without yielding one in his heart. She answered the compliments he made her but with tears, which seemed to stream in such abundance from her eyes that she could not keep her handkerchief from her face one moment. Being come into the chariot, *Beauplaisir* said a thousand handsome things to persuade her from giving way to so violent a grief, which, he told her, would not only be destructive to her beauty, but likewise her health. But all his endeavors for consolement appeared ineffectual, and he began to think he should have but a dull journey, in the company of one who seemed so obstinately devoted to the memory of her dead husband that there was no getting a word from her on any other theme.—But bethinking himself of the celebrated story of the *Ephesian* matron,[3] it came into his head to make trial, she who seemed equally susceptible of *sorrow*, might not also be so too of *love*: and having began a discourse on almost every other topic, and finding her still incapable of answering, resolved to put it to the proof, if this would have no more effect to rouse her sleeping spirits.—With a gay air, therefore, though accompanied with the greatest modesty and respect, he turned the conversation, as though without design, on that joy-

1. Stagecoach.
2. Unless.
3. In Petronius's *Satyricon,* a grieving widow who watches over her husband's burial vault is seduced by a soldier. When one of the bodies he was supposed to be guarding is stolen, she lets him replace it with her husband's.

giving passion, and soon discovered that was indeed the subject she was best pleased to be entertained with; for on his giving her a hint to begin upon, never any tongue run more voluble than hers, on the prodigious power it had to influence the souls of those possessed of it, to actions even the most distant from their intentions, principles, or humors.—From that she passed to a description of the happiness of mutual affection;—the unspeakable ecstasy of those who meet with equal ardency; and represented it in colors so lively, and disclosed by the gestures with which her words were accompanied, and the accent of her voice so true a feeling of what she said, that *Beauplaisir,* without being as stupid as he was really the contrary, could not avoid perceiving there were seeds of fire not yet extinguished in this fair widow's soul, which wanted but the kindling breath of tender sighs to light into a blaze.—He now thought himself as fortunate, as some moments before he had the reverse; and doubted not but that before they parted, he should find a way to dry the tears of this lovely mourner, to the satisfaction of them both. He did not, however, offer, as he had done to *Fantomina* and *Celia,* to urge his passion directly to her, but by a thousand little softening artifices, which he well knew how to use, gave her leave to guess he was enamored. When they came to the inn where they were to lie, he declared himself somewhat more freely, and perceiving she did not resent it past forgiveness, grew more encroaching still.—He now took the liberty of kissing away her tears, and catching the sighs as they issued from her lips; telling her if grief was infectious, he was resolved to have his share; protesting he would gladly exchange passions with her, and be content to bear her load of *sorrow,* if she would as willingly ease the burden of his *love.*—She said little in answer to the strenuous pressures with which at last he ventured to enfold her, but not thinking it decent, for the character she had assumed, to yield so suddenly, and unable to deny both his and her own inclinations, she counterfeited a fainting, and fell motionless upon his breast.—He had no great notion that she was in a real fit, and the room they supped in happening to have a bed in it, he took her in his arms and laid her on it, believing that whatever her distemper was, that was the most proper place to convey her to.—He laid himself down by her, and endeavored to bring her to herself; and she was too grateful to her kind physician at her returning sense, to remove from the posture he had put her in, without his leave.

It may, perhaps, seem strange that *Beauplaisir* should in such near intimacies continue still deceived. I know there are men who will swear it is an impossibility, and that no disguise could hinder them from knowing a woman they had once enjoyed. In answer to these scruples, I can only say, that besides the alteration which the change of dress made in her, she was so admirably skilled in the art of feigning that she had the power of putting on almost what face she pleased, and knew so exactly how to form her behavior to the character she represented that all the comedians[4] at both playhouses are infinitely short of her performances. She could vary her very glances, tune her voice to accents the most different imaginable from those in which she spoke when she appeared herself.—These aids from nature, joined to the wiles of art, and the distance between the places where the imagined *Fantomina* and *Celia* were, might very well prevent his having any thought

---

4. Actors.

that they were the same, or that the fair *widow* was either of them. It never so much as entered his head, and though he did fancy he observed in the face of the latter, features which were not altogether unknown to him, yet he could not recollect when or where he had known them;—and being told by her, that from her birth she had never removed from *Bristol*, a place where he never was, he rejected the belief of having seen her, and supposed his mind had been deluded by an idea of some other, whom she might have a resemblance of.

They passed the time of their journey in as much happiness as the most luxurious gratification of wild desires could make them; and when they came to the end of it, parted not without a mutual promise of seeing each other often.—He told her to what place she should direct a letter to him; and she assured him she would send to let him know where to come to her, as soon as she was fixed in lodgings.

She kept her promise; and charmed with the continuance of his eager fondness, went not home but into private lodgings, whence she wrote to him to visit her the first opportunity, and inquire for the Widow *Bloomer*.—She had no sooner dispatched this billet[5] than she repaired to the house where she had lodged as *Fantomina*, charging the people if *Beauplaisir* should come there, not to let him know she had been out of town. From thence she wrote to him, in a different hand, a long letter of complaint, that he had been so cruel in not sending one letter to her all the time he had been absent, entreated to see him, and concluded with subscribing herself his unalterably affectionate *Fantomina*. She received in one day answers to both these. The first contained these lines:

To the Charming Mrs. BLOOMER,

It would be impossible, my Angel! for me to express the thousandth part of that infinity of transport, the sight of your dear letter gave me.—Never was woman formed to charm like you: never did any look like you,—write like you,—bless like you;—nor did ever man adore as I do.—Since yesterday we parted, I have seemed a body without a soul; and had you not by this inspiring billet, gave me new life, I know not what by tomorrow I should have been.—I will be with you this evening about five.—O, 'tis an age till then!—But the cursed formalities of duty oblige me to dine with my lord—who never rises from table till that hour;—therefore adieu till then sweet lovely mistress of the soul and all the faculties of

> Your most faithful,
> BEAUPLAISIR.

The other was in this manner:

To the Lovely FANTOMINA,

If you were half so sensible as you ought of your own power of charming, you would be assured, that to be unfaithful or unkind to you would be among the things that are in their very natures impossibilities.—It was my misfortune, not my fault, that you were not persecuted every post with a declaration

---

5. Letter.

*of my unchanging passion; but I had unluckily forgot the name of the woman
at whose house you are, and knew not how to form a direction that it might
come safe to your hands.—And, indeed, the reflection how you might miscon-
strue my silence, brought me to town some weeks sooner than I intended—If
you knew how I have languished to renew those blessings I am permitted to
enjoy in your society, you would rather pity than condemn*

Your ever faithful,

BEAUPLAISIR.

P.S. *I fear I cannot see you till tomorrow; some business has unluckily fallen
out that will engross my hours till then.—Once more, my dear,* Adieu.

Traitor! (*cried she*) as soon as she had read them, 'tis thus our silly, fond,
believing sex are served when they put faith in man. So had I been deceived
and cheated, had I like the rest believed, and sat down mourning in absence,
and vainly waiting recovered tendernesses.—How do some women (*continued she*) make their life a hell, burning in fruitless expectations, and dreaming out their days in hopes and fears, then wake at last to all the horror of
despair?—But I have outwitted even the most subtle of the deceiving kind,
and while he thinks to fool me, is himself the only beguiled person.

She made herself, most certainly, extremely happy in the reflection on
the process of her stratagems; and while the knowledge of his inconstancy
and levity of nature kept her from having that real tenderness for him she
would else have had, she found the means of gratifying the inclination she
had for his agreeable person in as full a manner as she could wish. She had
all the sweets of love, but as yet had tasted none of the gall, and was in a
state of contentment which might be envied by the more delicate.

When the expected hour arrived, she found that her lover had lost no part
of the fervency with which he had parted from her; but when the next day
she received him as *Fantomina*, she perceived a prodigious difference; which
led her again into reflections on the unaccountableness of men's fancies,
who still[6] prefer the last conquest, only because it is the last.—Here was an
evident proof of it; for there could not be a difference in merit, because they
were the same person; but the Widow *Bloomer* was a more new acquaintance than *Fantomina*, and therefore esteemed more valuable. This, indeed,
must be said of *Beauplaisir*, that he had a greater share of good nature than
most of his sex, who, for the most part, when they are weary of an intrigue,
break it entirely off, without any regard to the despair of the abandoned
nymph. Though he retained no more than a bare pity and complaisance[7] for
Fantomina, yet believing she loved him to an excess, would not entirely forsake her, though the continuance of his visits was now become rather a penance than a pleasure.

The Widow *Bloomer* triumphed some time longer over the heart of this
inconstant, but at length her sway was at an end, and she sunk in this character to the same degree of tastelessness as she had done before in that of
Fantomina and *Celia*.—She presently perceived it, but bore it as she had
always done; it being but what she expected, she had prepared herself for it,
and had another project in *embryo* which she soon ripened into action. She

6. Always.   7. Indulgence.

did not, indeed, complete it altogether so suddenly as she had done the others, by reason there must be persons employed in it; and the aversion she had to any *confidants* in her affairs, and the caution with which she had hitherto acted, and which she was still determined to continue, made it very difficult for her to find a way without breaking through that resolution to compass what she wished.—She got over the difficulty at last, however, by proceeding in a manner, if possible, more extraordinary than all her former behavior.— Muffling herself up in her hood one day, she went into the park about the hour when there are a great many necessitous gentlemen, who think themselves above doing what they call little things for a maintenance, walking in the *Mall*, to take a *Camelion* treat,[8] and fill their stomachs with air instead of meat. Two of those, who by their physiognomy she thought most proper for her purpose, she beckoned to come to her; and taking them into a walk more remote from company, began to communicate the business she had with them in these words: I am sensible, gentlemen (*said she*), that, through the blindness of fortune and partiality of the world, merit frequently goes unrewarded, and that those of the best pretensions meet with the least encouragement.—I ask your pardon (*continued she*), perceiving they seemed surprised, if I am mistaken in the notion that you two may, perhaps, be of the number of those who have reason to complain of the injustice of fate; but if you are such as I take you for, I have a proposal to make you which may be of some little advantage to you. Neither of them made any immediate answer, but appeared buried in consideration for some moments. At length, We should, doubtless, madam (*said one of them*), willingly come into any measures to oblige you, provided they are such as may bring us into no danger, either as to our persons or reputations. That which I require of you (*resumed she*), has nothing in it criminal. All that I desire is *secrecy* in what you are entrusted, and to disguise yourselves in such a manner as you cannot be known, if hereafter seen by the person on whom you are to impose.—In fine, the business is only an innocent frolic, but if blazed abroad might be taken for too great a freedom in me.—Therefore, if you resolve to assist me, here are five pieces to drink my health and assure you, that I have not discoursed you on an affair I design not to proceed in; and when it is accomplished fifty more lie ready for your acceptance. These words, and above all the money, which was a sum which, 'tis probable, they had not seen of a long time, made them immediately assent to all she desired, and press for the beginning of their employment. But things were not yet ripe for execution; and she told them that the next day they should be let into the secret, charging them to meet her in the same place at an hour she appointed. 'Tis hard to say, which of these parties went away best pleased; *they*, that fortune had sent them so unexpected a windfall; or *she*, that she had found persons who appeared so well qualified to serve her.

Indefatigable in the pursuit of whatsoever her humor was bent upon, she had no sooner left her new-engaged emissaries than she went in search of a house for the completing her project.—She pitched on one very large and magnificently furnished, which she hired by the week, giving them the money beforehand to prevent any inquiries. The next day she repaired to the park, where she met the punctual squires of low degree; and ordering them

8. Chameleons supposedly fed on air. "The Mall": a fashionable promenade in St. James's Park.

to follow her to the house she had taken, told them they must condescend to appear like servants, and gave each of them a very rich livery. Then writing a letter to *Beauplaisir*, in a character vastly different from either of those she had made use of as *Fantomina*, or the fair Widow *Bloomer*, ordered one of them to deliver it into his own hands, to bring back an answer, and to be careful that he sifted out nothing of the truth.—I do not fear (*said she*), that you should discover to him who I am, because that is a secret of which you yourselves are ignorant; but I would have you be so careful in your replies, that he may not think the concealment springs from any other reasons than your great integrity to your trust.—Seem therefore to know my whole affairs; and let your refusing to make him partaker in the secret appear to be only the effect of your zeal for my interest and reputation. Promises of entire fidelity on the one side, and reward on the other, being past, the messenger made what haste he could to the house of *Beauplaisir*; and being there told where he might find him, performed exactly the injunction that had been given him. But never astonishment exceeding that which *Beauplaisir* felt at the reading this billet, in which he found these lines:

To the All-conquering BEAUPLAISIR.

I imagine not that 'tis a new thing to you, to be told you are the greatest charm in nature to our sex. I shall therefore, not to fill up my letter with any impertinent praises on your wit or person, only tell you that I am infinite in love with both, and if you have a heart not too deeply engaged, should think myself the happiest of my sex in being capable of inspiring it with some tenderness.— There is but one thing in my power to refuse you, which is the knowledge of my name, which believing the sight of my face will render no secret, you must not take it ill that I conceal from you.—The bearer of this is a person I can trust; send by him your answer; but endeavor not to dive into the meaning of this mystery, which will be impossible for you to unravel, and at the same time very much disoblige me.—But that you may be in no apprehensions of being imposed on by a woman unworthy of your regard, I will venture to assure you, the first and greatest men in the kingdom would think themselves blessed to have that influence over me you have, though unknown to yourself acquired.—But I need not go about to raise your curiosity, by giving you any idea of what my person is; if you think fit to be satisfied, resolve to visit me tomorrow about three in the afternoon; and though my face is hid, you shall not want sufficient dem- onstration that she who takes these unusual measures to commence a friend- ship with you is neither old, nor deformed. Till then I am,

Yours,
INCOGNITA.

He had scarce come to the conclusion before he asked the person who brought it, from what place he came;—the name of the lady he served;—if she were a wife, or widow, and several other questions directly opposite to the directions of the letter; but silence would have availed him as much as did all those testimonies of curiosity. No *Italian Bravo*,[9] employed in a business of the like nature, performed his office with more artifice; and the impatient

---

9. Ruffian for hire.

inquirer was convinced, that nothing but doing as he was desired could give him any light into the character of the woman who declared so violent a passion for him; and little fearing any consequence which could ensue from such an encounter, resolved to rest satisfied till he was informed of everything from herself, not imagining this *Incognita* varied so much from the generality of her sex as to be able to refuse the knowledge of anything to the man she loved with that transcendency of passion she professed, and which his many successes with the ladies gave him encouragement enough to believe. He therefore took pen and paper, and answered her letter in terms tender enough for a man who had never seen the person to whom he wrote. The words were as follows:

To the Obliging and Witty INCOGNITA.

Though to tell me I am happy enough to be liked by a woman such, as by your manner of writing, I imagine you to be, is an honor which I can never sufficiently acknowledge, yet I know not how I am able to content myself with admiring the wonders of your wit alone. I am certain a soul like yours must shine in your eyes with a vivacity which must bless all they look on.—I shall, however, endeavor to restrain myself in those bounds you are pleased to set me, till by the knowledge of my inviolable fidelity, I may be thought worthy of gazing on that heaven I am now but to enjoy in contemplation.—You need not doubt my glad compliance with your obliging summons. There is a charm in your lines which gives too sweet an idea of their lovely author to be resisted.—I am all impatient for the blissful moment which is to throw me at your feet, and give me an opportunity of convincing you that I am,

Your everlasting slave,
BEAUPLAISIR.

Nothing could be more pleased than she to whom it was directed, at the receipt of this letter; but when she was told how inquisitive he had been concerning her character and circumstances, she could not forbear laughing heartily to think of the tricks she had played him, and applauding her own strength of genius and force of resolution, which by such unthought-of ways could triumph over her lover's inconstancy, and render that very temper,[1] which to other women is the greatest curse, a means to make herself more blessed.—Had he been faithful to me (*said she, to herself*), either as *Fantomina*, or *Celia*, or the Widow *Bloomer*, the most violent passion, if it does not change its object, in time will wither. Possession naturally abates the vigor of desire, and I should have had, at best, but a cold, insipid, husband-like lover in my arms; but by these arts of passing on him as a new mistress whenever the ardor, which alone makes love a blessing, begins to diminish for the former one, I have him always raving, wild, impatient, longing, dying.—O that all neglected wives and fond abandoned nymphs would take this method!—Men would be caught in their own snare, and have no cause to scorn our easy, weeping, wailing sex! Thus did she pride herself as if secure she never should have any reason to repent the present gaiety of her humor. The hour drawing near in which he was to come, she dressed herself in as magnificent a man-

---

1. Habit of mind (inconstancy).

ner as if she were to be that night at a ball at court, endeavoring to repair the want of those beauties which the vizard[2] should conceal, by setting forth the others with the greatest care and exactness. Her fine shape, and air, and neck appeared to great advantage; and by that which was to be seen of her, one might believe the rest to be perfectly agreeable. *Beauplaisir* was prodigiously charmed, as well with her appearance as with the manner she entertained him. But though he was wild with impatience for the sight of a face which belonged to so exquisite a body, yet he would not immediately press for it, believing before he left her he should easily obtain that satisfaction.—A noble collation being over, he began to sue for the performance of her promise of granting everything he could ask, excepting the sight of her face, and knowledge of her name. It would have been a ridiculous piece of affectation in her to have seemed coy in complying with what she herself had been the first in desiring. She yielded without even a show of reluctance: and if there be any true felicity in an amour such as theirs, both here enjoyed it to the full. But not in the height of all their mutual raptures could he prevail on her to satisfy his curiosity with the sight of her face. She told him that she hoped he knew so much of her as might serve to convince him she was not unworthy of his tenderest regard; and if he could not content himself with that which she was willing to reveal, and which was the conditions of their meeting, dear as he was to her, she would rather part with him for ever than consent to gratify an inquisitiveness which, in her opinion, had no business with his love. It was in vain that he endeavored to make her sensible of her mistake; and that this restraint was the greatest enemy imaginable to the happiness of them both. She was not to be persuaded, and he was obliged to desist his solicitations, though determined in his mind to compass what he so ardently desired, before he left the house. He then turned the discourse wholly on the violence of the passion he had for her; and expressed the greatest discontent in the world at the apprehensions of being separated;—swore he could dwell for ever in her arms, and with such an undeniable earnestness pressed to be permitted to tarry with her the whole night, that had she been less charmed with his renewed eagerness of desire, she scarce would have had the power of refusing him; but in granting this request, she was not without a thought that he had another reason for making it besides the extremity of his passion, and had it immediately in her head how to disappoint him.

The hours of repose being arrived, he begged she would retire to her chamber; to which she consented, but obliged him to go to bed first; which he did not much oppose, because he supposed she would not lie in her mask, and doubted not but the morning's dawn would bring the wished discovery.— The two imagined servants ushered him to his new lodging; where he lay some moments in all the perplexity imaginable at the oddness of this adventure. But she suffered not these cogitations to be of any long continuance. She came, but came in the dark; which being no more than he expected by the former part of her proceedings, he said nothing of; but as much satisfaction as he found in her embraces, nothing ever longed for the approach of day with more impatience than he did. At last it came; but how great was his disappointment, when by the noises he heard in the street, the hurry of the coaches, and the cries of penny-merchants,[3] he was convinced it was night

---

2. Mask.   3. Street vendors.

nowhere but with him? He was still in the same darkness as before; for she had taken care to blind the windows in such a manner that not the least chink was left to let in day.—He complained of her behavior in terms that she would not have been able to resist yielding to, if she had not been certain it would have been the ruin of her passion.—She therefore answered him only as she had done before; and getting out of the bed from him, flew out of the room with too much swiftness for him to have overtaken her, if he had attempted it. The moment she left him, the two attendants entered the chamber, and plucking down the implements which had screened him from the knowledge of that which he so much desired to find out, restored his eyes once more to day.—They attended to assist him in dressing, brought him tea, and by their obsequiousness, let him see there was but one thing which the mistress of them would not gladly oblige him in.—He was so much out of humor, however, at the disappointment of his curiosity, that he resolved never to make a second visit.—Finding her in an outer room, he made no scruple of expressing the sense he had of the little trust she reposed in him, and at last plainly told her, he could not submit to receive obligations from a lady who thought him uncapable of keeping a secret, which she made no difficulty of letting her servants into.—He resented,—he once more entreated,—he said all that man could do, to prevail on her to unfold the mystery; but all his adjurations were fruitless; and he went out of the house determined never to re-enter it, till she should pay the price of his company with the discovery of her face and circumstances.—She suffered him to go with this resolution, and doubted not but he would recede from it, when he reflected on the happy moments they had passed together; but if he did not, she comforted herself with the design of forming some other stratagem, with which to impose on him a fourth time.

She kept the house and her gentlemen-equipage for about a fortnight, in which time she continued to write to him as *Fantomina* and the Widow *Bloomer*, and received the visits he sometimes made to each; but his behavior to both was grown so cold, that she began to grow as weary of receiving his now insipid caresses as he was of offering them. She was beginning to think in what manner she should drop these two characters, when the sudden arrival of her mother, who had been some time in a foreign country, obliged her to put an immediate stop to the course of her whimsical adventures.— That lady, who was severely virtuous, did not approve of many things she had been told of the conduct of her daughter; and though it was not in the power of any person in the world to inform her of the truth of what she had been guilty of, yet she heard enough to make her keep her afterwards in a restraint, little agreeable to her humor, and the liberties to which she had been accustomed.

But this confinement was not the greatest part of the trouble of this now afflicted lady. She found the consequences of her amorous follies would be, without almost a miracle, impossible to be concealed.—She was with child; and though she would easily have found means to have screened even this from the knowledge of the world, had she been at liberty to have acted with the same unquestionable authority over herself as she did before the coming of her mother, yet now all her invention was at a loss for a stratagem to impose on a woman of her penetration.—By eating little, lacing prodigious straight, and the advantage of a great hoop-petticoat, however, her bigness was not taken notice of, and, perhaps, she would not have been suspected till the time of her going into the country, where her mother designed to send her, and from whence she intended to make her escape to some place where she might be delivered with secrecy, if the time of it had not happened much sooner than she expected.—A ball being at court, the good old lady was willing she should partake of the diversion of it as a farewell to the town.— It was there she was seized with those pangs, which none in her condition are exempt from.—She could not conceal the sudden rack[4] which all at once invaded her; or had her tongue been mute, her wildly rolling eyes, the distortion of her features, and the convulsions which shook her whole frame, in spite of her, would have revealed she labored under some terrible shock of nature.—Everybody was surprised, everybody was concerned, but few guessed at the occasion.—Her mother grieved beyond expression, doubted not but she was struck with the hand of death; and ordered her to be carried home in a chair,[5] while herself followed in another.—A physician was immediately sent for; but he presently perceiving what was her distemper, called the old lady aside and told her, it was not a doctor of his sex, but one of her own, her daughter stood in need of.—Never was astonishment and horror greater than that which seized the soul of this afflicted parent at these words. She could not for a time believe the truth of what she heard; but he insisting on it, and conjuring her to send for a midwife, she was at length convinced of it.—All the pity and tenderness she had been for some moment before possessed of now vanished, and were succeeded by an adequate[6] shame and indignation.—She flew to the bed where her daughter was lying, and telling her what she had been informed of, and which she was now far from doubting, commanded her to reveal the name of the person whose insinuations[7] had drawn her to this dishonor.—It was a great while before she could be brought to confess anything, and much longer before she could be prevailed on to name the man whom she so fatally had loved; but the rack of nature growing more fierce, and the enraged old lady protesting no help should be afforded her while she persisted in her obstinacy, she, with great difficulty and hesitation in her speech, at last pronounced the name of *Beauplaisir*. She had no sooner satisfied her weeping mother, than that sorrowful lady sent messengers at the same time for a midwife, and for that gentleman who had occasioned the other's being wanted.—He happened by accident to be at home, and immediately obeyed the summons, though prodigiously surprised what business a lady so much a stranger to him could have to impart.—But how much greater was his amazement, when taking him into her closet,[8] she there acquainted him with her daughter's misfortune, of the discovery she had made, and how far he was concerned in it?—All the idea one can form of wild astonishment was mean to what he felt.—He assured her that the young lady her daughter was a person whom he had never, more than at a distance, admired;—that he had indeed spoke to her in public company, but that he never had a thought which tended to her dishonor.—His denials, if possible, added to the indignation she was before enflamed with.—She had no longer patience; and carrying him into the chamber, where she was just delivered of a fine girl, cried out, I will not be imposed on: the truth by one of you shall

4. Intense pain.
5. Carriage.
6. Equal.

7. Artful ways of winding into someone's favor.
8. Private room.

be revealed.—*Beauplaisir* being brought to the bedside, was beginning to address himself to the lady in it, to beg she would clear the mistake her mother was involved in; when she, covering herself with the clothes, and ready to die a second time with the inward agitations of her soul, shrieked out, Oh, I am undone!—I cannot live, and bear this shame!—But the old lady believing that now or never was the time to dive into the bottom of this mystery, forcing her to rear her head, told her she should not hope to escape the scrutiny of a parent she had dishonored in such a manner, and pointing to *Beauplaisir*, Is this the gentleman (*said she*), to whom you owe your ruin? or have you deceived me by a fictitious tale? Oh! no (*resumed the trembling creature*), he is indeed the innocent cause of my undoing.—Promise me your pardon (*continued she*), and I will relate the means. Here she ceased, expecting what she would reply, which, on hearing *Beauplaisir* cry out, What mean you, madam? I your undoing, who never harbored the least design on you in my life, she did in these words: Though the injury you have done your family (*said she*) is of a nature which cannot justly hope forgiveness, yet be assured, I shall much sooner excuse you when satisfied of the truth than while I am kept in a suspense, if possible, as vexatious as the crime itself is to me. Encouraged by this she related the whole truth. And 'tis difficult to determine if *Beauplaisir*, or the lady, were most surprised at what they heard; he, that he should have been blinded so often by her artifices; or she, that so young a creature should have the skill to make use of them. Both sat for some time in a profound reverie; till at length she broke it first in these words: Pardon, sir (*said she*), the trouble I have given you. I must confess it was with a design to oblige you to repair the supposed injury you had done this unfortunate girl, by marrying her, but now I know not what to say.—The blame is wholly hers, and I have nothing to request further of you, than that you will not divulge the distracted folly she has been guilty of.—He answered her in terms perfectly polite; but made no offer of that which, perhaps, she expected, though could not, now informed of her daughter's proceedings, demand. He assured her, however, that if she would commit the newborn lady to his care, he would discharge it faithfully. But neither of them would consent to that; and he took his leave, full of cogitations, more confused than ever he had known in his whole life. He continued to visit there, to inquire after her health every day; but the old lady perceiving there was nothing likely to ensue from these civilities but, perhaps, a renewing of the crime, she entreated him to refrain; and as soon as her daughter was in a condition, sent her to a monastery in *France*, the abbess of which had been her particular friend. And thus ended an intrigue which, considering the time it lasted, was as full of variety as any, perhaps, that many ages has produced.

1725

LADY MARY WORTLEY MONTAGU
1689–1762

In her early teens Lady Mary Pierrepont did something that well-bred young women were not supposed to do: she secretly taught herself Latin. The act reveals many of the traits that would also characterize her as a mature woman: curiosity, love of learning, intelligence, ambition, and independence of mind. The eldest daughter of a wealthy Whig peer (he later became marquess of Dorchester), she grew up amid a glittering London circle that included Addison, Steele, Congreve, and later Pope and Gay. But she was not content to live the life of a dutiful aristocratic daughter. Unlike most women in her time, she married for love, and when her husband, Edward Wortley Montagu, was appointed ambassador to Constantinople in 1716, she took advantage of the opportunity by traveling through Europe and studying the language and customs of Turkey. Returning home in 1718, she spent unhappy years that included bitter political quarrels with Pope and the gradual failure of her marriage. Then, in middle age, she fell in love with a young Italian author, Francesco Algarotti. In 1739 she traveled to Italy hoping to see him; but the passion that had kindled in their letters was soon quenched when he failed to join her. The rest of her life was passed abroad, in Avignon, France, and in Brescia and Venice, Italy. She died soon after her return to London, in 1762.

In a century that included many of the great letter writers in English—Gray, Horace Walpole, William Cowper, and others—Montagu is one of the greatest. She had saved her correspondence from 1716 to 1718, which centered on her experiences in the Ottoman empire, and in the year before she died, she deposited a manuscript version with a Protestant clergyman, intending it to be published. *Letters Written During Her Travels* appeared, posthumously, in 1763. "What fire, what ease, what knowledge of Europe and Asia!" the eminent historian Edward Gibbon exclaimed of the work. Montagu had traveled as a young woman with the deliberate ambition to gain such knowledge. Before arriving in Turkey, she undertook the project of understanding its culture in conversations with an Islamic scholar in Belgrade, and her curiosity led her to a multitude of revealing, provocative situations, on which she reflects with acuity and wit. She approvingly describes the liberties given to women by Turkish customs and institutions, such as the veils that rendered a woman incognito in the street (the better, she thought, to conduct secret love affairs). Letter XXXI explains the technique of smallpox inoculation in Turkey. Montagu would earn a place in medical history for her brave introduction of the practice to Britain on her return (her son and daughter were among the first to be inoculated), arousing resistance from doctors (as she predicts) and from fearful people in general. The admiring frankness of Montagu's description of the communal nudity of women in Turkish baths, in Letter XXVI, disturbed and shocked readers when the letters were finally published. Her correspondence presents two subjects to which many British readers at the time were unaccustomed: a complex, formidable civilization beyond Europe's borders, and the independent, brilliant perceptions of a woman able to view the norms of her own society critically in light of those of another.

From an early age Montagu had tried her hand at other literary forms as well: essays, poems, fiction, and even a translated play. In her own time she was especially admired as a poet. When Pope, after their quarrel, gave her the name "Sappho" (see *Epistle 2. To a Lady*, lines 24–26, p. 2774), he was doubtless betraying the nervousness that many men felt in the presence of intelligent women (the Greek poet Sappho, after all, preferred women to men); yet Pope was also associating her with the classic author of lyric verse. Montagu's poems, although often casual, reveal the mind of a woman who is not willing to accept the stereotypes imposed on her by men. Like her friend Mary Astell, Montagu puts her trust in education and reason, not in the opinions of others, and she insists on preserving her freedom of choice. A woman, her poems suggest, need not defer to a man who is less than her equal; she must look to her own satisfaction before she looks to his, and she retains the right to say no. The verse demands respect by virtue of its sexual candor and punishing wit. Like Montagu herself, it is never dull, and at its best it places her in that ideal community defined by E. M. Forster: "Not an aristocracy of power, based upon rank and influence, but an aristocracy of the sensitive, the considerate, and the plucky."

From Letters of the Right Honorable Lady M—y W——y M——e: Written During Her Travels in Europe, Asia and Africa, to Persons of Distinction [The Turkish Embassy Letters]

Letter XXVI, To Lady ———, *Adrianople,*[1] *1 April 1717*

["THE WOMEN'S COFFEE HOUSE"; OR, THE TURKISH BATHS]

I am now got into a new world, where every thing I see appears to me a change of scene; and I write to your ladyship with some content of mind, hoping, at least, that you will find the charm of novelty in my letters, and no longer reproach me that I tell you nothing extraordinary. I won't trouble you with a relation of our tedious journey; but I must not omit what I saw remarkable at Sophia,[2] one of the most beautiful towns in the Turkish empire and famous for its hot baths, that are resorted to both for diversion and health. I stopped here one day on purpose to see them; and designing to go *incognito,* I hired a Turkish coach. These voitures[3] are not at all like ours, but much more convenient for the country, the heat being so great that glasses[4] would be very troublesome. They are made a good deal in the manner of the Dutch coaches, having wooden lattices painted and gilded; the inside being painted with baskets and nosegays of flowers, intermixed commonly with little poetical mottos. They are covered all over with scarlet cloth, lined with silk, and very often richly embroidered and fringed. This covering entirely hides the persons in them, but may be thrown back at pleasure, and thus permit the ladies to peep through the lattices. They hold four people very conveniently, seated on cushions, but not raised.

In one of these covered wagons, I went to the bagnio[5] about ten o'clock. It was already full of women. It is built of stone, in the shape of a dome, with no windows but in the roof, which gives light enough. There were five of these domes joined together, the outmost being less[6] than the rest, and serving only as a hall, where the portress stood at the door. Ladies of quality generally give this woman the value of a crown or ten shillings, and I did not forget that ceremony. The next room is a very large one, paved with marble, and all round it raised two sofas of marble, one above another. There were four foun-

---

1. A city in western Turkey, named after the Roman emperor Hadrian and now called Edirne.
2. Sofia, now the capital of Bulgaria.
3. Carriages.
4. Windowpanes.
5. Bathhouse.
6. Smaller.

Unknown artist, *Mary Wortley Montagu in the Turkish Bath*, 1781. The scene in Montagu's *Letters* that most fascinated her European readers: the visit to the Turkish baths. From the frontispiece of *Letters . . . Written during her Travels in Europe, Asia, and Africa to Persons of Distinction, Men of Letters, &c. . . . which Contain . . . Accounts of the Policy & Manners of the Turks* (Berlin, 1781).

tains of cold water in this room, falling first into marble basins, and then running on the floor in little channels made for that purpose, which carried the streams into the next room, something less than this, with the same sort of marble sofas, but so hot with steams of sulphur proceeding from the baths joining to it, 'twas impossible to stay there with one's clothes on. The two other domes were the hot baths, one of which had cocks[7] of cold water turning into it, to temper it to what degree of warmth the bathers pleased to have.

I was in my traveling habit, which is a riding dress, and certainly appeared very extraordinary to them. Yet there was not one of them that showed the least surprise or impertinent curiosity, but received me with all the obliging civility possible. I know no European court where the ladies would have behaved themselves in so polite a manner to such a stranger. I believe, upon the whole, there were two hundred women, and yet none of those disdainful smiles or satirical whispers that never fail in our assemblies when anybody appears that is not dressed exactly in fashion. They repeated over and over to me, "Uzelle, pek uzelle," which is nothing but "charming, very charming."—The first sofas were covered with cushions and rich carpets, on which sat the ladies; and on the second, their slaves behind them, but without any distinction of rank by their dress, all being in the state of nature, that is, in plain English, stark naked, without any beauty or defect concealed.

7. Faucets.

Yet there was not the least wanton smile or immodest gesture amongst them. They walked and moved with the same majestic grace which Milton describes our General Mother[8] with. There were many amongst them as exactly proportioned as ever any goddess was drawn by the pencil of Guido or Titian,[9] and most of their skins shiningly white, only adorned by their beautiful hair, divided into many tresses hanging on their shoulders, braided either with pearl or ribbon, perfectly representing the figures of the graces.[1]

I was here convinced of the truth of a reflection I had often made, that if it were the fashion to go naked, the face would be hardly observed. I perceived that the ladies of the most delicate skins and finest shapes had the greatest share of my admiration, though their faces were sometimes less beautiful than those of their companions. To tell you the truth, I had wickedness enough to wish secretly that Mr. Gervase[2] could have been there invisible. I fancy it would have very much improved his art to see so many fine women naked in different postures, some in conversation, some working, others drinking coffee or sherbet, and many negligently lying on their cushions while their slaves (generally pretty girls of seventeen or eighteen) were employed in braiding their hair in several pretty fancies. In short, 'tis the women's coffee house, where all the news of the town is told, scandal invented, etc. They generally take this diversion once a week, and stay there at least four or five hours without getting cold, by immediate coming out of the hot bath into the cool room, which was very surprising to me. The lady that seemed the most considerable amongst them entreated me to sit by her, and would fain have undressed me for the bath. I excused myself with some difficulty. They being however all so earnest in persuading me, I was at last forced to open my skirt and show them my stays,[3] which satisfied them very well, for I saw they believed I was locked up in that machine, and that it was not in my own power to open it, which contrivance they attributed to my husband. I was charmed with their civility and beauty and should have been very glad to pass more time with them, but Mr. W[ortley] resolving to pursue his journey the next morning early, I was in haste to see the ruins of Justinian's church,[4] which did not afford me so agreeable a prospect as I had left, being little more than a heap of stones.

Adieu, Madam. I am sure I have now entertained you with an account of such a sight as you never saw in your life, and what no book of travels could inform you of, as 'tis no less than death for a man to be found in one of these places.

Letter XXXI, To Mrs. S. C. [Sarah Chiswell], Adrianople, 1 April 1717

[THE TURKISH METHOD OF INOCULATION FOR THE SMALL POX]

* * *

Apropos of distempers,[1] I am going to tell you a thing that will make you wish yourself here. The small pox, so fatal and so general amongst us, is here

---

8. Eve. See *Paradise Lost*, 4.492 and 8.42–43.
9. Guido Reni, Italian painter (1575–1642). Titian, Italian painter (ca. 1488–1576).
1. Three goddesses, daughters of Zeus, personifying grace and beauty.
2. Charles Jervas (1675–1739), English portrait

painter, friend of Montagu, Pope, and Swift.
3. Corset stiffened with strips of whalebone.
4. Roman emperor Justinian (483–565) built St. Sofia Church in the middle of the 6th century.
1. Montagu has just described a mild outbreak of the plague in the area.

entirely harmless by the invention of engrafting, which is the term they give it. There is a set of old women who make it their business to perform the operation, every autumn, in the month of September, when the great heat is abated. People send to one another to know if any of their family has a mind to have the small pox; they make parties for this purpose, and when they are met (commonly fifteen or sixteen together) the old woman comes with a nutshell full of the matter of the best sort of small pox,[2] and asks what veins you please to have opened. She immediately rips open that you offer to her, with a large needle (which gives you no more pain than a common scratch) and puts into the vein as much matter as can lie upon the head of her needle, and after that, binds up the little wound with a hollow bit of shell, and in this manner opens four or five veins. The Grecians have commonly the superstition of opening one in the middle of the forehead, one in each arm, and one on the breast to mark the sign of the cross; but this has a very ill effect, all these wounds leaving little scars, and is not done by those that are not superstitious, who choose to have them in the legs, or that part of the arm that is concealed. The children or young patients play together all the rest of the day and are in perfect health to the eighth. Then the fever begins to seize them, and they keep their beds two days, very seldom three. They have very rarely above twenty or thirty in their faces, which never mark, and in eight days' time they are as well as before their illness. Where they are wounded, there remains running sores during the distemper, which I don't doubt is a great relief to it. Every year thousands undergo this operation, and the French ambassador says pleasantly that they take the small pox here by way of diversion, as they take the waters in other countries. There is no example of anyone that has died in it, and you may believe I am very well satisfied of the safety of this experiment, since I intend to try it on my dear little son. I am patriot enough to take pains to bring this useful invention into fashion in England, and I should not fail to write to some of our doctors very particularly about it, if I knew any one of them that I thought had virtue enough to destroy such a considerable branch of their revenue, for the good of mankind. But that distemper is too beneficial to them, not to expose to all their resentment the hardy wight[3] that should undertake to put an end to it. Perhaps if I live to return, I may, however, have courage to war with them. Upon this occasion, admire the heroism in the heart of your friend, etc.

1717   1763

Epistle from Mrs. Yonge to Her Husband[1]

Think not this paper comes with vain pretense
To move your pity, or to mourn th' offense.

---

2. In inoculation or variolation, the milder form of the smallpox virus (*Variola minor*) is introduced to the skin of a healthy person; the localized nature of this infection stimulates the immune system in time for the body both to terminate it and to protect itself against the virus in the future.
3. Archaic word meaning "person," often implying misfortune.

1. In 1724 the notorious libertine William Yonge, separated from his wife, Mary, discovered that she (like him) had committed adultery. He sued her lover, Colonel Norton, for damages and collected £1500. Later that year, according to the law of the time, he petitioned the Houses of Parliament for a divorce. The case was tried in public, Mrs. Yonge's love letters were read aloud, and two men testified

Too well I know that hard obdurate heart;
No softening mercy there will take my part,
5   Nor can a woman's arguments prevail,
When even your patron's wise example fails.[2]
But this last privilege I still retain;
Th' oppressed and injured always may complain.
      Too, too severely laws of honor bind
10   The weak submissive sex of womankind.
If sighs have gained or force compelled our hand,
Deceived by art, or urged by stern command,
Whatever motive binds the fatal tie,
The judging world expects our constancy.
15   Just heaven! (for sure in heaven does justice reign,
Though tricks below that sacred name profane)
To you appealing I submit my cause,
Nor fear a judgment from impartial laws.
All bargains but conditional° are made;   *only conditionally*
20   The purchase void, the creditor unpaid;
Defrauded servants are from service free;
A wounded slave regains his liberty.
For wives ill used no remedy remains,
To daily racks condemned, and to eternal chains.
25   From whence is this unjust distinction grown?
Are we not formed with passions like your own?
Nature with equal fire our souls endued,
Our minds as haughty, and as warm our blood;
O'er the wide world your pleasures you pursue, ⎤
30   The change is justified by something new;   ⎬
But we must sigh in silence—and be true.   ⎦
Our sex's weakness you expose and blame
(Of every prattling fop the common theme),
Yet from this weakness you suppose is due
35   Sublimer virtue than your Cato[3] knew.
Had heaven designed us trials so severe,
It would have formed our tempers them to bear.
      And I have borne (oh what have I not borne!)
The pang of jealousy, the insults of scorn.
40   Wearied at length, I from your sight remove,
And place my future hopes in secret love.
In the gay bloom of glowing youth retired,
I quit the woman's joy to be admired,

---

that they had found her and Norton "together in naked bed." Yonge was granted the divorce, his wife's dowry, and the greater part of her fortune.

   Although the "Epistle" is obviously based on this sensational affair, it is also a work of imagination. Like Pope's *Eloisa to Abelard*—to which the author himself called Montagu's attention—it takes the form of a heroic epistle, the passionate outcry of an abandoned woman. The poet, entering into the feelings of Mary Yonge, justifies her conduct with reasons both of the heart and of the head. The objects of her attack include the institution of marriage, which binds wives in "eternal chains"; the double standard of morality, which requires chastity from women but not men; the hypocrisy of society, which condemns the very behavior it secretly lusts after; and the craven greed and cruelty of the husband himself. But 18th-century women seldom dared to speak like this in public, and the "Epistle" was not published until the 1970s.

2. Sir Robert Walpole, William Yonge's friend at court, was rumored to tolerate his own wife's infidelities.

3. The asceticism and self-discipline of the Roman statesman Cato were emphasized in Addison's famous tragedy *Cato* (1713).

With that small pension your hard heart allows,
45 Renounce your fortune, and release your vows.
To custom (though unjust) so much is due;
I hide my frailty from the public view.
My conscience clear, yet sensible of shame,
My life I hazard, to preserve my fame.
50 And I prefer this low inglorious state ⎫
To vile dependence on the thing I hate— ⎬
But you pursue me to this last retreat. ⎭
Dragged into light, my tender crime is shown
And every circumstance of fondness known.
55 Beneath the shelter of the law you stand,
And urge my ruin with a cruel hand,
While to my fault thus rigidly severe,
Tamely submissive to the man you fear.[4]

    This wretched outcast, this abandoned wife,
60 Has yet this joy to sweeten shameful life:
By your mean conduct, infamously loose,
You are at once my accuser and excuse.
Let me be damned by the censorious prude
(Stupidly dull, or spiritually lewd),
65 My hapless case will surely pity find
From every just and reasonable mind.
When to the final sentence I submit,
The lips condemn me, but their souls acquit.

    No more my husband, to your pleasures go,
70 The sweets of your recovered freedom know.
Go: court the brittle friendship of the great,
Smile at his board,° or at his levee[5] wait;   *dining table*
And when dismissed, to madam's toilet[6] fly,
More than her chambermaids, or glasses,° lie,   *mirrors*
75 Tell her how young she looks, how heavenly fair,
Admire the lilies and the roses there.
Your high ambition may be gratified,
Some cousin of her own be made your bride,
And you the father of a glorious race
80 Endowed with Ch—l's strength and Low—r's face.[7]

1724   1972

4. I.e., Walpole. Montagu suggests that the whole political establishment of England takes sides against Mary Yonge.
5. Morning reception of visitors.
6. It was fashionable for women like Lady Walpole to receive visitors during the last stages of dressing (their "toilet").
7. General Churchill was rumored to have had an affair with Lady Walpole. Antony Lowther was a notorious gallant. The author implies that William Yonge's next wife may be as untrue as his first. Mary Yonge remarried immediately after her divorce; five years later Yonge himself (whose divorce had made him rich) married the daughter of a baron.

Debating Women: Arguments in Verse

Satires on women are an ancient tradition. In many cultures, male writers have defined the nature of women, distinguished them sharply from men, laughed at their faults, looked into their hearts, and told them how to behave; and female writers such as Christine de Pisan (1363?–1431) have countered by pointing out the virtues of women and the unfairness of men. But the argument intensified in seventeenth- and eighteenth-century Britain. As literacy increased to unprecedented numbers, much of the reading public began to consist of women, whose concerns were addressed directly by Mary Astell and other women as well as by men. New forms of writing—the periodical essay, the conduct book, and above all the novel—developed to give women rules and models for living. But the early eighteenth century was also a great age of satire. Male satirists could not resist the urge to reflect on, or try to reform, women's follies; nor could female satirists resist the urge to reply that men were just as bad or worse and did not know what they were talking about. This led to a lively exchange in which women were not only the subject of the debate but also agents who spoke for themselves.

Jonathan Swift and Alexander Pope, who were lifelong bachelors and friends as well as brilliant satirists, represent two different positions. Swift's misogyny is part of his misanthropy. As a Christian he hates human pride, or the illusion that we can rise above the sinfulness and frailty that are our nature as impure, fallen creatures; and he never misses a chance to shatter that illusion. Hence women, associated romantically with beauty and love, must be dragged down to earth and have their cosmetics rubbed off. To Swift's admirers, this is realism; to his detractors, woman-hating. His focus on bodily functions in works like "The Lady's Dressing Room" has often been ascribed to a personal fixation or frustrated desire, as in Lady Mary Wortley Montagu's counterattack. It might also be regarded as the fury of an idealist when he looks at the world as it is.

Pope was far more comfortable with illusions; when he writes about a lady's dressing room, in *The Rape of the Lock,* it sparkles with glamour. Many readers have thought he had a feminine sensibility. Despite his patronizing attitude toward women, he certainly took a strong interest in female psychology; and his pleasure in delicate things and domestic arrangements appealed to many women. Anne Irwin and Mary Leapor argue with Pope's *Characters of Women,* but they are clearly influenced by the way he sees their world as well as by his poetic style. In this respect his satire might be thought more insidious than Swift's. The sympathy he expresses for women lends plausibility to his analysis of their flaws, and his distinctions between the sexes seem rooted in nature, not merely in custom. Thus Pope's shrewd portraits of the ways that women waste their lives can be very chilling.

Yet women could also write satire. The poets who respond to Swift and Pope poke fun at the smug assumption that men can tell women what women are thinking and feeling. Montagu's parody, one of many answers to Swift's poem, turns the tables on his disgust at the body; here the *man's* body falls short. (Some women agreed that men were Yahoos, though women were not.) Irwin suggests that Pope is the problem, not the solution: because lack of education makes all the difference between women and men, a truly good poet would devote himself to educating women, not to ridiculing faults they cannot help. Similarly, Leapor regards satire of women as blaming the victim; her characters resemble Pope's, but what dooms them is not the bad choices they make but the lack of any good choice in a man's world that turns all their dreams against them. The female satirists in this debate do not belong to any set, nor do they agree with each other's diagnoses. They do agree, however, on one main point: when the ways of women come into question, women must speak for themselves.

JONATHAN SWIFT

"The Lady's Dressing Room" is the first in a series of "excremental" poems in which Swift looks below the surface of women's allure. If one object of satire is the grossness of Celia, "the goddess," the romantic illusions of Strephon, her disabused lover, are far more absurd.

The Lady's Dressing Room

Five hours (and who can do it less in?)
By haughty Celia spent in dressing,
The goddess from her chamber issues,
Arrayed in lace, brocade, and tissues.
5 Strephon, who found the room was void,
And Betty otherwise employed,
Stole in, and took a strict survey
Of all the litter as it lay;
Whereof, to make the matter clear,
10 An inventory follows here.
    And first a dirty smock appeared,
Beneath the armpits well besmeared.
Strephon, the rogue, displayed it wide,
And turned it round on every side.
15 In such a case few words are best,
And Strephon bids us guess the rest;
But swears how damnably the men lie,
In calling Celia sweet and cleanly.
    Now listen while he next produces
20 The various combs for various uses,
Filled up with dirt so closely fixed,
No brush could force a way betwixt;
A paste of composition rare,
Sweat, dandruff, powder, lead, and hair;
25 A forehead cloth with oil upon't
To smooth the wrinkles on her front;
Here alum flower° to stop the steams   *styptic powder*
Exhaled from sour unsavory streams;
There night-gloves made of Tripsy's hide,

30   Bequeathed by Tripsy when she died,
        With puppy water,[1] beauty's help,
        Distilled from Tripsy's darling whelp;
        Here gallipots° and vials placed,   *small pots*
        Some filled with washes, some with paste,
35   Some with pomatum,° paints, and slops,   *pomade*
        And ointments good for scabby chops.
        Hard by a filthy basin stands,
        Fouled with the scouring of her hands;
        The basin takes whatever comes,
40   The scraping of her teeth and gums,
        A nasty compound of all hues,
        For here she spits, and here she spews.
            But oh! it turned poor Strephon's bowels,
        When he beheld and smelt the towels,
45   Begummed, bemattered, and beslimed,
        With dirt, and sweat, and earwax grimed.
        No object Strephon's eye escapes;
        Here petticoats in frowzy heaps,
        Nor be the handkerchiefs forgot,
50   All varnished o'er with snuff and snot.
        The stockings why should I expose,
        Stained with the marks of stinking toes,
        Or greasy coifs and pinners° reeking,   *nightcaps*
        Which Celia slept at least a week in?
55   A pair of tweezers next he found
        To pluck her brows in arches round,
        Or hairs that sink the forehead low,
        Or on her chin like bristles grow.
            The virtues we must not let pass
60   Of Celia's magnifying glass.
        When frighted Strephon cast his eye on't,
        It showed the visage of a giant—
        A glass that can to sight disclose
        The smallest worm in Celia's nose,
65   And faithfully direct her nail
        To squeeze it out from head to tail;
        For catch it nicely by the head,
        It must come out alive or dead.
            Why Strephon will you tell the rest?
70   And must you needs describe the chest?
        That careless wench! no creature warn her
        To move it out from yonder corner,
        But leave it standing full in sight,
        For you to exercise your spite.
75   In vain the workman showed his wit
        With rings and hinges counterfeit
        To make it seem in this disguise
        A cabinet to vulgar eyes;
        For Strephon ventured to look in,

---

1. A cosmetic made from the internal organs of a puppy (here from the whelp of Celia's former lapdog).

80 Resolved to go through thick and thin;
He lifts the lid, there needs no more,
He smelt it all the time before.
      As from within Pandora's box,
When Epimetheus oped the locks,
85 A sudden universal crew
Of human evils upward flew,
He still was comforted to find
That Hope at last remained behind;[2]
So Strephon, lifting up the lid
90 To view what in the chest was hid,
The vapors flew from out the vent,
But Strephon cautious never meant
The bottom of the pan to grope,
And foul his hands in search of Hope.
95 Oh never may such vile machine
Be once in Celia's chamber seen!
Oh may she better learn to keep
"Those secrets of the hoary deep"![3]
      As mutton cutlets, prime of meat,
100 Which though with art you salt and beat,
As laws of cookery require,
And roast them at the clearest fire,
If from adown the hopeful chops
The fat upon a cinder drops,
105 To stinking smoke it turns the flame,
Poisoning the flesh from whence it came,
And thence exhales a greasy stench,
For which you curse the careless wench;
So things which must not be expressed,
110 When plumped into the reeking chest,
Send up an excremental smell
To taint the parts from which they fell,
The petticoats and gown perfume,
And waft a stink round every room.
115   Thus finishing his grand survey,
The swain disgusted slunk away,
Repeating in his amorous fits,
"Oh! Celia, Celia, Celia shits!"
      But Vengeance, goddess never sleeping,
120 Soon punished Strephon for his peeping.
His foul imagination links
Each dame he sees with all her stinks,
And, if unsavory odors fly,
Conceives a lady standing by.
125 All women his description fits,
And both ideas jump like wits,[4]

2. Despite the warnings of his brother Prometheus, Epimetheus married Pandora, the first woman (according to Greek mythology). When the box that Zeus had given her was opened, all evils flew out into the world, and only hope remained.
3. *Paradise Lost* 2.891.
4. Coincide; after the proverb "Good wits jump" (i.e., great minds think alike).

By vicious fancy coupled fast,
And still appearing in contrast.
        I pity wretched Strephon, blind
130   To all the charms of womankind.
Should I the queen of love refuse
Because she rose from stinking ooze?[5]
To him that looks behind the scene,
Statira's but some pocky quean.[6]
135   When Celia in her glory shows,
If Strephon would but stop his nose,
Who now so impiously blasphemes
Her ointments, daubs, and paints, and creams,
Her washes, slops, and every clout°   rag
140   With which she makes so foul a rout,
He soon would learn to think like me,
And bless his ravished eyes to see
Such order from confusion sprung,
Such gaudy tulips raised from dung.

1732

---

5. The goddess Venus rose out of the sea.
6. Strumpet, with a pun on Nathaniel Lee's *Rival*

Queens (1677), a play in which Statira was a heroine.

LADY MARY WORTLEY MONTAGU

Montagu did not like Swift. She objected to his politics (he worked for Tories, she was a Whig), his friendship with Pope (with whom she had bitterly quarreled), his vanity (especially at knowing important people), and his defiant indecency (which she considered not only inappropriate for a clergyman but also a sign of low breeding). Her reply to "The Lady's Dressing Room" mimics its style, but substitutes vulgar names for its mock-pastoral (Betty instead of Celia) and personal pique for its moralistic conclusions. The poem was originally published anonymously in 1734 under the title "The Dean's Provocation for Writing the Lady's Dressing Room"; the version printed here is from a fair copy in Montagu's hand.

The Reasons That Induced Dr. Swift
to Write a Poem Called the Lady's Dressing Room

The Doctor in a clean starched band,°   clerical collar
His golden snuff box in his hand,
With care his diamond ring displays
And artful shows its various rays,
5   While grave he stalks down ——— Street,
His dearest Betty ——— to meet.
        Long had he waited for this hour,

Nor gained admittance to the bower,
Had joked and punned, and swore and writ,
10 Tried all his gallantry and wit,
Had told her oft what part he bore
In Oxford's[1] schemes in days of yore,
But bawdy, politics, nor satyr[2]
Could move this dull hard-hearted creature.
15 Jenny her maid could taste a rhyme
And grieved to see him lose his time,
Had kindly whispered in his ear,
"For twice two pound you enter here;
My lady vows without that sum
20 It is in vain you write or come."
 The destined offering now he brought
And in a paradise of thought
With a low bow approached the dame
Who smiling heard him preach his flame.
25 His gold she takes (such proofs as these
Convince most unbelieving shes)
And in her trunk rose up to lock it
(Too wise to trust it in her pocket)
And then, returned with blushing grace,
30 Expects the Doctor's warm embrace.
 But now this is the proper place
Where morals stare me in the face
And for the sake of fine expression
I'm forced to make a small digression.
35 Alas for wretched humankind,
With learning mad, with wisdom blind!
The ox thinks he's for saddle fit
(As long ago friend Horace writ)[3]
And men their talents still mistaking,
40 The stutterer fancies his is speaking.
With admiration oft we see
Hard features heightened by toupée,
The beau affects° the politician,   *poses as*
Wit is the citizen's[4] ambition,
45 Poor Pope philosophy displays on
With so much rhyme and little reason,
And though he argues ne'er so long
That all is right, his head is wrong.[5]
 None strive to know their proper merit
50 But strain for wisdom, beauty, spirit,
And lose the praise that is their due
While they've the impossible in view.
So have I seen the injudicious heir
To add one window the whole house impair.
55   Instinct the hound does better teach

---

1. Robert Harley, Earl of Oxford, headed the government from 1710 to 1714.
2. Satire (pronounced *say'tir*).
3. *Epistles* 1.14.43.

4. "A townsman; a man of trade; not a gentleman" (Johnson's *Dictionary*).
5. A parody of Pope's *Essay on Man* 1.292, which had just been published.

Who never undertook to preach;
The frighted hare from dogs does run
But not attempts to bear a gun.
Here many noble thoughts occur
60 But I prolixity abhor,
And will pursue the instructive tale
To show the wise in some things fail.
    The reverend lover with surprise ⎤
Peeps in her bubbies, and her eyes, ⎬
65 And kisses both, and tries—and tries. ⎦
The evening in this hellish play,
Beside his guineas thrown away,
Provoked the priest to that degree
He swore, "The fault is not in me.
70 Your damned close stool so near my nose,
Your dirty smock, and stinking toes,
Would make a Hercules as tame
As any beau that you can name."
    The nymph grown furious roared, "By God!
75 The blame lies all in sixty odd,"
And scornful pointing to the door
Cried, "Fumbler, see my face no more."
"With all my heart I'll go away,
But nothing done, I'll nothing pay.
80 Give back the money."—"How," cried she,
"Would you palm such a cheat on me!
For poor four pound to roar and bellow,
Why sure you want some new Prunella?"[6]
"I'll be revenged, you saucy quean"°   strumpet
85 (Replies the disappointed Dean),
"I'll so describe your dressing room
The very Irish shall not come."[7]
She answered short, "I'm glad you'll write,
You'll furnish paper when I shite."

1734

---

6. A name for a prostitute and a worsted cloth worn by clergymen.

7. A gibe at the supposed crassness of Irishmen (like Swift himself).

ALEXANDER POPE

"Epistle 2. To a Lady" is one of four poems that Pope grouped together under the title *Epistles to Several Persons* but that have usually been known by the less appropriate title *Moral Essays*. They were conceived as parts of Pope's ambitious "ethic work," of which only the first part, *An Essay on Man*, was completed. "Epistle 1" treats the characters of men and "Epistle 2," the characters of women. The other two epistles are concerned with the use of riches, a subject that engaged Pope's attention during the 1730s, because he distrusted the influence on private morals and public life of the rapidly growing wealth of England under the first Hanoverians.

"Epistle 2" combines two literary forms: the satire on women and the verse letter to a particular person—here Martha Blount (1690–1763), Pope's closest female friend, whose remark in line 2 sets the theme of the poem. The first section (to line 198) sketches a portrait gallery of ladies that illustrates their inconsistency and volatility. As an amateur painter, Pope is fascinated by the problem of catching such contrary types: the affected, the soft-natured, the cunning, the whimsical, the witty, and the silly. The next part of the poem (lines 199–248) develops Pope's favorite theory of the ruling passion—the idea that each person is driven by a single irresistible desire—and argues that women are limited to two passions: love of pleasure and love of power. The final part (line 249 to the end) describes an ideal woman, good-natured, sensible, and well balanced, who is identified with Blount herself.

Like every satire on women, "Epistle 2" is shaped by stereotypes: women are fickle, frail, and subordinate to men. Yet much of the poem undermines those prejudices by showing the real difficulties of women's lives. "By man's oppression cursed," they waste their talents on trivial pursuits and "die of nothing but a rage to live." The poem shares that restlessness. If women are full of contradictions, so are Pope's couplets, torn between sympathy and satiric bite. The poet finds himself strangely attracted to what he disapproves, and many female readers, then and now, have felt the same way about the poem.

Epistle 2. To a Lady

Of the Characters of Women

    Nothing so true as what you once let fall,
"Most women have no characters at all."
Matter too soft a lasting mark to bear,
And best distinguished by black, brown, or fair.
5   How many pictures[1] of one nymph we view,
All how unlike each other, all how true!
Arcadia's countess, here, in ermined pride,
Is, there, Pastora by a fountain side.
Here Fannia, leering on her own good man,
10   And there, a naked Leda with a swan.[2]
Let then the fair one beautifully cry,
In Magdalen's loose hair and lifted eye,
Or dressed in smiles of sweet Cecilia shine,[3]
With simpering angels, palms, and harps divine;
15   Whether the charmer sinner it, or saint it,
If folly grow romantic,° I must paint it.   *extravagant*
    Come then, the colors and the ground[4] prepare!
Dip in the rainbow, trick° her off in air;   *sketch*
Choose a firm cloud, before it fall, and in it
20   Catch, ere she change, the Cynthia[5] of this minute.

---

1. Ladies of the 17th and 18th centuries were often painted in the costumes and attitudes of fanciful, mythological, or historical characters.
2. Leda was seduced by Zeus, who approached her in the form of a swan.
3. St. Mary Magdalen and St. Cecilia were often painted in the manner described.
4. The first coatings of paint on the canvas before the figures in the picture are sketched in.
5. One of the names of Diana, goddess of the moon, a notoriously changeable heavenly body.

Rufa, whose eye quick-glancing o'er the park,
Attracts each light gay meteor of a spark,°   *beau*
Agrees as ill with Rufa studying Locke,
As Sappho's diamonds with her dirty smock,
25 Or Sappho at her toilet's greasy task,[6]
With Sappho fragrant at an evening masque:
So morning insects that in muck begun,
Shine, buzz, and flyblow[7] in the setting sun.
    How soft is Silia! fearful to offend,
30 The frail one's advocate, the weak one's friend:
To her, Calista proved her conduct nice,°   *refined*
And good Simplicius asks of her advice.
Sudden, she storms! she raves! You tip the wink,°   *look knowing*
But spare your censure; Silia does not drink.
35 All eyes may see from what the change arose,
All eyes may see—a pimple on her nose.
    Papillia,[8] wedded to her amorous spark,
Sighs for the shades—"How charming is a park!"
A park is purchased, but the fair he sees
40 All bathed in tears—"Oh, odious, odious trees!"
    Ladies, like variegated tulips, show;
'Tis to their changes half their charms we owe;
Their happy spots the nice admirer take,°   *captivate*
Fine by defect, and delicately weak.
45 'Twas thus Calypso[9] once each heart alarmed,
Awed without virtue, without beauty charmed;
Her tongue bewitched as oddly as her eyes,
Less wit than mimic, more a wit than wise;
Strange graces still, and stranger flights she had,
50 Was just not ugly, and was just not mad;
Yet ne'er so sure our passion to create,
As when she touched the brink of all we hate.
    Narcissa's[1] nature, tolerably mild,
To make a wash,° would hardly stew a child;   *cosmetic lotion*
55 Has even been proved to grant a lover's prayer,
And paid a tradesman once to make him stare,
Gave alms at Easter, in a Christian trim,
And made a widow happy, for a whim.
Why then declare good nature is her scorn,
60 When 'tis by that alone she can be borne?
Why pique all mortals, yet affect a name?
A fool to pleasure, yet a slave to fame:
Now deep in Taylor and the *Book of Martyrs*,[2]

6. Lady Mary Wortley Montagu, although beautiful as a young woman, became notorious for her slatternly appearance and personal uncleanliness. Both Sappho and Montagu were poets.
7. Deposit their eggs.
8. The name comes from Latin for "butterfly."
9. The name is borrowed from the fascinating goddess who detained Odysseus on her island for seven years after the fall of Troy, thus preventing his return to his kingdom, Ithaca.
1. Type of extreme self-love. Narcissus, a beautiful youth, fell in love with his own image when he saw it reflected in a fountain.
2. John Foxe's *Acts and Monuments*, usually referred to as Foxe's *Book of Martyrs*, was a household book in most Protestant families in the 17th and 18th centuries. A record of the Protestants who perished for their faith under the persecution of Mary Tudor (1553–58), it was instrumental in keeping anti-Catholic sentiments alive. Jeremy Taylor, 17th-century Anglican divine, whose *Holy Living and Holy Dying* was often reprinted in the 18th century.

Now drinking citron with his Grace and Chartres.[3]
65 Now conscience chills her, and now passion burns;
And atheism and religion take their turns;
A very heathen in the carnal part,
Yet still a sad, good Christian at her heart.
    See Sin in state, majestically drunk;
70 Proud as a peeress, prouder as a punk;°   *harlot*
Chaste to her husband, frank° to all beside,   *licentious*
A teeming mistress, but a barren bride.
What then? let blood and body bear the fault,
Her head's untouched, that noble seat of thought:
75 Such this day's doctrine—in another fit
She sins with poets through pure love of wit.
What has not fired her bosom or her brain?
Caesar and Tallboy, Charles[4] and Charlemagne.
As Helluo,[5] late dictator of the feast,
80 The nose of hautgout,[6] and the tip of taste,
Criticked your wine, and analyzed your meat,
Yet on plain pudding deigned at home to eat;
So Philomedé,[7] lecturing all mankind
On the soft passion, and the taste refined,
85 The address, the delicacy—stoops at once,
And makes her hearty meal upon a dunce.
    Flavia's a wit, has too much sense to pray;
To toast our wants and wishes, is her way;
Nor asks of God, but of her stars, to give
90 The mighty blessing, "while we live, to live."
Then all for death, that opiate of the soul!
Lucretia's dagger, Rosamonda's bowl.[8]
Say, what can cause such impotence of mind?
A spark too fickle, or a spouse too kind.
95 Wise wretch! with pleasures too refined to please,
With too much spirit to be e'er at ease,
With too much quickness ever to be taught,
With too much thinking to have common thought:
You purchase pain with all that joy can give,
100 And die of nothing but a rage to live.
    Turn then from wits; and look on Simo's mate,
No ass so meek, no ass so obstinate:
Or her, that owns her faults, but never mends,
Because she's honest, and the best of friends:
105 Or her, whose life the Church and scandal share,
Forever in a passion, or a prayer:
Or her, who laughs at hell, but (like her Grace)

---

3. Francis Charters was a debauchee often mentioned by Pope. "Citron": i.e., citron water; brandy flavored with lemon or orange peel. "His Grace" is usually said to be the Duke of Wharton, an old enemy of Swift's and a notorious libertine.
4. A generic name for a footman in the period. "Tallboy": a crude young man in Richard Brome's comedy *The Jovial Crew* (1641) or the opera adapted from the play (1731).
5. Glutton (Latin).

6. "Anything with a strong relish or strong scent, as overkept venison" (Johnson's *Dictionary*).
7. The name is Pope's adaptation of a Greek epithet meaning "laughter-loving," frequently applied to Aphrodite; the goddess of love.
8. According to tradition, the "fair Rosamonda," mistress of Henry II, was forced by Queen Eleanor to drink poison. Lucretia, violated by a son of Tarquin, committed suicide.

Cries, "Ah! how charming, if there's no such place!"
Or who in sweet vicissitude appears
110 Of mirth and opium, ratafie[9] and tears,
The daily anodyne, and nightly draught,
To kill those foes to fair ones, time and thought.
Woman and fool are two hard things to hit,
For true no-meaning puzzles more than wit.
115   But what are these to great Atossa's[1] mind?
Scarce once herself, by turns all womankind!
Who, with herself, or others, from her birth
Finds all her life one warfare upon earth:
Shines in exposing knaves, and painting fools,
120 Yet is whate'er she hates and ridicules.
No thought advances, but her eddy brain
Whisks it about, and down it goes again.
Full sixty years the world has been her trade,
The wisest fool much time has ever made.
125 From loveless youth to unrespected age,
No passion gratified except her rage.
So much the fury still outran the wit,
The pleasure missed her, and the scandal hit.
Who breaks with her, provokes revenge from hell,
130 But he's a bolder man who dares be well:°   *in her favor*
Her every turn with violence pursued,
Nor more a storm her hate than gratitude:
To that each passion turns, or soon or late;
Love, if it makes her yield, must make her hate:
135 Superiors? death! and equals? what a curse!
But an inferior not dependent? worse.
Offend her, and she knows not to forgive;
Oblige her, and she'll hate you while you live:
But die, and she'll adore you—Then the bust
140 And temple rise—then fall again to dust.
Last night, her lord was all that's good and great;
A knave this morning, and his will a cheat.
Strange! by the means defeated of the ends,
By spirit robbed of power, by warmth of friends,
145 By wealth of followers! without one distress
Sick of herself through very selfishness!
Atossa, cursed with every granted prayer,
Childless with all her children,[2] wants an heir.
To heirs unknown descends the unguarded store,
150 Or wanders, Heaven-directed, to the poor.
    Pictures like these, dear Madam, to design,
Asks no firm hand, and no unerring line;
Some wandering touches, some reflected light,
Some flying stroke alone can hit 'em right:
155 For how should equal colors do the knack?°   *do the trick*

---

9. "A fine liquor, prepared from the kernels of apricots and spirits" (Johnson's *Dictionary*).
1. Atossa, daughter of Cyrus, emperor of Persia (d. 529 B.C.E.). If the Duchess of Buckingham-shire is alluded to, the name is appropriate, for she was the natural daughter of James II.
2. The duchess's five children died before she did.

Chameleons who can paint in white and black?
  "Yet Chloe sure was formed without a spot—"
Nature in her then erred not, but forgot.
"With every pleasing, every prudent part,
160 Say, what can Chloe want?"—She wants a heart.
She speaks, behaves, and acts just as she ought;
But never, never, reached one generous thought.
Virtue she finds too painful an endeavor,
Content to dwell in decencies forever.
165 So very reasonable, so unmoved,
As never yet to love, or to be loved.
She, while her lover pants upon her breast,
Can mark° the figures on an Indian chest;   *pay attention to*
And when she sees her friend in deep despair,
170 Observes how much a chintz exceeds mohair.
Forbid it Heaven, a favor or a debt
She e'er should cancel—but she may forget.
Safe is your secret still in Chloe's ear;
But none of Chloe's shall you ever hear.
175 Of all her dears she never slandered one,
But cares not if a thousand are undone.
Would Chloe know if you're alive or dead?
She bids her footman put it in her head.
Chloe is prudent—Would you too be wise?
180 Then never break your heart when Chloe dies.
    One certain portrait may (I grant) be seen,
Which Heaven has varnished out, and made a *Queen*:
The same forever! and described by all
With truth and goodness, as with crown and ball.
185 Poets heap virtues, painters gems at will,
And show their zeal, and hide their want of skill.[3]
'Tis well—but, artists! who can paint or write,
To draw the naked is your true delight.
That robe of quality so struts and swells,
190 None see what parts of Nature it conceals:
The exactest traits of body or of mind,
We owe to models of an humble kind.
If Queensberry[4] to strip there's no compelling,
'Tis from a handmaid we must take a Helen.
195 From peer or bishop 'tis no easy thing
To draw the man who loves his God, or king:
Alas! I copy (or my draft would fail)
From honest Mah'met or plain Parson Hale.[5]
    But grant, in public men sometimes are shown,
200 A woman's seen in private life alone:
Our bolder talents in full light displayed;
Your virtues open fairest in the shade.
Bred to disguise, in public 'tis you hide;

---

3. Pope did not admire Queen Caroline.
4. The Duchess of Queensberry, whom Pope valued because of her kindness to his friend John Gay, had been a famous beauty.

5. Dr. Stephen Hales, an Anglican clergyman and friend of Pope. Mahomet was a Turkish servant of George I.

There, none distinguish 'twixt your shame or pride,
205 Weakness or delicacy; all so nice,
That each may seem a virtue, or a vice.
   In men, we various ruling passions find;
In women, two almost divide the kind;
Those, only fixed, they first or last obey,
210 The love of pleasure, and the love of sway.
   That, Nature gives;[6] and where the lesson taught
Is but to please, can pleasure seem a fault?
Experience, this; by man's oppression cursed,
They seek the second not to lose the first.
215   Men, some to business, some to pleasure take;
But every woman is at heart a rake;
Men, some to quiet, some to public strife;
But every lady would be queen for life.
   Yet mark the fate of a whole sex of queens!
220 Power all their end, but beauty all the means:
In youth they conquer, with so wild a rage,
As leaves them scarce a subject in their age:
For foreign glory, foreign joy, they roam;
No thought of peace or happiness at home.
225 But wisdom's triumph is well-timed retreat,
As hard a science to the fair as great![7]
Beauties, like tyrants, old and friendless grown,
Yet hate repose, and dread to be alone,
Worn out in public, weary every eye,
230 Nor leave one sigh behind them when they die.
   Pleasures the sex, as children birds, pursue,
Still out of reach, yet never out of view,
Sure, if they catch, to spoil the toy at most,
To covet flying, and regret when lost:
235 At last, to follies youth could scarce defend,
It grows their age's prudence to pretend;
Ashamed to own they gave delight before,
Reduced to feign it, when they give no more:
As hags hold sabbaths, less for joy than spite,
240 So these their merry, miserable night;[8]
Still round and round the ghosts of beauty glide,
And haunt the places where their honor died.
   See how the world its veterans rewards!
A youth of frolics, an old age of cards;
245 Fair to no purpose, artful to no end,
Young without lovers, old without a friend;
A fop their passion, but their prize a sot;
Alive, ridiculous, and dead, forgot!
   Ah friend! to dazzle let the vain design;
250 To raise the thought, and touch the heart be thine!

6. Women naturally love pleasure. Lines 213–14 say that experience teaches them a love of power ("sway").
7. Retreating is as hard for women to learn as it for great soldiers or statesmen.
8. I.e., evenings on which ladies entertained guests. "Sabbaths": obscene rites popularly supposed to be held by witches ("hags").

That charm shall grow, while what fatigues the Ring[9]
Flaunts and goes down, an unregarded thing:
So when the sun's broad beam has tired the sight,
All mild ascends the moon's more sober light,
255 Serene in virgin modesty she shines,
And unobserved the glaring orb declines.
　　　Oh! blest with temper, whose unclouded ray
Can make tomorrow cheerful as today;
She, who can love a sister's charms, or hear
260 Sighs for a daughter with unwounded ear;
She, who ne'er answers till a husband cools,
Or, if she rules him, never shows she rules;
Charms by accepting, by submitting sways,
Yet has her humor most, when she obeys;
265 Lets fops or fortune fly which way they will;
Disdains all loss of tickets° or Codille;[1]　　　*lottery tickets*
Spleen, vapors, or smallpox, above them all,
And mistress of herself, though China[2] fall.
　　　And yet, believe me, good as well as ill,
270 Woman's at best a contradiction still.
Heaven, when it strives to polish all it can
Its last best work, but forms a softer man;
Picks from each sex, to make the favorite blest,
Your love of pleasure, our desire of rest:
275 Blends, in exception to all general rules,
Your taste of follies, with our scorn of fools:
Reserve with frankness, art with truth allied,
Courage with softness, modesty with pride;
Fixed principles, with fancy ever new;
280 Shakes all together, and produces—you.
　　　Be this a woman's fame: with this unblest,
Toasts live a scorn, and queens may die a jest.
This Phoebus promised (I forget the year)
When those blue eyes first opened on the sphere;
285 Ascendant Phoebus watched that hour with care,
Averted half your parents' simple prayer;
And gave you beauty, but denied the pelf
That buys your sex a tyrant o'er itself.
The generous god, who wit and gold refines,
290 And ripens spirits as he ripens mines,[3]
Kept dross for duchesses, the world shall know it,
To you gave sense, good humor, and a poet.

1735, 1744

---

9. The fashionable drive in Hyde Park.
1. The loss of a hand at the card games of ombre or quadrille.
2. Pope refers punningly to the chinaware that fashionable women collected enthusiastically.

3. Phoebus Apollo, as god of poetry, "ripens wit"; as god of the sun, he "ripens mines," for respectable scientific theory held that the sun's rays mature precious metals in the earth.

ANNE INGRAM, VISCOUNTESS IRWIN

Lady Anne Howard (ca. 1696–1764) was raised on the Yorkshire estate of her father, third Earl of Carlisle; many years later she paid tribute to it and him in a poem, *Castle Howard* (1732). In 1717 she married Richard Ingram, fifth Viscount Irwin; and after he died of smallpox in 1721, she mourned him so long that she was reproached for it in verse by Lady Mary Wortley Montagu. Although the two women were friends, Irwin said that Montagu's "principles are as corrupt as her wit is entertaining"; and Montagu, who liked Irwin's good nature, was also amused by her "vanity and false pretensions." Irwin showed her independence by traveling alone in Holland and France in 1730. Later she served the Princess of Wales as a lady-in-waiting, but court life did not satisfy her; Pope's and Addison's works were "antidotes to preserve me from the contagion." In 1737, against the strong opposition of her family, she married Colonel William Douglas; he died in 1748. A young woman who knew her afterward was impressed by her learning and wit: "she wrote poetry, and every body was afraid of her." She died, in 1764, after a party at cards.

"An Epistle to Mr. Pope" reveals Irwin's keen attention to Pope's work as a whole, not only to his "Epistle 2. To a Lady"; it turns his verse technique as well as many of his principles against him. While many of Pope's couplets sharply contrast women's characters with men's, Irwin adapts the couplet form to emphasize what they have in common. In fact both sexes, she argues, want the same thing: love of power motivates them both. If women often trifle away their lives, the reason is poor education; not even Pope has taught them how to live. Irwin provides some positive models. Addressing Pope as an equal, in verse much like his own, she proves that men and women can think alike.

An Epistle to Mr. Pope,

Occasioned by his Characters of Women

Nec rude quid prosit video ingenium.[1]

> By custom doomed to folly, sloth and ease,
> No wonder Pope such female triflers sees.
> But would the satirist confess the truth,
> Nothing so like as male and female youth,
> 5 Nothing so like as man and woman old,
> Their joys, their loves, their hates, if truly told.
> Though different acts seem different sex's growth,
> 'Tis the same principle impels them both.
>   View daring men stung with ambition's fire,
> 10 The conquering hero, or the youthful 'squire,
> By different deeds aspire to deathless fame,
> One murthers° man, the other murthers game.   murders
> View a fair nymph blest with superior charms,
> Whose tempting form the coldest bosom warms;
> 15 No eastern monarch more despotic reigns

---

1. Nor can I see what good can come from untrained talent (Latin; Horace's *Art of Poetry* 410).

Than this fair tyrant of the Cyprian plains.[2]
Whether a crown or bauble we desire,
Whether to learning or to dress aspire,
Whether we wait with joy the trumpet's call,
20   Or wish to shine the fairest at a ball,
In either sex the appetite's the same,
For love of power is still° the love of fame.[3]   *always*
Women must in a narrow orbit move,
But power alike both males and females love.
25   What makes the difference then, you may inquire,
Between the hero and the rural 'squire,
Between the maid bred up with courtly care,
Or she who earns by toil her daily fare?
Their power is stinted, but not so their will;
30   Ambitious thoughts the humblest cottage fill;
Far as they can they push their little fame,
And try to leave behind a deathless name.
In education all the difference lies;
Women, if taught, would be as bold and wise
35   As haughty man, improved by art and rules;
Where God makes one, neglect makes twenty fools.
And though *Nugatrixes*° are daily found,   *female triflers*
Flutt'ring *Nugators*° equally abound;   *male triflers*
Such heads are toyshops,[4] filled with trifling ware,
40   And can each folly with each female share.
    A female mind like a rude fallow lies;
No seed is sown, but weeds spontaneous rise.
As well might we expect, in winter, spring,
As land untilled a fruitful crop should bring;
45   As well might we expect Peruvian ore
We should possess, yet dig not for the store.
Culture° improves all fruits, all sorts we find,   *cultivation, tillage*
Wit, judgment, sense—fruits of the human mind.
    Ask the rich merchant, conversant in trade,
50   How nature operates in the growing blade;
Ask the philosopher the price of stocks,
Ask the gay courtier how to manage flocks;
Inquire the dogmas of the learned schools
(From Aristotle down to Newton's rules),
55   Of the rough soldier, bred to boisterous war,
Or one still rougher, a true British tar:
They'll all reply, unpracticed in such laws,
The effect they know, though ignorant of the cause.
The sailor may perhaps have equal parts°   *abilities*
60   With him bred up to sciences and arts;
And he who at the helm or stern is seen,
Philosopher or hero might have been.
The whole in application is comprised,

2. Love. Aphrodite was worshiped on Cyprus.
3. Cf. Pope's "Epistle 2," lines 207–10.
4. A shop stocked with baubles and trifles (see

Pope's *Rape of the Lock,* Canto 1, line 100, p.
4850).

Reason's not reason, if not exercised;
65 Use, not possession, real good affords;
No miser's rich that dares not touch his hoards.
    Can female youth, left to weak woman's care,
Misled by custom (folly's fruitful heir),
Told that their charms a monarch may enslave,
70 That beauty like the gods can kill or save;
Taught the arcanas,[5] the mysterious art
By ambush dress to catch unwary hearts;
If wealthy born, taught to lisp French and dance,
Their morals left (Lucretius-like) to chance;[6]
75 Strangers to reason and reflection made,
Left to their passions, and by them betrayed;
Untaught the noble end of glorious truth,
Bred to deceive even from their earliest youth;
Unused to books, nor virtue taught to prize;
80 Whose mind a savage waste unpeopled lies,
Which to supply, trifles fill up the void,
And idly busy, to no end employed—
Can these, from such a school, more virtue show,
Or tempting vice treat like a common foe?
85 Can they resist, when soothing pleasure woos;
Preserve their virtue, when their fame° they lose?   reputation
Can they on other themes converse or write,
Than what they hear all day, and dream all night?
    Not so the Roman female fame was spread;
90 Not so was Clelia, or Lucretia bred;
Not so such heroines true glory sought;
Not so was Portia, or Cornelia[7] taught.
Portia! the glory of the female race;
Portia! more lovely by her mind than face.
95 Early informed by truth's unerring beam,
What to reject, what justly to esteem.
Taught by philosophy all moral good,
How to repel in youth the impetuous blood,
How her most favorite passions to subdue,
100 And fame through virtue's avenues pursue,
She tries herself, and finds even dolorous pain
Can't the close secret from her breast obtain.
To Cato born, to noble Brutus joined,
She shines invincible in form and mind.
105   No more such generous sentiments we trace
In the gay moderns of the female race,
No more, alas! heroic virtue's shown;

5. Profound secrets, as in alchemy. *Arcana* is the plural of the Latin *arcanum*, but some English writers added an *s*.
6. The Roman poet Lucretius was known as a materialist and atheist who taught that everything in the world results from the chance convergence of atoms.
7. Famous Roman paragons of virtue. Clelia (or Cloelia), given as a hostage to an enemy, Lars Porsenna, escaped to Rome by swimming the Tiber and was later set free by Porsenna for her bravery. Lucretia was raped by a son of King Tarquin and committed suicide, kindling a revolt that overthrew the Tarquins. Portia, the daughter of Cato and wife of Brutus, stabbed herself in the thigh to prove she was strong enough to keep her husband's secrets. Cornelia, mother of the Gracchi, was a model of maternal self-sacrifice.

Since knowledge ceased, philosophy's unknown.
No more can we expect our modern wives
110 Heroes should breed, who lead such useless lives.
Would you, who know the arcana of the soul,
The secret springs which move and guide the whole,
Would you, who can instruct as well as please,
Bestow some moments of your darling ease,
115 To rescue woman from this Gothic[8] state,
New passions raise, their minds anew create,
Then for the Spartan virtue[9] we might hope;
For who stands unconvinced by generous Pope?
Then would the British fair perpetual bloom,
120 And vie in fame with ancient Greece and Rome.

1736

8. Barbaric, as opposed to Greek or Roman. Cf. Pope's *Essay on Criticism* 3.692 (p. 2684).

9. Spartan women were known for their courage and contempt of pleasure.

MARY LEAPOR

A gardener's daughter, Mary Leapor (1722–1746) spent her short life in or near the small town of Brackley in Northamptonshire. When she was ten or eleven "she would often be scribbling," and poetry turned into a consuming interest. One of her poems describes her sitting "whole evenings, reading wicked plays" by candlelight; according to another, she lost employment as a cook-maid because she would not stop writing, even in the kitchen. Passed around the neighborhood, her verse impressed Bridget Freemantle, the daughter of a former Oxford don; she became Leapor's best friend and mentor. Together they planned to publish Leapor's work. A play was sent to Colley Cibber, the impresario and poet laureate, but it was returned stained by wine. Leapor's health was rarely good, and she died of measles at age twenty-four; she had never seen any of her poems in print. But Freemantle arranged an edition of Leapor's *Poems upon Several Occasions* (1748), with six hundred subscribers, and it was warmly received. Samuel Richardson admired the "sweetly easy poems" so much that he published a second volume; later, William Cowper thought they showed "more marks of a true poetical talent than I remember to have observed in the verses of any, whether male or female, so disadvantageously circumstanced." Recently Leapor's work has attracted renewed attention for its wit and skill as well as its sharp observations about the life of a working-class woman.

The preface to Leapor's *Poems* reports that "the author she most admired was Mr. Pope, whom she chiefly endeavored to imitate." "An Essay on Woman," like Irwin's epistle, reflects careful study of Pope's epistle on the "Characters of Women." But its view of female predicaments is very much darker. If women are living contradictions, as Pope had asserted, the reason is that whatever they are and whatever they do can be turned against them. Beauty will be betrayed, wit and learning will be shunned, and the pursuit of wealth will shrink the soul. Leapor's own situation gives her satire bite. As a gardener's daughter, she knows that the flower of womanhood costs money to cultivate and does not last; as someone witty, poor, infirm, and unattractive, she sees through romantic myths. In "An Epistle to a Lady" (another Popean title), she more autobiographically reflects on education, the main avenue of advancement for women proposed by reformers throughout the period (including Astell, Defoe, Addison, Irwin, and Johnson). Leapor's experience makes her pessimistic: her learning merely allows her to depict her bleak place in the world on an astronomically expanded scale; and homely, tattered images must intrude on her dreams of the wealth and leisure that she knows a genteel education and a poetic vocation require. But despite Leapor's stress on her frustrating social position and on the softness and weakness of women in general, her verse is strong. This poet never stops fighting against the traps in which she is caught.

An Essay on Woman

WOMAN—a pleasing but a short-lived flower,
Too soft for business and too weak for power:
A wife in bondage, or neglected maid;
Despised if ugly; if she's fair—betrayed.
5   'Tis wealth alone inspires every grace,
And calls the raptures to her plenteous[1] face.
What numbers for those charming features pine,
If blooming acres[2] round her temples twine?
Her lip the strawberry, and her eyes more bright
10   Than sparkling Venus in a frosty night;
Pale lilies fade and, when the fair appears,
Snow turns a negro[3] and dissolves in tears,
And where the charmer treads her magic toe,
On English ground Arabian odors grow;
15   Till mighty Hymen[4] lifts his sceptred rod,
And sinks her glories with a fatal nod,
Dissolves her triumphs, sweeps her charms away,
And turns the goddess to her native clay.
But, Artemisia,[5] let your servant sing
20   What small advantage wealth and beauties bring.
Who would be wise, that knew Pamphilia's fate?
Or who be fair, and joined to Sylvia's mate?
Sylvia, whose cheeks are fresh as early day,
As evening mild, and sweet as spicy May;
25   And yet that face her partial husband tires,
And those bright eyes, that all the world admires.
Pamphilia's wit who does not strive to shun,
Like death's infection or a dog-day's sun?
The damsels view her with malignant eyes,
30   The men are vexed to find a nymph so wise,
And wisdom only serves to make her know
The keen sensation of superior woe.
The secret whisper and the listening ear,
The scornful eyebrow and the hated sneer,

---

1. Not only blooming but wealthy.
2. Not only hair but property.
3. Black, when set against the fair one's skin. The hyperbolic comparisons throughout this passage are intentionally ironic, as in Shakespeare's Sonnet 130.
4. The god of marriage.
5. Bridget Freemantle, given the name of an ancient patron of the arts.

35 The giddy censures of her babbling kind,
With thousand ills that grate a gentle mind,
By her are tasted in the first degree,
Though overlooked by Simplicus and me.
Does thirst of gold a virgin's heart inspire,
40 Instilled by nature or a careful sire?
Then let her quit extravagance and play,
The brisk companion and expensive tea,
To feast with Cordia in her filthy sty
On stewed potatoes or on mouldy pie;
45 Whose eager° eyes stare ghastly at the poor,   *fierce*
And fright the beggars from the hated door;
In greasy clouts she wraps her smoky chin,
And holds that pride's a never-pardoned sin.
    If this be wealth, no matter where it falls;
50 But save, ye Muses, save your Mira's[6] walls:
Still give me pleasing indolence and ease,
A fire to warm me and a friend to please.
    Since, whether sunk in avarice or pride,
A wanton virgin or a starving bride,
55 Or wondering crowds attend her charming tongue,
Or deemed an idiot, ever speaks the wrong;
Though nature armed us for the growing ill
With fraudful cunning and a headstrong will,
Yet, with ten thousand follies to her charge,
60 Unhappy woman's but a slave at large.

1751

An Epistle to a Lady[1]

In vain, dear Madam, yes, in vain you strive,
Alas! to make your luckless Mira thrive;
For Tycho and Copernicus[2] agree,
No golden planet bent its rays on me.[3]

5 'Tis twenty winters, if it is no more,
To speak the truth it may be twenty four:
As many springs their 'pointed° space have run,   *appointed*
Since Mira's eyes first opened on the sun.
'Twas when the flocks on slabby° hillocks lie,   *muddy*
10 And the cold fishes rule the watery sky;[4]
But though these eyes the learned page explore,
And turn the ponderous volumes o'er and o'er,

6. Leapor's pen name.
1. The poem addresses her friend and patron, Bridget Freemantle.
2. Copernicus (1473–1543), Polish founder of modern astronomy, thought that Earth circled the sun. Tycho Brahe (1546–1601), Danish astronomer who thought the sun and moon revolved around the stationary Earth.
3. A "golden planet" would have marked Leapor's birth as auspicious.
4. Leapor was born in late winter, under the sign of Pisces (the "fishes").

I find no comfort from their systems flow,[5]
But am dejected more as more I know.
15 Hope shines a while, but like a vapor flies
(The fate of all the curious and the wise)
For, ah! cold Saturn[6] triumphed on that day,
And frowning Sol denied his golden ray.

You see I'm learned, and I show't the more,
20 That none may wonder when they find me poor.
Yet Mira dreams, as slumbering poets may,
And rolls in treasures till the breaking day:
While books and pictures in bright order rise,
And painted parlors swim before her eyes;
25 Till the shrill clock impertinently rings,
And the soft visions move their shining wings;
Then Mira wakes—her pictures are no more,
And through her fingers slides the vanished ore.
Convinced too soon, her eye unwilling falls
30 On the blue curtains and the dusty walls;
She wakes, alas! to business and to woes,
To sweep her kitchen, and to mend her clothes.[7]

But see pale sickness with her languid eyes,
At whose appearance all delusion flies:
35 The world recedes, its vanities decline,
Clorinda's features seem as faint as mine;
Gay robes no more the aching sight admires,
Wit grates the ear, and melting music tires;
Its wonted pleasures with each sense decay,
40 Books please no more, and paintings fade away,
The sliding joys in misty vapors end;
Yet let me still, ah! let me grasp a friend;
And when each joy, when each loved object flies,
Be you the last that leaves my closing eyes.

45 But how will this dismantled° soul appear,   *unclothed*
When stripped of all it lately held so dear,
Forced from its prison of expiring clay,
Afraid and shivering at the doubtful way?

Yet did these eyes a dying parent[8] see,
50 Loosed from all cares except a thought for me,
Without a tear resign her shortening breath,
And dauntless meet the lingering stroke of death.
Then at th'Almighty's sentence shall I mourn:
"Of dust thou art, to dust shalt thou return";[9]
55 Or shall I wish to stretch the line of fate,

---

5. I.e., no comfort flows from either the "systems" (bodies of doctrine) contained in books or the systems of stars and planets in the heavens.
6. The planet Saturn was thought to influence gloomy (hence "saturnine") temperaments.
7. Cf. Pope, *Eloisa to Abelard* 223–48.
8. Leapor's mother, Anne, died around 1742.
9. Genesis 3.19.

That the dull years may bear a longer date,
To share the follies of succeeding times
With more vexations and with deeper crimes?
Ah no—though Heav'n brings near the final day,
60   For such a life I will not, dare not pray;
But let the tear for future mercy flow,
And fall resigned beneath the mighty blow.
Nor I alone—for through the spacious ball,°   *Earth*
With me will numbers of all ages fall:
65   And the same day that Mira yields her breath,
Thousands may enter through the gates of death.

1748

JOHN GAY
1685–1732

The career of John Gay encompasses most of the ways that a talented but indigent writer of the early eighteenth century could try to make a living: publication, patronage, odd jobs at court, and the theater. After a good education at school in Devon, he went to London at seventeen to try his luck as apprentice to a dealer in silks. Five years later he became secretary to a friend from school, the writer and entrepreneur Aaron Hill, who introduced him to the publishing world and literary circles. Eventually, leading authors in London adopted Gay as a favorite; with Pope, Swift, Arbuthnot, and Thomas Parnell, he founded the Scriblerus Club, famous for its literary satires and practical jokes. Friends like these helped him obtain the patrons and political appointments that supported him. The same Scriblerian influence shaped the mixture of high Virgilian style and rustic humor in his first successful poem, *The Shepherd's Week* (1714), a burlesque pastoral. Here and in his other verse Gay shows off his special gifts: lightness of touch, a keen eye for homely details, and an irony that exposes the disparity between high poetic expectations and the coarse reality of the way people live. Two years later a mock georgic, *Trivia, or the Art of Walking the Streets of London,* revealed that the town could be as rough as the country, and far more corrupting. Gay's hopes for affluence were blasted by the collapse of South Sea stock in 1721. His popularity and financial security rose to new heights, however, with the phenomenal success of his verse *Fables* (1727; a second set was published posthumously in 1738) and above all *The Beggar's Opera* (1728), which made him rich. But he did not enjoy his prosperity for long. A sequel, *Polly* (1729), was banned from the stage by Walpole; and although the printed version sold very well, the tension may have precipitated the illness that led a few years later to his death.

Audiences have always loved *The Beggar's Opera.* Nothing quite like it had ever been seen on the London stage; when Congreve read the script, he said, "It would either take greatly, or be damned confoundedly." On opening night, according to Pope, Gay's friends were anxious, "till we were very much encouraged by overhearing the Duke of Argyle, who sat in the next box to us, say, 'It will do—it must do! I see it in the eyes of them.'" The duke was right. The play quickly became the talk of the town, it ran for a record sixty-two performances, and during the rest of the century it kept being revived. At first the shock of pleasure must have been sparked by daring thrusts at people and things in the news. Italian opera is one obvious target. Although it was preposterously artificial and costly, with lavish scenery and imported stars, opera had been the rage of fashionable London. Now Gay turned the music over to beggars, or actors playing thieves and whores, and gave them popular British tunes to sing instead of showy foreign arias.

On this stage, moreover, the underworld rose to the surface. Crime was a constant, brutal threat in early eighteenth-century London, and stories about notorious criminals (such as Moll Flanders) poured from the press. In the corrupt legal system, which rewarded racketeers for informing on (or "peaching") less powerful felons, the line between those who broke the law and those who enforced it was often smudged. Jonathan Wild, the "Thief-Taker General of Great Britain and Ireland," became rich and famous by manipulating this system (before the executioner caught up with him); he serves as a model for Peachum. By comparison, a forthright highwayman and killer like Macheath might seem rather gallant. But the electricity of the play comes from its superimposition of these criminals on heads of state, especially the prime minister, Robert Walpole. Playgoers recognized Walpole everywhere. In Act 2, scene 10, for instance, when Peachum and Lockit argue and conspire—"like great statesmen, we encourage those who betray their friends"— the audience roared at the allusion to Walpole and Lord Townshend, his ally and brother-in-law (at an early performance, Walpole himself is said to have won over the crowd by calling for an encore). Spectators saw a picture of their own times on the stage: a society driven by greed, where everything, including justice and love, was for sale.

Yet *The Beggar's Opera* has lasted beyond its age. The parallel between high life and low life turned out to be more than a trick; it still rings true when audiences reflect on those who hold power today. Brecht's and Weill's famous *Threepenny Opera* adapted Gay's story to the sinister conditions of Germany in the 1920s; gang lords, fascists, and capitalistic bosses all seem the same. Little people go to jail, the high ones get away. That worldly and cynical message, seasoned with wit, continues to make sense to people who compare their ideals of government, society, and law to things as they are.

Pope's epitaph on Gay, inscribed in Westminster Abbey, begins this way:

> Of manners gentle, of affections mild;
> In wit, a man; simplicity, a child;
> With native humor tempering virtuous rage,
> Formed to delight at once and lash the age.

But Gay's own epitaph is far less pious:

> Life is a jest, and all things show it;
> I thought so once, but now I know it.

The Beggar's Opera

DRAMATIS PERSONAE[1]

Men

PEACHUM	ROBIN OF BAGSHOT
LOCKIT	NIMMING NED
MACHEATH	HARRY PADDINGTON
FILCH	MATT OF THE MINT
JEMMY TWITCHER	BEN BUDGE
CROOK-FINGERED JACK	BEGGAR
WAT DREARY	PLAYER

CONSTABLES, DRAWER, TURNKEY, ETC.

Women

MRS. PEACHUM	MRS. VIXEN
POLLY PEACHUM	BETTY DOXY
LUCY LOCKIT	JENNY DIVER
DIANA TRAPES	MRS. SLAMMEKIN
MRS. COAXER	SUKY TAWDRY
DOLLY TRULL	MOLLY BRAZEN

Introduction

BEGGAR, PLAYER

BEGGAR If poverty be a title to poetry, I am sure nobody can dispute mine. I own myself of the Company of Beggars; and I make one at their weekly festivals at St. Giles's. I have a small yearly salary for my catches,[2] and am welcome to a dinner there whenever I please, which is more than most poets can say.

PLAYER As we live by the Muses, 'tis but gratitude in us to encourage poetical merit wherever we find it. The Muses, contrary to all other ladies, pay no distinction to dress, and never partially mistake the pertness of embroidery for wit, nor the modesty of want for dullness. Be the author who he will, we push his play as far as it will go. So (though you are in want) I wish you success heartily.

BEGGAR This piece I own was originally writ for the celebrating the marriage of James Chanter and Moll Lay, two most excellent ballad singers. I have introduced the similes that are in all your celebrated operas: the swallow, the moth, the bee, the ship, the flower, etc. Besides, I have a prison scene, which the ladies always reckon charmingly pathetic. As to the parts, I have observed such a nice impartiality to our two ladies, that

---

1. The names of characters reflect their trades. Peachum ("peach 'em") is an informer, Lockit a jailer, Macheath a "son of the heath" or highwayman, Twitcher and Diver pickpockets, Nimming Ned a thief, Budge a burglar, Trull and Doxy harlots. Dreary ("gory") suggests a cutthroat; Bagshot Heath was known for highway robberies; Paddington ("pad," a highwayman) was where criminals were hanged; the Mint was a sanctuary for outlaws. Trapes and Slammekin are slatterns.

2. Rounds, in which one singer follows or chases the words of another. St. Giles was a slum named after the patron saint of beggars and lepers.

it is impossible for either of them to take offense.[3] I hope I may be forgiven, that I have not made my opera throughout unnatural, like those in vogue; for I have no recitative.[4] Excepting this, as I have consented to have neither prologue nor epilogue, it must be allowed an opera in all its forms. The piece indeed hath been heretofore frequently represented by ourselves in our great room at St. Giles's, so that I cannot too often acknowledge your charity in bringing it now on the stage.

PLAYER But I see 'tis time for us to withdraw; the actors are preparing to begin. Play away the overture. [*Exeunt.*]

Act 1

SCENE 1 *Peachum's house*

PEACHUM *sitting at a table with a large book of accounts before him.*

AIR 1. An old woman clothed in gray[5]

> *Through all the employments of life*
> *Each neighbor abuses his brother;*
> *Whore and rogue they call husband and wife;*
> *All professions be-rogue one another.*
> *The priest calls the lawyer a cheat,*
> *The lawyer be-knaves the divine;*
> *And the statesman, because he's so great,*
> *Thinks his trade as honest as mine.*

A lawyer is an honest employment, so is mine. Like me too he acts in a double capacity, both against rogues and for 'em; for 'tis but fitting that we should protect and encourage cheats, since we live by them.

SCENE 2

PEACHUM, FILCH

FILCH Sir, Black Moll hath sent word her trial comes on in the afternoon, and she hopes you will order matters so as to bring her off.

PEACHUM Why, she may plead her belly[6] at worst; to my knowledge she hath taken care of that security. But as the wench is very active and industrious, you may satisfy her that I'll soften the evidence.

FILCH Tom Gagg, sir, is found guilty.

PEACHUM A lazy dog! When I took him the time before, I told him what he would come to if he did not mend his hand. This is death without reprieve. I may venture to book him. [*Writes.*] For Tom Gagg, forty pounds.[7] Let Betty Sly know that I'll save her from transportation,[8] for I can get more by her staying in England.

---

3. Two famous divas, Faustina and Cuzzoni, had recently feuded on stage.
4. Operatic declamation, midway between singing and speaking.
5. The name of the ballad whose tune Peachum sings.

6. Claim to be pregnant, hence not at risk of execution.
7. The reward when informing resulted in execution.
8. Criminals were sentenced to banishment abroad.

FILCH Betty hath brought more goods into our lock to-year[9] than any five of the gang; and in truth, 'tis a pity to lose so good a customer.

PEACHUM If none of the gang take her off,[1] she may, in the common course of business, live a twelve-month longer. I love to let women scape. A good sportsman always lets the hen partridges fly, because the breed of the game depends upon them. Besides, here the law allows us no reward; there is nothing to be got by the death of women—except our wives.

FILCH Without dispute, she is a fine woman! 'Twas to her I was obliged for my education, and (to say a bold word) she hath trained up more young fellows to the business than the gaming-table.

PEACHUM Truly, Filch, thy observation is right. We and the surgeons are more beholden to women than all the professions besides.[2]

AIR 2. The bonny gray-eyed morn

FILCH
'Tis woman that seduces all mankind,
By her we first were taught the wheedling arts:
Her very eyes can cheat; when most she's kind,
She tricks us of our money with our hearts.
For her, like wolves by night we roam for prey,
And practise every fraud to bribe her charms;
For suits of love, like law, are won by pay,
And beauty must be fee'd into our arms.

PEACHUM But make haste to Newgate,[3] boy, and let my friends know what I intend; for I love to make them easy one way or other.

FILCH When a gentleman is long kept in suspense, penitence may break his spirit ever after. Besides, certainty gives a man a good air upon his trial, and makes him risk another without fear or scruple. But I'll away, for 'tis a pleasure to be the messenger of comfort to friends in affliction.

SCENE 3

PEACHUM

But 'tis now high time to look about me for a decent execution against next Sessions.[4] I hate a lazy rogue, by whom one can get nothing 'till he is hanged. A register of the gang, [*reading*] Crook-fingered Jack. A year and a half in the service; let me see how much the stock owes to his industry: one, two, three, four, five gold watches, and seven silver ones. A mighty clean-handed fellow! Sixteen snuff-boxes, five of them of true gold. Six dozen of handkerchiefs, four silver-hilted swords, half a dozen of shirts, three tye-perriwigs, and a piece of broad cloth. Considering these are only the fruits of his leisure hours, I don't know a prettier fellow, for no man alive hath a more engaging presence of mind upon the road. Wat Dreary, alias Brown Will, an irregular dog, who hath an underhand way of disposing of his goods. I'll try him only for a Sessions or two longer upon his good behavior. Harry Paddington, a poor petty-larceny rascal, without the least genius; that fellow, though he were to live these six months, will

---

9. This year. "Lock": a house where stolen goods are kept.
1. Inform on her.

2. Surgeons treated venereal diseases.
3. The chief London prison.
4. Trials of criminals, held eight times a year.

never come to the gallows with any credit. Slippery Sam; he goes off the next Sessions, for the villain hath the impudence to have views of following his trade as a tailor, which he calls an honest employment. Matt of the Mint; listed[5] not above a month ago, a promising sturdy fellow, and diligent in his way; somewhat too bold and hasty, and may raise good contributions on the public, if he does not cut himself short by murder. Tom Tipple, a guzzling soaking sot, who is always too drunk to stand himself, or to make others stand.[6] A cart[7] is absolutely necessary for him. Robin of Bagshot, alias Gorgon, alias Bluff Bob, alias Carbuncle, alias Bob Booty.[8]

SCENE 4

PEACHUM, MRS. PEACHUM

MRS. PEACHUM   What of Bob Booty, husband? I hope nothing bad hath betided him. You know, my dear, he's a favorite customer of mine. 'Twas he made me a present of this ring.

PEACHUM   I have set his name down in the black-list, that's all, my dear; he spends his life among women, and as soon as his money is gone, one or other of the ladies will hang him for the reward, and there's forty pound lost to us forever.

MRS. PEACHUM   You know, my dear, I never meddle in matters of death; I always leave those affairs to you. Women indeed are bitter bad judges in these cases, for they are so partial to the brave that they think every man handsome who is going to the camp or the gallows.

AIR 3.   Cold and raw

If any wench Venus's girdle wear,
  Though she be never so ugly;
Lilies and roses will quickly appear,
  And her face look wond'rous smugly.
Beneath the left ear so fit but a cord,
  (A rope so charming a zone is!)
The youth in his cart hath the air of a lord,
  And we cry, "There dies an Adonis!"[9]

But really, husband, you should not be too hard hearted, for you never had a finer, braver set of men than at present. We have not had a murder among them all, these seven months. And truly, my dear, that is a great blessing.

PEACHUM   What a dickens is the woman always a-whimpering about murder for? No gentleman is ever looked upon the worse for killing a man in his own defense; and if business cannot be carried on without it, what would you have a gentleman do?

MRS. PEACHUM   If I am in the wrong, my dear, you must excuse me, for nobody can help the frailty of an over-scrupulous conscience.

PEACHUM   Murder is as fashionable a crime as a man can be guilty of. How many fine gentlemen have we in Newgate every year, purely upon

---

5. Enlisted.
6. Stand still; i.e., when held up.
7. Carriage to the gallows.
8. This became a nickname for Walpole.

9. Venus's lover. The magic powers of Venus's belt ("girdle"), which could make any woman sexy, are associated with the rope or belt ("zone") around a condemned man's neck.

that article! If they have wherewithal to persuade the jury to bring it in manslaughter, what are they the worse for it? So, my dear, have done upon this subject. Was Captain Macheath here this morning, for the bank notes he left with you last week?

MRS. PEACHUM   Yes, my dear; and though the bank hath stopped payment, he was so cheerful and so agreeable! Sure there is not a finer gentleman upon the road than the Captain! If he comes from Bagshot at any reasonable hour he hath promised to make one this evening with Polly and me, and Bob Booty, at a party of quadrille.[1] Pray, my dear, is the Captain rich?

PEACHUM   The Captain keeps too good company ever to grow rich. Marybone and the chocolate-houses[2] are his undoing. The man that proposes to get money by play should have the education of a fine gentleman, and be trained up to it from his youth.

MRS. PEACHUM   Really, I am sorry upon Polly's account the Captain hath not more discretion. What business hath he to keep company with lords and gentlemen? He should leave them to prey upon one another.

PEACHUM   Upon Polly's account! What, a plague, does the woman mean? Upon Polly's account!

MRS. PEACHUM   Captain Macheath is very fond of the girl.

PEACHUM   And what then?

MRS. PEACHUM   If I have any skill in the ways of women, I am sure Polly thinks him a very pretty man.

PEACHUM   And what then? You would not be so mad to have the wench marry him! Gamesters and highwaymen are generally very good to their whores, but they are very devils to their wives.

MRS. PEACHUM   But if Polly should be in love, how should we help her, or how can she help herself? Poor girl, I am in the utmost concern about her.

AIR 4.   Why is your faithful slave disdained?

> If love the virgin's heart invade,
> How, like a moth, the simple maid
>   Still plays about the flame!
> If soon she be not made a wife,
> Her honor's singed, and then for life,
>   She's—what I dare not name.

PEACHUM   Look ye, wife. A handsome wench in our way of business is as profitable as at the bar of a Temple[3] coffee-house, who looks upon it as her livelihood to grant every liberty but one. You see I would indulge the girl as far as prudently we can. In anything but marriage! After that, my dear, how shall we be safe? Are we not then in her husband's power? For a husband hath the absolute power over all a wife's secrets but her own. If the girl had the discretion of a court lady, who can have a dozen young fellows at her ear without complying with one, I should not matter it;[4] but Polly is tinder, and a spark will at once set her on a flame. Married! If the

---

1. A card game.
2. Popular haunts for gambling.
3. London college for lawyers.
4. Think it important.

wench does not know her own profit, sure she knows her own pleasure better than to make herself a property!⁵ My daughter to me should be, like a court lady to a minister of state, a key to the whole gang. Married! If the affair is not already done, I'll terrify her from it, by the example of our neighbors.

MRS. PEACHUM Mayhap, my dear, you may injure the girl. She loves to imitate the fine ladies, and she may only allow the Captain liberties in the view of interest.

PEACHUM But 'tis your duty, my dear, to warn the girl against her ruin, and to instruct her how to make the most of her beauty. I'll go to her this moment, and sift her. In the meantime, wife, rip out the coronets and marks of these dozen of cambric handkerchiefs, for I can dispose of them this afternoon to a chap in the City.

SCENE 5

MRS. PEACHUM

Never was a man more out of the way in an argument than my husband! Why must our Polly, forsooth, differ from her sex, and love only her husband? And why must Polly's marriage, contrary to all observation, make her the less followed by other men? All men are thieves in love, and like a woman the better for being another's property.

AIR 5. Of all the simple things we do

A maid is like the golden ore,
Which hath guineas intrinsical in't,
* Whose worth is never known, before*
It is tried and impressed in the Mint.
* A wife's like a guinea in gold,*
Stamped with the name of her spouse:
* Now here, now there, is bought, or is sold,*
And is current in every house.

SCENE 6

MRS. PEACHUM, FILCH

MRS. PEACHUM Come hither, Filch. I am as fond of this child, as though my mind misgave me he were my own. He hath as fine a hand at picking a pocket as a woman, and is as nimble-fingered as a juggler. If an unlucky Session does not cut the rope of thy life, I pronounce, boy, thou wilt be a great man in history. Where was your post last night, my boy?

FILCH I plied at the opera, madam; and considering 'twas neither dark nor rainy, so that there was no great hurry in getting chairs and coaches, made a tolerable hand on't. These seven handkerchiefs, madam.

MRS. PEACHUM Colored ones, I see. They are of sure sale from our warehouse at Redriff among the seamen.

FILCH And this snuffbox.

---

5. A husband had legal title to everything his wife possessed.

MRS. PEACHUM   Set in gold! A pretty encouragement this to a young beginner.

FILCH   I had a fair tug at a charming gold watch. Pox take the tailors for making the fobs so deep and narrow! It stuck by the way, and I was forced to make my escape under a coach. Really, madam, I fear I shall be cut off in the flower of my youth, so that every now and then (since I was pumped)[6] I have thoughts of taking up and going to sea.

MRS. PEACHUM   You should go to Hockley in the Hole,[7] and to Marybone, child, to learn valor. These are the schools that have bred so many brave men. I thought, boy, by this time, thou hadst lost fear as well as shame. Poor lad! How little does he know as yet of the Old Bailey![8] For the first fact I'll insure thee from being hanged; and going to sea, Filch, will come time enough upon a sentence of transportation. But now, since you have nothing better to do, even go to your book, and learn your catechism, for really a man makes but an ill figure in the Ordinary's paper,[9] who cannot give a satisfactory answer to his questions. But, hark you, my lad. Don't tell me a lie; for you know I hate a liar. Do you know of anything that hath passed between Captain Macheath and our Polly?

FILCH   I beg you, madam, don't ask me; for I must either tell a lie to you or to Miss Polly; for I promised her I would not tell.

MRS. PEACHUM   But when the honor of our family is concerned—

FILCH   I shall lead a sad life with Miss Polly, if ever she come to know that I told you. Besides, I would not willingly forfeit my own honor by betraying anybody.

MRS. PEACHUM   Yonder comes my husband and Polly. Come, Filch, you shall go with me into my own room, and tell me the whole story. I'll give thee a glass of a most delicious cordial that I keep for my own drinking.

SCENE 7

PEACHUM, POLLY

POLLY   I know as well as any of the fine ladies how to make the most of myself and of my man too. A woman knows how to be mercenary, though she hath never been in a court or at an assembly.[1] We have it in our natures, papa. If I allow Captain Macheath some trifling liberties, I have this watch and other visible marks of his favor to show for it. A girl who cannot grant some things, and refuse what is most material, will make but a poor hand of her beauty, and soon be thrown upon the common.[2]

AIR 6.   What shall I do to show how much I love her

Virgins are like the fair flower in its luster,
*   Which in the garden enamels the ground;*
Near it the bees in play flutter and cluster,
*   And gaudy butterflies frolic around.*
But, when once plucked, 'tis no longer alluring,

---

6. When pickpockets were caught, they were doused with water.
7. A place for brutal sports such as bear-baiting.
8. London's criminal court.
9. First offenders could escape the death sentence by pleading "benefit of clergy" if they passed a literacy test given by the ordinary or chaplain of Newgate.
1. A public social affair.
2. Common land; common law; and a name for a prostitute.

To Covent Garden³ 'tis sent (as yet sweet),
There fades, and shrinks, and grows past all enduring,
Rots, stinks, and dies, and is trod under feet.

PEACHUM   You know, Polly, I am not against your toying and trifling with a customer in the way of business, or to get out a secret, or so. But if I find out that you have played the fool and are married, you jade you, I'll cut your throat, hussy. Now you know my mind.

SCENE 8

PEACHUM, POLLY, MRS. PEACHUM

AIR 7.   Oh London is a fine town

MRS. PEACHUM [*In a very great passion.*]
Our Polly is a sad slut! nor heeds what we have taught her.
I wonder any man alive will ever rear a daughter!
For she must have both hoods and gowns, and hoops to swell her pride,
With scarfs and stays, and gloves and lace; and she will have men beside;
And when she's dressed with care and cost, all-tempting, fine and gay,
As men should serve a cowcumber,⁴ she flings herself away.
     Our Polly is a sad slut, etc.

You baggage! You hussy! You inconsiderate jade! Had you been hanged, it would not have vexed me, for that might have been your misfortune; but to do such a mad thing by choice! The wench is married, husband.

PEACHUM   Married! The Captain is a bold man, and will risk anything for money; to be sure he believes her a fortune. Do you think your mother and I should have lived comfortably so long together, if ever we had been married? Baggage!

MRS. PEACHUM   I knew she was always a proud slut; and now the wench hath played the fool and married, because forsooth she would do like the gentry. Can you support the expense of a husband, hussy, in gaming, drinking and whoring? Have you money enough to carry on the daily quarrels of man and wife about who shall squander most? There are not many husbands and wives who can bear the charges of plaguing one another in a handsome way. If you must be married, could you introduce nobody into our family but a highwayman? Why, thou foolish jade, thou wilt be as ill-used, and as much neglected, as if thou hadst married a lord!

PEACHUM   Let not your anger, my dear, break through the rules of decency, for the Captain looks upon himself in the military capacity, as a gentleman by his profession. Besides what he hath already, I know he is in a fair way of getting,⁵ or of dying; and both these ways, let me tell you, are most excellent chances for a wife. Tell me hussy, are you ruined or no?

MRS. PEACHUM   With Polly's fortune, she might very well have gone off to a person of distinction. Yes, that you might, you pouting slut!

---

3. A market where produce and prostitutes were bought.
4. Cucumber.
5. Acquiring wealth.

PEACHUM   What, is the wench dumb? Speak, or I'll make you plead by squeezing out an answer from you. Are you really bound wife to him, or are you only upon liking?[6] [*Pinches her.*]

POLLY   Oh! [*Screaming.*]

MRS. PEACHUM   How the mother is to be pitied who hath handsome daughters! Locks, bolts, bars, and lectures of morality are nothing to them; they break through them all. They have as much pleasure in cheating a father and mother as in cheating at cards.

PEACHUM   Why, Polly, I shall soon know if you are married, by Macheath's keeping from our house.

AIR 8.   Grim king of the ghosts

POLLY

> *Can love be controlled by advice?*
> > *Will Cupid our mothers obey?*
> *Though my heart were as frozen as ice,*
> > *At his flame 'twould have melted away.*
> *When he kissed me so closely he pressed,*
> > *'Twas so sweet that I must have complied;*
> *So I thought it both safest and best*
> > *To marry, for fear you should chide.*

MRS. PEACHUM   Then all the hopes of our family are gone for ever and ever!

PEACHUM   And Macheath may hang his father and mother-in-law, in hope to get into their daughter's fortune.

POLLY   I did not marry him (as 'tis the fashion) coolly and deliberately for honor or money. But I love him.

MRS. PEACHUM   Love him! Worse and worse! I thought the girl had been better bred. O husband, husband! Her folly makes me mad! My head swims! I'm distracted! I can't support myself—O! [*Faints.*]

PEACHUM   See, wench, to what a condition you have reduced your poor mother! A glass of cordial, this instant. How the poor woman takes it to heart! [POLLY *goes out, and returns with it.*] Ah hussy, now this is the only comfort your mother has left!

POLLY   Give her another glass, sir; my mama drinks double the quantity whenever she is out of order. This, you see, fetches[7] her.

MRS. PEACHUM   The girl shows such a readiness, and so much concern, that I could almost find in my heart to forgive her.

AIR 9.   O Jenny, O Jenny, where hast thou been

MRS. PEACHUM

> *Oh Polly, you might have toyed and kissed.*
> > *By keeping men off, you keep them on.*

POLLY

> > *But he so teased me,*
> > *And he so pleased me,*
> *What I did, you must have done.*

MRS. PEACHUM   Not with a highwayman. You sorry slut!

PEACHUM   A word with you, wife. 'Tis no new thing for a wench to take man without consent of parents. You know 'tis the frailty of woman, my dear.

---

6. On approval.   7. Revives.

MRS. PEACHUM   Yes, indeed, the sex is frail. But the first time a woman is frail, she should be somewhat nice[8] methinks, for then or never is the time to make her fortune. After that, she hath nothing to do but to guard herself from being found out, and she may do what she pleases.

PEACHUM   Make yourself a little easy; I have a thought shall soon set all matters again to rights. Why so melancholy, Polly? Since what is done cannot be undone, we must all endeavor to make the best of it.

MRS. PEACHUM   Well, Polly, as far as one woman can forgive another, I forgive thee. Your father is too fond of you, hussy.

POLLY   Then all my sorrows are at an end.

MRS. PEACHUM   A mighty likely speech in troth, for a wench who is just married!

AIR 10.   Thomas, I cannot

POLLY

I, like a ship in storms, was tossed,
Yet afraid to put in to land;
For seized in the port the vessel's lost,
Whose treasure is contraband.
   The waves are laid,
   My duty's paid.
O joy beyond expression!
   Thus, safe ashore,
   I ask no more,
My all is in my possession.

PEACHUM   I hear customers in t'other room. Go, talk with 'em, Polly; but come to us again as soon as they are gone. But, hark ye, child, if 'tis the gentleman who was here yesterday about the repeating-watch,[9] say, you believe we can't get intelligence of it, till tomorrow, for I lent it to Suky Straddle, to make a figure with it tonight at a tavern in Drury Lane. If t'other gentleman calls for the silver-hilted sword, you know beetle-browed Jemmy hath it on, and he doth not come from Tunbridge till Tuesday night, so that it cannot be had till then.

SCENE 9

PEACHUM, MRS. PEACHUM

PEACHUM   Dear wife, be a little pacified. Don't let your passion run away with your senses. Polly, I grant you, hath done a rash thing.

MRS. PEACHUM   If she had had only an intrigue with the fellow, why the very best families have excused and huddled up a frailty of that sort. 'Tis marriage, husband, that makes it a blemish.

PEACHUM   But money, wife, is the true fuller's earth[1] for reputations, there is not a spot or a stain but what it can take out. A rich rogue nowadays is fit company for any gentleman; and the world, my dear, hath not such a contempt for roguery as you imagine. I tell you, wife, I can make this match turn to our advantage.

---

8. Choosy.
9. A watch that strikes the hour and quarter

hour when a button is pressed.
1. Clay used for cleaning fabrics.

MRS. PEACHUM I am very sensible,[2] husband, that Captain Macheath is worth money, but I am in doubt whether he hath not two or three wives already, and then if he should die in a Session or two, Polly's dower would come into dispute.

PEACHUM That, indeed, is a point which ought to be considered.

AIR 11.   A soldier and a sailor

> *A fox may steal your hens, sir,*
> *A whore your health and pence, sir,*
> *Your daughter rob your chest, sir,*
> *Your wife may steal your rest, sir,*
>   *A thief your goods and plate.*
> *But this is all but picking,*
> *With rest, pence, chest, and chicken;*
> *It ever was decreed, sir,*
> *If lawyer's hand is fee'd, sir,*
>   *He steals your whole estate.*

The lawyers are bitter enemies to those in our way. They don't care that anybody should get a clandestine livelihood but themselves.

SCENE 10

MRS. PEACHUM, PEACHUM, POLLY

POLLY 'Twas only Nimming Ned. He brought in a damask window curtain, a hoop-petticoat, a pair of silver candlesticks, a perriwig, and one silk stocking, from the fire that happened last night.

PEACHUM There is not a fellow that is cleverer in his way, and saves more goods out of the fire than Ned. But now, Polly, to your affair; for matters must not be left as they are. You are married then, it seems?

POLLY Yes, sir.

PEACHUM And how do you propose to live, child?

POLLY Like other women, sir, upon the industry of my husband.

MRS. PEACHUM What, is the wench turned fool? A highwayman's wife, like a soldier's, hath as little of his pay as of his company.

PEACHUM And had not you the common views of a gentlewoman in your marriage, Polly?

POLLY I don't know what you mean, sir.

PEACHUM Of a jointure,[3] and of being a widow.

POLLY But I love him, sir. How then could I have thoughts of parting with him?

PEACHUM Parting with him! Why, that is the whole scheme and intention of all marriage articles. The comfortable estate of widowhood is the only hope that keeps up a wife's spirits. Where is the woman who would scruple to be a wife, if she had it in her power to be a widow whenever she pleased? If you have any views of this sort, Polly, I shall think the match not so very unreasonable.

2. Aware.
3. Property jointly held by a couple, hence inherited by the wife if her husband died.

POLLY   How I dread to hear your advice! Yet I must beg you to explain yourself.

PEACHUM   Secure what he hath got, have him peached the next Sessions, and then at once you are made a rich widow.

POLLY   What, murder the man I love! The blood runs cold at my heart with the very thought of it.

PEACHUM   Fie, Polly! What hath murder to do in the affair? Since the thing sooner or later must happen, I dare say, the Captain himself would like that we should get the reward for his death sooner than a stranger. Why, Polly, the Captain knows that as 'tis his employment to rob, so 'tis ours to take robbers; every man in his business. So that there is no malice in the case.

MRS. PEACHUM   Ay, husband, now you have nicked the matter.[4] To have him peached is the only thing could ever make me forgive her.

AIR 12.   Now Ponder well, ye parents dear

POLLY

> O, ponder well! be not severe;
>   So save a wretched wife!
> For on the rope that hangs my dear
>   Depends poor Polly's life.

MRS. PEACHUM   But your duty to your parents, hussy, obliges you to hang him. What would many a wife give for such an opportunity!

POLLY   What is a jointure, what is widowhood to me? I know my heart. I cannot survive him.

AIR 13.   Le printemps rappelle aux armes[5]

> The turtle[6] thus with plaintive crying,
>   Her lover dying,
> The turtle thus with plaintive crying,
>   Laments her dove.
> Down she drops quite spent with sighing,
> Paired in death, as paired in love.

Thus, sir, it will happen to your poor Polly.

MRS. PEACHUM   What, is the fool in love in earnest then? I hate thee for being particular.[7] Why, wench, thou art a shame to thy very sex.

POLLY   But hear me, mother. If you ever loved—

MRS. PEACHUM   Those cursed playbooks she reads have been her ruin. One word more, hussy, and I shall knock your brains out, if you have any.

PEACHUM   Keep out of the way, Polly, for fear of mischief, and consider of what is proposed to you.

MRS. PEACHUM   Away, hussy. Hang your husband, and be dutiful.

SCENE 11

MRS. PEACHUM, PEACHUM [POLLY listening]

MRS. PEACHUM   The thing, husband, must and shall be done. For the sake of intelligence[8] we must take other measures, and have him peached the

---

4. Hit the mark.
5. The spring calls to arms (French).
6. Turtledove.

7. Attached to one person; freakish.
8. Secret information.

next Session without her consent. If she will not know her duty, we know ours.

PEACHUM   But really, my dear, it grieves one's heart to take off a great man. When I consider his personal bravery, his fine stratagem,[9] how much we have already got by him, and how much more we may get, methinks I can't find in my heart to have a hand in his death. I wish you could have made Polly undertake it.

MRS. PEACHUM   But in a case of necessity—our own lives are in danger.

PEACHUM   Then, indeed, we must comply with the customs of the world, and make gratitude give way to interest. He shall be taken off.

MRS. PEACHUM   I'll undertake to manage Polly.

PEACHUM   And I'll prepare matters for the Old Bailey.

SCENE 12

POLLY

Now I'm a wretch, indeed. Methinks I see him already in the cart, sweeter and more lovely than the nosegay in his hand! I hear the crowd extolling his resolution and intrepidity! What volleys of sighs are sent from the windows of Holborn,[1] that so comely a youth should be brought to disgrace! I see him at the tree! The whole circle are in tears! Even butchers weep! Jack Ketch[2] himself hesitates to perform his duty, and would be glad to lose his fee, by a reprieve. What then will become of Polly! As yet I may inform him of their design, and aid him in his escape. It shall be so. But then he flies, absents himself, and I bar my self from his dear dear conversation![3] That too will distract me. If he keep out of the way, my papa and mama may in time relent, and we may be happy. If he stays, he is hanged, and then he is lost forever! He intended to lie concealed in my room, 'till the dusk of the evening. If they are abroad, I'll this instant let him out, lest some accident should prevent him.

[*Exit, and returns.*]

SCENE 13

POLLY, MACHEATH

AIR 14.   Pretty parrot, say

MACHEATH
> *Pretty Polly, say,*
> *When I was away,*
> *Did your fancy never stray*
> *To some newer lover?*

POLLY
> *Without disguise,*
> *Heaving sighs,*
> *Doating eyes,*
> *My constant heart discover.*
> *Fondly let me loll!*

MACHEATH
> *O pretty, pretty Poll.*

9. Guile.
1. The street that connects Newgate to the gallows ("tree") at Tyburn.

2. The hangman (after a famous 17th-century executioner).
3. Intimate contact.

POLLY   And are *you* as fond as ever, my dear?

MACHEATH   Suspect my honor, my courage, suspect anything but my love. May my pistols misfire, and my mare slip her shoulder while I am pursued, if I ever forsake thee!

POLLY   Nay, my dear, I have no reason to doubt you, for I find in the romance you lent me, none of the great heroes were ever false in love.

AIR 15.   Pray, fair one, be kind

MACHEATH
> *My heart was so free,*
> *It roved like the bee,*
> *'Till Polly my passion requited;*
> *I sipped each flower,*
> *I changed every hour,*
> *But here every flower is united.*

POLLY   Were you sentenced to transportation, sure, my dear, you could not leave me behind you—could you?

MACHEATH   Is there any power, any force that could tear me from thee? You might sooner tear a pension out of the hands of a courtier, a fee from a lawyer, a pretty woman from a looking glass, or any woman from quadrille. But to tear me from thee is impossible!

AIR 16.   Over the hills and far away

MACHEATH
> *Were I laid on Greenland's coast,*
> *And in my arms embraced my lass;*
> *Warm amidst eternal frost,*
> *Too soon the half year's night would pass.*

POLLY
> *Were I sold on Indian soil,*
> *Soon as the burning day was closed,*
> *I could mock the sultry toil,*
> *When on my charmer's breast reposed.*

MACHEATH   *And I would love you all the day,*

POLLY   *Every night would kiss and play,*

MACHEATH   *If with me you'd fondly stray*

POLLY   *Over the hills and far away.*

Yes, I would go with thee. But oh! How shall I speak it? I must be torn from thee. We must part.

MACHEATH   How? Part?

POLLY   We must, we must. My papa and mama are set against thy life. They now, even now, are in search after thee. They are preparing evidence against thee. Thy life depends upon a moment.

AIR 17.   Gin thou wert mine awn thing

> *Oh what pain it is to part!*
> *Can I leave thee, can I leave thee?*
> *Oh what pain it is to part!*
> *Can thy Polly ever leave thee?*
> *But lest death my love should thwart,*
> *And bring thee to the fatal cart,*

> *Thus I tear thee from my bleeding heart!*
> *Fly hence, and let me leave thee.*

One kiss and then—one kiss—begone—farewell.

MACHEATH   My hand, my heart, my dear, is so riveted to thine, that I cannot unloose my hold.

POLLY   But my papa may intercept thee, and then I should lose the very glimmering of hope. A few weeks, perhaps, may reconcile us all. Shall thy Polly hear from thee?

MACHEATH   Must I then go?

POLLY   And will not absence change your love?

MACHEATH   If you doubt it, let me stay—and be hanged.

POLLY   Oh how I fear! How I tremble! Go—but when safety will give you leave, you will be sure to see me again; for 'till then Polly is wretched.

AIR 18.   Oh the broom

[Parting, and looking back at each other with fondness; he at one door, she at the other.]

MACHEATH   *The miser thus a shilling sees,*
Which he's obliged to pay,
With sighs resigns it by degrees,
And fears 'tis gone for aye.

POLLY   *The boy, thus, when his sparrow's flown,*
The bird in silence eyes;
But soon as out of sight 'tis gone,
Whines, whimpers, sobs, and cries.

Act 2

SCENE 1 *A tavern near Newgate*

JEMMY TWITCHER, CROOK-FINGERED JACK, WAT DREARY, ROBIN OF BAGSHOT, NIMMING NED, HENRY PADDINGTON, MATT OF THE MINT, BEN BUDGE, *and the rest of the gang, at the table, with wine, brandy, and tobacco.*

BEN   But prithee, Matt, what is become of thy brother Tom? I have not seen him since my return from transportation.

MATT   Poor brother Tom had an accident this time twelve-month, and so clever a made fellow he was, that I could not save him from those flaying rascals the surgeons; and now, poor man, he is among the otamies[4] at Surgeon's Hall.

BEN   So it seems, his time was come.

JEMMY   But the present time is ours, and nobody alive hath more. Why are the laws levelled at us? Are we more dishonest than the rest of mankind? What we win, gentlemen, is our own by the law of arms and the right of conquest.

JACK   Where shall we find such another set of practical philosophers, who to a man are above the fear of death?

---

4. Skeletons ("anatomies"). The "accident" was hanging. "Clever a made": Well-made.

WAT   Sound men, and true!

ROBIN   Of tried courage, and indefatigable industry!

NED   Who is there here that would not die for his friend?

HARRY   Who is there here that would betray him for his interest?

MATT   Show me a gang of courtiers that can say as much.

BEN   We are for a just partition of the world, for every man hath a right to enjoy life.

MATT   We retrench the superfluities of mankind. The world is avaricious, and I hate avarice. A covetous fellow, like a jackdaw, steals what he was never made to enjoy, for the sake of hiding it. These are the robbers of mankind, for money was made for the free-hearted and generous, and where is the injury of taking from another what he hath not the heart to make use of?

JEMMY   Our several stations[5] for the day are fixed. Good luck attend us all. Fill the glasses.

AIR 19.   Fill every glass

MATT
> Fill every glass, for wine inspires us,
> > And fires us
> With courage, love, and joy.
> Women and wine should life employ.
> Is there ought else on earth desirous?

CHORUS
> Fill every glass, etc.

SCENE 2

To them enter MACHEATH

MACHEATH   Gentlemen, well met. My heart hath been with you this hour; but an unexpected affair hath detained me. No ceremony, I beg you.

MATT   We were just breaking up to go upon duty. Am I to have the honor of taking the air with you, sir, this evening upon the heath? I drink a dram now and then with the stagecoachmen in the way of friendship and intelligence; and I know that about this time there will be passengers upon the Western Road, who are worth speaking with.

MACHEATH   I was to have been of that party, but—

MATT   But what, sir?

MACHEATH   Is there any man who suspects my courage?

MATT   We have all been witnesses of it.

MACHEATH   My honor and truth to the gang?

MATT   I'll be answerable for it.

MACHEATH   In the division of our booty, have I ever shown the least marks of avarice or injustice?

MATT   By these questions something seems to have ruffled you. Are any of us suspected?

MACHEATH   I have a fixed confidence, gentlemen, in you all, as men of honor, and as such I value and respect you. Peachum is a man that is useful to us.

---

5. Individual posts.

MATT   Is he about to play us any foul play? I'll shoot him through the head.

MACHEATH   I beg you, gentlemen, act with conduct and discretion. A pistol is your last resort.

MATT   He knows nothing of this meeting.

MACHEATH   Business cannot go on without him. He is a man who knows the world, and is a necessary agent to us. We have had a slight difference, and till it is accommodated I shall be obliged to keep out of his way. Any private dispute of mine shall be of no ill consequence to my friends. You must continue to act under his direction, for the moment we break loose from him, our gang is ruined.

MATT   As a bawd to a whore, I grant you, he is to us of great convenience.

MACHEATH   Make him believe I have quitted the gang, which I can never do but with life. At our private quarters I will continue to meet you. A week or so will probably reconcile us.

MATT   Your instructions shall be observed. 'Tis now high time for us to repair to our several duties; so till the evening at our quarters in Moorfields[6] we bid you farewell.

MACHEATH   I shall wish myself with you. Success attend you. [*Sits down melancholy at the table.*]

AIR 20.   March in *Rinaldo*,[7] with drums and trumpets

MATT   *Let us take the road.*
     Hark I hear the sound of coaches!
     The hour of attack approaches,
    To your arms, brave boys, and load.
      See the ball I hold!
     Let the chemists[8] *toil like asses,*
     Our fire their fire surpasses,
      And turns all our lead to gold.

[*The gang, ranged in the front of the stage, load their pistols, and stick them under their girdles; then go off singing the first part in chorus.*]

SCENE 3

MACHEATH

What a fool is a fond wench! Polly is most confoundedly bit.[9] I love the sex. And a man who loves money might as well be contented with one guinea, as I with one woman. The town perhaps hath been as much obliged to me for recruiting it with free-hearted ladies, as to any recruiting officer in the army. If it were not for us and the other gentlemen of the sword, Drury Lane[1] would be uninhabited.

---

6. A district known as a "seminary of vice."
7. Opera by Handel.
8. Alchemists.

9. Taken in.
1. Associated with prostitutes.

AIR 21.   Would you have a young virgin

If the heart of a man is depressed with cares,
The mist is dispelled when a woman appears;
Like the notes of a fiddle, she sweetly, sweetly
Raises the spirits, and charms our ears,
Roses and lilies her cheeks disclose,
But her ripe lips are more sweet than those.
Press her,
Caress her,
With blisses,
Her kisses
Dissolve us in pleasure, and soft repose.

I must have women. There is nothing unbends the mind like them. Money is not so strong a cordial for the time. Drawer! [*Enter* DRAWER.] Is the porter gone for all the ladies, according to my directions?

DRAWER   I expect him back every minute. But you know, sir, you sent him as far as Hockley in the Hole, for three of the ladies, for one in Vinegar Yard, and for the rest of them somewhere about Lewkner's Lane. Sure some of them are below, for I hear the bar bell. As they come I will show them up. Coming, coming.

SCENE 4

MACHEATH, MRS. COAXER, DOLLY TRULL, MRS. VIXEN, BETTY DOXY, JENNY DIVER, MRS. SLAMMEKIN, SUKY TAWDRY, *and* MOLLY BRAZEN

MACHEATH   Dear Mrs. Coaxer, you are welcome. You look charmingly today. I hope you don't want the repairs of quality, and lay on paint.[2] Dolly Trull! Kiss me, you slut; are you as amorous as ever, hussy? You are always so taken up with stealing hearts, that you don't allow yourself time to steal anything else. Ah Dolly, thou wilt ever be a coquette! Mrs. Vixen, I'm yours, I always loved a woman of wit and spirit; they make charming mistresses, but plaguey wives. Betty Doxy! Come hither, hussy. Do you drink as hard as ever? You had better stick to good wholesome beer; for in troth, Betty, strong waters[3] will in time ruin your constitution. You should leave those to your betters. What! and my pretty Jenny Diver too! As prim and demure as ever! There is not any prude, though ever so high bred, hath a more sanctified look, with a more mischievous heart. Ah! Thou art a dear artful hypocrite. Mrs. Slammekin! As careless and genteel as ever! All you fine ladies, who know your own beauty, affect an undress.[4] But see, here's Suky Tawdry come to contradict what I was saying. Everything she gets one way she lays out upon her back. Why, Suky, you must keep at least a dozen tallymen.[5] Molly Brazen! [*She kisses him.*] That's well done. I love a free-hearted wench. Thou hast a most agreeable assurance, girl, and art as willing as a turtle. But hark! I hear music. The harper is at the door. "If music be the food of love, play on."[6] E'er you seat yourselves,

2. Cosmetics. "Quality": women of high social position.
3. Spirits.
4. Prefer casual clothes.
5. Suppliers of clothes on credit.
6. The opening line of *Twelfth Night*.

ladies, what think you of a dance? Come in. [*Enter* HARPER.] Play the
French tune that Mrs. Slammekin was so fond of.

> [*A dance a la ronde in the French manner; near the end of it this song
> and chorus.*]

AIR 22.   Cotillon

MACHEATH   *Youth's the season made for joys,*
        Love is then our duty,
       She alone who that employs,
        Well deserves her beauty.
          Let's be gay,
          While we may,
          Beauty's a flower despised in decay.

CHORUS   *Youth's the season etc.*

MACHEATH   *Let us drink and sport today,*
        Ours is not tomorrow.
   Love with youth flies swift away,
        Age is nought but sorrow.
          Dance and sing,
           Time's on the wing,
           Life never knows the return of spring.

CHORUS   *Let us drink etc.*

MACHEATH   Now, pray ladies, take your places. Here, fellow. [*Pays the*
HARPER.] Bid the drawer bring us more wine. [*Exit* HARPER.] If any of the
ladies choose gin, I hope they will be so free to call for it.

JENNY   You look as if you meant me. Wine is strong enough for me.
Indeed, sir, I never drink strong waters, but when I have the colic.

MACHEATH   Just the excuse of the fine ladies! Why, a lady of quality is
never without the colic. I hope, Mrs. Coaxer, you have had good success
of late in your visits among the mercers.[7]

MRS. COAXER   We have so many interlopers.[8] Yet with industry, one may
still have a little picking. I carried a silver flowered lute string and a
piece of black padesoy[9] to Mr. Peachum's lock but last week.

MRS. VIXEN   There's Molly Brazen hath the ogle of a rattlesnake. She riveted a linen draper's eye so fast upon her that he was nicked of three
pieces of cambric before he could look off.

MOLLY BRAZEN   Oh dear madam! But sure nothing can come up to your
handling of laces! And then you have such a sweet deluding tongue. To
cheat a man is nothing; but the woman must have fine parts indeed who
cheats a woman!

MRS. VIXEN   Lace, madam, lies in a small compass, and is of easy conveyance. But you are apt, madam, to think too well of your friends.

MRS. COAXER   If any woman hath more art than another, to be sure, 'tis
Jenny Diver. Though her fellow be never so agreeable, she can pick his
pocket as coolly, as if money were her only pleasure. Now that is a command of the passions uncommon in a woman!

---

7. Dealers in fabrics.
8. I.e., competitors in thievery.
9. Expensive silks.

JENNY I never go to the tavern with a man, but in the view of business. I have other hours, and other sort of men, for my pleasure. But had I your address,[1] madam—

MACHEATH Have done with your compliments, ladies; and drink about. You are not so fond of me, Jenny, as you use to be.

JENNY 'Tis not convenient, sir, to show my fondness among so many rivals. 'Tis your own choice, and not the warmth of my inclination, that will determine you.

AIR 23. All in a misty morning

Before the barn door crowing,
  The cock by hens attended,
His eyes around him throwing,
  Stands for a while suspended.
Then one he singles from the crew,
  And cheers the happy hen;
With how do you do, and how do you do,
  And how do you do again.

MACHEATH Ah Jenny! Thou art a dear slut.

DOLLY Pray, madam, were you ever in keeping?[2]

SUKY I hope, madam, I ha'nt been so long upon the town, but I have met with some good fortune as well as my neighbors.

DOLLY Pardon me, madam, I meant no harm by the question; 'twas only in the way of conversation.

SUKY Indeed, madam, if I had not been a fool, I might have lived very handsomely with my last friend. But upon his missing five guineas, he turned me off. Now I never suspected he had counted them.

MRS. SLAMMEKIN Who do you look upon, madam, as your best sort of keepers?

DOLLY That, madam, is thereafter as they be.[3]

MRS. SLAMMEKIN I, madam, was once kept by a Jew; and bating[4] their religion, to women they are a good sort of people.

SUKY Now for my part, I own I like an old fellow, for we always make them pay for what they can't do.

MRS. VIXEN A spruce prentice, let me tell you, ladies, is no ill thing, they bleed[5] freely. I have sent at least two or three dozen of them in my time to the plantations.[6]

JENNY But to be sure, sir, with so much good fortune as you have had upon the road, you must be grown immensely rich.

MACHEATH The road, indeed, hath done me justice, but the gaming table hath been my ruin.

AIR 24. When once I lay with another man's wife

JENNY   *The gamesters and lawyers are jugglers[7] alike,*
      If they meddle your all is in danger.
    Like gypsies, if once they can finger a souse,[8]

---

1. Adroitness.
2. A kept mistress.
3. Depends on their behavior.
4. Except for.

5. Spend.
6. The colonies, where convicts were transported.
7. Tricksters.
8. A negligible coin.

> *Your pockets they pick, and they pilfer your house,*
> *And give your estate to a stranger.*

A man of courage should never put anything to the risk but his life. These are the tools of a man of honor. Cards and dice are only fit for cowardly cheats, who prey upon their friends. [*She takes up his pistol.* SUKY *takes up the other.*]

SUKY This, sir, is fitter for your hand. Besides your loss of money, 'tis a loss to the ladies. Gaming takes you off from women. How fond could I be of you! But before company, 'tis ill bred.

MACHEATH Wanton hussies!

JENNY I must and will have a kiss to give my wine a zest.
    [*They take him about the neck, and make signs to* PEACHUM *and the constables, who rush in upon him.*]

SCENE 5

To them, PEACHUM *and constables.*

PEACHUM I seize you, sir, as my prisoner.

MACHEATH Was this well done, Jenny? Women are decoy ducks; who can trust them! Beasts, jades, jilts, harpies, furies, whores!

PEACHUM Your case, Mr. Macheath, is not particular. The greatest heroes have been ruined by women. But, to do them justice, I must own they are a pretty sort of creatures, if we could trust them. You must now, sir, take your leave of the ladies, and if they have a mind to make you a visit, they will be sure to find you at home. The gentleman, ladies, lodges in Newgate. Constables, wait upon the Captain to his lodgings.

AIR 25. When first I laid siege to my Chloris

MACHEATH   *At the tree I shall suffer with pleasure,*
                  At the tree I shall suffer with pleasure,
                      Let me go where I will,
                      In all kinds of ill,
                  I shall find no such Furies as these are.

PEACHUM Ladies, I'll take care the reckoning shall be discharged.
    [*Exit* MACHEATH, *guarded, with* PEACHUM *and the constables.*]

SCENE 6

The women remain.

MRS. VIXEN Look ye, Mrs. Jenny, though Mr. Peachum may have made a private bargain with you and Suky Tawdry for betraying the Captain, as we were all assisting, we ought all to share alike.

MRS. COAXER I think Mr. Peachum, after so long an acquaintance, might have trusted me as well as Jenny Diver.

MRS. SLAMMEKIN I am sure at least three men of his hanging, and in a year's time too (if he did me justice), should be set down to my account.

DOLLY Mrs. Slammekin, that is not fair. For you know one of them was taken in bed with me.

JENNY As far as a bowl of punch or a treat, I believe Mrs. Suky will join with me. As for anything else, ladies, you cannot in conscience expect it.

MRS. SLAMMEKIN   Dear madam—
DOLLY   I would not for the world[9]—
MRS. SLAMMEKIN   'Tis impossible for me—
DOLLY   As I hope to be saved, madam—
MRS. SLAMMEKIN   Nay, then I must stay here all night—
DOLLY   Since you command me.

[*Exeunt with great ceremony.*]

SCENE 7 *Newgate*

LOCKIT, *turnkeys,* MACHEATH, *constables.*

LOCKIT   Noble Captain, you are welcome. You have not been a lodger of mine this year and half. You know the custom, sir. Garnish,[1] Captain, garnish. Hand me down those fetters there.

MACHEATH   Those, Mr. Lockit, seem to be the heaviest of the whole set. With your leave, I should like the further pair better.

LOCKIT   Look ye, Captain, we know what is fittest for our prisoners. When a gentleman uses me with civility, I always do the best I can to please him. Hand them down I say. We have them of all prices, from one guinea to ten, and 'tis fitting every gentleman should please himself.

MACHEATH   I understand you, sir. [*Gives money.*] The fees here are so many, and so exorbitant, that few fortunes can bear the expense of getting off handsomely, or of dying like a gentleman.

LOCKIT   Those, I see, will fit the Captain better. Take down the further pair. Do but examine them, sir. Never was better work. How genteelly they are made! They will sit as easy as a glove, and the nicest man in England might not be ashamed to wear them. [*He puts on the chains.*] If I had the best gentleman in the land in my custody, I could not equip him more handsomely. And so, sir, I now leave you to your private meditations.

SCENE 8

MACHEATH.

AIR 26.   Courtiers, courtiers think it no harm

Man may escape from rope and gun;
Nay, some have outlived the doctor's pill;
Who takes a woman must he undone,
*   That basilisk[2] is sure to kill.*
The fly that sips treacle is lost in the sweets,
So he that tastes woman, woman, woman,
*   He that tastes woman, ruin meets.*

To what a woeful plight have I brought myself! Here must I (all day long, 'till I am hanged) be confined to hear the reproaches of a wench who lays her ruin at my door. I am in the custody of her father, and to be sure if he knows of the matter, I shall have a fine time on't betwixt this and my execution. But I promised the wench marriage. What signifies a promise

---

9. With exaggerated politeness, each gestures for the other to leave the room first.
1. Jailer's fee or bribe.

2. Mythical reptile whose breath and look were fatal.

to a woman? Does not man in marriage itself promise a hundred things that he never means to perform? Do all we can, women will believe us, for they look upon a promise as an excuse for following their own inclinations. But here comes Lucy, and I cannot get from her. Would I were deaf!

SCENE 9

MACHEATH, LUCY.

LUCY   You base man you! How can you look me in the face after what hath passed between us? See here, perfidious wretch, how I am forced to bear about the load of infamy[3] you have laid upon me. O Macheath! Thou hast robbed me of my quiet. To see thee tortured would give me pleasure!

AIR 27.   *A lovely lass to a friar came*

> *Thus when a good huswife sees a rat*
> *In her trap in the morning taken,*
> *With pleasure her heart goes pit a pat,*
> *In revenge for her loss of bacon.*
> *Then she throws him*
> *To the dog or cat,*
> *To be worried, crushed and shaken.*

MACHEATH   Have you no bowels,[4] no tenderness, my dear Lucy, to see a husband in these circumstances?

LUCY   A husband!

MACHEATH   In every respect but the form, and that, my dear, may be said over us at any time. Friends should not insist upon ceremonies. From a man of honor, his word is as good as his bond.

LUCY   'Tis the pleasure of all you fine men to insult the women you have ruined.

AIR 28.   *'Twas when the sea was roaring*

> *How cruel are the traitors,*
> *Who lie and swear in jest,*
> *To cheat unguarded creatures*
> *Of virtue, fame, and rest!*
> *Whoever steals a shilling,*
> *Through shame the guilt conceals;*
> *In love the perjured villain*
> *With boasts the theft reveals.*

MACHEATH   The very first opportunity, my dear (have but patience), you shall be my wife in whatever manner you please.

LUCY   Insinuating monster! And so you think I know nothing of the affair of Miss Polly Peachum. I could tear thy eyes out!

MACHEATH   Sure Lucy, you can't be such a fool as to be jealous of Polly!

LUCY   Are you not married to her, you brute, you?

---

3. Pregnancy.   4. Pity.

MACHEATH   Married! Very good. The wench gives it out only to vex thee, and to ruin me in thy good opinion. 'Tis true, I go to the house; I chat with the girl, I kiss her, I say a thousand things to her (as all gentlemen do) that mean nothing, to divert myself; and now the silly jade hath set it about that I am married to her, to let me know what she would be at. Indeed, my dear Lucy, these violent passions may be of ill consequence to a woman in your condition.

LUCY   Come, come, Captain, for all your assurance, you know that Miss Polly hath put it out of your power to do me the justice you promised me.

MACHEATH   A jealous woman believes everything her passion suggests. To convince you of my sincerity, if we can find the Ordinary,[5] I shall have no scruples of making you my wife; and I know the consequence of having two at a time.

LUCY   That you are only to be hanged, and so get rid of them both.

MACHEATH   I am ready, my dear Lucy, to give you satisfaction—if you think there is any in marriage. What can a man of honor say more?

LUCY   So then it seems you are not married to Miss Polly.

MACHEATH   You know, Lucy, the girl is prodigiously conceited. No man can say a civil thing to her, but (like other fine ladies) her vanity makes her think he's her own for ever and ever.

AIR 29.   The sun had loosed his weary teams

> The first time at the looking-glass
>   The mother sets her daughter,
> The image strikes the smiling lass
>   With self-love ever after.
> Each time she looks, she, fonder grown,
>   Thinks every charm grows stronger.
> But alas, vain maid, all eyes but your own
>   Can see you are not younger.

When women consider their own beauties, they are all alike unreasonable in their demands; for they expect their lovers should like them as long as they like themselves.

LUCY   Yonder is my father. Perhaps this way we may light upon the Ordinary, who shall try if you will be as good as your word. For I long to be made an honest woman.

SCENE 10

PEACHUM, LOCKIT *with an account book.*

LOCKIT   In this last affair, Brother Peachum, we are agreed. You have consented to go halves in Macheath.

PEACHUM   We shall never fall out about an execution. But as to that article, pray how stands our last year's account?

LOCKIT   If you will run your eye over it, you'll find 'tis fair and clearly stated.

PEACHUM   This long arrear[6] of the Government is very hard upon us! Can it be expected that we should hang our acquaintance for nothing, when

5. Chaplain.

6. Overdue reward money.

our betters will hardly save theirs without being paid for it. Unless the people in employment pay better, I promise them for the future, I shall let other rogues live besides their own.

LOCKIT Perhaps, brother, they are afraid these matters may be carried too far. We are treated too by them with contempt, as if our profession were not reputable.

PEACHUM In one respect indeed, our employment may be reckoned dishonest, because, like great statesmen, we encourage those who betray their friends.

LOCKIT Such language, brother, anywhere else, might turn to your prejudice. Learn to be more guarded, I beg you.

AIR 30.   How happy are we

> When you censure the age,
> Be cautious and sage,
> Lest the courtiers offended should be:
> If you mention vice or bribe,
> 'Tis so pat to all the tribe,
> Each cries, "That was leveled at me!"

PEACHUM Here's poor Ned Clincher's name, I see. Sure, brother Lockit, there was a little unfair proceeding in Ned's case; for he told me in the condemned hold,[7] that for value received, you had promised him a Session or two longer without molestation.

LOCKIT Mr. Peachum, this is the first time my honor was ever called in question.

PEACHUM Business is at an end if once we act dishonorably.

LOCKIT Who accuses me?

PEACHUM You are warm, brother.

LOCKIT He that attacks my honor, attacks my livelihood. And this usage, sir, is not to be born.

PEACHUM Since you provoke me to speak, I must tell you too that Mrs. Coaxer charges you with defrauding her of her information money, for the apprehending of curl-pated Hugh. Indeed, indeed, brother, we must punctually pay our spies, or we shall have no information.

LOCKIT Is this language to me, sirrah, who have saved you from the gallows, sirrah! [Collaring each other.]

PEACHUM If I am hanged, it shall be for ridding the world of an arrant rascal.

LOCKIT This hand shall do the office of the halter[8] you deserve, and throttle you—you dog!

PEACHUM Brother, brother, we are both in the wrong. We shall be both losers in the dispute—for you know we have it in our power to hang each other. You should not be so passionate.

LOCKIT Nor you so provoking.

PEACHUM 'Tis our mutual interest; 'tis for the interest of the world we should agree. If I said anything, brother, to the prejudice of your character, I ask pardon.

---

7. Prison cell.   8. Noose.

LOCKIT   Brother Peachum, I can forgive as well as resent. Give me your hand. Suspicion does not become a friend.

PEACHUM   I only meant to give you occasion to justify yourself. But I must now step home, for I expect the gentleman about this snuffbox, that Filch nimmed[9] two nights ago in the park. I appointed him at this hour.

SCENE 11

LOCKIT, LUCY

LOCKIT   Whence come you, hussy?

LUCY   My tears might answer that question.

LOCKIT   You have then been whimpering and fondling, like a spaniel, over the fellow that hath abused you.

LUCY   One can't help love; one can't cure it. 'Tis not in my power to obey you, and hate him.

LOCKIT   Learn to bear your husband's death like a reasonable woman. 'Tis not the fashion, nowadays, so much as to affect sorrow upon these occasions. No woman would ever marry, if she had not the chance of mortality for a release. Act like a woman of spirit, hussy, and thank your father for what he is doing.

AIR 31.   Of a noble race was Shenkin

LUCY

> *Is then his fate decreed, sir?*
> *Such a man can I think of quitting?*
> *When first we met, so moves me yet,*
> *Oh see how my heart is splitting!*

LOCKIT   Look ye, Lucy, there is no saving him. So I think you must even do like other widows: buy yourself weeds,[1] and be cheerful.

AIR 32.   You'll think e'er many days ensue

> *You'll think e'er many days ensue*
> *This sentence not severe;*
> *I hang your husband, child, 'tis true,*
> *But with him hang your care.*
> *Twang dang dillo dee.*

Like a good wife, go moan over your dying husband. That, child, is your duty. Consider, girl, you can't have the man and the money too. So make yourself as easy as you can, by getting all you can from him.

SCENE 12

LUCY, MACHEATH

LUCY   Though the Ordinary was out of the way today, I hope; my dear, you will, upon the first opportunity, quiet my scruples. Oh sir! My father's hard heart is not to be softened, and I am in the utmost despair.

MACHEATH   But if I could raise a small sum—would not twenty guineas, think you, move him? Of all the arguments in the way of business, the

---

9. Stole.   1. Mourning clothes.

perquisite[2] is the most prevailing. Your father's perquisites for the escape of prisoners must amount to a considerable sum in the year. Money well timed, and properly applied, will do any thing.

AIR 33.   London ladies

> *If you at an office solicit your due,*
> *And would not have matters neglected,*
> *You must quicken the clerk with the perquisite too,*
> *To do what his duty directed.*
> *Or would you the frowns of a lady prevent,*
> *She too has this palpable failing,*
> *The perquisite softens her into consent;*
> *That reason with all is prevailing.*

LUCY   What love or money can do shall be done; for all my comfort depends upon your safety.

SCENE 13

LUCY, MACHEATH, POLLY

POLLY   Where is my dear husband? Was a rope ever intended for this neck! Oh let me throw my arms about it, and throttle thee with love! Why dost thou turn away from me? 'Tis thy Polly! 'Tis thy wife!

MACHEATH   Was ever such an unfortunate rascal as I am!

LUCY   Was there ever such another villain!

POLLY   Oh Macheath! Was it for this we parted? Taken! Imprisoned! Tried! Hanged! Cruel reflection! I'll stay with thee 'till death. No force shall tear thy dear wife from thee now.—What means my love? Not one kind word! Not one kind look! Think what thy Polly suffers to see thee in this condition.

AIR 34.   All in the downs

> *Thus when the swallow, seeking prey,*
> *Within the sash[3] is closely pent,*
> *His consort, with bemoaning lay,*
> *Without sits pining for th' event.*
> *Her chattering lovers all around her skim;*
> *She heeds them not (poor bird!), her soul's with him.*

MACHEATH [*Aside.*]   I must disown her. The wench is distracted.

LUCY   Am I then bilked of my virtue? Can I have no reparation? Sure men were born to lie, and women to believe them! Oh villain! Villain!

POLLY   Am I not thy wife? Thy neglect of me, thy aversion to me, too severely proves it. Look on me. Tell me, am I not thy wife?

LUCY   Perfidious wretch!

POLLY   Barbarous husband!

LUCY   Hadst thou been hanged five months ago, I had been happy.

POLLY   And I too. If you had been kind to me 'till death, it would not have vexed me—and that's no very unreasonable request (though from a wife) to a man who hath not above seven or eight days to live.

---

2. Tip or bribe.   3. Window.

LUCY Art thou then married to another? Hast thou two wives, monster?

MACHEATH If women's tongues can cease for an answer, hear me.

LUCY I won't. Flesh and blood can't bear my usage.

POLLY Shall I not claim my own? Justice bids me speak.

AIR 35. Have you heard of a frolicsome ditty

MACHEATH *How happy could I be with either,*
Were t'other dear charmer away!
But while you thus tease me together,
To neither a word will I say,
But tol de rol, etc.

POLLY Sure, my dear, there ought to be some preference shown to a wife. At least she may claim the appearance of it. He must be distracted with his misfortunes, or he could not use me thus!

LUCY Oh villain, villain! Thou hast deceived me. I could even inform against thee with pleasure. Not a prude wishes more heartily to have facts[4] against her intimate acquaintance, than I now wish to have facts against thee. I would have her satisfaction, and they should all out.

AIR 36. Irish trot

POLLY *I'm bubbled.[5]*

LUCY *I'm bubbled.*

POLLY *O how I am troubled!*

LUCY *Bamboozled, and bit!*

POLLY *My distresses are doubled.*

LUCY *When you come to the tree, should the hangman refuse,*
These fingers, with pleasure, could fasten the noose.

POLLY *I'm bubbled, etc.*

MACHEATH Be pacified, my dear Lucy. This is all a fetch[6] of Polly's, to make me desperate with you in case I get off. If I am hanged, she would fain have the credit of being thought my widow. Really, Polly, this is no time for a dispute of this sort; for whenever you are talking of marriage, I am thinking of hanging.

POLLY And hast thou the heart to persist in disowning me?

MACHEATH And hast thou the heart to persist in persuading me that I am married? Why, Polly, dost thou seek to aggravate my misfortunes?

LUCY Really, Miss Peachum, you but expose yourself. Besides, 'tis barbarous in you to worry a gentleman in his circumstances.

AIR 37.

POLLY *Cease your funning;*
Force or cunning
Never shall my heart trapan.[7]
All these sallies
Are but malice
To seduce my constant man.

---

4. Incriminating information.
5. Cheated.

6. Ruse.
7. Beguile.

> *'Tis most certain,*
> *By their flirting*
> *Women oft have envy shown;*
> *Pleased to ruin*
> *Others wooing,*
> *Never happy in their own!*

Decency, madam, methinks might teach you to behave yourself with some reserve with the husband, while his wife is present.

MACHEATH But seriously, Polly, this is carrying the joke a little too far.

LUCY If you are determined, madam, to raise a disturbance in the prison, I shall be obliged to send for the turnkey to show you the door. I am sorry, madam, you force me to be so ill-bred.

POLLY Give me leave to tell you, madam, these forward airs don't become you in the least, madam. And my duty, madam, obliges me to stay with my husband, madam.

AIR 38.   Good morrow, gossip Joan

LUCY
> *Why how now, Madam Flirt?*
> *If you thus must chatter;*
> *And are for flinging dirt,*
> *Let's try who best can spatter,*
> *Madam Flirt!*

POLLY
> *Why how now, saucy jade?*
> *Sure the wench is tipsy!*

[To him.]
> *How can you see me made*
> *The scoff of such a gipsy?*

[To her.]
> *Saucy jade!*

SCENE 14

LUCY, MACHEATH, POLLY, PEACHUM

PEACHUM Where's my wench? Ah hussy! Hussy! Come you home, you slut; and when your fellow is hanged, hang yourself, to make your family some amends.

POLLY Dear, dear father, do not tear me from him. I must speak; I have more to say to him—Oh! Twist thy fetters about me, that he may not haul me from thee!

PEACHUM Sure all women are alike! If ever they commit the folly, they are sure to commit another by exposing themselves. Away, not a word more. You are my prisoner now, hussy.

AIR 39.   Irish howl

POLLY
> *No power on earth can e'er divide*
> *The knot that sacred love hath tied.*
> *When parents draw against our mind,*
> *The true-love's knot they faster bind.*
> *Oh, oh ray, oh Amborah—oh, oh, etc.*

[*Holding* MACHEATH, PEACHUM *pulling her.*]

SCENE 15

LUCY, MACHEATH

MACHEATH   I am naturally compassionate, wife, so that I could not use the wench as she deserved; which made you at first suspect there was something in what she said.

LUCY   Indeed, my dear, I was strangely puzzled.

MACHEATH   If that had been the case, her father would never have brought me into this circumstance. No, Lucy, I had rather die than be false to thee.

LUCY   How happy am I, if you say this from your heart! For I love thee so, that I could sooner bear to see thee hanged than in the arms of another.

MACHEATH   But couldst thou bear to see me hanged?

LUCY   O Macheath, I can never live to see that day.

MACHEATH   You see, Lucy, in the account of love you are in my debt, and you must now be convinced that I rather choose to die than be another's. Make me, if possible, love thee more, and let me owe my life to thee. If you refuse to assist me, Peachum and your father will immediately put me beyond all means of escape.

LUCY   My father, I know, hath been drinking hard with the prisoners, and I fancy he is now taking his nap in his own room. If I can procure the keys, shall I go off with thee, my dear?

MACHEATH   If we are together, 'twill be impossible to lie concealed. As soon as the search begins to be a little cool, I will send to thee. 'Till then my heart is thy prisoner.

LUCY   Come then, my dear husband, owe thy life to me. And though you love me not, be grateful. But that Polly runs in my head strangely.

MACHEATH   A moment of time may make us unhappy forever.

AIR 40.   The lass of Patie's mill

LUCY

> I like the fox shall grieve,
>   Whose mate hath left her side,
> Whom hounds, from morn to eve,
>   Chase o'er the country wide.
> Where can my lover hide?
>   Where cheat the weary pack?
> If love be not his guide,
>   He never will come back!

Act 3

SCENE 1 *Newgate*

LOCKIT, LUCY

LOCKIT   To be sure, wench, you must have been aiding and abetting to help him to this escape.

LUCY   Sir, here hath been Peachum and his daughter Polly, and to be sure they know the ways of Newgate as well as if they had been born and bred in the place all their lives. Why must all your suspicion light upon me?

LOCKIT   Lucy, Lucy, I will have none of these shuffling[8] answers.

LUCY   Well then—if I know anything of him I wish I may be burnt!

LOCKIT   Keep your temper, Lucy, or I shall pronounce you guilty.

LUCY   Keep yours, sir. I do wish I may be burnt. I do. And what can I say more to convince you?

LOCKIT   Did he tip handsomely? How much did he come down with? Come hussy, don't cheat your father, and I shall not be angry with you. Perhaps you have made a better bargain with him than I could have done. How much, my good girl?

LUCY   You know, sir, I am fond of him, and would have given money to have kept him with me.

LOCKIT   Ah Lucy! Thy education might have put thee more upon thy guard, for a girl in the bar of an ale house is always besieged.

LUCY   Dear sir, mention not my education, for 'twas to that I owe my ruin.

AIR 41.   If love's a sweet passion

When young at the bar you first taught me to score,
And bid me be free of my lips, and no more,
I was kissed by the parson, the squire, and the sot;
When the guest was departed, the kiss was forgot.
But his kiss was so sweet, and so closely he pressed,
That I languished and pined 'till I granted the rest.

If you can forgive me, sir, I will make a fair confession, for to be sure he hath been a most barbarous villain to me.

LOCKIT   And so you have let him escape, hussy, have you?

LUCY   When a woman loves, a kind look, a tender word can persuade her to anything. And I could ask no other bribe.

LOCKIT   Thou wilt always be a vulgar slut, Lucy. If you would not be looked upon as a fool, you should never do anything but upon the foot of interest. Those that act otherwise are their own bubbles.[9]

LUCY   But love, sir, is a misfortune that may happen to the most discreet woman, and in love we are all fools alike. Notwithstanding all he swore, I am now fully convinced that Polly Peachum is actually his wife. Did I let him escape (fool that I was!) to go to her? Polly will wheedle herself into his money, and then Peachum will hang him, and cheat us both.

LOCKIT   So I am to be ruined because, forsooth, you must be in love! A very pretty excuse!

LUCY   I could murder that impudent happy strumpet. I gave him his life, and that creature enjoys the sweets of it. Ungrateful Macheath!

AIR 42.   South Sea ballad

My love is all madness and folly,
Alone I lie,
Toss, tumble, and cry,
What a happy creature is Polly!
Was e'er such a wretch as I!
With rage I redden like scarlet,
That my dear inconstant varlet,

8. Evasive.   9. Dupes.

> *Stark blind to my charms,*
> *Is lost in the arms*
> *Of that jilt, that inveigling harlot!*
> *Stark blind to my charms,*
> *Is lost in the arms*
> *Of that jilt, that inveigling harlot!*
> *This, this my resentment alarms.*

LOCKIT   And so, after all this mischief, I must stay here to be entertained with your caterwauling, Mistress Puss! Out of my sight, wanton strumpet! You shall fast and mortify yourself into reason, with now and then a little handsome discipline to bring you to your senses. Go.

SCENE 2

LOCKIT

Peachum then intends to outwit me in this affair; but I'll be even with him. The dog is leaky[1] in his liquor, so I'll ply him that way, get the secret from him, and turn this affair to my own advantage. Lions, wolves, and vultures don't live together in herds, droves, or flocks. Of all animals of prey, man is the only sociable one. Every one of us preys upon his neighbor, and yet we herd together. Peachum is my companion, my friend. According to the custom of the world, indeed, he may quote thousands of precedents for cheating me. And shall not I make use of the privilege of friendship to make him a return?

AIR 43.   Packington's pound

> *Thus gamesters united in friendship are found,*
> *Though they know that their industry all is a cheat;*
> *They flock to their prey at the dice-box's sound,*
> *And join to promote one another's deceit.*
> *But if by mishap*
> *They fail of a chap,[2]*
> *To keep in their hands, they each other entrap.*
> *Like pikes, lank with hunger, who miss of their ends,*
> *They bite their companions, and prey on their friends.*

Now, Peachum, you and I, like honest tradesmen, are to have a fair trial which of us two can overreach the other. Lucy! [*Enter* LUCY] Are there any of Peachum's people now in the house?

LUCY   Filch, sir, is drinking a quartern[3] of strong waters in the next room with Black Moll.

LOCKIT   Bid him come to me.

SCENE 3

LOCKIT, FILCH

LOCKIT   Why, boy, thou lookest as if thou wert half starved, like a shotten herring.[4]

---

1. A blabbermouth.
2. Customer or sucker.
3. Quarter of a pint.
4. A herring exhausted by spawning.

FILCH   One had need have the constitution of a horse to go through the business. Since the favorite child-getter[5] was disabled by a mishap, I have picked up a little money by helping the ladies to a pregnancy against their being called down to sentence. But if a man cannot get an honest livelihood any easier way, I am sure 'tis what I can't undertake for another Session.

LOCKIT   Truly, if that great man should tip off,[6] 'twould be an irreparable loss. The vigor and prowess of a knight-errant never saved half the ladies in distress that he hath done. But, boy, can'st thou tell me where thy master is to be found?

FILCH   At his lock, sir, at the Crooked Billet.

LOCKIT   Very well. I have nothing more with you. [*Exit* FILCH.] I'll go to him there, for I have many important affairs to settle with him; and in the way of those transactions, I'll artfully get into his secret. So that Macheath shall not remain a day longer out of my clutches.

SCENE 4 *A gaming-house*

MACHEATH *in a fine tarnished coat,* BEN BUDGE, MATT OF THE MINT

MACHEATH   I am sorry, gentlemen, the road was so barren of money. When my friends are in difficulties, I am always glad that my fortune can be serviceable to them. [*Gives them money.*] You see, gentlemen, I am not a mere court friend, who professes everything and will do nothing.

AIR 44.   Lillibullero

The modes of the court so common are grown,
  That a true friend can hardly be met;
Friendship for interest is but a loan,
  Which they let out for what they can get.
    'Tis true, you find
    Some friends so kind,
Who will give you good counsel themselves to defend.
    In sorrowful ditty,
    They promise, they pity,
  But shift you for money, from friend to friend.

But we, gentlemen, have still honor enough to break through the corruptions of the world. And while I can serve you, you may command me.

BEN   It grieves my heart that so generous a man should be involved in such difficulties, as oblige him to live with such ill company, and herd with gamesters.

MATT   See the partiality of mankind! One man may steal a horse, better than another look over a hedge.[7] Of all mechanics,[8] of all servile handicraftsmen, a gamester is the vilest. But yet, as many of the quality are of the profession, he is admitted amongst the politest company. I wonder we are not more respected.

---

5. Stud.
6. Die.
7. I.e., a mere look at a horse can get some people in trouble.
8. Workers who use their hands.

MACHEATH   There will be deep play tonight at Marybone, and consequently money may be picked up upon the road. Meet me there, and I'll give you the hint who is worth setting.[9]

MATT   The fellow with a brown coat with a narrow gold binding, I am told, is never without money.

MACHEATH   What do you mean, Matt? Sure you will not think of meddling with him! He's a good honest kind of a fellow, and one of us.

BEN   To be sure, sir, we will put ourselves under your direction.

MACHEATH   Have an eye upon the moneylenders. A rouleau,[1] or two, would prove a pretty sort of an expedition. I hate extortion.

MATT   Those rouleaus are very pretty things. I hate your bank bills; there is such a hazard in putting them off.[2]

MACHEATH   There is a certain man of distinction, who in his time hath nicked me out of a great deal of the ready.[3] He is in my cash,[4] Ben. I'll point him out to you this evening, and you shall draw upon him for the debt. The company are met; I hear the dicebox in the other room. So, gentlemen, your servant. You'll meet me at Marybone.

SCENE 5 *Peachum's Lock*

A table with wine, brandy, pipes, and tobacco

PEACHUM, LOCKIT

LOCKIT   The Coronation account,[5] brother Peachum, is of so intricate a nature, that I believe it will never be settled.

PEACHUM   It consists indeed of a great variety of articles. It was worth to our people, in fees of different kinds, above ten installments.[6] This is part of the account, brother, that lies open before us.

LOCKIT   A lady's tail[7]—of rich brocade—that, I see, is disposed of.

PEACHUM   To Mrs. Diana Trapes, the tallywoman, and she will make a good hand on't in shoes and slippers, to trick out young ladies, upon their going into keeping.[8]

LOCKIT   But I don't see any article of the jewels.

PEACHUM   Those are so well known, that they must be sent abroad. You'll find them entered under the article of exportation. As for the snuffboxes, watches, swords, etc., I thought it best to enter them under their several heads.

LOCKIT   Seven and twenty women's pockets[9] complete, with the several things therein contained; all sealed, numbered, and entered.

PEACHUM   But, brother, it is impossible for us now to enter upon this affair. We should have the whole day before us. Besides, the account of the last half year's plate[1] is in a book by itself, which lies at the other office.

---

9. Robbing.
1. Rolls of gold coins.
2. Converting them into money.
3. Money.
4. He owes me.
5. Register of goods stolen during the coronation of George II (1727).

6. Public installations of the new Lord Mayor of London.
7. Train.
8. Becoming mistresses.
9. Purses worn around the waist.
1. Silver or gold utensils.

LOCKIT   Bring us then more liquor. Today shall be for pleasure, tomorrow for business. Ah brother, those daughters of ours are two slippery hussies. Keep a watchful eye upon Polly, and Macheath in a day or two shall be our own again.

AIR 45.   Down in the North Country

What gudgeons[2] are we men!
Every woman's easy prey.
Though we have felt the hook, again
We bite and they betray.

The bird that hath been trapped,
When he hears his calling mate,
To her he flies, again he's clapped
Within the wiry grate.

PEACHUM   But what signifies catching the bird, if your daughter Lucy will set open the door of the cage?

LOCKIT   If men were answerable for the follies and frailties of their wives and daughters, no friends could keep a good correspondence together for two days. This is unkind of you, brother; for among good friends, what they say or do goes for nothing.

[*Enter a* SERVANT.]

SERVANT   Sir, here's Mrs. Diana Trapes wants to speak with you.

PEACHUM   Shall we admit her, brother Lockit?

LOCKIT   By all means. She's a good customer, and a fine-spoken woman. And a woman who drinks and talks so freely, will enliven the conversation.

PEACHUM   Desire her to walk in.

[*Exit* SERVANT.]

SCENE 6

PEACHUM, LOCKIT, MRS. TRAPES

PEACHUM   Dear Mrs. Dye, your servant. One may know by your kiss that your gin is excellent.

MRS. TRAPES   I was always very curious[3] in my liquors.

LOCKIT   There is no perfumed breath like it. I have been long acquainted with the flavor of those lips, han't I, Mrs. Dye?

MRS. TRAPES   Fill it up. I take as large draughts of liquor, as I did of love. I hate a flincher in either.

AIR 46.   A shepherd kept sheep

In the days of my youth I could bill like a dove, fa, la, la, etc.
Like a sparrow at all times was ready for love, fa, la, la, etc.
The life of all mortals in kissing should pass,
Lip to lip while we're young—then the lip to the glass, fa, etc.

___

2. Minnows.   3. Choosy.

But now, Mr. Peachum, to our business. If you have blacks of any kind, brought in of late, mantoes[4]—velvet scarfs, petticoats—let it be what it will, I am your chap. For all my ladies are very fond of mourning.

PEACHUM   Why, look ye, Mrs. Dye, you deal so hard with us that we can afford to give the gentlemen who venture their lives for the goods little or nothing.

MRS. TRAPES The hard times oblige me to go very near[5] in my dealing. To be sure, of late years I have been a great sufferer by the Parliament—three thousand pounds would hardly make me amends. The Act for destroying the Mint[6] was a severe cut upon our business. 'Till then, if a customer stepped out of the way, we knew where to have her. No doubt you know Mrs. Coaxer. There's a wench now (till today) with a good suit of clothes of mine upon her back, and I could never set eyes upon her for three months together. Since the Act too against imprisonment for small sums,[7] my loss there too hath been very considerable, and it must be so, when a lady can borrow a handsome petticoat or a clean gown, and I not have the least hank[8] upon her! And o' my conscience, nowadays most ladies take a delight in cheating, when they can do it with safety.

PEACHUM   Madam, you had a handsome gold watch of us t'other day for seven guineas. Considering we must have our profit, to a gentleman upon the road, a gold watch will be scarce worth the taking.

MRS. TRAPES   Consider, Mr. Peachum, that watch was remarkable, and not of very safe sale. If you have any black velvet scarfs, they are a handsome winter wear, and take with most gentlemen who deal with my customers. 'Tis I that put the ladies upon a good foot. 'Tis not youth or beauty that fixes their price. The gentlemen always pay according to their dress, from half a crown to two guineas; and yet those hussies make nothing of bilking of me. Then too, allowing for accidents—I have eleven fine customers now down under the surgeon's hands. What with fees and other expenses, there are great goings-out, and no comings-in, and not a farthing to pay for at least a month's clothing. We run great risks, great risks indeed.

PEACHUM   As I remember, you said something just now of Mrs. Coaxer.

MRS. TRAPES   Yes, sir. To be sure I stripped her of a suit of my own clothes about two hours ago; and have left her as she should be, in her shift, with a lover of hers at my house. She called him upstairs, as he was going to Marybone in a hackney coach. And I hope, for her own sake and mine, she will persuade the Captain to redeem her, for the Captain is very generous to the ladies.

LOCKIT   What Captain?

MRS. TRAPES   He thought I did not know him. An intimate acquaintance of yours, Mr. Peachum. Only Captain Macheath—as fine as a lord.

PEACHUM   Tomorrow, dear Mrs. Dye, you shall set your own price upon any of the goods you like. We have at least half a dozen velvet scarfs, and all at your service. Will you give me leave to make you a present of this suit of night-clothes for your own wearing? But are you sure it is Captain Macheath?

---

4. Mantles or cloaks. "Blacks": mourning clothes.
5. Stingy.
6. The status of the Mint district as a sanctuary for outlaws had been undermined by recent statutes.
7. Previous to this act, someone could be arrested for owing any sum, however small.
8. Hold.

MRS. TRAPES   Though he thinks I have forgot him, nobody knows him better. I have taken a great deal of the Captain's money in my time at second hand, for he always loved to have his ladies well dressed.

PEACHUM   Mr. Lockit and I have a little business with the Captain—you understand me—and we will satisfy you for Mrs. Coaxer's debt.

LOCKIT   Depend upon it. We will deal like men of honor.

MRS. TRAPES   I don't inquire after your affairs, so whatever happens, I wash my hands on't. It hath always been my maxim, that one friend should assist another. But if you please, I'll take one of the scarfs home with me. 'Tis always good to have something in hand.

SCENE 7 *Newgate*

LUCY

Jealousy, rage, love, and fear are at once tearing me to pieces. How I am weather-beaten and shattered with distresses!

AIR 47. One evening, having lost my way

> *I'm like a skiff on the ocean tossed,*
> > *Now high, now low, with each billow born,*
> *With her rudder broke, and her anchor lost,*
> > *Deserted and all forlorn.*
> *While thus I lie rolling and tossing all night,*
> *That Polly lies sporting on seas of delight!*
> > *Revenge, revenge, revenge,*
> *Shall appease my restless sprite.*

I have the ratsbane[9] ready. I run no risk, for I can lay her death upon the gin, and so many die of that naturally that I shall never be called in question. But say I were to be hanged—I never could be hanged for anything that would give me greater comfort than the poisoning that slut.

[*Enter* FILCH.]

FILCH   Madam, here's our Miss Polly come to wait upon you.

LUCY   Show her in.

SCENE 8

LUCY, POLLY

LUCY   Dear madam, your servant. I hope you will pardon my passion when I was so happy to see you last. I was so overrun with the spleen[1] that I was perfectly out of myself. And really when one hath the spleen, everything is to be excused by a friend.

AIR 48.   Now Roger, I'll tell thee, because thou'rt my son

> *When a wife's in her pout,*
> *(As she's sometimes, no doubt!)*
> > *The good husband as meek as a lamb,*
> > *Her vapors[2] to still,*

---

9. Poison.
1. Fashionable seizure of peevishness or melancholy.
2. Ill humor or whims.

> *First grants her her will,*
> *And the quieting draught is a dram.*
> *Poor man! And the quieting draught is a dram.*

I wish all our quarrels might have so comfortable a reconciliation.

POLLY   I have no excuse for my own behavior, madam, but my misfortunes. And really, madam, I suffer too upon your account.

LUCY   But, Miss Polly, in the way of friendship, will you give me leave to propose a glass of cordial to you?

POLLY   Strong waters are apt to give me the headache. I hope, madam, you will excuse me.

LUCY   Not the greatest lady in the land could have better in her closet,[3] for her own private drinking. You seem mighty low in spirits, my dear.

POLLY   I am sorry, madam, my health will not allow me to accept of your offer. I should not have left you in the rude manner I did when we met last, madam, had not my papa hauled me away so unexpectedly. I was indeed somewhat provoked, and perhaps might use some expressions that were disrespectful. But really, madam, the Captain treated me with so much contempt and cruelty that I deserved your pity rather than your resentment.

LUCY   But since his escape, no doubt all matters are made up again. Ah Polly, Polly! 'Tis I am the unhappy wife, and he loves you as if you were only his mistress.

POLLY   Sure, madam, you cannot think me so happy as to be the object of your jealousy. A man is always afraid of a woman who loves him too well, so that I must expect to be neglected and avoided.

LUCY   Then our cases, my dear Polly, are exactly alike. Both of us indeed have been too fond.

AIR 49.   O Bessy Bell

POLLY   *A curse attends that woman's love,*
            Who always would be pleasing.
LUCY   *The pertness of the billing dove,*
            Like tickling, is but teasing.
POLLY   *What then in love can woman do?*
LUCY   *If we grow fond they shun us.*
POLLY   *And when we fly them, they pursue.*
LUCY   *But leave us when they've won us.*

Love is so very whimsical in both sexes, that it is impossible to be lasting. But my heart is particular, and contradicts my own observation.

POLLY   But really, Mistress Lucy, by his last behavior I think I ought to envy you. When I was forced from him, he did not show the least tenderness. But perhaps he hath a heart not capable of it.

AIR 50.   Would Fate to me Belinda give

> *Among the men, coquettes we find,*
> *Who court by turns all womankind;*
> *And we grant all their hearts desired,*
> *When they are flattered, and admired.*

---

3. Small private room.

The coquettes of both sexes are self-lovers, and that is a love no other whatever can dispossess. I fear, my dear Lucy, our husband is one of those.

LUCY   Away with these melancholy reflections. Indeed, my dear Polly, we are both of us a cup too low. Let me prevail upon you, to accept of my offer.

AIR 51.   Come, sweet lass

Come sweet lass,
Let's banish sorrow
'Till tomorrow;
Come, sweet lass,
Let's take a chirping⁴ glass.
Wine can clear
The vapors of despair,
And make us light as air;
Then drink, and banish care.

I can't bear, child, to see you in such low spirits. And I must persuade you to what I know will do you good. [*Aside.*] I shall now soon be even with the hypocritical strumpet.

SCENE 9

POLLY

All this wheedling of Lucy cannot be for nothing. At this time too, when I know she hates me! The dissembling of a woman is always the forerunner of mischief. By pouring strong waters down my throat, she thinks to pump some secrets out of me. I'll be upon my guard, and won't taste a drop of her liquor, I'm resolved.

SCENE 10

LUCY, *with strong waters.* POLLY

LUCY   Come, Miss Polly.

POLLY   Indeed, child, you have given yourself trouble to no purpose. You must, my dear, excuse me.

LUCY   Really, Miss Polly, you are so squeamishly affected about taking a cup of strong waters as a lady before company. I vow, Polly, I shall take it monstrously ill if you refuse me. Brandy and men (though women love them never so well) are always taken by us with some reluctance—unless 'tis in private.

POLLY   I protest, madam, it goes against me.—What do I see! Macheath again in custody! Now every glimmering of happiness is lost. [*Drops the glass of liquor on the ground.*]

LUCY [*Aside.*]   Since things are thus, I'm glad the wench hath escaped; for by this event, 'tis plain she was not happy enough to deserve to be poisoned.

4. Cheering.

SCENE 11[5]

LOCKIT, MACHEATH, PEACHUM, LUCY, POLLY

LOCKIT Set your heart to rest, Captain. You have neither the chance of love or money for another escape, for you are ordered to be called down upon your trial immediately.

PEACHUM Away, hussies! This is not a time for a man to be hampered with his wives. You see, the gentleman is in chains already.

LUCY O husband, husband, my heart longed to see thee; but to see thee thus distracts me!

POLLY Will not my dear husband look upon his Polly? Why hadst thou not flown to me for protection? With me thou hadst been safe.

AIR 52. The last time I went o'er the moor

POLLY	*Hither, dear husband, turn your eyes.*
LUCY	*Bestow one glance to cheer me.*
POLLY	*Think with that look, thy Polly dies.*
LUCY	*O shun me not, but hear me.*
POLLY	*'Tis Polly sues.*
LUCY	*—'Tis Lucy speaks.*
POLLY	*Is thus true love requited?*
LUCY	*My heart is bursting*
POLLY	*—Mine too breaks.*
LUCY	*Must I—*
POLLY	*—Must I be slighted?*

MACHEATH What would you have me say, ladies? You see, this affair will soon be at an end, without my disobliging either of you.

PEACHUM But the settling this point, Captain, might prevent a lawsuit between your two widows.

AIR 53. Tom Tinker's my true love

MACHEATH *Which way shall I turn me? How can I decide?*
Wives, the day of our death, are as fond as a bride.
One wife is too much for most husbands to hear,
But two at a time there's no mortal can bear.
This way, and that way, and which way I will,
What would comfort the one, t'other wife would take ill.

POLLY But if his own misfortunes have made him insensible to mine, a father sure will be more compassionate. Dear, dear sir, sink[6] the material evidence, and bring him off at his trial. Polly upon her knees begs it of you.

AIR 54. I am a poor shepherd undone

When my hero in court appears,
And stands arraigned for his life,
Then think of poor Polly's tears;

5. For an illustration of this scene by William Hogarth, see the color insert in this volume.

6. Suppress.

> For ah! Poor Polly's his wife.
> Like the sailor he holds up his hand,
>   Distressed on the dashing wave.
> To die a dry death at land,
> Is as had as a wat'ry grave.
> And alas, poor Polly!
> Alack, and well-a-day!
> Before I was in love,
>   Oh! every month was May.

LUCY   If Peachum's heart is hardened, sure you, sir, will have more compassion on a daughter. I know the evidence is in your power: how then can you be a tyrant to me? [*Kneeling.*]

AIR 55.   Ianthe the lovely

> When he holds up his hand arraigned for his life,
> Oh think of your daughter, and think I'm his wife!
> What are cannons, or bombs, or clashing of swords?
> For death is more certain by witnesses' words.
> Then nail up their lips, that dread thunder allay;
> And each month of my life will hereafter be May.

LOCKIT   Macheath's time is come, Lucy. We know our own affairs, therefore let us have no more whimpering or whining.

AIR 56.   A cobbler there was

> Ourselves, like the great, to secure a retreat,
> When matters require it, must give up our gang.
>   And good reason why,
>   Or, instead of the fry,
>   Even Peachum and I,
> Like poor petty rascals, might hang, hang;
> Like poor petty rascals, might hang.

PEACHUM   Set your heart at rest, Polly. Your husband is to die today. Therefore, if you are not already provided, 'tis high time to look about for another. There's comfort for you, you slut.

LOCKIT   We are ready, sir, to conduct you to the Old Bailey.

AIR 57.   Bonny Dundee

MACHEATH   The charge is prepared; the lawyers are met;
> The judges all ranged (a terrible show!).
> I go, undismayed, for death is a debt,
> A debt on demand. So take what I owe.
> Then farewell my love—dear charmers, adieu.
> Contented I die—'tis the better for you.
> Here ends all dispute the rest of our lives,
> For this way at once I please all my wives.

Now, gentlemen, I am ready to attend you.

SCENE 12

LUCY, POLLY, FILCH

POLLY Follow them, Filch, to the court. And when the trial is over, bring me a particular account of his behavior, and of everything that happened. You'll find me here with Miss Lucy. [*Exit* FILCH.] But why is all this music?

LUCY The prisoners whose trials are put off till next Session are diverting themselves.

POLLY Sure there is nothing so charming as music, I'm fond of it to distraction. But alas! Now all mirth seems an insult upon my affliction. Let us retire, my dear Lucy, and indulge our sorrows. The noisy crew, you see, are coming upon us.   [*Exeunt.*]

[*A Dance of Prisoners in Chains, etc.*]

SCENE 13 *The condemned hold*

MACHEATH, *in a melancholy posture*

AIR 58.   Happy groves

O cruel, cruel, cruel case!
Must I suffer this disgrace?

AIR 59.   Of all the girls that are so smart

Of all the friends in time of grief,
When threat'ning death looks grimmer,
Not one so sure can bring relief,
As this best friend, a brimmer.[7]   [*Drinks.*]

AIR 60.   Britons strike home

Since I must swing, I scorn, I scorn to wince or whine.   [*Rises.*]

AIR 61.   Chevy Chase

But now again my spirits sink;
I'll raise them high with wine.

                                                    [*Drinks a glass of wine.*]

AIR 62.   To old Sir Simon the King

But valor the stronger grows,
The stronger liquor we're drinking.
And how can we feel our woes,
When we've lost the trouble of thinking?   [*Drinks.*]

AIR 63.   Joy to great Caesar

If thus—A man can die
Much bolder with brandy.

                                                    [*Pours out a bumper of brandy.*]

---

7. Brimming goblet.

AIR 64.   There was an old woman

So I drink off this bumper. And now I can stand the test.
And my comrades shall see, that I die as brave as the best.   [*Drinks.*]

AIR 65.   Did you ever hear of a gallant sailor

But can I leave my pretty hussies,
Without one tear, or tender sigh?

AIR 66.   Why are mine eyes still flowing

Their eyes, their lips, their busses[8]
Recall my love. Ah must I die?

AIR 67.   Green sleeves

Since laws were made for every degree,
To curb vice in others, as well as me,
I wonder we han't better company,
Upon Tyburn Tree!
But gold from law can take out the sting;
And if rich men like us were to swing,
'Twould thin the land, such numbers to string
Upon Tyburn Tree!

JAILER   Some friends of yours, Captain, desire to be admitted. I leave you
together.

SCENE 14

MACHEATH, BEN BUDGE, MATT OF THE MINT

MACHEATH   For my having broke prison, you see, gentlemen, I am ordered
immediate execution. The sheriff's officers, I believe, are now at the door.
That Jemmy Twitcher should peach me, I own surprised me! 'Tis a plain
proof that the world is all alike, and that even our gang can no more trust
one another than other people. Therefore, I beg you, gentlemen, look well
to yourselves, for in all probability you may live some months longer.

MATT   We are heartily sorry, Captain, for your misfortune. But 'tis what
we must all come to.

MACHEATH   Peachum and Lockit, you know, are infamous scoundrels.
Their lives are as much in your power as yours are in theirs. Remember
your dying friend! 'Tis my last request. Bring those villains to the gallows
before you, and I am satisfied.

MATT   We'll do't.

JAILER   Miss Polly and Miss Lucy entreat a word with you.

MACHEATH   Gentlemen, adieu.

SCENE 15

LUCY, MACHEATH, POLLY

MACHEATH   Lucy, my dear Polly, whatsoever hath passed between us is
now at an end. If you are fond of marrying again, the best advice I can

8. Kisses.

give you, is to ship yourselves off for the West Indies,[9] where you'll have a fair chance of getting a husband apiece; or by good luck, two or three, as you like best.

POLLY   How can I support this sight!

LUCY   There is nothing moves one so much as a great man in distress.

AIR 68.   All you that must take a leap

LUCY	*Would I might be hanged!*
POLLY	*And I would so too!*
LUCY	*To be hanged with you.*
POLLY	*My dear, with you.*
MACHEATH	*O leave me to thought! I fear! I doubt!*
	I tremble! I droop! See, my courage is out.
	[Turns up the empty bottle.]
POLLY	*No token of love?*
MACHEATH	*See, my courage is out.*
	[Turns up the empty pot.]
LUCY	*No token of love?*
POLLY	*Adieu.*
LUCY	*Farewell.*
MACHEATH	*But hark! I hear the toll of the bell.*[1]
CHORUS	*Tol de rol lol, etc.*

JAILER   Four women more, Captain, with a child apiece! See, here they come. [*Enter women and children.*]

MACHEATH   What—four wives more! This is too much. Here—tell the sheriff's officers I am ready. [*Exit* MACHEATH *guarded.*]

SCENE 16

To them, enter PLAYER *and* BEGGAR

PLAYER   But, honest friend, I hope you don't intend that Macheath shall be really executed.

BEGGAR   Most certainly, sir. To make the piece perfect, I was for doing strict poetical justice. Macheath is to be hanged; and for the other personages of the drama, the audience must have supposed they were all either hanged or transported.

PLAYER   Why then, friend, this is a downright deep tragedy. The catastrophe is manifestly wrong, for an opera must end happily.

BEGGAR   Your objection, sir, is very just, and is easily removed. For you must allow that in this kind of drama 'tis no matter how absurdly things are brought about. So—you rabble there—run and cry a reprieve. Let the prisoner be brought back to his wives in triumph.

PLAYER   All this we must do, to comply with the taste of the town.

BEGGAR   Through the whole piece you may observe such a similitude of manners in high and low life, that it is difficult to determine whether (in the fashionable vices) the fine gentlemen imitate the gentlemen of the road, or the gentlemen of the road the fine gentlemen. Had the play

---

9. In the sequel to *The Beggar's Opera*, Polly does find a husband in the West Indies, where fortunes could be made.

1. Rung five minutes before the condemned were taken to Tyburn.

remained as I at first intended, it would have carried a most excellent moral. 'Twould have shown that the lower sort of people have their vices in a degree as well as the rich, and that they are punished for them.[2]

SCENE 17

To them, MACHEATH *with rabble, etc.*

MACHEATH   So, it seems, I am not left to my choice, but must have a wife at last. Look ye, my dears, we will have no controversy now. Let us give this day to mirth, and I am sure she who thinks herself my wife will testify her joy by a dance.

ALL   Come, a dance, a dance.

MACHEATH   Ladies, I hope you will give me leave to present a partner to each of you. And (if I may without offense) for this time, I take Polly for mine. [*To* POLLY.] And for life, you slut, for we were really married. As for the rest—But at present keep your own secret.

A DANCE

AIR 69.   Lumps of pudding

> *Thus I stand like the Turk, with his doxies around;*
> *From all sides their glances his passion confound;*
> *For black, brown, and fair, his inconstancy burns,*
> *And the different beauties subdue him by turns;*
> *Each calls forth her charms, to provoke his desires;*
> *Though willing to all, with but one he retires.*
> *But think of this maxim, and put off your sorrow,*
> *The wretch of today may be happy tomorrow.*

CHORUS   *But think of this maxim, etc.*

FINIS

1728

2. *Unlike* the rich.

WILLIAM HOGARTH
1697–1764

William Hogarth was a Londoner born and bred; the life of the city, both high and low, fills all his work. His early life was hard. When his father, a writer and teacher, failed in business, the family was confined to the area of the Fleet, the debtor's prison. Hogarth never forgot "the cruel treatment" of his father by booksellers, and he resolved to make his living without relying on dealers; he would always be aggressively independent. Apprenticed as an engraver, he trained himself to sketch scenes quickly or catch them in memory. He also learned to paint, studying with the Serjeant Painter to the King, Sir James Thornhill, whose daughter he married (late in life Hogarth himself would become Serjeant Painter). Gradually he won a reputation for portraits and conversation pieces—group portraits in which members of a family or assembly interact in a social situation. But his popular fame was forged by sets of pictures that told a story: *A Harlot's Progress* (1731–32), *A Rake's Progress* (1734–35), and *Marriage A-la-Mode* (1743–45). First Hogarth painted these Modern Moral Subjects (as he called them), then prints were made and sold in large editions. He also found new ways to market and protect his work; a copyright bill to ban cheap imitations of prints was known as "Hogarth's Act." Despite this success, however, his ambition to redefine British standards of art led to frustration. The high regard and high prices for continental old masters were too well entrenched to be undermined. Hogarth did not get prestigious commissions, and his *Analysis of Beauty* (1753), an effort to fix "the fluctuating ideas of taste" by appealing to practical observations, not academic rules, was poorly received. Political and aesthetic controversies embittered his final years.

Writers have always loved Hogarth's satiric art, and many have claimed him as one of their own. Swift, Fielding, and Sterne associated their work with his; Horace Walpole considered him more "a writer of comedy with a pencil" than a painter; Charles Lamb compared him to Shakespeare; and William Hazlitt included him among the great English comic writers. This emphasis may slight Hogarth's importance in the history of art. His attempts to found a British school that looked at life and nature directly, not through a haze of ideas or reverence for the past, and to give pleasure to common people, not only to critics and connoisseurs, opened the eyes of many artists to come. But Hogarth is also a great storyteller, someone to *read*. Like novels and plays, his pictures have plots and morals; they ask us not only to look but also to think. Yet looking and thinking are always intertwined. The mind delights in riddles, according to Hogarth; and as he revised his work he stuffed in more and more clues, like a mystery writer. A feast of interpretation draws the reader in. So many expressive details crowd the pictures, so many keys to character and meaning, that viewers often become obsessed with figuring them out. Even inanimate objects can speak; playwrights rely on words, as Walpole pointed out, but "it was reserved to Hogarth to write a scene of furniture."

The furniture is particularly eloquent in *Marriage A-la-Mode*; note, for example, the fallen chairs in Plates 2 and 6. Hogarth took special pains with this series. The audience at which he aimed, as well as the subject matter, belonged to high society; and the art too is highly refined. A sinuous line weaves through each picture, leading the reader on, and each piece of bric-a-brac carries a message of lavish excess. Yet the story itself is brutally straightforward. A disastrous forced marriage stands at the center: a rich but miserly merchant buys the worthless son of an aristocrat for his restless daughter, and with nothing in common the couple destroy one another. The crisis of values that Hogarth depicts was bringing about radical changes in English life. In the tension between a fading aristocracy, both morally and financially bankrupt, and an upwardly mobile middle class, greedy for power but culturally insecure, the marriage reflects a society that has lost all sense of right and wrong. The artist plays no favorites. The aristocratic Squanderfields are not only vain, effete, and dissipated but also lacking in taste; the wan mythological paintings on their walls are just the sort of pretentious, overpriced art that Hogarth hates. But the vulgar Dutch art on the merchant's walls (in Plate 6) seems even worse, and his daughter falls for every extravagant, spurious fashion (in Plate 4). Nor do the parasites who live off these easy marks offer any hope. Lawyer and doctor, bawd and servant pave the road to ruin. Hogarth's satire warns against the spreading corruption of modern times, when self-interest eats into marriage and old values die. Look hard, he tells the public. These objects make up the world we live in. We might become these people.

Many commentaries have been written on Hogarth's pictures. The notes printed here were supplied by the editors of this volume.

Marriage A-la-Mode

Plate 1. *The Marriage Contract*.   Lord Squanderfield points to the family tree, going back to William the Conquerer, that his son will bring to the marriage. Coronets are blazed all over the room, from the top of the canopy at the upper left to the side of the prostrate dog on the lower right. The earl, though hobbled by gout, is proud. But he has run out of money: construction has stopped on the Palladian mansion seen through the window. Sitting across from him, a squinting merchant grasps the marriage settlement. Some of the coins and banknotes he has placed on the table have been taken up by a scrawny usurer, who hands the earl a mortgage in return. At the right the betrothed sit back to back, uncaring as the dogs chained to each other below. The vacuous viscount pinches snuff and gazes at himself in a mirror, which ominously reflects the image of lawyer Silvertongue, who sharpens his pen as he bends unctuously over the bride-to-be. Pouting, she twirls her wedding ring in a handkerchief. Disasters from mythology cover the walls. A bombastic portrait of the earl as Jupiter, astride a cannon, dominates the room; and in a candle sconce on the right Medusa glowers over the scene.

Plate 2. *After the Marriage*.   By now the couple are used to ignoring each other. The morning after a spree, the rumpled, exhausted viscount slouches in a chair. His broken sword has dropped on the carpet, and a lapdog sniffs at a woman's cap in his pocket—souvenirs of the night. Lolling and stretching in an unladylike pose, his wife too is half asleep. She has spent the night home but not alone. *Hoyle on Whist* lies before her, cards are scattered on the floor, and the overturned chair, book of music, and violin cases suggest that some player may have departed in haste. A steward carries away a sheaf of bills—only one paid—and the household ledger; a Methodist (*Regeneration* is in his pocket), he petitions heaven to look down on these heathens. Oriental idols decorate the mantel over the fireplace, surmounted by a broken-nosed Roman bust that frowns like the steward and a painting of Cupid playing the bagpipes. On the left, amid the shrubbery of a rococo clock, a cat leers over fish and a Buddha smiles. In the next room, a dozing servant fails to notice that a candle has set fire to a chair. Next to a row of saints, a curtain does not quite cover a bawdy painting from which a naked foot peeps.

Plate 3. *The Scene with the Quack*.   The husband has come to this chamber of medical horrors in search of a cure. The pillbox he holds toward the quack has not done its job, and he raises his cane as if with a playful threat. Evidently the little girl who stands between his legs is infected. She dabs a sore on her lip, and her ageless face may hint that she is not as young and pure as she looks. Her cap resembles the cap in Plate 2; she is the husband's mistress. Perhaps the beauty spot on his neck also covers a sore. The bowlegged Monsieur de la Pillule comfortably wipes his glasses; he has seen all this before. Between the two men an angry woman, fortified by a massive hoop skirt, opens a knife. She may be the wife of the quack, defending her man, or else a bawd who resents the charge that her girls are damaged goods. Medical oddities and monstrosities clutter the room, along with portents of death. The viscount's cane points to a cabinet where a wigged head looks at a skeleton that seems to be groping a cadaver; the tripod above evokes a gallows tree. At the far left, in front of a laboratory door, are two of the doctor's inventions: machines for setting bones and uncorking bottles. Their similarity to instruments of torture hints at how useful the doctor's assistance will be.

Plate 4. ***The Countess's Levee.*** In her bedchamber at rising (*levée;* French), the countess receives some guests and puts on a show. Her husband is now earl (note the coronets), and they have a child (note the rattle on her chair). While a hairdresser curls her locks, she hangs on the words of Silvertongue, who makes himself at home (note his portrait on the upper right wall). Tonight they will be going to a masquerade ball, like the one on the screen he gestures toward; his left hand holds the tickets. At the far right a puffy, bedizened castrato sings, accompanied by a flute. His audience includes a self-absorbed dandy in curl-papers; a man who appreciatively smirks and opens his hand, from which a fan dangles; a snoring husband, holding his riding-crop like a baton; and his enraptured wife, who leans forward as if about to swoon. Unobserved by the others, a black servant, bearing a cup of chocolate, smiles in amazement at these precious airs. At the lower left another black servant, a boy in a turban, grins at gewgaws purchased at an auction. His finger points both to Actaeon's horns, the sign of a cuckold, and to the couple as they arrange their tryst. Wall paintings illustrate unnatural sex: Lot's seduction by his daughters, Jupiter embracing Io, and the rape of Ganymede.

Plate 5. *The Death of the Earl*. The melodramatic tableau at the center, as the earl totters toward death and the countess kneels to beg forgiveness, imitates paintings of Christ descending from the cross while Mary Magdalen mourns. But the surroundings are sordid. At a house of ill repute, the Turk's Head Bagnio, the countess and Silvertongue have been surprised in bed. The earl has broken in (key and socket on the floor) and drawn his sword, and the lawyer has run him through. As the horrified owner and constable enter, under a watchman's lantern, the killer, still in his nightshirt, flees through a window. A fire, outside the picture on the lower right, casts lurid light on the victim; the shadow of the tongs encircles the murder weapon. Costumed as a nun and friar, the lovers have come from a masquerade, and their discarded masks and clothes show they were in haste. Pills (presumably mercury, prescribed for venereal disease) have spilled from an overturned table on the right, beside an advertisement for the bagnio, a corset, and a bundle of firewood. The portrait of a streetwalker, a squirrel perched on her hand, leers over the countess; on the wall behind the earl an uplifted blade is about to sever a child, in the Judgment of Solomon. At the top left St. Luke, the patron of artists, inscribes these transgressions.

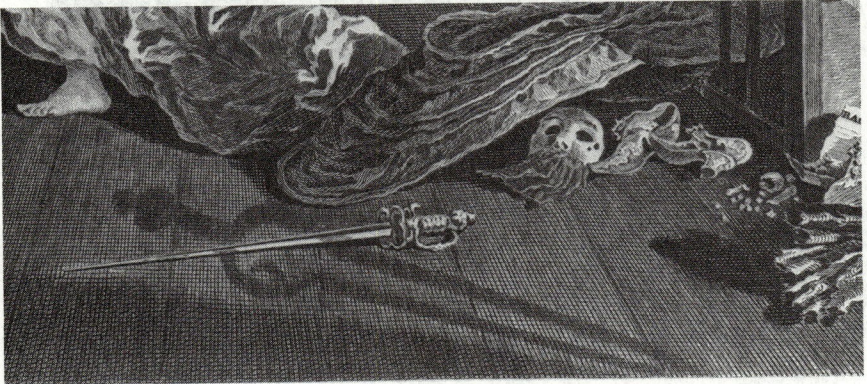

Plate 6. *The Death of the Countess*. "Counseller Silvertongues Last Dying Speech," a paper on the floor announces, and a bottle of laudanum has dropped beside it. News of her lover's execution has driven the countess to poison herself. Slumped in a chair, she is already dead; on the far right a doctor steals away. Her father calmly slides the ring from her finger. This is his house; a window with cobwebs and broken panes opens on London Bridge, in the heart of the City. No luxury here. The furnishings are sparse, the floor is bare, and the dining table holds only one egg and a few leftovers, including a pathetic boar's head from which a starving hound is tearing scraps. The art is equally cheap: a pissing boy, a jumbled still life, a pipe set alight by the glowing nose of a drunk. At the center, beneath a coatrack, a stout apothecary (stomach pump and julep in his pocket) points toward the empty bottle in reproof and pokes the servant who brought it—an idiot wearing a coat many sizes too large, the merchant's hand-me-down. The service staff is completed by a withered old woman who holds out the countess's little child for one last hug and kiss. But the mark on the child's cheek and the brace on its leg imply that disease has passed to the next generation. This noble family will have no heir.

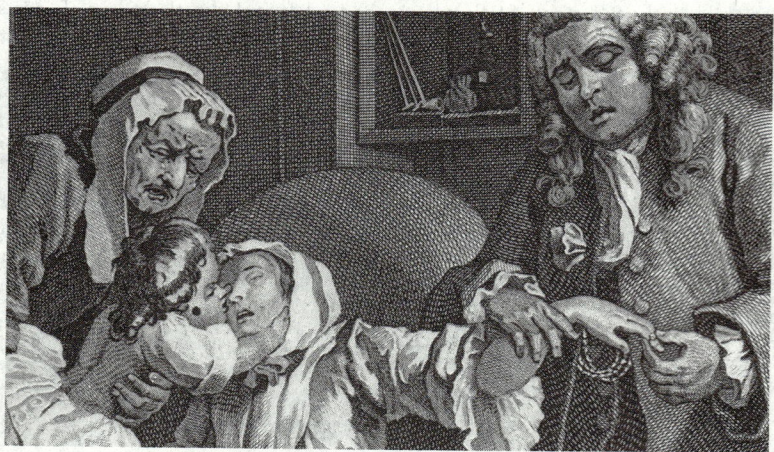

SAMUEL JOHNSON
1709–1784

Samuel Johnson was famous as a talker in his own time, and his conversation (preserved by James Boswell and others) has been famous ever since. But his wisdom survives above all in his writings: a few superb poems; the grave *Rambler* essays, which established his reputation as a stylist and a moralist; the lessons about life in *Rasselas* and the *Lives of the Poets*; and literary criticism that ranks among the best in English. The virtues of the talk and the writings are the same. They come hot from a mind well stored with knowledge, searingly honest, humane, and quick to seize the unexpected but appropriate image of truth. Johnson's wit is timeless, for it deals with the great facts of human experience, with hope and happiness and loss and duty and the fear of death. Whatever topic he addresses, whatever the form in which he writes, he holds to one commanding purpose: to see life as it is.

Two examples must suffice here. When Anna Williams wondered why a man should make a beast of himself through drunkenness, Johnson answered that "he who makes a beast of himself gets rid of the pain of being a man." In this reply Williams's tired metaphor is so charged with an awareness of the dark aspects of human life that it comes almost unbearably alive. Such moments characterize Johnson's writings as well. For instance, in reviewing the book of a fatuous would-be philosopher who blandly explained away the pains of poverty by declaring that a kindly providence compensates the poor by making them more hopeful, more healthy, more easily pleased, and less sensitive than the rich, Johnson retorted: "The poor indeed are insensible of many little vexations which sometimes embitter the possessions and pollute the enjoyments of the rich. They are not pained by casual incivility, or mortified by the mutilation of a compliment; but this happiness is like that of a malefactor who ceases to feel the cords that bind him when the pincers are tearing his flesh."

Johnson had himself known the pains of poverty. During his boyhood and youth in Lichfield, his father's bookshop and other businesses plunged into debt, so that he was forced to leave Oxford before he had taken a degree. An early marriage to a well-to-do widow, Elizabeth ("Tetty") Porter, more than twenty years older than he, enabled him to open a school. But the school failed, and he moved to London to make his way as a writer. The years between 1737, when he first arrived there with his pupil David Garrick (who later became the leading actor of his generation), and 1755, when the publication of the *Dictionary* established his reputation, were often difficult. He supported himself at first as best he could by doing hack work for the *Gentleman's Magazine*, but gradually his own original writings began to attract attention.

In 1747 Johnson published the Plan of his *Dictionary*, and he spent the next seven years compiling it—although he had expected to finish it in three. When in 1748 Dr. Adams, a friend from Oxford days, questioned his ability to carry out such a work alone so fast and reminded him that the *Dictionary* of the French Academy had needed forty academicians working for forty years, Johnson replied with humorous jingoism: "Sir, thus it is. This is the proportion. Let me see; forty times forty is sixteen hundred. As three to sixteen hundred, so is the proportion of an Englishman to a Frenchman."

Johnson's achievement in compiling the *Dictionary* seems even greater when we realize that he was writing some of his best essays and poems during the same period. Although the booksellers who published the *Dictionary* paid him what was then the large sum of £1575, it was not enough to enable him to support his household, buy materials, and pay the wages of the six assistants whom he employed year by year until the task was accomplished. He therefore had to earn more money by writing. In 1749, his early tragedy *Irene* (pronounced *I-re-nĕ*) was produced at long last by his old friend Garrick, by then the manager of Drury Lane. The play was not a success, although Johnson made some profit from it. In the same year appeared his finest poem, "The Vanity of Human Wishes." With the *Rambler* (1750–52) and the *Idler* (1758–60), two series of periodical essays, Johnson found a devoted audience, but his pleasure was tempered by the death of his wife in 1752. He never remarried.

Boswell said of the *Rambler* essays that "in no writings whatever can be found more bark and steel [i.e., quinine and iron] for the mind." Moral strength and health; the importance of applying reason to experience; the test of virtue by what we do, not what we say or "feel"; faith in God: these are the centers to which Johnson's moral writings always return. What Johnson uniquely offers us is the quality of his understanding of the human condition, based on wide reading but always ultimately referred to his own passionate and often anguished experience. Such understanding had to be fought for again and again.

Johnson is thought of as the great generalizer, but what gives his generalizations strength is that they are rooted in the particulars of his self-knowledge. He had constantly to fight against what he called "filling the mind" with illusions to avoid the call of duty, his own black melancholy, and the realities of life. The portrait (largely a self-portrait) of Sober in *Idler* 31 is revealing: he occupies his idle hours with crafts and hobbies and has now taken up chemistry—he "sits and counts the drops as they come from his retort, and forgets that, whilst a drop is falling, a moment flies away."

His theme of themes is expressed in the title "The Vanity of Human Wishes": the dangerous but all-pervasive power of wishful thinking, the feverish intrusion of desires and hopes that distort reality and lead to false expectations. Almost all of Johnson's major writings—verse satire, moral essay, or the prose fable *Rasselas* (1759)—express this theme. In *Rasselas* it is called "the hunger of imagination, which preys upon life," picturing things as one would like them to be, not as they are. The travelers who are the fable's protagonists pursue some formula for happiness; they reflect our naive hope, against the lessons of experience, that one choice of life will make us happy forever.

Johnson also developed a style of his own: balanced, extended sentences, phrases, or clauses moving to carefully controlled rhythms, in language that is characteristically general, often Latinate, and frequently polysyllabic. This style is far from Swift's simplicity or Addison's neatness, but it never becomes obscure or turgid, for even a very complex sentence reveals—as it should—the structure of the thought, and the learned words are always precisely used. While reading early scientists to collect words for the *Dictionary*, Johnson developed a new vocabulary: for example, *obtund, exuberate, fugacity,* and *frigorific.* But he used many of these strange words in conversation as well as in his writings, often with a peculiarly Johnsonian felicity, describing the operations of the mind with a scientific precision.

After Johnson received his pension in 1762, he no longer had to write for a living, and because he held that "no man but a blockhead" ever wrote for any other reason, he produced as little as he decently could during the last twenty years of his life. His edition of Shakespeare, long delayed, was published in 1765, with a fine preface and fascinating notes. His last important work is the *Lives of the Poets,* which came out in two parts in 1779 and 1781. These biographical and critical prefaces were commissioned by a group of booksellers who had joined together to publish a large collection of the English poets and who wished to give their venture the prestige that Johnson would lend it. The poets to be included (except for four insisted on by Johnson) were selected by the booksellers according to current fashions. Therefore the collection begins with Abraham Cowley and John Milton and ends with Thomas Gray, and it omits such standard poets as Chaucer, Spenser, Sidney, Donne, and Marvell.

In the *Lives of the Poets* and in the earlier *Life of Richard Savage* (1744), Johnson did much to advance the art of biography in England. Biography had long been associated with panegyrics or scandalous memoirs; and therefore, Johnson's insistence on truth, even about the subject's defects, and on concrete, often minute, details was a new departure. "The biographical part of literature is what I love most," Johnson said, for he found every biography useful in revealing the human nature that all of us share. His insistence on truth in biography (and knowing that Boswell intended to write his life, he insisted that he should write it truthfully) was owing to his conviction that only a truthful work can be trusted to help us with the business of living.

The ideal poet, according to Johnson, has a genius for making the things we see every day seem new. The same might be said of Johnson himself as a critic. Johnson is our great champion, in criticism, of common sense and the common reader. Without denying the right of the poet to flights of imagination, he also insists that poems must make sense, please readers, and help us not only understand the world but cope with it. Johnson holds poems to the truth, as he sees it: the principles of nature, logic, religion, and morality. Not even Shakespeare can be excused when "he sacrifices virtue to convenience" and "seems to write without any moral purpose." Yet Johnson is no worshiper of authority or mere "correctness." As a critic he is always the empiricist, testing theory by practice. His determination to judge literature by its truth to life, not by abstract rules, is perfectly illustrated by his treatment of the doctrine of the three unities in the Preface to Shakespeare. Johnson is never afraid to state the obvious, whether the lack of human interest in *Paradise Lost* or Shakespeare's temptation by puns. But at its best, as in the praise of Milton or Shakespeare, his criticism engages some of the deepest questions about literature: why it endures, and how it helps us endure.

The Vanity of Human Wishes

This poem is an imitation of Juvenal's *Satire 10*. Although it closely follows the order and the ideas of the Latin poem, it remains a very personal work, for Johnson has used the Roman Stoic's satire as a means of expressing his own sense of the tragic and comic in human life. He has tried to reproduce in English verse the qualities he thought especially Juvenalian: stateliness, pointed sentences, and declamatory grandeur. The poem is difficult because of the extreme compactness of the style: every line is forced to convey the greatest possible amount of meaning. Johnson believed that "great thoughts are always general," but he certainly did not intend that the general should fade into the abstract: observe, for example, how he makes personified nouns concrete, active, and dramatic by using them as subjects of active and dramatic verbs: "Hate *dogs* their flight, and Insult *mocks* their end" (line 78). But the difficulty of the poem is also related to its theme, the difficulty of seeing anything clearly on this earth. In a world of blindness and illusion, human beings must struggle to find a point of view that will not deceive them, and a happiness that can last.

The Vanity of Human Wishes

In Imitation of the Tenth Satire of Juvenal

Let Observation, with extensive view,
Survey mankind, from China to Peru;
Remark each anxious toil, each eager strife,
And watch the busy scenes of crowded life;
5   Then say how hope and fear, desire and hate
O'erspread with snares the clouded maze of fate,

Where wavering man, betrayed by venturous Pride
To tread the dreary paths without a guide,
As treacherous phantoms in the mist delude,
10 Shuns fancied ills, or chases airy good.
How rarely Reason guides the stubborn choice,
Rules the bold hand, or prompts the suppliant voice;
How nations sink, by darling schemes oppressed,
When Vengeance listens to the fool's request.
15 Fate wings with every wish the afflictive dart,
Each gift of nature, and each grace of art;
With fatal heat impetuous courage glows,
With fatal sweetness elocution flows,
Impeachment stops the speaker's powerful breath,
20 And restless fire precipitates on death.
   But scarce observed, the knowing and the bold
Fall in the general massacre of gold;
Wide-wasting pest! that rages unconfined,
And crowds with crimes the records of mankind;
25 For gold his sword the hireling ruffian draws,
For gold the hireling judge distorts the laws;
Wealth heaped on wealth, nor truth nor safety buys,
The dangers gather as the treasures rise.
   Let History tell where rival kings command,
30 And dubious title° shakes the madded land,   *claim of right*
When statutes glean the refuse of the sword,
How much more safe the vassal than the lord;
Low skulks the hind° beneath the rage of power,   *peasant*
And leaves the wealthy traitor in the Tower,[1]
35 Untouched his cottage, and his slumbers sound,
Though Confiscation's vultures hover round.
   The needy traveler, serene and gay,
Walks the wild heath, and sings his toil away.
Does envy seize thee? crush the upbraiding joy,
40 Increase his riches and his peace destroy;
New fears in dire vicissitude invade,
The rustling brake° alarms, and quivering shade,   *thicket*
Nor light nor darkness bring his pain relief,
One shows the plunder, and one hides the thief.
45   Yet still one general cry the skies assails,
And gain and grandeur load the tainted gales;
Few know the toiling statesman's fear or care,
The insidious rival and the gaping heir.
   Once more, Democritus,[2] arise on earth,
50 With cheerful wisdom and instructive mirth,
See motley life in modern trappings dressed,
And feed with varied fools the eternal jest:
Thou who couldst laugh where Want enchained Caprice,
Toil crushed Conceit, and man was of a piece;

---

1. I.e., the Tower of London, which served as a prison. Johnson first wrote "bonny traitor," recalling the Jacobite uprising of 1745 and the execution of four of its Scot leaders.

2. A Greek philosopher of the late 5th century B.C.E., remembered as the "laughing philosopher" because men's follies only moved him to mirth.

55 Where Wealth unloved without a mourner died;
And scarce a sycophant was fed by Pride;
Where ne'er was known the form of mock debate,
Or seen a new-made mayor's unwieldy state;[3]
Where change of favorites made no change of laws,

60 And senates heard before they judged a cause;
How wouldst thou shake at Britain's modish tribe,
Dart the quick taunt, and edge the piercing gibe?
Attentive truth and nature to descry,
And pierce each scene with philosophic eye.

65 To thee were solemn toys or empty show
The robes of pleasure and the veils of woe:
All aid the farce, and all thy mirth maintain,
Whose joys are causeless, or whose griefs are vain.
    Such was the scorn that filled the sage's mind,

70 Renewed at every glance on human kind;
How just that scorn ere yet thy voice declare,
Search every state, and canvass every prayer.
    Unnumbered suppliants crowd Preferment's gate,
Athirst for wealth, and burning to be great;

75 Delusive Fortune hears the incessant call,
They mount, they shine, evaporate,[4] and fall.
On every stage the foes of peace attend,
Hate dogs their flight, and Insult mocks their end.
Love ends with hope, the sinking statesman's door

80 Pours in the morning worshiper no more;[5]
For growing names the weekly scribbler lies,
To growing wealth the dedicator flies;
From every room descends the painted face,
That hung the bright palladium[6] of the place;

85 And smoked in kitchens, or in auctions sold,
To better features yields the frame of gold;
For now no more we trace in every line
Heroic worth, benevolence divine:
The form distorted justifies the fall,

90 And Detestation rids the indignant wall.
    But will not Britain hear the last appeal,
Sign her foes' doom, or guard her favorites' zeal?
Through Freedom's sons no more remonstrance rings,
Degrading nobles and controlling kings;

95 Our supple tribes repress their patriot throats,
And ask no questions but the price of votes;
With weekly libels and septennial ale,[7]
Their wish is full to riot and to rail.

---

3. Pomp. Mayors organized costly processions.
4. Disperse in vapors, like fireworks.
5. Statesmen gave interviews and received friends and petitioners at levees, or morning receptions.
6. An image of Pallas Athena, that fell from heaven and was preserved at Troy. Not until it was stolen by Diomedes could the city fall to the Greeks.

7. Ministers and even the king freely bought support by bribing members of Parliament, who in turn won elections by buying votes. "Weekly libels": politically motivated lampoons published in the weekly newspapers. "Septennial ale": the ale given away by candidates at parliamentary elections, held at least every seven years.

In full-blown dignity, see Wolsey[8] stand,
100　Law in his voice, and fortune in his hand:
To him the church, the realm, their powers consign,
Through him the rays of regal bounty shine;
Turned by his nod the stream of honor flows,
His smile alone security bestows:
105　Still to new heights his restless wishes tower,
Claim leads to claim, and power advances power;
Till conquest unresisted ceased to please,
And rights submitted, left him none to seize.
At length his sovereign frowns—the train of state
110　Mark the keen glance, and watch the sign to hate.
Where'er he turns, he meets a stranger's eye,
His suppliants scorn him, and his followers fly;
At once is lost the pride of awful state,
The golden canopy, the glittering plate,
115　The regal palace, the luxurious board,
The liveried army, and the menial lord.
With age, with cares, with maladies oppressed,
He seeks the refuge of monastic rest.
Grief aids disease, remembered folly stings,
120　And his last sighs reproach the faith of kings.
　　　Speak thou, whose thoughts at humble peace repine,
Shall Wolsey's wealth, with Wolsey's end be thine?
Or liv'st thou now, with safer pride content,
The wisest justice on the banks of Trent?
125　For why did Wolsey, near the steeps of fate,
On weak foundations raise the enormous weight?
Why but to sink beneath misfortune's blow,
With louder ruin to the gulfs below?
　　　What gave great Villiers[9] to the assassin's knife,
130　And fixed disease on Harley's closing life?
What murdered Wentworth, and what exiled Hyde,
By kings protected, and to kings allied?
What but their wish indulged in courts to shine,
And power too great to keep or to resign?
135　　　When first the college rolls receive his name,
The young enthusiast quits his ease for fame;
Through all his veins the fever of renown
Burns from the strong contagion of the gown:[1]
O'er Bodley's dome his future labors spread,
140　And Bacon's[2] mansion trembles o'er his head.

---

8. Thomas Cardinal Wolsey (ca. 1475–1530), lord chancellor and favorite of Henry VIII. Shakespeare dramatized his fall in *Henry VIII*.
9. George Villiers, first duke of Buckingham, favorite of James I and Charles I, was assassinated in 1628. Mentioned in the following lines: Robert Harley, earl of Oxford, chancellor of the exchequer and later lord treasurer under Queen Anne (1710–14), impeached and imprisoned by the Whigs in 1715. Thomas Wentworth, earl of Strafford, intimate and adviser of Charles I, impeached by the Long Parliament and executed

in 1641. Edward Hyde, earl of Clarendon ("to kings allied" because his daughter married James, duke of York), lord chancellor under Charles II (impeached in 1667, he fled to the Continent).
1. Academic robe; here associated with the poisoned shirt that tormented Hercules.
2. Roger Bacon (ca. 1214–1294), scientist and philosopher, taught at Oxford, where his study, according to tradition, would collapse if a man greater than he should appear at Oxford. "Bodley's dome": the Bodleian Library, Oxford.

Are these thy views? proceed, illustrious youth,
And Virtue guard thee to the throne of Truth!
Yet should thy soul indulge the generous heat,
Till captive Science° yields her last retreat;   *knowledge*
145 Should Reason guide thee with her brightest ray,
And pour on misty Doubt resistless day;
Should no false kindness lure to loose delight,
Nor praise relax, nor difficulty fright;
Should tempting Novelty thy cell refrain,
150 And Sloth effuse her opiate fumes in vain;
Should Beauty blunt on fops her fatal dart,
Nor claim the triumph of a lettered heart;
Should no disease thy torpid veins invade,
Nor Melancholy's phantoms haunt thy shade;
155 Yet hope not life from grief or danger free,
Nor think the doom of man reversed for thee:
Deign on the passing world to turn thine eyes,
And pause a while from letters, to be wise;
There mark what ills the scholar's life assail,
160 Toil, envy, want, the patron,[3] and the jail.
See nations slowly wise, and meanly just,
To buried merit raise the tardy bust.
If dreams yet flatter, once again attend,
Hear Lydiat's life, and Galileo's[4] end.
165   Nor deem, when Learning her last prize bestows,
The glittering eminence exempt from foes;
See when the vulgar 'scapes, despised or awed,
Rebellion's vengeful talons seize on Laud.[5]
From meaner minds, though smaller fines content,
170 The plundered palace or sequestered rent;[6]
Marked out by dangerous parts° he meets   *accomplishments*
     the shock,
And fatal Learning leads him to the block:
Around his tomb let Art and Genius weep,
But hear his death, ye blockheads, hear and sleep.
175   The festal blazes, the triumphal show,
The ravished standard, and the captive foe,
The senate's thanks, the gazette's pompous tale,
With force resistless o'er the brave prevail.
Such bribes the rapid Greek° o'er Asia whirled, *Alexander the Great*
180 For such the steady Romans shook the world;
For such in distant lands the Britons shine,
And stain with blood the Danube or the Rhine;
This power has praise that virtue scarce can warm,
Till fame supplies the universal charm.
185 Yet Reason frowns on War's unequal game,

3. In the first edition, "garret." For the reason of the change see Boswell's *Life of Johnson* (p. 2971).
4. Famous astronomer (1564–1642) who was imprisoned as a heretic by the Inquisition in 1633; he died blind. Thomas Lydiat (1572–1646), Oxford scholar, died impoverished because of his Royalist sympathies.

5. Appointed archbishop of Canterbury by Charles I, William Laud followed rigorously High Church policies and was executed by order of the Long Parliament in 1645.
6. During the Commonwealth, the estates of many Royalists were pillaged and their incomes confiscated ("sequestered") by the state.

Where wasted nations raise a single name,
And mortgaged states their grandsires' wreaths regret
From age to age in everlasting debt;
Wreaths which at last the dear-bought right convey
190 To rust on medals, or on stones decay.
　　On what foundation stands the warrior's pride?
How just his hopes, let Swedish Charles[7] decide;
A frame of adamant, a soul of fire,
No dangers fright him, and no labors tire;
195 O'er love, o'er fear, extends his wide domain,
Unconquered lord of pleasure and of pain;
No joys to him pacific scepters yield,
War sounds the trump, he rushes to the field;
Behold surrounding kings their powers combine,
200 And one capitulate, and one resign;[8]
Peace courts his hand, but spreads her charms in vain;
"Think nothing gained," he cries, "till naught remain,
On Moscow's walls till Gothic standards fly,
And all be mine beneath the polar sky."
205 The march begins in military state,
And nations on his eye suspended wait;
Stern Famine guards the solitary coast,
And Winter barricades the realms of Frost;
He comes, nor want nor cold his course delay—
210 Hide, blushing Glory, hide Pultowa's day:
The vanquished hero leaves his broken bands,
And shows his miseries in distant lands;
Condemned a needy supplicant to wait,
While ladies interpose, and slaves debate.
215 But did not Chance at length her error mend?
Did no subverted empire mark his end?
Did rival monarchs give the fatal wound?
Or hostile millions press him to the ground?
His fall was destined to a barren strand,
220 A petty fortress, and a dubious hand;[9]
He left the name at which the world grew pale,
To point a moral, or adorn a tale.
　　All times their scenes of pompous woes afford,
From Persia's tyrant to Bavaria's lord.[1]
225 In gay hostility, and barbarous pride,
With half mankind embattled at his side,
Great Xerxes comes to seize the certain prey,
And starves exhausted regions in his way;
Attendant Flattery counts his myriads o'er,

---

7. Charles XII of Sweden (1682–1718). Defeated by the Russians at Pultowa (1709), he escaped to Turkey and tried to form an alliance against Russia with the sultan. Returning to Sweden, he attacked Norway and was killed in the attack on Fredrikshald.
8. Frederick IV of Denmark capitulated to Charles in 1700. Augustus II of Poland resigned his throne to Charles in 1704.

9. It was disputed whether Charles was shot by the enemy or by his own aide-de-camp.
1. The Elector Charles Albert caused the War of the Austrian Succession (1740–48) when he contested the crown of the empire with Maria Theresa ("Fair Austria" in line 245). "Persia's tyrant": Xerxes invaded Greece and was totally defeated in the sea battle off Salamis, 480 B.C.E.

230　Till counted myriads soothe his pride no more;
　　Fresh praise is tried till madness fires his mind,
　　The waves he lashes, and enchains the wind;[2]
　　New powers are claimed, new powers are still bestowed,
　　Till rude resistance lops the spreading god;
235　The daring Greeks deride the martial show,
　　And heap their valleys with the gaudy foe;
　　The insulted sea with humbler thoughts he gains,
　　A single skiff to speed his flight remains;
　　The encumbered oar scarce leaves the dreaded coast
240　Through purple billows and a floating host.
　　　　The bold Bavarian, in a luckless hour,
　　Tries the dread summits of Caesarean power,
　　With unexpected legions bursts away,
　　And sees defenseless realms receive his sway;
245　Short sway! fair Austria spreads her mournful charms,
　　The queen, the beauty, sets the world in arms;
　　From hill to hill the beacon's rousing blaze
　　Spreads wide the hope of plunder and of praise;
　　The fierce Croatian, and the wild Hussar,[3]
250　With all the sons of ravage crowd the war;
　　The baffled prince in honor's flattering bloom
　　Of hasty greatness finds the fatal doom,
　　His foes' derision, and his subjects' blame,
　　And steals to death from anguish and from shame.
255　　　Enlarge my life with multitude of days!
　　In health, in sickness, thus the suppliant prays;
　　Hides from himself his state, and shuns to know,
　　That life protracted is protracted woe.
　　Time hovers o'er, impatient to destroy,
260　And shuts up all the passages of joy;
　　In vain their gifts the bounteous seasons pour,
　　The fruit autumnal, and the vernal flower;
　　With listless eyes the dotard views the store,
　　He views, and wonders that they please no more;
265　Now pall the tasteless meats, and joyless wines,
　　And Luxury with sighs her slave resigns.
　　Approach, ye minstrels, try the soothing strain,
　　Diffuse the tuneful lenitives of pain:°　　　　　　　　*painkillers*
　　No sounds, alas! would touch the impervious ear,
270　Though dancing mountains witnessed Orpheus[4] near;
　　Nor lute nor lyre his feeble powers attend,
　　Nor sweeter music of a virtuous friend,
　　But everlasting dictates crowd his tongue,
　　Perversely grave, or positively wrong.
275　The still returning tale, and lingering jest,
　　Perplex the fawning niece and pampered guest,
　　While growing hopes scarce awe the gathering sneer,

2. When storms destroyed Xerxes' boats, he commanded his men to punish the wind and sea.
3. Hungarian light cavalry.
4. A legendary poet who played on the lyre so beautifully that even stones were moved.

And scarce a legacy can bribe to hear;
The watchful guests still hint the last offense,
280 The daughter's petulance, the son's expense,
Improve° his heady rage with treacherous skill,   *increase*
And mold his passions till they make his will.
    Unnumbered maladies his joints invade,
Lay siege to life and press the dire blockade;
285 But unextinguished avarice still remains,
And dreaded losses aggravate his pains;
He turns, with anxious heart and crippled hands,
His bonds of debt, and mortgages of lands;
Or views his coffers with suspicious eyes,
290 Unlocks his gold, and counts it till he dies.
    But grant, the virtues of a temperate prime
Bless with an age exempt from scorn or crime;
An age that melts with unperceived decay,
And glides in modest innocence away;
295 Whose peaceful day Benevolence endears,
Whose night congratulating Conscience cheers;
The general favorite as the general friend:
Such age there is, and who shall wish its end?
    Yet even on this her load Misfortune flings,
300 To press the weary minutes' flagging wings;
New sorrow rises as the day returns,
A sister sickens, or a daughter mourns.
Now kindred Merit fills the sable bier,
Now lacerated Friendship claims a tear;
305 Year chases year, decay pursues decay,
Still drops some joy from withering life away;
New forms arise, and different views engage,
Superfluous lags the veteran[5] on the stage,
Till pitying Nature signs the last release,
310 And bids afflicted Worth retire to peace.
    But few there are whom hours like these await,
Who set unclouded in the gulfs of Fate.
From Lydia's monarch[6] should the search descend,
By Solon cautioned to regard his end,
315 In life's last scene what prodigies surprise,
Fears of the brave, and follies of the wise!
From Marlborough's eyes the streams of dotage flow,
And Swift[7] expires a driveler and a show.
    The teeming mother, anxious for her race,°   *family*
320 Begs for each birth the fortune of a face:
Yet Vane could tell what ills from beauty spring;
And Sedley[8] cursed the form that pleased a king.
Ye nymphs of rosy lips and radiant eyes,

---

5. I.e., of life, not of war.
6. Croesus, the wealthy and fortunate king, was warned by Solon not to count himself happy until he ceased to live. He lost his crown to Cyrus the Great of Persia.
7. Jonathan Swift, who passed the last four years of his life in utter senility. John Churchill, Duke

of Marlborough, England's brilliant general during most of the War of the Spanish Succession (1702–13).
8. Catherine Sedley, mistress of James II. Anne Vane, mistress of Frederick, Prince of Wales (son of George II).

Whom Pleasure keeps too busy to be wise,
325 Whom Joys with soft varieties invite,
By day the frolic, and the dance by night;
Who frown with vanity, who smile with art,
And ask the latest fashion of the heart;
What care, what rules your heedless charms shall save,
330 Each nymph your rival, and each youth your slave?
Against your fame with Fondness Hate combines,
The rival batters, and the lover mines.[9]
With distant voice neglected Virtue calls,
Less heard and less, the faint remonstrance falls;
335 Tired with contempt, she quits the slippery reign,
And Pride and Prudence take her seat in vain.
In crowd at once, where none the pass defend,
The harmless freedom, and the private friend.
The guardians yield, by force superior plied:
340 To Interest, Prudence; and to Flattery, Pride.
Now Beauty falls betrayed, despised, distressed,
And hissing Infamy proclaims the rest.
     Where then shall Hope and Fear their objects find?
Must dull Suspense° corrupt the stagnant mind?   *uncertainty*
345 Must helpless man, in ignorance sedate,
Roll darkling down the torrent of his fate?
Must no dislike alarm, no wishes rise,
No cries invoke the mercies of the skies?
Inquirer, cease; petitions yet remain,
350 Which Heaven may hear, nor deem religion vain.
Still raise for good the supplicating voice,
But leave to Heaven the measure and the choice.
Safe in his power, whose eyes discern afar
The secret ambush of a specious prayer.
355 Implore his aid, in his decisions rest,
Secure, whate'er he gives, he gives the best.
Yet when the sense of sacred presence fires,
And strong devotion to the skies aspires,
Pour forth thy fervors for a healthful mind,
360 Obedient passions, and a will resigned;
For love, which scarce collective man can fill;[1]
For patience sovereign o'er transmuted ill;
For faith, that panting for a happier seat,
Counts death kind Nature's signal of retreat:
365 These goods for man the laws of Heaven ordain,
These goods he grants, who grants the power to gain;
With these celestial Wisdom calms the mind,
And makes the happiness she does not find.

                                                              1749

---

9. Plants mines beneath, as in the siege of a fortress.

1. Which humankind as a whole can hardly over-task.

Rambler No. 5[1]

[ON SPRING]

TUESDAY, *April* 3, 1750

Et nunc omnis ager, nunc omnis parturit arbos,
Nunc frondent silvae, nunc formosissimus annus.
VIRGIL, *Eclogues* 3.5.56

Now ev'ry field, now ev'ry tree is green;
Now genial nature's fairest face is seen.
ELPHINSTON

Every man is sufficiently discontented with some circumstances of his present state, to suffer his imagination to range more or less in quest of future happiness, and to fix upon some point of time, in which, by the removal of the inconvenience which now perplexes him, or acquisition of the advantage which he at present wants, he shall find the condition of his life very much improved.

When this time, which is too often expected with great impatience, at last arrives, it generally comes without the blessing for which it was desired; but we solace ourselves with some new prospect, and press forward again with equal eagerness.

It is lucky for a man, in whom this temper prevails, when he turns his hopes upon things wholly put of his own power; since he forbears then to precipitate[2] his affairs, for the sake of the great event that is to complete his felicity, and waits for the blissful hour, with less neglect of the measures necessary to be taken in the mean time.

I have long known a person of this temper, who indulged his dream of happiness with less hurt to himself than such chimerical wishes commonly produce, and adjusted his scheme with such address, that his hopes were in full bloom three parts of the year, and in the other part never wholly blasted. Many, perhaps, would be desirous of learning by what means he procured to himself such a cheap and lasting satisfaction. It was gained by a constant practice of referring the removal of all his uneasiness to the coming of the next spring; if his health was impaired, the spring would restore it; if what he wanted was at a high price, it would fall in value in the spring.

The spring, indeed, did often come without any of these effects, but he was always certain that the next would be more propitious; nor was ever convinced that the present spring would fail him before the middle of summer; for he always talked of the spring as coming till it was past, and when it was once past, everyone agreed with him that it was coming.

By long converse with this man, I am, perhaps, brought to feel immoderate pleasure in the contemplation of this delightful season; but I have the satisfaction of finding many, whom it can be no shame to resemble, infected

---

1. The *Rambler*, almost wholly written by Johnson himself, appeared every Tuesday and Saturday from March 20, 1750, to March 14, 1752—years in which Johnson was writing the *Dictionary*. It is a successor of the *Tatler* and the *Spectator*, but it is much more serious in tone than the earlier periodicals. Johnson's reputation as a moralist and a stylist was established by these essays; because of them Boswell first conceived the ambition to seek Johnson's acquaintance.
2. "To hurry blindly or rashly" (Johnson's *Dictionary*).

with the same enthusiasm; for there is, I believe, scarce any poet of eminence, who has not left some testimony of his fondness for the flowers, the zephyrs, and the warblers of the spring. Nor has the most luxuriant imagination been able to describe the serenity and happiness of the golden age, otherwise than by giving a perpetual spring, as the highest reward of uncorrupted innocence.

There is, indeed, something inexpressibly pleasing, in the annual renovation of the world, and the new display of the treasures of nature. The cold and darkness of winter, with the naked deformity of every object on which we turn our eyes, make us rejoice at the succeeding season, as well for what we have escaped, as for what we may enjoy; and every budding flower, which a warm situation brings early to our view, is considered by us as a messenger to notify the approach of more joyous days.

The spring affords to a mind, so free from the disturbance of cares or passions as to be vacant[3] to calm amusements, almost every thing that our present state makes us capable of enjoying. The variegated verdure of the fields and woods, the succession of grateful odors, the voice of pleasure pouring out its notes on every side, with the gladness apparently conceived by every animal, from the growth of his food, and the clemency of the weather, throw over the whole earth an air of gaiety, significantly expressed by the smile of nature.

Yet there are men to whom these scenes are able to give no delight, and who hurry away from all the varieties of rural beauty, to lose their hours, and divert their thoughts by cards, or assemblies, a tavern dinner, or the prattle of the day.

It may be laid down as a position which will seldom deceive, that when a man cannot bear his own company there is something wrong. He must fly from himself, either because he feels a tediousness in life from the equipoise of an empty mind, which, having no tendency to one motion more than another but as it is impelled by some external power, must always have recourse to foreign objects; or he must be afraid of the intrusion of some unpleasing ideas, and, perhaps, is struggling to escape from the remembrance of a loss, the fear of a calamity, or some other thought of greater horror.

Those whom sorrow incapacitates to enjoy the pleasures of contemplation, may properly apply to such diversions, provided they are innocent, as lay strong hold on the attention; and those, whom fear of any future affliction chains down to misery, must endeavor to obviate the danger.

My considerations shall, on this occasion, be turned on such as are burthensome to themselves merely because they want subjects for reflection, and to whom the volume of nature is thrown open, without affording them pleasure or instruction, because they never learned to read the characters.

A French author has advanced this seeming paradox, that *very few men know how to take a walk*; and, indeed, it is true, that few know how to take a walk with a prospect of any other pleasure, than the same company would have afforded them at home.

There are animals that borrow their color from the neighboring body, and, consequently, vary their hue as they happen to change their place. In

---

3. "At leisure" (Johnson's *Dictionary*).

like manner it ought to be the endeavor of every man to derive his reflections from the objects about him; for it is to no purpose that he alters his position, if his attention continues fixed to the same point. The mind should be kept open to the access of every new idea, and so far disengaged from the predominance of particular thoughts, as easily to accommodate itself to occasional entertainment.

A man that has formed this habit of turning every new object to his entertainment, finds in the productions of nature an inexhaustible stock of materials upon which he can employ himself, without any temptations to envy or malevolence; faults, perhaps, seldom totally avoided by those, whose judgment is much exercised upon the works of art. He has always a certain prospect of discovering new reasons for adoring the sovereign author of the universe, and probable hopes of making some discovery of benefit to others, or of profit to himself. There is no doubt but many vegetables and animals have qualities that might be of great use, to the knowledge of which there is not required much force of penetration, or fatigue of study, but only frequent experiments, and close attention. What is said by the chemists of their darling mercury, is, perhaps, true of everybody through the whole creation, that if a thousand lives should be spent upon it, all its properties would not be found out.

Mankind must necessarily be diversified by various tastes, since life affords and requires such multiplicity of employments, and a nation of naturalists[4] is neither to be hoped, or desired; but it is surely not improper to point out a fresh amusement to those who languish in health, and repine in plenty, for want of some source of diversion that may be less easily exhausted, and to inform the multitudes of both sexes, who are burthened with every new day, that there are many shows which they have not seen.

He that enlarges his curiosity after the works of nature, demonstrably multiplies the inlets to happiness; and, therefore, the younger part of my readers, to whom I dedicate this vernal speculation, must excuse me for calling upon them, to make use at once of the spring of the year, and the spring of life; to acquire, while their minds may be yet impressed with new images, a love of innocent pleasures, and an ardor for useful knowledge; and to remember, that a blighted spring makes a barren year, and that the vernal flowers, however beautiful and gay, are only intended by nature as preparatives to autumnal fruits.

Idler No. 31[1]

[ON IDLENESS]

SATURDAY, *November* 18, 1758

Many moralists have remarked, that Pride has of all human vices the widest dominion, appears in the greatest multiplicity of forms, and lies hid under

4. "A student in physicks, or natural philosophy" (Johnson's *Dictionary*).

1. Johnson wrote and published the *Idler*, a peri-

odical similar to the *Rambler*, from 1758 until 1760.

the greatest variety of disguises; of disguises, which, like the moon's *veil of brightness*, are both *its luster and its shade*,[2] and betray it to others, though they hide it from ourselves.

It is not my intention to degrade Pride from this pre-eminence of mischief, yet I know not whether Idleness may not maintain a very doubtful and obstinate competition.

There are some that profess Idleness in its full dignity, who call themselves the Idle, as Busiris in the play "calls himself the Proud";[3] who boast that they do nothing, and thank their stars that they have nothing to do; who sleep every night till they can sleep no longer, and rise only that exercise may enable them to sleep again; who prolong the reign of darkness by double curtains, and never see the sun but to "tell him how they hate his beams";[4] whose whole labor is to vary the postures of indulgence, and whose day differs from their night but as a couch or chair differs from a bed.

These are the true and open votaries of Idleness, for whom she weaves the garlands of poppies, and into whose cup she pours the waters of oblivion; who exist in a state of unruffled stupidity, forgetting and forgotten; who have long ceased to live, and at whose death the survivors can only say, that they have ceased to breathe.

But Idleness predominates in many lives where it is not suspected; for being a vice which terminates in itself, it may be enjoyed without injury to others; and is therefore not watched like Fraud, which endangers property, or like Pride, which naturally seeks its gratifications in another's inferiority. Idleness is a silent and peaceful quality, that neither raises envy by ostentation, nor hatred by opposition; and therefore nobody is busy to censure or detect it.

As Pride sometimes is hid under humility, Idleness is often covered by turbulence and hurry. He that neglects his known duty and real employment, naturally endeavors to crowd his mind with something that may bar out the remembrance of his own folly, and does any thing but what he ought to do with eager diligence, that he may keep himself in his own favor.

Some are always in a state of preparation, occupied in previous measures, forming plans, accumulating materials, and providing for the main affair. These are certainly under the secret power of Idleness. Nothing is to be expected from the workman whose tools are forever to be sought. I was once told by a great master, that no man ever excelled in painting, who was eminently curious about pencils and colors.

There are others to whom Idleness dictates another expedient, by which life may be passed unprofitably away without the tediousness of many vacant hours. The art is, to fill the day with petty business, to have always something in hand which may raise curiosity, but not solicitude, and keep the mind in a state of action, but not of labor.

This art has for many years been practiced by my old friend Sober, with wonderful success. Sober is a man of strong desires and quick imagination, so exactly balanced by the love of ease, that they can seldom stimulate him to any difficult undertaking; they have, however, so much power, that they

---

2. Quoted from Samuel Butler's *Hudibras* 2.1.907–08.

3. Edward Young's *Busiris* (1719) 1.1.13.

4. *Paradise Lost* 4.37.

will not suffer him to lie quite at rest, and though they do not make him sufficiently useful to others, they make him at least weary of himself.

Mr. Sober's chief pleasure is conversation; there is no end of his talk or
his attention; to speak or to hear is equally pleasing; for he still fancies that
he is teaching or learning something, and is free for the time from his own
reproaches.

But there is one time at night when he must go home, that his friends may
sleep; and another time in the morning, when all the world agrees to shut
out interruption. These are the moments of which poor Sober trembles at
the thought. But the misery of these tiresome intervals, he has many means
of alleviating. He has persuaded himself that the manual arts are undeservedly overlooked; he has observed in many trades the effects of close thought,
and just ratiocination. From speculation he proceeded to practice, and
supplied himself with the tools of a carpenter, with which he mended his
coalbox very successfully, and which he still continues to employ, as he finds
occasion.

He has attempted at other times the crafts of the shoemaker, tinman,
plumber, and potter; in all these arts he has failed, and resolves to qualify
himself for them by better information. But his daily amusement is chemistry. He has a small furnace, which he employs in distillation, and which has
long been the solace of his life. He draws oils and waters, and essences and
spirits, which he knows to be of no use; sits and counts the drops as they
come from his retort, and forgets that, whilst a drop is falling, a moment
flies away.

Poor Sober![5] I have often teased him with reproof, and he has often promised reformation; for no man is so much open to conviction as the Idler, but
there is none on whom it operates so little. What will be the effect of this
paper I know not; perhaps he will read it and laugh, and light the fire in his
furnace; but my hope is that he will quit his trifles, and betake himself to
rational and useful diligence.

Rasselas Johnson wrote *Rasselas* in January 1759 during the evenings of one
week, a remarkable instance of his ability to write rapidly and brilliantly under the
pressure of necessity. His mother lay dying in Lichfield. Her son, famous for his *Dictionary*, was nonetheless oppressed by poverty and in great need of ready money with
which to make her last days comfortable, pay her funeral expenses, and settle her
small debts. He was paid £100 for the first edition of *Rasselas*, but not in time to
attend her deathbed or her funeral.

Rasselas is a philosophical fable cast in the popular form of an Oriental tale, a type
of fiction that owed its popularity to the vogue of the *Arabian Nights*, first translated
into English in the early eighteenth century. Because the work is a fable, we should
not approach it as a novel: psychologically credible characters and a series of intricately involved actions that lead to a necessary resolution and conclusion are not to
be found in *Rasselas*. Instead we are meant to reflect on the ideas and to savor the
melancholy resonance and intelligence of the stately prose that expresses them. Johnson arranges the incidents of the fable to test a variety of possible solutions to a problem: What choice of life will bring us happiness? (*The Choice of Life* was his working

5. Sober represents aspects of Johnson's own character. He was much given to indolence, and he performed chemical experiments in a small laboratory in his garret.

title for the book.) Many ways of life are examined in turn, and each is found wanting. Johnson does not pretend to have solved the problem. Rather, he locates the sources of discontent in a basic principle of human nature: the "hunger of imagination which preys incessantly upon life" (chapter 32) and which lures us to "listen with credulity to the whispers of fancy and pursue with eagerness the phantoms of hope" (chapter 1). The tale is a gentle satire on one of the perennial topics of satirists: the folly of all of us who stubbornly cling to our illusions despite the evidence of experience. *Rasselas* is not all darkness and gloom, for Johnson's theme invites comic as well as tragic treatment, and some of the episodes evoke that laughter of the mind that is the effect of high comedy. In its main theme, however—the folly of cherishing the dream of ever attaining unalloyed happiness in a world that can never wholly satisfy our desires—and in many of the sayings of its characters, especially of the sage Imlac, *Rasselas* expresses some of Johnson's own deepest convictions.

The History of Rasselas, Prince of Abyssinia

Chapter 1. Description of a Palace in a Valley

Ye who listen with credulity to the whispers of fancy, and pursue with eagerness the phantoms of hope; who expect that age will perform the promises of youth, and that the deficiencies of the present day will be supplied by the morrow—attend to the history of Rasselas, prince of Abyssinia.

Rasselas was the fourth son of the mighty emperor in whose dominions the Father of Waters[1] begins his course; whose bounty pours down the streams of plenty, and scatters over half the world the harvests of Egypt.

According to the custom which has descended from age to age among the monarchs of the torrid zone, Rasselas was confined in a private palace, with the other sons and daughters of Abyssinian royalty, till the order of succession should call him to the throne.

The place which the wisdom or policy of antiquity had destined for the residence of the Abyssinian princes was a spacious valley[2] in the kingdom of Amhara, surrounded on every side by mountains, of which the summits overhang the middle part. The only passage by which it could be entered was a cavern that passed under a rock, of which it has long been disputed whether it was the work of nature or of human industry. The outlet of the cavern was concealed by a thick wood, and the mouth which opened into the valley was closed with gates of iron, forged by the artificers of ancient days, so massy that no man could, without the help of engines, open or shut them.

From the mountains on every side rivulets descended that filled all the valley with verdure and fertility, and formed a lake in the middle, inhabited by fish of every species, and frequented by every fowl whom nature has taught to dip the wing in water. This lake discharged its superfluities by a stream, which entered a dark cleft of the mountain on the northern side, and fell with dreadful noise from precipice to precipice till it was heard no more.

The sides of the mountains were covered with trees, the banks of the brooks were diversified with flowers; every blast[3] shook spices from the rocks,

1. The Nile.
2. Johnson had read of the Happy Valley in the Portuguese Jesuit Father Lobo's book on Abyssinia, which he translated in 1735. This description also owes something to the description of the Garden in *Paradise Lost* 4, and Coleridge's "Kubla Khan" may owe something to it.
3. "A gust or puff of wind" (Johnson's *Dictionary*).

and every month dropped fruits upon the ground. All animals that bite the grass, or browse the shrub, whether wild or tame, wandered in this extensive circuit, secured from beasts of prey by the mountains which confined them. On one part were flocks and herds feeding in the pastures, on another all the beasts of chase frisking in the lawns; the sprightly kid was bounding on the rocks, the subtle monkey frolicking in the trees, and the solemn elephant reposing in the shade. All the diversities of the world were brought together, the blessings of nature were collected, and its evils extracted and excluded.

The valley, wide and fruitful, supplied its inhabitants with the necessaries of life, and all delights and superfluities were added at the annual visit which the emperor paid his children, when the iron gate was opened to the sound of music, and during eight days everyone that resided in the valley was required to propose whatever might contribute to make seclusion pleasant, to fill up the vacancies of attention, and lessen the tediousness of time. Every desire was immediately granted. All the artificers of pleasure were called to gladden the festivity; the musicians exerted the power of harmony, and the dancers showed their activity before the princes, in hope that they should pass their lives in this blissful captivity, to which those only were admitted whose performance was thought able to add novelty to luxury. Such was the appearance of security and delight which this retirement afforded, that they to whom it was new always desired that it might be perpetual; and as those on whom the iron gate had once closed were never suffered to return, the effect of longer experience could not be known. Thus every year produced new schemes of delight and new competitors for imprisonment.

The palace stood on an eminence, raised about thirty paces[4] above the surface of the lake. It was divided into many squares or courts, built with greater or less magnificence according to the rank of those for whom they were designed. The roofs were turned into arches of massy stone, joined with a cement that grew harder by time, and the building stood from century to century, deriding the solstitial rains and equinoctial hurricanes, without need of reparation.

This house, which was so large as to be fully known to none but some ancient officers, who successively inherited the secrets of the place, was built as if suspicion herself had dictated the plan. To every room there was an open and secret passage; every square had a communication with the rest, either from the upper stories by private galleries, or by subterranean passages from the lower apartments. Many of the columns had unsuspected cavities, in which a long race of monarchs had reposited their treasures. They then closed up the opening with marble, which was never to be removed but in the utmost exigencies of the kingdom, and recorded their accumulations in a book, which was itself concealed in a tower, not entered but by the emperor, attended by the prince who stood next in succession.

Chapter 2. The Discontent of Rasselas in the Happy Valley

Here the sons and daughters of Abyssinia lived only to know the soft vicissitudes of pleasure and repose, attended by all that were skillful to delight,

---

4. About 150 feet.

and gratified with whatever the senses can enjoy. They wandered in gardens of fragrance, and slept in the fortresses of security. Every art was practiced to make them pleased with their own condition. The sages who instructed them told them of nothing but the miseries of public life, and described all beyond the mountains as regions of calamity, where discord was always raging, and where man preyed upon man.

To heighten their opinion of their own felicity, they were daily entertained with songs, the subject of which was the *happy valley*. Their appetites were excited by frequent enumerations of different enjoyments, and revelry and merriment was the business of every hour, from the dawn of morning to the close of even.

These methods were generally successful; few of the princes had ever wished to enlarge their bounds, but passed their lives in full conviction that they had all within their reach that art or nature could bestow, and pitied those whom fate had excluded from this seat of tranquility, as the sport of chance and the slaves of misery.

Thus they rose in the morning and lay down at night, pleased with each other and with themselves; all but Rasselas, who, in the twenty-sixth year of his age, began to withdraw himself from their pastimes and assemblies, and to delight in solitary walks and silent meditation. He often sat before tables covered with luxury, and forgot to taste the dainties that were placed before him; he rose abruptly in the midst of the song, and hastily retired beyond the sound of music. His attendants observed the change, and endeavored to renew his love of pleasure. He neglected their officiousness, repulsed their invitations, and spent day after day on the banks of rivulets sheltered with trees, where he sometimes listened to the birds in the branches, sometimes observed the fish playing in the stream, and anon cast his eyes upon the pastures and mountains filled with animals, of which some were biting the herbage, and some sleeping among the bushes.

This singularity of his humor made him much observed. One of the sages, in whose conversation he had formerly delighted, followed him secretly, in hope of discovering the cause of his disquiet. Rasselas, who knew not that anyone was near him, having for some time fixed his eyes upon the goats that were browsing among the rocks, began to compare their condition with his own.

"What," said he, "makes the difference between man and all the rest of the animal creation? Every beast that strays beside me has the same corporal necessities with myself; he is hungry, and crops the grass, he is thirsty, and drinks the stream, his thirst and hunger are appeased, he is satisfied, and sleeps; he rises again, and he is hungry, he is again fed, and is at rest. I am hungry and thirsty like him, but when thirst and hunger cease, I am not at rest; I am, like him, pained with want, but am not, like him, satisfied with fullness. The intermediate hours are tedious and gloomy; I long again to be hungry that I may again quicken my attention. The birds peck the berries or the corn, and fly away to the groves, where they sit in seeming happiness on the branches, and waste their lives in tuning one unvaried series of sounds. I likewise can call the lutanist and the singer, but the sounds that pleased me yesterday weary me today, and will grow yet more wearisome tomorrow. I can discover within me no power of perception which is not glutted with its proper pleasure, yet I do not feel myself delighted. Man has surely some latent sense for which this place affords no gratification, or he has some desires distinct from sense, which must be satisfied before he can be happy."

After this he lifted up his head, and seeing the moon rising, walked towards the palace. As he passed through the fields, and saw the animals around him, "Ye," said he, "are happy, and need not envy me that walk thus among you, burthened with myself; nor do I, ye gentle beings, envy your felicity, for it is not the felicity of man. I have many distresses from which ye are free; I fear pain when I do not feel it; I sometimes shrink at evils recollected, and sometimes start at evils anticipated. Surely the equity of Providence has balanced peculiar sufferings with peculiar enjoyments."

With observations like these the prince amused himself as he returned, uttering them with a plaintive voice, yet with a look that discovered[5] him to feel some complacence in his own perspicacity, and to receive some solace of the miseries of life from consciousness of the delicacy with which he felt, and the eloquence with which he bewailed them. He mingled cheerfully in the diversions of the evening, and all rejoiced to find that his heart was lightened.

Chapter 3. The Wants of Him That Wants Nothing

On the next day his old instructor, imagining that he had now made himself acquainted with his disease of mind, was in the hope of curing it by counsel, and officiously sought an opportunity of conference, which the prince, having long considered him as one whose intellects were exhausted, was not very willing to afford. "Why," said he, "does this man thus intrude upon me; shall I be never suffered to forget those lectures which pleased only while they were new, and to become new again must be forgotten?" He then walked into the wood, and composed himself to his usual meditations; when, before his thoughts had taken any settled form, he perceived his pursuer at his side, and was at first prompted by his impatience to go hastily away; but, being unwilling to offend a man whom he had once reverenced and still loved, he invited him to sit down with him on the bank.

The old man, thus encouraged, began to lament the change which had been lately observed in the prince, and to inquire why he so often retired from the pleasures of the palace, to loneliness and silence. "I fly from pleasure," said the prince, "because pleasure has ceased to please; I am lonely because I am miserable, and am unwilling to cloud with my presence the happiness of others." "You, sir," said the sage, "are the first who has complained of misery in the *happy valley*. I hope to convince you that your complaints have no real cause. You are here in full possession of all that the emperor of Abyssinia can bestow; here is neither labor to be endured nor danger to be dreaded, yet here is all that labor or danger can procure or purchase. Look round and tell me which of your wants is without supply; if you want nothing, how are you unhappy?"

5. Showed.

"That I want nothing," said the prince, "or that I know not what I want, is the cause of my complaint; if I had any known want, I should have a certain wish; that wish would excite endeavor, and I should not then repine to see the sun move so slowly towards the western mountain, or lament when the day breaks, and sleep will no longer hide me from myself. When I see the kids and the lambs chasing one another, I fancy that I should be happy if I had something to pursue. But, possessing all that I can want, I find one day and one hour exactly like another, except that the latter is still more tedious than the former. Let your experience inform me how the day may now seem as short as in my childhood, while nature was yet fresh and every moment showed me what I never had observed before. I have already enjoyed too much; give me something to desire."

The old man was surprised at this new species of affliction and knew not what to reply, yet was unwilling to be silent. "Sir," said he, "if you had seen the miseries of the world you would know how to value your present state." "Now," said the prince, "you have given me something to desire. I shall long to see the miseries of the world, since the sight of them is necessary to happiness."

Chapter 4. The Prince Continues to Grieve and Muse

At this time the sound of music proclaimed the hour of repast, and the conversation was concluded. The old man went away sufficiently discontented to find that his reasonings had produced the only conclusion which they were intended to prevent. But in the decline of life shame and grief are of short duration; whether it be that we bear easily what we have born long, or that, finding ourselves in age less regarded, we less regard others; or, that we look with slight regard upon afflictions, to which we know that the hand of death is about to put an end.

The prince, whose views were extended to a wider space, could not speedily quiet his emotions. He had been before terrified at the length of life which nature promised him, because he considered that in a long time much must be endured; he now rejoiced in his youth, because in many years much might be done.

This first beam of hope, that had been ever darted into his mind, rekindled youth in his cheeks, and doubled the luster of his eyes. He was fired with the desire of doing something, though he knew not yet with distinctness, either end or means.

He was now no longer gloomy and unsocial; but, considering himself as master of a secret stock of happiness, which he could enjoy only by concealing it, he affected to be busy in all schemes of diversion, and endeavored to make others pleased with the state of which he himself was weary. But pleasures never can be so multiplied or continued, as not to leave much of life unemployed; there were many hours, both of the night and day, which he could spend without suspicion in solitary thought. The load of life was much lightened: he went eagerly into the assemblies, because he supposed the frequency of his presence necessary to the success of his purposes; he retired gladly to privacy, because he had now a subject of thought.

His chief amusement was to picture to himself that world which he had never seen; to place himself in various conditions; to be entangled in imaginary difficulties, and to be engaged in wild adventures: but his benevolence always terminated his projects in the relief of distress, the detection of fraud, the defeat of oppression, and the diffusion of happiness.

Thus passed twenty months of the life of Rasselas. He busied himself so intensely in visionary bustle, that he forgot his real solitude; and, amidst hourly preparations for the various incidents of human affairs, neglected to consider by what means he should mingle with mankind.

One day, as he was sitting on a bank, he feigned to himself an orphan virgin robbed of her little portion[6] by a treacherous lover, and crying after him for restitution and redress. So strongly was the image impressed upon his mind, that he started up in the maid's defense, and ran forward to seize the plunderer, with all the eagerness of real pursuit. Fear naturally quickens the flight of guilt. Rasselas could not catch the fugitive with his utmost efforts; but, resolving to weary, by perseverance, him whom he could not surpass in speed, he pressed on till the foot of the mountain stopped his course.

Here he recollected himself, and smiled at his own useless impetuosity. Then raising his eyes to the mountain, "This," said he, "is the fatal obstacle that hinders at once the enjoyment of pleasure, and the exercise of virtue. How long is it that my hopes and wishes have flown beyond this boundary of my life, which yet I never have attempted to surmount!"

Struck with this reflection, he sat down to muse, and remembered, that since he first resolved to escape from his confinement, the sun had passed twice over him in his annual course. He now felt a degree of regret with which he had never been before acquainted. He considered how much might have been done in the time which had passed, and left nothing real behind it. He compared twenty months with the life of man. "In life," said he, "is not to be counted the ignorance of infancy, or imbecility[7] of age. We are long before we are able to think, and we soon cease from the power of acting. The true period of human existence may be reasonably estimated as forty years, of which I have mused away the four and twentieth part. What I have lost was certain, for I have certainly possessed it; but of twenty months to come who can assure me?"

The consciousness of his own folly pierced him deeply, and he was long before he could be reconciled to himself. "The rest of my time," said he, "has been lost by the crime or folly of my ancestors, and the absurd institutions of my country; I remember it with disgust, yet without remorse: but the months that have passed since new light darted into my soul, since I formed a scheme of reasonable felicity, have been squandered by my own fault. I have lost that which can never be restored: I have seen the sun rise and set for twenty months, an idle gazer on the light of heaven. In this time the birds have left the nest of their mother, and committed themselves to the woods and to the skies: the kid has forsaken the teat, and learned by degrees to climb the rocks in quest of independent sustenance. I only have made no advances, but am still helpless and ignorant. The moon, by more than twenty changes, admonished me of the flux of life; the stream that rolled before my feet upbraided my inactivity. I sat feasting on intellectual luxury, regardless alike of the examples of the earth, and the instructions of the planets. Twenty months are past, who shall restore them!"

6. Money or goods.   7. Weakness.

These sorrowful meditations fastened upon his mind; he passed four months in resolving to lose no more time in idle resolves, and was awakened to more vigorous exertion by hearing a maid, who had broken a porcelain cup, remark that what cannot be repaired is not to be regretted.

This was obvious; and Rasselas reproached himself that he had not discovered it, having not known, or not considered, how many useful hints are obtained by chance, and how often the mind, hurried by her own ardor to distant views, neglects the truths that lie open before her. He, for a few hours, regretted his regret, and from that time bent his whole mind upon the means of escaping from the valley of happiness.

Chapter 5. The Prince Meditates His Escape

He now found that it would be very difficult to effect that which it was very easy to suppose effected. When he looked round about him, he saw himself confined by the bars of nature which had never yet been broken, and by the gate, through which none that once had passed it were ever able to return. He was now impatient as an eagle in a grate.[8] He passed week after week in clambering the mountains, to see if there was any aperture which the bushes might conceal, but found all the summits inaccessible by their prominence. The iron gate he despaired to open; for it was not only secured with all the power of art, but was always watched by successive sentinels, and was by its position exposed to the perpetual observation of all the inhabitants.

He then examined the cavern through which the waters of the lake were discharged; and, looking down at a time when the sun shone strongly upon its mouth, he discovered it to be full of broken rocks, which, though they permitted the stream to flow through many narrow passages, would stop anybody of solid bulk. He returned discouraged and dejected; but, having now known the blessing of hope, resolved never to despair.

In these fruitless searches he spent ten months. The time, however, passed cheerfully away: in the morning he rose with new hope, in the evening applauded his own diligence, and in the night slept sound after his fatigue. He met a thousand amusements which beguiled his labor, and diversified his thoughts. He discerned the various instincts of animals, and properties of plants, and found the place replete with wonders, of which he purposed to solace himself with the contemplation, if he should never be able to accomplish his flight; rejoicing that his endeavors, though yet unsuccessful, had supplied him with a source of inexhaustible enquiry.

But his original curiosity was not yet abated; he resolved to obtain some knowledge of the ways of men. His wish still continued, but his hope grew less. He ceased to survey any longer the walls of his prison, and spared to search by new toils for interstices which he knew could not be found, yet determined to keep his design always in view, and lay hold on any expedient that time should offer.

8. Barred cage.

Chapter 6. A Dissertation on the Art of Flying

Among the artists that had been allured into the happy valley, to labor for the accommodation and pleasure of its inhabitants, was a man eminent for his knowledge of the mechanic powers, who had contrived many engines[9] both of use and recreation. By a wheel, which the stream turned, he forced the water into a tower, whence it was distributed to all the apartments of the palace. He erected a pavillion in the garden, around which he kept the air always cool by artificial showers. One of the groves appropriated to the ladies, was ventilated by fans, to which the rivulet that run through it gave a constant motion; and instruments of soft music were placed at proper distances, of which some played by the impulse of the wind, and some by the power of the stream.

This artist was sometimes visited by Rasselas, who was pleased with every kind of knowledge, imagining that the time would come when all his acquisitions should be of use to him in the open world. He came one day to amuse himself in his usual manner, and found the master busy in building a sailing chariot: he saw that the design was practicable upon a level surface, and with expressions of great esteem solicited its completion. The workman was pleased to find himself so much regarded by the prince, and resolved to gain yet higher honors. "Sir," said he, "you have seen but a small part of what the mechanic sciences can perform. I have been long of opinion, that, instead of the tardy conveyance of ships and chariots, man might use the swifter migration of wings; that the fields of air are open to knowledge, and that only ignorance and idleness need crawl upon the ground."

This hint rekindled the prince's desire of passing the mountains; having seen what the mechanist had already performed, he was willing to fancy that he could do more; yet resolved to inquire further before he suffered hope to afflict him by disappointment. "I am afraid," said he to the artist, "that your imagination prevails over your skill, and that you now tell me rather what you wish than what you know. Every animal has his element assigned him; the birds have the air, and man and beasts the earth." "So," replied the mechanist, "fishes have the water, in which yet beasts can swim by nature, and men by art. He that can swim needs not despair to fly: to swim is to fly in a grosser fluid, and to fly is to swim in a subtler.[1] We are only to proportion our power of resistance to the different density of the matter through which we are to pass. You will be necessarily upborn by the air, if you can renew any impulse upon it, faster than the air can recede from the pressure."

"But the exercise of swimming," said the prince, "is very laborious; the strongest limbs are soon wearied; I am afraid the act of flying will be yet more violent, and wings will be of no great use, unless we can fly further than we can swim."

"The labor of rising from the ground," said the artist, "will be great, as we see it in the heavier domestic fowls; but, as we mount higher, the earth's attraction, and the body's gravity, will be gradually diminished, till we shall arrive at a region where the man will float in the air without any tendency to fall: no care will then be necessary, but to move forwards, which the gentlest impulse will effect. You, Sir, whose curiosity is so extensive, will easily con-

9. Machines. "Mechanic powers": the forces that cause things to move.

1. Thinner.

ceive with what pleasure a philosopher, furnished with wings, and hovering in the sky, would see the earth, and all its inhabitants, rolling beneath him, and presenting to him successively, by its diurnal motion, all the countries within the same parallel. How must it amuse the pendent spectator to see the moving scene of land and ocean, cities and deserts! To survey with equal security the marts of trade, and the fields of battle; mountains infested by barbarians, and fruitful regions gladdened by plenty, and lulled by peace! How easily shall we then trace the Nile through all his passage; pass over to distant regions, and examine the face of nature from one extremity of the earth to the other!"

"All this," said the prince, "is much to be desired, but I am afraid that no man will be able to breathe in these regions of speculation and tranquility. I have been told, that respiration is difficult upon lofty mountains, yet from these precipices, though

Unknown engraver, *Rasselas*, 1787. Rasselas pulls the artist to shore. *The History of Rasselas, Prince of Abissinia, a tale, in two volumes.*

so high as to produce great tenuity of the air, it is very easy to fall: therefore I suspect, that from any height, where life can be supported, there may be danger of too quick descent."

"Nothing," replied the artist, "will ever be attempted, if all possible objections must be first overcome. If you will favor my project I will try the first flight at my own hazard. I have considered the structure of all volant[2] animals, and find the folding continuity of the bat's wings most easily accommodated to the human form. Upon this model I shall begin my task tomorrow, and in a year expect to tower into the air beyond the malice or pursuit of man. But I will work only on this condition, that the art shall not be divulged, and that you shall not require me to make wings for any but ourselves."

"Why," said Rasselas, "should you envy others so great an advantage? All skill ought to be exerted for universal good; every man has owed much to others, and ought to repay the kindness that he has received."

"If men were all virtuous," returned the artist, "I should with great alacrity teach them all to fly. But what would be the security of the good, if the bad could at pleasure invade them from the sky? Against an army sailing through the clouds neither walls, nor mountains, nor seas, could afford any

2. Able to fly.

security. A flight of northern savages might hover in the wind, and light at once with irresistible violence upon the capital of a fruitful region that was rolling under them. Even this valley, the retreat of princes, the abode of happiness, might be violated by the sudden descent of some of the naked nations that swarm on the coast of the southern sea."

The prince promised secrecy, and waited for the performance, not wholly hopeless of success. He visited the work from time to time, observed its progress, and remarked many ingenious contrivances to facilitate motion, and unite levity with strength. The artist was every day more certain that he should leave vultures and eagles behind him, and the contagion of his confidence seized upon the prince.

In a year the wings were finished, and, on a morning appointed, the maker appeared furnished for flight on a little promontory: he waved his pinions a while to gather air, then leaped from his stand, and in an instant dropped into the lake. His wings, which were of no use in the air, sustained him in the water, and the prince drew him to land, half dead with terror and vexation.

Chapter 7. The Prince Finds a Man of Learning

The prince was not much afflicted by this disaster, having suffered himself to hope for a happier event, only because he had no other means of escape in view. He still persisted in his design to leave the happy valley by the first opportunity.

His imagination was now at a stand; he had no prospect of entering into the world; and, notwithstanding all his endeavors to support himself, discontent by degrees preyed upon him, and he began again to lose his thoughts in sadness, when the rainy season, which in these countries is periodical, made it inconvenient to wander in the woods.

The rain continued longer and with more violence than had been ever known; the clouds broke on the surrounding mountains, and the torrents streamed into the plain on every side, till the cavern was too narrow to discharge the water. The lake overflowed its banks, and all the level of the valley was covered with the inundation. The eminence, on which the palace was built, and some other spots of rising ground, were all that the eye could now discover. The herds and flocks left the pastures, and both the wild beasts and the tame retreated to the mountains.

This inundation confined all the princes to domestic amusements, and the attention of Rasselas was particularly seized by a poem, which Imlac rehearsed,[3] upon the various conditions of humanity. He commanded the poet to attend him in his apartment, and recite his verses a second time; then entering into familiar talk, he thought himself happy in having found a man who knew the world so well, and could so skillfully paint the scenes of life. He asked a thousand questions about things, to which, though common to all other mortals, his confinement from childhood had kept him a stranger. The poet pitied his ignorance, and loved his curiosity, and entertained him from day to day with novelty and instruction, so that the prince regretted the necessity of sleep, and longed till the morning should renew his pleasure.

3. Recited.

As they were sitting together, the prince commanded Imlac to relate his history, and to tell by what accident he was forced, or by what motive induced, to close his life in the happy valley. As he was going to begin his narrative, Rasselas was called to a concert, and obliged to restrain his curiosity till the evening.

Chapter 8. The History of Imlac

The close of the day is, in the regions of the torrid zone, the only season of diversion and entertainment, and it was therefore midnight before the music ceased, and the princesses retired. Rasselas then called for his companion and required him to begin the story of his life.

"Sir," said Imlac, "my history will not be long: the life that is devoted to knowledge passes silently away, and is very little diversified by events. To talk in public, to think in solitude, to read and to hear, to inquire, and answer inquiries, is the business of a scholar. He wanders about the world without pomp or terror, and is neither known nor valued but by men like himself.

"I was born in the kingdom of Goiama, at no great distance from the fountain of the Nile. My father was a wealthy merchant, who traded between the inland countries of Africk and the ports of the red sea. He was honest, frugal and diligent, but of mean sentiments, and narrow comprehension: he desired only to be rich, and to conceal his riches, lest he should be spoiled[4] by the governors of the province."

"Surely," said the prince, "my father must be negligent of his charge, if any man in his dominions dares take that which belongs to another. Does he not know that kings are accountable for injustice permitted as well as done? If I were emperor, not the meanest of my subjects should be oppressed with impunity. My blood boils when I am told that a merchant durst not enjoy his honest gains for fear of losing them by the rapacity of power. Name the governor who robbed the people, that I may declare his crimes to the emperor."

"Sir," said Imlac, "your ardor is the natural effect of virtue animated by youth: the time will come when you will acquit your father, and perhaps hear with less impatience of the governor. Oppression is, in the Abyssinian dominions, neither frequent nor tolerated; but no form of government has been yet discovered, by which cruelty can be wholly prevented. Subordination supposes power on one part and subjection on the other; and if power be in the hands of men, it will sometimes be abused. The vigilance of the supreme magistrate may do much, but much will still remain undone. He can never know all the crimes that are committed, and can seldom punish all that he knows."

"This," said the prince, "I do not understand, but I had rather hear thee than dispute. Continue thy narration."

"My father," proceeded Imlac, "originally intended that I should have no other education, than such as might qualify me for commerce; and discovering in me great strength of memory, and quickness of apprehension, often declared his hope that I should be some time the richest man in Abyssinia."

---

4. Robbed.

"Why," said the prince, "did thy father desire the increase of his wealth, when it was already greater than he durst discover or enjoy? I am unwilling to doubt thy veracity, yet inconsistencies cannot both be true."

"Inconsistencies," answered Imlac, "cannot both be right, but, imputed to man, they may both be true. Yet diversity is not inconsistency. My father might expect a time of greater security. However, some desire is necessary to keep life in motion, and he, whose real wants are supplied, must admit those of fancy."

"This," said the prince, "I can in some measure conceive. I repent that I interrupted thee."

"With this hope," proceeded Imlac, "he sent me to school; but when I had once found the delight of knowledge, and felt the pleasure of intelligence[5] and the pride of invention, I began silently to despise riches, and determined to disappoint the purpose of my father, whose grossness of conception raised my pity. I was twenty years old before his tenderness would expose me to the fatigue of travel, in which time I had been instructed, by successive masters, in all the literature of my native country. As every hour taught me something new, I lived in a continual course of gratifications; but, as I advanced towards manhood, I lost much of the reverence with which I had been used to look on my instructors; because, when the lesson was ended, I did not find them wiser or better than common men.

"At length my father resolved to initiate me in commerce, and, opening one of his subterranean treasuries, counted out ten thousand pieces of gold. 'This, young man,' said he, 'is the stock with which you must negotiate.[6] I began with less than the fifth part, and you see how diligence and parsimony have increased it. This is your own to waste or to improve. If you squander it by negligence or caprice, you must wait for my death before you will be rich: if, in four years, you double your stock, we will thenceforward let subordination cease, and live together as friends and partners; for he shall always be equal with me, who is equally skilled in the art of growing rich.'

"We laid our money upon camels, concealed in bales of cheap goods, and travelled to the shore of the Red Sea. When I cast my eye on the expanse of waters my heart bounded like that of a prisoner escaped. I felt an unextinguishable curiosity kindle in my mind, and resolved to snatch this opportunity of seeing the manners of other nations, and of learning sciences unknown in Abyssinia.

"I remembered that my father had obliged me to the improvement of my stock, not by a promise which I ought not to violate, but by a penalty which I was at liberty to incur; and therefore determined to gratify my predominant desire, and by drinking at the fountains of knowledge, to quench the thirst of curiosity.

"As I was supposed to trade without connection with my father, it was easy for me to become acquainted with the master of a ship, and procure a passage to some other country. I had no motives of choice to regulate my voyage; it was sufficient for me that, wherever I wandered, I should see a country which I had not seen before. I therefore entered a ship bound for Surat,[7] having left a letter for my father declaring my intention.

5. Information or knowledge.
6. Do business.

7. A port in India.

Chapter 9. The History of Imlac Continued

"When I first entered upon the world of waters, and lost sight of land, I looked round about me with pleasing terror, and thinking my soul enlarged by the boundless prospect, imagined that I could gaze round for ever without satiety; but, in a short time, I grew weary of looking on barren uniformity, where I could only see again what I had already seen. I then descended into the ship, and doubted for a while whether all my future pleasures would not end like this in disgust and disappointment. Yet, surely, said I, the ocean and the land are very different; the only variety of water is rest and motion, but the earth has mountains and valleys, deserts and cities: it is inhabited by men of different customs and contrary opinions; and I may hope to find variety in life, though I should miss it in nature.

"With this thought I quieted my mind; and amused myself during the voyage, sometimes by learning from the sailors the art of navigation, which I have never practiced, and sometimes by forming schemes for my conduct in different situations, in not one of which I have been ever placed.

"I was almost weary of my naval amusements when we landed safely at Surat. I secured my money, and purchasing some commodities for show, joined myself to a caravan that was passing into the inland country. My companions, for some reason or other, conjecturing that I was rich, and, by my inquiries and admiration, finding that I was ignorant, considered me as a novice whom they had a right to cheat, and who was to learn at the usual expense the art of fraud. They exposed me to the theft of servants, and the exaction of officers,[8] and saw me plundered upon false pretences, without any advantage to themselves, but that of rejoicing in the superiority of their own knowledge."

"Stop a moment," said the prince. "Is there such depravity in man, as that he should injure another without benefit to himself? I can easily conceive that all are pleased with superiority; but your ignorance was merely accidental, which, being neither your crime nor your folly, could afford them no reason to applaud themselves; and the knowledge which they had, and which you wanted, they might as effectually have shown by warning, as betraying you."

"Pride," said Imlac, "is seldom delicate, it will please itself with very mean advantages; and envy feels not its own happiness, but when it may be compared with the misery of others. They were my enemies because they grieved to think me rich, and my oppressors because they delighted to find me weak."

"Proceed," said the prince: "I doubt not of the facts which you relate, but imagine that you impute them to mistaken motives."

"In this company," said Imlac, "I arrived at Agra, the capital of Indostan, the city in which the great Mogul commonly resides. I applied myself to the language of the country, and in a few months was able to converse with the learned men; some of whom I found morose and reserved, and others easy and communicative; some were unwilling to teach another what they had with difficulty learned themselves; and some showed that the end of their studies was to gain the dignity of instructing.

"To the tutor of the young princes I recommended myself so much, that I was presented to the emperor as a man of uncommon knowledge. The

8. Officials or agents.

emperor asked me many questions concerning my country and my travels; and though I cannot now recollect any thing that he uttered above the power of a common man, he dismissed me astonished at his wisdom, and enamored of his goodness.

"My credit was now so high, that the merchants, with whom I had traveled, applied to me for recommendations to the ladies of the court. I was surprised at their confidence of solicitation, and gently reproached them with their practices on the road. They heard me with cold indifference, and showed no tokens of shame or sorrow.

"They then urged their request with the offer of a bribe; but what I would not do for kindness I would not do for money; and refused them, not because they had injured me, but because I would not enable them to injure others; for I knew they would have made use of my credit to cheat those who should buy their wares.

"Having resided at Agra till there was no more to be learned, I traveled into Persia, where I saw many remains of ancient magnificence, and observed many new accommodations[9] of life. The Persians are a nation eminently social, and their assemblies afforded me daily opportunities of remarking characters and manners, and of tracing human nature through all its variations.

"From Persia I passed into Arabia, where I saw a nation at once pastoral and warlike; who live without any settled habitation; whose only wealth is their flocks and herds; and who have yet carried on, through all ages, an hereditary war with all mankind, though they neither covet nor envy their possessions.

Chapter 10. Imlac's History Continued. A Dissertation upon Poetry

"Wherever I went, I found that poetry was considered as the highest learning, and regarded with a veneration somewhat approaching to that which man would pay to the angelic nature. And yet it fills me with wonder that, in almost all countries, the most ancient poets are considered as the best: whether it be that every other kind of knowledge is an acquisition gradually attained, and poetry is a gift conferred at once; or that the first poetry of every nation surprised them as a novelty, and retained the credit by consent which it received by accident at first; or whether, as the province of poetry is to describe nature and passion, which are always the same, the first writers took possession of the most striking objects for description and the most probable occurrences for fiction, and left nothing to those that followed them, but transcription of the same events, and new combinations of the same images—whatever be the reason, it is commonly observed that the early writers are in possession of nature, and their followers of art; that the first excel in strength and invention, and the latter in elegance and refinement.

"I was desirous to add my name to this illustrious fraternity. I read all the poets of Persia and Arabia, and was able to repeat by memory the volumes that are suspended in the mosque of Mecca.[1] But I soon found that no man

---

9. "Conveniences, things requisite to ease or refreshment" (Johnson's *Dictionary*).
1. In the 7th century, seven peerless Arabic poems were supposed to have been transcribed in gold and hung up in a mosque.

was ever great by imitation. My desire of excellence impelled me to transfer my attention to nature and to life. Nature was to be my subject, and men to be my auditors: I could never describe what I had not seen; I could not hope to move those with delight or terror, whose interests and opinions I did not understand.

"Being now resolved to be a poet, I saw everything with a new purpose; my sphere of attention was suddenly magnified; no kind of knowledge was to be overlooked. I ranged mountains and deserts for images and resemblances, and pictured upon my mind every tree of the forest and flower of the valley. I observed with equal care the crags of the rock and the pinnacles of the palace. Sometimes I wandered along the mazes of the rivulet, and sometimes watched the changes of the summer clouds. To a poet nothing can be useless. Whatever is beautiful, and whatever is dreadful, must be familiar to his imagination; he must be conversant with all that is awfully[2] vast or elegantly little. The plants of the garden, the animals of the wood, the minerals of the earth, and meteors of the sky, must all concur to store his mind with inexhaustible variety: for every idea[3] is useful for the enforcement or decoration of moral or religious truth; and he who knows most will have most power of diversifying his scenes, and of gratifying his reader with remote allusions and unexpected instruction.

"All the appearances of nature I was therefore careful to study, and every country which I have surveyed has contributed something to my poetical powers."

"In so wide a survey," said the prince, "you must surely have left much unobserved. I have lived till now within the circuit of these mountains, and yet cannot walk abroad without the sight of something which I have never beheld before, or never heeded."

"The business of a poet," said Imlac, "is to examine, not the individual, but the species; to remark general properties and large appearances; he does not number the streaks of the tulip, or describe the different shades in the verdure of the forest. He is to exhibit in his portraits of nature such prominent and striking features as recall the original to every mind, and must neglect the minuter discriminations, which one may have remarked and another have neglected, for those characteristics which are alike obvious to vigilance and carelessness.

"But the knowledge of nature is only half the task of a poet; he must be acquainted likewise with all the modes of life. His character requires that he estimate the happiness and misery of every condition; observe the power of all the passions in all their combinations, and trace the changes of the human mind, as they are modified by various institutions and accidental influences of climate or custom, from the sprightliness of infancy to the despondence of decrepitude. He must divest himself of the prejudices of his age or country; he must consider right and wrong in their abstracted and invariable state; he must disregard present laws and opinions, and rise to general and transcendental[4] truths, which will always be the same. He must, therefore, content himself with the slow progress of his name, contemn the applause of his own time, and commit his claims to the justice of posterity.

---

2. Awe-inspiringly.
3. Mental image.

4. "General; pervading many particulars" (Johnson's *Dictionary*).

He must write as the interpreter of nature and the legislator of mankind, and consider himself as presiding over the thoughts and manners of future generations, as a being superior to time and place.

"His labor is not yet at an end; he must know many languages and many sciences; and, that his style may be worthy of his thoughts, must by incessant practice familiarize to himself every delicacy of speech and grace of harmony."

Chapter 11. Imlac's Narrative Continued. A Hint on Pilgrimage

Imlac now felt the enthusiastic fit, and was proceeding to aggrandize his own profession, when the prince cried out: "Enough! thou hast convinced me that no human being can ever be a poet. Proceed with thy narration."

"To be a poet," said Imlac, "is indeed very difficult." "So difficult," returned the prince, "that I will at present hear no more of his labors. Tell me whither you went when you had seen Persia."

"From Persia," said the poet, "I traveled through Syria, and for three years resided in Palestine, where I conversed with great numbers of the northern and western nations of Europe, the nations which are now in possession of all power and all knowledge, whose armies are irresistible, and whose fleets command the remotest parts of the globe. When I compared these men with the natives of our own kingdom, and those that surround us, they appeared almost another order of beings. In their countries it is difficult to wish for anything that may not be obtained; a thousand arts, of which we never heard, are continually laboring for their convenience and pleasure; and whatever their own climate has denied them is supplied by their commerce."

"By what means," said the prince, "are the Europeans thus powerful, or why, since they can so easily visit Asia and Africa for trade or conquest, cannot the Asiatics and Africans invade their coasts, plant colonies in their ports, and give laws to their natural princes? The same wind that carries them back would bring us thither."

"They are more powerful, sir, than we," answered Imlac, "because they are wiser; knowledge will always predominate over ignorance, as man governs the other animals. But why their knowledge is more than ours, I know not what reason can be given, but the unsearchable will of the Supreme Being."

"When," said the prince with a sigh, "shall I be able to visit Palestine, and mingle with this mighty confluence of nations? Till that happy moment shall arrive, let me fill up the time with such representations as thou canst give me. I am not ignorant of the motive that assembles such numbers in that place, and cannot but consider it as the center of wisdom and piety, to which the best and wisest men of every land must be continually resorting."

"There are some nations," said Imlac, "that send few visitants to Palestine; for many numerous and learned sects in Europe concur to censure pilgrimage as superstitious, or deride it as ridiculous."

"You know," said the prince, "how little my life has made me acquainted with diversity of opinions. It will be too long to hear the arguments on both sides; you, that have considered them, tell me the result."

"Pilgrimage," said Imlac, "like many other acts of piety, may be reasonable or superstitious, according to the principles upon which it is performed. Long journeys in search of truth are not commanded. Truth, such as is necessary to the regulation of life, is always found where it is honestly sought. Change of place is no natural cause of the increase of piety, for it inevitably produces dissipation of mind. Yet, since men go every day to view the fields where great actions have been performed, and return with stronger impressions of the event, curiosity of the same kind may naturally dispose us to view that country whence our religion had its beginning; and I believe no man surveys those awful scenes without some confirmation of holy resolutions. That the Supreme Being may be more easily propitiated in one place than in another is the dream of idle superstition, but that some places may operate upon our own minds in an uncommon manner is an opinion which hourly experience will justify. He who supposes that his vices may be more successfully combated in Palestine, will, perhaps, find himself mistaken, yet he may go thither without folly; he who thinks they will be more freely pardoned, dishonors at once his reason and religion."

"These," said the prince, "are European distinctions. I will consider them another time. What have you found to be the effect of knowledge? Are those nations happier than we?"

"There is so much infelicity," said the poet, "in the world that scarce any man has leisure from his own distresses to estimate the comparative happiness of others. Knowledge is certainly one of the means of pleasure, as is confessed by the natural desire which every mind feels of increasing its ideas. Ignorance is mere privation, by which nothing can be produced; it is a vacuity in which the soul sits motionless and torpid for want of attraction; and, without knowing why, we always rejoice when we learn, and grieve when we forget. I am therefore inclined to conclude that if nothing counteracts the natural consequence of learning, we grow more happy as our minds take a wider range.

"In enumerating the particular comforts of life, we shall find many advantages on the side of the Europeans. They cure wounds and diseases with which we languish and perish. We suffer inclemencies of weather which they can obviate. They have engines for the despatch of many laborious works, which we must perform by manual industry. There is such communication between distant places that one friend can hardly be said to be absent from another. Their policy removes all public inconveniences; they have roads cut through their mountains, and bridges laid upon their rivers. And, if we descend to the privacies of life, their habitations are more commodious, and their possessions are more secure."

"They are surely happy," said the prince, "who have all these conveniencies, of which I envy none so much as the facility with which separated friends interchange their thoughts."

"The Europeans," answered Imlac, "are less unhappy than we, but they are not happy. Human life is everywhere a state in which much is to be endured, and little to be enjoyed."

Chapter 12. The Story of Imlac Continued

"I am not yet willing," said the prince, "to suppose that happiness is so parsimoniously distributed to mortals; nor can believe but that, if I had the choice of life, I should be able to fill every day with pleasure. I would injure no man, and should provoke no resentment: I would relieve every distress, and should enjoy the benedictions of gratitude. I would choose my friends among the wise, and my wife among the virtuous; and therefore should be in no danger from treachery, or unkindness. My children should, by my care, be learned and pious, and would repay to my age what their childhood had received. What would dare to molest him who might call on every side to thousands enriched by his bounty, or assisted by his power? And why should not life glide quietly away in the soft reciprocation of protection and reverence? All this may be done without the help of European refinements, which appear by their effects to be rather specious than useful. Let us leave them and pursue our journey."

"From Palestine," said Imlac, "I passed through many regions of Asia; in the more civilized kingdoms as a trader, and among the barbarians of the mountains as a pilgrim. At last I began to long for my native country, that I might repose after my travels, and fatigues, in the places where I had spent my earliest years, and gladden my old companions with the recital of my adventures. Often did I figure to myself those, with whom I had sported away the gay hours of dawning life, sitting round me in its evening, wondering at my tales, and listening to my counsels.

"When this thought had taken possession of my mind, I considered every moment as wasted which did not bring me nearer to Abyssinia. I hastened into Egypt, and, notwithstanding my impatience, was detained ten months in the contemplation of its ancient magnificence, and in enquiries after the remains of its ancient learning. I found in Cairo a mixture of all nations; some brought thither by the love of knowledge, some by the hope of gain, and many by the desire of living after their own manner without observation, and of lying hid in the obscurity of multitudes: for, in a city, populous as Cairo, it is possible to obtain at the same time the gratifications of society, and the secrecy of solitude.

"From Cairo I traveled to Suez, and embarked on the Red Sea, passing along the coast till I arrived at the port from which I had departed twenty years before. Here I joined myself to a caravan and re-entered my native country.

"I now expected the caresses of my kinsmen, and the congratulations of my friends, and was not without hope that my father, whatever value he had set upon riches, would own with gladness and pride a son who was able to add to the felicity and honor of the nation. But I was soon convinced that my thoughts were vain. My father had been dead fourteen years, having divided his wealth among my brothers, who were removed to some other provinces. Of my companions the greater part was in the grave, of the rest some could with difficulty remember me, and some considered me as one corrupted by foreign manners.

"A man used to vicissitudes is not easily dejected. I forgot, after a time, my disappointment, and endeavored to recommend myself to the nobles of the kingdom: they admitted me to their tables, heard my story, and dismissed me. I opened a school, and was prohibited to teach. I then resolved to sit down in the quiet of domestic life, and addressed a lady that was fond of my conversation, but rejected my suit, because my father was a merchant.

"Wearied at last with solicitation and repulses, I resolved to hide myself for ever from the world, and depend no longer on the opinion or caprice of others. I waited for the time when the gate of the *happy valley* should open, that I might bid farewell to hope and fear: the day came; my performance was distinguished with favor, and I resigned myself with joy to perpetual confinement."

"Hast thou here found happiness at last?" said Rasselas. "Tell me without reserve; art thou content with thy condition? or, dost thou wish to be again wandering and inquiring? All the inhabitants of this valley celebrate their lot, and, at the annual visit of the emperor, invite others to partake of their felicity."

"Great prince," said Imlac, "I shall speak the truth: I know not one of all your attendants who does not lament the hour when he entered this retreat. I am less unhappy than the rest, because I have a mind replete with images, which I can vary and combine at pleasure. I can amuse my solitude by the renovation of the knowledge which begins to fade from my memory, and by recollection of the accidents of my past life. Yet all this ends in the sorrowful consideration, that my acquirements are now useless, and that none of my pleasures can be again enjoyed. The rest, whose minds have no impression but of the present moment, are either corroded by malignant passions, or sit stupid in the gloom of perpetual vacancy."

"What passions can infest those," said the prince, "who have no trials? We are in a place where impotence precludes malice, and where all envy is repressed by community[5] of enjoyments."

"There may be community," said Imlac, "of material possessions, but there can never be community of love or of esteem. It must happen that one will please more than another; he that knows himself despised will always be envious; and still more envious and malevolent, if he is condemned to live in the presence of those who despise him. The invitations, by which they allure others to a state which they feel to be wretched, proceed from the natural malignity of hopeless misery. They are weary of themselves, and of each other, and expect to find relief in new companions. They envy the liberty which their folly has forfeited, and would gladly see all mankind imprisoned like themselves.

"From this crime, however, I am wholly free. No man can say that he is wretched by my persuasion. I look with pity on the crowds who are annually soliciting admission to captivity, and wish that it were lawful for me to warn them of their danger."

"My dear Imlac," said the prince, "I will open to thee my whole heart. I have long meditated an escape from the happy valley. I have examined the mountains on every side, but find myself insuperably barred: teach me the way to break my prison; thou shalt be the companion of my flight, the guide of my rambles, the partner of my fortune, and my sole director in the *choice of life*."

"Sir," answered the poet, "your escape will be difficult, and, perhaps, you may soon repent your curiosity. The world, which you figure to yourself smooth and quiet as the lake in the valley, you will find a sea foaming with tempests, and boiling with whirlpools: you will be sometimes overwhelmed by the waves of violence, and sometimes dashed against the rocks of treachery. Amidst wrongs and frauds, competitions and anxieties, you will wish a

5. Joint possession.

thousand times for these seats of quiet, and willingly quit hope to be free from fear."

"Do not seek to deter me from my purpose," said the prince: "I am impatient to see what thou hast seen; and, since thou art thyself weary of the valley, it is evident, that thy former state was better than this. Whatever be the consequence of my experiment, I am resolved to judge with my own eyes of the various conditions of men, and then to make deliberately my *choice of life.*"

"I am afraid," said Imlac, "you are hindered by stronger restraints than my persuasions; yet, if your determination is fixed, I do not counsel you to despair. Few things are impossible to diligence and skill."

Chapter 13. Rasselas Discovers the Means of Escape

The prince now dismissed his favorite to rest, but the narrative of wonders and novelties filled his mind with perturbation. He revolved all that he had heard, and prepared innumerable questions for the morning.

Much of his uneasiness was now removed. He had a friend to whom he could impart his thoughts, and whose experience could assist him in his designs. His heart was no longer condemned to swell with silent vexation. He thought that even the *happy valley* might be endured with such a companion, and that, if they could range the world together, he should have nothing further to desire.

In a few days the water was discharged, and the ground dried. The prince and Imlac then walked out together to converse without the notice of the rest. The prince, whose thoughts were always on the wing, as he passed by the gate, said, with a countenance of sorrow, "Why art thou so strong, and why is man so weak?"

"Man is not weak," answered his companion; "knowledge is more than equivalent to force. The master of mechanics laughs at strength. I can burst the gate, but cannot do it secretly. Some other expedient must be tried."

As they were walking on the side of the mountain, they observed that the conies,[6] which the rain had driven from their burrows, had taken shelter among the bushes, and formed holes behind them, tending upwards in an oblique line. "It has been the opinion of antiquity," said Imlac, "that human reason borrowed many arts from the instinct of animals; let us, therefore, not think ourselves degraded by learning from the coney. We may escape by piercing the mountain in the same direction. We will begin where the summit hangs over the middle part, and labor upward till we shall issue out beyond the prominence."

The eyes of the prince, when he heard this proposal, sparkled with joy. The execution was easy, and the success certain.

No time was now lost. They hastened early in the morning to choose a place proper for their mine. They clambered with great fatigue among crags and brambles, and returned without having discovered any part that favored their design. The second and the third day were spent in the same manner, and with the same frustration. But, on the fourth, they found a small cavern, concealed by a thicket, where they resolved to make their experiment.

---

6. Rabbits.

Imlac procured instruments proper to hew stone and remove earth, and they fell to their work on the next day with more eagerness than vigor. They were presently exhausted by their efforts, and sat down to pant upon the grass. The prince, for a moment, appeared to be discouraged. "Sir," said his companion, "practice will enable us to continue our labor for a longer time; mark, however, how far we have advanced, and you will find that our toil will some time have an end. Great works are performed, not by strength, but perseverance: yonder palace was raised by single stones, yet you see its height and spaciousness. He that shall walk with vigor three hours a day will pass in seven years a space equal to the circumference of the globe."

They returned to their work day after day, and, in a short time, found a fissure in the rock, which enabled them to pass far with very little obstruction. This Rasselas considered as a good omen. "Do not disturb your mind," said Imlac, "with other hopes or fears than reason may suggest: if you are pleased with prognostics of good, you will be terrified likewise with tokens of evil, and your whole life will be a prey to superstition. Whatever facilitates our work is more than an omen, it is a cause of success. This is one of those pleasing surprises which often happen to active resolution. Many things difficult to design prove easy to performance."

Chapter 14. Rasselas and Imlac Receive an Unexpected Visit

They had now wrought their way to the middle, and solaced their toil with the approach of liberty, when the prince, coming down to refresh himself with air, found his sister Nekayah standing before the mouth of the cavity. He started and stood confused, afraid to tell his design, and yet hopeless to conceal it. A few moments determined him to repose on her fidelity, and secure her secrecy by a declaration without reserve.

"Do not imagine," said the princess, "that I came hither as a spy: I had long observed from my window, that you and Imlac directed your walk every day towards the same point, but I did not suppose you had any better reason for the preference than a cooler shade, or more fragrant bank; nor followed you with any other design than to partake of your conversation. Since then not suspicion but fondness has detected you, let me not lose the advantage of my discovery. I am equally weary of confinement with yourself, and not less desirous of knowing what is done or suffered in the world. Permit me to fly with you from this tasteless tranquility, which will yet grow more loathsome when you have left me. You may deny me to accompany you, but cannot hinder me from following."

The prince, who loved Nekayah above his other sisters, had no inclination to refuse her request, and grieved that he had lost an opportunity of showing his confidence by a voluntary communication. It was therefore agreed that she should leave the valley with them; and that, in the mean time, she should watch, lest any other straggler should, by chance or curiosity, follow them to the mountain.

At length their labor was at an end; they saw light beyond the prominence, and, issuing to the top of the mountain, beheld the Nile, yet a narrow current, wandering beneath them.

The prince looked round with rapture, anticipated all the pleasures of travel, and in thought was already transported beyond his father's dominions.

Imlac, though very joyful at his escape, had less expectation of pleasure in the world, which he had before tried, and of which he had been weary.

Rasselas was so much delighted with a wider horizon, that he could not soon be persuaded to return into the valley. He informed his sister that the way was open, and that nothing now remained but to prepare for their departure.

Chapter 15. The Prince and Princess Leave the Valley, and See Many Wonders

The prince and princess had jewels sufficient to make them rich whenever they came into a place of commerce, which, by Imlac's direction, they hid in their clothes, and, on the night of the next full moon, all left the valley. The princess was followed only by a single favorite, who did not know whither she was going.

They clambered through the cavity, and began to go down on the other side. The princess and her maid turned their eyes towards every part, and, seeing nothing to bound their prospect, considered themselves as in danger of being lost in a dreary vacuity. They stopped and trembled. "I am almost afraid," said the princess, "to begin a journey of which I cannot perceive an end, and to venture into this immense plain where I may be approached on every side by men whom I never saw." The prince felt nearly the same emotions, though he thought it more manly to conceal them.

Imlac smiled at their terrors, and encouraged them to proceed; but the princess continued irresolute till she had been imperceptibly drawn forward too far to return.

In the morning they found some shepherds in the field, who set milk and fruits before them. The princess wondered that she did not see a palace ready for her reception, and a table spread with delicacies; but, being faint and hungry, she drank the milk and ate the fruits, and thought them of a higher flavor than the products of the valley.

They traveled forward by easy journeys, being all unaccustomed to toil or difficulty, and knowing, that though they might be missed, they could not be pursued. In a few days they came into a more populous region, where Imlac was diverted with the admiration which his companions expressed at the diversity of manners, stations and employments.

Their dress was such as might not bring upon them the suspicion of having any thing to conceal, yet the prince, wherever he came, expected to be obeyed, and the princess was frighted, because those that came into her presence did not prostrate themselves before her. Imlac was forced to observe them with great vigilance, lest they should betray their rank by their unusual behavior, and detained them several weeks in the first village to accustom them to the sight of common mortals.

By degrees the royal wanderers were taught to understand that they had for a time laid aside their dignity, and were to expect only such regard as liberality and courtesy could procure. And Imlac, having, by many admonitions, prepared them to endure the tumults of a port, and the ruggedness of the commercial race, brought them down to the seacoast.

The prince and his sister, to whom every thing was new, were gratified equally at all places, and therefore remained for some months at the port without any inclination to pass further. Imlac was content with their stay, because he did not think it safe to expose them, unpracticed in the world, to the hazards of a foreign country.

At last he began to fear lest they should be discovered, and proposed to fix a day for their departure. They had no pretensions to judge for themselves, and referred the whole scheme to his direction. He therefore took passage in a ship to Suez; and, when the time came, with great difficulty prevailed on the princess to enter the vessel. They had a quick and prosperous voyage, and from Suez traveled by land to Cairo.

Chapter 16. *They Enter Cairo, and Find Every Man Happy*

As they approached the city, which filled the strangers with astonishment, "This," said Imlac to the prince, "is the place where travelers and merchants assemble from all the corners of the earth. You will here find men of every character and every occupation. Commerce is here honorable. I will act as a merchant, and you shall live as strangers, who have no other end of travel than curiosity. It will soon be observed that we are rich; our reputation will procure us access to all whom we shall desire to know; you will see all the conditions of humanity, and enable yourself at leisure to make your *choice of life*."

They now entered the town, stunned by the noise, and offended by the crowds. Instruction had not yet so prevailed over habit, but that they wondered to see themselves pass undistinguished along the street, and met by the lowest of the people without reverence or notice. The princess could not at first bear the thought of being leveled with the vulgar,[7] and for some days continued in her chamber, where she was served by her favorite, Pekuah, as in the palace of the valley.

Imlac, who understood traffic,[8] sold part of the jewels the next day, and hired a house, which he adorned with such magnificence that he was immediately considered as a merchant of great wealth. His politeness attracted many acquaintance, and his generosity made him courted by many dependents. His table was crowded by men of every nation, who all admired his knowledge, and solicited his favor. His companions, not being able to mix in the conversation, could make no discovery[9] of their ignorance or surprise, and were gradually initiated in the world as they gained knowledge of the language.

The prince had, by frequent lectures, been, taught the use and nature of money; but the ladies could not for a long time comprehend what the merchants did with small pieces of gold and silver, or why things of so little use should be received as equivalent to the necessaries of life.

They studied the language two years, while Imlac was preparing to set before them the various ranks and conditions of mankind. He grew acquainted with all who had anything uncommon in their fortune or conduct. He frequented the voluptuous and the frugal, the idle and the busy, the merchants and the men of learning.

7. Ordinary people.
8. Commerce.

9. Exposure.

The prince being now able to converse with fluency, and having learned the caution necessary to be observed in his intercourse with strangers, began to accompany Imlac to places of resort, and to enter into all assemblies, that he might make his *choice of life*.

For some time he thought choice needless, because all appeared to him equally happy. Wherever he went he met gaiety and kindness, and heard the song of joy or the laugh of carelessness. He began to believe that the world overflowed with universal plenty, and that nothing was withheld either from want or merit; that every hand showered liberality, and every heart melted with benevolence: "And who then," says he, "will be suffered to be wretched?"

Imlac permitted the pleasing delusion, and was unwilling to crush the hope of inexperience, till one day, having sat awhile silent, "I know not," said the prince, "what can be the reason that I am more unhappy than any of our friends. I see them perpetually and unalterably cheerful, but feel my own mind restless and uneasy. I am unsatisfied with those pleasures which I seem most to court; I live in the crowds of jollity, not so much to enjoy company as to shun myself, and am only loud and merry to conceal my sadness."

"Every man," said Imlac, "may, by examining his own mind, guess what passes in the minds of others; when you feel that your own gaiety is counterfeit, it may justly lead you to suspect that of your companions not to be sincere. Envy is commonly reciprocal. We are long before we are convinced that happiness is never to be found, and each believes it possessed by others, to keep alive the hope of obtaining it for himself. In the assembly where you passed the last night, there appeared such sprightliness of air, and volatility of fancy, as might have suited beings of an higher order, formed to inhabit serener regions, inaccessible to care or sorrow; yet, believe me, prince, there was not one who did not dread the moment when solitude should deliver him to the tyranny of reflection."

"This," said the prince, "may be true of others, since it is true of me; yet, whatever be the general infelicity of man, one condition is more happy than another, and wisdom surely directs us to take the least evil in the *choice of life*."

"The causes of good and evil," answered Imlac, "are so various and uncertain, so often entangled with each other, so diversified by various relations, and so much subject to accidents which cannot be foreseen, that he who would fix his condition upon incontestable reasons of preference must live and die inquiring and deliberating."

"But, surely," said Rasselas, "the wise men, to whom we listen with reverence and wonder, chose that mode of life for themselves which they thought most likely to make them happy."

"Very few," said the poet, "live by choice. Every man is placed in his present condition by causes which acted without his foresight, and with which he did not always willingly cooperate; and therefore you will rarely meet one who does not think the lot of his neighbor better than his own."

"I am pleased to think," said the prince, "that my birth has given me at least one advantage over others, by enabling me to determine for myself. I have here the world before me. I will review it at leisure; surely happiness is somewhere to be found."

Chapter 17. The Prince Associates with Young Men of Spirit and Gaiety

Rasselas rose next day, and resolved to begin his experiments upon life. "Youth," cried he, "is the time of gladness: I will join myself to the young men, whose only business is to gratify their desires, and whose time is all spent in a succession of enjoyments."

To such societies he was readily admitted, but a few days brought him back weary and disgusted. Their mirth was without images,[1] their laughter without motive; their pleasures were gross and sensual, in which the mind had no part; their conduct was at once wild and mean; they laughed at order and at law, but the frown of power dejected, and the eye of wisdom abashed them.

The prince soon concluded, that he should never be happy in a course of life of which he was ashamed. He thought it unsuitable to a reasonable being to act without a plan, and to be sad or cheerful only by chance. "Happiness," said he, "must be something solid and permanent, without fear and without uncertainty."

But his young companions had gained so much of his regard by their frankness and courtesy, that he could not leave them without warning and remonstrance. "My friends," said he, "I have seriously considered our manners and our prospects, and find that we have mistaken our own interest. The first years of man must make provision for the last. He that never thinks never can be wise. Perpetual levity must end in ignorance; and intemperance, though it may fire the spirits for an hour, will make life short or miserable. Let us consider that youth is of no long duration, and that in maturer age, when the enchantments of fancy shall cease, and phantoms of delight dance no more about us, we shall have no comforts but the esteem of wise men, and the means of doing good. Let us, therefore, stop, while to stop is in our power: let us live as men who are sometime to grow old, and to whom it will be the most dreadful of all evils not to count their past years but by follies, and to be reminded of their former luxuriance of health only by the maladies which riot has produced."

They stared a while in silence one upon another, and, at last, drove him away by a general chorus of continued laughter.

The consciousness that his sentiments were just, and his intentions kind, was scarcely sufficient to support him against the horror of derision. But he recovered his tranquillity, and pursued his search.

Chapter 18. The Prince Finds a Wise and Happy Man

As he was one day walking in the street, he saw a spacious building which all were, by the open doors, invited to enter: he followed the stream of people, and found it a hall or school of declamation, in which professors read lectures to their auditory.[2] He fixed his eye upon a sage raised above the rest, who discoursed with great energy on the government of the passions. His look was venerable, his action graceful, his pronunciation clear, and his diction elegant. He showed with great strength of sentiment and variety of illustration that human nature is degraded and debased, when the lower faculties

1. Ideas.   2. Audience.

predominate over the higher; that when fancy, the parent of passion, usurps the dominion of the mind, nothing ensues but the natural effect of unlawful government, perturbation, and confusion; that she betrays the fortresses of the intellect to rebels, and excites her children to sedition against reason, their lawful sovereign. He compared reason to the sun, of which the light is constant, uniform and lasting; and fancy to a meteor, of bright but transitory luster, irregular in its motion, and delusive in its direction.

He then communicated the various precepts given from time to time for the conquest of passion, and displayed the happiness of those who had obtained the important victory, after which man is no longer the slave of fear, nor the fool of hope; is no more emaciated by envy, inflamed by anger, emasculated by tenderness, or depressed by grief; but walks on calmly through the tumults or the privacies of life, as the sun pursues alike his course through the calm or the stormy sky.

He enumerated many examples of heroes immovable by pain or pleasure, who looked with indifference on those modes or accidents to which the vulgar give the names of good and evil. He exhorted his hearers to lay aside their prejudices, and arm themselves against the shafts of malice or misfortune, by invulnerable patience; concluding that this state only was happiness, and that this happiness was in everyone's power.

Rasselas listened to him with the veneration due to the instructions of a superior being, and, waiting for him at the door, humbly implored the liberty of visiting so great a master of true wisdom. The lecturer hesitated a moment, when Rasselas put a purse of gold into his hand, which he received with a mixture of joy and wonder.

"I have found," said the prince at his return to Imlac, "a man who can teach all that is necessary to be known; who, from the unshaken throne of rational fortitude, looks down on the scenes of life changing beneath him. He speaks, and attention watches his lips. He reasons, and conviction closes his periods.[3] This man shall be my future guide; I will learn his doctrines, and imitate his life."

"Be not too hasty," said Imlac, "to trust or to admire the teachers of morality: they discourse like angels, but they live like men."

Rasselas, who could not conceive how any man could reason so forcibly without feeling the cogency of his own arguments, paid his visit in a few days, and was denied admission. He had now learned the power of money, and made his way by a piece of gold to the inner apartment, where he found the philosopher in a room half darkened, with his eyes misty and his face pale. "Sir," said he, "you are come at a time when all human friendship is useless; what I suffer cannot be remedied, what I have lost cannot be supplied. My daughter, my only daughter, from whose tenderness I expected all the comforts of my age, died last night of a fever. My views, my purposes, my hopes are at an end; I am now a lonely being, disunited from society."

"Sir," said the prince, "mortality is an event by which a wise man can never be surprised; we know that death is always near, and it should therefore always be expected." "Young man," answered the philosopher, "you speak like one that has never felt the pangs of separation." "Have you then forgot the precepts," said Rasselas, "which you so powerfully enforced? Has wisdom no

---

3. Completed sentences.

strength to arm the heart against calamity? Consider that external things are naturally variable, but truth and reason are always the same." "What comfort," said the mourner, "can truth and reason afford me? Of what effect are they now, but to tell me that my daughter will not be restored?"

The prince, whose humanity would not suffer him to insult misery with reproof, went away, convinced of the emptiness of rhetorical sound, and the inefficacy of polished periods and studied sentences.[4]

Chapter 19. A Glimpse of Pastoral Life

He was still eager upon the same inquiry; and having heard of a hermit that lived near the lowest cataract of the Nile, and filled the whole country with the fame of his sanctity, resolved to visit his retreat, and inquire whether that felicity which public life could not afford was to be found in solitude; and whether a man whose age and virtue made him venerable could teach any peculiar art of shunning evils, or enduring them.

Imlac and the princess agreed to accompany him, and, after the necessary preparations, they began their journey. Their way lay through fields, where shepherds tended their flocks and the lambs were playing upon the pasture. "This," said the poet, "is the life which has been often celebrated for its innocence and quiet; let us pass the heat of the day among the shepherds' tents, and know whether all our searches are not to terminate in pastoral simplicity."

The proposal pleased them, and they induced the shepherds, by small presents and familiar questions, to tell their opinion of their own state. They were so rude and ignorant, so little able to compare the good with the evil of the occupation, and so indistinct in their narratives and descriptions, that very little could be learned from them. But it was evident that their hearts were cankered with discontent; that they considered themselves as condemned to labor for the luxury of the rich, and looked up with stupid malevolence toward those that were placed above them.

The princess pronounced with vehemence that she would never suffer these envious savages to be her companions, and that she should not soon be desirous of seeing any more specimens of rustic happiness; but could not believe that all the accounts of primeval pleasures were fabulous, and was yet in doubt whether life had anything that could be justly preferred to the placid gratifications of fields and woods. She hoped that the time would come, when, with a few virtuous and elegant companions, she could gather flowers planted by her own hand, fondle the lambs of her own ewe, and listen, without care, among brooks and breezes, to one of her maidens reading in the shade.

Chapter 20. The Danger of Prosperity

On the next day they continued their journey, till the heat compelled them to look round for shelter. At a small distance they saw a thick wood, which they no sooner entered than they perceived that they were approaching the habitations of men. The shrubs were diligently cut away to open walks where

4. Maxims or moral axioms.

the shades were darkest; the boughs of opposite trees were artificially inter-woven; seats of flowery turf were raised in vacant spaces, and a rivulet, that wantoned along the side of a winding path, had its banks sometimes opened into small basins, and its stream sometimes obstructed by little mounds of stone heaped together to increase its murmurs.

They passed slowly through the wood, delighted with such unexpected accommodations, and entertained each other with conjecturing what, or who, he could be, that, in those rude and unfrequented regions, had leisure and art for such harmless luxury.

As they advanced, they heard the sound of music, and saw youths and virgins dancing in the grove; and, going still further, beheld a stately palace built upon a hill surrounded with woods. The laws of eastern hospitality allowed them to enter, and the master welcomed them like a man liberal and wealthy.

He was skilful enough in appearances soon to discern that they were no common guests, and spread his table with magnificence. The eloquence of Imlac caught his attention, and the lofty courtesy of the princess excited his respect. When they offered to depart he entreated their stay, and was the next day still more unwilling to dismiss them than before. They were easily persuaded to stop, and civility grew up in time to freedom and confidence.

The prince now saw all the domestics cheerful, and all the face of nature smiling round the place, and could not forbear to hope that he should find here what he was seeking; but when he was congratulating the master upon his possessions, he answered with a sigh, "My condition has indeed the appearance of happiness, but appearances are delusive. My prosperity puts my life in danger; the Bassa[5] of Egypt is my enemy, incensed only by my wealth and popularity. I have been hitherto protected against him by the princes of the country; but, as the favor of the great is uncertain, I know not how soon my defenders may be persuaded to share the plunder with the Bassa. I have sent my treasures into a distant country, and, upon the first alarm, am prepared to follow them. Then will my enemies riot in my mansion, and enjoy the gardens which I have planted."

They all joined in lamenting his danger, and deprecating his exile; and the princess was so much disturbed with the tumult of grief and indignation, that she retired to her apartment. They continued with their kind inviter a few days longer, and then went forward to find the hermit.

Chapter 21. The Happiness of Solitude. The Hermit's History

They came on the third day, by the direction of the peasants, to the hermit's cell: it was a cavern in the side of a mountain, over-shadowed with palm-trees; at such a distance from the cataract, that nothing more was heard than a gentle uniform murmur, such as composed the mind to pensive meditation, especially when it was assisted by the wind whistling among the branches. The first rude essay of nature had been so much improved by human labor, that the cave contained several apartments, appropriated to different uses, and often afforded lodging to travelers, whom darkness or tempests happened to overtake.

5. Pasha: a Turkish viceroy.

The hermit sat on a bench at the door, to enjoy the coolness of the evening. On one side lay a book with pens and papers, on the other mechanical instruments of various kinds. As they approached him unregarded, the princess observed that he had not the countenance of a man that had found, or could teach, the way to happiness.

They saluted him with great respect, which he repaid like a man not unaccustomed to the forms of courts. "My children," said he, "if you have lost your way, you shall be willingly supplied with such conveniencies for the night as this cavern will afford. I have all that nature requires, and you will not expect delicacies in a hermit's cell."

They thanked him, and, entering, were pleased with the neatness and regularity of the place. The hermit set flesh and wine before them, though he fed only upon fruits and water. His discourse was cheerful without levity, and pious without enthusiasm.[6] He soon gained the esteem of his guests, and the princess repented of her hasty censure.

At last Imlac began thus: "I do not now wonder that your reputation is so far extended; we have heard at Cairo of your wisdom, and came hither to implore your direction for this young man and maiden in the *choice of life*."

"To him that lives well," answered the hermit, "every form of life is good; nor can I give any other rule for choice, than to remove from all apparent evil."

"He will remove most certainly from evil," said the prince, "who shall devote himself to that solitude which you have recommended by your example."

"I have indeed lived fifteen years in solitude," said the hermit, "but have no desire that my example should gain any imitators. In my youth I professed arms, and was raised by degrees to the highest military rank. I have traversed wide countries at the head of my troops, and seen many battles and sieges. At last, being disgusted by the preferment of a younger officer, and feeling that my vigor was beginning to decay, I resolved to close my life in peace, having found the world full of snares, discord, and misery. I had once escaped from the pursuit of the enemy by the shelter of this cavern, and therefore chose it for my final residence. I employed artificers to form it into chambers, and stored it with all that I was likely to want.

"For some time after my retreat, I rejoiced like a tempest-beaten sailor at his entrance into the harbor, being delighted with the sudden change of the noise and hurry of war, to stillness and repose. When the pleasure of novelty went away, I employed my hours in examining the plants which grow in the valley, and the minerals which I collected from the rocks. But that inquiry is now grown tasteless and irksome. I have been for some time unsettled and distracted: my mind is disturbed with a thousand perplexities of doubt, and vanities of imagination, which hourly prevail upon me, because I have no opportunities of relaxation or diversion. I am sometimes ashamed to think that I could not secure myself from vice, but by retiring from the exercise of virtue, and begin to suspect that I was rather impelled by resentment, than led by devotion, into solitude. My fancy riots in scenes of folly, and I lament that I have lost so much, and have gained so little. In solitude, if I escape the

---

6. "A vain belief of private revelation; a vain confidence of divine favor or communication" (Johnson's *Dictionary*).

example of bad men, I want likewise the counsel and conversation of the good. I have been long comparing the evils with the advantages of society, and resolve to return into the world tomorrow. The life of a solitary man will be certainly miserable, but not certainly devout."

They heard his resolution with surprise, but, after a short pause, offered to conduct him to Cairo. He dug up a considerable treasure which he had hid among the rocks, and accompanied them to the city, on which, as he approached it, he gazed with rapture.

Chapter 22. The Happiness of a Life Led According to Nature

Rasselas went often to an assembly of learned men, who met at stated times to unbend their minds and compare their opinions. Their manners were somewhat coarse, but their conversation was instructive, and their disputations acute, though sometimes too violent, and often continued till neither controvertist remembered upon what question they began. Some faults were almost general among them; everyone was desirous to dictate to the rest, and everyone was pleased to hear the genius or knowledge of another depreciated.

In this assembly Rasselas was relating his interview with the hermit, and the wonder with which he heard him censure a course of life which he had so deliberately chosen, and so laudably followed. The sentiments of the hearers were various. Some were of opinion that the folly of his choice had been justly punished by condemnation to perpetual perseverance. One of the youngest among them, with great vehemence, pronounced him an hypocrite. Some talked of the right of society to the labor of individuals, and considered retirement as a desertion of duty. Others readily allowed that there was a time when the claims of the public were satisfied, and when a man might properly sequester himself, to review his life and purify his heart.

One, who appeared more affected with the narrative than the rest, thought it likely that the hermit would in a few years go back to his retreat, and perhaps, if shame did not restrain, or death intercept him, return once more from his retreat into the world. "For the hope of happiness," said he, "is so strongly impressed that the longest experience is not able to efface it. Of the present state, whatever it be, we feel and are forced to confess the misery; yet when the same state is again at a distance, imagination paints it as desirable. But the time will surely come when desire will be no longer our torment, and no man shall be wretched but by his own fault."

"This," said a philosopher who had heard him with tokens of great impatience, "is the present condition of a wise man. The time is already come when none are wretched but by their own fault. Nothing is more idle than to inquire after happiness, which nature has kindly placed within our reach. The way to be happy is to live according to nature, in obedience to that universal and unalterable law with which every heart is originally impressed; which is not written on it by precept, but engraven by destiny, not instilled by education, but infused at our nativity. He that lives according to nature will suffer nothing from the delusions of hope, or importunities of desire; he will receive and reject with equability of temper, and act or suffer as the reason of things shall alternately prescribe. Other men may amuse themselves with subtle definitions, or intricate ratiocination. Let them learn to be wise by easier means; let them observe the hind of the forest, and the linnet of the grove; let them consider the life of animals, whose motions are regulated by instinct; they obey their guide, and are happy. Let us therefore, at length, cease to dispute, and learn to live; throw away the encumbrance of precepts, which they who utter them with so much pride and pomp do not understand, and carry with us this simple and intelligible maxim, that deviation from nature is deviation from happiness."

When he had spoken, he looked round him with a placid air, and enjoyed the consciousness of his own beneficence. "Sir," said the prince with great modesty, "as I, like all the rest of mankind, am desirous of felicity, my closest attention has been fixed upon your discourse. I doubt not the truth of a position which a man so learned has so confidently advanced. Let me only know what it is to live according to nature."

"When I find young men so humble and so docile," said the philosopher, "I can deny them no information which my studies have enabled me to afford. To live according to nature, is to act always with due regard to the fitness arising from the relations and qualities of causes and effects; to concur with the great and unchangeable scheme of universal felicity; to co-operate with the general disposition and tendency of the present system of things."

The prince soon found that this was one of the sages whom he should understand less as he heard him longer. He therefore bowed and was silent; and the philosopher, supposing him satisfied, and the rest vanquished, rose up and departed with the air of a man that had co-operated with the present system.

Chapter 23. The Prince and His Sister Divide between Them the Work of Observation

Rasselas returned home full of reflections, doubtful how to direct his future steps. Of the way to happiness he found the learned and simple equally ignorant; but, as he was yet young, he flattered himself that he had time remaining for more experiments, and further inquiries. He communicated to Imlac his observations and his doubts, but was answered by him with new doubts, and remarks that gave him no comfort. He therefore discoursed more frequently and freely with his sister, who had yet the same hope with himself, and always assisted him to give some reason why, though he had been hitherto frustrated, he might succeed at last.

"We have hitherto," said she, "known but little of the world: we have never yet been either great or mean. In our own country, though we had royalty, we had no power, and in this we have not yet seen the private recesses of domestic peace. Imlac favors not our search, lest we should in time find him mistaken. We will divide the task between us: you shall try what is to be found in the splendor of courts, and I will range the shades of humbler life. Perhaps command and authority may be the supreme blessings, as they afford most opportunities of doing good: or, perhaps, what this world can give may be found in the modest habitations of middle fortune; too low for great designs, and too high for penury and distress."

Chapter 24. The Prince Examines the Happiness of High Stations

Rasselas applauded the design, and appeared next day with a splendid retinue at the court of the Bassa. He was soon distinguished for his magnificence, and admitted, as a prince whose curiosity had brought him from distant countries, to an intimacy with the great officers, and frequent conversation with the Bassa himself:

He was at first inclined to believe, that the man must be pleased with his own condition, whom all approached with reverence, and heard with obedience, and who had the power to extend his edicts to a whole kingdom. "There can be no pleasure," said he, "equal to that of feeling at once the joy of thousands all made happy by wise administration. Yet, since, by the law of subordination, this sublime delight can be in one nation but the lot of one, it is surely reasonable to think that there is some satisfaction more popular[7] and accessible, and that millions can hardly be subjected to the will of a single man, only to fill his particular breast with incommunicable content."

These thoughts were often in his mind, and he found no solution of the difficulty. But as presents and civilities gained him more familiarity, he found that almost every man who stood high in employment hated all the rest, and was hated by them, and that their lives were a continual succession of plots and detections, stratagems and escapes, faction and treachery. Many of those, who surrounded the Bassa, were sent only to watch and report his conduct; every tongue was muttering censure and every eye was searching for a fault.

At last the letters of revocation arrived, the Bassa was carried in chains to Constantinople, and his name was mentioned no more.

"What are we now to think of the prerogatives of power," said Rasselas to his sister; "is it without any efficacy to good? or, is the subordinate degree only dangerous, and the supreme safe and glorious? Is the Sultan the only happy man in his dominions? or, is the Sultan himself subject to the torments of suspicion, and the dread of enemies?"

In a short time the second Bassa was deposed. The Sultan, that had advanced him, was murdered by the Janisaries,[8] and his successor had other views and different favorites.

Chapter 25. The Princess Pursues Her Inquiry with More Diligence than Success

The princess, in the mean time, insinuated herself into many families; for there are few doors, through which liberality, joined with good humor, cannot find its way. The daughters of many houses were airy[9] and cheerful, but Nekayah had been too long accustomed to the conversation of Imlac and her brother to be much pleased with childish levity and prattle which had no meaning. She found their thoughts narrow, their wishes low, and their merriment often artificial. Their pleasures, poor as they were, could not be preserved pure, but were embittered by petty competitions and worthless emulation. They were always jealous of the beauty of each other; of a quality

7. Common.
8. Guards of the Turkish ruler.

9. "Gay; sprightly; full of mirth" (Johnson's *Dictionary*).

to which solicitude can add nothing, and from which detraction can take nothing away. Many were in love with triflers like themselves, and many fancied that they were in love when in truth they were only idle. Their affection was seldom fixed on sense or virtue, and therefore seldom ended but in vexation. Their grief, however, like their joy, was transient; everything floated in their mind unconnected with the past or future, so that one desire easily gave way to another, as a second stone cast into the water effaces and confounds the circles of the first.

With these girls she played as with inoffensive animals, and found them proud of her countenance,[1] and weary of her company.

But her purpose was to examine more deeply, and her affability easily persuaded the hearts that were swelling with sorrow to discharge their secrets in her ear: and those whom hope flattered, or prosperity delighted, often courted her to partake their pleasures.

The princess and her brother commonly met in the evening in a private summer-house on the bank of the Nile, and related to each other the occurrences of the day. As they were sitting together, the princess cast her eyes upon the river that flowed before her. "Answer," said she, "great father of waters, thou that rollest thy floods through eighty nations, to the invocations of the daughter of thy native king. Tell me if thou waterest, through all thy course, a single habitation from which thou dost not hear the murmurs of complaint?"

"You are then," said Rasselas, "not more successful in private houses than I have been in courts." "I have, since the last partition of our provinces,"[2] said the princess, "enabled myself to enter familiarly into many families, where there was the fairest show of prosperity and peace, and know not one house that is not haunted by some fury that destroys its quiet.

"I did not seek ease among the poor, because I concluded that there it could not be found. But I saw many poor whom I had supposed to live in affluence. Poverty has, in large cities, very different appearances: it is often concealed in splendor, and often in extravagance. It is the care of a very great part of mankind to conceal their indigence from the rest: they support themselves by temporary expedients, and every day is lost in contriving for the morrow.

"This, however, was an evil, which, though frequent, I saw with less pain, because I could relieve it. Yet some have refused my bounties; more offended with my quickness to detect their wants, than pleased with my readiness to succor them: and others, whose exigencies compelled them to admit my kindness, have never been able to forgive their benefactress. Many, however, have been sincerely grateful without the ostentation of gratitude, or the hope of other favors."

Chapter 26. The Princess Continues Her Remarks upon Private Life

Nekayah, perceiving her brother's attention fixed, proceeded in her narrative.

"In families where there is or is not poverty, there is commonly discord. If a kingdom be, as Imlac tells us, a great family, a family likewise is a little

1. Patronage, favor. 2. Division of our responsibilities.

kingdom, torn with factions and exposed to revolutions. An unpracticed observer expects the love of parents and children to be constant and equal; but this kindness seldom continues beyond the years of infancy: in a short time the children become rivals to their parents. Benefits are allayed[3] by reproaches, and gratitude debased by envy.

"Parents and children seldom act in concert; each child endeavors to appropriate the esteem or fondness of the parents, and the parents, with yet less temptation, betray each other to their children. Thus, some place their confidence in the father, and some in the mother, and by degrees the house is filled with artifices and feuds.

"The opinions of children and parents, of the young and the old, are naturally opposite, by the contrary effects of hope and despondence, of expectation and experience, without crime or folly on either side. The colors of life in youth and age appear different, as the face of nature in spring and winter. And how can children credit the assertions of parents, which their own eyes show them to be false?

"Few parents act in such a manner as much to enforce their maxims by the credit of their lives. The old man trusts wholly to slow contrivance and gradual progression; the youth expects to force his way by genius, vigor, and precipitance. The old man pays regard to riches, and the youth reverences virtue. The old man deifies prudence; the youth commits himself to magnanimity and chance. The young man, who intends no ill, believes that none is intended, and therefore acts with openness and candor; but his father, having suffered the injuries of fraud, is impelled to suspect, and too often allured to practice it. Age looks with anger on the temerity of youth, and youth with contempt on the scrupulosity[4] of age. Thus parents and children, for the greatest part, live on to love less and less; and, if those whom nature has thus closely united are the torments of each other, where shall we look for tenderness and consolation?"

"Surely," said the prince, "you must have been unfortunate in your choice of acquaintance: I am unwilling to believe that the most tender of all relations is thus impeded in its effects by natural necessity."

"Domestic discord," answered she, "is not inevitably and fatally necessary, but yet is not easily avoided. We seldom see that a whole family is virtuous; the good and evil cannot well agree, and the evil can yet less agree with one another. Even the virtuous fall sometimes to variance, when their virtues are of different kinds, and tending to extremes. In general, those parents have most reverence who most deserve it; for he that lives well cannot be despised.

"Many other evils infest private life. Some are the slaves of servants whom they have trusted with their affairs. Some are kept in continual anxiety to the caprice of rich relations, whom they cannot please, and dare not offend. Some husbands are imperious, and some wives perverse; and, as it is always more easy to do evil than good, though the wisdom or virtue of one can very rarely make many happy, the folly or vice of one may often make many miserable."

---

3. To allay is "to join anything to another, so as to abate its predominant qualities" (Johnson's Dictionary).

4. "Fear of acting in any manner" (Johnson's Dictionary).

"If such be the general effect of marriage," said the prince, "I shall for the future think it dangerous to connect my interest with that of another, lest I should be unhappy by my partner's fault."

"I have met," said the princess, "with many who live single for that reason; but I never found that their prudence ought to raise envy. They dream away their time without friendship, without fondness, and are driven to rid themselves of the day, for which they have no use, by childish amusements, or vicious delights. They act as beings under the constant sense of some known inferiority that fills their minds with rancor, and their tongues with censure. They are peevish at home, and malevolent abroad; and, as the outlaws of human nature, make it their business and their pleasure to disturb that society which debars them from its privileges. To live without feeling or exciting sympathy, to be fortunate without adding to the felicity of others, or afflicted without tasting the balm of pity, is a state more gloomy than solitude; it is not retreat but exclusion from mankind. Marriage has many pains, but celibacy has no pleasures."

"What then is to be done?" said Rasselas; "the more we inquire, the less we can resolve. Surely he is most likely to please himself that has no other inclination to regard."

Chapter 27. Disquisition upon Greatness

The conversation had a short pause. The prince, having considered his sister's observations, told her, that she had surveyed life with prejudice, and supposed misery where she did not find it. "Your narrative," says he, "throws yet a darker gloom upon the prospects of futurity: the predictions of Imlac were but faint sketches of the evils painted by Nekayah. I have been lately, convinced that quiet is not the daughter of grandeur, or of power: that her presence is not to be bought by wealth, nor enforced by conquest. It is evident, that as any man acts in a wider compass, he must be more exposed to opposition from enmity or miscarriage from chance; whoever has many to please or to govern, must use the ministry of many agents, some of whom will be wicked, and some ignorant; by some he will be misled, and by others betrayed. If he gratifies one he will offend another: those that are not favored will think themselves injured; and, since favors can be conferred but upon few, the greater number will be always discontented."

"The discontent," said the princess, "which is thus unreasonable, I hope that I shall always have spirit to despise, and you, power to repress."

"Discontent," answered Rasselas, "will not always be without reason under the most just or vigilant administration of public affairs. None, however attentive, can always discover that merit which indigence or faction may happen to obscure; and none, however powerful, can always reward it. Yet, he that sees inferior desert[5] advanced above him, will naturally impute that preference to partiality or caprice; and, indeed, it can scarcely be hoped that any man, however magnanimous by nature, or exalted by condition, will be able to persist for ever in fixed and inexorable justice of distribution: he will sometimes indulge his own affections, and sometimes those of his favorites; he will permit some to please him who can never serve him; he will discover

---

5. Merit; one deserving reward.

in those whom he loves qualities which in reality they do not possess; and to those, from whom he receives pleasure, he will in his turn endeavor to give it. Thus will recommendations sometimes prevail which were purchased by money, or by the more destructive bribery of flattery and servility.

"He that has much to do will do something wrong, and of that wrong must suffer the consequences; and, if it were possible that he should always act rightly, yet when such numbers are to judge of his conduct, the bad will censure and obstruct him by malevolence, and the good sometimes by mistake.

"The highest stations cannot therefore hope to be the abodes of happiness, which I would willingly believe to have fled from thrones and palaces to seats of humble privacy and placid obscurity. For what can hinder the satisfaction, or intercept the expectations, of him whose abilities are adequate to his employments, who sees with his own eyes the whole circuit of his influence, who chooses by his own knowledge all whom he trusts, and whom none are tempted to deceive by hope or fear? Surely he has nothing to do but to love and to be loved, to be virtuous and to be happy."

"Whether perfect happiness would be procured by perfect goodness," said Nekayah, "this world will never afford an opportunity of deciding. But this, at least, may be maintained, that we do not always find visible happiness in proportion to visible virtue. All natural and almost all political evils, are incident alike to the bad and good: they are confounded in the misery of a famine, and not much distinguished in the fury of a faction; they sink together in a tempest, and are driven together from their country by invaders. All that virtue can afford is quietness of conscience, a steady prospect of a happier state; this may enable us to endure calamity with patience; but remember that patience must suppose pain."

Chapter 28. Rasselas and Nekayah Continue Their Conversation

"Dear princess," said Rasselas, "you fall into the common errors of exaggeratory declamation, by producing, in a familiar disquisition,[6] examples of national calamities, and scenes of extensive misery, which are found in books rather than in the world, and which, as they are horrid, are ordained to be rare. Let us not imagine evils which we do not feel, nor injure life by misrepresentations. I cannot bear that querulous eloquence which threatens every city with a siege like that of Jerusalem,[7] that makes famine attend on every flight of locusts, and suspends pestilence on the wing of every blast that issues from the south.

"On necessary and inevitable evils, which overwhelm kingdoms at once, all disputation is vain: when they happen they must be endured. But it is evident, that these bursts of universal distress are more dreaded than felt: thousands and ten thousands flourish in youth, and wither in age, without the knowledge of any other than domestic evils, and share the same pleasures and vexations whether their kings are mild or cruel, whether the armies of their country pursue their enemies, or retreat before them. While courts are disturbed with intestine[8] competitions, and ambassadors are negotiating in foreign countries, the smith still plies his anvil, and the husbandman drives

---

6. Family discussion of a question.
7. In 70 c.e. the Romans, under Titus, besieged

and destroyed Jerusalem.
8. Internal, domestic.

his plow forward; the necessaries of life are required and obtained, and the successive business of the seasons continues to make its wonted revolutions.

"Let us cease to consider what, perhaps, may never happen, and what, when it shall happen, will laugh at human speculation. We will not endeavor to modify the motions of the elements, or to fix the destiny of kingdoms. It is our business to consider what beings like us may perform; each laboring for his own happiness, by promoting within his circle, however narrow, the happiness of others.

"Marriage is evidently the dictate of nature; men and women were made to be companions of each other, and therefore I cannot be persuaded but that marriage is one of the means of happiness."

"I know not," said the princess, "whether marriage be more than one of the innumerable modes of human misery. When I see and reckon the various forms of connubial infelicity, the unexpected causes of lasting discord, the diversities of temper, the oppositions of opinion, the rude collisons of contrary desire where both are urged by violent impulses, the obstinate contests of disagreeing virtues, where both are supported by consciousness of good intention, I am sometimes disposed to think with the severer casuists of most nations, that marriage is rather permitted than approved, and that none, but by the instigation of a passion too much indulged, entangle themselves with indissoluble compacts."

"You seem to forget," replied Rasselas, "that you have, even now, represented celibacy as less happy than marriage. Both conditions may be bad, but they cannot both be worst. Thus it happens when wrong opinions are entertained, that they mutually destroy each other, and leave the mind open to truth."

"I did not expect," answered the princess, "to hear that imputed to falsehood which is the consequence only of frailty. To the mind, as to the eye, it is difficult to compare with exactness objects vast in their extent, and various in their parts. Where we see or conceive the whole at once we readily note the discriminations and decide the preference: but of two systems, of which neither can be surveyed by any human being in its full compass of magnitude and multiplicity of complication, where is the wonder, that judging of the whole by parts, I am alternately affected by one and the other as either presses on my memory or fancy? We differ from ourselves just as we differ from each other, when we see only part of the question, as in the multifarious relations of politics and morality: but when we perceive the whole at once, as in numerical computations, all agree in one judgment, and none ever varies his opinion."

"Let us not add," said the prince, "to the other evils of life, the bitterness of controversy, nor endeavor to vie with each other in subtleties of argument. We are employed in a search, of which both are equally to enjoy the success, or suffer by the miscarriage. It is therefore fit that we assist each other. You surely conclude too hastily from the infelicity of marriage against its institution; will not the misery of life prove equally that life cannot be the gift of heaven? The world must be peopled by marriage, or peopled without it."

"How the world is to be peopled," returned Nekayah, "is not my care, and needs not be yours. I see no danger that the present generation should omit to leave successors behind them: we are not now inquiring for the world, but for ourselves."

Chapter 29. The Debate on Marriage Continued

"The good of the whole," says Rasselas, "is the same with the good of all its parts. If marriage be best for mankind it must be evidently best for individuals, or a permanent and necessary duty must be the cause of evil, and some must be inevitably sacrificed to the convenience of others. In the estimate which you have made of the two states, it appears that the incommodities of a single life are, in a great measure, necessary and certain, but those of the conjugal state accidental and avoidable.

"I cannot forbear to flatter myself that prudence and benevolence will make marriage happy. The general folly of mankind is the cause of general complaint. What can be expected but disappointment and repentance from a choice made in the immaturity of youth, in the ardor of desire, without judgment, without foresight, without inquiry after conformity of opinions, similarity of manners, rectitude of judgment, or purity of sentiment.

"Such is the common process of marriage. A youth and maiden meeting by chance, or brought together by artifice, exchange glances, reciprocate civilities, go home, and dream of one another. Having little to divert attention, or diversify thought, they find themselves uneasy when they are apart, and therefore conclude that they shall be happy together. They marry, and discover what nothing but voluntary blindness had before concealed; they wear out life in altercations, and charge nature with cruelty.

"From those early marriages proceeds likewise the rivalry of parents and children: the son is eager to enjoy the world before the father is willing to forsake it, and there is hardly room at once for two generations. The daughter begins to bloom before the mother can be content to fade, and neither can forbear to wish for the absence of the other.

"Surely all these evils may be avoided by that deliberation and delay which prudence prescribes to irrevocable choice. In the variety and jollity of youthful pleasures life may be well enough supported without the help of a partner. Longer time will increase experience, and wider views will allow better opportunities of inquiry and selection: one advantage, at least, will be certain; the parents will be visibly older than their children."

"What reason cannot collect," said Nekayah, "and what experiment has not yet taught, can be known only from the report of others. I have been told that late marriages are not eminently happy. This is a question too important to be neglected, and I have often proposed it to those, whose accuracy of remark, and comprehensiveness of knowledge, made their suffrages[9] worthy of regard. They have generally determined that it is dangerous for a man and woman to suspend their fate upon each other, at a time when opinions are fixed, and habits are established; when friendships have been contracted on both sides, when life has been planned into method, and the mind has long enjoyed the contemplation of its own prospects.

"It is scarcely possible that two traveling through the world under the conduct of chance should have been both directed to the same path, and it will not often happen that either will quit the track which custom has made pleasing. When the desultory levity of youth has settled into regularity, it is soon succeeded by pride ashamed to yield, or obstinacy delighting to con-

9. Opinions.

tend. And even though mutual esteem produces mutual desire to please, time itself, as it modifies unchangeably the external mien, determines likewise the direction of the passions, and gives an inflexible rigidity to the manners. Long customs are not easily broken: he that attempts to change the course of his own life very often labors in vain; and how shall we do that for others which we are seldom able to do for ourselves?"

"But surely," interposed the prince, "you suppose the chief motive of choice forgotten or neglected. Whenever I shall seek a wife, it shall be my first question, whether she be willing to be led by reason?"

"Thus it is," said Nekayah, "that philosophers are deceived. There are a thousand familiar[1] disputes which reason never can decide; questions that elude investigation, and make logic ridiculous; cases where something must be done, and where little can be said. Consider the state of mankind, and inquire how few can be supposed to act upon any occasions, whether small or great, with all the reasons of action present to their minds. Wretched would be the pair above all names of wretchedness, who should be doomed to adjust by reason every morning all the minute detail of a domestic day.

"Those who marry at an advanced age will probably escape the encroachments of their children; but, in diminution of this advantage, they will be likely to leave them, ignorant and helpless, to a guardian's mercy: or, if that should not happen, they must at least go out of the world before they see those whom they love best either wise or great.

"From their children, if they have less to fear, they have less also to hope, and they lose, without equivalent, the joys of early love, and the convenience of uniting with manners pliant and minds susceptible of new impressions, which might wear away their dissimilitudes by long cohabitation, as soft bodies, by continual attrition, conform their surfaces to each other.

"I believe it will be found that those who marry late are best pleased with their children, and those who marry early with their partners."

"The union of these two affections," said Rasselas, "would produce all that could be wished. Perhaps there is a time when marriage might unite them, a time neither too early for the father, nor too late for the husband."

"Every hour," answered the princess, "confirms my prejudice in favor of the position so often uttered by the mouth of Imlac, 'That nature sets her gifts on the right hand and on the left.' Those conditions, which flatter hope and attract desire, are so constituted that, as we approach one, we recede from another. There are goods so opposed that we cannot seize both, but, by too much prudence, may pass between them at too great a distance to reach either. This is often the fate of long consideration; he does nothing who endeavors to do more than is allowed to humanity. Flatter not yourself with contrarieties of pleasure. Of the blessings set before you make your choice, and be content. No man can taste the fruits of autumn, while he is delighting his scent with the flowers of the spring: no man can, at the same time, fill his cup from the source and from the mouth of the Nile."

1. Domestic.

Chapter 30. Imlac Enters, and Changes the Conversation

Here Imlac entered, and interrupted them. "Imlac," said Rasselas, "I have been taking from the princess the dismal history of private life, and am almost discouraged from further search."

"It seems to me," said Imlac, "that while you are making the choice of life, you neglect to live. You wander about a single city, which, however large and diversified, can now afford few novelties, and forget that you are in a country, famous among the earliest monarchies for the power and wisdom of its inhabitants; a country where the sciences first dawned that illuminate the world, and beyond which the arts cannot be traced of civil society or domestic life.

"The old Egyptians have left behind them monuments of industry and power before which all European magnificence is confessed to fade away. The ruins of their architecture are the schools of modern builders, and from the wonders which time has spared we may conjecture, though uncertainly, what it has destroyed."

"My curiosity," said Rasselas, "does not very strongly lead me to survey piles of stone, or mounds of earth; my business is with man. I came hither not to measure fragments of temples, or trace choked aqueducts, but to look upon the various scenes of the present world."

"The things that are now before us," said the princess, "require attention, and deserve it. What have I to do with the heroes or the monuments of ancient times? with times which never can return, and heroes, whose form of life was different from all that the present condition of mankind requires or allows."

"To know anything," returned the poet, "we must know its effects; to see men we must see their works, that we may learn what reason has dictated, or passion has incited, and find what are the most powerful motives of action. To judge rightly of the present we must oppose it to the past; for all judgment is comparative, and of the future nothing can be known. The truth is, that no mind is much employed upon the present: recollection and anticipation fill up almost all our moments. Our passions are joy and grief, love and hatred, hope and fear. Of joy and grief the past is the object, and the future of hope and fear; even love and hatred respect the past, for the cause must have been before the effect.

"The present state of things is the consequence of the former, and it is natural to inquire what were the sources of the good that we enjoy, or of the evil that we suffer. If we act only for ourselves, to neglect the study of history is not prudent: if we are entrusted with the care of others, it is not just. Ignorance, when it is voluntary, is criminal; and he may properly be charged with evil who refused to learn how he might prevent it.

"There is no part of history so generally useful as that which relates the progress of the human mind, the gradual improvement of reason, the successive advances of science, the vicissitudes of learning and ignorance, which are the light and darkness of thinking beings, the extinction and resuscitation of arts, and all the revolutions of the intellectual world. If accounts of battles and invasions are peculiarly the business of princes, the useful or elegant arts are not to be neglected; those who have kingdoms to govern, have understandings to cultivate.

"Example is always more efficacious than precept. A soldier is formed in war, and a painter must copy pictures. In this, contemplative life has the advantage: great actions are seldom seen, but the labors of art are always at hand for those who desire to know what art has been able to perform.

"When the eye or the imagination is struck with any uncommon work the next transition of an active mind is to the means by which it was performed. Here begins the true use of such contemplation; we enlarge our comprehension by new ideas, and perhaps recover some art lost to mankind, or learn what is less perfectly known in our own country. At least we compare our own with former times, and either rejoice at our improvements, or, what is the first motion towards good, discover our defects."

"I am willing," said the prince, "to see all that can deserve my search." "And I," said the princess, "shall rejoice to learn something of the manners of antiquity."

"The most pompous monument of Egyptian greatness, and one of the most bulky works of manual industry," said Imlac, "are the pyramids; fabrics[2] raised before the time of history, and of which the earliest narratives afford us only uncertain traditions. Of these the greatest is still standing, very little injured by time."

"Let us visit them tomorrow," said Nekayah. "I have often heard of the pyramids, and shall not rest, till I have seen them within and without with my own eyes."

Chapter 31. They Visit the Pyramids

The resolution being thus taken, they set out the next day. They laid tents upon their camels, being resolved to stay among the pyramids till their curiosity was fully satisfied. They traveled gently, turned aside to everything remarkable, stopped from time to time and conversed with the inhabitants, and observed the various appearances of towns ruined and inhabited, of wild and cultivated nature.

When they came to the great pyramid, they were astonished at the extent of the base, and the height of the top. Imlac explained to them the principles upon which the pyramidal form was chosen for a fabric intended to coextend its duration with that of the world; he showed that its gradual diminution gave it such stability as defeated all the common attacks of the elements, and could scarcely be overthrown by earthquakes themselves, the least resistible of natural violence. A concussion that should shatter the pyramid would threaten the dissolution of the continent.

They measured all its dimensions, and pitched their tents at its foot. Next day they prepared to enter its interior apartments, and having hired the common guides, climbed up to the first passage, when the favorite of the princess, looking into the cavity, stepped back and trembled. "Pekuah," said the princess, "of what art thou afraid?" "Of the narrow entrance," answered the lady, "and of the dreadful gloom. I dare not enter a place which must surely be inhabited by unquiet souls. The original possessors of these dreadful vaults will start up before us, and perhaps shut us in forever." She spoke, and threw her arms round the neck of her mistress.

2. Buildings.

"If all your fear be of apparitions," said the prince, "I will promise you safety. There is no danger from the dead; he that is once buried will be seen no more."

"That the dead are seen no more," said Imlac, "I will not undertake to maintain, against the concurrent and unvaried testimony of all ages, and of all nations. There is no people, rude or learned, among whom apparitions of the dead are not related and believed. This opinion, which perhaps prevails as far as human nature is diffused, could become universal only by its truth; those that never heard of one another would not have agreed in a tale which nothing but experience can make credible. That it is doubted by single cavil-ers can very little weaken the general evidence; and some who deny it with their tongues confess it by their fears.

"Yet I do not mean to add new terrors to those which have already seized upon Pekuah. There can be no reason why specters should haunt the pyra-mid more than other places, or why they should have power or will to hurt innocence and purity. Our entrance is no violation of their privileges; we can take nothing from them, how then can we offend them?"

"My dear Pekuah," said the princess, "I will always go before you, and Imlac shall follow you. Remember that you are the companion of the prin-cess of Abyssinia."

"If the princess is pleased that her servant should die," returned the lady, "let her command some death less dreadful than enclosure in this horrid cavern. You know I dare not disobey you; I must go if you command me, but if I once enter, I never shall come back."

The princess saw that her fear was too strong for expostulation or reproof, and, embracing her, told her that she should stay in the tent till their return. Pekuah was yet not satisfied, but entreated the princess not to pursue so dreadful a purpose as that of entering the recesses of the pyramid. "Though I cannot teach courage," said Nekayah, "I must not learn cowardice, nor leave at last undone what I came hither only to do."

Chapter 32. They Enter the Pyramid

Pekuah descended to the tents, and the rest entered the pyramid. They passed through the galleries, surveyed the vaults of marble, and examined the chest in which the body of the founder is supposed to have been repos-ited. They then sat down in one of the most spacious chambers to rest a while before they attempted to return.

"We have now," said Imlac, "gratified our minds with an exact view of the greatest work of man, except the wall of China.

"Of the wall it is very easy to assign the motive. It secured a wealthy and timorous nation from the incursions of barbarians, whose unskillfulness in arts made it easier for them to supply their wants by rapine than by industry, and who from time to time poured in upon the habitations of peaceful com-merce, as vultures descend upon domestic fowl. Their celerity and fierceness made the wall necessary, and their ignorance made it efficacious.

"But for the pyramids, no reason has ever been given adequate to the cost and labor of the work. The narrowness of the chambers proves that it could afford no retreat from enemies, and treasures might have been reposited at far less expense with equal security. It seems to have been erected only in compliance with that hunger of imagination which preys incessantly upon life, and must be always appeased by some employment. Those who have already all that they can enjoy must enlarge their desires. He that has built for use till use is supplied, must begin to build for vanity, and extend his plan to the utmost power of human performance, that he may not be soon reduced to form another wish.

"I consider this mighty structure as a monument of the insufficiency of human enjoyments. A king, whose power is unlimited, and whose treasures surmount all real and imaginary wants, is compelled to solace, by the erection of a pyramid, the satiety of dominion and tastelessness of pleasures, and to amuse the tediousness of declining life by seeing thousands laboring without end, and one stone, for no purpose, laid upon another. Whoever thou art, that, not content with a moderate condition, imaginest happiness in royal magnificence, and dreamest that command or riches can feed the appetite of novelty with perpetual gratifications, survey the pyramids, and confess thy folly!"

Chapter 33. *The Princess Meets with an Unexpected Misfortune*

They rose up, and returned through the cavity at which they had entered, and the princess prepared for her favorite a long narrative of dark labyrinths, and costly rooms, and of the different impressions which the varieties of the way had made upon her. But when they came to their train, they found every one silent and dejected: the men discovered[3] shame and fear in their countenances, and the women were weeping in the tents.

What had happened they did not try to conjecture, but immediately inquired. "You had scarcely entered into the pyramid," said one of the attendants, "when a troop of Arabs rushed upon us: we were too few to resist them, and too slow to escape. They were about to search the tents, set us on our camels, and drive us along before them, when the approach of some Turkish horsemen put them to flight; but they seized the lady Pekuah with her two maids, and carried them away: the Turks are now pursuing them by our instigation, but I fear they will not be able to overtake them."

The princess was overpowered with surprise and grief. Rasselas, in the first heat of his resentment, ordered his servants to follow him, and prepared to pursue the robbers with his saber in his hand. "Sir," said Imlac, "what can you hope from violence or valor? the Arabs are mounted on horses trained to battle and retreat; we have only beasts of burden. By leaving our present station we may lose the princess, but cannot hope to regain Pekuah."

In a short time the Turks returned, having not been able to reach the enemy. The princess burst out into new lamentations, and Rasselas could scarcely forbear to reproach them with cowardice; but Imlac was of opinion, that the escape of the Arabs was no addition to their misfortune, for, perhaps, they would have killed their captives rather than have resigned them.

---

3. Revealed, betrayed. "Train": retinue.

Chapter 34. They Return to Cairo without Pekuah

There was nothing to be hoped from longer stay. They returned to Cairo repenting of their curiosity, censuring the negligence of the government, lamenting their own rashness which had neglected to procure a guard, imagining many expedients by which the loss of Pekuah might have been prevented, and resolving to do something for her recovery, though none could find any thing proper to be done.

Nekayah retired to her chamber, where her women attempted to comfort her, by telling her that all had their troubles, and that lady Pekuah had enjoyed much happiness in the world for a long time, and might reasonably expect a change of fortune. They hoped that some good would befall her wheresoever she was, and that their mistress would find another friend who might supply her place.

The princess made them no answer, and they continued the form of condolence, not much grieved in their hearts that the favorite was lost.

Next day the prince presented to the Bassa a memorial[4] of the wrong which he had suffered, and a petition for redress. The Bassa threatened to punish the robbers, but did not attempt to catch them, nor, indeed, could any account or description be given by which he might direct the pursuit.

It soon appeared that nothing would be done by authority. Governors, being accustomed to hear of more crimes than they can punish, and more wrongs than they can redress, set themselves at ease by indiscriminate negligence, and presently[5] forget the request when they lose sight of the petitioner.

Imlac then endeavored to gain some intelligence by private agents. He found many who pretended to an exact knowledge of all the haunts of the Arabs, and to regular correspondence with their chiefs, and who readily undertook the recovery of Pekuah. Of these, some were furnished with money for their journey, and came back no more; some were liberally paid for accounts which a few days discovered to be false. But the princess would not suffer any means, however improbable, to be left untried. While she was doing something she kept her hope alive. As one expedient failed, another was suggested; when one messenger returned unsuccessful, another was dispatched to a different quarter.

Two months had now passed, and of Pekuah nothing had been heard; the hopes which they had endeavored to raise in each other grew more languid, and the princess, when she saw nothing more to be tried, sunk down inconsolable in hopeless dejection. A thousand times she reproached herself with the easy compliance by which she permitted her favorite to stay behind her. "Had not my fondness," said she, "lessened my authority, Pekuah had not dared to talk of her terrors. She ought to have feared me more than specters. A severe look would have overpowered her; a peremptory command would have compelled obedience. Why did foolish indulgence prevail upon me? Why did I not speak and refuse to hear?"

"Great princess," said Imlac, "do not reproach yourself for your virtue, or consider that as blameable by which evil has accidentally been caused. Your tenderness for the timidity of Pekuah was generous and kind. When we act

4. Statement of facts.   5. Immediately.

according to our duty, we commit the event to him by whose laws our actions are governed, and who will suffer none to be finally punished for obedience. When, in prospect of some good, whether natural or moral, we break the rules prescribed us, we withdraw from the direction of superior wisdom, and take all consequences upon ourselves. Man cannot so far know the connection of causes and events, as that he may venture to do wrong in order to do right. When we pursue our end by lawful means, we may always console our miscarriage by the hope of future recompense. When we consult only our own policy, and attempt to find a nearer way to good, by overleaping the settled boundaries of right and wrong, we cannot be happy even by success, because we cannot escape the consciousness of our fault; but, if we miscarry, the disappointment is irremediably embittered. How comfortless is the sorrow of him, who feels at once the pangs of guilt, and the vexation of calamity which guilt has brought upon him?

"Consider, princess, what would have been your condition, if the lady Pekuah had entreated to accompany you, and, being compelled to stay in the tents, had been carried away; or how would you have borne the thought, if you had forced her into the pyramid, and she had died before you in agonies of terror."

"Had either happened," said Nekayah, "I could not have endured life till now: I should have been tortured to madness by the remembrance of such cruelty, or must have pined away in abhorrence of myself."

"This at least," said Imlac, "is the present reward of virtuous conduct, that no unlucky consequence can oblige us to repent it."

Chapter 35. *The Princess Languishes for Want of Pekuah*

Nekayah, being thus reconciled to herself, found that no evil is insupportable but that which is accompanied with consciousness of wrong. She was, from that time, delivered from the violence of tempestuous sorrow, and sunk into silent pensiveness and gloomy tranquillity. She sat from morning to evening recollecting all that had been done or said by her Pekuah, treasured up with might recall to mind any little incident or careless conversation. The sentiments of her, whom she now expected to see no more, were treasured in her memory as rules of life, and she deliberated to no other end than to conjecture on any occasion what would have been the opinion and counsel of Pekuah.

The women, by whom she was attended, knew nothing of her real condition, and therefore she could not talk to them but with caution and reserve. She began to remit[6] her curiosity, having no great care to collect notions which she had no convenience of uttering. Rasselas endeavored first to comfort and afterwards to divert her; he hired musicians, to whom she seemed to listen, but did not hear them, and procured masters to instruct her in various arts, whose lectures, when they visited her again, were again to be repeated. She had lost her taste of pleasure and her ambition of excellence. And her mind, though forced into short excursions, always recurred to the image of her friend.

6. Slacken.

Imlac was every morning earnestly enjoined to renew his inquiries, and was asked every night whether he had yet heard of Pekuah, till not being able to return the princess the answer that she desired, he was less and less willing to come into her presence. She observed his backwardness, and commanded him to attend her. "You are not," said she, "to confound impatience with resentment, or to suppose that I charge you with negligence, because I repine at your unsuccessfulness. I do not much wonder at your absence; I know that the unhappy are never pleasing, and that all naturally avoid the contagion of misery. To hear complaints is wearisome alike to the wretched and the happy; for who would cloud by adventitious grief the short gleams of gaiety which life allows us? or who, that is struggling under his own evils, will add to them the miseries of another?

"The time is at hand, when none shall be disturbed any longer by the sighs of Nekayah: my search after happiness is now at an end. I am resolved to retire from the world with all its flatteries and deceits, and will hide myself in solitude, without any other care than to compose my thoughts, and regulate my hours by a constant succession of innocent occupations, till, with a mind purified from all earthly desires, I shall enter into that state, to which all are hastening, and in which I hope again to enjoy the friendship of Pekuah."

"Do not entangle your mind," said Imlac, "by irrevocable determinations, nor increase the burden of life by a voluntary accumulation of misery: the weariness of retirement will continue or increase when the loss of Pekuah is forgotten. That you have been deprived of one pleasure is no very good reason for rejection of the rest."

"Since Pekuah was taken from me," said the princess, "I have no pleasure to reject or to retain. She that has no one to love or trust has little to hope. She wants the radical principle of happiness. We may, perhaps, allow that what satisfaction this world can afford, must arise from the conjunction of wealth, knowledge and goodness: wealth is nothing but as it is bestowed, and knowledge nothing but as it is communicated: they must therefore be imparted to others, and to whom could I now delight to impart them? Goodness affords the only comfort which can be enjoyed without a partner, and goodness may be practised in retirement."

"How far solitude may admit goodness, or advance it, I shall not," replied Imlac, "dispute at present. Remember the confession of the pious hermit. You will wish to return into the world, when the image of your companion has left your thoughts." "That time," said Nekayah, "will never come. The generous frankness, the modest obsequiousness,[7] and the faithful secrecy of my dear Pekuah, will always be more missed, as I shall live longer to see vice and folly."

"The state of a mind oppressed with a sudden calamity," said Imlac, "is like that of the fabulous inhabitants of the new created earth, who, when the first night came upon them, supposed that day never would return. When the clouds of sorrow gather over us, we see nothing beyond them, nor can imagine how they will be dispelled: yet a new day succeeded to the night, and sorrow is never long without a dawn of ease. But they who restrain themselves from receiving comfort, do as the savages would have done, had they put out their eyes when it was dark. Our minds, like our bodies, are in con-

7. Obedience.

tinual flux; something is hourly lost, and something acquired. To lose much at once is inconvenient to either, but while the vital powers remain uninjured, nature will find the means of reparation. Distance has the same effect on the mind as on the eye, and while we glide along the stream of time, whatever we leave behind us is always lessening, and that which we approach increasing in magnitude. Do not suffer life to stagnate; it will grow muddy for want of motion: commit yourself again to the current of the world; Pekuah will vanish by degrees; you will meet in your way some other favorite, or learn to diffuse yourself in general conversation."

"At least," said the prince, "do not despair before all remedies have been tried: the inquiry after the unfortunate lady is still continued, and shall be carried on with yet greater diligence, on condition that you will promise to wait a year for the event, without any unalterable resolution."

Nekayah thought this a reasonable demand, and made the promise to her brother, who had been advised by Imlac to require it. Imlac had, indeed, no great hope of regaining Pekuah, but he supposed, that if he could secure the interval of a year, the princess would be then in no danger of a cloister.

Chapter 36. *Pekuah Is Still Remembered. The Progress of Sorrow*

Nekayah, seeing that nothing was omitted for the recovery of her favorite, and having, by her promise, set her intention of retirement at a distance, began imperceptibly to return to common cares and common pleasures. She rejoiced without her own consent at the suspension of her sorrows, and sometimes caught herself with indignation in the act of turning away her mind from the remembrance of her, whom yet she resolved never to forget.

She then appointed a certain hour of the day for meditation on the merits and fondness of Pekuah, and for some weeks retired constantly at the time fixed, and returned with her eyes swollen and her countenance clouded. By degrees she grew less scrupulous, and suffered any important and pressing avocation to delay the tribute of daily tears. She then yielded to less occasions; sometimes forgot what she was indeed afraid to remember, and, at last, wholly released herself from the duty of periodical affliction.

Her real love of Pekuah was yet not diminished. A thousand occurrences brought her back to memory, and a thousand wants, which nothing but the confidence of friendship can supply, made her frequently regretted. She, therefore, solicited Imlac never to desist from inquiry, and to leave no art of intelligence untried, that, at least, she might have the comfort of knowing that she did not suffer by negligence or sluggishness. "Yet what," said she, "is to be expected from our pursuit of happiness, when we find the state of life to be such, that happiness itself is the cause of misery? Why should we endeavor to attain that, of which the possession cannot be secured? I shall henceforward fear to yield my heart to excellence, however bright, or to fondness, however tender, lest I should lose again what I have lost in Pekuah."

Chapter 37. *The Princess Hears News of Pekuah*

In seven months, one of the messengers, who had been sent away upon the day when the promise was drawn from the princess, returned, after many unsuccessful rambles, from the borders of Nubia, with an account that

Pekuah was in the hands of an Arab chief, who possessed a castle or fortress on the extremity of Egypt. The Arab, whose revenue was plunder, was willing to restore her, with her two attendants, for two hundred ounces of gold.

The price was no subject of debate. The princess was in ecstasies when she heard that her favorite was alive, and might so cheaply be ransomed. She could not think of delaying for a moment Pekuah's happiness or her own, but entreated her brother to send back the messenger with the sum required. Imlac, being consulted, was not very confident of the veracity of the relator, and was still more doubtful of the Arab's faith, who might, if he were too liberally trusted, detain at once the money and the captives. He thought it dangerous to put themselves in the power of the Arab, by going into his district, and could not expect that the rover[8] would so much expose himself as to come into the lower country, where he might be seized by the forces of the Bassa.

It is difficult to negotiate where neither will trust. But Imlac, after some deliberation, directed the messenger to propose that Pekuah should be conducted by ten horsemen to the monastery of St. Anthony, which is situated in the deserts of Upper Egypt, where she should be met by the same number, and her ransom should be paid.

That no time might be lost, as they expected that the proposal would not be refused, they immediately began their journey to the monastery; and, when they arrived, Imlac went forward with the former messenger to the Arab's fortress. Rasselas was desirous to go with them, but neither his sister nor Imlac would consent. The Arab, according to the custom of his nation, observed the laws of hospitality with great exactness to those who put themselves into his power, and, in a few days, brought Pekuah with her maids, by easy journeys, to their place appointed, where receiving the stipulated price, he restored her with great respect to liberty and her friends, and undertook to conduct them back toward Cairo beyond all danger of robbery or violence.

The princess and her favorite embraced each other with transport too violent to be expressed, and went out together to pour the tears of tenderness in secret, and exchange professions of kindness and gratitude. After a few hours they returned into the refectory of the convent, where, in the presence of the prior and his brethren, the prince required of Pekuah the history of her adventures.

Chapter 38. The Adventures of the Lady Pekuah

"At what time, and in what manner, I was forced away," said Pekuah, "your servants have told you. The suddenness of the event struck me with surprise, and I was at first rather stupified than agitated with any passion of either fear or sorrow. My confusion was increased by the speed and tumult of our flight while we were followed by the Turks, who, as it seemed, soon despaired to overtake us, or were afraid of those whom they made a show of menacing.

"When the Arabs saw themselves out of danger they slackened their course, and, as I was less harassed by external violence, I began to feel more uneasiness in my mind. After some time we stopped near a spring shaded with trees in a pleasant meadow, where we were set upon the ground, and offered such

8. Robber.

refreshments as our masters were partaking. I was suffered to sit with my maids apart from the rest, and none attempted to comfort or insult us. Here I first began to feel the full weight of my misery. The girls sat weeping in silence, and from time to time looked on me for succor. I knew not to what condition we were doomed, nor could conjecture where would be the place of our captivity, or whence to draw any hope of deliverance. I was in the hands of robbers and savages, and had no reason to suppose that their pity was more than their justice, or that they would forbear the gratification of any ardor of desire, or caprice of cruelty. I, however, kissed my maids, and endeavored to pacify them by remarking, that we were yet treated with decency, and that, since we were now carried beyond pursuit, there was no danger of violence to our lives.

"When we were to be set again on horseback, my maids clung round me, and refused to be parted, but I commanded them not to irritate those who had us in their power. We traveled the remaining part of the day through an unfrequented and pathless country, and came by moonlight to the side of a hill, where the rest of the troop was stationed. Their tents were pitched, and their fires kindled, and our chief was welcomed as a man much beloved by his dependents.

"We were received into a large tent, where we found women who had attended their husbands in the expedition. They set before us the supper which they had provided, and I eat it rather to encourage my maids than to comply with any appetite of my own. When the meat was taken away they spread the carpets for repose. I was weary, and hoped to find in sleep that remission of distress which nature seldom denies. Ordering myself therefore to be undressed, I observed that the women looked very earnestly upon me, not expecting, I suppose, to see me so submissively attended. When my upper vest was taken off, they were apparently struck with the splendor of my clothes, and one of them timorously laid her hand upon the embroidery. She then went out, and, in a short time, came back with another woman, who seemed to be of higher rank, and greater authority. She did, at her entrance, the usual act of reverence, and, taking me by the hand, placed me in a smaller tent, spread with finer carpets, where I spent the night quietly with my maids.

"In the morning, as I was sitting on the grass, the chief of the troop came towards me: I rose up to receive him, and he bowed with great respect. 'Illustrious lady,' said he, 'my fortune is better than I had presumed to hope; I am told by my women that I have a princess in my camp.' 'Sir,' answered I, 'your women have deceived themselves and you; I am not a princess, but an unhappy stranger who intended soon to have left this country, in which I am now to be imprisoned for ever.' 'Whoever, or whencesoever, you are,' returned the Arab, 'your dress, and that of your servants, show your rank to be high, and your wealth to be great. Why should you, who can so easily procure your ransom, think yourself in danger of perpetual captivity? The purpose of my incursions is to increase my riches, or more properly to gather tribute. The sons of Ishmael[9] are the natural and hereditary lords of this part of the continent, which is usurped by late invaders, and low-born tyrants, from whom we are compelled to take by the sword what is denied to justice. The violence

9. Arabs, who claim descent from Ishmael, a son of Abraham.

of war admits no distinction; the lance that is lifted at guilt and power will sometimes fall on innocence and gentleness.'

"'How little,' said I, 'did I expect that yesterday it should have fallen upon me.'

"'Misfortunes,' answered the Arab, 'should always be expected. If the eye of hostility could learn reverence or pity, excellence like yours had been exempt from injury. But the angels of affliction spread their toils alike for the virtuous and the wicked, for the mighty and the mean. Do not be disconsolate; I am not one of the lawless and cruel rovers of the desert; I know the rules of civil life: I will fix your ransom, give a passport to your messenger, and perform my stipulation with nice punctuality.'[1]

"You will easily believe that I was pleased with his courtesy; and finding that his predominant passion was desire of money, I began now to think my danger less, for I knew that no sum would be thought too great for the release of Pekuah. I told him that he should have no reason to charge me with ingratitude, if I was used with kindness, and that any ransom, which could be expected for a maid of common rank, would be paid, but that he must not persist to rate me as a princess. He said, he would consider what he should demand, and then, smiling, bowed and retired.

"Soon after the women came about me, each contending to be more officious[2] than the other, and my maids themselves were served with reverence. We traveled onward by short journeys. On the fourth day the chief told me, that my ransom must be two hundred ounces of gold, which I not only promised him, but told him, that I would add fifty more, if I and my maids were honorably treated.

"I never knew the power of gold before. From that time I was the leader of the troop. The march of every day was longer or shorter as I commanded, and the tents were pitched where I chose to rest. We now had camels and other conveniencies for travel, my own women were always at my side, and I amused myself with observing the manners of the vagrant nations,[3] and with viewing remains of ancient edifices with which these deserted countries appear to have been, in some distant age, lavishly embellished.

"The chief of the band was a man far from illiterate: he was able to travel by the stars or the compass, and had marked in his erratic expeditions such places as are most worthy the notice of a passenger.[4] He observed to me, that buildings are always best preserved in places little frequented, and difficult of access: for, when once a country declines from its primitive splendor, the more inhabitants are left, the quicker ruin will be made. Walls supply stones more easily than quarries, and palaces and temples will be demolished to make stables of granite, and cottages of porphyry.

Chapter 39. The Adventures of Pekuah Continued

"We wandered about in this manner for some weeks, whether, as our chief pretended, for my gratification, or, as I rather suspected, for some convenience of his own. I endeavored to appear contented where sullenness and resentment would have been of no use, and that endeavor conduced much to

---

1. Scrupulous exactness. "Civil": civilized.
2. Ready to serve.
3. Nomads.
4. Traveler.

the calmness of my mind; but my heart was always with Nekayah, and the troubles of the night much overbalanced the amusements of the day. My women, who threw all their cares upon their mistress, set their minds at ease from the time when they saw me treated with respect, and gave themselves up to the incidental alleviations of our fatigue without solicitude or sorrow. I was pleased with their pleasure, and animated with their confidence. My condition had lost much of its terror, since I found that the Arab ranged the country merely to get riches. Avarice is an uniform and tractable vice: other intellectual distempers are different in different constitutions of mind; that which soothes the pride of one will offend the pride of another; but to the favor of the covetous there is a ready way, bring money and nothing is denied.

"At last we came to the dwelling of our chief, a strong and spacious house built with stone in an island of the Nile, which lies, as I was told, under the tropic. 'Lady,' said the Arab, 'you shall rest after your journey a few weeks in this place, where you are to consider yourself as sovereign. My occupation is war: I have therefore chosen this obscure residence, from which I can issue unexpected, and to which I can retire unpursued. You may now repose in security: here are few pleasures, but here is no danger.' He then led me into the inner apartments, and seating me on the richest couch, bowed to the ground. His women, who considered me as a rival, looked on me with malignity; but being soon informed that I was a great lady detained only for my ransom, they began to vie with each other in obsequiousness and reverence.

"Being again comforted with new assurances of speedy liberty, I was for some days diverted from impatience by the novelty of the place. The turrets overlooked the country to a great distance, and afforded a view of many windings of the stream. In the day I wandered from one place to another as the course of the sun varied the splendor of the prospect, and saw many things which I had never seen before. The crocodiles and river-horses[5] are common in this unpeopled region, and I often looked upon them with terror, though I knew that they could not hurt me. For some time I expected to see mermaids and tritons, which, as Imlac has told me, the European travelers have stationed in the Nile, but no such beings ever appeared, and the Arab, when I inquired after them, laughed at my credulity.

"At night the Arab always attended me to a tower set apart for celestial observations, where he endeavored to teach me the names and courses of the stars. I had no great inclination to this study, but an appearance of attention was necessary to please my instructor, who valued himself for his skill, and, in a little while, I found some employment requisite to beguile the tediousness of time, which was to be passed always amidst the same objects. I was weary of looking in the morning on things from which I had turned away weary in the evening: I therefore was at last willing to observe the stars rather than do nothing, but could not always compose my thoughts, and was very often thinking on Nekayah when others imagined me contemplating the sky. Soon after the Arab went upon another expedition, and then my only pleasure was to talk with my maids about the accident by which we were carried away, and the happiness that we should all enjoy at the end of our captivity."

5. Hippopotamuses.

"There were women in your Arab's fortress," said the princess, "why did you not make them your companions, enjoy their conversation, and partake their diversions? In a place where they found business or amusement, why should you alone sit corroded with idle melancholy? or why could not you bear for a few months that condition to which they were condemned for life?"

"The diversions of the women," answered Pekuah, "were only childish play, by which the mind accustomed to stronger operations could not be kept busy. I could do all which they delighted in doing by powers merely sensitive,[6] while my intellectual faculties were flown to Cairo. They ran from room to room as a bird hops from wire to wire in his cage. They danced for the sake of motion, as lambs frisk in a meadow. One sometimes pretended to be hurt that the rest might be alarmed, or hid herself that another might seek her. Part of their time passed in watching the progress of light bodies that floated on the river, and part in marking the various forms into which clouds broke in the sky.

"Their business was only needlework, in which I and my maids sometimes helped them; but you know that the mind will easily straggle from the fingers, nor will you suspect that captivity and absence from Nekayah could receive solace from silken flowers.

"Nor was much satisfaction to be hoped from their conversation: for of what could they be expected to talk? They had seen nothing; for they had lived from early youth in that narrow spot: of what they had not seen they could have no knowledge, for they could not read. They had no ideas but of the few things that were within their view, and had hardly names for anything but their clothes and their food. As I bore a superior character, I was often called to terminate their quarrels, which I decided as equitably as I could. If it could have amused me to hear the complaints of each against the rest, I might have been often detained by long stories, but the motives of their animosity were so small that I could not listen without intercepting the tale."

"How," said Rasselas, "can the Arab, whom you represented as a man of more than common accomplishments, take any pleasure in his seraglio, when it is filled only with women like these. Are they exquisitely beautiful?"

"They do not," said Pekuah, "want that unaffecting and ignoble beauty which may subsist without spriteliness or sublimity, without energy of thought or dignity of virtue. But to a man like the Arab such beauty was only a flower casually plucked and carelessly thrown away. Whatever pleasures he might find among them, they were not those of friendship or society. When they were playing about him he looked on them with inattentive superiority: when they vied for his regard he sometimes turned away disgusted. As they had no knowledge, their talk could take nothing from the tediousness of life: as they had no choice, their fondness, or appearance of fondness, excited in him neither pride nor gratitude; he was not exalted in his own esteem by the smiles of a woman who saw no other man, nor was much obliged by that regard, of which he could never know the sincerity, and which he might often perceive to be exerted not so much to delight him as to pain a rival. That which he gave, and they received, as love, was only a careless distribution of superfluous time, such love as man can bestow upon that which he despises, such as has neither hope nor fear, neither joy nor sorrow."

6. "Having sense or perception, but not reason" (Johnson's *Dictionary*).

"You have reason, lady, to think yourself happy," said Imlac, "that you have been thus easily dismissed. How could a mind, hungry for knowledge, be willing, in an intellectual famine, to lose such a banquet as Pekuah's conversation?"

"I am inclined to believe," answered Pekuah, "that he was for some time in suspense; for, notwithstanding his promise, whenever I proposed to dispatch a messenger to Cairo, he found some excuse for delay. While I was detained in his house he made many incursions into the neighboring countries, and, perhaps, he would have refused to discharge me, had his plunder been equal to his wishes. He returned always courteous, related his adventures, delighted to hear my observations, and endeavored to advance my acquaintance with the stars. When I imported him to send away my letters, he soothed me with professions of honor and sincerity; and, when I could be no longer decently denied, put his troop again in motion, and left me to govern in his absence. I was much afflicted by this studied procrastination, and was sometimes afraid that I should be forgotten; that you would leave Cairo, and I must end my days in an island of the Nile.

"I grew at last hopeless and dejected, and cared so little to entertain him, that he for a while more frequently talked with my maids. That he should fall in love with them, or with me, might have been equally fatal, and I was not much pleased with the growing friendship. My anxiety was not long; for, as I recovered some degree of cheerfulness, he returned to me, and I could not forbear to despise my former uneasiness.

"He still delayed to send for my ransom, and would, perhaps, never have determined, had not your agent found his way to him. The gold, which he would not fetch, he could not reject when it was offered. He hastened to prepare for our journey hither, like a man delivered from the pain of an intestine conflict. I took leave of my companions in the house, who dismissed me with cold indifference."

Nekayah, having heard her favorite's relation, rose and embraced her, and Rasselas gave her an hundred ounces of gold, which she presented to the Arab for the fifty that were promised.

Chapter 40. The History of a Man of Learning

They returned to Cairo, and were so well pleased at finding themselves together, that none of them went much abroad. The prince began to love learning, and one day declared to Imlac, that he intended to devote himself to science,[7] and pass the rest of his days in literary solitude.

"Before you make your final choice," answered Imlac, "you ought to examine its hazards, and converse with some of those who are grown old in the company of themselves. I have just left the observatory of one of the most learned astronomers in the world, who has spent forty years in unwearied attention to the motions and appearances of the celestial bodies, and has drawn out his soul in endless calculations. He admits a few friends once a month to hear his deductions and enjoy his discoveries. I was introduced as a man of knowledge worthy of his notice. Men of various ideas and fluent conversation are commonly welcome to those whose thoughts have been long

7. Knowledge.

fixed upon a single point, and who find the images of other things stealing away. I delighted him with my remarks, he smiled at the narrative of my travels, and was glad to forget the constellations, and descend for a moment into the lower world.

"On the next day of vacation[8] I renewed my visit, and was so fortunate as to please him again. He relaxed from that time the severity of his rule, and permitted me to enter at my own choice. I found him always busy, and always glad to be relieved. As each knew much which the other was desirous of learning, we exchanged our notions with great delight. I perceived that I had every day more of his confidence, and always found new cause of admiration in the profundity of his mind. His comprehension is vast, his memory capacious and retentive, his discourse is methodical, and his expression clear.

"His integrity and benevolence are equal to his learning. His deepest researches and most favorite studies are willingly interrupted for any opportunity of doing good by his counsel or his riches. To his closest retreat,[9] at his most busy moments, all are admitted that want his assistance: 'For though I exclude idleness and pleasure, I will never,' says he, 'bar my doors against charity. To man is permitted the contemplation of the skies, but the practice of virtue is commanded.'"

"Surely," said the princess, "this man is happy."

"I visited him," said Imlac, "with more and more frequency, and was every time more enamored of his conversation: he was sublime without haughtiness, courteous without formality, and communicative without ostentation. I was at first, great princess, of your opinion, thought him the happiest of mankind, and often congratulated him on the blessing that he enjoyed. He seemed to hear nothing with indifference but the praises of his condition, to which he always returned a general answer, and diverted the conversation to some other topic.

"Amidst this willingness to be pleased, and labor to please, I had quickly reason to imagine that some painful sentiment pressed upon his mind. He often looked up earnestly towards the sun, and let his voice fall in the midst of his discourse. He would sometimes, when we were alone, gaze upon me in silence with the air of a man who longed to speak what he was yet resolved to suppress. He would often send for me with vehement injunctions of haste, though, when I came to him, he had nothing extraordinary to say. And sometimes, when I was leaving him, he would call me back, pause a few moments and then dismiss me.

Chapter 41. *The Astronomer Discovers the Cause of His Uneasiness*

"At last the time came when the secret burst his reserve. We were sitting together last night in the turret of his house, watching the emersion of a satellite of Jupiter. A sudden tempest clouded the sky, and disappointed our observation. We sat a while silent in the dark, and then he addressed himself to me in these words: 'Imlac, I have long considered thy friendship as the greatest blessing of my life. Integrity without knowledge is weak and useless, and knowledge without integrity is dangerous and dreadful. I have found in thee all the qualities requisite for trust, benevolence, experience,

8. Leisure.

9. Most secluded place of privacy.

and fortitude. I have long discharged an office which I must soon quit at the call of nature, and shall rejoice in the hour of imbecility[1] and pain to devolve it upon thee.'

"I thought myself honored by this testimony, and protested that whatever could conduce to his happiness would add likewise to mine.

"'Hear, Imlac, what thou wilt not without difficulty credit. I have possessed for five years the regulation of weather, and the distribution of the seasons: the sun has listened to my dictates, and passed from tropic to tropic by my direction; the clouds, at my call, have poured their waters, and the Nile has overflowed at my command; I have restrained the rage of the dog-star, and mitigated the fervors of the crab.[2] The winds alone, of all the elemental powers, have hitherto refused my authority, and multitudes have perished by equinoctial tempests which I found myself unable to prohibit or restrain. I have administered this great office with exact justice, and made to the different nations of the earth an impartial dividend of rain and sunshine. What must have been the misery of half the globe, if I had limited the clouds to particular regions, or confined the sun to either side of the equator?'

Chapter 42. *The Opinion of the Astronomer Is Explained and Justified*

"I suppose he discovered in me, through the obscurity of the room, some tokens of amazement and doubt, for, after a short pause, he proceeded thus:

"'Not to be easily credited will neither surprise nor offend me; for I am, probably, the first of human beings to whom this trust has been imparted. Nor do I know whether to deem this distinction a reward or punishment; since I have possessed it I have been far less happy than before, and nothing but the consciousness of good intention could have enabled me to support the weariness of unremitted vigilance.'

"'How long, Sir,' said I, 'has this great office been in your hands?'

"'About ten years ago,' said he, 'my daily observations of the changes of the sky led me to consider, whether, if I had the power of the seasons, I could confer greater plenty upon the inhabitants of the earth. This contemplation fastened on my mind, and I sat days and nights in imaginary dominion, pouring upon this country and that the showers of fertility, and seconding every fall of rain with a due proportion of sunshine. I had yet only the will to do good, and did not imagine that I should ever have the power.

"'One day as I was looking on the fields withering with heat, I felt in my mind a sudden wish that I could send rain on the southern mountains, and raise the Nile to an inundation. In the hurry of my imagination I commanded rain to fall, and, by comparing the time of my command, with that of the inundation, I found that the clouds had listened to my lips.'

"'Might not some other cause,' said I, 'produce this concurrence? the Nile does not always rise on the same day.'

"'Do not believe,' said he with impatience, 'that such objections could escape me: I reasoned long against my own conviction, and labored against truth with the utmost obstinacy. I sometimes suspected myself of madness, and should not have dared to impart this secret but to a man like you, capable

---

1. Feebleness.
2. The fourth sign of the zodiac (Cancer). "The

dog-star": Sirius was supposed to cause the heat ("dog days") of summer.

of distinguishing the wonderful from the impossible, and the incredible from the false.'

"'Why, Sir,' said I, 'do you call that incredible, which you know, or think you know, to be true?'

"'Because,' said he, 'I cannot prove it by any external evidence; and I know too well the laws of demonstration to think that my conviction ought to influence another, who cannot, like me, be conscious of its force. I therefore shall not attempt to gain credit by disputation. It is sufficient that I feel this power, that I have long possessed, and every day exerted it. But the life of man is short, the infirmities of age increase upon me, and the time will soon come when the regulator of the year must mingle with the dust. The care of appointing a successor has long disturbed me; the night and the day have been spent in comparisons of all the characters which have come to my knowledge, and I have yet found none so worthy as thyself.

Chapter 43. The Astronomer Leaves Imlac His Directions

"'Hear therefore, what I shall impart, with attention, such as the welfare of a world requires. If the task of a king be considered as difficult, who has the care only of a few millions, to whom he cannot do much good or harm, what must be the anxiety of him, on whom depends the action of the elements, and the great gifts of light and heat!—Hear me therefore with attention.

"'I have diligently considered the position of the earth and sun, and formed innumerable schemes in which I changed their situation. I have sometimes turned aside the axis of the earth, and sometimes varied the ecliptic of the sun: but I have found it impossible to make a disposition by which the world may be advantaged; what one region gains, another loses by any imaginable alteration, even without considering the distant parts of the solar system with which we are unacquainted. Do not, therefore, in thy administration of the year, indulge thy pride by innovation; do not please thyself with thinking that thou canst make thyself renowned to all future ages, by disordering the seasons. The memory of mischief is no desirable fame. Much less will it become thee to let kindness or interest prevail. Never rob other countries of rain to pour it on thine own. For us the Nile is sufficient.'

"I promised that when I possessed the power, I would use it with inflexible integrity, and he dismissed me, pressing my hand. 'My heart,' said he, 'will be now at rest, and my benevolence will no more destroy my quiet: I have found a man of wisdom and virtue, to whom I can cheerfully bequeath the inheritance of the sun.'"

The prince heard this narration with very serious regard, but the princess smiled, and Pekuah convulsed herself with laughter. "Ladies," said Imlac, "to mock the heaviest of human afflictions is neither charitable nor wise. Few can attain this man's knowledge, and few practice his virtues; but all may suffer his calamity. Of the uncertainties of our present state, the most dreadful and alarming is the uncertain continuance of reason."

The princess was recollected, and the favorite was abashed. Rasselas, more deeply affected, inquired of Imlac, whether he thought such maladies of the mind frequent, and how they were contracted.

Chapter 44. The Dangerous Prevalence[3] of Imagination

"Disorders of intellect," answered Imlac, "happen much more often than superficial observers will easily believe. Perhaps, if we speak with rigorous exactness, no human mind is in its right state. There is no man whose imagination does not sometimes predominate over his reason, who can regulate his attention wholly by his will, and whose ideas will come and go at his command. No man will be found in whose mind airy notions do not sometimes tyrannize, and force him to hope or fear beyond the limits of sober probability. All power of fancy over reason is a degree of insanity; but while this power is such as we can control and repress, it is not visible to others, nor considered as any depravation of the mental faculties; it is not pronounced madness but when it comes ungovernable, and apparently influences speech or action.

"To indulge the power of fiction, and send imagination out upon the wing, is often the sport of those who delight too much in silent speculation. When we are alone we are not always busy; the labor of excogitation is too violent to last long; the ardor of inquiry will sometimes give way to idleness or satiety. He who has nothing external that can divert him must find pleasure in his own thoughts, and must conceive himself what he is not; for who is pleased with what he is? He then expatiates in boundless futurity, and culls from all imaginable conditions that which for the present moment he should most desire, amuses his desires with impossible enjoyments, and confers upon his pride unattainable dominion. The mind dances from scene to scene, unites all pleasures in all combinations, and riots in delights which nature and fortune, with all their bounty, cannot bestow.

"In time, some particular train of ideas fixes the attention; all other intellectual gratifications are rejected; the mind, in weariness or leisure, recurs constantly to the favorite conception, and feasts on the luscious falsehood, whenever she is offended with the bitterness of truth. By degrees the reign of fancy is confirmed; she grows first imperious, and in time despotic. Then fictions begin to operate as realities, false opinions fasten upon the mind, and life passes in dreams of rapture or of anguish.

"This, sir, is one of the dangers of solitude, which the hermit has confessed not always to promote goodness, and the astronomer's misery has proved to be not always propitious to wisdom."

"I will no more," said the favorite, "imagine myself the queen of Abyssinia. I have often spent the hours which the princess gave to my own disposal, in adjusting ceremonies and regulating the court; I have repressed the pride of the powerful, and granted the petitions of the poor; I have built new palaces in more happy situations, planted groves upon the tops of mountains, and have exulted in the beneficence of royalty, till, when the princess entered, I had almost forgotten to bow down before her."

"And I," said the princess, "will not allow myself any more to play the shepherdess in my waking dreams. I have often soothed my thoughts with the quiet and innocence of pastoral employments, till I have in my chamber heard the winds whistle, and the sheep bleat; sometimes freed the lamb entangled in the thicket, and sometimes with my crook encountered the wolf. I have a dress like that of the village maids, which I put on to help my

3. Predominance.

imagination, and a pipe on which I play softly, and suppose myself followed by my flocks."

"I will confess," said the prince, "an indulgence of fantastic delight more dangerous than yours. I have frequently endeavored to image the possibility of a perfect government, by which all wrong should be restrained, all vice reformed, and all the subjects preserved in tranquility and innocence. This thought produced innumerable schemes of reformation, and dictated many useful regulations and salutary edicts. This has been the sport, and sometimes the labor, of my solitude; and I start, when I think with how little anguish I once supposed the death of my father and my brothers."

"Such," says Imlac, "are the effects of visionary schemes; when we first form them, we know them to be absurd, but familiarize them by degrees, and in time lose sight of their folly."

Chapter 45. They Discourse with an Old Man

The evening was now far past, and they rose to return home. As they walked along the bank of the Nile, delighted with the beams of the moon quivering on the water, they saw at a small distance an old man, whom the prince had often heard in the assembly of the sages. "Yonder," said he, "is one whose years have calmed his passions, but not clouded his reason. Let us close the disquisitions of the night by inquiring what are his sentiments of his own state, that we may know whether youth alone is to struggle with vexation, and whether any better hope remains for the latter part of life."

Here the sage approached and saluted them. They invited him to join their walk, and prattled a while, as acquaintance that had unexpectedly met one another. The old man was cheerful and talkative, and the way seemed short in his company. He was pleased to find himself not disregarded, accompanied them to their house, and, at the prince's request, entered with them. They placed him in the seat of honor, and set wine and conserves before him.

"Sir," said the princess, "an evening walk must give to a man of learning like you pleasures which ignorance and youth can hardly conceive. You know the qualities and the causes of all that you behold, the laws by which the river flows, the periods in which the planets perform their revolutions. Everything must supply you with contemplation, and renew the consciousness of your own dignity."

"Lady," answered he, "let the gay and the vigorous expect pleasure in their excursions; it is enough that age can obtain ease. To me the world has lost its novelty; I look round, and see what I remember to have seen in happier days. I rest against a tree, and consider that in the same shade I once disputed upon the annual overflow of the Nile with a friend who is now silent in the grave. I cast my eyes upward, fix them on the changing moon, and think with pain on the vicissitudes of life. I have ceased to take much delight in physical truth; for what have I to do with those things which I am soon to leave?"

"You may at least recreate[4] yourself," said Imlac, "with the recollection of an honorable and useful life, and enjoy the praise which all agree to give you."

4. Refresh.

"Praise," said the sage with a sigh, "is to an old man an empty sound. I have neither mother to be delighted with the reputation of her son, nor wife to partake the honors of her husband. I have outlived my friends and my rivals. Nothing is now of much importance; for I cannot extend my interest beyond myself. Youth is delighted with applause, because it is considered as the earnest of some future good, and because the prospect of life is far extended; but to me, who am now declining to decrepitude, there is little to be feared from the malevolence of men, and yet less to be hoped from their affection or esteem. Something they may yet take away, but they can give me nothing. Riches would now be useless, and high employment would be pain. My retrospect of life recalls to my view many opportunities of good neglected, much time squandered upon trifles, and more lost in idleness and vacancy. I leave many great designs unattempted, and many great attempts unfinished. My mind is burthened with no heavy crime, and therefore I compose myself to tranquility; endeavor to abstract my thoughts from hopes and cares which, though reason knows them to be vain, still try to keep their old possession of the heart; expect,[5] with serene humility, that hour which nature cannot long delay; and hope to possess, in a better state, that happiness which here I could not find, and that virtue which here I have not attained."

He arose and went away, leaving his audience not much elated with the hope of long life. The prince consoled himself with remarking that it was not reasonable to be disappointed by this account; for age had never been considered as the season of felicity, and if it was possible to be easy in decline and weakness, it was likely that the days of vigor and alacrity might be happy; that the noon of life might be bright, if the evening could be calm.

The princess suspected that age was querulous and malignant, and delighted to repress the expectations of those who had newly entered the world. She had seen the possessors of estates look with envy on their heirs, and known many who enjoy pleasure no longer than they can confine it to themselves.

Pekuah conjectured that the man was older than he appeared, and was willing to impute his complaints to delirious dejection; or else supposed that he had been unfortunate, and was therefore discontented. "For nothing," said she, "is more common than to call our own condition the condition of life."

Imlac, who had no desire to see them depressed, smiled at the comforts which they could so readily procure to themselves, and remembered that, at the same age, he was equally confident of unmingled prosperity, and equally fertile of consolatory expedients. He forbore to force upon them unwelcome knowledge, which time itself would too soon impress. The princess and her lady retired; the madness of the astronomer hung upon their minds, and they desired Imlac to enter upon his office, and delay next morning the rising of the sun.

Chapter 46. The Princess and Pekuah Visit the Astronomer

The princess and Pekuah, having talked in private of Imlac's astronomer, thought his character at once so amiable and so strange, that they could not

5. Await.

be satisfied without a nearer knowledge, and Imlac was requested to find the means of bringing them together.

This was somewhat difficult; the philosopher had never received any visits from women, though he lived in a city that had in it many Europeans who followed the manners of their own countries, and many from other parts of the world that lived there with European liberty. The ladies would not be refused, and several schemes were proposed for the accomplishment of their design. It was proposed to introduce them as strangers in distress, to whom the sage was always accessible; but, after some deliberation, it appeared, that by this artifice, no acquaintance could be formed, for their conversation would be short, and they could not decently importune him often. "This," said Rasselas, "is true; but I have yet a stronger objection against the misrepresentation of your state. I have always considered it as treason against the great republic of human nature, to make any man's virtues the means of deceiving him, whether on great or little occasions. All imposture weakens confidence and chills benevolence. When the sage finds that you are not what you seemed, he will feel the resentment natural to a man who, conscious of great abilities, discovers that he has been tricked by understandings meaner than his own, and, perhaps, the distrust, which he can never afterwards wholly lay aside, may stop the voice of counsel, and close the hand of charity; and where will you find the power of restoring his benefactions to mankind, or his peace to himself?"

To this no reply was attempted, and Imlac began to hope that their curiosity would subside; but next day Pekuah told him, she had now found an honest pretense for a visit to the astronomer, for she would solicit permission to continue under him the studies in which she had been initiated by the Arab, and the princess might go with her either as a fellow-student, or because a woman could not decently come alone. "I am afraid," said Imlac, "that he will be soon weary of your company: men advanced far in knowledge do not love to repeat the elements of their art, and I am not certain, that even of the elements, as he will deliver them connected with inferences, and mingled with reflections, you are a very capable auditress." "That," said Pekuah, "must be my care: I ask of you only to take me thither. My knowledge is, perhaps, more than you imagine it, and by concurring always with his opinions I shall make him think it greater than it is."

The astronomer, in pursuance of this resolution, was told, that a foreign lady, traveling in search of knowledge, had heard of his reputation, and was desirous to become his scholar. The uncommonness of the proposal raised at once his surprise and curiosity, and when, after a short deliberation, he consented to admit her, he could not stay without impatience till the next day.

The ladies dressed themselves magnificently, and were attended by Imlac to the astronomer, who was pleased to see himself approached with respect by persons of so splendid an appearance. In the exchange of the first civilities he was timorous and bashful; but when the talk became regular, he recollected his powers, and justified the character which Imlac had given. Inquiring of Pekuah what could have turned her inclination towards astronomy, he received from her a history of her adventure at the pyramid, and of the time passed in the Arab's island. She told her tale with ease and elegance, and her conversation took possession of his heart. The discourse was then turned to astronomy: Pekuah displayed what she knew: he looked upon her as a prodigy of genius, and entreated her not to desist from a study which she had so happily begun.

They came again and again, and were every time more welcome than before. The sage endeavored to amuse them, that they might prolong their visits, for he found his thoughts grow brighter in their company; the clouds of solicitude vanished by degrees, as he forced himself to entertain them, and he grieved when he was left at their departure to his old employment of regulating the seasons.

The princess and her favorite had now watched his lips for several months, and could not catch a single word from which they could judge whether he continued, or not, in the opinion of his preternatural commission. They often contrived to bring him to an open declaration, but he easily eluded all their attacks, and on which side soever they pressed him escaped from them to some other topic.

As their familiarity increased they invited him often to the house of Imlac, where they distinguished him by extraordinary respect. He began gradually to delight in sublunary pleasures. He came early and departed late; labored to recommend himself by assiduity and compliance; excited their curiosity after new arts, that they might still want his assistance; and when they made any excursion of pleasure or inquiry, entreated to attend them.

By long experience of his integrity and wisdom, the prince and his sister were convinced that he might be trusted without danger; and lest he should draw any false hopes from the civilities which he received, discovered to him their condition, with the motives of their journey, and required his opinion on the choice of life.

"Of the various conditions which the world spreads before you, which you shall prefer," said the sage, "I am not able to instruct you. I can only tell that I have chosen wrong. I have passed my time in study without experience; in the attainment of sciences which can, for the most part, be but remotely useful to mankind. I have purchased knowledge at the expense of all the common comforts of life: I have missed the endearing elegance of female friendship, and the happy commerce of domestic tenderness. If I have obtained any prerogatives above other students, they have been accompanied with fear, disquiet, and scrupulosity; but even of these prerogatives, whatever they were, I have, since my thoughts have been diversified by more intercourse with the world, begun to question the reality. When I have been for a few days lost in pleasing dissipation, I am always tempted to think that my inquiries have ended in error, and that I have suffered much, and suffered it in vain."

Imlac was delighted to find that the sage's understanding was breaking through its mists, and resolved to detain him from the planets till he should forget his task of ruling them, and reason should recover its original influence.

From this time the astronomer was received into familiar friendship, and partook of all their projects and pleasures: his respect kept him attentive, and the activity of Rasselas did not leave much time unengaged. Something was always to be done; the day was spent in making observations which furnished talk for the evening, and the evening was closed with a scheme for the morrow.

The sage confessed to Imlac, that since he had mingled in the gay tumults of life, and divided his hours by a succession of amusements, he found the conviction of his authority over the skies fade gradually from his mind, and began to trust less to an opinion which he never could prove to others, and which he now found subject to variation from causes in which reason had no part. "If I am accidentally left alone for a few hours," said he, "my inveterate persuasion rushes upon my soul, and my thoughts are chained down by some irresistible violence, but they are soon disentangled by the prince's conversation, and instantaneously released at the entrance of Pekuah. I am like a man habitually afraid of specters, who is set at ease by a lamp, and wonders at the dread which harassed him in the dark, yet, if his lamp be extinguished, feels again the terrors which he knows that when it is light he shall feel no more. But I am sometimes afraid lest I indulge my quiet by criminal negligence, and voluntarily forget the great charge with which I am entrusted. If I favor myself in a known error, or am determined by my own ease in a doubtful question of this importance, how dreadful is my crime!"

"No disease of the imagination," answered Imlac, "is so difficult of cure, as that which is complicated with the dread of guilt: fancy and conscience then act interchangeably upon us, and so often shift their places, that the illusions of one are not distinguished from the dictates of the other. If fancy presents images not moral or religious, the mind drives them away when they give it pain, but when melancholic[6] notions take the form of duty, they lay hold on the faculties without opposition, because we are afraid to exclude or banish them. For this reason the superstitious are often melancholy, and the melancholy almost always superstitious.

"But do not let the suggestions of timidity overpower your better reason: the danger of neglect can be but as the probability of the obligation, which, when you consider it with freedom, you find very little, and that little growing every day less. Open your heart to the influence of the light, which, from time to time, breaks in upon you: when scruples importune you, which you in your lucid moments know to be vain, do not stand to parley, but fly to business or to Pekuah, and keep this thought always prevalent, that you are only one atom of the mass of humanity, and have neither such virtue nor vice, as that you should be singled out for supernatural favors or afflictions."

Chapter 47. The Prince Enters, and Brings a New Topic

"All this," said the astronomer, "I have often thought, but my reason has been so long subjugated by an uncontrollable and overwhelming idea, that it durst not confide in its own decisions. I now see how fatally I betrayed my quiet, by suffering chimeras to prey upon me in secret; but melancholy shrinks from communication, and I never found a man before, to whom I could impart my troubles, though I had been certain of relief. I rejoice to find my own sentiments confirmed by yours, who are not easily deceived, and can have no motive or purpose to deceive. I hope that time and variety will dissipate the gloom that has so long surrounded me, and the latter part of my days will be spent in peace."

"Your learning and virtue," said Imlac, "may justly give you hopes."

---

6. Obsessive. According to Johnson's *Dictionary*, one definition of melancholy is "a kind of madness in which the mind is always fixed on one object."

Rasselas then entered with the princess and Pekuah, and inquired whether they had contrived any new diversion for the next day. "Such," said Nekayah, "is the state of life, that none are happy but by the anticipation of change: the change itself is nothing; when we have made it, the next wish is to change again. The world is not yet exhausted; let me see something tomorrow which I never saw before."

"Variety," said Rasselas, "is so necessary to content, that even the happy valley disgusted me by the recurrence of its luxuries; yet I could not forbear to reproach myself with impatience, when I saw the monks of St. Anthony support without complaint, a life, not of uniform delight, but uniform hardship."

"Those men," answered Imlac, "are less wretched in their silent convent than the Abyssinian princes in their prison of pleasure. Whatever is done by the monks is incited by an adequate and reasonable motive. Their labor supplies them with necessaries; it therefore cannot be omitted, and is certainly rewarded. Their devotion prepares them for another state, and reminds them of its approach, while it fits them for it. Their time is regularly distributed; one duty succeeds another, so that they are not left open to the distraction of unguided choice, nor lost in the shades of listless inactivity. There is a certain task to be performed at an appropriated hour; and their toils are cheerful, because they consider them as acts of piety, by which they are always advancing towards endless felicity."

"Do you think," said Nekayah, "that the monastic rule is a more holy and less imperfect state than any other? May not he equally hope for future happiness who converses openly with mankind, who succors the distressed by his charity, instructs the ignorant by his learning, and contributes by his industry to the general system of life; even though he should omit some of the mortifications which are practiced in the cloister, and allow himself such harmless delights as his condition may place within his reach?"

"This," said Imlac, "is a question which has long divided the wise, and perplexed the good. I am afraid to decide on either part. He that lives well in the world is better than he that lives well in a monastery. But perhaps everyone is not able to stem the temptations of public life; and if he cannot conquer, he may properly retreat. Some have little power to do good, and have likewise little strength to resist evil. Many are weary of their conflicts with adversity, and are willing to eject those passions which have long busied them in vain. And many are dismissed by age and diseases from the more laborious duties of society. In monasteries the weak and timorous may be happily sheltered, the weary may repose, and the penitent may meditate. Those retreats of prayer and contemplation have something so congenial to the mind of man, that, perhaps, there is scarcely one that does not purpose to close his life in pious abstraction with a few associates serious as himself."

"Such," said Pekuah, "has often been my wish, and I have heard the princess declare, that she should not willingly die in a crowd."

"The liberty of using harmless pleasures," proceeded Imlac, "will not be disputed; but it is still to be examined what pleasures are harmless. The evil of any pleasure that Nekayah can image is not in the act itself, but in its consequences. Pleasure, in itself harmless, may become mischievous, by endearing to us a state which we know to be transient and probatory,[7] and

7. Serving as a trial or test.

withdrawing our thoughts from that, of which every hour brings us nearer to the beginning, and of which no length of time will bring us to the end. Mortification is not virtuous in itself, nor has any other use, but that it disengages us from the allurements of sense. In the state of future perfection, to which we all aspire, there will be pleasure without danger, and security without restraint."

The princess was silent, and Rasselas, turning to the astronomer, asked him, whether he could not delay her retreat, by showing her something which she had not seen before.

"Your curiosity," said the sage, "has been so general, and your pursuit of knowledge so vigorous, that novelties are not now very easily to be found: but what you can no longer procure from the living may be given by the dead. Among the wonders of this country are the catacombs, or the ancient repositories, in which the bodies of the earliest generations were lodged, and where, by the virtue of the gums which embalmed them, they yet remain without corruption."

"I know not," said Rasselas, "what pleasure the sight of the catacombs can afford; but, since nothing else is offered, I am resolved to view them, and shall place this with many other things which I have done, because I would do something."

They hired a guard of horsemen, and the next day visited the catacombs. When they were about to descend into the sepulchral caves, "Pekuah," said the princess, "we are now again invading the habitations of the dead; I know that you will stay behind; let me find you safe when I return." "No, I will not be left," answered Pekuah; "I will go down between you and the prince."

They then all descended, and roved with wonder through the labyrinth of subterraneous passages, where the bodies were laid in rows on either side.

Chapter 48. Imlac Discourses on the Nature of the Soul

"What reason," said the prince, "can be given, why the Egyptians should thus expensively preserve those carcasses which some nations consume with fire, others lay to mingle with the earth, and all agree to remove from their sight, as soon as decent rites can be performed?"

"The original of ancient customs," said Imlac, "is commonly unknown; for the practice often continues when the cause has ceased; and concerning superstitious ceremonies it is vain to conjecture; for what reason did not dictate reason cannot explain. I have long believed that the practice of embalming arose only from tenderness to the remains of relations or friends, and to this opinion I am more inclined, because it seems impossible that this care should have been general: had all the dead been embalmed, their repositories must in time have been more spacious than the dwellings of the living. I suppose only the rich or honorable were secured from corruption, and the rest left to the course of nature.

"But it is commonly supposed that the Egyptians believed the soul to live as long as the body continued undissolved, and therefore tried this method of eluding death."

"Could the wise Egyptians," said Nekayah, "think so grossly of the soul? If the soul could once survive its separation, what could it afterwards receive or suffer from the body?"

"The Egyptians would doubtless think erroneously," said the astronomer, "in the darkness of heathenism, and the first dawn of philosophy. The nature of the soul is still disputed amidst all our opportunities of clearer knowledge: some yet say, that it may be material, who, nevertheless, believe it to be immortal."

"Some," answered Imlac, "have indeed said that the soul is material, but I can scarcely believe that any man has thought it, who knew how to think; for all the conclusions of reason enforce the immateriality of mind, and all the notices of sense and investigations of science concur to prove the unconsciousness of matter.

"It was never supposed that cogitation is inherent in matter, or that every particle is a thinking being. Yet if any part of matter be devoid of thought, what part can we suppose to think? Matter can differ from matter only in form, density, bulk, motion, and direction of motion: to which of these, however varied or combined, can consciousness be annexed? To be round or square, to be solid or fluid, to be great or little, to be moved slowly or swiftly one way or another, are modes of material existence, all equally alien from the nature of cogitation. If matter be once without thought, it can only be made to think by some new modification, but all the modifications which it can admit are equally unconnected with cogitative powers."

"But the materialists," said the astronomer, "urge that matter may have qualities with which we are unacquainted."

"He who will determine," returned Imlac, "against that which he knows, because there may be something which he knows not; he that can set hypothetical possibility against acknowledged certainty, is not to be admitted among reasonable beings. All that we know of matter is, that matter is inert, senseless and lifeless; and if this conviction cannot be opposed but by referring us to something that we know not, we have all the evidence that human intellect can admit. If that which is known may be overruled by that which is unknown, no being, not omniscient, can arrive at certainty."

"Yet let us not," said the astronomer, "too arrogantly limit the Creator's power."

"It is no limitation of omnipotence," replied the poet, "to suppose that one thing is not consistent with another, that the same proposition cannot be at once true and false, that the same number cannot be even and odd, that cogitation cannot be conferred on that which is created incapable of cogitation."

"I know not," said Nekayah, "any great use of this question. Does that immateriality, which, in my opinion, you have sufficiently proved, necessarily include eternal duration?"

"Of immateriality," said Imlac, "our ideas are negative, and therefore obscure. Immateriality seems to imply a natural power of perpetual duration as a consequence of exemption from all causes of decay: whatever perishes, is destroyed by the solution of its contexture,[8] and separation of its parts; nor can we conceive how that which has no parts, and therefore admits no solution, can be naturally corrupted or impaired."

"I know not," said Rasselas, "how to conceive anything without extension: what is extended must have parts, and you allow, that whatever has parts may be destroyed."

---

8. Dissolution of its structure.

"Consider your own conceptions," replied Imlac, "and the difficulty will be less. You will find substance without extension. An ideal form is no less real than material bulk: yet an ideal form has no extension. It is no less certain, when you think on a pyramid, that your mind possesses the idea of a pyramid, than that the pyramid itself is standing. What space does the idea of a pyramid occupy more than the idea of a grain of corn? or how can either idea suffer laceration? As is the effect such is the cause; as thought is, such is the power that thinks; a power impassive and indiscerptible."[9]

"But the Being," said Nekayah, "whom I fear to name, the Being which made the soul, can destroy it."

"He, surely, can destroy it," answered Imlac, "since, however unperishable, it receives from a superior nature its power of duration. That it will not perish by any inherent cause of decay, or principle of corruption, may be shown by philosophy; but philosophy can tell no more. That it will not be annihilated by him that made it, we must humbly learn from higher authority."

The whole assembly stood a while silent and collected. "Let us return," said Rasselas, "from this scene of mortality. How gloomy would be these mansions of the dead to him who did not know that he shall never die; that what now acts shall continue its agency, and what now thinks shall think on for ever. Those that lie here stretched before us, the wise and the powerful of ancient times, warn us to remember the shortness of our present state: they were, perhaps, snatched away while they were busy, like us, in the choice of life."

"To me," said the princess, "the choice of life is become less important; I hope hereafter to think only on the choice of eternity."

They then hastened out of the caverns, and, under the protection of their guard, returned to Cairo.

Chapter 49. The Conclusion, in Which Nothing Is Concluded

It was now the time of the inundation of the Nile: a few days after their visit to the catacombs, the river began to rise.

They were confined to their house. The whole region being under water gave them no invitation to any excursions, and being well supplied with materials for talk, they diverted themselves with comparisons of the different forms of life which they had observed, and with various schemes of happiness which each of them had formed.

Pekuah was never so much charmed with any place as the convent of St. Anthony, where the Arab restored her to the princess, and wished only to fill it with pious maidens, and to be made prioress of the order; she was weary of expectation and disgust,[1] and would gladly be fixed in some unvariable state.

The princess thought that, of all sublunary things, knowledge was the best: she desired first to learn all sciences, and then purposed to found a college of learned women, in which she would preside, that, by conversing with the old and educating the young, she might divide her time between the acquisition and communication of wisdom, and raise up for the next age models of prudence, and patterns of piety.

---

9. Not to be separated.　　　　　1. Aversion.

The prince desired a little kingdom, in which he might administer justice in his own person, and see all the parts of government with his own eyes; but he could never fix the limits of his dominion, and was always adding to the number of his subjects.

Imlac and the astronomer were contented to be driven along the stream of life, without directing their course to any particular port.

Of these wishes that they had formed, they well knew that none could be obtained. They deliberated a while what was to be done, and resolved, when the inundation should cease, to return to Abyssinia.[2]

1759

Rambler No. 4

[ON FICTION]

Saturday, *March* 31, 1750

Simul et jucunda et idonea dicere vitae.
—HORACE, *Art of Poetry*, 334

And join both profit and delight in one.
—CREECH

The works of fiction with which the present generation seems more particularly delighted are such as exhibit life in its true state, diversified only by accidents that daily happen in the world, and influenced by passions and qualities which are really to be found in conversing with mankind.

This kind of writing may be termed, not improperly, the comedy of romance, and is to be conducted nearly by the rules of comic poetry. Its province is to bring about natural events by easy means, and to keep up curiosity without the help of wonder: it is therefore precluded from the machines[1] and expedients of the heroic romance, and can neither employ giants to snatch away a lady from the nuptial rites, nor knights to bring her back from captivity; it can neither bewilder its personages in deserts, nor lodge them in imaginary castles.

I remember a remark made by Scaliger upon Pontanus,[2] that all his writings are filled with the same images; and that if you take from him his lilies and his roses, his satyrs and his dryads, he will have nothing left that can be called poetry. In like manner, almost all the fictions of the last age will vanish if you deprive them of a hermit and a wood, a battle and a shipwreck.

Why this wild strain of imagination found reception so long in polite and learned ages, it is not easy to conceive; but we cannot wonder that while readers could be procured, the authors were willing to continue it; for when a man had by practice gained some fluency of language, he had no further care than to retire to his closet, let loose his invention, and heat his mind with incredibilities; a book was thus produced without fear of criticism, without the toil of study, without knowledge of nature, or acquaintance with life.

2. Probably not to the Happy Valley, which they earlier fled. Their future remains uncertain.

1. The technical term in neoclassical critical theory for the supernatural agents who intervene in human affairs in epic and tragedy.

2. Julius Caesar Scaliger (1484–1558) criticized the Latin poems of the Italian poet Jovianus Pontanus (1426–1503).

The task of our present writers is very different; it requires, together with that learning which is to be gained from books, that experience which can never be attained by solitary diligence, but must arise from general converse and accurate observation of the living world. Their performances have, as Horace expresses it, *plus oneris quanto veniae minus*,[3] little indulgence, and therefore more difficulty. They are engaged in portraits of which everyone knows the original, and can detect any deviation from exactness of resemblance. Other writings are safe, except from the malice of learning, but these are in danger from every common reader; as the slipper ill executed was censured by a shoemaker who happened to stop in his way at the Venus of Apelles.[4]

But the fear of not being approved as just copiers of human manners is not the most important concern that an author of this sort ought to have before him. These books are written chiefly to the young, the ignorant, and the idle, to whom they serve as lectures of conduct, and introductions into life. They are the entertainment of minds unfurnished with ideas, and therefore easily susceptible of impressions; not fixed by principles, and therefore easily following the current of fancy; not informed by experience, and consequently open to every false suggestion and partial account.

That the highest degree of reverence should be paid to youth, and that nothing indecent should be suffered to approach their eyes or ears, are precepts extorted by sense and virtue from an ancient writer by no means eminent for chastity of thought.[5] The same kind, though not the same degree, of caution, is required in everything which is laid before them, to secure them from unjust prejudices, perverse opinions, and incongruous combinations of images.

In the romances formerly written, every transaction and sentiment was so remote from all that passes among men that the reader was in very little danger of making any applications to himself; the virtues and crimes were equally beyond his sphere of activity; and he amused himself with heroes and with traitors, deliverers and persecutors, as with beings of another species, whose actions were regulated upon motives of their own, and who had neither faults nor excellencies in common with himself.

But when an adventurer is leveled with the rest of the world, and acts in such scenes of the universal drama as may be the lot of any other man, young spectators fix their eyes upon him with closer attention, and hope, by observing his behavior and success, to regulate their own practices when they shall be engaged in the like part.

For this reason these familiar histories may perhaps be made of greater use than the solemnities of professed morality, and convey the knowledge of vice and virtue with more efficacy than axioms and definitions. But if the power of example is so great as to take possession of the memory by a kind of violence, and produce effects almost without the intervention of the will, care ought to be taken that when the choice is unrestrained, the best examples only should be exhibited; and that which is likely to operate so strongly should not be mischievous or uncertain in its effects.

---

3. *Epistles* 2.1.170.
4. According to Pliny the Younger (*Naturalis Historia* 35.85), the Greek painter Apelles of Kos (4th century B.C.E.) corrected the drawing of a sandal after hearing a shoemaker criticize it as faulty, but when the flattered artisan dared to find fault with the drawing of a leg, the artist bade him "stick to his last."
5. Juvenal's *Satires* 14.1–58.

The chief advantage which these fictions have over real life is that their authors are at liberty, though not to invent, yet to select objects, and to cull from the mass of mankind those individuals upon which the attention ought most to be employed; as a diamond, though it cannot be made, may be polished by art, and placed in such situation as to display that luster which before was buried among common stones.

It is justly considered as the greatest excellency of art to imitate nature; but it is necessary to distinguish those parts of nature which are most proper for imitation: greater care is still required in representing life, which is so often discolored by passion or deformed by wickedness. If the world be promiscuously[6] described, I cannot see of what use it can be to read the account; or why it may not be as safe to turn the eye immediately upon mankind as upon a mirror which shows all that presents itself without discrimination.

It is therefore not a sufficient vindication of a character that it is drawn as it appears, for many characters ought never to be drawn; nor of a narrative that the train of events is agreeable to observation and experience, for that observation which is called knowledge of the world will be found much more frequently to make men cunning than good. The purpose of these writings is surely not only to show mankind, but to provide that they may be seen hereafter with less hazard; to teach the means of avoiding the snares which are laid by Treachery for Innocence, without infusing any wish for that superiority with which the betrayer flatters his vanity; to give the power of counteracting fraud without the temptation to practice it; to initiate youth by mock encounters in the art of necessary defense, and to increase prudence without impairing virtue.

Many writers, for the sake of following nature, so mingle good and bad qualities in their principal personages that they are both equally conspicuous; and as we accompany them through their adventures with delight, and are led by degrees to interest ourselves in their favor, we lose the abhorrence of their faults because they do not hinder our pleasure, or perhaps regard them with some kindness for being united with so much merit.[7]

There have been men indeed splendidly wicked, whose endowments threw a brightness on their crimes, and whom scarce any villainy made perfectly detestable because they never could be wholly divested of their excellencies; but such have been in all ages the great corrupters of the world, and their resemblance ought no more to be preserved than the art of murdering without pain.

Some have advanced, without due attention to the consequences of this notion, that certain virtues have their correspondent faults, and therefore that to exhibit either apart is to deviate from probability. Thus men are observed by Swift to be "grateful in the same degree as they are resentful." This principle, with others of the same kind, supposes man to act from a brute impulse, and pursue a certain degree of inclination without any choice of the object; for, otherwise, though it should be allowed that gratitude and resentment arise from the same constitution of the passions, it follows not that they will be equally indulged when reason is consulted; yet, unless that

---

6. Indiscriminately.
7. Johnson is probably thinking of such popular novels as Tobias Smollett's *Roderick Random* (1748) and Henry Fielding's *Tom Jones* (1749), as opposed to the model of virtue provided by Samuel Richardson's *Clarissa* (1747–48).

consequence be admitted, this sagacious maxim becomes an empty sound, without any relation to practice or to life.

Nor is it evident that even the first motions to these effects are always in the same proportion. For pride, which produces quickness of resentment, will obstruct gratitude by unwillingness to admit that inferiority which obligation implies; and it is very unlikely that he who cannot think he receives a favor will acknowledge or repay it.

It is of the utmost importance to mankind that positions of this tendency should be laid open and confuted; for while men consider good and evil as springing from the same root, they will spare the one for the sake of the other, and in judging, if not of others at least of themselves, will be apt to estimate their virtues by their vices. To this fatal error all those will contribute who confound the colors of right and wrong, and, instead of helping to settle their boundaries, mix them with so much art that no common mind is able to disunite them.

In narratives where historical veracity has no place, I cannot discover why there should not be exhibited the most perfect idea of virtue; of virtue not angelical, nor above probability (for what we cannot credit, we shall never imitate), but the highest and purest that humanity can reach, which, exercised in such trials as the various revolutions of things shall bring upon it, may, by conquering some calamities and enduring others, teach us what we may hope, and what we can perform. Vice (for vice is necessary to be shown) should always disgust; nor should the graces of gaiety, nor the dignity of courage, be so united with it as to reconcile it to the mind. Wherever it appears, it should raise hatred by the malignity of its practices, and contempt by the meanness of its stratagems: for while it is supported by either parts[8] or spirit, it will be seldom heartily abhorred. The Roman tyrant was content to be hated if he was but feared;[9] and there are thousands of the readers of romances willing to be thought wicked if they may be allowed to be wits. It is therefore to be steadily inculcated that virtue is the highest proof of understanding, and the only solid basis of greatness; and that vice is the natural consequence of narrow thoughts; that it begins in mistake, and ends in ignominy.

Rambler No. 60

[BIOGRAPHY]

Saturday, *October* 13, 1750

—*Quid sit pulchrum, quid turpe, quid utile, quid non,*
Plenius ac melius Chrysippo et Crantore dicit.
—HORACE, *Epistles,* 1.2.3–4

Whose works the beautiful and base contain,
Of vice and virtue more instructive rules,
Than all the sober sages of the schools.

—FRANCIS

---

8. Abilities.
9. The emperor Tiberius (see Suetonius's *Lives of the Caesars*).

All joy or sorrow for the happiness or calamities of others is produced by an act of the imagination, that realizes the event, however fictitious, or approximates it,[1] however remote, by placing us, for a time, in the condition of him whose fortune we contemplate; so that we feel, while the deception lasts, whatever motions would be excited by the same good or evil happening to ourselves.

Our passions are therefore more strongly moved, in proportion as we can more readily adopt the pains or pleasure proposed to our minds, by recognizing them as once our own, or considering them as naturally incident to our state of life. It is not easy for the most artful writer to give us an interest in happiness or misery, which we think ourselves never likely to feel, and with which we have never yet been made acquainted. Histories of the downfall of kingdoms, and revolutions of empires, are read with great tranquility; the imperial tragedy pleases common auditors only by its pomp of ornament, and grandeur of ideas; and the man whose faculties have been engrossed by business, and whose heart never fluttered but at the rise or fall of stocks, wonders how the attention can be seized, or the affections agitated, by a tale of love.

Those parallel circumstances, and kindred images to which we readily conform our minds, are, above all other writings, to be found in narratives of the lives of particular persons; and therefore no species of writing seems more worthy of cultivation than biography, since none can be more delightful or more useful, none can more certainly enchain the heart by irresistible interest, or more widely diffuse instruction to every diversity of condition.

The general and rapid narratives of history, which involve a thousand fortunes in the business of a day, and complicate[2] innumerable incidents in one great transaction, afford few lessons applicable to private life, which derives its comforts and its wretchedness from the right or wrong management of things, which nothing but their frequency makes considerable, *Parva si non fiunt quotidie*, says Pliny,[3] and which can have no place in those relations which never descend below the consultation of senates, the motions of armies, and the schemes of conspirators.

I have often thought that there has rarely passed a life of which a judicious and faithful narrative would not be useful. For, not only every man has in the mighty mass of the world great numbers in the same condition with himself, to whom his mistakes and miscarriages, escapes and expedients, would be of immediate and apparent use; but there is such an uniformity in the state of man, considered apart from adventitious and separable decorations and disguises, that there is scarce any possibility of good or ill, but is common to humankind. A great part of the time of those who are placed at the greatest distance by fortune, or by temper, must unavoidably pass in the same manner; and though, when the claims of nature are satisfied, caprice, and vanity, and accident, begin to produce discriminations and peculiarities, yet the eye is not very heedful or quick, which cannot discover the same causes still[4] terminating their influence in the same effects, though sometimes accelerated, sometimes retarded, or perplexed by multiplied combinations. We are

---

1. Brings it near.
2. Join.
3. Pliny the Younger's *Epistles* 3.1. Johnson trans- lates the phrase in the preceding clause.
4. Always.

all prompted by the same motives, all deceived by the same fallacies, all animated by hope, obstructed by danger, entangled by desire, and seduced by pleasure.

It is frequently objected to relations of particular lives, that they are not distinguished by any striking or wonderful vicissitudes. The scholar who passed his life among his books, the merchant who conducted only his own affairs, the priest whose sphere of action was not extended beyond that of his duty, are considered as no proper objects of public regard, however they might have excelled in their several stations, whatever might have been their learning, integrity, and piety. But this notion arises from false measures of excellence and dignity, and must be eradicated by considering, that in the esteem of uncorrupted reason, what is of most use is of most value.

It is, indeed, not improper to take honest advantages of prejudice, and to gain attention by a celebrated name; but the business of the biographer is often to pass slightly over those performances and incidents, which produce vulgar greatness, to lead the thoughts into domestic privacies, and display the minute details of daily life, where exterior appendages are cast aside, and men excel each other only by prudence and by virtue. The account of Thuanus[5] is, with great propriety, said by its author to have been written, that it might lay open to posterity the private and familiar character of that man, *cujus ingenium et candorem ex ipsius scriptis sunt olim semper miraturi*, whose candor and genius will to the end of time be by his writings preserved in admiration.

There are many invisible circumstances which, whether we read as inquirers after natural or moral knowledge, whether we intend to enlarge our science, or increase our virtue, are more important than public occurrences. Thus Sallust, the great master of nature, has not forgot, in his account of Catiline,[6] to remark that *his walk was now quick, and again slow*, as an indication of a mind revolving something with violent commotion. Thus the story of Melancthon[7] affords a striking lecture on the value of time, by informing us that when he made an appointment, he expected not only the hour, but the minute to be fixed, that the day might not run out in the idleness of suspense; and all the plans and enterprises of De Witt are now of less importance to the world, than that part of his personal character, which represents him as careful of his health, and negligent of his life.[8]

But biography has often been allotted to writers who seem very little acquainted with the nature of their task, or very negligent about the performance. They rarely afford any other account than might be collected from public papers, but imagine themselves writing a life when they exhibit a chronological series of actions or preferments; and so little regard the manners or behavior of their heroes, that more knowledge may be gained of a man's real character, by a short conversation with one of his servants, than from a formal and studied narrative, begun with his pedigree, and ended with his funeral.

5. Jacques-Auguste de Thou (1553–1617), an important French historian, of whom Nicholas Rigault wrote a brief biography, a sentence of which Johnson quotes and translates below.
6. Sallust, a Roman historian of the 1st century B.C.E., wrote an account of Catiline's conspiracy against the Roman state.
7. Camerarius wrote a life of Melancthon, a German theologian of the 16th century.
8. Sir William Temple, characterizing the Dutch statesman John De Witt.

If now and then they condescend to inform the world of particular facts, they are not always so happy as to select the most important. I know not well what advantage posterity can receive from the only circumstance by which Tickell has distinguished Addison from the rest of mankind, the irregularity of his pulse:[9] nor can I think myself overpaid for the time spent in reading the life of Malherbe, by being enabled to relate, after the learned biographer,[1] that Malherbe had two predominant opinions; one, that the looseness of a single woman might destroy all her boast of ancient descent; the other, that the French beggars made use very improperly and barbarously of the phrase *noble gentleman*, because either word included the sense of both.

There are, indeed, some natural reasons why these narratives are often written by such as were not likely to give much instruction or delight, and why most accounts of particular persons are barren and useless. If a life be delayed till interest and envy are at an end, we may hope for impartiality, but must expect little intelligence;[2] for the incidents which give excellence to biography are of a volatile and evanescent kind, such as soon escape the memory, and are rarely transmitted by tradition. We know how few can portray a living acquaintance, except by his most prominent and observable particularities, and the grosser features of his mind; and it may be easily imagined how much of this little knowledge may be lost in imparting it, and how soon a succession of copies will lose all resemblance of the original.

If the biographer writes from personal knowledge, and makes haste to gratify the public curiosity, there is danger lest his interest, his fear, his gratitude, or his tenderness, overpower his fidelity, and tempt him to conceal, if not to invent. There are many who think it an act of piety to hide the faults or failings of their friends, even when they can no longer suffer by their detection; we therefore see whole ranks of characters adorned with uniform panegyric, and not to be known from one another, but by extrinsic and casual circumstances. "Let me remember," says Hale, "when I find myself inclined to pity a criminal, that there is likewise a pity due to the country."[3] If we owe regard to the memory of the dead, there is yet more respect to be paid to knowledge, to virtue, and to truth.

A Dictionary of the English Language

Before Johnson, no standard dictionary of the English language existed. The lack had troubled speakers of English for some time, both because Italian and French academies had produced major dictionaries of their own tongues and because, in the absence of any authority, English seemed likely to change utterly from one generation to another. Many eighteenth-century authors feared that their own language would soon become obsolete: as Alexander Pope wrote in *An Essay on Criticism*,

> Our sons their fathers' failing language see,
> And such as Chaucer is, shall Dryden be.

A dictionary could help retard such change, and commercially it would be a book that everyone would need to buy. In 1746 a group of London publishers commissioned

9. From Thomas Tickell's preface to Addison's *Works* (1721).
1. The life of the French poet François de Malherbe (1555–1628) was written by Honorat de

Racan.
2. Information.
3. From Gilbert Burnet's *Life and Death of Sir Matthew Hale* (1682).

Johnson, still an unknown author, to undertake the project. He hoped to finish it in three years; it took him nine. But the quantity and quality of work he accomplished, aided only by six part-time assistants, made him famous as "Dictionary Johnson." The *Dictionary* remained a standard reference book for one hundred years.

Johnson's achievement is notable in three respects: its size (forty thousand words), the wealth of illustrative quotations, and the excellence of the definitions. No earlier English dictionary rivaled the scope of Johnson's two large folio volumes. About 114,000 quotations, gathered from the best English writers from Sidney to the eighteenth century, exemplify the usage of words as well as their meanings. Above all, it was the definitions, however, that established the authority of Johnson's *Dictionary*. A small selection is only too likely to concentrate on a few amusing or notorious definitions, but the great majority are full, clear, and totally free from eccentricity. Indeed, many of them are still repeated in modern dictionaries. Language, Johnson knew, cannot be fixed once and for all; many of the words he defines have radically changed meaning since the eighteenth century. Yet Johnson did more than any other person of his time to preserve the ideal of a standard English.

From A Dictionary of the English Language

From *Preface*

* * *

A large work is difficult because it is large, even though all its parts might singly be performed with facility; where there are many things to be done, each must be allowed its share of time and labor, in the proportion only which it bears to the whole; nor can it be expected that the stones which form the dome of a temple should be squared and polished like the diamond of a ring.

Of the event of this work, for which, having labored it with so much application, I cannot but have some degree of parental fondness, it is natural to form conjectures. Those who have been persuaded to think well of my design will require that it should fix our language, and put a stop to those alterations which time and chance have hitherto been suffered to make in it without opposition. With this consequence I will confess that I flattered myself for a while;[1] but now begin to fear that I have indulged expectation which neither reason nor experience can justify. When we see men grow old and die at a certain time one after another, from century to century, we laugh at the elixir that promises to prolong life to a thousand years; and with equal justice may the lexicographer be derided, who being able to produce no example of a nation that has preserved their words and phrases from mutability, shall imagine that his dictionary can embalm his language and secure it from corruption and decay, that it is in his power to change sublunary nature, or clear the world at once from folly, vanity, and affectation.

With this hope, however, academies have been instituted, to guard the avenues of their languages, to retain fugitives, and repulse intruders; but their vigilance and activity have hitherto been vain; sounds are too volatile and subtle for legal restraints; to enchain syllables, and to lash the wind, are

---

1. Johnson's Plan (1747) had called for "a dictionary by which the pronunciation of our language may be fixed, and its attainment facilitated; by which its purity may be preserved, its use ascertained, and its duration lengthened."

equally the undertakings of pride, unwilling to measure its desires by its strength. The French language has visibly changed under the inspection of the academy;[2] the style of Amelot's translation of father Paul is observed by Le Courayer to be *un peu passé*;[3] and no Italian will maintain that the diction of any modern writer is not perceptibly different from that of Boccace, Machiavel, or Caro.[4]

Total and sudden transformations of a language seldom happen; conquests and migrations are now very rare: but there are other causes of change, which, though slow in their operation, and invisible in their progress, are perhaps as much superior to human resistance as the revolutions of the sky, or intumescence[5] of the tide. Commerce, however necessary, however lucrative, as it depraves the manners, corrupts the language; they that have frequent intercourse with strangers, to whom they endeavor to accommodate themselves, must in time learn a mingled dialect, like the jargon which serves the traffickers[6] on the Mediterranean and Indian coasts. This will not always be confined to the exchange, the warehouse, or the port, but will be communicated by degrees to other ranks of the people, and be at last incorporated with the current speech.

There are likewise internal causes equally forcible. The language most likely to continue long without alteration would be that of a nation raised a little, and but a little, above barbarity, secluded from strangers, and totally employed in procuring the conveniencies of life; either without books, or, like some of the Mahometan countries, with very few: men thus busied and unlearned, having only such words as common use requires, would perhaps long continue to express the same notions by the same signs. But no such constancy can be expected in a people polished by arts, and classed by subordination, where one part of the community is sustained and accommodated by the labor of the other. Those who have much leisure to think, will always be enlarging the stock of ideas, and every increase of knowledge, whether real or fancied, will produce new words, or combinations of words. When the mind is unchained from necessity, it will range after convenience; when it is left at large in the fields of speculation, it will shift opinions; as any custom is disused, the words that expressed it must perish with it; as any opinion grows popular, it will innovate speech in the same proportion as it alters practice.

As by the cultivation of various sciences, a language is amplified, it will be more furnished with words deflected from their original sense; the geometrician will talk of a courtier's zenith, or the eccentric virtue of a wild hero, and the physician of sanguine expectations and phlegmatic delays.[7] Copiousness of speech will give opportunities to capricious choice, by which some words will be preferred, and others degraded; vicissitudes of fashion will enforce

2. The French academy, founded to purify the French language, had produced a dictionary in 1694; but revisions were necessary within a few years.
3. A bit old-fashioned (French). Le Courayer's translation (1736) of Father Paolo Sarpi's *History of the Council of Trent* superseded Amelot's (1683).
4. Like Boccaccio (1313–1375) and Machiavelli (1469–1527), Annibale Caro (1507–1566) was a classic Italian stylist whose work had preceded

the dictionary published in 1612 by the Italian academy.
5. Swelling.
6. Traders.
7. "Sanguine" and "phlegmatic" once referred only to the physiological predominance of blood or phlegm. "Zenith" (the point of the sky directly overhead) and "eccentric" (deviating from the center) were originally astronomical and geometrical terms.

the use of new, or extend the signification of known terms. The tropes[8] of poetry will make hourly encroachments, and the metaphorical will become the current sense: pronunciation will be varied by levity or ignorance, and the pen must at length comply with the tongue; illiterate writers will at one time or other, by public infatuation, rise into renown, who, not knowing the original import of words, will use them with colloquial licentiousness, confound distinction, and forget propriety. As politeness increases, some expressions will be considered as too gross and vulgar for the delicate, others as too formal and ceremonious for the gay and airy; new phrases are therefore adopted, which must, for the same reasons, be in time dismissed. Swift, in his petty treatise on the English language,[9] allows that new words must sometimes be introduced, but proposes that none should be suffered to become obsolete. But what makes a word obsolete, more than general agreement to forbear it? and how shall it be continued, when it conveys an offensive idea, or recalled again into the mouths of mankind, when it has once by disuse become unfamiliar, and by unfamiliarity unpleasing.

There is another cause of alteration more prevalent than any other, which yet in the present state of the world cannot be obviated. A mixture of two languages will produce a third distinct from both, and they will always be mixed, where the chief part of education, and the most conspicuous accomplishment, is skill in ancient or in foreign tongues. He that has long cultivated another language, will find its words and combinations crowd upon his memory; and haste or negligence, refinement or affectation, will obtrude borrowed terms and exotic expressions.

The great pest of speech is frequency of translation. No book was ever turned from one language into another, without imparting something of its native idiom; this is the most mischievous and comprehensive innovation; single words may enter by thousands, and the fabric of the tongue continue the same, but new phraseology changes much at once; it alters not the single stones of the building, but the order[1] of the columns. If an academy should be established for the cultivation of our style, which I, who can never wish to see dependence multiplied, hope the spirit of English liberty will hinder or destroy, let them, instead of compiling grammars and dictionaries, endeavor with all their influence to stop the license of translators, whose idleness and ignorance, if it be suffered to proceed, will reduce us to babble a dialect of France.

If the changes that we fear be thus irresistible, what remains but to acquiesce with silence, as in the other insurmountable distresses of humanity? It remains that we retard what we cannot repel, that we palliate what we cannot cure. Life may be lengthened by care, though death cannot be ultimately defeated: tongues, like governments, have a natural tendency to degeneration; we have long preserved our constitution, let us make some struggles for our language.

In hope of giving longevity to that which its own nature forbids to be immortal, I have devoted this book, the labor of years, to the honor of my country, that we may no longer yield the palm of philology without a contest

---

8. "A change of a word from its original signification" (Johnson's *Dictionary*).
9. "A Proposal for Correcting, Improving, and Ascertaining the English Tongue" (1712). "Petty": little.
1. Architectural mode (Doric, etc.), which determines the style and proportions of columns.

to the nations of the continent. The chief glory of every people arises from its authors: whether I shall add anything by my own writings to the reputation of English literature, must be left to time. Much of my life has been lost under the pressures of disease; much has been trifled away; and much has always been spent in provision for the day that was passing over me; but I shall not think my employment useless or ignoble, if by my assistance foreign nations, and distant ages, gain access to the propagators of knowledge, and understand the teachers of truth; if my labors afford light to the repositories of science, and add celebrity to Bacon, to Hooker, to Milton, and to Boyle.[2]

When I am animated by this wish, I look with pleasure on my book, however defective; and deliver it to the world with the spirit of a man that has endeavored well. That it will immediately become popular I have not promised to myself: a few wild blunders and risible absurdities, from which no work of such multiplicity was ever free, may for a time furnish folly with laughter, and harden ignorance in contempt; but useful diligence will at last prevail, and there never can be wanting some who distinguish desert;[3] who will consider that no dictionary of a living tongue ever can be perfect, since while it is hastening to publication, some words are budding, and some falling away; that a whole life cannot be spent upon syntax and etymology, and that even a whole life would not be sufficient; that he, whose design includes whatever language can express, must often speak of what he does not understand; that a writer will sometimes be hurried by eagerness to the end, and sometimes faint with weariness under a task, which Scaliger compares to the labors of the anvil and the mine;[4] that what is obvious is not always known, and what is known is not always present; that sudden fits of inadvertency will surprise vigilance, slight avocations[5] will reduce attention, and casual eclipses of the mind will darken learning; and that the writer shall often in vain trace his memory at the moment of need, for that which yesterday he knew with intuitive readiness, and which will come uncalled into his thoughts tomorrow.

In this work, when it shall be found that much is omitted, let it not be forgotten that much likewise is performed; and though no book was ever spared out of tenderness to the author, and the world is little solicitous to know whence proceeded the faults of that which it condemns; yet it may gratify curiosity to inform it, that the *English Dictionary* was written with little assistance of the learned, and without any patronage of the great;[6] not in the soft obscurities of retirement, or under the shelter of academic bowers, but amidst inconvenience and distraction, in sickness and in sorrow: and it may repress the triumph of malignant criticism to observe, that if our language is not here fully displayed, I have only failed in an attempt which no human powers have hitherto completed. If the lexicons of ancient tongues, now immutably fixed, and comprised in a few volumes, be yet, after the toil of successive ages, inadequate and delusive; if the aggregated knowledge and cooperating diligence

---

2. Leading physicist and chemist (1627–1691). "Science": knowledge. Richard Hooker wrote *The Laws of Ecclesiastical Polity* (1594–97), a famous defense of the Church of England.
3. Merit.
4. Joseph Justus Scaliger (1540–1609), a great

scholar and lexicographer, wrote Latin verses suggesting that criminals should be condemned to lexicography.
5. Whatever calls one aside.
6. See Johnson's letter to Lord Chesterfield in Boswell's *Life of Johnson* (pp. 2969–72).

of the Italian academicians did not secure them from the censure of Beni;[7] if the embodied critics of France, when fifty years had been spent upon their work, were obliged to change its economy,[8] and give their second edition another form, I may surely be contented without the praise of perfection, which, if I could obtain, in this gloom of solitude, what would it avail me? I have protracted my work till most of those whom I wished to please have sunk into the grave,[9] and success and miscarriage are empty sounds: I therefore dismiss it with frigid tranquility, having little to fear or hope from censure or from praise.

[SOME DEFINITIONS: A SMALL ANTHOLOGY][1]

ANTHO'LOGY. *n.*

1. A collection of flowers.

To CANT. *v.*

To talk in the jargon of particular professions, or in any kind of formal affected language, or with a peculiar and studied tone of voice.

> Men *cant* endlessly about *materia forma;* and hunt chimeras by rules of art, or dress up ignorance in words of bulk or sound, which may stop up the mouth of inquiry.—*Glanville's Scepsis Scientifica.*

ENTHU'SIASM. *n.*

1. A vain belief of private revelation; a vain confidence of divine favor or communication.

> *Enthusiasm* is founded neither on reason nor divine revelation, but rises from the conceits of a warmed or overweening brain.—*Locke.*

GE'NIUS. *n.*

1. The protecting or ruling power of men, places, or things.

> And as I awake, sweet music breathe,
> Sent by some spirit to mortals good,
> Or th' unseen *genius* of the wood.—*Milton.*

2. A man endowed with superior faculties.

3. Mental power or faculties.

4. Disposition of nature by which anyone is qualified for some peculiar employment.

5. Nature; disposition.

IMA'GINATION, *n.*

1. Fancy; the power of forming ideal pictures; the power of representing things absent to one's self or others.

2. Conception; image in the mind; idea.

3. Contrivance; scheme.

LEXICO'GRAPHER. *n.*

A writer of dictionaries; a harmless drudge, that busies himself in tracing the original, and detailing the signification of words.

MELANCHO'LY. *n.*

1. A disease, supposed to proceed from a redundance of black bile.

---

7. Paolo Beni's *L'Anticrusca* (1612) violently attacked the first edition of the *Vocabolario* (the Italian dictionary).
8. Organization.

9. Johnson's wife had died three years earlier.
1. Johnson's definitions include etymologies and illustrative quotations, some of which are omitted in this selection.

2. A kind of madness, in which the mind is always fixed on one object.

3. A gloomy, pensive, discontented temper.

NA'TURE. *n.*

1. An imaginary being supposed to preside over the material and animal world.

> Thou, *nature*, art my goddess; to thy law
> My services are bound.—*Shakespeare.*

2. The native state or properties of anything, by which it is discriminated from others.

3. The constitution of an animated body.

4. Disposition of mind; temper.

5. The regular course of things.

6. The compass of natural existence.

7. Natural affection, or reverence; native sensations.

8. The state or operation of the material world.

9. Sort; species.

10. Sentiments or images adapted to nature, or comfortable to truth and reality.

11. Physics; the science which teaches the qualities of things.

> *Nature* and *nature's* laws lay hid in night,
> God said, Let Newton be, and all was light.—*Pope.*

NE'TWORK. *n.*

Anything reticulated or decussated, at equal distances, with interstices between the intersections.

OATS. *n.*

A grain, which in England is generally given to horses, but in Scotland supports the people.

PA'STERN. *n.*

1. The knee of an horse.[2]

PA'TRON. *n.*

1. One who countenances, supports, or protects. Commonly a wretch who supports with insolence, and is paid with flattery.

PE'NSION. *n.*

An allowance made to anyone without an equivalent. In England it is generally understood to mean pay given to a state hireling for treason to his country.[3]

SA'TIRE. *n.*

A poem in which wickedness or folly is censured. Proper *satire* is distinguished, by the generality of the reflections, from a *lampoon*, which is aimed against a particular person; but they are too frequently confounded.

TO'RY. *n.*

One who adheres to the ancient constitution of the state, and the apostolical hierarchy of the church of England, opposed to a whig.

> The knight is more a *tory* in the country than the town, because it more advances his interest.—*Addison.*

---

2. "A lady once asked him how he came to define *Pastern* the *knee* of a horse: instead of making an elaborate defense, as she expected, he at once answered, 'Ignorance, Madam, pure ignorance'" (Boswell).

3. In 1762 Johnson was awarded a pension, but he did not revise the definition in later editions.

WHIG. *n.*

2. The name of a faction.

> Whoever has a true value for church and state, should avoid the extremes of *whig* for the sake of the former, and the extremes of tory on the account of the latter.—*Swift.*

WIT. *n.*

1. The powers of the mind; the mental faculties; the intellects. This is the original signification.
2. Imagination; quickness of fancy.
3. Sentiments produced by quickness of fancy.
4. A man of fancy.
5. A man of genius.
6. Sense; judgment.
7. In the plural. Sound mind; intellect not crazed.
8. Contrivance; stratagem; power of expedients.

1755

The Preface to Shakespeare This is the finest piece of Shakespeare criticism in the eighteenth century; it culminates a critical tradition that began with John Dryden's remarks on Shakespeare and continued as the plays were edited by Nicholas Rowe, Alexander Pope, Lewis Theobald, and William Warburton. Johnson addresses the standard topics: Shakespeare is the poet of nature, not learning; the creator of characters who spring to life; and a writer whose works express the full range of human passions. But the Preface also takes a fresh look not only at the plays but at the first principles of criticism. Resisting "bardolatry"—uncritical worship of Shakespeare—Johnson points out his faults as well as his virtues and finds that his truth to life, or "just representations of general nature," surpasses that of all other modern writers. The Preface is most original when it attacks the long-standing critical reverence for the unities of time and place. What seems real on the stage, Johnson argues, does not depend on artificial rules but on what the mind is willing to imagine.

Johnson's edition of Shakespeare also contained footnotes and brief introductions to each of the plays. Reprinted here are his afterwords to *Twelfth Night* and *King Lear*.

From The Preface to Shakespeare

[SHAKESPEARE'S EXCELLENCE, GENERAL NATURE]

That praises are without reason lavished on the dead, and that the honors due only to excellence are paid to antiquity, is a complaint likely to be always continued by those who, being able to add nothing to truth, hope for eminence from the heresies of paradox; or those who, being forced by disappointment upon consolatory expedients, are willing to hope from posterity what the present age refuses, and flatter themselves that the regard which is yet denied by envy will be at last bestowed by time.

Antiquity, like every other quality that attracts the notice of mankind, has undoubtedly votaries that reverence it not from reason but from prejudice. Some seem to admire indiscriminately whatever has been long preserved, without considering that time has sometimes cooperated with chance; all perhaps are more willing to honor past than present excellence; and the mind contemplates genius through the shades of age, as the eye surveys the sun through artificial opacity. The great contention of criticism is to find the faults of the moderns and the beauties of the ancients. While an author is yet living we estimate his powers by his worst performance; and when he is dead we rate them by his best.

To works, however, of which the excellence is not absolute and definite, but gradual and comparative; to works not raised upon principles demonstrative and scientific, but appealing wholly to observation and experience, no other test can be applied than length of duration and continuance of esteem. What mankind have long possessed they have often examined and compared; and if they persist to value the possession, it is because frequent comparisons have confirmed opinion in its favor. As among the works of nature no man can properly call a river deep or a mountain high, without the knowledge of many mountains and many rivers; so in the productions of genius, nothing can be styled excellent till it has been compared with other works of the same kind. Demonstration[1] immediately displays its power and has nothing to hope or fear from the flux of years; but works tentative and experimental must be estimated by their proportion to the general and collective ability of man, as it is discovered in a long succession of endeavors. Of the first building that was raised, it might be with certainty determined that it was round or square, but whether it was spacious or lofty must have been referred to time. The Pythagorean scale of numbers[2] was at once discovered to be perfect; but the poems of Homer we yet know not to transcend the common limits of human intelligence, but by remarking that nation after nation, and century after century, has been able to do little more than transpose his incidents, new name his characters, and paraphrase his sentiments.

The reverence due to writings that have long subsisted arises, therefore, not from any credulous confidence in the superior wisdom of past ages, or gloomy persuasion of the degeneracy of mankind, but is the consequence of acknowledged and indubitable positions, that what has been longest known has been most considered, and what is most considered is best understood.

The poet of whose works I have undertaken the revision may now begin to assume the dignity of an ancient and claim the privilege of established fame and prescriptive veneration. He has long outlived his century, the term commonly fixed as the test of literary merit.[3] Whatever advantages he might once derive from personal allusions, local customs, or temporary opinions, have for many years been lost; and every topic of merriment or motive of sorrow which the modes of artificial life afforded him now only obscure the scenes which they once illuminated. The effects of favor and competition are at an end; the tradition of his friendships and his enmities has perished; his works support no opinion with arguments nor supply any faction with invectives; they can neither indulge vanity nor gratify malignity; but are read without any other reason than the desire of pleasure, and are therefore praised only as pleasure is obtained; yet, thus unassisted by interest or passion, they have passed through variations of taste and changes of manners, and, as they

1. "The highest degree of deducible or argumental evidence" (Johnson's *Dictionary*).
2. Pythagoras discovered the ratios that determine the principal intervals of the musical scale.
3. Horace's *Epistles* 2.1.39.

devolved from one generation to another, have received new honors at every transmission.

But because human judgment, though it be gradually gaining upon certainty, never becomes infallible, and approbation, though long continued, may yet be only the approbation of prejudice or fashion, it is proper to inquire by what peculiarities of excellence Shakespeare has gained and kept the favor of his countrymen.

Nothing can please many, and please long, but just representations of general nature. Particular manners can be known to few, and therefore few only can judge how nearly they are copied. The irregular combinations of fanciful invention may delight awhile by that novelty of which the common satiety of life sends us all in quest; but the pleasures of sudden wonder are soon exhausted, and the mind can only repose on the stability of truth.

Shakespeare is, above all writers, at least above all modern writers, the poet of nature, the poet that holds up to his readers a faithful mirror of manners and of life. His characters are not modified by the customs of particular places, unpracticed by the rest of the world; by the peculiarities of studies or professions, which can operate but upon small numbers; or by the accidents of transient fashions or temporary opinions: they are the genuine progeny of common humanity, such as the world will always supply and observation will always find. His persons act and speak by the influence of those general passions and principles by which all minds are agitated and the whole system of life is continued in motion. In the writings of other poets a character is too often an individual: in those of Shakespeare it is commonly a species.

It is from this wide extension of design that so much instruction is derived. It is this which fills the plays of Shakespeare with practical axioms and domestic wisdom. It was said of Euripides[4] that every verse was a precept; and it may be said of Shakespeare that from his works may be collected a system of civil and economical prudence. Yet his real power is not shown in the splendor of particular passages, but by the progress of his fable[5] and the tenor of his dialogue; and he that tries to recommend him by select quotations will succeed like the pedant in Hierocles[6] who, when he offered his house to sale, carried a brick in his pocket as a specimen.

It will not easily be imagined how much Shakespeare excels in accommodating his sentiments to real life but by comparing him with other authors. It was observed of the ancient schools of declamation that the more diligently they were frequented, the more was the student disqualified for the world, because he found nothing there which he should ever meet in any other place. The same remark may be applied to every stage but that of Shakespeare. The theater, when it is under any other direction, is peopled by such characters as were never seen, conversing in a language which was never heard, upon topics which will never arise in the commerce of mankind. But the dialogue of this author is often so evidently determined by the incident

4. The Greek tragic poet (ca. 480–406 B.C.E.). The observation is Cicero's.
5. Plot. "The series or contexture of events which constitute a poem epic or dramatic" (Johnson's *Dictionary*).
6. Hierocles of Alexandria, a Greek philosopher of the 5th century C.E.

which produces it, and is pursued with so much ease and simplicity, that it seems scarcely to claim the merit of fiction, but to have been gleaned by diligent selection out of common conversation and common occurrences.

Upon every other stage the universal agent is love, by whose power all good and evil is distributed and every action quickened or retarded. To bring a lover, a lady, and a rival into the fable; to entangle them in contradictory obligations, perplex them with oppositions of interest, and harass them with violence of desires inconsistent with each other; to make them meet in rapture, and part in agony; to fill their mouths with hyperbolical joy and outrageous sorrow; to distress them as nothing human ever was distressed; to deliver them as nothing human ever was delivered, is the business of a modern dramatist. For this, probability is violated, life is misrepresented, and language is depraved. But love is only one of many passions; and as it has no great influence upon the sum of life, it has little operation in the dramas of a poet who caught his ideas from the living world and exhibited only what he saw before him. He knew that any other passion, as it was regular or exorbitant, was a cause of happiness or calamity.

Characters thus ample and general were not easily discriminated and preserved; yet perhaps no poet ever kept his personages more distinct from each other. I will not say with Pope that every speech may be assigned to the proper speaker,[7] because many speeches there are which have nothing characteristical; but perhaps though some may be equally adapted to every person, it will be difficult to find that any can be properly transferred from the present possessor to another claimant. The choice is right when there is reason for choice.

Other dramatists can only gain attention by hyperbolical or aggravated characters, by fabulous and unexampled excellence or depravity, as the writers of barbarous romances invigorated the reader by a giant and a dwarf; and he that should form his expectations of human affairs from the play or from the tale would be equally deceived. Shakespeare has no heroes; his scenes are occupied only by men, who act and speak as the reader thinks that he should himself have spoken or acted on the same occasion; even where the agency is supernatural, the dialogue is level with life. Other writers disguise the most natural passions and most frequent incidents so that he who contemplates them in the book will not know them in the world: Shakespeare approximates[8] the remote, and familiarizes the wonderful; the event which he represents will not happen, but, if it were possible, its effects would probably be such as he has assigned; and it may be said that he has not only shown human nature as it acts in real exigencies, but as it would be found in trials to which it cannot be exposed.

This therefore is the praise of Shakespeare, that his drama is the mirror of life; that he who has mazed his imagination in following the phantoms which other writers raise up before him, may here be cured of his delirious ecstasies by reading human sentiments in human language, by scenes from which a hermit may estimate the transactions of the world, and a confessor predict the progress of the passions.

7. In the preface to his edition of Shakespeare's plays (1725).

8. Brings near.

[SHAKESPEARE'S FAULTS. THE THREE DRAMATIC UNITIES]

Shakespeare with his excellencies has likewise faults, and faults sufficient to obscure and overwhelm any other merit. I shall show them in the proportion in which they appear to me, without envious malignity or superstitious veneration. No question can be more innocently discussed than a dead poet's pretensions to renown; and little regard is due to that bigotry which sets candor[9] higher than truth.

His first defect is that to which may be imputed most of the evil in books or in men. He sacrifices virtue to convenience, and is so much more careful to please than to instruct that he seems to write without any moral purpose. From his writings indeed a system of social duty may be selected, for he that thinks reasonably must think morally, but his precepts and axioms drop casually from him; he makes no just distribution of good or evil, nor is always careful to show in the virtuous a disapprobation of the wicked; he carries his persons indifferently through right and wrong, and at the close dismisses them without further care, and leaves their examples to operate by chance. This fault the barbarity of his age cannot extenuate; for it is always a writer's duty to make the world better, and justice is a virtue independent on time or place.

The plots are often so loosely formed that a very slight consideration may improve them, and so carelessly pursued that he seems not always fully to comprehend his own design. He omits opportunities of instructing or delighting which the train of his story seems to force upon him, and apparently rejects those exhibitions which would be more affecting for the sake of those which are more easy.

It may be observed that in many of his plays the latter part is evidently neglected. When he found himself near the end of his work, and in view of his reward, he shortened the labor to snatch the profit. He therefore remits his efforts where he should most vigorously exert them, and his catastrophe is improbably produced or imperfectly represented.

He had no regard to distinction of time or place, but gives to one age or nation, without scruple, the customs, institutions, and opinions of another, at the expense not only of likelihood but of possibility. These faults Pope has endeavored, with more zeal than judgment, to transfer to his imagined interpolators. We need not wonder to find Hector quoting Aristotle, when we see the loves of Theseus and Hippolyta combined with the Gothic mythology of fairies.[1] Shakespeare, indeed, was not the only violator of chronology, for in the same age Sidney, who wanted not the advantages of learning, has, in his *Arcadia*, confounded the pastoral with the feudal times, the days of innocence, quiet, and security with those of turbulence, violence, and adventure.

In his comic scenes he is seldom very successful when he engages his characters in reciprocations of smartness and contests of sarcasm; their jests are commonly gross, and their pleasantry licentious; neither his gentlemen nor his ladies have much delicacy, nor are sufficiently distinguished from his clowns[2] by any appearance of refined manners. Whether he represented the real conversation of his time is not easy to determine: the reign of Elizabeth

---

9. Kindness.
1. In *Troilus and Cressida* 2.2.166 and in *A Mid-*

summer Night's Dream, respectively.
2. Rustics.

is commonly supposed to have been a time of stateliness, formality, and reserve; yet perhaps the relaxations of that severity were not very elegant. There must, however, have been always some modes of gaiety preferable to others, and a writer ought to choose the best.

In tragedy his performance seems constantly to be worse as his labor is more. The effusions of passion, which exigence forces out, are for the most part striking and energetic; but whenever he solicits his invention, or strains his faculties, the offspring of his throes is tumor,[3] meanness, tediousness, and obscurity.

In narration he affects a disproportionate pomp of diction and a wearisome train of circumlocution, and tells the incident imperfectly in many words which might have been more plainly delivered in few. Narration in dramatic poetry is naturally tedious, as it is unanimated and inactive, and obstructs the progress of the action; it should therefore always be rapid and enlivened by frequent interruption. Shakespeare found it an encumbrance, and instead of lightening it by brevity, endeavored to recommend it by dignity and splendor.

His declamations or set speeches are commonly cold and weak, for his power was the power of nature; when he endeavored, like other tragic writers, to catch opportunities of amplification and, instead of inquiring what the occasion demanded, to show how much his stores of knowledge could supply, he seldom escapes without the pity or resentment of his reader.

It is incident to him to be now and then entangled with an unwieldy sentiment which he cannot well express, and will not reject; he struggles with it awhile, and, if it continues stubborn, comprises it in words such as occur, and leaves it to be disentangled and evolved[4] by those who have more leisure to bestow upon it.

Not that always where the language is intricate the thought is subtle, or the image always great where the line is bulky; the equality of words to things is very often neglected, and trivial sentiments and vulgar[5] ideas disappoint the attention, to which they are recommended by sonorous epithets and swelling figures.

But the admirers of this great poet have most reason to complain when he approaches nearest to his highest excellence, and seems fully resolved to sink them in dejection and mollify them with tender emotions by the fall of greatness, the danger of innocence, or the crosses of love. What he does best, he soon ceases to do. He is not long soft and pathetic without some idle conceit or contemptible equivocation. He no sooner begins to move than he counteracts himself; and terror and pity, as they are rising in the mind, are checked and blasted by sudden frigidity.

A quibble[6] is to Shakespeare what luminous vapors are to the traveler: he follows it at all adventures; it is sure to lead him out of his way, and sure to engulf him in the mire. It has some malignant power over his mind, and its fascinations are irresistible. Whatever be the dignity or profundity of his disquisitions, whether he be enlarging knowledge or exalting affection, whether he be amusing[7] attention with incidents, or enchaining it in suspense, let but

3. Inflated grandeur, false magnificence.
4. Unfolded.
5. "Mean; low; being of the common rate" (Johnson's *Dictionary*).

6. Pun.
7. "To entertain with tranquility; to fill with thoughts that engage the mind, without distracting it" (Johnson's *Dictionary*).

a quibble spring up before him, and he leaves his work unfinished. A quibble is the golden apple for which he will always turn aside from his career[8] or stoop from his elevation. A quibble, poor and barren as it is, gave him such delight that he was content to purchase it by the sacrifice of reason, propriety, and truth. A quibble was to him the fatal Cleopatra for which he lost the world, and was content to lose it.

It will be thought strange that in enumerating the defects of this writer, I have not yet mentioned his neglect of the unities; his violation of those laws which have been instituted and established by the joint authority of poets and critics.

For his other deviations from the art of writing, I resign him to critical justice without making any other demand in his favor than that which must be indulged to all human excellence: that his virtues be rated with his failings. But from the censure which this irregularity may bring upon him I shall, with due reverence to that learning which I must oppose, adventure to try how I can defend him.

His histories, being neither tragedies nor comedies, are not subject to any of their laws; nothing more is necessary to all the praise which they expect than that the changes of action be so prepared as to be understood; that the incidents be various and affecting, and the characters consistent, natural, and distinct. No other unity is intended, and therefore none is to be sought.

In his other works he has well enough preserved the unity of action. He has not, indeed, an intrigue regularly perplexed and regularly unraveled: he does not endeavor to hide his design only to discover it, for this is seldom the order of real events, and Shakespeare is the poet of nature: but his plan has commonly what Aristotle requires,[9] a beginning, a middle, and an end; one event is concatenated with another, and the conclusion follows by easy consequence. There are, perhaps, some incidents that might be spared, as in other poets there is much talk that only fills up time upon the stage; but the general system makes gradual advances, and the end of the play is the end of expectation.

To the unities of time and place he has shown no regard; and perhaps a nearer view of the principles on which they stand will diminish their value and withdraw from them the veneration which, from the time of Corneille,[1] they have very generally received, by discovering that they have given more trouble to the poet than pleasure to the auditor.

The necessity of observing the unities of time and place arises from the supposed necessity of making the drama credible. The critics hold it impossible that an action of months or years can be possibly believed to pass in three hours; or that the spectator can suppose himself to sit in the theater while ambassadors go and return between distant kings, while armies are levied and towns besieged, while an exile wanders and returns, or till he whom they saw courting his mistress shall lament the untimely fall of his son. The mind revolts from evident falsehood, and fiction loses its force when it departs from the resemblance of reality.

---

8. Course of action; the ground on which a race is run. In Greek legend Atalanta refused to marry any man who could not defeat her in a foot race. Hippomenes won her by dropping, as he ran, three of the golden apples of the Hesperides, which she paused to pick up.
9. *Poetics* 7.
1. Pierre Corneille (1606–1684), the French playwright, discussed the unities in his *Discours des trois unités* (1660).

From the narrow limitation of time necessarily arises the contraction of place. The spectator who knows that he saw the first act at Alexandria cannot suppose that he sees the next at Rome, at a distance to which not the dragons of Medea[2] could, in so short a time, have transported him; he knows with certainty that he has not changed his place; and he knows that place cannot change itself, that what was a house cannot become a plain, that what was Thebes can never be Persepolis.

Such is the triumphant language with which a critic exults over the misery of an irregular poet, and exults commonly without resistance or reply. It is time, therefore, to tell him by the authority of Shakespeare that he assumes, as an unquestionable principle, a position which, while his breath is forming it into words, his understanding pronounces to be false. It is false that any representation is mistaken for reality; that any dramatic fable in its materiality was ever credible or, for a single moment, was ever credited.

The objection arising from the impossibility of passing the first hour at Alexandria and the next at Rome supposes that when the play opens the spectator really imagines himself at Alexandria, and believes that his walk to the theater has been a voyage to Egypt, and that he lives in the days of Antony and Cleopatra. Surely he that imagines this may imagine more. He that can take the stage at one time for the palace of the Ptolemies may take it in half an hour for the promontory of Actium. Delusion, if delusion be admitted, has no certain limitation; if the spectator can be once persuaded that his old acquaintances are Alexander and Caesar, that a room illuminated with candles is the plain of Pharsalia or the bank of Granicus, he is in a state of elevation above the reach of reason or of truth, and from the heights of empyrean poetry may despise the circumscriptions of terrestrial nature. There is no reason why a mind thus wandering in ecstasy should count the clock, or why an hour should not be a century in that calenture[3] of the brain that can make the stage a field.

The truth is that the spectators are always in their senses, and know, from the first act to the last, that the stage is only a stage, and that the players are only players. They came to hear a certain number of lines recited with just gesture and elegant modulation. The lines relate to some action, and an action must be in some place; but the different actions that complete a story may be in places very remote from each other; and where is the absurdity of allowing that space to represent first Athens, and then Sicily, which was always known to be neither Sicily nor Athens but a modern theater?

By supposition, as place is introduced, time may be extended; the time required by the fable elapses, for the most part, between the acts; for, of so much of the action as is represented, the real and poetical duration is the same. If, in the first act, preparations for war against Mithridates are represented to be made in Rome, the event of the war may, without absurdity, be represented, in the catastrophe, as happening in Pontus; we know that there is neither war nor preparation for war; we know that we are neither in Rome nor Pontus, that neither Mithridates nor Lucullus are before us. The drama exhibits successive imitations of successive actions; and why may not

---

2. According to legend, Medea fled the scene of her crimes in a chariot drawn by dragons.
3. A delirium produced by tropical heat, which causes sailors to leap into the sea under the delusion that it is a green field.

the second imitation represent an action that happened years after the first, if it be so connected with it that nothing but time can be supposed to intervene? Time is, of all modes of existence, most obsequious[4] to the imagination; a lapse of years is as easily conceived as a passage of hours. In contemplation we easily contract the time of real actions, and therefore willingly permit it to be contracted when we only see their imitation.

It will be asked how the drama moves if it is not credited. It is credited with all the credit due to a drama. It is credited, whenever it moves, as a just picture of a real original; as representing to the auditor what he would himself feel if he were to do or suffer what is there feigned to be suffered or to be done. The reflection that strikes the heart is not that the evils before us are real evils, but that they are evils to which we ourselves may be exposed. If there be any fallacy, it is not that we fancy the players, but that we fancy ourselves, unhappy for a moment; but we rather lament the possibility than suppose the presence of misery, as a mother weeps over her babe when she remembers that death may take it from her. The delight of tragedy proceeds from our consciousness of fiction; if we thought murders and treasons real, they would please no more.

Imitations produce pain or pleasure, not because they are mistaken for realities, but because they bring realities to mind. When the imagination is recreated[5] by a painted landscape, the trees are not supposed capable to give us shade or the fountains coolness; but we consider how we should be pleased with such fountains playing beside us and such woods waving over us. We are agitated in reading the history of *Henry the Fifth*; yet no man takes his book for the field of Agincourt. A dramatic exhibition is a book recited with concomitants that increase or diminish its effect. Familiar[6] comedy is often more powerful on the theater than in the page; imperial tragedy is always less. The humor of Petruchio may be heightened by grimace; but what voice or what gesture can hope to add dignity or force to the soliloquy of Cato?[7]

A play read affects the mind like a play acted. It is therefore evident that the action is not supposed to be real; and it follows that between the acts a longer or shorter time may be allowed to pass, and that no more account of space or duration is to be taken by the auditor of a drama than by the reader of a narrative, before whom may pass in an hour the life of a hero or the revolutions of an empire.

Whether Shakespeare knew the unities and rejected them by design or deviated from them by happy ignorance, it is, I think, impossible to decide and useless to inquire. We may reasonably suppose that, when he rose to notice, he did not want[8] the counsels and admonitions of scholars and critics, and that he at last deliberately persisted in a practice which he might have begun by chance. As nothing is essential to the fable but unity of action, and as the unities of time and place arise evidently from false assumptions, and, by circumscribing the extent of the drama, lessen its variety, I cannot think it much to be lamented that they were not known by him, or not observed: nor, if such another poet could arise, should I very vehemently reproach him that

---

4. "Obedient; compliant" (Johnson's *Dictionary*).
5. Delighted.
6. Domestic.
7. In Addison's tragedy *Cato* (5.1), the hero solilo-

quizes on immortality shortly before committing suicide. Petruchio is the hero of Shakespeare's comedy *The Taming of the Shrew*.
8. Lack.

his first act passed at Venice and his next in Cyprus.[9] Such violations of rules merely positive[1] become the comprehensive genius of Shakespeare, and such censures are suitable to the minute and slender criticism of Voltaire.

> *Non usque adeo permiscuit imis*
> *Longus summa dies, ut non, si voce Metelli*
> *Serventur leges, malint a Caesare tolli.*[2]

Yet when I speak thus slightly of dramatic rules, I cannot but recollect how much wit and learning may be produced against me; before such authorities I am afraid to stand: not that I think the present question one of those that are to be decided by mere authority, but because it is to be suspected that these precepts have not been so easily received but for better reasons than I have yet been able to find. The result of my inquiries, in which it would be ludicrous to boast of impartiality, is that the unities of time and place are not essential to a just drama, that though they may sometimes conduce to pleasure, they are always to be sacrificed to the nobler beauties of variety and instruction; and that a play written with nice observation of critical rules is to be contemplated as an elaborate curiosity, as the product of superfluous and ostentatious art, by which is shown rather what is possible than what is necessary.

He that without diminution of any other excellence shall preserve all the unities unbroken deserves the like applause with the architect who shall display all the orders of architecture in a citadel without any deduction for its strength; but the principal beauty of a citadel is to exclude the enemy, and the greatest graces of a play are to copy nature and instruct life. * * *

[*TWELFTH NIGHT*]

This play is in the graver part elegant and easy, and in some of the lighter scenes exquisitely humorous. Ague-cheek is drawn with great propriety, but his character is, in a great measure, that of natural fatuity, and is therefore not the proper prey of a satirist. The soliloquy of Malvolio is truly comick; he is betrayed to ridicule merely by his pride. The marriage of Olivia, and the succeeding perplexity, though well enough contrived to divert on the stage, wants credibility, and fails to produce the proper instruction required in the drama, as it exhibits no just picture of life.

[*KING LEAR*]

The tragedy of *Lear* is deservedly celebrated among the dramas of Shakespeare. There is perhaps no play which keeps the attention so strongly fixed; which so much agitates our passions and interests our curiosity. The artful involutions[3] of distinct interests, the striking opposition of contrary characters, the sudden changes of fortune, and the quick succession of events, fill the mind with a perpetual tumult of indignation, pity, and hope. There is no scene which does not contribute to the aggravation of the distress or conduct of the action, and scarce a line which does not conduce to the progress

---

9. As is the case in *Othello*.
1. Arbitrary; not natural.
2. Lucan's *Pharsalia* 3.138–40: "The course of time has not wrought such confusion that the

laws would not rather be trampled on by Caesar than saved by Metellus."
3. Entanglements.

of the scene. So powerful is the current of the poet's imagination, that the mind, which once ventures within it, is hurried irresistibly along.

On the seeming improbability of Lear's conduct it may be observed, that he is represented according to histories at that time vulgarly[4] received as true. And perhaps if we turn our thoughts upon the barbarity and ignorance of the age to which this story is referred, it will appear not so unlikely as while we estimate Lear's manners by our own. Such preference of one daughter to another, or resignation of dominion on such conditions, would be yet credible, if told of a petty prince of Guinea or Madagascar. Shakespeare, indeed, by the mention of his earls and dukes, has given us the idea of times more civilized, and of life regulated by softer manners; and the truth is, that though he so nicely discriminates, and so minutely describes the characters of men, he commonly neglects and confounds the characters of ages, by mingling customs ancient and modern, English and foreign.

My learned friend Mr. Warton, who has in the *Adventurer* very minutely criticized this play,[5] remarks, that the instances of cruelty are too savage and shocking, and that the intervention of Edmund destroys the simplicity of the story. These objections may, I think, be answered, by repeating that the cruelty of the daughters is an historical fact, to which the poet has added little, having only drawn it into a series by dialogue and action. But I am not able to apologize with equal plausibility for the extrusion of Gloucester's eyes, which seems an act too horrid to be endured in dramatic exhibition, and such as must always compel the mind to relieve its distress by incredulity. Yet let it be remembered that our author well knew what would please the audience for which he wrote.

The injury done by Edmund to the simplicity of the action is abundantly recompensed by the addition of variety, by the art with which he is made to co-operate with the chief design, and the opportunity which he gives the poet of combining perfidy with perfidy, and connecting the wicked son with the wicked daughters, to impress this important moral, that villainy is never at a stop, that crimes lead to crimes, and at last terminate in ruin.

But though this moral be incidentally enforced, Shakespeare has suffered the virtue of Cordelia to perish in a just cause, contrary to the natural ideas of justice, to the hope of the reader, and, what is yet more strange, to the faith of chronicles. Yet this conduct is justified by the Spectator, who blames Tate for giving Cordelia success and happiness in his alteration, and declares that in his opinion, "the tragedy has lost half its beauty."[6] Dennis has remarked, whether justly or not, that to secure the favorable reception of *Cato*, "the town was poisoned with much false and abominable criticism,"[7] and that endeavors had been used to discredit and decry poetical justice. A play in which the wicked prosper, and the virtuous miscarry, may doubtless be good, because it is a just representation of the common events of human life: but since all reasonable beings naturally love justice, I cannot easily be persuaded, that the observation of justice makes a play worse; or, that if

4. Popularly.
5. Joseph Warton (1722–1800) contributed several papers to Johnson's periodical the *Adventurer*; nos. 113, 116, and 122 discuss *King Lear*.
6. Addison, *Spectator* 40. During the 18th century, *King Lear* was often performed with a happy ending, in the adaptation by Nahum Tate.
7. John Dennis, "Remarks upon *Cato, a Tragedy*" (1713). Dennis implies that Addison excuses the lack of poetic justice in *Lear* to justify the absence of poetic justice in his own play, *Cato*.

other excellencies are equal, the audience will not always rise better pleased from the final triumph of persecuted virtue.

In the present case the public has decided. Cordelia, from the time of Tate, has always retired with victory and felicity. And, if my sensations could add anything to the general suffrage, I might relate, that I was many years ago so shocked by Cordelia's death, that I know not whether I ever endured to read again the last scenes of the play till I undertook to revise them as an editor.

1765

FROM LIVES OF THE POETS

From Cowley[1]

[METAPHYSICAL WIT]

Wit, like all other things subject by their nature to the choice of man, has its changes and fashions, and at different times takes different forms. About the beginning of the seventeenth century appeared a race of writers that may be termed the metaphysical poets,[2] of whom in a criticism on the works of Cowley it is not improper to give some account.

The metaphysical poets were men of learning, and to show their learning was their whole endeavor; but, unluckily resolving to show it in rhyme, instead of writing poetry they only wrote verses, and very often such verses as stood the trial of the finger better than of the ear; for the modulation was so imperfect that they were only found to be verses by counting the syllables.

If the father of criticism[3] has rightly denominated poetry *tekhnē mimētikè, an imitative art*, these writers will without great wrong lose their right to the name of poets, for they cannot be said to have imitated anything: they neither copied nature nor life; neither painted the forms of matter nor represented the operations of intellect.

Those however who deny them to be poets allow them to be wits. Dryden confesses of himself and his contemporaries that they fall below Donne in wit, but maintains that they surpass him in poetry.[4]

If wit be well described by Pope as being "that which has been often thought, but was never before so well expressed,"[5] they certainly never attained nor ever sought it, for they endeavored to be singular in their thoughts, and were careless of their diction. But Pope's account of wit is undoubtedly erroneous; he depresses it below its natural dignity, and reduces it from strength of thought to happiness of language.

If by a more noble and more adequate conception that be considered as wit which is at once natural and new, that which though not obvious is,

---

1. Abraham Cowley (1618–1667) was much admired during the middle of the 17th century. His reputation began to decline before 1700, but he was remembered as a writer of false wit, especially in his love poems *The Mistress*.
2. Presumably Johnson took this now common designation from a hint in Dryden's "A Discourse Concerning the Original and Progress of Satire."

Dryden condemned Donne because "he affects the metaphysics . . . and perplexes the minds of the fair sex with nice speculations of philosophy, when he should engage their hearts, and entertain them with the softnesses of love."
3. Aristotle in his *Poetics*.
4. "A Discourse . . . of Satire."
5. *An Essay on Criticism*, lines 297–98.

upon its first production, acknowledged to be just; if it be that which he that never found it, wonders how he missed; to wit of this kind the metaphysical poets have seldom risen. Their thoughts are often new, but seldom natural; they are not obvious, but neither are they just;[6] and the reader, far from wondering that he missed them, wonders more frequently by what perverseness of industry they were ever found.

But wit, abstracted from its effects upon the hearer, may be more rigorously and philosophically considered as a kind of *discordia concors;*[7] a combination of dissimilar images, or discovery of occult resemblances in things apparently unlike. Of wit, thus defined, they have more than enough. The most heterogeneous ideas are yoked by violence together; nature and art are ransacked for illustrations, comparisons, and allusions; their learning instructs, and their subtlety surprises; but the reader commonly thinks his improvement dearly bought, and, though he sometimes admires, is seldom pleased.

From this account of their compositions it will be readily inferred that they were not successful in representing or moving the affections. As they were wholly employed on something unexpected and surprising, they had no regard to that uniformity of sentiment which enables us to conceive and to excite the pains and the pleasure of other minds: they never inquired what on any occasion they should have said or done, but wrote rather as beholders than partakers of human nature; as beings looking upon good and evil, impassive and at leisure; as Epicurean deities making remarks on the actions of men and the vicissitudes of life, without interest and without emotion. Their courtship was void of fondness and their lamentation of sorrow. Their wish was only to say what they hoped had been never said before.

Nor was the sublime more within their reach than the pathetic; for they never attempted that comprehension and expanse of thought which at once fills the whole mind, and of which the first effect is sudden astonishment, and the second rational admiration. Sublimity is produced by aggregation, and littleness by dispersion. Great thoughts are always general, and consist in positions not limited by exceptions, and in descriptions not descending to minuteness. It is with great propriety that subtlety, which in its original import means exility[8] of particles, is taken in its metaphorical meaning for nicety of distinction. Those writers who lay on the watch for novelty could have little hope of greatness; for great things cannot have escaped former observation. Their attempts were always analytic: they broke every image into fragments, and could no more represent by their slender conceits and labored particularities the prospects of nature or the scenes of life, than he who dissects a sunbeam with a prism can exhibit the wide effulgence of a summer noon.

What they wanted however of the sublime they endeavored to supply by hyperbole;[9] their amplification had no limits: they left not only reason but fancy behind them, and produced combinations of confused magnificence that not only could not be credited, but could not be imagined.

Yet great labor directed by great abilities is never wholly lost: if they frequently threw away their wit upon false conceits, they likewise sometimes struck out unexpected truth: if their conceits were farfetched, they were

---

6. Exact, proper.
7. A harmonious discord (Latin). Johnson is himself being witty in using this phrase, a familiar philosophical concept denoting the general har-

mony of God's creation despite its manifold and often contradictory particulars.
8. Thinness, smallness.
9. An image heightened beyond reality.

often worth the carriage.[1] To write on their plan it was at least necessary to read and think. No man could be born a metaphysical poet, nor assume the dignity of a writer by descriptions copied from descriptions, by imitations borrowed from imitations, by traditional imagery and hereditary similes, by readiness of rhyme and volubility of syllables.

1779

From Milton[1]

["LYCIDAS"]

One of the poems on which much praise has been bestowed is *Lycidas;* of which the diction is harsh, the rhymes uncertain, and the numbers[2] unpleasing. What beauty there is, we must therefore seek in the sentiments and images. It is not to be considered as the effusion of real passion; for passion runs not after remote allusions and obscure opinions. Passion plucks no berries from the myrtle and ivy, nor calls upon Arethuse and Mincius, nor tells of "rough satyrs and fauns with cloven heel." Where there is leisure for fiction there is little grief.

In this poem there is no nature, for there is no truth; there is no art, for there is nothing new. Its form is that of a pastoral, easy, vulgar, and therefore disgusting:[3] whatever images it can supply are long ago exhausted; and its inherent improbability always forces dissatisfaction on the mind. When Cowley tells of Hervey that they studied together,[4] it is easy to suppose how much he must miss the companion of his labors and the partner of his discoveries; but what image of tenderness can be excited by these lines!

> We drove afield, and both together heard
> What time the grayfly winds her sultry horn,
> Battening our flocks with the fresh dews of night.

We know that they never drove afield, and that they had no flocks to batten; and though it be allowed that the representation may be allegorical, the true meaning is so uncertain and remote that it is never sought because it cannot be known when it is found.

Among the flocks and copses and flowers appear the heathen deities, Jove and Phoebus, Neptune and Aeolus, with a long train of mythological imagery, such as a college easily supplies. Nothing can less display knowledge or less exercise invention than to tell how a shepherd has lost his companion and must now feed his flocks alone, without any judge of his skill in piping; and how one god asks another god what is become of Lycidas, and

---

1. In the *Life of Addison*, Johnson wrote: "A simile may be compared to lines converging at a point, and is more excellent as the lines approach from greater distance."

1. Johnson's treatment of Milton as man and poet offended many ardent Miltonians in his own day and damaged his reputation as a critic in the following century. He did not admire Milton's character, and he detested his politics and religion. But no one has praised *Paradise Lost* more handsomely. Especially offensive in the 19th century was his attack on "Lycidas." Johnson disliked modern pastorals, believing that the tradition had been worn threadbare. His views on the genre may be read in *Rambler* no. 36 and no. 37.

2. Versification.

3. Distasteful, because too facile and common.

4. Cowley's "On the Death of Mr. William Hervey" (1656).

how neither god can tell. He who thus grieves will excite no sympathy; he who thus praises will confer no honor.

This poem has yet a grosser fault. With these trifling fictions are mingled the most awful and sacred truths, such as ought never to be polluted with such irreverent combinations. The shepherd likewise is now a feeder of sheep, and afterwards an ecclesiastical pastor, a superintendent of a Christian flock. Such equivocations are always unskillful; but here they are indecent,[5] and at least approach to impiety, of which, however, I believe the writer not to have been conscious.

Such is the power of reputation justly acquired that its blaze drives away the eye from nice examination. Surely no man could have fancied that he read *Lycidas* with pleasure had he not known its author.

[*PARADISE LOST*]

Those little pieces may be dispatched without much anxiety; a greater work calls for greater care. I am now to examine *Paradise Lost*, a poem which, considered with respect to design, may claim the first place, and with respect to performance the second, among the productions of the human mind.

By the general consent of critics the first praise of genius is due to the writer of an epic poem, as it requires an assemblage of all the powers which are singly sufficient for other compositions. Poetry is the art of uniting pleasure with truth, by calling imagination to the help of reason. Epic poetry undertakes to teach the most important truths by the most pleasing precepts, and therefore relates some great event in the most affecting manner. History must supply the writer with the rudiments of narration, which he must improve and exalt by a nobler art, must animate by dramatic energy, and diversify by retrospection and anticipation; morality must teach him the exact bounds and different shades of vice and virtue; from policy and the practice of life he has to learn the discriminations of character and the tendency of the passions, either single or combined; and physiology[6] must supply him with illustrations and images. To put these materials to poetical use is required an imagination capable of painting nature and realizing fiction. Nor is he yet a poet till he has attained the whole extension of his language, distinguished all the delicacies of phrase, and all the colors of words, and learned to adjust their different sounds to all the varieties of metrical modulation.

Bossu is of opinion that the poet's first work is to find a *moral*, which his fable is afterwards to illustrate and establish.[7] This seems to have been the process only of Milton: the moral of other poems is incidental and consequent; in Milton's only it is essential and intrinsic. His purpose was the most useful and the most arduous: "to vindicate the ways of God to man";[8] to show the reasonableness of religion, and the necessity of obedience to the Divine Law.

To convey this moral there must be a *fable*, a narration artfully constructed, so as to excite curiosity and surprise expectation. In this part of his work Milton must be confessed to have equaled every other poet. He has

---

5. Unbecoming, lacking in decorum.
6. "The doctrine of the constitution of the works of nature" (Johnson's *Dictionary*).
7. René le Bossu's treatise on the epic poem, *Traité du Poëme Épique*, 1675, was much admired

in the late 17th and early 18th centuries.
8. Milton wrote "justify," not "vindicate" (*Paradise Lost* 1.26). It was Pope, in *An Essay on Man* 1.16, who used "vindicate."

involved in his account of the Fall of Man the events which preceded, and those that were to follow it: he has interwoven the whole system of theology with such propriety that every part appears to be necessary, and scarcely any recital is wished shorter for the sake of quickening the progress of the main action.

The subject of an epic poem is naturally an event of great importance. That of Milton is not the destruction of a city, the conduct of a colony, or the foundation of an empire. His subject is the fate of worlds, the revolutions of heaven and of earth; rebellion against the Supreme King raised by the highest order of created beings; the overthrow of their host and the punishment of their crime; the creation of a new race of reasonable creatures; their original happiness and innocence, their forfeiture of immortality, and their restoration to hope and peace.

Great events can be hastened or retarded only by persons of elevated dignity. Before the greatness displayed in Milton's poem all other greatness shrinks away. The weakest of his agents are the highest and noblest of human beings, the original parents of mankind; with whose actions the elements consented; on whose rectitude or deviation of will depended the state of terrestrial nature and the condition of all the future inhabitants of the globe.

Of the other agents in the poem, the chief are such as it is irreverence to name on slight occasions. The rest were lower powers;

> of which the least could wield
> Those elements, and arm him with the force
> Of all their regions;[9]

powers which only the control of Omnipotence restrains from laying creation waste, and filling the vast expanse of space with ruin and confusion. To display the motives and actions of beings thus superior, so far as human reason can examine them or human imagination represent them, is the task which this mighty poet has undertaken and performed.

In the examination of epic poems much speculation is commonly employed upon the *characters*. The characters in the *Paradise Lost* which admit of examination are those of angels and of man; of angels good and evil, of man in his innocent and sinful state.

Among the angels the virtue of Raphael is mild and placid, of easy condescension and free communication; that of Michael is regal and lofty, and, as may seem, attentive to the dignity of his own nature. Abdiel and Gabriel appear occasionally, and act as every incident requires; the solitary fidelity of Abdiel is very amiably painted.[1]

Of the evil angels the characters are more diversified. To Satan, as Addison observes, such sentiments are given as suit "the most exalted and most depraved being."[2] Milton has been censured by Clarke for the impiety which sometimes breaks from Satan's mouth. For there are thoughts, as he justly remarks, which no observation of character can justify, because no good man would willingly permit them to pass, however transiently, through his own mind.[3] To make Satan speak as a rebel, without any such expressions as might taint the reader's imagination, was indeed one of the great

9. *Paradise Lost* 6.221.
1. *Paradise Lost* 5.803ff.
2. *Spectator* 303.
3. John Clarke's *Essay upon Study* (1731).

difficulties in Milton's undertaking, and I cannot but think that he has extricated himself with great happiness. There is in Satan's speeches little that can give pain to a pious ear. The language of rebellion cannot be the same with that of obedience. The malignity of Satan foams in haughtiness and obstinacy; but his expressions are commonly general, and no otherwise offensive than as they are wicked.

The other chiefs of the celestial rebellion are very judiciously discriminated in the first and second books; and the ferocious character of Moloch appears, both in the battle and the council, with exact consistency.

To Adam and Eve are given during their innocence such sentiments as innocence can generate and utter. Their love is pure benevolence and mutual veneration; their repasts are without luxury and their diligence without toil. Their addresses to their Maker have little more than the voice of admiration and gratitude. Fruition left them nothing to ask, and Innocence left them nothing to fear.

But with guilt enter distrust and discord, mutual accusation, and stubborn self-defense; they regard each other with alienated minds, and dread their Creator as the avenger of their transgression. At last they seek shelter in his mercy, soften to repentance, and melt in supplication. Both before and after the Fall the superiority of Adam is diligently sustained.

Of the *probable* and the *marvelous*,[4] two parts of a vulgar epic poem which immerge the critic in deep consideration, the *Paradise Lost* requires little to be said. It contains the history of a miracle, of Creation and Redemption; it displays the power and the mercy of the Supreme Being: the probable therefore is marvelous, and the marvelous is probable. The substance of the narrative is truth; and as truth allows no choice, it is, like necessity, superior to rule. To the accidental or adventitious parts, as to every thing human, some slight exceptions may be made. But the main fabric is immovably supported.

It is justly remarked by Addison[5] that this poem has, by the nature of its subject, the advantage above all others, that it is universally and perpetually interesting. All mankind will, through all ages, bear the same relation to Adam and to Eve, and must partake of that good and evil which extend to themselves.

Of the *machinery*, so called from *theòs apò mēkhanēs*,[6] by which is meant the occasional interposition of supernatural power, another fertile topic of critical remarks, here is no room to speak, because every thing is done under the immediate and visible direction of Heaven; but the rule is so far observed that no part of the action could have been accomplished by any other means.

Of *episodes*[7] I think there are only two, contained in Raphael's relation of the war in heaven and Michael's prophetic account of the changes to happen in this world. Both are closely connected with the great action; one was necessary to Adam as a warning, the other as a consolation.

To the completeness or *integrity* of the design nothing can be objected; it has distinctly and clearly what Aristotle requires, a beginning, a middle, and an end. There is perhaps no poem of the same length from which so little

---

4. Actions in an epic poem that are wonderful because they exceed the probable.
5. *Spectator* 273.
6. Aristotle's *Poetics* 15.10. *Deus ex machina*, the intervention of supernatural powers into the affairs of humans.
7. Incidental but related narratives within an epic poem. Johnson is citing *Paradise Lost* 5.577ff. and 11.334ff.

can be taken without apparent mutilation. Here are no funeral games, nor is there any long description of a shield. The short digressions at the beginning of the third, seventh, and ninth books might doubtless be spared; but superfluities so beautiful who would take away? or who does not wish that the author of the *Iliad* had gratified succeeding ages with a little knowledge of himself? Perhaps no passages are more frequently or more attentively read than those extrinsic paragraphs; and since the end of poetry is pleasure, that cannot be unpoetical with which all are pleased.

The questions, whether the action of the poem be strictly *one*,[8] whether the poem can be properly termed *heroic*, and who is the hero, are raised by such readers as draw their principles of judgment rather from books than from reason. Milton, though he entitled *Paradise Lost* only a "poem," yet calls it himself "heroic song."[9] Dryden, petulantly and indecently, denies the heroism of Adam because he was overcome; but there is no reason why the hero should not be unfortunate except established practice, since success and virtue do not go necessarily together. Cato is the hero of Lucan, but Lucan's authority will not be suffered by Quintilian to decide. However, if success be necessary, Adam's deceiver was at last crushed; Adam was restored to his Maker's favor, and therefore may securely resume his human rank.

After the scheme and fabric of the poem must be considered its component parts, the sentiments, and the diction.

The *sentiments*, as expressive of manners or appropriated to characters, are for the greater part unexceptionably just. Splendid passages containing lessons of morality or precepts of prudence occur seldom. Such is the original formation of this poem that as it admits no human manners till the Fall, it can give little assistance to human conduct. Its end is to raise the thoughts above sublunary cares or pleasures. Yet the praise of that fortitude, with which Abdiel maintained his singularity of virtue against the scorn of multitudes, may be accommodated to all times; and Raphael's reproof of Adam's curiosity after the planetary motions, with the answer returned by Adam, may be confidently opposed to any rule of life which any poet has delivered.[1]

The thoughts which are occasionally called forth in the progress are such as could only be produced by an imagination in the highest degree fervid and active, to which materials were supplied by incessant study and unlimited curiosity. The heat of Milton's mind might be said to sublimate his learning, to throw off into his work the spirit of science,[2] unmingled with its grosser parts.

He had considered creation in its whole extent, and his descriptions are therefore learned. He had accustomed his imagination to unrestrained indulgence, and his conceptions therefore were extensive. The characteristic quality of his poem is sublimity. He sometimes descends to the elegant, but his element is the great. He can occasionally invest himself with grace; but his natural port is gigantic loftiness. He can please when pleasure is required; but it is his peculiar power to astonish.

He seems to have been well acquainted with his own genius, and to know what it was that Nature had bestowed upon him more bountifully than

---

8. I.e., a single action dealing with a single character.
9. *Paradise Lost* 9.25.

1. *Paradise Lost* 8.65ff.
2. Knowledge.

upon others; the power of displaying the vast, illuminating the splendid, enforcing the awful, darkening the gloomy, and aggravating the dreadful: he therefore chose a subject on which too much could not be said, on which he might tire his fancy without the censure of extravagance.

* * *

The defects and faults of *Paradise Lost*, for faults and defects every work of man must have, it is the business of impartial criticism to discover. As in displaying the excellence of Milton I have not made long quotations, because of selecting beauties there had been no end, I shall in the same general manner mention that which seems to deserve censure; for what Englishman can take delight in transcribing passages, which, if they lessen the reputation of Milton, diminish in some degree the honor of our country?

* * *

The plan of *Paradise Lost* has this inconvenience, that it comprises neither human actions nor human manners. The man and woman who act and suffer are in a state which no other man or woman can ever know. The reader finds no transaction in which he can be engaged, beholds no condition in which he can by any effort of imagination place himself; he has, therefore, little natural curiosity or sympathy.

We all, indeed, feel the effects of Adam's disobedience; we all sin like Adam, and like him must all bewail our offenses; we have restless and insidious enemies in the fallen angels, and in the blessed spirits we have guardians and friends; in the Redemption of mankind we hope to be included: in the description of heaven and hell we are surely interested, as we are all to reside hereafter either in the regions of horror or of bliss.

But these truths are too important to be new: they have been taught to our infancy; they have mingled with our solitary thoughts and familiar conversation, and are habitually interwoven with the whole texture of life. Being therefore not new they raise no unaccustomed emotion in the mind: what we knew before, we cannot learn; what is not unexpected, cannot surprise.

Of the ideas suggested by these awful scenes, from some we recede with reverence, except when stated hours require their association; and from others we shrink with horror, or admit them only as salutary inflictions, as counterpoises to our interests and passions. Such images rather obstruct the career of fancy than incite it.

Pleasure and terror are indeed the genuine sources of poetry; but poetical pleasure must be such as human imagination can at least conceive, and poetical terror such as human strength and fortitude may combat. The good and evil of Eternity are too ponderous for the wings of wit; the mind sinks under them in passive helplessness, content with calm belief and humble adoration.

Known truths however may take a different appearance, and be conveyed to the mind by a new train of intermediate images. This Milton has undertaken, and performed with pregnancy and vigor of mind peculiar to himself. Whoever considers the few radical[3] positions which the Scriptures

---

3. Original or primary.

afforded him will wonder by what energetic operation he expanded them to such extent and ramified them to so much variety, restrained as he was by religious reverence from licentiousness of fiction.

Here is a full display of the united force of study and genius; of a great accumulation of materials, with judgment to digest and fancy to combine them: Milton was able to select from nature or from story, from ancient fable or from modern science, whatever could illustrate or adorn his thoughts. An accumulation of knowledge impregnated his mind, fermented by study and exalted by imagination.

* * *

But original deficience cannot be supplied. The want of human interest is always felt. *Paradise Lost* is one of the books which the reader admires and lays down, and forgets to take up again. None ever wished it longer than it is. Its perusal is a duty rather than a pleasure. We read Milton for instruction, retire harassed and overburdened, and look elsewhere for recreation; we desert our master, and seek for companions.

* * *

Dryden remarks that Milton has some flats among his elevations.[4] This is only to say that all the parts are not equal. In every work one part must be for the sake of others; a palace must have passages, a poem must have transitions. It is no more to be required that wit should always be blazing than that the sun should always stand at noon. In a great work there is a vicissitude[5] of luminous and opaque parts, as there is in the world a succession of day and night. Milton, when he has expatiated in the sky, may be allowed sometimes to revisit earth; for what other author ever soared so high or sustained his flight so long?

* * *

The highest praise of genius is original invention. Milton cannot be said to have contrived the structure of an epic poem, and therefore owes reverence to that vigor and amplitude of mind to which all generations must be indebted for the art of poetical narration, for the texture of the fable, the variation of incidents, the interposition of dialogue, and all the stratagems that surprise and enchain attention. But of all the borrowers from Homer Milton is perhaps the least indebted. He was naturally a thinker for himself, confident of his own abilities and disdainful of help or hindrance; he did not refuse admission to the thoughts or images of his predecessors, but he did not seek them. From his contemporaries he neither courted nor received support; there is in his writings nothing by which the pride of other authors might be gratified or favor gained, no exchange of praise or solicitation of support. His great works were performed under discountenance and in blindness, but difficulties vanished at his touch; he was born for whatever is arduous; and his work is not the greatest of heroic poems, only because it is not the first.

1779

---

4. Preface to *Sylvae.*   5. Regular change.

From Pope

[POPE'S INTELLECTUAL CHARACTER. POPE AND DRYDEN COMPARED]

Of his intellectual character, the constituent and fundamental principle was good sense, a prompt and intuitive perception of consonance and propriety. He saw immediately, of his own conceptions, what was to be chosen, and what to be rejected; and, in the works of others, what was to be shunned, and what was to be copied.

But good sense alone is a sedate and quiescent quality, which manages its possessions well, but does not increase them; it collects few materials for its own operations, and preserves safety, but never gains supremacy. Pope had likewise genius; a mind active, ambitious, and adventurous, always investigating, always aspiring; in its widest searches still longing to go forward, in its highest flights still wishing to be higher; always imagining something greater than it knows, always endeavoring more than it can do.

To assist these powers, he is said to have had great strength and exactness of memory. That which he had heard or read was not easily lost; and he had before him not only what his own meditation suggested, but what he had found in other writers that might be accommodated to his present purpose.

These benefits of nature he improved by incessant and unwearied diligence; he had recourse to every source of intelligence, and lost no opportunity of information; he consulted the living as well as the dead; he read his compositions to his friends, and was never content with mediocrity when excellence could be attained. He considered poetry as the business of his life, and however he might seem to lament his occupation, he followed it with constancy: to make verses was his first labor, and to mend them was his last.

From his attention to poetry he was never diverted. If conversation offered anything that could be improved, he committed it to paper; if a thought, or perhaps an expression more happy than was common, rose to his mind, he was careful to write it; an independent distich was preserved for an opportunity of insertion, and some little fragments have been found containing lines, or parts of lines, to be wrought upon at some other time.

He was one of those few whose labor is their pleasure; he was never elevated to negligence, nor wearied to impatience; he never passed a fault unamended by indifference, nor quitted it by despair. He labored his works first to gain reputation, and afterwards to keep it.

Of composition there are different methods. Some employ at once memory and invention, and, with little intermediate use of the pen, form and polish large masses by continued meditation, and write their productions only when, in their own opinion, they have completed them. It is related of Virgil[1] that his custom was to pour out a great number of verses in the morning, and pass the day in retrenching exuberances and correcting inaccuracies. The method of Pope, as may be collected from his translation, was to write his first thoughts in his first words, and gradually to amplify, decorate, rectify, and refine them.

With such faculties and such dispositions, he excelled every other writer in *poetical prudence*; he wrote in such a manner as might expose him to

---

1. By Suetonius, in his brief life of the poet.

few hazards. He used almost always the same fabric of verse; and, indeed, by those few essays which he made of any other, he did not enlarge his reputation. Of this uniformity the certain consequence was readiness and dexterity. By perpetual practice, language had in his mind a systematical arrangement; having always the same use for words, he had words so selected and combined as to be ready at his call. This increase of facility he confessed himself to have perceived in the progress of his translation.

But what was yet of more importance, his effusions were always voluntary, and his subjects chosen by himself. His independence secured him from drudging at a task, and laboring upon a barren topic: he never exchanged praise for money, nor opened a shop of condolence or congratulation. His poems, therefore, were scarce ever temporary.[2] He suffered coronations and royal marriages to pass without a song, and derived no opportunities from recent events, nor any popularity from the accidental disposition of his readers. He was never reduced to the necessity of soliciting the sun to shine upon a birthday, of calling the Graces and Virtues to a wedding, or of saying what multitudes have said before him. When he could produce nothing new, he was at liberty to be silent.

His publications were for the same reason never hasty. He is said to have sent nothing to the press till it had lain two years under his inspection: it is at least certain that he ventured nothing without nice examination. He suffered the tumult of imagination to subside, and the novelties of invention to grow familiar. He knew that the mind is always enamored of its own productions, and did not trust his first fondness. He consulted his friends, and listened with great willingness to criticism; and, what was of more importance, he consulted himself, and let nothing pass against his own judgment.

He professed to have learned his poetry from Dryden, whom, whenever an opportunity was presented, he praised through his whole life with unvaried liberality; and perhaps his character may receive some illustration, if he be compared with his master.

Integrity of understanding and nicety of discernment were not allotted in a less proportion to Dryden than to Pope. The rectitude of Dryden's mind was sufficiently shown by the dismission of his poetical prejudices,[3] and the rejection of unnatural thoughts and rugged numbers. But Dryden never desired to apply all the judgment that he had. He wrote, and professed to write, merely for the people; and when he pleased others, he contented himself. He spent no time in struggles to rouse latent powers; he never attempted to make that better which was already good, nor often to mend what he must have known to be faulty. He wrote, as he tells us, with very little consideration; when occasion or necessity called upon him, he poured out what the present moment happened to supply, and, when once it had passed the press, ejected it from his mind; for when he had no pecuniary interest, he had no further solicitude.

Pope was not content to satisfy; he desired to excel, and therefore always endeavored to do his best: he did not court the candor,[4] but dared the judgment of his reader, and, expecting no indulgence from others, he showed none to himself. He examined lines and words with minute and punctilious

---

2. Topical or transitory.
3. Prepossessions. Dryden's early poems were

influenced by the metaphysical poets.
4. Kindness, sweetness of temper.

observation, and retouched every part with indefatigable diligence, till he had left nothing to be forgiven.

For this reason he kept his pieces very long in his hands, while he considered and reconsidered them. The only poems which can be supposed to have been written with such regard to the times as might hasten their publication were the two satires of *Thirty-Eight;* of which Dodsley[5] told me that they were brought to him by the author, that they might be fairly copied. "Almost every line," he said, "was then written twice over; I gave him a clean transcript, which he sent some time afterwards to me for the press, with almost every line written twice over a second time."

His declaration, that his care for his works ceased at their publication, was not strictly true. His parental attention never abandoned them; what he found amiss in the first edition, he silently corrected in those that followed. He appears to have revised the *Iliad*, and freed it from some of its imperfections; and the *Essay on Criticism* received many improvements after its first appearance. It will seldom be found that he altered without adding clearness, elegance, or vigor. Pope had perhaps the judgment of Dryden; but Dryden certainly wanted the diligence of Pope.

In acquired knowledge, the superiority must be allowed to Dryden, whose education was more scholastic, and who before he became an author had been allowed more time for study, with better means of information. His mind has a larger range, and he collects his images and illustrations from a more extensive circumference of science. Dryden knew more of man in his general nature, and Pope in his local manners. The notions of Dryden were formed by comprehensive speculation, and those of Pope by minute attention. There is more dignity in the knowledge of Dryden, and more certainty in that of Pope.

Poetry was not the sole praise of either; for both excelled likewise in prose; but Pope did not borrow his prose from his predecessor. The style of Dryden is capricious and varied, that of Pope is cautious and uniform; Dryden obeys the motions of his own mind, Pope constrains his mind to his own rules of composition; Dryden is sometimes vehement and rapid; Pope is always smooth, uniform, and gentle. Dryden's page is a natural field, rising into inequalities, and diversified by the varied exuberance of abundant vegetation; Pope's is a velvet lawn, shaven by the scythe, and leveled by the roller.

Of genius, that power which constitutes a poet; that quality without which judgment is cold and knowledge is inert; that energy which collects, combines, amplifies, and animates; the superiority must, with some hesitation, be allowed to Dryden. It is not to be inferred that of this poetical vigor Pope had only a little, because Dryden had more; for every other writer since Milton must give place to Pope; and even of Dryden it must be said that if he has brighter paragraphs, he has not better poems. Dryden's performances were always hasty, either excited by some external occasion, or extorted by domestic necessity; he composed without consideration, and published without correction. What his mind could supply at call, or gather in one excursion, was all that he sought, and all that he gave. The dilatory caution of Pope enabled him to condense his sentiments, to multiply his images, and to accumulate all that study might produce, or chance might supply. If the flights

5. Robert Dodsley, the publisher.

of Dryden therefore are higher, Pope continues longer on the wing. If of Dryden's fire the blaze is brighter, of Pope's the heat is more regular and constant. Dryden often surpasses expectation, and Pope never falls below it. Dryden is read with frequent astonishment, and Pope with perpetual delight.

This parallel will, I hope, when it is well considered, be found just; and if the reader should suspect me, as I suspect myself, of some partial fondness for the memory of Dryden, let him not too hastily condemn me; for meditation and inquiry may, perhaps, show him the reasonableness of my determination.

1781

JAMES BOSWELL
1740–1795

The discovery of a vast number of James Boswell's personal papers (believed until 1925 to have been destroyed by his literary executors) has made it possible to know the author of *The Life of Samuel Johnson* as well as we can know anybody, dead or living. His published letters and journals have made modern readers aware of the serious and absurd, the charming and repellent sides of his character. At twenty-three, when he met Johnson, he had already trained himself to listen, to observe, and to remember until he found time to write it all down. Only rarely did he take notes while a conversation was in progress, since doing this might have inhibited the speakers. His unusual memory and disciplined art enabled him to re-create and vividly preserve the many "scenes" that distinguish his journals as they do the *Life*.

Boswell was the elder son of Alexander Boswell of Auchinleck (pronounced *Affléck*) in Ayrshire, a judge who bore the courtesy title of Lord Auchinleck. As a member of an ancient family and heir to its large estate, Boswell was in the technical sense of the term a gentleman, with entrée into the best circles of Edinburgh and London. By temperament he was unstable, emotionally and sexually skittish. After attending the universities of Edinburgh and Glasgow and studying law in Holland, he made the grand tour of Europe; in Switzerland he met and succeeded in captivating the two foremost French men of letters, Jean-Jacques Rousseau and Voltaire. He visited the beleaguered hero of Corsica, General Pasquale de Paoli, whose revolt against Genoa seemed to European liberals to embody all the civic and military virtues of Republican Rome. Upon returning to England, Boswell wrote *An Account of Corsica* (1768). It was promptly translated into Dutch, German, French, and Italian, and its young author found himself with a modest European reputation.

By 1769, Boswell was established in what was to prove a successful law practice in Edinburgh and had married his cousin, Margaret Montgomerie. But he kept his ties to London and Johnson. In 1773 he persuaded Johnson to join him in a tour of the Highlands and the Hebrides. Almost every aspect of the adventure should have made it impossible. Johnson, far from young and after years of sedentary city living, found himself astride a horse in wild country or in open boats in autumn weather. As a devout Anglican, he was an outspoken enemy of the Presbyterian church. As a lover of London, he was a stranger to the primitive life of the Highlands. Moreover, for many years he had half-jestingly, half-seriously, made Scots the butt of his wit.

But such were Boswell's social tact and Johnson's vigor and curiosity that the tour was a great success. Johnson's *Journey to the Western Isles of Scotland* (1775) is a thoughtful account of the way that people live in the Hebrides (though some Scots were offended). Boswell's *Journal of a Tour to the Hebrides* (1785), a preliminary study for the *Life*, is a lively and entertaining diary that amused Johnson himself.

In 1788, four years after Johnson's death, Boswell abandoned his Scottish practice; moved to London; was admitted to the English bar (but never actually practiced); and, often depressed and drunken, began the *Life*. Fortunately he had the help and encouragement of the distinguished literary scholar Edmond Malone, without whose guidance he might never have finished his task.

Boswell had an overwhelming amount of material to deal with: his own journals, all of Johnson's letters that he could find, Johnson's voluminous writings, and every scrap of information that his friends would furnish—all of which had to be collected, verified, and somehow reduced to unity. The *Life* is a record not of Johnson alone but of literary England during the last half of the century. But Boswell wrote with his eye on the object, and that object was Samuel Johnson, toward whom such eminent persons as Sir Joshua Reynolds, Edmund Burke, Oliver Goldsmith, Lord Chesterfield—even the king himself—always face. Individual episodes are designed to reveal the great protagonist in a variety of aspects, and the world that Boswell created and populated is sustained by the vitality of his hero.

Boswell's gift is not only narrative but also dramatic. A gifted mimic, he often writes like a theatrical improviser, creating scenes with living people and playing simultaneously the roles of contriver of the dialogue, director of the plot, actor in the drama, and applauding audience—for Boswell kept an eye on his own performance. The quintessence of Boswell as both a social genius and a literary artist is to be found in his description of his visit to Voltaire: "I placed myself by him. I touched the keys in unison with his imagination. I wish you had heard the music."

Although the Johnson of popular legend is largely Boswell's creation, there was much in his life about which Boswell had no firsthand knowledge. At their first meeting, Johnson was fifty-four, a widower, already established as "Dictionary" Johnson and the author of the *Rambler*, and pensioned by the crown. Boswell knew nothing at firsthand of the long, hard years during which Johnson made his way painfully up from obscurity to fame. Hence the *Life* is the portrait of a sage. Its chief glory is conversation: the talk of a man who has experienced broadly, read widely, and observed and reflected on his observations; whose ideas are constantly brought to the test of experience; and whose experience is habitually transmuted into ideas. The book is as large as life and as human as its central character.

From Boswell on the Grand Tour

[BOSWELL INTERVIEWS VOLTAIRE][1]

And whence do I now write to you, my friend?[2] From the château of Monsieur de Voltaire. I had a letter for him from a Swiss colonel at The Hague. I came hither Monday and was presented to him. He received me with dignity

---

1. Voltaire was the name assumed by François-Marie Arouet (1694–1778), the most famous French writer of his generation. Playwright, poet, satirist, philosopher, enemy of the church, and irrepressible ironist, he (after a stormy career) was living in splendor at his chateau at Ferney near the border of Switzerland and France, just outside Geneva. His housekeeper and mistress was his niece Marie-Louise Denis. He and Jean-Jacques Rousseau, whom Boswell had just visited and flattered, were deadly enemies.

2. This passage is taken from a letter, dated December 28, 1764, written to Boswell's closest friend, a young clergyman named William Temple.

and that air of a man who has been much in the world which a Frenchman acquires in perfection. I saw him for about half an hour before dinner. He was not in spirits. Yet he gave me some brilliant sallies. He did not dine with us, and I was obliged to post away immediately after dinner, because the gates of Geneva shut before five and Ferney is a good hour from town. I was by no means satisfied to have been so little time with the monarch of French literature. A happy scheme sprung up in my adventurous mind. Madame Denis, the niece of Monsieur de Voltaire, had been extremely good to me. She is fond of our language. I wrote her a letter in English begging her interest to obtain for me the privilege of lodging a night under the roof of Monsieur de Voltaire, who, in opposition to our sun, rises in the evening. I was in the finest humor and my letter was full of wit. I told her, "I am a hardy and a vigorous Scot. You may mount me to the highest and coldest garret. I shall not even refuse to sleep upon two chairs in the bedchamber of your maid. I saw her pass through the room where we sat before dinner." I sent my letter on Tuesday by an express. It was shown to Monsieur de Voltaire, who with his own hand wrote this answer in the character of Madame Denis: "You will do us much honor and pleasure. We have few beds. But you will (*shall*) not sleep on two chairs. My uncle, though very sick, hath guessed at your merit. I know it better; for I have seen you longer." * * *

I returned yesterday to this enchanted castle. The magician appeared a very little before dinner. But in the evening he came into the drawing room in great spirits. I placed myself by him. I touched the keys in unison with his imagination. I wish you had heard the music. He was all brilliance. He gave me continued flashes of wit. I got him to speak English, which he does in a degree that made me now and then start up and cry, "Upon my soul this is astonishing!" When he talked our language he was animated with the soul of a Briton. He had bold flights. He had humor. He had an extravagance; he had a forcible oddity of style that the most comical of our *dramatis personae* could not have exceeded. He swore bloodily, as was the fashion when he was in England.[3] He hummed a ballad; he repeated nonsense. Then he talked of our Constitution with a noble enthusiasm. I was proud to hear this from the mouth of an illustrious Frenchman. At last we came upon religion. Then did he rage. The company went to supper. Monsieur de Voltaire and I remained in the drawing room with a great Bible before us; and if ever two mortal men disputed with vehemence, we did. Yes, upon that occasion he was one individual and I another. For a certain portion of time there was a fair opposition between Voltaire and Boswell. The daring bursts of his ridicule confounded my understanding. He stood like an orator of ancient Rome. Tully[4] was never more agitated than he was. He went too far. His aged frame trembled beneath him. He cried, "Oh, I am very sick; my head turns round," and he let himself gently fall upon an easy chair. He recovered. I resumed our conversation, but changed the tone. I talked to him serious and earnest. I demanded of him an honest confession of his real sentiments. He gave it me with candor and with a mild eloquence which touched my heart. I did not believe him capable of

3. In 1726, to avoid imprisonment because of a quarrel with a nobleman, Voltaire had gone into exile in England, where he remained for three years, meeting many distinguished English writers and statesmen and learning to admire the British Constitution and the English principle of religious toleration. His *Lettres philosophiques sur les Anglais* (1734) expressed his admiration of English institutions and indirectly criticized France.
4. Marcus Tullius Cicero.

thinking in the manner that he declared to me was "from the bottom of his heart." He expressed his veneration—his love—of the Supreme Being, and his entire resignation to the will of Him who is all-wise. He expressed his desire to resemble the Author of Goodness by being good himself. His sentiments go no farther. He does not inflame his mind with grand hopes of the immortality of the soul. He says it may be, but he knows nothing of it. And his mind is in perfect tranquility. I was moved; I was sorry. I doubted his sincerity. I called to him with emotion, "Are you sincere? are you really sincere?" He answered "Before God, I am." Then with the fire of him whose tragedies have so often shone on the theater of Paris, he said, "I suffer much. But I suffer with patience and resignation; not as a Christian—but as a man."

Temple, was not this an interesting scene? Would a journey from Scotland to Ferney have been too much to obtain such a remarkable interview? * * *

1764   1928

From The Life of Samuel Johnson, LL.D.

[PLAN OF THE *LIFE*]

* * * Had Dr. Johnson written his own life, in conformity with the opinion which he has given, that every man's life may be best written by himself;[1] had he employed in the preservation of his own history, that clearness of narration and elegance of language in which he has embalmed so many eminent persons, the world would probably have had the most perfect example of biography that was ever exhibited. But although he at different times, in a desultory manner, committed to writing many particulars of the progress of his mind and fortunes, he never had persevering diligence enough to form them into a regular composition. Of these memorials a few have been preserved; but the greater part was consigned by him to the flames, a few days before his death.

As I had the honor and happiness of enjoying his friendship for upwards of twenty years; as I had the scheme of writing his life constantly in view; as he was well apprised of this circumstance, and from time to time obligingly satisfied my inquiries, by communicating to me the incidents of his early years; as I acquired a facility in recollecting, and was very assiduous in recording, his conversation, of which the extraordinary vigor and vivacity constituted one of the first features of his character; and as I have spared no pains in obtaining materials concerning him, from every quarter where I could discover that they were to be found, and have been favored with the most liberal communications by his friends; I flatter myself that few biographers have entered upon such a work as this with more advantages; independent of literary abilities, in which I am not vain enough to compare myself with some great names who have gone before me in this kind of writing. * * *

Instead of melting down my materials into one mass, and constantly speaking in my own person, by which I might have appeared to have more merit in the execution of the work, I have resolved to adopt and enlarge upon the

1. *Idler* 84.

excellent plan of Mr. Mason, in his *Memoirs of Gray*.[2] Wherever narrative is necessary to explain, connect, and supply, I furnish it to the best of my abilities; but in the chronological series of Johnson's life, which I trace as distinctly as I can, year by year, I produce, wherever it is in my power, his own minutes, letters, or conversation, being convinced that this mode is more lively, and will make my readers better acquainted with him than even most of those were who actually knew him, but could know him only partially; whereas there is here an accumulation of intelligence from various points, by which his character is more fully understood and illustrated.

Indeed I cannot conceive a more perfect mode of writing any man's life than not only relating all the most important events of it in their order, but interweaving what he privately wrote, and said, and thought; by which mankind are enabled as it were to see him live, and to "live o'er each scene"[3] with him, as he actually advanced through the several stages of his life. Had his other friends been as diligent and ardent as I was, he might have been almost entirely preserved. As it is, I will venture to say that he will be seen in this work more completely than any man who has ever yet lived.

And he will be seen as he really was; for I profess to write, not his panegyric, which must be all praise, but his Life; which, great and good as he was, must not be supposed to be entirely perfect. To be as he was, is indeed subject of panegyric enough to any man in this state of being; but in every picture there should be shade as well as light, and when I delineate him without reserve, I do what he himself recommended, both by his precept and his example. * * *

I am fully aware of the objections which may be made to the minuteness on some occasions of my detail of Johnson's conversation, and how happily it is adapted for the petty exercise of ridicule, by men of superficial understanding and ludicrous fancy; but I remain firm and confident in my opinion, that minute particulars are frequently characteristic, and always amusing, when they relate to a distinguished man. I am therefore exceedingly unwilling that anything, however slight, which my illustrious friend thought it worth his while to express, with any degree of point, should perish. * * *

Of one thing I am certain, that considering how highly the small portion which we have of the table-talk and other anecdotes of our celebrated writers is valued, and how earnestly it is regretted that we have not more, I am justified in preserving rather too many of Johnson's sayings, than too few; especially as from the diversity of dispositions it cannot be known with certainty beforehand, whether what may seem trifling to some, and perhaps to the collector himself, may not be most agreeable to many; and the greater number that an author can please in any degree, the more pleasure does there arise to a benevolent mind. * * *

[JOHNSON'S EARLY YEARS, MARRIAGE AND LONDON]

[*1709*] Samuel Johnson was born at Lichfield, in Staffordshire, on the 18th of September, N.S.,[4] 1709; and his initiation into the Christian Church was not

2. William Mason, poet and dramatist, published his life of Thomas Gray in 1774:
3. Pope's Prologue to Addison's *Cato*, line 4.
4. New Style. In 1752, Great Britain adopted the

Gregorian calendar, introduced in 1582 by Pope Gregory XIII, to correct the accumulated inaccuracies of Julius Caesar's calendar, which had been in use since 46 B.C.E. By 1752, the error amounted

delayed; for his baptism is recorded, in the register of St. Mary's parish in that city, to have been performed on the day of his birth. His father is there styled *Gentleman*, a circumstance of which an ignorant panegyrist has praised him for not being proud; when the truth is, that the appellation of Gentleman, though now lost in the indiscriminate assumption of *Esquire*, was commonly taken by those who could not boast of gentility. His father was Michael Johnson, a native of Derbyshire, of obscure extraction, who settled in Lichfield as a bookseller and stationer. His mother was Sarah Ford, descended of an ancient race of substantial yeomanry in Warwickshire. They were well advanced in years when they married, and never had more than two children, both sons; Samuel, their first-born, who lived to be the illustrious character whose various excellence I am to endeavor to record, and Nathanael, who died in his twenty-fifth year.

Mr. Michael Johnson was a man of a large and robust body, and of a strong and active mind; yet, as in the most solid rocks veins of unsound substance are often discovered, there was in him a mixture of that disease, the nature of which eludes the most minute inquiry, though the effects are well known to be a weariness of life, an unconcern about those things which agitate the greater part of mankind, and a general sensation of gloomy wretchedness. From him then his son inherited, with some other qualities, "a vile melancholy," which in his too strong expression of any disturbance of the mind, "made him mad all his life, at least not sober." Michael was, however, forced by the narrowness of his circumstances to be very diligent in business, not only in his shop, but by occasionally resorting to several towns in the neighborhood, some of which were at a considerable distance from Lichfield. At that time booksellers' shops in the provincial towns of England were very rare, so that there was not one even in Birmingham, in which town old Mr. Johnson used to open a shop every market day. He was a pretty good Latin scholar, and a citizen so creditable as to be made one of the magistrates of Lichfield; and, being a man of good sense, and skill in his trade, he acquired a reasonable share of wealth, of which however he afterwards lost the greatest part, by engaging unsuccessfully in a manufacture of parchment. He was a zealous highchurch man and royalist, and retained his attachment to the unfortunate house of Stuart, though he reconciled himself, by casuistical arguments of expediency and necessity, to take the oaths imposed by the prevailing power. * * *

Johnson's mother was a woman of distinguished understanding. I asked his old schoolfellow, Mr. Hector,[5] surgeon of Birmingham, if she was not vain of her son. He said, "She had too much good sense to be vain, but she knew her son's value." Her piety was not inferior to her understanding; and to her must be ascribed those early impressions of religion upon the mind of her son, from which the world afterwards derived so much benefit. He told me that he remembered distinctly having had the first notice of Heaven, "a place to which good people went," and hell, "a place to which bad people went," communicated to him by her, when a little child in bed with her; and that it might be the better fixed in his memory, she sent him to repeat it to Thomas Jack-

---

to eleven days. Dates before September 2, 1752, must, therefore, be corrected by adding eleven days or by using the Julian date, followed by "O.S." (Old Style).

5. Edmund Hector, a lifelong friend of Johnson.

son, their manservant; he not being in the way, this was not done; but there was no occasion for any artificial aid for its preservation. * * *

[1728] That a man in Mr. Michael Johnson's circumstances should think of sending his son to the expensive University of Oxford, at his own charge, seems very improbable. The subject was too delicate to question Johnson upon. But I have been assured by Dr. Taylor[6] that the scheme never would have taken place had not a gentleman of Shropshire, one of his schoolfellows, spontaneously undertaken to support him at Oxford, in the character of his companion; though, in fact, he never received any assistance whatever from that gentleman.

He, however, went to Oxford, and was entered a Commoner of Pembroke College on the 31st of October, 1728, being then in his nineteenth year.

The Reverend Dr. Adams,[7] who afterwards presided over Pembroke College with universal esteem, told me he was present, and gave me some account of what passed on the night of Johnson's arrival at Oxford. On that evening, his father, who had anxiously accompanied him, found means to have him introduced to Mr. Jorden, who was to be his tutor. * * *

His father seemed very full of the merits of his son, and told the company he was a good scholar, and a poet, and wrote Latin verses. His figure and manner appeared strange to them; but he behaved modestly and sat silent, till upon something which occurred in the course of conversation, he suddenly struck in and quoted Macrobius; and thus he gave the first impression of that more extensive reading in which he had indulged himself.

His tutor, Mr. Jorden, fellow of Pembroke, was not, it seems, a man of such abilities as we should conceive requisite for the instructor of Samuel Johnson, who gave me the following account of him. "He was a very worthy man, but a heavy man, and I did not profit much by his instructions. Indeed, I did not attend him much. The first day after I came to college I waited upon him, and then stayed away four. On the sixth, Mr. Jorden asked me why I had not attended. I answered I had been sliding in Christ Church meadow. And this I said with as much *nonchalance* as I am now talking to you. I had no notion that I was wrong or irreverent to my tutor." BOSWELL: "That, Sir, was great fortitude of mind." JOHNSON: "No, Sir; stark insensibility." * * *

[1729] The "morbid melancholy," which was lurking in his constitution, and to which we may ascribe those particularities and that aversion to regular life, which, at a very early period, marked his character, gathered such strength in his twentieth year as to afflict him in a dreadful manner. While he was at Lichfield, in the college vacation of the year 1729, he felt himself overwhelmed with an horrible hypochondria,[8] with perpetual irritation, fretfulness, and impatience; and with a dejection, gloom, and despair, which made existence misery. From this dismal malady he never afterwards was perfectly relieved; and all his labors, and all his enjoyments, were but temporary interruptions of its baleful influence. He told Mr. Paradise[9] that he was sometimes so languid and inefficient that he could not distinguish the hour upon the town-clock. * * *

6. A well-to-do clergyman who had been Johnson's schoolfellow in Lichfield.
7. The Reverend William Adams, D.D., elected master of Pembroke in 1775.

8. Depression.
9. John Paradise, a member of the Essex Head Club, which Johnson founded in 1783.

To Johnson, whose supreme enjoyment was the exercise of his reason, the disturbance or obscuration of that faculty was the evil most to be dreaded. Insanity, therefore, was the object of his most dismal apprehension; and he fancied himself seized by it, or approaching to it, at the very time when he was giving proofs of a more than ordinary soundness and vigor of judgment. That his own diseased imagination should have so far deceived him, is strange; but it is stranger still that some of his friends should have given credit to his groundless opinion, when they had such undoubted proofs that it was totally fallacious; though it is by no means surprising that those who wish to depreciate him should, since his death, have laid hold of this circumstance, and insisted upon it with very unfair aggravation. * * *

Dr. Adams told me that Johnson, while he was at Pembroke College, "was caressed and loved by all about him, was a gay and frolicsome fellow, and passed there the happiest part of his life." But this is a striking proof of the fallacy of appearances, and how little any of us know of the real internal state even of those whom we see most frequently; for the truth is, that he was then depressed by poverty, and irritated by disease. When I mentioned to him this account as given me by Dr. Adams, he said, "Ah, Sir, I was mad and violent. It was bitterness which they mistook for frolic. I was miserably poor, and I thought to fight my way by my literature and my wit; so I disregarded all power and all authority." * * *

[1734] In a man whom religious education has secured from licentious indulgences, the passion of love, when once it has seized him, is exceedingly strong; being unimpaired by dissipation,[1] and totally concentrated in one object. This was experienced by Johnson, when he became the fervent admirer of Mrs. Porter, after her first husband's death. Miss Porter told me that when he was first introduced to her mother, his appearance was very forbidding: he was then lean and lank, so that his immense structure of bones was hideously striking to the eye, and the scars of the scrofula were deeply visible. He also wore his hair,[2] which was straight and stiff, and separated behind: and he often had, seemingly, convulsive starts and odd gesticulations, which tended to excite at once surprise and ridicule. Mrs. Porter was so much engaged by his conversation that she overlooked all these external disadvantages, and said to her daughter, "This is the most sensible man that I ever saw in my life."

[1735] Though Mrs. Porter was double the age of Johnson, and her person and manner, as described to me by the late Mr. Garrick,[3] were by no means pleasing to others, she must have had a superiority of understanding and talents, as she certainly inspired him with a more than ordinary passion; and she having signified her willingness to accept of his hand, he went to Lichfield to ask his mother's consent to the marriage, which he could not but be conscious was a very imprudent scheme, both on account of their disparity of years and her want of fortune. But Mrs. Johnson knew too well the ardor of her son's temper, and was too tender a parent to oppose his inclinations.

I know not for what reason the marriage ceremony was not performed at Birmingham; but a resolution was taken that it should be at Derby, for which

1. Scattered attention.
2. I.e., he wore no wig.
3. David Garrick (1717–1779), the most famous

actor of his day. In 1736 he was one of Johnson's three pupils in an unsuccessful school at Edial.

place the bride and bridegroom set out on horseback, I suppose in very good humor. But though Mr. Topham Beauclerk[4] used archly to mention Johnson's having told him, with much gravity, "Sir, it was a love marriage on both sides," I have had from my illustrious friend the following curious account of their journey to church upon the nuptial morn:

9th July: "Sir, she had read the old romances, and had got into her head the fantastical notion that a woman of spirit should use her lover like a dog. So, Sir, at first she told me that I rode too fast, and she could not keep up with me; and, when I rode a little slower, she passed me, and complained that I lagged behind. I was not to be made the slave of caprice; and I resolved to begin as I meant to end. I therefore pushed on briskly, till I was fairly out of her sight. The road lay between two hedges, so I was sure she could not miss it; and I contrived that she should soon come up with me. When she did, I observed her to be in tears." * * *

[1737] Johnson now thought of trying his fortune in London, the great field of genius and exertion, where talents of every kind have the fullest scope and the highest encouragement. It is a memorable circumstance that his pupil David Garrick went thither at the same time, with intention to complete his education, and follow the profession of the law, from which he was soon diverted by his decided preference for the stage.[5] * * *

[1744] * * * He produced one work this year, fully sufficient to maintain the high reputation which he had acquired. This was *The Life of Richard Savage*;[6] a man of whom it is difficult to speak impartially without wondering that he was for some time the intimate companion of Johnson; for his character was marked by profligacy, insolence, and ingratitude: yet, as he undoubtedly had a warm and vigorous, though unregulated mind, had seen life in all its varieties, and been much in the company of the statesmen and wits of his time, he could communicate to Johnson an abundant supply of such materials as his philosophical curiosity most eagerly desired; and as Savage's misfortunes and misconduct had reduced him to the lowest state of wretchedness as a writer for bread, his visits to St. John's Gate[7] naturally brought Johnson and him together.

It is melancholy to reflect that Johnson and Savage were sometimes in such extreme indigence that they could not pay for a lodging; so that they have wandered together whole nights in the streets. Yet in these almost incredible scenes of distress, we may suppose that Savage mentioned many of the anecdotes with which Johnson afterwards enriched the life of his unhappy companion, and those of other poets.

4. Pronounced *bo-clare*. A descendant of Charles II and the actress Nell Gwynn, he was brilliant and dissolute.
5. Johnson had hoped to complete his tragedy *Irene* and to get it produced, but this was not accomplished until Garrick staged it in 1749. Meanwhile Johnson struggled against poverty, at first as a writer and translator for Edward Cave's *Gentleman's Magazine*. He gradually won recognition but was never financially secure until he was pensioned in 1762. Garrick succeeded in the theater much more rapidly than did Johnson in literature.
6. The poet Richard Savage courted and gained notoriety by claiming to be the illegitimate son of Earl Rivers and the Countess of Macclesfield, whose husband had divorced her because of her unfaithfulness with Rivers. Savage publicized his claim and persecuted his alleged mother. Johnson and many others believed Savage's story and resented what they considered the lady's inhumanity. Savage was a gifted man, but he lived in poverty as a hack writer, although he was long assisted by Pope and others. He died in a debtor's prison in Bristol in 1743.
7. Where Cave published the *Gentleman's Magazine*.

He told Sir Joshua Reynolds that one night in particular, when Savage and he walked round St. James's Square for want of a lodging, they were not at all depressed by their situation; but in high spirits and brimful of patriotism, traversed the square for several hours, inveighed against the minister, and "resolved they would *stand by their country*." * * *

[1752] That there should be a suspension of his literary labors during a part of the year 1752[8] will not seem strange when it is considered that soon after closing his *Rambler*, he suffered a loss which, there can be no doubt, affected him with the deepest distress. For on the 17th of March, O.S., his wife died. * * *

The following very solemn and affecting prayer was found, after Dr. Johnson's decease, by his servant, Mr. Francis Barber, who delivered it to my worthy friend the Reverend Mr. Strahan, Vicar of Islington, who at my earnest request has obligingly favored me with a copy of it, which he and I compared with the original:

"April 26, 1752, being after 12 at night of the 25th.

"O Lord! Governor of heaven and earth, in whose hands are embodied and departed spirits, if thou hast ordained the souls of the dead to minister to the living, and appointed my departed wife to have care of me, grant that I may enjoy the good effects of her attention and ministration, whether exercised by appearance, impulses, dreams or in any other manner agreeable to thy government. Forgive my presumption, enlighten my ignorance, and however meaner agents are employed, grant me the blessed influences of thy holy Spirit, through Jesus Christ our Lord. Amen." * * *

One night when Beauclerk and Langton[9] had supped at a tavern in London, and sat till about three in the morning, if came into their heads to go and knock up Johnson, and see if they could prevail on him to join them in a ramble. They rapped violently at the door of his chambers in the Temple,[1] till at last he appeared in his shirt, with his little black wig on the top of his head, instead of a nightcap, and a poker in his hand, imagining, probably, that some ruffians were coming to attack him. When he discovered who they were, and was told their errand, he smiled, and with great good humor agreed to their proposal: "What, is it you, you dogs! I'll have a frisk with you." He was soon dressed, and they sallied forth together into Covent Garden, where the greengrocers and fruiterers were beginning to arrange their hampers, just come in from the country. Johnson made some attempts to help them; but the honest gardeners stared so at his figure and manner and odd interference, that he soon saw his services were not relished. They then repaired to one of the neighboring taverns, and made a bowl of that liquor called *Bishop*,[2] which Johnson had always liked; while in joyous contempt of sleep, from which he had been roused, he repeated the festive lines,

---

8. Johnson's important works written before the publication of the *Dictionary* are the poems "London" (1738) and "The Vanity of Human Wishes" (1749), the *Life of Savage* (1744), and the essays that made up his periodical the *Rambler* (1750–52).

9. Bennet Langton. As a boy he so much admired the *Rambler* that he sought Johnson's acquain-

tance. They became lifelong friends.

1. Because Johnson lived in Inner Temple Lane between 1760 and 1765, the "frisk" could not have taken place in the year of his wife's death, where Boswell, for his own convenience, placed it.

2. A drink made of wine, sugar, and either lemon or orange.

> Short, O short then be thy reign,
> And give us to the world again![3]

They did not stay long, but walked down to the Thames, took a boat, and rowed to Billingsgate. Beauclerk and Johnson were so well pleased with their amusement that they resolved to persevere in dissipation for the rest of the day: but Langton deserted them, being engaged to breakfast with some young ladies. Johnson scolded him for "leaving his social friends, to go and sit with a set of wretched *un-idea'd* girls." Garrick being told of this ramble, said to him smartly, "I heard of your frolic t' other night. You'll be in the *Chronicle*." Upon which Johnson afterwards observed, "*He* durst not do such a thing. His *wife* would not *let* him!" * * *

[THE LETTER TO CHESTERFIELD]

[1754] Lord Chesterfield,[4] to whom Johnson had paid the high compliment of addressing to his Lordship the *Plan* of his *Dictionary*, had behaved to him in such a manner as to excite his contempt and indignation. The world has been for many years amused with a story confidently told, and as confidently repeated with additional circumstances, that a sudden disgust was taken by Johnson upon occasion of his having been one day kept long in waiting in his Lordship's antechamber, for which the reason assigned was that he had company with him; and that at last, when the door opened, out walked Colley Cibber;[5] and that Johnson was so violently provoked when he found for whom he had been so long excluded, that he went away in a passion, and never would return. I remember having mentioned this story to George Lord Lyttelton, who told me he was very intimate with Lord Chesterfield; and holding it as a well-known truth, defended Lord Chesterfield, by saying, that Cibber, who had been introduced familiarly by the back stairs, had probably not been there above ten minutes. It may seem strange even to entertain a doubt concerning a story so long and so widely current, and thus implicitly adopted, if not sanctioned, by the authority which I have mentioned; but Johnson himself assured me that there was not the least foundation for it. He told me that there never was any particular incident which produced a quarrel between Lord Chesterfield and him; but that his Lordship's continued neglect was the reason why he resolved to have no connection with him. When the *Dictionary* was upon the eve of publication, Lord Chesterfield, who, it is said, had flattered himself with expectations that Johnson would dedicate the work to him, attempted, in a courtly manner, to soothe, and insinuate himself with the sage, conscious, as it should seem, of the cold indifference with which he had treated its learned author; and further attempted to conciliate him, by writing two papers in *The World*, in recommendation of the work; and it must be confessed that they contain some studied compliments, so finely turned, that if there had been no previous offense, it is probable that Johnson would have been highly delighted. Praise, in general,

3. Misquoted from Lansdowne's "Drinking Song to Sleep."
4. Philip Dormer Stanhope, earl of Chesterfield (1694–1773), statesman; wit, man of fashion. His *Letters*, written for the guidance of his natural son, are famous for their worldly good sense and for their expression of the ideal of an 18th-century gentleman.
5. Cibber (1671–1757), playwright, comic actor, and (after 1730) poet laureate. A fine actor but a very bad poet, Cibber was a constant object of ridicule by the wits of the town. Pope made him king of the Dunces in the *Dunciad* of 1743.

was pleasing to him; but by praise from a man of rank and elegant accomplishments, he was peculiarly gratified. * * *

This courtly device failed of its effect. Johnson, who thought that "all was false and hollow,"[6] despised the honeyed words, and was even indignant that Lord Chesterfield should, for a moment, imagine that he could be dupe of such an artifice. His expression to me concerning Lord Chesterfield, upon this occasion, was, "Sir, after making great professions, he had, for many years, taken no notice of me; but when my *Dictionary* was coming out, he fell a-scribbling in *The World* about it. Upon which, I wrote him a letter expressed in civil terms, but such as might show him that I did not mind what he said or wrote, and that I had done with him."

This is that celebrated letter of which so much has been said, and about which curiosity has been so long excited, without being gratified. I for many years solicited Johnson to favor me with a copy of it, that so excellent a composition might not be lost to posterity. He delayed from time to time to give it me; till at last in 1781, when we were on a visit at Mr. Dilly's,[7] at Southill in Bedfordshire, he was pleased to dictate it to me from memory. He afterwards found among his papers a copy of it, which he had dictated to Mr. Baretti,[8] with its title and corrections, in his own handwriting. This he gave to Mr. Langton; adding that if it were to come into print, he wished it to be from that copy. By Mr. Langton's kindness, I am enabled to enrich my work with a perfect transcript of what the world has so eagerly desired to see.

TO THE RIGHT HONORABLE THE EARL OF CHESTERFIELD

February 7, 1755

MY LORD,

I have been lately informed, by the proprietor of *The World*, that two papers, in which my Dictionary is recommended to the public, were written by your Lordship. To be so distinguished, is an honor, which, being very little accustomed to favors from the great, I know not well how to receive, or in what terms to acknowledge.

When, upon some slight encouragement, I first visited your Lordship, I was overpowered, like the rest of mankind, by the enchantment of your address; and could not forbear to wish that I might boast myself *Le vainqueur du vainqueur de la terre*[9]—that I might obtain that regard for which I saw the world contending; but I found my attendance so little encouraged that neither pride nor modesty would suffer me to continue it. When I had once addressed your Lordship in public, I had exhausted all the art of pleasing which a retired and uncourtly scholar can possess. I had done all that I could; and no man is well pleased to have his all neglected, be it ever so little.

Seven years, my Lord, have now passed since I waited in your outward rooms, or was repulsed from your door; during which time I have

---

6. *Paradise Lost* 2.112.
7. Southill was the country home of Charles and Edward Dilly, publishers. The firm published all of Boswell's serious works and shared in the publication of Johnson's *Lives of the Poets* (1779–81).
8. Giuseppe Baretti, an Italian writer and lexicographer whom Johnson introduced into his circle.
9. The conqueror of the conqueror of the earth (French). From the first line of Scudéry's epic *Alaric* (1654).

been pushing on my work through difficulties of which it is useless to complain, and have brought it, at last, to the verge of publication, without one act of assistance, one word of encouragement, or one smile of favor. Such treatment I did not expect, for I never had a patron before.

The shepherd in Virgil grew at last acquainted with Love, and found him a native of the rocks.[1]

Is not a patron, my Lord, one who looks with unconcern on a man struggling for life in the water, and, when he has reached ground, encumbers him with help? The notice which you have been pleased to take of my labors, had it been early, had been kind; but it has been delayed till I am indifferent, and cannot enjoy it; till I am solitary, and cannot impart it; till I am known, and do not want it. I hope it is no very cynical asperity not to confess obligations where no benefit has been received, or to be unwilling that the public should consider me as owing that to a patron which Providence has enabled me to do for myself.

Having carried on my work thus far with so little obligation to any favorer of learning, I shall not be disappointed though I should conclude it, if less be possible, with less; for I have been long wakened from that dream of hope in which I once boasted myself with so much exultation, my Lord, your Lordship's most humble, most obedient servant,

SAM. JOHNSON.

"While this was the talk of the town," says Dr. Adams, in a letter to me, "I happened to visit Dr. Warburton,[2] who finding that I was acquainted with Johnson, desired me earnestly to carry his compliments to him, and to tell him that he honored him for his manly behavior in rejecting these condescensions of Lord Chesterfield, and for resenting the treatment he had received from him, with a proper spirit. Johnson was visibly pleased with this compliment, for he had always a high opinion of Warburton. Indeed, the force of mind which appeared in this letter was congenial with that which Warburton himself amply possessed."

There is a curious minute circumstance which struck me, in comparing the various editions of Johnson's imitations of Juvenal. In the tenth satire, one of the couplets upon the vanity of wishes even for literary distinction stood thus:

> Yet think what ills the scholar's life assail,
> Toil, envy, want, the *garret*, and the jail.

But after experiencing the uneasiness which Lord Chesterfield's fallacious patronage made him feel, he dismissed the word *garret* from the sad group, and in all the subsequent editions the line stands

> Toil, envy, want, the *patron*, and the jail.

[1762] The accession of George the Third to the throne of these kingdoms[3] opened a new and brighter prospect to men of literary merit, who had been honored with no mark of royal favor in the preceding reign. His present Majesty's education in this country, as well as his taste and beneficence, prompted

1. *Eclogues* 8.44.
2. William Warburton, bishop of Gloucester, friend and literary executor of Pope, editor of Pope
and Shakespeare, theological controversialist.
3. In 1760.

him to be the patron of science and the arts; and early this year Johnson, having been represented to him as a very learned and good man, without any certain provision, his Majesty was pleased to grant him a pension of three hundred pounds a year. The Earl of Bute,[4] who was then Prime Minister, had the honor to announce this instance of his Sovereign's bounty, concerning which many and various stories, all equally erroneous, have been propagated: maliciously representing it as a political bribe to Johnson, to desert his avowed principles, and become the tool of a government which he held to be founded in usurpation. I have taken care to have it in my power to refute them from the most authentic information. Lord Bute told me that Mr. Wedderburne, now Lord Loughborough, was the person who first mentioned this subject to him. Lord Loughborough told me that the pension was granted to Johnson solely as the reward of his literary merit, without any stipulation whatever, or even tacit understanding that he should write for administration. His Lordship added that he was confident the political tracts which Johnson afterwards did write, as they were entirely consonant with his own opinions, would have been written by him though no pension had been granted to him.[5] * * *

[A MEMORABLE YEAR: BOSWELL MEETS JOHNSON]

[1763] This is to me a memorable year; for in it I had the happiness to obtain the acquaintance of that extraordinary man whose memoirs I am now writing; an acquaintance which I shall ever esteem as one of the most fortunate circumstances in my life. * * *

Mr. Thomas Davies the actor, who then kept a bookseller's shop in Russel Street, Covent Garden, told me that Johnson was very much his friend, and came frequently to his house, where he more than once invited me to meet him; but by some unlucky accident or other he was prevented from coming to us. * * *

At last, on Monday the 16th of May, when I was sitting in Mr. Davies's back parlor, after having drunk tea with him and Mrs. Davies, Johnson unexpectedly came into the shop; and Mr. Davies having perceived him through the glass door in the room in which we were sitting, advancing towards us— he announced his awful approach to me, somewhat in the manner of an actor in the part of Horatio, when he addresses Hamlet on the appearance of his father's ghost, "Look, my Lord, it comes." I found that I had a very perfect idea of Johnson's figure, from the portrait of him painted by Sir Joshua Reynolds soon after he had published his *Dictionary*, in the attitude of sitting in his easy chair in deep meditation, which was the first picture his friend did for him, which Sir Joshua very kindly presented to me, and from which an engraving has been made for this work. Mr. Davies mentioned my name, and respectfully introduced me to him. I was much agitated; and recollecting his prejudice against the Scotch, of which I had heard much, I said to Davies, "Don't tell where I come from."—"From Scotland," cried Davies roguishly.

4. An intimate friend of George III's mother, he early gained an ascendancy over the young prince and was largely responsible for the king's autocratic views. He was hated in England both as a favorite and as a Scot.

5. Johnson's few political pamphlets in the 1770s invariably supported the policies of the crown. The best known is his answer to the American colonies, "Taxation No Tyranny" (1775). His dislike of the Americans was in large part due to the fact they owned slaves.

"Mr. Johnson," said I, "I do indeed come from Scotland, but I cannot help it."
I am willing to flatter myself that I meant this as light pleasantry to soothe
and conciliate him, and not as an humiliating abasement at the expense of
my country. But however that might be, this speech was somewhat unlucky;
for with that quickness of wit for which he was so remarkable, he seized the
expression "come from Scotland," which I used in the sense of being of that
country; and, as if I had said that I had come away from it, or left it, retorted,
"That, Sir, I find, is what a very great many of your countrymen cannot help."
This stroke stunned me a good deal; and when we had sat down, I felt myself
not a little embarrassed, and apprehensive of what might come next. He then
addressed himself to Davies: "What do you think of Garrick? He has refused
me an order for the play for Miss Williams,[6] because he knows the house will
be full, and that an order would be worth three shillings." Eager to take any
opening to get into conversation with him, I ventured to say, "O Sir, I cannot
think Mr. Garrick would grudge such a trifle to you." "Sir," said he, with a
stern look, "I have known David Garrick longer than you have done: and I
know no right you have to talk to me on the subject." Perhaps I deserved this
check; for it was rather presumptuous in me, an entire stranger, to express
any doubt of the justice of his animadversion upon his old acquaintance and
pupil. I now felt myself much mortified, and began to think that the hope
which I had long indulged of obtaining his acquaintance was blasted. And, in
truth, had not my ardor been uncommonly strong, and my resolution uncommonly persevering, so rough a reception might have deterred me forever from
making any further attempts. Fortunately, however, I remained upon the
field not wholly discomfited. * * *

I was highly pleased with the extraordinary vigor of his conversation, and
regretted that I was drawn away from it by an engagement at another place.
I had, for a part of the evening, been left alone with him, and had ventured
to make an observation now and then, which he received very civilly; so
that I was satisfied that though there was a roughness in his manner, there
was no ill nature in his disposition. Davies followed me to the door, and
when I complained to him a little of the hard blows which the great man
had given me, he kindly took upon him to console me by saying, "Don't be
uneasy. I can see he likes you very well."

A few days afterwards I called on Davies, and asked him if he thought I
might take the liberty of waiting on Mr. Johnson at his chambers in the
Temple. He said I certainly might, and that Mr. Johnson would take it as a
compliment. So upon Tuesday the 24th of May, after having been enlivened
by the witty sallies of Messieurs Thornton, Wilkes, Churchill, and Lloyd,[7]
with whom I had passed the morning, I boldly repaired to Johnson. His
chambers were on the first floor of No. 1, Inner Temple Lane, and I entered
them with an impression given me by the Reverend Dr. Blair,[8] of Edinburgh,
who had been introduced to him not long before, and described his having
"found the giant in his den"; an expression, which, when I came to be pretty

---

6. Mrs. Anna Williams (1706–1783), a blind poet
and friend of Mrs. Johnson. She continued to live
in Johnson's house after his wife's death and
habitually sat up to make tea for him whenever he
came home.
7. Robert Lloyd, poet and essayist. Bonnell
Thornton, journalist. Charles Churchill, satirist.

For Wilkes, see p. 2982. The four were bound
together by a common love of wit and dissipation,
Boswell enjoyed their company in 1763.
8. The Reverend Hugh Blair (1718–1800), Scottish divine and professor of rhetoric and *belles
lettres* at the University of Edinburgh.

well acquainted with Johnson, I repeated to him, and he was diverted at this picturesque account of himself. Dr. Blair had been presented to him by Dr. James Fordyce.[9] At this time the controversy concerning the pieces published by Mr. James Macpherson, as translations of *Ossian*, was at its height.[1] Johnson had all along denied their authenticity; and, what was still more provoking to their admirers, maintained that they had no merit. The subject having been introduced by Dr. Fordyce, Dr. Blair, relying on the internal evidence of their antiquity, asked Dr. Johnson whether he thought any man of a modern age could have written such poems? Johnson replied, "Yes, Sir, many men, many women, and many children." Johnson, at this time, did not know that Dr. Blair had just published a dissertation, not only defending their authenticity, but seriously ranking them with the poems of Homer and Virgil; and when he was afterwards informed of this circumstance, he expressed some displeasure at Dr. Fordyce's having suggested the topic, and said, "I am not sorry that they got thus much for their pains. Sir, it was like leading one to talk of a book when the author is concealed behind the door."

He received me very courteously; but, it must be confessed that his apartment, and furniture, and morning dress, were sufficiently uncouth. His brown suit of clothes looked very rusty; he had on a little old shriveled unpowdered wig, which was too small for his head; his shirt neck and knees of his breeches were loose; his black worsted stockings ill drawn up; and he had a pair of unbuckled shoes by way of slippers. But all these slovenly particularities were forgotten the moment that he began to talk. Some gentlemen, whom I do not recollect, were sitting with him; and when they went away, I also rose; but he said to me, "Nay, don't go." "Sir," said I, "I am afraid that I intrude upon you. It is benevolent to allow me to sit and hear you." He seemed pleased with this compliment, which I sincerely paid him, and answered, "Sir, I am obliged to any man who visits me." I have preserved the following short minute of what passed this day:

"Madness frequently discovers itself merely by unnecessary deviation from the usual modes of the world. My poor friend Smart showed the disturbance of his mind by falling upon his knees, and saying his prayers in the street, or in any other unusual place. Now although, rationally speaking, it is greater madness not to pray at all than to pray as Smart did, I am afraid there are so many who do not pray, that their understanding is not called in question."

Concerning this unfortunate poet, Christopher Smart, who was confined in a madhouse, he had, at another time, the following conversation with Dr. Burney:[2] BURNEY. "How does poor Smart do, Sir; is he likely to recover?" JOHNSON. "It seems as if his mind had ceased to struggle with the disease; for he grows fat upon it." BURNEY. "Perhaps, Sir, that may be from want of exercise." JOHNSON. "No, Sir; he has partly as much exercise as he used to have, for he digs in the garden. Indeed, before his confinement, he used for exercise to walk to the ale house; but he was *carried* back again. I did not think he ought to be shut up. His infirmities were not noxious to society. He insisted

9. A Scottish preacher.

1. Macpherson had imposed on most of his contemporaries, Scottish and English, by convincing them of the genuineness of prose poems that he had concocted but that he claimed to have translated from the original Gaelic of Ossian, a blind epic poet of the 3rd century. The vogue of the poems both in Europe and in America was enormous.

2. Dr. Charles Burney (1726–1814), historian of music and father of the novelist and diarist Frances Burney, whom Johnson befriended in his old age.

on people praying with him; and I'd as lief pray with Kit Smart as anyone else. Another charge was that he did not love clean linen; and I have no passion for it."—Johnson continued. "Mankind have a great aversion to intellectual labor; but even supposing knowledge to be easily attainable, more people would be content to be ignorant than would take even a little trouble to acquire it."

Talking of Garrick, he said, "He is the first man in the world for sprightly conversation."

When I rose a second time he again pressed me to stay, which I did. * * *

[GOLDSMITH. SUNDRY OPINIONS. JOHNSON MEETS HIS KING]

As Dr. Oliver Goldsmith will frequently appear in this narrative, I shall endeavor to make my readers in some degree acquainted with his singular character. He was a native of Ireland, and a contemporary with Mr. Burke[3] at Trinity College, Dublin, but did not then give much promise of future celebrity. He, however, observed to Mr. Malone,[4] that "though he made no great figure in mathematics, which was a study in much repute there, he could turn an ode of Horace into English better than any of them." He afterwards studied physic[5] at Edinburgh, and upon the Continent; and I have been informed, was enabled to pursue his travels on foot, partly by demanding at universities to enter the lists as a disputant, by which, according to the custom of many of them, he was entitled to the premium of a crown, when luckily for him his challenge was not accepted; so that, as I once observed to Dr. Johnson, he *disputed* his passage through Europe. He then came to England, and was employed successively in the capacities of an usher[6] to an academy, a corrector of the press, a reviewer, and a writer for a newspaper. He had sagacity enough to cultivate assiduously the acquaintance of Johnson, and his faculties were gradually enlarged by the contemplation of such a model. To me and many others it appeared that he studiously copied the manner of Johnson, though, indeed, upon a smaller scale.

At this time I think he had published nothing with his name, though it was pretty generally known that *one Dr. Goldsmith* was the author of *An Enquiry into the Present State of Polite Learning in Europe*, and of *The Citizen of the World*, a series of letters supposed to be written from London by a Chinese. No man had the art of displaying, with more advantage as a writer, whatever literary acquisitions he made. *"Nihil quod tetigit non ornavit."*[7] His mind resembled a fertile, but thin soil. There was a quick, but not a strong vegetation, of whatever chanced to be thrown upon it. No deep root could be struck. The oak of the forest did not grow there; but the elegant shrubbery and the fragrant parterre[8] appeared in gay succession. It has been generally circulated and believed that he was a mere fool in conversation; but, in truth, this has been greatly exaggerated. He had, no doubt, a more than common share of that hurry of ideas which we often find in his countrymen, and which sometimes produces a laughable confu-

---

3. Edmund Burke (1729–1797), statesman, orator, and political philosopher.
4. Edmond Malone (1741–1812), distinguished editor and literary scholar. He helped Boswell in the writing and publication of the *Life*.
5. Medicine.

6. An assistant teacher; then a disagreeable and ill-paid job.
7. He touched nothing that he did not adorn (Latin). From Johnson's epitaph for Goldsmith's monument in Westminster Abbey.
8. A flower garden with beds laid out in patterns.

sion in expressing them. He was very much what the French call *un étourdi*,[9] and from vanity and an eager desire of being conspicuous wherever he was, he frequently talked carelessly without knowledge of the subject, or even without thought. His person was short, his countenance coarse and vulgar, his deportment that of a scholar awkwardly affecting the easy gentleman. Those who were in any way distinguished, excited envy in him to so ridiculous an excess that the instances of it are hardly credible. When accompanying two beautiful young ladies with their mother on a tour in France, he was seriously angry that more attention was paid to them than to him; and once at the exhibition of the *Fantoccini*[1] in London, when those who sat next him observed with what dexterity a puppet was made to toss a pike, he could not bear that it should have such praise, and exclaimed with some warmth, "Pshaw! I can do it better myself." * * *

I had as my guests this evening at the Mitre Tavern, Dr. Johnson, Dr. Goldsmith, Mr. Thomas Davies, Mr. Eccles, an Irish gentleman, for whose agreeable company I was obliged to Mr. Davies, and the Reverend Mr. John Ogilvie,[2] who was desirous of being in company with my illustrious friend, while I, in my turn, was proud to have the honor of showing one of my countrymen upon what easy terms Johnson permitted me to live with him. * * *

Mr. Ogilvie was unlucky enough to choose for the topic of his conversation the praises of his native country. He began with saying that there was very rich land round Edinburgh. Goldsmith, who had studied physic there, contradicted this, very untruly, with a sneering laugh. Disconcerted a little by this, Mr. Ogilvie then took new ground, where, I suppose, he thought himself perfectly safe; for he observed that Scotland had a great many noble wild prospects. JOHNSON. "I believe, Sir, you have a great many. Norway, too, has noble wild prospects; and Lapland is remarkable for prodigious noble wild prospects. But, Sir, let me tell you, the noblest prospect which a Scotchman ever sees, is the highroad that leads him to England!" This unexpected and pointed sally produced a roar of applause. After all, however, those who admire the rude grandeur of nature cannot deny it to Caledonia. * * *

At night Mr. Johnson and I supped in a private room at the Turk's Head Coffeehouse, in the Strand. "I encourage this house," said he, "for the mistress of it is a good civil woman, and has not much business.

"Sir, I love the acquaintance of young people; because, in the first place, I don't like to think myself growing old. In the next place, young acquaintances must last longest, if they do last; and then, Sir, young men have more virtue than old men: they have more generous sentiments in every respect. I love the young dogs of this age: they have more wit and humor and knowledge of life than we had; but then the dogs are not so good scholars. Sir, in my early years I read very hard. It is a sad reflection, but a true one, that I knew almost as much at eighteen as I do now. My judgment, to be sure, was not so good; but I had all the facts. I remember very well, when I was at Oxford, an old gentleman said to me, 'Young man, ply your book diligently now, and acquire a stock of knowledge; for when years come upon you, you will find that poring upon books will be but an irksome task.'" * * *

---

9. One who acts without thought.
1. Puppets (Italian).

2. A Presbyterian minister and poet.

He again insisted on the duty of maintaining subordination of rank. "Sir, I would no more deprive a nobleman of his respect than of his money. I consider myself as acting a part in the great system of society, and I do to others as I would have them to do to me. I would behave to a nobleman as I should expect he would behave to me, were I a nobleman and he Sam. Johnson. Sir, there is one Mrs. Macaulay[3] in this town, a great republican. One day when I was at her house, I put on a very grave countenance, and said to her, 'Madam, I am now become a convert to your way of thinking. I am convinced that all mankind are upon an equal footing; and to give you an unquestionable proof, Madam, that I am in earnest, here is a very sensible, civil, well-behaved fellow citizen, your footman; I desire that he may be allowed to sit down and dine with us.' I thus, Sir, showed her the absurdity of the leveling doctrine.[4] She has never liked me since. Sir, your levelers wish to level *down* as far as themselves; but they cannot bear leveling *up* to themselves. They would all have some people under them; why not then have some people above them?" * * *

At supper this night he talked of good eating with uncommon satisfaction. "Some people," he said, "have a foolish way of not minding, or pretending not to mind, what they eat. For my part, I mind my belly very studiously, and very carefully; for I look upon it that he who does not mind his belly will hardly mind anything else." He now appeared to me *Jean Bull philosophe*,[5] and he was, for the moment, not only serious but vehement. Yet I have heard him, upon other occasions, talk with great contempt of people who were anxious to gratify their palates; and the 206th number of his *Rambler* is a masterly essay against gulosity.[6] His practice, indeed, I must acknowledge, may be considered as casting the balance of his different opinions upon this subject; for I never knew any man who relished good eating more than he did. When at table, he was totally absorbed in the business of the moment; his looks seemed riveted to his plate; nor would he, unless when in very high company, say one word, or even pay the least attention to what was said by others, till he had satisfied his appetite, which was so fierce, and indulged with such intenseness, that while in the act of eating, the veins of his forehead swelled, and generally a strong perspiration was visible. To those whose sensations were delicate, this could not but be disgusting; and it was doubtless not very suitable to the character of a philosopher, who should be distinguished by self-command. But it must be owned that Johnson, though he could be rigidly *abstemious*, was not a *temperate* man either in eating or drinking. He could refrain, but he could not use moderately. He told me that he had fasted two days without inconvenience, and that he had never been hungry but once. They who beheld with wonder how much he eat upon all occasions when his dinner was to his taste, could not easily conceive what he must have meant by hunger; and not only was he remarkable for the extraordinary quantity which he eat, but he was, or affected to be, a man of very nice discernment in the science of cookery. * * *

---

3. Catharine Macaulay, a distinguished feminist, historian, and propounder of libertarian and egalitarian ideas.
4. Leveler: "One who destroys superiority; one who endeavours to bring all to the same state of equality" (Johnson's *Dictionary*).
5. I.e., John Bull (the typical hardheaded Englishman) in the role of philosopher.
6. Greediness.

[*1767*] In February, 1767, there happened one of the most remarkable incidents of Johnson's life, which gratified his monarchical enthusiasm, and which he loved to relate with all its circumstances, when requested by his friends. This was his being honored by a private conversation with his Majesty, in the library at the Queen's house. He had frequently visited those splendid rooms and noble collection of books, which he used to say was more numerous and curious than he supposed any person could have made in the time which the King had employed. Mr. Barnard, the librarian, took care that he should have every accommodation that could contribute to his ease and convenience, while indulging his literary taste in that place; so that he had here a very agreeable resource at leisure hours.

His Majesty having been informed of his occasional visits, was pleased to signify a desire that he should be told when Dr. Johnson came next to the library. Accordingly, the next time that Johnson did come, as soon as he was fairly engaged with a book, on which, while he sat by the fire, he seemed quite intent, Mr. Barnard stole round to the apartment where the King was, and, in obedience to his Majesty's commands, mentioned that Dr. Johnson was then in the library. His Majesty said he was at leisure, and would go to him; upon which Mr. Barnard took one of the candles that stood on the King's table, and lighted his Majesty through a suite of rooms, till they came to a private door into the library, of which his Majesty had the key. Being entered, Mr. Barnard stepped forward hastily to Dr. Johnson, who was still in a profound study, and whispered him, "Sir, here is the King." Johnson started up, and stood still. His Majesty approached him, and at once was courteously easy.

His Majesty began by observing that he understood he came sometimes to the library; and then mentioning his having heard that the Doctor had been lately at Oxford, asked him if he was not fond of going thither. To which Johnson answered that he was indeed fond of going to Oxford sometimes, but was likewise glad to come back again. The King then asked him what they were doing at Oxford. Johnson answered, he could not much commend their diligence, but that in some respects they were mended, for they had put their press under better regulations, and were at that time printing Polybius. He was then asked whether there were better libraries at Oxford or Cambridge. He answered, he believed the Bodleian was larger than any they had at Cambridge; at the same time adding, "I hope, whether we have more books or not than they have at Cambridge, we shall make as good use of them as they do." Being asked whether All Souls or Christ Church library was the largest, he answered, "All Souls library is the largest we have, except the Bodleian." "Aye," said the King, "that is the public library."

His Majesty inquired if he was then writing anything. He answered, he was not, for he had pretty well told the world what he knew, and must now read to acquire more knowledge. The King, as it should seem with a view to urge him to rely on his own stores as an original writer, and to continue his labors, then said "I do not think you borrow much from anybody." Johnson said he thought he had already done his part as a writer. "I should have thought so too," said the King, "if you had not written so well."—Johnson observed to me, upon this, that "No man could have paid a handsomer compliment; and it was fit for a king to pay. It was decisive." When asked by another friend, at Sir Joshua Reynolds's, whether he made any reply to this high compliment, he answered,

"No, Sir. When the King had said it, it was to be so. It was not for me to bandy civilities with my sovereign." Perhaps no man who had spent his whole life in courts could have shown a more nice and dignified sense of true politeness than Johnson did in this instance. * * *

[FEAR OF DEATH]

[1769] When we were alone, I introduced the subject of death, and endeavored to maintain that the fear of it might be got over. I told him that David Hume said to me, he was no more uneasy to think he should *not be* after this life, than that he *had not been* before he began to exist. JOHNSON. "Sir, if he really thinks so, his perceptions are disturbed; he is mad: if he does not think so, he lies. He may tell you, he holds his finger in the flame of a candle, without feeling pain; would you believe him? When he dies, he at least gives up all he has." BOSWELL. "Foote,[7] Sir, told me, that when he was very ill he was not afraid to die." JOHNSON. "It is not true, Sir. Hold a pistol to Foote's breast, or to Hume's breast, and threaten to kill them, and you'll see how they behave." BOSWELL. "But may we not fortify our minds for the approach of death?" Here I am sensible I was in the wrong, to bring before his view what he ever looked upon with horror; for although when in a celestial frame, in his *Vanity of Human Wishes*, he has supposed death to be "kind Nature's signal for retreat," from this stage of being to "a happier seat," his thoughts upon this awful change were in general full of dismal apprehensions. His mind resembled the vast amphitheater, the Colosseum at Rome. In the center stood his judgment, which, like a mighty gladiator, combated those apprehensions that, like the wild beasts of the arena, were all around in cells, ready to be let out upon him. After a conflict, he drove them back into their dens; but not killing them, they were still assailing him. To my question, whether we might not fortify our minds for the approach of death, he answered, in a passion, "No, Sir, let it alone. It matters not how a man dies, but how he lives. The act of dying is not of importance, it lasts so short a time." He added (with an earnest look), "A man knows it must be so, and submits. It will do him no good to whine."

I attempted to continue the conversation. He was so provoked that he said, "Give us no more of this"; and was thrown into such a state of agitation that he expressed himself in a way that alarmed and distressed me; showed an impatience that I should leave him, and when I was going away, called to me sternly, "Don't let us meet tomorrow." * * *

[OSSIAN. "TALKING FOR VICTORY"]

MR. BOSWELL TO DR. JOHNSON

Edinburgh, Feb. 2, 1775.

* * * As to Macpherson, I am anxious to have from yourself a full and pointed account of what has passed between you and him. It is confidently told here that before your book[8] came out he sent to you, to let you know that he understood you meant to deny the authenticity of

---

7. Samuel Foote, actor and dramatist, famous for his wit and his skill in mimicry.
8. Johnson's *Journey to the Western Islands*

(1775), in which he had publicly expressed his views on the Ossianic poems.

Ossian's poems; that the originals were in his possession; that you might have inspection of them, and might take the evidence of people skilled in the Erse language; and that he hoped, after this fair offer, you would not be so uncandid[9] as to assert that he had refused reasonable proof. That you paid no regard to his message, but published your strong attack upon him; and then he wrote a letter to you, in such terms as he thought suited to one who had not acted as a man of veracity. * * *

What words were used by Mr. Macpherson in his letter to the venerable sage, I have never heard; but they are generally said to have been of a nature very different from the language of literary contest. Dr. Johnson's answer appeared in the newspapers of the day, and has since been frequently republished; but not with perfect accuracy. I give it as dictated to me by himself, written down in his presence, and authenticated by a note in his own handwriting, *"This, I think, is a true copy."*

MR. JAMES MACPHERSON,

I received your foolish and impudent letter. Any violence offered me I shall do my best to repel; and what I cannot do for myself, the law shall do for me. I hope I shall never be deterred from detecting what I think a cheat, by the menaces of a ruffian.

What would you have me retract? I thought your book an imposture; I think it an imposture still. For this opinion I have given my reasons to the public, which I here dare you to refute. Your rage I defy. Your abilities, since your Homer, are not so formidable; and what I hear of your morals inclines me to pay regard not to what you shall say, but to what you shall prove. You may print this if you will.

SAM. JOHNSON.

Mr. Macpherson little knew the character of Dr. Johnson if he supposed that he could be easily intimidated; for no man was ever more remarkable for personal courage. He had, indeed, an awful dread of death, or rather, "of something after death";[1] and what rational man, who seriously thinks of quitting all that he has ever known, and going into a new and unknown state of being, can be without that dread? But his fear was from reflection; his courage natural. His fear, in that one instance, was the result of philosophical and religious consideration. He feared death, but he feared nothing else, not even what might occasion death. Many instances of his resolution may be mentioned. One day, at Mr. Beauclerk's house in the country, when two large dogs were fighting, he went up to them, and beat them till they separated; and at another time, when told of the danger there was that a gun might burst if charged with many balls, he put in six or seven, and fired it off against a wall. Mr. Langton told me that when they were swimming together near Oxford, he cautioned Dr. Johnson against a pool which was reckoned particularly dangerous; upon which Johnson directly swam into it. He told me himself that one night he was attacked in the street by four men, to whom he would not yield, but kept them all at bay, till the watch came up, and carried

9. Unfair, malicious.   1. *Hamlet* 3.1.80.

both him and them to the roundhouse.[2] In the playhouse at Lichfield, as Mr. Garrick informed me, Johnson having for a moment quitted a chair which was placed for him between the side-scenes, a gentleman took possession of it, and when Johnson on his return civilly demanded his seat, rudely refused to give it up; upon which Johnson laid hold of it, and tossed him and the chair into the pit. Foote, who so successfully revived the old comedy, by exhibiting living characters, had resolved to imitate Johnson on the stage, expecting great profits from his ridicule of so celebrated a man. Johnson being informed of his intention, and being at dinner at Mr. Thomas Davies's the bookseller, from whom I had the story, he asked Mr. Davies what was the common price of an oak stick; and being answered six-pence, "Why then, Sir," said he, "give me leave to send your servant to purchase me a shilling one. I'll have a double quantity; for I am told Foote means to *take me off*, as he calls it, and I am determined the fellow shall not do it with impunity." Davies took care to acquaint Foote of this, which effectually checked the wantonness of the mimic. Mr. Macpherson's menaces made Johnson provide himself with the same implement of defense; and had he been attacked, I have no doubt that, old as he was, he would have made his corporal prowess be felt as much as his intellectual. * * *

[1776] I mentioned a new gaming club, of which Mr. Beauclerk had given me an account, where the members played to a desperate extent. JOHNSON. "Depend upon it, Sir, this is mere talk. *Who* is ruined by gaming? You will not find six instances in an age. There is a strange rout made about deep play: whereas you have many more people ruined by adventurous trade, and yet we do not hear such an outcry against it." THRALE.[3] "There may be few people absolutely ruined by deep play; but very many are much hurt in their circumstances by it." JOHNSON. "Yes, Sir, and so are very many by other kinds of expense." I had heard him talk once before in the same manner; and at Oxford he said, he wished he had learnt to play at cards. The truth, however, is that he loved to display his ingenuity in argument; and therefore would sometimes in conversation maintain opinions which he was sensible were wrong, but in supporting which, his reasoning and wit would be most conspicuous. He would begin thus: "Why, Sir, as to the good or evil of card playing——" "Now," said Garrick, "he is thinking which side he shall take." He appeared to have a pleasure in contradiction, especially when any opinion whatever was delivered with an air of confidence; so that there was hardly any topic, if not one of the great truths of religion and morality, that he might not have been incited to argue, either for or against. Lord Elibank[4] had the highest admiration of his powers. He once observed to me, "Whatever opinion Johnson maintains, I will not say that he convinces me; but he never fails to show me that he has good reasons for it." I have heard Johnson pay his Lordship this high compliment: "I never was in Lord Elibank's company without learning something." * * *

---

2. "The constable's prison, in which disorderly persons, found in the street, are confined" (Johnson's *Dictionary*).
3. Johnson met Henry Thrale, the wealthy brewer, and his charming wife, Hester, in 1765. Thereafter he spent much of his time at their house at Streatham near London. There he enjoyed the good things of life, as well as the companionship of Mrs. Thrale and her children. Henry Thrale died in 1781. His widow's marriage to Gabriel Piozzi, an Italian musician, in 1784, caused Johnson to quarrel with her and darkened the last months of his life. "Rout": uproar.
4. Prominent in Scottish literary circles. Johnson, who admired him, had visited him on his tour of Scotland with Boswell in 1773.

[DINNER WITH WILKES]

My worthy booksellers and friends, Messieurs Dilly in the Poultry, at whose hospitable and well-covered table I have seen a greater number of literary men than at any other, except that of Sir Joshua Reynolds, had invited me to meet Mr. Wilkes[5] and some more gentlemen on Wednesday, May 15. "Pray," said I, "let us have Dr. Johnson."—"What, with Mr. Wilkes? not for the world," said Mr. Edward Dilly, "Dr. Johnson would never forgive me."—"Come," said I, "if you'll let me negotiate for you, I will be answerable that all shall go well." DILLY. "Nay, if you will take it upon you, I am sure I shall be very happy to see them both here."

Notwithstanding the high veneration which I entertained for Dr. Johnson, I was sensible that he was sometimes a little actuated by the spirit of contradiction, and by means of that I hoped I should gain my point. I was persuaded that if I had come upon him with a direct proposal, "Sir, will you dine in company with Jack Wilkes?" he would have flown into a passion, and would probably have answered, "Dine with Jack Wilkes, Sir! I'd as soon dine with Jack Ketch."[6] I therefore, while we were sitting quietly by ourselves at his house in an evening, took occasion to open my plan thus: "Mr. Dilly, Sir, sends his respectful compliments to you, and would be happy if you would do him the honor to dine with him on Wednesday next along with me, as I must soon go to Scotland." JOHNSON. "Sir, I am obliged to Mr. Dilly. I will wait upon him—" BOSWELL. "Provided, Sir, I suppose, that the company which he is to have, is agreeable to you." JOHNSON. "What do you mean, Sir? What do you take me for? Do you think I am so ignorant of the world as to imagine that I am to prescribe to a gentleman what company he is to have at his table?" BOSWELL. "I beg your pardon, Sir, for wishing to prevent you from meeting people whom you might not like. Perhaps he may have some of what he calls his patriotic[7] friends with him." JOHNSON. "Well, Sir, and what then? What care *I* for his *patriotic friends*? Poh!" BOSWELL. "I should not be surprised to find Jack Wilkes there." JOHNSON. "And if Jack Wilkes *should* be there, what is that to *me*, Sir? My dear friend, let us have no more of this. I am sorry to be angry with you; but really it is treating me strangely to talk to me as if I could not meet any company whatever, occasionally." BOSWELL. "Pray forgive me, Sir: I meant well. But you shall meet whoever comes, for me." Thus I secured him, and told Dilly that he would find him very well pleased to be one of his guests on the day appointed.

Upon the much-expected Wednesday, I called on him about half an hour before dinner, as I often did when we were to dine out together, to see that he was ready in time, and to accompany him. I found him buffeting his books, as upon a former occasion, covered with dust, and making no prepa-

---

5. John Wilkes (1727–1797) was disapproved of by the Christian and Tory Johnson in every way. He was profane and dissolute, and his personal life was a public scandal. For more than a decade he had been notorious as a courageous and resourceful opponent of the authoritarian policies of the king and his ministers and had been the envenomed critic of Lord Bute, to whom Johnson owed his pension. When Johnson met him he had totally defeated his enemies, had served as lord mayor, and was again a member of Parliament, a post from which he had been expelled and driven into exile as an outlaw in 1764. Boswell had found Wilkes a gay and congenial companion in Italy in 1764.

6. A famous public hangman.

7. In Tory circles the word had come to be used ironically of those who opposed the government. The "patriots" considered themselves the defenders of the ancient liberties of the English. They included the partisans of both Wilkes and the American colonists.

ration for going abroad. "How is this, Sir?" said I. "Don't you recollect that you are to dine at Mr. Dilly's?" JOHNSON. "Sir, I did not think of going to Dilly's: it went out of my head. I have ordered dinner at home with Mrs. Williams." BOSWELL. "But, my dear Sir, you know you were engaged to Mr. Dilly, and I told him so. He will expect you, and will be much disappointed if you don't come." JOHNSON. "You must talk to Mrs. Williams about this."

Here was a sad dilemma. I feared that what I was so confident I had secured would yet be frustrated. He had accustomed himself to show Mrs. Williams such a degree of humane attention as frequently imposed some restraint upon him; and I knew that if she should be obstinate, he would not stir. I hastened downstairs to the blind lady's room, and told her I was in great uneasiness, for Dr. Johnson had engaged to me to dine this day at Mr. Dilly's, but that he had told me he had forgotten his engagement, and had ordered dinner at home. "Yes, Sir," said she, pretty peevishly, "Dr. Johnson is to dine at home."—"Madam," said I, "his respect for you is such that I know he will not leave you unless you absolutely desire it. But as you have so much of his company, I hope you will be good enough to forgo it for a day; as Mr. Dilly is a very worthy man, has frequently had agreeable parties at his house for Dr. Johnson, and will be vexed if the Doctor neglects him today. And then, Madam, be pleased to consider my situation; I carried the message, and I assured Mr. Dilly that Dr. Johnson was to come, and no doubt he has made a dinner, and invited a company, and boasted of the honor he expected to have. I shall be quite disgraced if the Doctor is not there." She gradually softened to my solicitations, which were certainly as earnest as most entreaties to ladies upon any occasion, and was graciously pleased to empower me to tell Dr. Johnson that all things considered, she thought he should certainly go. I flew back to him, still in dust, and careless of what should be the event, "indifferent in his choice to go or stay";[8] but as soon as I had announced to him Mrs. Williams' consent, he roared, "Frank, a clean shirt," and was very soon dressed. When I had him fairly seated in a hackney coach with me, I exulted as much as a fortune hunter who has got an heiress into a post chaise with him to set out for Gretna Green.[9]

When we entered Mr. Dilly's drawing room, he found himself in the midst of a company he did not know. I kept myself snug and silent, watching how he would conduct himself. I observed him whispering to Mr. Dilly, "Who is that gentleman, Sir?"—"Mr. Arthur Lee."—JOHNSON. "Too, too, too" (under his breath), which was one of his habitual mutterings. Mr. Arthur Lee could not but be very obnoxious to Johnson, for he was not only a *patriot* but an *American*.[1] He was afterwards minister from the United States at the court of Madrid. "And who is the gentleman in lace?"—"Mr. Wilkes, Sir." This information confounded him still more; he had some difficulty to restrain himself, and taking up a book, sat down upon a window seat and read, or at least kept his eye upon it intently for some time, till he composed himself. His feelings, I dare say, were awkward enough. But he

---

8. Addison's *Cato* 5.1.40. Boswell cleverly adapts to his own purpose Cato's words, "Indifferent in his choice to sleep or die."
9. A village just across the Scottish border where runaway couples were married by the local innkeeper or the blacksmith.
1. Johnson was extremely hostile to the rebelling American colonists. On one occasion he said, "I am willing to love all mankind, except an American." Lee had been educated in England and Scotland, and had recently been admitted to the English bar. He had been a loyal supporter of Wilkes.

no doubt recollected his having rated me for supposing that he could be at all disconcerted by any company, and he, therefore, resolutely set himself to behave quite as an easy man of the world, who could adapt himself at once to the disposition and manners of those whom he might chance to meet.

The cheering sound of "Dinner is upon the table," dissolved his reverie, and we *all* sat down without any symptom of ill humor. There were present, beside Mr. Wilkes, and Mr. Arthur Lee, who was an old companion of mine when he studied physic at Edinburgh, Mr. (now Sir John) Miller, Dr. Lettsom, and Mr. Slater the druggist. Mr. Wilkes placed himself next to Dr. Johnson, and behaved to him with so much attention and politeness that he gained upon him insensibly. No man eat more heartily than Johnson, or loved better what was nice and delicate. Mr. Wilkes was very assiduous in helping him to some fine veal. "Pray give me leave, Sir—It is better here—A little of the brown—Some fat, Sir—A little of the stuffing—Some gravy—Let me have the pleasure of giving you some butter—Allow me to recommend a squeeze of this orange—or the lemon, perhaps, may have more zest."—"Sir, Sir, I am obliged to you, Sir," cried Johnson, bowing, and turning his head to him with a look for some time of "surly virtue," but, in a short while, of complacency.

Foote being mentioned, Johnson said, "He is not a good mimic." One of the company added, "A merry Andrew, a buffoon." JOHNSON. "But he has wit too, and is not deficient in ideas, or in fertility and variety of imagery, and not empty of reading; he has knowledge enough to fill up his part. One species of wit he has in an eminent degree, that of escape. You drive him into a corner with both hands; but he's gone, Sir, when you think you have got him—like an animal that jumps over your head. Then he has a great range for wit; he never lets truth stand between him and a jest, and he is sometimes mighty coarse. Garrick is under many restraints from which Foote is free." WILKES. "Garrick's wit is more like Lord Chesterfield's." JOHNSON. "The first time I was in company with Foote was at Fitzherbert's. Having no good opinion of the fellow, I was resolved not to be pleased; and it is very difficult to please a man against his will. I went on eating my dinner pretty sullenly, affecting not to mind him. But the dog was so very comical, that I was obliged to lay down my knife and fork, throw myself back upon my chair, and fairly laugh it out. No, Sir, he was irresistible. He upon one occasion experienced, in an extraordinary degree, the efficacy of his powers of entertaining. Amongst the many and various modes which he tried of getting money, he became a partner with a small-beer[2] brewer, and he was to have a share of the profits for procuring customers amongst his numerous acquaintance. Fitzherbert was one who took his small beer; but it was so bad that the servants resolved not to drink it. They were at some loss how to notify their resolution, being afraid of offending their master, who they knew liked Foote much as a companion. At last they fixed upon a little black boy, who was rather a favorite, to be their deputy, and deliver their remonstrance; and having invested him with the whole authority of the kitchen, he was to inform Mr. Fitzherbert, in all their names, upon a certain day, that they would drink Foote's small beer no longer. On that day Foote happened to dine at Fitzherbert's, and this boy served at table; he was so delighted with Foote's stories, and merriment, and gri-

---

2. Weak beer, served in the servants' hall.

mace, that when he went downstairs, he told them, 'This is the finest man I have ever seen. I will not deliver your message. I will drink his small beer.'"

Somebody observed that Garrick could not have done this. WILKES. "Garrick would have made the small beer still smaller. He is now leaving the stage; but he will play *Scrub*[3] all his life." I knew that Johnson would let nobody attack Garrick but himself, as Garrick once said to me, and I had heard him praise his liberality; so to bring out his commendation of his celebrated pupil, I said, loudly, "I have heard Garrick is liberal." JOHNSON. "Yes, Sir, I know that Garrick has given away more money than any man in England that I am acquainted with, and that not from ostentatious views. Garrick was very poor when he began life; so when he came to have money, he probably was very unskillful in giving away, and saved when he should not. But Garrick began to be liberal as soon as he could; and I am of opinion, the reputation of avarice which he has had, has been very lucky for him, and prevented his having many enemies. You despise a man for avarice, but do not hate him. Garrick might have been much better attacked for living with more splendor than is suitable to a player: if they had had the wit to have assaulted him in that quarter, they might have galled him more. But they have kept clamoring about his avarice, which has rescued him from much obloquy and envy."

Talking of the great difficulty of obtaining authentic information for biography, Johnson told us, "When I was a young fellow I wanted to write the *Life of Dryden*, and in order to get materials, I applied to the only two persons then alive who had seen him; these were old Swinney,[4] and old Cibber. Swinney's information was no more than this, that at Will's Coffeehouse Dryden had a particular chair for himself, which was set by the fire in winter, and was then called his winter chair; and that it was carried out for him to the balcony in summer, and was then called his summer chair. Cibber could tell no more but that he remembered him a decent old man, arbiter of critical disputes at Will's. You are to consider that Cibber was then at a great distance from Dryden, had perhaps one leg only in the room, and durst not draw in the other." BOSWELL. "Yet Cibber was a man of observation?" JOHNSON. "I think not." BOSWELL. "You will allow his *Apology* to be well done." JOHNSON. "Very well done, to be sure, Sir. That book is a striking proof of the justice of Pope's remark:

> Each might his several province well command,
> Would all but stoop to what they understand."[5]

BOSWELL. "And his plays are good." JOHNSON. "Yes; but that was his trade; *l'esprit du corps*: he had been all his life among players and play writers. I wondered that he had so little to say in conversation, for he had kept the best company, and learnt all that can be got by the ear. He abused Pindar to me, and then showed me an ode of his own, with an absurd couplet, making a linnet soar on an eagle's wing. I told him that when the ancients made a simile, they always made it like something real."

Mr. Wilkes remarked that "among all the bold flights of Shakespeare's imagination, the boldest was making Birnam Wood march to Dunsinane;[6]

---

3. The servant of Squire Sullen in Farquhar's *Beaux' Stratagem*, a favorite role of Garrick.
4. Owen Mac Swinney, a playwright.
5. *An Essay on Criticism* 1.66–67.
6. *Macbeth* 5.5.30–52.

creating a wood where there never was a shrub; a wood in Scotland! ha! ha! ha!" And he also observed, that "the clannish slavery of the Highlands of Scotland was the single exception to Milton's remark of 'The mountain nymph, sweet Liberty,'[7] being worshiped in all hilly countries."—"When I was at Inverary," said he, "on a visit to my old friend, Archibald, Duke of Argyle, his dependents congratulated me on being such a favorite of his Grace. I said, 'It is then, gentlemen, truly lucky for me; for if I had displeased the Duke, and he had wished it, there is not a Campbell among you but would have been ready to bring John Wilkes's head to him in a charger.[8] It would have been only

Off with his head! So much for Aylesbury.'[9]

I was then member for Aylesbury." * * *

Mr. Arthur Lee mentioned some Scotch who had taken possession of a barren part of America, and wondered why they should choose it. JOHNSON. "Why, Sir, all barrenness is comparative. The *Scotch* would not know it to be barren." BOSWELL. "Come, come, he is flattering the English. You have now been in Scotland, Sir, and say if you did not see meat and drink enough there." JOHNSON. "Why yes, Sir; meat and drink enough to give the inhabitants sufficient strength to run away from home." All these quick and lively sallies were said sportively, quite in jest, and with a smile, which showed that he meant only wit. Upon this topic he and Mr. Wilkes could perfectly assimilate; here was a bond of union between them, and I was conscious that as both of them had visited Caledonia, both were fully satisfied of the strange narrow ignorance of those who imagine that it is a land of famine. But they amused themselves with persevering in the old jokes. When I claimed a superiority for Scotland over England in one respect, that no man can be arrested there for a debt merely because another swears it against him; but there must first be the judgment of a court of law ascertaining its justice; and that a seizure of the person, before judgment is obtained, can take place only if his creditor should swear that he is about to fly from the country, or, as it is technically expressed, is *in meditatione fugae*: WILKES. "That, I should think, may be safely sworn of all the Scotch nation." JOHNSON (to Mr. Wilkes). "You must know, Sir, I lately took my friend Boswell and showed him genuine civilized life in an English provincial town. I turned him loose at Lichfield, my native city, that he might see for once real civility: for you know he lives among savages in Scotland, and among rakes in London." WILKES. "Except when he is with grave, sober, decent people like you and me." JOHNSON (smiling). "And we ashamed of him."

They were quite frank and easy. Johnson told the story of his asking Mrs. Macaulay to allow her footman to sit down with them, to prove the ridiculousness of the argument for the equality of mankind; and he said to me afterwards, with a nod of satisfaction, "You saw Mr. Wilkes acquiesced." * * *

This record, though by no means so perfect as I could wish, will serve to give a notion of a very curious interview, which was not only pleasing at the time, but had the agreeable and benignant effect of reconciling any animos-

---

7. "L'Allegro," line 36.
8. Platter.
9. "Off with his head! So much for Bucking-ham." A line in Cibber's version of Shakespeare's *Richard III*.

ity and sweetening any acidity, which in the various bustle of political contest, had been produced in the minds of two men, who, though widely different, had so many things in common—classical learning, modern literature, wit, and humor, and ready repartee—that it would have been much to be regretted if they had been forever at a distance from each other.

Mr. Burke gave me much credit for this successful "negotiation"; and pleasantly said that there was nothing to equal it in the whole history of the *Corps Diplomatique.* * * *

[DREAD OF SOLITUDE]

[*1777*] I talked to him of misery being "the doom of man" in this life, as displayed in his *Vanity of Human Wishes.* Yet I observed that things were done upon the supposition of happiness; grand houses were built, fine gardens were made, splendid places of public amusement were contrived, and crowded with company. JOHNSON. "Alas, Sir, these are all only struggles for happiness. When I first entered Ranelagh,[1] it gave an expansion and gay sensation to my mind, such as I never experienced anywhere else. But, as Xerxes wept when he viewed his immense army, and considered that not one of that great multitude would be alive a hundred years afterwards, so it went to my heart to consider that there was not one in all that brilliant circle that was not afraid to go home and think; but that the thoughts of each individual there, would be distressing when alone." * * *

["A BOTTOM OF GOOD SENSE." BET FLINT. "CLEAR YOUR MIND OF CANT"]

[*1781*] Talking of a very respectable author, he told us a curious circumstance in his life, which was that he had married a printer's devil.[2] REYNOLDS. "A printer's devil, Sir! Why, I thought a printer's devil was a creature with a black face and in rags." JOHNSON. "Yes, Sir. But I suppose, he had her face washed, and put clean clothes on her." Then looking very serious, and very earnest: "And she did not disgrace him; the woman had a bottom of good sense." The word *bottom* thus introduced was so ludicrous when contrasted with his gravity, that most of us could not forbear tittering and laughing; though I recollect that the Bishop of Killaloe kept his countenance with perfect steadiness, while Miss Hannah More[3] slyly hid her face behind a lady's back who sat on the same settee with her. His pride could not bear that any expression of his should excite ridicule, when he did not intend it; he therefore resolved to assume and exercise despotic power, glanced sternly around, and called out in a strong tone, "Where's the merriment?" Then collecting himself, and looking awful, to make us feel how he could impose restraint, and as it were searching his mind for a still more ludicrous word, he slowly pronounced, "I say the *woman* was *fundamentally* sensible"; as if he had said, "hear this now, and laugh if you dare." We all sat composed as at a funeral. * * *

He gave us an entertaining account of Bet Flint, a woman of the town, who, with some eccentric talents and much effrontery, forced herself upon

---

1. Pleasure gardens in Chelsea, where concerts were held, fireworks displayed, and food and drink sold.
2. Apprentice in a print shop.

3. Bluestocking and religious writer (1745–1833), one of the promoters of the Sunday School movement.

his acquaintance. "Bet," said he, "wrote her own Life in verse, which she brought to me, wishing that I would furnish her with a Preface to it" (laughing). "I used to say of her that she was generally slut and drunkard; occasionally, whore and thief. She had, however, genteel lodgings, a spinnet on which she played, and a boy that walked before her chair. Poor Bet was taken up on a charge of stealing a counterpane, and tried at the Old Bailey. Chief Justice———, who loved a wench, summed up favorably, and she was acquitted. After which Bet said, with a gay and satisfied air, 'Now that the counterpane is *my own*, I shall make a petticoat of it.'" * * *

[1783] I have no minute of any interview with Johnson till Thursday, May 15, when I find what follows: BOSWELL. "I wish much to be in Parliament, Sir." JOHNSON. "Why, Sir, unless you come resolved to support any administration, you would be the worse for being in Parliament, because you would be obliged to live more expensively." BOSWELL. "Perhaps, Sir, I should be the less happy for being in Parliament. I never would sell my vote, and I should be vexed if things went wrong." JOHNSON. "That's cant,[4] Sir. It would not vex you more in the house than in the gallery: public affairs vex no man." BOSWELL. "Have not they vexed yourself a little, Sir? Have not you been vexed by all the turbulence of this reign, and by that absurd vote of the House of Commons, 'That the influence of the Crown has increased, is increasing, and ought to be diminished?'" JOHNSON. "Sir, I have never slept an hour less, nor eat an ounce less meat. I would have knocked the factious dogs on the head, to be sure; but I was not *vexed*." BOSWELL. "I declare, Sir, upon my honor, I did imagine I was vexed, and took a pride in it; but it *was*, perhaps, cant; for I own I neither ate less, nor slept less." JOHNSON. "My dear friend, clear your *mind* of cant. You may *talk* as other people do: you may say to a man, 'Sir, I am your most humble servant.' You are *not* his most humble servant. You may say, 'These are bad times; it is a melancholy thing to be reserved to such times.' You don't mind the times. You tell a man, 'I am sorry you had such bad weather the last day of your journey, and were so much wet.' You don't care sixpence whether he is wet or dry. You may *talk* in this manner; it is a mode of talking in society: but don't *think* foolishly." * * *

[JOHNSON PREPARES FOR DEATH]

My anxious apprehensions at parting with him this year proved to be but too well founded; for not long afterwards he had a dreadful stroke of the palsy, of which there are very full and accurate accounts in letters written by himself, to show with what composure of mind, and resignation to the Divine Will, his steady piety enabled him to behave. * * *

Two days after he wrote thus to Mrs. Thrale:

> "On Monday, the 16th, I sat for my picture, and walked a considerable way with little inconvenience. In the afternoon and evening I felt myself light and easy, and began to plan schemes of life. Thus I went to bed, and in a short time waked and sat up, as has been long my custom, when I felt a confusion and indistinctness in my head, which lasted, I suppose, about half a minute. I was alarmed, and prayed God that however he might afflict my body, he would spare my understanding. This prayer,

---

4. "A whining pretension to goodness in formal and affected terms" (Johnson's *Dictionary*).

that I might try the integrity of my faculties, I made in Latin verse. The lines were not very good, but I knew them not to be very good: I made them easily, and concluded myself to be unimpaired in my faculties.

"Soon after I perceived that I had suffered a paralytic stroke, and that my speech was taken from me. I had no pain, and so little dejection in this dreadful state, that I wondered at my own apathy, and considered that perhaps death itself, when it should come, would excite less horror than seems now to attend it.

"In order to rouse the vocal organs, I took two drams. Wine has been celebrated for the production of eloquence. I put myself into violent motion, and I think repeated it; but all was vain. I then went to bed and strange as it may seem, I think, slept. When I saw light, it was time to contrive what I should do. Though God stopped my speech, he left me my hand; I enjoyed a mercy which was not granted to my dear friend Lawrence,[5] who now perhaps overlooks me as I am writing, and rejoices that I have what he wanted. My first note was necessarily to my servant, who came in talking, and could not immediately comprehend why he should read what I put into his hands.

"I then wrote a card to Mr. Allen,[6] that I might have a discreet friend at hand, to act as occasion should require. In penning this note, I had some difficulty; my hand, I knew not how nor why, made wrong letters. I then wrote to Dr. Taylor to come to me, and bring Dr. Heberden; and I sent to Dr. Brocklesby, who is my neighbor.[7] My physicians are very friendly, and give me great hopes; but you may imagine my situation. I have so far recovered my vocal powers as to repeat the Lord's Prayer with no very imperfect articulation. My memory, I hope, yet remains as it was; but such an attack produces solicitude for the safety of every faculty." * * *

[1784] To Mr. Henry White, a young clergyman, with whom he now formed an intimacy, so as to talk to him with great freedom, he mentioned that he could not in general accuse himself of having been an undutiful son. "Once, indeed," said he, "I was disobedient; I refused to attend my father to Uttoxeter market. Pride was the source of that refusal, and the remembrance of it was painful. A few years ago, I desired to atone for this fault; I went to Uttoxeter in very bad weather, and stood for a considerable time bareheaded in the rain, on the spot where my father's stall used to stand. In contrition I stood, and I hope the penance was expiatory."

"I told him," says Miss Seward,[8] "in one of my latest visits to him, of a wonderful learned pig, which I had seen at Nottingham; and which did all that we have observed exhibited by dogs and horses. The subject amused him. 'Then,' said he, 'the pigs are a race unjustly calumniated. *Pig* has, it seems, not been wanting to *man*, but *man* to *pig*. We do not allow *time* for his education, we kill him at a year old.' Mr. Henry White, who was present, observed that if this instance had happened in or before Pope's time, he would not have been justified in instancing the swine as the lowest degree of groveling

5. Dr. Thomas Lawrence, president of the Royal College of Physicians and Johnson's own doctor, had died paralyzed shortly before this was written.
6. Edmund Allen, a printer, Johnson's landlord and neighbor.
7. These two physicians attended Johnson on his deathbed.
8. Anna Seward, "the Swan of Lichfield," a poet.

instinct.[9] Dr. Johnson seemed pleased with the observation, while the person who made it proceeded to remark that great torture must have been employed, ere the indocility of the animal could have been subdued. 'Certainly,' said the Doctor; 'but,' turning to me, 'how old is your pig?' I told him, three years old. 'Then,' said he, 'the pig has no cause to complain; he would have been killed the first year if he had not been *educated*, and protracted existence is a good recompense for very considerable degrees of torture.'"

[JOHNSON FACES DEATH]

As Johnson had now very faint hopes of recovery, and as Mrs. Thrale was no longer devoted to him, it might have been supposed that he would naturally have chosen to remain in the comfortable house of his beloved wife's daughter,[1] and end his life where he began it. But there was in him an animated and lofty spirit, and however complicated diseases might depress ordinary mortals, all who saw him, beheld and acknowledged the *invictum animum Catonis*.[2] Such was his intellectual ardor even at this time that he said to one friend, "Sir, I look upon every day to be lost, in which I do not make a new acquaintance"; and to another, when talking of his illness, "I will be conquered; I will not capitulate." And such was his love of London, so high a relish had he of its magnificent extent, and variety of intellectual entertainment, that he languished when absent from it, his mind having become quite luxurious from the long habit of enjoying the metropolis; and, therefore, although at Lichfield, surrounded with friends, who loved and revered him, and for whom he had a very sincere affection, he still found that such conversation as London affords, could be found nowhere else. These feelings, joined, probably, to some flattering hopes of aid from the eminent physicians and surgeons in London, who kindly and generously attended him without accepting fees, made him resolve to return to the capital. * * * Death had always been to him an object of terror; so that, though by no means happy, he still clung to life with an eagerness at which many have wondered. At any time when he was ill, he was very much pleased to be told that he looked better. An ingenious member of the Eumelian Club[3] informs me that upon one occasion when he said to him that he saw health returning to his cheek, Johnson seized him by the hand and exclaimed, "Sir, you are one of the kindest friends I ever had." * * *

Dr. Heberden, Dr. Brocklesby, Dr. Warren, and Dr. Butter, physicians, generously attended him, without accepting any fees, as did Mr. Cruikshank, surgeon; and all that could be done from professional skill and ability was tried, to prolong a life so truly valuable. He himself, indeed, having, on account of his very bad constitution, been perpetually applying himself to medical inquiries, united his own efforts with those of the gentlemen who attended him; and imagining that the dropsical collection of water which oppressed him might be drawn off by making incisions in his body, he, with his usual resolute defiance of pain, cut deep, when he thought that his surgeon had done it too tenderly.

---

9. *An Essay on Man* 1.221.
1. Lucy Porter.
2. The unconquered soul of Cato (Latin). An

adaptation of a phrase in Horace's *Odes* 2.1.24.
3. A club to which Boswell and Reynolds belonged.

About eight or ten days before his death, when Dr. Brocklesby paid him his morning visit, he seemed very low and desponding, and said, "I have been as a dying man all night." He then emphatically broke out in the words of Shakespeare:

> "Canst thou not minister to a mind diseased;
> Pluck from the memory a rooted sorrow,
> Raze out the written troubles of the brain,
> And with some sweet oblivious antidote
> Cleanse the stuffed bosom of that perilous stuff
> Which weighs upon the heart?"

To which Dr. Brocklesby readily answered, from the same great poet:

> "—Therein the patient
> Must minister to himself."[4]

Johnson expressed himself much satisfied with the application. * * *

Amidst the melancholy clouds which hung over the dying Johnson, his characteristical manner showed itself on different occasions.

When Dr. Warren, in the usual style, hoped that he was better; his answer was, "No, Sir; you cannot conceive with what acceleration I advance towards death."

A man whom he had never seen before was employed one night to sit up with him. Being asked next morning how he liked his attendant, his answer was, "Not at all, Sir: the fellow's an idiot; he is as awkward as a turnspit[5] when first put into the wheel, and as sleepy as a dormouse."

Mr. Windham[6] having placed a pillow conveniently to support him, he thanked him for his kindness, and said, "That will do—all that a pillow can do." * * *

Johnson, with that native fortitude, which, amidst all his bodily distress and mental sufferings, never forsook him, asked Dr. Brocklesby, as a man in whom he had confidence, to tell him plainly whether he could recover. "Give me," said he, "a direct answer." The Doctor having first asked him if he could bear the whole truth, which way soever it might lead, and being answered that he could, declared that, in his opinion, he could not recover without a miracle. "Then," said Johnson, "I will take no more physic, not even my opiates; for I have prayed that I may render up my soul to God unclouded." In this resolution he persevered, and, at the same time, used only the weakest kinds of sustenance. Being pressed by Mr. Windham to take somewhat more generous nourishment, lest too low a diet should have the very effect which he dreaded, by debilitating his mind, he said, "I will take anything but inebriating sustenance."

The Reverend Mr. Strahan,[7] who was the son of his friend, and had been always one of his great favorites, had, during his last illness, the satisfaction of contributing to soothe and comfort him. That gentleman's house, at Islington, of which he is Vicar, afforded Johnson, occasionally and easily, an agree-

---

4. *Macbeth* 5.3.40–46.
5. "A dog kept to turn the roasting-spit by running within a tread-wheel connected to it" (*OED*).
6. William Windham, one of Johnson's younger

friends, later a member of Parliament.
7. The Reverend George Strahan (pronounced *Strawn*), who later published Johnson's *Prayers and Meditations*.

able change of place and fresh air; and he attended also upon him in town in the discharge of the sacred offices of his profession.

Mr. Strahan has given me the agreeable assurance that, after being in much agitation, Johnson became quite composed, and continued so till his death.

Dr. Brocklesby, who will not be suspected of fanaticism, obliged me with the following account:

> "For some time before his death, all his fears were calmed and absorbed by the prevalence of his faith, and his trust in the merits and *propitiation* of Jesus Christ." * * *

Johnson having thus in his mind the true Christian scheme, at once rational and consolatory, uniting justice and mercy in the Divinity, with the improvement of human nature, previous to his receiving the Holy Sacrament in his apartment, composed and fervently uttered this prayer:

> "Almighty and most merciful Father, I am now as to human eyes, it seems, about to commemorate, for the last time, the death of thy Son Jesus Christ, our Saviour and Redeemer. Grant, O Lord, that my whole hope and confidence may be in his merits, and thy mercy; enforce and accept my imperfect repentance; make this commemoration available to the confirmation of my faith, the establishment of my hope, and the enlargement of my charity; and make the death of thy Son Jesus Christ effectual to my redemption. Have mercy upon me, and pardon the multitude of my offenses. Bless my friends; have mercy upon all men. Support me, by thy Holy Spirit, in the days of weakness, and at the hour of death; and receive me, at my death, to everlasting happiness, for the sake of Jesus Christ. Amen."

Having * * * made his will on the 8th and 9th of December, and settled all his worldly affairs, he languished till Monday, the 13th of that month, when he expired, about seven o'clock in the evening, with so little apparent pain that his attendants hardly perceived when his dissolution took place. * * *

1791

FRANCES BURNEY
1752–1840

People have often made the mistake of underestimating Frances Burney. In person, as in her writing, she seemed a proper, self-effacing lady. Many readers still call her "Fanny," as if familiarity could make her harmless. But she saw through such poses. Sir Joshua Reynolds said that "if he was conscious to himself of any trick, or any affectation, there is nobody he should so much fear as this little Burney!" And Samuel Johnson teased her by claiming that "your shyness, & slyness, & pretending to know nothing, never took *me* in, whatever you may do with others. *I* always knew you for a *toadling!*" (according to legend, little toads may look submissive but actually carry poison). Although her writing crackles with humor, it can be relentless—and sometimes cruel—in exposing bad manners or a selfish heart.

She learned quite young how to hide in a crowd. A devoted daughter of Charles Burney, a popular teacher and historian of music, Frances grew up in a large family that gave her many opportunities to study character and mix discreetly in society. Her first novel, *Evelina, or A Young Lady's Entrance into the World* (1778), was written in secret and published anonymously. But delighted readers, including Johnson, Burke, and Hester Thrale, soon found her out and sang her praises; and a second novel, *Cecilia* (1782), confirmed her reputation. Her home life was less happy, however; she and her stepmother disliked each other, and she fell in love with a young clergyman who never got around to proposing. In 1786, to please her father, she accepted a place as a lady-in-waiting at court, where the paralyzing etiquette and lack of independence tormented her for the next five years, until she finally managed to resign. At forty-one she married a French émigré, General Alexandre-Gabriel-Jean-Baptiste d'Arblay. Despite the disapproval of her father—d'Arblay was penniless, Catholic, and politically liberal—the marriage was happy. Madame d'Arblay soon bore a son, and her novel *Camilla* (1796) brought in good money. After she joined her husband in France, in 1802, the Napoleonic wars prevented them from returning to England for ten years; the pain of an outcast dominates her last novel, *The Wanderer, or Female Difficulties* (1814). But she never stopped writing, producing a doctored version of her father's *Memoirs* (1832) and more of the diaries and letters that, edited after her death by a niece, made her famous again.

Burney wrote all her life—not only novels and plays but perpetual letters and journals, recording whatever she saw for friends and family as well as herself. Even the most informal pages display her gifts: a knack for catching character, a wonderful ear for dialogue, wry humor, and a swift pace that carries the reader along from moment to moment. Her special subject is embarrassment—often her own. In scenes like her flight from the king, where she is torn between opposite notions of the right thing to do, shame and comedy mingle. These trepidations can also be incredibly painful, as in her gripping account of a mastectomy. Despite her propriety, Burney looks at the world and its institutions with the clear eyes of an outsider, aware of the gaps between what people say and what they do. She frees herself to write with utter honesty by pretending, at first, that nobody is going to read her. But her private thoughts are reported so fully and faithfully that, in the end, every reader can share them.

From The Journal and Letters

[FIRST JOURNAL ENTRY]

Poland Street, London, March 27, 1768[1]

To have some account of my thoughts, manners, acquaintance and actions, when the hour arrives at which time is more nimble than memory, is the reason which induces me to keep a journal: a journal in which I must confess my *every* thought, must open my whole heart! But a thing of this kind ought to be addressed to somebody—I must imagine myself to be talking—talking to the most intimate of friends—to one in whom I should take delight in confiding, and feel remorse in concealment: but who must this

---

1. This is the first page of Burney's first journal, begun when she was fifteen.

friend be?—to make choice of one to whom I can but *half* rely, would be to frustrate entirely the intention of my plan. The only one I could wholly, totally confide in, lives in the same house with me, and not only never *has*, but never *will*, leave me one secret *to* tell her.[2] To whom, then *must* I dedicate my wonderful, surprising and interesting adventures?—to *whom* dare I reveal my private opinion of my nearest relations? the secret thoughts of my dearest friends? my own hopes, fears, reflections and dislikes—Nobody!

To Nobody, then, will I write my Journal! since To Nobody can I be wholly unreserved—to Nobody can I reveal every thought, every wish of my heart, with the most unlimited confidence, the most unremitting sincerity to the end of my life! For what chance, what accident can end my connections with Nobody? No secret *can* I conceal from No—body, and to No—body can I be *ever* unreserved. Disagreement cannot stop our affection, Time itself has no power to end our friendship. The love, the esteem I entertain for Nobody, No-body's self has not power to destroy. From Nobody I have nothing to fear, the secrets sacred to friendship, Nobody will not reveal, when the affair is doubtful, Nobody will not look towards the side least favourable.—

I will suppose you, then, to be my best friend; tho' God forbid you ever should! my dearest companion—and a romantick girl, for mere oddity may perhaps be more sincere—more *tender*—than if you were a friend in propria personae[3]—in as much as imagination often exceeds reality. In your breast my errors may create pity without exciting contempt; may raise your compassion, without eradicating your love.

From this moment, then, my dear girl—but why, permit me to ask, must a *female* be made Nobody? Ah! my dear, what were this world good for, *were* Nobody a female? And now I have done with *perambulation*.

[MR. BARLOW'S PROPOSAL]

About 2 o'clock, while I was dawdling in the study, and waiting for an opportunity to speak, John came in, and said "A gentleman is below, who asks for Miss Burney,—Mr. Barlow."[4]

I think I was never more distressed in my life—to have taken pains to avoid a private conversation so highly disagreeable to me, and at last to be forced into it at so unfavourable a juncture,—for I had now 2 letters from him, both unanswered and consequently open to his conjectures. I exclaimed "Lord!—how provoking! what shall I do?"

My father looked uneasy and perplexed:—he said something about not being hasty, which I did not desire him to explain. Terrified lest he should hint at the advantage of an early establishment—like Mr. Crisp[5]—quick from the study—but slow enough afterwards—I went down stairs.—I saw my mother pass from the front into the back parlour; which did not add to the *graciousness* of my reception of poor Mr. Barlow, who I found alone in the

2. Burney's younger sister Susanna. In 1773, when Burney spent the summer away from home, she began a journal for her sister, continuing it off and on until 1800, when Susanna died.
3. As a real person.
4. Thomas Barlow had met Burney early in May and immediately wrote to declare that he loved and admired her. She did not reciprocate her feel-

ings: "his language is stiff & uncommon, he has a great desire to please, but no elegance of manners; neither, though he may be very worthy, is he at all agreeable." Her family, however, approved of the match and encouraged her to accept him.
5. Samuel Crisp, an old family friend, had been a mentor to Burney. "Early establishment": marriage when young.

front parlor. I was not sorry that none of the family were there, as I now began to seriously dread any protraction of this affair.

He came up to me, and with an air of *tenderness* and satisfaction, began some anxious enquiries about my health, but I interrupted him with saying "I fancy, sir, you have not received a letter I—I—"

I stopt, for I could not say which I had *sent*!

"A letter?—no, ma'am!"

"You will have it, then, to-morrow, sir."

We were both silent for a minute or two, when he said "In consequence, I presume, ma'am, of the one I—"

"Yes, sir!" cried I.

"And pray—ma'am—Miss Burney!—may I—beg to ask the contents? that is—the—the—" he could not go on.

"Sir—I—it was only—it was merely—in short, you will see it tomorrow."

"But if you would favor me with the contents now, I could perhaps answer it at once?"

"Sir, it requires no answer!"

A second silence ensued. I was really distressed myself to see *his* distress, which was very apparent. After some time, he stammered out something of *hoping*—and *beseeching*,—which, gathering more firmness, I announced— "I am much obliged to you, sir, for the too good opinion you are pleased to have of me—but I should be sorry you should lose any more time upon my account—as I have no thoughts at all of changing my situation and abode."

* * *

He remonstrated very earnestly. "This is the severest decision!—Surely you must allow that the *social state* is what we were all meant for?—that we were created for one another?—that to form such a resolution is contrary to the design of our being?—"

"All this may be true,—" said I;—"I have nothing to say in contradiction to it—but you know there are many odd characters in the world—and perhaps I am one of them."

"O no, no, no,—that can never be!—but is it possible you can have so bad an opinion of the married state? It seems to me the *only* state for happiness!—"

"Well, sir, *you* are attached to the married life—*I* am to the single— therefore, *every man in his humor*[6]—do *you* follow *your* opinion,—and let *me* follow *mine*."

"But surely—is not this—*singular?*—"

"I give you leave, sir," cried I, laughing, "to think me singular—odd— queer—nay, even whimsical, if you please."

"But, my *dear* Miss Burney, only—"

"I entreat you, sir, to take my answer—You really pain me by being so urgent.—"

"That would not I do for the world!—I only beg you to suffer me— perhaps in future—"

"No, indeed; I shall never change—I do assure you you will find me very obstinate!"

6. Title of a play (1598) by Ben Jonson.

He began to lament his own destiny. I grew extremely tired of saying so often the same thing;—but I could not absolutely turn him out of the house, and indeed he seemed so dejected and unhappy, that I made it my study to soften my refusal as much as I could without leaving room for future expectation.

About this time, my mother came in. We both rose.—I was horridly provoked at my situation—

"I am only come in for a letter," cried she,—"pray don't let me disturb you.—" And away she went.

This could not but be encouraging to him, for she was no sooner gone, than he began again the same story, and seemed determined not to give up his cause. He hoped, at least, that I would allow him to enquire after my health?—

"I must beg you, sir, to send me no more letters."

He seemed much hurt.

"You had better, sir, think of me no more—if you study your own happiness—"

"I *do* study my own happiness—more than I have ever had any probability of doing before—!"

"You have made an unfortunate choice, sir; but you will find it easier to forget it than you imagine. You have only to suppose I was not at Mr. Burney's on May Day—and it was a mere chance my being there—and then you will be—"

"But if I *could*—could I also forget seeing you at old Mrs. Burney's?—and if I did—can I forget that I see you now?—"

"O yes!—in 3 months time you may forget you ever knew me. You will not find it so difficult as you suppose."

"You have heard, ma'am, of an old man being growed young?—perhaps you believe *that*?—But you will not deny me leave to sometimes see you?—"

"My father, sir, is seldom,—hardly ever, indeed, at home—"

"I have never seen the doctor—but I hope he would not refuse me permission to enquire after your health? I have no wish without his consent."

"Though I acknowledge myself to be *singular* I would not have you think me either *affected* or *trifling*,—and therefore I must assure you that I am *fixed* in the answer I have given you; *unalterably* fixed."

* * *

He then took his leave:—returned back—took leave—and returned again:—I now made a more formal reverence of the head, at the same time expressing my good wishes for his welfare, in a sort of way that implied I expected never to see him again—he would fain have taken a more *tender* leave of me,—but I repulsed him with great surprise and displeasure. I did not, however, as he was so terribly sorrowful, refuse him my hand, which he had made sundry vain attempts to take in the course of our conversation; but when I withdrew it, as I did presently, I rang the bell, to prevent him again returning from the door.

Though I was really sorry for the unfortunate and misplaced attachment which this young man professes for me, yet I could almost have *jumped* for joy when he was gone, to think that the affair was thus finally over.

Indeed I think it hardly possible for a woman to be in a more irksome situation, than when rejecting a worthy man who is all humility, respect and submission, and who throws himself and his fortune at her feet.

* * *

The next day—a day the remembrance of which will be never erased from my memory—my father first spoke to me *in favor* of Mr. Barlow! and desired me not to be *peremptory* in the answer I had still to write, though it was to appear written previously.

I scarce made any answer—I was terrified to death—I felt the utter impossibility of resisting not merely my father's *persuasion*, but even his *advice*.—I felt, too, that I had no *argumentative* objections to make to Mr. Barlow, his character—disposition—situation—I knew nothing against—but O!—I felt he was no companion for my heart!—I wept like an infant when alone—eat nothing—seemed as if already married—and passed the whole day in more misery than, merely on my own account, I ever passed one before in my life,—except when a child, upon the loss of my own beloved mother—and ever revered and most dear grandmother!

After supper, I went into the study, while my dear father was alone, to wish him good night, which I did as cheerfully as I could, though pretty evidently in dreadful uneasiness. When I had got to the door, he called me back, and asked some questions concerning a new court mourning,[7] kindly saying he would assist Susette and me in our fitting-out, which he accordingly did, and affectionately embraced me, saying "I wish I could do more for thee, Fanny!" "O Sir!—" cried I—"*I* wish for nothing!—only let me live with you!—"—"My life!" cried he, kissing me kindly, "Thee shalt live with me for ever, if thee wilt! Thou canst not think I meant to get rid of thee?"

"I could not, sir! I could not!" cried I, "I could not outlive such a thought—" and, as I kissed him—O! how gratefully and thankfully! with what a relief to my heart! I saw his dear eyes full of tears! a mark of his tenderness which I shall never forget!

"God knows"—continued he—"I wish not to part with my girls!—they are my greatest comfort!—only—do not be too hasty!—"

Thus relieved, restored to future hopes, I went to bed as light, happy and thankful as if escaped from destruction.

From that day to this, my father, I thank heaven, has never again mentioned Mr. Barlow.

["DOWN WITH HER, BURNEY"]

Streatham, September 15, 1778[8]

I was then looking over the "Life of Cowley," which he[9] had himself given me to read, at the same time that he gave to Mrs. Thrale that of Waller. They are

7. A period of general mourning had been ordered after the death of George III's sister Caroline, queen of Denmark.
8. *Evelina* was published in January 1778 and enthusiastically received. After her authorship became known, Burney was invited to Streatham

Park, the country house of Henry and Hester Lynch Thrale. Samuel Johnson spent much of his time there and was then writing his *Lives of the Poets*. He and Hester Thrale became fond of Burney.
9. Johnson.

now printed, though they will not be published for some time. But he bade me put it away.

"Do," cried he, "put away that now, and prattle with us; I can't make this little Burney prattle, and I am sure she prattles well; but I shall teach her another lesson than to sit thus silent before I have done with her."

"To talk," cried I, "is the only lesson I shall be backward to learn from you, sir."

* * *

Mrs. Thrale. "To morrow, Sir, Mrs. Montagu[1] dines here! and then you will have talk enough."

Dr. Johnson began to seesaw, with a countenance strongly expressive of *inward fun*,—and, after enjoying it some time in silence, he suddenly, and with great animation, turned to me, and cried "*Down* with her, Burney!—*down* with her!—spare her not! attack her, fight her, and *down* with her at once!—*You* are a *rising* wit,—*she* is at the *top*,—and when I was beginning the world, and was nothing and nobody, the joy of my life was to fire at all the established wits!—and then, every body loved to hallow[2] me on;—but there is no game *now*, and, *now*, every body would be glad to see me *conquered*: but *then*, when I was *new*,—to vanquish the great ones was all the delight of my poor little dear soul!—So at her, Burney!—at her, and *down* with her!"

O how we were all amused! By the way, I must tell you that Mrs. Montagu is in very great estimation here, even with Dr. Johnson himself, when others do not praise her *improperly*: Mrs Thrale ranks her as the *first of women*, in the literary way.

* * *

I should have told you that Miss Gregory, daughter of the Gregory who wrote the "Letters," or, "Legacy of Advice,"[3] lives with Mrs. Montagu, and was invited to accompany her.

"Mark, now," said Dr. Johnson, "if I contradict her tomorrow. I am determined, let her say what she will, that I will not contradict her."

Mrs. T.—Why, to be sure, sir, you did put her a little out of countenance last time she came. Yet you were neither rough, nor cruel, nor ill-natured; but still, when a lady changes color, we imagine her feelings are not quite composed.

Dr. J.—Why, madam, I won't answer that I shan't contradict her again, if she provokes me as she did then; but a less provocation I will withstand. I believe I am not high in her good graces already; and I begin (added he, laughing heartily) to tremble for my admission into her new house. I doubt I shall never see the inside of it.

(Mrs. Montagu is building a most superb house.)

Mrs. T.—Oh, I warrant you, she fears you, indeed; but that, you know, is nothing uncommon; and dearly I love to hear your disquisitions; for certainly she is the first woman for literary knowledge in England, and if in England, I hope I may say in the world.

---

1. Elizabeth Montagu, known as "Queen of the Blues" (or bluestockings), a group of intellectual women, was probably the most respected literary woman in England; she had written the famous *Essay on Shakespear* (1769).
2. A cry inciting hunters to the chase.
3. John Gregory, *A Father's Legacy to His Daughters* (1774).

Dr. J.—I believe you may, madam. She diffuses more knowledge in her conversation than any woman I know, or, indeed, almost any man.

Mrs. T.—I declare I know no man equal to her, take away yourself and Burke, for that art. And you who love magnificence, won't quarrel with her, as everybody else does, for her love of finery.

Dr. J.—No, I shall not quarrel with her upon that topic. (Then, looking earnestly at me,) "Nay," he added, "it's very handsome!"

"What, sir?" cried I, amazed.

"Why, your cap:—I have looked at it some time, and I like it much. It has not that vile bandeau[4] across it, which I have so often cursed."

Did you ever hear anything so strange? nothing escapes him. My Daddy Crisp[4] is not more minute in his attentions: nay, I think he is even less so.

Mrs. T.—Well, sir, that bandeau you quarreled with was worn by every woman at court the last birthday,[5] and I observed that all the men found fault with it.

Dr. J.—The truth is, women, take them in general, have no idea of grace. Fashion is all they think of. I don't mean Mrs. Thrale and Miss Burney, when I talk of women!—they are goddesses!—and therefore I except them.

Mrs. T.—Lady Ladd never wore the bandeau, and said she never would, because it is unbecoming.

Dr. J.—(Laughing.) Did not she? then is Lady Ladd a charming woman, and I have yet hopes of entering into engagements with her!

Mrs. T.—Well, as to that I can't say; but to be sure, the only similitude I have yet discovered in you, is in size: there you agree mighty well.

Dr. J.—Why, if anybody could have worn the bandeau, it must have been Lady Ladd; for there is enough of her to carry it off; but you are too little for anything ridiculous; that which seems nothing upon a Patagonian,[6] will become very conspicuous upon a Lilliputian, and of you there is so little in all, that one single absurdity would swallow up half of you.

Some time after, when we had all been a few minutes wholly silent, he turned to me and said:

"Come, Burney, shall you and I study our parts against[7] Mrs. Montagu comes?"

"Miss Burney," cried Mr. Thrale, "you must get up your courage for this encounter! I think you should begin with Miss Gregory; and down with her first."

Dr. J.—No, no, always fly at the eagle! down with Mrs. Montagu herself! I hope she will come full of "Evelina"!

[A YOUNG AND AGREEABLE INFIDEL]

Bath, June 1780

Miss White[8] is young and pleasing in her appearance, not pretty, but agreeable in her face, and soft, gentle and well bred in her manners. Our conversation, for some time, was upon the common Bath topics,—but when Mrs.

---

4. A narrow headband.
5. June 4, the king's birthday.
6. The Indians of Patagonia, whose average height was more than six feet, were commonly thought to be giants.

7. Before.
8. Lydia Rogers White (ca. 1763–1827) would become a well-known London hostess and wit.

Lambart left us,—called to receive more company, we went, insensibly, into graver matters.

As I soon found, by the looks and expressions of this young lady, that she was of a *peculiar cast*, I left all choice of subjects to herself, determined quietly to follow as she led. And very soon, and I am sure I know not how, we had for topics the follies and vices of mankind,—and indeed she spared not for lashing them!—The *women* she rather excused than defended, laying to the door of the *men* their faults and imperfections;—but the *men*, she said, were *all* bad,—*all*, in one word, and without exception, *sensualists*.

I stared much at a severity of speech for which her softness of manner had so ill prepared me,—and she, perceiving my surprise, said "I am sure I ought to apologise for speaking *my* opinion to *you*,—*you*, who have so just and so uncommon a knowledge of human nature,—I have long wished ardently to have the honour of conversing with you,—but your party has, altogether, been regarded as so formidable, that I have not had courage to approach it."

I made, as what could I do else, disqualifying speeches, and she then led to discoursing of happiness and misery;—the *latter* she held to be the *invariable* lot of us all,—and "*one* word," she added, "we have in our language, and in all other, for which there is never any essential necessity,—and that is *pleasure*." And her eyes filled with tears as she spoke.

"How you amaze me!" cried I: "I have met with *misanthropes* before, but never with so complete a one,—and I can hardly think I hear right when I see how young you are."

She then, in rather indirect terms, gave me to understand that she was miserable *at home*,—and in *very direct* terms that she was wretched *abroad*, and openly said that to affliction she was born, and in affliction she must die, for that the world was so vilely formed as to render happiness *impossible* for its inhabitants.

There was something in this freedom of repining that I could by no means approve, and as I found by all her manner that she had a disposition to even *respect* whatever I said, why I now grew very serious, and frankly told her that I could not think it consistent with either truth or religion to cherish such notions.

"One thing," answered she, "there is which I believe *might* make me happy,—but for that I have no inclination;—it is an amorous disposition. But that I do not possess; I can make myself no happiness by intrigue."

"I hope not, indeed!" cried I, almost confounded by her extraordinary notions and speeches,—"but surely there are worthier subjects of happiness attainable."—

"No, I believe there are not,—and the reason the men are happier than us, is because they are more sensual."

"I would not *think such thoughts*," cried I, clasping my hands with an involuntary vehemence, "for worlds!"—

The Miss Caldwells then interrupted us, and seated themselves next to us,—but Miss White paid them little attention at first, and soon after none at all, but, in a low voice, continued her discourse with me; recurring to the same subject of happiness and misery, upon which, after again asserting the folly of ever hoping for the former, she made this speech—

"There may be, indeed, *one moment* of happiness,—which must be the finding one worthy of exciting a passion which one should dare own to himself! *That* would, indeed, be a moment worth living for! but that can never happen,—I am sure not to *me*,—the men are so low, so vicious,—so worthless!—no, there is not one such to be found."

*   *   *

"Well,—you are a most extraordinary character indeed! I must confess I have seen *nothing like you!*"

"I hope, however, *I* shall find something like myself,—and, like the magnet rolling in the dust, attract some metal as I go."

"That you may *attract* what you please, is of all things most likely;—but if you wait to be happy for a friend resembling *yourself*, I shall no longer wonder at your despondency."

"O!" cried she, raising her eyes in ecstasy, "*could* I find such a one!—male or female,—for sex would be indifferent to me, with such a one I would go to *live* directly."

I half laughed,—but was perplexed in my own mind whether to be *sad* or *merry* at such a speech.

"But then," she continued, "after *making*—should I *lose* such a friend—I would not survive!"

"Not survive?" repeated I; "what can you mean?"

She looked down, but said nothing.

"Surely you cannot mean," said I, *very* gravely indeed, "to put a violent end to your life?"

"I should not," said she, again looking up, "hesitate a moment."

I was quite thunderstruck,—and for some time could not say a word;—but when I *did* speak, it was in a style of exhortation so serious and earnest I am ashamed to write it to you lest you should think it too much.

She gave me an attention that was even *respectful*, but when I urged her to tell me by what *right* she thought herself entitled to *rush unlicensed on Eternity*,[9] she said—"By the right of believing I shall be *extinct*."

I really felt *horror'd*!

"Where, for heaven's sake," I cried, "where have you picked up such dreadful reasoning?"

"In *Hume*," said she;—"I have read his *Essays*[1] repeatedly."

"I am sorry to find they have power to do so much mischief; you should not have read them, at least, till a man equal to Hume in *abilities* had answered him. Have you read any more infidel writers?"

"Yes,—Bolingbroke,[2]—the divinest of all writers!"

"And do you read nothing upon the *right* side?"

"Yes,—the Bible, till I was sick to death of it, every Sunday evening to my mother."

"Have you read Beattie on the immutability of Truth?"[3]

"No."

9. Burney echoes lines from William Mason's dramatic poem *Elfrida* (1752).
1. The edition of David Hume's *Essays* published in 1777, the year after his death, included two essays previously suppressed: "Of Suicide," which argues that suicide is not a transgression, and "Of the Immortality of the Soul," which argues that immortality is unlikely and cannot be proved.
2. The philosophical *Letters, or Essays, addressed*

to Alexander Pope (1754) by Henry St. John, Viscount Bolingbroke, advocates a religion and ethics based on nature rather than on the teachings of the established church.
3. James Beattie, *An Essay on the Nature and Immutability of Truth, in Opposition to Sophistry and Scepticism* (1770), attempts to refute Hume and other "infidels."

"Give me leave, then, to recommend it to you. After Hume's *Essays*, you *ought* to read it. And even, for *lighter* reading, if you were to look at Mason's elegy on Lady Coventry,[4] it might be of no disservice to you."

* * *

This was the chief of our conversation,—which indeed made an impression upon me I shall not easily get rid of, a young and agreeable *infidel* is even a shocking sight,—and with her romantic, flighty and unguarded turn of mind, what could happen to her that could surprise?

Poor misguided girl![5]

[ENCOUNTERING THE KING]

Kew Palace, Monday February 2, 1789

What an adventure had I this morning! one that has occasioned me the severest personal terror I ever experienced in my life.

Sir Lucas Pepys still persisting that exercise and air were absolutely necessary to save me from illness, I have continued my walks, varying my gardens from Richmond to Kew, according to the accounts I received of the movements of the King. For this I had her majesty's permission, on the representation of Sir Lucas.

This morning, when I received my intelligence of the king, from Dr. John Willis,[6] I begged to know where I might walk in safety? In Kew Garden, he said, as the king would be in Richmond.

"Should any unfortunate circumstance," I cried, "at any time, occasion my being seen by his majesty, do not mention my name, but let me run off, without call or notice."

This he promised. Everybody, indeed, is ordered to keep out of sight.

Taking, therefore, the time I had most at command, I strolled into the garden; I had proceeded, in my quick way, nearly half the round, when I suddenly perceived, through some trees, two or three figures. Relying on the instructions of Dr. John, I concluded them to be workmen, and gardeners;— yet tried to look sharp,—and in so doing, as they were less shaded, I thought I saw the person of his majesty!

Alarmed past all possible expression, I waited not to know more, but turning back, ran off with all my might—But what was my terror to hear myself pursued!—to hear the voice of the king himself, loudly and hoarsely calling after me "Miss Burney! Miss Burney!—"

I protest I was ready to die;—I knew not in what state he might be at the time; I only knew the orders to keep out of his way were universal; that the queen would highly disapprove any unauthorised meeting, and that the very action of my running away might deeply, in his present irritable state, offend him.

Nevertheless, on I ran,—too terrified to stop, and in search of some short passage, for the garden is full of little labyrinths, by which I might escape.

4. Burney quotes eight lines on immortality from William Mason's elegy "On the Death of a Lady" (1760).
5. A fictional version of the "young infidel" plays a major role in Burney's last novel, *The Wanderer* (1814).

6. In 1788, two years after Burney joined the court, George III began to have fits of madness or delirium (today diagnosed as resulting from porphyria, a hereditary disease). He was kept in isolation at Kew, under the control of two physicians, Francis and John Willis.

The steps still pursued me, and still the poor hoarse and altered voice rang in my ears:—more and more footsteps resounded frightfully behind me,—the attendants all running, to catch their eager master, and the voices of the two Doctor Willises loudly exhorting him not to heat himself so unmercifully.

Heavens how I ran!—I do not think I should have felt the hot lava from Vesuvius,—at least not the hot cinders, had I so ran during its eruption. My feet were not sensible that they even touched the ground.

Soon after, I heard other voices, shriller though less nervous, call out "Stop! Stop!—Stop!—"

I could by no means consent,—I knew not what was purposed,—but I recollected fully my agreement with Dr. John that very morning, that I should decamp if surprised, and not be named.

My own fears and repugnance, also, after a flight and disobedience like this, were doubled in the thought of not escaping; I knew not to what I might be exposed, should the malady be then high, and take the turn of resentment.

Still, therefore, on I flew,—and such was my speed, so almost incredible to relate, or recollect, that I fairly believe no one of the whole party could have overtaken me, if these words, from one of the attendants, had not reached me: "Dr. Willis begs you to stop!—"

"I cannot!—I cannot!—" I answered, still flying on,—when he called out "You *must*, ma'am, it hurts the king to run.—"

Then, indeed, I stopt!—in a state of fear really amounting to agony!—I turned round,—I saw the two doctors had got the king between them, and about 8 attendants of Dr. Willis's were hovering about. They all slacked their pace, as they saw me stand still,—but such was the excess of my alarm, that I was wholly insensible to the effects of a race which, at any other time, would have required an hour's recruit.[7]

As they approached, some little presence of mind happily came to my command; it occurred to me that, to appease the wrath of my flight, I must now show some confidence; I therefore faced them as undauntedly as I was able,—only charging the nearest of the attendants to stand by my side.

When they were within a few yards of me, the king called out "Why did you run away?—"

Shocked at a question impossible to answer, yet a little assured by the mild tone of his voice, I instantly forced myself forward, to meet him—though the internal sensation which satisfied me this was a step the most proper, to appease his suspicions and displeasure, was so violently combated by the tremor of my nerves, that I fairly think I may reckon it the greatest effort of personal courage I have ever made.

The effort answered,—I looked up, and met all his wonted benignity of countenance, though something still of wildness in his eyes. Think, however, of my surprise, to feel him put both his hands round my two shoulders, and then kiss my cheek!—I wonder I did not really sink, so exquisite was my affright when I saw him spread out his arms!—Involuntarily, I concluded he meant to crush me:—but the Willises, who have never seen him till this fatal illness, not knowing how very extraordinary an action this was from him,

7. Renewal of strength.

simply smiled and looked pleased, supposing, perhaps, it was his customary salutation!

I have reason, however, to believe it was but the joy of a heart unbridled, now, by the forms and proprieties of established custom, and sober reason. He looked almost in *rapture* at the meeting, from the moment I advanced; and to see any of his household thus by accident, seemed such a near approach to liberty and recovery, that who can wonder it should serve rather to elate[8] than lessen what yet remains of his disorder?—

He now spoke in such terms of his pleasure in seeing me, that I soon lost the whole of my terror, though it had threatened to almost lose *me*: astonishment to find him so nearly *well*, and gratification to see him so pleased, removed every uneasy feeling, and the joy that succeeded, in my conviction of his recovery, made me ready to throw myself at his feet to express it.

What a conversation followed!—when he saw me fearless, he grew more and more alive, and made me walk close by his side, away from the attendants, and even the Willises themselves, who, to indulge him, retreated. I own myself not completely *composed*, but *alarm* I could entertain no more.—

Everything that came uppermost in his mind he mentioned; he seemed to have just such remains of his flightiness, as heated his imagination, without deranging his reason, and robbed him of all control over his speech, though nearly in his perfect state of mind as to his opinions.

What did he not say!—He opened his whole heart to me,—expounded all his sentiments, and acquainted me with all his intentions.

* * *

He next talked to me a great deal of my dear father, and made a thousand inquiries concerning his history of music. This brought him to his favorite theme, Handel;[9] and he told me innumerable anecdotes of him, and particularly that celebrated tale of Handel's saying of himself, when a boy, "While that boy lives, my music will never want a protector—" And this, he said, I might relate to my father.

Then he ran over most of his oratorios, attempting to sing the subjects of several airs and choruses, but so dreadfully hoarse, that the sound was terrible.

Dr. Willis, quite alarmed at this exertion, feared he would do himself harm, and again proposed a separation. "No! no! no!" he exclaimed, "not yet,—I have something I must just mention first."

Dr. Willis, delighted to comply, even when uneasy at compliance, again gave way.

The good king then greatly affected me,—he began upon my revered old friend, Mrs. Delany![1]—and he spoke of her with such warmth, such kindness:—"She was my *friend*!" he cried, "and I *loved* her as a friend!—I have made a memorandum when I lost her!—I will show it you—"

He pulled out a pocketbook, and rummaged some time, but to no purpose—

8. Heighten.
9. From childhood, George III had been a devotee of George Frideric Handel (1685–1759), the great German-English composer. George III, who loved German music, took a keen interest in Charles Burney's pioneering work, *A General History of Music*; the third and fourth volumes were just about to be published.
1. Mary Delany, a figure at court and accomplished artist of works in cut paper, was regarded by Burney as "the pattern of a perfect fine lady," and had died the previous year.

The tears stood in his eyes,—he wiped them,—and Dr. Willis again became very anxious,—"Come, sir," he cried, "now do you come in, and let the lady go on her walk,—come, now you have talked a long while,—so will go in,—if your majesty pleases."

"No!—no!—" he cried, "I want to ask her a few questions,—I have lived so long out of the world, I know nothing!—"

This touched me to the heart.

* * *

What a scene! how variously was I affected by it!—but, upon the whole, how inexpressibly thankful to see him so nearly himself! so little removed from recovery.

[A MASTECTOMY]

Paris, March 22, 1812[2]

Separated as I have now so long—long been from my dearest father—brothers—sisters—nieces, and native friends, I would spare, at least, their kind hearts any grief for me but what they must inevitably feel in reflecting upon the sorrow of such an absence to one so tenderly attached to all her first and forever so dear and regretted ties—nevertheless, if they should hear that I have been dangerously ill from any hand but my own, they might have doubts of my perfect recovery which my own alone can obviate. And how can I hope they will escape hearing what has reached Seville to the south, and Constantinople to the east? from both I have had messages—yet nothing could urge me to this communication till I heard that M. de Boinville[3] had written it to his wife, without any precaution, because in ignorance of my plan of silence. Still I must hope it may never travel to my dearest father—But to you, my beloved Esther, who, living more in the world, will surely hear it ere long, to you I will write the whole history, certain that, from the moment you know any evil has befallen me your kind kind heart will be constantly anxious to learn its extent and its circumstances, as well as its termination.

About August, in the year 1810, I began to be annoyed by a small pain in my breast, which went on augmenting from week to week, yet, being rather heavy than acute, without causing me any uneasiness with respect to consequences: Alas, "what was the ignorance?" The most sympathizing of partners, however, was more disturbed: not a start, not a wry face, not a movement that indicated pain was unobserved, and he early conceived apprehensions to which I was a stranger. He pressed me to see some surgeon; I revolted from the idea, and hoped, by care and warmth, to make all succor unnecessary. Thus passed some months, during which Madame de Maisonneuve, my particularly intimate friend, joined with M. d'Arblay to press me to consent to an examination. I thought their fears groundless, and could not make so great a conquest over my repugnance. I relate this false confidence, now, as a warning to my dear Esther—my sisters and nieces,

---

2. Burney (now Madame D'Arblay) sent this letter to Esther Burney, her sister; it describes an operation performed the previous September.

3. Because Chastel de Boinville's wife was English, it was likely that news of the illness would spread to the Burney family in England.

should any similar sensations excite similar alarm. M. d'Arblay now revealed his uneasiness to another of our kind friends, Mme. de Tracy, who wrote to me a long and eloquent letter upon the subject, that began to awaken very unpleasant surmises; and a conference with her ensued, in which her urgency and representations, aided by her long experience of disease, and most miserable existence by art, subdued me, and, most painfully and reluctantly, I ceased to object, and M. d'Arblay summoned a physician—M. Bourdois? Maria will cry;—No, my dear Maria, I would not give your beau frere[4] that trouble; not him, but Dr. Jouart, the physician of Miss Potts. Thinking but slightly of my statement, he gave me some directions that produced no fruit—on the contrary, I grew worse, and M. d'Arblay now would take no denial to my consulting M. Dubois, who had already attended and cured me in an abscess of which Maria, my dearest Esther, can give you the history. M. Dubois, the most celebrated surgeon of France, was then appointed accoucheur to the empress, and already lodged in the Tuilleries,[5] and in constant attendance: but nothing could slacken the ardour of M. d'Arblay to obtain the first advice. Fortunately for his kind wishes, M. Dubois had retained a partial regard for me from the time of his former attendance, and, when applied to through a third person, he took the first moment of liberty, granted by a *promenade* taken by the empress, to come to me. It was now I began to perceive my real danger, M. Dubois gave me a prescription to be pursued for a month, during which time he could not undertake to see me again, and pronounced nothing—but uttered so many charges to me to be tranquil, and to suffer no uneasiness, that I could not but suspect there was room for terrible inquietude. My alarm was increased by the nonappearance of M. d'Arblay after his departure. They had remained together some time in the book room, and M. d'Arblay did not return—till, unable to bear the suspense, I begged him to come back. He, also, sought then to tranquilize me— but in words only; his looks were shocking! his features, his whole face displayed the bitterest woe. I had not, therefore, much difficulty in telling myself what he endeavored not to tell me—that a small operation would be necessary to avert evil consequences!—Ah, my dearest Esther, for this I felt no courage—my dread and repugnance, from a thousand reasons *besides* the pain, almost shook all my faculties, and, for some time, I was rather confounded and stupified than affrighted.—Direful, however, was the effect of this interview; the pains became quicker and more violent, and the hardness of the spot affected increased. I took, but vainly, my proscription, and every symptom grew more serious.

* * *

A physician was now called in, Dr. Moreau, to hear if he could suggest any new means: but Dr. Larrey[6] had left him no resources untried. A formal consultation now was held, of Larrey, Ribe, and Moreau—and, in fine, I was formally condemned to an operation by all three. I was as much astonished as

---

4. Brother-in-law. Maria (or Marianne), Esther Burney's daughter, had married Antoine Bourdois, whose brother was a prominent French physician.
5. The royal palace in Paris. "Accoucheur":

obstetrician.
6. Dominique-Jean Larrey, "Napoleon's surgeon," is remembered for his courage on the battlefield and his innovative procedures.

disappointed—for the poor breast was no where discoloured, and not much larger than its healthy neighbor. Yet I felt the evil to be deep, so deep, that I often thought if it could not be dissolved, it could only with life be extirpated. I called up, however, all the reason I possessed, or could assume, and told them that—if they saw no other alternative, I would not resist their opinion and experience:—the good Dr. Larrey, who, during his long attendance had conceived for me the warmest friendship, had now tears in his eyes; from my dread he had expected resistance.

* * *

All hope of escaping this evil now at an end, I could only console or employ my mind in considering how to render it less dreadful to M. d'Arblay. M. Dubois had pronounced "il faut s'attendre à souffrir, Je ne veux pas vous tromper—Vous souffrirez—vous souffrirez *beaucoup*!—"[7] M. Ribe had *charged* me to cry! to withhold or restrain myself might have seriously bad consequences, he said. M. Moreau, in echoing this injunction, inquired whether I had cried or screamed at the birth of Alexander—Alas, I told him, it had not been possible to do otherwise; Oh then, he answered, there is no fear!—What terrible inferences were here to be drawn! I desired, therefore, that M. d'Arblay might be kept in ignorance of the day till the operation should be over. To this they agreed, except M. Larrey, with high approbation: M. Larrey looked dissentient, but was silent. M. Dubois protested he would not undertake to act, after what he had seen of the agitated spirits of M. d'Arblay if he were present: nor would he suffer me to know the time myself over night; I obtained with difficulty a promise of 4 hours warning, which were essential to me for sundry regulations.

From this time, I assumed the best spirits in my power, *to meet the coming blow*;—and support my too sympathizing partner.

* * *

Sundry necessary works and orders filled up my time entirely till one o'clock, when all was ready—but Dr. Moreau then arrived, with news that M. Dubois could not attend till three. Dr. Aumont went away—and the coast was clear. This, indeed, was a dreadful interval. I had no longer any thing to do—I had only to think—two hours thus spent seemed never-ending. I would fain have written to my dearest father—to you, my Esther—to Charlotte James— Charles—Amelia Lock—but my arm prohibited me: I strolled to the salon—I saw it fitted with preparations, and I recoiled—But I soon returned; to what effect disguise from myself what I must so soon know?—yet the sight of the immense quantity of bandages, compresses, spunges, lint—made me a little sick:—I walked backwards and forwards till I quieted all emotion, and became by degrees, nearly stupid—torpid, without sentiment or consciousness;—and thus I remained till the clock struck three. A sudden spirit of exertion then returned,—I defied my poor arm, no longer worth sparing, and took my long banished pen to write a few words to M. d'Arblay— and a few more for Alex, in case of a fatal result. These short billets I could

---

7. You must expect to suffer. I do not want to deceive you—you will suffer—you will suffer *greatly* (French). Operations were then performed without anesthestics.

only deposit safely, when the cabriolets[8]—one—two—three—four—succeeded rapidly to each other in stopping at the door. Dr. Moreau instantly entered my room, to see if I were alive. He gave me a wine cordial, and went to the salon. I rang for my maid and nurses,—but before I could speak to them, my room, without previous message, was entered by 7 men in black, Dr. Larrey, M. Dubois, Dr. Moreau, Dr. Aumont, Dr. Ribe, and a pupil of Dr. Larrey, and another of M. Dubois. I was now awakened from my stupor—and by a sort of indignation—Why so many? and without leave?—But I could not utter a syllable. M. Dubois acted as commander in chief. Dr. Larrey kept out of sight; M. Dubois ordered a bedstead into the middle of the room. Astonished, I turned to Dr. Larrey, who had promised that an arm chair would suffice; but he hung his head, and would not look at me. Two *old mattresses* M. Dubois then demanded, and an old sheet. I now began to tremble violently, more with distaste and horror of the preparations even than of the pain. These arranged to his liking, he desired me to mount the bedstead. I stood suspended, for a moment, whether I should not abruptly escape—I looked at the door, the windows—I felt desperate—but it was only for a moment, my reason then took the command, and my fears and feelings struggled vainly against it. I called to my maid—she was crying, and the two nurses stood, transfixed, at the door. "Let those women all go!" cried M. Dubois. This order recovered me my voice—"No," I cried, "let them stay! *qu'elles restent!*" This occasioned a little dispute, that re-animated me—The maid, however, and one of the nurses ran off—I charged the other to approach, and she obeyed. M. Dubois now tried to issue his commands *en militaire,*[9] but I resisted all that were resistable—I was compelled, however, to submit to taking off my long robe de chambre,[1] which I had meant to retain—Ah, then, how did I think of my sisters!—not one, at so dreadful an instant, at hand, to protect—adjust—guard me—I regretted that I had refused Mme de Maisonneuve—Mme Chastel—no one upon whom I could rely—my departed angel![2]—how did I think of her!—how did I long—long for my Esther—my Charlotte!—My distress was, I suppose, apparent, though not my wishes, for M. Dubois himself now softened, and spoke soothingly. "Can *you,*" I cried, "feel for an operation that, to *you,* must seem so trivial?"—"Trivial?" he repeated—taking up a bit of paper, which he tore, unconsciously, into a million pieces, "*oui—c'est peu de chose—mais—*"[3] he stammered, and could not go on. No one else attempted to speak, but I was softened myself, when I saw even M. Dubois grow agitated, while Dr. Larrey kept always aloof, yet a glance showed me he was pale as ashes. I knew not, positively, then, the immediate danger, but every thing convinced me danger was hovering about me, and that this experiment could alone save me from its jaws. I mounted, therefore, unbidden, the bedstead—and M. Dubois placed me upon the mattress, and spread a cambric handkerchief upon my face. It was transparent, however, and I saw, through it, that the bedstead was instantly surrounded by the 7 men and my nurse. I refused to be held; but when, bright through the cambric, I saw the glitter of polished steel—I closed my eyes. I would not trust to convulsive fear the sight of the terrible incision. A silence the most profound ensued,

8. Carriages.
9. In military fashion (French). Most of the attending physicians had been army surgeons.
1. Dressing gown.

2. Susanna, Burney's favorite sister, had died in 1800.
3. Yes—it is not much—but— (French).

which lasted for some minutes, during which, I imagine, they took their orders by signs, and made their examination—Oh what a horrible suspension!—I did not breathe—and M. Dubois tried vainly to find any pulse. This pause, at length, was broken by Dr. Larrey, who in a voice of solemn melancholy, said "Qui me tiendra ce sein?—"[4]

No one answered; at least not verbally; but this aroused me from my passively submissive state, for I feared they imagined the whole breast infected— feared it too justly,—for, again through the cambric, I saw the hand of M. Dubois held up, while his forefinger first described a straight line from top to bottom of the breast, secondly a cross, and thirdly a circle; intimating that the whole was to be taken off. Excited by this idea, I started up, threw off my veil, and, in answer to the demand "Qui me tiendra ce sein?" cried "C'est moi, Monsieur!"[5] and I held my hand under it, and explained the nature of my sufferings, which all sprang from one point, though they darted into every part. I was heard attentively, but in utter silence, and M. Dubois then, re-placed me as before, and, as before, spread my veil over my face. How vain, alas, my representation! immediately again I saw the fatal finger describe the cross— and the circle—Hopeless, then, desperate, and self-given up, I closed once more my eyes, relinquishing all watching, all resistance, all interference, and sadly resolute to be wholly resigned.

My dearest Esther,—and all my dears to whom she communicates this doleful ditty, will rejoice to hear that this resolution once taken, was firmly adhered to, in defiance of a terror that surpasses all description, and the most torturing pain. Yet—when the dreadful steel was plunged into the breast— cutting through veins—arteries—flesh—nerves—I needed no injunctions not to restrain my cries. I began a scream that lasted unintermittingly during the whole time of the incision—and I almost marvel that it rings not in my ears still! so excruciating was the agony. When the wound was made, and the instrument was withdrawn, the pain seemed undiminished, for the air that suddenly rushed into those delicate parts felt like a mass of minute but sharp and forked poniards,[6] that were tearing the edges of the wound—but when again I felt the instrument—describing a curve—cutting against the grain, if I may so say, while the flesh resisted in a manner so forcible as to oppose and tire the hand of the operator, who was forced to change from the right to the left—then, indeed, I thought I must have expired. I attempted no more to open my eyes,—they felt as if hermetically shut, and so firmly closed, that the eyelids seemed indented into the cheeks. The instrument this second time withdrawn, I concluded the operation over,—Oh no! presently the terrible cutting was renewed—and worse than ever, to separate the bottom, the foundation of this dreadful gland from the parts to which it adhered—Again all description would be baffled—yet again all was not over,—Dr. Larrey rested but his own hand, and—Oh heaven!—I then felt the knife rackling[7] against the breast bone—scraping it!—This performed, while I yet remained in utterly speechless torture, I heard the voice of Mr. Larrey,—(all others guarded a dead silence) in a tone nearly tragic, desire every one present to pronounce if anything more remained to be done; or if he thought the operation complete. The general voice was yes,—but the finger of Mr. Dubois—

---

4. Who will hold this breast for me? (French).
5. *I* will (French).
6. Daggers.
7. Raking (?).

which I literally *felt* elevated over the wound, though I saw nothing, and though he touched nothing, so indescribably sensitive was the spot—pointed to some further requisition[8]—and again began the scraping!—and, after this, Dr. Moreau thought he discerned a peccant atom—and still, and still, M. Dubois demanded atom after atom—My dearest Esther, not for days, not for weeks, but for months I could not speak of this terrible business without nearly again going through it! I could not *think* of it with impunity! I was sick, I was disordered by a single question—even now, 9 months after it is over, I have a head ache from going on with the account! and this miserable account, which I began 3 months ago, at least, I dare not revise, nor read, the recollection is still so painful.

To conclude, the evil was so profound, the case so delicate, and the precautions necessary for preventing a return so numerous, that the operation, including the treatment and the dressing, lasted 20 minutes! a time, for sufferings so acute, that was hardly supportable—However, I bore it with all the courage I could exert, and never moved, nor stopped them, nor resisted, nor remonstrated, nor spoke—except once or twice, during the dressings, to say "Ah Messieurs! que je vous plains!—"[9] for indeed I was sensible to the feeling concern with which they all saw what I endured, though my speech was principally—*very* principally meant for Dr. Larrey. Except this, I uttered not a syllable, save, when so often they re-commenced, calling out "Avertissez moi, Messieurs! avertissez moi!—"[1] Twice, I believe, I fainted; at least, I have two total chasms in my memory of this transaction, that impede my tying together what passed. When all was done, and they lifted me up that I might be put to bed, my strength was so totally annihilated, that I was obliged to be carried, and could not even sustain my hands and arms, which hung as if I had been lifeless; while my face, as the nurse has told me, was utterly colorless. This removal made me open my eyes—and I then saw my good Dr. Larrey, pale nearly as myself, his face streaked with blood, and its expression depicting grief, apprehension, and almost horror.

When I was in bed,—my poor M. d'Arblay—who ought to write you himself his own history of this morning—was called to me—and afterwards our Alex.—

[M. D'ARBLAY'S POSTSCRIPT]

No! No my dearest and ever more dear friends, I shall not make a *fruitless* attempt. No language could convey what I felt in the deadly course of these seven hours. Nevertheless, every one *of you, my dearest dearest friends*, can guess, must even know it. Alexandre had no less feeling, but showed more fortitude. He, perhaps, will be more able to describe to you, nearly at least, the torturing state of my poor heart and soul. Besides, I must own, to you, that these details which were, till just now, quite unknown to me, have almost killed me, and I am only able to thank God that this more than half angel has had the sublime courage to deny herself the comfort I might have offered her, to spare me, not the sharing of her excruciating pains, that was impossible, but the witnessing so terrific a scene, and perhaps the remorse to

---

8. Necessity. Surgical practice of the time dictated that "the whole diseased structure" be cut out, no matter how long or painful the operation.

9. How I pity you! (French).
1. Give me warning! (French).

have rendered it more tragic. For I don't flatter myself I could have got through it—I must confess it.

Thank heaven! She is now surprisingly well, and in good spirits, and we hope to have many many still happy days. May that of peace soon arrive, and enable me to embrace better than with my pen my beloved and ever ever more dear friends of the town and country. Amen. Amen![2]

2. The wound healed without infection. Burney returned to England later in 1812 and lived for twenty-eight more years.

Liberty

No idea resonated more strongly in the minds of Britons in the eighteenth century than liberty. Writers explained its political significance in many, at times contradictory ways. It was seen by some as the natural right of every human being, and by others as a uniquely British birthright. Its origins were hotly debated: as their model of liberty, some took the ancient Roman Republic, others the ancient, "Gothic" constitution of pre-Norman England. To other minds, it was a distinctly modern product: either of the volatile, bloody period of the English civil wars and Commonwealth (when Milton's defense of liberty, "Areopagitica," appeared), or of the remarkably bloodless Glorious Revolution of 1688, which established the stability some felt was needed for true liberty to be enjoyed. Some thought liberty could prosper only in a society where power lay in the hands of independent landowners, while others felt it thrived best on the fluidity of commerce, markets, and credit. In different contexts throughout the eighteenth century, ideologues across the political spectrum, both Tories and Whigs, appealed to some understanding of British liberty as a fundamental, guiding principle.

But the concept of liberty applied far beyond the spheres of economics and politics. It became the basis for a new social ethos: as the influential philosopher Anthony Ashley Cooper, third earl of Shaftesbury (1671–1713), remarked, "all politeness is owing to liberty." And English literature itself derived its character from the elaboration of the concept. Most practically, the eighteenth century witnessed a growing respect for the freedom of the press and the end of prepublication censorship. As an abstract idea and a piece of political ideology, liberty also absorbed the attention of leading writers: Henry Fielding, William Collins, James Thomson, and Joseph Warton, among many others, wrote idealistic (and in Thomson's case, rather long) poems addressed to it in the 1730s and 1740s. Perhaps most profoundly, a reverence for liberty granted an imaginative, intellectual, and sentimental expansiveness to English literature: frequently contrasted with the French neoclassicists' supposedly slavish regard for the rules of good writing (which was thought to be of a piece with France's royal absolutism), the English love of liberty fostered literary naturalness, truth, and originality. In "The Preface to Shakespeare," Samuel Johnson defends Shakespeare's disregard of the unities of time and place in these terms, declaring that such violations of the rules suit "the comprehensive genius of Shakespeare."

It is, therefore, the most considerable of historical ironies that liberty-loving eighteenth-century Britain engaged as extensively as it did in the slave trade. In the early 1660s, when the events in Behn's *Oroonoko* are supposed to have taken place, this engagement was gathering momentum. Later, in 1713, the Treaty of Utrecht secured Great Britain the contract (*asiento*) to monopolize the export of slaves to Spain's American colonies. Bristol and then Liverpool developed into prosperous slave ports, trading manufactured goods to Africa for human cargo, which crossed the Atlantic on ships that returned to England with sugar and money. By the 1780s, when Britain shipped a third of a million slaves to the New World, the national economy depended on this so-called Triangle Trade. Though slavery was not new to Africa, the Middle Passage—the deadly voyage across the Atlantic—made the suffering and degradation it inflicted newly terrible, brutal, and global. The former slave Olaudah Equiano describes the experience of such a crossing in his autobiography.

The stark contradiction of Britons' love of liberty and their profit from slavery is reflected in English political philosophy and law. John Locke's chapter "Of Slavery" from the *Second Treatise of Civil Government* sets forth the idea that "the natural

William Blake, *Europe Supported by Africa & America,* 1796. Blake follows the allegorical tradition of representing the continents as beautiful women. The armbands on Africa and America signify their enslavement, but their strength supports Europe, and unlike hers, their eyes meet the viewer's. From John Stedman, *Narrative of a Five Years Expedition Against the Revolted Negroes of Surinam . . . from the Year 1772, to 1777* (1796).

liberty of man is to be free from any superior power on earth," but Locke also invested in the slave trade and upheld the notion that slavery was necessary in various writings. And though William Blackstone wrote in his commentaries on English law that "a slave or negro, the moment he lands in England, falls under the protection of the laws," and thus becomes a freeman, he later added another clause: "though the master's right to his service may probably still continue" (1769).

Yet the eighteenth-century language of liberty was not merely hypocritical. It provided terms in which a range of injustices, inequalities, and abridgements of rights could be attacked and thus became a language of world-transforming, even revolutionary importance. It helped stimulate the growth of feminism, as Mary Astell ironically explores its applicability to women, Mary Wortley Montagu laments the "eternal chains" of oppressive matrimony in "Epistle from Mrs. Yonge to Her Husband" (1724), and Mary Wollstonecraft later affirms that both genders deserve "to breathe the sharp invigorating air of freedom" in *A Vindication of the Rights of Woman* (1792). It also inspired the British abolitionist movement, which gained particular fervor in the 1780s; a bill abolishing the slave trade finally became law in Britain in 1807. That did not put an end, of course, to illegal trade, let alone to already existing slavery itself. The conflict between boasts of liberty and the enslavement of human beings then passed from Britain to America, where its consequences would be written in blood.

JOHN LOCKE

At Stowe in Buckinghamshire, the greatest of eighteenth-century English landscape gardens, a bust of John Locke appears in a temple with busts of Pope, Newton, Milton, Shakespeare, Queen Elizabeth I, and other "British Worthies." The inscription under his name says that he, "best of all philosophers, understood the powers of the human mind, the nature, end, and bounds of civil government; and with equal sagacity refuted the slavish system of usurped authority over the rights, the consciences, or the reason of mankind." Locke's reputation as the philosopher of political liberty in the eighteenth century was not always this easy to read, nor was it as pervasive as his influence as a philosopher of "the powers of the human mind" (see the selection from the *Essay Concerning Human Understanding*, p. 2280, for his program for the liberation of mankind's reason). Other Whig writers from Locke's era arguably influenced the developing discourse of liberty as much as or more than his *Two Treatises of Government* did (published 1690). Indeed, it is not clear the radicalism of the *Treatises* was always appreciated. Scholars have found they were mostly composed during the years 1679–81, before the Glorious Revolution (1688), not after it: the works represent not an after-the-fact justification of deposing a tyrannical king, James II, but rather a more dangerous meditation on the people's right to depose tyrants during the turbulent years of Charles II's reign. In any case, the inscription at Stowe, executed half a century later in the 1730s to buoy the Whig and Tory opposition to Robert Walpole's putatively corrupt, tyrannical Whig administration, attests to Locke's continuing relevance to defenders of liberty as eighteenth-century politics evolved. A classic articulation of the rights and freedoms of the individual, Locke's second *Treatise* has come to occupy a preeminent place in political theory.

The degree of Locke's own opposition to slavish systems was far from unambiguous, however. Though he maintains that all men are born free, he himself invested in the Royal Africa Company (formed 1672) and a group of "Bahamas Adventurers": both enterprises were predicated on slavery. Scholars have also argued that he helped draft "The Fundamental Constitutions of Carolina" (1669), with his employer Lord Ashley, which granted each freeman "absolute power and authority over his negro slaves." (Ashley would become the first Earl of Shaftesbury, himself the great Whig paragon of liberty.) The selection included here from the second *Treatise* indicates both Locke's detestation of the condition of slavery and his allowance for its justification: if he can somehow consider slaveholders the "lawful conquerors" of their slaves, who themselves may have committed some base act or other, Locke may defend the slave-owning and slave-trading societies he wished to legitimize. Over Britons, however, he believed that civil government should never be tyrannical, because of their natural rights to liberty and property. Locke's first *Treatise* (not printed here) attacked the writings of Sir Robert Filmer, who insisted that kings hold a patriarchal authority over their subjects ultimately derived from God's authority over all mankind. The second *Treatise* describes the origins and ends of legitimate political society, from the state of nature, in which mankind discovers the natural rights to liberty and property, to the institution of civil government, designed solely to protect these rights and allow them best to flourish.

From Two Treatises of Government

An Essay Concerning the True Original, Extent, and End of Civil Government

CHAPTER IV. OF SLAVERY

22. The natural liberty of man is to be free from any superior power on earth, and not to be under the will or legislative authority of man, but to have only the law of nature for his rule. The liberty of man in society is to be under no other legislative power, but that established, by consent, in the commonwealth; nor under the dominion of any will, or restraint of any law, but what that legislative shall enact, according to the trust put in it. Freedom then is not what *Sir R. F.* tells us, *O.A.* 55, "A liberty for every one to do what he lists, to live as he pleases, and not to be tied by any laws":[1] but freedom of men under government is to have a standing rule to live by, common to every one of that society, and made by the legislative power erected in it, a liberty to follow my own will in all things, where the rule prescribes not, [and] not to be subject to the inconstant, uncertain, unknown, arbitrary will of another man; as freedom of nature is to be under no other restraint but the law of nature.

23. This freedom from absolute, arbitrary power is so necessary to and closely joined with a man's preservation that he cannot part with it but by what forfeits his preservation and life together. For a man, not having the power of his own life,[2] cannot by compact or his own consent enslave himself to any one, nor put himself under the absolute, arbitrary power of another, to take away his life, when he pleases. Nobody can give more power than he has himself; and he that cannot take away his own life cannot give another power over it. Indeed having, by his fault, forfeited his own life by some act that deserves death; he to whom he has forfeited it may (when he has him in his power) delay to take it, and make use of him to his own service, and he does him no injury by it. For whenever he finds the hardship of his slavery outweigh the value of his life, 'tis in his power by resisting the will of his master to draw on himself the death he desires.

24. This is the perfect condition of slavery, which is nothing else but the state of war continued between a lawful conqueror and a captive. For if once compact enter between them[3] and make an agreement for a limited power on the one side, and obedience on the other, the state of war and slavery ceases, as long as the compact endures. For as has been said, no man can by agreement pass over to another that which he hath not in himself, a power over his own life.

I confess we find among the Jews as well as other nations that men did sell themselves; but, 'tis plain this was only to drudgery, not to slavery. For it is evident the person sold was not under an absolute, arbitrary, despotical power. For the master could not have power to kill him at any time whom at

---

1. Sir Robert Filmer (1588–1653), a defender of royal prerogative and the divine right of kings, is Locke's chief opponent in the first *Treatise*. Locke here refers to page 55 of the 1679 republication of Filmer's *Observations upon Aristotle's Politics* (originally published 1652).

2. In chapter 2, section 6 of the second *Treatise*,

Locke explained that the law of nature, which is essentially the will of God as our reason reveals it to us, dictates that human beings may not commit suicide.

3. That is, once their relationship attains the status of a legal agreement or contract.

a certain time he was obliged to let go free out of his service: and the master of such a servant was so far from having an arbitrary power over his life, that he could not, at pleasure, so much as maim him, but the loss of an eye, or tooth, set him free, *Exod*. XXI.

CHAPTER IX. OF THE ENDS OF POLITICAL SOCIETY AND GOVERNMENT

123. If man in the state of nature be so free, as has been said; if he be absolute lord of his own person[4] and possessions, equal to the greatest and subject to nobody, why will he part with his freedom? Why will he give up this empire, and subject himself to the dominion and control of any other power? To which 'tis obvious to answer that though in the state of nature he hath such a right, yet the enjoyment of it is very uncertain and constantly exposed to the invasion of others; for all being kings as much as he, every man his equal, and the greater part no strict observers of equity and justice, the enjoyment of the property he has in this state is very unsafe, very insecure. This makes him willing to quit this condition, which however free is full of fears and continual dangers: and 'tis not without reason that he seeks out and is willing to join in society with others who are already united or have a mind to unite for the mutual preservation of their lives, liberties, and estates, which I call by the general name, property.

124. The great and chief end therefore of men's uniting into commonwealths and putting themselves under government is the preservation of their property. To which in the state of nature there are many things wanting.

First, there wants an established, settled, known law, received and allowed by common consent to be the standard of right and wrong, and the common measure to decide all controversies between them. For though the law of nature be plain and intelligible to all rational creatures; yet men being biased by their interest, as well as ignorant for want of study of it, are not apt to allow of it as a law binding to them in the application of it to their particular cases.

125. Secondly, in the state of nature there wants a known and indifferent[5] judge, with authority to determine all differences according to the established law. For everyone in that state being both judge and executioner of the law of nature, men being partial to themselves, passion and revenge is very apt to carry them too far, and with too much heat in their own cases, as well as negligence and unconcernedness make them too remiss in other men's.

126. Thirdly, in the state of nature there often wants power to back and support the sentence when right, and to give it due execution. They who by any injustice offended will seldom fail where they are able by force to make good their injustice; such resistance many times makes the punishment dangerous and frequently destructive to those who attempt it.

127. Thus mankind, notwithstanding all the privileges of the state of nature, being but in an ill condition while they remain in it, are quickly driven into society. Hence it comes to pass that we seldom find any number

---

4. Body, physical being. Locke earlier defines "the state of nature," the "state all men are naturally in," as "a state of perfect freedom to order their actions and dispose of their possessions and persons as they think fit, within the bounds of the law of nature, without asking leave or depending upon the will of any other man" (chapter 2, section 4).

5. Impartial.

of men live any time together in this state. The inconveniencies that they are therein exposed to by the irregular and uncertain exercise of the power every man has of punishing the transgressions of others make them take sanctuary under the established laws of government, and therein seek the preservation of their property. 'Tis this makes them so willingly give up every one his single power of punishing to be exercised by such alone as shall be appointed to it amongst them; and by such rules as the community, or those authorized by them to that purpose, shall agree on. And in this we have the original right and rise of both the legislative and executive power,[6] as well as of the governments and societies themselves.

128. For in the state of nature, to omit the liberty he has of innocent delights, a man has two powers. The first is to do whatsoever he thinks fit for the preservation of himself and others within the permission of the law of nature; by which law common to them all, he and all the rest of mankind are one community, make up one society distinct from all other creatures, and were it not for the corruption and viciousness of degenerate men, there would be no need of any other, no necessity that men should separate from this great and natural community and associate into lesser combinations. The other power a man has in the state of nature is the power to punish the crimes committed against that law. Both these he gives up when he joins in a private, if I may so call it, or particular political society, and incorporates into any commonwealth[7] separate from the rest of mankind.

129. The first power, *viz.* of doing whatsoever he thought fit for the preservation of himself and the rest of mankind, he gives up to be regulated by laws made by the society, so far forth as the preservation of himself and the rest of that society shall require; which laws of the society in many things confine the liberty he had by the law of nature.

130. Secondly, the power of punishing he wholly gives up, and engages his natural force, which he might before employ in the execution of the law of nature, by his own single authority, as he thought fit, to assist the executive power of the society, as the law thereof shall require. For being now in a new state wherein he is to enjoy many conveniences from the labor, assistance, and society of others in the same community, as well as protection from its whole strength; he is to part also with as much of his natural liberty in providing for himself, as the good, prosperity, and safety of the society shall require; which is not only necessary but just, since the other members of the society do the like.

131. But though men when they enter into society give up the equality, liberty, and executive power they had in the state of nature into the hands of the society, to be so far disposed of by the legislative as the good of the society shall require; yet it being only with an intention in everyone, the better to preserve himself, his liberty, and property, (for no rational creature can be supposed to change his condition with an intention to be worse), the power of the society, or legislative constituted by them, can never be supposed to extend farther than the common good; but is obliged to secure everyone's property by providing against those three defects above-mentioned, that made the state of nature so unsafe and uneasy. And so whoever has the

6. A branch of government charged with executing the laws of a state.

7. A political unit formed for the common good of its members.

legislative or supreme power of any commonwealth is bound to govern by established standing laws, promulgated and known to the people, and not by extemporary decrees; by indifferent and upright judges, who are to decide controversies by those laws; and to employ the force of the community at home, only in the execution of such laws, or abroad to prevent or redress foreign injuries, and secure the community from inroads and invasion. And all this to be directed to no other end, but the peace, safety, and public good of the people.

1690

MARY ASTELL

Mary Astell challenged many orthodoxies, including the ideas that women should not be educated, that they are intellectually inferior to men, and that they ought to marry at practically any cost (see *Some Reflections upon Marriage*, p. 2421). Yet she was also a vigorous Tory controversialist who defended the doctrine of the divine right of kings, argued that English subjects owe (at least) "passive obedience" to their monarchs, and denounced toleration of Dissenters. Astell devoted much of her writing to political controversy: she published three substantial political pamphlets in 1704 alone. Her four-hundred-page magnum opus, *The Christian Religion as Profess'd by a Daughter of the Church of England* (1705), explicitly attacks Locke's *Two Treatises of Government;* at various places in her work, she criticizes his theological essay *The Reasonableness of Christianity* (1695); and she even mocks what she sees as the political tendency of his epistemology in his *Essay Concerning Human Understanding* (1689). Her Tory convictions also color her discussions of gender relations. In *Some Reflections upon Marriage*, she consistently draws parallels between a wife's duty of obedience to her husband and the obedience that subjects owe their sovereigns: a woman who marries "elects a monarch for life" and "gives him an authority she cannot recall however he misapply it." She devoutly held her belief in obedience, authority, and hierarchy—it was far more than a mere concession to the status quo—and this stance set her against the Whig theorists who supported the rights of subjects to disobey unjust power.

Yet Astell's involvement in contemporary political debate made certain ironies irresistible to her. Her most famous work, the "Preface, in Answer to Some Objections" added to the third edition of *Reflections upon Marriage* (1706; the word *some* was dropped from the title) is filled with the language of freedom, tyranny, rights, and slavery. In the Preface, she singles out some of Locke's pronouncements in the chapter "Of Slavery" from the *Second Treatise of Government* for ironic commentary. "If all men are born free, how is it that all women are born slaves?" she asks. Such questions expose the hypocrisy of male advocates of liberty who refuse to extend it to domestic relationships. And perhaps Astell's ironies do more. While she would never espouse the right to rebel against unjust authority in a marriage or a monarchy, some readers find in the Preface an awareness of domestic tyranny too keen to be piously constrained, and detect in Astell's deftly ironic repetition of the formulaic praises of liberty the seeds of women's liberation. Much of the Preface catalogs strong, sensible women from both the Old and New Testaments to prove that the Bible does not proclaim women's natural intellectual inferiority. In the paragraphs printed here, Astell approaches an outright denunciation of the "arbitrary power" that men exercise in families. Through the very sarcasm with which she accepts the subjection of wives in marriage, she draws close to applying a doctrine of English political liberty to women.

From A Preface, in Answer to Some Objections to *Reflections upon Marriage*

* * *

[T]his design, which is unfortunately accused of being so destructive to the government, of the men I mean, is entirely her own.[1] She neither advised with friends, nor turned over[2] ancient or modern authors, nor prudently submitted to the correction of such as are, or such as *think* they are good judges, but with an *English* spirit and genius set out upon the forlorn hope, meaning no hurt to anybody, nor designing any thing but the public good, and to retrieve, if possible, the native liberty, the rights and privileges of the subject.

Far be it from her to stir up sedition of any sort, none can abhor it more; and she heartily wishes that our masters[3] would pay their civil and ecclesiastical governors the same submission which they themselves exact from their domestic subjects. Nor can she imagine how she any way undermines the masculine empire or blows the trumpet of rebellion to the moiety[4] of mankind. Is it by exhorting women not to expect to have their own will in any thing, but to be entirely submissive when once they have made choice of a lord and master, though he happen not to be so wise, so kind, or even so just a governor as was expected?[5] She did not indeed advise them to think his folly wisdom, nor his brutality that love and worship he promised in his matrimonial oath, for this required a flight of wit and sense much above her poor ability, and proper only to masculine understandings. However she did not in any manner prompt them to resist or to abdicate the perjured spouse, though the laws of God and the land make special provision for it in a case wherein, as is to be feared, few men can truly plead not guilty.[6]

* * *

If mankind had never sinned, reason would always have been obeyed, there would have been no struggle for dominion, and brutal power would not have prevailed. But in the lapsed state of mankind, and now that men will not be guided by their reason but by their appetites, and do not what they *ought* but what they *can*, the reason, or that which stands for it, the will and pleasure of the governor, is to be the reason of those who will not be guided by their own, and must take place for order's sake, although it should not be conformable to right reason. Nor can there be any society great or little,

1. As in earlier editions, Astell does not put her name on the third edition's title page, but she here affirms that she, the author, is a woman (referring to herself in the third person).
2. Ransacked.
3. Men in general, masters of women.
4. Half; here referring to the female half of humankind.

5. Astell advises in the body of *Some Reflections upon Marriage* that women accept their marriages, no matter how tyrannical their husbands are.
6. In Astell's time, both ecclesiastical and civil law allowed wives the right to petition for legal separation (not divorce) from husbands who were egregiously, physically cruel to them.

from empires down to private families, without a last resort to determine the affairs of the society by an irresistible sentence.[7] Now unless this supremacy be fixed somewhere, there will be a perpetual contention about it, such is the love of dominion; and let the reason of things be what it may, those who have least force or cunning to supply it[8] will have the disadvantage. So that since women are acknowledged to have least bodily strength, their being commanded to obey is in pure kindness to them, and for their quiet and security, as well as for the exercise of their virtue.[9] But does it follow that domestic governors have more sense than their subjects, any more than that other governors have? We do not find any man thinks the worse of his own understanding because another has superior power; or concludes himself less capable of a post of honor and authority because he is not preferred[1] to it. How much time would lie on men's hands, how empty would the places of concourse be, and how silent most companies, did men forbear to censure their governors; that is, in effect, to think themselves wiser. Indeed, government would be much more desirable than it is did it invest the possessor with a superior understanding as well as power. And if mere power gives a right to rule, there can be no such thing as usurpation; but a highway-man, so long as he has strength to force, has also a right to require our obedience.

Again, if absolute sovereignty be not necessary in a state, how comes it to be so in a family? or if in a family why not in a state; since no reason can be alleged for the one that will not hold more strongly for the other? If the authority of the husband, so far as it extends, is sacred and inalienable, why not of the prince? The domestic sovereign is without dispute elected,[2] and the stipulations and contracts are mutual. Is it not then partial[3] in men to the last degree to contend for and practice that arbitrary dominion in their families which they abhor and exclaim against in the state? For if arbitrary power is evil in itself, and an improper method of governing rational and free agents, it ought not to be practiced anywhere. Nor is it less but rather more mischievous in families than in kingdoms, by how much 100,000 tyrants are worse than one. What though a husband can't deprive a wife of life without being responsible to the law, he may however do what is much more grievous to a generous mind, render life miserable, for which she has no redress, scarce pity, which is afforded to every other complainant; it being thought a wife's duty to suffer everything without complaint. If *all men are born free*, how is it that all women are born slaves? as they must be if the being subjected to the *inconstant, uncertain, unknown, arbitrary will* of men be the *perfect condition of slavery?* and if the essence of freedom consists, as our masters say it does, in having *a standing rule to live by?*[4] And why is slavery so much condemned and strove against in one case and so highly applauded and held so necessary and so sacred in another?

* * *

---

7. I.e., no society can subsist without vesting power in some ultimate authority that incontrovertibly decides contentious questions.
8. To occupy the place of supremacy.
9. Here Astell presents the crucial link between her politics and her feminism: women must look favorably on absolute sovereignty because political instability threatens them, the weakest members of society, the most.

1. Promoted.
2. The wife "elects" her husband when she consents to marry him.
3. Unfair, or biased.
4. The last three italicized phrases quote the first and third paragraphs of the chapter "Of Slavery" (sections 22 and 24) from John Locke's *Second Treatise of Government* (p. 3015).

Again, men are possessed of all places of power, trust, and profit; they make laws and exercise the magistracy. Not only the sharpest sword, but even all the swords and blunderbusses are theirs, which by the strongest logic in the world gives them the best title to everything they please to claim as their prerogative. Who shall contend with them? Immemorial prescription[5] is on their side in these parts of the world, ancient tradition and modern usage! Our fathers have all along both taught and practiced superiority over the weaker sex, and consequently women are by nature inferior to men, as was to be demonstrated. An argument which must be acknowledged unanswerable; for as well as I love my sex, I will not pretend a reply to *such* demonstration!

Only let me beg to be informed, to whom we poor fatherless maids and widows who have lost their masters owe subjection? It can't be to all men in general, unless all men were agreed to give the same commands. Do we then fall as strays to the first who finds us? By the maxims of some men and the conduct of some women, one would think so. But whoever he be that thus happens to become our master, if he allows us to be reasonable creatures and does not merely compliment us with that title, since no man denies our readiness to use our tongues, it would tend I should think to our master's advantage, and therefore he may please to be advised, to teach us to improve our reason. But if reason is only allowed us by way of raillery, and the secret maxim is that we have none, or little more than brutes, 'tis the best way to confine us with chain and block to the chimney-corner, which probably might save the estates of some families and the honor of others.

I do not propose this to prevent a rebellion, for women are not so well united as to form an insurrection. They are for the most part wise enough to love their chains and to discern how very becomingly they set. They think as humbly of themselves as their masters can wish with respect to the other sex, but in regard to their own they have a spice of masculine ambition: every one would lead, and none would follow—both sexes being too apt to envy and too backward in emulating, and take more delight in detracting from their neighbor's virtue than in improving their own. And therefore as to those women who find themselves born for slavery and are so sensible of their own meanness as to conclude it impossible to attain to anything excellent, since they are or ought to be best acquainted with their own strength and genius, she's a fool who would attempt their deliverance or improvement. No, let them enjoy the great honor and felicity of their tame, submissive, and depending temper! Let the men applaud and let them glory in this wonderful humility! Let them receive the flatteries and grimaces of the other sex, live unenvied by their own, and be as much beloved as one such woman can afford to love another! Let them enjoy the glory of treading in the footsteps of their predecessors, and of having the prudence to avoid that audacious attempt of soaring beyond their sphere! Let them housewife[6] or play, dress, and be pretty entertaining company! Or, which is better, relieve the poor to ease their own compassions, read pious books, say their prayers and go to church, because they have been taught and used to do so, without being able to give a better reason for their faith and practice! Let them not by any means aspire at being women of understanding, because no man can endure a woman of superior sense or would treat a reasonable woman civilly, but that he thinks he stands

---

5. Title or claim based on long possession.   6. Perform domestic duties.

on higher ground and that she is so wise as to make exceptions in his favor and to take her measures by his directions. They may pretend to sense indeed since mere pretences only render one the more ridiculous! Let them in short be what is called *very* women, for this is most acceptable to all sorts of men; or let them aim at the title of *good devout* women, since some men can bear with this; but let them not judge of the sex by their own scantling.[7] For the great Author of nature and fountain of all perfection never designed that the mean and imperfect, but that the most complete and excellent, of his creatures in every kind should be the standard to the rest.

* * *

1706

7. Small ability.

JAMES THOMSON

James Thomson's *Liberty* (1735–36), a poem of some thirty-five hundred lines that portrays British freedom as the culmination of the progress of European civilization, is now no longer much read. But his short ode "Rule, Britannia" remains one of the nation's most popular patriotic songs. Set to music by Thomas Arne, the poem was composed for *Alfred* (1740), a masque in honor of Frederick, Prince of Wales, whom opponents of Robert Walpole's administration such as Thomson, Bolingbroke, and Pope supported. Many writers of the era evoke the image of Alfred the Great (849–899) to locate the origins of British liberty in a Gothic past, free of modern corruption: the ode was originally sung by an actor dressed as an ancient bard, accompanied by a British harp. The poem's depiction of Britons as exceptionally unfit for slavery and willing to fight for their freedom at home and abroad both criticizes the contemporary antiwar policy of Walpole and contributes to a national self-image that will shape Britain's role in the world in the centuries to come.

T. Medland, *The Gothic Temple of Liberty*, engraving, 1796. New buildings like this one (ca. 1748) at Stowe Landscape Garden revived the ancient Gothic architectural style to recall the liberty enjoyed by the forebears of modern Britons, who feared their nation was becoming slavish and corrupt. From *Stowe. A Description of the House and Gardens* (1796).

Ode: Rule, Britannia

1

When *Britain* first, at heaven's command,
  Arose from out the azure main°   *open ocean*
This was the charter of the land,
  And guardian angels sung *this* strain:
5   "Rule, *Britannia*, rule the waves;
    Britons never will be slaves."

2

The nations, not so blest as thee,
  Must, in their turns, to tyrants fall:
While thou shalt flourish great and free,
10   The dread and envy of them all.
    "Rule," etc.

3

Still more majestic shalt thou rise,
  More dreadful, from each foreign stroke:
As the loud blast that tears the skies,
15   Serves but to root thy native oak.
    "Rule," etc.

4

Thee haughty tyrants ne'er shall tame:
  All their attempts to bend thee down
Will but arouse thy generous flame;
20   But work their woe, and thy renown.
    "Rule," etc.

5

To thee belongs the rural reign;
  Thy cities shall with commerce shine:
All thine shall be the subject main,
25   And every shore it circles thine.
    "Rule," etc.

6

The Muses, still° with freedom found,   *always*
  Shall to thy happy coast repair:
Blest isle! with matchless beauty crowned,
30   And manly hearts to guard the fair.
    "Rule, *Britannia*, rule the waves;
    Britons never will be slaves."

1740   1745–46

DAVID HUME

David Hume (1711–1776) declared that he "was seized very early with a passion for literature," which, he said, "has been the ruling passion of my life, and the great source of my enjoyments." Now we think of Hume as the most devastatingly brilliant of British philosophers. But epistemology and moral philosophy were only part of his larger literary enterprise, and in his time he was known better as a historian and an essayist on various topics—matters of taste, culture, politics, history, economics—than he was as the great philosophical skeptic who undermined commonsense notions of causation and personal identity. The selection printed here comes from Hume's first collection, *Essays, Moral and Political* (1741; rev. ed. 1742), which, though published anonymously, launched the body of writing that would soon establish his reputation after the disappointing indifference that greeted his massive, brilliant *Treatise of Human Nature* (1739–40). Hume went on to produce other collections of essays and the popular and influential *History of England* (1754–62) in six volumes, which surveyed the development of politics, commerce, and the arts and sciences in Great Britain from ancient times to the Revolution of 1688, for the first time, Hume thought, from a nonpartisan perspective. A Scot and a skeptic, Hume was in a position to survey British culture and history from a critical distance that sometimes produced anger or bafflement in his readers, though these reactions augmented more than mitigated his fame. His detractors brought up his reputed atheism when opportunities arose for him to take important public positions—on different occasions he was denied professorships in Scottish universities on these grounds—though his most probing religious writing, including the *Dialogues Concerning Natural Religion* (1779), was suppressed until after his death.

Hume's style as an essayist is familiar, polished, and urbane; he wears his learning lightly and gracefully. But even these performances reveal a subtle mind unwilling to accept any easy answer or comforting ideological piety. The selection included here celebrates the freedom of the press in Britain, upon which many of Hume's fellow subjects congratulated themselves, in contrast to the heavier legal restrictions imposed on writers on the Continent. But typically for Hume this liberty results less from a high-minded British embrace of rationalized principle than from passion, specifically the intense "jealousy" energizing Britain's mix of monarchy and republic. Later, indeed, he came to have second thoughts: the final version of the essay excises the last three paragraphs praising liberty and dourly concludes that "unbounded liberty of the press . . . is one of those evils, attending those mixed forms of government." The earlier version, reproduced here, offers a more positive view, but still a complex one, noting that the freedom to publish can help contain political rebelliousness even while allowing its expression. The essay is true to Hume's abiding belief that liberty produces a stronger, richer (if not more rational) social fabric.

Of the Liberty of the Press

There is nothing more apt to surprise a foreigner than the extreme liberty we enjoy in this country of communicating whatever we please to the public, and of openly censuring every measure which is entered into by the king or his ministers. If the administration resolve upon war, 'tis affirmed that either willfully or ignorantly they mistake the interest of the nation, and that peace in the present situation of affairs is infinitely preferable. If the passion of the ministers be for peace, our political writers breathe nothing but war and devastation, and represent the pacific conduct of the government as mean and pusillanimous. As this liberty is not indulged in any other government, either republican or monarchical, in Holland and Venice, no more than in France or Spain,[1] it may very naturally give occasion to these two questions: how it happens that Great Britain alone enjoys such a peculiar privilege? and, whether the unlimited exercise of this liberty be advantageous or prejudicial to the public?

As to the first question, why the laws indulge us in such an extraordinary liberty? I believe the reason may be derived from our mixed form of government, which is neither wholly monarchical, nor wholly republican. 'Twill be found, if I mistake not, a true observation in politics that the two extremes in government, of liberty and slavery, approach nearest to each other; and, that as you depart from the extremes, and mix a little of monarchy with liberty, the government becomes always the more free; and, on the other hand, when you mix a little of liberty with monarchy, the yoke becomes always the more grievous and intolerable.[2] In a government such as that of France, which is entirely absolute, and where laws, custom, and religion all concur to make the people fully satisfied with their condition, the monarch cannot entertain the least jealousy[3] against his subjects, and is therefore apt to indulge them in great liberties both of speech and action. In a government altogether republican such as that of Holland, where there is no magistrate[4] so eminent as to give jealousy to the state, there is also no danger in intrusting the magistrates with very large discretionary powers, and though many advantages result from such powers in the preservation of peace and order; yet they lay a considerable restraint on men's actions, and make every private subject pay a great respect to the government. Thus it is evident that the two extremes of absolute monarchy and of a republic approach very near to each other in the most material circumstances. In the first, the magistrate has no jealousy of the people: in the second, the people have no jealousy of the magistrate: which want of jealousy begets a mutual confidence and trust in both cases, and produces a species of liberty in monarchies and of arbitrary power in republics.

To justify the other part of the foregoing observation, that in every government the means are most wide of each other, and that the mixtures of monarchy and liberty render the yoke either more easy or more grievous; I must take notice of a remark of Tacitus with regard to the Romans under the emperors, that they neither could bear total slavery nor total liberty: Nec

---

1. The former pair typify republics; the latter, absolutist monarchies.
2. In the following examples, Hume argues that Holland and France exemplify the "extremes" of liberty and slavery, respectively, which in the final analysis resemble one another, while imperial Rome and modern Britain are described as political mixtures that prove to differ profoundly.
3. Suspicion as toward a competitor or rival; here for power in the state.
4. Governmental official.

totam servitutem, nec totam libertatem pati possunt.[5] This remark a famous poet has translated and applied to the English in his admirable description of Queen Elizabeth's policy and happy government.

> Et fit aimer son joug a l'Anglois indompté,
> Qui ne peut ni servir, ni vivre en liberté . . .
>   HENRIADE, *liv.* I.[6]

According to these remarks, therefore, we are to consider the Roman government as a mixture of despotism and liberty, where the despotism prevailed; and the English government as a mixture of the same kind, but where the liberty predominates. The consequences are exactly conformable to the foregoing observation; and such as may be expected from those mixed forms of government, which beget a mutual watchfulness and jealousy. The Roman emperors were, many of them, the most frightful tyrants that ever disgraced humanity; and 'tis evident their cruelty was chiefly excited by their jealousy, and by their observing that all the great men of Rome bore with impatience the dominion of a family which, but a little before, was noways superior to their own. On the other hand, as the republican part of the government prevails in England, though with a great mixture of monarchy, 'tis obliged for its own preservation to maintain a watchful jealousy over the magistrates, to remove all discretionary powers, and to secure every one's life and fortune by general and inflexible laws. No action must be deemed a crime but what the law has plainly determined to be such: no crime must be imputed to a man but from a legal proof before his judges; and even these judges must be his fellow-subjects, who are obliged by their own interest to have a watchful eye over the encroachments and violence of the ministers. From these causes it proceeds that there is as much liberty, and even, perhaps, licentiousness in Britain, as there were formerly slavery and tyranny in Rome.

These principles account for the great liberty of the press in these kingdoms, beyond what is indulged in any other government. 'Tis sufficiently known that despotic power would soon steal in upon us were we not extreme watchful to prevent its progress, and were there not an easy method of conveying the alarum from one end of the kingdom to the other. The spirit of the people must frequently be roused to curb the ambition of the court; and the dread of rousing this spirit must be employed to prevent that ambition. Nothing is so effectual to this purpose as the liberty of the press, by which all the learning, wit, and genius of the nation may be employed on the side of liberty, and every one be animated to its defense. As long, therefore, as the republican part of our government can maintain itself against the monarchical, it must be extreme jealous[7] of the liberty of the press, as of the utmost importance to its preservation.

Since therefore the liberty of the press is so essential to the support of our mixed government, this sufficiently decides the second question,

---

5. Hume translates the Latin in the preceding phrase. The quotation is from the *Histories* (1.16.28) of Roman historian Tacitus (55?–117?).
6. The famous poet is François-Marie Arouet, known as Voltaire (1694–1778). The lines on Eliz-

abeth are from his epic poem *La Henriade* (1728): She made her yoke agreeable to the unconquered English, who could neither serve nor live in freedom (French).
7. Here vigilant in guarding as a possession.

"Whether this liberty be advantageous or prejudicial?"; there being nothing of greater importance in every state than the preservation of the ancient government, especially if it be a free one. But I would fain go a step farther and assert that such a liberty is attended with so few inconveniencies that it may be claimed as the common right of mankind, and ought to be indulged them almost in every government: except the ecclesiastical, to which indeed it would be fatal. We need not dread from this liberty any such ill consequences as followed from the harangues of the popular demagogues of Athens and tribunes of Rome. A man reads a book or pamphlet alone and coolly. There is none present from whom he can catch the passion by contagion. He is not hurried away by the force and energy of action. And should he be wrought up to never so seditious a humor,[8] there is no violent resolution presented to him by which he can immediately vent his passion. The liberty of the press, therefore, however abused, can scarce ever excite popular tumults or rebellion. And as to those murmurs or secret discontents it may occasion, 'tis better they should get vent in words, that they may come to the knowledge of the magistrate before it be too late, in order to his providing a remedy against them. Mankind, 'tis true, have always a greater propension to believe what is said to the disadvantage of their governors than the contrary; but this inclination is inseparable from them whether they have liberty or not. A whisper may fly as quick and be as pernicious as a pamphlet. Nay, it will be more pernicious, where men are not accustomed to think freely, or distinguish betwixt truth and falsehood.

It has also been found as the experience of mankind increases that the people are no such dangerous monster as they have been represented, and that 'tis in every respect better to guide them like rational creatures than to lead or drive them like brute beasts. Before the United Provinces[9] set the example, toleration was deemed incompatible with good government; and 'twas thought impossible that a number of religious sects could live together in harmony and peace, and have all of them an equal affection to their common country, and to each other. England has set a like example of civil liberty; and though this liberty seems to occasion some small ferment at present, it has not as yet produced any pernicious effects; and it is to be hoped that men, being every day more accustomed to the free discussion of public affairs, will improve in their judgment of them and be with greater difficulty seduced by every idle rumor and popular clamor.

'Tis a very comfortable reflection to the lovers of liberty that this peculiar privilege of Britain is of a kind that cannot easily be wrested from us, but must last as long as our government remains in any degree free and independent. 'Tis seldom that liberty of any kind is lost all at once. Slavery has so frightful an aspect to men accustomed to freedom that it must steal in upon them by degrees, and must disguise itself in a thousand shapes in order to be received. But if the liberty of the press ever be lost, it must be lost all at once. The general laws against sedition and libeling are at present as strong as they possibly can be made. Nothing can impose a farther restraint, but either

8. Mood.   9. Holland, noted for its religious toleration.

the clapping an IMPRIMATUR[1] upon the press, or the giving very large discretionary powers to the court to punish whatever displeases them. But these concessions would be such a bare-faced violation of liberty that they will probably be the last efforts of a despotic government. We may conclude that the liberty of Britain is gone for ever when these attempts shall succeed.

1741, 1742

1. Let it be printed (Latin). This word was applied by the Vatican to indicate that a book may be published and is often employed, as here, to refer to the general practice of prepublication licensing of texts.

EDMUND BURKE

Edmund Burke (1729–1797) commanded both an acute capacity for political analysis and a confident, passionate, often poetic gift for dramatizing what he took to be the stakes of the great historical events of his time. Born and educated in Dublin, the son of an Anglican father and Catholic mother, he came to London in 1750 to study law. But he made his first mark in the world as a philosopher, publishing *A Philosophical Enquiry into the Origin of Our Ideas of the Sublime and the Beautiful* in 1757, a work that has exercised considerable influence on the study of aesthetics to the present day. Its main claim is that we respond with instinctive feeling to certain objects—beautiful ones with pleasure, sublime ones with a type of pain—before the intervention of reason. His insight into human passion deeply informed his later career in politics, both as an analyst of events and their causes and as the most moving orator of his day. Many of his twenty-nine years in Parliament were spent in opposition: he was a voice of conscience and protest not only against Tory governments in power but often against his fellow Whigs. Most of the time he fought for the losing side. He sought to reconcile Britain with its American colonies and avoid war; argued against the persecution of Irish Catholics; and presided over the trial of Warren Hastings, governor-general of India, whose administration Burke found rapacious and corrupt. To different degrees, such campaigns ended in failure. Some of Burke's most famous and lasting political thinking appears in his works opposing the French Revolution, including *Reflections on the Revolution in France* (1790). In it he denounces what he saw as the destructively "metaphysical," rationalistic spirit of the revolutionaries, which led them to neglect the ways in which history and human emotions knit the fabric of society together—a neglect that resulted in recklessness and cruelty.

Burke's speech recommending Britain's conciliation with its American colonies (1775), delivered on the eve of the American War for Independence, has powerfully resonated long past its historical moment. Burke both unfolds the complex origins of liberty in British history and shows how the idea helps establish the very political identity of the people soon to become the citizens of the United States. The speech has long been popular with Americans: in the early nineteenth century, for instance, anti-abolitionists were fond of citing Burke's depiction of the fierce commitment to liberty of the white South (though he had not meant that as praise). Most characteristic of Burke's political thinking is the speech's description of liberty as a complex, concrete reality, not as "abstract liberty," which, "like other mere abstractions, is not to be found." More than an ideal, the meaning of liberty emerges from a richly detailed weave of particular historical processes.

From Speech on the Conciliation with the American Colonies

* * *

In [the] character of the Americans a love of freedom is the predominating feature which marks and distinguishes the whole: and as an ardent is always a jealous affection, your colonies become suspicious, restive, and untractable, whenever they see the least attempt to wrest from them by force, or shuffle from them by chicane, what they think the only advantage worth living for. This fierce spirit of liberty is stronger in the English colonies, probably, than in any other people of the earth, and this from a great variety of powerful causes; which, to understand the true temper of their minds, and the direction which this spirit takes, it will not be amiss to lay open somewhat more largely.

First, the people of the colonies are descendants of Englishmen. England, Sir, is a nation which still, I hope, respects, and formerly adored, her freedom. The colonists emigrated from you when this part of your character was most predominant; and they took this bias and direction the moment they parted from your hands. They are therefore not only devoted to liberty, but to liberty according to English ideas and on English principles. Abstract liberty, like other mere abstractions, is not to be found. Liberty inheres in some sensible object[1] and every nation has formed to itself some favorite point, which by way of eminence becomes the criterion of their happiness. It happened, you know, Sir, that the great contests for freedom in this country were from the earliest times chiefly upon the question of taxing. Most of the contests in the ancient commonwealths turned primarily on the right of election of magistrates, or on the balance among the several orders of the state. The question of money was not with them so immediate. But in England it was otherwise. On this point of taxes the ablest pens and most eloquent tongues have been exercised, the greatest spirits have acted and suffered. In order to give the fullest satisfaction concerning the importance of this point, it was not only necessary for those who in argument defended the excellence of the English Constitution to insist on this privilege of granting money as a dry point of fact, and to prove that the right had been acknowledged in ancient parchments and blind usages to reside in a certain body called a House of Commons: they went much further: they attempted to prove, and they succeeded, that in theory it ought to be so, from the particular nature of a House of Commons, as an immediate representative of the people, whether the old records had delivered this oracle or not. They took infinite pains to inculcate, as a fundamental principle, that in all monarchies the people must in effect themselves, mediately or immediately, possess the power of granting their own money, or no shadow of liberty could subsist. The colonies draw from you, as with their life-blood, these ideas and principles. Their love of liberty, as with you, fixed and attached on this specific point of taxing. Liberty might be safe or might be endangered in twenty other particulars without their being much pleased or alarmed. Here they felt its pulse; and as they found that beat, they thought themselves sick or sound. I do not say whether they were right or wrong in applying your

1. I.e., an object perceived by the senses.

general arguments to their own case. It is not easy, indeed, to make a monopoly of theorems and corollaries. The fact is, that they did thus apply those general arguments; and your mode of governing them, whether through lenity or indolence, through wisdom or mistake, confirmed them in the imagination, that they, as well as you, had an interest in these common principles.

They were further confirmed in this pleasing error by the form of their provincial legislative assemblies. Their governments are popular in an high degree: some are merely[2] popular; in all, the popular representative is the most weighty; and this share of the people in their ordinary government never fails to inspire them with lofty sentiments, and with a strong aversion from whatever tends to deprive them of their chief importance.

If anything were wanting to this necessary operation of the form of government, religion would have given it a complete effect. Religion, always a principle of energy, in this new people is no way worn out or impaired; and their mode of professing it is also one main cause of this free spirit. The people are Protestants, and of that kind which is the most adverse to all implicit submission of mind and opinion. This is a persuasion not only favorable to liberty, but built upon it. I do not think, Sir, that the reason of this averseness in the dissenting churches from all that looks like absolute government is so much to be sought in their religious tenets as in their history. Every one knows that the Roman Catholic religion is at least coeval with most of the governments where it prevails, that it has generally gone hand in hand with them, and received a great favor and every kind of support from authority. The Church of England, too, was formed from her cradle under the nursing care of regular government. But the dissenting interests have sprung up in direct opposition to all the ordinary powers of the world, and could justify that opposition only on a strong claim to natural liberty. Their very existence depended on the powerful and unremitted assertion of that claim. All Protestantism, even the most cold and passive, is a sort of dissent. But the religion most prevalent in our northern colonies is a refinement on the principle of resistance: it is the dissidence of dissent, and the protestantism of the Protestant religion. This religion, under a variety of denominations agreeing in nothing but in the communion of the spirit of liberty, is predominant in most of the northern provinces, where the Church of England, notwithstanding its legal rights, is in reality no more than a sort of private sect, not composing, most probably, the tenth of the people. The colonists left England when this spirit was high, and in the emigrants was the highest of all; and even that stream of foreigners which has been constantly flowing into these colonies has, for the greatest part, been composed of dissenters from the establishments of their several countries, and have brought with them a temper and character far from alien to that of the people with whom they mixed.

Sir, I can perceive, by their manner, that some gentlemen object to the latitude of this description, because in the southern colonies the Church of England forms a large body, and has a regular establishment. It is certainly true. There is, however, a circumstance attending these colonies, which, in my opinion, fully counterbalances this difference, and makes the spirit of liberty still more high and haughty than in those to the northward. It is, that

2. Entirely. "Popular": elected by the people. In 18th-century England the masses could not vote.

in Virginia and the Carolinas they have a vast multitude of slaves. Where this is the case in any part of the world, those who are free are by far the most proud and jealous of their freedom. Freedom is to them not only an enjoyment, but a kind of rank and privilege. Not seeing there, that freedom, as in countries where it is a common blessing, and as broad and general as the air, may be united with much abject toil, with great misery, with all the exterior of servitude, liberty looks, amongst them, like something that is more noble and liberal. I do not mean, Sir, to commend the superior morality of this sentiment, which has at least as much pride as virtue in it,[3] but I cannot alter the nature of man. The fact is so; and these people of the southern colonies are much more strongly, and with an higher and more stubborn spirit, attached to liberty, than those to the northward. Such were all the ancient commonwealths; such were our Gothic ancestors; such in our days were the Poles;[4] and such will be all masters of slaves, who are not slaves themselves. In such a people, the haughtiness of domination combines with the spirit of freedom, fortifies it, and renders it invincible.

Permit me, Sir, to add another circumstance in our colonies, which contributes no mean part towards the growth and effect of this untractable spirit: I mean their education. In no country, perhaps, in the world is the law so general a study. * * * This study renders men acute, inquisitive, dexterous, prompt in attack, ready in defense, full of resources. In other countries, the people, more simple, and of a less mercurial cast, judge of an ill principle in government only by an actual grievance; here they anticipate the evil, and judge the pressure of the grievance by the badness of the principle. They augur misgovernment at a distance, and snuff the approach of tyranny in every tainted breeze.

The last cause of this disobedient spirit in the colonies is hardly less powerful than the rest, as it is not merely moral, but laid deep in the natural constitution of things. Three thousand miles of ocean lie between you and them. No contrivance can prevent the effect of this distance in weakening government. Seas roll, and months pass, between the order and the execution; and the want of a speedy explanation of a single point is enough to defeat an whole system. You have, indeed, winged ministers of vengeance, who carry your bolts in their pounces[5] to the remotest verge of the sea: but there a power steps in, that limits the arrogance of raging passions and furious elements, and says, "So far shalt thou go, and no farther."[6] Who are you, that should fret and rage, and bite the chains of Nature? Nothing worse happens to you than does to all nations who have extensive empire; and it happens in all the forms into which empire can be thrown. In large bodies, the circulation of power must be less vigorous at the extremities. Nature has said it. The Turk cannot govern Egypt, and Arabia, and Kurdistan, as he governs Thrace; nor has he the same dominion in Crimea and Algiers which he has at Brusa and Smyrna. Despotism itself is obliged to truck and huckster. The Sultan gets such obedience as he can. He governs with a loose rein, that he may govern at all; and the whole of the force and vigor of his

---

3. Burke himself passionately opposed slavery. In 1765 he had argued against American representation in Parliament on the ground that slave-owners had no right to make laws for free men.
4. Slavery was abolished in Poland in 1772.

5. Talons; gunpowder. Burke compares the ships of the British navy to Milton's avenging angels.
6. A reference to King Canute, who could not command the sea.

authority in his center is derived from a prudent relaxation in all his borders. Spain, in her provinces, is perhaps not so well obeyed as you are in yours. She complies, too; she submits; she watches times. This is the immutable condition, the eternal law, of extensive and detached empire.

Then, Sir, from these six capital sources, of descent, of form of government, of religion in the northern provinces, of manners in the southern, of education, of the remoteness of situation from the first mover of government—from all these causes a fierce spirit of liberty has grown up. It has grown with the growth of the people in your colonies, and increased with the increase of their wealth: a spirit, that, unhappily meeting with an exercise of power in England, which, however lawful, is not reconcilable to any ideas of liberty, much less with theirs, has kindled this flame that is ready to consume us.

* * *

1775

SAMUEL JOHNSON

Samuel Johnson detested slavery and the owners of slaves. Once, "in company with some very grave men at Oxford, his toast was, 'Here's to the next insurrection of the Negroes in the West Indies,'" and in his pamphlet *Taxation No Tyranny* (1775), he put the American rebels down with a devastating question: "How is it that we hear the loudest yelps for liberty among the drivers of Negroes?" Although slavery had been abolished in England in 1772, serfdom still existed in Scotland, and the British remained heavily involved in the slave trade. In 1777 a black slave, Joseph Knight, sued for freedom from the Scottish master he had escaped. On his behalf Johnson dictated this argument to Boswell.

[A Brief to Free a Slave]

It must be agreed that in most ages many countries have had part of their inhabitants in a state of slavery; yet it may be doubted whether slavery can ever be supposed the natural condition of man. It is impossible not to conceive that men in their original state were equal; and very difficult to imagine how one would be subjected to another but by violent compulsion. An individual may, indeed, forfeit his liberty by a crime; but he cannot by that crime forfeit the liberty of his children. What is true of a criminal seems true likewise of a captive. A man may accept life from a conquering enemy on condition of perpetual servitude; but it is very doubtful whether he can entail[1] that servitude on his descendants; for no man can stipulate without commission for another. The condition which he himself accepts, his son or grandson perhaps would have rejected. If we should admit, what perhaps

1. Settle unalterably.

may with more reason be denied, that there are certain relations between man and man which may make slavery necessary and just,[2] yet it can never be proved that he who is now suing for his freedom ever stood in any of those relations. He is certainly subject by no law, but that of violence, to his present master,[3] who pretends no claim to his obedience, but that he bought him from a merchant of slaves, whose right to sell him never was examined. It is said that, according to the constitutions of Jamaica, he was legally enslaved; these constitutions are merely positive;[4] and apparently injurious to the rights of mankind, because whoever is exposed to sale is condemned to slavery without appeal; by whatever fraud or violence he might have been originally brought into the merchant's power. In our own time princes have been sold, by wretches to whose care they were entrusted, that they might have an European education; but when once they were brought to a market in the plantations, little would avail either their dignity or their wrongs. The laws of Jamaica afford a Negro no redress. His color is considered as a sufficient testimony against him. It is to be lamented that moral right should ever give way to political convenience. But if temptations of interest are sometimes too strong for human virtue, let us at least retain a virtue where there is no temptation to quit it. In the present case there is apparent right on one side, and no convenience on the other. Inhabitants of this island can neither gain riches nor power by taking away the liberty of any part of the human species. The sum of the argument is this:—No man is by nature the property of another: The defendant is, therefore, by nature free: The rights of nature must be some way forfeited before they can be justly taken away: That the defendant has by any act forfeited the rights of nature we require to be proved; and if no proof of such forfeiture can be given, we doubt not but the justice of the court will declare him free.[5]

1777   1792

2. Boswell, who strongly disagreed with Johnson's "prejudice" against slavery, argued that "to abolish a *status*, which in all ages GOD has sanctioned, and man has continued, would not only be *robbery* to an innumerable class of our fellow subjects; but it would be extreme cruelty to the African savages."

3. Knight had been kidnapped as a child.

4. Arbitrarily instituted (opposed to *natural* laws).

5. Knight was set free by the Scottish court.

OLAUDAH EQUIANO

*T*he Interesting Narrative of the Life of Olaudah Equiano, or Gustavus Vassa, the African, Written by Himself, published in 1789, is the classic story of an eighteenth-century African's descent into slavery and rise to freedom. It describes how its author (ca. 1745–1797) was raised in an Ibo village (in modern Nigeria), kidnapped by African raiders, and sold into slavery. Particularly powerful is its account of the horrors of the Middle Passage to the New World. There, an English naval officer bought him to serve as a cabin boy and renamed him Gustavus Vassa, after a sixteenth-century Swedish hero who freed his people from the Danes (such names concealed the status of a slave, because slavery was frowned on by the British

Navy). During years at sea, as well as a period at a London school, Equiano acquired a basic education. He also underwent baptism, a ritual that many slaves expected to make them free. But his hopes were cruelly disappointed when, after six years' service, he was suddenly sold and shipped to the West Indies. There a Quaker merchant, Robert King, purchased him, employed him as a clerk and a seaman, and eventually allowed him, in 1766, to buy his freedom. Equiano went back to England, working first as a hairdresser and later voyaging all over the world, even taking part in an effort to find a passage to India by way of the North Pole. Scholars have raised doubts about the account that the *Interesting Narrative* gives of the early parts of Equiano's life: parish and British naval records indicate he was born not in Africa but in South Carolina and hence did not himself undergo the Middle Passage. Whether fact or fiction—scholars may never determine conclusively—the description of his days in Africa, abduction, and suffering in the slave ship gives a voice to countless Africans who faced such experiences and dramatizes the undeniable realities of the slave trade to a white readership. Equiano's publication of his story is a culmination of his involvement in the abolitionist movement through the 1780s and was an important contribution to that movement, not only for its explicit arguments against the slave trade but also for its demonstration that someone of African descent could be humane, intelligent, a good Christian, and a free and eloquent British subject. The book went through many editions and made Equiano famous. He married an Englishwoman, fathered two daughters, and died in London in 1797.

The *Life of Equiano* combines several literary genres. It is a captivity narrative, a spiritual autobiography, a travel memoir, an adventure story, and an abolitionist tract. The early chapters describe the healthy, cheerful, and virtuous life of Africans, contrasted with European inhumanity, and the later chapters show how much a black man can achieve, when given a chance. Equiano does not disguise the strains of his position as he is pulled between different identities and different worlds. His main purpose, however, is clearly to force his readers to face the ordeals a slave must endure—to live in his skin. If *Oroonoko* taught Europeans to sympathize with Africans, Equiano taught them that a black man could speak for himself.

William Blake, *A Coromantyn Free Negro, or Ranger, Armed,* 1796. Blake depicts the strength and independence of one of the African soldiers in Surinam promised their freedom for fighting with whites to suppress a slave rebellion. His scarlet cap signifies liberty. From John Stedman, *Narrative of a Five Years Expedition Against the Revolted Negroes of Surinam . . . from the Year 1772, to 1777* (1796).

From The Interesting Narrative of the Life of Olaudah Equiano, or Gustavus Vassa, the African, Written by Himself

[THE MIDDLE PASSAGE][1]

The first object which saluted my eyes when I arrived on the coast was the sea, and a slave ship, which was then riding at anchor, and waiting for its cargo. These filled me with astonishment, which was soon converted into terror when I was carried on board. I was immediately handled and tossed up to see if I were sound by some of the crew; and I was now persuaded that I had gotten into a world of bad spirits, and that they were going to kill me. Their complexions too differing so much from ours, their long hair, and the language they spoke, (which was very different from any I had ever heard) united to confirm me in this belief. Indeed such were the horrors of my views and fears at the moment, that, if ten thousand worlds had been my own, I would have freely parted with them all to have exchanged my condition with that of the meanest slave in my own country. When I looked round the ship too and saw a large furnace of copper boiling, and a multitude of black people of every description chained together, every one of their countenances expressing dejection and sorrow, I no longer doubted of my fate; and, quite overpowered with horror and anguish, I fell motionless on the deck and fainted. When I recovered a little I found some black people about me, who I believe were some of those who brought me on board, and had been receiving their pay; they talked to me in order to cheer me, but all in vain. I asked them if we were not to be eaten by those white men with horrible looks, red faces, and loose hair. They told me I was not; and one of the crew brought me a small portion of spirituous liquor in a wine glass; but, being afraid of him, I would not take it out of his hand. One of the blacks therefore took it from him and gave it to me, and I took a little down my palate, which, instead of reviving me, as they thought it would, threw me into the greatest consternation at the strange feeling it produced, having never tasted any such liquor before. Soon after this the blacks who brought me on board went off, and left me abandoned to despair. I now saw myself deprived of all chance of returning to my native country, or even the least glimpse of hope of gaining the shore, which I now considered as friendly; and I even wished for my former slavery in preference to my present situation, which was filled with horrors of every kind, still heightened by my ignorance of what I was to undergo. I was not long suffered to indulge my grief; I was soon put down under the decks, and there I received such a salutation in my nostrils as I had never experienced in my life; so that, with the loathsomeness of the stench, and crying together, I became so sick and low that I was not able to eat, nor had I the least desire to taste any thing. I now wished for the last friend, death, to relieve me; but soon, to my grief, two of the white men offered me eatables; and, on my refusing to eat, one of them held me fast by the hands, and laid me across I think the windlass, and tied my feet, while the other flogged me severely. I had never experienced any thing of

1. After his kidnapping, young Equiano passes from one African master to another. The last of these, a merchant, treats him like a member of the family, until one morning the boy is suddenly wakened and hurried away to the seacoast.

this kind before; and although, not being used to the water, I naturally feared that element the first time I saw it, yet nevertheless, could I have got over the nettings,[2] I would have jumped over the side, but I could not; and, besides, the crew used to watch us very closely who were not chained down to the decks, lest we should leap into the water; and I have seen some of these poor African prisoners most severely cut for attempting to do so, and hourly whipped for not eating. This indeed was often the case with myself. In a little time after, amongst the poor chained men, I found some of my own nation, which in a small degree gave ease to my mind. I inquired of these what was to be done with us; they gave me to understand we were to be carried to these white people's country to work for them. I then was a little revived, and thought, if it were no worse than working, my situation was not so desperate: but still I feared I should be put to death, the white people looked and acted, as I thought, in so savage a manner; for I had never seen among any people such instances of brutal cruelty; and this not only shewn towards us blacks, but also to some of the whites themselves. One white man in particular I saw, when we were permitted to be on deck, flogged so unmercifully with a large rope near the foremast, that he died in consequence of it; and they tossed him over the side as they would have done a brute. This made me fear these people the more; and I expected nothing less than to be treated in the same manner. I could not help expressing my fears and apprehensions to some of my countrymen: I asked them if these people had no country, but lived in this hollow place (the ship): they told me they did not, but came from a distant one. "Then," said I, "how comes it in all our country we never heard of them?" They told me because they lived so very far off. I then asked where were their women? had they any like themselves? I was told they had: "and why," said I, "do we not see them?" they answered, because they were left behind. I asked how the vessel could go? they told me they could not tell; but that there were cloths put upon the masts by the help of the ropes I saw, and then the vessel went on; and the white men had some spell or magic they put in the water when they liked in order to stop the vessel. I was exceedingly amazed at this account, and really thought they were spirits. I therefore wished much to be from amongst them, for I expected they would sacrifice me: but my wishes were vain; for we were so quartered that it was impossible for any of us to make our escape. While we stayed on the coast I was mostly on deck; and one day, to my great astonishment, I saw one of these vessels coming in with the sails up. As soon as the whites saw it, they gave a great shout, at which we were amazed; and the more so as the vessel appeared larger by approaching nearer. At last she came to an anchor in my sight, and when the anchor was let go I and my countrymen who saw it were lost in astonishment to observe the vessel stop; and were now convinced it was done by magic. Soon after this the other ship got her boats out, and they came on board of us, and the people of both ships seemed very glad to see each other. Several of the strangers also shook hands with us black people, and made motions with their hands, signifying I suppose we were to go to their country; but we did not understand them. At last, when the ship we were in had got in all her cargo, they made ready with many fearful noises, and we were all put under deck, so that we could not

---

2. A network of small ropes around the ship kept slaves from jumping overboard.

see how they managed the vessel. But this disappointment was the least of my sorrow. The stench of the hold while we were on the coast was so intolerably loathsome, that it was dangerous to remain there for any time, and some of us had been permitted to stay on the deck for the fresh air; but now that the whole ship's cargo were confined together, it became absolutely pestilential. The closeness of the place, and the heat of the climate, added to the number in the ship, which was so crowded that each had scarcely room to turn himself, almost suffocated us. This produced copious perspirations, so that the air soon became unfit for respiration, from a variety of loathsome smells, and brought on a sickness among the slaves, of which many died, thus falling victims to the improvident avarice, as I may call it, of their purchasers. This wretched situation was again aggravated by the galling of the chains, now become insupportable; and the filth of the necessary tubs,[3] into which the children often fell, and were almost suffocated. The shrieks of the women, and the groans of the dying, rendered the whole a scene of horror almost inconceivable. Happily perhaps for myself I was soon reduced so low here that it was thought necessary to keep me almost always on deck; and from[4] my extreme youth I was not put in fetters. In this situation I expected every hour to share the fate of my companions, some of whom were almost daily brought upon deck at the point of death, which I began to hope would soon put an end to my miseries. Often did I think many of the inhabitants of the deep much more happy than myself. I envied them the freedom they enjoyed, and as often wished I could change my condition for theirs. Every circumstance I met with served only to render my state more painful, and heighten my apprehensions, and my opinion of the cruelty of the whites. One day they had taken a number of fishes; and when they had killed and satisfied themselves with as many as they thought fit, to our astonishment who were on the deck, rather than give any of them to us to eat as we expected, they tossed the remaining fish into the sea again, although we begged and prayed for some as well as we could, but in vain; and some of my countrymen, being pressed by hunger, took an opportunity, when they thought no one saw them, of trying to get a little privately; but they were discovered, and the attempt procured them some very severe floggings.

One day, when we had a smooth sea and moderate wind, two of my wearied countrymen who were chained together (I was near them at the time), preferring death to such a life of misery, somehow made through the nettings and jumped into the sea; immediately another quite dejected fellow, who, on account of his illness, was suffered to be out of irons, also followed their example; and I believe many more would very soon have done the same if they had not been prevented by the ship's crew, who were instantly alarmed. Those of us that were the most active were in a moment put down under the deck, and there was such a noise and confusion amongst the people of the ship as I never heard before, to stop her, and get the boat out to go after the slaves. However two of the wretches were drowned, but they got the other, and afterwards flogged him unmercifully for thus attempting to prefer death to slavery. In this manner we continued to undergo more hardships than I can now relate, hardships which are inseparable from this

3. Latrines.
4. Because of.

accursed trade. Many a time we were near suffocation from the want of fresh air, which we were often without for whole days together. This, and the stench of the necessary tubs, carried off many. During our passage I first saw flying fishes, which surprised me very much: they used frequently to fly across the ship, and many of them fell on the deck. I also now first saw the use of the quadrant; I had often with astonishment seen the mariners make observations with it, and I could not think what it meant. They at last took notice of my surprise; and one of them, willing to increase it, as well as to gratify my curiosity, made me one day look through it. The clouds appeared to me to be land, which disappeared as they passed along. This heightened my wonder; and I was now more persuaded than ever that I was in another world, and that every thing about me was magic. At last we came in sight of the island of Barbados,[5] at which the whites on board gave a great shout, and made many signs of joy to us. We did not know what to think of this; but as the vessel drew nearer we plainly saw the harbor, and other ships of different kinds and sizes; and we soon anchored amongst them off Bridge Town. Many merchants and planters now came on board, though it was in the evening. They put us in separate parcels,[6] and examined us attentively. They also made us jump, and pointed to the land, signifying we were to go there. We thought by this we should be eaten by these ugly men, as they appeared to us; and, when soon after we were all put down under the deck again, there was much dread and trembling among us, and nothing but bitter cries to be heard all the night from these apprehensions, insomuch that at last the white people got some old slaves from the land to pacify us. They told us we were not to be eaten, but to work, and were soon to go on land, where we should see many of our country people. This report eased us much; and sure enough, soon after we were landed, there came to us Africans of all languages. We were conducted immediately to the merchant's yard, where we were pent up altogether like so many sheep in a fold, without regard to sex or age. As every object was new to me, every thing I saw filled me with surprise. What struck me first was that the houses were built with stories, and in every other respect different from those in Africa; but I was still more astonished on seeing people on horseback. I did not know what this could mean; and indeed I thought these people were full of nothing but magical arts. While I was in this astonishment one of my fellow prisoners spoke to a countryman of his about the horses, who said they were the same kind they had in their country. I understood them, though they were from a distant part of Africa, and I thought it odd I had not seen any horses there; but afterwards, when I came to converse with different Africans, I found they had many horses amongst them, and much larger than those I then saw. We were not many days in the merchant's custody before we were sold after their usual manner, which is this:—On a signal given (as the beat of a drum) the buyers rush at once into the yard where the slaves are confined, and make a choice of that parcel they like best. The noise and clamor with which this is attended, and the eagerness visible in the countenances of the buyers, serve not a little to increase the apprehensions of the terrified Africans, who may well be supposed to consider them as the ministers of that destruction to

---

5. The easternmost Caribbean island, then an important center for the trade of sugar and slaves.

6. Groups sorted to be sold as one lot.

which they think themselves devoted.[7] In this manner, without scruple, are relations and friends separated, most of them never to see each other again. I remember in the vessel in which I was brought over, in the men's apartment, there were several brothers, who, in the sale, were sold in different lots; and it was very moving on this occasion to see and hear their cries at parting. O, ye nominal Christians! might not an African ask you, learned you this from your God, who says unto you, Do unto all men as you would men should do unto you? Is it not enough that we are torn from our country and friends to toil for your luxury and lust of gain? Must every tender feeling be likewise sacrificed to your avarice? Are the dearest friends and relations, now rendered more dear by their separation from their kindred, still to be parted from each other, and thus prevented from cheering the gloom of slavery with the small comfort of being together and mingling their sufferings and sorrows? Why are parents to lose their children, brothers their sisters, or husbands their wives? Surely this is a new refinement in cruelty, which, while it has no advantage to atone for it, thus aggravates distress, and adds fresh horrors even to the wretchedness of slavery.

* * *

[A FREE MAN][8]

Every day now brought me nearer my freedom, and I was impatient till we proceeded again to sea, that I might have an opportunity of getting a sum large enough to purchase it. I was not long ungratified; for, in the beginning of the year 1766, my master bought another sloop, named the *Nancy*, the largest I had ever seen. She was partly laden, and was to proceed to Philadelphia; our Captain had his choice of three, and I was well pleased he chose this, which was the largest; for, from his having a large vessel, I had more room, and could carry a larger quantity of goods with me. Accordingly, when we had delivered our old vessel, the *Prudence*, and completed the lading of the *Nancy*, having made near three hundred per cent, by four barrels of pork I brought from Charlestown, I laid in as large a cargo as I could, trusting to God's providence to prosper my undertaking. With these views I sailed for Philadelphia. On our passage, when we drew near the land, I was for the first time surprised at the sight of some whales, having never seen any such large sea monsters before; and as we sailed by the land one morning I saw a puppy whale close by the vessel; it was about the length of a wherry boat, and it followed us all the day till we got within the Capes. We arrived safe and in good time at Philadelphia, and I sold my goods there chiefly to the Quakers. They always appeared to be a very honest discreet sort of people, and never attempted to impose on me; I therefore liked them, and ever after chose to deal with them in preference to any others.

One Sunday morning while I was here, as I was going to church, I chanced to pass a meeting house. The doors being open, and the house full of people,

---

7. Doomed.
8. Frustrated in his hope to be set free in England, Equiano is shipped to Montserrat, a British colony in the Leeward Islands of the West Indies. Robert King, a prosperous Quaker merchant from Philadelphia, buys him, treats him kindly, and values him as a reliable worker. By being useful to a friendly sea captain, Thomas Farmer, Equiano has opportunities to travel and trade goods for money. Eventually King promises to let him purchase his freedom for his original cost: forty pounds sterling.

it excited my curiosity to go in. When I entered the house, to my great surprise, I saw a very tall woman standing in the midst of them, speaking in an audible voice something which I could not understand. Having never seen anything of this kind before, I stood and stared about me for some time, wondering at this odd scene. As soon as it was over I took an opportunity to make inquiry about the place and people, when I was informed they were called Quakers.[9] I particularly asked what that woman I saw in the midst of them had said, but none of them were pleased to satisfy me; so I quitted them, and soon after, as I was returning, I came to a church crowded with people; the church-yard was full likewise, and a number of people were even mounted on ladders, looking in at the windows. I thought this a strange sight, as I had never seen churches, either in England or the West Indies, crowded in this manner before. I therefore made bold to ask some people the meaning of all this, and they told me the Rev. Mr. George Whitfield[1] was preaching. I had often heard of this gentleman, and had wished to see and hear him; but I had never before had an opportunity. I now therefore resolved to gratify myself with the sight, and I pressed in amidst the multitude. When I got into the church I saw this pious man exhorting the people with the greatest fervor and earnestness, and sweating as much as I ever did while in slavery on Montserrat beach. I was very much struck and impressed with this; I thought it strange I had never seen divines exert themselves in this manner before, and I was no longer at a loss to account for the thin congregations they preached to.

When we had discharged our cargo here, and were loaded again, we left this fruitful land once more, and set sail for Montserrat. My traffic had hitherto succeeded so well with me, that I thought, by selling my goods when we arrived at Montserrat, I should have enough to purchase my freedom. But, as soon as our vessel arrived there, my master came on board, and gave orders for us to go to St. Eustatia,[2] and discharge our cargo there, and from thence proceed for Georgia. I was much disappointed at this; but thinking, as usual, it was of no use to murmur at the decrees of fate, I submitted without repining, and we went to St. Eustatia. After we had discharged our cargo there we took in a live cargo, as we call a cargo of slaves. Here I sold my goods tolerably well; but, not being able to lay out all my money in this small island to as much advantage as in many other places, I laid out only part, and the remainder I brought away with me neat.[3] We sailed from hence for Georgia, and I was glad when we got there, though I had not much reason to like the place from my last adventure in Savannah;[4] but I longed to get back to Montserrat and procure my freedom, which I expected to be able to purchase when I returned. As soon as we arrived here I waited on my careful doctor, Mr. Brady, to whom I made the most grateful acknowledgments in my power for his former kindness and attention during my illness.

9. Quaker meetings are not led by clergy; any worshiper who feels inspired by God can rise to speak.
1. Whitefield (1714–1770), a famous evangelist who helped found Methodism, was in Britain, not Philadelphia, in 1766. It is possible that Equiano had heard him preach the previous year, in Savannah, Georgia. Equiano's later conversion to Methodism will become a dominant theme of his life story.
2. An island in the Netherlands Antilles (West Indies).
3. Intact.
4. The year before, a drunken slave owner and his servant had beaten Equiano so brutally that he nearly died.

While we were here an odd circumstance happened to the Captain and me, which disappointed us both a good deal. A silversmith, whom we had brought to this place some voyages before, agreed with the Captain to return with us to the West Indies, and promised at the same time to give the Captain a great deal of money, having pretended to take a liking to him, and being, as we thought, very rich. But while we stayed to load our vessel this man was taken ill in a house where he worked, and in a week's time became very bad. The worse he grew the more he used to speak of giving the Captain what he had promised him, so that he expected something considerable from the death of this man, who had no wife or child, and he attended him day and night. I used also to go with the Captain, at his own desire, to attend him; especially when we saw there was no appearance of his recovery; and, in order to recompense me for my trouble, the Captain promised me ten pounds, when he should get the man's property. I thought this would be of great service to me, although I had nearly money enough to purchase my freedom, if I should get safe this voyage to Montserrat. In this expectation I laid out above eight pounds of my money for a suit of superfine clothes to dance with at my freedom, which I hoped was then at hand. We still continued to attend this man, and were with him even on the last day he lived, till very late at night, when we went on board. After we were got to bed, about one or two o'clock in the morning, the Captain was sent for, and informed the man was dead. On this he came to my bed, and, waking me, informed me of it, and desired me to get up and procure a light, and immediately go to him. I told him I was very sleepy, and wished he would take somebody else with him, or else, as the man was dead, and could want no farther attendance, to let all things remain as they were till next morning. "No, no," said he, "we will have the money tonight, I cannot wait till tomorrow; so let us go." Accordingly I got up and struck a light, and away we both went and saw the man as dead as we could wish. The Captain said he would give him a grand burial, in gratitude for the promised treasure; and desired that all the things belonging to the deceased might be brought forth. Among others, there was a nest of trunks of which he had kept the keys whilst the man was ill, and when they were produced we opened them with no small eagerness and expectation; and as there were a great number within one another, with much impatience we took them one out of the other. At last, when we came to the smallest, and had opened it, we saw it was full of papers, which we supposed to be notes; at the sight of which our hearts leapt for joy; and that instant the Captain, clapping his hands, cried out, "Thank God, here it is." But when we took up the trunk, and began to examine the supposed treasure and long-looked-for bounty, (alas! alas! how uncertain and deceitful are all human affairs!) what had we found! While we were embracing a substance we grasped an empty nothing. The whole amount that was in the nest of trunks was only one dollar and a half; and all that the man possessed would not pay for his coffin. Our sudden and exquisite joy was now succeeded by as sudden and exquisite pain; and my Captain and I exhibited, for some time, most ridiculous figures—pictures of chagrin and disappointment! We went away greatly mortified, and left the deceased to do as well as he could for himself, as we had taken so good care of him when alive for nothing. We set sail once more for Montserrat, and arrived there safe; but much out of humor with our friend the silversmith. When we had unladen the vessel, and I had sold my venture, finding myself master of about forty-seven pounds, I consulted my true friend, the Captain, how I should proceed in offering my master the money for my freedom. He told me to come on a certain morning, when he and my master would be at breakfast together. Accordingly, on that morning I went, and met the Captain there, as he had appointed. When I went in I made my obeisance to my master, and with my money in my hand, and many fears in my heart, I prayed him to be as good as his offer to me, when he was pleased to promise me my freedom as soon as I could purchase it. This speech seemed to confound him; he began to recoil; and my heart that instant sank within me. "What," said he, "give you your freedom? Why, where did you get the money? Have you got forty pounds sterling?" "Yes, sir," I answered. "How did you get it?" replied he. I told him, very honestly. The Captain then said he knew I got the money very honestly and with much industry, and that I was particularly careful. On which my master replied, I got money much faster than he did; and said he would not have made me the promise he did if he had thought I should have got money so soon. "Come, come," said my worthy Captain, clapping my master on the back, "Come, Robert" (which was his name), "I think you must let him have his freedom; you have laid your money out very well; you have received good interest for it all this time, and here is now the principal at last. I know Gustavus has earned you more than an hundred a-year, and he will still save you money, as he will not leave you:—Come, Robert, take the money." My master then said, he would not be worse than his promise; and, taking the money, told me to go to the Secretary at the Register Office, and get my manumission[5] drawn up. These words of my master were like a voice from heaven to me: in an instant all my trepidation was turned into unutterable bliss; and I most reverently bowed myself with gratitude, unable to express my feelings, but by the overflowing of my eyes, while my true and worthy friend, the Captain, congratulated us both with a peculiar degree of heartfelt pleasure. As soon as the first transports of my joy were over, and that I had expressed my thanks to these my worthy friends in the best manner I was able, I rose with a heart full of affection and reverence, and left the room, in order to obey my master's joyful mandate of going to the Register Office. As I was leaving the house I called to mind the words of the Psalmist, in the 126th Psalm, and like him, "I glorified God in my heart, in whom I trusted." These words had been impressed on my mind from the very day I was forced from Deptford[6] to the present hour, and I now saw them, as I thought, fulfilled and verified. My imagination was all rapture as I flew to the Register Office, and in this respect, like the apostle Peter[7] (whose deliverance from prison was so sudden and extraordinary, that he thought he was in a vision), I could scarcely believe I was awake. Heavens! who could do justice to my feelings at this moment! Not conquering heroes themselves, in the midst of a triumph—Not the tender mother who had just regained her long-lost infant, and presses it to her heart—Not the weary hungry mariner, at the sight of the desired friendly port—Not the lover, when he once more embraces his beloved mistress, after she had been ravished from his arms!—All within my breast was tumult, wildness, and delirium! My feet scarcely touched the ground, for they were

---

5. Release from slavery.
6. The port near London from which Equiano was sold by his English master.
7. Acts, chap, xii, ver. 9 [Equiano's note].

winged with joy, and, like Elijah, as he rose to Heaven,[8] they "were with light-ning sped as I went on." Every one I met I told of my happiness, and blazed about the virtue of my amiable master and captain.

When I got to the office and acquainted the Register with my errand he congratulated me on the occasion, and told me he would draw up my manu-mission for half price, which was a guinea. I thanked him for his kindness; and having received it and paid him, I hastened to my master to get him to sign it, that I might be fully released. Accordingly he signed the manumis-sion that day, so that, before night, I who had been a slave in the morning, trembling at the will of another, was become my own master, and completely free. I thought this was the happiest day I had ever experienced; and my joy was still heightened by the blessings and prayers of the sable race, particu-larly the aged, to whom my heart had ever been attached with reverence.

As the form of my manumission has something peculiar in it, and expresses the absolute power and dominion one man claims over his fellow, I shall beg leave to present it before my readers at full length:

Montserrat.—To all men unto whom these presents shall come: I Robert King, of the parish of St. Anthony in the said island, merchant, send greet-ing: Know ye, that I the aforesaid Robert King, for and in consideration of the sum of seventy pounds current money of the said island,[9] to me in hand paid, and to the intent that a negro man-slave, named Gustavus Vassa, shall and may become free, have manumitted, emancipated, enfranchised, and set free, and by these presents do manumit, emancipate, enfranchise, and set free, the aforesaid negro man-slave, named Gustavus Vassa, for ever, hereby giving, granting, and releasing unto him, the said Gustavus Vassa, all right, title, dominion, sovereignty, and property, which, as lord and master over the aforesaid Gustavus Vassa, I had, or now I have, or by any means whatsoever I may or can hereafter possibly have over him the aforesaid negro, for ever. In witness whereof I the above-said Robert King have unto these presents set my hand and seal, this tenth day of July, in the year of our Lord one thousand seven hundred and sixty-six.

ROBERT KING

Signed, sealed, and delivered in the presence of Terrylegay, Montserrat.
Registered the within manumission at full length, this eleventh day of July, 1766, in liber D.[1]

TERRYLEGAY, REGISTER.

In short, the fair as well as black people immediately styled me by a new appellation, to me the most desirable in the world, which was Freeman, and at the dances I gave my Georgia superfine blue clothes made no indifferent appearance, as I thought.

* * *

1789

8. 2 Kings 2.11.
9. The equivalent of forty pounds in British money.
1. Book or register D.

JAMES THOMSON
1700–1748

James Thomson, the first and most popular nature poet of the century, did not see London until he was twenty-five years old. He grew up in the picturesque border country of Roxboroughshire in Scotland and, after studying divinity in Edinburgh, went to London in 1725, bringing with him, in addition to a memory well stored with images of the external world, the earliest version of his descriptive poem "Winter" in 405 lines of blank verse. Published in 1726, it soon became popular. Thomson went on to publish "Summer" (1727), "Spring" (1728), and "Autumn" in the first collected edition of *The Seasons* (1730), to which he added the "Hymn to the Seasons." During the next sixteen years, because of constant revisions and additions, the poem grew in length to 5,541 lines. *The Seasons* continued to be popular well into the Romantic period; between 1730 and 1800 it was printed fifty times. Thomson's last poem, *The Castle of Indolence* (1748), is a witty imitation of Spenser; it moves from a playful portrait of the idleness of the poet and his friends to a celebration of industry and progress.

The Seasons set the fashion for the poetry of natural description. Generations of readers learned to look at the external world through Thomson's eyes and with the emotions that he had taught them to feel. The *eye* dominates the literature of external nature during the eighteenth century as the *imagination* was to do in the poetry of William Wordsworth. And Thomson amazed his readers by his capacity to see: the general effects of light and cloud and foliage or the particular image of a leaf tossed in the gale or the slender feet of a robin or the delicate film of ice at the edge of a brook. He tries to view each season from every perspective, as it might be perceived by a bird in the sky or by the tiniest insect, by God or a painter or Milton or Sir Isaac Newton (whom Thomson commemorated in a popular ode). As the poem grew, it became an *omnium gatherum* of contemporary ideas and interests: natural history; ideas about the nature of man and society, primitive and civilized; the conception of created nature as a source of religious experience, as an object of religious veneration, and as a continuing revelation of a Creator whose presence fills the world.

From The Seasons

From *Autumn*

[EVENING AND NIGHT][1]

The western sun withdraws the shortened day;
And humid evening, gliding o'er the sky,
In her chill progress, to the ground condensed
1085   The vapors throws. Where creeping waters ooze,

---

1. This passage, like many in *The Seasons*, went through extensive revisions. The opening lines on the harvest moon shining through fog (1082–1102) originally belonged to "Winter"; the descriptions of the aurora borealis (1108–37) and wildfire (1150–64) first appeared in "Summer." Scientific and visionary, divine and human perspectives are contrasted and join together in an intricate harmony.

Where marshes stagnate, and where rivers wind,
Cluster the rolling fogs, and swim along
The dusky-mantled lawn. Meanwhile the moon,
Full-orbed and breaking through the scattered clouds,
1090 Shows her broad visage in the crimsoned east.
Turned to the sun direct, her spotted disk
(Where mountains rise, umbrageous dales descend,[2]
And caverns deep, as optic tube° descries) *telescope*
A smaller earth, gives all his blaze again,
1095 Void of its flame, and sheds a softer day.
Now through the passing cloud she seems to stoop,
Now up the pure cerulean rides sublime.
Wide the pale deluge° floats, and streaming mild *moonlight*
O'er the skied[3] mountain to the shadowy vale,
1100 While rocks and floods reflect the quivering gleam,
The whole air whitens with a boundless tide
Of silver radiance trembling round the world.
  But when, half blotted from the sky, her light
Fainting, permits the starry fires to burn
1105 With keener luster through the depth of heaven;
Or quite extinct her deadened orb appears,
And scarce appears, of sickly beamless white;
Oft in this season, silent from the north
A blaze of meteors[4] shoots—ensweeping first
1110 The lower skies, they all at once converge
High to the crown[5] of heaven, and, all at once
Relapsing quick, as quickly reascend,
And mix and thwart,° extinguish and renew, *cross*
All ether coursing[6] in a maze of light.
1115 From look to look, contagious through the crowd,
The panic runs, and into wondrous shapes
The appearance throws—armies in meet° array, *fitting*
Thronged with aerial spears and steeds of fire;
Till, the long lines of full-extended war
1120 In bleeding fight commixed, the sanguine flood
Rolls a broad slaughter o'er the plains of heaven.
As thus they scan the visionary scene,
On all sides swells the superstitious din,
Incontinent; and busy frenzy talks
1125 Of blood and battle; cities overturned,
And late at night in swallowing earthquake sunk,
Or hideous wrapped in fierce ascending flame;
Of sallow famine, inundation, storm;
Of pestilence, and every great distress;
1130 Empires subversed,° when ruling fate has struck *overthrown*
The unalterable hour; even nature's self

---

2. Observation of the moon had revealed shadows ("umbrageous dales"), hence an irregular surface.
3. I.e., seeming to touch the sky.
4. Not meteors as we think of them, but the aurora borealis, or northern lights (multicolored, streaming pulses of light in the upper atmosphere). The aurora had often been associated with cosmic battles, in both literature and popular superstition.
5. The corona or central ring of the aurora.
6. Running through all the upper sky.

Is deemed to totter on the brink of time.
Not so the man of philosophic eye
And inspect sage:° the waving brightness he   *wise examination*
1135 Curious surveys, inquisitive to know
The causes and materials, yet unfixed,[7]
Of this appearance beautiful and new.
    Now black and deep the night begins to fall,
A shade immense! Sunk in the quenching gloom,
1140 Magnificent and vast, are heaven and earth.
Order confounded lies, all beauty void,
Distinction lost, and gay variety
One universal blot—such the fair power
Of light to kindle and create the whole.
1145 Drear is the state of the benighted wretch
Who then bewildered wanders through the dark
Full of pale fancies and chimeras° huge;   *imaginary monsters*
Nor visited by one directive ray
From cottage streaming or from airy hall.
1150 Perhaps, impatient as he stumbles on,
Struck from the root of slimy rushes, blue
The wildfire[8] scatters round, or, gathered, trails
A length of flame deceitful o'er the moss;
Whither decoyed by the fantastic blaze,
1155 Now lost and now renewed, he sinks absorbed,
Rider and horse, amid the miry gulf—
While still, from day to day, his pining wife
And plaintive children his return await,
In wild conjecture lost. At other times,
1160 Sent by the better genius of the night,
Innoxious,° gleaming on the horse's mane,   *harmless*
The meteor[9] sits, and shows the narrow path
That winding leads through pits of death, or else
Instructs him how to take the dangerous ford.
1165   The lengthened night elapsed, the morning shines
Serene, in all her dewy beauty bright,
Unfolding fair the last autumnal day.
And now the mounting sun dispels the fog;
The rigid hoarfrost melts before his beam;
1170 And, hung on every spray, on every blade
Of grass, the myriad dewdrops twinkle round.

1730

---

7. Unexplained by science.
8. Will-o'-the-wisp or ignis fatuus, a flitting phosphorescent light thought to kindle from the gas of decaying swamp grasses ("slimy rushes").

9. The ignis lambens, or St. Elmo's fire, a halo of light that shines on the tips of certain objects during electrical storms.

THOMAS GRAY
1716–1771

The man who wrote the English poem most loved by those whom Samuel Johnson called "the common reader" was a scholarly recluse who lived the quiet life of a university professor in the stagnant atmosphere of mid-eighteenth-century Cambridge. Born in London, Thomas Gray was the only one of twelve children to survive, and his family life was desperately unhappy. At eight he left home for Eton, where he made intimate friends: Richard West, a fellow poet; Thomas Ashton; and Horace Walpole, the son of the prime minister. After four years at Cambridge, Gray left without a degree to take the grand tour of France and Italy as Walpole's guest. The death of West in 1742 desolated Gray, and memories of West haunt much of his verse. He spent the rest of his life in Cambridge, pursuing his studies and writing wonderful letters as well as a handful of poems. Two high-flown Pindaric odes, "The Progress of Poesy" (1754) and "The Bard" (1757), display his learning and his love of nature and the sublime.

Most of Gray's poems take part in a contemporary reaction against the wit and satiric elegance of Pope's couplets; poets sought a new style, at once intimate and prophetic. Gray was not easily satisfied; he constantly revised his poems and published very little. Because he held that "the language of the age is never the language of poetry," he often uses archaic words and a word order borrowed from Latin, where a verb can precede its subject (as in line 35 of the "Elegy Written in a Country Churchyard": "Awaits alike the inevitable hour"). But the "Elegy" stands alone in his work. It balances Latinate phrases with living English speech, and the learning of a scholar with a common humanity that everyone can share. Johnson, who did not usually like Gray's poetry, acknowledged that the "Elegy" would live on:

> The Churchyard abounds with images that find a mirror in every mind, and with sentiments to which every bosom returns an echo. The four stanzas beginning "Yet even these bones" are to me original: I have never seen the notions in any other place; yet he that reads them here, persuades himself that he has always felt them. Had Gray written often thus, it had been vain to blame, and useless to praise him.

Ode on a Distant Prospect of Eton College

Anthrōpos ikanē prophasis eis tò dustukheīn.[1]
MENANDER

Ye distant spires, ye antique towers,
  That crown the watery glade,
Where grateful Science° still adores   *Learning*
  Her Henry's holy shade;[2]
5 And ye, that from the stately brow

---

1. I am a man: sufficient reason for being miserable (Greek).
2. Henry VI founded Eton in 1440.

Of Windsor's heights[3] the expanse below
   Of grove, of lawn, of mead survey,
Whose turf, whose shade, whose flowers among
Wanders the hoary Thames along
10   His silver-winding way.

Ah happy hills, ah pleasing shade,
   Ah fields beloved in vain,
Where once my careless childhood strayed,
   A stranger yet to pain!
15 I feel the gales, that from ye blow,
A momentary bliss bestow,
   As waving fresh their gladsome wing,
My weary soul they seem to soothe,
And, redolent of joy and youth,
20   To breathe a second spring.

Say, Father Thames, for thou hast seen
   Full many a sprightly race
Disporting on thy margent° green   *bank*
   The paths of pleasure trace,
25 Who foremost now delight to cleave
With pliant arm thy glassy wave?
   The captive linnet which enthrall?°   *imprison*
What idle progeny succeed[4]
To chase the rolling circle's° speed,   *hoop's*
30   Or urge the flying ball?

While some on earnest business bent
   Their murmuring labors[5] ply
'Gainst graver hours, that bring constraint
   To sweeten liberty:
35 Some bold adventurers disdain
The limits of their little reign,
   And unknown regions dare descry:
Still as they run they look behind,
They hear a voice in every wind,
40   And snatch a fearful joy.

Gay hope is theirs by fancy fed,
   Less pleasing when possessed;
The tear forgot as soon as shed,
   The sunshine of the breast:
45 Theirs buxom° health of rosy hue,   *zestful, jolly*
Wild wit, invention ever new,
   And lively cheer of vigor born;
The thoughtless day, the easy night,
The spirits pure, the slumbers light,
50   That fly the approach of morn.

---

3. Windsor Castle, across the Thames valley
from Eton.

4. I.e., follow in succession Gray's generation.
5. Recited lessons for school.

Alas, regardless of their doom,
  The little victims play!
No sense have they of ills to come,
  Nor care beyond today.
55 Yet see how all around 'em wait
The ministers of human fate,
  And black Misfortune's baleful train!
Ah, show them where in ambush stand
To seize their prey the murderous band!
60   Ah, tell them they are men!

These shall the fury Passions tear,
  The vultures of the mind,
Disdainful Anger, pallid Fear,
  And Shame that skulks behind;
65 Or pining Love shall waste their youth,
Or Jealousy with rankling tooth,
  That inly gnaws the secret heart,
And Envy wan, and faded Care,
Grim-visaged comfortless Despair,
70   And Sorrow's piercing dart.

Ambition this shall tempt to rise,
  Then whirl the wretch from high,
To bitter Scorn a sacrifice,
  And grinning Infamy.
75 The stings of Falsehood those shall try,
And hard Unkindness' altered eye,
  That mocks the tear it forced to flow;
And keen Remorse with blood defiled,
And moody Madness laughing wild
80   Amid severest woe.

Lo, in the vale of years beneath
  A grisly troop are seen,
The painful family of Death,
  More hideous than their queen:
85 This racks the joints, this fires the veins,
That every laboring sinew strains,
  Those in the deeper vitals rage:
Lo, Poverty, to fill the band,
That numbs the soul with icy hand,
90   And slow-consuming Age.

To each his sufferings: all are men,
  Condemned alike to groan;
The tender for another's pain,
  The unfeeling for his own.
95 Yet ah! why should they know their fate?
Since sorrow never comes too late,
  And happiness too swiftly flies.
Thought would destroy their paradise.

No more; where ignorance is bliss,
100   'Tis folly to be wise.

1742   1747

Ode on the Death of a Favorite Cat[1]

Drowned in a Tub of Goldfishes

'Twas on a lofty vase's side,
Where China's gayest art had dyed
    The azure flowers that blow;°   bloom
Demurest of the tabby kind,
5   The pensive Selima reclined,
    Gazed on the lake below.

Her conscious tail her joy declared;
The fair round face, the snowy beard,
    The velvet of her paws,
10   Her coat, that with the tortoise vies,
Her ears of jet, and emerald eyes,
    She saw; and purred applause.

Still had she gazed; but 'midst the tide
Two angel forms were seen to glide,
15   The genii of the stream:
Their scaly armor's Tyrian° hue   purple
Through richest purple to the view
    Betrayed a golden gleam.

The hapless nymph with wonder saw:
20   A whisker first and then a claw,
    With many an ardent wish,
She stretched in vain to reach the prize.
What female heart can gold despise?
    What cat's averse to fish?

25   Presumptuous maid! with looks intent
Again she stretched, again she bent,
    Nor knew the gulf between.
(Malignant Fate sat by and smiled)
The slippery verge her feet beguiled,
30   She tumbled headlong in.

Eight times emerging from the flood
She mewed to every watery god,
    Some speedy aid to send.

1. Selima, one of Horace Walpole's cats, had recently drowned in a china cistern. Gray wrote this memorial at Walpole's request. For an illus- tration of this poem by William Blake, see the color insert in this volume.

No dolphin came, no nereid° stirred: *sea nymph*
35 Nor cruel Tom, nor Susan² heard.
  A favorite has no friend!

From hence, ye beauties, undeceived,
Know, one false step is ne'er retrieved,
  And be with caution bold.
40 Not all that tempts your wandering eyes
And heedless hearts is lawful prize;
  Nor all that glisters gold.

1747   1748

Elegy Written in a Country Churchyard

The curfew¹ tolls the knell of parting day,
 The lowing herd wind slowly o'er the lea,
The plowman homeward plods his weary way,
 And leaves the world to darkness and to me.

5 Now fades the glimmering landscape on the sight,
 And all the air a solemn stillness holds,
Save where the beetle wheels his droning flight,
 And drowsy tinklings lull the distant folds;

Save that from yonder ivy-mantled tower
10 The moping owl does to the moon complain
Of such, as wandering near her secret bower,
 Molest her ancient solitary reign.

Beneath those rugged elms, that yew tree's shade,
 Where heaves the turf in many a moldering heap,
15 Each in his narrow cell forever laid,
 The rude° forefathers of the hamlet sleep. *uneducated*

The breezy call of incense-breathing Morn,
 The swallow twittering from the straw-built shed,
The cock's shrill clarion, or the echoing horn,° *hunter's horn*
20 No more shall rouse them from their lowly bed.

For them no more the blazing hearth shall burn,
 Or busy housewife ply her evening care;
No children run to lisp their sire's return,
 Or climb his knees the envied kiss to share.

25 Oft did the harvest to their sickle yield,
 Their furrow oft the stubborn glebe° has broke; *soil*
How jocund did they drive their team afield!
 How bowed the woods beneath their sturdy stroke!

2. Servants' names.   1. A bell rung in the evening.

Let not Ambition mock their useful toil,
     30   Their homely joys, and destiny obscure;
Nor Grandeur hear with a disdainful smile
     The short and simple annals of the poor.

The boast of heraldry,° the pomp of power,   *noble birth*
     And all that beauty, all that wealth e'er gave,
     35   Awaits alike the inevitable hour.
     The paths of glory lead but to the grave.

Nor you, ye proud, impute to these the fault,
     If Memory o'er their tomb no trophies[2] raise,
Where through the long-drawn aisle and fretted[3] vault
     40   The pealing anthem swells the note of praise.

Can storied urn[4] or animated° bust   *lifelike*
     Back to its mansion call the fleeting breath?
Can Honor's voice provoke° the silent dust,   *call forth*
     Or Flattery soothe the dull cold ear of Death?

     45   Perhaps in this neglected spot is laid
     Some heart once pregnant with celestial fire;
Hands that the rod of empire might have swayed,°   *wielded*
     Or waked to ecstasy the living lyre.

But Knowledge to their eyes her ample page
     50   Rich with the spoils of time did ne'er unroll;
Chill Penury repressed their noble rage,°   *inspiration*
     And froze the genial° current of the soul.   *creative*

Full many a gem of purest ray serene,
     The dark unfathomed caves of ocean bear:
     55   Full many a flower is born to blush unseen,
     And waste its sweetness on the desert air.

Some village Hampden,[5] that with dauntless breast
     The little tyrant of his fields withstood;
Some mute inglorious Milton here may rest,
     60   Some Cromwell guiltless of his country's blood.

The applause of listening senates to command,
     The threats of pain and ruin to despise,
To scatter plenty o'er a smiling land,
     And read their history in a nation's eyes,

     65   Their lot forbade: nor circumscribed alone
     Their growing virtues, but their crimes confined;

---

2. An ornamental or symbolic group of figures depicting the achievements of the deceased.
3. Decorated with intersecting lines in relief.
4. A funeral urn with an epitaph or pictured story inscribed on it.

5. John Hampden (1594–1643), who, both as a private citizen and as a member of Parliament, zealously defended the rights of the people against the autocratic policies of Charles I.

Forbade to wade through slaughter to a throne,
    And shut the gates of mercy on mankind,

The struggling pangs of conscious truth to hide,
70   To quench the blushes of ingenuous shame,
Or heap the shrine of Luxury and Pride
    With incense kindled at the Muse's flame.

Far from the madding crowd's ignoble strife,
    Their sober wishes never learned to stray;
75 Along the cool sequestered vale of life
    They kept the noiseless tenor of their way.

Yet even these bones from insult to protect
    Some frail memorial still erected nigh,
With uncouth rhymes and shapeless sculpture decked,[6]
80   Implores the passing tribute of a sigh.

Their name, their years, spelt by the unlettered Muse,
    The place of fame and elegy supply:
And many a holy text around she strews,
    That teach the rustic moralist to die.

85 For who to dumb Forgetfulness a prey,
    This pleasing anxious being e'er resigned,
Left the warm precincts of the cheerful day,
    Nor cast one longing lingering look behind?

On some fond breast the parting soul relies,
90   Some pious drops the closing eye requires;
Even from the tomb the voice of Nature cries,
    Even in our ashes live their wonted fires.

For thee, who mindful of the unhonored dead
    Dost in these lines their artless tale relate;
95 If chance,° by lonely contemplation led,   *perchance*
    Some kindred spirit shall inquire thy fate,

Haply some hoary-headed swain may say,
    "Oft have we seen him at the peep of dawn
Brushing with hasty steps the dews away
100   To meet the sun upon the upland lawn.

"There at the foot of yonder nodding beech
    That wreathes its old fantastic roots so high,
His listless length at noontide would he stretch,
    And pore upon the brook that babbles by.

105 "Hard by yon wood, now smiling as in scorn,
    Muttering his wayward fancies he would rove,

---

6. Cf. "storied urn or animated bust" dedicated inside the church to "the proud" (line 41).

Now drooping, woeful wan, like one forlorn,
　　Or crazed with care, or crossed in hopeless love.

"One morn I missed him on the customed hill,
110　　Along the heath and near his favorite tree;
Another came; nor yet beside the rill,
　　Nor up the lawn, nor at the wood was he;

"The next with dirges due in sad array
　　Slow through the churchway path we saw him borne.
115 Approach and read (for thou canst read) the lay,
　　Graved on the stone beneath yon aged thorn."

The Epitaph

Here rests his head upon the lap of Earth
　　A youth to Fortune and to Fame unknown.
Fair Science° frowned not on his humble birth,　　　　　Learning
120　　*And Melancholy marked him for her own.*

Large was his bounty, and his soul sincere,
　　Heaven did a recompense as largely send:
He gave to Misery all he had, a tear,
　　He gained from Heaven ('twas all he wished) a friend.

125　*No farther seek his merits to disclose,*
　　Or draw his frailties from their dread abode
(There they alike in trembling hope repose),
　　The bosom of his Father and his God.

ca. 1742–50　　　　　　　　　　　　　　　　　　　　　　　1751

WILLIAM COLLINS
1721–1759

William Collins was born in Chichester and was educated at Winchester and Oxford. Coming up to London from the university, he tried to establish himself as an author, but he was given rather to planning than to writing books. He came to know Samuel Johnson, who later remembered him affectionately as a man of learning who "loved fairies, genii, giants, and monsters" and who "delighted to rove through the meanders of enchantment." In 1746 Collins published his *Odes on Several Descriptive and Allegorical Subjects*, his part in an undertaking, with his friend Joseph Warton, to create a new poetry, more lyrical and fanciful than that of Alexander Pope's generation. Collins's *Odes* address personified abstractions (Fear, Pity, the Passions), which are imagined as vivid presences that overwhelm the poet as he calls them to life. In form these poems represent a new version of the Great or

Cowleian Ode (see headnote to Ben Jonson's "Cary-Morison ode," p. 1551); Collins returns to Pindar's regularity of structure. But the originality of the *Odes* lies in their intensity of vision, which risks obscurity in quest of the sublime.

To his disappointment, contemporaries preferred his early *Persian Eclogues* to the more difficult *Odes*. Inheriting some money, the poet traveled for a while, but fits of depression gradually deepened into total debility. He spent his last years in Chichester, forgotten by all but a small circle of loyal friends. As the century progressed he gained in reputation. The Romantics admired his poems and felt akin to him. Coleridge said that "Ode on the Poetical Character" "has inspired and whirled me along with greater agitations of enthusiasm than any the most *impassioned* scene in Schiller or Shakespeare."

Ode on the Poetical Character   This ode, long disregarded, has lately been acclaimed by critics as an early, dramatic engagement with one of the central concerns of the Romantic age—the origin and role of the creative imagination and, indeed, of the poet himself.

In the strophe an analogy is drawn between the magic girdle of Venus, which only the chaste can wear, and the cest, or girdle, of Fancy, or the creative imagination. In the epode the creation of the world is presented as an act of the divine imagination. Inspired by God, Fancy gives birth to another sublime creation, the spirit of poetry.

In the antistrophe, John Milton is regarded as the type of poet divinely able to wear the girdle of Fancy. Collins pictures himself pursuing the "guiding steps" (line 71) of Milton, as of Edmund Spenser (in the strophe)—both poet-prophets. His movement away from the elegant school of Edmund Waller (and, by implication, that of Alexander Pope) is "In vain" (line 72), however, for he lives in an uninspired age.

Ode on the Poetical Character

Strophe

As once, if not with light regard,
I read aright that gifted bard
(Him[1] whose school above the rest
His loveliest Elfin Queen has blest),
5   One, only one, unrivaled fair
Might hope the magic girdle wear,
At solemn tourney hung on high,
The wish of each love-darting eye;[2]
Lo! to each other nymph in turn applied,
10   As if, in air unseen, some hovering hand,
Some chaste and angel-friend to virgin-fame,
    With whispered spell had burst the starting band,
It left unblest her loathed dishonored side;
    Happier, hopeless fair, if never
15   Her baffled hand with vain endeavor
Had touched that fatal zone° to her denied!   *girdle*
Young Fancy thus, to me divinest name,

---

1. Edmund Spenser.
2. *The Faerie Queene* 4.5 tells of the contest of many beautiful ladies for the girdle of Venus.

To whom, prepared and bathed in Heaven
The cest° of amplest power is given: *girdle*
20 To few the godlike gift assigns,
To gird their blest, prophetic loins,[3]
And gaze her visions wild, and feel unmixed her flame!

Epode

The band, as fairy legends say,
Was wove on that creating day,
25 When He,[4] who called with thought to birth
Yon tented sky, this laughing earth,
And dressed with springs, and forests tall,
And poured the main engirting all,
Long by the loved Enthusiast[5] wooed,
30 Himself in some diviner mood,
Retiring, sate with her alone,
And placed her on his sapphire throne;
The whiles, the vaulted shrine around,
Seraphic wires were heard to sound,
35 Now sublimest triumph swelling,
Now on love and mercy dwelling;
And she, from out the veiling cloud,
Breathed her magic notes aloud:
And thou, thou rich-haired Youth of Morn,[6]
40 And all thy subject life was born!
The dangerous Passions kept aloof,
Far from the sainted growing woof:
But near it sate ecstatic Wonder,
Listening the deep applauding thunder:
45 And Truth, in sunny vest arrayed,
By whose the tarsel's° eyes were made; *falcon's*
All the shadowy tribes of Mind,
In braided dance their murmurs joined,
And all the bright uncounted Powers
50 Who feed on Heaven's ambrosial flowers.
Where is the bard, whose soul can now
Its high presuming hopes avow?
Where he who thinks, with rapture blind,
This hallow'd work[7] for him designed?

Antistrophe

55 High on some cliff, to Heaven up-piled,
Of rude access, of prospect wild,
Where, tangled round the jealous° steep, *vigilant*
Strange shades o'erbrow the valleys deep,

3. Pronounced *lines*.
4. God, on the day of creation.
5. I.e., Fancy; literally, "enthusiast" means "one possessed by a god."

6. Apollo, god of the sun and of poetry, associated with the archetypal poet.
7. The girdle of Fancy.

And holy Genii guard the rock,
60 Its glooms embrown, its springs unlock,
    While on its rich ambitious head,
    An Eden, like his° own, lies spread: *Milton's*
    I view that oak, the fancied glades among,
    By which as Milton lay, his evening ear,
65 From many a cloud that dropped ethereal dew,
    Nigh sphered in Heaven its native strains could hear:
    On which that ancient trump he reached was hung;
        Thither oft, his glory greeting,
        From Waller's[8] myrtle shades retreating,
70 With many a vow from Hope's aspiring tongue,
    My trembling feet his guiding steps pursue;
        In vain—such bliss to one alone,°   *Milton*
        Of all the sons of soul was known,
        And Heaven, and Fancy, kindred powers,
75   Have now o'erturned the inspiring bowers,
    Or curtained close such scene from every future view.

                                                           1746

Ode to Evening[1]

    If aught of oaten stop,[2] or pastoral song,
    May hope, chaste Eve, to soothe thy modest ear,
        Like thy own solemn springs,
        Thy springs and dying gales,
5   O nymph reserved, while now the bright-haired sun
    Sits in yon western tent, whose cloudy skirts,
        With brede° ethereal wove,   *embroidery*
        O'erhang his wavy bed:
    Now air is hushed, save where the weak-eyed bat,
10 With short shrill shriek flits by on leathern wing,
        Or where the beetle winds
        His small but sullen horn,
    As oft he rises 'midst the twilight path,
    Against the pilgrim borne in heedless hum:
15   Now teach me, maid composed,
        To breathe some softened strain,
    Whose numbers,° stealing through thy darkening vale,   *measures*
    May not unseemly with its stillness suit,
        As, musing slow, I hail
20   Thy genial° loved return!   *life-giving*
    For when thy folding-star[3] arising shows
    His paly circlet, at his warning lamp

---

8. Edmund Waller (1606–1687). The myrtle is the symbol of love poetry; Waller's poetry is thought of as trivial compared with Milton's grandeur.
1. Collins borrowed the metrical structure and the rhymeless lines of this ode from Milton's translation of Horace, *Odes* 1.5 (1673). The text printed here is based on the revised version, published in Dodsley's *Miscellany* (1748).
2. Finger hole in a shepherd's flute.
3. The evening star, which signals the hour for herding the sheep into the sheepfold.

The fragrant Hours, and elves
Who slept in flowers the day,
25 And many a nymph who wreaths her brows with sedge,
And sheds the freshening dew, and, lovelier still,
    The pensive Pleasures sweet,
    Prepare thy shadowy car.
Then lead, calm vot'ress, where some sheety lake
30 Cheers the lone heath, or some time-hallowed pile
    Or upland fallows gray
    Reflect its last cool gleam.
But when chill blustering winds, or driving rain,
Forbid my willing feet, be mine the hut
35   That from the mountain's side
    Views wilds, and swelling floods,
And hamlets brown, and dim-discovered spires,
And hears their simple bell, and marks o'er all
    Thy dewy fingers draw
40   The gradual dusky veil.
While Spring shall pour his showers, as oft he wont,
And bathe thy breathing tresses, meekest Eve;
    While Summer loves to sport
    Beneath thy lingering light;
45 While sallow Autumn fills thy lap with leaves;
Or Winter, yelling through the troublous air,
    Affrights thy shrinking train,
    And rudely rends thy robes;
So long, sure-found beneath the sylvan shed,
50 Shall Fancy, Friendship, Science, rose-lipped Health,
    Thy gentlest influence own,
    And hymn thy favorite name!

1746, 1748

CHRISTOPHER SMART
1722–1771

In 1756 Christopher Smart, who had won prizes at Pembroke College, Cambridge, as a scholar and poet and was known in London as a wit and bon vivant, was seized by religious mania: "a preternatural excitement to prayer," according to Hester Thrale, "which he held it as a duty not to control or repress." If Smart had been content to pray in private, his life might have ended as happily as it began, but he insisted on kneeling down in the streets, in parks, and in assembly rooms. He became a public nuisance, and the public took its revenge. For most of the next seven years Smart was confined, first in St. Luke's hospital, then in a private madhouse. There, severed from his wife, his children, and his friends, he began to write a bold new sort of poetry:

vivid, concise, abrupt, syntactically daring. Few of his contemporaries noticed it. After Smart's release from the madhouse (1763) he fell into debt—he had always been profligate—and his masterpiece, *A Song to David* (1763), was almost completely ignored (for the complete text of *A Song to David*, see the supplemental ebook). He died, forgotten, in a debtor's prison. But in the nineteenth century his reputation revived, and since the publication of *Jubilate Agno* in 1939 his poems have become newly famous.

Jubilate Agno (Rejoice in the Lamb), written a few lines at a time during Smart's confinement, is (1) a record of his daily life and thoughts; (2) the notebook of a scholar, crammed with puns and obscure learning, which sets out elaborate correspondences between the world of the Bible and modern England; and (3) a personal testament or book of worship, antiphonally arranged in lines beginning alternately with *Let* and *For*, which seeks to join the material and spiritual universes in one unending prayer. It has also come to be recognized, since first published in 1939 by W. F. Stead, as a poem—a poem unique in English for its ecstatic sense of the presence of the divine spirit. The most famous passage describes Smart's cat, Jeoffry, his only companion during the years of confinement: "For I am possessed of a cat, surpassing in beauty, from whom I take occasion to bless Almighty God." At once a real cat, lovingly observed in all its frisks, and visible evidence of the providential plan, Jeoffry celebrates the Maker, as all things do, in his very being.

From Jubilate Agno

[MY CAT JEOFFRY]

For I will consider my Cat Jeoffry.
For he is the servant of the Living God duly and daily serving him.
For at the first glance of the glory of God in the East° he   sunrise
    worships in his way.
For is this done by wreathing his body seven times round with elegant
    quickness.
5 For then he leaps up to catch the musk, wch is the blessing of God
    upon his prayer.
For he rolls upon prank° to work it in.   prankishly
For having done duty and received blessing he begins to consider
    himself.
For this he performs in ten degrees.
For first he looks upon his fore-paws to see if they are clean.
10 For secondly he kicks up behind to clear away there.
For thirdly he works it upon stretch with the fore-paws extended.
For fourthly he sharpens his paws by wood.
For fifthly he washes himself.
For Sixthly he rolls upon wash.
15 For Seventhly he fleas himself, that he may not be interrupted upon
    the beat.
For Eighthly he rubs himself against a post.
For Ninthly he looks up for his instructions.
For Tenthly he goes in quest of food.
For having consider'd God and himself he will consider his neighbor.
20 For if he meets another cat he will kiss her in kindness.
For when he takes his prey he plays with it to give it a chance.

For one mouse in seven escapes by his dallying.
For when his day's work is done his business more properly begins.
For he keeps the Lord's watch in the night against the adversary.
25 For he counteracts the powers of darkness by his electrical skin &
  glaring eyes.
For he counteracts the Devil, who is death, by brisking about the life.
For in his morning orisons he loves the sun and the sun loves him.
For he is of the tribe of Tiger.
For the Cherub Cat is a term of the Angel Tiger.[1]
30 For he has the subtlety and hissing of a serpent, which in goodness he
  suppresses.
For he will not do destruction if he is well-fed, neither will he spit
  without provocation.
For he purrs in thankfulness, when God tells him he's a good Cat.
For he is an instrument for the children to learn benevolence upon.
For every house is incomplete without him & a blessing is lacking in
  the spirit.
35 For the Lord commanded Moses concerning the cats at the departure
  of the Children of Israel from Egypt.[2]
For every family had one cat at least in the bag.
For the English Cats are the best in Europe.
For he is the cleanest in the use of his fore-paws of any quadrupede.
For the dexterity of his defence is an instance of the love of God to
  him exceedingly.
40 For he is the quickest to his mark of any creature.
For he is tenacious of his point.
For he is a mixture of gravity and waggery.
For he knows that God is his Saviour.
For there is nothing sweeter than his peace when at rest.
45 For there is nothing brisker than his life when in motion.
For he is of the Lord's poor and so indeed is he called by benevolence
  perpetually—Poor Jeoffry! poor Jeoffry! the rat has bit thy throat.
For I bless the name of the Lord Jesus that Jeoffry is better.
For the divine spirit comes about his body to sustain it in compleat
  cat.
For his tongue is exceeding pure so that it has in purity what it wants
  in music.
50 For he is docile and can learn certain things.
For he can set up with gravity which is patience upon approbation.
For he can fetch and carry, which is patience in employment.
For he can jump over a stick which is patience upon proof positive.
For he can spraggle upon waggle[3] at the word of command.
55 For he can jump from an eminence into his master's bosom.
For he can catch the cork and toss it again.
For he is hated by the hypocrite and miser.
For the former is afraid of detection.
For the latter refuses the charge.
60 For he camels his back to bear the first notion of business.
For he is good to think on, if a man would express himself neatly.

---

1. As a cherub is a small angel, so a cat is a small
tiger.
2. No cats are mentioned in the Bible.

3. He can sprawl when his master waggles a finger or stick.

For he made a great figure in Egypt for his signal services.
For he killed the Icneumon-rat very pernicious by land.[4]
For his ears are so acute that they sting again.
65 For from this proceeds the passing° quickness of his   *surpassing*
        attention.
For by stroking of him I have found out electricity.
For I perceived God's light about him both wax and fire.
For the Electrical fire is the spiritual substance, which God sends
        from heaven to sustain the bodies both of man and beast.
For God has blessed him in the variety of his movements.
70 For, though he cannot fly, he is an excellent clamberer.
For his motions upon the face of the earth are more than any other
        quadrupede.
For he can tread to all the measures upon the music.
For he can swim for life.
For he can creep.

1759–63   1939

4. The ichneumon, which resembles a weasel, was venerated and domesticated by the ancient
Egyptians.

OLIVER GOLDSMITH
ca. 1730–1774

Oliver Goldsmith was born in Ireland, the son of an Anglican clergyman whose geniality he inherited and whose improvidence he imitated. Disfigured by smallpox, he grew up homely, ungainly, apparently stupid, and certainly idle. Nonetheless, he was sent to Trinity College, Dublin, as a sizar—i.e., a student who did menial jobs for well-to-do undergraduates—and took his A.B. in 1749. After studying medicine at the University of Edinburgh he wandered for a while on the Continent, visiting Holland, France, Italy, and Switzerland. He returned to England in 1756 with a mysteriously acquired M.D. and tried in vain to support himself as a physician among the poor in the borough of Southwark. Eventually he drifted into the profession of hack writer for Ralph Griffiths, the proprietor of the *Monthly Review*, and later worked for and with the benevolent publisher John Newbery. His first success, *An Inquiry into the Present State of Polite Learning in Europe* (1759), attributes the decline of the fine arts in mid-eighteenth-century Europe to the lack of enlightened patronage and to the malign influence of criticism and scholarship. Soon he became a famous author and an intimate of the brilliant circle around Samuel Johnson. Although his writings brought in a great deal of money, extravagance and generosity kept him always in debt. He died owing the prodigious sum (for a man whose only source of income was writing) of £2000.

The variety and excellence of Goldsmith's work are astonishing. His easy and pleasant prose style and shrewd observations of character and scene enliven his essays, especially those in the series *The Citizen of the World* (1762), and his popular novel *The Vicar of Wakefield* (1766). Two plays, *The Good-Natured Man* (1768) and *She Stoops to Conquer* (1773), achieve a sort of hearty and mirthful comedy— unspoiled by the fashionable sentimentality of the moment—that is unique in the century. His two major poems, *The Traveler, or A Prospect of Society* (1764) and *The Deserted Village*, are distinguished for the unforced grace of their couplets and for an air of simplicity that is far from simple to achieve.

The Deserted Village[1]

Sweet Auburn! loveliest village of the plain,
Where health and plenty cheered the laboring swain,
Where smiling spring its earliest visit paid,
And parting summer's lingering blooms delayed:
5   Dear lovely bowers of innocence and ease,
Seats of my youth, when every sport could please,
How often have I loitered o'er thy green,
Where humble happiness endeared each scene;
How often have I paused on every charm,
10   The sheltered cot,° the cultivated farm,   *cottage*
The never-failing brook, the busy mill,
The decent church that topped the neighboring hill,
The hawthorn bush, with seats beneath the shade,
For talking age and whispering lovers made;
15   How often have I blessed the coming day,°   *Sunday*
When toil remitting lent its turn to play,
And all the village train, from labor free,
Led up their sports beneath the spreading tree,
While many a pastime circled in the shade,
20   The young contending as the old surveyed;
And many a gambol frolicked o'er the ground,
And sleights of art and feats of strength went round;
And still as each repeated pleasure tired,
Succeeding sports the mirthful band inspired;
25   The dancing pair that simply sought renown,
By holding out to tire each other down;
The swain mistrustless of his smutted face,
While secret laughter tittered round the place;
The bashful virgin's sidelong looks of love,
30   The matron's glance that would those looks reprove:
These were thy charms, sweet village! sports like these,
With sweet succession, taught even toil to please;
These round thy bowers their cheerful influence shed,
These were thy charms—But all these charms are fled.
35   Sweet smiling village, loveliest of the lawn,
Thy sports are fled, and all thy charms withdrawn;
Amidst thy bowers the tyrant's hand is seen,

---

1. *The Deserted Village* is an idealization of English rural life mingled with poignant memories of the poet's own youth in Lissoy, Ireland. Goldsmith was seriously concerned about the effects of the agricultural revolution then in progress, which was being hastened by Enclosure Acts. Either for the sake of more profitable farming or to create vast private parks and landscape

Thomas Gainsborough, *The Cottage Door,* ca. 1778. Gainsborough painted several versions of this idealized, cozy view of home, motherhood, and childhood as experienced by peasants in rural Britain.

And desolation saddens all thy green:
One only master grasps the whole domain,
40 And half a tillage stints thy smiling plain;
No more thy glassy brook reflects the day,
But choked with sedges, works its weedy way;
Along thy glades, a solitary guest,
The hollow-sounding bittern guards its nest;
45 Amidst thy desert walks the lapwing flies,
And tires their echoes with unvaried cries.
Sunk are thy bowers, in shapeless ruin all,

---

gardens, arable land was being "enclosed"—i.e., taken out the hands of small proprietors—thus displacing yeoman farmers who, like their ancestors, had lived for generations in small villages, grazing their cattle on common land and raising food on small holdings. The only alternative available to many such people was to seek employment in the city or to migrate to America. In the poem, Goldsmith opposes "luxury" (the increase of wealth, the growth of cities, and the costly country estates of great noblemen and wealthy merchants) to "rural virtue" (the old agrarian economy that supported a sturdy population of independent peasants). His poem is thus at once a nostalgic lament for a doomed way of life and a denunciation of what he regarded as the corrupting, destructive force of new wealth.

And the long grass o'ertops the moldering wall;
And trembling, shrinking from the spoiler's hand,
50 Far, far away thy children leave the land.
 Ill fares the land, to hastening ills a prey,
Where wealth accumulates, and men decay;
Princes and lords may flourish, or may fade;
A breath can make them, as a breath has made;
55 But a bold peasantry, their country's pride.
When once destroyed, can never be supplied.
 A time there was, ere England's griefs began,
When every rood° of ground maintained its man;   *quarter acre*
For him light labor spread her wholesome store,
60 Just gave what life required, but gave no more:
His best companions, innocence and health;
And his best riches, ignorance of wealth.
 But times are altered; Trade's unfeeling train
Usurp the land and dispossess the swain;
65 Along the lawn, where scattered hamlets rose,
Unwieldy wealth, and cumbrous° pomp repose;   *oppressive*
And every want to opulence allied,
And every pang that folly pays to pride.
These gentle hours that plenty bade to bloom,
70 Those calm desires that asked but little room,
Those healthful sports that graced the peaceful scene,
Lived in each look, and brightened all the green;
These far departing seek a kinder shore,
And rural mirth and manners are no more.
75 Sweet Auburn! parent of the blissful hour,
Thy glades forlorn confess the tyrant's power.
Here, as I take my solitary rounds,
Amidst thy tangling walks, and ruined grounds,
And, many a year elapsed, return to view
80 Where once the cottage stood, the hawthorn grew,
Remembrance wakes with all her busy train,
Swells at my breast, and turns the past to pain.
 In all my wanderings round this world of care,
In all my griefs—and God has given my share—
85 I still had hopes my latest hours to crown,
Amidst these humble bowers to lay me down;
To husband out life's taper at the close,
And keep the flame from wasting by repose.
I still had hopes, for pride attends us still,
90 Amidst the swains to show my book-learned skill,
Around my fire an evening group to draw,
And tell of all I felt, and all I saw;
And, as an hare whom hounds and horns pursue,
Pants to the place from whence at first she flew,
95 I still had hopes, my long vexations past,
Here to return—and die at home at last.
 O blest retirement, friend to life's decline,
Retreats from care that never must be mine,
How happy he who crowns in shades like these,

100 A youth of labor with an age of ease;
Who quits a world where strong temptations try,
And, since 'tis hard to combat, learns to fly!
For him no wretches, born to work and weep,
Explore the mine, or tempt the dangerous deep;
105 No surly porter stands in guilty state
To spurn imploring famine from the gate;
But on he moves to meet his latter end,
Angels around befriending virtue's friend;
Bends to the grave with unperceived decay,
110 While Resignation gently slopes the way;
And, all his prospects brightening to the last,
His Heaven commences ere the world be passed!
    Sweet was the sound when oft at evening's close,
Up yonder hill the village murmur rose;
115 There, as I passed with careless steps and slow,
The mingling notes came softened from below;
The swain responsive as the milkmaid sung,
The sober herd that lowed to meet their young,
The noisy geese that gabbled o'er the pool,
120 The playful children just let loose from school;
The watchdog's voice that bayed the whispering wind,
And the loud laugh that spoke the vacant° mind;   *idle, carefree*
These all in sweet confusion sought the shade,
And filled each pause the nightingale had made.
125 But now the sounds of population fail,
No cheerful murmurs fluctuate in the gale,
No busy steps the grass-grown footway tread,
For all the bloomy flush of life is fled.
All but yon widowed, solitary thing
130 That feebly bends beside the plashy° spring;   *boggy*
She, wretched matron, forced, in age, for bread,
To strip the brook with mantling cresses spread,
To pick her wintry faggot from the thorn,
To seek her nightly shed, and weep till morn;
135 She only left of all the harmless train,
The sad historian of the pensive° plain.   *gloomy*
    Near yonder copse, where once the garden smiled,
And still where many a garden flower grows wild,
There, where a few torn shrubs the place disclose,
140 The village preacher's modest mansion rose.
A man he was, to all the country dear,
And passing rich with forty pounds a year;
Remote from towns he ran his godly race,
Nor e'er had changed, nor wished to change his place;
145 Unpracticed he to fawn, or seek for power,
By doctrines fashioned to the varying hour;
Far other aims his heart had learned to prize,
More skilled to raise the wretched than to rise.
His house was known to all the vagrant train,
150 He chid their wanderings, but relieved their pain;
The long-remembered beggar was his guest,

Whose beard descending swept his aged breast;
The ruined spendthrift, now no longer proud,
Claimed kindred there, and had his claims allowed;
155 The broken soldier, kindly bade to stay,
Sate by his fire, and talked the night away;
Wept o'er his wounds, or tales of sorrow done,
Shouldered his crutch, and showed how fields were won.
Pleased with his guests, the good man learned to glow,
160 And quite forgot their vices in their woe;
Careless their merits, or their faults to scan,
His pity gave ere charity began.
    Thus to relieve the wretched was his pride,
And even his failings leaned to Virtue's side;
165 But in his duty prompt at every call,
He watched and wept, he prayed and felt, for all.
And, as a bird each fond endearment tries,
To tempt its new-fledged offspring to the skies,
He tried each art, reproved each dull delay,
170 Allured to brighter worlds, and led the way.
    Beside the bed where parting life was laid,
And sorrow, guilt, and pain, by turns dismayed,
The reverend champion stood. At his control,
Despair and anguish fled the struggling soul;
175 Comfort came down the trembling wretch to raise,
And his last faltering accents whispered praise.
    At church, with meek and unaffected grace,
His looks adorned the venerable place;
Truth from his lips prevailed with double sway,
180 And fools, who came to scoff, remained to pray.
The service past, around the pious man,
With steady zeal each honest rustic ran;
Even children followed with endearing wile,
And plucked his gown, to share the good man's smile.
185 His ready smile a parent's warmth expressed,
Their welfare pleased him, and their cares distressed;
To them his heart, his love, his griefs were given,
But all his serious thoughts had rest in Heaven.
As some tall cliff that lifts its awful form,
190 Swells from the vale, and midway leaves the storm,
Though round its breast the rolling clouds are spread,
Eternal sunshine settles on its head.
    Beside yon straggling fence that skirts the way,
With blossomed furze unprofitably gay,
195 There, in his noisy mansion, skilled to rule,
The village master taught his little school;
A man severe he was, and stern to view,
I knew him well, and every truant knew;
Well had the boding tremblers learned to trace
200 The day's disasters in his morning face;
Full well they laughed with counterfeited glee,
At all his jokes, for many a joke had he;
Full well the busy whisper circling round,

Conveyed the dismal tidings when he frowned;
205 Yet he was kind, or if severe in aught,
The love he bore to learning was in fault;[2]
The village all declared how much he knew;
'Twas certain he could write, and cipher too;
Lands he could measure, terms and tides[3] presage,
210 And even the story ran that he could gauge.[4]
In arguing too, the parson owned his skill,
For even though vanquished, he could argue still;
While words of learned length, and thundering sound,
Amazed the gazing rustics ranged around;
215 And still they gazed, and still the wonder grew,
That one small head could carry all he knew.
    But past is all his fame. The very spot
Where many a time he triumphed, is forgot.
Near yonder thorn, that lifts its head on high,
220 Where once the signpost caught the passing eye,
Low lies that house where nut-brown draughts inspired,
Where graybeard Mirth and smiling Toil retired,
Where village statesmen talked with looks profound,
And news much older than their ale went round.
225 Imagination fondly stoops to trace
The parlor splendors of that festive place:
The whitewashed wall, the nicely sanded floor,
The varnished clock that clicked behind the door;
The chest contrived a double debt to pay,
230 A bed by night, a chest of drawers by day;
The pictures placed for ornament and use,
The twelve good rules, the royal game of goose;[5]
The hearth, except when winter chilled the day,
With aspen boughs, and flowers, and fennel gay,
235 While broken teacups, wisely kept for show,
Ranged o'er the chimney, glistened in a row.
    Vain transitory splendors! Could not all
Reprieve the tottering mansion from its fall!
Obscure it sinks, nor shall it more impart
240 An hour's importance to the poor man's heart;
Thither no more the peasant shall repair
To sweet oblivion of his daily care;
No more the farmer's news, the barber's tale,
No more the woodman's ballad shall prevail;
245 No more the smith his dusky brow shall clear,
Relax his ponderous strength, and lean to hear;
The host himself no longer shall be found
Careful to see the mantling bliss[6] go round;
Nor the coy maid, half willing to be pressed,

2. Because the *l* was silent, *fault* and *aught* rhymed perfectly.
3. Feasts and seasons in the church year. "Terms": dates on which rent, wages, etc. were due and tenancy began or ended.
4. Measure the content of casks and other vessels.

5. A game in which counters were moved on a board, according to the throw of the dice. "The twelve good rules" of conduct, attributed to Charles I, were printed in a broadside that was often seen on the walls of taverns.
6. Foaming bliss, i.e., foaming ale.

250   Shall kiss the cup to pass it to the rest.
       Yes! let the rich deride, the proud disdain,
    These simple blessings of the lowly train,
    To me more dear, congenial to my heart,
    One native charm, than all the gloss of art;
255   Spontaneous joys, where nature has its play,
    The soul adopts, and owns their first-born sway;
    Lightly they frolic o'er the vacant mind,
    Unenvied, unmolested, unconfined.
    But the long pomp, the midnight masquerade,
260   With all the freaks of wanton wealth arrayed,
    In these, ere triflers half their wish obtain,
    The toiling pleasure sickens into pain;
    And, even while fashion's brightest arts decoy,
    The heart distrusting asks, if this be joy.
265   Ye friends to truth, ye statesmen, who survey
    The rich man's joys increase, the poor's decay,
    'Tis yours to judge how wide the limits stand
    Between a splendid and an happy land.
    Proud swells the tide with loads of freighted ore,
270   And shouting Folly hails them from her shore;
    Hoards, even beyond the miser's wish abound,
    And rich men flock from all the world around.
    Yet count our gains. This wealth is but a name
    That leaves our useful products still the same.
275   Not so the loss. The man of wealth and pride
    Takes up a space that many poor supplied;
    Space for his lake, his park's extended bounds,
    Space for his horses, equipage, and hounds;
    The robe that wraps his limbs in silken sloth
280   Has robbed the neighboring fields of half their growth;
    His seat, where solitary sports are seen,
    Indignant spurns the cottage from the green;
    Around the world each needful product flies,
    For all the luxuries the world supplies.
285   While thus the land adorned for pleasure all
    In barren splendor feebly waits the fall.
       As some fair female unadorned and plain,
    Secure to please while youth confirms her reign,
    Slights every borrowed charm that dress supplies,
290   Nor shares with art the triumph of her eyes:
    But when those charms are past, for charms are frail,
    When time advances, and when lovers fail,
    She then shines forth, solicitous to bless,
    In all the glaring impotence of dress:
295   Thus fares the land, by luxury betrayed;
    In nature's simplest charms at first arrayed;
    But verging to decline, its splendors rise,
    Its vistas strike, its palaces surprise;
    While scourged by famine from the smiling land,
300   The mournful peasant leads his humble band;
    And while he sinks without one arm to save,

The country blooms—a garden, and a grave.
     Where then, ah where, shall Poverty reside,
To 'scape the pressure of contiguous Pride?
305 If to some common's fenceless limits strayed,
He drives his flock to pick the scanty blade,
Those fenceless fields the sons of wealth divide,
And even the bare-worn common is denied.
     If to the city sped—What waits him there?
310 To see profusion that he must not share;
To see ten thousand baneful arts combined
To pamper luxury, and thin mankind;
To see those joys the sons of pleasure know,
Extorted from his fellow creature's woe.
315 Here, while the courtier glitters in brocade,
There the pale artist° plies the sickly trade;   *artisan*
Here, while the proud their long-drawn pomps display,
There the black gibbet glooms beside the way.
The dome where Pleasure holds her midnight reign,
320 Here, richly decked, admits the gorgeous train;
Tumultuous grandeur crowds the blazing square,
The rattling chariots clash, the torches glare.
Sure scenes like these no troubles e'er annoy!
Sure these denote one universal joy!
325 Are these thy serious thoughts?—Ah, turn thine eyes
Where the poor houseless shivering female lies.
She once, perhaps, in village plenty blest,
Has wept at tales of innocence distressed;
Her modest looks the cottage might adorn,
330 Sweet as the primrose peeps beneath the thorn;
Now lost to all; her friends, her virtue fled,
Near her betrayer's door she lays her head,
And pinched with cold, and shrinking from the shower,
With heavy heart deplores that luckless hour,
335 When idly first, ambitious of the town,
She left her wheel° and robes of country brown.   *spinning wheel*
     Do thine, sweet Auburn, thine, the loveliest train,
Do thy fair tribes participate her pain?
Even now, perhaps, by cold and hunger led,
340 At proud men's doors they ask a little bread!
     Ah, no. To distant climes, a dreary scene,
Where half the convex world intrudes between,
Through torrid tracts with fainting steps they go,
Where wild Altama[7] murmurs to their woe.
345 Far different there from all that charmed before,
The various terrors of that horrid shore;
Those blazing suns that dart a downward ray,
And fiercely shed intolerable day;
Those matted woods where birds forget to sing,
350 But silent bats in drowsy clusters cling;
Those poisonous fields with rank luxuriance crowned,

7. The Altamaha River in Georgia.

Where the dark scorpion gathers death around;
Where at each step the stranger fears to wake
The rattling terrors of the vengeful snake;
355 Where crouching tigers[8] wait their hapless prey,
And savage men, more murderous still than they;
While oft in whirls the mad tornado flies,
Mingling the ravaged landscape with the skies.
Far different these from every former scene,
360 The cooling brook, the grassy-vested green,
The breezy covert of the warbling grove,
That only sheltered thefts of harmless love.

    Good Heaven! what sorrows gloomed that parting day,
That called them from their native walks away;
365 When the poor exiles, every pleasure past,
Hung round their bowers, and fondly looked their last,
And took a long farewell, and wished in vain
For seats like these beyond the western main;
And shuddering still to face the distant deep,
370 Returned and wept, and still returned to weep.
The good old sire, the first prepared to go
To new-found worlds, and wept for other's woe.
But for himself, in conscious virtue brave,
He only wished for worlds beyond the grave.
375 His lovely daughter, lovelier in her tears,
The fond companion of his helpless years,
Silent went next, neglectful of her charms,
And left a lover's for a father's arms.
With louder plaints the mother spoke her woes,
380 And blessed the cot where every pleasure rose;
And kissed her thoughtless babes with many a tear,
And clasped them close in sorrow doubly dear;
Whilst her fond husband strove to lend relief
In all the silent manliness of grief.

385   O luxury! Thou cursed by Heaven's decree,
How ill exchanged are things like these for thee!
How do thy portions, with insidious joy,
Diffuse their pleasures only to destroy!
Kingdoms, by thee, to sickly greatness grown,
390 Boast of a florid vigor not their own.
At every draught more large and large they grow,
A bloated mass of rank unwieldy woe;
Till sapped their strength, and every part unsound,
Down, down they sink, and spread a ruin round.

395   Even now the devastation is begun,
And half the business of destruction done;
Even now, methinks, as pondering here I stand,
I see the rural Virtues leave the land.
Down where yon anchoring vessel spreads the sail,
400 That idly waiting flaps with every gale,
Downward they move, a melancholy band,

---

8. Not the Asian tiger but the puma.

Pass from the shore, and darken all the strand.
Contented Toil, and hospitable Care,
And kind connubial Tenderness are there;
405 And Piety, with wishes placed above,
And steady Loyalty, and faithful Love:
And thou, sweet Poetry, thou loveliest maid,
Still° first to fly where sensual joys invade;   *always*
Unfit in these degenerate times of shame,
410 To catch the heart, or strike for honest fame;
Dear charming Nymph, neglected and decried,
My shame in crowds, my solitary pride;
Thou source of all my bliss, and all my woe,
That found'st me poor at first, and keep'st me so;
415 Thou guide by which the nobler arts excel,
Thou nurse of every virtue, fare thee well.
Farewell, and O! where'er thy voice be tried
On Torno's cliffs, or Pambamarca's side,[9]
Whether where equinoctial fervors glow,
420 Or winter wraps the polar world in snow,
Still let thy voice, prevailing over time,
Redress the rigors of the inclement clime;
Aid slighted truth, with thy persuasive strain
Teach erring man to spurn the rage of gain;
425 Teach him that states of native strength possessed,
Though very poor, may still be very blest;
That Trade's proud empire hastes to swift decay,
As ocean sweeps the labored mole[1] away;
While self-dependent power can time defy,
430 As rocks resist the billows and the sky.[2]

1770

9. The river Torne in Sweden falls into the Gulf of Bothnia. Pambamarca is a mountain in Ecuador.
1. The laboriously built breakwater.

2. Johnson composed the last four lines of the poem.

WILLIAM COWPER
1731–1800

There are no saner poems in the language than William Cowper's, yet they were written by a man who was periodically insane and who for forty years lived day to day with the possibility of madness. After attempting suicide in 1763, he believed that he was damned for having committed the unforgivable sin, the "sin against the Holy Ghost." From then on, a refugee from life, he looked for hope in Evangelicalism and found shelter first, in 1765, in the pious family of the clergyman Morley Unwin, and after Unwin's death, with his widow, Mary Unwin, who cared for Cowper until her death in 1796. Their move to rural Olney (pronounced *Own-y*) in 1768 brought them under the influence of the strenuous and fervent Evangelical minister John Newton, author of "Amazing Grace." With him Cowper wrote the famous *Olney Hymns*, still familiar to Methodists and other Nonconformists. But a second attack of madness, in 1773, not only frustrated his planned marriage to Mary Unwin but left him for the rest of his life with the assurance that he had been cast out by God. He never again attended services, and the main purpose of his life thereafter was to divert his mind from numb despair by every possible innocent device. He gardened, he kept pets, he walked, he wrote letters (some of the best of the century), he conversed, he read—and he wrote poetry. When it was published, it brought him a measure of fame that his modest nature could never have hoped for.

Cowper's major work is *The Task* (1785), undertaken at the bidding of Lady Austen, a friend who, when he complained that he had no subject, directed him to write about the sofa in his parlor. It began with a mock-heroic account of the development of the sofa from a simple stool, but it grew into a long meditative poem of more than five thousand lines. The poet describes his small world of country, village, garden, and parlor, and from time to time he glances toward the great world to condemn cities and worldliness, war and slavery, luxury and corruption. The tone is muted, the sensibility delicate, the language on the whole precise and clear. Cowper does not strive to be great, yet his contemporaries recognized their own concerns in his pious and humorous musings. Blake, Wordsworth, and Coleridge felt close to him, and so did many literary women. No eighteenth-century poet was more beloved.

From The Task

From *Book 1*

[A LANDSCAPE DESCRIBED. RURAL SOUNDS]

150 Thou[1] knowest my praise of nature most sincere,
     And that my raptures are not conjured up
     To serve occasions of poetic pomp,
     But genuine, and art partner of them all.
     How oft upon yon eminence our pace
155 Has slackened to a pause, and we have borne
     The ruffling wind, scarce conscious that it blew,
     While admiration, feeding at the eye,
     And still unsated, dwelt upon the scene.
     Thence with what pleasure have we just discerned
160 The distant plow slow moving, and beside
     His laboring team, that swerved not from the track,
     The sturdy swain diminished to a boy!
     Here Ouse,[2] slow winding through a level plain
     Of spacious meads with cattle sprinkled o'er,
165 Conducts the eye along its sinuous course
     Delighted. There, fast rooted in their bank,
     Stand, never overlooked, our favorite elms,
     That screen the herdsman's solitary hut;
     While far beyond, and overthwart the stream

1. Mary Unwin.
2. The village of Olney, where Cowper and Mary Unwin were living, is situated on the river Ouse.

170 That, as with molten glass, inlays the vale,
The sloping land recedes into the clouds;
Displaying on its varied side the grace
Of hedgerow beauties numberless, square tower,
Tall spire, from which the sound of cheerful bells
175 Just undulates upon the listening ear,
Groves, heaths, and smoking villages, remote.
Scenes must be beautiful, which, daily viewed,
Please daily, and whose novelty survives
Long knowledge and the scrutiny of years—
180 Praise justly due to those that I describe.
  Nor rural sights alone, but rural sounds,
Exhilarate the spirit, and restore
The tone of languid Nature. Mighty winds,
That sweep the skirt of some far-spreading wood
185 Of ancient growth, make music not unlike
The dash of ocean on his winding shore,
And lull the spirit while they fill the mind;
Unnumbered branches waving in the blast,
And all their leaves fast fluttering, all at once.
190 Nor less composure waits upon the roar
Of distant floods, or on the softer voice
Of neighboring fountain, or of rills that slip
Through the cleft rock, and, chiming as they fall
Upon loose pebbles, lose themselves at length
195 In matted grass, that with a livelier green
Betrays the secret of their silent course.
Nature inanimate employs sweet sounds,
But animated nature sweeter still,
To soothe and satisfy the human ear.
200 Ten thousand warblers cheer the day, and one
The livelong night: nor these alone, whose notes
Nice-fingered art[3] must emulate in vain,
But cawing rooks, and kites that swim sublime
In still repeated circles, screaming loud,
205 The jay, the pie,° and even the boding owl   magpie
That hails the rising moon, have charms for me.
Sounds inharmonious in themselves and harsh,
Yet heard in scenes where peace forever reigns,
And only there, please highly for their sake.

[CRAZY KATE]

There often wanders one, whom better days
535 Saw better clad, in cloak of satin trimmed
With lace, and hat with splendid ribband bound.
A servingmaid was she, and fell in love
With one who left her, went to sea, and died.
Her fancy followed him through foaming waves
540 To distant shores; and she would sit and weep

---

3. Refined skill, such as that of a flutist imitating the nightingale's song.

At what a sailor suffers; fancy, too,
Delusive most where warmest wishes are,
Would oft anticipate his glad return,
And dream of transports she was not to know.
545 She heard the doleful tidings of his death—
And never smiled again! And now she roams
The dreary waste; there spends the livelong day,
And there, unless when charity forbids,
The livelong night. A tattered apron hides,
550 Worn as a cloak, and hardly hides, a gown
More tattered still; and both but ill conceal
A bosom heaved with never-ceasing sighs.
She begs an idle pin of all she meets,
And hoards them in her sleeve; but needful food,
555 Though pressed with hunger oft, or comelier clothes,
Though pinched with cold, asks never.—Kate is crazed!

From *Book 3*

[THE STRICKEN DEER]

I was a stricken deer, that left the herd
Long since; with many an arrow deep infixed
110 My panting side was charged, when I withdrew
To seek a tranquil death in distant shades.
There was I found by one who had himself
Been hurt by the archers. In his side he bore,
And in his hands and feet, the cruel scars.
115 With gentle force soliciting[4] the darts,
He drew them forth, and healed, and bade me live.
Since then, with few associates, in remote
And silent woods I wander, far from those
My former partners of the peopled scene;
120 With few associates, and not wishing more.
Here much I ruminate, as much I may,
With other views of men and manners now
Than once, and others of a life to come.
I see that all are wanderers, gone astray
125 Each in his own delusions; they are lost
In chase of fancied happiness, still wooed
And never won. Dream after dream ensues;
And still they dream that they shall still succeed,
And still are disappointed. Rings the world
130 With the vain stir. I sum up half mankind
And add two-thirds of the remaining half,
And find the total of their hopes and fears
Dreams, empty dreams.

---

4. "To endeavor to draw out by the use of gentle force" (*OED*).

From *Book 4*

[THE WINTER EVENING: A BROWN STUDY]

Come evening once again, season of peace,
Return sweet evening, and continue long!
245 Methinks I see thee in the streaky west,
With matron-step slow-moving, while the night
Treads on thy sweeping train; one hand employed
In letting fall the curtain of repose
On bird and beast, the other charged for man
250 With sweet oblivion of the cares of day;
Not sumptuously adorned, nor needing aid
Like homely featured night, of clustering gems;
A star or two just twinkling on thy brow
Suffices thee; save that the moon is thine
255 No less than hers, not worn indeed on high
With ostentatious pageantry, but set
With modest grandeur in thy purple zone,[5]
Resplendent less, but of an ampler round.[6]
Come then and thou shalt find thy votary calm,
260 Or make me so. Composure is thy gift.
And whether I devote thy gentle hours
To books, to music, or the poet's toil,
To weaving nets for bird-alluring fruit;
Or twining silken threads round ivory reels
265 When they command whom man was born to please;[7]
I slight thee not, but make thee welcome still.
    Just when our drawing rooms begin to blaze
With lights by clear reflection multiplied
From many a mirror, in which he of Gath,
270 Goliah,[8] might have seen his giant bulk
Whole without stooping, towering crest and all,
My pleasures too begin. But me perhaps
The glowing hearth may satisfy awhile
With faint illumination that uplifts
275 The shadow to the ceiling, there by fits
Dancing uncouthly to the quivering flame.
Not undelightful is an hour to me
So spent in parlor twilight; such a gloom
Suits well the thoughtful or unthinking mind,
280 The mind contemplative, with some new theme
Pregnant, or indisposed alike to all.
Laugh ye, who boast your more mercurial powers
That never feel a stupor, know no pause,
Nor need one. I am conscious,° and confess,   *conscious of*

---

5. Encircling band. Evening is seen both as a personified goddess, whose "zone" is her royal belt, and as a natural phenomenon, where the "zone" is a stripe of color in the sky.
6. The moon looks larger at evening, when just over the horizon, than at night, when it is higher and brighter.
7. I.e., women.
8. Goliath, the giant of Gath slain by David (1 Samuel 17.19–51).

285   Fearless, a soul that does not always think.
Me oft has fancy ludicrous and wild
Soothed with a waking dream of houses, towers,
Trees, churches, and strange visages expressed
In the red cinders, while with poring eye
290   I gazed, myself creating what I saw.
Nor less amused have I quiescent watched
The sooty films that play upon the bars,[9]
Pendulous and foreboding, in the view
Of superstition prophesying still,
295   Though still deceived, some stranger's near approach.[1]
'Tis thus the understanding takes repose
In indolent vacuity of thought,
And sleeps and is refreshed. Meanwhile the face
Conceals the mood lethargic with a mask
300   Of deep deliberation, as° the man   *as if*
Were tasked to his full strength, absorbed and lost.
Thus oft reclined at ease, I lose an hour
At evening, till at length the freezing blast
That sweeps the bolted shutter, summons home
305   The recollected powers, and snapping short
The glassy threads with which the fancy weaves
Her brittle toys, restores me to myself.
How calm is my recess, and how the frost,
Raging abroad, and the rough wind, endear
310   The silence and the warmth enjoyed within.
I saw the woods and fields at close of day,
A variegated show; the meadows green,
Though faded; and the lands where lately waved
The golden harvest, of a mellow brown,
315   Upturned so lately by the forceful share.°   *plowshare*
I saw far off the weedy fallows[2] smile
With verdure not unprofitable, grazed
By flocks fast feeding and selecting each
His favorite herb; while all the leafless groves
320   That skirt the horizon wore a sable hue,
Scarce noticed in the kindred dusk of eve.
Tomorrow brings a change, a total change!
Which even now, though silently performed
And slowly, and by most unfelt, the face
325   Of universal nature undergoes.
Fast falls a fleecy shower. The downy flakes,
Descending and with never-ceasing lapse,[3]
Softly alighting upon all below,
Assimilate all objects. Earth receives
330   Gladly the thickening mantle, and the green

---

9. The grate of a fireplace.
1. The piece of soot that often flaps on the bars
of a grate was called a "stranger" and was supposed to portend an unexpected visitor. Cf. lines
272–310 with Coleridge's "Frost at Midnight."
2. Plowed but unseeded land.
3. Gentle downward glide.

And tender blade that feared the chilling blast,
Escapes unhurt beneath so warm a veil.

1785

The Castaway

Obscurest night involved the sky,
    The Atlantic billows roared,
When such a destined wretch as I,
    Washed headlong from on board,
5 Of friends, of hope, of all bereft,
His floating home forever left.

No braver chief[1] could Albion boast
    Than he with whom he went,
Nor ever ship left Albion's coast,
10   With warmer wishes sent.
He loved them both, but both in vain,
Nor him beheld, nor her again.

Not long beneath the whelming brine,
    Expert to swim, he lay;
15 Nor soon he felt his strength decline,
    Or courage die away;
But waged with death a lasting strife,
Supported by despair of life.

He shouted; nor his friends had failed
20   To check the vessel's course,
But so the furious blast prevailed,
    That, pitiless perforce,
They left their outcast mate behind,
And scudded still before the wind.

25 Some succor yet they could afford;
    And, such as storms allow,
The cask, the coop, the floated cord,
    Delayed not to bestow.
But he (they knew) nor ship, nor shore,
30 Whate'er they gave, should visit more.

Nor, cruel as it seemed, could he
    Their haste himself condemn,
Aware that flight, in such a sea,
    Alone could rescue them;

---

1. George, Lord Anson (1697–1762), in whose *Voyage* (1748) Cowper, years before writing this poem, had read the story of the sailor washed overboard in a storm.

35   Yet bitter felt it still to die
      Deserted, and his friends so nigh.

He long survives, who lives an hour
    In ocean, self-upheld;
And so long he, with unspent power,
40   His destiny repelled;
And ever, as the minutes flew,
Entreated help, or cried, "Adieu!"

At length, his transient respite past,
    His comrades, who before
45   Had heard his voice in every blast,
     Could catch the sound no more.
For then, by toil subdued, he drank
The stifling wave, and then he sank.

No poet wept him; but the page
50   Of narrative sincere,
That tells his name, his worth, his age,
    Is wet with Anson's tear.
And tears by bards or heroes shed
Alike immortalize the dead.

55   I therefore purpose not, or dream,
     Descanting on his fate,
To give the melancholy theme
    A more enduring date:
But misery still delights to trace
60   Its semblance in another's case.

No voice divine the storm allayed,
    No light propitious shone,
When, snatched from all effectual aid,
    We perished, each alone;
65   But I beneath a rougher sea,
And whelmed in deeper gulfs than he.

1799   1803

APPENDIXES

General Bibliography

This bibliography consists of a list of suggested general readings on English literature. Bibliographies for the authors in *The Norton Anthology of English Literature* are available online in the Supplemental Ebook.

Suggested General Readings

Histories of England and of English Literature

Even the most distinguished of the comprehensive general histories written in past generations have come to seem outmoded. Innovative research in social, cultural, and political history has made it difficult to write a single coherent account of England from the Middle Ages to the present, let alone to accommodate in a unified narrative the complex histories of Scotland, Ireland, Wales, and the other nations where writing in English has flourished. Readers who wish to explore the historical matrix out of which the works of literature collected in this anthology emerged are advised to consult the studies of particular periods listed in the appropriate sections of this bibliography. The multivolume *Oxford History of England* and *New Oxford History of England* are useful, as are the three-volume *Peoples of the British Isles: A New History*, ed. Stanford Lehmberg, 1992; the nine-volume *Cambridge Cultural History of Britain*, ed. Boris Ford, 1992; the three-volume *Cambridge Social History of Britain, 1750–1950*, ed. F. M. L. Thompson, 1992; and the multivolume *Penguin History of Britain*, gen. ed. David Cannadine, 1996–. For Britain's imperial history, readers can consult the five-volume *Oxford History of the British Empire*, ed. Roger Louis, 1998–99, as well as *Gender and Empire*, ed. Philippa Levine, 2004. Given the cultural centrality of London, readers may find particular interest in *The London Encyclopaedia*, ed. Ben Weinreb and Christopher Hibbert, rev. ed., 1993; Roy Porter, *London: A Social History*, 1994; and Jerry White, *London in the Nineteenth Century: "A Human Awful Wonder of God,"* 2007, and *London in the Twentieth Century: A City and Its People*, 2001.

Similar observations may be made about literary history. In the light of such initiatives as women's studies, new historicism, and postcolonialism, the range of authors deemed significant has expanded in recent years, along with the geographical and conceptual boundaries of literature in English. Attempts to capture in a unified account the great sweep of literature from *Beowulf* to the early twenty-first century have largely given way to studies of individual genres, carefully delimited time periods, and specific authors. For these more focused accounts, see the listings by period. Among the large-scale literary surveys, *The Cambridge Guide to Literature in English*, 1994, is useful, as is the seven-volume *Penguin History of Literature*, 1993–94. *The Feminist Companion to Literature in English*, ed. Virginia Blain, Isobel Grundy, and Patricia Clements, 1990, is an important resource, and the editorial materials in *The Norton Anthology of Literature by Women*, 3rd ed., 2007, ed. Sandra M. Gilbert and Susan Gubar, constitute a concise history and set of biographies of women authors since the Middle Ages. *Annals of English Literature, 1475–1950*, rev. 1961, lists important publications year by year, together with the significant literary events for each year. Five volumes have been published in the *Oxford English Literary History*, gen. ed. Jonathan Bate, 2002–: James Simpson, *1350–1547: Reform and*

Cultural Revolution; Philip Davis, *1830–1880: The Victorians*; Chris Baldick, *1830–1880: The Modern Movement*; Randall Stevenson, *1960–2000: The Last of England?*; and Bruce King, *1948–2000: The Internationalization of English Literature*. See also *The Cambridge History of Medieval English Literature*, ed. David Wallace, 1999; *The Cambridge History of Early Modern English Literature*, ed. David Loewenstein and Janel Mueller, 2002; *The Cambridge History of English Literature, 1660–1780*, ed. John Richetti, 2005; *The Cambridge History of English Romantic Literature*, ed. James Chandler, 2009; and *The Cambridge History of Twentieth-Century English Literature*, ed. Laura Marcus and Peter Nicholls, 2005.

Helpful treatments and surveys of English meter, rhyme, and stanza forms are Paul Fussell Jr., *Poetic Meter and Poetic Form*, rev. 1979; Donald Wesling, *The Chances of Rhyme: Device and Modernity*, 1980; Charles O. Hartman, *Free Verse: An Essay in Prosody*, 1983; John Hollander, *Rhyme's Reason: A Guide to English Verse*, rev. 1989; Derek Attridge, *Poetic Rhythm: An Introduction*, 1995; Robert Pinsky, *The Sounds of Poetry: A Brief Guide*, 1998; and Mark Strand and Eavan Boland, eds., *The Making of a Poem: A Norton Anthology of Poetic Forms*, 2000.

On the development and functioning of the novel as a form, see Ian Watt, *The Rise of the Novel*, 1957; Gérard Genette, *Narrative Discourse: An Essay in Method*, 1980; Peter Brooks, *Reading for the Plot: Design and Intention in Narrative*, 1984; *The Columbia History of the British Novel*, ed. John Richetti, 1994; Margaret Doody, *The True Story of the Novel*, 1996; *Theory of the Novel: A Historical Approach*, ed. Michael McKeon, 2000; and McKeon, *The Origins of the English Novel, 1600–1740*, 15th anniversary ed., 2002. On women novelists and readers, see Nancy Armstrong, *Desire and Domestic Fiction: A Political History of the Novel*, 1987; and Catherine Gallagher, *Nobody's Story: The Vanishing Acts of Women Writers in the Marketplace, 1670–1820*, 1994.

On the history of playhouse design, see Richard Leacroft, *The Development of the English Playhouse: An Illustrated Survey of Theatre Building in England from Medieval to Modern Times*, 1988. For a survey of the plays that have appeared on these and other stages, see Allardyce Nicoll, *British Drama*, rev. 1962; the eight-volume *Revels History of Drama in English*, gen. eds. Clifford Leech and T. W. Craik, 1975–83; and Alfred Harbage, *Annals of English Drama, 975–1700*, 3rd ed., 1989, rev. S. Schoenbaum and Sylvia Wagonheim.

On some of the key intellectual currents that are at once reflected in and shaped by literature and contemporary literary criticism, Arthur O. Lovejoy's classic studies *The Great Chain of Being*, 1936, and *Essays in the History of Ideas*, 1948, remain valuable, along with such works as Georg Simmel, *The Philosophy of Money*, 1907; Lovejoy and George Boas, *Primitivism and Related Ideas in Antiquity*, 1935; Norbert Elias, *The Civilizing Process*, orig. pub. 1939, English trans. 1969; Ernst Cassirer, *The Philosophy of Symbolic Forms*, 4 vols., 1953–96; Ernst Kantorowicz, *The King's Two Bodies: A Study in Medieval Political Theology*, 1957, new ed. 1997; Richard Popkin, *The History of Skepticism from Erasmus to Descartes*, 1960; M. H. Abrams, *Natural Supernaturalism: Tradition and Revolution in Romantic Literature*, 1971; Michel Foucault, *Madness and Civilization: A History of Insanity in the Age of Reason*, Eng. trans. 1965, and *The Order of Things: An Archaeology of the Human Sciences*, Eng. trans. 1970; Gaston Bachelard, *The Poetics of Space*, Eng. trans. 1969; Martin Jay, *The Dialectical Imagination: A History of the Frankfurt School and the Institute of Social Research, 1923–1950*, 1973, new ed. 1996; Hayden White, *Metahistory*, 1973; Roland Barthes, *The Pleasure of the Text*, Eng. trans. 1975; Jacques Derrida, *Of Grammatology*, Eng. trans. 1976, and *Dissemination*, Eng. trans. 1981; Richard Rorty, *Philosophy and the Mirror of Nature*, 1979; Gilles Deleuze and Félix Guattari, *A Thousand Plateaus* (1980); Raymond Williams, *Keywords: A Vocabulary of Culture and Society*, rev. 1983; Pierre Bourdieu, *Distinction: A Social Critique of the Judgment of Taste*, Eng. trans. 1984; Michel de Certeau, *The Practice of Every-*

day Life, Eng. trans. 1984; Hans Blumenberg, *The Legitimacy of the Modern Age*, Eng. trans. 1985; Jürgen Habermas, *The Philosophical Discourse of Moderntiy*, Eng. trans, 1987; Slavoj Žižek, *The Sublime Object of Ideology*, 1989; and Sigmund Freud, *Writings on Art and Literature*, ed. Neil Hertz, 1997.

Reference Works

The single most important tool for the study of literature in English is the *Oxford English Dictionary*, 2nd ed. 1989, 3rd ed. in process. The most current edition is available online to subscribers. The *OED* is written on historical principles: that is, it attempts not only to describe current word use but also to record the history and development of the language from its origins before the Norman conquest to the present. It thus provides, for familiar as well as archaic and obscure words, the widest possible range of meanings and uses, organized chronologically and illustrated with quotations. The *OED* can be searched as a conventional dictionary arranged a–z and also by subject, usage, region, origin, and timeline (the first appearance of a word). Beyond the *OED* there are many other valuable dictionaries, such as *The American Heritage Dictionary* (4th ed. 2000), *The Oxford Dictionary of Abbreviations, The Concise Oxford Dictionary of English Etymology, The Oxford Dictionary of English Grammar, A New Dictionary of Eponyms, The Oxford Essential Dictionary of Foreign Terms in English, The Oxford Dictionary of Idioms, The Concise Oxford Dictionary of Linguistics, The Oxford Guide to World English*, and *The Concise Oxford Dictionary of Proverbs*. Other valuable reference works include *The Cambridge Encyclopedia of the English Language*, ed. David Crystal, 1995; *The Concise Oxford Companion to the English Language; Pocket Fowler's Modern English Usage;* and the numerous guides to specialized vocabularies, slang, regional dialects, and the like.

There is a steady flow of new editions of most major and many minor writers in English, along with a ceaseless outpouring of critical appraisals and scholarship. James L. Harner's *Literary Research Guide: An Annotated List of Reference Sources in English Literary Studies* (5th ed., 2008; online ed. at www.mla.org/store/PID335) offers thorough, evaluative annotations of a wide range of sources. For the historical record of scholarship and critical discussion, *The New Cambridge Bibliography of English Literature*, ed. George Watson, 5 vols. (1969–77) and *The Cambridge Bibliography of English Literature*, ed. F. W. Bateson, 5 vols. (1941–57) are useful. The *MLA International Bibliography* (also online) is a key resource for following critical discussion of literatures in English. Ranging from 1926 to the present, it includes journal articles, essays, chapters from collections, books, and dissertations, and covers folklore, linguistics, and film. The *Annual Bibliography of English Language and Literature (ABELL)*, compiled by the Modern Humanities Research Association, lists monographs, periodical articles, critical editions of literary works, book reviews and collections of essays published anywhere in the world; unpublished doctoral dissertations are covered for the period 1920–99 (available online to subscribers and as part of Literature Online http://lion.chadwyck.com/marketing/index.jsp.)

For compact biographies of English authors, see the multivolume *Oxford Dictionary of National Biography (DNB)*, ed. H. C. G. Matthew and Brian Harrison, 2004; since 2004 the *DNB* has been extended online with three annual updates. Handy reference books of authors, works, and various literary terms and allusions include many volumes in the *Cambridge Companion* and *Oxford Companion* series (e.g., *The Cambridge Companion to Narrative*, ed David Herman, 2007; *The Oxford Companion to English Literature*, ed. Margaret Drabble, rev. 2009; *The Cambridge Companion to Allegory*, ed. Rita Copeland and Peter Struck, 2010; etc.). *The Oxford Companion to the Theatre*, ed. Phyllis Hartnoll, is available online to subscribers via Oxford Reference Online's Performing Arts collection (www.oxfordreference.com/pub/views/home.html). Likewise, *The New Princeton Encyclopedia of Poetry and Poetics*, ed. Alex Preminger and others, is available online to subscribers in Literature Online (http://lion.chadwyck.com/marketing/index.jsp). Handbooks that define and illustrate literary concepts and terms are *The Penguin Dictionary of Literary Terms and Literary Theory*, ed. J. A. Cuddon, 4th ed., 2000; W. F. Thrall and Addison Hibbard, *A Handbook to Literature*, ed. William Harmon and Hugh Holman, 8th ed., 1999 (companion website http://wps.prenhall.com/hss_harmon_handbook_10); *Critical Terms for Literary Study*, ed. Frank Lentricchia and Thomas McLaughlin, rev. 1995; and M. H. Abrams, *A Glossary of Literary Terms*, 9th ed., 2009. Also useful are Richard Lanham, *A Handlist of Rhetorical Terms*, 2nd ed., 1991; Arthur Quinn, *Figures of Speech: 60 Ways to Turn a Phrase*, 1993; and the *Barnhart Concise Dictionary of Etymology*, ed. Robert K. Barnhart, 1995.

On the Greek and Roman backgrounds, see *The Cambridge History of Classical Literature* (vol. 1: *Greek Literature*, 1982; vol. 2: *Latin Literature*, 1989), both available online; *The Oxford Companion to Classical Literature*, ed. M. C. Howatson, 2nd ed., 1989; Gian Biagio Conte, *Latin Literature: A History*, 1994; *The Oxford Classical Dictionary*, 3rd ed., rev. 2003, also available online; Richard Rutherford, *Classical Literature: A Concise History*, 2005; and Mark P. O. Morford, Robert J. Lenardon, and Michael Sham, *Classical Mythology*, 9th ed., 2010.

Digital resources in the humanities have vastly proliferated since the previous edition of *The Norton Anthology of English Literature* and are continuing to grow rapidly. The NAEL StudySpace (wwnorton.com/nael) is the gateway to an extensive array of annotated texts, images, and other materials especially designed for the readers of this anthology. Among other useful electronic resources for the study of English literature are enormous digital archives, available to subscribers: Early English Books Online (EEBO) http://eebo.chadwyck.com/home; Literature Online http://lion.chadwyck.com/marketing/index.jsp; and Eighteenth Century Collections Online (ECCO) http://mlr.com/DigitalCollections/products/ecco/. There are also numerous free sites of variable quality. Many of the best of these are period or author specific and hence are listed in the subsequent sections of this bibliography. Among the general sites, one of the most useful and wide-ranging is Voice of the Shuttle (http://vox.ucsb.edu), which includes in its aggregation links to Bartleby.com and Project Gutenberg.

Literary Criticism and Theory

Eight volumes of the *Cambridge History of Literary Criticism* have been published, 1989– : *Classical Criticism*, ed. George A. Kennedy; *The Middle Ages*, ed. Alastair Minnis and Ian Johnson; *The Renaissance*, ed. Glyn P. Norton; *The Eighteenth Century*, ed. H. B. Nisbet and Claude Rawson; *Romanticism*, ed. Marshall Brown; *Modernism and the New Criticism*, ed. A. Walton Litz, Louis Menand, and Lawrence Rainey; *From Formalism to Poststructuralism*, ed. Raman Selden; and *Twentieth-Century Historical, Philosophical, and Psychological Perspectives*, ed. Christa Knellwolf and Christopher Norris. See also M. H. Abrams, *The Mirror and the Lamp: Romantic Theory and the Critical Tradition*, 1953; William K. Wimsatt and Cleanth Brooks, *Literary Criticism: A Short History*, 1957; René Wellek, *A History of Modern Criticism: 1750–1950*, 9 vols., 1955–93; Frank Lentricchia, *After the New Criticism*, 1980; and J. Hillis Miller, *On Literature*, 2002. Raman Selden, Peter Widdowson, and Peter Brooker have written *A Reader's Guide to Contemporary Literary Theory*, 1997. Other useful resources include *The Johns Hopkins Guide to Literary Theory and Criticism*, ed. Michael Groden and Martin Kreiswirth, 1994 (also online); *Literary Theory, an Anthology*, ed. Julie Rivkin and Michael Ryan, 1998; and *The Norton Anthology of Theory and Criticism*, 2nd ed., gen. ed. Vincent Leitch, 2010.

Modern approaches to English literature and literary theory were shaped by certain landmark works: William Empson, *Seven Types of Ambiguity*, 1930, 3rd ed.

1953, *Some Versions of Pastoral*, 1935, rpt. 1986, and *The Structure of Complex Words*, 1951; F. R. Leavis, *Revaluation*, 1936, and *The Great Tradition*, 1948; Lionel Trilling, *The Liberal Imagination*, 1950; T. S. Eliot, *Selected Essays*, 3rd ed. 1951, and *On Poetry and Poets*, 1957; Erich Auerbach, *Mimesis: The Representation of Reality in Western Literature*, 1953; William K. Wimsatt, *The Verbal Icon*, 1954; Northrop Frye, *Anatomy of Criticism*, 1957; Wayne C. Booth, *The Rhetoric of Fiction*, 1961, rev. ed. 1983; and W. J. Bate, *The Burden of the Past and the English Poet*, 1970. René Wellek and Austin Warren, *Theory of Literature*, rev. 1970, is a useful introduction to the variety of scholarly and critical approaches to literature up to the time of its publication. Jonathan Culler's *Literary Theory: A Very Short Introduction*, 1997, discusses recurrent issues and debates.

Beginning in the late 1960s, there was a significant intensification of interest in literary theory as a specific field. Certain forms of literary study had already been influenced by the work of the Russian linguist Roman Jakobson and the Russian formalist Viktor Shklovsky and, still more, by conceptions that derived or claimed to derive from Marx and Engels, but the full impact of these theories was not felt until what became known as the "theory revolution" of the 1970s and '80s. For Marxist literary criticism, see Georg Lukacs, *Theory of the Novel*, 1920, trans. 1971; *The Historical Novel*, 1937, trans. 1983; and *Studies in European Realism*, trans. 1964; Walter Benjamin's essays from the 1920s and '30s represented in *Illuminations*, trans. 1986, and *Reflections*, trans. 1986; Mikhail Bakhtin's essays from the 1930s represented in *The Dialogic Imagination*, trans. 1981, and his *Rabelais and His World*, 1941, trans. 1968; *Selections from the Prison Notebooks of Antonio Gramsci*, ed. and trans. Quintin Hoare and Geoffrey Smith, 1971; Raymond Williams, *Marxism and Literature*, 1977; Fredric Jameson, *The Political Unconscious: Narrative as a Socially Symbolic Act*, 1981; and Terry Eagleton, *Literary Theory: An Introduction*, 1983, and *The Ideology of the Aesthetic*, 1990.

Structural linguistics and anthropology gave rise to a flowering of structuralist literary criticism; convenient introductions include Robert Scholes, *Structuralism in Literature: An Introduction*, 1974, and Jonathan Culler, *Structuralist Poetics*, 1975. Poststructuralist challenges to this approach are epitomized in such influential works as Jacques Derrida, *Writing and Difference*, 1967, trans. 1978, and Paul de Man, *Blindness and Insight: Essays in the Rhetoric of Contemporary Criticism*, 1971, 2nd ed., 1983. Poststructuralism is discussed in Jonathan Culler, *On Deconstruction*, 1982; Slavoj Žižek, *The Sublime Object of Ideology*, 1989; Fredric Jameson, *Postmodernism; or the Cultural Logic of Late Capitalism*, 1991; John McGowan, *Postmodernism and Its Critics*, 1991; and *Beyond Structuralism*, ed. Wendell Harris, 1996. A figure who greatly influenced both structuralism and poststructuralism is Roland Barthes, in *Mythologies*, trans. 1972, and *S/Z*, trans. 1974. Among other influential contributions to literary theory are the psychoanalytic approach in Harold Bloom, *The Anxiety of Influence*, 1973; and the reader-response approach in Stanley Fish, *Is There a Text in This Class?: The Authority of Interpretive Communities*, 1980. For a retrospect on the theory decades, see Terry Eagleton, *After Theory*, 2003.

Influenced by these theoretical currents but not restricted to them, modern feminist literary criticism was fashioned by such works as Patricia Meyer Spacks, *The Female Imagination*, 1975; Ellen Moers, *Literary Women*, 1976; Elaine Showalter, *A Literature of Their Own*, 1977; and Sandra Gilbert and Susan Gubar, *The Madwoman in the Attic*, 1979. More recent studies include Jane Gallop, *The Daughter's Seduction: Feminism and Psychoanalysis*, 1982; Luce Irigaray, *This Sex Which Is Not One*, trans. 1985; Gayatri Chakravorty Spivak, *In Other Worlds: Essays in Cultural Politics*, 1987; Sandra Gilbert and Susan Gubar, *No Man's Land: The Place of the Woman Writer in the Twentieth Century*, 3 vols., 1988–94; Barbara Johnson, *A World of Difference*, 1989; Judith Butler, *Gender Trouble*, 1990; and the critical views sampled in Elaine Showalter, *The New Feminist Criticism*, 1985; *The Hélène Cixous Reader*, ed. Susan Sellers, 1994; *Feminist Literary Theory: A Reader*, ed. Mary Eagleton, 2nd ed., 1995; and *Feminisms: An Anthology of Literary Theory and Criticism*, ed. Robyn R. Warhol and Diane Price Herndl, 2nd ed. 1997.

Gay literature and queer studies are represented in *Inside/Out: Lesbian Theories, Gay Theories*, ed. Diana Fuss, 1991; *The Lesbian and Gay Studies Reader*, ed. Henry Abelove, Michele Barale, and David Halperin, 1993; *The Columbia Anthology of Gay Literature: Readings from Western Antiquity to the Present Day*, ed. Byrne R. S. Fone, 1998; and by such books as Eve Sedgwick, *Between Men: English Literature and Male Homosocial Desire*, 1985, and *Epistemology of the Closet*, 1990; Diana Fuss, *Essentially Speaking: Feminism, Nature, and Difference*, 1989; Terry Castle, *The Apparitional Lesbian: Female Homosexuality and Modern Culture*, 1993; Leo Bersani, *Homos*, 1995; Gregory Woods, *A History of Gay Literature: The Male Tradition*, 1998; David Halperin, *How to Do the History of Homosexuality*, 2002; and Judith Halberstam, *In a Queer Time and Place: Transgender Bodies, Subcultural Lives*, 2005.

New historicism is represented in Stephen Greenblatt, *Learning to Curse*, 1990; in the essays collected in *The New Historicism Reader*, ed. Harold Veeser, 1993, and *New Historical Literary Study: Essays on Reproducing Texts, Representing History*, ed. Jeffrey N. Cox and Larry J. Reynolds, 1993; and in Catherine Gallagher and Stephen Greenblatt, *Practicing New Historicism*, 2000. The related social and historical dimension of texts is discussed in Jerome McGann, *Critique of Modern Textual Criticism*, 1983; and *Scholarly Editing: A Guide to Research*, ed. D. C. Greetham, 1995. Characteristic of new historicism is an expansion of the field of literary interpretation still further in cultural studies; for a broad sampling of the range of interests, see Lawrence Grossberg, Cary Nelson, and Paula Treichler, eds., *Cultural Studies*, 1992; *The Cultural Studies Reader*, ed. Simon During, 1993; and *A Cultural Studies Reader: History, Theory, Practice*, ed. Jessica Munns and Gita Rajan, 1997. This expansion of the field is similarly reflected in postcolonial studies: see Frantz Fanon, *Black Skin, White Masks*, 1952, new trans. 2008, and *The Wretched of the Earth*, 1961, new trans. 2004; Edward Said, *Orientalism*, 1978, and *Culture and Imperialism*, 1993; *The Post-Colonial Studies Reader*, ed. Bill Ashcroft, Gareth Griffiths, and Helen Tiffin, 1995; and such influential books as Ranajit Guha and Gayatri Chakravorty Spivak, *Selected Subaltern Studies*, 1988; Homi Bhabha, ed., *Nation and Narration*, 1990, and *The Location of Culture*, 1994; Anne McClintock, *Imperial Leather: Race, Gender, and Sexuality in the Colonial Contest*, 1995; Robert J. C. Young, *Postcolonialism: An Historical Introduction*, 2001; Bill Ashcroft, Gareth Griffiths, and Helen Tiffin, *The Empire Writes Back: Theory and Practice in Post-Colonial Literatures*, 1989, 2nd ed. 2002; Elleke Boehmer, *Colonial and Postcolonial Literature*, 1995, 2nd ed. 2005; and *The Cambridge History of Postcolonial Literature*, ed. Ato Quayson, 2011.

In the wake of the theory revolution, critics have focused on a wide array of topics, which can only be briefly surveyed here. One current of work, focusing on the history of emotion, is represented in Brian Massumi, *Parables for the Virtual*, 2002; Sianne Ngai, *Ugly Feelings*, 2005; and *The Affect Theory Reader*, eds. Melissa Gregg and Gregory J. Seigworth, 2010. A somewhat related current, examining the special role of traumatic memory in literature, is exemplified in Cathy Caruth, *Trauma: Explorations in Memory*, 1995; and Dominic LaCapra, *Writing History, Writing Trauma*, 2000. Work on the literary implications of cognitive science may be glimpsed in *Introduction to Cognitive Cultural Studies*, ed. Lisa Zunshine, 2010. A growing interest in quantitative approaches to literature has been sparked by Franco Moretti, *Graphs, Maps, Trees: Abstract Models for Literary History*, 2005. There is an ongoing flourishing of ecocriticism, or studies of literature and the environment, including *The Ecocriticism Reader: Landmarks in Literary Ecology*, ed. Cheryll Glotfelty and Harold Fromm, 1996; *Writing the Environment*, eds. Richard Kerridge and Neil

Sammells, 1998; and Jonathan Bate, *The Song of the Earth*, 2002. The relationship between literature and law is central to such works as *Interpreting Law and Literature: A Hermeneutic Reader*, ed. Sanford Levinson and Steven Mailloux, 1988; *Law's Stories: Narrative and Rhetoric in the Law*, ed. Peter Brooks and Paul Gerwertz, 1998; and *Literature and Legal Problem Solving: Law and Literature as Ethical Discourse*, Paul J. Heald, 1998. Ethical questions in literature have been usefully explored by, among others, Geoffrey Galt Harpham in *Getting It Right: Language, Literature, and Ethics*, 1997, and Derek Attridge in *The Singularity of Literature*, 2004. Finally, approaches to literature, such as formalism and literary biography, that had seemed superseded in the theoretical ferment of the late twentieth century, have had a powerful resurgence. A renewed interest in form is evident in Susan Stewart, *Poetry and the Fate of the Senses*, 2002, and *Reading for Form*, ed. Susan J. Wolfson and Marshall Brown, 2007. Revitalized interest in the history of the book has been spearheaded by D. F. McKenzie's *Bibliography and the Sociology of Texts*, 1986; and Roger Chartier's *The Order of Books: Readers, Authors, and Libraries in Europe Between the Fourteenth and Eighteenth Centuries*, 1994. See also *The Cambridge History of the Book in Britain*, 6 vols., 1998–2009; and *The Practice and Representation of Reading in England*, ed. James Raven, Helen Small, and Naomi Tadmor, 2007.

Anthologies representing a range of recent approaches include *Modern Criticism and Theory*, ed. David Lodge, 1988; *Contemporary Literary Criticism*, ed. Robert Con Davis and Ronald Schlieffer, rev. ed. 1998; and *The Norton Anthology of Theory and Criticism*, ed. Vincent Leitch, et al., 2nd ed. 2010.

Literary Terminology*

Using simple technical terms can sharpen our understanding and streamline our discussion of literary works. Some terms, such as the ones in section A, help us address the internal style, structure, form, and kind of works. Other terms, such as those in section B, provide insight into the material forms in which literary works have been produced.

In analyzing what they called "rhetoric," ancient Greek and Roman writers determined the elements of what we call "style" and "structure." Our literary terms are derived, via medieval and Renaissance intermediaries, from the Greek and Latin sources. In the definitions that follow, the etymology, or root, of the word is given when it helps illuminate the word's current usage.

Most of the examples are drawn from texts in this anthology.

Words **boldfaced** within definitions are themselves defined in this appendix. Some terms are defined within definitions; such words are *italicized*.

A. Terms of Style, Structure, Form, and Kind

accent (synonym "stress"): a term of **rhythm.** The special force devoted to the voicing of one syllable in a word over others. In the noun "accent," for example, the accent, or stress, is on the first syllable.

act: the major subdivision of a play, usually divided into **scenes.**

aesthetics (from Greek, "to feel, apprehend by the senses"): the philosophy of artistic meaning as a distinct mode of apprehending untranslatable truth, defined as an alternative to rational enquiry, which is purely abstract. Developed in the late eighteenth century by the German philosopher Immanuel Kant especially.

Alexandrine: a term of **meter.** In French verse a line of twelve syllables, and, by analogy, in English verse a line of six stresses. See **hexameter.**

allegory (Greek "saying otherwise"): saying one thing (the "vehicle" of the allegory) and meaning another (the allegory's "tenor"). Allegories may be momentary aspects of a work, as in **metaphor** ("John is a lion"), or, through extended metaphor, may constitute the basis of narrative, as in Bunyan's *Pilgrim's Progress*: this second meaning is the dominant one. See also **symbol** and **type.** Allegory is one of the most significant **figures of thought.**

alliteration (from Latin "litera," alphabetic letter): a **figure of speech.** The repetition of an initial consonant sound or consonant cluster in consecutive or closely positioned words. This pattern is often an inseparable part of the meter in Germanic languages, where the tonic, or accented **syllable,** is usually the first syllable. Thus all Old English poetry and some varieties of Middle English poetry use alliteration as part of their basic metrical practice. *Sir Gawain and the Green Knight,* line 1: "Sithen the sege and the assaut was sesed at Troye" (see vol. 1/A, p. 184). Otherwise used for local effects; Stevie Smith, "Pretty," lines 4–5: "And in the pretty pool the pike stalks / He stalks his prey . . ." (see vol. 2/F, p. 2604).

*This appendix was devised and compiled by James Simpson with the collaboration of all the editors. We especially thank Professor Lara Bovilsky of the University of Oregon at Eugene, who helped us reshape this appendix for this edition.

allusion: Literary allusion is a passing but illuminating reference within a literary text to another, well-known text (often biblical or **classical**). Topical allusions are also, of course, common in certain modes, especially **satire**.

anagnorisis (Greek "recognition"): the moment of **protagonist's** recognition in a narrative, which is also often the moment of moral understanding.

anapest: a term of **rhythm**. A three-syllable foot following the rhythmic pattern, in English verse, of two unstressed (uu) syllables followed by one stressed (/). Thus, for example, "Illinois."

anaphora (Greek "carrying back"): a **figure of speech**. The repetition of words or groups of words at the beginning of consecutive sentences, clauses, or phrases. Blake, "London," lines 5–8: "In every cry of every Man, / In every Infant's cry of fear, / In every voice, in every ban . . ." (see vol. 2/D, p. 132); Louise Bennett, "Jamaica Oman," lines 17–20: "Some backa man a push, some side-a / Man a hole him han, / Some a lick sense eena him head, / Some a guide him pon him plan!" (see vol. 2/F, p. 2729).

animal fable: a **genre**. A short narrative of speaking animals, followed by moralizing comment, written in a low style and gathered into a collection. Robert Henryson, "The Cock and the Fox" (see vol. 1/A, p. 501).

antithesis (Greek "placing against"): a **figure of thought**. The juxtaposition of opposed terms in clauses or sentences that are next to or near each other; Milton, *Paradise Lost* 1.777–80: "They but now who seemed / In bigness to surpass Earth's giant sons / Now less than smallest dwarfs, in narrow room / Throng numberless" (see vol. 1/B, p. 1964).

apostrophe (from Greek "turning away"): a **figure of thought**. An address, often to an absent person, a force, or a quality. For example, a poet makes an apostrophe to a Muse when invoking her for inspiration.

apposition: a term of **syntax**. The repetition of elements serving an identical grammatical function in one sentence. The effect of this repetition is to arrest the flow of the sentence, but in doing so to add extra semantic nuance to repeated elements. This is an especially important feature of Old English poetic style. See, for example, Caedmon's *Hymn* (vol. 1/A, p. 30), where the phrases "heaven-kingdom's Guardian," "the Measurer's might," "his mind-plans," and "the work of the Glory-Father" each serve an identical syntactic function as the direct objects of "praise."

assonance (Latin "sounding to"): a **figure of speech**. The repetition of identical or near identical stressed vowel sounds in words whose final consonants differ, producing half-rhyme. Tennyson, "The Lady of Shalott," line 100: "His broad clear brow in sunlight glowed" (see vol. 2/E, p. 1163).

aubade (originally from Spanish "alba," dawn): a **genre**. A lover's dawn song or lyric bewailing the arrival of the day and the necessary separation of the lovers; Donne, "The Sun Rising" (see vol. 1/B, p. 1376). Larkin recasts the genre in "Aubade" (see vol. 2/F, p. 2789).

autobiography (Greek "self-life writing"): a **genre**. A narrative of a life written by the subject; Wordsworth, *The Prelude* (see vol. 2/D, p. 349). There are subgenres, such as the spiritual autobiography, narrating the author's path to conversion and subsequent spiritual trials, as in Bunyan's *Grace Abounding*.

ballad stanza: a **verse form**. Usually a **quatrain** in alternating **iambic tetrameter** and **iambic trimeter** lines, rhyming abcb. See "Sir Patrick Spens" (vol. 2/D, p. 36); Louise Bennett's poems (vol. 2/F, pp. 2726–27); Eliot, "Sweeney among the Nightingales" (vol. 2/F, p. 2528); Larkin, "This Be the Verse" (vol. 2/F, p. 2789).

ballade: a **verse form.** A form consisting usually of three stanzas followed by a four-line envoi (French, "send off"). The last line of the first stanza establishes a **refrain,** which is repeated, or subtly varied, as the last line of each stanza. The form was derived from French medieval poetry; English poets, from the fourteenth to the sixteenth centuries especially, used it with varying stanza forms. Chaucer, "Complaint to His Purse" (see vol. 1/A, p. 345).

bathos (Greek "depth"): a **figure of thought.** A sudden and sometimes ridiculous descent of tone; Pope, *The Rape of the Lock* 3.157–58: "Not louder shrieks to pitying heaven are cast, / When husbands, or when lapdogs breathe their last" (see vol. 1/C, p. 2169).

beast epic: a **genre.** A continuous, unmoralized narrative, in prose or verse, relating the victories of the wholly unscrupulous but brilliant strategist Reynard the Fox over all adversaries. Chaucer arouses, only to deflate, expectations of the genre in *The Nun's Priest's Tale* (see vol. 1/A, p. 326).

biography (Greek "life-writing"): a **genre.** A life as the subject of an extended narrative. Thus Izaak Walton, *The Life of Dr. Donne* (see vol. 1/B, p. 1424).

blank verse: a **verse form.** Unrhymed **iambic pentameter** lines. Blank verse has no stanzas, but is broken up into uneven units (verse paragraphs) determined by sense rather than form. First devised in English by Henry Howard, Earl of Surrey, in his translation of two books of Virgil's *Aeneid* (see vol. 1/B, p. 669), this very flexible verse type became the standard form for dramatic poetry in the seventeenth century, as in most of Shakespeare's plays. Milton and Wordsworth, among many others, also used it to create an English equivalent to **classical epic.**

blazon: strictly, a heraldic shield; in rhetorical usage, a **topos** whereby the individual elements of a beloved's face and body are singled out for **hyperbolic** admiration. Spenser, *Epithalamion,* lines 167–84 (see vol. 1/B, p. 990). For an inversion of the **topos,** see Shakespeare, Sonnet 130 (vol. 1/B, p. 1183).

burlesque (French and Italian "mocking"): a work that adopts the **conventions** of a genre with the aim less of comically mocking the genre than of satirically mocking the society so represented (see **satire**). Thus Pope's *Rape of the Lock* (see vol. 1/C, p. 2157) does not mock **classical epic** so much as contemporary mores.

caesura (Latin "cut") (plural "caesurae"): a term of **meter.** A pause or breathing space within a line of verse, generally occurring between syntactic units; Louise Bennett, "Colonization in Reverse," lines 5–8: "By de hundred, by de tousan, / From country an from town, / By de ship-load, by de plane-load, / Jamaica is Englan boun" (see vol. 2/F, p. 2727), where the caesurae occur in lines 5 and 7.

canon (Greek "rule"): the group of texts regarded as worthy of special respect or attention by a given institution. Also, the group of texts regarded as definitely having been written by a certain author.

catastrophe (Greek "overturning"): the decisive turn in **tragedy** by which the plot is resolved and, usually, the **protagonist** dies.

catharsis (Greek "cleansing"): According to Aristotle, the effect of **tragedy** on its audience, through their experience of pity and terror, was a kind of spiritual cleansing, or catharsis.

character (Greek "stamp, impression"): a person, personified animal, or other figure represented in a literary work, especially in narrative and drama. The more a character seems to generate the action of a narrative, and the less he or she seems merely to serve a preordained narrative pattern, the "fuller," or more "rounded," a character is said to be. A "stock" character, common particularly in many comic genres, will perform a predictable function in different works of a given genre.

chiasmus (Greek "crosswise"): a **figure of speech.** The inversion of an already established sequence. This can involve verbal echoes: Pope, "Eloisa to Abelard," line 104, "The crime was common, common be the pain" (see vol. 1/C, p. 2180); or it can be purely a matter of syntactic inversion: Pope, *Epistle to Dr. Arbuthnot,* line 8: "They pierce my thickets, through my grot they glide" (see vol. 1/C, p. 2195).

classical, classicism, classic: Each term can be widely applied, but in English literary discourse, "classical" primarily describes the works of either Greek or Roman antiquity. "Classicism" denotes the practice of art forms inspired by classical antiquity, in particular the observance of rhetorical norms of **decorum** and balance, as opposed to following the dictates of untutored inspiration, as in Romanticism. "Classic" denotes an especially famous work within a given **canon.**

climax (Greek "ladder"): a moment of great intensity and structural change, especially in drama. Also a **figure of speech** whereby a sequence of verbally linked clauses is made, in which each successive clause is of greater consequence than its predecessor. Bacon, *Of Studies:* "Studies serve for pastimes, for ornaments, and for abilities. Their chief use for pastimes is in privateness and retiring; for ornament, is in discourse; and for ability, is in judgement" (see vol. 1/B, p. 1673).

comedy: a **genre.** A term primarily applied to drama, and derived from ancient drama, in opposition to **tragedy.** Comedy deals with humorously confusing, sometimes ridiculous situations in which the ending is, nevertheless, happy. A comedy often ends in one or more marriages. Shakespeare, *Twelfth Night* (see vol. 1/B, p. 1186).

comic mode: Many genres (e.g., **romance, fabliau, comedy**) involve a happy ending in which justice is done, the ravages of time are arrested, and that which is lost is found. Such genres participate in a comic mode.

connotation: To understand connotation, we need to understand **denotation.** While many words can denote the same concept—that is, have the same basic meaning—those words can evoke different associations, or connotations. Contrast, for example, the clinical-sounding term "depression" and the more colorful, musical, even poetic phrase "the blues."

consonance (Latin "sounding with"): a **figure of speech.** The repetition of final consonants in words or stressed syllables whose vowel sounds are different. Herbert, "Easter," line 13: "Consort, both heart and lute . . ." (see vol. 1/B, p. 1708).

convention: a repeatedly recurring feature (in either form or content) of works, occurring in combination with other recurring formal features, which constitutes a convention of a particular genre.

couplet: a **verse form.** In English verse two consecutive, rhyming lines usually containing the same number of stresses. Chaucer first introduced the **iambic pentameter** couplet into English (*Canterbury Tales*); the form was later used in many types of writing, including drama; imitations and translations of **classical epic** (thus *heroic couplet*); essays; and **satire** (see Dryden and Pope). The *distich* (Greek "two lines") is a couplet usually making complete sense; Aemilia Lanyer, *Salve Deus Rex Judaeorum,* lines 5–6: "Read it fair queen, though it defective be, / Your excellence can grace both it and me" (see vol. 1/B, p. 1431).

dactyl (Greek "finger," because of the finger's three joints): a term of **rhythm.** A three-syllable foot following the rhythmic pattern, in English verse, of one stressed followed by two unstressed syllables. Thus, for example, "Oregon."

decorum (Latin "that which is fitting"): a rhetorical principle whereby each formal aspect of a work should be in keeping with its subject matter and/or audience.

deixis (Greek "pointing"): relevant to **point of view.** Every work has, implicitly or explicitly, a "here" and a "now" from which it is narrated. Words that refer to or imply this point from which the voice of the work is projected (such as "here," "there," "this," "that," "now," "then") are examples of deixis, or "deictics." This technique is especially important in drama, where it is used to create a sense of the events happening as the spectator witnesses them.

denotation: A word has a basic, "prosaic" (factual) meaning prior to the associations it connotes (see **connotation**). The word "steed," for example, might call to mind a horse fitted with battle gear, to be ridden by a warrior, but its denotation is simply "horse."

denouement (French "unknotting"): the point at which a narrative can be resolved and so ended.

dialogue (Greek "conversation"): a **genre.** Dialogue is a feature of many genres, especially in both the **novel** and drama. As a genre itself, dialogue is used in philosophical traditions especially (most famously in Plato's *Dialogues*), as the representation of a conversation in which a philosophical question is pursued among various speakers.

diction, or **"lexis"** (from, respectively, Latin "dictio" and Greek "lexis," each meaning "word"): the actual words used in any utterance—speech, writing, and, for our purposes here, literary works. The choice of words contributes significantly to the style of a given work.

didactic mode (Greek "teaching mode"): **Genres** in a didactic mode are designed to instruct or teach, sometimes explicitly (e.g., sermons, philosophical **discourses, georgic**), and sometimes through the medium of fiction (e.g., **animal fable, parable**).

diegesis (Greek for "narration"): a term that simply means "narration," but is used in literary criticism to distinguish one kind of story from another. In a *mimetic* story, the events are played out before us (see **mimesis**), whereas in diegesis someone recounts the story to us. Drama is for the most part *mimetic,* whereas the novel is for the most part diegetic. In novels the narrator is not, usually, part of the action of the narrative; s/he is therefore extradiegetic.

dimeter (Greek "two measure"): a term of **meter.** A two-stress line, rarely used as the meter of whole poems, though used with great frequency in single poems by Skelton, e.g., "The Tunning of Elinour Rumming" (see vol. 1/B, p. 567). Otherwise used for single lines, as in Herbert, "Discipline," line 3: "O my God" (see vol. 1/B, p. 1724).

discourse (Latin "running to and fro"): broadly, any nonfictional speech or writing; as a more specific genre, a philosophical meditation on a set theme. Thus Newman, *The Idea of a University* (see vol. 2/E, p. 1078).

dramatic irony: a feature of narrative and drama, whereby the audience knows that the outcome of an action will be the opposite of that intended by a **character.**

dramatic monologue (Greek "single speaking"): a **genre.** A poem in which the voice of a historical or fictional **character** speaks, unmediated by any narrator, to an implied though silent audience. See Tennyson, "Ulysses" (vol. 2/E, p. 1170); Browning, "The Bishop Orders His Tomb" (vol. 2/E, p. 1286); Eliot, "The Love Song of J. Alfred Prufrock" (vol. 2/F, p. 2525); Carol Ann Duffy, "Medusa" and "Mrs Lazarus" (vol. 2/F, pp. 3044–45).

ecphrasis (Greek "speaking out"): a **topos** whereby a work of visual art is represented in a literary work. Auden, "Musée des Beaux Arts" (see vol. 2/F, p. 2686).

elegy: a **genre.** In **classical** literature elegy was a form written in elegiac **couplets** (a **hexameter** followed by a **pentameter**) devoted to many possible topics. In Ovidian elegy a lover meditates on the trials of erotic desire (e.g., Ovid's *Amores*). The **sonnet** sequences of both Sidney and Shakespeare exploit this genre, and, while it was still practiced in classical tradition by Donne ("On His Mistress" [see vol. 1/B, p. 1392]), by the later seventeenth century the term came to denote the poetry of loss, especially through the death of a loved person. See Tennyson, *In Memoriam* (vol. 2/E, p. 1187); Yeats, "In Memory of Major Robert Gregory" (vol. 2/F, p. 2034); Auden, "In Memory of W. B. Yeats" (see vol. 2/F, p. 2686); Heaney, "Clearances" (vol. 2/F, p. 2963).

emblem (Greek "an insertion"): a **figure of thought.** A picture allegorically expressing a moral, or a verbal picture open to such interpretation. Donne, "A Hymn to Christ," lines 1–2: "In what torn ship soever I embark, / That ship shall be my emblem of thy ark" (see vol. 1/B, p. 1416).

end-stopping: the placement of a complete syntactic unit within a complete line, fulfilling the metrical pattern; Auden, "In Memory of W. B. Yeats," line 42: "Earth, receive an honoured guest" (see vol. 2/F, p. 2688). Compare **enjambment.**

enjambment (French "striding," encroaching): The opposite of **end-stopping,** enjambment occurs when the syntactic unit does not end with the end of the line and the fulfillment of the metrical pattern. When the sense of the line overflows its meter and, therefore, the line break, we have enjambment; Auden, "In Memory of W. B. Yeats," lines 44–45: "Let the Irish vessel lie / Emptied of its poetry" (see vol. 2/F, p. 2688).

epic (synonym, *heroic poetry*): a **genre.** An extended narrative poem celebrating martial heroes, invoking divine inspiration, beginning in medias res (see **order**), written in a high style (including the deployment of **epic similes;** on high style, see **register**), and divided into long narrative sequences. Homer's *Iliad* and Virgil's *Aeneid* were the prime models for English writers of epic verse. Thus Milton, *Paradise Lost* (see vol. 1/B, p. 1943); Wordsworth, *The Prelude* (see vol. 2/D, p. 349); and Walcott, *Omeros* (see vol. 2/F, p. 2806). With its precise repertoire of stylistic resources, epic lent itself easily to **parodic** and **burlesque** forms, known as **mock epic;** thus Pope, *The Rape of the Lock* (see vol. 1/C, p. 2157).

epigram: a **genre.** A short, pithy poem wittily expressed, often with wounding intent. See Jonson, *Epigrams* (see vol. 1/B, p. 1539).

epigraph (Greek "inscription"): a **genre.** Any formal statement inscribed on stone; also the brief formulation on a book's title page, or a quotation at the beginning of a poem, introducing the work's themes in the most compressed form possible.

epistle (Latin "letter"): a **genre.** The letter can be shaped as a literary form, involving an intimate address often between equals. The *Epistles* of Horace provided a model for English writers from the sixteenth century. Thus Wyatt, "Mine own John Poins" (see vol. 1/B, p. 659), or Pope, "Epistle to a Lady" (vol. 1/C, p. 2245). Letters can be shaped to form the matter of an extended fiction, as the eighteenth-century epistolary **novel** (e.g., Samuel Richardson's *Pamela*).

epitaph: a **genre.** A pithy formulation to be inscribed on a funeral monument. Thus Ralegh, "The Author's Epitaph, Made by Himself" (see vol. 1/B, p. 1030).

epithalamion (Greek "concerning the bridal chamber"): a **genre.** A wedding poem, celebrating the marriage and wishing the couple good fortune. Thus Spenser, *Epithalamion* (see vol. 1/B, p. 990).

epyllion (plural "epyllia") (Greek: "little epic"): a **genre.** A relatively short poem in the meter of epic poetry. See, for example, Marlowe, *Hero and Leander*.

essay (French "trial, attempt"): a **genre.** An informal philosophical meditation, usually in prose and sometimes in verse. The journalistic periodical essay was developed in the early eighteenth century. Thus Addison and Steele, periodical essays (see vol. 1/C, p. 2113); Pope, *An Essay on Criticism* (see vol. 1/C, p. 2141).

euphemism (Greek "sweet saying"): a **figure of thought.** The figure by which something distasteful is described in alternative, less repugnant terms (e.g., "he passed away").

exegesis (Greek "leading out"): interpretation, traditionally of the biblical text, but, by transference, of any text.

exemplum (Latin "example"): an example inserted into a usually nonfictional writing (e.g., sermon or **essay**) to give extra force to an abstract thesis. Thus Johnson's example of "Sober" in his essay "On Idleness" (see vol. 1/C, p. 2326).

fabliau (French "little story," plural *fabliaux*): a **genre.** A short, funny, often bawdy narrative in low style (see **register**) imitated and developed from French models most subtly by Chaucer; see *The Miller's Prologue and Tale* (vol. 1/A, p. 264).

farce (French "stuffing"): a **genre.** A play designed to provoke laughter through the often humiliating antics of stock **characters.** Congreve's *The Way of the World* (see vol. 1/C, p. 1832) draws on this tradition.

figures of speech: Literary language often employs patterns perceptible to the eye and/or to the ear. Such patterns are called "figures of speech"; in classical rhetoric they were called "schemes" (from Greek "schema," meaning "form, figure").

figures of thought: Language can also be patterned conceptually, even outside the rules that normally govern it. Literary language in particular exploits this licensed linguistic irregularity. Synonyms for figures of thought are "trope" (Greek "twisting," referring to the irregularity of use) and "conceit" (Latin "concept," referring to the fact that these figures are perceptible only to the mind). Be careful not to confuse **trope** with **topos** (a common error).

first-person narration: relevant to **point of view,** a narrative in which the voice narrating refers to itself with forms of the first-person pronoun ("I," "me," "my," etc., or possibly "we," "us," "our"), and in which the narrative is determined by the limitations of that voice. Thus Mary Wollstonecraft Shelley, *Frankenstein.*

frame narrative: Some narratives, particularly collections of narratives, involve a frame narrative that explains the genesis of, and/or gives a perspective on, the main narrative or narratives to follow. Thus Chaucer, *Canterbury Tales;* Mary Wollstonecraft Shelley, *Frankenstein;* or Conrad, *Heart of Darkness.*

free indirect style: relevant to **point of view,** a narratorial voice that manages, without explicit reference, to imply, and often implicitly to comment on, the voice of a **character** in the narrative itself. Virginia Woolf, "A Sketch of the Past," where the voice, although strictly that of the adult narrator, manages to convey the child's manner of perception: "—I begin: the first memory. This was of red and purple flowers on a black background—my mother's dress."

genre and mode: The **style,** structure, and, often, length of a work, when coupled with a certain subject matter, raise expectations that a literary work conforms to a certain **genre** (French "kind"). Good writers might upset these expectations, but they remain aware of the expectations and thwart them purposefully. Works in different genres may nevertheless participate in the same **mode,** a broader category designating the fundamental perspectives governing various genres of writing. For mode, see **tragic, comic, satiric,** and **didactic modes.** Genres are fluid, sometimes very fluid (e.g., the **novel**); the word "usually" should be added to almost every account of the characteristics of a given genre!

georgic (Greek "farming"): a **genre.** Virgil's *Georgics* treat agricultural and occasionally scientific subjects, giving instructions on the proper management of farms. Unlike **pastoral,** which treats the countryside as a place of recreational idleness among shepherds, the georgic treats it as a place of productive labor. For an English poem that critiques both genres, see Crabbe, "The Village" (vol. 1/C, p. 1932).

hermeneutics (from the Greek god Hermes, messenger between the gods and humankind): the science of interpretation, first formulated as such by the German philosophical theologian Friedrich Schleiermacher in the early nineteenth century.

heroic poetry: see **epic.**

hexameter (Greek "six measure"): a term of **meter.** The hexameter line (a six-stress line) is the meter of **classical** Latin **epic;** while not imitated in that form for epic verse in English, some instances of the hexameter exist. See, for example, the last line of a Spenserian stanza, *Faerie Queene* 1.1.2: "O help thou my weake wit, and sharpen my dull tong" (vol. 1/B, p. 781), or Yeats, "The Lake Isle of Innisfree," line 1: "I will arise and go now, and go to Innisfree" (vol. 2/F, p. 2088).

homily (Greek "discourse"): a **genre.** A sermon, to be preached in church; *Book of Homilies* (see vol. 1/B, p. 692). Writers of literary fiction sometimes exploit the homily, or sermon, as in Chaucer, *The Pardoner's Tale* (see vol. 1/A, p. 310).

homophone (Greek "same sound"): a **figure of speech.** A word that sounds identical to another word but has a different meaning ("bear" / "bare").

hyperbaton (Greek "overstepping"): a term of **syntax.** The rearrangement, or inversion, of the expected word order in a sentence or clause. Gray, "Elegy Written in a Country Churchyard," line 38: "If Memory o'er their tomb no trophies raise" (vol. 1/C, p. 2524). Poets can suspend the expected syntax over many lines, as in the first sentences of the *Canterbury Tales* (vol. 1/A, p. 243) and of *Paradise Lost* (vol. 1/B, p. 1943).

hyperbole (Greek "throwing over"): a **figure of thought.** Overstatement, exaggeration; Marvell, "To His Coy Mistress," lines 11–12: "My vegetable love would grow / Vaster than empires, and more slow" (see vol. 1/B, p. 1797); Auden, "As I Walked Out One Evening," lines 9–12: "'I'll love you, dear, I'll love you / Till China and Africa meet / And the river jumps over the mountain / And the salmon sing in the street" (see vol. 2/F, p. 2684).

hypermetrical (adj.; Greek "over measured"): a term of **meter;** the word describes a breaking of the expected metrical pattern by at least one extra syllable.

hypotaxis, or **subordination** (respectively Greek and Latin "ordering under"): a term of **syntax.** The subordination, by the use of subordinate clauses, of different elements of a sentence to a single main verb. Milton, *Paradise Lost* 9.513–15: "As when a ship by skillful steersman wrought / Nigh river's mouth or foreland, where the wind / Veers oft, as oft so steers, and shifts her sail; So varied he" (vol. 1/B, p. 2102). The contrary principle to **parataxis.**

iamb: a term of **rhythm.** The basic foot of English verse; two syllables following the rhythmic pattern of unstressed followed by stressed and producing a rising effect. Thus, for example, "Vermont."

imitation: the practice whereby writers strive ideally to reproduce and yet renew the **conventions** of an older form, often derived from **classical** civilization. Such a practice will be praised in periods of classicism (e.g., the eighteenth century) and repudiated in periods dominated by a model of inspiration (e.g., Romanticism).

irony (Greek "dissimulation"): a **figure of thought.** In broad usage, irony designates the result of inconsistency between a statement and a context that undermines the statement. "It's a beautiful day" is unironic if it's a beautiful day; if, however, the weather is terrible, then the inconsistency between statement and context is ironic. The effect is often amusing; the need to be ironic is sometimes produced by censorship of one kind or another. Strictly, irony is a subset of allegory: whereas allegory says one thing and means another, irony says one thing and means its opposite. For an extended example of irony, see Swift's "Modest Proposal." See also **dramatic irony.**

journal (French "daily"): a **genre.** A diary, or daily record of ephemeral experience, whose perspectives are concentrated on, and limited by, the experiences of single days. Thus Pepys, *Diary* (see vol. 1/C, p. 1732).

lai: a **genre.** A short narrative, often characterized by images of great intensity; a French term, and a form practiced by Marie de France (see vol. 1/A, p. 142).

legend (Latin "requiring to be read"): a **genre.** A narrative of a celebrated, possibly historical, but mortal **protagonist.** To be distinguished from **myth.** Thus the "Arthurian legend" but the "myth of Proserpine."

lexical set: Words that habitually recur together (e.g., January, February, March, etc.; or red, white, and blue) form a lexical set.

litotes (from Greek "smooth"): a **figure of thought.** Strictly, understatement by denying the contrary; More, *Utopia:* "differences of no slight import" (see vol. 1/B, p. 575). More loosely, understatement; Swift, "A Tale of a Tub": "Last week I saw a woman flayed, and you will hardly believe how much it altered her person for the worse" (see vol. 1/C, p. 1956). Stevie Smith, "Sunt Leones," lines 11–12: "And if the Christians felt a little blue— / Well people being eaten often do" (see vol. 2/F, p. 2600).

lullaby: a **genre.** A bedtime, sleep-inducing song for children, in simple and regular meter. Adapted by Auden, "Lullaby" (see vol. 2/F, p. 2680).

lyric (from Greek "lyre"): Initially meaning a song, "lyric" refers to a short poetic form, without restriction of meter, in which the expression of personal emotion, often by a voice in the first person, is given primacy over narrative sequence. Thus "The Wife's Lament" (see vol. 1/A, p. 120); Yeats, "The Wild Swans at Coole" (see vol. 2/F, p. 2096).

masque: a **genre.** Costly entertainments of the Stuart court, involving dance, song, speech, and elaborate stage effects, in which courtiers themselves participated.

metaphor (Greek "carrying across," etymologically parallel to Latin "translation"): One of the most significant **figures of thought,** metaphor designates identification or implicit identification of one thing with another with which it is not literally identifiable. Blake, "London," lines 11–12: "And the hapless Soldier's sigh / Runs in blood down Palace walls" (see vol. 2/D, p. 132).

meter: Verse (from Latin "versus," turned) is distinguished from prose (from Latin "prorsus," straightforward) as a more compressed form of expression, shaped by metrical norms. **Meter** (Greek "measure") refers to the regularly recurring sound pattern of verse lines. The means of producing sound patterns across lines differ in different poetic traditions. Verse may be **quantitative,** or determined by the quantities of syllables (set patterns of long and short syllables), as in Latin and Greek poetry. It may be **syllabic,** determined by fixed numbers of syllables in the line, as in the verse of Romance languages (e.g., French and Italian). It may be **accentual,** determined by the number of accents, or stresses in the line, with variable numbers of syllables, as in Old English and some varieties of Middle English alliterative verse. Or it may be **accentual-syllabic,** determined by the numbers of accents, but possessing a regular pattern of stressed and unstressed syllables, so as to produce regular numbers of syllables per line. Since Chaucer, English verse has worked primarily within the many possibilities of accentual-syllabic meter. The unit of meter is the **foot.** In English verse the number of feet per line corresponds to the number of accents in a line. For the types and examples of different meters, see **monometer, dimeter, trimester, tetrameter, pentameter,** and **hexameter.** In the definitions below, "u" designates one unstressed syllable, and "/" one stressed syllable.

metonymy (Greek "change of name"): one of the most significant **figures of thought.** Using a word to **denote** another concept or other concepts, by virtue of habitual association. Thus "The Press," designating printed news media. Fictional names often work by associations of this kind. Closely related to **synecdoche.**

mimesis (Greek for "imitation"): A central function of literature and drama has been to provide a plausible imitation of the reality of the world beyond the literary work; mimesis is the representation and imitation of what is taken to be reality.

mise-en-abyme (French for "cast into the abyss"): Some works of art represent themselves in themselves; if they do so effectively, the represented artifact also represents itself, and so ad infinitum. The effect achieved is called "*mise-en-abyme.*" Hoccleve's *Complaint,* for example, represents a depressed man reading about a depressed man. This sequence threatens to become a *mise-en-abyme.*

monometer (Greek "one measure"): a term of **meter.** An entire line with just one stress; *Sir Gawain and the Green Knight,* line 15, "most (u) grand (/)" (see vol. 1/A, p. 186).

myth: a **genre.** The narrative of **protagonists** with, or subject to, superhuman powers. A myth expresses some profound foundational truth, often by accounting for the origin of natural phenomena. To be distinguished from **legend.** Thus the "Arthurian legend" but the "myth of Proserpine."

novel: an extremely flexible **genre** in both form and subject matter. Usually in prose, giving high priority to narration of events, with a certain expectation of length, novels are preponderantly rooted in a specific, and often complex, social world; sensitive to the realities of material life; and often focused on one **character** or a small circle of central characters. By contrast with chivalric **romance** (the main European narrative genre prior to the novel), novels tend to eschew the marvelous in favor of a recognizable social world and credible action. The novel's openness allows it to participate in all modes, and to be co-opted for a huge variety of subgenres. In English literature the novel dates from the late seventeenth century and has been astonishingly successful in appealing to a huge readership, particularly in the nineteenth and twentieth centuries. The English and Irish tradition of the novel includes, for example, Fielding, Austen, the Brontë sisters, Dickens, George Eliot, Conrad, Woolf, Lawrence, Joyce, to name but a few very great exponents of the genre.

novella: a **genre.** A short **novel,** often characterized by imagistic intensity. Conrad, *Heart of Darkness* (see vol. 2/F, p. 1954).

occupatio (Latin "taking possession"): a **figure of thought.** Denying that one will discuss a subject while actually discussing it; also known as "praeteritio" (Latin "passing by"). See Chaucer, *Nun's Priest's Tale,* lines 414–32 (see vol. 1/A, p. 335).

ode (Greek "song"): a **genre.** A **lyric** poem in elevated, or high style (see **register**), often addressed to a natural force, a person, or an abstract quality. The Pindaric ode in English is made up of **stanzas** of unequal length, while the Horatian ode has stanzas of equal length. For examples of both types, see, respectively, Wordsworth, "Ode: Intimations of Immortality" (vol. 2/D, p. 335); and Marvell, "An Horatian Ode" (vol. 1/B, p. 1806), or Keats, "Ode on Melancholy" (vol. 2/D, p. 931). For a fuller discussion, see the headnote to Jonson's "Ode on Cary and Morison" (vol. 1/B, p. 1551).

omniscient narrator (Latin "all-knowing narrator"): relevant to **point of view.** A narrator who, in the fiction of the narrative, has complete access to both the deeds and the thoughts of all **characters** in the narrative. Thus Thomas Hardy, "On the Western Circuit" (see vol. 2/F, p. 1917).

onomatopoeia (Greek "name making"): a **figure of speech.** Verbal sounds that imitate and evoke the sounds they denotate. Hopkins, "Binsey Poplars," lines 10–12 (about some felled trees): "O if we but knew what we do / When we delve [dig] or hew— / Hack and rack the growing green!" (see vol. 2/E, p. 1552).

order: A story may be told in different narrative orders. A narrator might use the sequence of events as they happened, and thereby follow what **classical** rhetoricians called the *natural order;* alternatively, the narrator might reorder the sequence of events, beginning the narration either in the middle or at the end of the sequence of events, thereby following an *artificial order.* If a narrator begins in the middle of events, he or she is said to begin *in medias res* (Latin "in the middle of the matter"). For a brief discussion of these concepts, see Spenser, *Faerie Queene,* "A Letter of the Authors" (vol. 1/B, p. 777). Modern narratology makes a related distinction, between *histoire* (French "story") for the natural order that readers mentally reconstruct, and *discours* (French, here "narration") for the narrative as presented. See also **plot** and **story.**

ottava rima: a **verse form.** An eight-line stanza form, rhyming abababcc, using **iambic pentameter;** Yeats, "Sailing to Byzantium" (see vol. 2/F, p. 2103). Derived from the Italian poet Boccaccio, an eight-line stanza was used by fifteenth-century English poets for inset passages (e.g., Christ's speech from the Cross in Lydgate's *Testament,* lines 754–897). The form in this rhyme scheme was used in English poetry for long narrative by, for example, Byron (*Don Juan;* see vol. 2/D, p. 672).

oxymoron (Greek "sharp blunt"): a **figure of thought.** The conjunction of normally incompatible terms; Milton, *Paradise Lost* 1.63: "darkness visible" (see vol. 1/B, p. 1947).

panegyric: a **genre.** Demonstrative, or epideictic (Greek "showing"), rhetoric was a branch of **classical** rhetoric. Its own two main branches were the rhetoric of praise on the one hand and of vituperation on the other. Panegyric, or eulogy (Greek "sweet speaking"), or encomium (plural *encomia*), is the term used to describe the speeches or writings of praise.

parable: a **genre.** A simple story designed to provoke, and often accompanied by, **allegorical** interpretation, most famously by Christ as reported in the Gospels.

paradox (Greek "contrary to received opinion"): a **figure of thought.** An apparent contradiction that requires thought to reveal an inner consistency. Chaucer, "Troilus's Song," line 12: "O sweete harm so quainte" (see vol. 1/A, p. 344).

parataxis, or **coordination** (respectively Greek and Latin "ordering beside"): a term of **syntax.** The coordination, by the use of coordinating conjunctions, of different main clauses in a single sentence. Malory, "Morte Darthur": "So Sir Lancelot departed and took his sword under his arm, and so he walked in his mantel, that noble knight, and put himself in great jeopardy" (see vol. 1/A, p. 484). The opposite principle to **hypotaxis.**

parody: a work that uses the **conventions** of a particular genre with the aim of comically mocking a **topos,** a genre, or a particular exponent of a genre. Shakespeare parodies the topos of **blazon** in Sonnet 130 (see vol. 1/B, p. 1183).

pastoral (from Latin "pastor," shepherd): a **genre.** Pastoral is set among shepherds, making often refined **allusion** to other apparently unconnected subjects (sometimes politics) from the potentially idyllic world of highly literary if illiterate shepherds. Pastoral is distinguished from **georgic** by representing recreational rural idleness, whereas the georgic offers instruction on how to manage rural labor. English writers had classical models in the *Idylls* of Theocritus in Greek and Virgil's *Eclogues* in Latin. Pastoral is also called bucolic (from the Greek word for "herdsman"). Thus Spenser, *Shepheardes Calender* (see vol. 1/B, p. 769).

pathetic fallacy: the attribution of sentiment to natural phenomena, as if they were in sympathy with human feelings. Thus Milton, *Lycidas,* lines 146–47: "With cowslips wan that hang the pensive head, / And every flower that sad embroidery wears" (see vol. 1/B, p. 1922). For critique of the practice, see Ruskin (who coined the term), "Of the Pathetic Fallacy" (vol. 2/E, p. 1340).

pentameter (Greek "five measure"): a term of **meter.** In English verse, a five-stress line. Between the late fourteenth and the nineteenth centuries, this meter, frequently employing an iambic rhythm, was the basic line of English verse. Chaucer, Shakespeare, Milton, and Wordsworth each, for example, deployed this very flexible line as their primary resource; Milton, *Paradise Lost* 1.128: "O Prince, O Chief of many thronèd Powers" (see vol. 1/B, p. 1949).

performative: Verbal expressions have many different functions. They can, for example, be descriptive, or constative (if they make an argument), or performative, for example. A performative utterance is one that makes something happen in the world by virtue of its utterance. "I hereby sentence you to ten years in prison," if uttered in the appropriate circumstances, itself performs an action; it makes something happen in the world. By virtue of its performing an action, it is called a "performative." See also **speech act.**

peripeteia (Greek "turning about"): the sudden reversal of fortune (in both directions) in a dramatic work.

periphrasis (Greek "declaring around"): a **figure of thought.** Circumlocution; the use of many words to express what could be expressed in few or one; Sidney, *Astrophil and Stella* 39.1–4 (vol. 1/B, p. 1091).

persona (Latin "sound through"): originally the mask worn in the Roman theater to magnify an actor's voice; in literary discourse persona (plural *personae*) refers to the narrator or speaker of a text, whose voice is coherent and whose person need have no relation to the person of the actual author of a text. Eliot, "The Love Song of J. Alfred Prufrock" (see vol. 2/F, p. 2525).

personification, or **prosopopoeia** (Greek "person making"): a **figure of thought.** The attribution of human qualities to nonhuman forces or objects; Shakespeare, *King Lear* 3.2.1: "Blow winds and crack your cheeks, rage! Blow!" (see vol. 1/B, p. 1295).

plot: the sequence of events in a story as narrated, as distinct from **story,** which refers to the sequence of events as we reconstruct them from the plot. See also **order.**

point of view: All of the many kinds of writing involve a point of view from which a text is, or seems to be, generated. The presence of such a point of view may be powerful and explicit, as in many novels, or deliberately invisible, as in much drama. In some genres, such as the **novel,** the narrator does not necessarily tell the story from a position we can predict; that is, the needs of a particular story, not the **conventions** of the genre, determine the narrator's position. In other genres, the narrator's position is fixed by convention; in certain kinds of love poetry, for example, the narrating voice is always that of a suffering lover. Not only does the point of view significantly inform the style of a work, but it also informs the structure of that work.

protagonist (Greek "first actor"): the hero or heroine of a drama or narrative.

pun: a **figure of thought.** A sometimes irresolvable doubleness of meaning in a single word or expression; Shakespeare, Sonnet 135, line 1: "Whoever hath her wish, thou hast thy *Will*" (see vol. 1/B, p. 1183).

quatrain: a **verse form.** A stanza of four lines, usually rhyming abcb, abab, or abba. Of many possible examples, see Crashaw, "On the Wounds of Our Crucified Lord" (see vol. 1/B, p. 1746).

refrain: usually a single line repeated as the last line of consecutive stanzas, sometimes with subtly different wording and ideally with subtly different meaning as the poem progresses. See, for example, Wyatt, "Blame not my lute" (vol. 1/B, p. 656).

register: The register of a word is its stylistic level, which can be distinguished by degree of technicality but also by degree of formality. We choose our words from different registers according to context, that is, audience and/or environment. Thus a chemist in a laboratory will say "sodium chloride," a cook in a kitchen "salt." A formal register designates the kind of language used in polite society (e.g., "Mr. President"), while an informal or colloquial register is used in less formal or more relaxed social situations (e.g., "the boss"). In **classical** and medieval rhetoric, these registers of formality were called *high style* and *low style.* A *middle style* was defined as the style fit for narrative, not drawing attention to itself.

rhetoric: the art of verbal persuasion. **Classical** rhetoricians distinguished three areas of rhetoric: the forensic, to be used in law courts; the deliberative, to be used in political or philosophical deliberations; and the demonstrative, or epideictic, to be used for the purposes of public praise or blame. Rhetorical manuals covered all the skills required of a speaker, from the management of style and structure to delivery. These manuals powerfully influenced the theory of poetics as a separate branch of verbal practice, particularly in the matter of style.

rhyme: a **figure of speech.** The repetition of identical vowel sounds in stressed syllables whose initial consonants differ ("dead" / "head"). In poetry, rhyme often links the end of one line with another. *Masculine rhyme:* full rhyme on the final syllable of the line ("decays" / "days"). *Feminine rhyme:* full rhyme on syllables that are followed by unaccented syllables ("fountains" / "mountains"). *Internal rhyme:* full rhyme within a single line; Coleridge, *The Rime of the Ancient Mariner,* line 7: "The guests are met, the feast is set" (see vol. 2/D, p. 444). *Rhyme riche:* rhyming on **homophones;** Chaucer, *General Prologue,* lines 17–18: "seeke" / "seke." *Off rhyme* (also known as *half rhyme, near rhyme,* or *slant rhyme*): differs from perfect rhyme in changing the vowel sound and/or the concluding consonants expected of perfect rhyme; Byron, "They say that Hope is Happiness," lines 5–7: "most" / "lost." *Pararhyme:* stressed vowel sounds differ but are flanked by identical or similar consonants; Owen, "Miners," lines 9–11: "simmer" / "summer" (see vol. 2/F, p. 2037).

rhyme royal: a **verse form.** A **stanza** of seven **iambic pentameter** lines, rhyming ababbcc; first introduced by Chaucer and called "royal" because the form was used by James I of Scotland for his *Kingis Quair* in the early fifteenth century. Chaucer, "Troilus's Song" (see vol. 1/A, p. 344).

rhythm: Rhythm is not absolutely distinguishable from **meter.** One way of making a clear distinction between these terms is to say that rhythm (from the Greek "to flow") denotes the patterns of sound within the feet of verse lines and the combination of those feet. Very often a particular meter will raise expectations that a given rhythm will be used regularly through a whole line or a whole poem. Thus in English verse the pentameter regularly uses an iambic rhythm. Rhythm, however, is much more fluid than meter, and many lines within the same poem using a single meter will frequently exploit different rhythmic possibilities. For examples of different rhythms, see **iamb, trochee, anapest, spondee,** and **dactyl.**

romance: a **genre.** From the twelfth to the sixteenth century, the main form of European narrative, in either verse or prose, was that of chivalric romance. Romance, like the later **novel,** is a very fluid genre, but romances are often characterized by (i) a tripartite structure of social integration, followed by disintegration, involving moral tests and often marvelous events, itself the prelude to reintegration in a happy ending, frequently of marriage; and (ii) aristocratic social milieux. Thus *Sir Gawain and the Green Knight* (see vol. 1/A, p. 186); Spenser's (unfinished) *Faerie Queene* (vol. 1/B, p. 775). The immensely popular, fertile genre was absorbed, in both domesticated and undomesticated form, by the novel. For an adaptation of romance, see Chaucer, *Wife of Bath's Tale* (vol. 1/A, p. 282).

sarcasm (Greek "flesh tearing"): a **figure of thought.** A wounding expression, often expressed ironically; Boswell, *Life of Johnson:* Johnson [asked if any man of the modern age could have written the **epic** poem *Fingal*] replied, "Yes, Sir, many men, many women, and many children" (see vol. 1/C, p. 2446).

satire (Latin for "a bowl of mixed fruits"): a **genre.** In Roman literature (e.g., Juvenal), the communication, in the form of a letter between equals, complaining of the ills of contemporary society. The genre in this form is characterized by a first-person narrator exasperated by social ills; the letter form; a high frequency of contemporary reference; and the use of invective in **low-style** language. Pope practices the genre thus in the *Epistle to Dr. Arbuthnot* (see vol. 1/C, p. 2193). Wyatt's "Mine own John Poins" (see vol. 1/B, p. 659) draws ultimately on a gentler, Horatian model of the genre.

satiric mode: Works in a very large variety of genres are devoted to the more or less savage attack on social ills. Thus Swift's travel narrative *Gulliver's Travels* (see vol. 1/C, p. 1959), his **essay** "A Modest Proposal" (vol. 1/C, p. 2105), Pope's mock-**epic** *The Dunciad* (vol. 1/C, p. 2204), and Gay's *Beggar's Opera* (vol. 1/C, p. 2261), to look no further than the eighteenth century, are all within a satiric mode.

scene: a subdivision of an **act,** itself a subdivision of a dramatic performance and/or text. The action of a scene usually occurs in one place.

sensibility (from Latin, "capable of being perceived by the senses"): as a literary term, an eighteenth-century concept derived from moral philosophy that stressed the social importance of fellow feeling and particularly of sympathy in social relations. The concept generated a literature of "sensibility," such as the sentimental **novel** (the most famous of which was Goethe's *Sorrows of the Young Werther* [1774]), or sentimental poetry, such as Cowper's passage on the stricken deer in *The Task* (see vol. 1/C, p. 2546).

short story: a **genre.** Generically similar to, though shorter and more concentrated than, the **novel;** often published as part of a collection. Thus Mansfield, "The Daughters of the Late Colonel" (see vol. 2/F, p. 2569).

simile (Latin "like"): a **figure of thought.** Comparison, usually using the word "like" or "as," of one thing with another so as to produce sometimes surprising analogies. Donne, "The Storm," lines 29–30: "Sooner than you read this line did the gale, / Like shot, not feared till felt, our sails assail." Frequently used, in extended form, in **epic** poetry; Milton, *Paradise Lost* 1.338–46 (see vol. 1/B, p. 1954).

soliloquy (Latin "single speaking"): a **topos** of drama, in which a **character,** alone or thinking to be alone on stage, speaks so as to give the audience access to his or her private thoughts. Thus Viola's soliloquy in Shakespeare, *Twelfth Night* 2.2.17–41 (vol. 1/B, p. 1205).

sonnet: a **verse form.** A form combining a variable number of units of rhymed lines to produce a fourteen-line poem, usually in rhyming **iambic pentameter** lines. In English there are two principal varieties: the Petrarchan sonnet, formed by an octave (an eight-line stanza, often broken into two **quatrains** having the same rhyme scheme, typically abba abba) and a sestet (a six-line stanza, typically cdecde or cdcdcd); and the Shakespearean sonnet, formed by three quatrains (abab cdcd efef) and a **couplet** (gg). The declaration of a sonnet can take a sharp turn, or "volta," often at the decisive formal shift from octave to sestet in the Petrarchan sonnet, or in the final couplet of a Shakespearean sonnet, introducing a trenchant counterstatement. Derived from Italian poetry, and especially from the poetry of Petrarch, the sonnet was first introduced to English poetry by Wyatt, and initially used principally for the expression of unrequited erotic love, though later poets used the form for many other purposes. See Wyatt, "Whoso list to hunt" (vol. 1/B, p. 649); Sidney, *Astrophil and Stella* (vol. 1/B, p. 1084); Shakespeare, *Sonnets* (vol. 1/B, p. 1169); Wordsworth, "London, 1802" (vol. 2/D, p. 346); McKay, "If We Must Die" (vol. 2/F, p. 2724); Heaney, "Clearances" (vol. 2/F, p. 2963).

speech act: Words and deeds are often distinguished, but words are often (perhaps always) themselves deeds. Utterances can perform different speech acts, such as promising, declaring, casting a spell, encouraging, persuading, denying, lying, and so on. See also **performative.**

Spenserian stanza: a **verse form.** The stanza developed by Spenser for *The Faerie Queene*; nine **iambic** lines, the first eight of which are **pentameters,** followed by one **hexameter,** rhyming ababbcbcc. See also, for example, Shelley, *Adonais* (vol. 2/D, p. 839), and Keats, *The Eve of St. Agnes* (vol. 2/D, p. 912).

spondee: a term of **meter.** A two-syllable foot following the rhythmic pattern, in English verse, of two stressed syllables. Thus, for example, "Utah."

stanza (Italian "room"): groupings of two or more lines, though "stanza" is usually reserved for groupings of at least four lines. Stanzas are often joined by rhyme, often in sequence, where each group shares the same metrical pattern and, when rhymed, rhyme scheme. Stanzas can themselves be arranged into larger groupings. Poets often invent new **verse forms,** or they may work within established forms.

story: a narrative's sequence of events, which we reconstruct from those events as they have been recounted by the narrator (i.e., the **plot**). See also **order.**

stream of consciousness: usually a **first-person** narrative that seems to give the reader access to the narrator's mind as it perceives or reflects on events, prior to organizing those perceptions into a coherent narrative. Thus (though generated from a **third-person** narrative) Joyce, *Ulysses*, "Penelope" (see vol. 2/F, p. 2475).

style (from Latin for "writing instrument"): In literary works the manner in which something is expressed contributes substantially to its meaning. The expressions "sun," "mass of helium at the center of the solar system," "heaven's golden orb" all designate "sun," but do so in different manners, or styles, which produce different meanings. The manner of a literary work is its "style," the effect of which is its "tone." We often can intuit the tone of a text; from that intuition of tone we can analyze the stylistic resources by which it was produced. We can analyze the style of literary works through consideration of different elements of style; for example, **diction, figures of thought, figures of speech, meter and rhythm, verse form, syntax, point of view.**

sublime: As a concept generating a literary movement, the sublime refers to the realm of experience beyond the measurable, and so beyond the rational, produced especially by the terrors and grandeur of natural phenomena. Derived especially from the first-century Greek treatise *On the Sublime,* sometimes attributed to Longinus, the notion of the sublime was in the later eighteenth century a spur to Romanticism.

syllable: the smallest unit of sound in a pronounced word. The syllable that receives the greatest stress is called the *tonic* syllable.

symbol (Greek "token"): a **figure of thought.** Something that stands for something else, and yet seems necessarily to evoke that other thing. In Neoplatonic, and there-fore Romantic, theory, to be distinguished from **allegory** thus: whereas allegory involves connections between vehicle and tenor agreed by convention or made explicit, the meanings of a symbol are supposedly inherent to it. For discussion, see Coleridge, "On Symbol and Allegory" (vol. 2/D, p. 502).

synecdoche (Greek "to take with something else"): a **figure of thought.** Using a part to express the whole, or vice versa; e.g., "all hands on deck." Closely related to **metonymy.**

syntax (Greek "ordering with"): Syntax designates the rules by which sentences are constructed in a given language. Discussion of meter is impossible without some reference to syntax, since the overall effect of a poem is, in part, always the product of a subtle balance of meter and sentence construction. Syntax is also essential to the understanding of prose style, since prose writers, deprived of the full shaping possibilities of meter, rely all the more heavily on syntactic resources. A working command of syntactical practice requires an understanding of the parts of speech (nouns, verbs, adjectives, adverbs, conjunctions, pronouns, prepositions, and inter-jections), since writers exploit syntactic possibilities by using particular combina-tions and concentrations of the parts of speech.

taste (from Italian "touch"): Although medieval monastic traditions used eating and tasting as a metaphor for reading, the concept of taste as a personal ideal to be cultivated by, and applied to, the appreciation and judgment of works of art in gen-eral was developed in the eighteenth century.

tercet: a **verse form.** A stanza or group of three lines, used in larger forms such as **terza rima,** the **Petrarchan sonnet,** and the **villanelle.**

terza rima: a **verse form.** A sequence of rhymed **tercets** linked by rhyme thus: aba bcb cdc, etc. first used extensively by Dante in *The Divine Comedy,* the form was adapted in English **iambic pentameters** by Wyatt and revived in the nineteenth century. See Wyatt, "Mine own John Poins" (vol. 1/B, p. 659); Shelley, "Ode to the West Wind" (vol. 2/D, p. 791); and Morris, "The Defence of Guinevere" (vol. 2/E, p. 1513). For modern adaptations see Eliot, lines 78–149 (though unrhymed) of "Little Gidding" (vol. 2/F, pp. 2548); Heaney, "Station Island" (vol. 2/F, p. 2961); Walcott, *Omeros* (vol. 2/F, p. 2806).

tetrameter (Greek "four measure"): a term of **meter.** A line with four stresses. Coleridge, *Christabel,* line 31: "She stole along, she nothing spoke" (see vol. 2/D, p. 462).

theme (Greek "proposition"): In literary criticism the term designates what the work is about; the theme is the concept that unifies a given work of literature.

third-person narration: relevant to **point of view.** A narration in which the narrator recounts a narrative of **characters** referred to explicitly or implicitly by third-person pronouns ("he," "she," etc.), without the limitation of a **first-person narration.** Thus Johnson, *The History of Rasselas.*

topographical poem (Greek "place writing"): a **genre.** A poem devoted to the meditative description of particular places. Thus Gray, "Ode on a Distant Prospect of Eton College" (see vol. 1/C, p. 2519).

topos (Greek "place," plural *topoi*): a commonplace in the content of a given kind of literature. Originally, in **classical** rhetoric, the topoi were tried-and-tested stimuli to literary invention: lists of standard headings under which a subject might be investigated. In medieval narrative poems, for example, it was commonplace to begin with a description of spring. Writers did, of course, render the commonplace uncommon, as in Chaucer's spring scene at the opening of *The Canterbury Tales* (see vol. 1/A, p. 243).

tradition (from Latin "passing on"): A literary tradition is whatever is passed on or revived from the past in a single literary culture, or drawn from others to enrich a writer's culture. "Tradition" is fluid in reference, ranging from small to large referents: thus it may refer to a relatively small aspect of texts (e.g., the tradition of **iambic pentameter**), or it may, at the other extreme, refer to the body of texts that constitute a **canon.**

tragedy: a **genre.** A dramatic representation of the fall of kings or nobles, beginning in happiness and ending in catastrophe. Later transferred to other social milieux. The opposite of **comedy,** Shakespeare, *King Lear* (see vol. 1/B, p. 1251).

tragic mode: Many genres (**epic** poetry, **legend**ary chronicles, **tragedy,** the **novel**) either do or can participate in a tragic mode, by representing the fall of noble **protagonists** and the irreparable ravages of human society and history.

tragicomedy: a **genre.** A play in which potentially tragic events turn out to have a happy, or **comic,** ending. Thus Shakespeare, *Measure for Measure.*

translation (Latin "carrying across"): the rendering of a text written in one language into another.

trimeter (Greek "three measure"): a term of **meter.** A line with three stresses. Herbert, "Discipline," line 1: "Throw away thy rod" (see vol. 1/B, p. 1724).

triplet: a **verse form.** A **tercet** rhyming on the same sound. Pope inserts triplets among heroic **couplets** to emphasize a particular thought; see *Essay on Criticism*, 315–17 (vol. 1/C, p. 2148).

trochee: a term of **rhythm.** A two-syllable foot following the pattern, in English verse, of stressed followed by unstressed syllable, producing a falling effect. Thus, for example, "Texas."

type (Greek "impression, figure"): a **figure of thought** In Christian allegorical interpretation of the Old Testament, pre-Christian figures were regarded as "types," or foreshadowings, of Christ or the Christian dispensation. *Typology* has been the source of much visual and literary art in which the parallelisms between old and new are extended to nonbiblical figures; thus the virtuous plowman in *Piers Plowman* becomes a type of Christ.

unities: According to a theory supposedly derived from Aristotle's *Poetics,* the events represented in a play should have unity of time, place, and action: that the play take up no more time than the time of the play, or at most a day; that the space of action should be within a single city; and that there should be no subplot. See Johnson, *The Preface to Shakespeare* (vol. 1/C, p. 2408).

vernacular (from Latin "verna," servant): the language of the people, as distinguished from learned and arcane languages. From the later Middle Ages especially, the "vernacular" languages and literatures of Europe distinguished themselves from the learned languages and literatures of Latin, Greek, and Hebrew.

verse form: The terms related to **meter** and **rhythm** describe the shape of individual lines. Lines of verse are combined to produce larger groupings, called verse forms. These larger groupings are in the first instance **stanzas.** The combination of a certain meter and stanza shape constitutes the verse form, of which there are many standard kinds.

villanelle: a **verse form.** A fixed form of usually five **tercets** and a **quatrain** employing only two rhyme sounds altogether, rhyming aba for the tercets and abaa for the quatrain, with a complex pattern of two **refrains.** Derived from a French fixed form. Thomas, "Do Not Go Gentle into That Good Night" (see vol. 2/F, p. 2704).

wit: Originally a synonym for "reason" in Old and Middle English, "wit" became a literary ideal in the Renaissance as brilliant play of the full range of mental resources. For eighteenth-century writers, the notion necessarily involved pleasing expression, as in Pope's definition of true wit as "Nature to advantage dressed, / What oft was thought, but ne'er so well expressed" (*Essay on Criticism,* lines 297–98; see vol. 1/C, p. 2147). See also Johnson, *Lives of the Poets,* "Cowley," on "metaphysical wit" (see vol. 1/C, p. 2419). Romantic theory of the imagination deprived wit of its full range of apprehension, whence the word came to be restricted to its modern sense, as the clever play of mind that produces laughter.

zeugma (Greek "a yoking"): a **figure of thought.** A figure whereby one word applies to two or more words in a sentence, and in which the applications are surprising, either because one is unusual, or because the applications are made in very different ways; Pope, *Rape of the Lock* 3.7–8, in which the word "take" is used in two senses: "Here thou, great Anna! whom three realms obey, / Dost sometimes counsel take—and sometimes tea" (see vol. 1/C, p. 2166).

B: Publishing History, Censorship

By the time we read texts in published books, they have already been treated—that is, changed by authors, editors, and printers—in many ways. Although there are differences across history, in each period literary works are subject to pressures of many kinds, which apply before, while, and after an author writes. The pressures might be financial, as in the relations of author and patron; commercial, as in the marketing of books; and legal, as in, during some periods, the negotiation through official and unofficial censorship. In addition, texts in all periods undergo technological processes, as they move from the material forms in which an author produced them to the forms in which they are presented to readers. Some of the terms below designate important material forms in which books were produced, disseminated, and surveyed across the historical span of this anthology. Others designate the skills developed to understand these processes. The anthology's introductions to individual periods discuss the particular forms these phenomena took in different eras.

bookseller: In England, and particularly in London, commercial bookmaking and-selling enterprises came into being in the early fourteenth century. These were loose organizations of artisans who usually lived in the same neighborhoods (around St. Paul's Cathedral in London). A bookseller or dealer would coordinate the production of hand-copied books for wealthy patrons (see **patronage**), who would order books to be custom-made. After the introduction of **printing** in the late fifteenth century, authors generally sold the rights to their work to booksellers, without any further **royalties.** Booksellers, who often had their own shops, belonged to the **Stationers' Company.** This system lasted into the eighteenth century. In 1710, however, authors were for the first time granted **copyright,** which tipped the commercial balance in their favor, against booksellers.

censorship: The term applies to any mechanism for restricting what can be published. Historically, the reasons for imposing censorship are heresy, sedition, blasphemy, libel, or obscenity. External censorship is imposed by institutions having legislative sanctions at their disposal. Thus the pre-Reformation Church imposed the Constitutions of Archbishop Arundel of 1409, aimed at repressing the Lollard "heresy." After the Reformation, some key events in the history of censorship are as follows: 1547, when anti-Lollard legislation and legislation made by Henry VIII concerning treason by writing (1534) were abolished; the Licensing Order of 1643, which legislated that works be licensed, through the Stationers' Company, prior to publication; and 1695, when the last such Act stipulating prepublication licensing lapsed. Postpublication censorship continued in different periods for different reasons. Thus, for example, British publication of D. H. Lawrence's *Lady Chatterley's Lover* (1928) was obstructed (though unsuccessfully) in 1960, under the Obscene Publications Act of 1959. Censorship can also be international: although not published in Iran, Salman Rushdie's *Satanic Verses* (1988) was censored in that country, where the leader, Ayatollah Ruhollah Khomeini, proclaimed a fatwa (religious decree) promising the author's execution. Very often censorship is not imposed externally, however: authors or publishers can censor work in anticipation of what will incur the wrath of readers or the penalties of the law. Victorian and Edwardian publishers of **novels,** for example, urged authors to remove potentially offensive material, especially for serial publication in popular magazines.

codex: the physical format of most modern books and medieval manuscripts, consisting of a series of separate leaves gathered into quires and bound together, often with a cover. In late antiquity, the codex largely replaced the scroll, the standard form of written documents in Roman culture.

copy text: the particular text of a work used by a textual editor as the basis of an edition of that work.

copyright: the legal protection afforded to authors for control of their work's publication, in an attempt to ensure due financial reward. Some key dates in the history of copyright in the United Kingdom are as follows: 1710, when a statute gave authors the exclusive right to publish their work for fourteen years, and fourteen years more if the author were still alive when the first term had expired; 1842, when the period of authorial control was extended to forty-two years; and 1911, when the term was extended yet further, to fifty years after the author's death. In 1995 the period of protection was harmonized with the laws in other European countries to be the life of the author plus seventy years. In the United States no works first published before 1923 are in copyright. Works published since 1978 are, as in the United Kingdom, protected for the life of the author plus seventy years.

folio: the leaf formed by both sides of a single page. Each folio has two sides: a *recto* (the front side of the leaf, on the right side of a double-page spread in an open codex), and a *verso* (the back side of the leaf, on the left side of a double-page spread). Modern book pagination follows the pattern 1, 2, 3, 4, while medieval manuscript pagination follows the pattern 1r, 1v, 2r, 2v. "Folio" can also designate the size of a printed book. Books come in different shapes, depending originally on the number of times a standard sheet of paper is folded. One fold produces a large volume, a *folio* book; two folds produce a *quarto*, four an *octavo*, and six a very small *duodecimo*. Generally speaking, the larger the book, the grander and more expensive. Shakespeare's plays were, for example, first printed in quartos, but were gathered into a folio edition in 1623.

foul papers: versions of a work before an author has produced, if she or he has, a final copy (a "fair copy") with all corrections removed.

incunabulum (plural "incunabula"): any printed book produced in Europe before 1501. Famous incunabula include the Gutenberg Bible, printed in 1455.

manuscript (Latin, "written by hand"): Any text written physically by hand is a manuscript. Before the introduction of **printing** with moveable type in 1476, all texts in England were produced and reproduced by hand, in manuscript. This is an extremely labor-intensive task, using expensive materials (e.g., **vellum,** or **parchment**); the cost of books produced thereby was, accordingly, very high. Even after the introduction of printing, many texts continued to be produced in manuscript. This is obviously true of letters, for example, but until the eighteenth century, poetry written within aristocratic circles was often transmitted in manuscript copies.

paleography (Greek "ancient writing"): the art of deciphering, describing, and dating forms of handwriting.

parchment: animal skin, used as the material for handwritten books before the introduction of paper. See also **vellum.**

patronage, patron (Latin "protector"): Many technological, legal, and commercial supports were necessary before professional authorship became possible. Although some playwrights (e.g., Shakespeare) made a living by writing for the theater, other authors needed, principally, the large-scale reproductive capacities of **printing** and the security of **copyright** to make a living from writing. Before these conditions obtained, many authors had another main occupation, and most authors had to rely on patronage. In different periods, institutions or individuals offered material support, or patronage, to authors. Thus in Anglo-Saxon England, monasteries afforded the conditions of writing to monastic authors. Between the twelfth and the seventeenth centuries, the main source of patronage was the royal court. Authors offered patrons prestige and ideological support in return for financial support. Even as the conditions of professional authorship came into being at the beginning of the eighteenth century, older forms of direct patronage were not altogether displaced until the middle of the century.

periodical: Whereas journalism, strictly, applies to daily writing (from French "jour," day), periodical writing appears at larger, but still frequent, intervals, characteristically in the form of the **essay.** Periodicals were developed especially in the eighteenth century.

printing: Printing, or the mechanical reproduction of books using moveable type, was invented in Germany in the mid-fifteenth century by Johannes Gutenberg; it quickly spread throughout Europe. William Caxton brought printing into England from the Low Countries in 1476. Much greater powers of reproduction at much lower prices transformed every aspect of literary culture.

publisher: the person or company responsible for the commissioning and publicizing of printed matter. In the early period of **printing,** publisher, printer, and bookseller were often the same person. This trend continued in the ascendancy of the **Stationers' Company,** between the middle of the sixteenth and the end of the seventeenth centuries. Toward the end of the seventeenth century, these three functions began to separate, leading to their modern distinctions.

quire: When medieval manuscripts were assembled, a few loose sheets of parchment or paper would first be folded together and sewn along the fold. This formed a quire (also known as a "gathering" or "signature"). Folded in this way, four large sheets of parchment would produce eight smaller manuscript leaves. Multiple quires could then be bound together to form a codex.

royalties: an agreed-upon proportion of the price of each copy of a work sold, paid by the publisher to the author, or an agreed-upon fee paid to the playwright for each performance of a play.

scribe: In **manuscript** culture, the scribe is the copyist who reproduces a text by hand.

scriptorium (plural "scriptoria"): a place for producing written documents and manuscripts.

serial publication: generally referring to the practice, especially common in the nineteenth-century, of publishing novels a few chapters at a time, in periodicals.

Stationers' Company: The Stationers' Company was an English guild incorporating various tradesmen, including printers, publishers, and booksellers, skilled in the production and selling of books. It was formed in 1403, received its royal charter in 1557, and served as a means both of producing and of regulating books. Authors would sell the manuscripts of their books to individual stationers, who incurred the risks and took the profits of producing and selling the books. The stationers entered their rights over given books in the Stationers' Register. They also regulated the book trade and held their monopoly by licensing books and by being empowered to seize unauthorized books and imprison resisters. This system of licensing broke down in the social unrest of the Civil War and Interregnum (1640–60), and it ended in 1695. Even after the end of licensing, the Stationers' Company continued to be an intrinsic part of the **copyright** process, since the 1710 copyright statute directed that copyright had to be registered at Stationers' Hall.

subscription: An eighteenth-century system of bookselling somewhere between direct **patronage** and impersonal sales. A subscriber paid half the cost of a book before publication and half on delivery. The author received these payments directly. The subscriber's name appeared in the prefatory pages.

textual criticism: Works in all periods often exist in many subtly or not so subtly different forms. This is especially true with regard to manuscript textual reproduction, but it also applies to printed texts. Textual criticism is the art, developed from the fifteenth century in Italy but raised to new levels of sophistication from the eighteenth century, of deciphering different historical states of texts. This art involves the analysis of textual **variants,** often with the aim of distinguishing authorial from scribal forms.

variant: differences that appear among different manuscripts or printed editions of the same text.

vellum: animal skin, used as the material for handwritten books before the introduction of paper. See also **parchment.**

watermark: the trademark of a paper manufacturer, impressed into the paper but largely invisible unless held up to light.

Geographic Nomenclature

The British Isles refers to the prominent group of islands off the northwest coast of Europe, especially to the two largest, **Great Britain** and **Ireland**. At present these comprise two sovereign states: **the Republic of Ireland**, or **Éire**, and **the United Kingdom of Great Britain and Northern Ireland**—known for short as the **United Kingdom** or the **U.K.** Most of the smaller islands are part of the **U.K.** but a few, like the **Isle of Man** and the tiny **Channel Islands**, are largely independent. The **U.K.** is often loosely referred to as "Britain" or "Great Britain" and is sometimes called simply, if inaccurately, "England." For obvious reasons, the latter usage is rarely heard among the inhabitants of the other countries of the **U.K.**—**Scotland, Wales,** and **Northern Ireland** (sometimes called **Ulster**). England is by far the most populous part of the kingdom, as well as the seat of its capital, London.

From the first to the fifth century C.E. most of what is now **England** and **Wales** was a province of the Roman Empire called **Britain** (in Latin, **Britannia**). After the fall of Rome, much of the island was invaded and settled by peoples from northern Germany and Denmark speaking what we now call Old English. These peoples are collectively known as the Anglo-Saxons, and the word **England** is related to the first element of their name. By the time of the Norman Conquest (1066) most of the kingdoms founded by the Anglo-Saxons and subsequent Viking invaders had coalesced into the kingdom of **England,** which, in the latter Middle Ages, conquered and largely absorbed the neighboring Celtic kingdom of **Wales.** In 1603 James VI of **Scotland** inherited the island's other throne as James I of **England,** and for the next hundred years—except for the brief period of Puritan rule—**Scotland** (both its English-speaking **Lowlands** and its Gaelic-speaking **Highlands**) and **England** (with **Wales**) were two kingdoms under a single king. In 1707 the Act of Union welded them together as **the United Kingdom of Great Britain. Ireland,** where English rule had begun in the twelfth century and been tightened in the sixteenth, was incorporated by the 1800–1801 Act of Union into **the United Kingdom of Great Britain and Ireland**. With the division of Ireland and the establishment of **the Irish Free State** after World War I, this name was modified to its present form, and in 1949 **the Irish Free State** became **the Republic of Ireland.** In 1999 **Scotland** elected a separate parliament it had relinquished in 1707, and **Wales** elected an assembly it lost in 1409; neither Scotland nor Wales ceased to be part of the **United Kingdom.**

The **British Isles** are further divided into counties, which in **Great Britain** are also known as shires. This word, with its vowel shortened in pronunciation, forms the suffix in the names of many counties, such as **Yorkshire, Wiltshire, Somersetshire.**

The Latin names **Britannia (Britain), Caledonia (Scotland),** and **Hibernia (Ireland)** are sometimes used in poetic diction; so too is **Britain's** ancient Celtic name, **Albion.** Because of its accidental resemblance to *albus* (Latin for "white"), **Albion** is especially associated with the chalk cliffs that seem to gird much of the English coast like defensive walls.

The **British Empire** took its name from **the British Isles** because it was created not only by the **English** but also by the **Irish, Scots,** and **Welsh,** as well as by civilians and servicemen from other constituent countries of the empire. Some of the empire's **overseas colonies,** or **crown colonies,** were populated largely by settlers of European origin and their descendants. These predominantly white **settler colonies,** such as **Canada, Australia,** and **New Zealand,** were allowed significant self-government in the nineteenth century and recognized as **dominions** in the early twentieth century. The **white dominions** became members of **the Commonwealth of Nations**, also called **the Commonwealth, the British Commonwealth**, and **"the Old Commonwealth"** at different times, an association of sovereign states under the symbolic leadership of the British monarch.

Other **overseas colonies** of the empire had mostly indigenous populations (or, in the Caribbean, the descendants of imported slaves, indentured servants, and others). These **colonies** were granted political independence after World War II, later than the **dominions**, and have often been referred to since as **postcolonial** nations. In South and Southeast Asia, **India** and **Pakistan** gained independence in 1947, followed by other countries including **Sri Lanka** (formerly Ceylon), **Burma** (now **Myanmar**), **Malaya** (now **Malaysia**), and **Singapore**. In West and East Africa, the **Gold Coast** was decolonized as **Ghana** in 1957, **Nigeria** in 1960, **Sierra Leone** in 1961, **Uganda** in 1962, **Kenya** in 1963, and so forth, while in southern Africa, the white minority government of **South Africa** was already independent in 1931, though majority rule did not come until 1994. In the Caribbean, **Jamaica** and **Trinidad and Tobago** won independence in 1962, followed by **Barbados** in 1966, and other islands of the British West Indies in the 1970s and '80s. Other regions with nations emerging out of British colonial rule included Central America (**British Honduras**, now **Belize**), South America (**British Guiana**, now **Guyana**), the Pacific islands (**Fiji**), and Europe (**Cyprus, Malta**). After decolonization, many of these nations chose to remain within a newly conceived **Commonwealth** and are sometimes referred to as **"New Commonwealth"** countries. Some nations, such as **Ireland**, **Pakistan**, and **South Africa**, withdrew from the **Commonwealth**, though **South Africa** and **Pakistan** eventually rejoined, and others, such as **Burma** (**Myanmar**), gained independence outside the **Commonwealth**. Britain's last major overseas colony, **Hong Kong**, was returned to Chinese sovereignty in 1997, but while Britain retains only a handful of dependent territories, such as **Bermuda** and **Montserrat**, the scope of the **Commonwealth** remains vast, with 30 percent of the world's population.

British Money

One of the most dramatic changes to the system of British money came in 1971. In the system previously in place, the pound consisted of 20 shillings, each containing 12 pence, making 240 pence to the pound. Since 1971, British money has been calculated on the decimal system, with 100 pence to the pound. Britons' experience of paper money did not change very drastically: as before, 5- and 10-pound notes constitute the majority of bills passing through their hands (in addition, 20- and 50- pound notes have been added). But the shift necessitated a whole new way of thinking about and exchanging coins and marked the demise of the shilling, one of the fundamental units of British monetary history. Many other coins, still frequently encountered in literature, had already passed. These include the groat, worth 4 pence (the word "groat" is often used to signify a trifling sum); the angel (which depicted the archangel Michael triumphing over a dragon), valued at 10 shillings; the mark, worth in its day two-thirds of a pound or 13 shillings 4 pence; and the sovereign, a gold coin initially worth 22 shillings 6 pence, later valued at 1 pound, last circulated in 1932. One prominent older coin, the guinea, was worth a pound and a shilling; though it has not been minted since 1813, a very few quality items or prestige awards (like the purse in a horse race) may still be quoted in guineas. (The table below includes some other well-known, obsolete coins.) Colloquially, a pound was (and is) called a quid; a shilling a bob; sixpence, a tanner; a copper could refer to a penny, a half-penny, or a farthing (¼ penny).

Old Currency	*New Currency*
1 pound note	1 pound coin (or note in Scotland)
10 shilling (half-pound note)	50 pence
5 shilling (crown)	
2½ shilling (half crown)	20 pence
2 shilling (florin)	10 pence
1 shilling	5 pence
6 pence	
2½ pence	1 penny
2 pence	
1 penny	
½ penny	
¼ penny (farthing)	

In recent years, the British government and people have been contemplating and debating a change even greater than the shift to the decimal system. Britain, a member of the European Union, may adopt the EU's common currency, the Euro, and eventually see the pound itself become obsolete. More than many other EU-member countries, Britain has resisted this change: many people strongly identify their country with its rich commercial history and tend to view their currency patriotically as a national symbol.

Even more challenging than sorting out the values of obsolete coins is calculating for any given period the purchasing power of money, which fluctuates over time by its very nature. At the beginning of the twentieth century, 1 pound was worth about 5 American dollars, though those bought three to four times what they now do. Now, the pound buys anywhere from $1.50 to $1.90. As difficult as it is to generalize, it is clear that money used to be worth much more than it is currently. In Anglo-Saxon times, the most valuable circulating coin was the silver penny: four would buy a sheep. Beyond long-term inflationary trends, prices varied from times of plenty to those marked by poor harvests; from peacetime to wartime; from the country to the metropolis (life in London has always been very expensive); and wages varied according to the availability of labor (wages would sharply rise, for instance, during the devastating Black Death in the fourteenth century). The chart below provides a glimpse of some actual prices of given periods and their changes across time, though all the variables mentioned above prevent them from being definitive. Even from one year to the next, an added tax on gin or tea could drastically raise prices, and a lottery ticket could cost much more the night before the drawing than just a month earlier. Still, the prices quoted below do indicate important trends, such as the disparity of incomes in British society and the costs of basic commodities. In the chart below, the symbol £ is used for pound, s. for shilling, d. for a penny (from Latin *denarius*); a sum would normally be written £2.19.3, i.e., 2 pounds, 19 shillings, 3 pence. (This is Leopold Bloom's budget for the day depicted in Joyce's novel *Ulysses* [1922]; in the new currency, it would be about £2.96.)

circa	1390	1590	1650	1750	1815	1875	1950
food and drink	gallon (8 pints) of ale, 1.5d.	tankard of beer, .5d.	coffee, 1d. a dish	"drunk for a penny, dead drunk for two-pence" (gin shop sign in Hogarth print)	ounce of laudanum, 3d.	pint of beer, 3d.	pint of Guinness stout, 11d.
	gallon (8 pints) of wine, 3 to 4d.	pound of beef, 2s. 5d.	chicken, 1s. 4d.	dinner at a steakhouse, 1s.	ham and potato dinner for two, 7s.	dinner in a good hotel, 5s.	pound of beef, 2s. 2d.
	pound of cinnamon, 1 to 3s.	pound of cinnamon, 10s. 6d.	pound of tea, £3 10s.	pound of tea, 16s.	Prince Regent's dinner party for 2000, £12.000	pound of tea, 2s.	dinner on railway car, 7s. 6d.
entertainment	no cost to watch a cycle play	admission to public theater, 1 to 3d.	falcon, £11s. 5d.	theater tickets, 1 to 5s.	admission to Covent Garden theater, 1 to 7s.	theater tickets, 6d. to 7s.	admission to Old Vic theater, 1s. 6d. to 10s. 6d.
	contributory admission to professional troupe theater	cheap seat in private theater, 6d.	billiard table, £25	admission to Vauxhall Gardens, 1s.	annual subscription to Almack's (exclusive club), 10 guineas	admission to Madam Tussaud's waxworks, 1s.	admission to Odeon cinema, Manchester, 1s 3d.
	maintenance for royal hounds at Windsor, .75d. a day	"to see a dead Indian" (quoted in *The Tempest*), 1.25d. (ten "doits")	three-quarter length portrait painting, £31	lottery ticket, £20 (shares were sold)	Jane Austen's piano, 30 guineas	annual fees at a gentleman's club, 7 to 10 guineas	tropical fish tank, £4 4s.

circa	1390	1590	1650	1750	1815	1875	1950
reading	cheap romance, 1s.; a Latin Bible, 2 to £4; payment for illuminating a liturgical book, £22 9s.	play quarto, 6d.; Shakespeare's *First Folio* (1623), £1; Foxe's *Acts and Monuments*, 24s.	pamphlet, 1 to 6d.; student Bible, 6s.; Hobbes's *Leviathan*, 8s.	issue of The *Gentleman's Magazine*, 6d.; cheap edition of Milton, 2s.; Johnson's *Dictionary*, folio, 2 vols., £4 10s.	issue of *Edinburgh Review*, 6s.; membership in circulating library (3rd class), £1 4s. a year; 1st edition of Austen's *Pride and Prejudice*, 18s.	copy of *The Times*, 3d.; illustrated edition of *Through the Looking-glass*, 6s.; 1st edition of Trollope's *The Way We Live Now*, 2 vols., £1 1s.	copy of *The Times*, 3d.; issue of *Eagle* comics, 4.5d.; Orwell's *Nineteen Eighty Four*, paperback, 3s. 6d.
transportation	night's supply of hay for horse, 2d.; coach, £8; quality horse, £10.	wherry (whole boat) across Thames, 1d.; hiring a horse for a day, 12d.; hiring a coach for a day, 10s.	day's journey, coach, 10s.; coach horse, £30; fancy carriage, £170.	boat across Thames, 4d.; coach fare, London to Edinburgh, £4 10s.; transport to America, £5.	coach ride, outside, 2 to 3d. a mile; inside, 4 to 5d. a mile; palanquin transport in Madras, 5s. a day; passage, Liverpool to New York, £10.	15-minute journey in a London cab, 1s. 6d.; railway, 3rd class, London to Plymouth, 18s.; 8d. (about 1d. a mile); passage to India, 1st class, £50.	London tube fare, about 2d. a mile; petrol, 3s. a gallon; midsize Austin sedan, £449 plus £188 4s. 2d. tax.
clothes	clothing allowance for peasant, 3s. a year.	shoes with buckles, 8d.	footman's frieze coat, 15s.	working woman's gown, 6s. 6d.	checked muslin, 7s. per yard.	flannel for a cheap petticoat, 1s. 3d. a yard.	woman's sun frock, £3 13s. 10d.

shoes for gentry wearer, 4d.	woman's gloves, £1 5s.	falconer's hat, 10s.	gentleman's suit, £8	hiring a dressmaker for a pelisse, 8s.	overcoat for an Eton schoolboy, £1 1s.	tweed sports jacket, £3 16s. 6d.
hat for gentry wearer, 10d.	fine cloak, £16	black cloth for mourning household of an earl, £100	very fine wig, £30	ladies silk stockings, 12s.	set of false teeth, £2 10s.	"Teddy boy" drape suit, £20

labor/incomes							
	hiring a skilled building worker, 4d. a day	actor's daily wage during playing season, 1s.	agricultural laborer, 6s. 5d. a week	price of boy slave, £32	lowest-paid sailor on Royal Navy ship, 10s. 9d. a month	seasonal agricultural laborer, 14s. a week	minimum wage, agricultural laborer, £4 14s. per 47-hour week
	wage for professional scribe, £2 3s. 4d. a year + cloak	household servant 2 to £5 a year + food, clothing	tutor to noble-man's children, £30 a year	housemaid's wage, £6 to £8 a year	contributor to *Quarterly Review*, 10 guineas per sheet	housemaid's wage, £10 to £25 a year	shorthand typist, £367 a year
	minimum income to be called gentleman £10 a year; for knighthood, 40 to £400	minimum income for eligibility for knighthood, £30 a year	Milton's salary as Secretary of Foreign Tongues, £288 a year	Boswell's allowance, £200 a year	minimum income for a "genteel" family, £100 a year	income of the "comfortable" classes, £800 and up a year	middle manager's salary, £1,480 a year
	income from land of richest magnates, £3,500 a year	income from land of average earl, £4000 a year	Earl of Bedford's income, £8,000 a year	Duke of New-castle's income, £40,000 a year	Mr. Darcy's income, *Pride and Prejudice*, £10,000	Trollope's income, £4,000 a year	barrister's salary, £2,032 a year

The British Baronage

The English monarchy is in principle hereditary, though at times during the Middle Ages the rules were subject to dispute. In general, authority passes from father to eldest surviving son, from daughters in order of seniority if there is no son, to a brother if there are no children, and in default of direct descendants to collateral lines (cousins, nephews, nieces) in order of closeness. There have been breaks in the order of succession (1066, 1399, 1688), but so far as possible the usurpers have always sought to paper over the break with a legitimate, i.e., hereditary, claim. When a queen succeeds to the throne and takes a husband, he does not become king unless he is in the line of blood succession; rather, he is named prince consort, as Albert was to Victoria. He may father kings, but is not one himself.

The original Saxon nobles were the king's thanes, ealdormen, or earls, who provided the king with military service and counsel in return for booty, gifts, or landed estates. William the Conqueror, arriving from France, where feudalism was fully developed, considerably expanded this group. In addition, as the king distributed the lands of his new kingdom, he also distributed dignities to men who became known collectively as "the baronage." "Baron" in its root meaning signifies simply "man," and barons were the king's men. As the title was common, a distinction was early made between greater and lesser barons, the former gradually assuming loftier and more impressive titles. The first English "duke" was created in 1337; the title of "marquess," or "marquis" (pronounced "markwis"), followed in 1385, and "viscount" ("vyekount") in 1440. Though "earl" is the oldest title of all, an earl now comes between a marquess and a viscount in order of dignity and precedence, and the old term "baron" now designates a rank just below viscount."Baronets" were created in 1611 as a means of raising revenue for the crown (the title could be purchased for about £1000); they are marginal nobility and have never sat in the House of Lords.

Kings and queens are addressed as "Your Majesty," princes and princesses as "Your Highness," the other hereditary nobility as "My Lord" or "Your Lordship." Peers receive their titles either by inheritance (like Lord Byron, the sixth baron of that line) or from the monarch (like Alfred Lord Tennyson, created first Baron Tennyson by Victoria). The children, even of a duke, are commoners unless they are specifically granted some other title or inherit their father's title from him. A peerage can be forfeited by act of attainder, as for example when a lord is convicted of treason; and, when forfeited, or lapsed for lack of a successor, can be bestowed on another family. Thus in 1605 Robert Cecil was made first earl of Salisbury in the third creation, the first creation dating from 1149, the second from 1337, the title having been in abeyance since 1539. Titles descend by right of succession and do not depend on tenure of land; thus, a title does not always indicate where a lord dwells or holds power. Indeed, noble titles do not always refer to a real place at all. At Prince Edward's marriage in 1999, the queen created him earl of Wessex, although the old kingdom of Wessex has had no political existence since the Anglo-Saxon period, and the name was all but forgotten until it was resurrected by Thomas Hardy as the setting of his novels. (This is perhaps but one of many ways in which the world of the aristocracy increasingly resembles the realm of literature.)

The king and queen	(These are all of the royal line.)
Prince and princess	
Duke and duchess	(These may or may not be of the royal
Marquess and marchioness	line, but are ordinarily remote from the
Earl and countess	succession.)
Viscount and viscountess	
Baron and baroness	
Baronet and lady	

Scottish peers sat in the parliament of Scotland, as English peers did in the parliament of England, till at the Act of Union (1707) Scottish peers were granted sixteen seats in the English House of Lords, to be filled by election. (In 1963, all Scottish lords were allowed to sit.) Similarly, Irish peers, when the Irish parliament was abolished in 1801, were granted the right to elect twenty-eight of their number to the House of Lords in Westminster. (Now that the Republic of Ireland is a separate nation, this no longer applies.) Women members (peeresses) were first allowed to sit in the House as nonhereditary Life Peers in 1958 (when that status was created for members of both genders); women first sat by their own hereditary right in 1963. Today the House of Lords still retains some power to influence or delay legislation, but its future is uncertain. In 1999, the hereditary peers (then amounting to 750) were reduced to 92 temporary members elected by their fellow peers. Holders of Life Peerages remain, as do senior bishops of the Church of England and high-court judges (the "Law Lords").

Below the peerage the chief title of honor is "knight." Knighthood, which is not hereditary, is generally a reward for services rendered. A knight (Sir John Black) is addressed, using his first name, as "Sir John"; his wife, using the last name, is "Lady Black"—unless she is the daughter of an earl or nobleman of higher rank, in which case she will be "Lady Arabella." The female equivalent of a knight bears the title of "Dame." Though the word itself comes from the Anglo-Saxon *cniht*, there is some doubt as to whether knighthood amounted to much before the arrival of the Normans. The feudal system required military service as a condition of land tenure, and a man who came to serve his king at the head of an army of tenants required a title of authority and badges of identity—hence the title of knighthood and the coat of arms. During the Crusades, when men were far removed from their land (or even sold it in order to go on crusade), more elaborate forms of fealty sprang up that soon expanded into orders of knighthood. The Templars, Hospitallers, Knights of the Teutonic Order, Knights of Malta, and Knights of the Golden Fleece were but a few of these companionships; not all of them were available at all times in England.

Gradually, with the rise of centralized government and the decline of feudal tenures, military knighthood became obsolete, and the rank largely honorific; sometimes, as under James I, it degenerated into a scheme of the royal government for making money. For hundreds of years after its establishment in the fourteenth century, the Order of the Garter was the only English order of knighthood, an exclusive courtly companionship. Then, during the late seventeenth, the eighteenth, and the nineteenth centuries, a number of additional orders were created, with names such as the Thistle, Saint Patrick, the Bath, Saint Michael and Saint George, plus a number of special Victorian and Indian orders. They retain the terminology, ceremony, and dignity of knighthood, but the military implications are vestigial.

Although the British Empire now belongs to history, appointments to the Order of the British Empire continue to be conferred for services to that empire at home or abroad. Such honors (commonly referred to as "gongs") are granted by the monarch in her New Year's and Birthday lists, but the decisions are now made by the government in power. In recent years there have been efforts to popularize and democratize the dispensation of honors, with recipients including rock stars and actors. But this does not prevent large sectors of British society from regarding both knighthood and the peerage as largely irrelevant to modern life.

The Royal Lines of England and Great Britain

England

SAXONS AND DANES

Egbert, king of Wessex	802–839
Ethelwulf, son of Egbert	839–858
Ethelbald, second son of Ethelwulf	858–860
Ethelbert, third son of Ethelwulf	860–866
Ethelred I, fourth son of Ethelwulf	866–871
Alfred the Great, fifth son of Ethelwulf	871–899
Edward the Elder, son of Alfred	899–924
Athelstan the Glorious, son of Edward	924–940
Edmund I, third son of Edward	940–946
Edred, fourth son of Edward	946–955
Edwy the Fair, son of Edmund	955–959
Edgar the Peaceful, second son of Edmund	959–975
Edward the Martyr, son of Edgar	975–978 (murdered)
Ethelred II, the Unready, second son of Edgar	978–1016
Edmund II, Ironside, son of Ethelred II	1016–1016
Canute the Dane	1016–1035
Harold I, Harefoot, natural son of Canute	1035–1040
Hardecanute, son of Canute	1040–1042
Edward the Confessor, son of Ethelred II	1042–1066
Harold II, brother-in-law of Edward	1066–1066 (died in battle)

HOUSE OF NORMANDY

William I the Conqueror	1066–1087
William II, Rufus, third son of William I	1087–1100 (shot from ambush)
Henry I, Beauclerc, youngest son of William I	1100–1135

HOUSE OF BLOIS

Stephen, son of Adela, daughter of William I	1135–1154

HOUSE OF PLANTAGENET

Henry II, son of Geoffrey Plantagenet by Matilda, daughter of Henry I	1154–1189
Richard I, Coeur de Lion, son of Henry II	1189–1199
John Lackland, son of Henry II	1199–1216
Henry III, son of John	1216–1272
Edward I, Longshanks, son of Henry III	1272–1307
Edward II, son of Edward I	1307–1327 (deposed)
Edward III of Windsor, son of Edward II	1327–1377
Richard II, grandson of Edward III	1377–1399 (deposed)

HOUSE OF LANCASTER

Henry IV, son of John of Gaunt, son of Edward III	1399–1413
Henry V, Prince Hal, son of Henry IV	1413–1422
Henry VI, son of Henry V	1422–1461 (deposed), 1470–1471 (deposed)

HOUSE OF YORK

Edward IV, great-great-grandson of Edward III	1461–1470 (deposed), 1471–1483
Edward V, son of Edward IV	1483–1483 (murdered)
Richard III, Crookback	1483–1485 (died in battle)

HOUSE OF TUDOR

Henry VII, married daughter of Edward IV	1485–1509
Henry VIII, son of Henry VII	1509–1547
Edward VI, son of Henry VIII	1547–1553
Mary I, "Bloody," daughter of Henry VIII	1553–1558
Elizabeth I, daughter of Henry VIII	1558–1603

HOUSE OF STUART

James I (James VI of Scotland)	1603–1625
Charles I, son of James I	1625–1649 (executed)

COMMONWEALTH & PROTECTORATE

Council of State	1649–1653
Oliver Cromwell, Lord Protector	1653–1658
Richard Cromwell, son of Oliver	1658–1660 (resigned)

HOUSE OF STUART (RESTORED)

Charles II, son of Charles I	1660–1685
James II, second son of Charles I	1685–1688

(INTERREGNUM, 11 DECEMBER 1688 TO 13 FEBRUARY 1689)

William III of Orange, by	
Mary, daughter of Charles I	1689–1701
and Mary II, daughter of James II	–1694
Anne, second daughter of James II	1702–1714

Great Britain

HOUSE OF HANOVER

George I, son of Elector of Hanover and	
Sophia, granddaughter of James I	1714–1727
George II, son of George I	1727–1760
George III, grandson of George II	1760–1820
George IV, son of George III	1820–1830
William IV, third son of George III	1830–1837
Victoria, daughter of Edward, fourth son	
of George III	1837–1901

HOUSE OF SAXE-COBURG AND GOTHA

Edward VII, son of Victoria	1901–1910

HOUSE OF WINDSOR (NAME ADOPTED 17 JULY 1917)

George V, second son of Edward VII	1910–1936
Edward VIII, eldest son of George V	1936–1936 (abdicated)
George VI, second son of George V	1936–1952
Elizabeth II, daughter of George VI	1952–

Religions in England

In the sixth century C.E., missionaries from Ireland and the Continent introduced Christianity to the Anglo-Saxons—actually, reintroduced it, since it had briefly flourished in the southern parts of the British Isles during the Roman occupation, and even after the Roman withdrawal had persisted in the Celtic regions of Scotland and Wales. By the time the earliest poems included in the *Norton Anthology* were composed, therefore, the English people had been Christians for hundreds of years; such Anglo-Saxon poems as "The Dream of the Rood" bear witness to their faith. Our knowledge of the religion of pre-Christian Britain is sketchy, but it is likely that vestiges of paganism assimilated into, or coexisted with, the practice of Christianity: fertility rites were incorporated into the celebration of Easter resurrection, rituals commemorating the dead into All-Hallows Eve and All Saints Day, and elements of winter solstice festivals into the celebration of Christmas. In English literature such "folkloric" elements often elicit romantic nostalgia. Geoffrey Chaucer's Wife of Bath looks back to a magical time before the arrival of Christianity in which the land was "fulfilled of fairye." Hundreds of years later, the seventeenth-century writer Robert Herrick honors the amalgamation of Christian and pagan elements in agrarian British culture in such poems as "Corinna's Gone A-Maying" and "The Hock Cart."

Medieval Christianity was fairly uniform across Western Europe—hence called "catholic," or universally shared—and its rituals and expectations, common to the whole community, permeated everyday life. The Catholic Church was also an international power structure. In its hierarchy of pope, cardinals, archbishops, and bishops, it resembled the feudal state, but the church power structure coexisted alongside a separate hierarchy of lay authorities with a theoretically different sphere of social responsibilities. The sharing out of lay and ecclesiastical authority in medieval England was sometimes a source of conflict. Chaucer's pilgrims are on their way to visit the memorial shrine to one victim of such struggle: Thomas a Becket, Archbishop of Canterbury, who opposed the policies of King Henry III, was assassinated on the king's orders in 1120 and later made a saint. As an international organization, the church conducted its business in the universal language of Latin, and thus although statistically in the period the largest segment of literate persons were monks and priests, the clerical contribution to great writing in English was relatively modest. Yet the lay writers of the period reflect the importance of the church as an institution and the pervasiveness of religion in everyday life.

Beginning in 1517 the German monk Martin Luther, in Wittenberg, Germany, openly challenged many aspects of Catholic practice and by 1520 had completely repudiated the authority of the Pope, setting in train the Protestant Reformation. Luther argued that the Roman Catholic Church had strayed far from the pattern of Christianity laid out in scripture. He rejected Catholic doctrines for which no biblical authority was to be found, such as the belief in Purgatory, and translated the Bible into German, on the grounds that the importance of scripture for all Christians made its translation into the vernacular tongue essential. Luther was not the first to advance such views—followers of the Englishman John Wycliffe had translated the Bible in the fourteenth century. But Luther, protected by powerful German rulers, was able to speak out with impunity and convert others to his views, rather than suffer the persecution usually meted out to heretics. Soon other reformers were following in Luther's footsteps: of these, the Swiss Ulrich Zwingli and the French Jean Calvin would be especially influential for English religious thought.

At first England remained staunchly Catholic. Its king, Henry VIII, was so severe to heretics that the Pope awarded him the title "Defender of the Faith," which British monarchs have retained to this day. In 1534, however, Henry rejected the authority of the Pope to prevent his divorce from his queen, Catherine of Aragon, and his marriage to his mistress, Ann Boleyn. In doing so, Henry appropriated to himself ecclesiastical as well as secular authority. Thomas More, author of *Utopia*, was executed for refusing to endorse Henry's right to govern the English church. Over the following six years, Henry consolidated his grip on the ecclesiastical establishment by dissolving the powerful, populous Catholic monasteries and redistributing their massive landholdings to his own lay followers. Yet Henry's church largely retained Catholic doctrine and liturgy. When Henry died and his young son, Edward, came to the throne in 1547, the English church embarked on a more Protestant path, a direction abruptly reversed when Edward died and his older sister Mary, the daughter of Catherine of Aragon, took the throne in 1553 and attempted to reintroduce Roman Catholicism. Mary's reign was also short, however, and her successor, Elizabeth I, the daughter of Ann Boleyn, was a Protestant. Elizabeth attempted to establish a "middle way" Christianity, compromising between Roman Catholic practices and beliefs and reformed ones.

The Church of England, though it laid claim to a national rather than panEuropean authority, aspired like its predecessor to be the universal church of all English subjects. It retained the Catholic structure of parishes and dioceses and the Catholic hierarchy of bishops, though the ecclesiastical authority was now the Archbishop of Canterbury and the Church's "Supreme Governor" was the monarch. Yet disagreement and controversy persisted. Some members of the Church of England wanted to retain many of the ritual and liturgical elements of Catholicism. Others, the Puritans, advocated a more thoroughgoing reformation. Most Puritans remained within the Church of England, but a minority, the "Separatists" or "Congregationalists," split from the established church altogether. These dissenters no longer the ideal church thought of as an organization to which everybody belonged; instead, they conceived it as a more exclusive group of likeminded people, one not necessarily attached to a larger body of believers.

In the seventeenth century, the succession of the Scottish king James to the English throne produced another problem. England and Scotland were separate nations, and in the sixteenth century Scotland had developed its own national Presbyterian church, or "kirk," under the leadership of the reformer John Knox. The kirk retained fewer Catholic liturgical elements than did the Church of England, and its authorities, or "presbyters," were elected by assemblies of their fellow clerics, rather than appointed by the king. James I and his son Charles I, especially the latter, wanted to bring the Scottish kirk into conformity with Church of England practices. The Scots violently resisted these efforts, with the collaboration of many English Puritans, in a conflict that eventually developed into the English Civil War in the mid-seventeenth century. The effect of these disputes is visible in the poetry of such writers as John Milton, Robert Herrick, Henry Vaughan, and Thomas Traherne, and in the prose of Thomas Browne, Lucy Hutchinson, and Dorothy Waugh. Just as in the mid-sixteenth century, when a succession of monarchs with different religious commitments destabilized the church, so the seventeenth century endured spiritual whiplash. King Charles I's highly ritualistic Church of England was violently overturned by the Puritan victors in the Civil War—until 1660, after the death of the Puritan leader, Oliver Cromwell, when the Church of England was restored along with the monarchy.

The religious and political upheavals of the seventeenth century produced Christian sects that de-emphasized the ceremony of the established church and rejected as well its top-down authority structure. Some of these groups were ephemeral, but the Baptists (founded in 1608 in Amsterdam by the English expatriate John Smyth) and Quakers, or Society of Friends (founded by George Fox in the 1640s), flourished outside the established church, sometimes despite cruel persecution. John Bunyan, a Baptist, wrote the Christian allegory *Pilgrim's Progress* while in prison. Some dissenters, like the Baptists, shared the reformed reverence for the absolute authority of scripture but interpreted the scriptural texts differently from their fellow Protestants. Others, like the Quakers, favored, even over the authority of the Bible, the "inner light" or voice of individual conscience, which they took to be the working of the Holy Spirit in the lives of individuals.

The Protestant dissenters were not England's only religious minorities. Despite crushing fines and the threat of imprisonment, a minority of Catholics under Elizabeth and James openly refused to give their allegiance to the new church, and others remained secret adherents to the old ways. John Donne was brought up in an ardently Catholic family, and several other writers converted to Catholicism as adults—Ben Jonson for a considerable part of his career, Elizabeth Carey and Richard Crashaw permanently, and at profound personal cost. In the eighteenth century, Catholics remained objects of suspicion as possible agents of sedition, especially after the "Glorious Revolution" in 1688 deposed the Catholic James II in favor of the Protestant William and Mary. Anti-Catholic prejudice affected John Dryden, a Catholic convert, as well as the lifelong Catholic Alexander Pope. By contrast, the English colony of Ireland remained overwhelmingly Roman Catholic, the fervor of its religious commitment at least partly inspired by resistance to English occupation. Starting in the reign of Elizabeth, England shored up its own authority in Ireland by encouraging Protestant immigrants from Scotland to settle in northern Ireland, producing a virulent religious divide the effects of which are still playing out today.

A small community of Jews had moved from France to London after 1066, when the Norman William the Conqueror came to the English throne. Although despised and persecuted by many Christians, they were allowed to remain as moneylenders to the Crown, until the thirteenth century, when the king developed alternative sources of credit. At this point, in 1290, the Jews were expelled from England. In 1655 Oliver Cromwell permitted a few to return, and in the late seventeenth and early eighteenth centuries the Jewish population slowly increased, mainly by immigration from Germany. In the mid-eighteenth century some prominent Jews had their children brought up as Christians so as to facilitate their full integration into English society: thus the nineteenth-century writer and politician Benjamin Disraeli, although he and his father were members of the Church of England, was widely considered a Jew insofar as his ancestry was Jewish.

In the late seventeenth century, as the Church of England reasserted itself, Catholics, Jews, and dissenting Protestants found themselves subject to significant legal restrictions. The Corporation Act, passed in 1661, and the Test Act, passed in 1673, excluded all who refused to take communion in the Church of England from voting, attending university, or working in government or in the professions. Members of religious minorities, as well as Church of England communicants, paid mandatory taxes in support of Church of England ministers and buildings. In 1689 the dissenters gained the right to worship in public, but Jews and Catholics were not permitted to do so.

During the eighteenth century, political, intellectual, and religious history remained closely intertwined. The Church of England came to accommodate a good deal of variety. "Low church" services resembled those of the dissenting Protestant churches, minimizing ritual and emphasizing the sermon; the "high church" retained more elaborate ritual elements, yet its prestige was under attack on several fronts. Many Enlightenment thinkers subjected the Bible to rational critique and found it wanting: the philosopher David Hume, for instance, argued that the "miracles" described therein were more probably lies or errors than real breaches of the laws of nature. Within the Church of England, the "broad church" Latitudinarians welcomed this rationalism, advocating theological openness and an emphasis on ethics rather than dogma. More radically, the Unitarian movement rejected the divinity of Christ while professing to accept his ethical teachings. Taking a different tack, the preacher John Wesley, founder of Methodism, responded to the rationalists' challenge with a newly fervent call to evangelism and personal discipline; his movement was particularly successful in Wales. Revolutions in America and France at the end of the century generated considerable millenarian excitement and fostered more new religious ideas, often in conjunction with a radical social agenda. Many important writers of the Romantic period were indebted to traditions of protestant dissent: Unitarian and rationalist protestant ideas influenced William Hazlitt, Anna Barbauld, Mary Wollstonecraft, and the young Samuel Taylor Coleridge. William Blake created a highly idiosyncratic poetic mythology loosely indebted to radical strains of Christian mysticism. Others were even more heterodox: Lord Byron and Robert Burns, brought up as Scots Presbyterians, rebelled fiercely, and Percy Shelley's writing of an atheistic pamphlet resulted in his expulsion from Oxford.

Great Britain never erected an American-style "wall of separation" between church and state, but in practice religion and secular affairs grew more and more distinct during the nineteenth century. In consequence, members of religious minorities no longer seemed to pose a threat to the commonweal. A movement to repeal the Test Act failed in the 1790s, but a renewed effort resulted in the extension of the franchise to dissenting Protestants in 1828 and to Catholics in 1829. The numbers of Roman Catholics in England were swelled by immigration from Ireland, but there were also some prominent English adherents. Among writers, the converts John Newman and Gerard Manley Hopkins are especially important. The political participation and social integration of Jews presented a thornier challenge. Lionel de Rothschild, repeatedly elected to represent London in Parliament during the 1840s and 1850s, was not permitted to take his seat there because he refused to take his oath of office "on the true faith of a Christian"; finally, in 1858, the Jewish Disabilities Act allowed him to omit these words. Only in 1871, however, were Oxford and Cambridge opened to non-Anglicans.

Meanwhile geological discoveries and Charles Darwin's evolutionary theories increasingly cast doubt on the literal truth of the Creation story, and close philological analysis of the biblical text suggested that its origins were human rather than divine. By the end of the nineteenth century, many writers were bearing witness to a world in which Christianity no longer seemed fundamentally plausible. In his poetry and prose, Thomas Hardy depicts a world devoid of benevolent providence. Matthew Arnold's poem "Dover Beach" is in part an elegy to lost spiritual assurance, as the "Sea of Faith" goes out like the tide: "But now I only hear / Its melancholy, long, withdrawing roar / Retreating." For Arnold, literature must replace religion as a source of spiritual truth, and intimacy between individuals substitute for the lost communal solidarity of the universal church.

The work of many twentieth-century writers shows the influence of a religious upbringing or a religious conversion in adulthood. T. S. Eliot and W. S. Auden embrace Anglicanism, William Butler Yeats spiritualism. James Joyce repudiates Irish Catholicism but remains obsessed with it. Yet religion, or lack of it, is a matter of individual choice and conscience, not social or legal mandate. In the past fifty years, church attendance has plummeted in Great Britain. Although 71 percent of the population still identified itself as "Christian" on the 2000 census, only about 7 percent of these regularly attend religious services of any denomination. Meanwhile, immigration from former British colonies has swelled the ranks of religions once alien to the British Isles—Muslim, Sikh, Hindu, Buddhist—though the numbers of adherents remain small relative to the total population.

THE UNIVERSE ACCORDING TO PTOLEMY

Ptolemy was a Roman astronomer of Greek descent, born in Egypt during the second century C.E.; for nearly fifteen hundred years after his death his account of the design of the universe was accepted as standard. During that time, the basic pattern underwent many detailed modifications and was fitted out with many astrological and pseudoscientific trappings. But in essence Ptolemy's followers portrayed the earth as the center of the universe, with the sun, planets, and fixed stars set in transparent spheres orbiting around it. In this scheme of things, as modified for Christian usage, Hell was usually placed under the earth's surface at the center of the cosmic globe, while Heaven, the abode of the blessed spirits, was in the outermost, uppermost circle, the empyrean. But in 1543 the Polish astronomer Copernicus proposed an alternative hypothesis—that the earth rotates around the sun, not vice versa; and despite theological opposition, observations with the new telescope and careful mathematical calculations insured ultimate acceptance of the new view.

The map of the Ptolemaic universe below is a simplified version of a diagram in Peter Apian's *Cosmography* (1584). In such a diagram, the Firmament is the sphere that contained the fixed stars; the Crystalline Sphere, which contained no heavenly bodies, is a late innovation, included to explain certain anomalies in the observed movement of the heavenly bodies; and the Prime Mover is the sphere that, itself put into motion by God, imparts rotation around the earth to all the other spheres.

Milton, writing in the mid-seventeenth century, used two universes. The Copernican universe, though he alludes to it, was too large, formless, and unfamiliar to be the setting for the war between Heaven and Hell in *Paradise Lost*. He therefore used the Ptolemaic cosmos, but placed Heaven well outside this smaller earth-centered universe, Hell far beneath it, and assigned the vast middle space to Chaos.

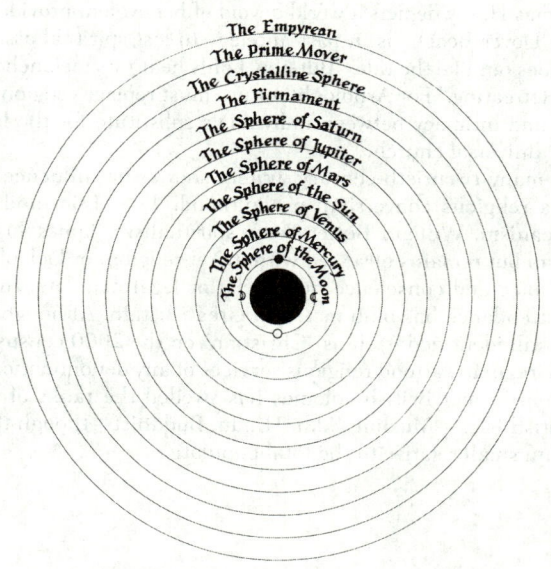

The Empyrean
The Prime Mover
The Crystalline Sphere
The Firmament
The Sphere of Saturn
The Sphere of Jupiter
The Sphere of Mars
The Sphere of the Sun
The Sphere of Venus
The Sphere of Mercury
The Sphere of the Moon

A LONDON PLAYHOUSE OF SHAKESPEARE'S TIME

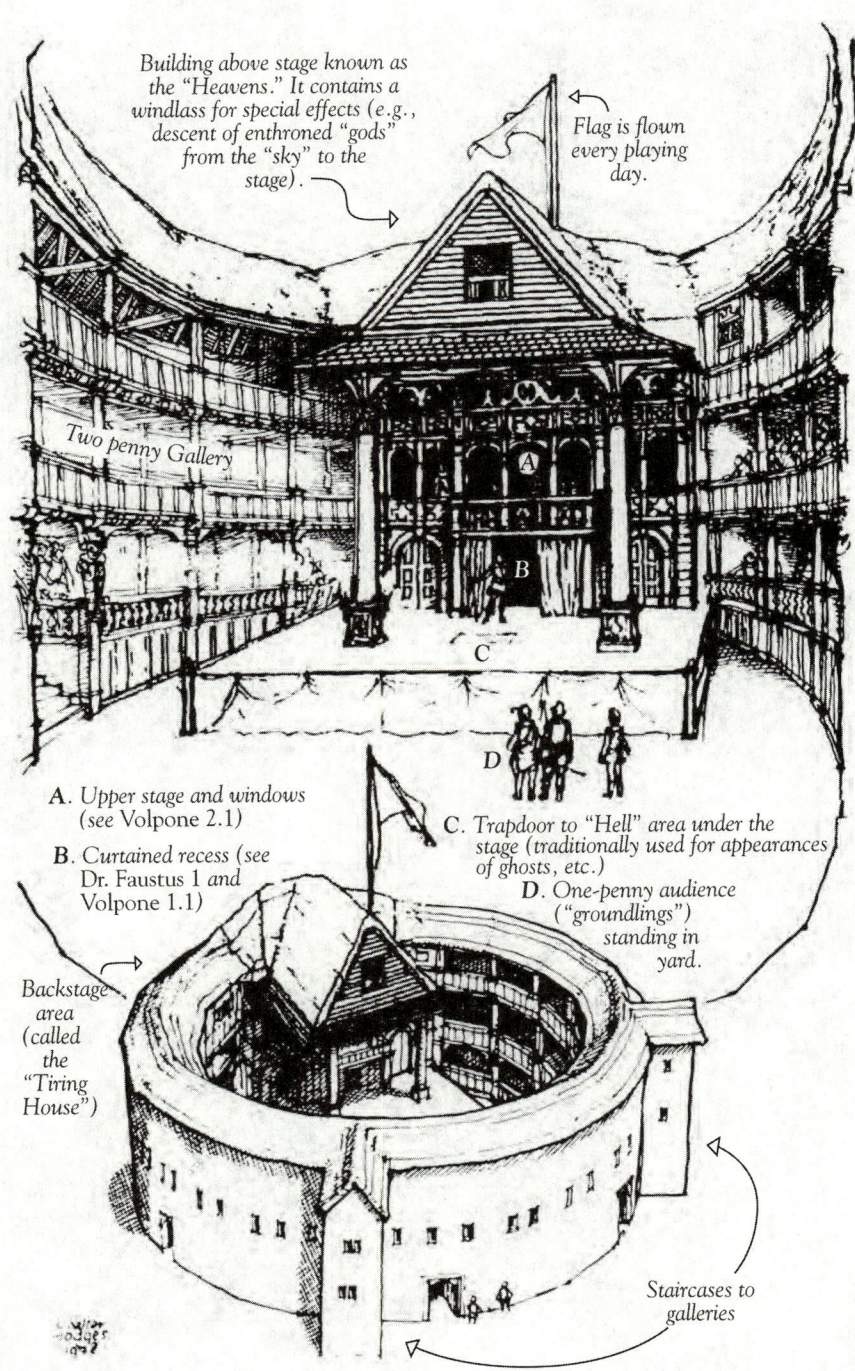

Building above stage known as the "Heavens." It contains a windlass for special effects (e.g., descent of enthroned "gods" from the "sky" to the stage).

Flag is flown every playing day.

Two penny Gallery

A. *Upper stage and windows (see Volpone 2.1)*

B. *Curtained recess (see Dr. Faustus 1 and Volpone 1.1)*

C. *Trapdoor to "Hell" area under the stage (traditionally used for appearances of ghosts, etc.)*

D. *One-penny audience ("groundlings") standing in yard.*

Backstage area (called the "Tiring House")

Staircases to galleries

PERMISSIONS ACKNOWLEDGMENTS

TEXT CREDITS

Ancrene Riwle: "The Sweetness and Pains of Enclosure" from THE ANCRENE RIWLE, translated by M. B. Salu, 1990. Reprinted by permission of the University of Exeter Press.

Aphra Behn: *The Complete Text of OROONOKO,* edited by Joanna Lipking. Copyright © 1993 by Joanna Lipking and W. W. Norton & Company, Inc. Reprinted by permission of W. W. Norton & Company, Inc.

Beowulf: From BEOWULF, translated by Seamus Heaney. Copyright © 2000 by Seamus Heaney. Used with permission of W. W. Norton & Company, Inc.

James Boswell: *Boswell Interviews Voltaire* from BOSWELL ON THE GRAND TOUR: GERMANY AND SWITZERLAND, 1764, edited by F. A. Pottle. Reprinted with the permission of Yale Boswell Editions.

Margaret Lucas Cavendish: Extracts from THE BLAZING WORLD are from Margaret Cavendish, Duchess of Newcastle, THE DESCRIPTION OF A NEW WORLD CALLED THE BLAZING WORLD AND OTHER WRITINGS, edited by Kate Lilley (London: Pickering & Chatto 1992). Pp. 24,122–25, 180–81, 184–86. Reprinted by permission of the publisher.

Geoffrey Chaucer: All excerpts are from CHAUCER'S POETRY: AN ANTHOLOGY FOR THE MODERN READER, 2nd ed., edited by E. T. Donaldson. Copyright © 1958, 1975 by Judith Anderson and Deirdre Donaldson. Used by permission of W. W. Norton & Company, Inc.

Edward De Vere, Earl of Oxford: "The lively lark stretched forth her wing" edited by Dr. Glen Black. Used with permission of Dr. Glen Black.

Dream of the Rood: Translated by Alfred David. Copyright © 2012 by Alfred David. Reprinted by permission of the translator.

Early Irish Lyrics: From EARLY IRISH LYRICS, edited and translated by Gerard Murphy, Four Courts Press, 1998. Reproduced with permission from Gerard Murphy and Four Courts Press.

Queen Elizabeth: *On Monsieur's Departure* from THE POEMS OF QUEEN ELIZABETH I, edited by Leicester Bradner. Copyright © 1964 by Brown University. Reprinted by permission of the University Press of New England. *Letter to Sir Amyes Paulet* and *Letter to King James VI of Scotland* from THE LETTERS OF QUEEN ELIZABETH, edited by G. B. Harrison (Cassell, 1935). Reprinted by permission of David Higham Associates. *The Golden Speech* from THE PUBLIC SPEAKING OF QUEEN ELIZABETH: SELECTIONS FROM HER OFFICIAL ADDRESSES, edited by George P. Rice, Jr. (AMS Press, 1966). Reprinted with the permission of AMS Press, Inc.

Stephen Greenblatt et al.: Footnotes to *King Lear* by Stephen Greenblatt, copyright © 1997 by W. W. Norton & Company, Inc., from THE NORTON SHAKESPEARE: BASED ON THE OXFORD EDITION, edited by Stephen Greenblatt et al. Reprinted by permission of W. W. Norton & Company, Inc.

Robert Henryson: *The Cock and the Fox* from ROBERT HENRYSON: THE POEMS, edited by Denton Fox (1980). Reprinted by permission of Oxford University Press.

Robert Herrick: *How the Roses Came Red* by Robert Herrick, from BEN JONSON AND THE CAVALIER POETS: A Norton Critical Edition by Hugh Maclean, editor. Copyright © 1974 by W. W. Norton & Company, Inc. Reprinted by permission of W. W. Norton & Company, Inc.

Thomas Hoccleve: "My Compleinte" from 'MY COMPLEINTE' AND OTHER POEMS by Thomas Hoccleve, edited by Roger Ellis, 2001. Reprinted by permission of the University of Exeter Press.

Judith: From OLD & MIDDLE ENGLISH translated by Elaine Treharne. Reprinted with the permission of the translator.

Julian of Norwich: Excerpts reprinted from Julian of Norwich, A BOOK OF SHOWINGS, edited by Edmund Colledge and James Walsh, by permission of the publisher. Copyright © 1978 by the Pontifical Institute of Mediaeval Studies, Toronto.

Margery Kempe: All excerpts including bibliographical citation excerpts from THE BOOK OF MARGERY KEMPE, edited by Lynn Staley (Kalamazoo, MI: Medieval Institute Publications). Copyright © 1996 by the Board of The Medieval Institute. Reprinted by permission of the publisher.

William Langland: Excerpts from PIERS PLOWMAN: AN ALLITERATIVE VERSE TRANSLATION by William Langland, translated by E. Talbot Donaldson. Translation © 1990 by W. W. Norton & Company, Inc. Reprinted by permission of W. W. Norton & Company, Inc.

Layamon: Excerpts from Layamon's BRUT, translated by Rosamund Allen. Reprinted by permission of The Orion Publishing Group Ltd. on behalf of the publisher, Everyman.

Marie de France: Translation of LANVAL by Alfred David. Copyright © 2000 by Alfred David. Reprinted with the permission of the translator. "Milun," and "Chevrefoil" from THE LAIS OF MARIE DE FRANCE translated by Robert Hanning and Joan Ferrante. Copyright © 1978 by Robert W. Hanning and Joan M. Ferrante. Reprinted by permission of Baker Academic, a division of Baker Publishing Group.

Medieval English Lyrics: "Foweles in the Frith" from MEDIEVAL ENGLISH LYRICS edited by Theodore Silverstein (London: Arnold, 1971), copyright © 1971. Reproduced by permission of Hodder Education.

John Milton: Excerpts from *Areopagitica* from THE COMPLETE POETRY AND MAJOR PROSE OF MILTON, edited by Merritt Y. Hughes, copyright © 1957. Reprinted by permission of Prentice-Hall, Inc., Upper Saddle River, NJ. Complete text and endnotes from PARADISE LOST: A Norton Critical Edition, Second Edition, by John Milton edited by Scott Elledge. Copyright © 1993, 1975 by W. W. Norton & Company, Inc. Reprinted by permission of W. W. Norton & Company, Inc.

Lady Mary Wortley Montagu: Poems from LADY MARY WORTLEY MONTAGU, ESSAYS AND POEMS, 1977, revised 1993, edited by R. Halsband and I. Grundy. Reprinted with permission.

Sir Thomas More: from UTOPIA: A Norton Critical Edition, Second Edition, by Sir Thomas More, translated by Robert M. Adams. Copyright © 1992, 1975 by W. W. Norton & Company, Inc. Used by permission of W. W. Norton & Company, Inc.

Mystery Plays: *The Wakefield Second Shepherd's Play* based on the edition by A. C. Cawley and Martin Stevens. Copyright © 1994. Reprinted by permission of Oxford University Press.

Samuel Pepys: Excerpts from THE DIARY OF SAMUEL PEPYS, 11 volumes, edited by Robert Latham and William Matthews. Copyright © 1972, 1986 by The Master, Fellows and Scholars of Magdalen College, Cambridge, Robert Latham, and the Executors of William Matthews. Copyright © 2000 by the Regents of the University of California. Reprinted by permission of the publisher, the University of California Press and HarperCollins Publishers Ltd.

Petrarch: Reprinted by permission of the publisher from PETRARCH'S LYRIC POEMS: THE *RIME SPARSE* AND OTHER LYRICS, translated and edited by Robert M. Durling, pp. 272, 284, 310, 334, 336, 488. Cambridge, Mass.: Harvard University Press. Copyright © 1976 by Robert M. Durling.

Katherine Philips: *A Married State* from NLW Orielton Collection, box 24. Courtesy of The National Library of Wales.

William Shakespeare: *Twelfth Night,* edited by Barbara A. Mowat and Paul Werstine. 1993 © The Folger Shakespeare Library. Text of *King Lear,* edited by Barbara Lewalski. Copyright © 1993 by W. W. Norton & Company, Inc., from THE NORTON ANTHOLOGY OF ENGLISH LITERATURE, SIXTH EDITION, VOLUME 1, edited by M. H. Abrams et al. Reprinted by permission of W. W. Norton & Company, Inc.

Sir Gawain and the Green Knight: From SIR GAWAIN AND THE GREEN KNIGHT: A NEW VERSE TRANSLATION translated by Simon Armitage. Copyright © 2007 by Simon Armitage. Used by permission of W. W. Norton & Company, Inc.

Christopher Smart: *My Cat Jeoffry* from JUBILATE AGNO, edited by W. H. Bond. Reprinted by permission of HarperCollins Publishers Ltd.

Tain Epic: *Cuchulainn's Boyhood Deeds* from THE TAIN translated by Thomas Kinsella. Copyright © 1969 by Thomas Kinsella. Used by permission of the translator.

The Wanderer: Translated by Alfred David. Copyright © 2012 by Alfred David. Reprinted by permission of the translator.

The Wife's Lament: Translated by Alfred David. Copyright © 2012 by Alfred David. Reprinted by permission of the translator.

Mary Wroth: from THE POEMS OF LADY MARY WROTH, edited by Josephine A. Roberts. Reprinted by permission of Louisiana State University Press.

Every effort has been made to contact the copyright holders of each of the selections. Rights holders of any selections not credited should contact W. W. Norton & Company, Inc., 500 Fifth Avenue, New York, NY 10110, in order for a correction to be made in the next reprinting of our work.

IMAGE CREDITS

Pp. 2–3 The British Library, MS Royal 18 D II, Folio 148; **7** British Library, London, UK / © British Library Board. All Rights Reserved / The Bridgeman Art Library; **11** ARTstor, Centre Guillaume le Conquérant, Bayeux, France; **14** ARTstor, SCALA, Florence / ART RESOURCE, NY; **17** Réunion des Musées Nationaux /Art Resource, NY; **37** British Library, London, Great Britain/HIP/Art Resource, NY; **38** © The Trustees of the British Museum/Art Resource, NY; **133** Art Resource, NY; **141** The British Library, London, UK / © British Library Board. All Rights Reserved / The Bridgeman Art Library International; **184** Musee Conde, Chantilly, France / Giraudon / The Bridgeman Art Library International; **210** British Library, London, UK / The Bridgeman Art Library International; **239** National Gallery, London, UK / The Bridgeman Art Library International; **282** Ellesmere Manuscript, facsimile edition, 1911, English School, (15th century) (after) / Private Collection / The Bridgeman Art Library International; **310** Louvre, Paris, France / Giraudon / The Bridgeman Art Library International; **359** British Library, London, UK / © British Library Board. All Rights Reserved / The Bridgeman Art Library International; **371** Prado, Madrid, Spain / The Bridgeman Art Library International; **372** Prado, Madrid, Spain / Giraudon / The Bridgeman Art Library International; **412** Österreichische Nationalbibliothek, (Vienna, Austria), Codex Vindobonensis 1857, fols. 14v-15r; **501** Jost Amman/THO Special Collections Rare Books/OSU. **530–31** The Granger Collection, NYC—All rights reserved; **536** Bridgeman Art Library; **559** The Bridgeman Art Library; **543** © The Gallery Collection / Corbis; **545** University of Toronto Wenceslaus Hollar Digital Collection / Wikimedia Commons; **556** The Bridgeman Art Library; **675** Houghton Library / Harvard; **689** Henry E. Huntington Library and Art Gallery; **731** Universal Images Group / Getty Images; **748** The Art Archive; **1001** Project Gutenberg; **1002** Glasgow University; **1187** Everett Collection; **pp. 1340–41** Scala / Art Resource; National Portrait Gallery London; **1350** The Great Chain of Being from *Retorica Christiana* by Didacus Valades, printed in 1579 (woodcut) (b/w photo), Italian School (16th century) / Private Collection / The Bridgeman Art Library International ; **1363** Snark / Art Resource, NY; **1442** The Granger Collection; **1444** Alciato's Book of Emblems, 189; **1561** Norton Literature Online; **1649** George Wither; **1687** Princeton University; **1752** Alinari Archives / Getty Images; **1807** National Portrait Gallery London; **1897** National Portrait Gallery London. **2176–77** Giraudon / Art Resource; **2186** City of London/Heritage-Images; **2191** National Portrait Gallery (London); **2197** R. Bentley; **2203** Lewis Walpole Library; **2289** William Hogarth; **2303** © The Gallery Collection/ Corbis; **2355** © Hulton-Deutsch Collection / CORBIS; **2650** Francesco Bartolozzi (1727–1815) / Private Collection / The Bridgeman Art Library International; **2436** Charles Gildon, The History of the Athenian Society ; **2454** Time & Life Pictures / Getty Images; **2458** Tate Collection, London / Art Resource; **2761** Art Resource; **2835–40** Reproduced by permission of the Print Collection, Miriam and Ira D. Wallach Division of Art, Prints and Photographs, The New York Public Library, Astor, Lenox and Tilden Foundations; **3013** William Blake / John Gabriel Stedman/Private Collection / Archives Charmet / The Bridgeman Art Library International; **3034** William Blake / John Gabriel Stedman / Private Collection / Archives Charmet / The Bridgeman Art Library International; **3063** © The Huntington Library, Art Collections & Botanical Gardens / The Bridgeman Art Library International.

COLOR INSERT CREDITS

C1 The British Museum, London / Brieman Art Library; C2 The British Library, Cotton Nero C. IV, Folio 11; C3 The Pierpont Morgan Library / Art Resource NY; C4 The British Library, Folio 170r from the Luttrell Psalter, MS additional 42130; C5 National Gallery, London / Art Resource NY; C6 Corpus Christi College, University of Oxford, MS 394; C7 The British Library, MS Harley 4866, Folio 88; C7 The British Library, MS Royal 18 D II, Folio 148; C8 Bodleian Library, University of Oxford, MS Douce 338, Folio 60, 56, 78. C9 National Gallery London; C10 Frick Collection; C10 National Portrait Gallery, London; C11 British Museum; C11 The Royal Collection © 2011 Her Majesty Queen Elizabeth II / The Bridgeman Art Library International; C12 Tate Gallery; C13 National Portrait Gallery, London; C13 National Portrait Gallery, London; C14 Victoria and Albert Museum; C14 The Stapleton Collection; C15 Private Collection / Bridgeman C16 SCALA / Art Resource; C17 Erich Lessing / Art Resource; C18 Scala / Art Resource; C18 Camaraphoto / Art Resource; C19 Private Collection / Bridgeman Art Library; C20 Viscount De L'Isle, from his private collection at Penhurst Place; C21 Woburn Abbey, Bedfordshire, UK / Bridgeman Art Library; C22 Scala / Art Resource; C23 National Gallery London / Bridgeman Art Library; C24 Reunion des Musees / Art Resource. C25 National Gallery of Scotland / Bridgeman Art Library; C26 Museum of London / Bridgeman Art Library; C27 Reunion des Musees Nationaux / Art Resource; C28 Bristol City Museum and Art Gallery UK / Bridgeman Art Library; C28 Private Collection / Bridgeman Art Library; C29 Tate Gallery / Art Resource; C30 Somerset Maugham Theatre Collection / Bridgeman Art Library; C30 Giraudon / Art Resource; C31 Private Collection / Phillips, Fine Art Auctioneers / Bridgeman Art Library; C31 State Hermitage Museum, St. Petersburg, Russia; C32 Yale Center for British Art, Paul Mellon Collection / Bridgeman Art Library.

Index